HILLTOP ELEMENTARY SCHOOL

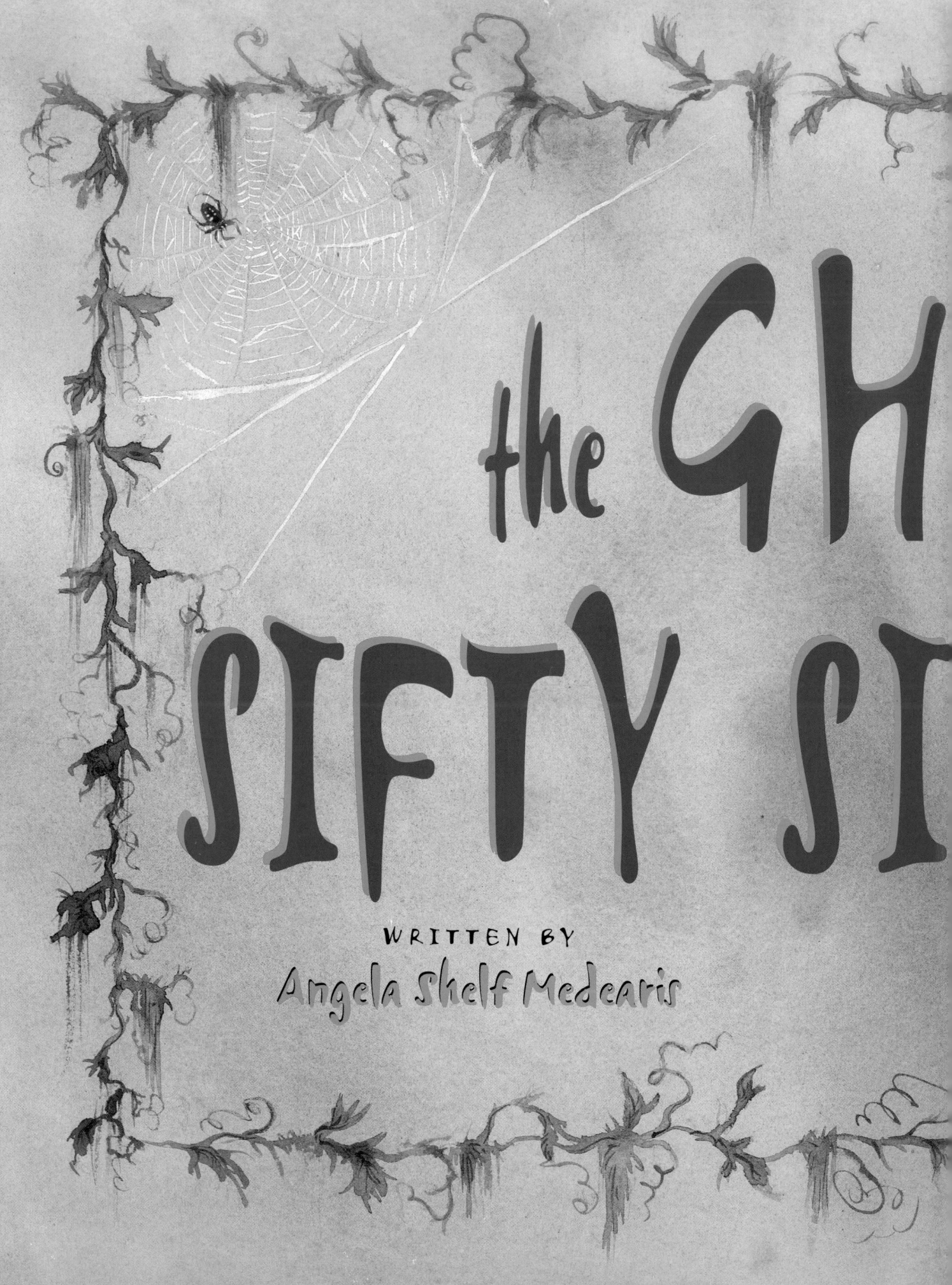

the GH
SIFTY SI

WRITTEN BY
Angela Shelf Medearis

OST of
FTY SAM

ILLUSTRATED BY

Jacqueline Rogers

Scholastic Press   New York

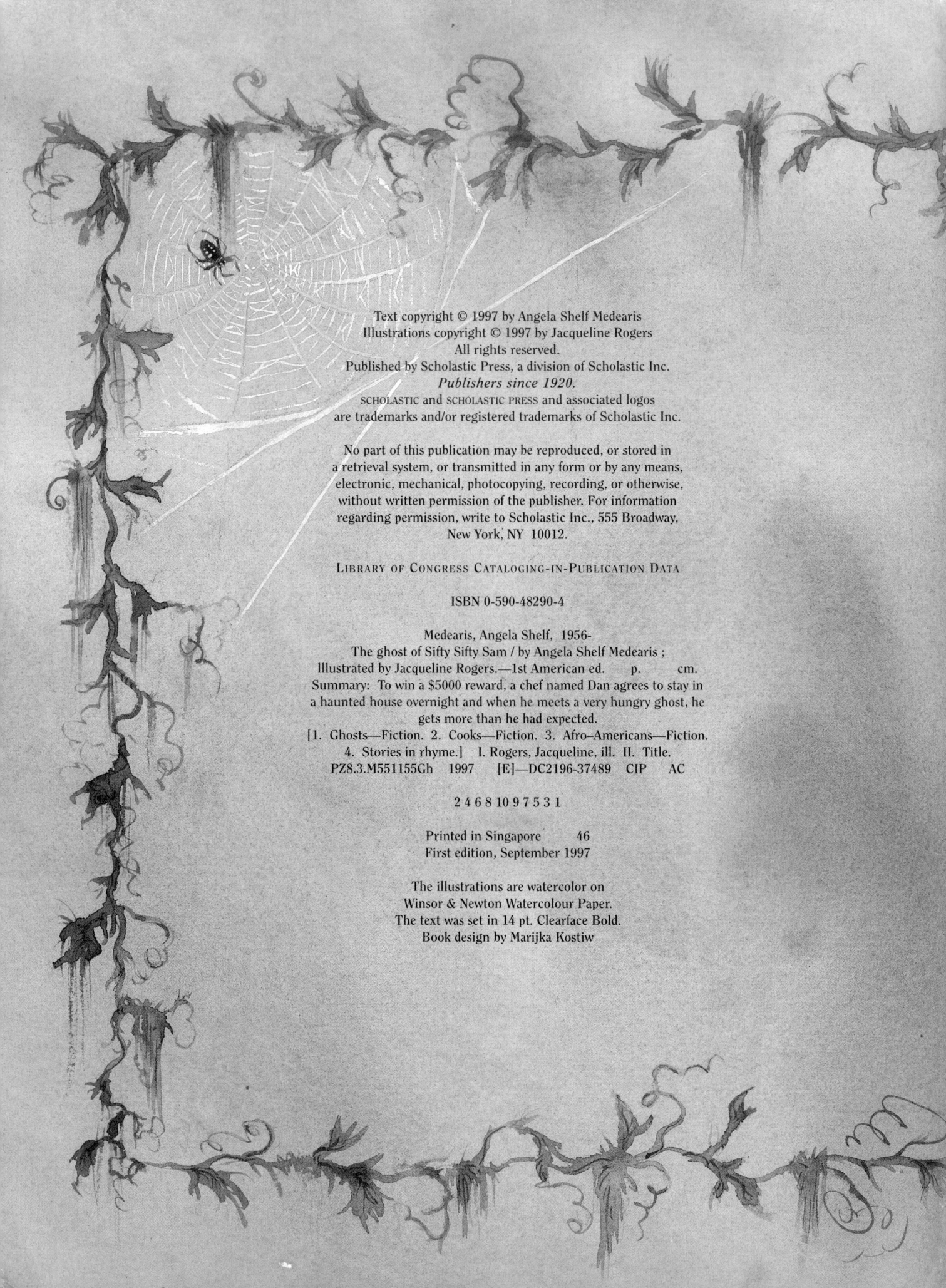

Published by Scholastic Press, a division of Scholastic Inc.
Publishers since 1920.
SCHOLASTIC and SCHOLASTIC PRESS and associated logos
are trademarks and/or registered trademarks of Scholastic Inc.

LIBRARY OF CONGRESS CATALOGING-IN-PUBLICATION DATA

ISBN 0-590-48290-4

Medearis, Angela Shelf, 1956-
The ghost of Sifty Sifty Sam / by Angela Shelf Medearis ;
Illustrated by Jacqueline Rogers.—1st American ed.   p.   cm.
Summary: To win a $5000 reward, a chef named Dan agrees to stay in
a haunted house overnight and when he meets a very hungry ghost, he
gets more than he had expected.
[1. Ghosts—Fiction. 2. Cooks—Fiction. 3. Afro-Americans—Fiction.
4. Stories in rhyme.]   I. Rogers, Jacqueline, ill. II. Title.
PZ8.3.M551155Gh 1997   [E]—DC2196-37489 CIP   AC

2 4 6 8 10 9 7 5 3 1

Printed in Singapore   46
First edition, September 1997

The illustrations are watercolor on
Winsor & Newton Watercolour Paper.
The text was set in 14 pt. Clearface Bold.
Book design by Marijka Kostiw

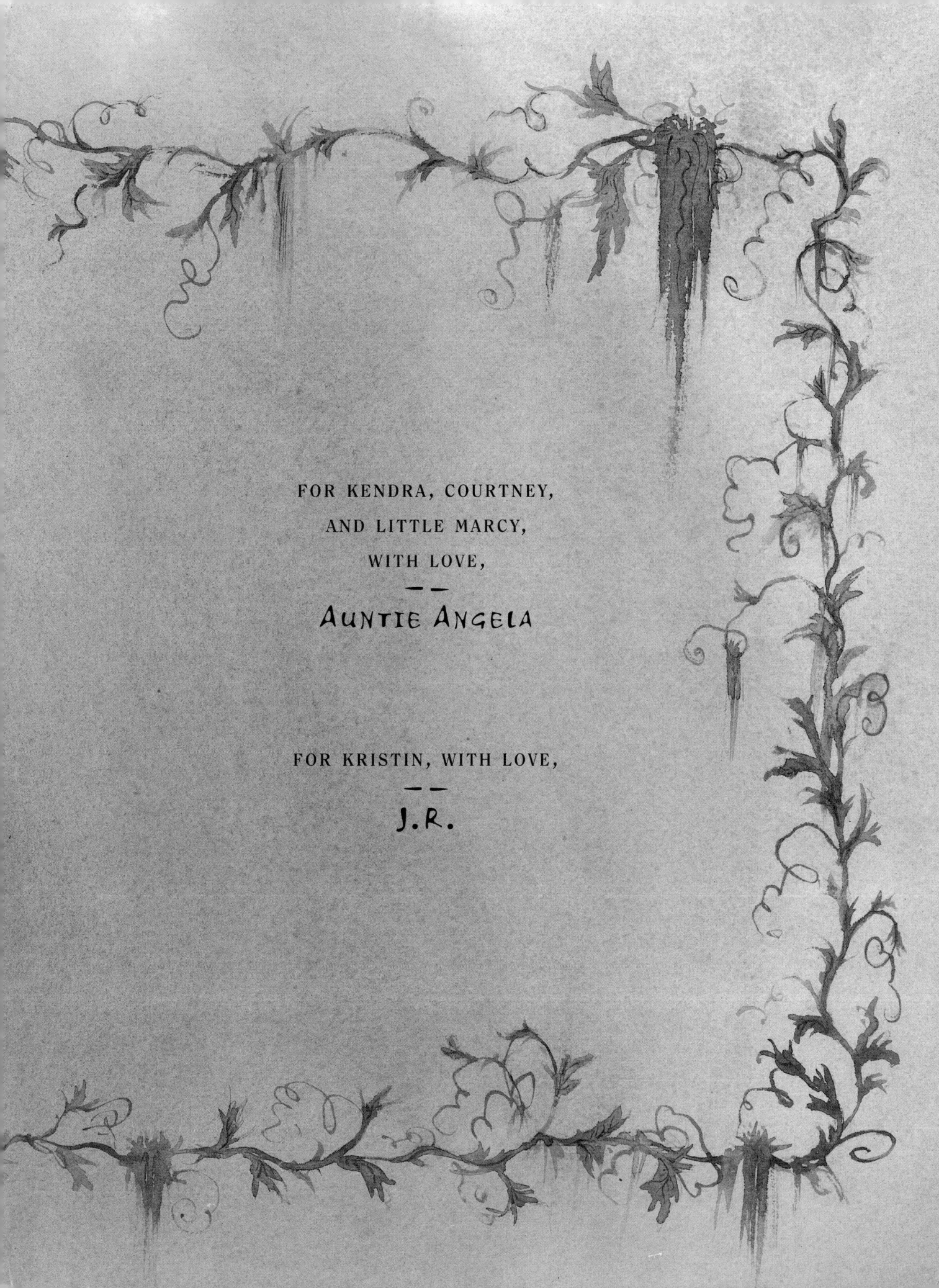

FOR KENDRA, COURTNEY,
AND LITTLE MARCY,
WITH LOVE,
– –
AUNTIE ANGELA

FOR KRISTIN, WITH LOVE,
– –
J.R.

DEEP DOWN in the East Texas woods,
where the wind wails through the tall pine trees,
there stands a beautiful old house.
That old house sits by a lake that's so clear,
the moon uses it for a mirror.
Now folks in those parts say
that the house is haunted
by the ghost of Sifty Sifty Sam.

When everything is still and dark,
old Sam appears.
That's when all the mischief starts.
He wails and he howls and he rattles his chains.
Then he screeches so loud it shakes the windowpanes.
Old Sam roams around that house every night,
scaring anyone who comes into sight.

A realtor man had been trying to sell
that old place for many a year.
He finally offered a $5,000 reward
to anyone brave enough
and smart enough
and crafty enough
to stay in the house all night long.
Folks thought, if anyone came out the next morning
alive and kicking,
that would rid the house of the ghost
of Sifty Sifty Sam.

$5000.00
REWARD
TO RID THIS HOUSE OF
THE GHOST OF SIFTY SIFTY SAM
JUST SPEND 1 NIGHT!

DAN'S
crispy delicious batter dipped fish
BISCUITS
GUMBO
PIES

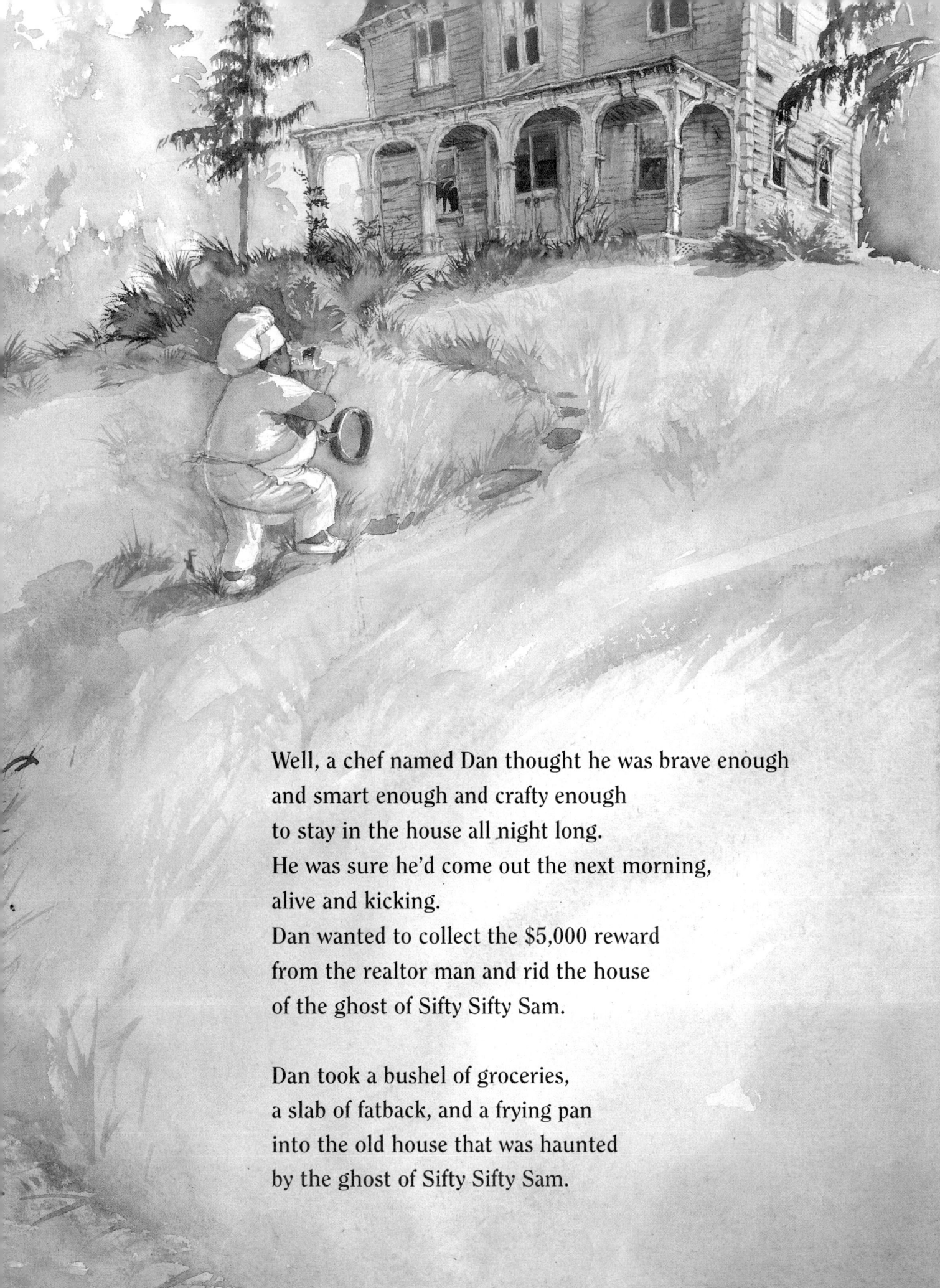

Well, a chef named Dan thought he was brave enough
and smart enough and crafty enough
to stay in the house all night long.
He was sure he'd come out the next morning,
alive and kicking.
Dan wanted to collect the $5,000 reward
from the realtor man and rid the house
of the ghost of Sifty Sifty Sam.

Dan took a bushel of groceries,
a slab of fatback, and a frying pan
into the old house that was haunted
by the ghost of Sifty Sifty Sam.

The sun had already drifted
out of sight.
Soon, the moon rose,
round and full and bright.
Dan closed the curtains
and locked all the doors.
Then he looked in each closet,
hoping and praying
he wouldn't come face to face
with the ghost of Sifty Sifty Sam,
who was haunting that place.

Dan sliced up his fatback
and made a fire in the grate.
He cooked his meat to a sizzle
and got himself a plate . . .
when suddenly,
Dan thought he heard a sound,
but he wasn't certain.
A cool breeze blew into the room
and gently parted the curtains.

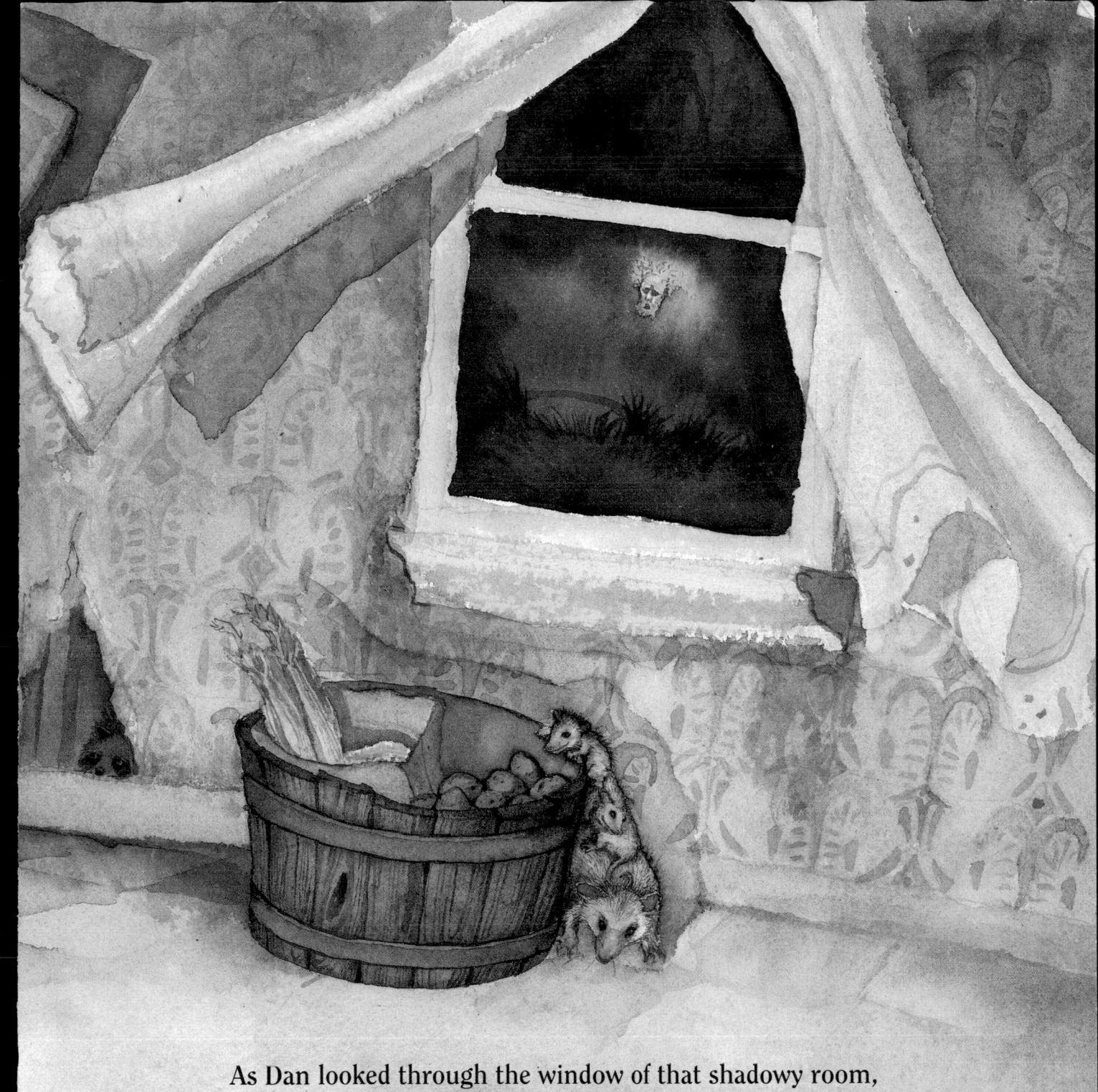

As Dan looked through the window of that shadowy room,
he saw a boat just beyond the edge of the land
and what looked like the head of a man.
Just the head of a man!
But it was hard to see in all the dark and gloom.
Then a voice whispered in the wind,
"I'm the ghost of Sifty Sifty Sam.
I'm on the lake near the man."

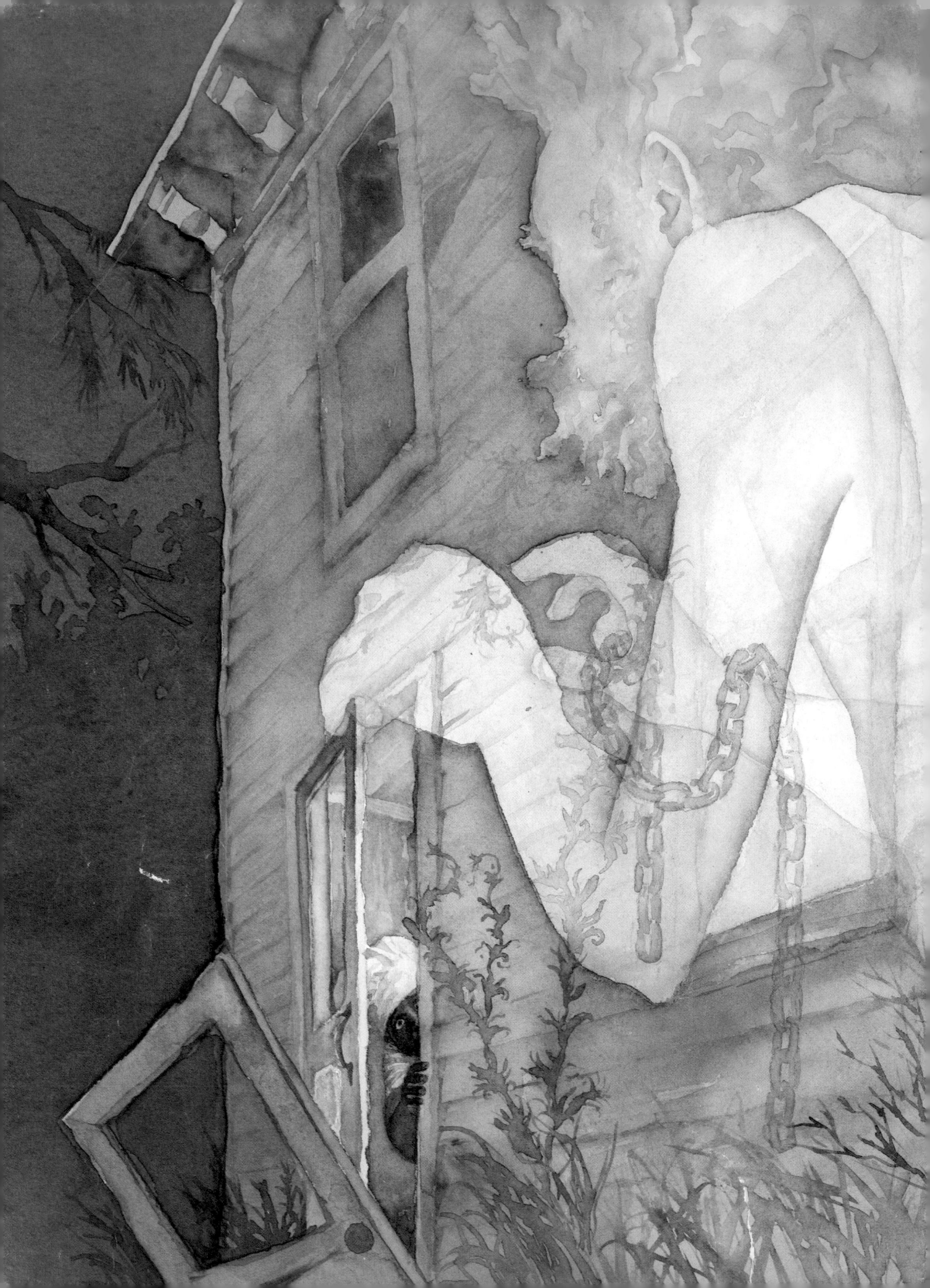

Well, Dan had his pride and he wanted to win
that $5,000 reward from the realtor man.
So he closed the curtains and tried to pretend
that what he heard and saw were only the wind.

Then Dan heard that voice again,
but it was louder this time.
So he slipped over to the door,
cracked it open a little bit,
and scrunched up his eye
to peer through the slit.
Out on the porch there stood a man
about seven feet tall
with a head and shoulders and chest and arms . . .
but no legs! No legs at all!
Then a wave of cold air whistled through the room.
A loud voice said to Dan,
**"I'M THE GHOST OF SIFTY SIFTY SAM.
I'M ON THE PORCH NEAR THE MAN."**

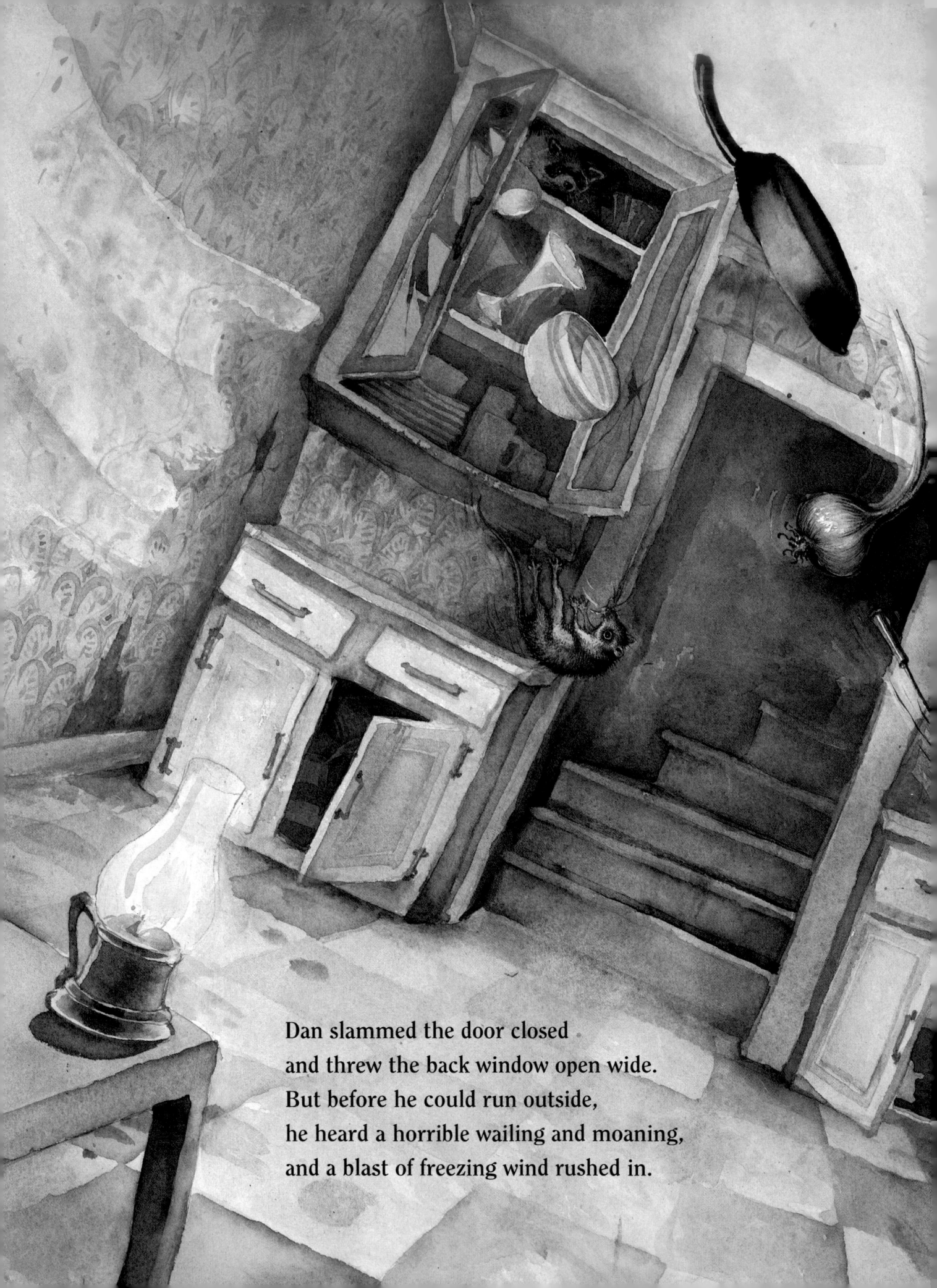

Dan slammed the door closed
and threw the back window open wide.
But before he could run outside,
he heard a horrible wailing and moaning,
and a blast of freezing wind rushed in.

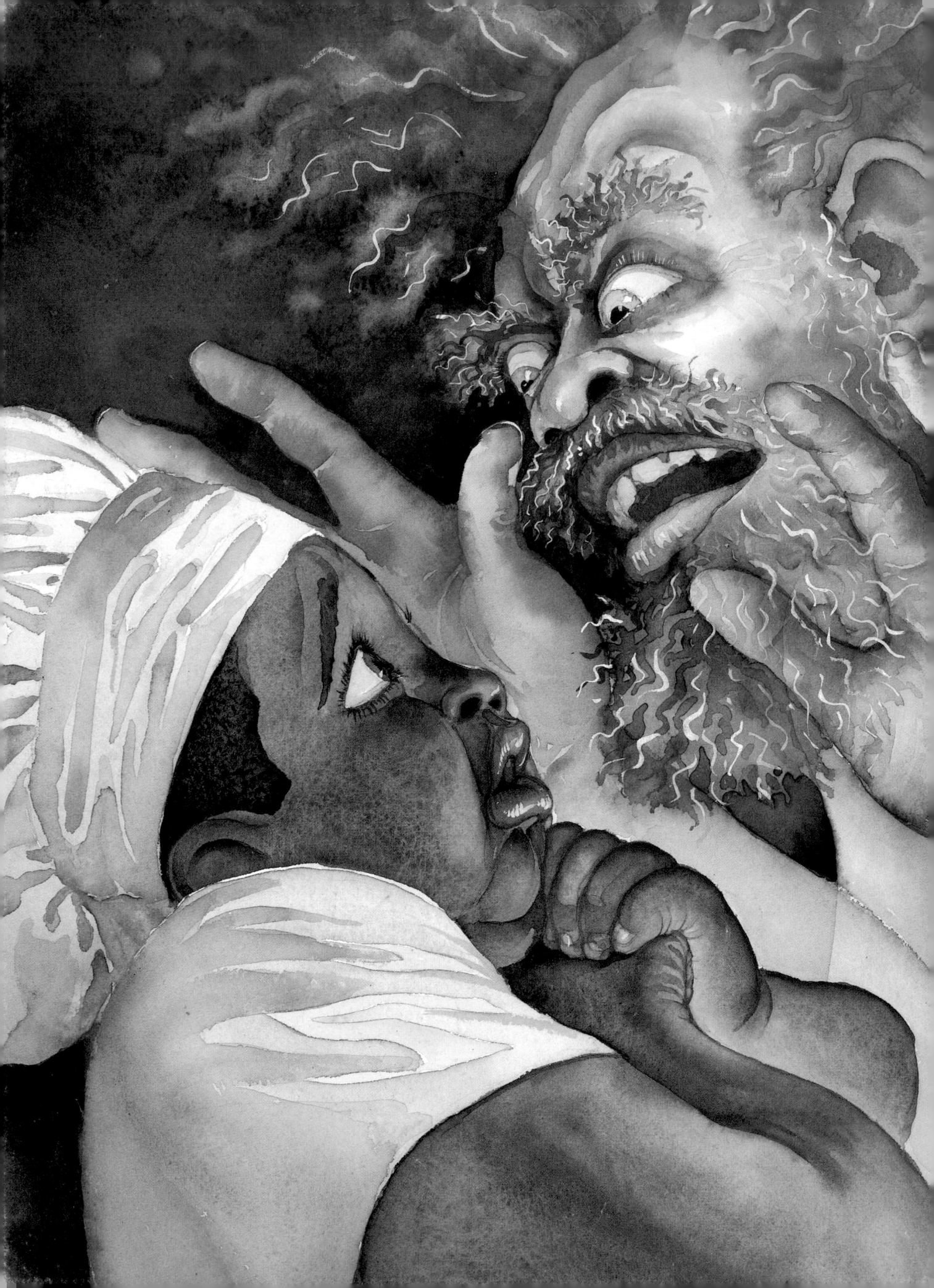

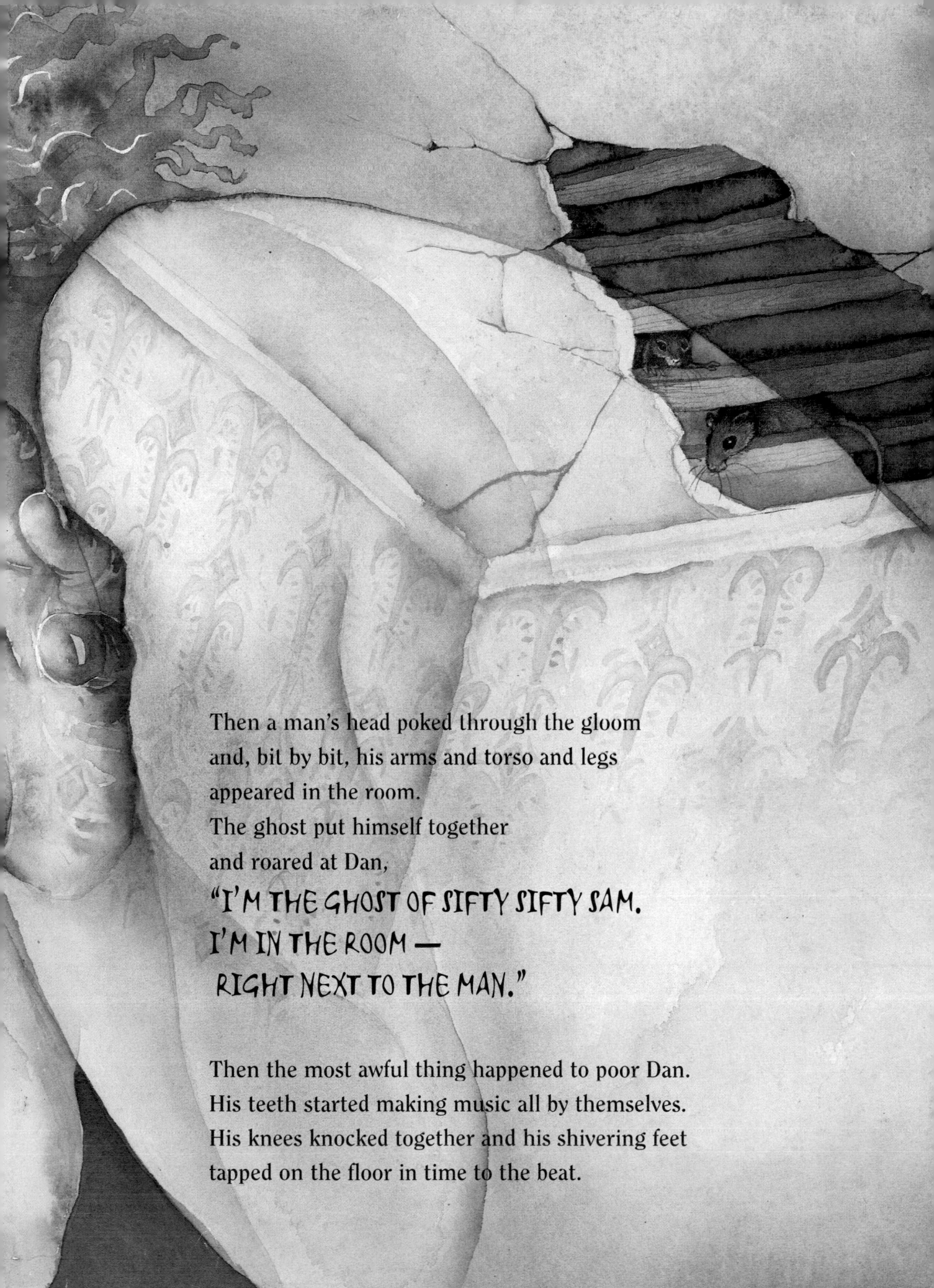

Then a man's head poked through the gloom
and, bit by bit, his arms and torso and legs
appeared in the room.
The ghost put himself together
and roared at Dan,
"I'M THE GHOST OF SIFTY SIFTY SAM.
I'M IN THE ROOM —
RIGHT NEXT TO THE MAN."

Then the most awful thing happened to poor Dan.
His teeth started making music all by themselves.
His knees knocked together and his shivering feet
tapped on the floor in time to the beat.

The ghost sniffed the air
and snatched the frying pan from the grate.
He ate and he ate and he ate.
Then he drank all that burning hot grease down,
without making a single, solitary sound.
When he had finished all of Dan's meat,
he looked around for something else to eat.

But there was nothing left.
The ghost had eaten every bite.
So he turned to Dan
and roared with all his might,
"I'M THE GHOST OF SIFTY SIFTY SAM
AND I WANT SOME MORE!"
Well, Dan was so scared he jumped out of his shoes.
But when he landed on the floor again,
he knew exactly what to do.

First, he grabbed some potatoes,
some ground meat, and tomatoes,
and with potato peels flying every which way,
Dan cooked up a hash for that ghost in a flash.

"MORE!" cried the ghost,
as he gobbled it all down.
He looked at Dan with a horrible frown.
Dan's hands shook as he scrambled a dozen eggs
and buttered and toasted a loaf of bread.

"MORE! MORE!" cried the ghost
with a mighty bellow.
"GIVE ME MORE FOOD
BECAUSE I'M ONE HUNGRY FELLOW!"
Dan trembled all over from head to toe
and whipped up a pan of spicy gumbo.

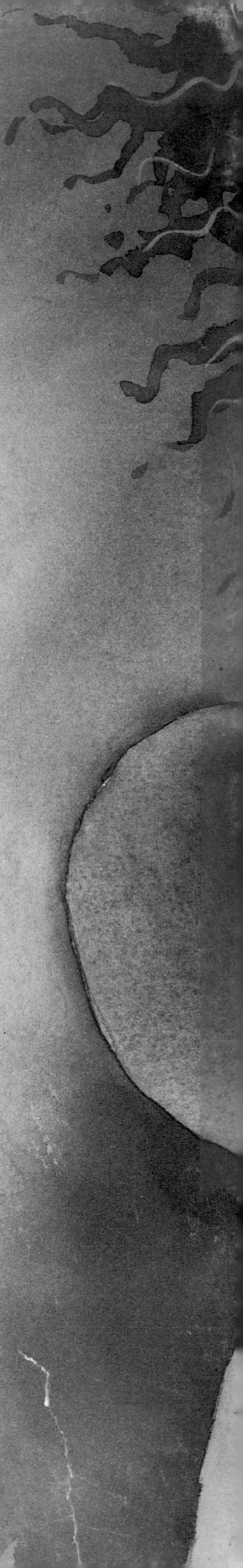

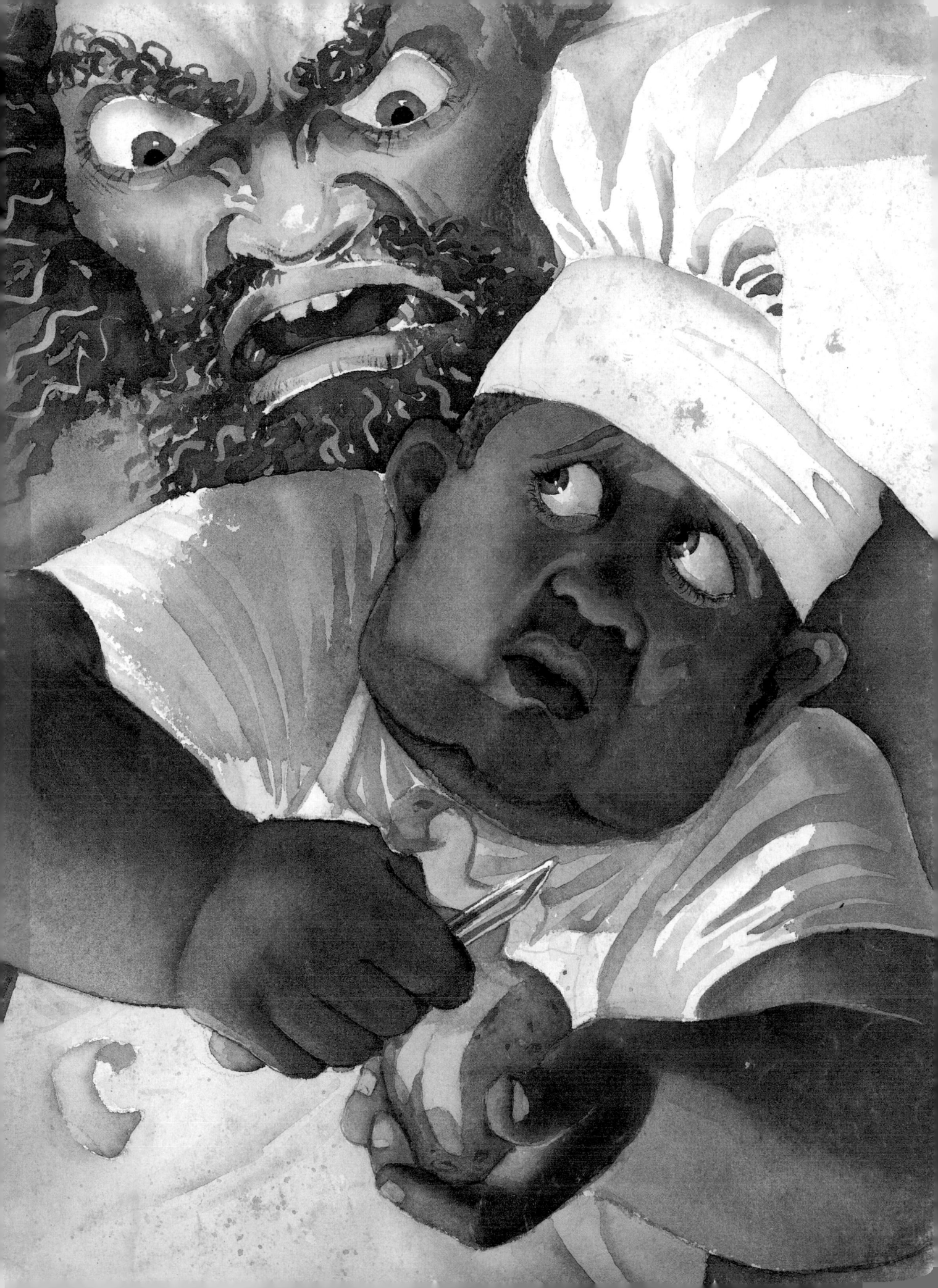

"MORE! MORE! MORE!" cried the ghost
as he wiped his plate clean.
"GIVE ME MORE FOOD RIGHT NOW!
I'M FEELING HUNGRY AND MEAN!"

Poor Dan cooked and cooked
until the pan was red-hot,
but that ghost kept eating
around the clock.
He ate fried chicken and pancakes,
squash and french fries,
heaps of vegetables, mounds of potatoes,
and six kinds of pies.
He ate spaghetti and corn bread
and dish after dish
of Dan's crispy, delicious,
batter-dipped fish.

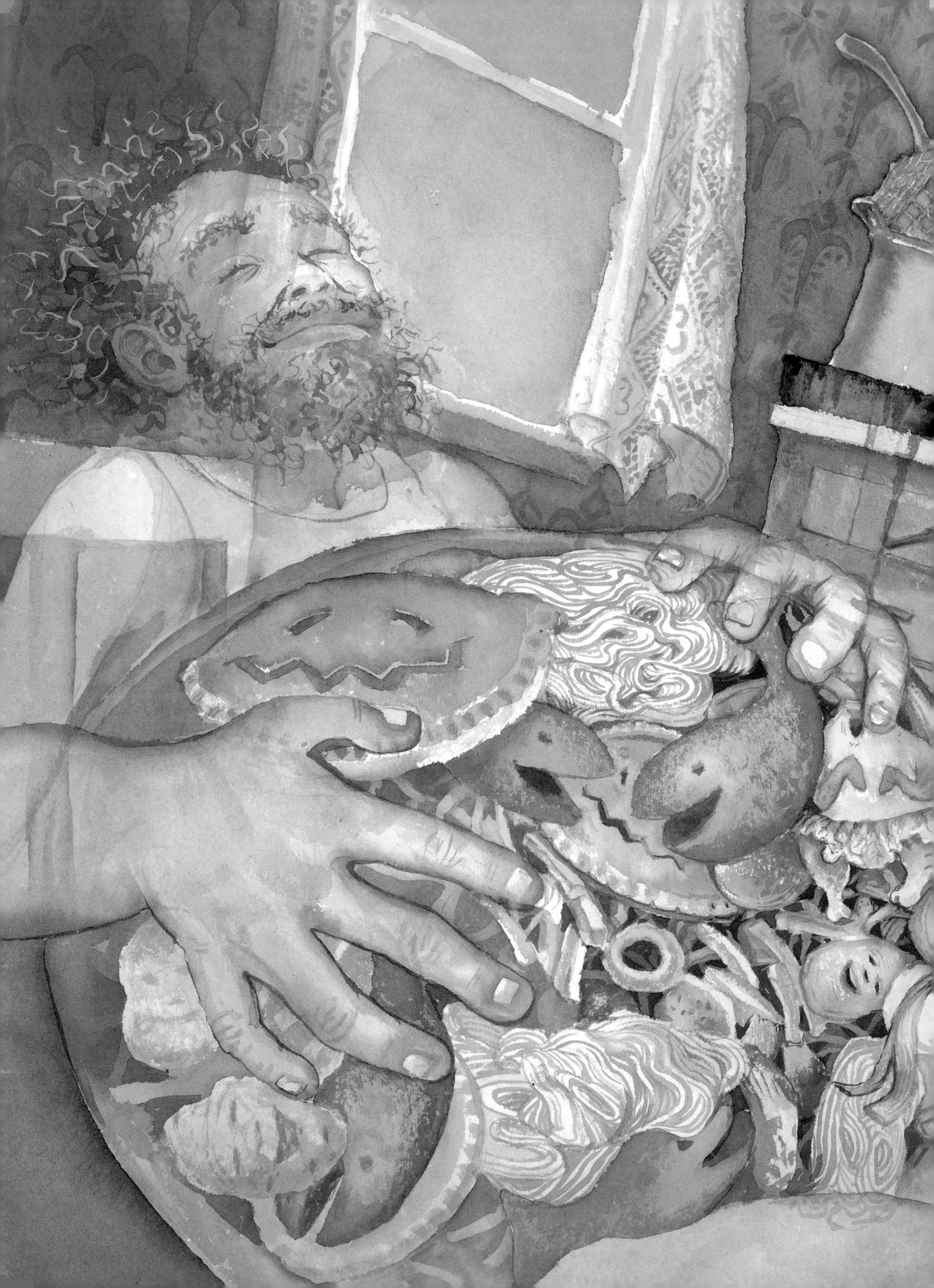

As the pale pink of morning
crept into the sky,
Old Sam rubbed his huge belly,
belched, and said with a sigh,
"I've been hungry for the last twenty years.
It's so hard to find a good meal around here.
I sure appreciate all the wonderful food.
I'd love to stay around here.
Is there something I can do?"

Dan thought awhile,
then he whispered in the ghost's ear.
When old Sam heard his request,
he moaned and trembled with fear.
"Oh well," said the ghost,
as he licked a few crumbs from a dish.
"I'll do anything
to get some more of that fish!"
Then, as the sun turned night into day,
the ghost grabbed a doughnut and faded away.

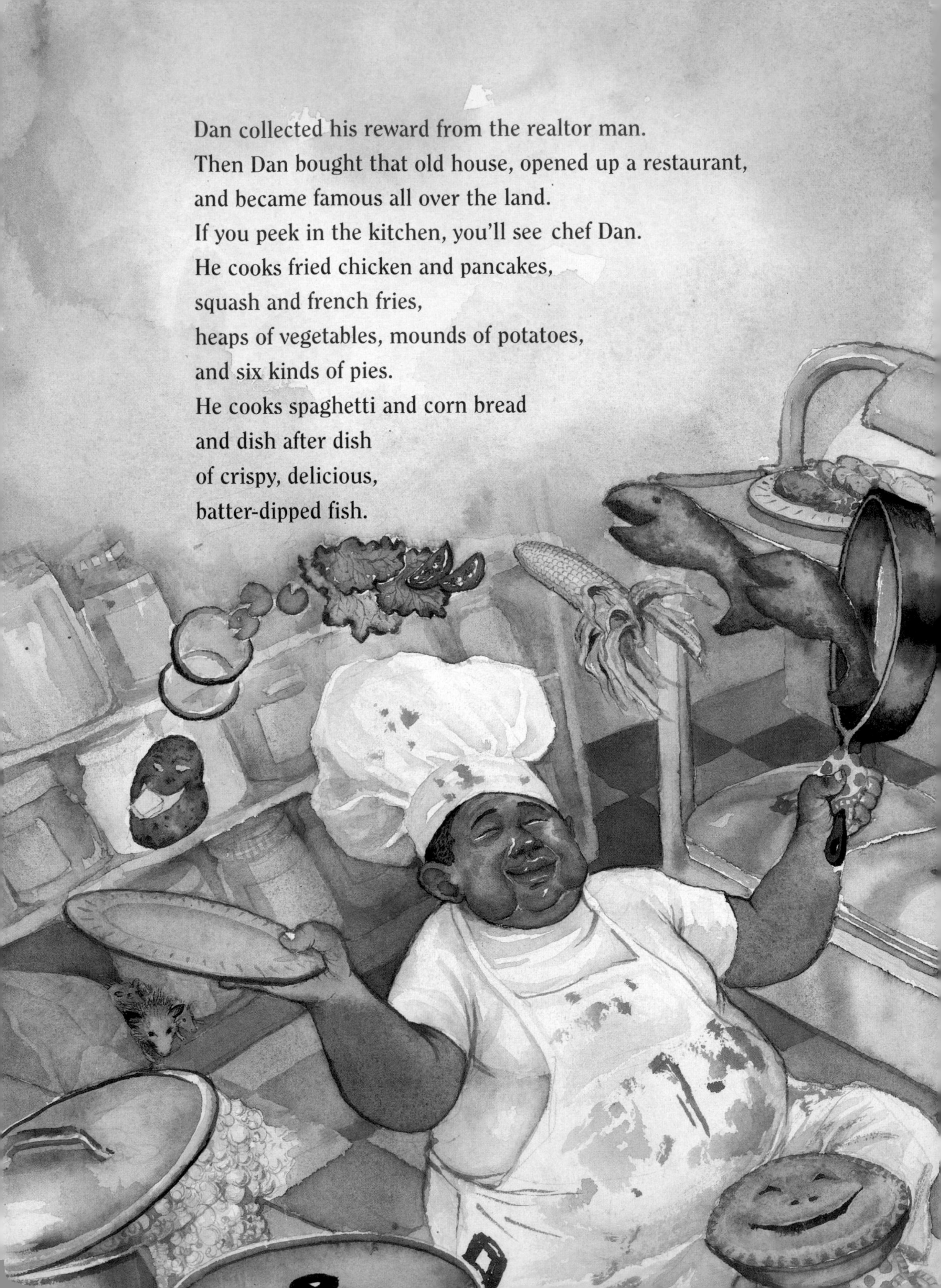

Dan collected his reward from the realtor man.
Then Dan bought that old house, opened up a restaurant,
and became famous all over the land.
If you peek in the kitchen, you'll see chef Dan.
He cooks fried chicken and pancakes,
squash and french fries,
heaps of vegetables, mounds of potatoes,
and six kinds of pies.
He cooks spaghetti and corn bread
and dish after dish
of crispy, delicious,
batter-dipped fish.

And over by the sink,
the ghost of Sifty Sifty Sam
is washing every messy pot, dish, and pan.
Dan never wanted to wash dishes again,
and he got his wish.

After old Sam has washed every last dish,
Dan rewards him with crispy, delicious,
batter-dipped fish.

HILLTOP ELEMENTARY SCHOOL

W9-CDI-457

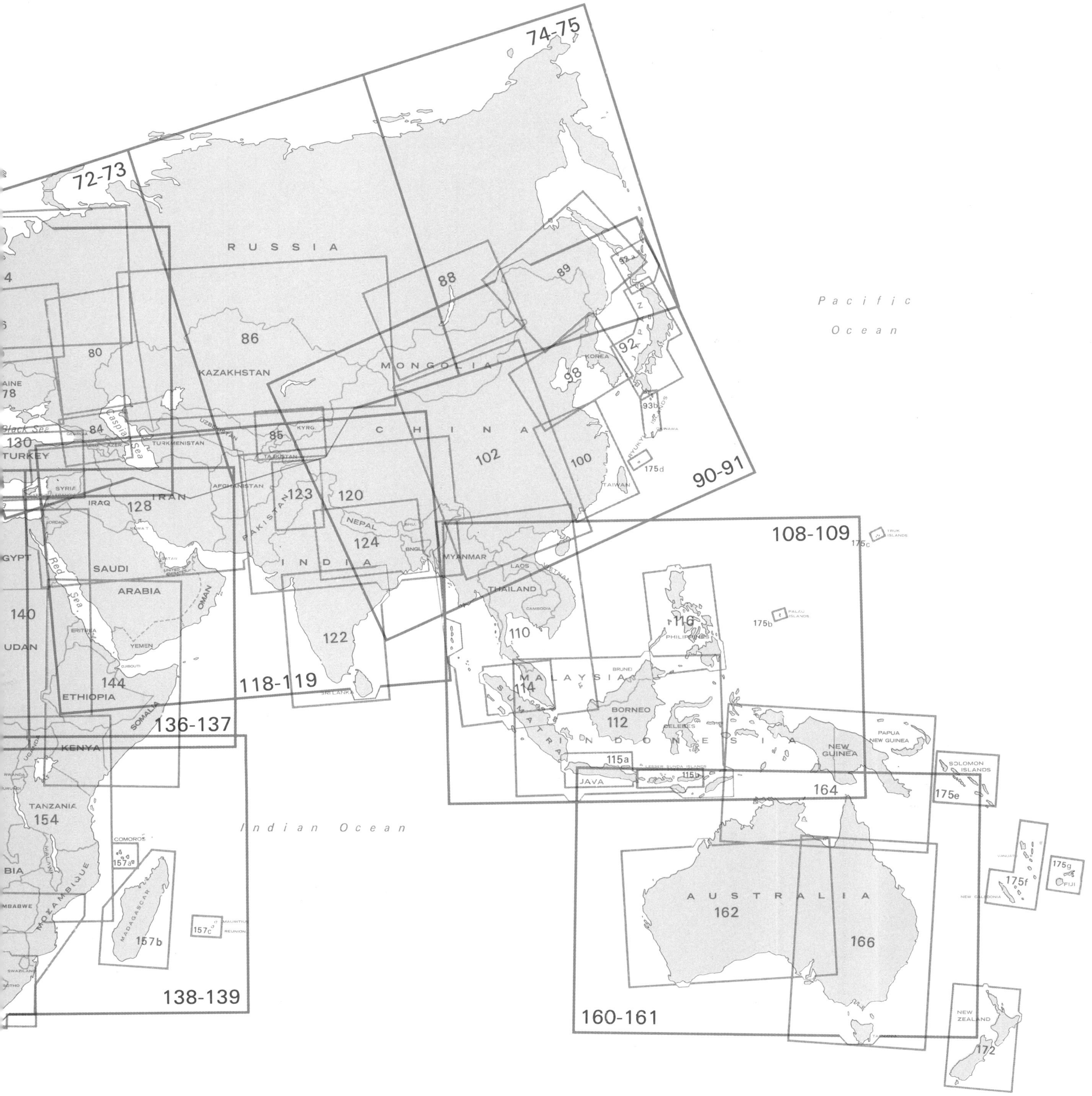

74-75

72-73

R U S S I A

4

88

89

92

80

86

Pacific

Ocean

KAZAKHSTAN

MONGOLIA

82

KOREA

130

84

85

KYRG

C H I N A

98

TURKEY

TURKMENISTAN

TAJIKISTAN

93b

90-91

TURKEY

IRAN

AFGHANISTAN

128

PAKISTAN

123

120

102

100

TAIWAN

175d

SYRIA

IRAQ

NEPAL

108-109

175c

EGYPT

SAUDI

Red Sea

ARABIA

OMAN

YEMEN

INDIA

124

BNGL

MYANMAR

LAOS

THAILAND

CAMBODIA

PALAU ISLANDS

116

175b

PHILIPPINES

140

122

118-119

SRI LANKA

110

UDAN

ERITREA

DJIBOUTI

114

SUMATRA

MALAYSIA

BRUNEI

144

ETHIOPIA

SOMALIA

136-137

112

BORNEO

CELEBES

I N D O N E S I A

PAPUA NEW GUINEA

KENYA

UGANDA

115a

NEW GUINEA

SOLOMON ISLANDS

TANZANIA

154

Indian Ocean

JAVA

115b

164

175e

COMOROS

157a

BIA

MBABWE

157b

157c

MADAGASCAR

MAURITIUS

REUNION

A U S T R A L I A

162

VANUATU

175f

175g

FIJI

NEW CALEDONIA

MOZAMBIQUE

166

LESOTHO

SWAZILAND

138-139

160-161

NEW ZEALAND

172

A-510000-964 -4 -6 -3 -21

Other features of the atlas

List of Places

The following list gives the location, by page number, at which the best-scale depiction of an entire country or its chief administrative subdivisions (for Australia, Canada, United Kingdom, and United States) can be found.

For complete listing of places, including such physical features as seas, mountain ranges, lakes, and rivers, see the SELECTED MAP REFERENCES, p. *xvi*.

Britannica Atlas

Encyclopædia Britannica, Inc.

CHICAGO

AUCKLAND • LONDON • MADRID • MANILA • PARIS

ROME • SEOUL • SYDNEY • TOKYO • TORONTO

INTERNATIONAL PLANNING CONFERENCE
INTERNATIONALE BERATER-KONFERENZ
CONFERENCIA INTERNACIONAL DE CONSULTORES
CONFÉRENCE INTERNATIONALE DE CONSEILLERS
CONFERÉNCIA INTERNACIONAL DE CONSULTORES

Dr. Manlio Castiglioni
Chief Editor, Touring Club Italiano, Milano
Dr. S. P. Chatterjee
Chairman (1970-1972), National Committee for Geography, India
Dr. Arch C. Gerlach
Chief Geographer, United States Geological Survey
Dr. Ir. Cornelis Koeman
Professor of Cartography, State University of Utrecht
Dr. André Libault
Department of Geography, Universidade de São Paulo
Brig. D. E. O. Thackwell
President (1964-1968), International Cartographic Association
Robert J. Voskuil
Adviser on Cartography, United States Department of State
Dr. Akira Watanabe
Chairman, National Committee of Geography, Science Council of Japan

CARTOGRAPHIC FIRMS
KARTOGRAPHISCHE FIRMEN
FIRMAS CARTOGRÁFICAS
MAISONS D'ÉDITIONS CARTOGRAPHIQUES
CASA DE EDIÇÕES CARTOGRÁPHICAS

RAND McNALLY & COMPANY, Chicago
  Russell L. Voisin, Vice-President, Cartography
  Jon M. Leverenz, Cartographic Editor
MONDADORI-McNALLY GmbH, Stuttgart
  Helmut Schaub, Cartographic Editor
CARTOGRAPHIA, Budapest
  Ervin Földi, Coordinator
ESSELTE MAP SERVICE, Stockholm
  Gösta Lundqvist General Supervisor
  Paul R. Kraske, Head of Editorial Staff
GEORGE PHILIP & SON LIMITED, London
  Harold Fullard, Director and Cartographic Editor
TEIKOKU-SHOIN CO., LTD., Tokyo
  Kimio Moriya, General Supervisor

MAP ADVISERS
KARTOGRAPHISCHE BERATER
CONSEJEROS CARTOGRÁFICOS
CONSEILLERS CARTOGRAPHES
CONSELHEIROS CARTOGRÁFICOS

Europe
Prof. Dr. Emil Meynen
Direktor des Instituts für Landeskunde, Bonn

Prof. Sándor Radó
Director, Department of Cartography, National Office of Lands and Mapping, Budapest

Dr. Hisashi Sato
Science Faculty, Geographical Institute, Tokyo University

Australia
Prof. R. O. Buchanan
Professor Emeritus, London School of Economics and Political Science, University of London

Anglo-America
Dr. Arch C. Gerlach
Chief Geographer, United States Geological Survey

Latin America
Dr. André Libault
Department of Geography, Universidade de São Paulo

Dra. Consuelo Soto Mora
Directora del Instituto de Geografía, Universidad Nacional Autónoma de México

Dr. Jorge A. Vivó Escoto
Centro de Investigaciones Geográficas, Facultad de Filosofía y Letras, Universidad Nacional de México

Metropolitan Area Maps
Prof. Harold M. Mayer
Department of Geography, University of Wisconsin, Milwaukee

World Scene
Prof. Norton S. Ginsburg,
Prof. Chauncy D. Harris,
Prof. Marvin W. Mikesell
Department of Geography, University of Chicago

CONTRIBUTORS—WORLD SCENE
MITARBEITER—WELT-PANORAMA
COLABORADORES—PERSPECTIVA DEL MUNDO
COLLABORATEURS—LE MONDE AUJOURD'HUI
COLABORADORES—PERSPECTIVA DO MUNDO

Robert C. Bergstrom
Department of Geology-Geography, Morton College, Cicero, Illinois

Nathaniel B. Guyol
Consulting Economist on Energy, Interenergie, San Rafael, California

Prof. Edwin H. Hammond
Department of Geography, University of Tennessee, Knoxville

Robert D. Hodgson
The Geographer (1970-1979), United States Department of State

Prof. A. W. Küchler
Department of Geography-Meteorology, The University of Kansas

Prof. G. Etzel Pearcy
Department of Geography, California State College, Los Angeles

Prof. David E. Sopher
Department of Geography, Syracuse University

Prof. Richard S. Thoman
Department of Geography, California State University, Hayward

Mrs. Evelyn Z. Thoman

Dr. William Van Royen
Director, Division of Environmental Sciences, United States Army Research Office, Durham, North Carolina

Prof. Philip L. Wagner
Department of Geography, Simon Fraser University, British Columbia

Maps for the World Scene were designed especially for *Encyclopædia Britannica* by David L. Burke

EDITORS
HERAUSGEBER
REDACTORES
ÉDITEURS
EDITORES

William A. Cleveland
  Editor

Staff:
Sujata Banerjee
David I. Gandolfo
Rosaline Jackson Keys
W. Peter Kindel
Stephen Neher
Marino P. PeBenito
Joseph R. Sturgis
Edward F. Vowell

ENCYCLOPÆDIA BRITANNICA, INC.

Peter B. Norton, *President and Chief Executive Officer*
Joseph J. Esposito, *President, Encyclopædia Britannica North America*
Robert McHenry, *Editor in Chief*
Karen M. Barch, *Executive Vice President, Operations*
Elizabeth O'Connor, *Executive Director, Finance and Operations*
Anne Long Dimopoulos, *Director, Editorial Development*

Foreword

Throughout history, educators have pointed out that a deep gulf may separate knowledge of something from the understanding of it. The *Britannica Atlas* presents the latest facts about the present-day world at the same time that it attempts to add substantially to man's understanding of it. To produce a work that may give a reader this deeper insight, the editors have departed from traditional atlas-making in two important particulars: (1) greater internationalism of content and (2) complete comparability among the maps.

Internationalism: Too often an atlas will cater to local prejudices and tastes. To avoid this pitfall, the publishers of this atlas—Encyclopædia Britannica, Inc., and Rand McNally & Company—assured the truly international character of the content at the earliest planning stage by inviting a group of eminent scholars and cartographic houses from various parts of the world to participate in the work. The original planning group included members from France, Germany, India, Italy, Japan, the Netherlands, Sweden, the United Kingdom, and the United States. Actual compilation of the maps was carried out in six countries—Germany, Hungary, Japan, Sweden, the United Kingdom, and the United States.

In keeping with the international outlook of the atlas, the metric system of measurement has been used throughout the reference maps, rather than the British-U.S. system. Map scales and elevation and depth scales on the map pages are given in both systems of measurement. In the Legend to Maps meter-foot and kilometer-mile equivalents are given.

Most of the atlas carries parallel texts in English, German, Spanish, French, and Portuguese. Names of inhabited places and of physical features situated within the boundaries of one country appear on the maps in the local language; where space permits, the English alternate also is given if the local name is likely to be unfamiliar. The names of countries are in English, because some country names are extremely unfamiliar in the local language—Druk-Yul (Bhutan), Magyarország (Hungary), Nihon (Japan). On the larger-scale maps, however, the local form of a country name is shown also. The names of large bodies of water, mountain ranges, and other major physical features that extend across international boundaries are given in English on smaller-scale maps, but on large-scale maps both the English and local forms will be found. In transliterating place names into English from languages not written in the roman alphabet, every effort has been made to use internationally accepted systems of transliteration.

Geographical terms such as lake, mountain, island, etc., appear on the maps in the local language. Five-language glossaries of selected terms used on a map are printed in the margins of most pages, and a glossary of all terms appears on pages 289-295.

In the index, symbols are given with all entries except those naming cities or towns, to aid in identifying the features, e.g., ∧ for mountain, ≻ for cape, ≃ for river. The symbols represent graphically the broad categories of the features named. A five-language key at the bottom of the index pages associates each symbol with the class of terms it represents.

The World Scene is a separate section of topical maps. These maps summarize in cartographic form the patterns of man's physical environment and some of his more important economic activities, political alignments, and cultural distributions. Several maps are concerned with recent political history. In the maps that show climate, surface configurations, soils, natural vegetation, and drainage, the reader may identify the influence of the natural habitat on human settlement and activity.

Finally, the effort to ensure the international character of the atlas is manifest in the balanced coverage of the world's regions. The *Britannica Atlas* allots to each region of the world a map coverage that takes into account the region's economic and cultural significance, its population, and its surface area. Aproximately two-thirds of the map pages are devoted to Anglo-America, Asia, and Europe, and about one-third to Africa, Australia/Oceania, Latin America, and the former Soviet Union. A world map on pp. xiv-xv has blocked out on it the areas and page numbers of the various maps.

Comparability. All atlases have attempted, with varying degrees of success, to use uniform map scales wherever practical. This atlas has been prepared with a minimal number of map scales, selected to permit valid areal comparisons between all parts of the earth. At the beginning of the atlas there appear political and physical maps of the world at 1:75,000,000, maps of the oceans at 1:48,000,000, and relief maps of the continents at 1:24,000,000. Next, the major world regions are uniformly presented at 1:12,000,000 (190 miles to the inch).

Virtually the entire land area of the earth is portrayed again, in sections, at one of two larger scales. The less densely populated regions are at 1:6,000,000 (95 miles to the inch), and Europe, most of North America, and the most densely populated sections of South and East Asia are at 1:3,000,000 (47 miles to the inch). The 1:3,000,000 and 1:6,000,000 series are thoroughly comparable with one another. Both indicate the chief natural and man-made features of each region, showing elevations, rivers, major railroads and airports, two classes of highways, and even selected offshore water depths.

Finally, the scale of 1:1,000,000 (16 miles to the inch) has been used in presenting 50 key regions of the continents characterized by exceptional economic importance, high concentration of population, complexity of transportation development, or some combination of these. This scale is unusually large for a general atlas, and is ordinarily reserved for small inset maps dealing with special subjects. Its use in this atlas permits the inclusion of a multitude of place names and many other local details such as waterfalls, ruins, parks, bird and wildlife sanctuaries, shipyards, military installations, dams, and reservoirs.

At the back of the atlas is a 29-page section of 60 maps of the world's major urban centers, all at a scale of 1:300,000 (just under 5 miles to the inch). These maps display the land-use patterns and other local features of great metropolitan agglomerations. Nearly all of the most populous world metropolitan areas are shown, and a number of smaller but important areas are also included. Grouping these metropolitan maps in a separate section following the regional maps facilitates comparison between them and avoids interrupting continuity of the regional maps.

The arrangement of the maps is such that the reader gets a progressively more detailed, but always comparable, view of the earth's surface. There is first a global view of the world and of the oceans, then an overall survey of the continents, shown in hemispheres or quadrants of the earth. There follows a closer view of all regions within the continents, in maps that are primarily political. The regions are next shown in sections at a larger scale, with emphasis on the relationships between physical and cultural features. At a still larger scale, the cultural features of densely populated areas are shown in great detail. Finally, the close-up maps of cities and their environs include even more detail. A three-page Legend to Maps appears on pp. x-xii.

Collection and analysis of the map data have benefited from the recent accelerated progress in aerial and satellite surveying, radar and sonar technology, and electronic data processing. The shaded relief technique was used to give the maps the effect of a third dimension. All the resources of modern graphic arts were utilized to give form to the editorial plan.

Vorwort

Pädagogen haben schon immer darauf hingewiesen, dass blosses Wissen und wahres Verstehen zwei ganz verschiedene Dinge sein können. Der *Britannica Atlas* nun versucht, nicht nur die letzten Errungenschaften der Wissenschaft darzulegen, sondern auch das Verständnis der Welt bedeutend zu vertiefen. Um dem Leser diesen tieferen Einblick zu gewähren, sind die Herausgeber von der beim Zusammenstellen von Atlanten üblichen Methode in zwei wichtigen Punkten abgegangen: sie haben erstens einen grösseren Internationalismus des Inhalts, zweitens eine vollkommene Vergleichbarkeit der einzelnen Karten untereinander angestrebt.

Internationalismus. Es geschieht allzu oft, dass ein Atlas national und provinziell anmutet. Um dies zu vermeiden, haben die Verleger des vorliegenden Atlasses—Encyclopædia Britannica, Inc., und Rand McNally & Company—den internationalen Charakter des Inhalts dadurch gewährleistet, dass sie eminente Wissenschaftler und kartographische Firmen aus aller Welt von Anfang an mit dem Unternehmen assoziiert haben. Die ursprüngliche Planungsgruppe zählte Mitglieder aus Frankreich, Deutschland, Indien, Italien, Japan, den Niederlanden, Schweden, Grossbritannien und den Vereinigten Staaten. Zusammengestellt wurden die Karten in sechs Ländern: in Deutschland, Ungarn, Japan, Schweden, Grossbritannien und in den Vereinigten Staaten.

Das metrische und nicht das angelsächsische Masssystem wird in den Karten benutzt. Die Massstäbe der Karten sowie die Farbskalen für Höhen und Tiefen am Rand jeder Karte werden in beiden Masssystemen angeführt. In die Zeichenerklärung wird die Gleichwertigkeit zwischen Metern und "feet" sowie zwischen Kilometern und Meilen gegeben.

Fast alle Texte des Atlasses sind zugleich in Englisch, Deutsch, Spanisch, Französisch und Portugiesisch gedruckt. Die Namen bewohnter Orte und physischer Gepräge, die innerhalb der Grenzen eines Staates liegen, erscheinen auf den Karten in der Landessprache; wo es der Platz erlaubte, ist der englische Name dann hinzugefügt, wenn der landessprachliche wahrscheinlich unbekannt ist. Die Namen der Länder werden in Englisch wiedergegeben, da manche Ländernamen in ihrer landessprachlichen Form überhaupt nicht geläufig sind—Druk-Yul (Bhutan), Magyarország (Ungarn), Nihon (Japan). Auf den Karten in grösserem Massstab findet sich jedoch auch die lokale Form eines Ländernamens. Die Namen grosser Gewässer, die Namen von Gebirgen und anderen grösseren physischen Geprägen, die sich über das Gebiet mehrerer Staaten erstrecken, sind auf den Karten in kleinerem Massstab nur auf Englisch eingezeichnet, auf den Karten in grösserem Massstab ist jedoch die landessprachliche Form hinzugefügt. Viel Mühe wurde darauf verwendet, international anerkannte Transliterationssysteme zu benutzen, um Ortsnamen aus Sprachen mit nichtlateinischen Schriftzeichen in Englisch wiederzugeben.

Geographische Begriffe wie See, Berg, Insel usw, sind auf den Karten in der Landessprache gedruckt. Am Rand der meisten Karten befinden sich fünfsprachige Glossare der wichtigsten Begriffe, die in den Karten vorkommen. Ein Verzeichnis aller Begriffe ist auf den Seiten 289-295.

Neben allen Namen, die im Register enthalten sind, ausgenommen Grossstädte und Städte, steht das entsprechende Symbol, das jeden Namen einer physischen Gegebenheit zuordnet: z.B. ∧ für Berg, ≻ für Kap, ≃ für Fluss. Die Symbole drücken in graphischer Form die Kategorien für die genannten physischen Gegebenheiten aus. Am Fuss der Registerseite befindet sich ein fünfsprachiges Verzeichnis, in dem jedes Symbol dem Begriff zugeordnet wird, den es darstellt.

Das World Scene (Welt-Panorama) ist eine besondere Reihe von thematischen Karten. Diese Karten stellen in kartographischer Weise die Gebilde der natürlichen Umgebung des Menschen dar. Sie zeigen ausserdem einige der bedeutenderen Wirtschaftsformen, politischen Verbände und Kulturgruppen. Die Reihe enthält einige Karten zur politischen Geschichte der jüngsten Vergangenheit. Mit Hilfe der Karten über Klima, Oberflächenformen, Bodenarten, natürliche Vegetation und Entwässerung kann der Leser den Einfluss der natürlichen Umbebung des Menschen auf menschliche Siedlungsformen und Tätigkeiten feststellen. Für diese Kartenreihe wurden die modernsten Informationen verwendet, die erhältlich waren.

Schliesslich zeigt die Auswahl der Karten das Bemühen um den internationalen Charakter des Atlasses. Der Kartenanteil, den der *Britannica Atlas* jeder Region einräumt, beachtet die ökonomische und kulturelle Bedeutung des Gebietes, seine Bevölkerungszahl und die Grösse des Territoriums. Ungefähr zwei Drittel der Kartenseiten stellen Anglo-Amerika, Asien und Europa dar, ungefähr ein Drittel Afrika, Australien/Ozeanien, Latein-Amerika und die ehemalige Sowjetunion. Auf den Seiten xiv-xv sind die Gebiete und Seitenzahlen der verschiedenen Karten auf einer Erdkarte skizziert.

Vergleichsmöglichkeiten. Mit unterschiedlichem Erfolg haben alle Atlanten versucht, wo es praktisch erschien, einheitliche Massstäbe für Karten zu verwenden. Dieser Atlas gebraucht eine sehr geringe Zahl von Massstäben, um fundierte Vergleiche zwischen Gebieten aus allen Teilen der Erde zu ermöglichen. Am Anfang des Atlasses stehen politische und physische Erdkarten im Massstab 1:75 000 000, Ozeankarten im Massstab 1:48 000 000 und Reliefkarten der Erdteile im Massstab 1:24 000 000. Als nächstes werden die Hauptgebiete der Erde alle im Massstab 1:12 000 000 (1 cm = 120 km) dargestellt.

Fast das gesamte Landgebiet der Erde wird in Ausschnitten in einem der beiden grösseren Massstäbe dargestellt. Die weniger dicht besiedelten Gebiete der Erde werden in 1:6 000 000 (1 cm = 60 km) abgebildet; Europa, der grösste Teil Nordamerikas und die am dichtesten besiedelten Regionen von Süd- und Ostasien werden in 1:3 000 000 (1 cm = 30 km) dargestellt. Diese beiden Kartenreihen sind miteinander vollständig vergleichbar. Beide Reihen stellen die wichtigsten natürlichen Gebilde und die von Menschenhand ausgeführten Konstruktionen jeder Region dar sowie Erhebungen, Flüsse, grössere Eisenbahnlinien und Flughäfen, zwei Klassen von Autostrassen und sogar manche Meerestiefen.

Der Massstab 1:1 000 000 (1 cm = 10 km) wird schliesslich verwendet, um 50 Schlüsselgebiete darzustellen, die eine oder mehrere der folgenden Besonderheiten zeigen: ausserordentliche wirtschaftliche Bedeutung, dichte Besiedlung und Komplexität des Verkehrsnetzes. Dieser Massstab ist für einen allgemeinen Atlas ungewöhnlich gross und ist normalerweise nur für kleine Nebenkarten reserviert, die spezielle Themen darstellen. Er wird jedoch in diesem Atlas verwendet, um viele Ortsnamen verzeichnen zu können sowie andere lokale Einzelheiten, z.B. Wasserfälle, Ruinen, Naturschutzgebiete, Werften, Militäranlagen, Talsperren und Wasserreservoirs.

Am Schluss des Kartenteils dieses Atlasses befindet sich eine Reihe von 60 Karten, die auf 29 Seiten im Massstab 1:300 000 (1 cm = 3 km) die grössten städtischen Siedlungsgebiete der Erde abbilden. Diese Karten zeigen die Bodennutzung und andere örtliche Gebilde innerhalb der Stadtregionen. Die meist besiedelten Stadtregionen der

Erde sind fast alle abgebildet sowie auch eine Anzahl kleinerer und dennoch wichtiger Stadtregionen. Die Zusammenfassung dieser Stadtregionen in einem besonderen Kartenteil erleichtert den Vergleich zwischen ihnen, ausserdem wird die Folge der Regionalkarten nicht unterbrochen.

Die Karten sind so angeordnet, dass der Leser eine fortschreitend detailliertere, aber immer vergleichbare Ansicht der Erdoberfläche bekommt, Zuerst findet er eine globale Darstellung der Welt und der Ozeane, dann eine allgemeine Übersicht der Erdteile, die in Hemisphären oder Quadranten der Erde gezeigt werden. Darauf folgt eine detailliertere Darstellung aller Regionen jedes Erdteils auf Karten, die vorwiegend politisch sind. In grösserem Massstab werden danach die Regionen in Ausschnitten abgebildet, wobei die Beziehungen zwischen physischen und kulturellen Gebieten betont werden. In noch grösserem Massstab wird sehr detailliert das kulturelle Gepräge dicht besiedelter Gebiete vorgeführt. Schliesslich gibt die Kartenreihe der Städte und ihrer Umgebungen eine noch mehr in Einzelheiten gehende Darstellung. Die Zeichenerklärung ist auf den Seiten x-xii zu finden.

Sammlung und Analyse der Karteninformation hat von dem rapiden Fortschritt in der Technik der Luft- und Satellitenaufnahmen, in der Radar-und Sonartechnik und in der elektronischen Datenverarbeitung profitiert. Die sogenannte Schummerungstechnik, die den Karten einen dreidimensionalen Effekt gibt, wurde verwand. Alle Mittel der modernen Graphik wurden gebraucht, um dem Plan der Herausgeber Gestalt zu verleihen.

Prefacio

A través de la historia, los pedagogos han sabido muy bien, que el mero conocimiento y el legítimo entendimiento son conceptos que, pueden hallarse separados por un verdadero abismo. Una simple acumulación de datos muy bien puede resultar de escaso valor si el significado de los mismos y su interrelación no se comprenden plenamente.

Además de reflejar los últimos conocimientos que nos ofrece la ciencia, el *Britannica Atlas* tiene por meta el incrementar sustancialmente el grado de comprensión con que el hombre moderno mira a su mundo. Para lograr este fin, los editores se han apartado del curso tradicional en dos importantes sentidos: (1) más internacionalismo en cuanto al contenido y (2) una paridad metódica en el diseño de los mapas que permite su mejor comparación.

Internacionalismo. Frecuentemente, muchos atlas, tratan de satisfacer gustos y prejuicios locales. Para evitar esto, los responsables de la creación de esta obra—Encyclopædia Britannica, Inc., y Rand McNally & Company—desde un principio aseguraron el carácter verdaderamente internacional de su contenido al invitar a un grupo de eminentes geógrafos y firmas cartográficas de distintas partes del mundo a colaborar en su preparación. El grupo que participó en el proyecto original quedó constituido por representantes de Francia, Alemania, India, Italia, Japón, los Países Bajos, Suecia, el Reino Unido y los Estados Unidos de Norteamérica. La realización de los mapas en sí tuvo lugar en seis países—Alemania, Hungría, Japón, Suecia, el Reino Unido y los Estados Unidos de Norteamérica.

El sistema métrico ha sido usado en todos los mapas topográficos, en lugar del sistema anglo-norteamericano de medidas. Las escalas horizontales y las escalas verticales (alturas y profundidades) en las páginas de mapas se expresan en ambos sistemas, y en la Leyenda para los Mapas se ofrecen las equivalencias metro-pie y kilómetro-milla.

El inglés, el alemán, el español, el francés y el portugués se utilizan paralelamente en la mayor parte de la obra. Los nombres de los lugares habitados y de los accidentes geográficos situados dentro de los límites de un país dado se escriben en la lengua local; de permitirlo el espacio disponible, también se da el equivalente inglés si el nombre local no es fácilmente reconocible. Los nombres de los países se dan en inglés, puesto que algunos son muy difíciles de identificar si se expresan en el idioma local—Druk-Yul (Bhután), Magyarország (Hungría), Nihon (Japón). Ahora bien, en los mapas a mayor escala la forma local del nombre del país también se expresa. En cuanto a los nombres de grandes mares o lagos, cordilleras, u otros accidentes mayores que se extienden a través de las fronteras internacionales, éstos se dan en inglés en los mapas a escala reducida, y tanto en las formas locales como en inglés, en los mapas a mayor escala. A los efectos de "trasliterar" al inglés los nombres de lugares cuyas grafías originales no se escriben por medio del alfabeto latino, se ha puesto el mayor esfuerzo en seguir la guía de los sistemas de "trasliteración" más aceptados internacionalmente.

Términos geográficos tales como lago, monte, isla, etc., aparecen en los mapas en el idioma local. Sobre los márgenes de la mayor parte de las páginas se hallarán glosarios en cinco idiomas que incluyen la mayoría de las voces utilizadas en cada mapa, y en las páginas 289-295 se incluye un glosario completo.

Todas las entradas del índice, a excepción de las ciudades o poblaciones, van acompañadas de un símbolo gráfico que las identifica a primera vista como nombre de, v. gr., montaña ∧, cabo ≻, río ≃, etc. Y al pie de cada página del índice se hallará una clave en cinco idiomas en la que se equiparan los símbolos con las amplias categorías de accidentes geográficos que representan.

La World Scene (Perspectiva del Mundo) constituye una sección aparte dedicada a mapas especializados. Estos mapas compendian cartográficamente el medio físico en que habita la humanidad, y algunas de sus actividades económicas, alineamientos políticos y aspectos culturales más importantes. Varios de los mapas se ocupan de la historia política más reciente. En los mapas que se ocupan de aspectos de geografía física tales como la distribución de climas, las estructuras geológicas, los suelos, la flora, el régimen de vertientes, podrá el lector observar la influencia que sobre el asiento de las comunidades humanas y sus actividades ha tenido el medio físico.

Por último, *Britannica Atlas* pone de manifiesto el esfuerzo de asegurarle a la obra su carácter internacional cubriendo de forma equilibrada todas las regiones del mundo. Provee un mapa que abarca todas las regiones a nivel mundial, cuyo contenido toma en cuenta la importancia de su situación económica, demográfica y cultural además de sus dimensiones territoriales. La América Latina junto con África, Australia/Oceanía y la ex-Unión Soviética comprenden una tercera parte de los mapas; el resto es dedicado a la América anglosajona, Asia y Europa. Véase el mapamundi en las paginas *xiv-xv*, en el cual se han trazado las zonas, e indicado los folios a que corresponden los distintos mapas.

Paridad de escalas. Todos los atlas intentan, con mayor o menor éxito, y siempre que sea práctico, utilizar escalas uniformes. En este atlas se ha utilizado el mínimo posible de escalas, y éstas se han escogido de manera que permitan la comparación entre todas las porciones de la tierra en cuanto a su extensión superficial. En la sección inicial aparecen varios grandes mapas: mapamundis con información política y fisiográfica, a una escala de 1:75 000 000; mapas oceánicos, a 1:48 000 000; y mapas topográficos de los continentes, a 1:24 000 000. Seguidamente se agrupan las principales regiones del mundo, a una escala uniforme de 1:12 000 000 (o sea, cada centímetro corresponde a 120 kilómetros).

El resto de la superficie terrestre, en su casi totalidad, queda representado, por secciones, a base de una u otra de dos escales mayores. La de 1:6 000 000 (60 kms. por cm.) se aplica a las regiones menos pobladas, y la de 1:3 000 000 (30 kms. por cm.), a Europa, casi toda la América del Norte y las regiones más densamente pobladas del Asia meridional y del extremo Oriente. Las dos series son perfectamente comparables entre sí, pues ambas indican los principales rasgos de cada región, tanto naturales como artificales, tales como las cumbres más elevadas, las corrientes fluviales, los principales aeropuertos y vías ferroviarias, dos tipos de carreteras, y aun profundidades marinas representativas.

Por último, la escala de 1:1 000 000 (10 kms. por cm.) se ha destinado a la representación de 50 regiones estratégicas, escogidas atendiendo a su excepcional importancia económica, su gran densidad de población, la complejidad de sus redes de communicaciones, o alguna combinación de estos factores. Esta escala es mucho mayor de la que se acostumbra utilizar en atlas generales, y a lo sumo se reserva para pequeños recuadros especializados que se insertan dentro del marco de mapas mayores. Su uso en esta obra permite abundar en una verdadera riqueza de detalles—saltos de agua, restos arqueológicos, parques forestales y santuarios de flora y fauna, astilleros, instalaciones militares, presas y embalses, además de muchas poblaciones.

Al final de la obra hay una sección de 29 páginas que contiene 60 planos de los principales complejos urbanos, trazados todos a una escala de 1:300 000 (tres kms. por cm.). En estos mapas se muestran, entre otras, las características demográfico-territoriales de las grandes aglomeraciones urbanas. Casi todas las metrópolis más populosas de la Tierra están representadas, así como algunas menores pero realmente importantes. Estos mapas se han agrupado al final del atlas a fin de facilitar la comparación entre sí y para no interrumpir la continuidad de los mapas regionales.

Los mapas están ordenados de modo que el lector vaya obteniendo progresivamente imágenes cada vez más detalladas, si bien siempre comparables de la superficie terrestre. Primero, la visión global del mundo y sus océanos; seguidamente, una visión panorámica de los continentes, mostrados en sus respectivos hemisferios o cuadrantes terrestres. A continuación, la vista más cercana de todas las regiones dentro de los continentes, con énfasis principalmente político. Después, las subregiones, a mayor escala, con énfasis principalmente en las relaciones entre los rasgos físicos y los culturales. A escala aun mayor, se muestran en gran detalle los rasgos culturales de las zonas densamente pobladas. Y por último, los planos de las ciudades y sus alrededores, que incluyen aun más detalles. La sección denominada Leyenda para los Mapas ocupa las tres páginas x a xii.

La compilación y el análisis de datos cartográficos se han beneficiado con el reciente y aceleradísimo progreso logrado en las técnicas del reconocimiento aéreo, y del efectuado por medio de satélites, del radar o del sonar, así como del procesamiento de datos por medios electrónicos. Se ha aprovechado plenamente el sombreado al relieve, que produce un efecto tridimensional en el mapa forzosamente plano de un atlas. Todos los más modernos recursos de las artes gráficas se han puesto en juego al estructurar el plan editorial.

Avant-propos

Tout au long de l'histoire, les éducateurs ont déploré le fossé profond qui sépare trop souvent le savoir accumulatif de la compréhension. Aussi *Britannica Atlas* ne se contente-t-il pas de rassembler les connaissances les plus récentes concernant la physionomie de la planète; il s'efforce d'élargir la compréhension qu'acquiert l'homme du monde au sein duquel il vit. Afin de dégager pour le lecteur le sens intime des faits, les éditeurs se sont écartés des méthodes traditionnelles: (1) par la présentation d'un contenu plus largement international; (2) en proposant une systématique complète de comparaison entre les cartes.

Caractère international. On constate souvent qu'en s'inspirant d'un certain esprit de clocher, tel atlas en arrive à ne plus guère refléter que les vues d'un nationalisme étriqué. Soucieux d'éviter cet écueil, c'est d'entrée de jeu que les éditeurs ont tenu à affirmer le caractère fondamentalement international du nouvel ouvrage. D'éminents spécialistes et plusieurs maisons d'éditions cartographiques du monde entier ont été invités à collaborer à cette œuvre. Des personnalités d'Allemagne, des États-Unis, de France, de Grande-Bretagne, de l'Inde, d'Italie, du Japon, des Pays-Bas et de Suède ont formé le groupe initial. Les documents cartographiques proviennent de six pays: l'Allemagne, les États-Unis, la Grande-Bretagne, la Hongrie, le Japon et la Suède.

On a utilisé dans l'ensemble des cartes les unités de mesure du système métrique de préférence à leurs équivalents anglo-américains. Toutefois, les échelles des cartes et les échelles altimétriques et bathymétriques sont indiquées dans les deux systèmes, métrique et anglo-américain. On trouvera, dans la légende des cartes, les rapports respectifs du mètre et du pied, du kilomètre et du mille.

La plupart des textes de l'Atlas sont présentés en cinq langues: anglais, allemand, espagnol, français et portugais. Les noms de lieux et de particularités géographiques sont, pour chaque pays, transcrits dans leur forme locale. Néanmoins, chaque fois que celle-ci risquait de paraître insolite, on l'a complétée par la variante anglaise pour autant que le permettait l'échelle de la carte. En ce qui concerne les noms de pays, on a eu recours à l'anglais, la version locale de certains d'entre eux risquant de demeurer hermétique au lecteur. Tel est le cas de Magyarország (Hongrie), Nihon (Japon) et Druk-Yul (Bhoutan). Cependant, les noms locaux apparaissent aussi sur les cartes à grande échelle. Dans le cas des océans, des

chaînes de montagnes et des autres unités géographiques qui ignorent les frontières politiques, les cartes à petite échelle ne font état que de la seule appellation anglaise, tandis que les projections à grande échelle comportent les deux versions, locale et anglaise. La transcription correspondant à la graphie et à la phonétique anglaises de caractères étrangers à l'alphabet romain a été établie avec le souci de respecter au plus près les systèmes de translittération internationalement reconnus.

On a conservé leur forme locale aux termes génériques s'appliquant à des unités géographiques telles que lac, montagne, île. C'est pourquoi des glossaires succincts en cinq langues figurent en marge de la grande majorité des cartes. En outre, ces renseignements sont complétés aux pages 289-295 par un lexique exhaustif.

Exception faite pour les noms de villes, tous les mots figurant à l'index sont identifiés à l'aide de signes conventionnels représentant graphiquement les traits évocateurs des catégories considérées; c'est ainsi qu'on trouvera Λ pour montagne, ≻ pour cap, ≏ pour rivière. Une clé de cinq langues rappelle, en bas des pages d'index, la classe des termes associés à chaque signe conventionnel utilisé.

Une section séparée, intitulée World Scene (Le Monde Aujourd'hui), contient une série de cartes thématiques. Ces cartes présentent synthétiquement les différents types d'environnement physique auxquels l'homme se trouve associé et quelques-unes des activités économiques, dépendances politiques et aires culturelles les plus notables. Plusieurs cartes touchent à l'histoire politique récente. Dans les cartes consacrées aux climats, aux configurations de surface, aux sols, à la végétation naturelle et à l'hydrographie, le lecteur aura tout loisir de reconnaître les influences d'ordre écologique sur l'implantation et l'activité humaines.

Enfin, on retrouve ce caractère international de l'Atlas jusque dans l'équilibre respecté dans la représentation des différentes régions de la Terre. *Britannica Atlas* accorde à chaque région du monde une couverture cartographique tenant compte de son importance économique et culturelle, de sa densité démographique, de sa superficie. C'est ainsi qu'environ les deux tiers des pages de cartes portent sur le monde anglo-américain, l'Asie et l'Europe, tandis que le tiers restant se partage entre l'Afrique, l'Amérique latine, l'Australie et l'Océanie, et l'ancienne Union soviétique. La repérage et l'identification des surfaces cartographiées dans l'Atlas sont assurés par une mappemonde avec renvoi aux pages où elles figurent (voir pages xiv et xv).

Systématique de comparaison. Avec un succès plus ou moins affirmé, tous les atlas ont jusqu'ici tendu à utiliser une gamme d'échelles uniformisées, dans la mesure où l'opération était techniquement possible. *Britannica Atlas* comporte un nombre restreint d'échelles soigneusement déterminées, propres à rendre vraiment significatives les comparaisons entre les différentes parties du monde. Les premières planches de l'Atlas permettent une vue d'ensemble sur le monde physique et politique grâce à des cartes au 1:75 000 000. Des projections au 1:48 000 000 sont consacrées aux océans, tandis que la figuration du relief des continents est reproduite au 1:24 000 000 (1 cm = 240 km). Ensuite, les vastes régions du globe sont toutes uniformément représentées au 1:12 000 000 (1 cm = 120 km).

Dans un découpage à plus grande échelle, la quasi-totalité des régions du monde est présentée de nouveau à l'échelle de 1:6 000 000 (1 cm = 60 km), pour les régions de moindre population, et à celle de 1:3 000 000 (1 cm = 30 km), pour l'Europe, la plus grande partie de l'Amérique du Nord et pour les régions les plus peuplées du Sud et de l'Est de l'Asie. Les séries au 1:6 000 000 et au 1:3 000 000 sont parfaitement comparables. L'une et l'autre indiquent les accidents naturels et les aspects proprement humains de chaque région: l'altitude, le système fluvial, les grands réseaux ferroviaires, les principaux aéroports, deux catégories de réseaux routiers et même les indications bathymétriques marquantes au large des côtes.

Enfin, on a fait appel à l'échelle de 1:1 000 000 (1 cm = 10 km) pour représenter 50 régions essentielles, choisies soit pour leur importance économique exceptionnelle, leur forte densité démographique, la complexité de leur réseau de transports, soit pour telle ou telle combinaison de ces facteurs. C'est une échelle inhabituellement grande dans les atlas généraux; on la réserve, d'ordinaire, aux cartons illustrant des études particulières. Elle a permis d'introduire quantité de noms de lieux ainsi que de multiples particularités locales: chutes d'eau, ruines, parcs, réserves ornithologiques et zoologiques, chantiers navals, installations militaires, barrages et réservoirs.

À la fin de l'Atlas, une section de 29 pages comprend 60 cartes au 1:300 000 (1 cm = 3 km) des centres urbains les plus importants. On y trouve l'aménagement et les traits caractéristiques des grandes agglomérations urbaines. Les principales concentrations urbaines y sont presque toutes comprises. Il s'y ajoute quelques agglomérations moins compactes mais non sans importance. Ce regroupement des zones citadines à la suite des cartes par régions offre l'avantage d'éviter toute rupture dans la succession de ces dernières.

La succession des cartes a été ordonnée de telle sorte que la surface de la Terre se dévoile progressivement du général au particulier, sans que le lecteur cesse de disposer de termes de comparaison. C'est d'abord une vue d'ensemble de la planète et de ses océans; puis, un survol général des continents présentés par hémisphère ou par quadrant terrestre. Suit l'examen plus poussé, sur des cartes principalement politiques, de toutes les régions qu'ils englobent. Celles-ci sont à leur tour projetées à grande échelle; l'accent est alors mis sur les relations de l'évolution culturelle et de l'environnement. Sous un verre plus grossissant apparaissent dans le détail les particularités culturelles des zones de forte densité démographique. Enfin, les gros plans des métropoles et de leurs agglomérations apportent au lecteur un faisceau d'informations plus détaillées. Les pages x à xii présentent la légende des cartes.

La collecte et l'analyse des données d'ordre physique destinées à la réalisation des cartes ont bénéficié des progrès de plus en plus rapides qui interviennent dans le domaine de l'observation aérienne et par satellites, de la technologie du radar et du sonar, enfin du traitement électronique de l'information. Le "relief ombré" a permis de conférer à nos cartes un aspect tridimensionnel. En un mot, toutes les ressources de l'art graphique contemporain ont été mises en œuvre afin d'atteindre le but que s'étaient fixé les éditeurs.

Prefácio

Ao longo da história, sabem-no muito bem os pedagogos, o conhecimento das coisas e a sua compreensão são conceitos que podem estar separados por um verdadeiro abismo. Uma simples acumulação de dados pode valer muito pouco se o seu significado e sua inter-relação não forem plenamente compreendidos.

Além de refletir os mais recentes fatos em relação ao mundo de hoje, o *Britannica Atlas* tem por meta aumentar substancialmente o grau de compreensão que o homem moderno tem do mundo em que vive. Para atingir esse objetivo, os editores afastaram-se dos caminhos tradicionais em dois importantes aspectos: (1) maior internacionalismo de conteúdo, e (2) perfeita comparabilidade dos mapas.

Internacionalismo. Freqüentemente, muitos atlas procuram satisfazer gostos e preconceitos locais. Para evitar esse defeito, os responsáveis por esta obra—Encyclopaedia Britannica, Inc. e Rand McNally & Company—desde o princípio asseguraram o caráter verdadeiramente internacional de seu conteúdo convidando um grupo de eminentes geógrafos e firmas cartográficas de diversas partes do mundo para colaborar em seu preparo. O grupo que participou foi constituído por representantes do Brasil e Ibero-América, da França, Alemanha, Índia, Itália, Japão, Países Baixos, Suécia, Reino Unido, e os Estados Unidos.

O sistema métrico foi usado em todos os mapas topográficos em lugar do sistema anglo-americano de medidas. As escalas horizontais e verticais (altitudes e profundidades) são expressas, nas páginas dos mapas, em ambos os sistemas, e na *Legendas dos Mapas* figuram as equivalências metro-pé e quilômetro-milha.

O inglês, o alemão, o espanhol, o francês e o português são utilizados paralelamente na maior parte da obra. Os nomes dos lugares habitados e dos acidentes geográficos situados dentro dos limites de um dado país são escritos na língua local; se o espaço disponível o permitir, apresenta-se também o equivalente inglês, caso o nome local não seja facilmente reconhecível. Os nomes dos países são apresentados em inglês, uma vez que alguns são muito difíceis de identificar quando expressos na língua local: Druk-Yul (Butã), Magyarország (Hungria), Nihon (Japão). Contudo, nos mapas em escala maior figura também a forma local do nome do país. Os nomes dos grandes mares ou lagos, cordilheiras ou outros acidentes maiores, que se estendem através de fronteiras internacionais, são apresentados em inglês nos mapas em escala reduzida, e tanto nas formas locais como em inglês nos mapas em escala maior. Para fins de transliteração para o inglês dos topônimos em línguas que não utilizam o alfabeto latino, fez-se o maior esforço para seguir os sistemas de transliteração mais aceitos internacionalmente.

Termos geográficos tais como lago, monte, ilha etc., aparecem nos mapas na língua local. À margem da maior parte das páginas acham-se glossários, em cinco línguas, que incluem a maioria dos termos utilizados em cada mapa; um glossário completo figura às páginas 289-295.

Todas as entradas no índice, exceto as de cidades ou outros centros urbanos, são acompanhadas de um símbolo gráfico que os identifica, como, por exemplo, montanha Λ, cabo ≻, rio ≏ etc., e ao pé de cada página, encontra-se, em cinco línguas, a chave da equivalência dos símbolos às categorias maiores de acidentes geográficos que representam.

Esforço para assegurar à obra seu caráter internacional fez-se evidente no tratamento equilibrado dado às diversas regiões do mundo. O *Britannica Atlas* reparte entre as regiões do mundo o seu conteúdo cartográfico, levando em conta sua significação cultural, econômica, demográfica e territorial. A América Latina, juntamente com a África, Austrália/Oceania e a antiga União Soviética, compreendem, aproximadamente, a terça parte dos mapas, sendo os restantes dois terços dedicados à Anglo-América, Ásia e Europa. No mapa-múndi nas páginas xii-xv foram traçadas as zonas e indicadas as páginas a que correspondem os diversos mapas.

Comparabilidade. Todos os atlas, com êxito maior ou menor, e sempre que possível procuram utilizar escalas uniformes. No *Britannica Atlas* utilizou-se o menor número possível de escalas, e estas foram escolhidas de modo a permitir a comparabilidade de todas as partes da Terra no tocante à área. Na seção inicial do Atlas, aparecem vários mapas grandes: mapasmúndi, com informações políticas e fisiográficas, em escala de 1:75 000 000; mapas oceânicos, em escala de 1:48 000 000; e mapas dos continentes, em escala 1:24 000 000. A seguir, agrupam-se as principais regiões do mundo a uma escala uniforme de 1:12 000 000 (seja, cada centímetro corresponde a 120 quilômetros).

O restante da superfície terrestre, em sua quase totalidade, foi representada por seções, utilizando-se uma ou outra das duas escalas maiores. A de 1:6 000 000 (60 km por cm) aplica-se às regiões menos povoadas, e a de 1:3 000 000 (30 km por cm), à Europa, quase toda a América do Norte e às regiões mais densamente povoadas da Ásia Meridional e do Extremo Oriente. As duas séries são perfeitamente comparáveis entre si, pois ambas indicam os principais acidentes de cada região, tanto naturais como artificiais, tais como os picos mais elevados, os rios, os principais aeroportos a ferrovias, duas categorias de rodovias, e, ainda, as profundidades submarinas mais representativas.

Por último, a escala de 1:1 000 000 (10 km por cm) foi destinada à representação de 50 regiões estratégicas, escolhidas de acordo com a excepcional importância econômica, grande densidade demográfica, complexidade da rede de comunicações, ou alguma combinação desses fatores. Essa escala, muito maior que a habitualmente utilizada em atlas gerais, costuma ser reservada aos mapas que focalizam temas especiais insertos em mapas maiores. Seu uso nesta obra proporciona uma grande riqueza de detalhes, tais como quedas d'água, sítios arqueológicos, parques florestais, reservas militares e biológicas, estaleiros, instalações militares, represas e barragens, além de muitos centros urbanos menores.

No final do Atlas figura uma seção de 29 páginas que contêm 60/mapas dos principais centros urbanos, traçados à escala única de 1:300 000 (3 km por cm). Esses mapas mostram a forma de uso do solo e outras características demográfico-territoriais das grandes aglomerações urbanas. Quase todas as áreas metropolitanas mais populosas do Mundo estão aí representadas, assim como algumas menores, mas igualmente importantes. Esses mapas foram agrupados em uma seção especial no final do Atlas para fins de comparabilidade, bem como para evitar a interrupção da continuidade dos mapas regionais.

Os mapas estão ordenados de modo a permitir ao leitor uma visão progressivamente mais detalhada, mas sempre comparável, da superfície terrestre. Primeiro, vem uma visão global do Mundo e dos oceanos; em seguida, uma visão panorâmica dos continentes, apresentados em seus respectivos hemisférios ou quadrantes terrestres. Segue-se uma visão mais próxima de todas as regiões dentro dos continentes, em mapas primordialmente políticos. Depois, as subregiões, em escala maior, com ênfase principalmente nas relações entre os acidentes físicos e os culturais. A escala ainda maior, apresentam-se, em grande detalhe, os acidentes culturais das zonas densamente povoadas. E por último, os mapas das cidades e seus arredores, que incluem ainda mais detalhes. A seção denominada *Legendas dos Mapas* ocupa a três páginas, de x a xii.

A compilação e a análise dos dados cartográficos beneficiaram-se com o recente e aceleradíssimo progresso alcançado pelas técnicas dos levantamentos aerofotogramétricos e por meio de satélites, pela tecnologia do radar e do sonar, e pelo processamento electrônico de dados. Utilizou-se a técnica do sombreado para o relevo, com o objetivo de dar aos mapas um efeito tridimensional. Todos os recursos das artes gráficas atuais foram empregados na execução do projeto editorial.

List of Maps

Kartenverzeichnis

* Massstab in Millionen

Lista de Mapas

*Escala en millones

Liste des Cartes

Lista de Mapas

Legend to Maps / Zeichenerklärung
Leyendas Para Mapas / Légende des Cartes / Legendas dos Mapas

The design and color of the map symbols are consistent throughout the Regional and Metropolitan Area maps, although the size of the symbol varies with scale. An asterisk marks those symbols which appear only on the 1:300,000 scale maps. Symbols for inhabited localities, boundaries, and capitals are given on page xi.

The symbol 80-81→ in the margin of a map directs the reader to a map of the adjoining area.

A separate legend on page 1 identifies the land and submarine features which appear on the World, Ocean, and Continent maps.

Der Entwurf und die Farbe der Kartensymbole sind einheitlich für alle Regionalkarten und Karten von Stadtregionen, während die Grösse des Symbols sich mit dem Massstab ändert. Ein Stern kennzeichnet diejenigen Symbole, welche nur auf den Karten im Massstab 1:300 000 erscheinen. Symbole für bewohnte Orte, für Grenzen und Hauptstädte sind auf Seite xi angeführt.

Kennzeichen 80-81→ am Rande einer Karte ist ein Hinweis für den Leser, die Karte eines angrenzenden Gebietes nachzuschlagen.

Eine andere Legende auf Seite 1 identifiziert die Land- und untermeerischen Phänomene, die auf den Weltkarten, Karten der Ozeane und Erdteile erscheinen.

El diseño y el color de los símbolos cartográficos son uniformes para todas los mapas regionales y de las áreas metropolitanas, aunque el tamaño del símbolo varía según la escala. Un asterisco distingue los símbolos que aparecen sólo en los mapas a 1:300 000. Los símbolos de lugares poblados, de límites y de capitales se hallan en la página xi.

El símbolo 80-81→ al margen de un mapa dirige al lector a un mapa del área adyacente.

Otra leyenda, en la página 1, identifica la topografía terrestre y submarina que se encuentra en los mapas del Mundo, Océanos y Continentes.

La couleur et la forme des symboles cartographiques des cartes régionales et des cartes des zones métropolitaines sont identiques, bien que la grandeur des signes varie selon l'échelle. Un astérisque accompagne les symboles qui n'apparaissent que sur les cartes au 1:300 000. La légende des signes conventionnels pour les lieux habités, les frontières et les capitales se trouve à la page xi.

Le symbole 80-81→ en marge d'une carte renvoie le lecteur à une carte de la région voisine.

Pour les cartes du monde, des océans et des continents une légende séparée, à la page 1, donne le sens des symboles représentant les paysages continentaux et les formes de relief sous-marin.

A cor e a forma dos símbolos cartográficos dos mapas regionais e das áreas metropolitanas são idênticos, ainda que a dimensão do símbolo varie segundo a escala. Um asterisco distingue os símbolos que só aparecem nos mapas da escala de 1:300 000. As legendas dos símbolos convencionais dos lugares povoados, fronteiras e capitais encontram-se à pág. xi.

O símbolo 80-81→ à margem de um mapa, remete o leitor a um mapa da região vizinha.

Nos mapas do mundo, dos oceanos e dos continentes uma legenda separada, na pág. 1, indica o sentido dos símbolos representativos das paisagens continentais e das formas do relevo submarino.

Hydrographic Features / Hydrographische Objekte / Elementos Hidrográficos
Données Hydrographiques / Acidentes Hidrográficos

Shoreline/Uferlinie Línea costanera/Trait de côte Linha costeira	Canal du Midi — Navigable Canal/Schiffbarer Kanal Canal navegable/Canal navigable Canal navegável
Undefined or Fluctuating Shoreline Unbestimmte oder Veränderliche Uferlinie Línea costanera indefinida o fluctuante Trait de côte indéfini ou fluctuant Linha costeira indefinida ou flutuante	Irrigation or Drainage Canal Be- oder Entwässerungskanal Canal de irrigación o desagüe Canal d'irrigation ou de drainage Canal de irrigação ou drenagem
Amur — River, Stream/Fluss, Strom Río, Corriente/Rivière, Cours d'eau Rio, curso d'água	Los Angeles Aqueduct — Aqueduct/Aquädukt Acueducto/Aqueduc Aqueduto
Intermittent Stream/Periodischer Fluss Corriente intermitente/Cours d'eau périodique Rio, curso d'água intermitente	Pier, Breakwater/Landungsbrücke, Wellenbrecher Embarcadero, Rompeolas/Jetée, Brise-lames Cais, Quebra-mar
SALTO ANGEL — Rapids, Falls/Stromschnellen, Wasserfälle Rápidos, Cascadas/Rapides, Chutes d'eau Corredeiras, quedas d'água	GREAT BARRIER REEF — Reef/Riff Arrecife/Récif Recife
764 ▽ Depth of Water/Wassertiefe Profundidad del aqua/Profondeur bathymétrique Profundidade da água	Kumdah⊅ — Uninhabited Oasis/Unbewohnte Oase Oasis deshabitado/Oasis inhabitée Oásis desabitado
8428 ▼ Greatest Depth (Atlantic, Indian, Pacific oceans) Grösste Tiefe (Atlantischer, Indischer, Pazifischer Ozean) Profundidad más grande (Océanos Atlántico, Índico, Pacífico) Profondeur maximum (océans Atlantique, Indien, Pacifique) Profundidade máxima (oceanos Atlântico, Índico, Pacífico)	

L. Victoria — Lake, Reservoir/See, Stausee Lago, Embalse/Lac, Réservoir Lago, reservatório (represa)	
Intermittent Lake, Reservoir Periodischer See, Stausee Lago o Embalse intermitente Lac ou Réservoir périodique Lago, reservatório (represa) intermitente	
Tuz Gölü — Salt Lake/Salzsee Lago salado/Lac salé Lago salgado	
Dry Lake Bed/Trockener Seeboden Lecho de lago seco/Fond de lac asséché Leito de lago seco	
The Everglades — Swamp/Sumpf Pantano/Marais Pântano	
RIMO GLACIER — Glacier/Gletscher Glaciar/Glacier Geleira	
(395) — Lake Surface Elevation Seehöhe Elevación del lago Cote du niveau du lac Altitude do nível do lago	

Topographic Features / Topographische Objekte / Elementos Topográficos
Données Topographiques / Acidentes Topográficos

Matterhorn 4478 △ Elevation Above Sea Level Höhe über dem Meeresspiegel Elevation sobre el nivel del mar Cote au-dessus du niveau de la mer Altitude acima do nível do mar	Khyber Pass 1067 — Mountain Pass/Pass Paso/Col de montagne Passo (de montanha)	ANDES / KUNLUN SHAN — Mountain Range, Plateau, Valley, etc. Gebirge, Hochebene, Tal, usw. Sierra, Meseta, Valle, etc. Chaîne de montagnes, Plateau, Vallée, etc. Cadeia de montanhas. Planalto, Vale etc.
	∗ Rock/Fels Roca/Rocher Rocha	
76 ▽ Elevation Below Sea Level Höhe unter dem Meeresspiegel Elevación bajo del nivel del mar Cote au-dessous du niveau de la mer Altitude abaixo do nível do mar	Lava/Lava Lava/Lave Lava	BAFFIN ISLAND / NUNIVAK ISLAND — Island Insel Isla Île Ilha
Mount Cook 3764 ▲ Highest Elevation in Country Höchster Punkt des Landes Elevación más alta en el país Cote la plus élevée d'un pays Altitude mais elevada de um país	Sand Area/Sandgebiet Area de arena/Région sableuse, Erg Região arenosa, Erg	POLUOSTROV KAMČATKA / CABO DE HORNOS — Peninsula, Cape, Point, etc. Halbinsel, Kap, Landspitze, usw. Península, Cabo, Punta, etc. Péninsule, Cap, Pointe, etc. Península, Cabo, Ponta etc.
133 ▾ Lowest Elevation in Country Tiefster Punkt des Landes Elevación más baja en el país Cote la plus basse d'un pays Altitude mais baixa de um país	Salt Flat/Salzebene Salar/Dépression salée Depressão salgada	
(106) Elevation of City Höhenangabe einer Stadt Elevación de ciudad Altitude d'une ville Altitude de uma cidade	Elevations and depths are given in meters Höhen und Tiefen sind in Metern angegeben Elevaciones y profundidades se dan en metros Cotes et profondeurs sont indiquées en mètres Altitudes e profundidades são apresentadas em metros	Highest Elevation and Lowest Elevation of a continent are underlined Höchster und tiefster Punkt innerhalb eines Erdteils sind unterstrichen Elevación más alta y más baja de un continente se subrayan La cote la plus haute et la cote la plus basse d'un continent sont soulignées As altitudes mais e menos elevadas de um continente são sublinhadas

Inhabited Localities / Bewohnte Orte / Lugares Poblados / Lieux Habités / Lugares Habitados

The symbol represents the number of inhabitants within the locality/Die Signatur entspricht der Einwohnerzahl des Ortes
El símbolo representa el número de habitantes dentro del lugar/Le symbole représente le nombre d'habitants de la localité
O símbolo representa o número de habitantes do lugar

1:300,000 1:1,000,000		1:12,000,000		1:24,000,000	
1:3,000,000 1:6,000,000	. 0—10,000		. 0—50,000	1:48,000,000	. 0—100,000
	o 10,000—25,000		⊙ 50,000—100,000		⊙ 100,000—1,500,000
	⊙ 25,000—100,000		⊡ 100,000—250,000		■ >1,500,000
	⊡ 100,000—250,000		▣ 250,000—1,000,000		
	▣ 250,000—1,000,000		■ >1,000,000		
	■ >1,000,000				

The size of type indicates the relative economic and political importance of the locality
Die Schriftgrösse entspricht der relativen wirtschaftlichen und politischen Bedeutung des Ortes
El tamaño del tipo de imprenta indica la relativa importancia económica y política del lugar
La dimension des caractères indique l'importance économique et politique relative d'une localité
A dimensão dos caracteres tipográficos indica a importância econômica e política relativa do lugar

Écommoy	Lisieux	**Rouen**
Trouville	**Orléans**	**PARIS**

Hollywood □
Westminster
Section of a City, Neighborhood/Stadtteil, Nachbarschaft
Sección de una ciudad, Barrio/Arrondissement, Quartier
Seção de uma cidade, Bairro

Northland ■
Center
* Major Shopping Center/Haupteinkaufszentrum/Mercado principal
Centre commercial important/Centro comercial importante

BYRD □ Scientific Station/Wissenschaftliche Station/Estación científica
Station scientifique/Estação científica

Bi'r Safâjah ° Inhabited Oasis/Bewohnte Oase/Oasis habitado
Oasis habitée/Oásis habitado

Kumdah ° Uninhabited Oasis/Unbewohnte Oase/Oasis deshabitado
Oasis inhabitée/Oásis desabitado

Urban Area (area of continuous industrial, commercial, and residential development)
Stadtgebiet (ausgedehntes industrie-, Geschäfts- und Wohngebiet)
Zona urbanizada (área de desarrollo industrial, comercial y residencial)
Zone urbanisée (zone d'occupation continue par des industries, des commerces, des habitations)
Zona urbanizada (área de ocupação contínua por indústrias, estabelecimentos comerciais e habitações)

* Major Industrial Area/Hauptindustriegebiet/Zona principal industrial
Région industrielle importante/Zona industrial importante

* Wooded Area/Wald/Área de bosque
Région boisée/Área verde

* Local Park or Recreational Area/Park oder Erholungsgebiet
Parque municipal o área de recreo/Parc municipal ou zone de loisirs
Parque municipal ou área de lazer

Political Boundaries / Politische Grenzen / Límites Políticos / Frontières Politiques / Fronteiras e Limites

International (First-order political unit) /Staatsgrenze (Politische Einheit erster Ordnung)
Internacionales (Unidad política de primer orden) /Internationales (Entités politiques de premier ordre)
Internacionais (Unidade política de primeiro nível)

Capitals of Political Units
Hauptstädte politischer Einheiten
Capitales de Unidades Políticas
Capitales d'Entités Politiques
Capitais de Unidades Políticas

1:1,000,000	1:300,000 1:3,000,000 1:6,000,000	1:24,000,000 1:48,000,000	1:12,000,000	

HUNGARY

Demarcated, Undemarcated, and Administrative
Markiert, unmarkiert, verwaltungstechnisch
Demarcado, No demarcado, y Administrativo
Délimitées, Non-délimitées, Administratives
Delimitados, Não delimitados, Administrativos

Disputed de facto/Umstritten de facto
Disputado de hecho/Contestées de facto
Contestados de fato

Disputed de jure/Umstritten de jure
Disputado de derecho/Contestées de jure
Contestados de direito

Indefinite or Undefined/Unklar oder Unbestimmt
Indefinido o No determinado/Imprécises ou Non définies
Imprecisos ou Não definidos

Demarcation Line/Demarkationslinie
Línea de demarcación/Ligne de démarcation
Linha de demarcação

BUDAPEST Independent Nation
Unabhängiger Staat
Nación independiente
État indépendant
Estado independente

Cayenne Dependency
(Colony, protectorate, etc.)
Abhängiges Gebiet
(Kolonie, Protektorat, usw.)
Dependencia
(Colonia, protectorado, etc.)
Territoire dépendant
(Colonie, protectorat, etc.)
Dependência
(Colônia, protetorado, etc.)

GALAPAGOS (Ecuador) Administering Country
Verwaltender Staat
País administrador
Pays administrateur
País administrador

Internal/Verwaltungsgrenze/Internos/Intérieures/Limites Internos

PERNAMBUCO

State, Province, etc. (Second-order political unit)
Land, Provinz, usw. (Politische Einheit zweiter Ordnung)
Estado, Provincia, etc. (Unidad política de segundo orden)
État, Province, etc. (Subdivision administrative de deuxième ordre)
Estado, Província, etc. (Unidade política de segundo nível)

Recife State, Province, etc./Land, Provinz, usw.
Estado, Provincia, etc./État, Province, etc.
Estado, Província, etc.

SIENA WESTCHESTER
County, Oblast, etc. (Third-order political unit)/Grafschaft, Oblast, usw. (Politische Einheit dritter Ordnung)
Condado, Oblast, etc. (Unidad política de tercer orden)
Comté, Oblast, etc. (Subdivision administrative de troisième ordre)
Condado, Oblast, etc. (Unidade política de terceiro nível)

Ambāla
Johnstown County, Oblast, etc./Grafschaft, Oblast, usw.
Condado, Oblast, etc./Comté, Oblast, etc.
Condado, Oblast, etc.

ISERLOHN
Okrug, Kreis, etc. (Fourth-order political unit)/Okrug, Kreis, usw. (Politische Einheit vierter Ordnung)
Okrug, Kreis, etc. (Unidad política de cuarto orden)
Okrug, Kreis, etc. (Subdivision administrative de quatrième ordre)
Okrug, Kreis, etc. (Unidade política de quarto nível)

Iserlohn Okrug, Kreis, etc./Okrug, Kreis, usw.
Okrug, Kreis, etc./Okrug, Kreis, etc.
Okrug, Kreis, etc.

City or Municipality (may appear in combination with another boundary symbol)
Stadt oder Gemeinde (kann zusammen mit einem anderen Begrenzungssymbol erscheinen)
Ciudad o Municipio (puede aparecer en combinación con otro símbolo de límite)
Ville ou Municipalité (peut paraître en combinaison avec un autre symbole de limites politiques)
Cidade ou Municipalidade (Pode aparecer em combinação com outro símbolo de limite político)

NORMANDIE
Historical Region (No boundaries indicated)
Historische Landschaft (Grenzen werden nicht gezeigt)
Región Histórica (Sin indicación de límites)
Région Historique (Sans indication de frontières)
Região Histórica (Sem indicação de fronteiras)

Legend to Maps/Zeichenerklärung
Leyendas Para Mapas/Légende des Cartes/Legendas dos Mapas

Transportation / Verkehr / Transporte / Transports / Transporte

	1:300,000	1:1,000,000	1:3,000,000 1:6,000,000	1:12,000,000
Road/Strasse/Camino/Route/Rodovia				
Primary/Erster Ordnung/Principal/de premier ordre/Principal	PASSAIC EXPWY. (I-80)	PENNSYLVANIA TURNPIKE		
Secondary/Zweiter Ordnung/Secundario/de second ordre/Secundária	BERLINER RING			
Tertiary/Dritter Ordnung/Terciario/de troisième ordre/Terciária				
Minor Road, Trail/Weg, Pfad Rodera, Vereda/Route secondaire, Piste/Caminho, trilha				

Railway/Eisenbahn/Ferrocarril/Voie ferrée/Ferrovia

Primary/Hauptbahn/Principal/Principale/Principal	CANADIAN NATIONAL	SANTA FE		
Secondary/Sonstige Bahn/Secundario/Secondaire/Secundária				

*Rapid Transit/Schnellverkehr/Tránsito rápido/Métro/Trânsito rápido (metrô)

Airport/Flughafen/Aeropuerto/Aéroport/Aeroporto — LONDON (HEATHROW) AIRPORT — DULLES INTERNATIONAL AIRPORT

*Rail or Air Terminal/Bahnhof oder Flughafengebäude
Terminal ferroviaria o aéro/Gare ou aérogare
Terminal ferroviário ou aéreo (estação) — SÜD-BAHNHOF

REICHS-BRÜCKE — Bridge/Brücke/Puente/Pont/Ponte

GREAT ST. BERNARD TUNNEL — Tunnel/Tunnel/Túnel/Tunnel/Túnel

Houston Ship Channel — Shipping Channel/Schiffahrtsrinne Canal marítimo/Chenal maritime Canal marítimo

Canal du Midi — Navigable Canal/Schiffbarer Kanal Canal navegable/Canal navigable Canal navegável

Intracoastal Waterway/Küstenschiffahrtsweg Via fluvial Intracostera/Canal côtier Via costeira interna

TO MALMÖ — Ferry/Fähre Balsadera/Bac Balsa

Miscellaneous Cultural Features / Sonstige Objekte / Elementos Culturales Misceláneos
Éléments Culturels Divers / Acidentes Culturais Diversos

PARQUE NACIONAL LANÍN — National or State Park or Monument
National- oder Naturpark oder Denkmal
Parque o Monumento nacional o provincial
Parc ou Monument national ou régional
Parque ou Monumento nacional ou regional

EDISON NAT. HIST. SITE — National or State Historic(al) Site, Memorial
Historische Stätte, Gedenkstätte
Sitio histórico nacional o provincial, Monumento
Site historique national ou régional, Mémorial
Sítio histórico nacional ou regional, Monumento histórico

SEMINOLE IND. RES. — Indian Reservation/Indianerreservation
Reserva de indios/Réserve indienne
Reserva Indígena

FORT DIX — Military Installation/Militäranlage
Instalación militar/Installation militaire
Instalação militar

GREENWOOD CEMETERY — *Cemetery/Friedhof
Cementerio/Cimetière/Cemitério

SORBONNE — Point of Interest (Battlefield, museum, temple, university, etc.)
Sehenswürdigkeit (Schlachtfeld, Museum, Tempel, Universität, usw.)
Punto de interés (Campo de batalla, museo, templo, universidad, etc.)
Curiosité (Champ de bataille, musée, temple, université, etc.)
Pontos de interesse (Campo de batalha, museu, templo, universidade, etc.)

STEPHANSDOM — Church, Monastery/Kirche, Kloster
Iglesia, Monasterio/Église, Monastère
Igreja, Mosteiro

UXMAL — Ruins/Ruinen/Ruinas/Ruines/Ruínas

WINDSOR CASTLE — Castle/Burg, Schloss/Castillo/Château/Castelo

*Lighthouse/Leuchtturm
Faro/Phare/Farol

ASWÂN DAM — Dam/Damm/Presa/Barrage
Represa (barragem)

*Lock/Schleuse/Esclusa
Écluse/Eclusa

Crib — *Water Intake Crib/Wasseraufnahmestation
Toma de agua/Prise d'eau/Captação de água

Quarry or Surface Mine
Steinbruch oder Tagebau
Cantera o Mina de hoyo abierto
Carrière ou Mine à ciel ouvert
Pedreira ou mina a céu aberto

Subsurface Mine/Bergwerk
Mina subterránea/Mine souterraine
Mina subterrânea

*Oil Well/Ölbohrturm
Pozo de petróleo/Puits de pétrole
Poço de petróleo

Metric-English Equivalents / Umrechnung metrischer Masse in englische Masse / Métrico-Equivalentes Ingleses
Equivalences métriques des mesures anglaises / Equivalentes métricos das medidas inglesas

Areas represented by one square centimeter at various map scales
Flächen die einem cm² in den verschiedenen Kartenmassstäben entsprechen
Áreas representados por un centímetro cuadrado a varias escalas de mapas
Surface représentée par un cm² aux échelles indiquées
Áreas representadas por cm² nas escalas indicadas nos mapas

Meter=3.28 feet
Kilometer=0.62 mile

Meter² (m²)=10.76 square feet
Kilometer² (km²)=0.39 square mile

1:300,000
9 km²
3.48 square miles

1:1,000,000
100 km²
39 square miles

1:3,000,000
900 km²
348 square miles

1:6,000,000
3,600 km²
1,390 square miles

1:12,000,000
14,400 km²
5,558 square miles

1:24,000,000
57,600 km²
22,234 square miles

1:48,000,000
230,400 km²
88,934 square miles

Elevation tints shown only on 1:3,000,000 and 1:6,000,000 scale maps
Höhenschichten erscheinen nur auf Karten im Massstab 1:3 000 000 und 1:6 000 000
Se indica las tintas de elevación sólo en los mapas de escala 1:3 000 000 y 1:6 000 000
Teintes hypsométriques exprimées seulement sur cartes à 1:3 000 000 et 1:6 000 000
Indicaram-se as graduações de cor hipsométricas somente nos mapas de escalas 1:3 000 000 e 1:6 000 000

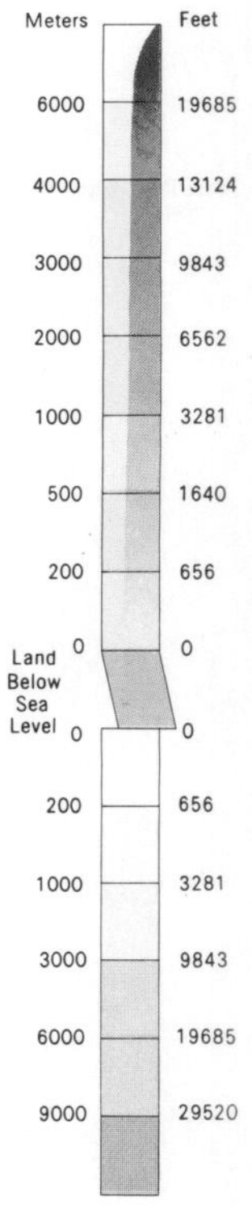

Meters	Feet
6000	19685
4000	13124
3000	9843
2000	6562
1000	3281
500	1640
200	656
Land Below Sea Level 0	0
0	0
200	656
1000	3281
3000	9843
6000	19685
9000	29520

Alternate Names / Alternative Namensformen / Nombres Alternativos
Variantes Toponymiques / Variantes Toponímicas

MOSKVA MOSCOW
Basel Bâle

English or second official language names are shown in reduced size lettering
Englische Namen oder Namen in einer zweiten offiziellen Sprache erscheinen in kleineren Schriftgrössen
Los nombres en inglés o un segundo idioma oficial se muestran en tipo de imprenta mas pequeño
Les toponymes en anglais ou dans la seconde langue officielle sont indiqués en caractères plus petits
Os topônimos em inglês ou num segundo idioma oficial aparecem em tipologia menor

VOLGOGRAD (STALINGRAD)
Ventura (San Buenaventura)

Historical or other alternates in the local language are shown in parentheses
Historische oder alternative Namensformen einheimischen Sprache erscheinen in Klammern
Los nombres históricos y alternativos locales se muestran en paréntesis
Les noms historiques de lieux ou les variantes toponymiques locales sont mis entre parenthèses
Os topônimos históricos ou as variantes toponímicas locais aparecem entre parênteses

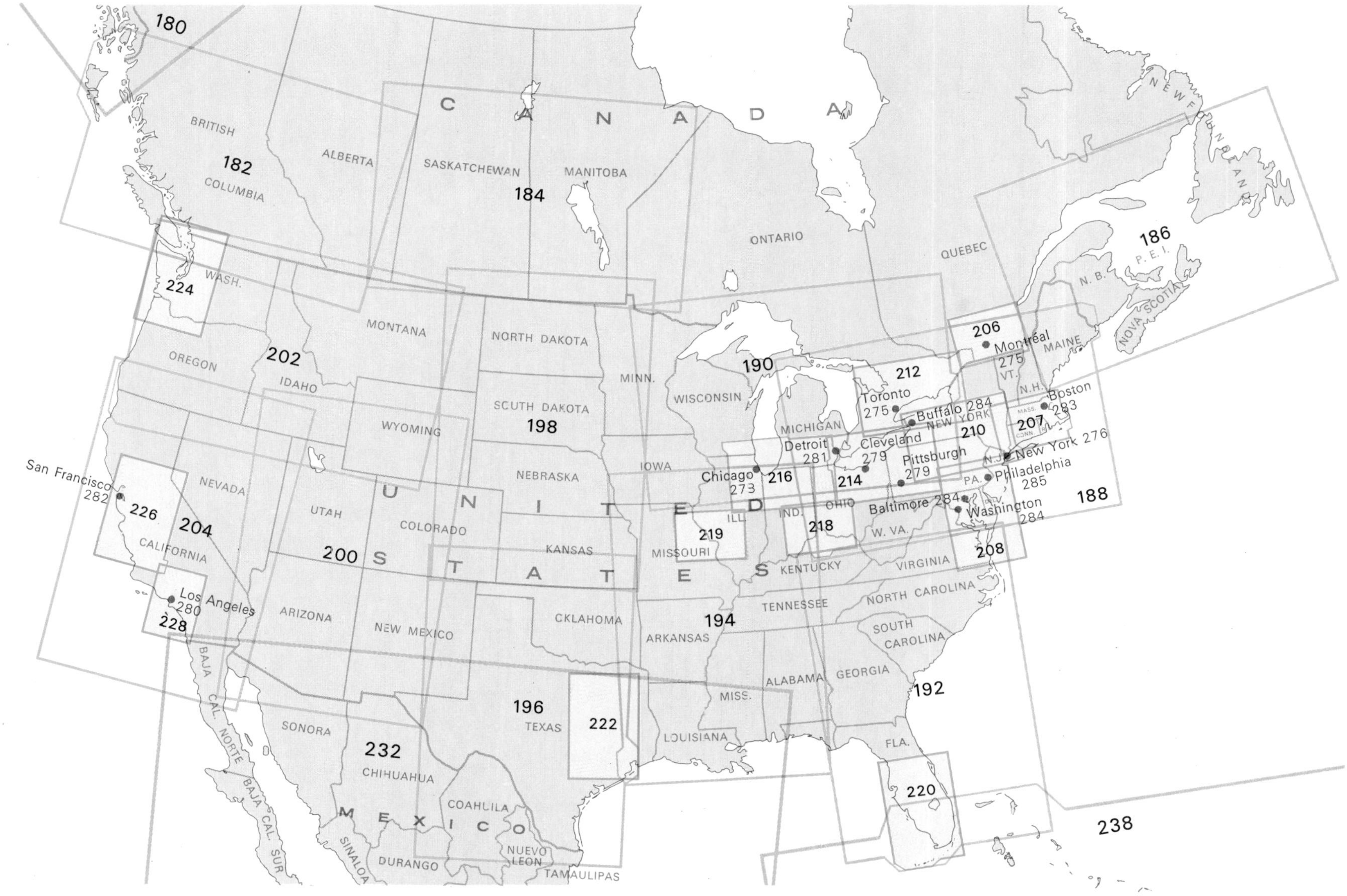
180
CANADA
BRITISH COLUMBIA
182
ALBERTA
SASKATCHEWAN
MANITOBA
184
ONTARIO
QUEBEC
NEWFOUNDLAND
186
P. E. I.
N. B.
NOVA SCOTIA
224
WASH.
MONTANA
NORTH DAKOTA
202
OREGON
IDAHO
190
206
Montréal
275
MAINE
VT.
N.H.
212
Toronto
275
Buffalo 284
NEW YORK
Boston
283
207
210
MINN.
WISCONSIN
MICHIGAN
SOUTH DAKOTA
198
WYOMING
Detroit
281
Cleveland
279
Pittsburgh
279
New York 276
N.J.
PA.
Philadelphia
285
San Francisco
282
NEVADA
NEBRASKA
IOWA
Chicago
273
216
214
UNITED STATES
226
UTAH
COLORADO
ILL.
IND.
OHIO
218
Baltimore 284
Washington
284
188
204
CALIFORNIA
219
W. VA.
200
KANSAS
MISSOURI
KENTUCKY
VIRGINIA
208
Los Angeles
280
228
ARIZONA
NEW MEXICO
OKLAHOMA
194
ARKANSAS
TENNESSEE
NORTH CAROLINA
SOUTH CAROLINA
BAJA CAL. NORTE
ALABAMA
GEORGIA
192
MISS.
196
TEXAS
222
SONORA
232
CHIHUAHUA
LOUISIANA
FLA.
220
MEXICO
COAHUILA
BAJA CAL. SUR
SINALOA
DURANGO
NUEVO LEON
TAMAULIPAS
238

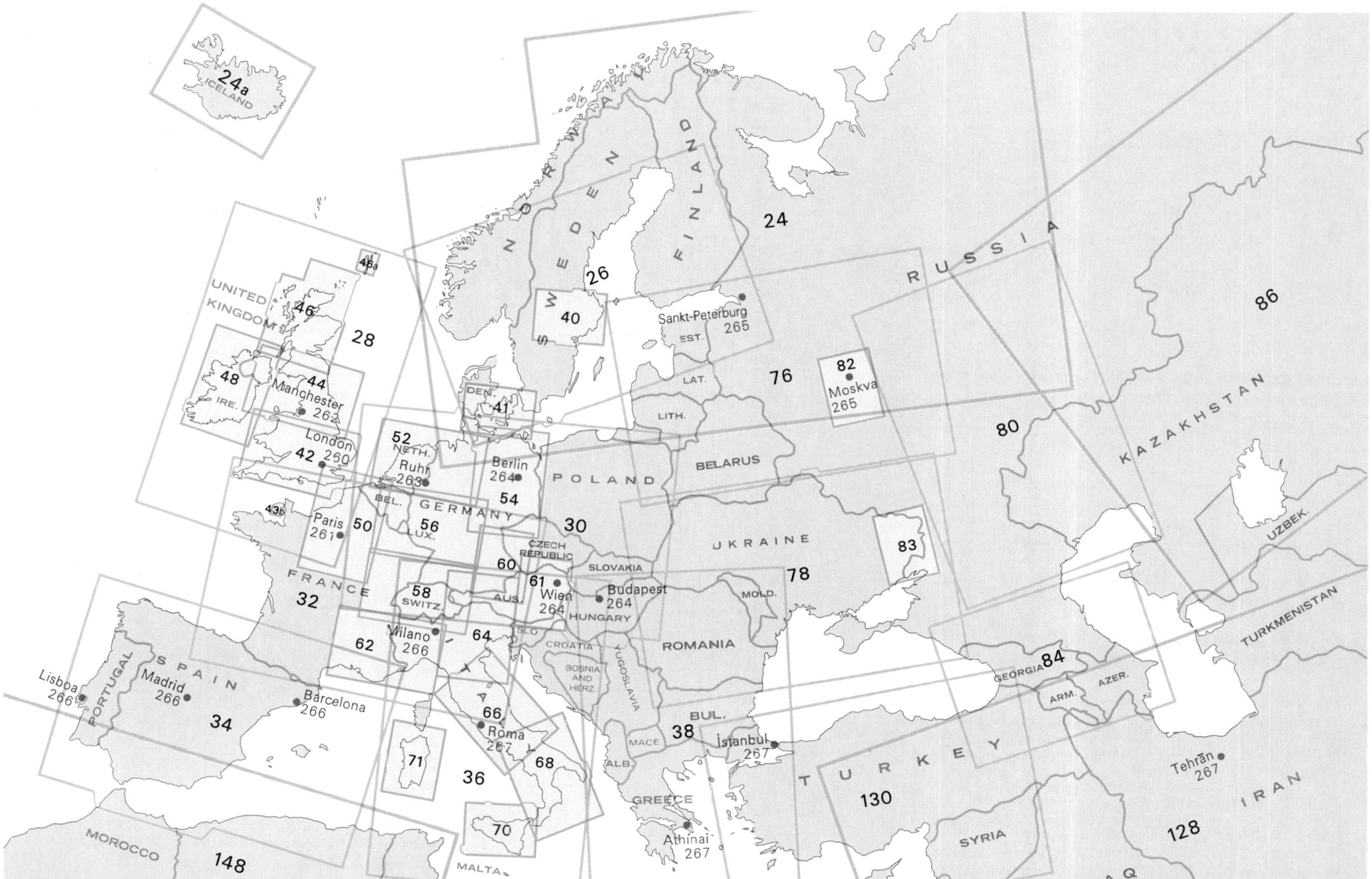
24a
ICELAND
NORWAY
SWEDEN
FINLAND
24
26
40
46a
UNITED KINGDOM
46
28
Sankt-Peterburg
265
EST.
RUSSIA
86
48
IRE.
44
Manchester
262
DEN.
41
LAT.
76
82
Moskva
265
LITH.
80
KAZAKHSTAN
London
260
42
52
NETH.
Ruhr
263
Berlin
264
BELARUS
POLAND
54
BEL.
GERMANY
43b
Paris
261
50
56
LUX.
30
CZECH REPUBLIC
UKRAINE
83
UZBEK.
FRANCE
32
60
SLOVAKIA
58
SWITZ.
61
Wien
264
AUS.
Budapest
264
HUNGARY
78
MOLD.
62
Milano
266
64
SLO.
CROATIA
ROMANIA
TURKMENISTAN
SPAIN
Lisboa
266
PORTUGAL
Madrid
266
BOSNIA AND HERZ.
YUGOSLAVIA
GEORGIA
84
AZER.
ARM.
Barcelona
266
34
66
Roma
267
ITALY
BUL.
38
MACE.
İstanbul
267
ALB.
71
68
36
TURKEY
130
Tehrān
267
IRAN
GREECE
70
Athínai
267
SYRIA
128
MOROCCO
148
MALTA
ALGERIA
TUNISIA
CYPRUS
LEBANON
IRAQ
Copyright © by Rand McNally & Co.
A-515300-964 -4 3-10

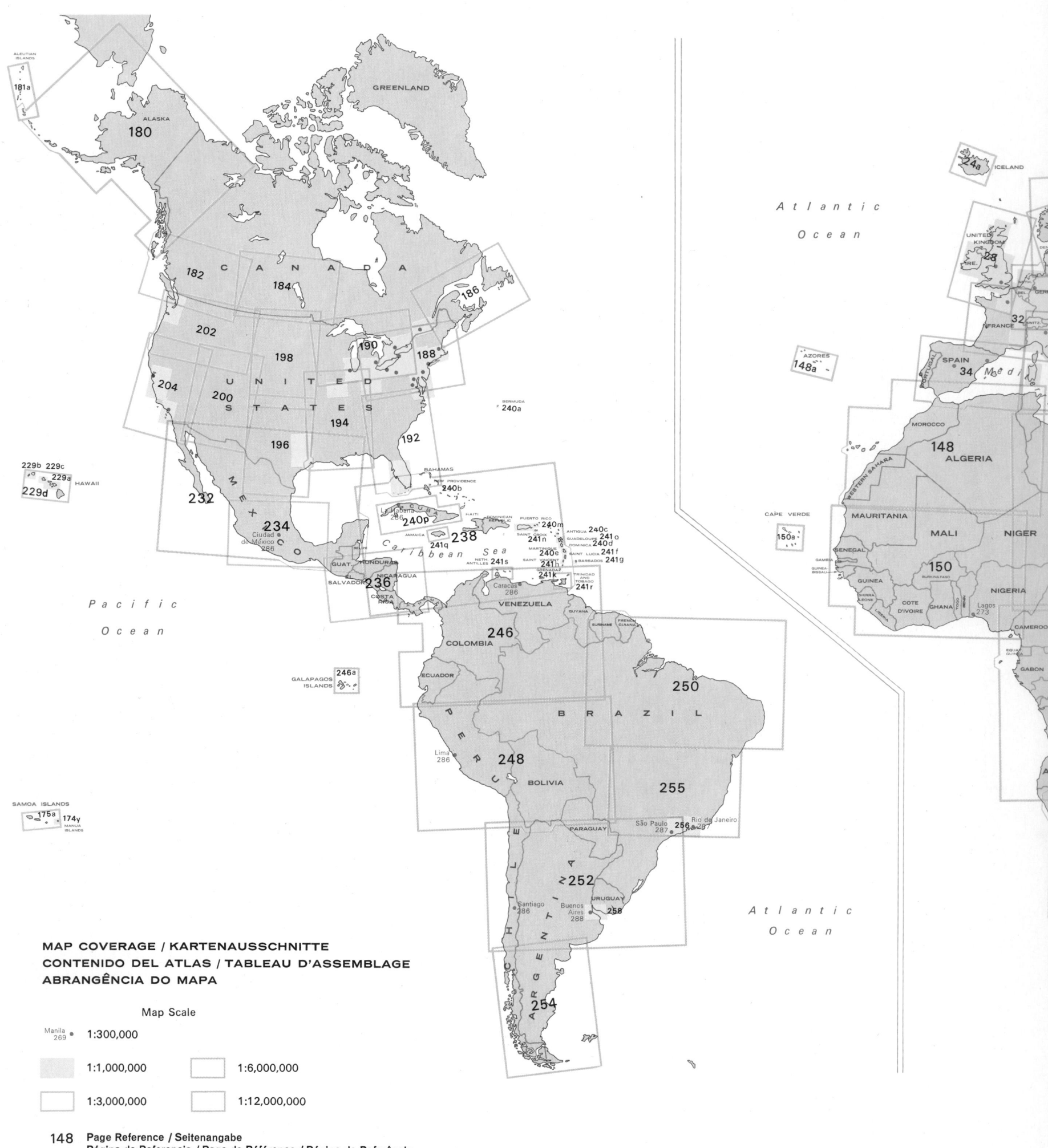

MAP COVERAGE / KARTENAUSSCHNITTE
CONTENIDO DEL ATLAS / TABLEAU D'ASSEMBLAGE
ABRANGÊNCIA DO MAPA

Map Scale

Manila
269 • 1:300,000

1:1,000,000   1:6,000,000

1:3,000,000   1:12,000,000

148 Page Reference / Seitenangabe
      Página de Referencia / Page de Référence / Página de Referência

Enlarged maps of Anglo-America and Europe on page xiii.
Vergrösserte Karten von Anglo-Amerika und Europa auf Seite xiii.
Mapas aumentados de América Anglosajona y Europa, página xiii.
Cartes à grande échelle de l'Ámerique anglo-saxonne et de l'Europe à la page xiii.
Mapas ampliados da América Anglo-saxônica e da Europa, página xiii.

World, Ocean, and Continent maps on pages 2-19.
Weltkarten, Karten der Ozeane und Erdteile auf Seiten 2-19.
Mapas del Mundo, Océanos y Continentes, páginas 2-19.
Cartes du Monde, des Océans et des Continents aux pages 2-19.
Mapas do Mundo, dos Oceanos e dos Continentes, páginas 2-19.

Additional Pacific Ocean Island maps on pages 174-175.
Zusätzliche Karten der Inseln des Pazifischen Ozeans auf Seite 174-175.
Mapas adicionales de las Islas del Océano Pacífico, páginas174-175.
Cartes supplémentaires des Îles de l'Océan Pacifique aux pages 174-175.
Mapas suplementares das ilhas do Oceano Pacífico, páginas 174-175.

R U S S I A
24
76
80
86
88
89
KAZAKHSTAN
M O N G O L I A
C H I N A
102
100
104
105
98
106
107
92
93b
94
96
92a
Pacific
Ocean
UKRAINE
78
Black Sea
84
85
TURKEY
130
TURKMENISTAN
UZBEKISTAN
AFGHANISTAN
KYRG.
TAJIKISTAN
Caspian Sea
Tehrān
267
IRAN
128
IRAQ
SYRIA
132
142
EGYPT
SAUDI
ARABIA
OMAN
YEMEN
Red Sea
140
SUDAN
144
ETHIOPIA
SOMALIA
KENYA
TANZANIA
154
ZAMBIA
MOZAMBIQUE
ZIMBABWE
MADAGASCAR
157b
157a
157c
COMOROS
MAURITIUS
REUNION
123
120
PAKISTAN
NEPAL
Delhi
272
124
I N D I A
Calcutta
272
126
Bombay
272
122
SRI LANKA
MYANMAR
LAOS
VIETNAM
THAILAND
Krung Thep
(Bangkok)
269
CAMBODIA
Thanh-pho Ho Chi Minh
(Saigon)
269
110
Beijing
(Peking)
271
KOREA
Shanghai
269
T'aipei
269
TAIWAN
Hong Kong
271
OKINAWA
174m
175d
175c
TRUK ISLANDS
175b
PALAU ISLANDS
Manila
269
116
PHILIPPINES
M A L A Y S I A
BRUNEI
114
Singapore
271
BORNEO
112
CELEBES
SUMATRA
I N D O N E S I A
Jakarta
269
115a
115b
JAVA
LESSER SUNDA ISLANDS
PAPUA
NEW GUINEA
164
SOLOMON ISLANDS
175e
Indian Ocean
A U S T R A L I A
162
166
171a
168a
168b
170
171b
169
Sydney
274
Melbourne
TASMANIA
VANUATU
175f
NEW CALEDONIA
175g
FIJI
NEW ZEALAND
172

176
178
230
242
244

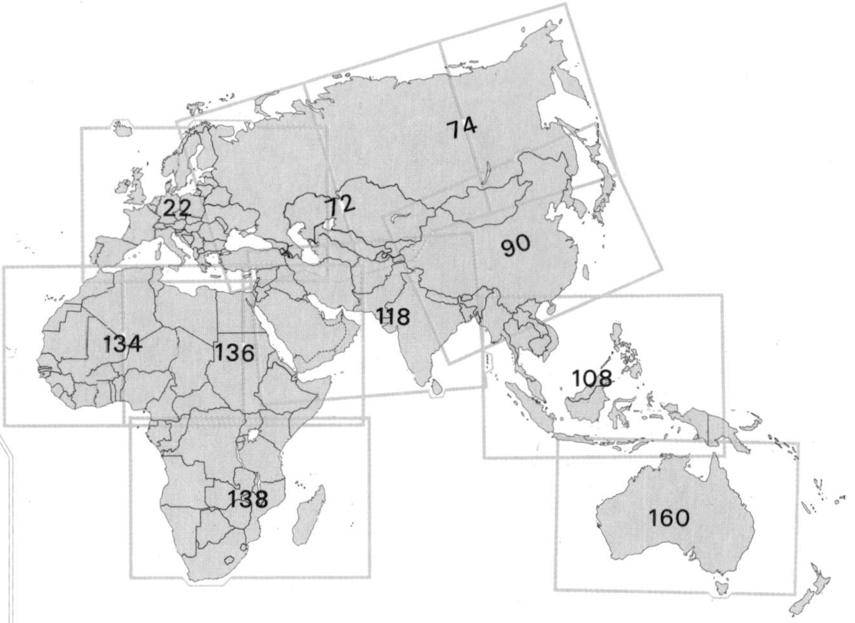
74
22
72
90
134
136
118
108
138
160

World Scene

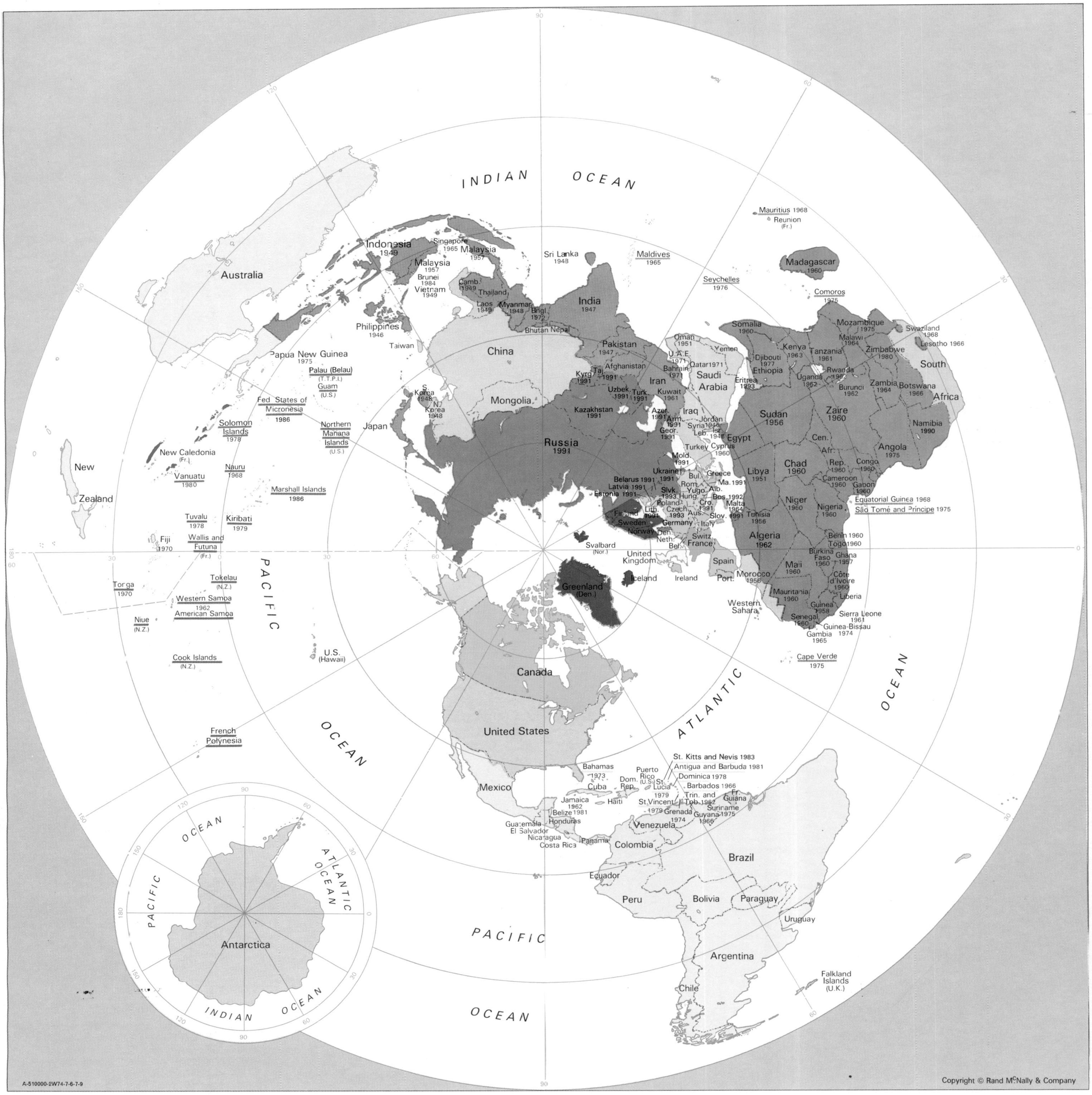

INDIAN OCEAN

Australia

Indonesia 1949

Singapore 1965
Malaysia 1957
Malaysia 1957

Sri Lanka 1948

Maldives 1965

Mauritius 1968
Réunion (Fr.)

Seychelles 1976

Madagascar 1960

Comoros 1975

Philippines 1946

Brunei 1984
Vietnam 1949
Camb. 1949
Thailand
Laos 1949
Myanmar 1948
Bngl. 1971
Bhutan Nepal

India 1947

Mozambique 1975
Malawi 1964
Swaziland 1968
Lesotho 1966

Somalia 1960
Kenya 1963
Tanzania 1961
Zimbabwe 1980

South Africa

Taiwan

Papua New Guinea 1975

China

Pakistan 1947

Oman 1951
U.A.E. 1971
Qatar 1971
Bahrain 1971
Yemen

Djibouti 1977
Ethiopia
Uganda 1962
Rwanda 1962
Burundi 1962
Zambia 1964
Botswana 1966

Palau (Belau) (T.T.P.I.)
Guam (U.S.)

Fed. States of Micronesia 1986

Northern Mariana Islands (U.S.)

Japan

S. Korea 1948
N. Korea 1948

Mongolia

Afghanistan
Kyrg. 1991
Iran
Uzbek. 1991
Turk. 1991
Kuwait 1961

Saudi Arabia

Eritrea 1993

Namibia 1990

Angola 1975

Cen. Afr. Rep. 1960
Congo 1960
Gabon 1960

Equatorial Guinea 1968
São Tomé and Príncipe 1975

New Caledonia (Fr.)

Nauru 1968

Solomon Islands 1978

Vanuatu 1980

Marshall Islands 1986

New Zealand

Tuvalu 1978
Kiribati 1979

Fiji 1970

Wallis and Futuna (Fr.)

Kazakhstan 1991

Azer. 1991
Arm. 1991
Geor. 1991

Iraq
Jordan 1946
Syria 1946
Leb. 1946

Sudan 1956

Zaire 1960

Russia 1991

Egypt

Turkey Cyprus
Mold. 1991

Ukraine 1991

Chad 1960

Niger 1960

Nigeria 1960

Benin 1960
Togo 1960

PACIFIC OCEAN

Tonga 1970

Western Samoa 1962
American Samoa

Niue (N.Z.)

Tokelau (N.Z.)

Belarus 1991
Latvia 1991
Estonia 1991

Lith. 1991

Bul.
Rom.
Greece
Ma. 1991

Libya 1951

Algeria 1962

Mali 1960

Burkina Faso 1960
Ghana 1957
Côte d'Ivoire 1960

Liberia

Guinea 1958
Sierra Leone 1961

Finland
Sweden
Norway Den.
Neth.
Bel.

Slvk. 1993
Hung.
Yugo. Alb.
Bos. 1992
Cro. 1991
Slov. 1991
Malta 1964
Tunisia 1956

Poland
Czech. 1993
Aus.
Switz.
France
Italy
Germany

Svalbard (Nor.)

United Kingdom

Iceland

Ireland

Spain

Port.

Morocco 1956

Western Sahara

Mauritania 1960

Senegal 1960

Gambia 1965
Guinea-Bissau 1974

Cook Islands (N.Z.)

U.S. (Hawaii)

Greenland (Den.)

Cape Verde 1975

French Polynesia

Canada

United States

ATLANTIC OCEAN

Mexico

Bahamas 1973
Cuba

Puerto Rico (U.S.)
Dom. Rep.
Haiti

St. Kitts and Nevis 1983
Antigua and Barbuda 1981
Dominica 1978
St. Lucia 1979
Barbados 1966
St.Vincent 1979
Grenada 1974
Trin. and Tob. 1962
Guyana 1966
Suriname 1975
Fr. Guiana

Jamaica 1962
Belize 1981
Guatemala
El Salvador
Honduras
Nicaragua
Costa Rica
Panama

Venezuela

Colombia

Ecuador

Brazil

Peru

Bolivia

Paraguay

Uruguay

Argentina

Chile

Falkland Islands (U.K.)

PACIFIC OCEAN

PACIFIC OCEAN

ATLANTIC OCEAN

Antarctica

INDIAN OCEAN

A-510000-2W74-7-6-7-9

Intergovernmental Organizations: December 1, 1993

The admission of scores of new countries to the world community after World War II, indicated on the map above by the dates of their independence, created certain opportunities for these new countries that had formerly been the prerogative of a much smaller community of independent states. Until the 19th century, the countries to which international law was applicable was confined to the principal states of Europe and such others, like those of the Americas, as had asserted their independence and right to be treated as equals, or those older kingdoms and states like Siam and Ethiopia that had preserved their independence in an era of colonialism and had,

perforce, to be treated as equals in treaty relationships. But equality as a matter of international law does not constitute equality of opportunity, identity of national interest, or safety from aggression. Consequently, despite the aims and achievements of the United Nations, there remains the need for intergovernmental organizations as a means for small and large countries to promote economic advancement, military security, or to assert their cultural identity with a stronger voice than a single country might possess. The organizations shown represent some of the principal regional and mutual-interest organizations created to advance those interests.

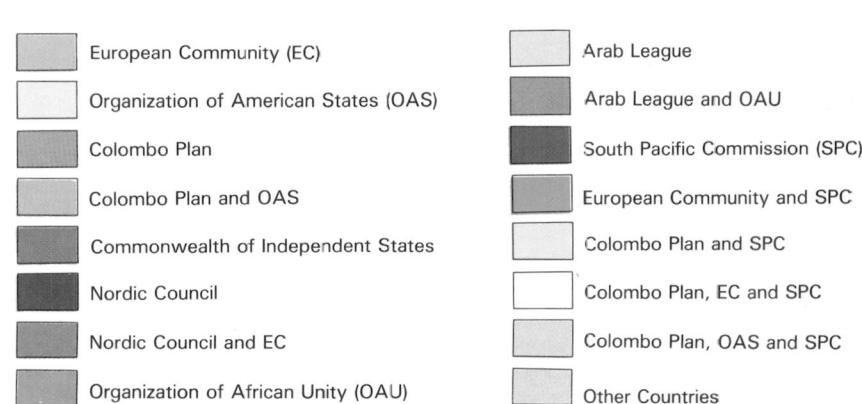

European Community (EC)

Organization of American States (OAS)

Colombo Plan

Colombo Plan and OAS

Commonwealth of Independent States

Nordic Council

Nordic Council and EC

Organization of African Unity (OAU)

Arab League

Arab League and OAU

South Pacific Commission (SPC)

European Community and SPC

Colombo Plan and SPC

Colombo Plan, EC and SPC

Colombo Plan, OAS and SPC

Other Countries

Seaward Claims

Common territorial sea claims

3 nautical miles
6 nautical miles
12 nautical miles

Less common claims

4 nautical miles
10 nautical miles
Over 12 nautical miles
Unusual claim

Other features

Landlocked countries
Continental shelf

Note: Territorial claims of outlying islands to their offshore waters are the same as those of the administering country.

The growth of international law on the legal status of the portions of the seas claimed by coastal states probably began in the early 17th century, when conflicting claims to parts of the high seas by colonial and exploring European sea powers induced the Dutch jurist Hugo Grotius to write *Mare liberum* (1609), on the concept of the "free, or open, sea." His work was answered in 1617-18 by John Selden's *Mare clausum*, proposing that the seas were as subject to property rights and claims as land areas. The first successful synthesis of the two positions was Cornelis van Bynkershoek's *De dominio maris* (1702) in which he suggested that the seaward limit of a national claim should be that of its effective land-based control (the distance of a cannon-shot, three nautical miles). Though never universally accepted, that standard persisted well into the twentieth century.

After World War II, however, both traditional sea-based economic activity—fishing, commercial navigation—and activities made newly possible or intensified by technological change—exploitation of the seabed, pollution, scientific investigation—led coastal states to make increasingly wider claims to both territorial seas, those wholly subject to national law, and to zones in which some, but not all, sovereign rights were claimed, usually to protect economic, but especially fishing, interests. The first Law of the Sea Conference in 1958 attempted under UN auspices to codify international law in these areas. More than 14 years later at the final meeting of the Third Conference, a text representing the efforts of some 150 countries was opened for signature on Dec. 10, 1982 as the *United Nations Convention on the Law of the Sea*. Accessions were deposited that day by 119 states to a document providing definitions, guidelines, procedures, and institutions to govern a wide range of maritime law and activities.

Among the subjects relating to sovereignty delimited by the Convention were sections defining the rights, jurisdiction, and duties of coastal states in matters relating to the territorial sea, the right of innocent passage, international straits, archipelagic (island) states, exclusive economic zones (EEZ's), the continental shelf, the high seas, as well as access to, and use of, areas of the sea beyond the jurisdiction of a single national power.

Territorial sea may be claimed up to a distance of 12 nautical miles (n.m.) from either the shoreline of a coastal state (measured from low water on navigational charts), or from a straight baseline defined by the state when its shoreline is very irregular, as is that of Norway. Waters directly connected to the sea behind this baseline are called internal waters, and include bays (which may be closed at the mouth by a single baseline if they are less than 24 n.m. wide, and river mouths and estuaries. A zone contiguous to the territorial sea not wider than 24 n.m. beyond the baselines defining the territorial sea is defined in which states may exercise *limited* control for customs, immigration, fiscal, or sanitary reasons. Another zone, defined in relation to the continental shelf (the seaward prolongation of the coastal landmass beneath the sea) permits extension of the national sovereignty over the seabed and subsoil of the zone to the edge of the continental margin (the lower termination of the continental slope and rise) for purposes of exploration, scientific study, or economic exploitation of either biological or mineral resources.

In areas of the seas where coastal states lie in close proximity, the seaward extension of a national boundary may necessitate the drawing or negotiation of an international boundary in the sea. Where claims permissible under the Convention overlap, as in the Persian Gulf, median lines must be drawn so as to accommodate each state's maximum claim without disadvantaging bordering states.

The table opposite provides a description of the nature of current national claims to territorial seas and of the economic, usually fishing, zones that have been declared *within* the permissible 200-n.m. limits of the potential EEZ permitted by the Convention.

Offshore zones

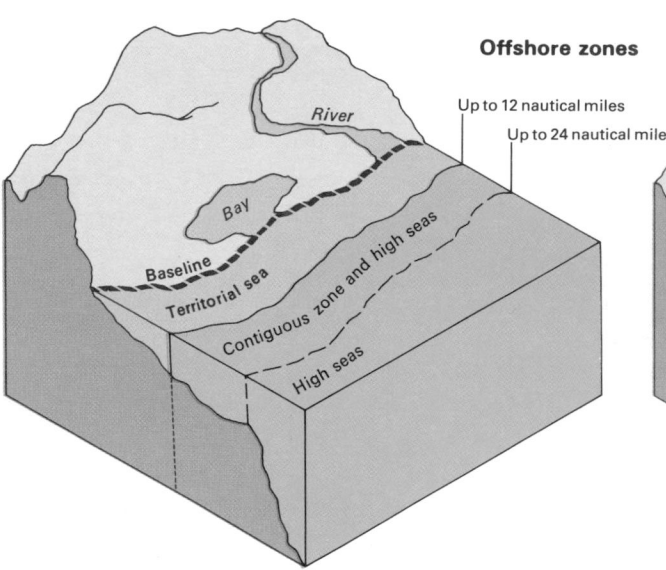

Up to 12 nautical miles
Up to 24 nautical miles

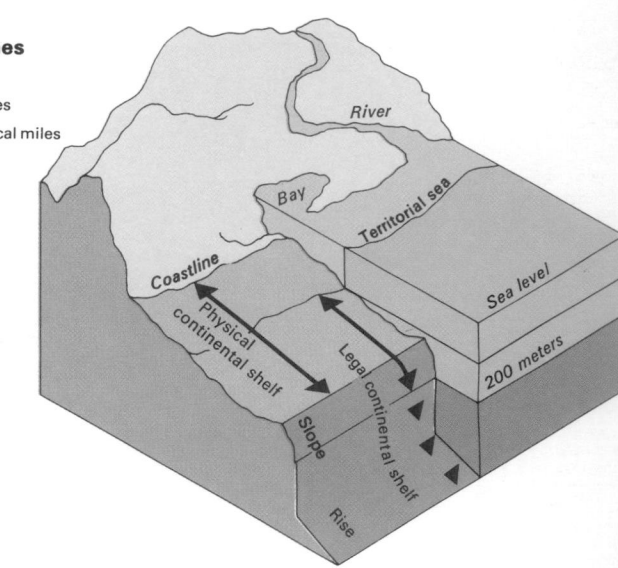

Irregular coastline of Norway

Norway measures its territorial sea from a straight baseline, which in general runs along the outer fringe of offshore islands and coastal promontories. The Law of the Sea Convention permits this type of claim in the case of highly irregular coastlines fringed with islands. In other cases the coastal features do not justify such claims to additional waters, and the claims may not be recognized.

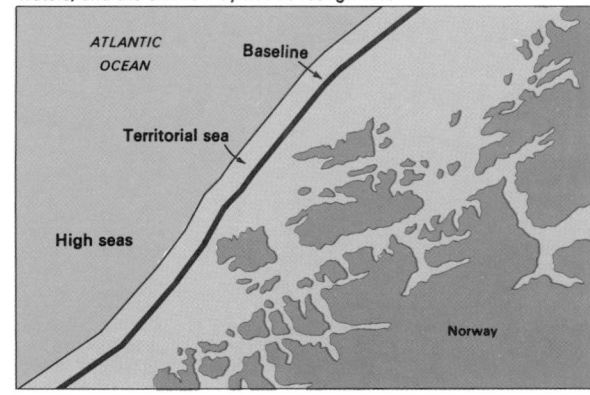

Overlapping claims in the Persian Gulf

The waters of the Persian Gulf are less than 200 meters in depth and the entire seabed is continental shelf. To determine the extent of jurisdiction that each state has over the resources of the seabed beyond its territorial sea, the Law of the Sea Convention provides for median lines, measured from the same baseline as the territorial sea. The median lines divide the continental shelf between opposite and adjacent states.

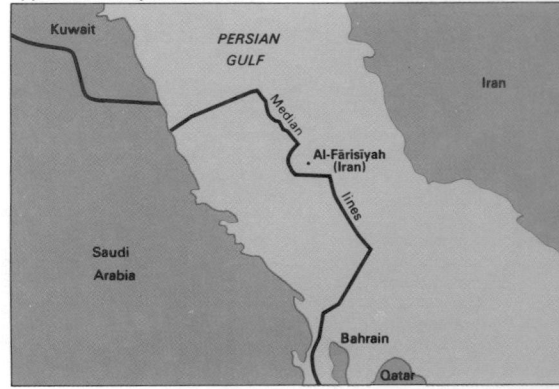

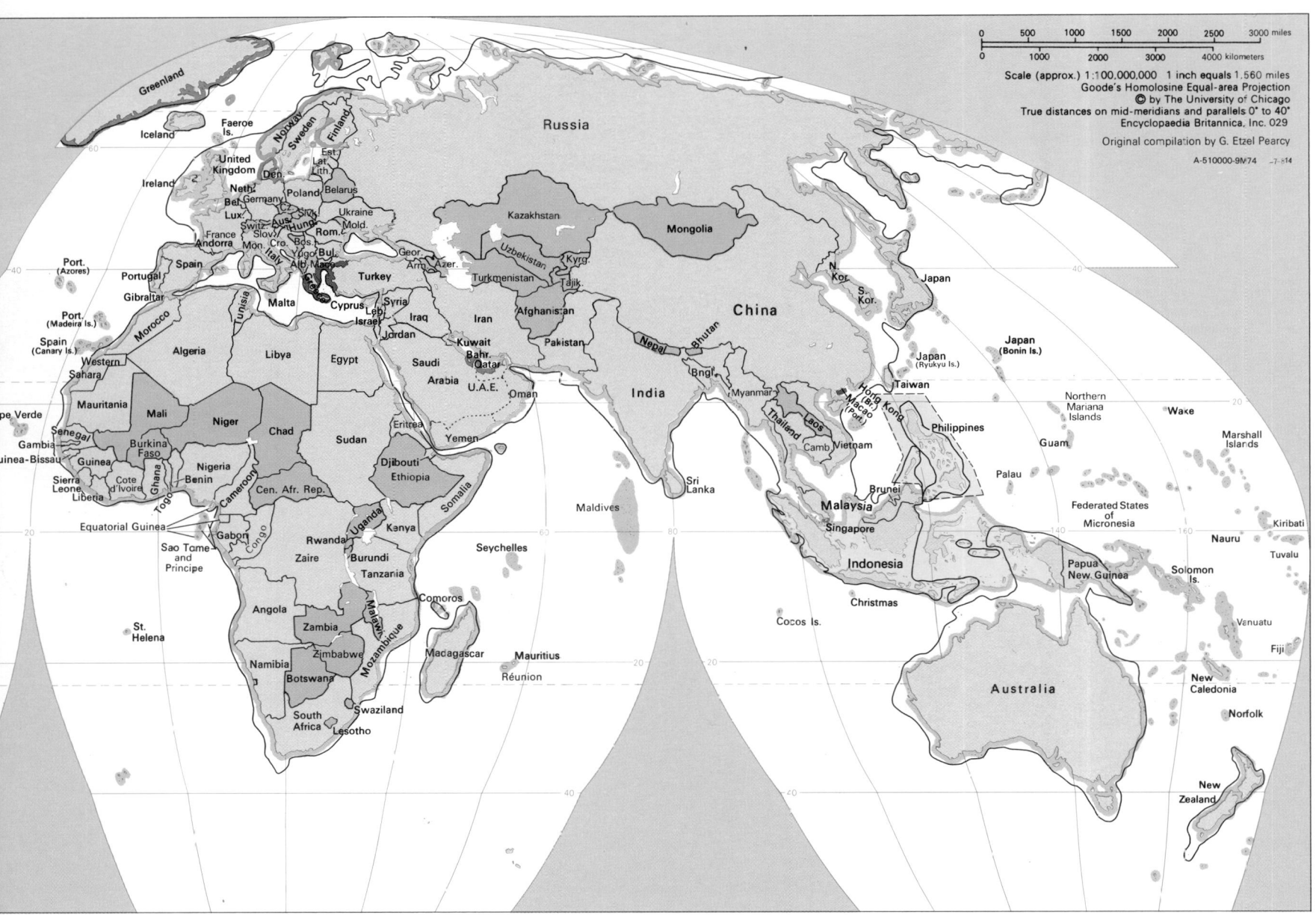

Scale (approx.) 1:100,000,000 1 inch equals 1,560 miles
Goode's Homolosine Equal-area Projection
© by The University of Chicago
True distances on mid-meridians and parallels 0° to 40°
Encyclopaedia Britannica, Inc. 029

Original compilation by G. Etzel Pearcy

A-510000-9M-74   -7- =14

Political unit	Territorial sea claim*	Fishing claim*†	Political unit	Territorial sea claim*	Fishing claim*†	Political unit	Territorial sea claim*	Fishing claim*†
Albania	12 A		Greece	6		Oman	12 A	200 D
Algeria	12 A		Greenland	3 B	200	Pakistan	12	200 D
Angola	20 A	200	Grenada	12	200 D	Palau	12 B	200 D
Antigua and Barbuda	12	200 D	Guatemala	12 A	200 D	Panama	200 A	
Argentina	12 A	200 D	Guinea	12 A	200 D	Papua New Guinea	12 C	200
Aruba	12 B		Guinea-Bissau	12 A	200 D	Peru	200	
Australia	12 A	200	Guyana	12	200	Philippines		200 D
Bahamas	3 -	200	Haiti	12 A	200 D	Poland	12 A	E
Bahrain	3		Honduras	12	200 D	Portugal	12 A	200 D
Bangladesh	12 A	200 D	Hong Kong	3 B		Puerto Rico	12 B	200 D
Barbados	12	200 D	Iceland	12 A	200 D	Qatar	3	E
Belgium	12	E	India	12	200 D	Romania	12	200 D
Belize	3		Indonesia	12 C	200 D	St. Kitts and Nevis	12	200 D
Benin	200		Iran	12 A	50	St. Lucia	12	200 D
Bermuda	3 B	200	Iraq	12		St. Pierre and Miquelon	12 B	200 D
Brazil	200 A		Ireland	12 A	200	St. Vincent and the Grenadines	12	200 D
Brunei	12	200	Israel	12		Sao Tome and Principe	12 C	200 D
Bulgaria	12 A	200 D	Italy	12		Saudi Arabia	12 A	
Cambodia	12 A	200 D	Jamaica	12		Senegal	12 A	200 D
Cameroon	50 A		Japan	12	200	Seychelles	12	200 D
Canada	12 A	200	Jordan	3		Sierra Leone	200	
Cape Verde	12 C	200 D	Kenya	12 A	200 D	Singapore	3	
Chile	12 A	200 D	Kiribati	12	200 D	Solomon Islands	12 C	200 D
China	12 A		Korea, North	12	200 D	Somalia	200 A	
Colombia	12 A	200 D	Korea, South	12 A		South Africa	12	200
Comoros	12 C	200 D	Kuwait	12 A		Soviet Union (former)	12 A	200 D
Congo	200		Lebanon	12		Spain	12 AC	200 D
Cook Islands	12 B	200 D	Liberia	200		Sri Lanka	12 A	200 D
Costa Rica	12	200 D	Libya	12 A		Sudan	12 A	
Cote d'Ivoire	12	200 D	Madagascar	12 A	200 D	Suriname	12	200 D
Cuba	12 A	200 D	Malaysia	12 A	200 D	Sweden	12 A	E
Cyprus	12		Maldives	12	37-310 D	Syria	35 A	
Denmark	3 A	200	Malta	12 A	25	Taiwan	12	200 D
Djibouti	12	200 D	Marshall Islands	12	200 D	Tanzania	12 A	200 D
Dominica	12	200 D	Mauritania	12 A	200 D	Thailand	12 A	200 D
Dominican Republic	6 A	200 D	Mauritius	12 A	200 D	Togo	30	200 D
Ecuador	200 A		Mexico	12 A	200 D	Tonga	12 A	200 D
Egypt	12 A	200 D	Micronesia, Fed. States of	12	200 D	Trinidad and Tobago	12	200 D
El Salvador	200		Monaco	12		Tunisia	12	
Equatorial Guinea	12	200 D	Morocco	12 A	200 D	Turkey	6-12 A	12
Eritrea	12 A		Mozambique	12 A	200 D	Tuvalu	12	200 D
Faeroe Islands	3 B	200	Myanmar	12 A	200 D	United Arab Emirates	3	F
Falkland Islands	3	200	Namibia	12	200 D	United Kingdom	12 A	200
Fiji	12 C	200 D	Nauru	12	200	United States	12 A	
Finland	4 A	12	Netherlands	12 A	200	Uruguay	200	
France	12 A	200 D	Netherlands Antilles	12		Vanuatu	12 C	200 D
French Guiana	12 B	200 D	New Caledonia	12 B	200 D	Venezuela	12 A	200 D
French Polynesia	12 B	200 D	New Zealand	12	200 D	Vietnam	12 A	200 D
Gabon	12	200 D	Nicaragua	200		Western Samoa	12	200 D
Gambia	12	200	Nigeria	30	200 D	Yemen	12	
Germany	3-16 A	200	Northern Mariana Islands	12 B	200 D	Yugoslavia	12 A	
Ghana	12	200 D	Norway	4 A	200 D	Zaire	12	200 D
Gibraltar	3 B							

* Nautical miles
† When claim is beyond the territorial sea.
Data as of December 31, 1990.

A. Measured from a straight baseline.
B. Same as that of administering country.
C. Extends beyond a perimeter drawn around archipelago.

D. Exclusive economic zone.
E. Fishing rights extend to median line with neighboring countries.
F. Exclusive econ. zone extends to median line with neighboring countries.

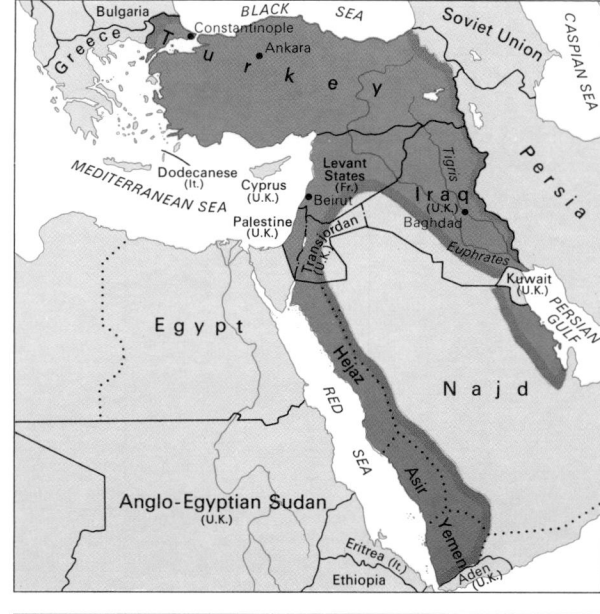

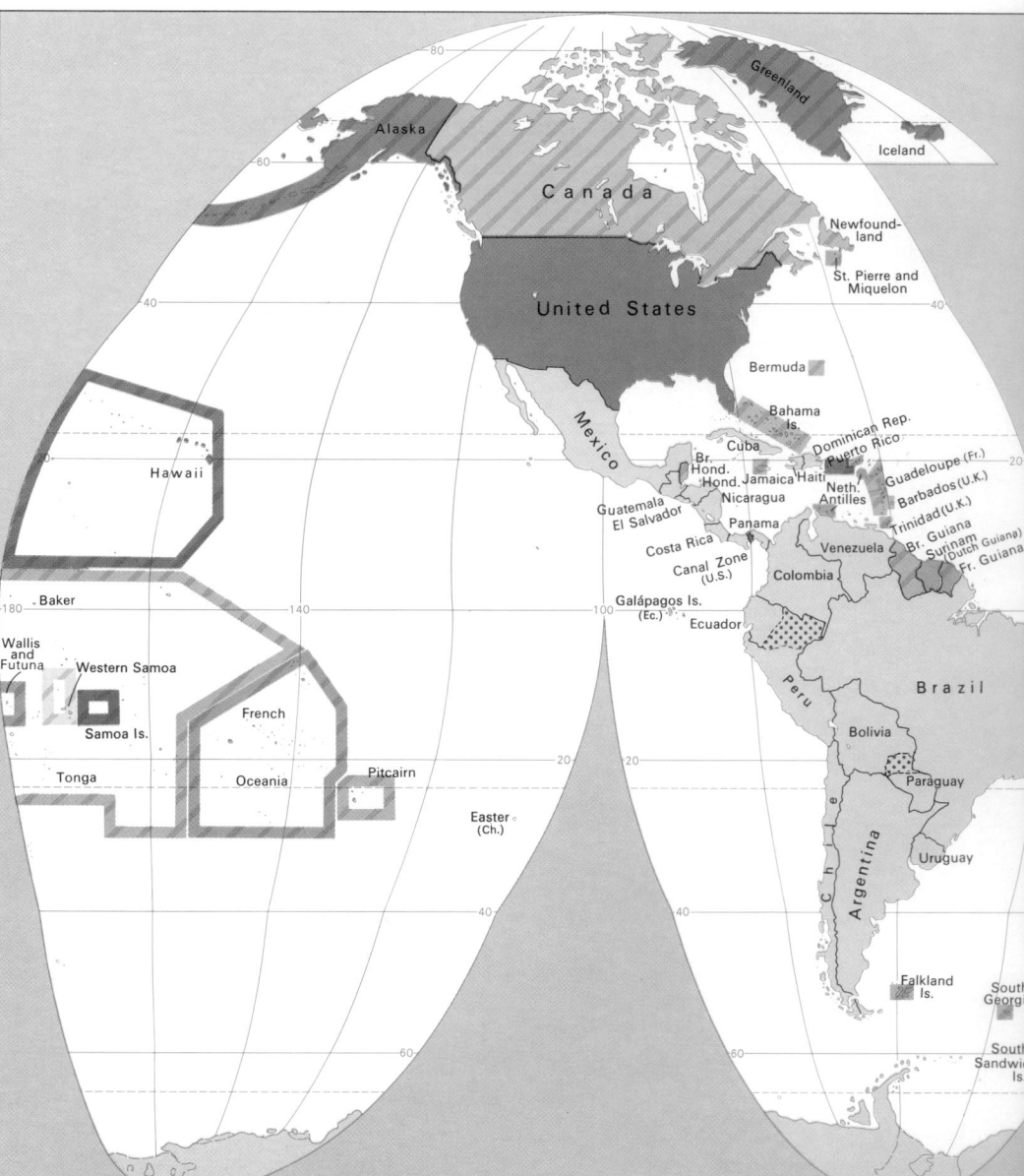

Dissolution of the Ottoman Empire

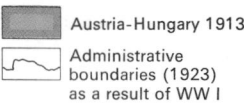

Ottoman Empire 1913

Administrative boundaries (1923) as a result of WW I settlements; dotted are indefinite

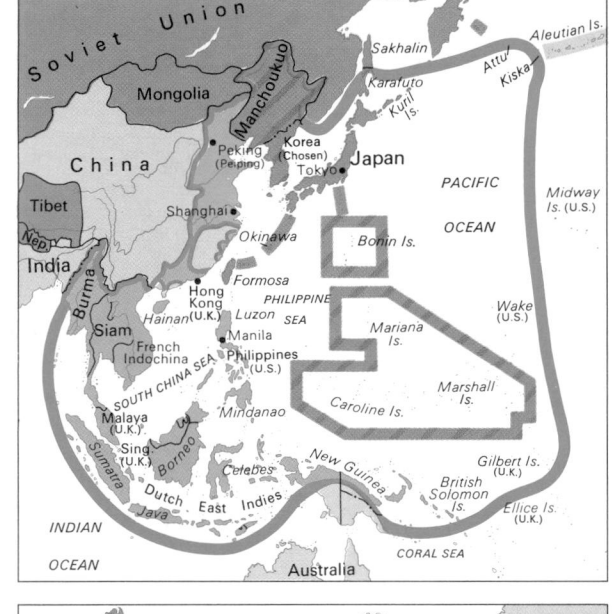

Dissolution of Austria-Hungary

Austria-Hungary 1913

Administrative boundaries (1923) as a result of WW I settlements

Japanese Expansion World War II

Japan 1939

Japanese dependencies 1939

Maximum occupation

Neutral states

States joining Allies 1945

Axis Expansion World War II

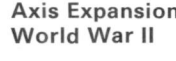

Germany 1939

Other Axis Powers 1940-45

Maximum occupation

Neutral states

States joining Allies 1943-45

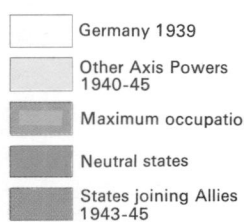

*Occupied by Allies

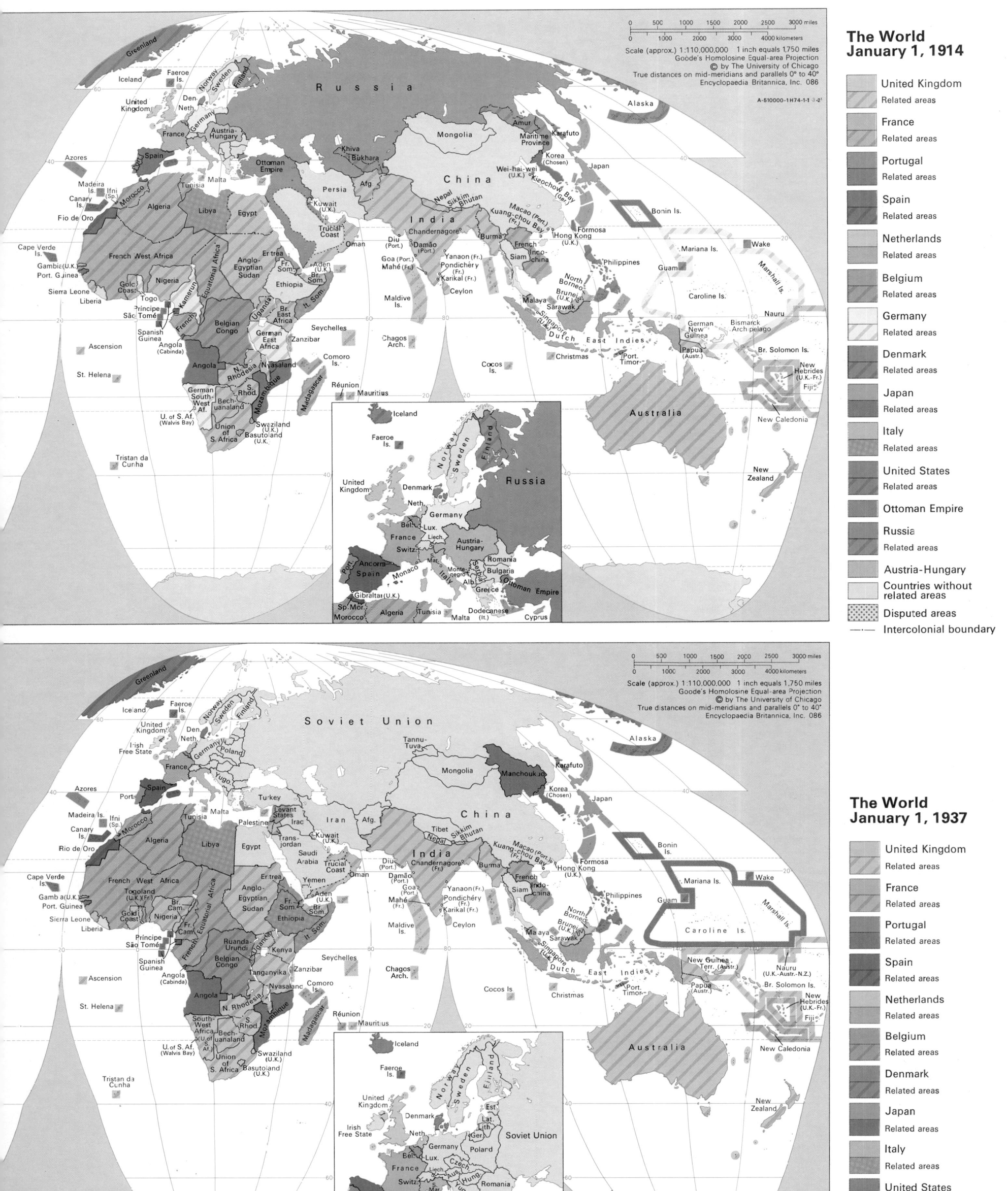

The World
January 1, 1914

Scale (approx.) 1:110,000,000   1 inch equals 1,750 miles
Goode's Homolosine Equal-area Projection
© by The University of Chicago
True distances on mid-meridians and parallels 0° to 40°
Encyclopaedia Britannica, Inc. 086

A-510000-1H74-1-1-2

United Kingdom
Related areas
France
Related areas
Portugal
Related areas
Spain
Related areas
Netherlands
Related areas
Belgium
Related areas
Germany
Related areas
Denmark
Related areas
Japan
Related areas
Italy
Related areas
United States
Related areas
Ottoman Empire
Russia
Related areas
Austria-Hungary
Countries without related areas
Disputed areas
Intercolonial boundary

The World
January 1, 1937

Scale (approx.) 1:110,000,000   1 inch equals 1,750 miles
Goode's Homolosine Equal-area Projection
© by The University of Chicago
True distances on mid-meridians and parallels 0° to 40°
Encyclopaedia Britannica, Inc. 086

United Kingdom
Related areas
France
Related areas
Portugal
Related areas
Spain
Related areas
Netherlands
Related areas
Belgium
Related areas
Denmark
Related areas
Japan
Related areas
Italy
Related areas
United States
Related areas
Countries without related areas
Disputed areas
Intercolonial boundary

Population

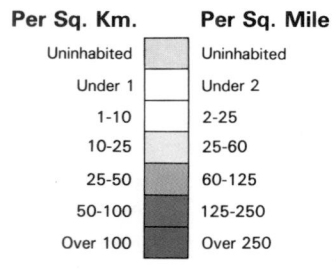

Per Sq. Km.	Per Sq. Mile
Uninhabited	Uninhabited
Under 1	Under 2
1-10	2-25
10-25	25-60
25-50	60-125
50-100	125-250
Over 100	Over 250

● Metropolitan areas over 2,000,000 population
○ Metropolitan areas 1,000,000 to 2,000,000 population

Some cities are identified by initial letter only.

The numbers and distribution of human beings on their planet and the forms that their occupance takes are controlled by a variety of factors. The main population map opposite focuses on identifying the location and density of the most populous regions and cities of the earth. The Urbanization inset highlights the propensity of man to congregate in cities and the group of "age pyramids" below illustrates some of the diversity that is concealed within apparently simple population totals.

Population

The patterns of distribution shown display certain characteristics worldwide: relative densities decline with altitude (and the capacity of the land to support higher densities); settlement patterns follow rivers, or focus on harbours opening on large bodies of water connecting populous, economically interrelated areas; populations tend to fill up contiguous areas of similar topographical and climatic opportunity, whether in coastal plains, intermontane basins, along railroad right-of-ways, or in biologically and climatically defined regions of similar soil, vegetative response, or access from more populous areas.

The main map also identifies the largest cities of the world, distinguishing between those of 1-2 million and more than 2 million population. The selection of cities is determined by the concept of "city proper," that is, usually the smallest contiguous civilly or adminstratively defined and named entity. The meaning of the concept in terms of local practice worldwide, however, is considerable. A city of 100,000 may in one country be a single social, economic, and administrative place, bound together fully by its transportation infrastructure and representing a single *urban* entity in its population's collective mind. A city of the same apparent size in another country, however, might represent something more nearly characterizable as 100 villages of 1,000 persons, pursuing separate economic activities in separate neighbourhoods, often poorly interconnected, sometimes still predominately rural in terms of economic activity, and perhaps not universally understood by its own people as the greater place seen by others.

Urbanization

The concept of "urban" exemplified on the inset map of urbanization is particularly elusive in international studies of population, as most countries have their own definition of the concept, appropriate to local conditions and discourse, but often unsuitable for international comparisons. It is that local concept which is mapped here. Size is a useful indicator as to whether a place is classifiable as "urban," but as indicated above, the "size" of a place, even in the presence of administrative requirements may be misleading. Japan defines a place as "urban" if it has 50,000 or more population and meets certain criteria for their location within the city. A smaller country with a less hospitable landscape, like Iceland or Norway, might, by the same token, define a place as small as 200 as "urban" if it had predominately non-rural employment patterns, administrative function, or its houses were closer together than some set distance. The concept of "metropolitan area," or urban areas contiguous with a central city that are economically dependent on it is also complex and interpreted differently throughout the world. The inset map of urbanization extends the city proper concept of the main map by showing metropolitan areas of more than 2 million. As can be seen from comparison of the two maps, sometimes high urbanization may correlate with relatively low numbers or densities of population. This occurs when the majority of a population lives in large settlements, rather than distributed across an entire landscape and may happen either because of localized economic and employment opportunities in the city, or because the countryside is unsuitable for agricultural or other exploitation. The strong correlation, however, is still between highly populous areas and large cities.

Age and sex composition

Among the characteristics of a population having the greatest significance both in terms of current needs and future trends, the age and sex composition of a population is perhaps the most important. Several examples are presented at the right of a graphic called an "age pyramid," which summarizes the relative proportion of males and females in each age cohort of a population. These examples, drawn by five-year age groups, often illuminate the effects on the whole population of the recent history of the relative growth or diminution of smaller parts of the whole: war losses, emigration of the young for work abroad, natural causes like disasters. The origins of the concern of many countries and organizations with uncontrolled population growth may be inferred from examples like Brazil, where the high proportion of young people means enormous numbers (both absolutely and relatively) in or near their childbearing years resulting in growth rates for the total population that can outrun the far more difficult-to-attain economic growth rates that determine the relative prosperity of a country. Japan, on the other hand, shows a pattern typical of a demographically mature population, that is, a population which is growing slowly or not at all, resulting in lower, more predictable, and more economically supportable demographic rates, but also foreshadowing the movement of large numbers of its people into the pensionable and financially dependent age groups without large numbers of younger workers to support them. The Japanese example also shows, in a somewhat smoothed form, the effects of some of the viscissitudes of Twentieth century history on the relative size of certain age groups.

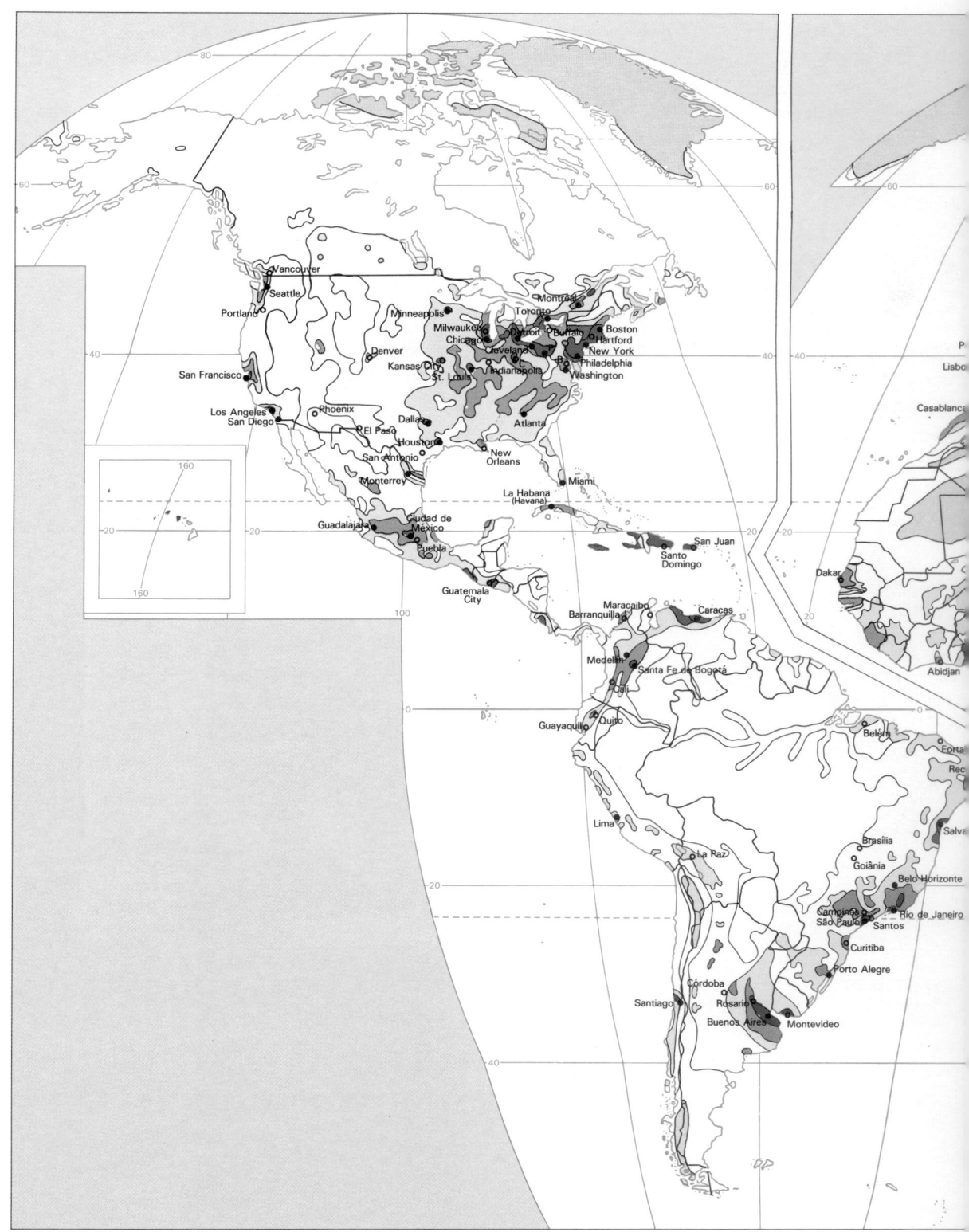

Age and sex composition

■ Male
■ Female

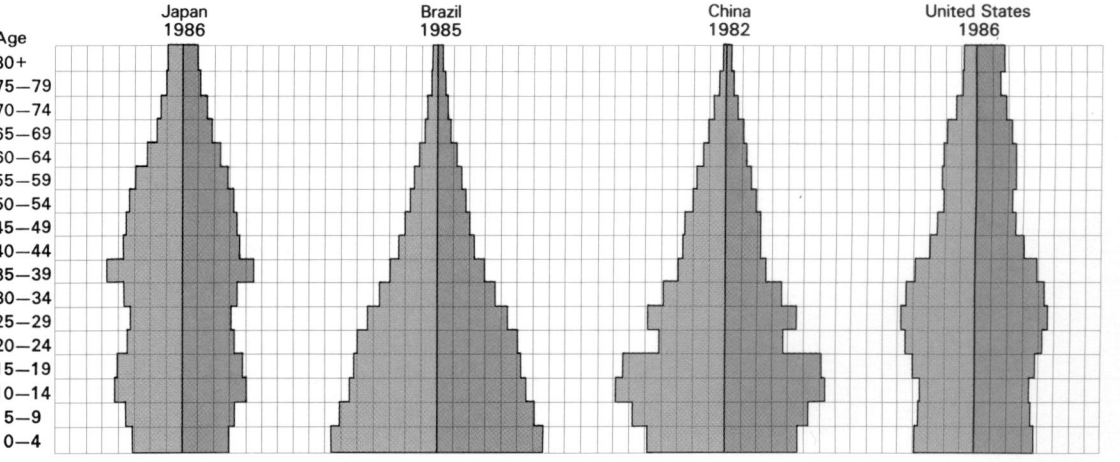

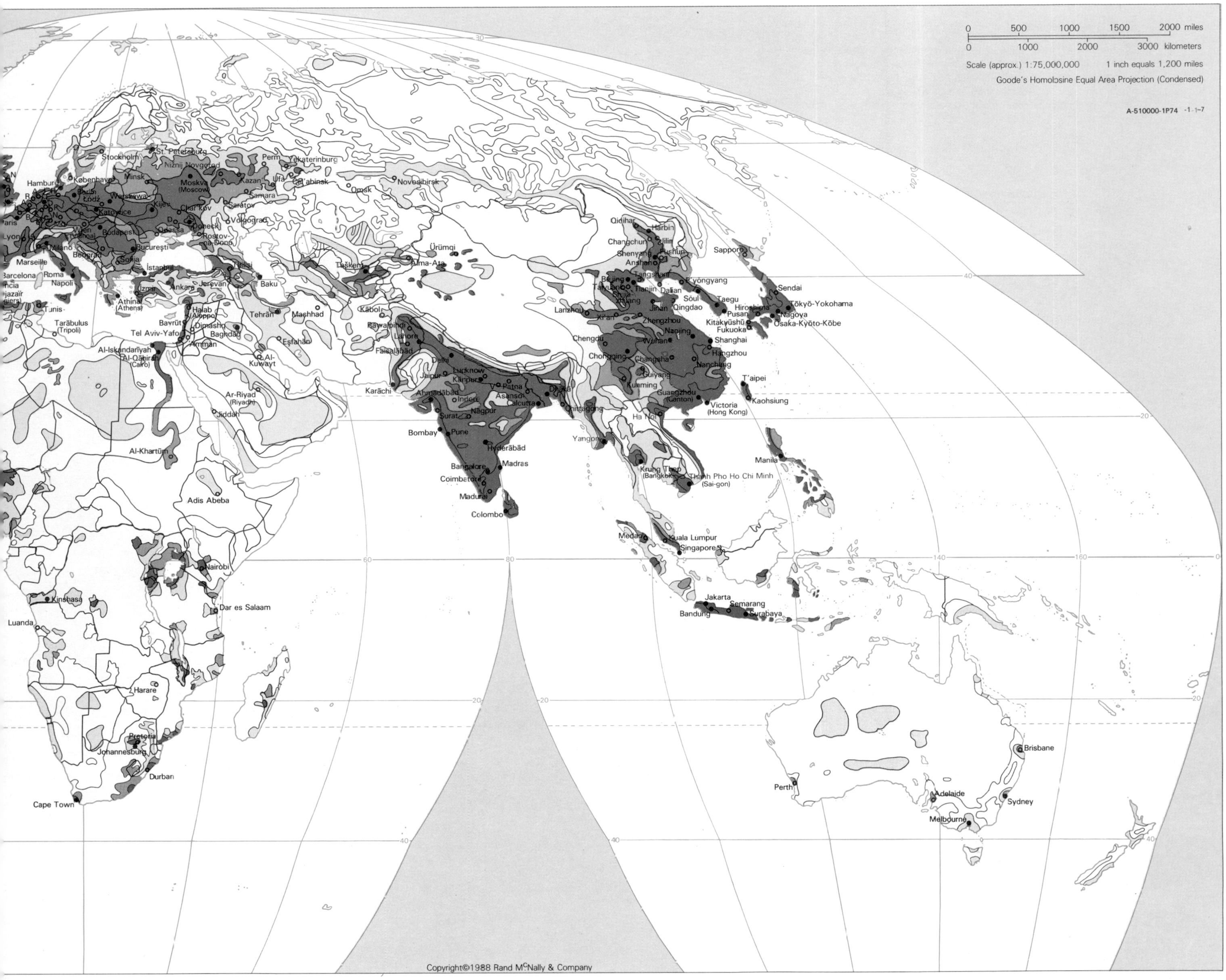

Scale (approx.) 1:75,000,000   1 inch equals 1,200 miles
Goode's Homolosine Equal Area Projection (Condensed)

A-510000-1P74   -1-1-7

Copyright©1988 Rand McNally & Company

Urbanization

World Av. 42% →

- >60%
- 45-60
- 30-45
- 15-30
- <15
- Uninhabited or sparsely populated

● Metropolitan areas over 5,000,000 population

○ Metropolitan areas 2,000,000 to 5,000,000 population

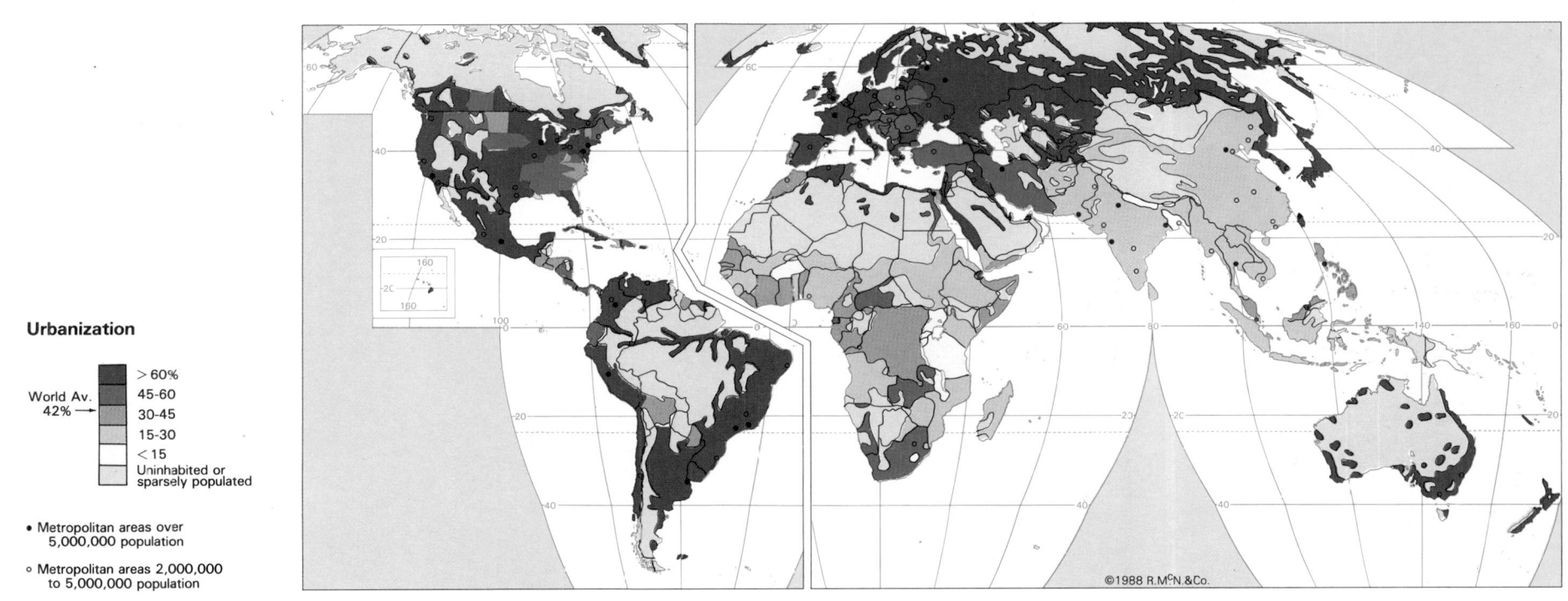

©1988 R.M⁽c⁾N.&Co.

Religions

The majority of the inhabitants in each of the areas colored on the map share the religious tradition indicated. Letter symbols show religious traditions shared by at least 25% of the inhabitants within areal units no smaller than one thousand square miles. Therefore minority religions of city-dwellers have generally not been represented.

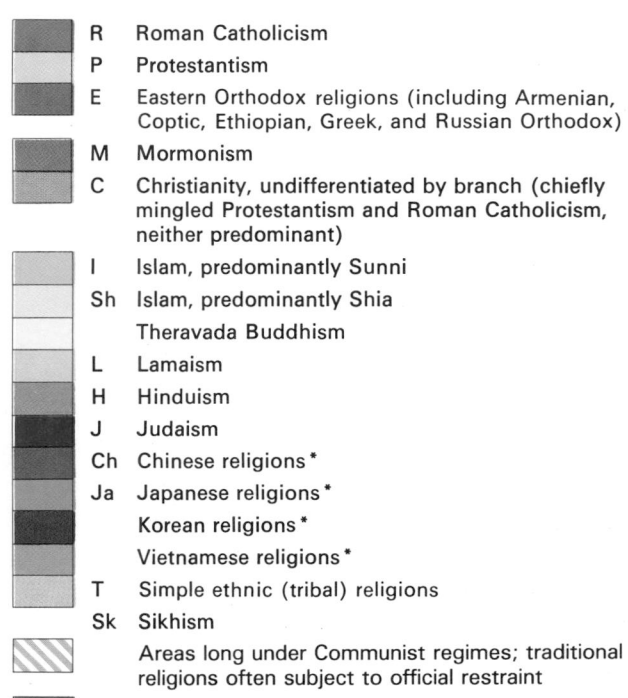

New World religions copyright by Encyclopaedia Britannica, Inc. Old World religions adapted by permission from *Geography of Religions*, D. E. Sopher, copyright, 1967, by Prentice-Hall, Inc.

R	Roman Catholicism
P	Protestantism
E	Eastern Orthodox religions (including Armenian, Coptic, Ethiopian, Greek, and Russian Orthodox)
M	Mormonism
C	Christianity, undifferentiated by branch (chiefly mingled Protestantism and Roman Catholicism, neither predominant)
I	Islam, predominantly Sunni
Sh	Islam, predominantly Shia
	Theravada Buddhism
L	Lamaism
H	Hinduism
J	Judaism
Ch	Chinese religions *
Ja	Japanese religions *
	Korean religions *
	Vietnamese religions *
T	Simple ethnic (tribal) religions
Sk	Sikhism
	Areas long under Communist regimes; traditional religions often subject to official restraint
	Uninhabited

*In certain Eastern Asian areas, most of the people have plural religious affiliations. Chinese, Korean, and Vietnamese religions include Mahayana Buddhism, Taoism, Confucianism, and folk cults. The Japanese religions include Shinto and Mahayana Buddhism.

Languages

Languages of Europe

The following languages are ranked in descending order by number of speakers. Languages spoken by more than 4.5 million people are indicated by color. Others listed, spoken by fewer than 4.5 million persons, are named on the map.

Russian	Norwegian	Basque	Karelian
German	Lithuanian	Irish-Gaelic	Icelandic
Italian	Chuvash	Mari	Adyge
English	Slovenian	Welsh	Scots-Gaelic
French	Macedonian	Friulian	Romansh
Ukrainian	Latvian	Komi	Lappish
Polish	Mordvinian	Frisian	Lusatian
Spanish	Estonian	Sardinian	Ladin
Romanian	Breton	Maltese	
Serbo-Croatian			
Dutch-Flemish			
Hungarian			
Portuguese			
Czech			
Belorussian			
Greek			
Bulgarian			
Swedish			
Catalan			
Danish			
Turkish			
Slovak			
Albanian			
Finnish			
All others			

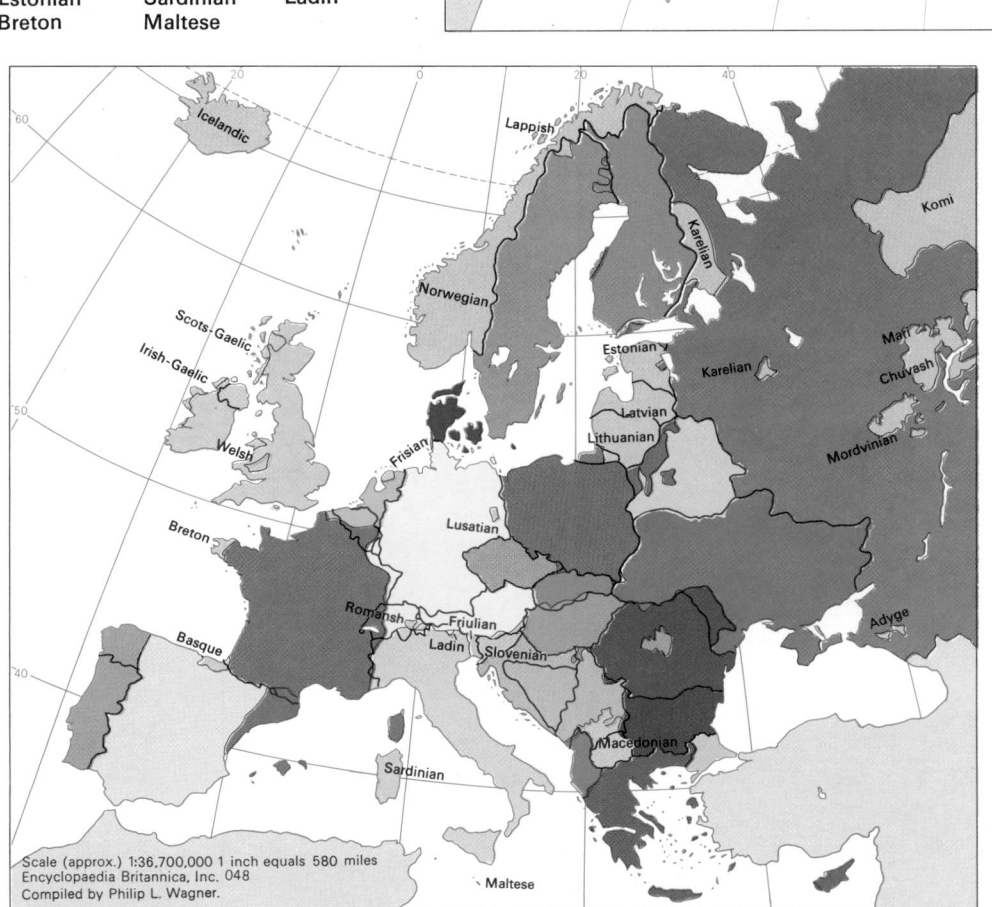

Scale (approx.) 1:36,700,000 1 inch equals 580 miles
Encyclopaedia Britannica, Inc. 048
Compiled by Philip L. Wagner.

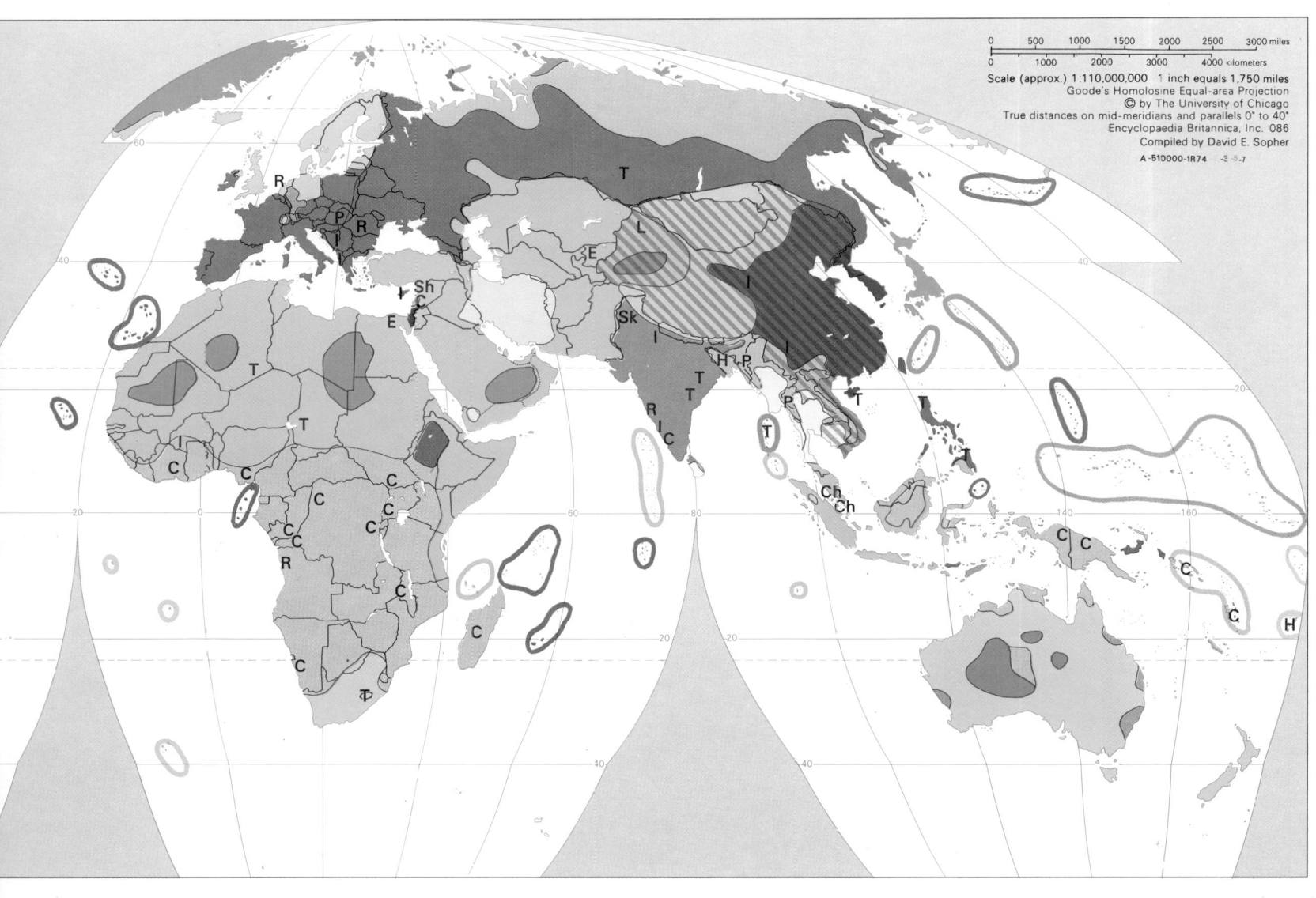

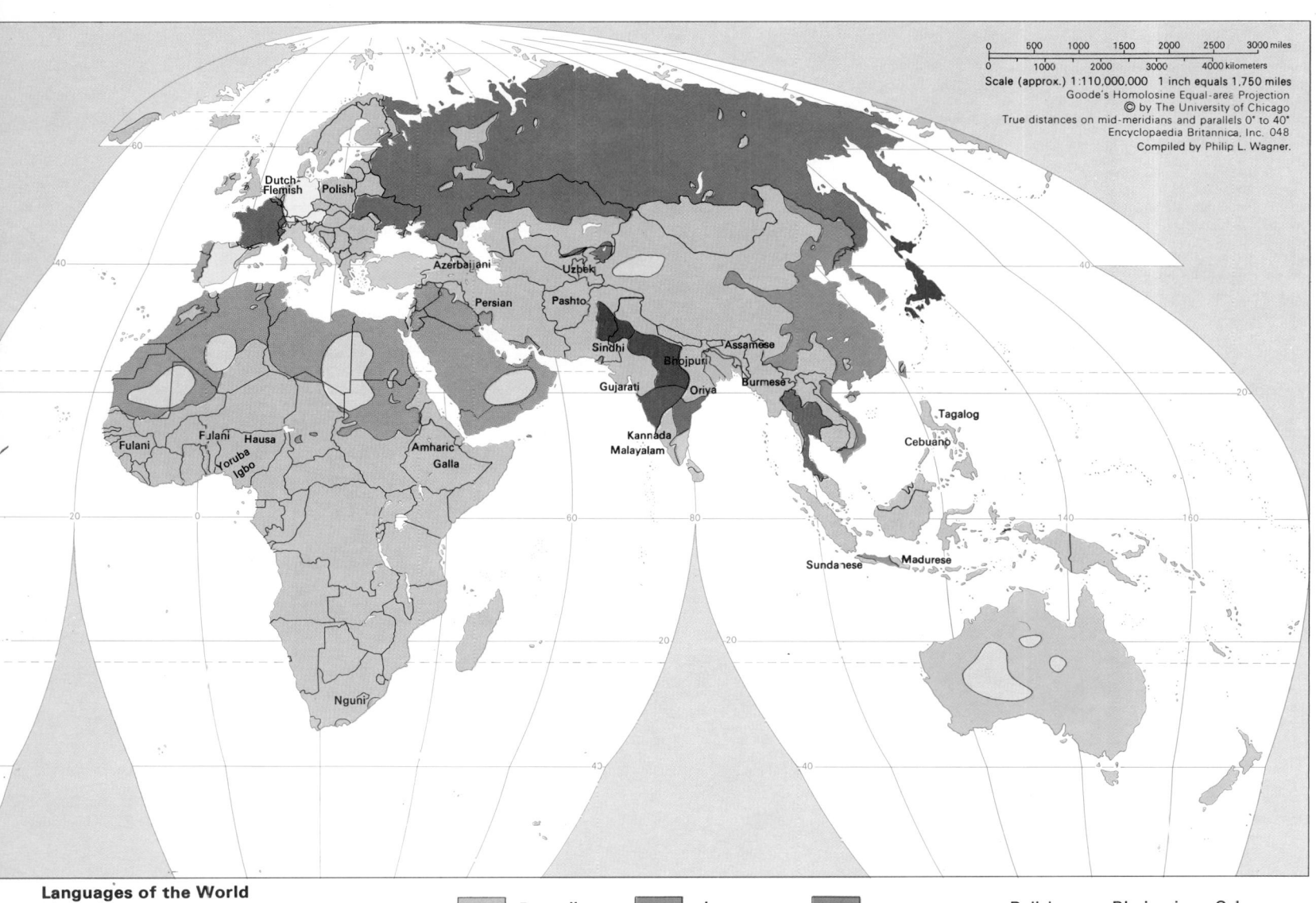

Languages of the World

The following languages are ranked in descending order by number of speakers. Languages spoken by more than 40 million persons are indicated by color. Others listed, spoken by 10-40 million persons, are named on the map.

Chinese

Spanish

English

Hindi

Bengali
Arabic
Russian
Portuguese
Japanese
German
Punjabi

Javanese
Korean
Telugu
Marathi
French
Italian
Tamil

Vietnamese
Urdu
Turkish
Ukrainian
Thai
All others
Uninhabited

Polish	Bhojpuri	Cebuano
Gujarati	Yoruba	Azerbaijani
Malayalam	Dutch-	Nguni
Kannada	Flemish	Tagalog
Oriya	Pashtu	Assamese
Burmese	Fulani	Sindhi
Persian	Igbo	Amharic
Hausa	Uzbek	Madurese
Sundanese	Galla	

Agricultural Regions

- Cash crop and livestock farming
- Cash crop farming, grain or cotton dominant
- Crop and livestock farming with cash products minor
- Livestock ranching
- Dairying
- Mediterranean agriculture
- Specialized horticulture
- Plantation agriculture
- Intensive subsistence tillage, rice dominant
- Intensive subsistence tillage, with no dominant crop
- Rudimental sedentary farming
- Shifting cultivation
- Nomadic herding
- No agriculture

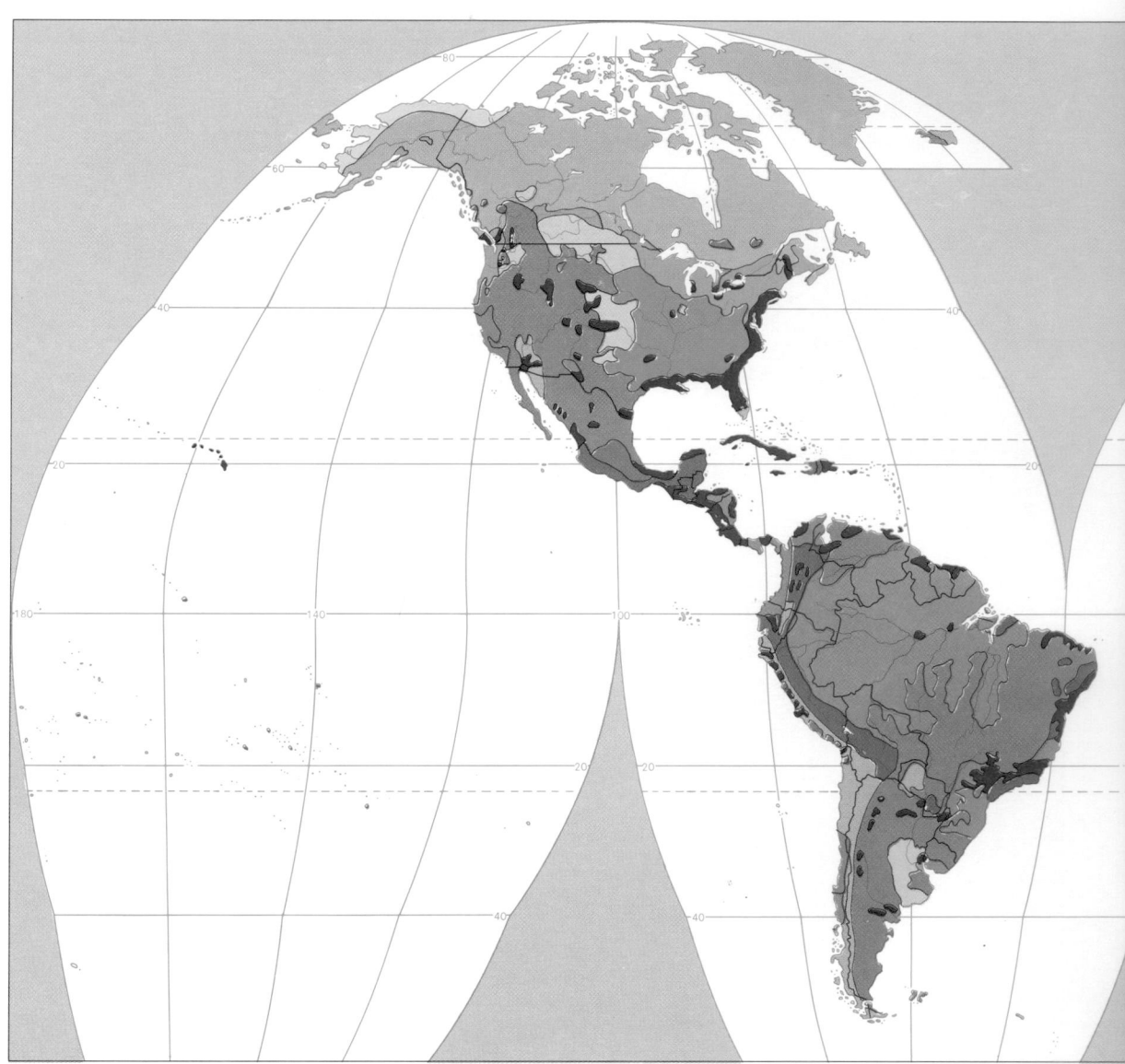

The agricultural systems classified and mapped here represent the primary *agricultural*, rather than economic, activity in the areas shown, since in many developed countries farm population may now constitute less than 5 percent of the total population. No particular level of technology is implied by the classification, as reindeer herding can be carried out with dogs or snowmobiles, crops be irrigated with bucket wheels or electric pumps, dairy cows milked by hand or by machine. Much of the activity shown is controlled, or more specifically, limited by topography and climate. Thus while it is easier to farm on flat land, terracing can create flat land where none exists; intermediate slopes can either be cropped by special techniques, as in Switzerland, or planted in a crop like tea or wine grapes for which slope, or attitude toward the sun and other climatic elements might determine the crop's success. Density of natural vegetation usually declines with altitude and rainfall and so livestock ranching can take place in the compass of a North American feedlot, an Australian cattle station, or a Papua New Guinean butterfly farm. Among the types of occupance listed, "Mediterranean" agriculture may be the least familiar to North Americans. It refers to a system developed in the Mediterranean basin's hot, dry summers that concentrates on hardy tree crops (olive, citrus) or vines (grape), interspersed with small plantings of vegetables or grain; few livestock are kept except in uplands, though small ruminants like goats may be kept lower down.

Forests and Fisheries

Forests

- Conifers: cedar, fir, hemlock, pine, redwood, spruce
- Regions of exploitation

- Tropical hardwoods: ebony, mahogany, rosewood, teak
- Regions of exploitation

- Temperate hardwoods: hickory, maple, oak, poplar, walnut, and some mixed hardwoods and conifers
- Regions of exploitation

Fisheries

- Pelagic fishing regions: anchoveta, anchovy, herring, menhaden, pilchard, sardine, sprat, tuna
- Ground fishing regions: cod, haddock, hake, horse mackerel, mackerel, pollack, redfish
- Mixed ground and pelagic fishing regions
- Shellfish: clam, crab, lobster, mussel, oyster, scallop, shrimp, squid

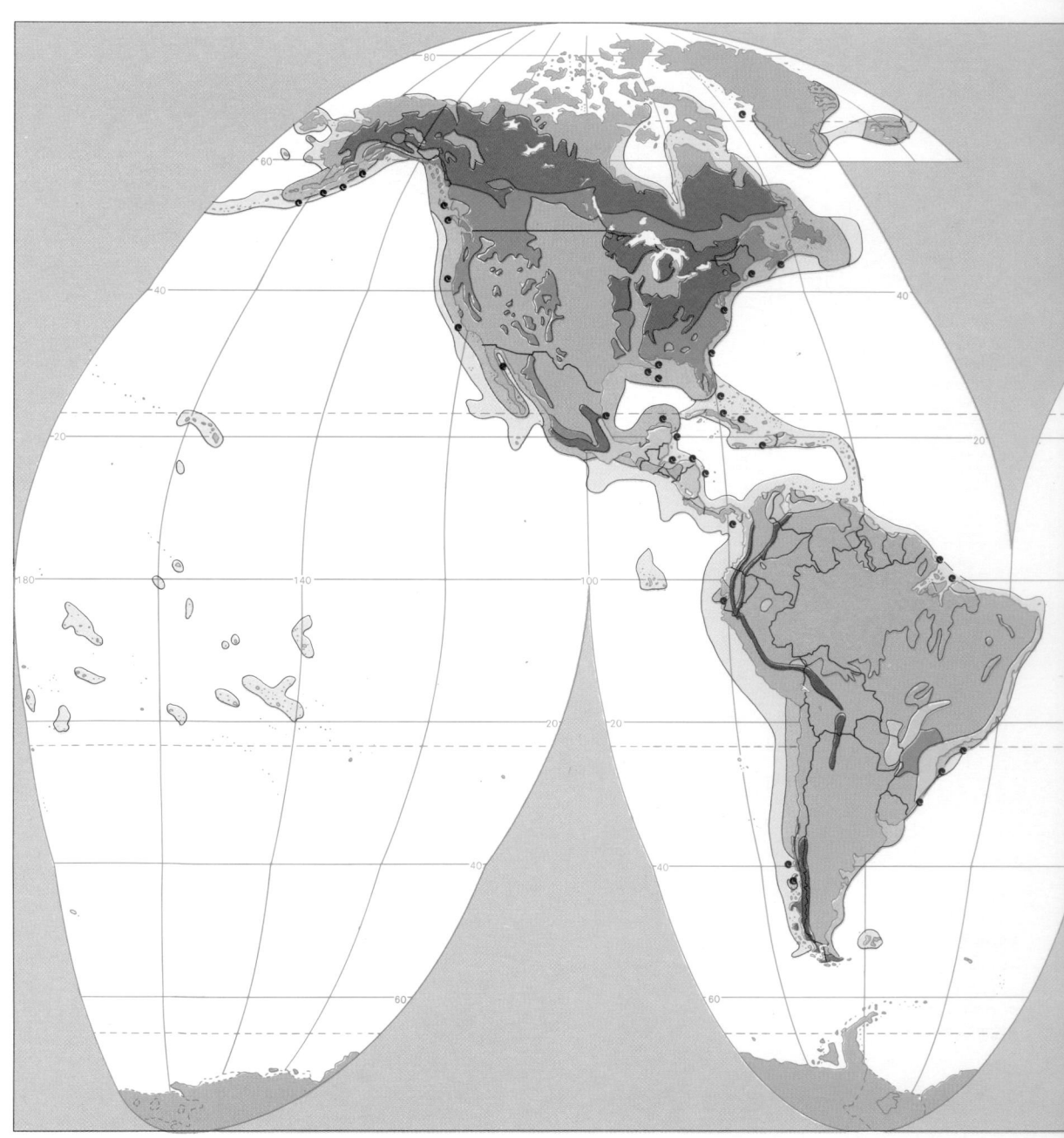

Two principal *commercial* activities are summarized on the map opposite: forestry, classified by type of forests exploited, and fisheries, classified by type of fishing grounds. Three forest types are shown, classified by the woods of chief economic interest within them, rather than by the predominant vegetation. For example, while the softwood conifers listed may actually predominate in many of the regions shown, there are very few areas where the temperate or tropical hardwoods listed will actually constitute the predominant or characteristic tree. Commercial exploitation concentrates on regions where the tree stock has reached economically significant size, is not diluted by other, uneconomical woods, and where transportation infrastructure permits economical removal.

Of the ocean fisheries shown, the term 'Pelagic' refers to near-surface fisheries, either near-shore or on the high seas. 'Ground' fisheries are those which exploit bottom-dwelling fish, or shellfish but should not be confused with the term 'fishing grounds,' which may be either pelagic or ground. The types of fish listed are the principal species exploited in terms of quantities landed. Ocean areas of greatest biological diversity may support both kinds of fish populations, such as those of the Grand Banks of Newfoundland. Commercial whaling is no longer significant although some traditional whaling from small boats still takes place.

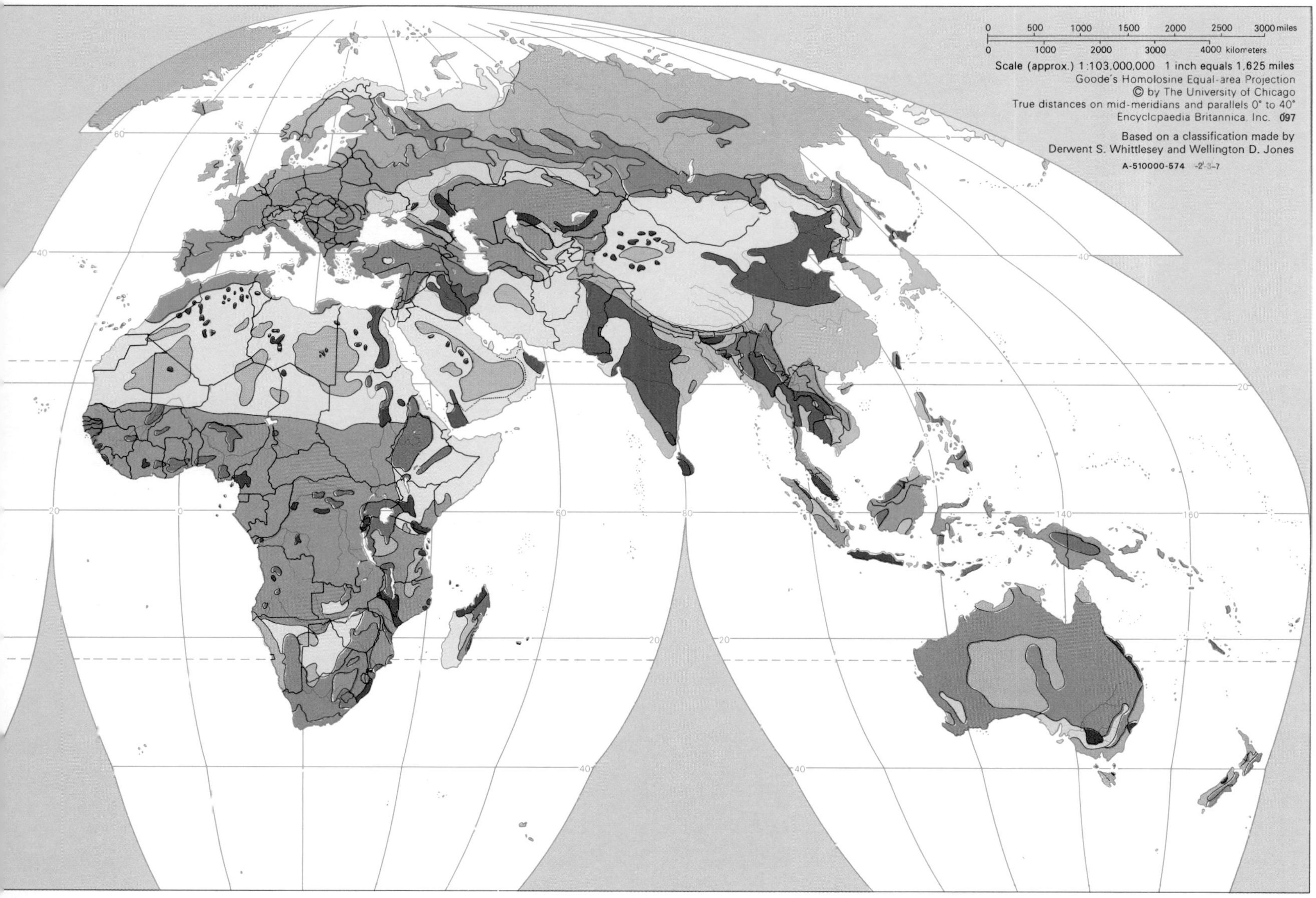

Scale (approx.) 1:103,000,000 1 inch equals 1,625 miles
Goode's Homolosine Equal-area Projection
© by The University of Chicago
True distances on mid-meridians and parallels 0° to 40°
Encyclopaedia Britannica, Inc. 097

Based on a classification made by
Derwent S. Whittlesey and Wellington D. Jones

A-510000-574 -2-3-7

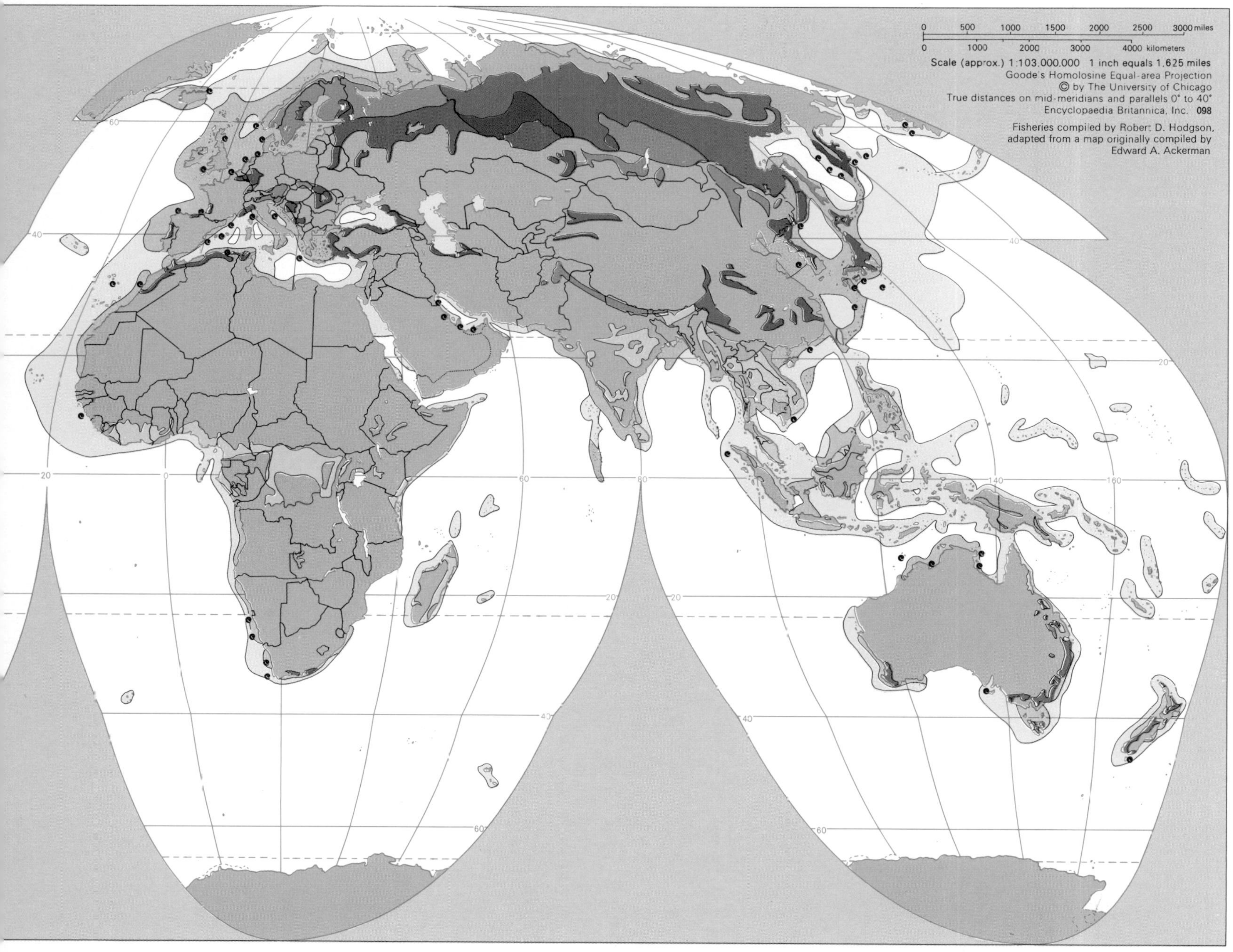

Scale (approx.) 1:103,000,000 1 inch equals 1,625 miles
Goode's Homolosine Equal-area Projection
© by The University of Chicago
True distances on mid-meridians and parallels 0° to 40°
Encyclopaedia Britannica, Inc. 098

Fisheries compiled by Robert D. Hodgson,
adapted from a map originally compiled by
Edward A. Ackerman

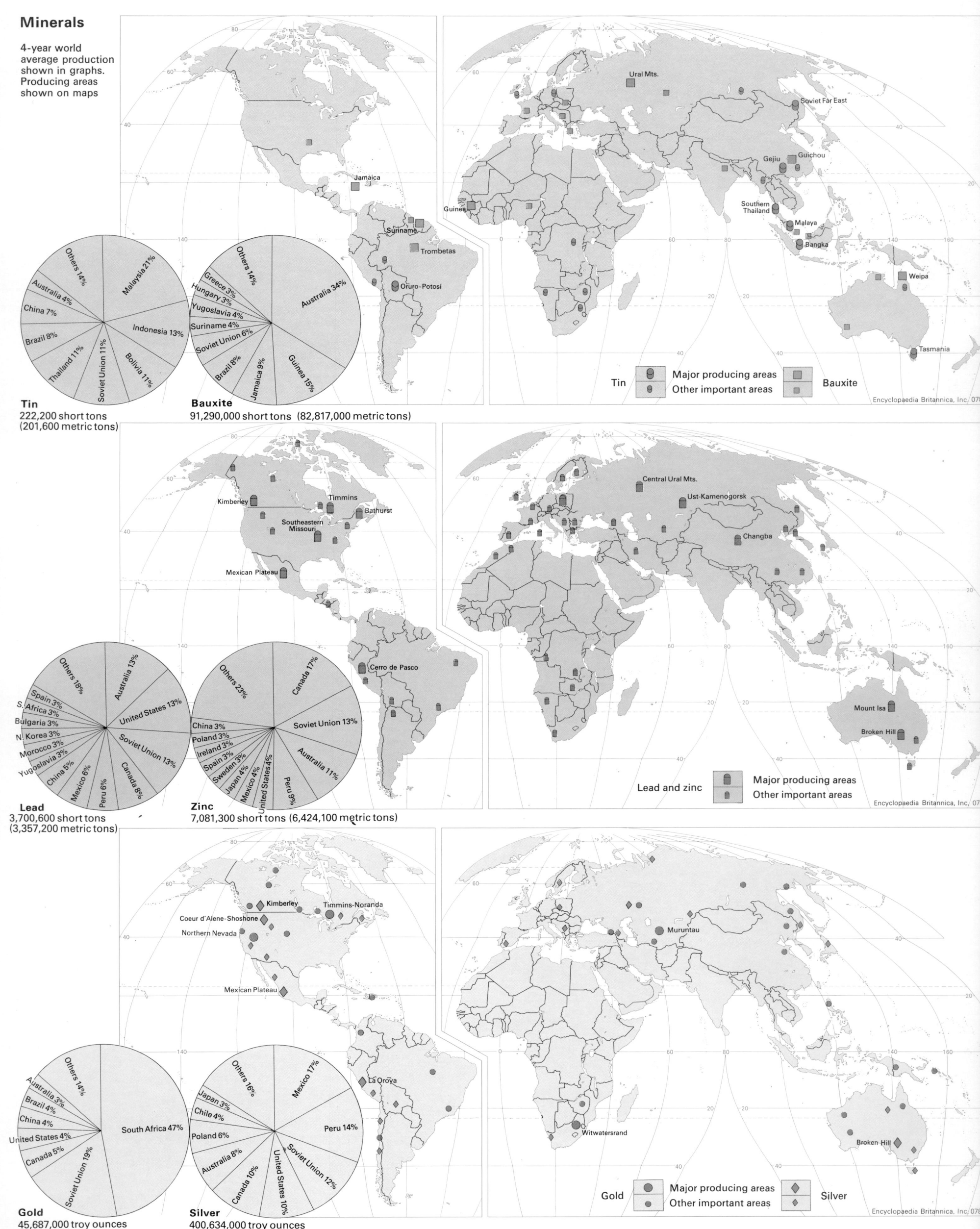

Minerals

4-year world average production shown in graphs. Producing areas shown on maps

Tin
Others 14%
Malaysia 21%
Australia 4%
China 7%
Brazil 8%
Indonesia 13%
Thailand 11%
Soviet Union 11%
Bolivia 11%

Tin
222,200 short tons
(201,600 metric tons)

Bauxite
Others 14%
Greece 3%
Hungary 3%
Yugoslavia 4%
Suriname 4%
Soviet Union 6%
Brazil 8%
Jamaica 9%
Guinea 15%
Australia 34%
Indonesia 13%

Bauxite
91,290,000 short tons (82,817,000 metric tons)

Jamaica
Suriname
Trombetas
Guinea
Oruro-Potosí

Ural Mts.
Soviet Far East
Gejiu
Guichou
Southern Thailand
Malaya
Bangka
Weipa
Tasmania

Tin — Major producing areas / Other important areas   Bauxite

Encyclopaedia Britannica, Inc. 078

Lead
Others 18%
Australia 13%
Spain 3%
United States 13%
S. Africa 3%
Bulgaria 3%
N. Korea 3%
Soviet Union 13%
Morocco 3%
Yugoslavia 3%
China 5%
Mexico 6%
Peru 6%
Canada 8%

Lead
3,700,600 short tons
(3,357,200 metric tons)

Zinc
Others 23%
Canada 17%
China 3%
Poland 3%
Soviet Union 13%
Ireland 3%
Spain 3%
Australia 11%
Sweden 4%
Japan 4%
Mexico 4%
United States 4%
Peru 9%

Zinc
7,081,300 short tons (6,424,100 metric tons)

Kimberley
Timmins
Bathurst
Southeastern Missouri
Mexican Plateau
Cerro de Pasco

Central Ural Mts.
Ust-Kamenogorsk
Changba
Mount Isa
Broken Hill

Lead and zinc — Major producing areas / Other important areas

Encyclopaedia Britannica, Inc. 078

Gold
Others 14%
Australia 3%
Brazil 4%
China 4%
United States 4%
Canada 5%
South Africa 47%
Soviet Union 19%

Gold
45,687,000 troy ounces
(1,421,000 kilograms)

Silver
Others 16%
Mexico 17%
Japan 3%
Chile 4%
Poland 6%
Peru 14%
Australia 8%
Soviet Union 12%
Canada 10%
United States 10%

Silver
400,634,000 troy ounces
(12,461,000 kilograms)

Kimberley
Timmins-Noranda
Coeur d'Alene-Shoshone
Northern Nevada
Mexican Plateau
La Oroya
Muruntau
Witwatersrand
Broken Hill

Gold — Major producing areas / Other important areas   Silver

Encyclopaedia Britannica, Inc. 078

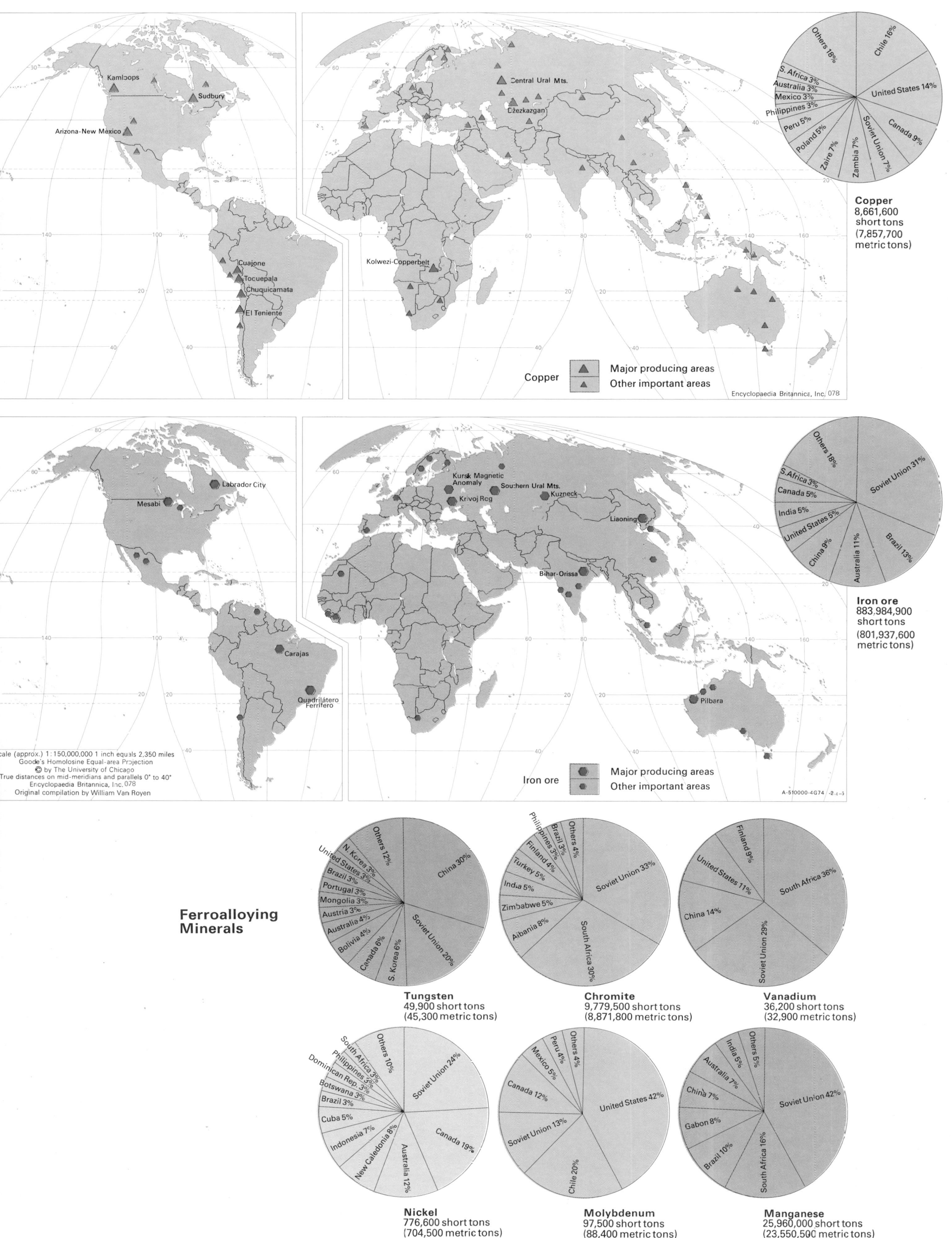

Copper
8,661,600
short tons
(7,857,700
metric tons)

Chile 16%
United States 14%
Canada 9%
Soviet Union 7%
Zambia 7%
Zaire 7%
Poland 5%
Peru 5%
Philippines 3%
Mexico 3%
Australia 3%
S. Africa 3%
Others 18%

Kamloops
Sudbury
Arizona-New Mexico
Central Ural Mts.
Czezkazgan
Cuajone
Tocuepala
Chuquicamata
El Teniente
Kolwezi-Copperbelt

Copper ▲ Major producing areas
        ▲ Other important areas

Encyclopaedia Britannica, Inc. 078

Iron ore
883.984,900
short tons
(801,937,600
metric tons)

Soviet Union 31%
Brazil 13%
Australia 11%
China 9%
United States 5%
India 5%
Canada 5%
S. Africa 3%
Others 18%

Labrador City
Mesabi
Kursk Magnetic Anomaly
Southern Ural Mts.
Krivoj Rog
Kuzneck
Liaoning
Bihar-Orissa
Carajas
Quadrilátero Ferrífero
Pilbara

scale (approx.) 1:150,000,000 1 inch equals 2,350 miles
Goode's Homolosine Equal-area Projection
© by The University of Chicago
True distances on mid-meridians and parallels 0° to 40°
Encyclopaedia Britannica, Inc. 078
Original compilation by William Van Royen

Iron ore ⬡ Major producing areas
          ⬡ Other important areas

A-510000-4G74 -2-4-3

Ferroalloying Minerals

China 30%
Soviet Union 20%
S. Korea 6%
Canada 6%
Bolivia 4%
Australia 4%
Austria 3%
Mongolia 3%
Portugal 3%
Brazil 3%
United States 3%
N. Korea 3%
Others 12%

Tungsten
49,900 short tons
(45,300 metric tons)

Soviet Union 33%
South Africa 30%
Albania 8%
Zimbabwe 5%
India 5%
Turkey 5%
Finland 4%
Philippines 3%
Brazil 3%
Others 4%

Chromite
9,779,500 short tons
(8,871,800 metric tons)

South Africa 36%
Soviet Union 29%
China 14%
United States 11%
Finland 9%

Vanadium
36,200 short tons
(32,900 metric tons)

Soviet Union 24%
Canada 19%
Australia 12%
New Caledonia 8%
Indonesia 7%
Cuba 5%
Brazil 3%
Botswana 3%
Dominican Rep. 3%
Philippines 3%
South Africa 3%
Others 10%

Nickel
776,600 short tons
(704,500 metric tons)

United States 42%
Chile 20%
Soviet Union 13%
Canada 12%
Mexico 5%
Peru 4%
Others 4%

Molybdenum
97,500 short tons
(88,400 metric tons)

Soviet Union 42%
South Africa 16%
Brazil 10%
Gabon 8%
China 7%
Australia 7%
India 5%
Others 5%

Manganese
25,960,000 short tons
(23,550,500 metric tons)

Energy Production and Consumption
Unit of measure is metric tons coal equivalent (m.t.c.e.)

Production

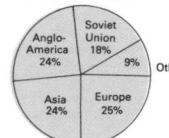

Coal and lignite
World total: 2,712,000,000

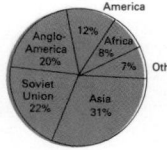

Crude petroleum
World total: 4,035,000,000

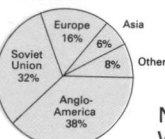

Natural gas
World total: 1,852,000,000

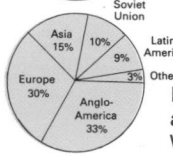

Primary electricity (hydro-, geothermal, and nuclear)
World total: 334,000,000

Table of equivalents

Coal, anthracite and bituminous	1 metric ton = 1.0 m.t.c.e.
Lignite	1 metric ton = 0.3 – 0.6 m.t.c.e.
Petroleum	1 metric ton = 1.5 m.t.c.e.
Natural gas	1,000 cubic meters = 1.33 m.t.c.e.
Hydro-, geothermal, and nuclear electricity	1.0 megawatt-hour = 0.125 m.t.c.e.

Potential energy of 1 metric ton of coal equals 28,000,000 B.T.U.

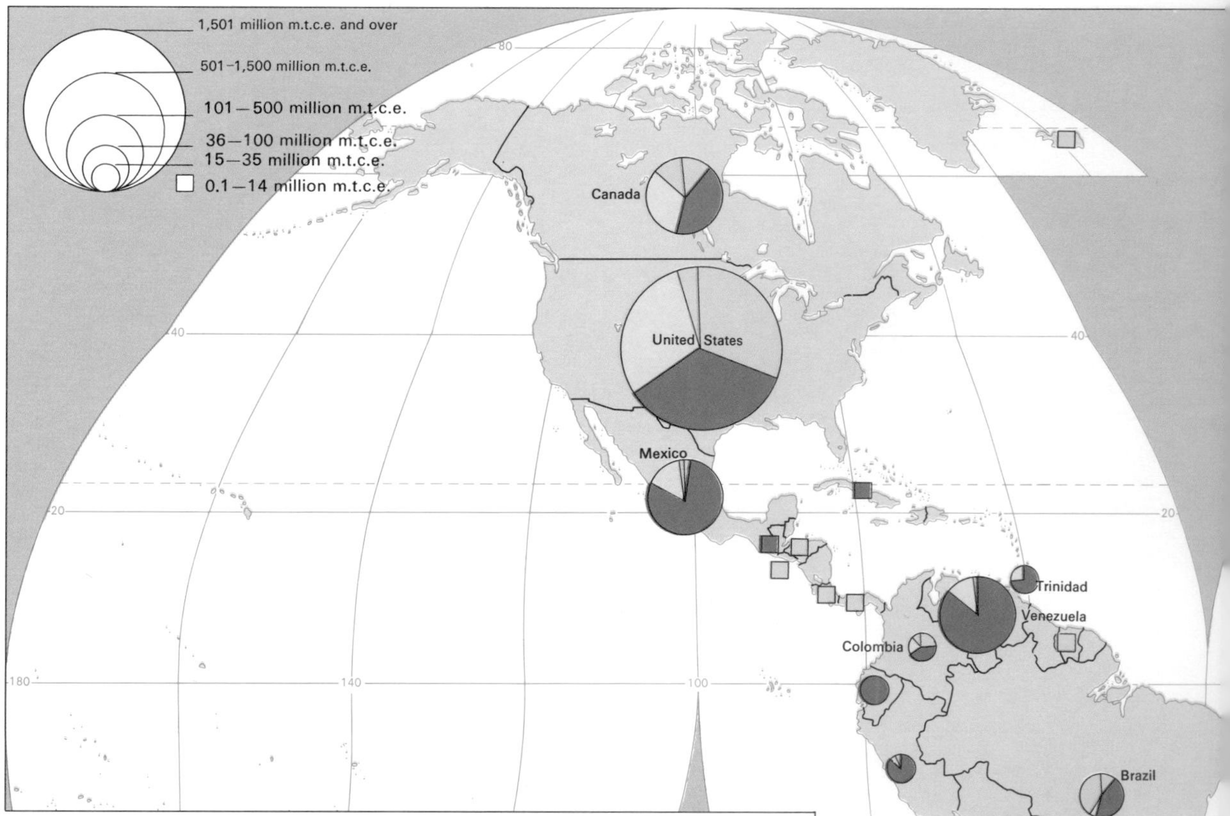

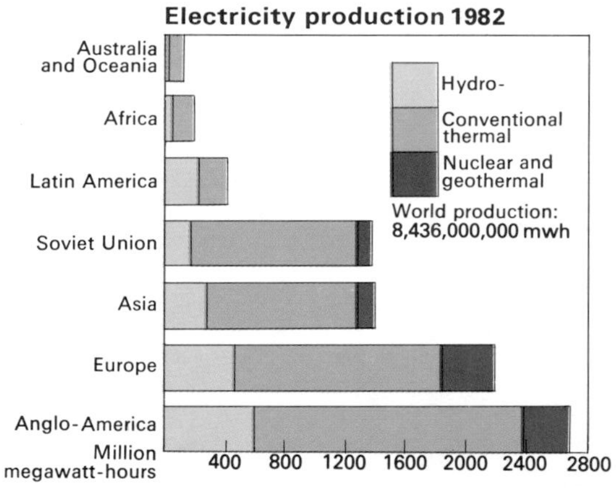

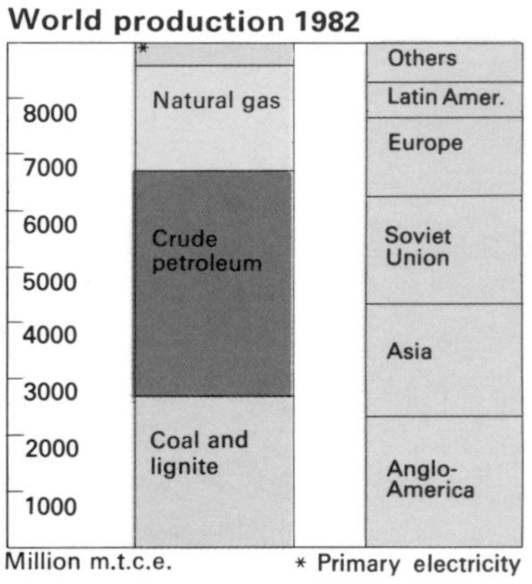

Consumption

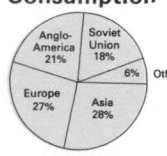

Solid fuels
World total: 2,693,000,000

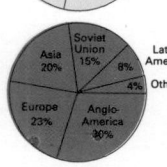

Liquid fuels
World total: 3,543,000,000

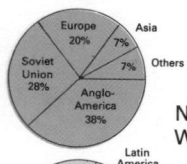

Natural and manufactured gas
World total: 1,836,000,000

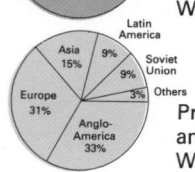

Primary electricity (hydro-, geothermal, and nuclear)
World total: 334,000,000

Consumption totals exclude noncommercial fuels, fuels consumed by vessels engaged in international trade, and nonfuel petroleum products.

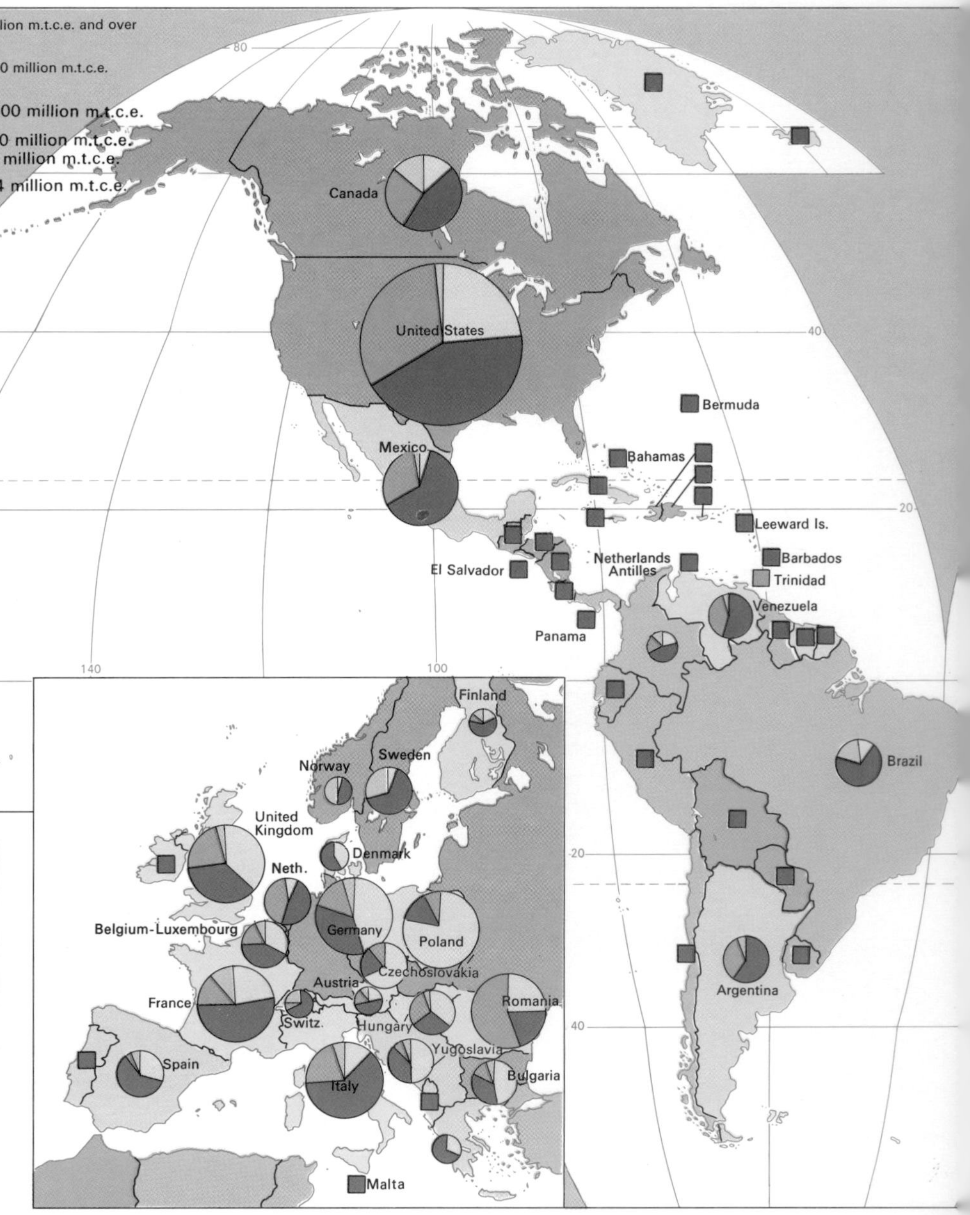

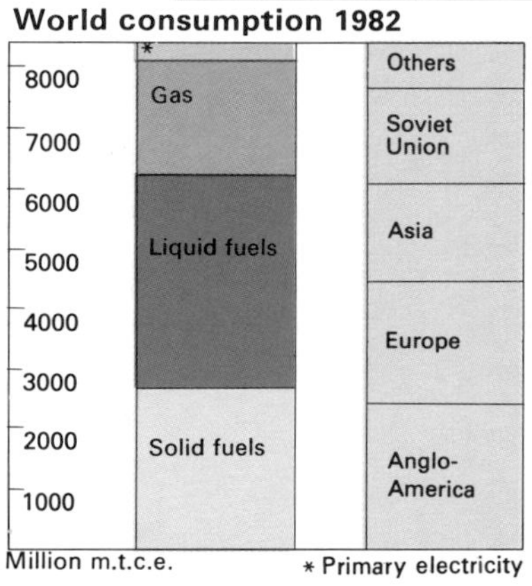

Per capita consumption

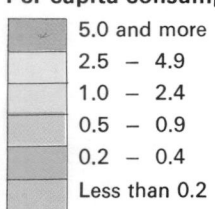

- 5.0 and more
- 2.5 – 4.9
- 1.0 – 2.4
- 0.5 – 0.9
- 0.2 – 0.4
- Less than 0.2

Map legend (top)

1,501 million m.t.c.e. and over
501–1,500 million m.t.c.e.
101–500 million m.t.c.e.
36–100 million m.t.c.e.
15–35 million m.t.c.e.
0.1–14 million m.t.c.e.

Canada
United States
Mexico
Trinidad
Venezuela
Colombia
Brazil
Argentina

Electricity production 1982

- Hydro-
- Conventional thermal
- Nuclear and geothermal

World production: 8,436,000,000 mwh

Australia and Oceania
Africa
Latin America
Soviet Union
Asia
Europe
Anglo-America

Million megawatt-hours   400 800 1200 1600 2000 2400 2800

World production 1982

Natural gas
Crude petroleum
Coal and lignite

8000
7000
6000
5000
4000
3000
2000
1000
Million m.t.c.e.

*Others
Latin Amer.
Europe
Soviet Union
Asia
Anglo-America

* Primary electricity

Map legend (bottom)

1,501 million m.t.c.e. and over
501–1,500 million m.t.c.e.
101–500 million m.t.c.e.
36–100 million m.t.c.e.
15–35 million m.t.c.e.
0.1–14 million m.t.c.e.

Canada
United States
Mexico
Bermuda
Bahamas
Leeward Is.
El Salvador
Netherlands Antilles
Barbados
Trinidad
Venezuela
Panama
Brazil
Argentina

American Samoa

Finland
Norway
Sweden
United Kingdom
Denmark
Neth.
Belgium-Luxembourg
Germany
Poland
France
Austria
Czechoslovakia
Switz.
Hungary
Romania
Spain
Italy
Yugoslavia
Bulgaria
Malta

World consumption 1982

Gas
Liquid fuels
Solid fuels

8000
7000
6000
5000
4000
3000
2000
1000
Million m.t.c.e.

*Others
Soviet Union
Asia
Europe
Anglo-America

* Primary electricity

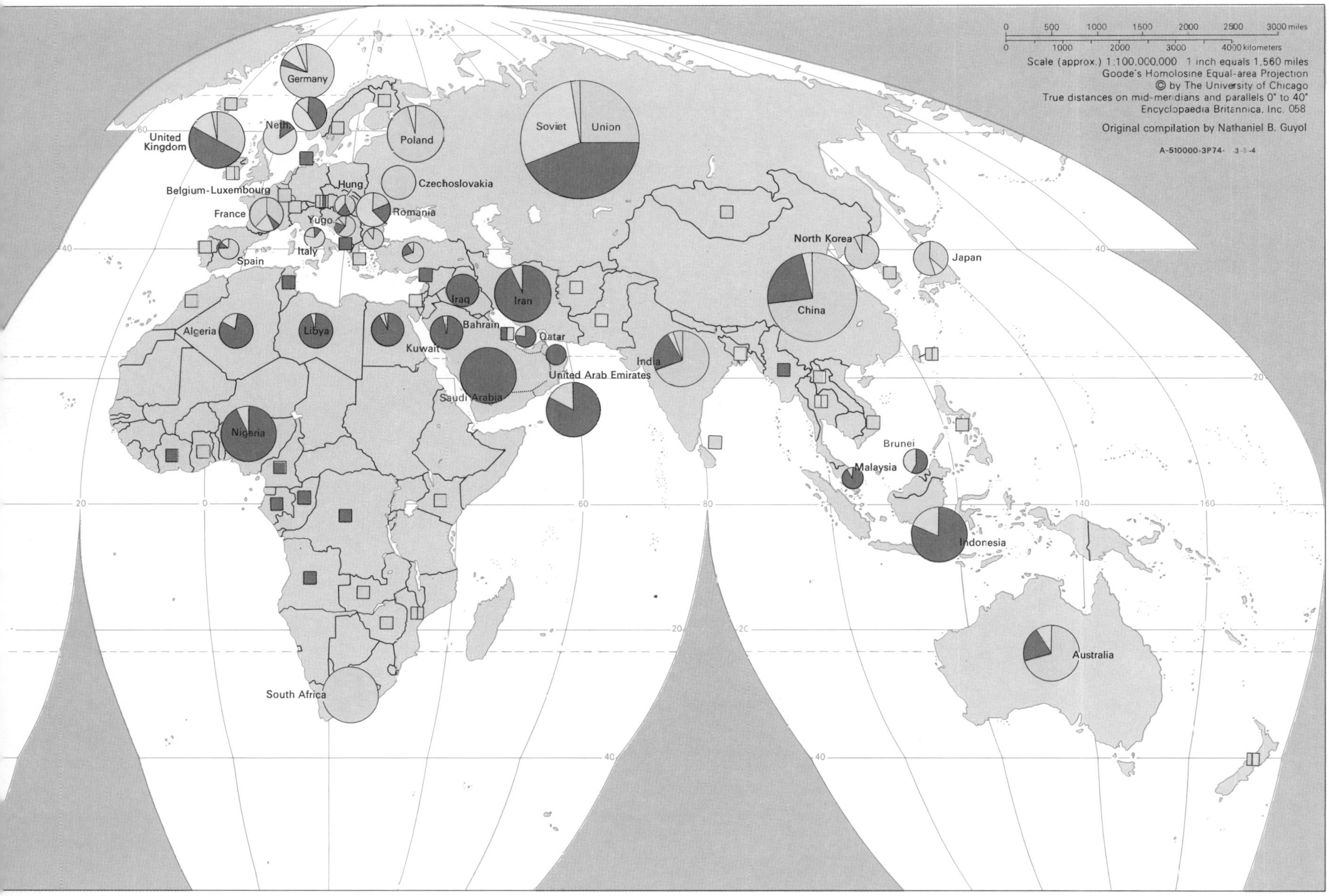

0   500   1000   1500   2000   2500   3000 miles

0   1000   2000   3000   4000 kilometers
Scale (approx.) 1:100,000,000   1 inch equals 1,560 miles
Goode's Homolosine Equal-area Projection
© by The University of Chicago
True distances on mid-meridians and parallels 0° to 40°
Encyclopaedia Britannica, Inc. 058

Original compilation by Nathaniel B. Guyol

A-510000-3P74· 3·0·4

Germany

United
Kingdom

Neth

Poland

Soviet   Union

Belgium-Luxembourg

Hung   Czechoslovakia

France   Romania

Yugo

Italy

Spain

North Korea   Japan

Iraq   Iran

China

Algeria   Libya   Bahrain

Kuwait   Qatar

India

United Arab Emirates

Saudi Arabia

Nigeria

Brunei

Malaysia

Indonesia

Australia

South Africa

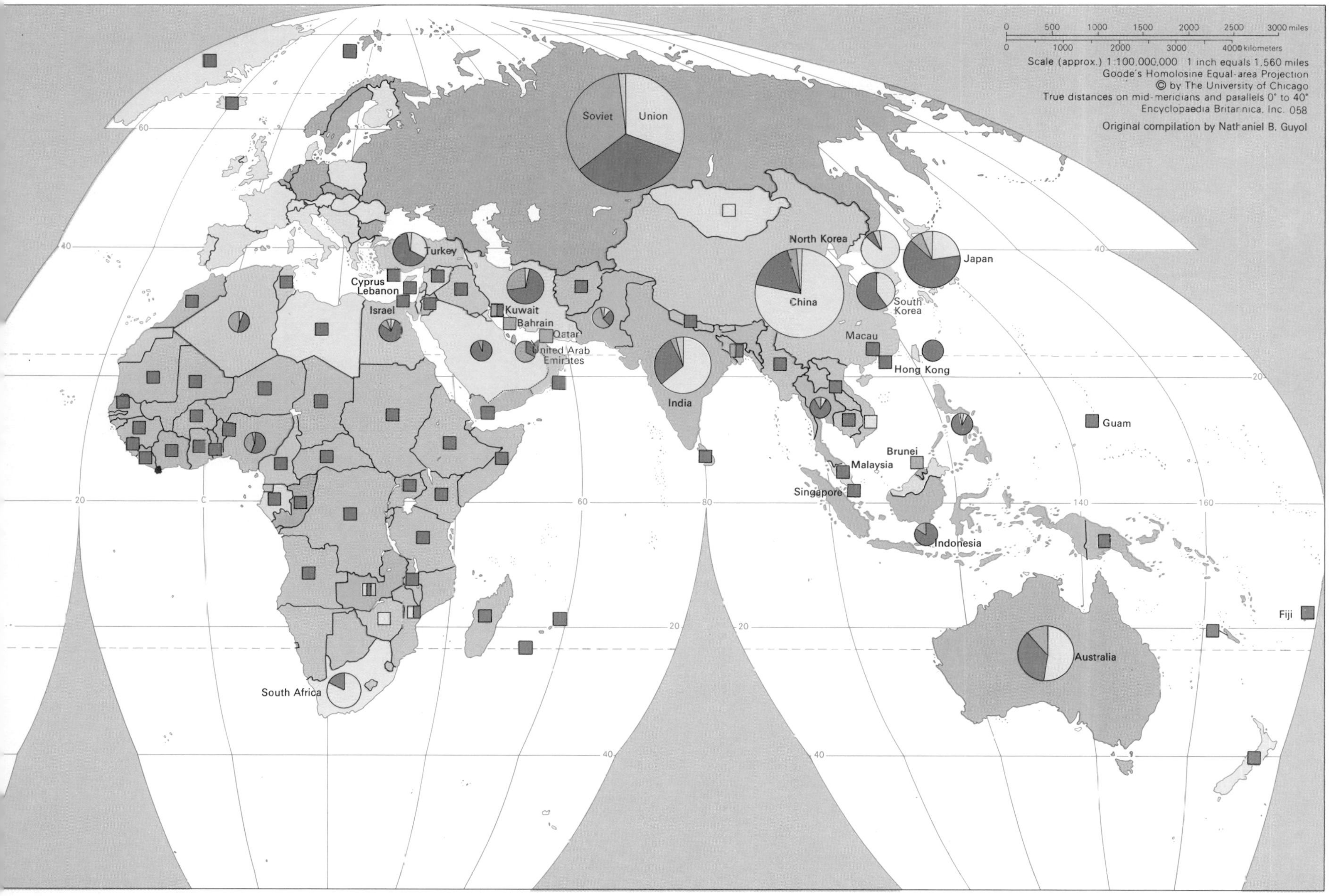

0   500   1000   1500   2000   2500   3000 miles

0   1000   2000   3000   4000 kilometers
Scale (approx.) 1:100,000,000   1 inch equals 1,560 miles
Goode's Homolosine Equal-area Projection
© by The University of Chicago
True distances on mid-meridians and parallels 0° to 40°
Encyclopaedia Britannica, Inc. 058

Original compilation by Nathaniel B. Guyol

Soviet   Union

Turkey

Cyprus
Lebanon

North Korea   Japan

Israel

Kuwait   China   South
Korea

Bahrain

Qatar   Macau

United Arab
Emirates   Hong Kong

India

Thailand

Brunei

Malaysia

Singapore   Guam

Indonesia

Fiji

Australia

South Africa

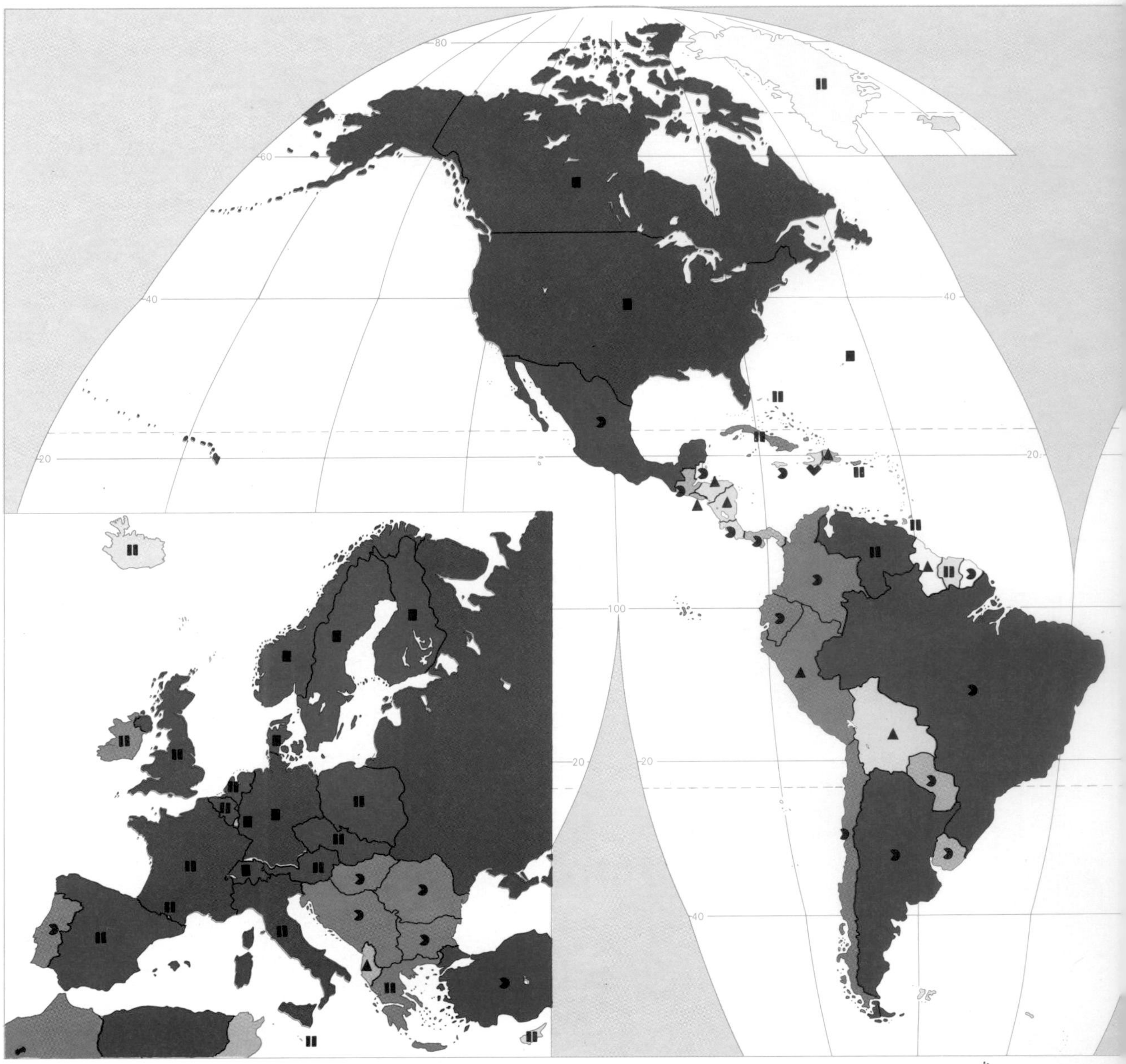

Gross National Product

Total per country at market price
In billions of U.S. dollars

		Number of countries
	300–3,670	9
	50–300	26
	10–50	28
	3–10	34
	1–3	32
	Less than 1	21
	No data available	

Per capita
In U.S. dollars

▪	10,000–22,300	19
‖	3,000–10,000	33
☽	1,000–3,000	32
▲	400–1,000	30
❤	200–400	27
●	Less than 200	15

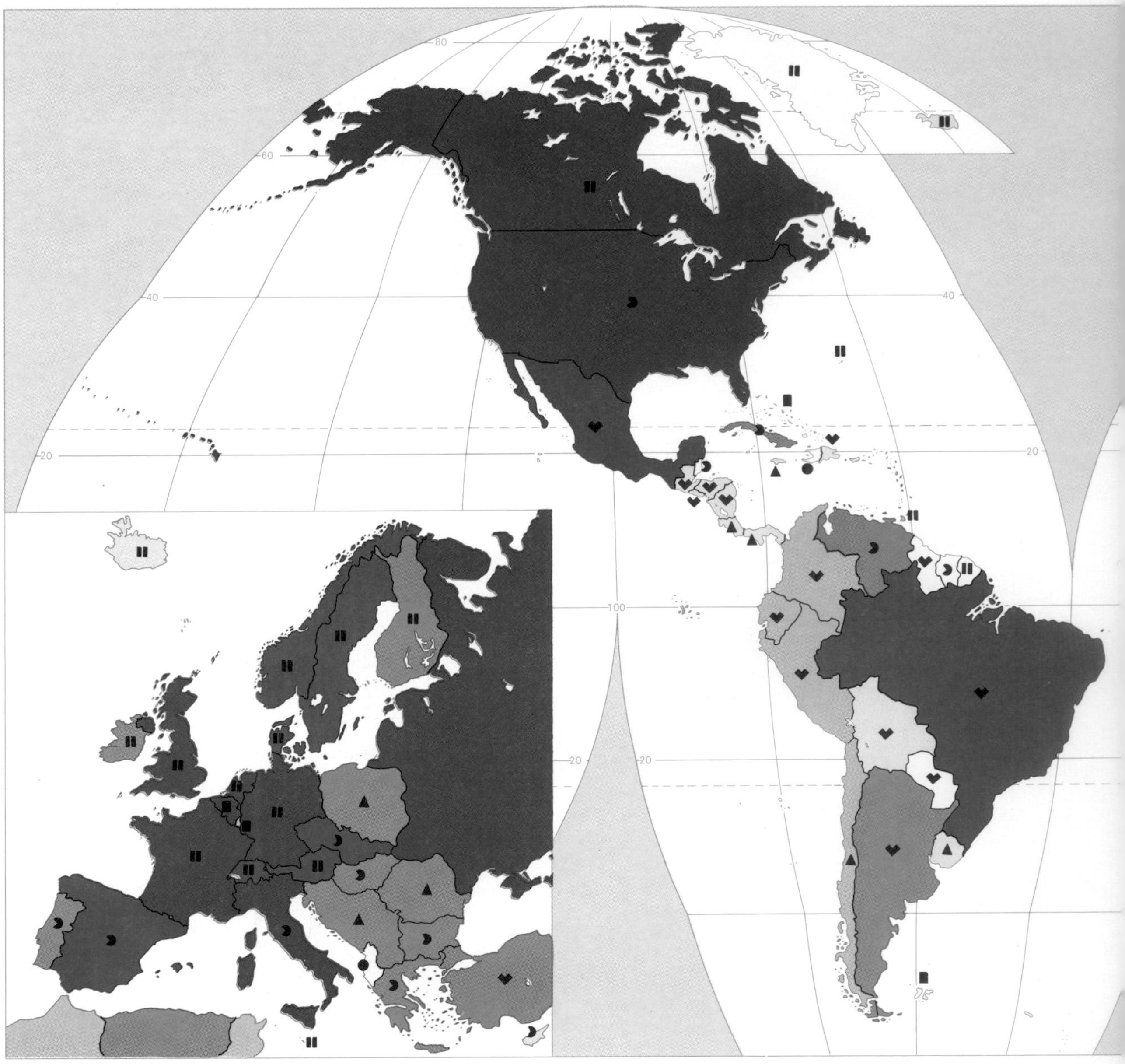

International Trade

Total per country
In billions of U.S. dollars

		Number of countries
	100–560	10
	30–100	18
	10–30	25
	3–10	19
	1–3	33
	Less than 1	46
	No data available	

Per capita
In U.S. dollars

▪	10,000–45,000	11
‖	3,000–10,000	25
☽	1,000–3,000	27
▲	500–1,000	18
❤	200–500	36
●	Less than 200	39

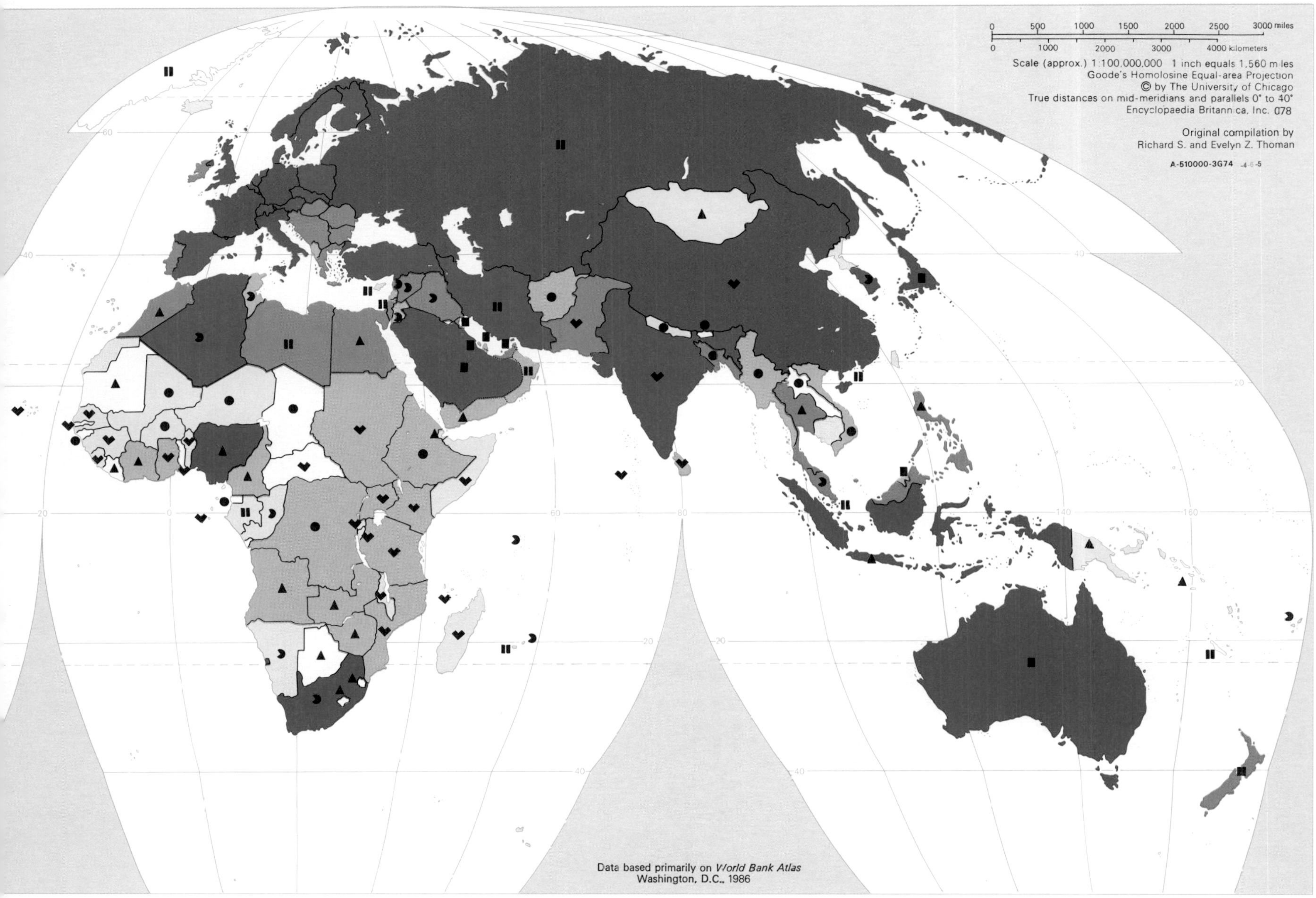

Scale (approx.) 1:100,000,000 1 inch equals 1,560 miles
Goode's Homolosine Equal-area Projection
© by The University of Chicago
True distances on mid-meridians and parallels 0° to 40°
Encyclopaedia Britannica, Inc. 078

Original compilation by
Richard S. and Evelyn Z. Thoman

A-510000-3G74 -4-4-5

Data based primarily on *World Bank Atlas*
Washington, D.C., 1986

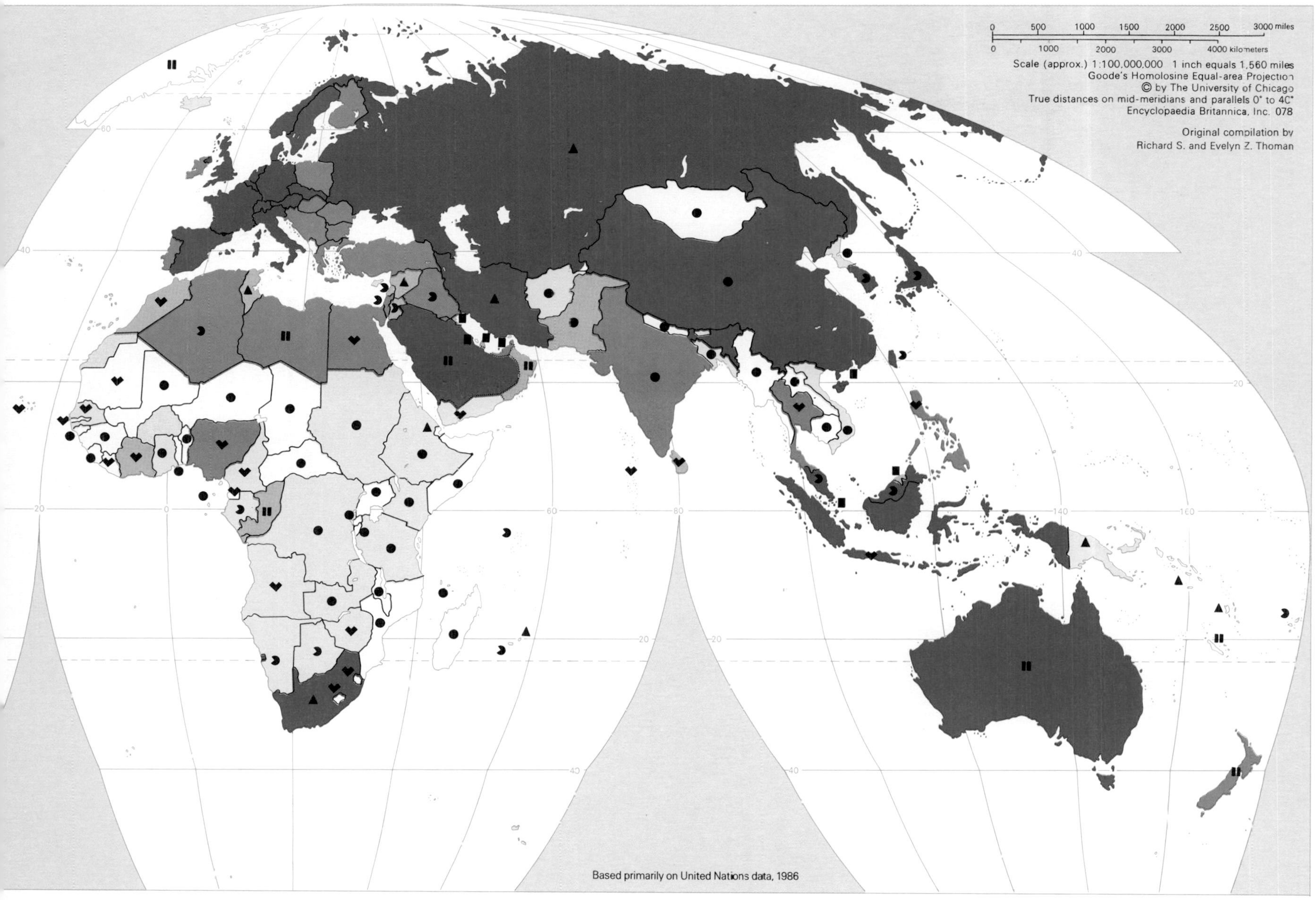

Scale (approx.) 1:100,000,000 1 inch equals 1,560 miles
Goode's Homolosine Equal-area Projection
© by The University of Chicago
True distances on mid-meridians and parallels 0° to 4C°
Encyclopaedia Britannica, Inc. 078

Original compilation by
Richard S. and Evelyn Z. Thoman

Based primarily on United Nations data, 1986

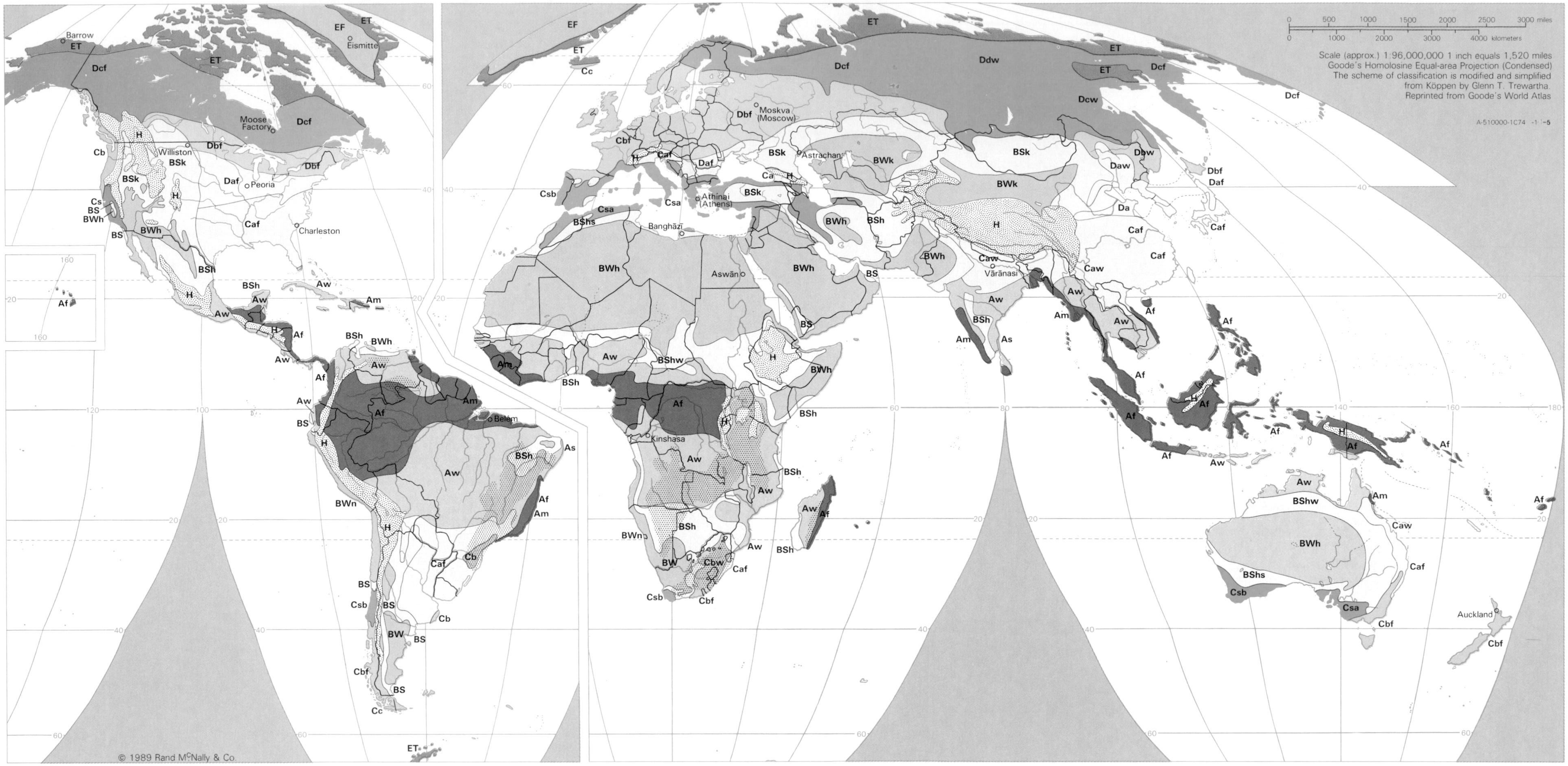

Climate

A. Tropical Rainy Climates
- Tropical Rainforest (**Af**, **Am**)
- Tropical Savanna (**Aw**)
  Cooler uplands stippled

B. Dry Climates
- Steppe (**BS**)
  Tropical and Subtropical Steppe (**BSh**)
  Middle latitude Steppe (**BSk**)
- Desert (**BW**)
  Tropical and Subtropical Desert (**BWh**)
  Middle latitude Desert (**BWk**)

C. Humid Mesothermal Climates
- Mediterranean or Dry Summer Subtropical (**Cs**)
- Humid Subtropical (**Ca**, warm summer)
- Marine West Coast (**Cb**, **Cc**, cool summer)

D. Humid Microthermal Climates
- Humid Continental, Warm Summer (**Da**)
- Humid Continental, Cool Summer (**Db**)
- Subarctic (**Dc**, **Dd**)

E. Polar Climates
- Tundra (**ET**)
- Ice Cap (**EF**)

H. Extensive Uplands
Undifferentiated Highlands
Two types of higher elevation climatic region are shown: (1) lower and flatter 'extensive uplands' areas above 2000 feet (600 meters), which, though cooler and wetter, contain no topographic barriers to climatic regions around them, and are thus classifiable with them; and (2) 'undifferentiated highlands,' mountainous regions of great elevation (forming barriers to regional atmospheric circulation) and great local relief, creating microclimates effectively unmappable at this scale.

Type Regions and Subtypes

A – Tropical forest climates: coolest month above 64.4°F. (18°C.).

B – Dry climates
 BS – Steppe or semiarid climate.
 BW – Desert or arid climate.

*C – Mesothermal forest climates: coldest month above 32°F. (0°C.) but below 64.4°F. (18°C.); warmest month above 50°F. (10°C.).

*D – Microthermal, snow-forest climates: coldest month below 32°F. (0°C.); warmest month above 50°F. (10°C.).

E – Polar climates: warmest month below 50°F. (10°C.).
 ET – Tundra climate: warmest month below 50°F. (10°C.) but above 32°F. (0°C.).
 EF – Perpetual frost: all months below 32°F. (0°C.).

a – Warmest month above 71.6°F. (22°C.).
b – Warmest month below 71.6°F. (22°C.).
c – Less than four months over 50°F. (10°C.).
d – Same as "c", but coldest month below -36.4°F. (-38°C.).
f – Constantly moist; precipitation all through the year.
*h – Hot and dry; all months above 32°F. (0°C.).
*k – Cold and dry; at least one month below 32°F. (0°C.)
m – Monsoon rain; short dry season, but total rainfall sufficient to support rainforest.
n – Frequent fog.
s – Dry season in summer.
w – Dry season in winter.

* Modification of Köppen definition

Curves show Fahrenheit temperature; vertical bars show precipitation in inches.

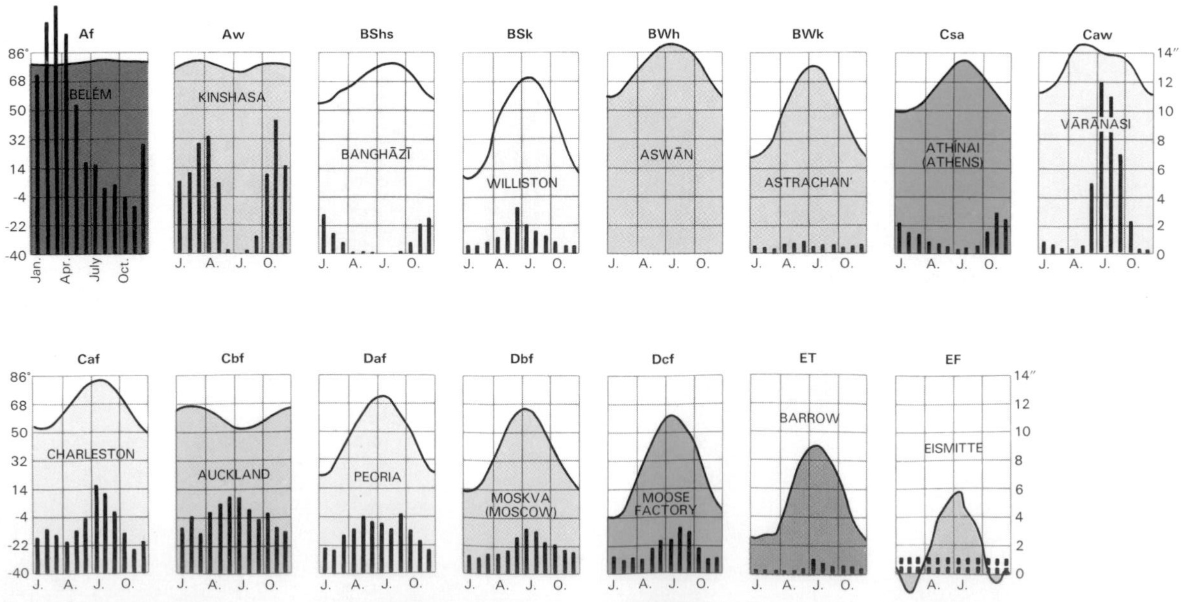

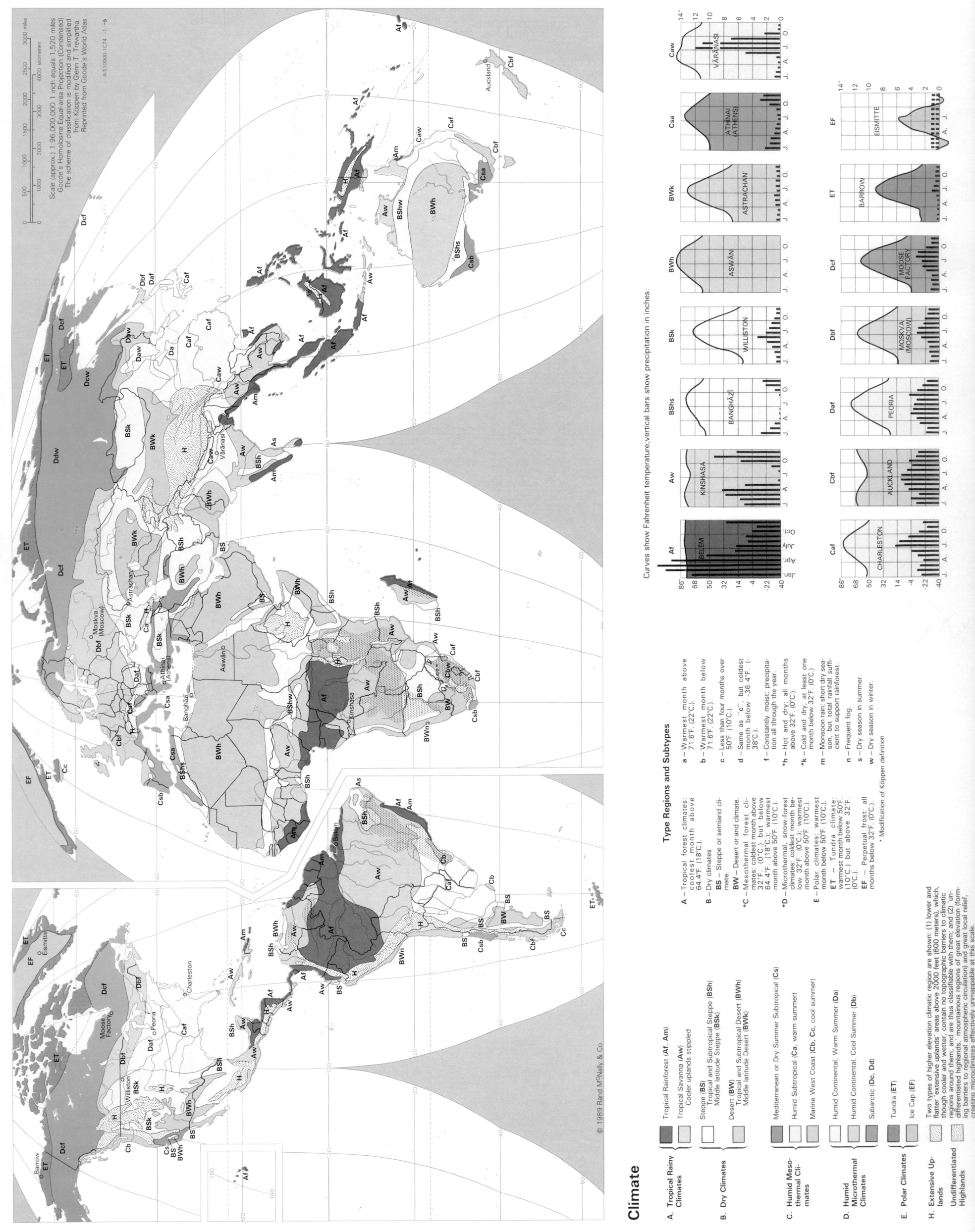

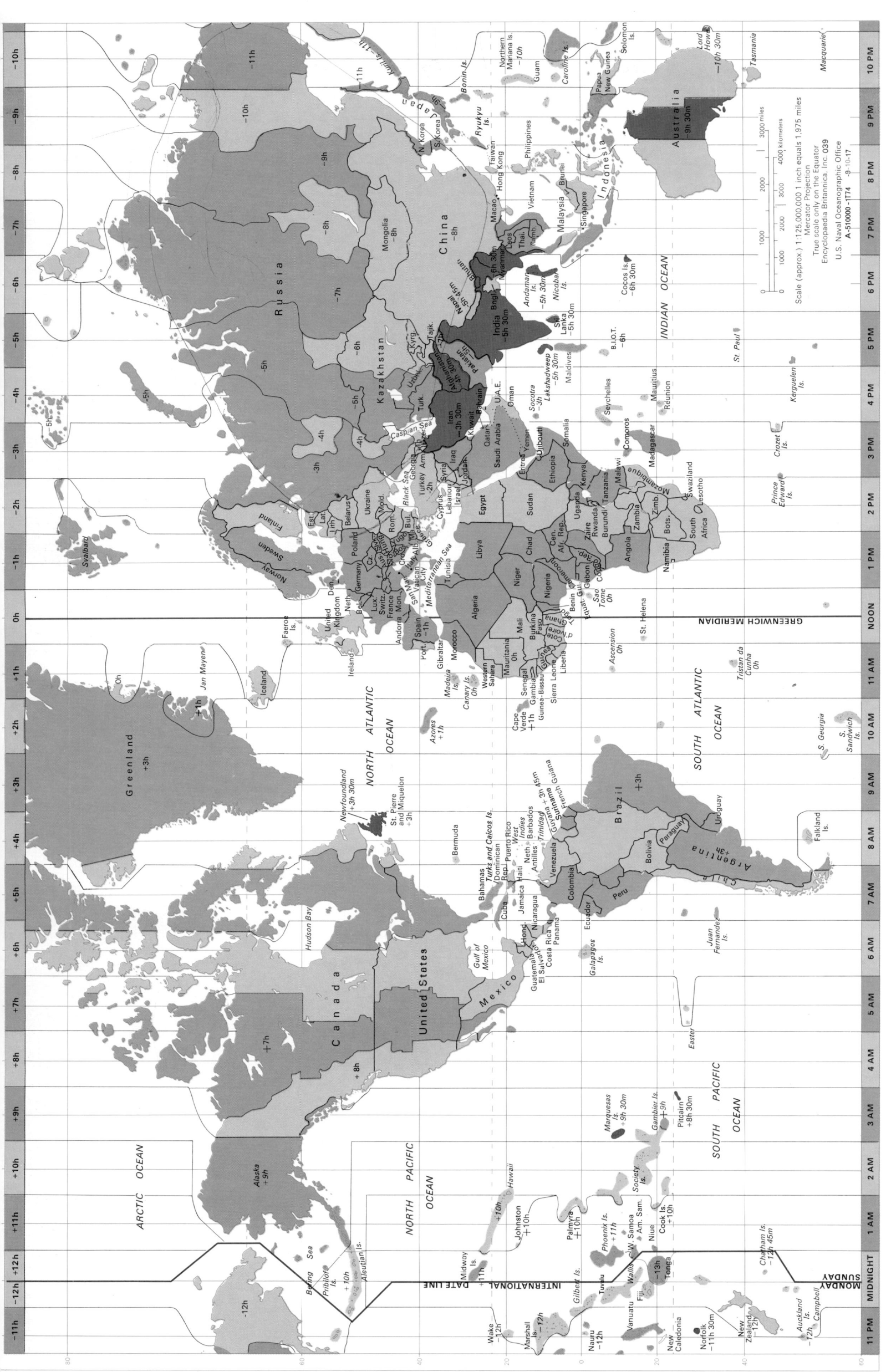

Time Zones

The standard time zone system, fixed by international agreement and by law in each country, is based on a theoretical division of the globe into 24 zones of 15° longitude each. The mid-meridian of each zone fixes the hour for the entire zone. The zero time zone extends 7½° east and 7½° west of the Greenwich meridian, 0° longitude. Since the earth rotates toward the east, time zones to the west of Greenwich are earlier, to the east, later.

Plus and minus hours at the top of the map are added to or subtracted from local time to find Greenwich time. Local standard time can be determined for any area in the world by adding one hour for each time zone counted in an easterly direction from one's own, or by subtracting one hour for each zone counted in a westerly direction. To separate one day from the next, the 180th meridian has been designated as the international date line. On both sides of the line the time of day is the same, but west of the line it is one day later than it is to the east. Countries that adhere to the international zone system adopt the zone applicable to their location. Some countries, however, establish time zones based on political boundaries, or adopt the time zone of a neighboring unit. For all or part of the year some countries also advance their time by one hour, thereby utilizing more daylight hours each day.

| h m | hours, minutes |

Standard time zone of even-numbered hours from Greenwich time

Standard time zone of odd-numbered hours from Greenwich time

Time varies from the standard time zone by half an hour

Time varies from the standard time zone by other than half an hour

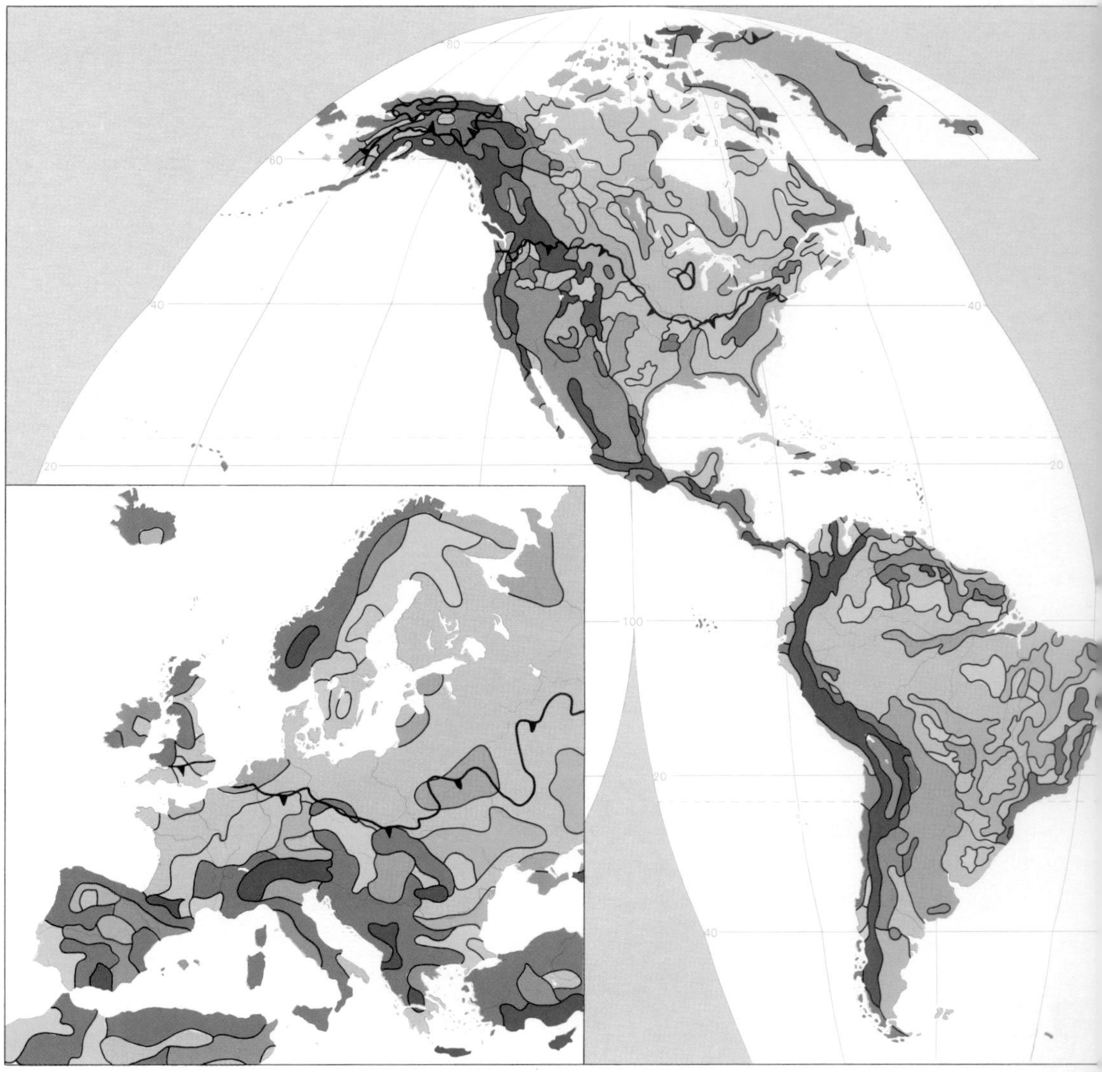

Surface Configuration

Smooth lands

- Level plains: nearly all slopes gentle; local relief less than 100 ft. (30 m.)
- Irregular plains: majority of slopes gentle; local relief 100-300 ft. (30-90 m.)

Broken lands

- Tablelands and plateaus: majority of slopes gentle, with the gentler slopes on the uplands; local relief more than 300 ft. (90 m.)
- Hill-studded plains: majority of slopes gentle, with the gentler slopes in the lowlands; local relief 300-1,000 ft. (90-300 m.)
- Mountain-studded plains: majority of slopes gentle, with the gentler slopes in the lowlands; local relief more than 1,000 ft. (300 m.)

Rough lands

- Hill lands: steeper slopes predominate; local relief less than 1,000 ft. (300 m.)
- Mountains: steeper slopes predominate; local relief 1,000-5,000 ft. (300-1,500 m.)
- Mountains of great relief: steeper slopes predominate; local relief more than 5,000 ft. (1,500 m.)

Other surfaces

- Ice caps: permanent ice
- Maximum extent of glaciation

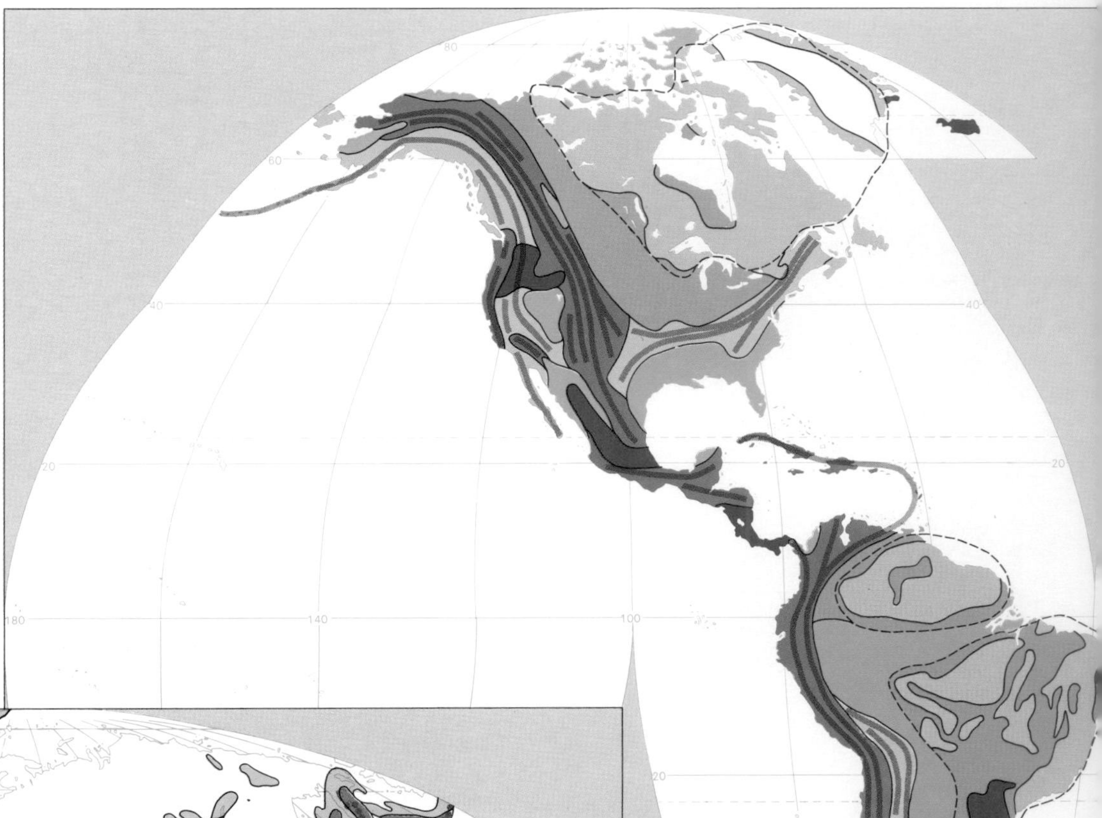

Earth Structure and Tectonics

- Precambrian stable shield areas
- Exposed Precambrian rock
- Paleozoic and Mesozoic flat-lying sedimentary rocks
- Principal Paleozoic and Mesozoic folded areas
- Cenozoic sedimentary rocks
- Principal Cenozoic folded areas
- Lava plateaus
- Major trends of folding

Geologic time chart

Precambrian—from formation of the earth (at least 4 billion years ago) to 600 million years ago

Paleozoic—from 600 million to 200 million years ago

Mesozoic—from 200 million to 70 million years ago

Cenozoic—from 70 million years ago to present time

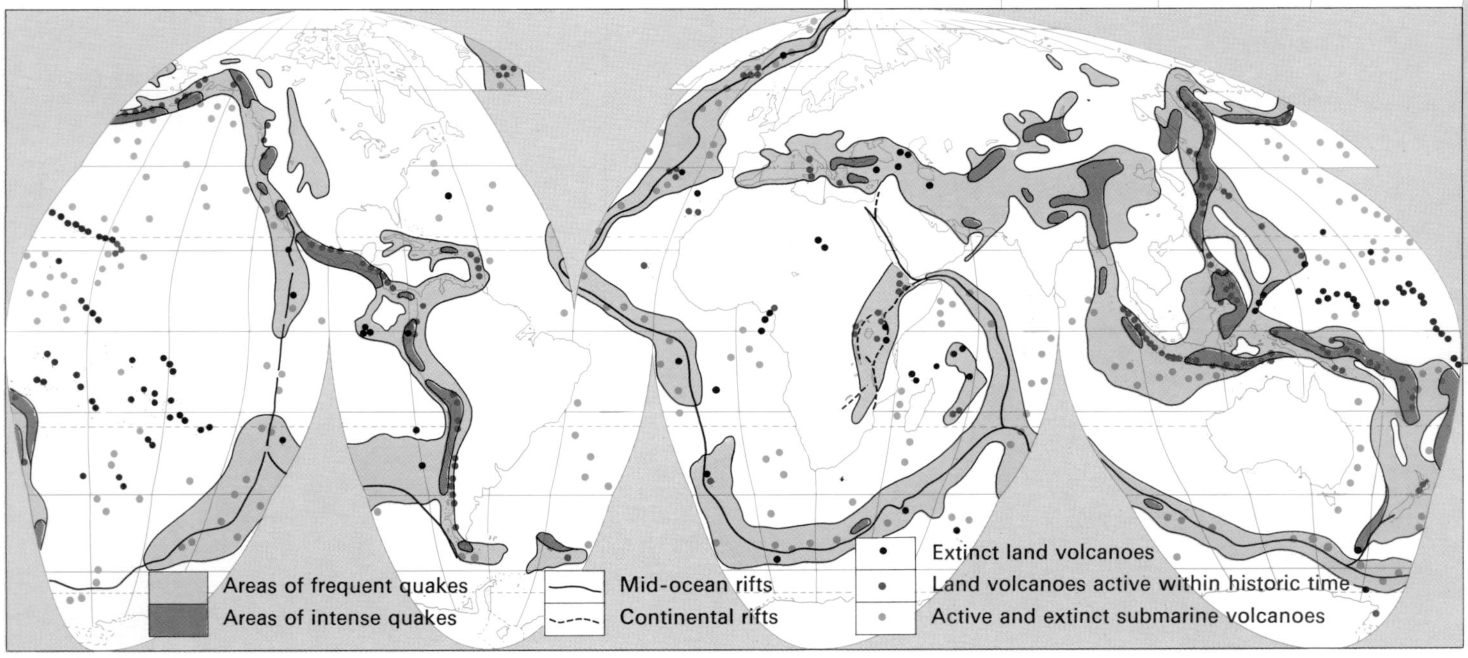

- Areas of frequent quakes
- Areas of intense quakes
- Mid-ocean rifts
- Continental rifts
- Extinct land volcanoes
- Land volcanoes active within historic time
- Active and extinct submarine volcanoes

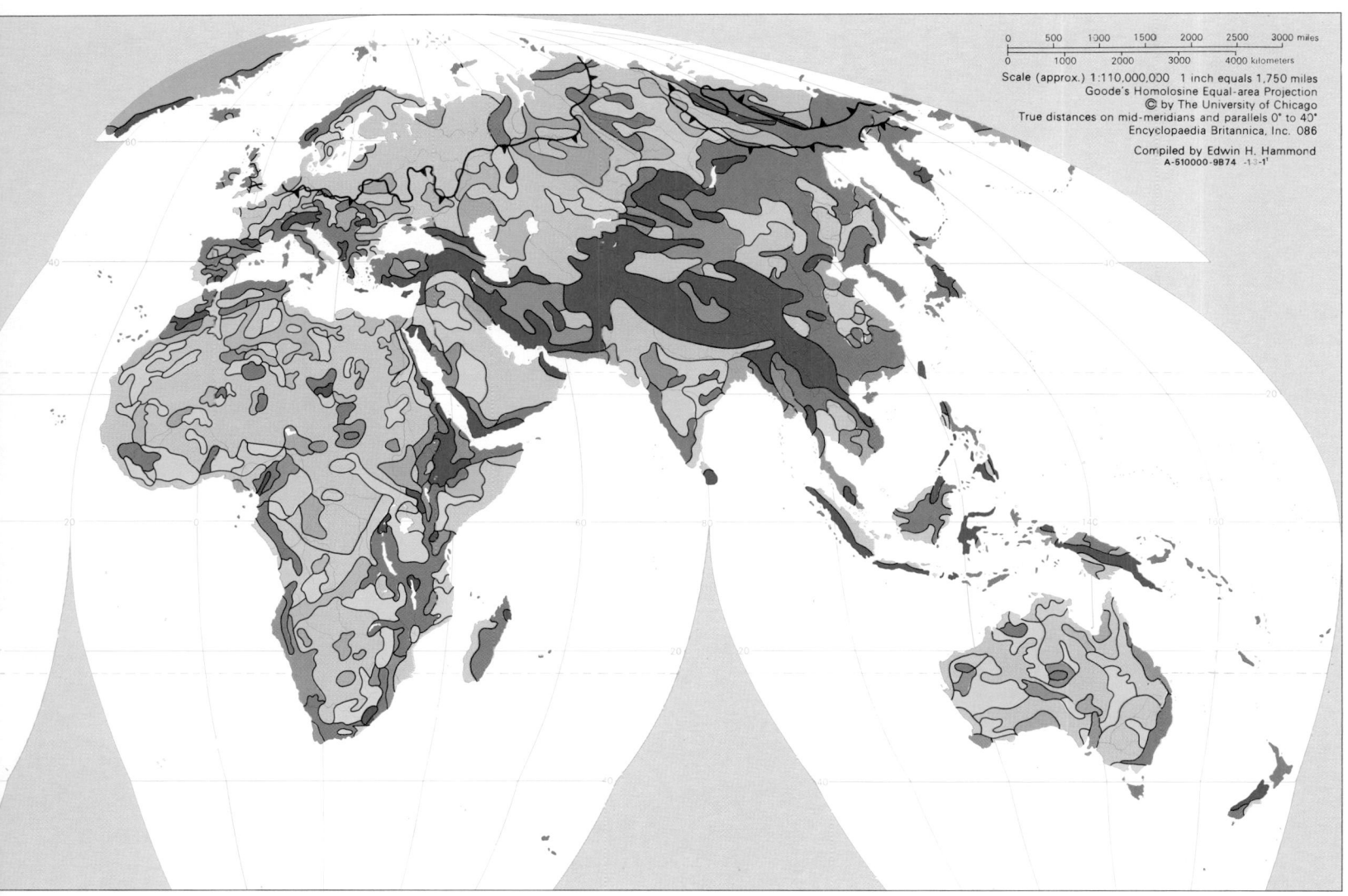

Scale (approx.) 1:110,000,000 1 inch equals 1,750 miles
Goode's Homolosine Equal-area Projection
© by The University of Chicago
True distances on mid-meridians and parallels 0° to 40°
Encyclopaedia Britannica, Inc. 086

Compiled by Edwin H. Hammond
A-510000-9B74 -1 -1'

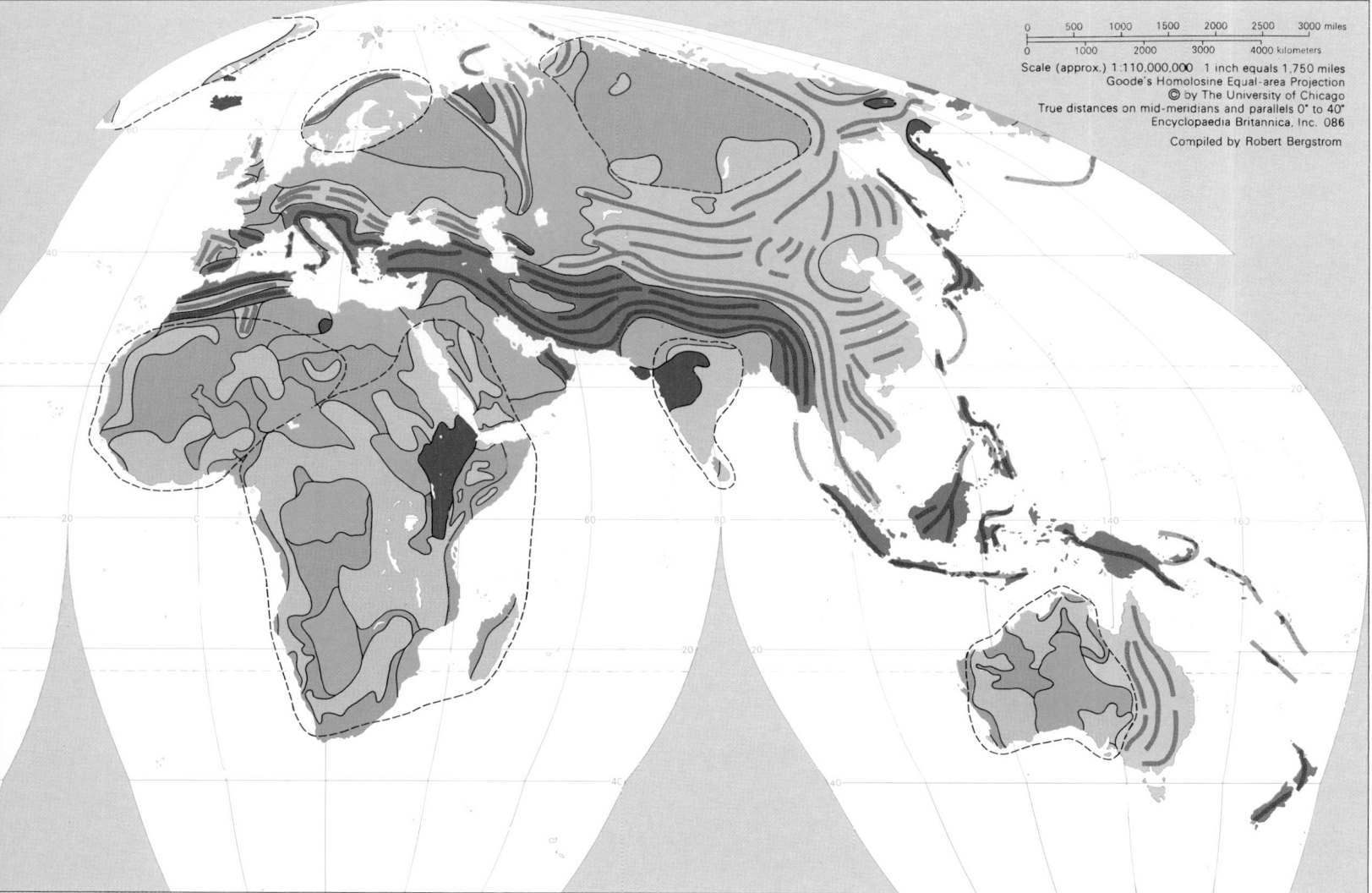

Scale (approx.) 1:110,000,000 1 inch equals 1,750 miles
Goode's Homolosine Equal-area Projection
© by The University of Chicago
True distances on mid-meridians and parallels 0° to 40°
Encyclopaedia Britannica, Inc. 086

Compiled by Robert Bergstrom

Development of the earth's structure

The earth is in process of constant transformation. Movements in the hot, dense interior of the earth result in folding and fracture of the crust and transfer of molten material to the surface. As a result, large structures such as mountain ranges, volcanoes, lava plateaus, and rift valleys are created. The forces that bring about these structural changes are called *tectonic forces*.

The present continents have developed from stable nuclei, or *shields*, of ancient (Precambrian) rock. Erosive forces such as water, wind, and ice have worn away particles of the rock, depositing them at the edges of the shields, where they have accumulated and ultimately become sedimentary rock. Subsequently, in places, these extensive areas of flat-lying rock have been elevated, folded, or warped, by the action of tectonic forces, to form mountains. The shape of these mountains has been altered by later erosion. Where the forces of erosion have been at work for a long time, the mountains tend to have a low relief and rounded contours, like the Appalachians. Mountains more recently formed are high and rugged, like the Himalayas.

The map above depicts some of the major geologic structures of the earth and identifies them according to the period of their formation. A geologic time chart is included in the legend. The inset map shows the most important areas of earthquakes, rifts, and volcanic activity. Comparison of all the maps will show the close correlation between present-day mountain systems, recent (Cenozoic) mountain-building, and the areas of frequent earthquakes and active volcanoes.

Natural Vegetation

Broad-leaved evergreen vegetation

Broad-leaved evergreen forest

Broad-leaved evergreen shrub formation

Scattered broad-leaved evergreen shrubs

Scattered broad-leaved evergreen dwarf shrubs

Broad-leaved deciduous vegetation

Broad-leaved deciduous forest

Broad-leaved deciduous shrub formation

Scattered broad-leaved deciduous shrubs

Scattered broad-leaved deciduous dwarf shrubs

Coniferous vegetation

Needle-leaved evergreen forest

Scattered needle-leaved evergreen trees

Needle-leaved deciduous forest

Mixed vegetation without grass

Forest of broad-leaved evergreen and deciduous trees

Forest of broad-leaved and needle-leaved evergreen trees

Broad-leaved deciduous forests with broad-leaved evergreen shrubs

Forest of broad-leaved deciduous and needle-leaved evergreen trees

Mixed vegetation with grass

Grassland with scattered broad-leaved evergreen trees

Grassland with broad-leaved evergreen shrubs

Grassland with scattered broad-leaved deciduous trees

Grassland with broad-leaved deciduous shrubs

Grassland, tundra, barren

Grassland

Patches of grass

Lichens and grasses

Lichens and mosses

Barren

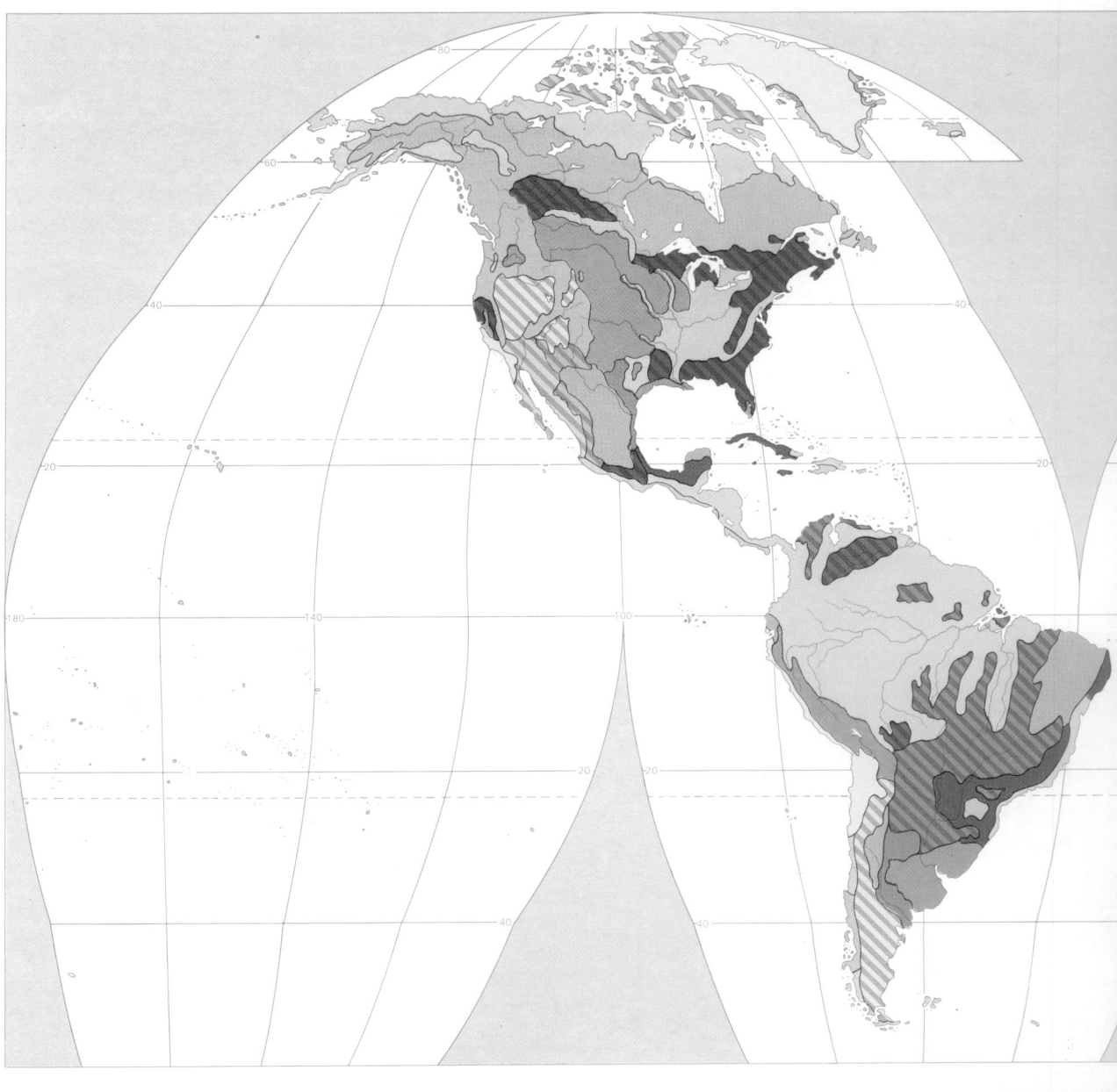

Soils

Tundra soils of frigid climates; commonly with permanently frozen subsoil; supports dwarf shrubs, mosses, and lichens; some used for reindeer pasture

Podzolic soils of humid, cool climates; covered with predominantly coniferous forest; some farming, mainly subsistence

Podzolic soils of humid, temperate climates; originally covered with predominantly deciduous forest, much of it removed to accommodate extensive general farming, industry, and cities

Podzolic soils of humid, warm climates; covered with coniferous or mixed forest; general farming

Chernozemic soils of subhumid and semiarid, cool to tropical climates; supports mainly grasslands; extensive grain and livestock farming

Latosolic soils of humid or wet-dry tropical and subtropical climates; supports forest or savanna; shifting cultivation with some plantation agriculture

Grumusolic soils of humid to semiarid and temperate to tropical climates, with distinct wet and dry seasons; mainly grass-covered; livestock and grain farming

Desertic soils of arid climates; includes many areas of shallow, stony soils; sparse cover of shrubs and grass, some suitable for grazing; fertile if irrigated; dry farming possible in some areas

Mountain soils of all climates; shallow, stony; barren, grass-covered, or forested, depending on climate; includes many areas of other soils

Alluvial soils of all climates; deposited by water in flood plains and deltas of rivers; intensive farming in most temperate and some tropical regions (many smaller areas not shown)

Ice cap of polar regions

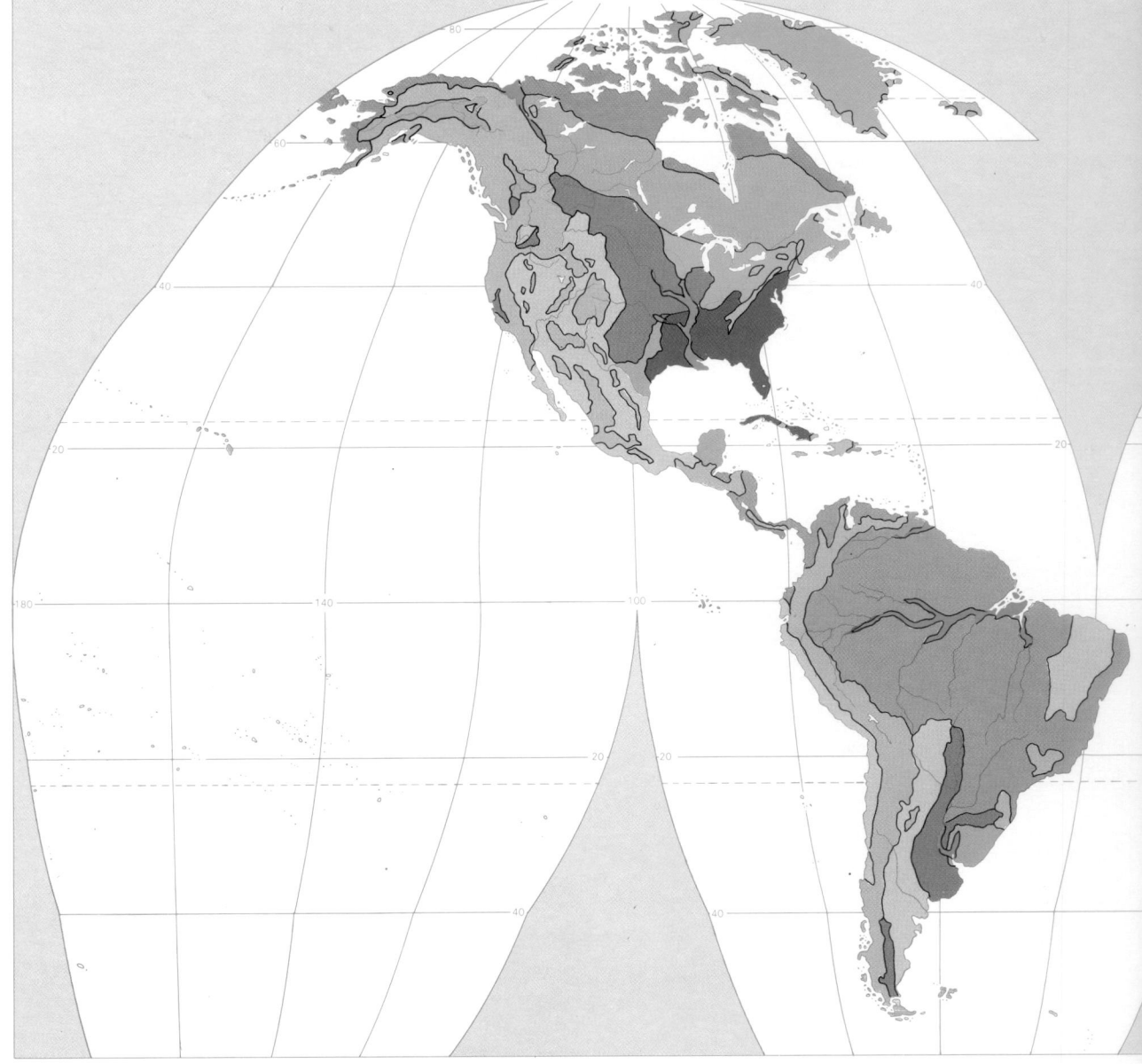

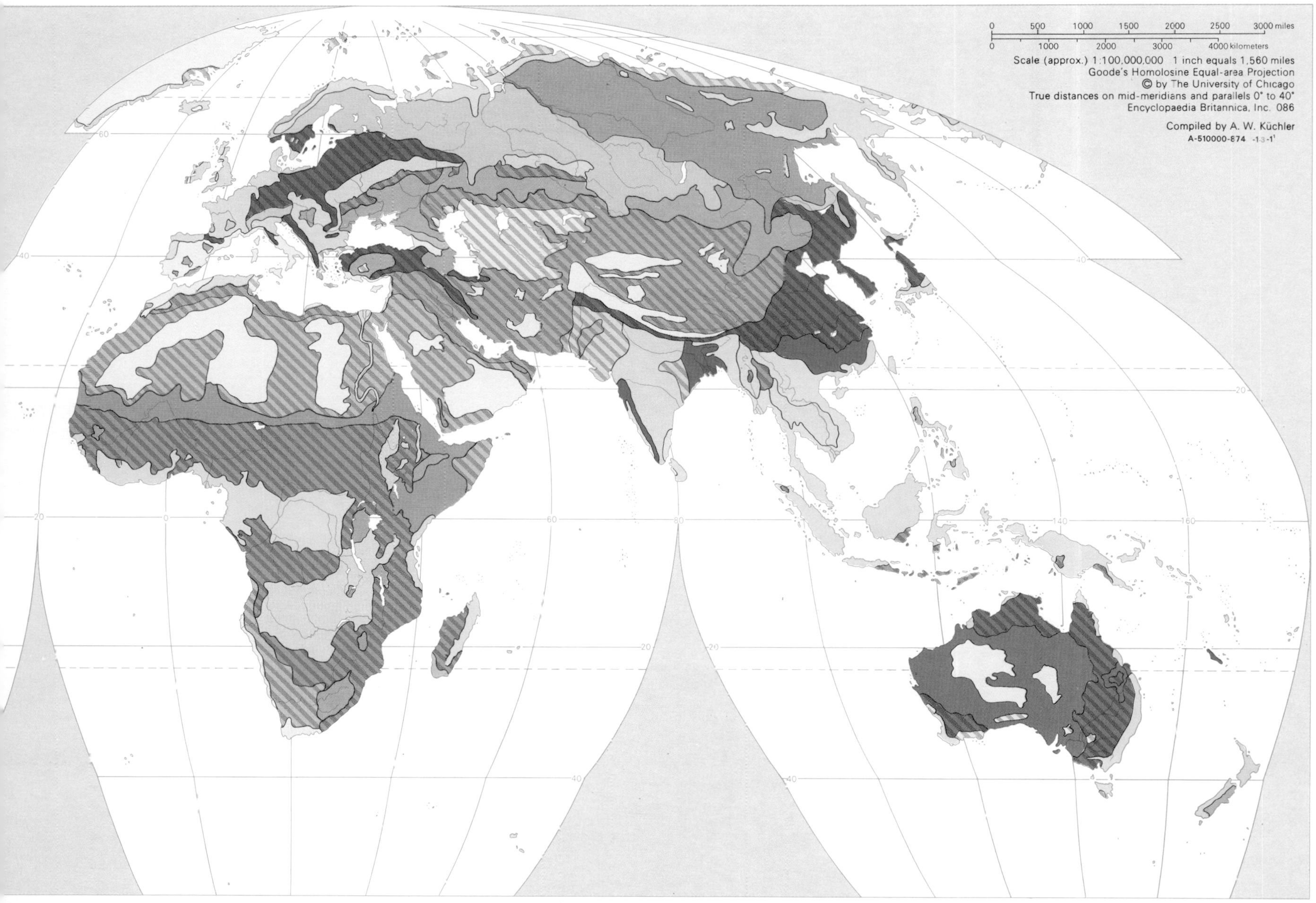

Scale (approx.) 1:100,000,000 1 inch equals 1,560 miles
Goode's Homolosine Equal-area Projection
© by The University of Chicago
True distances on mid-meridians and parallels 0° to 40°
Encyclopaedia Britannica, Inc. 086

Compiled by A. W. Küchler
A-510000-874 -1.9-1'

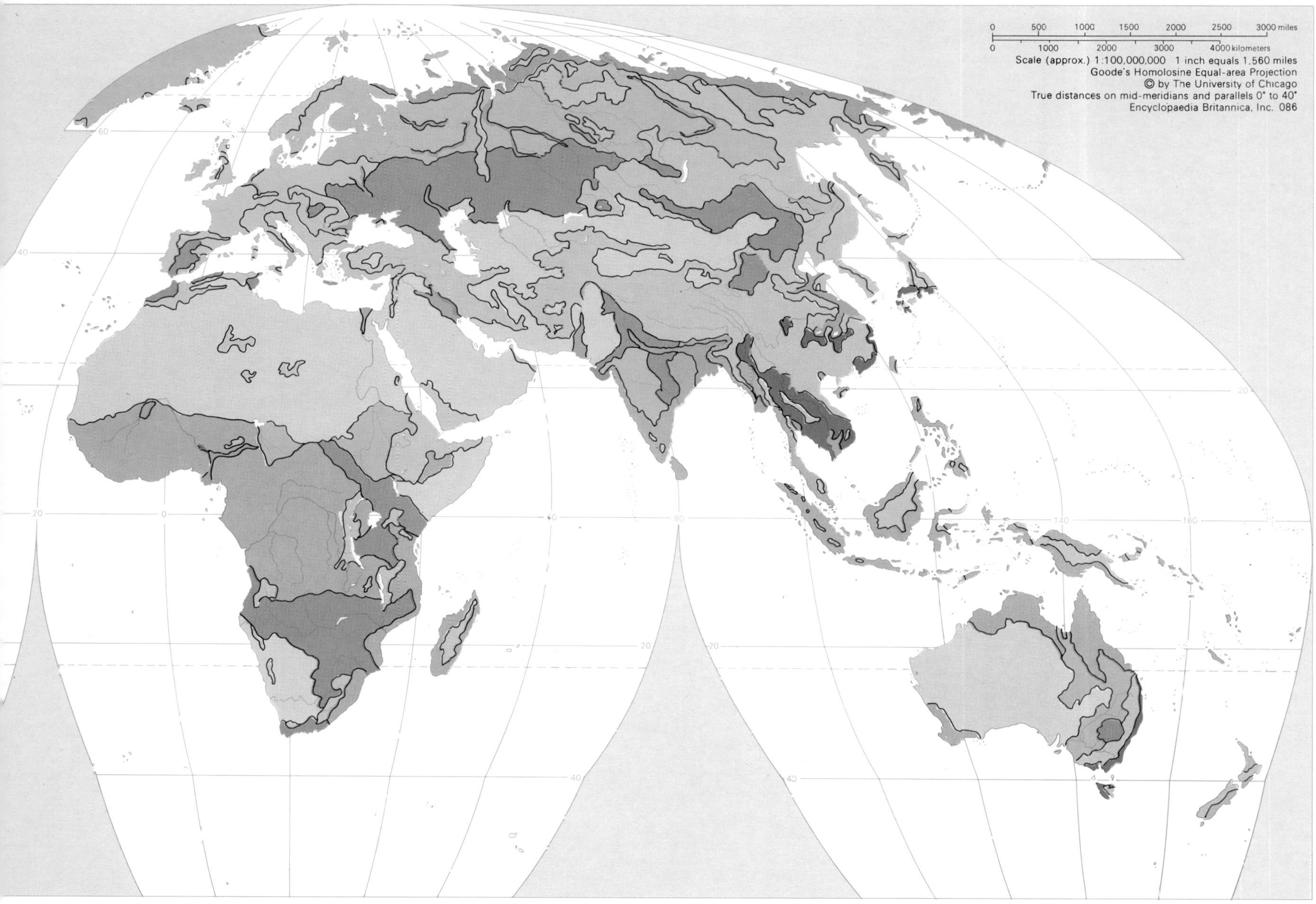

Scale (approx.) 1:100,000,000 1 inch equals 1,560 miles
Goode's Homolosine Equal-area Projection
© by The University of Chicago
True distances on mid-meridians and parallels 0° to 40°
Encyclopaedia Britannica, Inc. 086

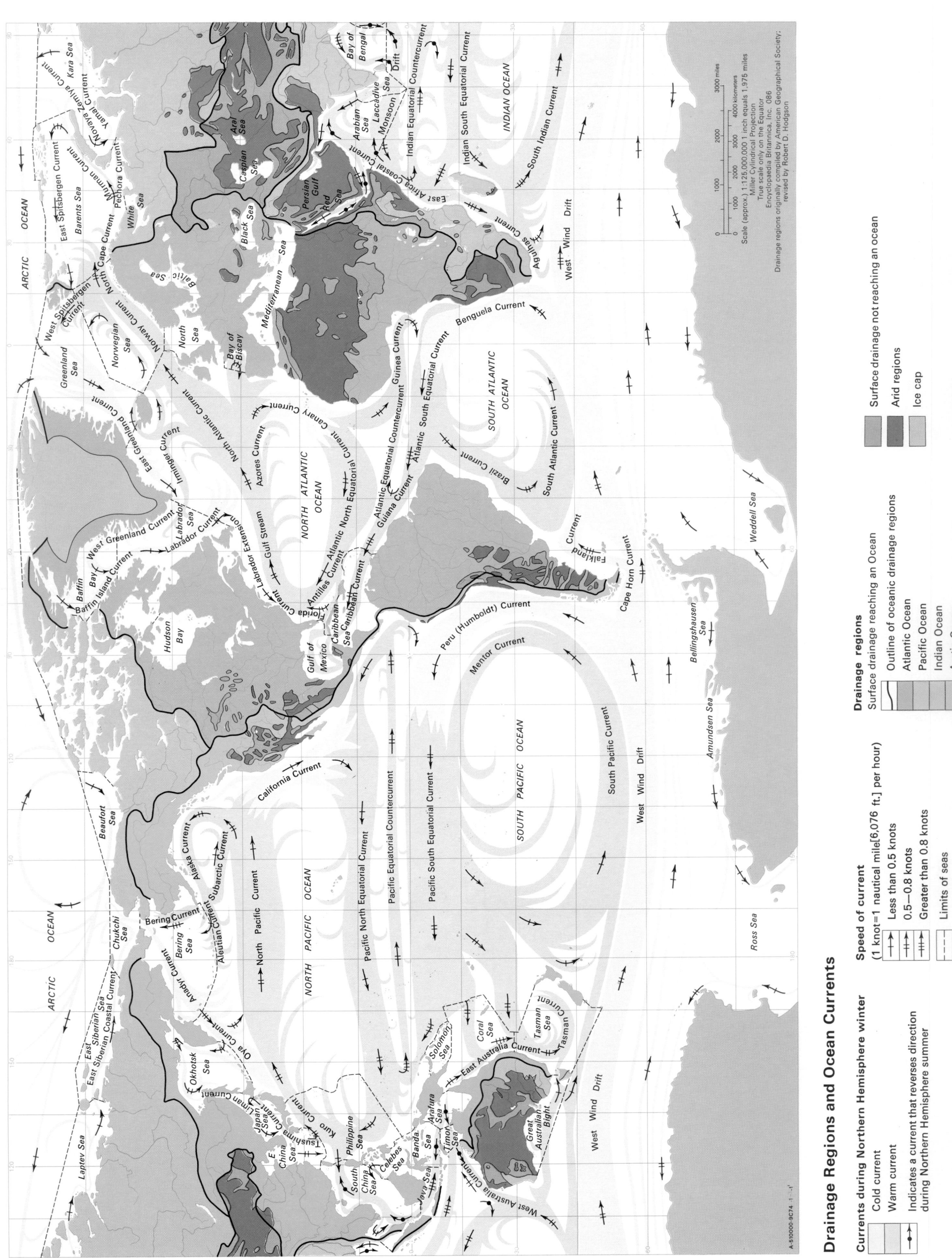

Drainage Regions and Ocean Currents

Currents during Northern Hemisphere winter

Cold current

Warm current

Indicates a current that reverses direction during Northern Hemisphere summer

Speed of current

(1 knot=1 nautical mile[6,076 ft.] per hour)

Less than 0.5 knots

0.5—0.8 knots

Greater than 0.8 knots

Limits of seas

Drainage regions

Surface drainage reaching an Ocean

Outline of oceanic drainage regions

Atlantic Ocean

Pacific Ocean

Indian Ocean

Arctic Ocean

Surface drainage not reaching an ocean

Arid regions

Ice cap

Scale (approx.) 1:125,000,000 1 inch equals 1,975 miles
Miller Cylindrical Projection
True scale only on the Equator
Encyclopaedia Britannica, Inc. 086
Drainage regions originally compiled by American Geographical Society; revised by Robert D. Hodgson

A-510000-9C74 -1- -1'

World, Ocean, and Continent Maps / Weltkarten, Karten der Ozeane und Erdteile
Mapas del Mundo, Océanos y Continentes / Cartes du Monde, des Océans et des Continents
Mapas do Mundo, dos Oceanos e dos Continentes

1

THIS SECTION OPENS with World Political and World Physical maps at the scale of 1:75,000,000. There follow maps of the Pacific, Indian, and Atlantic oceans at the scale 1:48,000,000, the largest scale at which the total expanse of these bodies of water could be portrayed. Finally, a series of continent relief maps at the scale of 1:24,000,000 show a global view of the earth as it would appear from about 4,000 miles in space. The Azimuthal Equal-Area projection is used for the 1:24,000,000 maps, the scale being approximately that of a globe 20 inches in diameter.

The colors of the continent maps portray the land areas as if viewed from space during the growing season, without regard to the fact that the growing seasons are not concurrent in all areas. Underwater features and varying water depths are represented by shaded relief and different color tones. The result is a strong physical portrait of the earth's major land and submarine forms. The legend below shows how these different kinds of terrain and vegetation have been represented. The names of physical features—plateaus, basins, mountain ranges, seas, rivers, lakes, gulfs, trenches, bays, islands—predominate on these maps.

DIESER KARTENTEIL BEGINNT mit politischen und physischen Weltkarten im Massstab 1:75 Millionen. Dann folgen Karten des Pazifischen, Indischen und Atlantischen Ozeans in 1:48 Millionen, dem grössten Massstab, in dem diese Wasserflächen in ihrer ganzen Ausdehnung abgebildet werden konnten. Schliesslich folgt eine Reihe von Reliefkarten der Erdteile in 1:24 Millionen. Sie geben eine Übersicht der Erde, wie sie aus einer Entfernung von ungefähr 6 400 Kilometer aus dem Weltraum gewonnen würde. Den Karten im Massstab 1:24 Millionen liegt ein flächentreuer azimutaler Entwurf zugrunde, dieser Massstab entspricht ungefähr dem eines Globus von 50 cm Durchmesser.

Die Farben der Erdteilkarten bilden jedes Landgebiet so ab, wie es in der Vegetationsperiode aus der Vogelperspektive erschiene, ohne zu berücksichtigen, dass die Vegetationsperioden nicht in allen Gebieten gleichzeitig eintreten. Die Gliederung des Meeresbodens und die unterschiedlichen Meerestiefen werden durch Schummerung und verschiedene Farbstufen dargestellt. Das Ergebnis ist eine anschauliche physische Darstellung der wichtigsten terrestrischen und untermeerischen Formen der Erde. Die untenstehende Zeichenerklärung zeigt, wie diese verschiedenen Geländeformen und Vegetationsgebiete veranschaulicht werden. Namen physischer Objekte—Hochebenen, Becken, Gebirgszüge, Meere, Flüsse, Seen, Buchten, Gräben, Inseln—herrschen in diesen Karten vor.

ESTA SECCIÓN DA PRINCIPIO con los Mapas Políticos y Físicos del Mundo, a una escala de 1:75 000 000. A continuación están los mapas de los océanos Pacífico, Indico y Atlántico a una escala de 1:48 000 000, que es la mayor escala utilizable para la representación de esas masas de agua en toda su extensión. Por último, una serie de mapas del relieve de los continentes, a una escala de 1:24 000 000, proporcionan una vista global de la tierra tal como se apreciaría desde el espacio a una distancia aproximada de 6 400 kilómetros. La proyección azimutal equiárea se usa, para los mapas de 1:24 000 000, a una escala según la cual la tierra se reduciría a un globo de unos 50 cm de diámetro.

Los colores utilizados en los mapas de los continentes representan las diversas regiones de la tierra tal como se verían desde el espacio durante la estación en que la vegetación se desarrolla, sin tomar en cuenta que este fenómeno no se produce simultáneamente en todas las áreas. Las estructuras características del fondo marino y las variaciones de profundidad de los océanos se representan mediante relieve sombreado y distintos matices de color. El resultado es una imagen elocuente de las formas terrestres y submarinas más notables del planeta. La leyenda abajo explica cómo se representan estos diferentes tipos de terreno y vegetación. En estos mapas predomina la nomenclatura de elementos físicos: mesetas, cuencas, sierras, mares, ríos, lagos, golfos, bahías, trincheras, islas.

CETTE PARTIE comprend d'abord des cartes du monde politique et du monde physique à l'échelle de 1:75 000 000. Viennent ensuite les cartes des océans Pacifique, Indien et Atlantique à l'échelle de 1:48 000 000, la plus grande échelle qui a permis la reproduction complète de ces étendues d'eau. Pour terminer, une série de cartes en relief des continents à l'échelle de 1:24 000 000 donne une vue globale de la terre, telle qu'elle apparaîtrait vue de l'espace à une distance d'environ 6 400 kilomètres.

La projection azimutale équivalente a été utilisée pour les cartes au 1:24 000 000e, dont l'échelle équivaut à celle d'un globe de 50 cm de diamètre environ.

Les couleurs des cartes font apparaître les continents tels qu'on les verrait de l'espace, pendant la saison de croissance végétale, mais sans tenir compte du fait que cette saison n'apparaît pas partout simultanément. Le relief sous-marin est représenté par un estompage et la profondeur des océans par une variation de la couleur. Il en résulte une reproduction vigoureuse des principaux paysages continentaux et des principales formes sousmarines. La légende ci-dessous indique de quelle façon ils sont cartographiés. Les noms d'éléments topographiques tels que plateaux, bassins, chaînes de montagnes, mers, cours d'eau, lacs, golfes, baies, crêtes, îles et fosses océaniques, prédominent dans ces cartes.

ESTA SEÇÃO PRINCIPIA com os mapas políticos e físicos do Mundo, em escala de 1:75 000 000. Seguem-se os mapas dos oceanos Pacífico, Índico e Atlântico na escala de 1:48 000 000, a maior escala que se pode utilizar para a representação dessas massas de água em toda a sua extensão. Finalmente, uma série de mapas de relevo dos continentes, na escala de 1:24 000 000, proporciona uma visão global da Terra tal como apareceria do espaço a uma distância aproximada de cerca de 6 400 km. A projeção azimutal equiárea foi usada para os mapas da escala de 1:24 000 000, segundo a qual a Terra se apresentaria como um globo de cerca de 50 cm de diâmetro.

As cores utilizadas nos mapas dos continentes representam as massas terrestres tal como apareceriam vistas do espaço durante a estação do crescimento vegetal, sem levar em conta que este fenómeno não se produz simultaneamente em todas as regiões. As características do fundo do mar e as variações de profundidade das águas são representadas por um relevo sombreado e por diferentes matizes de cor. O resultado proporciona uma imagem física eloqüente das principais formas terrestres e submarinas da Terra. As legendas abaixo explicam como foram representados os diversos tipos de terreno e de vegetação. Nestes mapas predomina a nomenclatura dos elementos físicos: planaltos, bacias, cadeias de montanhas, mares, rios, lagos, golfos, baías, fossas, ilhas.

Land Features / Land Phänomene / Elementos de la Tierra Paysages Continentaux / Acidentes Continentais

Submarine Features / Untermeerische Phänomene Elementos Submarinos / Formes de Relief Sous-marin / Acidentes do Revelo Submarino

Ice and Snow
Eis und Schnee
Hielo y nieve
Glace et neige
Gelo e neve

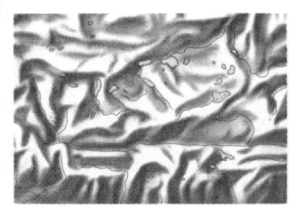

High Barren Area
Hochgebirgswüste
Alta zona árida
Région haute et aride
Alta zona árida

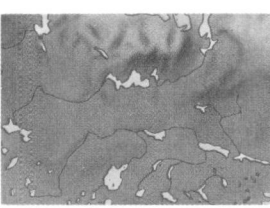

Tundra and Alpine
Tundra und Alpine Vegetation
Tundra y alpina
Toundra et végétation alpine
Tundra e vegetação alpina

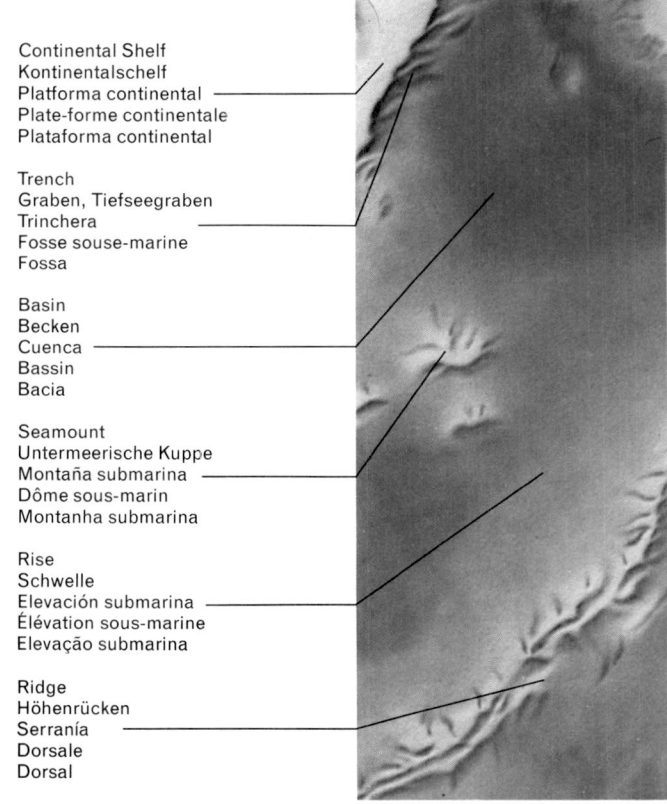

Continental Shelf
Kontinentalschelf
Platforma continental
Plate-forme continentale
Plataforma continental

Trench
Graben, Tiefseegraben
Trinchera
Fosse souse-marine
Fossa

Basin
Becken
Cuenca
Bassin
Bacia

Seamount
Untermeerische Kuppe
Montaña submarina
Dôme sous-marin
Montanha submarina

Rise
Schwelle
Elevación submarina
Élévation sous-marine
Elevação submarina

Ridge
Höhenrücken
Serranía
Dorsale
Dorsal

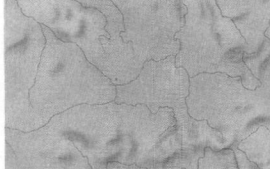

Needleleaf Trees
Nadelwälder
Coníferas
Forêt de conifères
Coníferas

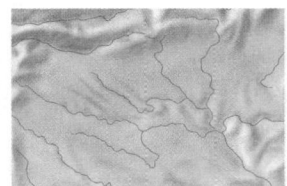

Broadleaf Trees
Laubwälder
Árboles de hojas anchas
Forêt à feuilles caduques
Árvores de folhas caducas

Tropical Rainforest
Tropischer Regenwald
Bosque tropical lluvioso
Forêt tropicale humide
Floresta tropical úmida

Grassland
Grasland
Pradera
Formations herbacées
Pradaria

Dry Scrub
Trockenes Buschland
Matorral
Brousse sèche
Caatinga

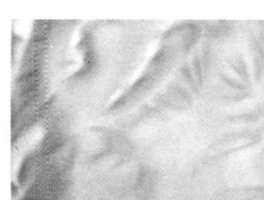

Desert
Wüste
Desierto
Désert
Deserto

ARCTIC OCEAN
Beaufort Sea
GREENLAND
(Den.)
Greenland Sea
Baffin Bay
BAFFIN ISLAND
VICTORIA ISLAND
Thule
Godhavn
Godthåb
Angmagssalik
Reykjavík
ICELAND
Davis Strait
Denmark Strait
RUSSIA
Bering Strait
UNITED STATES
Arctic Circle
Nome
Yukon
Fairbanks
Anchorage
Mount McKinley
6194
Inuvik
Yellowknife
Bering Sea
Gulf of Alaska
ALEUTIAN ISLANDS
Hudson Bay
Churchill
Juneau
ROCKY MOUNTAINS
CANADA
Edmonton
Calgary
Winnipeg
Vancouver
Seattle
Portland
Lake Superior
Lake Huron
Québec
Montreal
Ottawa
NEWFOUNDLAND
St. John's
Halifax
Minneapolis
Toronto
DETROIT
CHICAGO
Boston
NEW YORK
PHILADELPHIA
WASHINGTON
Lake Michigan
NORTH AMERICA
Salt Lake City
Denver
UNITED STATES
SAN FRANCISCO
St. Louis
APPALACHIAN MOUNTAINS
LOS ANGELES
San Diego
Phoenix
Mississippi
El Paso
Dallas
Atlanta
Houston
New Orleans
Miami
BAHAMAS
Monterrey
Gulf of Mexico
Tropic of Cancer
CABO SAN LUCAS
MEXICO
Guadalajara
CIUDAD DE MÉXICO
MEXICO CITY
LA HABANA
CUBA
HAITI
DOMINICAN REPUBLIC
PUERTO RICO (U.S.)
Port-au-Prince
SANTO DOMINGO
SAN JUAN
JAMAICA
Kingston
GUADELOUPE (Fr.)
MARTINIQUE (Fr.)
BARBADOS
TRINIDAD AND TOBAGO
Port of Spain
BELIZE
GUATEMALA
HONDURAS
Tegucigalpa
San Salvador
EL SALVADOR
NICARAGUA
Managua
Caribbean Sea
SAN JOSÉ
COSTA RICA
Panamá
PANAMA
CARACAS
VENEZUELA
GUYANA
Georgetown
Paramaribo
SURINAME
FRENCH GUIANA
Medellín
SANTA FE DE BOGOTÁ
Cali
COLOMBIA
QUITO
ECUADOR
Guayaquil
Iquitos
Manaus
Amazon
Belém
Fortaleza
CABO DE SÃO ROQUE
Natal
Recife
BRAZIL
PERU
ANDES
Trujillo
LIMA
SOUTH AMERICA
Salvador
Arequipa
LA PAZ
BOLIVIA
Sucre
Goiânia
BRASÍLIA
Belo Horizonte
PARAGUAY
Asunción
SÃO PAULO
RIO DE JANEIRO
Santos
Curitiba
Antofagasta
CHILE
Co. Aconcagua
6959
Córdoba
Paraná
Porto Alegre
Valparaíso
SANTIAGO
Rosario
URUGUAY
BUENOS AIRES
MONTEVIDEO
ARGENTINA
Concepción
Mar del Plata
Bahía Blanca
FALKLAND ISLANDS
(U.K.)
Punta Arenas
CABO DE HORNOS
CAPE HORN
SOUTH GEORGIA
(U.K.)
Drake Passage
SOUTH ORKNEY ISLANDS
(U.K.)
ANTARCTIC PENINSULA
Bellingshausen Sea
Weddell Sea
Ross Sea
ROSS ICE SHELF
MARIE BYRD LAND
Vinson Massif
4897
ANTAR
Antarctic Circle
PACIFIC OCEAN
PACIFIC OCEAN
ATLANTIC OCEAN
ATLANTIC OCEAN
Equator
Tropic of Capricorn
MIDWAY ISLANDS
(U.S.)
HAWAIIAN ISLANDS
(U.S.)
Honolulu
JOHNSTON ATOLL
(U.S.)
POLYNESIA
ÎLE CLIPPERTON
(Fr.)
ARCHIPIÉLAGO DE COLÓN
GALAPAGOS ISLANDS
(Ec.)
KIRIBATI
PHOENIX ISLANDS
TOKELAU
(N.Z.)
ÎLES MARQUISES
WALLIS AND FUTUNA
(Fr.)
W. SAMOA
AM. SAMOA
Apia
FIJI
ÎLES TUAMOTU
NIUE
(N.Z.)
COOK ISLANDS
(N.Z.)
FRENCH POLYNESIA
TONGA
PITCAIRN
(U.K.)
ISLA DE PASCUA
EASTER ISLAND
(Chile)
ISLA SAN AMBROSIO
(Chile)
ARCHIPIÉLAGO JUAN FERNÁNDEZ
(Chile)
International Date Line
CHATHAM ISLANDS
(N.Z.)
BERMUDA
(U.K.)
AÇORES AZORES
(Port.)
ARQUIPÉLAGO DA MADEIRA
(Port.)
ISLAS CANARIAS
CANARY ISLANDS
(Sp.)
CAPE VERDE
PORTUGAL
Porto
LISBOA
GIBRALTAR
(U.K.)
RABAT
Casablanca
MOROCCO
WESTERN SAHARA
MAURITANIA
Nouakchott
Tombouctou
SENEGAL
DAKAR
GAMBIA
Banjul
GUINEA-BISSAU
Bamako
GUINEA
Conakry
Freetown
SIERRA LEONE
Monrovia
LIBERIA
ABIDJAN
IRELAND
DUBLIN
Glasgow
FAEROE ISLANDS
(Den.)
SAINT HELENA
(U.K.)
Equator
180°
165°
150°
135°
120°
105°
90°
75°
60°
45°
30°
15°
0°

Kilometers 0 1000 2000 3000 Km.
Statute Miles 0 1000 2000 3000 Mi.

One centimeter represents 750 kilometers.
One inch represents approximately 1200 miles.
Robinson Projection
Scale 1:75,000,000

ARCTIC OCEAN
Beaufort Sea
Chukchi Sea
Bering Sea
ALEUTIAN BASIN
ALEUTIAN TRENCH
Gulf of Alaska
UNITED STATES
BROOKS RANGE
ALASKA RANGE
Mount McKinley 6194
Mount Logan 5959
Arctic Circle
QUEEN ELIZABETH ISLANDS
ELLESMERE ISLAND
GRØNLAND
Baffin Bay
BAFFIN BASIN
BAFFIN ISLAND
Davis Strait
Hudson Bay
Hudson Strait
Great Bear Lake
Great Slave Lake
Lake Athabasca
Lake Winnipeg
C A N A D A
N O R T H
A M E R I C A
UNITED STATES
ROCKY MOUNTAINS
COAST MTS
CASCADE RANGE
SIERRA NEVADA
GREAT BASIN
Great Salt Lake
Mount Whitney 4418
Pikes Peak 4301
GREAT PLAINS
OZARK PLATEAU
APPALACHIAN MOUNTAINS
Lake Superior
Lake Michigan
Lake Huron
Lake Erie
Lake Ontario
CHICAGO
NEW YORK
Montréal
LOS ANGELES
Houston
Mississippi
Missouri
Colorado
Rio Grande
Gulf of Mexico
MEXICO BASIN
Tropic of Cancer
M E X I C O
SIERRA MADRE OCCIDENTAL
SIERRA MADRE ORIENTAL
Pico de Orizaba 5610
CIUDAD DE MÉXICO
LABRADOR BASIN
Labrador Sea
NEWFOUNDLAND BASIN
NORTH AMERICAN BASIN
BERMUDA ISLANDS
Sargasso Sea
ATLANTIC
OCEAN
MID-ATLANTIC RIDGE
AZORES PLATEAU
WEST EUROPEAN BASIN
ICELAND
Greenland Sea
CUBA
GREATER ANTILLES
WEST INDIES
HISPANIOLA
JAMAICA
PUERTO RICO
Caribbean Sea
VENEZUELAN BASIN
CAYMAN TRENCH
MIDDLE AMERICA TRENCH
CAPE VERDE BASIN
GUIANA BASIN
SIERRA LEONE BASIN
VENEZUELA
COLOMBIA
LLANOS
Orinoco
Equator
Amazon
SELVAS
S O U T H
B R A Z I L
A M E R I C A
Chimborazo 6310
Nevado Huascarán 6746
LIMA
ANDES
BOLIVIA
Lago Titicaca
PERU
GRAN CHACO
PARAGUAY
SÃO PAULO
RIO DE JANEIRO
BRAZIL BASIN
URUGUAY
BUENOS AIRES
PAMPA
Cerro Aconcagua 6959
SANTIAGO
Nevado Ojos del Salado 6893
ARGENTINA
PATAGONIA
CHILE
ARGENTINE BASIN
Golfo San Matías
Golfo San Jorge
FALKLAND ISLANDS
FALKLAND PLATEAU
Drake Passage
Scotia Sea
SOUTH SHETLAND ISLANDS
SOUTH ORKNEY ISLANDS
Weddell Sea
Bellingshausen Sea
Amundsen Sea
Ross Sea
ROSS ICE SHELF
MARIE BYRD LAND
Mount Sidley 4181
Vinson Massif 4897
RONNE ICE SHELF
FILCHNER ICE SHELF
COATS LAND
NEW SCHWABENLAND
Antarctic Circle
P A C I F I C
O C E A N
PACIFIC OCEAN
MENDOCINO FRACTURE ZONE
MURRAY FRACTURE ZONE
CLARION FRACTURE ZONE
CLIPPERTON FRACTURE ZONE
HAWAIIAN ISLANDS
HAWAIIAN RIDGE
CENTRAL PACIFIC BASIN
CHRISTMAS RIDGE
P O L Y N E S I A
ÎLES MARQUISES
NORTHERN COOK ISLANDS
SOUTHERN COOK ISLANDS
AUSTRAL SEAMOUNTS
Tropic of Capricorn
International Date Line
TONGA TRENCH
KERMADEC TRENCH
EAST PACIFIC RISE
CHILE RISE
SOUTHWEST PACIFIC BASIN
SOUTHEAST PACIFIC BASIN
CHATHAM ISLANDS
ARCHIPIÉLAGO DE COLÓN
ISLA DE PASCUA
ARCHIPIÉLAGO JUAN FERNÁNDEZ
COCOS RIDGE
180° 165° 150° 135° 120° 105° 90° 75° 60° 45° 30° 15° 0°
75° 60° 45° 30° 15° 0° 15° 30° 45° 60° 75° 90°

One centimeter represents 750 kilometers.
One inch represents approximately 1200 miles.
Robinson Projection
Scale 1:75,000,000

GREENLAND
ICELAND
Greenland Sea
Norwegian Sea
Barents Sea
Arctic Circle
FAEROE IS.
ROCKALL RISE
IRELAND
UNITED KINGDOM
North Sea
NORWAY
SWEDEN
FINLAND
DENMARK
POLAND
GERMANY
FRANCE
SPAIN
ITALY
AUSTRIA
HUNGARY
ROMANIA
BULGARIA
UKRAINE
BELARUS
MOSKVA
SANKT-PETERBURG
URAL'SKIJE GORY
URAL MOUNTAINS
ZAPADNO-SIBIRSKAJA RAVNINA
SIBERIA
SREDNESIBIRSKOJE PLOSKOGORJE
R U S S I A
Laptevych
Sea of Okhotsk
KAZAKHSTAN
Caspian Sea
Black Sea
MEDITERRANEAN SEA
TURKEY
SYRIA
IRAQ
IRAN
JORDAN
SAUDI ARABIA
ARABIAN PENINSULA
AFGHANISTAN
PAKISTAN
INDIA
NEPAL
BHUTAN
HIMALAYAS
TIENSHAN
MONGOLIA
GOBI
CHINA
KUNLUN SHAN
QING ZANG GAOYUAN
JAPAN
Sea of Japan
Yellow Sea
East China Sea
SOUTH KOREA
N. KOREA
TAIWAN
PHILIPPINES
Philippine Sea
South China Sea
INDOCHINA
THAILAND
VIETNAM
MYANMAR
Bay of Bengal
ARABIAN SEA
SRI LANKA
MALDIVES
MALAYSIA
SINGAPORE
INDONESIA
GREATER SUNDA ISLANDS
JAVA TRENCH
NEW GUINEA
PAPUA NEW GUINEA
Arafura Sea
Timor Sea
Gulf of Carpentaria
AUSTRALIA
GREAT SANDY DESERT
GIBSON DESERT
GREAT VICTORIA DESERT
Great Australian Bight
GREAT DIVIDING RANGE
TASMANIA
LIBYA
EGYPT
SAHARA
Tropic of Cancer
SUDAN
ETHIOPIA
SOMALIA
KENYA
TANZANIA
ZAMBIA
ZIMBABWE
MOZAMBIQUE
BOTSWANA
SOUTH AFRICA
MADAGASCAR
Mozambique Channel
Equator
Tropic of Capricorn
I N D I A N
O C E A N
MID-INDIAN RIDGE
MID-INDIAN BASIN
NINETY-EAST RIDGE
CHAGOS-LACCADIVE PLATEAU
SOMALI BASIN
MASCARENE BASIN
WHARTON BASIN
NORTH AUSTRALIAN BASIN
PERTH BASIN
MADAGASCAR BASIN
SOUTHWEST INDIAN RIDGE
CROZET BASIN
AGULHAS BASIN
SOUTHERN OCEAN
SOUTHEAST INDIAN RIDGE
SOUTH AUSTRALIAN BASIN
SOUTH INDIAN BASIN
ATLANTIC-INDIAN RIDGE
ATLANTIC-INDIAN BASIN
KERGUELEN PLATEAU
Antarctic Circle
ENDERBY LAND
WILKES LAND
AMERICAN HIGHLAND
A N T A R C T I C A

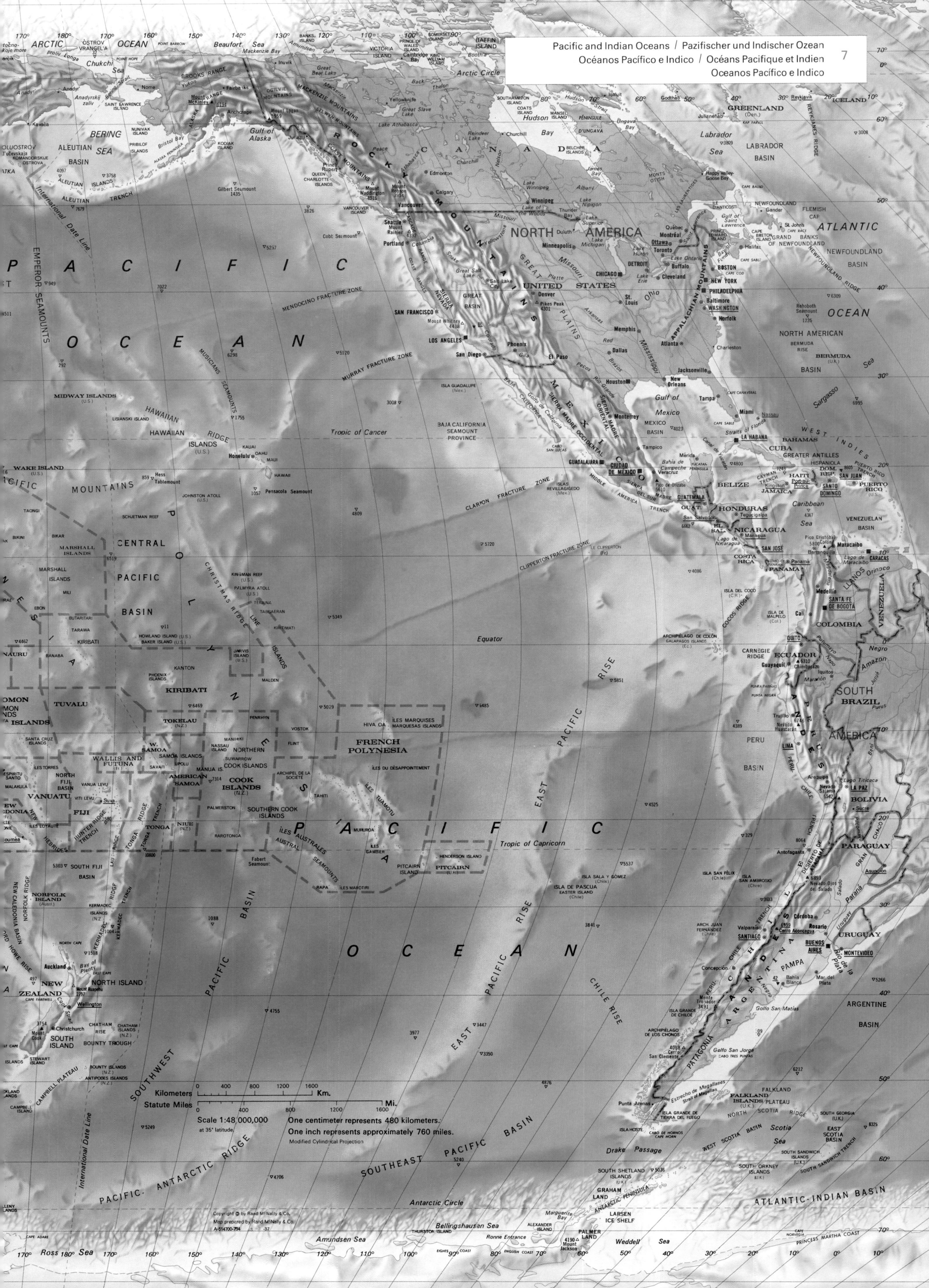

Pacific and Indian Oceans / Pazifischer und Indischer Ozean
Océanos Pacífico e Indico / Océans Pacifique et Indien
Oceanos Pacífico e Indico

7

ARCTIC OCEAN

PACIFIC OCEAN

NORTH AMERICA

UNITED STATES

MEXICO

ATLANTIC OCEAN

CENTRAL PACIFIC BASIN

MIDWAY ISLANDS (U.S.)

HAWAIIAN ISLANDS (U.S.)

Honolulu

Tropic of Cancer

Equator

FRENCH POLYNESIA

SOUTH AMERICA

BRAZIL

PERU

BOLIVIA

Tropic of Capricorn

EAST PACIFIC RISE

CHILE RISE

PACIFIC OCEAN

NEW ZEALAND

ARGENTINE BASIN

Kilometers

Statute Miles

Scale 1:48,000,000
at 35° latitude.

One centimeter represents 480 kilometers.
One inch represents approximately 760 miles.
Modified Cylindrical Projection

SOUTHEAST PACIFIC BASIN

PACIFIC-ANTARCTIC RIDGE

Antarctic Circle

ATLANTIC-INDIAN BASIN

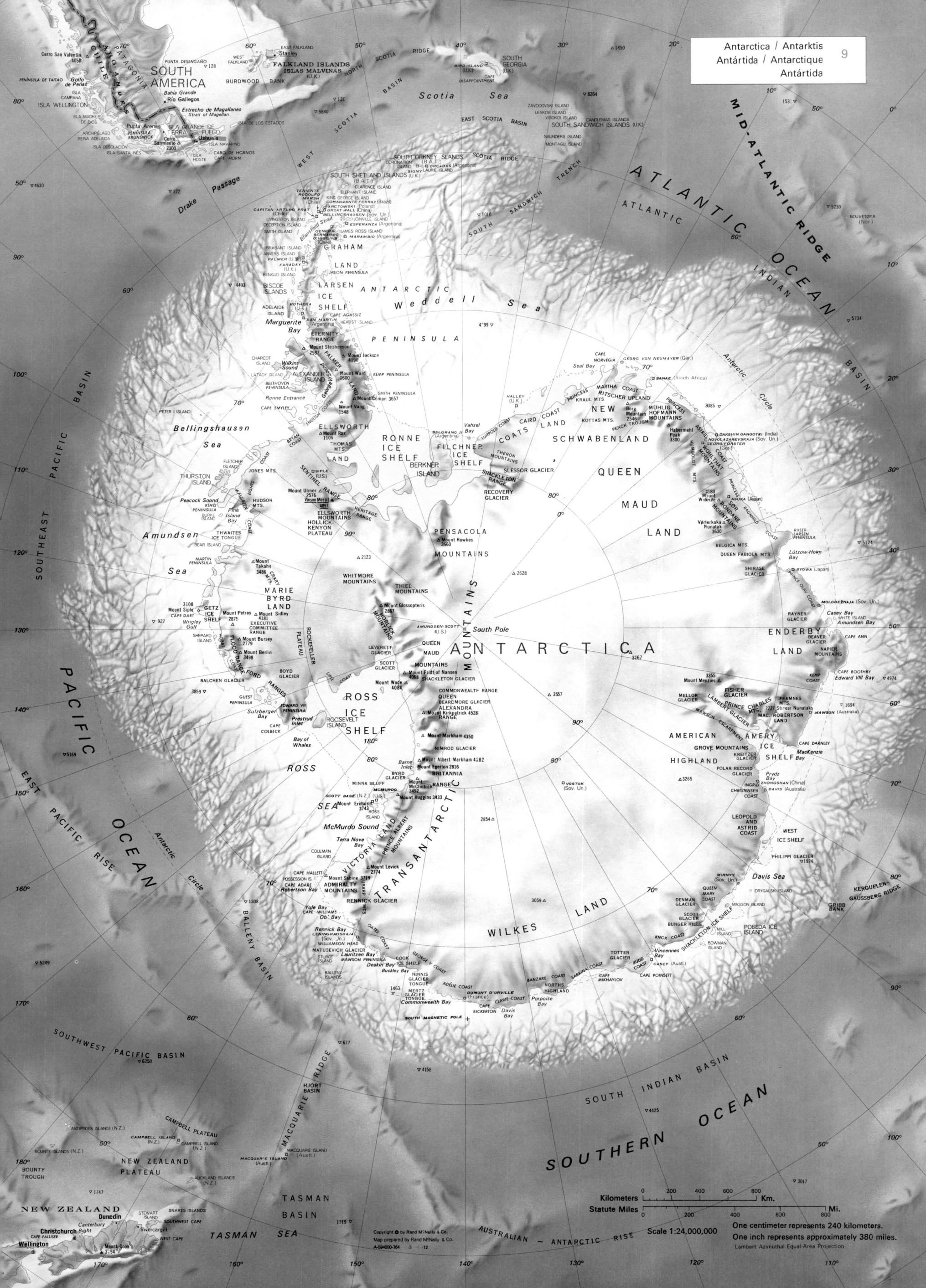

Antarctica / Antarktis
Antártida / Antarctique
Antártida

9

CANADA
GREENLAND
Davis Strait
Labrador Sea
LABRADOR BASIN
IRMINGER BASIN
REYKJANES RIDGE
ICELAND BASIN
ROCKALL RISE
Denmark Strait
ICELAND
Reykjavík
GREENLAND BASIN
Greenland Sea
LOFOTEN BASIN
NORWEGIAN BASIN
Norwegian Sea
JAN MAYEN
SPITSBERGEN
SVALBARD
BARENTS TROUGH
Barents Sea
MURMANSK RISE
Arctic Circle
ATLANTIC OCEAN
MID-ATLANTIC RIDGE
WEST EUROPEAN BASIN
AZORES
AZORES-GIBRALTAR RIDGE
PLATEAU
CANARY BASIN
CELTIC SHELF
FAEROE ISLANDS
HEBRIDES
IRELAND
DUBLIN
UNITED KINGDOM
LONDON
Edinburgh
Glasgow
Belfast
Manchester
Liverpool
Birmingham
Cardiff
Plymouth
Cork
English Channel
North Sea
NORWAY
Oslo
Bergen
Trondheim
SWEDEN
STOCKHOLM
Göteborg
FINLAND
HELSINKI
Gulf of Bothnia
Baltic Sea
DENMARK
KØBENHAVN
Malmö
Hamburg
BERLIN
GERMANY
Essen
Köln
Bonn
Frankfurt
Stuttgart
München
Leipzig
AMSTERDAM
Rotterdam
Antwerpen
BRUXELLES
Lille
PARIS
FRANCE
Nantes
Brest
Bordeaux
Lyon
Marseille
Nice
Bay of Biscay
SPAIN
MADRID
BARCELONA
Valencia
Bilbao
La Coruña
ANDORRA
PORTUGAL
LISBOA
Porto
Strait of Gibraltar
Gibraltar
Tanger
RABAT
CASABLANCA
Marrakech
Fès
MOROCCO
ATLAS MOUNTAINS
EL DJAZAÏR
ALGIERS
ALGERIA
TUNIS
TUNISIA
TARĀBULUS
TRIPOLI
LIBYA
SWITZ.
Zürich
Basel
Genève
ALPS
AUSTRIA
WIEN
VIENNA
Graz
ITALY
MILANO
Torino
Venezia
ROMA
Napoli
Palermo
Cagliari
Tyrrhenian Sea
Adriatic Sea
Ionian Sea
MALTA
Mediterranean Sea
CZECH REP.
PRAHA
POLAND
WARSZAWA
Gdańsk
Kraków
Katowice
SLOVAKIA
HUNGARY
BUDAPEST
SLO.
CROATIA
Zagreb
BOSNIA AND HERZ.
YUGO.
BEOGRAD
ALBANIA
Tiranë
MACE.
GREECE
ATHÍNAI
Thessaloníki
Aegean Sea
BULGARIA
SOFIJA
ROMANIA
BUCUREŞTI
MOLD.
Kišin'ov
UKRAINE
KIJEV
CHAR'KOV
ODESSA
L'vov
BELARUS
MINSK
LITH.
Vilnius
LAT.
RIGA
EST.
Tallinn
EUROPE
RUSSIA
MOSKVA
MOSCOW
SANKT-PETERBURG
ST. PETERSBURG
Murmansk
Archangel'sk
White Sea
Volga
Don
Dnepr
VOLGOGRAD
Samara
Kazan'
Perm'
Ufa
URAL'SKIJE GORY
URAL MOUNTAINS
JEKATERINBURG
Čel'abinsk
Omsk
Rostov-na-Donu
Black Sea
Sevastopol'
Caspian Sea
KAZAKHSTAN
UZBEKISTAN
TURKMENISTAN
Aral'skoje more
Aral Sea
BOL'ŠOJ KAVKAZ
CAUCASUS
GEORGIA
TBILISI
ARM.
JEREVAN
AZER.
BAKU
TURKEY
ANKARA
İSTANBUL
İzmir
ASIA MINOR
CYPRUS
SYRIA
DIMASHQ
LEBANON
BAYRŪT
ISRAEL
Tel Aviv-Yafo
JORDAN
'AMMAN
IRAQ
BAGHDĀD
MESOPOTAMIA
Tigris
Euphrates
IRAN
TEHRĀN
Mashhad
Eşfahān
AL-KUWAYT
KUWAIT
BAHRAIN
QATAR
UNITED ARAB EMIRATES
OMAN
Gulf of Oman
Persian Gulf
SAUDI ARABIA
AR-RIYĀD
Al-Madīnah
Makkah
Jiddah
Red Sea
EGYPT
AL-QĀHIRAH
CAIRO
AL-ISKANDARĪYAH
ALEXANDRIA
Nile
Aswān
SAHARA
WESTERN SAHARA
MAURITANIA
Nouakchott
CAPE VERDE
Tropic of Cancer
ISLAS CANARIAS
CANARY ISLANDS
Santa Cruz
Las Palmas
Funchal
ARQUIPÉLAGO DA MADEIRA
ASIA
ZAPADNO-SIBIRSKAJA RAVNINA
MALI
NIGER

Europe and Africa / Europa und Afrika
Europa y África / Europe et Afrique   11
Europa e África

INDIAN OCEAN

SOMALI BASIN

SEYCHELLES

MASCARENE BASIN

MAURITIUS
RÉUNION (Fr.)

MADAGASCAR BASIN

SOUTHWEST INDIAN RIDGE

SOMALIA

Gulf of Aden
Djibouti
DJIBOUTI
Mugdisho
Mogadishu

ETHIOPIA
ADIS ABEBA

OGADEN

RIFT VALLEY

White Nile
Blue Nile

AS-SUDD

UGANDA
KAMPALA
KENYA
NAIROBI
Mombasa
Lake Victoria
Lake Rudolf
Lake Albert
SERENGETI

RWANDA
Kigali
BURUNDI
Bujumbura

DAR ES SALAAM
Zanzibar

TANZANIA

COMOROS
MAYOTTE (Fr.)

Antananarivo
ANTANANARIVO
Toamasina

MADAGASCAR

Mozambique Channel

Tropic of Capricorn

A F R I C A

CENTRAL AFRICAN REPUBLIC

Bangui

ZAIRE
BASIN
Kisangani
STANLEY FALLS

CONGO

Lake Tanganyika
Lake Nyasa
Lake Malawi

MALAWI
Lilongwe
Blantyre

MOZAMBIQUE

Beira

Zambezi

ZAMBIA
Lusaka
Ndola
Lubumbashi

Lake Kariba
VICTORIA FALLS
Livingstone

ZIMBABWE
HARARE
Bulawayo

Limpopo

MAPUTO

NATAL BASIN

MOZAMBIQUE PLATEAU

N'Djamena

CAMEROON
Yaoundé
Douala

EQUAT. GUI.

GABON
Libreville

CONGO
Brazzaville
KINSHASA
Matadi
CABINDA (Angola)
Pointe-Noire

ANGOLA

LUANDA

Lobito

NAMIBIA
Windhoek

NAMIB DESERT

KALAHARI DESERT

BOTSWANA
Gaborone

SOUTH AFRICA

PRETORIA
JOHANNESBURG
Bloemfontein

LESOTHO
SWAZILAND

Port Elizabeth
East London

GREAT KARROO

CAPE TOWN
CAPE OF GOOD HOPE

AGULHAS PLATEAU

NIGERIA
Abuja
LAGOS
Ibadan
Kano
Kaduna
Enugu
Aba
Port Harcourt

SÃO TOMÉ AND PRÍNCIPE
Bight of Biafra

Gulf of Guinea

BENIN
TOGO
GHANA
ACCRA
Kumasi
Sekondi-Takoradi

BURKINA FASO
Ouagadougou

CÔTE D'IVOIRE
ABIDJAN
Bouaké

LIBERIA
Monrovia

SIERRA LEONE
Freetown

GUINEA
Conakry

GUINEA-BISSAU
Bissau

Bamako

Niamey

GUINEA BASIN

GUINEA RISE

SAINT HELENA (U.K.)

ANGOLA BASIN

ANGOLA RISE

WALVIS RIDGE

CAPE BASIN

A T L A N T I C   O C E A N

Equator

TRISTAN DA CUNHA GROUP
(St. Helena)

GOUGH ISLAND (St. Helena)

Tropic of Capricorn

M I D - A T L A N T I C   R I D G E

BRAZIL BASIN

Mi.
800
600
400
200
0
One centimeter represents 240 kilometers.
One inch represents approximately 380 miles.
Lambert Azimuthal Equal-Area Projection

Km.
800
600
400
200
0

Scale 1:24,000,000

Kilometers
Statute Miles

Copyright © by Rand McNally & Co.
A-518994-784
Map prepared by Rand McNally & Co.

ATLANTIC OCEAN
ARCTIC OCEAN
North Pole
GREENLAND
ICELAND
Reykjavík
Greenland Sea
Norwegian Sea
Barents Sea
Kara Sea
Laptev Sea
East Siberian Sea
Chukchi Sea
Bering Sea
Bering Strait
Sea of Okhotsk
Sea of Japan
Yellow Sea
EAST CHINA SEA
Caspian Sea
Black Sea
Aral Sea
Baltic Sea
North Sea
UNITED STATES
UNITED KINGDOM
IRELAND
NORWAY
SWEDEN
FINLAND
DENMARK
NETHERLANDS
GERMANY
POLAND
BELARUS
UKRAINE
ROMANIA
HUNGARY
BULGARIA
TURKEY
SYRIA
IRAQ
IRAN
SAUDI ARABIA
AFGHANISTAN
KAZAKHSTAN
UZBEKISTAN
TURKMENISTAN
KYRGYZSTAN
TAJIKISTAN
RUSSIA
MONGOLIA
NORTH KOREA
SOUTH KOREA
JAPAN
EUROPE
ASIA
SIBERIA
URAL'SKIJE GORY
URAL MOUNTAINS
ZAPADNO-SIBIRSKAJA RAVNINA
SREDNESIBIRSKOJE PLOSKOGORJE
CHREBET ČERSKOGO
SAJAN MOUNTAINS
ALTAI
TIEN SHAN
PAMIR
HINDU KUSH
KUNLUN SHAN
TARIM PENDI
GOBI
DA HINGGAN LING
SEVERNAJA ZEML'A
NOVAJA ZEML'A
ZEML'A FRANCA-IOSIFA
FRANZ JOSEF LAND
SVALBARD
NOVOSIBIRSKIJE OSTROVA
OSTROV VRANGEL'A
KURIL'SKIJE OSTROVA
KURIL ISLANDS
ALEUTIAN ISLANDS
OSTROV SACHALIN
LONDON
DUBLIN
OSLO
STOCKHOLM
HELSINKI
KØBENHAVN
BERLIN
WARSZAWA
PRAHA
WIEN
BUDAPEST
BUCUREŞTI
SOFIJA
BEOGRAD
KIJEV
MINSK
MOSKVA
SANKT-PETERBURG
RIGA
VILNIUS
TALLINN
ISTANBUL
ANKARA
TBILISI
JEREVAN
BAKU
TEHRĀN
BAGHDĀD
DIMASHQ
AMMĀN
BAYRŪT
AL-KUWAYT
KĀBOL
TAŠKENT
ALMA-ATA
AŠCHABAD
DUŠANBE
ULAANBAATAR
BEIJING
TIANJIN
SHENYANG
P'YONGYANG
SŎUL
SHANGHAI
NANJING
WUHAN
XI'AN
Novosibirsk
Omsk
Jekaterinburg
Čel'abinsk
Krasnojarsk
Irkutsk
Jakutsk
Magadan
Vladivostok
Chabarovsk
Murmansk
Archangel'sk
Volgograd
Samara
Kazan'
Nižnij Novgorod
Saratov
Perm'
Ufa
Tomsk
Barnaul
Kemerovo
Novokuzneck
Harbin
Changchun
Qiqihar
Sapporo
Sendai
Nagoya
Ōsaka
Kyōto
Hiroshima
Fukuoka
Kagoshima
Pusan
Taegu
Dalian
Qingdao
Jinan
Zhengzhou
Lanzhou
Yinchuan
Taiyuan
Ürümqi
Kashi
Yining
Samarkand
Mashhad
Yazd
Eşfahān
Tabrīz
Halab
Adana
Izmir
Odessa
Doneck
Char'kov
Rostov-na-Donu
Kraków
Katowice
Gdańsk
Hamburg
Essen
Köln
Frankfurt
Stuttgart
München
Leipzig
Glasgow
Edinburgh
Belfast
Liverpool
Manchester
Birmingham
Cardiff
Bergen
Trondheim
Göteborg
Amur
Lena
Ob'
Jenisej
Volga
Don
Dnepr
Irtyš
Angara
Huang
Chang
Arctic Circle

AUSTRALIA

PHILIPPINE
Sea

CHINA
SEA

SOUTH

Philippine
Sea

Celebes Sea

SUNDA

INDONESIA
ISLANDS

GREATER

JAKARTA

JAVA TRENCH

NORTH
AUSTRALIAN
BASIN

CHRISTMAS
ISLAND

WHARTON

BASIN

PERTH

BASIN

Perth

INDOCHINA

THAILAND

KRUNG
THEP
BANGKOK

CAMBODIA

VIETNAM

LAOS

Gulf of
Thailand

MYANMAR
(BURMA)

YANGON
RANGOON

MALAY
PENINSULA
MALAYSIA

KUALA
LUMPUR

SINGAPORE

SUMATRA

COCOS
ISLANDS

Andaman
Sea

ANDAMAN

Bay of
Bengal

ANDAMAN
ISLANDS
(India)

NICOBAR
ISLANDS
(India)

BROKEN RIDGE

NINETYEAST RIDGE

BANGLADESH

DHAKA

CALCUTTA

INDIA

MADRAS

SRI LANKA

COLOMBO

MID-

INDIAN

BASIN

I N D I A N

O C E A N

BOMBAY

BANGALORE

LACCADIVE PLATEAU

LAKSHADWEEP
(India)

MALDIVES

CHAGOS

CHAGOS
ARCHIPELAGO

DIEGO GARCIA

PAKISTAN

KARACHI

ARABIAN
SEA

ARABIAN
BASIN

CARLSBERG RIDGE

OWEN FRACTURE ZONE

MID- INDIAN RIDGE

SOUTHWEST

INDIAN

RIDGE

OMAN

ARABIAN
PENINSULA

AR-RUB'AL-KHĀLĪ

YEMEN

Gulf of Aden

DJIBOUTI

SOMALIA

ETHIOPIA

SOMALI

BASIN

SEYCHELLES

SEYCHELLES
BANK

SAYA DE MALHA
BANK

NAZARETH
BANK

CARGADOS CARAJOS
ISLANDS

MASCARENE

PLATEAU

MASCARENE

BASIN

MAURITIUS

REUNION

MADAGASCAR

ANTANANARIVO

Red Sea

Scale 1:24,000,000

One centimeter represents 240 kilometers.
One inch represents approximately 380 miles.

Lambert Azimuthal Equal-Area Projection

Statute Miles

Kilometers

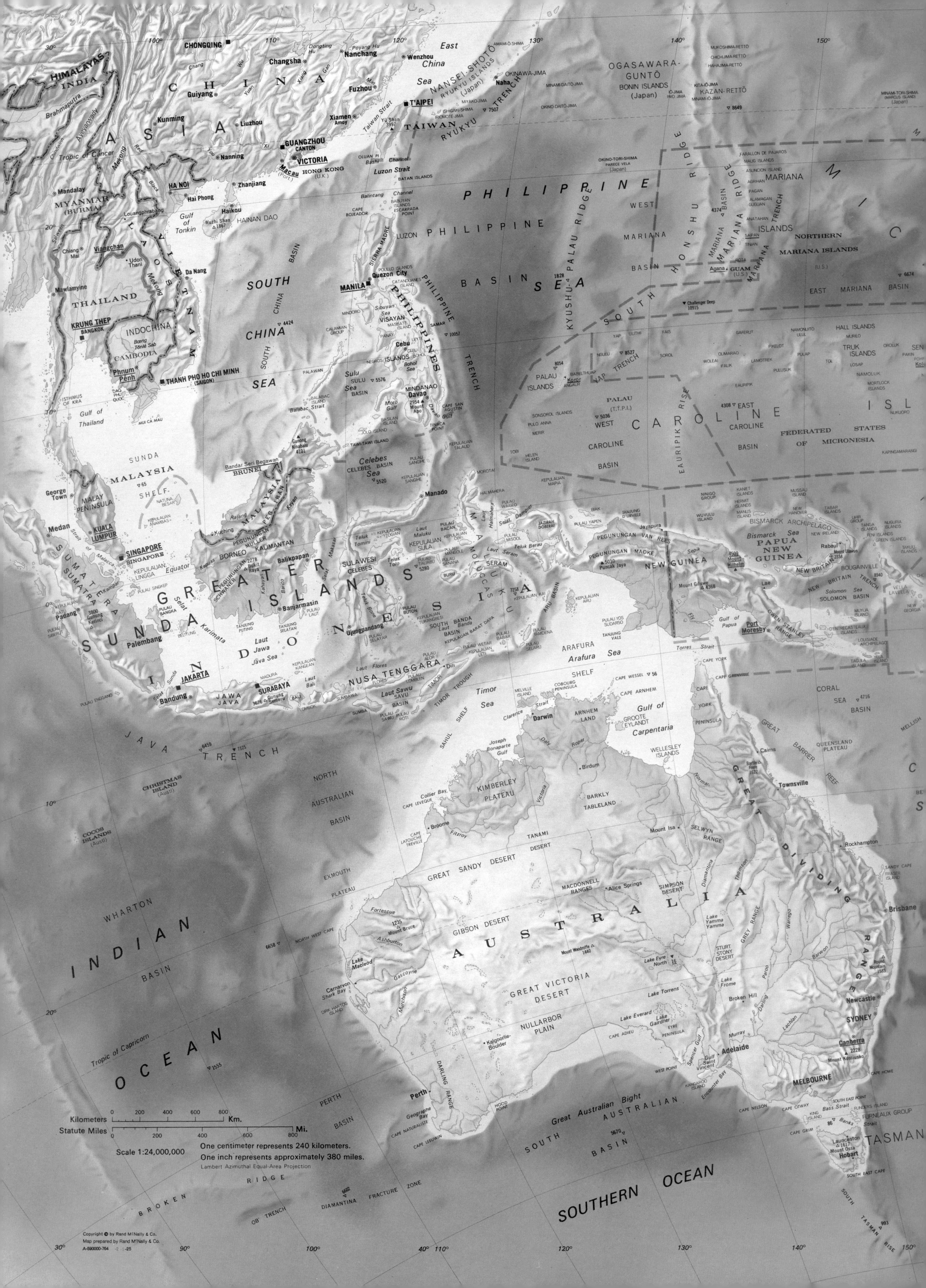
ASIA
CHINA
CHONGQING
Changsha
Nanchang
Wenzhou
Fuzhou
Guiyang
Kunming
Liuzhou
Nanning
GUANGZHOU
CANTON
VICTORIA
HONG KONG
(U.K.)
Macau
(Port.)
Zhanjiang
HA NOI
Hai Phong
Haikou
HAINAN DAO
Gulf of Tonkin
East China Sea
NANSEI-SHOTŌ
RYUKYU ISLANDS
(Japan)
Naha
RYUKYU TRENCH
T'AIPEI
TAIWAN
Taiwan Strait
Luzon Strait
Xiamen
Amoy
HIMALAYAS
INDIA
Brahmaputra
Tropic of Cancer
Mekong
Mandalay
MYANMAR
(BURMA)
LAOS
VIETNAM
Viangchan
Da Nang
THAILAND
KRUNG THEP
BANGKOK
INDOCHINA
CAMBODIA
Phnum Pénh
THANH PHO HO CHI MINH
(SAIGON)
Gulf of Thailand
SOUTH CHINA SEA
SOUTH CHINA BASIN
PHILIPPINE SEA
PHILIPPINE BASIN
WEST MARIANA BASIN
KYUSHU-PALAU RIDGE
SOUTH HONSHU RIDGE
MARIANA TRENCH
MARIANA ISLANDS
NORTHERN MARIANA ISLANDS
(U.S.)
Agana
GUAM
Challenger Deep
EAST MARIANA BASIN
OGASAWARA-GUNTŌ
BONIN ISLANDS
(Japan)
KAZAN-RETTŌ
PHILIPPINES
LUZON
Quezon City
MANILA
VISAYAN
Cebu
MINDANAO
Davao
PHILIPPINE TRENCH
Sulu Sea
Celebes Sea
PALAU ISLANDS
Koror
YAP TRENCH
CAROLINE ISLANDS
WEST CAROLINE BASIN
EAST CAROLINE BASIN
EAURIPIK RISE
FEDERATED STATES OF MICRONESIA
MALAYSIA
SUNDA SHELF
George Town
MALAY PENINSULA
KUALA LUMPUR
SINGAPORE
Medan
SUMATERA
SUMATRA
Padang
Palembang
Bandar Seri Begawan
BRUNEI
Kuching
BORNEO
KALIMANTAN
Balikpapan
Banjarmasin
GREATER SUNDA ISLANDS
SULAWESI
CELEBES
Manado
MALUKU
MOLUCCAS
INDONESIA
Laut Jawa
Java Sea
JAKARTA
Bandung
JAWA
JAVA
SURABAYA
Ujungpandang
NUSA TENGGARA
TIMOR
Dili
Laut Banda
PEGUNUNGAN MAOKE
Puncak Jaya
NEW GUINEA
Jayapura
PAPUA NEW GUINEA
Bismarck Sea
BISMARCK ARCHIPELAGO
NEW BRITAIN
Rabaul
Lae
Port Moresby
Gulf of Papua
OWEN STANLEY RANGE
Torres Strait
ARAFURA SEA
Arafura Sea
Timor Sea
Darwin
ARNHEM LAND
GROOTE EYLANDT
Gulf of Carpentaria
CAPE YORK PENINSULA
CORAL SEA BASIN
GREAT BARRIER REEF
QUEENSLAND PLATEAU
Cairns
Townsville
KIMBERLEY PLATEAU
BARKLY TABLELAND
Broome
Mount Isa
TANAMI DESERT
GREAT SANDY DESERT
Alice Springs
MACDONNELL RANGES
SIMPSON DESERT
GIBSON DESERT
AUSTRALIA
GREAT DIVIDING RANGE
Rockhampton
Brisbane
Lake Eyre North
GREAT VICTORIA DESERT
NULLARBOR PLAIN
Kalgoorlie-Boulder
Perth
DARLING RANGE
Broken Hill
Lake Torrens
Adelaide
Newcastle
SYDNEY
Canberra
Mount Kosciusko
MELBOURNE
Bass Strait
Hobart
TASMAN
Great Australian Bight
SOUTH AUSTRALIAN BASIN
SOUTHERN OCEAN
JAVA TRENCH
CHRISTMAS ISLAND
(Austl.)
COCOS ISLANDS
(Austl.)
NORTH AUSTRALIAN BASIN
EXMOUTH PLATEAU
WHARTON BASIN
INDIAN OCEAN
Tropic of Capricorn
Shark Bay
PERTH BASIN
BROKEN RIDGE
DIAMANTINA FRACTURE ZONE
Kilometers
Km.
Statute Miles
Mi.
Scale 1:24,000,000
One centimeter represents 240 kilometers.
One inch represents approximately 380 miles.
Lambert Azimuthal Equal-Area Projection
Copyright © by Rand McNally & Co.
Map prepared by Rand McNally & Co.

Australia and Oceania / Australien und Ozeanien
Australia y Oceanía / Australie et Océanie
Austrália e Oceania   15

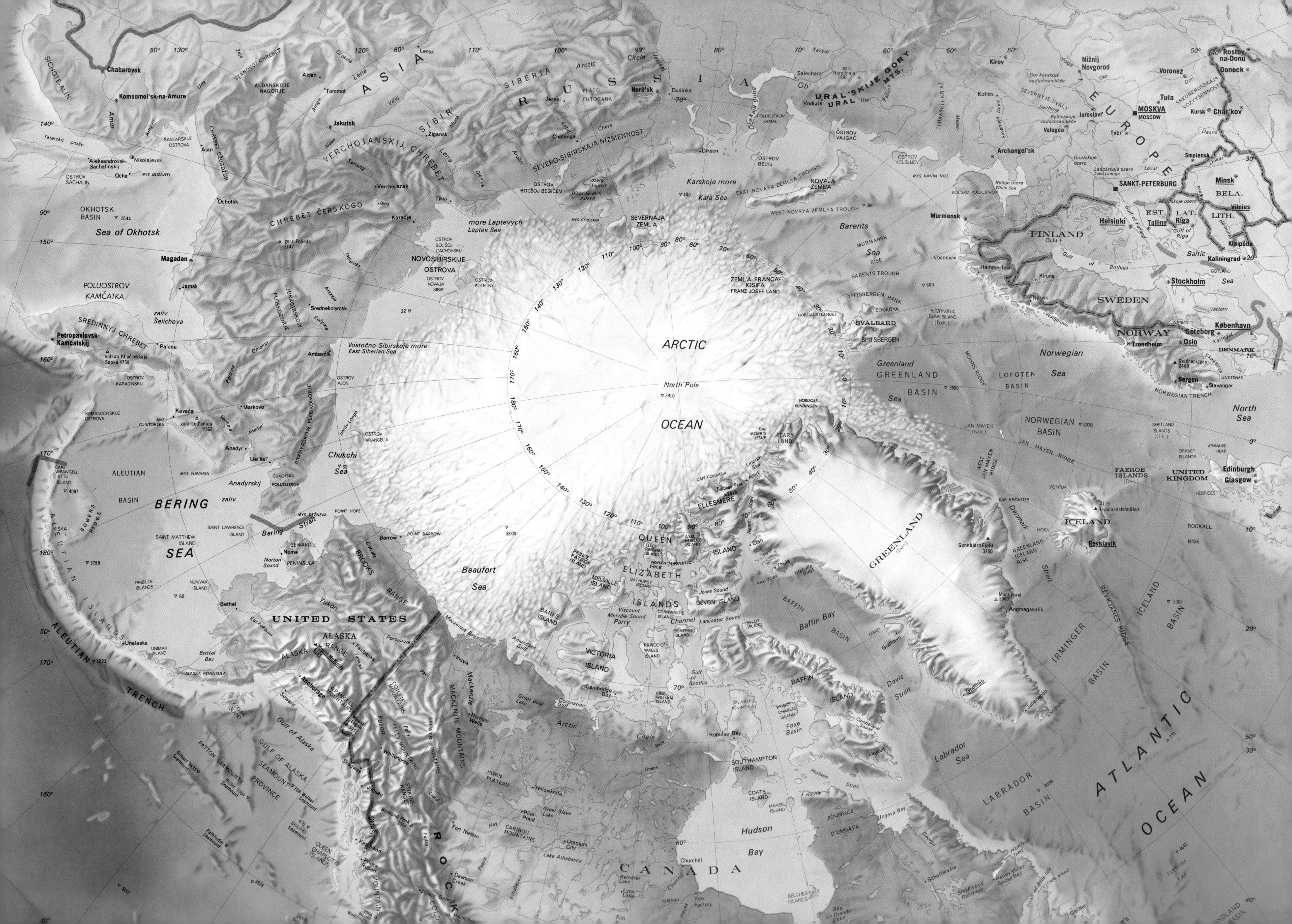
ARCTIC
OCEAN
North Pole
3910
ASIA
RUSSIA
SIBERIA
EUROPE
UNITED STATES
ALASKA
CANADA
GREENLAND
(Den.)
ICELAND
ATLANTIC
OCEAN
SWEDEN
NORWAY
FINLAND
DENMARK
UNITED KINGDOM
Norwegian Sea
Greenland Sea
Barents Sea
Karskoje more
Kara Sea
more Laptevych
Laptev Sea
Vostočno-Sibirskoje more
East Siberian Sea
Chukchi Sea
Beaufort Sea
BERING SEA
Sea of Okhotsk
Baffin Bay
Hudson Bay
Labrador Sea
North Sea
Gulf of Alaska
Bering Strait
Davis Strait
Denmark Strait
QUEEN ELIZABETH ISLANDS
ELLESMERE
DEVON ISLAND
BAFFIN ISLAND
VICTORIA ISLAND
BANKS ISLAND
SVALBARD
ZEML'A FRANCA-IOSIFA
FRANZ JOSEF LAND
SEVERNAJA ZEML'A
NOVAJA ZEML'A
NOVOSIBIRSKIJE OSTROVA
POLUOSTROV KAMČATKA
ALEUTIAN TRENCH
ALEUTIAN ISLANDS
BROOKS RANGE
ALASKA RANGE
MACKENZIE MOUNTAINS
URAL'SKIJE GORY
URAL MTS.
CHREBET ČERSKOGO
VERCHOJANSKIJ CHREBET
MOSKVA
MOSCOW
SANKT-PETERBURG
Helsinki
Stockholm
Oslo
København
Reykjavík
Murmansk
Anchorage
Fairbanks
Magadan
Jakutsk
Noril'sk
Churchill
Edinburgh
Glasgow

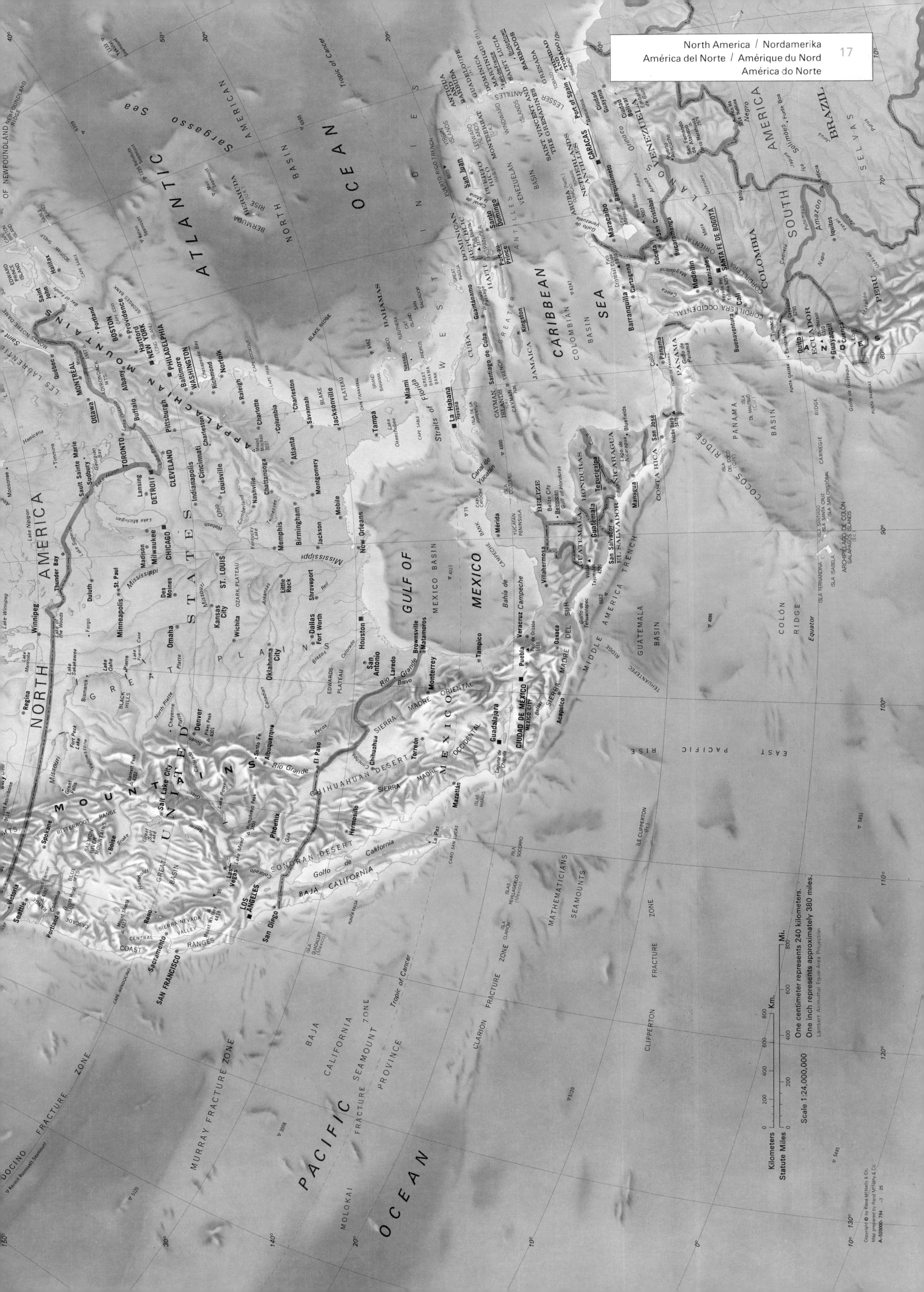
NORTH AMERICA
UNITED STATES
ATLANTIC OCEAN
PACIFIC OCEAN
GULF OF MEXICO
CARIBBEAN SEA
Sargasso Sea
WEST INDIES
SOUTH AMERICA
MEXICO
CUBA
BAHAMAS
JAMAICA
HAITI
DOMINICAN REPUBLIC
PUERTO RICO
BELIZE
GUATEMALA
HONDURAS
EL SALVADOR
NICARAGUA
COSTA RICA
PANAMA
COLOMBIA
VENEZUELA
ECUADOR
PERU
BRAZIL
GREAT PLAINS
ROCKY MOUNTAINS
APPALACHIAN MOUNTAINS
SIERRA MADRE OCCIDENTAL
SIERRA MADRE ORIENTAL
SIERRA MADRE DEL SUR
CHIHUAHUAN DESERT
SONORAN DESERT
GREAT BASIN
BAJA CALIFORNIA
Golfo de California
Tropic of Cancer
Equator
WASHINGTON
NEW YORK
PHILADELPHIA
BOSTON
CHICAGO
DETROIT
CLEVELAND
TORONTO
MONTRÉAL
Ottawa
ST. LOUIS
New Orleans
Houston
Dallas
Denver
LOS ANGELES
SAN FRANCISCO
Seattle
CIUDAD DE MÉXICO
Guadalajara
Monterrey
La Habana
Kingston
CARACAS
SANTA FE DE BOGOTÁ
Quito
Panamá
San José
Kilometers
Statute Miles
Scale 1:24,000,000
One centimeter represents 240 kilometers.
One inch represents approximately 380 miles.
Lambert Azimuthal Equal-Area Projection

NORTH AMERICA
UNITED STATES
ROCKY MTS.
APPALACHIAN MOUNTAINS
GREAT PLAINS
OZARK PLATEAU
EDWARDS PLATEAU
CHICAGO
CLEVELAND
NEW YORK
PHILADELPHIA
WASHINGTON
Baltimore
Pittsburgh
Indianapolis
Cincinnati
Charleston
Louisville
Nashville
Chattanooga
Memphis
Birmingham
Atlanta
Richmond
Norfolk
Raleigh
Charlotte
Columbia
Charleston
Savannah
Montgomery
Jackson
Mobile
New Orleans
Jacksonville
Tampa
Miami
Lake Okeechobee
Omaha
Des Moines
Kansas City
ST. LOUIS
Wichita
Oklahoma City
Little Rock
Dallas
Fort Worth
Shreveport
Houston
San Antonio
Laredo
Brownsville
Denver
Cheyenne
Pikes Peak 4301
Santa Fe
Albuquerque
El Paso
Mississippi
Missouri
Ohio
Arkansas
Red
Brazos
Colorado
Pecos
Rio Grande
Bravo
North Platte
South Platte
Platte
Canadian
Wabash
Cumberland
Tennessee
Kentucky Lake
2037 Mt. Mitchell
Chesapeake Bay
LONG ISLAND
GEORGES BANK
CAPE HATTERAS
CAPE LOOKOUT
CAPE FEAR
CAPE CANAVERAL
CAPE SABLE
BLAKE PLATEAU
BLAKE RIDGE
MEXICO
SIERRA MADRE ORIENTAL
SIERRA MADRE DEL SUR
Monterrey
Matamoros
Torreón
Tampico
Guadalajara
Laguna de Chapala
CIUDAD DE MÉXICO
MEXICO CITY
Puebla
Veracruz
Pico de Orizaba 5610
Oaxaca
Acapulco
Villahermosa
Mérida
YUCATAN PENINSULA
Bahía de Campeche
CAMPECHE BANK
Golfo de Tehuantepec
GULF OF MEXICO
MEXICO BASIN
Canal de Yucatán
Straits of Florida
BAHAMAS
GRAND BAHAMA
GREAT BAHAMA BANK
ABACO
ELEUTHERA
CAT ISLAND
SAN SALVADOR
ANDROS
Nassau
CUBA
La Habana
Havana
ISLA DE LA JUVENTUD
Santiago de Cuba
Guantánamo
CAYMAN ISLANDS (U.K.)
CAYMAN TRENCH
Windward Passage
HISPANIOLA
HAITI
Port-au-Prince
DOMINICAN REPUBLIC
Santo Domingo
Pico Duarte 3175
JAMAICA
Kingston
PUERTO RICO
San Juan
PUERTO RICO TRENCH
GREAT INAGUA
VIRGIN ISLANDS
WEST INDIES
GREATER ANTILLES
LESSER ANTILLES
LEEWARD ISLANDS
WINDWARD ISLANDS
ANTIGUA AND BARBUDA
MONTSERRAT (U.K.)
GUADELOUPE (Fr.)
DOMINICA
MARTINIQUE (Fr.)
Fort-de-France
SAINT LUCIA
BARBADOS
Bridgetown
SAINT VINCENT AND THE GRENADINES
GRENADA
TRINIDAD AND TOBAGO
Port of Spain
NETHERLANDS ANTILLES
ARUBA (Neth.)
CURAÇAO
BONAIRE
CARIBBEAN SEA
VENEZUELAN BASIN
COLOMBIAN BASIN
BELIZE
Belize City
Belmopan
Gulf of Honduras
GUATEMALA
Guatemala
Volcán Tajumulco 4220
HONDURAS
Tegucigalpa
EL SALVADOR
San Salvador
NICARAGUA
Managua
Lago de Nicaragua
Bluefields
COSTA RICA
San José
PANAMA
Panamá
Golfo de Panamá
Colón
ISTMO DE PANAMÁ
Volcán Barú 3475
MIDDLE AMERICA TRENCH
TEHUANTEPEC RIDGE
GUATEMALA BASIN
PANAMA BASIN
COCOS RIDGE
ISLA DEL COCO (C.R.)
ISLA DE MALPELO (Col.)
COLÓN RIDGE
CARNEGIE RIDGE
ARCHIPIÉLAGO DE COLÓN
GALAPAGOS ISLANDS (Ec.)
ISLA ISABELA
ISLA FERNANDINA
ISLA SANTA CRUZ
ISLA SAN CRISTÓBAL
Equator
Tropic of Cancer
NORTH AMERICAN BASIN
BERMUDA (U.K.)
BERMUDA RISE
Sargasso Sea
ATLANTIC OCEAN
MID-ATLANTIC RIDGE
AZORES PLATEAU
AÇORES
AZORES (Port.)
FLORES
TERCEIRA
PICO
SÃO MIGUEL
SANTA MARIA
Great Meteor Tablemount 269
Kelvin Seamount
Rehoboth Seamount 1235
Muir Seamount
Yakutat Seamount 1133
CAPE VERDE BASIN
GUIANA BASIN
VENEZUELA
CARACAS
Maracaibo
Lago de Maracaibo
Golfo de Venezuela
Barquisimeto
Barcelona
Ciudad Bolívar
Ciudad Guayana
Embalse de Guri
SALTO ÁNGEL
ANGEL FALLS
Orinoco
Apure
Arauca
Meta
LLANOS
Puerto Ayacucho
San Fernando de Atabapo
Cerro Marahuaca
Pico Bolívar 5007
San Cristóbal
Cúcuta
COLOMBIA
SANTA FE DE BOGOTÁ
Barranquilla
Cartagena
Pico Cristóbal Colón 5800
Medellín
Manizales
Cali
Buenaventura
Nevado del Tolima 5215
CORDILLERA OCCIDENTAL
CORDILLERA ORIENTAL
Bucaramanga
Magdalena
Cauca
Guaviare
Mitú
Tumaco
Esmeraldas
PUNTA GALERA
ECUADOR
Quito
Cayambe 5790
Chimborazo 6310
Guayaquil
Golfo de Guayaquil
Cuenca
Loja
ANDES
PERU
LIMA
Chiclayo
Trujillo
Cajamarca
Huaraz
Nevado Huascarán 6746
Nevado Yerupajá 6634
Cerro de Pasco
Huancayo
Pucallpa
Iquitos
Cuzco
Ica
Puerto Maldonado
Lago Titicaca
PERU-CHILE TRENCH
GUYANA
Georgetown
KAIETEUR FALL
Mount Roraima 2875
PAKARAIMA MTS.
Essequibo
Cuyuni
SURINAME
Paramaribo
FRENCH GUIANA
Cayenne
Oiapoque
TUMUC-HUMAC MTS.
CABO ORANGE
Amapá
ILHA DE MARACÁ
Macapá
ILHA CAVIANA DE FORA
CABO MAGUARI
ILHA DE MARAJÓ
Belém
SOUTH AMERICA
BRAZIL
SELVAS
Manaus
Boa Vista
Pico da Neblina 3014
Negro
Branco
Represa Balbina
Amazon
Amazonas
Solimões
Japurá
Caquetá
Putumayo
Napo
Marañón
Ucayali
Javari
Yavari
Leticia
Içá
Fonte Boa
Juruá
Purus
Madeira
Aripuanã
Tapajós
Xingu
Iriri
Jari
Pará
Tocantins
Araguaia
Óbidos
Santarém
Porto de Moz
SA. DO CACHIMBO
São Manuel
SA. FORMOSA
Juruena
Guaporé
Itenes
Mamoré
Beni
Madre de Dios
Porto Velho
Rio Branco
Cobija
Riberalta
Guajará-Mirim
Trinidad
Mato Grosso
Cuiabá
PLANALTO
ILHA DO BANANAL
CHAPADA DAS MANGABEIRAS
Marabá
Carolina
Porto Nacional
Barra
Represa de Sobradinho
Juazeiro
São Francisco
Pico das Almas 1836
Paraguaçu
Parnaíba
São Luís
Teresina
Fortaleza
ATOL DAS ROCAS
ILHA FERNANDO DE NORONHA (Braz.)
CABO DE SÃO ROQUE
Natal
João Pessoa
PONTA DO SEIXAS
Recife
Campina Grande
Caruaru
Paulistana
Maceió
Penedo
Aracaju
Salvador

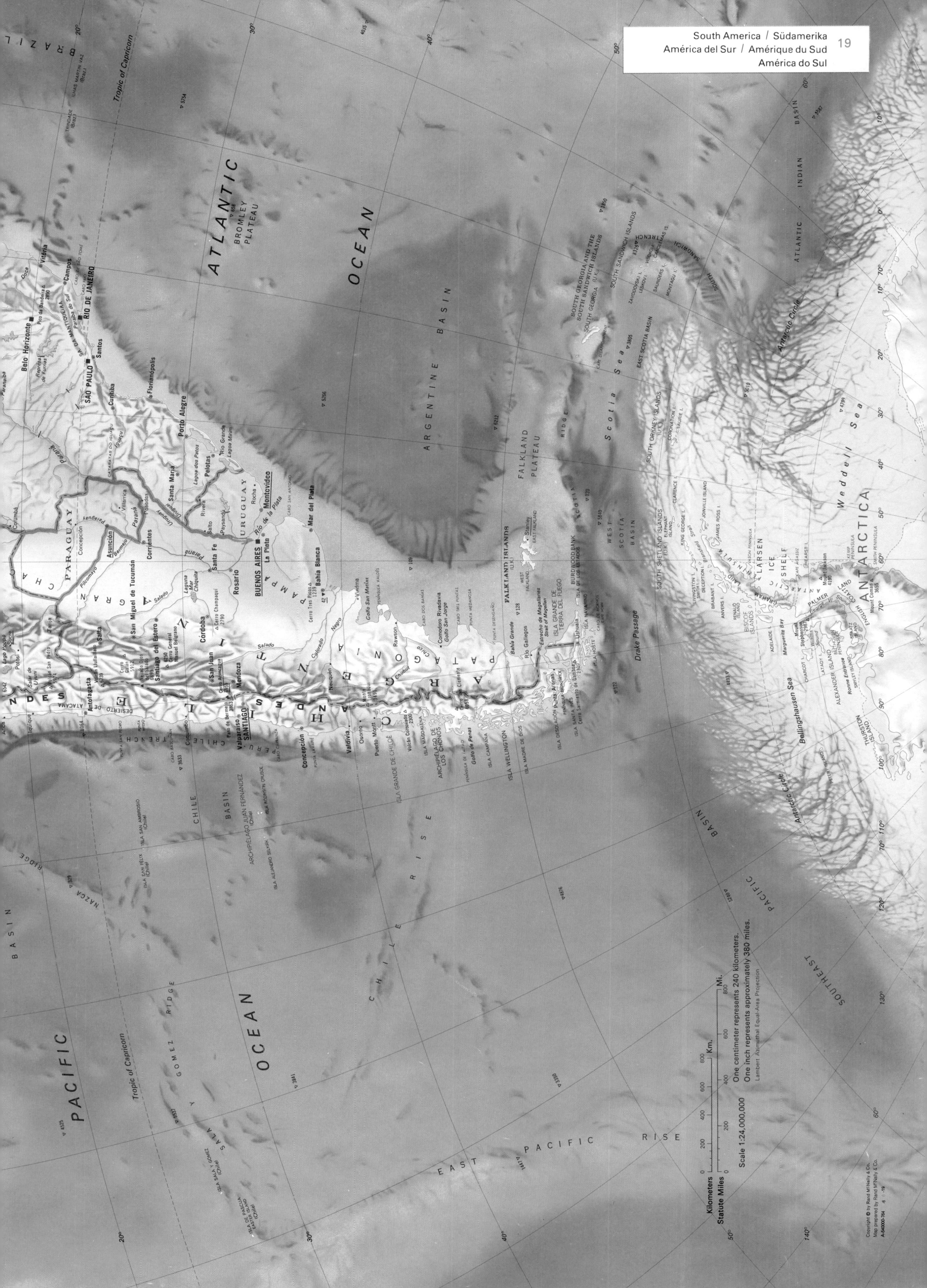

ATLANTIC

OCEAN

BROMLEY
PLATEAU

ARGENTINE BASIN

ATLANTIC

INDIAN BASIN

SOUTH GEORGIA AND THE
SOUTH SANDWICH ISLANDS

SOUTH GEORGIA (U.K.)

SOUTH SANDWICH ISLANDS

Scotia Sea

EAST SCOTIA BASIN

Weddell Sea

FALKLAND
PLATEAU

WEST SCOTIA BASIN

SOUTH ORKNEY ISLANDS
(U.K.)

ANTARCTICA

FALKLAND ISLANDS
(U.K.)

WEST
FALKLAND

EAST
FALKLAND

Stanley

SOUTH SHETLAND ISLANDS

LARSEN ICE SHELF

BRAZIL

Tropic of Capricorn

Belo Horizonte

Vitória

Pico da Bandeira
2890

Campos

SÃO PAULO

RIO DE JANEIRO

Santos

Curitiba

Florianópolis

Porto Alegre

Santa Maria

Pelotas

Rio Grande

Lagoa dos Patos

Lagoa Mirim

URUGUAY

Rivera

Salto

Paysandú

Montevideo

Rocha

CABO SAN ANTONIO

Mar del Plata

PARAGUAY

Asunción

Concepción

Corrientes

Santa Fe

Rosario

BUENOS AIRES

La Plata

Río de la Plata

Bahía Blanca

GRAN CHACO

San Miguel de Tucumán

Córdoba

Santiago del Estero

Salta

San Juan

Mendoza

San Antonio

PAMPA

Cerro Tres Picos
1239

Neuquén

PATAGONIA

Río Negro

Colorado

Golfo San Matías

PENÍNSULA VALDÉS

Rawson

Golfo San Jorge

Comodoro Rivadavia

ANDES

Antofagasta

ATACAMA

DESIERTO DE ATACAMA

ANDES

Valparaíso

SANTIAGO

Concepción

Valdivia

Osorno

Puerto Montt

CHILE

ISLA GRANDE DE CHILOÉ

ARCHIPIÉLAGO DE LOS CHONOS

Golfo de Penas

ISLA WELLINGTON

ARGENTINA

PATAGONIA

Río Gallegos

Bahía Grande

Estrecho de Magallanes
Strait of Magellan

ISLA GRANDE DE
TIERRA DEL FUEGO

Ushuaia

BURDWOOD BANK

Drake Passage

GRAHAM LAND

PALMER LAND

ALEXANDER ISLAND

Bellingshausen Sea

THURSTON ISLAND

ENGLISH COAST

PACIFIC

OCEAN

CHILE BASIN

NAZCA BASIN

NAZCA RIDGE

CHILE RISE

GOMEZ RIDGE

SALA Y GOMEZ RIDGE

Tropic of Capricorn

EAST PACIFIC RISE

SOUTHEAST PACIFIC BASIN

Mi.

Km.

One centimeter represents 240 kilometers.
One inch represents approximately 380 miles.
Lambert Azimuthal Equal-Area Projection

Scale 1:24,000,000

Kilometers

Statute Miles

THE REGIONAL MAPS consist of three basic series, each distinctive in style, but using common symbols to ensure ease of understanding (see Legend to Maps, pages x-xii). Every major land region, continent or subcontinent, is introduced by one or more maps at the scale of 1:12,000,000. There follow maps at 1:6,000,000 and 1:3,000,000 which cover the region in sections, in greater detail. Except for scale, the 1:6,000,000 and 1:3,000,000 maps are alike. Finally, selected areas of special importance in the region are shown at 1:1,000,000. Each scale is identified by a color bar, and a locater map with the same color may be found in the margin of the map page. A sample area at each of the scales, including centimeter-kilometer and inch-mile equivalents, appears on page 21.

The three basic series differ in content and emphasis. The 1:12,000,000 maps, which are primarily political, present an overview of each region. They show national boundaries and, in some cases, subordinate administrative subdivisions as well. These introductory maps make it possible to compare location, areal extent, and shape among the nations of the world. The distribution of cities, towns and metropolitan areas is shown in the context of broad physical configurations. A selection of the most important railways and highways also appears.

The 1:6,000,000 and 1:3,000,000 maps together constitute about half of the map pages and provide the basic reference coverage of the Atlas. They show sections of regions in great detail—in some cases individual countries (Japan and New Zealand), in others, parts of countries (central Mexico), in still others, larger regions (the Middle East). The more densely settled areas appear at the larger 1:3,000,000 scale, the remaining areas at 1:6,000,000. Maps at these two scales present political and cultural information against the background of a detailed physical portrait of the terrain, which is depicted by both shaded relief and a spectrum of altitude tints. Bathymetric tints are used to show offshore water depths. The transportation pattern shown includes major railways, two classes of roads, and airports that offer either international or jet service. The names and boundaries of political subdivisions are given for selected countries.

In the 1:1,000,000 series, strategic areas that are of special interest because of economic importance, dense settlement, or both, appear in even greater detail. This series is designed to show the pattern of cities, towns, roads, railways, bridges, airports, dams, reservoirs, and other interrelated features reflecting man's dense occupancy in these areas. The most important parks, places of historical interest, and recreational facilities are indicated. Three classes of highways and two classes of railways are shown, and major roads are named. All features are portrayed against a topographic background of shaded relief.

Inhabited places on the regional maps are classified in two distinct ways. Cities and towns of different *population size* are distinguished by the *size and shape of the symbol* that locates the place. The symbol reflects the population within the municipal or corporate limits, exclusive of any suburbs. In countries where the limits of a municipality include rural areas, the symbol represents only the urban or agglomerated population. The *relative political and economic importance* of a place which may be independent of the number of its inhabitants, is indicated by the *size of type* in which its name appears.

DIE REGIONALKARTEN bestehen aus drei Serien, die im Stil verschieden sind, der besseren Lesbarkeit halber aber gemeinsame Kartensignaturen verwenden (siehe "Zeichenerklärung" S. x-xii). Jede Grossregion, jeder Kontinent oder Subkontinent werden durch eine oder mehrere Karten im Massstab 1:12 Millionen eingeleitet. Es folgen sodann Karten in den Massstäben 1:6 und 1:3 Millionen, welche die Region in Teilen und grösseren Einzelheiten darstellen. Die Karten in 1:6 Millionen und 1:3 Millionen unterscheiden sich nur im Massstab. Schliesslich werden ausgewählte Gebiete von besonderer Bedeutung innerhalb der Region in 1:1 Million dargestellt. Jede Massstabsangabe ist durch ein Farbfeld gekennzeichnet, und ein Lagekärtchen in derselben Farbe erscheint am Rand der Kartenseite. Kartenausschnitte als Beispiele für jeden Massstäbe mit Angabe des Verhältnisses Zentimeter zu Kilometer und Zoll zu Meilen sind auf Seite 21 aufgeführt.

Die drei Kartenreihen unterscheiden sich in Inhalt und Betonung. Die Karten im Massstab 1:12 Millionen, die vor allem politische Karten sind, geben einen Überblick über jede Region. Sie zeigen die Staatsgrenzen und in manchen Fällen auch die Grenzen von nachgeordneten Verwaltungseinheiten. Diese einführenden Karten ermöglichen einen Vergleich der Lage, Ausdehnung und Gestalt der Staaten der Erde. Die Verteilung der städtischen Ballungsgebiete, Grossstädte und Städte wird in ihrem Zusammenhang mit dem grossräumigen Formenschatz des Reliefs dargestellt. Gezeigt wird auch eine Auswahl der wichtigsten Eisenbahnlinien und Fernverkehrsstrassen.

Die Karten 1:6 Millionen und 1:3 Millionen machen zusammen mehr als die Hälfte der Kartenseiten aus und bilden den grundlegenden Teil des Atlas. Sie zeigen sehr inhaltsreiche Ausschnitte von Regionen—in einigen Fällen einzeln Länder (Japan und Neuseeland), in anderen Landesteile (Zentralmexiko) und wieder anderen Grossräume (Mittlerer Osten).

Die dichter besiedelten Gebiete sind im Massstab 1:3 Millionen dargestellt, die übrigen Gebiete im Massstab 1:6 Millionen. Die Karten in diesen beiden Massstäben liefern politische und kulturgeographische Informationen vor dem Hintergrund einer detaillierten Geländedarstellung, gekennzeichnet durch Reliefschummerung und eine Skala von Höhenschichten. Tiefenstufen werden verwendet, um die Meerestiefen jenseits der Küsten zu gliedern. Das abgebildete Verkehrsnetz umfasst wichtige Eisenbahnlinien, zwei Klassen von Strassen und Flughäfen, die entweder im internationalen Verkehr oder von Düsenflugzeugen angeflogen werden. Die Verwaltungsgliederung wird für eine grosse Zahl von Staaten gezeigt.

In der Kartenserie 1:1 Million sind mit noch zahlreicheren Einzelheiten zentrale Räume dargestellt, denen infolge ihrer wirtschaftlichen Bedeutung, dichten Besiedlung oder durch beide Faktoren bedingt besonderes Interesse zukommt. Diese Kartenserie wurde entwickelt, um die Verteilung der Grossstädte, Städte, Strassen, Eisenbahnen, Brücken, Flughäfen, Dämme, Stauseen und anderer Objekte zu zeigen, die Ausdruck sind für die dichte Besiedlung. Verzeichnet sind auch die wichtigsten Parks, Örtlichkeiten von historischem Interesse und Erholungsstätten. Drei Strassenklassen und zwei Klassen von Eisenbahnlinien werden unterschieden. Die Darstellung ist mit einer Reliefschummerung unterlegt.

Die Siedlungen auf den Regionalkarten sind auf zwei bestimmte Arten klassifiziert. Grossstädte und Städte unterschiedlicher *Einwohnerzahl* sind durch *Grösse und Form der Signatur* unterschieden, die den Ort lokalisiert. Die Signatur entspricht der Zahl der Einwohner innerhalb der Stadtgrenzen, schliesst also nicht eingemeindete Vororte aus. In Staaten, in denen ländliche Gebiete in die Stadtgemeinden einbezogen sind, entsprechen die Signaturen nur der in den zentralen Siedlungen ansässigen Bevölkerung. Die *relative politische und wirtschaftliche Bedeutung* eines Ortes, die von der Zahl seiner Einwohner unabhängig sein kann, ist ausgedrückt durch die *Schriftgrösse*, in welcher der Ortsname erscheint.

LOS MAPAS REGIONALES integran tres series básicas, cada una con su estilo propio; pero los símbolos usados son en todas los mismos para facilitar su comprensión (véanse las Leyendas para Mapas, páginas x-xii). Cada una de las grandes regiones, continentes o subcontinentes, se presenta a través de uno o varios mapas a la escala de 1:12 000 000. A continuación hay mapas a escalas de 1:6 000 000 y 1:3 000 000 que presentan la región correspondiente en secciones, con mayores detalles. Con excepción de su escala, los mapas de 1:6 000 000 y 1:3 000 000 tienen las mismas características. Por ultimo, aparecen a la escala de 1:1 000 000 áreas de cada región seleccionadas por su importancia. Cada escala se identifica por una barra de color, y un mapa-guía con el mismo color se presenta en el margen de la página de cada mapa. La página 21 ofrece como ejemplo un área-muestra a cada una de las escalas, incluyendo equivalentes en centímetros-kilómetros y pulgadas-millas.

Las tres series básicas son diferentes en contenido y en énfasis. Los mapas a escala de 1:12 000 000, fundamentalmente políticos, ofrecen una vista general de cada región. Indican las fronteras nacionales y, en algunos casos, las subdivisiones administrativas secundarias. Son mapas introductivos que permiten comparar la ubicación, extensión territorial y forma de las distintas naciones. La distribución de ciudades, poblados y áreas metropolitanas se aprecia en un contexto físico esbozado a grandes rasgos. Los detalles incluyen una selección de las vías férras y las carreteras más importantes.

Las series de mapas a 1:6 000 000 y a 1:3 000 000 ocupan entre ambas cerca de la mitad de los mapas del atlas y en ellas se concentra el material de consulta básico de la obra. Los mapas muestran secciones de regiones en gran detalle: en algunos casos países enteros, como Japón y Nueva Zelandia; en otros, partes de países, como el centro de México; y en otros, regiones mas extensas, como el Medio Oriente. Las áreas con mayor densidad de establecimientos humanos se presentan a una escala mayor, la de 1:3 000 000, y las demás a la escala de 1:6 000 000. En estas dos escalas los mapas contienen información política y cultural, sobre un fondo que ilustra en detalle la configuración física del terreno, utilizando sombreado para el relieve y toda una gama de tintes para indicar las altitudes. Un colorido batimétrico señala las variaciones de profundidad en el suelo marino. El esquema de las vías de comunicación incluye las principales vías férreas, dos clases de caminos, y los aeropuertos que ofrecen servicio nacional o internacional de jets. Las subdivisiones políticas secundarias se dan para una selección de varios países.

En la serie de mapas de 1:1 000 000, las áreas estratégicas de especial interés por su importancia económica, su densidad de población, o ambos factores combinados, aparecen aún con mayor detalle. Esta serie se diseñó para mostrar la distribución de ciudades, poblados, caminos, vías férreas, puentes, aeropuertos, presas, embalses y otros elementos similares, que reflejan la densidad de la ocupación humana. También se consignan los parques más importantes, los sitios de interés histórico, los campos de recreo, tres clases de carreteras, y dos de ferrocarriles, se da los nombres de los caminos más importantes. Todos estos elementos aparecen sobre un fondo topográfico de relieve sombreado.

En los mapas regionales se hacen dos clasificaciones distintas de los lugares habitados. Las ciudades y las poblaciones *de diferente densidad de habitantes* se distinguen por la *forma y tamaño del símbolo* que las localiza en el mapa. Este símbolo refleja el tamaño de la poblacióin dentro de sus límites municipales, sin tomar en cuenta los suburbios. En los países donde los límites de una municipalidad incluyen áreas rurales, el símbolo se limita a representar el conglomerado urbano de habitantes. La *importancia económica y política de un lugar,* la cual puede ser independiente del número de sus habitantes, se indica mediante el *tamaño del tipo de imprenta* en que aparece su nombre.

LES CARTES RÉGIONALES sont de trois types principaux, chacun d'un style différent mais avec des symboles communs pour faciliter la compréhension (voir la légende des cartes pages x-xii). Chaque grande région, continent ou subcontinent, est représentée par une ou plusieurs cartes à l'échelle de 1:12 000 000ᵉ. Viennent ensuite des cartes au 1:6 000 000ᵉ et au 1:3 000 000ᵉ qui couvrent la région par sections plus détaillées; hormis la différence d'échelle, ces cartes sont semblables. Enfin, des secteurs particulièrement importants sont représentés au 1:1 000 000ᵉ. À chaque échelle correspond une bande colorée et une carte repère de même couleur, dans la marge de chaque page. Un échantillon de cartes aux diverses échelles est représenté à droite. Chaque carte est accompagnée d'une double échelle graphique donnant les rapports centimètre/kilomètre et inch/mille correspondants.

Les trois catégories de cartes diffèrent par le contenu et par ce qu'elles mettent en relief. Les cartes au 1:12 000 000ᵉ, qui sont essentiellement politiques, donnent un aperçu général de chaque région. Elles indiquent les frontières nationales et, dans certains cas, les subdivisions administratives intérieures. Ces cartes d'introduction permettent de comparer la localisation, la superficie et la forme des pays du monde. La répartition des villes et des zones métropolitaines y apparaît dans le cadre des grandes régions naturelles. Les routes et les voies ferrées les plus importantes y figurent également.

Les cartes au 1:6 000 000ᵉ et au 1:3 000 000ᵉ forment la moitié de l'Atlas et en constituent la série cartographique essentielle. Elles représentent de façon plus détaillée une partie de pays (centre du Mexique), ou encore des régions plus vastes (Moyen-Orient) ou, parfois, des pays entiers (Japon, Nouvelle-Zélande). Les régions les plus peuplées sont représentées à plus grande échelle (1;3 000 000ᵉ) que les autres (1:6 000 000ᵉ). Ces cartes offrent des informations d'ordre politique et culturel sur un fond topographique précis où le relief est indiqué à la fois par un estompage et par des variations de couleur. Différentes teintes de bleu sont utilisées pour symboliser les profondeurs marines. Les réseaux de transport représentés comprennent les principales voies ferrées, deux catégories de routes et les aéroports internationaux ou desservis par des avions à réaction. Les subdivisions politiques d'un certain nombre de pays sont aussi tracées.

Dans la série de cartes au 1:1 000 000ᵉ, des régions très importantes, soit du fait de leur densité de population, soit du fait de leur rôle économique, sont représentées d'une manière encore plus détaillée. L'objectif de cette série de cartes est de montrer la répartition des villes, routes, voies ferrées, ponts, aéroports, barrages, lacs de barrages et autres données associées qui traduisent la densité de l'occupation humaine dans ces régions. Les parcs les plus importants, les sites historiques essentiels et les centres de loisirs sont indiqués. Toutes les informations se détachent sur un fond topographique où le relief apparaît en estompage.

Les centres urbains des cartes régionales sont classés de deux manières différentes. *L'importance de la population* des villes est indiquée par *la dimension et la forme du symbole* qui les situe sur la carte. Seule la population comprise dans les limites municipales est prise en considération; dans les pays où des espaces ruraux sont inclus dans les limites d'une municipalité, seule la population urbaine entre en ligne de compte. *L'importance politique et économique relative* d'une ville, qui n'est pas nécessairement liée au nombre d'habitants, est indiquée par la dimension des caractères qui composent son nom.

OS MAPAS REGIONAIS compreendem três séries básicas, cada uma em estilo diferente, mas que empregam os mesmos símbolos para facilitar sua compreensão (Ver as *Legendas dos mapas*, pág. x-xii). Os mapas de cada uma das principais regiões terrestres, continentes ou subcontinentes, são introduzidos por um ou mais mapas na escala 1:12 000 000. Em seguida, vêm mapas, nas escalas de 1:6 000 000 e 1:3 000 000, que apresentam, com maiores detalhes, seções da região considerada. Exceto quanto à escala, os mapas de 1:6 000 000 e 1:3 000 000 têm as mesmas características. Finalmente, aparecem, na escala de 1:1 000 000, os mapas das áreas mais importantes da região considerada. A cada escala corresponde uma barra colorida e um indicador da mesma cor, que se encontra à margem da página de cada mapa. À página 21, acha-se um exemplo de cada escala, bem como a equivalência das relações centímetro/quilômetro e polegada/milha.

As três séries básicas de mapas são diferentes quanto ao conteúdo e à apresentação. Os mapas em escala de 1:12 000 000, que são essencialmente políticos, oferecem uma visão geral de cada região. Indicam as fronteiras nacionais e, em alguns casos, as subdivisões administrativas internas. Esses mapas servem de introdução e permitem avaliar e comparar a posição, superfície e forma dos países do Mundo. Neles está claramente indicada a distribuição das cidades e outros centros urbanos, bem como as principais características da configuração do solo. Encontra-se neles também uma seleção das ferrovias e rodovias mais importantes.

A série de mapas das escalas de 1:6 000 000 e de 1:3 000 000 constituem o principal material de referência do Atlas e representa cerca de metade do conjunto de mapas. Entre eles há mapas detalhados de parte de um país (centro do México), de um país inteiro (Japão e a Nova Zelândia) ou de uma região mais extensa (Oriente Médio). As áreas de maior densidade demográfica são apresentadas em escala maior, a de 1:3 000 000, e as demais, na de 1:6 000 000. Nessas duas escalas, os mapas fornecem informações de ordem política e cultural sobre um fundo que indica a configuração detalhada das particularidades físicas do solo, cujo relevo se destaca por contrastes de sombras e cores. Diversos matizes do azul traduzem o mapa batimétrico da profundidade ao largo das costas. Indicam também os aeroportos internacionais, as principais ferrovias, duas categorias de rodovias. As subdivisões políticas internas de numerosos países estão igualmente assinalados.

Na série de mapas da escala de 1:1 000 000, certas áreas, de interesse estratégico conjugado à importância econômica, densidade demográfica, ou ambos os elementos combinados, aparecem em forma ainda mais detalhada. O objetivo dessa série é representar a distribuição dos grandes centros urbanos, cidades, rodovias, ferrovias, pontes, aeroportos, represas, reservatórios e outras características associadas às grandes densidades demográficas. Indicam-se, também, os parques mais importantes, os lugares de interesse histórico, as áreas de lazer, três categorias de rodovias, e duas de ferrovias; e a nomenclatura dos grandes itinerários rodoviários. Todos esses elementos destacam-se sobre um fundo topográfico do relevo, executado em matizes das diversas cores.

Nos mapas regionais, assinalam-se os centros urbanos de dois modos. A *grandeza da população* das grandes cidades e dos centros urbanos secundários é representada pela *dimensão e forma do símbolo* que as localiza no mapa. O símbolo só reflete a população situada dentro de limites administrativos, sem levar em conta os subúrbios. Nos países onde os limites de uma municipalidade incluem zonas rurais, o símbolo representa apenas a população. A *importância política e econômica* de uma cidade, que não se relaciona necessariamente com o número de seus habitantes, é indicada pela *dimensão* dos caracteres tipográficos com que se compõe o seu nome.

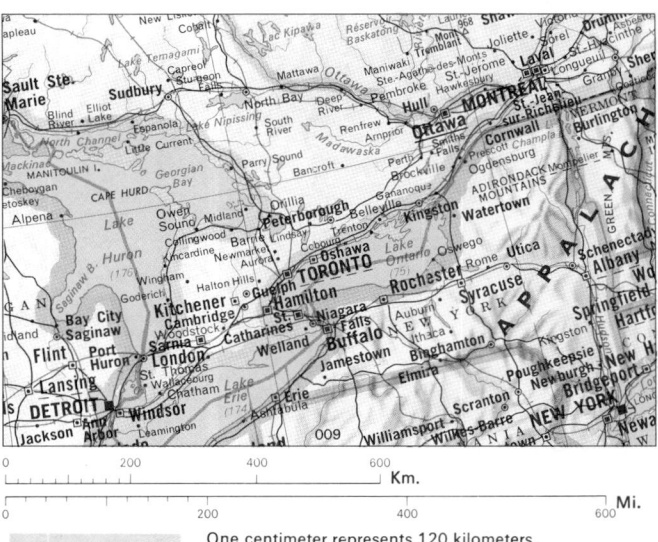

Scale 1:12,000,000

One centimeter represents 120 kilometers.
One inch represents approximately 190 miles.

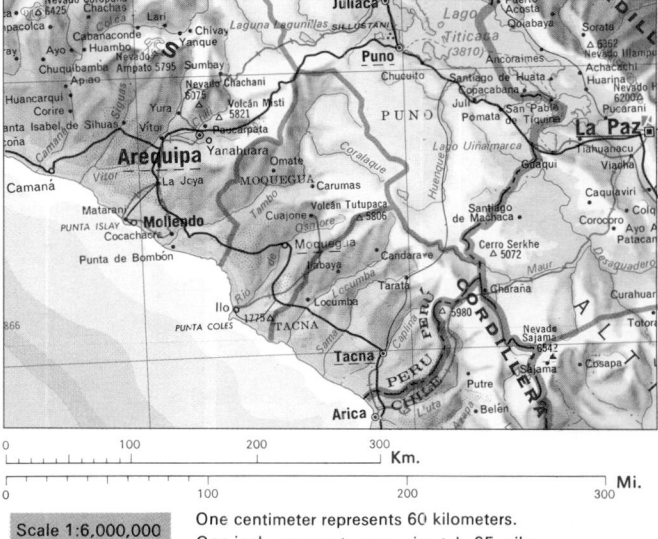

Scale 1:6,000,000

One centimeter represents 60 kilometers.
One inch represents approximately 95 miles.

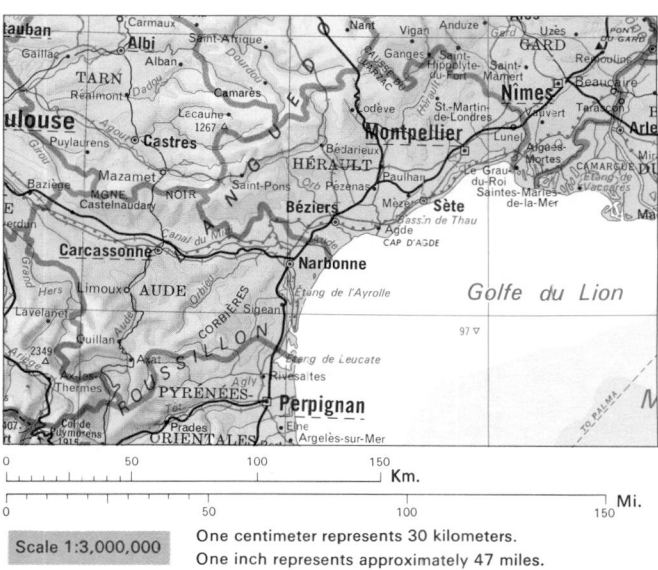

Scale 1:3,000,000

One centimeter represents 30 kilometers.
One inch represents approximately 47 miles.

Scale 1:1,000,000

One centimeter represents 10 kilometers.
One inch represents approximately 16 miles.

Map continues
pages 134-135

MAP FORM	-älven	gora	île	islands	-gya	ozero	sea	vodochranilišče
ENGLISH	river	mountain	island	islands	island	lake	sea	reservoir
DEUTSCH	Fluss	Berg	Insel	Inseln	Insel	See	Meer	Stausee
ESPAÑOL	rio	montaña	isla	islas	isla	lago	mar	embalse
FRANÇAIS	rivière	montagne	île	îles	île	lac	mer	réservoir
PORTUGUÊS	rio	montanha	ilha	ilhas	ilha	lago	mar	reservatório

Copyright © by Rand McNally & Co.
Map prepared by Esselte Map Service AB, Stockholm.
A-550000-064   -15 -16 -27

BARENTS SEA

POLUOSTROV

White Sea
Beloje More

FINLAND

KARELIJA

RUSSIA

ESTONIA

LATVIA

LITHUANIA

BELARUS

UKRAINE

MOLDOVA

ROMANIA

BULGARIA

Murmansk
Archangel'sk
Severodvinsk
Syktyvkar

HELSINKI
Tallinn
SANKT-PETERBURG
ST. PETERSBURG
LENINGRAD
RIGA
Novgorod
Pskov
Vologda
Jaroslavl'
Ivanovo
Nižnij Novgorod (Gor'kij)
MOSCOW MOSKVA
Podol'sk
Kolomna
Tula
R'azan'
Tambov
Lipeck
Voronež
Penza
Saratov
Engel's
Volgograd (Stalingrad)
Kazan'
Ul'janovsk
Samara (Kujbyšev)
Toljatti
Orenburg
Ufa
Perm'
Iževsk
Jekaterinburg (Sverdlovsk)
Nižnij Tagil
Čel'abinsk
Magnitogorsk

URAL'SKIE GORY
URAL MOUNTAINS

ZAPADNO SIBIRSKAJA RAVNINA

KAZACHSTAN

UZBEK.

KALMYKIJA

TATARIJA

MORDOVIJA

MINSK
Mogil'ov
Gomel'
WARSAW WARSZAWA
Lublin
L'vov
KIJEV KIEV
Char'kov
DONECK
Rostov-na-Donu
Zaporožje
Odessa
KIŠINOV
BUCUREŞTI BUCHAREST

BLACK SEA

Azovskoje more
Sea of Azov

CASPIAN SEA

Astrachan'
Baku Baky
AZERBAIJAN
TBILISI
GEORGIA
ARMENIA
JEREVAN
BOL'ŠOJ KAVKAZ CAUCASUS

SOFIJA BULGARIA
Plovdiv
Thessaloniki
ATHINAI ATHENS

İstanbul
ANKARA
TURKEY
İzmir
Konya
Adana

CYPRUS
NORTH CYPRUS
N.cosia

SYRIA
Halab Aleppo
IRAQ
BAGHDAD

IRAN
TEHRAN
Tabriz

TURKMENISTAN

Map continues
pages 72-73

Map continues
pages 118-119

Kilometers 0 200 400 600 Km.
Statute Miles 0 200 400 600 Mi.

Scale 1:12,000,000
One centimeter represents 120 kilometers.
One inch represents approximately 190 miles.
Miller Oblated Stereographic Projection

MAP FORM	-älven	-fjorden	guba	-joki	-jökull	lääni	-øya	ozero
ENGLISH	river	fjord, lake	bay	river	glacier	province	island	lake
DEUTSCH	Fluss	Fjord, See	Bucht	Fluss	Gletscher	Provinz	Insel	See
ESPAÑOL	rio	fiordo, lago	bahia	rio	glaciar	provincia	isla	lago
FRANÇAIS	rivière	fjord, lac	baie	rivière	glacier	province	île	lac
PORTUGUÊS	rio	fiorde, lago	baia	rio	geleira	provincia	ilha	lago

Meters / Feet

6000 — 19685
4000 — 13124
3000 — 9843
2000 — 6562
1000 — 3281
500 — 1640
200 — 656
0 — 0

Land Below Sea Level

0 — 0
200 — 656
1000 — 3281
3000 — 9843
6000 — 19685
9000 — 29520

Map continues
pages 86-87

Map continues
pages 76-77

Kilometers ⊢⊢⊢⊢⊢ 100   200   300   Km.
Statute Miles   100   200   300   Mi.

Scale 1:6,000,000
One centimeter represents 60 kilometers.
One inch represents approximately 95 miles.
Lambert Conformal Conic Projection

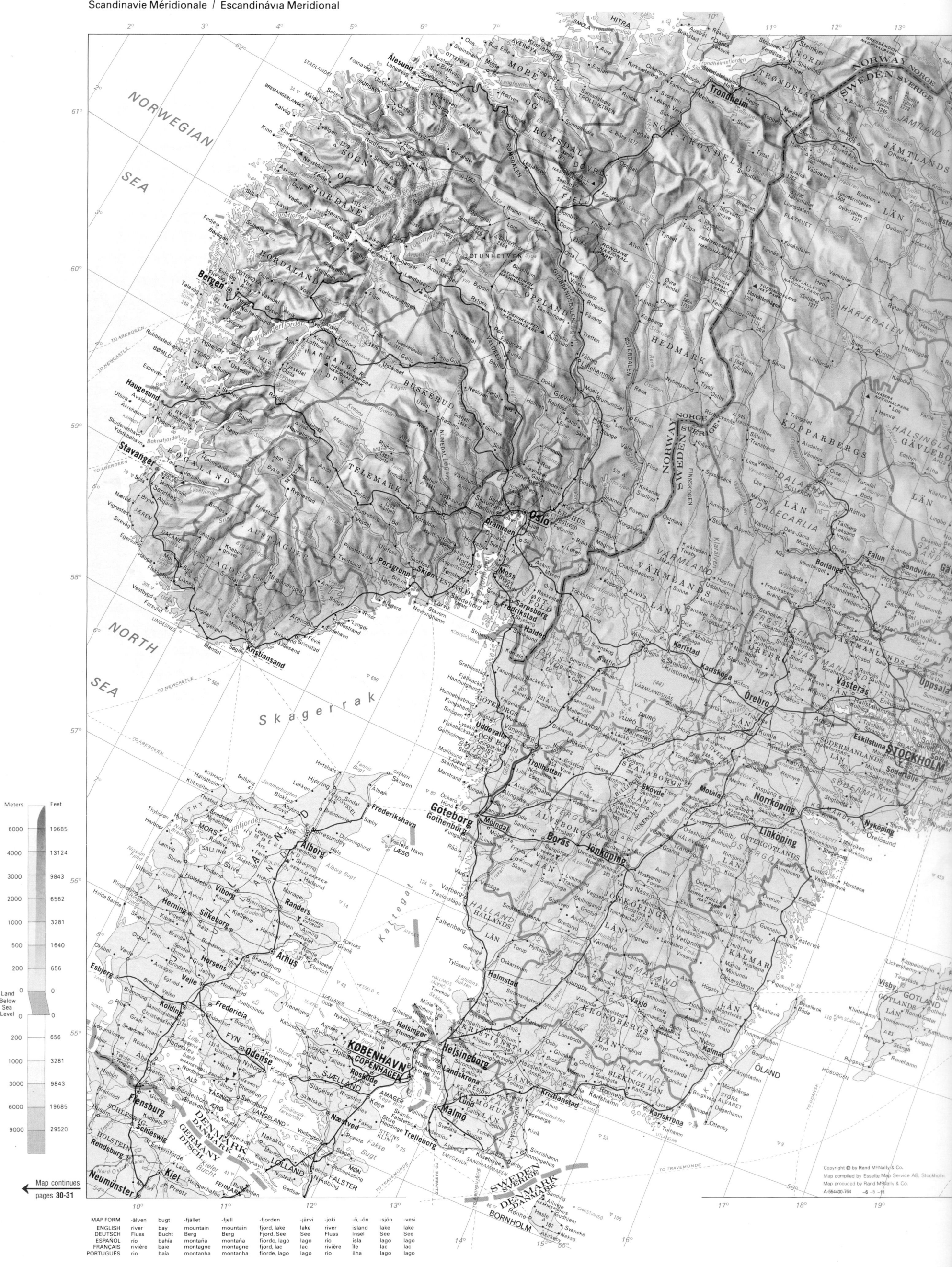

← Map continues
pages 30-31

MAP FORM	-älven	bugt	-fjället	-fjell	-fjorden	-järvi	-joki	-ö, -ön	-sjön	-vesi
ENGLISH	river	bay	mountain	mountain	fjord, lake	lake	river	island	lake	lake
DEUTSCH	Fluss	Bucht	Berg	Berg	Fjord, See	See	Fluss	Insel	See	See
ESPAÑOL	río	bahía	montaña	montaña	fiordo, lago	lago	río	isla	lago	lago
FRANÇAIS	rivière	baie	montagne	montagne	fjord, lac	lac	rivière	île	lac	lac
PORTUGUÊS	rio	baía	montanha	montanha	fiorde, lago	lago	rio	ilha	lago	lago

Copyright © by Rand McNally & Co.
Map compiled by Esselte Map Service AB, Stockholm.
Map produced by Rand McNally & Co.
A-554400-764   –6 –5 –11

Kilometers

Statute Miles

Scale 1:3,000,000

One centimeter represents 30 kilometers.
One inch represents approximately 47 miles.
Conic Projection, Two Standard Parallels

Map continues pages 24-25

Map continues pages 76-77

Map continues pages 76-77

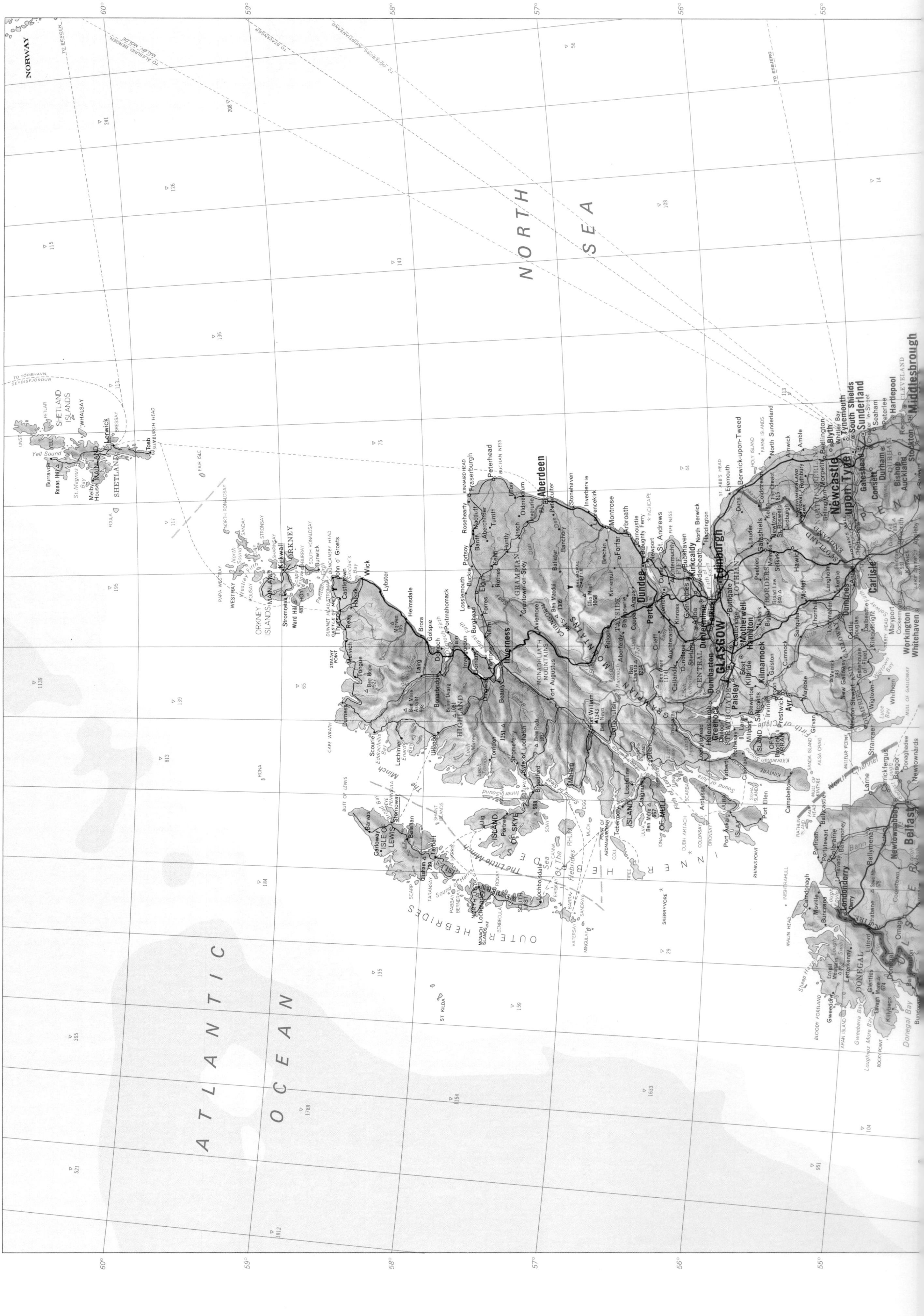
NORTH SEA
ATLANTIC OCEAN
NORWAY
SHETLAND ISLANDS
ORKNEY ISLANDS
OUTER HEBRIDES
Lerwick
Kirkwall
Wick
Thurso
Inverness
Aberdeen
Dundee
Perth
St Andrews
Edinburgh
GLASGOW
Paisley
Kilmarnock
Ayr
Stranraer
Dumfries
Carlisle
Newcastle upon Tyne
Sunderland
Middlesbrough
Hartlepool
Durham
Workington
Whitehaven
Belfast
Londonderry
Larne
Bangor
Stornoway
ISLE OF SKYE
ST KILDA
Fort William
Oban
Campbeltown
Peterhead
Fraserburgh
Montrose
Arbroath
Berwick-upon-Tweed
DONEGAL
Donegal Bay

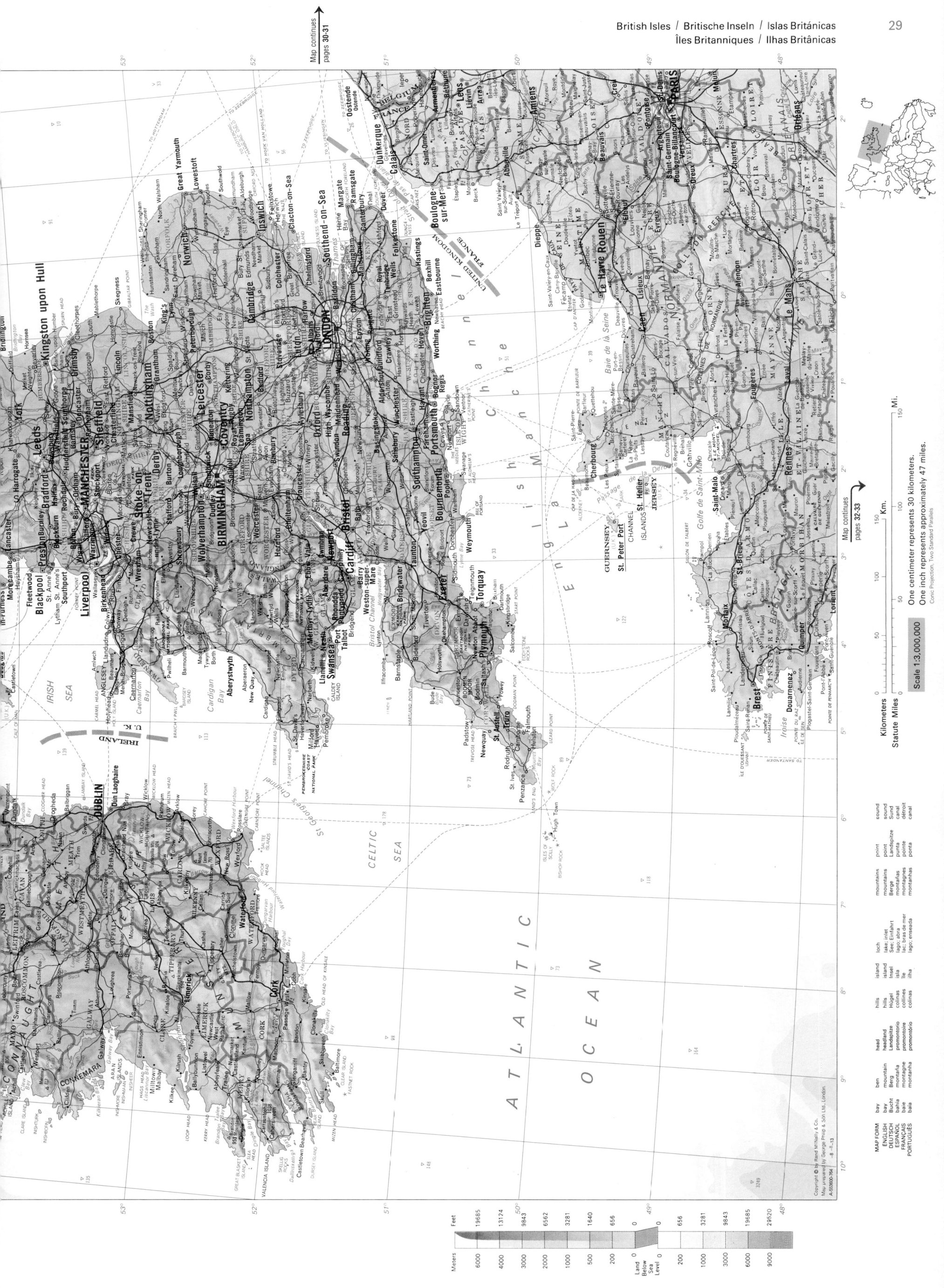

Map continues pages 30-31

Map continues pages 32-33

Scale 1:3,000,000

One centimeter represents 30 kilometers.
One inch represents approximately 47 miles.

Conic Projection. Two Standard Parallels

Kilometers
Statute Miles

MAP FORM	bay	ben	head	hills	island	loch	mountains	point	sound
ENGLISH	bay	mountain	headland	hills	island	lake; inlet	mountains	point	sound
DEUTSCH	Bucht	Berg	Landspitze	Hügel	Insel	See; Einfahrt	Berge	Landspitze	Sund
ESPAÑOL	bahía	montaña	promontorio	colinas	isla	lago; entrada	montañas	punta	canal
FRANÇAIS	baie	montagne	promontoire	collines	île	lac; bras de mer	montagnes	pointe	détroit
PORTUGUÊS	baía	montanha	promontório	colinas	ilha	lago; enseada	montanhas	ponta	canal

Feet
19685   6000
13124   4000
9843   3000
6562   2000
3281   1000
1640   500
656   200
0   0
Land Below Sea Level
0
656   200
3281   1000
9843   3000
19685   6000
29520   9000
Meters

Map continues
pages 26-27

Map continues
pages 28-29

MAP FORM	Bucht	Gebirge	jezioro	Kanal	park narodowy	See	Wald
ENGLISH	bay	range	lake, lagoon	canal	national park	lake	forest, mountains
DEUTSCH	Bucht	Gebirge	See, Haff	Kanal	Nationalpark	See	Wald
ESPAÑOL	bahía	sierra	lago, laguna	canal	parque national	lago	bosque, montañas
FRANÇAIS	baie	chaîne	lac, lagune	canal	parc national	lac	forêt, montagnes
PORTUGUÊS	baia	serra	lago, laguna	canal	parque nacional	lago	floresta, montar has

Kilometers

Statute Miles

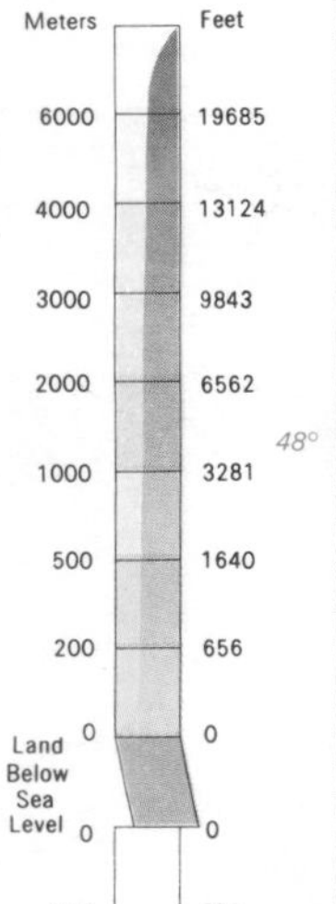

Meters	Feet
6000	19685
4000	13124
3000	9843
2000	6562
1000	3281
500	1640
200	656
Land Below Sea Level 0	0
0	0
200	656
1000	3281
3000	9843
6000	19685
9000	29520

Scale 1:3,000,000

One centimeter represents 30 kilometers.
One inch represents approximately 47 miles.
Conic Projection, Two Standard Parallels.

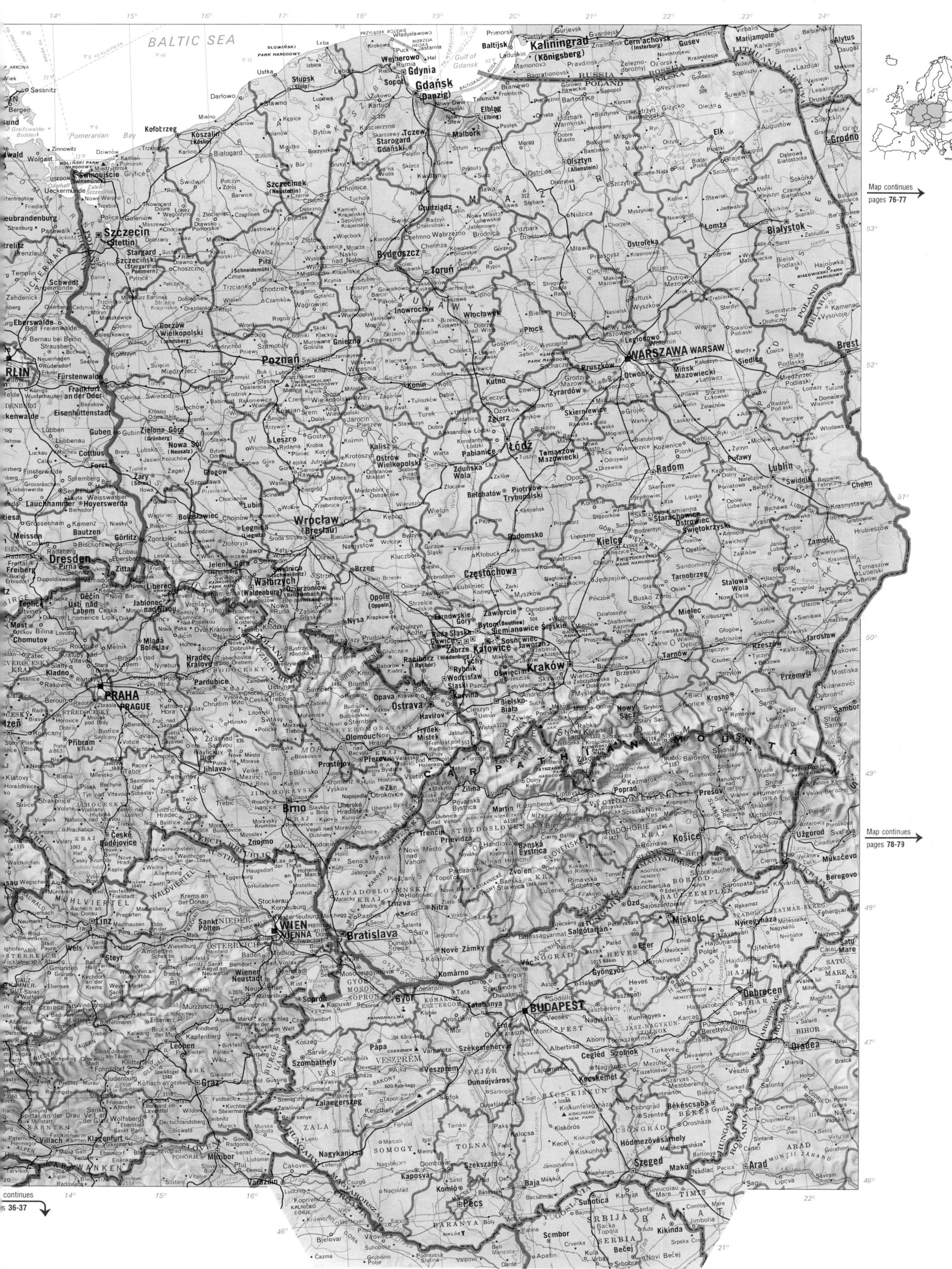

Map continues
pages 76-77

Map continues
pages 78-79

continues
36-37

Map continues
pages 28-29

Map continues
pages 34-35

	MAP FORM	canal	cap	île	lago	mont (e)	monts	pointe	See
	ENGLISH	canal	cape	island	lake	mount	mountains	point	lake
	DEUTSCH	Kanal	Kap	Insel	See	Berg	Berge	Landspitze	See
	ESPAÑOL	canal	cabo	isla	lago	monte	montes	punta	lago
	FRANÇAIS	canal	cap	île	lac	mont	monts	pointe	lac
	PORTUGUÊS	canal	cabo	ilha	lago	monte	montes	ponta	lago

Meters	Feet
6000	19685
4000	13124
3000	9843
2000	6562
1000	3281
500	1640
200	656
Land Below Sea Level	0
0	0
200	656
1000	3281
3000	9843
6000	19685
9000	29520

Map continues
pages 30-31

Map continues
pages 36-37

Kilometers   0   50   100   150   Km.

Statute Miles   0   50   100   150   Mi.

Scale 1:3,000,000

One centimeter represents 30 kilometers.
One inch represents approximately 47 miles.

Lambert Conformal Conic Projection

Spain and Portugal / Spanien und Portugal / España y Portugal
Espagne et Portugal / Espanha e Portugal

Meters	Feet
6000	19685
4000	13124
3000	9843
2000	6562
1000	3281
500	1640
200	656
0	0
Land Below Sea Level	
0	0
200	656
1000	3281
3000	9843
6000	19685
9000	29520

Copyright © by Rand McNally & Co.
Map prepared by Rand McNally GmbH, Stuttgart.
A-559900-764   —6   —5 —12

ESPAÑOL	bahía	cabo	isla	embalse	puerto	punta	ría	sierra
ENGLISH	bay	cape	island	reservoir	port	point	estuary	mountains
DEUTSCH	Bucht	Kap	Insel	Stausee	Hafen	Landspitze	Trichtermündung	Berge
FRANÇAIS	baie	cap	île	réservoir	port	pointe	estuaire	montagnes
PORTUGUÊS	baía	cabo	ilha	reservatório	porto	ponta	estuário	serra

Map continues
pages 32-33

Golfe du Lion

MEDITERRANEAN SEA

ILLES BALEARS
BALEARIC ISLANDS

BALEARS

MENORCA
MINORCA

MALLORCA
MAJORCA

EIVISSA
IBIZA

Map continues
pages 148-149

Kilometers   0   50   100   150   Km.

Statute Miles   0   50   100   150   Mi.

Scale 1:3,000,000
One centimeter represents 30 kilometers.
One inch represents approximately 47 miles.
Conic Projection, Two Standard Parallels

Map continues
pages 38-39

Map continues
pages 30-31

Map continues
pages 32-33

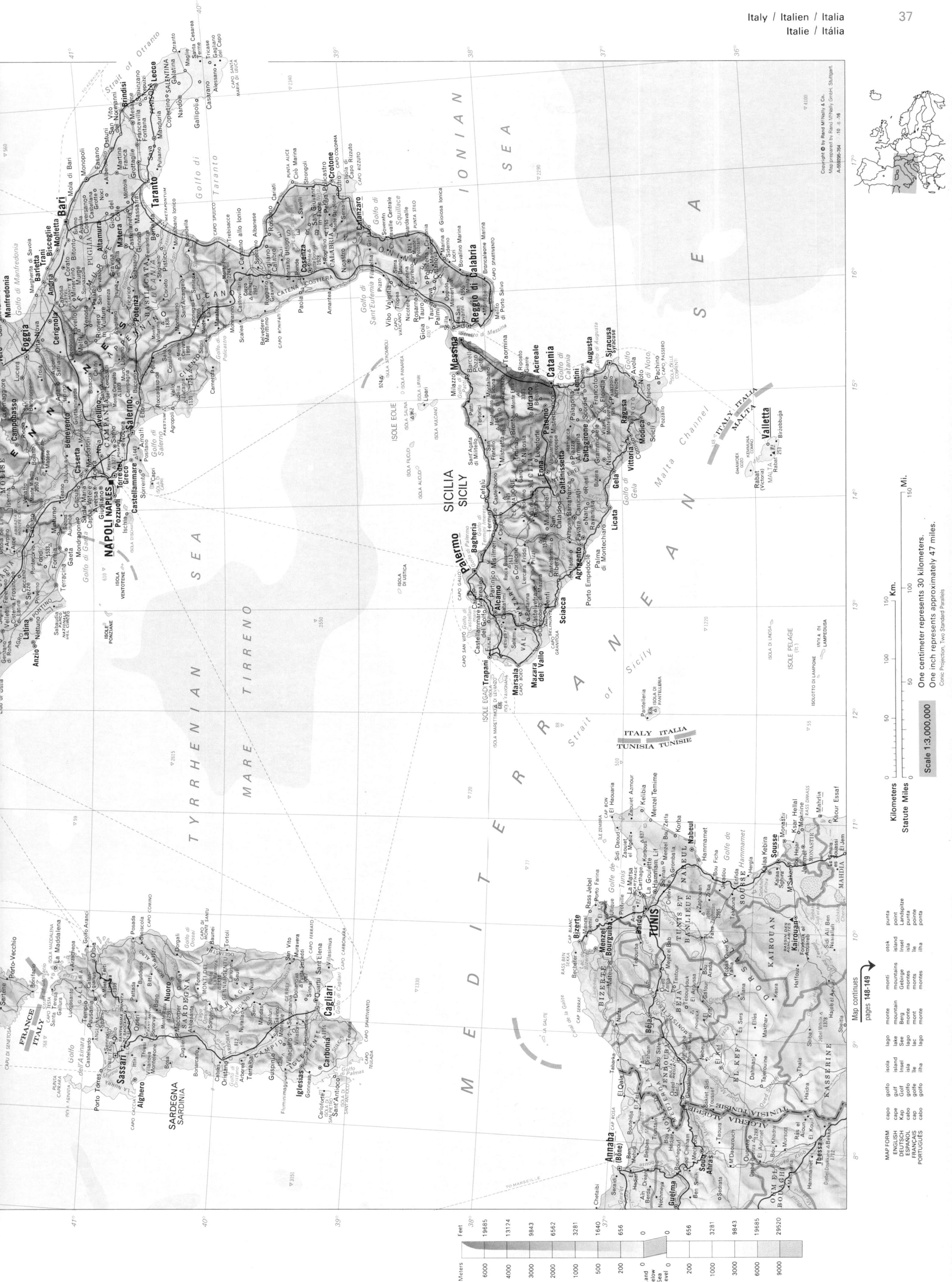

I O N I A N   S E A

Strait of Otranto

Lecce
Brindisi
Taranto
Bari
Foggia
Manfredonia
Golfo di Manfredonia
Golfo di Taranto
Campobasso
Benevento
NAPOLI NAPLES
Salerno
Golfo di Salerno
Golfo di Gaeta
Cosenza
Catanzaro
Reggio di Calabria
Messina
CALABRIA
Crotone

M A R E   T I R R E N O
T Y R R H E N I A N   S E A

ISOLE EOLIE

SICILIA
SICILY
Palermo
Bagheria
Catania
Siracusa
Ragusa
Gela
Marsala
Mazara del Vallo
Trapani
Agrigento
Sciacca

Malta Channel

ITALY ITALIA
MALTA
Valletta

M E D I T E R R A N E A N   S E A

Strait of Sicily

ISOLE PELAGE (It.)

ITALY ITALIA
TUNISIA TUNISIE

TUNIS
Bizerte
Sousse
Nabeul
Kairouan

ALGERIA ALGÉRIE

Annaba (Bône)

SARDEGNA
SARDINIA
Cagliari
Sassari
Nuoro
Oristano
Iglesias
Carbonia
Alghero

FRANCE
ITALY

Map continues
pages 148-149

MAP FORM				
ENGLISH	cape	gulf	island	lake
DEUTSCH	Kap	Golf	Insel	See
ESPAÑOL	cabo	golfo	isla	lago
FRANÇAIS	cap	golfe	île	lac
PORTUGUÊS	cabo	golfo	ilha	lago

monte	mountain	monti	mountains
Berg		Berg	
monte		montes	
mont		monts	
monte		montes	

otok	island
Insel	
isla	
île	
ilha	

punta	point
Landspitze	
punta	
pointe	
ponta	

Scale 1:3,000,000

One centimeter represents 30 kilometers.
One inch represents approximately 47 miles.
Conic Projection, Two Standard Parallels

Kilometers   0   50   100   150 Km.
Statute Miles   0   50   100   150 Mi.

Copyright © by Rand McNally & Co.
Map prepared by Rand McNally & Co., Stuttgart.

Meters   Feet
6000 19685
4000 13124
3000 9843
2000 6562
1000 3281
500   1640
200   656
0   0
Land
Below
Sea
Level
200   656
1000 3281
3000 9843
6000 19685
9000 29520

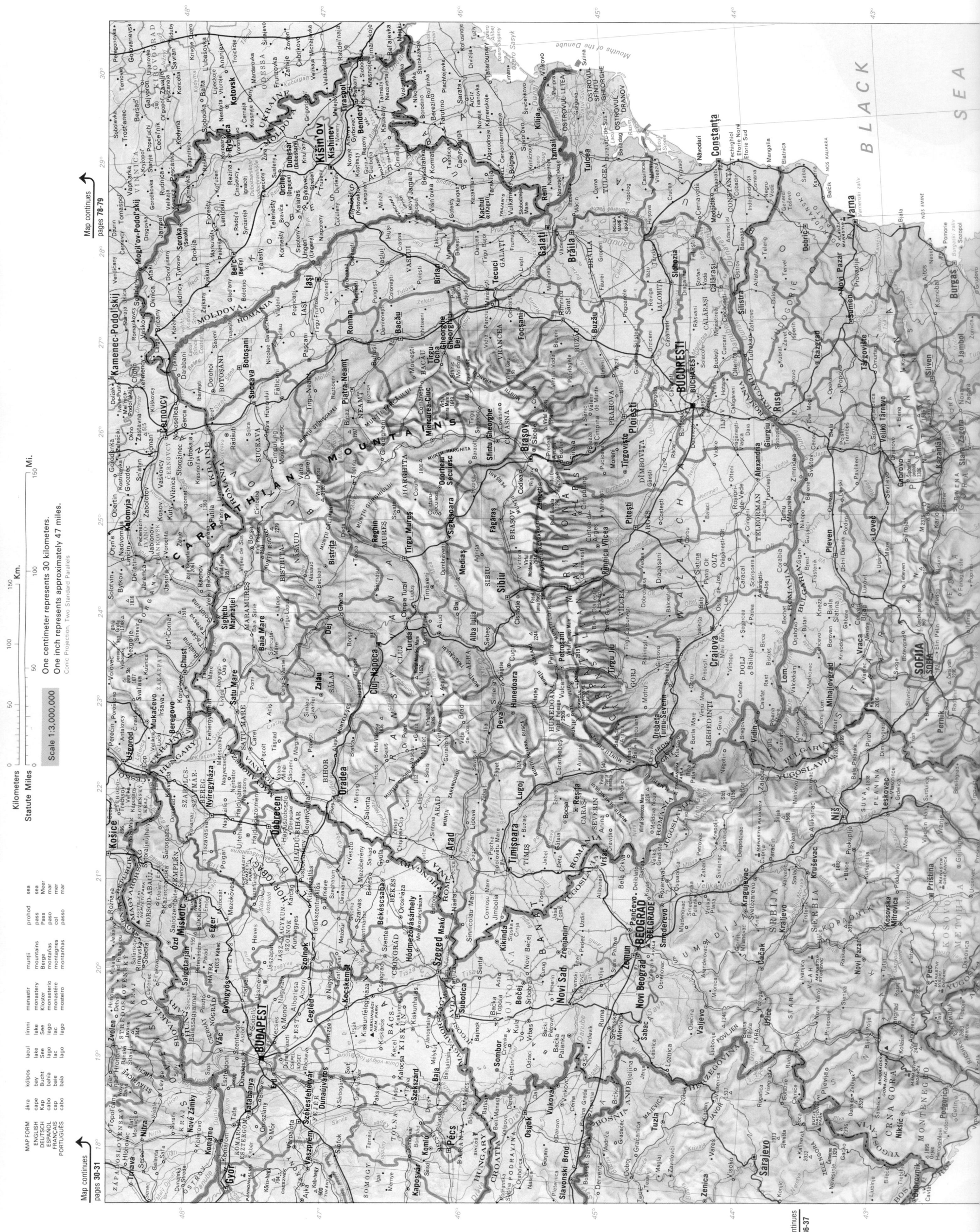

Map continues
pages 78-79

Map continues
pages 30-31

Map continues
pages 36-37

Scale 1:3,000,000

One centimeter represents 30 kilometers.
One inch represents approximately 47 miles.
Conic Projection; Two Standard Parallels

MAP FORM ENGLISH DEUTSCH ESPAÑOL FRANÇAIS PORTUGUÊS
ákra cape Kap cabo cap cabo
kólpos bay Bucht bahía baie baía
lacul lake See lago lac lago
limni lake See lago lac lago
manastir monastery Kloster monasterio monastère mosteiro
munţii mountains Berge montañas montagnes montanhas
prohod pass Pass paso col passo
sea sea Meer mar mer mar
Statute Miles
BLACK SEA
CARPATHIAN MOUNTAINS
BUDAPEST
BUCUREŞTI
BEOGRAD
SOFIJA

Map continues
pages 130-131

Major labels

ISTANBUL
Bursa
İzmir / Smyrna
Çanakkale
Balıkesir
Manisa
Aydın
Muğla
Denizli
Kütahya
Uşak
Edirne
Tekirdağ
Bandırma
Ródhos / Rhodes
RÓDHOS / RHODES

TURKEY / TÜRKIYE
GREECE / ELLÁS

DHODHEKÁNISOS
DODECANESE

THESSALONÍKI / Salonika
KAVÁLA
SÉRRAI
Xánthi
Komotiní
Alexandroúpolis

LÉSVOS / LESBOS
Mitilíni
Khíos / CHÍOS
SÁMOS
IKARÍA

KIKLÁDHES
CYCLADES
NÁXOS
ÁNDROS
TÍNOS
PÁROS
MÍLOS

ATHÍNAI / ATHENS
Piraiévs / Piraeus
Khalkís
EVVOIA

KRÍTI / CRETE
Iráklion
Khaniá
Réthimnon

A E G E A N   S E A

Kritikón Pélagos
Sea of Crete

IÓNIOI NÍSOI
IONIAN ISLANDS

I O N I A N   S E A

A D R I A T I C   S E A

M E D I T E R R A N E A N   S E A

Strait of Otranto

ITALY

ALBANIA / SHQIPËRI
Tiranë
Durrës
Vlorë
Fier
Elbasan
Korçë
Gjirokastër

Kérkira / CORFU

Ioánnina
Préveza
Árta
Agrínion
Mesolóngion
Pátrai
Pírgos
Kalámai
Spárti
Trípolis
Kórinthos
Návplion
Kalamáta

PELOPÓNNISOS

Lárisa
Vólos
Tríkala
Véroia
Kateríni
Lamía
Khalkís

MAKEDONIJA
BULGARIA
Bitola
Titov Veles
Prilep
Strumica
Štip

Scale

Feet		
19685	13124	9843
6562	3281	1640
656	0	

Meters		
6000	4000	3000
2000	1000	500
200	0	
Land Below Sea Level		
0	200	656
1000	3000	6000
9000		

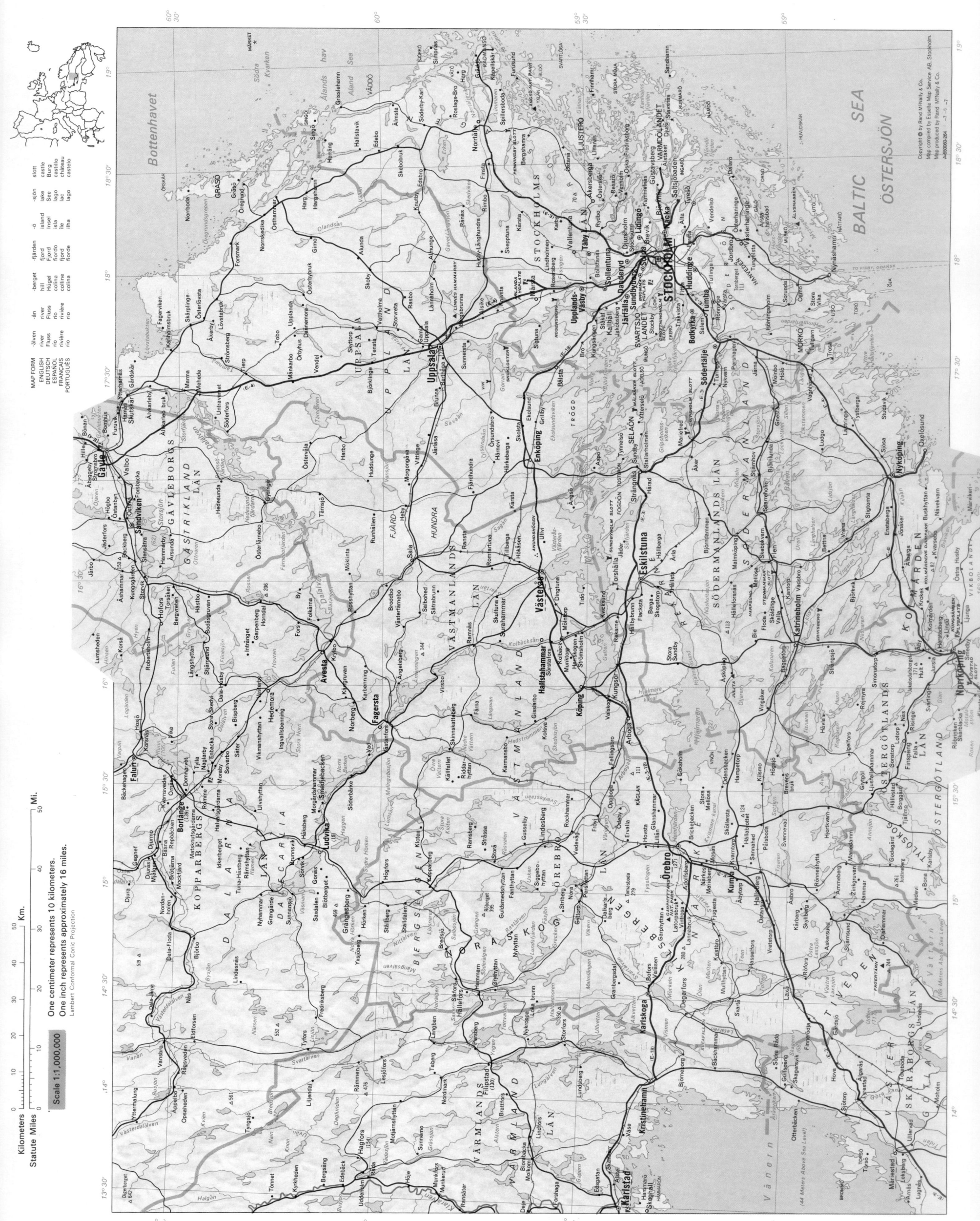

Copyright © by Rand McNally & Co.
Map compiled by Esselte Map Service AB, Stockholm.
Map produced by Rand McNally & Co.
A050060/264   -7 -5 -7

Kilometers
Statute Miles

Scale 1:1,000,000

One centimeter represents 10 kilometers.
One inch represents approximately 16 miles.
Lambert Conformal Conic Projection

MAP FORM		
ENGLISH	DEUTSCH	ESPAÑOL
FRANÇAIS	PORTUGUÊS	

-älven	river	Fluss
	río	rivière
	rio	

-ån	river	Fluss
	río	rivière
	rio	

-berget	hill	Hügel
	colina	colline
	colina	

-fjärden	fjord	Fjord
	fiordo	fiord
	fiorde	

-ö	island	Insel
	isla	île
	ilha	

-sjön	lake	See
	lago	lac
	lago	

slott	castle	Burg
	castillo	château
	castelo	

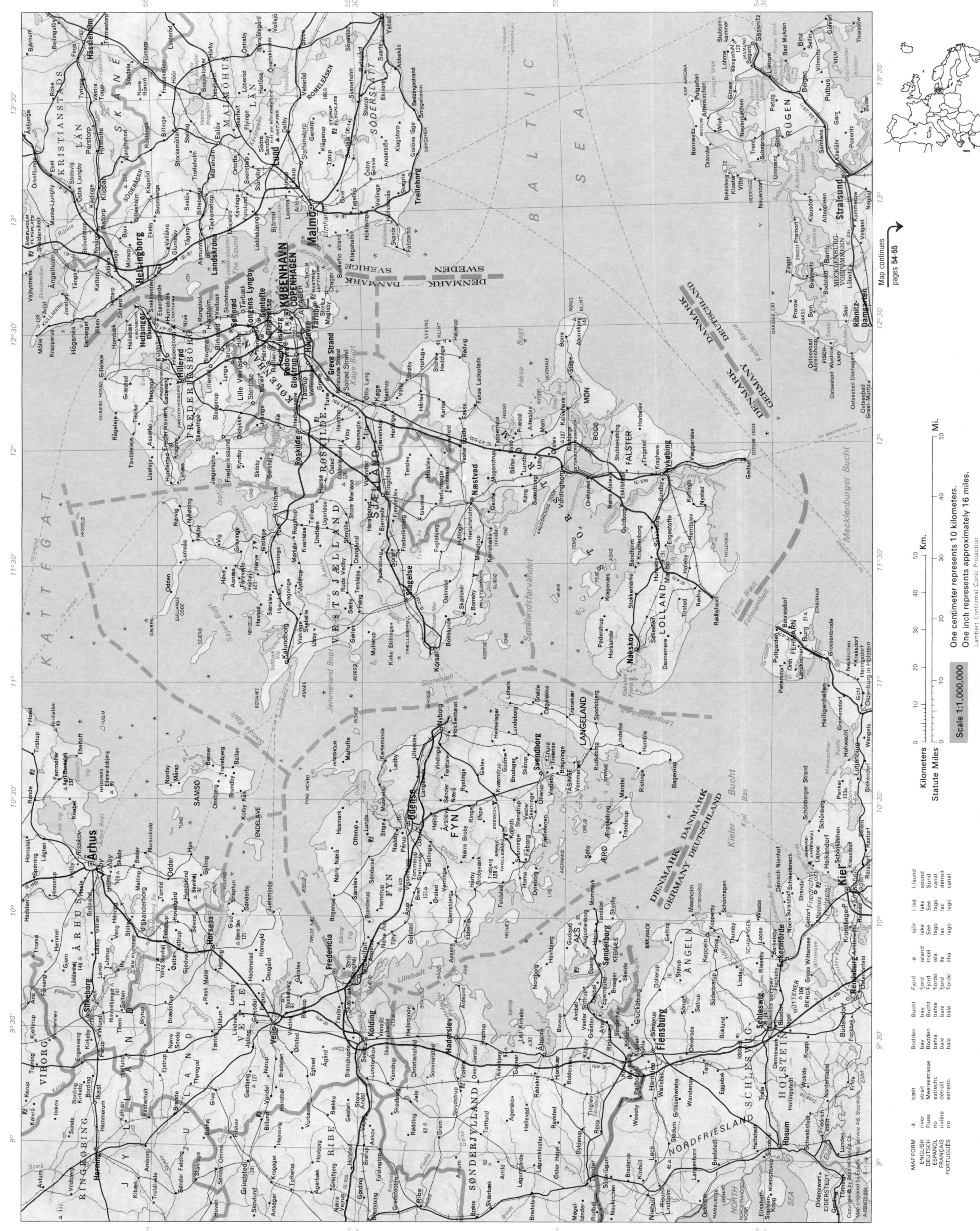

Map continues
pages 54-55

Scale 1:1,000,000

Kilometers

Statute Miles

One centimeter represents 10 kilometers.
One inch represents approximately 16 miles.

Lambert Conformal Conic Projection

MAP FORM						
ENGLISH	river	bay	Bucht	Fjord	island	lake	sound
DEUTSCH	Fluss	Boden	bay	fjord	island	lake	Sund
DEUTSCH	Meeresstrasse	Bodden	Bucht	Fjord	Insel	See	Sund
ESPAÑOL	rio	estrecho	bahia	fiordo	isla	lago	canal
FRANÇAIS	rivière	detroit	baie	fjord	île	lac	detroit
PORTUGUÊS	rio	estreito	bala	fiorde	ilha	lago	canal

← Map continues
pages 48-49

a

ISLES OF SCILLY

TRESCO   ST. MARTIN'S
BRYHER   EASTERN ISLES
SAMPSON   ST. MARY'S
              Hugh Town
ANNET   ST. AGNES
BISHOP ROCK

ATLANTIC OCEAN

ENGLISH	bay	drain	fo·rest	head	hill	isle	marsh	point	vale
DEUTSCH	Bucht	Abzugsgraben	Wald	Landspitze	Hügel	Insel	Marsch	Landspitze	Tal
ESPAÑOL	bahía	acquia	bosque	promontorio	colina	isla	pantano	punta	valle
FRANÇAIS	baie	drainage	fo·rêt	promontoire	colline	île	marais	pointe	dépression
PORTUGUÊS	baia	drenagem	floresta	promontório	colina	ilha	pântano	ponta	vale

Copyright © by Rand McNally & Co.
Map prepared by Rand McNally & Co.
A-856900-264

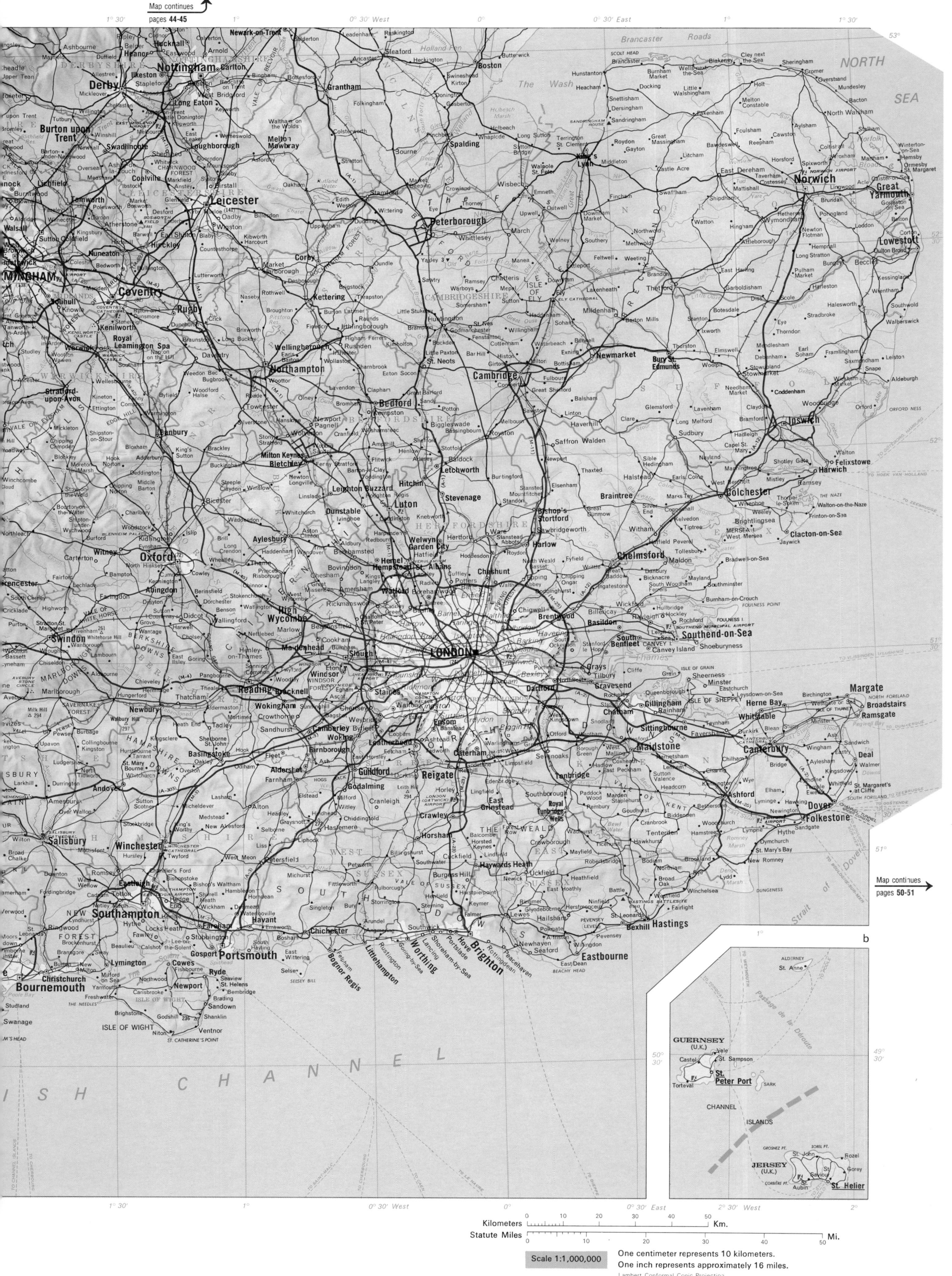

Map continues
pages 44-45

Map continues
pages 50-51

Kilometers

Statute Miles

Scale 1:1,000,000

One centimeter represents 10 kilometers.
One inch represents approximately 16 miles.

Lambert Conformal Conic Projection

Map continues
pages 46-47

Map continues
pages 48-49

NORTHERN IRELAND

NORTH CHANNEL

IRISH SEA

ISLE OF MAN (U.K.)

DONEGAL

NORTHERN IRELAND

MONAGHAN

CAVAN

LOUTH

MEATH

KILDARE

WICKLOW

WICKLOW MOUNTAINS

CARLOW

WEXFORD

ANGLESEY

SNOWDONIA NATIONAL PARK

LLEYN PENINSULA

STRATHCLYDE

THE GLENKENS

GALLOWAY

THE RHINS

THE MACHARS

Londonderry Derry 393

Coleraine

Portrush

Ballymena

Larne

Belfast
BELFAST (ALDERGROVE) AIRPORT

Newtownabbey

Bangor

Newtownards

Carrickfergus

Lisburn

Lurgan

Portadown

Armagh

Banbridge

Downpatrick

Newry

Newcastle

Dundalk
Dún Dealgan

Drogheda
Droichead Átha

Navan

Balbriggan

Skerries

Swords

Malahide

Portmarnock

Howth

DUBLIN BAILE ÁTHA CLIATH
DUBLIN (COLLINSTOWN) AIRPORT

Dún Laoghaire

Bray

Greystones

Wicklow

Arklow

Holyhead

Llandudno

Colwyn Bay

Rhyl

Bangor

Caernarfon

IRELAND ÉIRE
UNITED KINGDOM

IRELAND ÉIRE

Kilmarnock

Ayr

Irvine

Troon
PRESTWICK AIRPORT

Prestwick

Dumfries

Stranraer

Portpatrick

Girvan

Ballantrae

ISLAND OF ARRAN

Campbeltown

KINTYRE

Workington

Whitehaven

St. Bees

Barrow-in-Furness

Douglas

Ramsey

Peel

Port Erin

Castletown
ISLE OF MAN (RONALDSWAY) AIRPORT

Lough Foyle

Lough Neagh

Strangford Lough

MOURNE MTS.

Slieve Donard 850

Luce Bay

Solway Firth

Firth of Clyde

Copyright © by Rand McNally & Co.
Map prepared by Rand McNally & Co.
A-656800-264 —11-9 —14

MAP FORM								
ENGLISH	bay	dale	firth	forest	head	lake; inlet	moor	water (lake, river)
DEUTSCH	Bucht	Weites Tal	Trichtermündung	Wald	Landspitze	See; Einfahrt	Moor	See, Fluss
ESPAÑOL	bahía	valle	estuario	bosque	promontorio	lago; abra	páramo	lago, río
FRANÇAIS	baie	vallée	estuaire	forêt	promontoire	lac; bras de mer	lande	lac, rivière
PORTUGUÊS	baía	vale	estuário	floresta	promontório	lago; enseada	pântano	lago, rio

Map continues
pages 42-43

Kilometers
Statute Miles

Scale 1:1,000,000   One centimeter represents 10 kilometers.
One inch represents approximately 16 miles.
Lambert Conformal Conic Projection

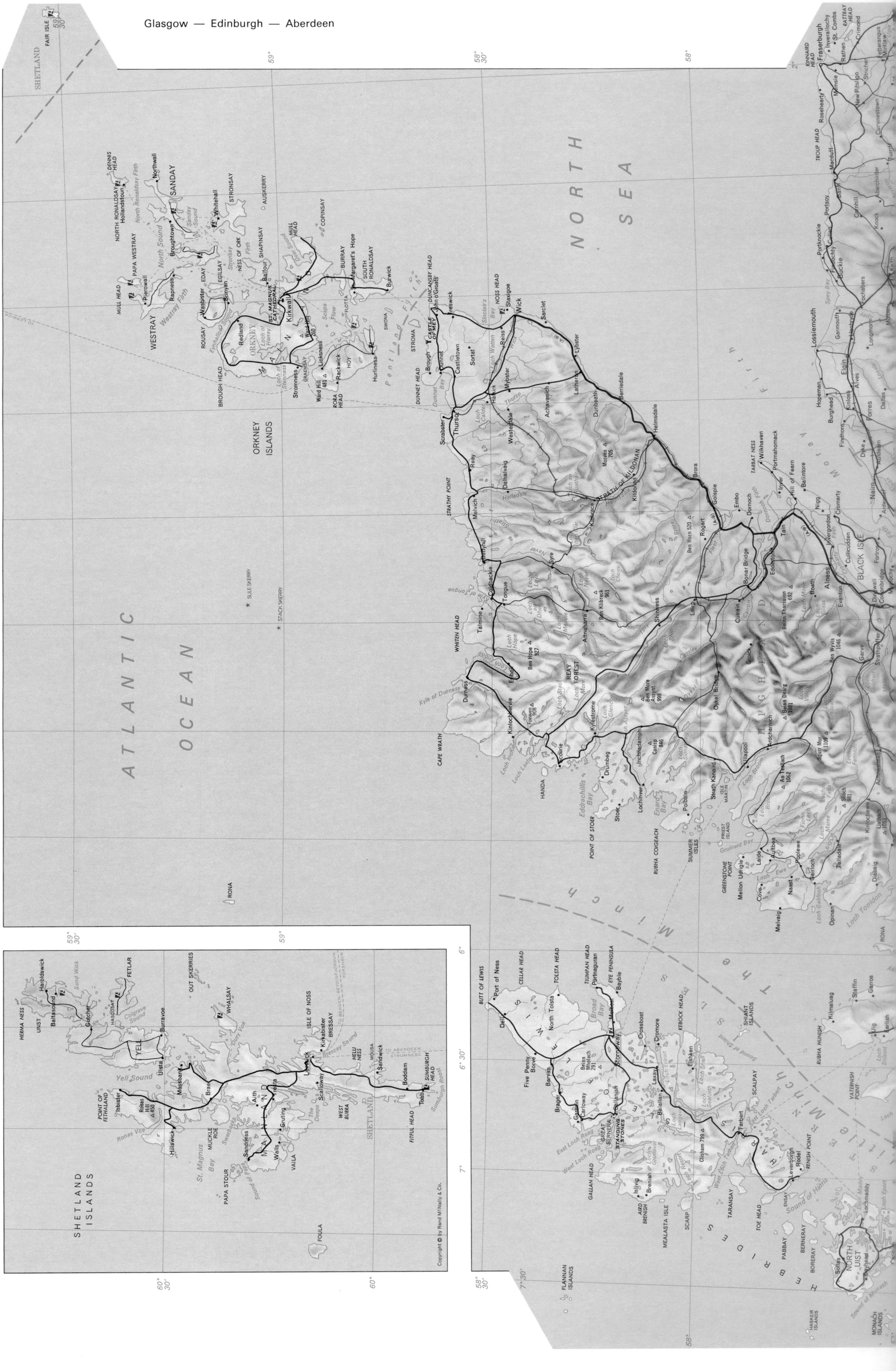
ATLANTIC OCEAN
NORTH SEA
ORKNEY ISLANDS
SHETLAND ISLANDS
ORKNEY
SHETLAND
WESTRAY
SANDAY
STRONSAY
SHAPINSAY
ROUSAY
EDAY
HOY
Kirkwall
Stromness
Pentland Firth
Thurso
Wick
John o'Groats
Castletown
Helmsdale
Brora
Golspie
Dornoch
Tain
Lairg
Tongue
Durness
Kinlochbervie
Scourie
Lochinver
Ullapool
Gairloch
Moray Firth
Lossiemouth
Elgin
Forres
Nairn
Fraserburgh
BLACK ISLE
HIGHLANDS
The Minch
Little Minch
OUTER HEBRIDES
LEWIS
HARRIS
NORTH UIST
Stornoway
Tarbert
Leverburgh
Butt of Lewis
Lerwick
Scalloway
Sumburgh Head
UNST
YELL
FETLAR
WHALSAY
MAINLAND
FOULA
FAIR ISLE
RONA
SULE SKERRY
STACK SKERRY
Copyright © by Rand McNally & Co.

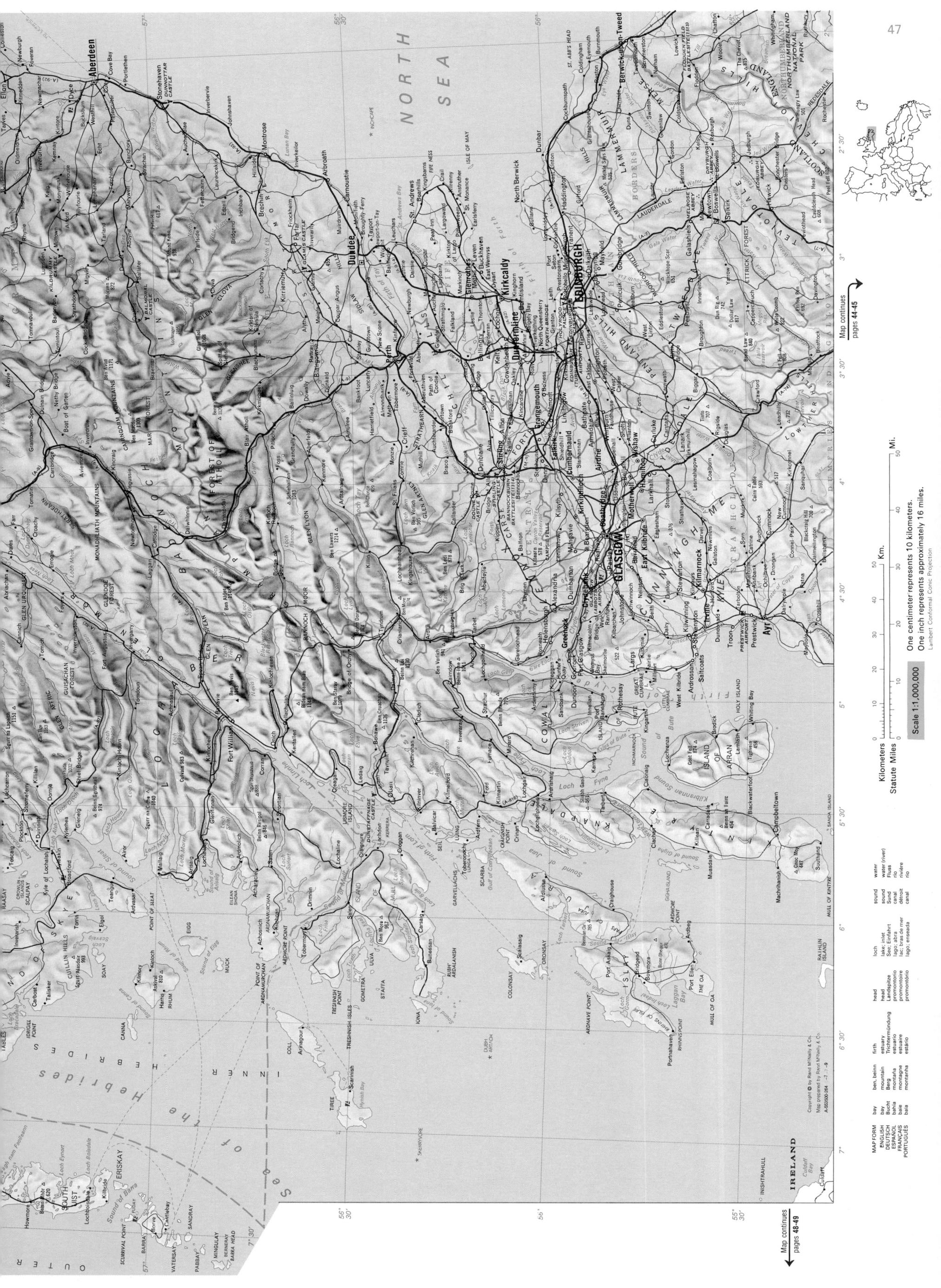

NORTH SEA

INNER HEBRIDES

OUTER HEBRIDES

IRELAND

Map continues pages 44-45

Map continues pages 48-49

Scale 1:1,000,000

One centimeter represents 10 kilometers.
One inch represents approximately 16 miles.
Lambert Conformal Conic Projection

Kilometers
Statute Miles

Km.
Mi.

MAPFORM				
ENGLISH	bay	ben, ben, beinn	firth	head	loch	sound	water
DEUTSCH	Bucht	Berg	Trichtermündung	Landspitze	See; Einfahrt	Sund	Fluss
ESPAÑOL	bahía	montaña	estuario	promontorio	lago; abra	canal	río
FRANÇAIS	baie	montagne	estuaire	promontoire	lac; bras de mer	détroit	rivière
PORTUGUÊS	baía	montanha	estuário	promontório	lago; enseada	canal	río

mountain
Berg
montaña
montagne
montanha

water (river)
Fluss
río
rivière
río

Copyright © by Rand McNally & Co.
Map prepared by Rand McNally & Co.
A-555500-264

Map continues
pages 46-47

Map continues
pages 44-45

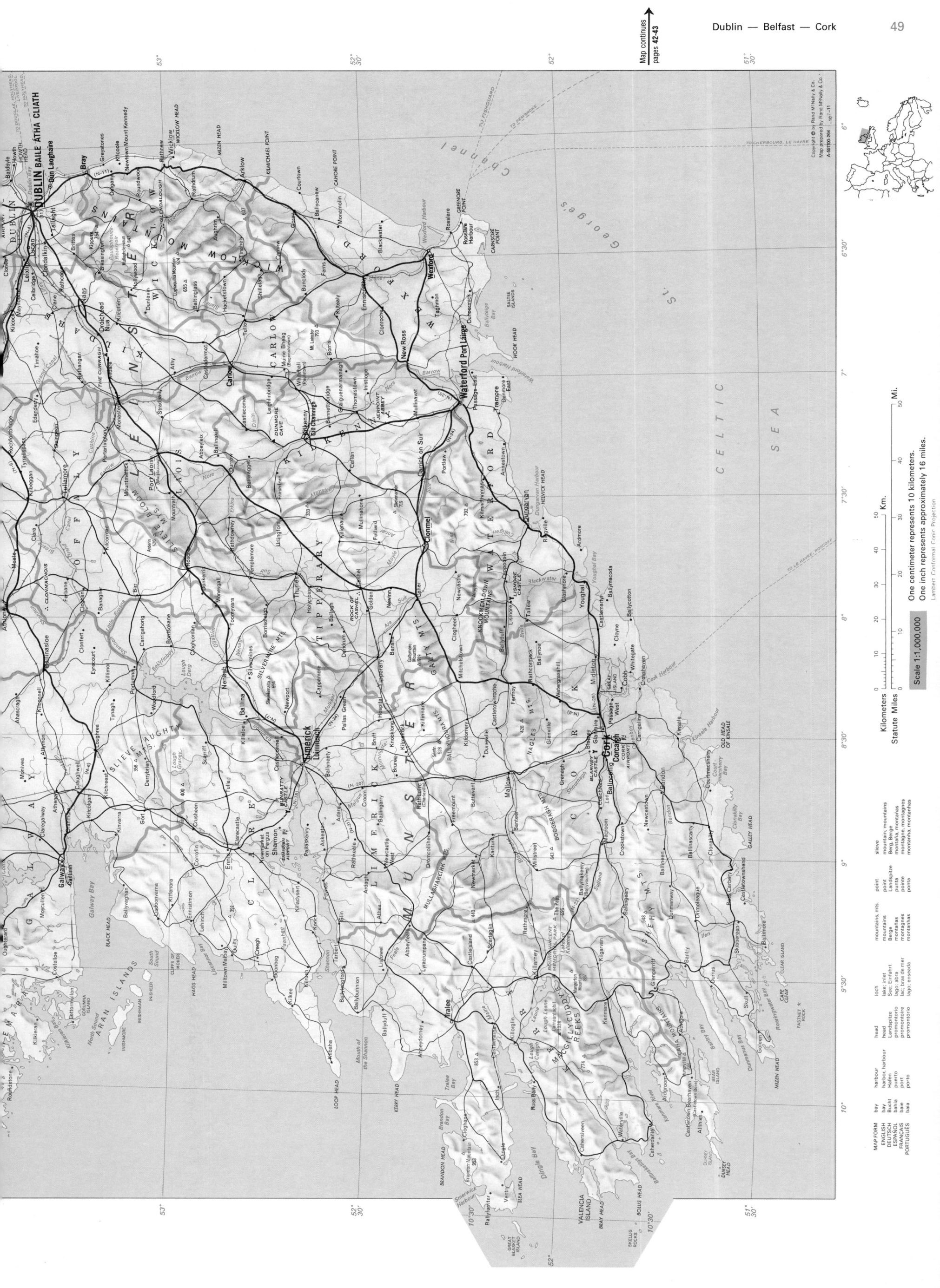

Map continues
pages 42-43

Scale 1:1,000,000

One centimeter represents 10 kilometers.
One inch represents approximately 16 miles.

Lambert Conformal Conic Projection

Kilometers

Statute Miles

Km.

Mi.

MAP FORM	bay	harbour, harbour	head	loch	mountains, mts.	point	slieve
ENGLISH	bay	harbor, harbour	head	lake; inlet	mountains	point	mountain, mountains
DEUTSCH	Bucht	Hafen	Landspitze	See; Einfahrt	Berge	Spitze	Berg, Berge
ESPAÑOL	bahía	puerto	promontorio	lago; abra	montañas	punta	montaña, montañas
FRANÇAIS	baie	port	promontoire	lac; bras de mer	montagnes	pointe	montagne, montagnes
PORTUGUÉS	baía	porto	promontório	lago; enseada	montanhas	ponta	montanha, montanhas

DUBLIN BAILE ÁTHA CLIATH

CELTIC   SEA

St. George's   Channel

ATLANTIC OCEAN

Map continues pages 56-57

Map continues pages 52-53

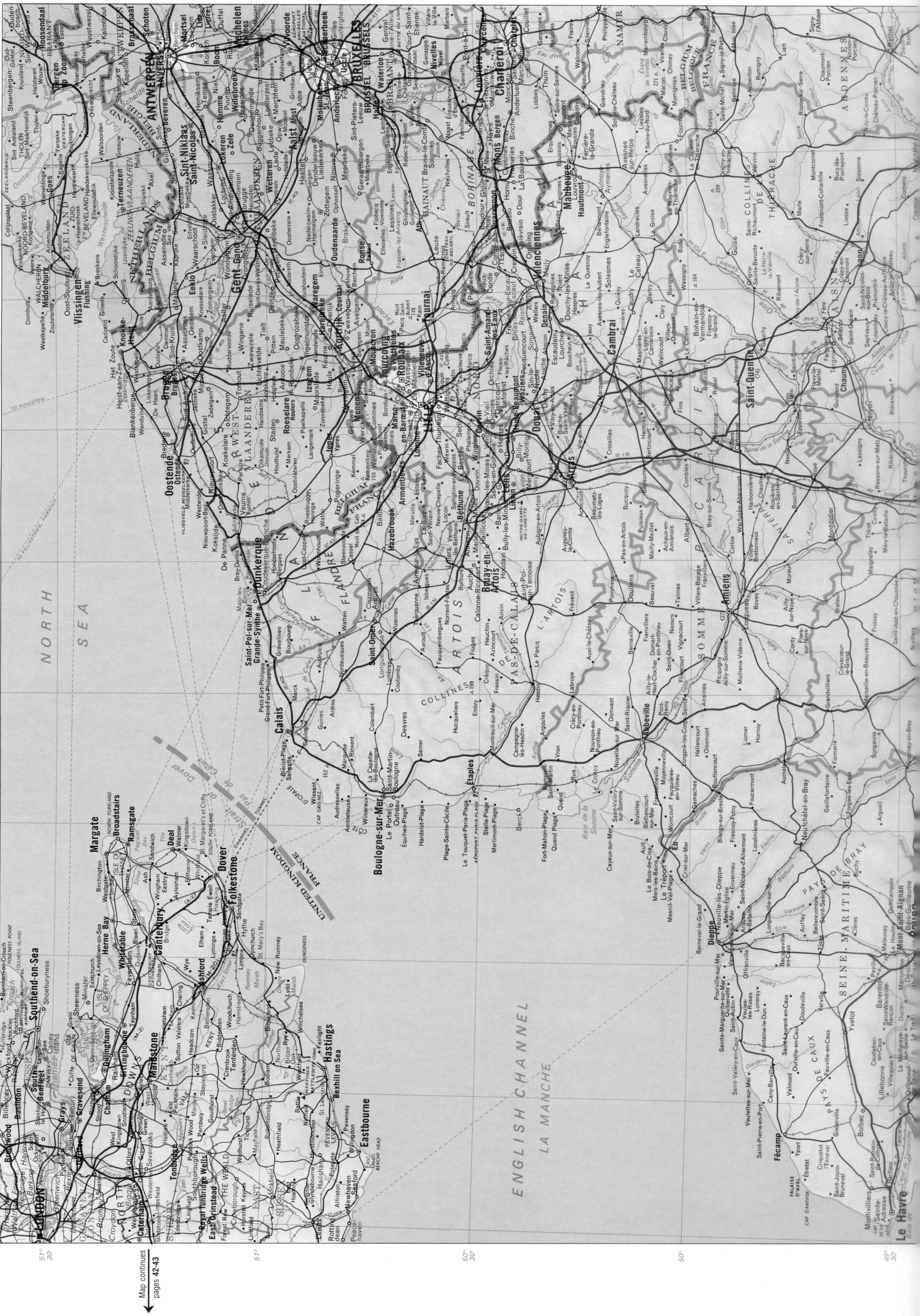

Map continues pages 42-43

NORTH SEA

ENGLISH CHANNEL — LA MANCHE

NETHERLAND

BELGIUM — BELGIË

FRANCE

UNITED KINGDOM

ANTWERPEN · BRUSSELS · BRUXELSL · Gent Gand · Oostende Ostende · Charleroi · NAMUR · Mons Bergen · Valenciennes · Cambrai · Saint-Quentin · Amiens · Abbeville · Dieppe · Le Havre · Boulogne-sur-Mer · Calais · Dunkerque · LONDON · Canterbury · Dover · Folkestone · Margate · Ramsgate · Hastings · Eastbourne · Maidstone · Southend-on-Sea · Lille · Roubaix · Tournai · Béthune · Lens · Douai · Arras

Map continues pages 58-59

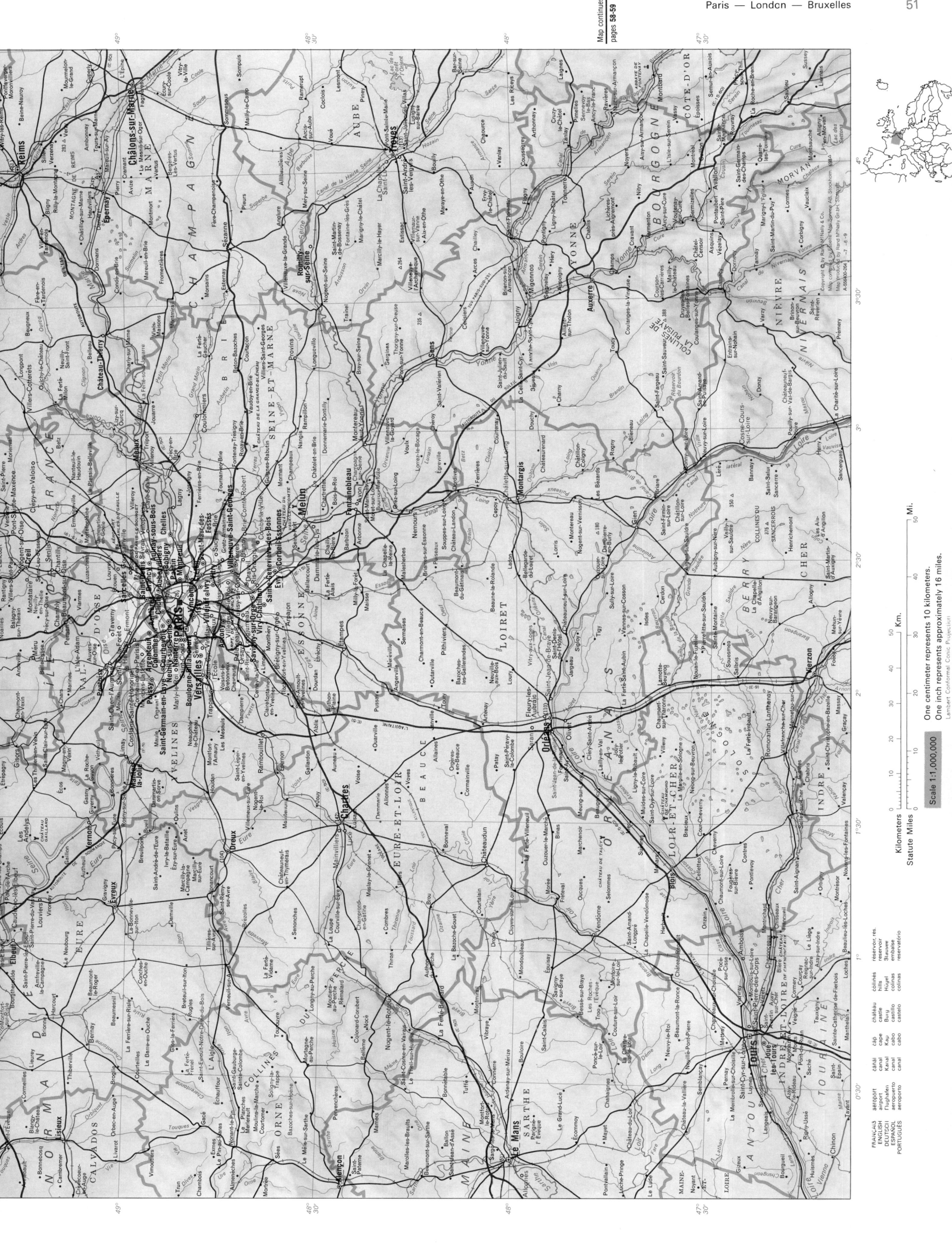

Scale 1:1,000,000

One centimeter represents 10 kilometers.
One inch represents approximately 16 miles.

Lambert Conformal Conic Projection

Kilometers

Statute Miles

Km.

Mi.

FRANÇAIS	aéroport	cap	château	colines	reservoir, rés.
ENGLISH	airport	cape	castle	hills	reservoir
DEUTSCH	Flughafen	Kap	Burg	Hügel	Stausee
ESPAÑOL	aeropuerto	cabo	castillo	colinas	embalse
PORTUGUÊS	aeroporto	cabo	castelo	colinas	reservatorio

← Map continues pages 50-51

Map continues pages 56-57

DEUTSCH	Gebirge	Kanal	Moor	Naturpark	Stausee	Talsperre	Wald
ENGLISH	range	canal	moor	reserve	reservoir	dam	forest, mountains
ESPAÑOL	sierra	canal	páramo	reserva	embalse	presa	bosque, montañas
FRANÇAIS	chaîne	canal	lande	réserve	réservoir	barrage	forêt, montagnes
PORTUGUÊS	serra	canal	pântano	reserva natural	reservatório	represa	floresta, montanhas

Map continues
pages 54-55

Kilometers
Statute Miles

Scale 1:1,000,000

One centimeter represents 10 kilometers.
One inch represents approximately 16 miles.

Lambert Conformal Conic Projection

BALTIC SEA

Pomeranian Bay

POMERANIA

Szczecin (Stettin)

Police

Świnoujście

USEDOM

RÜGEN

Sassnitz

Bergen

Stralsund

Greifswald

Anklam

Neubrandenburg

Neustrelitz

Prenzlau

Eberswalde

UCKERMARK

BARNIM

BERLIN

Oranienburg

Falkensee

HAVELLAND

Neuruppin

PRIGNITZ

MECKLENBURG-VORPOMMERN

MECKLENBURGISCHE SEENPLATTE

Waren

Güstrow

Rostock

Ribnitz–Damgarten

Wismar

Schwerin

Parchim

Ludwigslust

Wittenberge

Stendal

ALTMARK

WENDLAND

Salzwedel

Uelzen

Lüneburg

LÜNEBURGER HEIDE

HAMBURG

Geesthacht

Lübeck

Bad Schwartau

Neustadt in Holstein

Eutin

Kiel

Mecklenburger Bucht

Kieler Bucht

POLAND

GERMANY

DEUTSCHLAND

POLSKA

Oder

Elbe

Map continues page 41

Map continues pages 52-53

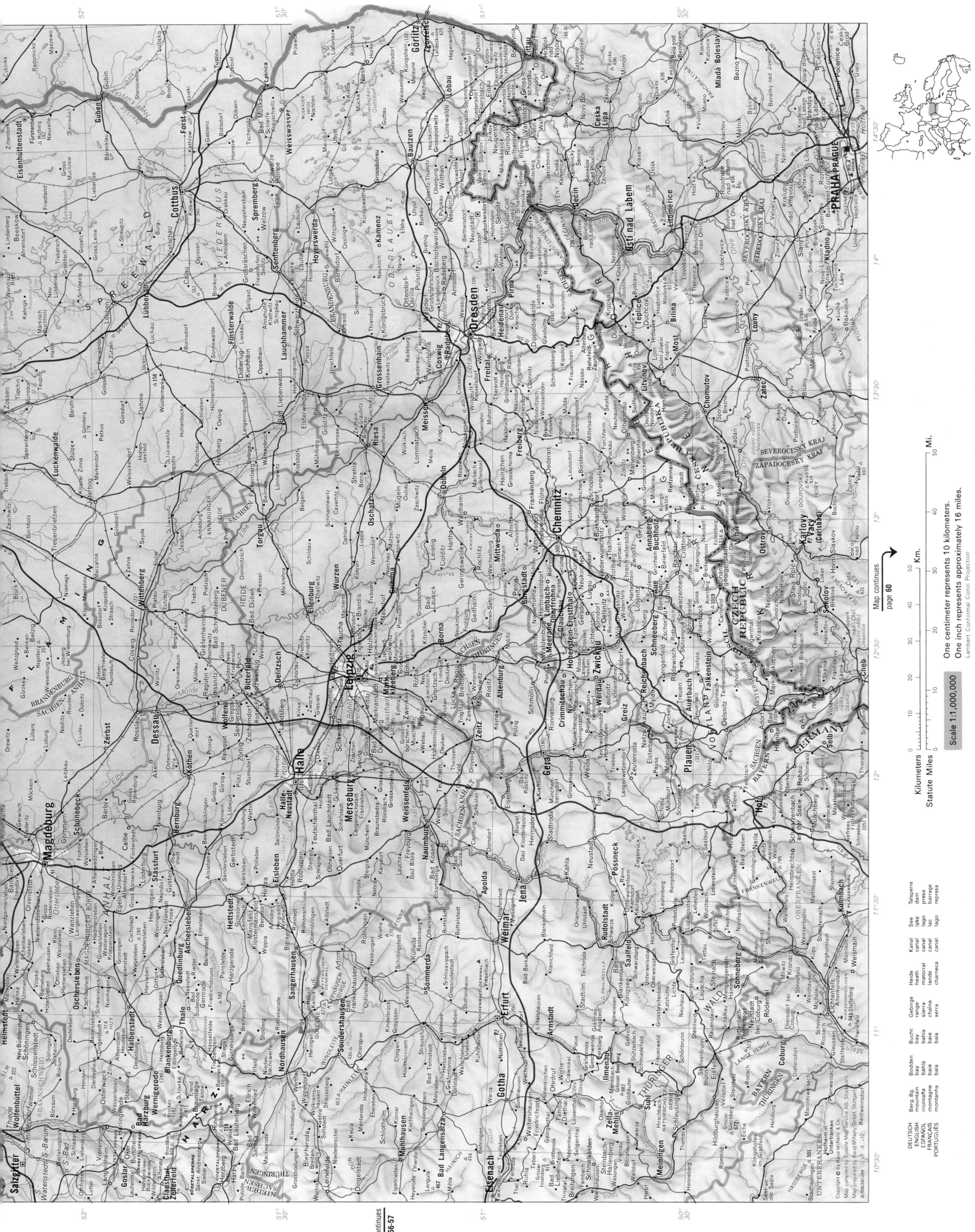

Map continues
pages 56-57

Map continues
page 60

Mi.

Km.

Kilometers

Statute Miles

Scale 1:1,000,000

One centimeter represents 10 kilometers.
One inch represents approximately 16 miles.
Lambert Conformal Conic Projection

DEUTSCH	Berg, Bg.	Bodden	Bucht	Gebirge	Heide	Kanal	See	Talsperre
ENGLISH	mountain	bay	bay	range	heath	canal	lake	dam
ESPAÑOL	montaña	bahía	bahía	sierra	matorral	canal	lago	presa
FRANÇAIS	montagne	baie	baie	chaîne	lande	canal	lac	barrage
PORTUGUÊS	montanha	baía	baía	serra	charneca	canal	lago	represa

Copyright © by Rand McNally & Co.
Map completed by Geodata Mapservice AB, Stockholm
Map prepared by Rand McNally Gmbh, Stuttgart
A-556XX-94   2 4 -12

Map continues
pages 52-53

Map continues
pages 50-51

Map continues
pages 58-59

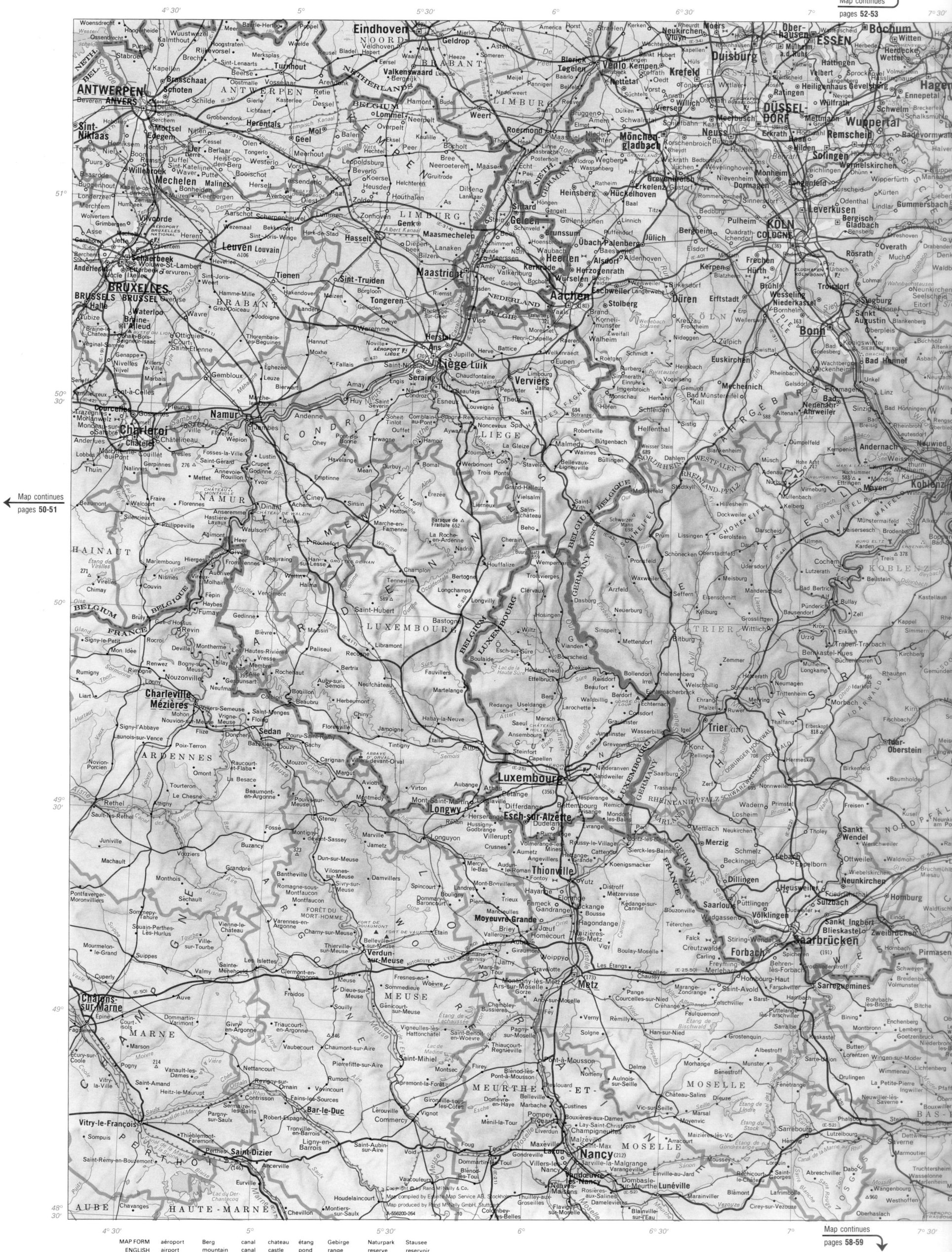

MAP FORM	aéroport	Berg	canal	chateau	étang	Gebirge	Naturpark	Stausee
ENGLISH	airport	mountain	canal	castle	pond	range	reserve	reservoir
DEUTSCH	Flughafen	Berg	Kanal	Burg	Teich	Gebirge	Naturpark	Stausee
ESPAÑOL	aeropuerto	montaña	canal	castillo	charca	cordillera	reserva	embalse
FRANÇAIS	aéroport	montagne	canal	château	étang	chaîne	réserve	réservoir
PORTUGUÊS	aeroporto	montanha	canal	castelo	lagoa	cordilheira	reserva	reservatório

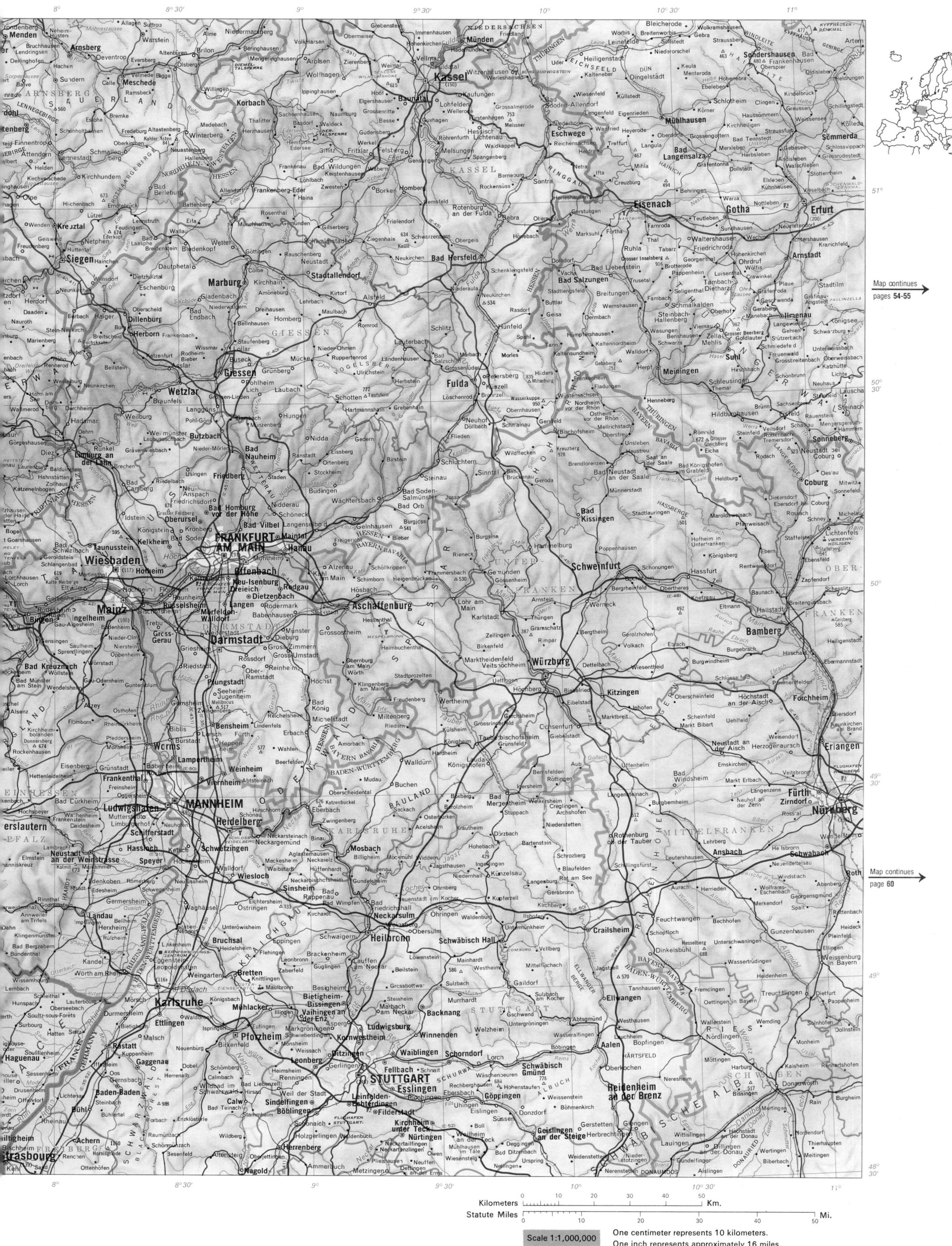

Map continues
pages 54-55

Map continues
page 60

Kilometers   Km.
Statute Miles   Mi.

Scale 1:1,000,000   One centimeter represents 10 kilometers.
One inch represents approximately 16 miles.
Lambert Conformal Conic Projection

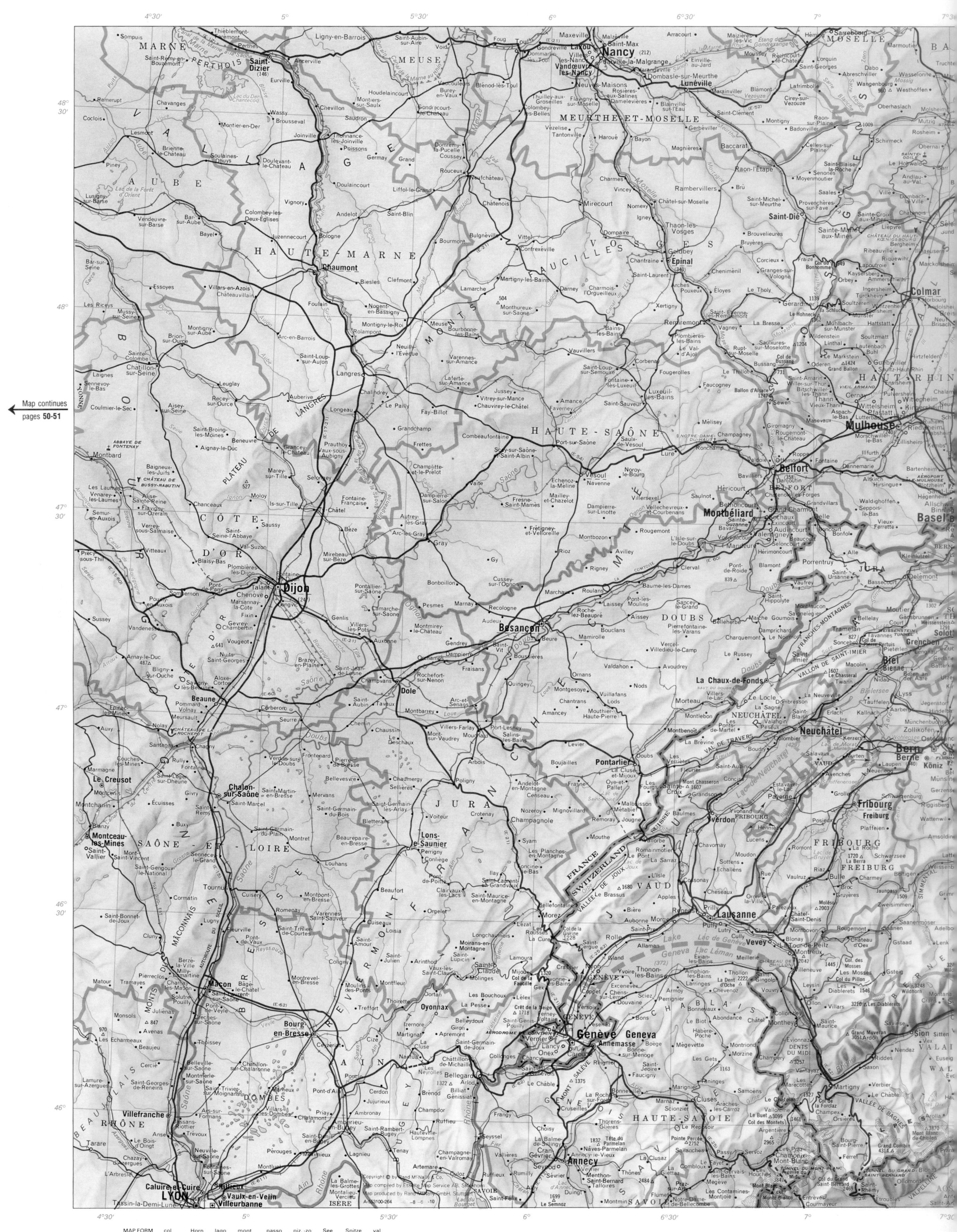

← Map continues
pages 50-51

MAP FORM	col	Horn	lago	mont	passo	piz, -zo	See	Spitze	val
ENGLISH	pass	peak	lake	mount	peak	peak	lake	peak	valley
DEUTSCH	Pass	Horn	See	Berg	Pass	Gipfel	See	Spitze	Tal
ESPAÑOL	paso	pico	lago	monte	paso	pico	lago	pico	valle
FRANÇAIS	col	cime	lac	mont	col	cime	lac	cime	val
PORTUGUÊS	passo	pico	lago	monte	passo	pico	lago	pico	vale

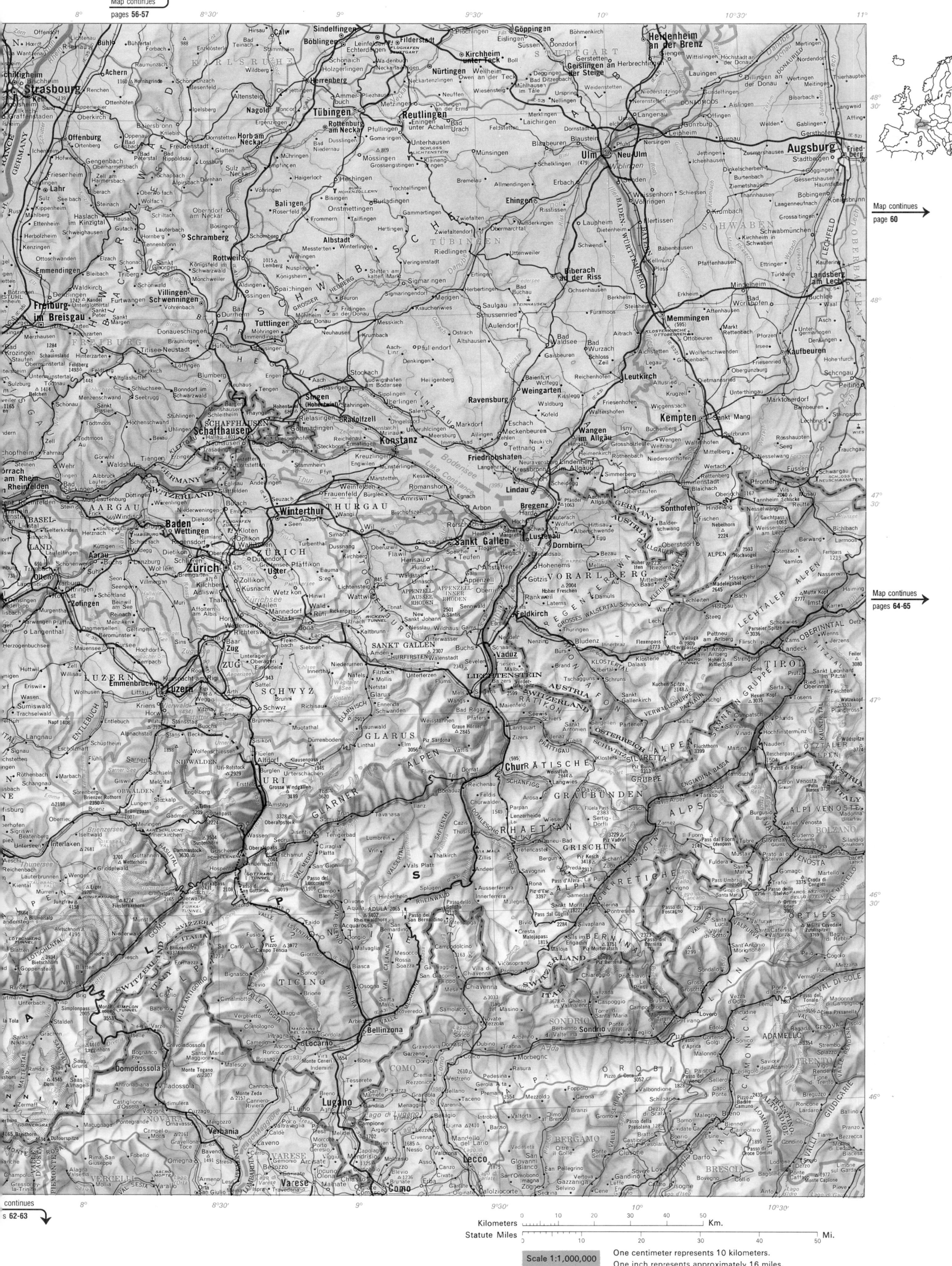

Map continues
pages 56-57

Map continues
page 60

Map continues
pages 64-65

continues
s 62-63

Kilometers
Statute Miles

Scale 1:1,000,000

One centimeter represents 10 kilometers.
One inch represents approximately 16 miles.

Lambert Conformal Conic Projection

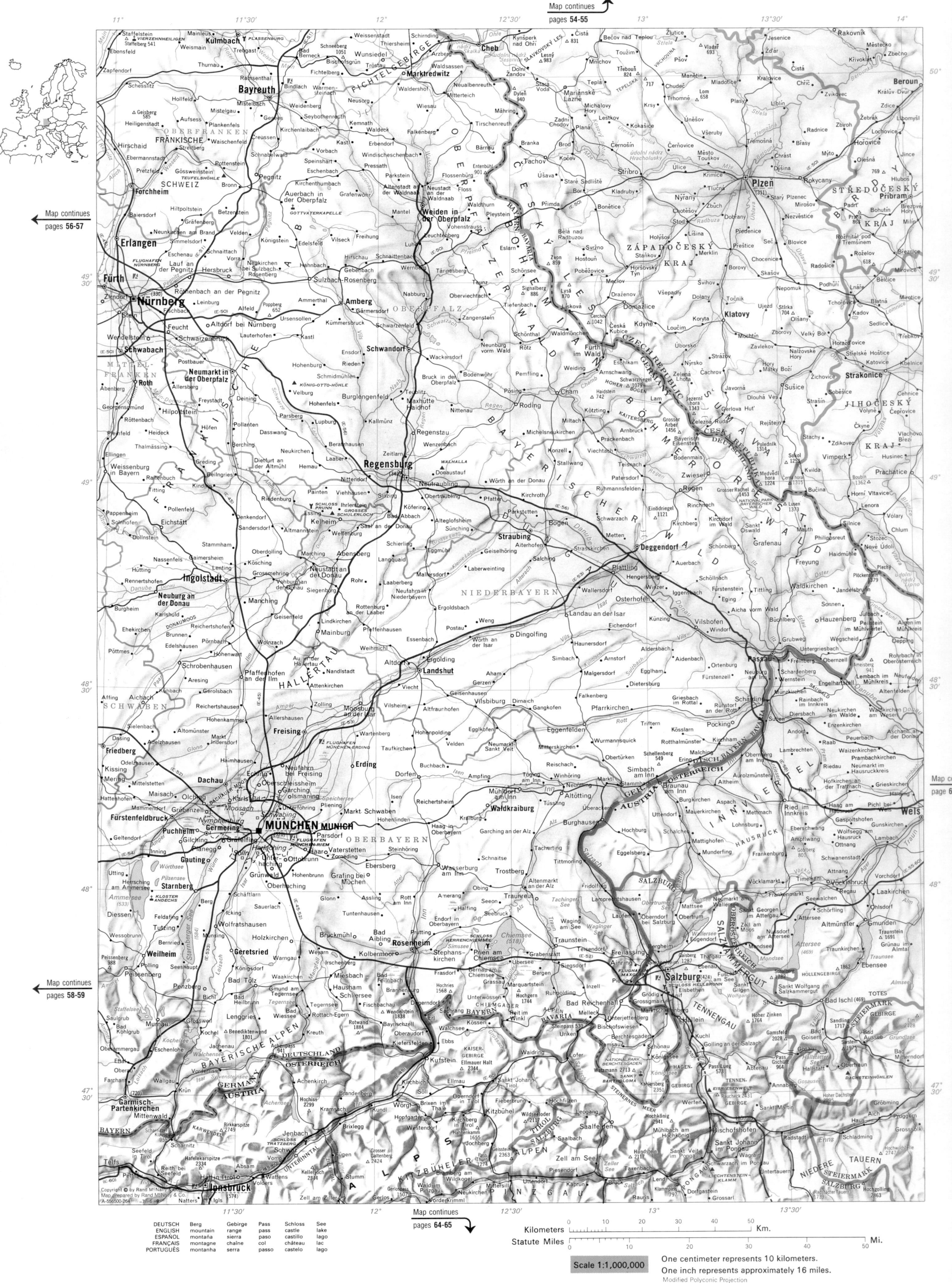

Map continues pages 54-55

Map continues pages 56-57

Map continues pages 58-59

Map continues pages 64-65

Map continues page 61

DEUTSCH	Berg	Gebirge	Pass	Schloss	See
ENGLISH	mountain	range	pass	castle	lake
ESPAÑOL	montaña	sierra	paso	castillo	lago
FRANÇAIS	montagne	chaîne	col	château	lac
PORTUGUÊS	montanha	serra	passo	castelo	lago

Kilometers
Km.
Statute Miles
Mi.

Scale 1:1,000,000
One centimeter represents 10 kilometers.
One inch represents approximately 16 miles.
Modified Polyconic Projection

Copyright © by Rand McNally
Map prepared by Rand McNally & Co.
A-556500-204

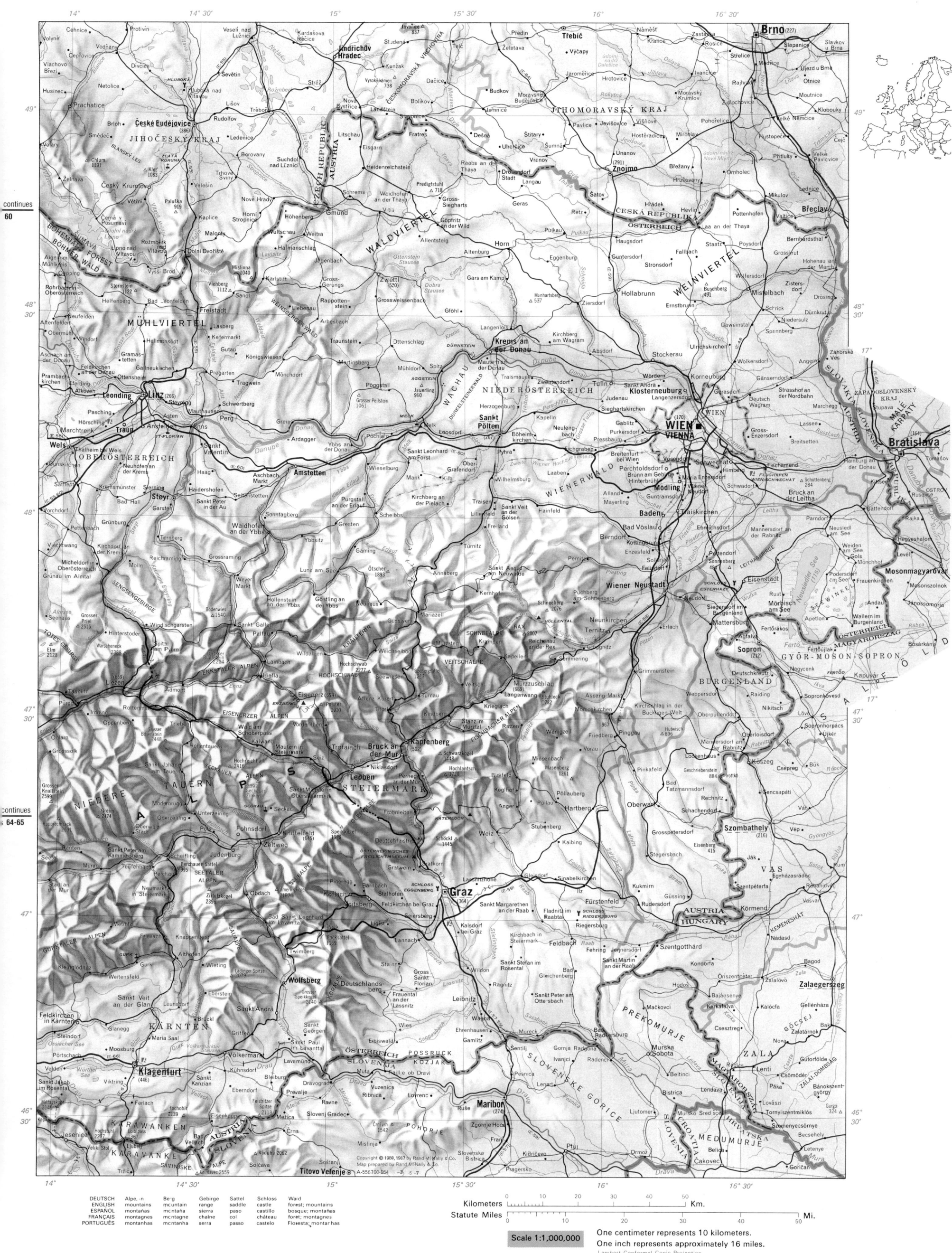

DEUTSCH	Alpe,-n	Be'g	Gebirge	Sattel	Schloss	Wald
ENGLISH	mountains	mountain	range	saddle	castle	forest; mountains
ESPAÑOL	montañas	montaña	sierra	paso	castillo	bosque; montañas
FRANÇAIS	montagnes	montagne	chaîne	col	château	forêt; montagnes
PORTUGUÊS	montanhas	montanha	serra	passo	castelo	Floresta; montanhas

Kilometers

Statute Miles

Scale 1:1,000,000

One centimeter represents 10 kilometers.
One inch represents approximately 16 miles.
Lambert Conformal Conic Projection

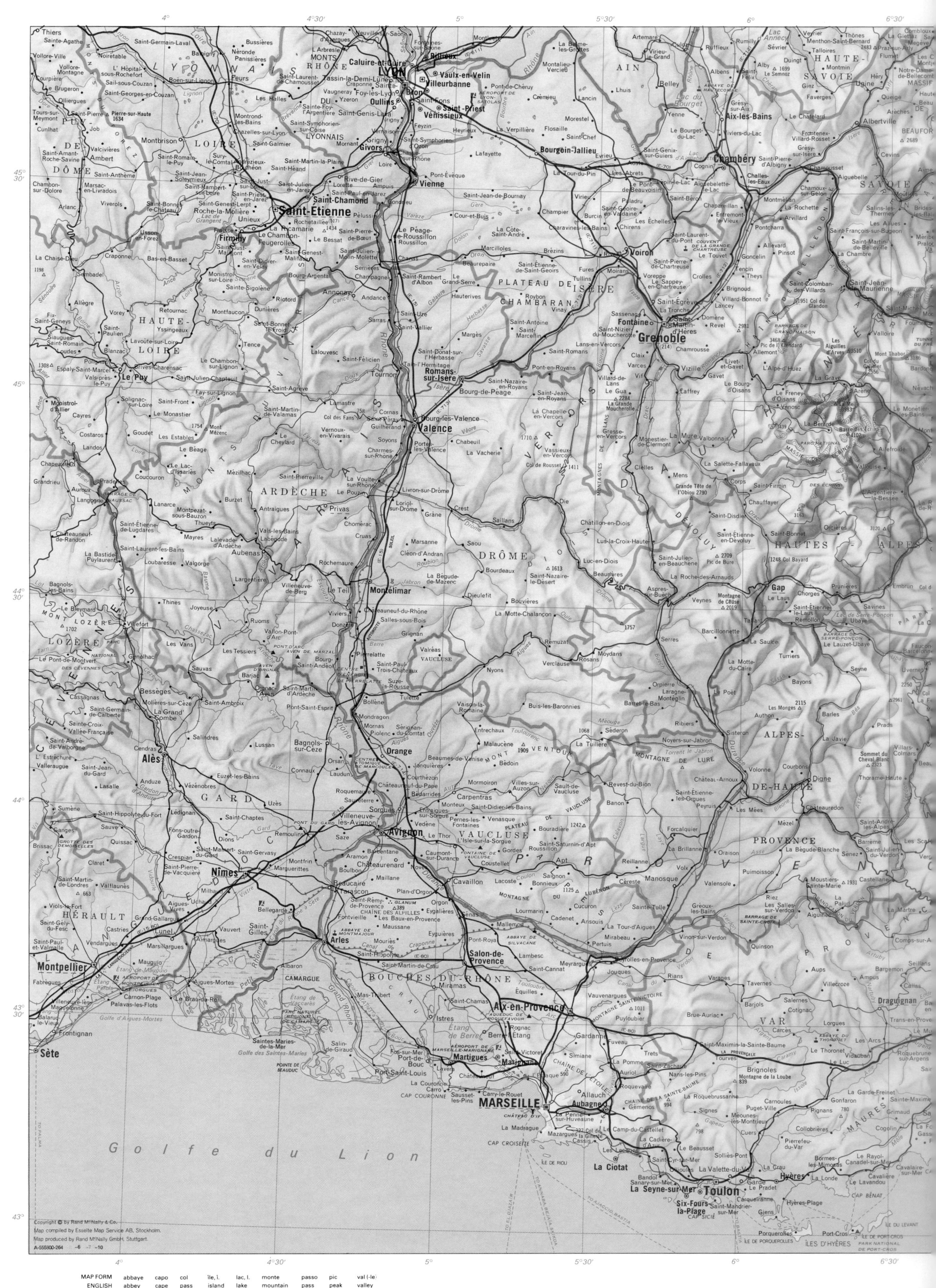

MAP FORM	abbaye	capo	col	île, l.	lac, l.	monte	passo	pic	val (-le)
ENGLISH	abbey	cape	pass	island	lake	mountain	pass	peak	valley
DEUTSCH	Abtei	Kap	Pass	Insel	See	Berg	Pass	Gipfel	Tal
ESPAÑOL	abadía	cabo	paso	isla	lago	montaña	paso	pico	valle
FRANÇAIS	abbaye	cap	col	île	lac	montagne	col	cime	val
PORTUGUÊS	abadia	cabo	passo	ilha	lago	montanha	passo	pico	vale

Map continues
pages **58-59**

Map continues
pages **64-65**

Kilometers

Statute Miles

Scale 1:1,000,000   One centimeter represents 10 kilometers.
One inch represents approximately 16 miles.
Lambert Conformal Conic Projection

Map continues
page 61

Map continues
page 60

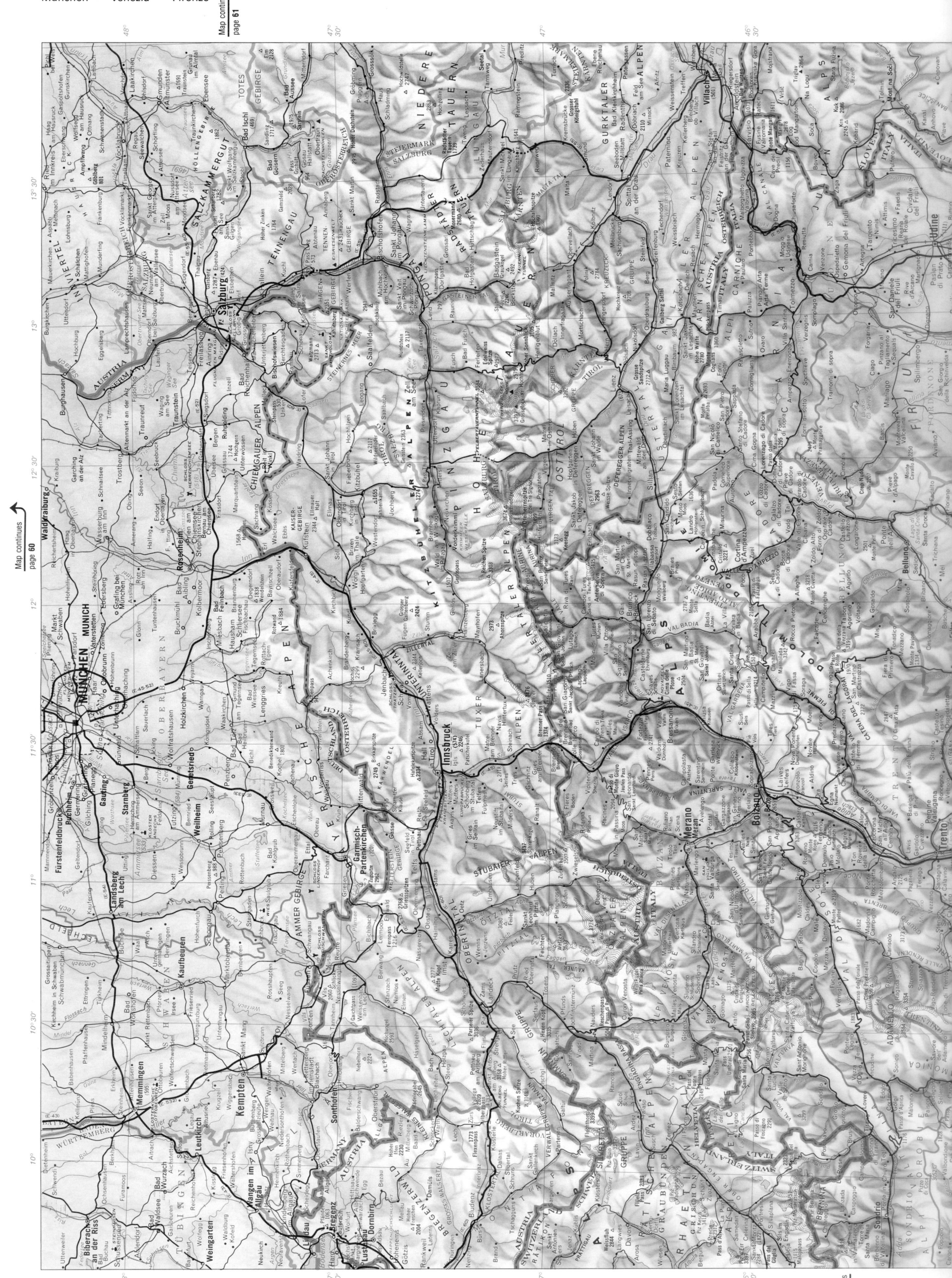

Map continues
pages 58-59

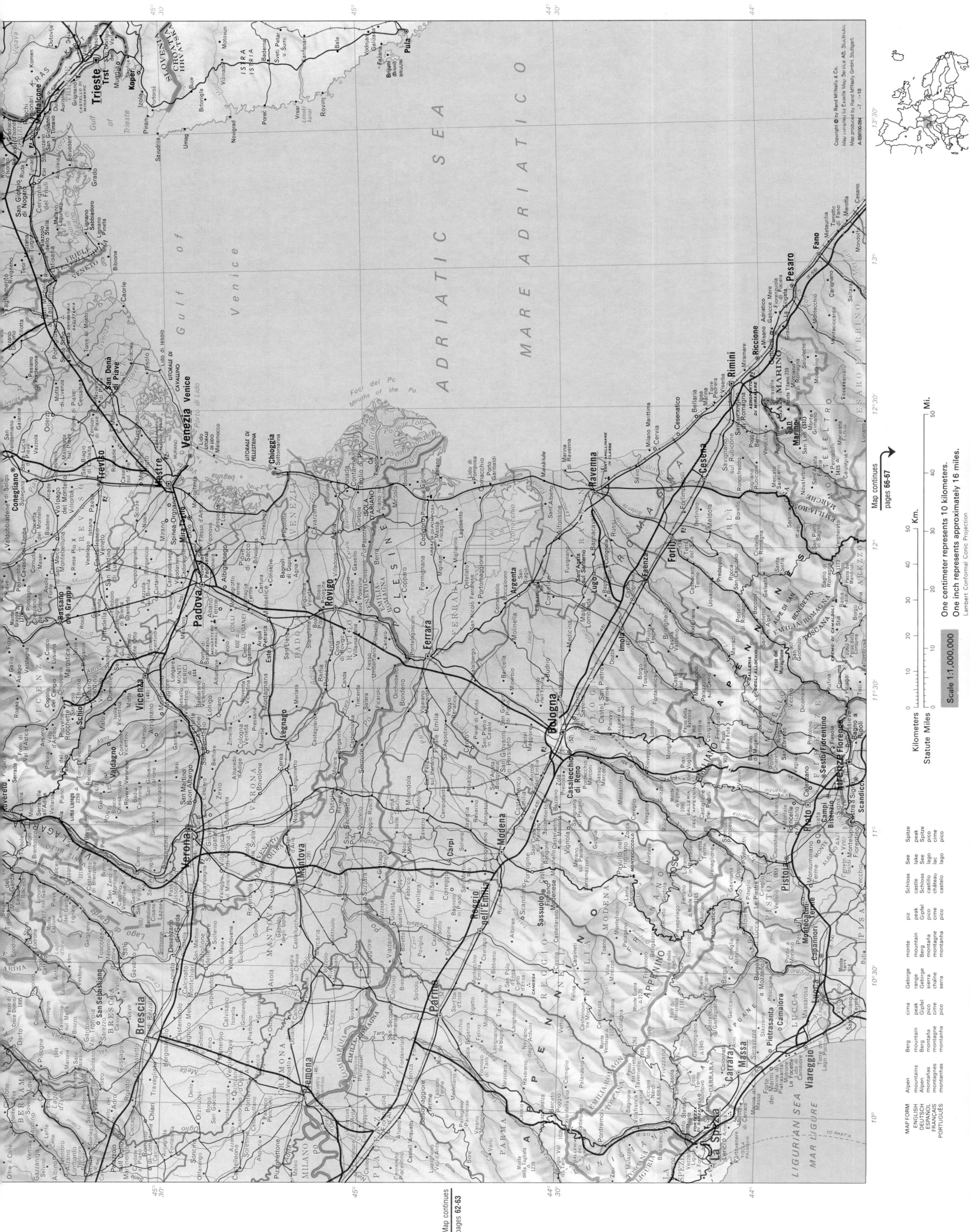

ADRIATIC SEA

MARE ADRIATICO

Gulf of Venice

LIGURIAN SEA

MAR LIGURE

Trieste

Venezia Venice

Padova

Vicenza

Verona

Brescia

Mantova

Cremona

Parma

Reggio nell'Emilia

Modena

Bologna

Ferrara

Rovigo

Ravenna

Forlì

Cesena

Rimini

Riccione

San Marino

Pesaro

Fano

Firenze Florence

Prato

Pistoia

Lucca

Viareggio

Massa

Carrara

La Spezia

Treviso

Conegliano

Bassano del Grappa

Schio

Valdagno

Legnano

Pula

Map continues pages 66-67

Map continues pages 62-63

Scale 1:1,000,000

One centimeter represents 10 kilometers.
One inch represents approximately 16 miles.

Kilometers
Statute Miles

Km.
Mi.

Lambert Conformal Conic Projection

Copyright © by Rand McNally & Co.
Map produced by Kartographie...
A-069100364

MAP FORM						
ENGLISH	Alps	Mountains	mountain	mountain range	peak	lake	castle
DEUTSCH	Alpen	Berg	cima	Gebirge	Gipfel	Spitze	See	Schloss
ESPAÑOL		Berg	montaña	sierra	pico	pico	lago	castillo
FRANÇAIS		montañas	montagne	chaîne	pico	cime	lac	château
PORTUGUÊS		montanhas	montagne	serra	pico	pico	lago	castelo

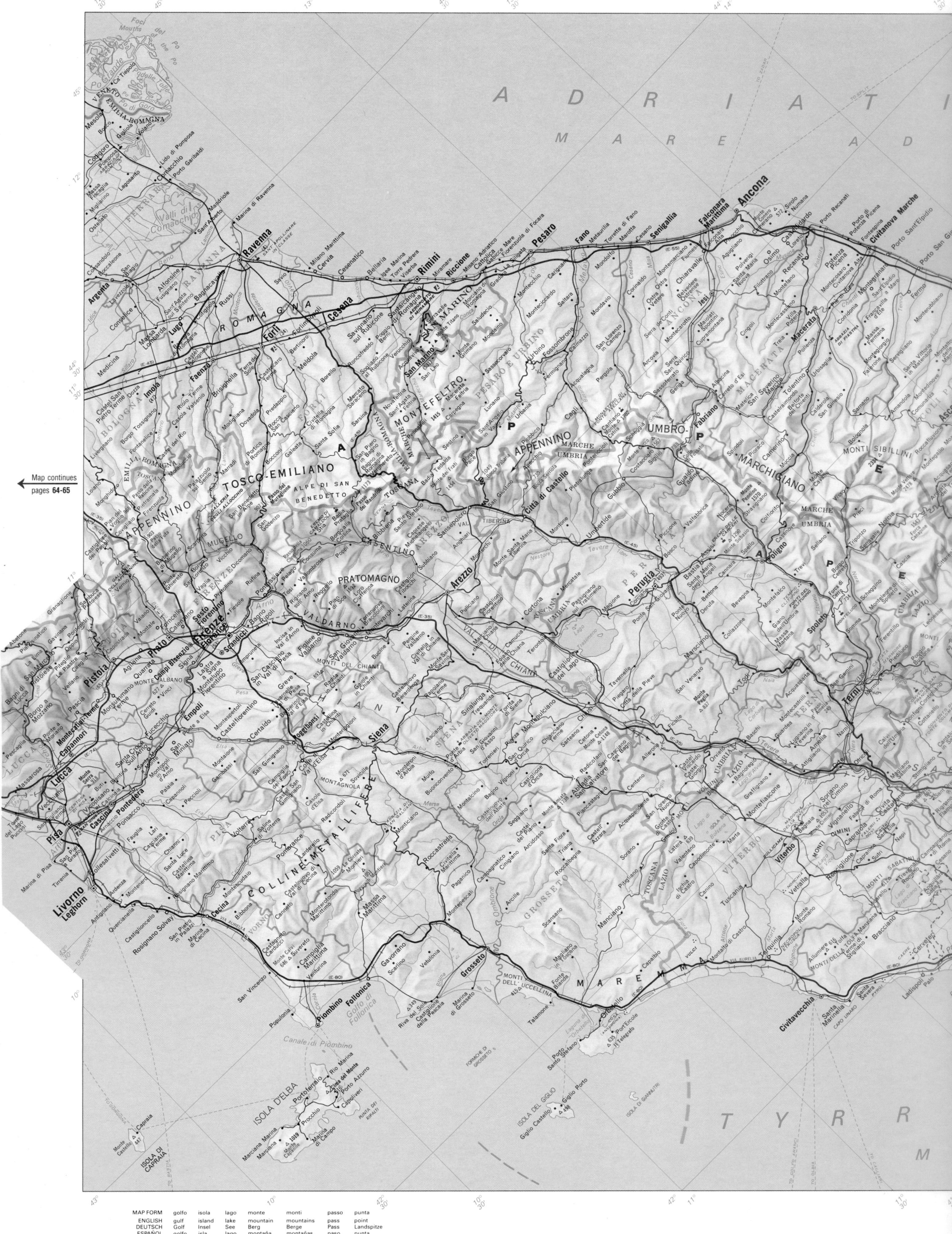

← Map continues pages 64-65

MAP FORM	golfo	isola	lago	monte	monti	passo	punta
ENGLISH	gulf	island	lake	mountain	mountains	pass	point
DEUTSCH	Golf	Insel	See	Berg	Berge	Pass	Landspitze
ESPAÑOL	golfo	isla	lago	montaña	montañas	paso	punta
FRANÇAIS	golfe	île	lac	montagne	montagnes	col	pointe
PORTUGUÊS	golfo	ilha	lago	montanha	montanhas	passo	ponta

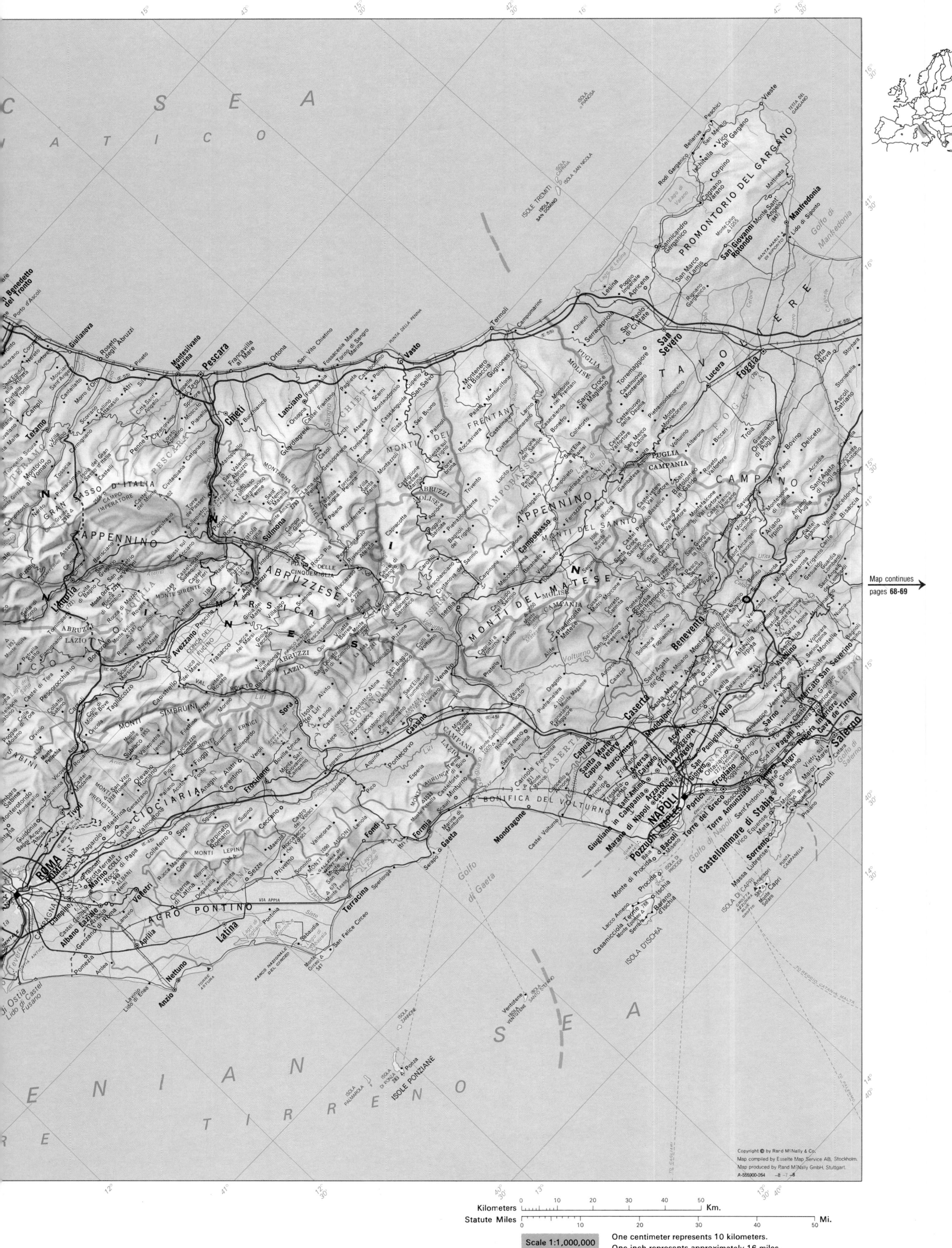

Map continues
pages 68-69

Copyright © by Rand McNally & Co.
Map compiled by Esselte Map Service AB, Stockholm.
Map produced by Rand McNally GmbH, Stuttgart.
A-585900-264

Kilometers
Statute Miles

Scale 1:1,000,000   One centimeter represents 10 kilometers.
One inch represents approximately 16 miles.
Lambert Conformal Conic Projection

← Map continues pages 66-67

MAP FORM	capo	golfo	isola	lago	monte	monti	punta
ENGLISH	cape	gulf	island	lake	mountain	mountains	point
DEUTSCH	Kap	Golf	Insel	See	Berg	Berge	Landspitze
ESPAÑOL	cabo	golfo	isla	lago	montaña	montañas	punta
FRANÇAIS	cap	golfe	île	lac	montagne	montagnes	pointe
PORTUGUÊS	cabo	golfo	ilha	lago	montanha	montanhas	ponta

Strait of Otranto

Golfo
di
Taranto

PENISOLA SALENTINA

Lecce
Galatina
Nardò
Copertino

MURGE

IONIAN SEA
MARE IONIO

MARE
TIRRENO

Ciro Marina

Crotone

CAPO COLONNA

SILA GRANDE

COSENZA

Cosenza

SILA PICCOLA

Catanzaro

Golfo di
Squillace

Nicastro

Golfo di
Sant'Eufemia

Golfo
di Gioia

Reggio
di Calabria

CALABRIA
SICILIA

Messina

SICILIA

Map continues
page 70

Kilometers   0 10 20 30 40 50   Km.
Statute Miles 0   10   20   30   40   50   Mi.

Scale 1:1,000,000
One centimeter represents 10 kilometers.
One inch represents approximately 16 miles.
Lambert Conformal Conic Projection

Map continues
pages 68-69

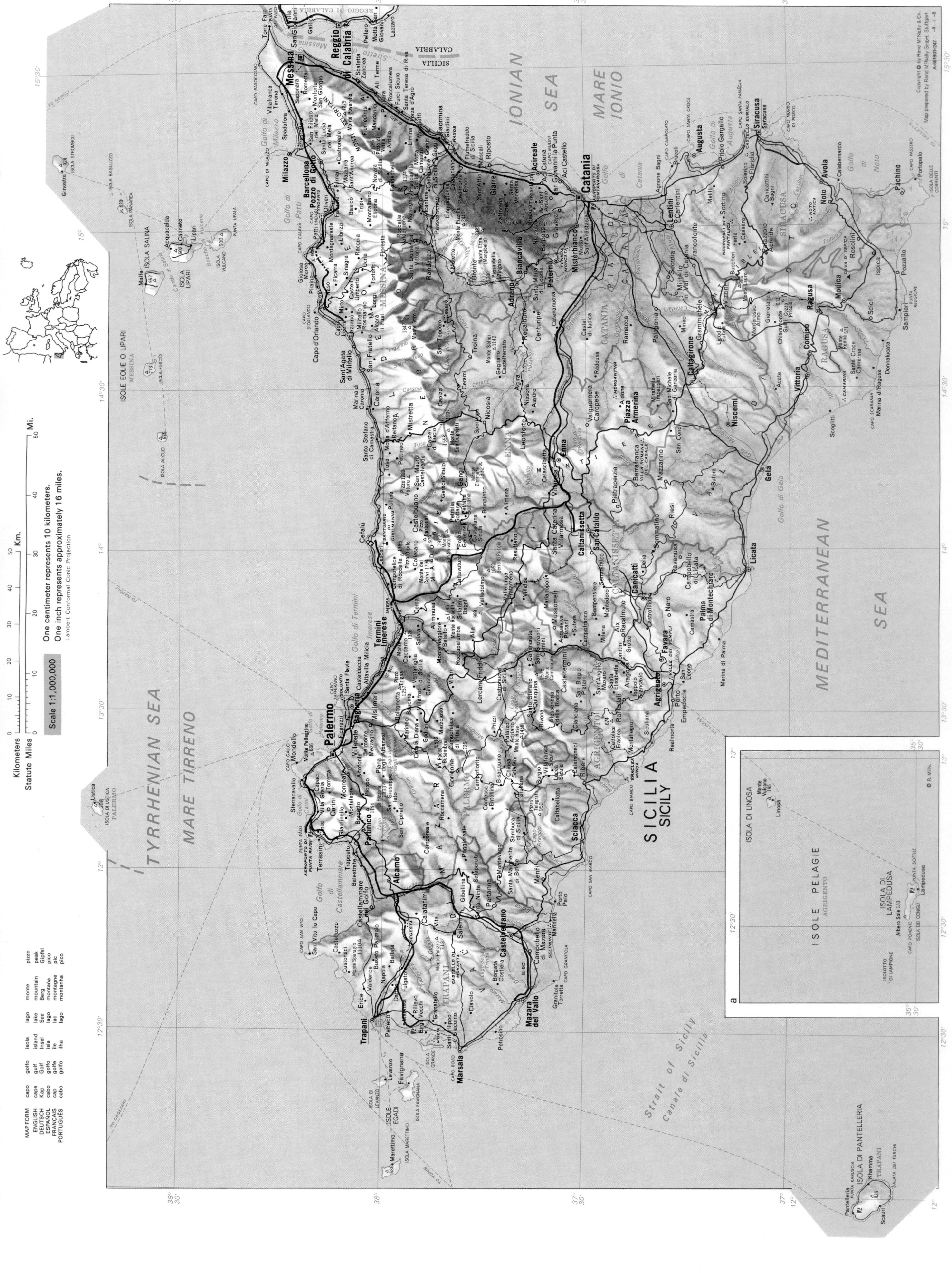

Kilometers

Statute Miles

Mi.
Km.

One centimeter represents 10 kilometers.
One inch represents approximately 16 miles.
Lambert Conformal Conic Projection

Scale 1:1,000,000

MAP FORM				
ENGLISH	capo	golfo	isola	lago	monte	pizzo
DEUTSCH	cape	gulf	island	lake	mountain	peak
ESPAÑOL	Kap	Golf	Insel	See	Berg	Gipfel
FRANÇAIS	cabo	golfo	isla	lago	montaña	pico
PORTUGUÊS	cabo	golfe	île	lac	montagne	pic
	cabo	golfo	ilha	lago	montanha	pico

TYRRHENIAN SEA

MARE TIRRENO

ISOLE EOLIE O LIPARI

ISOLA STROMBOLI

ISOLA SALINA
ISOLA LIPARI
ISOLA VULCANO

ISOLA DI USTICA
USTICA

Palermo
Mondello
Termini Imerese
Bagheria

Milazzo
Barcellona
Pozzo di Gotto
Messina

REGGIO DI CALABRIA
Reggio di Calabria

CALABRIA
SICILIA

IONIAN SEA
MARE IONIO

Catania
Acireale
Giarre
Taormina

Siracusa
Augusta
Lentini

Avola
Noto
Pachino

Paternò
Adrano
Biancavilla
Misterbianco

Enna
Caltanissetta
Piazza Armerina
Caltagirone

Ragusa
Modica
Comiso
Vittoria
Niscemi
Gela

SICILIA
SICILY

Agrigento
Favara
Canicattì
Licata

Sciacca
Mazara del Vallo
Marsala
Trapani
Erice
Alcamo
Castelvetrano

MEDITERRANEAN SEA

Strait of Sicily
Canale di Sicilia

Cefalù

ISOLE PELAGIE

ISOLA DI LINOSA
Linosa
Monte Vulcano

ISOLA DI LAMPEDUSA
Lampedusa

Pantelleria
ISOLA DI PANTELLERIA

Copyright © by Rand McNally & Co.
Map prepared by Rand McNally GmbH, Stuttgart

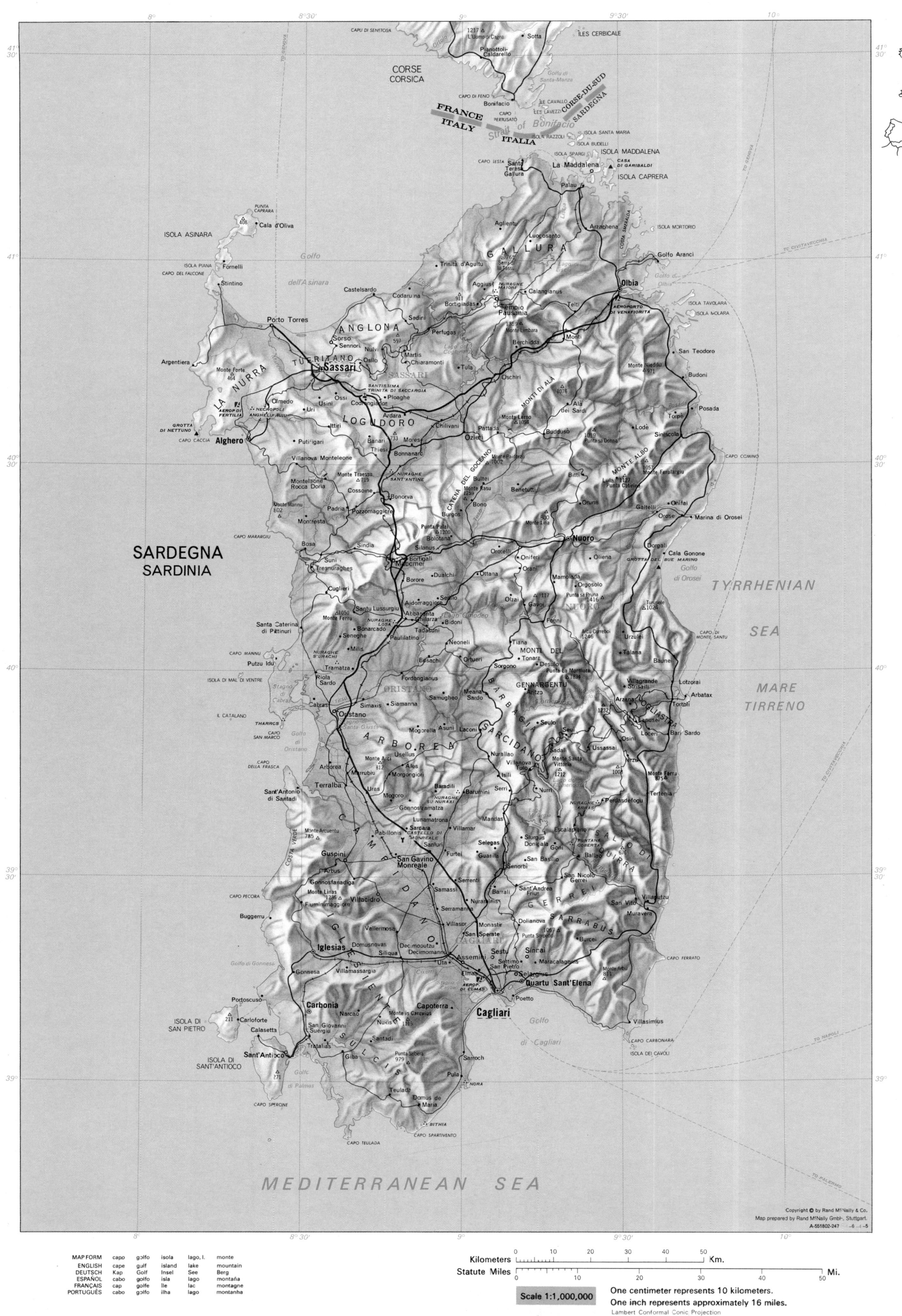

SARDEGNA
SARDINIA

TYRRHENIAN
SEA

MARE
TIRRENO

MEDITERRANEAN SEA

MAP FORM	capo	golfo	isola	lago, l.	monte
ENGLISH	cape	gulf	island	lake	mountain
DEUTSCH	Kap	Golf	Insel	See	Berg
ESPAÑOL	cabo	golfo	isla	lago	montaña
FRANÇAIS	cap	golfe	île	lac	montagne
PORTUGUÊS	cabo	golfo	ilha	lago	montanha

Kilometers 0 10 20 30 40 50 Km.
Statute Miles 0 10 20 30 40 50 Mi.

Scale 1:1,000,000   One centimeter represents 10 kilometers.
One inch represents approximately 16 miles.
Lambert Conformal Conic Projection

← Map continues pages **22-23**

← Map continues pages **118-119**

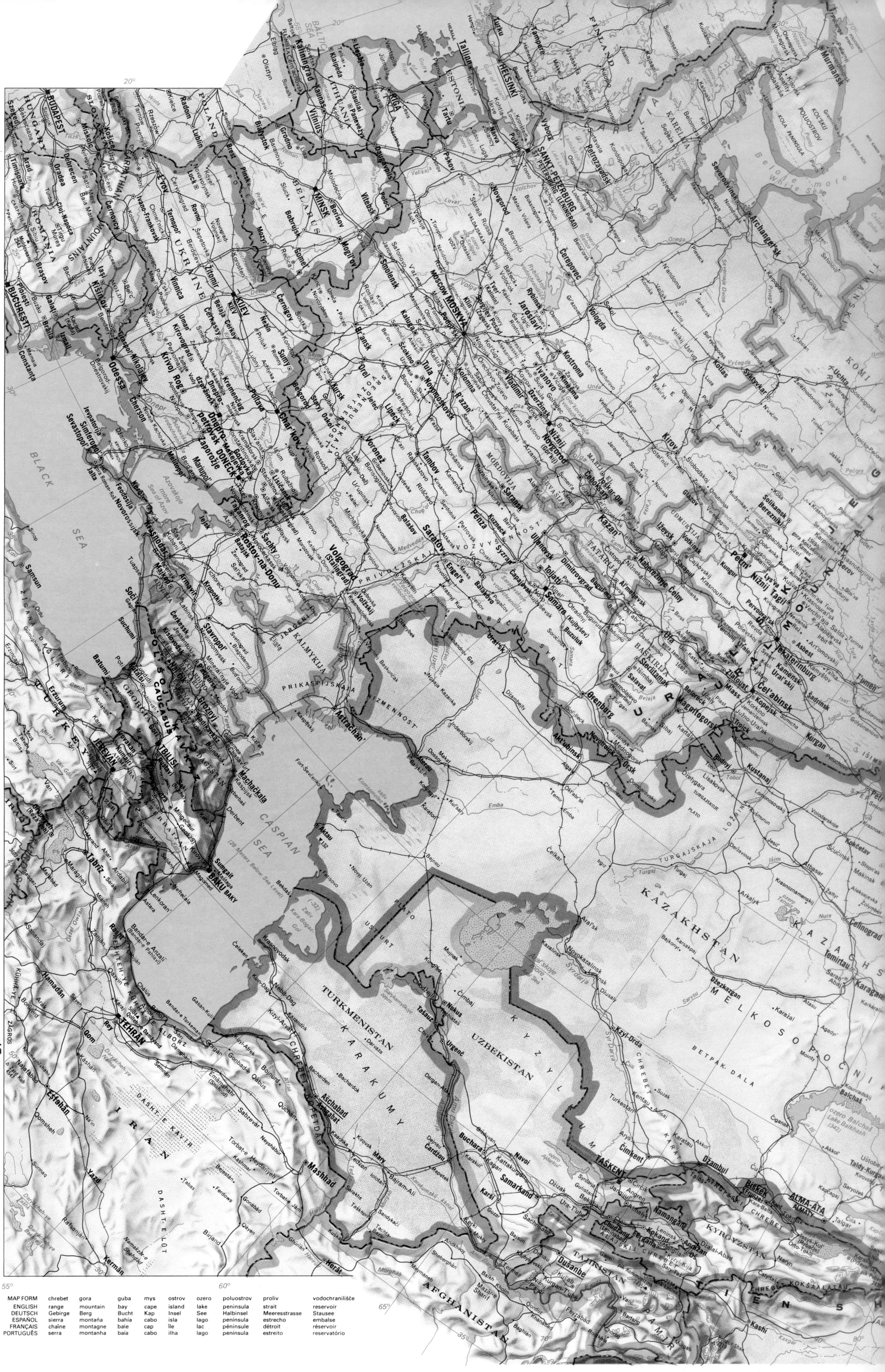

MAP FORM	chrebet	gora	guba	mys	ostrov	ozero	poluostrov	proliv	vodochranilišče
ENGLISH	range	mountain	bay	cape	island	lake	peninsula	strait	reservoir
DEUTSCH	Gebirge	Berg	Bucht	Kap	Insel	See	Halbinsel	Meeresstrasse	Stausee
ESPAÑOL	sierra	montaña	bahía	cabo	isla	lago	península	estrecho	embalse
FRANÇAIS	chaîne	montagne	baie	cap	île	lac	péninsule	détroit	réservoir
PORTUGUÊS	serra	montanha	baia	cabo	ilha	lago	península	estreito	reservatório

Map continues
pages 74-75

Map continues
pages 90-91

Kilometers
Statute Miles

Scale 1:12,000,000

One centimeter represents 120 kilometers.
One inch represents approximately 190 miles.
Lambert Conformal Conic Projection

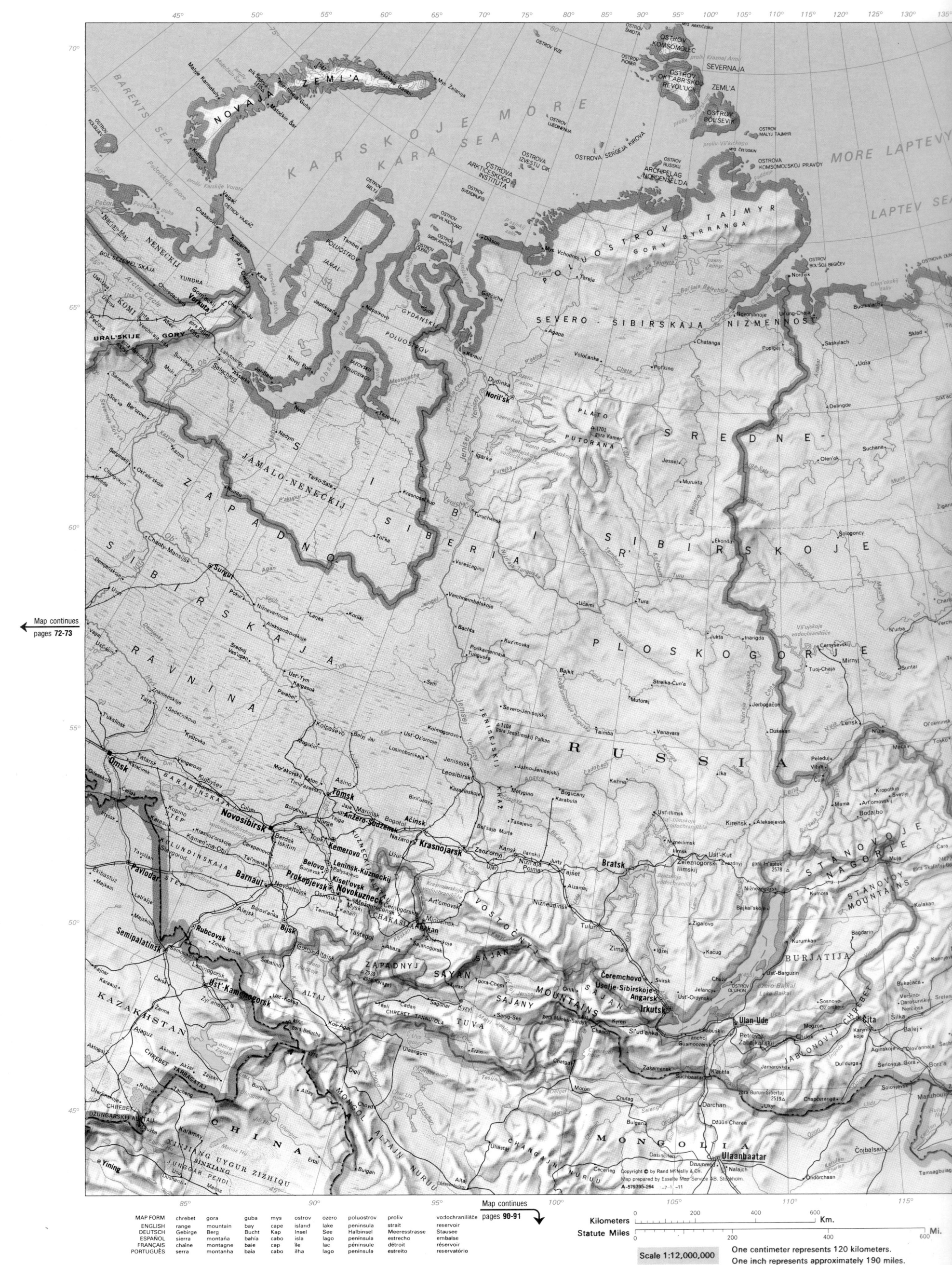

← Map continues
  pages 72-73

Map continues
pages 90-91 ↓

MAP FORM	chrebet	gora	guba	mys	ostrov	ozero	poluostrov	proliv	vodochranilišče
ENGLISH	range	mountain	bay	cape	island	lake	peninsula	strait	reservoir
DEUTSCH	Gebirge	Berg	Bucht	Kap	Insel	See	Halbinsel	Meeresstrasse	Stausee
ESPAÑOL	sierra	montaña	bahía	cabo	isla	lago	península	estrecho	embalse
FRANÇAIS	chaîne	montagne	baie	cap	île	lac	péninsule	détroit	réservoir
PORTUGUÊS	serra	montanha	baía	cabo	ilha	lago	península	estreito	reservatório

Kilometers

Statute Miles

Scale 1:12,000,000

One centimeter represents 120 kilometers.
One inch represents approximately 190 miles.

Lambert Conformal Conic Projection

ALASKA
UNITED STATES

Chukchi Sea

Bering Sea

Bering Strait

SAINT LAWRENCE ISLAND

NUNIVAK ISLAND

OSTROVA

OSTROVA ANŽU

OSTROV KOTEL'NYJ

VOSTOČNO-SIBIRSKOJE MORE

EAST SIBERIAN SEA

OSTROV NOVAJA SIBIR'

OSTROV VRANGEL'A

proliv Longa

SIBIRSKIJE OSTROVA

L'ACHOVSKIJE OSTROVA

Janskij zaliv

KOLYMSKAJA NIZMENNOST'

AN'UJSKIJ CHREBET

EKIATAPSKIJ CHREBET

ANADYRSKOJE

BLOSKOGORJE

JAKUTIJA

SIBERIA

CHREBET

CHREBET ČERSKOGO

MOMSKIJ CHREBET

JUKAGIRSKOJE

LOSKOGORJE

Verchjansk

Jakutsk

Lena

CHREBET SUNTAR-CHAJATA

CHREBET SETE-DABAN

PENŽINSKIJ CHREBET

KORAKSKOJE NAGORJE

SREDINNYJ CHREBET

KOMANDORSKIJE OSTROVA

Magadan

ALDANSKOJE NAGORJE

CHREBET DŽUGDŽUR

Ochotsk

POLUOSTROV KAMČATKA

KAMČATKA

Petropavlovsk-Kamčatskij

STANOVOJ CHREBET

Ajan

SEA OF OKHOTSK

OCHOTSKOJE MORE

Aldan

Tyndinskij

Skovorodino

Komsomol'sk na-Amure

Svobodnyj

OSTROV SACHALIN

SACHALIN

KURIL'SKIJE OSTROVA

KURIL ISLANDS

Pervyj Kuril'skij proliv

Severo-Kuril'sk

OSTROV PARAMUŠIR

OSTROV ONEKOTAN

OSTROV ŠIAŠKOTAN

OSTROV ŠIMUŠIR

OSTROV SIMUŠIR

OSTROV KETOJ

OSTROV URUP

proliv Frizа

OSTROV ITURUP

Kuril'sk

OSTROV KUNAŠIR

proliv Jekaterina

Belogorsk

Blagoveščensk

SICHOTE-ALIN'

BUREINSKIJ CHREBET

Chabarovsk

JEVREJ

Uglegorsk

Sovetskaja Gavan'

Južno-Sachalinsk

Birobidžan

DA HINGGAN LING

NEI MONGGOL ZIZHIQU

MONGOLIA

HEILONGJIANG

Bei'an

Yichun

Hegang

Jiamusi

Shuangyashan

Qiqihar Tsitsihar

MANCHURIA

CHINA

Harbin

La Perouse Strait

Wakkanai

Monbetsu

Asahikawa

Kushiro

Obihiro

HOKKAIDO

Otaru

Sapporo

Tomakomai

Muroran

Hakodate

Mudanjiang

Art'om

Ussurijsk

Nachodka

Vladivostok

Petra Velikogo

JILIN

SEA OF JAPAN

Aomori

Hachinohe

Hirosaki

Akita

Morioka

Miyako

JAPAN

HONSHŪ

PACIFIC OCEAN

Habomai, Shikotan, Kunashiri, and Etorofu, occupied since 1945, are claimed by Japan pending a final peace treaty.

Map continues
pages 26-27

Map continues
pages 30-31

MAP FORM	gr'ada	ostrov, o.	ozero, o.	vodochranilišče, vdchr.	vozvyšennost', vozv.	zaliv	zapovednik, zapov.
ENGLISH	ridge	island	lake	reservoir	upland	gulf; bay	reserve
DEUTSCH	Höhenrücken	Insel	See	Stausee	Bergland	Golf; Bucht	Reservat
ESPAÑOL	lomerío	isla	lago	embalse	tierras altas	golfo; bahía	reserva
FRANÇAIS	crête	île	lac	réservoir	hautes terres	golfe; baie	réserve
PORTUGUÊS	cordilheira	ilha	lago	reservatório	terras altas	golfo; baía	reserva

Baltic and Moscow Regions / Baltenland und Mittelrussland / Regiones de Báltico y de Moscú
Républiques Baltes et la Région de Moscou / Regiões do Báltico e de Moscou

77

Map continues
pages 24-25

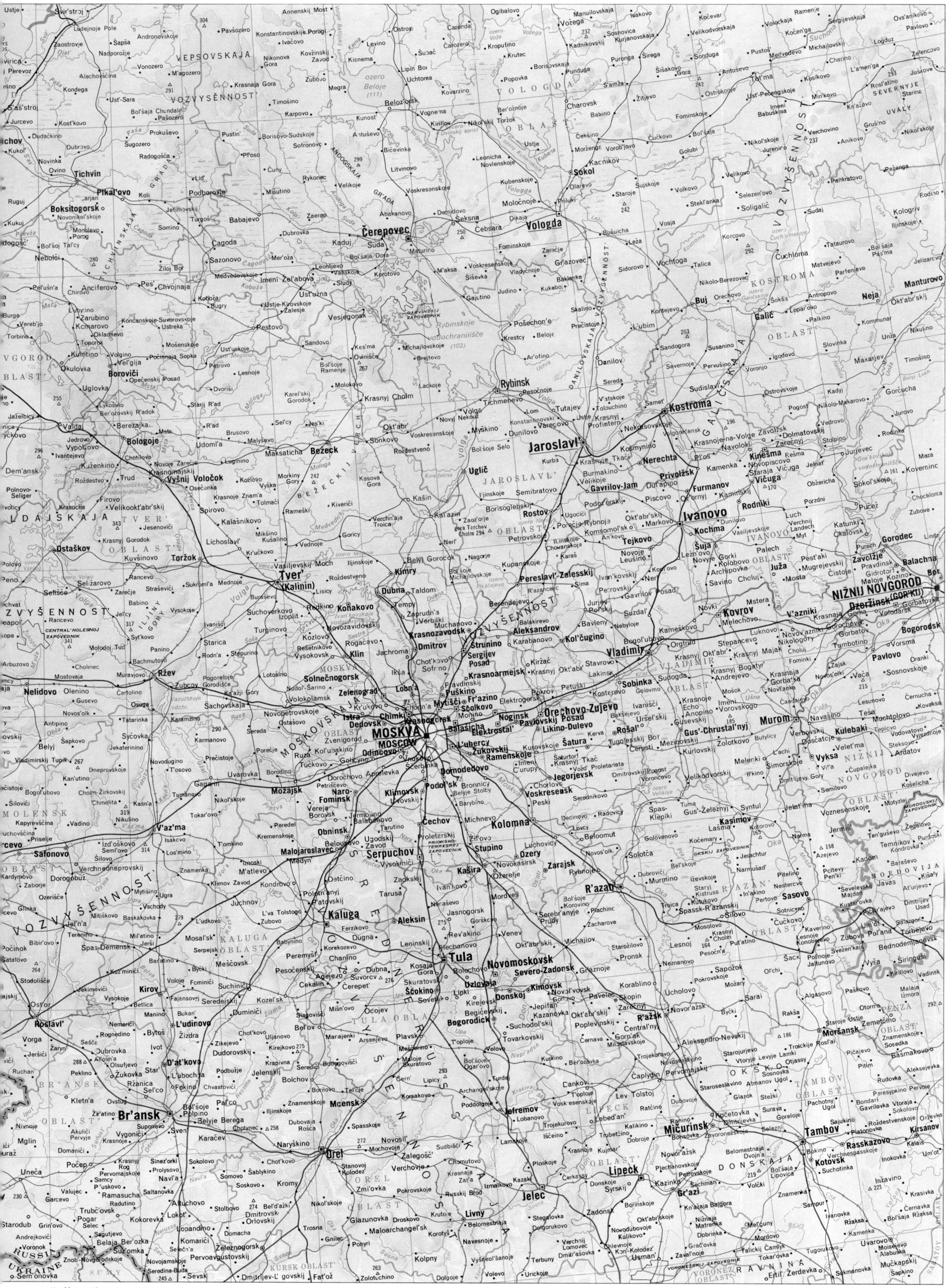

Map continues
pages 80-81

Map continues
pages 78-79

Kilometers
Statute Miles

Scale 1:3,000,000

One centimeter represents 30 kilometers.
One inch represents approximately 47 miles.

Lambert Conformal Conic Projection

Ukraine / Ukraine / Ucrania
Ukraine / Ucrânia

Map continues
pages 30-31

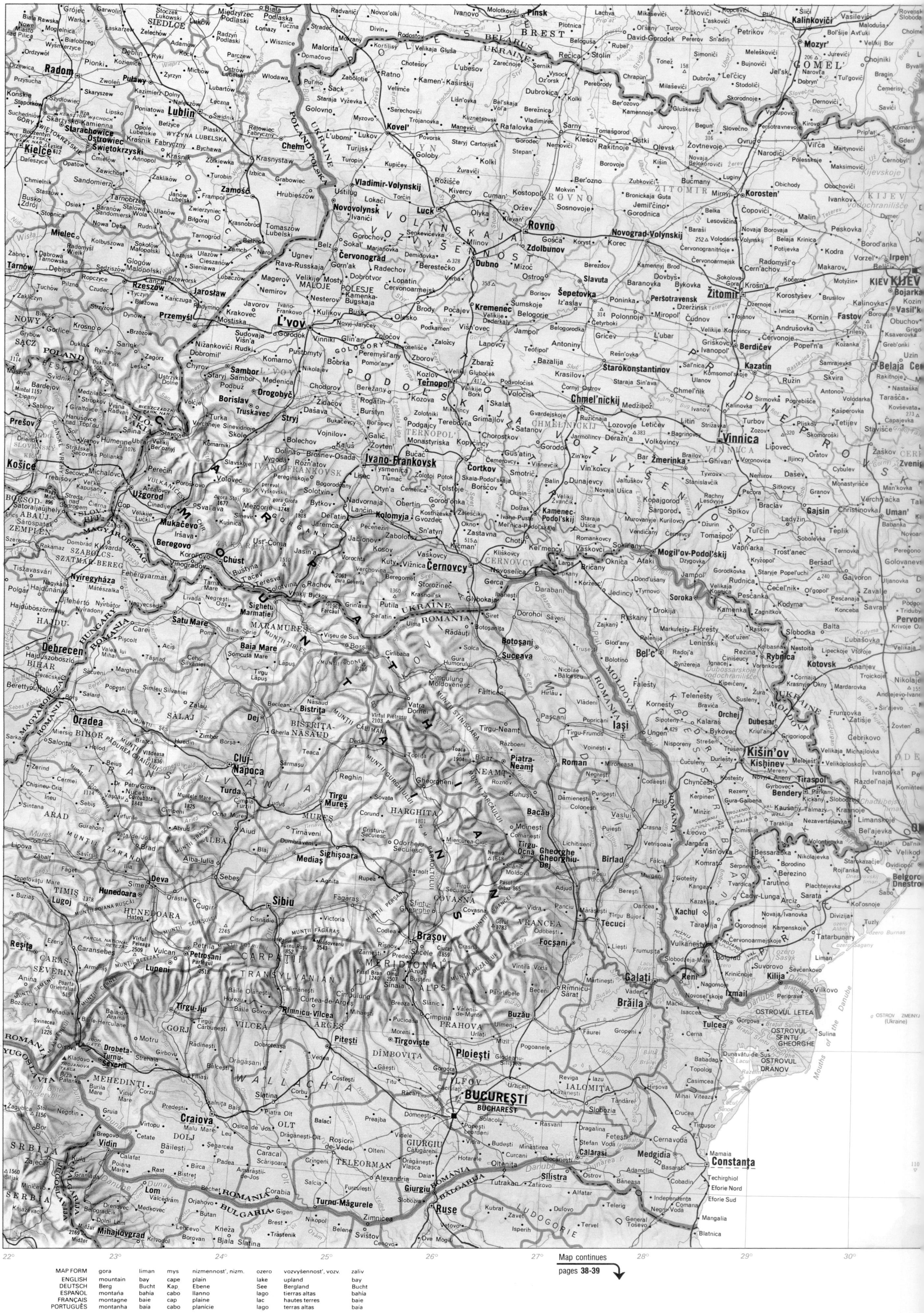

Map continues
pages 38-39

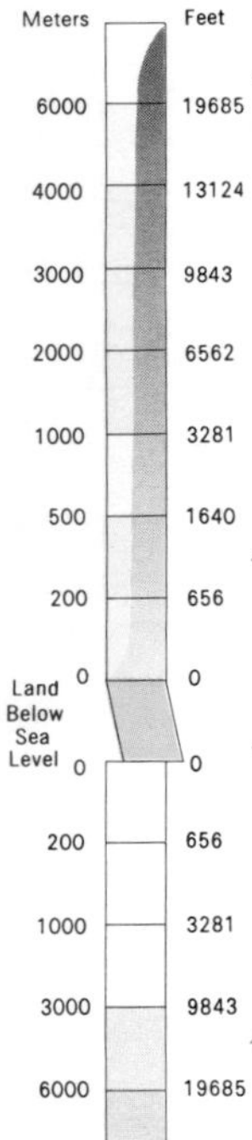

	Meters	Feet
	6000	19685
	4000	13124
	3000	9843
	2000	6562
	1000	3281
	500	1640
	200	656
Land Below Sea Level	0	0
	0	0
	200	656
	1000	3281
	3000	9843
	6000	19685
	9000	29520

MAP FORM	gora	liman	mys	nizmennost', nizm.	ozero	vozvyšennost', vozv.	zaliv
ENGLISH	mountain	bay	cape	plain	lake	upland	bay
DEUTSCH	Berg	Bucht	Kap	Ebene	See	Bergland	Bucht
ESPAÑOL	montaña	bahía	cabo	llano	lago	tierras altas	bahía
FRANÇAIS	montagne	baie	cap	plaine	lac	hautes terres	baie
PORTUGUÊS	montanha	baía	cabo	planície	lago	terras altas	baía

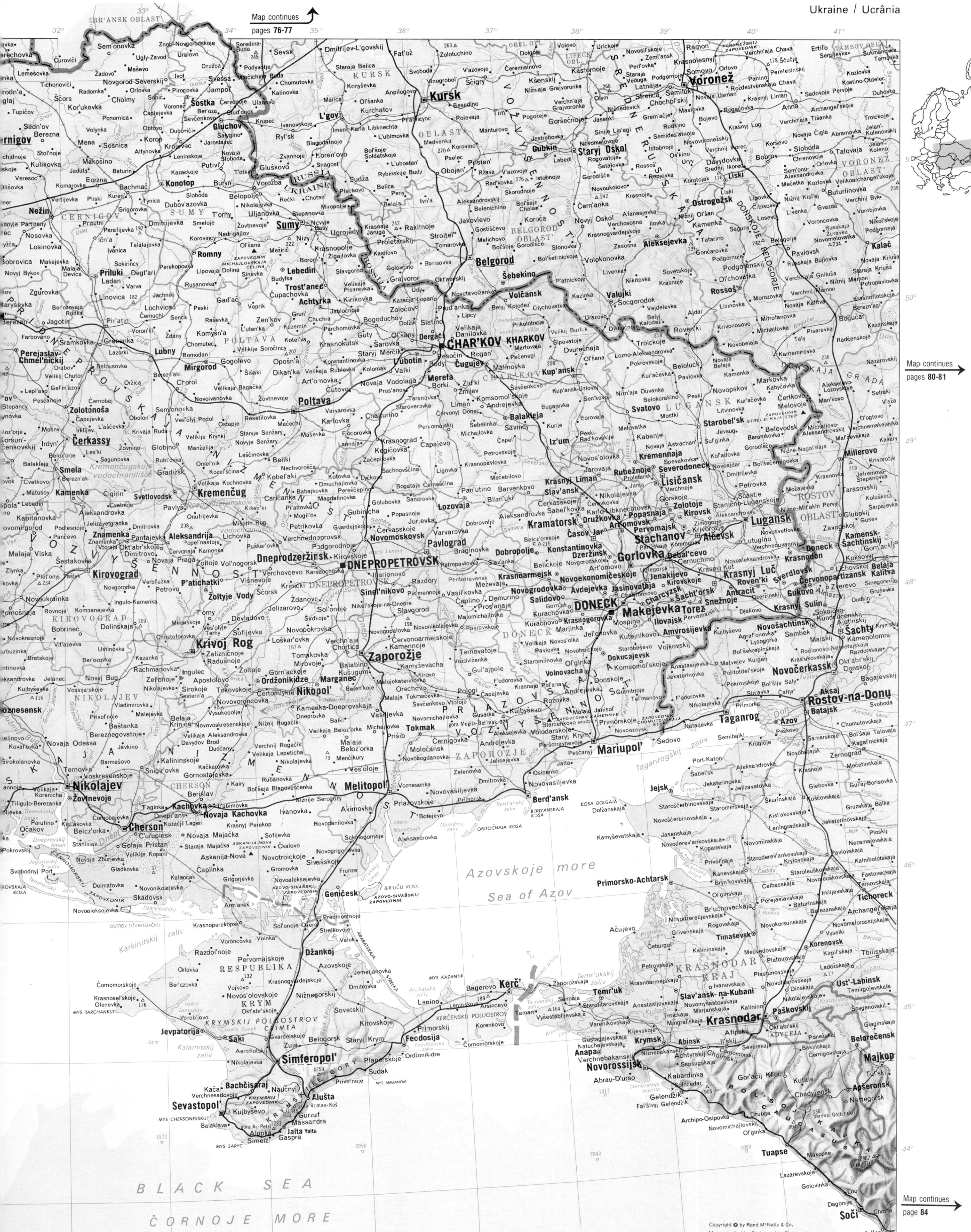

Map continues
pages 76-77

Map continues
pages 80-81

Map continues
page 84

Major labels

KURSK OBLAST

BELGOROD OBLAST

VORONEZ OBLAST

DONSKAJA GRADA

ROSTOV OBLAST

KRASNODAR KRAJ

RUSSIA
UKRAINE

CERNIGOV
SUMY
POLTAVA
CHARKOV
LUGANSK
DONECK
DNEPROPETROVSK
KIROVOGRAD
NIKOLAJEV
CHERSON
ZAPOROZJE
PRIAZOVSKAJA VOZVYSENNOST
PRICERNOMORSKAJA NIZMENNOST
RESPUBLIKA KRYM
KRYMSKIJ POLUOSTROV / CRIMEA
KRYMSKIJE GORY
ADYGEJA
KAVKAZ

Cities

Voronez
Kursk
Staryj Oskol
Belgorod
Sumy
Romny
Priluki
Lebedin
CHAR'KOV KHARKOV
Kup'ansk
Poltava
Mirgorod
Čerkassy
Kremenčug
Svatovo
Starobel'sk
Lisičansk
Severodoneck
Lugansk
Stachanov
Alčevsk
Kramatorsk
Gorlovka
Krasnyj Luč
Sverdlovsk
Kirovograd
Dneprodzeržinsk
DNEPROPETROVSK
Pavlograd
Novomoskovsk
Lozovaja
DONECK
Makejevka torez
Amvrosijevka
Krivoj Rog
Nikopol'
Zaporožje
Marganec
Ordžonikidze
Volnovacha
Novočerkassk
Rostov-na-Donu
Taganrog
Azov
Nikolajev
Cherson
Melitopol'
Berd'ansk
Mariupol'
Primorsko-Achtarsk
Jejsk
Tichoreck
Novaja Kachkovka
Geničesk
Džankoj
Krasnoperekopsk
Kerč'
Temr'uk
Slav'ansk-na-Kubani
Ust'-Labinsk
Paškovskij
Krasnodar
Belorečensk
Majkop
Jevpatorija
Saki
Simferopol'
Bachčisaraj
Sevastopol'
Feodosija
Sudak
Alušta
Jalta Yalta
Anapa
Novorossijsk
Apšeronsk
Tuapse
Soči

Seas

Azovskoje more
Sea of Azov

BLACK SEA
ČORNOJE MORE

Taganrogskij zaliv

Kalamitskij zaliv

Karkinitskij zaliv

Scale

Kilometers 0 50 100 150 Km.
Statute Miles 0 50 100 150 Mi.

Scale 1:3,000,000
One centimeter represents 30 kilometers.
One inch represents approximately 47 miles.
Lambert Conformal Conic Projection

Copyright © by Rand McNally & Co.
Map compiled by Cartographia, Budapest.
Map produced by Rand McNally & Co.
A-571900-764 -7 -6 -13

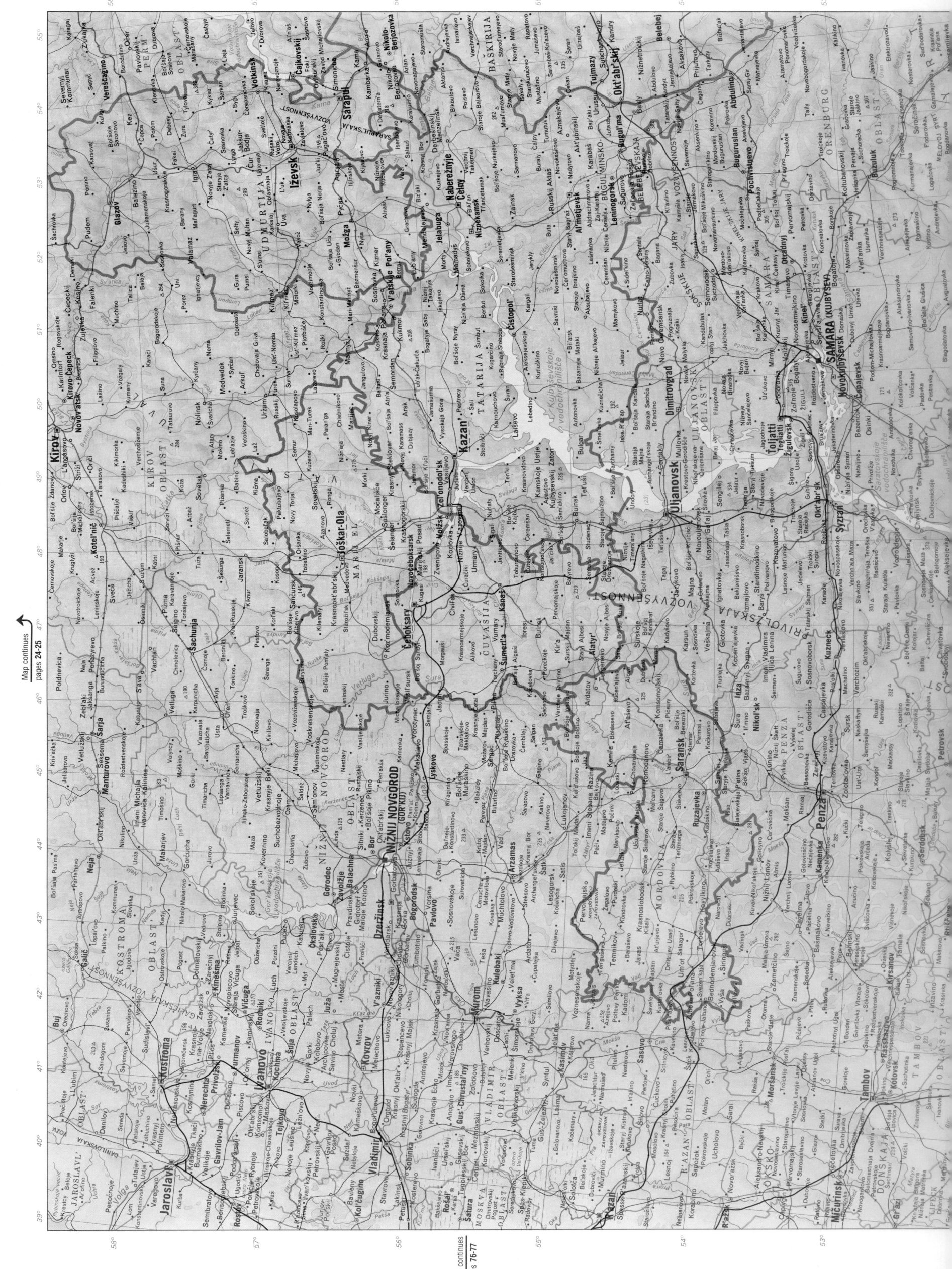

Map continues
pages 24-25

Map continues
pages 76-77

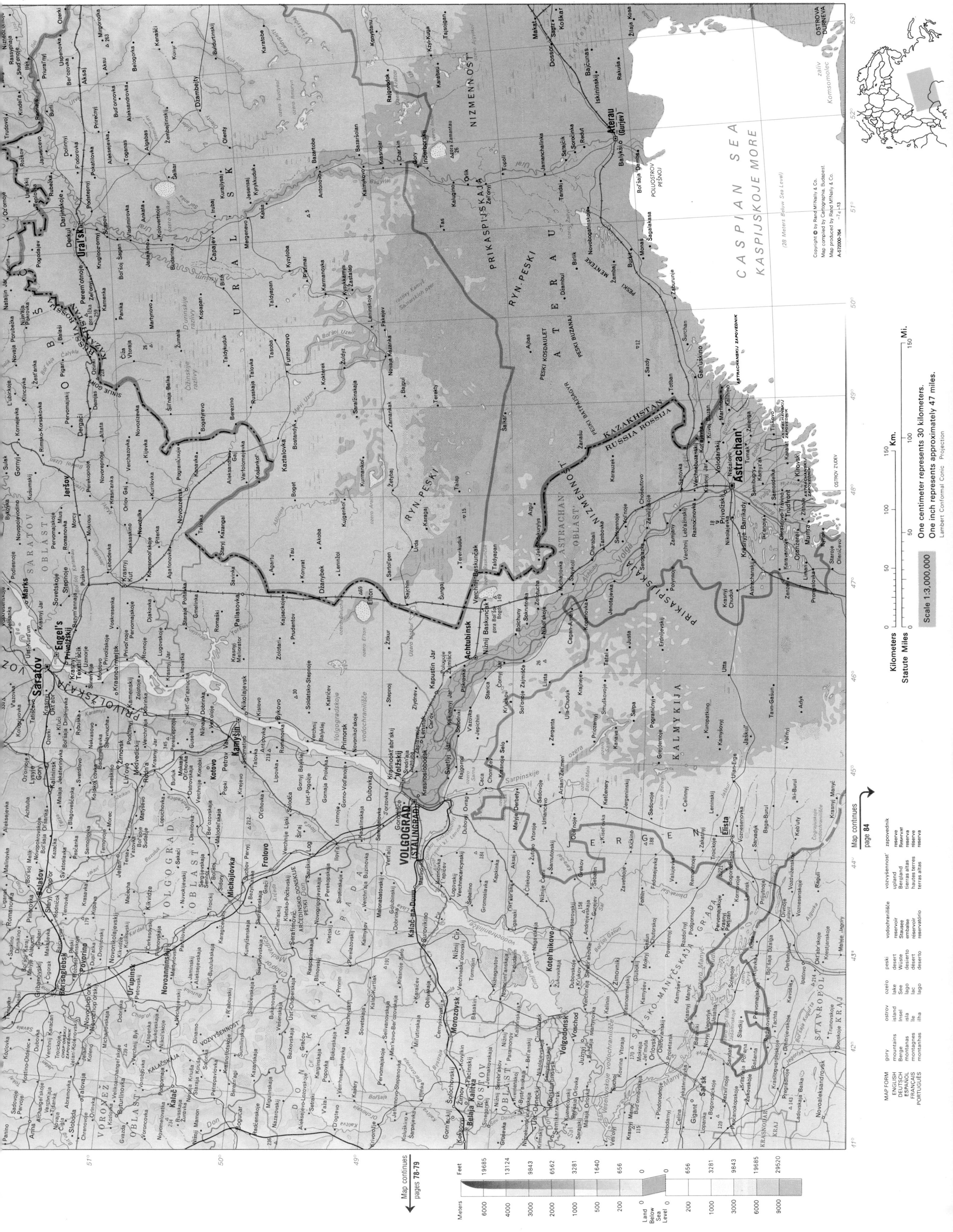

Map continues pages 86-87

Map continues pages 78-79

Map continues page 84

CASPIAN SEA
KASPIJSKOJE MORE

NIZMENNOST

URAL'SK

PRIKASPIJSKAJA

RYN-PESKI

KAZACHSTAN
RUSSIA ROSSIJA

ASTRACHAN' OBLAST'

NIZMENNOST

Atyrau (Gur'ev)

Astrachan'

KALMYKIJA

Elista

SARATOV OBLAST'

PRIVOLŽSKAJA VOZVYŠENNOST'

Saratov

Engel's Pokrovsk

Marks

Jeršov

VOLGOGRAD OBLAST'

VOLGOGRAD STALINGRAD

Kamyšin

Michajlovka

Frolovo

Kalač-na-Donu

Kotel'nikovo

Volgodonsk

Novoanninskij

Uŕjupinsk

Borisoglebsk

Kalač

ROSTOV OBLAST'

Belaja Kalitva

Morozovsk

Sal'sk

KRASNODAR KRAJ

STAVROPOL' KRAJ

VORONEŽ OBLAST'

Achtubinsk

Nižnij Baskunčak

Verchnij Baskunčak

Kapustin Jar

Volžskij

Primorsk

Ural'sk

OSTROVA DURNEVA

POLUOSTROV PEŠNOJ

ASTRACHANSKIJ ZAPOVEDNIK

OSTROV ŽDOV

Copyright © by Rand McNally & Co.
Map compiled by Cartographia, Budapest.
Map produced by Rand McNally & Co.
A-07000-764   -74+13

(28 Meters Below Sea Level)

Scale 1:3,000,000

One centimeter represents 30 kilometers.
One inch represents approximately 47 miles.
Lambert Conformal Conic Projection

Kilometers
Statute Miles
Km.
Mi.
0   50   100   150

MAP FORM						
ENGLISH	mountains	island	lake	desert	reservoir	upland	reserve
DEUTSCH	Berge	Insel	See	Wüste	Stausee	Bergland	Reservat
ESPAÑOL	montañas	isla	lago	desierto	embalse	tierras altas	reserva
FRANÇAIS	montagnes	île	lac	désert	réservoir	hautes terres	réserve
PORTUGUÊS	montanhas	ilha	lago	deserto	reservatório	terras altas	reserva
	gory	ostrov	ozero	peski	vodochranilišče	vozvyšennost'	zapovednik

Feet	Meters
19685	6000
13124	4000
9843	3000
6562	2000
3281	1000
1640	500
656	200
Land Below Sea Level	0
0	200
656	1000
3281	3000
9843	6000
19685	9000
29520	

Don

Volga

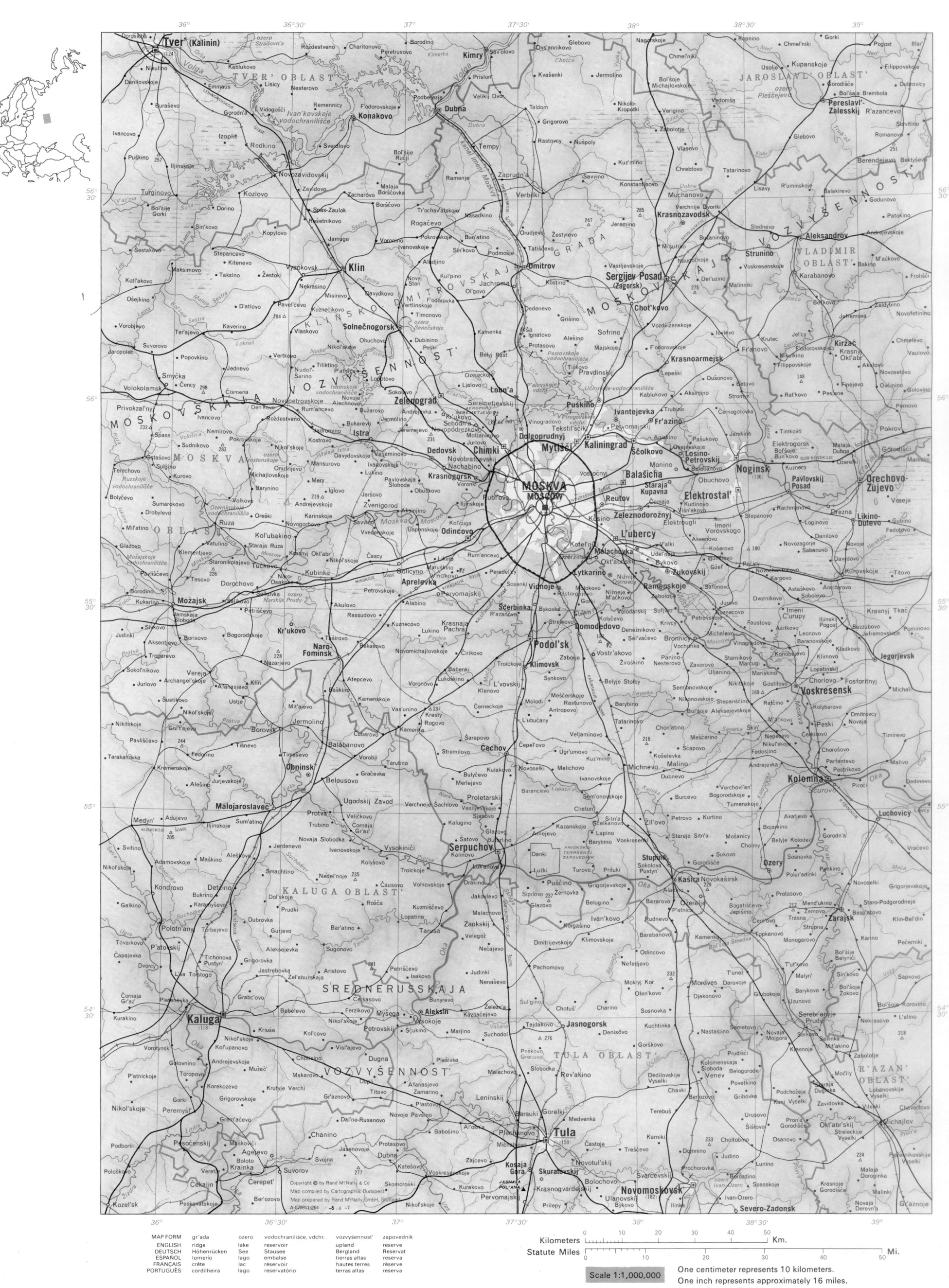

MAP FORM	gr'ada	ozero	vodochranilišče, vdchr.	vozvyšennost'	zapovednik
ENGLISH	ridge	lake	reservoir	upland	reserve
DEUTSCH	Höhenrücken	See	Stausee	Bergland	Reservat
ESPAÑOL	lomerio	lago	embalse	tierras altas	reserva
FRANÇAIS	crête	lac	réservoir	hautes terres	réserve
PORTUGUÊS	cordilheira	lago	reservatório	terras altas	reserva

Kilometers   0 10 20 40 50 Km.
Statute Miles   0   10   20   30   40 50 Mi.

Scale 1:1,000,000   One centimeter represents 10 kilometers.
One inch represents approximately 16 miles.
Lambert Conformal Conic Projection

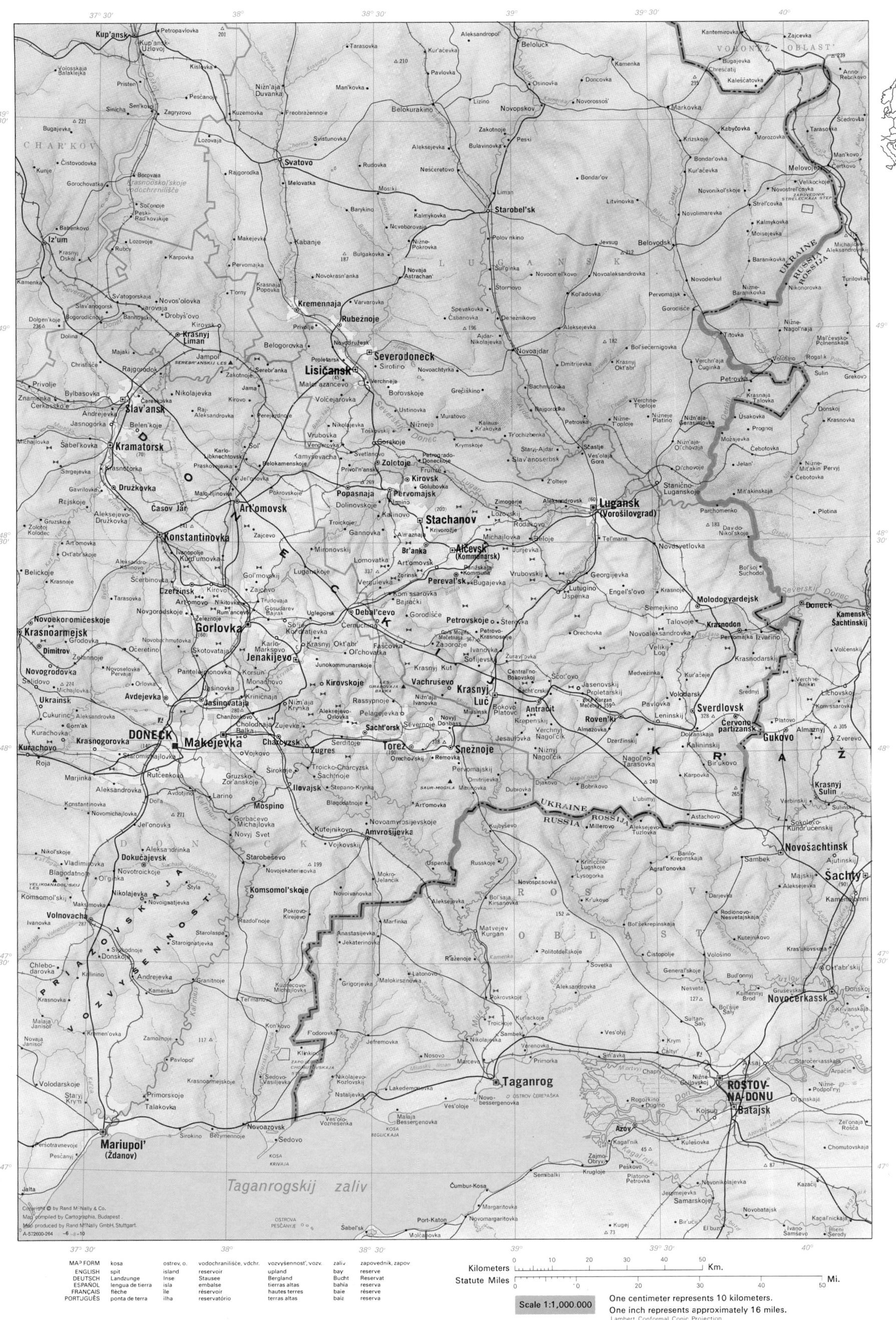

Caucasus and Transcaucasia / Kaukasus und Transkaukasien / Cáucaso y Transcaucasia
Caucasie et Transcaucasie / Cáucaso e Transcaucásia

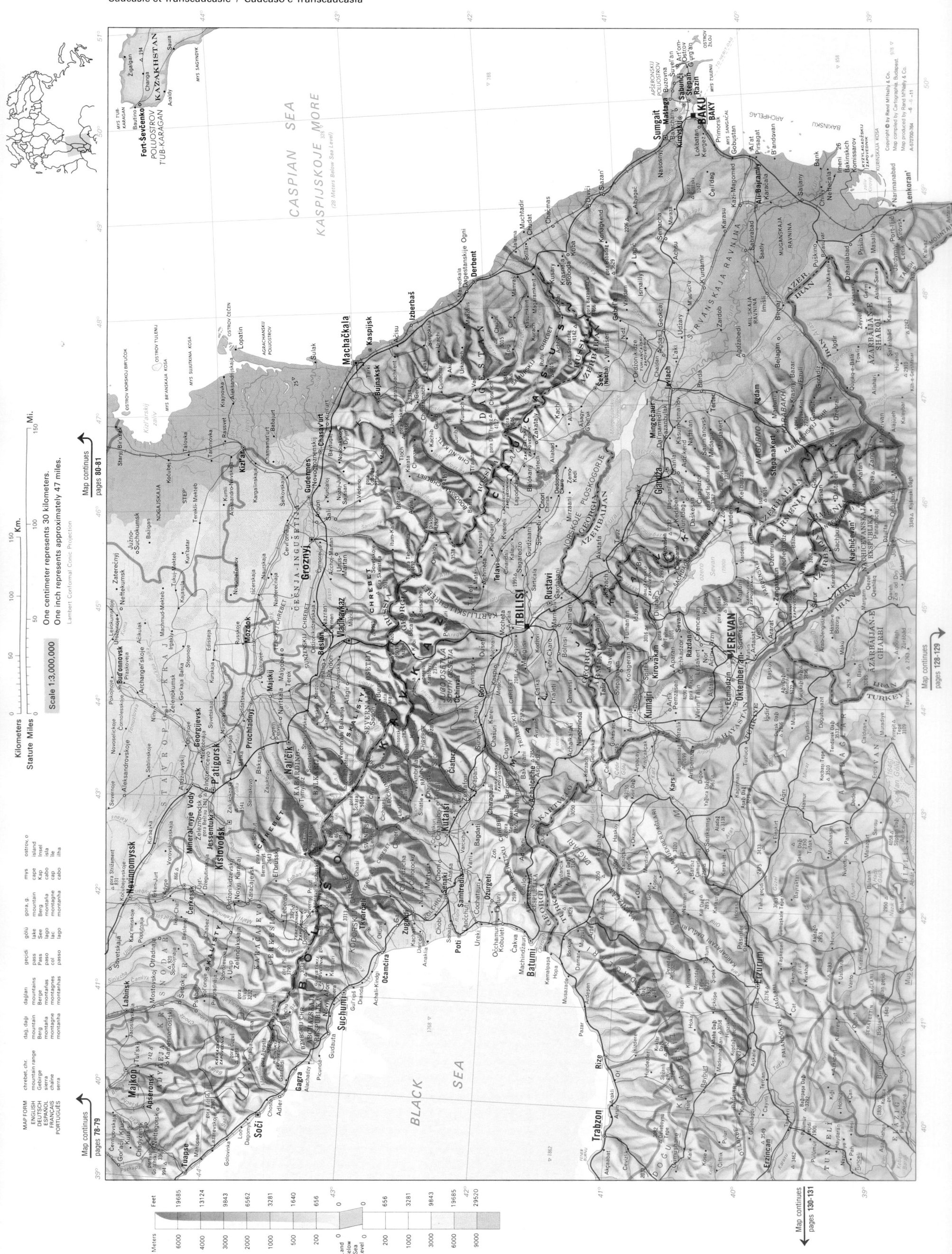

CASPIAN SEA

KASPIJSKOJE MORE

(28 Meters Below Sea Level)

BLACK SEA

BLACK SEA

Map continues pages 80-81

Map continues pages 78-79

Map continues pages 128-129

Map continues pages 130-131

Kilometers

Statute Miles

Scale 1:3,000,000

One centimeter represents 30 kilometers.
One inch represents approximately 47 miles.

Lambert Conformal Conic Projection

BAKU
BAKY

TBILISI

JEREVAN

Machačkala

Groznyj

Majkop

Nevinnomyssk

Suchumi

Batumi

Trabzon

Erzurum

Sumgait

MAP FORM | chrebet, chr. | dag, dağı | dağları | geçidi | gölü | gora, g. | mys | ostrov, o
ENGLISH | mountain range | mountain | mountains | pass | lake | mountain | cape | island
DEUTSCH | Gebirge | Berg | Berge | Pass | See | Berg | Kap | Insel
ESPAÑOL | sierra | montaña | montañas | paso | lago | montaña | cabo | isla
FRANÇAIS | chaîne | montagne | montagnes | col | lac | montagne | cap | île
PORTUGUÊS | serra | montanha | montanhas | passo | lago | montanha | cabo | ilha
Copyright © by Rand McNally & Co.
Map compiled by Cartographia, Budapest.
Map produced by Rand McNally & Co.

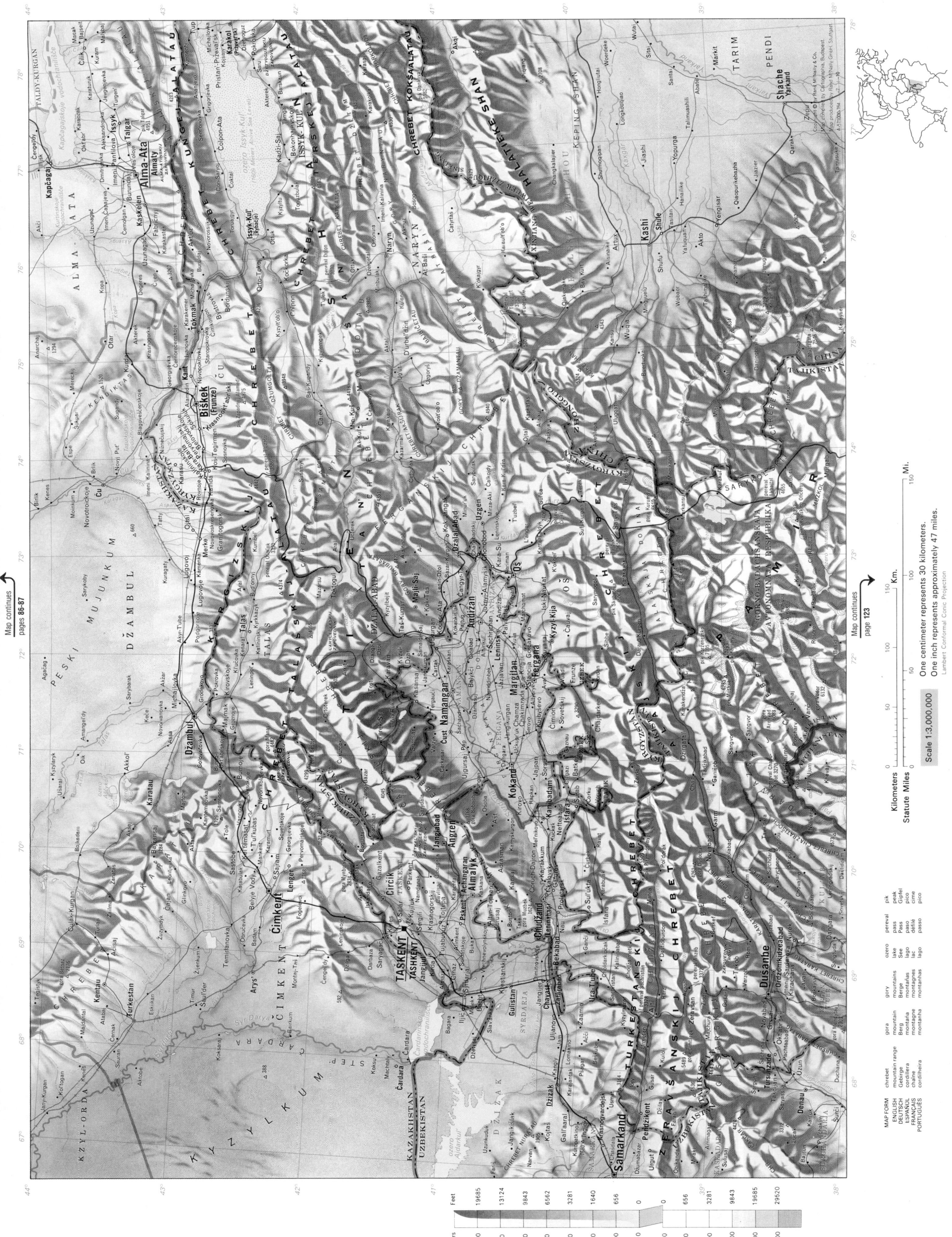

Map continues
pages 86-87

Map continues
page 123

Kilometers
Statute Miles

Scale 1:3,000,000

One centimeter represents 30 kilometers.
One inch represents approximately 47 miles.

Lambert Conformal Conic Projection

MAP FORM					
ENGLISH	mountain range	mountain	mountains	lake	pass	peak
DEUTSCH	Gebirge	Berg	Berge	See	Pass	Gipfel
ESPAÑOL	cordillera	montaña	montañas	lago	paso	pico
FRANÇAIS	chaîne	montagne	montagnes	lac	défilé	cime
PORTUGUÊS	cordilheira	montanha	montanhas	lago	passo	pico
	chrebet	gora	gory	ozero	pereval	pik

Feet
19685
13124
9843
6562
3281
1640
656
0
0
656
3281
9843
19685
29520

Meters
6000
4000
3000
2000
1000
500
200
0
Land
Below
Sea
Level
0
200
1000
3000
6000
9000

86

Central Russia and Kazakhstan / Mittelrussland und Kasachstan / Rusia Central e Kazajstan
Russie Centrale et Kazakhstan / Rússia Central e Casaquistão

Map continues
pages 72-73

Map continues
pages 24-25

Map continues
pages 80-81

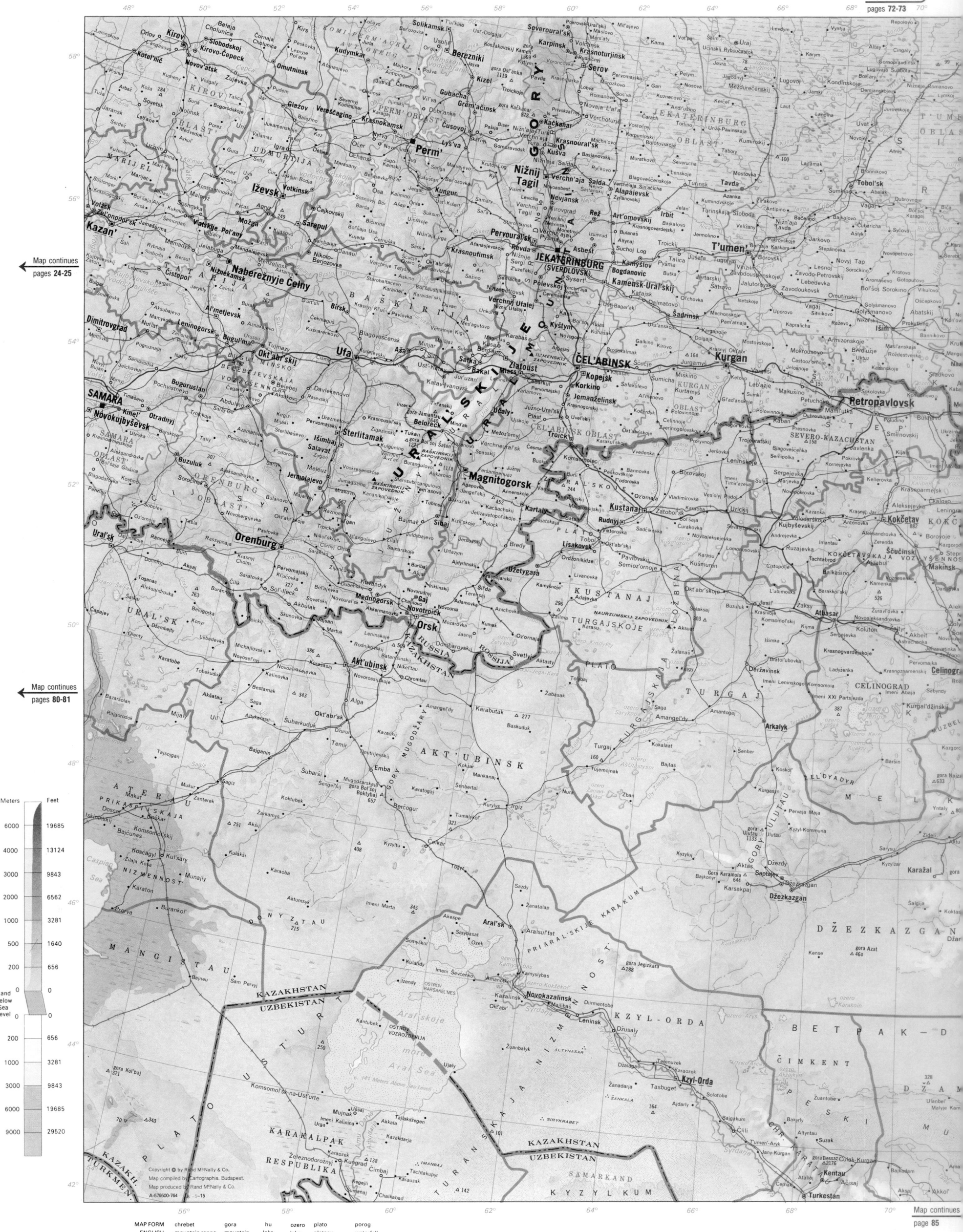

Map continues

page 85

MAP FORM	chrebet	gora	hu	ozero	plato	porog
ENGLISH	mountain range	mountain	lake	lake	plateau	waterfall
DEUTSCH	Gebirge	Berg	See	See	Hochebene	Wasserfall
ESPAÑOL	cordillera	montaña	lago	lago	meseta	cascada
FRANÇAIS	chaîne	montagne	lac	lac	plateau	chute d'eau
PORTUGUÊS	cordilheira	montanha	lago	lago	planalto	queda d'água

Meters | Feet
6000 | 19685
4000 | 13124
3000 | 9843
2000 | 6562
1000 | 3281
500 | 1640
200 | 656
Land Below Sea Level | 0 — 0
200 | 656
1000 | 3281
3000 | 9843
6000 | 19685
9000 | 29520

Central Russia and Kazakhstan / Mittelrussland und Kasachstan / Rusia Central e Kazajstan
Russie Centrale et Kazakhstan / Rússia Central e Casaquistão

87

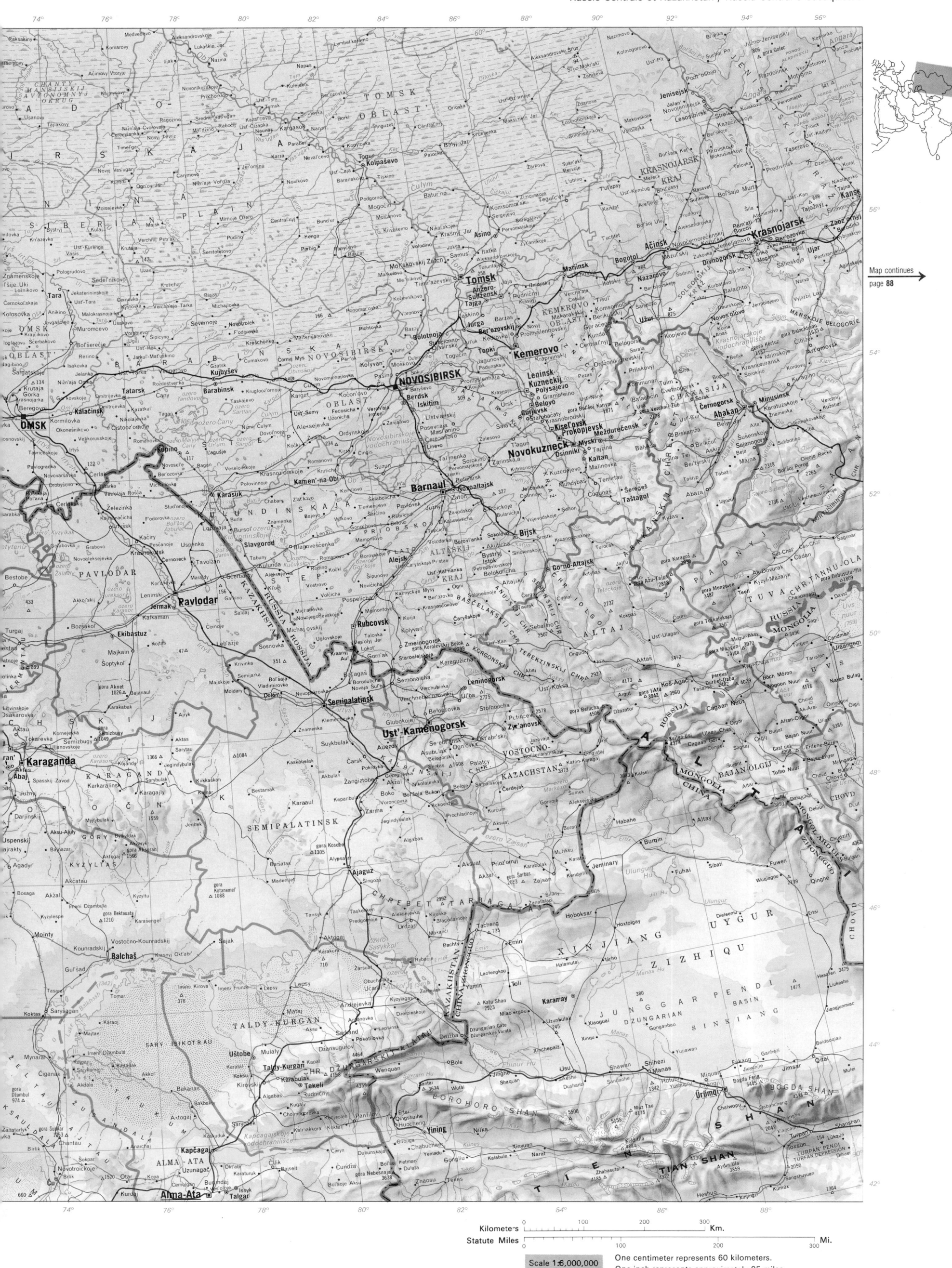

Map continues
page 88

Kilometers 0   100   200   300 Km.

Statute Miles 0   100   200   300 Mi.

Scale 1:6,000,000

One centimeter represents 60 kilometers.
One inch represents approximately 95 miles.

Lambert Conformal Conic Projection

Lake Baikal Region / Baikalseegebiet / Región del Lago Baikal
Région du Lac Baïkal / Região do Lago Baikal

Map continues page 89

Map continues pages 74-75

Map continues pages 102-103

Map continues pages 86-87

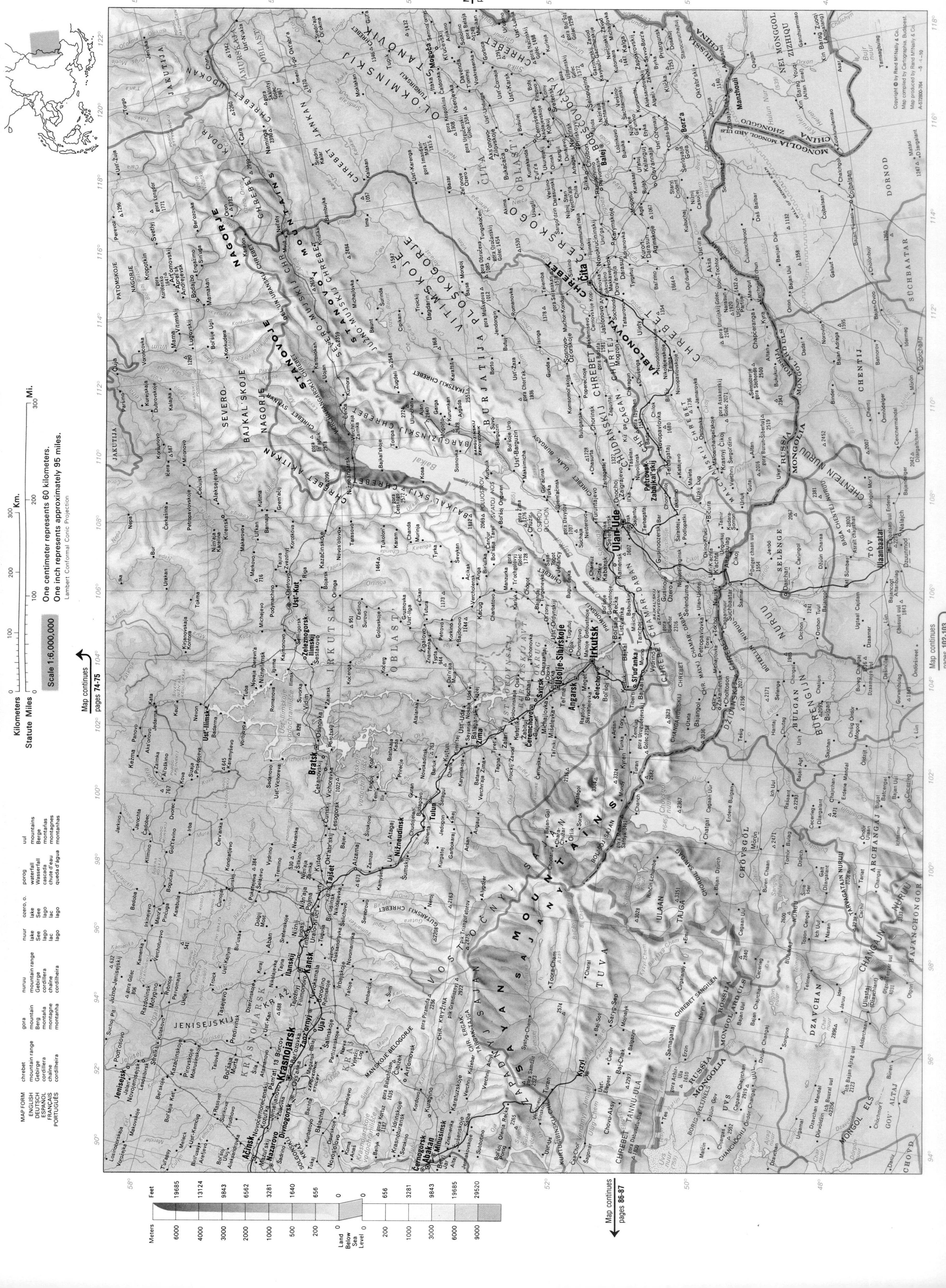

Scale 1:6,000,000

One centimeter represents 60 kilometers.
One inch represents approximately 95 miles.

Lambert Conformal Conic Projection

Kilometers

Statute Miles

Mi.

Km.

MAP FORM				
ENGLISH	chrebet	gora	nuruu	nuur
DEUTSCH	Gebirge	Berg	mountain range	lake
ESPAÑOL	cordillera	montaña	Gebirge	See
FRANÇAIS	chaîne	montagne	cordillera	lago
PORTUGUÊS	cordilheira	montanha	chaîne	lac

ozero, o.	porog	uul
lake	waterfall	mountains
See	Wasserfall	Berge
lago	cascada	montañas
lac	chute d'eau	montagnes
lago	queda d'água	montanhas

Feet
19685
13124
9843
6562
3281
1640
656
0
656
3281
9843
19685
29520

Meters
6000
4000
3000
2000
1000
500
200
0
200
1000
3000
6000
9000

Land Below Sea Level

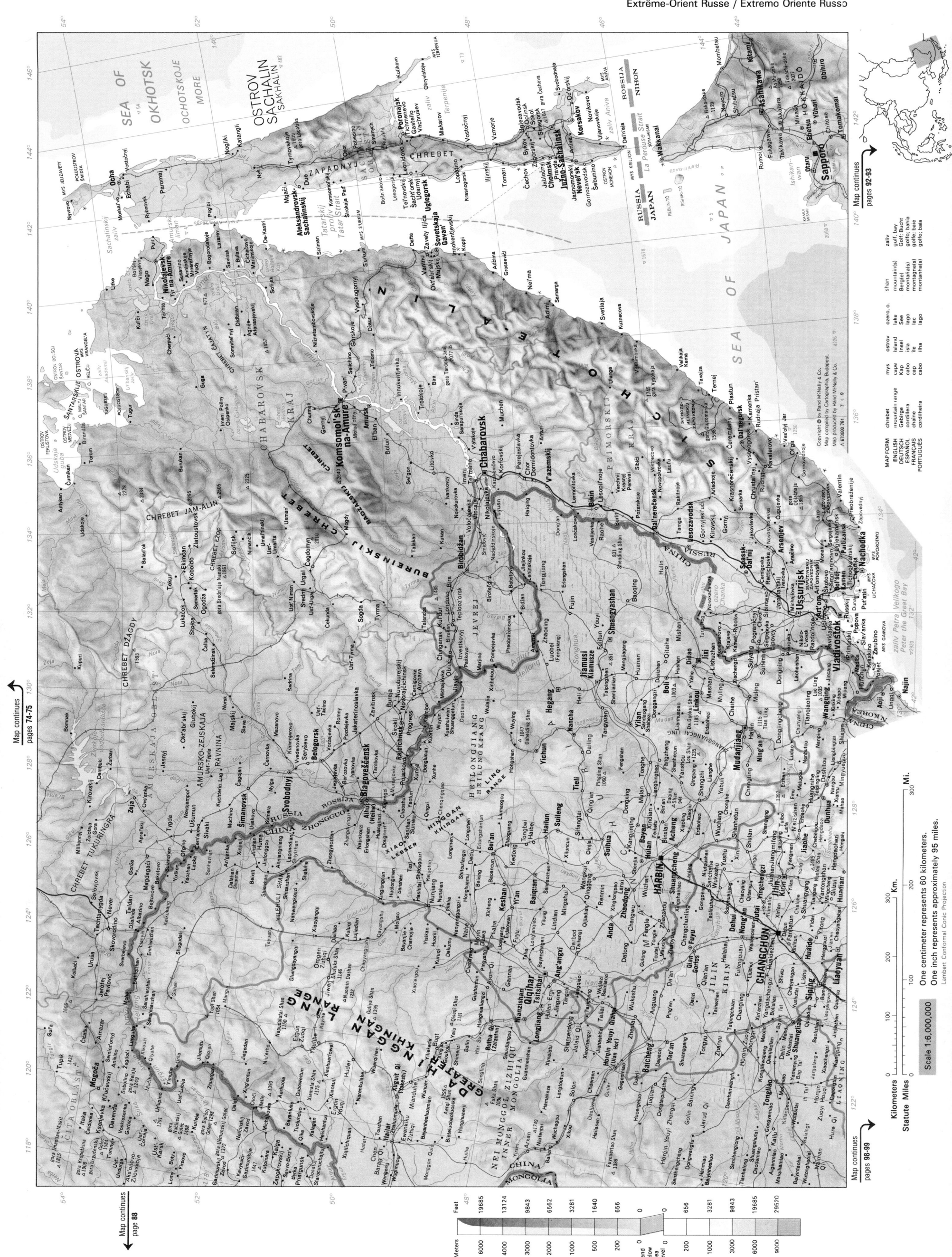

Map continues
pages 74-75

Map continues
page 88

Map continues
pages 98-99

Map continues
pages 92-93

MAP FORM		
ENGLISH	chrebet	mountain range
DEUTSCH	Gebirge	
ESPAÑOL	cordillera	
FRANÇAIS	cordillère	
PORTUGUÊS	cordilheira	

mys	cape	ostrov	island
Kap	Kap	Insel	Insel
cabo	cabo	isla	isla
cap	cap	île	ilha
cabo	cabo	ilha	

ozero, o.	lake	shan	mountain(s)
See	See	Berg(e)	Berg(e)
lago	lago	montaña(s)	montaña(s)
lac	lac	montagnes	montagnes
lago	lago	montanha(s)	montanha(s)

zaliv	gulf, bay
Golf, Bucht	Golf, Bucht
golfo, bahía	golfo, bahía
golfe	golfe
golfo, baía	golfo, baía

Copyright © by Rand McNally & Co.
Map compiled by Cartographia, Budapest.
Map produced by Rand McNally & Co.
A 72000 781

One centimeter represents 60 kilometers.
One inch represents approximately 95 miles.
Lambert Conformal Conic Projection

Scale 1:6,000,000

SEA OF OKHOTSK / OCHOTSKOJE MORE

OSTROV SACHALIN / SAKHALIN

SEA OF JAPAN

CHABAROVSK KRAJ

PRIMORSKIJ KRAJ

AMURSKAJA OBLAST'

CHITA OBLAST'

RUSSIA / ROSSIJA

CHINA / ZHONGGUO

HEILONGJIANG / HEILUNG KIANG

JILIN / KIRIN

NEI MONGGOL ZIZHIQU / INNER MONGOLIA

GREATER KHINGAN RANGE / DA HINGGAN LING

LESSER KHINGAN RANGE / XIAO HINGGAN LING

HARBIN

CHANGCHUN

Vladivostok

Chabarovsk

Komsomol'sk na-Amure

Map continues
pages **74-75**

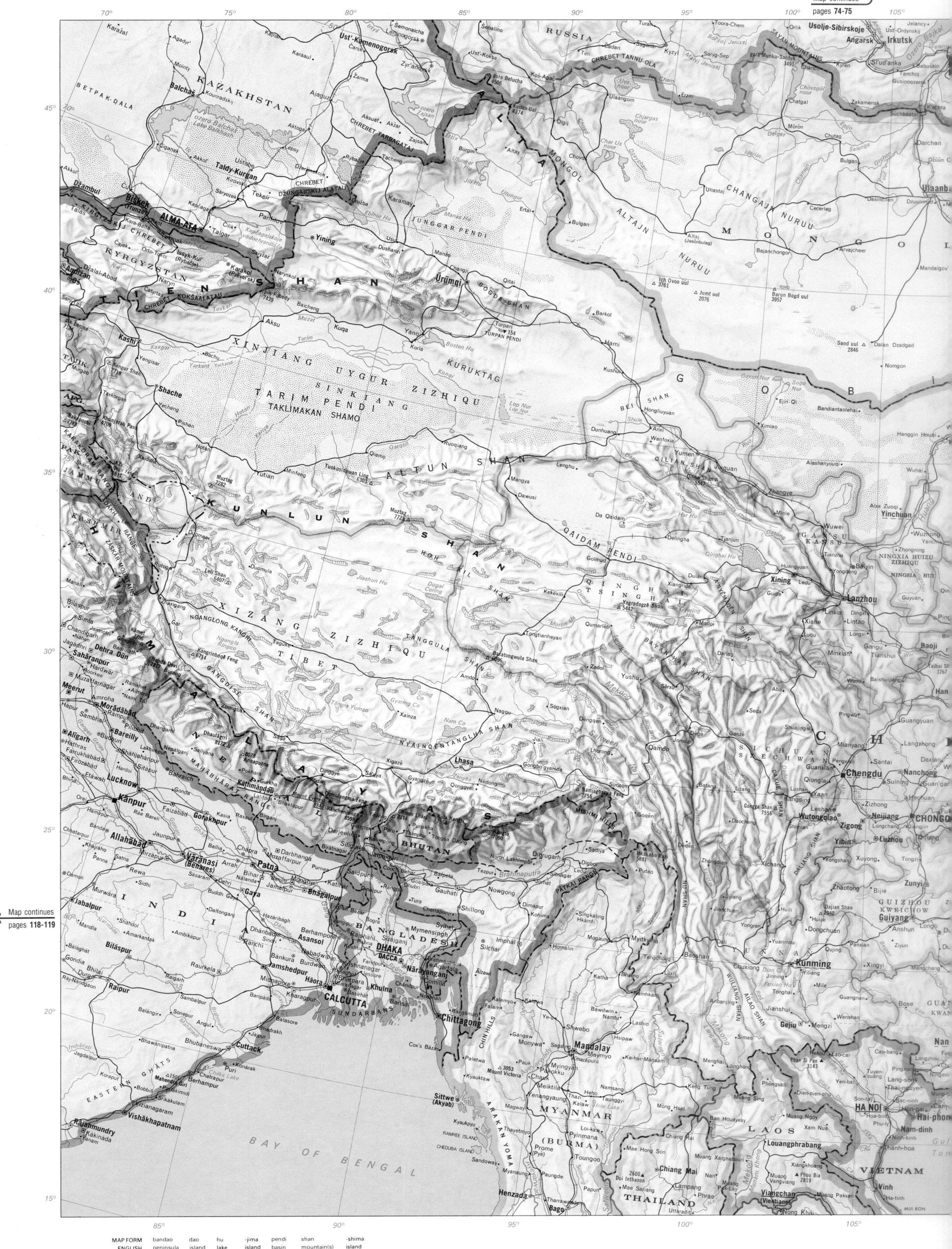

← Map continues
pages **118-119**

MAP FORM	bandao	dao	hu	-jima	pendi	shan	-shima
ENGLISH	peninsula	island	lake	island	basin	mountain(s)	island
DEUTSCH	Halbinsel	Insel	See	Insel	Becken	Berg(e)	Insel
ESPAÑOL	península	isla	lago	isla	cuenca	montaña(s)	isla
FRANÇAIS	péninsule	île	lac	île	bassin	montagne(s)	île
PORTUGUÊS	península	ilha	lago	ilha	bacia	montanha(s)	ilha

RUSSIA

SEA OF OKHOTSK

OSTROV SACHALIN
SAKHALIN

Južno-Sachalinsk

Čita
Blagoveščensk
Chabarovsk

DA HINGGAN LING
HEILONGJIANG
HEILUNGKIANG
MANCHURIA

Qiqihar
Tsitsihar
Harbin
Baicheng

NEI MONGGOL ZIZHIQU
INNER MONGOLIA

Changchun
JILIN
KIRIN
Vladivostok
Nachodka

HOKKAIDO
Asahikawa
Sapporo
Otaru
Muroran
Hakodate

Aomori
Hachinohe
Hirosaki
Morioka
Akita

Baotou
Hohhot

Zhangjiakou
Kalgan
BEIJING SHI
Datong
BEIJING
PEKING
Tianjin
TIANJIN
TIENTSIN

SHENYANG
MUKDEN
Fushun
Anshan
Jinzhou
Dandong

NORTH KOREA
P'YONGYANG
Hamhung
Wonsan

SEA OF JAPAN

JAPAN
HONSHU
Niigata
Kanazawa
TOKYO
Kawasaki
Yokohama
Nagoya
OSAKA
Kyoto
KOBE

SHANXI
SHANSI
Taiyuan
Shijiazhuang

Dalian
Lüshun
(Port Arthur)

Korea Bay

Bo Hai

SOUTH KOREA
SEOUL
Inch'on
Taejon
Taegu
Pusan
Kwangju
Mokp'o

Hiroshima
Kitakyushu
Fukuoka
Matsuyama
SHIKOKU

Jinan
Tsinan
SHANDONG
SHANTUNG
Qingdao
Tsingtao

Yellow Sea

Nagasaki
KYUSHU
Kumamoto
Miyazaki
Kagoshima

HENAN
HONAN
Zhengzhou
Luoyang
Kaifeng

JIANGSU
KIANGSU
Xuzhou

EAST CHINA SEA

Nanjing
Hefei
ANHUI
ANHWEI
SHANGHAI
Suzhou
Wuxi

WUHAN
HUBEI
HUPEH
Hangzhou
Ningbo
ZHEJIANG
CHEKIANG
Wenzhou

RYUKYU ISLANDS (Japan)
NANSEI-SHOTO

HUNAN
Changsha
Nanchang
JIANGXI
KIANGSI

Fuzhou

Naha
OKINAWA-JIMA

Tropic of Cancer

GUANGDONG
KWANGTUNG
Guangzhou
CANTON

FUJIAN
FUKIEN
Xiamen
Amoy

T'AIPEI
Chilung
Hsinchu
T'aichung
TAIWAN
T'ainan
Kaohsiung

PACIFIC OCEAN

HONG KONG (U.K.)
VICTORIA
Macau

Haikou
HAINAN

SOUTH CHINA SEA

PHILIPPINES
LUZON

PHILIPPINE SEA

Map continues pages 108-109

Kilometers
Statute Miles

Scale 1:12,000,000
One centimeter represents 120 kilometers.
One inch represents approximately 190 miles.
Lambert Conformal Conic Projection

Copyright © by Rand McNally & Co.
Map prepared by Esselte Map Service AB, Stockholm.

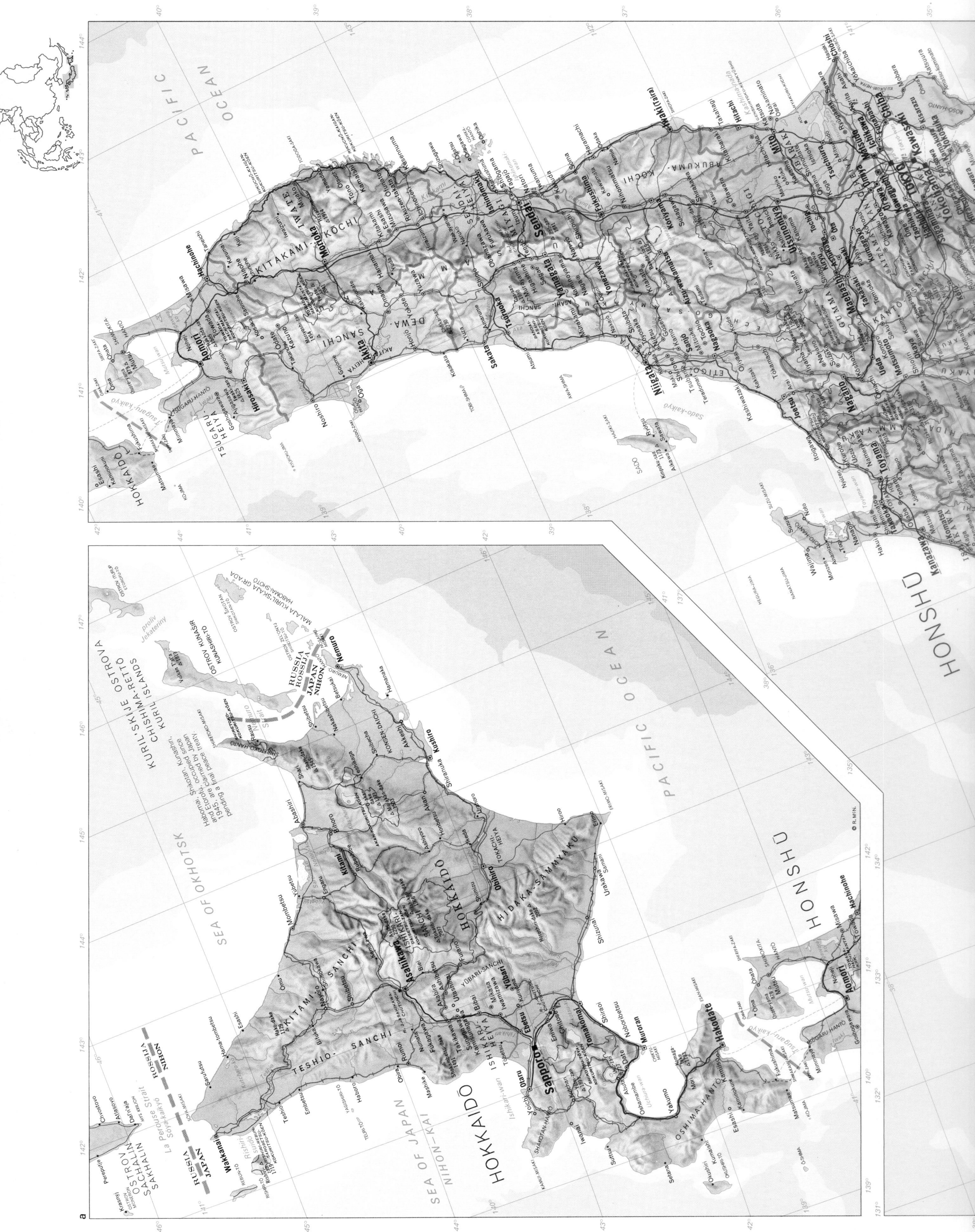

PACIFIC OCEAN

HONSHŪ

HOKKAIDO

SEA OF OKHOTSK

KURIL'SKIJE OSTROVA
CHISHIMA-RETTO
KURIL ISLANDS

RUSSIA ROSSIJA
JAPAN NIHON

PACIFIC OCEAN

SEA OF JAPAN
NIHON-KAI

OSTROV SACHALIN
SAKHALIN

RUSSIA
JAPAN

Wakkanai

Sapporo

Hakodate

Aomori

Hachinohe

Asahikawa

Kushiro

Nemuro

Muroran

Tomakomai

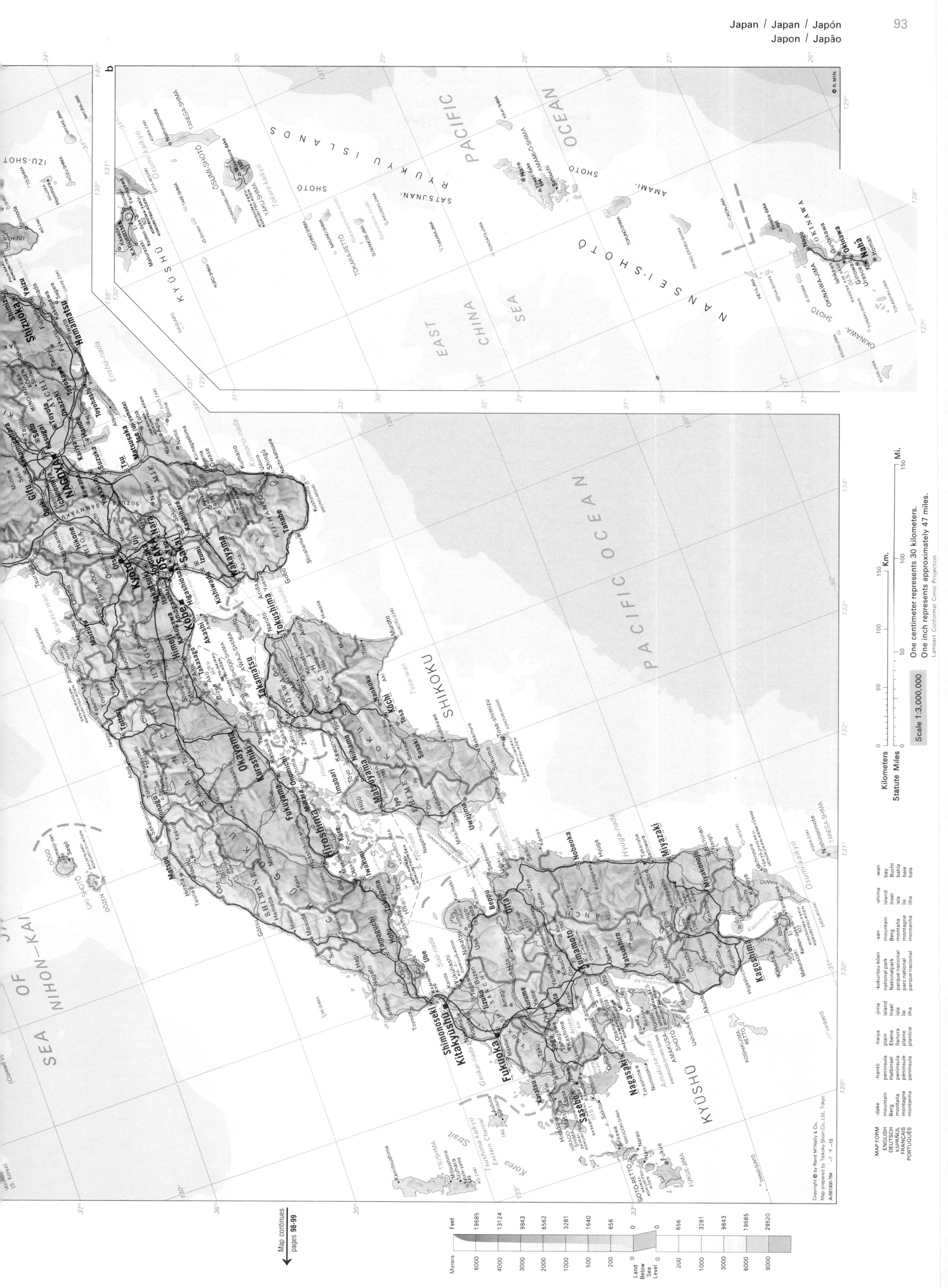
PACIFIC OCEAN
SHIKOKU
KYŪSHŪ
EAST CHINA SEA
RYUKYU ISLANDS
NANSEI-SHOTŌ
OKINAWA
Naha
Nagasaki
Fukuoka
Kitakyūshū
Shimonoseki
Hiroshima
Okayama
Kōbe
Ōsaka
Kyōto
Nagoya
Kagoshima
Kumamoto
Miyazaki
Matsuyama
Takamatsu
Kōchi
Tokushima
Wakayama
Kilometers
Statute Miles
Scale 1:3,000,000
One centimeter represents 30 kilometers.
One inch represents approximately 47 miles.
Lambert Conformal Conic Projection
Map continues pages 98-99
Meters
Feet
Land Below Sea Level
Copyright © by Rand McNally & Co.
Map prepared by Teikoku Shoin Co., Ltd., Tokyo

← Map continues pages 96-97

MAP FORM	-dake	-hantō	-kokutei-kōen	-misaki	-san	-tōge	-wan	-yama	-zaki
ENGLISH	mountain	peninsula	national park	cape	mountain	pass	bay	mountain	point
DEUTSCH	Berg	Halbinsel	Nationalpark	Kap	Berg	Pass	Bucht	Berg	Landspitze
ESPAÑOL	montaña	península	parque nacional	cabo	montaña	paso	bahía	montaña	punta
FRANÇAIS	montagne	péninsule	parc national	cap	montagne	col	baie	montagne	pointe
PORTUGUÊS	montanha	península	parque nacional	cabo	montanha	passo	baía	montanha	ponta

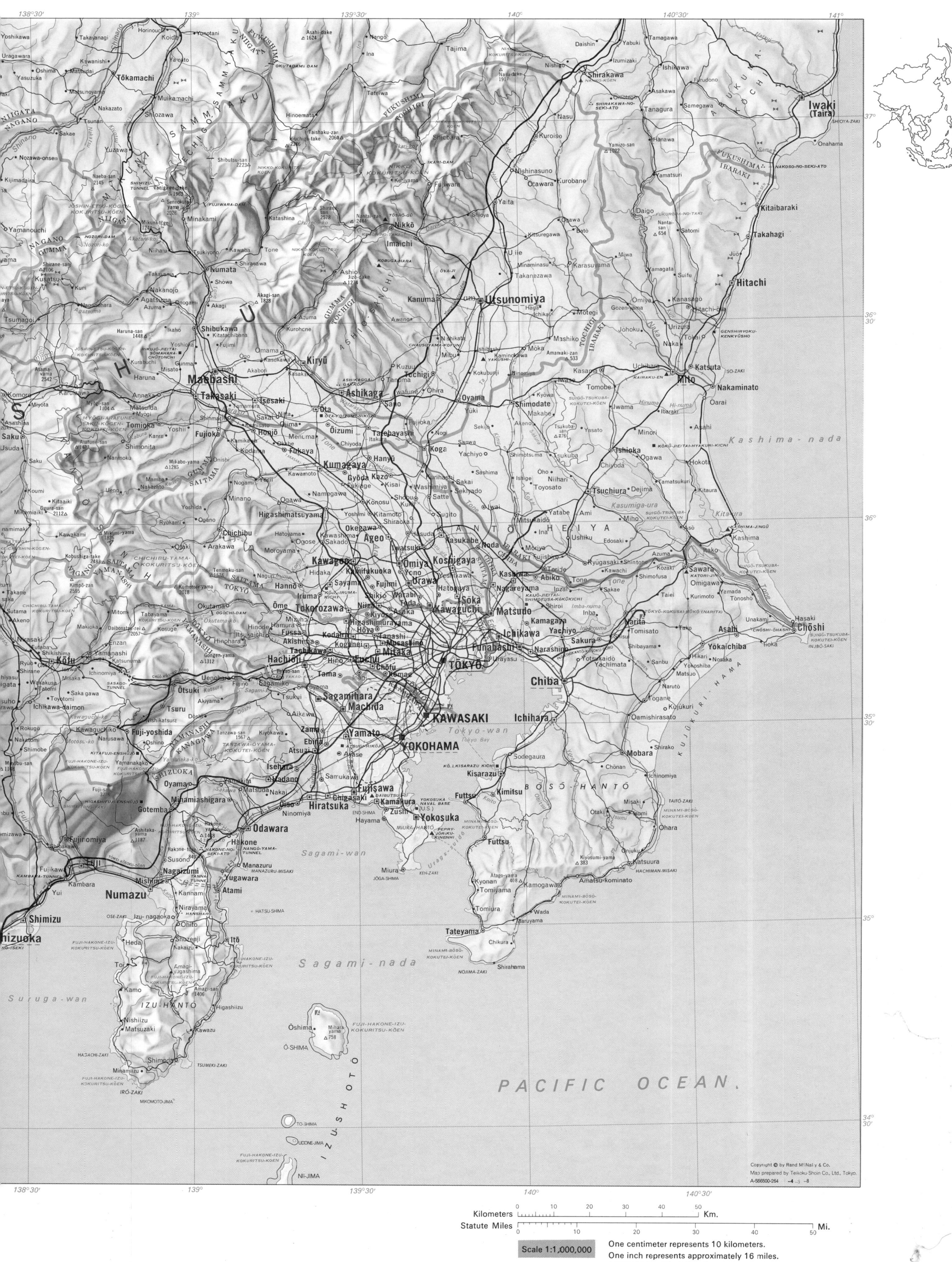

Kilometers
Statute Miles

Scale 1:1,000,000   One centimeter represents 10 kilometers.
One inch represents approximately 16 miles.
Lambert Conformal Conic Projection

SEA OF JAPAN

NIHON-KAI

HIROSHIMA

FUKUOKA

KITAKYŪSHŪ

Shimonoseki

Yamaguchi

KYŪSHŪ

Kurume

Ōita

Beppu

Suō-nada

Iyo-nada

Uwa-kai

MAP FORM	-jima	-misaki	-san	-sen	-shima	-tōge	-yama	-zen
ENGLISH	island	cape	mountain	mountain	island	pass	mountain	mountain
DEUTSCH	Insel	Kap	Berg	Berg	Insel	Pass	Berg	Berg
ESPAÑOL	isla	cabo	montaña	montaña	isla	paso	montaña	montaña
FRANÇAIS	île	cap	montagne	montagne	île	col	montagne	montagne
PORTUGUÊS	ilha	cabo	montanha	montanha	ilha	passo	montanha	montanha

Map continues
pages 94-95

Kilometers
Statute Miles

Scale 1:1,000,000 One centimeter represents 10 kilometers.
One inch represents approximately 16 miles.
Lambert Conformal Conic Projection

Copyright © by Rand McNally & Co.
Map prepared by Teikoku-Shoin Co., Ltd., Tokyo.
A-566600-264 -4 -5 -6

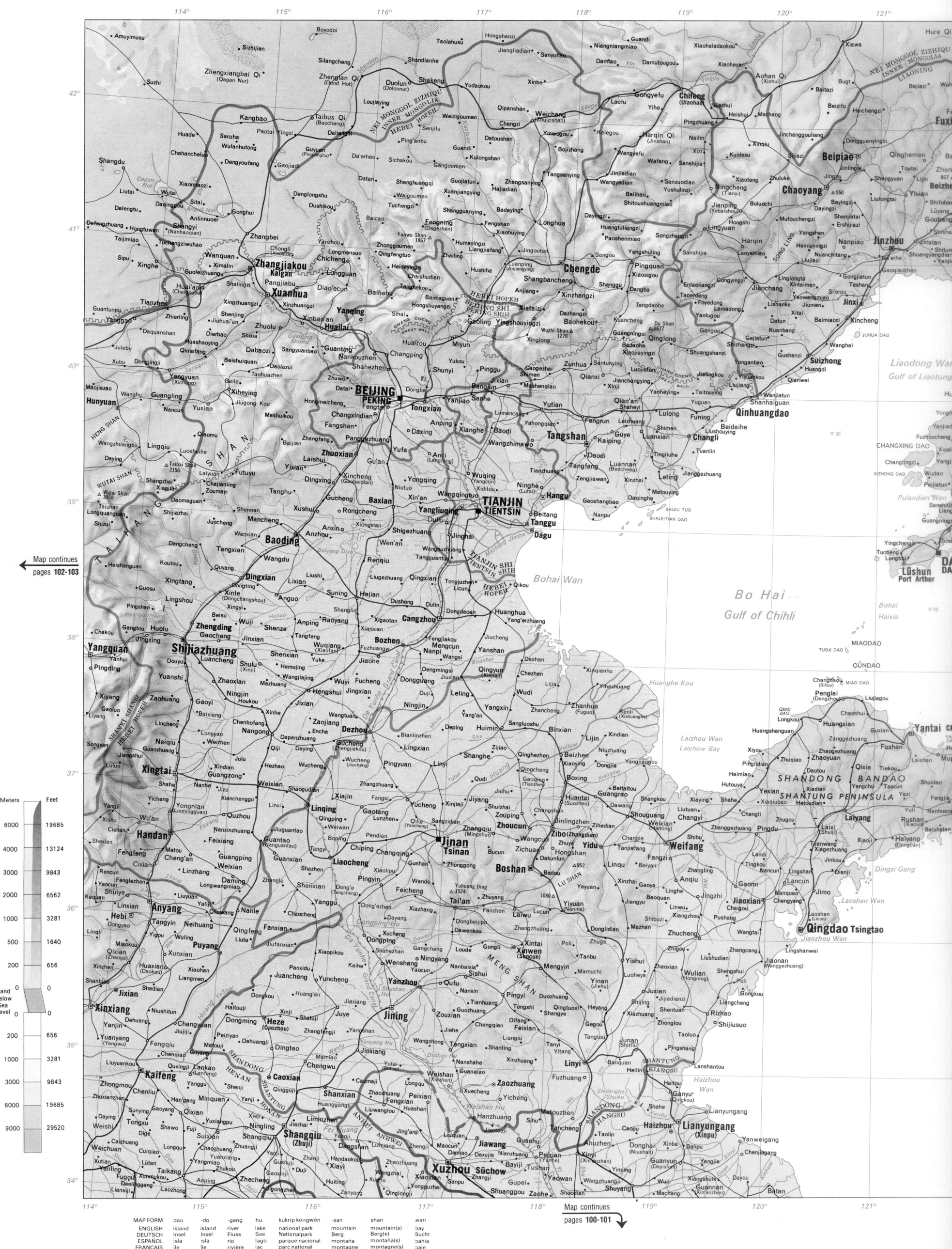

Map continues
pages 102-103

Map continues
pages 100-101

MAP FORM	dao	-do	-gang	hu	kukrip kongwŏn	-san	shan	-wan
ENGLISH	island	island	river	lake	national park	mountain	mountain(s)	bay
DEUTSCH	Insel	Insel	Fluss	See	Nationalpark	Berg	Berg(e)	Bucht
ESPAÑOL	isla	isla	río	lago	parque nacional	montaña	montaña(s)	bahía
FRANÇAIS	île	île	rivière	lac	parc national	montagne	montagne(s)	baie
PORTUGUÊS	ilha	ilha	rio	lago	parque nacional	montanha	montanha(s)	baía

Scale 1:3,000,000
One centimeter represents 30 kilometers.
One inch represents approximately 47 miles.
Lambert Conformal Conic Projection

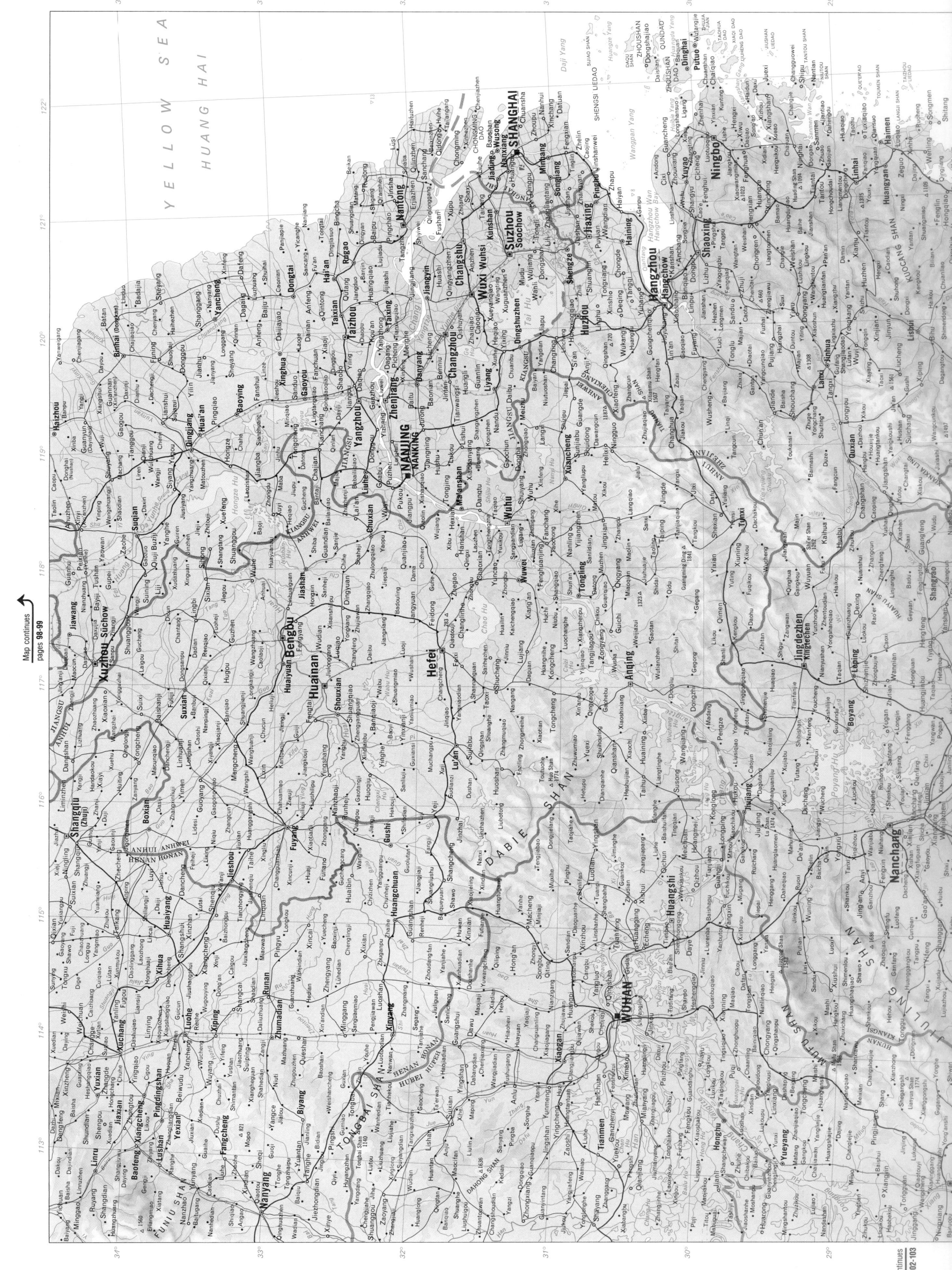

Map continues
pages 98-99

Map continues
pages 102-103

East and Southeast China / Ost- und Südostchina / Este y Sudeste de la China
Chine de l'Est et du Sud-Est / Leste e Sudeste da China
101

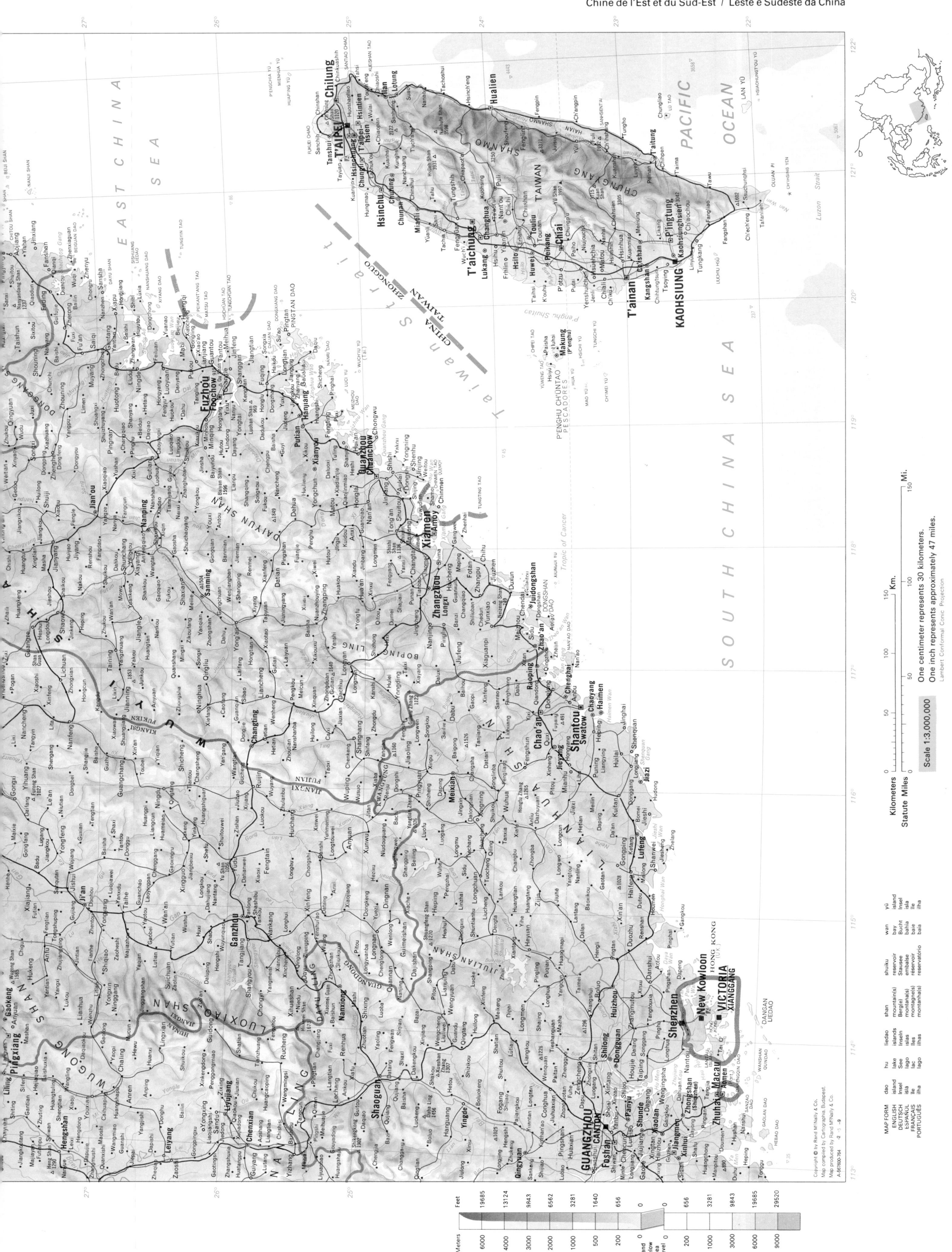

Map continues pages 98-99

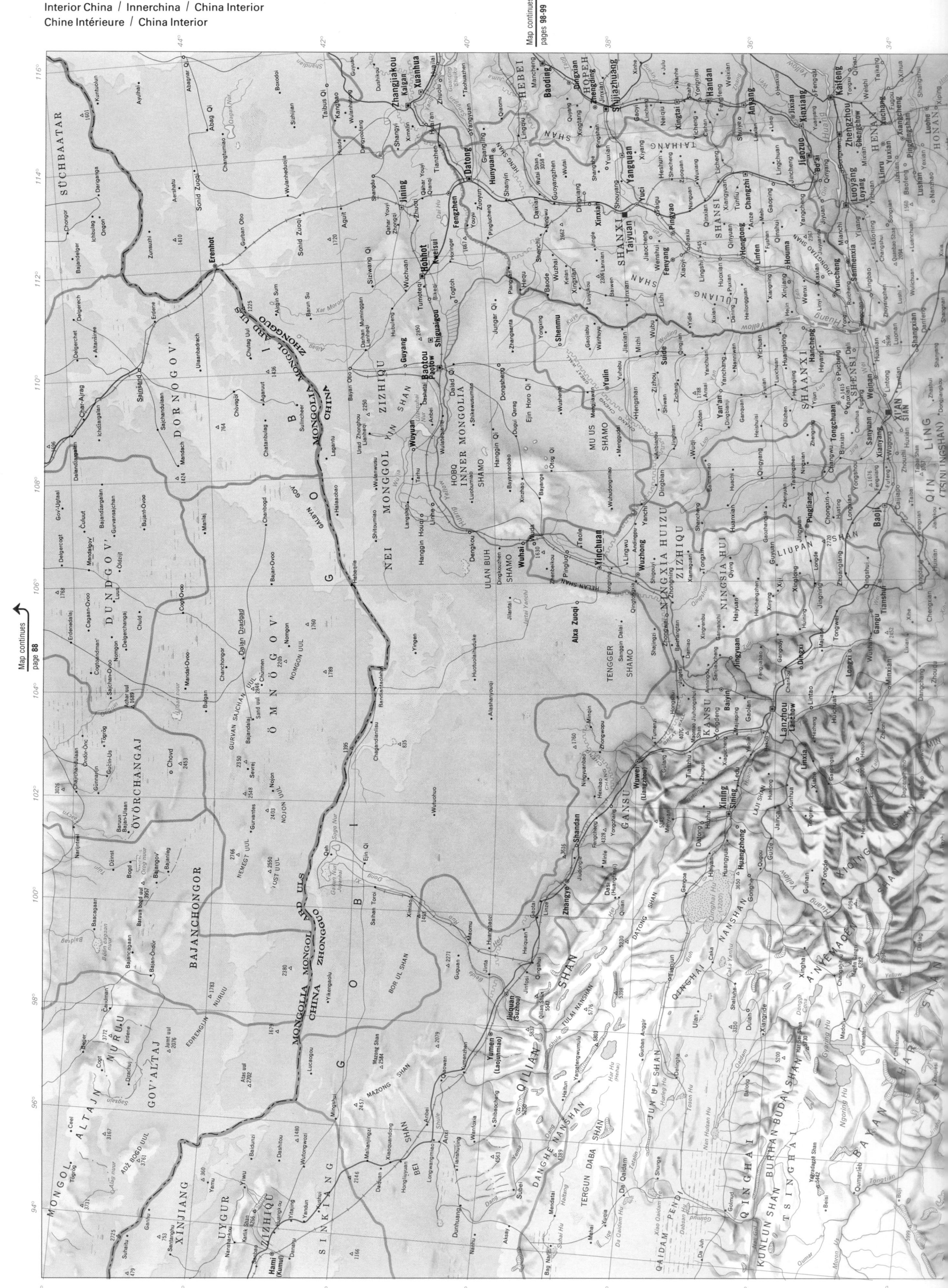
INNER MONGOLIA
NEI MONGGOL ZIZHIQU
GANSU
KANSU
NINGXIA HUIZU ZIZHIQU
NINGSIA HUI
SHAANXI
SHENSI
SHANXI
SHANSI
HENAN
HONAN
HEBEI
HOPEH
QINGHAI
TSINGHAI
XINJIANG
SINKIANG
UYGUR ZIZHIQU
MONGOLIA
MONGOL ARD ULS
CHINA
ZHONGGUO
G O B I
ÖMNÖGOV'
DUNDGOV'
DORNOGOV'
SÜCHBAATAR
ÖVÖRCHANGAJ
BAJANCHONGOR
GOV'ALTAJ
QILIAN SHAN
QIN LING (TSINLINGSHAN)
BAYAN HAR SHAN
KUNLUN SHAN
QAIDAM PENDI
TENGGER SHAMO
MU US SHAMO
HOBQ SHAMO
ULAN BUH SHAMO
Lanzhou
Lanchow
Xining
Sining
Yinchuan
Hohhot
Baotou
Taiyuan
Xi'an
Zhengzhou
Shijiazhuang
Datong
Erenhot
Hami (Kumul)

Map continues page 88

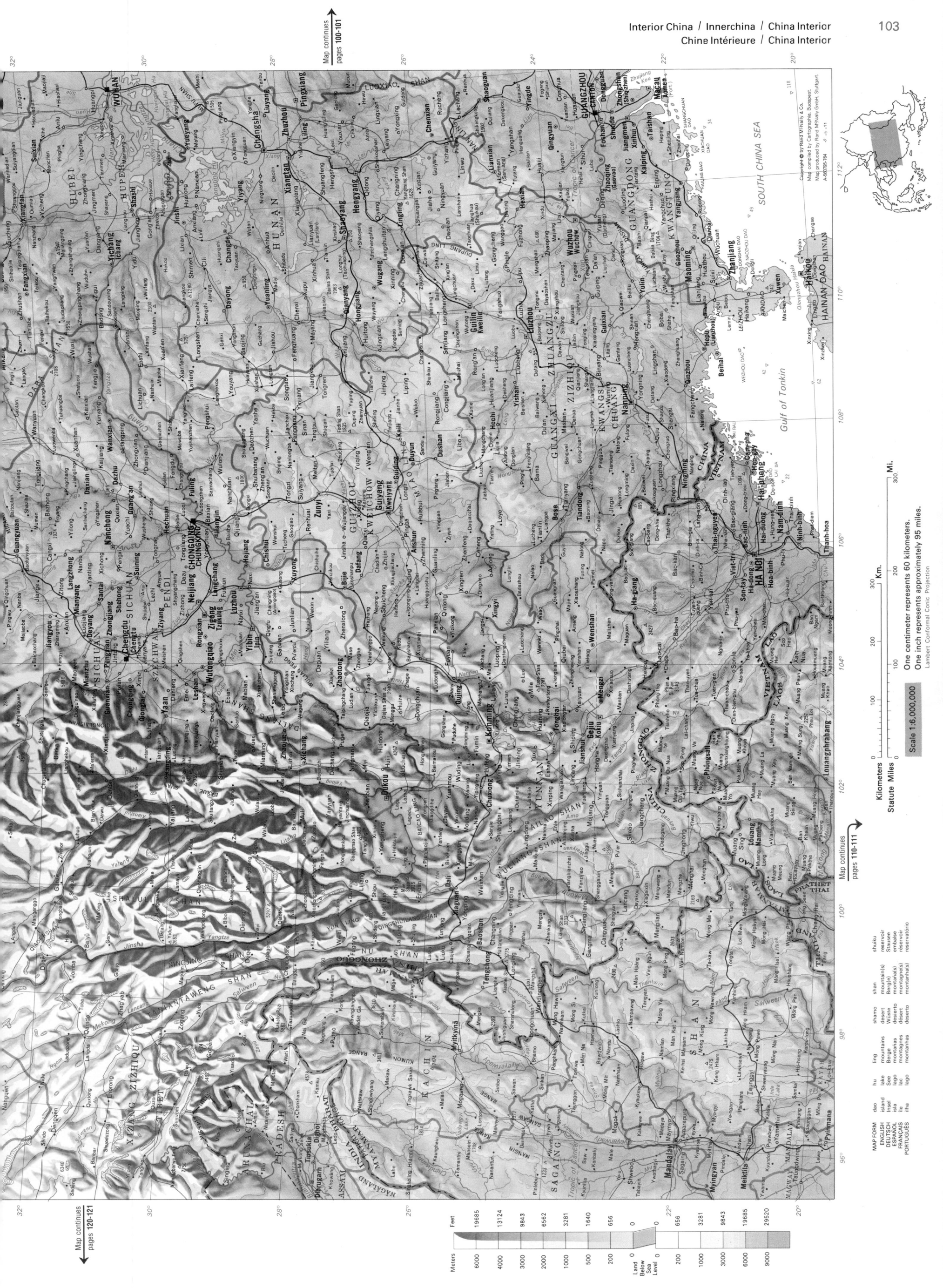

Map continues
pages 100-101

Map continues
pages 110-111

Map continues
pages 120-121

SOUTH CHINA SEA

Gulf of Tonkin

Kilometers

Statute Miles

Scale 1:6,000,000

One centimeter represents 60 kilometers.
One inch represents approximately 95 miles.

Lambert Conformal Conic Projection

Copyright © by Rand McNally & Co.
Map compiled by Cartographia, Budapest.
Map produced by Rand McNally GmbH, Stuttgart.

MAP FORM					
ENGLISH	island	lake	mountains	desert	mountain(s)	reservoir
DEUTSCH	Insel	See	Berge	Wüste	Berg(e)	Stausee
ESPAÑOL	isla	lago	montañas	desierto	montaña(s)	embalse
FRANÇAIS	île	lac	montagnes	désert	montagne(s)	réservoir
PORTUGUÊS	ilha	lago	montanhas	deserto	montanha(s)	reservatório
	dao	hu	ling	shamo	shan	shuiku

Feet	Meters
19685	6000
13124	4000
9843	3000
6562	2000
3281	1000
1640	500
656	200
0	Land 0 Below Sea Level
656	200
3281	1000
9843	3000
19685	6000
29520	9000

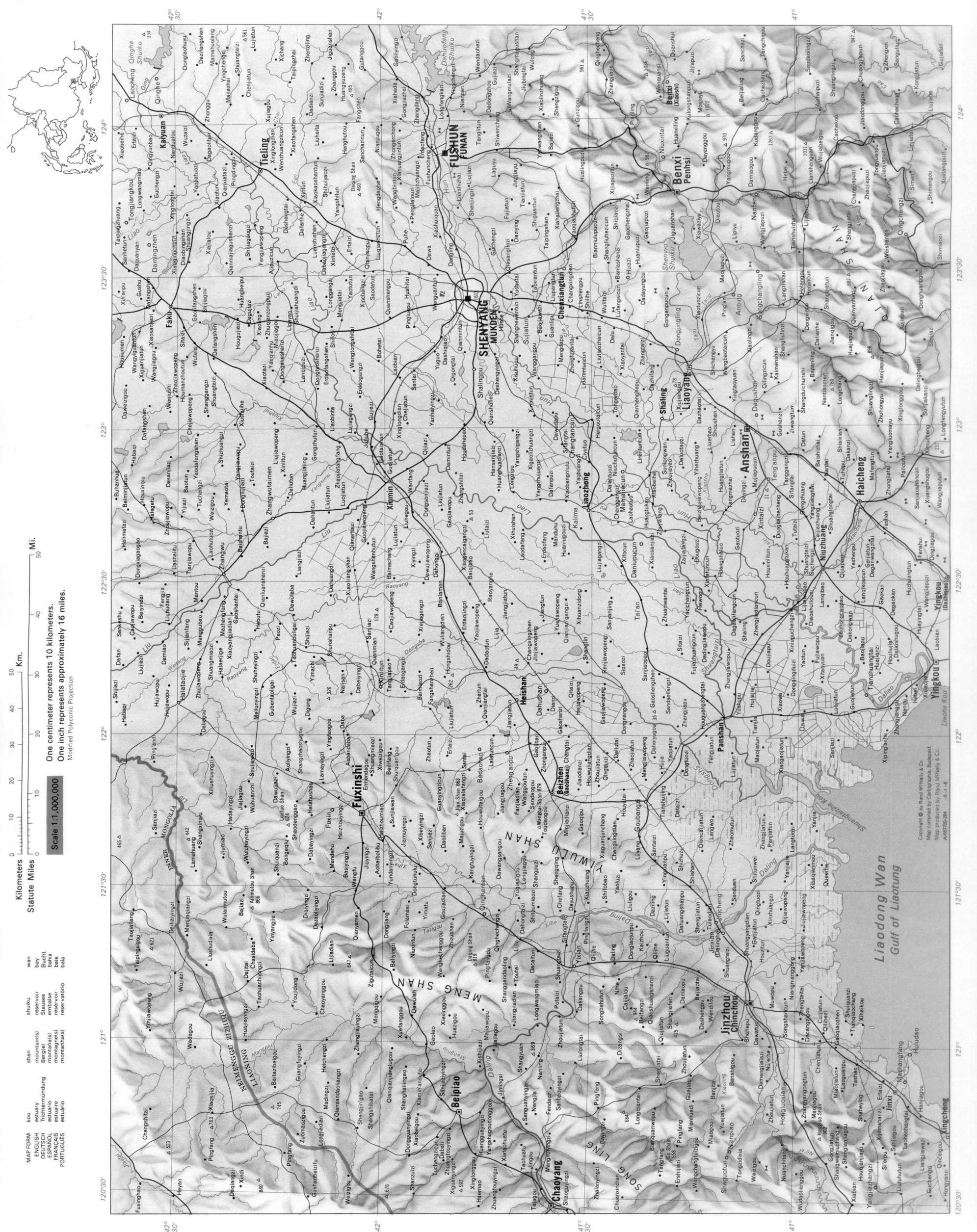

Kilometers
Statute Miles

Mi.

One centimeter represents 10 kilometers.
One inch represents approximately 16 miles.
Modified Polyconic Projection

Scale 1:1,000,000

MAP FORM
ENGLISH
DEUTSCH
ESPAÑOL
FRANÇAIS
PORTUGUÊS

kou   estuary
             Trichtermündung
             estuario
             estuaire
             estuário

shan   mountain(s)
             Berg(e)
             montaña(s)
             montagne(s)
             montanha(s)

shuku   reservoir
             Stausee
             embalse
             réservoir
             reservatório

wan   bay
             Bucht
             bahía
             baie
             baía

Copyright © by Rand McNally & Co.
Map produced by Cartographia, Budapest.
Map compiled by Cartographia, Budapest / Rand McNally & Co.
A-467195395

Bohai Wan

Scale 1:1,000,000

One centimeter represents 10 kilometers.
One inch represents approximately 16 miles.
Modified Polyconic Projection

MAP FORM	hai	shan	shuiku	wa
ENGLISH	lake	mountain(s)	reservoir	marsh
DEUTSCH	See	Berg(e)	Stausee	Marsch
ESPAÑOL	lago	montaña(s)	embalse	pantano
FRANÇAIS	lac	montagne(s)	réservoir	marais
PORTUGUÊS	lago	montanha(s)	reservatório	pântano

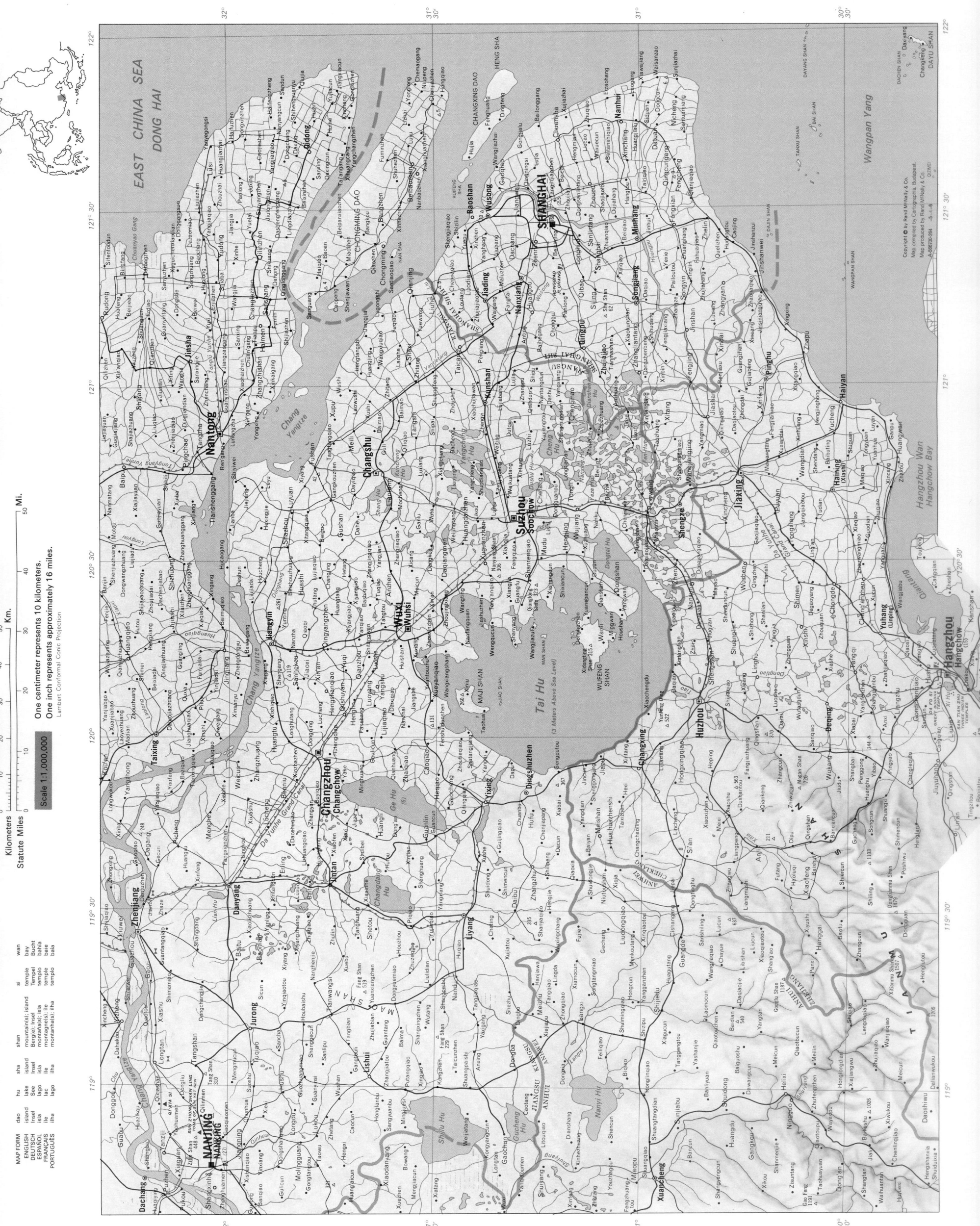

EAST CHINA SEA
DONG HAI

Wangpan Yang

Mi.
Km.

Statute Miles

One centimeter represents 10 kilometers.
One inch represents approximately 16 miles.
Lambert Conformal Conic Projection

Scale 1:1,000,000

Kilometers Miles

MAP FORM					
ENGLISH	dao	hu	sha	shan	si	wan
DEUTSCH	island	lake	island	mountain(s); island	temple	bay
ESPAÑOL	Insel	See	Insel	Berg(e); Insel	Tempel	Bucht
FRANÇAIS	isla	lago	isla	montaña(s); isla	templo	bahía
PORTUGUÊS	île	lac	île	montagnes; île	temple	baie
	ilha	lago	ilha	montanhas; ilha	templo	baía

NANJING
NANKING

Zhenjiang

Nantong

Changzhou
Changchow

Wuxi
Wuhsi

Suzhou
Soochow

SHANGHAI

Hangzhou
Hangchow

Tai Hu

Copyright © by Rand McNally & Co.
Map compiled by Cartographia, Budapest.
Map produced by Rand McNally & Co.

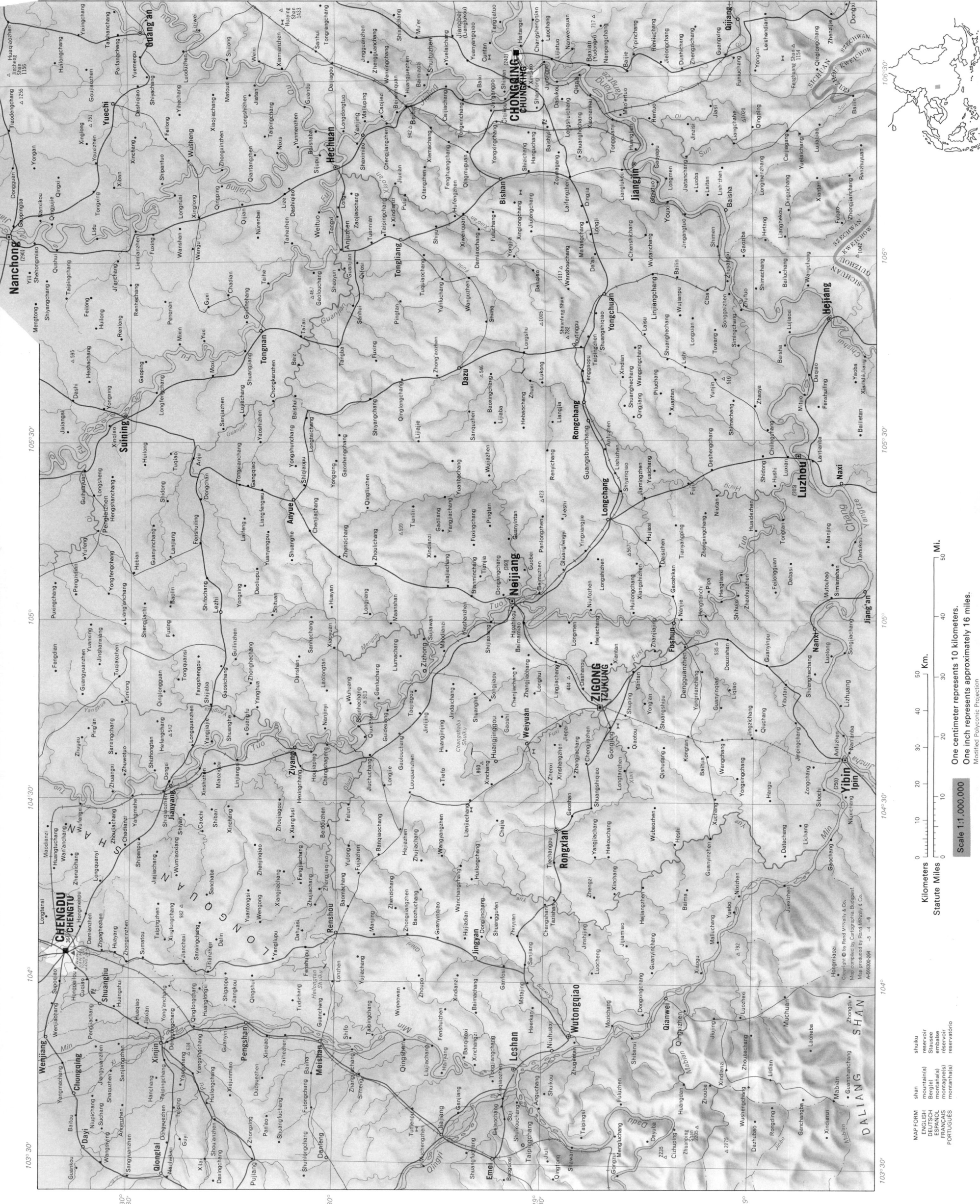

Scale 1:1,000,000

One centimeter represents 10 kilometers.
One inch represents approximately 16 miles.
Modified Polyconic Projection

MAP FORM
ENGLISH   shan   shuiku
DEUTSCH   mountain(s) reservoir
ESPAÑOL   Berg(e)   Stausee
FRANÇAIS   montaña(s) embalse
PORTUGUÊS   montanha(s) réservoir
             montanha(s) reservatório

Copyright © by Rand McNally & Co.
Map prepared by Cartographia, Budapest
Map produced in Hungary by Rand McNally & Co.
A66000095R   -3 - 4 - 4

Map continues
pages 90-91

Map continues
pages 118-119

MAP FORM	gulf	gunung	island	kepulauan	pulau	sea	selat	strait
ENGLISH	gulf	mountain	island	islands	island	sea	strait	strait
DEUTSCH	Golf	Berg	Insel	Inseln	Insel	Meer	Meeresstrasse	Meeresstrasse
ESPAÑOL	golfo	montaña	isla	islas	isla	mar	estrecho	estrecho
FRANÇAIS	golfe	montagne	île	îles	île	mer	détroit	détroit
PORTUGUÊS	golfo	montanha	ilha	ilhas	ilha	mar	estreito	estreito

Copyright © by Rand McNally & Co.
Map prepared by Esselte Map Service AB, Stockholm.
A-569800-264   -11-5 -16

Map continues
pages 160-161

Kilometers 0 200 400 600 Km.

Statute Miles 0 200 400 600 Mi.

Scale 1:12,000,000   One centimeter represents 120 kilometers.
One inch represents approximately 190 miles.
Lambert Conformal Conic Projection

Kilometers
Statute Miles
0 100 200 300 Km.
0 100 200 300 Mi.
Scale 1:6,000,000
One centimeter represents 60 kilometers.
One inch represents approximately 95 miles.
Lambert Conformal Conic Projection
Map continues pages 102-103
Map continues pages 120-121
MAP FORM dao gunung island kepulauan khao kyun pulau shan
ENGLISH island mountain island islands mountain island island mountain(s)
DEUTSCH Insel Berg Insel Inseln Berg Insel Insel Berg(e)
ESPAÑOL isla montaña isla islas montaña isla isla montaña(s)
FRANÇAIS île montagne île îles montagne île île montagne(s)
PORTUGUÊS ilha montanha ilha ilhas montanha ilha ilha montanha(s)
SOUTH CHINA SEA
Gulf of Tonkin
BAY OF BENGAL
Gulf of Martaban
HAINAN DAO
Mouths of the Irrawaddy
Preparis North Channel
Preparis South Channel
Coco Channel
COCO ISLANDS
YANGON RANGOON
Mandalay
HA NOI
Viangchan (Vientiane)
Da Nang
Kunming
Nanning
Guiyang
Chittagong
BANGLADESH
MYANMAR
INDIA
CHINA
LAOS
VIETNAM
THAILAND
PRATHET THAI
KAMPUCHEA
YUNNAN
GUANGXI ZHUANGZU ZIZHIQU
GUIZHOU
QUANGDONG KWANGTUNG
HAINAN
HUNAN
SHAN
PEGU YOMA
ARAKAN YOMA
CHIN HILLS
NAGA HILLS
MANIPUR
ASSAM
MIZORAM
SAGAING
MAGWAY
MANDALAY
KACHIN
KAYAH
KAYIN
MON
BAGO
AYEYARWADY
RAKHINE
PLATEAU DES BOLOVENS
Tropic of Cancer

Myanmar, Thailand and Indochina/Myanmar, Thailand und Indochina/Myanmar, Siam e Indochina
Myanmar, Thaïlande et Indochine/Myanmar, Tailândia e Indochina

111

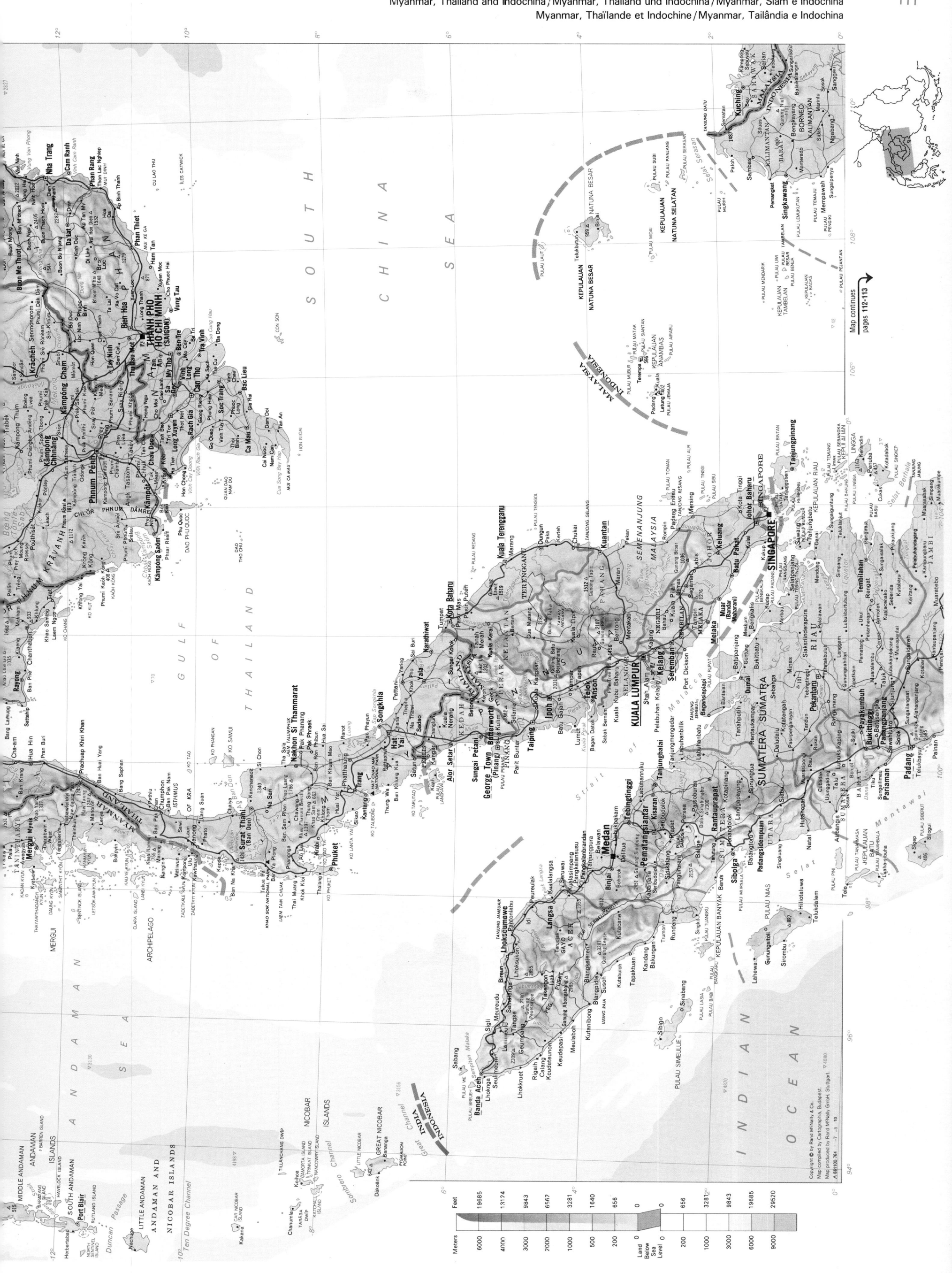

Map continues
pages 112-113

S O U T H   C H I N A   S E A

A N D A M A N   S E A

G U L F   O F   T H A I L A N D

I N D I A N   O C E A N

MALAYSIA
INDONESIA

SINGAPORE

KUALA LUMPUR

THANH PHO
HO CHI MINH
(SAIGON)

Phnum Pénh

THAILAND

MYANMAR

ANDAMAN
ISLANDS

NICOBAR
ISLANDS

ANDAMAN AND
NICOBAR ISLANDS

MERGUI
ARCHIPELAGO

Feet	Meters
19685	6000
13174	4000
9843	3000
6567	2000
3281	1000
1640	500
656	200
0	0 Land
0	0 Below Sea Level
656	200
3281	1000
9843	3000
19685	6000
29520	9000

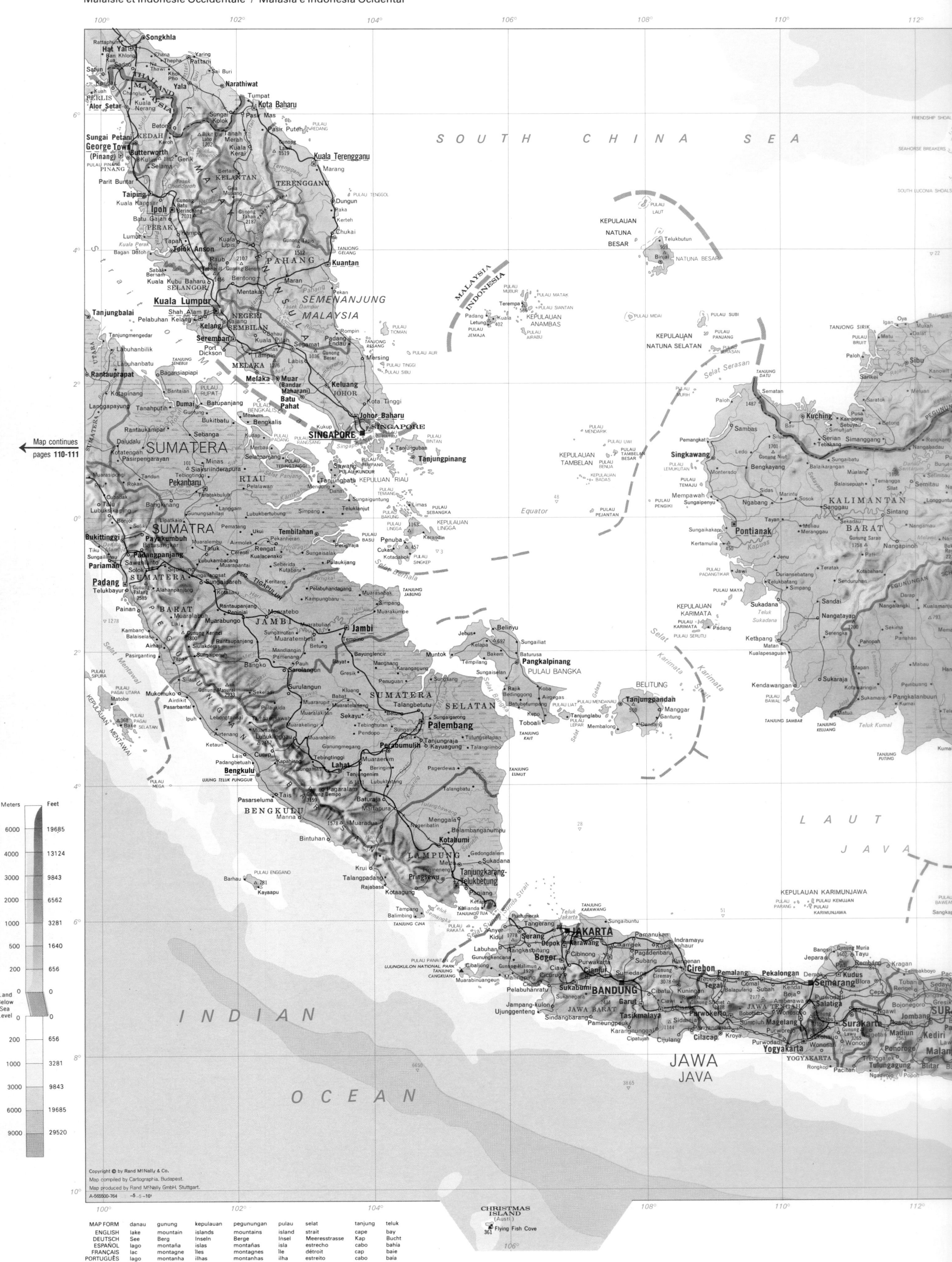

Map continues
← pages 110-111

Meters	Feet
6000	19685
4000	13124
3000	9843
2000	6562
1000	3281
500	1640
200	656
0	0
Land Below Sea Level	0
200	656
1000	3281
3000	9843
6000	19685
9000	29520

Copyright © by Rand McNally & Co.
Map compiled by Cartographia, Budapest.
Map produced by Rand McNally GmbH, Stuttgart.
A-565500-764   -5 - .5 -10°

MAP FORM	danau	gunung	kepulauan	pegunungan	pulau	selat	tanjung	teluk
ENGLISH	lake	mountain	islands	mountains	island	strait	cape	bay
DEUTSCH	See	Berg	Inseln	Berge	Insel	Meeresstrasse	Kap	Bucht
ESPAÑOL	lago	montaña	islas	montañas	isla	estrecho	cabo	bahía
FRANÇAIS	lac	montagne	îles	montagnes	île	détroit	cap	baie
PORTUGUÊS	lago	montanha	ilhas	montanhas	ilha	estreito	cabo	baia

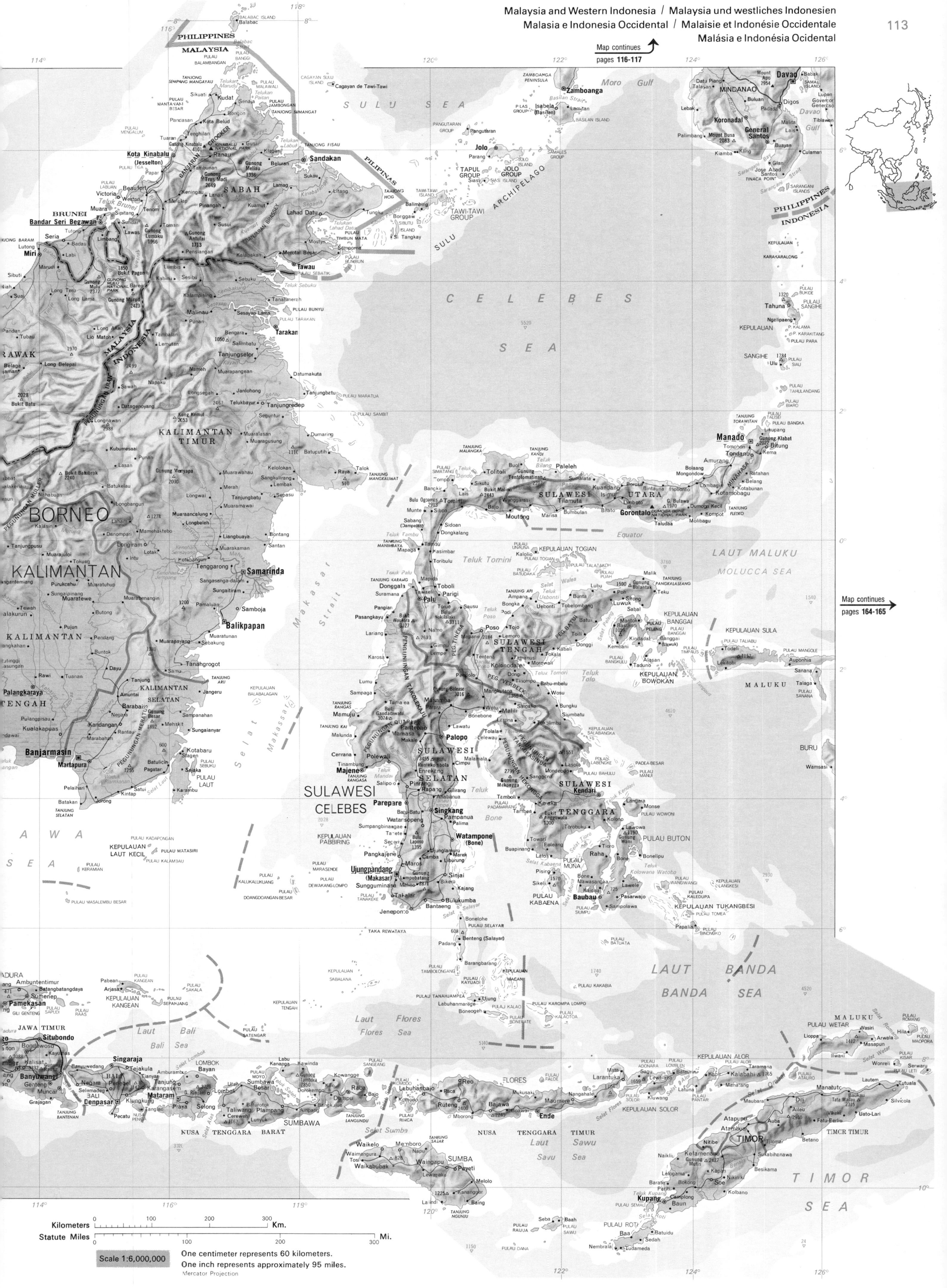

Malaysia and Western Indonesia / Malaysia und westliches Indonesien
Malasia e Indonesia Occidental / Malaisie et Indonésie Occidentale
Malásia e Indonésia Ocidental

113

Map continues
pages 116-117

Map continues
pages 164-165

PHILIPPINES
MALAYSIA
BRUNEI
Bandar Seri Begawan
Miri
SABAH
Kota Kinabalu
(Jesselton)
Sandakan
Tawau
PILIPINAS

SULU SEA

MINDANAO
Davao
Zamboanga
General Santos
Koronadal
Jolo

PHILIPPINES
INDONESIA

CELEBES SEA

BORNEO
KALIMANTAN
KALIMANTAN TIMUR
KALIMANTAN SELATAN
Samarinda
Balikpapan
Tarakan
Banjarmasin
Martapura
Palangkaraya

Manado
Gorontalo
Tondano

SULAWESI UTARA
SULAWESI TENGAH
SULAWESI SELATAN
SULAWESI TENGGARA
SULAWESI
CELEBES
Palu
Poso
Palopo
Majene
Parepare
Singkang
Watampone (Bone)
Ujungpandang (Makasar)
Kendari
Baubau

LAUT MALUKU
MOLUCCA SEA
MALUKU
BURU

Makasar Strait
Selat Makasar

JAWA SEA

LAUT BANDA
BANDA SEA

Laut Flores
Flores Sea

Laut Bali
Bali Sea

JAWA TIMUR
BALI
Denpasar
Mataram
LOMBOK
SUMBAWA
NUSA TENGGARA BARAT
NUSA TENGGARA TIMUR
FLORES
Ende
SUMBA
Waingapu
TIMOR
TIMOR TIMUR
Kupang
Dili

Laut Savu
Sawu Sea

TIMOR SEA

Kilometers
Statute Miles

Scale 1:6,000,000
One centimeter represents 60 kilometers.
One inch represents approximately 95 miles.
Mercator Projection

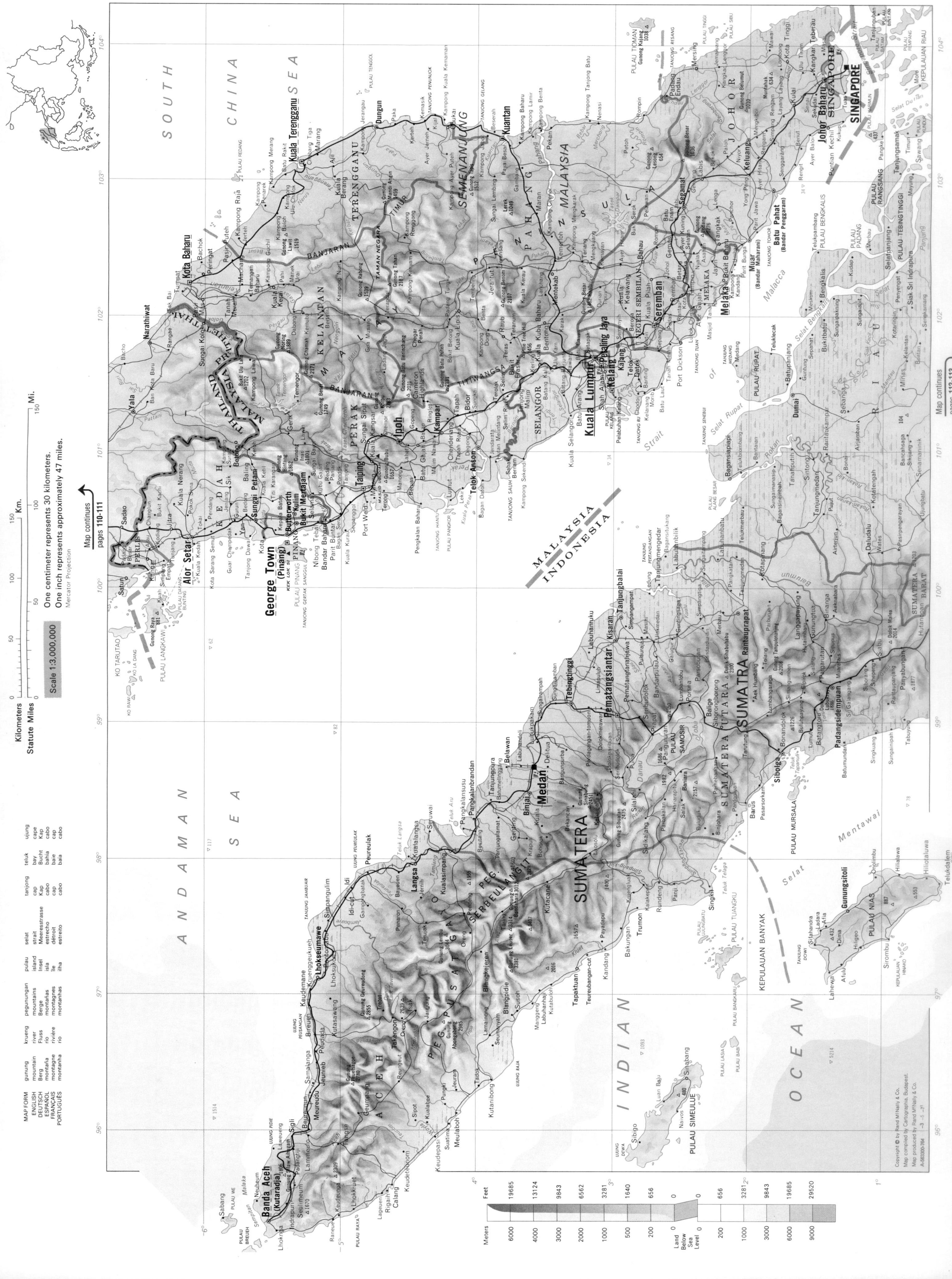
Kilometers
Statute Miles
Scale 1:3,000,000
One centimeter represents 30 kilometers.
One inch represents approximately 47 miles.
Mercator Projection
Map continues pages 110-111
Map continues pages 112-113
MAP FORM
ENGLISH
DEUTSCH
ESPAÑOL
FRANÇAIS
PORTUGUÊS
gunung mountain Berg montaña montagne montanha
krueng river Fluss rio rivière rio
pegunungan mountains Berge montañas montagnes montanhas
pulau island Insel isla île ilha
selat strait Meeresstrasse estrecho détroit estreito
tanjong cap Kap cabo cap cabo
teluk bay Bucht bahía baie baía
ujung cape Kap cabo cap cabo
SOUTH CHINA SEA
ANDAMAN SEA
INDIAN OCEAN
MALAYSIA
INDONESIA
THAILAND
SINGAPORE
SUMATERA
Kuala Lumpur
George Town (Pinang)
Medan
Johor Baharu
Kuala Terengganu
Kota Baharu
Kuantan
Ipoh
Melaka
Seremban
Banda Aceh (Kutaradja)
Strait of Malacca
Meters
Feet
Land Below Sea Level
Copyright © by Rand McNally & Co.

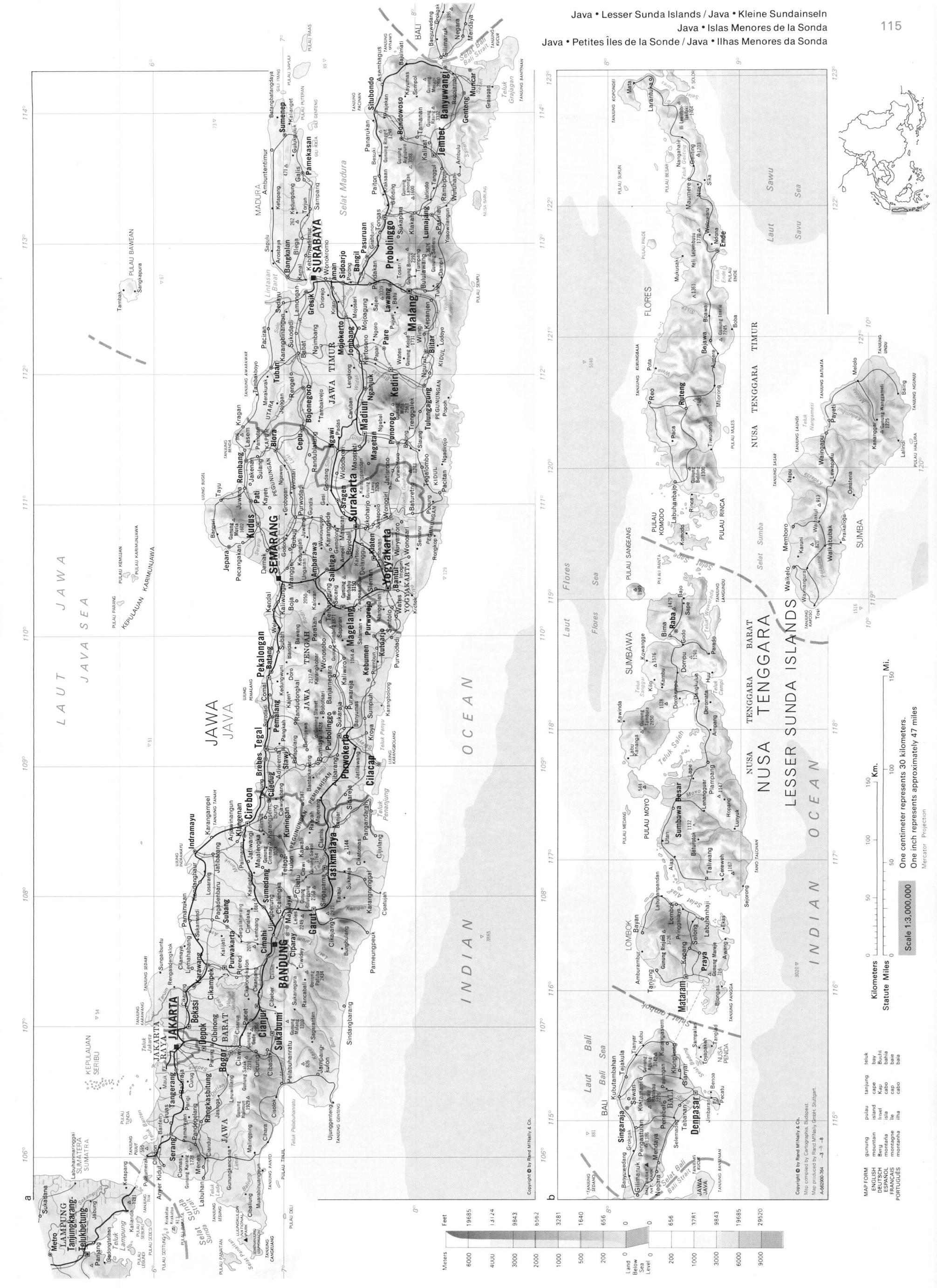

Java • Lesser Sunda Islands / Java • Kleine Sundainseln
Java • Islas Menores de la Sonda
Java • Petites Îles de la Sonde / Java • Ilhas Menores da Sonda

115

a

LAUT JAWA
JAVA SEA

JAWA
JAVA

INDIAN OCEAN

JAKARTA RAYA

BANDUNG

SEMARANG

SURABAYA

YOGYAKARTA

MADURA

Selat Madura

b

Laut Bali
Bali Sea

Laut Flores
Flores Sea

NUSA TENGGARA BARAT

NUSA TENGGARA TIMUR

LESSER SUNDA ISLANDS

NUSA TENGGARA

Laut Sawu
Savu Sea

INDIAN OCEAN

BALI

LOMBOK

SUMBAWA

FLORES

SUMBA

Denpasar

Mataram

Ende

Scale 1:3,000,000

One centimeter represents 30 kilometers.
One inch represents approximately 47 miles.

Mercator Projection

Kilometers
Statute Miles

Km.
Mi.

MAP FORM					
ENGLISH	gunung	pulau	tanjung	teluk	
DEUTSCH	mountain	island	cape	bay	
ESPAÑOL	Berg	Insel	Kap	Bucht	
FRANÇAIS	montaña	isla	cabo	bahía	
PORTUGUÊS	montagne	île	cap	baie	
	montanha	ilha	cabo	baía	

Copyright © by Rand McNally & Co.

Feet
19685
13124
9843
6562
3281
1640
656
0
200
656
3281
9843
19685
29520

Meters
6000
4000
3000
2000
1000
500
200
0
Land Below Sea Level
200
1000
3000
6000
9000

Copyright © by Rand McNally & Co.
Map compiled by Cartographia, Budapest.
Map produced by Rand McNally Grpbh, Stuttgart.
A-662300-764   -3 -3 -8

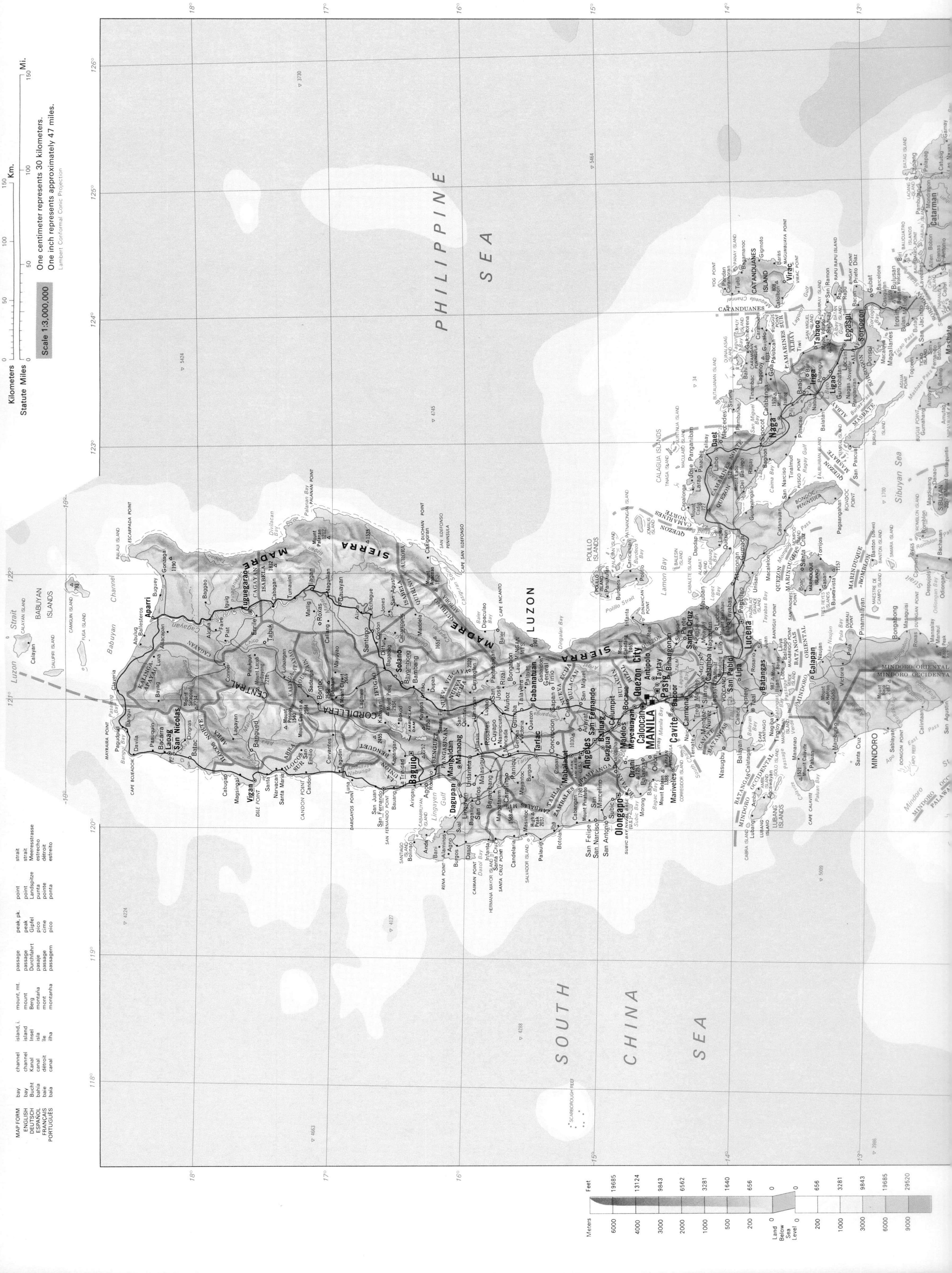

Kilometers
Statute Miles

Scale 1:3,000,000

One centimeter represents 30 kilometers.
One inch represents approximately 47 miles.

Lambert Conformal Conic Projection

MAP FORM									
ENGLISH	bay	channel	island, i.	mount, mt.	passage	peak, pk.	point	strait	
DEUTSCH	Bucht	Kanal	Insel	Berg	Durchfahrt	Gipfel	Landspitze	Meerenge	
ESPAÑOL	bahía	canal	isla	montaña	pasaje	pico	punta	estrecho	
FRANÇAIS	baie	détroit	île	mont	passage	cime	pointe	détroit	
PORTUGUÊS	baía	canal	ilha	montanha	passagem	pico	ponta	estreito	

PHILIPPINE SEA

SOUTH CHINA SEA

Sibuyan Sea

LUZON

SIERRA MADRE

CORDILLERA CENTRAL

MANILA
Quezon City
Baguio
Laoag
San Nicolas
Vigan
Dagupan
Tarlac
Angeles
San Fernando
Caloocan
Cavite
Batangas
Lucena
San Pablo
Calapan
Olongapo
Aparri
Tuguegarao
Legaspi
Naga
Sorsogon
Virac
Daet
Calamba
Antipolo

MINDORO
MINDORO ORIENTAL
MINDORO OCCIDENTAL

MASBATE

MARINDUQUE

CATANDUANES

CAMARINES NORTE
CAMARINES SUR

BABUYAN ISLANDS

Luzon Strait

Babuyan Channel

Lingayen Gulf

Manila Bay

Feet	Meters
19685	6000
13124	4000
9843	3000
6562	2000
3281	1000
1640	500
656	200
0	0 Land Below Sea Level
656	200
3281	1000
9843	3000
19685	6000
29520	9000

MINDANAO

Davao

Cagayan de Oro

Zamboanga

General Santos

Cotabato

Iloilo

Bacolod

Cebu

Tacloban

Puerto Princesa

PALAWAN

NEGROS

PANAY

BOHOL

LEYTE

SAMAR

CELEBES SEA

SULU SEA

Bohol Sea

Moro Gulf

Visayan Sea

Sulu Sea

BORNEO

KALIMANTAN

Sandakan

PHILIPPINES · PILIPINAS
MALAYSIA

SULU ARCHIPELAGO

Jolo

BASILAN ISLAND

TAWI-TAWI

Map continues pages 112-113 ►

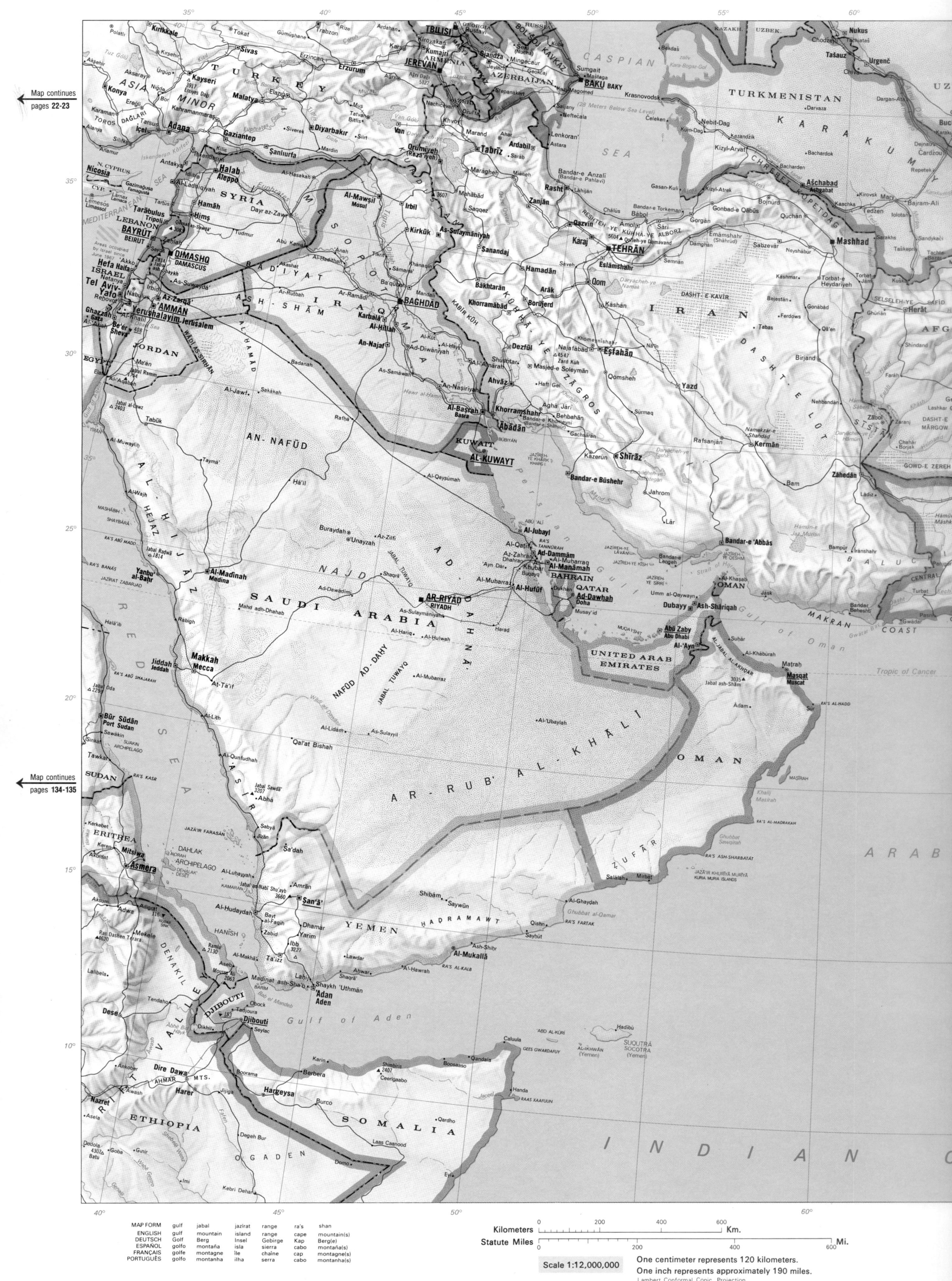

Map continues pages 22-23

Map continues pages 134-135

MAP FORM	gulf	jabal	jazirat	range	ra's	shan
ENGLISH	gulf	mountain	island	range	cape	mountain(s)
DEUTSCH	Golf	Berg	Insel	Gebirge	Kap	Berg(e)
ESPAÑOL	golfo	montaña	isla	sierra	cabo	montaña(s)
FRANÇAIS	golfe	montagne	île	chaîne	cap	montagne(s)
PORTUGUÊS	golfo	montanha	ilha	serra	cabo	montanha(s)

Kilometers   0   200   400   600   Km.

Statute Miles   0   200   400   600   Mi.

Scale 1:12,000,000   One centimeter represents 120 kilometers.
One inch represents approximately 190 miles.
Lambert Conformal Conic Projection

India, Pakistan and Southwest Asia / Indien, Pakistan und Südwestasien / India, Pakistán y Asia Sud-occidental
nde, Pakistan et Asie du Sud-Ouest / Índia, Paquistão e Ásia do Sudoeste

119

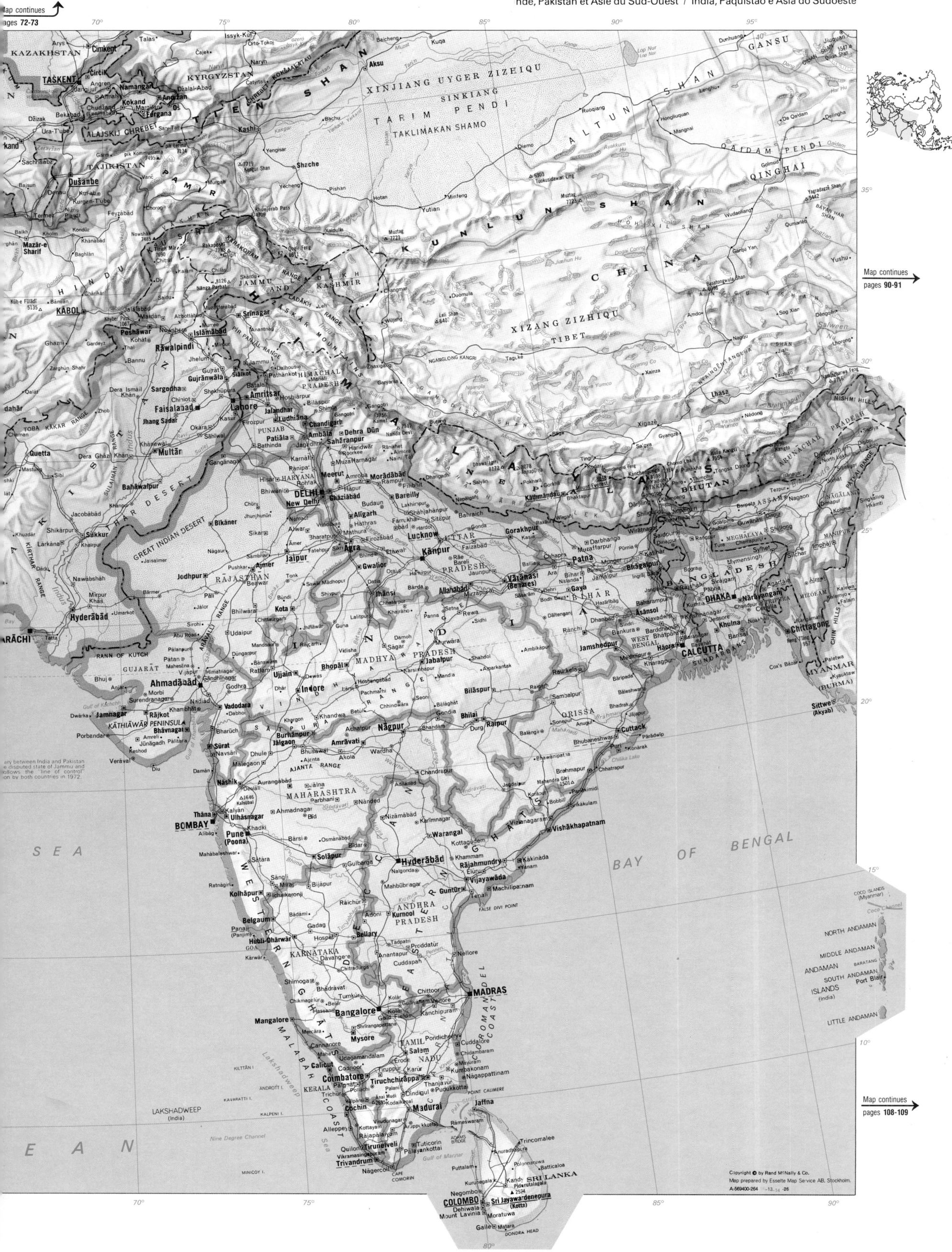

Map continues
ages 72-73

Map continues
pages 90-91

Map continues
pages 108-109

Copyright © by Rand McNally & Co.
Map prepared by Esselte Map Service AB, Stockholm.
A-569400-264   -13, 14 -26

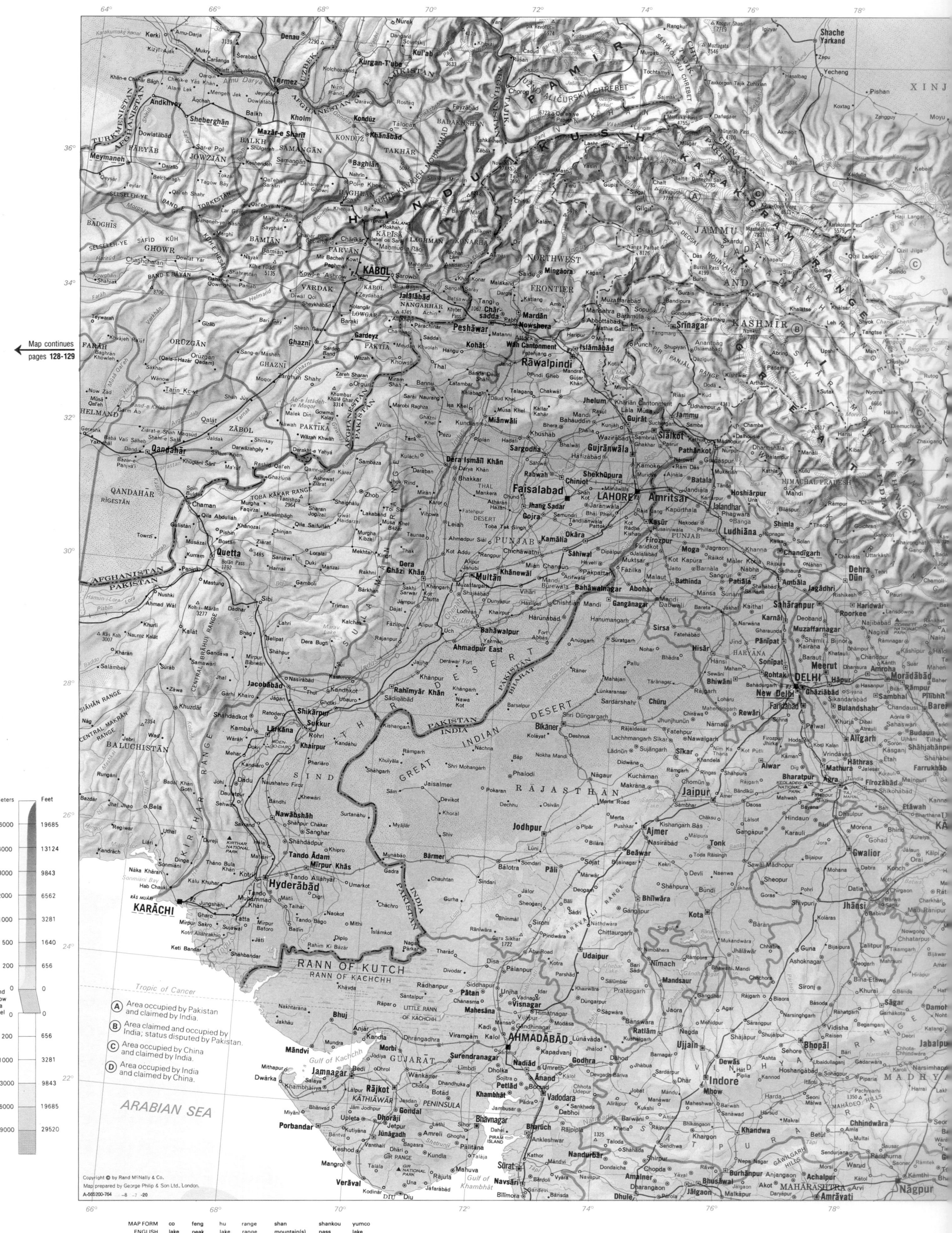

Map continues
pages **128–129**

Meters | Feet
6000 | 19685
4000 | 13124
3000 | 9843
2000 | 6562
1000 | 3281
500 | 1640
200 | 656
Land 0 | 0
Below
Sea
Level 0 | 0
200 | 656
1000 | 3281
3000 | 9843
6000 | 19685
9000 | 29520

Ⓐ Area occupied by Pakistan and claimed by India.

Ⓑ Area claimed and occupied by India; status disputed by Pakistan.

Ⓒ Area occupied by China and claimed by India.

Ⓓ Area occupied by India and claimed by China.

Tropic of Cancer

ARABIAN SEA

Copyright © by Rand McNally & Co.
Map prepared by George Philip & Son Ltd., London.
A-565200-764   –8 –7 –20

MAP FORM	co	feng	hu	range	shan	shankou	yumco
ENGLISH	lake	peak	lake	range	mountain(s)	pass	lake
DEUTSCH	See	Gipfel	See	Gebirge	Berg(e)	Pass	See
ESPAÑOL	lago	pico	lago	sierra	montaña(s)	paso	lago
FRANÇAIS	lac	cime	lac	chaîne	montagne(s)	col	lac
PORTUGUÉS	lago	pico	lago	serra	montanha(s)	passo	lago

Northern India and Pakistan / Nordindien und Pakistan / India Septentrional y Pakistán
Inde Septentrionale et Pakistan / Índia Setentrional e Paquistão

121

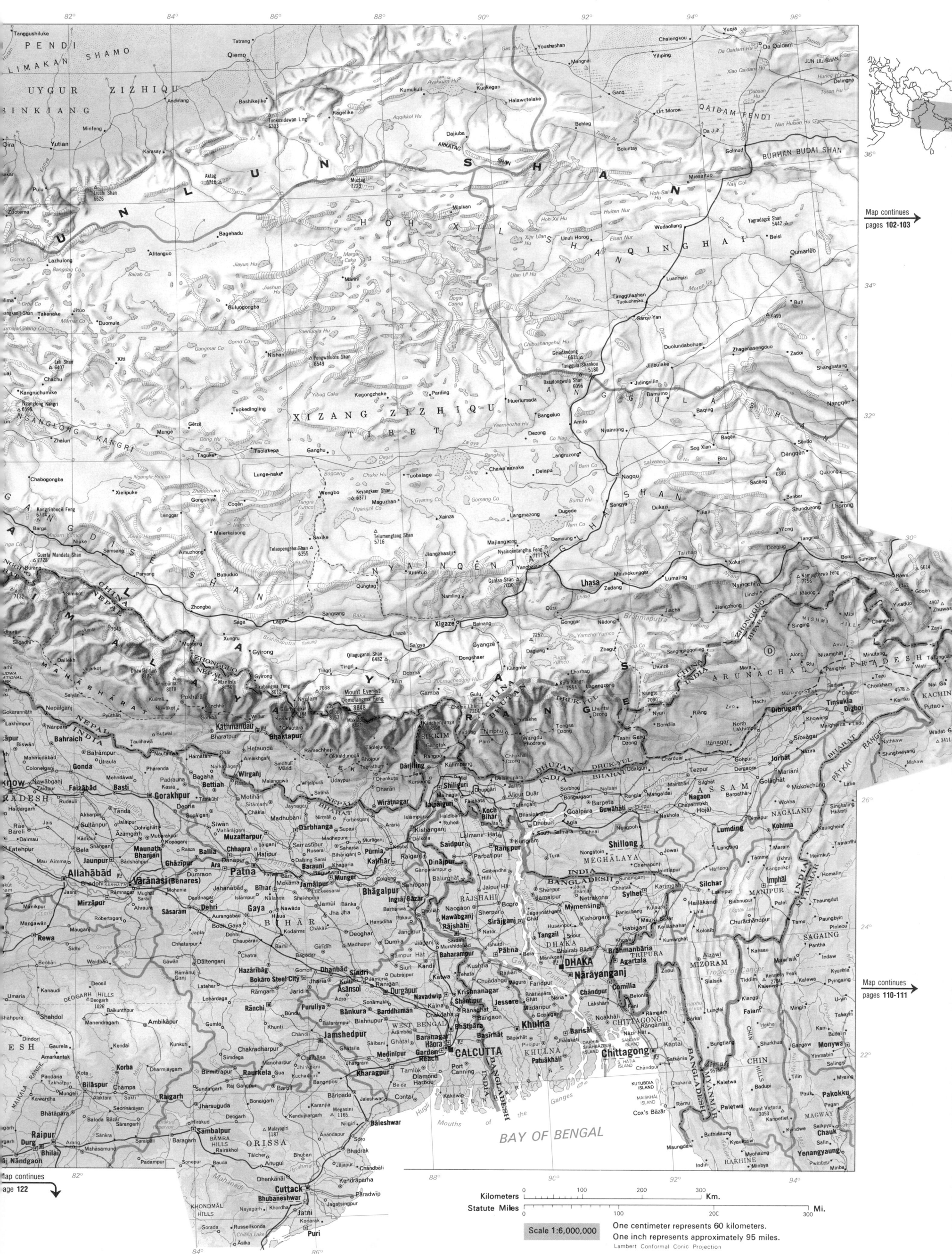

Map continues
pages 120-121

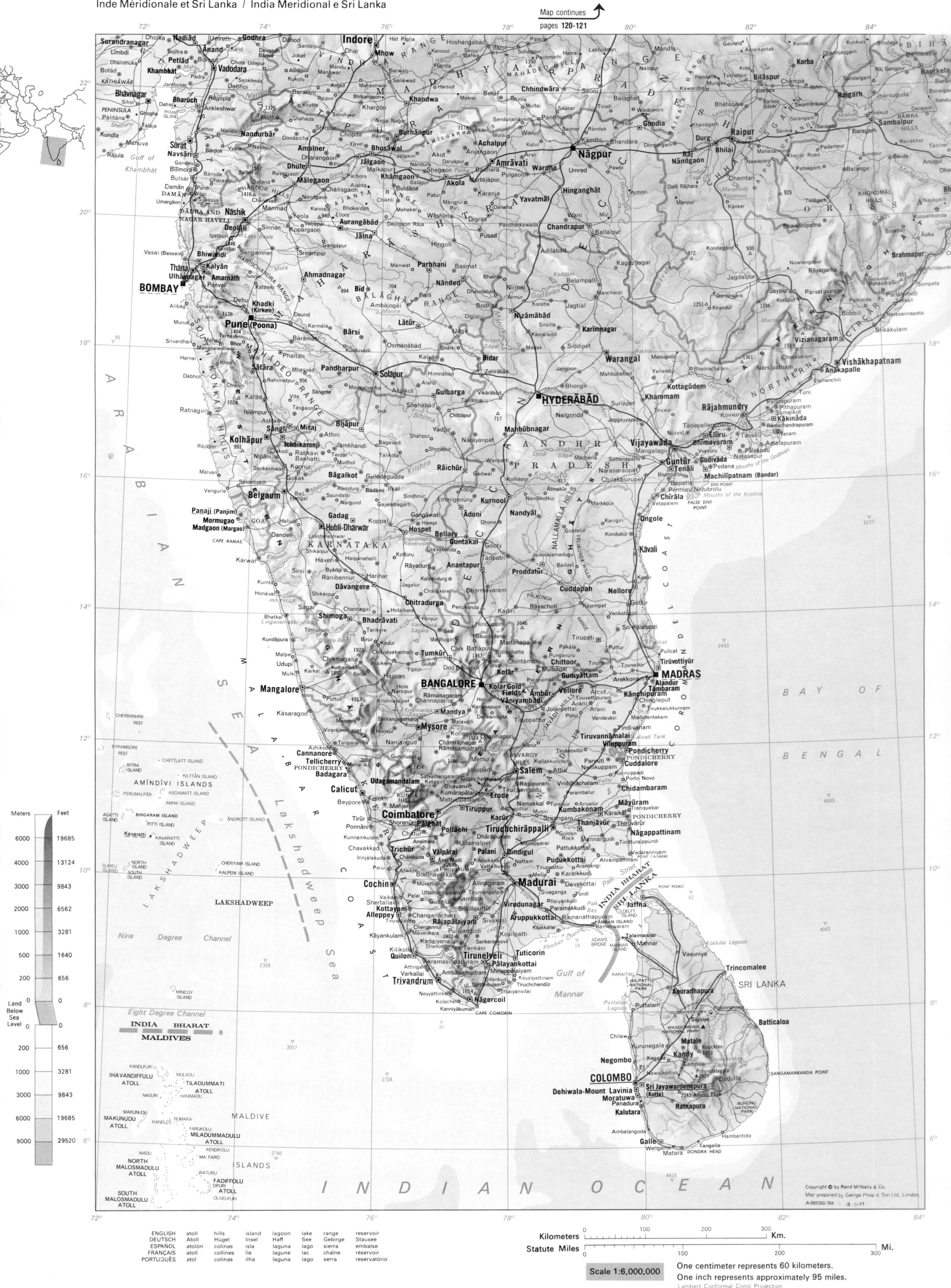

Meters   Feet
6000   19685
4000   13124
3000   9843
2000   6562
1000   3281
500   1640
200   656
Land   0
Below
Sea
Level   0
200   656
1000   3281
3000   9843
6000   19685
9000   29520

ENGLISH	atoll	hills	island	lagoon	lake	range	reservoir
DEUTSCH	Atoll	Hügel	Insel	Haff	See	Gebirge	Stausee
ESPAÑOL	atolón	colinas	isla	laguna	lago	sierra	embalse
FRANÇAIS	atoll	collines	île	lagune	lac	chaîne	réservoir
PORTUGUÊS	atol	colinas	ilha	laguna	lago	serra	reservatório

Kilometers
Statute Miles

One centimeter represents 60 kilometers.
One inch represents approximately 95 miles.

Scale 1:6,000,000

Lambert Conformal Conic Projection

Copyright © by Rand McNally & Co.
Map prepared by George Philip & Son Ltd., London
A-565300-764   -3 - 5 -11

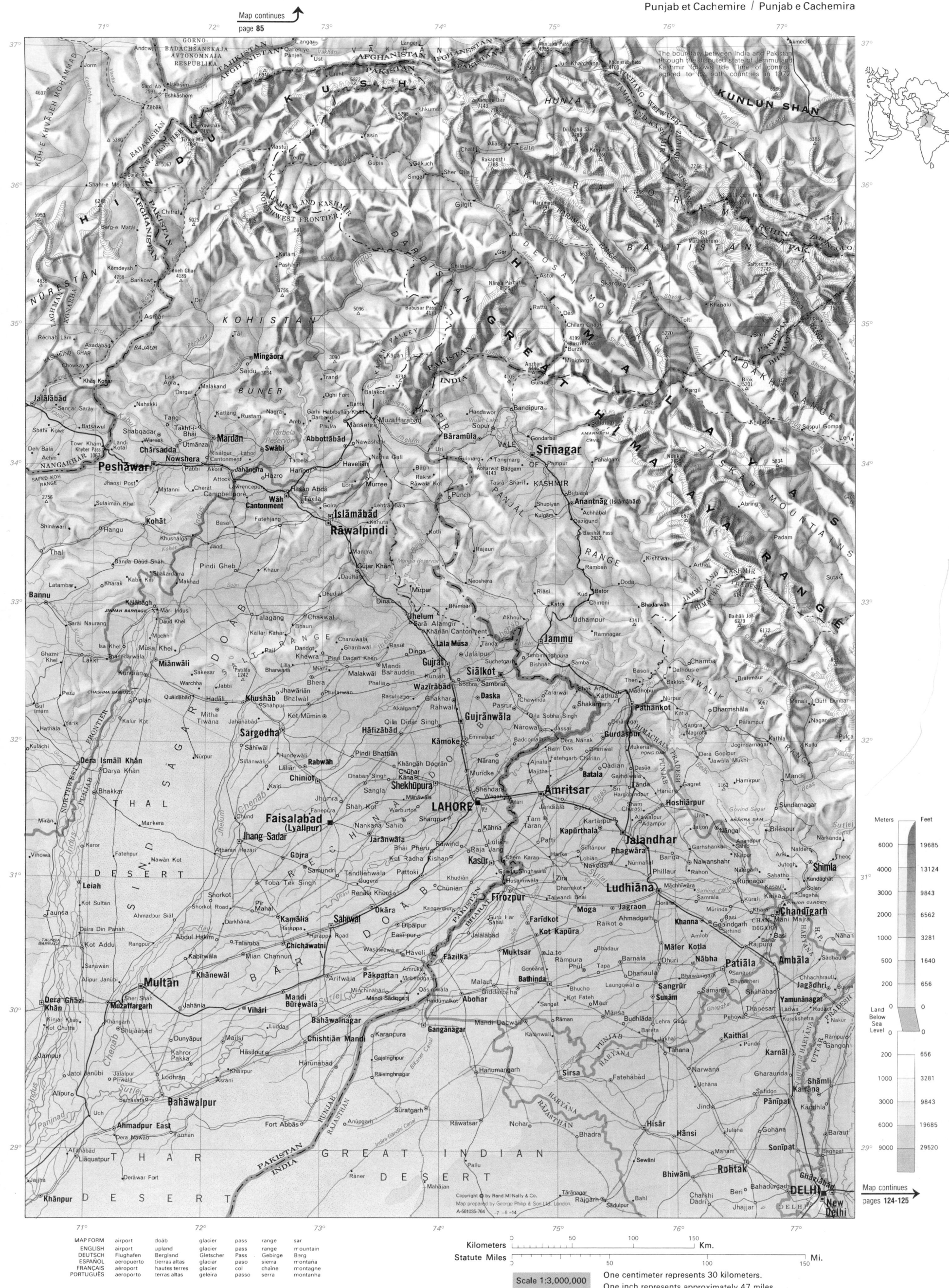

Map continues
page 85

The boundary between India and Pakistan through the disputed state of Jammu and Kashmir follows the "line of control agreed by the both countries in 1972.

Map continues
pages 124-125

Meters	Feet
6000	19685
4000	13124
3000	9843
2000	6562
1000	3281
500	1640
200	656
0 Land Below Sea Level 0	
200	656
1000	3281
3000	9843
6000	19685
9000	29520

MAP FORM						
ENGLISH	airport	doāb	glacier	pass	range	sar
ENGLISH	airport	upland	glacier	pass	range	mountain
DEUTSCH	Flughafen	Bergland	Gletscher	Pass	Gebirge	Berg
ESPAÑOL	aeropuerto	tierras altas	glaciar	paso	sierra	montaña
FRANÇAIS	aéroport	hautes terres	glacier	col	chaîne	montagne
PORTUGUÊS	aeroporto	terras altas	geleira	passo	serra	montanha

Kilometers 0 50 100 150 Km.

Statute Miles 0 50 100 150 Mi.

Scale 1:3,000,000

One centimeter represents 30 kilometers.
One inch represents approximately 47 miles.

Lambert Conformal Conic Projection

Copyright © by Rand McNally & Co.
Map prepared by George Philip & Son Ltd., London.
A-561035-764   7 -6 -14

Map continues page 123

MAP FORM	hills	plains	plateau	range	shan	yumco
ENGLISH	hills	plains	plateau	range	mountains	lake
DEUTSCH	Hügel	Ebenen	Hochebene	Gebirge	Berge	See
ESPAÑOL	colinas	llanos	meseta	sierra	montañas	lago
FRANÇAIS	collines	plaines	plateau	chaîne	montagnes	lac
PORTUGUÊS	colinas	planícies	planalto	serra	montanhas	lago

Kilometers
Statute Miles

Scale 1:3,000,000

One centimeter represents 30 kilometers.
One inch represents approximately 47 miles.

Lambert Conformal Conic Projection

Ganges Lowland and Nepal / Gangestiefland und Nepal / Llanuras del Ganges y Nepal
Plaine du Gange et Népal / Planície do Ganges e Nepal

125

MAP FORM	bay	canal	char	delta	island	plain
ENGLISH	bay	canal	island	delta	island	plain
DEUTSCH	Bucht	Kanal	Insel	Delta	Insel	Ebene
ESPAÑOL	bahía	canal	isla	delta	isla	llanura
FRANÇAIS	baie	canal	île	delta	île	plaine
PORTUGUÊS	baía	canal	ilha	delta	ilha	planície

Kilometers
Statute Miles

Scale 1:1,000,000

One centimeter represents 10 kilometers.
One inch represents approximately 16 miles.
Lambert Conformal Conic Projection

Map continues
page **84**

Map continues
pages **130–131**

Map continues
pages **140–141**

Map continues
pages **144–145**

MEDITERRANEAN SEA

RED SEA

Gulf of Suez

The Turkish Republic of
Northern Cyprus unilaterally
declared its independence
on November 15, 1983.

Area occupied by Israel
since June 1967

Administrative
Boundary

Area administered
by Sudan

Tropic of Cancer

Scale legend

Meters		Feet
6000		19685
4000		13124
3000		9843
2000		6562
1000		3281
500		1640
200		656
Land Below Sea Level	0	0
200		656
1000		3281
3000		9843
6000		19685
9000		29520

MAP FORM	harrat	jabal	jazireh	küh	ra's	sabkhat	wâdi
ENGLISH	lava flow	mountain	island	mountain	cape	salt marsh	wadi
DEUTSCH	Lavastrom	Berg	Insel	Berg	Kap	Salzmarsch	Wadi
ESPAÑOL	corriente de lava	montaña	isla	montaña	cabo	pantano salado	uadi
FRANÇAIS	coulée de lave	montagne	île	montagne	cap	marais salé	wadi
PORTUGUÊS	corrente de lava	montanha	ilha	montanha	cabo	pântano salgado	uádi

Kilometers ⊢——————100——————200——————300—— Km.

Statute Miles ⊢——————100——————200——————300—— Mi.

Scale 1:6,000,000   One centimeter represents 60 kilometers.
One inch represents approximately 95 miles.
Lambert Conformal Conic Projection

Copyright © by Rand McNally & Co.
Map prepared by George Philip & Son Ltd., London.
A-589495-764 -13 16 -25

Map continues
pages 120-121

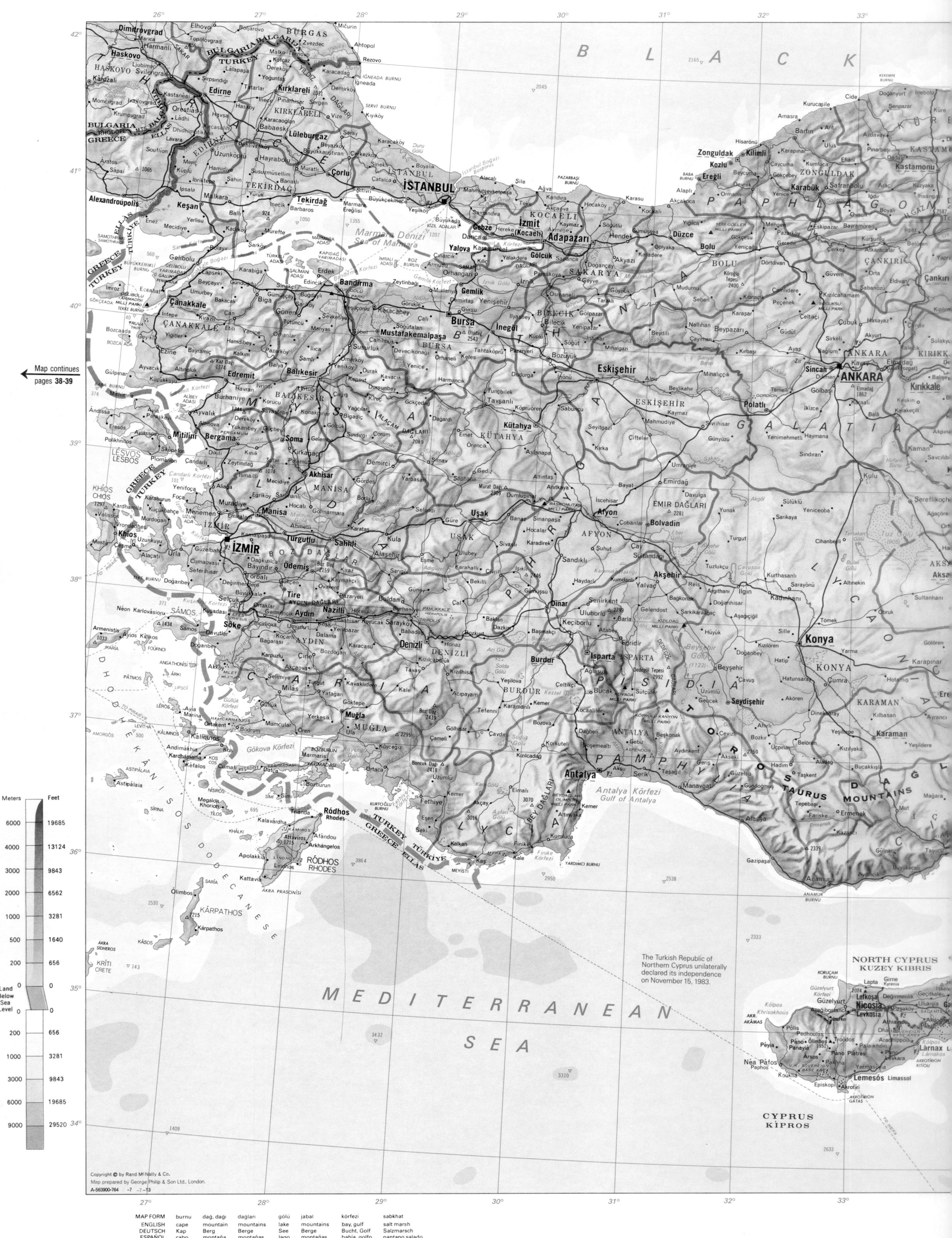

Map continues
pages **38-39**

The Turkish Republic of
Northern Cyprus unilaterally
declared its independence
on November 15, 1983.

MAP FORM	burnu	dağ, dağı	dağları	gölü	jabal	körfezi	sabkhat
ENGLISH	cape	mountain	mountains	lake	mountains	bay, gulf	salt marsh
DEUTSCH	Kap	Berg	Berge	See	Berge	Bucht, Golf	Salzmarsch
ESPAÑOL	cabo	montaña	montañas	lago	montañas	bahía, golfo	pantano salado
FRANÇAIS	cap	montagne	montagnes	lac	montagnes	baie, golfe	marais salé
PORTUGUÊS	cabo	montanha	montanhas	lago	montanhas	baía, golfo	pântano salgado

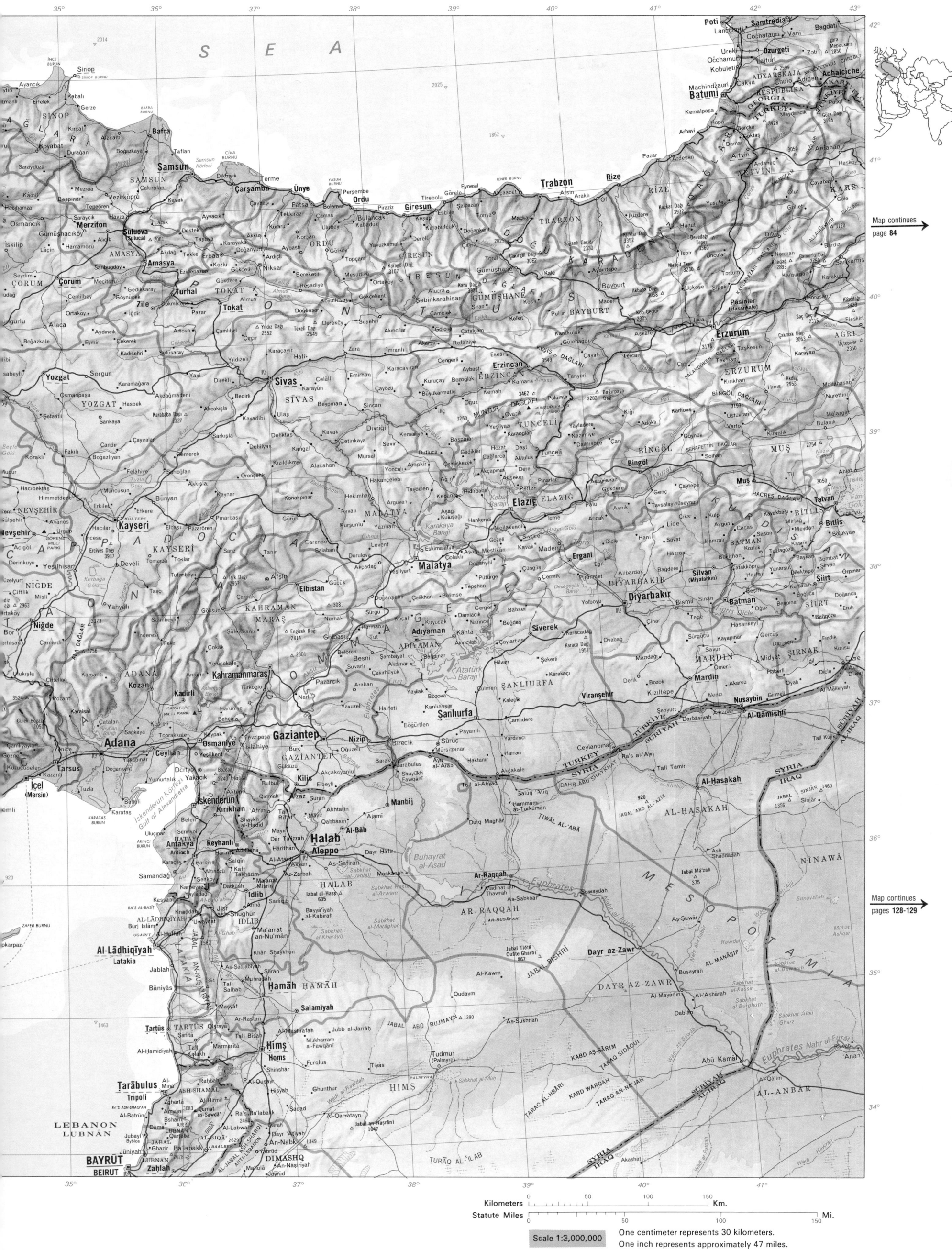

Map continues
page 84

Map continues
pages 128-129

Kilometers
Statute Miles

Scale 1:3,000,000

One centimeter represents 30 kilometers.
One inch represents approximately 47 miles.
Conic Projection, Two Standard Parallels

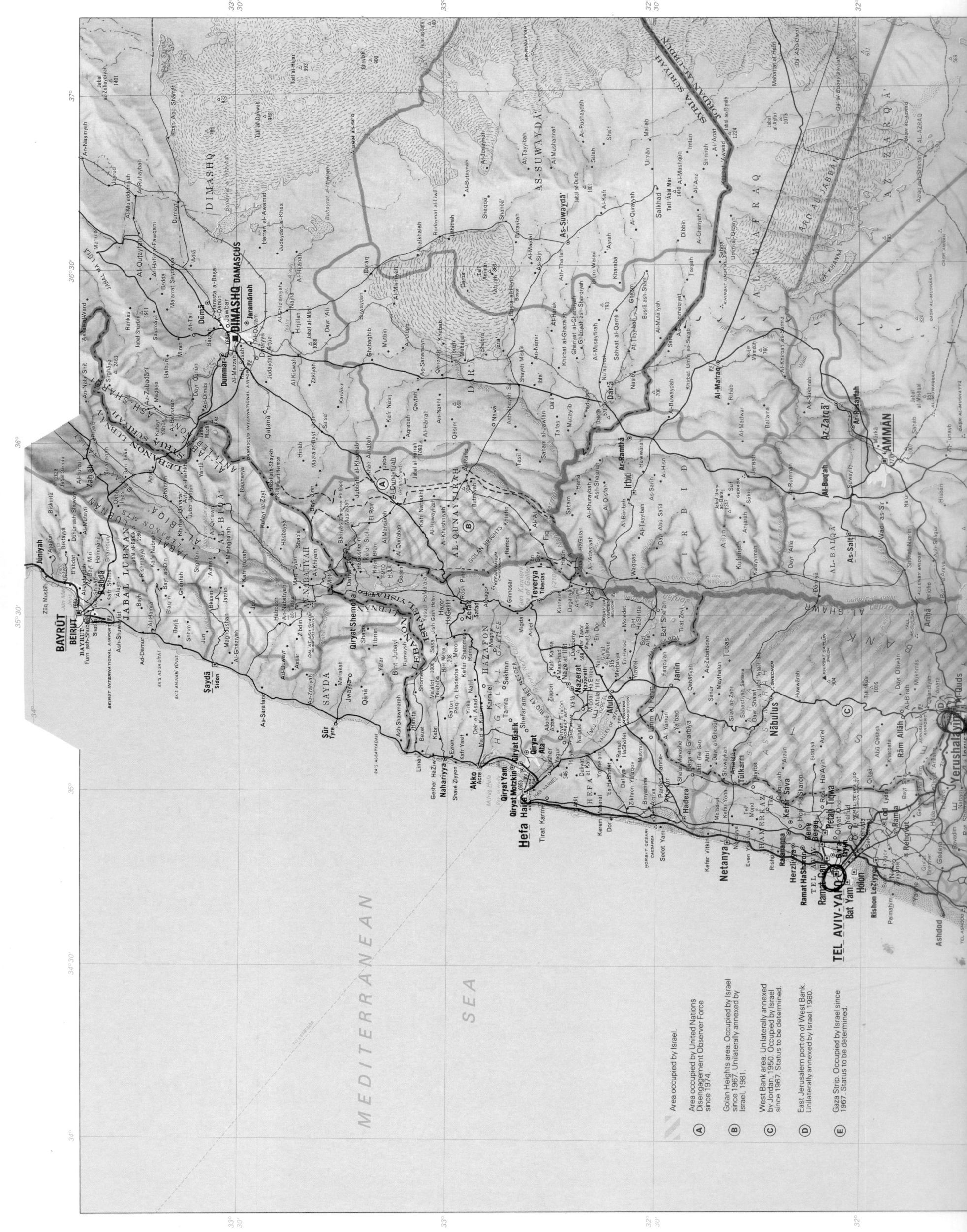

A   Area occupied by Israel.

Ⓐ   Area occupied by United Nations
      Disengagement Observer Force
      since 1974.

Ⓑ   Golan Heights area. Occupied by Israel
      since 1967. Unilaterally annexed by
      Israel, 1981.

Ⓒ   West Bank area. Unilaterally annexed
      by Jordan, 1950. Occupied by Israel
      since 1967. Status to be determined.

Ⓓ   East Jerusalem portion of West Bank.
      Unilaterally annexed by Israel, 1980.

Ⓔ   Gaza Strip. Occupied by Israel since
      1967. Status to be determined.

Ghazzah
Gaza
Jabalyah
Khān Yūnus
Rafah
Al-'Arīsh
Be'er Sheva
Qiryat Gat
Al-Khalīl
Hebron
Dimona
'Arad
HADAROM
HANEGEV
NEGEV DESERT
HOLOT HALUZA
Mizpe Ramon
Yotvata
Elat
Al-'Aqabah
Dead Sea
Yam HaMelah
Al-Bahr al-Mayyit
Al-Karak
AL-KARAK
AT-TAFILAH
Aṭ-Ṭafīlah
Ma'ān
MA'AN
Ash-Shawbak
Wadi Musa
JIBĀL AL-BATRĀ'
WADI AL-'ARABA
HA'ARAVA
ISRAEL
JORDAN
AL-URDUN
EGYPT
MIṢR
SAUDI ARABIA
AL-'ARABIYAH AS-SU'ŪDIYAH
SINAI PENINSULA
SĪNĀ'
Al-Jafr
QĀ' AL-JAFR
JIBĀL AṬ-ṬUBAYQ

MAP FORM	har	jabal	nahr	ra's	sede-te'ufa	tall	wadi
ENGLISH	mountain	mountain(s)	river	cape	airport	mountain	wadi
DEUTSCH	Berg	Berg(e)	Fluss	Kap	Flughafen	Berg	Wadi
ESPAÑOL	montaña	montaña(s)	río	cabo	aeropuerto	montaña	uadi
FRANÇAIS	montagne	montagne(s)	rivière	cap	aéroport	montagne	wadi
PORTUGUÊS	montanha	montanha(s)	rio	cabo	aeroporto	montanha	uádi

Kilometers 0 10 20 30 40 50 Km.

Statute Miles 0 10 20 30 40 50 Mi.

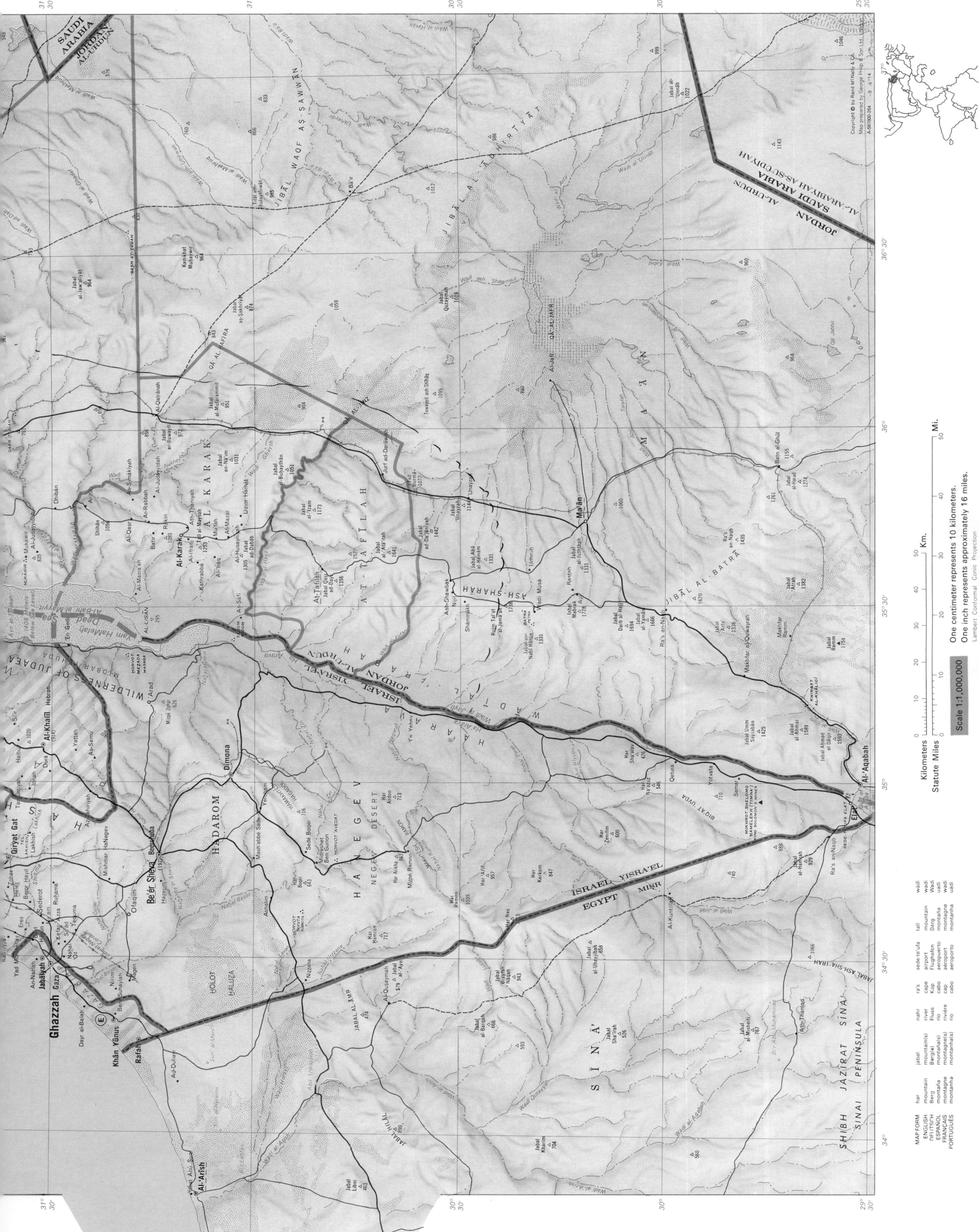

Scale 1:1,000,000

One centimeter represents 10 kilometers.

One inch represents approximately 16 miles.

Lambert Conformal Conic Projection

Western Sahara has been occupied by Morocco

MAP FORM

	bahr, baḥr	chott	jabal	lake	mountains	oued	wahāt
ENGLISH	river, sea	salt marsh	mountain(s)	lake	mountains	wadi	oasis
DEUTSCH	Fluss, Meer	Salzmarsch	Berg(e)	See	Berge	Wadi	Oase
ESPAÑOL	rio, mar	pantano salado	montaña(s)	lago	montañas	uadi	oasis
FRANÇAIS	rivière, mer	marais salé	montagne(s)	lac	montagnes	wadi	oasis
PORTUGUÊS	rio, mar	pântano salgado	montanha(s)	lago	montanhas	uádi	oásis

Western North Africa / West Nordafrika / Región Occidental de Africa Septentrional
Afrique du Nord Occidentale / África do Norte Ocidental

135

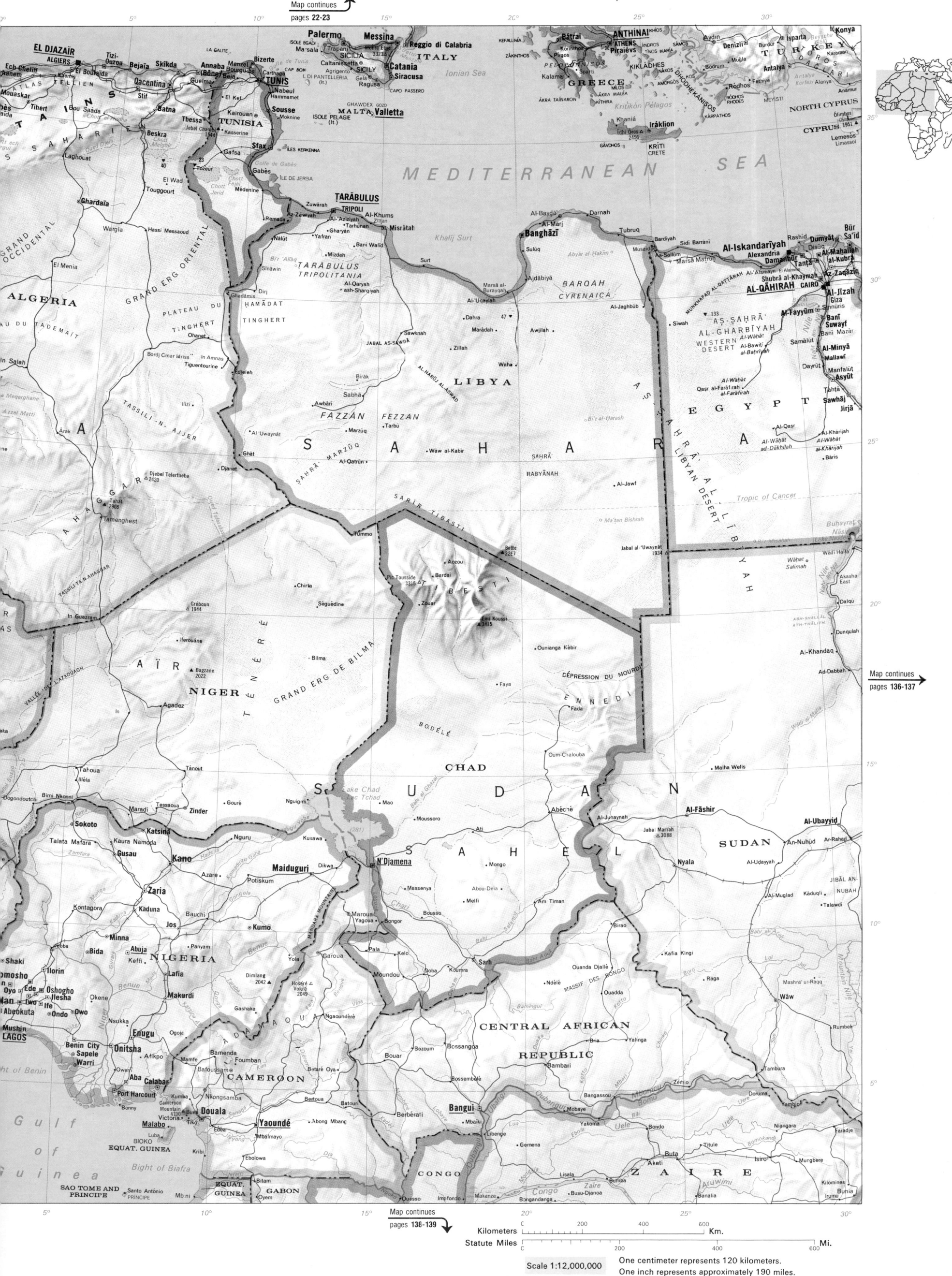

Map continues
pages 22-23

Map continues
pages 136-137

Map continues
pages 138-139

Kilometers
Statute Miles

Scale 1:12,000,000

One centimeter represents 120 kilometers.
One inch represents approximately 190 miles.
Miller Oblated Stereographic Projection

136

Eastern North Africa / Ost Nordafrika / Región Oriental de Africa Septentrional
Afrique du Nord Orientale / África do Norte Oriental

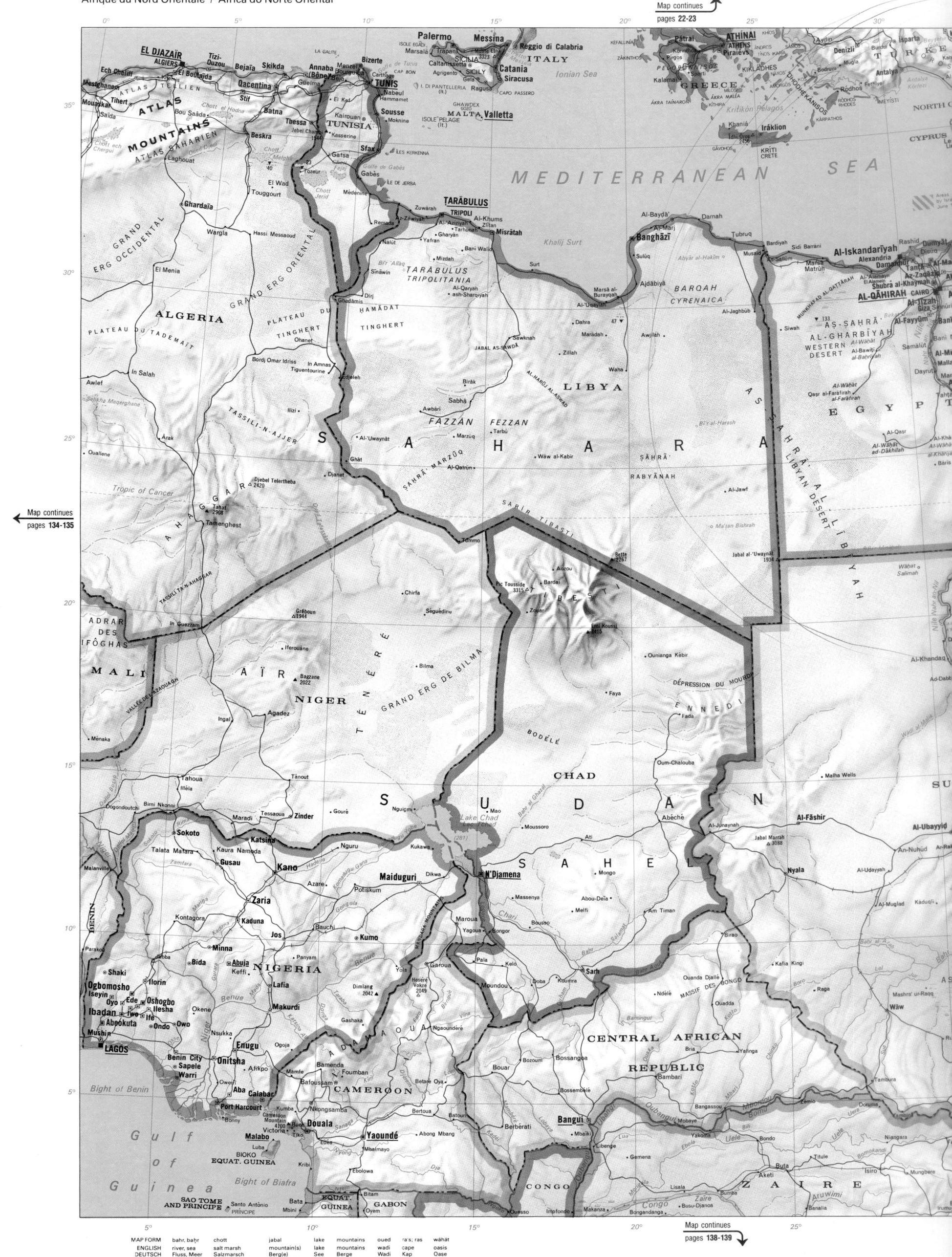

Map continues
pages 22-23

Map continues
pages 134-135

Map continues
pages 138-139

MAP FORM	bahr, baḥr	chott	jabal	lake	mountains	oued	ra's; ras	wāhāt
ENGLISH	river, sea	salt marsh	mountain(s)	lake	mountains	wadi	cape	oasis
DEUTSCH	Fluss, Meer	Salzmarsch	Berg(e)	See	Berge	Wadi	Kap	Oase
ESPAÑOL	río, mar	pantano salado	montaña(s)	lago	montañas	uadi	cabo	oasis
FRANCAIS	rivière, mer	marais salé	montagne(s)	lac	montagnes	wadi	cap	oasis
PORTUGUÊS	rio, mar	pântano salgado	montanha(s)	lago	montanhas	uádi	cabo	oásis

Eastern North Africa / Ost Nordafrika / Región Oriental de Africa Septentrional
Afrique du Nord Orientale / África do Norte Oriental

137

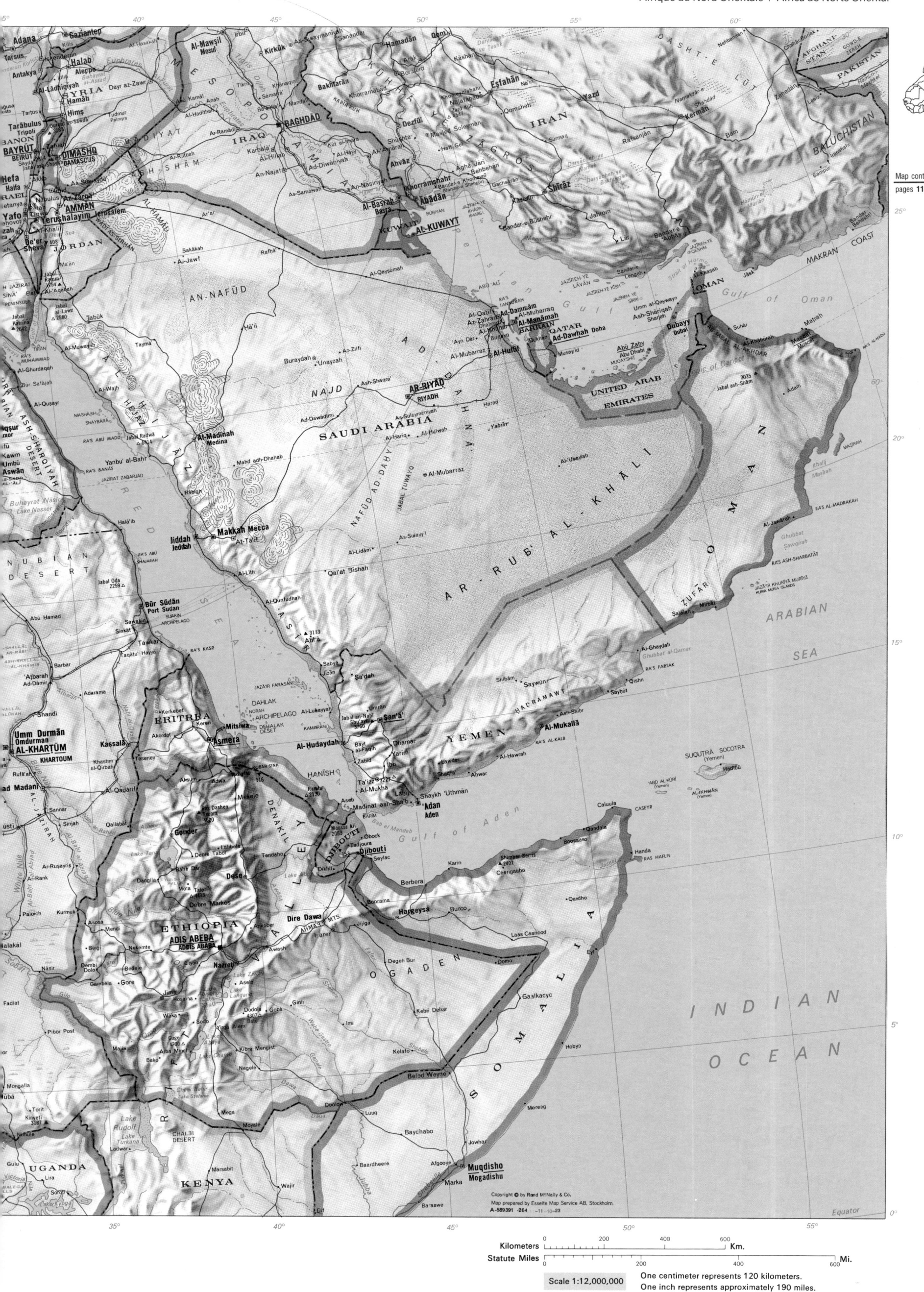

Map continues
pages 118-119

Kilometers
0   200   400   600
Km.

Statute Miles
0   200   400   600
Mi.

Scale 1:12,000,000

One centimeter represents 120 kilometers.
One inch represents approximately 190 miles.
Miller Oblated Stereographic Projection

Map continues
pages 136-137

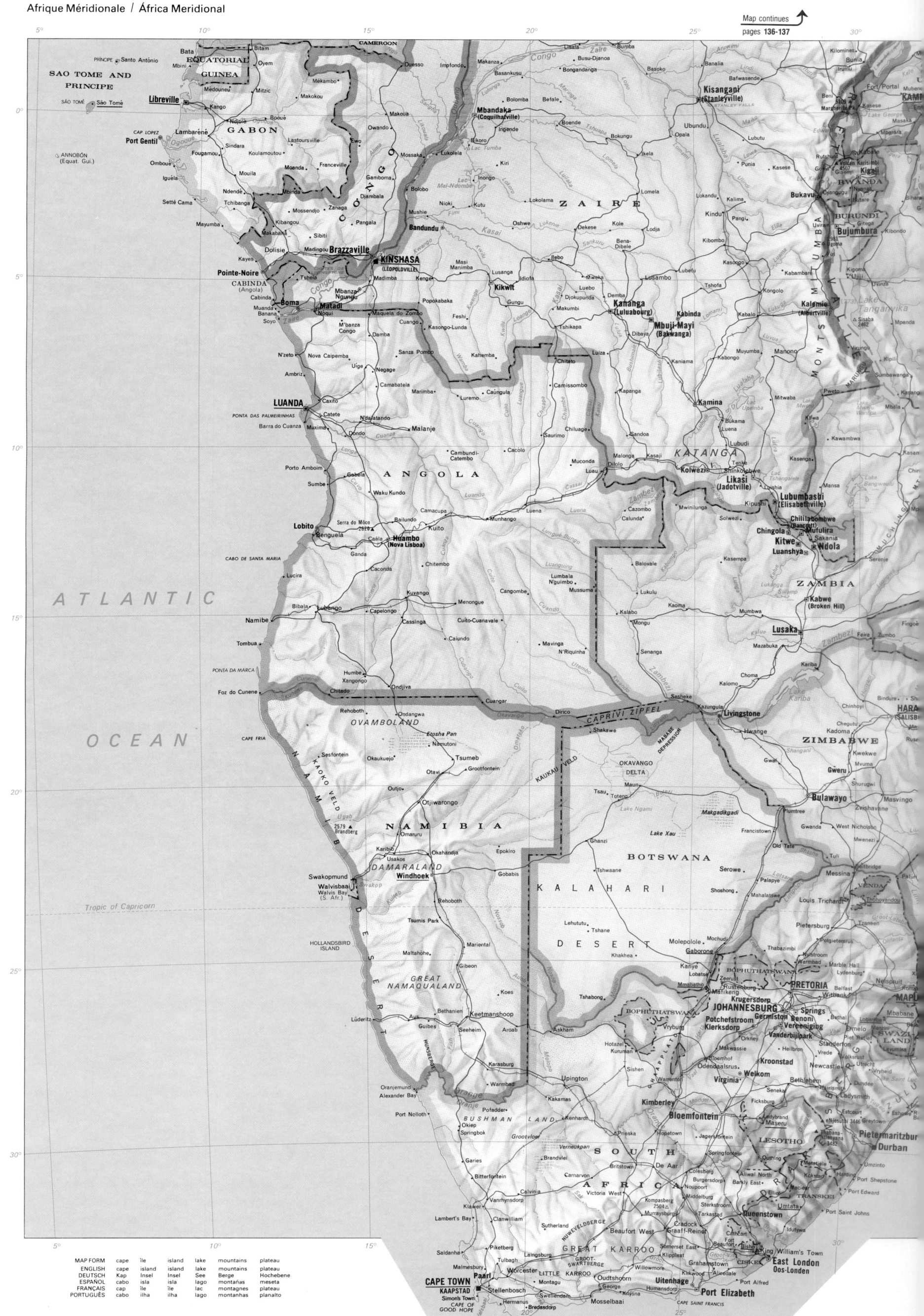

MAP FORM   cape   île   island   lake   mountains   plateau
ENGLISH   cape   île   island   lake   mountains   plateau
DEUTSCH   Kap   Insel   Insel   See   Berge   Hochebene
ESPAÑOL   cabo   isla   isla   lago   montañas   meseta
FRANÇAIS   cap   île   île   lac   montagnes   plateau
PORTUGUÊS   cabo   ilha   ilha   lago   montanhas   planalto

Equator

INDIAN OCEAN

SOMALIA

KENYA
Kisumu
NAIROBI
Mombasa

MASAI
STEPPE
Zanzibar
Bagamoyo
DAR ES SALAAM

ANZANIA

MAFIA ISLAND
Kilindoni

SEYCHELLES
PRASLIN ISLAND LA DIGUE
SILHOUETTE Victoria
MAHÉ ISLAND

AMIRANTE ISLANDS (Sey.) ÎLE DESROCHES (Sey.) PLATTE ISLAND (Sey.)

COETIVY ISLAND (Sey.)

ALPHONSE ISLAND (Sey.)

PROVIDENCE ISLAND (Sey.)

MALAWI
Lilongwe

ALDABRA ISLAND (Sey.)
ASSUMPTION ISLAND (Sey.)

COSMOLEDO I. (Sey.)
ASTOVE ISLAND (Sey.)

SAINT PIERRE ISLAND (Sey.) CERF ISLAND (Sey.)

FARQUHAR GROUP (Sey.)

AGALEGA ISLANDS (Mauritius)

Lindi
Mtwara
CABO DELGADO
Palma
Moçimboa da Praia

Ibo
Quissanga
Pemba

Moroni NDZUDJA COMOROS
Fomboni Mutsamudu NZWANI
MWALI

ÎLES GLORIEUSES (Fr.)

CAP D'AMBRE
CAP SAINT-SÉBASTIEN Antsiranana

ARCHIPEL DES COMORES

MAYOTTE (Fr.) Dzaoudzi

NOSY MITSIO

Montepuez
Lúrio
Namapa

NOSY BE
Hell-Ville Ambilobe
Vohimarina

MASSIF DU TSARATANANA
Maromokotro 2876 Sambava

Ambanja
Doany
Ancapa Antalaha

Nacala

Moçambique

NOSY LAVA
Analalava Befandriana
Analalava Antsohihy

MOZAMBIQUE

Nampula
Mogincual
Quinga
Angoche
ILHA ANGOCHE

Helodranon' i Mahajamba

Mahajanga Port-Bergé Mandritsara NOSY BORAHA
Marovoay Mampikony Mananara Ambodifototra

CAP EST
PRESQU' ÎLE DE MASOALA

Baie de Narinda

Baie d'Antongil

Moma

CAP SAINT-ANDRÉ
NOSY CHESTERFIELD (Madag.)

Soalala Tsaratanana
Maevatanana

Fenoarivo Atsinanana

ÎLE TROMELIN (Fr.)

Quelimane
Sena Vila Fontes
Marromeu
Chinde

ILE JUAN DE NOVA (Fr.)
Tambohorano

Morafenobe

Andriamena Ambatondrazaka

Toamasina

Manica
Dondo
Beira

NOSY BARREN

Maintirano
Ankazobe ANTANANARIVO

MADAGASCAR
Tsiroanomandidy Vohidiany
Ankavandra

Vatomandry

Nova Sofala
Nova Mambone
Bartolomeu Dias

BASSAS DA INDIA (Fr.)
ILHA DO BAZARUTO

Belo Mandiavazo Ambatolampy
Morondava Mahabo Antsirabe
Malaimbandy Mahanoro

ANKARATRA

Vilanculos
PONTA SÃO SEBASTIÃO

Mandabe Ambositra
Manja Nosy Varika
Morombe Ambosondra Mananjary

Port Louis
Curepipe Mahébourg
MAURITIUS

PONTA DA BARRA FALSA

ILE EUROPA (Fr.)
CAP SAINT-VINCENT

Beroroha Fianarantsoa
Ambalavao

Le Port
Saint-Paul Saint-Denis
RÉUNION (Fr.)
Saint-Pierre

Funhalouro
Massinga
Morrumbene
PONTA DA BARRA
Inhambane

Ankazoabo
Pic Boby 2658

Manakara

MASCARENE ISLANDS

Maxixe

Ihosy Toliara Betroka
Farafangana

Mancaze
Inharrime

Betioky Vangaindrano
Bekily Midongy Sud

Tropic of Capricorn

Ampanihy
Androka Tsihombe
Ambovombe Faradofay

CAP SAINTE-MARIE

INDIAN OCEAN

Kilometers 200 400 600 Km.
Statute Miles 200 400 600 Mi.

Scale 1:12,000,000
One centimeter represents 120 kilometers.
One inch represents approximately 190 miles.
Miller Oblated Stereographic Projection

Map continues pages 128-129

MEDITERRANEAN SEA
RED SEA
AL BAHR AL-AHMAR
Khalij as-Suways
Gulf of Suez
Gulf of Aqaba
AL-ISKANDARIYAH
ALEXANDRIA
AL-QAHIRAH
CAIRO
AL-JIZAH
Bur Sa'id Port Said
As-Suways Suez
Aswan
Luxor
Asyut
Al-Minya
TEL AVIV-YAFO
Yerushalayim
Jerusalem
AMMAN
Al-'Aqabah
Al-Madinah
Medina
Jiddah
Makkah
Mecca
Bur Sudan
Port Sudan
Marsa Matruh
Siwah
Tubruq
Tobruk
EGYPT
MISR
SUDAN
LIBYA
LIBIYA
CHAD
TCHAD
WESTERN DESERT
ARABIAN DESERT
LIBYAN DESERT
NUBIAN DESERT
AS-SAHRA AL-LIBIYAH
AS-SAHRA ASH-SHARQIYAH
AS-SAHRA AL-GHARBIYAH
LIBYAN PLATEAU
BARQAH
CYRENAICA
SINAI PENINSULA
Tropic of Cancer
Nile
AN-NAFUD
AL-HIJAZ
MIDIAN
JORDAN
SAUDI ARABIA
ISRAEL
IRAQ

Map continues pages 144-145

Map continues pages 154-155

Map continues pages 146-147

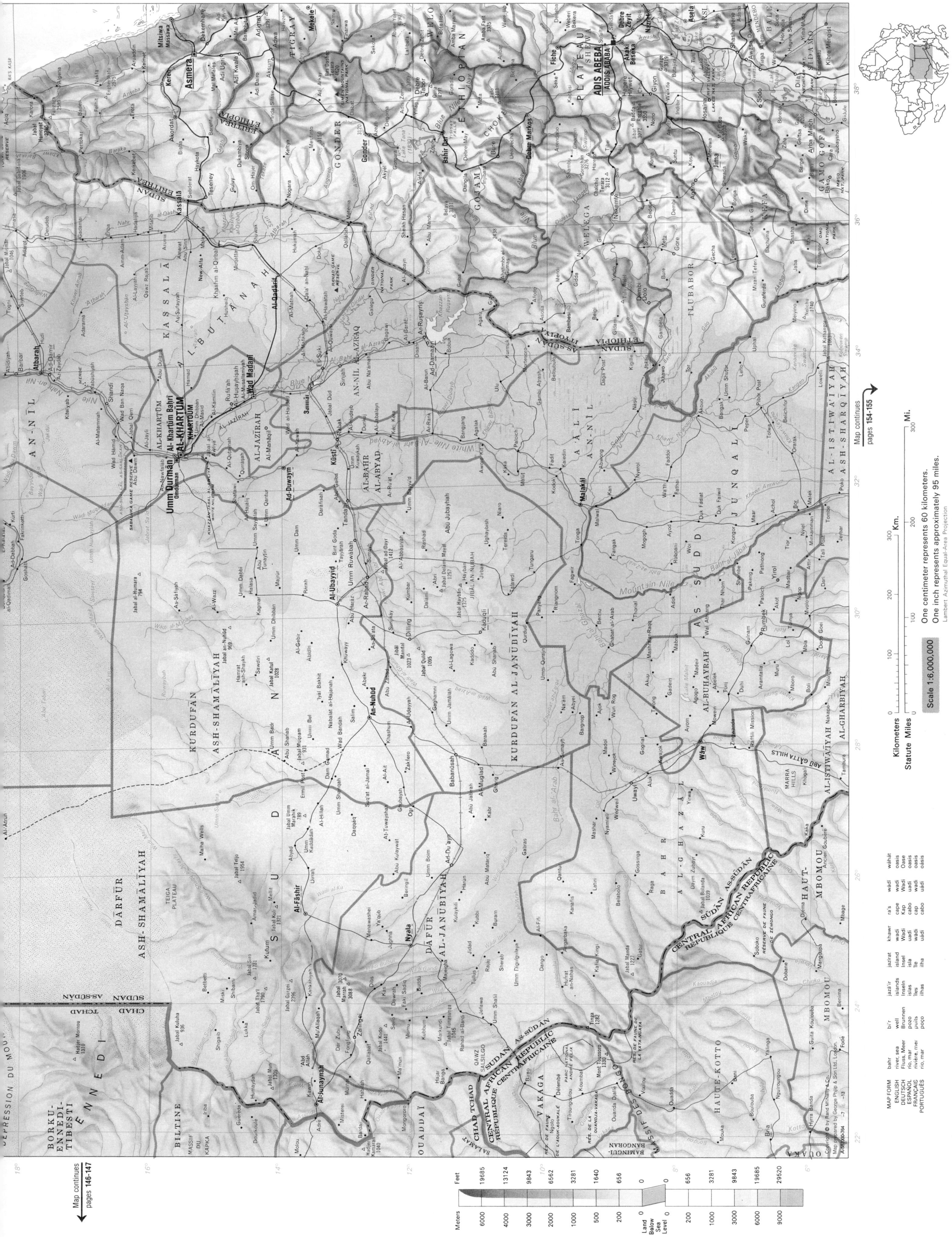

Scale 1:6,000,000

One centimeter represents 60 kilometers.
One inch represents approximately 95 miles.
Lambert Azimuthal Equal-Area Projection

Kilometers
0   100   200   300   Km.

Statute Miles
0   100   200   300   Mi.

MAP FORM	bahr	b'r	jazā'ir	jazīrat	khawr	ra's	wadi	wāhāt
ENGLISH	river, sea	well	islands	island	wadi	cape	wadi	oasis
DEUTSCH	Fluss, Meer	Brunnen	Inseln	Insel	Wadi	Kap	Wadi	Oase
ESPAÑOL	rio, mar	pozo	islas	isla	uadi	cabo	uadi	oasis
FRANÇAIS	rivière, mer	puits	îles	île	uadi	cap	uadi	oasis
PORTUGUÊS	rio, mar	poço	ilhas	ilha	uadi	cabo	uadi	oásis

Feet	Meters
19685	6000
13124	4000
9843	3000
6562	2000
3281	1000
1640	500
656	200
0	0
Land Below Sea Level	
0	0
656	200
3281	1000
9843	3000
19685	6000
29520	9000

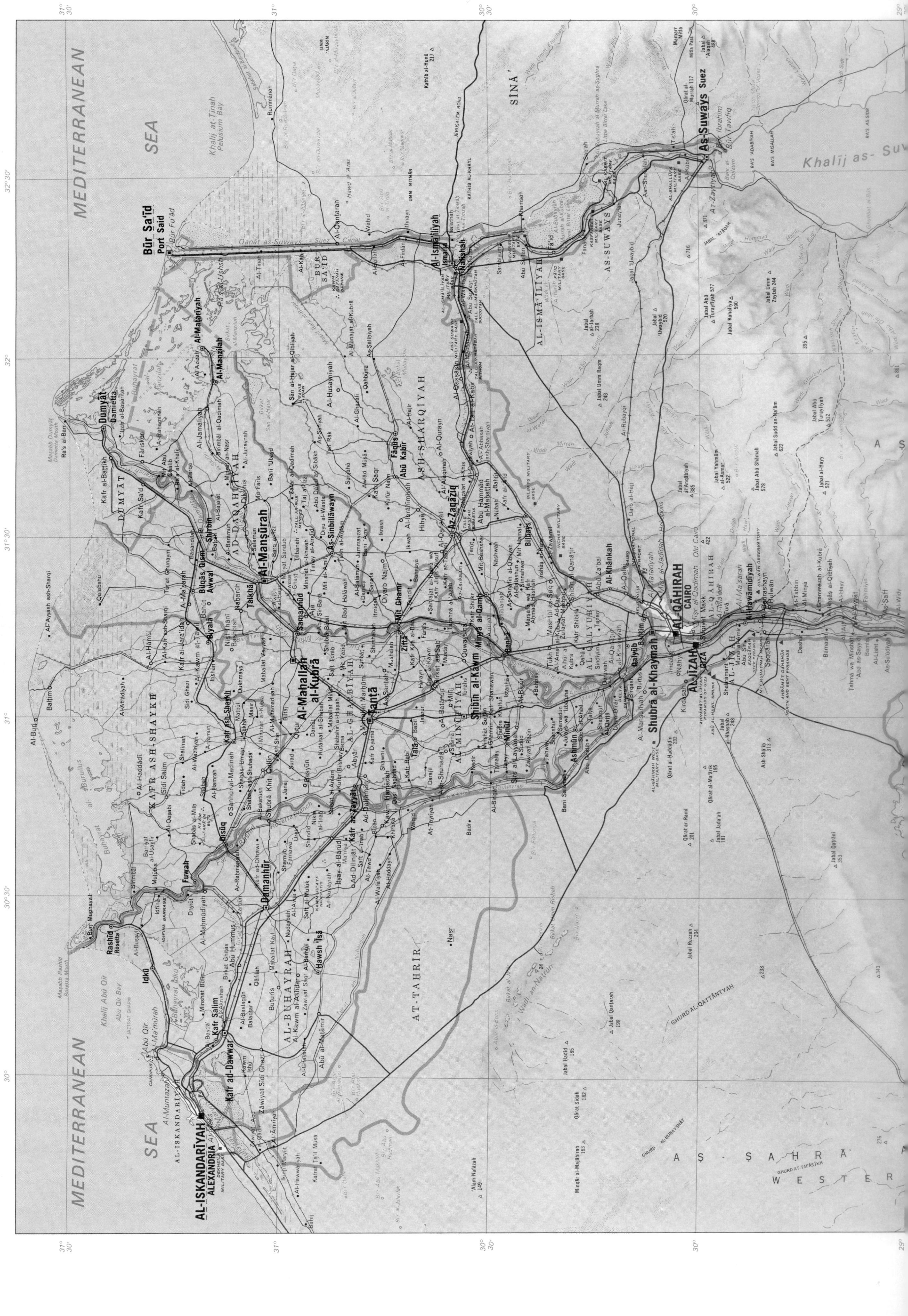
MEDITERRANEAN
SEA
MEDITERRANEAN
SEA
Khalīj at-Tīnah
Pelusium Bay
Khalīj Abū Qīr
Abu Qir Bay
Būr Sa'īd
Port Said
As-Suways Suez
Khalīj as-Suways
Al-Ismā'īlīyah
Dumyāṭ
Damietta
Rashīd
Rosetta
AL-ISKANDARĪYAH
ALEXANDRIA
AL-QĀHIRAH
CAIRO
AL-JĪZAH
GIZA
Shubrā al-Khaymah
Al-Manṣūrah
Al-Maḥallah al-Kubrā
Ṭanṭā
Az-Zaqāzīq
Damanhūr
Kafr ad-Dawwār
Kafr ash-Shaykh
Shibīn al-Kawm
Banhā
Bilbays
Ḥulwān
Al-Khānkah
Fāqūs
Abū Kabīr
Al-Manzilah
Al-Maṭarīyah
SĪNĀ'
AS-SUWAYS
AL-ISMĀ'ĪLĪYAH
ASH-SHARQĪYAH
AD-DAQAHLĪYAH
DUMYĀṬ
KAFR ASH-SHAYKH
AL-GHARBĪYAH
AL-MINŪFĪYAH
AL-QALYŪBĪYAH
AL-BUḤAYRAH
AL-ISKANDARĪYAH
AL-QĀHIRAH
AL-JĪZAH
AT-TAḤRĪR
AṢ-ṢAḤRĀ' WESTER
31° 30'
31°
30° 30'
30°
29°
32° 30'
32°
31° 30'
31°
30° 30'
30°

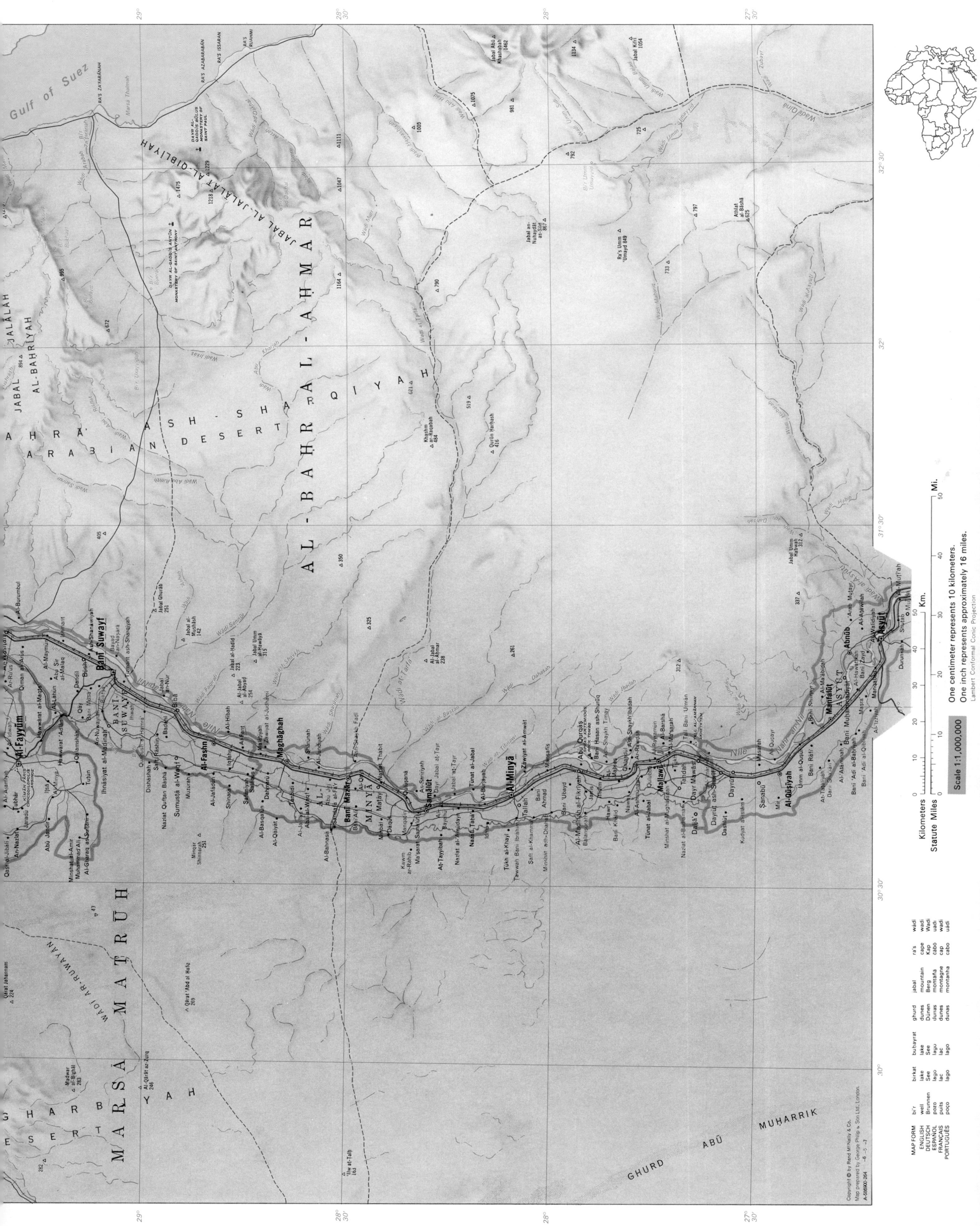

Gulf of Suez

JABAL AL-BAHRĪYAH

JABAL AL-JALĀLAT AL-QIBLĪYAH

DAYR AL-QADĪS ANTŪN
MONASTERY OF SAINT ANTHONY

DAYR AL-
QADDĪS BŪLUS
MONASTERY OF
SAINT PAUL

AL-BAHR AL-AHMAR

ASH-SHARQĪYAH

ARABIAN DESERT

SAHRĀ

JABAL AL-BAHRĪYAH

MARSA MATRŪH

WĀDĪ AR-RUWAYYĀN

GHARBĪYAH

DESERT

GHURD ABŪ MUHARRIK

Bani Suwayf
Al-Fayyūm
BANI SUWAYF
Al-Fashn
Maghāghah
AL-MINYĀ
Al-Minyā
Samālūt
Mallawī
Al-Qūsīyah
Manfalūt
ASYŪT
Asyūt
Abnūb

Scale 1:1,000,000

One centimeter represents 10 kilometers.
One inch represents approximately 16 miles.
Lambert Conformal Conic Projection

Kilometers
0   10   20   30   40   50   Km.

Statute Miles
0   10   20   30   40   50   Mi.

MAP FORM						
ENGLISH	bi'r	birkat	buhayrat	ghurd	jabal	ra's	wadi
	well	lake	lake	dunes	mountain	cape	wadi
DEUTSCH	Brunnen	See	See	Dünen	Berg	Kap	Wadi
ESPAÑOL	pozo	laguna	laguna	dunas	montaña	cabo	uadi
FRANÇAIS	puits	lac	lac	dunes	montagne	cap	uadi
PORTUGUÊS	poço	lago	lago	dunas	montanha	cabo	uadi

Copyright © by Rand McNally & Co.
Map prepared by George Philip & Son, Ltd., London.
A-599300-284   —8—5 —7

Map continues
pages 128-129

Map continues
pages 140-141

Ethiopia, Somalia and Yemen / Äthiopien, Somalia und Jemen / Etiopía, Somalía y Yemen
Ethiopie, Somalie et Yemen / Etiópia, Somália e Iémen

145

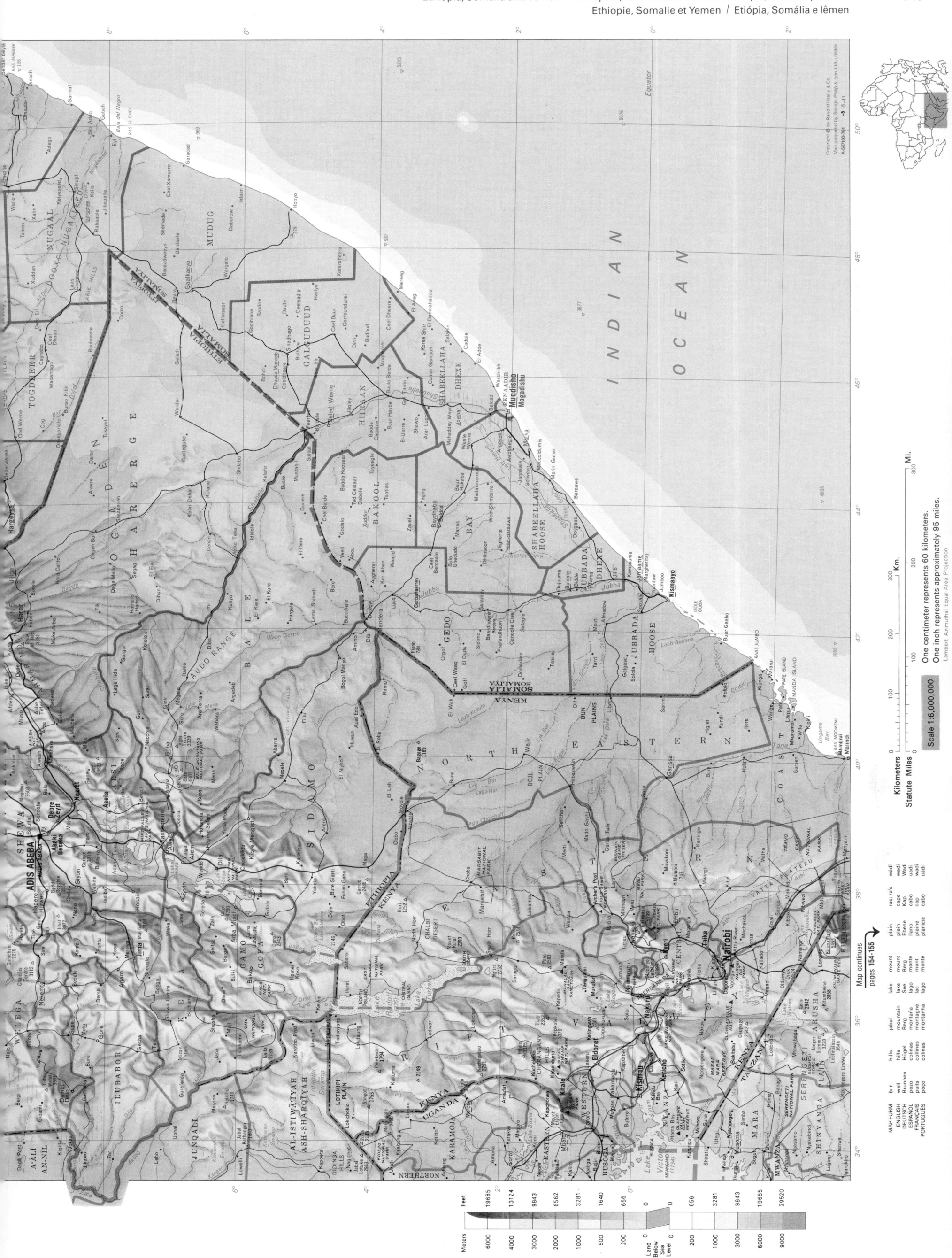

INDIAN OCEAN

ADIS ABEBA

Muqdisho
Mogadishu

Nairobi

Kismaayo

Map continues
pages 154-155

Scale 1:6,000,000

One centimeter represents 60 kilometers.
One inch represents approximately 95 miles.

Lambert Azimuthal Equal-Area Projection

Kilometers
Statute Miles

Km.
Mi.

MAP·UHM					
ENGLISH	b/r	hills	jabal	lake	mount
DEUTSCH	Brunnen	Hügel	Berg	See	Berg
ESPAÑOL	pozo	colinas	montaña	lago	monte
FRANCAIS	puits	colines	montagne	lac	monte
PORTUGUÊS	poço	colinas	montanha	lago	monte

plain	ras·ra's	wadi
plain	cape	wadi
Ebene	Kap	Wadi
llano	cabo	uadi
plaine	cabo	uadi
planicie	cabo	uadi

Feet
Meters

Land Below Sea Level

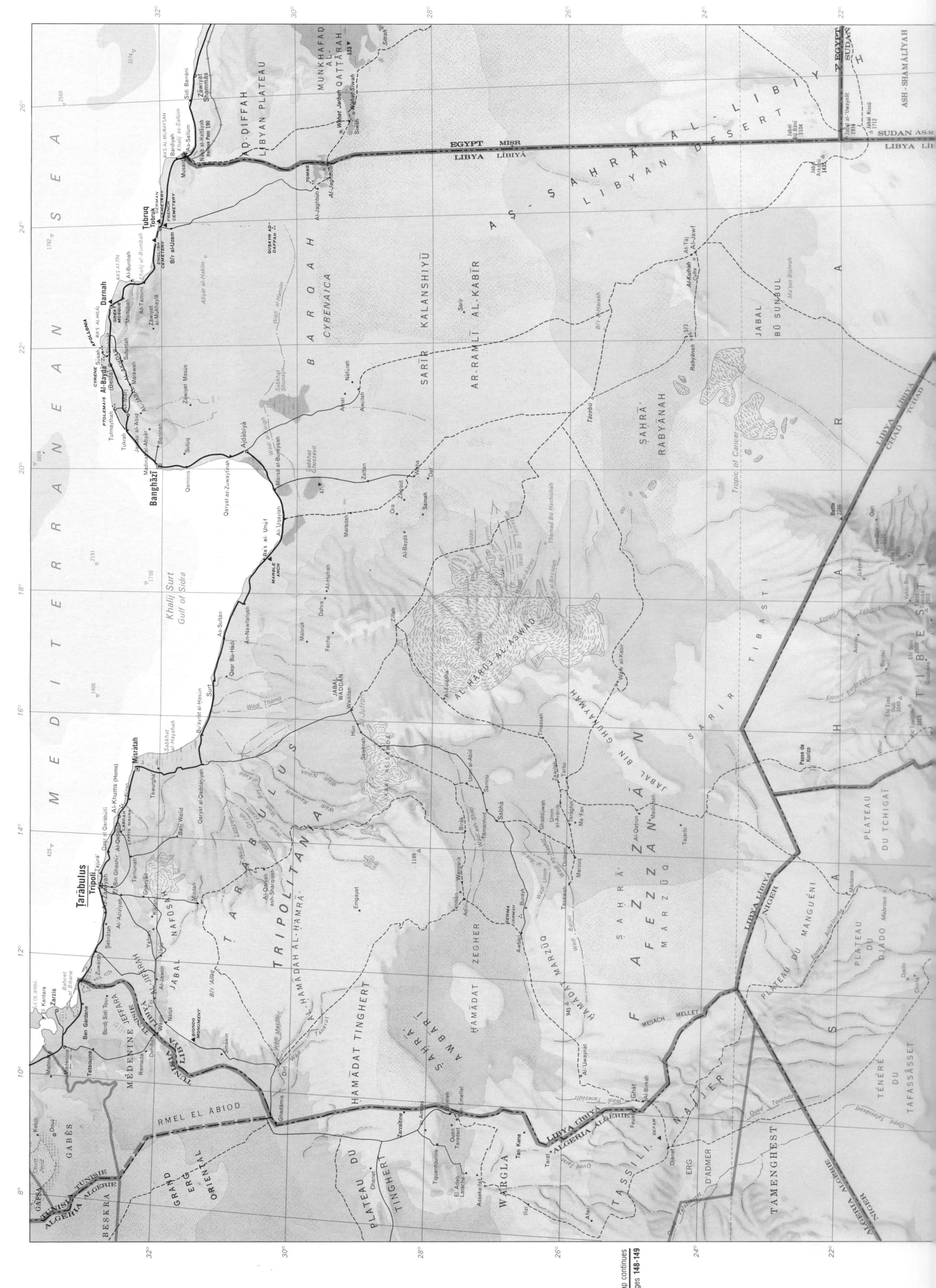
MEDITERRANEAN SEA
Tarābulus
Tripoli
Banghāzī
Misrātah
Darnah
Tubruq
Al-Bayḍā'
Ajdābiyā
Surt
Sabhā
Ghadāmis
Murzuq
Khalij Surt
Gulf of Sidra
TRIPOLITANIA
CYRENAICA
FEZZAN
BARQAH
AS-SAHRĀ' AL-LĪBIYAH
LIBYAN DESERT
SARĪR KALANSHIYŪ
AR-RAMLĪ AL-KABĪR
AL-HARŪJ AL-ASWAD
AL-HAMĀDAH AL-HAMRĀ'
HAMĀDAT TINGHERT
ṢAḤRĀ' RABYĀNAH
SAHRĀ' MARZŪQ
JABAL NAFŪSAH
TIBESTI
EGYPT MISR
LIBYA LĪBIYĀ
SUDAN
NIGER
ALGERIA
TUNISIA
Tropic of Cancer

Map continues pages 148–149

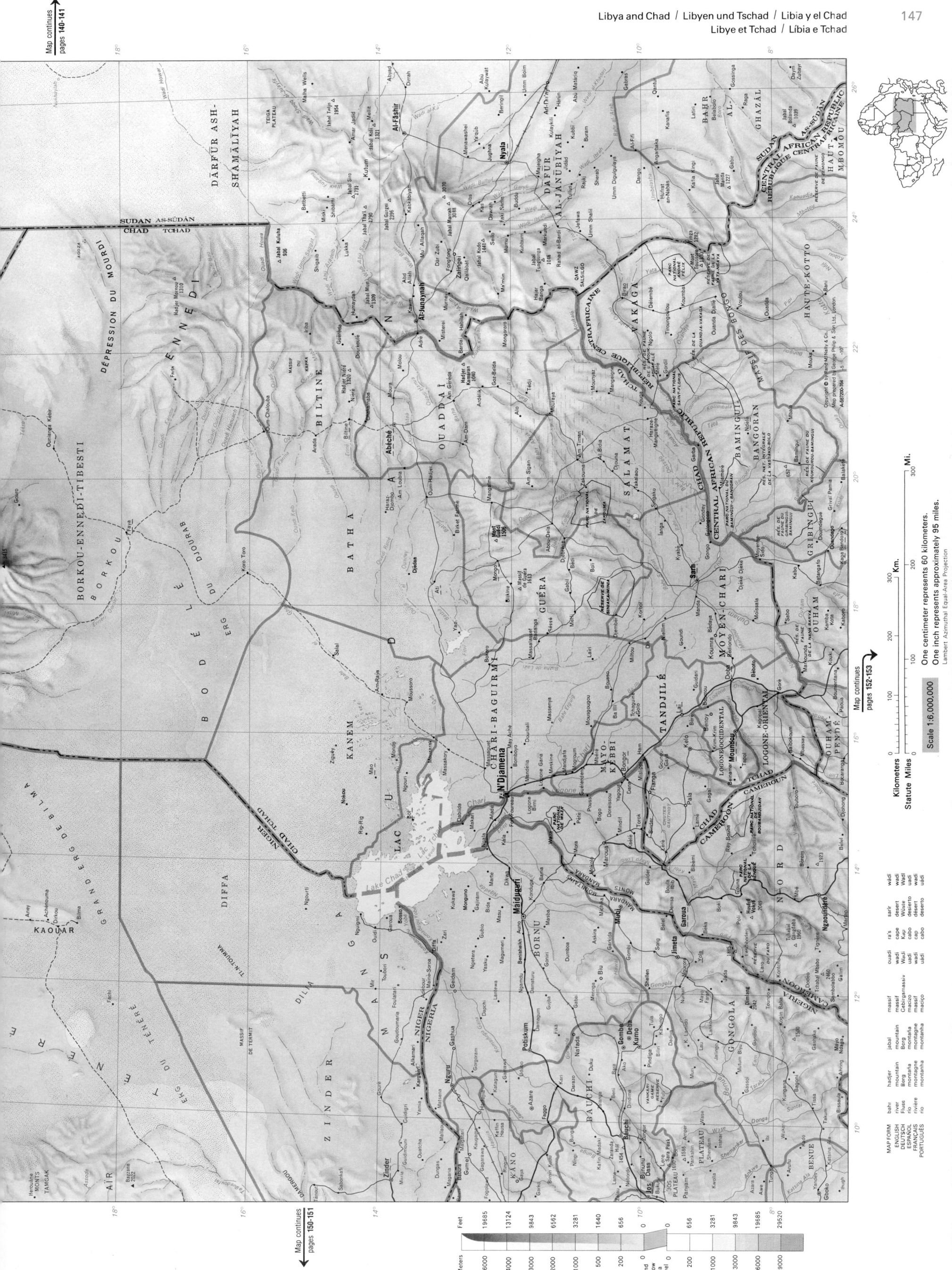

Map continues
pages 140-141

Map continues
pages 150-151

Map continues
pages 152-153

Scale 1:6,000,000

One centimeter represents 60 kilometers.
One inch represents approximately 95 miles.
Lambert Azimuthal Equal-Area Projection

Kilometers   Km.
Statute Miles   Mi.

MAP FORM						
ENGLISH	bahr	hadjer	jabal	massif	ra's	saïr	wâdi
DEUTSCH	river	mountain	mountain	massif	cape	desert	wadi
ESPAÑOL	Fluss	Berg	Berg	Gebirgsmassiv	Kap	Wüste	Wadi
FRANÇAIS	río	montaña	montaña	macizo	cabo	desierto	uadi
PORTUGUÊS	riviére	montagne	montagne	massif	cap	désert	uadi
	rio	montanha	montanha	maciço	cabo	deserto	uádi

Feet
19685
13124
9843
6562
3281
1640
656
0

Meters
6000
4000
3000
2000
1000
500
200
0
Land Below Sea Level
0
200
1000
3000
6000
9000

656
3281
9843
19685
29520

Northwestern Africa / Nordwestafrika / África Nor-occidental
Afrique du Nord-Ouest / África Norte-ocidental

Map continues
pages 34-35

Meters **Feet**
6000 19685
4000 13124
3000 9843
2000 6562
1000 3281
500 1640
200 656
0 0
Land Below Sea Level 0
200 656
1000 3281
3000 9843
6000 19685
9000 29520

a

ATLANTIC OCEAN

CORVO
FLORES
Santa Cruz das Flores

GRACIOSA
Santa Cruz da Graciosa
TERCEIRA
Praia da Vitória
Angra do Heroísmo
FAIAL
Velas SÃO JORGE
Horta 235
São Mateus Peala do Pico
PICO

A Z O R E S

SÃO MIGUEL
Ribeira Grande
Povoação
Ponta Delgada

(Port.)

SANTA MARIA
Vila do Porto

© R. MTN.

ATLANTIC OCEAN

ARQUIPÉLAGO DA MADEIRA
MADEIRA ISLANDS
(Port.)
PORTO SANTO
Pico Ruivo 1862
MADEIRA
Funchal Machico
ILHAS DESERTAS

ILHAS SELVAGENS (Mad. Is.)

ISLAS CANARIAS
CANARY ISLANDS (Sp.)

ISLA ALEGRANZA
ISLA GRACIOSA
LANZAROTE
Arrecife

LA PALMA
Los Llanos
Pico de la Cruz
TENERIFE
La Orotava
San Cristóbal de la Laguna
Santa Cruz de Tenerife
GOMERA
San Sebastián de la Gomera
San Miguel
San Nicolás
Arucas
Las Palmas de Gran Canaria
Telde
GRAN CANARIA
HIERRO
Valverde
FERRO

ISLA DE LOBOS
Puerto del Rosario
Tuineje
FUERTEVENTURA

CAP JUBY
Tarfaya
LA'YOUN
Sebkha Tah

ATLANTIC OCEAN

Western Sahara has been occupied by Morocco.

Lemsid
CAP BOUJDOUR

Dakhla
Bir Enzaran
Khlij Oued edh Dheheb
Tropic of Cancer

Golfe de Cintra

CAP BARBAS

Nouâdhibou
La Gouèra
RAS NOUÂDHIBOU
RAS AGADIR

WESTERN SAHARA
MAURITANIA MAURITANIE
DAKHLET NOUÂDHIBOU
INCHIRI

MOROCCO AL-MAGREB
WESTERN SAHARA

El Aaiún
La'youn

Smara
Hawza
Al Mahbas

ALGERIA ALGÉRIE
MAURITANIA MAURITANIE

Bir Mogreïn (Fort-Trinquet)
Galtat Zemmour

ZEMMOUR

TIRIS ZEMMOUR

Fdérik
Zouérat
Kediet ej Jill

EL HAMMAMI
EL KHATT

Passe de Ouarata
Choûm
Sebkhet Chemchâm
Richât
Ouadâne

ADRAR
Atâr
Chinguetti

MAQTEIR

OUARÂNE

ADRAR

HODH ECH CHARGUI

Copyright © by Rand McNally & Co.
Map prepared by George Philip & Son Ltd. London
A-589791-764

PORTUGAL
SPAIN ESPAÑA

Odemira
Almodôvar
BEJA
Serpa
Córdoba

CABO DE SÃO VICENTE
Lagos
Faro
Huelva
Sevilla
Golfo de Cádiz
Jerez de la Frontera
Cádiz
CAP SPARTEL
Ceuta
Tanger Tangier
Tétouan
Larache
Ksar-el-Kebir
Ouezzane

Salé
RABAT
Kenitra
Meknès
Fès
CASABLANCA
DAR-EL-BEIDA
Mohammedia (Fedala)
El-Jadida (Mazagan)
Settat
Khouribga
Oued-Zem
Beni-Mellal
Safi
Essaouira (Mogador)
Marrakech
Agadir

HAUT ATLAS

Ouarzazate
Tiznit
Sidi Ifni
IFNI

MOROCCO AL-MAGREB
ALGERIA ALGÉRIE

HAMADA DU DRÂA

Oued Drâa

EL EGLAB

Sebkha de Tindouf
Tindouf

IGUIDI

EL KHNÂCHICH

TOMBOU

Map continues
pages 150-151

MAP FORM	cap	chott	djebel	erg	hamada	jbel	oued	sebkha
ENGLISH	cape	intermittent lake	mountain	sand desert	desert	mountain	wadi	salt flat
DEUTSCH	Kap	periodischer See	Berg	Sandwüste	Wüste	Berg	Wadi	Salzebene
ESPAÑOL	cabo	lago intermitente	montaña	desierto arenoso	desierto	montaña	uadi	salar
FRANÇAIS	cap	lac périodique	montagne	désert de sable	désert	montagne	wadi	saline
PORTUGUÊS	cabo	lago intermitente	montanha	deserto arenoso	deserto	montanha	uádi	salina

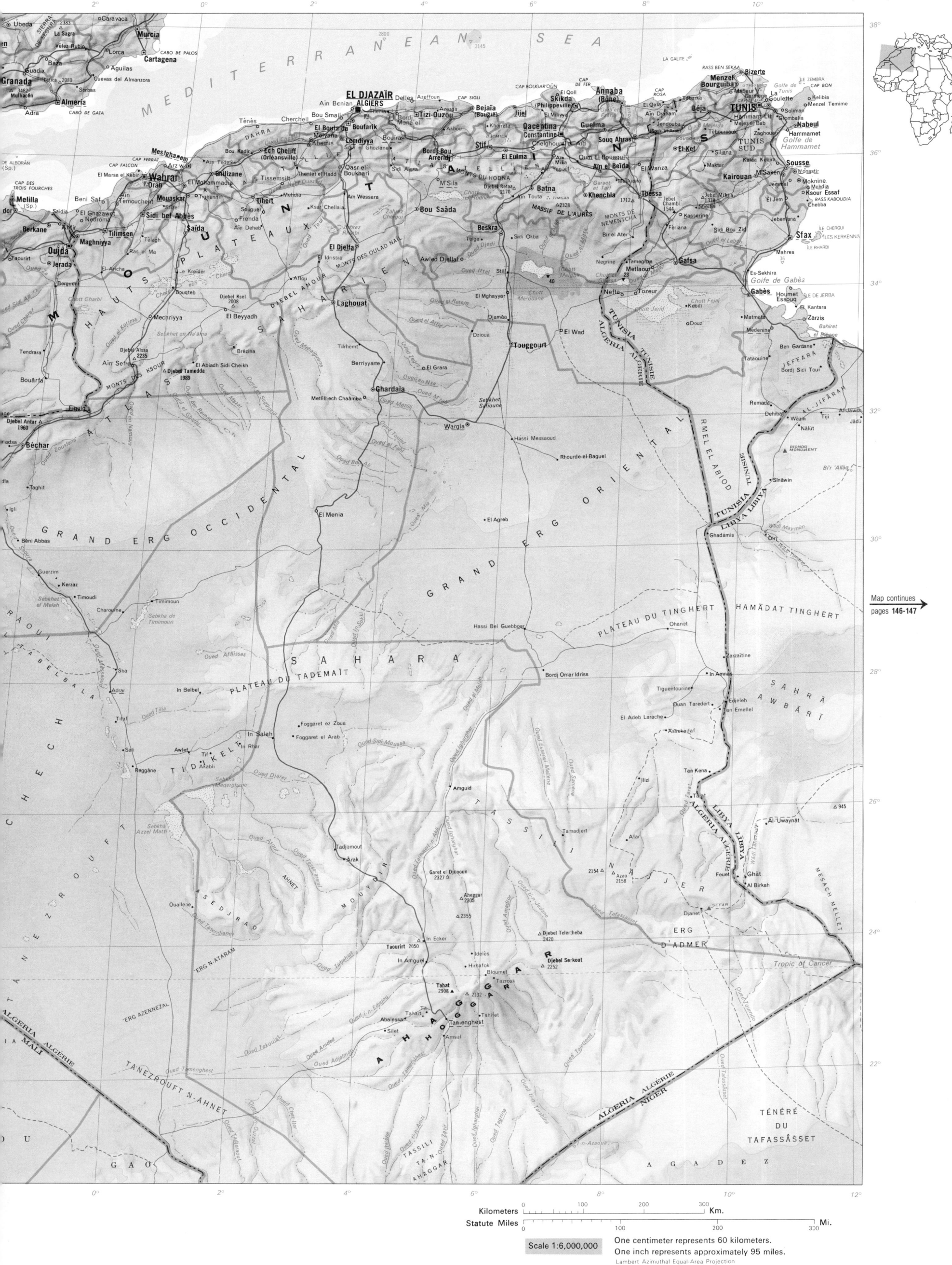

Map continues
pages 146-147

Kilometers
Statute Miles

Scale 1:6,000,000

One centimeter represents 60 kilometers.
One inch represents approximately 95 miles.
Lambert Azimuthal Equal-Area Projection

	MAP FORM	coast	dhar	game reserve	ilha	lac	monts	mountains	vallée
	ENGLISH	coast	escarpment	game reserve	island	lake	mountains	mountains	valley
	DEUTSCH	Küste	Landstufe	Wildpark	Insel	See	Berge	Berge	Tal
	ESPAÑOL	costa	escarpa	vedado de caza	isla	lago	montes	montañas	valle
	FRANÇAIS	côte	escarpa	réserve à gibier	île	lac	monts	montagnes	vallée
	PORTUGUÊS	costa	escarpa	reserva de caça	ilha	lago	montes	montanhas	vale

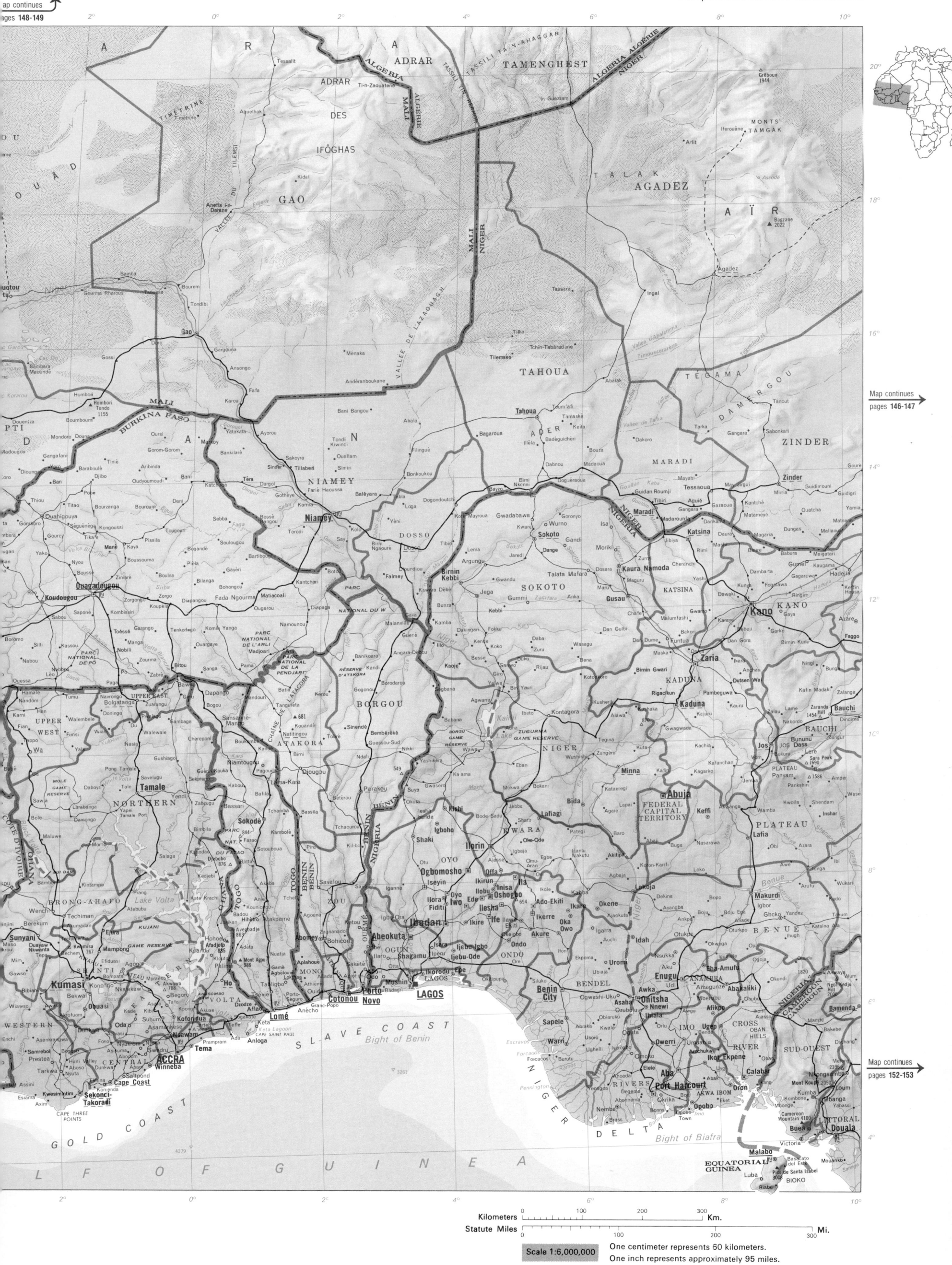

Map continues
pages 148-149

Map continues
pages 146-147

Map continues
pages 152-153

Kilometers
Statute Miles

Scale 1:6,000,000

One centimeter represents 60 kilometers.
One inch represents approximately 95 miles.
Lambert Azimuthal Equal-Area Projection

Map continues
pages 146-147

Map continues
pages 150-151

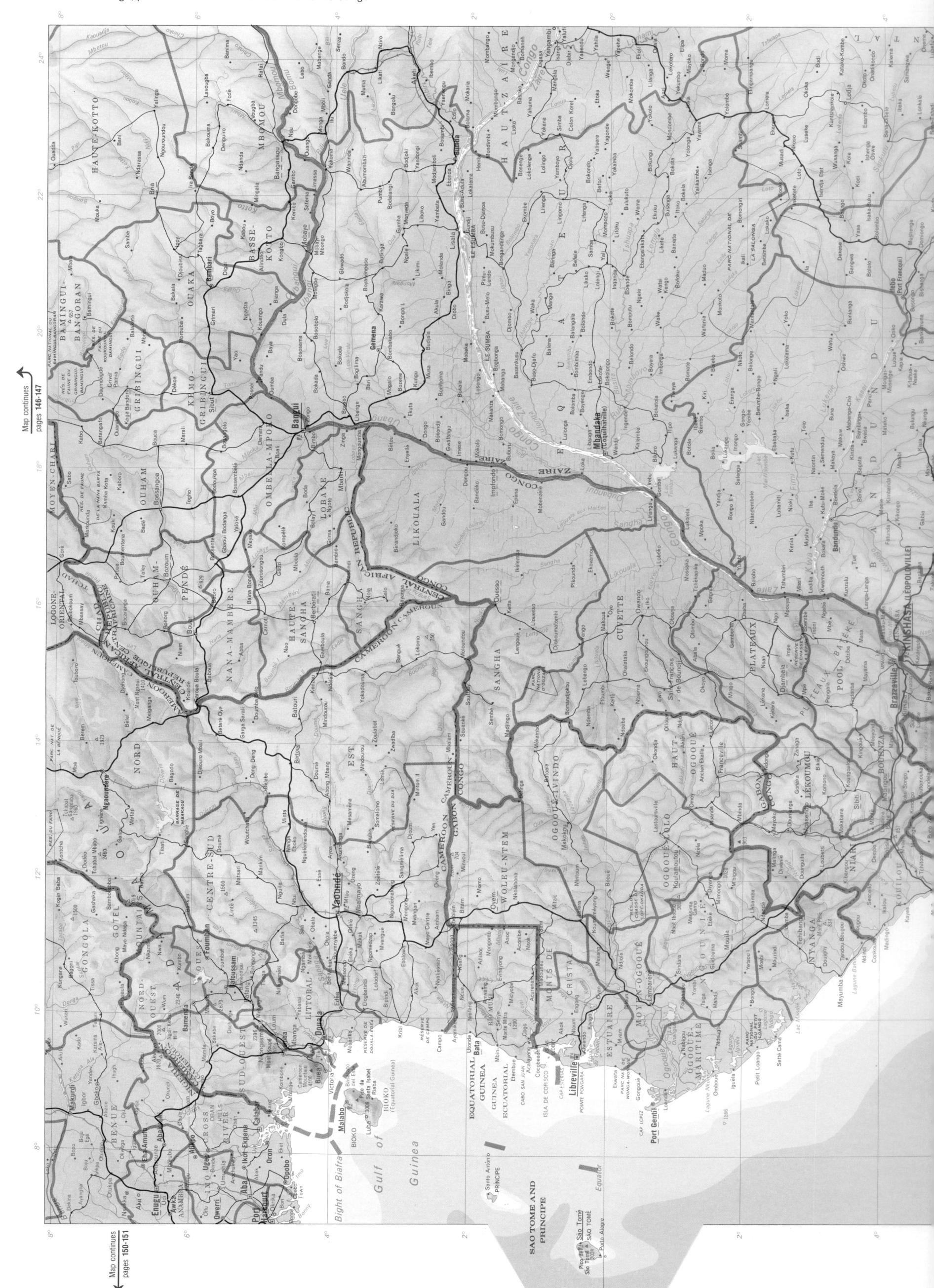

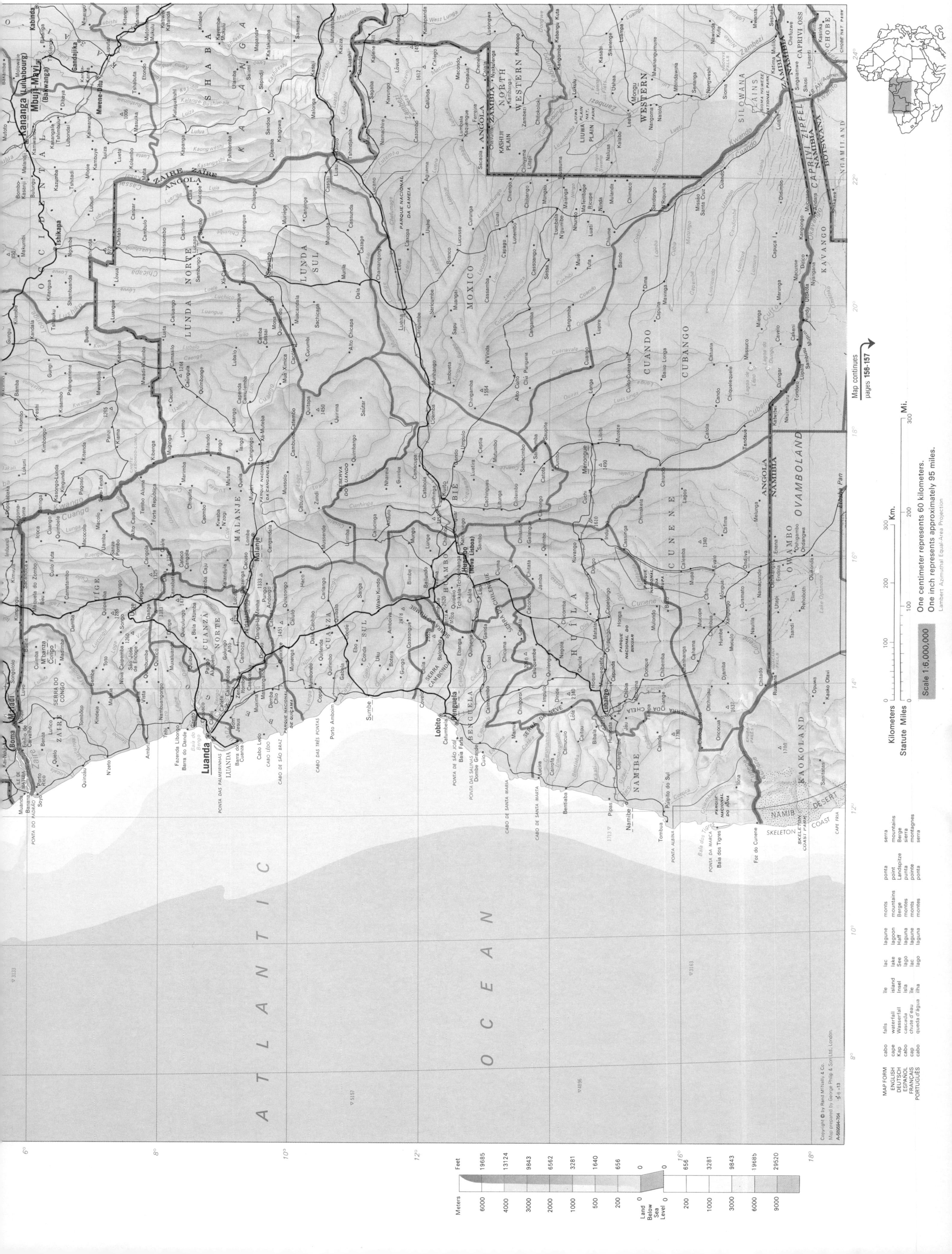

Western Congo Basin / Westliches Kongobecken / Cuenca Occidental del Congo
Bassin du Congo, partie Occidentale / Bacia Ocidental do Congo

153

Map continues
pages **154-155**

Map continues
pages **156-157**

Scale 1:6,000,000

Kilometers

Statute Miles

One centimeter represents 60 kilometers.
One inch represents approximately 95 miles.

Lambert Azimuthal Equal-Area Projection

MAP FORM									
ENGLISH	cape	falls	island	lake	lagoon	mountains	point	mountains	mountains
DEUTSCH	Kap	Wasserfall	Insel	See	Haff	Berge	Landspitze	Berge	Berge
ESPAÑOL	cabo	cascada	isla	lago	laguna	montes	punta	sierra	sierra
FRANÇAIS	cap	chute d'eau	île	lac	lagune	monts	pointe	montagnes	montagnes
PORTUGUÊS	cabo	queda d'água	ilha	lago	laguna	montes	ponta	serra	serra

Feet	Meters
19685	6000
13124	4000
9843	3000
6562	2000
3281	1000
1640	500
656	200
0	0 Land Below Sea Level
0	0
656	200
3281	1000
9843	3000
19685	6000
29520	9000

A T L A N T I C   O C E A N

Copyright © by Reed International Books
Map compiled by George Philip & Son Ltd., London

154

East Africa and Eastern Congo Basin / Ostafrika und Östliches Kongobecken / África Oriental y Cuenca Oriental del Congo
Afrique Orientale et Bassin du Congo, partie Orientale / África Oriental e Bacia Oriental do Congo

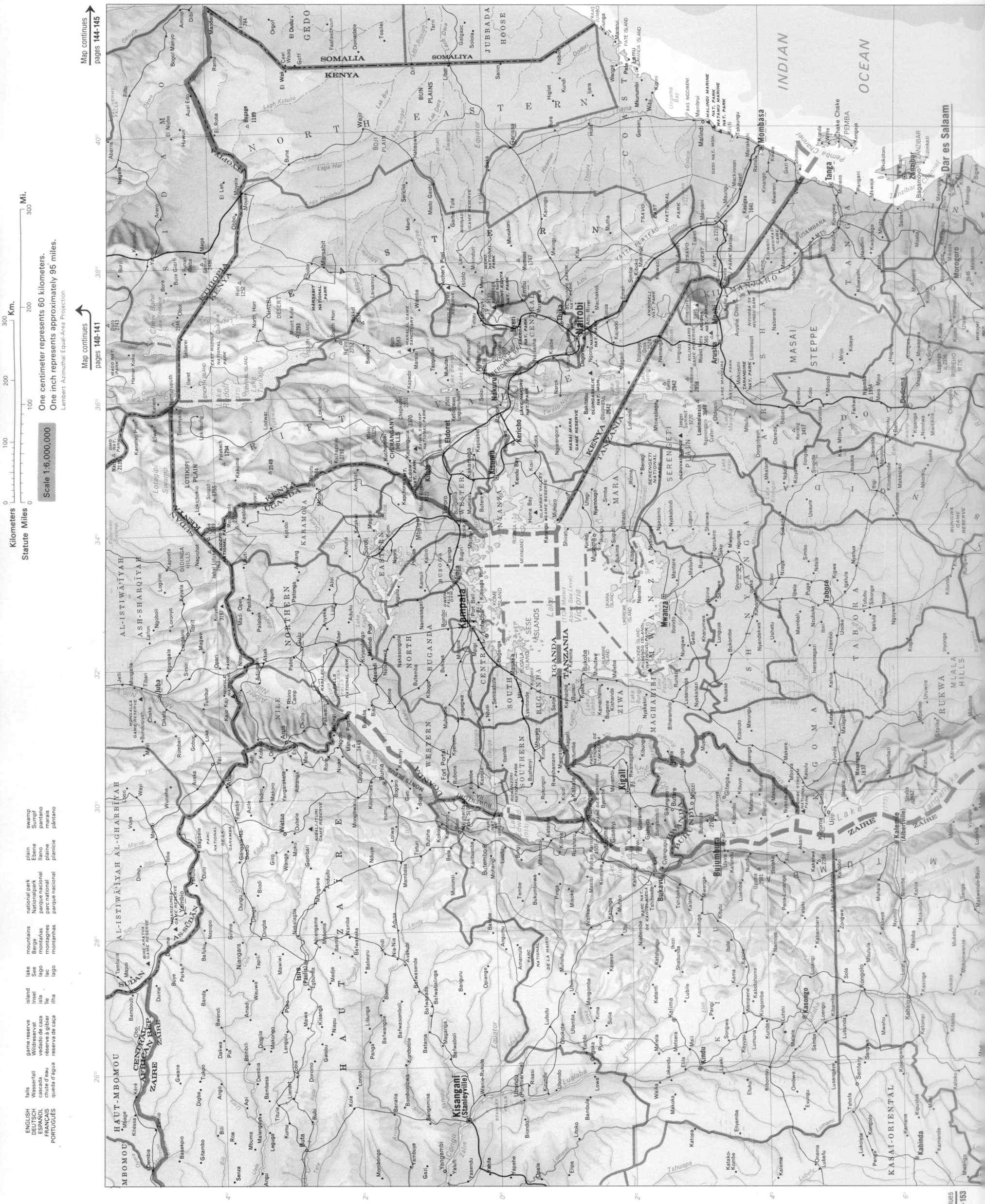

Map continues pages 144-145
Map continues pages 140-141
Map continues pages 152-153

Kilometers

Statute Miles

Mi.

Km.

One centimeter represents 60 kilometers.
One inch represents approximately 95 miles.
Lambert Azimuthal Equal-Area Projection

Scale 1:6,000,000

ENGLISH
DEUTSCH
ESPAÑOL
FRANÇAIS
PORTUGUÊS

falls	game reserve	national park	plain	swamp
Wasserfall	Wildreservat	Nationalpark	Ebene	Sumpf
cascada	vedado de caza	parque nacional	llano	pantano
chute d'eau	réserve à gibier	parc national	plaine	marais
queda de água	reserva de caça	parque nacional	planície	pântano

mountains	lake	island
Gebirge	See	Insel
montañas	lago	isla
montagnes	lac	île
montanhas	lago	ilha

East Africa and Eastern Congo Basin / Ostafrika und Östliches Kongobecken / África Oriental y Cuenca Oriental del Congo
Afrique Orientale et Bassin du Congo, partie Orientale / África Oriental e Bacia Oriental do Congo

155

Map continues
pages 156-157

Southern Africa and Madagascar / Südafrika und Madagaskar / África Meridional y Madagascar
Afrique Méridionale et Madagascar / África Meridional e Madagascar

Map continues
pages 152-153

MAP FORM	bay	berg, berge	cape	game reserve	ilha	lake	national park
ENGLISH	bay	mountain, mountains	cape	game reserve	island	lake	national park
DEUTSCH	Bucht	Berg, Berge	Kap	Wildpark	Insel	See	Nationalpark
ESPAÑOL	bahía	montaña, montañas	cabo	vedado de caza	isla	lago	parque nacional
FRANÇAIS	baie	montagne, montagnes	cap	réserve à gibier	île	lac	parc national
PORTUGUÊS	baía	montanha, montanhas	cabo	reserva de caça	ilha	lago	parque nacional

Kilometers
Statute Miles

Scale 1:6,000,000

One centimeter represents 60 kilometers.
One inch represents approximately 95 miles.

Lambert Azimuthal Equal-Area Projection

Meters   Feet
6000   19685
4000   13124
3000   9843
2000   6562
1000   3281
500   1640
200   656
0   0
Land Below Sea Level
0   0
200   656
1000   3281
3000   9843
6000   19685
9000   29520

Southern Africa and Madagascar / Südafrika und Madagaskar / África Meridional y Madagascar
Afrique Méridionale et Madagascar / África Meridional e Madagascar

157

Map continues
pages 154-155

Bophuthatswana, Ciskei, Transkei, and Venda
are not internationally recognized.

Tropic of Capricorn

Map continues
pages 156-157

MAP FORM	bay	berge	cape	dam	game reserve	national park	pass	point
ENGLISH	bay	mountains	cape	dam	game reserve	national park	pass	point
DEUTSCH	Bucht	Berge	Kap	Damm	Wildpark	Nationalpark	Pass	Landspitze
ESPAÑOL	bahía	montañas	cabo	presa	vedado de caza	parque nacional	paso	punta
FRANÇAIS	baie	montagnes	cap	barrage	réserve à gibier	parc national	col	pointe
PORTUGUÊS	baía	montanhas	cabo	represa	reserva de caça	parque nacional	passo	ponta

MOZAMBIQUE

SWAZILAND

Maputo
(Lourenço Marques)

LESOTHO

TRANSVAAL

NATAL

SOUTH AFRICA
SUID-AFRIKA

TRANSKEI

GRIQUALAND

CISKEI

BOPHUTHATSWANA

DRAKENSBERG

WILD COAST

PONDOLAND

Bophuthatswana, Ciskei, Transkei, and Venda
are not internationally recognized.

INDIAN

OCEAN

JOHANNESBURG
Pretoria
Soweto
Krugersdorp
Vereeniging
Potchefstroom
Klerksdorp
Kroonstad
Welkom
Virginia
Bethlehem
Harrismith
Ladysmith
Dundee
Pietermaritzburg
DURBAN
Richard's Bay
Umtata
East London
Oos-Londen
Queenstown
King William's Town
Grahamstown
Elizabeth
Maseru
Mbabane
Manzini
Piet Retief

Kilometers 0 50 100 150 Km.
Statute Miles 0 50 100 150 Mi.

Scale 1:3,000,000
One centimeter represents 30 kilometers.
One inch represents approximately 47 miles.
Lambert Conformal Conic Projection

Map continues
pages 108-109

ENGLISH	bay	cape	island	lake	mount	point	range	reef
DEUTSCH	Bucht	Kap	Insel	See	Berg	Landspitze	Gebirge	Riff
ESPAÑOL	bahía	cabo	isla	lago	montaña	punta	cordillera	arrecife
FRANÇAIS	baie	cap	île	lac	mont	pointe	chaîne	récif
PORTUGUÊS	baia	cabo	ilha	lago	monte	ponta	cordilheira	recife

Scale 1:12,000,000

One centimeter represents 120 kilometers.
One inch represents approximately 190 miles.
Lambert Conformal Conic Projection

Meters	Feet
6000	19685
4000	13124
3000	9843
2000	6562
1000	3281
500	1640
200	656
0	0
Land Below Sea Level	
0	0
200	656
1000	3281
3000	9843
6000	19685
9000	29520

ENGLISH	bay	cape	creek, cr.	island, i.	lake, l.	mount	point	range
DEUTSCH	Bucht	Kap	Bach	Insel	See	Berg	Landspitze	Gebirge
ESPAÑOL	bahía	cabo	riachuelo	isla	lago	montaña	punta	cordillera
FRANÇAIS	baie	cap	crique	île	lac	mont	pointe	chaîne
PORTUGUÊS	baía	cabo	riacho	ilha	lago	monte	ponta	cordilheira

Western and Central Australia / West- und Mittelaustralien / Australia Centro-occidental
Australie Occidentale et Centrale / Austrália Ocidental e Central

163

Map continues
pages 164-165

Map continues
pages 166-167

Kilometers
Statute Miles

Scale 1:6,000,000
One centimeter represents 60 kilometers.
One inch represents approximately 95 miles.
Lambert Conformal Conic Projection

Map continues
pages 112-113

Map continues
pages 162-163

MAP FORM	bay	cape	island	kepulauan	mount	pulau	range	tanjung
ENGLISH	bay	cape	island	islands	mount	island	range	cape
DEUTSCH	Bucht	Kap	Insel	Inseln	Berg	Insel	Gebirge	Kap
ESPAÑOL	bahía	cabo	isla	islas	montaña	isla	cordillera	cabo
FRANÇAIS	baie	cap	île	îles	mont	île	chaîne	cap
PORTUGUÊS	baía	cabo	ilha	ilhas	monte	ilha	cordilheira	cabo

Northern Australia and New Guinea / Nordaustralien und Neuguinea / Australia Septentrional y Nueva Guinea
Australie Septentrionale et Nouvelle Guinée / Austrália Setentrional e Nova Guiné

165

Map continues
pages 166-167

Kilometers 0   100   200   300 Km.

Statute Miles 0   100   200   300 Mi.

Scale 1:6,000,000

One centimeter represents 60 kilometers.
One inch represents approximately 95 miles.
Lambert Conformal Conic Projection

Copyright © by Rand McNally & Co.
Map prepared by George Philip & Son Ltd., London.
A-593000-764   -7 -5 -13

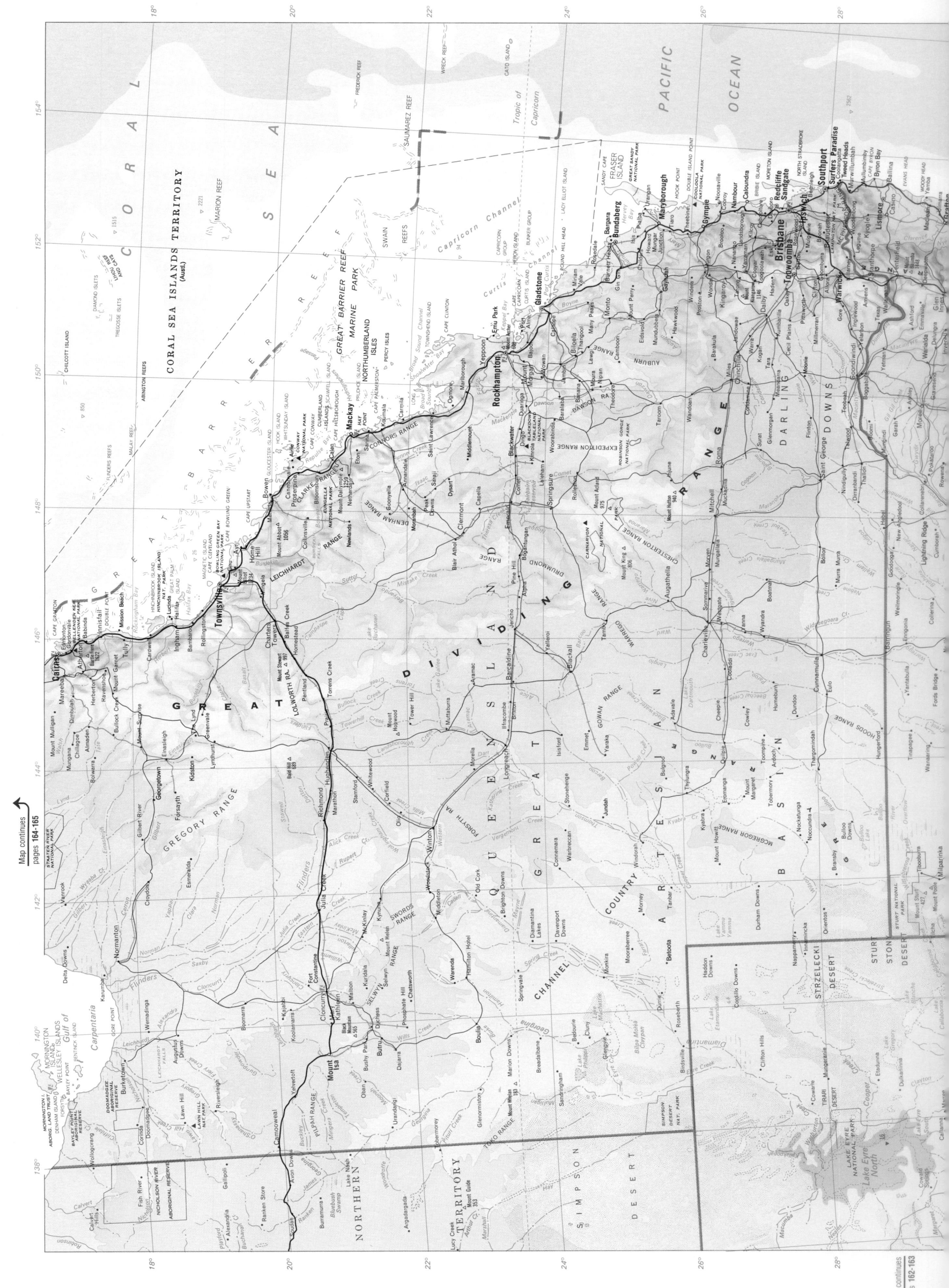

Map continues
pages 164-165

Map continues
pages 162-163

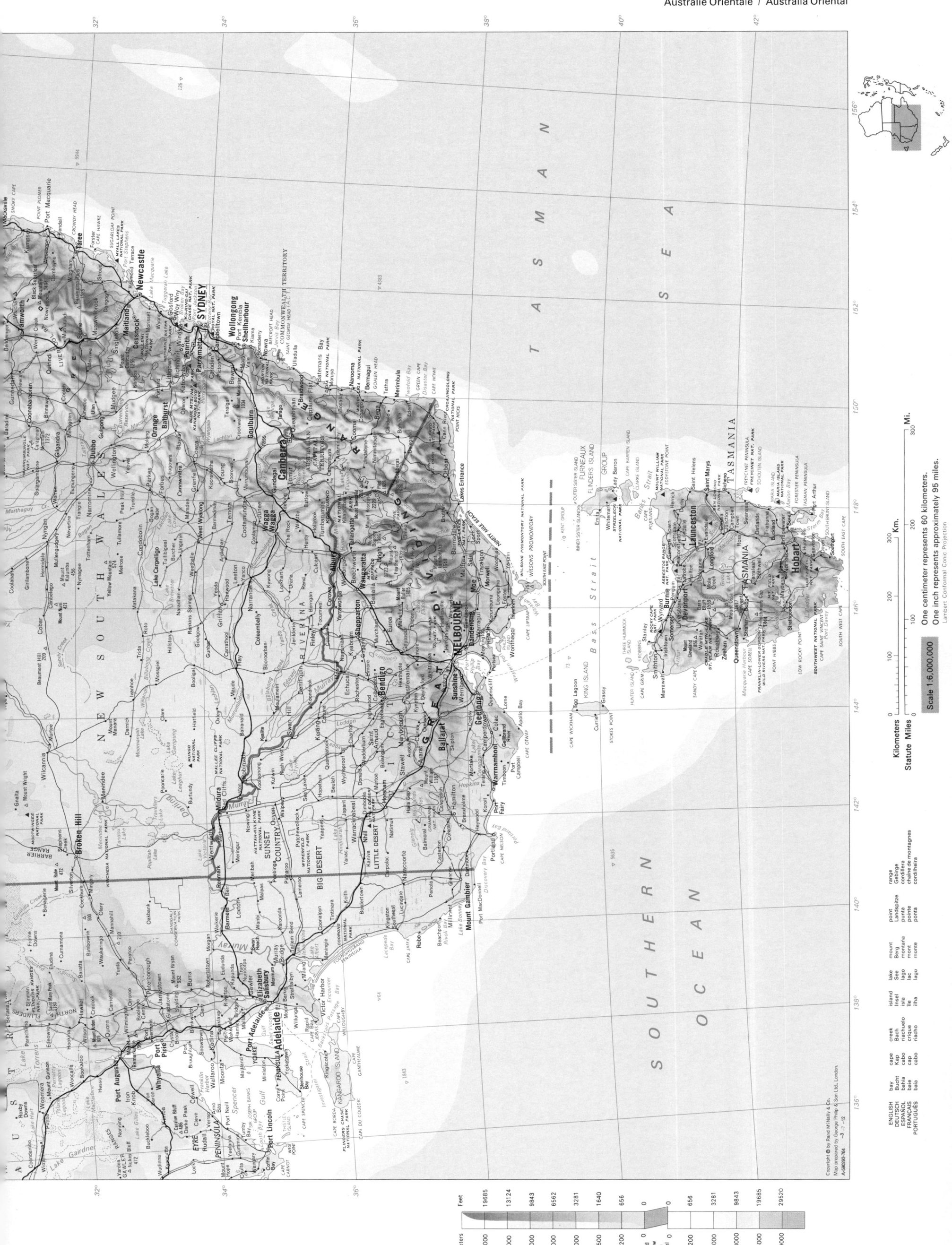

TASMAN SEA

SOUTHERN OCEAN

Bass Strait

Copyright © by Rand McNally & Co.
Map prepared by George Philip & Son Ltd., London.
A-590200-784   -3 -7 --12

ENGLISH	bay	cape	creek	island	lake	mount	point	range
DEUTSCH	Bucht	Kap	Bach	Insel	See	Berg	Landspitze	Gebirge
ESPAÑOL	bahía	cabo	riachuelo	isla	lago	montaña	punta	cordillera
FRANÇAIS	baie	cap	crique	île	lac	mont	pointe	chaîne de montagnes
PORTUGUÊS	baía	cabo	riacho	ilha	lago	monte	ponta	cordilheira

Kilometers

Statute Miles

Scale 1:6,000,000

One centimeter represents 60 kilometers.
One inch represents approximately 95 miles.

Lambert Conformal Conic Projection

Mi.   300

Km.   300   200   100   0

Feet
19685
13124
9843
6562
3281
1640
656
0

Land
Below
Sea
Level   0
656
3281
9843
19685
29520

Meters
6000
4000
3000
2000
1000
500
200
0

0
200
1000
3000
6000
9000

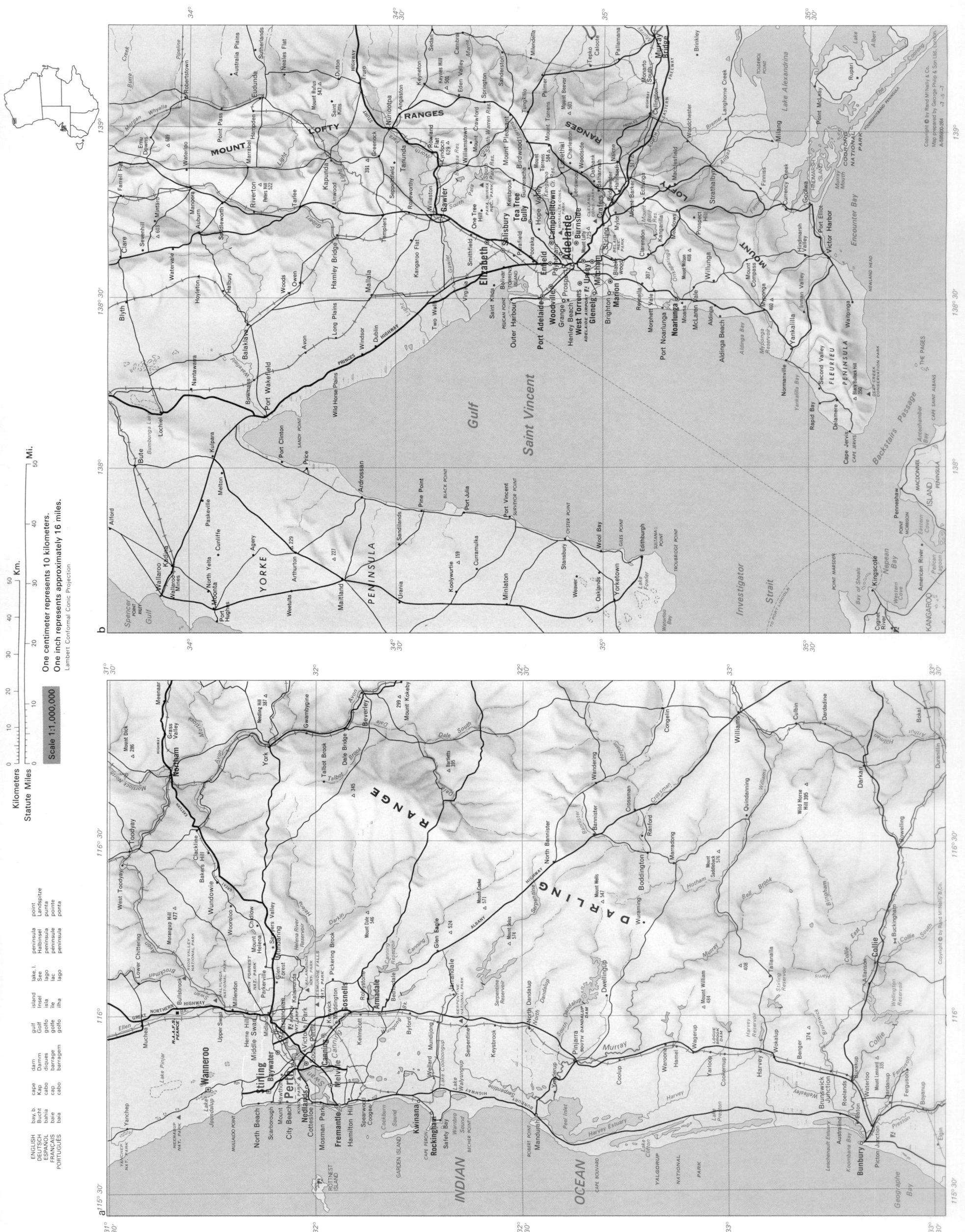

Kilometers

Statute Miles

Scale 1:1,000,000

One centimeter represents 10 kilometers.
One inch represents approximately 16 miles.

Lambert Conformal Conic Projection

ENGLISH	DEUTSCH	ESPAÑOL	FRANÇAIS	PORTUGUÊS
bay, b.	Bucht	bahia	baie	baía
cape	Kap	cabo	cap	cabo
dam	Damm	dique	barrage	barragem
gulf	Golf	golfo	golfe	golfo
island	Insel	isla	île	ilha
lake, l.	See	lago	lac	lago
peninsula	Halbinsel	peninsula	péninsule	peninsula
point	Landspitze	punta	pointe	ponta

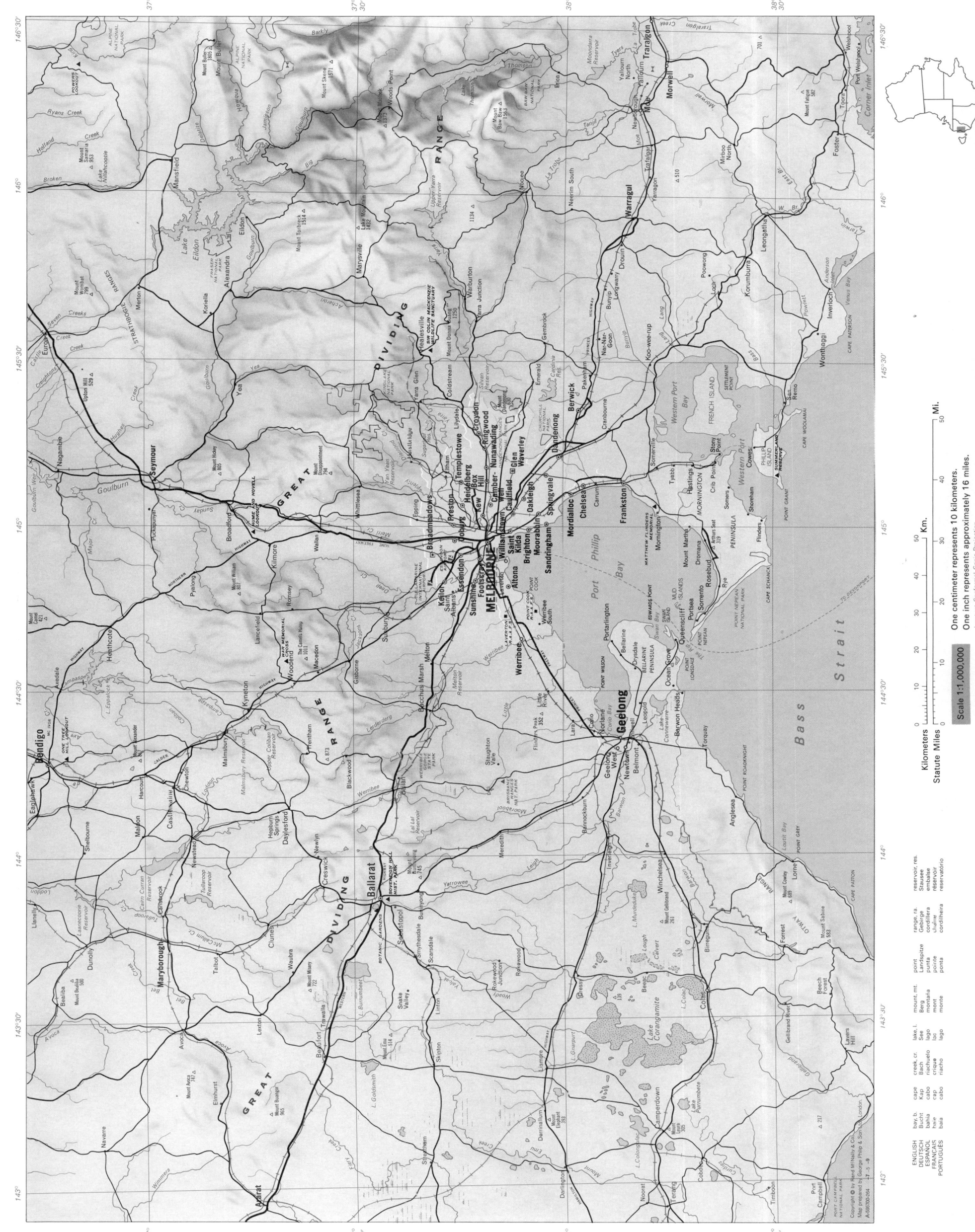

One centimeter represents 10 kilometers.
One inch represents approximately 16 miles.
Lambert Conformal Conic Projection

Scale 1:1,000,000

Kilometers

Statute Miles

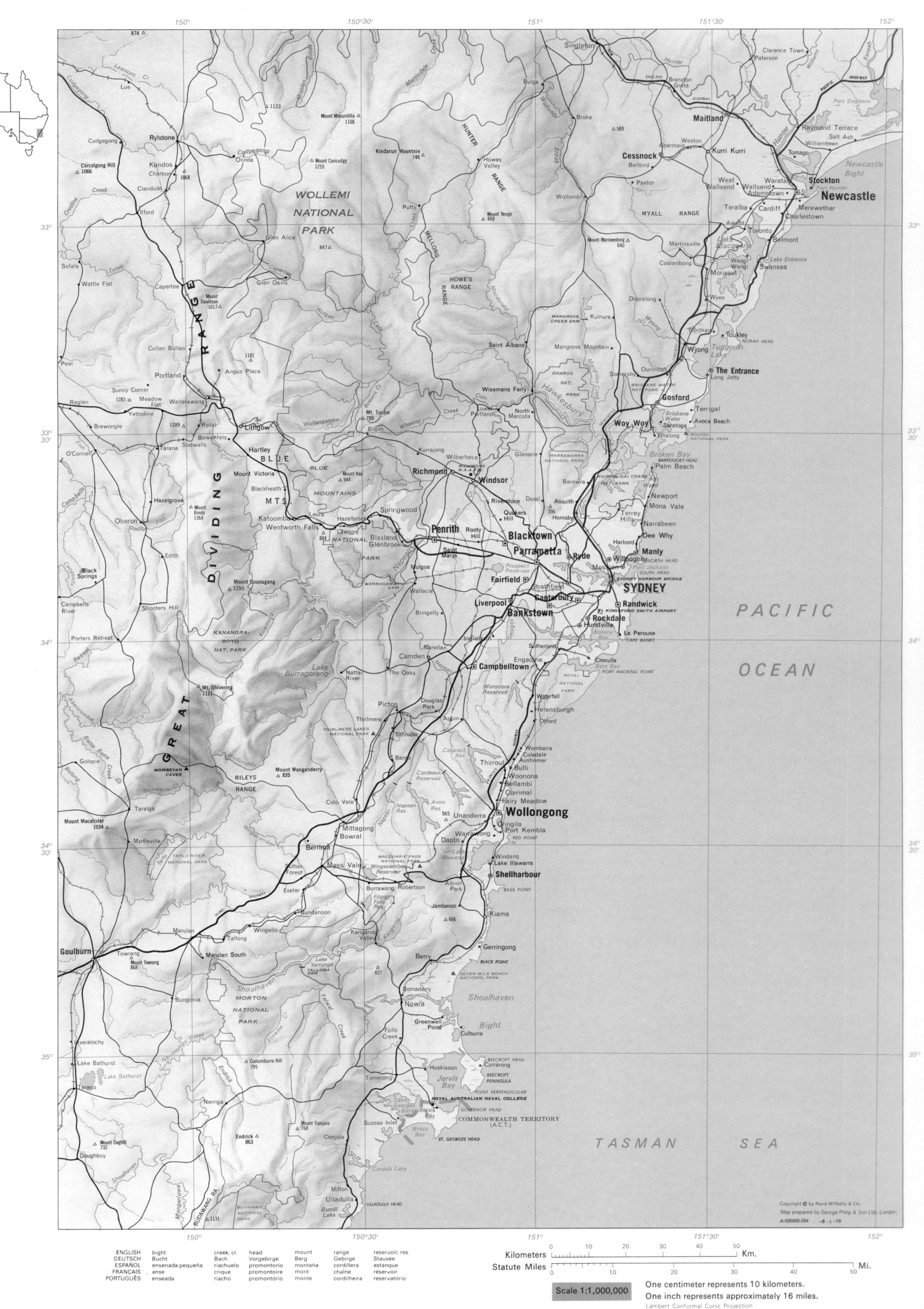

ENGLISH   bight   creek, cr.   head   mount   range   reservoir, res.
DEUTSCH   Bucht   Bach   Vorgebirge Berg   Gebirge   Stausee
ESPAÑOL   ensenada pequeña riachuelo   promontorio montaña   cordillera   estanque
FRANÇAIS   anse   crique   promontoire mont   chaîne   réservoir
PORTUGUÊS   enseada   riacho   promontório monte   cordilheira reservatório

Kilometers

Statute Miles

Scale 1:1,000,000

One centimeter represents 10 kilometers.
One inch represents approximately 16 miles.
Lambert Conformal Conic Projection

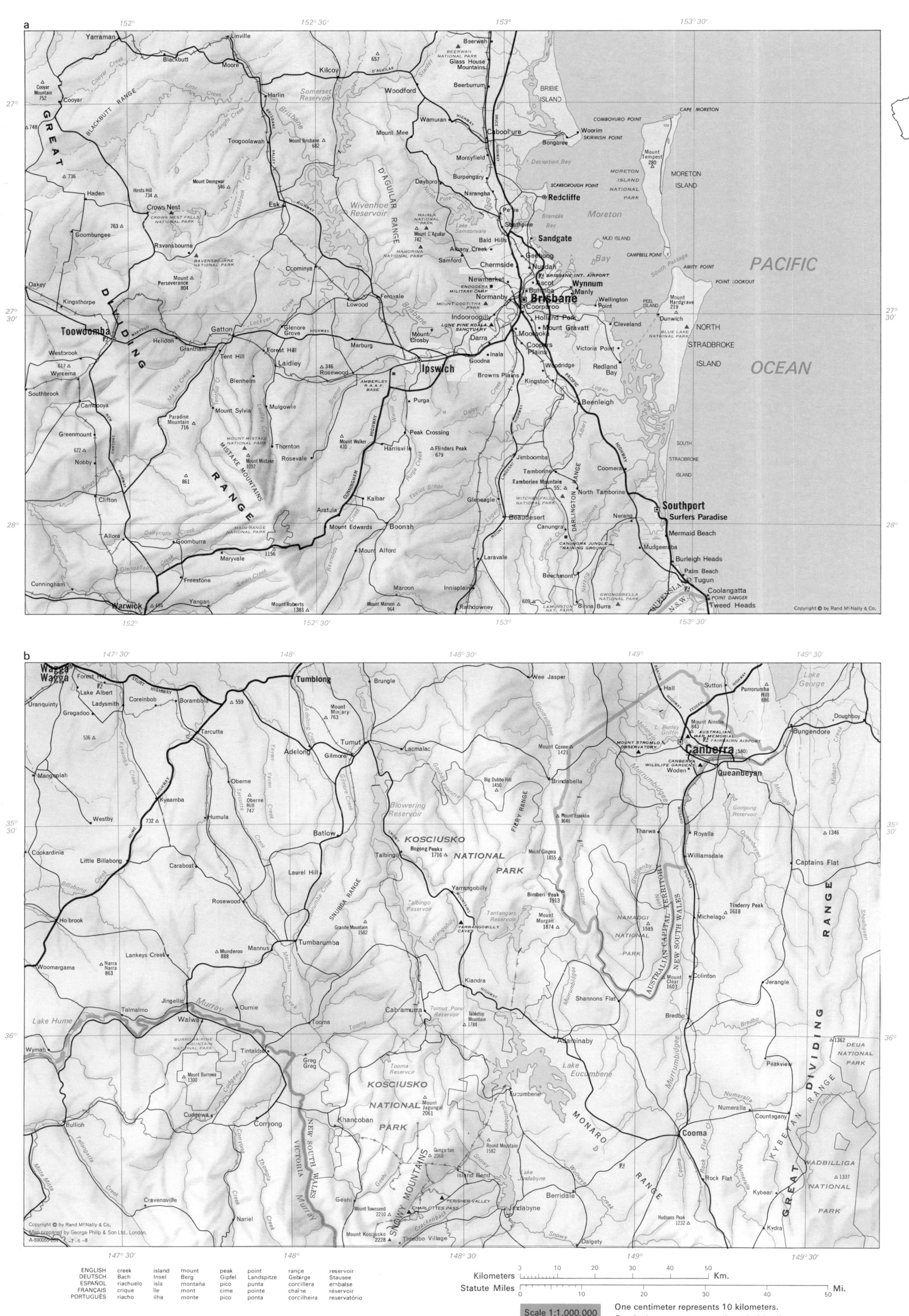

a

Yarraman
Linville
Blackbutt
Moore
Kilcoy
Beerwah
BEERWAH
NATIONAL PARK
Glass House
Mountains
Cooyar
Mountain
752
Cooyar
Harlin
D'AGUILAR
Woodford
Beerburrum
BRIBIE
ISLAND
Haden
Hirsts Hill
734
Crows Nest
CROWS NEST FALLS
NATIONAL PARK
Toogoolawah
Mount Brisbane
682
Wamuran
Caboolture
Woorim
SKIRMISH POINT
Bongaree
COMBOYURO POINT
CAPE MORETON

Toowoomba
Ipswich
Brisbane
Redcliffe
Sandgate

PACIFIC
OCEAN

Warwick
Tweed Heads

Copyright © by Rand McNally & Co.

b

Wagga
Wagga
Tumblong
Canberra
Queanbeyan

Cooma

Copyright © by Rand McNally & Co.
Map prepared by George Philip & Son Ltd., London.

ENGLISH	creek	island	mount	peak	point	range	reservoir
DEUTSCH	Bach	Insel	Berg	Gipfel	Landspitze	Gebirge	Stausee
ESPAÑOL	riachuelo	isla	montaña	pico	punta	corcillera	embalse
FRANÇAIS	crique	île	mont	cime	pointe	chaîne	réservoir
PORTUGUÊS	riacho	ilha	monte	pico	ponta	corcilheira	reservatório

Kilometers   Km.
Statute Miles   Mi.

Scale 1:1,000,000

One centimeter represents 10 kilometers.
One inch represents approximately 16 miles.
Lambert Conformal Conic Projection

New Zealand / Neuseeland / Nueva Zelanda
Nouvelle Zélande / Nova Zelândia

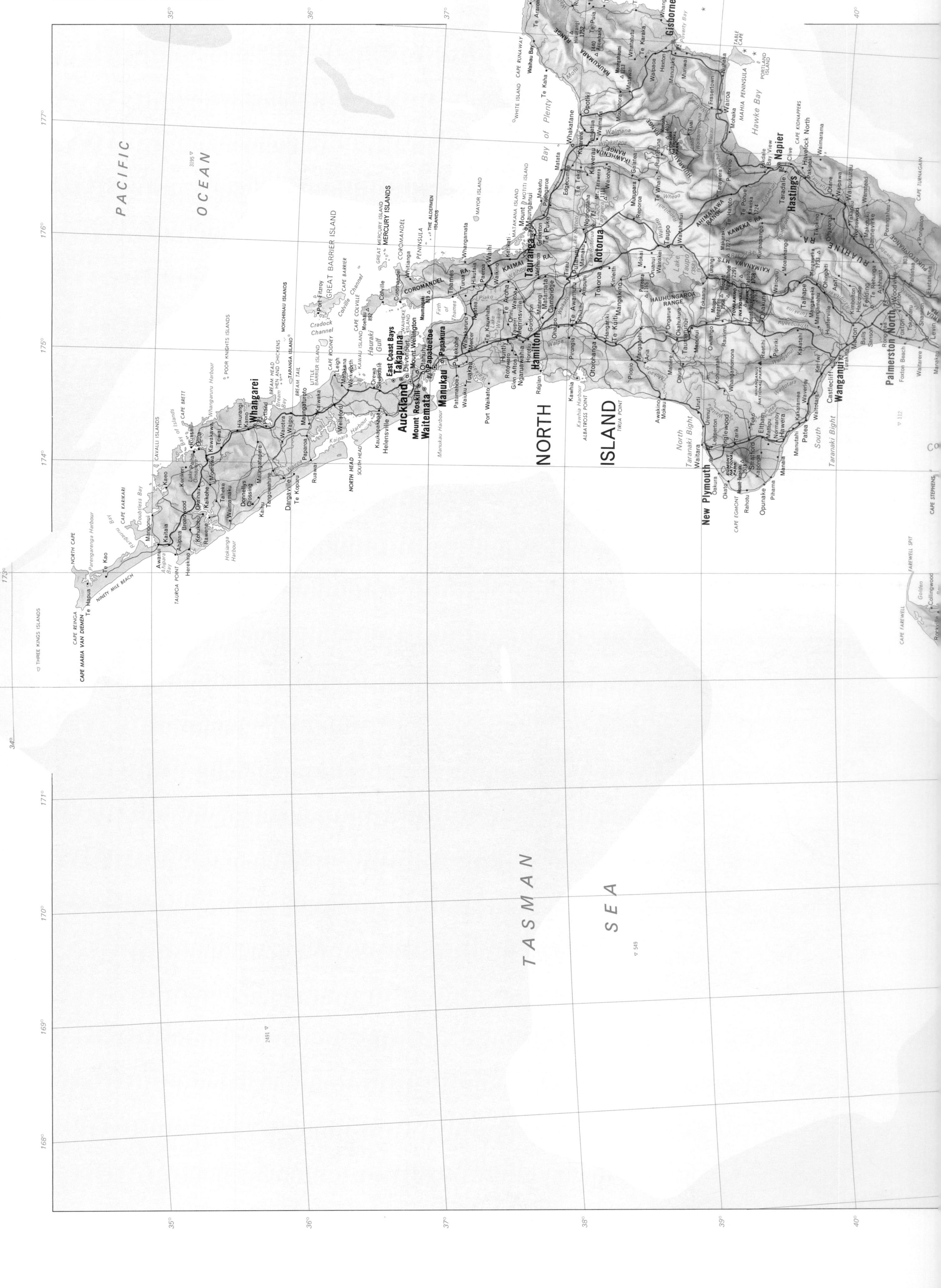
PACIFIC
OCEAN
TASMAN
SEA
NORTH
ISLAND
Auckland
Hamilton
Tauranga
Rotorua
Gisborne
Napier
Hastings
New Plymouth
Wanganui
Palmerston North
Whangarei
Manukau
Waitemata
Takapuna
East Coast Bays
Papakura
Papatoetoe
Mount Roskill
Mount Wellington
GREAT BARRIER ISLAND
Hauraki Gulf
Bay of Plenty
Hawke Bay
North Taranaki Bight
South Taranaki Bight
NORTH CAPE
CAPE REINGA
CAPE MARIA VAN DIEMEN
THREE KINGS ISLANDS
NINETY MILE BEACH
MERCURY ISLANDS
Dargaville
Kaitaia
Thames
Taupo
Whakatane
Cambridge
Te Awamutu
Te Kuiti
Wairoa
Hawera
Stratford
Whitianga
Coromandel
Waihi
Opotiki

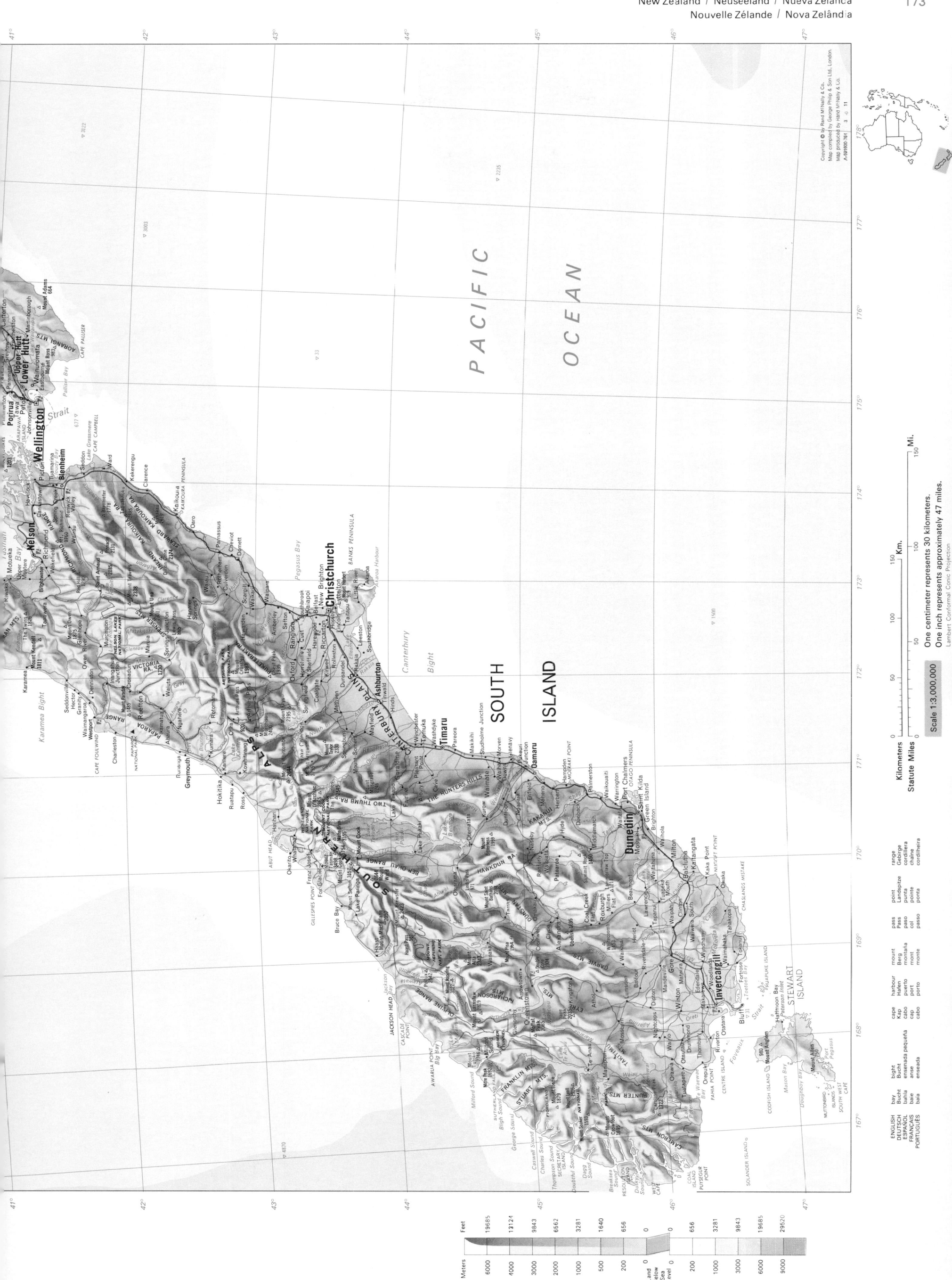

PACIFIC

OCEAN

SOUTH   ISLAND

STEWART
ISLAND

Kilometers
Statute Miles

Scale 1:3,000,000

One centimeter represents 30 kilometers.
One inch represents approximately 47 miles.
Lambert Conformal Conic Projection

ENGLISH	bay	bight	cape	harbour	mount	pass	point	range
DEUTSCH	Bucht	Bucht	Kap	Hafen	Berg	Pass	Landspitze	Gebirge
ESPAÑOL	bahía	ensenada pequeña	cabo	puerto	montaña	paso	punta	cordillera
FRANÇAIS	baie	anse	cap	port	mont	col	pointe	chaîne
PORTUGUÊS	baía	ensaada	cabo	porto	monte	passo	ponta	cordilheira

Feet	Meters
19685	6000
13124	4000
9843	3000
6562	2000
3281	1000
1640	500
656	200
0	0 Land Below Sea Level
0	0
656	200
3281	1000
9843	3000
19685	6000
29620	9000

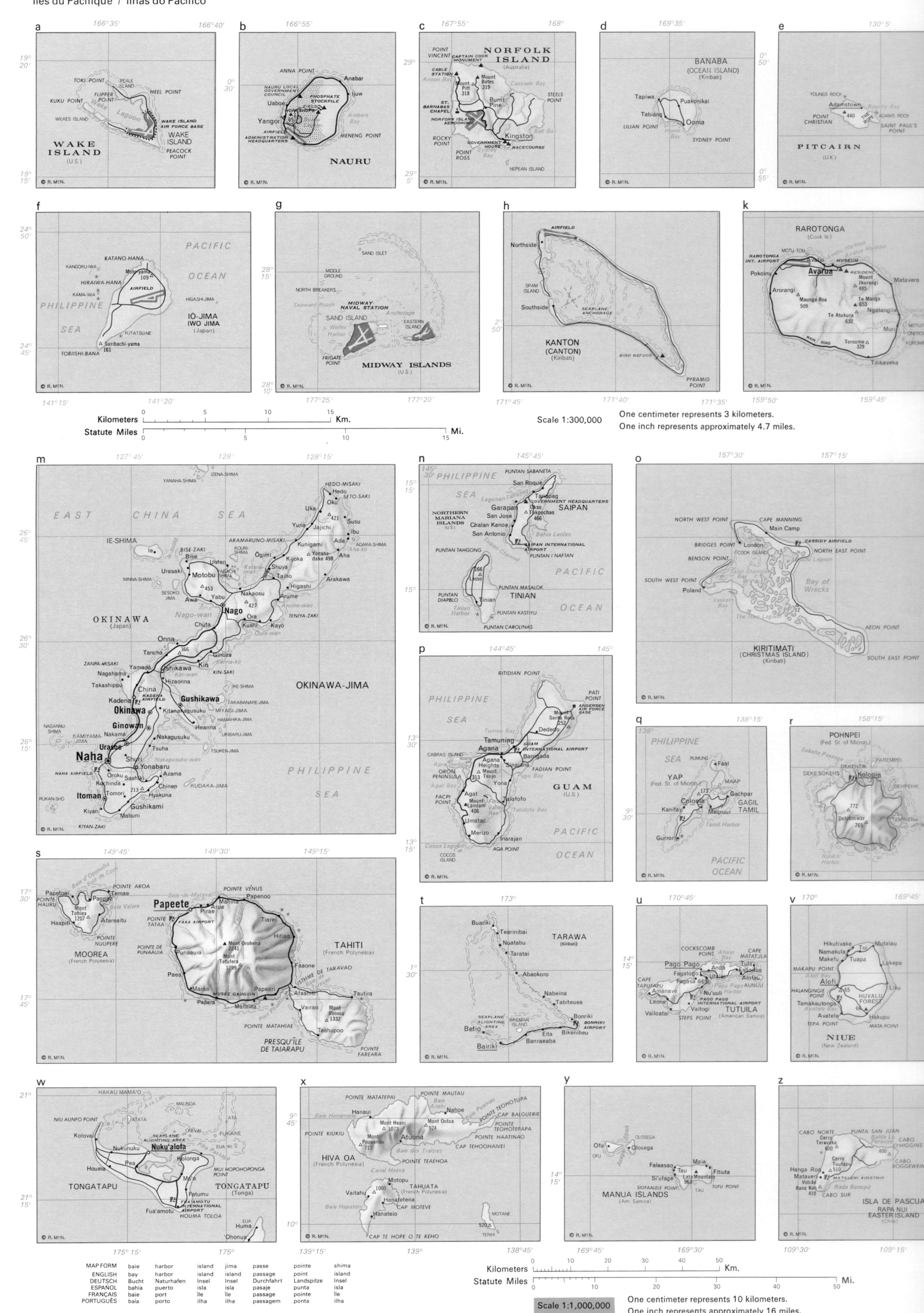

Scale 1:300,000
One centimeter represents 3 kilometers.
One inch represents approximately 4.7 miles.

MAP FORM	baie	harbor	island	jima	passe	pointe	shima
ENGLISH	bay	harbor	island	island	passage	point	island
DEUTSCH	Bucht	Naturhafen	Insel	Insel	Durchfahrt	Landspitze	Insel
ESPAÑOL	bahía	puerto	isla	isla	pasaje	punta	isla
FRANÇAIS	baie	port	île	île	passage	pointe	île
PORTUGUÊS	baía	porto	ilha	ilha	passagem	ponta	ilha

Kilometers
Statute Miles

Scale 1:1,000,000
One centimeter represents 10 kilometers.
One inch represents approximately 16 miles.
Transverse Mercator Projection

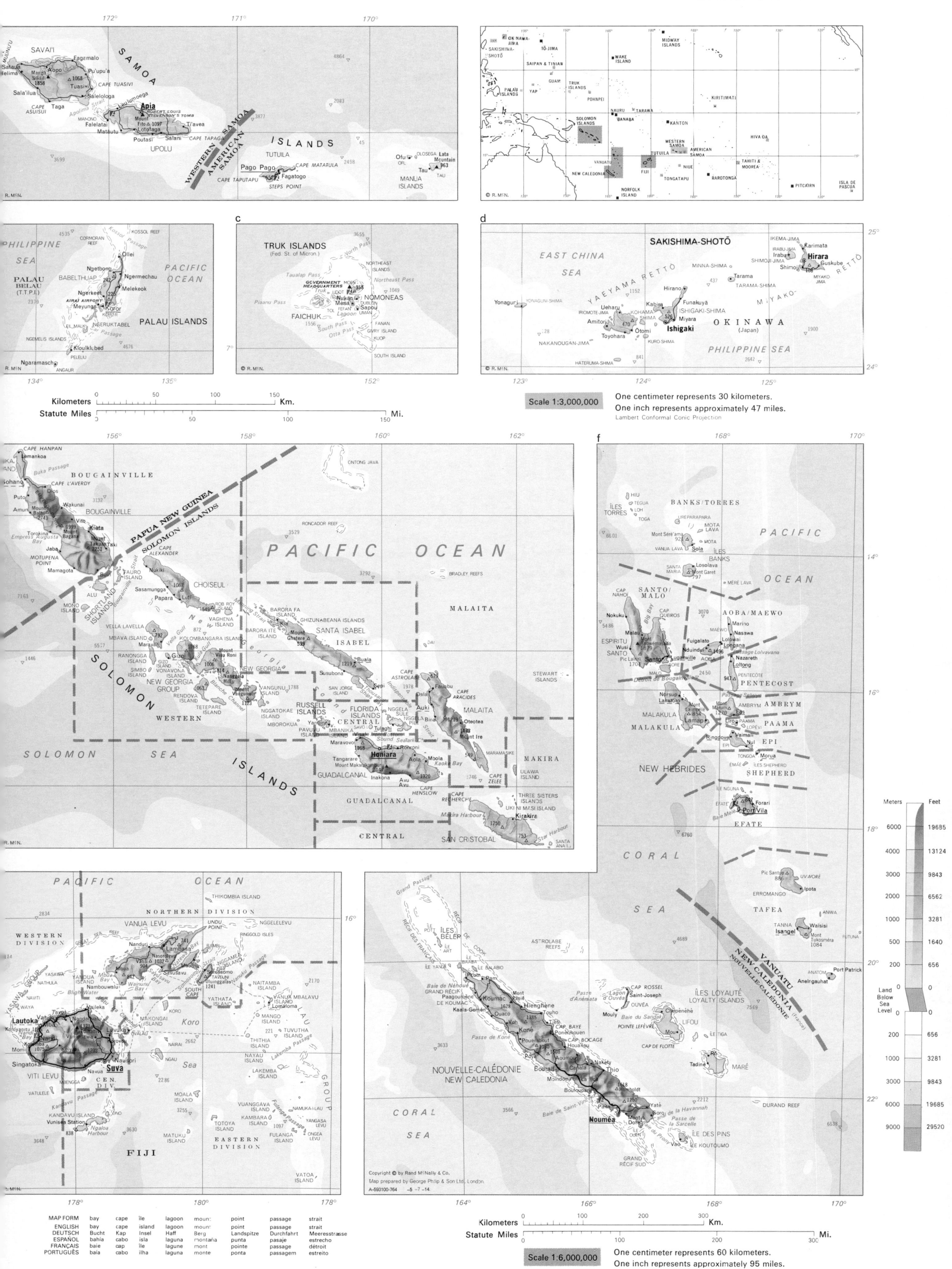

Scale 1:3,000,000
One centimeter represents 30 kilometers.
One inch represents approximately 47 miles.
Lambert Conformal Conic Projection

Copyright © by Rand MCNally & Co.
Map prepared by George Philip & Son Ltd., London.
A-593100-764   -5 - 7 -14.

Scale 1:6,000,000
One centimeter represents 60 kilometers.
One inch represents approximately 95 miles.
Lambert Conformal Conic Projection

MAP FORM	bay	cape	île	lagoon	moun:	point	passage	strait
ENGLISH	bay	cape	island	lagoon	moun:	point	passage	strait
DEUTSCH	Bucht	Kap	Insel	Haff	Berg	Landspitze	Durchfahrt	Meerestrasse
ESPAÑOL	bahía	cabo	isla	laguna	montaña	punta	pasaje	estrecho
FRANÇAIS	baie	cap	île	lagune	mont	pointe	passage	détroit
PORTUGUÊS	baía	cabo	ilha	laguna	monte	ponta	passagem	estreito

Meters	Feet
6000	19685
4000	13124
3000	9843
2000	6562
1000	3281
500	1640
200	656
Land Below Sea Level 0	0
200	656
1000	3281
3000	9843
6000	19685
9000	29520

ENGLISH	bay	cape	island	lake, l.	mountains, mts.	point	range	strait
DEUTSCH	Bucht	Kap	Insel	See	Berge	Landspitze	Gebirge	Meeresstrasse
ESPAÑOL	bahia	cabo	isla	lago	montañas	punta	sierra	estrecho
FRANÇAIS	baie	cap	île	lac	montagnes	pointe	chaîne	détroit
PORTUGUÊS	baia	cabo	ilha	lago	montanhas	ponta	serra	estreito

Kilometers |_____| Km.
0   200   400   600

Statute Miles |_____| Mi.
0   200   400   600

Scale 1:12,000,000   One centimeter represents 120 kilometers.
One inch represents approximately 190 miles.
Lambert Conformal Conic Projection

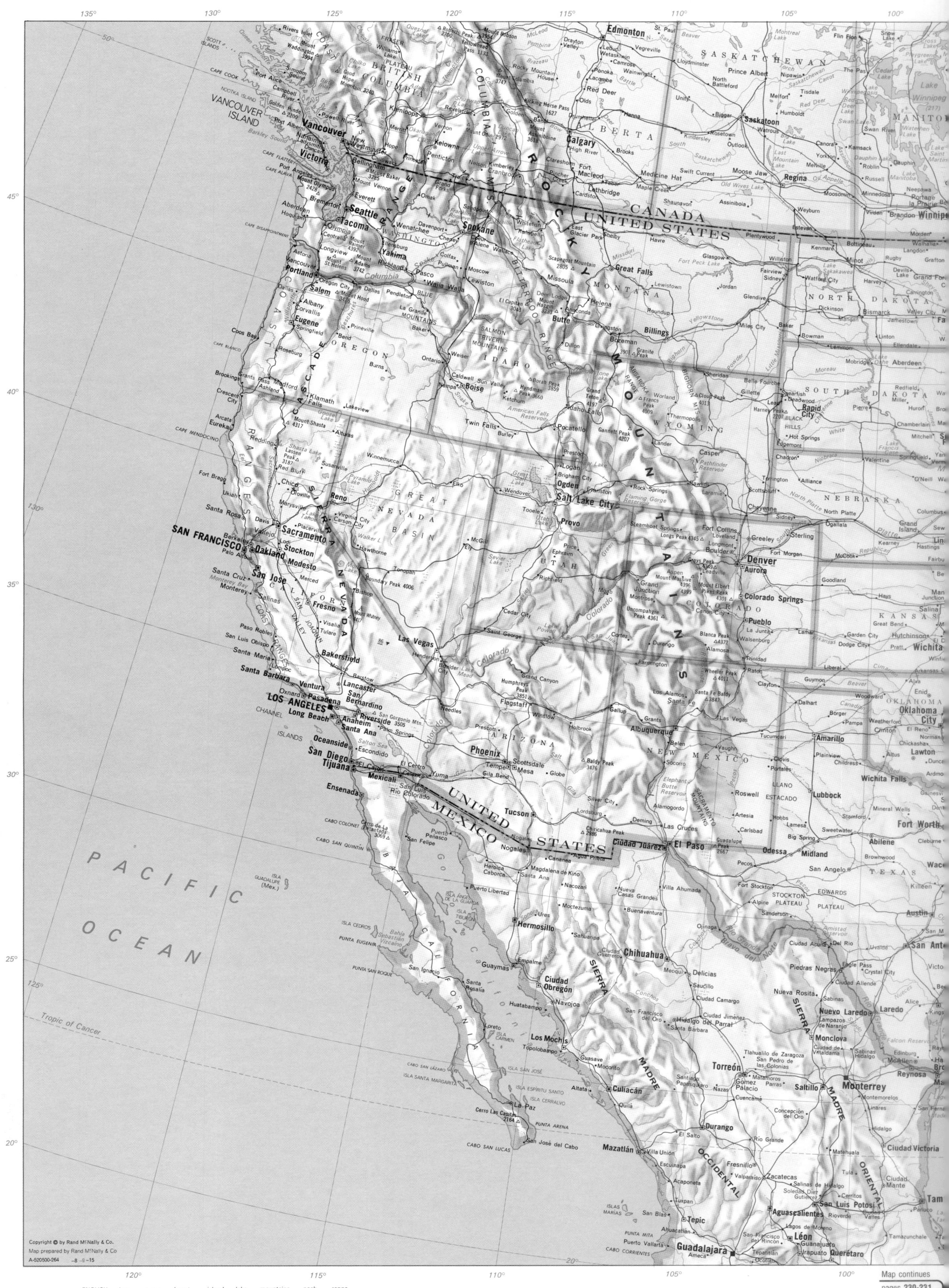

PACIFIC OCEAN

Tropic of Cancer

ENGLISH	bay	cape	desert	island	lake	mountains	peak	range
DEUTSCH	Bucht	Kap	Wüste	Insel	See	Berge	Gipfel	Gebirge
ESPAÑOL	bahía	cabo	desierto	isla	lago	montañas	pico	sierra
FRANÇAIS	baie	cap	désert	île	lac	montagnes	cime	chaîne
PORTUGUÊS	baia	cabo	deserto	ilha	lago	montanhas	pico	serra

Map continues
pages 230-231

Map continues
pages 176-177

Kilometers
Statute Miles

0   200   400   600   Km.
0   200   400   600   Mi.

Scale 1:12,000,000   One centimeter represents 120 kilometers.
One inch represents approximately 190 miles.
Albers Conical Equal-Area Projection

ENGLISH	bay	cape	island, i.	lake, l.	mount, mt.	peak, pk.	point		volca
DEUTSCH	Bucht	Kap	Insel	See	Berg	Gipfel	Landspitze		Vulka
ESPAÑOL	bahia	cabo	isla	lago	monte	pico	punta		vulca
FRANÇAIS	baie	cap	île	lac	mont	cime	pointe		volca
PORTUGUÊS	baía	cabo	ilha	lago	monte	pico	ponta		vulca

Scale 1:6,000,000

One centimeter represents 60 kilometers.
One inch represents approximately 95 miles.
Lambert Conformal Conic Projection

Map continues
pages 176-177

Map continues
pages 182-183

Southwestern Canada / Südwestkanada / Canadá Sud-occidental
Sud-Ouest du Canada / Canadá: Sudoeste

Map continues
pages 180-181

Meters	Feet
6000	19685
4000	13124
3000	9843
2000	6562
1000	3281
500	1640
200	656
0	0
Land Below Sea Level	
0	0
200	656
1000	3281
3000	9843
6000	19685
9000	29520

Copyright © by Rand McNally & Co.
Map prepared by Rand McNally & Co.
A-530020-764   -5 -1 -9

ENGLISH	creek	Indian reserve	inlet	island	lake, l.	mountain	peak	provincial park	sound
DEUTSCH	Bach	Indianerreservation	Einfahrt	Insel	See	Berg	Gipfel	Provinz-Park	Sund
ESPAÑOL	riachuelo	reserva de Indios	abra	isla	lago	montaña	pico	parque de provincia	sonda
FRANÇAIS	crique	réserve indienne	bras de mer	île	lac	montagne	cime	parc provincial	détroit
PORTUGUÊS	riacho	reserva indígena	enseada	ilha	lago	montanha	pico	parque provincial	estreito

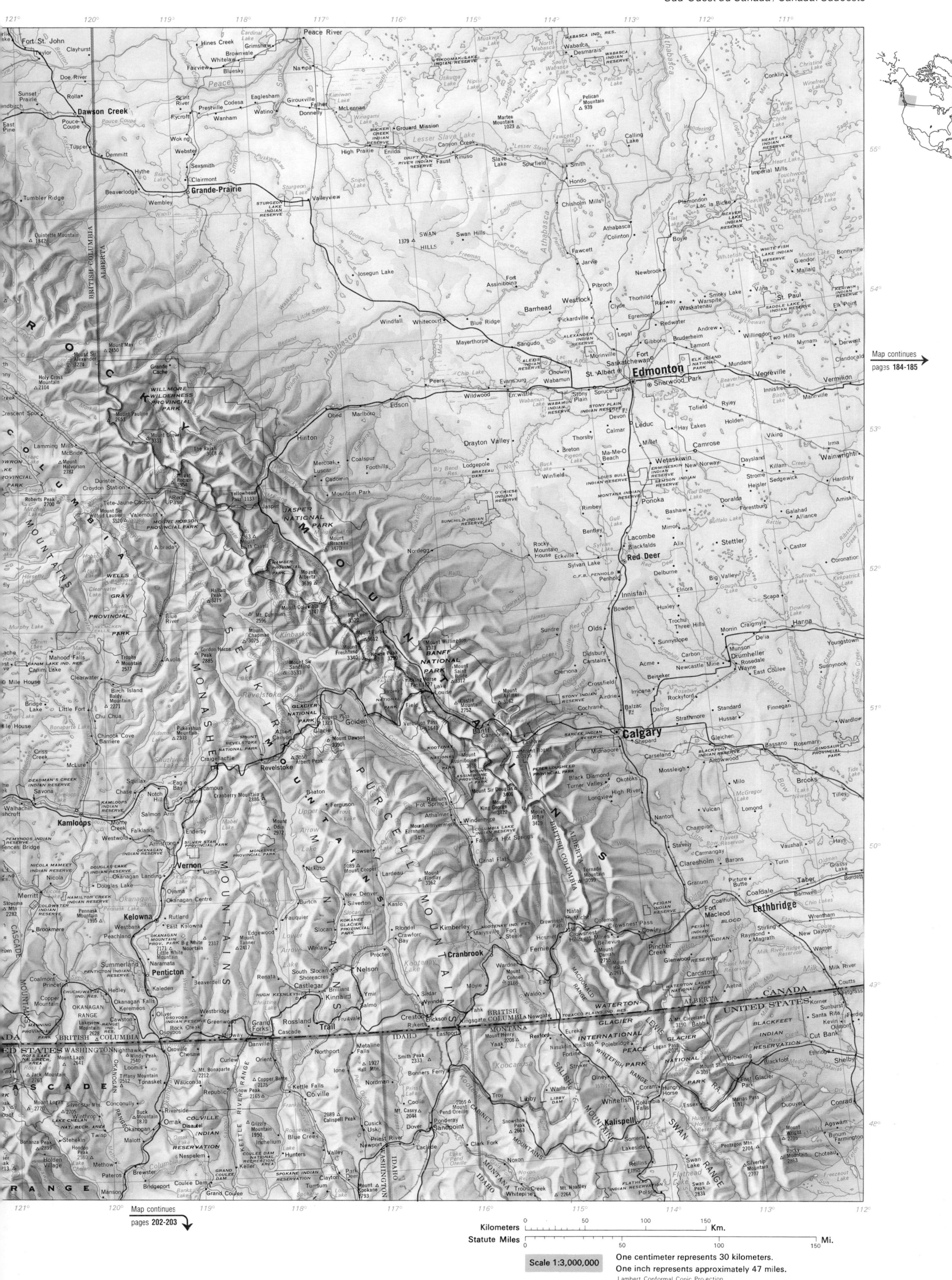

Map continues
pages 184-185

Map continues
pages 202-203

Kilometers

Statute Miles

Scale 1:3,000,000

One centimeter represents 30 kilometers.
One inch represents approximately 47 miles.

Lambert Conformal Conic Projection

184

South-Central Canada / Südliches Mittelkanada / Centro Meridional del Canadá
Canada Central, partie Méridionale / Canadá Central, parte meridional

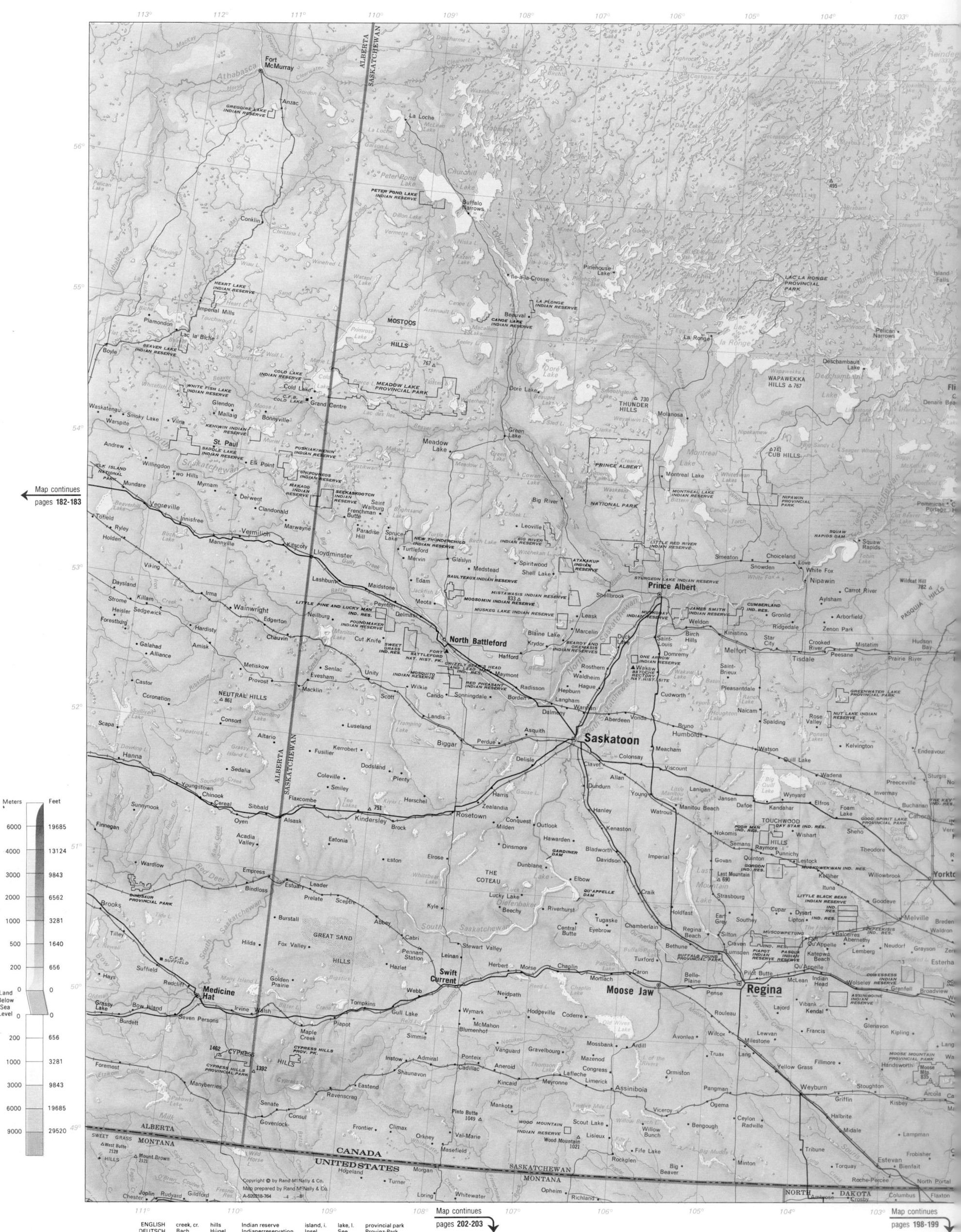

◄ Map continues
pages **182-183**

Map continues
pages **202-203** ▼

Map continues
pages **198-199** ▼

		Meters	Feet
		6000	19685
		4000	13124
		3000	9843
		2000	6562
		1000	3281
		500	1640
		200	656
		0	0
Land Below Sea Level		0	0
		200	656
		1000	3281
		3000	9843
		6000	19685
		9000	29520

	ENGLISH	DEUTSCH	ESPAÑOL	FRANÇAIS	PORTUGUÊS
	creek, cr.	Bach	riachuelo	crique	riacho
	hills	Hügel	colinas	collines	colinas
	Indian reserve	Indianerreservation	reserva de Indios	réserve indienne	reserva indigena
	island, i.	Insel	isla	ile	ilha
	lake, l.	See	lago	lac	lago
	provincial park	Provinz-Park	parque de provincia	parc provincial	parque provincial

South-Central Canada / Südliches Mittelkanada / Centro Meridional del Canadá
Canada Central, partie Méridionale / Canadá Central, parte meridional

185

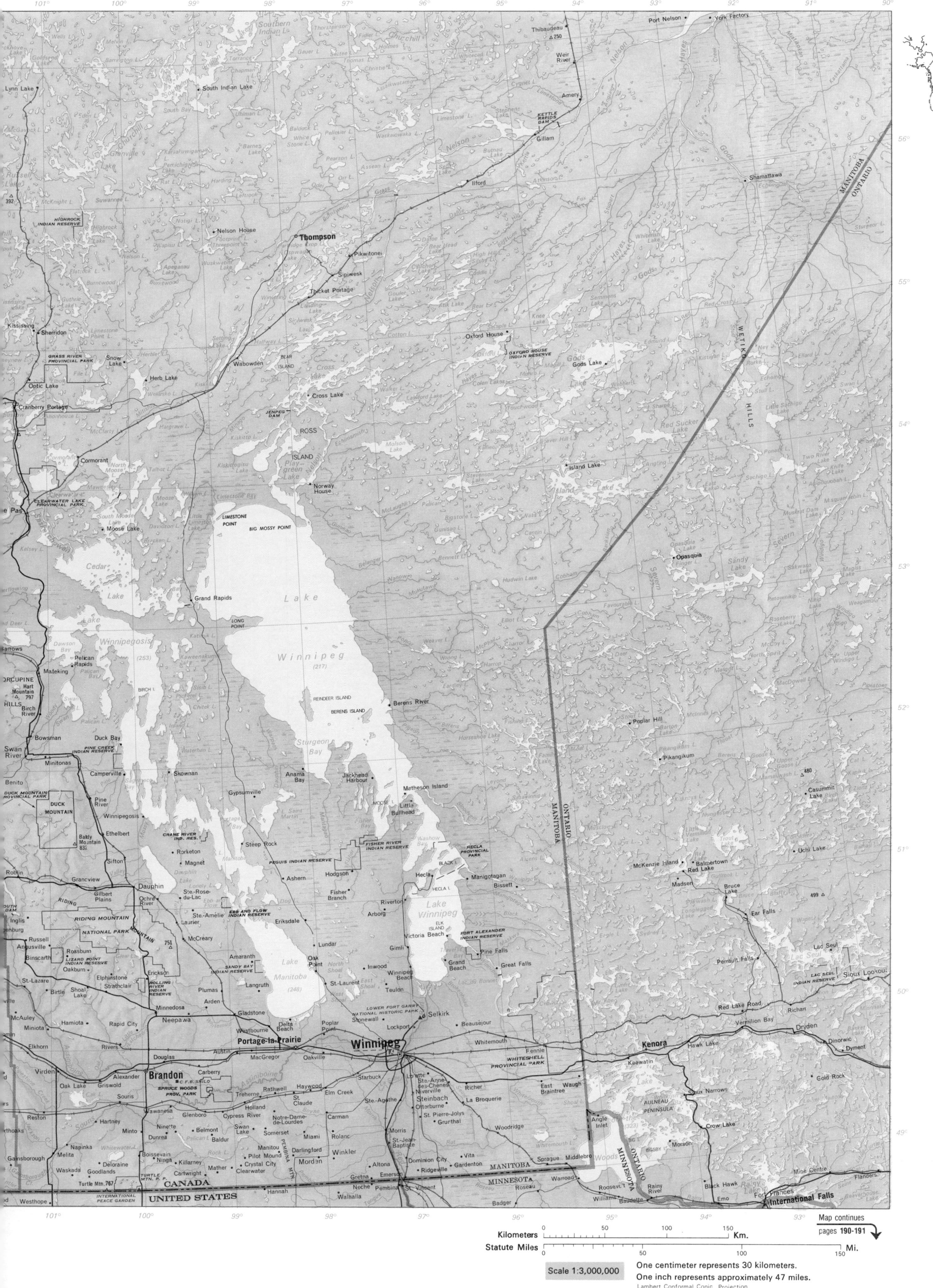

Kilometers
Statute Miles

Map continues
pages **190-191**

Scale 1:3,000,000

One centimeter represents 30 kilometers.
One inch represents approximately 47 miles.

Lambert Conformal Conic Projection

ENGLISH	bay	cape	dam	island	lake, l.	mountain	point	strait
DEUTSCH	Bucht	Kap	Damm	Insel	See	Berg	Landspitze	Meeresstrasse
ESPAÑOL	bahía	cabo	presa	isla	lago	montaña	punta	estrecho
FRANÇAIS	baie	cap	barrage	île	lac	montagne	pointe	détroit
PORTUGUÊS	baía	cabo	represa	ilha	lago	montanha	ponta	estreito

LABRADOR
SEA

ATLANTIC

OCEAN

NEWFOUNDLAND

Corner Brook

St. John's

SAINT PIERRE
AND MIQUELON
(France)
SAINT-PIERRE-
ET-MIQUELON

Saint-
Pierre
SAINT-PIERRE

Gulf
of
Lawrence

Cabot   Strait

Sydney
North Sydney
Glace Bay
CAPE BRETON
ISLAND

SABLE ISLAND
(N.S.)

Kilometers   0   50   100   150   Km.

Statute Miles   0   50   100   150   Mi.

Scale 1:3,000,000

One centimeter represents 30 kilometers.
One inch represents approximately 47 miles.
Lambert Conformal Conic Projection

Copyright © by Rand McNally & Co.
Map prepared by Rand McNally & Co.
A-520219-764   3 5 -8°

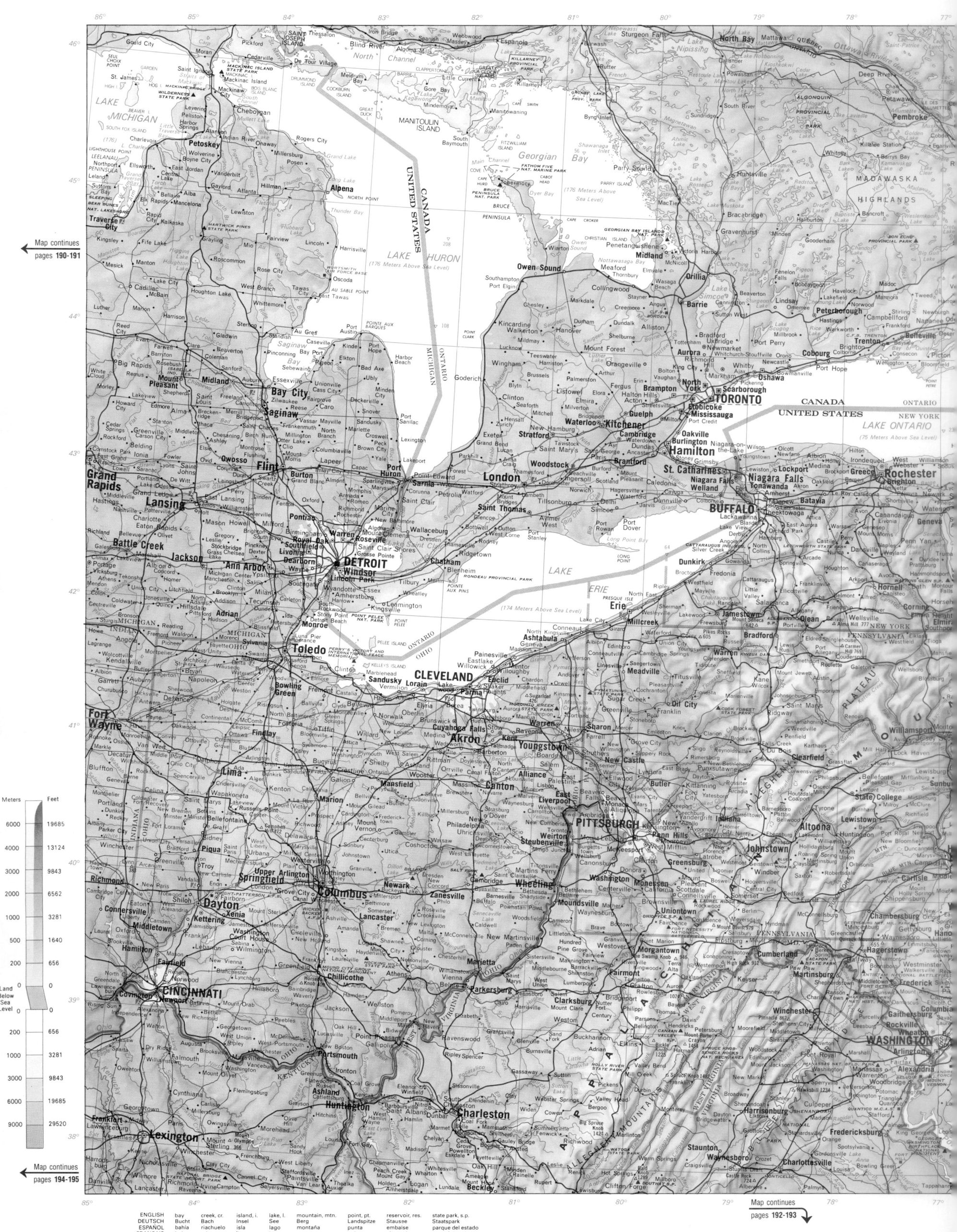

← Map continues
pages **190-191**

← Map continues
pages **194-195**

Map continues
pages **192-193** →

ENGLISH	bay	creek, cr.	island, i.	lake, l.	mountain, mtn.	point, pt.	reservoir, res.	state park, s.p.
DEUTSCH	Bucht	Bach	Insel	See	Berg	Landspitze	Stausee	Staatspark
ESPAÑOL	bahía	riachuelo	isla	lago	montaña	punta	embalse	parque del estado
FRANÇAIS	baie	crique	île	lac	montagne	pointe	réservoir	parc régional
PORTUGUÊS	baia	riacho	ilha	lago	montanha	ponta	reservatório	parque estadual

Northeastern United States / Nordöstliche Vereinigte Staaten / Nor-este de los Estados Unidos
Nord-Est des États-Unis / Estados Unidos: Nordeste

189

Map continues
pages 186-187

Kilometers

Statute Miles

Scale 1:3,000,000

One centimeter represents 30 kilometers.
One inch represents approximately 47 miles.
Albers Conical Equal-Area Projection

Map continues
pages 184-185

Map continues
pages 198-199

Map continues
pages 194-195

ENGLISH	bay	creek, cr.	Indian reservation	island, i.	lake, l.	point	reservoir, res.	state park, s.p.
DEUTSCH	Bucht	Bach	Indianerreservation	Insel	See	Landspitze	Stausee	Staatspark
ESPAÑOL	bahía	riachuelo	reserva de Indios	isla	lago	punta	embalse	parque del estado
FRANÇAIS	baie	crique	réserve indienne	île	lac	pointe	réservoir	parc régional
PORTUGUÊS	baía	riacho	reserva indígena	ilha	lago	ponta	reservatório	parque estadual

Copyright by Rand McNally & Co.
Map prepared by Rand McNally & Co.
A-521000-766

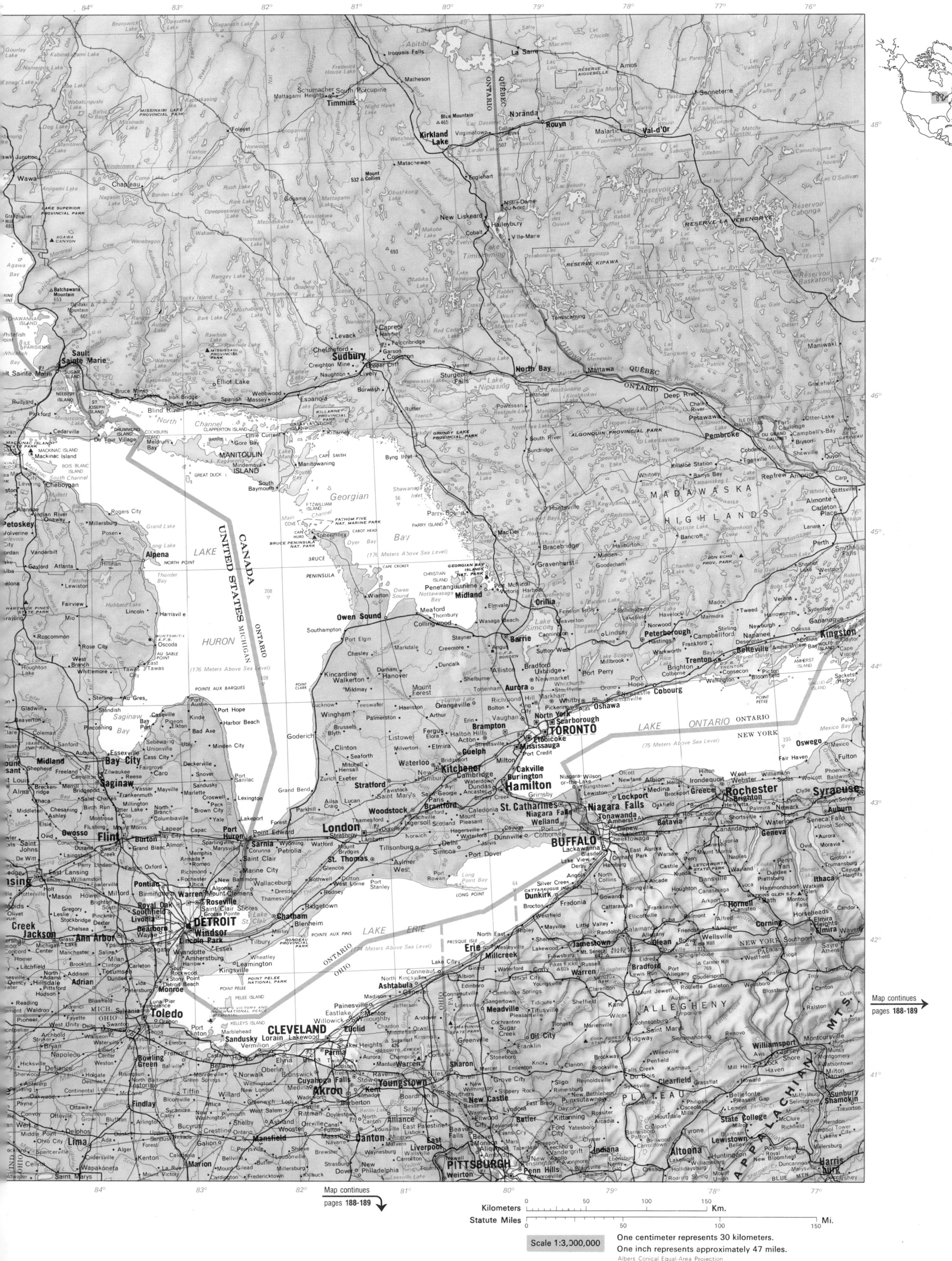

Map continues
pages 188-189

Map continues
pages 188-189

Kilometers

Statute Miles

0   50   100   150

Km.

Mi.

Scale 1:3,000,000

One centimeter represents 30 kilometers.
One inch represents approximately 47 miles.
Albers Conical Equal-Area Projection

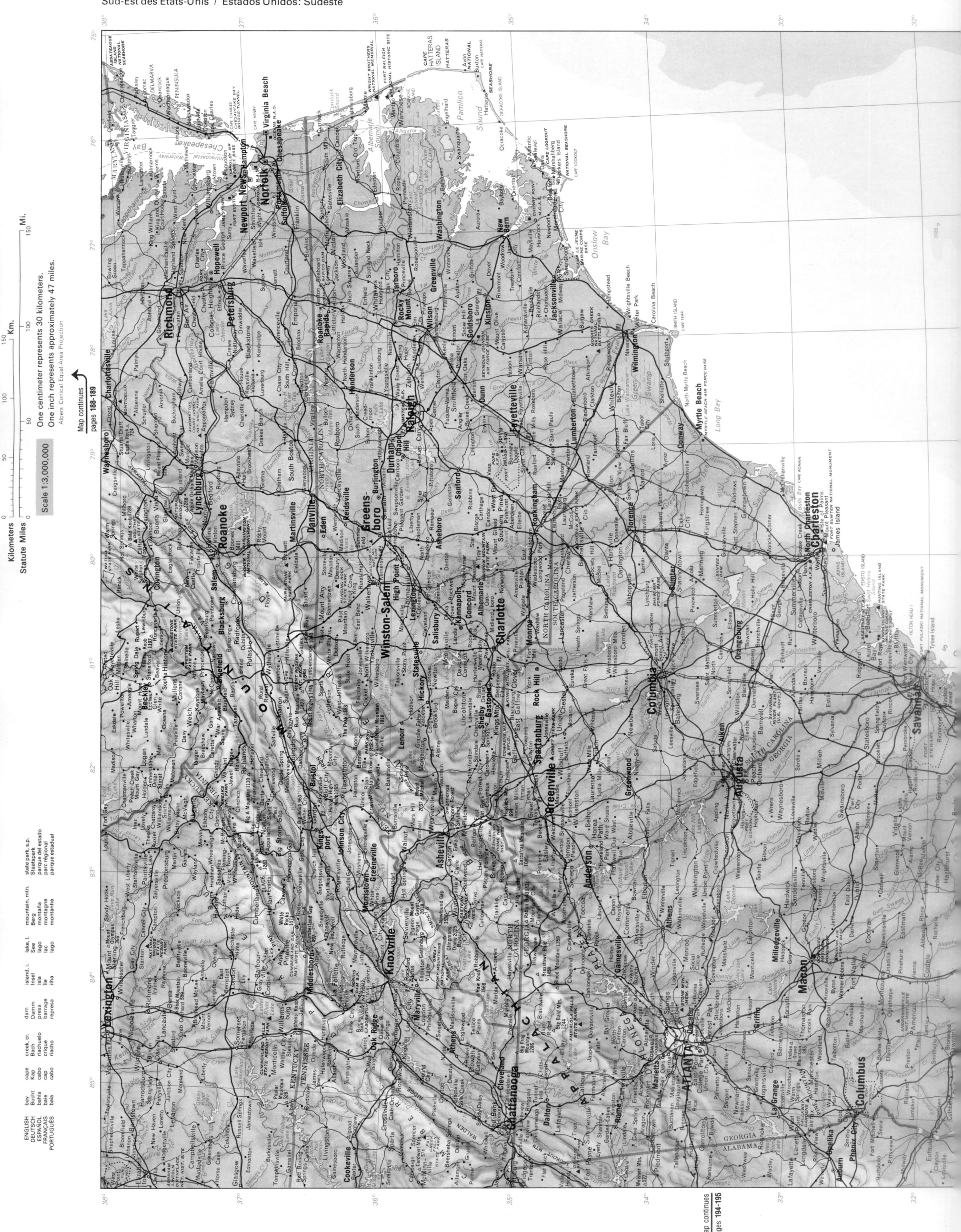

Scale 1:3,000,000

One centimeter represents 30 kilometers.
One inch represents approximately 47 miles.

Albers Conical Equal-Area Projection

Map continues
pages 188-189

Map continues
pages 194-195

Southeastern United States / Südöstliche Vereinigte Staaten / Sud-este de los Estados Unidos
Sud-Est des États-Unis / Estados Unidos: Sudeste

193

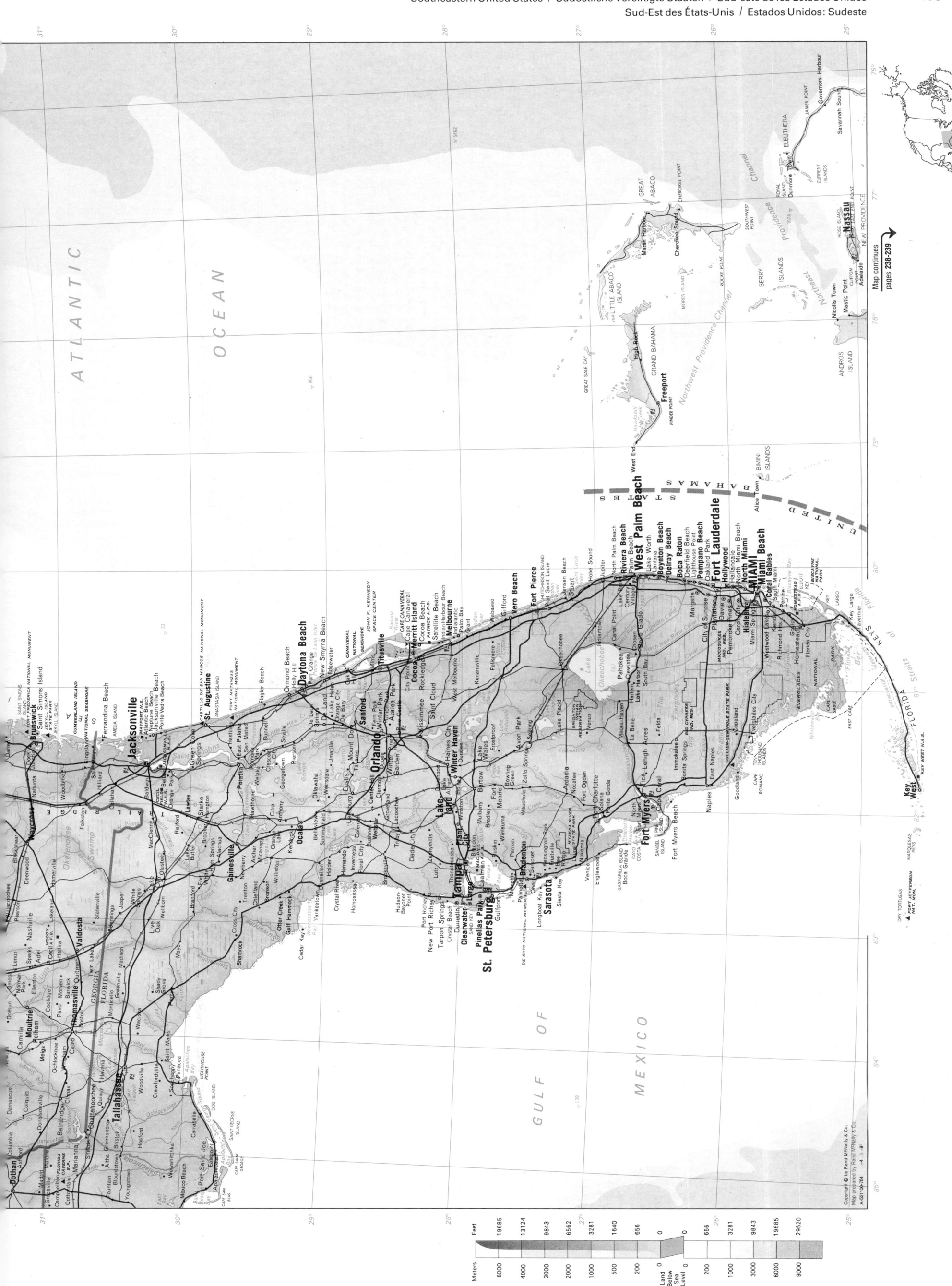

Map continues
pages 238-239

Feet										
19685	13124	9843	6562	3281	1640	656	0			

Meters								Land Below Sea Level				
6000	4000	3000	2000	1000	500	200	0	0	200	1000	3000	6000	9000

0	656	3281	9843	19685	29520

Copyright © by Rand McNally & Co.
Map prepared by Rand McNally & Co.
A-521100-764   -4-3-5P

Map continues pages 188-189

Map continues pages 190-191

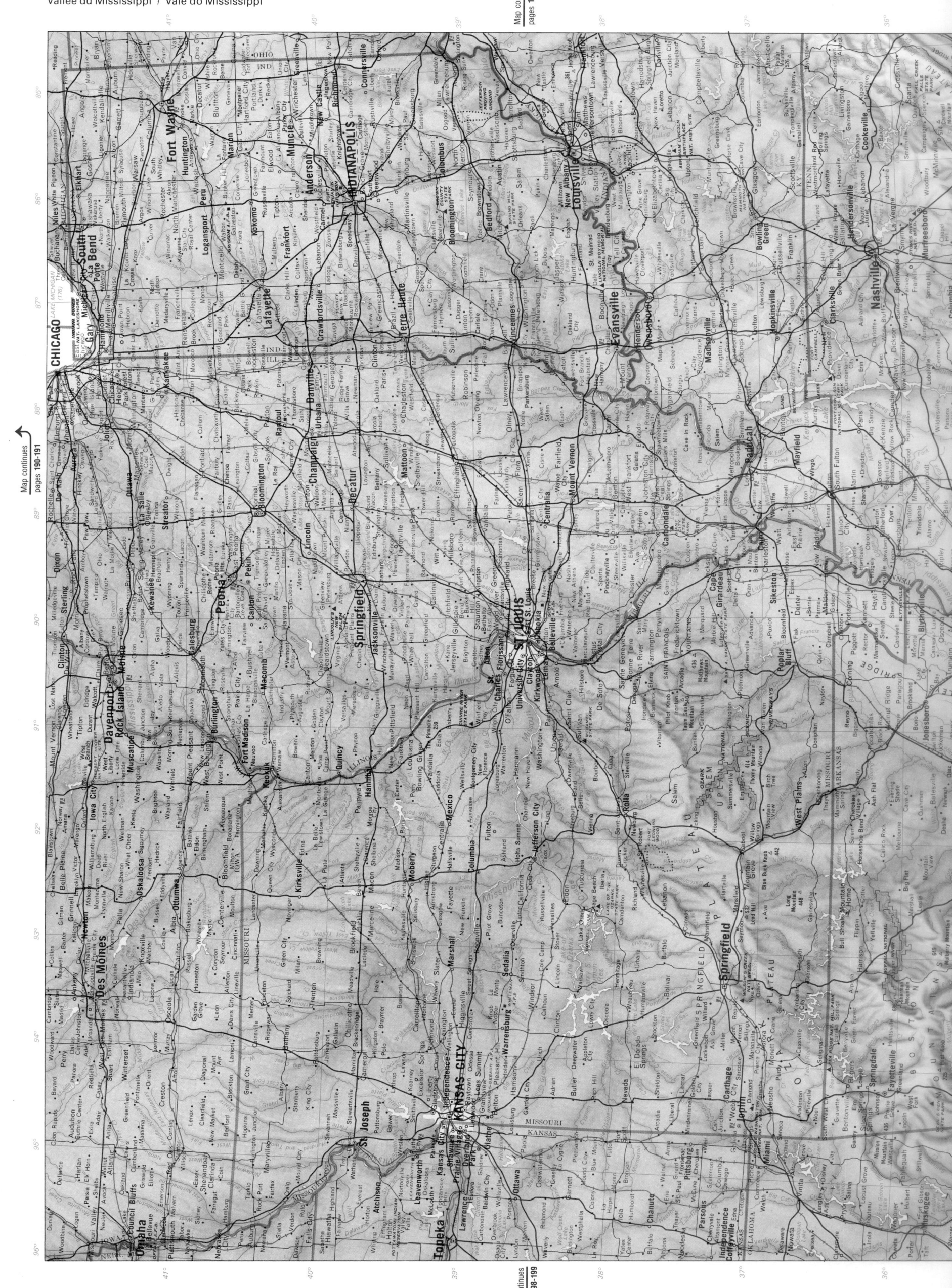

Map continues pages 198-199

Map continues
pages 192-193

Map continues
pages 196-197

Copyright © by Rand McNally & Co.
Map prepared by Rand McNally & Co.

GULF OF MEXICO

GULF OF MEXICO

ENGLISH	bay	bayou, bay	creek, cr.	dam	lake	mountain, mtn.	reservoir, res.	state park, s.p.
DEUTSCH	Bucht	Bayou	Bach	Damm	See	Berg	Stausee	Staatspark
ESPAÑOL	bahía	ensenada	riachuelo	presa	lago	montaña	embalse	parque del estado
FRANÇAIS	baie	bayou	crique	barrage	lac	montagne	réservoir	parc régional
PORTUGUÊS	baía	enseada	riacho	represa	lago	montanha	reservatório	parque estadual

Kilometers
Statute Miles
Mi.
Km.

Scale 1:3,000,000
Albers Conical Equal-Area Projection

One centimeter represents 30 kilometers.
One inch represents approximately 47 miles.

| Feet | 19685 | 13124 | 9843 | 6562 | 3281 | 1640 | 656 | 0 | 0 | 656 | 3281 | 9843 | 19685 | 29520 |
| Meters | 6000 | 4000 | 3000 | 2000 | 1000 | 500 | 200 | 0 | 0 | 200 | 1000 | 3000 | 6000 | 9000 |

Land Below Sea Level

196

Southern Great Plains / Südliche Grosse Ebenen / Grandes Llanos: zona meridional
Grandes Plaines, partie Méridionale / Grandes Planícies: zona meridional

Map continues pages 194-195

Map continues pages 198-199

Map continues pages 200-201

Southern Great Plains / Südliche Grosse Ebenen / Grandes Llanos: zona meridional
Grandes Plaines, partie Méridionale / Grandes Planícies: zona meridional
197

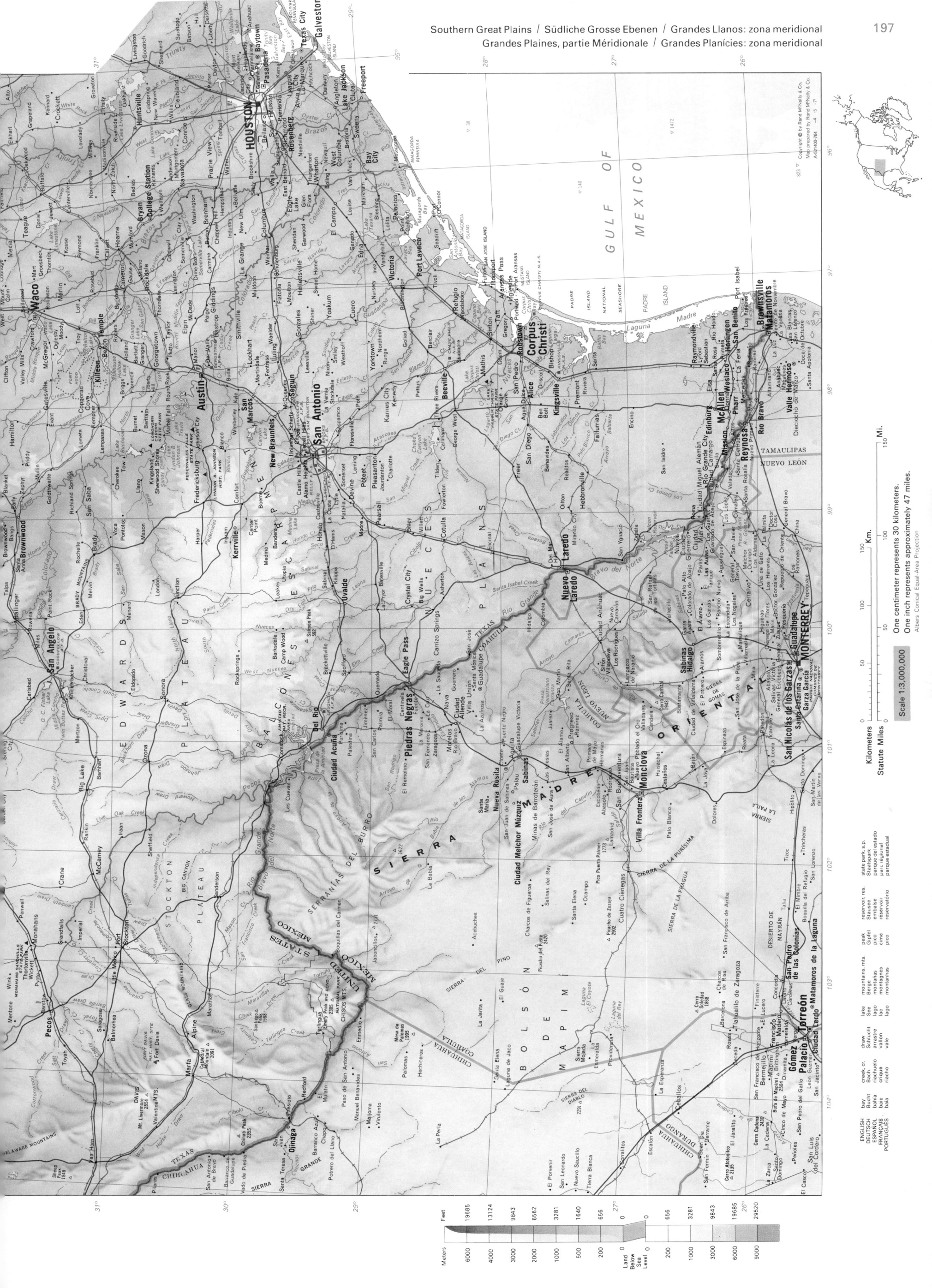

Scale 1:3,000,000

One centimeter represents 30 kilometers.
One inch represents approximately 47 miles.

Albers Conical Equal-Area Projection

ENGLISH	DEUTSCH	ESPAÑOL	FRANÇAIS	PORTUGUÊS
bay	Bucht	bahía	baie	baía
creek, cr.	Bach	riachuelo	crique	riacho
draw	Schlucht	arrastre	ravin	vale
lake	See	lago	lac	lago
mountains, mts.	Berge	montañas	montagnes	montanhas
peak	Gipfel	pico	cime	pico
reservoir, res.	Stausee	embalse	réservoir	reservatório
state park, s.p.	Staatspark	parque del estado	parc du état	parque estadual

Map continues
pages 190–191

Map continues
pages 184–185

Map continues
pages 202–203

Northern Great Plains / Nördliche Grosse Ebenen / Grandes Llanos: zona septentrional
Grandes Plaines, partie Septentrionale / Grandes Planícies: zona setentrional

199

Map continues
pages 194-195

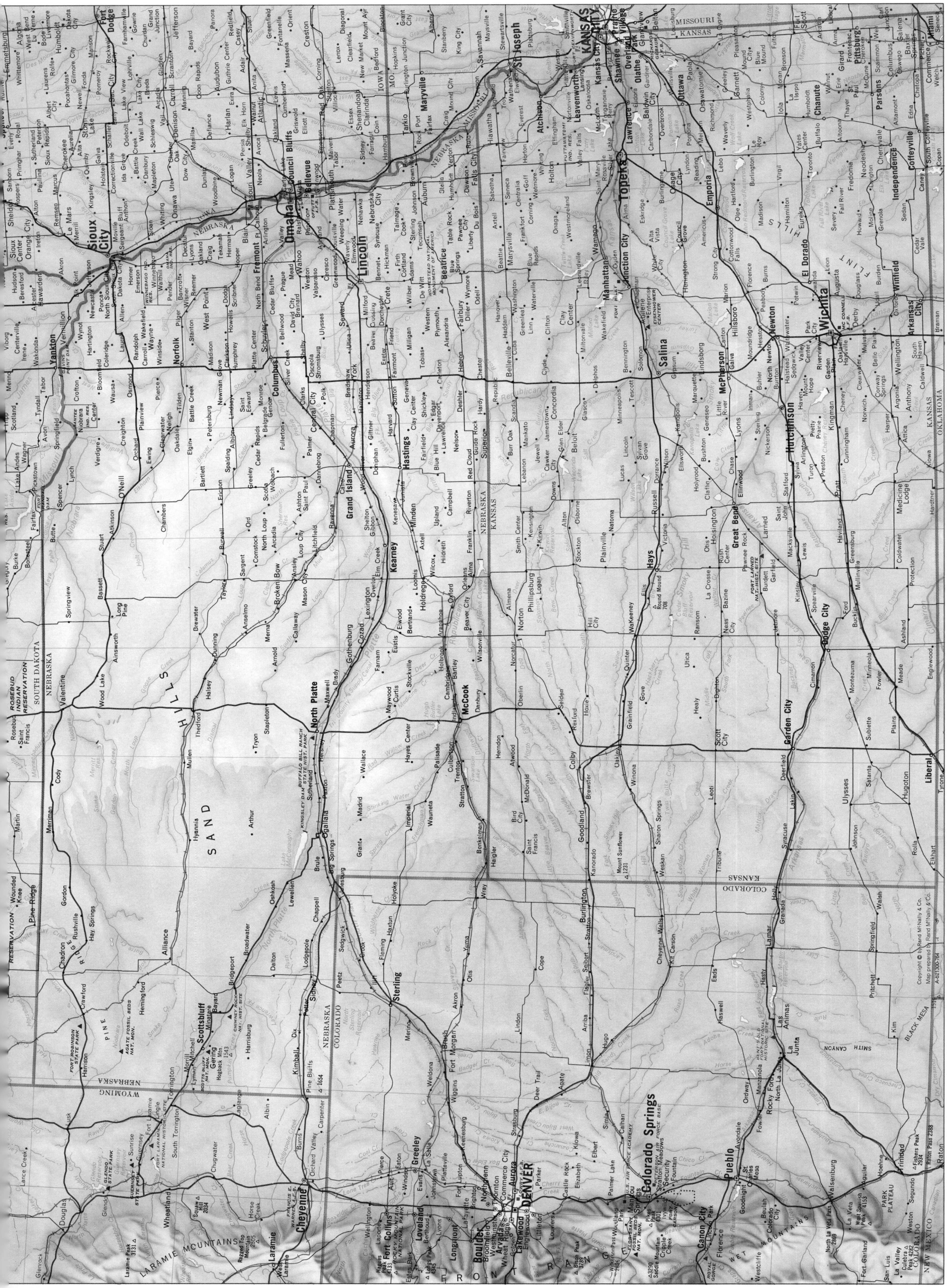

Map continues
pages 196-197

Map continues
pages 200-201

Scale 1:3,000,000

Kilometers
Km.

Statute Miles
Mi.

One centimeter represents 30 kilometers.
One inch represents approximately 47 miles.
Albers Conical Equal-Area Projection

Copyright by Rand McNally & Co.
Map prepared by Rand McNally & Co.
A-697306-314

ENGLISH	creek, cr.	dam	Indian reservation, Ind. res.	lake, l.	mountain, mtn.	peak	reservoir, res.	state park
DEUTSCH	Bach	Damm	Indianerreservation	See	Gebirge	Gipfel	Stausee	Staatspark
ESPAÑOL	riachuelo	presa	reserva de indios	lago	sierra	pico	embalse	parque del estado
FRANÇAIS	crique	barrage	réserve indienne	lac	montagne	cime	réservoir	parc régional
PORTUGUÊS	riacho	barragem	reserva indígena	lago	montanha	pico	reservatório	parque estadual

Feet / Meters elevation scale:
19685 / 6000
13124 / 4000
9843 / 3000
6562 / 2000
3281 / 1000
1640 / 500
656 / 200
0 / Land / Below Sea Level
0
656 / 200
3281 / 1000
9843 / 3000
19685 / 6000
29520 / 9000

Southern Rocky Mountains / Südliches Felsengebirge / Montañas Rocosas: zona meridional
Montagnes Rocheuses, partie Méridionale / Montanhas Rochosas: zona meridional

Map continues pages 198-199

Map continues pages 202-203

Map continues pages 204-205

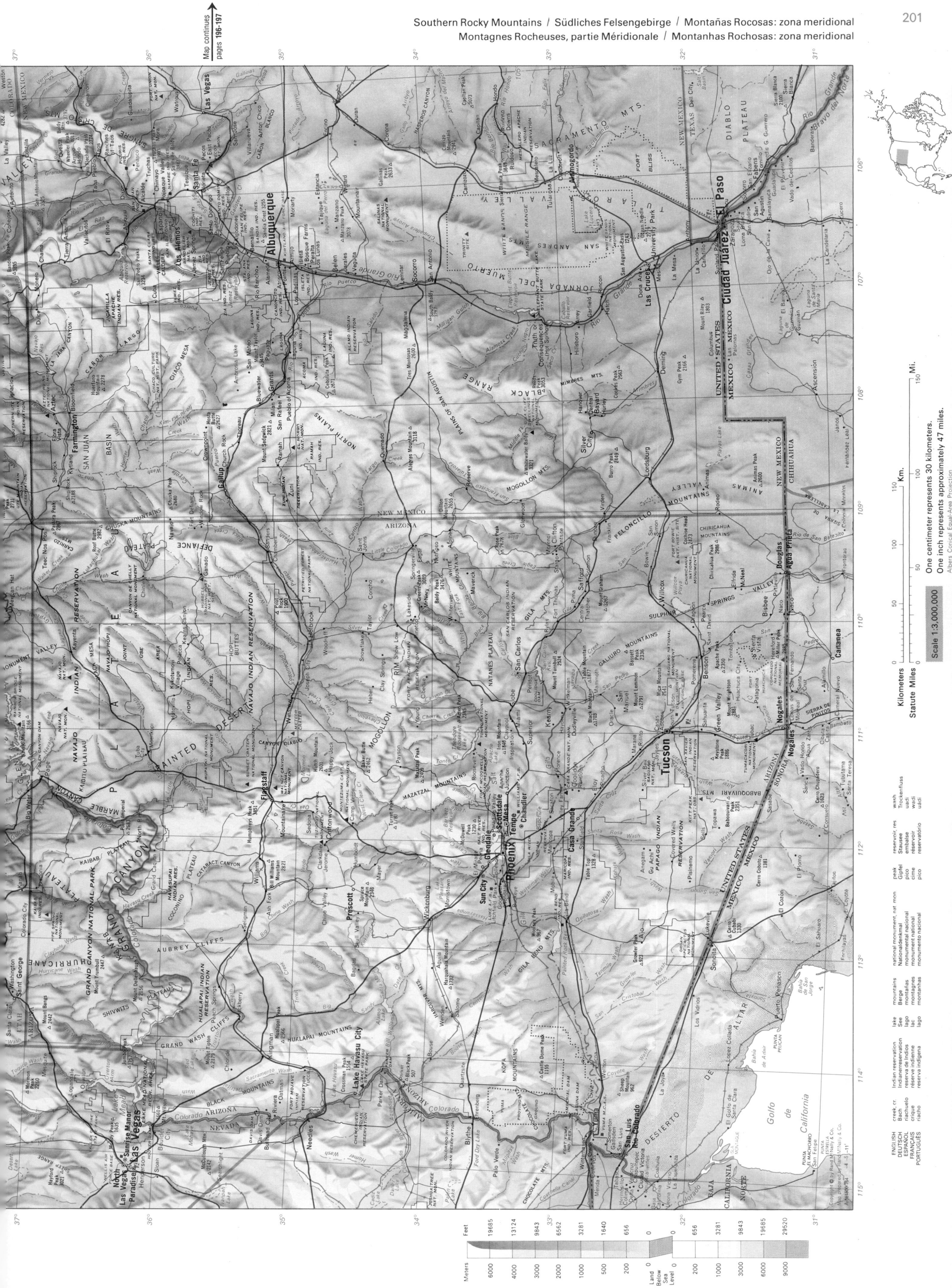
Southern Rocky Mountains / Südliches Felsengebirge / Montañas Rocosas: zona meridional
Montagnes Rocheuses, partie Méridionale / Montanhas Rochosas: zona meridional

201

Map continues
pages 196-197

Scale 1:3,000,000

Albers Conical Equal-Area Projection

One centimeter represents 30 kilometers.
One inch represents approximately 47 miles.

Kilometers
Km.
Statute Miles
Mi.

ENGLISH	DEUTSCH	ESPAÑOL	FRANÇAIS	PORTUGUÊS

wash — Trockenfluss — wadi — wadi — uádi

reservoir, res — Stausee — reservoir — réservoir — reservatório

peak — Gipfel — pico — cime — pico

national monument, nat mon — Nationaldenkmal — monumento nacional — monument national — monumento nacional

mountains — Berge — montañas — montagnes — montanhas

lake — See — lago — lac — lago

Indian reservation — Indianerreservation — reserva de Indios — réserve indienne — reserva indígena

creek, cr — Bach — riachuelo — crique — riacho

202

Northwestern United States / Nordwestliche Vereinigte Staaten / Nor-oeste de los Estados Unidos
Nord-Ouest des États-Unis / Noroeste dos Estados Unidos

Map continues
pages 182-183

Map continues
pages 204-205

ENGLISH	creek, cr.	Indian reservation	lake, l.	mountain, mtn.	pass	peak	range	reservoir, res.
DEUTSCH	Bach	Indianerreservation	See	Berg	Pass	Gipfel	Gebirge	Stausee
ESPAÑOL	riachuelo	reserva de Indios	lago	montaña	paso	pico	sierra	embalse
FRANÇAIS	crique	réserve indienne	lac	montagne	col	cime	chaîne	réservoir
PORTUGUÊS	riacho	reserva indígena	lago	montanha	passo	pico	serra	reservatório

Northwestern United States / Nordwestliche Vereinigte Staaten / Nor-oeste de los Estados Unidos
Nord-Ouest des États-Unis / Noroeste dos Estados Unidos

203

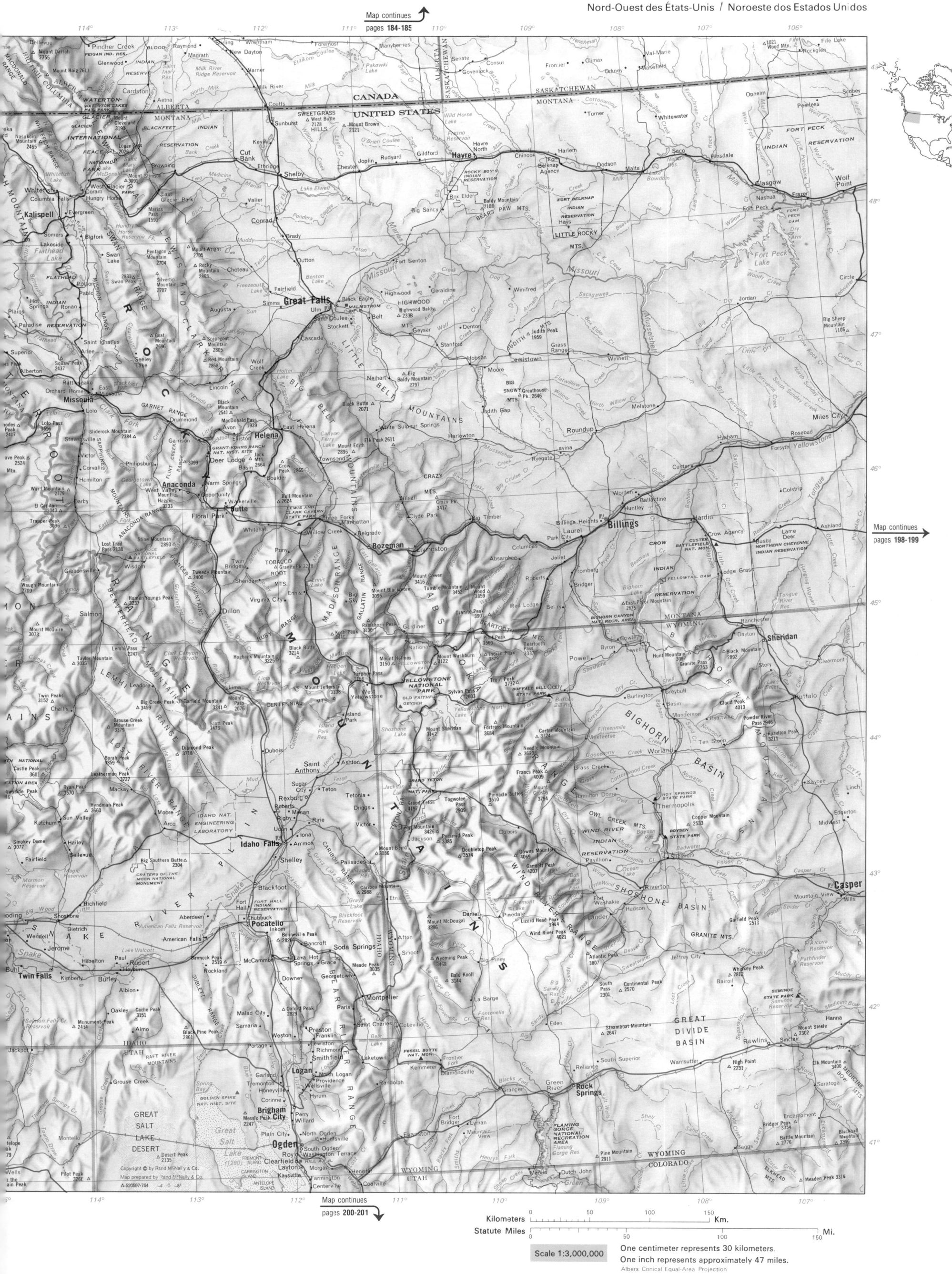

Map continues
pages 184-185

Map continues
pages 198-199

Map continues
pages 200-201

Kilometers

Statute Miles

Scale 1:3,000,000
One centimeter represents 30 kilometers.
One inch represents approximately 47 miles.
Albers Conical Equal-Area Projection

Map continues pages 200-201

Map continues pages 202-203

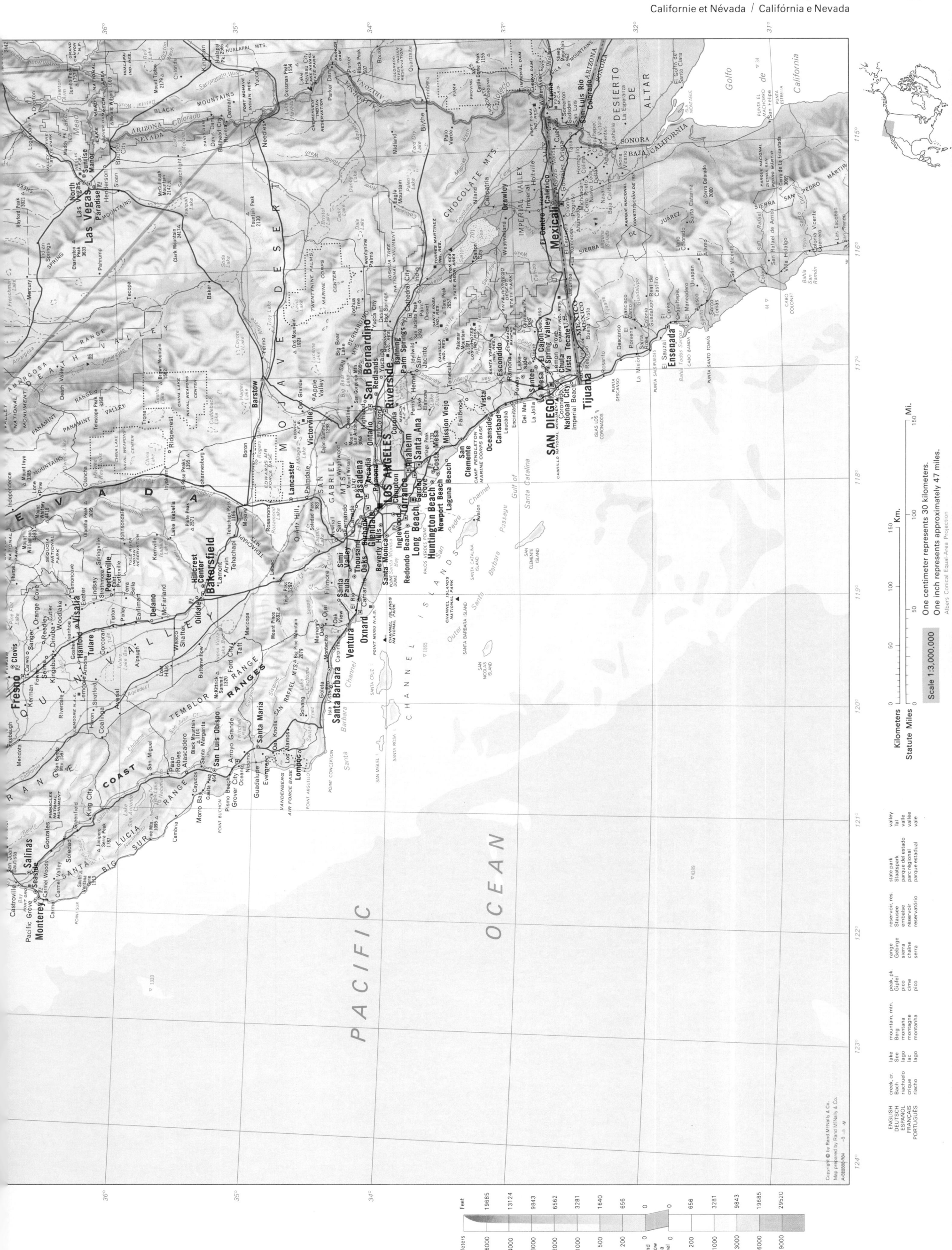

Copyright © by Rand McNally & Co.
Map prepared by Rand McNally & Co.
A-602000-984

Scale 1:3,000,000

One centimeter represents 30 kilometers.
One inch represents approximately 47 miles.

Albers Conical Equal-Area Projection

ENGLISH	creek, cr.	lake	mountain, mtn.	peak, pk.	range	reservoir, res.	state park	valley
DEUTSCH	Bach	See	Berg	Gipfel	Gebirge	Stausee	Staatspark	Tal
ESPAÑOL	riachuelo	lago	montaña	pico	sierra	embalse	parque del estado	valle
FRANÇAIS	crique	lac	montagne	cime	chaîne	reservoir	parc régional	vallée
PORTUGUÊS	riacho	lago	montanha	pico	serra	reservatório	parque estadual	vale

Feet	Meters
19685	6000
13124	4000
9843	3000
6562	2000
3281	1000
1640	500
656	200
0	Land Below Sea Level 0
656	200
3281	1000
9843	3000
19685	6000
29520	9000

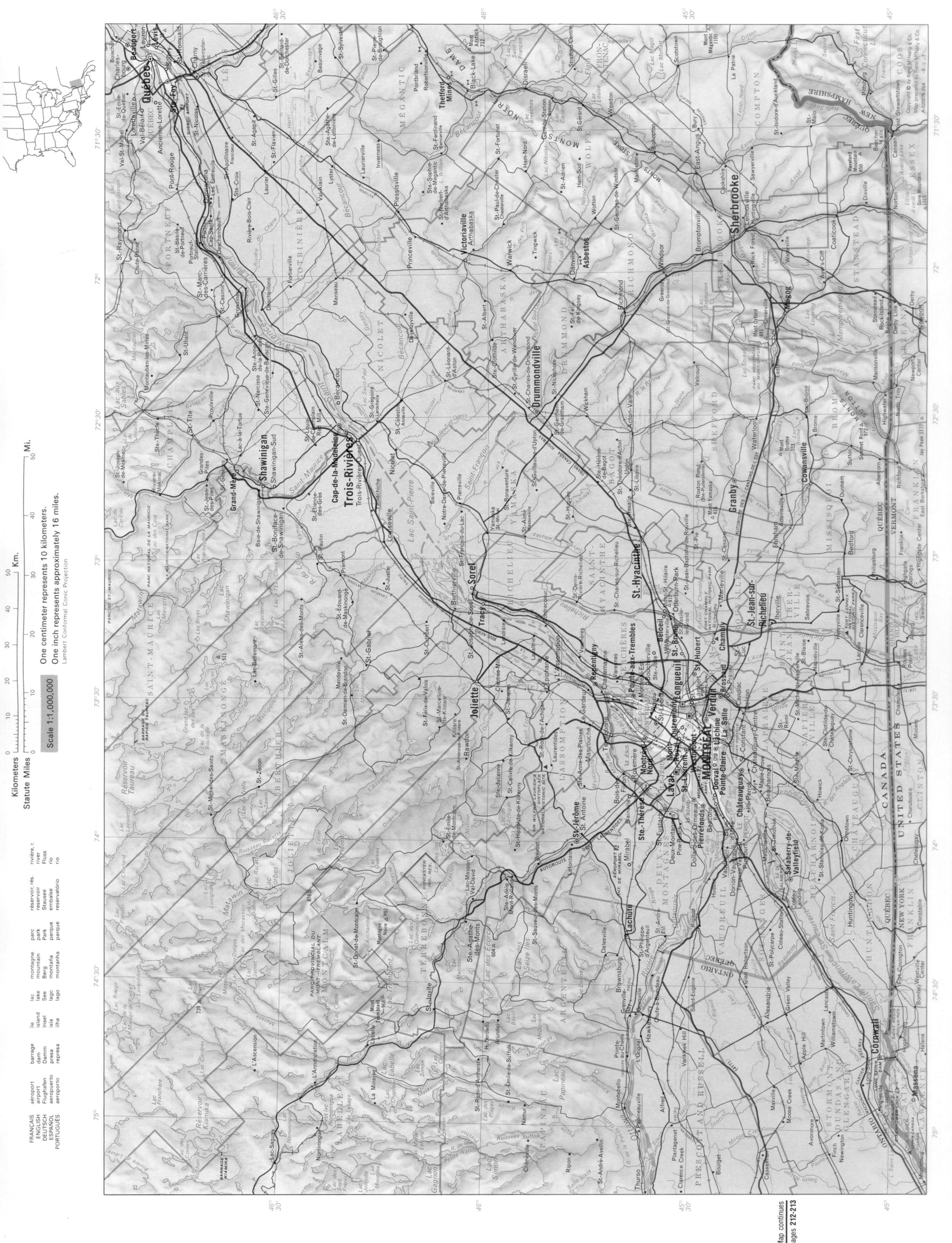

Kilometers

Statute Miles

One centimeter represents 10 kilometers.
One inch represents approximately 16 miles.
Lambert Conformal Conic Projection

Scale 1:1,000,000

FRANÇAIS	aéroport	île	lac	montagne	parc	réservoir, rés.	rivière, r.
ENGLISH	airport	island	lake	mountain	park	reservoir	river
DEUTSCH	Flughafen	Insel	See	Berg	Park	Stausee	Fluss
ESPAÑOL	aeropuerto	isla	lago	montaña	parque	embalse	río
PORTUGUÊS	aeroporto	ilha	lago	montanha	parque	reservatório	rio

Map continues
pages 212-213

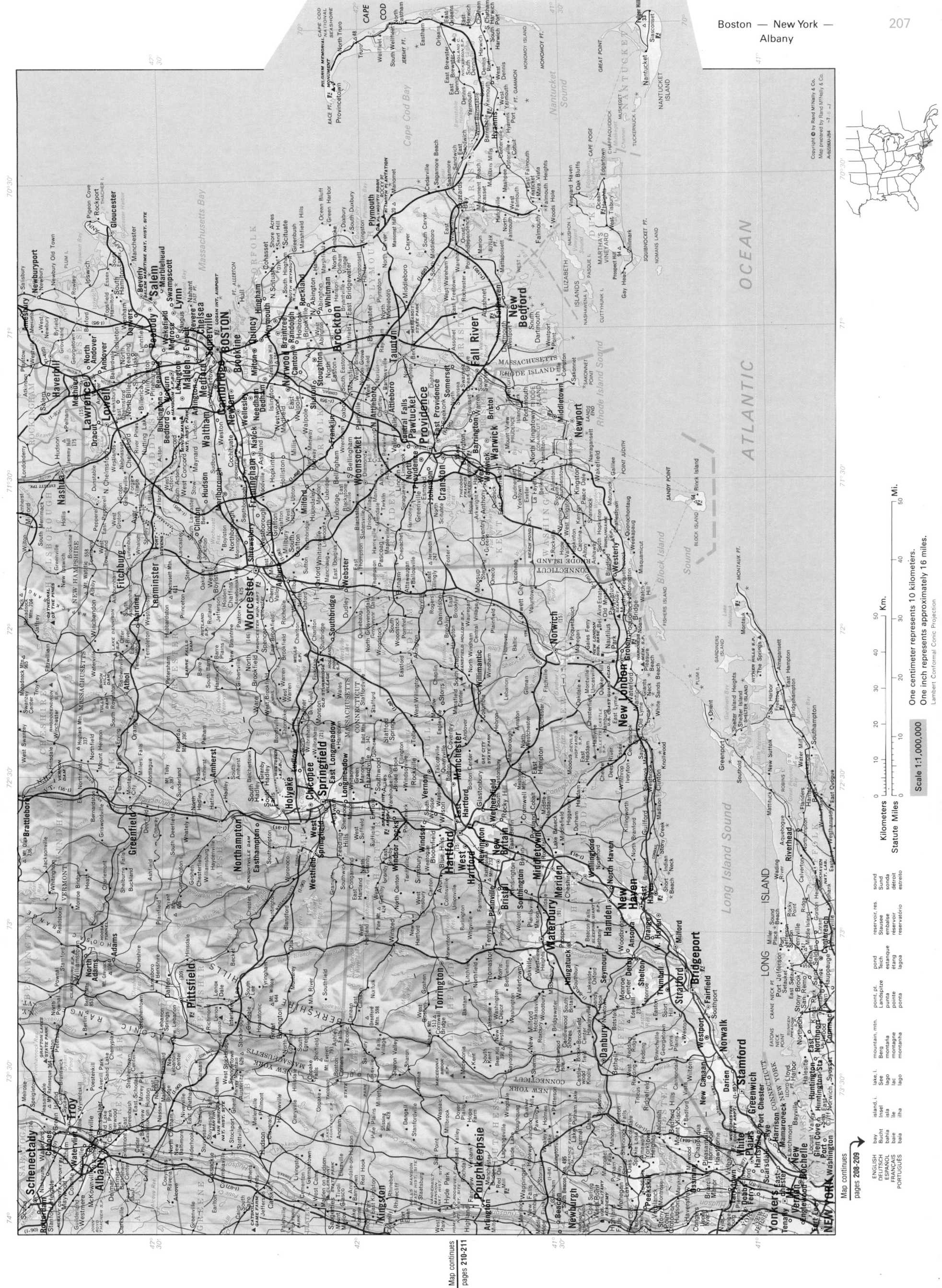

ATLANTIC OCEAN

Massachusetts Bay

Cape Cod Bay

Nantucket Sound

Long Island Sound

Rhode Island Sound

Block Island Sound

LONG ISLAND

BOSTON

Worcester

Providence

Springfield

Hartford

New Haven

Bridgeport

Stamford

Albany

Schenectady

Troy

Pittsfield

New Bedford

Fall River

New London

Norwich

Newport

Poughkeepsie

NEW YORK

Yonkers

Waterbury

Meriden

Danbury

Norwalk

Brockton

Plymouth

Taunton

Lawrence

Lowell

Nashua

Haverhill

Newburyport

Gloucester

Salem

Lynn

Quincy

Cambridge

Newton

Framingham

Fitchburg

Leominster

Gardner

Greenfield

Northampton

Holyoke

Chicopee

Manchester

Brattleboro

North Adams

Torrington

Map continues
pages 210-211

Map continues
pages 208-209

Scale 1:1,000,000

One centimeter represents 10 kilometers.
One inch represents approximately 16 miles.
Lambert Conformal Conic Projection

Kilometers

Statute Miles

Km.

Mi.

0 10 20 30 40 50

ENGLISH	bay	island, i.	lake, l.	mountain, mtn.	point, pt.	pond	reservoir, res.	sound
DEUTSCH	Bucht	Insel	See	Berg	Landspitze	Teich	Stausee	Sund
ESPAÑOL	bahia	isla	lago	montaña	punta	estanque	embalse	sonda
FRANÇAIS	baie	île	lac	montagne	pointe	étang	réservoir	détroit
PORTUGUÊS	baía	ilha	lago	montanha	ponta	lagoa	reservatório	estreito

Map continues pages 210-211

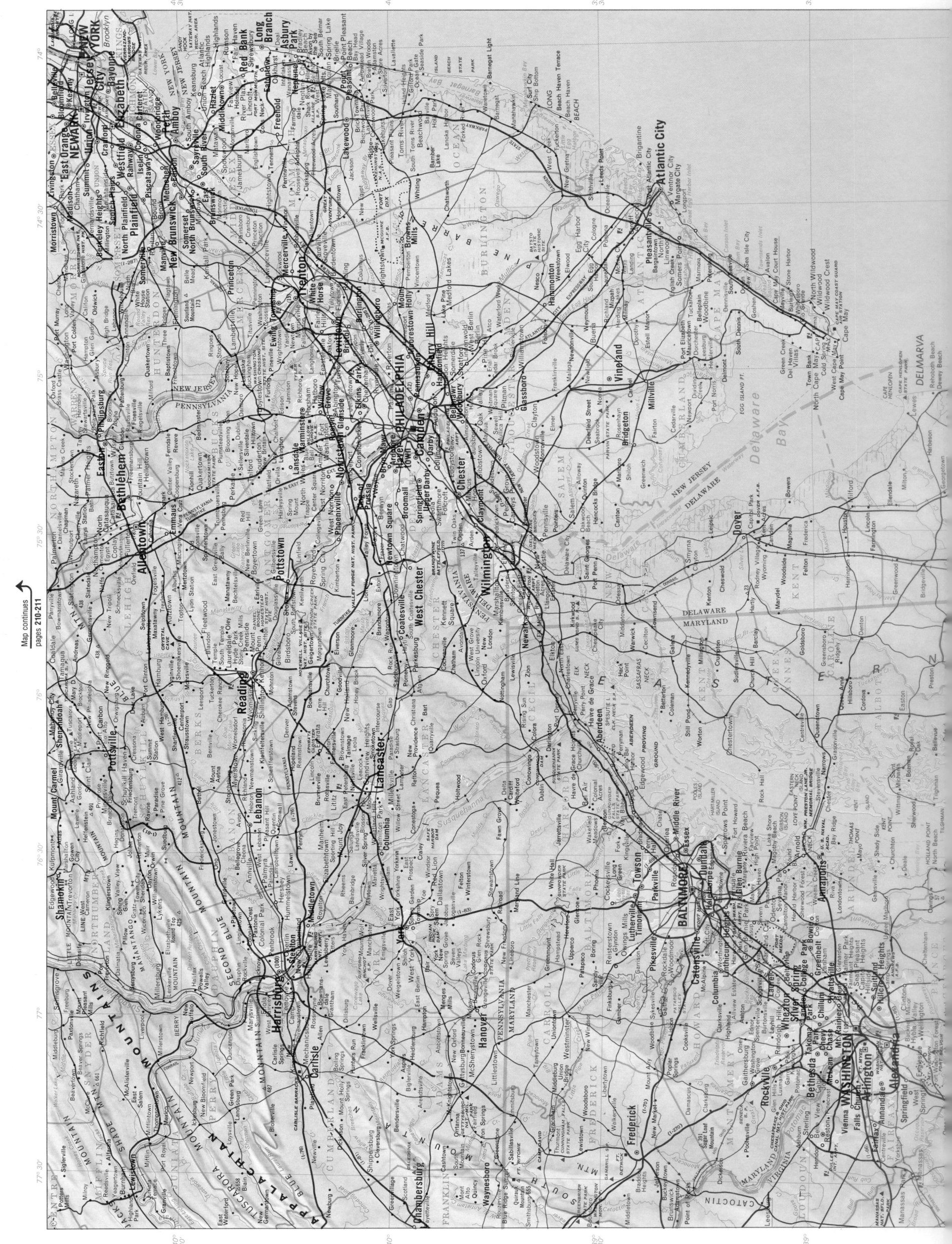
NEW YORK
NEWARK
Elizabeth
Jersey City
Atlantic City
Trenton
PHILADELPHIA
Camden
Wilmington
Chester
Allentown
Bethlehem
Reading
Lancaster
Harrisburg
York
BALTIMORE
WASHINGTON
Alexandria
Arlington
Annapolis
Frederick
Dover
Vineland
Delaware Bay
OCEAN
DELMARVA
NEW JERSEY
PENNSYLVANIA
DELAWARE
MARYLAND
VIRGINIA

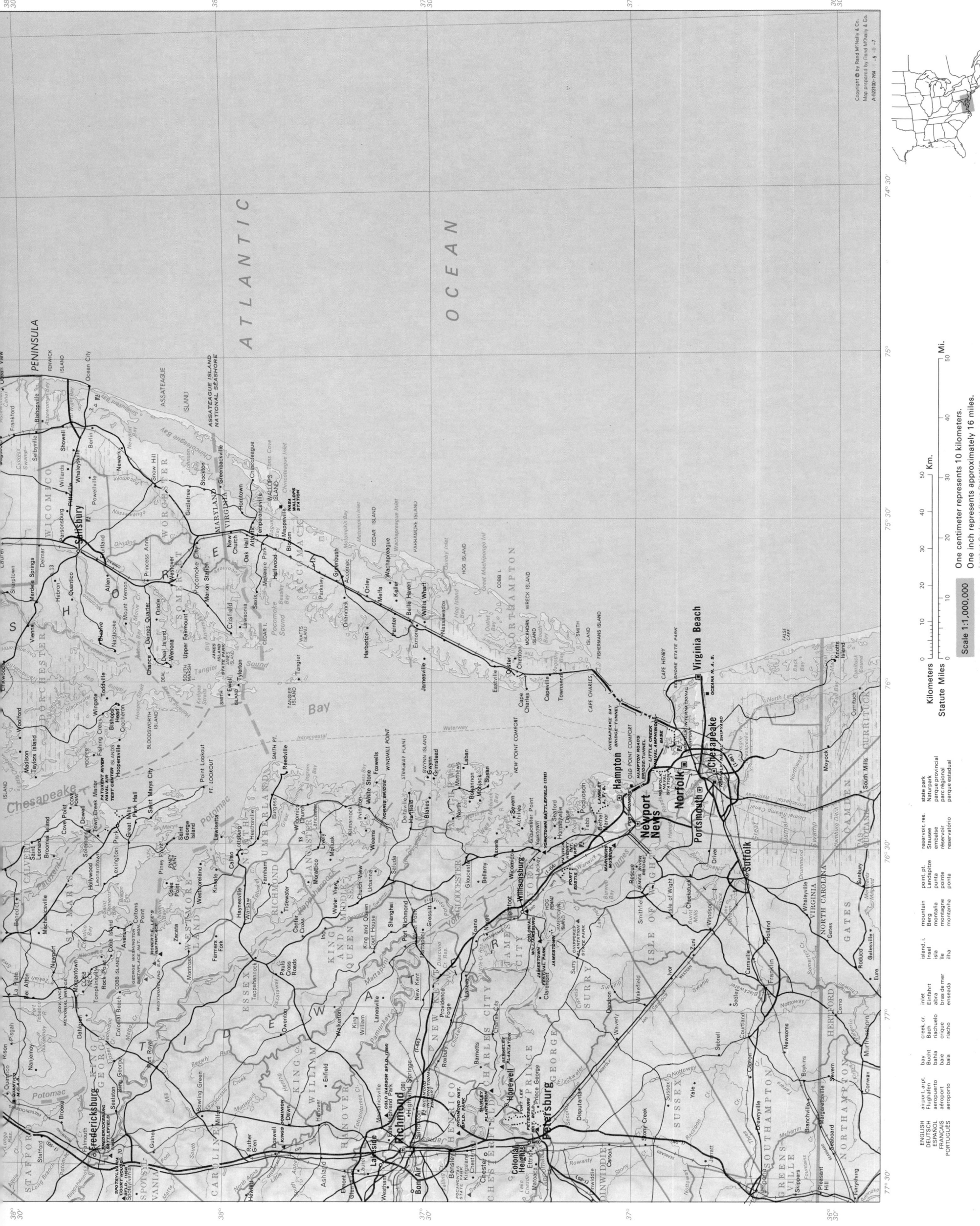

Scale 1:1,000,000

One centimeter represents 10 kilometers.
One inch represents approximately 16 miles.

Lambert Conformal Conic Projection

Kilometers

Statute Miles

ENGLISH	airport, arpt.	bay	creek, cr.	inlet	island, i.	mountain	point, pt.	reservoir, res.	state park
DEUTSCH	Flughafen	Bucht	Bach	Einfahrt	Insel	Berg	Landspitze	Stausee	Naturpark
ESPAÑOL	aeropuerto	bahía	riachuelo	abra	isla	montaña	punta	embalse	parque provincial
FRANÇAIS	aéroport	baie	crique	bras de mer	île	montagne	pointe	reservoir	parc régional
PORTUGUÊS	aeroporto	baía	riacho	enseada	ilha	montanha	ponta	reservatório	parque estadual

Map continues
pages 212-213

Map continues
pages 214-215

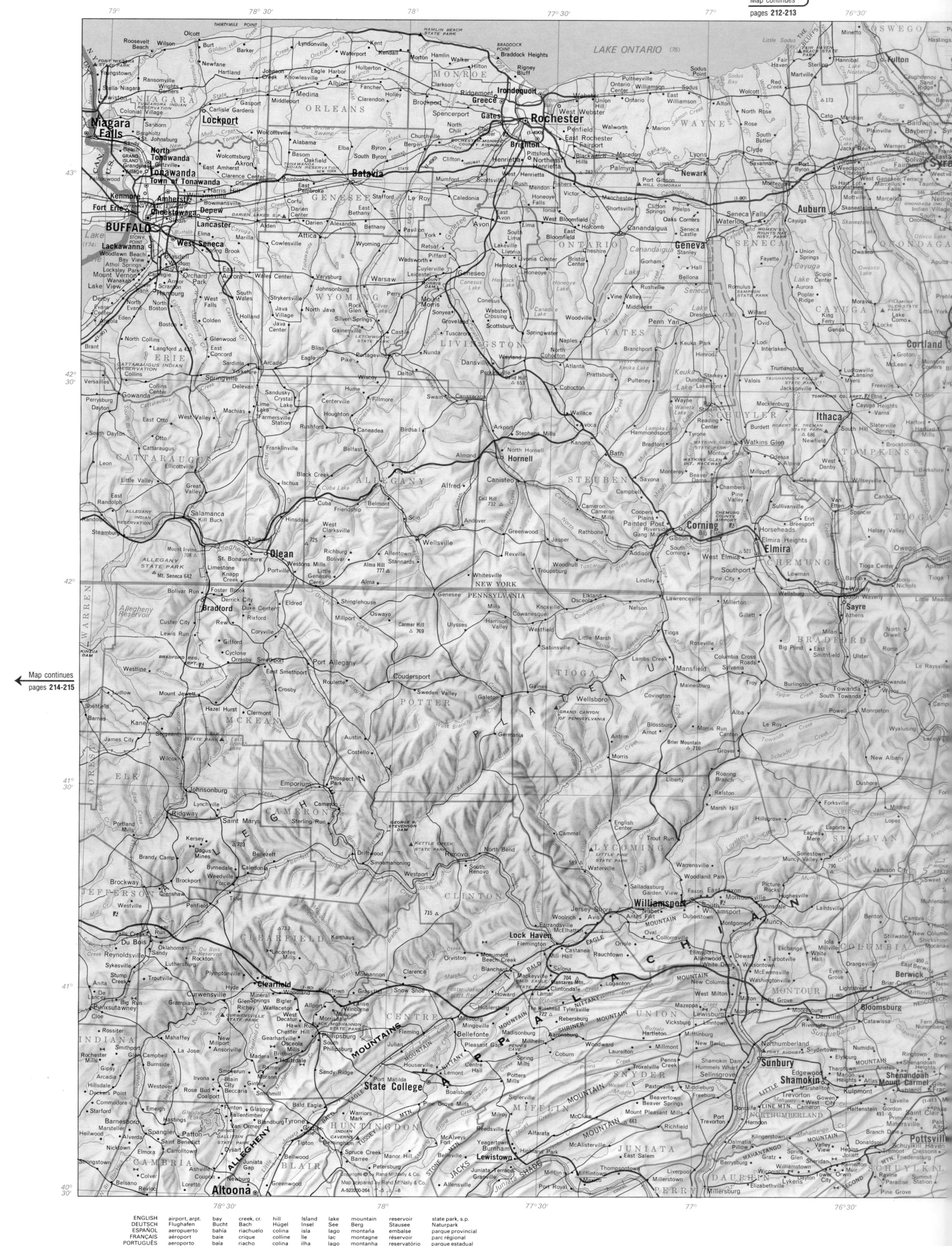

ENGLISH	airport, arpt.	bay	creek, cr.	hill	island	lake	mountain	reservoir	state park, s.p.
DEUTSCH	Flughafen	Bucht	Bach	Hügel	Insel	See	Berg	Stausee	Naturpark
ESPAÑOL	aeropuerto	bahía	riachuelo	colina	isla	lago	montaña	embalse	parque provincial
FRANÇAIS	aéroport	baie	crique	colline	île	lac	montagne	réservoir	parc régional
PORTUGUÊS	aeroporto	baía	riacho	colina	ilha	lago	montanha	reservatório	parque estadual

Map continues
page **207**

Map continues
pages **208-209**

Kilometers

Statute Miles

Scale 1:1,000,000   One centimeter represents 10 kilometers.
One inch represents approximately 16 miles.
Lambert Conformal Conic Projection

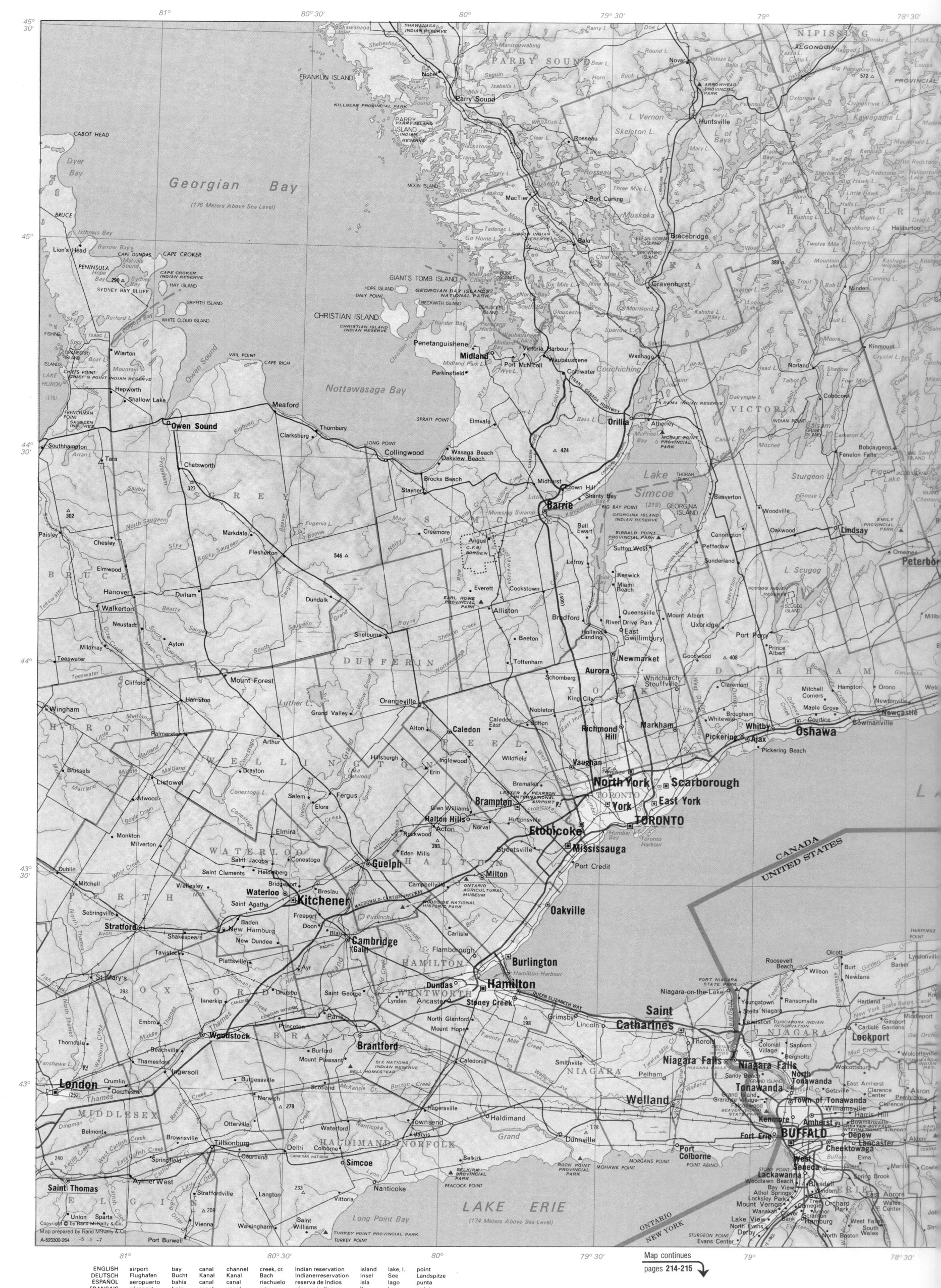

Map continues
pages 214-215 →

	ENGLISH	airport	bay	canal	channel	creek, cr.	Indian reservation	island	lake, l.	point
	DEUTSCH	Flughafen	Bucht	Kanal	Kanal	Bach	Indianerreservation	Insel	See	Landspitze
	ESPAÑOL	aeropuerto	bahía	canal	canal	riachuelo	reserva de Indios	isla	lago	punta
	FRANÇAIS	aéroport	baie	canal	canal	crique	réserve indienne	île	lac	pointe
	PORTUGUÊS	aeroporto	baía	canal	canal	riacho	reserva indígena	ilha	lago	ponta

Map continues
page 206

Map continues
pages 210-211

Kilometers
Statute Miles

Scale 1:1,000,000

One centimeter represents 10 kilometers.
One inch represents approximately 16 miles.

Lambert Conformal Conic Projection

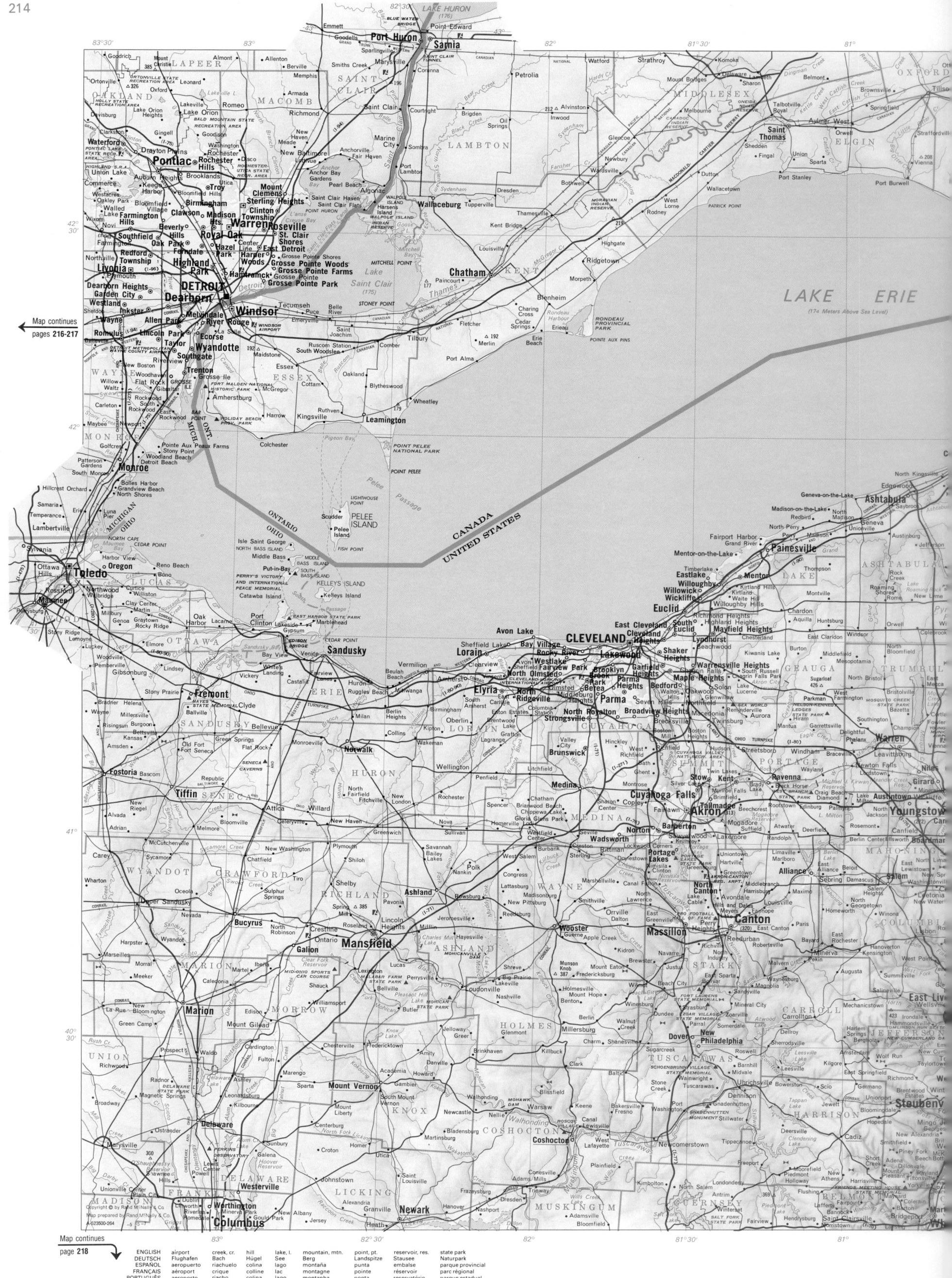

← Map continues pages 216-217

Map continues page 218 ↓

LAKE HURON (176)

LAKE ERIE (174 Meters Above Sea Level)

CANADA
UNITED STATES

ENGLISH	airport	creek, cr.	hill	lake, l.	mountain, mtn.	point, pt.	reservoir, res.	state park
DEUTSCH	Flughafen	Bach	Hügel	See	Berg	Landspitze	Stausee	Naturpark
ESPAÑOL	aeropuerto	riachuelo	colina	lago	montaña	punta	embalse	parque provincial
FRANÇAIS	aéroport	crique	colline	lac	montagne	pointe	réservoir	parc régional
PORTUGUÊS	aeroporto	riacho	colina	lago	montanha	ponta	reservatório	parque estadual

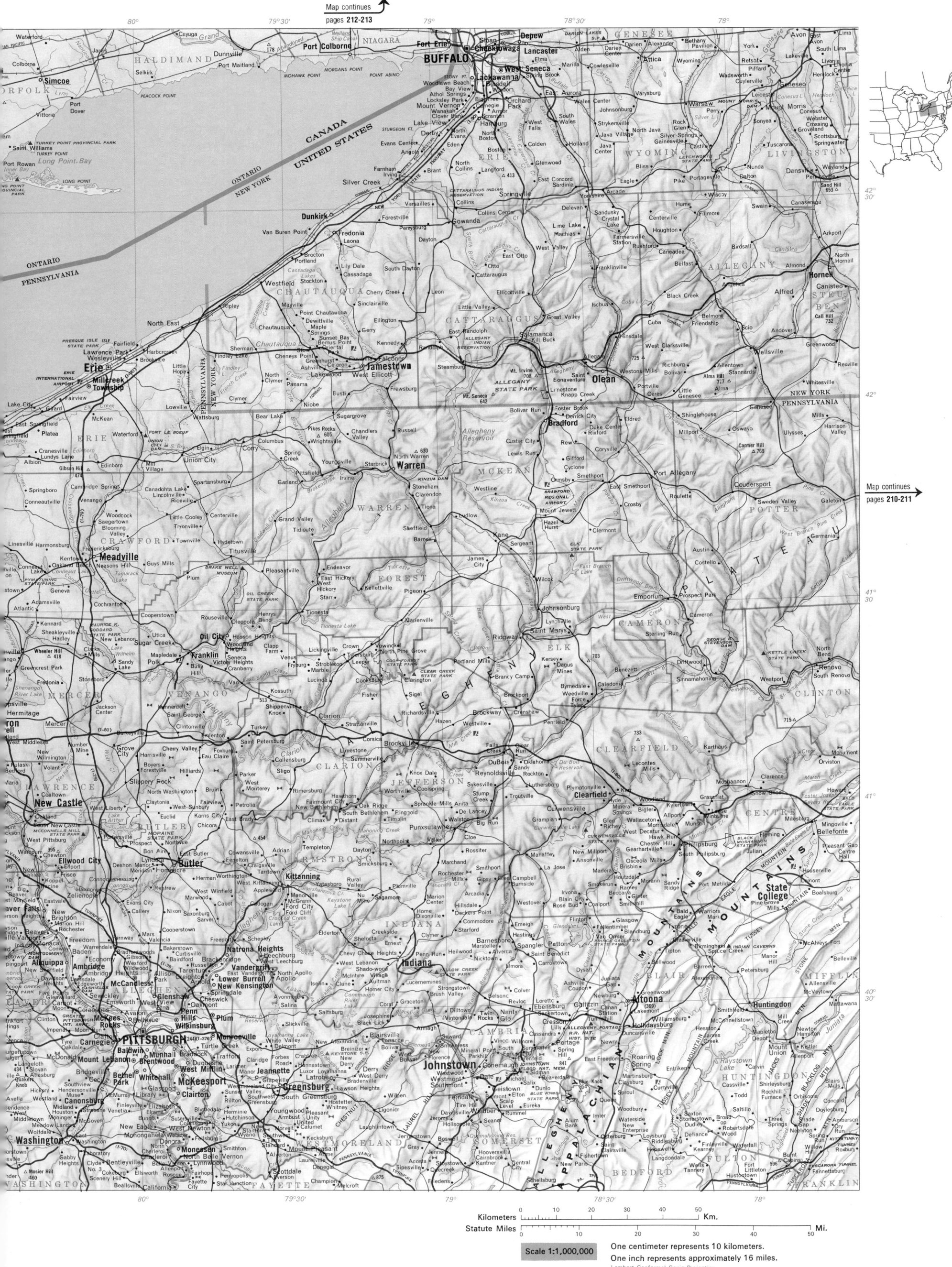

Map continues
pages 212-213

Map continues
pages 210-211

Kilometers

Statute Miles

Scale 1:1,000,000   One centimeter represents 10 kilometers.
One inch represents approximately 16 miles.
Lambert Conformal Conic Projection

Map continues
page 219

ENGLISH	airport	creek, cr.	ditch	lake, l.	reservoir	state park, s.p.
DEUTSCH	Flughafen	Bach	Graben	See	Stausee	Naturpark
ESPAÑOL	aeropuerto	riachuelo	acequia	lago	embalse	parque provincial
FRANÇAIS	aéroport	crique	fossé	lac	réservoir	parc régional
PORTUGUÊS	aeroporto	riacho	fosso	lago	reservatório	parque estadual

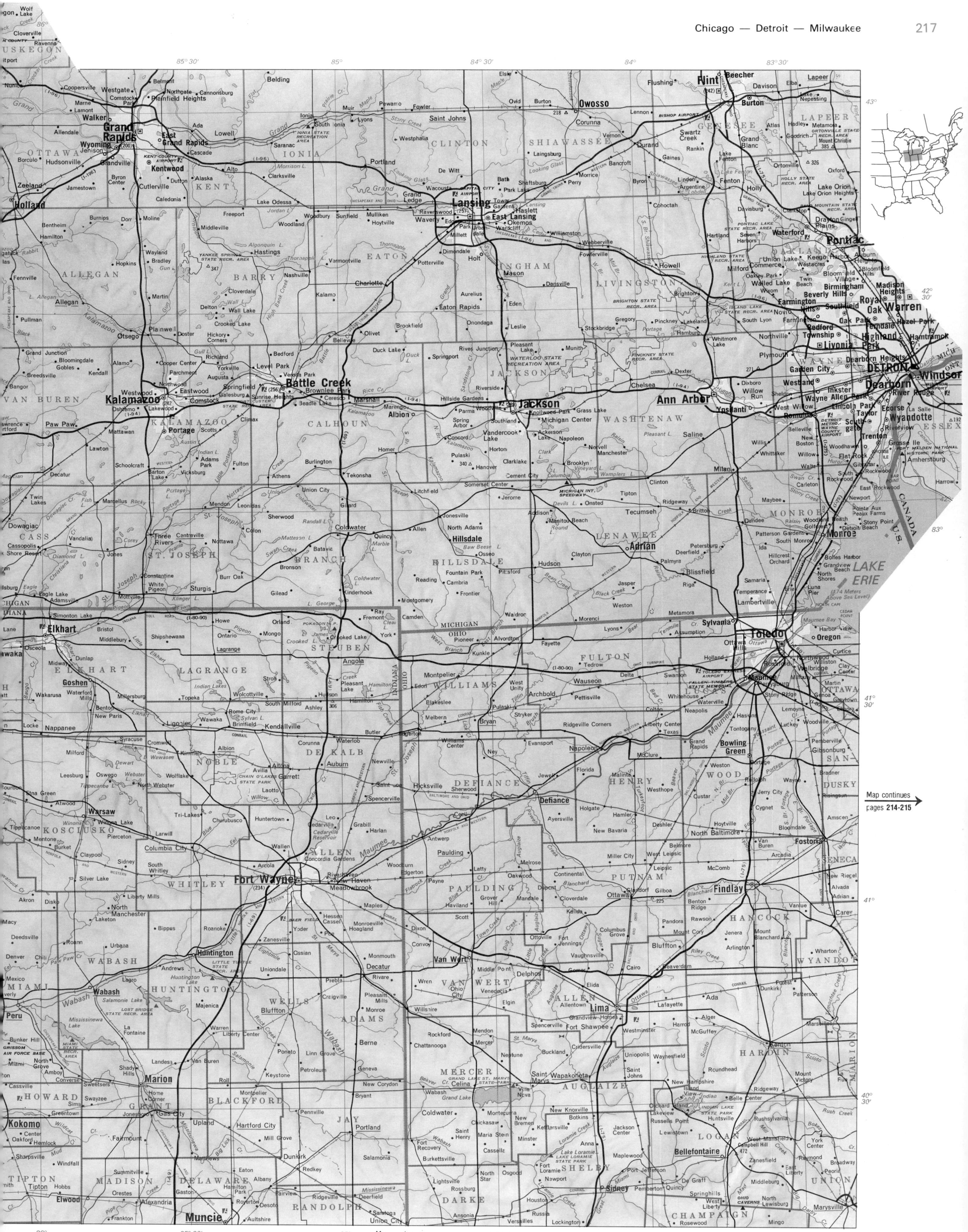

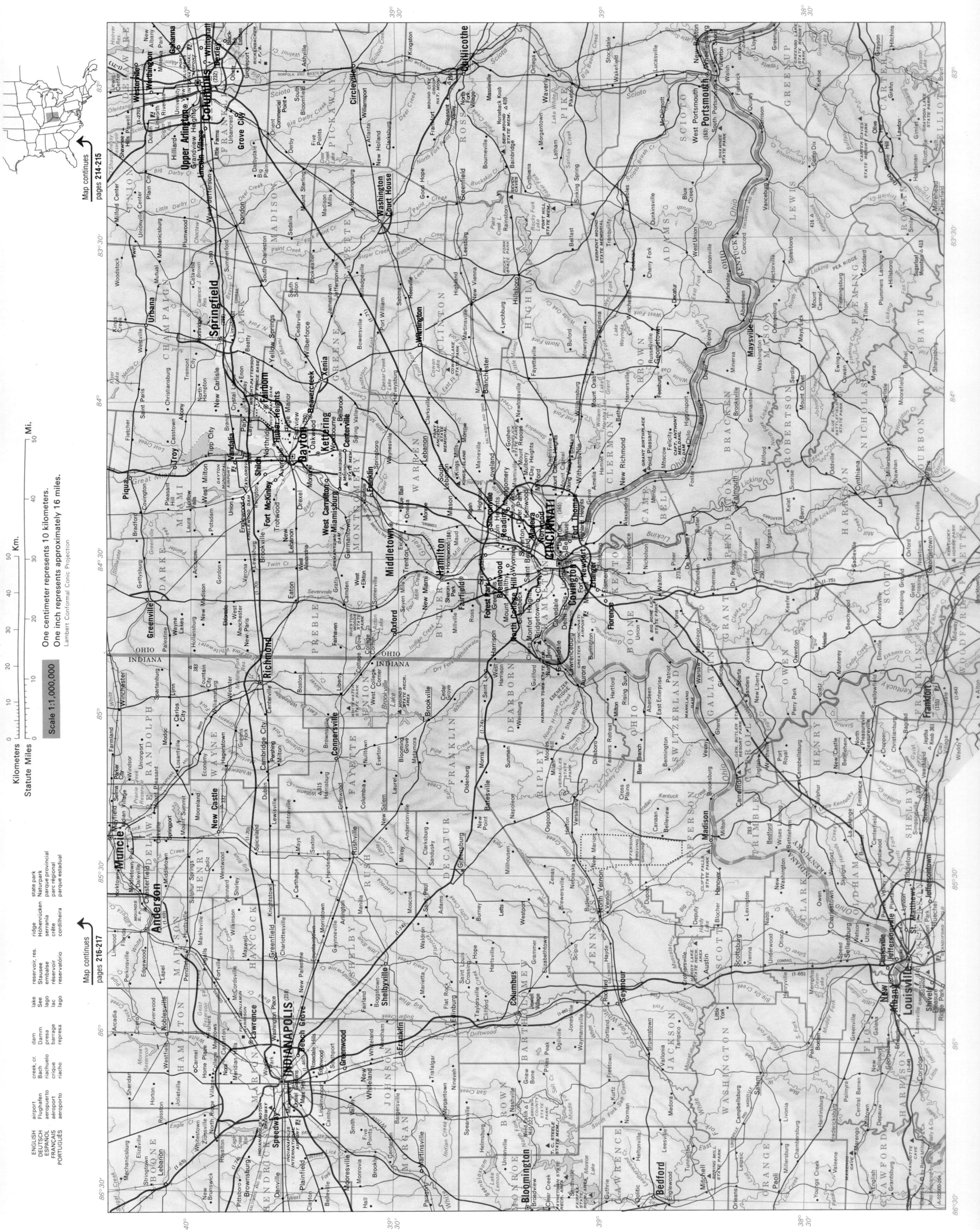

Mi.
50
40
Km.
50
40
30
20
10
Kilometers
Statute Miles
0
10
20
30
40
50

One centimeter represents 10 kilometers.
One inch represents approximately 16 miles.
Lambert Conformal Conic Projection

Scale 1:1,000,000

ENGLISH   airport
DEUTSCH   Flughafen
ESPAÑOL   aeropuerto
FRANÇAIS   aéroport
PORTUGUÊS   aeroporto

creek, cr.
Bach
riachuelo
crique
riacho

dam
Damm
presa
barrage
represa

lake
See
lago
lac
lago

reservoir, res.
Stausee
embalse
réservoir
reservatorio

ridge
Höhenrücken
serranía
crête
cordilheira

state park
Naturpark
parque provincial
parc regional
parque estadual

Map continues
pages 214–215

Map continues
pages 216–217

Map continues
pages 216–217

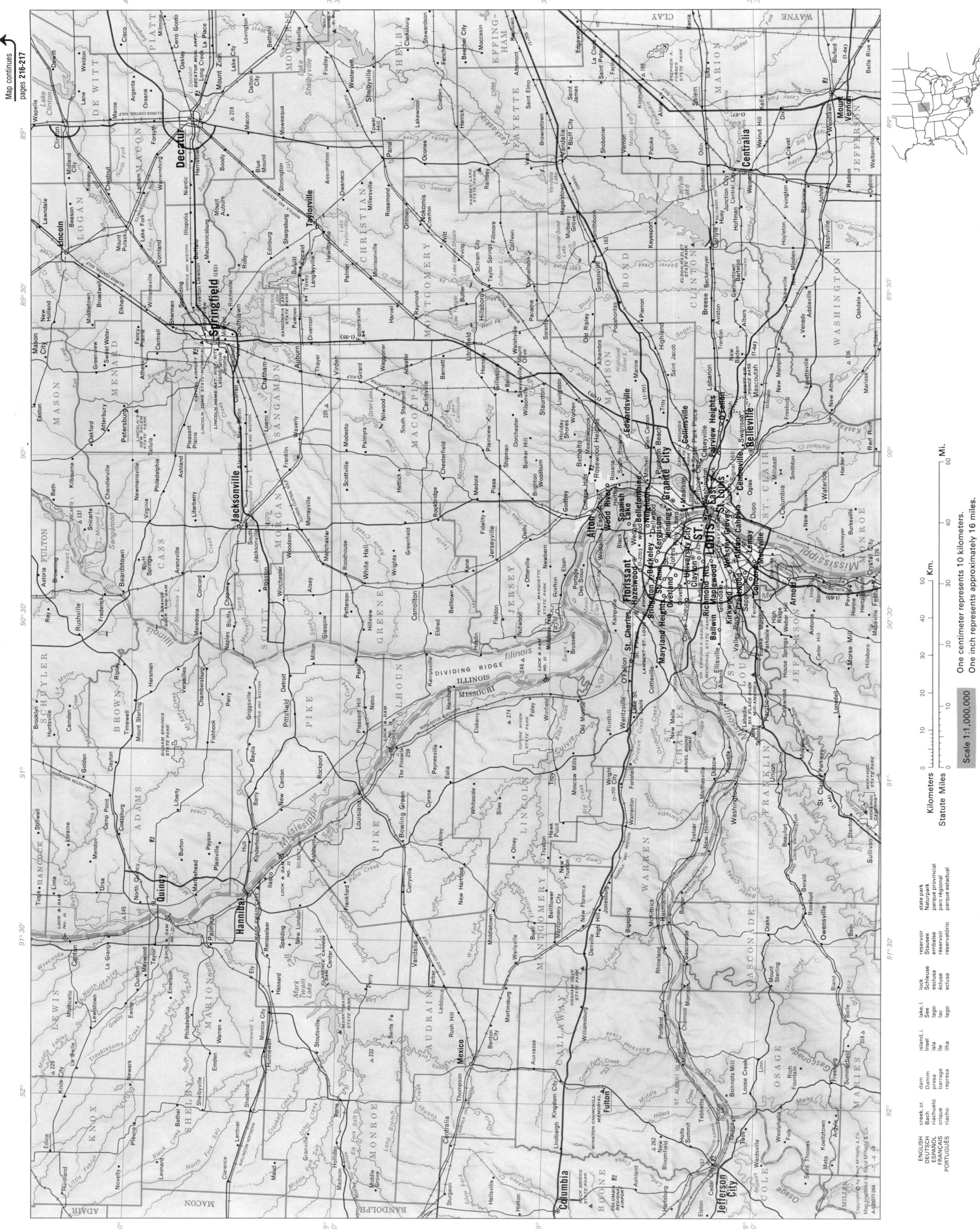

Map continues
pages 216-217

Scale 1:1,000,000

One centimeter represents 10 kilometers.
One inch represents approximately 16 miles.

Lambert Conformal Conic Projection

ENGLISH	creek, cr.	island, i.	lake, l.	lock	reservoir	state park
DEUTSCH	Bach	Insel	See	Schleuse	Stausee	Naturpark
ESPAÑOL	riachuelo	isla	lago	esclusa	embalse	parque provincial
FRANÇAIS	ruisseau	île	lac	écluse	barrage	parque regional
PORTUGUÊS	riacho	ilha	lago	eclusa	reservatório	parque estadual

Kilometers 0 10 20 30 40 50 Km.
Statute Miles 0 10 20 30 40 50 Mi.

Scale 1:1,000,000

One centimeter represents 10 kilometers.
One inch represents approximately 16 miles.
Lambert Conformal Conic Projection

ENGLISH	bay	canal	cape	creek, cr.	inlet	island	key	lake, l.	swamp
DEUTSCH	Bucht	Kanal	Kap	Bach	Einfahrt	Insel	Klippe	See	Sumpf
ESPAÑOL	bahía	canal	cabo	riachuelo	abra	isla	cayo	lago	pantano
FRANÇAIS	baie	canal	cap	ruisseau	bras de mer	île	caye	lac	marais
PORTUGUÊS	baía	canal	cabo	riacho	enseada	ilha	recife	lago	pântano

West Palm Beach
Palm Beach
Lake Worth
Boynton Beach
Delray Beach
Boca Raton
Deerfield Beach
Pompano Beach
Fort Lauderdale
Hollywood
Hallandale
North Miami Beach
North Miami
MIAMI
Miami Beach
Hialeah
Coral Gables
South Miami
Homestead
Florida City
Key Largo
Plantation
Islamorada
Marathon
Key West
Naples
East Naples
Golden Gate
Fort Myers
Cape Coral
Immokalee
Clewiston
Belle Glade
La Belle
Everglades City
Flamingo
PALM BEACH
BROWARD
HENDRY
COLLIER
LEE
DADE
MONROE
EVERGLADES NATIONAL PARK
BIG CYPRESS NATIONAL PRESERVE
Florida Bay
FLORIDA KEYS
GULF OF MEXICO
DRY TORTUGAS
Copyright © by Rand McNally & Co.
Map prepared by Rand McNally & Co.

33°
32° 30'
32°
31° 30'
94° 30'
95°
95° 30'
96°
96° 30'
97°
97° 30'
CASS
MARION
HARRISON
PANOLA
MORRIS
TITUS
CAMP
UPSHUR
GREGG
RUSK
NACOGDOCHES
ANGELINA
FRANKLIN
WOOD
SMITH
CHEROKEE
HOPKINS
RAINS
VAN ZANDT
HENDERSON
ANDERSON
HOUSTON
TRINITY
HUNT
KAUFMAN
NAVARRO
FREESTONE
LEON
COLLIN
ROCKWALL
DALLAS
ELLIS
LIMESTONE
DENTON
TARRANT
JOHNSON
HILL
MCLENNAN
FALLS
WISE
PARKER
HOOD
SOMERVELL
BOSQUE
CORYELL
Marietta
Hughes Springs
Avinger
Naples
Omaha
Daingerfield
Lone Star
Mount Pleasant
Pittsburg
Longview
Kilgore
Henderson
Marshall
Tyler
Jacksonville
Nacogdoches
Lufkin
Palestine
Athens
Corsicana
Mexia
Groesbeck
Waco
Sulphur Springs
Greenville
Terrell
Kaufman
Ennis
Waxahachie
Hillsboro
Cleburne
Dallas
Mesquite
Garland
Irving
Grand Prairie
Arlington
Fort Worth
Denton
McKinney
Plano
Richardson
Carrollton
Lewisville
Weatherford
Decatur
Bridgeport
Granbury
Glen Rose
Meridian
Clifton
Gatesville
Killeen
Temple
Marlin
Fairfield
Teague
Crockett
Rusk
Mineola
Canton
Grand Saline
Wills Point
Emory
Quitman
Winnsboro
Gilmer
Gladewater
Big Sandy
Lake o' the Pines
Sam Rayburn Reservoir
Lake Tawakoni
Cedar Creek Reservoir
Lake Palestine
Lake Whitney
Lake Limestone
Lewisville Lake
Lavon Lake
Lake Ray Hubbard
Sabine
Neches
Trinity
Brazos

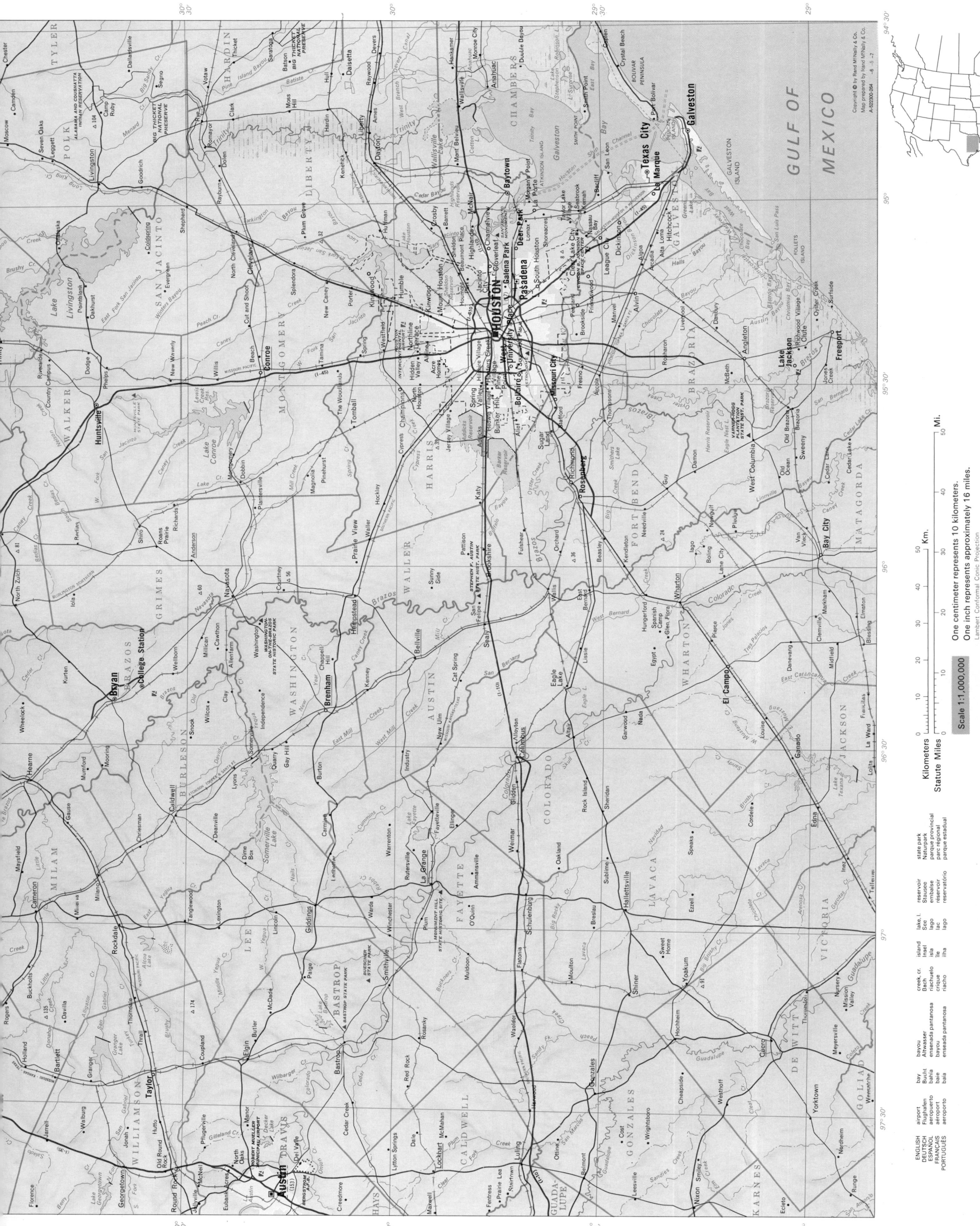

Copyright © by Rand McNally & Co.
Map prepared by Rand McNally & Co.
A-52230-354

GULF OF MEXICO

Scale 1:1,000,000

One centimeter represents 10 kilometers.
One inch represents approximately 16 miles.
Lambert Conformal Conic Projection

ENGLISH	DEUTSCH	ESPAÑOL	FRANÇAIS	PORTUGUÊS
airport	Flughafen	aeropuerto	aéroport	aeroporto
bay	Bucht	bahia	baie	baía
bayou	Altwasser	ensenada pantanosa	bayou	ensenada pantanosa
creek, cr.	Bach	riachuelo	crique	riacho
island	Insel	isla	île	ilha
lake, l.	See	lago	lac	lago
reservoir	Stausee	embalse	réservoir	reservatório
state park	Naturpark	parque provincial	parc régional	parque estadual

VANCOUVER
New Westminster
Burnaby
North Vancouver
Richmond
Victoria
Oak Bay
Esquimalt
Nanaimo
Port Alberni
Bellingham
Mount Vernon
Anacortes
Everett
SEATTLE
Bremerton
Tacoma
Renton
Port Angeles
Port Townsend
Chilliwack
Strait of Georgia
Strait of Juan de Fuca
Haro Strait
SAN JUAN ISLANDS
VANCOUVER ISLAND
OLYMPIC MOUNTAINS
CASCADE MOUNTAINS
BRITISH COLUMBIA
WASHINGTON
CANADA
UNITED STATES
Puget Sound
49°
48° 30'
48°
47° 30'
121°
121° 30'
122°
122° 30'
123°
123° 30'
124°
124° 30'

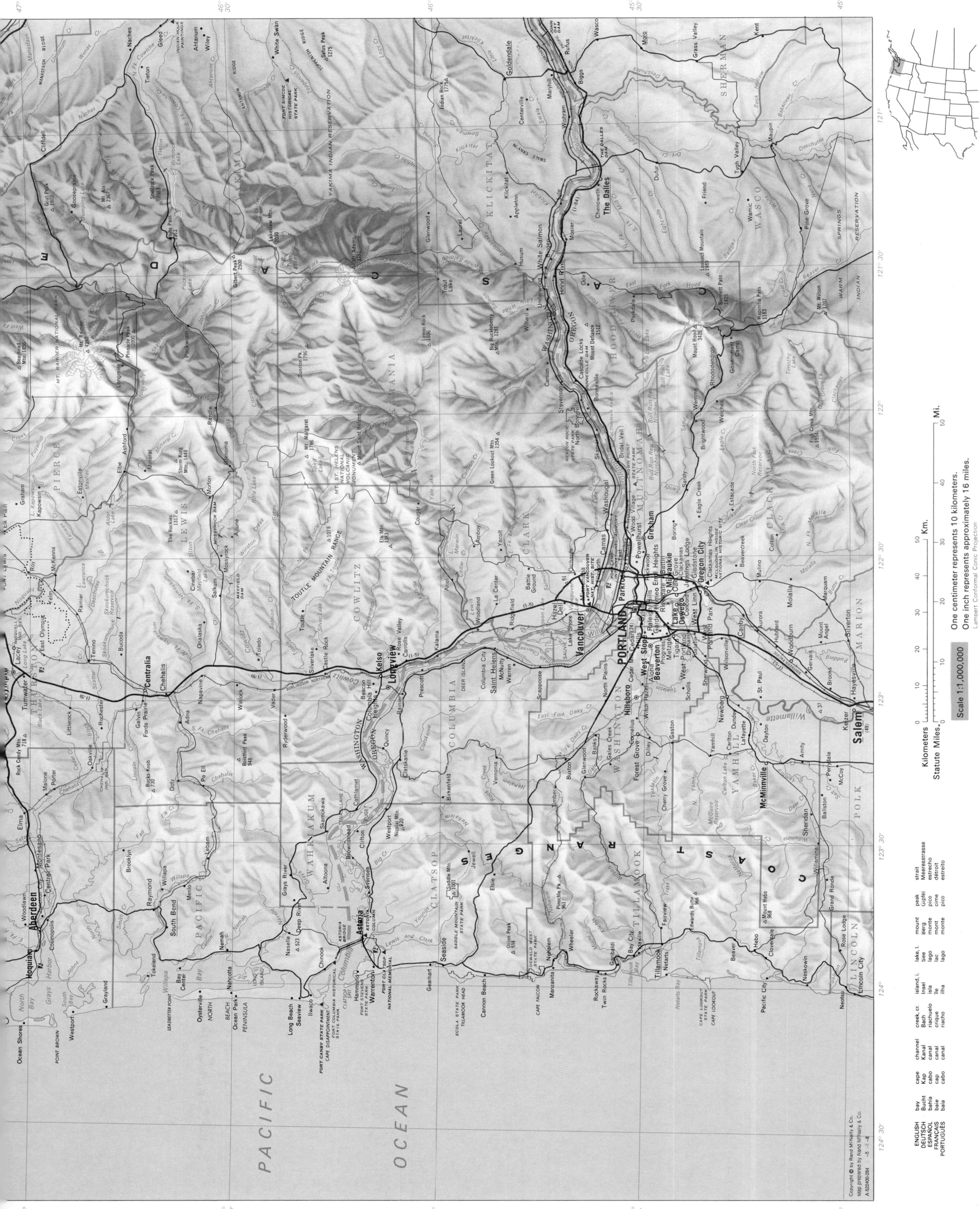

ENGLISH	bay	cape	channel	creek, cr.	island, i.	lake, l.	mount	peak	strait
DEUTSCH	Bucht	Kap	Kanal	Bach	Insel	See	Berg	Gipfel	Meeresstrasse
ESPAÑOL	bahía	cabo	canal	riachuelo	isla	lago	monte	pico	estrecho
FRANÇAIS	baie	cap	canal	crique	île	lac	mont	cime	détroit
PORTUGUÊS	baía	cabo	canal	riacho	ilha	lago	monte	pico	estreito

Kilometers 0   10   20   30   40   50   Km.

Statute Miles 0   10   20   30   40   50   Mi.

Scale 1:1,000,000

One centimeter represents 10 kilometers.
One inch represents approximately 16 miles.
Lambert Conformal Conic Projection

Reno
Sparks
Carson City
Yerington
Lake Tahoe
South Lake Tahoe
SIERRA NEVADA
PINE NUT MOUNTAINS
SWEETWATER MTS.
CARSON RANGE
CARSON VALLEY
DOUGLAS
LYON
WASHOE
STOREY
ALPINE
MONO
TUOLUMNE
CALAVERAS
AMADOR
EL DORADO
PLACER
NEVADA
YUBA
SUTTER
BUTTE
GLENN
COLUSA
YOLO
SOLANO
NAPA
SONOMA
LAKE
MARIN
SAN JOAQUIN
STANISLAUS
MARIPOSA
CONTRA COSTA
ALAMEDA
SACRAMENTO VALLEY
YOSEMITE NATIONAL PARK
CATHEDRAL RANGE
Sacramento
Stockton
Modesto
Lodi
Marysville
Yuba City
Oroville
Roseville
Auburn
Placerville
Davis
Woodland
Fairfield
Vacaville
Vallejo
Napa
Santa Rosa
Petaluma
Novato
Concord
Walnut Creek
Berkeley
Oakland
Alameda
San Leandro
Hayward
Fremont
Pleasanton
Livermore
Tracy
Manteca
Antioch
Pittsburg
Richmond
SAN FRANCISCO
Daly City
San Mateo
Redwood City
Sonora
Jackson
Grass Valley
Nevada City
Truckee
Colusa
Willows

Map continues
page 228

Scale 1:1,000,000

One centimeter represents 10 kilometers.
One inch represents approximately 16 miles.

Lambert Conformal Conic Projection

Kilometers

Statute Miles

Mi.

Km.

ENGLISH	bay	creek, cr.	lake, l.	mountain, mtn.	pass	range	reservoir	slough
DEUTSCH	Bucht	Bach	See	Berg	Pass	Gebirge	Stausee	verlandete Wasserfläche
ESPAÑOL	bahía	riachuelo	lago	montaña	paso	sierra	embalse	pantano
FRANÇAIS	baie	crique	lac	montagne	col	chaîne	réservoir	fondrière
PORTUGUÊS	baía	riacho	lago	montanha	passo	serra	reservatório	pântano

PACIFIC OCEAN

Fresno

Bakersfield

San Luis Obispo

Salinas

Santa Cruz

Monterey

Visalia

Tulare

Hanford

Madera

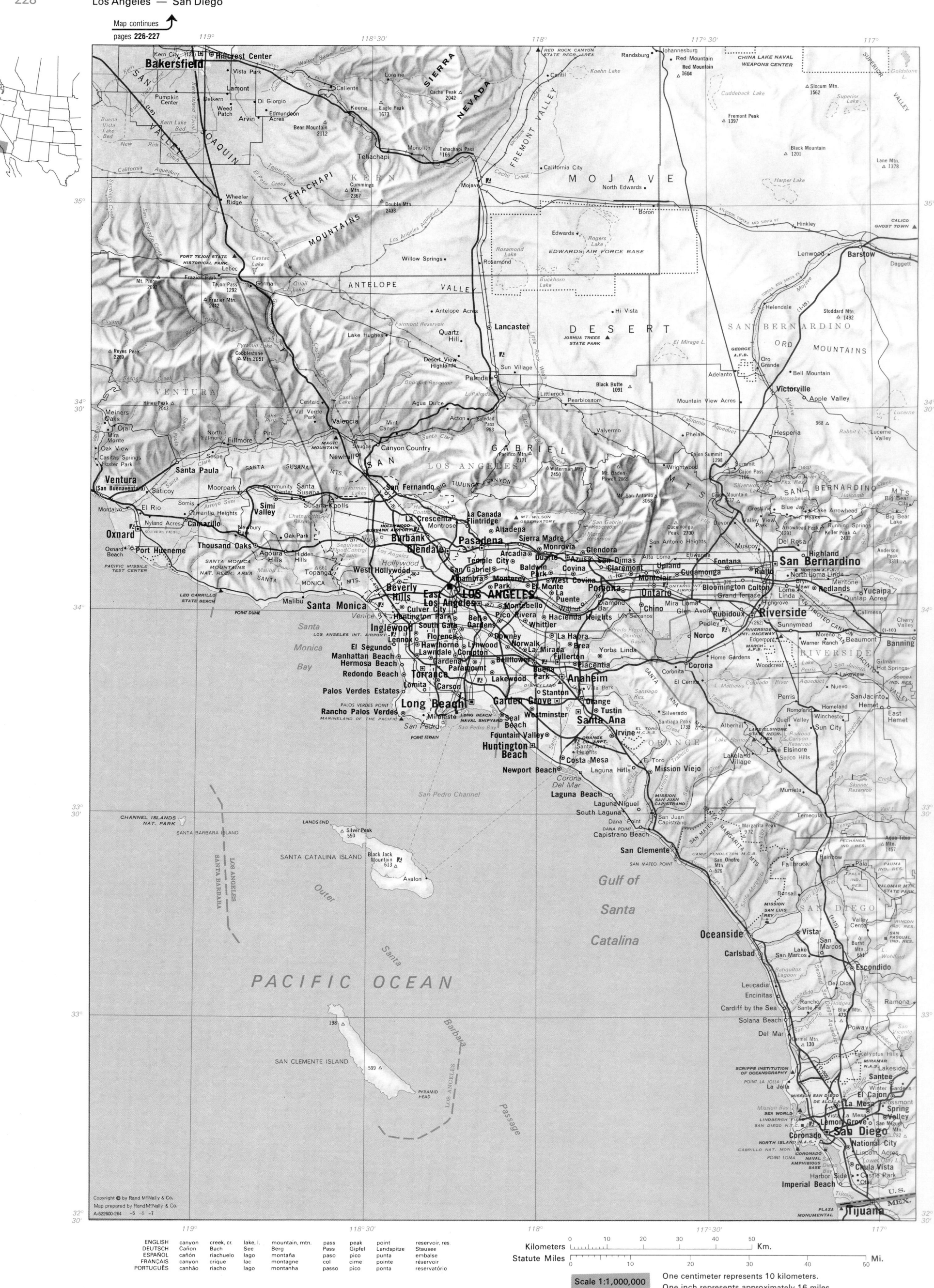

Map continues
pages 226-227

ENGLISH	creek, cr.	lake, l.	mountain, mtn.	pass	peak	point
DEUTSCH	Cañon	Bach	See	Berg	Pass	Gipfel	Landspitze
ESPAÑOL	cañon	riachuelo	lago	montaña	paso	pico	punta
FRANÇAIS	canyon	crique	lac	montagne	col	cime	pointe
PORTUGUÊS	canhão	riacho	lago	montanha	passo	pico	ponta

		res
	reservoir, res
Stausee
embalse
réservoir
reservatório

Kilometers 0 10 20 30 40 50 Km.

Statute Miles 0 10 20 30 40 50 Mi.

Scale 1:1,000,000
One centimeter represents 10 kilometers.
One inch represents approximately 16 miles.
Lambert Conformal Conic Projection

Copyright © by Rand McNally & Co.
Map prepared by Rand McNally & Co.
A-522600-264   −5 −6 −7

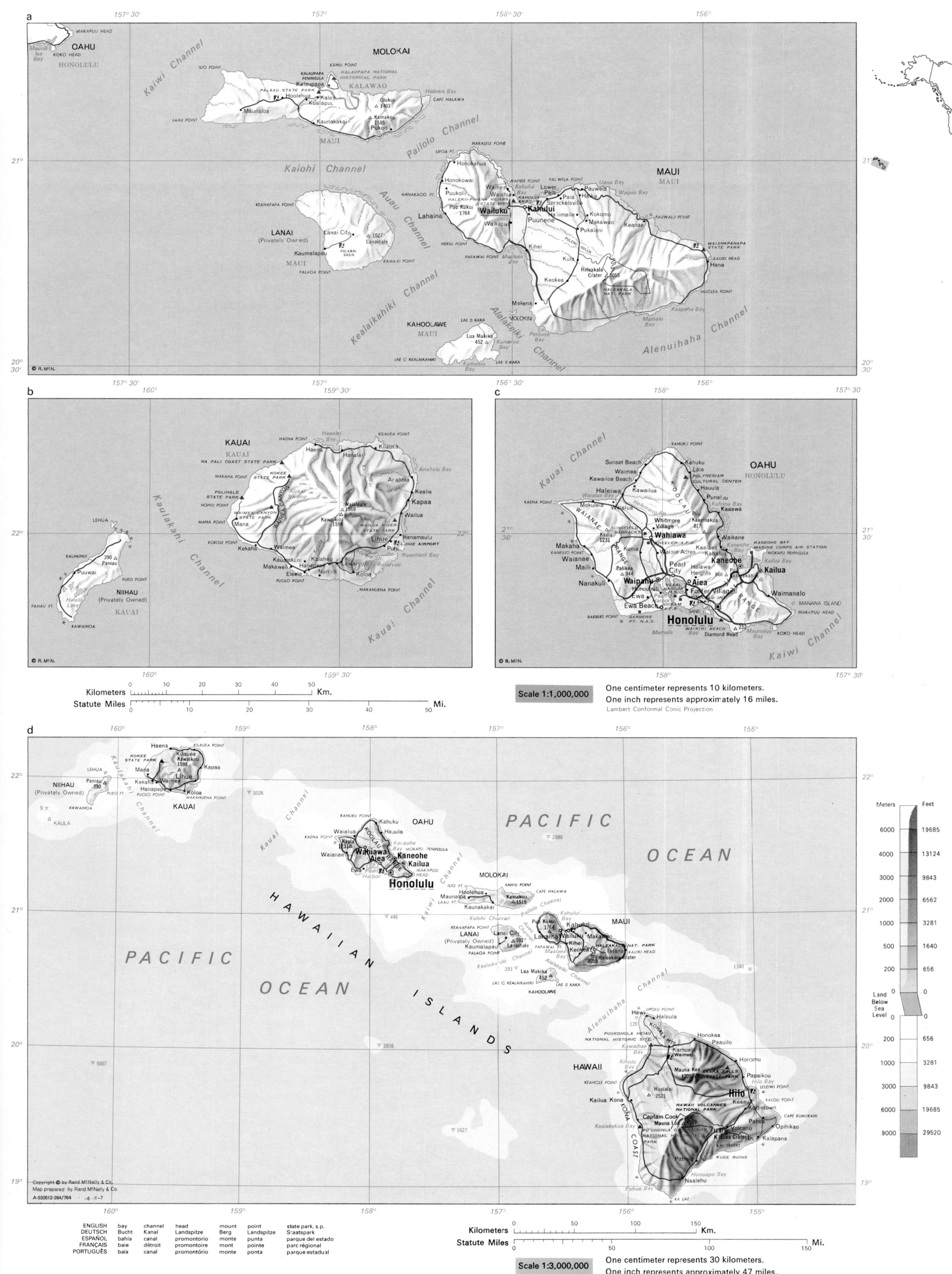

Scale 1:1,000,000

One centimeter represents 10 kilometers.
One inch represents approximately 16 miles.
Lambert Conformal Conic Projection

ENGLISH	bay	channel	head	mount	point	state park, s.p.
DEUTSCH	Bucht	Kanal	Landspitze	Berg	Landspitze	S?aatspark
ESPAÑOL	bahia	canal	promontorio	monte	punta	parque del estado
FRANÇAIS	baie	détroit	promontoire	mont	pointe	parc régional
PORTUGUÊS	baía	canal	promontório	monte	ponta	parque estadual

Scale 1:3,000,000

One centimeter represents 30 kilometers.
One inch represents approximately 47 miles.
Lambert Conformal Conic Projection

Meters	Feet
6000	19685
4000	13124
3000	9843
2000	6562
1000	3281
500	1640
200	656
0	0
Land Below Sea Level	
0	0
200	656
1000	3281
3000	9843
6000	19685
9000	29520

Map continues
pages 178-179

ESPAÑOL	cabo	cordillera	golfo	isla, i.	lago, l.	punta	sierra	volcán, vol.
ENGLISH	cape	mountains	gulf	island	lake	point	mountains	volcano
DEUTSCH	Kap	Berge	Golf	Insel	See	Landspitze	Berge	Vulkan
FRANÇAIS	cap	montagnes	golfe	île	lac	pointe	montagnes	volcan
PORTUGUÊS	cabo	cordilheira	golfo	ilha	lago	ponta	serra	vulcão

Middle America / Mittelamerika / México, Centroamérica y Las Antillas
Mexique, Amérique Centrale et Région des Caraïbes / México, América Central e Antilhas

231

Kilometers
Statute Miles

Scale 1:12,000,000

One centimeter represents 120 kilometers.
One inch represents approximately 190 miles.

Oblique Conic Conformal Projection

ESPAÑOL	bahía	cerro	isla	laguna	presa	punta	río	sierra
ENGLISH	bay	mountain	island	lagoon	reservoir	point	river	mountains
DEUTSCH	Bucht	Berg	Insel	Haff	Stausee	Landspitze	Fluss	Berge
FRANÇAIS	baie	montagne	île	lagune	réservoir	pointe	rivière	montagnes
PORTUGUÊS	baía	montanha	ilha	laguna	reservatório	ponta	rio	serra

Kilometers

Statute Miles

Scale 1:6,000,000

One centimeter represents 60 kilometers.
One inch represents approximately 95 miles.
Lambert Conformal Conic Projection

Meters / Feet

Meters	Feet
6000	19685
4000	13124
3000	9843
2000	6562
1000	3281
500	1640
200	656
Land Below Sea Level 0	0
0	0
200	656
1000	3281
3000	9843
6000	19685
9000	29520

Map continues
pages 238-239

GULF

OF

MEXICO

Tropic of Cancer

Bahía de Campeche

GUATEMALA

Map continues
pages 236-237

Map continues
pages 232-233

PACIFIC OCEAN

Meters	Feet
6000	19685
4000	13124
3000	9843
2000	6562
1000	3281
500	1640
200	656
0	0
Land Below Sea Level	
0	0
200	656
1000	3281
3000	9843
6000	19685
9000	29520

ESPAÑOL	arroyo	boca	cerro	lago	laguna	punta	rio	sierra	volcán
ENGLISH	brook	entrance	butte	lake	lagoon	point	river	ranges	volcano
DEUTSCH	Bach	Einfahrt	Restberg	See	Haff	Landspitze	Fluss	Bergketten	Vulkan
FRANÇAIS	ruisseau	entrée	butte	lac	lagune	pointe	rivière	chaîne	volcan
PORTUGUÊS	riacho	entrada	cerro	lago	laguna	ponta	rio	serra	vulcão

Map continues
pages 232-233

Map continues
pages 236-237

Kilometers
Statute Miles

Scale 1:3,000,000

One centimeter represents 30 kilometers.
One inch represents approximately 47 miles.
Lambert Conformal Conic Projection

Central America / Zentralamerika / América Central
Amérique Centrale / América Central

Map continues
pages 232-233

Map continues
pages 234-235

PACIFIC

OCEAN

Meters	Feet
6000	19685
4000	13124
3000	9843
2000	6562
1000	3281
500	1640
200	656
0	0
Land Below Sea Level 0	0
200	656
1000	3281
3000	9843
6000	19685
9000	29520

ESPAÑOL	bahía	cerro	cordillera	isla	lago	laguna	punta	sierra	volcán
ENGLISH	bay	mountain	mountains	island	lake	lagoon	point	mountains	volcano
DEUTSCH	Bucht	Berg	Berge	Insel	See	Haff	point	Berge	Vulkan
FRANÇAIS	baie	montagne	montagnes	île	lac	lagune	pointe	montagnes	Vulkan
PORTUGUÊS	baía	montanha	cordilheira	ilha	lago	laguna	ponta	serra	vulcão

Map continues
pages 246-247

Kilometers

Statute Miles

Scale 1:3,000,000

One centimeter represents 30 kilometers.

One inch represents approximately 47 miles.

Lambert Conformal Conic Projection

Caribbean Region / Mittelamerikanische Inselwelt / Región del Caribe
Région des Caraïbes / Região do Caribe

← Map continues
pages 232-233

← Map continues
pages 236-237

Meters		Feet
6000		19685
4000		13124
3000		9843
2000		6562
1000		3281
500		1640
200		656
Land Below Sea Level		0
		0
200		656
1000		3281
3000		9843
6000		19685
9000		29520

MAP FORM	bahia	cabo	cerro	channel	golfo	isla	passage	pico	punta
ENGLISH	bay	cape	mountain	channel	gulf	isle	passage	peak	point
DEUTSCH	Bucht	Kap	Berg	Kanal	Golf	Insel	Durchfahrt	Gipfel	Landspitze
ESPAÑOL	bahía	cabo	cerro	canal	golfo	isla	pasaje	pico	punta
FRANÇAIS	baie	cap	montagne	détroit	golfe	île	passage	cime	pointe
PORTUGUÊS	baía	cabo	montanha	canal	golfo	ilha	passagem	pico	ponta

72°   70°   68°   66°   64°   62°   60°

24°

A T L A N T I C

O C E A N

Sargasso   Sea

Tropic of Cancer

22°

▽ 5486

▽ 6960

SAMANA CAY

EAST POINT

MAYAGUANA

CAICOS ISLANDS
NORTH CAICOS

TURKS AND CAICOS ISLANDS
(U.K.)

▽ 2853
LITTLE INAGUA

▽ 5420

Kew
MIDDLE CAICOS
PROVIDENCIALES
WEST CAICOS   EAST CAICOS
CAICOS
BANK   TURKS
ISLANDS
Grand
Turk
SEAL
CAYS

NORTH EAST POINT

▽ 3877

GREAT INAGUA

MOUCHOIR BANK
MOUCHOIR BANK

20°

I   N   D   I   E   S

SILVER BANK

SILVER BANK

▽ 53

HAITI
HAÏTI

Île de la Tortue
Port-de-Paix   Manzanillo Bay
Cap-Haïtien   Monte Cristi
La Limbe   Fort-Liberté
Gonaïves   Dajabón
Saint-Marc   Mao
Hinche
1788   Moca
HISPANIOLA
Comendador
Bani
Azua

CABO ISABELA
Puerto Plata   CABO MACORIS
CABO FRANCÉS VIEJO
Santiago   1249
La Vega   Bahía
Escocesa
San Francisco
de Macorís   CABO SAMANA
Cotuí   Sabana de la Mar
3175   Sánchez
Pico Duarte   Samaná
Bonao   Bahía de Samaná
SANTO   Hato   Miches
DOMINGO   Mayor   El Seibo
Bandera   Higüey
2630
La Romana   CABO
ENGANO

▽ 8165

PUERTO RICO
(U.S.)

Aguadilla   Arecibo   SAN
Mayagüez   Manatí   JUAN
San Germán   Utuado   Bayamón   Caguas
Yauco   Ponce   Cayey   Humacao
Guayama

▽ 3292

BRITISH
VIRGIN
ISLANDS   ANEGADA

VIRGIN   Virgin
ISLANDS   Gorda
(U.S.)   Road Town
ISLA DE   172
CULEBRA   Charlotte
SAINT   Amalie
THOMAS   SAINT JOHN

▽ 7433

LEEWARD

ANGUILLA
DOG I.   The Valley
SOMBRERO   ISLANDS
Marigot   SAINT-MARTIN
(Guad and Neth Ant.)
Philipsburg   SAINT BARTHÉLEMY
(Guad.)

18°

DOMINICAN REPUBLIC
REPÚBLICA DOMINICANA

▽ 5197

Christiansted   870
Frederiksted   SAINT CROIX
(U.S.)

SABA
(Neth. Ant.)
SABA BANK   SAINT EUSTATIUS
(Neth. Ant.)   BARBUDA
Sandy Point   SAINT CHRISTOPHER
SAINT KITTS
Basseterre   ANTIGUA
Charlestown   AND
SAINT KITTS AND NEVIS   NEVIS   Saint John's   BARBUDA
REDONDA   ANTIGUA

▽ 4096

A   N   T   I   L   L   E   S

MONTSERRAT
(U.K.)   Plymouth

GRANDE-TERRE
Le Moule
LA DÉSIRADE
Pointe-à-Pitre
Soufrière   GUADELOUPE
1467
Basse-Terre
BASSE-TERRE   MARIE-GALANTE
LES SAINTES   Grand-Bourg

16°

S   E   A

▽ 2121

▽ 4200

▽ 5630

▽ 603

ISLA DE AVES
(Ven.)

DOMINICA
Morne
Diablotins
1433   Marigot
Roseau
Berekua

Montagne
Pelée   La Trinité
Saint-Pierre   1397
Fort-de-France   Le Lamentin
MARTINIQUE
(Fr.)   Martinique
Channel
Castries   POINTE DU CAP
Mount Gimie   Vieux Fort
(951)

14°

▽ 5102

SAINT LUCIA

Windward   Soufrière
1234   Bathsheba
Kings-   Georgetown   Speightstown
town   SAINT VINCENT

SAINT VINCENT
AND THE
GRENADINES   BEQUIA

Bridgetown
BARBADOS
1742

12°

▽ 4069
▽ 475

ARUBA
(Neth.)   NETHERLANDS ANTILLES
NEDERLANDSE ANTILLEN
Oranjestad   CURAÇAO   BONAIRE
Willemstad   Kralendijk

L   E   S   S   E   R   A   N   T   I   L   L   E   S

Victoria   GRENADA
CANOUAN
CARRIACOU
Saint George's

Bahía Honda   Punta Gallinas
Bahía Portete   Punta Espada
Puerto Bolívar   Puerto Estrella
CABO DE LA VELA   PENÍNSULA DE
LA GUAJIRA   Pueblo Nuevo
LA GUAJIRA   Punto Fijo   Coro
Riohacha   Uribia
Albania   Maicao   Sinamaica   La Vela
de Coro
San Carlos   Dabajuro   Capatárida
del Zulia   Mene de
Mauroa
Maracaibo   FALCÓN
Cabimas
Ciudad   Churuguara
Ojeda   Barquisimeto

ISLAS LAS AVES
(Ven.)   ISLA LA ORCHILA
(Ven.)   ISLA BLANQUILLA (Ven.)   ▽ 570   Speyside   TOBAGO
ISLAS LOS ROQUES   ISLAS LOS HERMANOS   Scarborough
(Ven.)   (Ven.)   TRINIDAD
▽ 1902   ISLAS LOS TESTIGOS   GALERA   AND
(Ven.)   POINT   TOBAGO

ISLA DE MARGARITA
(Ven.)   PENÍNSULA DE
NUEVA   Juangriego   La Asunción   PARIA
ESPARTA   Porlamar   Río   Port of Spain
ISLA LA TORTUGA   Punta de Piedras   Caribe   PUNTA
(Ven.)   ISLA COCHE   Carúpano   PIEDRAS   San
ISLA CUBAGUA   El Pilar   Yaguaraparo   TRINIDAD   Fernando
▽ 1353   Cumaná   Casanay   Point   GALEOTA POINT
Puerto   CABO CODERA   Araya   Güiria   Fortín   Princes Town   Gulf of
Cumarebo   Maiquetía   Carenero   SUCRE   Irapa Yoco   Siparia   Paria   Serpents Mouth
Puerto   Petare   El Guapo   Cumanacoa   Caripito
San Juan de los Cayos   Cabello   CARACAS   Guarenas   Río   Quiriquire   Pedernales
Tucacas   PARQUE   Guatire   Chico   Puerto la Cruz   Tunapui   DELTA
NACIONAL   Los Teques   Barcelona   Maturín
Morón   Maracay   Pozuelos   Caripe   DEL
Chichiriviche   HENRI   MIRANDA   Bergantín   Quiocata   AMACURO
PITTIER   Ocumare   2596   Punta de Araya   Aragua de Maturín   Tucupita   ORINOCO
Valencia   del Tuy   Barbacoa   Uracoa
San Felipe   Altagracia   Onoto   San Antonio   ISLA TOBEJUBA
Los Morros   de Orituco   de Maturín
PARQUE   Guanape   Aragua   MONAGAS
NACIONAL   San Juan de   Clarines   de Barcelona
Valencia   los Morros   Santa Ana
San Carlos   Tinaco   El Pao   Lezama   Chaguaramas   Anaco   DELTA
Acarigua   Parapara   ANZOÁTEGUI   Cantaura
Valle de la Pascua   San Diego   San Tomé   Temblador
COJEDES   El Sombrero   de Cabrutica   El Tigre   San José de Guanipa
GUÁRICO   Santa María   Barrancas
Las Mercedes   de Ipire   Grande
El Calvario   El Socorro   Pariaguán

10°

CARIBBEAN   SEA

A   N   T   I   L   L   E   S

COLOMBIA   VENEZUELA
ZULIA   Lago de
Maracaibo
NORTE DE
SANTANDER   TRUJILLO
Valera   PORTUGUESA

Map continues
pages 246-247 →

Kilometers   0   100   200   300   Km.
Statute Miles   0   100   200   300   Mi.

Scale 1:6,000,000   One centimeter represents 60 kilometers.
One inch represents approximately 95 miles.
Lambert Conformal Conic Projection

Islands of the West Indies / Westindische Inseln / Islas de las Antillas
Îles des Antilles / Ilhas do Caribe (Índias Ocidentais)

a — BERMUDA (U.K.)
ATLANTIC OCEAN
SAINT GEORGE'S ISLAND / Saint George / SAINT DAVID'S ISLAND
KINDLEY FIELD / U.S. NAVAL AIR STATION
Castle Harbour
SPANISH PT. / FT. / Spanish Pt. / Town Hill
SOMERSET ISLAND / Platts
Hamilton

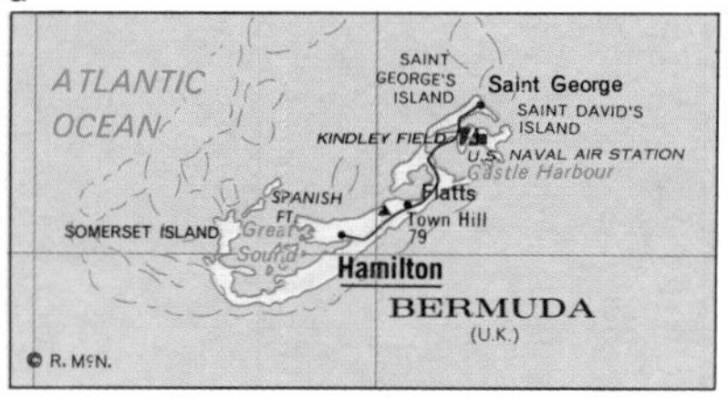

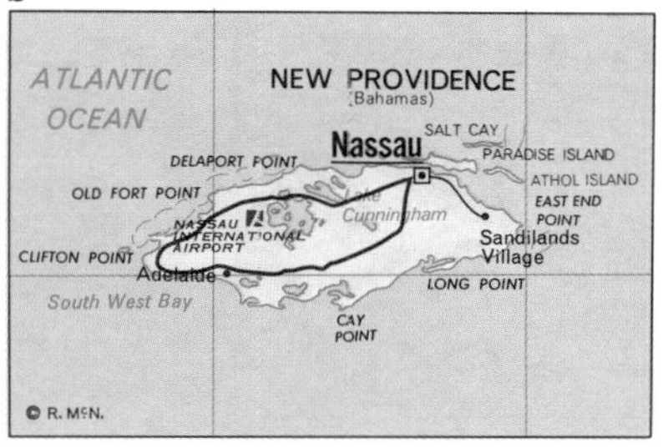

b — NEW PROVIDENCE (Bahamas)
ATLANTIC OCEAN
SALT CAY / CAY SAL
DELAPORT POINT / Nassau / PARADISE ISLAND / ATHOL ISLAND / EAST END POINT
OLD FORT POINT / Cunningham / NASSAU INTERNATIONAL AIRPORT
CLIFTON POINT / Adelaide / Sandilands Village / LONG POINT
South West Bay / CAY POINT

c — ANTIGUA AND BARBUDA
CARIBBEAN SEA
BOON POINT / LONG ISLAND (North Sound)
ANTIGUA / PRICKLY PEAR / GUANA ISLAND
Saint John's / Parham / INDIAN TOWN POINT
FULLERTON POINT / Willikies / Dunbar's Bay
FIVE ISLANDS HARBOUR / PEARNS POINT / Bolans / All Saints / Liberta
Boggy Peak / SOLDIER POINT
URLINGS / JOHNSONS POINT / Old Road / Freetown / NELSON'S DOCKYARD
Willoughby Bay
Guadeloupe

d — DOMINICA
ATLANTIC OCEAN
CAPUCIN / Morne aux Diables / Vieille Case
PRINCE RUPERT BLUFF POINT / Portsmouth / CROMPTON POINT
Prince Rupert Bay / POINTE RONDE / MELVILLE HALL AIRPORT / Wesley / Marigot
Coulibistri / Morne Diablotins / Castle Bruce
Salisbury / POINTE À PEINE
Saint Joseph
Mahaut / Morne Trois Pitons / La Plaine
Roseau / NATIONAL PARK / Watt Mtn. / POINTE GIRAUD
Delices
CARIBBEAN SEA
Soufrière Bay / Berekua
SCOTTS HEAD / POINTE DES FOUS
Martinique Passage

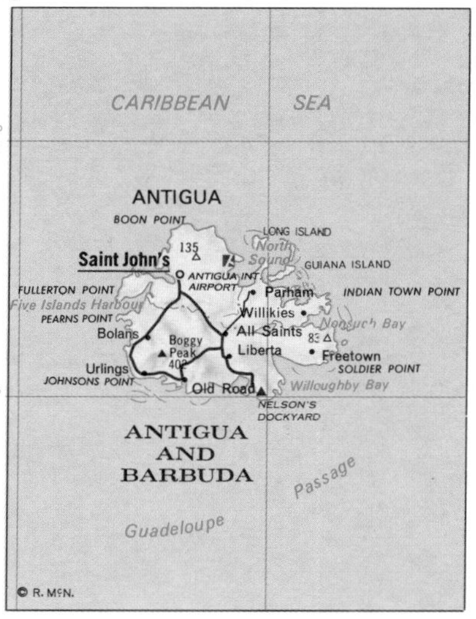

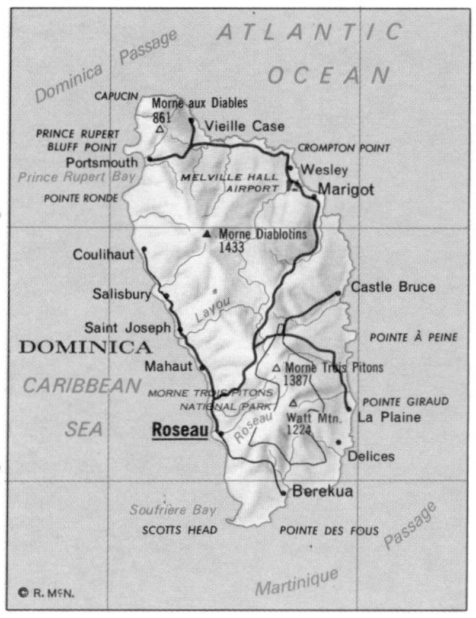

e — MARTINIQUE
ATLANTIC OCEAN
Martinique Passage / POINTE DE MACOUBA
Grand' Rivière / CAP SAINT-MARTIN / Basse-Pointe
Le Prêcheur / Montagne Pelée / Le Lorrain
Saint-Pierre / Sainte-Marie / POINTE DU DIABLE
Le Carbet / Pitons du Carbet / La Trinité / PRESQU'ÎLE DE LA CARAVELLE
Bellefontaine / Gros-Morne / Havre du Robert
Case-Pilote / Saint-Joseph / Le Robert
Schoelcher / Le Lamentin / François
Fort-de-France / Baie de Fort-de-France / Le Saint-Esprit
Les Trois-Îlets / Morne Bigot / Rivière-Salée / Le Vauclin
Les Anses-d'Arlets / Saint-Luce / Rivière-Pilote
Le Diamant / POINTE BORGNESSE / CAP FERRÉ
MARTINIQUE / POINTE DU DIAMANT / Sainte-Anne
CARIBBEAN SEA / POINTE DES SALINES
Saint Lucia Channel

m — PUERTO RICO (U.S.)
ATLANTIC OCEAN
San Antonio / Isabela / Camuy / PUNTA LAS TUNAS / SAN JUAN
PUNTA AGUJEREADA / Quebradillas / Hatillo / Arecibo / Vega Baja / Poblado Cerro Gordo
Feliciano / Barceloneta / Dorado / Levittown / Cantaño
Aguadilla / El Coto / La Cuesta / Palo Blanco / Bayamón / Carolina
Pueblo de Ponce / Pueblo Nuevo / Manatí / Vega Alta / Guaynabo / Trujillo Alto
Aguada / Moca / Charco Hondo / Asomante / El Campamento / Río Grande / Fajardo
Rincón / San Sebastián / Dos Bocas / Corozal / Naranjito / El Yunque / Luquillo
Córcega / Lares / Morovis / Aguas Buenas / Las Piñas / Playa de Fajardo
Mayagüez / Utuado / Ciales / Comerío / Caguas / Humacao
Añasco / Las Marías / Orocovis / Cidra / Cayey / Las Piedras
Maricao / Adjuntas / Barranquitas / Aibonito / San Lorenzo / Yabucoa
San Germán / Yauco / Juana Díaz / Coamo / Salinas / Arroyo
Sabana Grande / Guayanilla / Ponce / Santa Isabel / Guayama / Patillas / Maunabo
Cabo Rojo / Lajas / Guánica / Playa de Ponce / Las Mareas
Ensenada / CABO ROJO
PUERTO RICO / CORDILLERA CENTRAL / SIERRA DE CAYEY
ISLA DE VIEQUES / ISLA DE CULEBRA
CARIBBEAN

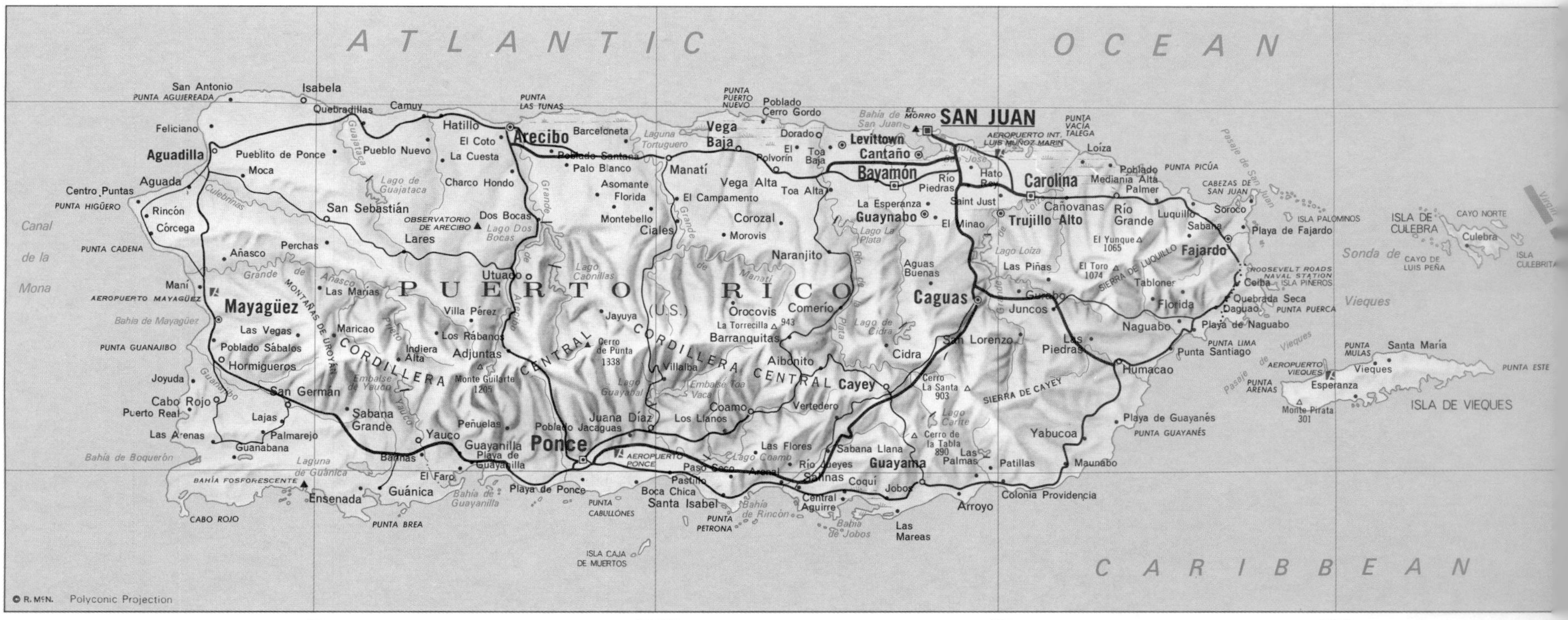

p — CUBA
GULF OF MEXICO
LA HABANA (HAVANA) / Matanzas / Cárdenas
Mariel / Bauta / San José de las Lajas / Varadero
San Antonio de los Baños / Güines / Colón / Sagua la Grande
Artemisa / Bejucal / Jovellanos / Santa Clara
Pinar del Río / Güira de Melena / Unión de Reyes / Cienfuegos / Placetas
Consolación del Sur / Batabanó / Aguada de Pasajeros / Sancti Spíritus
San Cristóbal / Jagüey Grande / Trinidad / Ciego de Ávila
Nueva Gerona / Cienfuegos / Morón
ISLA DE LA JUVENTUD (ISLA DE PINOS)
CARIBBEAN SEA
CAYMAN ISLANDS (U.K.)

MAP FORM								
ENGLISH	bay	cay	channel	bayou	gulf	island	mount	passage	point
DEUTSCH	Bucht	Klippe	Kanal	Altwasser	Golf	Insel	Berg	Durchfahrt	Landspitze
ESPAÑOL	bahía	cayo	canal	ensenada	golfo	isla	montaña	pasaje	punta
FRANÇAIS	baie	caye	détroit	bayou	golfe	île	mont	passage	pointe
PORTUGUÊS	baía	baixio	canal	enseada	golfo	ilha	montanha	passagem	ponta

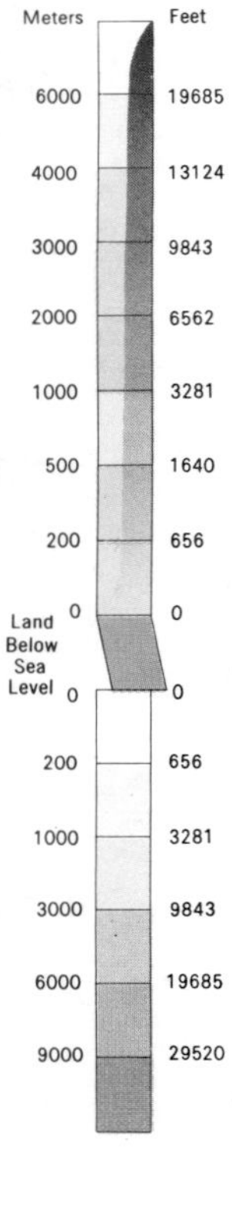

Meters	Feet
6000	19685
4000	13124
3000	9843
2000	6562
1000	3281
500	1640
200	656
0	0
Land Below Sea Level	
200	656
1000	3281
3000	9843
6000	19685
9000	29520

Copyright © by Rand McNally & Co.
Map prepared by Rand McNally & Co.
A-533200-264/764   -8-6 -15

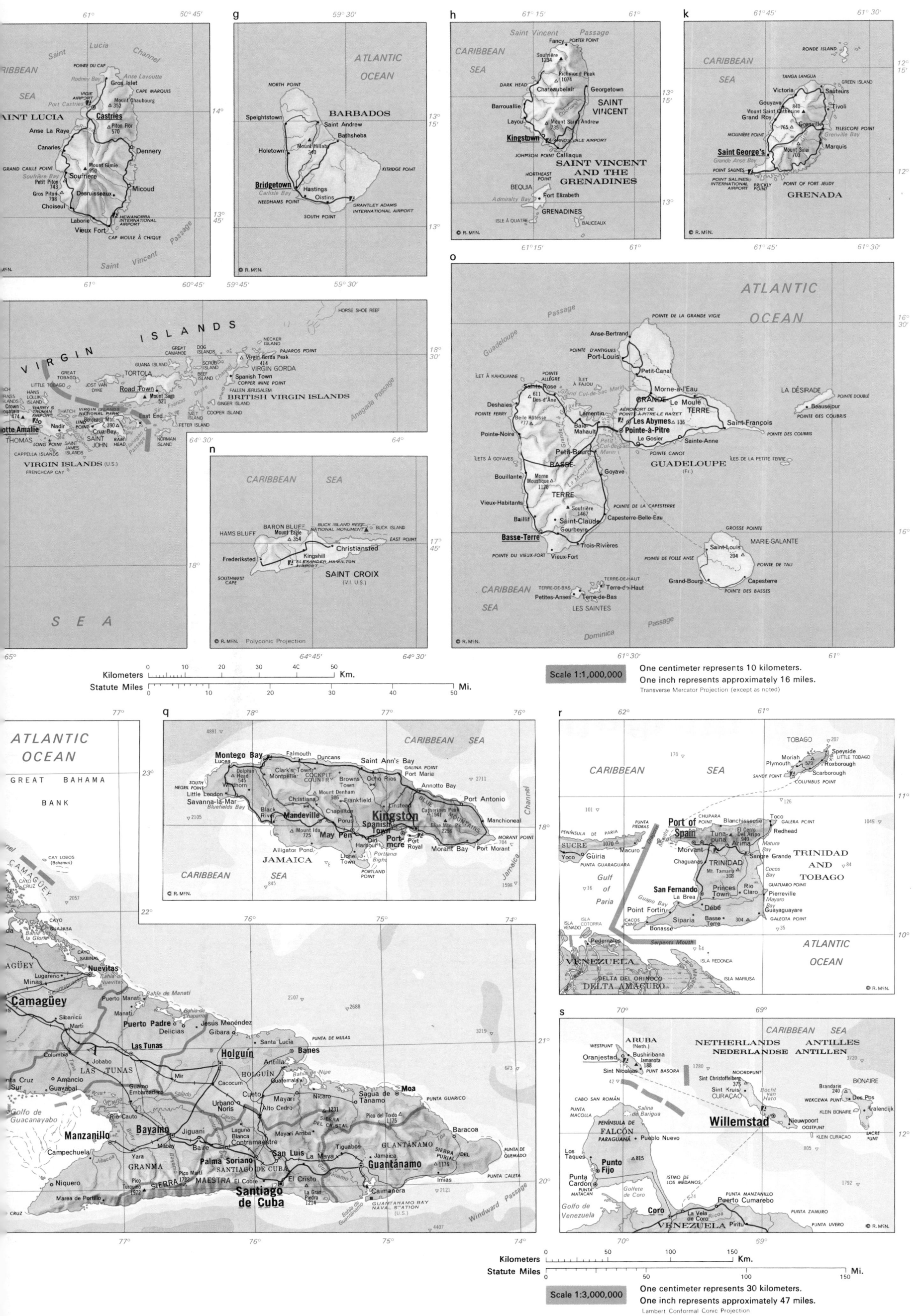

One centimeter represents 10 kilometers.
One inch represents approximately 16 miles.
Transverse Mercator Projection (except as noted)

Scale 1:1,000,000

One centimeter represents 30 kilometers.
One inch represents approximately 47 miles.
Lambert Conformal Conic Projection

Scale 1:3,000,000

Northern South America / Südamerika, nördlicher Teil / América del Sur: zona septentrional
Amérique du Sud Septentrionale / América do Sul: zona setentrional

Map continues
pages 230-231

CARIBBEAN SEA

PACIFIC OCEAN

NICARAGUA

COSTA RICA

PANAMA

COLOMBIA

ECUADOR

PERU

VENEZUELA

AMAZONAS

SELVA

ACRE

RONDÔNIA

BOLIVIA

CHILE

ARGENTINA

LESSER ANTILLES

NETHERLANDS ANTILLES

SAINT VINCENT AND THE GRENADINES

TRINIDAD

CORDILLERA OCCIDENTAL

CORDILLERA CENTRAL

CORDILLERA ORIENTAL

CORDILLERA REAL

Equator

Copyright © by Rand McNally & Co.
Map prepared by Esselte Map Service AB, Stockholm.
A-549100-254   -8 -6 -16

Kilometers   0   200   400   600   Km.
Statute Miles   0   200   400   600   Mi.

Scale 1:12,000,000

One centimeter represents 120 kilometers.
One inch represents approximately 190 miles.
Oblique Conic Conformal Projection

Northern South America / Südamerika, nördlicher Teil / América del Sur: zona septentrional
Amérique du Sud Septentrionale / América do Sul: zona setentrional

243

ATLANTIC OCEAN

Georgetown

Paramaribo

Cayenne

FRENCH
GUIANA

SURINAME

AMAPÁ

Macapá

ILHA DE MARAJÓ

Belém

São Luís

Parnaíba

Fortaleza

Santarém

PARÁ

Represa
de
Tucuruí

MARANHÃO

Teresina

Imperatriz

Marabá

PIAUÍ

CEARÁ

Mossoró

Natal

RIO GRANDE DO NORTE

SERRA DO CACHIMBO

Juazeiro
do Norte

Campina Grande

João Pessoa

Olinda

Recife

PERNAMBUCO

PARAÍBA

TOCANTINS

Petrolina
Juazeiro

Paulo
Afonso

ALAGOAS

Maceió

Arapiraca

B R A Z I L

ILHA
DO
BANANAL

SERGIPE

Aracaju

MATO GROSSO

BAHIA

Feira de Santana

Alagoinhas

Salvador

PLANALTO DO

MATO GROSSO

Cuiabá

GOIÁS

Vitória
da Conquista

Ilhéus
Itabuna

BRASÍLIA

Anápolis

Goiânia

PLANALTO

CENTRAL

Montes
Claros

Rondonópolis

MINAS GERAIS

Corumbá

MATO GROSSO
DO SUL

Araguari

Uberlândia

Uberaba

Governador
Valadares

ESPÍRITO
SANTO

Belo
Horizonte

Vitória
Vila Velha

Campo Grande

Barretos

Divinópolis

Campos

Ribeirão
Preto

São José
do Rio Preto

Araçatuba

SÃO PAULO

Presidente Prudente

Campinas

RIO DE JANEIRO

SÃO PAULO

Santos

Tropic of Capricorn

Map continues
pages 244-245

MAP FORM						
ENGLISH	cerro	cordillera	ilha	lago	nevado	península	serra
	mountain	range	island	lake	mountain	peninsula	mountains
DEUTSCH	Berg	Gebirge	Insel	See	Berg	Halbinsel	Berge
ESPAÑOL	montaña	cordillera	isla	lago	montaña	península	montañas
FRANÇAIS	montagne	chaîne	île	lac	montagne	péninsule	montagnes
PORTUGUÊS	montanha	cordilheira	ilha	lago	montanha	península	montanhas

Map continues
pages 242-243

MAP FORM	cerro, co.	golfo	ilha	isla	lago	lagoa	monte	salar
ENGLISH	butte	gulf	island	isle	lake	lake	mountain	saltflat
DEUTSCH	Restberg	Golf	Insel	Insel	See	See	Berg	Salzebene
ESPAÑOL	cerro	golfo	isla	isla	lago	lago	montaña	salina
FRANÇAIS	butte	golfe	île	île	lac	lac	montagne	salobral
PORTUGUÊS	colina	golfo	ilha	ilha	lago	lago	montanha	salina

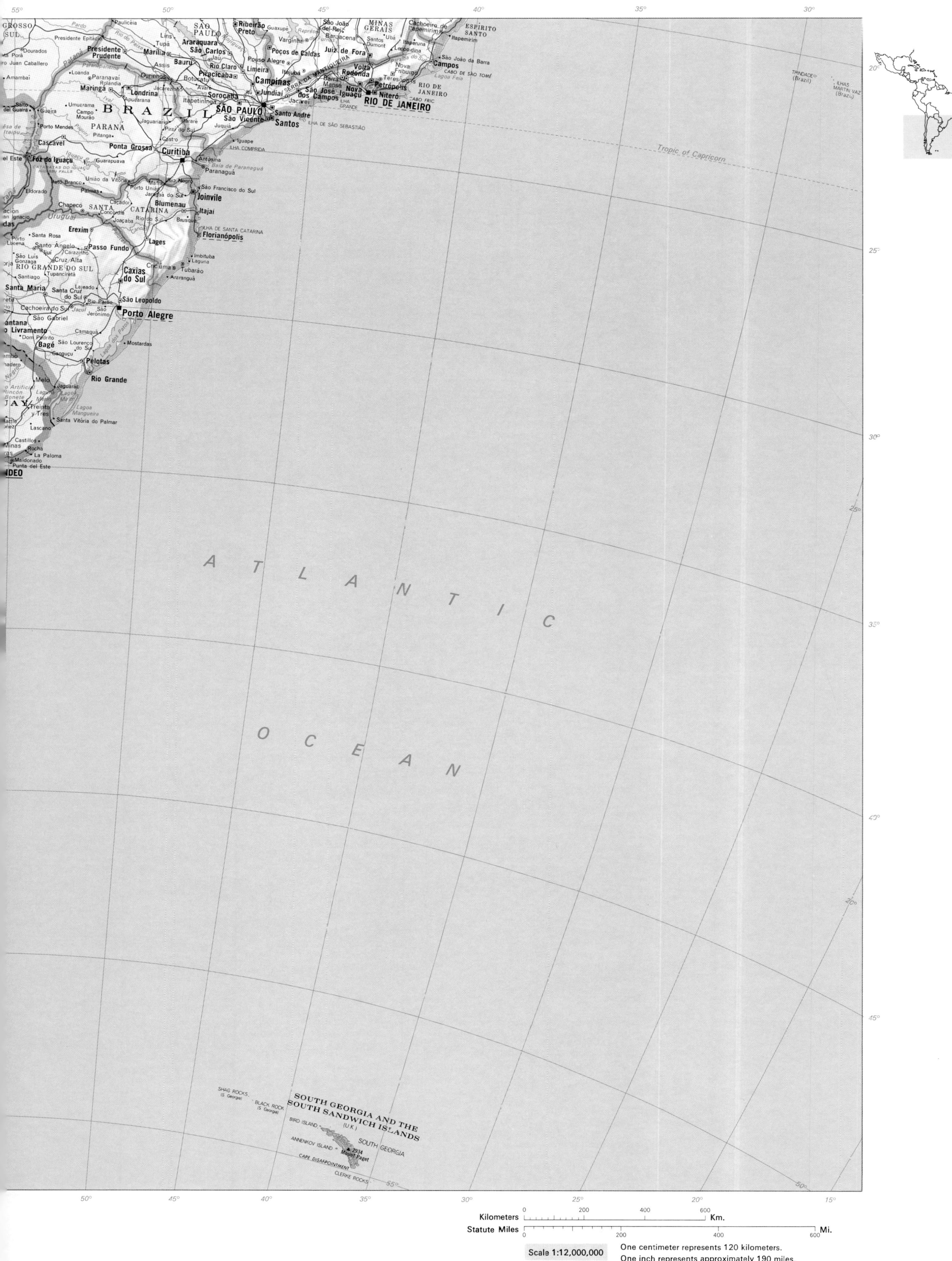

Kilometers | 0   200   400   600 | Km.
Statute Miles | 0   200   400   600 | Mi.

Scale 1:12,000,000   One centimeter represents 120 kilometers.
One inch represents approximately 190 miles.
Oblique Conic Conformal Projection

Map continues
pages 238-239

Map continues
pages 248-249

MAP FORM	bahía	cabo	cerro, co.	golfo	igarapé	isla, i.	lago, l.	punta	volcán, vol.
ENGLISH	bay	cape	butte	gulf	river	island	lake	point	volcano
DEUTSCH	Bucht	Kap	Restberg	Golf	Fluss	Insel	See	Landspitze	Vulkan
ESPAÑOL	bahía	cabo	cerro	golfo	río	isla	lago	punta	volcán
FRANÇAIS	baie	cap	butte	golfe	rivière	île	lac	pointe	volcan
PORTUGUÊS	baía	cabo	colina	golfo	rio	ilha	lago	ponta	vulcão

Copyright © by Rand McNally & Co.
Map prepared by Rand McNally & Co.
A-649700-764   -10 -7 -16

Colombia, Ecuador, Venezuela and Guyana / Kolumbien, Ecuador, Venezuela und Guayana / Colombia, Ecuador, Venezuela y Guyana
Colombie, Equateur, Venezuela et Guyane / Colômbia, Equador, Venezuela e Guiana

247

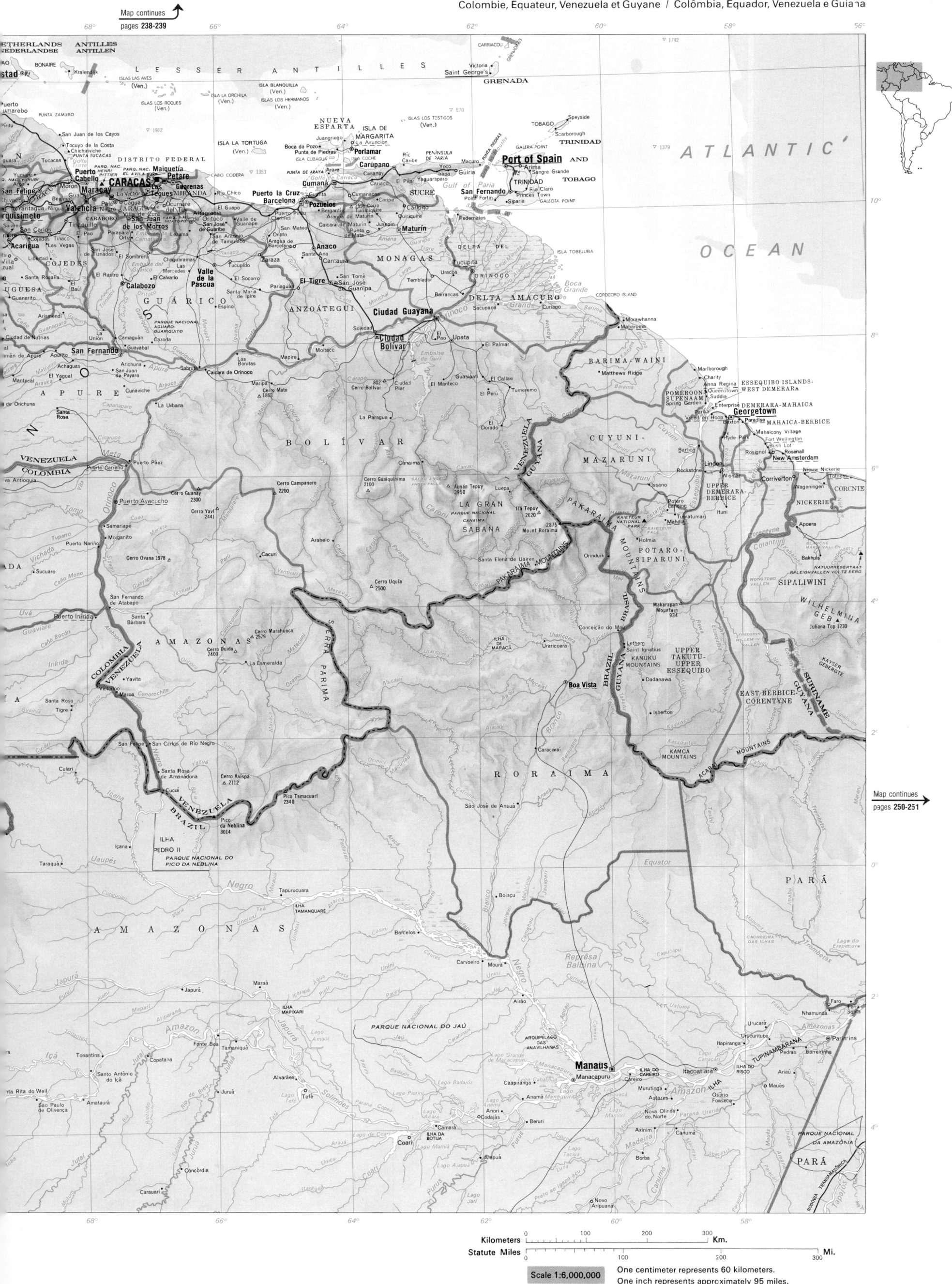

Map continues
pages 238-239

Map continues
pages 250-251

Kilometers
Statute Miles

Scale 1:6,000,000

One centimeter represents 60 kilometers.
One inch represents approximately 95 miles.
Oblique Conic Conformal Projection

Peru, Bolivia and Western Brazil / Peru, Bolivien und westliches Brasilien / Perú, Bolivia y Brasil Occidental
Pérou, Bolivie et Brésil Occidental / Peru, Bolívia e Brasil Ocidental

Meters	Feet
6000	19685
4000	13124
3000	9843
2000	6562
1000	3281
500	1640
200	656
0	0
Land Below Sea Level	
0	0
200	656
1000	3281
3000	9843
6000	19685
9000	29520

Copyright © by Rand McNally & Co.
Map prepared by Rand McNally & Co.
A-549792-764   -6 -7 -9

MAP FORM	cerro	cordillera	isla, i.	lago, l.	nevado	punta	rio	serra
ENGLISH	mountain	mountains	island	lake	mountain	point	river	mountains
DEUTSCH	Berg	Berge	Insel	See	Berg	Landspitze	Fluss	Berge
ESPAÑOL	montaña	montañas	isla	lago	nevado	punta	rio	sierra
FRANÇAIS	montagne	montagnes	île	lac	montagne	pointe	rivière	montagnes
PORTUGUÊS	montanha	montanhas	ilha	lago	pico nevado	ponta	rio	serra

Peru, Bolivia and Western Brazil / Peru, Bolivien und westliches Brasilien / Perú, Bolivia y Brasil Occidental
Pérou, Bolivie et Brésil Occidental / Peru, Bolívia e Brasil Ocidental

249

Map continues
pages 246-247

Map continues
pages 250-251

Map continues
page 255

Map continues
pages 252-253

Kilometers
Statute Miles

Scale 1:6,000,000

One centimeter represents 60 kilometers.
One inch represents approximately 95 miles.
Oblique Conic Conformal Projection

Mahaicony
Village
Fort Wellington
Bush Lot
Rosehall
New Amsterdam
Rosignol
Corriverton
WANICA
COMME-WIJNE
Paramaribo
Lelydorp
MAROWIJNE
Mana
Iracoubo
Sinnamary
Kourou
ÎLE DU DIABLE
DEVILS ISLAND
Saint-Laurent-du-Maroni
Cayenne
Remire
Matoury
Roura

Wageningen
Nieuw Nickerie Totness
CORONIE
NICKERIE
Groningen
Onverwacht
Paranam
Kwakoegron
Berg en Dal
Brokopondo
Apatou
Saint-Élie
Tonate
Pointe Behague
Kaw
Guisanbourg
Regina

Nieuw Amsterdam
PARA
SARAMACCA
Moengo
Albina
Grand-Santi
Maripasoula

BROKO-PONDO
NATUURPARK
BROWNSBERG
Brokopondo
Stuwmeer

CABO ORANGE
Saint-Georges
Oiapoque
Clevelândia do Norte
Monte Tipoca △ 430
Vila Velha
Cunani
Calçoene
Lourenço

NATUURPARK
BROWNSBERG
VOLTZ BERG
NATUURRESERVAAT
RALEIGHVALLEN
VOLTZ BERG

Bakhuis

Tafelberg △ 1026
Juliana Top △ 1230
WILHELMINA GEB.

SIPALIWINI
KAYSER
GEBERGTE

SURINAME
FRENCH GUIANA
GUYANE FRANÇAISE
BRASIL
BRAZIL
CAYENNE

EAST
BERBICE-CORENTYNE
SURINAME
GUYANA

TUMUC-HUMAC MOUNTAINS

830 △

PARQUE NACIONAL
DO CABO ORANGE

Saul

GUYANA
BRAZIL
BRASIL

AMAPÁ

ILHA DE MARACÁ
ILHA JIPIOCA
CABO NORTE
Sucuriju
Amapá

Serra do Navio
Ferreira Gomes
Pôrto Grande
ILHA DO CURUÁ
Aporema
ILHA BAILIQUE
Bailique

Lago Maruani
18 ▽
ILHA JANAUCU

Equator
Equador

Macapá
Pôrto Santana
Mazagão
Mazagão Velho
ILHA DO
CARÁ
ILHA
QUEIMADA
ILHA DO PARÁ
ILHA DE JURUPARI
ILHA CAVIANA
DE FORA
ARQUIPÉLAGO JURUPARI
ILHA MEXIANA
CABO MAGUARI

Afuá
Chaves
Canal do Sul
Baía de
Marajó
Salinópolis

ILHA
CHARAPUCU
Anajás
ILHA DE MARAJÓ
Lago Arari
São Caetano
de Odivelas
Soure
Salvaterra
Joanes
Colares
Mosqueiro
Marapanim
Primavera
Curuçá

Itatupa
Gurupá
ILHA GRANDE
DO GURUPÁ
ILHA DO
MUTUTI
Cachoeira do Arari
Muaná
Condeixa
Vigia
Igarapé-Açu
Capanema
Bragança
Viseu

Bôca
do Jari
ILHA
CURUAÍ
São Miguel dos Macacos
Ponta de Pedras
Americano
Castanhal
Marapanim
Nova Timboteua
São José
do Pirá

ILHA URURICAIA
Aruman-duba
Aimerim
Pôrto de Moz
Carrazedo
Vilarinho do
Monte
ILHA DOS
MACACOS
Breves
Piriá
São Sebastião
da Boa Vista
Belém
Ananindeua
Val-de-Cães
Guajará-Açu
Tentugal
São Miguel
do Guamá
Ourém
Capitão-Poço
Irituia
São José
do Gurupi

Almeirim
Carrazedo
Porto de Moz
Veiros
Portel
Bagre
Curuçambaba
Abaetetuba
Moju
Acará
São Domingos
do Capim
Camiranga

Prainha
Monte Alegre
ILHA DA
LAGUNA
Melgaço
Portel
Deiras
Cametá
Curuçambaba
Mocajuba
Tomé-Açu
Santa Helena

Óbidos
Alenquer
Terra Santa
Faro
Nhamundá
AMAZONAS
ILHA ARAPIRI
ILHA GRANDE
DO TAPARÁ
Santarém
Belterra
Juruti
Óbidos
Oriximiná

Lago do
Curuaí
Lago do Erepecu

Amazon
Amazonas
Parintins
Urucará
Itapiranga
Pedras
Barreirinha
Maués
Urucurituba
Nhamundá

Boim
Aveiro
Vitória
Senador José
Porfírio
Altamira

ILHA DO
RISCO
Itacoatiara
Ariaú
Osório Fonseca

Brasília Legal
Itaituba
PARQUE NACIONAL
DA AMAZÔNIA
TRANSAMAZÔNICA
228
RODOVIA

PARÁ

Tucuruí
Represa
de
Tucuruí

Jacundá
MARANHÃO
Itupiranga
Acailândia

SERRA
DOS
CARAJÁS
Marabá
São João
do Araguaia
Araguatins
Itaguatins
Imperatriz
Amarante do
Maranhão
Montes
Altos
Sítio Novo
Grajaú
Barra do Cor

Carajás
△ 898
Santa Isabel do Araguaia
Xambioá
Tocantinópolis
Nazaré
Porto Franco
Paranaitu
640 △
Resplande

Araguaína
Babaçulândia
Carolina
Riachão
Balsas
Ribe
Gonçalv

Conceição
SERRA
DO
CACHIMBO
Gradaús
Conceição do
Araguaia
Itaporã
de Goiás
Couto de Magalhães
Pequizeiro
Araguacema
Itacajá
593
Fortaleza
dos Nogueiras
São Raimundo
das Mangabeiras

TOCANTINS
SERRA
DO
ESTRONDO
CHAPADA
DAS
MANGABEIRAS

Cachimbo
Alta Floresta
SERRA DOS APIACÁS
192
Dois Irmãos
de Goiás
Pedro Afonso
Alto Parnaíba
Santa Filome

PARQUE
NACIONAL
DO ARAGUAIA
Santa Terezinha
Cristalândia
Piurn
Pôrto
Nacional
Monte
do Carmo
Ponte Alta
do Norte
Pindorama de Goiás
Brejinho
de Nazaré
Monte Alegre
do Piauí
Curupá

MATO GROSSO
Sinop
FORMOSA
SERRA DO RONCADOR
ILHA DO
BANANAL
São Félix do
Araguaia
Luciara
Dueré
Palmas
Miracema do Tocantins
Tocantínia
Formiga

SERRA DO TOMBADOR
Pôrto dos Gaúchos
Jauru
Gurupi
Peixe
Natividade
Almas
Dianópolis
Conceição
do Norte
Ponte Alta do Bom Jesus
Taguatinga

Map continues
pages 246-247

Map continues
pages 248-249

Map continues
page 255

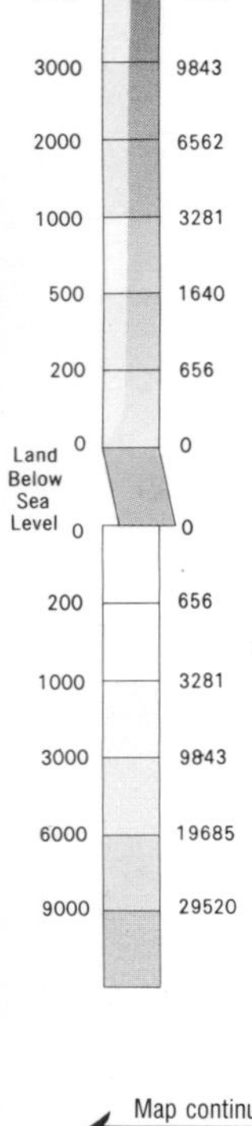

Meters	Feet
6000	19685
4000	13124
3000	9843
2000	6562
1000	3281
500	1640
200	656
0	0
Land Below Sea Level 0	0
200	656
1000	3281
3000	9843
6000	19685
9000	29520

MAP FORM	cabo	cachoeira, cach.	ilha, i.	lago, l.	riacho	ribeirão, rão.	rio, r.	serra, sa.
ENGLISH	cape	waterfall	island	lake	creek	creek	river	mountains
DEUTSCH	Kap	Wasserfall	Insel	See	Bach	Bach	Fluss	Berge
ESPAÑOL	cabo	cascada	isla	lago	riachuelo	riachuelo	río	montañas
FRANÇAIS	cap	chute d'eau	île	lac	crique	crique	rivière	montagnes
PORTUGUÊS	cabo	queda d'água	ilha	lago	riacho	riacho	rio	montanhas

ATLANTIC

OCEAN

Kilometers
Statute Miles

Km.

Mi.

Scale 1:6,000,000

One centimeter represents 60 kilometers.
One inch represents approximately 95 miles.
Oblique Conic Corformal Projection

Copyright © by Rand McNally & Co.
Map prepared by Rand McNally & Co.
A-540396-764   -6-8-10

Central Argentina and Chile / Mittelargentinien und Mittelchile / Argentina y Chile: zonas centrales
Argentine et Chili, parties Centrales / Argentina e Chile: zonas centrais

Map continues
pages 248-249

Map continues
page 254

MAP FORM	cabo	cerro	cuchilla	ilha	laguna	punta	salar	sierra	volcán
ENGLISH	cape	mountain	hills	island	lagoon; lake	point	saltflat	mountains	volcano
DEUTSCH	Kap	Berg	Hügel	Insel	Haff; See	Landspitze	Salzebene	Berge	Vulkan
ESPAÑOL	cabo	cerro	cuchilla	isla	laguna	punta	salobral	sierra	volcán
FRANÇAIS	cap	montagne	collines	île	lagune; lac	pointe	salina	montagnes	volcan
PORTUGUÊS	cabo	montanha	colina	ilha	laguna	ponta	salina	serra	vulcão

Copyright © by Rand McNally & Co.
Map prepared by Rand McNally & Co.
A-540191-764   -4-7-8

Central Argentina and Chile / Mittelargentinien und Mittelchile / Argentina y Chile: zonas centrales
Argentine et Chili, parties Centrales / Argentina e Chile: zonas centrais

253

Map continues
page 255

Kilometers
Statute Miles

Scale 1:6,000,000

One centimeter represents 60 kilometers.
One inch represents approximately 95 miles.
Oblique Conic Conformal Projection

Southern Argentina and Chile / Südliches Argentinien und südliches Chile / Argentina y Chile: zonas meridionales
Argentine et Chili, parties Méridionales / Argentina e Chile: zonas meridionais

Map continues pages **252-253**

PACIFIC OCEAN

ATLANTIC OCEAN

FALKLAND ISLANDS (U.K.)

Meters	Feet
6000	19685
4000	13124
3000	9843
2000	6562
1000	3281
500	1640
200	656
Land Below Sea Level 0	0
200	656
1000	3281
3000	9843
6000	19685
9000	29520

MAP FORM	bahia	cabo	cerro	isla	lago	monte	punta
ENGLISH	bay	cape	mountain, hill	isle	lake	mount	point
DEUTSCH	Bucht	Kap	Berg, Hügel	Insel	See	Berg	Landspitze
ESPAÑOL	bahía	cabo	cerro	isla	lago	monte	punta
FRANÇAIS	baie	cap	montagne, colline	île	lac	montagne	pointe
PORTUGUÊS	baía	cabo	montanha, colina	ilha	lago	monte	ponta

Kilometers 0   100   200   300 Km.
Statute Miles 0   100   200   300 Mi.

Scale 1:6,000,000   One centimeter represents 60 kilometers.
One inch represents approximately 95 miles.
Oblique Conic Conformal Projection

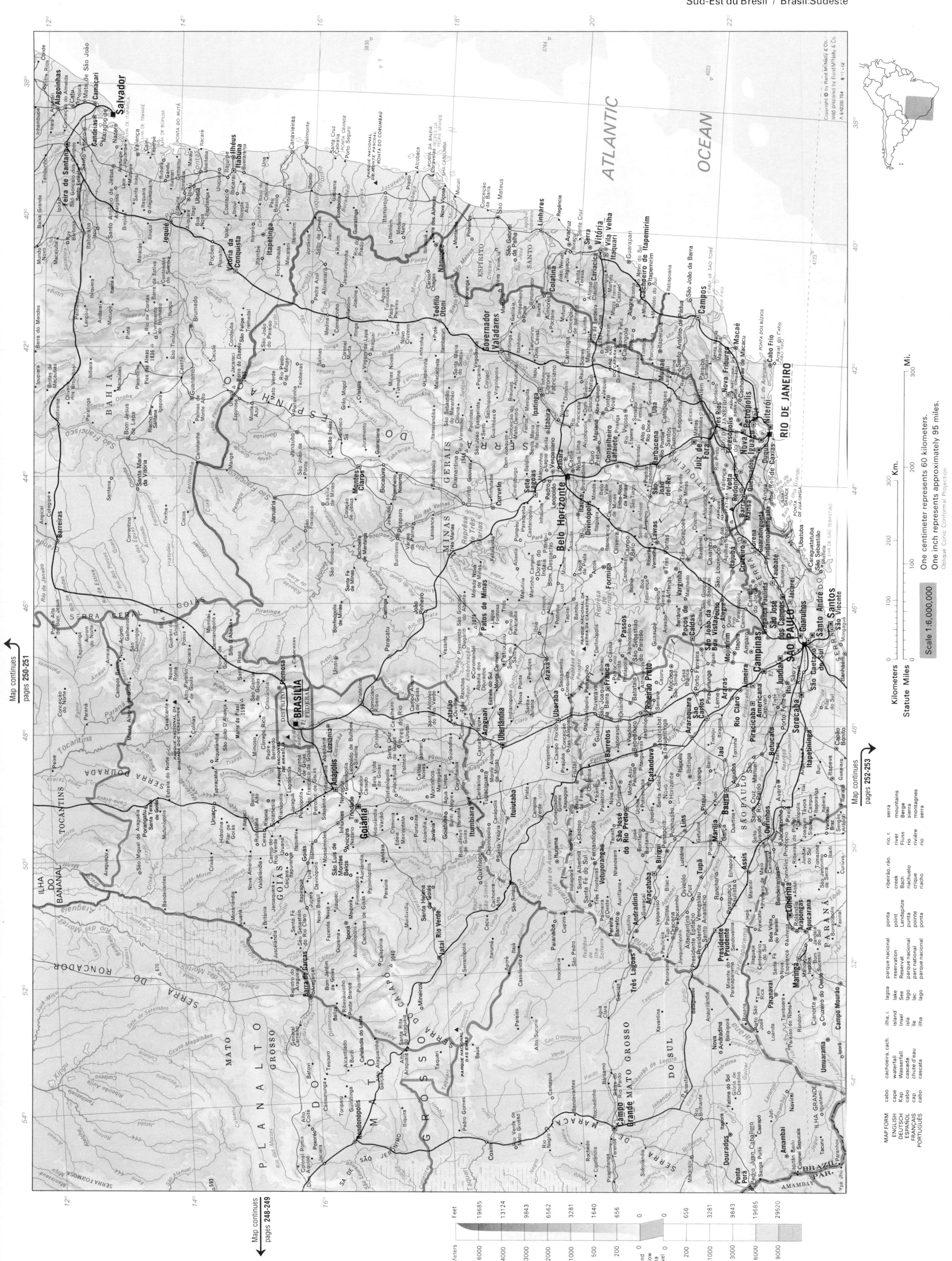

ATLANTIC OCEAN

BAHIA

ESPINHAÇO

MINAS GERAIS

ESPÍRITO SANTO

Salvador

Belo Horizonte

BRASÍLIA
DISTRITO FEDERAL

Goiânia

GOIÁS

MATO GROSSO

MATO GROSSO DO SUL

SÃO PAULO

SÃO PAULO

RIO DE JANEIRO

PARANÁ

SERRA DO RONCADOR

ILHA DO BANANAL

SERRA DOS CAIAPÓS

PLANALTO DO MATO GROSSO

Map continues pages 250-251

Map continues pages 248-249

Map continues pages 252-253

Scale 1:6,000,000

One centimeter represents 60 kilometers.
One inch represents approximately 95 miles.
Oblique Conic Conformal Projection

Kilometers   0   100   200   300   Km.

Statute Miles   0   100   200   300   Mi.

MAP FORM				
ENGLISH	cabo	cachoeira, cach.	ilha, i.	lagoa
DEUTSCH	Kap	waterfall	island	lake
ESPAÑOL	cabo	Wasserfall	Insel	See
FRANÇAIS	cap	cascada	isla	lago
PORTUGUÊS	cabo	chute d'eau	île	lac
		cascata	ilha	lago

parque nacional	ponta	ribeirão, rão.	rio, r.
reservation	point	creek	river
Reservat	Landspitze	Bach	Fluss
punta	punta	riachuelo	río
parc national	pointe	crique	rivière
parque nacional	ponta	riacho	rio

serra		
mountains		
Gebirge		
sierra		
montagnes		
serra		

Feet
19685
13124
9843
6562
3281
1640
656
0

Meters
6000
4000
3000
2000
1000
500
200
Land
Below
Sea
Level 0

0
200
656
1000
3281
3000
9843
6000
19685
9000
29520

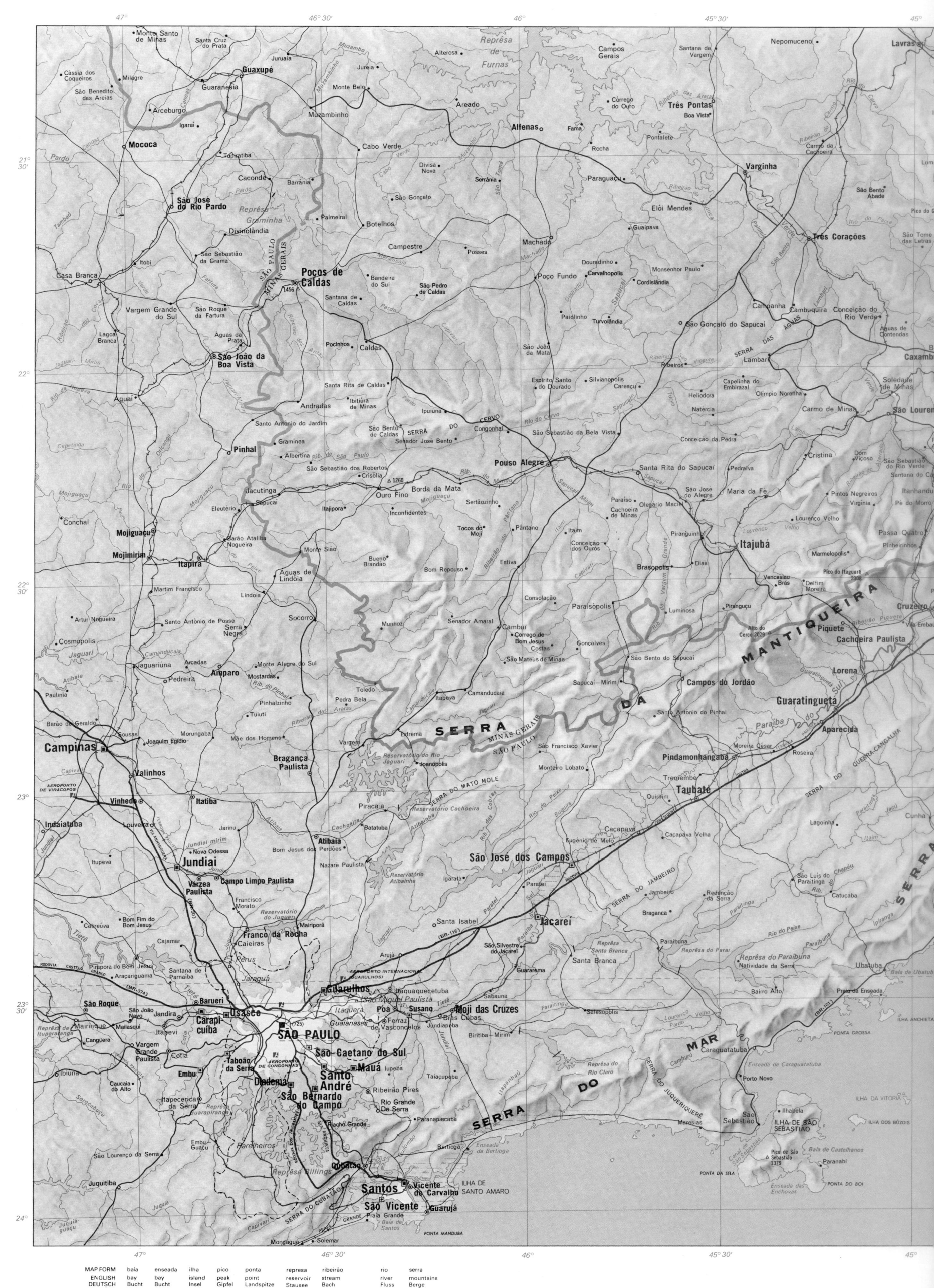

MAP FORM	baía	enseada	ilha	pico	ponta	represa	ribeirão	rio	serra
ENGLISH	bay	bay	island	peak	point	reservoir	stream	river	mountains
DEUTSCH	Bucht	Bucht	Insel	Gipfel	Landspitze	Stausee	Bach	Fluss	Berge
ESPAÑOL	bahía	bahía	isla	pico	punta	estanque	corriente de agua	río	sierra
FRANÇAIS	baie	baie	île	cime	pointe	réservoir	cours d'eau	rivière	montagnes
PORTUGUÊS	baía	enseada	ilha	pico	ponta	represa	ribeirão	rio	serra

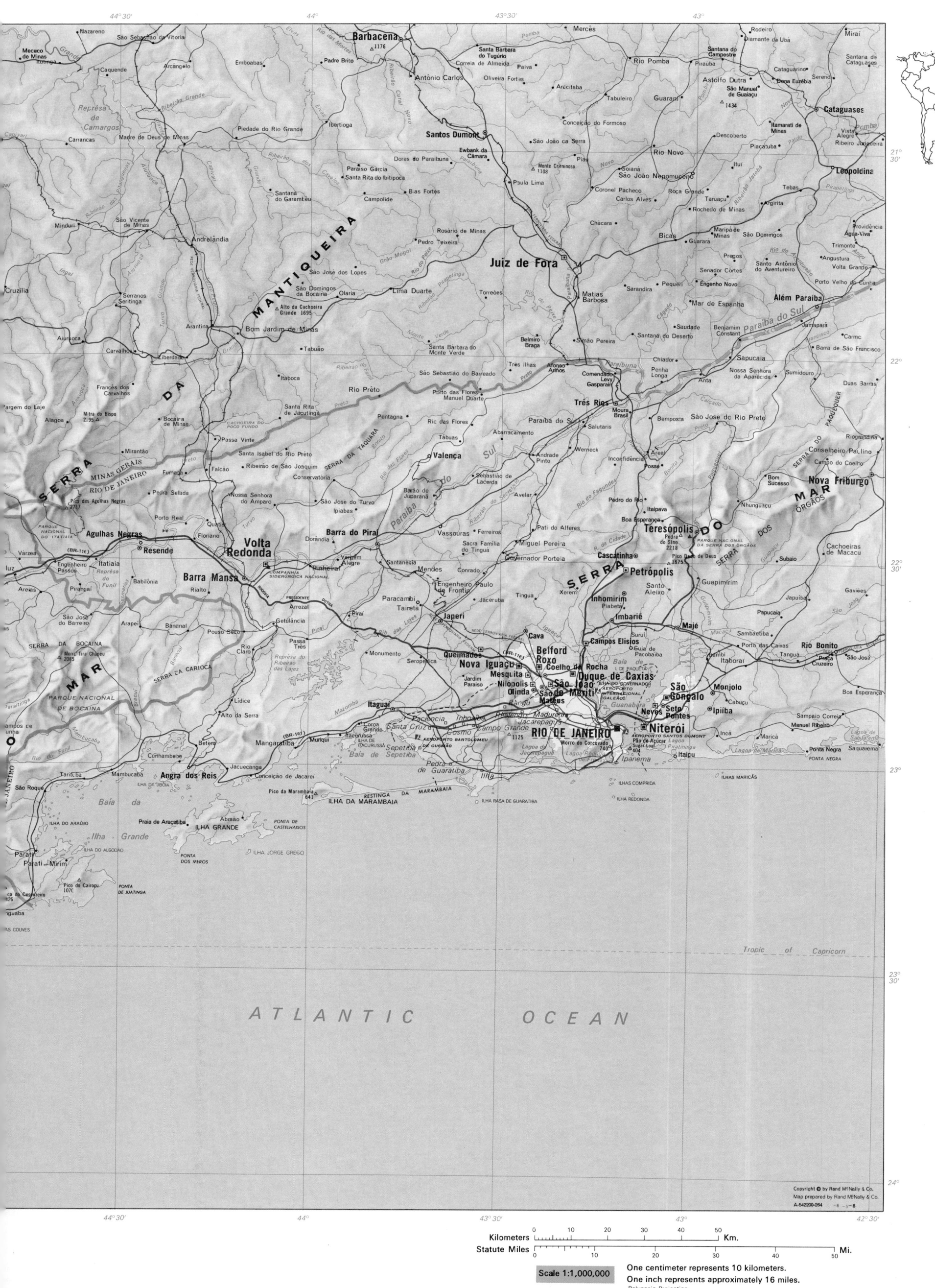

Scale 1:1,000,000

One centimeter represents 10 kilometers.
One inch represents approximately 16 miles.
Polyconic Projection

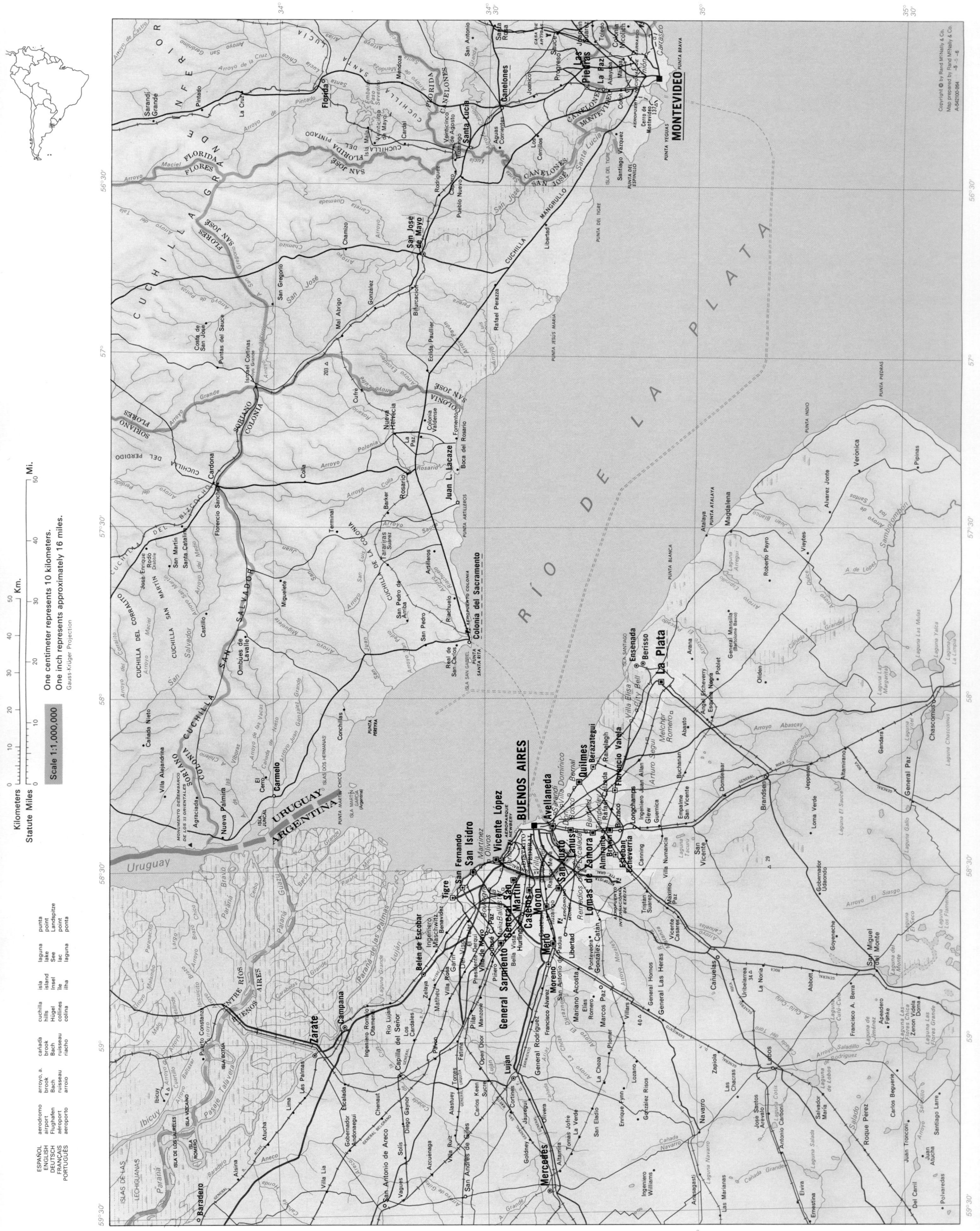

Kilometers 0 10 20 30 40 50 Km.
Statute Miles 0 10 20 30 40 50 Mi.
Scale 1:1,000,000
One centimeter represents 10 kilometers.
One inch represents approximately 16 miles.
Gauss-Krüger Projection
ESPAÑOL / ENGLISH / DEUTSCH / FRANÇAIS / PORTUGUÊS
aerodromo / airport / Flughafen / aéroport / aeroporto
arroyo, a. / brook / Bach / ruisseau / arroio
cañada / brook / Bach / ruisseau / riacho
cuchilla / hills / Hügel / collines / colina
isla / island / Insel / île / ilha
laguna / lake / See / lac / laguna
punta / point / Landspitze / point / ponta
BUENOS AIRES
MONTEVIDEO
RÍO DE LA PLATA
Uruguay
URUGUAY
ARGENTINA
ENTRE RÍOS
BUENOS AIRES
Baradero
Zárate
Campana
Mercedes
Luján
Tigre
San Fernando
San Isidro
Vicente López
General Sarmiento
General San Martín
Caseros
Morón
Merlo
Moreno
San Justo
Lanús
Avellaneda
Lomas de Zamora
Quilmes
Berazategui
Florencio Varela
Ensenada
Berisso
La Plata
Magdalena
Chascomús
Carmelo
Nueva Palmira
Colonia del Sacramento
Juan L. Lacaze
Rosario
Nueva Helvecia
San José de Mayo
Florida
Santa Lucía
Canelones
Las Piedras
La Paz
Copyright © by Rand McNally & Co.
Map prepared by Rand McNally & Co.
A-542100-264

Metropolitan Area Maps/Karten von Stradtregionen
Mapas de las Areas Metropolitanas/Cartes des Zones Métropolitaines
Mapas das Áreas Metropolitanas

259

THIS SECTION CONSISTS of 60 maps of the world's major metropolitan areas, at the scale of 1:300,000. The maps show the generalized land-use patterns in and around each city—the total urban extent, major industrial areas, parks and preserves, and wooded areas. Airports are shown, as are many details of the highway and rail transportation networks. Selected points of interest appear, such as Fisherman's Wharf and Chinatown in San Francisco, the Welcome monument in Jakarta, the Temple of the Jade Buddha in Shanghai, and the Cristo Redentor statue in Rio de Janeiro.

The maps name and locate a great number of towns, villages, and suburbs, and also sections or neighborhoods within limits of the larger cities. Prominent physical fea-tures, including elevations, named and unnamed, have been indicated to give a general impression of the local topography. Shaded relief has been omitted, however, to permit display of such details as streams, parks, airport runways, important public buildings and monuments, and the names of major streets. The corporate limits of major cities are also outlined. For the symbols used on these maps see the Legend to Maps.

Maps of major world cities usually vary widely in scale, and heretofore have not been consistent in design and coverage. For this section, a special effort has been made to portray these varied metropolitan areas in as standard and comparable a fashion as possible. However, for a few cities (notably several in Asia) there has not been adequate source material to include certain information, such as major industrial areas and corporate limits.

The order of presentation is generally regional, with some exceptions where for ease of comparison major capitals or industrial centers or cities located in similar physical surroundings have been juxtaposed. Many American cities and some European cities, with their lower densities and more extensive areas, require larger maps than do Asiatic cities of comparable population. The total land area and population within the confines of each map are stated in the margin as a further aid to comparison.

DIESER KARTENTEIL UMFASST 60 Karten der bedeutendsten Stadtregionen der Erde im Massstab 1:300 000. Die Karten zeigen in generalisierter Form die Landnutzung in und um jede Stadt: die gesamte Ausdehnung des verstädterten Gebietes, wichtige Industriegebiete, Parks, Landflächen in Gemeinbesitz und Wald. Flughäfen werden ebenso dargestellt wie viele Einzelheiten des Strassen- und Eisenbahnnetzes. Bekannte Sehenswürdigkeiten sind eingetragen wie die "Fisherman's Wharf" und "Chinatown" in San Francisco, das Willkomm-Denkmal in Jakarta, der Tempel des Jade-Buddhas in Shanghai und die "Cristo Redentor"-Statue in Rio de Janeiro.

Die Karten verzeichnen Name und Lage einer grossen Zahl von Städten, Dörfern, Vororten ebenso wie eingemeindete Ortsteile bei grösseren Städten. Hervortretende physische Formen wie benannte und unbenannte Erhebungen sind aufgenommen, um eine allgemeine Vor-stellung des lokalen Reliefs zu geben. Auf die Schummerung wurde jedoch verzichtet, um klar solche Einzelheiten wie Flüsse, Parks, Start- und Landebahnen der Flughäfen, bedeutende öffentliche Gebäude und Denkmäler sowie die Namen der wichtigsten Strassen herausstellen zu können. Eingetragen sind ferner die Gemeindegrenzen der wichtigsten Städte. Zu den auf diesen Karten verwendeten Signaturen siehe "Zeichenerklärung".

Karten der bedeutendsten Weltstädte differieren normalerweise sehr stark in ihren Massstäben und sind daher uneinheitlich in ihrer Gestaltung und Begrenzung. Deshalb wurde in diesem Kartenteil besonderer Wert darauf gelegt, die verschiedenen städtischen Ballungsgebiete in möglichst einheitlicher und vergleichbarer Form darzustellen. Für einige Städte, vor allem mehrere asiatische, war das Quellenmaterial jedoch nicht ausreichend genug, um gewisse Informationen wie Hauptindustriegebiete oder Stadtgrenzen einzutragen.

Im allgemeinen sind diese Karten nach regionalen Gesichtspunkten geordnet. Um Vergleiche zu erleichtern wurden einige Ausnahmen gemacht, indem wichtige Hauptstädte, Industriezentren oder Städte in vergleichbarer landschaftlicher Lage einander gegenübergestellt wurden. Viele amerikanische und einige europäische Städte mit ihrer geringen Bevölkerungsdichte, aber ausgedehnteren Fläche erfordern eine grössere Kartenfläche als asiatische Städte von vergleichbarer Bevölkerungszahl. Die gesamte Landfläche und die Bevölkerung innerhalb des dargestellten Gebietes ist am Kartenrand verzeichnet als ein weiteres Hilfsmittel für Vergleiche.

INTEGRAN ESTA SECCION 60 mapas de las áreas metropolitanas más importantes del mundo, a la escala de 1:300 000. Los mapas muestran los patrones de uso del suelo dentro de cada ciudad y en sus alrededores—la extensión total del conglomerado urbano, las principales áreas industriales, parques y reservas, y zonas boscosas. Aparecen los aeropuertos, así como muchos otros detalles de las redes de carreteras y ferrocarriles. Se seleccionaron también puntos de interés, como el Muelle de los Pescadores y el Barrio Chino de San Francisco, el monumento de Bienvenida de Jakarta, el Templo del Buda de Jade de Shanghai y la estatua del Cristo Redentor de Rio de Janeiro.

Los mapas incluyen los nombres y la ubicación de gran número de ciudades, poblaciones menores, suburbios, e inclusive barrios y distritos de algunas de las ciudades más importantes. Las características físicas sobresalientes, e incluso algunas elevaciones con o sin nombre, están indicados para dar una impresión general de la topografía local. Se omitió sin embargo el relieve sombreado, lo cual permite mostrar detalles como ríos y arroyos, parques, pistas de aterrizaje, edificios y monumentos públicos notables y los nombres de las calles principales. También están marcados los límites territoriales de las ciudades más grandes. Para la interpretación de los símbolos usados en estos mapas, véanse Leyendas para Mapas.

Los mapas de las ciudades más importantes del mundo varían generalmente en escala, y hasta ahora no han sido consistentes ni en diseño ni en contenido. En esta sección hemos hecho un esfuerzo de presentar las distintas áreas metropolitanas en la forma más uniforme posible, para facilitar sus comparaciones. Para algunas ciudades (la mayoría de ellas en Asia), no fué posible obtener de las propias fuentes material adecuado para la inclusión de ciertos datos, tales como las mayores áreas industriales y los límites municipales.

Los mapas de áreas metropolitanas se presentan por regiones, a excepción de unos cuantos que aparecen yuxtapuestos para facilitar la comparación entre grandes capitales, o centros comerciales, o ciudades ubicadas en contextos físicos similares. Muchas ciudades de América y algunas ciudades de Europa, por su baja densidad de población y su área extensa, requieren mapas más grandes que los ocupados por ciudades asiáticas con poblaciones comparables. Al margen de cada mapa se anotaron el área total y la población de territorio representado, lo cual facilita también las comparaciones.

CETTE PARTIE COMPREND 60 cartes des principales zones métropolitaines à l'échelle du 1:300 000ᵉ. Les cartes représentent les principaux types d'occupation du sol des villes et de leurs environs, c'est-à-dire de toute la zone urbanisée, les principales zones industrielles, les parcs et réserves naturelles, et les régions boisées. Les aéroports sont aussi représentés ainsi que de nombreux éléments des réseaux routier et ferroviaire. Certains lieux particulièrement intéressants sont indiqués, tels que le quai des pêcheurs et la ville chinoise à San Francisco, le monument de la Bienvenue à Jakarta, le temple du Bouddha de Jade à Shanghai et la statue du Christ Rédempteur à Rio de Janeiro.

Les cartes permettent de localiser un grand nombre de villes, villages et banlieues, ainsi que des quartiers de grandes villes. Les caractéristiques topographiques nota-bles, comme les hauteurs sont indiquées même si elles ne portent pas de nom, pour donner une idée du site de l'aire métropolitaine. L'estompage du relief est omis cependant pour permettre de représenter cours d'eau, parcs, pistes d'envol des aéroports, monuments et bâtiments publics importants, noms des principales rues, ainsi que les limites municipales des grandes villes. (Pour la signification des symboles voir légende.)

En général, les échelles des cartes des grandes villes du monde varient considérablement, et jusqu'ici la présentation et le contenu de ces cartes n'étaient pas comparables. Dans cette partie de l'Atlas, un effort spécial a été fait pour représenter les diverses zones métropolitaines de manière aussi homogène que possible. Cependant, dans certains cas (en Asie notamment), les documents de base n'étaient pas assez complets pour qu'il fût possible d'inclure avec préci-sion des données comme les zones industrielles et les limites municipales.

L'ordre de présentation est régional, avec des exceptions quand, pour faciliter les comparaisons, de grandes capitales de grands centres industriels ou encore des villes possédant un même environnement naturel, sont juxtaposés. Beaucoup de villes américaines et quelques villes européennes ont une faible densité de population et une étendue considérable; elles requièrent, par conséquent, des cartes plus grandes que des villes asiatiques de population similaire. La superficie et la population de chaque carte sont indiquées dans la marge.

INTEGRAM ESTA SEÇÃO 60 mapas das áreas metropolitanas mais importantes do mundo, em escala de 1:300 000. Os mapas mostram os principais tipos de uso do solo em cada cidade e seus arredores, seja, a extensão total da zona urbanizada, as principais áreas industriais, os parques e reservas, e as áreas florestais. Mostram os aeroportos, e muitos detalhes das redes rodo e ferroviária. Indicam também pontos de interesse, selecionados, tais como o Cais dos Pescadores e o Bairro Chinês de San Francisco, o monumento de Boasvindas, em Jakarta, o templo do Buda de Jade, em Shanghai, e a Estátua do Cristo Redentor, no Rio de Janeiro.

Os mapas apresentam o nome e a localização de grande número de cidades, vilas e subúrbios, e incluem bairros das cidades mais importantes. Foram indicadas as características físicas principais, inclusive elevações, com ou sem nome, com o objetivo de proporcionar uma idéia geral da topografia local. No entanto, omitiu-se o sombreado do relevo, para permitir a indicação de detalhes tais como cursos d'água, parques, pistas de aeroportos, edifícios públicos e monumentos notáveis, e os nomes das principais ruas, bem como os limites municipais das grandes cidades. Para a interpretação dos símbolos usados nesses mapas, ver as *Legendas dos mapas*.

Os mapas das cidades mais importantes do mundo variam consideravelmente, de modo geral, quanto à escala, e até o presente não são comparáveis nem na forma de apresentação nem no conteúdo. Nesta seção, fez-se um esforço especial para representar as diversas áreas metropolitanas do modo mais uniforme e comparável possível. No entanto, para algumas cidades, a maioria das quais da Ásia, não foi possível obter fontes fidedignas de informações, tais como áreas industriais principais e limites municipais.

A ordem de apresentação dos mapas das áreas metropolitanas é geralmente regional, exceto em certos casos em que, para facilidade de comparação, capitais ou centros industriais e cidades importantes localizadas em meio físico semelhante foram justapostos. Muitas cidades da América e algumas da Europa, por sua baixa densidade demográfica e áreas mais extensas, exigem mapas maiores que as cidades asiáticas de população comparável. À margem de cada mapa indicam-se a área terrestre e a população total do território representado, também para maior facilidade de comparação.

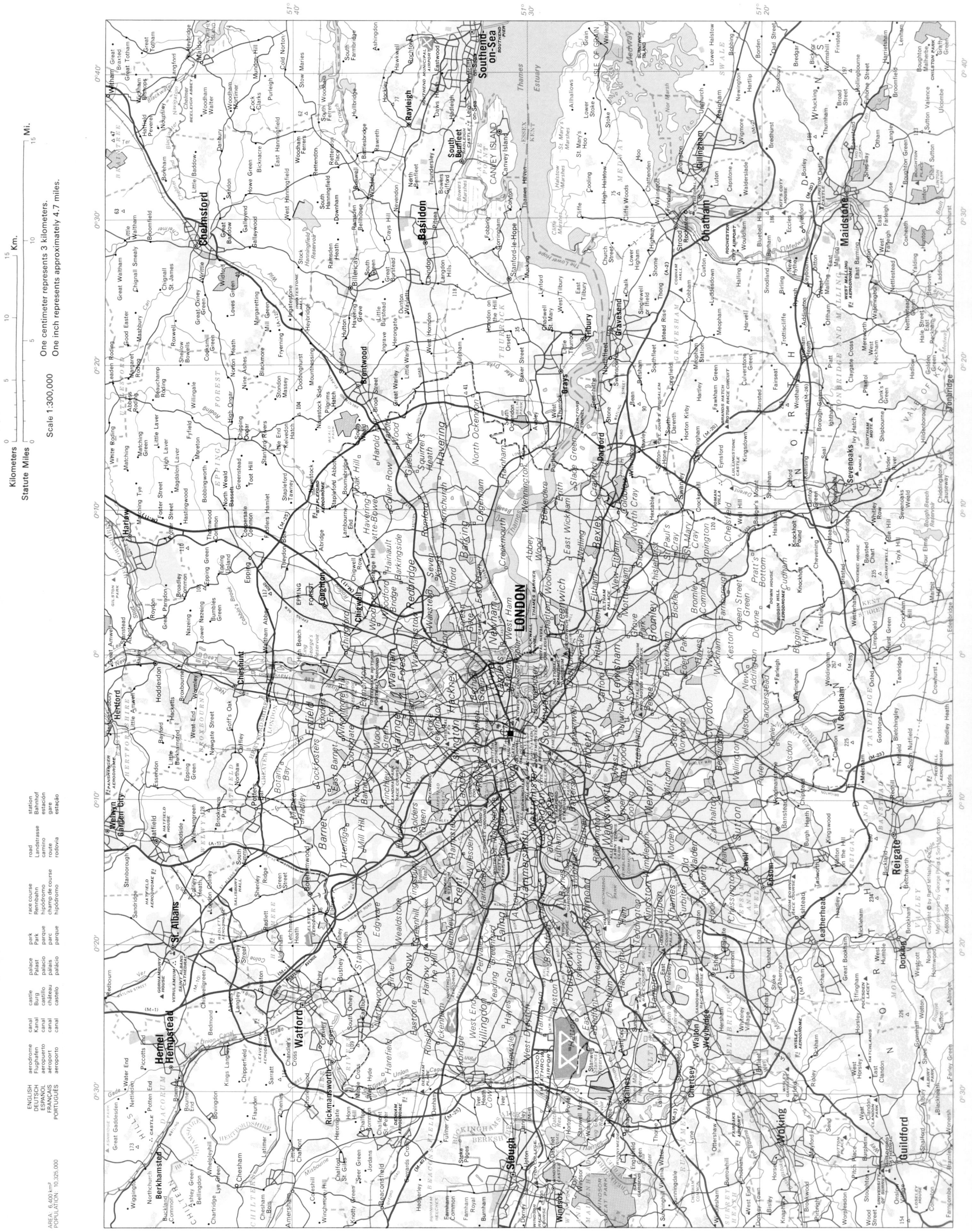

AREA 6,400 km²
POPULATION 10,325,000

Scale 1:300,000

One centimeter represents 3 kilometers.
One inch represents approximately 4.7 miles.

Kilometers

Statute Miles

ENGLISH	aerodrome	canal	castle	palace	park	race course	station
DEUTSCH	Flughafen	Kanal	Burg	Palast	Park	Rennbahn	Bahnhof
ESPAÑOL	aeropuerto	canal	castillo	palacio	parque	hipódromo	estación
FRANÇAIS	aéroport	canal	château	palais	parc	champ de course	gare
PORTUGUÊS	aeroporto	canal	castelo	palácio	parque	hipódromo	estação

road
Landstrasse
camino
route
rodovia

Scale 1:300,000

One centimeter represents 3 kilometers.
One inch represents approximately 4.7 miles.

Kilometers
Statute Miles

AREA 6,500 km²
POPULATION 9,800,000

FRANÇAIS	aérodrome	bois	château	étang	forêt	ruisseau
ENGLISH	airport	woods	castle	pond	forest	brook
DEUTSCH	Flughafen	Gehölz	Burg	Teich	Wald	Bach
ESPAÑOL	aeropuerto	bosques	castillo	charca	bosque	arroyo
PORTUGUÊS	aeroporto	bosques	castelo	lagoa	floresta	arroio

AREA: 5,650 km²
POPULATION: 6,275,000

ENGLISH	bank	canal	hill	moor	park	railway station	reservoir	tower
DEUTSCH	Bank	Kanal	Hügel	Ried	Park	Bahnhof	Stausee	Turm
ESPAÑOL	banco	canal	colina	páramo	parque	terminal ferroviaria	estanque	torre
FRANÇAIS	banc	canal	colline	lande	parc	gare	réservoir	tour
PORTUGUÊS	banco	canal	colina	charneca	parque	estação ferroviária	reservatório	torre

Kilometers 0 5 10 15 Km.
Statute Miles 0 5 10 15 Mi.
Scale 1:300,000
One centimeter represents 3 kilometers.
One inch represents approximately 4.7 miles.

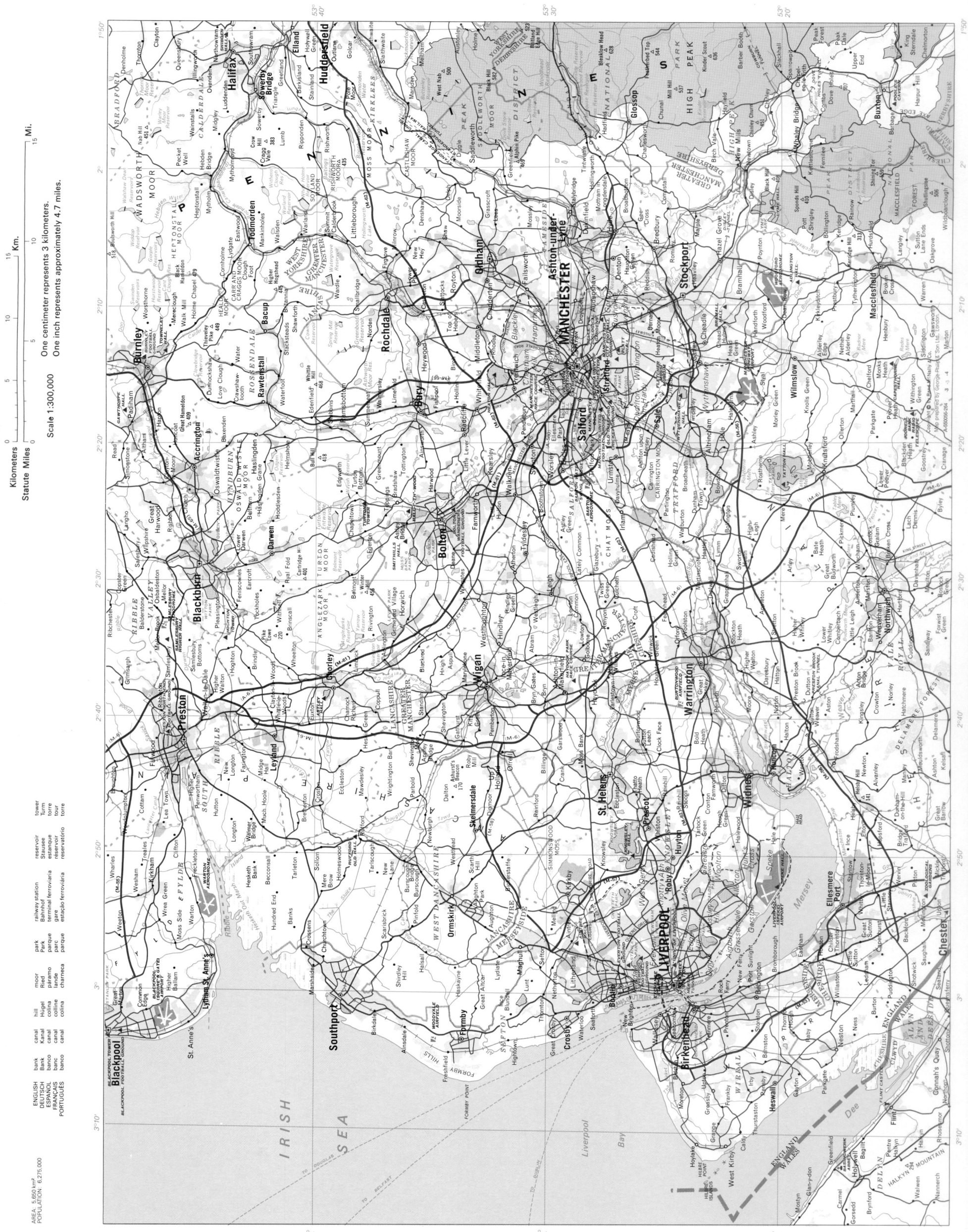
IRISH SEA
Liverpool Bay
Blackpool
Preston
Blackburn
Burnley
Accrington
Halifax
Huddersfield
Southport
Rochdale
Bury
Bolton
Wigan
Oldham
MANCHESTER
Salford
Ashton-under-Lyne
St. Helens
LIVERPOOL
Birkenhead
Warrington
Widnes
Runcorn
Stockport
Wilmslow
Macclesfield
Northwich
Ellesmere Port
Chester
Buxton
Glossop

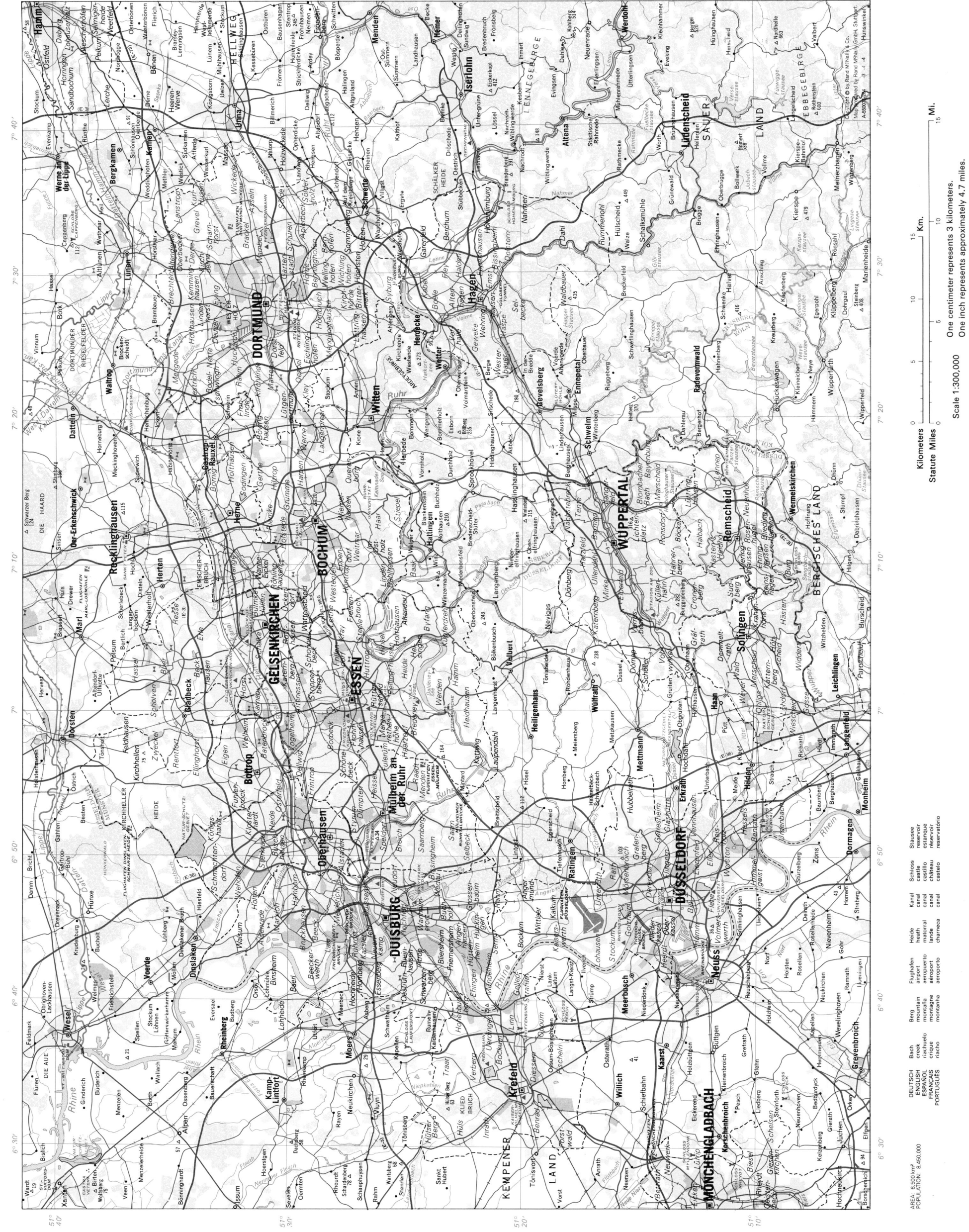

Scale 1:300,000

One centimeter represents 3 kilometers.
One inch represents approximately 4.7 miles.

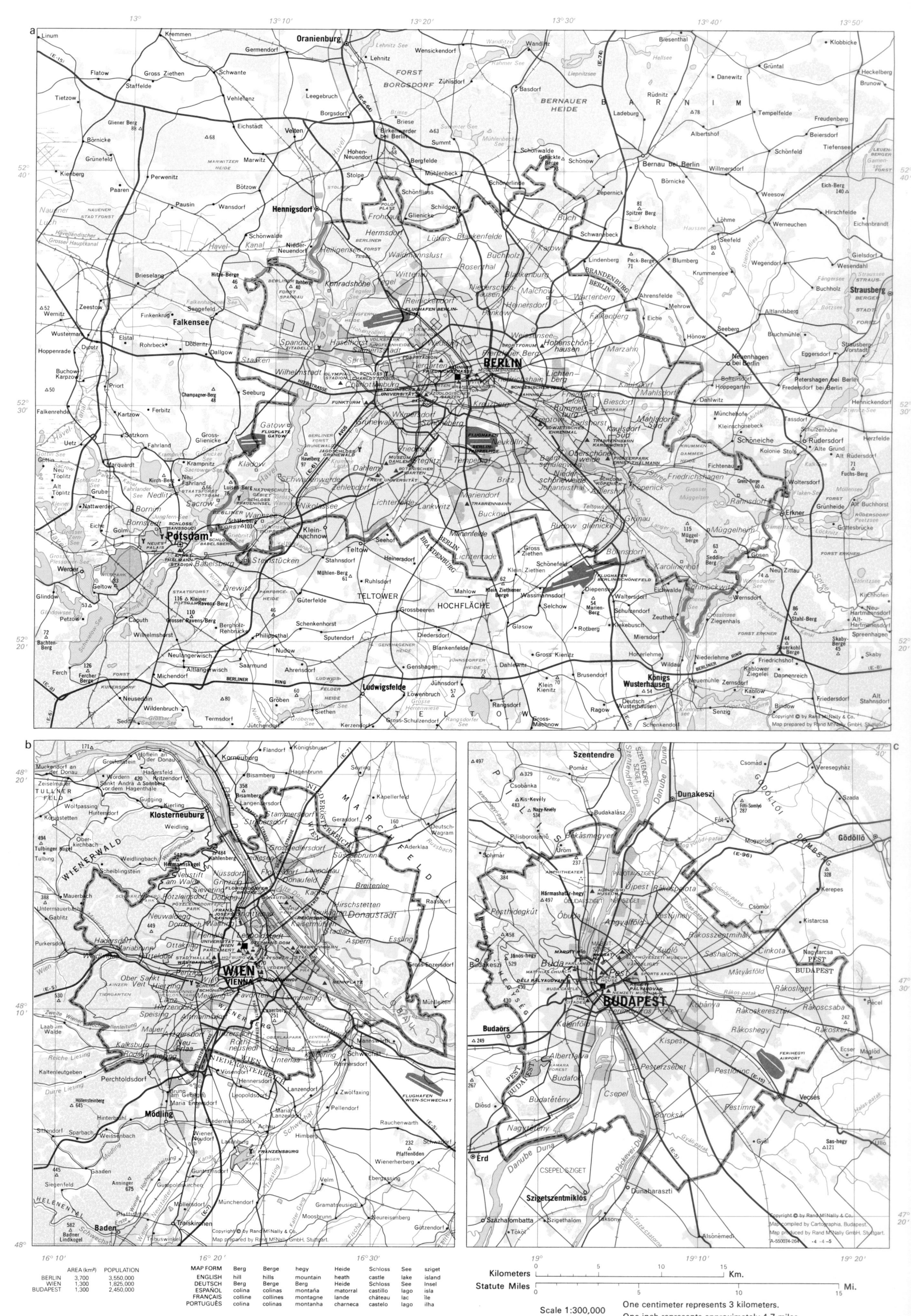

	AREA (km²)	POPULATION
BERLIN	3,700	3,550,000
WIEN	1,300	1,825,000
BUDAPEST	1,300	2,450,000

MAP FORM	Berg	Berge	hegy	Heide	Schloss	See	sziget
ENGLISH	hill	hills	mountain	heath	castle	lake	island
DEUTSCH	Berg	Berge	Berg	Heide	Schloss	See	Insel
ESPAÑOL	colina	colinas	montaña	matorral	castillo	lago	isla
FRANÇAIS	colline	collines	montagne	lande	château	lac	île
PORTUGUÊS	colina	colinas	montanha	charneca	castelo	lago	ilha

Kilometers

Statute Miles

Scale 1:300,000

One centimeter represents 3 kilometers.
One inch represents approximately 4.7 miles.

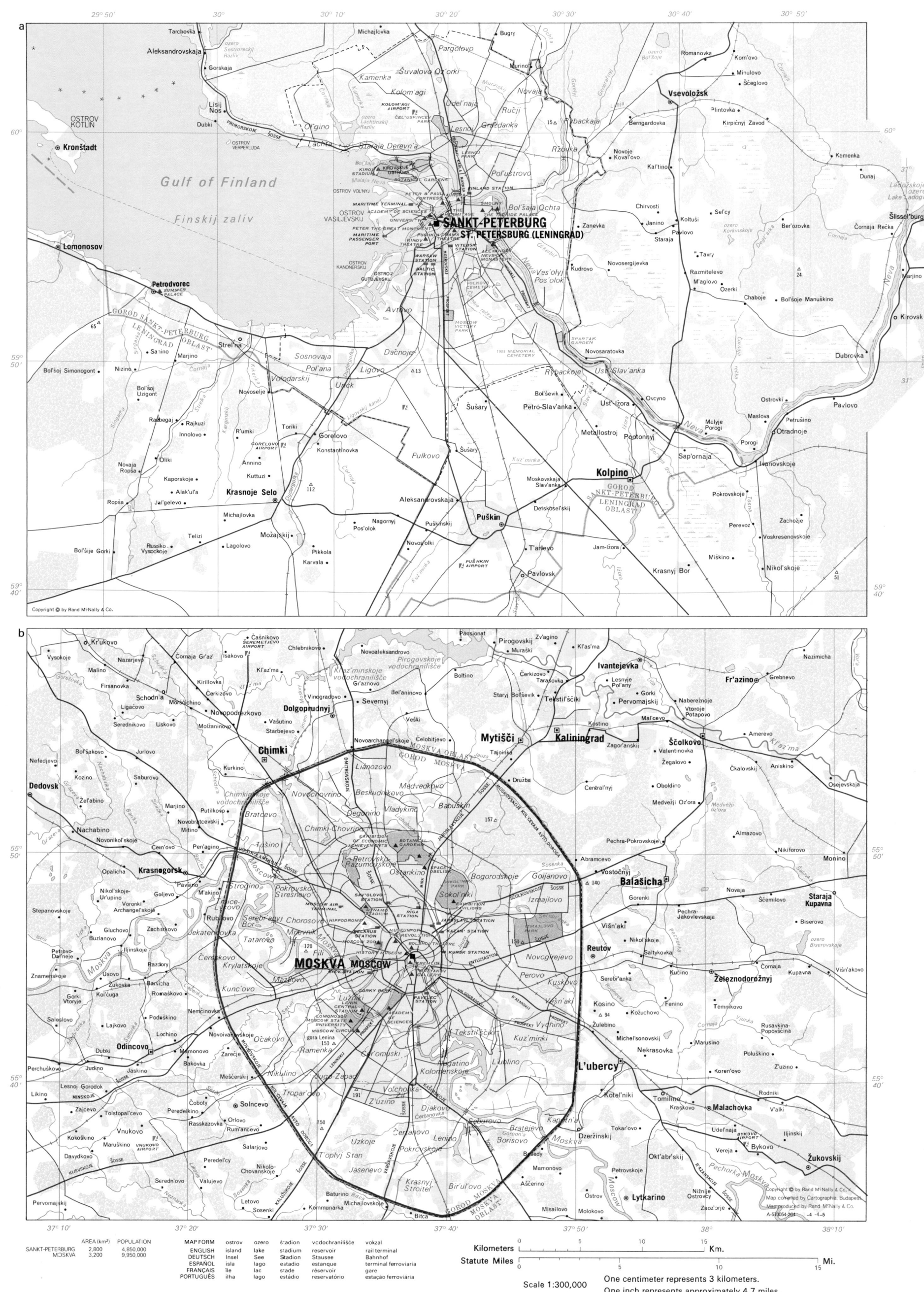

a

29° 50'   30°   30° 10'   30° 20'   30° 30'   30° 40'   30° 50'

Tarchovka
Aleksandrovskaja
Michajlovka
Bugry
Pargolovo
Romanovka
Kom'ovo
Gorskaja
Šuvalovo Oz'orki
Murino
Minulovo
Ščeglovo
OSTROV
KOTLIN
Kamenka
Kolom'agi
Udel'naja
Ručji
Novaja
Berngardovka
Kirpičnyj Zavod
Vsevoložsk
Kronštadt
Lisij
Nos
Dubki
KOLOM'AGI
AIRPORT
ozero
Lachtinskij
Razliv
ČEL'USPINCEV
PARK
Lesnoj Graždanka
15△
Arbackaja
Novoje
Koval'ovo
Kal'tino
Plintovka
Dunaj
Kamenka
Orgino
Lachta
Staraja Derevn'a
LESNOJ
PARK
Rž'ovka
Novoje
Seľco
Ber'ozovka
Čornaja Rečka
Šlissel'burg
Gulf of Finland
KIROV
STADIUM
KIROVSKOE
BOTANICAL GARDENS
FINLAND STATION
Pol'ustrovo
Chirvosti
Janino
Koltuši
ozero
Korkinskoe
Finskij zaliv
OSTROV VOLYNJ
PETER & PAUL
FORTRESS
SMOLNY
Bol'šaja Ochta
Zanevka
ozero
Ladožskoe
Lake Ladoga
MARITIME TERMINAL
ACADEM OF SCIENCES
UNIVERSI
PETER THE GREAT MONUMENT
Kudrovo
Novosergijevka
Razmitelevo
△24
Lomonosov
OSTROV VASIL'EVSKIJ
PETER THE GREAT
MONUMENT
SANKT-PETERBURG
ST. PETERSBURG (LENINGRAD)
Vas'olyj Pos'olok
M'aglovo
Ozerki
Marjino
Chaboje
Bol'šoje Manuškino
K'rovsk
Petrodvorec
SUMMER
PALACE
OSTROV KANONERSKIJ
WARSAW
STATION
BALTIC
STATION
VOLKOVO
CEMETERY
Neva
Novosaratovka
Dubrovka
GOROD SANKT-PETERBURG
LENINGRAD OBLAST'
65△
Strel'na
Avtovo
MOSCOW
VICTORY
PARK
1905 MEMORIAL
CEMETERY
SPARTAK
GARDEN
Rybackoje
Ust' Slav'anka
Ostrovki
Pavlovo
59° 50'
Bol'šoj Simonogont
Nizino
Sašino
Marjino
Sosnovaja
Pol'ana
Ligovo
Dačnoje
Urick
△13
Volodarskij
Bol'ševik
Ust' Ižora
Ovcyno
Petrušino
Otradnoje
Porogi
Bol'šoj Uzigont
Novoselje
Šušary
Petro-Slav'anka
Metallostroj
Malyje Porogi
Maslova
Razbegaj
Rajkuzi
R'umki
Toriki
Gorelovo
Pulkovo
Šušary
Poptonnyj
Sapornaja
Ivanovskoje
Innolovo
GORELOVO
AIRPORT
Konstantinovka
Kuz' minka
Moskovskaja
Slav'anka
Kolpino
Pokrovskoje
Zachozje
Novaja
Ropsa
Oliki
Kaporskoje
Annino
Kuttuzi
Aleksanarovskaja
Detskosel'skij
GOROD SANKT-PETERBURG
LENINGRAD OBLAST'
Perevoz
Ropša
Jal'gelevo
Alak'ul'a
△112
Krasnoje Selo
Michajlovka
Nagornyj
Pos'olok
Puškinskij
Puškin
T'arlevo
Jam-Ižora
Voskresenovskoje
Bol'šije Gorki
Russko-Vysockoje
Telizi
Možajskij
Novos'olki
Miškino
Nikol'skoje
Lagolovo
Pikkola
Karvala
PUŠKIN
AIRPORT
Krasnyj Bor
Pavlovsk
△51

Copyright © by Rand McNally & Co.

b

37° 10'   37° 20'   37° 30'   37° 40'   37° 50'   38°   38° 10'

Kr'ukovo
Čašnikovo
ŠEREMETJEVO
AIRPORT
Chlebnikovo
Novoaleksandrovo
Pansionat
Pirogovskoje
Zv'agino
Pirogovskoje
vodochranilišče
Vysokoje
Nazarjevo
Čornaja Gr'az'
Isakovo
Mel'niki
Piri
Muraški
Kl'as'ma
Nazimicha
Malino
Firsanovka
Kirillovka
Knäž'minskoje
vodochranilišče
Gr'aznovo
Boltino
Čerkizovo
Tarasovka
Staryj Bol'ševik
Lesnyje Pol'any
Gorki
Pervomajskij
Ivantejevka
Grebnevo
Fr'azino
Schodn'a
Morščichino
Čerkizovo
Vinogradovo
Severnyj
Žel'aninov
Textil'ščiki
Naberežnoje
Vtoroje
Potapovo
Ligacovo
Srednikovo
Liskovo
Novopodrezkovo
Vašutino
Starbejevo
Veški
Kostino
Mal'cevo
Amerevo
Ščolkovo
Dolgoprudnyj
Molžaninovo
Novoarchangel'skoje
Čelobitjevo
GOROD MOSKVA
Mytišči
Kaliningrad
Zagor'anskij
Valentinovka
Oboldino
Čkalovskij
Aniskino
Nefedjevo
Bol'šovo
Jurlovo
Kurkino
Lianozovo
MOSKVA OBLAST'
Tajomino
Družba
Central'nyj
Medveži
oz'ora
Almazovo
Dedovsk
Kozino
Saburovo
Chimkinskoje
vodochranilišče
Novochovrino
Beskudnikovo
Medvedkovo
Babuškin
157△
Pechra-Pokrovskoje
Nikiforovo
Žel'abino
Marjino
Putilkovo
Bratcevo
Chimki-Chovrino
Degonino
Vladykino
Monino
Nachabino
Novobratcevskij
Mitino
EXHIBITION OF ECONOMIC ACHIEVEMENTS
BOTANICAL GARDENS
Abramcevo
△140
Novonikol'skoje
Čern'ovo
Pen'agino
Tušino
Petrovsko
Razumovskoje
Ostankino
SPACE
OBELISK
Bogorodskoje
Gojanovo
Vostočnyj
Balašicha
Opalicha
Krasnogorsk
Pavšino
M'akino
Strogino
Pokrovskoje
Streshnevo
SAV'OLOVO
STATION
Sokol'niki
Izmajlovo
Gorenki
Novaja
Ščemilovo
Staraja
Kupavna
Nikol'skoje-
Ur'upino
Voronki
Archangel'skoje
MOSCOW AIR
TERMINAL
DYNAMO
STADIUM
RIGA
STATION
JAROSLAVL'
STATION
KAZAN STATION
Višn'aki
Nikol'skoje
Saltykovka
Biserovo
Stepanovskoje
Rublovo
Chorosovo
HIPPODROME
KRESTOVSKY
Perovo
Kuskovo
Serebr'anka
Kučino
Železnodorožnyj
Serebr'anyj
Bor
Mnevnik
BELORUS
STATION
DRUZ' MOSCOW ZOO
HISTORY MUSEUM
MUZIMPORT
KIEV
STATION
KURSK STATION
Novogirejevo
Višn'akovo
Jekaterovka
Tatarovo
△120
Fili
MOSKVA
MOSKVA
REKA STATION
KREMLIN
BOLSHOI THEATRE
ENTUZIASTOV ŠOSSE
Reutov
Kosino
Fenino
Temnikovo
Rusavkina-
Popovščina
Čerebkovo
Krylatskoje
Kunc'ovo
GORKY PARK
PAVELEC STATION
150△
Kuz'minki
Kožuchovo
Žulebino
Michel'sonovskij
Marusino
Mežovo
Razdory
Romaškovo
LENIN
CENTRAL
STADIUM
LOMONOSOV STATE
UNIVERSITY
ACADEM OF SCIENCES
△94
Nekrasovka
Poluškino
Gorki
Vtoryje
Kol'cuga
Novoivankovskoje
Očakovo
gora Lenina
MOSCOW CIRCUS
153△
L'ubercy
Koren'ovo
Z'uzino
Saloslovo
Lajkovo
Lochino
Zarečje
Bakovka
Mešcerskij
Ramenka
Jugo-Zapad
Ljublino
Odincovo
Dubki
Mamonovo
Nikulino
Tropar'ovo
Bratejevo
Saburovo
Kapotn'a
Malachovka
Perchuškovo
Judino
Jaskino
Volchonka
△191
Leščanovo
Kotel'niki
Tomilina
BYKOVO
AIRPORT
Likino
Lesnoj Gorodok
Peredelkino
Orlovo
Rum'ancevo
△250
Čertanovo
Lenino
Djakovo
Dzeržinskij
Kraskovo
Iljinskij
Davydkovo
Kokoškino
Maruškino
VNUKOVO
AIRPORT
Uzkoje
Pokrovskoje
Gorod Moskva
Ostrov
Okt'abr'skij
Vereja
Bykovo
Pervomajskij
Vnukovo
Solncevo
Toplyj Stan
Jasenevo
Krasnyj
Stroitel'
Bir'ulovo
Mamonovo
Aščerino
Tokar'ovo
Lytkarino
Misajlovo
Molokovo
Žukovskij

Copyright © by Rand McNally & Co.
Map covered by Cartographia, Budapest
Map produced by Rand McNally & Co.
A-570054-266   4-4-5

	AREA (km²)	POPULATION
SANKT-PETERBURG	2,800	4,850,000
MOSKVA	3,200	9,950,000

MAP FORM					
	ostrov	ozero	s'adion	vcdochranilišče	vokzal
ENGLISH	island	lake	stadium	reservoir	rail terminal
DEUTSCH	Insel	See	Stadion	Stausee	Bahnhof
ESPAÑOL	isla	lago	estadio	estanque	terminal ferroviaria
FRANÇAIS	île	lac	stade	réservoir	gare
PORTUGUÊS	ilha	lago	estádio	reservatório	estação ferroviária

Kilometers   0   5   10   15
Statute Miles   0   5   10   15

Km.
Mi.

Scale 1:300,000

One centimeter represents 3 kilometers.
One inch represents approximately 4.7 miles.

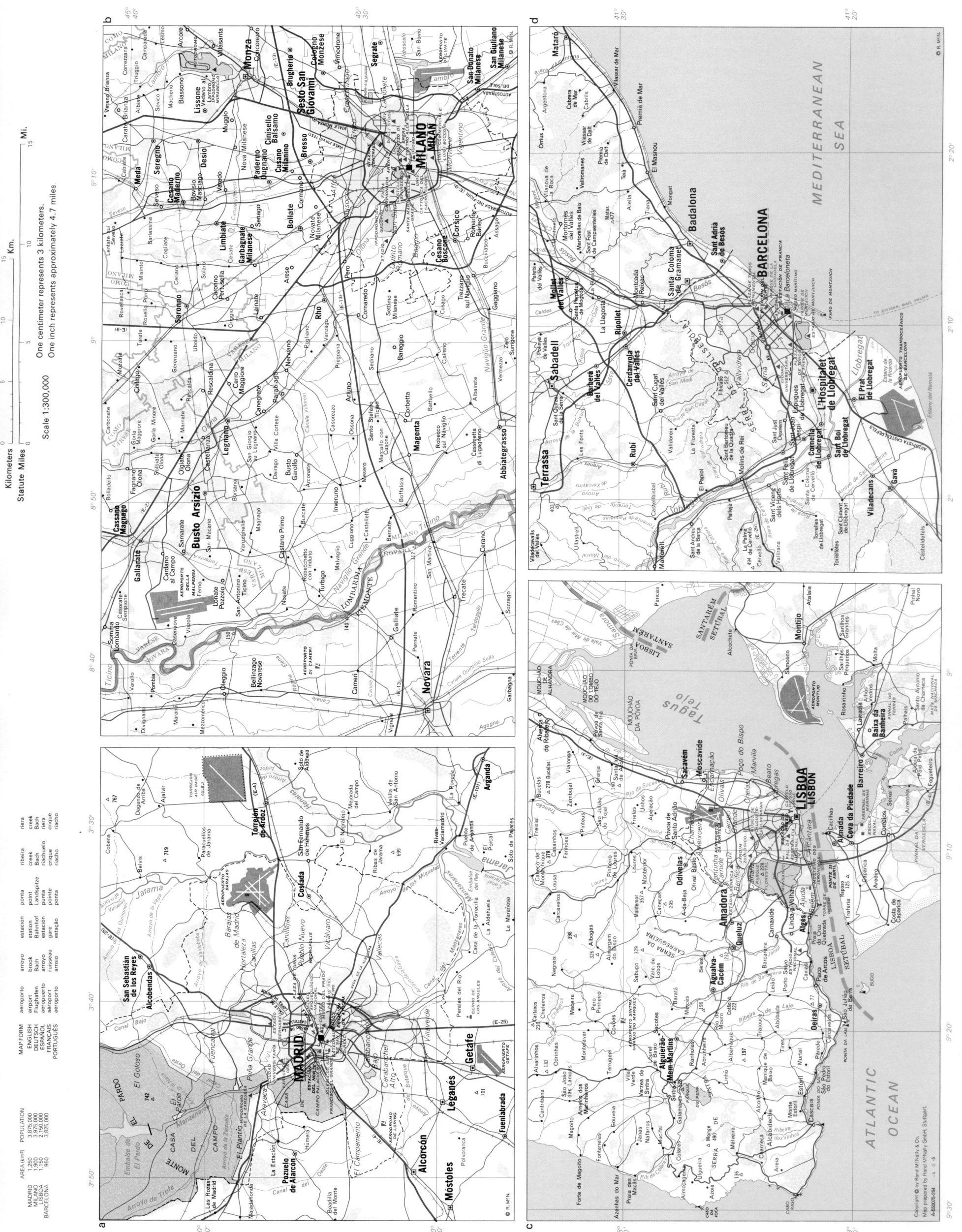

Kilometers
Statute Miles

Scale 1:300,000

One centimeter represents 3 kilometers.
One inch represents approximately 4.7 miles.

MAP FORM
ENGLISH
DEUTSCH
ESPAÑOL
FRANÇAIS
PORTUGUÊS

	aeropuerto	arroyo	estación	punta	ribeira
	airport	brook	station	point	creek
	Flughafen	Bach	Bahnhof	Landspitze	Bach
	aeropuerto	arroyo	estación	punta	riachuelo
	aéroport	ruisseau	gare	pointe	crique
	aeroporto	arroio	estação	ponta	riacho

		riera
		creek
		Bach
		riera
		crique
		riacho

	AREA (km²)	POPULATION
MADRID	1,250	3,875,000
MILANO	1,900	3,975,000
LISBOA	1,550	3,150,000
BARCELONA	1,950	3,325,000

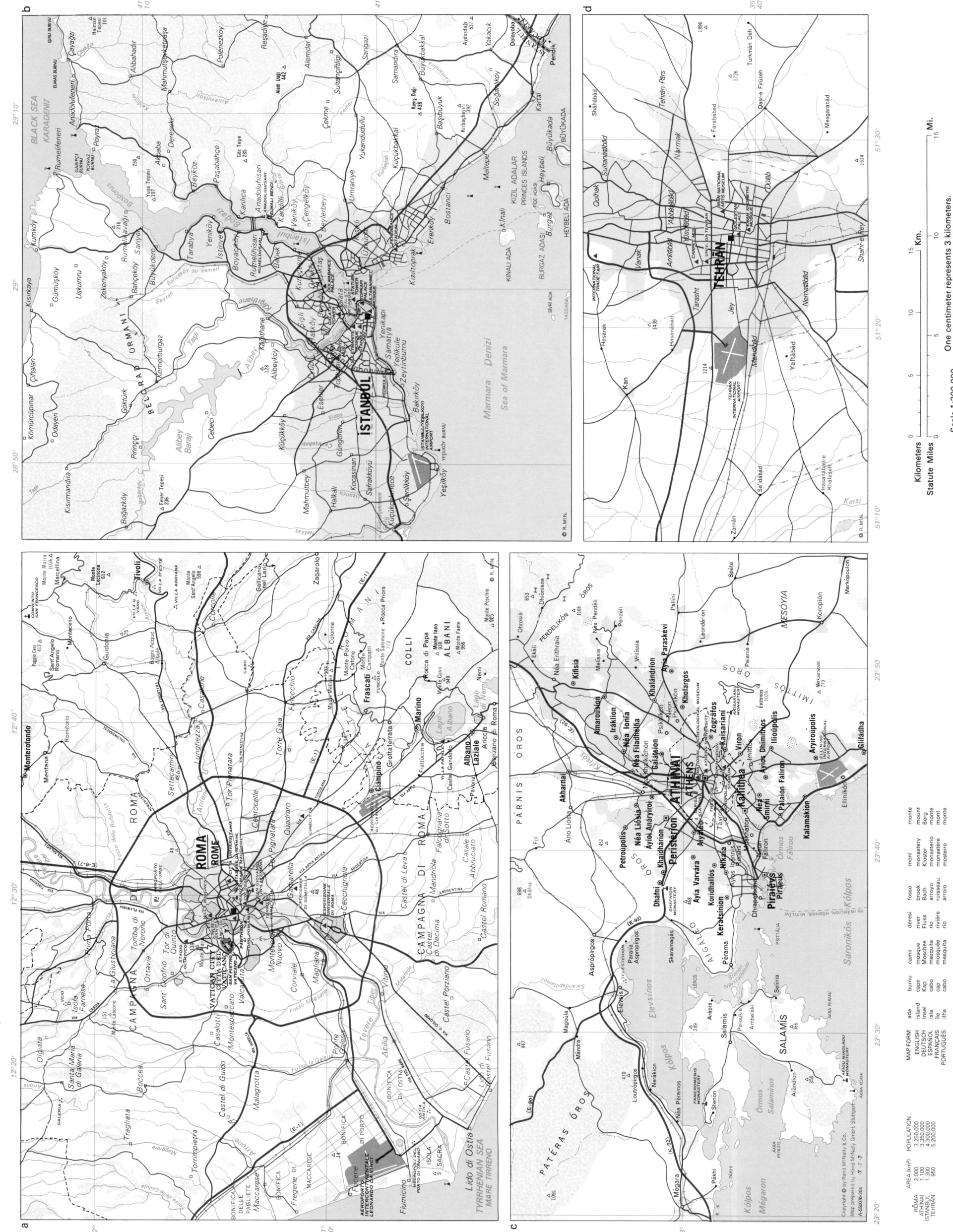

Scale 1:300,000

Kilometers
Km.

Statute Miles
Mi.

One centimeter represents 3 kilometers.
One inch represents approximately 4.7 miles.

Copyright © by Rand McNally & Co.
Map prepared by Hand McNally GmbH, Stuttgart.
A-550026-264   -7 - 7 -7

	AREA (km²)	POPULATION
RŌMA	2,000	3,250,000
ATHÍNAI	1,100	3,360,000
İSTANBUL	1,300	4,300,000
TEHRĀN	950	5,200,000

MAP FORM						
ENGLISH	island	cape	mosque	river	brook	mount	monastery
DEUTSCH	Insel	Kap	Moschee	Fluss	Bach	Berg	Kloster
ESPAÑOL	isla	cabo	mezquita	rio	arroyo	monte	monasterio
FRANÇAIS	île	cap	mosquée	rivière	ruisseau	mont	monastère
PORTUGUÊS	ilha	cabo	mesquita	rio	arroio	monte	mosteiro
	ada	burnu	camii	deresi	fosso	moni	

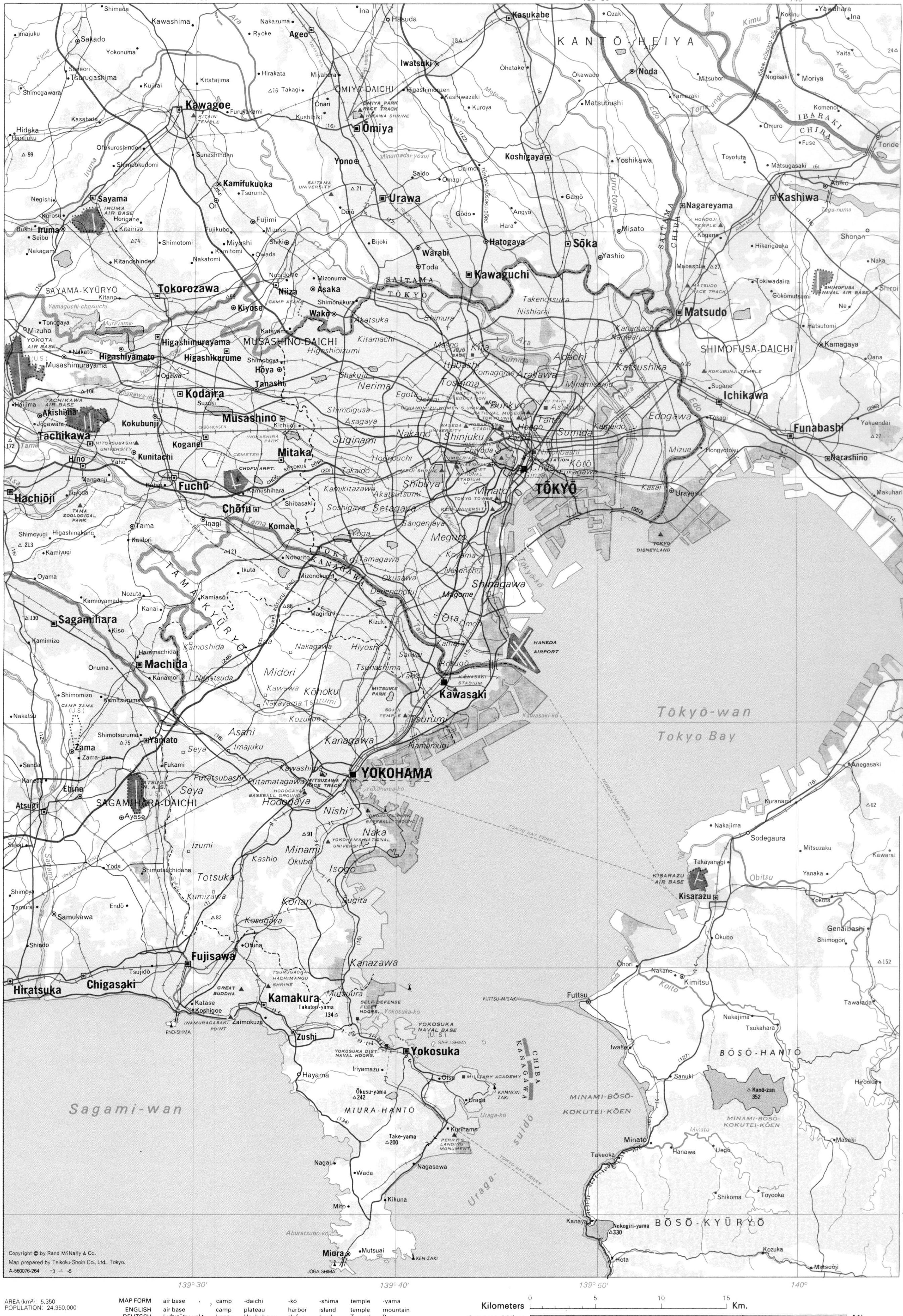

AREA (km²): 5,350
POPULATION: 24,350,000

MAP FORM	air base	camp	-daichi	-kō	-shima	temple	-yama
ENGLISH	air base	camp	plateau	harbor	island	temple	mountain
DEUTSCH	Luftstützpunkt	Lager	Hochebene	Hafen	Insel	Tempel	Berg
ESPAÑOL	base aérea	campo	meseta	puerto	isla	templo	montaña
FRANÇAIS	base aérienne	camp	plateau	port	île	temple	montagne
PORTUGUÊS	base aérea	campo	planalto	porto	ilha	templo	montanha

Kilometers 0 5 10 15 Km.
Statute Miles 0 5 10 15 Mi.

Scale 1:300,000

One centimeter represents 3 kilometers.
One inch represents approximately 4.7 miles.

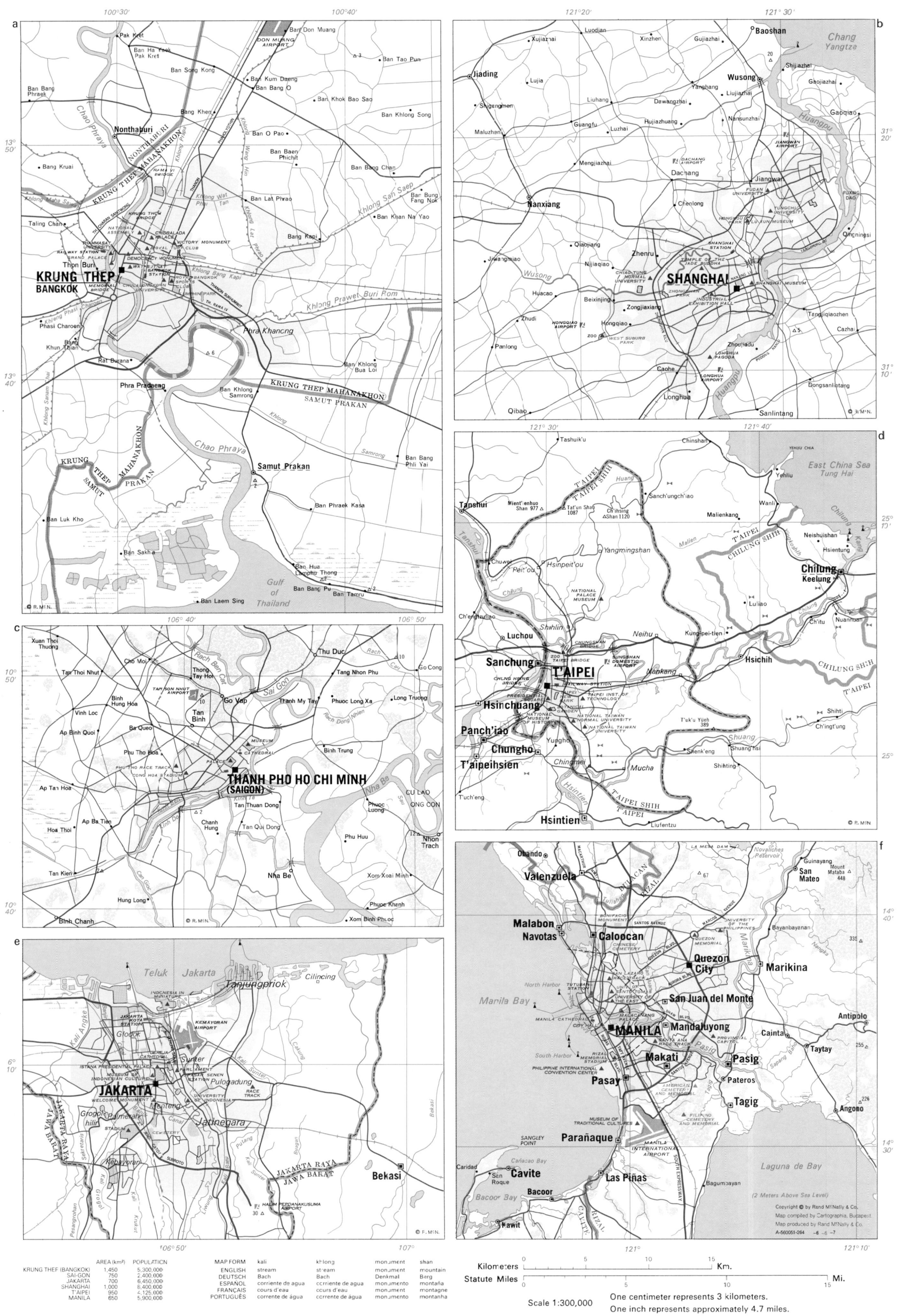

	AREA (km²)	POPULATION
KRUNG THEP (BANGKOK)	1,450	5,300,000
SAI-GON	750	2,400,000
JAKARTA	700	6,450,000
SHANGHAI	1,900	6,400,000
T'AIPEI	960	4,125,000
MANILA	650	5,900,000

MAP FORM	kali	khlong	monument	shan
ENGLISH	stream	stream	monument	mountain
DEUTSCH	Bach	Bach	Denkmal	Berg
ESPAÑOL	corriente de agua	corriente de agua	monumento	montaña
FRANÇAIS	cours d'eau	cours d'eau	monument	montagne
PORTUGUÊS	corrente de água	corrente de água	monumento	montanha

Kilometers

Statute Miles

Scale 1:300,000

One centimeter represents 3 kilometers.
One inch represents approximately 4.7 miles.

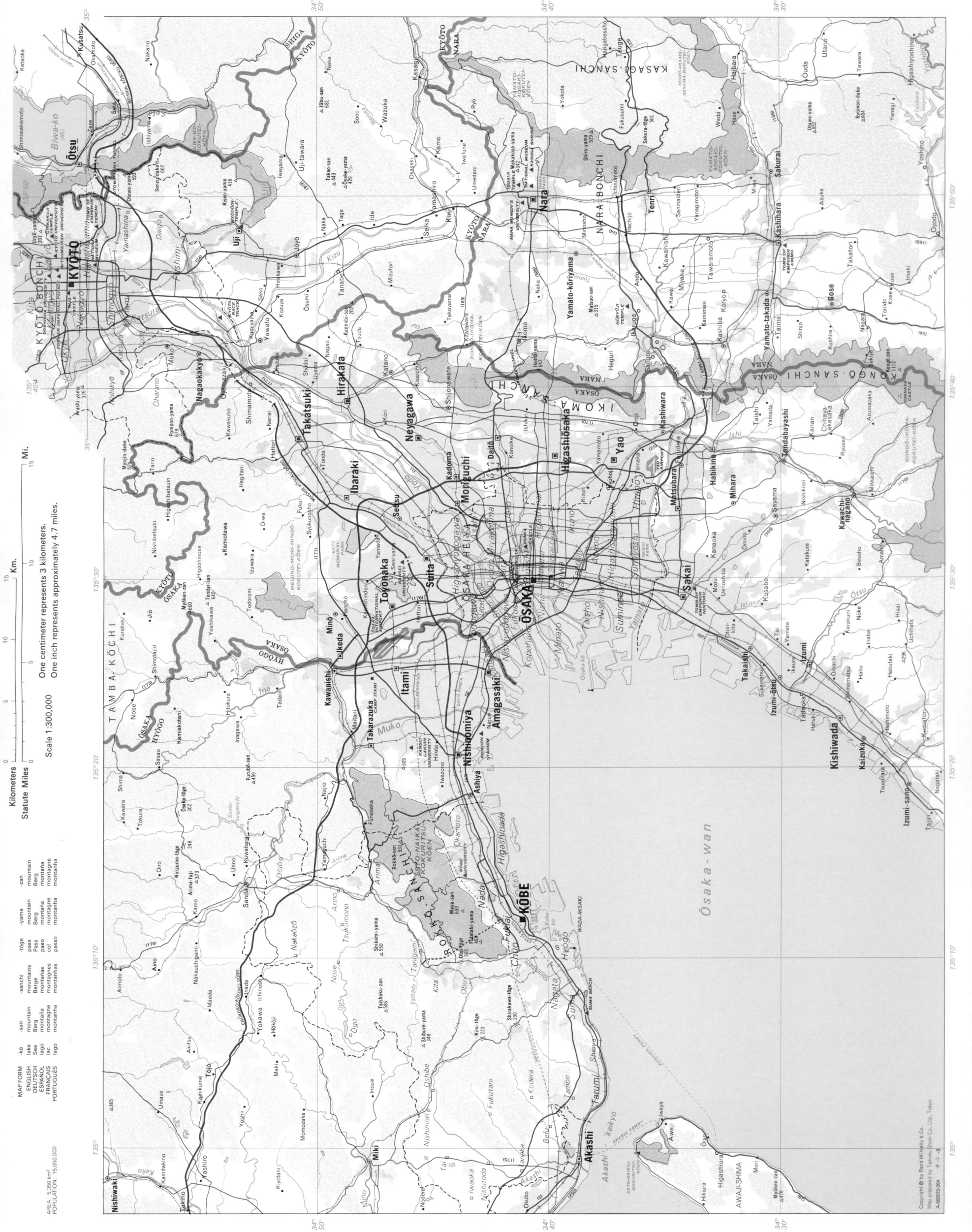

AREA 5,350 km²
POPULATION 15,050,000

Scale 1:300,000
One centimeter represents 3 kilometers.
One inch represents approximately 4.7 miles.

Kilometers

Statute Miles

MAP FORM				
ENGLISH	-kō lake	-san mountain	-yama mountain	-sanchi mountains	-tōge pass	-zan mountain
DEUTSCH	See	Berg	Berg	Berge	Pass	Berg
ESPAÑOL	lago	montaña	montaña	montañas	paso	montaña
FRANÇAIS	lac	montagne	montagne	montagnes	col	montagne
PORTUGUÊS	lago	montanha	montanha	montanhas	passo	montanha

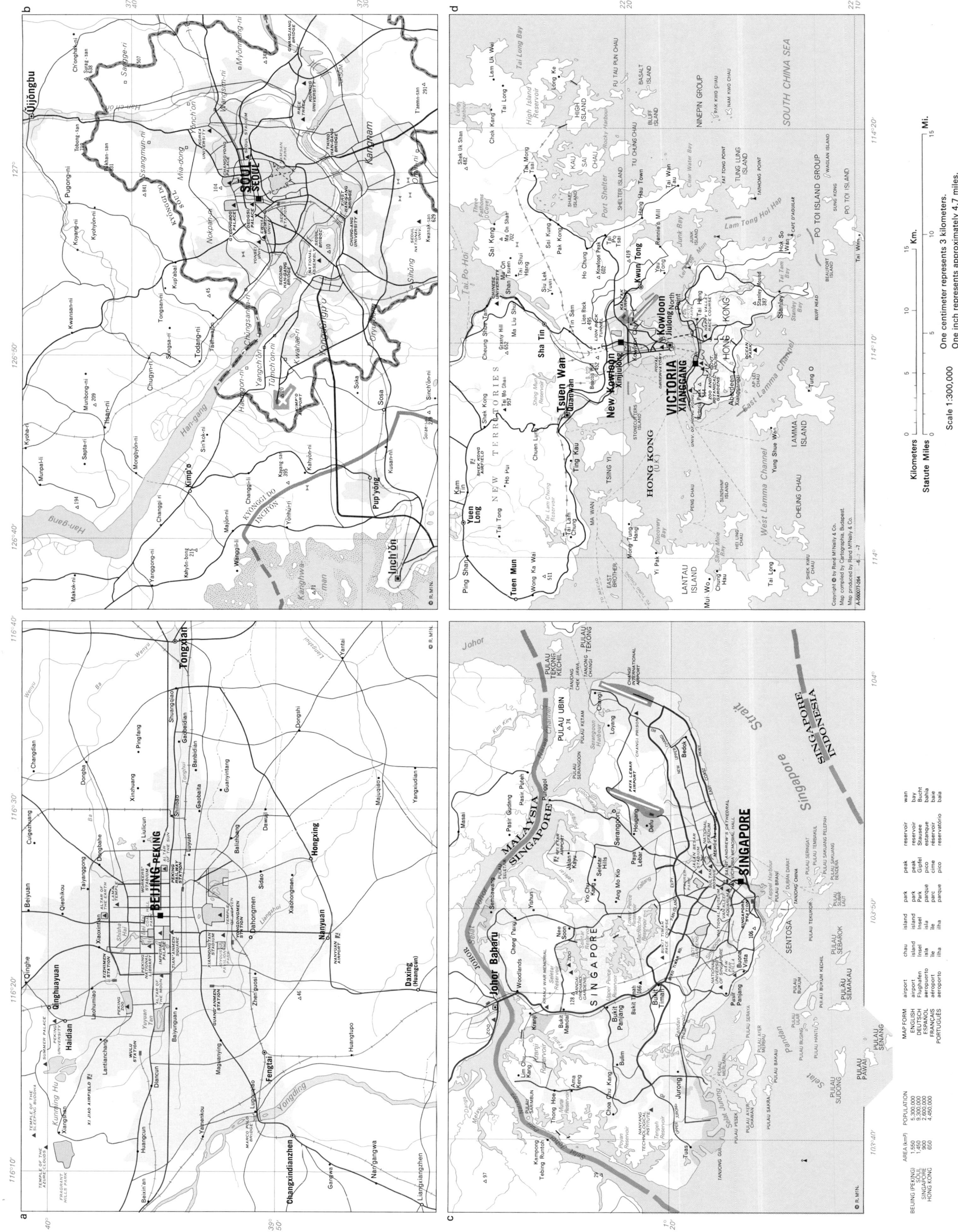

Scale 1:300,000

One centimeter represents 3 kilometers.
One inch represents approximately 4.7 miles.

Kilometers 0 5 10 15 Km.

Statute Miles 0 5 10 15 Mi.

Scale 1:300,000

One centimeter represents 3 kilometers.
One inch represents approximately 4.7 miles.

	AREA (km²)	POPULATION
DELHI	1,400	5,500,000
BOMBAY	1,050	8,250,000
CALCUTTA	3,100	11,200,000

ENGLISH	airport	dock	island	lake	point	railroad station	road	temple
DEUTSCH	Flughafen	Dock	Insel	See	Punkt	Bahnhof	Landstrasse	Tempel
ESPAÑOL	aeropuerto	muelle	isla	lago	punta	terminal ferroviaria	camino	templo
FRANÇAIS	aéroport	quai	île	lac	pointe	gare	route	temple
PORTUGUÊS	aeroporto	cais	ilha	lago	ponta	estação ferroviária	rodovia	templo

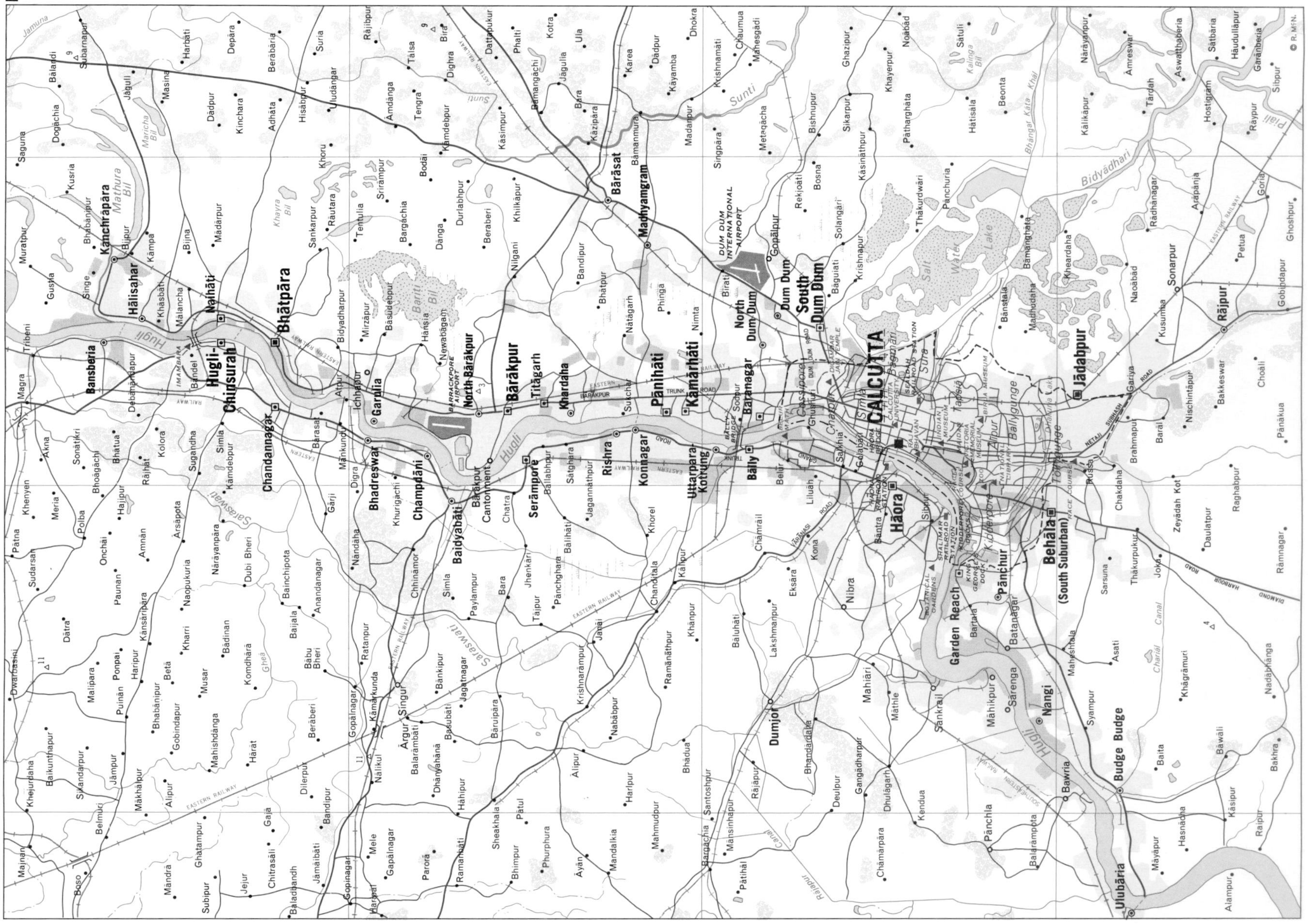

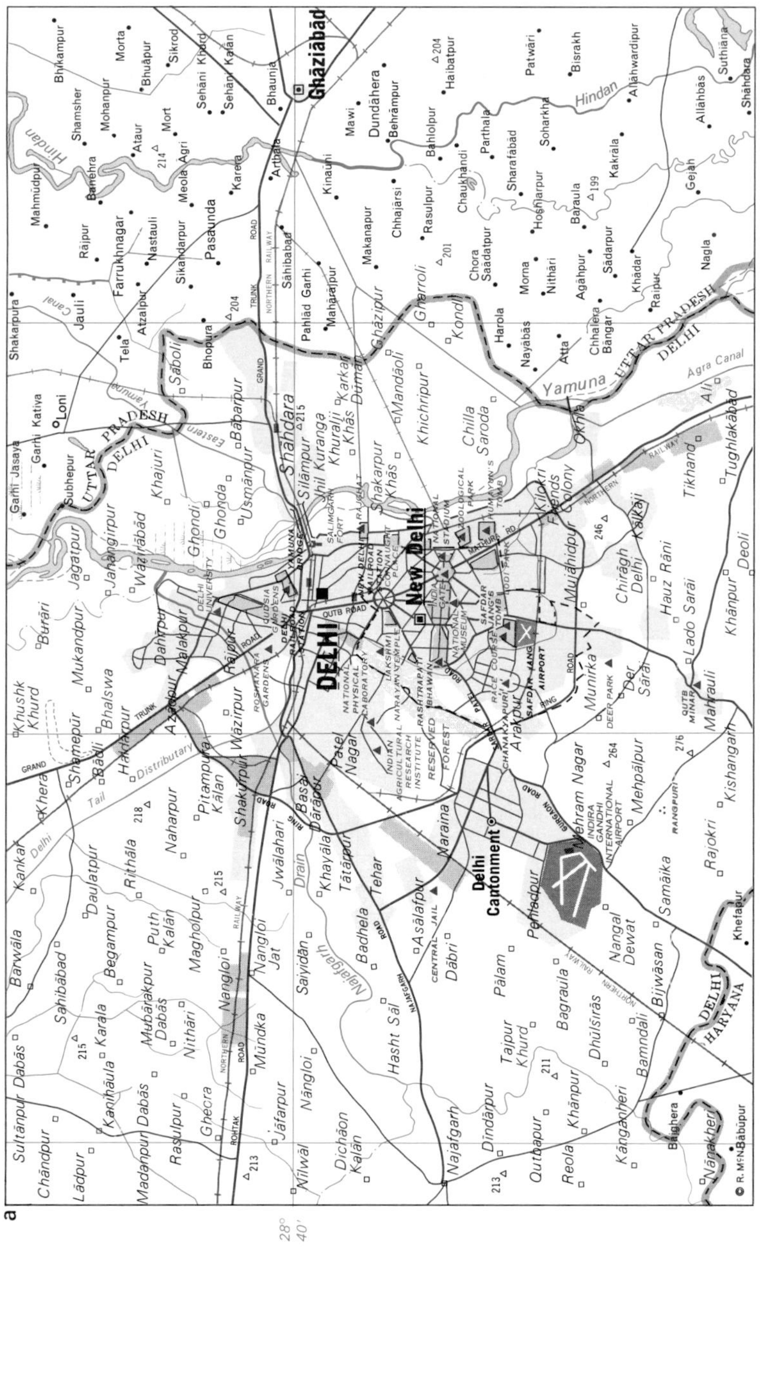

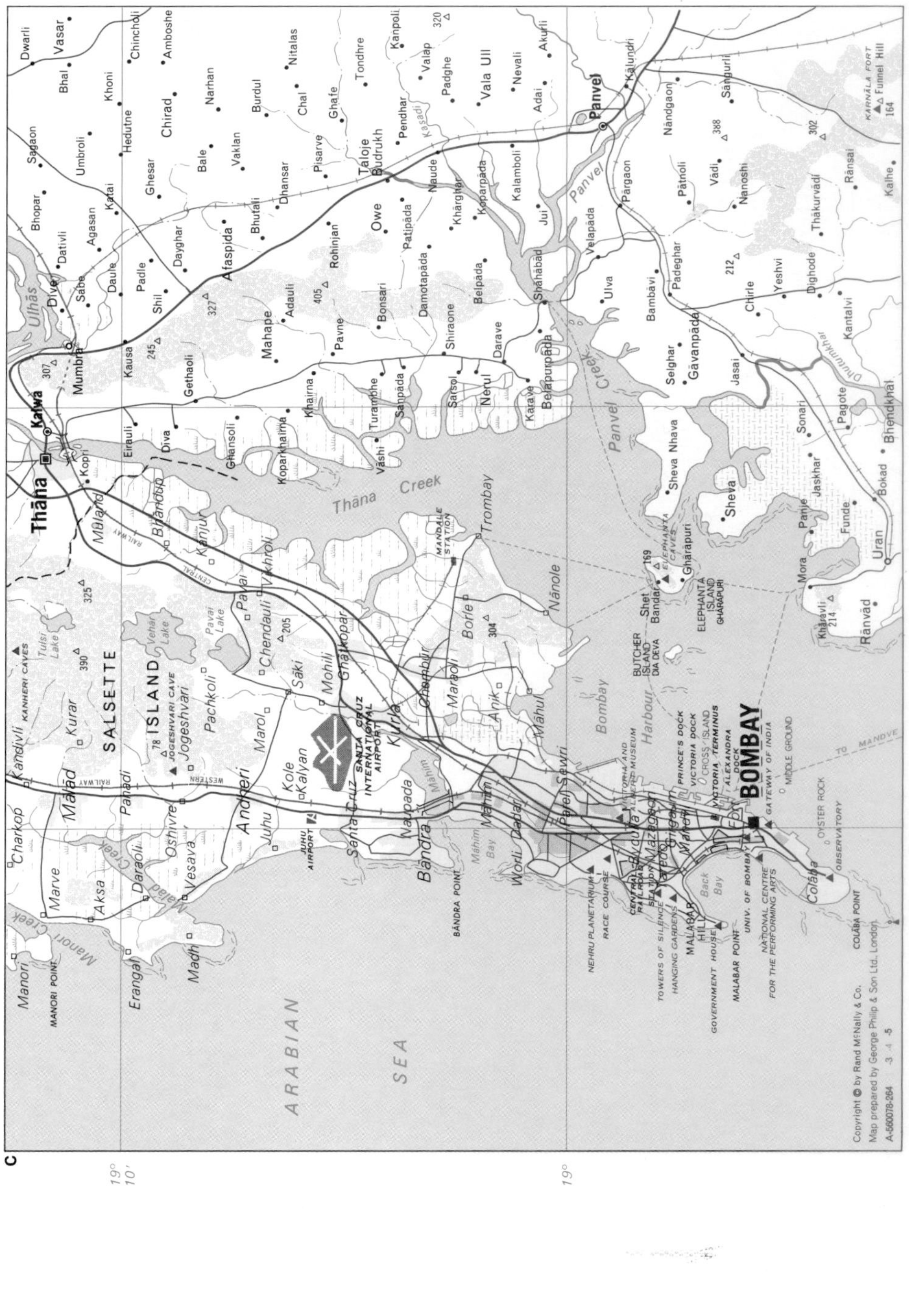

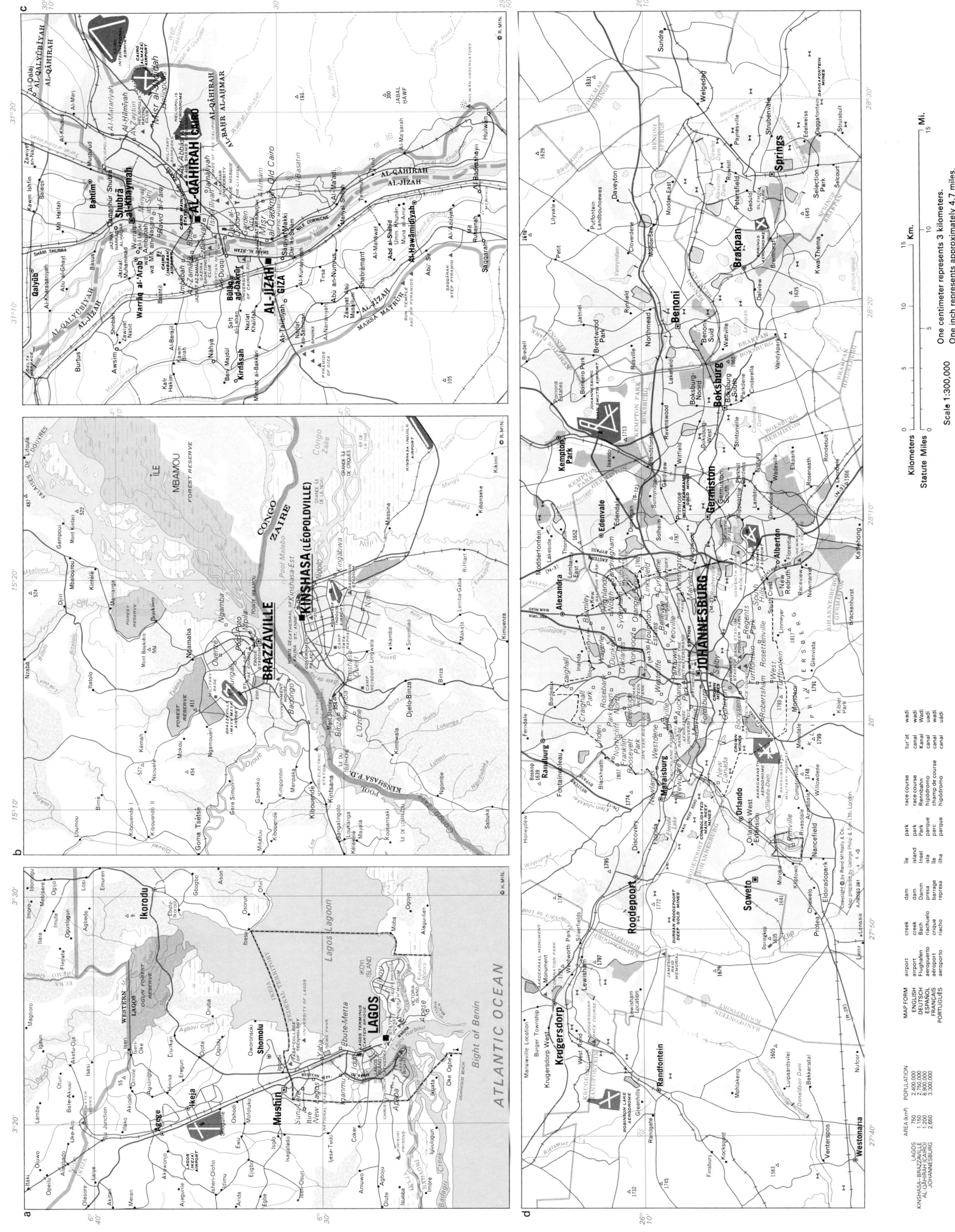

			MAP FORM						
airport	creek	dam	île	park	race course	tur'at	wadi
airport	creek	dam	island	park	race course	canal	wadi
Flughafen	Bach	Damm	Insel	Park	Rennbahn	Kanal	Wadi
aeropuerto	riachuelo	presa	isla	parque	hipódromo	canal	uadi
aeroport	crique	barrage	île	parc	champ de course	canal	wadi
aeroporto	riacho	represa	ilha	parque	hipódromo	canal	uádi

	AREA (km²)	POPULATION
LAGOS	750	2.400.000
KINSHASA—BRAZZAVILLE	1.150	2.750.000
AL-QĀHIRAH (CAIRO)	1.200	8.900.000
JOHANNESBURG	2.660	3.300.000

Scale 1:300,000

Kilometers
Statute Miles

One centimeter represents 3 kilometers.
One inch represents approximately 4.7 miles.

Km.

Mi.

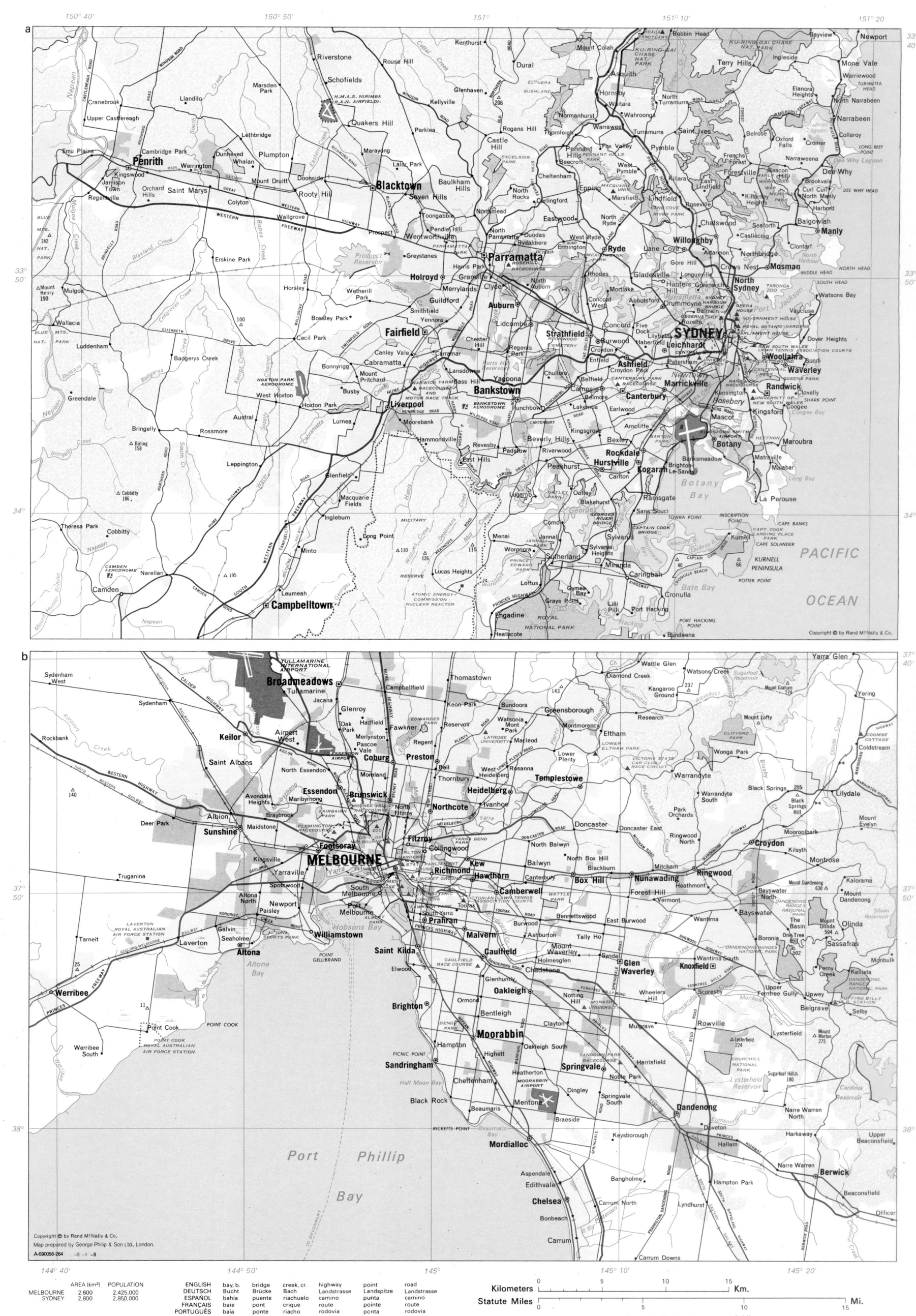

a

150° 40'   150° 50'   151°   151° 10'   151° 20'

33° 40'

Newport
Bayview
Ingleside
Mona Vale
Warriewood
Elanora Heights
North Narrabeen
Narrabeen
Collaroy
LONG REEF POINT
DEE WHY HEAD
Dee Why Lagoon

Kenthurst
Riverstone
Rouse Hill
Dural
Mount Colah
Bobbin Head
KU-RING-GAI CHASE NAT. PARK
Terry Hills
Frenchs Forest
Belrose
Cromer

Schofields
Marsden Park
H.M.A.S. NIRIMBA R.A.N. AIRFIELD
Kellyville
Hornsby
Asquith
BUSHLAND

Cranebrook
Llandilo
Glenhaven
Normanhurst
Waitara
Wahroonga
Saint Ives
Pymble
Killara
East Lindfield
Killarney Heights
Beacon Hill
Brookvale
Narraweena
Narrabeen

Upper Castlereagh
Quakers Hill
Parklea
Castle Hill
Pennant Hills
Beecroft
West Pymble
Lindfield
Roseville
Forestville
Seaforth
North Manly
Harbord

Cambridge Park
Dunheved
Whalan
Plumpton
Marayong
EXCELSIOR RESERVE
Rogans Hill
North Rocks
Carlingford
Eastwood
Marsfield
North Ryde
Chatswood
Castlecrag
Balgowlah
Manly

Emu Plains
Penrith
Werrington
Mount Druitt
Doonside
Rooty Hill
Blacktown
Baulkham Hills
Seven Hills
Toongabbie
North Parramatta
Dundas
Rydalmere
Ryde
Lane Cove
Willoughby
Northbridge
Mosman
NORTH HEAD

Kingswood
Jamison Town
Regentville
Orchard Hills
Saint Marys
Colyton
Wallgrove
WESTERN HIGHWAY
Prospect
Wentworthville
Pendle Hill
Greystanes
Harris Park
Parramatta
West Ryde
Ermington
Concord West
Drummoyne
Rozelle
SYDNEY HARBOUR BRIDGE
Gore Hill
Crows Nest
North Sydney
Port Jackson
SOUTH HEAD
MIDDLE HEAD

33° 50'

BLUE MTS. NAT.
242
Erskine Park
Prospect Reservoir
Holroyd
Merrylands
Granville
Clyde
Auburn
North Auburn
Lidcombe
Concord
Mortlake
Abbotsford
Gladesville
Hunters Hill
Longueville
Balmain
SYDNEY
OBSERVATORY
ROYAL BOTANIC GARDENS
GOVERNMENT HOUSE
Watsons Bay
Dover Heights

Mount Henry 190
Mulgoa
Wetherill Park
Horsley
Guildford
Smithfield
Yennora
Chester Hill
Regents Park
Strathfield
Burwood
Croydon
Enfield
Ashfield
Leichhardt
Newtown
NEW SOUTH WALES UNIVERSITY
Woollahra
Vaucluse

Wallacia
Luddenham
BLUE NAT.
Baggerys Creek
Bossley Park
Cecil Park
Canley Vale
Carramar
Five Dock
Haberfield
Petersham
Camperdown
Randwick
Clovelly
Bondi

Greendale
Bonnyrigg
Cabramatta
Mount Pritchard
Bass Hill
Chullora
Belfield
Canterbury
Marrickville
Kensington
Kingsford
Coogee Bay

Badgerys Creek
Birling 158
Fairfield
Lansdowne
WARWICK FARM RACECOURSE
Yagoona
Campsie
Belmore
Roseberry
University
SHARK POINT
COOGEE

West Hoxton
HOXTON PARK AERODROME
Busby
Bankstown
BANKSTOWN RACECOURSE
Punchbowl
Lakemba
Earlwood
Mascot
KINGSFORD SMITH AIRPORT

Austral
Lurnea
Liverpool
NEWBRIDGE ROAD
BANKSTOWN AERODROME
Moorebank
Revesby
Beverly Hills
Kingsgrove
Arncliffe
Botany
Maroubra

Bringelly
Rossmore
Hammondville
Padstow
Bexley
Riverwood
Rockdale
Brighton-Le-Sands
Matraville
Malabar

Leppington
Glenfield
East Hills
Peakhurst
Hurstville
Carlton
Kogarah
BANKSMEADOW
Long Bay

Cobbitty 186
Macquarie Fields
Ingleburn
Oatley
Blakehurst
Ramsgate
Botany Bay
La Perouse
INSCRIPTION POINT
CAPE BANKS

Theresa Park
Cobbitty
Long Point
Minto
Sans Souci
Towra Point
CAPE SOLANDER

34°
Camden
CAMDEN AERODROME
Narellan
195
Menai
Jannali
Sutherland
Sylvania Heights
Miranda
Caringbah
KURNELL PENINSULA
66
PACIFIC
OCEAN

MILITARY RESERVE
Lucas Heights
PRINCE EDWARD PARK
Loftus
Gymea Bay
Cronulla
Bate Bay
POTTER POINT

Leumeah
ATOMIC ENERGY COMMISSION NUCLEAR REACTOR
Engadine
Grays Point
Port Hacking
PORT HACKING POINT

Campbelltown
ROYAL NATIONAL PARK
Heathcote
Bundeena

Copyright © by Rand McNally & Co.

b

37° 40'
Yarra Glen
Yering

TULLAMARINE INTERNATIONAL AIRPORT

Sydenham West
Wattle Glen
Watsons Creek
Sugarloaf
Sydenham
Thomastown
Diamond Creek
Kangaroo Ground
Mount Lofty 234

Rockbank
Broadmeadows
Tullamarine
Jacana
Campbellfield
Keon Park
Bundoora
Greensborough
Research
Mount Lofty
COOMBE COTTAGE

Keilor
Glenroy
Oak Park
Hadfield
Fawkner
Reservoir
Watsonia
Macleod
Montmorency
Eltham
CLIFFORD PARK
Coldstream

Saint Albans
Airport West
Merlynston
Pascoe Vale
Regent
LATROBE UNIVERSITY
Lower Plenty
Warrandyte
Black Springs

Deer Park
Albion
North Essendon
Coburg
Moreland
Bell
West Heidelberg
Rosanna
Warrandyte South
Lilydale

Sunshine
Avondale Heights
Essendon
Brunswick
North Fitzroy
Thornbury
Heidelberg
Ivanhoe
Templestowe
Park Orchards
Mount Evelyn

Maidstone
Maribyrnong
Northcote
Doncaster
Doncaster East
Ringwood North
Montrose

Truganina
FLEMINGTON RACECOURSE
Fitzroy
Collingwood
North Balwyn
Mitcham
Croydon
Kilsyth

MELBOURNE
Richmond
Kew
Hawthorn
Balwyn
North Box Hill
Nunawading
Ringwood
Kalorama

Kingsville
Footscray
Yarraville
MELBOURNE CRICKET GROUND
Camberwell
Canterbury
Box Hill
Forest Hill
Vermont
Bayswater North
Mount Dandenong 630

Spotswood
South Melbourne
Toorak
Burwood
Ashburton
Tally Ho
Wantirna
Bayswater
The Basin

Newport
Paisley
Port Melbourne
Prahran
South Yarra
Malvern
East Burwood
Mount Waverley
Boronia
Olinda

Altona North
Williamstown
Saint Kilda
Caulfield
CAULFIELD RACE COURSE
Chadstone
Holmesglen
Syndal
Wantirna South
Sassafras

Galvin
Seaholme
Elwood
Glenhuntly
Glen Waverley
Knoxfield
Upper Ferntree Gully
Upwey

Laverton
LAVERTON ROYAL AUSTRALIAN AIR FORCE STATION
ALTONA SPORTS PARK
Brighton
Ormond
Bentleigh
Clayton
Notting Hill
MONASH UNIVERSITY
Wheelers Hill
Scoresby
Ferny Creek
Belgrave

Tarneit
Altona Bay
POINT GELLIBRAND
Moorabbin
Oakleigh
Mulgrave
Rowville
Lysterfield
Selby

Werribee
Point Cook
POINT COOK ROYAL AUSTRALIAN AIR FORCE STATION
Hampton
Highett
Oakleigh South
SANDOWN PARK
Harrisfield
CHURCHILL NATIONAL PARK

Werribee South
Sandringham
MOORABBIN AIRPORT
Cheltenham
Heatherton
Dingley
Springvale
Springvale South
Noble Park
Sugarloaf Hill 180

Black Rock
Beaumaris
Mentone
Keysborough
Dandenong
Narre Warren North

Port Phillip Bay
RICKETTS POINT
Mordialloc
Aspendale
Edithvale
Bangholme
Hampton Park
Berwick

Chelsea
Carrum North
Lyndhurst
Hallam
Harkaway
Upper Beaconsfield

Bonbeach
Carrum
Carrum Downs
Beaconsfield
Officer

Copyright © by Rand McNally & Co.
Map prepared by George Philip & Son Ltd., London.
A-590056-264   –5–4– –8

144° 40'   144° 50'   145°   145° 10'   145° 20'

37° 50'

38°

	AREA (km²)	POPULATION
MELBOURNE	2,600	2,425,000
SYDNEY	2,800	2,850,000

	bay, b.	creek, cr.	highway	point
ENGLISH	bay, b.	creek, cr.	highway	point
DEUTSCH	Bucht	Bach	Landstrasse	Landspitze
ESPAÑOL	bahia	riachuelo	camino	punta
FRANÇAIS	baie	crique	route	pointe
PORTUGUÊS	baia	riacho	rodovia	ponta

	bridge	road
ENGLISH	bridge	road
DEUTSCH	Brücke	Landstrasse
ESPAÑOL	puente	camino
FRANÇAIS	pont	route
PORTUGUÊS	ponte	rodovia

Kilometers 0   5   10   15 Km.

Statute Miles 0   5   10   15 Mi.

Scale 1:300,000
One centimeter represents 3 kilometers.
One inch represents approximately 4.7 miles.

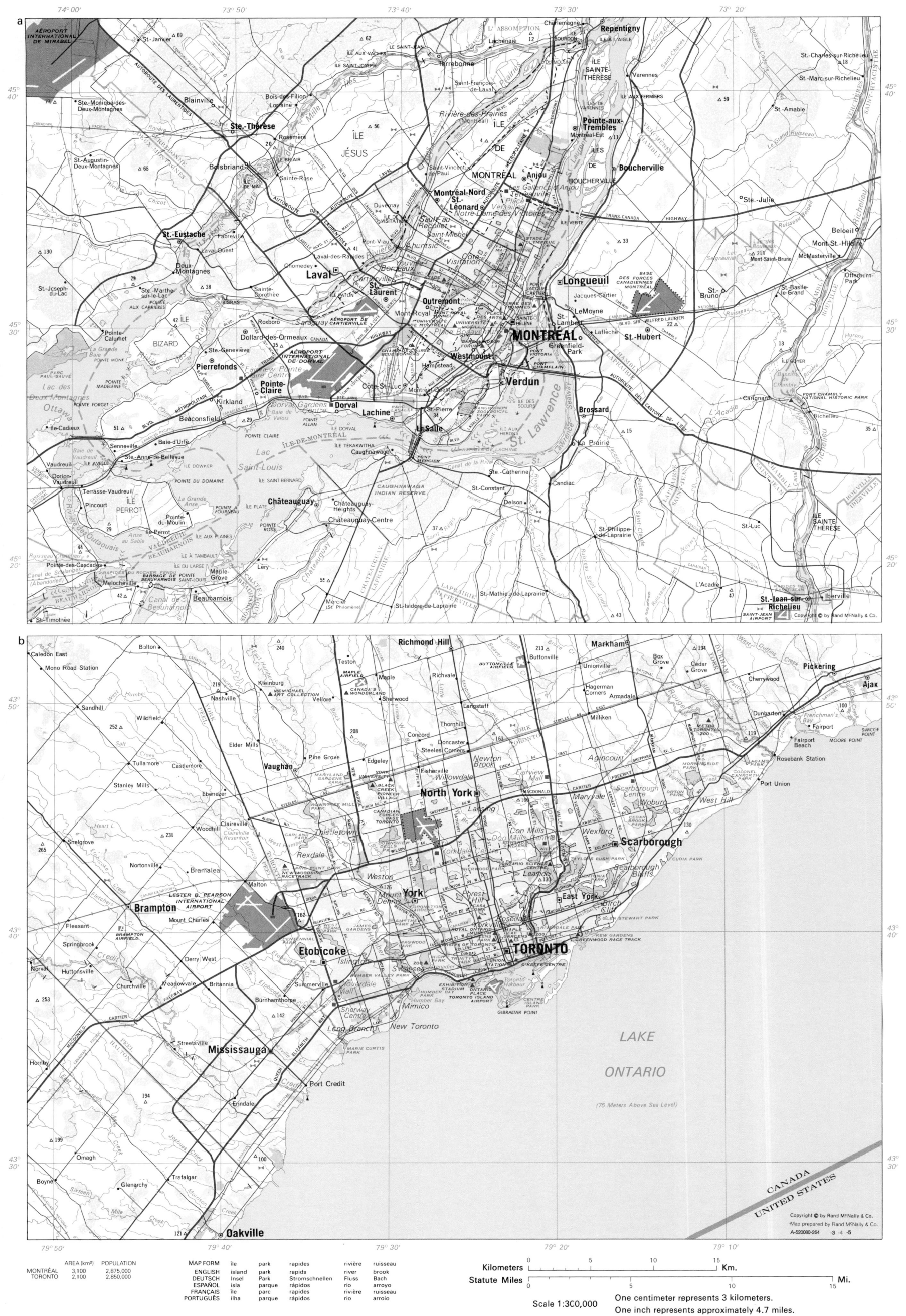

a

b

	AREA (km²)	POPULATION
MONTRÉAL	3,100	2,875,000
TORONTO	2,100	2,850,000

MAP FORM				
ENGLISH	Île	park	rapides	rivière	ruisseau
DEUTSCH	island	park	rapids	river	brook
ESPAÑOL	Insel	Park	Stromschnellen	Fluss	Bach
FRANÇAIS	isla	parque	rápidos	rio	arroyo
PORTUGUÊS	Île	parc	rapides	rivière	ruisseau
	ilha	parque	rápidos	rio	arroio

Kilometers 0   5   10   15 Km.

Statute Miles 0   5   10   15 Mi.

Scale 1:300,000

One centimeter represents 3 kilometers.
One inch represents approximately 4.7 miles.

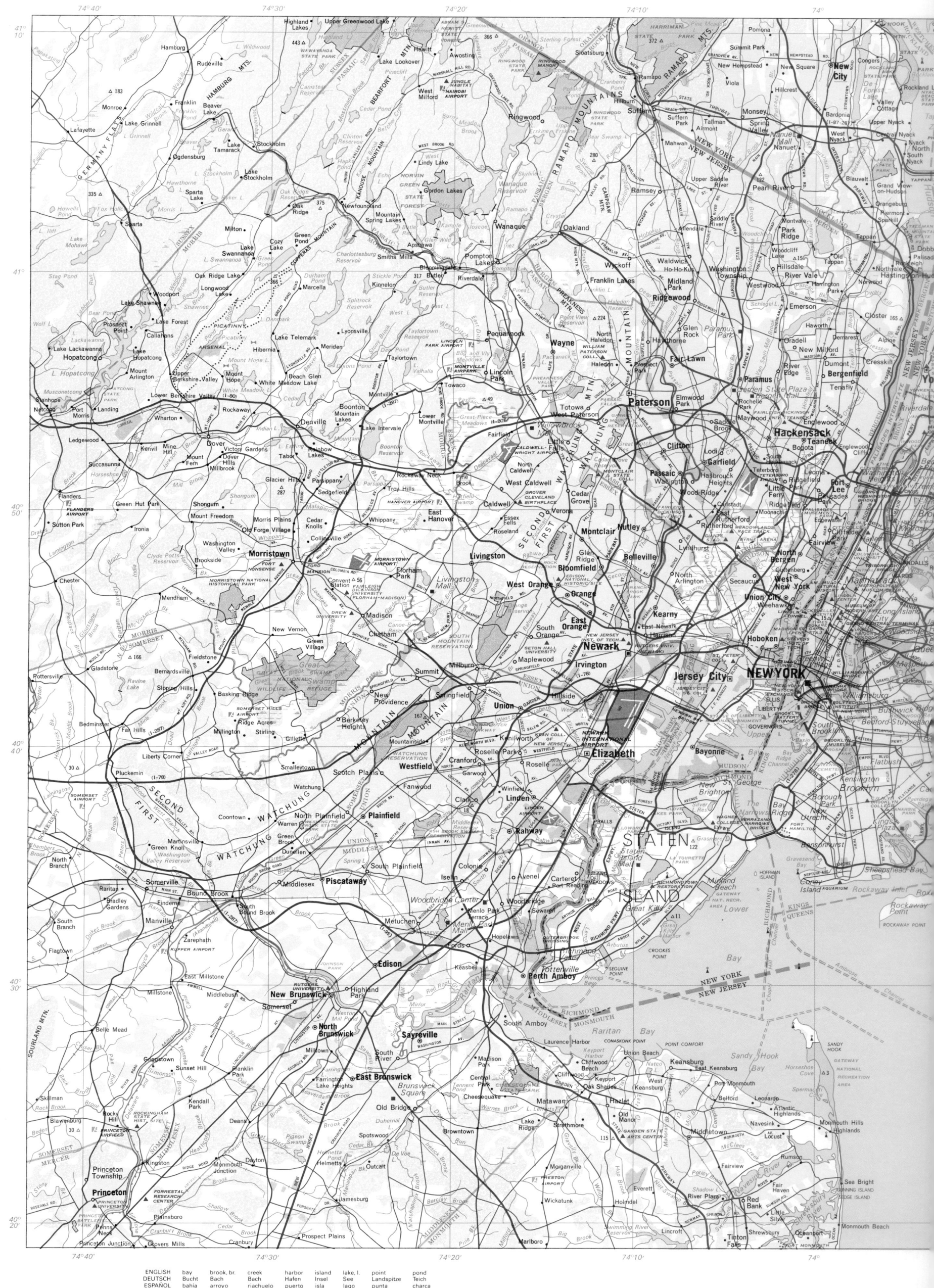

ENGLISH   bay   brook, br.   creek   harbor   island   lake, l.   point   pond
DEUTSCH   Bucht   Bach   Bach   Hafen   Insel   See   Landspitze Teich
ESPAÑOL   bahía   arroyo   riachuelo puerto   isla   lago   punta   charca
FRANÇAIS   baie   ruisseau   crique   port   île   lac   pointe   étang
PORTUGUÊS   baía   arroio   riacho   porto   ilha   lago   ponta   lagoa
For complete glossary see page 1·1.

Kilometers 0 5 10 15 Km.

Statute Miles 0 5 10 15 Mi.

Scale 1:300,000

One centimeter represents 3 kilometers.
One inch represents approximately 4.7 miles.

ENGLISH   airport   creek, cr.   harbor   lake, l.   park   woods
DEUTSCH   Flughafen   Bach   Hafen   See   Park   Gehölz
ESPAÑOL   aeropuerto   riachuelo   puerto   lago   parque   bosques
FRANÇAIS   aéroport   crique   port   lac   parc   bois
PORTUGUÊS aeroporto   riacho   porto   lago   parque   bosques

Kilometers 0   5   10   15   Km.

Statute Miles 0   5   10   15   Mi.

Scale 1:300,000

One centimeter represents 3 kilometers.
One inch represents approximately 4.7 miles.

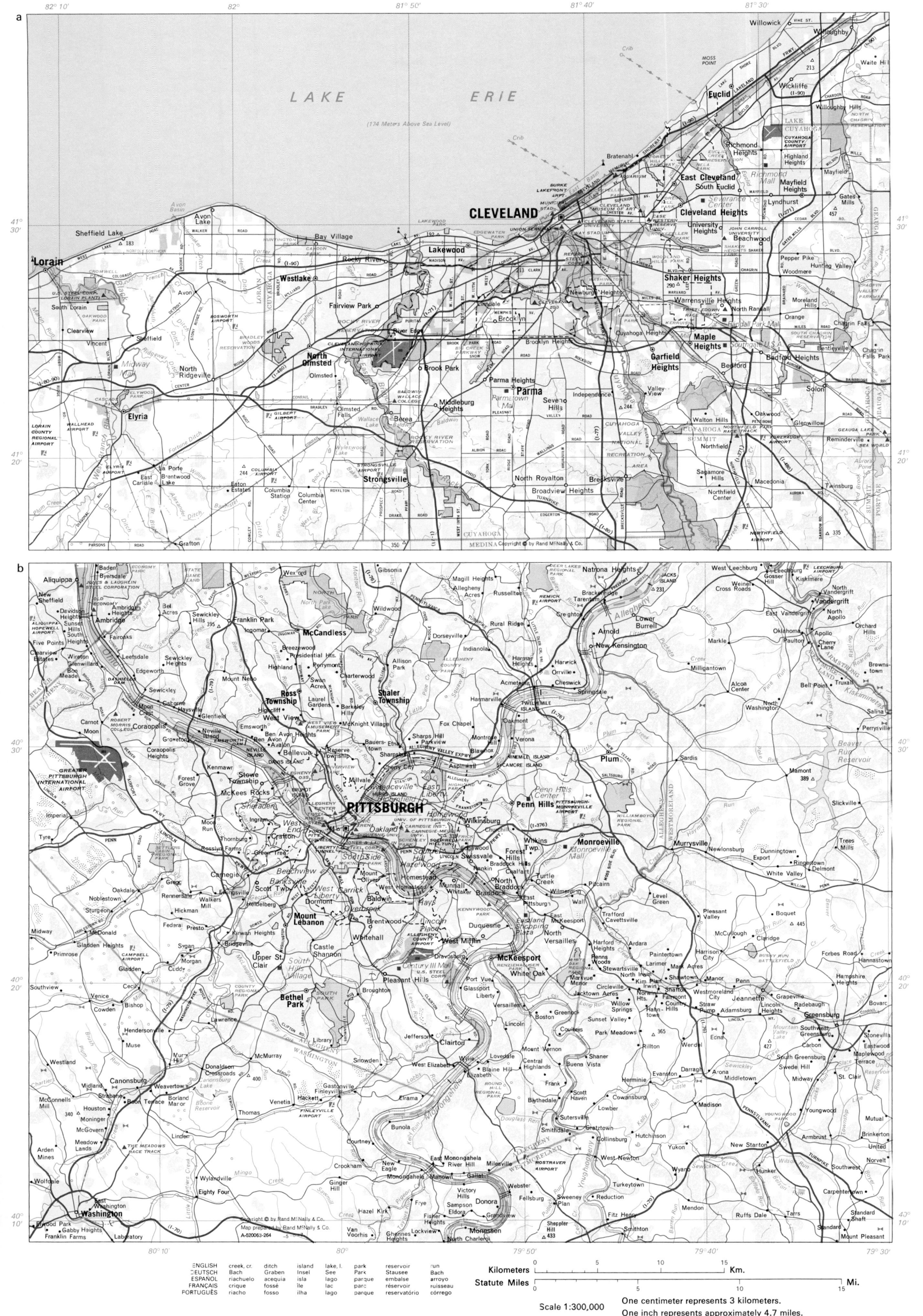

ENGLISH   creek, cr.   ditch   island   lake, l.   park   reservoir   run
DEUTSCH   Bach   Graben   Insel   See   Park   embalse   Bach
ESPAÑOL   riachuelo   acequia isla   lago   parque embalse   arroyo
FRANÇAIS crique   fossé   île   lac   parc   réservoir   ruisseau
PORTUGUÊS riacho   fosso   ilha   lago   parque reservatório córrego

Kilometers
Statute Miles

Scale 1:300,000
One centimeter represents 3 kilometers.
One inch represents approximately 4.7 miles.

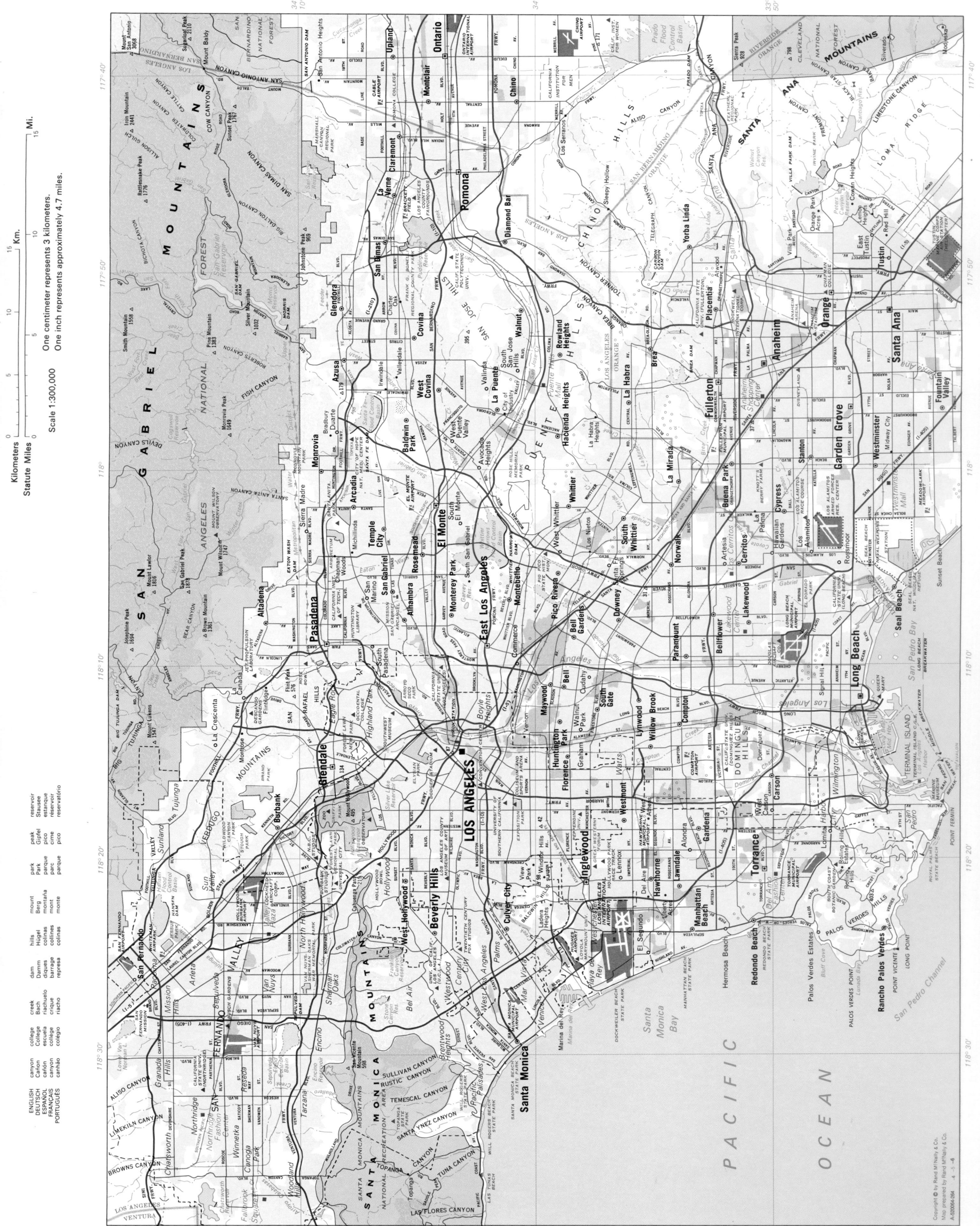

Kilometers
Statute Miles

ENGLISH   canyon   creek   dam   hills   mount   park   peak   reservoir
DEUTSCH   Cañon   Bach   Damm   Hügel   Berg   Park   Gipfel Stausee
ESPAÑOL   cañon   riachuelo presa colinas monte   parque pico   estanque
FRANÇAIS   canyon   crique   barrage collines montagne parc   cime   reservoir
PORTUGUÊS canhão   riacho   represa colinas monte   parque pico   reservatório

Scale 1:300,000

One centimeter represents 3 kilometers.
One inch represents approximately 4.7 miles.

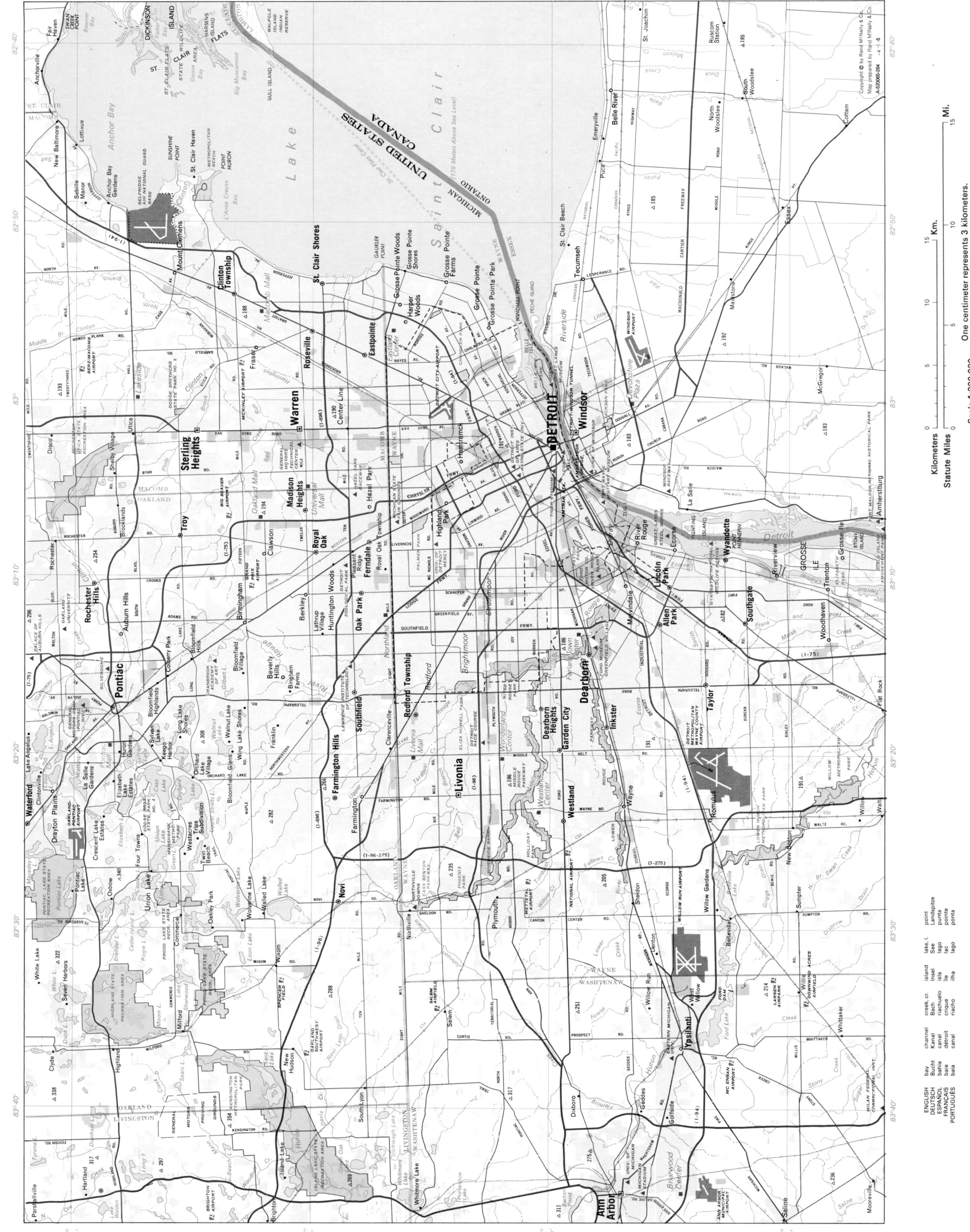

One centimeter represents 3 kilometers.
One inch represents approximately 4.7 miles.

Scale 1:300,000

Mi.

Km.

Kilometers

Statute Miles

ENGLISH	bay	channel	creek, cr.	island	lake, l.	point
DEUTSCH	Bucht	Kanal	Bach.	Insel	See	Landspitze
ESPAÑOL	bahía	canal	riachuelo	isla	lago	punta
FRANÇAIS	baie	canal	crique	île	lac	pointe
PORTUGUÊS	baía	canal	riacho	ilha	lago	ponta

Copyright © by Rand McNally & Co.
Map prepared by Rand McNally & Co.
A-500066-284   -4 -1 -5

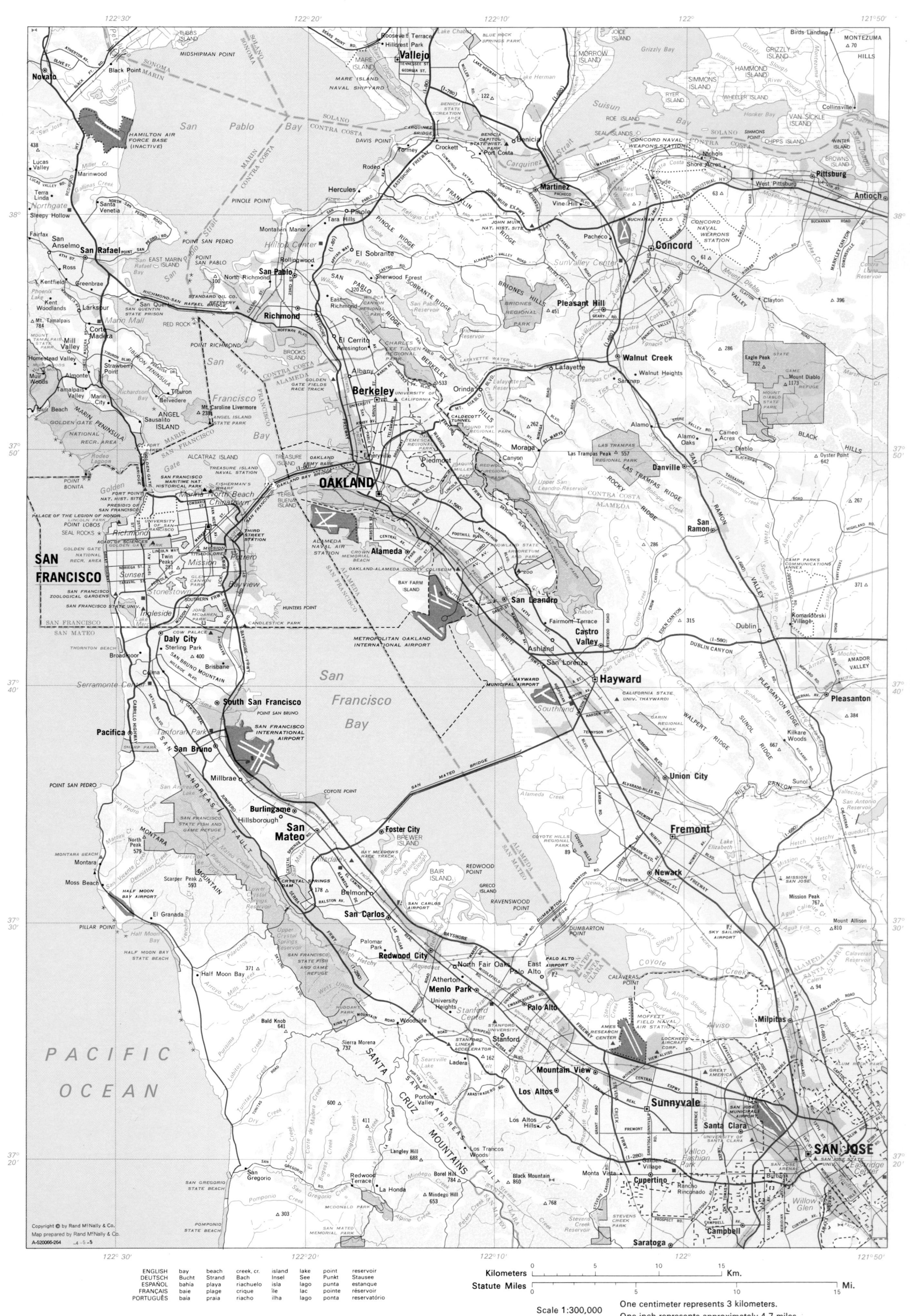

Copyright © by Rand McNally & Co.
Map prepared by Rand McNally & Co.
A-520066-264   -4 -5 -5

ENGLISH	bay	beach	creek, cr.	island	lake	point	reservoir
DEUTSCH	Bucht	Strand	Bach	Insel	See	Punkt	Stausee
ESPAÑOL	bahía	playa	riachuelo	isla	lago	punta	estanque
FRANÇAIS	baie	plage	crique	île	lac	pointe	réservoir
PORTUGUÊS	baía	praia	riacho	ilha	lago	ponta	reservatório

Kilometers

Statute Miles

Scale 1:300,000
One centimeter represents 3 kilometers.
One inch represents approximately 4.7 miles.

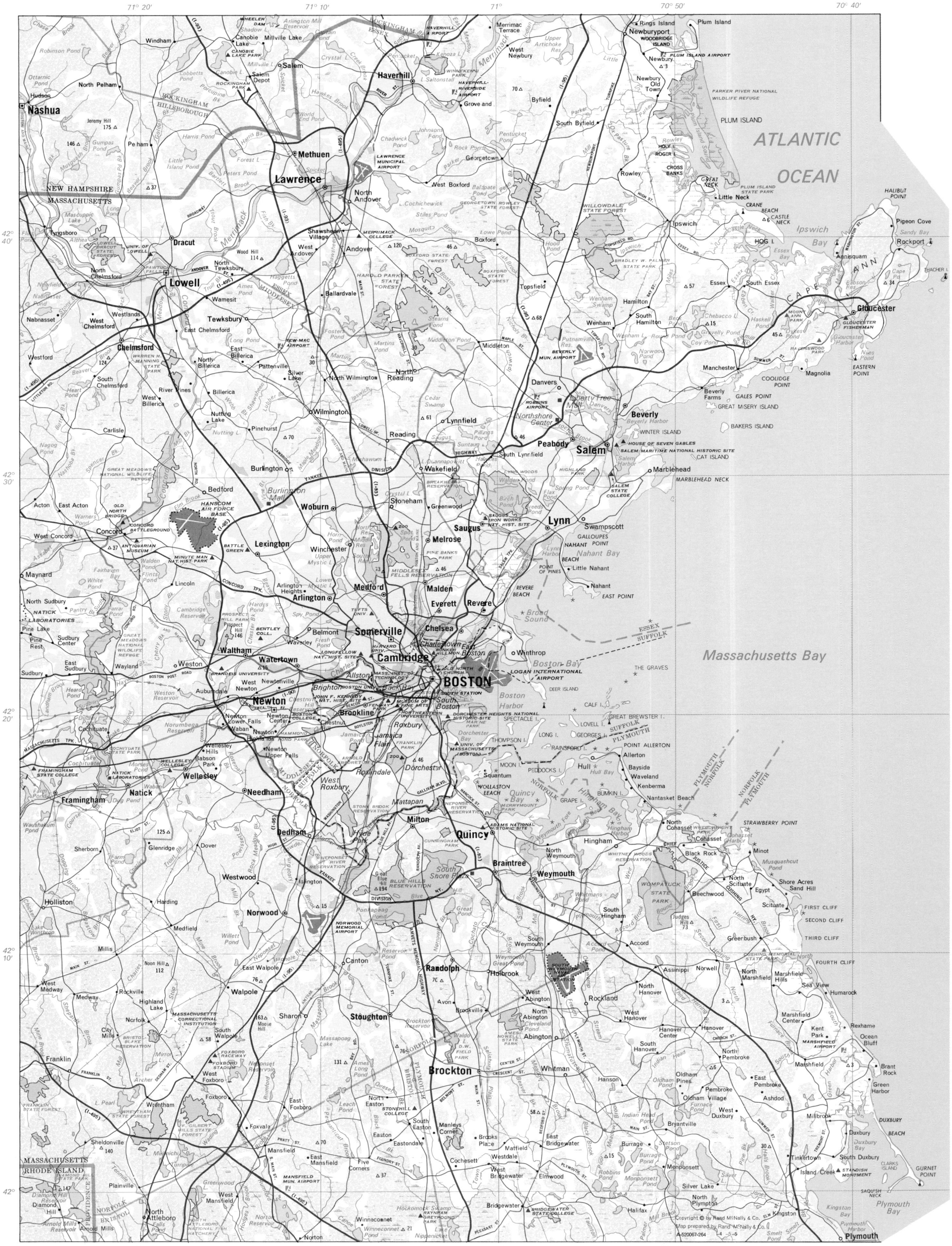

NEW HAMPSHIRE
MASSACHUSETTS

MASSACHUSETTS
RHODE ISLAND

ATLANTIC OCEAN

Massachusetts Bay

Boston Bay

Boston Harbor

Nashua · North Pelham · Windham · Hudson · Windham

Methuen · Lawrence · North Andover · Andover · Haverhill · Newburyport · Plum Island · Rowley · Ipswich · Rockport · Gloucester · Essex · Manchester · Beverly · Salem · Peabody · Marblehead · Lynn · Swampscott · Nahant

Lowell · Dracut · Chelmsford · Tewksbury · Billerica · Wilmington · Reading · Wakefield · Stoneham · Melrose · Saugus · Woburn · Burlington · Bedford · Lexington · Winchester · Medford · Malden · Everett · Revere · Chelsea · Somerville · Cambridge

Concord · Lincoln · Waltham · Watertown · Belmont · Arlington · Newton · Brighton · BOSTON · Winthrop · Logan International Airport · Deer Island

Framingham · Natick · Wellesley · Needham · Dedham · Brookline · Roxbury · Jamaica Plain · Dorchester · Quincy · Hull · Nantasket Beach · Cohasset · Scituate

Norwood · Westwood · Milton · Braintree · Weymouth · Hingham · Accord

Holliston · Medfield · Walpole · Canton · Randolph · Holbrook · Rockland · Hanover · Marshfield

Franklin · Wrentham · Foxboro · Mansfield · Stoughton · Brockton · Whitman · Abington · Hanson · Pembroke · Duxbury · Plymouth

Blue Hills Reservation · Wompatuck State Park · Myles Standish State Forest

---

ENGLISH	bay	brook	island, i.	lake, l.	point	pond	reservation
DEUTSCH	Bucht	Bach	Insel	See	Landspitze	Teich	Reservat
ESPAÑOL	bahía	arroyo	isla	lago	punta	charca	parque naciona
FRANÇAIS	baie	ruisseau	île	lac	pointe	étang	réservation
PORTUGUÊS	baía	arroio	ilha	lago	ponta	lagoa	parque naciona

Kilometers 0   5   10   15   Km.

Statute Miles 0   5   10   15   Mi.

Scale 1:300,000

One centimeter represents 3 kilometers.
One inch represents approximately 4.7 miles.

Kilometers 0 5 10 15 Km.
Statute Miles 0 5 10 15 Mi.

Scale 1:300,000
One centimeter represents 3 kilometers.
One inch represents approximately 4.7 miles.

ENGLISH	airport	bridge	creek, cr.	island, i.	park	point	run	university
DEUTSCH	Flughafen	Brücke	Bach	Insel	Park	Landspitze	Bach	Universität
ESPAÑOL	aeropuerto	puente	riachuelo	isla	parque	punta	arroyo	universidad
FRANÇAIS	aéroport	pont	crique	île	parc	pointe	ruisseau	université
PORTUGUÊS	aeroporto	ponte	riacho	ilha	parque	ponta	córrego	universidade

b

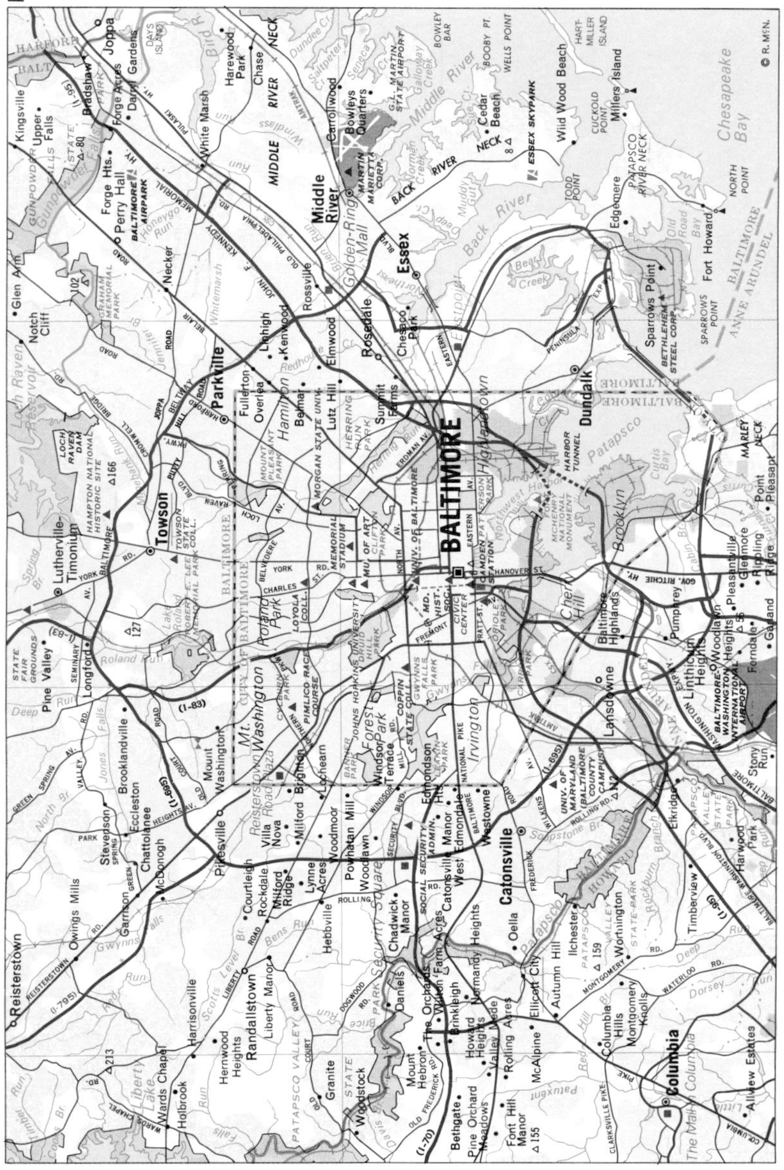

c

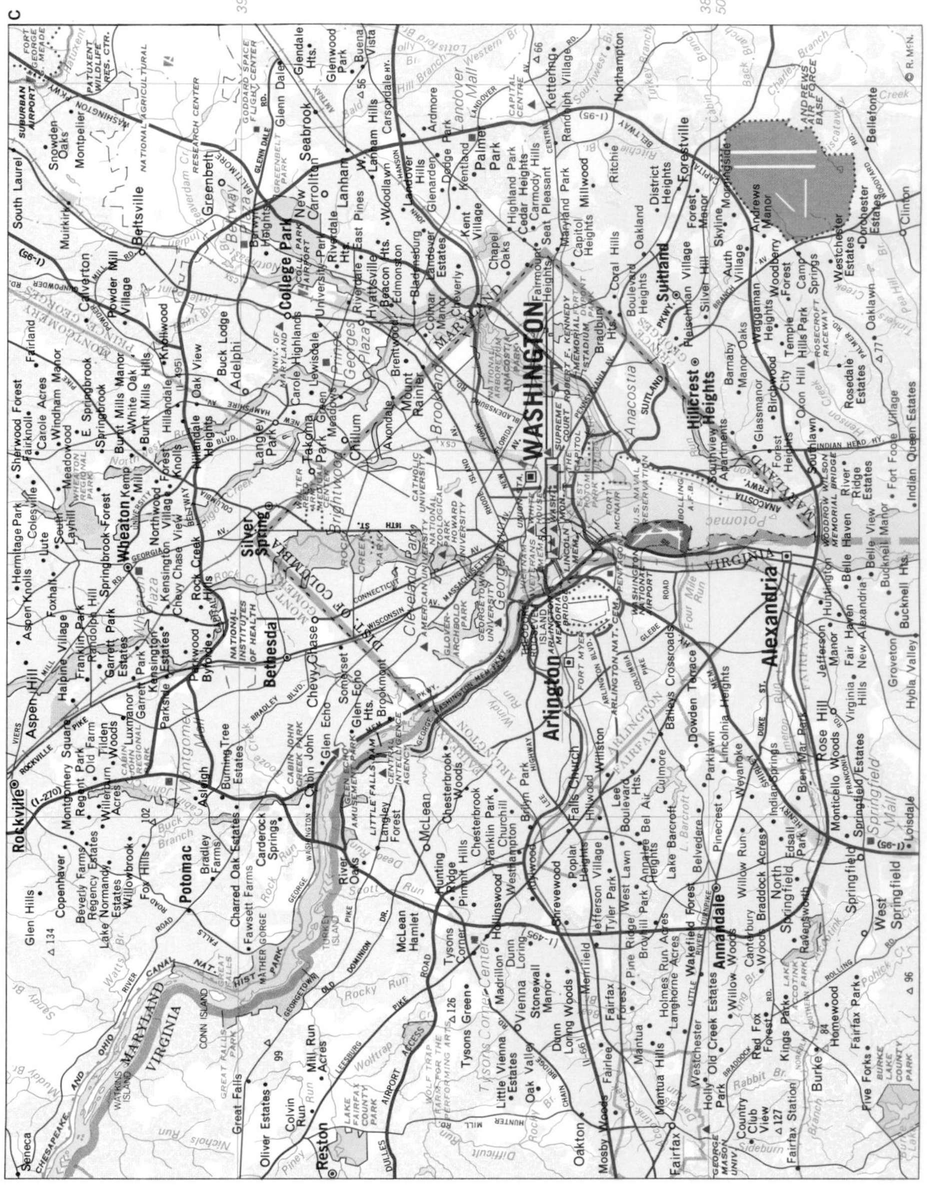

a

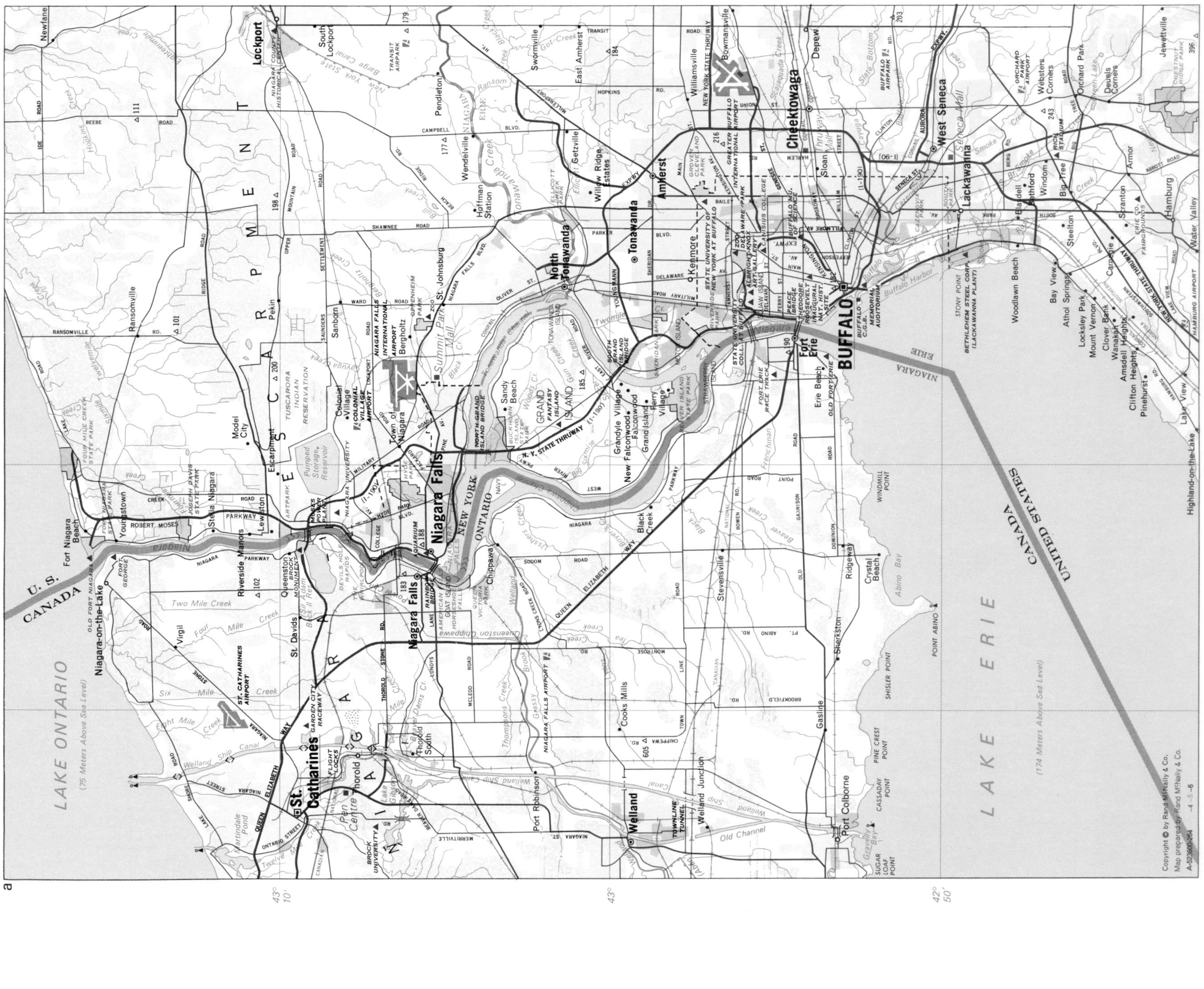

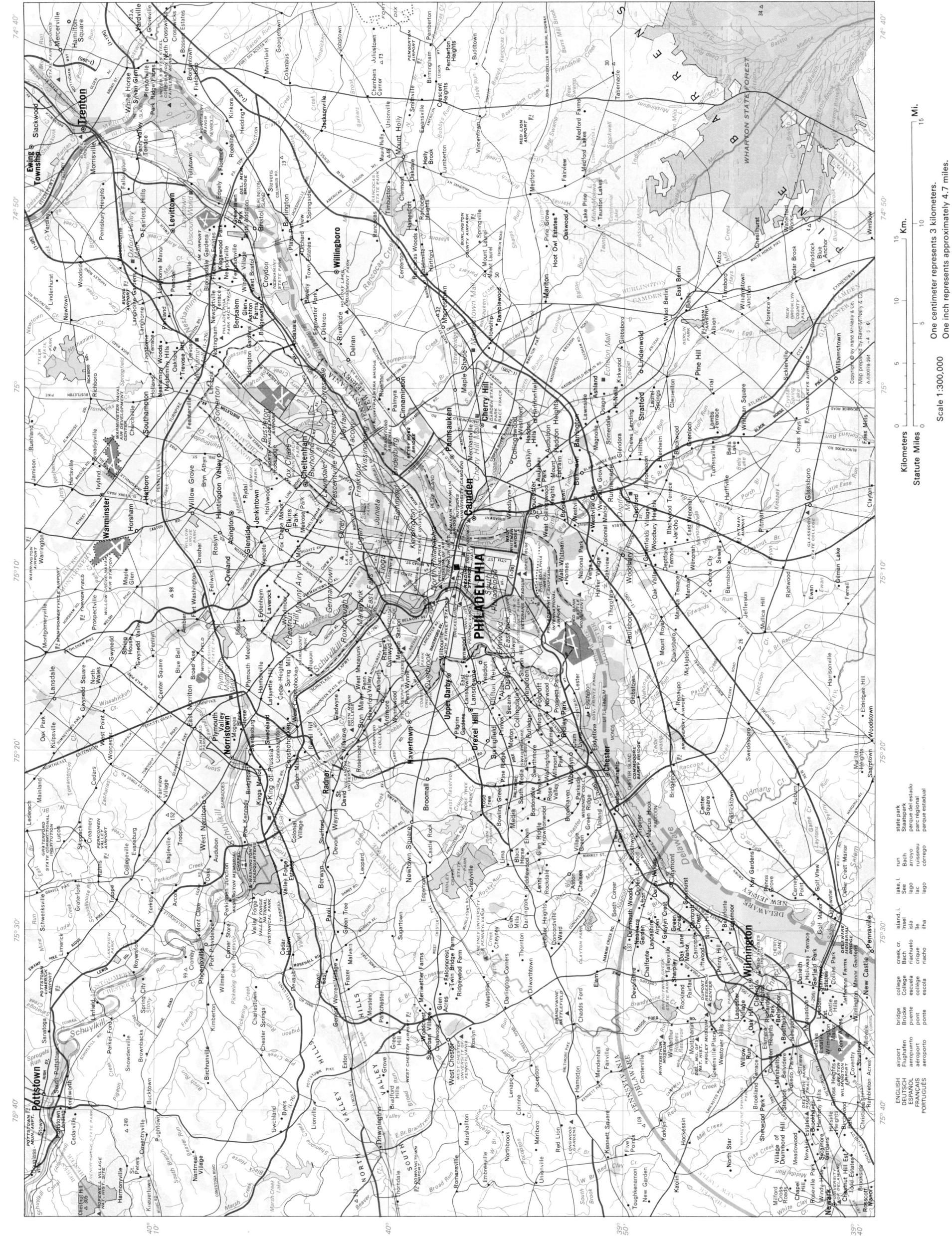

Scale 1:300,000

Kilometers
Statute Miles

One centimeter represents 3 kilometers.
One inch represents approximately 4.7 miles.

ENGLISH	airport	bridge	college	island, i.	lake, l.	run	state park
DEUTSCH	Flughafen	Brücke	College	Insel	See	Bach	Staatspark
ESPAÑOL	aeropuerto	puente	escuela	isla	lago	arroyo	parque del estado
FRANCAIS	aéroport	pont	collège	île	lac	russeau	parc régional
PORTUGUÊS	aeroporto	ponte	escola	ilha	lago	riacho	parque estadual

| creek, cr. |
| Bach |
| riachuelo |
| crique |
| riacho |

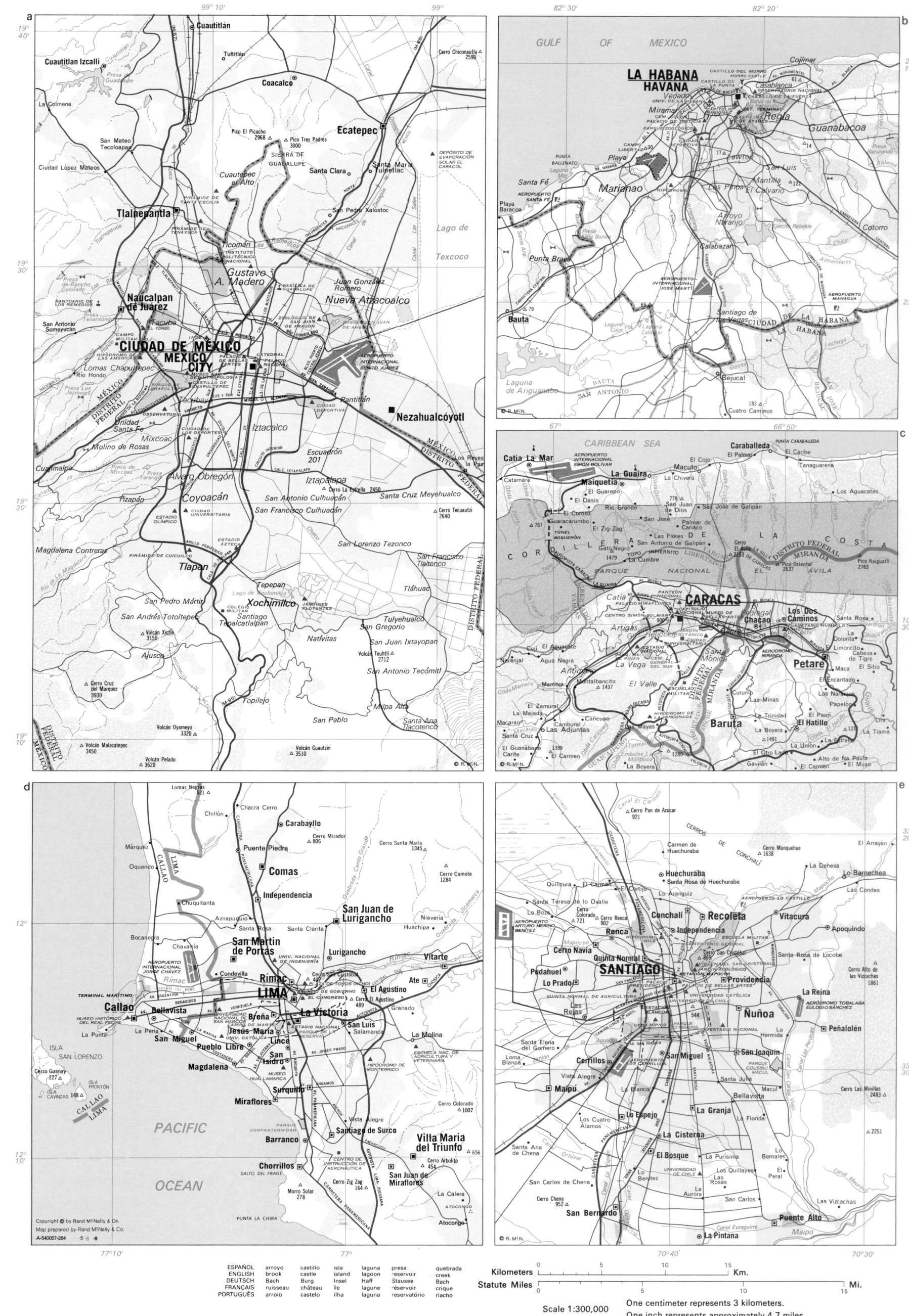

ESPAÑOL	arroyo	castillo	isla	laguna	presa	quebrada
ENGLISH	brook	castle	island	lagoon	reservoir	creek
DEUTSCH	Bach	Burg	Insel	Haff	Stausee	Bach
FRANÇAIS	ruisseau	château	île	lagune	réservoir	crique
PORTUGUÊS	arroio	castelo	ilha	laguna	reservatório	riacho

Kilometers   0   5   10   15   Km.

Statute Miles   0   5   10   15   Mi.

Scale 1:300,000
One centimeter represents 3 kilometers.
One inch represents approximately 4.7 miles.

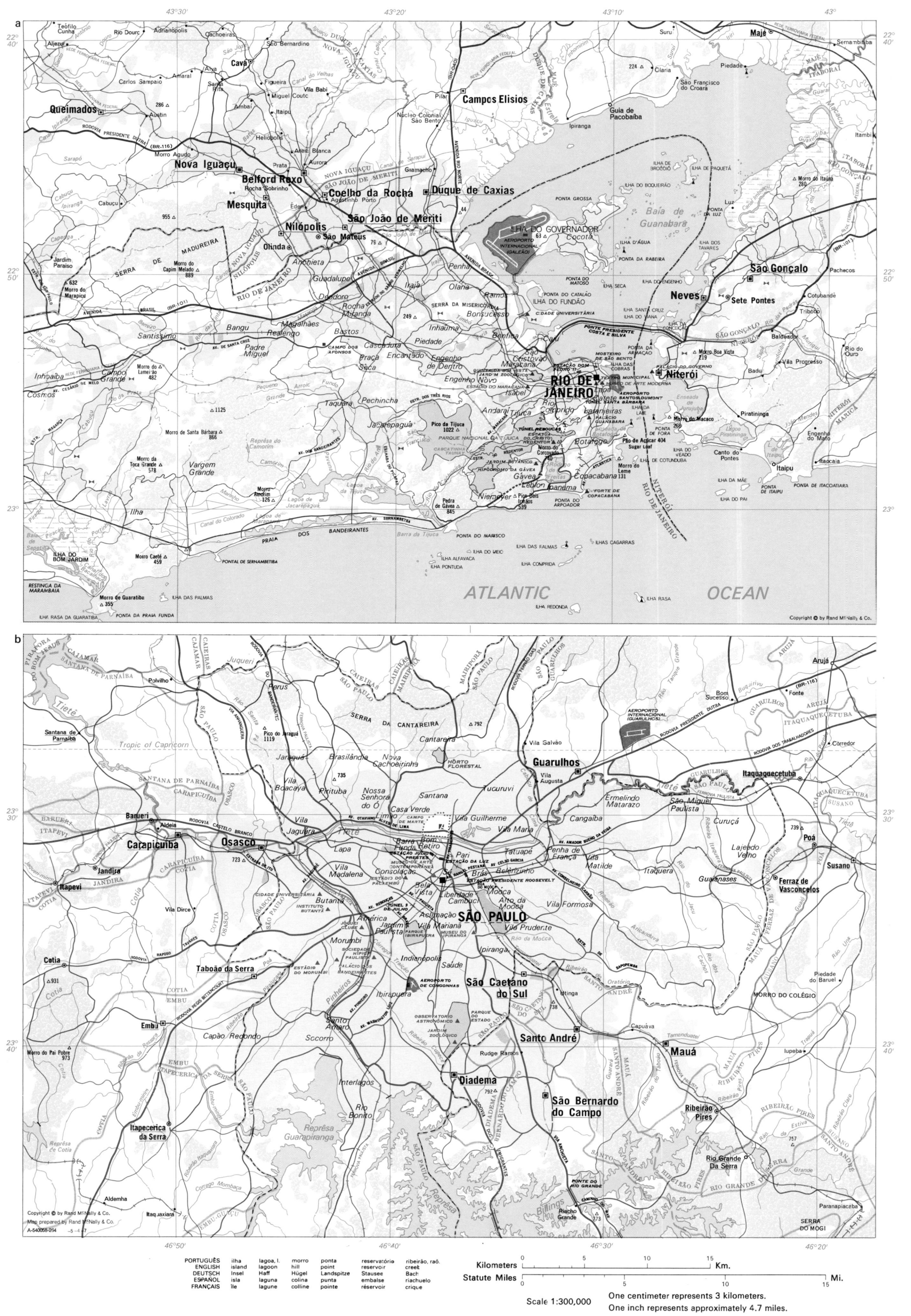

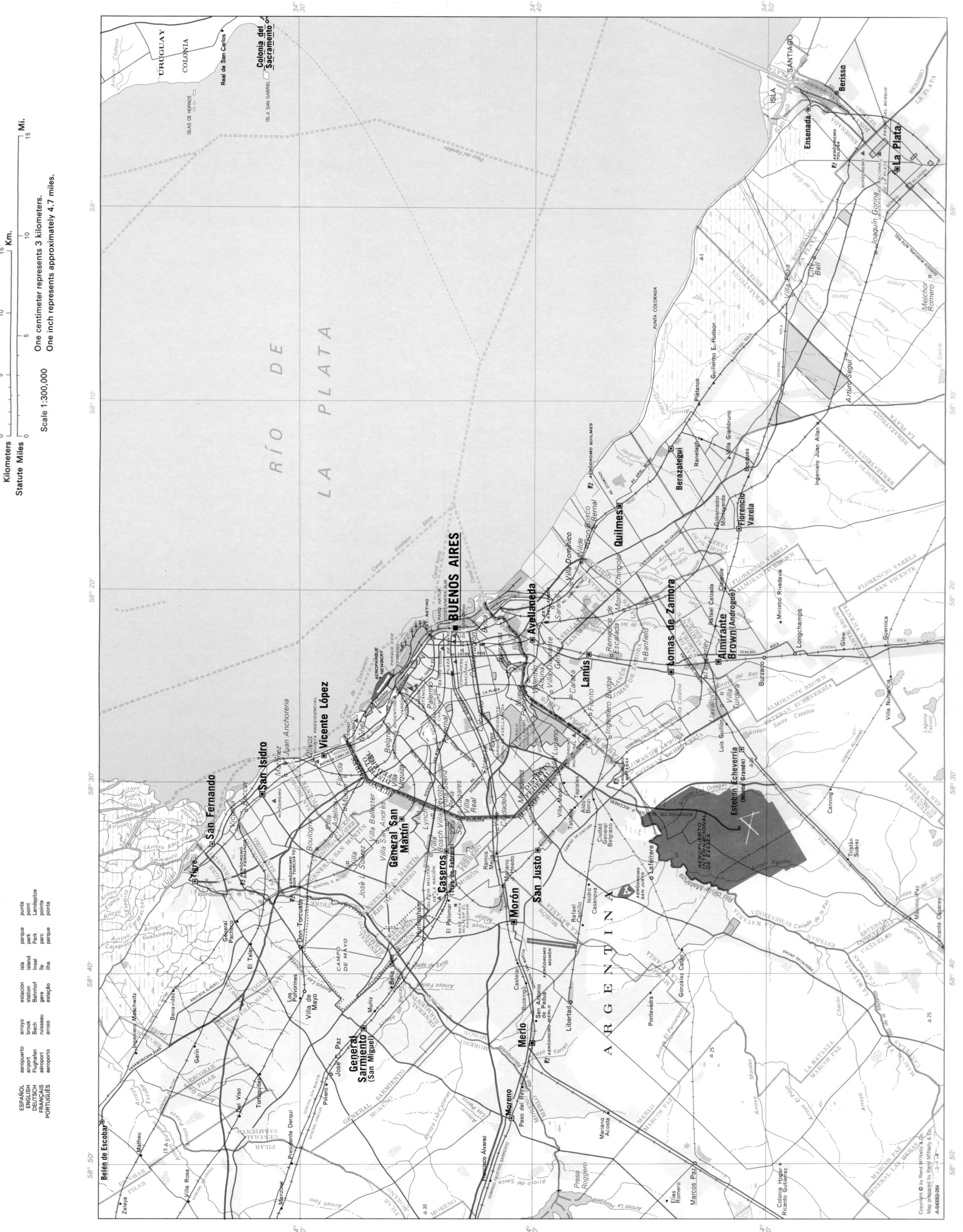

THE MAP FORM column of the glossary lists in alphabetical order the geographical terms, including any abbreviations, that appear on the maps. Terms preceded by a hyphen are those which commonly appear as endings in map names (for example, -san in Fuji-san, -älven in Dalälven). The languages of the terms are identified by abbreviations in *italics* (see Abbreviations of Language Names below). The glossary provides the English, German, Spanish, French, and Portuguese equivalent for each term.

As a rule, the translations were made from the map form to English, then from English into the other four languages. Since the glossary terms and translations refer to specific map features, some may vary from the customary dictionary definitions of the terms.

IN DER SPALTE "Geographische Begriffe" werden alle Begriffe und Abkürzungen in alphabetischer Ordnung aufgeführt, die in den Karten erscheinen. Begriffe mit vorgesetztem Bindestrich erscheinen normalerweise als Wortendungen in Kartennamen (z.B. -san in Fuji-san, -älven in Dalälven). In *Kursivschrift* sind die jeweiligen Abkürzungen angegeben für die Sprachen, in denen der Begriff wiedergegeben ist (siehe unten: Abkürzungen der Sprachen). Das Verzeichnis gibt für jeden Begriff den entsprechenden Ausdruck in englisch, deutsch, spanisch, französisch, und portugiesisch.

In der Regel wurde der Begriff in der Karte ins Englische übersetzt und dann vom Englischen in die vier anderen Sprachen. Da die Begriffe und Übersetzungen sich auf bestimmte Objekte in der Karte beziehen, können einige von ihnen von den in den üblichen Wörterbüchern aufgeführten Begriffsbestimmungen abweichen.

LOS TÉRMINOS GEOGRÁFICOS que aparecen en los mapas, incluyendo abreviaciones, son presentados en la columna de Términos Geográficas del Glosario, en orden alfabético. Los términos que están precedidos por un guión aparecen frecuentemente como terminaciones de los nombres en los mapas (por ejemplo, -san en Fuji-san, -älvan en Dalälven). Los idiomas que representan los términos están identificados por medio de abreviaciones en *cursiva* (véase abajo, Abreviaciones de los Idiomas Extranjeros). El Glosario provee el equivalente para cada término en inglés, alemán, español, francés y portugués.

Generalmente las traducciones están hechas de las formas originales de la terminología de los mapas que aparecen primero en inglés, y luego se traducen a las otras cuatro lenguas. Algunos términos y traducciones pueden aparecer distintas a las usadas en los diccionarios generales porque se refieren a los rasgos particulares de los mapas.

LE GLOSSAIRE cite par ordre alphabétique les termes géographiques et les abréviations utilisées. Les mots précédés d'un tiret sont des suffixes (par exemple, -san dans Fuji-san, -älven dans Dalälven). La langue d'origine du nom cité est indiquée par une abréviation en *italique* (voir Abréviations des noms de langues, ci-dessous). Le Glossaire donne chaque nom en anglais, allemand, espagnol, français, et portugais.

En général, les termes géographiques des cartes ont d'abord été traduits en anglais, puis de l'anglais dans les quatre autres langues. Les définitions de certains termes sont adaptées aux particularités de l'Atlas. Il peut arriver qu'elles diffèrent des définitions habituelles données par les dictionnaires.

A COLUNA 'TERMINOLOGIA', do *Glossário*, contém todos os termos geográficos que figuram nos mapas, em ordem alfabética e com as respectivas abreviações. Os termos precedidos por um hífen são os que freqüentemente aparecem nos mapas como sufixos de nomes tais como *-san* (em Fuji-san), *-älven* (em Dalälven). As línguas em que os termos são expressos estão identificadas por abreviações em *grifo* (ver abaixo, 'Abreviações das línguas estrangeiras'). O Glossário fornece o equivalente de cada termo em inglês, alemão, espanhol, português e francês.

De modo geral, as traduções foram feitas das formas originais da terminologia usada nos mapas para o inglês, e, em seguida, do inglês para as outras quatro línguas. Uma vez que os termos geográficos e traduções do *Glossário* referem-se a acidentes específicos de cada mapa, é possível que algumas definições sejam diferentes das consignadas nos dicionários gerais das línguas.

Abbreviations of Language Names / Abkürzungen der Nationalsprachen / Abreviaciones de los Idiomas Extranjeros
Abréviations des Noms de Langues / Abreviações dos Idiomas Estrangeiros

	ENGLISH	DEUTSCH	ESPAÑOL	FRANÇAIS	PORTUGUÊS
Afk.	Afrikaans	Afrikaans	Africano	Afrikaans	Afrikaans
Alb.	Albanian	Albanisch	Albanesa	Albanais	Albanês
Ara.	Arabic	Arabisch	Árabe	Arabe	Árabe
Ber.	Berber	Berberisch	Bereber	Berbère	Berbere
Ben.	Bengali	Bengali	Bengali	Bengali	Bengali
Blg.	Bulgarian	Bulgarisch	Búlgaro	Bulgare	Búlgaro
Bur.	Burmese	Burmanisch	Birmano	Birman	Birmanês
Cat.	Catalan	Katalanisch	Catalán	Catalan	Catalão
Cbd.	Cambodian	Kambodschanisch	Camboyano	Cambodgien	Cambojano
Ch.	Chinese	Chinesisch	Chino	Chinois	Chinês
Czech	Czech	Tschechisch	Checo	Tchèque	Tcheco
Dan.	Danish	Dänisch	Danés	Danois	Dinamarquês
Du.	Dutch	Niederländisch	Holandés	Néerlandais	Holandês
Eng.	English	Englisch	Inglés	Anglais	Inglês
Est.	Estonian	Estnisch	Estonio	Esthonien	Estoniano
Finn.	Finnish	Finnisch	Finés	Finnois	Finlandês
Flm.	Flemish	Flämisch	Flamenco	Flamand	Flamengo
Fr.	French	Französisch	Francés	Français	Francês
Gae.	Gaelic	Gälisch	Gaélico	Gaélique	Gaélico
Ger.	German	Deutsch	Alemán	Allemand	Alemão
Gr.	Greek	Griechisch	Griego	Grec	Grego
Hau.	Hausa	Haussa	Hausa	Haoussa	Haussa
Heb.	Hebrew	Hebräisch	Hebreo	Hébreu	Hebraico
Hung.	Hungarian	Ungarisch	Húngaro	Hongrois	Húngaro
Ice.	Icelandic	Isländisch	Islandés	Islandais	Islandês
Indon.	Indonesian	Indonesisch	Indonesio	Indonésien	Indonésio
It.	Italian	Italienisch	Italiano	Italien	Italiano
Jap.	Japanese	Japanisch	Japonés	Japonais	Japonês
Kor.	Korean	Koreanisch	Coreano	Coréen	Coreano
Lao.	Laotian	Laotisch	Laosiano	Laotien	Laosiano
Lapp.	Lappish	Lappisch	Lapón	Lapon	Lapão
Latv.	Latvian	Lettisch	Letón	Letton	Letão
Lith.	Lithuanian	Litauisch	Lituano	Lithuanien	Lituano
Mal.	Malay	Malaiisch	Malayo	Malais	Malaio
Mong.	Mongolian	Mongolisch	Mogol	Mongol	Mongol
Nor.	Norwegian	Norwegisch	Norvego	Norvégien	Norueguês
Pas.	Pashto	Paschtu	Pushtu	Pachtou	Pachtu
Per.	Persian	Persisch	Persa	Persan	Persa
Pol.	Polish	Polnisch	Polaco	Polonais	Polonês
Poly.	Polynesian	Polynesisch	Polinesio	Polynésien	Polinésio
Port.	Portuguese	Portugiesisch	Portugués	Portugais	Português
Rom.	Romanian	Rumänisch	Rumano	Roumain	Romeno
Rus.	Russian	Russisch	Ruso	Russe	Russo
S./C.	Serbo-Croatian	Serbokroatisch	Servio-croata	Serbo-croate	Servo-croata
Sin.	Sinhalese	Singhalesisch	Cingalés	Cinghalais	Cingalês
Slo.	Slovak	Slowakisch	Eslovaco	Slovaque	Eslovaco
Sp.	Spanish	Spanisch	Español	Espagnol	Espanhol
Swe.	Swedish	Schwedisch	Sueco	Suédois	Sueco
Thai	Thai	Thai	Tai	Thaï	Tailandês
Tib.	Tibetan	Tibetisch	Tibetano	Tibétain	Tibetano
Tur.	Turkish	Türkisch	Turco	Turc	Turco
Viet.	Vietnamese	Vietnamesisch	Vietnamita	Vietnamien	Vietnamita
Welsh	Welsh	Walisisch	Galés	Gallois	Galês

ENGLISH	DEUTSCH	Map Form Geographische Begriffe Términos Geográficos Termes Géographiques Termos Geográficos	ESPAÑOL	FRANÇAIS	PORTUGUÊS
			A		
river	Fluss	**-å** *Dan., Nor., Swe.*	río	rivière	rio
brook	Bach	**a., arroyo** *Sp.*	arroyo	ruisseau	córrego
river	Fluss	**āb** *Per.*	río	rivière	rio
army base	Heeresstützpunkt	**a.b., army base** *Eng.*	base del ejército	base d'armée	base militar
well	Brunnen	**ābār** *Ara.*	pozo	puits	poço
abbey	Abtei	**abb., abbazia** *It.*	abadía	abbaye	abadia
abbey	Abtei	**abbaye** *Fr.*	abadía	abbaye	abadia
abbey	Abtei	**abbazia** *It.*	abadía	abbaye	abadia
abbey	Abtei	**abbey** *Eng.*	abadía	abbaye	abadia
aboriginal reserve	Eingeborenenschutzgebiet	**aboriginal reserve** *Eng.*	zona de aborígenes	réserve d'indigènes	reserva indígena
abbey	Abtei	**Abtei** *Ger.*	abadía	abbaye	abadia
ditch	Graben	**acequia** *Sp.*	acequia	fossé	fosso
reservoir	Stausee	**ačude** *Port.*	embalse	réservoir	açude
island(s)	Insel(n)	**ada(lar)** *Tur.*	isla(s)	île(s)	ilha(s)
island	Insel	**adası** *Tur.*	isla	île	ilha
mountains	Berge	**adrar** *Ber.*	montañas	montagnes	montanhas
Atomic Energy Commission	Atomenergiekommission	**A.E.C., Atomic Energy Commission** *Eng.*	Comisión de Energía Atomica	Commission de l'Énergie Atomique	Comissão de Energia Atômica
airport	Flughafen	**aérd., aérodrome** *Fr.*	aeródromo	aérodrome	aeródromo
airport	Flughafen	**aeródromo** *Port., Sp.*	aeródromo	aérodrome	aeródromo
airport	Flughafen	**aeroparque** *Sp.*	aeroparque	aéroport	aeroporto
airport	Flughafen	**aéroport** *Fr.*	aeropuerto	aéroport	aeroporto
airport	Flughafen	**aeroporto** *It., Port.*	aeropuerto	aéroport	aeroporto
airport	Flughafen	**aeropuerto** *Sp.*	aeropuerto	aéroport	aeroporto
air force base	Luftwaffenstützpunkt	**a.f.b., air force base** *Eng.*	base aeronáutica	base aérienne	base aérea
wadi	Wadi	**ahzar** *Ara.*	uadi	wadi	uádi
peak	Gipfel	**aiguille** *Fr.*	pico	aiguille	pico
air base	Luftstützpunkt	**air base** *Eng.*	base aérea	base aérienne	base aérea
airfield	Flugplatz	**airfield** *Eng.*	camp de aviación	aérodrome	campo de pouso
air force base	Luftwaffenstützpunkt	**air force base** *Eng.*	base aeronáutica	base aérienne	base aérea
airport	Flughafen	**airport** *Eng.*	aeropuerto	aéroport	aeroporto
cape	Kap	**ákra, akrotírion** *Gr.*	cabo	cap	cabo
hill	Hügel	**'alam, 'alāmat** *Ara.*	colina	colline	colina
avenue	Allee	**alameda** *Sp.*	alameda	avenue	avenida
alps	Alpen	**alpes** *Fr.*	alpes	alpes	alpes
alps	Alpen	**alpi** *It.*	alpes	alpes	alpes
mountains, hills	Berge, Hügel	**altos** *Sp.*	altos	montagnes, collines	montanhas, colinas
river	Fluss	**-älv,-älven** *Swe.*	río	rivière	rio
amusement park	Vergnügungspark	**amusement park** *Eng.*	parque de diversiones	parc récréatif	parque de diversões
river	Fluss	**-ån** *Swe.*	río	rivière	rio
anchorage	Ankerplatz	**anchorage** *Eng.*	ancladero	ancrage	ancoradouro
bay	Bucht	**angra** *Sp.*	angra	baie	baía
cove	kleine Bucht	**anse** *Fr.*	ensenada	anse	enseada
bay	Bucht	**ao** *Ch.*	bahía	baie	baía
bay	Bucht	**ao** *Thai*	bahía	baie	baía
aqueduct	Aquädukt	**aqueduc** *Fr.*	acueducto	aqueduc	aqueduto
aqueduct	Aquädukt	**aqueduct** *Eng.*	acueducto	aqueduc	aqueduto
archipelago	Archipel	**archipel** *Fr.*	archipiélago	archipel	arquipélago
archipelago	Archipel	**archipelag** *Rus.*	archipiélago	archipel	arquipélago
archipelago	Archipel	**archipelago** *Eng.*	archipiélago	archipel	arquipélago
archipelago	Archipel	**archipiélago** *Sp.*	archipiélago	archipel	arquipélago
arm	Arm	**arm** *Eng.*	brazo	bras	braço de rio
army base	Heeresstützpunkt	**army base** *Eng.*	base del ejército	base d'armée	base militar
airport	Flughafen	**arpt., aéroport** *Fr.* **aeroporto** **aeropuerto** **airport**	aeropuerto	aéroport	aeroporto
archipelago	Archipel	**arquipélago** *Port.*	archipiélago	archipel	arquipélago
reef	Riff	**arrecife** *Sp.*	arrecife	récif	recife
brook	Bach	**arroyo** *Sp.*	arroyo	ruisseau	córrego, arroio
hills	Hügel	**-ås,-åsen** *Swe.*	colinas	collines	colinas
ridge	Höhenrücken	**'assâbet** *Ara.*	sierra	crête	serra
atoll	Atoll	**atol** *Port.*	atolón	atoll	atol
atoll	Atoll	**atoll** *Eng., Fr.*	atolón	atoll	atol
auditorium	Auditorium	**aud., auditorium** *Eng.*	auditorio	auditorium	auditório
race course	Rennbahn	**autodrome** *Fr.*	autódromo	autodrome	autódromo
race course	Rennbahn	**autodromo** *It.*	autódromo	autodrome	autódromo
expressway	Autobahn	**autopista** *Sp.*	autopista	autoroute	via expressa

290 Glossary and Abbreviations of Geographical Terms / Verzeichnis und Abkürzungen Geographischer Begriffe
Glosario y Abreviaciones de Términos Geográficos / Glossaire et Abréviations de Termes Géographiques
Glossário e Abreviações de Termos Geográficos

ENGLISH	DEUTSCH	Map Form Geographische Begriffe Términos Geográficos Termes Géographiques Termos Geográficos	ESPAÑOL	FRANÇAIS	PORTUGUÊS
avenue	Allee	**av., avenida** *Port., Sp.* **avenue**	avenida	avenue	avenida
channel	Kanal	**ava** *Poly.*	canal, estrecho	canal, détroit	canal, estreito
avenue	Allee	**avenida** *Port., Sp.*	avenida	avenue	avenida
spring	Quelle	**'ayn** *Ara.*	manantial	source	manancial, fonte

B

ENGLISH	DEUTSCH	Map Form	ESPAÑOL	FRANÇAIS	PORTUGUÊS
bay	Bucht	**baai** *Du.*	bahía	baie	baía
strait	Meeresstrasse	**bab** *Ara.*	estrecho	détroit	estreito
brook, creek	Bach	**Bach** *Ger.*	arroyo, riachuelo	ruisseau, crique	córrego, arroio
hill	Hügel	**-backen** *Swe.*	colina	colline	colina
bay	Bucht	**badia** *Cat.*	bahía	baie	baía
desert	Wüste	**bādiyat** *Ara.*	desierto	désert	deserto
strait	Meeresstrasse	**bælt** *Dan.*	estrecho	détroit	estreito
bay	Bucht	**bahía** *Sp.*	bahía	baie	baía
inlet	Einfahrt	**bahiret** *Ara.*	abra	bras de mer	enseada, estuário
railroad station	Bahnhof	**Bahnhof** *Ger.*	estacíon de ferrocarril	gare	estação ferroviária
river, sea	Fluss, Meer	**bahr, bahr** *Ara.*	río, mar	rivière, mer	rio, mar
reservoir	Stausee	**baḥrat** *Ara.*	embalse	réservoir	reservatório
bay	Bucht	**baía** *Port.*	bahía	baie	baía
bay	Bucht	**baie** *Fr.*	bahía	baie	baía
reef, sand bar	Riff, Sandbarre	**bajo** *Sp.*	bajo	récif, banc de sable	recife, banco de areia
gorge	Schlucht	**balka** *Rus.*	garganta	gorge	garganta
dome	Kuppe	**ballon** *Fr.*	domo	ballon	domo
marsh	Marsch	**balta** *Rom.*	pantano	marais	pântano
cape	Kap	**-bana** *Jpn.*	cabo	cap	cabo
marsh	Marsch	**bañados** *Sp.*	bañados	marais	pântano
island	Insel	**-banare** *Jpn.*	isla	île	ilha
bank	Bank	**banco** *Sp.*	banco	banc	banco
peninsula	Halbinsel	**bandao** *Ch.*	península	péninsule	península
bank	Bank	**bank** *Eng.*	banco	banc	banco
shoal	Untiefe	**-banken** *Swe.*	bajo	haut-fond	escolho
sand bar	Sandbarre	**barra** *Sp.*	barra	banc de sable	banco de areia
dam	Damm	**barrage** *Fr.*	presa	barrage	represa
ravine	Tobel	**barranca** *Sp.*	barranca	ravin	ravina
air base	Luftstützpunkt	**base aérea** *Sp.*	base aérea	base aérienne	base aérea
basilica	Basilika	**basílica** *Sp.*	basílica	basilique	basílica
basilica	Basilika	**basilique** *Fr.*	basílica	basilique	basílica
basin	Becken	**basin** *Eng.*	cuenca	bassin	bacia
basin	Becken	**bassin** *Fr.*	cuenca	bassin	bacia
marsh	Marsch	**batakliği** *Tur.*	pantano	marais	pântano
river	Fluss	**batang** *Indon.*	río	rivière	rio
river	Fluss	**batha** *Ara.*	río	rivière	rio
marsh	Marsch	**bāṭlāq** *Per.*	pantano	marais	pântano
battlefield	Schlachtfeld	**battlefield** *Eng.*	campo de batalla	champ de bataille	campo de batalha
mountain	Berg	**batu** *Mal.*	montaña	montagne	montanha
bay	Bucht	**bay** *Eng.*	bahía	baie	baía
bayou	Altwasser	**bayou** *Fr., Eng.*	ensenada pantanosa	bayou	enseada pantanosa
beach	Strand	**beach** *Eng.*	playa	plage	praia
mountain	Berg	**bein, beinn** *Gae.*	montaña	montagne	montanha
snowcapped mountains	Schneegipfel	**belogorje** *Rus.*	nevados	montagnes neigeuses	picos nevados
mountain	Berg	**ben** *Gae.*	montaña	montagne	montanha
mountain, hill	Berg	**Berg** *Ger.*	montaña, colina	montagne, colline	montanha, colina
mountains	Gebirge	**-berg** *Afk.*	montañas	montagnes	montanhas
hill(s), mountain(s)	Hügel, Berg(e)	**-berg** *Swe.*	colina(s), montaña(s)	colline(s), montagne(s)	colina(s), montanha(s)
mountains	Berge	**Berge** *Ger.*	montañas	montagnes	montanhas
mountains	Berge	**-berge** *Afk.*	montañas	montagnes	montanhas
hills, mountains	Hügel, Berge	**-bergen** *Swe.*	colinas, montañas	collines, montagnes	colinas, montanhas
hill, mountain	Hügel, Berg	**-berget** *Swe.*	colina, montaña	colline, montagne	colina, montanha
upland	Bergland	**Bergland** *Ger.*	tierras altas	hautes terres	terras altas
battlefield	Schlachtfeld	**bfld., battlefield** *Eng.*	campo de batalla	champ de bataille	campo de batalha
mountain, hill	Berg	**Bg., Berg** *Ger.*	montaña, colina	montagne, colline	montanha, colina
bridge	Brücke	**bge., bridge** *Eng.*	puente	pont	ponte
bight (bay)	Bucht	**bight** *Eng.*	bahía	baie	baía, enseada
bill (point)	Landspitze	**bill** *Eng.*	punta	pointe	ponta
valley	Tal	**biq'at** *Heb.*	valle	vallée	vale
well	Brunnen	**bi'r** *Ara.*	pozo	puits	poço
lake	See	**birkat** *Ara.*	lago	lac	lago
mountains	Berge	**bjeshkët** *Alb.*	montañas	montagnes	montanhas
brook	Bach	**bk., brook** *Eng.*	arroyo	ruisseau	córrego, arroio
upland	Bergland	**blaenau** *Welsh*	tierras altas	hautes terres	terras altas
bluff(s)	Steilufer	**bluff(s)** *Eng.*	acantilado(s)	falaise(s)	falésia(s)
boulevard	Boulevard	**blvd., boulevard** *Fr., Eng.*	boulevar	boulevard	bulevar
mountain	Berg	**b'nom** *Viet.*	montaña	montagne	montanha
river mouth	Flussmündung	**boca** *Sp.*	boca	embouchure	foz
river mouth, pass	Flussmündung, Pass	**bocca** *It.*	boca, paso	embouchure, col	foz, passo
bay	Bucht	**bocht** *Du.*	bahía	baie	baía
bay	Bodden	**Bodden** *Ger.*	bahía	baie	baía
lake	See	**bœng** *Cbd.*	lago	lac	lago
bog	Moor	**bog** *Eng.*	pantano	fondrière	pântano
strait	Meeresstrasse	**boğazı** *Tur.*	estrecho	détroit	estreito
range	Gebirge	**bogd** *Mong.*	sierra	chaîne	cordilheira
woods	Gehölz	**bois** *Fr.*	bosque	bois	bosque
enclosed basin	Becken	**bolsón** *Sp.*	bolsón	bassin fermée	bacia fechada
forest	Wald	**bory** *Pol.*	bosque	forêt	floresta
forest	Wald	**bosque** *Sp.*	bosque	forêt	floresta
boulevard	Boulevard	**boulevard** *Fr., Eng.*	boulevar	boulevard	bulevar
branch	Arm	**br., branch** *Eng.*	brazo	bras	braço
stream distributary	Flussarm	**braţul** *Rom.*	brazo de río	bras	braço de rio
breakwater	Wellenbrecher	**breakwater** *Eng.*	rompeolas	brise-lames	quebra-mar
glacier	Gletscher	**-breen** *Nor.*	glaciar	glacier	geleria
bridge	Brücke	**bridge** *Eng.*	puente	pont	ponte
marsh	Bruch	**Bruch** *Ger.*	pantano	marais	pântano
bridge	Brücke	**Brücke** *Ger.*	puente	pont	ponte
bridge	Brücke	**brug** *Du.*	puente	pont	ponte
bay	Bucht	**Bucht** *Ger.*	bahía	baie	baía
bay	Bucht	**buchta** *Rus.*	bahía	baie	baía
mountain	Berg	**bufa** *Sp.*	bufa	montagne	montanha
bay	Bucht	**bugt** *Dan.*	bahía	baie	baía
lake	See	**buḥayrah** *Ara.*	lago	lac	lago
lake, lagoon	See, Lagune, Haff	**buḥayrat** *Ara.*	lago, laguna	lac, lagune	lago, laguna
mountain, hill	Berg, Hügel	**bukit** *Indon., Mal.*	montaña, colina	montagne, colline	montanha, colina
bay	Bucht	**-bukten** *Swe.*	bahía	baie	baía
mountain	Berg	**bulu** *Indon.*	montaña	montagne	montanha
castle	Burg	**Burg** *Ger.*	castillo	château	castelo
hill	Hügel	**burj** *Ara.*	colina	colline	colina
brook	Bach	**burn** *Gae.*	riachuelo	crique	riacho
cape	Kap	**burnu, burun** *Tur.*	cabo	cap	cabo
bay	Busen	**Busen** *Ger.*	bahía	baie	baía
butte(s)	Restberg(e)	**butte(s)** *Eng., Fr.*	butte(s)	butte(s)	colina, outeiro

C

ENGLISH	DEUTSCH	Map Form	ESPAÑOL	FRANÇAIS	PORTUGUÊS
cape	Kap	**c. , cabo** *Sp.* **cap cape**	cabo	cap	cabo
street	Strasse	**c., calle** *Sp.*	calle	rue	rua
peaks	Gipfel	**cabezas** *Sp.*	cabezas	cimes	picos
cape	Kap	**cabo** *Port., Sp.*	cabo	cap	cabo
waterfall	Wasserfall	**cachoeira** *Port.*	cascada	chute d'eau	cachoeira
street	Strasse	**calle** *Sp.*	calle	rue	rua
parkway	Ferienstrasse	**calzada** *Sp.*	calzada	allée de parc	alameda de parque
mosque	Moschee	**camıı** *Tur.*	mezquita	mosqée	mesquita
road	Landstrasse	**camino** *Sp.*	camino	route	rodovia
camp	Lager	**camp** *Eng., Fr.*	campo	camp	campo
plain	Ebene	**campo** *It.*	llanura	plaine	planície
brook, ravine	Bach, Tobel	**cañada** *Sp.*	cañada	ruisseau, ravin	ravina
canal	Kanal	**canal** *Eng.*	canal	canal	canal
canal, channel	Kanal	**canal** *Fr., Port., Sp.*	canal	canal	canal
canal, channel	Kanal	**canale** *It.*	canal	canal	canal
stream distributary	Flussarm	**caño** *Sp.*	caño	bras	braço de rio, igarapé
canyon	Cañon	**cañón** *Sp.*	cañón	canyon	canhão
canyon	Cañon	**canyon** *Eng.*	cañón	canyon	canhão
plateau	Hochebene	**cao nguyen** *Viet.*	meseta	plateau	planalto
cape	Kap	**cap** *Fr., Cat.*	cabo	cap	cabo
cape	Kap	**cape** *Eng.*	cabo	cap	cabo
capitol	Kapitol	**capitolio** *Sp.*	capitolio	capitole	capitólio
cape	Kap	**capo** *It.*	cabo	cap	cabo
captain	Kapitän	**capt., captain** *Eng.*	capitán	capitaine	capitão
highway	Strasse	**carretera** *Sp.*	carretera	route	rodovia
valley	Tal	**carse** *Gae.*	valle	vallée	vale
waterfall	Wasserfall	**cascada** *Sp.*	cascada	chute d'eau	queda d'água
waterfall	Wasserfall	**cascata** *It.*	cascada	chute d'eau	queda d'água
castle	Burg, Schloss	**castel, castello** *It.*	castillo	château	castelo
castle	Burg, Schloss	**castelo** *Port.*	castillo	château	castelo
castle	Burg, Schloss	**castillo** *Sp.*	castillo	château	castelo
castle	Burg, Schloss	**castle** *Eng.*	castillo	château	castelo
cataracts	Katarakten	**cataratas** *Port., Sp.*	cataratas	cataractes	cataratas
cathedral	Kathedrale	**catedral** *Sp.*	catedral	cathédrale	catedral
range	Gebirge	**catena** *Sp.*	catena	chaîne	cordilheira
cathedral	Kathedrale	**cathedral** *Eng.*	catedral	cathédrale	catedral
causeway	Dammweg	**causeway** *Eng.*	calzada	chaussée	calçada
upland	Bergland	**causse** *Fr.*	tierras altas	causse	terras altas
cave(s)	Höhle(n)	**cave(s)** *Eng.*	cueva(s)	caverne(s)	caverna(s)
cay (islet)	Klippe	**cay** *Eng.*	cayo	caye	baixio
cay(s), islet(s)	Klippe(n)	**cayo(s)** *Sp.*	cayo(s)	caye(s)	baixio(s)
cemetery	Friedhof	**cementerio** *Sp.*	cementerio	cimetière	cemitério
cemetery	Friedhof	**cemetery** *Eng.*	cementerio	cimetière	cemitério
mountain(s), hill(s)	Berg(e), Hügel	**cerro(s)** *Sp.*	cerro(s)	montagne(s), colline(s)	montanha(s), colina(s)
range	Gebirge	**chaîne** *Fr.*	sierra	chaîne	cordilheira
channel	Kanal	**channel** *Eng.*	canal, estrecho	canal, détroit	canal, estreito
hills	Hügel	**chapada** *Port.*	colinas	collines	chapada
island	Insel	**char** *Ben.*	isla	île	ilha
castle	Burg, Schloss	**château** *Fr.*	castillo	château	castelo
road	Landstrasse	**chemin** *Fr.*	camino	chemin	rodovia
bay	Bucht	**chhâk** *Cbd.*	bahía	baie	baía
lake	See	**chi** *Ch.*	lago	lac	lago
harbor, harbour	Hafen	**chiang** *Ch.*	puerto	port	porto
cape	Kap	**chiao** *Ch.*	cabo	cap	cabo
road	Landstrasse	**chin., chemin** *Fr.*	camino	chemin	rodovia
river	Fluss	**-ch'ŏn** *Kor.*	río	rivière	rio
reservoir	Stausee	**-chŏsuji** *Kor.*	embalse	réservoir	reservatório
intermittent lake, salt marsh	periodischer See, Salzmarsch	**chott** *Ara.*	lago intermitente, pantano salado	lac périodique, marais salé	lago intermitente, pântano salgado
range	Gebirge	**chr., chrebet** *Rus.*	sierra	chaîne	cordilheira
mountains	Berge	**chuŏr phnum** *Cbd.*	montañas	montagnes	montanhas
church	Kirche	**church** *Eng.*	iglesia	église	igreja
waterfalls	Wasserfälle	**chutes** *Fr.*	cascadas	chutes d'eau	quedas d'água
marsh	Marsch	**ciénaga** *Sp.*	ciénaga	marais	pântano
peak	Gipfel	**cima** *It., Sp.*	cima	cime	pico
peak	Gipfel	**cime** *Fr.*	cima	cime	pico
cemetery	Friedhof	**cimetière** *Fr.*	cementerio	cimetière	cemitério
city	Stadt	**città** *It.*	ciudad	ville	cidade
city	Stadt	**city** *Eng.*	ciudad	ville	cidade
city	Stadt	**ciudad** *Sp.*	ciudad	ville	cidade
claypan	Tonpfanne	**claypan** *Eng.*	capa de arcilla	couche argilleuse	camada de argila
cliff(s)	Kliff(e)	**cliff(s)** *Eng.*	risco(s)	falaise(s)	falésia(s)
lake	See	**co** *Tib.*	lago	lac	lago
mountain	Berg	**co** *Viet.*	montaña	montagne	montanha
mountain, hill	Berg, Hügel	**co., cerro** *Sp.*	cerro	montagne, colline	montanha, colina
coast	Küste	**coast** *Eng.*	costa	côte	costa
coast guard station	Küstenwacht-station	**coast guard station** *Eng.*	estación de los guardacostas	station des gardescôte	estação de guarda costeira
pass	Pass	**col** *Fr.*	paso	col	passo
college	Hochschule	**colegio** *Sp.*	colegio	collège	colégio
hill(s)	Hügel	**colina(s)** *Sp.*	colina(s)	colline(s)	colina(s)
college	Hochschule	**coll., college** *Eng.*	colegio	collège	colégio
hills	Hügel	**colli** *It.*	colinas	collines	colinas
hills	Hügel	**colline** *It.*	colinas	collines	colinas
hills	Hügel	**collines** *Fr.*	colinas	collines	colinas
common	Gemeindeland	**common** *Eng.*	campo común	commune	terra comum
islands	Inseln	**con** *Viet.*	islas	îles	ilhas
plain	Ebene	**conca** *It.*	llanura	plaine	planície
convent	Nonnenkloster	**convent** *Eng.*	convento	couvent	convento
convent	Nonnenkloster	**convento** *It., Port., Sp.*	convento	couvent	convento
range	Gebirge	**cord., cordillera** *Sp.*	cordillera	chaîne	cordilheira
mountain	Berg	**corno** *It.*	montaña	montagne	montanha
brook	Bach	**córrego** *Port.*	arroyo	ruisseau	córrego
coast	Küste	**costa** *Sp.*	costa	côte	costa
coast, hills	Küste, Hügel	**côte** *Fr.*	costa, colinas	côte	costa, colinas
hills	Hügel	**coteau** *Fr.*	colinas	coteau	colinas
coulee	breite Schlucht	**coulee** *Eng.*	rambla	coulée	barranco
coulee	breite Schlucht	**coulée** *Fr.*	rambla	coulée	barranco
county park	Park	**county park** *Eng.*	parque del condado	parc de comté	parque de condado
convent	Nonnenkloster	**couvent** *Fr.*	convento	couvent	convento
cove	kleine Bucht	**cove** *Eng.*	ensenada	anse	enseada
brook	Bach	**cr., creek** *Eng.*	riachuelo	crique	riacho
crag	Felsspitze	**crag** *Eng.*	despeñadero	pointe de rocher	despenhadeiro
crater	Krater	**crater** *Eng.*	cráter	cratère	cratera
crater	Krater	**cratère** *Fr.*	cráter	cratère	cratera
creek	Bach	**creek** *Eng.*	riachuelo	crique	riacho
peak	Gipfel	**croda** *It.*	pico	cime	pico
canal	Kanal	**csatorna** *Hung.*	canal	canal	canal
bay	Bucht	**cua** *Viet.*	bahía	baie	baía
hills, ridge	Hügel, Höhenrücken	**cuchilla** *Sp.*	cuchilla	collines, crête	coxilha
caves	Höhen	**cuevas** *Sp.*	cuevas	cavernes	cavernas
cove	kleine Bucht	**cul-de-sac** *Fr.*	ensenada	cul-de-sac	enseada
mountains	Berge	**culmea** *Rom.*	montañas	montagnes	montanhas
summit	Gipfel	**cumbre** *Sp.*	cumbre	sommet	cume

D

ENGLISH	DEUTSCH	Map Form	ESPAÑOL	FRANÇAIS	PORTUGUÊS
mountain	Berg	**dağ, dağı** *Tur.*	montaña	montagne	montanha
mountains	Berge	**dāgh** *Per.*	montañas	montagnes	montanhas
mountains	Berge	**dağlar, dağları** *Tur.*	montañas	montagnes	montanhas
hill	Hügel	**ḍahr** *Ara.*	colina	colline	colina
plateau	Hochebene	**-dai, -daichi** *Jpn.*	meseta	plateau	planalto
mountain	Berg	**-dake** *Jpn.*	montaña	montagne	montanha
valley	Tal	**-dal, -dalen** *Nor., Swe.*	valle	vallée	vale
dale	weites Tal	**dale** *Eng.*	valle ancho	vallée large	vale aberto
dam	Damm	**dam** *Eng.*	presa	barrage	represa
lake	See	**danau** *Indon.*	lago	lac	lago
island	Insel	**dao** *Ch., Viet.*	isla	île	ilha
marsh	Marsch	**daqq** *Per.*	pantano	marais	pântano
lake	See	**daryācheh** *Per.*	lago	lac	lago
desert	Wüste	**dasht** *Per.*	desierto	désert	deserto
monastery	Kloster	**dayr** *Ara.*	monasterio	monastère	mosteiro

Glossary and Abbreviations of Geographical Terms / Verzeichnis und Abkürzungen Geographischer Begriffe
Glosario y Abreviaciones de Términos Geográficos / Glossaire et Abréviations de Termes Géographiques
Glossário e Abreviações de Termos Geográficos
291

ENGLISH	DEUTSCH	Map Form / Geographische Begriffe / Términos Geográficos / Termes Géographiques / Termos Geográficos	ESPAÑOL	FRANÇAIS	PORTUGUÊS
deep	Tiefe	**deep** *Eng.*	fosa marina	fossé marin	fossa submarina
delta	Delta	**delta** *Eng., Fr., Sp.*	delta	delta	delta
sea	Meer	**deniz, denizi** *Tur.*	mar	mer	mar
monument	Denkmal	**Denkmal** *Ger.*	monumento	monument	monumento
pass	Pass	**deo** *Viet.*	paso	col	passo
depression	Senke	**depression** *Eng.*	depresión	dépression	depressão
river	Fluss	**deresi** *Tur.*	río	rivière	rio
desert	Wüste	**desert** *Eng.*	desierto	désert	deserto
desert	Wüste	**desierto** *Sp.*	desierto	désert	deserto
strait	Meeresstrasse	**détroit** *Fr.*	estrecho	détroit	estreito
escarpment	Landstufe	**dhar** *Ara.*	escarpa	escarpement	escarpa
canal	Kanal	**dhiórix** *Gr.*	canal	canal	canal
lake, marsh	See, Marsch	**dian** *Ch.*	lago, pantano	lac, marais	lago, pântano
channel	Kanal	**diep** *Du.*	canal, estrecho	canal, détroit	canal, estreito
dike	Deich	**dijk** *Du.*	dique	digue	dique
district	Distrikt	**district** *Eng.*	distrito	district	distrito
district	Distrikt	**distrito** *Sp.*	distrito	district	distrito
ditch	Graben	**ditch** *Eng.*	acequia	fossé	fosso
mountain(s)	Berg(e)	**djebel** *Ara.*	montaña(s)	montagne(s)	montanha(s)
fjord	Fjord	**-djúp** *Ice.*	fiordo	fjord	fiorde
channel, sound	Kanal, Sund	**-djupet** *Swe.*	canal, sonda	canal, détroit	canal, estreito
zoo	Zoo	**djurpark** *Swe.*	parque zoológico	zoo	jardim zoológico
island	Insel	**-do** *Kor.*	isla	île	ilha
interfluve	Erhebung	**doāb** *Per.*	interfluvio	interfluve	interflúvio
dock	Dock	**dock** *Eng.*	muelle	quai	doca
mountain	Berg	**doi** *Thai*	montaña	montagne	montanha
valley	Tal	**dolina** *Rus.*	valle	vallée	vale
mountain	Berg	**dolok** *Indon.*	montaña	montagne	montanha
hills	Hügel	**dombrovidék** *Hung.*	colinas	collines	colinas
hills	Hügel	**dombvidék** *Hung.*	colinas	collines	colinas
peak	Gipfel	**dos** *Fr.*	pico	dos	pico
downs (hills)	Hügelland	**downs** *Eng.*	colinas	collines	terras baixas (colinas)
drive	Fahrweg	**dr., drive** *Eng.*	calzada	avenue	avenida
drain (water-course)	Abzugsgraben	**drain** *Eng.*	desaguadero	drainage	escoadouro
draw (ravine)	kleines Tal	**draw** *Eng.*	valle pequeño	ravine	bacia, vale
drive	Fahrweg	**drive** *Eng.*	calzada	avenue	avenida
dry lake	Trockensee	**dry lake** *Eng.*	lago seco	lac asséché	lago seco
dunes	Dünen	**dunes** *Eng., Fr.*	dunas	dunes	dunas

E

ENGLISH	DEUTSCH	Map Form	ESPAÑOL	FRANÇAIS	PORTUGUÊS
east	Ost	**e., east** *Eng.*	este	est	leste
school	Schule	**école** *Fr.*	escuela	école	escola
mountain	Berg	**-egga** *Nor.*	montaña	montagne	montanha
memorial	Ehrenmal	**Ehrenmal** *Ger.*	monumento	memorial	monumento
river	Fluss	**-elv,-elva** *Nor.*	río	rivière	rio
reservoir	Stausee	**embalse** *Sp.*	embalse	réservoir	reservatório
pier	Landungsbrücke	**embarcadero** *Sp.*	embarcadero	jetée	cais
valley	Tal	**'emeq** *Heb.*	valle	vallée	vale
monument	Denkmal	**emlékmü** *Hung.*	monumento	monument	monumento
spring	Quelle	**'en** *Heb.*	manantial	source	fonte, manancial
cove	kleine Bucht	**enseada** *Port.*	ensenada	anse	enseada
cove	kleine Bucht	**ensenada** *Sp.*	ensenada	anse	enseada
entrance	Einfahrt	**entrance** *Eng.*	entrada	entrée	entrada
forest	Wald	**erdö** *Hung.*	bosque	forêt	floresta
sand desert	Sandwüste	**erg** *Ara.*	desierto arenoso	désert de sable	deserto arenoso
escarpment	Landstufe	**escarpment** *Eng.*	escarpa	escarpement	escarpa
school	Schule	**escuela** *Sp.*	escuela	école	escola
highland	Hochland	**espigão** *Port.*	región montañosa	pays montagneux	espigão
station	Bahnhof, Stützpunkt	**est., estação** *Port.* **estación**	estación	station	estação
stadium	Stadion	**estadio** *Sp.*	estadio	stade	estádio
reservoir	Stausee	**estanque** *Sp.*	estanque	réservoir	reservatório
estuary	Trichtermündung	**estero** *Sp.*	estero	estuaire	estuário
road	Landstrasse	**estr., estrada** *Port.*	camino	route	estrada
strait	Meeresstrasse	**estrecho** *Sp.*	estrecho	détroit	estreito
estuary	Trichtermündung	**estuary** *Eng.*	estuario	estuaire	estuário
pond	Teich	**étang** *Fr.*	charca	étang	lagoa, açude
expressway	Autobahn	**expy., expressway** *Eng.*	autopista	autoroute	via expressa
island	Insel	**-ey** *Ice.*	isla	île	ilha
lake	See	**ežeras** *Lith.*	lago	lac	lago
lake	See	**ezers** *Latv.*	lago	lac	lago

F

ENGLISH	DEUTSCH	Map Form	ESPAÑOL	FRANÇAIS	PORTUGUÊS
faculty (school)	Fakultät	**faculté** *Fr.*	facultad	faculté	faculdade
fairground	Ausstellungsgelände	**fairground** *Eng.*	campo para ferias	champ de foire	terreno para feiras
cliff	Kliff	**falaise** *Fr.*	risco	falaise	falésia
fall(s) (waterfall)	Wasserfall	**falls(s)** *Eng.*	cascada	chute d'eau	queda d'agua
waterfall	Fall	**Fall** *Ger.*	cascada	chute d'eau	queda d'água
waterfall	Wasserfall	**-fallet** *Swe.*	cascada	chute d'eau	queda d'água
river	Fluss	**far'** *Ara.*	río	rivière	rio
lighthouse	Leuchtturm	**faro** *Sp.*	faro	phare	farol
upland	Bergland	**farsh** *Ara.*	tierras altas	hautes terres	terras altas
fell (mountain, hill)	ödes Hügelland	**fell** *Eng.*	colina rocosa	colline rocheuse	colina rochosa
mountain	Berg	**-fell** *Ice.*	montaña	montagne	montanha
mountain	Berg	**feng** *Ch.*	montaña	montagne	montanha
upland	Bergland	**fennsík** *Hung.*	tierras altas	hautes terres	terras altas
ferry	Fähre	**ferry** *Eng.*	balsadera	bac	balsa
lake	See	**fertö** *Hung.*	lago	lac	lago
fortress	Feste	**Feste** *Ger.*	fortaleza	fort	fortaleza
estuary, strait	Trichtermündung, Meeresstrasse	**firth** *Gae.*	estuario, estrecho	estuaire, détroit	estuário, estreito
mountain(s)	Berg(e)	**fjäll(en)** *Swe.*	montaña(s)	montagne(s)	montanha(s)
mountain	Berg	**fjället** *Swe.*	montaña	montagne	montanha
fjord	Fjord	**fjärden** *Swe.*	fiordo	fjord	fiorde
mountain	Berg	**-fjell, -fjellet** *Nor.*	montaña	montagne	montanha
mountain	Berg	**-fjöll** *Ice.*	montaña	montagne	montanha
fjord	Fjord	**-fjord** *Nor.*	fiordo	fjord	fiorde
fjord, lake	Fjord, See	**-fjorden** *Nor., Swe.*	fiordo, lago	fjord, lac	fiorde, lago
fjord, bay	Fjord, Bucht	**-fjörður** *Ice.*	fiordo, bahía	fjord, baie	fiorde, baía
fork	Arm	**fk., fork** *Eng.*	brazo	bras	braço de rio
flat	Flachland	**flat** *Eng.*	llano	plat	planície
river	Fluss	**-fljót** *Ice.*	río	rivière	rio
bay	Bucht	**-flói** *Ice.*	bahía	baie	baía
flood control basin	Hochwasserrückhaltebecken	**flood control basin** *Eng.*	cuenca para controlar la inundación	bassin de contrôle d'inondation	bacia de controle de inundações
airport	Flugplatz	**Flughafen** *Ger.*	aeropuerto	aéroport	aeroporto
airport	Flugplatz	**Flugplatz** *Ger.*	aeropuerto	aérodrome	aeroporto
airport	Flughafen	**flygplats** *Swe.*	aeródromo	aérodrome	aeródromo
river mouth, pass	Flussmündung, Pass	**foce** *It.*	desembocadura, paso	embouchure, col	desembocadura, foz, passo
canal	Kanal	**föcsatorna** *Hung.*	canal	canal	canal
glacier	Gletscher	**-fonn** *Nor.*	glaciar	glacier	geleira
spring	Quelle	**fontaine** *Fr.*	manantial	fontaine	fonte, manancial
pass	Pass	**forca** *It.*	paso	col	passo

ENGLISH	DEUTSCH	Map Form / Geographische Begriffe / Términos Geográficos / Termes Géographiques / Termos Geográficos	ESPAÑOL	FRANÇAIS	PORTUGUÊS
inlet	Förde	**Förde** *Ger.*	abra	bras de mer	enseada, estuário
foreland	Vorland	**foreland** *Eng.*	promontorio	promontoire	promontório
forest	Wald	**forest** *Eng.*	bosque	forêt	floresta
forest reserve	Waldreservat	**forest reserve** *Eng.*	reserva de bosque	réserve forestière	reserva florestal
forest	Wald	**forêt** *Fr.*	bosque	forêt	floresta
waterfall	Wasserfall	**-forsen** *Swe.*	cascada	chute d'eau	queda d'água
forest	Forst	**Forst** *Ger.*	bosque	forêt	floresta
fort	Fort	**fort** *Eng., Fr.*	fuerte	fort	forte
waterfall	Wasserfall	**-foss** *Ice.*	cascada	chute d'eau	queda d'água
waterfall	Wasserfall	**-fossen** *Nor.*	cascada	chute d'eau	queda d'água
brook	Bach	**fosso** *It.*	arroyo	ruisseau	córrego
pass	Pass	**foum** *Ara.*	paso	col	passo
fracture zone	Bruchzone	**fracture zone** *Eng.*	zona de fractura	zone de faille	zona de fratura
freeway	Autobahn	**frwy., freeway** *Eng.*	autopista	autoroute	via expressa
fort	Fort	**ft., fort** *Eng., Fr.*	fuerte	fort	forte
stream distributary	Flussarm	**furo** *Port.*	brazo de río	bras	furo

G

ENGLISH	DEUTSCH	Map Form	ESPAÑOL	FRANÇAIS	PORTUGUÊS
mountain, hill	Berg, Hügel	**g., gora** *Rus.*	montaña, colina	montagne, colline	montanha, colina
mountain	Berg	**g., gunong** *Mal.* **gunung**	montaña	montagne	montanha
mountain	Berg	**-gai'sa** *Lapp.*	montaña	montagne	montanha
tunnel	Tunnel	**galleria** *It.*	túnel	tunnel	túnel
gallery	Galerie	**gallery** *Eng.*	galería	galerie	galeria
game farm	Wildfarm	**game farm** *Eng.*	criadero de caza	ferme de gibier	fazenda de caça
game park	Wildpark	**game park** *Eng.*	vedado de caza	parc à gibier	parque de caça
game refuge	Wildgehege	**game refuge** *Eng.*	refugio de caza	refuge de gibier	refúgio de caça
game reserve	Wildreservat	**game reserve** *Eng.*	vedado de caza	réserve à gibier	reserva de caça
game sanctuary	Wildschutzgebiet	**game sanctuary** *Eng.*	vedado de caza	réserve à gibier	santuario de caça
bay	Bucht	**gang** *Ch.*	bahía	baie	baía
river	Fluss	**-gang** *Kor.*	río	rivière	rio
gap	Pass	**gap** *Eng.*	paso	col	passo
intermittent lake	periodischer See	**garaet** *Ara.*	lago intermitente	lac périodique	lago intermitente
garden	Garten	**gard., garden** *Eng.*	jardín	jardin	jardim
gardens	Gärten	**gardens** *Eng.*	jardines	jardins	jardins
mountain	Berg	**garet** *Ara.*	montaña	montagne	montanha
lake	See	**-gata** *Jpn.*	lago	lac	lago
gate	Tor	**gate** *Eng.*	puerta	porte	portão
mountain torrent	Wildbach	**gave** *Fr.*	torrente	gave	torrente
range	Gebirge	**gebergte** *Du.*	sierra	chaîne	cordilheira
range	Gebirge	**Gebirge** *Ger.*	sierra	chaîne	cordilheira
pass	Pass	**geçidi** *Tur.*	paso	col	passo
oasis, well	Oase, Brunnen	**ghadīr** *Ara.*	oasis, pozo	oasis, puits	oásis, poço
mountains	Gebirge	**ghar** *Pas.*	montañas	montagnes	montanhas
spring	Quelle	**ghayl** *Ara.*	manantial	source	manancial
bay	Bucht	**ghubbat** *Ara.*	bahía	baie	baía
dunes	Dünen	**ghurd** *Ara.*	dunas	dunes	dunas
island	Insel	**gili** *Indon.*	isla	île	ilha
peak	Gipfel	**Gipfel** *Ger.*	pico	cime	pico
hill	Hügel	**giva't** *Heb.*	colina	colline	colina
bay	Bucht	**gji** *Alb.*	bahía	baie	baía
glacier	Gletscher	**glacier** *Eng., Fr.*	glaciar	glacier	geleira
lake	See	**göl** *Tur.*	lago	lac	lago
bald mountains	kahle Berge	**gol'cy** *Rus.*	montañas calvas	monts chauves	montanhas calvas
gulf	Golf	**golf** *Cat.*	golfo	golfe	golfo
golf course	Golfplatz	**golf course** *Eng.*	campo de golf	champ de golf	campo de golfe
gulf	Golf	**golfe** *Fr.*	golfo	golfe	golfo
bay	Bucht	**golfete** *Sp.*	golfete	baie	baía
gulf	Golf	**golfo** *It., Sp.*	golfo	golfe	golfo
lake	See	**gölü** *Tur.*	lago	lac	lago
mountain, hill	Berg, Hügel	**gora** *Rus.*	montaña, colina	montagne, colline	montanha, colina
mountains	Berge	**gora** *S./C.*	montañas	montagnes	montanhas
mountain	Berg	**góra** *Pol.*	montaña	montagne	montanha
gorge	Schlucht	**gorge** *Eng., Fr.*	garganta	gorge	garganta
mountains, hills	Berge, Hügel	**gorje** *S./C.*	montañas, colinas	montagnes, collines	montanhas, colinas
ruins	Ruinen	**gorodišče** *Rus.*	ruinas	ruines	ruínas
mountains, hills	Berge, Hügel	**gory** *Rus.*	montañas, colinas	montagnes, collines	montanhas, colinas
mountains	Berge	**góry** *Pol.*	montañas	montagnes	montanhas
sinkhole	Schluckloch	**gouffre** *Fr.*	sumidero	gouffre	sumidouro
wadi	Wadi	**goulbin** *Hau.*	uadi	wadi	uádi
ditch	Graben	**Graben** *Ger.*	acequia	fossé	fosso
ridge	Höhenrücken	**gr'ada** *Rus.*	sierra	crête	cordilheira
mountain	Berg	**gradište** *Blg.*	montaña	montagne	montanha
ridges	Höhenrücken	**gr'ady** *Rus.*	sierras	crêtes	cordilheira
general	General	**gral., general** *Eng., Sp.*	general	général	geral
ridge	Grat	**Grat** *Ger.*	sierra	crête	cordilheira
grotto	Grotte	**grotta** *It.*	gruta	grotte	gruta
grotto	Grotte	**grotte** *Fr.*	gruta	grotte	gruta
group	Gruppe	**group** *Eng.*	grupo	groupe	grupo
island	Insel	**-grund** *Swe.*	isla	île	ilha
group	Gruppe	**grupo** *Sp.*	grupo	groupe	grupo
group	Gruppe	**groppo** *It.*	grupo	groupe	grupo
pass	Pass	**guan** *Ch.*	paso	col	passo
bay	Bucht	**guba** *Rus.*	bahía	baie	baía
mountain	Berg	**guelb** *Ara.*	montaña	montagne	montanha
gulch	Wildbachschlucht	**gulch** *Eng.*	quebrada	ravin	quebrada
gulf	Golf	**gulf** *Eng.*	golfo	golfe	golfo
mountain	Berg	**gunong** *Mal.*	montaña	montagne	montanha
mountain	Berg	**gunung** *Indon.*	montaña	montagne	montanha
islands	Inseln	**-guntō** *Jpn.*	islas	îles	ilhas

H

ENGLISH	DEUTSCH	Map Form	ESPAÑOL	FRANÇAIS	PORTUGUÊS
upland	Bergland	**hadabat** *Ara.*	tierras altas	hautes terres	terras altas
mountain	Berg	**hadjer** *Ara.*	montaña	montagne	montanha
lagoon	Haff	**Haff** *Ger.*	laguna	lagune	laguna
sea, lake	Meer, See	**hai** *Ch.*	mar, lago	mer, lac	mar, lago
strait	Meeresstrasse	**haixia** *Ch.*	estrecho	détroit	estreito
reef	Riff	**hakau** *Poly.*	arrecife	récif	recife
peninsula	Halbinsel	**Halbinsel** *Ger.*	península	péninsule	península
hall	Halle	**hall** *Eng., Fr.*	salón	hall	hall
peninsula	Halbinsel	**-halvøya** *Nor.*	península	péninsule	península
beach	Strand	**-hama** *Jpn.*	playa	plage	praia
desert	Wüste	**hamada** *Ara.*	desierto	désert	deserto
plateau	Hochebene	**hammādat** *Ara.*	meseta	plateau	planalto
lake, marsh	See, Marsch	**hāmūn** *Per.*	lago, pantano	lac, marais	lago, pântano
point	Landspitze	**-hana** *Jpn.*	punta	pointe	ponta
peninsula	Halbinsel	**-hantō** *Jpn.*	península	péninsule	península
mountain, hill	Berg, Hügel	**har** *Heb.*	montaña, colina	montagne, colline	montanha, colina
harbor, harbour	Hafen	**harbor, harbour** *Eng.*	puerto	port	porto
mountains, hills	Berge, Hügel	**hare** *Heb.*	montañas, colinas	montagnes, collines	montanhas, colinas
ridge	Höhenrücken	**-harju** *Finn.*	sierra	crête	cordilheira
lava flow	Lavastrom	**harrat** *Ara.*	corriente de lava	coulée de lave	corrente de lava
hills	Hügel	**hauteurs** *Fr.*	colinas	hauteurs	colinas
sea, bay	Meer, Bucht	**-hav** *Swe.*	mar, bahía	mer, baie	mar, baía
harbor, harbour	Hafen	**havre** *Fr.*	puerto	havre	porto
oasis	Oase	**hawd** *Ara.*	oasis	oasis	oásis
lake	See	**hawr** *Ara.*	lago	lac	lago

292 Glossary and Abbreviations of Geographical Terms / Verzeichnis und Abkürzungen Geographischer Begriffe
Glosario y Abreviaciones de Términos Geográficos / Glossaire et Abréviations de Termes Géographiques
Glossário e Abreviações de Termos Geográficos

ENGLISH	DEUTSCH	Map Form Geographische Begriffe Términos Geográficos Termes Géographiques Termos Geográficos	ESPAÑOL	FRANÇAIS	PORTUGUÊS
harbor, harbour	Hafen	**hbr., harbor, harbour** *Eng.*	puerto	port	porto
headquarters	Hauptquartier	**hdqrs., headquarters** *Eng.*	cuartel general	guartier général	quartel-general
river	Fluss	**he** *Ch.*	río	rivière	rio
head (headland)	Landspitze	**head** *Eng.*	promontorio	promontoire	promontório
heath	Heide	**heath** *Eng.*	matorral	lande	charneca
mountain(s)	Berg(e)	**hegy(ség)** *Hung.*	montaņa(s)	montagne(s)	montanha(s)
heath	Heide	**Heide** *Ger.*	matorral	lande	charneca
plain	Ebene	**-heiya** *Jpn.*	llanura	plaine	planície
hills	Hügel	**-heuwells** *Afk.*	colinas	collines	colinas
highland	Hochland	**highland** *Eng.*	región montañosa	pays montagneux	terras altas
highway	Strasse	**highway** *Eng.*	carretera	route	rodovia
hill(s)	Hügel	**hill(s)** *Eng.*	colina(s)	colline(s)	colina(s)
race course	Rennbahn	**hipódromo** *Sp.*	hipódromo	hippodrome	hipódromo
race course	Rennbahn	**hippodrome** *Fr.*	hipódromo	hippodrome	hipódromo
historical	historisch	**hist., historical** *Eng.*	histórico	historique	histórico
historical park	historischer Park	**historical park** *Eng.*	parque histórico	parc historique	parque histórico
historic(al) site	historische Stätte	**historic(al) site** *Eng.*	sitio histórico	site historique	sítio histórico
Her Majesty's Air Station (U.K.)	Luftwaffen-stützpunkt (V.K.)	**H.M.A.S., Her Majesty's Air Station** *Eng.*	Real Estación Aeronáutica (R.U.)	Station Aérienne Royale (R.U.)	Estação Aérea Real (R.U.)
river	Fluss	**ho** *Ch.*	río	rivière	rio
reservoir	Stausee	**-ho** *Kor.*	embalse	réservoir	reservatório
mountain	Berg	**-hø** *Nor.*	montaña	montagne	montanha
plateau	Hochebene	**Hochebene** *Ger.*	meseta	plateau	planalto
forest	Hochwald	**Hochwald** *Ger.*	bosque	forêt	floresta
mountain	Berg	**-högarna** *Swe.*	montaña	montagne	montanha
height	Höhe	**Höhe** *Ger.*	altura	hauteur	elevação
cave(s)	Höhle(n)	**Höhle(n)** *Ger.*	cueva(s)	caverne(s)	caverna(s)
island	Insel	**-holm** *Dan.*	isla	île	ilha
hook	Haken	**hook** *Eng.*	gancho	crochet	cabo, promontório
mountain	Berg	**hora** *Czech, Slo.*	montaña	montagne	montanha
point, peak	Horn	**Horn** *Ger.*	punta, pico	pointe, cime	ponta, pico
ruin	Ruine	**ḩorva** *Heb.*	ruina	ruine	ruína
mountains	Berge	**hory** *Czech, Slo.*	montañas	montagnes	montanhas
hospital	Krankenhaus	**hospital** *Eng., Sp.*	hospital	hôpital	hospital
point	Landspitze	**houma** *Poly.*	punta	pointe	ponta
house	Haus	**house** *Eng.*	casa	maison	casa
island	Insel	**hsü** *Ch.*	isla	île	ilha
lake, reservoir	See, Stausee	**hu** *Ch.*	lago, embalse	lac, réservoir	lago, reservatório
hill	Hügel	**Hügel** *Ger.*	colina	colline	colina
cape	Huk	**Huk** *Ger.*	cabo	cap	cabo
cape	Huk	**-huk** *Swe.*	cabo	cap	cabo
highway	Strasse	**hy., highway** *Eng.*	carretera	route	rodovia

I

island	Insel	**i., isla** *Sp.* **island**	isla	île	ilha
icefield	Eisdecke	**icefield** *Eng.*	helero	champ de glace	geleira
ice shelf	Schelfeis	**ice shelf** *Eng.*	corniza glacial	barrière de glace	banco de gelo
ice tongue	Eiszunge	**ice tongue** *Eng.*	lengua de glaciar	langue glaciaire	língua de geleira
dunes	Dünen	**idehan** *Ber.*	dunas	dunes	dunas
river	Fluss	**ig., igarapé** *Port.*	río	rivière	igarapé
church	Kirche	**iglesia** *Sp.*	iglesia	église	igreja
lake	See	**-ike** *Jpn.*	lago	lac	lago
island(s)	Insel(n)	**île(s)** *Fr.*	isla(s)	île(s)	ilha(s)
islet(s)	kleine Insel(n)	**îlet(s)** *Fr.*	isleta(s)	îlet(s)	ilhota(s)
island(s)	Insel(n)	**ilha(s)** *Port.*	isla(s)	île(s)	ilha(s)
islet(s)	kleine Insel(n)	**ilhéu(s)** *Port.*	isleta(s)	îlot(s)	ilhéu(s)
island	Insel	**illa** *Cat.*	isla	île	ilha
islands	Inseln	**illes** *Cat.*	islas	îles	ilhas
hill, upland	Hügel, Bergland	**ʻilw** *Ara.*	colina, tierras altas	colline, hautes terres	colina, terras altas
hill	Hügel	**ʻilwat** *Ara.*	colina	colline	colina
Indian reservation	Indianer-reservation	**Ind. res., Indian reservation** *Eng.*	reserva de Indios	réserve indienne	reserva indígena
inlet	Einfahrt	**inlet** *Eng.*	abra	bras de mer	enseada
island(s)	Insel(n)	**Insel(n)** *Ger.*	isla(s)	île(s)	ilha(s)
institute	Institut	**inst., institute** *Eng.*	instituto	institut	instituto
international	international	**int., international** *Eng.*	internacional	international	internacional
race course	Rennbahn	**ippodromo** *It.*	hipódromo	hippodrome	hipódromo
wadi	Wadi	**irhazer** *Ber.*	uadi	wadi	uádi
dunes	Dünen	**ʻirq** *Ara.*	dunas	dunes	dunas
islands	Inseln	**is., islands** *Eng.* **islas**	islas	îles	ilhas
island	Insel	**isla** *Sp.*	isla	île	ilha
island(s)	Insel(n)	**island(s)** *Eng.*	isla(s)	île(s)	ilha(s)
islands	Inseln	**islas** *Sp.*	islas	îles	ilhas
isle(s)	Insel(n)	**isle(s)** *Eng.*	isla(s)	île(s)	ilha(s)
islet(s)	kleine Insel(n)	**islet(s)** *Eng.*	isleta(s)	îlot(s)	ilhota(s)
islet	kleine Insel	**islote** *Sp.*	islote	îlot	ilhota
island	Insel	**isola** *It.*	isla	île	ilha
islands	Inseln	**isole** *It.*	islas	îles	ilhas
islet	kleine Insel	**isolotto** *It.*	isleta	îlot	ilhota
isthmus	Landenge	**isthme** *Fr.*	istmo	isthme	istmo
isthmus	Landenge	**isthmus** *Eng.*	istmo	isthme	istmo
isthmus	Landenge	**istmo** *Sp.*	istmo	isthme	istmo
island	Insel	**-iwa** *Jpn.*	isla	île	ilha

J

mountain(s)	Berg(e)	**jabal** *Ara.*	montaņa(s)	montagne(s)	montanha(s)
cave	Höhle	**jama** *S./C.*	cueva	caverne	caverna
caves	Höhlen	**jame** *S./C.*	cuevas	cavernes	cavernas
garden	Garten	**jardin** *Fr.*	jardín	jardin	jardim
garden	Garten	**jardín** *Sp.*	jardín	jardin	jardim
gardens	Gärten	**jardines** *Sp.*	jardines	jardins	jardins
lake	See	**järv** *Est.*	lago	lac	lago
lake	See	**-järvi** *Finn.*	lago	lac	lago
mountains	Berge	**jary** *Rus.*	montañas	montagnes	montanhas
lake	See	**-jaur** *Lapp.*	lago	lac	lago
islands	Inseln	**jazā'ir** *Ara.*	islas	îles	ilhas
peninsula	Halbinsel	**jazirah** *Indon.*	península	péninsule	península
island	Insel	**jazīrat** *Ara.*	isla	île	ilha
island	Insel	**jazīreh** *Per.*	isla	île	ilha
reservoir	Stausee	**jazovir** *Blg.*	embalse	réservoir	reservatório
mountain(s)	Berg(e)	**jbel** *Ara.*	montaņa(s)	montagne(s)	montanha(s)
lake	See	**jezero** *S./C.*	lago	lac	lago
lake, lagoon	See, Lagune, Haff	**jezioro** *Pol.*	lago, laguna	lac, lagune	lago, laguna
river	Fluss	**jiang** *Ch.*	río	rivière	rio
cape	Kap	**jiao** *Ch.*	cabo	cap	cabo
mountains	Berge	**jibāl** *Ara.*	montañas	montagnes	montanhas
island	Insel	**-jima** *Jpn.*	isla	île	ilha
saddle (pass)	Joch	**Joch** *Ger.*	paso	col	passo
river	Fluss	**-joki** *Finn.*	río	rivière	rio
glacier	Gletscher	**-jøkulen** *Nor.*	glaciar	glacier	geleria
glacier	Gletscher	**-jökull** *Ice.*	glaciar	glacier	geleria
gulf	Golf	**jūras līcis** *Latv.*	golfo	golfe	golfo
islands	Inseln	**juzur** *Ara.*	islas	îles	ilhas

K

ENGLISH	DEUTSCH	Map Form Geographische Begriffe Términos Geográficos Termes Géographiques Termos Geográficos	ESPAÑOL	FRANÇAIS	PORTUGUÊS
mountains	Berge	**kabīr** *Per.*	montañas	montagnes	montanhas
dunes	Dünen	**kahal** *Ara.*	dunas	dunes	dunas
sea	Meer	**-kai** *Jpn.*	mar	mer	mar
strait	Meeresstrasse	**-kaikyō** *Jpn.*	estrecho	détroit	estreito
mountain	Berg	**-kaise** *Lapp.*	montaña	montagne	montanha
navy installation	Anlage de Marine	**ka.j., kaijō-jieitai** *Jpn.*	estación de la marina	installation navale	instalação naval
brook	Bach	**kali** *Indon.*	riachuelo	crique	riacho
mountain	Berg	**kalns** *Latv.*	montaña	montagne	montanha
ridge	Kamm	**Kamm** *Ger.*	sierra	crête	serra
canal	Kanal	**kanaal** *Du.*	canal	canal	canal
canal, channel	Kanal	**Kanal** *Ger.*	canal	canal	canal
canal, channel	Kanal	**kanal** *Rus., S./C., Swe.*	canal	canal	canal
canal, channel	Kanal	**kanał** *Pol.*	canal	canal	canal
canal, channel	Kanal	**kanalen** *Swe.*	canal	canal	canal
canal, channel	Kanal	**kanava** *Finn.*	canal	canal	canal
pass	Pass	**kandao** *Pas.*	paso	col	passo
river	Fluss	**-kang** *Kor.*	río	rivière	rio
moor	Moor	**-kangas** *Finn.*	páramo	lande	charneca
national park	Nationalpark	**kansallis-puisto** *Finn.*	parque nacional	parc national	parque nacional
island	Insel	**kaŏh** *Cbd.*	isla	île	ilha
cape	Kap	**Kap** *Ger.*	cabo	cap	cabo
gorge	Schlucht	**kapija** *S./C.*	garganta	gorge	garganta
cape	Kap	**-kapp** *Nor.*	cabo	cap	cabo
dunes	Dünen	**kathīb** *Ara.*	dunas	dunes	dunas
desert	Wüste	**kavīr** *Per.*	desierto	désert	deserto
mountain	Berg	**kawlat** *Ara.*	montaña	montagne	montanha
hill	Hügel	**kawm** *Ara.*	colina	colline	colina
mountain	Berg	**kedīet** *Ara.*	montaña	montagne	montanha
lake	See	**kenohan** *Indon.*	lago	lac	lago
cape	Kap	**kep** *Alb.*	cabo	cap	cabo
islands	Inseln	**kepulauan** *Indon.*	islas	îles	ilhas
key(s), cay(s)	Klippe(n)	**key(s)** *Eng.*	cayo(s)	caye(s)	baixio(s)
intermittent lake	periodischer See	**khabrat** *Ara.*	lago intermitente	lac périodique	lago intermitente
gulf	Golf	**khalīj** *Ara.*	golfo	golfe	golfo
mountain	Berg	**khao** *Bur., Thai*	montaña	montagne	montanha
mountain	Berg	**khashm** *Ara.*	montaña	montagne	montanha
wadi	Wadi	**khatt** *Ara.*	uadi	wadi	uádi
wadi, river	Wadi, Fluss	**khawr** *Ara.*	uadi, río	wadi, rivière	uádi, rio
dam	Damm	**khazzān** *Ara.*	presa	barrage	represa
river, canal	Fluss, Kanal	**khlong** *Thai*	río, canal	rivière, canal	rio, canal
dunes	Dünen	**khubb** *Ara.*	dunas	dunes	dunas
kill (river, channel)	Fluss, Kanal	**kill** *Eng.*	río, canal	rivière, canal	rio, canal
cemetery	Friedhof	**kladb., kladbišče** *Rus.*	cementerio	cimetière	cemitério
cloister	Kloster	**klasztory** *Pol.*	claustro	cloître	claustro, convento
cloister, monastery	Kloster	**Kloster** *Ger.*	claustro, monasterio	cloître, monastère	claustro, mosteiro
knob	Kuppe	**knob** *Eng.*	protuberancia	bosse	cerro, colina
island	Insel	**ko** *Thai*	isla	île	ilha
lake, lagoon	See, Lagune, Haff	**-ko** *Jpn.*	lago, laguna	lac, lagune	lago, laguna
harbor, harbour	Hafen	**-kō** *Jpn.*	puerto	port	porto
highland	Hochland	**-kōchi** *Jpn.*	región montañosa	pays montagneux	terras altas
mountain	Kogel	**Kogel** *Ger.*	montaña	montagne	montanha
plateau	Hochebene	**-kogen** *Jpn.*	meseta	plateau	planalto
mountains	Berge	**koh** *Per.*	montañas	montagnes	montanhas
air force installation	Anlage der Luftwaffe	**ko.j., kōkū-jieitai** *Jpn.*	estación aeronáutica	installation aérienne	instalação da força aérea
national park	Nationalpark	**-kokuritsu-kōen** *Jpn.*	parque nacional	parc national	parque nacional
national park	Nationalpark	**-kokutei-kōen** *Jpn.*	parque nacional	parc national	parque nacional
bay	Bucht	**kólpos** *Gr.*	bahía	baie	baía
mountain	Berg	**kong** *Indon.*	montaña	montagne	montanha
peak	Kopf	**Kopf** *Ger.*	pico	cime	pico
bridge	Brücke	**köprüsü** *Tur.*	puente	pont	ponte
gulf, bay	Golf, Bucht	**körfezi** *Tur.*	golfo, bahía	golfe, baie	golfo, baía
spit	Landzunge	**kosa** *Rus.*	lengua de tierra	flèche	ponta de terra
rapids	Stromschnellen	**-koski** *Finn.*	rápidos	rapides	rápidos
pass	Pass	**kotal** *Per.*	paso	col	passo
basin	Becken	**kotlina** *Pol.*	cuenca	bassin	bacia
bay, pass	Bucht, Pass	**kou** *Ch.*	bahía, paso	baie, col	baía, passo
ridge	Höhenrücken	**kr'až** *Rus.*	sierra	crête	serra
escarpment	Landstufe	**kreb** *Ara.*	escarpa	escarpement	escarpa
fort	Fort	**krepost'** *Rus.*	fuerte	fort	forte
national park	Nationalpark	**krk., kokuritsu-kōen** *Jpn.*	parque nacional	parc national	parque nacional
national park	Nationalpark	**ktk., kokutei-kōen** *Jpn.*	parque nacional	parc national	parque nacional
bay	Bucht	**kuala** *Mal.*	bahía	baie	baía
mountain(s)	Berg(e)	**kūh(ha)** *Per.*	montaņa(s)	montagne(s)	montanha(s)
hill	Hügel	**-kulle** *Swe.*	colina	colline	colina
dome	Kuppe	**Kuppe** *Ger.*	domo	dôme	domo
strait	Meeresstrasse	**-kurkku** *Finn.*	estrecho	détroit	estreito
channel	Kanal	**kyle** *Gae.*	canal, estrecho	canal, détroit	canal, estreito
island	Insel	**kyun** *Bur.*	isla	île	ilha
hills	Hügel	**-kyūryū** *Jpn.*	colinas	collines	colinas

L

lake	See	**l., lac** *Fr.* **lago** **lagoa** **lake**	lago	lac	lago, lagoa
pass	Pass	**la** *Tib.*	paso	col	passo
province	Provinz	**lääni** *Finn.*	provincia	province	província
lake(s)	See(n)	**lac(s)** *Fr.*	lago(s)	lac(s)	lago(s)
lake	See	**lacul** *Rom.*	lago	lac	lago
cape	Kap	**laem** *Thai*	cabo	cap	cabo
lagoon, lake	Lagune, Haff, See	**lag., laguna** *Sp.*	laguna	lagune, lac	laguna
lake	See	**lago** *It., Port., Sp.*	lago	lac	lago
lake, lagoon	See, Lagune, Haff	**lagoa** *Port.*	lago, laguna	lac, lagune	lagoa
lagoon	Lagune, Haff	**lagoon** *Eng.*	laguna	lagune	laguna
lakes	Seen	**lagos** *Port., Sp.*	lagos	lacs	lagos
lagoon, lake	Lagune, Haff, See	**laguna** *Sp.*	laguna	lagune, lac	laguna, lago
lagoon	Lagune, Haff	**lagune** *Fr.*	laguna	lagune	laguna
bay	Bucht	**laht** *Est.*	bahía	baie	baía
gulf	Golf	**-lahti** *Finn.*	golfo	golfe	golfo
lake(s)	See(n)	**lake(s)** *Eng.*	lago(s)	lac(s)	lago(s)
county	Grafschaft	**län** *Swe.*	condado	comté	condado
lake	Lanke (See)	**Lanke** *Ger.*	lago	lac	lago
sea	Meer	**laut** *Indon.*	mar	mer	mar
lava flow	Lavastrom	**lava flow** *Eng.*	corriente de lava	coulée de lave	corrente de lava
hill, mountain	Hügel, Berg	**law** *Gae.*	colina, montaña	colline, montagne	colina, montanha
mountains, forest	Berge, Wald	**les** *Czech*	montañas, bosque	montagnes, forêt	montanhas, floresta
forest	Wald	**les** *Rus.*	bosque	forêt	floresta
level (plain)	Niveau (Ebene)	**level** *Eng.*	nivel (llano)	niveau (plaine)	planície
islands	Inseln	**liedao** *Ch.*	islas	îles	ilhas
lighthouse	Leuchtturm	**lighthouse** *Eng.*	faro	phare	farol
estuary	Trichter-mündung	**liman** *Rus.*	estuario	estuaire	estuário
bay	Bucht	**limanı** *Tur.*	bahía	baie	baía
lake	See	**límni** *Gr.*	lago	lac	lago
mountain(s), peak	Berg(e), Gipfel	**ling** *Ch.*	montaña(s), pico	montagne(s), pic	montanha(s), pico
plain(s)	Ebene(n)	**llano(s)** *Sp.*	llano(s)	plaine(s)	planície(s)

Glossary and Abbreviations of Geographical Terms / Verzeichnis und Abkürzungen Geographischer Begriffe
Glosario y Abreviaciones de Términos Geográficos / Glossaire et Abréviations de Termes Géographiques
Glossário e Abreviações de Termos Geográficos

293

ENGLISH	DEUTSCH	Map Form / Geographische Begriffe / Términos Geográficos / Termes Géographiques / Termos Geográficos	ESPAÑOL	FRANÇAIS	PORTUGUÊS
lake, reservoir	See, Stausee	**llyn** *Welsh*	lago, embalse	lac, réservoir	lago, reservatório
lake, inlet	See, Einfahrt	**loch** *Gae.*	lago, abra	lac, bras de mer	lago, angra
lock	Schleuse	**lock** *Eng.*	esclusa	écluse	eclusa
lock and dam	Damm mit Schleuse	**lock and dam** *Eng.*	presa y esclusa	écluse et barrage	represa e eclusa
gorge	Schlucht	**log** *Rus.*	garganta	gorge	garganta
mountain	Berg	**loi** *Bur.*	montaña	montagne	montanha
hills	Hügel	**lomas** *Sp.*	lomas	collines	colinas
lake	See	**lough** *Gae.*	lago	lac	lago
lowland	Tiefland	**lowland** *Eng.*	tierra baja	terrain bas	terras baixas
marsh	Luch (Bruch)	**Luch** *Ger.*	pantano	marais	pântano
island	Insel	**-luoto** *Finn.*	isla	île	ilha

M

ENGLISH	DEUTSCH	Map Form	ESPAÑOL	FRANÇAIS	PORTUGUÊS
mountains	Berge	**m., munţii** *Rom.*	montañas	montagnes	montanhas
island	Insel	**-maa** *Est.*	isla	île	ilha
strait	Meeresstrasse	**maḍīq** *Ara.*	estrecho	détroit	estreito
river	Fluss	**mae** *Thai*	río	rivière	rio
depression	Senke	**makhtesh** *Heb.*	depresión	dépression	depressão
bay	Bucht	**-man** *Kor.*	bahía	baie	baía
monastery	Kloster	**manastir** *S./C.*	monasterio	monastère	mosteiro
sea	Meer	**mar** *Sp., It.*	mar	mer	mar
marsh	Marsch	**marais** *Fr.*	pantano	marais	pântano
sea	Meer	**mare** *It.*	mar	mer	mar
marine corps air station	Flugstützpunkt des Marine-Corps	**marine corps air station** *Eng.*	estación aeronáutica de la infantería de marina	station aérienne de fusiliers marins	estação aérea de fuzileiros navais
marine corps base	Marine-Corps-Stützpunkt	**marine corps base** *Eng.*	base de la infantería de marina	base de fusiliers marins	base de fuzileiros navais
bay	Bucht	**marsā** *Ara.*	bahía	baie	baía
marsh	Marsch	**Marsch** *Ger.*	pantano	marais	pântano
marsh(es)	Marsch(en)	**marsh(es)** *Eng.*	pantano(s)	marais	pântano(s)
river mouth	Flussmündung	**maṣabb** *Ara.*	desembocadura	embouchure	desembocadura
canal	Kanal	**masrif** *Ara.*	canal	canal	canal
massif	Gebirgsmassiv	**massif** *Eng., Fr.*	macizo	massif	maciço
marine corps air station	Flugstützpunkt des Marine-Corps	**m.c.a.s., marine corps air station**	estación aeronáutica de la infantería de marina	station aérienne de fusiliers marins	estação aérea de fuzileiros navais
marine corps base	Marine-Corps-Stützpunkt	**m.c.b., marine corps base** *Eng.*	base de la infantería de marina	base de fusiliers marins	base de fuzileiros navais
meadow	Wiese	**meadow** *Eng.*	prado	prairie	pradaria
dunes	Dünen	**médanos** *Sp.*	médanos	dunes	dunas
sea, lake	Meer	**Meer** *Ger.*	mar, lago	mer, lac	mar, lago
sea, lake	Meer	**-meer** *Afk., Du.*	mar, lago	mer, lac	mar, lago
hills	Hügel	**melkosopočnik** *Rus.*	colinas	collines	colinas
memorial	Gedenkstätte	**mem., memorial** *Eng.*	monumento	mémorial	monumento
peninsula	Halbinsel	**menanjung** *Indon.*	península	péninsule	península
sea	Meer	**mer** *Fr.*	mar	mer	mar
mesa	Tafelberg	**mesa** *Sp.*	mesa	mesa	mesa
plateau	Hochebene	**meseta** *Sp.*	meseta	plateau	planalto
middle	Mittel-	**mid., middle** *Eng.*	medio	moyen	médio, central
spit	Landzunge	**mierzeja** *Pol.*	lengua de tierra	flèche	ponta de terra
bay	Bucht	**mifraz** *Heb.*	bahía	baie	baía
mines	Bergwerke	**mikhrot** *Heb.*	minas	mines	minas
military	militärisch	**mil., military** *Eng.*	militar	militaire	militar
harbor, harbour	Hafen	**-minato** *Jpn.*	puerto	port	porto
mine	Bergwerk	**mine** *Eng., Fr.*	mina	mine	mina
mountain	Berg	**-mine** *Jpn.*	montaña	montagne	montanha
cliff	Kliff	**minqār** *Ara.*	risco	falaise	falésia
cape	Kap	**-misaki** *Jpn.*	cabo	cap	cabo
mission	Mission	**mission** *Eng., Fr.*	misión	mission	missão
monument	Denkmal	**mon., monument** *Eng., Fr.*	monumento	monument	monumento
monastery	Kloster	**monasterio** *Sp.*	monasterio	monastère	mosteiro
monastery	Kloster	**monastero** *It.*	monasterio	monastère	mosteiro
monastery	Kloster	**monastery** *Eng.*	monasterio	monastère	mosteiro
monastery	Kloster	**moní** *Gr.*	monasterio	monastère	mosteiro
mount	Berg	**mont** *Fr.*	monte	mont	monte
mountain	Berg	**montagna** *It.*	montaña	montagne	montanha
mountain(s)	Berg(e)	**montagne(s)** *Fr.*	montaña(s)	montagne(s)	montanha(s)
mountain(s)	Berg(e)	**montaña(s)** *Sp.*	montaña(s)	montagne(s)	montanha(s)
mount	Berg	**monte** *It., Port., Sp.*	monte	mont	monte
mountains	Berge	**montes** *Port., Sp.*	montes	monts	montes
mountains	Berge	**monti** *It.*	montes	monts	montes
mountains	Berge	**monts** *Fr.*	montes	monts	montes
monument	Denkmal	**monument** *Eng., Fr.*	monumento	monument	monumento
moor	Moor	**moor** *Eng.*	páramo	lande	pântano
moor	Moor	**Moor** *Ger.*	páramo	lande	pântano
sea	Meer	**more** *Rus.*	mar	mer	mar
mountain	Berg	**-mori** *Jpn.*	montaña	montagne	montanha
mountain	Berg	**morne** *Fr.*	montaña	morne	montanha
hill, mountain	Hügel, Berg	**morro** *Port., Sp.*	morro	colline, montagne	morro
mosque	Moschee	**mosque** *Eng.*	mezquita	mosquée	mesquita
island, rock	Insel, Fels	**motu** *Poly.*	isla, roca	île, rocher	ilha, rochedo
island	Insel	**mouchão** *Port.*	isla	île	mouchão
mound	Erdhügel	**mound** *Eng.*	montículo	tertre	montículo
mount	Berg	**mount** *Eng.*	monte	mont	monte
mountain(s)	Berg(e)	**mountain(s)** *Eng.*	montaña(s)	montagne(s)	montanha(s)
mouth (river mouth)	Mündung	**mouth** *Eng.*	desembocadura	embouchure	desembocadura
mount	Berg	**mt., mount** *Eng.*	monte	mont	monte
mountain	Berg	**mtn., mountain** *Eng.*	montaña	montagne	montanha
mountains	Berge	**mts., mountains** *Eng.*	montañas	montagnes	montanhas
point	Landspitze	**mui** *Viet.*	punta	pointe	ponta
headland	Landspitze	**mull** *Gae.*	promontorio	promontoire	promontório
depression	Senke	**munkhafaḍ** *Ara.*	depresión	dépression	depressão
mountain	Berg	**muntele** *Rom.*	montaña	montagne	montanha
mountains	Berge	**munţii** *Rom.*	montañas	montagnes	montanhas
museum	Museum	**museo** *It., Sp.*	museo	musée	museu
museum	Museum	**Museum** *Ger.*	museo	musée	museu
museum	Museum	**museum** *Eng.*	museo	musée	museu
museum	Museum	**múzeum** *Hung.*	museo	musée	museu
museum	Museum	**muzej** *Rus.*	museo	musée	museu
cape	Kap	**mys** *Rus.*	cabo	cap	cabo

N

ENGLISH	DEUTSCH	Map Form	ESPAÑOL	FRANÇAIS	PORTUGUÊS
north	Nord	**n., north** *Eng.*	norte	nord	norte
sea, gulf	Meer, Golf	**-nada** *Jpn.*	mar, golfo	mer, golfe	mar, golfo
desert	Wüste	**nafūd** *Ara.*	desierto	désert	deserto
plateau, mountains	Hochebene, Berge	**nagorje** *Rus.*	meseta, montañas	plateau, montagnes	planalto, montanhas
river	Fluss	**nahr** *Ara.*	río	rivière	rio
sea	Meer	**-naikai** *Jpn.*	mar	mer	mar
salt flat	Salzebene	**namakzār** *Per.*	salar	saline	salina
narrows	Meeresenge	**narrows** *Eng.*	angostura	goulet	estreito
peninsula	Halbinsel	**-näs** *Swe.*	península	péninsule	península
naval air station	Flugstützpunkt der Marine	**n.a.s., naval air station** *Eng.*	estación aeronáutica de la marina	station de forces aériennes navales	estação aérea da marinha
National Aeronautics and Space Administration	Nationale Aeronautik-und Weltraum-Behörde	**N.A.S.A., National Aeronautics and Space Administration** *Eng.*	Administración Nacional Aeronáutica y Espacial	Administration Nationale de l'Espace et Aéronautique	Administração Nacional do Espaço e Aeronáutica
national park	Nationalpark	**nasjonal park** *Nor.*	parque nacional	parc national	parque nacional
national	national	**nat., national** *Eng., Fr.*	nacional	national	nacional
national battlefield site	Schlachtfeld	**national battlefield site** *Eng.*	campo de batalla nacional	champ de bataille national	campo de batalha nacional
national cemetery	Nationalfriedhof	**national cemetery** *Eng.*	cementerio nacional	cimetière national	cemitério nacional
national forest	Wald in Gemeinbesitz	**national forest** *Eng.*	bosque nacional	forêt nationale	floresta nacional
national historical park	Park an historischer Stätte	**national historical park** *Eng.*	parque histórico nacional	parc historique national	parque histórico nacional
national historical site	historische Stätte	**national historical site** *Eng.*	lugar histórico nacional	site historique national	sítio histórico nacional
national laboratory	staatliche Forschungsanstalt	**national laboratory** *Eng.*	laboratorio nacional	laboratoire national	laboratório nacional
national memorial	nationale Gedenkstätte	**national memorial** *Eng.*	monumento nacional	memorial national	monumento nacional
national military park	Park bei einem Schlachtfeld	**national military park** *Eng.*	parque militar nacional	parc militaire national	parque militar nacional
national monument	Nationaldenkmal	**national monument** *Eng.*	monumento nacional	monument national	monumento nacional
national park	Nationalpark	**national park** *Eng.*	parque nacional	parc nationale	parque nacional
national recreation area	Ausflugsgebiet	**national recreation area** *Eng.*	campo nacional de recreo	région de récréation national	área de lazer nacional
national seashore	öffentlicher Badestrand	**national seashore** *Eng.*	playa nacional	plage nationale	praia nacional
reserve	Naturpark	**Naturpark** *Ger.*	reserva natural	réserve naturelle	reserva natural
nature reserve	Naturschutzgebiet	**Naturschutzgebiet** *Ger.*	reserva natural	réserve naturelle	reserva natural
naval air station	Flugstützpunkt der Marine	**naval air station** *Eng.*	estación aeronáutica de la marina	station de forces aériennes navales	estação aérea da marinha
naval base	Flottenstützpunkt	**naval base** *Eng.*	base naval	base navale	base naval
naval station	Marinestation	**naval station** *Eng.*	estación naval	station navale	estação naval
naval base	Flottenstützpunkt	**n.b., naval base** *Eng.*	base naval	base navale	base naval
rock	Fels	**-ne** *Jpn.*	roca	rocher	rochedo
neck	Landenge	**neck** *Eng.*	istmo	isthme	istmo
necropolis (cemetery)	Friedhof	**necrópolis** *Sp.*	necrópolis	nécropole	necrópole
cape	Kap	**neem** *Est.*	cabo	cap	cabo
peninsula, point	Halbinsel, Landspitze	**-nes** *Ice., Nor.*	península, punta	péninsule, pointe	península, ponta
promontory	Vorgebirge	**ness** *Gae.*	promontorio	promontoire	promontório
snowcapped mountain(s)	Schneegipfel	**nev.(s)., nevado(s)** *Sp.*	nevado(s)	montagne(s) neigeuse(s)	pico(s) nevado(s)
mountain	Berg	**ngoc** *Viet.*	montaña	montagne	montanha
cape	Kap	**nina** *Est.*	cabo	cap	cabo
islands	Inseln	**nísoi** *Gr.*	islas	îles	ilhas
island	Insel	**nísos** *Gr.*	isla	île	ilha
lowland	Tiefland	**nizina** *Rus.*	tierra baja	terrain bas	terras baixas
lowland	Tiefland	**nižina** *Slo.*	tierra baja	terrain bas	terras baixas
lowland	Tiefland	**nizmennost'** *Rus.*	tierra baja	terrain bas	terras baixas
cape	Kap	**nos** *Blg.*	cabo	cap	cabo
naval station	Marinestation	**n.s., naval station** *Eng.*	estación naval	station navale	estação naval
nature reserve	Naturschutzgebiet	**Nsg., Naturschutzgebiet** *Ger.*	reserva natural	réserve naturelle	reserva natural
mountain	Berg	**nui** *Viet.*	montaña	montagne	montanha
lake	See	**-numa** *Jpn.*	lago	lac	lago
mountains	Berge	**nuruu** *Mong.*	montañas	montagnes	montanhas
island	Insel	**nusa** *Indon.*	isla	île	ilha
lake	See	**nuur** *Mong.*	lago	lac	lago

O

ENGLISH	DEUTSCH	Map Form	ESPAÑOL	FRANÇAIS	PORTUGUÊS
island	Insel	**-ø** *Dan., Nor.*	isla	île	ilha
island	Insel	**-ö** *Swe.*	isla	île	ilha
island	Insel	**o., ostrov** *Rus.*	isla	île	ilha
islands	Inseln	**-öarna** *Swe.*	islas	îles	ilhas
oasis	Oase	**oasis** *Eng., Fr., Sp.*	oasis	oasis	oásis
observatory	Observatorium	**observatorio** *Sp.*	observatorio	observatoire	observatório
observatory	Observatorium	**observatory** *Eng.*	observatorio	observatoire	observatório
ocean	Ozean	**ocean** *Eng.*	océano	océan	oceano
island	Insel	**-ön** *Swe.*	isla	île	ilha
mountains	Berge	**óri** *Gr.*	montañas	montagnes	montanhas
bay	Bucht	**órmos** *Gr.*	bahía	baie	baía
mountain(s)	Berg(e)	**óros** *Gr.*	montaña(s)	montagne(s)	montanha(s)
island(s)	Insel(n)	**ostrov(a)** *Rus.*	isla(s)	île(s)	ilha(s)
island	Insel	**ostrovul** *Rom.*	isla	île	ilha
islands	Inseln	**otoci** *S./C.*	islas	îles	ilhas
island	Insel	**otok** *S./C.*	isla	île	ilha
wadi	Wadi	**ouadi** *Ara.*	uadi	wadi	uádi
wadi	Wadi	**oued** *Ara.*	uadi	wadi	uádi
outlet	Abfluss	**outlet** *Eng.*	desagüe	débouché	escoadouro
island	Insel	**-øy, -øya** *Nor.*	isla	île	ilha
lake	See	**oz., ozero** *Rus.*	lago	lac	lago
lakes	Seen	**ozera** *Rus.*	lagos	lacs	lagos

P

ENGLISH	DEUTSCH	Map Form	ESPAÑOL	FRANÇAIS	PORTUGUÊS
hills	Hügel	**pahorkatina** *Czech*	colinas	collines	colinas
palace	Palast	**pal., palace** *Eng.*	palacio	palais	palácio
palace	Palast	**palacio** *Sp.*	palacio	palais	palácio
palace	Palast	**palais** *Fr.*	palacio	palais	palácio
palace	Palast	**palazzo** *It.*	palacio	palais	palácio
palace	Palast	**paleis** *Du.*	palacio	palais	palácio
railroad station	Bahnhof	**pályaudvar** *Hung.*	estacíon ferrocarril	gare	estação ferroviária
monument	Denkmal	**pam'atnik** *Rus.*	monumento	monument	monumento
plain	Ebene	**pampa** *Sp.*	pampa	plaine	pampa
basin	Becken	**pánev** *Czech*	cuenca	bassin	bacia
swamp	Sumpf	**pantanal** *Port., Sp.*	pantanal	marais	pantanal
marsh, swamp, reservoir	Marsch, Sumpf, Stausee	**pantano** *Sp.*	pantano	marais, réservoir	Pântano
moor	Moor	**páramo** *Sp.*	páramo	lande	pântano
park	Park	**parc** *Fr.*	parque	parc	parque
national park	Nationalpark	**parc national** *Fr.*	parque nacional	parc national	parque nacional
park	Park	**parco** *It.*	parque	parc	parque
national park	Nationalpark	**parco nazionale** *It.*	parque nacional	parc national	parque nacional
provincial park	Naturpark	**parc provincial** *Fr.*	parque de la provincia	parc provincial	parque provincial
park	Park	**Park** *Ger.*	parque	parc	parque
park	Park	**park** *Eng.*	parque	parc	parque
national park	Nationalpark	**park narodowy** *Pol.*	parque nacional	parc national	parque nacional
parkway	Ferienstrasse	**parkway** *Eng.*	calzada	allée de parc	alameda de parque
park	Park	**parque** *Port., Sp.*	parque	parc	parque
national park	Nationalpark	**parq. nac., parque nacional** *Port., Sp.*	parque nacional	parc national	parque nacional
beach	Strand	**part** *Hung.*	playa	plage	praia
strait	Meeresstrasse	**pas** *Fr.*	estrecho	détroit	estreito
passage	Durchfahrt	**pasaje** *Sp.*	pasaje	passage	passagem
pass	Pass	**paso** *Sp.*	paso	col	passo
pass	Pass	**Pass** *Ger.*	paso	col	passo
pass	Pass	**pass** *Eng.*	paso	col	passo
passage	Durchfahrt	**passage** *Eng., Fr.*	pasaje	passage	passagem
passage	Durchfahrt	**passe** *Fr.*	pasaje	passe	passagem
pass	Pass	**passo** *It.*	paso	col	passo
pass	Pass	**pasul** *Rom.*	paso	col	passo
brook	Bach	**patak** *Hung.*	riachuelo	crique	riacho
peak(s)	Gipfel	**peak(s)** *Eng.*	pico(s)	pic(s)	pico(s)
cave	Höhle	**pećina** *S./C.*	cueva	caverne	caverna
mountain	Berg	**pedra** *Port.*	montaña	montagne	montanha

294 Glossary and Abbreviations of Geographical Terms / Verzeichnis und Abkürzungen Geographischer Begriffe
Glosario y Abreviaciones de Términos Geográficos / Glossaire et Abréviations de Termes Géographiques
Glossário e Abreviacões de Termos Geográficos

ENGLISH	DEUTSCH	Map Form Geographische Begriffe Términos Geográficos Termes Géographiques Termos Geográficos	ESPAÑOL	FRANÇAIS	PORTUGUÊS
mountains	Berge	**peg., pegunungan** *Indon.*	montañas	montagnes	montanhas
sea	Meer	**pélagos** *Gr.*	mar	mer	mar
peninsula	Halbinsel	**pen., peninsula** *Eng.*	península	péninsule	península
peak, rock	Gipfel, Fels	**peña** *Sp.*	peña	pic, rocher	penha
peak, large rock	Gipfel, grosser Fels	**peñasco** *Sp.*	peñasco	pic, rocher	penhasco
basin	Becken	**pendi** *Ch.*	cuenca	bassin	bacia
peninsula	Halbinsel	**peninsula** *Eng.*	península	péninsule	península
peninsula	Halbinsel	**península** *Sp.*	península	péninsule	península
peninsula	Halbinsel	**péninsule** *Fr.*	península	péninsule	península
rock	Fels	**peñón** *Sp.*	peñón	rocher	rochedo
pass	Pass	**pereval** *Rus.*	paso	col	passo
strait	Meeresstrasse	**pertuis** *Fr.*	estrecho	pertuis	estreito
sand desert	Sandwüste	**peski** *Rus.*	desierto arenoso	désert de sable	deserto arenoso
mountain	Berg	**phnum** *Cbd.*	montaña	montagne	montanha
mountain	Berg	**phou** *Lao.*	montaña	montagne	montanha
mountain	Berg	**phu** *Thai*	montaña	montagne	montanha
cape	Kap	**pi** *Ch.*	cabo	cap	cabo
plain	Ebene	**piano** *It.*	llanura	plaine	planície
peak	Gipfel	**pic** *Fr.*	pico	pic	pico
peak	Gipfel	**picacho** *Sp.*	picacho	pic	pico
peak	Gipfel	**picco** *It.*	pico	pic	pico
peak(s)	Gipfel	**pico(s)** *Port., Sp.*	pico(s)	pic(s)	pico(s)
pier	Landungsbrücke	**pier** *Eng.*	embarcadero	jetée	cais
mountain	Berg	**-piggen** *Nor.*	montaña	montagne	montanha
peak	Gipfel	**pik** *Rus.*	pico	pic	pico
forest	Wald	**pinhal** *Port.*	bosque	forêt	pinhal
peak	Gipfel	**pique** *Fr.*	pico	pique	pico
pyramid	Pyramide	**pirámide** *Sp.*	pirámide	pyramide	pirâmide
peak(s)	Gipfel	**piton(s)** *Fr.*	pico(s)	piton(s)	pico(s)
peak	Gipfel	**piz, pizzo** *It.*	pico	pic	pico
peak	Gipfel	**pk., peak** *Eng.*	pico	pic	pico
parkway	Ferienstrasse	**pkwy., parkway** *Eng.*	calzada	allée de parc	avenida
plain	Ebene	**plain** *Eng.*	llanura	plaine	planície
plain	Ebene	**plaine** *Fr.*	llanura	plaine	planície
plains	Ebenen	**plains** *Eng.*	llanura	plaines	planícies
plateau	Hochebene	**planalto** *Port.*	meseta	plateau	planalto
planetarium	Planetarium	**planetario** *Sp.*	planetario	planétarium	planetário
planetarium	Planetarium	**planetarium** *Eng.*	planetario	planétarium	planetário
mountain, range	Berg, Gebirge	**planina** *S./C.*	montaña, sierra	montagne, chaîne	montanha, cordilheira
plateau	Hochebene	**plateau** *Eng., Fr.*	meseta	plateau	planalto
plateau	Hochebene	**plato** *Afk., Blg., Rus.*	meseta	plateau	planalto
beach	Strand	**playa** *Sp.*	playa	plage	praia
square	Platz	**plaza** *Sp.*	plaza	place	praça
plateau	Hochebene	**plošina** *Czech*	meseta	plateau	planalto
plateau	Hochebene	**ploskogorje** *Rus.*	meseta	plateau	planalto
pass	Pass	**poarta** *Rom.*	paso	col	passo
hill	Hügel	**poggio** *It.*	colina	colline	colina
point	Landspitze	**point** *Eng.*	punta	pointe	ponta
point	Landspitze	**pointe** *Fr.*	punta	pointe	ponta
island	Insel	**pol** *Du.*	isla	île	ilha
plain, basin	Ebene, Becken	**polje** *S./C.*	llanura, cuenca	plaine, bassin	planície, bacia
peninsula	Halbinsel	**poluostrov** *Rus.*	península	péninsule	península
peninsula	Halbinsel	**poluotok** *S./C.*	península	péninsule	península
pond	Teich	**pond** *Eng.*	charca	étang	lago
peak	Gipfel	**-pong** *Kor.*	pico	cime	pico
bridge	Brücke	**pont** *Fr.*	puente	pont	ponte
point	Landspitze	**ponta, pontal** *Port.*	punta	pointe	ponta, pontal
bridge	Brücke	**ponte** *Port.*	puente	pont	ponte
pool	Tümpel	**pool** *Eng.*	charco	étang	charco
rapids	Stromschnellen	**porog** *Rus.*	rápidos	rapides	rápidos
port	Hafen	**port** *Eng., Fr.*	puerto	port	porto
port	Hafen	**porto** *It.*	puerto	port	porto
strait	Meeresstrasse	**porthmós** *Gr.*	estrecho	détroit	estreito
provincial park	Naturpark	**p.p., provincial park** *Eng.*	parque de la provincia	parc provincial	parque provincial
beach	Strand	**praia** *Port.*	playa	plage	praia
reservoir	Stausee	**přehr., přehradová nádrž** *Czech*	embalse	réservoir	reservatório
reservoir, dam	Stausee, Damm	**presa** *Sp.*	presa	réservoir, barrage	represa
peninsula	Halbinsel	**presqu'île** *Fr.*	península	presqu'île	península
reservoir	Stausee	**priehradová nádrz** *Slo.*	embalse	réservoir	reservatório
pass	Pass	**priesmyk** *Slo.*	paso	col	passo
prison	Gefängnis	**prison** *Eng.*	prisión	prison	prisão
pass	Pass	**prohod** *Blg.*	paso	col	passo
strait	Meeresstrasse	**proliv** *Rus.*	estrecho	détroit	estreito
promontory	Vorgebirge	**promontorio** *It., Sp.*	promontorio	promontoire	promontório
promontory	Vorgebirge	**promontory** *Eng.*	promontorio	promontoire	promontório
provincial park	Naturpark	**prov. park, provincial park** *Eng.*	parque de la provincia	parc provincial	parque provincial
reservoir	Stausee	**prudy** *Rus.*	embalse	réservoir	reservatório
pass	Pass	**průsmyk** *Czech*	paso	col	passo
pass	Pass	**przełęcz** *Pol.*	paso	col	passo
cape	Kap	**przylądek** *Pol.*	cabo	cap	cabo
point	Landspitze	**pt., point** *Eng.*	punta	pointe	ponta
railroad station	Bahnhof	**pu., pályaudvar** *Hung.*	estación de ferrocarril	gare	estação ferroviária
port	Hafen	**puerto** *Sp.*	puerto	port	porto
peak	Gipfel	**puig** *Cat.*	pico	cime	pico
island	Insel	**pulau** *Indon., Mal.*	isla	île	ilha
upland	Bergland	**puna** *Sp.*	puna	hautes terres	terras altas
peak	Gipfel	**puncak** *Indon.*	pico	cime	pico
point	Landspitze	**punt** *Du.*	punta	pointe	ponta
point, peak	Landspitze, Gipfel	**punta** *It., Sp.*	punta	pointe, cime	ponta
point	Landspitze	**puntilla** *Sp.*	puntilla	pointe	ponta pequena
forest	Wald	**puszcza** *Pol.*	bosque	forêt	floresta
pyramid	Pyramide	**pyramid** *Eng.*	pirámide	pyramide	pirâmide

Q

ENGLISH	DEUTSCH	Map Form	ESPAÑOL	FRANÇAIS	PORTUGUÊS
salt flat	Salzebene	**qā'** *Ara.*	salar	saline	salina
canal	Kanal	**qanāt** *Ara.*	canal	canal	canal
hill	Hügel	**qārat** *Ara.*	colina	colline	colina
hills	Hügel	**qārāt** *Ara.*	colinas	collines	colinas
dunes	Dünen	**qawz** *Ara.*	dunas	dunes	dunas
brook	Bach	**qbda., quebrada** *Sp.*	quebrada	crique	arroio
mountain	Berg	**qolleh** *Per.*	montaña	montagne	montanha
canal	Kanal	**-qu** *Ch.*	canal	canal	canal
quarry	Steinbruch	**quarry** *Eng.*	cantera	carrière	pedreira
brook	Bach	**quebrada** *Sp.*	quebrada	crique	arroio
rapids	Stromschnellen	**quedas** *Port.*	rápidos	rapides	quedas
islands	Inseln	**qundao** *Ch.*	islas	îles	ilhas
hill	Hügel	**qūr** *Ara.*	colina	colline	colina
mountain	Berg	**qurnat** *Ara.*	montaña	montagne	montanha

R

ENGLISH	DEUTSCH	Map Form	ESPAÑOL	FRANÇAIS	PORTUGUÊS
river	Fluss	**r., rio** *Port.* **río** **river** **rivière**	río	rivière	rio
range	Gebirge	**ra., range** *Eng.*	sierra	chaîne	cordilheira
Royal Australian Air Force Station	Luftwaffenstützpunkt (Austl.)	**R.A.A.F.S., Royal Australian Air Force Station** *Eng.*	Real Estación Aeronáutica (Austl.)	Station Aérienne Royale (Austl.)	Real Estação da Força Aérea Australiana
race course	Rennbahn	**race course** *Eng.*	hipódromo	champ de course	hipódromo
race track	Rennbahn	**race track** *Eng.*	hipódromo	champ de course	hipódromo
raceway	Rennbahn	**raceway** *Eng.*	hipódromo	champ de course	hipódromo
river	Fluss	**rach** *Viet.*	río	rivière	rio
anchorage	Ankerplatz	**rada** *Sp.*	rada	ancrage	ancoradouro
cape	Kap	**rags** *Latv.*	cabo	cap	cabo
railroad	Eisenbahn	**railroad** *Eng.*	ferrocarril	chemin de fer	ferrovia
railway	Eisenbahn	**railway** *Eng.*	ferrocarril	chemin de fer	ferrovia
railway station	Bahnhof	**railway station** *Eng.*	estacíon de ferrocarril	gare	estação ferroviária
dunes	Dünen	**ramlat** *Ara.*	dunas	dunes	dunas
range(s)	Gebirge	**range(s)** *Eng.*	sierra(s)	chaîne(s)	cordilheira(s)
river	Fluss	**rão., ribeirão** *Port.*	río	rivière	rio, ribeirão
rapids	Stromschnellen	**rapides** *Fr.*	rápidos	rapides	rápidos
rapids	Stromschnellen	**rapids** *Eng.*	rápidos	rapides	rápidos
wadi	Wadi	**raqabat** *Ara.*	uadi	wadi	uádi
cape	Kap	**ras, ra's** *Ara.*	cabo	cap	cabo
cape	Kap	**rās** *Per.*	cabo	cap	cabo
ravine	Tobel	**ravine** *Eng.*	barranca	ravin	ravina
plain	Ebene	**ravnina** *Rus.*	llanura	plaine	planície
canal	Kanal	**rayyāh** *Ara.*	canal	canal	canal
flood plain	Überschwemmungsebene	**razlivy** *Rus.*	llanura de inundación	lit d'inondation	planície de inundação
road	Landstrasse	**rd., road** *Eng.*	camino	route	rodovia
reef	Riff	**récif** *Fr.*	arrecife	récif	recife
reefs	Riffe	**recifes** *Port.*	arrecifes	récifs	recifes
reefs	Riffe	**récifs** *Fr.*	arrecifes	récifs	recifes
reef(s)	Riff(e)	**reef(s)** *Eng.*	arrecife(s)	récif(s)	recife(s)
regional park	Regionalpark	**regional park** *Eng.*	parque regional	parc régional	parque regional
mountain	Berg	**-rei** *Jpn.*	montaña	montagne	montanha
race course	Rennbahn	**Rennbahn** *Ger.*	hipódromo	champ de course	hipódromo
dam, reservoir	Damm, Stausee	**represa** *Port.*	presa, embalse	barrage, réservoir	represa
airport	Flughafen	**repülötér** *Hung.*	aeropuerto	aéroport	aeroporto
reservoir	Stausee	**res., reservoir** *Eng.*	embalse	réservoir	reservatório
reservation	Reservat	**reservation** *Eng.*	reservación	réservation	reserva
reservoir	Stausee	**reservatório** *Port.*	embalse	réservoir	reservatório
reserve	Reservat	**reserve** *Eng.*	reserva	réserve	reserva
reserve	Reservat	**réserve** *Fr.*	reserva	réserve	reserva
game reserve	Wildreservat	**réserve de chasse** *Fr.*	vedado de caza	réserve de chasse	reserva de caça
reservoir	Stausee	**reservoir** *Eng.*	embalse	réservoir	reservatório
reservoir	Stausee	**réservoir** *Fr.*	embalse	réservoir	reservatório
beach	Strand	**restinga** *Port.*	playa	plage	praia
islands	Inseln	**-retto** *Jpn.*	islas	îles	ilhas
ria (inlet)	Ria	**ría** *Sp.*	ría	ria	ria
brook	Bach	**riacho** *Port., Sp.*	riacho	crique	riacho
brook	Bach	**riachuelo** *Sp.*	riachuelo	crique	riacho
brook	Bach	**rib., ribeira** *Port.*	riachuelo	crique	ribeira
river	Fluss	**ribeirão** *Port.*	río	rivière	ribeirão
ridge	Höhenrücken	**ridge** *Eng.*	sierra	crête	serra
moor	Ried	**Ried** *Ger.*	páramo	lande	pântano
brook	Bach	**riera** *Sp., Cat.*	riera	crique	riacho
national museum	Reichsmuseum	**rijksmuseum** *Du.*	museo nacional	musée national	museu nacional
army installation	Anlage des Heeres	**rikujō-jieitai** *Jpn.*	estación del ejército	installation militaire	instalação militar
river	Fluss	**rio** *Port.*	río	rivière	rio
river	Fluss	**río** *Sp.*	río	rivière	rio
river	Fluss	**riozinho** *Port.*	río	rivière	riozinho
rise (submarine)	Schwelle (untermeerische)	**rise** *Eng.*	elevación (submarina)	élévation (sous-marine)	elevação (submarina)
river	Fluss	**river** *Eng.*	río	rivière	rio
brook	Bach	**rivera** *Sp.*	rivera	ruisseau	córrego
coast	Küste	**riviera** *It.*	costa	côte	costa
river	Fluss	**rivière** *Fr.*	río	rivière	rio
army installation	Anlage des Heeres	**r.j., rikujō-jieitai** *Jpn.*	estación del ejército	installation militaire	instalação do exército
road	Landstrasse	**road** *Eng.*	camino	route	rodovia
roads (anchorage)	Ankerplatz	**roads** *Eng.*	ancladero	ancrage	ancoradouro
rock	Fels	**roca** *Sp.*	roca	rocher	rochedo
rock, mountain	Fels, Berg	**rocca** *It.*	roca, montaạa	rocher, montagne	rochedo, montanha
rock(s)	Fels(en)	**rock(s)** *Eng.*	roca(s)	rocher(s)	rochedo(s)
cape	Kap	**rt** *S./C.*	cabo	cap	cabo
brook	Bach	**rû** *Fr.*	arroyo	rû	córrego
mountains	Berge	**rudohorie** *Slo.*	montañas	montagnes	montanhas
brook	Bach	**ruisseau** *Fr.*	arroyo	ruisseau	córrego
mountain	Berg	**rujm** *Ara.*	montaña	montagne	montanha
run (stream)	Bach	**run** *Eng.*	arroyo	ruisseau	córrego

S

ENGLISH	DEUTSCH	Map Form	ESPAÑOL	FRANÇAIS	PORTUGUÊS
south	Süd	**s., south** *Eng.*	sur	sud	sul
range	Gebirge	**sa., serra** *Port.*	sierra	chaîne	cordilheira
island	Insel	**saar** *Est.*	isla	île	ilha
savanna	Savanne	**sabana** *Sp.*	sabana	savane	savana
salt marsh, lagoon	Salzmarsch, Lagune, Haff	**sabkhat** *Ara.*	pantano salado, laguna	marais salé, lagune	pântano salgado, laguna
dam	Damm	**sadd** *Ara.*	presa	barrage	represa
wadi	Wadi	**saguia** *Ara.*	uadi	wadi	uádi
desert	Wüste	**şahrā'** *Ara.*	desierto	désert	deserto
cape	Kap	**-saki** *Jpn.*	cabo	cap	cabo
salt flat	Salzebene	**salar** *Sp.*	salar	saline	salina
salt marsh, salt flat	Salzmarsch, Salzebene	**salina(s)** *Sp.*	salina(s)	marais salé, saline	salina(s)
salt marsh, salt flat	Salzmarsch, Salzebene	**salines** *Fr.*	pantano salado, salinas, salar	salines	pântano salgado, salinas
salt flat	Salzebene	**salt flat** *Eng.*	salar	saline	salina
salt lake	Salzsee	**salt lake** *Eng.*	lago salado	lac salé	lago salgado
salt marsh	Salzmarsch	**salt marsh** *Eng.*	pantano salado	marais salé	pântano salgado
waterfall	Wasserfall	**salto(s)** *Port., Sp.*	salto(s)	chute d'eau	salto(s)
reservoir	Stausee	**samudra** *Sin.*	embalse	réservoir	reservatório
range	Gebirge	**-sammyaku** *Jpn.*	sierra	chaîne	cordilheira
mountain	Berg	**-san** *Jpn., Kor.*	montaña	montagne	montanha
mountains	Berge	**-sanchi** *Jpn.*	montañas	montagnes	montanhas
mountains	Berge	**-sanmaek** *Kor.*	montañas	montagnes	montanhas
shrine	Schrein	**santuario** *It., Sp.*	santuario	châsse	santuário
mountain	Berg	**sar** *Pas.*	montaña	montagne	montanha
island	Insel	**sari** *Est.*	isla	île	ilha
desert	Wüste	**sarīr** *Ara.*	desierto	désert	deserto
saddle (pass)	Sattel	**Sattel** *Ger.*	paso	col	passo
strait	Meeresstrasse	**šaurums** *Latv.*	estrecho	détroit	estreito
waterfall	Wasserfall	**saut** *Fr.*	cascada	saut	queda d'água
castle	Schloss	**Schloss** *Ger.*	castillo	château	castelo
gorge	Schlucht	**Schlucht** *Ger.*	garganta	gorge	garganta
school	Schule	**school** *Eng.*	escuela	école	escola
sea	Meer	**sea** *Eng.*	mar	mer	mar
seamount	untermeerische Kuppe	**seamount** *Eng.*	montaña submarina	montagne sous-marine	montanha submarina
sea scarp	Abbruch	**sea scarp** *Eng.*	cantil	escarpement sous-marine	escarpa submarina
dry lake	Trockensee	**sebjet** *Ara.*	lago seco	lac asséché	lago seco
salt flat	Salzebene	**sebkha** *Ara.*	salar	saline	salina
intermittent lake	periodischer See	**sebkra** *Ara.*	lago intermitente	lac périodique	lago intermitente
salt marsh	Salzmarsch	**sebkret** *Ara.*	pantano salado	marais salé	pântano salgado
airport	Flughafen	**sede-te'ufa** *Heb.*	aeropuerto	aéroport	aeroporto
saddle (pass)	Sattel	**sedlo** *Czech*	paso	col	passo
lake(s)	See(n)	**See(n)** *Ger.*	lago(s)	lac(s)	lago(s)
strait	Meerestrasse	**selat** *Indon.*	estrecho	détroit	estreito
peninsula	Halbinsel	**semenanjung** *Indon.*	península	péninsule	península
seminary	Seminar	**seminary** *Eng.*	seminario	séminaire	seminário
mountain	Berg	**-sen** *Jpn.*	montaña	montagne	montanha
sound	Sund	**seno** *Sp.*	seno	détroit	estreito

Glossary and Abbreviations of Geographical Terms / Verzeichnis und Abkürzungen Geographischer Begriffe
Glosario y Abreviaciones de Términos Geográficos / Glossaire et Abréviations de Termes Géographiques
Glossário e Abreviações de Termos Geográficos 295

ENGLISH	DEUTSCH	Map Form / Geographische Begriffe / Términos Geográficos / Termes Géographiques / Termos Geográficos	ESPAÑOL	FRANÇAIS	PORTUGUÊS
mountains	Gebirge	**serra** *Cat.*	montañas	montagnes	montanhas
range, mountain	Gebirge, Berg	**serra** *Port.*	sierra	chaîne, montagne	serra
ridge(s)	Höhenrücken	**serranía(s)** *Sp.*	serranía(s)	crête(s)	serrania(s)
island	Insel	**sha** *Ch.*	isla	île	ilha
rapids	Stromschnellen	**shallāl** *Ara.*	rápidos	rapides	rápidos
desert	Wüste	**shamo** *Ch.*	desierto	désert	deserto
mountain(s), island	Berg(e), Insel	**shan** *Ch.*	montaña(s), isla	montagne(s), île	montanha(s), ilha
pass	Pass	**shankou** *Ch.*	paso	col	passo
mountains	Berge	**shanmo** *Ch.*	montañas	montagnes	montanhas
bay	Bucht	**sharm** *Ara.*	bahía	baie	baía
peninsula	Halbinsel	**shibh jazīrat** *Ara.*	península	péninsule	península
island	Insel	**-shima** *Jpn.*	isla	île	ilha
reef	Riff	**-shō** *Jpn.*	arrecife	récif	recife
shoal(s)	Untiefe(n)	**shoal(s)** *Eng.*	bajo(s)	haut-fond(s)	baixio(s)
islands	Inseln	**-shotō** *Jpn.*	islas	îles	ilhas
shrine	Schrein	**shrine** *Eng.*	santuario	châsse	santuário
river	Fluss	**shui** *Ch.*	río	rivière	rio
reservoir	Stausee	**shuiku** *Ch.*	embalse	réservoir	reservatório
strait	Meeresstrasse	**shuitao** *Ch.*	estrecho	détroit	estreito
temple	Tempel	**si** *Ch.*	templo	temple	templo
range, ridge	Gebirge, Höhenrücken	**sierra** *Sp.*	sierra	chaîne, crête	serra
rapids	Stromschnellen	**šivera** *Rus.*	rápidos	rapides	rápidos
lake	See	**-sjø** *Nor.*	lago	lac	lago
lakes	Seen	**-sjöarna** *Swe.*	lagos	lacs	lagos
lake	See	**-sjøen** *Nor.*	lago	lac	lago
lake, bay	See, Bucht	**-sjön** *Swe.*	lago, bahía	lac, baie	lago, baía
island	Insel	**skär** *Swe.*	isla	île	ilha
forest	Wald	**-skog, -skogen** *Swe.*	bosque	forêt	floresta
mountain	Berg	**slieve** *Gae.*	montaña	montagne	montanha
castle	Schloss	**slot** *Du.*	castillo	château	castelo
castle	Schloss	**slott** *Swe.*	castillo	château	castelo
slough (swamp)	verlandende Wasserfläche	**slough** *Eng.*	pantano	fondrière	pântano, brejo
ridge	Höhenrücken	**snía., serranía** *Sp.*	serranía	crête	serrania
snowfield	Schneefeld	**snowfield** *Eng.*	ventisquero	champ de neige	campo de neve
lake	See	**-sø** *Dan.*	lago	lac	lago
sound	Sund	**sonda** *Sp.*	sonda	détroit	estreito
sound	Sund	**sound** *Eng.*	sonda	détroit	estreito
cave, tunnel	Höhle, Tunnel	**souterrain** *Fr.*	cueva, túnel	souterrain	caverna, túnel
state park	Naturpark	**s.p., state park** *Eng.*	parque provincial	parc régional	parque estadual
cave	Höhle	**špilja** *S./C.*	cueva	caverne	caverna
spit	Landzunge	**spit** *Eng.*	lengua de tierra	flèche	ponta de terra
peak	Spitze	**Spitze** *Ger.*	pico	cime	pico
spring	Quelle	**spr., spring** *Eng.*	manantial	source	fonte, manancial
square	Platz	**sq., square** *Eng.*	plaza	place	praça
range, ridge	Gebirge, Höhenrücken	**srra., sierra** *Sp.*	sierra	chaîne, crête	serra
saint	Sankt	**st., saint** *Eng., Fr.*	san, santa, santo	saint	são, santa, santo
street	Strasse	**st., street** *Eng.*	calle	rue	rua
saint	Sankt	**sta., santa** *Port., Sp.*	santa	sainte	santa
station	Bahnhof, Stützpunkt	**sta., station** *Eng., Fr.*	estación	station	estação
stadium	Stadion	**stad., stadium** *Eng.*	estadio	stade	estádio
stadium	Stadion	**stadio** *It.*	estadio	stade	estádio
stadium	Stadion	**Stadion** *Ger.*	estadio	stade	estádio
stadium	Stadion	**stadion** *Rus.*	estadio	stade	estádio
stadium	Stadion	**stadium** *Eng.*	estadio	stade	estádio
state beach	öffentlicher Badestrand	**state beach** *Eng.*	playa provincial	plage régionale	praia estadual
state forest	Wald in Gemeinbesitz	**state forest** *Eng.*	bosque provincial	forêt régionale	floresta estadual
state historical park	Park an historischer Stätte	**state historical park** *Eng.*	parque histórico provincial	parc historique régional	parque histórico estadual
state park	Naturpark	**state park** *Eng.*	parque provincial	parc régional	parque estadual
state recreation area	Ausflugsgebiet	**state recreation area** *Eng.*	zona de recreo provincial	zone récréative regionale	área de lazer estadual
station	Bahnhof, Stützpunkt	**station** *Eng., Fr.*	estación	station	estação
reservoir	Stausee	**Stausee** *Ger.*	embalse	réservoir	reservatório
station	Bahnhof, Stützpunkt	**stazione** *It.*	estación	station	estação
saint	Sankt	**ste., sainte** *Fr.*	santa	sainte	santa
mountains	Berge	**stěny** *Czech*	montañas	montagnes	montanhas
steppe	Steppe	**step'** *Rus.*	estepa	steppe	estepe
peak	Gipfel	**štít** *Slo.*	pico	cime	pico
saint	Sankt	**sto., santo** *Port., Sp.*	santo	saint	santo
strait(s)	Meeresstrasse	**strait(s)** *Eng.*	estrecho	détroit	estreito
stream	Strom	**stream** *Eng.*	corriente de agua	cours d'eau	curso d'água
street	Strasse	**street** *Eng.*	calle	rue	rua
strait	Meeresstrasse	**stretto** *It.*	estrecho	détroit	estreito
stream	Strom	**Strom** *Ger.*	corriente de agua	cours d'eau	curso d'água
stream	Strom	**-ström, -strömmen** *Swe.*	corriente de agua	cours d'eau	curso d'água
river	Fluss	**-su** *Kor.*	río	rivière	rio
channel	Kanal	**-suidō** *Jpn.*	canal, estrecho	canal, détroit	canal, estreito
sound	Sund	**Sund** *Ger.*	sonda	détroit	estreito
sound	Sund	**-sund** *Swe.*	sonda	détroit	estreito
swamp	Sumpf	**swamp** *Eng.*	pantano	marais	pântano
ridge	Höhenrücken	**syrt** *Tur.*	sierra	crête	serra
island	Insel	**sziget** *Hung.*	isla	île	ilha

T

ENGLISH	DEUTSCH	Map Form	ESPAÑOL	FRANÇAIS	PORTUGUÊS
tableland	Tafelland	**tableland** *Eng.*	mesa, altiplano	plateau	planalto
woods	Gehölz	**taillis** *Fr.*	bosque	taillis	bosque
reef	Riff	**taka** *Indon.*	arrecife	récif	recife
mountain	Berg	**-take** *Jpn.*	montaña	montagne	montanha
waterfall	Wasserfall	**-taki** *Jpn.*	cascada	chute d'eau	queda d'água
valley	Tal	**Tal** *Ger.*	valle	vallée	vale
mountain	Berg	**tall** *Ara.*	montaña	montagne	montanha
mountain, hill	Berg, Hügel	**tallat** *Ara.*	montaña, colina	montagne, colline	montanha, colina
hills	Hügel	**tallāt** *Ara.*	colinas	collines	colinas
dam	Talsperre	**Talsperre** *Ger.*	presa	barrage	represa
point	Landspitze	**-tangar, -tangi** *Ice.*	punta	pointe	ponta
cape	Kap	**tanjong** *Mal.*	cabo	cap	cabo
cape	Kap	**tanjung** *Indon.*	cabo	cap	cabo
island	Insel	**tao** *Ch.*	isla	île	ilha
hills	Hügel	**taraq** *Ara.*	colinas	collines	colinas
lake	See	**tasek** *Mal.*	lago	lac	lago
lake	See	**tasik** *Indon.*	lago	lac	lago
plateau	Hochebene	**tassili** *Ber.*	meseta	plateau	planalto
mountain	Berg	**taung** *Bur.*	montaña	montagne	montanha
range	Gebirge	**taungdan** *Bur.*	sierra	chaîne	cordilheira
theatre	Theater	**teatro** *It., Sp.*	teatro	théâtre	teatro
bay	Bucht	**teluk** *Indon.*	bahía	baie	baía
temple	Tempel	**temple** *Eng., Fr.*	templo	temple	templo
church	Kirche	**templom** *Hung.*	iglesia	église	igreja
desert	Wüste	**ténéré** *Ber.*	desierto	désert	deserto
peak, hill	Gipfel, Hügel	**tepe, tepesi** *Tur.*	pico, colina	cime, colline	pico, colina
territory	Territorium	**territory** *Eng.*	territorio	territoire	território
lagoon	Lagune, Haff	**thale** *Thai*	laguna	lagune	laguna
mountains	Berge	**thiu khao** *Thai*	montañas	montagnes	montanhas
mountain	Berg	**-tind, -tinderne** *Nor.*	montaña	montagne	montanha
ridge	Höhenrücken	**ţiwāl** *Ara.*	sierra	crête	serra
mountain	Berg	**-tjåkko, tjöure** *Lapp.*	montaña	montagne	montanha
island	Insel	**-to** *Kor.*	isla	île	ilha
island	Insel	**-tō** *Jpn.*	isla	île	ilha
lake	See	**tó** *Hung.*	lago	lac	lago
pass	Pass	**-tōge** *Jpn.*	paso	col	passo
island	Insel	**tokong** *Mal.*	isla	île	ilha
lake	See	**tônlé** *Cbd.*	lago	lac	lago
mountain torrent	Wildbach	**torrente** *It., Sp.*	torrente	torrent	torrente
tower	Turm	**tower** *Eng.*	torre	tour	torre
turnpike	gebührenpflichtige Autobahn	**tpk., turnpike** *Eng.*	camino con peaje	grande route à péage	rodovia com pedágio
lake	See	**-träsk** *Swe.*	lago	lac	lago
trench	Tiefseegraben	**trench** *Eng.*	trinchera	tranchée	fossa submarina
trough	Tiefseegraben	**trough** *Eng.*	trinchera	tranchée	fossa submarina
volcano	Vulkan	**tulūl** *Ara.*	volcán	volcan	vulcão
tunnel	Tunnel	**túnel** *Sp.*	túnel	tunnel	túnel
tunnel	Tunnel	**tunnel** *Eng., Fr.*	túnel	tunnel	túnel
hill, mountain	Hügel, Berg	**-tunturi** *Finn.*	colina, montaña	colline, montagne	colina, montanha
island	Insel	**tuo** *Ch.*	isla	île	ilha
canal	Kanal	**tur'at** *Ara.*	canal	canal	canal
turnpike	gebührenpflichtige Autobahn	**turnpike** *Eng.*	camino con peaje	grande route à péage	rodovia com pedágio

U-V

ENGLISH	DEUTSCH	Map Form	ESPAÑOL	FRANÇAIS	PORTUGUÊS
cape	Kap	**ujung** *Indon.*	cabo	cap	cabo
lagoon	Lagune, Haff	**-umi** *Jpn.*	laguna	lagune	laguna
United Nations	Vereinte Nationen	**U.N., United Nations** *Eng.*	Naciones Unidas	Nations Unies	Nações Unidas
canal	Kanal	**-unga** *Jpn.*	canal	canal	canal
university	Universität	**univ., universidad** *Sp.* **universidade** **università** **university**	universidad	université	universidade
university	Universität	**Universität** *Ger.*	universidad	université	universidade
university	Universität	**université** *Fr.*	universidad	université	universidade
university	Universität	**universitet** *Rus.*	universidad	université	universidade
upland	Bergland	**upland** *Eng.*	tierras altas	hautes terres	terras altas
lake	See	**-ura** *Jpn.*	lago	lac	lago
mountain(s)	Berg(e)	**uul** *Mong.*	montaña(s)	montagne(s)	montanha(s)
elevation(s)	Höhe(n)	**uval(y)** *Rus.*	altura(s)	élévation(s)	elevação(ões)
spring	Quelle	**'uyūn** *Ara.*	manantial	source	fonte, manancial
hill	Hügel	**-vaara** *Finn.*	colina	colline	colina
strait	Meeresstrasse	**väin** *Est.*	estrecho	détroit	estreito
valley	Tal	**val** *Fr., It.*	valle	val	vale
valley	Tal	**valle** *It., Sp.*	valle	vallée	vale
valley	Tal	**vallée** *Fr.*	valle	vallée	vale
waterfall	Wasserfall	**vallen** *Du.*	cascada	chute d'eau	queda d'água
valley	Tal	**valley** *Eng.*	valle	vallée	vale
valley	Tal	**vallon** *Fr.*	valle	vallon	vale
lake	See	**-vatn** *Ice., Nor.*	lago	lac	lago
lake	See	**-vatnet** *Nor.*	lago	lac	lago
lake	See	**-vattnett** *Swe.*	lago	lac	lago
reservoir	Stausee	**vdchr., vodochranilišče** *Rus.*	embalse	réservoir	reservatório
hills	Hügel	**-veden** *Swe.*	colinas	collines	colinas
upland	Bergland	**verch** *Rus.*	tierras altas	hautes terres	terras altas
lake	See	**-vesi** *Finn.*	lago	lac	lago
viaduct	Viadukt	**viaducto** *Sp.*	viaducto	viaduc	viaduto
plateau	Hochebene	**-vidda** *Nor.*	meseta	plateau	planalto
gulf	Golf	**-viken** *Swe.*	golfo	golfe	golfo
bay	Bucht	**vinh** *Viet.*	bahía	baie	baía
mountain	Berg	**vîrful** *Rom.*	montaña	montagne	montanha
airport	Flughafen	**vliegveld** *Du.*	aeropuerto	aéroport	aeroporto
channel	Kanal	**vliet** *Du.*	canal, estrecho	canal, détroit	canal, estreito
canal	Kanal	**vodnyj put'** *Rus.*	canal	canal	canal
reservoir	Stausee	**vodochranilišče** *Rus.*	embalse	réservoir	reservatório
railroad station	Bahnhof	**vokzal** *Rus.*	estación de ferrocarril	gare	estação ferroviária
volcano	Vulkan	**vol., volcán** *Sp.* **volcano**	volcán	volcan	vulcão
pass	Pass	**vorota** *Rus.*	paso	col	passo
upland	Bergland	**vozvyšennost'** *Rus.*	tierras altas	hautes terres	terras altas
mountain	Berg	**vrâh** *Blg.*	montaña	montagne	montanha
mountains	Berge	**vrchovina** *Czech, Slo.*	montañas	montagnes	montanhas
mountains	Berge	**vrchy** *Slo.*	montañas	montagnes	montanhas
peak	Gipfel	**vrh** *S./C.*	pico	cime	pico
volcano	Vulkan	**vulkan** *Rus.*	volcán	volcan	vulcão
bay	Bucht	**vung** *Viet.*	bahía	baie	baía
mountain, hill	Berg, Hügel	**-vuori** *Finn.*	montaña, colina	montagne, colline	montanha, colina

W-Z

ENGLISH	DEUTSCH	Map Form	ESPAÑOL	FRANÇAIS	PORTUGUÊS
west	West	**w., west** *Eng.*	oeste	ouest	oeste
marsh	Marsch	**wa** *Ch.*	pantano	marais	pântano
wadi	Wadi	**wādī** *Ara.*	uadi	wadi	uádi
oasis	Oase	**wāhat, wāhāt** *Ara.*	oasis	oasis	oásis
forest, mountains	Wald	**Wald** *Ger.*	bosque, montañas	forêt, montagnes	floresta, montanhas
bay	Bucht	**wan** *Ch., Jap.*	bahía	baie	baía
wash	Wadi	**wash** *Eng.*	uadi	wadi	uádi
waterfalls	Wasserfälle	**Wasserfälle** *Ger.*	cascadas	chutes d'eau	quedas d'água
water (lake, river)	Wasser (See, Fluss)	**water** *Eng.*	agua (lago, río)	eau (lac, rivière)	água (lago, rio)
waterway	Wasserstrasse	**waterway** *Eng.*	canal	canal	canal
pond	Weiher	**Weiher** *Ger.*	charca	étang	charco
well	Brunnen	**well** *Eng.*	pozo	puits	poço
bay	Wiek	**Wiek** *Ger.*	bahía	baie	baía
woods	Gehölz	**woods** *Eng.*	bosque	bois	bosque
water (lake, river)	Wasser (See, Fluss)	**wr., water** *Eng.*	agua (lago, río)	eau (lac, rivière)	água (lago, rio)
strait	Meeresstrasse	**xia** *Ch.*	estrecho	détroit	estreito
lake, sea	See, Meer	**yam** *Heb.*	lago, mar	lac, mer	lago, mar
mountain	Berg	**-yama** *Jpn.*	montaña	montagne	montanha
bay	Bucht	**yang** *Ch.*	bahía	baie	baía
peninsula	Halbinsel	**yarımadası** *Tur.*	península	péninsule	península
mountain	Berg	**yebel** *Ara.*	montaña	montagne	montanha
rock, island	Fels, Insel	**yen** *Ch.*	roca, isla	rocher, île	rochedo, ilha
mountains	Berge	**yoma** *Bur.*	montañas	montagnes	montanhas
island	Insel	**yu** *Ch.*	isla	île	ilha
lake	See	**yumco** *Tib.*	lago	lac	lago
canal	Kanal	**yunhe** *Ch.*	canal	canal	canal
intermittent lake	periodischer See	**zahrez** *Ara.*	lago intermitente	lac périodique	lago intermitente
point	Landspitze	**-zaki** *Jpn.*	punta	pointe	ponta
lagoon	Lagune, Haff	**zalew** *Pol.*	laguna	lagune	laguna
gulf, bay	Golf, Bucht	**zaliv** *Rus.*	golfo, bahía	golfe, baie	golfo, baía
reserve	Reservat	**zapov., zapovednik** *Rus.*	reserva	réserve	reserva
sea, lake	Meer, See	**zee** *Du.*	mar, lago	mer, lac	mar, lago
autonomous province	autonome Provinz	**zizhiqu** *Ch.*	provincia autónoma	province autonome	província autônoma
zoo	Zoo	**zoo** *Eng.*	parque zoológico	zoo	jardim zoológico

THIS TABLE gives the area, population, population density, capital, and political status for every country in the world. The political units listed are categorized by political status in the last column of the table, as follows: A—independent countries; B—internally independent political entities which are under the protection of another country in matters of defense and foreign affairs; C—colonies and other dependent political units; and D—the major administrative subdivisions of Australia, Canada, China, the United Kingdom, and the United States. For comparison, the table also includes the continents and the world. For units categorized B, the names of protecting countries are specified in the political-status column. For units categorized C, the names of administering countries are given in parentheses in the first column.

The populations are estimates for January 1, 1993, made by Rand McNally on the basis of official data, United Nations estimates, and other available information.

IN DIESER ÜBERSICHT sind Fläche, Bevölkerung, Bevölkerungsdichte, Hauptstadt und politischer Status für jedes Land der Erde aufgeführt. Die politischen Einheiten sind in der letzten Spalte der Tabelle nach ihrem politischen Status wie folgt gegliedert: A—souveräne Staaten; B—innenpolitisch unabhängige Länder unter der Protektion eines anderen Landes in Angelegenheiten der Aussenpolitik und Verteidigung; C—Kolonien oder anderweitig abhängige Gebiete; D—die wichtigsten Verwaltungseinheiten von Australien, Kanada, China, dem Vereinigten Königreich und den Vereinigten Staaten. Für Vergleiche enthält die Übersicht auch Angaben über die Kontinente und die Welt. Für die unter B eingestuften Einheiten ist der Name des Schutzstaates in der Spalte Politischer Status aufgeführt. Für die unter C eingestuften Gebiete steht der Name des die Verwaltung ausübenden Landes in Klammern in der ersten Spalte.

Die Bevölkerungsangaben sind Schätzungen zum 1. Januar 1993, die Rand McNally auf der Grundlage amtlicher Zahlen, Schätzungen der Vereinten Nationen und anderer zugänglicher Informationen berechnet hat.

EL CUADRO ABAJO incluye la extensión, población y densidad de población, la capital y el estado político de todos los países del mundo. Las entidades políticas nombradas están clasificadas de acuerdo a su estado político en la última columna de la tabla, de esta manera: A—países independientes; B—entidades políticas internamente independientes las cuales se encuentran bajo la protección de otro país en cuanto a asuntos de defensa nacional y relaciones con el extranjero; C—colonias y otras entidades políticas dependientes; y D—las mayores subdivisiones administrativas de Australia, Canadá, China, el Reino Unido, y los Estados Unidos. Para servir de medida comparativa, el cuadro también incluye los continentes y el mundo. Para las entidades de la clasificación B, los nombres de los países protectores están especificados en la columna de estado político. Para las unidades bajo la categoría C, los nombres de los países administradores se encuentran entre paréntesis en la primera columna.

Las poblaciones son los estimados de Rand McNally, tomados el 1o. de Enero de 1993, en base a datos oficiales, estimados de las Naciones Unidas y varias otras informaciones disponibles.

CETTE TABLE donne, pour chaque pays du monde, les renseignements suivants: superficie, population, densité de population, capitale, statut politique. Les entités politiques sont classées, selon leur statut, dans la dernière colonne du tableau: A—pays indépendants; B—entités politiques indépendants intérieurement, mais qui se trouvent sous la protection d'un autre pays pour leur défense et leurs relations extérieures; C—colonies et autres entités politiques dépendantes; D—principales subdivisions administratives de l'Australie, du Canada, de la Chine, du Royaume-Uni, des États-Unis. Pour permettre les comparaisons, la table comprend aussi les continents et le monde. Pour les entités politiques de la catégorie B, les noms des pays protecteurs sont spécifiés dans la colonne "statut politique". Pour celles de la catégorie C, les noms des pays administrateurs sont mis entre parenthèses dans la première colonne.

Les chiffres concernant la population sont des estimations au 1er janvier 1993, établies par Rand McNally, d'après les sources officielles, les estimations des Nations Unies et autres informations disponibles.

A TABELA que se segue apresenta a área, a população, a densidade demográfica, a capital e o estatuto político de todos os países do mundo. As unidades políticas relacionadas na tabela estão classificadas de acordo com o respectivo estatuto político na última coluna, do seguinte modo: A—países independentes; B—unidades políticas internamente independentes mas que se encontram sob a proteção de outro país no tocante a assuntos de defesa nacional e negócios extrenos; C—colônias e outras unidades políticas dependentes; e D—subdivisões administrativas principais da Austrália, Canadá, China, Reino Unido e Estados Unidos. Para fins de comparabilidade, a tabela também inclui os continentes e o mundo. No tocante ás unidades classificadas em B, os nomes dos países protetores estão especificados na coluna relativa ao estatuto político. Para as unidades da categoria C, os nomes dos países administradores figuram entre parênteses na primeira coluna.

Os dados relativos à população são estimativas de Rand McNally para 1 de janeiro de 1993, com base em dados oficiais, estimativas das Nações Unidas e outras informações disponíveis.

NAME / NAME / NOMBRE / NOM / NOME — English / Englisch / Inglés / Anglais / Inglês	Local / Einheimisch / Local / Local / Local	AREA / FLÄCHE / AREA / SUPERFICIE / ÁREA — sq. km.	sq. mi.	POPULATION / BEVÖLKERUNG / POBLACIÓN / POPULATION / POPULAÇÃO	DENSITY PER / BEVÖLKERUNGSDICHTE PRO / DENSIDAD POR / DENSITÉ / DENSIDADE POR — sq. km.	sq. mi.	CAPITAL / HAUPSTADT / CAPITAL / CAPITALE / CAPITAL	POLITICAL STATUS / POLITISCHER STATUS / ESTADO POLITICO / STATUS POLITIQUE / ESTATUTO POLITICO
†Afghanistan	Afghānestān	652,225	251,826	16,290,000	25	65	Kābol	A
Africa	. . .	30,300,000	11,700,000	668,700,000	22	57	. . .	. . .
Alabama, U.S.	Alabama	135,775	52,423	4,128,000	30	79	Montgomery	D
Alaska, U.S.	Alaska	1,700,139	656,424	564,000	0.3	0.9	Juneau	D
†Albania	Shqipëri	28,748	11,100	3,305,000	115	298	Tiranë	A
Alberta, Can.	Alberta	661,190	255,287	2,839,000	4.3	11	Edmonton	D
†Algeria	Algérie (French) / Djazaïr (Arabic)	2,381,741	919,595	26,925,000	11	29	El Djazaïr (Algiers)	A
American Samoa (U.S.)	American Samoa (English) / Amerika Samoa (Samoan)	199	77	52,000	261	675	Pago Pago	C
†Andorra	Andorra	453	175	56,000	124	320	Andorra	B(Sp., Fr.)
†Angola	Angola	1,246,700	481,354	10,735,000	8.6	22	Luanda	A
Anguilla	Anguilla	91	35	7,000	77	200	The Valley	B(U.K.)
Anhwei, China	Anhui	139,000	53,668	58,440,000	420	1,089	Hefei	D
Antarctica	. . .	14,000,000	5,400,000	[1]	. . .	. . .	. . .	. . .
†Antigua and Barbuda	Antigua and Barbuda	442	171	77,000	174	450	St. John's	A
†Argentina	Argentina	2,780,400	1,073,519	32,950,000	12	31	Buenos Aires and Viedma [5]	A
Arizona, U.S.	Arizona	295,276	114,006	3,872,000	13	34	Phoenix	D
Arkansas, U.S.	Arkansas	137,742	53,182	2,410,000	17	45	Little Rock	D
†Armenia	Hayastan	29,800	11,506	3,429,000	115	298	Jerevan	A
Aruba	Aruba	193	75	65,000	337	867	Oranjestad	B(Neth.)
Asia	. . .	44,900,000	17,300,000	3,337,800,000	74	193	. . .	. . .
†Australia	Australia	7,682,300	2,966,155	16,965,000	2.2	5.7	Canberra	A
Australian Capital Territory, Austl.	Australian Capital Territory	2,400	927	282,000	118	304	Canberra	D
†Austria	Österreich	83,856	32,377	7,899,000	94	244	Wien (Vienna)	A
†Azerbaijan	Azerbajdžan	86,600	33,436	7,510,000	87	225	Baku (Baky)	A
†Bahamas	Bahamas	13,939	5,382	265,000	19	49	Nassau	A
†Bahrain	Al-Baḥrayn	691	267	561,000	812	2,101	Al-Manāmah	A
†Bangladesh	Bangladesh	143,998	55,598	120,850,000	839	2,174	Dhaka (Dacca)	A
†Barbados	Barbados	430	166	258,000	600	1,554	Bridgetown	A
†Belarus	Byelarus'	207,600	80,155	10,400,000	50	130	Minsk	A
†Belgium	Belgique (French) / België (Flemish)	30,518	11,783	10,030,000	329	851	Bruxelles (Brussels)	A
†Belize	Belize	22,963	8,866	186,000	8.1	21	Belmopan	A
†Benin	Bénin	112,600	43,475	5,083,000	45	117	Porto-Novo and Cotonou	A
Bermuda (U.K.)	Bermuda	54	21	60,000	1,111	2,857	Hamilton	C
†Bhutan	Druk-Yul	46,500	17,954	1,680,000	36	94	Thimphu	B(India)
†Bolivia	Bolivia	1,098,581	424,165	7,411,000	6.7	17	La Paz and Sucre	A
Bophuthatswana [2]	Bophuthatswana	40,509	15,641	2,525,000	62	161	Mmabatho	B(S. Afr.)
†Bosnia and Herzegovina	Bosna i Hercegovina	51,129	19,741	4,375,000	86	222	Sarajevo	A
†Botswana	Botswana	582,000	224,711	1,379,000	2.4	6.1	Gaborone	A
†Brazil	Brasil	8,511,996	3,286,500	159,630,000	19	49	Brasília	A
British Columbia, Can.	British Columbia (English) / Colombie-Britannique (French)	947,800	365,948	3,665,000	3.9	10	Victoria	D
British Indian Ocean Territory (U.K.)	British Indian Ocean Territory	60	23	[1]	. . .	. . .	. . .	C
British Virgin Islands (U.K.)	British Virgin Islands	153	59	13,000	85	220	Road Town	C
†Brunei	Brunei	5,765	2,226	273,000	47	123	Bandar Seri Begawan	A
†Bulgaria	Bâlgarija	110,912	42,823	8,842,000	80	206	Sofija (Sofia)	A
†Burkina Faso	Burkina Faso	274,200	105,869	9,808,000	36	93	Ouagadougou	A
†Burundi	Burundi	27,830	10,745	6,118,000	220	569	Bujumbura	A
California, U.S.	California	424,002	163,707	31,310,000	74	191	Sacramento	D
†Cambodia	Kâmpŭchéa	181,035	69,898	8,928,000	49	128	Phnum Pénh (Phnom Penh)	A
†Cameroon	Cameroun (French) / Cameroon (English)	475,442	183,569	12,875,000	27	70	Yaoundé	A
†Canada	Canada	9,970,610	3,849,674	30,530,000	3.1	7.9	Ottawa	A
†Cape Verde	Cabo Verde	4,033	1,557	404,000	100	259	Praia	A
Cayman Islands (U.K.)	Cayman Islands	259	100	29,000	112	290	George Town	C
†Central African Republic	République centrafricaine	622,984	240,535	3,068,000	4.9	13	Bangui	A
†Chad	Tchad	1,284,000	495,755	5,297,000	4.1	11	N'Djamena	A
Chekiang, China	Zhejiang	101,800	39,305	43,150,000	424	1,098	Hangzhou	D
†Chile	Chile	756,626	292,135	13,635,000	18	47	Santiago	A
†China (excl. Taiwan)	Zhongguo	9,556,100	3,689,631	1,179,030,000	123	320	Beijing (Peking)	A
Christmas Island (Austl.)	Christmas Island	135	52	900	6.7	17	The Settlement	C
Ciskei [2]	Ciskei	7,760	2,996	1,105,000	142	369	Bisho	B(S. Afr.)
Cocos (Keeling) Islands (Austl.)	Cocos (Keeling) Islands	14	5.4	500	36	93	. . .	C
†Colombia	Colombia	1,141,748	440,831	34,640,000	30	79	Santa Fe de Bogotá	A
Colorado, U.S.	Colorado	269,620	104,100	3,410,000	13	33	Denver	D
†Comoros (excl. Mayotte)	Comores (French) / Al-Qumur (Arabic)	2,235	863	503,000	225	583	Moroni	A
†Congo	Congo	342,000	132,047	2,413,000	7.1	18	Brazzaville	A
Connecticut, U.S.	Connecticut	14,358	5,544	3,358,000	234	606	Hartford	D
Cook Islands	Cook Islands	236	91	18,000	76	198	Avarua	B(N.Z.)
†Costa Rica	Costa Rica	51,100	19,730	3,225,000	63	163	San José	A
†Cote d'Ivoire	Côte d'Ivoire	322,500	124,518	13,765,000	43	111	Abidjan and Yamoussoukro [5]	A
†Croatia	Hrvatska	56,538	21,829	4,793,000	85	220	Zagreb	A
†Cuba	Cuba	110,861	42,804	10,900,000	98	255	La Habana (Havana)	A
†Cyprus (excl. North Cyprus)	Kípros (Greek) / Kıbrıs (Turkish)	5,896	2,276	527,000	89	232	Nicosia (Levkosía)	A
Cyprus, North	Kuzey Kıbrıs	3,355	1,295	193,000	58	149	Nicosia (Lefkoşa)	A

NAME / NAME / NOMBRE / NOM / NOME English / Englisch Inglés / Anglais / Inglês	Local / Einheimisch Local / Local / Local	AREA / FLÄCHE AREA / SUPERFICIE / ÁREA sq. km.	sq. mi.	POPULATION BEVÖLKERUNG POBLACIÓN POPULATION POPULAÇÃO	DENSITY PER BEVÖLKERUNGSDICHTE PRO / DENSIDAD POR DENSITÉ / DENSIDADE POR sq. km.	sq. mi.	CAPITAL HAUPSTADT CAPITAL CAPITALE CAPITAL	POLITICAL STATUS POLITISCHER STATUS ESTADO POLITICO STATUS POLITIQUE ESTATUTO POLITICO
†Czech Republic	Česká Republika	78,864	30,450	10,335,000	131	339	Praha (Prague)	A
Delaware, U.S.	Delaware	6,447	2,489	692,000	107	278	Dover	D
†Denmark	Danmark	43,093	16,638	5,169,000	120	311	København (Copenhagen)	A
District of Columbia, U.S.	District of Columbia	177	68	590,000	3,333	8,676	Washington	D
†Djibouti	Djibouti	23,200	8,958	396,000	17	44	Djibouti	A
†Dominica	Dominica	790	305	88,000	111	289	Roseau	A
†Dominican Republic	República Dominicana	48,442	18,704	7,591,000	157	406	Santo Domingo	A
†Ecuador	Ecuador	283,561	109,484	11,055,000	39	101	Quito	A
†Egypt	Misr	1,001,449	386,662	57,050,000	57	148	Al-Qāhirah (Cairo)	A
†El Salvador	El Salvador	21,041	8,124	5,635,000	268	694	San Salvador	A
England, U.K.	England	130,478	50,378	48,235,000	370	957	London	D
†Equatorial Guinea	Guinea Ecuatorial	28,051	10,831	394,000	14	36	Malabo	A
†Eritrea	Eritrea	93,679	36,170	3,425,000	37	95	Asmera	A
†Estonia	Eesti	45,100	17,413	1,613,000	36	93	Tallinn	A
†Ethiopia	Ityopiya	1,157,603	446,953	51,715,000	45	116	Adis Abeba	A
Europe	. . .	9,900,000	3,800,000	694,900,000	70	183	. . .	
Faeroe Islands	Føroyar	1,399	540	49,000	35	91	Tórshavn	B(Den.)
Falkland Islands (U.K.) (3)	Falkland Islands	12,173	4,700	2,100	0.2	0.4	Stanley	C
†Fiji	Fiji (French / Viti (Fijian)	18,274	7,056	754,000	41	107	Suva	A
†Finland	Suomi (Finnish) / Finland (Swedish)	338,145	130,559	5 074,000	15	39	Helsinki (Helsingfors)	A
Florida, U.S.	Florida	170,313	65,758	13 630,000	80	207	Tallahassee	D
†France (excl. Overseas Departments)	France	547,026	211,208	57,570,000	105	273	Paris	A
French Guiana (Fr.)	Guyane française	91,000	35,135	131,000	1.4	3.7	Cayenne	C
French Polynesia (Fr.)	Polynésie française	3,521	1,359	208,000	59	153	Papeete	C
Fukien, China	Fujian	120,000	46,332	31,160,000	260	673	Fuzhou	D
†Gabon	Gabon	267,667	103,347	1,115,000	4.2	11	Libreville	A
†Gambia	Gambia	10,689	4,127	916,000	86	222	Banjul	A
Georgia, U.S.	Georgia	153,953	59,441	6,795,000	44	114	Atlanta	D
†Georgia	Sakartvelo	69,700	26,911	5,593,000	80	208	Tbilisi	A
†Germany	Deutschland	356,955	137,822	80,590,000	226	585	Berlin and Bonn	A
†Ghana	Ghana	238,533	92,098	16,445,000	69	179	Accra	A
Gibraltar (U.K.)	Gibraltar	6.0	2.3	32,000	5,333	13,913	Gibraltar	C
†Greece	Ellás	131,957	50,949	10,075,000	76	198	Athínai (Athens)	A
Greenland	Kalaallit Nunaat (Eskimo) / Grønland (Danish)	2,175,600	840,000	57,000	. . .	0.1	Godthåb (Nuuk)	B(Den.)
†Grenada	Grenada	344	133	97,000	282	729	St. George's	A
Guadeloupe (incl. Dependencies) (Fr.)	Guadeloupe	1,780	687	413,000	232	601	Basse-Terre	C
Guam (U.S.)	Guam	541	209	143,000	264	684	Agana	C
†Guatemala	Guatemala	108,889	42,042	9,705,000	89	231	Guatemala	A
Guernsey (incl. Dependencies)	Guernsey	78	30	58,000	744	1,933	St. Peter Port	B(U.K.)
†Guinea	Guinée	245,857	94,926	7,726,000	31	81	Conakry	A
†Guinea-Bissau	Guiné-Bissau	36,125	13,948	1,060,000	29	76	Bissau	A
†Guyana	Guyana	214,969	83,000	737,000	3.4	8.9	Georgetown	A
Hainan, China	Hainan	34,000	13,127	6,820,000	201	520	Haikou	D
†Haiti	Haïti	27,750	10,714	6,509,000	235	608	Port-au-Prince	A
Hawaii, U.S.	Hawaii	28,313	10,932	1,159,000	41	106	Honolulu	D
Heilungkiang, China	Heilongjiang	469,000	181,082	36,685,000	78	203	Harbin	D
Honan, China	Henan	167,000	64,479	88,890,000	532	1,379	Zhengzhou	D
†Honduras	Honduras	112,088	43,277	5,164,000	46	119	Tegucigalpa	A
Hong Kong (U.K.)	Hong Kong (English) / Xianggang (Chinese)	1,072	414	5,580,000	5,205	13,478	Hong Kong (Victoria)	C
Hopeh, China	Hebei	190,000	73,359	63,500,000	334	866	Shijiazhuang	D
Hunan, China	Hunan	210,000	81,081	63,140,000	301	779	Changsha	D
†Hungary	Magyarország	93,033	35,920	10,305,000	111	287	Budapest	A
Hupeh, China	Hubei	187,400	72,356	56,090,000	299	775	Wuhan	D
†Iceland	Ísland	103,000	39,769	260,000	2.5	6.5	Reykjavík	A
Idaho, U.S.	Idaho	216,456	83,574	1,026,000	4.7	12	Boise	D
Illinois, U.S.	Illinois	150,007	57,918	11,640,000	78	201	Springfield	D
†India (incl. part of Jammu and Kashmir)	India (English) / Bharat (Hindi)	3,203,975	1,237,062	873,850,000	273	706	New Delhi	A
Indiana, U.S.	Indiana	94,328	36,420	5,667,000	60	156	Indianapolis	D
†Indonesia	Indonesia	1,948,732	752,410	186,180,000	96	247	Jakarta	A
Inner Mongolia, China	Nei Monggol	1,183,000	456,759	22,340,000	19	49	Hohhot	D
Iowa, U.S.	Iowa	145,754	56,276	2,821,000	19	50	Des Moines	D
†Iran	Īrān	1,638,057	632,457	60,500,000	37	96	Tehrān	A
†Iraq	Al-'Irāq	438,317	169,235	18,815,000	43	111	Baghdād	A
†Ireland	Ireland (English) / Éire (Gaelic)	70,285	27,137	3,525,000	50	130	Dublin (Baile Átha Cliath)	A
Isle of Man	Isle of Man	572	221	70,000	122	317	Douglas	B(U.K.)
†Israel (excl. Occupied Areas)	Yisra'el (Hebrew) / Isrā'īl (Arabic)	20,770	8,019	4,593,000	221	573	Yerushalayim (Jerusalem)	A
Israeli Occupied Areas (4)	. . .	7,632	2,947	2,461,000	322	835	. . .	. . .
†Italy	Italia	301,277	116,324	56,550,000	188	486	Roma (Rome)	A
†Jamaica	Jamaica	10,991	4,244	2,412,000	219	568	Kingston	A
†Japan	Nihon	377,801	145,870	124,710,000	330	855	Tōkyō	A
Jersey	Jersey	116	45	85,000	733	1,889	St. Helier	B(U.K.)
†Jordan	Al-Urdun	91,000	35,135	3,632,000	40	103	'Ammān	A
Kansas, U.S.	Kansas	213,110	82,282	2,539,000	12	31	Topeka	D
Kansu, China	Gansu	450,000	173,746	23,280,000	52	134	Lanzhou	D
†Kazakhstan	Kazakhstan	2,717,300	1,049,156	17,190,000	6.3	16	Alma-Ata (Almaty)	A
Kentucky, U.S.	Kentucky	104,665	40,411	3,745,000	36	93	Frankfort	D
†Kenya	Kenya	582,646	224,961	26,655,000	46	118	Nairobi	A
Kiangsi, China	Jiangxi	166,600	64,325	39,270,000	236	610	Nanchang	D
Kiangsu, China	Jiangsu	102,600	39,614	69,730,000	680	1,760	Nanjing (Nanking)	D
Kiribati	Kiribati	811	313	76,000	94	243	Bairiki	A
Kirin, China	Jilin	187,000	72,201	25,630,000	137	355	Changchun	D
†Korea, North	Chosŏn-minjujuŭi-inmīn-konghwaguk	120,538	46,540	22,450,000	186	482	P'yŏngyang	A
†Korea, South	Taehan-min'guk	99,016	38,230	43,660,000	441	1,142	Sŏul (Seoul)	A
†Kuwait	Al-Kuwayt	17,818	6,880	2,388,000	134	347	Al-Kuwayt (Kuwait)	A
Kwangsi Chuang, China	Guangxi Zhuangzu	236,300	91,236	43,975,000	186	482	Nanning	D
Kwangtung, China	Guangdong	178,000	68,726	65,380,000	367	951	Guangzhou (Canton)	D
Kweichow, China	Guizhou	170,000	65,637	33,745,000	199	514	Guiyang	D
†Kyrgyzstan	Kyrgyzstan	198,500	76,641	4,613,000	23	60	Biškek (Frunze)	A
†Laos	Lao	236,800	91,429	4,507,000	19	49	Viangchan (Vientiane)	A
†Latvia	Latvija	63,700	24,595	2,737,000	43	111	Rīga	A
†Lebanon	Lubnān	10,400	4,015	3,467,000	333	864	Bayrūt (Beirut)	A
†Lesotho	Lesotho	30,355	11,720	1,873,000	62	160	Maseru	A
Liaoning, China	Liaoning	145,700	56,255	41,035,000	282	729	Shenyang (Mukden)	D
†Liberia	Liberia	99,067	38,250	2,869,000	29	75	Monrovia	A
†Libya	Lībīyā	1,759,540	679,362	4,552,000	2.6	6.7	Tarābulus (Tripoli)	A
†Liechtenstein	Liechtenstein	160	62	30,000	188	484	Vaduz	A
†Lithuania	Lietuva	65,200	25,174	3,804,000	58	151	Vilnius	A
Louisiana, U.S.	Louisiana	134,275	51,843	4,282,000	32	83	Baton Rouge	D
†Luxembourg	Luxembourg (French) / Lezebuurg (Luxembourgish)	2,586	998	392,000	152	393	Luxembourg	A
Macau (Port.)	Macau	17	6.6	477,000	28,059	72,273	Macau	C
†Macedonia	Makedonija	25,713	9,928	2,179,000	85	219	Skopje	A
†Madagascar	Madagasikara (Malagasy) / Madagascar (French)	587,041	226,658	12,800,000	22	56	Antananarivo	A
Maine, U.S.	Maine	91,653	35,387	1,257,000	14	36	Augusta	D
†Malawi	Malaŵi	118,484	45,747	9,691,000	82	212	Lilongwe	A
†Malaysia	Malaysia	334,758	129,251	18,630,000	56	144	Kuala Lumpur	A
†Maldives	Maldives	298	115	235,000	789	2,043	Male'	A
†Mali	Mali	1,248,574	482,077	8,754,000	7.0	18	Bamako	A
†Malta	Malta	316	122	360,000	1,139	2,951	Valletta	A
Manitoba, Can.	Manitoba	649,950	250,947	1,221,000	1.9	4.9	Winnipeg	D
†Marshall Islands	Marshall Islands	181	70	51,000	282	729	Majuro (island)	A
Martinique (Fr.)	Martinique	1,100	425	372,000	338	875	Fort-de-France	C
Maryland, U.S.	Maryland	32,135	12,407	4,975,000	155	401	Annapolis	D
Massachusetts, U.S.	Massachusetts	27,337	10,555	6,103,000	223	578	Boston	D

NAME / NAME / NOMBRE / NOM / NOME		AREA / FLÄCHE AREA / SUPERFICIE / ÁREA		POPULATION BEVÖLKERUNG POBLACIÓN POPULATION POPULAÇÃO	DENSITY PER BEVÖLKERUNGSDICHTE PRO / DENSIDAD POR DENSITÉ / DENSIDADE POR		CAPITAL HAUPSTADT CAPITAL CAPITALE CAPITAL	POLITICAL STATUS POLITISCHER STATUS ESTADO POLÍTICO STATUS POLITIQUE ESTATUTO POLÍTICO
English / Englisch Inglés / Anglais / Inglês	Local / Einheimisch Local / Local / Local	sq. km.	sq. mi.		sq. km.	sq. mi.		
†Mauritania	Mauritanie (French) / Mūrītāniyā (Arabic)	1,025,520	395,956	2,092,000	2.0	5.3	Nouakchott	A
†Mauritius (incl. Dependencies)	Mauritius	2,040	788	1,096,000	537	1,391	Port Louis	A
Mayotte (Fr.) [6]	Mayotte	374	144	89,000	238	618	Dzaoudzi and Mamoudzou [5]	C
†Mexico	México	1,967,183	759,534	86,170,000	44	113	Ciudad de México (Mexico City)	A
Michigan, U.S.	Michigan	250,738	96,810	9,488,000	38	98	Lansing	D
†Micronesia, Federated States of	Federated States of Micronesia	702	271	117,000	167	432	Kolonia and Paliker [5]	A
Midway Islands (U.S.)	Midway Islands	5.2	2.0	500	96	250	. . .	C
Minnesota, U.S.	Minnesota	225,182	86,943	4,513,000	20	52	St. Paul	D
Mississippi, U.S.	Mississippi	125,443	48,434	2,616,000	21	54	Jackson	D
Missouri, U.S.	Missouri	180,546	69,709	5,231,000	29	75	Jefferson City	D
†Moldova	Moldova	33,700	13,012	4,474,000	133	344	Kišin'ov (Chişinău)	A
†Monaco	Monaco	1.9	0.7	31,000	16,316	44,286	Monaco	A
†Mongolia	Mongol Ard Uls	1,566,500	604,829	2,336,000	1.5	3.9	Ulaanbaatar (Ulan Bator)	A
Montana, U.S.	Montana	380,850	147,046	821,000	2.2	5.6	Helena	D
Montserrat (U.K.)	Montserrat	102	39	13,000	127	333	Plymouth	C
†Morocco (excl. Western Sahara)	Al-Magrib	446,550	172,414	27,005,000	60	157	Rabat	A
†Mozambique	Moçambique	799,380	308,642	15,795,000	20	51	Maputo	A
†Myanmar	Myanmar	676,577	261,228	43,070,000	64	165	Yangon (Rangoon)	A
†Namibia (excl. Walvis Bay)	Namibia	823,144	317,818	1,603,000	1.9	5.0	Windhoek	A
Nauru	Nauru (English) / Naoero (Nauruan)	21	8.1	10,000	476	1,235	Yaren District	A
Nebraska, U.S.	Nebraska	200,358	77,358	1,615,000	8.1	21	Lincoln	D
†Nepal	Nepāl	147,181	56,827	20,325,000	138	358	Kāthmāndau	A
†Netherlands	Nederland	41,864	16,164	15,190,000	363	940	Amsterdam and 's-Gravenhage (The Hague)	A
Netherlands Antilles	Nederlandse Antillen	800	309	191,000	239	618	Willemstad	B(Neth.)
Nevada, U.S.	Nevada	286,368	110,567	1,308,000	4.6	12	Carson City	D
New Brunswick, Can.	New Brunswick (English) / Nouveau-Brunswick (French)	73,440	28,355	824,000	11	29	Fredericton	D
New Caledonia (Fr.)	Nouvelle-Calédonie	19,058	7,358	177,000	9.3	24	Nouméa	C
Newfoundland, Can.	Newfoundland (English) / Terre-Neuve (French)	405,720	156,649	641,000	1.6	4.1	St. John's	D
New Hampshire, U.S.	New Hampshire	24,219	9,351	1,154,000	48	123	Concord	D
New Jersey, U.S.	New Jersey	22,590	8,722	7,898,000	350	906	Trenton	D
New Mexico, U.S.	New Mexico	314,939	121,598	1,590,000	5.0	13	Santa Fe	D
New South Wales, Austl.	New South Wales	801,600	309,500	5,770,000	7.2	19	Sydney	D
New York, U.S.	New York	141,089	54,475	18,350,000	130	337	Albany	D
†New Zealand	New Zealand	270,534	104,454	3,477,000	13	33	Wellington	A
†Nicaragua	Nicaragua	129,640	50,054	3,932,000	30	79	Managua	A
†Niger	Niger	1,267,000	489,191	8,198,000	6.5	17	Niamey	A
†Nigeria	Nigeria	923,768	356,669	91,700,000	99	257	Lagos and Abuja	A
Ningsia Hui, China	Ningxia Huizu	66,400	25,637	4,820,000	73	188	Yinchuan	D
Niue	Niue	258	100	1,700	6.6	17	Alofi	B(N.Z.)
Norfolk Island (Austl.)	Norfolk Island	36	14	2,600	72	186	Kingston	C
North America	. . .	24,700,000	9,500,000	438,200,000	18	46	. . .	. . .
North Carolina, U.S.	North Carolina	139,397	53,821	6,846,000	49	127	Raleigh	D
North Dakota, U.S.	North Dakota	183,123	70,704	632,000	3.5	8.9	Bismarck	D
Northern Ireland, U.K.	Northern Ireland	14,121	5,452	1,604,000	114	294	Belfast	D
Northern Mariana Islands	Northern Mariana Islands	477	184	48,000	101	261	Saipan (island)	B(U.S.)
Northern Territory, Austl.	Northern Territory	1,346,200	519,771	176,000	0.1	0.3	Darwin	D
Northwest Territories, Can.	Northwest Territories (English) / Territoires du Nord-Ouest (French)	3,426,320	1,322,910	61,000	. . .	. . .	Yellowknife	D
†Norway (incl. Svalbard and Jan Mayen)	Norge	386,975	149,412	4,308,000	11	29	Oslo	A
Nova Scotia, Can.	Nova Scotia (English) / Nouvelle-Écosse (French)	55,490	21,425	1,007,000	18	47	Halifax	D
Oceania (incl. Australia)	. . .	8,500,000	3,300,000	26,700,000	3.1	8.1	. . .	. . .
Ohio, U.S.	Ohio	116,103	44,828	11,025,000	95	246	Columbus	D
Oklahoma, U.S.	Oklahoma	181,049	69,903	3,205,000	18	46	Oklahoma City	D
†Oman	'Umān	212,457	82,030	1,617,000	7.6	20	Masqat (Muscat)	A
Ontario, Can.	Ontario	1,068,580	412,581	11,265,000	11	27	Toronto	D
Oregon, U.S.	Oregon	254,819	98,386	2,949,000	12	30	Salem	D
†Pakistan (incl. part of Jammu and Kashmir)	Pākistān	879,902	339,732	123,490,000	140	363	Islāmābād	A
Palau	Palau (English) / Belau (Palauan)	508	196	16,000	31	82	Koror and Melekeok [5]	B(U.S.)
†Panama	Panamá	75,517	29,157	2,555,000	34	88	Panamá	A
†Papua New Guinea	Papua New Guinea	462,840	178,704	3,737,000	8.1	21	Port Moresby	A
†Paraguay	Paraguay	406,752	157,048	5,003,000	12	32	Asunción	A
Peking, China	Beijing	16,800	6,487	11,290,000	672	1,740	Beijing (Peking)	D
Pennsylvania, U.S.	Pennsylvania	119,291	46,058	12,105,000	101	263	Harrisburg	D
†Peru	Perú	1,285,216	496,225	22,995,000	18	46	Lima	A
†Philippines	Philippines (English) / Pilipinas (Tagalog)	300,000	115,831	65,500,000	218	565	Manila	A
Pitcairn (incl. Dependencies) (U.K.)	Pitcairn	49	19	50	1.0	2.6	Adamstown	C
†Poland	Polska	312,683	120,728	38,330,000	123	317	Warszawa (Warsaw)	A
†Portugal	Portugal	91,985	35,516	10,660,000	116	300	Lisboa (Lisbon)	A
Prince Edward Island, Can.	Prince Edward Island (English) / Île-du Prince-Édouard (French)	5,660	2,185	152,000	27	70	Charlottetown	D
Puerto Rico	Puerto Rico	9,104	3,515	3,594,000	395	1,022	San Juan	B(U.S.)
†Qatar	Qatar	11,427	4,412	492,000	43	112	Ad-Dawhah (Doha)	A
Quebec, Can.	Québec	1,540,680	594,860	7,725,000	5.0	13	Québec	D
Queensland, Austl.	Queensland	1,727,200	666,876	3,000,000	1.7	4.5	Brisbane	D
Reunion (Fr.)	Réunion	2,510	969	633,000	252	653	Saint-Denis	C
Rhode Island, U.S.	Rhode Island	4,002	1,545	1,026,000	256	664	Providence	D
†Romania	România	237,500	91,699	23,200,000	98	253	Bucureşti (Bucharest)	A
†Russia	Rossija	17,075,400	6,592,849	150,500,000	8.8	23	Moskva (Moscow)	A
†Rwanda	Rwanda	26,338	10,169	7,573,000	288	745	Kigali	A
St. Helena (incl. Dependencies) (U.K.)	St. Helena	314	121	7,000	22	58	Jamestown	C
†St. Kitts and Nevis	St. Kitts and Nevis	269	104	40,000	149	385	Basseterre	A
†St. Lucia	St. Lucia	616	238	153,000	248	643	Castries	A
St. Pierre and Miquelon (Fr.)	Saint-Pierre-et-Miquelon	242	93	7,000	29	75	Saint-Pierre	C
†St. Vincent and the Grenadines	St. Vincent and the Grenadines	388	150	116,000	299	773	Kingstown	A
†San Marino	San Marino	61	24	23,000	377	958	San Marino	A
†Sao Tome and Principe	São Tomé e Príncipe	964	372	134,000	139	360	São Tomé	A
Saskatchewan, Can.	Saskatchewan	652,330	251,866	1,099,000	1.7	4.4	Regina	D
†Saudi Arabia	Al-'Arabīyah as-Su'ūdīyah	2,149,690	830,000	15,985,000	7.4	19	Ar-Riyād (Riyadh)	A
Scotland, U.K.	Scotland	78,789	30,421	5,145,000	65	169	Edinburgh	D
†Senegal	Sénégal	196,712	75,951	7,849,000	40	103	Dakar	A
†Seychelles	Seychelles	453	175	70,000	155	400	Victoria	A
Shanghai, China	Shanghai	6,200	2,394	13,875,000	2,238	5,796	Shanghai	D
Shansi, China	Shanxi	156,000	60,232	29,865,000	191	496	Taiyuan	D
Shantung, China	Shandong	153,000	59,074	87,840,000	574	1,487	Jinan	D
Shensi, China	Shaanxi	205,000	79,151	34,215,000	167	432	Xi'an (Sian)	D
†Sierra Leone	Sierra Leone	72,325	27,925	4,424,000	61	158	Freetown	A
†Singapore	Singapore	636	246	2,812,000	4,421	11,431	Singapore	A
Sinkiang Uighur, China	Xinjiang Uygur	1,600,000	617,764	15,755,000	9.8	26	Ürümqi	D
†Slovakia	Slovenská Republika	49,035	18,933	5,287,000	108	279	Bratislava	A
†Slovenia	Slovenija	20,251	7,819	1,965,000	97	251	Ljubljana	A
†Solomon Islands	Solomon Islands	28,370	10,954	366,000	13	33	Honiara	A
†Somalia	Somaliya	637,657	246,201	6,000,000	9.4	24	Muqdisho (Mogadishu)	A
†South Africa (incl. Walvis Bay)	South Africa (English) / Suid-Afrika (Afrikaans)	1,123,226	433,680	33,040,000	29	76	Pretoria, Cape Town, and Bloemfontein	A

World Information Table / Welt-Informationstabelle / Table de Información Mundial
Table d'Informations Mondiales / Tabela de Informação Mundial

299

| NAME / NAME / NOMBRE / NOM / NOME | | AREA / FLÄCHE AREA / SUPERFICIE / ÁREA | | POPULATION BEVÖLKERUNG POBLACIÓN POPULATION POPULAÇÃO | DENSITY PER BEVÖLKERUNGSDICHTE PRO / DENSIDAD POR DENSITÉ / DENSIDADE POR | | CAPITAL HAUPSTADT CAPITAL CAPITALE CAPITAL | POLITICAL STATUS POLITISCHER STATUS ESTADO POLITICO STATUS POLITIQUE ESTATUTO POLITICO |
English / Englisch Inglés / Anglais / Inglês	Local / Einheimisch Local / Local / Local	sq. km.	sq. mi.		sq. km.	sq. mi.		
South America	...	17,800,000	6,900,000	310,700,000	17	45	...	...
South Australia, Austl.	South Australia	984,000	379,925	1,410,000	1.4	3.7	Adelaide	D
South Carolina, U.S.	South Carolina	82,898	32,007	3,616,000	44	113	Columbia	D
South Dakota, U.S.	South Dakota	199,745	77,121	718,000	3.6	9.3	Pierre	D
South Georgia and the South Sandwich Islands (U.K.)	South Georgia and the South Sandwich Islands	3,755	1,450	(1)	...	...	...	C
†Spain	España	504,750	194,885	39,155,000	78	201	Madrid	A
Spanish North Africa (Sp.) (7)	Plazas de Soberanía en el Norte de África	32	12	144,000	4,500	12,000	...	C
†Sri Lanka	Sri Lanka	64,652	24,962	17,740,000	274	711	Colombo and Sri Jayawardenapura	A
†Sudan	As-Sūdān	2,505,813	967,500	28,760,000	11	30	Al-Khartūm (Khartoum)	A
†Suriname	Suriname	163,820	63,251	413,000	2.5	6.5	Paramaribo	A
†Swaziland	Swaziland	17,364	6,704	925,000	53	138	Mbabane and Lobamba	A
†Sweden	Sverige	449,964	173,732	8,619,000	19	50	Stockholm	A
Switzerland	Schweiz (German) / Suisse (French) / Svizzera (Italian)	41,293	15,943	6,848,000	166	430	Bern (Berne)	A
†Syria	Sūrīyah	185,180	71,498	14,070,000	76	197	Dimashq (Damascus)	A
Szechwan, China	Sichuan	570,000	220,078	111,470,000	196	507	Chengdu	D
Taiwan	T'aiwan	36,002	13,900	20,985,000	583	1,510	T'aipei	A
†Tajikistan	Tajikistan	143,100	55,251	5,765,000	40	104	Dušanbe	A
†Tanzania	Tanzania	945,087	364,900	28,265,000	30	77	Dar es Salaam and Dodoma	A
Tasmania, Austl.	Tasmania	67,800	26,178	456,000	6.7	17	Hobart	D
Tennessee, U.S.	Tennessee	109,158	42,146	5,026,000	46	119	Nashville	D
Texas, U.S.	Texas	695,676	268,601	17,610,000	25	66	Austin	D
†Thailand	Prathet Thai	513,115	198,115	58,030,000	113	293	Krung Thep (Bangkok)	A
Tibet, China	Xizang	1,220,000	471,045	2,235,000	1.8	4.7	Lhasa	D
Tientsin, China	Tianjin	11,300	4,363	9,170,000	812	2,102	Tianjin (Tientsin)	D
†Togo	Togo	56,785	21,925	4,030,000	71	184	Lomé	A
Tokelau (N.Z.)	Tokelau	12	4.6	1,800	150	391	...	C
Tonga	Tonga	747	288	103,000	138	358	Nuku'alofa	A
Transkei (2)	Transkei	43,553	16,816	4,845,000	111	288	Umtata	B(S. Afr.)
†Trinidad and Tobago	Trinidad and Tobago	5,128	1,980	1,307,000	255	660	Port of Spain	A
Tsinghai, China	Qinghai	720,000	277,994	4,585,000	6.4	16	Xining	D
†Tunisia	Tunisie (French) / Tunis (Arabic)	163,610	63,170	8,495,000	52	134	Tunis	A
†Turkey	Türkiye	779,452	300,948	58,620,000	75	195	Ankara	A
†Turkmenistan	Turkmenistan	488,100	188,456	3,884,000	8.0	21	Ašchabad (Ashgabat)	A
Turks and Caicos Islands (U.K.)	Turks and Caicos Islands	500	193	13,000	26	67	Grand Turk	C
Tuvalu	Tuvalu	26	10	10,000	385	1,000	Funafuti	A
†Uganda	Uganda	241,139	93,104	17,410,000	72	187	Kampala	A
†Ukraine	Ukrayina	603,700	233,090	51,990,000	86	223	Kijev (Kiev)	A
†United Arab Emirates	Al-Imārāt al-'Arabīyah al-Muttahidah	83,600	32,278	2,590,000	31	80	Abū Zaby (Abu Dhabi)	A
†United Kingdom	United Kingdom	244,154	94,269	57,890,000	237	614	London	A
†United States	United States	9,809,431	3,787,425	256,420,000	26	68	Washington	A
†Uruguay	Uruguay	177,414	68,500	3,151,000	18	46	Montevideo	A
Utah, U.S.	Utah	219,902	84,904	1,795,000	8.2	21	Salt Lake City	D
†Uzbekistan	Ūzbekiston	447,400	172,742	21,885,000	49	127	Taškent (Toshkent)	A
†Vanuatu	Vanuatu	12,190	4,707	157,000	13	33	Port Vila	A
Vatican City	Città del Vaticano	0.4	0.2	800	2,000	4,000	Città del Vaticano (Vatican City)	A
Venda (2)	Venda	6,198	2,393	732,000	118	306	Thohoyandou	B(S. Afr.)
†Venezuela	Venezuela	912,050	352,145	19,085,000	21	54	Caracas	A
Vermont, U.S.	Vermont	24,903	9,615	590,000	24	61	Montpelier	D
Victoria, Austl.	Victoria	227,600	87,877	4,273,000	19	49	Melbourne	D
†Vietnam	Viet Nam	330,036	127,428	69,650,000	211	547	Ha Noi	A
Virginia, U.S.	Virginia	110,771	42,769	6,411,000	58	150	Richmond	D
Virgin Islands (U.S.)	Virgin Islands	344	133	104,000	302	782	Charlotte Amalie	C
Wake Island (U.S.)	Wake Island	7.8	3.0	200	26	67	...	C
Wales, U.K.	Wales	20,766	8,018	2,906,000	140	362	Cardiff	D
Wallis and Futuna (Fr.)	Wallis et Futuna	255	98	17,000	67	173	Mata-Utu	C
Washington, U.S.	Washington	184,674	71,303	5,052,000	27	71	Olympia	D
Western Australia, Austl.	Western Australia	2,525,500	975,101	1,598,000	0.6	1.6	Perth	D
Western Sahara		266,000	102,703	200,000	0.8	1.9	El Aaiún (Laayone)	...
†Western Samoa	Western Samoa (English) / Samoa i Sisifo (Samoan)	2,831	1,093	197,000	70	180	Apia	A
West Virginia, U.S.	West Virginia	62,759	24,231	1,795,000	29	74	Charleston	D
Wisconsin, U.S.	Wisconsin	169,653	65,503	5,000,000	29	76	Madison	D
Wyoming, U.S.	Wyoming	253,349	97,818	462,000	1.8	4.7	Cheyenne	D
†Yemen	Al-Yaman	527,968	203,850	12,215,000	23	60	Ṣan'ā'	A
Yugoslavia	Jugoslavija	102,173	39,449	10,670,000	104	270	Beograd (Belgrade)	A
Yukon Territory, Can.	Yukon Territory	483,450	186,661	31,000	0.1	0.2	Whitehorse	D
Yunnan, China	Yunnan	394,000	152,124	38,450,000	98	253	Kunming	D
†Zaire	Zaïre	2,345,095	905,446	39,750,000	17	44	Kinshasa	A
†Zambia	Zambia	752,614	290,586	8,475,000	11	29	Lusaka	A
†Zimbabwe	Zimbabwe	390,759	150,873	10,000,000	26	66	Harare (Salisbury)	A
WORLD	...	150,100,000	57,900,000	5,477,000,000	36	95	...	...

† Member of the United Nations (1993).
. . . None, or not applicable.
(1) No permanent population.
(2) Bophuthatswana, Ciskei, Transkei, and Venda are not recognized by the United Nations.
(3) Claimed by Argentina.
(4) Includes West Bank, Golan Heights, and Gaza Strip.
(5) Future capital.
(6) Claimed by Comoros.
(7) Comprises Ceuta, Melilla, and several small islands.

† Mitglied der Vereinten Nationen (1993).
. . . Kein(e), oder nicht anwendbar.
(1) Bevölkerungszahl schwankend.
(2) Bophuthatswana, Ciskei, Transkei und Venda von Vereinten Nationen nicht anerkannt.
(3) Von Argentinien beansprucht.
(4) Westufer, Golan-Höhen und Gazastreifen einbegriffen.
(5) Zukünftige Hauptstadt.
(6) Von Komoren beansprucht.
(7) Umfasst Ceuta, Melilla und mehrere kleine Inseln.

† Miembro de las Naciones Unidas (1993).
. . . Ninguno, o no se aplica.
(1) Sin población permanente.
(2) Bophuthatswana, Ciskei, Transkei y Venda no reconocido por las Naciones Unidas.
(3) Reclamado por la Argentina.

(4) Incluye la ribera oeste, las alturas de Golán y la franja de Gaza.
(5) Capital futura.
(6) Reclamado por las Comores.
(7) Comprende Ceuta, Melilla y various islas pequeñas.

† Membre des Nations Unies (1993).
. . . Pas d'information, ou pas applicable.
(1) Pas de population permanente.
(2) Bophuthatswana, Ciskei, Transkei et Venda non reconnaissent pas les Nations Unies.
(3) Revendiqué par l'Argentine.
(4) Y compris Cisjordanie, hauteurs de Golan et la bande de Gaza.
(5) Capitale future.
(6) Revendiqué par les Comores.
(7) Inclus Ceuta, Melilla et plusieurs petites îles.

† Membro das Nações Unidas (1993).
. . . Inexistente ou não aplicável.
(1) Sem população permanente.
(2) Bophuthatswana, Ciskei, Transkei e Venda não son reconhecido pelas Nações Unidas.
(3) Reivindicado pela Argentina.
(4) Incluindo a margem oeste, as colinas de Golan e a faixa de Gaza.
(5) Capital futuro.
(6) Reivindicado pelas Comores.
(7) Compreende Ceuta, Melilla e várias ilhas pequenas.

THIS TABLE lists the major metropolitan areas of the world according to their estimated population on January l, 1993. For convenience in reference, the areas are grouped by major region with the total for each region given. The number of areas by population classification is given in parentheses with each size group.

For ease of comparison, each metropolitan area has been defined by Rand McNally according to consistent rules. A metropolitan area includes a central city, neighboring communities linked to it by continuous built-up areas, and more distant communities if the bulk of their population is supported by commuters to the central city. Some metropolitan areas have more than one central city; in such cases each central city is listed.

IN DIESER TABELLE sind die Hauptmetropolen der Welt verzeichnet, gemessen nach ihrer Bevölkerung, die nach dem Stand vom 1. Januar 1993 geschätzt wurde. Zur besseren Übersicht sind die Zonen nach grösseren Regionen gruppiert, wobei die Gesamtzahl für jede Region angegeben ist. Die Anzahl der Zonen ist nach Bevölkerung klassifiziert und in Klammern hinter denen nach Grössen sortierten Gruppen angegeben.

Zum einfacheren Vergleich ist jede Metropole von Rand McNally nach übereinstimmenden Massstäben definiert worden. Eine Metropole schliesst eine zentrale Stadt mit benachbarten Gemeinden, die mit ihr durch ununterbrochen bebaute Gebiete verbunden sind ein, sowie weiter entfernte Gemeinden, wenn der grösste Teil ihrer Bevölkerung von den Pendlern unterhalten wird. Einige Metropolen haben mehr als eine zentrale Stadt; in solchen Fällen ist jede dieser zentralen Städte angeführt.

ESTA TABLA indica las principales áreas metropolitanas del mundo, de acuerdo con su población calculada al 1 de enero de 1993. Para facilitar las referencias, las áreas se han agrupado por regiones principales, indicándose el total para cada región. El número de áreas, clasificadas por población, se indica entre paréntesis en los grupos de cada tamaño.

Para facilitar las comparaciones, Rand McNally ha definido cada área metropolitana de acuerdo con reglas consistentes. Un área metropolitana incluye una ciudad central, localidades vecinas vinculadas con ella mediante sectores construídos y contínuos, y localidades más distantes, si el grueso de su población lo constituye un núcleo que diariamente viaja a la ciudad central. Algunas áreas metropolitanas incluyen más de una ciudad central; en tales casos se indica cada una dichas ciudades.

CETTE TABLE contient la liste des aires métropolitaines les plus considérables dans le monde pour ce qui est du peuplement a la date du 1 er janvier 1993. Afin de faciliter la consultation, on a groupé les aires par grandes régions en indiquant la population totale pour chaque région, et, entre parenthéses, le nombre d'aires comprises dans celle-ci.

Afin de rendre plus faciles les comparaisons, Rand McNally a défini chaque aire métropolitaine selorègles cohérentes: une aire métropolitaine englobe une cité centrale ou métropole et l'environnement urbain continu qui s'y rattache; elle inclut également les agglomérations éloignées de la métropole lorsque la population de ces dernières est pour sa májorité constituée d'habitants se rendant quotidiennement dans la cité ou est situé le lieu de travail de ceux-ci. On trouvera quelques aires métropolitaines pourvues de plus d'une métropole. Dans ce cas, chaque métropole est mentionnée.

A TABELA que se segúe relaciona as principais áreas metropolitanas do mundo, de acordo com as respectivas populações, estimadas para 1 de janeiro de 1993. Para facilidade de referência, as áreas metropolitanas foram agrupadas dentro das regiões maiores, indicando-se, entre parênteses, os totais de cada região maior e o número de áreas metropolitanas, classificadas segundo a população, compreendidas em cada uma.

Para fins de comparabilidade, Rand McNally definiu cada área metropolitana de acordo com regras uniformes. Uma área metropolitana inclui uma cidade central, as localidades vizinhas ligadas a ela por áreas construídas contínuas, e as localidades mais distantes, desde que a maior parte de suas respectivas populações dependa economicamente da cidade central e que para ela viaje diariamente. Algumas áreas metropolitanas incluem mais de uma cidade central; em tais casos, indicam-se ambas as cidades.

CLASSIFICATION KLASSIFIZIERT CLASIFICADAS CLASSIFICATION CLASSIFICAÇÃO	ANGLO-AMERICA ANGLO-AMERIKA AMÉRICA ANGLOSAJONA AMÉRIQUE ANGLO-SAXONNE AMÉRICA ANGLO-SAXÔNICA	LATIN AMERICA LATEIN-AMERIKA AMÉRICA LATINA AMÉRIQUE LATINE AMÉRICA LATINA	WESTERN EUROPE WESTEUROPA EUROPA OCCIDENTAL EUROPE OCCIDENTALE EUROPA OCIDENTALE	EASTERN EUROPE-RUSSIA OSTEUROPA-RUSSLAND EUROPA ORIENTAL-RUSIA EUROPE ORIENTALE-RUSSIE EUROPA ORIENTAL-RÚSSIA	WEST ASIA WESTASIEN ASIA OCCIDENTAL ASIE OCCIDENTALE ÁSIA OCIDENTAL	EAST ASIA OSTASIEN ASIA ORIENTAL ASIE ORIENTALE ÁSIA ORIENTAL	AFRICA-OCEANIA AFRIKA-OZEANIEN AFRICA-OCEANIA AFRIQUE-OCÉANIE ÁFRICA-OCEANIA
Over 15,000,000 (6)	New York	Ciudad de México (Mexico City) São Paulo				Ōsaka-Kōbe-Kyōto Sŏul (Seoul) Tōkyō-Yokohama	
10,000,000-15,000,000 (13)	Los Angeles	Buenos Aires Rio de Janeiro	London Paris	Moskva (Moscow)	Bombay Calcutta Delhi-New Delhi	Jakarta Manila Shanghai	Al-Qāhirah (Cairo)
5,000,000-10,000,000 (21)	Chicago Philadelphia-Trenton- Wilmington San Francisco- Oakland-San Jose	Lima Santa Fe de Bogotá Santiago	Essen-Dortmund- Duisburg (Ruhr Area)	Sankt-Peterburg (St. Petersburg)	Dhaka (Dacca) İstanbul Karāchi Madras Tehrān	Beijing (Peking) Krung Thep (Bangkok) Nagoya T'aipei Tianjin (Tientsin) Victoria (Hong Kong)	Johannesburg Lagos
3,000,000- 5,000,000 (37)	Boston Dallas-Fort Worth Detroit-Windsor Houston Miami-Fort Lauderdale Montréal San Diego-Tijuana Toronto Washington	Belo Horizonte Caracas Guadalajara Porto Alegre	Barcelona Berlin Madrid Milano (Milan) Roma (Rome)	Athínai (Athens) Kijev (Kiev)	Ahmadābād Baghdād Bangalore Hyderābād Lahore	Guangzhou (Canton) Pusan Shenyang (Mukden) Singapore Thanh Pho Ho Chi Minh (Saigon) Wuhan Yangon (Rangoon)	Al-Iskandarīyah (Alexandria) Casablanca Kinshasa Melbourne Sydney
2,000,000- 3,000,000 (64)	Atlanta Baltimore Cleveland Minneapolis-St. Paul Phoenix Pittsburgh St. Louis Seattle-Tacoma	Fortaleza La Habana (Havana) Medellín Monterrey Recife Salvador San Juan Santo Domingo	Amsterdam Birmingham Bruxelles (Brussels) Frankfurt am Main Hamburg Leeds-Bradford Lisboa (Lisbon) Liverpool Manchester München (Munich) Napoli (Naples) Stuttgart Wien (Vienna)	Bucureşti (Bucharest) Budapest Char'kov (Kharkov) Doneck-Makejevka Katowice-Bytom- Gliwice Nižnij Novgorod (Gorky) Warszawa (Warsaw)	Ankara Baku Colombo Dimashq (Damascus) İzmir Kānpur Pune (Poona) Taškent	Bandung Changchun Chengdu (Chengtu) Chongqing (Chungking) Dalian (Dairen) Fukuoka Harbin Kuala Lumpur Nanjing (Nanking) P'yongyang Sapporo-Otaru Surabaya Taegu Xi'an (Sian)	Abidjan Adis Abeba Al-Khartūm-Umm Durmān (Khartoum- Omdurman) Cape Town Durban El Djazaïr (Algiers)
1,500,000- 2,000,000 (48)	Cincinnati Denver El Paso-Ciudad Juárez Portland Vancouver	Brasília Cali Curitiba Guatemala Guayaquil Montevideo San José	Glasgow København (Copenhagen) Köln (Cologne) Mannheim Stockholm	Beograd (Belgrade) Dnepropetrovsk Jekaterinburg (Sverdlovsk) Minsk Novosibirsk	'Amman Ar-Riyad (Riyadh) Bayrūt (Beirut) Chittagong Faisalabad Halab (Aleppo) Jaipur Jiddah Kābol (Kabul) Lucknow Mashhad Nāgpur Rāwalpindi- Islāmābād Surat Tbilisi Tel Aviv-Yafo	Hiroshima-Kure Jinan (Tsinan) Kaohsiung Kitakyūshū- Shimonoseki Medan Qingdao (Tsingtao) Taiyuan	Accra Dakar Rabat-Salé
1,000,000- 1,500,000 (119)	Buffalo-Niagara Falls- St. Catharines Columbus Hartford-New Britain Indianapolis Kansas City Milwaukee New Orleans Norfolk-Newport News Sacramento St. Petersburg- Clearwater San Antonio	Asuncion Barranquilla Belém Campinas Córdoba Goiânia La Paz Manaus Maracaibo Puebla Quito Rosario San Salvador Santos Valencia Vitória	Antwerpen (Antwerp) Dublin (Baile Átha Cliath) Düsseldorf Hannover Helsinki Lille-Roubaix Lyon Marseille Newcastle-Sunderland Nürnberg Porto Rotterdam Sevilla Torino (Turin) Valencia	Čel'abinsk (Chelyabinsk) Łódź Kazan' Kraków Krasnojarsk Odessa Omsk Perm Praha (Prague) Rīga Rostov-na-Donu Samara (Kuybyshev) Saratov Sofija (Sofia) Ufa Volgograd Voronež	Adana Agra Allahābād Al-Kuwayt (Kuwait) Alma-Ata Asansol Bhopāl Cochin Coimbatore Esfahān Indore Jerevan Ludhiāna Madurai Patna Shīrāz Tabrīz Vadodara Vārānasi (Benares) Vishākhapatnam	Anshan Baotou Changsha Fushun Guiyang Hangzhou Ha Noi Jilin (Kirin) Kunming Kwangju Lanzhou Nanchang Palembang Qiqihar (Tsitsihar) Semarang Sendai Shijiazhuang Shizuoka-Shimizu Taejŏn Tangshan Ujungpandang Ürümqi Zhengzhou Zibo	Adelaide Antananarivo Brisbane Dar es Salaam Douala Harare Ibadan Kampala Luanda Lusaka Maputo Nairobi Perth Pretoria Tarābulus (Tripoli) Tunis
Total/Gesamtzahl Total/Total/Total (308)	38	42	41	33	57	64	33

ALL URBAN CENTERS of 50,000 or more population and many other important or well-known cities and towns are listed in the following table. The populations are from recent censuses (designated C) or official estimates (designated E) for the dates specified. For a few cities, only unofficial estimates are available (designated U). For comparison, the total population of each country is also given. For each country, the date stated for the total population also applies to the cities, except those for which another date is specified.

Population estimates for 1993 for countries may be found in the World Information Table.

A population figure in parentheses and preceded by a star (★) is the population of a city's entire metropolitan area. To permit meaningful comparisons of metropolitan areas, these have been defined by Rand McNally according to consistent rules (see introduction to Metropolitan Areas Table), and in some cases may differ somewhat from the officially recognized metropolitan areas. Where a town is located within the metropolitan area of another city, that city's name is given in parentheses preceded by a star (★). The capital of a country is denoted by CAPITAL letters.

ALLE STÄDTISCHEN ZENTREN mit 50 000 oder mehr Einwohnern und zahlreiche andere bedeutende oder bekannte Städte sind in der folgenden Tabelle zusammengestellt. Die Bevölkerungszahlen stammen von neuesten Zählungen (mit C gekennzeichnet) oder amtlichen Schätzungen (E) zu den angegebenen Zeitpunkten. Für einige wenige Städte waren lediglich inoffizielle Schätzungen erhältlich (U). Zu Vergleichszwecken ist ferner die Gesamtbevölkerung jedes Landes angegeben. Das Bezugsjahr für die Einwohnerzahl eines Landes betrifft auch die Städte mit Ausnahme jener, bei denen ein anderes Datum angegeben ist.

Schätzungen der Bevölkerungszahlen der Länder für 1993 finden sich in der Welt-Informationstabelle.

Bevölkerungszahlen in Klammern mit vorangestelltem Stern (★) beziehen sich auf die gesamte Stadtregion einer Stadt. Um sinnvolle Vergleiche von Stadtregionen zu ermöglichen, wurden diese von Rand McNally nach einheitlichen Regeln festgelegt (siehe Einleitung: Tabelle der Stadtregionen), weshalb sie in einigen Fällen etwas von der offiziellen Abgrenzung von Stadtregionen abweichen können. Ist eine Stadt in die Stadtregion einer anderen Grossstadt einbezogen, so wird der Name der Stadtregion mit vorangestelltem Stern (★) in Klammern aufgeführt. Die Haupstadt eines Landes wird durch GROSSBUCHSTABEN hervorgehoben.

TODAS LOS CENTROS URBANOS de 50 000 habitantes o más y muchos otros de importancia así como bien conocidas ciudades y pueblos están incluídos en la tabla que se presenta a continuación. El número de habitantes indicados está tomado del censo más reciente (cifras identificadas con la letra C) o estimados oficiales (E) para las fechas especificadas. Para algunas ciudades, sólo existen informes no oficiales (U). Para medida de comparación, la población total de cada país se encuentra incluída también.

Para permitir una comparación, se da la población total de cada país, referente al mismo año que se usa para las ciudades principles, excepto para aquellas en las que se especifica otra fecha. El número de habitantes para 1993 para los países, se encuentra en la Tabla de Información Mundial.

La segunda cifra para la población que aparece en paréntesis y está precedida por una estrella (★) constituye la población de un área metropolitana entera. Para permitir comparaciones validas de áreas metropolitanas, éstas fueron definidas por Rand McNally siguiendo las reglas establecidas para estos propósitos (véase la Introducción a la Tabla de las Areas Metropolitanas), y en algunas ocasiones pueden ser un poco distintas de las áreas metropolitanas oficialmente reconocidas. Cuando una población se encuentra dentro de los límites de un área metropolitana de otra ciudad, el nombre de ésta se da entre paréntesis precedido por una (★). La capital de un país se indica con letras MAYÚSCULAS.

TOUTES LES VILLES de plus de 50 000 habitants et des villes moins peuplées, mais célèbres ou importantes, sont mentionnées dans la table ci-dessous. Les chiffres donnant la population proviennent de recensements récents (référence C), ou d'estimations officielles (référence E), aux dates indiquées. Pour quelques villes, on dispose seulement d'estimations non officielles (référence U). La population totale de chaque pays est également donnée, ce qui permet des comparaisons. Dans chaque pays, la date des renseignements est identique pour les villes et le pays, sauf indication contraire.

On trouvera dans la table d'informations mondiales les estimations de la population en 1993 pour chaque pays.

Les chiffres entre parenthèses, précédés d'une étoile (★), indiquent la population de l'ensemble de la zone métropolitaine. Pour permettre d'établir des comparaisons significatives entre les zones métropolitaines, ces dernières ont été définies selon des critères uniformes par Rand McNally & Company (voir l'introduction à la table des zones métropolitaines). Parfois, les limites des zones métropolitaines ainsi définies diffèrent des limites officielles. Quand une ville fait partie de la zone métropolitaine d'une autre ville, le nom de celle-ci, précédé d'une étoile (★), est mis entre parenthèses. Le nom des capitales de pays est écrit en lettres MAJUSCULES.

TODOS OS CENTROS URBANOS de 50 000 habitantes e mais, bem como muitas outras cidades e vilas importantes ou muito conhecidas figuram na tabela que se apresenta em sequida. Os dados relativos à população referem-se a censos recentes (identificadas com a letra C), ou a estimativas oficiais (E) nas datas indicadas. Para algumas cidades só existem estimativas não oficiais (U). Para fins de comparabilidade, apresenta-se também a população total de cada país.

Para cada país, a data de referência da população total aplica-se também às cidades exceto quando especificado em contrário. As estimativas da população dos países para 1993 encontra-se na *Tabela de informaçoes mundiais.*

Um dado de população apresentado entre parênteses e precedido por uma estrela (★), refere-se à população de toda a área metropolitana. Para fins de comparabilidade, as áreas metropolitanas foram definidas por Rand McNally segundo regras coerentes (ver a 'Introdução' à *Tabela das áreas metropolitanas),* e em certos casos podem ser um pouco diferentes das áreas metropolitanas oficialmente reconhecidas. Quando um centro urbano esta localizado dentro dos limites da área metropolitana de outro, seu nome figura entre parênteses precedido por uma estrela (★). A capital de um país é indicada por letras MAIÚSCULAS.

AFGHANISTAN / Afghānestān

1988 E	17,672,000
Herāt	177,300
Jalālābād (1982E)	58,000
• KĀBOL	1,424,400
Kondūz (1982E)	57,000
Mazār-e Sharīf	130,600
Qandahār	225,500

ALBANIA / Shqipëri

1989 C	3,182,400
Durrës	82,700
Elbasan	80,700
Korçë	63,600
Shkodër	79,900
• TIRANË	238,100
Vlorë	71,700

ALGERIA / Algérie / Djazaïr

1987 C	23,038,942
Aïn el Beïda	61,997
Aïn Oussera	44,270
Aïn Témouchent	47,479
Annaba (Bône)	305,526
Bab Ezzouar (★El Djazaïr)	55,211
Barika	56,488
Batna	181,601
Béchar	107,311
Bejaïa (Bougie)	114,534
Beskra	128,281
Bordj Bou Arreridj	84,264
Bordj el Kiffan (★El Djazaïr)	61,035
Boufarik	41,305
Bou Saâda	66,688
Ech Cheliff (Orléansville)	129,976
El Boulaïda	170,935
• EL DJAZAÏR (ALGIERS) (★2,547,983)	1,507,241
El Djelfa	84,207
El Eulma	67,933
El Wad	70,073
Ghardaïa	89,415
Ghilizane	80,091
Guelma	77,821
Jijel	62,793
Khemis	55,335
Khenchla	69,743
Laghouat	67,214
Lemdiyya	85,195
Maghniyya	52,275
Messaad	47,460
Mestghanem	114,037
Mouaskar	64,691
M'Sila	65,805
Qacentina	440,842
Saïda	80,825
Sidi bel Abbès	152,778
Skikda	128,747
Souq Ahras	83,015
Stif	170,182
Tbessa	107,559
Tihert	95,821
Tilimsen	126,882
Tizi-Ouzou	61,163
Touggourt	70,645
Wahran	628,558
Wargla	81,721

AMERICAN SAMOA / Amerika Samoa

1980 C	32,279
• PAGO PAGO	3,075

ANDORRA

1991 E	54,507
• ANDORRA	20,437

ANGOLA

1989 E	9,739,100
Benguela (1983E)	155,000
Huambo (Nova Lisboa) (1983E)	203,000
Lobito (1983E)	150,000
• LUANDA	1,459,900
Lubango (1984E)	95,915
Namibe (1981E)	100,000

ANGUILLA

1984 C	6,680
South Hill	961
• THE VALLEY	1,042

ANTIGUA AND BARBUDA

1977 E	72,000
• SAINT JOHN'S	24,359

ARGENTINA

1991 C	32,608,687
Almirante Brown (★Buenos Aires)	449,105
Avellaneda (★Buenos Aires)	346,620
Bahía Blanca	271,467
Berazategui (★Buenos Aires)	243,690
Berisso (★Buenos Aires)	74,012
• BUENOS AIRES (★10,800,000)	2,960,976
Campana (★Buenos Aires)	71,360
Caseros (Tres de Febrero) (★Buenos Aires)	349,221
Comodoro Rivadavia (1980C)	96,817
Concordia (1980C)	94,222
Córdoba (★1,260,000)	1,179,067
Corrientes (1990E)	222,772
Ensenada (★Buenos Aires)	48,524
Esteban Echeverría (★Buenos Aires)	276,017
Florencio Varela (★Buenos Aires)	253,554
Formosa (1990E)	124,997
General San Martín (★Buenos Aires)	407,506
General Sarmiento (San Miguel) (★Buenos Aires)	646,891
Godoy Cruz (★Mendoza)	179,502
Gualeguaychú (1980C)	51,400
Junín (▲84,324)	69,700
Lanús (★Buenos Aires)	466,755
La Plata (★Buenos Aires)	542,567
La Rioja (1980C)	67,043
Las Heras (▲156,543) (★Mendoza)	132,200
Lomas de Zamora (★Buenos Aires)	572,769
Mar del Plata (1990E)	523,178
Mendoza (★650,000)	121,696
Mercedes (1980C)	50,992
Merlo (★Buenos Aires)	390,031
Moreno (★Buenos Aires)	287,188
Morón (★Buenos Aires)	641,541
Necochea (▲84,684)	59,400
Neuquén (1990E)	135,464
Olavarría (▲98,078)	70,700
Paraná (1990E)	194,452
Pergamino (▲95,021)	78,300
Pilar (★Buenos Aires)	130,177
Posadas (1990E)	188,642
Presidencia Roque Sáenz Peña (1980C)	49,341
Punta Alta	59,715
Quilmes (★Buenos Aires)	509,445
Rafaela (▲124,075)	62,800
Resistencia (1980C)	220,104
Río Cuarto (1990E)	130,907
Rosario (★1,190,000)	1,078,374
Salta (1990E)	342,316
San Carlos de Bariloche (1980C)	48,980
San Fernando (★Buenos Aires)	144,761
San Fernando del Valle de Catamarca (★90,000) (1980C)	78,799
San Francisco (★58,536) (1980C)	51,932
San Isidro (★Buenos Aires)	299,022
San Juan (★300,000)	119,399
San Justo (★Buenos Aires)	1,121,164
San Lorenzo (▲130,242) (★Rosario)	114,900
San Luis (1980C)	70,999
San Miguel de Tucumán (★600,000)	474,314
San Nicolás de los Arroyos (1990E)	131,079
San Rafael (▲148,410)	78,100
San Salvador de Jujuy (1990E)	165,783
Santa Fe (1990E)	338,013
Santiago del Estero (★255,000) (1990E)	190,863
San Vincente (★Buenos Aires)	74,890
Tandil (▲101,231)	88,100
Tigre (★Buenos Aires)	256,005
Trelew (1980C)	52,372
Venado Tuerto (▲172,008)	53,600
Vicente López (★Buenos Aires)	289,142
Villa Krause (▲90,492) (★San Juan)	79,800
Villa María (▲105,302)	76,500
Villa Nueva (★Mendoza)	222,081
Zárate (▲91,820)	79,900

ARMENIA / Hayastan

1989 C	3,283,000
Abovjan (1987E)	53,000
Ečmiadzin (★Jerevan) (1987E)	53,000
• JEREVAN (★1,315,000)	1,199,000
Kirovakan (1987E)	169,000
Kumajri	120,000
Razdan (1987E)	56,000

ARUBA

1987 E	64,763
• ORANJESTAD	19,800

AUSTRALIA

1991 C	16,850,330
Adelaide (★1,023,597)	14,843
Albury (★72,871)	40,154
Auburn (★Sydney)	48,566
Ballarat (★78,342)	34,501
Bankstown (★Sydney)	153,904
Bayswater (★Perth)	44,010
Bendigo (★67,315)	30,134
Berwick (★Melbourne)	69,144
Blacktown (★Sydney)	211,710
Blue Mountains (★Sydney)	69,420
Box Hill (★Melbourne)	45,139
Brisbane (★1,334,017)	751,115
Broadmeadows (★Melbourne)	102,996
Brunswick (★Melbourne)	39,886
Camberwell (★Melbourne)	83,799
Campbelltown (★Sydney)	137,879
CANBERRA (★303,846)	276,162
Canning (★Perth)	65,967
Canterbury (★Sydney)	129,232
Caulfield (★Melbourne)	67,776
Coburg (★Melbourne)	50,625
Cockburn (★Perth)	50,380
Coffs Harbour	51,520
Dandenong (★Melbourne)	57,275
Darwin (★78,400)	70,072
Doncaster (★Melbourne)	102,898
Enfield (★Adelaide)	61,502
Essendon (★Melbourne)	52,721
Fairfield (★Sydney)	175,099
Footscray (★Melbourne)	46,844
Frankston (★Melbourne)	84,986
Geelong (★145,325)	13,036
Gosford	128,956
Gosnells (★Perth)	69,560

▲ Population of an entire municipality, commune, or district, including rural area.
• Largest city in country.
★ Population or designation of the metropolitan area, including suburbs.
C Census. **E** Official estimate. **U** Unofficial estimate.

▲ Bevölkerung eines ganzen städtischen Verwaltungsgebietes, eines Kommunalbezirkes oder eines Distrikts, einschliesslich ländlicher Gebiete.
• Grösste Stadt des Landes.
★ Bevölkerung oder Bezeichnung der Stadtregion einschliesslich Vororte.
C Volkszählung. **E** Offizielle Schätzung. **U** Inoffizielle Schätzung.

▲ Población de un municipio, comuna o distrito entero, incluyendo sus áreas rurales.
• Ciudad más grande de un país.
★ Población o designación de un área metropolitana, incluyendo los suburbios.
C Censo. **E** Estimado oficial. **U** Estimado no oficial.

▲ Population d'une municipalité, d'une commune ou d'un district, zone rurale incluse.
• Ville la plus peuplée du pays.
★ Population de l'agglomération (ou nom de la zone métropolitaine englobante).
C Recensement. **E** Estimation officielle. **U** Estimation non officielle.

▲ População de um municipio, comuna ou distrito, inclusive as respectivas áreas rurais.
• Maior cidade de um país.
★ População ou indicação de uma área metropolitana.
C Censo. **E** Estimativa oficial. **U** Estimativa não oficial.

Heidelberg (★Melbourne)	60,468
Hobart (★181,832)	47,106
Holroyd (★Sydney)	79,132
Hurstville (★Sydney)	63,757
Ipswich (★Brisbane)	73,299
Keilor (★Melbourne)	106,076
Knox (★Melbourne)	121,982
Kogarah (★Sydney)	46,518
Lake Macquarie (★Newcastle)	162,026
Launceston (★93,581)	59,646
Leichhardt (★Sydney)	58,484
Liverpool (★Sydney)	98,203
Logan (★Brisbane)	142,595
Mackay (★53,934)	23,052
Malvern (★Melbourne)	41,340
Marion (★Adelaide)	73,942
Marrickville (★Sydney)	78,023
Melbourne (★3,022,439)	60,476
Melville (★Perth)	84,838
Mitcham (★Adelaide)	60,939
Moorabbin (★Melbourne)	94,161
Newcastle (★427,824)	131,305
Noarlunga (★Adelaide)	80,882
Northcote (★Melbourne)	46,547
North Sydney (★Sydney)	50,446
Nunawading (★Melbourne)	91,468
Oakleigh (★Melbourne)	55,151
Parramatta (★Sydney)	132,798
Penrith (★Sydney)	149,630
Perth (★1,143,249)	80,517
Prahran (★Melbourne)	42,193
Preston (★Melbourne)	76,996
Randwick (★Sydney)	115,349
Redcliffe (★Brisbane)	47,799
Rockdale (★Sydney)	84,074
Rockhampton (★62,797)	59,394
Ryde (★Sydney)	90,197
Saint Kilda (★Melbourne)	45,481
Salisbury (★Adelaide)	106,007
Shoalhaven	68,287
Southport (★324,429)	157,857
South Sydney (★Sydney)	77,818
Springvale (★Melbourne)	89,478
Stirling (★Perth)	172,731
Sunshine (★Melbourne)	94,020
• Sydney (★3,538,749)	13,501
Tea Tree Gully (★Adelaide)	83,969
Toowoomba	81,043
Townsville (★101,398)	87,288
Wagga Wagga	53,447
Wanneroo (★Perth)	167,873
Waverley (★Melbourne)	118,265
Waverley (★Sydney)	59,095
West Torrens (★Adelaide)	42,863
Willoughby (★Sydney)	51,503
Wollongong (★235,966)	173,764
Woodville (★Adelaide)	78,824
Woollahra (★Sydney)	49,904

AUSTRIA / Österreich

1991 C	7,795,786
Bruck an der Mur (★50,000)	14,046
Graz (★265,000)	237,810
Innsbruck (★200,000)	118,112
Klagenfurt (★118,000)	89,415
Leoben (★47,600)	28,897
Linz (★352,000)	203,044
Neunkirchen (★45,000)	10,216
Salzburg (★185,000)	143,978
Sankt Pölten (★69,500)	50,026
Steyr (★58,000)	39,337
Villach (★66,500)	54,640
Wels (★68,000)	52,594
• WIEN (VIENNA) (★1,900,000)	1,539,848

AZERBAIJAN

1991 E	7,136,600
Ali-Bajramly	61,500
• BAKU (BAKY) (★2,020,000)	1,080,500
Gjandža	282,200
Mingečaur	90,900
Nachičevan'	61,700
Šeki (Nucha)	57,800
Stepanakert	55,200
Sumgait (★Baku)	236,200

BAHAMAS

1990 C	254,685
Freeport (▲171,542)	28,200
• NASSAU	141,000

BAHRAIN / Al-Baḥrayn

1988 E	473,000
• AL-MANĀMAH (★273,000) (1986E)	82,700
Al-Muḥarraq (★Al-Manāmah)	78,000
Jidd Ḥafṣ (★Al-Manāmah)	48,000

BANGLADESH

1991 C	104,766,143
Barisāl	180,014
Begamganj (1981C)	69,623
Bhairab Bāzār	75,747
Bogra	93,114
Brāhmanbāria	114,297
Chāndpur	84,067
Chittagong (★2,342,662)	1,566,070
Chuādanga	65,222
Comilla (1981C)	164,509
• DHAKA (DACCA) (★6,537,308)	3,637,892
Dinājpur	136,657
Farīdpur	72,927
Gopālpur	45,174
Gulshan (★Dhaka) (1981C)	215,444
Jamālpur	108,416
Jessore	176,398
Jhenida	69,501
Khulna (★966,096)	601,051
Kishorganj	64,676
Kurīgrām	62,075
Kushtia	71,706
Mādārīpur	46,842
Mīrpur (★Dhaka) (1981C)	349,031
Mymensingh	138,662
Naogaon	109,156
Nārāyanganj (★Dhaka)	288,008
Narsinghdi	100,120
Nawābganj	131,260
Noākhāli	73,766
Pābna	113,146
Patuākhāli	50,344
Rājshāhi (★560,013)	324,532
Rangpur	220,849
Saidpur	110,494
Sātkhira	81,199
Sherpur	63,030
Sirājganj	100,003
Sītākunda (★Chittagong) (1981C)	237,520
Sylhet	114,284
Tangail	111,783
Tongi (★Dhaka)	165,099

BARBADOS

1980 C	244,228
• BRIDGETOWN (★115,000)	7,466

BELARUS / Byelarus'

1991 E	10,260,400
Baranoviči	166,700
Bobrujsk	223,000
Borisov	150,200
Brest	277,000
Gomel'	503,300
Grodno	284,800
Kobrin	48,300
Lida	95,000
• MINSK (★1,694,000)	1,633,600
Mogil'ov	363,000
Molodečno	93,500
Mozyr'	103,000
Novopolock	96,600
Orša	125,300
Pinsk	123,800
Polock	78,700
Rečica	69,400
Sluck	60,100
Soligorsk	96,000
Vitebsk	361,500
Žlobin	60,800
Žodino	56,000

BELGIUM / België / Belgique

1987 E	9,864,751
Aalst (Alost) (★Bruxelles)	77,113
Anderlecht (★Bruxelles)	88,849
Antwerpen (★1,100,000)	479,748
Bastogne (▲11,699)	6,900
Brugge (Bruges) (★223,000)	117,755
• BRUXELLES (★2,385,000)	136,920
Charleroi (★480,000)	209,395
Etterbeek (★Bruxelles)	44,240
Forest (★Bruxelles)	48,266
Genk (★Hasselt)	61,391
Gent (Gand) (★465,000)	233,856
Hasselt (★290,000)	65,563
Ixelles (★Bruxelles)	76,241
Kortrijk (Courtrai) (★202,000)	76,216
La Louvière (★147,000)	76,340
Leuven (Louvain) (★173,000)	84,583
Liège (Luik) (★750,000)	200,891
Mechelen (Malines) (★121,000)	75,808
Molenbeek-St.-Jean (★Bruxelles)	69,764
Mons (Bergen) (★242,000)	89,697
Mouscron (★Lille, France)	53,713
Namur (★147,000)	102,670
Oostende (Ostende) (★122,000)	68,318
Roeselare (Roulers)	51,963
Saint-Gilles (★Bruxelles)	42,482
Schaerbeek (★Bruxelles)	104,919
Seraing (★Liège)	61,731
Sint-Niklaas (Saint-Nicolas)	68,082
Spa	9,645
Tournai (Doornik) (▲66,998)	44,900
Uccle (★Bruxelles)	75,876
Verviers (★101,000)	53,498
Waterloo (★Bruxelles)	25,232
Woluwe-Saint-Lambert (Sint-Lambrechts-Woluwe) (★Bruxelles)	47,887

BELIZE

1990 C	184,340
• Belize City	43,621
BELMOPAN	5,256

BENIN / Bénin

1984 E	3,825,000
Abomey	53,000
• COTONOU (1992C)	533,212
Parakou	92,000
PORTO-NOVO	164,000

BERMUDA

1985 E	56,000
• HAMILTON (★15,000)	1,676

BHUTAN / Druk-Yul

1982 E	1,333,000
• THIMPHU	12,000

BOLIVIA

1990 E	7,314,000
Cochabamba	413,300
• LA PAZ	1,125,600
Montero (1988E)	84,100
Oruro	207,700
Potosí	120,100
Santa Cruz de la Sierra	696,100
SUCRE	101,400
Tarija	74,600
Trinidad	51,900

BOPHUTHATSWANA

1987 E	1,819,242
• Ga-Rankuwa (1980C)	48,300
Mafikeng (★16,000) (1980C)	6,500
MMABATHO (★Mafikeng) (1977E)	9,062

BOSNIA AND HERZEGOVINA / Bosna i Hercegovina

1987 E	4,400,464
Banja Luka (▲193,890)	130,900
• SARAJEVO (▲479,688)	341,200
Tuzla (▲129,967)	67,300
Zenica (▲144,869)	67,500

BOTSWANA

1991 C	1,326,796
Francistown	65,244
• GABORONE	133,468
Selebi Phikwe	39,772

BRAZIL / Brasil

1991 C	146,917,459
Abaetetuba (▲100,016)	55,442
Abreu e Lima (▲76,568)	70,099
Alagoinhas (▲116,740)	97,819
Alegrete (▲78,879)	67,505
Almirante Tamandaré (▲66,090)	51,240
Altamira (▲120,441)	48,452
Alvorada (▲142,020) (★Porto Alegre)	132,582
Americana	153,592
Ananindeua (▲88,035)	73,941
Anápolis (▲239,047)	222,400
Anil (▲695,199)	81,879
Antônio Bezerra (▲1,765,794) (★Fortaleza)	193,682
Aparecida de Goiânia (▲178,326)	48,804
Apucarana (▲94,914)	80,048
Aracaju	401,676
Araçatuba (▲159,499)	146,977
Araguaína (▲103,396)	81,729
Araguari (▲91,202)	80,568
Arapiraca (▲165,379)	131,449
Arapongas (▲64,531)	59,996
Araraquara (▲166,732)	101,302
Araras (▲87,355)	79,002
Araucária (▲61,767)	53,522
Araxá	67,919
Arcoverde (▲55,790)	49,479
Assis (▲85,265)	72,004
Atibaia (▲86,193)	74,658
Avaré (▲61,063)	56,232
Bacabal (▲98,875)	64,844
Bagé (▲118,736)	89,372
Barbacena (▲99,895)	80,682
Barra Alegre (▲179,710)	58,445
Barra do Piraí (▲78,426)	59,202
Barra Mansa (▲171,671) (★Volta Redonda)	145,112
Barreiras (▲92,439)	70,701
Barreiros (▲139,318) (★Florianópolis)	58,694
Barretos (▲95,538)	88,935
Barueri (▲130,383)	66,722
Bauru	254,690
Bayeux (★João Pessoa)	77,047
Bebedouro (▲67,752)	60,792
Belém (★1,355,000)	765,476
Belford Roxo (▲1,293,611) (★Rio de Janeiro)	337,698
Belo Horizonte (★3,340,000)	1,529,566
Betim (★Belo Horizonte)	162,462
Birigui	70,547
Blumenau (▲211,862)	185,200
Boa Vista (▲142,902)	118,928
Botucatu (▲90,620)	81,528
Bragança Paulista (▲108,602)	88,336
Brás Cubas (▲273,255)	65,538
BRASÍLIA	1,513,470
Brusque	53,438
Cabo (▲126,756)	68,594
Cabo Frio (▲84,635)	70,251
Caçapava (▲65,889)	58,145
Cáceres (▲77,475)	51,891
Cachoeira do Sul (▲89,148)	69,780
Cachoeirinha (★Porto Alegre)	87,976
Cachoeiro de Itapemirim (▲143,763)	112,099
Camaçari (▲113,615)	88,302
Camarajibe	99,431
Cambé (▲73,803)	66,767
Campina Grande	298,331
Campinas (★1,290,000)	759,032
Campo Comprido (▲1,313,094) (★Curitiba)	105,631
Campo Grande	516,403
Campo Mourão (▲82,280)	69,966
Campos (▲388,747)	277,482
Campos Elisios (▲665,343) (★Rio de Janeiro)	197,833
Candeias (▲67,936)	61,432
Canoas (★Porto Alegre)	269,234
Capuáva (▲615,112)	92,950
Carapicuíba (▲283,653) (★São Paulo)	207,264
Carapina (▲221,510) (★Vit2oria)	141,234
Carazinho (▲58,770)	49,010
Cariacica (▲274,455) (★Vitória)	91,888
Caruaru (▲213,573)	180,654
Cascatinha (▲255,261)	56,890
Cascavel (▲192,884)	175,332
Castanhal (▲101,963)	90,364
Catanduva	88,024
Caucaia (▲165,015) (★Fortaleza)	66,379
Cava (▲1,293,611)	59,506
Cavaleiro (▲486,774) (★Recife)	120,065
Caxias (▲146,730)	85,332
Caxias do Sul (▲290,969)	262,983
Chapecó (▲122,889)	93,697
Codó (▲111,679)	58,163
Coelho da Rocha (▲424,689) (★Rio de Janeiro)	152,045
Colatina (▲106,712)	71,094
Colombo (▲117,658) (★Curitiba)	110,161
Conselheiro Lafaiete (▲88,843)	82,619
Contagem (▲448,991) (★Belo Horizonte)	195,705
Corumbá (▲88,290)	75,235
Cotia (▲106,822)	90,469
Coxipó da Ponte (▲401,303)	140,130
Crato (▲91,413)	56,374
Criciúma (▲146,162)	99,375
Cruz Alta (▲68,784)	61,860
Cruzeiro	65,935
Cubatão (★Santos)	90,572
Cuiabá (▲401,303)	252,784
Curitiba (★1,815,000)	841,882
Diadema (★São Paulo)	305,068
Divinópolis (▲151,382)	141,984
Dourados (▲135,786)	116,817
Dracena (▲39,576)	33,856
Duque de Caxias (▲665,343) (★Rio de Janeiro)	325,903
Embu (★São Paulo)	155,851
Erechim (▲72,292)	61,509
Esteio (★Porto Alegre)	70,449
Eunápolis (▲70,561)	63,553
Feira de Santana (▲405,848)	340,034
Fernandópolis (▲56,125)	51,216
Ferraz de Vasconcelos (▲95,973) (★São Paulo)	65,319
Florianópolis (★420,000)	191,664
Formosa (▲62,974)	49,135
Fortaleza (★2,040,000)	743,335
Foz do Iguaçu	186,362
Franca	227,613
Francisco Morato	83,361
Franco da Rocha	79,534
Garanhuns (▲103,365)	86,593
Goiabeiras (▲258,243) (★Vitória)	74,086
Goiânia (★1,130,000)	912,136
Governador Valadares (▲230,403)	210,396
Gravataí (▲181,019) (★Porto Alegre)	166,954
Guaíba (▲83,119)	72,739
Guarapari (▲61,594)	54,994
Guaratinguetá (▲102,005)	84,660
Guarujá (▲209,814) (★Santos)	98,918
Guarulhos (▲786,355) (★São Paulo)	546,417
Gurupi (▲56,741)	51,005
Hortolândia (▲226,225)	78,011
Ibes (▲265,251) (★Vitória)	91,071
Icoraci (▲1,244,688) (★Belém)	67,458
Igapó (▲606,681)	117,251
Igarassu (▲79,713) (★Recife)	48,598
Ijuí (▲75,169)	58,627
Ilhéus (▲223,482)	135,117
Imbariê (▲665,343)	100,687
Imperatriz (▲276,440)	209,970
Indaiatuba (▲100,816)	91,752
Inhomirim (▲191,249)	76,031
Ipatinga (★179,710)	120,025
Ipiíba (▲778,831) (★Rio de Janeiro)	121,785
Itabira (▲85,284)	71,287
Itaboraí (▲161,398)	72,410
Itabuna (▲185,165)	170,434
Itaguaí (▲113,019)	48,274
Itaipu (▲435,658)	35,072
Itaituba (▲116,541)	62,278
Itajaí	114,558
Itajubá (▲74,618)	68,469
Itambi (▲161,398)	48,891
Itapecerica da Serra (▲92,854) (★São Paulo)	84,479
Itaperuna (▲78,017)	55,484
Itapetininga (▲105,071)	84,703
Itapeva (▲81,858)	55,658
Itapevi (★São Paulo)	107,983
Itaquaquecetuba (★São Paulo)	164,665
Itaquari (▲274,455) (★Vitória)	169,145
Itatiba (▲61,587)	54,044
Itaúna	61,891
Itú (▲107,176)	88,838
Ituiutaba (▲84,581)	78,211
Itumbiara (▲79,457)	68,673
Jaboatão (▲486,774) (★Recife)	81,178
Jaboticabal (▲59,130)	53,027
Jacareí (▲163,843)	144,141
Jandira	62,573
Japeri (▲1,293,611)	65,576
Jaraguá do Sul (▲76,994)	62,578
Jardim Presidente Dutra (▲786,355) (★São Paulo)	229,987
Jataí (▲65,921)	53,431
Jaú (▲94,138)	80,331
Jequié (▲144,572)	114,542
Ji-Paraná (▲97,719)	75,384
João Monlevade	57,413
João Pessoa (★670,000)	497,308
Joinvile	326,208
Juàzeiro128,691) (★Petrolina)	95,676
Juazeiro do Norte	163,527
Juiz de Fora	377,538
Jundiaí (▲288,644)	265,599
Jurema (▲165,015) (★Fortaleza)	75,463
Justinópolis (▲143,696) (★Belo Horizonte)	85,452
Lages (▲151,100)	137,169
Lavras (▲65,857)	60,690
Leme	64,525
Limeira (▲207,416)	177,591
Linhares (▲119,501)	73,082
Lins (▲59,218)	54,868
Londrina (▲389,959)	355,062
Lorena (▲73,167)	67,766
Luziânia (▲207,425)	194,128
Macaé (▲100,642)	57,581
Macapá (▲179,252)	146,523
Maceió (▲628,241)	554,727
Manaus	1,005,634
Marabá (▲122,231)	102,364
Marília (▲160,872)	144,906
Maringá	225,516
Matão	59,694
Mauá (★São Paulo)	294,631
Mesquita (▲1,293,611) (★Rio de Janeiro)	141,326
Messejana (▲1,765,794) (★Fortaleza)	229,507
Mogi das Cruzes (▲273,255) (★São Paulo)	138,995
Mogi-Guaçu (▲107,440)	92,440
Mogimirim (▲64,750)	57,395
Mojiguaçu (▲107,440)	87,300
Mojimirim (▲64,746)	53,400
Mondubim (▲1,765,794) (★Fortaleza)	331,591
Monjolo (▲778,831) (★Rio de Janeiro)	137,974
Montes Claros (▲249,565)	223,046
Mossoró (▲191,959)	177,020
Muriaé (▲84,507)	65,406
Muribeca dos Guararapes (▲486,774) (★Recife)	217,905
Natal (▲606,681)	459,827
Neves (▲778,831) (★Rio de Janeiro)	151,067
Nilópolis (▲157,936) (★Rio de Janeiro)	104,671
Niterói (▲435,658) (★Rio de Janeiro)	400,586
Nossa Senhora do Socorro	67,443
Nova Brasilia (▲178,326) (★Goiânia)	126,701
Nova Friburgo (▲166,975)	111,020
Nova Iguaçu (▲1,293,611) (★Rio de Janeiro)	562,062
Nova Veneza (▲226,225)	82,203
Novo Hamburgo (★Porto Alegre)	201,334
Novo Mundo (▲1,313,094) (★Curitiba)	71,508
Olinda (★Recife)	341,059
Olinda (▲157,936)	53,265
Osasco (★São Paulo)	566,949
Ourinhos (▲76,912)	70,690
Palhoça (▲68,298) (★Florianópolis)	58,097
Paracatu (▲62,709)	49,656
Pará de Minas (▲61,066)	51,679
Paranaguá (▲107,601)	88,110
Paranavaí (▲71,173)	61,043
Parangaba (▲1,765,794) (★Fortaleza)	267,679
Parnaíba (▲127,992)	105,131
Parnamirim (▲63,253)	48,534
Parque Industrial (▲448,991) (★Belo Horizonte)	223,660
Passo do Sabão (▲169,079) (★Porto Alegre)	63,140
Passo Fundo (▲147,239)	135,158
Passos (▲84,618)	74,218
Patos (▲81,292)	76,378

▲ Population of an entire municipality, commune, or district, including rural area.
• Largest city in country.
★ Population or designation of the metropolitan area, including suburbs.
C Census. **E** Official estimate. **U** Unofficial estimate.

▲ Bevölkerung eines ganzen städtischen Verwaltungsgebietes, eines Kommunalbezirkes oder eines Distrikts, einschliesslich ländlicher Gebiete.
• Grösste Stadt des Landes.
★ Bevölkerung oder Bezeichnung der Stadtregion einschliesslich Vororte.
C Volkszählung. **E** Offizielle Schätzung. **U** Inoffizielle Schätzung.

Patos de Minas (▲102,765)	83,670
Paulista (▲211,017) (★Recife)	53,566
Paulo Afonso (▲86,594)	74,326
Pelotas (▲290,660)	260,510
Petrolina (★300,000)	123,857
Petrópolis (▲255,261) (★Rio de Janeiro)	164,849
Pindamonhangaba (▲101,939)	71,449
Pinhais (▲106,764) (★Curitiba)	71,973
Pinheirinho (▲1,313,094) (★Curitiba)	117,516
Piracicaba (▲283,634)	223,170
Poá (★São Paulo)	72,151
Poços de Caldas	105,223
Ponta Grossa	219,955
Porto Alegre (★2,850,000)	1,247,352
Porto Velho (▲161,611)	56,973
Porto Velho (▲286,471)	226,196
Pouso Alegre (▲81,776)	73,875
Praia da Conceição (▲211,017) (★Recife)	97,635
Praia Grande (▲123,494)	97,173
Presidente Prudente	157,618
Queimados (▲1,293,611) (★Rio de Janeiro)	124,121
Recife (★2,880,000)	1,296,995
Resende (▲91,605)	52,261
Ribeirão Pires	62,240
Ribeirão Preto	416,186
Rio Branco (▲196,871)	136,457
Rio Claro	130,364
Rio de Janeiro (★11,050,000)	5,473,909
Rio Grande (▲172,408)	157,608
Rio Verde (▲95,894)	76,818
Rondonópolis (▲126,082)	87,307
Salto	72,076
Salvador (★2,340,000)	2,070,296
Santa Bárbara d'Oeste	141,230
Santa Cruz do Sul (▲117,779)	74,295
Santa Felicidade (▲1,313,094) (★Curitiba)	53,560
Santa Inês (▲64,655)	54,006
Santa Maria (▲217,604)	193,294
Santana do Livramento (▲80,145)	72,950
Santarém (▲264,779)	168,153
Santa Rita (▲94,412) (★João Pessoa)	74,396
Santa Rosa (▲58,262)	48,211
Santo André (▲615,112) (★São Paulo)	518,272
Santo Ângelo (▲76,461)	59,688
Santo Antônio de Jesus (▲64,198)	52,770
Santos (★1,165,000)	415,554
São Benedito (▲137,686) (★Belo Horizonte)	91,733
São Bernardo do Campo (★São Paulo)	550,030
São Borja (▲63,766)	52,493
São Caetano do Sul (★São Paulo)	149,203
São Carlos (▲158,186)	100,502
São Cristóvão	46,172
São Gabriel (▲59,024)	47,668
São Gonçalo (▲778,831) (★Rio de Janeiro)	296,021
São João da Boa Vista (▲69,090)	60,845
São João del-Rei (▲72,741)	63,680
São João de Meriti (▲424,689) (★Rio de Janeiro)	220,742
São José do Rio Preto	263,454
São José dos Campos (▲442,009)	385,879
São José dos Pinhais (▲128,170) (★Curitiba)	99,154
São Leopoldo (★Porto Alegre)	160,228
São Lourenco da Mata (▲85,889) (★Recife)	68,479
São Luís (★710,000)	164,334
São Mateus (▲424,689)	51,902
• São Paulo (★16,925,000)	9,393,753
São Vicente (★Santos)	268,467
Sapiranga (▲58,522)	51,387
Sapucaia do Sul (★Porto Alegre)	104,626
Serra (▲221,510)	62,398
Sertãozinho (▲78,753)	68,874
Sete Lagoas	139,910
Sete Pontes (▲778,831) (★Rio de Janeiro)	71,984
Sobral (▲127,459)	92,805
Sorocaba	348,952
Sumaré (▲226,225)	64,673
Susano (▲159,142) (★São Paulo)	110,414
Taboão da Serra (★São Paulo)	159,894
Tatuí (▲76,662)	68,808
Taubaté (▲206,416)	185,790
Teixeira de Freitas (▲85,227)	73,107
Telêmaco Borba (▲64,854)	50,774
Teófilo Otoni (▲140,676)	96,382
Teresina (★665,000)	556,073
Teresópolis (▲120,712)	96,516
Timon (▲107,394) (★Teresina)	90,577
Timóteo (▲58,393)	48,340
Toledo (▲94,857)	67,343
Três Corações (▲57,053)	49,138
Três Lagoas (▲68,067)	60,716
Três Rios (▲81,163)	60,201
Tubarão (▲95,058)	83,262
Tucuruí (▲81,635)	46,011
Tupã (▲61,290)	53,282
Ubá (▲66,422)	52,673
Uberaba (▲211,356)	198,565
Uberlândia	355,191
Umbará (▲1,313,094) (★Curitiba)	64,523
Umuarama (▲100,185)	66,995
Uruguaiana (▲117,437)	103,160
Valinhos (▲67,867)	59,896
Varginha (▲88,045)	82,263
Várzea Grande (▲161,611)	96,379
Várzea Paulista	67,911
Venda Nova (▲2,017,127) (★Belo Horizonte)	481,470
Viamão (▲169,079)	75,782
Vicente de Carvalho (▲209,814) (★Santos)	110,881
Vila Dirce (▲283,653)	59,144
Vila Velha (▲265,251) (★Vitória)	113,664
Vila Xavier (▲166,732)	50,922
Vitória (★810,000)	184,157
Vitória da Conquista (▲224,896)	179,868
Vitória de Santo Antão (▲106,661)	84,116
Volta Redonda (★430,000)	219,988
Votorantim	79,150
Votuporanga (▲66,037)	59,604

BRITISH VIRGIN ISLANDS

1980 C	12,034
• ROAD TOWN	2,479

BRUNEI

1981 C	192,832
• BANDAR SERI BEGAWAN (★64,000)	22,777
Seria	23,415

BULGARIA / Bâlgarija

1989 E	8,986,636
Asenovgrad	58,568
Blagoevgrad	74,236
Burgas	200,464
Dimitrovgrad	57,102
Dobrič	112,582
Gabrovo	80,930
Haskovo	93,609
Jambol	97,414
Kărdžali	58,995
Kazanlâk	63,776
Kjustendil	55,620
Loveč	50,872
Mihajlovgrad	55,203
Pazardžik	83,451
Pernik	97,930
Pleven	136,287
Plovdiv	364,162
Razgrad	56,494
Ruse	190,720
Silistra	56,907
Sliven	109,432
• SOFIJA (★1,205,000)	1,136,875
Stara Zagora	158,151
Šumen	107,973
Varna	306,300
Veliko Târnovo	71,709
Vidin	65,892
Vraca	81,992

BURKINA FASO

1985 C	7,964,705
Bobo Dioulasso	228,668
Koudougou	51,926
• OUAGADOUGOU	441,514
Ouahigouya	38,902

BURUNDI

1990 C	5,356,266
• BUJUMBURA	226,628

CAMBODIA / Kâmpŭchéa

1990 E	8,567,582
Bătdâmbâng	94,412
Kâmpóng Saôm	67,452
• PHNUM PENH	620,000
Prey Vêng	41,456
Siĕmréab	76,434
Ta Khmau	34,947

CAMEROON / Cameroun

1986 E	10,446,409
Bafoussam (1985E)	89,000
Bamenda (1985E)	72,000
• Douala	1,029,731
Foumban (1985E)	50,000
Garoua (1985E)	96,000
Kumba (1985E)	67,000
Maroua	103,653
Ngaoundéré (1985E)	61,000
Nkongsamba	123,149
YAOUNDÉ	653,670

CANADA

1991 C	27,296,859

CANADA: ALBERTA

1991 C	2,545,553
Calgary (★754,033)	710,677
Edmonton (★839,924)	616,741
Lethbridge	60,974
Medicine Hat (★52,681)	43,625
Red Deer	58,134

CANADA: BRITISH COLUMBIA

1991 C	3,282,061
Burnaby (★Vancouver)	158,858
Chilliwack (★60,251)	49,531
Delta (★Vancouver)	95,577
Kamloops (★67,856)	67,057
Kelowna (★111,846)	75,950
Matsqui (★113,562)	68,064
Nanaimo (★73,547)	60,129
Prince George	69,653
Richmond (★Vancouver)	126,624
Saanich (★Victoria)	245,173
Surrey (★Vancouver)	84,021
Vancouver (★1,602,502)	471,844
Victoria (★287,897)	71,228

CANADA: MANITOBA

1991 C	1,091,942
Winnipeg (★652,354)	616,790

CANADA: NEW BRUNSWICK

1991 C	723,900
Fredericton (★71,869)	46,466
Moncton (★106,503)	57,010
Saint John (★124,981)	74,969

CANADA: NEWFOUNDLAND

1991 C	568,474
Saint John's (★171,859)	95,770

CANADA: NORTHWEST TERRITORIES

1991 C	57,649
Yellowknife	15,179

CANADA: NOVA SCOTIA

1991 C	899,942
Dartmouth (★Halifax)	67,798
Halifax (★320,501)	114,455
Sydney (★116,100)	26,063

CANADA: ONTARIO

1991 C	10,084,885
Ajax (★Toronto)	57,350
Barrie (★92,165)	62,728
Brampton (★Toronto)	234,445
Brantford (★97,106)	81,997
Burlington (★Hamilton)	129,575
Cambridge (Galt) (★Kitchener)	92,772
Cornwall (★53,545)	47,137
East York (★Toronto)	102,696
Etobicoke (★Toronto)	309,993
Gloucester (★Ottawa)	101,677
Guelph (★97,213)	87,976
Hamilton (★599,760)	318,499
Kingston (★136,401)	56,597
Kitchener (★356,421)	168,282
Leamington (★35,792)	14,182
London (★381,522)	303,165
Markham (★Toronto)	153,811
Mississauga (★Toronto)	463,388
Nepean (★Ottawa)	107,627
Newcastle	49,479
Niagara Falls (★Saint Catharines)	75,399
North Bay (★63,285)	55,405
North York (★Toronto)	562,564
Oakville (★Toronto)	114,670
Oshawa (★240,104)	129,344
OTTAWA (★920,857)	313,987
Peterborough (★98,060)	68,371
Pickering (★Toronto)	68,631
Richmond Hill (★Toronto)	80,142
Saint Catharines (★364,552)	129,300
Sarnia (★87,870)	74,376
Sault Sainte Marie (★101,800)	81,476
Scarborough (★Toronto)	524,598
Stoney Creek (★Hamilton)	49,968
Sudbury (★157,613)	92,884
Thunder Bay (★124,427)	113,946
• Toronto (★3,893,046)	635,395
Vaughan (★Toronto)	111,359
Waterloo (★Kitchener)	71,181
Whitby (★Oshawa)	61,281
Windsor (★262,075)	191,435
York (★Toronto)	140,525

CANADA: PRINCE EDWARD ISLAND

1991 C	129,765
Charlottetown (★57,472)	15,396

CANADA: QUÉBEC

1991 C	6,895,963
Beauport (★Québec)	69,158
Brossard (★Montréal)	64,793
Charlesbourg (★Québec)	70,788
Chicoutimi (★160,928)	62,670
Drummondville (★60,092)	35,462
Gatineau (★Ottawa)	92,284
Hull (★Ottawa)	60,707
Jonquière (★Chicoutimi)	57,933
La Salle (★Montréal)	73,804
Laval (★Montréal)	314,398
Lévis (★Québec)	39,452
Longueuil (★Montréal)	129,874
Montreal (★3,127,242)	1,017,666
Montréal-Nord (★Montréal)	85,516
Pierrefonds (★Montréal)	48,735
Québec (★645,550)	167,517
Repentigny (★Montréal)	49,630
Sainte-Foy (★Québec)	71,133
Saint-Hubert (★Montréal)	74,027
Saint-Jean-sur-Richelieu (★68,378)	37,607
Saint-Laurent (★Montréal)	72,402
Saint-Léonard (★Montréal)	73,120
Shawinigan (★61,672)	19,931
Sherbrooke (★139,194)	76,429
Trois-Rivières (★136,303)	49,426
Verdun (★Montréal)	61,307

CANADA: SASKATCHEWAN

1991 C	988,928
Regina (★191,692)	179,178
Saskatoon (★210,023)	186,058

CANADA: YUKON

1991 C	27,797
Whitehorse	17,925

CAPE VERDE / Cabo Verde

1990 C	341,491
Mindelo	47,109
• PRAIA	61,644

CAYMAN ISLANDS

1988 E	25,900
• GEORGE TOWN	13,700

CENTRAL AFRICAN REPUBLIC / République centrafricaine

1984 E	2,517,000
• BANGUI	473,817
Bouar (1982E)	48,000

CHAD / Tchad

1988 E	5,428,000
Abéché	40,000
Moundou	100,000
• N'DJAMENA	500,000
Sarh	76,835

CHILE

1982 C	11,329,736
Antofagasta (1990E)	218,800
Apoquindo (★Santiago)	175,735
Arica (1990E)	177,300
Calama	81,684
Cerrillos (★Santiago)	67,013
Cerro Navia (★Santiago)	137,777
Chillán (1990E)	146,000
Concepción (★710,000) (1990E)	306,500
Conchalí (★Santiago)	157,884
Copiapó	69,045
Coquimbo	62,186
Coronel (★Concepción)	65,918
Curicó	60,550
El Bosque (★Santiago)	143,717
Huechuraba (★Santiago)	56,313
Independencia (★Santiago)	86,724
Iquique (1990E)	148,500
La Cisterna (★Santiago)	95,863
La Florida (★Santiago)	191,883
La Granja (★Santiago)	109,168
La Pintana (★Santiago)	73,932
La Reina (★Santiago)	80,452
La Serena (1990E)	105,600
Las Rejas (★Santiago)	147,918
Linares	46,433
Lo Espejo (★Santiago)	124,462
Lo Prado (★Santiago)	103,575
Los Ángeles	70,529
Lota (★Concepción)	47,133
Macul (★Santiago)	113,100
Maipú (★Santiago)	114,117
Ñuñoa (★Santiago)	168,919
Osorno (1990E)	117,400
Ovalle	43,023
Pedro Aguirre Cerda (★Santiago)	145,207
Peñalolén (★Santiago)	137,298
Providencia (★Santiago)	115,449
Pudahuel (★Santiago)	97,578
Puente Alto (★Santiago) (1990E)	187,400
Puerto Montt (1990E)	106,500
Punta Arenas (1990E)	120,000
Quilpué (★Valparaíso) (1990E)	107,400
Quinta Normal (★Santiago)	128,989
Rancagua (1990E)	190,400
Recoleta (★Santiago)	164,292
Renca (★Santiago)	93,928
San Antonio	61,486
San Bernardo (★Santiago) (1990E)	188,200
San Joaquín (★Santiago)	123,904
San Miguel (★Santiago)	88,764
San Ramón (★Santiago)	99,410
• SANTIAGO (★4,100,000)	232,667
Talca (1990E)	164,500
Talcahuano (★Concepción) (1990E)	246,900
Temuco (1990E)	211,700
Valdivia (1990E)	113,500
Vallenar	38,375
Valparaíso (★690,000) (1990E)	276,800
Villa Alemana (★Valparaíso)	55,766
Viña del Mar (★Valparaíso) (1990E)	281,100
Vitacura (★Santiago)	72,038

CHINA / Zhongguo

1988 E	999,999,999
Abagnar Qi (▲100,700) (1986E)	71,700
Acheng (1985E)	100,304
Aihui (▲135,000) (1986E)	76,700
Aksu (▲345,900) (1986E)	143,100
Altay (▲141,700) (1986E)	62,800
Anci (Langfang) (▲522,800) (1986E)	122,100
Anda (▲425,500) (1986E)	130,200
Ankang (1985E)	89,188
Anqing (▲433,900) (1986E)	213,200
Anshan	1,330,000
Anshun (▲214,700) (1986E)	128,800
Anyang (▲541,900) (1986E)	361,200
Baicheng (▲282,000) (1986E)	198,600
Baiquan (1985E)	50,996
Baiyin (▲301,900) (1986E)	157,100
Baoding (▲535,100) (1986E)	423,200
Baoji (▲359,500) (1986E)	286,200
Baoshan (▲688,400) (1986E)	52,300
Baotou (Paotow)	1,130,000
Baoying (1985E)	50,479
Bei'an (▲440,500) (1986E)	199,500
Beihai (▲175,900) (1986E)	119,000
BEIJING (PEKING) (★7,320,000)	6,710,000
Beipiao (▲603,700) (1986E)	180,900
Bengbu (▲612,600) (1986E)	403,900
Benxi (Penhsi)	860,000
Bijie (1985E)	54,871
Binxian (▲177,900) (1986E)	86,700
Binxian (1982C)	127,326
Boli (1985E)	61,990
Bose (▲271,400) (1986E)	82,000
Boshan (1975U)	100,000
Boxian (1985E)	63,222
Boxing (1982C)	57,554
Boyang (1985E)	60,688
Butha Qi (Zalantun) (▲339,500) (1986E)	111,300
Cangshan (Bianzhuang) (1982C)	79,334
Cangzhou (▲293,600) (1986E)	196,700
Changchun (▲2,000,000)	1,822,000
Changde (▲220,800) (1986E)	178,200
Changge (1982C)	67,002
Changji (▲233,400) (1986E)	110,500
Changqing (1982C)	65,094
Changsha	1,230,000
Changshou (1985E)	51,923
Changshu (▲998,000) (1986E)	281,300
Changtu (1985E)	49,937
Changyi (1982C)	64,513
Changzhi (▲463,400) (1986E)	273,000
Changzhou (Changchow) (1986E)	522,700
Chao'an (▲1,214,500) (1986E)	265,400
Chaoxian (▲739,500) (1986E)	116,800
Chaoyang, Guangdong prov. (1985E)	85,968
Chaoyang, Liaoning prov. (▲318,900) (1986E)	180,300
Chengde (▲330,400) (1986E)	226,600
Chengdu (Chengtu) (▲2,960,000)	1,884,000
Chenghai (1985E)	50,631
Chenxian (▲191,900) (1986E)	143,500
Chifeng (Ulanhad) (▲882,900) (1986E)	299,000
Chongqing (Chungking) (▲2,890,000)	2,502,000
Chuxian (▲365,000) (1986E)	113,300
Chuxiong (▲379,400) (1986E)	67,700
Da'an (1985E)	70,552
Dachangzhen (1975U)	50,000
Dalian (Dairen)	2,280,000
Dandong (1986E)	579,800
Daqing (▲880,000) (1986E)	640,000
Dashiqiao (1985E)	68,898
Datong (1985E)	55,529
Datong (▲1,040,000)	810,000
Dawa (1985E)	142,581
Daxian (▲209,400) (1986E)	142,000
Dehui (1985E)	60,247
Dengfeng (1982C)	49,746
Deqing (1982C)	48,726
Deyang (▲753,400) (1986E)	184,800
Dezhou (▲276,200) (1986E)	161,300
Didao (1975U)	50,000
Dinghai (1985E)	50,161
Dongchuan (Xincun) (▲275,100) (1986E)	67,400
Dongguan (▲1,208,500) (1986E)	254,900
Dongsheng (▲121,300) (1986E)	57,500
Dongtai (1985E)	65,788
Dongying (▲514,400) (1986E)	178,100
Dukou (▲551,200) (1986E)	380,200
Dunhua (▲448,000) (1986E)	217,100
Duyun (▲386,600) (1986E)	123,800
Echeng (▲938,000) (1986E)	217,400

▲ Población de un municipio, comuna o distrito entero, incluyendo sus áreas rurales.
• Ciudad más grande de un país.
★ Población o designación de un área metropolitana, incluyendo los suburbios.
C Censo. E Estimado oficial. U Estimado no oficial.

▲ Population d'une municipalité, d'une commune ou d'un district, zone rurale incluse.
• Ville la plus peuplée du pays.
★ Population de l'agglomération (ou nom de la zone métropolitaine englobante).
C Recensement. E Estimation officielle. U Estimation non officielle.

▲ População de um municipio, comuna ou distrito, inclusive as respectivas áreas rurais.
• Maior cidade de um país.
★ População ou indicação de uma área metropolitana.
C Censo. E Estimativa oficial. U Estimativa não oficial.

Enshi (▲679,000) (1986E)	84,300
Erenhot (1986E)	7,200
Ergun Zuoqi (1985E)	55,970
Feixian (1982C)	73,246
Fengcheng (1985E)	66,745
Foshan (▲312,700) (1986E)	243,500
Fujin (1985E)	60,948
Fuling (▲973,500) (1986E)	166,300
Fushun (Funan)	1,290,000
Fuxian (Wafangdian) (▲960,700) (1986E)	246,200
Fuxin	700,000
Fuyang (▲195,200) (1986E)	143,400
Fuyu, Heilongjiang prov. (1985E)	48,670
Fuyu, Jilin prov. (1985E)	98,373
Fuzhou, Fujian prov. (▲1,240,000)	910,000
Fuzhou, Jiangxi prov. (▲171,800) (1986E)	106,700
Gaixian (1985E)	67,587
Ganhe (1985E)	48,128
Ganzhou (▲346,000) (1986E)	191,600
Gaoqing (Tianzhen) (1982C)	70,411
Gaoyou (1985E)	57,844
Gejiu (Kokiu) (▲341,700) (1986E)	193,600
Golmud (1986E)	60,300
Gongchangling (1982C)	49,281
Guanghua (▲420,000) (1986E)	104,400
Guangyuan (▲805,500) (1986E)	162,200
Guangzhou (Canton) (▲3,420,000)	3,100,000
Guanxian, Shandong prov. (1982C)	49,782
Guanxian, Sichuan prov. (1985E)	65,039
Guilin (Kweilin) (▲457,500) (1986E)	324,200
Guixian (1985E)	61,970
Guiyang (Kweiyang) (▲1,430,000)	1,030,000
Haicheng (▲984,800) (1986E)	210,700
Haifeng (1985E)	50,401
Haikou (▲289,600) (1986E)	209,200
Hailar (▲163,549) (1986E)	180,000
Hailin (1985E)	58,909
Hailong (Meihekou) (▲534,200) (1986E)	117,500
Hailun (1985E)	83,448
Haiyang (Dongcun) (1982C)	77,098
Hami (Kumul) (▲270,300) (1986E)	146,400
Hancheng (▲304,200) (1986E)	66,600
Handan (▲1,030,000)	870,000
Hangu (1975U)	100,000
Hangzhou (Hangchow)	1,290,000
Hanzhong (▲415,000) (1986E)	151,700
Harbin	2,710,000
Hebi (▲321,600) (1986E)	158,500
Hechi (▲266,800) (1986E)	74,400
Hechuan (1985E)	65,237
Hefei (▲930,000)	740,000
Hegang (1986E)	588,300
Helong (1985E)	62,665
Hengshui (▲286,500) (1986E)	83,100
Hengyang (▲601,300) (1986E)	419,200
Heshan (▲109,600) (1986E)	42,000
Heze (Caozhou) (▲1,001,500) (1986E)	115,400
Hohhot (▲830,000)	670,000
Hongjiang (▲67,000) (1986E)	54,300
Horqin Youyi Qianqi (Ulan Hot) (▲192,100) (1986E)	129,100
Hotan (▲122,800) (1986E)	71,700
Houma (▲158,500) (1986E)	67,000
Huadian (1985E)	75,183
Huai'an (1985E)	65,673
Huaibei (▲447,200) (1986E)	252,100
Huaide (▲899,400) (1986E)	187,600
Huaihua (▲427,100) (1986E)	102,000
Huainan (▲1,110,000)	700,000
Huaiyin (Wangying) (▲382,500) (1986E)	201,700
Huanan (1985E)	66,596
Huanggang (1982C)	65,961
Huangshi (1986E)	451,900
Huayun (Huarong) (▲313,500) (1986E)	81,000
Huinan (Chaoyang) (1985E)	52,429
Huizhou (▲182,100) (1986E)	117,000
Hulan (1985E)	74,989
Hunjiang (Badaojiang) (▲687,700) (1986E)	442,600
Huzhou (▲964,400) (1986E)	208,500
Jiading (1985E)	60,718
Jiamusi (Kiamusze) (▲557,700) (1986E)	429,800
Ji'an (▲184,300) (1986E)	132,200
Jiangling (1985E)	77,887
Jiangmen (▲231,700) (1986E)	168,800
Jiangyin (1985E)	66,476
Jiangyou (1985E)	72,663
Jian'ou (1985E)	55,180
Jiaohe (1985E)	51,504
Jiaojiang (▲385,200) (1986E)	82,300
Jiaoxian (1985E)	51,869
Jiaozuo (▲509,900) (1986E)	335,400
Jiawang (1975U)	50,000
Jiaxing (▲686,500) (1986E)	210,200
Jiayuguan (▲102,100) (1986E)	73,800
Jiexiu (1985E)	51,300
Jieyang (1985E)	98,531
Jilin (Kirin)	1,200,000
Jinan (Tsinan) (▲2,140,000)	1,546,000
Jinchang (Baijiazui) (▲136,000) (1986E)	90,500
Jincheng (▲612,700) (1986E)	99,900
Jingdezhen (Kingtechen) (▲569,700) (1986E)	304,000
Jingmen (▲946,500) (1986E)	227,000
Jinhua (▲799,900) (1986E)	147,800
Jining, Nei Monggol prov. (1986E)	163,300
Jining, Shandong prov. (▲765,700) (1986E)	222,600
Jinshi (▲219,700) (1986E)	73,700
Jinxi (▲634,300) (1986E)	223,100
Jinxian (1985E)	95,761
Jinzhou (Chinchou) (▲810,000)	710,000
Jishou (▲194,500) (1986E)	59,500
Jishu (1985E)	75,587
Jiujiang (▲382,300) (1986E)	248,500
Jiuquan (Suzhou) (▲269,900) (1986E)	56,300
Jiutai (1985E)	63,021
Jixi (▲820,000)	700,000
Jixian (1985E)	59,725
Juancheng (1982C)	54,110
Junan (Shizilu) (1982C)	90,222
Junxian (▲423,400) (1986E)	97,000
Juxian (1982C)	51,666
Kaifeng (▲629,100) (1986E)	458,800
Kaili (▲342,100) (1986E)	96,600
Kaiping (1985E)	54,145
Kaiyuan (▲342,100) (1986E)	96,600
Kaiyuan (1985E)	85,762
Karamay (▲168,868) (1986E)	185,300
Kashi (▲194,500) (1986E)	146,300
Keshan (1985E)	65,088
Korla (▲219,000) (1986E)	129,400
Kunming (▲1,550,000)	1,310,000
Kunshan (1985E)	44,645
Kuqa (1985E)	63,847
Kuytun (1986E)	60,200
Laiwu (▲1,041,800) (1986E)	143,500
Langxiang (1985E)	64,658
Lanxi (1985E)	53,236
Lanxi (▲606,800) (1986E)	70,500
Lanzhou (Lanchow) (▲1,420,000)	1,297,000
Lechang (1986E)	56,913
Lengshuijiang (▲277,600) (1986E)	101,700
Lengshuitan (▲362,000) (1986E)	60,900
Leshan (▲972,300) (1986E)	307,300
Lhasa (▲107,700) (1986E)	84,400
Lianyungang (Xinpu) (▲459,400) (1986E)	288,000
Liaocheng (▲724,300) (1986E)	119,000
Liaoyang (▲576,900) (1986E)	442,600
Liaoyuan (1986E)	370,400
Liling (▲856,300) (1986E)	107,100
Linfen (▲530,100) (1986E)	157,600
Lingling (▲515,300) (1986E)	72,700
Lingyuan (1985E)	66,825
Linhai (1985E)	52,653
Linhe (▲365,900) (1986E)	99,800
Linkou (1985E)	52,936
Linqing (▲603,000) (1986E)	87,000
Linqu (1982C)	84,196
Linxia (▲150,200) (1986E)	72,900
Linyi (▲1,365,000) (1986E)	190,000
Liuzhou	680,000
Longjiang (1985E)	51,156
Longyan (▲378,500) (1986E)	114,500
Loudi (▲254,300) (1986E)	84,200
Lu'an (▲163,400) (1986E)	122,600
Lufeng (1985E)	53,015
Luohe (▲159,100) (1986E)	102,300
Luoyang (Loyang) (▲1,090,000)	760,000
Luzhou (▲360,300) (1986E)	237,800
Ma'anshan (▲367,000) (1986E)	258,900
Manzhouli (1986E)	116,600
Maoming (▲434,900) (1986E)	118,600
Meixian (▲740,600) (1986E)	169,000
Mengyin (1982C)	70,602
Mianyang, Sichuan prov. (▲848,500) (1986E)	233,900
Minhang (1975U)	60,000
Mishan (1985E)	54,919
Mixian (1982C)	64,776
Mudanjiang	650,000
Nahe (1985E)	49,725
N'aizishen (1985E)	51,982
Nancha (1975U)	50,000
Nanchang (▲1,260,000)	1,090,000
Nanchong (▲238,100) (1986E)	158,000
Nanjing (Nanking)	2,390,000
Nanning (▲1,000,000)	720,000
Nanpiao (1982C)	67,274
Nanping (▲420,800) (1986E)	157,100
Nantong (▲411,000) (1986E)	308,800
Nanyang (▲294,800) (1986E)	199,400
Neihuang (1982C)	56,039
Neijiang (▲298,500) (1986E)	191,100
Ning'an (1985E)	49,334
Ningbo (▲1,050,000)	570,000
Ningyang (1982C)	55,424
Nong'an (1985E)	55,966
Nunjiang (1985E)	59,276
Orogen Zizhiqi (1985E)	48,042
Panshan (▲343,100) (1986E)	248,100
Panshi (1985E)	59,270
Pingdingshan (▲819,900) (1986E)	363,200
Pingliang (▲362,500) (1986E)	85,400
Pingxiang, Jiangxi prov. (▲1,286,700) (1986E)	368,700
Pingyi (1982C)	89,373
Pingyin (1982C)	62,827
Potou (▲456,100) (1986E)	59,000
Puqi (1985E)	65,239
Putian (▲265,400) (1986E)	64,600
Putuo (1985E)	50,962
Puyang (▲1,086,100) (1986E)	131,000
Qian Gorlos (1985E)	79,494
Qingdao (Tsingtao)	1,300,000
Qinggang (1985E)	43,075
Qingjiang, Jiangsu prov. (▲246,617) (1982C)	150,000
Qingjiang, Jiangxi prov. (1985E)	42,698
Qingyuan (1985E)	51,756
Qinhuangdao (Chinwangtao) (▲436,000) (1986E)	307,500
Qinzhou (▲923,400) (1986E)	97,100
Qiqihar (Tsitsihar) (▲1,330,000)	1,180,000
Qitaihe (▲309,900) (1986E)	166,400
Qixia (1982C)	54,158
Qixian (1982C)	53,041
Quanzhou (Chuanchou) (▲436,000) (1986E)	157,000
Qujing (▲758,000) (1986E)	135,000
Quxian (▲704,800) (1986E)	124,000
Raoping (1985E)	54,831
Rizhao (▲970,300) (1986E)	93,300
Rongcheng (1982C)	52,878
Rugao (1985E)	50,643
Rui'an (1985E)	57,993
Sanmenxia (Shanxian) (▲150,000) (1986E)	79,000
Sanming (▲214,300) (1986E)	144,900
• Shanghai (★9,300,000)	7,220,000
Shangqiu (Zhuji) (▲199,400) (1986E)	135,400
Shangrao (▲142,500) (1986E)	113,000
Shangshui (1982C)	50,191
Shantou (Swatow) (▲790,000)	560,000
Shanwei (1985E)	61,234
Shaoguan (1986E)	363,100
Shaowu (▲266,700) (1986E)	81,400
Shaoxing (▲250,900) (1986E)	167,100
Shaoyang (▲465,900) (1986E)	218,600
Shashi (1986E)	253,700
Shenxian (1982C)	50,208
Shenyang (Mukden) (▲4,370,000)	3,910,000
Shenzhen (▲231,900) (1986E)	189,600
Shiguaigou (1975U)	50,000
Shihezi (▲549,300) (1987E)	304,700
Shijiazhuang	1,220,000
Shiyan (▲332,600) (1986E)	227,300
Shizuishan (▲317,400) (1986E)	225,500
Shouguang (1982C)	83,400
Shuangcheng (1985E)	91,163
Shuangliao (1985E)	67,326
Shuangyashan (1986E)	427,300
Shuicheng (▲2,216,500) (1986E)	363,500
Shulan (1986E)	50,582
Shunde (1985E)	50,262
Siping (▲357,800) (1986E)	280,100
Sishui (1982C)	82,990
Songjiang (1985E)	71,864
Songjianghe (1985E)	53,023
Suifenhe (▲21,700) (1986E)	13,900
Suihua (▲732,100) (1986E)	200,400
Suileng (1985E)	68,399
Suining (▲1,174,900) (1986E)	118,500
Suixian (▲1,281,600) (1986E)	187,700
Suqian (1985E)	50,742
Suxian (▲218,600) (1986E)	123,300
Suzhou (Soochow)	740,000
Tai'an (▲1,325,400) (1986E)	215,900
Taiyuan (▲1,980,000)	1,700,000
Taizhou (▲210,800) (1987E)	143,200
Tancheng (1982C)	61,857
Tangshan (▲1,440,000)	1,080,000
Tao'an (1985E)	76,269
Tengxian (1985E)	53,254
Tianjin (Tientsin) (▲5,540,000)	4,950,000
Tianshui (▲953,200) (1986E)	209,500
Tiefa (▲146,367) (1982C)	60,000
Tieli (1985E)	102,527
Tieling (▲454,100) (1986E)	326,100
Tongchuan (▲393,200) (1986E)	268,900
Tonghua (▲367,400) (1986E)	290,200
Tongliao (▲253,100) (1986E)	190,100
Tongling (▲216,400) (1986E)	182,900
Tongren (1985E)	50,307
Tongxian (1985E)	97,168
Tumen (▲99,700) (1986E)	77,600
Tunxi (▲104,500) (1986E)	61,800
Turpan (▲196,800) (1986E)	52,300
Ürümqi	1,060,000
Wangkui (1985E)	52,021
Wangqing (1985E)	61,237
Wanxian (▲280,800) (1986E)	138,700
Weifang (▲1,042,200) (1986E)	312,500
Weihai (▲220,800) (1986E)	83,000
Weinan (▲699,400) (1986E)	111,300
Weishan (Xiazhen) (1982C)	57,932
Weixian (Hanting) (1982C)	50,180
Wenzhou (▲530,600) (1986E)	372,200
Wuchang (1985E)	64,403
Wuhai (1986E)	266,000
Wuhan	3,570,000
Wuhu (▲502,200) (1986E)	396,000
Wulian (Hongning) (1982C)	51,718
Wusong (1982C)	64,017
Wuwei (Liangzhou) (▲804,000) (1986E)	115,500
Wuxi (Wuhsi)	880,000
Wuzhong (▲402,400) (1986E)	48,600
Wuzhou (Wuchow) (▲261,500) (1986E)	194,800
Xiaguan (▲395,800) (1986E)	112,100
Xiamen (Amoy) (▲546,400) (1986E)	343,700
Xi'an (Sian) (▲2,580,000)	2,210,000
Xiangfan (▲421,200) (1986E)	314,900
Xiangtan (▲511,100) (1986E)	389,500
Xianning (▲402,200) (1986E)	122,200
Xianyang (▲641,800) (1986E)	285,900
Xiaogan (▲1,204,400) (1986E)	125,500
Xiaoshan (1985E)	63,074
Xichang (▲161,000) (1986E)	105,000
Xinghua (1985E)	75,573
Xinglongzhen (1982C)	52,961
Xingtai (▲350,800) (1986E)	265,600
Xinhui (1985E)	77,381
Xining (Sining)	620,000
Xinmin (1985E)	47,900
Xintai (▲1,157,300) (1986E)	171,400
Xinwen (Suncun) (1975U)	50,000
Xinxian (▲398,600) (1986E)	74,200
Xinxiang (▲540,500) (1986E)	411,000
Xinyang (▲234,200) (1986E)	169,100
Xinyu (▲610,600) (1986E)	140,200
Xuancheng (1985E)	52,387
Xuanhua (1975U)	140,000
Xuanwei (1982C)	70,081
Xuchang (▲247,200) (1986E)	167,800
Xuguit Qi (Yakeshi) (1986E)	390,000
Xuzhou (Süchow)	860,000
Yaan (▲277,600) (1986E)	89,200
Yan'an (▲259,800) (1986E)	86,700
Yancheng (▲1,251,400) (1986E)	258,400
Yangcheng (1982C)	57,255
Yangjiang (1986E)	91,433
Yangquan (▲478,900) (1986E)	295,100
Yangzhou (▲417,300) (1986E)	321,500
Yanji (▲216,900) (1986E)	175,000
Yanji (Longjing) (1985E)	55,035
Yanling (1982C)	52,679
Yantai (Chefoo) (▲717,300) (1986E)	327,000
Yanzhou (1985E)	48,972
Yaxian (Sanya) (▲321,700) (1986E)	70,500
Yi'an (1986E)	54,253
Yibin (Ipin) (▲636,500) (1986E)	218,800
Yichang (Ichang) (1986E)	410,500
Yichuan (1982C)	58,914
Yichun, Heilongjiang prov.	840,000
Yichun, Jiangxi prov. (▲770,200) (1986E)	132,600
Yidu (1985E)	54,838
Yilan (1985E)	50,436
Yima (▲84,800) (1986E)	53,700
Yinan (Jiehu) (1982C)	67,803
Yinchuan (▲396,900) (1986E)	268,200
Yingchengzi (1985E)	59,072
Yingkou (▲480,000) (1986E)	366,900
Yingtan (▲116,200) (1986E)	64,500
Yining (Kuldja) (▲232,000) (1986E)	153,200
Yiyang (▲365,000) (1986E)	155,300
Yiyuan (Nanma) (1982C)	53,800
Yong'an (▲269,000) (1986E)	105,100
Yongchuan (1985E)	70,444
Yuci (▲420,700) (1986E)	171,000
Yueyang (▲411,300) (1986E)	239,500
Yulin, Guangxi Zhuangzu prov. (▲1,228,800) (1986E)	115,600
Yulin, Shaanxi prov. (1985E)	51,610
Yumen (Laojunmiao) (▲160,100) (1986E)	84,300
Yuncheng, Shandong prov. (1982C)	54,262
Yuncheng, Shansi prov. (▲434,900) (1986E)	87,000
Yunyang (1982C)	54,903
Yushu (1985E)	57,222
Yuyao (▲772,700) (1986E)	169,700
Zaozhuang (▲1,592,000) (1986E)	292,200
Zhangjiakou (Kalgan) (▲640,000)	500,000
Zhangye (▲394,200) (1986E)	73,000
Zhangzhou (Longxi) (▲310,400) (1986E)	159,400
Zhanjiang (▲920,900) (1986E)	335,500
Zhaodong (1985E)	99,836
Zhaoqing (Gaoyao) (▲187,600) (1986E)	145,700
Zhaotong (▲546,600) (1986E)	77,500
Zhaoyuan (1985E)	42,426
Zhaoyuan (1982C)	56,389
Zhengzhou (Chengchow) (▲1,580,000)	1,150,000
Zhenjiang (1986E)	412,400
Zhongshan (Shiqizhen) (▲1,059,700) (1986E)	238,700
Zhoucun (1975U)	50,000
Zhoukouzhen (▲220,400) (1986E)	110,500
Zhuhai (▲155,000) (1986E)	88,800
Zhumadian (▲149,500) (1986E)	99,400
Zhuoxian (1985E)	54,523
Zhuzhou (Chuchow) (▲499,600) (1986E)	344,800
Zibo (Zhangdian) (▲2,370,000)	840,000
Zigong (Tzukung) (▲909,300) (1986E)	361,700
Zixing (▲334,300) (1986E)	97,100
Ziyang (1985E)	57,349
Zouping (1982C)	49,274
Zouxian (1985E)	61,578
Zunyi (▲347,600) (1986E)	236,600

CISKEI

1986 E	882,200
BISHO	2,850
• Mdantsane (★East London, S. Afr.)	242,823

COLOMBIA

1985 C	27,867,326
Armenia	187,130
Barrancabermeja	137,406
Barranquilla (★1,140,000)	899,781
Bello (★Medellín)	212,861
Bucaramanga (★550,000)	352,326
Buenaventura	160,342
Buga	82,992
Cali (★1,400,000)	1,350,565
Cartagena	531,426
Cartago	97,791
Ciénaga	56,860
Cúcuta (★445,000)	379,478
Dos Quebradas (★Pereira)	101,480
Duitama	56,390
Envigado (★Medellín)	91,391
Florencia	66,430
Floridablanca (★Bucaramanga)	143,824
Girardot	70,078
Ibagué	292,965
Itagüí (★Medellín)	137,623
Magangué	49,160
Maicao	46,033
Malambo (★Barranquilla)	52,584
Manizales (★330,000)	299,352
Medellín (★2,095,000)	1,468,089
Montería	157,466
Neiva	194,556
Ocaña	51,443
Palmira	175,186
Pasto	197,407
Pereira (★390,000)	233,271
Popayán	141,964
• SANTA FE DE BOGOTÁ (★4,260,000)	3,982,941
Santa Marta	177,922
Sincelejo	120,537
Soacha (★Santa Fe de Bogotá)	109,051
Sogamoso	64,437
Soledad (★Barranquilla)	165,791
Tuluá	99,721
Tunja	93,792
Valledupar	142,771
Villa Rosario (★Cúcuta)	63,615
Villavicencio	178,685
Zipaquirá	45,676

COMOROS / Al-Qumur / Comores

1990 E	452,742
• MORONI	23,432

CONGO

1989 C	2,188,367
• BRAZZAVILLE	693,712
Dolisie	57,991
Pointe-Noire	350,139

COOK ISLANDS

1986 C	18,155
• AVARUA	9,678

COSTA RICA

1988 E	2,851,000
Alajuela (▲147,400)	33,800
Desamparados (★San José) (1984C)	43,352
Puerto Limón (▲62,600)	40,400
Puntarenas (▲86,400)	34,100
• SAN JOSÉ (★1,355,000)	278,600

CÔTE D'IVOIRE (IVORY COAST)

1988 C	10,815,694
Abengourou	59,114
• ABIDJAN	1,929,079
Agboville	46,045
Bouaké	329,850
Daloa	121,842
Divo	72,350
Gagnoa	85,563
Korhogo	109,445
Man	89,575
San Pédro	70,611
YAMOUSSOUKRO	106,786

CROATIA / Hrvatska

1987 E	4,673,517
Osijek (▲162,490)	106,800
Rijeka (▲199,282)	166,400
Split	191,074
• ZAGREB	697,925

▲ Population of an entire municipality, commune, or district, including rural area.
• Largest city in country.
★ Population or designation of the metropolitan area, including suburbs.
C Census. **E** Official estimate. **U** Unofficial estimate.

▲ Bevölkerung eines ganzen städtischen Verwaltungsgebietes, eines Kommunalbezirkes oder eines Distrikts, einschliesslich ländlicher Gebiete.
• Grösste Stadt des Landes.
★ Bevölkerung oder Bezeichnung der Stadtregion einschliesslich Vororte.
C Volkszählung. **E** Offizielle Schätzung. **U** Inoffizielle Schätzung.

Population of Cities and Towns / Einwohnerzahlen von Grossstädten / Habitantes en las Ciudades y Poblaciones
Population des Grands Centres et des Villes / População dos Centros Urbanos 305

CUBA

1991 E	10,694,465
Bayamo	139,061
Camagüey	286,404
Cárdenas (▲84,590)	69,800
Ciego de Ávila	101,620
Cienfuegos	136,233
Florida	51,442
Guantánamo	215,864
Holguín	236,967
• LA HABANA (HAVANA) (★2,210,000)	2,119,059
Las Tunas	126,678
Manzanillo	108,668
Matanzas	119,510
Morón	49,793
Palma Soriano (▲124,543)	66,600
Pinar del Río	136,303
Sancti Spíritus	97,522
Santa Clara	203,753
Santiago de Cuba	434,541

CYPRUS / Kıbrıs / Kípros

1982 C	512,097
Lárnax (Larnaca) (★48,330)	35,823
Lemesós (Limassol) (★107,161)	74,782
• NICOSIA (LEVKOSÍA) (★185,000)	48,221

CYPRUS, NORTH / Kuzey Kıbrıs

1985 E	160,287
Gazimağusa (Famagusta)	19,428
• NICOSIA (LEFKOŞA)	37,400

CZECH REPUBLIC / Česká Republika

1991 C	10,298,731
Brno (★450,000)	387,986
Česká Lípa	39,667
České Budějovice (★114,000)	97,283
Český Těšín (★Třinec)	28,737
Cheb	31,847
Chomutov (★80,000)	53,191
Děčín (★72,000)	55,112
Frýdek-Místek (★Ostrava)	65,067
Havířov (★Ostrava)	86,267
Hodonín	30,736
Hradec Králové (★113,000)	99,889
Jablonec nad Nisou (★Liberec)	45,918
Jihlava	52,271
Karlovy Vary (Carlsbad)	56,291
Karviná (★Ostrava)	68,368
Kladno (★88,500)	71,735
Kolín	31,582
Kroměříž (★38,500)	28,962
Liberec (★175,000)	101,934
Litvínov (★Most)	29,085
Mladá Boleslav	44,471
Most (★135,000)	70,675
Nový Jičín	29,028
Olomouc (★126,000)	105,690
Opava (★78,000)	63,601
Orlová (★Ostrava)	36,307
Ostrava (★760,000)	327,553
Pardubice	94,857
Písek	29,542
Plzeň (★210,000)	173,129
• PRAHA (★1,328,000)	1,212,010
Přerov	51,341
Příbram	36,869
Prostějov	50,102
Šumperk	30,446
Tábor (★55,500)	36,329
Teplice (★94,000)	53,039
Třebíč	39,348
Třinec (★87,500)	45,189
Trutnov	31,957
Ústí nad Labem (★115,000)	99,739
Valašské Meziříčí	28,153
Vsetín	31,584
Zlín (★124,000)	84,634
Znojmo	39,910

DENMARK / Danmark

1992 E	5,162,126
Ålborg (▲156,614)	115,200
Århus (▲267,873)	207,300
Ballerup (★København)	45,476
Esbjerg (▲81,843)	72,200
Fredericia (▲46,617)	28,700
Frederiksberg (★København)	86,372
Gentofte (★København)	66,077
Gladsakse (★København)	60,604
Helsingør (Elsinore) (★København)	56,794
Horsens (▲55,123)	47,200
Hvidovre (★København)	48,754
• KØBENHAVN (★1,670,000)	464,566
Kolding (▲57,982)	42,700
Kongens Lyngby (★København)	49,612
Odense (▲179,487)	142,800
Randers	61,440
Rønne	15,236
Roskilde (▲50,158) (★København)	40,700
Vejle (▲51,845)	45,700

DJIBOUTI

1991 E	508,541
• DJIBOUTI	329,337

DOMINICA

1984 E	77,000
• ROSEAU	9,348

DOMINICAN REPUBLIC / República Dominicana

1990 E	7,169,800
Barahona	80,400
La Romana	147,800
La Vega	192,300
Mao	58,400
Puerto Plata	94,900
San Cristóbal	137,500
San Francisco de Macorís	165,300
San Juan [de la Maguana]	129,700
San Pedro de Macorís	144,300
Santiago [de los Caballeros]	489,500
• SANTO DOMINGO	2,411,900

ECUADOR

1990 C	9,648,189
Ambato	124,166
Babahoyo	50,285
Cuenca	194,981
Eloy Alfaro (★Guayaquil)	82,359
Esmeraldas	98,558
• Guayaquil	1,508,444
Ibarra	80,991
La Libertad	50,108
Loja	94,305
Machala	144,197
Manta	125,505
Milagro	93,637
Portoviejo	132,937
Quevedo	86,910
QUITO (★1,300,000)	1,100,847
Riobamba	94,505
Santo Domingo de los Colorados	114,422

EGYPT / Miṣr

1986 C	48,205,049
Abnūb	48,519
Abū Kabīr	69,509
Abū Tīj	48,711
Akhmīm	70,602
Al-ʿArīsh	67,638
Al-Fayyūm	212,523
Al-Ḥawāmidīyah (★Al-Qāhirah)	73,060
Al-Iskandarīyah (Alexandria) (★3,350,000)	2,917,327
Al-Ismāʿīlīyah (★235,000)	212,567
Al-Jīzah (Giza) (★Al-Qāhirah)	1,870,508
Al-Maḥallah al-Kubrā	358,844
Al-Manṣūrah (★375,000)	316,870
Al-Manzilah	55,090
Al-Maṭarīyah	74,554
Al-Minyā	179,136
• AL-QĀHIRAH (CAIRO) (★9,300,000)	6,052,836
Al-Qanāṭir al-Khayrīyah	48,909
Al-Uqṣur (Luxor)	125,404
Armant	54,650
Ashmūn	54,450
As-Sinbillāwayn	60,285
As-Suways (Suez)	326,820
Aswān	191,461
Asyūṭ	273,191
Az-Zaqāzīq	245,496
Bahtīm (★Al-Qāhirah)	275,807
Banhā	115,571
Banī Mazār	47,964
Banī Suwayf	151,813
Bilbays	96,540
Bilqās Qism Awwal	73,162
Biyalā	47,781
Būlāq ad-Dakrūr (★Al-Qāhirah)	148,787
Būr Saʿīd (Port Said)	399,793
Būsh	54,482
Damanhūr	190,840
Disūq	78,119
Dumyāṭ (Damietta)	89,498
Fāqūs	48,625
Ḥawsh ʿĪsā	53,619
Idkū	70,729
Jirjā	70,899
Kafr ad-Dawwār (★Al-Iskandarīyah)	195,102
Kafr ash-Shaykh	102,910
Kafr az-Zayyāt	58,061
Kawm Umbū	52,131
Maghāghah	50,807
Mallawī	99,062
Manfalūṭ	52,644
Marsā Maṭrūḥ	43,192
Minūf	69,883
Mīt Ghamr (★100,000)	93,253
Qalyūb	86,684
Qinā	119,794
Rashīd (Rosetta)	52,014
Rummānah	50,014
Samālūṭ	62,404
Sāqiyat Makkī	51,062
Sawhāj	132,965
Shibīn al-Kawm	132,751
Shubrā al-Khaymah (★Al-Qāhirah)	710,794
Sinnūris	55,323
Ṭahṭā	58,516
Ṭalkhā (★Al-Manṣūrah)	55,757
Ṭanṭā	334,505
Ṭimā	47,223
Warrāq al-ʿArab (★Al-Qāhirah)	127,108
Ziftā (★Mīt Ghamr)	69,050

EL SALVADOR

1985 E	5,337,896
Delgado (★San Salvador)	67,684
Mejicanos (★San Salvador)	91,465
Nueva San Salvador (★San Salvador)	53,688
San Miguel	88,520
• SAN SALVADOR (★920,000)	462,652
Santa Ana	137,879
Soyapango (★San Salvador)	60,000

EQUATORIAL GUINEA / Guinea Ecuatorial

1983 C	300,000
• MALABO	31,630

ERITREA

1987 E	2,951,000
• ASMERA (1990E)	358,100
Mitsiwa (1986E)	16,576

ESTONIA / Eesti

1991 E	1,581,800
Kohtla-Järve	74,700
Narva	83,000
Pärnu	54,200
• TALLINN	481,500
Tartu	115,300

ETHIOPIA / Ityopiya

1986 E	44,927,000
• ADIS ABEBA (★1,990,000) (1990E)	1,912,500
Akaki Beseka (★Adis Abeba)	58,977
Awasa	39,693
Bahir Dar	59,951
Debre Zeyit	55,706
Dese	77,459
Dire Dawa (1990E)	127,400
Gonder	88,000
Harer	68,000
Jima	67,470
Mekele	66,640
Nazret	83,091

FAEROE ISLANDS / Føroyar

1990 E	47,946
• TÓRSHAVN	14,767

FALKLAND ISLANDS

1991 C	2,050
• STANLEY	1,557

FIJI

1986 C	715,375
Lautoka (★39,057)	28,728
• SUVA (★141,273)	69,665

FINLAND / Suomi

1992 E	5,029,002
Espoo (Esbo) (★Helsinki)	175,670
• HELSINKI (HELSINGFORS) (★1,040,000)	497,542
Joensuu	48,182
Jyväskylä (★93,000) (1990E)	67,026
Kotka	56,515
Kouvola (★53,821)	32,066
Kuopio	81,593
Lahti (★108,000)	93,414
Lappeenranta	55,358
Oulu (★121,000) (1990E)	102,280
Pori	76,432
Tampere (★241,000)	173,797
Turku (Åbo) (★228,000)	159,403
Vaasa (Vasa)	53,764
Vantaa (Vanda) (★Helsinki)	157,274

FRANCE

1990 C	56,614,493
Aix-en-Provence (★Marseille)	123,842
Ajaccio	58,315
Albi (★54,359)	46,579
Alès (★76,856)	41,037
Amiens (★156,120)	131,872
Angers (★208,282)	141,404
Angoulême (★102,908)	42,876
Annecy (★126,729)	49,644
Antibes (★Cannes)	63,248
Antony (★Paris)	57,771
Argenteuil (★Paris)	93,096
Arles (★54,309)	39,000
Armentières (★57,738)	25,219
Arras (★79,607)	38,983
Asnières [-sur-Seine] (★Paris)	71,850
Aubervilliers (★Paris)	67,557
Aulnay-sous-Bois (★Paris)	82,314
Avignon (★181,136)	86,939
Bastia (★52,446)	37,845
Bayonne (★164,378)	40,051
Beauvais (★57,704)	54,190
Belfort (★77,844)	50,125
Besançon (★122,623)	113,828
Béthune (★261,535)	24,556
Béziers (★76,304)	70,996
Blois (★65,132)	49,318
Bondy (★Paris)	46,676
Bordeaux (★760,000)	210,336
Boulogne-Billancourt (★Paris)	101,743
Boulogne-sur-Mer (★91,249)	43,678
Bourg-en-Bresse (★55,784)	40,972
Bourges (★94,731)	75,609
Brest (★201,480)	147,956
Brive-la-Gaillarde (★64,379)	49,765
Bruay-en-Artois (★Béthune)	24,927
Caen (★191,490)	112,846
Calais (★101,768)	75,309
Cambrai (★48,133)	33,092
Cannes (★335,647)	68,676
Carcassonne	43,470
Castres (★46,482)	44,812
Châlons-sur-Marne (★61,452)	48,423
Chalon-sur-Saône (★77,764)	54,575
Chambéry (★103,283)	54,120
Champigny-sur-Marne (★Paris)	79,486
Charleville-Mézières (★67,213)	57,008
Chartres (★85,933)	39,595
Châteauroux (★67,090)	50,969
Châtellerault (★36,298)	34,678
Cherbourg (★92,045)	27,121
Cholet	55,132
Clamart (★Paris)	47,227
Clermont-Ferrand (★254,416)	136,181
Clichy (★Paris)	48,030
Cognac (★27,468)	19,528
Colmar (★83,816)	63,498
Colombes (★Paris)	78,513
Compiègne (★67,057)	41,896
Courbevoie (★Paris)	65,389
Creil (★97,119)	31,956
Créteil (★Paris)	82,088
Denain (★Valenciennes)	19,544
Dieppe (★43,348)	35,894
Dijon (★230,451)	146,703
Douai (★199,562)	42,175
Drancy (★Paris)	60,707
Dunkerque (★190,879)	70,331
Elbeuf (★53,886)	16,604
Épinal (★62,140)	36,732
Épinay-sur-Seine (★Paris)	48,762
Évreux (★57,968)	49,103
Évry (★Paris)	45,531
Fontainebleau (★35,706)	15,714
Fontenay-sous-Bois (★Paris)	51,868
Forbach (★98,758)	27,076
Fréjus (★73,967)	41,486
Gennevilliers (★Paris)	44,818
Grenoble (★404,733)	150,758
Hagondange (★112,061)	8,222
Hayange (★Thionville)	15,638
Issy-les-Moulineaux (★Paris)	46,127
Ivry-sur-Seine (★Paris)	53,619
La Rochelle (★100,264)	71,094
La Seyne-sur-Mer (★Toulon)	59,968
Laval (★56,855)	50,473
Le Blanc-Mesnil (★Paris)	46,956
Le Havre (★253,627)	195,854
Le Mans (★189,107)	145,502
Lens (★323,174)	35,017
Le Puy (★43,499)	21,743
Levallois-Perret (★Paris)	47,548
Lille (★1,050,000)	172,142
Limoges (★170,065)	133,464
Longwy (★41,300)	15,439
Lorient (★115,488)	59,271
Lourdes	16,300
Lyon (★1,335,000)	415,487
Mâcon (★46,714)	37,275
Maisons-Alfort (★Paris)	53,375
Mantes-la-Jolie (★Paris)	45,087
Marseille (★1,225,000)	800,550
Martigues (★Marseille)	31,300
Maubeuge (★102,772)	34,989
Meaux (★63,006)	48,305
Melun (★107,705)	35,319
Menton (★Monaco, Monaco)	29,141
Mérignac (★Bordeaux)	57,273
Metz (★193,117)	119,594
Meudon (★Paris)	45,339
Montargis (★52,804)	15,020
Montbéliard (★117,510)	29,005
Montceau-les-Mines (★47,283)	22,999
Montluçon (★63,018)	44,248
Montpellier (★248,303)	207,996
Montreuil-sous-Bois (★Paris)	94,754
Moulins (★41,715)	22,799
Moyeuvre-Grande (★Hagondange)	9,203
Mulhouse (Mülhausen) (★223,856)	108,357
Nancy (★329,447)	99,351
Nanterre (★Paris)	84,565
Nantes (★496,078)	244,995
Neuilly-sur-Seine (★Paris)	61,768
Nevers (★58,915)	41,968
Nice (★516,740)	342,439
Nîmes (★138,527)	128,471
Niort (★65,792)	57,012
Noisy-le-Grand (★Paris)	54,032
Noisy-le-Sec (★Paris)	36,309
Orléans (★243,153)	105,111
Orly (★Paris)	21,646
Pantin (★Paris)	47,303
• PARIS (★10,275,000)	2,152,423
Pau (★144,674)	82,157
Périgueux (★63,322)	30,280
Perpignan (★157,873)	105,983
Pessac (★Bordeaux)	51,055
Poissy (★Paris)	36,745
Poitiers (★107,625)	78,894
Quimper (★65,954)	59,437
Reims (★206,437)	180,620
Rennes (★245,065)	197,536
Roanne (★77,160)	41,756
Rodez (★39,017)	24,701
Romans-sur-Isère (★49,212)	32,734
Roubaix (★Lille)	97,746
Rouen (★380,161)	102,723
Rueil-Malmaison (★Paris)	66,401
Saint-Brieuc (★83,861)	44,752
Saint-Chamond (★81,795)	38,878
Saint-Denis (★Paris)	89,988
Saint-Dizier (★40,097)	33,552
Saint-Étienne (★313,338)	199,396
Saint-Lô (★2,760)	21,546
Saint-Malo	48,057
Saint-Maur-des-Fossés (★Paris)	77,206
Saint-Nazaire (★131,511)	64,812
Saint-Ouen (★Paris)	42,343
Saint-Quentin (★71,113)	60,644
Sarcelles (★Paris)	56,833
Sartrouville (★Paris)	50,329
Sevran	48,478
Soissons (★46,168)	29,829
Strasbourg (★415,000)	252,338
Suresnes (★Paris)	35,998
Tarbes (★77,787)	47,566
Thionville (★132,413)	39,712
Toulon (★437,553)	167,619
Toulouse (★650,000)	358,688
Tourcoing (★Lille)	93,765
Tours (★282,152)	129,509
Troyes (★122,763)	59,255
Valence (★107,965)	63,437
Valenciennes (★338,392)	38,441
Vénissieux (★Lyon)	60,444
Verdun-sur-Meuse (★26,711)	20,753
Versailles (★Paris)	87,789
Vichy (★61,566)	27,714
Villefranche (★55,249)	29,542
Villejuif (★Paris)	48,405
Villeneuve-d'Ascq (★Lille)	65,320
Villeurbanne (★Lyon)	116,872
Vitry-sur-Seine (★Paris)	82,400
Wattrelos (★Lille)	43,675

FRENCH GUIANA / Guyane française

1982 C	73,022
• CAYENNE	38,091

FRENCH POLYNESIA / Polynésie française

1988 C	188,814
• PAPEETE (★80,000)	23,555

GABON

1985 E	1,312,000
Franceville	58,800
Lambaréné	49,500
• LIBREVILLE	235,700
Port Gentil	124,400

GAMBIA

1983 C	687,817
• BANJUL (★160,000)	44,188
Brikama	19,624

GEORGIA / Sakartvelo

1991 E	5,464,200
Batumi	137,500
Gori	70,100
Kutaisi	238,200
Poti	51,100
Rustavi (★Tbilisi)	161,900
Suchumi	120,000
• TBILISI (★1,460,000)	1,279,000
Zugdidi	50,600

GERMANY / Deutschland

1991 E	79,753,227
Aachen (★540,000)	241,861
Aalen (★78,000)	64,781
Ahlen	54,169
Albstadt	49,021
Alsdorf (★Aachen)	46,935
Altenburg	48,926
Amberg	43,111
Arnsberg	75,864
Aschaffenburg (★150,000)	64,098
Augsburg (★420,000)	256,877
Baden-Baden	51,849
Bad Homburg (★Frankfurt am Main)	51,820
Bad Oeynhausen	46,475
Bad Salzuflen (★Herford)	53,771
Bamberg (★122,000)	70,521
Bautzen	48,588
Bayreuth (★87,000)	72,345

▲ Población de un municipio, comuna o distrito entero, incluyendo sus áreas rurales.
• Ciudad más grande de un país.
★ Población o designación de un área metropolitana, incluyendo los suburbios.
C Censo. **E** Estimado oficial. **U** Estimado no oficial.

▲ Population d'une municipalité, d'une commune ou d'un district, zone rurale incluse.
• Ville la plus peuplée du pays.
★ Population de l'agglomération (ou nom de la zone métropolitaine englobante).
C Recensement. **E** Estimation officielle. **U** Estimation non officielle.

▲ População de um municipio, comuna ou distrito, inclusive as respectivas áreas rurais.
• Maior cidade de um país.
★ População ou indicação de uma área metropolitana.
C Censo. **E** Estimativa oficial. **U** Estimativa não oficial.

Bergheim (★Köln)	58,146
Bergisch Gladbach (★Köln)	104,037
Bergkamen (★Essen)	49,761
BERLIN (★4,150,000)	3,433,695
Bielefeld (★535,000)	319,037
Bitterfeld (★105,000)	17,988
Bocholt	68,936
Bochum (★Essen)	396,486
BONN (★575,000)	292,234
Bottrop (★Essen)	118,936
Brandenburg	89,889
Braunschweig (★320,000)	258,833
Bremen (★790,000)	551,219
Bremerhaven (★180,000)	130,446
Castrop-Rauxel (★Essen)	79,037
Celle	72,260
Chemnitz (★500,000)	294,244
Coburg	44,246
Cottbus	125,891
Cuxhaven	56,090
Dachau (★München)	35,387
Darmstadt (★315,000)	138,920
Delmenhorst (★Bremen)	75,154
Dessau (★138,000)	96,754
Detmold	70,074
Dinslaken (★Essen)	65,313
Dormagen (★Köln)	58,260
Dorsten (★Essen)	78,035
Dortmund (★Essen)	599,055
Dresden (★870,000)	490,571
Duisburg (★Essen)	535,447
Düren (★108,000)	86,508
Düsseldorf (★1,225,000)	575,794
Eberswalde	52,586
Eisenach	45,220
Eisenhüttenstadt	50,216
Emden	50,735
Erfurt	208,989
Erlangen (★Nürnberg)	102,440
Eschweiler (★Aachen)	54,675
• Essen (★5,050,000)	626,973
Esslingen (★Stuttgart)	91,685
Euskirchen	49,654
Flensburg (★98,000)	86,977
Frankenthal (★Mannheim)	46,966
Frankfurt am Main (★1,935,000)	644,865
Frankfurt an der Oder	86,131
Freiberg	48,609
Freiburg (★235,000)	191,029
Friedrichshafen	54,129
Fulda (★74,000)	56,289
Fürth (★Nürnberg)	103,362
Garbsen (★Hannover)	60,776
Garmisch-Partenkirchen	26,837
Gelsenkirchen (★Essen)	293,714
Gera	129,037
Giessen (★155,000)	74,497
Gladbeck (★Essen)	80,267
Göppingen (★155,000)	54,957
Görlitz	72,237
Goslar (★72,000)	46,251
Gotha	54,525
Göttingen	121,831
Greifswald	66,251
Grevenbroich (★Düsseldorf)	60,835
Gummersbach	50,965
Gütersloh (★Bielefeld)	86,807
Hagen (★Essen)	214,449
Halberstadt	45,364
Halle (★455,000)	310,234
Hamburg (★2,385,000)	1,652,363
Hameln (★65,000)	58,539
Hamm	179,639
Hanau (★Frankfurt am Main)	86,913
Hannover (★1,000,000)	513,010
Hattingen (★Essen)	58,241
Heidelberg (★Mannheim)	136,796
Heidenheim (★80,000)	50,532
Heilbronn (★245,000)	115,843
Herford (★120,000)	63,893
Herne (★Essen)	178,132
Herten (★Essen)	69,245
Hilden (★Düsseldorf)	54,782
Hildesheim (★126,000)	105,291
Hof	52,913
Hoyerswerda	64,888
Hürth (★Köln)	50,808
Ingolstadt (★145,000)	105,489
Iserlohn	96,314
Jena	102,518
Kaiserslautern (★130,000)	99,351
Kamen (★Essen)	46,160
Karlsruhe (★505,000)	275,061
Kassel (★375,000)	194,268
Kempten (Allgäu)	61,906
Kerpen (★Köln)	57,337
Kiel (★325,000)	245,567
Kleve	45,963
Koblenz (★170,000)	108,733
Köln (★1,810,000)	953,551
Konstanz	75,089
Krefeld (★Essen)	244,020
Landshut	59,066
Langenfeld (★Düsseldorf)	53,455
Langenhagen (★Hannover)	47,432
Leipzig (★720,000)	511,079
Leverkusen (★Köln)	160,919
Lingen	49,137
Lippstadt	62,345
Lübeck (★250,000)	214,758
Lüdenscheid	79,401
Ludwigsburg (★Stuttgart)	82,343
Ludwigshafen (★Mannheim)	162,173
Lüneburg	61,870
Lünen (★Essen)	87,845
Magdeburg (★400,000)	278,807
Mainz (★Wiesbaden)	179,486
Mannheim (★1,525,000)	310,411
Marburg	74,146
Marl (★Essen)	91,467
Meerbusch (★Düsseldorf)	52,104
Menden	56,527
Merseburg (★Halle)	42,905
Minden (★121,000)	78,145
Moers (★Essen)	104,595
Mönchengladbach (★410,000)	259,436
Mülheim an der Ruhr (★Essen)	177,681
München (Munich) (★1,900,000)	1,229,026
Münster	259,438
Neubrandenburg	89,284
Neumünster	80,743
Neunkirchen/Saar (★125,000)	51,536
Neuss (★Düsseldorf)	147,019
Neustadt an der Weinstrasse	51,988
Neu-Ulm (★Ulm)	46,264
Neuwied (★157,000)	62,075
Norderstedt (★Hamburg)	68,450
Nordhausen	46,422
Nordhorn	49,359
Nürnberg (★1,065,000)	493,692
Oberhausen (★Essen)	223,840
Offenbach (★Frankfurt am Main)	114,992
Offenburg	52,964
Oldenburg	143,131
Osnabrück (★270,000)	163,168
Paderborn	120,680
Passau	50,328
Peine	46,654
Pforzheim (★230,000)	112,944
Pirmasens	47,680
Pirna (★Dresden)	41,798
Plauen	71,774
Potsdam (★Berlin)	139,794
Ratingen (★Düsseldorf)	91,007
Ravensburg (★75,000)	45,650
Recklinghausen (★Essen)	125,060
Regensburg (★180,000)	121,691
Remscheid (★Wuppertal)	123,155
Reutlingen (★170,000)	103,687
Rheine	70,452
Riesa	45,440
Rosenheim	56,340
Rostock	248,088
Rüsselsheim (★Wiesbaden)	59,430
Saarbrücken (★365,000)	191,694
Saarlouis (★115,000)	38,160
Salzgitter	114,355
Sankt Augustin (★Bonn)	51,886
Schwäbisch Gmünd	60,081
Schwedt	50,633
Schweinfurt (★105,000)	54,483
Schwerin	127,447
Schwerte (★Essen)	50,696
Siegburg (★175,000)	35,441
Siegen (★192,000)	109,174
Sindelfingen (★Stuttgart)	58,805
Solingen (★Wuppertal)	165,401
Speyer	46,553
Stendal	48,532
Stolberg (★Aachen)	57,231
Stralsund	72,780
Stuttgart (★2,005,000)	579,988
Suhl	54,731
Trier (★122,000)	97,835
Troisdorf (★Siegburg)	64,430
Tübingen	80,372
Ulm (★215,000)	110,529
Unna (★Essen)	61,552
Velbert (★Essen)	89,253
Viersen (★Mönchengladbach)	77,453
Villingen-Schwenningen	78,218
Weimar	60,326
Wesel	59,631
Wetzlar (★96,000)	51,737
Wiesbaden (★790,000)	260,301
Wilhelmshaven (★122,000)	90,561
Wismar	55,509
Witten (★Essen)	105,403
Wittenberg	49,682
Wolfenbüttel (★Braunschweig)	52,032
Wolfsburg	128,510
Worms (★Mannheim)	76,503
Wuppertal (★845,000)	383,660
Würzburg (★195,000)	127,777
Zweibrücken (★100,000)	33,918
Zwickau (★180,000)	114,632

GHANA

1987 E	13,577,538
• ACCRA (★1,390,000)	949,113
Ashiaman (★Accra) (1984C)	49,427
Cape Coast (1984C)	86,620
Koforidua (1984C)	54,400
Kumasi (★540,000)	385,192
Obuasi (1984C)	60,146
Sekondi (★175,352) (1984C)	32,355
Tafo (★Kumasi) (1984C)	50,432
Takoradi (★Sekondi) (1984C)	61,527
Tamale (★171,661)	151,069
Tema (★179,076) (★Accra)	109,975
Teshie (★Accra) (1984C)	62,954

GIBRALTAR

1988 E	30,077
• GIBRALTAR	30,077

GREECE / Ellás

1991 C	10,264,156
Aiyáleo (★Athínai)	79,560
Akharnai	60,062
Amaroúsion (★Athínai)	63,619
Ampelókipoi (★Thessaloníki) (1981C)	40,033
• ATHÍNAI (ATHENS) (★3,096,775)	748,110
Áyios Dhimítrios (★Athínai)	57,387
Ermoúpolis (★16,008)	12,987
Galátsion (★Athínai)	56,972
Glifádha (★Athínai)	62,310
Ilioúpolis (★Athínai)	72,623
Ioánnina	56,496
Iráklion (★127,600)	117,167
Kalámai (★45,090)	43,838
Kalamariá (★Thessaloníki) (1981C)	51,676
Kallithéa (★Athínai)	110,738
Kardhítsa	30,451
Kateríni (★48,021)	46,304
Kavála	58,576
Keratsínion (★Athínai)	71,845
Khalándrion (★Athínai)	72,286
Khalkís	51,482
Khaniá (★65,519)	50,077
Khíos (★27,405)	21,261
Koridhallós (★Athínai)	63,033
Kórinthos (Corinth)	28,903
Lárisa (★125,623)	113,426
Návplion	11,453
Néa Ionía (★Athínai)	60,364
Néa Liósia (★Athínai)	78,029
Neápolis (★Thessaloníki) (1981C)	31,464
Néa Smírni (★Athínai)	69,319
Níkaia (★Athínai)	87,924
Palaión Fáliron (★Athínai)	60,974
Pátrai (★172,763)	155,180
Peristérion (★Athínai)	145,854
Piraiévs (Piraeus) (★Athínai)	169,622
Ródhos (Rhodes)	43,619
Sérrai	50,875
Spárti (Sparta) (★15,496)	14,043
Thessaloníki (Salonika) (★739,998)	377,951
Tríkala	48,810
Trípolis	21,772
Véroia	38,871
Víron (★Athínai)	57,149
Vólos (★106,142)	77,907
Zográfos (★Athínai)	78,570

GREENLAND / Grønland / Kalaallit Nunaat

1990 E	55,558
Egedesminde (Aasiaat)	3,308
• GODTHÅB (NUUK)	12,217
Holsteinsborg (Sisimiut)	4,871

GRENADA

1991 C	90,691
• SAINT GEORGE'S (★25,000)	4,439

GUADELOUPE

1982 C	328,400
BASSE-TERRE (★26,600)	13,656
Les Abymes (★Pointe-à-Pitre)	56,165
• Pointe-à-Pitre (★83,000)	25,310

GUAM

1990 C	133,152
• AGANA (★50,000)	1,139

GUATEMALA

1989 E	8,935,395
Escuintla	60,673
• GUATEMALA (★1,400,000)	1,057,210
Quetzaltenango	88,769

GUERNSEY

1991 C	58,867
• SAINT PETER PORT (★36,000)	16,648

GUINEA / Guinée

1986 E	6,225,000
• CONAKRY	800,000
Kankan	100,000
Kindia	80,000
Labé	110,000
Nzérékoré (1983C)	55,356

GUINEA-BISSAU / Guiné-Bissau

1988 E	945,000
• BISSAU	125,000

GUYANA

1983 E	918,000
• GEORGETOWN (★188,000)	78,500

HAITI / Haïti

1987 E	5,531,802
Cap-Haïtien	72,161
Gonaïves	37,034
• PORT-AU-PRINCE (★880,000)	797,000

HONDURAS

1988 C	4,443,721
Choluteca	54,481
El Progreso	60,058
La Ceiba	68,764
San Pedro Sula (★375,000)	287,350
• TEGUCIGALPA	576,661

HONG KONG

1986 C	5,395,997
Kowloon (Jiulong) (★Victoria)	774,781
Kwai Chung (★Victoria)	131,362
New Kowloon (Xinjiulong) (★Victoria)	1,526,910
Sha Tin (★Victoria)	355,810
Sheung Shui	87,206
Tai Po	119,679
Tsuen Wan (Quanwan) (★Victoria)	514,241
Tuen Mun (★Victoria)	262,458
• VICTORIA (★4,770,000) (1991C)	1,250,993
Yuen Long	75,740

HUNGARY / Magyarország

1990 C	10,374,823
Békéscsaba	67,609
• BUDAPEST (★2,515,000)	2,016,774
Debrecen	212,235
Dunaújváros	59,028
Eger	61,892
Győr	129,338
Hódmezővásárhely	51,180
Kaposvár	71,788
Kecskemét	102,516
Miskolc	196,442
Nagykanizsa	54,052
Nyíregyháza	114,152
Ózd	43,592
Pécs	170,039
Salgótarján	47,822
Sopron	55,083
Szeged	175,301
Székesfehérvár	108,958
Szolnok	78,328
Szombathely	85,617
Tatabánya	74,277
Vác	34,015
Veszprém	63,867
Zalaegerszeg	62,212

ICELAND / Ísland

1991 E	259,577
Akureyri	14,436
• REYKJAVÍK (★149,482)	99,623

INDIA / Bharat

1991 C	844,324,222
Abohar	107,016
Achalpur	96,216
Ādilābād	84,233
Adītyapur (★Jamshedpur)	78,184
Ādoni	135,718
Agartala	157,636
Āgra (★955,684)	899,195
Āgra Cantonment (★Āgra)	49,975
Ahmadābād (★3,297,655)	2,872,865
Ahmadnagar (★221,710)	181,015
Āīzawl	154,343
Ajmer	401,930
Akola	327,946
Akot	65,670
Alandur (★Madras)	125,009
Alīgarh	479,978
Ālīpur Duār (★103,512)	65,945
Allahābād (★858,213)	806,447
Alleppey (★264,887)	174,606
Alwal (★Hyderābād)	66,064
Alwar (★211,162)	206,107
Amalner	76,406
Ambājogāi	57,054
Ambāla	119,535
Ambāla Cantonment (★Ambāla Sadar)	48,903
Ambāla Sadar (★139,615)	90,712
Ambāsamudram (★59,527)	33,860
Ambattur (★Madras)	223,332
Ambikāpur (★53,228)	50,278
Āmbūr	75,728
Amrāvati	433,746
Amreli (★69,279)	67,740
Amritsar	709,456
Amroha	136,893
Anakāpalle	84,362
Ānand (★168,776)	110,144
Anantapur	174,792
Anjār	51,207
Ankleshwar (★78,064)	51,708
Ara	156,871
Arakkonam	71,500
Arcot (★114,884)	45,193
Arni	54,881
Aruppukkottai	78,184
Asansol (★763,845)	261,836
Ashoknagar-Kalyangarh (★Hābra)	96,315
Āttūr	55,529
Auraiya	50,771
Aurangābād (★592,052)	572,034
Avadi (★Madras)	180,291
Āzamgarh	78,382
Badagara (★102,429)	72,441
Bagaha	64,574
Bāgalkot	76,819
Bahādurgarh (★57,195)	56,484
Baharampur (★126,303)	115,036
Bahraich	135,352
Baidyabāti (★Calcutta)	90,601
Bālāghāt (★67,113)	62,164
Balāngīr	70,014
Bāleshwar (★102,504)	86,116
Ballarpur (★92,438)	83,511
Ballia	84,758
Bālly (★Calcutta)	73,265
Bālly (★Calcutta)	181,978
Balrāmpur	60,077
Bālurghāt (★126,199)	119,829
Bānda	97,227
Bangalore (★4,086,548)	2,650,659
Bangaon	79,433
Bānkura	114,927
Bansberia (★Calcutta)	93,447
Bānswāra (★67,952)	66,676
Banūr	55,660
Bāpatla	62,688
Bārākpur (★Calcutta)	133,429
Bārān	57,703
Baranagar (★Calcutta)	223,770
Bārāsat (★Calcutta)	102,648
Baraut	67,673
Barddhamān	244,789
Bareilly (★607,652)	583,473
Bargarh	51,135
Bāripada (★68,895)	49,569
Bārmer	69,385
Barnāla	75,387
Bārsi	88,774
Basīrhāt	101,652
Basti	87,512
Batala (★106,062)	88,896
Bathinda	159,114
Beāwar (★106,715)	105,357
Begusarai (★83,907)	71,362
Bela	66,845
Belampalli	66,608
Belgaum (★401,619)	325,639
Bellary	245,758
Bettiah	92,583
Betūl	63,489
Bhadohi	63,590
Bhadrak	76,390
Bhadrāvati (★149,131)	55,413
Bhadrāvati New Town (★Bhadrāvati)	74,864
Bhadreswar (★Calcutta)	72,414
Bhāgalpur (★261,855)	254,993
Bhandāra	71,762
Bharatpur (★156,844)	148,506
Bharūch (★138,246)	132,312
Bhātpāra (★Calcutta)	304,298
Bhavāni (★97,020)	35,202
Bhāvnagar (★403,521)	400,636
Bhawānipatna	51,014
Bhilai (★688,670)	389,601
Bhīlwāra	183,791
Bhīmavaram	125,495
Bhind	109,731
Bhiwandi (★391,670)	378,546
Bhiwāni	121,449
Bhopāl	1,063,662
Bhubaneshwar	411,542
Bhuj (★110,734)	91,901
Bhusāwal (★159,459)	144,804
Bīd	112,351
Bīdar (★130,804)	107,542
Bihār	200,976
Bijāpur (★193,038)	186,846
Bijnor (★73,570)	66,156
Bīkāner	415,355
Bilāspur (★233,570)	190,911
Bīlīmora (★50,940)	46,366
Birlapur (★65,333)	20,239
Birnagar (★92,108)	20,014
Bishnupur	56,119
Bodhan	64,386
Bodināyakkanūr	66,028
Bokāro Steel City (★415,686)	350,540
Bolpur	52,866
• Bombay (★12,571,720)	9,909,547
Botād	64,491
Brahmapur	210,585
Brajrajnagar	69,548
Budaun	116,706
Budge Budge (★Calcutta)	73,361
Bulandshahr	126,737
Buldāna	52,738
Bulsār (★111,759)	57,903
Būndi	65,016
Burhānpur	172,809
Calcutta (★11,605,833)	4,388,262
Calicut (★800,913)	419,531
Cannanore (★Tellicherry)	65,233
Chāībāsa	56,657
Chākdaha	74,780
Chakradharpur (★48,329)	33,263
Chālisgaon	77,346
Champdāni (★Calcutta)	98,818
Chandannagar (★Calcutta)	122,351
Chandausi	82,733

▲ Population of an entire municipality, commune, or district, including rural area.
• Largest city in country.
★ Population or designation of the metropolitan area, including suburbs.
C Census. **E** Official estimate. **U** Unofficial estimate.

▲ Bevölkerung eines ganzen städtischen Verwaltungsgebietes, eines Kommunalbezirkes oder eines Distrikts, einschliesslich ländlicher Gebiete.
• Grösste Stadt des Landes.
★ Bevölkerung oder Bezeichnung der Stadtregion einschliesslich Vororte.
C Volkszählung. **E** Offizielle Schätzung. **U** Inoffizielle Schätzung.

Population of Cities and Towns / Einwohnerzahlen von Grossstädten / Habitantes en las Ciudades y Poblaciones
Population des Grands Centres et des Villes / População dos Centros Urbanos
307

Chandīgarh (★574,646)	502,992
Chāndpur	55,829
Chandrapur	225,841
Changanācheri	52,448
Channapatna	55,210
Chāpra	136,824
Chās	65,146
Chhatarpur (★75,515)	72,745
Chhindwāra (★96,852)	93,731
Chidambaram (★68,819)	58,927
Chikmagalūr	60,814
Chilakalūrupet	79,081
Chingleput	53,784
Chintāmani	50,376
Chīrāla (★142,654)	80,837
Chitradurga (★103,345)	87,053
Chittaranjan (★58,338)	47,148
Chittaurgarh	71,566
Chittoor	133,233
Chopda	49,112
Chūru (★82,818)	82,430
Cochin (★1,139,543)	564,038
Coimbatore (★1,135,549)	853,402
Contai	53,425
Coonoor (★99,615)	47,100
Cuddalore	143,774
Cuddapah (★215,545)	121,422
Cuttack (★439,273)	402,390
Dabgram	146,917
Dabhoi	50,619
Dāhod (★96,568)	66,444
Dāltenganj	56,408
Damoh (★105,032)	95,553
Dānāpur (★Patna)	84,104
Dandeli	52,699
Darbhanga	218,274
Darjiling	73,088
Datia	65,565
Dāvangere (★287,114)	265,971
Dehra Dūn (★367,411)	270,028
Dehri	94,526
Delhi (★8,375,188)	7,174,755
Delhi Cantonment (★Delhi)	94,326
Deoband	62,461
Deoghar (★85,846)	76,322
Deolāli Cantonment (★Nāsik)	51,115
Deoria	81,943
Dewās	163,699
Dhamtari	69,273
Dhanbad (★817,549)	151,334
Dhār	59,089
Dhārāpuram	48,392
Dharmapuri	59,070
Dharmavaram	78,747
Dhaulpur	68,524
Dholka (★54,351)	49,855
Dhorāji (★79,414)	77,683
Dhrāngadhra	54,281
Dhuburi	65,861
Dhule	277,957
Dibrugarh (★123,885)	118,374
Dimāpur	56,918
Dindigul	182,293
Dīsa	61,888
Dod Ballāpur	54,468
Dum Dum (★Calcutta)	40,942
Durg (★Bhilai)	150,513
Durgāpur	415,986
Elūru	212,918
Erode (★357,427)	158,774
Etah	78,424
Etāwah	124,032
Faizābād (★177,505)	125,012
Farīdābād New Township (★Delhi)	613,828
Farīdkot	56,038
Farrukhābād (★207,783)	193,624
Fatehpur	117,203
Fathpur	66,398
Fāzilka	57,386
Firozābād (★270,534)	215,089
Firozpur	77,505
Firozpur Cantonment	53,691
Gadag	133,918
Gandhidham	104,392
Gāndhinagar	121,746
Ganga Ghat	50,520
Gangānagar	161,377
Gangāpur (★68,982)	53,784
Gangāwati (★81,108)	64,807
Gangtok	24,971
Gārulia (★Calcutta)	80,872
Gaya (★293,971)	291,220
Ghāziābād (★519,508)	460,949
Ghāzīpur	77,069
Girīdīh	77,912
Godhra (★100,363)	96,514
Gokāk	52,037
Gonda	106,078
Gondal (★81,533)	80,506
Gondia	109,271
Gopichettipālaiyam	48,349
Gorakhpur	489,850
Gudivāda	101,635
Gudiyāttam (★89,966)	82,652
Gūdūr	55,962
Gulbarga (★309,962)	303,139
Guna	100,389
Guntakal	107,560
Guntūr	471,020
Gurdāspur	54,575
Gurgaon (★134,639)	120,790
Guruvayur (★118,626)	20,209
Guwāhāti	577,591
Gwalior (★720,068)	692,982
Hābra (★196,457)	100,142
Hājīpur	87,669
Haldwāni	102,744
Hālisahar (★Calcutta)	113,670
Hānsi	59,638
Hanumāngarh (★82,717)	78,504
Hāora (★Calcutta)	946,732
Hāpur	146,591
Hardoi	88,632
Haridwār (★188,961)	148,882
Harihar	66,660
Hassan (★108,458)	90,719
Hāthras	113,653
Hazārībāg	97,712
Himatnagar	50,929
Hindaun	60,761
Hindupur	104,635
Hinganghāt	78,709
Hingoli	54,444
Hisār (★180,774)	172,873
Hoshangābād	70,820
Hoshiārpur	122,528
Hospet (★134,935)	96,499
Hubli-Dhārwār	647,640
Hugli-Chinsurah (★Calcutta)	142,388
Hyderābād (★4,280,261)	2,991,884
Ichalkaranji (★235,854)	214,835
Imphāl (★200,615)	196,268
Indore (★1,104,065)	1,086,673
Ingrāj Bāzār (★176,991)	139,018
Itānagar	17,320
Itārsi (★85,706)	78,700
Jabalpur (★887,188)	739,961
Jabalpur Cantonment (★Jabalpur)	56,742
Jagādhri (★Yamunānagar)	67,371
Jagdalpur (★84,553)	65,544
Jagtiāl	67,965
Jahānābād	51,846
Jaipur (★1,514,425)	1,454,678
Jalandhar	519,530
Jālgaon	241,603
Jālna	174,958
Jalpāiguri	67,495
Jamālpur	86,123
Jamkhandi	48,111
Jammu (★223,361) (1981C)	206,135
Jamnagar (★365,464)	325,475
Jamshedpur (★834,535)	461,212
Jaora (★55,986)	54,960
Jaunpur	136,287
Jaypur	65,582
Jetpur (★95,290)	73,556
Jhānsi (★368,590)	301,304
Jharia (★Dhanbād)	69,542
Jhārsuguda	65,022
Jhunjhunūn	71,972
Jīnd	85,307
Jodhpur	648,621
Jorhāt (★111,584)	57,998
Jūnāgadh (★166,755)	130,132
Kadaiyanallūr	68,805
Kadiri	63,428
Kagaznagar	57,653
Kairāna	56,083
Kaithal	71,294
Kākināda (★327,407)	279,875
Kalamassery (★Cochin)	54,313
Kālol (★92,320)	81,916
Kalyān (★Bombay)	1,014,062
Kāmāreddi	48,641
Kāmārhāti (★Calcutta)	266,625
Kambam	51,987
Kāmthi (★131,837)	78,586
Kānchipuram (★169,813)	145,028
Kānchrāpāra (★Calcutta)	100,059
Kānnangād (★118,180)	57,133
Kannauj	59,650
Kānpur (★2,111,284)	1,958,282
Kānpur Cantonment (★Kānpur)	93,109
Kapra (★Hyderābād)	87,607
Kapūrthala	63,083
Karād	56,705
Kāraikāl	61,875
Kāraikkudi (★110,473)	71,599
Kāranja	48,857
Karauli	48,961
Karīmnagar	148,349
Karnāl (★176,120)	173,742
Karūr (★110,605)	73,428
Kārwār	51,011
Kāsaragod	50,123
Kāsganj	75,610
Kāshīpur	69,889
Katihār (★154,101)	135,348
Kātwa	55,535
Kāvali	65,804
Kāyankulam	67,170
Keshod	50,164
Khadki Cantonment (★Pune)	78,046
Khambhāt (★89,813)	76,724
Khāmgaon	73,705
Khammam (★148,646)	127,812
Khandwa	145,111
Khanna	72,140
Kharagpur (★279,736)	189,101
Kharagpur Railway Settlement (★Kharagpur)	881,253
Khardaha	88,278
Khargone	66,776
Khurja	80,384
Kishanganj	64,462
Kishangarh Bās	81,944
Koch Bihār (★92,628)	71,028
Kodarma	53,560
Kohīma	53,122
Kolār	83,219
Kolār Gold Fields (★156,398)	72,481
Kolhāpur (★417,286)	405,118
Konnagar (★Calcutta)	62,214
Korba	124,365
Kota	536,444
Kot Kapūra	62,403
Kottagūdem (★102,061)	80,420
Kottayam (★166,178)	62,829
Kovilpatti	77,967
Krishnagiri	60,252
Krishnanagar	120,918
Kukatpalle (★Hyderābād)	185,378
Kulti (★Asansol)	108,930
Kumārapālaiyam (★Bhavāni)	57,532
Kumbakonam (★150,502)	139,449
Kundla (★65,732)	64,762
Kurasia (★71,638)	15,828
Kurichi (★Coimbatore)	63,688
Kurnool (★274,795)	236,313
Lādnūn	48,174
Lakhīmpur	79,549
Lalitpur	79,891
Lalitpur	79,891
Lātūr	197,164
Luckeesarai	53,198
Lucknow (★1,642,134)	1,592,010
Lucknow Cantonment (★Lucknow)	50,124
Ludhiāna	1,012,062
Machilīpatnam (Bandar)	159,007
Madanapalle	73,729
Madgaon (Margao) (★72,070)	58,745
Mādhavaram (★Madras)	49,005
Madhubani	53,543
Madras (★5,361,468)	3,795,028
Madurai (★1,093,702)	951,696
Mahbūbnagar	116,775
Mahesāna (★109,540)	87,889
Mahoba	56,152
Mahuva (★63,837)	59,675
Mainpuri	76,696
Makrāna (★66,654)	59,648
Malappuram (★142,203)	49,690
Malaut	56,856
Mālegaon	342,431
Māler Kotla	88,587
Malkajgiri (★Hyderābād)	126,066
Malkāpur	51,302
Mancheriyal	52,626
Mandsaur	95,758
Mandya	119,970
Mangalagiri	59,276
Mangalore (★425,785)	272,819
Mango (★Jamshedpur)	110,024
Manjeri	69,335
Manmād	61,257
Mannārgudi	56,563
Mānsa	55,088
Mathura (★233,235)	226,850
Maunath Bhanjan	136,447
Mawāna	51,644
Māyūram	77,042
Medinīpur	125,098
Meerut (★846,954)	752,078
Meerut Cantonment (★Meerut)	94,876
Melappālaiyam (★Tirunelveli)	68,318
Mettuppālaiyam	63,217
Mhow (★83,649)	74,852
Mira Bhayandar (★Bombay)	175,372
Miraj (★Sāngli)	121,564
Miryalaguda	65,836
Mirzāpur	169,368
Modinagar (★124,197)	102,307
Moga (★110,867)	108,213
Mokāma	59,519
Morādābād (★432,434)	416,836
Morbi (★120,107)	90,349
Morena	147,095
Mormugao (★91,285)	83,209
Motihāri (★82,965)	77,440
Mubārakpur (★62,721)	45,388
Muktsar	66,377
Munger	150,042
Murwāra	163,390
Muzaffarnagar (★247,729)	240,057
Muzaffarpur	240,450
Mysore (★652,246)	480,006
Nābha	54,079
Nadiād (★170,018)	166,852
Nagaon	93,324
Nāgappattinam (★99,024)	86,155
Nāgaur	68,088
Nagda	79,405
Nāgercoil	189,482
Nagīna	58,494
Nāgpur (★1,661,409)	1,622,225
Naihāti (★Calcutta)	132,032
Najībābād	66,842
Nalasopara (★Bombay)	67,548
Nalgonda	84,674
Nānded (★308,853)	274,626
Nandurbār	78,364
Nandyāl	120,171
Nangi (★Calcutta)	52,909
Narasapur	56,358
Narasaraopet	88,766
Nārnaul	51,880
Nāshik (★722,139)	646,896
Navadwīp (★156,117)	125,247
Navsāri (★190,019)	125,980
Nawābganj (★77,613)	64,719
Nawāda	53,075
Nawalgarh	51,168
Nedumangād	49,864
Neemuch (★90,460)	81,397
Nellore	316,445
New Bārākpur (★Calcutta)	63,857
New Bombay (★Bombay)	307,297
NEW DELHI (★Delhi)	294,149
Neyveli (★126,494)	117,471
Nipāni	51,622
Nirmal	57,777
Nizāmābād	240,924
North Bārākpur (★Calcutta)	100,513
North Dum Dum (★Calcutta)	151,298
Ongole (★128,128)	100,544
Orai	98,640
Osmānābād	67,980
Pālakodu	56,972
Palani (★75,948)	68,747
Pālanpur (★90,231)	80,620
Pālayankottai (★Tirunelveli)	97,662
Pālghāt (★179,695)	122,964
Pāli	136,797
Pallavaram (★Madras)	111,194
Palwal	59,127
Palwancha	52,892
Panaji (Panjim) (★85,199)	42,915
Pandharpur	79,798
Pānihāti (★Calcutta)	275,359
Pānīpat	191,010
Panruti	51,424
Panvel	58,845
Paramakkudi	72,105
Parbhani	190,235
Parli	72,573
Pātan (★97,025)	96,109
Pathānkot (★147,130)	142,862
Patiāla (★268,521)	253,341
Patna (★1,098,572)	916,980
Pattukkottai	57,909
Payyannūr	64,011
Periyakulam	46,739
Petlād	48,546
Phagwāra (★88,855)	83,702
Pīlībhīt	106,329
Pilkhua	50,218
Pimpri-Chinchwad (★Pune)	515,962
Pollāchi (★127,180)	87,012
Pondicherry (★401,337)	202,648
Ponmalai (★Tiruchchirāppalli)	70,196
Ponnāni	51,754
Ponnūru Nidubrolu	54,352
Porbandar (★160,043)	116,546
Port Blair	74,810
Proddatūr	133,860
Pudukkottai	98,619
Puliyangudi	53,206
Pune (Poona) (★2,485,014)	1,559,558
Pune Cantonment (★Pune)	81,978
Puri	124,835
Pūrnia (★135,995)	114,189
Puruliya	92,574
Pusad	55,977
Quilon (★362,402)	139,717
Qutubullapur (★Hyderābād)	105,380
Rabkavi Banhatti	60,607
Rāe Bareli	130,101
Rāichūr (★170,500)	157,477
Raiganj (★159,675)	151,454
Raigarh (★92,569)	89,166
Raipur (★461,851)	437,887
Rājahmundry (★403,781)	326,071
Rājapālaiyam	114,042
Rajendranagar (★Hyderābād)	83,849
Rajhara-Jharandalli	55,928
Rājkot (★651,007)	556,137
Rāj Nāndgaon	125,394
Rājpur (★86,390)	61,121
Rājpura	70,886
Rāmanagaram	50,411
Rāmanāthapuram	52,654
Rāmgarh (★82,186)	51,138
Rāmpur	242,752
Rānāghāt (★126,611)	64,244
Rānchi (★614,454)	598,498
Rānībennur	67,419
Rānīganj (★155,644)	62,014
Ratangarh	55,078
Ratlām (★195,752)	183,370
Ratnāgiri	56,512
Raurkela (★398,692)	215,489
Raurkela Civil Township (★Raurkela)	140,192
Rāyagāda	48,352
Rewa	128,918
Rewāri	75,294
Rishīkesh (★71,510)	44,399
Rishra (★Calcutta)	102,649
Robertson Pet (★Kolār Gold Fields)	67,900
Rohtak	215,844
Roorkee (★90,116)	80,236
Rudrapur	61,067
Sāgar (★256,878)	195,106
Sahāranpur	373,904
Saharsa	80,071
Sahaswān	51,067
Sāhibganj	49,133
Salem (★573,685)	363,934
Sāmalkot	48,727
Sambalpur (★192,917)	130,766
Sambhal	150,012
Sangamner	48,895
Sangareddi	50,098
Sāngli (★363,728)	193,181
Sangrūr	56,374
Sankarankovil	48,739
Sardārshahr	67,969
Sarni	84,201
Sāsarām	98,220
Sātāra	95,133
Satna (★160,191)	156,321
Sawāi Mādhopur (★77,561)	72,037
Secunderābād Cantonment (★Hyderābād)	167,461
Sehore	71,437
Seoni	64,302
Serampore (★Calcutta)	137,087
Serilungampalle (★Hyderābād)	72,648
Shahdol (★60,572)	55,554
Shāhjahānpur (★260,260)	237,663
Shāmli	70,347
Shāntipur	109,911
Shikohābād	63,240
Shiliguri	226,677
Shillong (★222,273)	130,691
Shimoga (★192,647)	178,882
Shivpuri	108,271
Shrirampur (★79,042)	71,356
Siddhapur (★51,586)	50,858
Siddipet	54,020
Sikandarābād	61,035
Sīkar	148,235
Silchar	115,045
Silvassa	11,720
Simla (★109,860)	81,463
Sindri (★Dhānbād)	72,349
Sircilla	50,012
Sirsa	112,542
Sītāmarhi (★67,320)	44,910
Sītāpur	120,595
Siuri	54,274
Sivakāsi (★102,139)	65,556
Siwān	81,092
Solāpur (★620,499)	603,870
Sonīpat	142,992
South Dum Dum (★Calcutta)	230,507
Srīkākulam	88,684
Srikalahasti	61,575
Srīnagar (★606,002) (1981C)	594,775
Srīrangam (★Tiruchchirāppalli)	69,928
Srīvilliputtūr	68,543
Sujāngarh	70,393
Sultānpur	76,567
Sūrat (★1,517,076)	1,496,943
Surendranagar (★166,309)	105,973
Suriāpet	60,563
Tādepallegūdem	88,979
Tādpatri	71,043
Talipparamba	60,242
Tāmbaram (★Madras)	106,590
Tānda	69,989
Tanuku	62,877
Tellicherry (★463,951)	103,577
Tenāli	143,836
Tenkāsi	55,044
Tezpur	54,999
Thāna (★Bombay)	796,620
Thānesar	81,275
Thanjāvūr	200,216
Theni-Allinagaram	65,958
Thiruvārūr	49,194
Thrippunithura (★Cochin)	51,032
Tīkamgarh	54,130
Tindivanam	61,715
Tinsukia	73,760
Tiruchchirāppalli (★711,120)	386,628
Tiruchengodu	62,903
Tirunelveli (★365,932)	135,762
Tirupati (★189,030)	174,393
Tiruppattūr	54,884
Tiruppur (★305,546)	235,076
Tirūr	49,450
Tiruvalla	54,745
Tiruvannāmalai	108,291
Tiruvottiyūr (★Madras)	167,851
Tītāgarh (★Calcutta)	113,831
Tonk	100,020
Trichūr (★274,898)	73,849
Trivandrum (★825,682)	523,733
Ttruchchendūr (★75,400)	27,363
Tumkūr (★179,497)	138,598
Tuticorin (★284,193)	205,105
Udagamandalam	81,726
Udaipur	307,682
Udamalpet	58,643
Udgīr	70,409
Ujjain	366,787
Ulhāsnagar (★Bombay)	368,822
Ulubāria	155,188
Unjha	50,947
Unnāo	107,246
Upleta	51,553

▲ Población de un municipio, comuna o distrito entero, incluyendo sus áreas rurales.
• Ciudad más grande de un país.
★ Población o designación de un área metropolitana, incluyendo los suburbios.
C Censo. **E** Estimado oficial. **U** Estimado no oficial.

▲ Population d'une municipalité, d'une commune ou d'un district, zone rurale incluse.
• Ville la plus peuplée du pays.
★ Population de l'agglomération (ou nom de la zone métropolitaine englobante).
C Recensement. **E** Estimation officielle. **U** Estimation non officielle.

▲ População de um município, comuna ou distrito, inclusive as respectivas áreas rurais.
• Maior cidade de um país.
★ População ou indicação de uma área metropolitana.
C Censo. **E** Estimativa oficial. **U** Estimativa não oficial.

Uppal Kalan (★Hyderābād)	75,039
Uttarpara-Kotrung (★Calcutta)	100,867
Vadodara (★1,115,390)	1,021,084
Vālpārai	106,289
Vāniyambādi (★92,097)	72,282
Vārānasi (Benares) (★1,026,467)	925,962
Vasai (Bassein) (★83,572)	39,741
Veerappanchattiram (★Erode)	61,598
Vejalpur (★Ahmadābād)	89,053
Vellore (★304,713)	172,467
Verāval (★119,995)	93,826
Vidisha	92,917
Vijayawāda (★845,305)	701,351
Vikramasingapuram	49,034
Viluppuram	88,916
Viramgām	51,089
Virār (★Bombay)	57,581
Virudunagar	70,951
Vishākhapatnam (★1,051,918)	750,024
Visnagar (★59,693)	57,834
Vizianagaram (★176,125)	159,461
Vriddhāchalam	52,763
Wadhwan (★Surendranager)	49,773
Warangal (★466,877)	446,760
Wardha	102,974
Wāshīm	49,133
Yamunānagar (★219,642)	144,250
Yavatmāl (★121,834)	108,591
Yemmiganur	65,118

INDONESIA

1990 C	179,378,946
Ambon (▲275,888)	205,193
Balikpapan	344,147
Banda Aceh (Kuturaja) (▲184,650)	143,360
Bandung (★2,220,000)	2,058,122
Banjarmasin	480,737
Bantul (▲696,944)	13,700
Banyuwangi (▲1,455,010)	92,800
Batang (▲591,647)	55,200
Bekasi (▲951,509) (★Jakarta)	146,400
Bengkulu	170,183
Binjai (▲181,866)	127,184
Blitar (★150,000)	118,933
Bogor (★620,000)	271,341
Bojonegoro (▲1,104,031)	63,700
Brebes (▲1,521,835)	49,500
Bukittinggi	83,753
Cianjur (▲1,420,228)	108,700
Cibinong (▲1,812,734)	264,100
Cikampek (▲1,152,405)	91,200
Cilacap (▲1,487,308)	141,900
Ciledug (▲1,244,151)	293,000
Cimahi (▲1,909,459) (★Bandung)	196,900
Ciparay (▲1,909,456)	135,300
Cirebon (★315,000)	254,477
Denpasar (▲663,390)	209,500
Depok (▲1,812,734) (★Jakarta)	382,000
Dili (▲123,475)	12,900
Dumai (▲904,375)	71,500
Garut (▲1,478,757)	145,900
Genteng (▲1,455,010)	60,900
Gorontalo (▲119,745)	94,058
Gresik (▲856,853)	102,000
Indramayu (▲1,226,609)	32,700
• JAKARTA (★10,200,000)	8,227,746
Jambi	339,786
Jayapura (Sukarnapura) (▲246,389)	101,200
Jember (▲2,062,554)	190,000
Jepara (▲827,657)	36,200
Jombang (▲1,048,805)	65,700
Karawang (▲1,152,405)	143,300
Kebumen (▲1,120,982)	48,300
Kediri	249,538
Kendari (▲488,471)	70,700
Kisaran (▲884,594)	66,600
Klangenang (▲1,035,575)	291,200
Klaten (▲1,056,135)	120,400
Kudus (▲631,322)	182,600
Kuningan (▲739,360)	33,100
Kupang (▲522,944)	111,300
Lumajang (▲924,894)	62,100
Madiun (★200,000)	170,050
Magelang (★180,000)	123,156
Majalaya (▲1,909,459)	176,600
Malang	695,089
Manado	320,600
Mataram (▲859,273)	276,300
Medan	1,730,052
Mojokerto	99,707
Muncar (▲1,455,010)	48,100
Padang (▲631,263)	477,064
Padangsidempuan (▲954,184)	72,100
Palangkaraya	112,511
Palembang	1,144,047
Palu (▲784,647)	56,500
Pangkalpinang	113,129
Pare (▲1,343,125)	51,400
Parepare (▲101,421)	84,093
Pasuruan (★190,000)	152,075
Pati (▲1,064,115)	54,900
Payakumbuh (▲90,838)	50,475
Pekalongan (★430,000)	242,714
Pekanbaru	398,621
Pemalang (▲1,114,228)	86,200
Pematangsiantar (★250,000)	219,316
Perabumulih (▲582,396)	59,500
Ponorogo (▲837,055)	59,500
Pontianak	396,658
Pringsewu (▲1,825,040)	58,300
Probolinggo (▲176,906)	131,077
Purwakarta (▲437,327)	62,300
Purwokerto (▲1,348,825)	158,300
Purworejo (▲700,788)	38,600
Salatiga	98,012
Samarinda (▲407,174)	334,851
Semarang	1,249,230
Serang (▲1,201,742)	84,900
Sibolga	71,559
Sidoarjo (▲1,167,467)	76,800
Singaraja (▲540,150)	59,200
Singkawang (▲574,156)	64,000
Situbondo (▲574,156)	63,800
Sorong (▲199,085)	77,900
Subang (▲1,037,394)	52,700
Sukabumi (★250,000)	119,938
Sumedang (▲718,488)	42,900
Sumenep (▲933,746)	53,300
Surabaya	2,473,272
Surakarta (★590,000)	503,827
Taman (▲1,167,467)	88,100
Tangerang (▲1,244,151)	99,100
Tanjungbalai	107,751
Tanjungkarang-Telukbetung (▲636,418)	457,927
Tanjungpinang	105,820
Tarakan (▲232,494)	61,300
Tasikmalaya (▲1,444,242)	194,000
Tebingtinggi	116,749
Tegal (★510,000)	229,553
Tembilahan (▲4,878,066)	62,700
Tuban (▲977,716)	54,700
Tulungagung (▲890,032)	97,000
Ujungpandang (Makasar)	944,372
Yogyakarta (★540,000)	412,059

IRAN / Īrān

1986 C	49,445,010
Ābādān	21,879
Ābhar	41,628
Āghā Jārī	64,102
Ahar	62,145
Ahvāz	579,826
Alīgūdarz	53,843
Āmol	118,242
Andīmeshk	56,288
Arāk	265,349
Ardabīl	281,973
Bābol	115,320
Bākhtarān (Kermānshāh)	560,514
Bam	50,709
Bandar-e 'Abbās	201,642
Bandar-e Anzalī (Bandar-e Pahlavī)	87,063
Bandar-e Būshehr	120,787
Bandar-e Māh Shahr	71,808
Behbahān	78,694
Behshahr	52,461
Bīrjand	81,798
Bojnūrd	93,392
Borāzjān	67,061
Borūjerd	183,879
Dezfūl	151,420
Do Gonbadān	51,107
Do Rūd	62,517
Emāmshahr (Shāhrūd)	78,950
Eşfahān (★1,175,000)	986,753
Eslāmābād	73,362
Eslāmshahr (★Tehrān)	215,129
Fasā	64,771
Ganāveh	41,883
Gonbad-e Qābūs	87,100
Gorgān	139,430
Hamadān	272,499
Īlām	89,035
Jahrom	77,174
Karaj (★Tehrān)	275,100
Kāshān	138,599
Kāshmar	49,259
Kāzerūn	73,444
Kermān	257,284
Khomeynīshahr (★Eşfahān)	104,647
Khorramābād	208,592
Khorramshahr (1976C)	146,706
Khvoy	115,343
Mahābād	75,238
Malāyer	103,640
Marāgheh	100,679
Marand	71,394
Marv Dasht	79,132
Mashhad	1,463,508
Masjed-e Soleymān	104,787
Mīāndoāb	59,551
Mīāneh	65,959
Nahāvand	52,265
Najafābād	129,058
Naqadeh	52,275
Neyshābūr	109,258
Orūmīyeh (Reẕā'īyeh)	300,746
Qā'emshahr	109,288
Qazvīn	248,591
Qom	543,139
Qomsheh	73,367
Qūchān	66,531
Rafsanjān	66,498
Rasht	290,897
Sabzevār	129,103
Salmās	50,573
Sanandaj	204,537
Saqqez	81,351
Sārī	141,020
Sāveh	64,081
Semnān	64,891
Shahr-e Kord	75,080
Shīrāz	848,289
Shīrvān	48,688
Shūshtar	65,840
Sīrjān	90,072
Tabrīz	971,482
• TEHRĀN (★7,500,000)	6,042,584
Torbat-e Ḩeydarīyeh	72,068
Varāmīn	58,311
Yazd	230,483
Zābol	75,105
Zāhedān	281,923
Zanjān	215,261

IRAQ / Al 'Irāq

1985 E	15,584,987
Ad-Dīwānīyah (1970E)	62,300
Al-'Amārah	131,785
Al-Başrah	616,700
Al-Ḩillah	215,249
Al-Kūt	73,022
Al-Mawşil	570,926
An-Najaf	242,603
An-Nāşirīyah	138,842
Ar-Ramādī	137,388
As-Samāwah	75,293
As-Sulaymānīyah	279,424
• BAGHDĀD (1987C)	3,841,268
Ba'qūbah	114,516
Irbīl	333,903
Karbalā'	184,574
Kirkūk (1970E)	207,900

IRELAND / Éire

1986 C	3,540,643
Cork (★173,694)	133,271
• DUBLIN (BAILE ÁTHA CLIATH) (★1,140,000)	502,749
Dún Laoghaire (★Dublin)	54,715
Galway	47,104
Limerick (★76,557)	56,279
Waterford (★41,054)	39,529

ISLE OF MAN

1991 C	69,788
• DOUGLAS (★30,000)	22,214

ISRAEL / Isrā'īl / Yisra'el

1991 E	4,713,800
Ashdod	83,900
Ashqelon	59,700
Bat Yam (★Tel Aviv-Yafo)	141,300
Be'ér Sheva (Beersheba)	122,000
Bene Beraq (★Tel Aviv-Yafo)	116,700
Elat	26,300
Giv'atayim (★Tel Aviv-Yafo)	46,600
Ḩefa (★450,000)	245,900
Herzliyya (★Tel Aviv-Yafo)	77,200
Ḩolon (★Tel Aviv-Yafo)	156,700
Kefar Sava (★Tel Aviv-Yafo)	61,100
Lod (Lydda) (★Tel Aviv-Yafo)	43,300
Nazerat (Nazareth) (★77,000)	53,600
Netanya (★Tel Aviv-Yafo)	132,200
Petaḩ Tiqwa (★Tel Aviv-Yafo)	144,000
Ra'anana (★Tel Aviv-Yafo)	53,600
Ramat Gan (★Tel Aviv-Yafo)	119,500
Reḩovot (★Tel Aviv-Yafo)	80,300
Rishon LeẒiyyon (★Tel Aviv-Yafo)	139,500
• Tel Aviv-Yafo (★1,735,000)	339,400
YERUSHALAYIM (AL-QUDS) (JERUSALEM) (★560,000)	524,500

ISRAELI OCCUPIED TERRITORIES

1991 E	1,704,900
Al-Quds (Jerusalem) (★Yerushalayim) (1976E)	90,000
Arīḩā (Jericho) (1967C)	6,829
Bayt Laḩm (Bethlehem) (1971E)	25,000
• Ghazzah (1967C)	118,272
Khān Yūnis (1967C)	52,997
Nābulus (1971E)	64,000
Rafaḩ (1967C)	49,812

ITALY / Italia

1991 C	56,411,290
Afragola (★Napoli)	59,940
Alessandria (▲93,351)	74,000
Altamura	57,462
Ancona	103,268
Andria	82,556
Arezzo (▲91,623)	74,200
Asti (▲74,497)	62,800
Avellino	54,343
Aversa (★Napoli)	50,361
Bari (★475,000)	341,273
Barletta	86,215
Benevento (▲62,683)	51,900
Bergamo (★345,000)	115,655
Biella	50,993
Bitonto	49,792
Bologna (★525,000)	411,803
Bolzano	100,380
Brescia	196,766
Brindisi	91,778
Busto Arsizio (★Milano)	77,001
Cagliari (★305,000)	211,719
Caltanissetta	62,853
Campobasso (▲51,307)	44,400
Carpi (▲60,794)	49,600
Carrara (★Massa)	68,480
Caserta	68,811
Casoria (▲79,315) (★Napoli)	57,800
Castellammare di Stabia (★Napoli)	68,720
Catania (★550,000)	330,037
Catanzaro	103,802
Cava de' Tirreni (★Salerno)	52,610
Cerignola	54,971
Cesena (▲89,497)	72,200
Chieti	57,535
Cinisello Balsamo (★Milano)	75,606
Civitavecchia	50,856
Collegno (★Torino)	47,192
Cologno Monzese (★Milano)	50,853
Como (★165,000)	85,955
Cosenza (★150,000)	104,483
Cremona	75,160
Crotone (▲61,813)	54,300
Cuneo (▲55,838)	47,900
Empoli (▲42,790)	32,300
Ercolano (★Napoli)	60,869
Ferrara (▲140,600)	110,700
Firenze (★640,000)	402,316
Foggia	155,042
Foligno (▲53,518)	42,500
Forlì (▲109,755)	90,600
Gela	79,718
Genova (Genoa) (★805,000)	675,639
Giugliano in Campania (★Napoli)	59,091
Grosseto (▲71,373)	57,000
Imola (▲62,352)	48,800
Imperia	41,278
L'Aquila (▲67,818)	43,100
La Spezia (★185,000)	101,701
Latina (▲105,543)	72,700
Lecce	102,344
Lecco	45,859
Legnano (★Milano)	50,068
Livorno	171,265
Lucca	86,437
Manfredonia	58,157
Mantova (▲54,228)	46,800
Marsala	77,218
Massa (★145,000)	67,779
Matera	54,872
Messina	274,846
Mestre (▲317,837) (★Venezia)	181,900
• Milano (Milan) (★3,750,000)	1,371,008
Modena	177,501
Molfetta	66,658
Moncalieri (★Torino)	58,433
Monopoli (▲43,019)	33,100
Monza (★Milano)	121,151
Napoli (Naples) (★2,875,000)	1,024,601
Nicastro (▲69,660)	53,700
Nocera Inferiore	49,021
Novara	103,349
Padova (★270,000)	218,186
Palermo	697,162
Parma	173,991
Pavia	80,073
Perugia (▲150,576)	109,500
Pesaro (▲90,341)	78,700
Pescara	128,553
Piacenza	102,252
Pisa	101,500
Pistoia (▲87,275)	73,900
Pordenone	50,222
Portici (★Napoli)	67,824
Potenza (▲68,499)	58,800
Pozzuoli (▲75,706) (★Napoli)	67,100
Prato (★215,000)	165,364
Quartu Sant'Elena	60,852
Ragusa	69,423
Ravenna (▲136,724)	87,000
Reggio di Calabria	178,496
Reggio nell'Emilia (▲131,880)	108,800
Rho (★Milano)	51,646
Rimini (▲130,896)	114,800
Rivoli (★Torino)	51,884
ROMA (★3,175,000)	2,693,383
Salerno (★250,000)	153,436
San Benedetto del Tronto	45,220
San Giorgio a Cremano (★Napoli)	62,168
San Remo	59,247
San Severo	55,376
Sassari	120,011
Savona (★112,000)	68,997
Scandicci (★Firenze)	53,264
Sesto Fiorentino (★Firenze)	46,899
Sesto San Giovanni (★Milano)	85,175
Siena	57,745
Siracusa	125,444
Taranto	232,200
Teramo (▲52,490)	36,100
Terni (▲109,809)	93,400
Torino (★1,550,000)	961,916
Torre Annunziata (★Napoli)	50,346
Torre del Greco (★Napoli)	101,456
Trani	49,337
Trapani (▲69,273)	59,700
Trento (▲102,124)	83,100
Treviso	83,886
Trieste (Triest) (Trst)	231,047
Udine (★126,000)	98,322
Varese	85,461
Venezia (Venice) (★420,000)	85,100
Vercelli	50,207
Verona	258,946
Viareggio (▲60,559)	51,500
Vicenza	109,333
Vigevano	61,380
Viterbo (▲60,213)	48,700
Vittoria	56,970

JAMAICA

1990 E	2,392,000
• KINGSTON (★820,000)	661,600
Montego Bay (▲155,700)	80,500
Portmore (★Kingston) (1982C)	73,426
Spanish Town (▲358,600) (★Kingston)	96,100

JAPAN / Nihon

1990 C	123,611,167
Abiko (★Tōkyō)	120,628
Ageo (★Tōkyō)	194,947
Aizu-wakamatsu	119,080
Akashi (★Ōsaka)	270,722
Akigawa (★Tōkyō)	50,387
Akishima (★Tōkyō)	105,372
Akita	302,362
Akō	51,131
Amagasaki (★Ōsaka)	498,999
Anan (▲59,044)	47,000
Anjō	142,251
Aomori	287,808
Arao (★Ōmuta)	59,507
Asahikawa	359,071
Asaka (★Tōkyō)	103,617
Ashikaga	167,686
Ashiya (★Ōsaka)	87,524
Atami	47,291
Atsugi (★Tōkyō)	197,282
Ayase (★Tōkyō)	77,926
Beppu	130,334
Bisai (★Nagoya)	55,880
Chiba (★Tōkyō)	829,455
Chichibu	60,915
Chigasaki (★Tōkyō)	201,675
Chikushino (★Fukuoka)	70,303
Chiryū (★Nagoya)	54,059
Chita (★Nagoya)	75,433
Chitose	78,946
Chōfu (★Tōkyō)	197,677
Chōshi	85,138
Daitō (★Ōsaka)	126,460
Dazaifu (★Fukuoka)	62,402
Ebetsu (★Sapporo)	97,201
Ebina (★Tōkyō)	105,822
Eniwa	55,615
Fuchū (★Tōkyō)	209,396
Fuchū	45,739
Fuchū	50,060
Fuji (★370,000)	222,490
Fujieda (★Shizuoka)	119,815
Fujiidera (★Ōsaka)	65,922
Fujimi (★Tōkyō)	94,864
Fujinomiya (★Fuji)	117,092
Fujioka (▲60,981)	50,100
Fujisawa (★Tōkyō)	350,330
Fuji-yoshida	54,804
Fukaya (▲94,017)	75,600
Fukuchiyama (▲66,506)	56,700
Fukui	252,743
Fukuoka (★1,750,000)	1,237,062
Fukushima	277,528
Fukuyama	365,612
Funabashi (★Tōkyō)	533,270
Furukawa (▲64,230)	51,200
Fussa (★Tōkyō)	58,062
Gamagōri	84,819
Gifu	410,324
Ginowan	75,905
Gotemba	79,557
Gushikawa	54,018
Gyōda	83,181
Habikino (★Ōsaka)	115,049
Hachinohe	241,057
Hachiōji (★Tōkyō)	466,347
Hadano (★Tōkyō)	155,620
Hagi	50,618
Hakodate	307,249
Hamada	49,135
Hamakita	81,157
Hamamatsu	534,620
Hanamaki (▲70,514)	55,000
Handa (★Nagoya)	99,550
Hannō (★Tōkyō)	73,214
Hashima	61,460
Hasuda (★Tōkyō)	59,706
Hatogaya (★Tōkyō)	56,440
Hatsukaichi (★Hiroshima)	63,441
Hekinan	65,899
Higashihiroshima (★Hiroshima)	94,209
Higashikurume (★Tōkyō)	113,818
Higashimatsuyama	84,394
Higashimurayama (★Tōkyō)	134,002
Higashiōsaka (★Ōsaka)	518,319
Higashiyamato (★Tōkyō)	75,132
Hikari (★Tokuyama)	47,611
Hikone	99,519
Himeji (★660,000)	454,360
Himi (▲60,766)	51,400
Hino (★Tōkyō)	165,928
Hirakata (★Ōsaka)	390,788
Hiratsuka (★Tōkyō)	245,950
Hirosaki (★174,704)	133,800

▲ Population of an entire municipality, commune, or district, including rural area.
• Largest city in country.
★ Population or designation of the metropolitan area, including suburbs.
C Census. **E** Official estimate. **U** Unofficial estimate.

▲ Bevölkerung eines ganzen städtischen Verwaltungsgebietes, eines Kommunalbezirkes oder eines Distrikts, einschliesslich ländlicher Gebiete.
• Grösste Stadt des Landes.
★ Bevölkerung oder Bezeichnung der Stadtregion einschliesslich Vororte.
C Volkszählung. **E** Offizielle Schätzung. **U** Inoffizielle Schätzung.

Population of Cities and Towns / Einwohnerzahlen von Grossstädten / Habitantes en las Ciudades y Poblaciones
Population des Grands Centres et des Villes / População dos Centros Urbanos 309

Hiroshima (★1,575,000)	1,085,705
Hita (▲64,695)	57,100
Hitachi	202,141
Hōfu	117,634
Honjō	59,098
Hōya (★Tōkyō)	95,146
Hyūga	58,442
Ibaraki (★Ōsaka)	254,078
Ichihara (★Tōkyō)	257,716
Ichikawa (★Tōkyō)	436,596
Ichinomiya (★Nagoya)	262,434
Ichinoseki (▲61,967)	50,100
Iida (▲91,859)	64,700
Iizuka (★110,000)	83,131
Ikeda (★Ōsaka)	104,218
Ikoma (★Ōsaka)	99,604
Imabari	123,114
Imari (▲60,882)	50,000
Ina (▲60,062)	49,500
Inagi (★Tōkyō)	58,635
Inazawa (★Nagoya)	96,274
Inuyama (★Nagoya)	69,801
Iruma (★Tōkyō)	137,585
Isahaya	90,683
Ise (Uji-yamada)	104,164
Isehara (★Tōkyō)	89,567
Isesaki	115,938
Ishinomaki	121,976
Itami (★Ōsaka)	186,134
Itō	71,223
Iwaki (Taira)	355,812
Iwakuni	109,530
Iwamizawa	80,417
Iwata	83,521
Iwatsuki (★Tōkyō)	106,462
Izumi (★Sendai)	124,216
Izumi (★Ōsaka)	146,127
Izumi-ōtsu (★Ōsaka)	67,035
Izumi-sano (★Ōsaka)	88,866
Izumo (▲82,679)	69,600
Joetsu	130,116
Jōyō (★Ōsaka)	84,770
Kadoma (★Ōsaka)	142,297
Kaga	69,196
Kagoshima	536,752
Kainan (★Wakayama)	48,596
Kaizuka (★Ōsaka)	79,234
Kakamigahara	129,680
Kakegawa (▲72,795)	59,000
Kakogawa (★Ōsaka)	239,803
Kamagaya (★Tōkyō)	95,052
Kamaishi	52,484
Kamakura (★Tōkyō)	174,307
Kameoka	85,283
Kamifukuoka (★Tōkyō)	58,761
Kanazawa	442,868
Kani (★Nagoya)	80,012
Kanoya (▲77,655)	61,500
Kanuma (▲90,043)	74,900
Karatsu (▲79,207)	70,500
Kariya (★Nagoya)	120,126
Kasai	51,784
Kasaoka (▲59,619)	52,700
Kashihara (★Ōsaka)	115,554
Kashiwa (★Tōkyō)	305,058
Kashiwara (★Ōsaka)	76,819
Kashiwazaki (▲88,309)	75,300
Kasuga (★Fukuoka)	88,699
Kasugai (★Nagoya)	266,599
Kasukabe (★Tōkyō)	188,823
Katano (★Ōsaka)	65,308
Katsuta	109,825
Kawachi-nagano (★Ōsaka)	108,767
Kawagoe (★Tōkyō)	304,854
Kawaguchi (★Tōkyō)	438,680
Kawanishi (★Ōsaka)	141,253
Kawasaki (★Tōkyō)	1,173,603
Kesennuma	65,578
Kimitsu (▲89,242)	76,100
Kiryū	126,446
Kisarazu	123,433
Kishiwada (★Ōsaka)	188,563
Kitaibaraki	51,093
Kitakyūshū (★1,525,000)	1,026,455
Kitami	107,247
Kitamoto (★Tōkyō)	63,929
Kiyose (★Tōkyō)	67,539
Kōbe (★Ōsaka)	1,477,410
Kōchi	317,069
Kodaira (★Tōkyō)	164,013
Kōfu	200,626
Koga (★Tōkyō)	58,231
Koganei (★Tōkyō)	105,899
Kokubunji (★Tōkyō)	100,982
Komae (★Tōkyō)	74,189
Komaki (★Nagoya)	124,441
Komatsu	106,075
Kōnan (★Nagoya)	93,837
Kōnosu (★Tōkyō)	72,435
Kōriyama	314,642
Koshigaya (★Tōkyō)	285,259
Kudamatsu (★Tokuyama)	53,030
Kuki (★Tōkyō)	66,852
Kumagaya	152,124
Kumamoto	579,306
Kunitachi (★Tōkyō)	65,833
Kurashiki	414,693
Kure (★Hiroshima)	216,723
Kuroiso (▲52,344)	41,900
Kurume	228,347
Kusatsu (★Ōsaka)	94,767
Kushiro	205,639
Kuwana (★Nagoya)	97,909
Kyōto (★Ōsaka)	1,461,103
Machida (★Tōkyō)	349,050
Maebashi	286,261
Maizuru	96,333
Marugame	75,606
Matsubara (★Ōsaka)	135,919
Matsudo (★Tōkyō)	456,210
Matsue	142,956
Matsumoto	200,715
Matsusaka	118,725
Matsuyama	443,322
Mihara	85,518
Miki (★Ōsaka)	76,501
Minō (★Ōsaka)	122,120
Misato (★Tōkyō)	128,376
Mishima (★Numazu)	105,418
Mitaka (★Tōkyō)	165,564
Mito	234,968
Miura (★Tōkyō)	52,440
Miyako	58,503
Miyakonojō (▲130,153)	106,200
Miyazaki	287,352
Mobara	83,437
Moriguchi (★Ōsaka)	157,372
Morioka	235,434
Moriyama	58,561
Mukō (★Ōsaka)	52,928
Munakata	68,265
Muroran (★195,000)	117,855
Musashimurayama (★Tōkyō)	65,562
Musashino (★Tōkyō)	139,077
Mutsu	48,470
Nabari	68,933
Nagahama	55,485
Nagano	347,026
Nagaoka	185,938
Nagaokakyō (★Ōsaka)	77,191
Nagareyama (★Tōkyō)	140,059
Nagasaki	444,599
Nagoya (★4,800,000)	2,154,793
Naha	304,836
Nakama (★Kitakyūshū)	49,216
Nakatsu	66,388
Nakatsugawa	53,722
Nanao	50,103
Nara (★Ōsaka)	349,349
Narashino (★Tōkyō)	151,471
Narita	86,708
Naruto	64,575
Naze	46,306
Neyagawa (★Ōsaka)	256,524
Niigata	486,097
Niihama	129,149
Niitsu (▲63,999)	55,700
Niiza (★Tōkyō)	138,919
Nishinomiya (★Ōsaka)	426,909
Nishio	95,197
Nobeoka	130,624
Noboribetsu (★Muroran)	55,571
Noda (★Tōkyō)	114,475
Nōgata	62,530
Noshiro (▲55,915)	47,800
Numazu (★495,000)	211,732
Obihiro	167,384
Ōbu (★Nagoya)	69,720
Ōdate (▲68,195)	58,500
Odawara	193,417
Ōgaki	148,281
Ōita	408,501
Ōkawa	45,704
Okaya	59,849
Okayama	593,730
Okazaki	306,822
Okegawa (★Tōkyō)	69,029
Okinawa	105,845
Okinawa	105,852
Ōme (★Tōkyō)	125,960
Ōmi-hachiman (★Ōsaka)	66,066
Ōmiya (★Tōkyō)	403,776
Ōmura	73,435
Ōmuta (★225,000)	150,453
Ōnojō (★Fukuoka)	75,214
Onomichi	97,103
Ōsaka (★16,900,000)	2,623,801
Ōta	139,801
Otaru (★Sapporo)	163,211
Ōtsu (★Ōsaka)	260,018
Owariashi (★Nagoya)	65,675
Oyama (▲142,262)	120,000
Sabae	62,283
Saga	169,963
Sagamihara (★Tōkyō)	531,542
Saijō	56,821
Saiki	52,323
Sakado (★Tōkyō)	95,740
Sakai (★Ōsaka)	807,765
Sakaide	63,876
Sakata	100,811
Saku (▲62,003)	50,000
Sakura (★Tōkyō)	144,688
Sakurai	60,262
Sanda (▲64,560) (★Ōsaka)	54,500
Sanjō	85,823
Sano	83,484
Sapporo (★1,900,000)	1,671,742
Sasebo	244,677
Satte	54,342
Sayama (★Tōkyō)	157,309
Sayama (★Ōsaka)	54,319
Seki	68,386
Sendai, Kagoshima pref. (▲71,735)	58,000
Sendai, Miyagi pref. (★1,175,000)	918,398
Sennan (★Ōsaka)	60,065
Seto	126,340
Settsu (★Ōsaka)	87,453
Shibata (▲78,170)	63,600
Shijōnawate (★Ōsaka)	50,035
Shiki (★Tōkyō)	63,491
Shimada (▲73,810)	64,500
Shimizu (★Shizuoka)	241,523
Shimodate (▲66,028)	54,100
Shimonoseki (★Kitakyūshū)	262,635
Shiogama (★Sendai)	62,025
Shizuoka (★975,000)	472,196
Sōka (★Tōkyō)	206,132
Suita (★Ōsaka)	345,206
Suwa	52,464
Suzuka	174,105
Tachikawa (★Tōkyō)	152,824
Tagajō (★Sendai)	58,456
Tagawa	57,700
Tajimi (★Nagoya)	94,036
Takaishi (★Ōsaka)	65,086
Takamatsu	329,684
Takaoka (★220,000)	175,466
Takarazuka (★Ōsaka)	201,862
Takasago (★Ōsaka)	93,273
Takasaki	236,461
Takatsuki (★Ōsaka)	359,867
Takayama	65,243
Takefu	70,187
Takikawa	49,591
Tama (★Tōkyō)	144,489
Tamano	73,238
Tanabe (▲69,859)	59,100
Tanashi (★Tōkyō)	75,144
Tatebayashi	76,221
Tenri	68,815
Tochigi	86,216
Toda (★Tōkyō)	87,599
Tōkai (★Nagoya)	97,358
Toki	64,946
Tokoname (★Nagoya)	51,784
Tokorozawa (★Tōkyō)	303,040
Tokushima	263,356
Tokuyama (★250,000)	110,900
• TŌKYŌ (★30,300,000)	8,163,573
Tomakomai	160,118
Tondabayashi (★Ōsaka)	110,447
Toride (★Tōkyō)	81,665
Tosu	55,877
Tottori	142,467
Toyama	321,254
Toyoake (★Nagoya)	62,160
Toyohashi	337,982
Toyokawa	111,730
Toyonaka (★Ōsaka)	409,837
Toyota	332,336
Tsu	157,177
Tsuchiura	127,471
Tsuruga	68,041
Tsuruoka	99,889
Tsushima (★Nagoya)	59,343
Tsuyama	89,400
Ube (★230,000)	175,053
Ueda	119,435
Ueno (▲60,242)	51,400
Uji (★Ōsaka)	177,010
Uozu	49,514
Urasoe	89,994
Urawa (★Tōkyō)	418,271
Urayasu (★Tōkyō)	115,675
Usa (▲50,829)	38,600
Ushiku	60,693
Utsunomiya	426,795
Uwajima	68,034
Wakayama (★495,000)	396,553
Wakkanai	48,232
Wakō (★Tōkyō)	56,890
Warabi (★Tōkyō)	73,620
Yachiyo (★Tōkyō)	148,615
Yaizu (★Shizuoka)	112,186
Yamagata	249,487
Yamaguchi	129,461
Yamato (★Tōkyō)	194,866
Yamato-kōriyama (★Ōsaka)	92,949
Yamato-takada (★Ōsaka)	68,237
Yao (★Ōsaka)	277,568
Yashio (★Tōkyō)	72,473
Yatsushiro (▲108,135)	88,300
Yawata (★Ōsaka)	75,758
Yokkaichi	274,180
Yokohama (★Tōkyō)	3,220,331
Yokosuka (★Tōkyō)	433,358
Yonago	131,453
Yonezawa	94,760
Yono (★Tōkyō)	79,060
Yotsukaidō (★Tōkyō)	72,157
Yukuhashi	65,711
Zama (★Tōkyō)	112,102
Zushi (★Tōkyō)	56,704

JERSEY

1991 C	84,082
• SAINT HELIER (★46,500)	28,123

JORDAN / Al-Urdun

1989 E	3,111,000
Al-Baq'ah (★'Ammān)	63,985
• 'AMMĀN (★1,625,000)	936,300
Ar-Ruṣayfah (★'Ammān)	72,580
As-Salṭ	47,585
Az-Zarqā' (★'Ammān)	318,055
Irbid	167,785

KAZAKHSTAN

1991 E	16,793,100
Aktau	169,000
Akt'ubinsk	265,300
• ALMA-ATA (ALMATY) (★1,190,000)	1,156,200
Arkalyk	64,900
Aterau	152,500
Balchaš	87,600
Čelinograd	286,000
Čimkent	407,900
Džambul	312,300
Džetygara	48,900
Džezkazgan	111,100
Ekibastuz	138,900
Karaganda	608,600
Kentau	65,100
Kokčetav	143,300
Kustanaj	233,900
Kzyl-Orda	158,200
Leninogorsk	69,500
Leninsk	73,000
Pavlodar	342,500
Petropavlovsk	247,400
Rudnyj	128,800
Šachtinsk	65,300
Saptajev	61,400
Šaran'	62,600
Ščučinsk	56,000
Semipalatinsk	344,700
Taldy-Kurgan	124,500
Turkestan	81,200
Ural'sk	214,000
Ust'-Kamenogorsk	332,900
Žanatas	53,000
Zyr'anovsk	53,800

KENYA

1990 E	24,870,000
Eldoret (1979C)	50,503
Kisumu (1984E)	167,100
Machakos (1983E)	92,300
Meru (1979C)	72,049
Mombasa	537,000
• NAIROBI	1,505,000
Nakuru (1984E)	101,700

KIRIBATI

1990 C	72,298
BAIRIKI	2,226
• Bikenibeu	5,055

KOREA, NORTH / Chosŏn-minjujuŭi-inmīn-konghwaguk

1981 E	18,317,000
Ch'ŏngjin	490,000
Haeju (1983E)	213,000
Hamhŭng (1970E)	150,000
Hŭngnam (1976E)	260,000
Kaesŏng	259,000
Kanggye (1967E)	130,000
Kimch'aek (Sŏngjin) (1967E)	265,000
Namp'o	241,000
• P'YŎNGYANG	2,355,000
Sinŭiju	305,000
Songnim (1944C)	53,035
Wŏnsan	398,000

KOREA, SOUTH / Taehan-min'guk

1990 C	43,520,199
Andong	116,932
Ansan (★Sŏul)	252,157
Anyang (★Sŏul)	480,668
Bucheon (★Sŏul)	667,777
Changsŭngp'o	48,614
Changwŏn (★Masan)	323,138
Chech'ŏn	102,037
Cheju	232,687
Chinhae	120,207
Chinju	258,365
Chŏmch'ŏn	47,802
Ch'ŏnan	211,382
Ch'ŏngju	497,429
Chŏnju	86,850
Chŏnju, Chŏlla Pukdo prov.	517,104
Ch'unch'ŏn	174,153
Ch'ungju	129,994
Ch'ungmu	92,159
Hanam (★Sŏul)	101,278
Inch'ŏn (★Sŏul)	1,818,293
Iri	203,401
Kangnŭng	152,605
Kimch'ŏn	81,349
Kimhae	106,166
Kimje	55,136
Kongju	65,195
Kumi	206,101
Kŭmsŏng (1985C)	58,897
Kunp'o (★Sŏul)	99,956
Kunsan	218,216
Kwachŏn (★Sŏul)	72,328
Kwangju	1,144,695
Kwangmyŏng (★Sŏul)	328,803
Kyŏngju	141,895
Kyŏngsan	60,524
Masan (★625,000)	496,639
Mikŭm (★Sŏul)	74,688
Miryang	52,995
Mokp'o	253,423
Naju	55,306
Namwŏn	63,121
Ŏnyang	66,379
Osan	59,492
P'ohang	318,595
Pusan (★3,800,000)	3,797,566
P'yŏngt'aek	79,238
Samch'ŏnp'o	62,824
Sangju	51,875
Sihŭng (★Sŏul)	107,190
Sŏgwipo	88,292
Sŏkch'o	73,796
Sŏngnam (★Sŏul)	540,764
Songtan	77,460
Sŏsan	55,930
• SŎUL (★15,850,000)	10,627,790
Sunch'ŏn	167,209
Suwŏn (★Sŏul)	644,968
T'aebaek	89,770
Taech'ŏn	56,922
Taegu	2,228,834
Taejŏn	1,062,084
Tongduchŏn	71,448
Tonghae	89,162
Tongkwang	70,118
Ŭijŏngbu (★Sŏul)	212,368
Ŭiwang	96,892
Ulsan	682,978
Wŏnju	173,013
Yŏch'ŏn	63,802
Yŏngch'ŏn	48,890
Yŏngju	84,335
Yŏsu	173,164

KUWAIT / Al-Kuwayt

1985 C	1,697,301
Abraq Khīṭān (★Al-Kuwayt)	45,120
Al-Aḥmadī (★285,000)	26,899
Al-Farwānīyah (★Al-Kuwayt)	68,701
Al-Fuḥayḥīl (★Al-Aḥmadī)	50,081
Al-Jahrah (★Al-Kuwayt)	111,222
• AL-KUWAYT (★1,375,000)	44,335
As-Sālimīyah (★Al-Kuwayt)	153,359
Aṣ-Ṣulaybīyah (★Al-Kuwayt)	51,314
Ḥawallī (★Al-Kuwayt)	145,126
Qalīb ash-Shuyūkh (★Al-Kuwayt)	114,771
South Khīṭān (★Al-Kuwayt)	69,256
Subahiya (★Al-Aḥmadī)	60,787

KYRGYZSTAN

1991 E	4,422,200
• BIŠKEK	631,300
Džalal-Abad	74,200
Kara-Balta	55,000
Karakol (Prževal'sk)	64,300
Oš	218,700
Tokmak	71,200

LAOS / Lao

1985 C	3,584,803
Savannakhét (1975E)	53,000
• VIANGCHAN (VIENTIANE)	377,409

LATVIA / Latvija

1991 E	2,680,500
Daugavpils	129,000
Jelgava	74,500
Jūrmala (★Rīga)	66,500
Liepāja	114,900
• RĪGA (★1,005,000)	910,200
Ventspils	50,400

LEBANON / Lubnān

1982 E	2,637,000
• BAYRŪT (★1,675,000)	509,000
Saydā	105,000
Ṣūr (Tyre) (1970E)	12,500
Tarābulus (Tripoli) (★950,000)	198,000

LESOTHO

1986 C	1,577,536
• MASERU	109,382

LIBERIA

1986 E	2,221,000
• MONROVIA	465,000

LIBYA / Lībiyā

1988 E	3,772,500
Al-Bayḍā (Beida) (1984C)	67,120
Banghāzī	446,250
Darnah (1984C)	62,179
Misrātah	121,669
• ṬARĀBULUS (TRIPOLI)	591,062
Ṭubruq (Tobruk) (1984C)	75,282

▲ Población de un municipio, comuna o distrito entero, incluyendo sus áreas rurales.
• Ciudad más grande de un país.
★ Población o designación de un área metropolitana, incluyendo los suburbios.
C Censo. E Estimado oficial. U Estimado no oficial.

▲ Population d'une municipalité, d'une commune ou d'un district, zone rurale incluse.
• Ville la plus peuplée du pays.
★ Population de l'agglomération (ou nom de la zone métropolitaine englobante).
C Recensement. E Estimation officielle. U Estimation non officielle.

▲ População de um município, comuna ou distrito, inclusive as respectivas áreas rurais.
• Maior cidade de um país.
★ População ou indicação de uma área metropolitana.
C Censo. E Estimativa oficial. U Estimativa não oficial.

LIECHTENSTEIN

1992 E	29,386
• VADUZ	4,887

LITHUANIA / Lietuva

1992 E	3,746,400
Alytus	77,500
Kaunas	433,600
Klaipėda (Memel)	208,300
Marijampole	52,300
Panevėžys	132,300
Šiauliai	149,000
VILNIUS	596,900

LUXEMBOURG

1991 C	384,062
Esch-sur-Alzette (★83,000)	24,012
• LUXEMBOURG (★136,000)	75,377

MACAU

1989 E	452,300
• MACAU	452,300

MACEDONIA / Makedonija

1987 E	2,064,581
Bitola (▲143,090)	76,200
• SKOPJE (▲547,214)	444,900

MADAGASCAR / Madagasikara

1988 E	11,238,000
• ANTANANARIVO	1,250,000
Antsirabe (▲100,000)	52,700
Antsiranana	220,000
Fianarantsoa	300,000
Mahajanga	200,000
Toamasina	230,000
Toliara	150,000

MALAWI / Malaŵi

1987 C	7,988,507
• Blantyre	333,120
LILONGWE	223,318
Mzuzu	51,904

MALAYSIA

1980 C	13,136,109
Alor Setar	69,435
Batu Pahat	64,727
Butterworth (★George Town)	77,982
George Town (Pinang) (★495,000)	248,241
Ipoh	293,849
Johor Baharu (★Singapore, Singapore)	246,395
Kelang	192,080
Keluang	50,315
Kota Baharu	167,872
Kota Kinabalu (Jesselton)	55,997
• KUALA LUMPUR (★1,475,000)	919,610
Kuala Terengganu	180,296
Kuantan	131,547
Kuching	72,555
Melaka	87,494
Miri	52,125
Muar (Bandar Maharani)	65,151
Petaling Jaya (★Kuala Lumpur)	207,805
Sandakan	70,420
Seremban	132,911
Sibu	85,231
Taiping	146,000
Telok Anson	49,148

MALDIVES

1990 C	213,215
• MALE'	55,130

MALI

1987 C	7,696,348
• BAMAKO	658,275
Gao	55,266
Kayes	50,993
Koutiala	48,698
Mopti	74,771
Ségou	88,135
Sikasso	73,859
Tombouctou (Timbuktu)	31,962

MALTA

1991 E	355,910
• VALLETTA (★215,000)	9,199

MARSHALL ISLANDS

1980 C	30,873
• Jarej-Uliga-Delap	8,583

MARTINIQUE

1982 C	328,566
• FORT-DE-FRANCE (★116,017)	99,844

MAURITANIA / Mauritanie / Mūrītāniyā

1987 E	2,007,000
• NOUAKCHOTT	285,000

MAURITIUS

1989 E	1,081,669
Beau Bassin-Rose Hill (★Port Louis)	94,236
Curepipe (★Port Louis)	66,704
• PORT LOUIS (★420,000)	141,870
Quatre Bornes (★Port Louis)	65,759
Vacoas-Phoenix (★Port Louis)	56,335

MAYOTTE

1985 E	67,205
• DZAOUDZI (★6,979)	5,865

MEXICO / México

1990 C	81,249,645
Acámbaro	52,248
Acapulco [de Juárez]	515,374
Aguascalientes	440,425
Apatzingán de la Constitución	76,643
Apodaca	103,364
Atlixco	74,233
Buenavista	114,653
Campeche	150,518
Cancún	167,730
Cárdenas	61,017
Celaya	214,856
Chalco (★Ciudad de México)	224,190
Chetumal	94,158
Chicoloapan de Juárz	57,306
Chihuahua	516,153
Chilpancingo de los Bravo	97,165
Chimalhuacán	235,587
Cholula [de Rivadabia] (★Puebla)	53,673
Ciudad Acuña	52,983
Ciudad del Carmen	83,806
• CIUDAD DE MÉXICO (★14,100,000)	8,235,744
Ciudad Guzmán	72,619
Ciudad Hidalgo	48,476
Ciudad Juárez (★El Paso, Tex., U.S.A.)	789,522
Ciudad Lerdo (★Torreón)	46,593
Ciudad López Mateos	315,059
Ciudad Madero (★Tampico)	160,331
Ciudad Mante	76,799
Ciudad Obregón	219,980
Ciudad Valles	91,402
Ciudad Victoria	194,996
Coacalco	151,255
Coatzacoalcos	198,817
Colima	106,967
Comitan de Dominguez	48,299
Córdoba	130,695
Cortazar	45,579
Cuauhtémoc	6,938
Cuautitlán Izcalli (★Ciudad de México)	313,238
Cuernavaca	279,187
Culiacán	415,046
Delicias	87,412
Durango	348,036
Ecatepec (★Ciudad de México)	1,218,135
Ensenada	169,426
Fresnillo	75,118
Garza García (★Monterrey)	113,017
General Escobedo	96,962
Gómez Palacio (★Torreón)	164,092
Guadalajara (★2,430,000)	1,650,042
Guadalupe	46,433
Guadalupe (★Monterrey)	535,332
Guamúchil	49,635
Guanajuato	73,108
Guasave	49,338
Guaymas	87,484
Hermosillo	406,417
Heroica Zitácuaro	66,983
Hidalgo del Parral	88,197
Iguala	83,412
Irapuato	265,042
Ixtapaluca	115,711
Jiutepec	82,845
Juchitán de Zaragoza	53,666
Lagos de Moreno	63,646
La Paz	137,641
La Piedad de Cabadas	62,625
Las Choapas	43,868
León	758,279
Los Mochis	162,659
Los Reyes la Paz	134,544
Manzanillo	67,697
Matamoros (★Brownsville, Tex., U.S.A.)	266,055
Matehuala	54,713
Mazatlán	262,705
Mérida	523,422
Metepec	116,203
Mexicali (★460,000)	438,377
Minatitlán	142,060
Monclova	177,792
Monterrey (★2,015,000)	1,068,996
Morelia	428,486
Naucalpan de Juárez (★Ciudad de México)	845,960
Navojoa	82,618
Nezahualcóyotl (★Ciudad de México)	1,255,456
Nogales	105,873
Nuevo Laredo (★Laredo, Tex., U.S.A.)	218,413
Oaxaca [de Juárez]	212,818
Ocotlán	62,595
Orizaba (★215,000)	114,216
Pachuca	174,013
Papantla [de Olarte]	46,075
Piedras Negras	96,178
Poza Rica	151,739
Puebla (★1,200,000)	1,007,170
Puerto Vallarta	93,503
Querétaro	385,503
Reynosa	265,663
Río Bravo	67,092
Sahuayo de José María Morelos	50,463
Salamanca	123,190
Salina Cruz	61,656
Saltillo	420,947
San Andrés Tuxtla	49,658
San Cristóbal de las Casas	73,388
San Francisco del Rincón	52,291
San Juan del Río	61,652
San Luis Potosí (★600,000)	489,238
San Luis Río Colorado	95,461
San Martín Texmelucan	57,519
San Miguel de Allende	48,935
San Nicolás de los Garza (★Monterrey)	436,603
San Pablo de las Salinas	84,217
Santa Catarina (★Monterrey)	162,707
Silao	50,828
Soledad de Graciano Sanchez	123,943
Tampico (★440,000)	272,690
Tapachula	138,858
Tecomán	60,938
Tehuacán	139,450
Temixco	65,058
Tepatitlán de Morelos	54,036
Tepic	206,967
Texcoco [de Mora] (★Ciudad de México)	74,194
Tijuana (★San Diego, Calif., U.S.A.)	698,752
Tlalnepantla (★Ciudad de México)	702,270
Tlaquepaque (★Guadalajara)	328,031
Tlaxcala [de Xicoténcatl]	50,486
Toluca [de Lerdo]	327,865
Tonalá	151,190
Torreón (★690,000)	439,436
Tulancingo	75,477
Tuxpan	69,224
Tuxtepec	62,788
Tuxtla Gutiérrez	289,626
Uruapan del Progreso	187,623
Valle de Santiago	56,009
Veracruz [Llave] (★540,000)	438,821
Villa Frontera	58,216
Villahermosa	261,231
Villa Nicolás Romero	148,342
Xalapa	279,451
Zacatecas	100,051
Zamora de Hidalgo	109,751
Zapopan (★Guadalajara)	668,323

MICRONESIA, FEDERATED STATES OF

1985 E	94,534
• KOLONIA	6,306

MOLDOVA

1991 E	4,366,300
Bel'c'	161,800
Bendery	133,000
• KIŠIN'OV	676,700
Rybnica	62,900
Tiraspol'	186,000

MONACO

1990 C	29,972
• MONACO (★87,000)	29,972

MONGOLIA / Mongol Ard Uls

1989 E	2,040,000
Darchan (1985E)	69,800
• ULAANBAATAR	548,400

MONTSERRAT

1980 C	11,606
• PLYMOUTH	1,568

MOROCCO / Al-Magreb

1982 C	20,419,555
Agadir	110,479
Beni-Mellal	95,003
Berkane	60,490
• Casablanca (Dar-el-Beida) (★2,475,000)	2,139,204
El-Jadida (Mazagan)	81,455
Fès (★535,000)	448,823
Kenitra	188,194
Khemisset	58,925
Khouribga	127,181
Ksar-el-Kebir	73,541
Larache	63,893
Marrakech (★535,000)	439,728
Meknès (★375,000)	319,783
Mohammedia (Fedala) (★Casablanca)	105,120
Nador	62,040
Oued-Zem	58,744
Oujda	260,082
RABAT (★980,000)	518,616
Safi	197,309
Salé (★Rabat)	289,391
Settat	65,203
Sidi Kacem	55,833
Sidi Slimane	50,457
Tanger (Tangier) (★370,000)	266,346
Tan-Tan	41,451
Taza	77,216
Temera (★Rabat)	48,644
Tétouan	199,615

MOZAMBIQUE / Moçambique

1989 E	15,326,476
Beira	291,604
Chimoio (1986E)	86,928
Inhambane (1986E)	64,274
• MAPUTO	1,069,727
Nacala	101,615
Nampula	197,379
Pemba (1986E)	50,215
Quelimane	78,520
Tete (1986E)	56,178
Xai-Xai (1986E)	51,620

MYANMAR (BURMA)

1983 C	34,124,908
Bago (Pegu)	150,528
Chauk	51,437
Dawei (Tavoy)	69,882
Henzada	82,005
Kale	52,628
Lashio	88,590
Magway	54,881
Mandalay	532,949
Mawlamyine (Moulmein)	219,961
Maymyo	63,782
Meiktila	96,496
Mergui (Myeik)	88,600
Mogok	49,392
Monywa	106,843
Myingyan	77,060
Myitkyinā	56,427
Nyaunglebin	55,194
Pakokku	71,860
Pathein (Bassein)	144,096
Prome (Pyè)	83,332
Pyinmana	52,962
Sagaing	46,212
Shwebo	52,185
Sittwe (Akyab)	107,621
Taunggyi	108,231
Thaton	61,790
Toungoo	65,861
• YANGON (RANGOON) (★2,800,000)	2,705,039
Yenangyaung	62,582

NAMIBIA

1988 E	1,760,000
• WINDHOEK	114,500

NAURU / Naoero

1987 E	8,000

NEPAL / Nepāl

1981 C	15,022,839
Bhaktapur	48,472
• KĀTHMĀNḌAU (★320,000)	235,160
Wirāṭnagar	93,544

NETHERLANDS / Nederland

1992 E	15,129,150
Alkmaar (★124,000)	91,817
Almelo	63,383
Alphen aan den Rijn	63,573
Amersfoort	104,390
Amstelveen (★Amsterdam)	71,939
• AMSTERDAM (★1,875,000)	713,407
Apeldoorn	148,745
Arnhem (★305,000)	132,928
Assen	50,880
Bergen op Zoom	47,259
Breda (★165,000)	126,709
Delft (★'s-Gravenhage)	90,066
Den Helder	61,225
Deventer	68,004
Dordrecht (★209,000)	111,791
Ede (▲96,044)	50,700
Eindhoven (★384,000)	193,966
Emmen (▲93,107)	37,000
Enschede (★252,000)	147,199
Geleen (★179,000)	33,922
Gouda	67,416
Groningen (★208,000)	169,387
Haarlem (★Amsterdam)	149,788
Haarlemmermeer (▲100,659) (★Amsterdam)	14,000
Heerlen (★267,500)	53,600
Helmond	70,574
Hengelo (★Enschede)	76,726
Hilversum (★Amsterdam)	84,674
Hoorn	59,028
IJmuiden (★Amsterdam)	61,506
Kerkrade (★Heerlen)	53,364
Leeuwarden	86,405
Leiden (★190,000)	112,976
Maastricht (★163,000)	118,152
Nieuwegein (★Utrecht)	58,882
Nijmegen (★242,000)	146,344
Oss	52,132
Purmerend (★Amsterdam)	62,504
Ridderkerk (★Rotterdam)	45,834
Rijswijk (★'s-Gravenhage)	47,456
Roosendaal	61,354
Rotterdam (★1,120,000)	589,707
Schiedam (★Rotterdam)	71,117
'S-GRAVENHAGE (THE HAGUE) (★773,000)	445,287
's-Hertogenbosch (★200,000)	93,171
Soest (★Amersfoort)	41,693
Spijkenisse (★Rotterdam)	69,655
Tilburg (★235,000)	160,618
Utrecht (★528,000)	232,705
Veenendaal	50,791
Venlo (★88,000)	64,890
Vlaardingen (★Rotterdam)	73,893
Vlissingen (Flushing) (▲43,913)	25,000
Zaanstad (★Amsterdam)	131,273
Zeist (★Utrecht)	59,211
Zoetermeer (★'s-Gravenhage)	100,623
Zwolle	97,131

NETHERLANDS ANTILLES / Nederlandse Antillen

1990 E	189,687
• WILLEMSTAD (★130,000) (1981C)	31,883

NEW CALEDONIA / Nouvelle-Calédonie

1989 C	164,173
• NOUMÉA (★97,581)	65,110

NEW ZEALAND

1991 C	3,434,950
• Auckland (★855,571)	315,668
Christchurch (★307,179)	292,858
Dunedin	116,577
Hamilton (★148,625)	101,448
Invercargill	56,148
Lower Hutt (★Wellington)	94,540
Manukau (★Auckland)	226,147
Napier (★110,216)	51,645
Palmerston North (★70,951)	70,318
Rotorua (★53,702)	45,144
Takapuna (★Auckland)	74,360
Tauranga (★70,803)	46,308
Waitemata (★Auckland)	136,716
WELLINGTON (★375,000)	150,301
Whangarei (★44,183)	40,101

NICARAGUA

1985 E	3,272,100
Chinandega	75,000
Granada (1981E)	64,642
León	101,000
• MANAGUA	682,000
Masaya	75,000
Matagalpa	68,000

NIGER

1988 C	7,250,383
Agadez	50,164
Maradi	112,965
• NIAMEY	398,265
Tahoua	51,607
Zinder	120,892

NIGERIA

1987 E	101,907,000
Aba	239,800
Abakaliki	56,800
Abeokuta	341,300
ABUJA (1993U)	250,000
Ado-Ekiti	287,000
Afikpo	65,790
Agege	83,810
Akure	129,600
Amaigbo	53,690
Apomu	49,570
Aramoko	48,280
Asaba	47,410
Awka	88,800
Azare	50,020
Bauchi	68,840
Benin City	183,200
Bida	100,200
Calabar	139,800
Deba	110,600
Duku	52,880
Ede	245,200
Effon-Alaiye	122,300
Ejigbo	84,570
Emure-Ekiti	58,750
Enugu	252,500
Epe	80,560
Erin-Oshogbo	59,940
Eruwa	49,140
Fiditi	49,440
Gboko	49,390
Gbongan	53,990
Gombe	86,120
Gusau	126,200
Ibadan	1,144,000
Idah	50,550
Idanre	56,080

▲ Population of an entire municipality, commune, or district, including rural area.
• Largest city in country.
★ Population or designation of the metropolitan area, including suburbs.
C Census. **E** Official estimate. **U** Unofficial estimate.

▲ Bevölkerung eines ganzen städtischen Verwaltungsgebietes, eines Kommunalbezirkes oder eines Distrikts, einschliesslich ländlicher Gebiete.
• Grösste Stadt des Landes.
★ Bevölkerung oder Bezeichnung der Stadtregion einschliesslich Vororte.
C Volkszählung. **E** Offizielle Schätzung. **U** Inoffizielle Schätzung.

Ife	237,000
Ifon-Oshogbo	65,980
Igbasa-Odo	48,040
Igboho	85,230
Igbo-Ora	68,060
Igede-Ekiti	56,570
Ihiala	73,240
Ijebu-Igbo	78,680
Ijebu-Ode	124,900
Ijero-Ekiti	76,420
Ikare	112,500
Ikerre	195,400
Ikire	94,450
Ikirun	144,900
Ikole	71,860
Ikorodu	147,700
Ikot Ekpene	69,440
Ila	210,800
Ilawe-Ekiti	147,300
Ilesha	302,100
Ilobu	159,000
Ilorin	380,000
Inisa	95,630
Ipoti-Ekiti	53,220
Ise-Ekiti	82,580
Iseyin	173,500
Iwo	289,100
Jega (1985E)	47,000
Jimeta	66,130
Jos	164,700
Kaduna	273,200
Kano	538,300
Katsina	165,000
Kaura Namoda	52,910
Keffi	57,790
Kishi	77,210
Kumo	118,200
Lafia	97,810
Lafiagi	57,580
• LAGOS (★3,800,000)	1,213,000
Lalupon	56,130
Lere	49,670
Maiduguri	255,100
Makurdi	98,350
Minna	109,300
Mubi	51,190
Mushin (★Lagos)	266,100
Nguru	78,770
Nsukka	47,760
Ode-Ekiti	48,910
Offa	157,500
Ogbomosho	582,900
Oka	114,400
Oke-Mesi	55,040
Okwe	52,550
Olupona	65,720
Ondo	135,300
Onitsha	298,200
Opobo	64,620
Oron	62,260
Oshogbo	380,800
Owerri (1985E)	37,000
Owo	146,600
Oyan	50,930
Oyo	204,700
Pindiga	64,130
Port Harcourt	327,300
Potiskum	56,490
Sapele	111,200
Shagamu	93,610
Shaki	139,000
Shomolu (★Lagos)	120,700
Sokoto	163,700
Ugep	81,910
Umuahia	52,550
Uyo	60,500
Warri	100,700
Zaria	302,800

NIUE

1989 C	2,267
• ALOFI	706

NORTHERN MARIANA ISLANDS

1980 C	16,780
• Chalan Kanoa	2,678
Garapan	2,063

NORWAY / Norge

1987 E	4,190,000
Bærum (★Oslo) (1985E)	83,000
Bergen (★239,000)	209,320
Drammen (★73,000) (1985E)	50,700
Fredrikstad (★52,000) (1983E)	27,618
Hammerfest (1983E)	7,208
Kristiansand (1985E)	62,200
Narvik (1983E)	19,080
• OSLO (★720,000)	452,415
Skien (★77,981) (1985E)	46,700
Stavanger (★132,000) (1985E)	94,200
Tromsø (1985E)	47,800
Trondheim	135,010

OMAN / 'Umān

1983 E	1,131,000
• MASQAT (MUSCAT)	30,000
Maṭraḥ (1971E)	14,000
Şūr	30,000

PAKISTAN / Pākistān

1981 C	84,253,644
Abbottābād (★65,996)	32,188
Ahmadpur East	56,979
Attock (★39,986)	26,233
Bahāwalnagar	74,533
Bahāwalpur (★180,263)	152,009
Bannu (★43,210)	35,170
Bhakkar	41,934
Chārsadda	62,530
Chīchāwatni	50,241
Chiniot	105,559
Chishtiān Mandi	61,959
Daska	55,555
Dera Ghāzi Khān	102,007
Dera Ismāīl Khān (★68,145)	64,358
Drigh Road Cantonment (★Karāchi)	56,742
Faisalabad (Lyallpur)	1,104,209
Gojra	68,000
Gujrānwāla (★658,753)	600,993
Gujrānwāla Cantonment (★Gujrānwāla)	57,760
Gujrāt	155,058
Hāfizābād	83,464
Hyderābād (★800,000)	702,539
Hyderābād Cantonment (★Hyderābād)	48,990
ISLĀMĀBĀD (★Rāwalpind)	204,364
Jacobābād	79,365
Jarānwāla	69,459
Jhang Sadar	195,558
Jhelum (★106,462)	92,646
Kamālia	61,107
Kāmoke	71,097
• Karāchi (★5,300,000)	4,901,627
Karāchi Cantonment (★Karāchi)	181,981
Kasūr	155,523
Khairpur	61,447
Khānewāl	89,090
Khānpur	70,589
Khāriān Cantonment (★51,506)	16,042
Khushāb	56,274
Kohāt (★77,604)	55,832
Lahore (★3,025,000)	2,707,215
Lahore Cantonment (★Lahore)	245,474
Lārkāna	123,890
Leiah	51,482
Malir Cantonment (★Karāchi)	47,588
Mandi Būrewāla	86,311
Mardān (★147,977)	141,842
Miānwāli	59,159
Mingāora	88,078
Mīrpur Khās	124,371
Multān (★732,070)	696,316
Muzaffargarh	53,000
Nawābshāh	102,139
Nowshera (★74,913)	38,875
Okāra (★153,483)	127,455
Pākpattan	69,820
Peshāwar (★566,248)	506,896
Peshāwar Cantonment (★Peshāwar)	59,352
Quetta (★285,719)	244,842
Rahīmyār Khān (★132,635)	119,036
Rāwalpindi (★1,040,000)	457,091
Rāwalpindi Cantonment (★Rāwalpindi)	337,752
Sādiqābād	63,935
Sāhīwal	150,954
Sargodha (★291,362)	231,895
Sargodha Cantonment (★Sargodha)	59,467
Shekhūpura	141,168
Shikārpur	88,138
Shorkot (★50,568)	18,533
Siālkot (★302,009)	258,147
Sukkur	190,551
Tando Ādam	62,744
Turbat	52,337
Vihāri	53,799
Wāh Cantonment	122,335
Wazīrābād	62,725

PALAU / Belau

1986 C	13,873
• KOROR	8,629

PANAMA / Panamá

1990 C	2,315,047
Balboa (★Panamá)	1,214
Colón (★96,000)	54,469
David	65,635
• PANAMÁ (★770,000)	411,549
San Miguelito (★Panamá)	242,529

PAPUA NEW GUINEA

1990 C	3,534,038
Lae	78,265
• PORT MORESBY	193,242
Rabaul	16,883

PARAGUAY

1992 C	4,123,550
• ASUNCIÓN (★700,000)	502,426
Caaguazú	38,200
Capiatá	83,189
Ciudad del Este	133,896
Encarnación	55,359
Fernando de la Mora (★Asunción)	95,287
Lambaré (★Asunción)	99,681
Pedro Juan Caballero	53,601
San Lorenzo (★Asunción)	133,311

PERU / Perú

1981 C	17,031,221
Arequipa (★446,942)	108,023
Ayacucho (★69,533)	57,432
Barranco (★Lima)	46,478
Breña (★Lima)	112,398
Cajamarca	62,259
Callao (★Lima)	264,133
Cerro de Pasco (★66,373)	55,597
Chiclayo (★279,527)	213,095
Chimbote	223,341
Chorrillos (★Lima)	141,881
Chosica	65,139
Cuzco (★184,550)	89,563
Huacho	43,398
Huancayo (★164,954)	84,845
Huánuco	61,812
Ica	114,786
Iquitos	178,738
Jesús María (★Lima)	83,179
Juliaca	87,651
La Victoria (★Lima)	270,778
• LIMA (★4,608,010)	371,122
Lince (★Lima)	80,456
Magdalena (★Lima)	55,535
Miraflores (★Lima)	103,453
Pisco	55,604
Piura (★207,934)	144,609
Pucallpa	112,263
Pueblo Libre (★Lima)	83,985
Puno	67,397
Rímac (★Lima)	184,484
San Isidro (★Lima)	71,203
San Martín de Porras (★Lima)	404,856
Santiago de Surco (★Lima)	146,636
Sullana	89,037
Surquillo (★Lima)	134,158
Tacna	97,173
Talara	57,351
Trujillo (★354,301)	202,469
Tumbes	47,936
Vitarte (★Lima)	145,504

PHILIPPINES / Pilipinas

1990 C	60,477,000
Angeles	236,000
Antipolo (▲68,912) (1980C)	54,117
Bacolod	364,000
Bacoor (★Manila) (1980C)	90,364
Baguio	183,000
Baliuag (1980C)	70,555
Biñan (★Manila) (1980C)	83,684
Binangonan (1980C)	80,980
Bislig (▲81,615) (1980C)	49,498
Bocaue (1980C)	49,693
Butuan (▲228,000)	99,000
Cabanatuan (▲173,000)	75,700
Cagayan de Oro (▲340,000)	255,000
Cainta (★Manila) (1980C)	59,025
Calamba (▲121,175) (1980C)	72,359
Caloocan (★Manila)	746,000
Carmona (★Manila) (1980C)	65,014
Cavite (★195,000)	92,000
Cebu (★825,000)	610,000
Cotabato	127,000
Dagupan	122,000
Davao (▲850,000)	569,300
Dumaguete	80,000
General Santos (Dadiangas) (▲250,000)	157,600
Guagua (1980C)	72,609
Iloilo	311,000
Isabela (Basilan) (▲49,891) (1980C)	11,491
Jolo (1980C)	52,429
Lapu-Lapu (Opon)	146,000
Las Piñas (★Manila) (1984E)	190,364
Legaspi (▲121,000)	63,000
Lucena	151,000
Mabalacat (▲80,966) (1980C)	54,988
Makati (★Manila) (1984E)	408,991
Malabon (★Manila) (1984E)	212,930
Malolos (1980C)	95,699
Mandaluyong (★Manila) (1984E)	226,670
Mandaue (★Cebu)	180,000
Mangaldan (1980C)	50,434
• MANILA (★9,650,000)	1,587,000
Marawi	92,000
Marikina (★Manila) (1984E)	248,183
Meycauayan (★Manila) (1980C)	83,579
Muntinglupa (★Manila) (1984E)	172,421
Naga	115,000
Navotas (★Manila) (1984E)	146,899
Olongapo	192,000
Pagadian (▲107,000)	52,400
Parañaque (★Manila) (1984E)	252,791
Pasay (★Manila)	354,000
Pasig (★Manila) (1984E)	318,853
Puerto Princesa (▲92,000)	52,000
Quezon City (★Manila)	1,632,000
San Fernando (1980C)	110,891
San Juan del Monte (★Manila) (1984E)	139,126
San Pablo (▲161,000)	83,900
San Pedro (1980C)	74,556
Santa Cruz (1980C)	60,620
Santa Rosa (★Manila) (1980C)	64,325
Tacloban	138,000
Tagbilaran	56,000
Tagig (★Manila) (1984E)	130,719
Taytay (★Manila) (1980C)	75,328
Valenzuela (★Manila) (1984E)	275,725
Zamboanga (▲444,000)	107,000

PITCAIRN

1988 C	59
• ADAMSTOWN	59

POLAND / Polska

1991 E	38,183,200
Będzin (★Katowice)	76,200
Bełchatów	57,400
Biała Podlaska	53,100
Białystok	270,600
Bielsko-Biała	181,300
Bydgoszcz	381,500
Bytom (Beuthen) (★Katowice)	231,200
Chełm	66,400
Chorzów (★Katowice)	131,900
Częstochowa	258,000
Dąbrowa Górnicza (★Katowice)	136,900
Dzierżoniów (Reichenbach) (★89,000)	38,000
Elbląg (Elbing)	126,100
Ełk	52,400
Gdańsk (Danzig) (★909,000)	465,100
Gdynia (★Gdańsk)	251,500
Gliwice (Gleiwitz) (★Katowice)	214,200
Głogów	73,300
Gniezno	70,400
Gorzów Wielkopolski (Landsberg an der Warthe)	124,300
Grudziądz	102,300
Inowrocław	77,700
Jastrzębie-Zdrój	103,700
Jaworzno (★Katowice)	99,500
Jelenia Góra (Hirschberg)	93,400
Kalisz	106,200
• Katowice (★2,778,000)	366,800
Kędzierzyn Kozle	71,700
Kielce	214,200
Konin	80,300
Koszalin (Köslin)	108,700
Kraków (★828,000)	750,500
Krosno	49,700
Kutno	50,400
Legionowo (★Warszawa)	50,800
Legnica (Liegnitz)	105,200
Leszno	58,300
Łódź (★1,061,000)	848,200
Łomża	59,300
Lubin	82,300
Lublin (★389,000)	351,400
Mielec	61,800
Mysłowice (★Katowice)	93,800
Nowy Sącz	78,200
Olsztyn (Allenstein)	162,900
Opole (Oppeln)	128,400
Ostrołęka	50,700
Ostrowiec Świętokrzyski	78,600
Ostrów Wielkopolski	73,300
Pabianice (★Łódź)	75,200
Piekary Śląskie (★Katowice)	68,500
Piła (Schneidemühl)	72,300
Piotrków Trybunalski	81,000
Płock	123,400
Poznań (★672,000)	590,100
Pruszków (★Warszawa)	53,700
Przemyśl	68,500
Puławy	85,700
Racibórz (Ratibor)	64,400
Radom	228,500
Radomsko	50,400
Ruda Śląska (★Katowice)	171,000
Rybnik	144,000
Rzeszów	153,000
Siedlce	72,000
Siemianowice Śląskie (★Katowice)	81,100
Skarżysko-Kamienna	50,900
Słupsk (Stolp)	101,200
Sopot (★Gdańsk)	46,700
Sosnowiec (★Katowice)	259,400
Stalowa Wola	70,000
Starachowice	56,600
Stargard Szczeciński (Stargard in Pommern)	71,000
Starogard Gdański	49,500
Suwałki	61,300
Świdnica (Schweidnitz)	63,300
Świętochłowice (★Katowice)	60,500
Świnoujście (Swinemünde)	43,300
Szczecin (Stettin) (★449,000)	413,400
Tarnów	121,200
Tarnowskie Góry (★Katowice)	74,100
Tczew	59,500
Tomaszów Mazowiecki	69,900
Toruń	202,300
Tychy (★Katowice)	191,700
Wałbrzych (Waldenburg) (★207,000)	141,000
WARSZAWA (★2,323,000)	1,655,700
Włocławek	122,200
Wodzisław Śląski	111,800
Wrocław (Breslau)	643,200
Zabrze (Hindenburg) (★Katowice)	205,000
Zamość	61,800
Zawiercie	56,600
Zgierz (★Łódź)	59,000
Zielona Góra (Grünberg)	114,100
Żory	67,000

PORTUGAL

1981 C	9,833,014
Amadora (★Lisboa)	95,518
Barreiro (★Lisboa)	50,863
Braga	63,033
Coimbra	74,616
• LISBOA (★2,250,000)	807,167
Ponta Delgada	21,187
Porto (★1,225,000)	327,368
Setúbal	77,885
Vila Nova de Gaia (★Porto)	62,469

PUERTO RICO

1990 C	3,522,037
Arecibo (★160,500)	49,545
Bayamón (▲220,262) (★San Juan)	202,103
Caguas (▲133,447) (★San Juan)	92,429
Carolina (▲177,806) (★San Juan)	162,404
Guaynabo (▲92,886) (★San Juan)	73,385
Mayagüez (★200,600)	83,010
Ponce (★232,700)	159,151
• SAN JUAN (★1,877,000)	426,832

QATAR / Qaṭar

1986 C	369,079
• AD-DAWḤAH (DOHA) (★310,000)	217,294
Ar-Rayyān (★Ad-Dawḥah)	91,996

REUNION / Réunion

1982 C	515,814
• SAINT-DENIS (▲109,072)	84,400

ROMANIA / România

1992 C	22,760,449
Alba Iulia	71,254
Alexandria	58,582
Arad	190,088
Bacău	204,495
Baia Mare	148,815
Bîrlad	77,009
Bistrița	87,793
Botoșani	126,204
Brăila	234,706
Brașov	323,835
• BUCUREȘTI (BUCHAREST) (★2,300,000)	2,064,474
Buzău	148,247
Călărași	76,886
Cluj-Napoca	328,008
Constanța	350,476
Craiova	303,520
Deva	78,366
Drobeta-Turnu Severin	115,526
Focșani	101,296
Galați	325,788
Giurgiu	74,236
Hunedoara	81,198
Iași	342,994
Lugoj	50,983
Medgidia	46,586
Mediaș	64,488
Miercurea-Ciuc	46,029
Onești	59,008
Oradea	220,848
Petroșani (★76,000)	52,532
Piatra Neamț	123,175
Pitești	179,479
Ploiești (★310,000)	252,073
Reșița	96,798
Rîmnicu Vîlcea	113,356
Roman	80,192
Satu Mare	131,859
Sfîntu-Gheorghe	68,070
Sibiu	169,696
Slatina	85,336
Slobozia	55,614
Suceava	114,355
Tecuci	46,735
Timișoara	334,278
Tîrgoviște	97,876
Tîrgu Jiu	98,267
Tîrgu-Mureș	163,625
Tulcea	97,500
Turda	61,135
Vaslui	80,151
Zalău	68,322

RUSSIA

1991 E	148,542,700
Abakan	157,300
Achtubinsk	50,800
Ačinsk	122,000
Alapajevsk	50,300

▲ Población de un municipio, comuna o distrito entero, incluyendo sus áreas rurales.
• Ciudad más grande de un país.
★ Población o designación de un área metropolitana, incluyendo los suburbios.
C Censo. **E** Estimado oficial. **U** Estimado no oficial.

▲ Population d'une municipalité, d'une commune ou d'un district, zone rurale incluse.
• Ville la plus peuplée du pays.
★ Population de l'agglomération (ou nom de la zone métropolitaine englobante).
C Recensement. **E** Estimation officielle. **U** Estimation non officielle.

▲ População de um municipio, comuna ou distrito, inclusive as respectivas áreas rurais.
• Maior cidade de um país.
★ População ou indicação de uma área metropolitana.
C Censo. **E** Estimativa oficial. **U** Estimativa não oficial.

Alatyr'	47,700
Aleksandrov	68,600
Aleksin	74,200
Al'metjevsk	132,700
Amursk	59,600
Anapa	55,900
Angarsk	268,500
Anžero-Sudžensk	107,000
Apatity	88,600
Archangel'sk	420,400
Armavir	162,200
Arsenjev	71,200
Art'om	70,100
Arzamas	111,800
Asbest	84,900
Astrachan'	511,900
Azov	80,700
Balakovo	201,300
Balašicha (★Moskva)	137,600
Balašov	97,300
Barnaul (★673,000)	606,800
Batajsk (★Rostov-na-Donu)	93,300
Belebej	54,500
Belgorod	311,400
Belogorsk	74,300
Belorečensk	51,900
Beloreck	73,100
Belovo	92,900
Berdsk (★Novosibirsk)	80,400
Berezniki	199,700
Berezovskiy	51,900
Bijsk	234,600
Birobidžan	86,300
Blagoveščensk	211,000
Bor (★Nižnij Novgorod)	64,500
Borisoglebsk	72,100
Boroviči	62,800
Br'ansk	458,900
Bratsk	259,400
Bud'onnovsk	57,500
Bugul'ma	91,100
Buguruslan	54,100
Buj	62,900
Bujnaksk	57,900
Buzuluk	85,100
Čajkovskij	88,300
Čapajevsk	96,000
Čebarkul'	50,700
Čeboksary	436,000
Čechov	60,200
Čel'abinsk (★1,325,000)	1,148,300
Čeremchovo	73,600
Čerepovec	315,900
Čerkessk	117,000
Černogorsk	79,700
Chabarovsk	613,300
Chasavjurt	72,800
Chimki (★Moskva)	135,500
Cholmsk	51,800
Čistopol'	66,600
Čita	376,300
Čusovoj	58,000
Derbent	81,500
Dimitrovgrad	127,000
Dmitrov	65,600
Dolgoprudnyj (★Moskva)	71,100
Domodedovo (★Moskva)	56,300
Doneck	48,900
Dubna	67,200
Dzeržinsk (★Nižnij Novgorod)	286,700
Elektrostal'	153,000
Elista	92,700
Engel's (★Saratov)	183,600
Fr'azino (★Moskva)	54,000
Furmanov	45,900
Gatčina (★Sankt-Peterburg)	80,600
Gelendžik	48,600
Georgijevsk	63,700
Georgiu-Dež	54,600
Glazov	106,000
Gorno-Altajsk	47,500
Gr'azi	47,700
Groznyj	401,400
Gubkin	76,400
Gukovo	67,700
Gus'-Chrustal'nyj	77,000
Inta	60,900
Irbit	51,300
Irkutsk	640,500
Išim	65,900
Išimbaj	71,000
Iskitim	68,700
Ivanovo	482,200
Ivantejevka (★Moskva)	53,200
Iževsk	646,800
Jakutsk	193,300
Jarcevo	54,000
Jaroslavl'	638,100
Jefremov	56,600
Jegorjevsk	74,200
Jejsk	79,400
Jelec	121,300
Jelizovo	48,700
Jermolajevo	65,600
Jessentuki	86,300
Joškar-Ola	247,800
Jurga	94,000
Južno-Sachalinsk	164,000
Kaliningrad (Königsberg)	408,100
Kaliningrad (★Moskva)	161,500
Kaluga	315,500
Kamensk-Šachtinskij	73,100
Kamensk-Ural'skij	208,700
Kamyšin	124,400
Kanaš	56,100
Kandalakša	54,300
Kansk	109,900
Kaspijsk	61,900
Kazan' (★1,165,000)	1,107,300
Kemerovo	520,700
Kimry	62,000
Kinel'	33,800
Kinešma	104,900
Kingisepp	50,600
Kiriši	53,100
Kirov	491,200
Kirovo-Čepeck	95,600
Kisel'ovsk (★Prokopjevsk)	126,900
Kislovodsk	116,800
Kizel	36,600
Klimovsk (★Moskva)	57,600
Klin	95,100
Klincy	71,200
Kogalym	48,200
Kol'čugino	45,600
Kolomna	163,500
Kolpino (★Sankt-Peterburg)	144,500
Komsomol'sk-na-Amure	318,800
Kopejsk (★Čel'abinsk)	78,300
Korkino	44,800
Korsakov	45,300
Kostroma	281,800
Kotlas	68,900
Kovrov	161,900
Krasnodar	631,200
Krasnogorsk (★Moskva)	91,700
Krasnojarsk	924,400
Krasnokamensk	57,800
Krasnokamsk	67,000
Krasnoturjinsk	67,200
Krasnoufimsk	46,100
Krasnoural'sk	34,800
Krasnyj Sulin	43,200
Kropotkin	76,600
Krymsk	51,100
Kstovo (★Nižnij Novgord)	65,300
Kujbyšev	51,600
Kungur	81,800
Kurgan	363,800
Kursk	433,300
Kušva	43,300
Kuzneck	100,000
Kyzyl	88,000
Labinsk	58,600
Leninogorsk	63,300
Leninsk-Kuzneckij	133,400
Lesosibirsk	69,300
Lipeck	460,100
Livny	52,600
Lobn'a (★Moskva)	61,000
L'ubercy (★Moskva)	164,900
Lys'va	77,800
Lytkarino (★Moskva)	51,700
Machačkala	333,500
Magadan	154,900
Magnitogorsk	443,900
Majkop	152,500
Mcensk	49,200
Meleuz	55,200
Meždurečensk	107,500
Miass	169,700
Michajlovka	58,700
Mičurinsk	109,400
Mineral'nyje Vody	72,500
Minusinsk	74,200
Mončegorsk	68,100
Moršansk	50,500
• MOSKVA (MOSCOW) (★13,150,000)	8,801,500
Murmansk	472,900
Murom	126,000
Mytišči (★Moskva)	153,900
Naberežnyje Čelny	510,100
Nachodka	164,500
Nadym	52,200
Nal'čik	240,600
Naro-Fominsk	58,800
Nazarovo	65,200
Neftejugansk	65,500
Ner'ungri	77,200
Nevinnomyssk	123,300
Nikolo-Berjozovka	110,500
Nižnekamsk	196,200
Nižnevartovsk	247,400
Nižnij Novgorod (Gorky) (★2,025,000)	1,445,000
Nižnij Tagil	439,200
Njagan	59,800
Noginsk	122,700
Nojabr'sk	88,900
Noril'sk	169,000
Novgorod	233,800
Novoaltajsk (★Barnaul)	55,200
Novočeboksarsk	119,300
Novočerkassk	188,500
Novodvinsk	50,300
Novokujbyševsk (★Samara)	113,200
Novokuzneck	601,900
Novomoskovsk, Tula oblast' (★365,000)	145,800
Novorossijsk	188,600
Novošachtinsk	107,300
Novosibirsk (★1,600,000)	1,446,300
Novotroick	107,600
Novyj Urengoj	93,600
Obninsk	103,700
Odincovo (★Moskva)	128,400
Okt'abr'skij	106,700
Omsk (★1,190,000)	1,166,800
Orechovo-Zujevo (★205,000)	136,800
Orel	345,200
Orenburg	556,500
Orsk	272,200
Osinniki	63,200
Otradnyj	49,600
Partizansk	50,000
P'atigorsk	131,100
Pavlovo	72,200
Pavlovskij Posad	70,800
Pečora	65,500
Penza	551,100
Perm' (★1,180,000)	1,110,400
Pervoural'sk	143,700
Petrodvorec (★Sankt-Peterburg)	83,800
Petropavlovsk-Kamčatskij	272,900
Petrozavodsk	277,400
Podol'sk (★Moskva)	208,500
Polevskoj	71,900
Prochladnyj	58,500
Prokopjevsk (★410,000)	272,600
Pskov	207,500
Puškin (★Sankt-Peterburg)	95,300
Puškino (★Moskva)	75,800
Ramenskoje	88,800
Rasskazovo	49,800
R'azan'	527,200
Reutov (★Moskva)	68,900
Revda	66,000
Roslavl'	60,700
Rossoš'	58,900
Rostov-na-Donu (★1,165,000)	1,027,600
Rubcovsk	172,500
Ruzajevka	52,100
Rybinsk	252,600
Ržev	70,900
Šachty	227,700
Šadrinsk	87,500
Safonovo	56,300
Sajanogorsk	53,000
Salavat	151,400
Sal'sk	61,700
Samara (★1,505,000)	1,257,300
Sankt-Peterburg (Saint Petersburg) (★5,525,000)	4,466,800
Saransk	319,600
Sarapul	110,600
Saratov (★1,155,000)	911,100
Šatka	51,100
Ščelkovo (★Moskva)	109,600
Ščokino	68,800
Šelechov	48,600
Sergijev Posad (Zagorsk)	115,600
Serov	103,800
Serpuchov	141,200
Severodvinsk	251,500
Severomorsk	66,200
Slav'ansk-Na-Kubani	58,500
Smolensk	349,800
Soči	341,500
Sokol	46,700
Solikamsk	110,200
Solnečnogorsk (★Moskva)	56,700
Sosnovyj Bor	56,700
Spassk-Dal'nij	61,100
Staryj Oskol	181,900
Stavropol'	328,300
Sterlitamak	252,200
Stupino	74,600
Šuja	69,000
Surgut	261,100
Sverdlovsk (★1,629,000)	1,375,400
Svetlogorsk	71,600
Svobodnyj	80,900
Syktyvkar	224,000
Syzran'	174,900
Taganrog	293,600
Talnach	65,600
Tambov	309,600
Temirtau	213,100
Tichoreck	67,600
Tichvin	71,800
Tobol'sk	96,800
Toljatti	654,700
Tomsk	505,600
Toržok	50,500
Troick	89,800
Tuapse	63,800
Tujmazy	59,800
Tula (★640,000)	543,600
Tulun	53,700
T'umen'	494,200
Tver'	455,300
Tyndinskij	64,700
Uchta	112,100
Ufa (★1,118,000)	1,097,000
Uglič	40,000
Ulan-Ude	362,400
Uljanovsk	648,300
Usinsk	52,300
Usolje-Sibirskoje	106,800
Ussurijsk	160,200
Ust'-Ilimsk	112,200
Ust'-Kut	61,800
Uzlovaja (★Novomoskovsk)	64,000
V'az'ma	59,900
Velikije Luki	115,400
Verchn'aja Pyšma (★Sverdlovsk)	53,500
Verchn'aja Salda	55,100
Vičuga	49,700
Vidnoje (★Moskva)	56,900
Vladikavkaz	306,000
Vladimir	355,600
Vladivostok	648,000
Volchov	50,100
Volgodonsk	180,700
Volgograd (Stalingrad) (★1,360,000)	1,007,300
Vologda	289,200
Vol'sk	65,500
Volžsk	62,000
Volžskij (★Volgograd)	278,400
Vorkuta	117,400
Voronež	900,000
Voskresensk	81,400
Votkinsk	104,500
Vyborg	81,100
Vyksa	62,200
Vyšnij Voločok	64,600
Zarinsk	51,800
Zelenograd (★Moskva)	162,700
Železnodorožnyj (★Moskva)	99,300
Železnogorsk	89,200
Zel'onodol'sk	97,000
Žigulevsk	45,000
Zlatoust	208,200
Žukovskij	101,300

RWANDA

1991 C	6,762,145
• KIGALI	232,733

SAINT HELENA

1987 C	5,644
• JAMESTOWN	1,413

SAINT KITTS AND NEVIS

1980 C	44,404
• BASSETERRE	14,725
Charlestown	1,771

SAINT LUCIA

1987 C	142,342
• CASTRIES	53,933

SAINT PIERRE AND MIQUELON / Saint-Pierre-et-Miquelon

1982 C	6,041
• SAINT-PIERRE	5,371

SAINT VINCENT AND THE GRENADINES

1987 E	112,589
• KINGSTOWN (★28,936)	19,028

SAN MARINO

1989 E	23,000
• SAN MARINO	2,794

SAO TOME AND PRINCIPE / São Tomé e Príncipe

1991 C	117,504
• SÃO TOMÉ	5,245

SAUDI ARABIA / Al-'Arabīyah as-Su'ūdīyah

1980 E	9,229,000
Abhā (1974C)	30,150
Ad-Dammām	200,000
Al-Hufūf (1974C)	101,271
Al-Khubar (1974C)	48,817
Al-Madīnah (Medina)	290,000
Al-Mubarraz (1974C)	54,325
AR-RIYĀḌ (RIYADH)	1,250,000
Aṭ-Ṭā'if	300,000
Buraydah (1974C)	69,940
Hā'il (1974C)	40,502
• Jiddah (Jeddah)	1,300,000
Khamīs Mushayṭ (1974C)	49,581
Makkah (Mecca)	550,000
Najrān (1974C)	47,501
Tabūk (1974C)	74,825

SENEGAL / Sénégal

1988 C	6,892,720
• DAKAR	1,490,450
Diourbel	77,548
Kaolack	152,007
Louga	52,763
Saint-Louis	160,689
Thiès	184,902
Ziguinchor	124,283

SEYCHELLES

1984 E	64,718
• VICTORIA	23,000

SIERRA LEONE

1985 C	3,515,812
Bo	59,768
• FREETOWN (★525,000)	469,776
Kenema	52,473
Koidu	82,474
Makeni	49,038

SINGAPORE

1990 C	2,690,100
• SINGAPORE (★3,025,000)	2,690,100

SLOVAKIA / Slovenská Republika

1991 C	5,268,935
Banská Bystrica	85,007
• BRATISLAVA	441,453
Komárno	37,370
Košice	234,840
Martin	58,338
Michalovce	38,866
Nitra	89,888
Nové Zámky	42,851
Poprad	52,878
Považská Bystrica	39,801
Prešov	87,788
Prievidza	53,393
Spišská Nová Ves	39,187
Trenčín	56,733
Trnava	71,641
Žilina	83,853
Zvolen	41,935

SLOVENIA / Slovenija

1987 E	1,936,606
• LJUBLJANA (▲316,607)	233,200
Maribor (▲187,651)	107,400

SOLOMON ISLANDS

1986 C	285,176
• HONIARA	30,413

SOMALIA / Somaliya

1984 E	5,423,000
Berbera	65,000
Hargeysa	70,000
Kismaayo	70,000
Marka	60,000
• MUQDISHO	600,000

SOUTH AFRICA / Suid-Afrika

1985 C	23,385,645
Alberton (★Johannesburg)	66,155
Alexandra (★Johannesburg)	67,276
Atteridgeville (★Pretoria)	73,439
Bellville (★Cape Town)	68,915
Benoni (★Johannesburg)	94,926
Bloemfontein (★235,000)	104,381
Boksburg (★Johannesburg)	110,832
Botshabelo (★Bloemfontein)	95,625
Brakpan (★Johannesburg)	46,416
CAPE TOWN (KAAPSTAD) (★1,790,000)	776,617
Carletonville (★120,499)	97,874
Daveyton (★Johannesburg)	99,056
Diepmeadow (★Johannesburg)	192,682
Durban (★1,550,000)	634,301
East London (Oos-Londen) (★320,000)	85,699
Edendale (★Pietermaritzburg)	47,001
Elsies River (★Cape Town)	70,067
Empumalanga (★Durban)	47,938
Evaton (★Vereeniging)	52,559
Galeshewe (★Kimberley)	63,238
Germiston (★Johannesburg)	116,718
Grassy Park (★Cape Town)	50,193
Guguleto (★Cape Town)	63,893
• Johannesburg (★3,650,000)	632,369
Kagiso (★Johannesburg)	50,647
Katlehong (★Johannesburg)	137,745
Kayamnandi (★Port Elizabeth)	220,548
Kempton Park (★Johannesburg)	87,721
Kimberley (★145,000)	74,061
Klerksdorp (★205,000)	48,947
Krugersdorp (★Johannesburg)	73,767
Kwa Makuta (★Durban)	71,378
Kwa Mashu (★Durban)	111,593
Kwanobuhle (★Port Elizabeth)	52,376
Kwa-Thema (★Johannesburg)	78,640
Ladysmith (★31,670)	25,102
Lekoa (Shapeville) (★Vereeniging)	218,392
Madadeni (★Newcastle)	65,832
Mamelodi (★Pretoria)	127,033
Mangaung (★Bloemfontein)	79,851
Ntuzuma (★Durban)	61,834
Nyanga (★Cape Town)	148,882
Osizweni (★Newcastle)	51,934
Paarl (★Cape Town)	63,671
Parow (★Cape Town)	60,294
Pietermaritzburg (★230,000)	133,809
Pinetown (★Durban)	55,770
Port Elizabeth (★690,000)	272,844
PRETORIA (★960,000)	443,059
Randburg (★Johannesburg)	74,347
Randfontein (★Johannesburg)	43,763
Roodepoort-Maraisburg (★Johannesburg)	141,764
Sandton (★Johannesburg)	86,089
Soshanguve (★Pretoria)	68,598
Soweto (★Johannesburg)	521,948
Springs (★Johannesburg)	68,235
Tembisa (★Johannesburg)	149,282
Thabong (★Welkom)	43,470
Uitenhage (★Port Elizabeth)	54,987

▲ Population of an entire municipality, commune, or district, including rural area.
• Largest city in country.
★ Population or designation of the metropolitan area, including suburbs.
C Census. **E** Official estimate. **U** Unofficial estimate.

▲ Bevölkerung eines ganzen städtischen Verwaltungsgebietes, eines Kommunalbezirkes oder eines Distrikts, einschliesslich ländlicher Gebiete.
• Grösste Stadt des Landes.
★ Bevölkerung oder Bezeichnung der Stadtregion einschliesslich Vororte.
C Volkszählung. **E** Offizielle Schätzung. **U** Inoffizielle Schätzung.

Population of Cities and Towns / Einwohnerzahlen von Grossstädten / Habitantes en las Ciudades y Poblaciones
Population des Grands Centres et des Villes / População dos Centros Urbanos 313

Umlazi (★Durban)	194,933
Vanderbijlpark (★Vereeniging)	59,865
Vereeniging (★525,000)	60,584
Verwoerdburg (★Pretoria)	49,891
Vosloosrus (★Johannesburg)	52,061
Walvisbaai (Walvis Bay) (★16,607)	9,687
Welkom (★215,000)	54,488
Westonaria (★Johannesburg)	46,523

SPAIN / España

1988 E	39,217,804
Alacant (Alicante)	261,051
Albacete	125,997
Alcalá de Guadaira	50,935
Alcalá de Henares (★Madrid)	150,021
Alcobendas (★Madrid)	73,455
Alcoi (Alcoy)	66,074
Alcorcón (★Madrid)	139,796
Algeciras	99,528
Almería	157,644
Avilés (★131,000)	87,811
Badajoz (▲122,407)	106,400
Badalona (★Barcelona)	225,229
Baracaldo (★Bilbao)	113,502
Barcelona (★4,040,000)	1,714,355
Bilbao (★985,000)	384,733
Burgos	160,561
Cáceres	71,598
Cádiz (★240,000)	156,591
Cartagena (▲172,710)	70,000
Castelló de la Plana	131,809
Ciudad Real	56,300
Córdoba	302,301
Cornellà de Llobregat (★Barcelona)	86,866
Coslada (★Madrid)	68,765
Donostia (San Sebastián) (★285,000)	177,622
Dos Hermanas (▲68,456)	60,600
Elda	56,756
El Ferrol del Caudillo (★129,000)	86,503
El Prat de Llobregat (★Barcelona)	64,193
El Puerto de Santa María (▲62,285)	49,900
Elx (Elche) (▲180,256)	158,300
Fuenlabrada (★Madrid)	128,872
Gernika-Lumo (Guernica y Luno) (▲17,836) (1981C)	12,214
Getafe (★Madrid)	135,367
Gijón	262,156
Granada	263,334
Granollers (★Barcelona)	49,045
Guadalajara	61,309
Huelva	137,826
Irún	54,886
Jaén	106,435
Jerez de la Frontera (▲183,007)	156,200
La Coruña	248,862
La Línea	60,956
Las Palmas de Gran Canaria (▲366,347)	319,000
Leganés (★Madrid)	168,403
León (★159,000)	136,558
L'Hospitalet de Llobregat (★Barcelona)	278,449
Linares	58,622
Lleida (Lérida) (▲109,795)	91,500
Logroño	119,038
Lugo (▲78,795)	68,700
• MADRID (★4,650,000)	3,102,846
Málaga	574,456
Manresa	65,607
Mataró	100,817
Mérida	52,368
Móstoles (★Madrid)	181,648
Murcia (▲314,124)	149,800
Orense	106,042
Oviedo (▲190,073)	168,900
Palencia	76,692
Palma (▲314,608)	249,000
Pamplona	180,598
Parla (★Madrid)	66,253
Portugalete (★Bilbao)	57,813
Puertollano	52,284
Reus	83,800
Rubí (★Barcelona)	48,807
Sabadell (★Barcelona)	189,489
Salamanca	159,342
San Baudilio de Llobrega (★Barcelona)	77,502
San Cristóbal de la Laguna (▲111,533)	25,900
San Fernando (★Cádiz)	81,975
San Sebastián de los Reyes (★Madrid)	51,653
Santa Coloma de Gramanet (★Barcelona)	136,042
Santa Cruz de Tenerife	215,228
Santander (▲190,795)	166,800
Santiago de Compostela (▲88,110)	68,800
Santurce-Antiguo (★Bilbao)	52,334
Segovia	54,402
Sevilla (★945,000)	663,132
Talavera de la Reina	68,158
Tarragona (▲109,586)	63,500
Tarrasa (★Barcelona)	161,410
Toledo	59,551
Torrejón de Ardoz (★Madrid)	83,267
Torrent (★València)	55,751
València (★1,270,000)	743,933
Valladolid	331,461
Vigo (▲271,128)	179,500
Vitoria (Gasteiz)	204,264
Zamora	62,047
Zaragoza	582,239

SPANISH NORTH AFRICA / Plazas de Soberanía en el Norte de África

1988 E	122,905
• Ceuta	67,188
Melilla	55,717

SRI LANKA

1989 E	16,806,000
Battaramulla (★Colombo) (1981C)	56,535
Batticaloa	50,000
• COLOMBO (★2,050,000)	612,000
Dehiwala-Mount Lavinia (★Colombo)	193,000
Galle	83,000
Jaffna	128,000
Kandy	103,000
Moratuwa (★Colombo)	166,000
Negombo	64,000
SRI JAYAWARDENEPURA (KOTTE) (★Colombo)	108,000
Trincomalee	49,000

SUDAN / As-Sūdān

1983 C	20,594,197
Al-Fāshir	84,298
• AL-KHARṬŪM (★1,450,000)	473,597
Al-Kharṭūm Baḥrī (★Al-Kharṭūm)	340,857
Al-Qaḍārif	116,876
Al-Ubayyiḍ	137,582
'Aṭbarah	72,836
Būr Sūdān (Port Sudan)	206,038
Jūbā	84,377
Kassalā	141,429
Kūstī	89,135
Nyala	111,693
Umm Durmān (Omdurman) (★Al-Kharṭūm)	526,192
Wad Madanī	145,015
Wāw	90,960

SURINAME

1988 E	392,000
• PARAMARIBO (★296,000)	241,000
Wanica (★Paramaribo)	55,000

SWAZILAND

1986 C	712,131
LOBAMBA	
Manzini (★30,000)	18,084
• MBABANE	38,290

SWEDEN / Sverige

1991 E	8,590,630
Borås (▲101,766)	59,400
Eskilstuna (▲89,765)	59,800
Gävle (▲88,568)	67,300
Göteborg (★710,894)	433,042
Halmstad (▲80,061)	48,900
Helsingborg (▲109,267)	82,000
Huddinge (★Stockholm)	73,829
Järfälla (★Stockholm)	56,359
Jönköping (▲111,486)	76,300
Karlstad (▲76,467)	53,100
Linköping (▲122,268)	82,700
Luleå (▲68,412)	42,700
Lund (▲87,681) (★Malmö)	63,700
Malmö (★475,224)	233,887
Mölndal (★Göteborg)	52,028
Nacka (★Stockholm)	64,056
Norrköping (▲120,522)	82,600
Örebro (▲120,944)	86,000
Södertälje (▲81,786) (★Stockholm)	58,100
Sollentuna (★Stockholm)	51,377
Solna (★Stockholm)	51,841
• STOCKHOLM (★1,491,726)	674,452
Sundsvall (▲93,808)	50,300
Täby (★Stockholm)	56,714
Trollhättan (▲51,047)	41,000
Tumba (★Stockholm)	68,542
Umeå (▲91,258)	61,300
Uppsala (▲167,508)	110,000
Västerås (▲119,761)	98,300
Växjö (▲69,547)	48,000

SWITZERLAND / Schweiz / Suisse / Svizzera

1990 C	6,873,687
Aarau (★59,500)	16,481
Arbon (★41,400)	11,043
Baden (★73,200)	15,718
Basel (Bâle) (★587,000)	178,428
BERN (BERNE) (★300,400)	136,338
Biel (Bienne) (★83,100)	51,893
Fribourg (Freiburg) (★62,500)	36,355
Genève (Geneva) (★470,000)	171,042
Lausanne (★265,000)	128,112
Locarno (★42,200)	13,796
Lugano (★94,700)	25,344
Luzern (★165,000)	61,034
Neuchâtel (★67,500)	33,579
Sankt Gallen (★127,000)	75,237
Schaffhausen (★53,800)	34,225
Thun (★79,500)	38,211
Vevey (★65,900)	15,968
Winterthur (★110,500)	86,959
Zug (★69,000)	21,705
• Zürich (★870,000)	365,043

SYRIA / Sūrīyah

1988 E	11,338,000
Al-Ḥasakah (1981C)	73,426
Al-Lādhiqīyah (Latakia)	249,000
Al-Qāmishlī	126,236
Ar-Raqqah	113,000
As-Suwaydā'	46,844
Dar'ā (1981C)	49,534
Dārayyā (★Dimashq)	53,204
Dayr az-Zawr	112,000
• DIMASHQ (DAMASCUS) (★2,000,000)	1,326,000
Dūmā (★Dimashq)	66,130
Ḥalab (Aleppo) (★1,335,000)	1,261,000
Ḥamāh	222,000
Ḥimṣ	447,000
Idlib (1981C)	51,682
Jaramānah (★Dimashq)	96,681
Kābir aṣ Ṣaghīr	47,728
Madīnat ath Thawrah	58,151
Ṭarṭūs (1981C)	52,589

TAIWAN / T'aiwan

1991 E	20,352,966
Changhua (▲215,224)	165,000
Chiai (1992E)	258,713
Chilung (1992E)	357,000
Chungho (★T'aipei)	374,339
Chungli	269,804
Chutung (1988E)	104,797
Fangshan (★Kaohsiung)	290,777
Fengyüan (▲151,642)	121,100
Hsichih (★T'aipei) (1980C)	70,031
Hsinchu (1992E)	330,576
Hsinchuang (★T'aipei)	299,174
Hsintien (★T'aipei)	225,517
Hualien	107,552
Ilan (▲81,751) (1980C)	70,900
Kangshan (1980C)	78,049
Kaohsiung (★1,845,000) (1992E)	1,401,239
Lotung (1980C)	57,925
Lukang (1980C)	72,019
Miaoli (1980C)	81,500
Nant'ou (1980C)	84,038
P'ingchen (★T'aipei)	147,030
P'ingtung (▲210,801)	172,400
Sanchung (★T'aipei)	375,996
Shulin (★T'aipei)	111,993
Tach'i (1980C)	67,209
T'aichung (1992E)	785,182
T'ainan (1992E)	692,116
• T'AIPEI (★6,130,000) (1992)	2,706,453
T'aipeihsien (★T'aipei)	538,954
T'aitung (▲108,196)	79,100
Taoyüan	241,263
T'oufen (1980C)	66,536
T'uch'eng (▲136,928) (★T'aipei)	80,300
Yangmei (1980C)	84,353
Yüanlin (▲121,251)	53,200
Yungho (★T'aipei)	249,736
Yungkang (▲136,705)	70,900

TAJIKISTAN

1991 E	5,358,300
Chudžand (Leninabad)	164,500
• DUŠANBE	582,400
Kul'ab	79,300
Kurgan-T'ube	58,400

TANZANIA

1985 E	21,733,000
Arusha (1984E)	69,000
• DAR ES SALAAM	1,096,000
DODOMA	85,000
Iringa (1984E)	67,000
Kigoma (1978C)	50,044
Mbeya	194,000
Morogoro (1984E)	72,000
Moshi (1984E)	62,000
Mtwara (1978C)	48,510
Mwanza	252,000
Tabora	214,000
Tanga	172,000
Ujiji (1967C)	21,369
Zanzibar	133,000

THAILAND / Prathet Thai

1990 C	54,532,000
Chiang Mai	167,000
Chon Buri (1988E)	47,286
Hat Yai (1988E)	138,046
Khon Kaen (1988E)	131,340
• KRUNG THEP (BANGKOK) (★7,060,000)	5,876,000
Nakhon Ratchasima (1988E)	204,982
Nakhon Sawan (1988E)	105,220
Nakhon Si Thammarat (1988E)	72,407
Nonthaburi (★Krung Thep) (1988E)	218,354
Pattaya (1988E)	56,402
Phitsanulok	85,000
Phra Nakhon Si Ayutthaya (1988E)	60,847
Phuket	49,000
Sakon Nakhon	26,000
Samut Prakan (★Krung Thep) (1988E)	73,327
Samut Sakhon (1988E)	53,984
Saraburi (1988E)	61,206
Songkhla (1988E)	84,433
Trang (1988E)	48,042
Ubon Ratchathani (1988E)	100,374
Udon Thani	81,000
Yala (1988E)	67,383

TOGO

1987 E	3,148,000
• LOMÉ	500,000
Sokodé	55,000

TOKELAU

1986 C	1,690

TONGA

1986 C	94,535
• NUKU'ALOFA	21,265

TRANSKEI

1987 E	3,081,770
• UMTATA (1978E)	30,000

TRINIDAD AND TOBAGO

1990 C	1,234,388
• PORT OF SPAIN (★370,000)	50,878
San Fernando (★75,000)	30,092

TUNISIA / Tunis / Tunisie

1984 C	6,975,450
Ariana (★Tunis)	98,655
Bardo (★Tunis)	65,669
Ben Arous (★Tunis)	52,105
Bizerte	94,509
Gabès	92,258
Gafsa	60,970
Hammam Lif (★Tunis)	47,009
Houmt Essouk	92,269
Kairouan	72,254
Kasserine	47,606
La Goulette (★Tunis)	61,609
Menzel Bourguiba	51,399
Sfax (★310,000)	231,911
Sousse (★160,000)	83,509
• TUNIS (★1,225,000)	596,654
Zarzis	49,063

TURKEY / Türkiye

1990 C	56,473,035
Adana	916,150
Adapazarı	171,225
Adıyaman	100,045
Afyon	95,643
Ağrı	58,038
Akhisar	73,944
Aksaray	90,698
Akşehir	51,746
Alanya	52,460
Amasya	57,288
ANKARA (★2,650,000)	2,559,471
Antakya (Antioch)	123,871
Antalya	378,208
Aydın	107,011
Bafra	65,600
Balıkesir	170,589
Bandırma	77,444
Batman	147,347
Bilecik	23,273
Bolu	60,789
Burdur	56,432
Bursa	834,576
Çanakkale	53,995
Ceyhan	85,308
Cizre	50,023
Çorlu	74,681
Çorum	116,810
Darıca	53,560
Denizli	204,118
Diyarbakır	381,144
Düzce	61,878
Edirne	102,345
Elazığ	204,603
Elbistan	54,741
Ereğli, Konya prov.	74,283
Ereğli, Zonguldak prov.	63,987
Erzincan	91,772
Erzurum	242,391
Esenyurt (★İstanbul)	70,280
Eskişehir	413,082
Gaziantep	603,434
Gebze (★İstanbul)	159,116
Gelibolu	18,670
Gemlik	50,237
Giresun	67,604
Gölcük	64,911
Gümüşhane	26,014
Hakkâri	30,407
İçel (Mersin)	422,357
İnegöl	71,120
İskenderun	154,807
Isparta	112,117
• İstanbul (★7,550,000)	6,620,241
İzmir (★1,900,000)	1,757,414
İzmit	256,882
Kadirli	55,061
Kahramanmaraş	228,129
Karabük	105,373
Karaman	76,525
Kars	78,455
Kastamonu	51,560
Kayseri	421,362
Kilis	82,882
Kırıkkale	185,431
Kırşehir	73,538
Kızıltepe	60,134
Konya	513,346
Körfez	65,786
Kozan	54,451
Kütahya	130,994
Lüleburgaz	52,384
Malatya	281,776
Manisa	158,928
Mardin	53,005
Muş	44,019
Nazilli	80,277
Nevşehir	52,719
Niğde	55,035
Nizip	58,604
Nusaybin	49,671
Ödemiş	51,620
Ordu	102,107
Osmaniye	123,307
Polatlı	60,158
Rize	52,031
Salihli	70,861
Samsun	303,979
Şanlıurfa	276,528
Siirt	68,320
Silvan (Miyafarkin)	59,865
Sinop	25,537
Sivas	221,512
Siverek	63,049
Söke	50,866
Soma	49,977
Sultanbeyli (★İstanbul)	82,298
Tarsus	187,508
Tatvan	54,071
Tekirdağ	80,442
Tokat	83,058
Trabzon	143,941
Tunceli	24,513
Turgutlu	73,634
Turhal	68,384
Uşak	105,270
Van	153,111
Viranşehir	57,461
Yalova (★İstanbul)	65,823
Yozgat	50,335
Zonguldak (★220,000)	116,725

TURKMENISTAN

1991 E	3,714,100
• AŠCHABAD (ASHGABAT)	412,200
Čardžou	166,400
Krasnovodsk	59,500
Mary	94,900
Nebit-Dag	89,100
Tašauz	117,000

TURKS AND CAICOS ISLANDS

1990 C	11,465
• GRAND TURK	3,691

TUVALU

1979 C	7,349
• FUNAFUTI	2,191

UGANDA

1991 C	16,582,700
Jinja	60,979
• KAMPALA	773,463
Masaka	49,070
Mbale	53,634

UKRAINE / Ukrayina

1991 E	5,194,440
Achtyrka	52,000
Alčevsk (★Stachanov)	126,000
Aleksandrija	104,900
Antracit (★Krasnyj Luč)	72,800
Art'omovsk	90,800
Belaja Cerkov'	204,400
Belgorod-Dnestrovskij	56,800
Berd'ansk	135,200
Berdičev	93,400
Borispol' (★Kijev)	52,700
Br'anka (★Stachanov)	64,500
Brovary (★Kijev)	84,800
Čerkassy	302,200
Černigov	305,700
Černovcy	258,800
Červonograd	74,000
Charcyzsk (★Doneck)	69,300

▲ Población de un municipio, comuna o distrito entero, incluyendo sus áreas rurales.
• Ciudad más grande de un país.
★ Población o designación de un área metropolitana, incluyendo los suburbios.
C Censo. **E** Estimado oficial. **U** Estimado no oficial.

▲ Population d'une municipalité, d'une commune ou d'un district, zone rurale incluse.
• Ville la plus peuplée du pays.
★ Population de l'agglomération (ou nom de la zone métropolitaine englobante).
C Recensement. **E** Estimation officielle. **U** Estimation non officielle.

▲ População de um municipio, comuna ou distrito, inclusive as respectivas áreas rurais.
• Maior cidade de um país.
★ População ou indicação de uma área metropolitana.
C Censo. **E** Estimativa oficial. **U** Estimativa não oficial.

Char'kov (★2,050,000)	1,622,800
Cherson	365,400
Chmel'nickij	244,500
Dimitrov (★Krasnoarmejsk)	63,800
Dneprodzeržinsk (★Dnepropetrovsk)	284,400
Dnepropetrovsk (★1,600,000)	1,189,300
Doneck (★2,125,000)	1,121,300
Drogobyč	79,200
Družkovka (★Kramatorsk)	74,400
Džankoj	54,500
Dzeržinsk (★Gorlovka)	50,500
Energodar	51,500
Fastov	54,400
Feodosija	85,600
Gorlovka (★700,000)	336,600
Iljičovsk (★Odessa)	56,000
Ivano-Frankovsk	225,800
Izmail	95,100
Iz'um	64,800
Jalta	89,300
Jenakijevo (★Gorlovka)	120,100
Jevpatorija	110,500
Kaluš	69,400
Kamenec-Podol'skij	104,900
Kerč'	178,300
• KIJEV (★3,250,000)	2,635,000
Kirovograd	277,900
Kolomyja	66,200
Komsomol'sk	53,000
Konotop	97,700
Konstantinovka	107,800
Korosten'	67,500
Kovel'	69,700
Kramatorsk (★515,000)	201,300
Krasnoarmejsk (★180,000)	73,300
Krasnodon (★165,000)	54,800
Krasnyj Luč (★320,000)	113,400
Kremenčug	240,600
Krivoj Rog	724,000
Lisičansk (★415,000)	126,400
Lozovaja	74,100
Lubny	60,300
Luck	209,500
Lugansk (Vorošilovgrad) (★650,000)	503,900
L'vov	802,200
Makejevka (★Doneck)	423,900
Marganec	54,700
Mariupol' (Ždanov)	521,800
Melitopol'	176,900
Mukačevo	88,000
Nežin	82,000
Nikolajev	511,600
Nikopol'	159,000
Novaja Kachovka	59,000
Novograd-Volynskij	56,100
Novomoskovsk, Dnepropetrosvk oblast'	76,600
Novovolynsk	56,400
Odessa (★1,185,000)	1,100,700
Pavlograd	134,300
Pervomajsk	83,800
Pervomajsk (★Stachanov)	52,000
Poltava	320,100
Priluki	72,900
Romny	57,300
Roven'ki	58,500
Rovno	239,300
Rubežnoje (★Lisičansk)	75,100
Šacht'orsk (★Torez)	73,100
Šepetovka	51,900
Sevastopol'	366,200
Severodoneck (★Lisičansk)	133,300
Simferopol'	352,600
Slav'ansk (★Kramatorsk)	137,100
Smela	81,100
Snežnoje (★Torez)	68,900
Šostka	95,200
Stachanov (★700,000)	112,700
Stryj	68,200
Sumy	300,900
Sverdlovsk, Vorosilovgrad oblast' (★145,000)	83,700
Svetlovodsk	57,900
Ternopol'	218,400
Torez (★320,000)	88,100
Uman'	92,700
Užgorod	122,600
Vinnica	380,900
Zaporožje	896,600
Žitomir	297,500
Žoltyje Vody	63,900

UNITED ARAB EMIRATES / Al-Imārāt al-'Arabīyah al-Muttaḥidah

1980 C	980,000
ABŪ ẒABY (ABU DHABI)	242,975
Al-'Ayn	101,663
Ash-Shāriqah	125,149
• Dubayy	265,702
Ra's al-Khaymah	42,000

UNITED KINGDOM

1981 C	55,678,079

UNITED KINGDOM: ENGLAND

1981 C	46,220,955
Aldershot (★London)	53,665
Ashton-under-Lyne (★Manchester)	43,605
Aylesbury	51,999
Barnsley	76,783
Barrow-in-Furness	50,174
Basildon (★London)	94,800
Basingstoke	73,027
Bath	84,283
Bebington (★Liverpool)	62,618
Bedford	75,632
Beeston and Stapleford (★Nottingham)	64,785
Benfleet (★London)	50,783
Birkenhead (★Liverpool)	99,075
Birmingham (★2,675,000)	1,013,995
Blackburn (★221,900)	109,564
Blackpool (★280,000)	146,297
Bognor Regis	50,323
Bolton (★Manchester)	143,960
Bootle	70,860
Bournemouth (★315,000)	142,829
Bracknell (★London)	52,257
Bradford (★Leeds)	293,336
Brentwood (★London)	51,212
Brighton (★420,000)	134,581
Bristol (★630,000)	413,861
Burnley (★160,000)	76,365
Burton upon Trent	59,040
Bury (★Manchester)	61,785
Bury Saint Edmunds	30,563
Cambridge	87,111
Cannock (★Birmingham)	54,503
Canterbury	34,546
Carlisle	72,206
Carlton (★Nottingham)	46,053
Chatham (★London)	65,835
Cheadle and Gatley (★Manchester)	59,478
Chelmsford (★London)	91,109
Cheltenham	87,188
Cheshunt (★London)	49,616
Chester	80,154
Chesterfield (★127,000)	73,352
Clacton-on-Sea	39,618
Colchester	87,476
Corby	48,704
Coventry (★645,000)	318,718
Crawley (★London)	80,113
Crewe	59,097
Crosby (★Liverpool)	54,103
Darlington	85,519
Dartford (★London)	62,032
Derby (★275,000)	218,026
Dewsbury (★Leeds)	49,612
Doncaster	74,727
Dover	33,461
Dudley (★Birmingham)	186,513
Dunstable (★Luton)	48,436
Durham	38,105
Eastbourne	86,715
Eastleigh (★Southampton)	58,585
Ellesmere Port (★Liverpool)	65,829
Epsom and Ewell (★London)	65,830
Esher / Molesey (★London)	46,688
Exeter	88,235
Fareham / Portchester (★Portsmouth)	55,563
Farnborough (★London)	48,063
Folkestone	42,949
Frimley and Camberley (★London)	45,108
Gateshead (★Newcastle)	91,429
Gillingham (★London)	92,531
Gloucester (★115,000)	106,526
Gosport (★Portsmouth)	69,664
Gravesend (★London)	53,450
Grays (★London)	45,881
Greasby / Moreton (★Liverpool)	56,410
Great Yarmouth	54,777
Grimsby (★145,000)	91,532
Guildford (★London)	61,509
Halesowen (★Birmingham)	57,533
Halifax	76,675
Harlow (★London)	79,150
Harrogate	63,637
Hartlepool (★Middlesbrough)	91,749
Hastings	74,979
Havant (★Portsmouth)	50,098
Hemel Hempstead (★London)	80,110
Hereford	48,277
Hertford (★London)	21,350
High Wycombe (▲156,800)	69,575
Hove (★Brighton)	65,587
Huddersfield (▲377,400)	147,825
Huyton-with-Roby (★Liverpool)	62,011
Ipswich	129,661
Keighley (★Leeds)	49,188
Kidderminster	50,385
Kingston upon Hull (★350,000)	322,144
Kingswood (★Bristol)	54,736
Kirkby (★Liverpool)	52,825
Lancaster	43,902
Leeds (★1,540,000)	445,242
Leicester (★495,000)	324,394
Lincoln	79,980
Littlehampton	46,028
Liverpool (★1,525,000)	538,809
• LONDON (★11,100,000)	6,574,009
Loughborough	44,895
Lowestoft	59,430
Luton (★220,000)	163,209
Macclesfield	47,525
Maidenhead (★London)	59,809
Maidstone	86,067
Manchester (★2,775,000)	437,612
Mansfield (★198,000)	71,325
Margate	53,137
Middlesbrough (★580,000)	158,516
Middleton (★Manchester)	51,373
Milton Keynes	36,886
Newcastle-under-Lyme (★Stoke-on-Trent)	73,208
Newcastle upon Tyne (★1,300,000)	199,064
Northampton	154,172
Norwich (★230,000)	169,814
Nottingham (★655,000)	273,300
Nuneaton (★Coventry)	60,337
Oldbury / Smethwick (★Birmingham)	153,268
Oldham (★Manchester)	107,095
Oxford (★230,000)	113,847
Penzance	18,501
Peterborough	113,404
Plymouth (★290,000)	238,583
Poole (★Bournemouth)	122,815
Portsmouth (★485,000)	174,218
Preston (★250,000)	166,675
Ramsgate	36,678
Reading (★200,000)	194,727
Redditch (★Birmingham)	61,639
Reigate / Redhill (★London)	48,241
Rochdale (★Manchester)	97,292
Rotherham (★Sheffield)	122,374
Royal Leamington Spa (★Coventry)	56,552
Royal Tunbridge Wells	57,699
Rugby	59,039
Runcorn (★Liverpool)	63,995
Saint Albans (★London)	76,709
Saint Helens	114,397
Sale (★Manchester)	57,872
Salford (★Manchester)	96,525
Salisbury	36,890
Scarborough	36,665
Scunthorpe	79,043
Sheffield (★710,000)	470,685
Shrewsbury	57,731
Slough (★London)	106,341
Solihull (★Birmingham)	93,940
Southampton (★415,000)	211,321
Southend-on-Sea (★London)	155,720
Southport (★Liverpool)	88,596
South Shields (★Newcastle)	86,488
Stafford	60,915
Staines (★London)	51,949
Stevenage	74,757
Stockport (★Manchester)	135,489
Stockton-on-Tees (★Middlesbrough)	86,699
Stoke-on-Trent (★440,000)	272,446
Stourbridge (★Birmingham)	55,136
Stratford-upon-Avon	20,941
Stretford (★Manchester)	47,522
Sunderland (★Newcastle)	195,064
Sutton Coldfield (★Birmingham)	102,572
Swindon	127,348
Tanworth	63,260
Taunton	47,793
Torquay (★112,400)	54,430
Wakefield (★Leeds)	74,764
Wallasey (★Liverpool)	62,465
Walsall (★Birmingham)	177,923
Walton and Weybridge (★London)	50,031
Warrington	81,366
Washington (★Newcastle)	48,856
Waterlooville (★Portsmouth)	57,296
Watford (★London)	109,503
West Bromwich (★Birmingham)	153,725
Weston-super-Mare	60,821
Widnes	55,973
Wigan (★Manchester)	88,725
Woking (★London)	92,667
Wolverhampton (★Birmingham)	263,501
Worcester	75,466
Worthing (★Brighton)	90,687
York (★145,000)	123,126

UNITED KINGDOM: NORTHERN IRELAND

1990 E	1,589,400
Bangor (★Belfast)	72,600
Belfast (★685,000)	295,100
Castlereagh (★Belfast)	58,100
Londonderry (Derry)	100,500
Lurgan (★63,000) (1981C)	20,991
Newtownabbey (★Belfast)	72,900

UNITED KINGDOM: SCOTLAND

1990 E	5,102,400
Aberdeen	211,080
Ayr (★100,000) (1981C)	48,493
Clydebank (★Glasgow) (1981C)	51,832
Coatbridge (1981C)	50,831
Cumbernauld (★Glasgow)	50,700
Dundee	172,860
Dunfermline (★125,817) (1981C)	52,105
East Kilbride (★Glasgow)	70,500
Edinburgh (★630,000)	434,520
Falkirk (★148,171) (1981C)	36,372
Glasgow (★1,800,000)	689,210
Greenock (★101,000) (1981C)	58,436
Hamilton (★Glasgow) (1981C)	51,666
Irvine (★94,000)	56,000
Kilmarnock (★84,000) (1981C)	51,799
Kirkcaldy (★148,171) (1981C)	46,356
Motherwell (★Glasgow) (1981C)	30,616
Paisley (★Glasgow) (1981C)	84,330
Perth (1981C)	41,916
Stirling (★61,000) (1981C)	36,640

UNITED KINGDOM: WALES

1981 C	2,790,462
Cardiff (★625,000)	262,313
Cwmbran (★Newport)	44,592
Llanelli	45,336
Merthyr Tydfil	38,893
Neath (★Swansea)	48,687
Newport (★310,000)	115,896
Pontypool (★Newport)	36,064
Port Talbot (★130,000)	40,078
Rhondda (★Cardiff)	70,980
Swansea (★275,000)	172,433
Wrexham	39,929

UNITED STATES

1990 C	248,709,873

UNITED STATES: ALABAMA

1990 C	4,040,587
Anniston (★116,034)	26,623
Auburn (★61,100)	33,830
Birmingham (★907,810)	265,968
Decatur (★131,556)	48,761
Dothan (★130,964)	53,589
Florence (★131,327)	36,426
Gadsden (★99,840)	42,523
Huntsville (★238,912)	159,789
Mobile (★476,923)	196,278
Montgomery (★292,517)	187,106
Tuscaloosa (★150,522)	77,759

UNITED STATES: ALASKA

1990 C	550,043
Anchorage (★248,400)	226,338
Fairbanks (★59,500)	30,843
Juneau	26,751

UNITED STATES: ARIZONA

1990 C	3,665,228
Chandler (★Phoenix)	90,533
Glendale (★Phoenix)	148,134
Mesa (★Phoenix)	288,091
Nogales (★Nogales, Mexico)	19,489
Phoenix (★2,122,101)	900,013
Scottsdale (★Phoenix)	130,069
Tempe (★Phoenix)	141,865
Tucson (★666,880)	405,390
Yuma (★106,895)	54,923

UNITED STATES: ARKANSAS

1990 C	2,350,725
Fayetteville (★113,409)	42,099
Fort Smith (★175,911)	72,798
Hot Springs National Park (★56,500)	32,462
Jonesboro (★49,300)	46,535
Little Rock (★513,117)	175,795
North Little Rock (★Little Rock)	61,741
Pine Bluff (★85,487)	57,140

UNITED STATES: CALIFORNIA

1990 C	29,760,021
Alameda (★Oakland)	76,459
Alhambra (★Los Angeles)	82,106
Anaheim (★2,410,556) (★Los Angeles)	266,406
Antioch (★Oakland)	62,195
Arden (★Sacramento)	62,900
Bakersfield (★543,477)	174,820
Baldwin Park (★Los Angeles)	69,330
Bellflower (★Los Angeles)	61,815
Berkeley (★Oakland)	102,724
Buena Park (★Anaheim)	68,784
Burbank (★Los Angeles)	93,643
Calexico (★Mexicali, Mexico)	18,633
Camarillo (★Oxnard)	52,303
Carlsbad (★San Diego)	63,126
Carmichael (★Sacramento)	48,702
Carson (★Los Angeles)	83,995
Cerritos (★Los Angeles)	53,240
Chico (★182,120)	40,079
Chino (★Riverside)	59,682
Chula Vista (★San Diego)	135,163
Citrus Heights (★Sacramento)	112,800
Clovis (★Fresno)	50,323
Compton (★Los Angeles)	90,454
Concord (★Oakland)	111,348
Corona (★Riverside)	76,095
Costa Mesa (★Anaheim)	96,357
Cucamonga (★Riverside)	101,409
Daly City (★San Francisco)	92,311
Diamond Bar (★Los Angeles)	53,672
Downey (★Los Angeles)	91,444
East Los Angeles (★Los Angeles)	126,379
El Cajon (★San Diego)	88,693
El Monte (★Los Angeles)	106,209
El Toro (★Anaheim)	62,685
Escondido (★San Diego)	108,635
Eureka (★89,800)	27,025
Fairfield (★Vallejo)	77,211
Fontana (★Riverside)	87,535
Fountain Valley (★Anaheim)	53,691
Fremont (★Oakland)	173,339
Fresno (★667,490)	354,202
Fullerton (★Anaheim)	114,144
Gardena (★Los Angeles)	49,847
Garden Grove (★Anaheim)	143,050
Glendale (★Los Angeles)	180,038
Hacienda Heights (★Los Angeles)	58,200
Hawthorne (★Los Angeles)	71,349
Hayward (★Oakland)	111,498
Hemet (★Riverside)	36,094
Huntington Beach (★Anaheim)	181,519
Huntington Park (★Los Angeles)	56,065
Inglewood (★Los Angeles)	109,602
Irvine (★Anaheim)	110,330
La Habra (★Anaheim)	51,266
Lakewood (★Los Angeles)	73,557
La Mesa (★San Diego)	52,931
Lancaster (★189,300) (★Los Angeles)	97,291
Livermore (★Oakland)	56,741
Lodi (★Stockton)	51,874
Lompoc (★Santa Barbara)	37,649
Long Beach (★Los Angeles)	429,433
Los Angeles (★14,531,529)	3,485,398
Lynwood (★Los Angeles)	61,945
Merced (★178,403)	56,216
Milpitas (★San Jose)	50,686
Mission Viejo (★Anaheim)	72,820
Modesto (★370,522)	164,730
Montebello (★Los Angeles)	59,564
Monterey (★Salinas)	31,954
Monterey Park (★Los Angeles)	60,738
Mountain View (★San Jose)	67,460
Napa (★Vallejo)	61,842
National City (★San Diego)	54,249
Newport Beach (★Anaheim)	66,643
Norwalk (★Los Angeles)	94,279
Oakland (★2,082,914) (★San Francisco)	372,242
Oceanside (★San Diego)	128,398
Ontario (★Riverside)	133,179
Orange (★Anaheim)	110,658
Oxnard (★669,016) (★Los Angeles)	142,216
Palm Springs (★Riverside)	40,181
Palo Alto (★San Jose)	55,900
Pasadena (★Los Angeles)	131,591
Pico Rivera (★Los Angeles)	59,177
Pleasanton (★Oakland)	50,553
Pomona (★Los Angeles)	131,723
Porterville (★Visalia)	29,563
Rancho Cordova (★Sacramento)	48,731
Redding (★147,036)	66,462
Redlands (★Riverside)	60,394
Redondo Beach (★Los Angeles)	60,167
Redwood City (★San Francisco)	66,072
Rialto (★Riverside)	72,388
Richmond (★Oakland)	87,425
Riverside (★2,588,793) (★Los Angeles)	226,505
Rosemead (★Los Angeles)	51,638
Sacramento (★1,481,102)	369,365
Salinas (★355,660)	108,777
San Bernardino (★Riverside)	164,164
San Diego (★2,949,000)	1,110,549
San Francisco (★6,253,311)	723,959
San Jose (★1,497,577) (★San Francisco)	782,248
San Leandro (★Oakland)	68,223
San Mateo (★San Francisco)	85,486
Santa Ana (★Anaheim)	293,742
Santa Barbara (★369,608)	85,571
Santa Clara (★San Jose)	93,613
Santa Cruz (★229,734) (★San Francisco)	49,040
Santa Maria (★Santa Barbara)	61,284
Santa Monica (★Los Angeles)	86,905
Santa Rosa (★388,222) (★San Francisco)	113,313
Santee (★San Diego)	52,902
Simi Valley (★Oxnard)	100,217
South Gate (★Los Angeles)	86,284
South San Francisco (★San Francisco)	54,312
South Whittier (★Los Angeles)	51,100
Spring Valley (★San Diego)	54,600
Stockton (★480,628)	210,943
Sunnyvale (★San Jose)	117,229
Thousand Oaks (★Oxnard)	104,352
Torrance (★Los Angeles)	133,107
Tustin (★Anaheim)	50,689
Union City (★Oakland)	53,762
Upland (★Riverside)	63,374
Vacaville (★Vallejo)	71,479
Vallejo (★451,186) (★San Francisco)	109,199
Ventura (San Buenaventura) (★Oxnard)	92,575
Visalia (★311,921)	75,636
Vista (★San Diego)	71,872
Walnut Creek (★Oakland)	60,569
Watsonville (★Santa Cruz)	31,099
West Covina (★Los Angeles)	96,086
Westminster (★Anaheim)	78,118
Whittier (★Los Angeles)	77,671
Yorba Linda (★Anaheim)	52,422
Yuba City (★122,643)	27,437

▲ Population of an entire municipality, commune, or district, including rural area.
• Largest city in country.
★ Population or designation of the metropolitan area, including suburbs.
C Census. **E** Official estimate. **U** Unofficial estimate.

▲ Bevölkerung eines ganzen städtischen Verwaltungsgebietes, eines Kommunalbezirkes oder eines Distrikts, einschliesslich ländlicher Gebiete.
• Grösste Stadt des Landes.
★ Bevölkerung oder Bezeichnung der Stadtregion einschliesslich Vororte.
C Volkszählung. **E** Offizielle Schätzung. **U** Inoffizielle Schätzung.

Population of Cities and Towns / Einwohnerzahlen von Grossstädten / Habitantes en las Ciudades y Poblaciones
Population des Grands Centres et des Villes / População dos Centros Urbanos
315

UNITED STATES: COLORADO

1990 C	3,294,394
Arvada (★Denver)	89,235
Aurora (★Denver)	222,103
Boulder (★225,339) (★Denver)	83,312
Colorado Springs (★397,014)	281,140
Denver (★1,848,319)	467,610
Fort Collins (★186,136)	87,758
Grand Junction (★85,200)	29,034
Greeley (★131,821)	60,536
Lakewood (★Denver)	126,481
Longmont (★Boulder)	51,555
Loveland (★Fort Collins)	37,352
Pueblo (★123,051)	98,640
Thornton (★Denver)	55,031
Westminster (★Denver)	74,625

UNITED STATES: CONNECTICUT

1990 C	3,287,116
Bridgeport (★443,722) (★New York, N.Y.)	141,686
Bristol (★79,488) (★Hartford)	60,640
Danbury (★187,867) (★New York, N.Y.)	65,585
East Hartford (★Hartford)	50,452
Fairfield (★Bridgeport)	53,418
Greenwich (★Stamford)	58,441
Hamden (★New Haven)	53,100
Hartford (★1,085,837)	139,739
Manchester (★Hartford)	51,000
Meriden (★New Haven)	59,479
Milford (★Bridgeport)	48,168
New Britain (★148,188) (★Hartford)	75,491
New Haven (★530,180)	130,474
New London (★266,819)	28,540
Norwalk (★127,378) (★New York, N.Y.)	78,331
Stamford (★202,557) (★New York, N.Y.)	108,056
Stratford (★Bridgeport)	49,389
Torrington (★58,800)	33,687
Waterbury (★221,629)	108,961
West Hartford (★Hartford)	59,100
West Haven (★New Haven)	54,021

UNITED STATES: DELAWARE

1990 C	666,168
Dover (★78,900)	27,630
Wilmington (★Philadelphia, Pa.)	71,529

UNITED STATES: DISTRICT OF COLUMBIA

1990 C	606,900
WASHINGTON (★3,923,574)	606,900

UNITED STATES: FLORIDA

1990 C	12,937,926
Boca Raton (★West Palm Beach)	61,492
Brandon (★Tampa)	57,985
Cape Coral (★Fort Myers)	74,991
Carol City (★Miami)	52,800
City of Sunrise (★Fort Lauderdale)	64,407
Clearwater (★Tampa)	98,784
Daytona Beach (★370,712)	61,921
De Land (★Daytona Beach)	16,491
Fort Lauderdale (★1,255,488) (★Miami)	149,377
Fort Myers (★335,113)	45,206
Fort Pierce (★251,071)	36,830
Fort Walton Beach (★143,776)	21,471
Gainesville (★204,111)	84,770
Hialeah (★Miami)	188,004
Hollywood (★Fort Lauderdale)	121,697
Jacksonville (★906,727)	635,230
Kendall (★Miami)	53,100
Lakeland (★405,382)	70,576
Largo (★Tampa)	65,674
Melbourne (★398,978)	59,646
Miami (★3,192,582)	358,548
Miami Beach (★Miami)	92,639
Naples (★152,099)	19,505
Ocala (★194,833)	42,045
Orlando (★1,072,748)	164,693
Panama City (★126,994)	34,378
Pembroke Pines (★Fort Lauderdale)	65,452
Pensacola (★344,406)	58,165
Plantation (★Fort Lauderdale)	66,692
Pompano Beach (★Fort Lauderdale)	72,411
Saint Petersburg (★Tampa)	238,629
Sarasota (★277,776)	50,961
Tallahassee (★233,598)	124,773
Tampa (★2,067,959)	280,015
Venice (★Sarasota)	16,922
West Palm Beach (★863,518)	67,643
Winter Haven (★Lakeland)	24,725

UNITED STATES: GEORGIA

1990 C	6,478,216
Albany (★112,561)	78,122
Athens (★156,267)	45,734
Atlanta (★2,833,511)	394,017
Augusta (★396,809)	44,639
Columbus (★243,072)	178,681
Macon (★281,103)	106,612
Rome (★74,900)	30,326
Savannah (★242,622)	137,560
Valdosta (★64,000)	39,806
Warner Robins (★Macon)	43,726

UNITED STATES: HAWAII

1990 C	1,108,229
Hilo (★47,600)	37,808
Honolulu (★836,231)	365,272

UNITED STATES: IDAHO

1990 C	1,006,749
Boise (★205,775)	125,738
Idaho Falls (★72,700)	43,929
Lewiston (★44,300)	28,082
Nampa (★70,500)	28,365
Pocatello (★56,700)	46,080

UNITED STATES: ILLINOIS

1990 C	11,430,602
Arlington Heights (★Chicago)	75,460
Aurora (★356,884) (★Chicago)	99,581
Bloomington (★129,180)	51,972
Champaign (★173,025)	63,502
Chicago (★8,065,633)	2,783,726
Cicero (★Chicago)	67,436
Danville (★68,000)	33,828
Decatur (★117,206)	83,885
De Kalb (★52,200)	34,925
Des Plaines (★Chicago)	53,223
East Saint Louis (★Saint Louis, Mo.)	40,944
Elgin (★Aurora)	77,010
Evanston (★Chicago)	73,233
Galesburg (★40,600)	33,530
Joliet (★389,650) (★Chicago)	76,836
Kankakee (★96,255)	27,575
Mount Prospect (★Chicago)	53,170
Naperville (★Chicago)	85,351
Oak Lawn (★Chicago)	56,182
Oak Park (★Chicago)	53,648
Peoria (★339,172)	113,504
Quincy (★50,600)	39,681
Rockford (★283,719)	139,426
Schaumburg (★Chicago)	68,586
Skokie (★Chicago)	59,432
Springfield (★189,550)	105,227
Waukegan (★Chicago)	69,392
Wheaton (★Chicago)	51,464

UNITED STATES: INDIANA

1990 C	5,544,159
Anderson (★130,669)	59,459
Bloomington (★108,978)	60,633
Columbus (★59,000)	31,802
Elkhart (★156,198)	43,627
Evansville (★278,990)	126,272
Fort Wayne (★363,811)	173,072
Gary (★604,526) (★Chicago, Il.)	116,646
Hammond (★Gary)	84,236
Indianapolis (★1,249,822)	731,327
Kokomo (★96,946)	44,962
Lafayette (★130,598)	43,764
Marion (★76,900)	32,618
Michigan City (★55,600)	33,822
Muncie (★119,659)	71,035
Richmond (★64,100)	38,705
South Bend (★247,052)	105,511
Terre Haute (★130,812)	57,483

UNITED STATES: IOWA

1990 C	2,776,755
Ames (★65,400)	47,198
Cedar Rapids (★168,767)	108,751
Clinton (★39,600)	29,201
Council Bluffs (★Omaha, Ne.)	54,315
Davenport (★350,861)	95,333
Des Moines (★392,928)	193,187
Dubuque (★86,403)	57,546
Iowa City (★96,119)	59,738
Mason City	29,040
Sioux City (★115,018)	80,505
Waterloo (★146,611)	66,467

UNITED STATES: KANSAS

1990 C	2,477,574
Hutchinson (★46,800)	39,308
Kansas City (★Kansas City, Mo.)	149,767
Lawrence (★81,798)	65,608
Manhattan (★47,400)	37,712
Olathe (★Kansas City, Mo.)	63,352
Overland Park (★Kansas City, Mo.)	111,790
Salina (★42,700)	42,303
Topeka (★160,976)	119,883
Wichita (★485,270)	304,011

UNITED STATES: KENTUCKY

1990 C	3,685,296
Bowling Green (★59,100)	40,641
Covington (★Cincinnati, Oh.)	43,264
Frankfort	25,968
Lexington (★348,428)	225,366
Louisville (★952,662)	269,063
Owensboro (★87,189)	53,549
Paducah (★63,000)	27,256

UNITED STATES: LOUISIANA

1990 C	4,219,973
Alexandria (★131,556)	49,188
Baton Rouge (★528,264)	219,531
Bossier City (★Shreveport)	52,721
Houma (★182,842)	96,982
Kenner (★New Orleans)	72,033
Lafayette (★208,740)	94,440
Lake Charles (★168,134)	70,580
Metairie (★New Orleans)	149,428
Monroe (★142,191)	54,909
New Iberia (★49,000)	31,828
New Orleans (★1,238,816)	496,938
Shreveport (★334,341)	198,525

UNITED STATES: MAINE

1990 C	1,227,928
Augusta (★56,700)	21,325
Bangor (★88,745)	33,181
Lewiston (★88,141)	39,757
Portland (★215,281)	64,358

UNITED STATES: MARYLAND

1990 C	4,781,468
Annapolis (★Baltimore)	33,187
Baltimore (★2,382,172)	736,014
Bethesda (★Washington, D.C.)	62,936
Columbia (★Baltimore)	75,883
Cumberland (★101,643)	23,706
Dundalk (★Baltimore)	65,800
Hagerstown (★121,393)	35,445
Salisbury (★72,400)	20,592
Silver Spring (★Washington, D.C.)	76,046
Towson (★Baltimore)	49,445
Wheaton (★Washington, D.C.) (1989)	58,300

UNITED STATES: MASSACHUSETTS

1990 C	6,016,425
Amherst (★44,700)	17,824
Boston (★4,171,643)	574,283
Brockton (★189,478) (★Boston)	92,788
Brookline (★Boston)	54,718
Cambridge (★Boston)	95,802
Chicopee (★Springfield)	56,632
Fall River (★157,272) (★Providence, R.I.)	92,703
Fitchburg (★102,797)	41,194
Framingham (★Boston)	64,989
Haverhill (★Lawrence)	51,418
Lawrence (★393,516) (★Boston)	70,207
Lowell (★273,067) (★Boston)	103,439
Lynn (★Salem)	81,245
Malden (★Boston)	53,884
Medford (★Boston)	57,407
New Bedford (★175,641)	99,922
Newton (★Boston)	82,585
Northampton (★Springfield)	29,289
Pittsfield (★79,250)	48,622
Quincy (★Boston)	84,985
Somerville (★Boston)	76,210
Springfield (★529,519)	156,983
Taunton (★59,700)	49,832
Waltham (★Boston)	57,878
Weymouth (★Boston)	54,063
Worcester (★436,905)	169,759

UNITED STATES: MICHIGAN

1990 C	9,295,297
Ann Arbor (★282,937) (★Detroit)	109,592
Battle Creek (★135,982)	53,540
Benton Harbor (★161,378)	12,818
Clinton Township (★Detroit)	77,900
Dearborn (★Detroit)	89,286
Dearborn Heights (★Detroit)	60,838
Detroit (★4,665,236)	1,027,974
East Lansing (★Lansing)	50,677
Farmington Hills (★Detroit)	74,652
Flint (★430,459)	140,761
Grand Rapids (★688,399)	189,126
Holland (★Grand Rapids)	30,745
Jackson (★149,756)	37,446
Kalamazoo (★223,411)	80,277
Lansing (★432,674)	127,321
Livonia (★Detroit)	100,850
Monroe (★62,600) (★Detroit)	22,902
Muskegon (★158,983)	40,283
Pontiac (★Detroit)	71,166
Port Huron (★Sarnia, Canada)	33,694
Redford Township (★Detroit)	54,387
Roseville (★Detroit)	51,412
Royal Oak (★Detroit)	65,410
Saginaw (★399,320)	69,512
Saint Clair Shores (★Detroit)	68,107
Sault Sainte Marie	14,689
Southfield (★Detroit)	75,728
Sterling Heights (★Detroit)	117,810
Taylor (★Detroit)	70,811
Troy (★Detroit)	72,884
Warren (★Detroit)	144,864
Westland (★Detroit)	84,724
Wyoming (★Grand Rapids)	63,891

UNITED STATES: MINNESOTA

1990 C	4,375,099
Bloomington (★Minneapolis)	86,335
Brooklyn Park (★Minneapolis)	56,381
Burnsville (★Minneapolis)	51,288
Coon Rapids (★Minneapolis)	52,978
Duluth (★239,971)	85,493
Mankato (★48,400)	31,477
Minneapolis (★2,464,124)	368,383
Plymouth (★Minneapolis)	50,889
Rochester (★106,470)	70,745
Saint Cloud (★190,921)	48,812
Saint Paul (★Minneapolis)	272,235

UNITED STATES: MISSISSIPPI

1990 C	2,573,216
Biloxi (★197,125)	46,319
Columbus (★52,100)	23,799
Greenville (★48,500)	45,226
Gulfport (★Biloxi)	40,775
Hattiesburg (★71,600)	41,882
Jackson (★395,396)	196,637
Laurel (★47,300)	18,827
Meridian (★60,600)	41,036
Natchez (★45,700)	19,460
Pascagoula (★115,243)	25,899
Vicksburg (★43,500)	20,908

UNITED STATES: MISSOURI

1990 C	5,117,073
Cape Girardeau (★59,100)	34,438
Columbia (★112,379)	69,101
Florissant (★Saint Louis)	51,206
Independence (★Kansas City)	112,301
Jefferson City (★60,100)	35,481
Joplin (★134,910)	40,961
Kansas City (★1,566,280)	435,146
Saint Charles (★Saint Louis)	54,555
Saint Joseph (★83,083)	71,852
Saint Louis (★2,444,099)	396,685
Springfield (★240,593)	140,494

UNITED STATES: MONTANA

1990 C	799,065
Billings (★113,419)	81,151
Butte (★33,900)	33,336
Great Falls (★77,691)	55,097
Helena	24,569
Missoula (★65,700)	42,918

UNITED STATES: NEBRASKA

1990 C	1,578,385
Grand Island (★42,200)	39,386
Lincoln (★213,641)	191,972
Omaha (★618,262)	335,795

UNITED STATES: NEVADA

1990 C	1,201,833
Carson City	40,443
Henderson (★Las Vegas)	64,942
Las Vegas (★741,459)	258,295
Paradise (★Las Vegas)	124,682
Reno (★254,667)	133,850
Sparks (★Reno)	53,367
Sunrise Manor (★Las Vegas)	95,362

UNITED STATES: NEW HAMPSHIRE

1990 C	1,109,252
Concord (★73,300)	36,006
Manchester (★147,809)	99,567
Nashua (★180,557) (★Boston, Ma.)	79,662
Portsmouth (★223,578)	25,925

UNITED STATES: NEW JERSEY

1990 C	7,730,188
Atlantic City (★319,416)	37,986
Bayonne (★Jersey City)	61,444
Bloomfield (★Newark)	45,061
Brick Township (★New York, N.Y.)	66,473
Camden (★Philadelphia, Pa.)	87,492
Cherry Hill (★Philadelphia, Pa.)	69,319
Clifton (★New York, N.Y.)	71,742
East Orange (★Newark)	73,552
Edison (★New York, N.Y.)	88,680
Elizabeth (★Newark)	110,002
Irvington (★Newark)	59,774
Jersey City (★553,099) (★New York, N.Y.)	228,537
Middletown (★New York, N.Y.)	62,298
Newark (★1,824,321) (★New York, N.Y.)	275,221
Passaic (★New York, N.Y.)	58,041
Paterson (★New York, N.Y.)	140,891
Trenton (★325,824) (★Philadelphia, Pa.)	88,675
Union (★Newark)	50,024
Union City (★Jersey City)	58,012
Vineland (★138,053) (★Philadelphia, Pa.)	54,780

UNITED STATES: NEW MEXICO

1990 C	1,515,069
Albuquerque (★480,577)	384,736
Farmington (★50,300)	33,997
Las Cruces (★135,510)	62,126
Roswell (★50,600)	44,654
Santa Fe (★117,043)	55,859

UNITED STATES: NEW YORK

1990 C	17,990,455
Albany (★874,304)	101,082
Auburn (★52,900)	31,258
Binghamton (★264,497)	53,008
Buffalo (★1,189,288)	328,123
Cheektowaga (★Buffalo)	84,387
Elmira (★95,195)	33,724
Glens Falls (★118,539)	15,023
Hempstead (★New York)	49,453
Irondequoit (★Rochester)	52,322
Ithaca (★82,700)	29,541
Jamestown (★141,895)	34,681
Kingston (★88,200)	23,095
Levittown (★New York)	53,286
Lockport (★57,500) (★Buffalo)	24,426
Mount Vernon (★New York)	67,153
Newburgh (★102,300) (★New York)	26,454
New Rochelle (★New York)	67,265
• New York (★18,087,251)	7,322,564
Niagara Falls (★220,756) (★Buffalo)	61,840
Poughkeepsie (★259,462)	28,844
Rochester (★1,002,410)	231,636
Schenectady (★Albany)	65,566
Syracuse (★659,864)	163,860
Troy (★Albany)	54,269
Utica (★316,633)	68,637
West Seneca (★Buffalo)	47,866
Yonkers (★New York)	188,082

UNITED STATES: NORTH CAROLINA

1990 C	6,628,637
Asheville (★174,821)	61,607
Burlington (★108,213)	39,498
Charlotte (★1,162,093)	395,934
Durham (★Raleigh)	136,611
Fayetteville (★274,566)	75,695
Gastonia (★Charlotte)	54,732
Goldsboro (★94,200)	40,709
Greensboro (★942,091)	183,521
Hickory (★221,700)	28,301
High Point (★Greensboro)	69,496
Jacksonville (★149,838)	30,013
Kannapolis (★Charlotte)	29,696
Raleigh (★735,480)	207,951
Rocky Mount (★83,400)	48,997
Salisbury (★Charlotte)	23,087
Wilmington (★120,284)	55,530
Winston-Salem (★Greensboro)	143,485

UNITED STATES: NORTH DAKOTA

1990 C	638,800
Bismarck (★83,831)	49,256
Fargo (★153,296)	74,111
Grand Forks (★70,683)	49,425
Minot (★39,800)	34,544

UNITED STATES: OHIO

1990 C	10,347,115
Akron (★657,575) (★Cleveland)	223,019
Alliance (★Canton)	23,376
Ashtabula (★40,900)	21,633
Brunswick (★Cleveland)	28,230
Canton (★394,106)	84,161
Cincinnati (★1,744,124)	364,040
Cleveland (★2,759,823)	505,616
Cleveland Heights (★Cleveland)	54,052
Columbus (★1,377,419)	632,910
Dayton (★951,270)	182,044
East Liverpool (★44,400)	13,654
Elyria (★Lorain)	56,746
Euclid (★Cleveland)	54,875
Hamilton (★291,479) (★Cincinnati)	61,368
Kettering (★Dayton)	60,569
Lakewood (★Cleveland)	59,718
Lancaster (★Columbus)	34,507
Lima (★154,340)	45,549
Lorain (★271,126) (★Cleveland)	71,245
Mansfield (★126,137)	50,627
Marion (★53,900)	34,075
Middletown (★107,200) (★Cincinnati)	46,022
Newark (★Columbus)	44,389
Parma (★Cleveland)	87,876
Portsmouth (★64,300)	22,676
Sandusky (★79,800)	29,764
Springfield (★Dayton)	70,487
Steubenville (★142,523)	22,125
Toledo (★614,128)	332,943
Warren (★Youngstown)	50,793
Youngstown (★492,619)	95,732
Zanesville (★67,800)	26,778

UNITED STATES: OKLAHOMA

1990 C	3,145,585
Broken Arrow (★Tulsa)	58,043
Edmond (★Oklahoma City)	52,315
Enid (★56,735)	45,309
Lawton (★111,486)	80,561
Midwest City (★Oklahoma City)	52,267
Muskogee (★49,500)	37,708
Norman (★Oklahoma City)	80,071
Oklahoma City (★958,839)	444,719

▲ Población de un municipio, comuna o distrito entero, incluyendo sus áreas rurales.
• Ciudad más grande de un país.
★ Población o designación de un área metropolitana, incluyendo los suburbios.
C Censo. E Estimado oficial. U Estimado no oficial.

▲ Population d'une municipalité, d'une commune ou d'un district, zone rurale incluse.
• Ville la plus peuplée du pays.
★ Population de l'agglomération (ou nom de la zone métropolitaine englobante).
C Recensement. E Estimation officielle. U Estimation non officielle.

▲ População de um municipio, comuna ou distrito, inclusive as respectivas áreas rurais.
• Maior cidade de um país.
★ População ou indicação de uma área metropolitana.
C Censo E Estimativa oficial. U Estimativa não oficial.

Tulsa (★708,954)	367,302

UNITED STATES: OREGON

1990 C	2,842,321
Beaverton (★Portland)	53,310
Corvallis (★98,700)	44,757
Eugene (★282,912)	112,669
Gresham (★Portland)	68,235
Medford (★146,389)	46,951
Portland (★1,477,895)	437,319
Salem (★278,024)	107,786

UNITED STATES: PENNSYLVANIA

1990 C	11,881,643
Abington (★Philadelphia)	59,300
Allentown (★686,688)	105,090
Altoona (★130,542)	51,881
Bensalem (★Philadelphia)	56,788
Bethlehem (★Allentown)	71,428
Bristol (★Philadelphia)	57,129
Butler (★86,500)	15,714
Coatesville (★93,400) (★Philadelphia)	11,038
Erie (★275,572)	108,718
Hanover (★York)	14,399
Harrisburg (★587,986)	52,376
Haverford (★Philadelphia)	49,848
Hazleton (★Scranton)	24,730
Johnstown (★241,247)	28,134
Lancaster (★422,822)	55,551
Lebanon (★Harrisburg)	24,800
Lower Merion Township (★Philadelphia)	58,003
New Castle (★68,400)	28,334
Oil City (★42,000)	11,949
Penn Hills (★Pittsburgh)	51,430
Philadelphia (★5,899,345)	1,585,577
Pittsburgh (★2,242,798)	369,879
Pottstown (★88,300) (★Philadelphia)	21,831
Pottsville (★54,200)	16,603
Reading (★336,523)	78,380
Scranton (★734,175)	81,805
Sharon (★121,003)	17,493
State College (★123,786)	38,923
Uniontown (★53,200) (★Pittsburgh)	12,034
Upper Darby (★Philadelphia)	84,054
Washington (★66,000) (★Pittsburgh)	15,864
Wilkes-Barre (★Scranton)	47,523
Williamsport (★118,710)	31,933
York (★417,848)	42,192

UNITED STATES: RHODE ISLAND

1990 C	1,003,464
Cranston (★Providence)	76,060
East Providence (★Providence)	50,380
Newport (★64,500)	28,227
Pawtucket (★329,384) (★Providence)	72,644
Providence (★1,141,510)	160,728
Warwick (★Providence)	85,427

UNITED STATES: SOUTH CAROLINA

1990 C	3,486,703
Anderson (★145,196)	26,184
Charleston (★506,875)	80,414
Columbia (★453,331)	98,052
Florence (★114,344)	29,813
Greenville (★640,861)	58,282
North Charleston (★Charleston)	70,218
Rock Hill (★Charlotte, N.C.)	41,643
Spartanburg (★Greenville)	43,467
Sumter (★90,300)	41,943

UNITED STATES: SOUTH DAKOTA

1990 C	696,004
Pierre	12,906
Rapid City (★81,343)	54,523
Sioux Falls (★123,809)	100,814

UNITED STATES: TENNESSEE

1990 C	4,877,185
Bristol (★Johnson City)	23,421
Chattanooga (★433,210)	152,466
Clarksville (★169,439)	75,494
Jackson (★77,982)	48,949
Johnson City (★436,047)	49,381
Kingsport (★Johnson City)	36,365
Knoxville (★604,816)	165,121
Memphis (★981,747)	610,337
Murfreesboro (★Nashville)	44,922
Nashville (★985,026)	487,969

UNITED STATES: TEXAS

1990 C	16,986,510
Abilene (★119,655)	106,654
Amarillo (★187,547)	157,615
Arlington (★Fort Worth)	261,721
Austin (★781,572)	465,622
Baytown (★Houston)	63,850
Beaumont (★361,226)	114,323
Brownsville (★460,000)	98,962
Bryan (★121,862)	55,002
Carrollton (★Dallas)	82,169
College Station (★Bryan)	52,456
Corpus Christi (★349,894)	257,453
Dallas (★3,885,415)	1,006,877
Denton (★Dallas)	66,270
El Paso (★650,000)	515,342
Fort Worth (★1,332,053) (★Dallas)	447,619
Freeport (★88,600) (★Houston)	11,389
Galveston (★217,399) (★Houston)	59,070
Garland (★Dallas)	180,650
Grand Prairie (★Dallas)	99,616
Harlingen (★Brownsville)	48,735
Houston (★3,711,043)	1,630,553
Irving (★Dallas)	155,037
Killeen (★255,301)	63,535
Laredo (★354,000)	122,899
Longview (★162,431)	70,311
Lubbock (★222,636)	186,206
Lufkin (★56,000)	30,206
McAllen (★383,545)	84,021
Mesquite (★Dallas)	101,484
Midland (★106,611)	89,443
Odessa (★118,934)	89,699
Pasadena (★Houston)	119,363
Plano (★Dallas)	128,713
Port Arthur (★Beaumont)	58,724
Richardson (★Dallas)	74,840
San Angelo (★98,458)	84,474
San Antonio (★1,302,099)	935,933
Sherman (★95,021)	31,601
Temple (★Killeen)	46,109
Texarkana (★120,132)	31,656
Tyler (★151,309)	75,450
Victoria (★74,361)	55,076
Waco (★189,123)	103,590
Wichita Falls (★122,378)	96,259

UNITED STATES: UTAH

1990 C	1,722,850
Logan (★60,300)	32,762
Ogden (★Salt Lake City)	63,909
Orem (★Provo)	67,561
Provo (★263,590)	86,835
Salt Lake City (★1,072,227)	159,936
Sandy (★Salt Lake City)	75,058
West Valley City (★Salt Lake City)	86,976

UNITED STATES: VERMONT

1990 C	562,758
Burlington (★131,439)	39,127
Montpelier (★52,800)	8,247
Rutland (★53,000)	18,230

UNITED STATES: VIRGINIA

1990 C	6,187,358
Alexandria (★Washington, D.C.)	111,183
Annandale (★Washington, D.C.)	50,975
Arlington (★Washington, D.C.)	170,936
Charlottesville (★131,107)	40,341
Chesapeake (★Norfolk)	151,976
Danville (★108,711)	53,056
Hampton (★Norfolk)	133,793
Lynchburg (★142,199)	66,049
Martinsville (★67,100)	16,162
Newport News (★Norfolk)	170,045
Norfolk (★1,396,107)	261,229
Portsmouth (★Norfolk)	103,907
Richmond (★865,640)	203,056
Roanoke (★224,477)	96,397
Suffolk (★Norfolk)	52,141
Virginia Beach (★Norfolk)	393,069

UNITED STATES: WASHINGTON

1990 C	4,866,692
Bellevue (★Seattle)	86,874
Bellingham (★127,780)	52,179
Bremerton (★189,731)	38,142
Everett (★Seattle)	69,961
Lakes District (★Tacoma)	58,412
Longview (★67,100)	31,499
Olympia (★161,238)	33,840
Pasco (★Richland)	20,337
Seattle (★2,559,164)	516,259
Spokane (★361,364)	177,196
Tacoma (★586,203) (★Seattle)	176,664
Yakima (★188,823)	54,827

UNITED STATES: WEST VIRGINIA

1990 C	1,793,477
Beckley (★64,300)	18,296
Charleston (★250,454)	57,287
Clarksburg (★53,800)	18,059
Fairmont (★53,700)	20,210
Huntington (★312,529)	54,844
Morgantown (★71,500)	25,879
Parkersburg (★149,169)	33,862
Wheeling (★159,301)	34,882

UNITED STATES: WISCONSIN

1990 C	4,891,769
Appleton (★315,121)	65,695
Beloit (★Janesville)	35,573
Eau Claire (★137,543)	56,856
Fond du Lac (★52,400)	37,757
Green Bay (★194,594)	96,466
Janesville (★139,510)	52,133
Kenosha (★128,181) (★Chicago, Il.)	80,352
La Crosse (★97,904)	51,003
Madison (★367,085)	191,262
Manitowoc (★57,300)	32,520
Milwaukee (★1,607,183)	628,088
Oshkosh (★Appleton)	55,006
Racine (★175,034) (★Milwaukee)	84,298
Sheboygan (★103,877)	49,676
Waukesha (★Milwaukee)	56,958
Wausau (★115,400)	37,060
Wauwatosa (★Milwaukee)	49,366
West Allis (★Milwaukee)	63,221

UNITED STATES: WYOMING

1990 C	453,588
Casper (★61,226)	46,742
Cheyenne (★73,142)	50,008

URUGUAY

1985 C	2,955,241
Las Piedras (★Montevideo)	58,288
Melo	42,615
Mercedes	36,702
Minas	34,661
• MONTEVIDEO (★1,550,000)	1,251,647
Paysandú	76,191
Rivera	57,316
Salto	80,823

UZBEKISTAN

1991 E	20,708,200
Almalyk	116,400
Andižan	298,300
Angren	132,600
Bekabad	82,800
Buchara	249,600
Çhodžejli	61,200
Čirčik (★Taškent)	158,400
Denau	49,300
Džizak	109,700
Fergana	193,700
Gulistan	54,500
Jangijul'	56,900
Kagan	49,800
Karši	168,000
Kattakurgan	59,600
Kokand	175,000
Margilan	124,900
Namangan	319,200
Navoi	111,600
Nukus	179,600
Şachrichan	47,600
Šachrisabz	53,200
Samarkand	370,500
• TAŠKENT (TASHKENT) (★2,325,000)	2,113,300
Termez	90,400
Urgenč	130,400

VANUATU

1989 C	142,944
• PORT VILA (★23,000)	19,311

VATICAN CITY / Città del Vaticano

1988 E	766

VENDA

1985 C	459,819
Makwarela	3,712
• Shayandima	4,853
THOHOYANDOU	3,641

VENEZUELA

1990 C	18,105,265
Acarigua	116,551
Anaco	61,386
Araure	55,299
Barcelona	221,792
Barinas	153,630
Barquisimeto	625,450
Baruta (★Caracas)	182,941
Cabimas	165,755
Cagua	73,465
Calabozo	79,578
• CARACAS (★4,000,000)	1,822,465
Carora	70,715
Carúpano	92,333
Catia La Mar (★Caracas)	100,104
Chacao (★Caracas)	66,897
Ciudad Bolívar	225,340
Ciudad Guayana	453,047
Ciudad Ojeda (Lagunillas)	73,473
Coro	124,506
Cumaná	212,432
El Limón	90,030
El Tigre	93,229
Guacara	100,766
Guanare	84,904
Guarenas (★Caracas)	134,158
La Asunción	16,552
La Victoria	77,326
Los Dos Caminos (★Caracas)	59,141
Los Teques (★Caracas)	140,617
Maiquetía (★Caracas)	62,834
Maracaibo	1,249,670
Maracay	354,196
Mariara	69,404
Maturín	206,654
Mérida	170,902
Palo Negro	50,718
Petare (★Caracas)	338,417
Porlamar	62,732
Pozuelos (1981C)	80,342
Puerto Ayacucho	36,107
Puerto Cabello	128,825
Puerto la Cruz	115,731
Punto Fijo	88,681
San Carlos	50,708
San Cristóbal	220,675
San Felipe	65,509
San Fernando	72,716
San Juan de los Morros	67,791
Trujillo	33,241
Tucupita	41,117
Turmero	174,280
Valencia	903,621
Valera	97,012
Valle de la Pascua	67,100
Villa de Cura	51,096

VIETNAM / Viet Nam

1989 C	64,411,668
Bac Giang	50,879
Bac Lieu	83,483
Bien Hoa	273,879
Buon Me Thuot	97,044
Ca Mau	81,901
Cam Pha	105,336
Can Tho	208,078
Chau Doc	50,935
Da Lat	102,583
Da Nang	369,734
Hai Duong	53,370
Hai Phong (▲1,447,523)	351,919
HA NOI (★1,275,000)	905,939
Hoa Binh	69,323
Hon Gai	123,102
Hue	211,718
Long Xuyen	128,814
Minh Hai (1979C)	72,517
My Tho	104,724
Nam Dinh	165,629
Nha Trang	213,460
Phan Rang	71,111
Phan Thiet	114,236
Play Cu	76,991
Qui Nhon	159,852
Rach Gia	137,784
Sa Dec	50,733
Soc Trang	87,899
Soc Trang	87,899
Tan An	50,288
Thai Binh	57,640
Thai Nguyen	124,871
Thanh Hoa	84,951
• Thanh Pho Ho Chi Minh (Saigon) (★3,300,000)	2,796,229
Tra Vinh	47,785
Tuy Hoa	54,081
Uong Bi	49,595
Viet Tri	73,347
Vinh	110,793
Vinh Long	81,620
Vung Tau	123,528
Yen Bai	58,645

VIRGIN ISLANDS OF THE UNITED STATES

1990 C	101,809
• CHARLOTTE AMALIE (★32,000)	12,331

WALLIS AND FUTUNA / Wallis et Futuna

1983 E	12,408
• MATÂ'UTU	815
Ono (1976C)	624

WESTERN SAHARA

1982 E	142,000
• EL AAIÚN	93,875

WESTERN SAMOA / Samoa i Sisifo

1981 C	156,349
• APIA	33,170

YEMEN / Al-Yaman

1990 E	15,267,000
ʻAdan (★318,000) (1984E)	176,100
Al-Ḥudaydah (1986C)	155,110
Al-Mukallā (1984E)	58,000
• ṢANʻĀʼ (1986C)	427,150
Taʻizz (1986C)	178,043

YUGOSLAVIA / Jugoslavija

1991 C	10,337,920
• BEOGRAD (★1,554,826)	1,136,786
Čačak	72,392
Kragujevac	146,607
Kraljevo	56,616
Kruševac	58,114
Leskovac	61,963
Niš	175,555
Novi Pazar	51,906
Novi Sad	178,896
Pančevo (★Beograd)	72,717
Podgorica	118,059
Priština (▲244,830) (1987E)	125,400
Šabac	54,829
Smederevo	64,257
Sombor	48,789
Subotica1)	100,219
Užice	53,666
Valjevo	58,324
Vranje	51,695
Zrenjanin	81,382

ZAIRE / Zaïre

1984 C	30,729,443
Bandundu	63,642
Beni	44,141
Boma	197,617
Bukavu	167,950
Bumba	51,197
Bunia	59,598
Butembo	73,312
Gandajika	64,878
Gbadolite	27,063
Gemena	63,052
Goma	77,908
Ilebo (Port-Francqui)	53,887
Isiro	78,268
Kalemie (Albertville)	73,528
Kamina	62,789
Kananga (Luluabourg)	298,693
Kikwit	149,296
Kindu	66,812
• KINSHASA (LÉOPOLDVILLE) (1986E)	3,000,000
Kipushi	53,207
Kisangani (Stanleyville)	317,581
Kolwezi	416,122
Likasi (Jadotville)	213,862
Lubumbashi (Élisabethville)	564,830
Matadi	138,798
Mbandaka (Coquilhatville)	137,291
Mbuji-Mayi (Bakwanga)	486,235
Mwene-Ditu	94,560
Tshikapa	116,016
Uvira	74,432

ZAMBIA

1990 C	7,818,447
Chililabombwe (Bancroft) (★76,848)	35,200
Chingola	167,954
Kabwe (Broken Hill)	166,519
Kalulushi	75,197
Kitwe (★338,207)	247,100
Livingstone	82,218
Luanshya (★146,275)	79,500
• LUSAKA	982,362
Mufulira (★152,944)	85,000
Ndola	376,311

ZIMBABWE

1983 E	7,740,000
Bulawayo	429,000
Chitungwiza (★Harare)	202,000
Gweru (1982C)	78,940
• HARARE (★890,000)	681,000
Mutare (1982C)	75,358

▲ Population of an entire municipality, commune, or district, including rural area.

• Largest city in country.
★ Population or designation of the metropolitan area, including suburbs.
C Census. **E** Official estimate. **U** Unofficial estimate.

▲ Bevölkerung eines ganzen städtischen Verwaltungsgebietes, eines Kommunalbezirkes oder eines Distrikts, einschliesslich ländlicher Gebiete.
• Grösste Stadt des Landes.
★ Bevölkerung oder Bezeichnung der Stadtregion einschliess lich Vororte.
C Volkszählung. **E** Offizielle Schätzung. **U** Inoffizielle Schätzung.

▲ Población de un municipio, comuna o distrito entero, incluyendo sus áreas rurales.

• Ciudad más grande de un país.
★ Población o designación de un área metropolitana, incluyendo los suburbios.
C Censo. **E** Estimado oficial. **U** Estimado no oficial.

▲ Population d'une municipalité, d'une commune ou d'un district, zone rurale incluse.

• Ville la plus peuplée du pays.
★ Population de l'agglomération (ou nom de la zone métropolitaine englobante).
C Recensement. **E** Estimation officielle. **U** Estimation non officielle.

▲ População de um municipio, comuna ou distrito, inclusive as respectivas áreas rurais.

• Maior cidade de um país.
★ População ou indicação de uma área metropolitana.
C Censo. **E** Estimativa oficial. **U** Estimativa não oficial.

The index includes in a single alphabetical list some 170,000 names appearing on the maps. Each name is followed by a page reference to one or more maps and by the location of the feature on the map, in coordinates of latitude and longitude. If a page contains several maps, a lowercase letter identifies the particular map. The page reference for two-page maps is always to the left-hand page.

Most map features are indexed to the largest-scale map on which they appear. However, a feature usually is not indexed to a Metropolitan Area map if it is also shown on another map where it can be seen in a broader setting. Countries, mountain ranges, and other extensive features are generally indexed to the largest-scale map that shows them in their entirety.

The order in which index information is presented is shown in the English, German, Spanish, French, and Portuguese headings at the center of each two-page spread.

For example:

ENGLISH

Name	Page	Lat.°′	Long.°′

The features indexed are of three types: *point*, *areal*, and *linear*. For *point* features (for example, cities, mountain peaks, dams), latitude and longitude coordinates give the location of the point on the map. For *areal* features (countries, mountain ranges, etc.), the coordinates generally indicate the approximate center of the feature. For *linear* features (rivers, canals, aqueducts), the coordinates locate a terminating point—for example, the mouth of a river, or the point at which a feature reaches the map margin.

Name Forms Names in the index, as on the maps, are generally in the local language and insofar as possible are spelled according to official practice. Diacritical marks are included, except that those used to indicate tone, as in Vietnamese, are usually not shown. Most features that extend beyond the boundaries of one country have no single official name, and these are usually named in English. Many English, German, Spanish, French, and Portuguese names, which may not be shown on the maps, appear in the index as cross references. All cross references are indicated by the symbol →. A name that appears in a shortened version on the map due to space limitations is given in full in the index, with the portion that is omitted on the map enclosed in brackets, for example, Acapulco [de Juárez].

Transliteration For names in languages not written in the Roman alphabet, the locally official transliteration system has been used where one exists. Thus, names in Russia and Bulgaria have been transliterated according to the systems adopted by the academies of science of these countries. Similarly, the transliteration for mainland Chinese names follows the Pinyin system, which has been officially adopted in mainland China. For languages with no one locally accepted transliteration system, notably Arabic, transliteration in general follows closely a system adopted by the United States Board on Geographic Names.

Alphabetization Names are alphabetized in the order of the letters of the English alphabet. Spanish *ll* and *ch*, for example, are not treated as distinct letters. Furthermore, diacritical marks are disregarded in alphabetization—German or Scandinavian *ä* or *ö* are treated as *a* or *o*.

The names of physical features may appear inverted, since they are always alphabetized under the proper, not the generic, part of the name, thus: "Gibraltar, Strait of ʊ." Otherwise every entry, whether consisting of one word or more, is alphabetized as a single continuous entity. "Lakeland," for example, appears after "La Crosse" and before "La Salle." Names beginning with articles (Le Havre, Den Helder, Al-Qāhirah, As-Suways) are not inverted. Names beginning with "St." and "Sainte" are alphabetized as though spelled "Saint."

In the case of identical names, towns are listed first, then political divisions, then physical features. Entries that are completely identical (including symbols, discussed below) are distinguished by abbreviations of their official country names and are sequenced alphabetically by country name. The many duplicate names in Canada, the United Kingdom, and the United States are further distinguished by abbreviations of the names of their primary subdivisions. (See list of abbreviations on pages 319-320).

Abbreviation and Capitalization Abbreviation and styling have been standardized for all languages. A period is used after every abbreviation even when this may not be the local practice. The abbreviation "St." is used only for "Saint." "Sankt" and other forms of the term are spelled out.

All names are written with an initial capital letter except for a few Dutch names, such as 's-Gravenhage. Capitalization of noninitial words in a name generally follows local practice.

Symbols The symbols that appear in the index represent graphically the broad categories of the features named, for example, ∧ for mountain (Everest, Mount ∧). An abbreviated key to the symbols, in the five atlas languages, appears at the foot of each pair of index pages. Superior numbers following some symbols in the index indicate finer distinctions, for example, $\wedge^{1}$ for volcano (Fuji-san $\wedge^{1}$). A complete list of the symbols and superior numbers is given on page I•1.

Das Register umfasst in alphabetischer Anordnung etwa 170 000 in den Karten erscheinende Namen. Nach jedem Namen folgt die Seitenangabe zu einer oder mehreren Karten und die Lageangabe des Objektes in der Karte mit geographischer Länge und Breite. Enthält eine Seite mehrere Karten, so wird die betreffende Karte durch einen Kleinbuchstaben gekennzeichnet. Die Seitenangabe für Doppelseiten bezieht sich immer auf die linke Seite.

Die Verweise für die meisten Objekte in den Karten beziehen sich auf die Karte mit dem grössten Massstab. Normalerweise werden jedoch Verweise auf Objekte in den Karten der Stadtregionen nicht gegeben, wenn sie auf einer anderen Karte in grösserem Zusammenhang dargestellt sind. Die Lageangaben für Länder, Gebirgszüge und andere ausgedehnte Objekte beziehen sich allgemein auf die Karte grössten Massstabes, die sie in ihrer ganzen Ausdehnung zeigt.

Die Anordnung, in welcher die Lageangabe erfolgt, geht aus den englischen, deutschen, spanischen, französischen und portugiesischen Überschriften in der Mitte jeder Doppelseite hervor.

Zum Beispiel:

DEUTSCH

Name	Seite	Breite°′	Länge°′ E = Ost

Die aufgeführten Objekte gliedern sich in drei Gruppen: *punkt-*, *flächen-* und *linienförmige* Objekte. Bei *punktförmigen* Objekten (z.B. Städte, Berge, Dämme) beziehen sich die Angaben nach Länge und Breite auf die Signatur in der Karte. Bei *flächenhaften* Objekten (Länder, Gebirgszüge usw.) verweisen die Koordinaten im allgemeinen auf das ungefähre Zentrum des Objektes. Bei *linienhaften* Objekten (Flüsse, Kanäle, Wasserleitungen) beziehen sich die Koordinaten auf einen bestimmten Punkt, z.B. die Mündung eines Flusses oder den Punkt, an dem das Objekt den Kartenrand schneidet.

Namengebung Wie in den Karten so sind auch im Register die Namen im allgemeinen in der örtlichen Namensform wiedergegeben und soweit als möglich in der amtlichen Schreibweise. Diakritische Zeichen wurden gesetzt; sie wurden nur dort weggelassen, wo sie, wie im Vietnamesischen, Tonhöhen kennzeichnen. Meist haben Objekte, die sich über die Grenzen eines Landes hinaus erstrecken, keinen einzelnen offiziellen Namen; normalerweise sind sie daher englisch beschriftet. Viele englische, deutsche, spanische, französische und portugiesische Namensformen, die nicht in den Karten enthalten sind, erscheinen im Register als Kreuzverweis. Alle Kreuzverweise werden durch das Symbol → gekennzeichnet. Namen, die aus Platzgründen in abgekürzter Form in der Karte erscheinen, werden im Register voll ausgeschrieben, wobei der auf der Karte weggelassene Teil in Klammern gesetzt ist, z.B. Acapulco [de Juárez].

Transkription Für die Transkription von Namen aus Sprachen, die nicht im lateinischen Alphabet geschrieben werden, wurde das offizielle Transkriptionssystem benutzt, sofern ein solches vorhanden ist. So wurden die Namen in Russland und in Bulgarien nach dem von den wissenschaftlichen Akademien dieser Länder angewandten System transkribiert. Entsprechend wurden die Namen auf dem chinesischen Festland nach dem Pinyin-System übertragen, das offiziell in der Volksrepublik China eingeführt wurde. Bei Sprachen, für die ein allgemein anerkanntes Transkriptionssystem nicht vorliegt, vor allem für Arabisch, erfolgte die Transkription in enger Anlehnung an das vom United States Board on Geographic Names angewandte System.

Alphabetische Ordnung Die alphabetische Ordnung der Namen entspricht der Reihenfolge der Buchstaben im englischen Alphabet. So werden z.B. das spanische *ll* und *ch* nicht als besondere Buchstaben behandelt. Ferner wurden diakritische Zeichen beim Alphabetisieren nicht berücksichtigt, das deutsche oder skandinavische *ä* oder *ö* als *a* oder *o* behandelt.

Physische Objekte können umgestellt erscheinen, da sie immer nach dem Eigennamen und nicht nach dem Gattungsbegriff eingeordnet wurden, z.B. "Gibraltar, Strait of ʊ." Ansonsten wurde jeder Eintrag, ob er aus einem Wort oder aus mehreren besteht, als eine einzige Einheit behandelt. So ist z.B. "Lakeland" nach "La Crosse," aber vor "La Salle" aufgeführt. Namen, die mit einem Artikel beginnen, wurden nicht umgestellt (Le Havre, Den Helder, Al-Qāhirah, As-Suways). Namen, die mit "St." und "Sainte" beginnen, sind der Schreibweise "Saint" nach eingeordnet.

Wo Namensgleichheit besteht, werden zunächst die Städte aufgeführt, dann politische Einheiten und schliesslich physische Objekte. Eintragungen, die vollkommen identisch sind (einschliesslich der weiter unten erläuterten Symbole), werden durch Hinzufügung der Abkürzung des offiziellen Ländernamens unterschieden und sind den Ländernamen nach alphabetisch geordnet. Die zahlreichen identischen Namen in Kanada, dem Vereinigten Königreich und den Vereinigten Staaten sind darüber hinaus noch durch Abkürzungen der obersten Verwaltungseinheit unterschieden. (Siehe Verzeichnis der Abkürzungen, Seite 319-320).

Abkürzungen und Grossschreibung Abkürzung und Schreibweise wurden für alle Sprachen vereinheitlicht. Nach jeder Abkürzung steht ein Punkt, auch wenn dies nicht der jeweiligen Gepflogenheit entspricht. Die Abkürzung "St." wird ausschliesslich für "Saint" gebraucht. "Sankt" und andere Formen dieses Begriffes werden ausgeschrieben.

Der erste Buchstabe eines Namens wird gross geschrieben, ausgenommen einige holländische Namen wie 's-Gravenhage. Die Grossschreibung der weiteren Worte eines zusammengesetzten Namens folgt im allgemeinen der landesüblichen Schreibweise.

Symbole Die im Register verwendeten Symbole veranschaulichen graphisch die zahlreichen Kategorien der benannten Objekte, z.B. ∧ = Berg (Everest, Mount ∧). Eine kurzgefasste Erläuterung der Symbole erscheint in jeder der fünf Sprachen des Atlas am Fusse jeder Doppelseite des Registers. Hochgestellte Ziffern hinter Symbolen im Register bezeichnen feinere Unterscheidungen, z.B. $\wedge^{1}$ = Vulkan (Fuji-san $\wedge^{1}$). Eine vollständige Übersicht der Symbole und hochgestellten Ziffern findet sich auf Seite I•1.

El índice contiene en una sola lista alfabética, alrededor de 170 000 nombres que aparecen en los mapas. Después de cada nombre está indicada la página o las páginas de referencia, en los cuales se encuentran los mismos, y las coordinadas de la latitud y la longitud del lugar del rasgo. Si una página contiene various mapas, letras minúsculas identifican el mapa correspondiente. Para mapas que ocupan dos páginas, la página de referencia siempre es la de la izquierda.

La mayoría de los nombres que figuran en el índice, se efiere a los mapas en la escala más grande. Sin embargo, un nombre no se refiere en un mapa metropolitano si ya aparece en otro mapa, donde se muestra en un marco de mayor proporción. Los países, sierras y otros rasgos extensivos se refieren generalmente en el índice en los mapas de escalas mayores en que se muestran completos.

En orden en que la información del índice se presenta, aparece en un encabezamiento al centro de cada par de páginas, en inglés, alemán, español, francés y portugués.

Por ejemplo:

ESPAÑOL

Nombre	Página	Lat.°′	Long.°′ W = Oeste

Los rasgos anotados en el índice son de tres tipos: *el punto, el área y la extensión linear.* Para rasgos que indican *el punto* (como por ejemplo, las ciudades, picos de montañas, presas), las coordinadas de latitud y longitud indican la posición exacta del punto sobre el mapa. Respecto a *las áreas* (como países, sierras, etc.), las coordinadas indican usualmente el centro aproximado del rasgo particular. En cuanto a *los rasgos lineares* (ríos, canales, acueductos) las coordinadas indican los puntos terminales, por ejemplo, la boca de un río, o el punto en que un rasgo físico alcanza el margen del mapa.

Las Formas de los Nombres Los nombres que aparecen en el índice, así como también en los mapas, se dan en general en el idioma local, y en tanto que es posible siguen la ortografía oficialmente aceptada. Incluímos también marcas diacríticas, excepto las que se usan para indicar tono, como en la lengua vietnamita. A causa de que la mayoría de los rasgos que se extienden más allá de las fronteras de un país no tienen un solo nombre oficial, éstos se denominan usualmente en inglés. Muchos nombres, en inglés, alemán, español, francés y portugués, que pueden no figurar en el mapa, se dan como referencia de una página a otra en el índice. Todas las referencias que pasan a otras páginas se indican con el símbolo →. Un nombre que aparece en el mapa en forma abreviada, debido a la limitación de espacio, en el índice figura en su forma completa, poniendo entre paréntesis angulares la parte omitida en el mapa, por ejemplo Acapulco [de Juárez].

"Trasliteración" Para los nombres escritos en los idiomas que no usan el alfabeto latino, el sistema oficial de trasliteración ha sido utilizado donde localmente existe. Así, los nombres de Rusia y de Bulgaria se trasliteran conforme a los sistemas aceptados por las academias de las ciencias de sus respectivos países. De la misma manera, la trasliteración de los nombres en chino continental siguen el sistema Pinyin que ha sido oficialmente adoptado en este país. Para idiomas sin ningún sistema localmente aceptado de trasliteración, particularmente para el árabe, éstos se trasliteran usando por lo general un sistema adoptado por el United States Board on Geographic Names.

Alfabetización Los nombres se han ordenado de acuerdo con el alfabeto inglés. Las letras del alfabeto en español *ll* y *ch* por ejemplo, no se han considerado letras separadas. Además, los signos diacríticos no se toman en cuenta en la alfabetización — en alemán o escadinavo letras *ä* u *ö* se tratan como *a* u *o*.

Los nombres de los rasgos físicos algunas veces se invierten, ya que se ordenan alfabéticamente según la parte propia y no genérica del nombre. Así por ejemplo, en el caso del Estrecho de Gibraltar aparece: Gibraltar, Strait of ⊔. Por lo demás, cada renglón, sea una palabra o una frase, se alfabetiza como una unidad. Por ejemplo, "Lakeland" aparece después de "La Crosse" y antes de "La Salle." Los nombres que comienzan con artículos (Le Havre, Den Helder, Al-Qāhirah, As-Suways) no están invertidos. Nombres que empiezan con "St." y "Sainte" se alfabetizan como "Saint".

En los casos de nombres idénticos, las poblaciones aparecen primero, las divisiones políticas después y finalmente los rasgos físicos. En caso de ser completamente idénticos (incluyendo los símbolos, discutidos más abajo) se distinguen por medio de abreviaciones de los nombres oficiales de los países a que pertenecen y son puestos en orden alfabético, de acuerdo al nombre de cada país. Hay muchos nombres duplicados en Canadá, el Reino Unido y los Estados Unidos de América, y éstos se distinguen además, por sus subdivisiones primarias. (Vease abajo, la lista de abreviaciones en las páginas 319-320).

Abreviaciones y Mayúsculas Las abreviaciones y el uso de las mayúsculas se han hecho uniformes para todos los idiomas. Se usa un punto al final de la abreviación, aun cuando en algunos casos no sea ésta la práctica local. La abreviación "St." se usa sólo para "Saint." Las otras formas del mismo término, como "Sankt," se escriben completas.

La mayúscula se usa al comienzo de todos los nombres a excepción de algunos holandeses, como 's-Gravenhage. Las palabras que no son iniciales, se dan con mayúscula o minúscula, según la práctica local.

Símbolos Los símbolos que aparecen en el índice representan gráficamente las grandes categorías de los rasgos que se han ido nombrando, por ejemplo, ▲ para montaña (Everest, Mount ▲). Una clave abreviada para los símbolos aparece en los cinco idiomas del atlas al pie de cada par de páginas del índice. Los números que siguen más arriba del símbolo indican alguna diferencia más precisa, pro ejemplo, ▲^{1} para un volcán (Fuji- san ▲^{1}). Una lista completa de símbolos y números superiores aparece en la página I•1.

L'index rassemble en une seule liste alphabétique, quelque 170 000 noms qui figurent sur les cartes. Chaque nom est suivi d'un renvoi à une ou plusieurs pages de cartes et de coordonnées géographiques qui permettent de localiser ce qu'il désigne. Si une page contient plusieurs cartes, une lettre minuscule permet d'identifier chaque carte. Pour les cartes en double page, la référence indiquée est toujours celle de la page de gauche.

En général, l'index renvoie aux cartes où l'information recherchée est reproduite à la plus grande échelle; cependant, les cartes de zones métropolitaines ne sont pas utilisées si le terme géographique figure sur une autre carte dans un contexte plus large. Pour les éléments de grande dimension comme les pays et les chaînes de montagnes, l'index renvoie généralement à la carte à grande échelle qui les représente en entier.

L'ordre des informations de l'index est rappelé en tête de chaque double page dans les cinq langues: anglais, allemand, espagnol, français et portugais.

Par exemple:

FRANÇAIS

Nom	Page	Lat.°′	Long.°′ W = Ouest

Les termes de l'index désignent des réalités géographiques de type *ponctuel, spatial* ou *linéaire*. Leur position est déterminée par les coordonnées géographiques du lieu quand les données sont de type *ponctuel* (villes, sommets, barrages, etc.), quand elles sont de type *spatial* (pays, chaînes de montagnes, etc.) par les coordonnées du centre approximatif de la zone considérée, et, quand elles sont du type *linéaire* (aqueducs, canaux, etc.) par les coordonnées soit d'un point terminal comme l'embouchure d'un cours d'eau, soit du point où les limites de la carte les interrompent.

Forme des Toponymes Les noms de l'index comme ceux des cartes sont généralement reproduits dans la langue locale et, dans la mesure du possible, selon leur orthographe officielle. Les signes diacritiques sont conservés, à l'exclusion de ceux qui servent à indiquer le ton, comme en vietnamien. La plupart des données géographiques qui s'étendent au-delà des frontières d'un pays sont nommées souvent en anglais, car elles n'ont pas de nom officiel unique. Beaucoup de noms anglais, allemands, espagnols, français et portugais, qui ne se trouvent pas sur les cartes, sont cités dans l'index sous forme de renvois. Tous les renvois sont signalés par le symbole (→). Un nom écrit sur la carte sous forme abrégée, par manque de place, figure en entier dans l'index; la partie omise est entre crochets, par exemple: Acapulco [de Juárez].

Transcription des Noms Pour les noms qui viennent de langues n'utilisant pas l'alphabet romain, le système local et officiel de transcription a été utilisé là où il existait. Ainsi, les noms russes et bulgares ont été transcrits selon les systèmes adoptés par les académies des sciences de ces pays. De même, pour la transcription des noms de la Chine continentale, on a employé le système Pinyin, officiellement adopté en Chine continentale. Pour les langues qui n'ont pas de système officiel de transcription en alphabet romain, notamment l'arabe, la transcription suit généralement de près le système adopté par le United States Board on Geographic Names (Comité américain pour les noms géographiques).

Ordre Alphabétique Les noms sont classés dans l'ordre de l'alphabet anglais. Les *ll* et *ch* espagnols, par exemple, ne sont pas traités comme des lettres séparées. De plus, on ne tient pas compte des signes diacritiques: le *ä* et le *ö* allemand ou scandinave correspondent au *a* et *o* sans tréma.

Les noms des données physiques peuvent se trouver inversés car ils sont toujours classés suivant le nom propre. Exemple: "Gibraltar, Strait of ⊔." Par ailleurs, les noms composés d'un ou plusieurs mots sont considérés comme une seule entité. Exemple: "Lakeland" est inscrit après "La Crosse" et avant "La Salle." Les noms qui commencent par un article (Le Havre, Den Helder, Al-Qāhirah, As-Suways) ne sont pas inversés. Les noms qui commencent par "St." ou "Sainte" sont classés comme s'ils s'écrivaient "Saint."

Dans le cas de noms identiques, les villes sont inscrites d'abord, puis les divisions politiques, et ensuite les données physiques. Les noms qui sont tout à fait identiques (y compris les symboles qui s'y rapportent) se distinguent par leur pays d'origine, noté en abrégé dans l'ordre alphabétique. Les noms que l'on rencontre plusieurs fois, au Canada, au Royaume-Uni et aux Etats-Unis se distinguent grâce à l'abréviation de la première subdivision administrative de ce pays (voir la liste des abréviations de la page 319-320).

Abréviations et Majuscules L'usage des abréviations a été standardisé pour toutes les langues. Un point suit chaque abréviation, même quand ce n'est pas l'usage dans certaines langues. L'abréviation "St." sert uniquement pour le mot "Saint." "Sankt" et les autres formes du mot "Saint" sont écrites en entier.

Tous les noms commencent par une majuscule, sauf quelques noms des Pays-Bas comme 's-Gravenhage. Certains noms prennent une majuscule, même s'ils ne se trouvent pas au début du terme; on a adopté, en général, l'orthographe locale.

Symboles Les symboles utilisés dans l'index donnent une représentation graphique des réalités géographiques mentionnées. Par exemple, ▲ pour une montagne (Everest, Mount ▲). Une explication abrégée des symboles dans les cinq langues de l'Atlas se trouve au bas de chaque double page de l'index. Les indices qui accompagnent certains symboles permettent une distinction plus précise. Par exemple, ▲^{1} pour volcan (Fujisan ▲^{1}). Une liste complète des symboles et indices est donnée à la page I•1.

O Índice contém, numa só lista alfabética, cerca de 170,000 nomes que figuram nos mapas. Segue-se a cada nome a referência a um ou mais mapas e a localização do acidente geográfico no mapa pelas respectivas coordenadas de latitude e longitude. A referência a mapas que ocupam duas páginas fica sempre na página da esquerda. A maior parte dos acidentes geográficos estão indexados no mapa em que aparecem em escala maior. No entanto, um acidente geográfico não é geralmente indexado num mapa de Área Metropolitana se também figura em outro mapa em que aparece em contexto mais amplo. Os países, cordilheiras e outros acidentes geográficos de maior extensão estão geralmente indexados no mapa em escala maior que os apresente em seu todo.

A ordem em que as informações são apresentadas no Índice figura no cabeçalho, a cada duas páginas, em inglês, alemão, espanhol, francês e PORTUGUÊS.

Por exemplo:

PORTUGUÊS

Nome	Página	Lat.°′	Long.°′ W = Oeste

Os acidentes indexados são de três tipos: *Ponto, espacial* (área) e *linear* (extensão). Para acidentes que indicam *pontos* (como, por exemplo, cidades, picos de montanhas, represas), as coordenadas de latitude e longitude indicam a posição exata do ponto no mapa. No que se refere aos *acidentes espaciais* (como países, cordilheiras etc.), as coordenadas geralmente indicam o centro aproximado do acidente específico. Quanto aos *acidentes lineares* (rios, canais, aquedutos), as coordenadas localizam os pontos terminais, como, por exemplo, a foz de um rio, ou o ponto em que um acidente físico atinge a margem do mapa.

Formas dos nomes Os nomes que aparecem no Índice, assim como também nos mapas, são geralmente apresentados na língua local, e tanto quanto possível, seguem a ortografia oficial. Usam-se, também, os sinais diacríticos, exceto os que indicam tom, como na língua vietnamita. A maioria dos acidentes geográficos que se estendem além das fronteiras de um só país não possuem um nome oficial único; nesses casos, estão geralmente indicados em inglês. Muitos nomes em inglês, alemão, espanhol, português e francês podem não figurar nos mapas, mas aparecem no Índice como referências remissivas. Todas essas referências são indicadas pelo símbolo (→). Um nome que aparece no mapa em forma abreviada devido a limitações de espaço, figura no Índice em sua forma completa, com a parte omitida no mapa entre chaves (por exemplo, Acapulco [de Juárez]).

Transliteração Para os nomes escritos em línguas que não usam o alfabeto latino, foi utilizado o sistema oficial de transliteração, sempre que este existia. Assim, os nomes da Rússia e da Bulgária foram transliterados de acordo com os sistemas adotados pelas academias de ciências desses países. Do mesmo modo, a transliteração dos nomes da China continental seguem o sistema Pinyin, que foi oficialmente adotado nesse país. Para as línguas que não possuem um sistema de transliteração adotado oficialmente, em especial o árabe, a transliteração geralmente segue de perto o sistema adotado pelo Conselho de Nomes Geográficos dos Estados Unidos (United States Board on Geographic Names).

Alfabetação Os nomes foram ordenados de acordo com o alfabeto inglês. Por exemplo, o espanhol *ll* e *ch* não foram considerados como letras separadas. Ademais, os sinais diacríticos não foram considerados na alfabetação. Por exemplo, em alemão ou escandinavo as letras *ä* ou *ö* foram tratradas como *a* ou *o*.

Os nomes dos acidentes físicos podem aparecer, às vezes, invertidos, já que foram sempre alfabetados pela parte específica e não genérica do nome, como, por exemplo, *Gibraltar, estreito de* ⊔. Por outro lado, cada entrada do Índice, quer constituída por uma só palavra ou mais de uma, foi alfabetada como uma unidade contínua. Por exemplo, "Lakeland" aparece depois de "La Grosse" e antes de "La Salle". Os nomes que começam por artigo (Le Havre, Den Helder, Al-Qāhirah, As-Suways) não são invertidos. Os nomes que começam por "St." e "Sainte" são alfabetados como se fossem soletrados "Saint".

Nos casos de nomes idênticos, as cidades estão relacionadas em primeiro lugar; depois as divisões políticas e em seguida os acidentes físicos. As entradas completamente idênticas (inclusive símbolos, mencionados mais abaixo), distinguem-se pelas abreviaturas dos nomes oficiais dos países a que pertencem e são arrolados na ordem alfabética do nome do país. Os muitos nomes repetidos no Canadá, no Reino Unido e nos Estados Unidos, são ainda diferenciados pelas abreviaturas dos nomes das respectivas subdivisões primárias (Ver a lista de abreviaturas, das páginas 319-320).

Abreviações e uso de maiúsculas As abreviaturas e o estilo foram normalizados em todas as línguas. Usa-se um ponto depois de cada abreviatura, mesmo que não seja essa a prática local. A abreviatura "St." só é usada para "Saint". As outras formas do termo, tal como "Sankt", são escritas por extenso.

Todos os nomes são escritos com a inicial maiúscula exceto em alguns nomes holandeses, como 's-Gravenhage. O uso de maiúsculas em palavras não iniciais de um nome segue geralmente a prática local.

Símbolos Os símbolos que aparecem no Índice representam graficamente as grandes categorias dos acidentes indicados, por exemplo, ▲ para montanha (Everest, Mount ▲). Uma chave abreviada dos símbolos nas cinco línguas do Atlas figura no pé de cada par de páginas do Índice. Os números altos que acompanham certos símbolos do Índice indicam diferenças mais precisas, como, por examplo, ▲^{1} para vulcão (Fuji-san ▲^{1}). Uma lista completa de símbolos e números altos aparece à pág. I•1.

List of Abbreviations / Verzeichnis der Abkürzungen 319
Lista de Abreviaciones / Liste des Abréviations / Lista de Abreviaturas

	LOCAL NAME	ENGLISH	DEUTSCH	ESPAÑOL	FRANÇAIS	PORTUGUÊS
Ab., Can.	Alberta	Alberta	Alberta	Alberta	Alberta	Alberta
Afg.	Afghānestān	Afghanistan	Afghanistan	Afganistán	Afghanistan	Afeganistão
Afr.	. . .	Africa	Afrika	Africa	Afrique	África
Ak., U.S.	Alaska	Alaska	Alaska	Alaska	Alaska	Alasca
Al., U.S.	Alabama	Alabama	Alabama	Alabama	Alabama	Alabama
Alg.	Algérie / Djazaïr	Algeria	Algerien	Argelia	Algérie	Argélia
Am. Sam.	American Samoa / Amerika Samoa	American Samoa	Amerikanisch-Samoa	Samoa Americana	Samoa américaines	Samoa Americana
And.	Andorra	Andorra	Andorra	Andorra	Andorre	Andorra
Ang.	Angola	Angola	Angola	Angola	Angola	Angola
Anguilla	Anguilla	Anguilla	Anguilla	Anguilla	Anguilla	Anguilla
Ant.	. . .	Antarctica	Antarktis	Antártida	Antarctique	Antártida
Antig.	Antigua and Barbuda	Antigua and Barbuda	Antigua und Barbuda	Antigua y Barbuda	Antigua-et-Barbuda	Antígua e Barbuda
Ar., U.S.	Arkansas	Arkansas	Arkansas	Arkansas	Arkansas	Arkansas
Arg.	Argentina	Argentina	Argentinien	Argentina	Argentine	Argentina
Ar. Su.	Al-ʿArabīyah as-Suʿūdīyah	Saudi Arabia	Saudi-Arabien	Arabia Saudita	Arabie saoudite	Arábia Saudita
Aruba	Aruba	Aruba	Aruba	Aruba	Aruba	Aruba
Asia	. . .	Asia	Asien	Asia	Asie	Ásia
Austl.	Australia	Australia	Australien	Australia	Australie	Austrália
Az., U.S.	Arizona	Arizona	Arizona	Arizona	Arizona	Arizona
Azer.	Azerbaijan	Azerbaijan	Aserbaidschan	Azerbaiján	Azerbaïdjan	Azerbaijão
Ba.	Bahamas	Bahamas	Bahamas	Bahamas	Bahamas	Bahamas
Bahr.	Al-Baḥrayn	Bahrain	Bahrain	Bahrein	Bahreïn	Bahrein
Barb.	Barbados	Barbados	Barbados	Barbados	Barbade	Barbados
B.C., Can.	British Columbia / Colombie-Britannique	British Columbia	Britisch Kolumbien	Columbia Británica	Colombie-britannique	Colúmbia Britânica
Bdi.	Burundi	Burundi	Burundi	Burundi	Burundi	Burundi
Bel.	Belgique / België	Belgium	Belgien	Bélgica	Belgique	Bélgica
Belize	Belize	Belize	Belize	Belice	Bélize	Belize
Bela.	Belarus	Belarus	Belorussland	Bielorrusia	Biélorussie	Bielorrússia
Bénin	Bénin	Benin	Benin	Benin	Bénin	Benin
Ber.	Bermuda	Bermuda	Bermuda	Bermudas	Bermudes	Bermudas
B.I.O.T.	British Indian Ocean Territory	British Indian Ocean Territory	Britisch-Indien Ozean-Territorium	Territorio Británico del Océano Indico	Territoire britannique de l'océan Indien	Território Britânico do Oceano Indico
Blg.	Bâlgarija	Bulgaria	Bulgarien	Bulgaria	Bulgarie	Bulgária
Bngl.	Bangladesh	Bangladesh	Bangladesch	Bangladesh	Bangladesh	Bangladesh
Bol.	Bolivia	Bolivia	Bolivien	Bolivia	Bolivie	Bolívia
Boph.	Bophuthatswana	Bophuthatswana	Bophuthatswana	Bophuthatswana	Bophuthatswana	Bophuthatswana
Bos.	Bosna i Hercegovina	Bosnia and Hercegovina	Bosnien und Herzegowina	Bosnia y Herzegovina	Bosnie et Herzégovine	Bósnia e Herzegovina
Bots.	Botswana	Botswana	Botswana	Botswana	Botswana	Botsuana
Bra.	Brasil	Brazil	Brasilien	Brasil	Brésil	Brasil
Bru.	Brunei	Brunei	Brunei	Brunei	Brunéi	Brunei
Br. Vir. Is.	British Virgin Islands	British Virgin Islands	Britische Jungferninseln	Islas Vírgenes Británicas	Îles Vierges britanniques	Virgens Britânicas, Ilhas
Burkina	Burkina Faso	Burkina Faso	Burkina Faso	Burkina Faso	Burkina Faso	Burkina Faso
Ca., U.S.	California	California	Kalifornien	California	Californie	Califórnia
Cam.	Cameroun / Cameroon	Cameroon	Kamerun	Camerún	Cameroun	Camarão
Can.	Canada	Canada	Kanada	Canadá	Canada	Canadá
Cay. Is.	Cayman Islands	Cayman Islands	Caiman-Inseln	Islas Caimán	Îles Caïmanes	Cayman, Ilhas
Centraf.	République centrafricaine	Central African Republic	Zentralafrikanische Republik	República Centroafricana	République centrafricaine	Centro-Africana, República
Česká Rep.	Česká Republika	Czech Republic	Tschechische Republik	República Checa	République Tcheque	República Tcheca
Chile	Chile	Chile	Chile	Chile	Chili	Chile
Christ. I.	Christmas Island	Christmas Island	Weihnachtsinsel	Isla Christmas	Île Christmas	Christmas, Ilha
Ciskei	Ciskei	Ciskei	Ciskei	Ciskei	Ciskei	Ciskei
C. Iv.	Côte d'Ivoire	Côte d'Ivoire	Côte d'Ivoire	Côte d'Ivoire	Côte d'Ivoire	Côte d'Ivoire
C.M.I.K.	Chosŏn-minjujuŭi-inmīn-konghwaguk	Korea, North	Nordkorea	Corea del Norte	Corée du Nord	Coréia do Norte
Co., U.S.	Colorado	Colorado	Colorado	Colorado	Colorado	Colorado
Cocos Is.	Cocos (Keeling) Islands	Cocos (Keeling) Islands	Kokos-Inseln	Islas Cocos (Keeling)	Îles Cocos (Keeling)	Cocos (Keeling), Ilhas
Col.	Colombia	Colombia	Kolumbien	Colombia	Colombie	Colômbia
Comores	Comores / Al-Qumur	Comoros	Komoren	Comoras	Comores	Comores
Congo	Congo	Congo	Kongo	Congo	Congo	Congo
Cook Is.	Cook Islands	Cook Islands	Cook-Inseln	Islas Cook	Îles Cook	Cook, Ilhas
C.R.	Costa Rica	Costa Rica	Costa Rica	Costa Rica	Costa Rica	Costa Rica
Ct., U.S.	Connecticut	Connecticut	Connecticut	Connecticut	Connecticut	Connecticut
Cuba	Cuba	Cuba	Kuba	Cuba	Cuba	Cuba
C.V.	Cabo Verde	Cape Verde	Kap Verde	Cabo Verde	Cap-Vert	Cabo Verde
Dan.	Danmark	Denmark	Dänemark	Dinamarca	Danemark	Dinamarca
D.C., U.S.	District of Columbia	District of Columbia	District of Columbia	District of Columbia	District of Columbia	Distrito de Columbia
De., U.S.	Delaware	Delaware	Delaware	Delaware	Delaware	Delaware
Dji.	Djibouti	Djibouti	Djibouti	Djibouti	Djibouti	Djibouti
Dom.	Dominica	Dominica	Dominica	Dominica	Dominique	Dominica
Dtsch.	Deutschland	Germany	Deutschland	Alemania	Allemagne	Alemanha
D.Y.	Druk-Yul	Bhutan	Bhutan	Bhután	Bhoutan	Butã
Ec.	Ecuador	Ecuador	Ecuador	Ecuador	Équateur	Equador
Eesti	Eesti	Estonia	Estland	Estonia	Estonie	Estónia
Ellás	Ellás	Greece	Griechenland	Grecia	Grèce	Grécia
El Sal.	El Salvador	El Salvador	El Salvador	El Salvador	El Salvador	El Salvador
Eng., U.K.	England	England	England	Inglaterra	Angleterre	Inglaterra
Erit.	Eritrea	Eritrea	Eritrea	Eritrea	Erythrée	Eritréia
Esp.	España	Spain	Spanien	España	Espagne	Espanha
Europe	. . .	Europe	Europa	Europa	Europe	Europa
Falk. Is.	Falkland Islands	Falkland Islands	Falkland-Inseln	Islas Malvinas	Îles Falkland	Falkland, Ilhas
Fiji	Fiji	Fiji	Fidschi	Fiji	Fidji	Fiji (Fidji)
Fl., U.S.	Florida	Florida	Florida	Florida	Floride	Flórida
Før.	Føroyar	Faeroe Islands	Färöer	Islas Feroe	Îles Féroé	Faeroe, Ilhas
Fr.	France	France	Frankreich	Francia	France	França
Ga., U.S.	Georgia	Georgia	Georgia	Georgia	Georgie	Geórgia
Gabon	Gabon	Gabon	Gabun	Gabón	Gabon	Gabão
Gam.	Gambia	Gambia	Gambia	Gambia	Gambie	Gâmbia
Ghana	Ghana	Ghana	Ghana	Ghana	Ghana	Gana
Gib.	Gibraltar	Gibraltar	Gibraltar	Gibraltar	Gibraltar	Gibraltar
Gren.	Grenada	Grenada	Grenada	Granada	Grenade	Grenada
Guad.	Guadeloupe	Guadeloupe	Guadeloupe	Guadalupe	Guadeloupe	Guadalupe
Guam	Guam	Guam	Guam	Guam	Guam	Guam
Guat.	Guatemala	Guatemala	Guatemala	Guatemala	Guatemala	Guatemala
Guernsey	Guernsey	Guernsey	Guernsey	Guernsey	Guernesey	Guernsey
Gui.-B.	Guiné-Bissau	Guinea-Bissau	Guinea-Bissau	Guinea-Bissau	Guinée-Bissau	Guiné-Bissau
Gui. Ecu.	Guinea Ecuatorial	Equatorial Guinea	Äquatorial-guinea	Guinea Ecuatorial	Guinée équatoriale	Guiné Equatorial
Guinée	Guinée	Guinea	Guinea	Guinea	Guinée	Guiné
Guy.	Guyana	Guyana	Guyana	Guyana	Guyane	Guiana
Guy. fr.	Guyane française	French Guiana	Französisch-Guayana	Guayana Francesa	Guyane française	Guiana Francesa
Haï.	Haïti	Haiti	Haiti	Haití	Haïti	Haiti
Haya.	Hayastan	Armenia	Armenien	Armenia	Arménie	Arménia
Hi., U.S.	Hawaii	Hawaii	Hawaii	Hawaii	Hawaii	Havaí
H.K.	Hong Kong	Hong Kong	Hongkong	Hong Kong	Hong-Kong	Hong Kong
Hond.	Honduras	Honduras	Honduras	Honduras	Honduras	Honduras
Hrv.	Hrvatska	Croatia	Kroatien	Croacia	Croatie	Croácia
Ia., U.S.	Iowa	Iowa	Iowa	Iowa	Iowa	Iowa
I.A.M.	Al-Imārāt al-ʿArabīyah al-Muttaḥidah	United Arab Emirates	Vereinigte Arabische Emirate	Emiratos Arabes Unidos	Émirats arabes unis	Emirados Árabes Unidos

	LOCAL NAME	ENGLISH	DEUTSCH	ESPAÑOL	FRANÇAIS	PORTUGUÊS
Id., U.S.	Idaho	Idaho	Idaho	Idaho	Idaho	Idaho
Il., U.S.	Illinois	Illinois	Illinois	Illinois	Illinois	Illinois
In., U.S.	Indiana	Indiana	Indiana	Indiana	Indiana	Indiana
India	India / Bharat	India	Indien	India	Inde	Índia
Indon.	Indonesia	Indonesia	Indonesien	Indonesia	Indonésie	Indonésia
I. of Man	Isle of Man	Isle of Man	Insel Man	Isla de Man	Île de Man	Man, Ilha de
Īrān	Īrān	Iran	Iran	Irán	Iran	Irã
ʿĪrāq	Al-ʿĪrāq	Iraq	Irak	Iraq	Iraq	Iraque
Ire.	Ireland / Éire	Ireland	Irland	Irlanda	Irlande	Irlanda
Ísland	Ísland	Iceland	Island	Islandia	Islande	Islândia
Isr. Occ.	. . .	Israeli Occupied Areas	Von Israel besetztes Gebiet	Áreas ocupadas por Israel	Territoires occupés par Israël	Áreas occupadas por Israel
It.	Italia	Italy	Italien	Italia	Italie	Itália
Ityo.	Ityopiya	Ethiopia	Äthiopien	Etiopía	Éthiopie	Etiópia
Jam.	Jamaica	Jamaica	Jamaika	Jamaica	Jamaïque	Jamaica
Jersey	Jersey	Jersey	Jersey	Jersey	Jersey	Jersey
Jugo.	Jugoslavija	Yugoslavia	Jugoslawien	Yugoslavia	Yougoslavie	Iugoslávia
Kal. Nun.	Kalaallit Nunaat / Grønland	Greenland	Grönland	Groenlandia	Groenland	Groenlândia
Kâm.	Kâmpŭchéa	Cambodia	Kambodscha	Camboya	Cambodge	Camboja
Kaz.	Kazachstan	Kazakhstan	Kasachstan	Kazajstán	Kazakhstan	Cazaquistão
Kenya	Kenya	Kenya	Kenia	Kenya	Kenya	Quênia
Kıbrıs	Kuzey Kıbrıs	Cyprus, North	Türkische Republik Nordzypern	República Turca de Chipre del Norte	République turque du Nord de Chypre	República Turca do Norte de Chipre
Kípros	Kípros / Kıbrıs	Cyprus	Zypern	Chipre	Chypre	Chipre
Kiribati	Kiribati	Kiribati	Kiribati	Kiribati	Kiribati	Kiribati
Ks., U.S.	Kansas	Kansas	Kansas	Kansas	Kansas	Kansas
Kuwayt	Al-Kuwayt	Kuwait	Kuwait	Kuwait	Koweït	Kuwait
Ky., U.S.	Kentucky	Kentucky	Kentucky	Kentucky	Kentucky	Kentucky
Kyrg.	Kyrgyzstan	Kyrgyzstan	Kirgisistan	Kirguizia	Kirghizistan	Quirguistão
La., U.S.	Louisiana	Louisiana	Louisiana	Luisiana	Louisiane	Louisiana
Lao	Lao	Laos	Laos	Laos	Laos	Lao
Lat.	Latvija	Latvia	Lettland	Letonia	Lettonie	Letónia
Leso.	Lesotho	Lesotho	Lesotho	Lesotho	Lesotho	Lesoto
Liber.	Liberia	Liberia	Liberia	Liberia	Libéria	Libéria
Lībiyā	Lībiyā	Libya	Libyen	Libia	Libye	Líbia
Liech.	Liechtenstein	Liechtenstein	Liechtenstein	Liechtenstein	Liechtenstein	Liechtenstein
Liet.	Lietuva	Lithuania	Litauen	Lituania	Lithuanie	Lituânia
Lubnān	Lubnān	Lebanon	Libanon	Líbano	Liban	Líbano
Lux.	Luxembourg	Luxembourg	Luxemburg	Luxemburgo	Luxembourg	Luxemburgo
Ma., U.S.	Massachusetts	Massachusetts	Massachusetts	Massachusetts	Massachusetts	Massachusetts
Macau	Macau	Macao	Macao	Macao	Macao	Macau
Madag.	Madagasikara / Madagascar	Madagascar	Madagaskar	Madagascar	Madagascar	Madagascar
Magreb	Al-Magreb	Morocco	Marokko	Marruecos	Maroc	Marrocos
Magy.	Magyarország	Hungary	Ungarn	Hungría	Hongrie	Hungria
Mak.	Makedonija	Macedonia	Makedonien	Macedonia	Macédoine	Macedonia
Malaŵi	Malaŵi	Malawi	Malawi	Malawi	Malawi	Malaui
Malay.	Malaysia	Malaysia	Malaysia	Malasia	Malaisie	Malásia
Mald.	Maldives	Maldives	Malediven	Maldivas	Maldives	Maldivas
Mali	Mali	Mali	Mali	Malí	Mali	Mali
Malta	Malta	Malta	Malta	Malta	Malte	Malta
Marsh. Is.	Marshall Islands	Marshall Islands	Marshall Islands	Islas Marshall	Îles Marshall	Marshall Islands
Mart.	Martinique	Martinique	Martinique	Martinica	Martinique	Martinica
Maur.	Mauritanie / Mūrītāniyā	Mauritania	Mauretanien	Mauritania	Mauritanie	Mauritânia
Maus.	Mauritius	Mauritius	Mauritius	Mauricio	Maurice	Maurício
Mayotte	Mayotte	Mayotte	Mayotte	Mayotte	Mayotte	Mayotte
Mb., Can.	Manitoba	Manitoba	Manitoba	Manitoba	Manitoba	Manitoba
Md., U.S.	Maryland	Maryland	Maryland	Maryland	Maryland	Maryland
Me., U.S.	Maine	Maine	Maine	Maine	Maine	Maine
Méx.	México	Mexico	Mexiko	México	Mexique	México
Mi., U.S.	Michigan	Michigan	Michigan	Michigan	Michigan	Michigan
Micron.	Federated States of Micronesia	Micronesia, Federated States of	Federated States of Micronesia	Estado Federal de Micronesia	États fédérés de Micronésie	Federated States of Micronesia
Mid. Is.	Midway Islands	Midway Islands	Midway-Inseln	Islas Midway	Îles Midway	Midway, Ilhas
Mişr	Mişr	Egypt	Ägypten	Egipto	Égypte	Egito
Mn., U.S.	Minnesota	Minnesota	Minnesota	Minnesota	Minnesota	Minnesota
Mo., U.S.	Missouri	Missouri	Missouri	Misuri	Missouri	Missouri
Moç.	Moçambique	Mozambique	Mosambik	Mozambique	Mozambique	Moçambique
Mol.	Moldova	Moldova	Moldawien	Moldavia	Moldavie	Moldávia
Monaco	Monaco	Monaco	Monaco	Mónaco	Monaco	Mônaco
Mong.	Mongol Ard Uls	Mongolia	Mongolei	Mongolia	Mongolie	Mongólia
Monts.	Montserrat	Montserrat	Montserrat	Montserrat	Montserrat	Montserrat
Ms., U.S.	Mississippi	Mississippi	Mississippi	Misisipí	Mississippi	Mississippi
Mt., U.S.	Montana	Montana	Montana	Montana	Montana	Montana
Mya.	Myanmar	Myanmar	Myanmar	Myanmar	Myanmar	Myanmar
N.A.	. . .	North America	Nordamerika	América del Norte	Amérique du Nord	América do Norte
Namibia	Namibia	Namibia	Namibia	Namibia	Namibie	Namíbia
Nauru	Nauru / Naoero	Nauru	Nauru	Nauru	Nauru	Nauru
N.B., Can.	New Brunswick / Nouveau-Brunswick	New Brunswick	Neubraunschweig	Nueva Brunswick	Nouveau-Brunswick	Nova Brunswick
N.C., U.S.	North Carolina	North Carolina	Nord Karolina	Carolina del Norte	Caroline du Nord	Carolina do Norte
N. Cal.	Nouvelle-Calédonie	New Caledonia	Neukaledonien	Nueva Caledonia	Nouvelle Calédonie	Nova Caledônia
N.D., U.S.	North Dakota	North Dakota	Nord Dakota	Dakota del Norte	Dakota du Nord	Dakota do Norte
Ne., U.S.	Nebraska	Nebraska	Nebraska	Nebraska	Nebraska	Nebraska
Ned.	Nederland	Netherlands	Niederlande	Países Bajos	Pays-Bas	Países Baixos
Ned. Ant.	Nederlandse Antillen	Netherlands Antilles	Niederländische Antillen	Antillas Neerlandesas	Antilles néerlandaises	Antilhas Holandesas
Nepāl	Nepāl	Nepal	Nepal	Nepal	Népal	Nepal
Nf., Can.	Newfoundland / Terre-Neuve	Newfoundland	Neufundland	Terranova	Terre-Neuve	Terra Nova
N.H., U.S.	New Hampshire	New Hampshire	New Hampshire	Nuevo Hampshire	New Hampshire	Nova Hampshire
Nic.	Nicaragua	Nicaragua	Nicaragua	Nicaragua	Nicaragua	Nicarágua
Nig.	Nigeria	Nigeria	Nigeria	Nigeria	Nigéria	Nigéria
Niger	Niger	Niger	Niger	Níger	Niger	Níger
Nihon	Nihon	Japan	Japan	Japón	Japon	Japão
N. Ire., U.K.	Northern Ireland	Northern Ireland	Nordirland	Irlanda del Norte	Irlande du Nord	Irlanda do Norte
Niue	Niue	Niue	Niue	Niue	Nioué	Niue
N.J., U.S.	New Jersey	New Jersey	New Jersey	Nueva Jersey	New Jersey	Nova Jersey
N.M., U.S.	New Mexico	New Mexico	New Mexico	Nuevo México	Nouveau-Mexique	Nova México
N. Mar. Is.	Northern Mariana Islands	Northern Mariana Islands	Northern Mariana Islands	Islas Marianas	Îles Mariannes du Nord	Northern Mariana Islands
Nor.	Norge	Norway	Norwegen	Noruega	Norvège	Noruega
Norf. I.	Norfolk Island	Norfolk Island	Norfolk-Insel	Isla Norfolk	Île Norfolk	Norfolk, Ilha
N.S., Can.	Nova Scotia / Nouvelle-Écosse	Nova Scotia	Neu Schottland	Nueva Escocia	Nouvelle-Écosse	Nova Scotia
N.T., Can.	Northwest Territories / Territoires du Nord-Ouest	Northwest Territories	Nord-West Territorien	Territorios del Noroeste	Territoires du Nord-Ouest	Territórios do Noroeste
Nv., U.S.	Nevada	Nevada	Nevada	Nevada	Nevada	Nevada
N.Y., U.S.	New York	New York	New York	Nueva York	New York	Nova York
N.Z.	New Zealand	New Zealand	Neuseeland	Nueva Zelanda	Nouvelle-Zélande	Nova Zelândia
Oc.	. . .	Oceania	Ozeanien	Oceanía	Océanie	Oceania
Oh., U.S.	Ohio	Ohio	Ohio	Ohio	Ohio	Ohio

	LOCAL NAME	ENGLISH	DEUTSCH	ESPAÑOL	FRANÇAIS	PORTUGUÊS
Ok., U.S.	Oklahoma	Oklahoma	Oklahoma	Oklahoma	Oklahoma	Oklahoma
On., Can.	Ontario	Ontario	Ontario	Ontario	Ontario	Ontário
Or., U.S.	Oregon	Oregon	Oregon	Oregón	Oregon	Oregon
Öst.	Österreich	Austria	Österreich	Austria	Autriche	Austria
Pa., U.S.	Pennsylvania	Pennsylvania	Pennsylvanien	Pensilvania	Pennsylvanie	Pennsylvania
Pák.	Pākistān	Pakistan	Pakistan	Pakistán	Pakistan	Paquistão
Palau	Palau / Belau	Palau	Palau	Palau	Palau (Belau)	Palau
Pan.	Panamá	Panama	Panama	Panamá	Panama	Panamá
Pap. N. Gui.	Papua New Guinea	Papua New Guinea	Papua-Neuguinea	Papua Nueva Guinea	Papouasie-Nouvelle Guinée	Papua-Nova Guiné
Para.	Paraguay	Paraguay	Paraguay	Paraguay	Paraguay	Paraguai
P.E., Can.	Prince Edward Island / Île-du-Prince-Édouard	Prince Edward Island	Prinz Edward-Insel	Isla Príncipe Eduardo	Île-du-Prince Édouard	Príncipe Eduardo, Ilha do
Perú	Perú	Peru	Peru	Perú	Pérou	Peru
Pil.	Pilipinas / Philippines	Philippines	Philippinen	Filipinas	Philippines	Filipinas
Pit.	Pitcairn	Pitcairn	Pitcairn	Pitcairn	Pitcairn	Pitcairn
Pol.	Polska	Poland	Polen	Polonia	Pologne	Polónia
Poly. fr.	Polynésie française	French Polynesia	Französisch-Polynesien	Polinesia Francesa	Polynésie française	Polinésia Francesa
Port.	Portugal	Portugal	Portugal	Portugal	Portugal	Portugal
P.Q., Can.	Québec	Quebec	Quebec	Quebec	Québec	Québec
P.R.	Puerto Rico	Puerto Rico	Puerto Rico	Puerto Rico	Porto Rico	Porto Rico
P.S.N.Á.	Plazas de Soberanía en el Norte de África	Spanish North Africa	Spanisch-Nordafrika	Plazas de Soberanía en el Norte de África	Afrique du Nord espagnole	África do Norte Espanhola
Qatar	Qatar	Qatar	Katar	Qatar	Qatar	Qatar
Rep. Dom.	República Dominicana	Dominican Republic	Dominikanische Republik	República Dominicana	République dominicaine	Dominicana, República
Réu.	Réunion	Reunion	Réunion	Reunión	Réunion	Reunião
R.I., U.S.	Rhode Island	Rhode Island	Rhode Island	Rhode Island	Rhode Island	Rhode Island
Rom.	România	Romania	Rumänien	Rumanía	Roumanie	Roménia
Ross.	Rossija	Russia	Russland	Rusia	Russie	Rússia
Rw.	Rwanda	Rwanda	Ruanda	Rwanda	Rwanda	Ruanda
S.A.	. . .	South America	Südamerika	América del Sur	Amérique du Sud	América do Sul
S. Afr.	South Africa / Suid-Afrika	South Africa	Südafrika	Sudáfrica	Afrique du Sud	África do Sul
Sak.	Sakartvelo	Georgia	Georgien	Georgia	Géorgie	Geórgia
S.C., U.S.	South Carolina	South Carolina	Süd Karolina	Carolina del Sur	Caroline du Sud	Carolina do Sul
Schw.	Schweiz / Suisse / Svizzera	Switzerland	Schweiz	Suiza	Suisse	Suíça
Scot., U.K.	Scotland	Scotland	Schottland	Escocia	Écosse	Escócia
S.D., U.S.	South Dakota	South Dakota	Süd Dakota	Dakota del Sur	Dakota du Sud	Dakota do Sul
Sén.	Sénégal	Senegal	Senegal	Senegal	Sénégal	Senegal
Sey.	Seychelles	Seychelles	Seschellen	Seychelles	Seychelles	Seychelles
Shq.	Shqipëri	Albania	Albanien	Albania	Albanie	Albânia
Sing.	Singapore	Singapore	Singapur	Singapur	Singapour	Cingapura
Sk., Can.	Saskatchewan	Saskatchewan	Saskatchewan	Saskatchewan	Saskatchewan	Saskatchewan
S.L.	Sierra Leone	Sierra Leone	Sierra Leone	Sierra Leona	Sierra Leone	Serra Leoa
S. Lan.	Sri Lanka	Sri Lanka	Sri Lanka	Sri Lanka	Sri Lanka	Sri Lanka
Slvk.	Slovensko	Slovakia	Slowakei	Eslovaquia	Slovaquie	Eslováquia
Slvn.	Slovenija	Slovenia	Slowenien	Eslovenia	Slovénie	Eslovênia
S. Mar.	San Marino	San Marino	San Marino	San Marino	Saint-Marin	San Marino
Sol. Is.	Solomon Islands	Solomon Islands	Salomonen	Islas Salomón	Îles Salomon	Salomão, Ilhas
Som.	Somaliya	Somalia	Somalia	Somalia	Somalie	Somália
St. Hel.	St. Helena	St. Helena	Sankt Helena	Santa Elena	Sainte-Hélène	Santa Helena
St. K./N.	St. Kitts and Nevis	St. Kitts and Nevis	Sankt Kitts und Nevis	San Kitts y Nevis	Saint-Kitts-et-Nevis	São Kitts e Nevis
St. Luc.	St. Lucia	St. Lucia	Sankt Lucia	Santa Lucía	Sainte-Lucie	Santa Lúcia
S. Tom./P.	São Tomé e Príncipe	Sao Tome and Principe	São Tomé und Principe	Santo Tomé y Príncipe	Sao Tomé-et-Principe	São Tomé e Príncipe
St. P./M.	Saint-Pierre-et-Miquelon	St. Pierre and Miquelon	Saint-Pierre und Miquelon	San Pedro y Miquelón	Saint-Pierre-et-Miquelon	São Pedro e Miquelon
St. Vin.	St. Vincent and the Grenadines	St. Vincent and the Grenadines	Sankt Vincent und die Grenadinen	San Vicente y las Granadinas	Saint-Vincent-et-Grenadines	São Vicente e Granadinas
Süd.	As-Sūdān	Sudan	Sudan	Sudán	Soudan	Sudão
Suomi	Suomi / Finland	Finland	Finnland	Finlandia	Finlande	Finlândia

	LOCAL NAME	ENGLISH	DEUTSCH	ESPAÑOL	FRANÇAIS	PORTUGUÊS
Sur.	Suriname	Suriname	Suriname	Suriname	Suriname	Suriname
Sürïy.	Sūrïyah	Syria	Syrien	Siria	Syrie	Síria
Sve.	Sverige	Sweden	Schweden	Suecia	Suéde	Suécia
Swaz.	Swaziland	Swaziland	Swasiland	Swazilandia	Swaziland	Suazilândia
T.a.a.f.	Terres australes et antarctiques françaises	French Southern and Antarctic Territories	Französische Süd- und Antarktis-Gebiete	Tierras Australes y Antárticas Francesas	Terres australes et antarctiques françaises	Terras Austrais e Antárticas Francesas
Taehan	Taehan-min'guk	Korea, South	Südkorea	Corea del Sur	Corée du Sud	Coréia do Sul
T'aiwan	T'aiwan	Taiwan	Taiwan	Taiwán	Taïwan	Taiwan (Formosa)
Taj.	Tajikistan	Tajikistan	Tadschikistan	Tadjikistán	Tadjikistan	Tajiquistão
Tan.	Tanzania	Tanzania	Tansania	Tanzanía	Tanzanie	Tanzânia
Tchad	Tchad	Chad	Tschad	Chad	Tchad	Tchad
T./C. Is.	Turks and Caicos Islands	Turks and Caicos Islands	Turks- und Caicos-Inseln	Islas Turcas y Caicos	Îles Turques et Caïques	Turcas e Caicos, Ilhas
Thai	Prathet Thai	Thailand	Thailand	Tailandia	Thaïlande	Tailândia
Tn., U.S.	Tennessee	Tennessee	Tennessee	Tennessee	Tennessee	Tennessee
Togo	Togo	Togo	Togo	Togo	Togo	Togo
Tok.	Tokelau	Tokelau	Tokelau	Tokelau	Tokélaou	Tokelau
Tonga	Tonga	Tonga	Tonga	Tonga	Tonga	Tonga
Transkei	Transkei	Transkei	Transkei	Transkei	Transkei	Transkei
Trin.	Trinidad and Tobago	Trinidad and Tobago	Trinidad und Tobago	Trinidad y Tabago	Trinité-et-Tobago	Trinidad e Tobago
Tun.	Tunisie / Tunis	Tunisia	Tunesien	Túnez	Tunisie	Tunísia
Tür.	Türkiye	Turkey	Türkei	Turquía	Turquie	Turquia
Turk.	Turkmenistan	Turkmenistan	Turkmenistan	Turkmenia	Turkménistan	Turquemenistão
Tuvalu	Tuvalu	Tuvalu	Tuvalu	Tuvalu	Tuvalu	Tuvalu
Tx., U.S.	Texas	Texas	Texas	Texas	Texas	Texas
Ug.	Uganda	Uganda	Uganda	Uganda	Ouganda	Uganda
U.K.	United Kingdom	United Kingdom	Vereinigtes Königreich	Reino Unido	Royaume-Uni	Reino Unido
Ukr.	Ukraina	Ukraine	Ukraine	Ucrania	Ukraine	Ucrânia
'Umān	'Umān	Oman	Oman	Omán	Oman	Omã
Ur.	Uruguay	Uruguay	Uruguay	Uruguay	Uruguay	Uruguai
Urd.	Al-Urdun	Jordan	Jordanien	Jordania	Jordanie	Jordânia
U.S.	United States	United States	Vereinigte Staaten	Estados Unidos	États-Unis	Estados Unidos
Ut., U.S.	Utah	Utah	Utah	Utah	Utah	Utah
Uzb.	Uzbekistan	Uzbekistan	Usbekistan	Uzbekistán	Ouzbekistan	Usbequistão
Va., U.S.	Virginia	Virginia	Virginia	Virginia	Virginie	Virgínia
Vanuatu	Vanuatu	Vanuatu	Vanuatu	Vanuatu	Vanuatu	Vanuatu
Vat.	Città del Vaticano	Vatican City	Vatikanstadt	Ciudad del Vaticano	Cité du Vatican	Vaticano
Ven.	Venezuela	Venezuela	Venezuela	Venezuela	Venezuela	Venezuela
Venda	Venda	Venda	Venda	Venda	Venda	Venda
Viet	Viet Nam	Vietnam	Vietnam	Viet Nam	Viet Nam	Vietnam
Vir. Is., U.S.	Virgin Islands (U.S.)	Virgin Islands (U.S.)	Amerikanische Jungferninseln	Islas Vírgenes (americanas)	Îles Vierges (américaines)	Virgens Americanas, Ilhas
Vt.	Vermont	Vermont	Vermont	Vermont	Vermont	Vermont
Wa., U.S.	Washington	Washington	Washington	Washington	Washington	Washington
Wake I.	Wake Island	Wake Island	Wake	Isla Wake	Île Wake	Wake
Wales, U.K.	Wales	Wales	Wales	Gales	Galles	Gales
Wal./F.	Wallis et Futuna	Wallis and Futuna	Wallis und Futuna	Wallis y Futuna	Wallis et Futuna	Wallis e Futuna
Wi., U.S.	Wisconsin	Wisconsin	Wisconsin	Wisconsin	Wisconsin	Wisconsin
W. Sah.	. . .	Western Sahara	Westliche Sahara	Sahara Occidental	Sahara occidental	Saara Ocidental
W. Sam.	Western Samoa / Samoa i Sisifo	Western Samoa	Westsamoa	Samoa Occidental	Samoa-Occidental	Samoa Ocidental
W.V., U.S.	West Virginia	West Virginia	West Virginia	Virginia Occidental	Virginie Occidentale	Virgínia Ocidental
Wy., U.S.	Wyoming	Wyoming	Wyoming	Wyoming	Wyoming	Wyoming
Yaman	Al-Yaman	Yemen	Jemen	Yemen	Yémen	Iêmen
Yis.	Yisra'el / Isrā'īl	Israel	Israel	Israel	Israël	Israel
Yk., Can.	Yukon Territory	Yukon Territory	Yukon	Yukón	Yukon	Yukon
Zaïre	Zaïre	Zaire	Zaire	Zaire	Zaïre	Zaire
Zam.	Zambia	Zambia	Sambia	Zambia	Zambie	Zâmbia
Zhg.	Zhongguo	China	China	China	Chine	China
Zimb.	Zimbabwe	Zimbabwe	Simbabwe	Zimbabwe	Zimbabwe	Zimbabwe

Key to Index Symbols

The symbols below represent the categories into which the physical and cultural features are classified in the Index. Broad categories appear in **boldface** type. Symbols with superior numbers identify subcategories.

Schlüssel zu den Symbolen des Registers

Die folgenden Symbole veranschaulichen die Kategorien, nach denen physische und kulturgeographische Objekte im Register geordnet sind. Die Oberbegriffe sind in **Fettdruck** hervorgehoben. Symbole mit hochgestellten Nummern kennzeichnen Unterbegriffe.

Clave de los Símbolos del Índice

Los símbolos abajo representan las categorías dentro de las cuales están clasificados los rasgos físicos y culturales que están incluidos en el Índice. Las grandes categorías aparecen en **negrilla**. Los símbolos que tienen números en su parte superior identifican las subcategorías.

Signification des Symboles de l'Index

Les symboles ci-dessous représentent les catégories sous lesquelles les données physiques et culturelles sont classées dans l'index. Les symboles en caractèter **gras** correspondent aux catégories principales. Ceux suivis d'un indice désignent les subdivisions d'une même catégorie.

Chave dos Símbolos do Índice

Os símbolos abaixo representam as categorias em que estão classificados os acidentes físicos e culturais no Índice. As grandes categorias aparecem em **negrito**. Os símbolos acompanhados de números altos identificam as subcategorias.

ENGLISH	DEUTSCH	ESPANOL	FRANCAIS	PORTUGUES
Mountain	**Berg**	**Montaña**	**Montagne**	**Montanha**
Volcano	Vulkan	Volcán	Volcan	Vulcão
Hill	Hügel	Colina	Colline	Colina
Mountains	**Gebirge**	**Montañas**	**Montagnes**	**Montanhas**
Plateau	Hochebene	Meseta	Plateau	Plaralto
Hills	Hügel	Colinas	Collines	Colinas
Pass	**Paß**	**Paso**	**Col**	**Passo**
Valley, Canyon	**Tal, Cañon**	**Valle, Cañón**	**Vallée, Canyon**	**Vale, Canhão**
Plain	**Ebene**	**Llano**	**Plaine**	**Planície**
Basin	Becken	Cuenca	Bassin	Bacia
Delta	Delta	Delta	Delta	Delta
Cape	**Kap**	**Cabo**	**Cap**	**Cabo**
Peninsula	Halbinsel	Península	Péninsule	Peninsula
Spit, Sand Bar	Landzunge, Sandbarre	Lengua de Tierra, Bajo	Flèche, Banc de sable	Ponta de Terra, Banco de Areia
Island	**Insel**	**Isla**	**Île**	**Ilha**
Atoll	Atoll	Atolón	Atoll	Atol
Rock	Fels	Roca	Rocher	Rochedo
Islands	**Inseln**	**Islas**	**Îles**	**Ilhas**
Rocks	Felsen	Rocas	Rochers	Rochedos
Other Topographic Features	**Andere Topographische Objekte**	**Otros Elementos Topográficos**	**Autres données topographiques**	**Outros Acidentes Topográficos**
Continent	Erdteil	Continente	Continent	Continente
Coast, Beach	Küste, Strand	Costa, Playa	Côte, Plage	Costa, Praia
Isthmus	Landenge	Istmo	Isthme	Istmo
Cliff	Kliff	Risco	Falaise	Falésia
Cave, Caves	Höhle, Höhlen	Cueva, Cuevas	Caverne, Cavernes	Caverna, Cavernas
Crater	Krater	Cráter	Cratère	Cratera
Depression	Senke	Depresión	Dépression	Depressão
Dunes	Dünen	Dunas	Dunes	Dunas
Lava Flow	Lavastrom	Corriente de Lava	Coulée de lave	Corrente de Lava
River	**Fluß**	**Río**	**Rivière, Fleuve**	**Rio**
River Channel	Flussarm	Brazo de Río	Bras de rivière	Canal de Rio
Canal	**Kanal**	**Canal**	**Canal**	**Canal**
Aqueduct	Aquädukt	Acueducto	Aqueduc	Aqueduto
Waterfall, Rapids	**Wasserfall, Stromschnellen**	**Cascada, Rápidos**	**Chute d'eau, Rapides**	**Quedas d'água, Rápidos**
Strait	**Meeresstraße**	**Estrecho**	**Détroit**	**Estreito**
Bay, Gulf	**Bucht, Golf**	**Bahía, Golfo**	**Baie, Golfe**	**Baía, Golfo**
Estuary	Trichtermündung	Estuario	Estuaire	Estuário
Fjord	Fjord	Fiordo	Fjord	Fiorce
Bight	Bucht	Bahía	Baie	Enseada
Lake, Lakes	**See, Seen**	**Lago, Lagos**	**Lac, Lacs**	**Lago, Lagos**
Reservoir	Stausee	Embalse	Réservoir, Retenue	Reservatório
Swamp	**Sumpf**	**Pantano**	**Marais**	**Pântano**
Ice Features, Glacier	**Eis- und Gletscherformen**	**Accidentes Glaciales, Glaciar**	**Formes glaciaires, Glacier**	**Acidentes Glaciares, Geleira**
Other Hydrographic Features	**Andere Hydrographische Objekte**	**Otros Elementos Hidrográficos**	**Autres données hydrographiques**	**Outros Acidentes Hidrográficos**
Ocean	Ozean	Océano	Océan	Oceano
Sea	Meer	Mar	Mer	Mar
Anchorage	Ankerplatz	Ancladero	Ancrage	Ancoradouro
Oasis, Well, Spring	Oase, Brunnen, Quelle	Oasis, Pozo, Manantial	Oasis, Puits, Source	Oásis, Poço, Fonte, Manancial

ENGLISH	DEUTSCH	ESPANOL	FRANCAIS	PORTUGUES
Submarine Features	**Untermeerische Objekte**	**Accidentes Submarinos**	**Formes de relief sous-marin**	**Acidentes Submarinos**
Depression	Senke	Depresión	Dépression	Depressão
Reef, Shoal	Riff, Untiefe	Arrecife, Bajo	Récif, Haut-fond	Recife, Baixio
Mountain, Mountains	Berg, Gebirge	Montaña, Montañas	Montagne, Montagnes	Montanha, Montanhas
Slope, Shelf	Abhang, Schelf	Talud, Plataforma	Talus, Plateau continental	Talude, Plataforma
Political Unit	**Politische Einheit**	**Unidad Política**	**Entité politique**	**Unidade Política**
Independent Nation	Unabhängiger Staat	Nación Independiente	État indépendant	País Independente
Dependency	Abhängiges Gebiet	Dependencia	Dépendance	Dependência
State, Canton, Republic	Land, Kanton, Republik	Estado, Cantón, República	État, Canton, République	Estado, Cantão, República
Province, Region, Oblast	Provinz, Landschaft, Oblast	Provincia, Región, Oblast	Province, Région, Oblast	Província, Região, Oblast
Department, District, Prefecture	Département, Distrikt, Präfektur	Departamento, Distrito, Prefectura	Département, District, Préfecture	Departamento, Distrito, Prefeitura
County	Grafschaft	Condado	Comté	Condado
City, Municipality	Stadt, Stadtkreis	Ciudad, Municipalidad	Ville, Municipalité	Cidade, Municipalidade
Miscellaneous	Verschiedenes	Misceláneo	Divers	Diversos
Historical	Historisch	Histórico	Historique	Sítio Histórico
Cultural Institution	**Kulturelle Institution**	**Institución Cultural**	**Institution culturelle**	**Instituição Cultural**
Religious Institution	Religiöse Institution	Institución Religiosa	Institution religieuse	Instituição Religiosa
Educational Institution	Erziehungsinstitution	Institución Educacional	Établissement d'éducation	Estabelecimento de Ensino
Scientific, Industrial Facility	Wissenschaftliche, Industrielle Anlage	Institución Científica o Industrial	Établissement scientifique ou industriel	Estabelecimento Científico ou Industrial
Historical Site	**Historische Stätte**	**Sitio Históric**	**Site historique**	**Sítio Histórico**
Recreational Site	**Erholungs- und Ferienort**	**Sitio de Recreo**	**Centre de loisirs**	**Área de Lazer**
Airport	**Flughafen**	**Aeropuerto**	**Aéroport**	**Aeroporto**
Military Installation	**Militäranlage**	**Instalación Militar**	**Installation militaire**	**Instalação Militar**
Miscellaneous	**Verschiedenes**	**Misceláneo**	**Divers**	**Diversos**
Region	Region	Región	Région	Região
Desert	Wüste	Desierto	Désert	Deserto
Forest, Moor	Wald, Moor	Bosque, Páramo	Forêt, Lande	Floresta, Pântano
Reserve, Reservation	Reservat	Reserva, Reservación	Réserve	Reserva
Transportation	Verkehr	Transporte	Transport	Transporte
Dam	Damm	Presa	Barrage	Represa
Mine, Quarry	Bergwerk, Steinbruch	Mina, Cantera	Mine, Carrière	Mina, Pedreira
Neighborhood	Nachbarschaft	Barrio	Quartier	Arredores, Vizinhança
Shopping Center	Einkaufszentrum	Mercado	Centre commercial	Shopping Center

<table continues as gazetteer index — partial transcription>

A

Name								
Aa ≊	50	51.01 N	2.06 E					
Aach	54	47.50 N	8.51 E					
Aachen	56	50.47 N	6.05 E					
Aach im Allgäu	58	47.31 N	9.58 E					
Aach-Linz	58	47.54 N	9.11 E					
Aadorf	58	47.30 N	8.54 E					
Aaiun — El Aaiún	148	27.09 N	13.12 W					
Aalen	58	48.50 N	10.05 E					
A'Āli an-Nīl □⁴	140	9.30 N	31.00 E					
Aalsmeer	52	52.16 N	4.45 E					
Aalst (Alost), Bel.	50	50.56 N	4.02 E					
Aalst, Ned.	52	51.23 N	5.29 E					
Aalten	52	51.56 N	6.35 E					
Aalter	50	51.05 N	3.27 E					
Aalwynsfontein	158	30.27 S	18.38 E					
Äänekoski	26	62.36 N	25.44 E					
Aansluit	158	26.44 S	22.28 E					
Aar ≊	56	50.23 N	8.00 E					
Aarau	58	47.23 N	8.03 E					
Aarberg	58	47.03 N	7.16 E					
Aarburg	58	47.19 N	7.54 E					
Aardenburg	52	51.16 N	3.27 E					
Aare ≊	58	47.37 N	8.13 E					
Aareschlucht ♦	58	46.44 N	8.12 E					
Aargau □³	58	47.30 N	8.10 E					
Aarie-Rixtel	52	51.31 N	5.38 E					
Aaronsburg	210	40.54 N	77.27 W					
Aarschot	50	50.59 N	4.50 E					
Aarwangen	58	47.15 N	7.46 E					
Aazanén	38	35.13 N	3.10 W					
Aba, Nig.	150	5.06 N	7.21 E					
Aba, Zaïre	154	3.52 N	30.14 E					
Aba, Zng.	102	33.06 N	101.59 E					
Abā al-Bawl, Qurayn ʌ²	128	24.56 N	51.13 E					
Abā al-Waqf	142	28.35 N	30.46 E					
Abā as-Su'ūd	144	17.29 N	44.08 E					

Abacaxis ≊	242	3.54 S	58.47 W
Abaco I	238	26.28 N	77.05 W
Abacou, Pointe ⟩	238	18.03 N	73.47 W
Abadab, Jabal ʌ	140	18.53 N	35.59 E
Abādān	128	30.20 N	48.16 E
Ābādeh	128	31.10 N	52.37 E
Abadia dos Dourados	255	18.28 S	47.24 W
Abadiânia	255	16.06 S	48.48 W
Abadla	148	31.01 N	2.44 W
Abaeté	255	19.09 S	45.27 W
Abaeté ≊	255	18.02 S	45.12 W
Abaetetuba	250	1.42 S	48.54 W
Abagajtuj	88	49.35 N	117.49 E
Abagnar Qi	102	43.58 N	116.04 E
Abag Qi	102	43.53 N	114.33 E
Abaí	252	26.01 S	55.57 W
Abaj, Kaz.	86	49.38 N	72.52 E
Abaj, Ross.	86	50.27 N	85.05 E
Abajo Mountains ⟋	200	37.50 N	109.25 W
Abajo Peak ʌ	200	37.51 N	109.28 W
Abakaliki	150	4.57 N	7.47 E
Abakan	86	53.43 N	91.26 E
Abakan ≊	86	53.43 N	91.30 E
Abakanovo	76	59.18 N	37.39 E
Abakanskij chrebet ⟋	86	52.20 N	88.50 E
Abala, Congo	152	1.21 S	15.30 E
Abala, Niger	150	14.56 N	3.26 E
Abalak, Ross.	86	58.08 N	68.36 E
Abalemma, Vallée d' V	150	15.34 N	6.23 E
Abalessa	148	22.54 N	4.50 E
Aban	88	56.41 N	96.04 E
Abancay	248	13.35 S	72.55 W
Abanga ≊	152	0.20 S	10.30 E
Abano Terme	64	45.21 N	11.47 E
Abaokoro	174t	1.29 N	173.02 E
Abar Irir	144	4.53 N	46.10 E
Abar Kūh	128	31.08 N	53.17 E
Abarra	144	5.23 N	39.58 E
Abasa	84	42.12 N	42.13 E

Abascay, Arroyo ≊	258	35.17 S	58.07 W
Abashiri	92a	44.01 N	144.17 E
Abasolo, Méx.	196	27.12 N	101.24 W
Abasolo, Méx.	196	25.57 N	100.24 W
Abasolo, Méx.	204	32.39 N	115.21 W
Abasolo, Méx.	196	25.18 N	104.40 W
Abasolo, Méx.	232	24.04 N	98.22 W
Abasolo, Méx.	234	20.27 N	101.12 W
Abasolo del Valle	234	17.44 N	95.29 W
Abasto	258	34.58 S	58.06 W
Abastumani	84	41.46 N	42.50 E
Abate	85	39.03 N	77.36 E
Abate Alonia, Lago di ⊕	68	41.01 N	15.45 E
Abatimbo el Gumas	144	10.36 N	35.13 E
Abatskij	86	56.18 N	70.28 E
Abau	164	10.11 S	148.42 E
Abava ≊	76	57.06 N	21.54 E
Abay			
— Blue Nile ≊	140	15.38 N	32.31 E
Abaya, Lake ⊕	144	6.20 N	37.55 E
Abayuba	258	34.51 S	56.14 W
Abaza	86	52.39 N	90.06 E
Abba	152	5.20 N	15.11 E
Abbabach ≊	263	51.28 N	7.41 E
Abbadia San Salvatore	66	42.53 N	11.41 E
'Abbāsābād □³	267d	35.44 N	51.25 E
Abbasanta	71	40.08 N	8.49 E
Abbé, Lac (Lake Abe) ⊕	144	11.06 N	41.50 E
Abbehausen	63	53.29 N	8.26 E
Abbekås	41	55.24 N	13.36 E
Abbensen	63	52.23 N	10.11 E
Abbeville, Fr.	50	50.06 N	1.50 E
Abbeville, Ga., U.S.	192	31.59 N	83.18 W
Abbeville, La., U.S.	194	29.58 N	92.08 W
Abbeville, Ms., U.S.	194	34.30 N	89.30 W
Abbeville, S.C., U.S.	192	34.10 N	82.22 W
Abbey	184	50.43 N	108.45 W

Abbeydorney	48	52.19 N	9.41 W
Abbeyfeale	48	52.24 N	9.18 W
Abbey Head ⟩	44	54.46 N	3.58 W
Abbeyleix	48	52.55 N	7.20 W
Abbey Peak ʌ	164	14.18 S	144.29 E
Abbey Wood ⊶⁸	260	51.29 N	0.08 E
Abbiategrasso	62	45.24 N	8.54 E
Abbot, Mount ʌ	166	20.03 S	147.45 E
Abbots Bromley	42	52.48 N	1.52 W
Abbotsbury	42	50.40 N	2.36 W
Abbotsford, Austl.	274a	33.51 S	151.08 E
Abbotsford, B.C., Can.	224	49.03 N	122.17 W
Abbotsford, Wi., U.S.	190	44.56 N	90.18 W
Abbots Langley	42	51.43 N	0.25 W
Abbott, Arg.	258	35.17 S	58.48 W
Abbott, Tx., U.S.	222	31.53 N	97.04 W
Abbottābād	123	34.09 N	73.13 E
Abbott Butte ʌ	202	42.57 N	122.33 W
Abbottstown	208	39.53 N	76.59 W
Abchazskaja Respublika □³	84	43.10 N	41.00 E
Abcoude	52	52.16 N	4.59 E
'Abd al-'Azīz, Jabal ʌ	130	36.25 N	40.20 E
'Abd al-Hafiz, Qārat ʌ²	142	28.53 N	30.08 E
'Abd al-Kūrī I	112	12.12 N	52.13 E
'Abd Allāh, Khawr ≊	128	29.50 N	48.20 E
'Abd al-Shāhīd ʌ	273c	29.53 N	51.13 E
Abdānān	128	32.58 N	47.26 E
Ābdēra □	38	40.59 N	24.58 E
Abdrachmanovo	80	54.46 N	52.30 E
Abdul Hakīm	123	30.33 N	72.07 E
Abdulino	80	53.42 N	53.40 E
Abdurahmanovka	80	54.16 N	48.27 E
Abebsa Roding	260	51.47 N	0.17 E
Abe, Lake (Lac Abbé) ⊕	144	11.06 N	41.50 E
Abéché	152	13.49 N	20.49 E
Abejar	34	41.48 N	2.47 W
Abejonal, Cerro ʌ	236	11.39 N	86.10 W
Abejorral	246	5.47 N	75.26 W

Abekr	140	12.43 N	28.55 E
Abelek	140	7.23 N	28.46 E
Abel Tasman National Park ♦	172	40.55 S	173.00 E
Abelti	144	8.10 N	37.34 E
Abemama I¹	14	0.21 N	173.51 E
Abenberg	58	49.14 N	10.57 E
Abengourou	150	6.44 N	3.29 W
Abeno ⊶⁸	270	34.38 N	135.32 E
Abenōjar	34	38.53 N	4.21 W
Ābenrā	41	55.02 N	9.26 E
Ābenrā Fjord c	41	55.03 N	9.34 E
Abens ≊	60	48.51 N	11.46 E
Abensberg	60	48.49 N	11.51 E
Abeokuta	150	7.10 N	3.26 E
Aber	154	2.12 N	32.21 E
Aberaeron	42	52.15 N	4.15 W
Aberaman	42	51.42 N	3.25 W
Aberavon — Port Talbot	42	51.36 N	3.47 W
Abercarn	42	51.39 N	3.08 W
Aberchirder	46	57.33 N	2.38 W
Abercorn, P.Q., Can.	206	45.02 N	72.40 W
Abercorn — Mbala, Zam.	154	8.50 S	31.22 E
Abercrombie ≊	170	34.09 S	149.40 E
Aberdare	42	51.43 N	3.27 W
Aberdare National Park ♦	154	0.30 S	36.45 E
Aberdare Range ⟋	154	0.25 S	36.38 E
Aberdeen, S. Afr.	158	32.29 S	24.05 E
Aberdeen, Scot., U.K.	46	57.10 N	2.04 W
Aberdeen, Id., U.S.	202	42.56 N	112.50 W
Aberdeen, Md., U.S.	208	39.30 N	76.09 W
Aberdeen, Ms., U.S.	194	33.49 N	88.32 W
Aberdeen, N.C., U.S.	192	35.07 N	79.25 W
Aberdeen, S.D., U.S.	198	45.27 N	98.29 W
Aberdeen, Wa., U.S.	224	46.58 N	123.49 W

Aberdeen Lake ⊕	176	64.27 N	99.00 W
Aberdeen Lake ⊕ ¹	194	33.55 N	88.30 W
Aberdeen Proving Ground ⟋	208	39.25 N	76.10 W
Aberdour	46	56.03 N	3.19 W
Aberdulais	42	51.41 N	3.48 W
Aberdyfi	42	52.33 N	4.02 W
Aberfeldy	46	56.37 N	3.54 W
Aberfoyle	46	56.11 N	4.23 W
Abergavenny	42	51.50 N	3.00 W
Abergele	44	53.17 N	3.34 W
Abergwaun — Fishguard	42	52.00 N	4.59 W
Abergynolwyn	42	52.40 N	3.58 W
Aberjona ≊	283	42.27 N	71.08 W
Abernathy	222	33.50 N	101.50 W
Abernathy, Sk., Can.	184	50.45 N	103.25 W
Abernethy, Scot., U.K.	46	56.20 N	3.19 W
Aberporth	42	52.08 N	4.33 W
Abersoch	42	52.50 N	4.29 W
Aberystwyth	42	52.25 N	4.05 W
Abessinien, Hochland von — Ethiopien			
Abetone	66	44.08 N	10.40 E
Abez	24	66.32 N	61.42 E
Abhar	128	36.09 N	49.13 E
Abharwat ʌ	123	34.02 N	74.25 E
Abhayāpuri	124	26.20 N	90.40 E
Abiad, Ra's ⟩	132	23.01 N	35.00 E
Abiata Shala National Park ♦	144	7.35 N	38.35 E
Abiata Creek ≊	194	33.45 N	93.42 W
Abid, Oued el ≊	148	32.18 N	7.03 W
Abidjan	150	5.19 N	4.02 W
'Abidīyah	140	18.14 N	33.57 E
Abijatta ≊	150	5.19 N	4.02 W
'Ābid Mār, Tall ʌ	132	32.26 N	36.42 E
Abiengama	154	2.35 N	27.46 E

River	Fluß	Río	Rivière	Rio
Canal	Kanal	Canal	Canal	Canal
Waterfall, Rapids	Wasserfall, Stromschnellen	Cascada, Rápidos	Chute d'eau, Rapides	Cascata, Rápidos
Strait	Meeresstraße	Estrecho	Détroit	Estreito
Bay, Gulf	Bucht, Golf	Bahía, Golfo	Baie, Golfe	Baía, Golfo
Lake, Lakes	See, Seen	Lago, Lagos	Lac, Lacs	Lago, Lagos
Swamp	Sumpf	Pantano	Marais	Pântano
Ice Features, Glacier	Eis- und Gletscherformen	Accidentes Glaciales	Formes glaciaires	Acidentes glaciares
Other Hydrographic Features	Andere Hydrographische Objekte	Otros Elementos Hidrográficos	Autres données hydrographiques	Outros acidentes hidrográficos
Submarine Features	Untermeerische Objekte	Accidentes Submarinos	Formes de relief sous-marin	Acidentes submarinos
Political Unit	Politische Einheit	Unidad Política	Entité politique	Unidade política
Cultural Institution	Kulturelle Institution	Institución Cultural	Institution culturelle	Instituição cultural
Historical Site	Historische Stätte	Sitio Histórico	Site historique	Sítio histórico
Recreational Site	Erholungs- und Ferienort	Sitio de Recreo	Centre de loisirs	Area de Lazer
Airport	Flughafen	Aeropuerto	Aéroport	Aeroporto
Military Installation	Militäranlage	Instalación Militar	Installation militaire	Instalação militar
Miscellaneous	Verschiedenes	Misceláneo	Divers	Diversos

		ENGLISH				DEUTSCH		
		Name	Page	Lat.⁰ʳ	Long.⁰ʳ	Name	Seite	Breite⁰ʳ / Länge⁰ʳ E = Ost

---

Symbol	English	Deutsch	Español	Français	Português
∧	Mountain	Berg	Montaña	Montagne	Montanha
⟋	Mountains	Gebirge	Montañas	Montagnes	Montanhas
)(	Pass	Paß	Paso	Col	Passo
∨	Valley, Canyon	Tal, Cañon	Valle, Cañón	Vallée, Canyon	Vale, Canhão
≃	Plain	Ebene	Llano	Plaine	Planicie
≏	Cape	Kap	Cabo	Cap	Cabo
I	Island	Insel	Isla	Île	Ilha
II	Islands	Inseln	Islas	Îles	Ilhas
⊥	Other Topographic Features	Andere Topographische Objekte	Otros Elementos Topográficos	Autres données topographiques	Outros acidentes topográficos

ESPAÑOL				FRANÇAIS				PORTUGUÊS			
Nombre	Página	Lat.°'	Long.°' W=Oeste	Nom	Page	Lat.°'	Long.°' W=Ouest	Nome	Página	Lat.°'	Long.°' W=Oeste

The legend at the foot of the page:

		(Fluß)	(Río)	(Rivière)	(Rio)
≈	River	Fluß	Río	Rivière	Rio
≍	Canal	Kanal	Canal	Canal	Canal
L	Waterfall, Rapids	Wasserfall, Stromschnellen	Cascada, Rápidos	Chute d'eau, Rapides	Cascada, Rápidos
L	Strait	Meeresstraße	Estrecho	Détroit	Estreito
c	Bay, Gulf	Bucht, Golf	Bahía, Golfo	Baie, Golfe	Baía, Golfo
�	Lake, Lakes	See, Seen	Lago, Lagos	Lac, Lacs	Lago, Lagos
≋	Swamp	Sumpf	Pantano	Marais	Pântano
⊞	Ice Features, Glacier	Eis- und Gletscherformen	Accidentes Glaciales	Formes glaciaires	Acidentes glaciares
⊤	Other Hydrographic Features	Andere Hydrographische Objekte	Otros Elementos Hidrográficos	Autres données hydrographiques	Outros acidentes hidrográficos

⊹	Submarine Features	Untermeerische Objekte	Accidentes Submarinos	Formes de relief sous-marin	Acidentes submarinos
▪	Political Unit	Politische Einheit	Unidad Política	Entité politique	Unidade política
⚘	Cultural Institution	Kulturelle Institution	Institución Cultural	Institution culturelle	Instituição cultural
⌂	Historical Site	Historische Stätte	Sitio Histórico	Site historique	Sítio histórico
⚑	Recreational Site	Erholungs- und Ferienort	Sitio de Recreo	Centre de loisirs	Area de Lazer
✈	Airport	Flughafen	Aeropuerto	Aéroport	Aeroporto
⚔	Military Installation	Militäranlage	Instalación Militar	Installation militaire	Instalação militar
◆	Miscellaneous	Verschiedenes	Misceláneo	Divers	Diversos

ENGLISH: Name | Page | Lat.°' | Long.°'

DEUTSCH: Name | Seite | Breite°' | Länge°' E = Ost

Name	Page	Lat.°'	Long.°'
Aksu, Zhg.	90	41.10 N	80.20 E
Aksu ≃, Asia	85	43.22 N	73.54 E
Aksu ≃, Kaz.	86	46.20 N	78.15 E
Aksu ≃, Tür.	130	37.25 N	36.54 E
Aksu ≃, Tür.	130	36.51 N	30.54 E
Aksu-Ajuly	86	48.47 N	73.40 E
Aksuart, ozero ⊜	86	51.24 N	64.28 E
Aksuat, Kaz.	86	51.32 N	64.34 E
Aksuat, Kaz.	86	47.45 N	82.40 E
Aksuat, Kaz.	86	48.16 N	83.50 E
Aksubajevo	80	54.52 N	50.50 E
Aksu-Džabaglinskij zapovednik ♠	85	42.20 N	70.35 E
Aksum	144	14.08 N	38.43 E
Aktag ∧	120	36.45 N	84.40 E
Aktal	85	41.25 N	75.03 E
Aktanyš	80	55.43 N	54.05 E
Aktas, Kaz.	85	42.57 N	70.04 E
Aktas, Kaz.	86	48.02 N	66.21 E
Aktas, Kaz.	86	49.47 N	72.59 E
Aktas, Kaz.	86	50.06 N	76.40 E
Aktaš, Ross.	86	50.18 N	87.44 E
Aktaš, Uzb.	85	41.38 N	69.44 E
Aktaş Gölü ⊜	84	41.15 N	43.12 E
Aktasty	86	50.44 N	61.43 E
Aktau, Kaz.	72	43.35 N	51.05 E
Aktau, Kaz.	86	50.16 N	73.02 E
Aktau, gora ∧	86	48.00 N	71.45 E
Aktepe	130	36.44 N	36.27 E
Akterek, Kaz.	85	43.22 N	75.18 E
Akterek, Kyrg.	85	42.14 N	77.45 E
Akto	85	39.08 N	75.57 E
Aktobe	85	43.13 N	67.46 E
Aktogaj, Kaz.	86	44.27 N	76.42 E
Aktogaj, Kaz.	86	48.18 N	74.58 E
Aktogaj, Kaz.	86	46.57 N	79.40 E
Aktubek	86	48.37 N	71.06 E
Akt'ubinsk	86	50.17 N	57.10 E
Akt'ubinsk □[8]	86	48.30 N	58.30 E
Akt'ubinskij	80	54.49 N	52.47 E
Aktuluk	130	39.03 N	39.32 E
Aktumsyk	86	46.40 N	57.19 E
Akt'uz	85	42.54 N	76.07 E
Aku	150	6.42 N	7.20 E
Akūbū (Akobo) ≃	140	7.47 N	33.03 E
Akui ≃	96	34.06 N	134.33 E
Akula	152	2.22 N	20.11 E
Akuliči Pervyje	76	53.11 N	33.13 E
Akulovo, Ross.	82	55.31 N	36.42 E
Akulovo, Ross.	82	56.05 N	38.59 E
Akumadan	150	7.24 N	1.57 W
Akune	92	32.01 N	130.11 E
Akun Island I	180	54.12 N	165.35 W
Akure	150	7.15 N	5.12 E
Akureyri	24a	65.44 N	18.08 W
Akurli	272c	19.01 N	73.08 E
Akuša	84	42.17 N	47.21 E
Akuse	150	6.06 N	0.08 E
Akuseki-jima I	93b	29.27 N	129.37 E
Akutan	180	54.08 N	165.46 W
Akutan Island I	180	54.10 N	165.55 W
Akutan Pass ⊔	180	54.00 N	166.10 W
Akuticha	86	52.27 N	84.29 E
Akwa Ibom □[3]	150	4.50 N	7.50 E
Akwanga	150	8.55 N	8.23 E
Akwatia	150	6.04 N	0.49 W
Akwawa ∧[2]	150	6.27 N	0.25 W
Akwaya	152	6.30 N	9.40 E
Akyab → Sittwe	110	20.09 N	92.54 E
Akyazı	130	40.41 N	30.37 E
Akyel	144	12.33 N	37.04 E
Akyr-T'ube	85	42.59 N	72.07 E
Akyurt	130	40.08 N	33.06 E
Akžajkyn, ozero ⊜	86	44.55 N	67.46 E
Akžal, Kaz.	86	47.47 N	74.02 E
Akžal, Kaz.	86	49.13 N	81.25 E
Akžar, Kaz.	85	43.08 N	71.38 E
Akžar, Kaz.	86	47.35 N	83.42 E
Akžaryk	86	48.34 N	75.30 E
Ål	26	60.38 N	8.34 E
Ala	64	45.45 N	11.00 E
Ala ≃	86	42.42 N	89.12 E
Alà, Monti di ⋀	71	40.40 N	9.14 E
Al-Ab'ādīyah	142	31.22 N	31.07 E
Alabama	210	43.06 N	78.23 W
Alabama □[3], U.S.	178	32.50 N	87.00 W
Alabama □[3], U.S.	194	32.50 N	87.00 W
Alabama ≃	194	31.08 N	87.57 W
Alabama and Coushatta Indian Reservation ⬥[4]	222	30.43 N	94.42 W
Alabaster	194	33.14 N	86.48 W
Alabat Island I	116	14.07 N	122.03 E
Al-'Abbāsah ash-Sharqīyah	142	30.32 N	31.43 E
Al-'Abbāsīyah	140	12.10 N	31.18 E
Al-'Abbāsīyah ⬥[8]	273c	30.04 N	31.17 E
Alabino	82	55.31 N	37.01 E
Āl-'Ābis	144	18.04 N	43.10 E
Alabuga ≃	85	41.26 N	74.41 E
Ala-Buka	85	41.23 N	71.30 E
Alaca	130	40.10 N	34.51 E
Alacahan	130	39.07 N	37.37 E
Alacalı	130	41.11 N	29.27 E
Alaçam	130	41.37 N	35.37 E
Alaçam Dağları ⋀	130	39.20 N	28.32 E
Alacant	34	38.21 N	0.29 W
Alacant □[4]	34	38.30 N	0.45 W
Alaçatı	130	38.16 N	26.23 E
Alachadzy	84	43.14 N	40.18 E
Alachua	192	29.47 N	82.29 W
Alacrán, Arrecífe ✣[2]	232	22.24 N	89.42 W
Alacranes, Presa ⊜[1]	240p	22.45 N	80.08 W
Aladağ	130	37.02 N	32.41 E
Aladağ ∧, Tür.	84	40.11 N	42.49 E
Aladağ ∧, Tür.	130	37.44 N	35.09 E
Aladağlar ⋀, Tür.	84	39.20 N	43.35 E
Ala Dağlar ⋀, Tür.	130	37.55 N	35.13 E
Al-'Adasīyah	132	32.40 N	35.37 E
Alà dei Sardi	71	40.39 N	9.20 E
Aladino	82	54.49 N	38.12 E
Aladinskij, porog ⌞	86	58.24 N	95.29 E
Ala di Stura	62	45.19 N	7.19 E
Aladjino	82	56.21 N	37.04 E
Aladža manastir ʊ[1]	38	43.17 N	28.01 E
Alafia ≃	220	27.52 N	82.23 W
Alafia, South Prong ≃	220	27.51 N	82.08 W
Alagbado	273a	6.41 N	3.18 E
Alagna Valsesia	62	45.51 N	7.56 E
Alag nuur ⊜	102	45.09 N	94.28 E
Alagoa	256	22.10 S	44.38 W
Alagoa Grande	250	7.03 S	35.38 W
Alagoa Nova	250	7.04 S	35.46 W
Alagoas □[3]	250	9.00 S	36.00 W
Alagoinhas	255	12.07 S	38.26 W
Alagón	34	41.46 N	1.07 W
Alagón ≃	34	39.44 N	6.53 W
Alaguntan	273a	6.26 N	3.30 E
Alah ≃	116	6.53 N	124.33 E
Alahanpanjang	112	1.05 S	100.47 E
Alahärmä	26	63.14 N	22.51 E
Alaior	34	39.56 N	4.08 E
Al-Ait	140	12.22 N	27.27 E
Al-'Ajamīyīn	142	29.20 N	30.43 E
Alajärvi	26	63.00 N	23.49 E
Alajku	85	40.18 N	74.25 E
Alajõe	76	59.01 N	27.26 E
Alajskaja dolina V	85	39.30 N	73.00 E
Alajskij chrebet ⋀	85	39.45 N	72.00 E
Alajuela	236	10.01 N	84.13 W
Alajuela □[4]	236	10.30 N	84.30 W
Alajuela, Lago ⊜[1]	236	9.15 N	79.35 W
Ālājūjeh	84	38.57 N	46.41 E
Alakai Swamp ⩸	229b	22.08 N	159.35 W
Alakamisy	157b	21.19 S	47.14 E
Alakanuk	180	62.41 N	164.37 W
Alaknanda ≃	124	30.08 N	78.36 E
Alakol', ozero ⊜	86	46.10 N	81.45 E
Al-'Akrīshah	142	31.08 N	30.09 E
Alaktara	124	22.01 N	82.26 E
Alak'ul'a	265a	59.44 N	29.56 E
Alakurtti	24	66.57 N	30.18 E
Al-'Āl	132	32.48 N	35.44 E
Alalakeiki Channel ⊔	229a	20.35 N	156.30 W
Al-'Alamayn	140	30.49 N	28.57 E
Al-'Alāqimah	142	30.37 N	31.38 E
Alalaú ≃	246	0.30 S	61.09 W
Al-'Amādīyah	128	37.06 N	43.29 E
Alamagan I	108	17.36 N	145.50 E
Al-'Amārah	128	31.50 N	47.09 E
Al-'Amār al-Kubrā	142	30.21 N	31.08 E
Alamata	144	12.25 N	39.33 E
Alamdānga	124	23.46 N	88.57 E
Alameda, Esp.	34	37.12 N	4.39 W
Alameda, Ca., U.S.	226	37.45 N	122.14 W
Alameda, N.M., U.S.	200	35.11 N	106.37 W
Alameda □[6]	226	37.35 N	121.55 W
Alameda, Estación ⬥[5]	286e	33.27 S	70.41 W
Alameda Creek ≃	226	37.35 N	122.09 W
Alameda Naval Air Station ■	226	37.47 N	122.18 W
Alamedin	85	42.54 N	74.37 E
Alamein → Al-'Alamayn	140	30.49 N	28.57 E
Alamillo	200	31.02 N	110.35 W
Alaminos	116	16.10 N	119.59 E
Al-'Āmirīyah	142	31.01 N	29.48 E
'Alam Lek	128	37.02 N	65.57 E
Álamo, Méx.	234	20.55 N	97.41 W
Alamo, Ca., U.S.	226	37.51 N	122.02 W
Alamo, Ga., U.S.	192	32.08 N	82.46 W
Alamo, Mi., U.S.	216	42.22 N	85.43 W
Alamo, Nv., U.S.	204	37.21 N	115.09 W
Alamo, Tn., U.S.	194	35.47 N	89.07 W
Alamo ≃	204	33.14 N	115.39 W
Alamo Creek ≃	282	37.42 N	121.55 W
Alamo Creek, West Branch ≃	282	37.45 N	121.55 W
Alamogordo	200	32.53 N	105.57 W
Alamogordo Creek ≃	196	34.40 N	104.23 W
Alamo Heights	196	29.29 N	98.27 W
Alamo Indian Reservation ⬥[4]	200	34.30 N	107.30 W
Alamo Lake ⊜[1]	200	34.20 N	113.30 W
Alamo Oaks	282	37.51 N	121.59 W
Alamor	246	4.02 S	80.02 W
Alamos, Méx.	196	26.25 N	100.25 W
Álamos, Méx.	232	27.01 N	108.56 W
Álamos, Río de los ≃	196	27.53 N	101.12 W
Alamosa	200	37.28 N	105.52 W
Alamosa ≃	200	37.22 N	105.46 W
Alamosa Creek ≃, N.M., U.S.	196	34.26 N	103.58 W
Alamosa Creek ≃, N.M., U.S.	200	33.20 N	107.21 W
Alamosa East	200	37.28 N	105.49 W
Álamos de Márquez	232	28.40 N	103.30 W
Ālampur, Bngl.	126	23.49 N	89.06 E
Alampur, India	272b	22.25 N	88.08 E
Alanäs	26	64.10 N	15.42 E
Al-'Ānāt	132	32.21 N	36.48 E
Al-Anbār □[4]	128	33.45 N	41.45 E
Aland	122	17.34 N	76.34 E
Åland (Ahvenanmaa) II	26	60.15 N	20.00 E
Aland ≃	54	53.02 N	11.34 E
Åland-Inseln → Åland II	26	60.15 N	20.00 E
Ålands hav ⊤[2]	26	60.00 N	19.30 E
Alandur	122	13.02 N	80.15 E
Alangalang	116	11.12 N	124.51 E
Alang-besar, Pulau I	114	2.12 N	100.39 E
Alanje	236	8.24 N	82.33 W
Alano di Piave	64	45.55 N	11.52 E
Alanson	190	45.26 N	84.47 W
Alanya	130	36.33 N	32.01 E
Al-'Anz	132	32.23 N	36.38 E
Alaotra, Lac ⊜	157b	17.30 S	48.30 E
Alapaha	192	31.23 N	83.13 W
Alapaha ≃	192	30.26 N	83.06 W
Alapajevsk	86	57.52 N	61.42 E
Alaplı	130	41.11 N	31.24 E
Al-'Aqabah	132	29.31 N	35.00 E
'Alaqah, Jabal ∧	142	29.59 N	32.53 E
Alaquines	234	22.08 N	99.36 W
Al-'Arabīyah as-Su'ūdīyah → Saudi Arabia □[1]	118	25.00 N	45.00 E
Alarcón	34	39.33 N	2.05 W
Alarcón, Embalse de ⊜[1]	34	39.36 N	2.10 W
Al-'Arīsh	132	31.08 N	33.48 E
Al-'Armah ⋀[1]	128	25.30 N	46.30 E
Alarobia Vohiposa	157b	20.59 S	47.09 E
Alas	115b	8.32 S	117.00 E
Alas ≃, Indon.	114	3.05 N	97.55 E
Alaš ≃, Ross.	86	51.15 N	90.54 E
Alas, Selat ⊔	115b	8.40 S	116.40 E
Alasan	112	1.45 S	123.19 E
Alasdair, Sgurr ∧	46	57.12 N	6.14 W
Alaşehir	130	38.21 N	28.32 E
Alashanyouqi	102	40.02 N	103.33 E
Al-'Ashārah	130	34.55 N	40.34 E
Al-Ashmūnayn	142	27.47 N	30.49 E
Alaska	216	42.50 N	85.29 W
Alaska □[3]	180	65.00 N	153.00 W
Alaska, Gulf of ⊂	16	58.00 N	146.00 W
Alaska Peninsula ›[1]	180	57.00 N	158.00 W
Alaska Range ⋀	180	62.30 N	150.00 W
Al-'Assāfīyah	128	28.21 N	39.08 E
Alassio	62	44.00 N	8.10 E
Alastaro	26	60.56 N	22.55 E
Alastuey	258	34.25 S	59.13 W
Al'at, Azer.	84	39.57 N	49.25 E
Alat, Uzb.	128	39.26 N	63.48 E
Al-'Atāminah	142	27.20 N	30.50 E
Alatan'aola → Xin Barag Youqi	88	48.41 N	116.53 E
Al-Atārib	130	36.08 N	36.49 E
Al-Aṭāwilah	142	27.14 N	31.13 E
Al-'Aṭf	142	29.39 N	31.16 E
Al-'Athāmīn ⋀	128	30.22 N	43.40 E
Alatna ≃	180	66.34 N	152.34 W
Alatri	66	41.43 N	13.21 E
Al-'Aṭrūn	140	18.11 N	26.36 E
Alatyr'	80	54.51 N	46.36 E
Alatyr' ≃	80	54.52 N	46.36 E
Alausí	246	2.12 S	78.50 W
Alava, Cape ›	224	48.10 N	124.43 W
Alaverdi	84	41.08 N	44.39 E
Alavieska	26	64.10 N	24.18 E
Alavus	26	62.35 N	23.37 E
Alaw ≃	44	53.18 N	4.32 W
Alaw, Llyn ⊜[1]	44	53.20 N	4.22 W
Alawa	150	10.20 N	6.39 E
Alāwalpur	123	31.26 N	75.39 E
Al-'Awjā'	142	30.58 N	30.32 E
Al-'Awsajīyah	128	26.49 N	41.41 E
'Ālayh	132	33.48 N	35.36 E
Al-'Ayn	128	24.13 N	55.46 E
Al-'Ayn ⊤[4]	140	16.36 N	29.19 E
Al-'Ayyāsh ash-Sharqī	142	31.33 N	31.13 E
Al-'Ayyāṭ	142	29.37 N	31.15 E
Alazani ≃	84	41.05 N	46.40 E
Alazeja ≃	74	70.51 N	153.34 E
Al-Azhar University ʊ[2]	273c	30.03 N	31.16 E
Al'Azīzah	142	31.11 N	31.57 E
Al-'Azīzīyah, Lībiyā	146	32.32 N	13.01 E
Al-'Azīzīyah, Miṣr	142	30.29 N	31.18 E
Al-'Azīzīyah, Miṣr	273c	29.52 N	31.15 E
Al-Azraq ⬥[1]	132	31.52 N	36.50 E
Alb ≃	58	47.35 N	8.08 E
Alba, It.	62	44.42 N	8.02 E
Alba, Mi., U.S.	190	44.58 N	84.58 W
Alba, Pa., U.S.	210	41.42 N	76.50 W
Alba, Tx., U.S.	222	32.48 N	95.38 W
Alba □[6]	38	46.15 N	23.30 E
Alba, Foum de ⋊	148	20.27 N	3.36 W
Al-Bāb	130	36.22 N	37.31 E
Albacete	34	38.59 N	1.51 W
Albacete □[4]	34	38.50 N	1.50 W
Albachten	52	51.55 N	7.31 E
Albacina	66	43.21 N	13.01 E
Al-Bad'	128	28.25 N	35.04 E
Al-Badārī	140	26.59 N	31.25 E
Alba de Tormes	34	40.49 N	5.31 W
Al-Badrashayn	142	29.51 N	31.16 E
Ålbæk	26	57.36 N	10.25 E
Al-Bahnasā	142	28.32 N	30.39 E
Al-Baḥr al-Abyaḍ □[4]	140	13.15 N	32.25 E
Al-Baḥr al-Aḥmar □[4], Miṣr	142	28.45 N	32.00 E
Al-Baḥr al-Aḥmar □[4], Sūd.	140	20.00 N	35.15 E
Al-Baḥrayn → Bahrain □[1]	128	26.00 N	50.30 E
Albaida	34	38.51 N	0.31 W
Albairate	266b	45.25 N	8.56 E
Alba Iulia	38	46.04 N	23.35 E
Al-Bajalāt	142	31.10 N	31.37 E
Al-Bājūr	142	30.26 N	31.02 E
Al-Bakātūsh	142	31.03 N	30.48 E
Al-Balāmūn	142	30.49 N	31.26 E
Al-Balāshūn	142	30.26 N	31.26 E
Al-Ballaḥ	142	30.46 N	32.19 E
Al-Ballāṣ	140	26.01 N	32.46 E
Al-Balqā' □[8]	132	32.00 N	35.40 E
Al-Bālū'ah ⊜	130	35.55 N	36.28 E
Al-Balyanā	140	26.14 N	32.00 E
Alban	32	43.54 N	2.28 E
Albanel, Lac ⊜	176	50.55 N	73.12 W
Albanella	68	40.30 N	15.08 E
Albani, Colli ⋀[2]	66	41.45 N	12.45 E
Albania, Col.	246	11.01 N	72.40 W
Albania, Col.	246	1.21 N	75.57 W
Albania (Shqipëri) □[1], Europe	22	41.00 N	20.00 E
Albania (Shqipëri) □[1], Europe	38	41.00 N	20.00 E
Albanie → Albania □[1]	38	41.00 N	20.00 E
Albanien → Albania □[1]	38	41.00 N	20.00 E
Albano, Lago ⊜	66	41.45 N	12.40 E
Albano, Monte ⋀	66	43.50 N	10.58 E
Albano di Lucania	68	40.35 N	16.02 E
Albano Laziale	66	41.44 N	12.39 E
Albany, Austl.	162	35.02 S	117.53 E
Albany, Ca., U.S.	226	37.53 N	122.17 W
Albany, Ga., U.S.	192	31.34 N	84.09 W
Albany, Il., U.S.	190	41.47 N	90.13 W
Albany, In., U.S.	216	40.18 N	85.14 W
Albany, Ky., U.S.	194	36.41 N	85.08 W
Albany, Mn., U.S.	190	45.37 N	94.34 W
Albany, Mo., U.S.	194	40.14 N	94.19 W
Albany, N.Y., U.S.	210	42.39 N	73.45 W
Albany, Oh., U.S.	188	39.13 N	82.12 W
Albany, Or., U.S.	202	44.38 N	123.06 W
Albany, Tx., U.S.	196	32.43 N	99.17 W
Albany, Wi., U.S.	190	42.42 N	89.26 W
Albany □[6]	210	42.39 N	73.45 W
Albany ≃	176	52.17 N	81.31 W
Albany County Airport ⊠	210	42.45 N	73.48 W
Albany Creek	171a	27.21 S	152.58 E
Albany Park ⬥[8]	278	41.58 N	87.43 W
Al-Baq'ah	132	32.05 N	35.53 E
Al-Barājīl	273c	30.04 N	31.09 E
Al-Barāmūn	142	31.07 N	31.26 E
Albardón	252	31.26 S	68.32 W
Albaredo d'Adige	64	45.19 N	11.16 E
Al-Bāriḥah	132	32.34 N	35.50 E
Al-Barnūjī	142	30.56 N	30.23 E
Albaron	62	43.37 N	4.28 E
Albaron ∧	62	45.20 N	7.07 E
Albarracín	34	40.25 N	1.26 W
Al-Barrah	128	24.55 N	45.52 E
Albarraque	266c	38.46 N	9.21 W
Al-Barshā	142	27.43 N	30.54 E
Al-Barun	140	11.44 N	33.30 E
Al-Basāṭīn ⬥[8]	273c	29.59 N	31.16 E
Al-Baslaqūn	142	31.06 N	30.08 E
Al-Basqalūn	142	28.42 N	30.44 E
Al-Baṣrah (Basra)	128	30.30 N	47.47 E
Al-Baṣrah □[4]	128	30.20 N	47.35 E
Al-Batānūn	142	30.37 N	30.59 E
Al-Baṭḥā'	128	31.06 N	45.53 E
Al-Bāṭinah ⬥[1]	128	23.45 N	57.20 E
Albatross Bay ⊂	164	12.45 S	141.43 E
Albatross Point ›	172	38.06 S	174.41 E
Al-Batrūn	130	34.15 N	35.39 E
Al-Baṭrūnah	132	33.39 N	36.02 E
Al-Bauga	140	18.16 N	33.55 E
Al-Bawīṭī	140	28.21 N	28.52 E
Albay □[4]	116	13.00 N	123.40 E
Al-Bayahū	142	28.16 N	30.44 E
Al-Bayḍā (Beida), Lībiyā	146	28.22 N	18.55 E
Al-Bayḍā' (Beida), Lībiyā	146	32.46 N	21.43 E
Al-Bayḍā', Miṣr	142	31.10 N	30.05 E
Albay Gulf ⊂	116	13.10 N	124.00 E
Albazino	89	53.23 N	124.05 E
Albbruck	58	47.35 N	8.07 E
Albegna ≃	66	42.30 N	11.11 E
Albemarle	192	35.13 N	80.13 W
Albemarle and Chesapeake Canal ≍	208	36.43 N	76.15 W
Albemarle Sound ⊔	192	36.03 N	76.12 W
Albenga	62	44.03 N	8.13 E
Albens	62	45.47 N	5.57 E
Alberche ≃	34	39.58 N	4.46 W
Alberdi	252	26.10 S	58.09 W
Alberene	192	37.53 N	78.37 W
Alberga, Austl.	162	27.12 S	135.28 E
Ålberga, Sve.	40	58.44 N	16.34 E
Alberga Creek ≃	162	27.06 S	135.33 E
Albergaria-a-Velha	34	40.42 N	8.29 W
Alberhill	228	33.44 N	117.23 W
Alberic	34	39.07 N	0.31 W
Alberni Inlet ⊂	182	49.07 N	124.50 W
Alberobello	68	40.47 N	17.15 E
Alberona	68	41.26 N	15.07 E
Albero Sole ∧	70a	35.31 N	12.32 E
Albers	219	38.33 N	89.37 W
Alberschwende	58	47.27 N	9.49 E
Albersloh	52	51.52 N	7.43 E
Albert	50	50.00 N	2.39 E
Albert ≃	171a	27.42 S	153.15 E
Albert, Lake ⊜, Afr.	154	1.40 N	31.00 E
Albert, Lake ⊜, Austl.	166	35.38 S	139.17 E
Alberta	194	32.13 N	87.24 W
Alberta □[4], Can.	176	54.00 N	113.00 W
Alberta □[4], Can.	182	54.00 N	113.00 W
Alberta, Mount ∧	182	52.18 N	117.28 W
Albert Canyon	182	51.08 N	117.52 W
Albert City	198	42.46 N	94.56 W
Albert Edward, Mount ∧	164	8.23 S	147.24 E
Albert Edward Bay ⊂	176	69.32 N	103.00 W
Albert Falls	158	29.27 S	30.25 E
Albertfalva ⬥[8]	264c	47.27 N	19.02 E
Alberti	252	35.02 S	60.16 W
Al'bertin	76	53.05 N	25.23 E
Albertina	256	22.12 S	46.37 W
Albertinia	158	34.13 S	21.36 E
Albertirsa	30	47.15 N	19.38 E
Albert Kanaal (Canal Albert) ≍	56	50.39 N	5.37 E
Albert Lea	190	43.38 N	93.22 W
Albert Markham, Mount ∧	9	81.23 S	158.12 E
Albert Nile ≃	154	3.36 N	32.02 E
Alberto, Lago → Albert, Lake ⊜	154	1.40 N	31.00 E
Alberto Eduardo → Albert Edward, Mount ∧	164	8.23 S	147.24 E
Alberton, P.E., Can.	186	46.49 N	64.04 W
Alberton, S. Afr.	273d	26.16 S	28.08 E
Alberton, Mt., U.S.	202	47.00 N	114.29 W
Albert Park ♠	274b	37.51 S	144.57 E
Albert Peak ∧	182	51.02 N	117.51 W
Albertshof	264a	52.42 N	13.40 E
Albertson	276	40.46 N	73.38 W
Albertson Brook ≃	285	39.41 N	74.43 W
Albertson Brook, Blue Anchor Branch ≃	285	39.42 N	74.49 W
Albertson Brook, Pump Branch ≃	285	39.42 N	74.49 W
Albertville, Fr.	62	45.41 N	6.23 E
Albertville, Al., U.S.	194	34.16 N	86.12 W
Albertville → Kalemie, Zaïre	154	5.56 S	29.12 E
Albestroff	56	48.56 N	6.51 E
Albettone	64	45.21 N	11.35 E
Albi	32	43.56 N	2.09 E
Albia, Ia., U.S.	190	41.01 N	92.48 W
Albia, N.Y., U.S.	210	42.43 N	73.39 W
Albiate	266b	45.39 N	9.15 E
Al Bidia	146	10.33 N	20.13 E
Albidona	68	39.55 N	16.28 E
Albignasego	64	45.21 N	11.52 E
Albin	198	41.25 N	104.05 W
Albina	250	5.30 N	54.03 W
Albina, Ponta ›	152	15.51 S	11.44 E
Albinea	64	44.37 N	10.36 E
Albino	62	45.46 N	9.47 E
Albion, Austl.	274b	37.47 S	144.49 E
Albion, B.C., Can.	224	49.11 N	122.33 W
Albion, Ca., U.S.	204	39.13 N	123.46 W
Albion, Id., U.S.	202	42.24 N	113.34 W
Albion, Il., U.S.	194	38.22 N	88.03 W
Albion, In., U.S.	216	41.23 N	85.25 W
Albion, Ia., U.S.	190	42.06 N	92.59 W
Albion, Mi., U.S.	216	42.14 N	84.45 W
Albion, Ne., U.S.	198	41.41 N	98.00 W
Albion, N.J., U.S.	285	39.47 N	74.56 W
Albion, N.Y., U.S.	210	43.14 N	78.11 W
Albion, Pa., U.S.	214	41.53 N	80.22 W
Albion, R.I., U.S.	207	41.57 N	71.27 W
Albion, Wa., U.S.	202	46.47 N	117.14 W
Albion, Wi., U.S.	216	42.52 N	89.04 W
Albion Airstrip ⊠	285	39.46 N	74.58 W
Albion Park	170	34.34 S	150.47 E
Al-Biqā' □[4]	130	34.00 N	36.00 E
Al-Biqā' V	128	33.50 N	36.00 E
Al-Bi'r	128	28.50 N	36.19 E
Al-Bīrah	132	31.54 N	35.13 E
Al-Birīgāt	142	30.30 N	30.49 E
Al-Birk	144	18.13 N	41.33 E
Al-Birkah	146	24.54 N	10.11 E
Al-Birkah ⊤[4]	144	22.12 N	40.43 E
Albisola Marina	62	44.19 N	8.30 E
Albisola Superiore	62	44.20 N	8.31 E
Albizzate	62	45.43 N	8.44 E
Alblasserdam	52	51.52 N	4.40 E
Albo, Monte ∧	71	40.32 N	9.35 E
Albocàsser	34	40.21 N	0.02 E
Albogas	266c	38.51 N	9.15 W
Alborán, Isla de I	34	35.58 N	3.02 W
Alborán Sea ⊤[2]	34	36.00 N	3.00 W
Ålborg	26	57.03 N	9.56 E
Ålborg Bugt ⊂	26	56.45 N	10.30 E
Alborz, Reshteh-ye Kūhhā-ye (Elburz Mountains) ⋀	128	36.00 N	53.00 E
Albreda	182	52.38 N	119.09 W
Albright-Knox Art Gallery ʊ	284a	42.56 N	78.53 W
Albrighton	42	52.38 N	2.16 W
Albstadt	58	48.13 N	9.01 E
Albuch ⋀	56	48.15 N	9.50 E
Albuera	116	10.55 N	124.42 E
Albufeira	34	37.05 N	8.15 W
Ālbū Gharz, Sabkhat ⊜	130	34.45 N	41.15 E
Al-Buḥayrah □[4], Miṣr	142	30.59 N	30.12 E
Al-Buḥayrah □[4], Sūd.	140	7.30 N	29.30 E
Albula ≃	58	46.42 N	9.27 E
Al-Bunbah	146	32.24 N	23.08 E
Albuñol	34	36.47 N	3.12 W
Albuquerque, Bra.	248	19.23 S	57.26 W
Albuquerque, N.M., U.S.	200	35.05 N	106.39 W
Albuquerque, Cayos de II	236	12.10 N	81.50 W
Al-Buraymī	128	24.15 N	55.45 E
Alburg	206	44.58 N	73.18 W
Al-Burj	142	31.35 N	30.59 E
Al-Burjāyah	142	28.09 N	30.44 E
Alburno, Monte ∧	68	40.33 N	15.17 E
Alburquerque	34	39.13 N	7.00 W
Alburtis	208	40.31 N	75.36 W
Al-Burumbul	142	29.19 N	31.14 E
Albury, Austl.	166	36.05 S	146.55 E
Albury, N.Z.	172	44.14 S	170.52 E
Albury, Eng., U.K.	260	51.13 N	0.30 W
Albury Park ♠	260	51.13 N	0.29 W
Al-Buṣaylī	142	31.20 N	30.24 E
Al-Busayṭā' ≚	128	29.30 N	38.45 E
Al-Buṭānah ⬥[1]	140	15.00 N	34.40 E
Al-Buṭaynah	132	32.57 N	36.42 E
Al-Buwayḍah	132	32.28 N	36.04 E
Al-Buzūn	144	15.35 N	50.55 E
Albuzzano	62	45.11 N	9.16 E
Alby, Fr.	62	45.49 N	6.01 E
Alby, Sve.	26	62.30 N	15.28 E
Alca	248	15.08 S	72.46 W
Alcabideche	266c	38.44 N	9.24 W
Alcácer do Sal	34	38.22 N	8.30 W
Alcains	34	39.55 N	7.27 W
Alcala	116	17.54 N	121.39 E
Alcalá de Guadaira	34	37.20 N	5.50 W
Alcalá de Henares	34	40.29 N	3.22 W
Alcalá la Real	34	37.28 N	3.56 W
Alcalde	200	36.05 N	106.03 W
Alcamachi ≃	248	16.08 S	66.50 W
Alcamo	70	37.59 N	12.58 E
Alčan ≃	89	46.38 N	134.22 E
Alcanadre ≃	34	41.37 N	0.12 E
Alcanar	34	40.33 N	0.29 E
Alcañices	34	41.42 N	6.21 W
Alcañiz	34	41.03 N	0.08 W
Alcântara, Bra.	250	2.24 S	44.24 W
Alcántara, Esp.	34	39.43 N	6.53 W
Alcantara, Pil.	116	12.16 N	122.03 E
Alcântara ⬥[8]	266c	38.42 N	9.10 W
Alcantara ≃	70	37.49 N	15.16 E
Alcántara, Embalse de ⊜[1]	34	39.45 N	6.25 W
Alcantarilla	34	37.58 N	1.13 W
Alcantilado	255	16.23 S	53.31 W
Alcara li Fusi	70	38.01 N	14.42 E
Alcaraz	34	38.40 N	2.29 W
Alcarrache ≃	34	38.16 N	7.24 W
Alcatraz Island I	282	37.49 N	122.26 W
Alcaudete	34	37.36 N	4.05 W
Alcázar de San Juan	34	39.24 N	3.12 W
Alcazarquivir → Er-Rachidia	148	31.58 N	4.25 W
Alcester, Eng., U.K.	42	52.13 N	1.52 W
Alcester, S.D., U.S.	198	43.01 N	96.37 W
Alcester Island I	164	9.35 S	152.25 E
Alčevsk	83	48.30 N	38.47 E
Alcira (Gigena)	252	32.45 S	64.20 W
Alcoa	192	35.47 N	83.58 W
Alcoa Center	279b	40.33 N	79.39 W
Alcoa Lake ⊜[1]	222	30.34 N	97.03 W
Alcobaça, Bra.	255	17.30 S	39.13 W
Alcobaça, Port.	34	39.33 N	8.59 W
Alcobaça ≃	255	17.32 S	39.12 W
Alcobendas	34	40.32 N	3.38 W
Alcochete	266c	38.45 N	8.58 W
Alcockspruit	158	27.55 S	30.01 E
Alcoi	34	38.42 N	0.28 W
Alcoi ≃	34	38.59 N	0.09 W
Alcoitão	266c	38.44 N	9.24 W
Alcolea del Pinar	34	41.02 N	2.28 W
Alcolu	192	33.45 N	80.12 W
Alcomunga	234	18.25 N	97.02 W
Alconbury Brook ≃	42	52.19 N	0.12 W
Alconchel	34	38.31 N	7.04 W
Alcony	218	40.01 N	84.04 W
Alcorcón	266a	40.21 N	3.50 W
Alcorn	194	31.52 N	91.09 W
Alcorta	252	33.32 S	61.07 W
Alcoutim	34	37.28 N	7.28 W
Alcova Reservoir ⊜[1]	200	42.32 N	106.45 W
Alcove	210	42.28 N	73.55 W
Alcove Reservoir ⊜[1]	210	42.29 N	73.57 W
Alcovy ≃	192	33.26 N	83.50 W
Alcubierre	34	41.48 N	0.27 W
Alcúdia	34	39.52 N	3.07 E
Alcúdia, Badia d' ⊂	34	39.48 N	3.13 E
Alcyon Lake ⊜	285	39.44 N	75.08 W
Aldabra Island I	138	9.25 S	46.22 E
Aldama, Méx.	232	28.51 N	105.54 W
Aldama, Méx.	234	22.55 N	98.04 W
Aldama, Arroyo ≃	286b	23.05 N	82.15 W
Aldan, Ross.	74	58.37 N	125.24 E
Aldan, Pa., U.S.	285	39.55 N	75.17 W
Aldan ≃	74	63.28 N	129.35 E
Aldanskoje nagorje ⋀[1]	74	57.00 N	127.00 E
Aldbourne	42	51.31 N	1.37 W
Aldbrough	44	53.50 N	0.07 W
Aldbury	42	51.48 N	0.36 W
Alde ≃	42	52.03 N	1.28 E
Aldea Apeleg	254	44.41 S	70.51 W
Aldeburgh	42	52.09 N	1.35 E
Aldeia de Paio Pires	266c	38.38 N	9.05 W
Aldeia Nova de Santo Bento	34	37.55 N	7.25 W
Aldeia Velha	256	22.47 S	42.55 W
Aldemha	287b	23.45 S	46.53 W
Alden, Il., U.S.	216	42.27 N	88.31 W
Alden, Ia., U.S.	190	42.31 N	93.22 W
Alden, Mn., U.S.	190	43.40 N	93.34 W
Alden, N.Y., U.S.	210	42.54 N	78.29 W
Alden, Pa., U.S.	210	41.10 N	76.00 W
Alden Center	212	42.55 N	78.32 W
Aldenham	260	51.40 N	0.21 W
Aldenhoven	56	50.53 N	6.16 E
Aldenrade ⬥[8]	263	51.31 N	6.44 E
Alder, Ben ∧	46	56.48 N	4.28 W
Alder Creek ≃	202	45.50 N	119.56 W
Aldergrove	224	49.04 N	122.28 W
Alder Lake ⊜[1]	224	46.45 N	122.15 W
Alderley Edge	44	53.18 N	2.15 W
Aldermaston	42	51.23 N	1.09 W
Alderney I	43b	49.43 N	2.12 W
Alder Peak ∧	226	35.53 N	121.22 W
Aldersbach	60	48.36 N	13.05 E
Aldershot	42	51.15 N	0.47 W
Alderson	192	37.44 N	80.38 W
Alderton	224	47.10 N	122.14 W
Alderwood Manor	224	47.49 N	122.17 W
Aldine	222	29.54 N	95.24 W
Aldinga	168b	35.17 S	138.29 E
Aldinga Bay ⊂	168b	35.20 S	138.25 E
Aldinga Beach	168b	35.18 S	138.27 E
Aldingen	58	48.05 N	8.41 E
Aldino	64	46.23 N	11.20 E
Aldo Bonzi	288	34.42 S	58.31 W
Aldridge	42	52.36 N	1.55 W
Aldwell, Lake ⊜[1]	224	48.05 N	123.34 W
Alechovščina	76	60.25 N	33.52 E
Aled ≃	44	53.14 N	3.34 W
Aledo, Il., U.S.	190	41.11 N	90.44 W
Aledo, Tx., U.S.	222	32.42 N	97.36 W
Alefa	144	11.57 N	36.52 E
Aleg	150	17.03 N	13.55 W
Alegranza, Isla I	148	29.23 N	13.30 W
Alegre	255	20.46 S	41.32 W
Alegre ≃	248	15.01 S	59.57 W
Alegres Mountain ∧	200	34.09 N	108.11 W
Alegrete	252	29.46 S	55.46 W
Alej ≃	86	52.52 N	83.36 E
Alejandría → Al-Iskandarīyah	142	31.12 N	29.54 E
Alejandro, Isla → Alexander Island I	9	71.00 S	70.00 W
Alejandro Roca	252	33.21 S	63.43 W
Alejandro Selkirk, Isla (Isla Más Afuera) I	244	33.45 S	80.46 W
Alejo Ledesma	252	33.37 S	62.37 W
Alejsk	86	52.28 N	82.45 E
Aleknagik	180	59.17 N	158.38 W
Aleknagik, Lake ⊜	180	59.20 N	158.45 W
Aleksandrija	78	48.40 N	33.07 E
Aleksandrijskaja	84	43.54 N	47.08 E
Aleksandrinka	83	47.47 N	37.41 E
Aleksandro-Kalinovo	83	48.25 N	37.40 E
Aleksandro-Nevskaja	84	43.55 N	46.35 E
Aleksandro-Nevskij	80	53.28 N	40.13 E
Aleksandropol'	83	49.42 N	38.50 E
Aleksandrov	82	56.24 N	38.43 E
Aleksandrov Gaj	80	50.09 N	48.34 E
Aleksandrovka, Kaz.	80	50.47 N	52.59 E
Aleksandrovka, Kaz.	85	43.27 N	77.20 E
Aleksandrovka, Kaz.	86	53.07 N	69.50 E
Aleksandrovka, Ross.	78	46.47 N	39.01 E
Aleksandrovka, Ross.	80	52.36 N	50.37 E
Aleksandrovka, Ross.	83	47.26 N	39.13 E
Aleksandrovka, Ross.	86	52.43 N	54.17 E
Aleksandrovka, Ross.	86	56.32 N	90.47 E
Aleksandrovka, Ukr.	78	48.43 N	36.55 E
Aleksandrovka, Ukr.	78	48.57 N	32.14 E
Aleksandrovka, Ukr.	78	47.42 N	31.16 E
Aleksandrovka, Ukr.	78	46.32 N	35.29 E
Aleksandrovka, Ukr.	83	47.55 N	37.35 E
Aleksandrovka, Ukr.	83	48.05 N	37.27 E
Aleksandrovsk	83	48.35 N	39.12 E
Aleksandrovskaja, Ross.	265a	60.03 N	29.59 E
Aleksandrovskaja, Ross.	265a	59.44 N	30.21 E
Aleksandrovskij	78	51.03 N	36.44 E
Aleksandrovskij Šl'uz	86	59.26 N	89.20 E
Aleksandrovskij Zavod	88	50.55 N	117.57 E
Aleksandrovskoje, Ross.	84	44.42 N	43.00 E
Aleksandrovskoje, Ross.	86	56.44 N	85.23 E
Aleksandrovskoje, Ross.	86	60.26 N	77.50 E
Aleksandrovsk-Sachalinskij	89	50.54 N	142.10 E
Aleksandrów Kujawski	30	52.52 N	18.42 E
Aleksandrów Łódzki	30	51.49 N	19.19 E
Aleksaskino	80	50.57 N	47.42 E
Aleksejevka, Kaz.	80	50.58 N	52.25 E
Aleksejevka, Kaz.	86	48.25 N	85.40 E
Aleksejevka, Kaz.	86	53.31 N	69.30 E
Aleksejevka, Kaz.	86	51.59 N	70.59 E
Aleksejevka, Kaz.	86	47.16 N	81.34 E
Aleksejevka, Ross.	78	50.37 N	38.42 E
Aleksejevka, Ross.	80	52.35 N	51.17 E
Aleksejevka, Ross.	80	53.15 N	50.30 E
Aleksejevka, Ross.	80	53.02 N	42.46 E
Aleksejevka, Ross.	80	51.49 N	43.56 E
Aleksejevka, Ross.	80	52.18 N	48.01 E
Aleksejevka, Ross.	82	54.41 N	36.34 E
Aleksejevka, Ross.	83	47.38 N	38.49 E
Aleksejevka, Ross.	83	47.41 N	39.54 E
Aleksejevka, Ross.	86	52.30 N	79.33 E
Aleksejevka, Ross.	86	54.31 N	81.08 E
Aleksejevka, Ross.	86	55.22 N	72.03 E
Aleksejevka, Ukr.	78	47.14 N	36.32 E
Aleksejevka, Ukr.	83	49.25 N	38.46 E
Aleksejevka, Ukr.	83	49.01 N	39.11 E
Aleksejevo-Družkovka	83	48.34 N	37.36 E
Aleksejevo-Lozovskoje	78	49.24 N	40.39 E
Aleksejevo-Orlovka ⬥[8]	83	48.04 N	38.25 E
Aleksejevo-Tuzlovka	83	47.50 N	39.24 E
Aleksejevsk	88	57.50 N	108.23 E
Aleksejevskaja	80	50.17 N	42.11 E
Aleksejevskoje	80	55.18 N	50.06 E
Aleksin	82	54.31 N	37.05 E
Aleksinac	38	43.32 N	21.43 E
Alella	266d	41.30 N	2.18 E
Alemanha → Germany □[1]	30	51.00 N	10.00 E
Alemania	252	25.36 S	65.38 W
Alemania → Germany □[1]	30	51.00 N	10.00 E
Alem Dağı ∧	267b	41.04 N	29.12 E
Alemdar ⬥[8]	267b	41.03 N	29.14 E
Além Paraíba	256	21.52 S	42.41 W
Alençon	50	48.26 N	0.05 E
Alenquer	250	1.56 S	54.46 W
Alentejo □[9]	34	38.00 N	8.00 W
Alenuihaha Channel ⊔	229a	20.26 N	156.00 W
Aléoutiennes, Îles → Aleutian Islands II	180	52.00 N	176.00 W
Alep → Ḥalab	130	36.12 N	37.10 E
Aleppo → Ḥalab	130	36.12 N	37.10 E
Aléria	36	42.05 N	9.30 E
Alert	16	82.29 N	62.22 W
Alert Bay	182	50.35 N	126.55 W
Alès, Fr.	62	44.08 N	4.05 E
Ales, It.	71	39.46 N	8.49 E
Aleşd	38	47.04 N	22.24 E
Alešino, Ross.	82	56.09 N	37.45 E
Alešino, Ross.	82	55.04 N	36.05 E
Aleški	80	51.38 N	41.46 E
Aleškovo	82	54.53 N	36.23 E
Alessandria	62	44.54 N	8.37 E
Alessandria □[4]	62	44.49 N	8.42 E
Alessandria del Carretto	68	39.57 N	16.23 E
Alessandria della Rocca	70	37.34 N	13.27 E
Alessano	68	39.53 N	18.20 E
Ålestrup	26	56.42 N	9.30 E
Ålesund	26	62.28 N	6.09 E
Aletschhorn ∧	58	46.28 N	8.00 E
Alëuten → Aleutian Islands II	180	52.00 N	176.00 W
Aleutianas, Islas → Aleutian Islands II	180	52.00 N	176.00 W
Aleutian Basin ✣[1]	16	57.00 N	177.00 E
Aleutian Islands II	180	52.00 N	176.00 W
Aleutian Range ⋀	180	59.00 N	155.00 W
Aleutian Trench ✣[1]	6	51.00 N	170.00 W
Aleutka	74	45.57 N	150.10 E
Alevina, mys ›	74	58.50 N	151.20 E
Ale Water ≃	46	55.31 N	2.35 W
Alex	196	34.54 N	97.46 W
Alexander, Mb., Can.	184	49.50 N	100.17 W
Alexander, Il., U.S.	219	39.43 N	90.02 W
Alexander, N.Y., U.S.	210	42.54 N	78.16 W
Alexander, N.D., U.S.	198	47.50 N	103.38 W
Alexander ≃	132	32.24 N	34.52 E
Alexander, Cape ›	175e	6.35 S	156.30 E
Alexander, Mount ∧, Austl.	162	22.39 S	115.32 E
Alexander, Mount ∧, Austl.	169	36.59 S	144.18 E
Alexander Archipelago II	180	56.30 N	134.00 W
Alexander Bay	156	28.40 S	16.30 E
Alexander City	194	32.56 N	85.57 W
Alexander Dam ⊜[1]	273d	26.13 S	28.25 E
Alexander Ditch ≍	279a	41.20 N	82.05 W
Alexander Hamilton Airport ⊠	241n	17.42 N	64.48 W
Alexander Indian Reserve ⬥[4]	182	53.48 N	113.58 W
Alexander Island I	9	71.00 S	70.00 W
Alexander Nevsky Monastery ʊ[1]	265a	59.55 N	30.24 E
Alexandra, Austl.	169	37.12 S	145.43 E
Alexandra, N.Z.	172	45.15 S	169.24 E
Alexandra, S. Afr.	273d	26.06 S	28.05 E
Alexandra ≃	166	18.14 S	139.54 E
Alexandra Canal ≍	274a	33.56 S	151.10 E
Alexandra Falls ⌞	176	60.29 N	116.18 W
Alexandra Park ♠	262	53.27 N	2.15 W
Alexandra Park Race Course ♠	260	51.36 N	0.08 W
Alexandretta → İskenderun	130	36.37 N	36.07 E
Alexandretta, Gulf of → İskenderun Körfezi ⊂	130	36.30 N	35.40 E
Alexandria, Austl.	166	19.05 S	136.40 E
Alexandria, Bra.	250	6.25 S	38.01 W
Alexandria, B.C., Can.	182	52.38 N	122.27 W
Alexandria, On., Can.	206	45.19 N	74.38 W
Alexandria → Al-Iskandarīyah, Miṣr	142	31.12 N	29.54 E
Alexandria, Rom.	38	43.58 N	25.20 E
Alexandria, S. Afr.	158	33.40 S	26.24 E
Alexandria, Scot., U.K.	46	55.59 N	4.36 W
Alexandria, In., U.S.	216	40.15 N	85.40 W
Alexandria, Ky., U.S.	218	38.57 N	84.23 W
Alexandria, La., U.S.	194	31.18 N	92.26 W
Alexandria, Mn., U.S.	198	45.53 N	95.22 W
Alexandria, Mo., U.S.	194	40.21 N	91.27 W
Alexandria, Ne., U.S.	198	40.14 N	97.23 W
Alexandria, Oh., U.S.	214	40.05 N	82.37 W
Alexandria, Pa., U.S.	214	40.34 N	78.06 W
Alexandria, S.D., U.S.	198	43.39 N	97.46 W
Alexandria, Tn., U.S.	194	36.04 N	86.02 W
Alexandria, Va., U.S.	208	38.48 N	77.02 W
Alexandria Bay	212	44.20 N	75.55 W
Alexandrie → Al-Iskandarīyah	142	31.12 N	29.54 E
Alexandrina, Lake ⊜	168b	35.26 S	139.10 E
Alexandroúpolis	38	40.50 N	25.52 E
Alexis	190	41.03 N	90.33 W
Alexis Creek	182	52.05 N	123.17 W
Alexis Indian Reserve ⬥[4]	182	53.46 N	114.30 W
Alezio	68	40.04 N	18.03 E
Alf	56	50.03 N	7.07 E
Ālfādānga	126	23.18 N	89.42 E
Al-Fahmīyīn	142	29.36 N	31.17 E
Al-Fallūjah	128	33.20 N	43.46 E
Alfambra	34	40.33 N	1.02 W
Alfambra ≃	34	40.21 N	1.07 W
Al-Fant	142	28.46 N	30.53 E
Alfarata	208	40.39 N	77.27 W
Al-Farḍah	144	14.51 N	48.27 E
Alfaro	34	42.11 N	1.45 W
Alfarràs	34	41.49 N	0.35 E
Al-Fāshir	140	13.38 N	25.21 E
Al-Fashn	142	28.49 N	30.54 E
Alfatar	38	43.57 N	27.17 E
Alfavaca, Ilha I	287a	23.02 S	43.18 W
Al-Fāw	128	29.58 N	48.29 E
Al-Fayyūm	142	29.19 N	30.50 E
Al-Fayyūm □[4]	142	29.19 N	30.48 E
Al-Fāzah	144	14.08 N	43.05 E
Alfbach ≃	56	50.03 N	7.08 E
Alfedena	66	41.44 N	14.02 E
Alfeld, Dtsch.	52	51.59 N	9.50 E
Alfeld, Dtsch.	60	49.26 N	11.33 E
Alfenas	256	21.25 S	45.57 W

Symbols in the index entries represent the broad categories identified in the key at the right. Symbols with superior numbers (⋀[1]) identify subcategories (see complete key on page I · 1).

Symbole im Register stellen die rechts im Schlüssel erklärten Kategorien dar. Symbole mit hochgestellten Ziffern (⋀[1]) bezeichnen Unterabteilungen einer Kategorie (vgl. vollständiger Schlüssel auf Seite I · 1).

Los símbolos incluídos en el texto del índice representan las grandes categorías identificadas con la clave a la derecha. Los símbolos con numeros en su parte superior (⋀[1]) identifican las subcategorías (véase la clave completa en la página I · 1).

Les symboles de l'index représentent les catégories indiquées dans la légende à droite. Les symboles suivis d'un indice (⋀[1]) représentent des sous-catégories (voir légende complète à la page I · 1).

Os símbolos incluídos no texto do índice representam as grandes categorias identificadas com a chave à direita. Os símbolos com números em sua parte superior (⋀[1]) identificam as subcategorias (veja-se a chave completa à página I · 1).

Symbol	English	Deutsch	Español	Français	Português
∧	Mountain	Berg	Montaña	Montagne	Montanha
⋀	Mountains	Gebirge	Montañas	Montagnes	Montanhas
⋊	Pass	Paß	Paso	Col	Passo
V	Valley, Canyon	Tal, Cañon	Valle, Cañón	Vallée, Canyon	Vale, Canhão
≚	Plain	Ebene	Llano	Plaine	Planície
›	Cape	Kap	Cabo	Cap	Cabo
I	Island	Insel	Isla	Île	Ilha
II	Islands	Inseln	Islas	Îles	Ilhas
±	Other Topographic Features	Andere Topographische Objekte	Otros Elementos Topográficos	Autres données topographiques	Outros acidentes topográficos

ESPAÑOL · FRANÇAIS · PORTUGUÊS

Nombre / Nom / Nome	Página / Page	Lat.°′	Long.°′ W = Oeste / W = Ouest
Alfianello	64	45.16 N	10.10 E
Al-Fifi	140	10.03 N	25.01 E
Alfiós ≏	38	37.40 N	21.33 E
Al-Firdān	142	30.41 N	32.20 E
Alföld ≚	30	47.00 N	20.00 E
Alfonsine	66	44.30 N	12.03 E
Alford, Austl.	168b	33.49 S	137.49 E
Alford, Eng., U.K.	44	53.16 N	0.10 E
Alford, Scot., U.K.	46	57.13 N	2.42 W
Alfortville	261	48.49 N	2.25 E
Ålfotbreen ⊓	26	61.45 N	5.40 E
Alfred, On., Can.	206	45.34 N	74.53 W
Alfred, Me., U.S.	188	43.28 N	70.43 W
Alfred, N.Y., U.S.	210	42.15 N	77.47 W
Alfred National Park ♦	166	37.35 S	149.20 E
Alfredo M. Terrazas	234	21.28 N	98.51 W
Alfreton	44	53.06 N	1.23 W
Alfriston	42	50.48 N	0.10 E
Alfta	26	61.21 N	16.05 E
Al-Fujayrah	128	25.06 N	56.21 E
Al-Fuqahā'	146	27.50 N	16.22 E
Al-Furzul	132	33.52 N	35.56 E
Alga	86	49.46 N	57.20 E
Algabas, Kaz.	80	50.39 N	52.07 E
Algabas, Kaz.	86	44.41 N	78.06 E
Algabas, Kaz.	86	48.21 N	81.39 E
Algači	88	50.43 N	117.47 E
Älgarås	40	58.48 N	14.14 E
Ålgård	26	58.46 N	5.51 E
Al-Garef	140	12.03 N	34.19 E
Algarrobal	252	28.08 S	70.39 W
Algarrobo, Arg.	252	38.53 S	63.08 W
Algarrobo, Arg.	252	31.44 S	68.18 W
Algarrobo, Chile	252	33.22 S	71.40 W
Algarrobo del Águila	252	36.26 S	67.09 W
Algarve □[9]	34	37.10 N	8.15 W
Algás ≏	34	41.08 N	0.39 E
Algasovo	76	53.41 N	41.40 E
Al-Gebir	140	13.43 N	29.49 E
Algeciras, Col.	246	2.35 N	75.18 W
Algeciras, Esp.	34	36.08 N	5.30 W
Algemesí	34	39.11 N	0.26 W
Algena	144	17.19 N	38.31 E
Alger → El Djazaïr, Alg.	148	36.47 N	3.03 E
Alger, Oh., U.S.	216	40.42 N	83.50 W
Alger, Baie d' C	34	36.50 N	3.15 E
Algeria (Algérie) □[1], Afr.	134	28.00 N	3.00 E
Algeria (Algérie) □[1], Afr.	148	28.00 N	3.00 E
Algérie → Algeria □[1]	148	28.00 N	3.00 E
Algerien → Algeria □[1]	148	28.00 N	3.00 E
Algermissen	52	52.15 N	9.58 E
Algés	266c	38.42 N	9.13 W
Al-Ghāb ⊜	130	35.30 N	36.18 E
Al-Gharaq as-Sulṭānī	142	29.08 N	30.42 E
Al-Gharbīyah □[4]	142	30.45 N	31.00 E
Al-Ghāriyah	132	32.23 N	36.39 E
Al-Ghāṭ	128	26.00 N	45.03 E
Al-Ghawr V	132	31.50 N	35.30 E
Al-Ghayatah	142	30.57 N	30.06 E
Al-Ghayḍah	118	16.12 N	52.15 E
Al-Ghazālah	128	26.48 N	41.19 E
Al-Ghazālī	142	30.49 N	31.49 E
Al-Ghāzīyah	132	33.31 N	35.22 E
Alghero	71	40.34 N	8.19 E
Al-Ghurayfah	128	24.00 N	56.29 E
Al-Ghurdaqah	140	27.14 N	33.50 E
Algier → El Djazaïr	148	36.47 N	3.03 E
Algiers → El Djazaïr	148	36.47 N	3.03 E
Alginet	34	39.16 N	0.28 W
Algoa	222	29.24 N	95.11 W
Algoabaai C	158	33.50 S	25.50 E
Algodão, Ilha do I	256	23.13 S	44.36 W
Algodón ≏	246	2.23 S	71.56 W
Algodones	200	35.22 N	106.28 W
Algodor ≏	34	39.55 N	3.53 W
Algoma	190	44.36 N	87.25 W
Algoma Mills	190	46.10 N	82.50 W
Algona, Ia., U.S.	190	43.04 N	94.13 W
Algona, Wa., U.S.	224	47.16 N	122.15 W
Algonac	214	42.37 N	82.31 W
Algonquin	216	42.09 N	88.17 W
Algonquin Lake ⊜	216	42.40 N	85.20 W
Algonquin Provincial Park ♦	190	45.45 N	78.26 W
Algood	194	36.11 N	85.26 W
Algorta, Esp.	34	43.22 N	3.01 W
Algorta, Ur.	252	32.25 S	57.23 W
Alguierão-Mem Martins	266c	38.48 N	9.20 W
Al-Ḥaddādī	142	31.20 N	30.47 E
Al-Ḥaddayn	142	30.44 N	30.38 E
Al-Ḥadīthah	128	34.07 N	42.23 E
Al-Ḥaḍr	128	35.35 N	42.44 E
Al-Ḥaffah	130	35.35 N	36.02 E
Al-Ḥafīr Al-Fawqānī	132	33.42 N	36.28 E
Al-Ḥajālīj	140	14.36 N	31.54 E
Al-Ḥajarah ◆[1]	128	30.00 N	44.00 E
Al-Ḥajar al-Gharbī ⋏	128	24.10 N	56.15 E
Al-Ḥajar ash-Sharqī ⋏	128	22.45 N	59.00 E
Al Hajeb	148	33.43 N	5.13 W
Al-Ḥājir	142	30.41 N	31.49 E
Al-Ḥalfāyah	128	31.49 N	47.26 E
Al-Ḥamād ≚	128	32.00 N	39.30 E
Alhama de Granada	34	37.00 N	3.59 W
Alhama de Murcia	34	37.51 N	1.25 W
Al-Hamal ◆[1]	128	23.30 N	49.45 E
Alhambra, Ca., U.S.	228	34.05 N	118.07 W
Alhambra, Il., U.S.	219	38.53 N	89.44 W
Al-Ḥamīdīyah	130	34.43 N	35.56 E
Al-Ḥammām	140	30.50 N	29.23 E
Al-Ḥamrā', Ar. Su.	128	23.57 N	38.52 E
'Al-Ḥamrā', Lubnān	132	33.42 N	35.27 E
Al-Ḥamrah	142	31.10 N	30.52 E
Al-Ḥāmūl	142	31.19 N	31.10 E
Alhandra	250	7.26 S	34.54 W
Alhandra, Mouchão de I	266c	38.54 N	9.00 W
Al-Ḥarāk	132	32.44 N	36.18 E
Al-Ḥarīq	128	23.37 N	46.31 E
Al-Ḥārrah	132	33.03 N	36.00 E
Al-Ḥarrah ≗[5]	128	31.00 N	38.30 E
Al-Harūj al-Aswad ⋏[2]	146	27.00 N	17.10 E
Al-Ḥasakah	130	36.29 N	40.45 E
Al-Ḥasakah □[8]	130	36.30 N	41.00 E
Al-Ḥasānī I	128	24.58 N	37.05 E
Alhaurín el Grande	34	36.38 N	4.41 W
Al-Ḥawāmidīyah	273c	29.54 N	31.15 E
Al-Hawātah	140	13.25 N	34.38 E
Al-Ḥawātikah	142	27.16 N	31.01 E
Al-Ḥawrah	144	13.49 N	47.37 E
Al-Ḥawṭah	144	15.50 N	48.27 E
Al-Ḥawwārīyah	142	30.58 N	29.41 E
Al-Ḥayy, 'Irāq	128	32.10 N	46.03 E
Al-Ḥayy, Miṣr	142	29.39 N	31.16 E
Al-Ḥayyānīyah	128	28.38 N	42.45 E
Al-Ḥayz	140	28.02 N	28.39 E
Al-Hībah	142	28.45 N	30.55 E
Al-Ḥijānah	132	33.21 N	36.33 E
Al-Ḥijāz ⋏[1]	118	24.30 N	38.30 E
Al-Ḥillah, 'Irāq	128	32.29 N	44.25 E
Al-Ḥillah, Sūd.	140	13.27 N	27.08 E
Al-Ḥilmīyah ◆[8]	273c	30.07 N	31.17 E
Al-Hindīyah	128	32.33 N	44.13 E
Al-Hirmil	132	34.23 N	36.23 E
Al-Ḥiṣn	132	32.29 N	35.52 E
Al Hoceïma	148	35.15 N	3.55 W
Al-Hoceïma □[4]	148	35.00 N	4.30 W
Al Hoceïma, Baie d' C	34	35.20 N	3.50 W
Alhos Vedros	266c	38.39 N	9.02 W
Alhucemas, Peñón de I	34	35.13 N	3.53 W
Al-Huḍayb	140	13.00 N	32.50 E
Al-Ḥudaydah	144	14.48 N	42.57 E
Al-Hufrah	146	29.10 N	18.02 E
Al-Ḥufrah ◆[1]	128	28.40 N	38.30 E
Al-Hufūf	128	25.22 N	49.34 E
Al-Ḥulwah	128	23.27 N	46.47 E
Al-Humayshah	144	13.41 N	45.52 E
Al-Ḥumrah ◆[1]	128	23.20 N	54.30 E
Al-Ḥuṣayḥiṣah	140	14.44 N	33.18 E
Al-Ḥusaynīyah	142	30.52 N	31.55 E
Al-Ḥuṣaynīyah ∓[4]	144	17.48 N	44.27 E
Al-Huwaylizah	132	33.02 N	35.51 E
Al-Huwaymī	144	14.05 N	47.44 E
Al-Ḥuwayyiṭ	128	25.36 N	40.23 E
Alì	70	38.02 N	15.25 E
Ali ◆[8]	272a	28.31 N	77.18 E
'Ālī, As-Sadd al- (Aswān High Dam) ◆[6]	140	23.58 N	32.52 E
Alía, Esp.	34	39.27 N	5.13 W
Alia, It.	70	37.47 N	13.43 E
Aliabad, Azer.	84	41.29 N	46.37 E
'Alīābād, Īrān	128	36.57 N	54.59 E
Alīābād, Pāk.	123	36.18 N	74.37 E
Aliade	150	7.16 N	8.28 E
Aliaga, Esp.	34	40.40 N	0.42 W
Aliağa, Tür.	130	38.48 N	26.59 E
Aliákmon ≏	38	40.30 N	22.36 E
Aliákmonos, Tekhnití Límni ⊜[1]	38	40.15 N	22.00 E
Aliaksin, Cape ≻	180	55.30 N	160.43 W
'Alī al-Gharbī	128	32.27 N	46.41 E
Aliança	250	7.35 S	35.13 W
Aliano	68	40.19 N	16.14 E
Alībāg	122	18.39 N	72.54 E
Alibahadır ◆[8]	267b	41.11 N	29.12 E
Ali-Bajramly	84	39.56 N	48.56 E
Alibardak	130	38.06 N	40.25 E
Alibates Flint Quarries National Monument ♦	196	35.35 N	101.39 W
Alibej, ozero ⊜	78	45.48 N	30.02 E
Alibejli	84	41.23 N	46.49 E
Alibey ≏	267b	41.03 N	28.56 E
Alibey Adası I	130	39.20 N	26.38 E
Alibey Barajı ⊜[1]	267b	41.07 N	28.55 E
Alibeyköy ◆[8]	267b	41.04 N	28.56 E
Alibijaban Island I	116	13.20 N	122.43 E
Alibori ≏	150	11.56 N	3.17 E
Al-Ibrāhīmīyah	142	30.57 N	31.35 E
Alibunar	38	45.05 N	20.58 E
Alicante → Alacant	34	38.21 N	0.29 W
Alice, Ciskei	158	32.47 S	26.50 E
Alice, Tx., U.S.	196	27.45 N	98.04 W
Alice ≏, Austl.	164	15.22 S	141.58 E
Alice ≏, Austl.	166	24.02 S	144.50 E
Alice, Punta ≻	68	39.24 N	17.10 E
Alice Arm	182	55.29 N	129.29 W
Alicedale	158	33.19 S	26.05 E
Alice Downs	162	17.45 S	127.56 E
Alice Springs	162	23.42 S	133.53 E
Alice Superiore	62	45.28 N	7.47 E
Alice Town	238	25.44 N	79.17 W
Aliceville	194	33.07 N	88.09 W
Alicia, Pil.	116	16.45 N	121.42 E
Alicia, Pil.	116	7.30 N	122.55 E
Alıcık	130	40.49 N	35.21 E
Alick Creek ≏	166	20.25 S	142.00 E
Alicudi, Isola I	70	38.32 N	14.21 E
Alicurá, Embalse de ⊜[1]	254	40.40 S	71.00 W
Al-'Idwah	142	29.21 N	30.55 E
Alief	222	29.43 N	95.35 W
Alife	68	41.20 N	14.20 E
Al-Ifranj	132	31.11 N	35.41 E
Alīganj, India	124	28.07 N	80.36 E
Alīganj, India	124	27.30 N	79.11 E
Alīgarh	124	27.53 N	78.05 E
Alignements de Carnac ⊥	32	47.35 N	3.05 W
Alīgūdarz	128	33.24 N	49.41 E
Alijos, Islas II	232	24.57 N	115.44 W
'Alī Kheyl	120	33.57 N	69.43 E
Al-Ikhṣāṣ al-Qiblīyah	142	29.42 N	31.17 E
Al-Ikhwān II	118	12.08 N	53.10 E
Alikovo	80	55.45 N	46.45 E
Alima ≏	152	1.36 S	16.36 E
Al-Imām ◆[8]	273c	30.01 N	31.10 E
Al-Imārāt al-'Arabīyah al-Muttaḥidah → United Arab Emirates □[1]	128	24.00 N	54.00 E
Al-'Imārīyah	142	27.37 N	30.53 E
Alimena	70	37.42 N	14.07 E
Alimini Grande ⊜	68	40.12 N	18.27 E
Alimini Piccolo ⊜	68	40.10 N	18.27 E
Aliminusa	70	37.52 N	13.47 E
Alim Island I	164	2.55 S	147.05 E
Alimkent	85	40.58 N	69.11 E
Alimodian	116	10.49 N	122.26 E
Alindao	152	5.02 N	21.13 E
Alingsås	26	57.56 N	12.31 E
Ālipur, India	272b	22.43 N	88.12 E
Alipur, India	272b	22.55 N	88.11 E
Alīpur, Pāk.	123	29.23 N	70.55 E
Ālīpur ◆[8]	126	22.31 N	88.20 E
Ālīpur Duār	124	26.29 N	89.44 E
Alīpur Janūbi	123	30.13 N	71.18 E
Aliquippa	214	40.38 N	80.14 W
Aliquippa-Hopewell Airport ⊠	279b	40.35 N	80.17 W
Alīrājpur	120	22.19 N	74.21 E
Al-'Irāq	132	31.05 N	35.39 E
Al-'Īrāq → Iraq □[1]	128	33.00 N	44.00 E
Al-'Irqah	144	13.30 N	47.22 E
Ali-Sabieh	144	11.09 N	42.42 E
Al-'Īsāwīyah	128	30.38 N	37.53 E
Aliseda	34	39.26 N	6.41 W
Alise-Sainte-Reine	58	47.32 N	4.29 E
Alīshārī	84	39.02 N	47.15 E
Al-Iskandarīyah (Alexandria)	142	31.12 N	29.54 E
Al-Iskandarīyah □[4]	142	31.10 N	29.53 E
Al-Ismā'īlīyah (Ismailia)	142	30.35 N	32.16 E
Al-Ismā'īlīyah □[4]	142	30.30 N	32.15 E
Al-Ismā'īlīyah Military Base ■	142	30.35 N	32.14 E
Aliso Canyon V, Ca., U.S.	280	34.18 N	118.33 W
Aliso Canyon V, Ca., U.S.	280	33.53 N	117.40 W
Aliso Creek ≏	228	33.31 N	117.45 W
Al-Istiwā'īyah al-Gharbīyah □[4]	140	5.55 N	28.15 E
Al-Istiwā'īyah ash-Sharqīyah □[4]	154	4.30 N	33.00 E
Alistráti	38	41.04 N	23.57 E
Alitak, Cape ≻	180	56.51 N	154.21 W
Alitak Bay C	180	57.00 N	154.05 W
Alitanguo	120	35.10 N	83.35 E
Alì Terme	70	38.01 N	15.26 E
Alivérion	38	38.24 N	24.02 E
Aliwal North	158	30.45 S	26.45 E
Alix	182	52.24 N	113.11 W
Al-'Izzīyah	142	27.13 N	30.59 E
Al-Jabal al-Abyaḍ ∧[2]	142	28.46 N	31.00 E
Al-Jabal al-Aḥmar ∧[2]	142	28.19 N	31.07 E
Al-Jabalayn	140	12.36 N	33.48 E
Al-Jadīdah	140	25.34 N	28.51 E
Al-Jafr	132	30.18 N	36.13 E
Al-Jāfūrah ◆[2]	128	24.14 N	50.00 E
Al-Jaghbūb	146	29.45 N	24.31 E
Al-Jaghbūb ∓[4]	146	29.40 N	24.43 E
Al-Jamālīyah	142	31.11 N	31.51 E
Al-Jarnūs	142	28.38 N	30.43 E
Al-Jawf, Ar. Su.	128	29.50 N	39.52 E
Al-Jawf, Lībiyā	146	24.11 N	23.19 E
Al-Jawsh	146	32.00 N	11.40 E
Al-Jaylī	140	16.01 N	32.36 E
Al-Jazā'ir → Algeria □[1]	148	28.00 N	3.00 E
Al-Jazīrah □[4]	140	14.30 N	33.20 E
Al-Jazīrah ◆[1]	140	14.25 N	33.00 E
Aljezur, Bra.	287a	22.40 S	43.36 W
Aljezur, Port.	34	37.19 N	8.48 W
Al-Jibāb	132	33.06 N	36.15 E
Al-Jifārah	128	23.59 N	45.11 E
Al-Jifārah (Jeffara) ≚	146	32.30 N	11.45 E
Al-Jīzah (Giza), Miṣr	142	30.01 N	31.13 E
Al-Jīzah, Urd.	132	31.43 N	35.58 E
Al-Jīzah □[4]	142	29.46 N	31.18 E
Al-Jubayl	128	27.01 N	49.40 E
Al-Jubayn	140	12.07 N	35.10 E
Aljucén ≏	34	38.56 N	6.25 W
Al-Judaydah	132	33.54 N	35.34 E
Al-Judayyidah, Urd.	132	31.15 N	35.49 E
Al-Judayyidah, Urd.	132	31.32 N	35.39 E
Al-Jufrah ∓[4]	146	29.10 N	16.00 E
Al-Julaydah ∓[4]	128	29.03 N	45.38 E
Al-Junaynah, Miṣr	142	31.06 N	31.41 E
Al-Junaynah, Sūd.	140	13.27 N	22.27 E
Al-Junaynah, Sūrīy.	132	32.54 N	36.44 E
Al-Jundīyah	142	28.34 N	30.50 E
Aljustrel	34	37.52 N	8.10 W
Al-Kāb	142	30.57 N	32.18 E
Al-Kabrit Military Base ■	142	30.15 N	32.29 E
Al-Kafr	132	32.38 N	36.38 E
Al-Kafr ash-Sharqī	142	37.17 N	31.10 E
Al-Kahfah	128	27.04 N	43.02 E
Alkali Creek ≏, Ab., Can.	184	50.52 N	110.30 W
Alkali Creek ≏, Wy., U.S.	202	43.16 N	107.40 W
Alkali Lake	182	51.47 N	122.14 W
Alkali Lake ⊜, Nv., U.S.	204	41.42 N	119.50 W
Alkali Lake ⊜, Or., U.S.	202	42.58 N	120.02 W
Alkamari	146	13.24 N	11.07 E
Al-Kāmilīn	140	15.05 N	33.11 E
Al-Karabah	140	18.33 N	33.42 E
Al-Karak	132	31.11 N	35.42 E
Al-Karak □[8]	132	31.10 N	35.45 E
Al-Karnak	140	25.43 N	32.39 E
Al-Kawah	140	13.44 N	32.30 E
Al-Kawd	144	13.05 N	45.22 E
Al-Kawm	130	35.11 N	38.52 E
Al-Kawm al-Akhḍar	142	30.58 N	30.17 E
Al-Kawm Aṭ-Ṭawīl	142	31.12 N	31.05 E
Alken	56	50.15 N	7.26 E
Al-Khabrā'	128	26.04 N	43.33 E
Al-Khābūrah	128	23.59 N	57.08 E
Al-Khafaqān ⊜	128	23.24 N	40.24 E
Al-Khalīl (Hebron)	132	31.32 N	35.06 E
Al-Khālis	128	33.49 N	44.32 E
Al-Khandaq	140	18.36 N	30.34 E
Al-Khānkah	142	30.13 N	31.21 E
Al-Kharaqānīyah	273c	30.10 N	31.10 E
Al-Khārijah	140	25.26 N	30.33 E
Al-Kharṭūm (Khartoum)	140	15.36 N	32.32 E
Al-Kharṭūm □[4]	140	15.45 N	32.30 E
Al-Kharṭūm Baḥrī	140	15.38 N	32.33 E
Al-Khaṣab	123	26.12 N	56.15 E
Al-Khatam ◆[1]	128	24.00 N	55.10 E
Al-Khirbah as-Samrā'	132	32.11 N	36.10 E
Al-Khiyām	132	33.19 N	35.36 E
Al-Khubar	128	26.17 N	50.12 E
Al-Khums (Homs)	146	32.39 N	14.16 E
Al-Khuraybah, Urd.	132	32.40 N	35.52 E
Al-Khuraybah, Yaman	144	15.06 N	48.19 E
Al-Khurmah	144	21.54 N	42.03 E
Al-Khushnīyah	132	33.00 N	35.48 E
Al-Khuṣūṣ	273c	30.09 N	31.19 E
Al-Kifl	128	32.14 N	44.22 E
Al-Kiswah	132	33.21 N	36.14 E
Alkmaar	52	52.37 N	4.44 E
Alkoven	61	48.17 N	14.06 E
Al-Kūbrī	142	30.02 N	32.33 E
Al-Kūfah	128	32.02 N	44.24 E
Al-Kufrah (Cufra) ∓[4]	146	24.20 N	23.15 E
Al-Kunayyisah	273c	29.59 N	31.11 E
Al-Kuntillah	140	30.00 N	34.41 E
Al-Kūt	128	32.25 N	45.49 E
Al-Kuwayt	128	29.20 N	47.59 E
Al-Kuwayt → Kuwait □[1]	128	29.30 N	47.45 E
Alkvettern ⊜	40	59.25 N	14.21 E
Allaben	210	42.07 N	74.22 W
Al-Labwah	130	34.12 N	36.21 E
Allacapan	116	18.15 N	121.35 E
Allach-Jun'	74	61.08 N	138.03 E
Allada	150	6.39 N	2.09 E
Al-Lādhiqīyah (Latakia)	130	35.31 N	35.47 E
Al-Lādhiqīyah □[8]	130	35.30 N	36.00 E
Allagash ≏	186	47.05 N	69.02 W
Allagen	56	51.28 N	8.14 E
Al-Lagowa	140	11.24 N	29.08 E
Allahābād, India	124	25.27 N	81.51 E
Allāhābād, Pāk.	123	28.57 N	70.53 E
Allāhbās	272a	28.31 N	77.25 E
Allahüekber Dağları ⋏	130	40.35 N	42.32 E
Al-Lāhūn	142	29.13 N	30.59 E
Allāhwardipur	272a	28.33 N	77.26 E
Allaines	50	48.12 N	1.50 E
Allaire State Park ♦	208	40.08 N	74.08 W
Allakaket	180	66.34 N	152.41 W
Allaman	58	46.28 N	6.24 E
Allamuchy	210	40.55 N	74.48 W
Allan	184	51.53 N	106.04 W
Allan, Pointe ≻	275a	45.26 N	73.45 W
Allanche	32	45.14 N	2.56 E
Alland	61	48.03 N	16.05 E
Allan Island I	224	48.28 N	122.42 W
Allanmyo	110	19.22 N	95.13 E
Allanridge	158	27.55 S	26.44 E
Allanson	168a	33.20 S	116.06 E
Allanton	46	55.47 N	3.51 W
Allan Water ≏	46	56.08 N	3.56 W
Allapattah Flats ≚	220	27.29 N	82.34 W
'Allāq, Bi'r ∓[4]	146	31.05 N	11.42 E
'Allāqī, Wādī al- V	140	22.42 N	33.12 E
Allard, Lac ⊜	186	50.32 N	63.31 W
Allardt	194	36.22 N	84.53 W
Allariz	34	42.11 N	7.48 W
Allatoona Lake ⊜[1]	192	34.08 N	84.38 W
Allauch	62	43.20 N	5.29 E
Al-Layyah	140	16.16 N	35.25 E
Alldays	156	22.44 S	29.04 E
Alle, Bel.	56	49.51 N	4.58 E
Alle, Schw.	58	47.26 N	7.08 E
Allèberg ∧[2]	26	58.08 N	13.36 E
Allegan	216	42.31 N	85.51 W
Allegan □[6]	216	42.35 N	85.53 W
Allegan, Lake ⊜	216	42.35 N	86.00 W
Allegany	210	42.05 N	78.29 W
Allegany □[6]	210	42.13 N	78.02 W
Allegany Indian Reservation ◆[4]	210	42.10 N	78.47 W
Allegany State Park ♦	210	42.04 N	78.44 W
Alleghany	226	39.28 N	120.51 W
Alleghe	64	46.24 N	12.01 E
Allegheny □[6]	214	40.28 N	80.00 W
Allegheny ≏	214	40.27 N	80.00 W
Allegheny Acres	279b	40.37 N	79.53 W
Allegheny Center ◆	279b	40.27 N	80.01 W
Allegheny County Airport ⊠	279b	40.21 N	79.56 W
Allegheny County Park ♦	279b	40.34 N	79.55 W
Allegheny Mountains ⋏	188	38.30 N	80.00 W
Allegheny Observatory ʋ[3]	279b	40.29 N	80.01 W
Allegheny Plateau ⋏[1]	188	41.30 N	78.00 W
Allegheny Portage Railroad National Historic Site ⊥	214	40.28 N	78.32 W
Allegheny Reservoir ⊜[1]	214	42.00 N	78.56 W
Allègre	62	45.12 N	3.42 E
Allègre, Pointe ≻	241o	16.22 N	61.45 W
Allemagne → Germany □[1]	30	51.00 N	10.00 E
Allemands, Lac Des ⊜	194	29.55 N	90.35 W
Allemanskraaldam ⊜[1]	158	28.16 S	27.07 E
Allemant	261	48.45 N	1.37 E
Allemont	62	45.08 N	6.02 E
Allen, Arg.	252	38.58 S	67.50 W
Allen, Pil.	116	12.30 N	124.17 E
Allen, Md., U.S.	208	38.17 N	75.41 W
Allen, Mi., U.S.	216	41.57 N	84.46 W
Allen, Ne., U.S.	198	42.24 N	96.50 W
Allen, Ok., U.S.	196	34.52 N	96.24 W
Allen, Pa., U.S.	208	40.10 N	77.05 W
Allen, S.D., U.S.	198	43.16 N	101.55 W
Allen, Tx., U.S.	222	33.06 N	96.40 W
Allen, Wa., U.S.	224	48.31 N	122.23 W
Allen □[6], In., U.S.	216	41.04 N	85.09 W
Allen □[6], Oh., U.S.	216	40.46 N	84.06 W
Allen ≏	44	54.58 N	2.19 W
Allen, Lough ⊜	48	54.08 N	8.08 W
Allen, Mount ∧, N.Z.	172	47.05 S	167.48 E
Allen, Mount ∧, Ak., U.S.	180	62.14 N	142.13 W
Allenby Bridge ◆[5]	132	31.52 N	35.52 E
Allendale, Il., U.S.	194	38.32 N	87.43 W
Allendale, Mi., U.S.	216	42.58 N	85.57 W
Allendale, N.J., U.S.	276	41.02 N	74.07 W
Allendale, S.C., U.S.	192	33.00 N	81.18 W
Allendale Town	44	54.54 N	2.15 W
Allende, Méx.	232	28.20 N	100.51 W
Allende, Méx.	234	18.09 N	94.16 W
Allendorf	56	51.02 N	8.38 E
Allenfarm	222	30.24 N	96.14 W
All England Lawn Tennis Club ♦	260	51.26 N	0.13 W
Allen Grove	216	42.35 N	88.41 W
Allen Park	216	42.15 N	83.12 W
Allenport, Pa., U.S.	214	40.20 N	77.53 W
Allenport, Pa., U.S.	214	40.06 N	79.51 W
Allensbach	58	47.43 N	9.03 E
Allenstein → Olsztyn	30	53.48 N	20.29 E
Allensville	214	40.32 N	77.49 W
Allenton, Mi., U.S.	214	42.55 N	82.57 W
Allenton, R.I., U.S.	207	41.32 N	71.28 W
Allentown, N.J., U.S.	208	40.10 N	74.35 W
Allentown, N.Y., U.S.	210	42.05 N	78.03 W
Allentown, Oh., U.S.	216	40.46 N	84.12 W
Allentown, Pa., U.S.	208	40.36 N	75.28 W
Allentsteig	61	48.42 N	15.20 E
Allenwood, N.J., U.S.	208	40.12 N	74.13 W
Allenwood, N.Y., U.S.	276	40.48 N	73.44 W
Allenwood, Pa., U.S.	210	41.07 N	76.54 W
Alleppey	122	9.29 N	76.19 E
Aller ≏	30	52.57 N	9.11 E
Allerona	66	42.49 N	11.58 E
Allersberg	60	49.15 N	11.15 E
Allershausen	60	48.26 N	11.36 E
Allerslev	41	55.05 N	12.03 E
Allerton, Ia., U.S.	190	40.42 N	93.21 W
Allerton, Ma., U.S.	283	42.18 N	70.53 W
Allerton ◆[8]	262	53.22 N	2.53 W
Allerton, Point ≻	207	42.18 N	70.53 W
Allestree	42	52.57 N	1.29 W
Allevard	62	45.24 N	6.04 E
Alley Park ♦	276	40.45 N	73.44 W
Alleyton	222	29.43 N	96.29 W
Allgäu ◆[1]	58	47.35 N	10.10 E
Allgäuer Alpen ⋏	58	47.20 N	10.25 E
Allhallows	260	51.28 N	0.39 E
Alli ≏	68	38.51 N	16.40 E
Alliance, Ab., Can.	182	52.26 N	111.47 W
Alliance, Ne., U.S.	198	42.12 N	102.58 W
Alliance, Oh., U.S.	214	40.54 N	81.06 W
Allibaudières	50	48.35 N	4.07 E
Al-Lidām	144	20.29 N	44.50 E
Allier □[5]	32	46.25 N	3.00 E
Allier ≏	32	46.58 N	3.04 E
Alligator ≏	192	35.58 N	75.58 W
Alligator Creek ≏, Ga., U.S.	192	31.58 N	82.22 W
Alligator Creek ≏, Tx., U.S.	222	30.42 N	97.07 W
Alligator Lake ⊜	220	28.13 N	81.13 W
Alligator Pond	241q	17.52 N	77.34 W
Alligny-en-Morvan	50	47.12 N	4.10 E
Allihies	48	51.38 N	10.03 W
Allinagaram	122	10.02 N	77.30 E
Allinge	26	55.16 N	14.49 E
Allington Castle ⊥	260	51.17 N	0.31 E
Al-Lisān ≻[1]	132	31.17 N	35.28 E
Al-Lisht	142	29.34 N	31.14 E
Allison	190	42.45 N	92.47 W
Allison, Mount ∧	282	37.30 N	121.52 W
Allison Gulch V	280	34.16 N	117.44 W
Allison Park	214	40.34 N	79.57 W
Alliste	68	39.57 N	18.05 E
Alliston	212	44.09 N	79.52 W
Al-Līth	144	20.09 N	40.16 E
Allmendingen	58	48.20 N	9.43 E
Alloa	46	56.07 N	3.49 W
Allochio, Galleria degli ◆[5]	66	44.03 N	11.30 E
Allogny	50	47.13 N	2.19 E
Allonby	44	54.46 N	3.25 W
Allоné Abba	132	32.44 N	35.10 E
Allonnes, Fr.	50	47.58 N	0.09 E
Allonnes, Fr.	50	48.20 N	1.40 E
Allora	171a	28.02 S	151.59 E
Allos	62	44.14 N	6.38 E
Allos, Col d')(	62	44.18 N	6.36 E
Allott, Mount ∧[2]	162	26.06 S	124.46 E
Allouez	190	44.28 N	88.00 W
Alloway	208	39.33 N	75.21 W
Alloway Creek ≏	208	39.27 N	75.30 W
Allport	214	40.58 N	78.12 W
Allred Peak ∧	200	40.32 N	108.33 W
All Saints	240c	17.03 N	61.48 W
Allschwil	58	47.33 N	7.33 E
Allstedt	54	51.24 N	11.23 E
Allston ◆[8]	283	42.22 N	71.08 W
Alluets, Forêt des ♦	261	48.55 N	1.55 E
Al-Luḥayyah	144	15.42 N	42.42 E
Allumette Lake ⊜	190	45.53 N	77.13 W
Allumettes, Île des I	190	45.50 N	77.05 W
Allumiere	66	42.09 N	11.54 E
Allview Estates	208	39.12 N	76.51 W
Allyn	224	47.23 N	122.49 W
Alma, N.B., Can.	186	45.36 N	64.57 W
Alma, P.Q., Can.	186	48.33 N	71.39 W
Alma, Ar., U.S.	194	35.28 N	94.13 W
Alma, Ga., U.S.	192	31.32 N	82.27 W
Alma, Il., U.S.	219	38.43 N	88.55 W
Alma, Ks., U.S.	198	39.01 N	96.17 W
Alma, Mi., U.S.	190	43.22 N	84.39 W
Alma, Ne., U.S.	198	40.05 N	99.21 W
Alma, Wi., U.S.	190	44.19 N	91.54 W
Al-Ma'ādī ◆[8]	142	29.58 N	31.15 E
Alma-Ata (Almaty)	85	43.15 N	76.57 E
Alma-Ata □[8]	86	44.00 N	77.00 E
Alma-Atinskij zapovednik ♦	85	43.10 N	77.25 E
Alma Center	190	44.26 N	90.54 W
Almada	34	38.41 N	9.09 W
Almaden, Austl.	166	17.20 S	144.41 E
Almadén, Esp.	34	38.46 N	4.50 W
Almadén de la Plata	34	37.52 N	6.04 W
Al-Madīnah (Medina)	128	24.28 N	39.36 E
Al-Madīnah al-Fikrīyah	142	27.56 N	30.49 E
Al-Madwar	132	32.17 N	36.00 E
Al-Mafāzah	140	13.36 N	34.33 E
Al-Mafraq	132	32.21 N	36.12 E
Al-Mafraq □[8]	132	32.15 N	36.30 E
Almafuerte	252	32.12 S	64.15 W
Al-Maghārīm	144	15.01 N	47.51 E
Al-Maghrah ∓[4]	140	30.14 N	28.56 E
Almagor	132	32.55 N	35.36 E
Almagre, Laguna C	234	23.48 N	97.48 W
Al-Magreb → Morocco □[1]	148	32.00 N	5.00 W
Almagro	34	38.53 N	3.43 W
Almagro Island I	116	11.56 N	124.18 E
Al-Maḥallah al-Kubrā	142	30.58 N	31.10 E
Al-Maḥārīq	140	25.37 N	30.39 E
Al Mahbas	148	27.13 N	9.44 W
Alma Hill ∧[2]	210	42.03 N	78.01 W
Al-Maḥmūdīyah	142	31.11 N	30.32 E
Al-Mahraṣ	142	27.49 N	30.48 E
Al-Maḥsamah	142	30.34 N	32.01 E
Al-Majdal	132	32.47 N	36.30 E
Al-Majma'ah	128	25.54 N	45.20 E
Almăjului, Munții ⋏	38	44.43 N	22.12 E
Al-Maks ◆[8]	142	31.09 N	29.51 E
Al-Mālikīyah	130	37.10 N	42.08 E
Almalyk	85	40.50 N	69.35 E
Al-Ma'mūrah ◆[8]	142	31.18 N	30.03 E
Al-Manāmah	128	26.13 N	50.35 E
Al-Manāqil	140	14.15 N	32.59 E
Al-Manāṣif ◆[1]	130	35.17 N	40.50 E
Al-Manāwāt	273c	29.55 N	31.14 E
Almanor, Lake ⊜	204	40.15 N	121.08 W
Almansa	34	38.52 N	1.05 W
Al-Manshāh	140	26.28 N	31.48 E
Al-Manṣūrah, Isr. Occ	132	33.08 N	35.48 E
Al-Manṣūrah, Miṣr	142	31.03 N	31.23 E
Al-Manṣūrīyah	142	30.08 N	31.05 E
Almanza	34	42.39 N	5.02 W
Al-Manzilah	142	31.09 N	31.56 E
Almanzor ∧	34	40.15 N	5.18 W
Almanzora ≏	34	37.14 N	1.46 W
Almar ≏	34	40.54 N	5.29 W
Al-Marāghah	140	26.42 N	31.36 E
Almargem do Bispo	266c	38.51 N	9.16 W
Al-Marj	146	32.30 N	20.54 E
Al-Marj ◆[8]	273c	30.09 N	31.20 E
Almas	250	11.33 S	47.09 W
Almaș ≏	38	47.14 N	23.19 E
Almas, Pico das ∧	255	13.33 S	41.56 W
Al-Ma'ṣarah, Miṣr	142	27.42 N	30.52 E
Al-Ma'ṣarah, Miṣr	142	31.13 N	31.19 E
Al-Ma'sarah ◆[8]	142	29.54 N	31.17 E
Al-Mashqūq	132	32.24 N	36.43 E
Al-Mashrafah	130	34.50 N	36.52 E
Al-Masīd	140	15.15 N	32.57 E
Almassora	34	39.57 N	0.03 W
Al-Matammah	140	16.43 N	33.22 E
Al-Maṭarīyah	142	31.11 N	32.02 E
Al-Maṭarīyah ◆[8]	142	30.07 N	31.19 E
Al-Matnah	140	13.47 N	35.03 E
Al-Mawṣil (Mosul)	128	36.20 N	43.08 E
Al-Mayādīn	130	35.01 N	40.27 E
Al-Maymūn	142	29.14 N	31.12 E
Almazán	34	41.29 N	2.32 W
Al-Mazār, Urd.	132	31.04 N	35.42 E
Almazar, Uzb.	85	40.59 N	68.54 E
Almaznaja ◆[8]	83	48.31 N	38.35 E
Almaznyj	83	48.02 N	40.03 E
Almazovka ◆[8]	83	48.04 N	39.18 E
Almazovo	265b	55.51 N	38.02 E
Al-Mazra'ah	132	31.16 N	35.31 E
Al-Mazzah	132	33.30 N	36.15 E
Alme	56	51.28 N	8.37 E
Almeer	52	52.20 N	5.14 E
Almeida	34	40.43 N	6.54 W
Almeirim, Bra.	250	1.32 S	52.34 W
Almeirim, Port.	34	39.12 N	8.38 W
Almelo	52	52.21 N	6.39 E
Almena	198	39.53 N	99.42 W
Almenara	255	16.11 S	40.42 W
Almenar de Soria	34	41.41 N	2.12 W
Almendares ≏	286b	23.08 N	82.25 W
Almendra, Embalse de ⊜[1]	34	41.15 N	6.10 W
Almendralejo	34	38.41 N	6.24 W
Almenêches	50	48.42 N	0.07 E
Al'menevo	86	54.57 N	63.34 E
Almenno San Salvatore	62	45.45 N	9.35 E
Almería	34	36.50 N	2.27 W
Almería □[4]	34	37.10 N	2.25 W
Almería, Golfo de C	34	36.46 N	2.30 W
Al'metjevsk	80	54.53 N	52.20 E
Al'mež	24	60.03 N	48.03 E
Älmhult	26	56.33 N	14.08 E
Al-Midhnab	128	25.54 N	44.14 E
Al-Mīnā'	130	34.27 N	35.49 E
Almina, Punta ≻	34	35.53 N	5.15 W
Almino Afonso	250	6.09 S	37.46 W
Al-Minshāt al-Kubrā	142	31.03 N	30.54 E
Al-Minūfīyah □[4]	142	30.30 N	31.00 E
Al-Minyā, Miṣr	142	28.06 N	30.45 E
Al-Minyā, Miṣr	142	29.45 N	31.18 E
Al-Minyā, Miṣr	142	29.14 N	30.45 E
Al-Minyā □[4]	142	28.26 N	30.42 E
Al-Miqdādīyah	128	33.59 N	44.56 E
Almira	202	47.42 N	118.56 W
Almirantazgo, Islas → Admiralty Islands II	164	2.10 S	147.00 E
Almirantazgo, Montes → Admiralty Mountains ⋏	9	71.45 S	168.30 E
Almirante	236	9.18 N	82.24 W
Almirante, Bahía de C	236	9.20 N	82.18 W
Almirante Brown	258	34.48 S	58.23 W
Almirante Brown □[5]	288	34.50 S	58.20 W
Almirante Guillermo Brown, Parque ♦	288	34.40 S	58.28 W
Almirante Latorre	252	29.38 S	70.58 W
Almirante Montt, Golfo ꓤ	254	51.55 S	72.45 W
Almirós	38	39.11 N	22.46 E
Almiroú, Kólpos C	38	35.23 N	24.20 E
Al-Mismīyah	132	33.08 N	36.23 E
Almo	202	42.06 N	113.37 W
Almoçageme	266c	38.48 N	9.28 W
Almodôvar	34	37.31 N	8.04 W
Almodóvar del Campo	34	38.43 N	4.10 W
Almolonga	236	14.49 N	91.30 W
Almond, N.Y., U.S.	210	42.19 N	77.44 W
Almond, Wi., U.S.	190	44.15 N	89.24 W
Almond ≏, Scot., U.K.	46	56.25 N	3.27 W
Almond ≏, Scot., U.K.	46	55.58 N	3.18 W
Almondbank	46	56.24 N	3.33 W
Almondsbury	42	51.34 N	2.34 W
Almonesson	208	39.49 N	75.06 W
Almont	214	42.55 N	83.02 W
Almont ≏	261	48.28 N	2.40 E
Almonte, On., Can.	212	45.14 N	76.12 W
Almonte, Esp.	34	37.15 N	6.31 W
Almonte, Ca., U.S.	282	37.53 N	122.30 W
Almora	124	29.37 N	79.40 E
Almsee ⊜	58	47.45 N	13.57 E
Almsta	40	59.58 N	18.48 E
Al-Mu'addamīyah	132	33.45 N	36.39 E
Al-Mubarraz, Ar. Su.	128	25.25 N	49.35 E
Al-Mubarraz, Ar. Su.	144	22.17 N	46.44 E
Al-Mudawwarah	128	29.19 N	35.59 E
Almudébar	34	42.03 N	0.35 W
Al-Muglad	140	11.02 N	27.44 E
Al-Muḥarraq	128	26.16 N	50.37 E
Al-Mukallā	144	14.32 N	49.08 E
Al-Mukhā (Mocha)	144	13.19 N	43.15 E
Al-Munā ăt al-Kubrā	142	30.50 N	32.01 E
Almuñécar	34	36.43 N	3.41 W
Almunge	40	59.53 N	18.03 E
Al-Muntazah ◆[8]	142	31.17 N	30.01 E
Almus	130	40.23 N	36.55 E
Al-Musallamīyah	140	14.34 N	33.21 E
Al-Musayfirah	132	32.37 N	36.20 E
Al-Musayjīd	128	24.05 N	39.06 E
Al-Musayyib	128	32.47 N	44.18 E
Almus Barajı ⊜[1]	130	40.20 N	37.00 E
Al-Mushannaf	132	32.44 N	36.46 E
Al-Musharrak Qiblī	142	29.23 N	30.34 E
Al-Mutā'yah	132	32.29 N	36.17 E
Al-Mu'tamadīyah	142	31.02 N	31.05 E
Al-Mutayn	132	33.54 N	35.44 E
Al-Muthannā □[4]	128	30.30 N	45.15 E
Al-Muṭī'ah	142	27.08 N	31.18 E
Al-Muwaqqar ⊥	132	31.49 N	36.06 E
Al-Muwassam	144	16.25 N	42.20 E
Al-Muwayh	144	22.45 N	41.36 E
Al-Muwaylih	128	27.41 N	35.27 E
Aln ≏	44	55.23 N	1.37 W
Alnarp	41	55.39 N	13.05 E
Al-Narrārīyah	273c	29.58 N	31.10 E
Al'n'aš	80	56.44 N	54.43 E
Alnaši	80	56.11 N	52.28 E
Al-Nasser	140	24.32 N	32.55 E
Alne ≏	42	52.13 N	1.52 W
Alness	46	57.41 N	4.15 W
Alnmouth	44	55.23 N	1.36 W
Alnön I	26	62.25 N	17.26 E
Alnor	41	54.55 N	9.36 E
Alnwick	44	55.25 N	1.42 W
Alnwick Indian Reserve ◆[4]	212	44.10 N	78.06 W
Alo	146	11.47 N	20.53 E
Aloândia	255	17.43 S	49.29 W
Alofau	174u	14.16 S	170.36 W
Alofi	174v	19.01 S	169.55 W
Alofi, Île I	14	14.21 S	178.02 W
Alofi Bay C	174v	19.01 S	169.56 W
Aloha	224	45.29 N	122.51 W
Aloha, Lake ⊜	226	38.52 N	120.09 W
Aloi	154	2.17 N	33.10 E
Aloja	76	57.46 N	24.53 E
Alondra	280	33.55 N	118.15 W
Along	120	28.18 N	94.39 E
Alónnisos	38	39.08 N	23.50 E
Alónnisos I	38	39.13 N	23.55 E
Alor, Kepulauan II	112	8.15 S	124.30 E
Alor, Pulau I	112	8.15 S	124.45 E
Alor, Selat ꓤ	112	8.20 S	123.48 E
Álora	34	36.48 N	4.42 W
Alor Gajah	114	2.23 N	102.13 E
Alor Setar	114	6.07 N	100.22 E
Alor Star → Alor Setar	114	6.07 N	100.22 E
Alorton	219	38.36 N	90.08 W
Al'oškino	88	58.35 N	100.32 E
Al'ošn'a, Ross.	76	53.38 N	33.29 E
Al'ošn'a, Ross.	82	54.14 N	37.16 E
Alosno	34	37.33 N	7.07 W
Alost → Aalst	50	50.56 N	4.02 E
Alotau	164	10.14 S	150.30 E
Alouette ≏	224	49.16 N	122.42 W
Alouette Lake ⊜	224	49.19 N	122.28 W
Alovo	80	54.38 N	46.27 E
Aloxe-Corton	58	47.04 N	4.52 E
Aloysius, Mount ∧	162	26.01 S	128.34 E
Alpachiri	252	37.22 S	63.46 W
Alpaugh	226	35.53 N	119.29 W
Alpen	52	51.35 N	6.30 E
Alpen → Alps ⋏	32	46.25 N	10.00 E
Alpena, Ar., U.S.	194	36.17 N	93.17 W
Alpena, Mi., U.S.	190	45.03 N	83.25 W
Alpena, S.D., U.S.	198	44.10 N	98.21 W
Alpercatas ≏	250	6.02 S	44.19 W
Alpes → Alps ⋏	32	46.25 N	10.00 E
Alpes-de-Haute-Provence □[5]	62	44.10 N	6.00 E
Alpes Dináricos → Dinara ⋏	36	43.50 N	16.35 E
Alpes-Maritimes □[5]	62	44.00 N	7.10 E
Alpes Marítimos → Maritime Alps ⋏	62	44.15 N	7.10 E
Alpes Transilvanos → Carpații Meridionali ⋏	38	45.30 N	24.15 E
Alpha, Austl.	166	23.39 S	146.38 E
Alpha, Il., U.S.	190	41.12 N	90.23 W
Alpha, Mi., U.S.	190	46.02 N	88.22 W
Alpha, N.J., U.S.	210	40.40 N	75.09 W
Alpharetta	192	34.04 N	84.17 W
Alphen aan den Rijn	52	52.07 N	4.40 E
Alphington	42	50.42 N	3.31 W
Alphin Pike ∧[2]	262	53.31 N	2.00 W
Alphonse Island I	138	7.00 S	52.45 E
Alpi → Alps ⋏	32	46.25 N	10.00 E
Alpi, Monte ∧	68	40.07 N	15.59 E
Alpiarça	34	39.15 N	8.35 W
Alpi Dinariche → Dinara ⋏	36	43.50 N	16.35 E
Alpignano	62	45.06 N	7.31 E
Alpilles, Chaîne des ⋏[2]	62	43.45 N	4.50 E
Alpine, Az., U.S.	200	33.50 N	109.08 W
Alpine, Ca., U.S.	204	32.50 N	116.47 W
Alpine, N.J., U.S.	276	40.57 N	73.55 W
Alpine, N.Y., U.S.	210	42.19 N	76.44 W
Alpine, Tx., U.S.	196	30.21 N	103.39 W
Alpine □[6]	226	38.41 N	119.47 W
Alpine Creek ≏	282	37.19 N	122.17 W
Alpine National Park ♦	166	37.00 S	147.15 E
Alpinópolis	255	20.52 S	46.23 W
Alpi Retiche → Rhaetian Alps ⋏	58	46.30 N	10.00 E
Alpirsbach	58	48.21 N	8.23 E
Alplaus Kill ≏	210	42.51 N	73.54 W
Alpnachstad	58	46.57 N	8.17 E
Alps ⋏	22	46.25 N	10.00 E
Alpsee ⊜	58	47.34 N	10.10 E
Alpu	130	39.47 N	30.58 E
Al-Qābil	128	23.57 N	55.48 E
Al-Qābūn	132	33.33 N	36.20 E
Al-Qadam	132	33.28 N	36.17 E
Al-Qaḍārif	140	14.02 N	35.24 E
Al-Qadīmah	144	22.21 N	39.09 E
Al-Qādisīyah □[4]	128	31.55 N	45.00 E
Al-Qāhirah (Cairo), Miṣr	142	30.03 N	31.15 E
Al-Qāhirah (Cairo), Miṣr	273c	30.03 N	31.15 E
Al-Qāhirah □[4]	142	30.02 N	31.17 E
Al-Qāhirah West Military Base ■	142	30.06 N	30.56 E
Al-Qaḥmah	144	18.00 N	41.41 E
Al-Qā'im	128	34.21 N	41.07 E
Al-Qā'īyah ∓[4]	128	24.18 N	45.35 E
Al-Qāīyāt	142	28.40 N	30.41 E
Al-Qalaj	128	28.43 N	42.40 E
Al-Qalībah	128	28.32 N	37.42 E
Al-Qalyūbīyah □[4]	142	30.20 N	31.15 E
Al-Qāmishlī	130	37.02 N	41.14 E
Al-Qanāṭir al-Khayrīyah	142	30.12 N	31.08 E
Al-Qanāyāt	142	30.37 N	31.28 E
Al-Qanṭarah	142	30.52 N	32.19 E
Al-Qaryah ash-Sharqīyah	146	30.24 N	13.36 E
Al-Qaryatayn	130	34.14 N	37.14 E
Al-Qaṣabāt	146	32.35 N	14.04 E
Al-Qaṣābī	132	31.16 N	30.41 E
Al-Qaṣr, Miṣr	140	25.42 N	28.53 E
Al-Qaṣr, Urd.	132	31.19 N	35.45 E

Symbol	English	Deutsch	Español	Français	Português
≏	River	Fluß	Río	Rivière	Rio
≖	Canal	Kanal	Canal	Canal	Canal
⌊	Waterfall, Rapids	Wasserfall, Stromschnellen	Cascada, Rápidos	Chute d'eau, Rapids	Cascata, Rápidos
ꓤ	Strait	Meeresstraße	Estrecho	Detroit	Estreito
C	Bay, Gulf	Bucht, Golf	Bahía, Golfo	Baie, Golfe	Baía, Golfo
⊜	Lake, Lakes	See, Seen	Lago, Lagos	Lac, Lacs	Lago, Lagos
≚	Swamp	Sumpf	Pantano	Marais	Pântano
⊓	Ice Features, Glacier	Eis- und Gletscherformen	Accidentes Glaciales	Formes glaciaires	Acidentes glaciares
∓	Other Hydrographic Features	Andere Hydrographische Objekte	Otros Elementos Hidrográficos	Autres données hydrographiques	Outros acidentes hidrográficos
+	Submarine Features	Untermeerische Objekte	Accidentes Submarinos	Formes de relief sous-marin	Acidentes submarinos
□	Political Unit	Politische Einheit	Unidad Política	Entité politique	Unidade política
ʋ	Cultural Institution	Kulturelle Institution	Institución Cultural	Institution culturelle	Instituição cultural
⊥	Historical Site	Historische Stätte	Sitio Histórico	Site historique	Sitio histórico
♦	Recreational Site	Erholungs- und Ferienort	Sitio de Recreo	Centre de loisirs	Area de Lazer
⊠	Airport	Flughafen	Aeropuerto	Aéroport	Aeroporto
■	Military Installation	Militäranlage	Instalación Militar	Installation militaire	Instalação militar
◆	Miscellaneous	Verschiedenes	Misceláneo	Divers	Diversos

Name	Page	Lat.°′	Long.°′
Al-Qaṣṣāṣīn	142	30.34 N	31.56 E
Al-Qaṭīf	128	26.33 N	50.00 E
Al-Qaṭrānah	132	31.15 N	36.03 E
Al-Qaṭrūn	146	24.56 N	14.38 E
Al-Qaṭṭā	142	30.13 N	30.58 E
Al-Qaṭṭāwīyah	142	30.33 N	31.40 E
Al-Qays	142	28.29 N	30.47 E
Al-Qayṣūmah	128	28.16 N	46.03 E
Al-Qir'awn	132	33.34 N	35.43 E
Al-Qiṣfah	132	32.38 N	35.52 E
Al-Quds			
→ Yerushalayim	132	31.46 N	35.14 E
Alquízar	240p	22.48 N	82.35 W
Al-Qun'abah	132	33.08 N	35.40 E
Al-Qunayṭirah	132	33.07 N	35.49 E
Al-Qunayṭirah □[8]	132	33.00 N	35.50 E
Al-Qunfudhah	144	19.08 N	41.05 E
Al-Qurayn	142	30.37 N	31.44 E
Al-Qurayyah	132	32.32 N	36.36 E
Al-Qurnah	128	31.00 N	47.26 E
Al-Quṣaymah	132	30.40 N	34.22 E
Al-Quṣayr, Miṣr	128	26.06 N	34.17 E
Al-Quṣayr, Miṣr	142	27.27 N	30.52 E
Al-Quṣayr, Sūrīy.	130	34.31 N	36.35 E
Al-Qūṣīyah	142	27.26 N	30.49 E
Al-Quṭayfah	132	33.44 N	36.36 E
Al-Quṭaynah	140	14.52 N	32.21 E
Al-Quway'īyah	128	24.03 N	45.15 E
Al-Quwaysī	140	13.20 N	34.05 E
Alrø I	41	55.51 N	10.05 E
Alroy Downs	162	19.18 S	136.04 E
Als I	41	54.59 N	9.55 E
Alsace □[9]	58	48.30 N	7.30 E
Alsace, Ballon d' ∧	58	47.50 N	6.51 E
Alsager	44	53.06 N	2.17 W
Alsask	184	51.23 N	109.59 W
Alsasua	34	42.54 N	2.10 W
Alsdorf	56	50.53 N	6.10 E
Alsea	202	44.22 N	123.35 W
Alsea ≐	202	44.26 N	124.05 W
Alsek ≐	180	59.10 N	138.10 W
Alsen	198	48.37 N	98.42 W
Alseno	64	44.54 N	9.59 E
Alsenz	56	49.43 N	7.49 E
Alsenz ≐	56	49.49 N	7.51 E
Alsey	219	39.34 N	90.25 W
Alsfeld	56	50.45 N	9.16 E
Als Fjord c[2]	41	55.02 N	9.38 E
Alsh, Loch c	46	57.15 N	5.39 W
Al-Shallūfa Military			
Base ■	142	30.03 N	32.32 E
Alsike	40	59.45 N	17.45 E
Alsina	252	33.54 S	59.23 W
Alsip	216	41.40 N	87.44 W
Alsleben	54	51.42 N	11.41 E
Alsónémedi	264c	47.19 N	19.10 E
Alstaden ◈[8]	263	51.28 N	6.50 E
Ålstäket	40	59.20 N	18.28 E
Alstätte	52	52.08 N	6.55 E
Alstead ≐	184	55.50 N	107.26 W
Alster	40	59.24 N	13.36 E
Alster ≐	52	53.36 N	9.59 E
Alsterbro	26	56.57 N	15.55 E
Alstern ⊜	40	59.40 N	13.55 E
Alston	44	54.49 N	2.26 W
Alsunga	76	56.59 N	21.34 E
Alswede	52	52.20 N	8.33 E
Alt ≐	44	53.32 N	3.03 W
Alta, Nor.	24	69.55 N	23.12 E
Älta, Sve.	40	59.16 N	18.11 E
Alta, Ca., U.S.	226	39.12 N	120.49 W
Alta, Ia., U.S.	198	42.40 N	95.17 W
Alta, Cachoeira ↳	250	5.46 S	54.28 W
Alta, Mount ∧	172	44.30 S	168.58 E
Altadena	228	34.11 N	118.07 W
Alta Floresta	250	9.57 S	56.06 W
Alta Gracia, Arg.	252	31.40 S	64.26 W
Altagracia, Nic.	236	11.34 N	85.35 W
Altagracia, Ven.	246	10.43 N	71.32 W
Altagracia de Orituco	246	9.52 N	66.23 W
Alta Hill	226	39.14 N	121.04 W
Al Tahoe	226	38.57 N	119.59 W
Altai ⩘	90	48.00 N	90.00 E
Altair	222	29.34 N	96.28 W
Altaj, Mong.	86	48.18 N	89.35 E
Altaj (Jesönbulag),			
Mong.	90	46.20 N	96.18 E
Altaj, Ross.	86	53.27 N	91.48 E
Altaj □[3]	86	51.00 N	86.00 E
Altajskij	86	51.58 N	85.22 E
Alta Loma, Ca., U.S.	228	34.07 N	117.36 W
Alta Loma, Tx., U.S.	222	29.22 N	95.04 W
Altamaha ≐	192	31.19 N	81.17 W
Altamira, Arg.	258	34.40 S	59.22 W
Altamira, Bra.	250	3.12 S	52.12 W
Altamira, Chile	252	25.47 S	69.51 W
Altamira, C.R.	236	10.30 N	84.23 W
Altamira, Méx.	234	22.24 N	97.55 W
Altamira, Las Cuevas			
de ⫠[5]	34	43.18 N	4.08 W
Altamirano, Arg.	258	35.21 S	58.09 W
Altamirano, Méx.	196	25.55 N	97.47 W
Altamont, Il., U.S.	219	39.03 N	88.44 W
Altamont, Ks., U.S.	198	37.11 N	95.17 W
Altamont, N.Y., U.S.	210	42.42 N	74.02 W
Altamont, Or., U.S.	202	42.12 N	121.44 W
Altamont, Tn., U.S.	194	35.25 N	85.43 W
Altamonte Springs	220	28.39 N	81.21 W
Altamura	68	40.50 N	16.33 E
Altamura, Isla I	232	25.00 N	108.10 W
Altan, Ross.	88	49.31 N	111.32 E
Altan, Ross.	88	49.53 N	109.04 E
Altanbulag, Mong.	88	47.41 N	106.22 E
Altanbulag, Mong.	88	50.19 N	106.30 E
Altan-Cögor	86	49.03 N	90.27 E
Altanširee	102	45.35 N	110.27 E
Altar	232	30.43 N	111.44 W
Altar ≐	232	30.39 N	111.53 W
Altar, Desierto de ◈[2]	232	31.50 N	114.15 W
Altar de Los			
Sacrificios ⊥	232	16.28 N	90.32 W
Altare	62	44.20 N	8.20 E
Altario	184	51.55 N	110.09 W
Altarnun	42	50.37 N	4.30 W
Altar of the Earth ʋ[1]	271a	39.57 N	116.24 E
Altar of the Moon ʋ[1]	271a	39.55 N	116.20 E
Altar of the Sun ʋ[1]	271a	39.54 N	116.27 E
Altar Wash V	200	32.05 N	111.19 W
Altaskij Kraj □[8]	86	52.30 N	83.00 E
Altastenberg	56	51.11 N	8.28 E
Altata, Méx.	232	24.38 N	107.55 W
Altata, Ross.	80	51.07 N	48.44 E
Alta Verapaz □[5]	236	15.40 N	90.00 W
Altavilla Irpina	68	41.00 N	14.47 E
Altavilla Milicia	70	38.02 N	13.32 E
Altavilla Silentina	68	40.32 N	15.08 E
Altaville	226	38.05 N	120.33 W
Alta Vista, Ks., U.S.	198	38.51 N	96.29 W
Altavista, Va., U.S.	192	37.06 N	79.17 W
Altay, Ross.	86	60.20 N	68.58 E
Altay, Zhg.	86	47.52 N	88.07 E
Altay			
→ Altaj □[3]	86	51.00 N	86.00 E
Alt Buchhorst	264a	52.26 N	13.51 E
Altdöbern	54	51.39 N	14.02 E
Altdorf, Dtsch.	60	48.34 N	12.07 E
Altdorf, Schw.	58	46.53 N	8.39 E
Altdorf bei Nürnberg	60	49.23 N	11.21 E
Alte Donau ⊜	264b	48.14 N	16.26 E
Alteelva ≐	24	69.58 N	23.23 E
Altefähr	54	54.20 N	13.07 E
Alteglofsheim	60	48.55 N	12.12 E
Alte Grund	264a	52.28 N	13.47 E
Altena	56	51.17 N	7.40 E
Altenahr	56	50.31 N	6.59 E
Altenau	52	51.48 N	10.26 E
Altenbeken	52	51.46 N	8.56 E
Altenberg	54	50.46 N	13.45 E
Altenberge	52	52.03 N	7.27 E
Altenbruch	52	53.49 N	8.46 E
Altenbüren	56	51.23 N	8.30 E
Altenburg, Dtsch.	54	50.59 N	12.26 E
Altenburg, Öst.	61	48.38 N	15.35 E
Altenderne			
Oberbecker ◈[8]	263	51.35 N	7.33 E
Altendorf	263	51.29 N	7.40 E
Altendorf ◈[8]	263	51.25 N	7.06 E
Altendorf-Ulfkotte	263	51.38 N	7.00 E
Altenesch	52	53.08 N	8.37 E
Altenessen ◈[8]	263	51.29 N	7.00 E
Altenfelden	60	48.29 N	13.58 E
Altengamme ◈[8]	52	53.25 N	10.16 E
Altenhagen, Dtsch.	52	52.03 N	8.38 E
Altenhagen, Dtsch.	54	53.45 N	13.06 E
Altenhagen ◈[8]	263	51.22 N	7.28 E
Altenhof	54	52.55 N	13.43 E
Altenholz	41	54.24 N	10.07 E
Altenkirchen, Dtsch.	54	54.38 N	13.20 E
Altenkirchen			
(Westerwald),			
Dtsch.	56	50.41 N	7.38 E
Altenkrempe	54	54.08 N	10.49 E
Altenkunstadt	54	50.07 N	11.14 E
Altenmarkt an der Alz	60	48.00 N	12.32 E
Altenoythe	52	53.02 N	7.52 E
Altenpleen	54	54.21 N	12.57 E
Altenstadt an der			
Waldnaab	60	49.48 N	12.10 E
Altensteig	56	48.35 N	8.37 E
Altentreptow	54	53.42 N	13.14 E
Altenvoerde	263	51.18 N	7.22 E
Altenwalde	52	53.49 N	8.40 E
Altenweddingen	54	52.00 N	11.31 E
Alte Oder ≐	54	52.52 N	14.09 E
Alter do Chão	34	39.12 N	7.40 W
Alterosa	256	21.15 S	46.08 W
Alter Rhein ≐	263	51.35 N	6.36 E
Altes Land ◈[1]	52	53.33 N	9.38 E
Altevatnet ⊜	24	68.32 N	19.30 E
Altfraunhofen	60	48.27 N	12.10 E
Altfriedland	54	52.38 N	14.12 E
Altglashütten	58	47.51 N	8.06 E
Alt-Glienicke ◈[8]	264a	52.25 N	13.32 E
Altgruland	263	51.27 N	7.41 E
Altha	192	30.34 N	85.07 W
Altham	262	53.47 N	2.21 W
Alt-Hartmannsdorf	264a	52.21 N	13.50 E
Althea Lake ⊜	283	42.40 N	71.23 W
Altheim	60	48.15 N	13.13 E
Altheimer	194	34.19 N	91.50 W
Althofen	61	46.54 N	14.27 E
Altınekin	130	38.19 N	32.53 E
Altinho	250	8.29 S	36.04 W
Altınoluk	130	39.34 N	26.44 E
Altinópolis	255	21.02 S	47.23 W
Altınova	130	39.13 N	26.47 E
Altınözü	130	36.08 N	36.12 E
Altıntaş	130	39.04 N	30.07 E
Altınyaka	130	36.34 N	30.21 E
Altiplano ⩘[1]	248	18.00 S	68.00 W
Alt Käbelich	54	53.29 N	13.29 E
Altkirch	58	47.37 N	7.15 E
Altlandsberg	54	52.33 N	13.43 E
Altlangerwisch	264a	52.19 N	13.04 E
Altlewin	54	52.42 N	14.16 E
Altlüdersdorf	54	53.02 N	13.11 E
Altlünen	52	51.38 N	7.31 E
Altmannsdorf ◈[8]	264b	48.10 N	16.20 E
Altmannstein	60	48.54 N	11.39 E
Altmar	212	43.31 N	76.00 W
Altmark ◈[1]	54	52.40 N	11.20 E
Altmittweida	54	50.58 N	12.57 E
Altmühl ≐	60	48.54 N	11.54 E
Altmünster	64	47.54 N	13.45 E
Altnaharra	46	58.16 N	4.27 W
Alto, Mi., U.S.	216	42.51 N	85.22 W
Alto, Tx., U.S.	222	31.39 N	95.04 W
Alto, Cerro ∧, Méx.	234	20.50 N	100.22 W
Alto, Cerro ∧, Ca.,			
U.S.	226	35.25 N	120.43 W
Alto Anapu ≐	250	2.15 S	51.27 W
Alto Araguaia	255	17.19 S	53.12 W
Alto Cauale	152	7.34 S	16.16 E
Alto Cedro	240p	20.31 N	75.58 W
Alto Chicapa	152	10.53 S	19.14 E
Alto Coité	255	15.47 S	54.20 W
Alto Cuito	152	13.27 S	18.49 E
Alto da Moóca ◈[8]	287b	23.34 S	46.35 W
Alto da Serra	256	22.53 S	44.14 W
Alto de las			
Vizcachas, Cerro ∧	286e	33.25 S	70.26 W
Alto del Carmen	252	28.46 S	70.30 W
Alto de Ña Paula	286c	10.24 N	66.48 W
Alto do Rio Doce	255	21.02 S	43.25 W
Altofonte	70	38.03 N	13.18 E
Alto Garças	255	16.56 S	53.32 W
Alto Ligonha	154	15.30 S	38.20 E
Alto Longá	250	5.15 S	42.12 W
Alto Lucero	234	19.37 N	96.43 W
Alto Molócuè	154	15.38 S	37.42 E
Altomonte	68	39.42 N	16.08 E
Altomünster	60	48.23 N	11.15 E
Alton, On., Can.	212	43.52 N	80.04 W
Alton, Eng., U.K.	42	51.09 N	0.59 W
Alton, Il., U.S.	219	38.53 N	90.11 W
Alton, Ia., U.S.	198	42.59 N	96.00 W
Alton, Ks., U.S.	198	39.28 N	98.56 W
Alton, Ky., U.S.	218	38.04 N	84.55 W
Alton, Mo., U.S.	194	36.41 N	91.23 W
Alton, N.H., U.S.	188	43.27 N	71.13 W
Alton, N.Y., U.S.	210	43.13 N	76.59 W
Alton, R.I., U.S.	207	41.26 N	71.43 W
Altona, Austl.	162	27.34 S	120.00 E
Altona, Austl.	169	37.52 S	144.50 E
Altona, Mb., Can.	184	49.06 N	97.33 W
Altona, In., U.S.	216	41.21 N	85.09 W
Altona ◈[8]	52	53.32 N	9.56 E
Altona Bay c	274b	37.53 S	144.51 E
Altona North	274b	37.50 S	144.51 E
Altona Sports Park ♠	274b	37.52 S	144.52 E
Altoona, Al., U.S.	194	34.01 N	86.19 W
Altoona, Fl., U.S.	220	28.57 N	81.38 W
Altoona, Ia., U.S.	190	41.39 N	93.28 W
Altoona, Ks., U.S.	198	37.31 N	95.39 W
Altoona, Pa., U.S.	214	40.31 N	78.23 W
Altoona, Wa., U.S.	224	46.16 N	123.39 W
Altoona, Wi., U.S.	190	44.48 N	91.26 W
Alto Pacajá ≐	250	3.07 S	50.20 W
Alto Paraguai	248	14.30 S	56.31 W
Alto Paraguay □[5]	248	21.00 S	58.45 W
Alto Paraíso de Goiás	255	14.07 S	47.31 W
Alto Paraná □[5]	252	25.00 S	54.50 W
Alto Parnaíba	250	9.06 S	45.57 W
Alto Purús ≐	248	9.34 S	70.36 W
Alto Río Mayo	254	45.35 S	71.06 W
Alto Río Senguer	254	45.02 S	70.50 W
Altos	250	5.03 S	42.28 W
Alto Santo	250	5.31 S	38.15 W
Alto Sucuriú	255	19.19 S	52.47 W
Altotonga	234	19.46 N	97.14 W
Altötting	60	48.13 N	12.40 E
Alto Volta			
→ Burkina Faso □[1]	150	13.00 N	1.30 W
Alto Yurua ≐	248	9.24 S	72.43 W
Altrincham	44	53.24 N	2.21 W
Alt Rüdersdorf	264a	52.28 N	13.49 E
Altruppin	54	52.56 N	12.50 E
Altshausen	58	47.56 N	9.32 E
Alt Stahnsdorf	264a	52.17 N	13.53 E
Altstätten	58	47.23 N	9.33 E
Alt Töplitz	264a	52.26 N	12.55 E
Altuchovo	76	52.40 N	34.20 E
Āltūn Kūprī	128	35.45 N	44.09 E
Altun Shan ⩘	90	38.00 N	88.00 E
Alturas	204	41.29 N	120.32 W
Altus, Ar., U.S.	194	35.26 N	93.45 W
Altus, Ok., U.S.	196	34.38 N	99.20 W
Altus, Lake ⊜[1]	196	34.56 N	99.18 W
Altus Air Force Base			
■	196	34.40 N	99.16 W
Altusried	58	47.48 N	10.13 E
Altyagač	84	40.50 N	48.54 E
Altyaryk	85	40.23 N	71.30 E
Altykarasu	86	49.12 N	55.52 E
Altynaj	86	57.04 N	62.00 E
Altynasar ⊥	86	45.10 N	63.07 E
Altynkul'	85	40.48 N	72.10 E
Altynovka	78	51.27 N	33.10 E
Altyntau	86	44.08 N	68.03 E
Altyn-Topkan	85	40.38 N	69.35 E
Alu I	175e	7.02 S	155.47 E
Al-Ubayyiḍ	140	13.11 N	30.13 E
Alubijid	116	8.35 N	124.29 E
Alucra	130	40.20 N	38.46 E
Al-'Udaysāt	140	25.35 N	32.29 E
Al-Uḍayyah	140	12.03 N	28.17 E
Aluk	140	8.26 N	27.27 E
Alūksne	76	57.25 N	27.03 E
Al-'Ulā	128	26.37 N	37.52 E
Alum Bank	214	40.14 N	78.34 W
Alum Creek ≐	218	39.53 N	82.54 W
Alum Creek Lake ⊜[1]	214	40.15 N	82.58 W
Aluminé	254	39.13 S	70.57 W
Aluminé ≐	254	39.50 S	70.53 W
Aluminé, Lago ⊜	252	38.55 S	71.09 W
Alum Rock	226	37.21 N	121.49 W
Alum Rock Park ♠	282	37.24 N	121.49 W
Alunda	40	60.04 N	18.05 E
Alunitdag	84	40.32 N	46.03 E
Alupka	78	44.26 N	34.03 E
Al-'Uqaylah	146	30.16 N	19.12 E
Al-'Uqayr	128	25.39 N	50.12 E
Al-Uqṣur (Luxor)	140	25.41 N	32.39 E
Al-'Urayq ⫠[8]	128	29.10 N	39.15 E
Al-'Urayq ◈[1]	128	24.47 N	42.55 E
Al-Urdun			
→ Jordan □[1]	128	31.00 N	36.00 E
Al-Urdunn			
→ Jordan ≐	132	31.46 N	35.33 E
Alušta	78	44.42 N	34.24 E
Al-'Uṭayshān ⫟[4]	140	16.25 N	34.30 E
Al-'Uwaynāt	146	25.46 N	10.34 E
Al-'Uwaynidhīyah I	128	26.37 N	36.05 E
Al-'Uyaynah	128	24.54 N	46.23 E
Alva, Scot., U.K.	46	56.09 N	3.48 W
Alva, Fl., U.S.	220	26.42 N	81.36 W
Alva, Ok., U.S.	196	36.48 N	98.39 W
Alva ≐	34	40.18 N	8.15 W
Alvada	214	41.03 N	83.24 W
Alvaiázere	34	39.49 N	8.23 W
Alvaneu-Bad	58	46.40 N	9.39 E
Älvängen	26	57.58 N	12.07 E
Alvanley	262	53.16 N	2.45 W
Alvarado, Méx.	234	18.46 N	95.46 W
Alvarado, Tx., U.S.	222	32.24 N	97.12 W
Alvarado, Lake ⊜[1]	222	32.23 N	97.15 W
Alvarães	246	3.12 S	64.50 W
Álvarez Jonte	258	35.19 S	57.28 W
Alvarinhos	266c	38.54 N	9.22 W
Álvaro Obregón	234	19.50 N	101.05 W
Álvaro Obregón ◈[8]	286a	19.21 N	99.12 W
Álvaro Obregón,			
Presa ⊜[1]	232	27.55 N	109.52 W
Alvastra ⊥	26	58.18 N	14.39 E
Alvdal	26	62.07 N	10.39 E
Älvdalen	26	61.14 N	14.02 E
Alvear	252	29.06 S	56.33 W
Alvechurch	42	52.21 N	1.57 W
Alverca	34	38.54 N	9.02 W
Alverda	214	40.38 N	78.52 W
Alvernia, Mount ∧[2]	238	24.15 N	75.24 W
Alverton	214	40.08 N	79.35 W
Alves	46	57.38 N	3.27 W
Alvesta	26	56.54 N	14.33 E
Alveston	42	51.36 N	2.32 W
Alviano, Lago di ⊜[1]	66	42.36 N	12.15 E
Ålvik, Nor.	26	60.26 N	6.26 E
Alvik, Sve.	26	62.25 N	17.24 E
Alvin, Il., U.S.	216	40.19 N	87.37 W
Alvin, Tx., U.S.	222	29.25 N	95.14 W
Alvinópolis	255	20.06 S	43.03 W
Alvinston	214	42.49 N	81.52 W
Alviso ◈[8]	282	37.26 N	121.58 W
Alviso Slough ≐	282	37.27 N	122.02 W
Alvito, It.	66	41.41 N	13.45 E
Alvito, Port.	34	38.15 N	7.59 W
Älvkarleby	40	60.34 N	17.27 E
Älvkarleö bruk	40	60.32 N	17.24 E
Alvord	196	33.22 N	97.42 W
Alvord Desert ◈[2]	202	42.30 N	118.25 W
Alvord Lake ⊜	202	42.23 N	118.36 W
Alvordton	216	41.40 N	84.26 W
Alvra, Pass d')(	58	46.35 N	9.50 E
Älvros	26	62.03 N	14.39 E
Älvsborgs Län □[6]	26	58.00 N	12.30 E
Älvsbyn	24	65.39 N	20.59 E
Älvsnabben ⊥	40	58.59 N	18.10 E
Al-Wafā'īyah	142	30.46 N	30.36 E
Al-Wajh	128	26.15 N	36.26 E
Al-Wakrah	128	25.10 N	51.36 E
Al-Walīdīyah	142	27.12 N	31.10 E
Alwar	124	27.34 N	76.36 E
Alwar Hills ⩘[2]	124	27.20 N	76.15 E
Al-Wāṣifīyah	142	30.35 N	32.10 E
Al-Wāsiṭah	142	29.20 N	31.12 E
Alwaye	122	10.07 N	76.21 E
Al-Wazīrīyah	142	31.11 N	30.57 E
Al-Wazz	140	15.01 N	30.10 E
Alwen ≐	44	52.58 N	3.24 W
Al-Widy	142	29.31 N	31.16 E
Alxa Zuoqi	102	38.50 N	105.32 E
Al-Yamāmah			
→ As-			
Sulaymānīyah	128	24.09 N	47.19 E
Al-Yaman			
→ Yemen □[1]	144	15.00 N	47.00 E
Al Yāmūn	132	32.29 N	35.14 E
Alygdžer	88	53.38 N	98.16 E
Alyn and Deeside □[8]	262	53.16 N	3.02 W
Alypsatar	86	48.03 N	80.21 E
Alyth	46	56.37 N	3.13 W
Alytus	76	54.24 N	24.03 E
Alz ≐	60	48.16 N	12.49 E
Alzamaj	88	55.33 N	98.39 E
Alzano Lombardo	62	45.44 N	9.43 E
Al-Zarqa	142	31.13 N	31.38 E
Alzenau	56	50.05 N	9.04 E
Alzette ≐	56	49.52 N	6.07 E
Alzey	56	49.45 N	8.07 E
Alzira (Alcira)	34	39.09 N	0.26 W
Amab, Khawr V	140	17.08 N	34.51 E
Amacayacu, Parque			
Nacional ♠	246	3.45 S	70.10 W
Amacuro ≐	246	8.32 N	60.28 W
Amacuzac ≐	234	17.53 N	99.12 W
Amadeus, Lake ⊜	162	24.50 S	130.45 E
Āmādi, Bngl.	126	22.28 N	89.19 E
Amadi, Zaïre	154	3.35 N	26.47 E
Amadjuak Lake ⊜	176	65.00 N	71.00 W
Amador □[6]	226	38.21 N	120.46 W
Amadora	266c	38.45 N	9.14 W
Amador City	226	38.25 N	120.56 W
Amador Valley V	282	37.41 N	121.51 W
Amagansett	207	40.58 N	72.08 W
Amagasaki	96	34.43 N	135.25 E
Amagase	96	33.15 N	131.02 E
Amager I	41	55.37 N	12.37 E
Amagi	96	33.25 N	130.39 E
Amagi-san ∧	94	34.51 N	139.00 E
Amagi-yugashima	94	34.53 N	138.56 E
Amagoi-dake ∧	94	35.01 N	136.23 E
Amagunze	150	6.20 N	7.40 E
Amahai	164	3.20 S	128.55 E
Amaichá del Valle	252	26.36 S	65.55 W
Amaimon	164	5.10 S	145.25 E
Amajac ≐	234	21.15 N	98.46 W
Amaka ≐	236	14.14 N	85.07 W
Ama Keng	271c	1.24 N	103.42 E
Amak Island I	180	55.25 N	163.07 W
Amakusa-nada ⫟[2]	92	32.35 N	130.05 E
Amakusa-shotō II	92	32.20 N	130.15 E
Amakuso-Shimo-			
shima I	92	32.20 N	130.05 E
Amal, Lībiyā	146	29.25 N	21.10 E
Åmål, Sve.	26	59.03 N	12.42 E
Amalāpuram	122	16.35 N	82.01 E
Amalat ≐	88	54.49 N	115.12 E
Amalfi, Col.	246	6.55 N	75.04 W
Amalfi, It.	68	40.38 N	14.36 E
Amalia	158	27.16 S	25.03 E
Amaliás	38	37.49 N	21.23 E
Amalner	120	21.03 N	75.04 E
Amamaki-zan ∧	94	36.25 N	140.09 E
Amambaí	255	23.05 S	55.13 W
Amambaí ≐	255	23.22 S	53.56 W
Amambay □[5]	252	23.00 S	56.00 W
Amami-Ō-shima I	93b	28.15 N	129.20 E
Amami-shotō II	93b	28.16 N	129.21 E
Amamula	154	0.18 S	27.50 E
Amana	190	41.48 N	91.52 W
Amanã ≐, Bra.	250	4.25 S	57.34 W
Amana ≐, Ven.	238	9.45 N	62.39 W
Amaná, Lago ⊜	246	2.35 S	64.40 W
Amanab	164	3.35 S	141.13 E
Amanave	174u	14.19 S	170.49 W
Amance	58	47.48 N	6.04 E
Amancey	58	47.02 N	6.05 E
Amancio	240p	20.49 N	77.35 W
Amanda	188	39.38 N	82.44 W
Amanda Park	224	47.28 N	123.54 W
Amandola	66	42.59 N	13.21 E
Amānganj	124	24.26 N	80.02 E
Amangel'dy, Kaz.	85	43.43 N	71.07 E
Amangel'dy, Kaz.	86	50.10 N	65.13 E
Amangel'dy, Kaz.	86	49.52 N	59.00 E
Åmänningen ⊜	40	59.57 N	15.56 E
Amano	270	34.26 N	135.33 E
Amanotkel'	86	46.07 N	61.34 E
Amantea	68	39.08 N	16.05 E
Amantogaj	86	50.22 N	65.33 E
Amanu I[1]	14	17.48 S	140.46 W
Amanzimtofi	158	30.03 S	30.53 E
Amapá	250	2.03 N	50.48 W
Amapá □[3]	250	1.00 N	52.00 W
Amapa ≐	234	18.18 N	96.19 W
Amapala	236	13.17 N	87.40 W
Amapala, Punta de ›	236	13.10 N	87.54 W
Amapari ≐	250	0.43 N	51.32 W
Amaraji	250	8.24 S	35.27 W
Amaral	287a	22.42 S	43.29 W
Amaramba, Lago ⊜	154	14.30 S	35.55 E
Amarante	250	6.14 S	42.50 W
Amarante do			
Maranhão	250	5.36 S	46.45 W
Amaranth	184	50.36 N	98.43 W
Amarapura	110	21.54 N	96.03 E
Amărăştii-de-Jos	38	43.59 N	24.10 E
'Amārat Abū Sinn	140	15.21 N	35.45 E
Amarāvati ≐	122	10.51 N	78.11 E
Amarda	126	21.47 N	87.08 E
Amareleja	34	38.12 N	7.14 W
Amares	34	41.38 N	8.21 W
Amargosa	255	13.02 S	39.36 W
Amargosa ≐	204	36.13 N	116.48 W
Amargosa Range ⩘	204	36.15 N	116.45 W
Amarillo	196	35.13 N	101.49 W
Amarillo, Mar			
→ Yellow Sea ⫟[2]	90	36.00 N	123.00 E
'Amar Jadīd	140	14.28 N	25.14 E
Amarkantak	124	22.40 N	81.45 E
Amarnāth	122	19.11 N	73.10 E
Amarnāth Cave ⫠[5]	123	34.13 N	75.31 E
Amaro, Monte ∧	66	42.05 N	14.05 E
Amaroni	68	38.47 N	16.27 E
Amaroúsion	267c	38.03 N	23.49 E
Amarpātan	124	24.19 N	80.59 E
Amarube-saki ›	96	35.40 N	134.32 E
Amarume	92	38.50 N	139.55 E
Amarwāra	124	22.18 N	79.10 E
Amasa	190	46.13 N	88.26 W
Amaseno ≐	66	41.19 N	13.11 E
Amasija	84	40.58 N	43.46 E
Amasra	130	41.45 N	32.24 E
Amasya	130	40.39 N	35.51 E
Amasya □[4]	130	40.45 N	35.30 E
Amataurá	246	3.29 S	68.06 W
Amatignak Island I	181a	51.15 N	179.08 W
Amatikulu	158	29.06 S	31.27 E
Amatique, Bahía de c	236	15.55 N	88.45 W
Amatitán	234	20.50 N	103.43 W
Amatitlán	236	14.29 N	90.37 W
Amatitlán, Lago de ⊜	236	14.27 N	90.34 W
Amatlán de Cañas	234	20.52 N	104.27 W
Amatlán de los			
Reyes	234	18.50 N	96.55 W
Amatrice	66	42.38 N	13.17 E
Amatsu-kominato	94	35.07 N	140.10 E
Amau	164	10.02 S	148.34 E
Amausi	124	26.46 N	80.51 E
Amawalk	210	41.17 N	73.46 W
Amay	56	50.33 N	5.19 E
Ama-zaki ›	94	37.08 N	136.40 E
Amazar	89	53.54 N	120.53 E
Amazon (Solimões)			
(Amazonas) ≐	242	0.10 S	49.00 W
Amazonas □[3]	242	5.00 S	63.00 W
Amazonas □[5], Col.	246	1.00 S	72.00 W
Amazonas □[5], Perú	248	5.30 S	78.00 W
Amazonas □[8]	246	3.30 N	66.00 W
Amazonas			
→ Amazon ≐	242	0.10 S	49.00 W
Amazônia, Parque			
Nacional da ♠	250	4.30 S	56.30 W
Amb	123	34.19 N	72.51 E
Ambāh	124	26.43 N	78.14 E
Ambahikily	157b	21.36 S	43.41 E
Ambahita	157b	24.01 S	45.16 E
Ambaí	287a	22.43 S	43.28 W
Ambājogāi	122	18.44 N	76.23 E
Ambakaka	157b	24.10 S	46.17 E
Ambāla	124	30.21 N	76.50 E
Ambāla Airport ⊠	123	30.22 N	76.50 E
Ambalabe	157b	18.24 S	49.10 E
Ambalafany	157b	22.32 S	47.36 E
Ambalangoda	122	6.14 N	80.03 E
Ambalanjanakomby	157b	16.42 S	47.05 E
Ambalavao	157b	21.50 S	46.56 E
Ambam	152	2.23 N	11.17 E
Amba Maryam	144	11.26 N	39.17 E
Ambanja	157b	13.41 S	48.27 E
Ambar	248	10.44 S	77.16 W
Ambararata	157b	15.03 S	48.33 E
Ambarawa	115a	7.15 S	110.24 E
Ambarčik, Ross.	74	69.39 N	162.20 E
Ambarčik, Ross.	88	55.09 N	95.46 E
Ambargasta, Salinas			
de ≚	252	29.15 S	64.30 W
Ambarijeby	157b	14.56 S	47.41 E
Ambarnyj	24	65.56 N	33.43 E
Ambaro, Baie d' c	157b	13.23 S	48.38 E
Ambāsamudram	122	8.42 N	77.28 E
Ambassador Bridge			
◈[5]	281	42.20 N	83.05 W
Ambato, Ec.	246	1.15 S	78.37 W
Ambato, Madag.	157b	13.24 S	48.29 E
Ambato Boeny	157b	16.28 S	46.43 E
Ambatofinandrahana	157b	20.33 S	46.48 E
Ambatolampy	157b	19.23 S	47.25 E
Ambatomainty	157b	17.41 S	45.40 E
Ambatomanoina	157b	18.18 S	47.37 E
Ambatondrazaka	157b	17.50 S	48.25 E
Ambatosoratra	157b	17.34 S	48.32 E
Ambeláki	267c	37.57 N	23.32 E
Ambelau, Pulau I	164	3.51 S	127.12 E
Ámbelos, Ákra ›	38	39.56 N	23.55 E
Ambenja	157b	15.17 S	46.58 E
Amber ≐	44	53.04 N	1.29 W
Amberes			
→ Antwerpen	50	51.13 N	4.25 E
Amberg, Dtsch.	60	49.27 N	11.52 E
Amberg, Wi., U.S.	190	45.30 N	87.59 W
Ambergris Cay I	232	18.03 N	87.56 W
Ambérieu-en-Bugey	58	45.57 N	5.21 E
Amberley	172	43.10 S	172.44 E

ENGLISH

Name	Page	Lat.°′	Long.°′
Amberley Royal			
Australian Air			
Force Base ■	171a	27.37 S	152.41 E
Amberson	214	40.10 N	77.41 W
Ambert	62	45.33 N	3.45 E
Ambevongo	157b	15.27 S	47.27 E
Ambia	216	40.29 N	87.31 W
Ambidédi	150	14.35 N	11.47 W
Ambikānagar	126	22.57 N	86.46 E
Ambikāpur	124	23.07 N	83.12 E
Ambil	116	13.49 N	120.20 E
Ambil Island I	116	13.48 N	120.18 E
Ambilobe	157b	13.12 S	49.04 E
Ambinanindrano	157b	20.20 S	48.19 E
Ambinanitelo	157b	15.21 S	49.35 E
Ambinda	157b	16.25 S	45.52 E
Ambivy	157b	21.31 S	44.02 E
Ambjörby	26	60.30 N	13.10 E
Ambla	76	59.11 N	25.51 E
Amble	44	55.20 N	1.34 W
Ambler, Ak., U.S.	180	67.05 N	157.52 W
Ambler, Pa., U.S.	208	40.09 N	75.13 W
Ambleside	44	54.26 N	2.58 W
Ambleteuse	50	50.49 N	1.36 E
Amblève ≐	56	50.28 N	5.36 E
Ambo	248	10.07 S	76.10 W
Amboahangy	157b	24.15 S	46.22 E
Amboasary, Madag.	157b	18.26 S	48.16 E
Amboasary, Madag.	157b	25.02 S	46.23 E
Ambodifototra	157b	16.59 S	49.52 E
Ambodilazana	157b	18.06 S	49.10 E
Ambodiriana	157b	17.55 S	49.18 E
Ambohibary	157b	19.20 S	46.17 E
Ambohidratrimo	157b	18.50 S	47.26 E
Ambohidray	157b	18.36 S	48.18 E
Ambohimahamasina	157b	21.56 S	47.11 E
Ambohimahasoa	157b	21.07 S	47.13 E
Ambohimanga du			
Sud	157b	20.52 S	47.36 E
Ambohimitombo	157b	20.43 S	47.26 E
Amboina			
→ Ambon	164	3.43 S	128.12 E
Amboise	50	47.25 N	0.59 E
Amboíva	152	11.32 S	14.44 E
Ambon	164	3.43 S	128.12 E
Ambon, Pulau I	164	3.40 S	128.10 E
Ambondro	157b	25.13 S	45.44 E
Ambonnay	50	49.04 N	4.10 E
Amboseli, Lake ⊜	154	2.37 S	37.08 E
Amboseli National			
Park ♠	154	2.30 S	37.15 E
Amboshe	272c	19.09 N	73.08 E
Ambositra	157b	20.31 S	47.15 E
Ambovombe	157b	25.11 S	46.05 E
Amboy, Il., U.S.	190	41.42 N	89.19 W
Amboy, In., U.S.	216	40.36 N	85.55 W
Amboy, Mn., U.S.	190	43.53 N	94.09 W
Amboy, Wa., U.S.	224	45.54 N	122.26 W
Ambre, Cap d' ›	157b	11.57 S	49.17 E
Ambre, Montagne d'			
∧	157b	12.30 S	49.10 E
Ambridge	214	40.35 N	80.13 W
Ambridge Heights	214	40.36 N	80.13 W
Ambridge Reservoir			
⊜[1]	214	40.34 N	80.21 W
Ambrières	32	48.24 N	0.38 W
Ambriz	152	7.50 S	13.06 E
Ambrolauri	84	42.31 N	43.09 E
Ambronay	58	46.00 N	5.21 E
Ambrose	198	48.57 N	103.28 W
Ambrose Brook ≐	276	40.33 N	74.32 W
Ambrose Channel ⊎	276	40.32 N	74.02 W
Ambrosia Lake	200	35.25 N	107.49 W
Ambrym □[8]	175f	16.15 S	168.12 E
Ambrym I	175f	16.15 S	168.10 E
Ambuklao Dam ◈[6]	116	16.28 N	120.45 E
Ambulong Island I	116	12.12 N	121.01 E
Ambulu	115a	8.21 S	113.36 E
Ambuntentimur	115a	6.54 S	113.45 E
Ambunti	164	4.14 S	142.50 E
Āmbūr	122	12.47 N	78.42 E
Amburambur	115b	8.15 S	116.18 E
Amburayan Nabunga			
≐	116	16.55 N	120.27 E
Amby	56	50.53 N	5.44 E
Amchitka Island I	181a	51.30 N	179.00 E
Amchitka Pass ⊎	181a	51.30 N	179.30 W
'Amd	144	15.18 N	48.00 E
Am-Dam	146	12.46 N	20.29 E
Āmdānga	272b	22.49 N	88.31 E
Amded, Oued V	148	22.09 N	3.15 E
Amden	58	47.09 N	9.11 E
Amderma	72	69.45 N	61.39 E
Amdo	120	32.18 N	91.04 E
Ameagle	188	37.56 N	81.25 W
Ameca	234	20.33 N	104.02 W
Ameca ≐	234	20.41 N	105.18 W
Amecameca [de			
Juárez]	234	19.07 N	98.46 W
Ameghino	252	34.50 S	62.27 W
Ameglia	64	44.04 N	9.57 E
Ameisberg ∧	60	48.33 N	13.50 E
Ameixoeira ◈[8]	266c	38.47 N	9.10 W
Ameland I	52	53.25 N	5.45 E
Amele	164	5.16 S	145.42 E
Amelia, It.	66	42.33 N	12.25 E
Amelia, Oh., U.S.	218	39.01 N	84.13 W
Amelia, Passo d')(	66	42.36 N	12.32 E
Amelia Court House	192	37.20 N	77.58 W
Amelia Earhart Peak			
∧	226	37.47 N	119.17 W
Amelia Island I	192	30.37 N	81.27 W
Amelinghausen	52	53.08 N	10.13 E
Amelsbüren	52	51.53 N	7.37 E
Amendolara	68	39.57 N	16.35 E
Ameng	102	23.50 N	104.32 E
Amenia	210	41.50 N	73.33 W
Amenucourt	261	49.06 N	1.39 E
Āmer	120	26.59 N	75.52 E
Amerang	60	48.00 N	12.18 E
Amerevo	265b	55.55 N	38.03 E
America	52	51.26 N	5.59 E
América del Norte			
→ North America			
⫠[1]	16	45.00 N	100.00 W
América del Sur			
→ South America			
⫠[1]	18	15.00 S	60.00 W
American ≐, Ca.,			
U.S.	226	38.36 N	121.30 W
American ≐, Wa.,			
U.S.	224	46.58 N	121.08 W
American, Middle			
Fork ≐	226	38.55 N	121.02 W
American, North Fork			
≐	226	38.43 N	121.09 W
American, South			
Fork ≐	226	38.43 N	121.09 W
Americana	255	22.45 S	47.20 W
American Canyon	226	38.10 N	122.15 W
American Cemetery			
and Memorial ◈	269f	14.33 N	121.03 E
American Falls	202	42.47 N	112.51 W
American Falls ↳	284a	43.05 N	79.04 W
American Falls			
Reservoir ⊜[1]	202	42.45 N	112.45 W
American Fork	200	40.22 N	111.47 W
American Highland			
⩘[1]	9	72.30 S	78.00 E
American Lake ⊜	224	47.07 N	122.34 W
American Museum of			
Natural History ʋ	276	40.47 N	73.59 W
Americano	250	1.19 S	48.04 W
American River	168b	35.47 S	137.47 E
American Samoa □[2],			
Oc.	14	14.20 S	170.00 W
American Samoa □[2],			
Oc.	175a	14.20 S	170.00 W
American University			
ʋ[2]	284c	38.56 N	77.05 W

DEUTSCH

Name	Seite	Breite°′	Länge°′ E = Ost
Américas, Hipódromo			
de las ♠	286a	19.26 N	99.13 W
Americus, Ga., U.S.	192	32.04 N	84.13 W
Americus, Ks., U.S.	198	38.30 N	96.15 W
Amerikanisches			
Hochland			
→ American			
Highland ⩘[1]	9	72.30 S	78.00 E
Ameringkogel ∧	61	47.04 N	14.48 E
Amérique du Nord			
→ North America			
⫠[1]	16	45.00 N	100.00 W
Amern	56	51.14 N	6.15 E
Amerongen	52	52.00 N	5.27 E
Amersfoort, Ned.	52	52.09 N	5.24 E
Amersfoort, S. Afr.	158	27.01 S	29.51 E
Amersham	42	51.40 N	0.38 W
Amery, Austl.	162	31.09 S	117.05 E
Amery, Mb., Can.	184	56.34 N	94.03 W
Amery, Wi., U.S.	190	45.18 N	92.21 W
Amery Ice Shelf ⊓	9	69.30 S	72.00 E
Ames, Ia., U.S.	190	42.02 N	93.37 W
Ames, N.Y., U.S.	210	42.50 N	74.36 W
Ames, Tx., U.S.	222	30.03 N	94.46 W
Amesbury, Eng., U.K.	42	51.10 N	1.45 W
Amesbury, Ma., U.S.	207	42.51 N	70.55 W
Ames Long Pond ⊜	283	42.05 N	71.07 W
Ames Nowell State			
Park ♠	283	42.07 N	70.59 W
Ames Pond ⊜	283	42.38 N	71.13 W
Ames Research			
Center ʋ[3]	282	37.25 N	122.04 W
Amet Sound ⊎	186	45.47 N	63.13 W
Amfíklia	38	38.38 N	22.35 E
Amfilokhía	38	38.51 N	21.10 E
Ámfissa	38	38.31 N	22.24 E
Amfreville-la-			
Campagne	50	49.13 N	0.57 E
Amfreville-les-			
Champs	50	49.19 N	1.19 E
Amga	74	60.53 N	132.00 E
Amga ≐	74	62.38 N	134.32 E
Am Géréda	146	12.52 N	21.10 E
Amguema	180	66.58 N	179.16 W
Amguema ≐	180	68.10 N	177.40 W
Amguid	148	26.26 N	5.22 E
Amgun' ≐	89	52.56 N	139.40 E
Amherst, N.S., Can.	186	45.49 N	64.14 W
Amherst, Ma., U.S.	207	42.22 N	72.31 W
Amherst, N.H., U.S.	207	42.51 N	71.37 W
Amherst, N.Y., U.S.	210	42.58 N	78.48 W
Amherst, Oh., U.S.	214	41.23 N	82.13 W
Amherst, Tx., U.S.	196	34.01 N	102.25 W
Amherst, Va., U.S.	192	37.35 N	79.03 W
Amherst, Wi., U.S.	190	44.27 N	89.17 W
Amherst, Mount ∧	162	18.11 S	126.59 E
Amherstburg	214	42.06 N	83.06 W
Amherstdale	188	37.47 N	81.48 W
Amherst Island I	212	44.08 N	76.45 W
Amherstview	212	44.13 N	76.38 W
Ami	94	36.02 N	140.14 E
Amianan Island I	108	21.07 N	121.57 E
Amiata, Monte ∧	66	42.53 N	11.37 E
Amicalola Falls State			
Park ♠	192	34.33 N	84.15 W
Amidon	198	46.28 N	103.19 W
Amiens, Austl.	166	28.35 S	151.49 E
Amiens, Fr.	50	49.54 N	2.18 E
Amili, India	120	28.26 N	95.52 E
Amili, Zhg.	120	28.25 N	95.52 E
Amīn as-Samālūsī,			
Bi'r ⫟[4]	142	29.52 N	30.02 E
Amīndīvi Islands II	122	11.23 N	72.23 E
Aminga	252	28.50 S	66.54 W
Amini Island I	122	11.07 N	72.44 E
Amino, Ityo.	144	4.31 N	41.49 E
Amino, Nihon	96	35.41 N	135.02 E
Aminuis	156	23.43 S	19.21 E
Amīrābād	128	36.04 N	54.10 E
Amīrābād ◈[8]	267d	35.43 N	51.23 E
Amirante Islands II	138	6.00 S	53.10 E
Amirauté, Îles de l'			
→ Admiralty			
Islands II	164	2.10 S	147.00 E
Amisk	182	52.33 N	111.04 W
Amisk Lake ⊜	184	54.35 N	102.13 W
Amistad, Parque			
Internacional de la			
♠	236	9.25 N	83.10 W
Amistad, Presa de la			
(Amistad Reservoir)			
⊜[1]	196	29.34 N	101.15 W
Amistad National			
Recreation Area ♠	196	29.32 N	101.12 W
Amistad Reservoir			
(Presa de la			
Amistad) ⊜[1]	196	29.34 N	101.15 W
Amite	194	30.43 N	90.30 W
Amite ≐	194	30.12 N	90.35 W
Amite, East Fork ≐	194	30.58 N	90.51 W
Amiterno ⊥	66	42.21 N	13.19 E
Amitori	175d	24.18 N	123.41 E
Amity, Ar., U.S.	194	34.15 N	93.27 W
Amity, Oh., U.S.	214	40.03 N	83.17 W
Amity, Or., U.S.	224	45.06 N	123.12 W
Amity Point ›	171a	27.24 S	153.27 E
Amityville	276	40.40 N	73.25 W
Amixtlán	234	20.03 N	97.48 W
Amizmiz	148	31.14 N	8.14 W
Āmjhori ∧	126	21.51 N	86.19 E
Āmjhupi	126	23.45 N	88.42 E
Āmla, Bngl.	126	23.54 N	88.56 E
Āmla, India	124	21.56 N	78.07 E
Āmlāgora	126	22.50 N	87.20 E
Amlekhgañj	124	27.17 N	84.59 E
Åmli	26	58.47 N	8.30 E
Amlia Island I	180	52.06 N	173.30 W
Amloh	124	30.37 N	76.14 E
Am Loubia	146	13.39 N	20.08 E
Amlwch	44	53.25 N	4.20 W
'Amm-Adām	140	16.22 N	36.06 E
Ammagan	85	38.56 N	67.15 E
'Ammān	132	31.57 N	35.56 E
'Ammān □[8]	132	31.45 N	36.15 E
Ammanford	42	51.48 N	3.59 W
Ämmänsaari	26	64.53 N	28.55 E
Ammansville	222	29.47 N	96.51 W
'Ammār, Tall ∧[2]	132	32.53 N	36.29 E
Ammarnäs	24	65.56 N	16.09 E
Ammaroo	162	21.45 S	135.15 E
Åmmeberg	40	58.52 N	15.00 E
Ammeloe	52	52.05 N	6.47 E
Ammendorf ◈[8]	54	51.25 N	11.59 E
Ammer ≐	64	47.57 N	11.08 E
Ammerån ≐	26	63.09 N	16.13 E
Ammerbuch	56	48.33 N	8.58 E
Ammer Gebirge ⩘	64	47.35 N	10.55 E
Ammerland ◈[1]	52	53.15 N	8.00 E
Ammerman Mountain			
∧	180	68.21 N	141.03 W
Ammerschwihr	58	48.07 N	7.17 E
Ammersee ⊜	60	48.00 N	11.08 E
Ammerthal	60	49.26 N	11.45 E
Ammon	202	43.28 N	111.57 W
Ammonoosuc ≐	188	44.10 N	72.02 W
Amnān	272b	22.56 N	88.18 E
Amnat Charoen	110	15.51 N	104.38 E
Amnay ≐	116	12.58 N	120.46 E
Amne Machin Shan			
→ A'nyêmaqên			
Shan ⩘	102	34.30 N	100.00 E
Amnicon ≐	190	46.41 N	91.52 W
Amnok-kang (Yalu) ≐	98	39.55 N	124.22 E
Amo ≐, Asia	124	26.16 N	89.36 E
Amo ≐, Zhg.	102	22.58 N	101.44 E
Āmol	128	36.23 N	52.20 E
Amolar	248	18.01 S	57.30 W
Amöneburg	56	50.48 N	8.55 E
Amorbach	56	49.39 N	9.13 E
Amorgós	38	36.50 N	25.54 E
Amorgós I	38	36.50 N	25.59 E

Symbols in the index entries represent the broad categories identified in the key at the right. Symbols with superior numbers (⩘[1]) identify subcategories (see complete key on page *I · 1*).

Symbole im Register stellen die rechts im Schlüssel erklärten Kategorien dar. Symbole mit hochgestellten Ziffern (⩘[1]) bezeichnen Unterabteilungen einer Kategorie (vgl. vollständiger Schlüssel auf Seite *I · 1*).

Los símbolos incluídos en el texto del índice representan las grandes categorías identificadas con la clave a la derecha. Los símbolos con numeros en su parte superior (⩘[1]) identifican las subcategorías (véase la clave completa en la página *I · 1*).

Les symboles de l'index représentent les catégories indiquées dans la légende à droite. Les symboles suivis d'un indice (⩘[1]) représentent des sous-catégories (voir légende complète à la page *I · 1*).

Os símbolos incluídos no texto do índice representam as grandes categorias identificadas com a chave à direita. Os símbolos com números em sua parte superior (⩘[1]) identificam as subcategorias (veja-se a chave completa à página *I · 1*).

∧ Mountain	Berg	Montaña	Montagne	Montanha
⩘ Mountains	Gebirge	Montañas	Montagnes	Montanhas
)(Pass	Paß	Paso	Col	Passo
V Valley, Canyon	Tal, Cañon	Valle, Cañón	Vallée, Canyon	Vale, Canhão
≚ Plain	Ebene	Llano	Plaine	Planície
› Cape	Kap	Cabo	Cap	Cabo
I Island	Insel	Isla	Île	Ilha
II Islands	Inseln	Islas	Îles	Ilhas
⫠ Other Topographic Features	Andere Topographische Objekte	Otros Elementos Topográficos	Autres données topographiques	Outros acidentes topográficos

Amor-Anno I · 7

ESPAÑOL — Nombre / Página / Lat.°′ / Long.°′ W = Oeste
FRANÇAIS — Nom / Page / Lat.°′ / Long.°′ W = Ouest
PORTUGUÊS — Nome / Página / Lat.°′ / Long.°′ W = Oeste

Amorim, Morro ▲² 287a 23.00 S 43.26 W
Amorinópolis 255 16.36 S 51.08 W
Amorosi 68 41.12 N 14.28 E
Amory 194 33.59 N 88.29 W
Amos 190 48.35 N 78.07 W
Åmose ≃ 41 55.35 N 11.18 E
Åmot, Nor. 26 59.35 N 8.00 E
Åmot, Nor. 26 59.54 N 9.54 E
Åmotfors 26 59.46 N 12.22 E
Amour
 → Amur ≃ 74 52.56 N 141.10 E
Amour, Djebel ⋏ 148 34.00 N 2.15 E
Amoy
 → Xiamen 100 24.28 N 118.07 E
Amozoc 234 19.02 N 98.03 W
Ampana 112 0.51 S 121.32 E
Ampanavoana 157b 15.41 S 50.22 E
Ampang 115b 8.47 S 118.00 E
Ampanihy 157b 24.42 S 44.45 E
Ampaoid, Mount ▲ 116 7.57 N 125.41 E
Amparafaravola 157b 17.35 S 48.13 E
Amparihy, Madag. 157b 16.40 S 44.49 E
Amparihy, Madag. 157b 23.57 S 47.20 E
Amparo 256 22.42 S 46.45 W
Ampasibe 157b 22.56 S 46.58 E
Ampasinambo 157b 20.31 S 48.00 E
Ampasindava, Baie d' C 157b 13.16 S 48.43 E
Ampasindava, Presqu'île d' ›¹ 157b 13.45 S 48.00 E
Ampato, Nevado ▲ 248 15.50 S 71.52 W
Ampel 115a 7.27 S 110.32 E
Amper 150 9.20 N 9.43 E
Amper ≃ 60 48.30 N 11.58 E
Ampezzo 64 46.25 N 12.48 E
Ampezzo, Valle d' V 64 46.30 N 12.10 E
Ampfing 60 48.16 N 12.25 E
Ampflwang 64 48.05 N 13.34 E
Amphion-les-Bains 58 46.23 N 6.32 E
Ampisikina 157b 12.57 S 49.49 E
Ampleforth 44 54.12 N 1.06 W
Ampollino, Lago ⊜ 68 39.12 N 16.37 E
Ampombiantambo 157b 12.42 S 43.57 E
Amposta 34 40.43 N 0.35 E
Ampotaka 157b 25.03 S 44.41 E
Ampoza 157b 22.20 S 44.44 E
Ampthill 42 52.02 N 0.30 W
Ampuis 62 45.29 N 4.49 E
Ampus 62 43.36 N 6.23 E
Amqui 186 48.28 N 67.26 W
Åmr, Jabal al- ⋏ 132 30.45 N 34.20 E
Amraoti
 → Amrāvati 120 20.56 N 77.45 E
Amrāvati 120 20.56 N 77.45 E
Am-Raya 146 14.00 N 16.35 E
Amreli 120 21.37 N 71.14 E
Āmreswar 272b 22.28 N 88.34 E
Amriswil 58 47.33 N 9.18 E
Amritsar 123 31.35 N 74.53 E
Amroha 124 28.55 N 78.28 E
Amrūka 123 30.19 N 73.53 E
Amrum I 30 54.39 N 8.21 E
Amsdell Heights 284a 42.45 N 78.54 W
Amsden 214 41.13 N 83.20 W
Åmsel 148 22.37 N 5.26 E
Åmsele 26 64.32 N 19.20 E
Am Sigan 146 11.41 N 19.51 E
Amsoldingen 58 46.43 N 7.35 E
Amsteg 58 46.46 N 8.41 E
Amstel ≃ 52 52.22 N 4.54 E
Amstelmeer ⊜ 52 52.52 N 4.45 E
Amstelveen 52 52.18 N 4.51 E
Amsterdam, Ned. 52 52.22 N 4.54 E
Amsterdam, S. Afr. 158 26.35 S 30.45 E
Amsterdam, N.Y., U.S. 210 42.56 N 74.11 W
Amsterdam, Oh., U.S. 214 40.28 N 80.55 W
Amsterdam, Île I 6 37.52 S 77.32 E
Amsterdam-Rijnkanaal ≅ 52 51.57 N 5.20 E
Amstetten 61 48.07 N 14.53 E
Amston 207 41.37 N 72.20 W
Āmta 126 22.35 N 88.01 E
Amt'ae-do I 98 34.50 N 126.07 E
Āmtala 126 23.55 N 88.27 E
Āmtāli 126 22.08 N 90.14 E
Am Timan 146 11.02 N 20.17 E
Amtrak Station ◆⁵ 281 42.19 N 83.04 W
Amubri 236 9.31 N 82.56 W
'Āmūdah 130 37.05 N 40.54 E
Amu-Darja 128 37.53 N 65.15 E
Amu Darya (Amudarja) ≃ 72 43.40 N 59.01 E
Amudat 154 1.57 N 34.57 E
Amugulang
 → Xin Barag Zuoqi 88 48.14 N 118.18 E
Amukta Island I 180 52.29 N 171.15 W
Amukta Pass Ʉ 180 52.25 N 172.00 W
Amulree 46 56.30 N 3.47 W
Amun 175e 5.57 S 154.45 E
Amundsen Bay C 9 66.55 S 50.00 E
Amundsen Gulf C 176 71.00 N 124.00 W
Amundsen-Scott ▿³ 9 90.00 S 0.00
Amundsen Sea ∓² 9 72.30 S 112.00 W
Amung, Mount ▲ 164 7.26 S 146.36 E
Amungen ⊜ 26 61.09 N 15.39 E
Amuntai 112 2.26 S 115.15 E
Amur (Heilong) ≃ 74 52.56 N 141.10 E
'Amūr, Wādī V 140 18.56 N 33.34 E
Amurang 112 1.11 N 124.35 E
Amuria 154 2.01 N 33.38 E
Amursk 89 50.13 N 136.52 E
Amurskaja Oblast' ▫⁸ 89 53.00 N 129.00 E
Amurskij liman C 89 52.45 N 141.40 E
Amursko-Zejskaja ravnina ⋏¹ 89 52.30 N 128.30 E
Amurzet 89 47.42 N 131.05 E
Amutag 116 12.23 N 123.16 E
Amuwo 273a 6.28 N 3.18 E
Amuyimusu 98 42.25 N 113.21 E
Amuzhong 120 30.33 N 84.28 E
Amvamg 152 1.45 N 10.29 E
Amvrakikós Kólpos C 38 39.00 N 21.00 E
Amvrosijevka 83 47.47 N 38.29 E
Amwom, Khawr V 140 7.50 N 31.13 E
Amyl ≃ 86 53.47 N 92.54 E
Amyūn 130 34.18 N 35.49 E
Amz'a 80 56.13 N 54.23 E
Amzi, Oued ti-n- V 148 20.30 N 4.35 E
An 110 19.47 N 94.02 E
Anaa I¹ 14 17.25 S 145.30 W
Anabanua 112 3.57 S 120.04 E
Anabar 174b 0.30 S 166.57 E
Anabar ≃ 74 73.08 N 113.36 E
'Anabtā 132 32.19 N 35.07 E
Anabuki 96 34.02 N 134.11 E
Anacapri 68 40.33 N 14.13 E
Anaco 246 9.27 N 64.28 W
Anacoco 194 31.15 N 93.20 W
Anacoco, Bayou ≃ 194 30.52 N 93.34 W
Anaconda 202 46.07 N 112.56 W
Anaconda Range ⋏ 202 45.55 N 113.30 W
Anacortes 224 48.30 N 122.36 W
Anacostia ◆⁸ 284c 38.52 N 76.59 W
Anacostia ≃ 284c 38.52 N 77.01 W
Anacostia, Little Paint Branch ≃ 284c 39.01 N 76.56 W
Anacostia, Northeast Branch ≃ 284c 38.57 N 76.57 W
Anacostia, Paint Branch ≃ 284c 38.58 N 76.55 W
Anacostia Park ♦ 284c 38.54 N 76.58 W
Anacuao, Mount ▲ 116 16.16 N 121.53 E
Anadarko 196 35.04 N 98.14 W
Anadia 250 9.42 S 36.18 W
Anadolufeneri ◆⁸ 267b 41.12 N 29.09 E
Anadoluhisarı ⊥ 267b 41.04 N 29.03 E
Anadyr' 180 64.45 N 177.29 E
Anadyr' ≃ 74 64.55 N 176.05 E
Anadyrskaja nizmennost' ≡ 180 65.30 N 176.00 E
Anadyrskij liman C 180 64.30 N 177.45 E
Anadyrskij zaliv C 180 64.00 N 179.00 W
Anadyrskoje ploskogorje ⋏¹ 180 67.00 N 174.00 E
Anáfi I 38 36.21 N 25.50 E
Anagni 66 41.44 N 13.09 E
'Ānah 128 34.28 N 41.56 E
Anaheim 228 33.50 N 117.54 W
Anaheim Arena ♦ 280 33.48 N 117.52 W
Anaheim Shopping Center ◆⁹ 280 33.51 N 117.56 W
Anaheim Stadium ♦ 280 33.51 N 117.57 W
Anaheim Union Canal ≅ 280 33.54 N 117.52 W
Anahi, Baie C 174x 9.45 S 138.56 W
Anahim Lake 182 52.28 N 125.18 W
Anahola 229b 22.08 N 159.18 W
Anahola Bay C 229b 22.09 N 159.18 W
Anáhuac, Méx. 196 25.48 N 97.45 W
Anáhuac, Méx. 232 27.14 N 100.09 W
Anáhuac, Méx. 232 28.25 N 106.40 W
Anahuac, Tx., U.S. 222 29.46 N 94.41 W
Anahuac, Lake ⊜ 222 29.48 N 94.41 W
Anaimala 122 10.35 N 76.56 E
Ānai Mudi ▲ 122 10.10 N 77.04 E
Anajás 250 0.59 S 49.57 W
Anajás, Ilha I 250 0.20 S 50.30 W
Anajatuba 250 3.16 S 44.37 W
Anakāpalle 122 17.41 N 83.01 E
Anaklia 84 42.24 N 41.34 E
Anaktuvuk ≃ 180 69.32 N 151.30 W
Anaktuvuk Pass 180 68.10 N 151.50 W
Analalava 157b 14.38 S 47.45 E
Analapatsy 157b 25.10 S 46.42 E
Analavoka 157b 22.33 S 46.30 E
Analomink 210 41.03 N 75.13 W
Anamā 246 3.35 S 61.22 W
Anamã, Lago ⊜ 246 3.32 S 61.35 W
Anama Bay 184 51.56 N 98.05 W
Ana María, Cayos de II 240p 21.29 N 78.46 W
Ana María, Golfo de C 240p 21.25 N 78.40 W
Anambas, Kepulauan II 112 3.00 N 106.00 E
Anambra ▫³ 150 6.30 N 7.20 E
Anambra ≃ 150 6.11 N 6.46 E
Anamizu 94 37.14 N 136.54 E
Anamoose 198 47.52 N 100.14 W
Anamosa 190 42.06 N 91.17 W
Anamu ≃ 250 0.56 N 57.03 W
Anamur 130 36.06 N 32.50 E
Anamur Burnu › 130 36.03 N 32.48 E
Anan, Nihon 94 35.19 N 137.49 E
Anan, Nihon 96 33.55 N 134.39 E
Ānand 120 22.34 N 72.56 E
Ananda 150 7.17 N 4.16 W
Anandanagar 272b 22.51 N 88.16 E
Ānandapur, India 120 21.14 N 86.07 E
Anandapur, India 126 22.34 N 87.25 E
Anandpur Sahib 123 31.15 N 76.30 E
Ananea 248 14.42 S 69.33 W
Ananindeua 250 1.22 S 48.23 W
Anan'jev 78 47.40 N 29.55 E
Ananjevo 85 42.45 N 77.40 E
Anantapur 122 14.41 N 77.36 E
Anantnāg (Islāmābād) 123 33.44 N 75.09 E
Anao-aon 116 9.47 N 125.25 E
Anapa 78 44.53 N 37.19 E
Anapo ≃ 70 37.03 N 15.15 E
Anápolis 255 16.20 S 48.58 W
Anapu ≃ 250 1.53 S 50.53 W
Anapurus 250 3.40 S 43.06 W
Anār, Īrān 128 30.53 N 55.18 E
Anar, Kaz. 86 50.38 N 72.27 E
Anāra 126 23.28 N 86.33 E
Anārak 128 33.20 N 53.42 E
Anarchaj 85 44.02 N 75.15 E
Anār Darreh 128 32.46 N 61.39 E
Anaš 86 54.52 N 91.00 E
Anasagasti 258 35.01 S 59.24 W
Añasco 240m 18.17 N 67.08 W
Ånäset 26 64.16 N 21.03 E
Anastácio 255 21.31 S 54.08 W
Anastasia Island I 192 29.48 N 81.16 W
Anastasijevka 83 47.34 N 38.31 E
Anastasijevskaja 78 45.13 N 37.53 E
'Anātā 132 31.49 N 35.16 E
Anatahan I 108 16.22 N 145.40 E
Anatoljevka 78 46.48 N 31.13 E
Anatom I 175f 20.12 S 169.45 E
Añatuya 252 28.28 S 62.50 W
Anauá ≃ 246 0.58 N 61.21 W
Anaurilândia 255 22.03 S 52.45 W
Anavilhanas, Arquipélago das II 246 2.42 S 60.45 W
Anawalt 192 37.20 N 81.26 W
Anbanjing 102 23.57 N 100.55 E
Anbei, Zhg. 102 40.45 N 96.06 E
Anbei, Zhg. 102 40.49 N 108.56 E
Anbianbu 102 37.39 N 108.11 E
Anbo 98 39.51 N 122.19 E
Anbu 100 23.28 N 116.44 E
Anbyŏn 98 39.03 N 127.32 E
Ancarano 66 42.50 N 13.44 E
Ancash ▫⁵ 248 9.30 S 77.45 W
Ancaster, On., Can. 212 43.12 N 80.00 W
Ancaster, Eng., U.K. 44 52.59 N 0.32 W
Ancasti 252 28.49 S 65.30 W
Ancasti, Sierra de ⋏ 252 28.50 S 65.39 W
Ance ≃, Fr. 62 44.58 N 3.40 E
Ance ≃, Fr. 62 45.17 N 4.08 E
Ancenis 32 47.22 N 1.11 W
Ancerville 58 48.38 N 5.02 E
Anchang 100 30.09 N 120.30 E
Anchau 150 10.59 N 8.23 E
Anchieta ◆⁸ 287a 22.49 S 43.24 W
Anchieta, Ilha I 256 23.33 S 45.04 W
Anch'ing
 → Anqing 100 30.31 N 117.02 E
Ancho, Canal Ʉ 254 49.54 S 74.23 W
Ancholme ≃ 44 53.41 N 0.32 W
Anchor 216 40.34 N 88.32 W
Anchorage 180 61.13 N 149.54 W
Anchor Bay C 214 42.38 N 82.45 W
Anchor Bay Gardens 214 42.39 N 82.49 W
Anchorena 252 35.41 S 65.27 W
Anchor Point 180 59.46 N 151.52 W
Anchor Point › 180 59.47 N 151.52 W
Anchorville 214 42.42 N 82.41 W
Anchuras 34 39.29 N 4.50 W
Anci (Langfang) 105 39.31 N 116.41 E
Ancien Ekalla 152 1.27 S 14.00 E
Ancien Goubéré 140 5.51 N 26.46 E
Ancienne-Lorette 206 46.48 N 71.21 W
Anciferovo, Ross. 76 58.58 N 34.01 E
Anciferovo, Ross. 82 55.33 N 38.49 E
Ancipa, Lago di ⊜ 70 37.50 N 14.34 E
Anclitas, Cayo I 240p 20.48 N 78.54 W
Anclote ≃ 220 39.59 N 88.49 W
Anclote Keys II 220 28.12 N 82.51 W
Ancón, Méx. 234 22.35 N 101.11 W
Ancón, Perú 248 11.47 S 77.11 W
Ancona, It. 66 43.38 N 13.30 E
Ancona, S. Afr. 158 27.40 S 26.32 E
Ancona ▫⁴ 66 43.33 N 13.10 E
Ancón de Sardinas, Bahía de C 246 1.30 N 79.00 W
Ancoraimes 248 15.54 S 68.58 W
Ancram 210 42.03 N 73.38 W
Ancre ≃ 50 49.54 N 2.28 E
Ancrum 46 55.31 N 2.35 W
Ancuabe 154 12.58 S 39.54 E
Ancud 254 41.52 S 73.50 W
Ancud, Golfo de C 254 42.05 S 73.00 W
Ancy-le-Franc 50 47.46 N 4.10 E
Ancy-sur-Moselle 56 49.03 N 6.04 E
Anda, Pil. 116 16.17 N 119.57 E
Anda, Zhg. 89 46.24 N 125.19 E
Andacollo, Arg 252 37.11 S 70.41 W
Andacollo, Chile 252 30.14 S 71.06 W
Andahuaylas 248 13.39 S 73.23 W
Andaingo 157b 18.12 S 48.17 E
Andāl 124 23.36 N 87.12 E
Andalgalá 252 27.36 S 66.19 W
Andalo 64 46.10 N 11.00 E
Åndalsnes 26 62.34 N 7.42 E
Andalucía ▫⁴ 34 37.30 N 4.30 W
Andalucía ▫⁹ 34 37.36 N 4.30 W
Andalusia, Al., U.S. 194 31.19 N 86.29 W
Andalusia, Pa., U.S. 285 40.04 N 74.58 W
Andaman and Nicobar Islands ▫⁸ 110 11.00 N 93.00 E
Andaman Basin ✢¹ 12 10.00 N 94.00 E
Andamanen
 → Andaman Islands II 110 12.00 N 92.45 E
Andaman Islands II 110 12.00 N 92.45 E
Andaman Sea ∓² 110 10.00 N 95.00 E
Andamarca, Bol. 248 18.49 S 67.31 W
Andamarca, Perú 248 11.46 S 74.44 W
Andamooka 166 30.27 S 137.12 E
Andance 62 45.14 N 4.47 E
Andapa 157b 14.39 S 49.39 E
Andara 152 18.03 S 21.27 E
Andaraí 255 12.48 S 41.20 W
Andaraí ◆⁸ 287a 22.56 S 43.15 W
Andarax ≃ 34 36.48 N 2.26 W
Andaray 248 15.49 S 72.50 W
Andau 61 47.46 N 17.02 E
Andechs, Kloster ▿¹ 64 47.58 N 11.10 E
Andeer 58 46.36 N 9.26 E
Andelfingen 58 47.36 N 8.41 E
Andelle ≃ 50 49.19 N 1.14 E
Andelot 58 48.15 N 5.18 E
Andelot-en-Montagne 58 46.51 N 5.56 E
Andelu 261 48.53 N 1.50 E
Anden
 → Andes ⋏ 18 20.00 S 67.00 W
Andenes 24 69.16 N 16.08 E
Andenne 56 50.29 N 5.06 E
Andéranboukane 150 15.26 N 3.02 E
Ånderdalen Nasjonalpark ♦ 24 69.14 N 17.17 E
Anderlecht 50 50.50 N 4.18 E
Anderlues 50 50.24 N 4.16 E
Andermatt 58 46.38 N 8.36 E
Andernach 56 50.26 N 7.24 E
Andersen Air Force Base ■ 174p 13.35 N 144.56 E
Anderslöv 41 55.26 N 13.22 E
Anderson, Al., U.S. 194 34.55 N 87.15 W
Anderson, Ak., U.S. 180 64.21 N 149.10 W
Anderson, Ca., U.S. 204 40.26 N 122.17 W
Anderson, In., U.S. 218 40.06 N 85.40 W
Anderson, Mo., U.S. 194 36.39 N 94.26 W
Anderson, S.C., U.S. 192 34.30 N 82.39 W
Anderson, Tx., U.S. 222 30.29 N 95.59 W
Anderson ▫⁶, Ky., U.S. 218 38.05 N 84.55 W
Anderson ▫⁶, Tx., U.S. 222 31.47 N 95.40 W
Anderson ≃ 180 69.43 N 128.58 W
Anderson, Mount ▲ 224 47.43 N 123.20 W
Anderson Creek ≃ 194 33.18 N 94.26 W
Anderson Dam 202 43.30 N 115.30 W
Anderson Inlet C 169 38.39 S 145.48 E
Anderson Island I 224 47.10 N 122.42 W
Anderson Lake ⊜ 182 50.41 N 122.07 W
Anderson Lake ⊜¹ 226 37.11 N 121.37 W
Anderson Peak ▲ 228 34.08 N 116.53 W
Anderson Ranch Reservoir ⊜¹ 202 43.25 N 115.20 W
Andersonville 218 39.30 N 85.17 W
Andersonville National Historic Site ⊥ 192 32.12 N 84.07 W
Anderstorp 26 57.17 N 13.38 E
Anderten 52 52.21 N 9.51 E
Anderton 262 53.17 N 2.32 W
Andes, Col. 246 5.40 N 75.53 W
Andes, N.Y., U.S. 210 42.12 N 74.47 W
Andes ⋏ 18 20.00 S 67.00 W
Andes, Lake ⊜ 198 43.11 N 98.27 W
Andeville 50 49.15 N 2.10 E
Andevoranto 157b 18.57 S 49.06 E
Andfjorden Ʉ 24 69.10 N 16.20 E
Andheri ◆⁸ 272c 19.07 N 72.51 E
Andhra Lake ⊜ 122 18.54 N 73.32 E
Andhra Pradesh ▫³ 122 16.00 N 79.00 E
Andijk 52 52.45 N 5.12 E
Andijskoje Kojsu ≃ 84 42.47 N 46.48 E
Andikíthira I 38 35.52 N 23.18 E
Andilamena 157b 17.01 S 48.35 E
Andimákhia 38 36.48 N 27.07 E
Andīmeshk 128 32.27 N 48.21 E
Andingpu 102 37.58 N 107.02 E
Anding Zhan 105 39.38 N 116.29 E
Andíparos I 38 37.00 N 25.03 E
Andirá ≃ 250 2.45 S 56.49 W
Andirá, Riozinho do ≃ 248 9.21 S 67.31 W
Andırın 130 37.34 N 36.20 E
Andirlang 120 37.36 N 83.50 E
Andisleben 54 51.04 N 10.56 E
Ándissa 38 39.14 N 25.59 E
Andižan 85 40.45 N 72.22 E
Andižan ▫⁴ 85 40.45 N 72.15 E
Andkhvoy 120 36.56 N 65.08 E
Andlau-au-Val 58 48.23 N 7.25 E
Ando 270 34.37 N 135.46 E
Andoam 164 12.40 S 141.55 E
Andoas 246 2.50 S 76.30 W
Andoga ≃ 76 59.10 N 37.27 E
Andogskaja gr'ada ▲ 76 59.25 N 37.30 E
Andolsheim 58 48.04 N 7.25 E
Andomskij Pogost 24 61.14 N 36.36 E
Andong, Taehan 98 36.35 N 128.44 E
Andong, Zhg. 100 30.16 N 121.13 E
Andong-chŏsuji ⊜¹ 98 36.41 N 128.49 E
Andong-ni 98 39.28 N 127.27 E
Andora 62 43.59 N 8.08 E
Andorf 60 48.23 N 13.35 E
Andorno Micca 62 45.37 N 8.03 E
Andorra 34 42.30 N 1.31 E
Andorra ▫¹, Europe 22 42.30 N 1.30 E
Andorra ▫¹, Europe 34 42.30 N 1.30 E
Andorre
 → Andorra ▫¹ 34 42.30 N 1.30 E
Andover, Eng., U.K. 42 51.13 N 1.28 W
Andover, Ct., U.S. 207 41.44 N 72.22 W
Andover, Me., U.S. 188 44.38 N 70.45 W
Andover, Ma., U.S. 207 42.39 N 71.08 W
Andover, N.J., U.S. 210 40.59 N 74.44 W
Andover, N.Y. U.S. 210 42.09 N 77.47 W
Andover, Oh., U.S. 214 41.36 N 80.34 W
Andover, S.D., U.S. 198 45.24 N 97.54 W
Andowj 123 37.02 N 71.27 E
Andøya I 24 69.08 N 15.54 E
Andradas 256 22.04 S 46.34 W
Andrade Pinto 256 22.14 S 43.22 W
Andradina 255 20.54 S 51.23 W
Andramasina 157b 19.11 S 47.35 E
Andranopasy 157b 21.17 S 43.44 E
Andranovory 157b 23.08 S 44.10 E
Andrate 62 45.32 N 7.53 E
Andreafsky ≃ 180 62.02 N 163.16 W
Andreafsky, East Fork ≃ 180 62.03 N 163.07 W
Andreanof Islands II 180 52.00 N 176.00 W
Andreapol' 76 56.39 N 32.15 E
Andreas, I. of Man 44 54.22 N 4.26 W
Andreas, Pa., U.S 208 40.45 N 75.48 W
André Félix, Parc National ♦ 146 9.25 N 23.20 E
Andrejevka, Kaz. 86 52.59 N 67.23 E
Andrejevka, Kaz. 86 45.50 N 80.35 E
Andrejevka, Ross. 80 55.42 N 54.23 E
Andrejevka, Ross. 80 52.19 N 51.55 E
Andrejevka, Ross. 82 55.07 N 38.37 E
Andrejevka, Ross. 82 55.59 N 37.08 E
Andrejevka, Ukr. 78 49.32 N 36.38 E
Andrejevka, Ukr. 78 47.06 N 36.35 E
Andrejevka, Ukr. 83 48.49 N 37.33 E
Andrejevka, Ukr. 83 47.28 N 37.39 E
Andrejevo 80 55.56 N 41.08 E
Andrejevo-Ivanovka 78 47.28 N 30.28 E
Andrejevsk 88 58.06 N 114.08 E
Andrejevskaja 80 47.21 N 43.02 E
Andrejevskoje, Ross. 82 54.23 N 36.12 E
Andrejevskoje, Ross. 82 56.24 N 39.01 E
Andrejevskoje, Ross. 82 55.46 N 36.35 E
Andrejkoviči 76 52.25 N 33.00 E
Andrelândia 256 21.44 S 44.18 W
Andrésy 261 48.59 N 2.04 E
Andretta 68 40.56 N 15.19 E
Andrew 182 53.53 N 112.21 W
Andrew, Mount ▲ 162 32.52 S 122.56 E
Andrews, In., U.S. 216 40.51 N 85.36 W
Andrews, Mi., U.S. 216 41.57 N 86.22 W
Andrews, N.C., U.S. 192 35.12 N 83.49 W
Andrews, S.C., U.S. 192 33.18 N 79.17 W
Andrews, Tx., U.S. 196 32.19 N 102.32 W
Andrews Air Force Base ■ 208 38.48 N 76.52 W
Andrews Manor 284c 38.49 N 76.54 W
Andrezel 261 48.37 N 2.49 E
Andrézieux Bouthéon 62 45.32 N 4.16 E
Andria 68 41.13 N 16.18 E
Andriamena 157b 17.26 S 47.30 E
Andriandampy 157b 22.45 S 45.41 E
Andriba 157b 17.36 S 46.55 E
Andrija, Otok I 36 43.02 N 15.45 E
Andrijevica 38 42.44 N 19.46 E
Androka 157b 25.02 S 44.05 E
Andronovskoje 76 60.39 N 34.46 E
Andropov
 → Rybinsk 76 58.03 N 38.52 E
Ándros 38 37.50 N 24.57 E
Andros I, Ba. 238 24.26 N 77.57 W
Ándros I, Ellás 38 37.45 N 24.42 E
Androscoggin ≃ 188 43.55 N 69.55 W
Androsovka 80 52.41 N 49.35 E
Andros Town 238 24.43 N 77.47 W
Āndrott Island I 122 10.50 N 73.41 E
Andrupene 76 56.11 N 27.23 E
Andr'ušino 86 59.12 N 62.59 E
Andrušovka 78 50.01 N 29.01 E
Andrychów 30 49.52 N 19.21 E
Andudu 154 2.29 N 28.41 E
Andújar 34 38.03 N 4.04 W
Andulo 152 11.30 S 16.45 E
Anduze 62 44.03 N 3.59 E
Andžijevskij 84 44.14 N 43.05 E
Âne, Dos d' ▲ 241o 16.19 N 61.46 W
Aneby 26 57.50 N 14.48 E
Anécho 150 6.14 N 1.36 E
Anecón Grande, Cerro ▲ 254 41.25 S 70.16 W
Anefis i-n-Darane 150 18.03 N 0.36 E
Anegada I 238 18.45 N 64.20 W
Anegada, Bahía C 254 40.15 S 62.15 W
Anegada Passage Ʉ 238 18.30 N 63.40 W
Anegam 200 32.22 N 112.01 W
Anegasaki 268 35.28 N 140.02 E
Anelngauhat 175f 20.14 S 169.44 E
Añelo 252 38.21 S 68.47 W
Anémata, Passe d' Ʉ 175f 20.31 S 166.12 E
Anepahan Peak ▲ 116 9.40 N 118.25 E
Aneroid 184 49.43 N 107.20 W
Anet 50 48.51 N 1.26 E
Aneta 198 47.40 N 97.59 W
Aneto, Pico de ▲ 34 42.38 N 0.40 E
Aney 146 19.24 N 12.56 E
Anfeng, Zhg. 100 33.06 N 120.08 E
Anfeng, Zhg. 100 32.44 N 120.24 E
Anfengqiao 100 26.41 N 118.08 E
Anfo 64 45.46 N 10.29 E
Anfu 100 27.23 N 114.37 E
Anfuzhen, Zhg. 107 28.47 N 104.41 E
Anfuzhen, Zhg. 107 29.21 N 105.28 E
Anga 88 53.58 N 106.12 E
Angamacutiro [de la Unión] 234 20.10 N 101.41 W
Angamos, Punta › 252 23.01 S 70.32 W
Angangueo 234 19.37 N 100.18 W
Ang'angxi 89 47.09 N 123.48 E
An'ganka 89 52.18 N 126.17 E
Angao 100 33.08 N 112.22 E
Angar 164 3.39 S 130.50 E
Angara ≃ 88 58.06 N 93.00 E
Angara-Débou 150 11.19 N 3.03 E
Angarbaka 140 9.44 N 24.44 E
Āngāria 126 22.29 N 90.22 E
Angarsk 88 52.34 N 103.54 E
Angas ≃ 168b 35.23 S 138.59 E
Angas Downs 162 24.49 S 132.14 E
Angas Hills ⋏² 162 22.55 S 128.00 E
Angastaco 252 25.38 S 66.11 W
Angaston 168b 34.30 S 139.02 E
Angat ≃ 116 14.53 N 120.46 E
Angatuba 255 23.29 S 48.25 W
Angaul 88 53.49 N 100.18 E
Angaur I 175b 6.54 N 134.09 E
Angden Pass)(124 29.43 N 86.17 E
Angduo 102 32.20 N 98.55 E
Ånge 26 62.31 N 15.37 E
Ángel, Salto (Angel Falls) ⌊ 246 5.57 N 62.30 W
Angel City 220 28.20 N 80.40 W
Ángel de la Guarda, Isla I 232 29.20 N 113.25 W
Angeles 116 15.09 N 120.35 E
Angeles National Forest ♦ 280 34.15 N 117.56 W
Angel Etcheverry 258 35.02 S 58.04 W
Angel Falls
 → Ángel, Salto ⌊ 246 5.57 N 62.30 W
Ängelholm 41 56.15 N 12.51 E
Ängelholm flygplats ⊠ 41 56.20 N 12.51 E
Angelica 210 42.18 N 78.00 W
Angelina ▫⁶ 222 31.17 N 94.42 W
Angelina ≃ 194 30.53 N 94.12 W
Angelina, East Fork ≃ 222 31.50 N 94.56 W
Angel Island I 282 37.52 N 122.26 W
Angellala Creek ≃ 166 26.40 S 146.08 E
Angeln ◆¹ 41 54.39 N 9.44 E
Angelo ≃ 162 23.43 S 117.45 E
Angel R. Cabaca 234 18.35 N 95.26 W
Ängelsberg 40 59.58 N 16.00 E
Angels Camp 226 38.04 N 120.33 W
Angels Creek ≃ 226 38.01 N 120.33 W
Angelus, Lake ⊜ 281 42.41 N 83.20 W
Angemuk ▲ 164 3.30 S 138.34 E
Anger 61 47.16 N 15.42 E
Angera 62 45.46 N 8.35 E
Angerbach ≃ 263 51.23 N 6.44 E
Angereb ≃ 144 13.51 N 36.08 E
Angeren 52 51.55 N 5.58 E
Angerhausen ◆⁸ 263 51.23 N 6.44 E
Ångermanälven ≃ 26 62.48 N 17.56 E
Ångermanland ▫⁹ 26 63.30 N 18.05 E
Angermund ◆⁸ 263 51.20 N 6.47 E
Angermünde 54 53.01 N 14.00 E
Angern, Dtsch. 54 52.21 N 11.44 E
Angern, Öst. 61 48.22 N 16.50 E
Angers 32 47.28 N 0.33 W
Angerville 50 48.19 N 2.00 E
Angervilliers 261 48.36 N 2.04 E
Ängesön I 26 63.43 N 20.55 E
Angevillers 56 49.23 N 6.02 E
Anggowala, Bukit ▲ 112 4.15 S 121.44 E
Anghelu Ruiu, Necropoli ⊥ 71 40.38 N 8.20 E
Anghiari 66 43.32 N 12.03 E
Angical 255 12.00 S 44.42 W
Angical do Piauí 250 6.05 S 42.44 W
Angicos 250 5.40 S 36.36 W
Angier 192 35.30 N 78.44 W
Angijak Island I 176 65.40 N 62.15 W
Angikuni Lake ⊜ 176 62.13 N 99.50 W
Angke, Kali ≃ 269e 6.06 S 106.46 E
Angkor Wat ⊥ 110 13.26 N 103.52 E
Ângk Tasaôm 110 11.01 N 104.41 E
Anglais, Baie des C 186 49.15 N 68.07 W
Anglais, Jardin ♦ 261 48.38 N 1.49 E
Anglais, Rivière des (English) ≃ 206 45.13 N 73.50 W
Angle 42 51.41 N 5.06 W
Angle Inlet 198 49.21 N 95.04 W
Anglem, Mount ▲ 172 46.44 S 167.56 E
Anglesea 169 38.25 S 144.11 E
Anglesey I 44 53.17 N 4.22 W
Anglet 32 43.29 N 1.31 W
Angleterre
 → England ▫⁸ 28 52.30 N 1.30 W
Angleton 222 29.10 N 95.25 W
Anglezarke Moor ◆³ 262 53.40 N 2.33 W
Anglezarke Reservoir ⊜¹ 262 53.39 N 2.35 W
Angling ≃ 184 56.45 N 93.36 W
Angling Lake ⊜ 184 53.55 N 93.52 W
Anglona ◆¹ 71 40.50 N 8.45 E
Anglo-Normandes, Îles
 → Channel Islands II 28 49.20 N 2.20 W
Anglure 50 48.35 N 3.49 E
Angmagssalik 176 65.36 N 37.41 W
Angmering 42 50.48 N 0.28 W
Ang Mo Kio 271c 1.22 N 103.51 E
Ango 154 4.02 N 25.52 E
Angoche 154 16.15 S 39.54 E
Angoche, Ilha I 154 16.20 S 39.50 E
Angohrān 128 26.35 N 57.54 E
Angol 252 37.48 S 72.43 W
Angola, In., U.S. 216 41.38 N 84.59 W
Angola, N.Y., U.S. 210 42.38 N 79.01 W
Angola ▫¹, Afr. 138 12.30 S 18.30 E
Angola ▫¹, Afr. 152 12.30 S 18.30 E
Angola Basin ✢¹ 10 15.00 S 3.00 E
Angola Lake Shore 214 42.37 N 79.05 W
Angono 269f 14.31 N 121.09 E
Angoon 180 57.30 N 134.35 W
Angora
 → Ankara 130 39.56 N 32.52 E
Angoram 164 4.04 S 144.04 E
Angostura, Méx. 232 25.22 N 108.11 W
Angostura
 → Ciudad Bolívar, Ven. 246 8.08 N 63.33 W
Angostura, Presa de la ⊜¹ 234 16.10 N 92.40 W
Angostura Reservoir ⊜¹ 198 43.18 N 103.27 W
Angoulême 32 45.39 N 0.09 E
Angoumois ▫⁹ 32 45.30 N 0.05 W
Angra, Meos I 164 2.42 S 134.50 E
Angra do Heroísmo 148a 38.39 N 27.13 W
Angra do Heroísmo ▫⁵ 148a 38.50 N 27.30 W
Angra dos Reis 256 23.00 S 44.18 W
Angren 85 41.01 N 70.12 E
Angren ≃ 85 40.48 N 68.53 E
Angri 68 40.44 N 14.34 E
Angrignon Zoological Park ♦ 275a 45.26 N 73.36 W
Angrogna 62 44.50 N 7.13 E
Ängsö 40 59.32 N 16.51 E
Ängsö Nationalpark ♦ 40 59.39 N 18.44 E
Ang Thong 110 14.35 N 100.27 E
Angu 154 3.33 N 24.28 E
Angu ≃ 256 21.48 S 42.30 W
Angualasto 252 30.03 S 69.09 W
Anguang 89 45.31 N 123.45 E
Anguchang 107 29.30 N 103.39 E
Anguciana, Cerro ▲ 236 8.50 N 83.07 W
Anguilas, Arroyo ≃ 288 34.26 S 58.31 W
Anguilla 194 32.58 N 90.49 W
Anguilla ▫², N.A. 230 18.15 N 63.05 W
Anguilla ▫², N.A. 238 18.15 N 63.05 W
Anguilla Cays II 238 23.31 N 79.33 W
Anguillara Sabazia 66 42.05 N 12.16 E
Anguillara Veneta 64 45.08 N 11.53 E
Anguille, Cape › 186 47.55 N 59.25 W
Anguli Nur ⊜ 98 41.13 N 114.32 E
Angumu 154 0.07 S 27.42 E
Anguo 98 38.25 N 115.19 E
Anguozhuang 105 39.44 N 117.59 E
Anguruga 164 14.00 S 136.29 E
Angus 212 44.19 N 79.53 W
Angus Place 170 33.20 S 150.06 E
Angustura 256 21.45 S 42.41 W
Angusville 184 50.44 N 101.01 W
Angwa ≃ 154 15.51 S 30.35 E
Angwin 226 38.34 N 122.26 W
Angyalföld ◆⁸ 264c 47.33 N 19.05 E
Angyō 268 35.51 N 139.46 E
An Hai, Viet 110 15.13 N 108.56 E
Anhai, Zhg. 100 24.45 N 118.27 E
Anhalt ▫⁹ 54 52.00 N 11.30 E
Anholt 52 51.52 N 6.27 E
Anholt I 26 56.42 N 11.34 E
Anhovo 64 46.03 N 13.37 E
Anhua 102 28.18 N 111.14 E
Anhuai 100 33.04 N 117.50 E
Anhui (Anhwei) ▫⁴ 100 32.00 N 117.00 E
Anhŭng 98 36.41 N 126.10 E
Anhwei
 → Anhui ▫⁴ 100 32.00 N 117.00 E
Aniak 180 61.35 N 159.33 W
Aniak ≃ 180 61.34 N 159.30 W
Aniakchak National Monument ♦ 180 56.50 N 157.50 W
Anibare Bay C 174b 0.32 S 166.57 E
Aniche 50 50.20 N 3.15 E
Anicuns 255 16.28 S 49.58 W
Anié 150 7.45 N 1.12 E
Anié ≃ 150 7.40 N 1.18 E
Anie, Pic d' ▲ 32 42.57 N 0.43 W
Aniene ≃ 66 41.56 N 12.30 E
Anif 64 47.45 N 13.04 E
Anik ◆⁸ 272c 19.02 N 72.53 E
Anikino, Ross. 86 56.32 N 73.56 E
Anikino, Ross. 88 53.26 N 120.20 E
Anikovo 76 59.23 N 43.45 E
Anil 250 2.32 S 44.14 W
Anil, Rio do ≃ 287a 22.59 S 43.21 W
Animas 200 31.56 N 108.48 W
Animas ≃ 200 36.43 N 108.13 W
Animas Peak ▲ 200 31.35 N 108.47 W
Animas Valley V 200 31.45 N 108.50 W
Anin 110 15.40 N 97.46 E
Anina 38 45.05 N 21.51 E
Anipemza 84 40.27 N 43.37 E
Aniskino 82 55.54 N 38.06 E
Añisoc 152 1.51 N 10.46 E
Anita, Ia., U.S. 198 41.26 N 94.45 W
Anita, Pa., U.S. 214 41.00 N 78.58 W
Anıtkaya 130 38.57 N 30.18 E
Aniva 89 46.43 N 142.32 E
Aniva, mys › 89 46.01 N 143.25 E
Aniva, zaliv C 89 46.16 N 142.48 E
Anivorano 157b 18.44 S 48.58 E
Anivorano Nord 157b 12.44 S 49.13 E
Aniwa I 175f 19.17 S 169.35 E
Anizy-le-Château 50 49.30 N 3.27 E
Anjad 120 22.02 N 75.03 E
Anjan 26 63.41 N 12.49 E
Anjangaon 120 21.10 N 77.18 E
Anjār, India 120 23.08 N 70.01 E
'Anjar, Lubnān 132 33.42 N 35.54 E
'Anjarah 132 32.18 N 35.45 E
Anjavimihavana 157b 12.32 S 49.16 E
Anji 106 30.43 N 119.41 E
Anjiabe 157b 12.07 S 49.20 E
Anjiang 105 40.45 N 117.38 E
Anjigami Lake ⊜ 190 47.51 N 84.34 W
Anjō 94 34.57 N 137.05 E
Anjou 206 45.36 N 73.33 W
Anjou ▫⁹ 32 47.20 N 0.30 W
Anjozorobe 157b 18.24 S 47.52 E
Anju, C.M.I.K. 98 39.36 N 125.40 E
Anju, Zhg. 100 31.45 N 113.11 E
Anju, Zhg. 107 30.21 N 105.27 E
Anjudin 24 62.33 N 58.12 E
Anjuzhen 107 29.59 N 106.02 E
Anka 150 12.07 N 5.55 E
Ankang 102 32.42 N 109.05 E
Ankara 130 39.56 N 32.52 E
Ankara ▫⁴ 130 39.50 N 32.50 E
Ankara ≃ 130 39.51 N 31.55 E
Ankaramena 157b 21.57 S 46.39 E
Ankaratra ⋏ 157b 19.25 S 47.12 E
Ankarimbelo 157b 22.08 S 47.20 E
Ankaroaka ▲ 157b 17.48 S 48.32 E
Ankarsrum 26 57.42 N 16.19 E
Ankasakasa 157b 16.21 S 44.52 E
Ankata 80 50.44 N 51.34 E
Ankavandra 157b 18.46 S 45.18 E
Ankazoabo 157b 22.18 S 44.31 E
Ankazobe 157b 18.21 S 47.07 E
Ankazomiriotra 157b 19.38 S 46.32 E
Ankeny 190 41.43 N 93.36 W
An Khe 110 13.57 N 108.39 E
Ankilimalinika 157b 22.58 S 43.45 E
Ankilizato 157b 20.25 S 45.01 E
Anking
 → Anqing 100 30.31 N 117.02 E
Ankisabe 157b 19.17 S 46.29 E
Anklam 54 53.51 N 13.41 E
Ankleshwar 120 21.36 N 73.00 E
Ankober 144 9.35 N 39.44 E
Ankoro 154 6.45 S 26.57 E
Ankororoka 157b 25.30 S 45.11 E
Ankou 100 25.03 N 113.24 E
An'kovo 80 56.57 N 39.57 E
Ankpa 150 7.23 N 7.37 E
Ankum 52 52.32 N 7.52 E
Ankwe ≃ 150 8.03 N 9.26 E
Anlinnuoer 98 41.11 N 114.31 E
Anliu 100 23.42 N 115.42 E
Anloga 150 5.47 N 0.50 E
Anlong 102 25.02 N 105.31 E
Ânlóng Vêng 110 14.14 N 104.05 E
Anlu 100 31.17 N 113.40 E
Anma-do I 98 35.21 N 126.02 E
Anmyŏn-do I 98 36.30 N 126.22 E
Ånn ⊜ 26 63.16 N 12.34 E
Ann, Cape ›, Ant. 9 66.10 S 51.22 E
Ann, Cape ›, Ma., U.S. 283 42.39 N 70.38 W
Anna, Ross. 78 51.29 N 40.25 E
Anna, Il., U.S. 194 37.27 N 89.14 W
Anna, Oh., U.S. 216 40.23 N 84.10 W
Anna, Tx., U.S. 196 33.21 N 96.33 W
Anna, Lake ⊜¹ 188 38.04 N 77.45 W
Annaba (Bône) 148 36.54 N 7.46 E
Annaba ▫⁵ 148 36.50 N 8.00 E
An-Nabatīyah ▫⁴ 132 33.20 N 35.30 E
An-Nabatīyah at-Tahtā 132 33.23 N 35.29 E
Annaberg, Öst. 61 47.52 N 15.22 E
Annaberg, Öst. 64 47.31 N 13.26 E
Annaberg-Buchholz 54 50.35 N 13.00 E
An-Nabī Shīt 132 33.52 N 36.07 E
An-Nabk 130 34.01 N 36.44 E
An-Nabqīyah I 128 26.44 N 36.01 E
Annaburg 54 51.44 N 13.03 E
Annaburger Heide ◆³ 54 51.40 N 13.05 E
An-Nafūd ◆² 128 28.30 N 41.00 E
Annagassan 48 53.53 N 6.20 W
Annahütte 54 51.34 N 13.53 E
An-Najaf 128 31.59 N 44.20 E
An-Najaf ▫⁴ 128 31.00 N 44.00 E
Annaka 94 36.19 N 138.54 E
An-Nakhl, Misr 140 29.55 N 33.45 E
An-Nakhl, Sūrīy. 132 33.00 N 36.07 E
Annalee ≃ 48 54.03 N 7.24 W
Annalee Heights 208 38.51 N 77.10 W
Annalong 48 54.06 N 5.53 W
Annam
 → Trung Phan ▫⁹ 110 15.00 N 108.00 E
Anna Maria 220 27.31 N 82.44 W
Anna Maria Island I 220 27.30 N 82.43 W
An-Nāmir 132 32.47 N 36.13 E
Annamitique, Chaîne ⋏ 110 17.00 N 106.00 E
Annan 44 54.59 N 3.16 W
Annan ≃ 44 54.59 N 3.16 W
Annanberg 164 4.55 S 144.40 E
Annandale, Austl. 166 21.57 S 148.22 E
Annandale, Mn., U.S. 190 45.15 N 94.07 W
Annandale, N.J., U.S. 210 40.38 N 74.52 W
Annandale, Va., U.S. 208 38.49 N 77.11 W
Annandale V 44 55.10 N 3.25 W
Annandale-on-Hudson 210 42.01 N 73.54 W
Anna Pink, Bahía C 254 45.50 S 74.50 W
Anna Plains 162 19.17 S 121.37 E
Anna Point › 174b 0.30 S 166.56 E
Annapolis 208 38.58 N 76.29 W
Annapolis Basin C 186 44.39 N 65.42 W
Annapolis Royal 186 44.45 N 65.31 W
Annapūrna ▲ 124 28.34 N 83.50 E
Annapūrnapratham ▲ 124 28.31 N 84.08 E
An-Naqīrah ∓⁴ 128 27.53 N 48.15 E
Ann Arbor 216 42.16 N 83.43 W
Ann Arbor Municipal Airport ⊠ 281 42.14 N 83.45 W
Anna Regina 246 7.16 N 58.30 W
Annaricken Brook ≃ 285 40.03 N 74.42 W
An-Nāṣirīyah, 'Irāq 128 31.02 N 46.16 E
An-Nāṣirīyah, Sūrīy. 130 33.52 N 36.49 E
Annaspan ⊜ 158 28.33 S 25.47 E
An-Nawfalīb 140 15.52 N 32.32 E
An-Nawfalīyah 146 30.47 N 17.50 E
An-Nazlah 132 31.32 N 34.29 E
An-Nazlat 142 29.19 N 30.39 E
Annbank 44 55.28 N 4.30 W
Annean, Lake ⊜ 162 26.54 S 118.14 E
Anne Arundel ▫⁶ 208 38.59 N 76.30 W
Annebault 50 49.15 N 0.04 E
Annecy 58 45.54 N 6.07 E
Annecy, Lac d' ⊜ 58 45.51 N 6.11 E
Annecy-le-Vieux 58 45.55 N 6.09 E
Annemasse 58 46.12 N 6.15 E
Annen 263 51.27 N 7.22 E
Annenkov Island I 244 54.29 S 37.05 W
Annenskij Most 76 60.45 N 37.10 E
Annenskoje 86 53.08 N 60.26 E
Anner ≃ 48 52.22 N 7.39 W
Annestown 48 52.08 N 7.17 W
Annet I 42a 49.54 N 6.21 W
Annet-sur-Marne 261 48.56 N 2.43 E
Annette 182 55.03 N 131.34 W
Annette Island I 182 55.10 N 131.28 W
Annevoie-Rouillon 56 50.21 N 4.50 E
Annezin 50 50.32 N 2.37 E
Annfield Plain 44 54.51 N 1.45 W
An Nhon 110 13.53 N 109.06 E
Anniangniang 89 51.33 N 125.49 E
Annicco 62 45.14 N 9.52 E
An-Nīl ▫⁴ 140 19.00 N 33.00 E
An-Nīl al-Azraq ▫⁴ 140 12.00 N 34.00 E
Anning 102 24.59 N 102.18 E
Anningdu 102 36.56 N 104.31 E
Anninger ▲ 264b 48.03 N 16.15 E
Annino 265a 59.46 N 30.03 E
Anninskije Mineral'nyje Vody 89 52.44 N 140.12 E
Annisquam 283 42.39 N 70.41 W
Annisquam ≃ 283 42.39 N 70.41 W
Anniston 194 33.39 N 85.49 W
Annobón I 138 1.25 S 5.36 E
Annonay 62 45.14 N 4.40 E

≃ River — Fluß — Río — Rivière — Rio
≅ Canal — Kanal — Canal — Canal — Canal
⌊ Waterfall, Rapids — Wasserfall, Stromschnellen — Cascada, Rápidos — Chute d'eau, Rapides — Cascata, Rápidos
Ʉ Strait — Meeresstraße — Estrecho — Détroit — Estreito
C Bay, Gulf — Bucht, Golf — Bahía, Golfo — Baie, Golfe — Baía, Golfo
⊜ Lake, Lakes — See, Seen — Lago, Lagos — Lac, Lacs — Lago, Lagos
≡ Swamp — Sumpf — Pantano — Marais — Pântano
⊓ Ice Features, Glacier — Eis- und Gletscherformen — Accidentes Glaciales — Formes glaciaires — Acidentes glaciares
∓ Other Hydrographic Features — Andere Hydrographische Objekte — Otros Elementos Hidrográficos — Autres données hydrographiques — Outros acidentes hidrográficos

✢ Submarine Features — Untermeerische Objekte — Accidentes Submarinos — Formes de relief sous-marin — Acidentes submarinos
▫ Political Unit — Politische Einheit — Unidad Politica — Entité politique — Unidade política
▿ Cultural Institution — Kulturelle Institution — Institución Cultural — Institution culturelle — Instituição cultural
⊥ Historical Site — Historische Stätte — Sitio Histórico — Site historique — Sitio histórico
♦ Recreational Site — Erholungs- und Ferienort — Sitio de Recreo — Centre de loisirs — Area de Lazer
⊠ Airport — Flughafen — Aeropuerto — Aéroport — Aeroporto
■ Military Installation — Militäranlage — Instalación Militar — Installation militaire — Instalação militar
◆ Miscellaneous — Verschiedenes — Misceláneo — Divers — Diversos

	English	Berg	Montaña	Montanha	Montagne
∧	Mountain	Berg	Montaña	Montanha	Montagne
∧	Mountains	Gebirge	Montañas	Montanhas	Montagnes
⋏	Pass	Paß	Paso	Passo	Col / Passo
V	Valley, Canyon	Tal, Cañon	Valle, Cañón	Vale, Canhão	Vallée, Canyon
≃	Plain	Ebene	Llano	Planície	Plaine
›	Cape	Kap	Cabo	Cabo	Cap
I	Island	Insel	Isla	Ilha	Île
II	Islands	Inseln	Islas	Ilhas	Îles
⊥	Other Topographic Features	Andere Topographische Objekte	Otros Elementos Topográficos	Outros acidentes topográficos	Autres données topographiques

ESPAÑOL

Nombre	Página	Lat.°′	Long.°′ W = Oeste
Arbél	132	32.49 N	35.29 E
Arbesbach	61	48.29 N	14.57 E
Arbia ≃	66	43.08 N	11.28 E
Arboga	40	59.24 N	15.50 E
Arbogaån ≃	40	59.26 N	16.04 E
Arbois	58	46.54 N	5.46 E
Arboledas	252	36.53 S	61.29 W
Arboletes	246	8.51 N	76.26 W
Arbolito, Cerro ∧[2]	286d	12.10 S	76.57 W
Arbon	58	47.31 N	9.26 E
Arbonne	50	48.25 N	2.34 E
Arborea	71	39.46 N	8.35 E
Arborea ◆[1]	71	39.50 N	8.50 E
Arborfield	184	53.06 N	103.39 W
Arborg	184	50.55 N	97.15 W
Arbrå	26	61.29 N	16.23 E
Arbroath	46	56.34 N	2.35 W
Arbu, Monte ∧	71	39.15 N	9.27 E
Arbuckle	226	39.01 N	122.03 W
Arbuckle, Lake ⊜	220	27.41 N	81.24 W
Arbuckle Creek ≃	220	27.26 N	81.17 W
Arbuckle Mountains ⋏	196	34.25 N	97.20 W
Arbuckles, Lake of the ⊜[1]	196	34.25 N	97.00 W
Arbury Hills	216	41.33 N	87.51 W
Arbus	71	39.32 N	8.36 E
Arbutus Lake ⊜	276	40.31 N	74.10 W
Arbuzinka	78	47.53 N	31.19 E
Arbuzovo	76	56.21 N	32.27 E
Arc ≃, Fr.	62	43.31 N	5.07 E
Arc ≃, Fr.	62	45.34 N	6.12 E
Arc, Bayou des ≃	194	35.00 N	91.30 W
Arcachon	32	44.37 N	1.12 W
Arcachon, Bassin d' c	32	44.40 N	1.10 W
Arcadas	256	22.42 S	46.52 W
Arcade, It.	64	45.47 N	12.13 E
Arcade, Ca., U.S.	226	34.02 N	118.15 W
Arcade, N.Y., U.S.	210	42.32 N	78.25 W
Arcadia, Ca., U.S.	228	34.08 N	118.02 W
Arcadia, Fl., U.S.	220	27.12 N	81.51 W
Arcadia, In., U.S.	218	40.10 N	86.01 W
Arcadia, Ia., U.S.	198	42.01 N	95.02 W
Arcadia, Ks., U.S.	198	37.38 N	94.37 W
Arcadia, La., U.S.	194	32.32 N	92.55 W
Arcadia, Mi., U.S.	190	44.29 N	86.13 W
Arcadia, Mo., U.S.	194	37.35 N	90.37 W
Arcadia, Ne., U.S.	198	41.25 N	99.07 W
Arcadia, Oh., U.S.	216	41.06 N	83.31 W
Arcadia, Pa., U.S.	214	40.47 N	78.51 W
Arcadia, S.C., U.S.	192	34.57 N	81.59 W
Arcadia, Tx., U.S.	222	29.23 N	95.07 W
Arcadia, Wi., U.S.	190	44.15 N	91.30 W
Arcângelo	256	21.18 S	44.19 W
Arcanum	218	39.59 N	84.33 W
Arcas, Cayos II	232	20.12 N	91.58 W
Arcata	204	40.52 N	124.04 W
Arcatao	236	14.05 N	88.45 W
Arc de Triomphe ⊥	261	48.53 N	2.17 E
Arc Dome ∧	204	38.50 N	117.21 W
Arce	66	41.35 N	13.34 E
Arceburgo	256	21.22 S	46.56 W
Arčeda ≃	80	49.52 N	43.10 E
Arčedinsko-Donskije peski ◆[2]	80	49.33 N	43.15 E
Arcelia	234	18.17 N	100.16 W
Arcen	52	51.29 N	6.11 E
Arc-en-Barrois	58	47.57 N	5.00 E
Arces	50	48.05 N	3.36 E
Arc-et-Senans	58	47.02 N	5.46 E
Arcevia	66	43.30 N	12.56 E
Archambault, Lac ⊜	206	46.18 N	74.15 W
Archangaj □[8]	88	48.00 N	101.30 E
Archangel → Archangel'sk	24	64.34 N	40.32 E
Archangel'sk	24	64.34 N	40.32 E
Archangel'skaja	78	45.41 N	40.15 E
Archangel'sk Oblast' □[4]	24	63.00 N	42.00 E
Archangel'skoje, Ross.	76	53.16 N	37.42 E
Archangel'skoje, Ross.	78	51.27 N	40.55 E
Archangel'skoje, Ross.	80	55.13 N	44.05 E
Archangel'skoje, Ross.	80	54.26 N	48.40 E
Archangel'skoje, Ross.	82	55.19 N	35.58 E
Archangel'skoje, Ross.	84	44.37 N	44.05 E
Archangel'skoje, Ross.	265b	55.47 N	37.18 E
Archara	89	49.27 N	130.07 E
Archara ≃	89	49.13 N	129.53 E
Archbald	210	41.29 N	75.32 W
Archbold	216	41.31 N	84.18 W
Archdale	192	35.54 N	79.58 W
Archer	192	29.31 N	82.31 W
Archer ≃	164	13.28 S	141.41 E
Archer, Lake ⊜	283	42.04 N	71.20 W
Archer, Mount ∧	166	23.20 S	150.34 E
Archer Bay c	164	13.25 S	141.43 E
Archer Bend National Park ♠	164	13.30 S	142.20 E
Archer City	196	33.35 N	98.37 W
Archer's Post	154	0.39 N	37.41 E
Arches	58	48.07 N	6.32 E
Arches National Park ♠	200	38.42 N	109.45 W
Archi	66	42.05 N	14.23 E
Archiac	32	45.31 N	0.18 W
Archidona	34	37.05 N	4.23 W
Archipo-Osipovka	78	44.22 N	38.33 E
Archipovka	80	56.38 N	41.14 E
Archipovo	24	66.26 N	45.52 E
Archonskaja	84	43.07 N	44.30 E
Archshofen	56	49.27 N	10.04 E
Archville	276	41.07 N	73.52 W
Arci, Monte ∧	71	39.47 N	8.44 E
Arcidosso	66	42.52 N	11.33 E
Arcille	66	42.48 N	11.15 E
Arcinazzo Romano	66	41.48 N	13.12 E
Arcisate	62	45.54 N	8.52 E
Arcis-sur-Aube	50	48.32 N	4.08 E
Arciz	78	46.00 N	29.26 E
Arckaringa	162	27.56 S	134.45 E
Arckaringa Creek ≃	162	28.10 S	135.22 E
Arc-les-Gray	58	47.27 N	5.35 E
Arco, It.	64	45.55 N	10.53 E
Arco, Id., U.S.	202	43.38 N	113.17 W
Arco de Baúlhe	34	41.29 N	7.58 W
Arcola, Sk., Can.	184	49.37 N	102.30 W
Arcola, It.	64	44.07 N	9.54 E
Arcola, Il., U.S.	194	39.41 N	88.18 W
Arcola, In., U.S.	216	41.06 N	85.17 W
Arcola, Ms., U.S.	194	33.16 N	90.52 W
Arcola, Pa., U.S.	285	40.09 N	75.27 W
Arcola, Tx., U.S.	222	29.31 N	95.27 W
Arconate	266b	45.32 N	8.51 E
Arcore	266b	45.38 N	9.19 E
Arcos	255	20.17 S	45.32 W
Arcos de la Frontera	34	36.45 N	5.48 W
Arcot	122	12.54 N	79.20 E
Arcoverde	250	8.25 S	37.04 W
Arctic Bay	176	73.02 N	85.11 W
Arctic Ocean ⍑[1]	16	85.00 N	170.00 E
Arctic Red ≃	180	67.27 N	133.46 W
Arctic Red River	180	67.27 N	133.46 W
Arctic Village	180	68.08 N	145.19 W
Arctique, Océan Glacial → Arctic Ocean ⍑[1]	16	85.00 N	170.00 E
Arctowski ʊ[3]	9	62.09 S	58.28 W
Arcturus	154	17.47 S	31.20 E
Arcueil	261	48.48 N	2.20 E
Arcuentu, Monte ∧	71	39.35 N	8.33 E
Arcvašen	84	40.38 N	45.32 E

FRANÇAIS

Nom	Page	Lat.°′	Long.°′ W = Ouest
Arcy-sur-Cure	50	47.36 N	3.45 E
Ard, Loch ⊜	46	56.11 N	4.28 W
Arḑ, Ra's al- ›	128	29.21 N	48.05 E
Arda ≃, Europe	38	41.39 N	26.29 E
Arda ≃, It.	64	45.02 N	10.02 E
Ardabīl	128	38.15 N	48.18 E
Ardagger	61	48.11 N	14.50 E
Ardagh	48	52.28 N	9.04 W
Ardahan	130	41.07 N	42.41 E
Ardakān, Īrān	128	30.16 N	52.01 E
Ardakān, Īrān	128	32.19 N	53.59 E
Ardal	128	31.59 N	50.39 E
Ardalanish, Rubh' ›	46	56.17 N	6.18 W
Årdalsfjorden c[2]	26	61.12 N	7.30 E
Årdalstangen	26	61.14 N	7.43 E
Ardanuç	130	41.08 N	42.04 E
Ardara, Ire.	48	54.46 N	8.25 W
Árdara, It.	71	40.37 N	8.48 E
Ardara, Pa., U.S.	279b	40.22 N	79.44 W
Ardarroch	46	57.25 N	5.38 W
Ardatov, Ross.	80	55.15 N	43.06 E
Ardatov, Ross.	80	54.51 N	46.13 E
Ardbeg	46	55.39 N	6.05 W
Ardcharnich	46	57.51 N	5.05 W
Ardea	66	41.36 N	12.33 E
Ardèche □[5]	62	44.40 N	4.20 E
Ardèche ≃	62	44.16 N	4.39 E
Ardee	48	53.52 N	6.33 W
Ardélik	146	12.26 N	21.25 E
Arden, Mb., Can.	184	50.17 N	99.14 W
Arden, Ca., U.S.	226	38.36 N	121.23 W
Arden, De., U.S.	208	39.48 N	75.29 W
Arden, Forest of ◆[3]	42	52.23 N	1.42 W
Arden, Mount ∧	166	32.09 S	137.59 E
Ardenay-sur-Mérize	50	48.00 N	0.25 E
Arden Mines	279b	40.12 N	80.17 W
Ardennes □[5]	32	49.40 N	4.40 E
Ardennes ◆[1]	56	50.10 N	5.45 E
Ardennes, Canal des ≊	50	49.26 N	4.02 E
Ardenno	58	46.10 N	9.39 E
Ardentinny	46	56.03 N	4.55 W
Ardenza	66	43.31 N	10.19 E
Arderin ∧[2]	48	53.02 N	7.40 W
Ardersier	46	57.34 N	4.02 W
Ardeşen	130	41.12 N	41.00 E
Ardestān	128	33.22 N	52.23 E
Ardey	263	51.28 N	7.43 E
Ardeygebirge ⋏[2]	263	51.25 N	7.23 E
Ardez	58	46.46 N	10.11 E
Ardfern	46	56.10 N	5.32 W
Ardglass	48	54.16 N	5.37 W
Ardgroom	48	51.42 N	9.52 W
Ardıçlı	130	40.40 N	37.00 E
Ardila ≃	34	38.12 N	7.28 W
Ardill	184	49.53 N	105.49 W
Ardino	38	41.35 N	25.08 E
Ardlethan	166	34.21 S	146.54 E
Ardlui	46	56.18 N	4.43 W
Ardlussa	46	56.02 N	5.47 W
Ardmolich	46	56.49 N	5.41 W
Ardmore, Ire.	48	51.57 N	7.43 W
Ardmore, Al., U.S.	194	34.59 N	86.50 W
Ardmore, In., U.S.	216	41.41 N	86.19 W
Ardmore, Md., U.S.	284c	38.56 N	76.51 W
Ardmore, Ok., U.S.	196	34.10 N	97.08 W
Ardmore, Pa., U.S.	208	40.01 N	75.18 W
Ardmore Point ›, Scot., U.K.	46	56.39 N	6.07 W
Ardmore Point ›, Scot., U.K.	46	55.42 N	6.01 W
Ardnamurchan ›[1]	46	56.43 N	6.00 W
Ardnamurchan, Point of ›	46	56.44 N	6.13 W
Ardnaree	48	54.06 N	9.08 W
Ardnave Point ›	46	55.54 N	6.20 W
Ardoch	166	27.26 S	144.08 E
Ardon, Ross.	84	43.12 N	44.18 E
Ardon, Schw.	58	46.13 N	7.15 E
Ardon ≃	84	43.17 N	44.18 E
Ardon, Har ∧	132	30.38 N	34.57 E
Ardooie	50	50.59 N	3.12 E
Ardore	68	38.11 N	16.10 E
Ardoux ≃	50	47.42 N	1.35 E
Ardoz, Arroyo de ≃	266a	40.26 N	3.27 W
Ardres	50	50.51 N	1.59 E
Ardres ≃	50	49.18 N	3.40 E
Ardrishaig	46	56.01 N	5.27 W
Ardrossan, Austl.	168b	34.25 S	137.55 E
Ardrossan, Scot., U.K.	46	55.39 N	4.49 W
Ardsley, Eng., U.K.	44	53.32 N	1.28 W
Ardsley, N.Y., U.S.	276	41.00 N	73.50 W
Ardtalnaig	46	56.31 N	4.06 W
Arduan Island I	140	19.55 N	30.22 E
Ardusson ≃	50	48.30 N	3.32 E
Ardvasar	46	57.04 N	5.54 W
Åre	26	63.24 N	13.04 E
Areado	256	21.21 S	46.09 W
Areal	256	22.14 S	43.07 W
Arèches	62	45.41 N	6.34 E
Arecibo	240m	18.28 N	66.43 W
Arecibo, Observatorio de ʊ[3]	240m	18.20 N	66.46 W
Areco ≃	258	33.56 S	59.16 W
Areeiro	266c	38.39 N	9.12 W
Arefjevo	86	57.01 N	90.40 E
Areguá	252	25.18 S	57.25 W
Areia, Bra.	250	6.58 S	35.42 W
Areia, Port.	266c	38.43 N	9.08 W
Areia, Ribeirão da ≃	255	16.07 S	45.52 W
Areia Branca, Bra.	250	4.56 S	37.07 W
Areia Branca, Bra.	287a	22.44 S	43.25 W
Areias	256	22.35 S	44.42 W
Arena	68	38.34 N	16.13 E
Arena, Point ›	204	38.57 N	123.44 W
Arena, Punta ›	232	23.33 N	109.28 W
Arena de la Ventana, Punta ›	232	24.04 N	109.52 W
Arena Island I	116	9.14 N	120.46 E
Arenal, C.R.	236	10.29 N	84.53 W
Arenal, P.R.	240m	17.59 N	66.19 W
Arenal, Laguna de ⊜	236	10.32 N	84.56 W
Arenal, Volcán ∧[1]	236	10.28 N	84.44 W
Arenápolis	248	14.26 S	56.49 W
Arenas, Cayo I	232	22.08 N	91.24 W
Arenas, Punta ›	240m	18.07 N	65.35 W
Arenas, Punta de ›	254	53.09 S	68.13 W
Arenas de San Pedro	34	40.12 N	5.05 W
Arendal	26	58.27 N	8.48 E
Arendonk	56	51.19 N	5.05 E
Arendsee	54	52.53 N	11.30 E
Arendsee ⊜	54	52.53 N	11.30 E
Arendtsville	208	39.55 N	77.18 W
Arenes ≃	266d	41.29 N	2.02 E
Arenig Fawr ∧	42	52.55 N	3.45 W
Arenillas	246	3.33 S	80.04 W
Arenosa Creek ≃	196	28.52 N	96.44 W
Arenys de Mar	34	41.35 N	2.33 E
Arenzano	62	44.24 N	8.41 E
Arenzville	219	39.53 N	90.22 W
Arequipa	248	16.24 S	71.33 W
Arequipa □[5]	248	16.00 S	72.15 W
Arequito	252	33.09 S	61.28 W
Arero	144	4.45 N	38.49 E
Arês, Bra.	250	6.11 S	35.09 W
Arès, Fr.	32	44.46 N	1.08 W
Arese	266b	45.33 N	9.05 E
Aresing	60	48.32 N	11.18 E
Åreskutan ∧	26	63.26 N	13.06 E
Areuse ≃	58	46.56 N	6.53 E
Arévalo	34	41.04 N	4.43 W
Arezzo	66	43.25 N	11.53 E
Arezzo □[4]	66	43.32 N	11.50 E
Arfa', Jabal ∧	132	29.51 N	35.27 E
'Arfā', Wādī al- ∨	132	30.16 N	36.34 E
Arga ≃	34	42.18 N	1.47 W
Argada	88	54.14 N	110.41 E
Argadargada	166	21.40 S	136.40 E
Argajaš	86	55.29 N	60.52 E

PORTUGUÊS

Nome	Página	Lat.°′	Long.°′ W = Oeste
Argamasilla de Alba	34	39.07 N	3.06 W
Arganda	34	40.18 N	3.26 W
Argao	116	9.52 N	123.36 E
Arga-Sala ≃	74	68.30 N	112.12 E
Argedeb	144	6.10 N	41.10 E
Argegno	58	45.56 N	9.08 E
Argel → El Djazaïr	148	36.47 N	3.03 E
Argelès-Gazost	32	43.01 N	0.06 W
Argelès-sur-Mer	32	42.33 N	3.01 E
Argelia → Algeria □[1]	148	28.00 N	3.00 E
Argen ≃	58	47.35 N	9.33 E
Argens ≃	62	43.24 N	6.44 E
Argent	158	26.04 S	28.50 E
Argent, Côte d' ±[2]	32	43.30 N	1.30 W
Argenta, It.	66	44.37 N	11.50 E
Argenta, Il., U.S.	219	39.58 N	88.49 W
Argentan	32	48.45 N	0.01 W
Argentat	32	45.06 N	1.56 E
Argentera	62	44.24 N	6.57 E
Argentera ∧	62	44.10 N	7.18 E
Argenteuil	50	48.57 N	2.15 E
Argenteuil □[6]	206	45.45 N	74.30 W
Argentia	186	47.18 N	53.59 W
Argentiera	71	40.44 N	8.09 E
Argentière	58	45.59 N	6.56 E
Argentières	261	48.39 N	2.52 E
Argentina □[1]	244	34.00 S	64.00 W
Argentina ≃	62	43.50 N	7.51 E
Argentine	216	42.47 N	83.51 W
Argentine → Argentina □[1]	244	34.00 S	64.00 W
Argentine Basin ✣[1]	18	45.00 S	45.00 W
Argentinien → Argentina □[1]	244	34.00 S	64.00 W
Argentino, Hipódromo ♠	288	34.34 S	58.26 W
Argentino, Lago ⊜	254	50.13 S	72.25 W
Argentona	266d	41.33 N	2.24 E
Argentona, Riera d' ≃	266d	41.31 N	2.26 E
Argenton-Château	32	46.59 N	0.27 W
Argenton-sur-Creuse	32	46.35 N	1.31 E
Argentré	32	48.05 N	0.39 W
Argent-sur-Sauldre	50	47.33 N	2.27 E
Argeș □[6]	38	45.00 N	24.45 E
Argeș ≃	38	44.04 N	26.37 E
Arghandāb ≃	128	31.27 N	64.23 E
Arghastān ≃	120	31.23 N	65.45 E
Argirita	256	21.37 S	42.50 W
Argıthanı	130	38.17 N	31.43 E
Argo	140	19.31 N	30.25 E
Ārgoal	126	21.58 N	87.38 E
Argo Island I	140	19.25 N	30.27 E
Argolikós Kólpos c	38	37.33 N	22.45 E
Argonia	198	37.15 N	97.45 W
Argonne	190	45.39 N	88.52 W
Argonne ◆[1]	56	49.30 N	5.00 E
Argonne National Laboratory ʊ[3]	216	41.43 N	87.58 W
Argopuro, Gunung ∧	115a	7.57 S	113.33 E
Árgos, Ellás	38	37.39 N	22.44 E
Argos, In., U.S.	216	41.14 N	86.15 W
Árgos Orestikón	38	40.28 N	21.16 E
Argostólion	38	38.10 N	20.30 E
Argoules	50	50.21 N	1.50 E
Argueil	50	49.32 N	1.31 E
Arguello, Point ›	204	34.35 N	120.39 W
Argun	84	43.16 N	45.52 E
Argun ≃	84	43.22 N	45.55 E
Argun' (Ergun) ≃, Asia	74	53.20 N	121.28 E
Argungu	150	12.45 N	4.31 E
Arguni, Teluk c	164	3.06 S	133.42 E
Ārgur	272b	22.48 N	88.13 E
Argut	86	49.51 N	87.03 E
Argut ≃	86	50.16 N	86.43 E
Arguvan	130	38.47 N	38.17 E
Argyle, Austl.	162	33.32 S	115.46 E
Argyle, Mn., U.S.	198	48.19 N	96.49 W
Argyle, Mo., U.S.	219	38.18 N	92.02 W
Argyle, N.Y., U.S.	210	43.14 N	73.30 W
Argyle, Tx., U.S.	222	33.07 N	97.11 W
Argyle, Lake ⊜[1]	164	16.15 S	128.45 E
'Arhāb, Wādī ∨	142	28.55 N	31.09 E
Arhavi	130	41.22 N	41.16 E
Arhéa Epídavros ⊥	38	37.37 N	23.02 E
Århus	41	56.09 N	10.13 E
Århus □[6]	41	56.15 N	10.05 E
Århus Bugt c	41	56.09 N	10.18 E
Aria	172	38.33 S	174.59 E
Aria ≃	164	5.45 S	149.15 E
Ariadnoje	89	45.08 N	134.25 E
Ariah	126	23.33 N	86.20 E
Ariake-kai c	92	33.00 N	130.20 E
Ariāl Khān ≃	126	23.56 N	90.46 E
Ariamácina, Lago di ⊜[1]	68	39.20 N	16.32 E
Ariamsvlei	156	28.07 S	19.49 E
Ariana	36	36.52 N	10.12 E
Ariano, Isola d' I	64	45.00 N	12.10 E
Ariano Irpino	68	41.09 N	15.05 E
Ariano nel Polesine	64	44.56 N	12.07 E
Ariari ≃	246	2.35 N	72.47 W
Arias	252	33.38 S	62.25 W
Arias, Arroyo de ≃	258	34.17 S	56.06 W
Arias, Cañada ≃	258	34.39 S	58.59 W
Ariaú	250	3.11 S	57.14 W
Aribinda	150	14.14 N	0.52 W
Arica, Chile	248	18.29 S	70.20 W
Arica, Col.	246	2.08 S	71.47 W
Arıcak	130	38.33 N	39.48 E
Aricanduva, Ribeirão ≃	287b	23.32 S	46.33 W
Ariccia	66	41.43 N	12.40 E
Arichat	186	45.31 N	61.01 W
Arichuna	246	7.42 N	67.08 W
Arid, Cape ›	162	34.00 S	123.09 E
Arida, Nig.	273a	6.34 N	3.16 E
Arida, Nihon	96	34.05 N	135.07 E
Arida ≃	96	34.05 N	135.06 E
Aridal, Sabkhat ⊜	148	26.12 N	14.05 W
Aridhaía	38	40.59 N	22.03 E
Ariège □[5]	32	43.00 N	1.30 E
Ariège ≃	32	43.31 N	1.25 E
Ari'el, Isr. Occ	132	32.06 N	35.06 E
Ariel, Wa., U.S.	224	45.57 N	122.34 W
Arienzo	68	41.01 N	14.30 E
Arieș ≃	38	46.26 N	23.59 E
'Arif, Har ∧	132	30.26 N	34.44 E
Ārifwāla	123	30.17 N	73.04 E
Ariguanabo, Laguna de ⊜	286b	22.56 N	82.33 W
Ariguaní ≃	246	9.35 N	73.46 W
Arīḩā (Jericho), Isr. Occ	132	31.52 N	35.27 E
Arīḩā, Sūrīy.	130	35.48 N	36.36 E
Arīḩā, Urd.	132	31.25 N	35.47 E
Arikaree ≃	198	40.01 N	101.56 W
Arikaree, North Fork ≃	198	39.39 N	102.57 W
Arikawa	92	32.59 N	129.07 E
Arikha, Har ∧[2]	132	30.39 N	34.47 E
Arild	41	56.16 N	12.34 E
Arima	241r	10.38 N	61.17 W
Arima ◆[8]	270	34.48 N	135.15 E
Arima ≃	270	34.52 N	135.15 E
Arima-fuji ∧[2]	270	34.55 N	135.14 E
Arimine-dam ◆[6]	94	36.29 N	137.27 E
Arinagour	46	56.37 N	6.31 W
Aringay	116	16.26 N	120.21 E
Arino ◆[8]	270	34.50 N	135.14 E
Arinos ≃	248	10.25 S	58.20 W
Arinthod	58	46.23 N	5.34 E
Ario de Rosales	234	19.12 N	101.43 W
Ariogala	76	55.16 N	23.30 E
Aripeka	220	28.25 N	82.39 W
Ariporo ≃	246	6.03 N	69.54 W
Aripuanã	248	9.10 S	60.38 W

Aripuanã ≃	248	5.07 S	60.24 W
Ariquemes	248	9.56 S	63.04 W
Arisa ≃	246	7.32 N	64.00 W
Arisaig	46	56.51 N	5.51 W
Arisaig, Sound of c	46	56.51 N	5.51 W
'Arīsh, Wādī al- ∨	140	31.09 N	33.49 E
Arismendi	246	8.29 N	68.22 W
Aristazabal Island I	182	52.30 N	129.05 W
Aristes	210	40.49 N	76.20 W
Aristizábal, Cabo ›	254	45.13 S	66.31 W
Aristovo	82	54.37 N	36.40 E
Arıt	130	41.41 N	32.39 E
Aritao	116	16.18 N	121.02 E
Ariton	194	31.36 N	85.43 W
Aritzo	71	39.57 N	9.12 E
Arivonimamo	157b	19.01 S	47.15 E
Ariyalūr	122	11.08 N	79.05 E
Arizaro, Salar de ≚	252	24.42 S	67.45 W
Arizgoiti	34	43.13 N	2.54 W
Arizona	252	35.43 S	65.13 W
Arizona □[3], U.S.	178	34.00 N	112.00 W
Arizona □[3], U.S.	200	34.00 N	112.00 W
Arizpe	232	30.20 N	110.10 W
Arja	80	57.30 N	46.00 E
Årjäng	26	59.23 N	12.08 E
Arjasa	112	6.51 S	115.16 E
Arjawinangun	115a	6.39 S	108.24 E
Arjay	192	36.48 N	83.38 W
Arjeplog	24	66.00 N	17.58 E
Arjona, Col.	246	10.15 N	75.21 W
Arjona, Esp.	34	37.56 N	4.03 W
Arka	74	60.03 N	142.12 E
Arkabutla Lake ⊜[1]	194	34.45 N	90.06 W
Arkadak	80	51.58 N	43.28 E
Arkadelphia	194	34.07 N	93.03 W
Arkaig, Loch ⊜	46	56.58 N	5.08 W
Arkalyk	86	50.13 N	66.50 E
Arkansas □[3], U.S.	178	34.50 N	92.30 W
Arkansas □[3], U.S.	194	34.50 N	92.30 W
Arkansas ≃	178	33.48 N	91.04 W
Arkansas, Salt Fork ≃	196	36.36 N	97.03 W
Arkansas City, Ar., U.S.	194	33.36 N	91.12 W
Arkansas City, Ks., U.S.	198	37.03 N	97.02 W
Arkansas Post National Memorial ⊥	194	33.55 N	91.26 W
Arkanū, Jabal ∧	146	22.13 N	24.41 E
Arkatag Shan ⋏	120	36.48 N	89.10 E
Arken-Ahon ∧	146	20.05 N	18.25 E
Arkhangélos	38	36.12 N	28.08 E
Arkhangel'sk → Archangel'sk	24	64.34 N	40.32 E
Arki	123	31.09 N	76.58 E
Árki I	38	37.22 N	26.45 E
Arkit	85	41.47 N	71.58 E
Arklow	48	52.48 N	6.09 W
Arkoma	194	35.21 N	94.26 W
Arkona, Kap ›	54	54.41 N	13.26 E
Arkösund	26	58.30 N	16.56 E
Arkport	210	42.23 N	77.41 W
Arktičeskij, mys ›	74	81.15 N	95.45 E
Arktičeskogo Instituta, ostrova II	74	75.20 N	81.55 E
Arkul'	80	57.17 N	50.03 E
Arkville	210	42.08 N	74.37 W
Arkwright	207	41.43 N	71.33 W
Ärla	40	59.17 N	16.40 E
Arlan	80	55.58 N	54.15 E
Arlan, gora ∧	128	39.40 N	54.33 E
Arlanc	62	45.25 N	3.44 E
Arlanda flygplats ⊠	40	59.37 N	17.55 E
Arlanza ≃	34	42.06 N	4.09 W
Arlanzón ≃	34	42.03 N	4.17 W
Arlbergpass)(	64	47.08 N	10.12 E
Arlberg-Tunnel ◆[5]	64	47.08 N	10.12 E
Arlee	202	47.09 N	114.05 W
Arles	62	43.40 N	4.38 E
Arles à Port de Bouc, Canal d' ≊	62	43.40 N	4.37 E
Arlesey	42	52.01 N	0.14 W
Arlesheim	58	47.30 N	7.37 E
Arleta ◆[8]	280	34.15 N	118.26 W
Arleux	50	50.17 N	3.06 E
Arley	262	53.19 N	2.30 W
Arli	150	11.35 N	1.28 E
Arli, Parc National de l' ♠	150	11.35 N	1.30 E
Arlington, S. Afr.	158	28.06 S	27.54 E
Arlington, Ga., U.S.	192	31.26 N	84.43 W
Arlington, In., U.S.	218	39.38 N	85.34 W
Arlington, Ia., U.S.	190	42.44 N	91.40 W
Arlington, Ks., U.S.	198	37.53 N	98.10 W
Arlington, Ky., U.S.	194	36.47 N	89.00 W
Arlington, Ma., U.S.	207	42.24 N	71.09 W
Arlington, Mn., U.S.	190	44.36 N	94.04 W
Arlington, Ne., U.S.	198	41.27 N	96.21 W
Arlington, N.Y., U.S.	210	41.41 N	73.53 W
Arlington, Oh., U.S.	216	40.53 N	83.39 W
Arlington, Or., U.S.	202	45.43 N	120.11 W
Arlington, S.D., U.S.	198	44.21 N	97.07 W
Arlington, Tn., U.S.	194	35.18 N	89.40 W
Arlington, Tx., U.S.	222	32.44 N	97.06 W
Arlington, Vt., U.S.	210	43.04 N	73.09 W
Arlington, Va., U.S.	208	38.52 N	77.06 W
Arlington, Wa., U.S.	224	48.11 N	122.07 W
Arlington □[6]	284c	38.50 N	77.10 W
Arlington, Lake ⊜[1]	222	32.42 N	97.13 W
Arlington Heights, Il., U.S.	216	42.05 N	87.58 W
Arlington Heights, Ma., U.S.	283	42.25 N	71.11 W
Arlington International Race Course ♠	278	42.05 N	88.00 W
Arlington Memorial Bridge ◆[5]	284c	38.53 N	77.03 W
Arlington Mill Reservoir ⊜[1]	283	42.48 N	71.13 W
Arlington National Cemetery ◆	284c	38.53 N	77.04 W
Arlit	150	19.00 N	7.38 E
Arlod	58	46.06 N	5.49 E
Arlon	56	49.41 N	5.49 E
Arlöv	41	55.39 N	13.05 E
Arltunga	162	23.26 S	134.41 E
Arl'uk	86	55.26 N	84.50 E
Arluno	62	45.30 N	8.56 E
Arly ≃	62	45.40 N	6.23 E
Arlyn Oaks	276	40.40 N	73.27 W
Arm ≃	184	50.46 N	105.00 W
Arma	198	37.32 N	94.42 W
Armação, Ponta da ›	287a	22.53 S	43.08 W
Armada	214	42.50 N	82.53 W
Armadale, Austl.	168a	32.09 S	116.00 E
Armadale, On., Can.	275b	43.50 N	79.15 W
Armadale, S. Afr.	273d	26.17 S	27.57 E
Armadale, Scot., U.K.	46	55.54 N	3.42 W
Arma di Taggia	62	43.50 N	7.51 E
Armageddon → Tel Megiddo ⊥	132	32.35 N	35.11 E
Armagh, N. Ire., U.K.	48	54.21 N	6.39 W
Armagh, Pa., U.S.	214	40.27 N	79.02 W
Armagnac □[9]	32	43.45 N	0.10 E
Armah, Wādī ∨	144	18.12 N	51.02 E
Armainvilliers, Étang d' ⊜	261	48.45 N	2.44 E
Armainvilliers, Forêt d' ♠	261	48.45 N	2.45 E
Armance ≃	50	47.59 N	3.43 E
Armançon ≃, Fr.	50	47.57 N	3.30 E
Armançon ≃, Fr.	58	47.33 N	4.17 E
Arm'ansk	78	46.07 N	33.41 E
Armant	140	25.37 N	32.32 E
Armavir	72	45.00 N	41.08 E
Armazém	252	28.16 S	49.01 W
Armbrust	214	40.13 N	79.33 W
Armells Creek ≃	202	47.37 N	108.40 W
Armenia	246	4.31 N	75.41 W

Armenia □[9]	84	40.30 N	43.30 E
Armenia □[1], Asia	72	40.00 N	45.00 E
Armenia (Hayastan) □[1], Asia	84	40.00 N	45.00 E
Armenija → Armenia □[1]	72	40.00 N	45.00 E
Armeniș	38	45.12 N	22.19 E
Armenistís	38	37.36 N	26.08 E
Armeniya → Armenia □[1]	72	40.00 N	45.00 E
Armeno	62	45.49 N	8.26 E
Armenonville-les-Gâtineaux	261	48.33 N	1.39 E
Armentières	50	50.41 N	2.53 E
Armento	68	40.18 N	16.04 E
Armería	234	18.56 N	103.58 W
Armería ≃	234	18.52 N	103.59 W
Armero	246	4.58 N	74.54 W
Armidale	166	30.31 S	151.39 E
Armijo	200	35.03 N	106.40 W
Armitage	42	52.44 N	1.53 W
Armit Lake ⊜	176	64.10 N	91.32 W
Armizonskoje	86	55.57 N	67.42 E
Armona	226	36.19 N	119.42 W
Armonk	276	41.07 N	73.42 W
Armor	210	42.44 N	78.48 W
Armori	122	20.28 N	79.59 E
Armour	198	43.19 N	98.20 W
Armoy, Fr.	58	46.21 N	6.31 E
Armoy, N. Ire., U.K.	48	55.07 N	6.20 W
Armstrong, Arg.	252	32.47 S	61.36 W
Armstrong, B.C., Can.	182	50.27 N	119.12 W
Armstrong, Il., U.S.	216	40.18 N	87.53 W
Armstrong, Ia., U.S.	198	43.23 N	94.28 W
Armstrong, Mo., U.S.	194	39.16 N	92.42 W
Armstrong □[6]	214	40.49 N	79.32 W
Armstrong ≃	164	16.46 S	131.12 E
Armstrong, Mount ∧	180	63.12 N	133.16 W
Armstrong Station	176	50.18 N	89.02 W
Armthorpe	44	53.32 N	1.03 W
Ārmūr	122	18.48 N	78.17 E
Armutlu	130	40.31 N	28.50 E
Arnå ≃	41	54.57 N	8.53 E
Arnaccio	66	43.40 N	10.27 E
Arnaía	38	40.29 N	23.35 E
Arnarfjörður c[2]	24a	65.45 N	23.40 W
Arnäs	40	58.41 N	13.35 E
Arnaud ≃	176	59.59 N	69.46 W
Arnaudville	194	30.24 N	91.56 W
Arnavad, gora ∧	85	38.33 N	71.31 E
Arnavutköy ≃	267b	41.13 N	29.12 E
Arnay-le-Duc	58	47.08 N	4.29 E
Arnaz	62	45.38 N	7.43 E
Arnborg	41	56.01 N	8.59 E
Arnbruck	60	49.08 N	13.00 E
Arncliffe	274a	33.56 S	151.09 E
Arneburg	54	52.40 N	12.00 E
Arnedo	34	42.13 N	2.06 W
Arneiro dos Marinheiros	266c	38.51 N	9.25 W
Arneiroz	250	6.20 S	40.08 W
Arnejevo	82	54.58 N	37.35 E
Arnemuiden	52	51.30 N	3.41 E
Årnes	26	60.09 N	11.28 E
Arnett	196	36.08 N	99.46 W
Arney ≃	48	54.16 N	7.37 W
Arnhem	52	51.59 N	5.55 E
Arnhem, Cape ›	164	12.21 S	136.21 E
Arnhem Bay c	164	12.20 S	136.12 E
Arnhem Land ◆[1]	164	13.10 S	134.30 E
Arnhem Land Aboriginal Reserve ◆[4]	164	13.10 S	134.30 E
Arni	64	44.04 N	10.15 E
Arnis	41	54.38 N	9.56 E
Árnissa	38	40.48 N	21.50 E
Arno I[1]	14	7.05 N	171.41 E
Arno ≃	66	43.41 N	10.17 E
Arno, Torrente ≃	266b	45.42 N	8.48 E
Arno Bay	166	33.54 S	136.34 E
Arnold, B.C., Can.	224	49.08 N	122.03 W
Arnold, Eng., U.K.	44	53.00 N	1.08 W
Arnold, Ca., U.S.	204	38.15 N	120.21 W
Arnold, Md., U.S.	208	39.01 N	76.30 W
Arnold, Mn., U.S.	190	46.52 N	92.05 W
Arnold, Mo., U.S.	219	38.25 N	90.22 W
Arnold, Ne., U.S.	198	41.25 N	100.11 W
Arnold, Pa., U.S.	214	40.34 N	79.46 W
Arnold ≃	164	15.19 S	134.06 E
Arnold Arboretum ♠	283	42.18 N	71.08 W
Arnold Mills	283	41.58 N	71.23 W
Arnold Mills Reservoir ⊜[1]	283	41.59 N	71.25 W
Arnolds Park	198	43.22 N	95.08 W
Arnoldstein	64	46.33 N	13.43 E
Arnon ≃	50	47.13 N	2.01 E
Arnos Vale Airport ⊠	241h	13.09 N	61.13 W
Arnot	210	41.39 N	77.07 W
Arnouville-lès-Gonesse	261	49.00 N	2.25 E
Arnouville-lès-Mantes	261	48.55 N	1.44 E
Arnoya ≃	34	42.15 N	8.09 W
Arnprior	212	45.26 N	76.21 W
Arnsberg	56	51.24 N	8.03 E
Arnsberg □[5]	52	51.20 N	8.00 E
Arnschwang	60	49.16 N	12.49 E
Arnsdorf	54	51.05 N	13.59 E
Arnside	44	54.12 N	2.50 W
Arnstadt	54	50.50 N	10.57 E
Arnstein	56	49.58 N	9.58 E
Arnstorf	60	48.34 N	12.49 E
Arnum	41	55.15 N	8.59 E
Årø I	41	55.15 N	9.45 E
Aro ≃	246	8.01 N	64.11 W
Aroa	246	10.26 N	68.54 W
Aroa ≃	246	10.40 N	68.19 W
Aroa, Pointe ›	174s	17.28 S	149.46 W
Aroab	156	26.47 S	19.40 E
Aroali	126	24.03 N	87.56 E
Arochukwu	150	5.23 N	7.55 E
Aroeiras	250	7.31 S	35.41 W
Ar'ofino	80	58.16 N	39.15 E
Arolla	58	46.02 N	7.29 E
Arolsen	56	51.23 N	9.01 E
Aroma	140	15.49 N	36.08 E
Aroma Park	216	41.04 N	87.48 W
Aromas	226	36.53 N	121.39 W
Aromaševo	86	56.52 N	68.39 E
Arona, It.	62	45.46 N	8.34 E
Arona, Pap. N. Gui.	164	6.20 S	146.00 E
Arona, Pa., U.S.	279b	40.16 N	79.39 W
Aroostook ≃	186	46.48 N	67.45 W
Arop Island I	164	5.20 S	147.05 E
Aropuk Lake ⊜	180	61.12 N	163.50 W
Arorae I	14	2.38 S	176.49 E
Arorangi	174k	21.13 S	159.49 W
Aroroy	116	12.31 N	123.24 E
Aros ≃	232	29.09 N	109.40 W
Arosa	58	46.47 N	9.41 E
Arosa, Ría de c[1]	34	42.28 N	8.57 W
Arosbaya	115a	6.56 S	112.51 E
Årøsund	41	55.16 N	9.45 E
Aro Usu, Tanjung ›	164	8.20 S	130.45 E
Arowhana ∧	172	38.07 S	177.52 E
Arp	222	32.13 N	95.03 W
Arpa ≃	84	39.28 N	44.57 E
Arpaçay	84	40.52 N	43.20 E
Arpaçay (Achur'an) ≃	84	40.06 N	43.39 E
Arpačin	83	47.14 N	40.11 E
Arpaia	68	41.02 N	14.33 E
Arpajon	50	48.35 N	2.15 E
Ārpāra	126	23.23 N	89.23 E
Arpino	66	41.39 N	13.36 E
Arpoador, Ponta do ›	287a	22.59 S	43.12 W
Arquà Petrarca	64	45.16 N	11.43 E
Arquà Polesine	64	45.01 N	11.45 E
Arquata del Tronto	66	42.46 N	13.18 E
Arquata Scrivia	62	44.41 N	8.53 E
Arque	248	17.48 S	66.23 W

Arques	50	50.44 N	2.17 E
Arques-la-Bataille	50	49.53 N	1.08 E
Ar-Rabaḑ	128	23.11 N	39.32 E
Ar-Rabbah	132	31.16 N	35.44 E
Arracourt	58	48.44 N	6.32 E
Ar-Radīsīyah Baḩrī	140	24.57 N	32.53 E
Ar-Rafīd	132	32.57 N	35.53 E
Arraga	252	28.04 S	64.14 W
Arrah	150	6.40 N	3.58 W
Ar-Rahad	140	12.43 N	30.39 E
Ar-Raḩāminah	142	31.18 N	31.45 E
Ar-Raḩmānīyah	142	31.06 N	30.38 E
Arraial do Cabo	255	22.58 S	42.01 W
Arraias	255	12.56 S	46.57 W
Arraias ≃, Bra.	250	11.10 S	53.35 W
Arraias ≃, Bra.	255	12.28 S	47.18 W
'Arrām, Wādī ∨	132	32.55 N	36.10 E
Ar-Ramādī	128	33.25 N	43.17 E
Ar-Ramthā	132	32.34 N	36.00 E
Arran, Island of I	46	55.35 N	5.15 W
Ar-Rank	140	11.45 N	32.48 E
Arran Lake ⊜	212	44.29 N	81.16 W
Ar-Raqqah	130	35.56 N	39.01 E
Ar-Raqqah □[8]	130	36.00 N	39.00 E
Arras	50	50.17 N	2.47 E
Arras, Nuraghe ⊥	71	39.40 N	9.25 E
Ar-Rāshidah	140	25.35 N	28.56 E
Ar-Rass	128	25.52 N	43.28 E
Ar-Rastan	130	34.55 N	36.44 E
Arrats ≃	32	44.06 N	0.52 E
Ar-Rawḑah, Ar. Su.	128	26.05 N	40.37 E
Ar-Rawḑah, Miṣr	142	27.48 N	30.52 E
Ar-Rawḑah, Miṣr	142	29.27 N	31.00 E
Ar-Rawḑah, Yaman	144	14.28 N	47.17 E
Ar-Rāwuk	144	15.45 N	48.54 E
Ar-Rayramūn	142	27.45 N	30.52 E
Ar-Rayyāḩ ar-Minūfīya ≊	142	30.20 N	31.00 E
Ar-Rayyāḩ at-Tawfīqī ≊	142	30.11 N	31.07 E
Ar-Rayyān	128	25.18 N	51.27 E
Arrecife	148	28.57 N	13.32 W
Arrecifes	252	34.03 S	60.07 W
Arrée, Montagnes d' ⋏	32	48.26 N	3.55 W
Arregui, Laguna ⊜	258	35.05 S	57.33 W
Arrentela	266c	38.38 N	9.06 W
Arresø ⊜	41	55.58 N	12.08 E
Arrey	200	32.50 N	107.19 W
Arriaga	234	16.14 N	93.54 W
Arriba	198	39.17 N	103.16 W
Arrild	41	55.09 N	8.58 E
Ar-Riyāḑ (Riyadh)	128	24.38 N	46.43 E
Arrochar	46	56.12 N	4.44 W
Arroio Grande	252	32.14 S	53.05 W
Arrojado ≃	255	13.24 S	44.20 W
Arronches	34	39.07 N	7.17 W
Arrone ≃, It.	66	41.52 N	12.11 E
Arrone ≃, It.	66	42.18 N	11.38 E
Arros ≃	32	43.40 N	0.02 W
Arroscia ≃	62	44.03 N	8.11 E
Arroux ≃	32	46.29 N	3.58 E
Arrow ≃, Eng., U.K.	42	52.12 N	2.43 W
Arrow ≃, Eng., U.K.	42	52.09 N	1.53 W
Arrow, Lough ⊜	48	54.04 N	8.21 W
Arrow Creek ≃	202	47.43 N	109.50 W
Arrowhead, Lake ⊜[1], Ca., U.S.	228	34.15 N	117.11 W
Arrowhead, Lake ⊜[1], Tx., U.S.	196	33.40 N	98.20 W
Arrowhead Peak ∧	228	34.13 N	117.16 W
Arrowhead Provincial Park ♠	212	45.24 N	79.13 W
Arrowhead Village	208	40.04 N	74.07 W
Arrow Lake ⊜	190	48.08 N	90.18 W
Arrowrock Reservoir ⊜[1]	202	43.36 N	115.51 W
Arrowsmith	216	40.27 N	88.38 W
Arrowsmith, Mount ∧, Austl.	166	30.09 S	141.50 E
Arrowsmith, Mount ∧, B.C., Can.	224	49.13 N	124.36 W
Arrowsmith, Mount ∧, N.Z.	172	43.21 S	170.59 E
Arrowtown	172	44.56 S	168.50 E
Arrowwood	182	50.44 N	113.09 W
Arroyan, Arroyo ≃[1]	288	34.24 S	58.32 W
Arroyito	252	31.25 S	63.03 W
Arroyo	240m	17.58 N	66.04 W
Arroyo de la Luz	34	39.29 N	6.35 W
Arroyo Grande, Ca., U.S.	204	35.07 N	120.35 W
Arroyo Grande → Ismael Cortinas, Ur.	258	33.58 S	57.06 W
Arroyo Hondo	200	36.32 N	105.40 W
Arroyo Naranjo ◆[8]	286b	23.02 N	82.23 W
Arroyo Seco	252	33.14 S	60.50 W
Arroyo Seco Park ♠	280	34.06 N	118.12 W
Arroyos y Esteros	252	25.04 S	57.06 W
Arrozal	256	22.37 S	44.03 W
Ar-Ru'at	140	12.21 N	32.17 E
Ar-Rub' al-Khālī ◆[2]	118	20.00 N	51.00 E
Ar-Rubayqī	142	30.10 N	31.46 E
Ar-Ruḩaybah	132	33.45 N	36.42 E
Ar-Rukhaymīyah ⍑[4]	128	29.14 N	45.35 E
Ar-Rumaythah	128	31.32 N	45.12 E
Ar-Rummān	132	32.10 N	35.50 E
Ar-Ruqayyah ⊥	132	32.47 N	37.05 E
Ar-Ruṣāfah ⊥	130	35.37 N	38.45 E
Ar-Ruṣayfah	132	32.01 N	36.03 E
Ar-Ruṣayriṣ	140	11.51 N	34.23 E
Ar-Rushaydah	132	32.40 N	36.50 E
Ar-Ruṭbah	128	33.02 N	40.17 E
Ar-Ru'ūs	142	29.21 N	31.04 E
Ar-Ruways	128	26.08 N	51.13 E
Års	26	56.48 N	9.32 E
Aršan, Ross.	88	51.54 N	102.27 E
Aršan, Ross.	88	53.54 N	99.54 E
Arsanjān	128	29.56 N	53.18 E
Aršan'-Zel'men'	80	47.36 N	44.36 E
Ārsāpota	272b	22.55 N	88.18 E
Arsbeck	56	51.08 N	6.12 E
Arsenal de Marinha ■	266c	38.39 N	9.09 W
Arsenal Football Club ♠	260	51.33 N	0.06 W
Arsenault Lake ⊜	184	55.06 N	108.30 W
Arsenjev	89	44.10 N	133.15 E
Arsenjevka ≃	89	44.54 N	133.35 E
Arsenjevo	76	53.44 N	36.40 E
Ars-en-Ré	32	46.12 N	1.31 W
Arsi □[4]	144	8.00 N	39.40 E
Arsiè	64	45.59 N	11.45 E
Arsiero	64	45.48 N	11.21 E
Arsikere	122	13.20 N	76.15 E
Arsin	130	40.58 N	39.56 E
Aršincevo	78	45.17 N	36.25 E
Arsk	80	56.06 N	49.54 E
Arslanbob	85	41.21 N	72.56 E
Årslev	41	55.18 N	10.29 E
Arso	164	2.56 S	140.47 E
Arsoli	66	42.02 N	13.01 E
Ársos	130	34.50 N	32.46 E
Ars-sur-Formans	58	45.59 N	4.49 E
Ars-sur-Moselle	56	49.05 N	6.04 E
Årsta havsbad	40	59.05 N	18.10 E
Arsufhsa ≃	84	39.08 N	46.50 E
Arsunda	40	60.32 N	16.44 E
Art, Île I	175f	19.43 S	163.38 E
Árta, Ellás	38	39.09 N	20.59 E
Artà, Esp.	34	39.42 N	3.21 E
Artarmon	274a	33.49 S	151.11 E
Artašat	84	39.59 N	44.33 E
Arta Terme	64	46.28 N	13.01 E
Arteaga	234	18.28 N	102.25 W
Arteche	116	12.17 N	125.22 E
Arte Contemporânea, Museu de ʊ	287b	23.32 S	46.38 W
Artegna	64	46.14 N	13.09 E
Artemare	62	45.52 N	5.42 E

≃ River	Fluß	Río	Rivière	Rio
≊ Canal	Kanal	Canal	Canal	Canal
ʟ Waterfall, Rapids	Wasserfall, Stromschnellen	Cascada, Rápidos	Chute d'eau, Rapides	Cascata, Rápidos
ʯ Strait	Meeresstraße	Estrecho	Détroit	Estreito
c Bay, Gulf	Bucht, Golf	Bahía, Golfo	Baie, Golfe	Baía, Golfo
⊜ Lake, Lakes	See, Seen	Lago, Lagos	Lac, Lacs	Lago, Lagos
≡ Swamp	Sumpf	Pantano	Marais	Pântano
⩊ Ice Features, Glacier	Eis- und Gletscherformen	Accidentes Glaciales	Formes glaciaires	Acidentes glaciares
⍑ Other Hydrographic Features	Andere Hydrographische Objekte	Otros Elementos Hidrográficos	Autres données hydrographiques	Outros acidentes hidrográficos

✣ Submarine Features	Untermeerische Objekte	Accidentes Submarinos	Formes de relief sous-marin	Acidentes submarinos
□ Political Unit	Politische Einheit	Unidad Politica	Entité politique	Unidade política
ʊ Cultural Institution	Kulturelle Institution	Institución Cultural	Institution culturelle	Instituição cultural
⊥ Historical Site	Historische Stätte	Sitio Histórico	Site historique	Sitio histórico
♠ Recreational Site	Erholungs- und Ferienort	Sitio de Recreo	Centre de loisirs	Area de Lazer
⊠ Airport	Flughafen	Aeropuerto	Aéroport	Aeroporto
■ Military Installation	Militäranlage	Instalación Militar	Installation militaire	Instalação militar
◆ Miscellaneous	Verschiedenes	Misceláneo	Divers	Diversos

I · 10 Arte-Athe

ENGLISH: Name / Page / Lat.°′ / Long.°′ — DEUTSCH: Name / Seite / Breite°′ / Länge°′ E = Ost

Name	Page	Lat.	Long.
Artemisa	240p	22.49 N	82.46 W
Artemón	38	36.59 N	24.43 E
Artémou	150	15.31 N	12.16 W
Artemovsk → Art'omovsk	83	48.35 N	38.00 E
Artèn	64	46.00 N	11.50 E
Artenay	50	48.05 N	1.53 E
Artern	54	51.22 N	11.17 E
Artesia → Mosomane, Bots.	156	24.04 S	26.15 E
Artesia, Ca., U.S.	280	33.51 N	118.04 W
Artesia, Ms., U.S.	194	33.24 N	88.38 W
Artesia, N.M., U.S.	196	32.50 N	104.24 W
Artesia Lake ⊜	226	38.57 N	119.22 W
Artesian	198	44.00 N	97.55 W
Arth	58	47.04 N	8.31 E
Arthabaska	206	46.02 N	71.55 W
Arthabaska □6	206	46.05 N	72.00 W
Arthal	123	33.16 N	76.11 E
Arthala	272a	28.40 N	77.24 E
Arthies	261	49.06 N	1.48 E
Arthonnay	50	47.56 N	4.13 E
Arthur, On., Can.	212	43.50 N	80.32 W
Arthur, Il., U.S.	194	39.43 N	88.28 W
Arthur, Ne., U.S.	198	41.34 N	101.41 W
Arthur, N.D., U.S.	198	47.06 N	97.13 W
Arthur, Tn., U.S.	192	36.32 N	83.40 W
Arthur ≃, Austl.	166	41.03 S	144.40 E
Arthur ≃, Austl.	168a	33.31 S	116.50 E
Arthur, Lake ⊜1	214	40.57 N	80.05 W
Arthur Creek ≃	162	22.55 S	136.45 E
Arthur Kill ⊔	276	40.30 N	74.15 W
Arthurs Pass	172	42.57 S	171.34 E
Arthurs Pass)(	172	42.54 S	171.34 E
Arthur's Pass National Park ♠	172	42.50 S	171.40 E
Arthurs Seat ∧2	169	38.21 S	144.57 E
Arthur's Town	238	24.38 N	75.42 W
Arthurton	168b	34.16 S	137.45 E
Arti	86	56.26 N	58.32 E
Artibonite ≃	238	19.15 N	72.47 W
Artico, Océano → Arctic Ocean ⫟1	16	85.00 N	170.00 E
Artigas	252	30.24 S	56.28 W
Artigas ⊷8	286c	10.30 N	66.56 W
Artigas, Casa de ⊥	258	34.39 S	56.03 W
Artik	84	40.37 N	43.59 E
Artilleros	258	34.22 S	57.34 W
Artilleros, Punta ›	258	34.28 S	57.32 W
Artillery Lake ⊜	176	63.09 N	107.52 W
Artlenburg	52	53.22 N	10.29 E
Artney, Glen V	46	56.20 N	4.04 W
Artois □9	50	50.30 N	2.30 E
Artois, Collines de l' ⋏2	50	50.25 N	2.10 E
Art'om	89	43.22 N	132.13 E
Art'om-Ostrov	84	40.28 N	50.20 E
Art'omovka, Ukr.	78	49.46 N	35.04 E
Art'omovka, Ukr.	83	47.53 N	38.38 E
Art'omovka, Ukr.	83	48.29 N	37.23 E
Art'omovo	83	48.22 N	37.53 E
Art'omovsk, Ross.	86	54.21 N	93.26 E
Art'omovsk, Ukr.	83	48.27 N	38.42 E
Art'omovsk, Ukr.	83	48.35 N	38.00 E
Art'omovskij, Ross.	86	57.21 N	61.54 E
Art'omovskij, Ross.	88	58.12 N	114.45 E
Art'omovskij, Ross.	89	43.27 N	132.22 E
Artova	130	40.03 N	36.19 E
Artpark ♠	284a	43.10 N	79.03 W
Artrutx, Cap d' ›	34	39.56 N	3.48 E
Artuby ≃	62	43.44 N	6.22 E
Artur Nogueira	256	22.35 S	47.09 W
Arturo Merino Benítez, Aeropuerto ⊠	286e	33.23 S	70.49 W
Arturo Segui ⊷8	258	34.51 S	58.09 W
Artvin	130	41.11 N	41.49 E
Artvin □4	130	41.05 N	42.00 E
Artybaš	86	51.48 N	87.16 E
Artyk	74	64.12 N	145.06 E
Aru, Kepulauan II	164	6.00 S	134.30 E
Aru, Tanjung ›	112	2.10 S	116.34 E
Aru, Teluk C	114	4.09 N	98.12 E
Arua	154	3.01 N	30.55 E
Aruã ≃	250	2.39 S	55.38 W
Aruaddin	144	16.15 N	38.43 E
Aruanã	255	14.54 S	51.05 W
Aruângua (Luangwa) ≃	154	15.36 S	30.25 E
Aruba □2, N.A.	230	12.30 N	69.58 W
Aruba □2, N.A.	241s	12.30 N	69.58 W
Aru Basin ✢1	14	5.00 S	134.00 E
Arucas	148	28.07 N	15.31 W
Arue	174s	17.32 S	149.32 W
Arufu	150	7.50 N	9.14 E
Arujá	256	23.24 S	46.20 W
Arujá □7	287b	23.24 S	46.20 W
Arumanduba	250	1.29 S	52.29 W
Arume	174m	26.36 N	128.07 E
Arume-wan C	174m	26.35 N	128.08 E
Arun (Pong) ≃, Asia	124	26.49 N	87.09 E
Arun ≃, Eng., U.K.	42	50.48 N	0.33 W
Arunāchal Pradesh □3	120	28.30 N	95.00 E
Arundel, P.Q., Can.	206	45.58 N	74.37 W
Arundel, Eng., U.K.	42	50.51 N	0.34 W
Arun Qi	89	48.07 N	123.28 E
Årup	41	55.23 N	10.04 E
Aruppukkottai	122	9.31 N	78.06 E
Arurandeua ≃	250	3.43 S	48.50 W
Arusha	154	3.22 S	36.41 E
Arusha □4	154	4.00 S	36.15 E
Arusha Chini	154	3.35 S	37.20 E
Arusha National Park ♠	154	3.17 S	36.56 E
Arut ≃	112	2.42 S	111.34 E
Aruvi ≃	122	8.49 N	79.55 E
Aruwimi ≃	138	1.13 N	23.36 E
Arvada	200	39.48 N	105.05 W
Arvagh	48	53.55 N	7.34 W
Arvajcheer	90	46.15 N	102.48 E
Arve ≃	58	46.12 N	6.08 E
Arverne ⊷8	276	40.35 N	73.48 W
Arves, Les Aiguilles d' ∧	62	45.08 N	6.21 E
Arvi	120	20.59 N	78.14 E
Arvida	186	48.25 N	71.11 W
Arvidsjaur	24	65.35 N	19.07 E
Arvier	62	45.42 N	7.11 E
Arvieux	62	44.46 N	6.44 E
Arvika	26	59.39 N	12.36 E
Arvillard	62	45.27 N	6.07 E
Arvin	228	35.12 N	118.49 W
Arvo, Lago ⊜	68	39.14 N	16.29 E
Arvon, Mount ∧	190	46.45 N	88.09 W
Arvonia	192	37.40 N	78.20 W
Arvorezinha	252	28.53 S	52.10 W
Arwal	124	25.15 N	84.41 E
Arwala	112	7.41 S	126.49 E
Arxan	89	47.11 N	119.57 E
Aryamūn	142	31.11 N	30.54 E
Aryiroúpolis	267c	37.54 N	23.45 E
Arys'	85	42.26 N	68.48 E
Arys' ≃	85	42.48 N	68.12 E
Arys, ozero ⊜	86	45.50 N	66.20 E
Arzachena	71	41.05 N	9.23 E
Arzamas	80	55.23 N	43.50 E
Arzana	71	39.55 N	9.31 E
Arzano	68	40.55 N	14.16 E
Arzberg	60	50.04 N	12.12 E
Arzew, Golfe d' C	34	35.50 N	0.10 W
Arzew, Salines d' ⊜	34	35.40 N	0.15 W
Arzfeld	56	50.05 N	6.16 E
Arzignano	64	45.31 N	11.20 E
Arziw	148	35.51 N	0.19 W
Arz Lubnān ⊷3	130	34.14 N	36.03 E
Arzni	84	40.19 N	44.36 E
Arzon ≃	62	45.11 N	3.54 E
Arzúa	34	42.56 N	8.09 W
As, Bel.	56	51.01 N	5.35 E
Aš, Česká Rep.	54	50.10 N	12.10 E
Ås, Nor.	26	59.40 N	10.48 E
Asa, Nihon	96	34.33 N	132.26 E
Aša, Ross.	86	55.00 N	57.16 E
Asa ≃, Nihon	94	35.39 N	139.26 E
Asa ≃, Nihon	96	34.01 N	131.09 E
Asa ≃, Ven.	246	6.50 N	63.18 W
Asab	156	25.29 S	17.59 E
Asaba, Nig.	150	6.12 N	6.44 E
Asaba, Nihon	94	34.42 N	137.56 E
Asad, Buḥayrat al- ⊜1	130	36.00 N	38.10 E
Asadābād, Afg.	120	34.52 N	71.09 E
Asadābād, Īrān	128	34.47 N	48.07 E
Asafo	150	6.11 N	0.28 W
Asaga Strait ⊔	174y	14.11 S	169.40 W
Asagaya ⊷8	268	35.42 N	139.38 E
Aşağibostancı	130	35.10 N	33.00 E
Aşağıçiğil	130	38.03 N	31.52 E
Aşağı Dağ ∧	84	40.01 N	43.11 E
Aşağı Kuluşağı	130	38.39 N	38.39 E
Aşağılahan	130	38.50 N	39.59 E
Aşağı Mestikân	130	38.25 N	38.46 E
Ašagy-G'ojn'uk	84	41.18 N	47.00 E
Asahan	114	2.23 N	102.33 E
Asahan ≃	114	3.02 N	99.52 E
Asahi, Nihon	94	35.14 N	137.22 E
Asahi, Nihon	94	35.43 N	140.39 E
Asahi, Nihon	94	35.59 N	136.07 E
Asahi, Nihon	94	36.05 N	137.21 E
Asahi, Nihon	94	36.14 N	140.31 E
Asahi, Nihon	94	35.02 N	136.40 E
Asahi, Nihon	94	36.07 N	137.52 E
Asahi, Nihon	94	36.57 N	137.34 E
Asahi, Nihon	96	34.59 N	133.50 E
Asahi, Nihon	96	34.51 N	132.16 E
Asahi, Nihon	96	34.17 N	131.28 E
Asahi ⊷8, Nihon	268	35.29 N	139.33 E
Asahi ⊷8, Nihon	270	34.44 N	135.34 E
Asahi ≃	96	34.36 N	133.58 E
Asahi-dake ∧, Nihon	92a	43.40 N	142.51 E
Asahi-dake ∧, Nihon	94	37.14 N	139.21 E
Asahigawa → Asahikawa	92a	43.46 N	142.22 E
Asahi-gawa-daiichi-dam ⊷6	96	34.53 N	133.22 E
Asahikawa	92a	43.46 N	142.22 E
Asahikawa-chūtonchi, Rikujō-Jieitai- ■	92a	43.49 N	142.25 E
Asahi-ko ⊜1	96	34.56 N	133.51 E
Asahi-sanchi ⋏	92	38.25 N	139.50 E
Asaka	94	35.48 N	139.36 E
Asaka, Camp ■	268	35.47 N	139.36 E
Asakanskij Golec, gora ∧	88	50.18 N	109.55 E
Asakawa	94	37.05 N	140.25 E
Asake ≃	94	35.00 N	136.41 E
Asako	96	35.14 N	134.48 E
Asakura	96	33.23 N	130.44 E
Asakusa ⊷8	268	35.43 N	139.49 E
Asālafpur ⊷8	272a	28.38 N	77.05 E
Asale	144	14.22 N	40.32 E
Asale, Lake ⊜	144	14.19 N	40.18 E
Asamankese	150	5.52 N	0.42 W
Asama-yama ∧	94	36.24 N	138.31 E
Asanbani, India	126	22.43 N	86.20 E
Asanbāni, India	126	24.07 N	87.27 E
Asani	154	4.25 S	29.05 E
Asankrangwa	150	5.48 N	2.26 W
Asan-man C	98	36.56 N	126.51 E
Āsānsol, India	126	24.14 N	87.17 E
Āsānsol, India	126	23.41 N	86.59 E
Ašap	86	57.07 N	56.30 E
Asar	88	47.56 N	117.38 E
Åsarna	26	62.39 N	14.21 E
Asarum	26	56.12 N	14.50 E
Asashina	94	36.16 N	138.25 E
Āsāsuni	126	22.32 N	89.10 E
Asati	272b	22.29 N	88.14 E
Asa-yama ∧	96	34.47 N	132.23 E
Asayita	144	11.33 N	41.30 E
Asbach	56	50.40 N	7.25 E
Asbeck	263	51.21 N	7.18 E
Asberg	263	51.26 N	6.40 E
Asbesberg ⋏	158	28.55 S	23.15 E
Asbest	86	57.00 N	61.30 E
Asbestos	206	45.46 N	71.57 W
Asbestos Range National Park ♠	166	41.08 S	146.39 E
Asbe Teferi	144	9.02 N	40.58 E
Åsbro	40	59.00 N	15.03 E
Asbury	210	40.41 N	75.00 W
Asbury Park	208	40.13 N	74.01 W
Ascea	68	40.08 N	15.11 E
Ascensión	232	31.06 N	107.59 W
Ascension I	10	7.57 S	14.22 W
Ascent	158	27.12 S	29.03 E
Aščerino	265b	55.36 N	37.46 E
Asch	58	47.57 N	10.49 E
Aschabad (Ashgabat)	128	37.57 N	58.23 E
Aschach an der Donau	61	48.22 N	14.02 E
Aschaffenburg	56	49.59 N	9.09 E
Aschbach Markt	61	48.04 N	14.45 E
Ascheberg, Dtsch.	52	51.47 N	7.37 E
Ascheberg, Dtsch.	54	54.08 N	10.20 E
Aschendorf	52	53.04 N	7.22 E
Aschersleben	54	51.45 N	11.27 E
Asciano	66	43.14 N	11.33 E
Aščikol', ozero ⊜	86	45.05 N	67.15 E
Aščiozek ≃	80	49.12 N	48.06 E
Aščitastysor, ozero ⊜	86	49.19 N	63.59 E
Ascoli Piceno	66	42.51 N	13.34 E
Ascoli Piceno □4	66	43.01 N	13.34 E
Ascoli Satriano	68	41.12 N	15.34 E
Ascona	58	46.09 N	8.46 E
Ascope	248	7.43 S	79.07 W
Ascot, Austl.	171a	27.26 S	153.04 E
Ascot, Eng., U.K.	42	51.25 N	0.41 W
Ascot ≃	206	45.21 N	71.51 W
Ascotán	252	21.44 S	68.18 W
Ascros	62	43.55 N	7.01 E
Aščykol', ozero ⊜	85	43.32 N	70.35 E
Aščysu ≃	86	49.54 N	78.58 E
Aseb	144	13.00 N	42.45 E
Åseda	26	57.10 N	15.20 E
Asedjrad ⋏1	148	24.28 N	1.52 E
Asekejevo	80	53.36 N	52.49 E
Asela	144	7.59 N	39.08 E
Åsele	26	64.10 N	17.20 E
Asem ≃	115a	6.14 S	107.42 E
Asembagus	115a	7.45 S	114.14 E
Asembourg	56	49.43 N	6.02 E
Åsen	26	63.36 N	11.03 E
Asendabo	144	9.50 N	37.33 E
Asendorf	52	52.46 N	9.00 E
Asenovgrad	38	42.01 N	24.52 E
Åsensbruk	26	58.48 N	12.25 E
Aseri	76	59.27 N	26.52 E
Aṣfar, Jabal al- ∧	132	32.12 N	36.54 E
Asfordby	42	52.46 N	0.57 W
Aṣfūn al-Maṭāʿinah	140	25.23 N	32.32 E
Åsgårdstrand	26	59.21 N	10.28 E
Ash, Eng., U.K.	42	51.17 N	1.16 E
Ash, Eng., U.K.	42	51.15 N	0.44 W
Ashalim	132	30.58 N	34.40 E
Åshammar	40	60.39 N	16.32 E
Ashanti □4	150	6.45 N	1.30 W
ʿAsharah, Wādī al- V	142	30.21 N	32.15 E
Asharoken	276	40.56 N	73.22 W
Ashaway	207	41.25 N	71.47 W
Ashbourne, Ire.	48	53.31 N	6.24 W
Ashbourne, Eng., U.K.	44	53.02 N	1.44 W
Ash Brook Swamp Reservation ♠	276	40.37 N	74.21 W
Ashburn, Ga., U.S.	192	31.42 N	83.39 W
Ashburn, Mo., U.S.	219	39.33 N	91.10 W
Ashburn, Va., U.S.	208	39.02 N	77.29 W
Ashburnham	207	42.38 N	71.54 W
Ashburton, Austl.	274b	37.52 S	145.05 E
Ashburton, N.Z.	172	43.55 S	171.45 E
Ashburton, Eng., U.K.	42	50.31 N	3.45 W
Ashburton ≃, Austl.	162	21.40 S	114.56 E
Ashburton ≃, N.Z.	172	44.04 S	171.48 E
Ashburton, North Branch ≃	172	43.54 S	171.44 E
Ashburton, South Branch ≃	172	43.44 S	171.32 E
Ashburton Downs	162	23.24 S	117.04 E
Ashby	207	42.40 N	71.49 W
Ashby, Lake ⊜	220	28.56 N	81.07 W
Ashby-de-la-Zouch	42	52.46 N	1.28 W
Ashchurch	42	52.00 N	2.07 W
Ash Creek ≃, Ca., U.S.	204	41.05 N	121.08 W
Ash Creek ≃, Ct., U.S.	276	41.08 N	73.14 W
Ashcroft	182	50.43 N	121.17 W
Ashdod, Ma., U.S.	283	42.04 N	70.45 W
Ashdod, Yis.	132	31.49 N	34.40 E
Ashdod, Tel ⊥	132	31.45 N	34.40 E
Ashdot Yaʿaqov	132	32.40 N	35.35 E
Ashdown	194	33.40 N	94.07 W
Asheboro	192	35.42 N	79.48 W
Ashern	184	51.11 N	98.21 W
Asherton	196	28.26 N	99.45 W
Asheville	192	35.36 N	82.33 W
Ashewat Ziārat	120	31.22 N	68.32 E
Asheweig ≃	176	54.17 N	87.12 W
Ashfield, Austl.	274a	33.53 S	151.08 E
Ashfield, Ma., U.S.	207	42.31 N	72.47 W
Ash Flat	194	36.13 N	91.36 W
Ashford, Austl.	166	29.20 S	151.06 E
Ashford, Eng., U.K.	42	51.08 N	0.53 E
Ashford, Eng., U.K.	260	51.26 N	0.27 W
Ashford, Al., U.S.	194	31.10 N	85.14 W
Ashford, Wa., U.S.	224	46.46 N	122.02 W
Ashford Airport ⊠	42	51.04 N	1.01 E
Ash Fork	200	35.13 N	112.28 W
Ash Grove	194	37.18 N	93.35 W
Ashhurst	172	40.18 S	175.45 E
Ashibe	92	33.48 N	129.46 E
Ashibetsu	92a	43.31 N	142.11 E
Ashida ≃	96	34.26 N	133.25 E
Ashikaga	94	36.20 N	139.27 E
Ashikagga-gakkō ⊥	94	36.22 N	139.30 E
Ashingdon	260	51.36 N	0.42 E
Ashington	44	55.12 N	1.35 W
Ashino-ko ⊜	94	35.13 N	139.00 E
Ashio	94	36.38 N	139.27 E
Ashio-sanchi ⋏	94	36.35 N	139.30 E
Ashippun	216	43.14 N	88.31 W
Ashippun ≃	216	43.10 N	88.33 W
Ashitaka-yama ∧	94	35.12 N	138.49 E
Ashiya, Nihon	96	33.53 N	130.40 E
Ashiya, Nihon	96	34.43 N	135.17 E
Ashiya ≃	270	34.43 N	135.18 E
Ashiyasu	94	35.38 N	138.23 E
Ashiyoro	92a	43.15 N	143.30 E
Ashizuri-misaki ›	92	32.44 N	133.01 E
Ashizuri-Uwakai-kokuritsu-kōen ♠, Nihon	92	32.45 N	132.45 E
Ashizuri-Uwakai-kokuritsu-kōen ♠, Nihon	96	33.07 N	132.27 E
Ashkhabad → Aschabad	128	37.57 N	58.23 E
Ashkum	216	40.53 N	87.57 W
Ashland, Al., U.S.	194	33.16 N	85.50 W
Ashland, Ca., U.S.	226	37.41 N	122.06 W
Ashland, Il., U.S.	219	39.53 N	90.00 W
Ashland, Ks., U.S.	198	37.11 N	99.45 W
Ashland, Ky., U.S.	188	38.28 N	82.38 W
Ashland, Me., U.S.	186	46.37 N	68.24 W
Ashland, Ma., U.S.	207	42.15 N	71.27 W
Ashland, Ms., U.S.	194	34.49 N	89.10 W
Ashland, Mo., U.S.	219	38.46 N	92.15 W
Ashland, Mt., U.S.	202	45.35 N	106.16 W
Ashland, Ne., U.S.	198	41.02 N	96.22 W
Ashland, N.H., U.S.	188	43.41 N	71.37 W
Ashland, N.J., U.S.	285	39.51 N	75.00 W
Ashland, N.Y., U.S.	210	42.18 N	74.20 W
Ashland, Oh., U.S.	214	40.52 N	82.19 W
Ashland, Or., U.S.	202	42.11 N	122.42 W
Ashland, Pa., U.S.	210	40.46 N	76.20 W
Ashland, Va., U.S.	208	37.45 N	77.28 W
Ashland, Wi., U.S.	190	46.35 N	90.53 W
Ashland □6	214	40.52 N	82.19 W
Ashland, Mount ∧	202	42.05 N	122.43 W
Ashland City	194	36.16 N	87.03 W
Ashley, Austl.	166	29.19 S	149.49 E
Ashley, Eng., U.K.	262	53.21 N	2.20 W
Ashley, Il., U.S.	219	38.20 N	89.11 W
Ashley, In., U.S.	216	41.32 N	85.04 W
Ashley, Mi., U.S.	190	43.11 N	84.28 W
Ashley, Mo., U.S.	219	39.15 N	91.14 W
Ashley, N.D., U.S.	198	46.01 N	99.22 W
Ashley, Oh., U.S.	214	40.24 N	82.57 W
Ashley, Pa., U.S.	210	41.12 N	75.53 W
Ashley ≃	172	43.16 S	172.43 E
Ashley Creek ≃	200	40.21 N	109.22 W
Ashley Falls	207	42.03 N	73.20 W
Ashley Green	260	51.44 N	0.35 W
Ashmore	194	39.32 N	88.01 W
Ashmore Islands II	160	12.14 S	123.05 E
Ashmūn	142	30.18 N	30.58 E
Ashokan Reservoir ⊜1	210	41.58 N	74.10 W
Ashoknagar	120	24.34 N	77.43 E
Ashqelon	132	31.40 N	34.35 E
Ashridge Park ♠	260	51.48 N	0.34 W
Ash-Shabakah	128	30.49 N	43.39 E
Ash-Shabb ⫟4	140	22.19 N	29.46 E
Ash-Shaddādah	130	36.02 N	40.45 E
Ash-Shāgūr	132	31.50 N	35.39 E
Ash-Shāʿib ∧2	142	29.50 N	30.56 E
Ash-Shajarah	132	32.39 N	35.56 E
Ash-Shallūfah	142	30.07 N	32.34 E
Ash-Shamāl □4	130	34.30 N	36.00 E
Ash-Shamālīyah □4	140	19.15 N	29.00 E
Ash-Shāmīyah	128	31.57 N	44.36 E
Ash-Shanāwīyah	142	29.08 N	31.08 E
Ash-Sharāh ⊷1	132	30.20 N	35.30 E
Ash-Shāriqah	128	25.22 N	55.23 E
Ash-Sharmah	128	28.01 N	35.18 E
Ash-Sharqāṭ	128	35.27 N	43.16 E
Ash-Sharqīyah □4	142	30.48 N	31.48 E
Ash-Sharqīyah ⊷1	128	27.00 N	49.00 E
Ash-Shaṭrah	128	31.25 N	46.10 E
Ash-Shawāshinah	142	29.22 N	30.36 E
Ash-Shawbak	132	30.32 N	35.34 E
Ash-Shawmarah	132	33.07 N	35.08 E
Ash-Shaykh Faḍl	142	28.29 N	30.50 E
Ash-Shaykh ʿIbādah	142	27.48 N	30.52 E
Ash-Shaykh Saʿd	132	32.50 N	36.02 E
Ash-Shaykh Timay	142	27.53 N	30.51 E
Ash-Shiḥr	144	14.44 N	49.35 E
Ash-Shīn	142	31.01 N	30.53 E
Ash-Shināfīyah	128	31.35 N	44.39 E
Ash-Shīyāḥ	132	33.51 N	35.30 E
Ash-Shufayyah	128	23.50 N	39.08 E
Ash-Shuhadāʾ	142	30.36 N	30.54 E
Ash-Shumlul	128	26.31 N	47.19 E
Ash-Shuqayq	144	17.43 N	42.01 E
Ash-Shurayf	128	25.43 N	39.14 E
Ash-Shurayk	140	18.48 N	33.34 E
Ash-Shuwayfāt	132	33.49 N	35.31 E
Ash Slough ≃	226	37.02 N	120.32 W
Ashta, India	122	16.57 N	74.24 E
Ashta, India	124	23.01 N	76.43 E
Ashtabula	214	41.51 N	80.47 W
Ashtabula □6	214	41.44 N	80.46 W
Ashtabula ≃	214	41.55 N	80.47 W
Ashtabula, East Branch ≃	214	41.48 N	80.37 W
Ashtabula, Lake ⊜1	198	47.11 N	97.58 W
Ashtabula, West Branch ≃	214	41.48 N	80.37 W
Ashtead	42	51.19 N	0.18 W
Ashton, S. Afr.	158	33.50 S	20.05 E
Ashton, Eng., U.K.	262	53.13 N	2.45 W
Ashton, Id., U.S.	202	44.04 N	111.26 W
Ashton, Il., U.S.	190	41.51 N	89.13 W
Ashton, Ia., U.S.	198	43.18 N	95.47 W
Ashton, Md., U.S.	208	39.08 N	77.00 W
Ashton, Ne., U.S.	198	41.14 N	98.47 W
Ashton, R.I., U.S.	207	41.46 N	71.25 W
Ashton-in-Makerfield	44	53.29 N	2.39 W
Ashton-under-Lyne	44	53.29 N	2.06 W
Ashton upon Mersey	262	53.26 N	2.19 W
Ashuanipi Lake ⊜	176	52.35 N	66.10 W
Ashuelot ≃	188	42.46 N	72.29 W
Ashurst's Beacon ∧2	262	53.34 N	2.45 W
Ashville, Al., U.S.	194	33.52 N	86.17 W
Ashville, N.Y., U.S.	214	42.06 N	79.23 W
Ashville, Oh., U.S.	218	39.42 N	82.57 W
Ashville, Pa., U.S.	214	40.34 N	78.33 W
Ashwater	42	50.44 N	4.16 W
Ashwaubenon	190	44.30 N	88.06 W
Ashworth Moor Reservoir ⊜1	262	53.38 N	2.16 W
Asi (Nahr al-ʿĀṣī) ≃	130	36.02 N	35.58 E
Asia ≗1	4	50.00 N	100.00 E
Asia ≗1	12	50.00 N	100.00 E
Asia, Kepulauan II	108	1.03 N	131.18 E
Asiago	64	45.52 N	11.30 E
Asia Menor → Asia Minor □9	22	39.00 N	32.00 E
Asia Minor □9	22	39.00 N	32.00 E
Asid Gulf C	116	12.07 N	123.30 E
Asie → Asia ≗1	12	50.00 N	100.00 E
Asie Mineure → Asia Minor □9	22	39.00 N	32.00 E
Asien → Asia ≗1	12	50.00 N	100.00 E
āsika	120	19.36 N	84.39 E
Asikuma	150	5.35 N	1.00 W
Asilah	148	35.32 N	6.00 W
Asinara, Golfo dell' C	71	41.00 N	8.32 E
Asinara, Isola I	71	41.04 N	8.16 E
Asinaro ≃	70	36.53 N	15.08 E
Asino	86	57.00 N	86.09 E
Asipoquobah Lake ⊜	184	53.40 N	91.15 W
ʿAsīr ⊷1	144	19.00 N	42.00 E
Ašitkovo	82	55.26 N	38.36 E
Aşkale	130	39.55 N	40.42 E
Askam in Furness	44	54.11 N	3.13 W
Askanija-Nova	78	46.27 N	33.52 E
Askanija-nova zapovednik ♠	78	46.37 N	33.54 E
Askarovo	86	53.21 N	58.30 E
Askeaton	48	52.36 N	8.58 W
Asker	26	59.50 N	10.26 E
Askern	44	53.37 N	1.09 W
Askersund	40	58.53 N	14.54 E
Askham	158	26.59 S	20.47 E
Askim	26	59.35 N	11.10 E
Askino	86	56.05 N	56.34 E
Askira	146	10.39 N	12.55 E
Askival ∧	46	56.59 N	6.17 W
Askiz	86	53.08 N	90.32 E
Askja ∧1	24a	65.00 N	16.48 W
Askø I	41	54.54 N	11.30 E
Äsköping	40	59.09 N	16.04 E
Askov	41	55.28 N	9.06 E
Askraal	158	34.09 S	20.52 E
Askrigg	44	54.19 N	2.04 W
Askvoll	26	61.21 N	5.04 E
Aslanapa	130	39.13 N	29.52 E
Aslan-Sara	84	39.02 N	48.16 E
Aslantaş Barajı ⊜1	130	37.20 N	36.15 E
Asleigh	284c	39.01 N	77.10 W
Asljunga	41	56.19 N	13.22 E
Ašlyk	86	57.33 N	68.40 E
Ašlyk ≃	86	57.50 N	69.12 E
Asmār	120	35.02 N	71.22 E
Asmara → Asmera	144	15.20 N	38.53 E
Asmera	144	15.20 N	38.53 E
Asmundtorp	41	55.53 N	12.56 E
Asnæs	41	55.49 N	11.31 E
Asnæs ›1	41	55.40 N	11.00 E
Asnebumskit Hill ∧2	207	42.18 N	71.54 W
Åsnen ⊜	26	56.38 N	14.42 E
Asni	148	31.14 N	7.55 W
Asnières [-sur-Seine]	50	48.55 N	2.17 E
Asō, Nihon	94	35.59 N	140.29 E
Aso, Nihon	96	32.58 N	131.02 E
Aso ≃	66	43.06 N	13.51 E
Asoc	152	1.26 N	11.18 E
Aso-kokuritsu-kōen ♠	92	33.00 N	131.07 E
Asola	64	45.13 N	10.24 E
Asolo	64	45.48 N	11.54 E
Asomante	240m	18.23 N	66.36 W
Ason	273a	6.34 N	3.31 E
Asosa	144	10.03 N	34.32 E
Aso-san ∧	92	32.53 N	131.06 E
Asoteriba, Jabal ∧	140	21.51 N	36.30 E
Asotin	202	46.20 N	117.02 W
Asouf, Oued V	148	25.51 N	1.33 E
Asowsches Meer → Azovskoje more ⫟2	78	46.00 N	36.00 E
Asp	34	38.21 N	0.46 W
Aspach	60	48.11 N	13.18 E
Aspach-le-Bas	58	47.46 N	7.09 E
Aspang Markt	61	47.33 N	16.06 E
Aspara ≃	85	43.17 N	73.28 E
Aspatria	44	54.46 N	3.20 W
Aspe, Gave d' ≃	32	43.12 N	0.36 W
Aspen	200	39.11 N	106.49 W
Aspen Butte ∧	202	42.19 N	122.05 W
Aspendale	274b	38.02 S	145.07 E
Aspendos ⊥	130	37.00 N	31.10 E
Aspen Hill	284c	39.04 N	77.04 W
Aspen Knolls	284c	39.05 N	77.05 W
Aspen Lake ⊜	202	42.18 N	122.00 W
Asperg	56	48.54 N	9.07 E
Aspermont	196	33.08 N	100.13 W
Aspern ⊷8	264b	48.13 N	16.29 E
Aspers	208	39.59 N	77.13 W
Asperup	41	55.29 N	9.55 E
Aspid, Mount ∧	180	53.30 N	167.33 W
Aspindza	84	41.36 N	43.15 E
Aspinwall → Colón, Pan.	236	9.22 N	79.54 W
Aspinwall, Pa., U.S.	279b	40.29 N	79.54 W
Aspiring, Mount ∧	172	44.23 S	168.44 E
Aspö	40	59.29 N	17.02 E
Aspres-sur-Buëch	62	44.31 N	5.45 E
Aspromonte ⋏	68	38.10 N	15.55 E
Asprópirgos	267c	38.04 N	23.35 E
Aspull	262	53.34 N	2.35 W
Aspy Bay C	186	46.55 N	60.25 W
Asquins	50	47.29 N	3.45 E
Asquith, Austl.	274a	33.41 S	151.06 E
Asquith, Sk., Can.	184	52.08 N	107.13 W
Asralt chajrchan ∧	88	48.29 N	107.24 E
Asrāni	123	29.31 N	72.07 E
Assa, Kaz.	85	43.02 N	71.10 E
Assa, Magreb	148	28.34 N	9.27 W
Assa ≃, Kaz.	85	43.55 N	70.25 E
Assa ≃, Ross.	84	43.13 N	45.25 E
As-Saʿata	140	13.37 N	29.59 E
Assab → Aseb	144	13.00 N	42.45 E
Assabet ≃	283	42.28 N	71.21 W
As-Sabkhah	130	35.48 N	39.15 E
Aṣ-Ṣadārah	144	14.30 N	48.04 E
As-Saʿdīyah	128	34.11 N	45.07 E
Aṣ-Ṣaff	140	29.34 N	31.17 E
As-Saffānīyah	128	27.58 N	48.47 E
Aṣ-Ṣāfī	132	31.02 N	35.28 E
As-Safīrah	130	36.04 N	37.22 E
Aṣ-Ṣāfiyah	140	15.31 N	30.07 E
Assago	266b	45.24 N	9.08 E
Assaí	255	23.22 S	50.49 W
Aṣ-Ṣaʿīd □9	140	26.00 N	32.00 E
Assaikwatamo ≃	184	56.52 N	95.50 W
Assal, Lac ⊜	144	11.41 N	42.25 E
ʿAssāl al-Ward	132	33.52 N	36.24 E
Aṣ-Ṣāliḥīyah	142	30.47 N	31.59 E
As-Salīmah	144	14.02 N	45.46 E
As-Sallūm	140	31.34 N	25.09 E
As-Salmān	128	30.30 N	44.32 E
As-Salṭ	132	32.03 N	35.44 E
Assam □3	120	26.00 N	93.00 E
As-Samāwah	128	31.18 N	45.17 E
As-Samūʿ	132	31.24 N	35.04 E
Assam Valley V	124	26.30 N	90.30 E
ʿAssān	130	36.05 N	37.14 E
Aṣ-Ṣanāfīn Al-Qiblīyah	142	30.27 N	31.18 E
Aṣ-Ṣanamayn	132	33.05 N	36.10 E
As-Santah	142	30.45 N	31.08 E
Assaq, Oued V	148	25.41 N	14.40 W
Aṣ-Ṣaqlabiyah	130	35.22 N	36.23 E
Aṣ-Ṣarafand	132	33.27 N	35.18 E
Assaré	250	6.52 S	39.52 W
Aṣ-Ṣarīḥ	132	32.30 N	35.54 E
As-Sarīrīyah	142	28.20 N	30.45 E
Assateague Island I	208	38.05 N	75.10 W
Assateague Island National Seashore ♠	208	38.00 N	75.15 W
Assawoman Bay C	208	38.25 N	75.05 W
Assawoman Canal ≋	208	38.31 N	75.04 W
Assawompset Pond ⊜	207	41.50 N	70.55 W
Asse	50	50.55 N	4.12 E
Asse ≃	62	43.53 N	5.53 E
Assean Lake ⊜	184	56.13 N	96.30 W
Assebroek	50	51.12 N	3.16 E
Assekaifaf	148	27.08 N	8.50 E
Assel	52	53.41 N	9.25 E
Asseln ⊷8	263	51.32 N	7.35 E
Assembleia Nacional, Palacio da ⊍	266c	38.43 N	9.09 W
Assemini	71	39.17 N	9.00 E
Assen	52	52.59 N	6.34 E
Assendelft	52	52.27 N	4.45 E
Assenede	50	51.14 N	3.45 E
Assens	41	55.16 N	9.55 E
Asserbo	41	56.01 N	12.01 E
Assergi	66	42.25 N	13.30 E
Asseria ⊥	36	44.02 N	15.39 E
As-Sīb	128	23.41 N	58.11 E
As-Sidr	128	23.27 N	39.45 E
As-Sijn	132	32.47 N	36.28 E
As-Simākīyah	132	31.18 N	35.48 E
As-Sinbillāwayn	142	30.53 N	31.27 E
Assíni ⊥	38	37.36 N	22.48 E
Assiniboia	184	49.38 N	105.59 W
Assiniboine ≃	184	49.53 N	97.08 W
Assiniboine, Mount ∧	182	50.52 N	115.39 W
Assiniboine Indian Reserve ⊷4	184	50.21 N	103.28 W
Assinika ≃	184	52.37 N	96.10 W
Assinippi	283	42.09 N	70.51 W
Assis	255	22.40 S	50.25 W
Assis Chateaubriand	252	24.29 S	53.32 W
Assiscunk Creek ≃	208	40.05 N	74.51 W
Assisi	66	43.04 N	12.37 E
Asslar	56	50.35 N	8.28 E
Assling	60	48.00 N	12.00 E
Asso	62	45.52 N	9.16 E
Assodé ⫟4	150	18.26 N	8.28 E
Assomada	150a	15.06 N	23.41 W
Assonet	207	41.47 N	71.04 W
Assoro	70	37.37 N	14.25 E
As-Subūʿ ⊥	140	22.45 N	32.34 E
As-Sūdān → Sudan □1	140	15.00 N	30.00 E
As-Sudd ⊷1	140	8.00 N	31.00 E
As-Sufāl	144	14.06 N	48.42 E
Aṣ-Ṣufayyah	140	15.30 N	34.42 E
Aṣ-Ṣūfīyah	142	30.55 N	31.46 E
As-Sukhnah, Sūrīy.	130	34.52 N	38.52 E
As-Sukhnah, Urd.	132	32.08 N	36.04 E
As-Sulaymānīyah, Ar. Su.	128	24.09 N	47.19 E
As-Sulaymānīyah, ʿIrāq	128	35.33 N	45.26 E
As-Sulaymānīyah □4	128	35.30 N	45.25 E
As-Sulaymī	128	26.17 N	41.21 E
As-Sulayyil	144	20.27 N	45.34 E
As-Sulṭān	146	31.07 N	17.10 E
As-Sumayḥ	140	9.49 N	27.39 E
Aṣ-Ṣummān ⊷1	128	25.00 N	47.00 E
As-Summāqīyāt	132	32.26 N	36.24 E
Assumption, Il., U.S.	219	39.31 N	89.02 W
Assumption, Oh., U.S.	216	41.40 N	83.54 W
Assumption Island I	138	9.45 S	46.30 E
Assunpink Creek ≃	285	40.13 N	74.46 W
As-Suʿūdīyah	142	29.33 N	31.14 E
Aṣ-Ṣuwār	130	35.30 N	40.39 E
As-Suwaydāʾ	132	32.42 N	36.34 E
As-Suwaydāʾ □8	132	32.45 N	36.45 E
As-Suways (Suez)	142	29.58 N	32.33 E
As-Suways □4	142	30.12 N	32.30 E
Assynt, Loch ⊜	46	58.11 N	5.06 W
Ašt	85	40.41 N	70.20 E
Asta, Cima d' ∧	64	46.10 N	11.36 E
Astachovo	83	47.52 N	39.37 E
Astaffort	32	44.04 N	0.40 E
Astakós	38	38.32 N	21.05 E
Āstāneh, Īrān	128	37.17 N	49.59 E
Āstāneh, Īrān	128	33.53 N	49.22 E
Astara, Azer.	84	38.28 N	48.52 E
Āstārā, Īrān	128	38.26 N	48.52 E
Aštarak	84	40.18 N	44.22 E
Astaškovo	82	55.32 N	38.38 E
Astatula	220	28.43 N	81.44 W
Asten, Ned.	52	51.24 N	5.45 E
Asten, Öst.	61	48.13 N	14.25 E
Asti	62	44.54 N	8.12 E
Asti □4	62	44.55 N	8.10 E
Astica	252	30.56 S	67.23 W
Astico ≃	64	45.37 N	11.37 E
Astillero	34	43.24 N	3.49 W
Astipálaia	38	36.30 N	26.30 E
Astipálaia I	38	36.35 N	26.25 E
Astley Bridge	262	53.36 N	2.26 W
Astley Green	262	53.29 N	2.27 W
Astley Hall ⊥	262	53.39 N	2.38 W
Astola Island I	128	25.07 N	63.51 E
Astolfo Dutra	256	21.19 S	42.52 W
Aston, Eng., U.K.	262	53.18 N	2.40 W
Aston, Pa., U.S.	285	39.52 N	75.26 W
Aston Clinton	42	51.48 N	0.44 W
Aston-on-Trent	42	52.52 N	1.23 W
Astor	123	35.22 N	74.51 E
Astor ≃	123	35.34 N	74.41 E
Astorga, Bra.	255	23.13 S	51.40 W
Astorga, Esp.	34	42.27 N	6.03 W
Astorga, Pil.	116	6.54 N	125.27 E
Astoria, Il., U.S.	219	40.13 N	90.21 W
Astoria, Or., U.S.	224	46.11 N	123.49 W
Astoria ⊷8	276	40.46 N	73.55 W
Astoria Bridge ⊷5	224	46.13 N	123.52 W
Astoria Column ⊥	224	46.11 N	123.50 W
Åstorp	41	56.08 N	12.57 E
Astove Island I	138	10.06 S	47.45 E
Astra	254	45.44 S	67.30 W
Astrachan'	80	46.21 N	48.03 E
Astrachanka	86	51.33 N	69.47 E
Astrachan' Oblast' □4	80	47.00 N	47.30 E
Astrachanskij	80	46.12 N	47.16 E
Astrachanskij zapovednik ⊷4	80	46.00 N	48.32 E
Astrakhan → Astrachan'	80	46.21 N	48.03 E
Astrodome ♠	222	29.41 N	95.25 W
Astrolabe, Cape ›	175e	8.20 S	160.34 E
Astrolabe Bay C	164	5.20 S	145.50 E
Astrolabe Reefs ✢2	175f	19.48 S	165.37 E
Astudillo	34	42.12 N	4.18 W
Astura, Torre ⊥	66	41.24 N	12.46 E
Asturias	116	10.34 N	123.43 E
Asturias □4, Esp.	34	43.20 N	6.00 W
Asturias □4, Esp.	34	43.20 N	6.00 W
Astwood Bank	42	52.15 N	1.56 W
Asubulak	86	49.31 N	83.03 E
Asuisui, Cape ›	175a	13.47 S	172.29 W
Asuka	96	34.28 N	135.50 E
Asuka ⊍3	9	71.32 S	24.08 E
Asuke	94	35.08 N	137.19 E
Asunción	252	25.16 S	57.40 W
Asunción, Bahía C	232	27.06 N	114.11 W
Asuncion Island I	108	19.40 N	145.24 E
Asunción Ixtaltepec	234	16.30 N	95.03 W
Asunción Mita	236	14.20 N	89.43 W
Asunción Nochixtlán	234	17.28 N	97.14 W
Åsunden ⊜, Sve.	26	57.58 N	15.50 E
Åsunden ⊜, Sve.	26	57.44 N	13.22 E
Asunga, Wādī V	146	13.21 N	22.17 E
Asuni	71	39.52 N	8.56 E
ʿĀṣūr, Tall ∧	132	31.59 N	35.17 E
Asuwa	94	36.01 N	136.16 E
Asuwa ≃	94	36.04 N	136.11 E
Aswad, Ar-Raʾs al- ›	144	21.22 N	39.08 E
Aswān	140	24.05 N	32.53 E
Aswān High Dam → ʿĀli, As-Sadd al- ⊷6	140	23.58 N	32.52 E
Aswatthaberia	272b	22.26 N	88.32 E
Asy ≃	85	43.31 N	78.20 E
Asyūṭ	142	27.11 N	31.11 E
Asyūṭ □4	142	27.20 N	30.50 E
Asyūṭī, Wādī al- V	142	27.11 N	31.16 E
Aszód	30	47.39 N	19.31 E
ʻAta I, Tonga	14	22.20 S	176.12 W
Ata I, Tonga	174w	21.03 S	175.00 W
Atabaj	85	43.30 N	68.20 E
Atabapo ≃	246	4.03 N	67.42 W
Atabasca → Athabasca ≃	176	58.40 N	110.50 W
Atabasca, Lago → Athabasca, Lake ⊜	176	59.07 N	110.00 W
Atabey	130	37.57 N	30.39 E
Atacama □4	252	27.30 S	70.00 W
Atacama, Desierto de ⊷2	18	24.30 S	69.15 W
Atacama, Puna de ⋏1	252	24.30 S	67.30 W
Atacama, Salar de ≚	252	23.30 S	68.15 W
Ataco	246	3.35 N	75.23 W
Atacora, Chaîne de l' ⋏	150	10.45 N	1.30 E
Atacuari ≃	246	3.47 S	70.44 W
Atafu I1	14	8.33 S	172.30 W
Atagaj	88	55.06 N	99.23 E
Atago-yama ∧, Nihon	94	35.07 N	139.59 E
Atago-yama ∧, Nihon	96	35.03 N	135.37 E
Ātāi ≃1	126	22.51 N	89.33 E
ʿAṭāʿiṭah, Jabal al- ∧	132	30.40 N	35.39 E
Atakakup Indian Reserve ⊷4	184	53.24 N	106.55 W
Atakano-seki ⊥	94	36.24 N	136.25 E
Ataki	38	48.25 N	27.47 E
Atakora □5	150	10.00 N	1.35 E
Atakora, Réserve d' ⊷4	150	11.30 N	2.10 E
Atakpamé	150	7.32 N	1.08 E
Atalaia, Bra.	250	9.31 S	36.02 W
Atalaia, Port.	266c	38.42 N	8.55 W
Atalándi	38	38.39 N	23.00 E
Atalanka	88	54.50 N	103.05 E
Atalaya, Arg.	258	35.02 S	57.32 W
Atalaya, Pan.	236	8.03 N	80.56 W
Atalaya, Perú	248	10.44 S	73.45 W
Atalaya, Cerro ∧, Chile	254	52.45 S	72.42 W
Atalaya, Cerro ∧, Perú	248	12.38 S	71.56 W
Atalaya, Punta ›	258	35.01 S	57.31 W
Atamanovka	88	51.56 N	113.37 E
Atamanovo	86	56.24 N	93.36 E
Atambua	112	9.07 S	124.54 E
Atami	94	35.05 N	139.04 E
Atapupu	112	9.00 S	124.51 E
ʿAtāq	144	14.33 N	46.48 E
ʿAtāqah, Jabal ⋏	142	29.58 N	32.20 E
Atâr	150	20.31 N	13.03 W
Ataram, 'Erg n- ⊷2	148	23.46 N	1.44 E
Atarés, Castillo de ⊥	286b	23.08 N	82.21 W
Atāri	123	31.36 N	74.35 E
Atary	80	57.32 N	49.18 E
Atascadero	226	35.29 N	120.40 W
Atascosa ≃	196	28.26 N	98.12 W
At'aševo	80	54.36 N	46.06 E
Atasu	86	48.42 N	71.38 E
Atas uul ∧	102	43.18 N	96.36 E
Atata I	174w	21.03 S	175.15 W
Atatürk Barajı ⊜1	130	37.30 N	38.30 E
Ataturk Tower ⊥	267b	41.00 N	28.59 E
Ataur	272a	28.43 N	77.24 E
Atauro, Pulau I	112	8.13 S	125.35 E
Atbara (ʿAṭbarah) ≃	140	17.40 N	33.56 E
ʿAṭbarah	140	17.42 N	33.59 E
ʿAṭbarah (Atbara) ≃	140	17.40 N	33.56 E
Atbasar	86	51.48 N	68.20 E
At-Baši	85	41.10 N	75.48 E
Atbaši ≃	85	41.24 N	75.38 E
Atbaši, chrebet ⋏	85	40.55 N	75.40 E
Atchafalaya ≃	194	29.53 N	91.28 W
Atchafalaya Bay C	194	29.25 N	91.20 W
Atchison	198	39.33 N	95.07 W
Atco	208	39.46 N	74.53 W
Ate	286d	12.03 S	76.58 W
Atebubu	150	7.45 N	0.59 W
Ateca	34	41.20 N	1.47 W
Atelchu ≃	255	12.05 S	53.46 W
Ateleta	66	41.51 N	14.12 E
Ateli	124	28.06 N	76.17 E
Atella	68	40.52 N	15.39 E
Atemajac de Brizuela	234	20.11 N	103.42 W
Atemar	80	54.11 N	45.24 E
Atemble	164	5.05 S	144.45 E
Atena Lucana	68	40.27 N	15.33 E
Atenango del Río	234	18.05 N	99.06 W
Atenas → Athínai	38	37.58 N	23.43 E
Atencingo	234	18.30 N	98.36 W
Atengo ≃	234	21.50 N	104.43 W
Atenguillo	234	20.25 N	104.31 W
Atenguillo ≃	234	20.55 N	104.38 W
Atenquique	234	19.31 N	103.30 W
Atepcevo	82	55.20 N	36.46 E
Aterau	80	47.07 N	51.56 E
Aterau □4	80	47.30 N	51.00 E
Aterno ≃	66	42.11 N	13.51 E
Aterrado, Ribeirão do ≃	256	22.09 S	45.03 W
Atessa	66	42.04 N	14.27 E
Aṭfīḥ	142	29.24 N	31.15 E
Aṭfīḥī, Wādī al- V	142	29.23 N	31.16 E
Ātgharia	126	24.06 N	89.14 E
Atglen	208	39.57 N	75.58 W
Ath	50	50.38 N	3.47 E
Athabasca	182	54.43 N	113.17 W
Athabasca ≃	176	58.40 N	110.50 W
Athabasca, Lake ⊜	176	59.07 N	110.00 W
Athalmer	182	50.32 N	116.02 W
Athapapuskow Lake ⊜	184	54.33 N	101.40 W
Athārabānki ≃1	126	22.49 N	89.39 E
Athārān Hazāri	123	31.11 N	72.06 E
Athboy	48	53.37 N	6.55 W
Athea	48	52.28 N	9.17 W
Athen → Athínai	38	37.58 N	23.43 E
Athena	202	45.48 N	118.29 W
Athènes → Athínai	38	37.58 N	23.43 E
Athenry	48	53.18 N	8.45 W
Athens, On., Can.	212	44.38 N	75.57 W
Athens → Athínai, Ellás	38	37.58 N	23.43 E

Symbols in the index entries represent the broad categories identified in the key at the right. Symbols with superior numbers (⋏1) identify subcategories (see complete key on page *I · 1).*

Symbole im Register stellen die rechts im Schlüssel erklärten Kategorien dar. Symbole mit hochgestellten Ziffern (⋏1) bezeichnen Unterabteilungen einer Kategorie (vgl. vollständiger Schlüssel auf Seite *I · 1).*

Los símbolos incluídos en el texto del índice representan las grandes categorías identificadas con la clave a la derecha. Los símbolos con numeros en su parte superior (⋏1) identifican las subcategorías (véase la clave completa en la página *I · 1).*

Les symboles de l'index représentent les catégories indiquées dans la légende à droite. Les symboles suivis d'un indice (⋏1) représentent des sous-catégories (voir légende complète à la page *I · 1).*

Os símbolos incluídos no texto do índice representam as grandes categorias identificadas com a chave à direita. Os símbolos com números em sua parte superior (⋏1) identificam as subcategorias (veja-se a chave completa à página *I · 1).*

Symbol	English	Deutsch	Español	Français	Português
∧	Mountain	Berg	Montaña	Montagne	Montanha
⋏	Mountains	Gebirge	Montañas	Montagnes	Montanhas
)(	Pass	Paß	Paso	Col	Passo
V	Valley, Canyon	Tal, Cañon	Valle, Cañón	Vallée, Canyon	Vale, Canhão
≚	Plain	Ebene	Llano	Plaine	Planície
›	Cape	Kap	Cabo	Cap	Cabo
I	Island	Insel	Isla	Île	Ilha
II	Islands	Inseln	Islas	Îles	Ilhas
≗	Other Topographic Features	Andere Topographische Objekte	Otros Elementos Topográficos	Autres données topographiques	Outros acidentes topográficos

ESPAÑOL Nombre	Página	Lat.°'	Long.°' W=Oeste
FRANÇAIS Nom	Page	Lat.°'	Long.°' W=Ouest
PORTUGUÊS Nome	Página	Lat.°'	Long.°' W=Oeste

Athens, Al., U.S. 194 34.48 N 86.58 W
Athens, Ga., U.S. 192 33.57 N 83.22 W
Athens, Il., U.S. 219 39.57 N 89.43 W
Athens, La., U.S. 192 32.39 N 93.01 W
Athens, Mi., U.S. 216 42.05 N 85.14 W
Athens, N.Y., U.S. 210 42.15 N 73.48 W
Athens, Oh., U.S. 188 39.19 N 82.06 W
Athens, Pa., U.S. 210 41.57 N 76.31 W
Athens, Tn., U.S. 192 35.26 N 84.35 W
Athens, Tx., U.S. 222 32.12 N 95.51 W
Athens, W.V., U.S. 192 37.25 N 81.00 W
Athens, Wi., U.S. 190 45.01 N 90.04 W
Athenstedt 54 51.56 N 10.55 E
Athens University 267 37.59 N 23.44 E
Atherley 212 44.36 N 79.22 W
Atherstone 42 52.35 N 1.31 W
Atherton, Austl. 166 17.16 S 145.29 E
Atherton, Eng., U.K. 44 53.31 N 2.31 W
Atherton, Ca., U.S. 226 37.27 N 122.11 W
Athi ≈ 154 2.59 S 38.31 E
Athiaïnou 130 35.04 N 33.32 E
Athiémé 106 6.35 N 1.40 E
Athies-sous-Laon 50 49.34 N 3.41 E
Athinaí (Athens), Ellás 38 37.58 N 23.43 E
Athinaí (Athens), Ellás 267c 37.58 N 23.43 E
Athiopien → Ethiopia ▫ 144 9.00 N 41.00 E
Athi River 154 1.27 S 36.59 E
Athis-Mons 261 48.43 N 2.24 E
Athlat al-Bāshā ✶ 132 27.31 N 32.20 E
Athleague 48 53.34 N 8.15 W
Athlone 48 53.25 N 7.56 W
Athni 122 16.44 N 75.04 E
Athok, N.Z. 172 45.31 S 168.35 E
Athol, Ma., U.S. 207 42.35 N 72.13 W
Athol Bay c 262 34.57 S 77.15 W
Athol Island I 240b 25.05 N 77.16 W
Athol, Forest of ➤ 56 56.50 N 4.00 W
Athol Springs 210 42.46 N 78.52 W
Áthos 38 40.09 N 24.19 E

...

ENGLISH — Name | Page | Lat.°′ | Long.°′
DEUTSCH — Name | Seite | Breite°′ | Länge°′ E = Ost

Ayer Hitam, Malay. 114 1.55 N 103.11 E
Ayer Hitam, Malay. 114 2.56 N 102.24 E
Ayer Jerneh 114 4.24 N 103.24 E
Ayer Kuning Selatan 114 2.30 N 102.28 E
Ayer Merbau, Pulau I 271c 1.16 N 103.43 E
Ayers Cliff 206 45.10 N 72.03 W
Ayers Rock ∧ 162 25.23 S 131.05 E
Ayersville 216 41.14 N 84.17 W
Ayeyarwady □[8] 110 17.00 N 95.00 E
Ayeyarwady (Irrawaddy) ≃ 110 15.50 N 95.06 E
Aygün 130 38.26 N 41.17 E
Ayía Marína 38 37.09 N 26.52 E
Ayía Paraskeví, Ellás 38 39.15 N 26.16 E
Ayía Paraskeví, Ellás 267c 38.01 N 23.50 E
Ayiássos 38 39.05 N 26.23 E
Ayía Varvára 267c 37.59 N 23.39 E
Ayina ≃ 152 1.48 N 13.10 E
Áyioi Anáryiroi 267c 38.02 N 23.43 E
Áyion Óros □[8] 38 40.15 N 24.15 E
Áyion Óros ›[1] 38 40.15 N 24.15 E
Áyios Dhimítrios 267c 37.56 N 23.44 E
Áyios Evstrátios I 38 39.31 N 25.00 E
Áyios Ioánnis Réndis 267c 37.58 N 23.40 E
Áyios Kírikos 38 37.37 N 26.14 E
Áyios Nikólaos 38 35.11 N 25.42 E
Ayiou Nikolaou Monastery ⱱ[1] 267c 37.53 N 23.27 E
Ayíou Órous, Kólpos ⊂ 38 40.12 N 24.03 E
Ayl 132 30.13 N 35.32 E
Aylesbury 42 51.50 N 0.50 W
Aylesford 42 51.18 N 0.29 E
Aylesham 42 51.13 N 1.13 E
Aylmer 188 45.26 N 75.50 W
Aylmer, Lake ⊜ 206 45.50 N 71.22 W
Aylmer, Mount ∧ 182 51.19 N 115.26 W
Aylmer-East 212 45.26 N 75.50 W
Aylmer Lake ⊜ 176 64.05 N 108.30 W
Aylmer West 212 42.46 N 80.59 W
Aylsham, Sk., Can. 184 53.11 N 103.49 W
Aylsham, Eng., U.K. 42 52.49 N 1.15 E
ʻAyn al-ʻArab 130 36.54 N 38.21 E
ʻAyn Dār 128 25.59 N 49.23 E
ʻAyn Dīwār 130 37.17 N 42.11 E
ʻAynīn ⊤[4] 144 20.48 N 41.39 E
Aynor 192 33.59 N 79.11 W
ʻAynūnah 128 28.05 N 35.08 E
Ayo 248 15.41 S 72.16 W
Ayo Ayo 248 17.05 S 68.00 W
Ayod 140 8.07 N 31.26 E
Ayodhya 124 26.48 N 82.12 E
Ayo El Chico 234 20.32 N 102.21 W
Ayom 140 7.52 N 28.23 E
Ayorou 150 14.44 N 0.55 E
Ayos 152 3.54 N 12.31 E
'Ayoûn el 'Atroûs 150 16.40 N 9.37 W
Ayr, Austl. 166 19.35 S 147.24 E
Ayr, On., Can. 212 43.17 N 80.27 W
Ayr, Scot., U.K. 44 55.28 N 4.38 W
Ayr ≃ 44 55.29 N 4.28 W
ʻAyrah 132 32.37 N 36.32 E
Ayrancı 130 37.22 N 33.42 E
Ayre, Point of › 44 54.26 N 4.22 W
Aysgarth 44 54.17 N 2.00 W
Aysha 144 10.46 N 42.37 E
ʻAytā al-Fakhkhār 132 33.38 N 35.54 E
ʻAytanīt 132 33.34 N 35.40 E
Ayton, Austl. 164 15.56 S 145.22 E
Ayton, On., Can. 212 44.03 N 80.56 W
Ayton, Eng., U.K. 44 54.14 N 0.29 W
Ayu, Kepulauan II 108 0.28 N 131.03 E
Ayubnagar 126 23.46 N 90.23 E
Ayulhai 102 44.36 N 115.36 E
Ayuñgon 116 9.51 N 123.08 E
Ayuquila ≃ 234 19.23 N 103.51 W
Ayutla 234 20.07 N 104.22 W
Ayutla de los Libres 234 16.54 N 99.13 W
Ayvacık, Tür. 130 39.36 N 26.24 E
Ayvacık, Tür. 130 41.00 N 36.39 E
Ayvalı 130 38.44 N 37.38 E
Ayvalık 130 39.18 N 26.41 E
Aywaille 56 50.28 N 5.40 E
Azabarabān, Ra's › 142 28.51 N 32.43 E
Azacualpa, Hond. 236 14.27 N 86.09 W
Azacualpa, Hond. 236 15.19 N 88.33 W
Azādpur ◆[8] 272a 28.43 N 77.11 E
Azai 94 35.26 N 136.18 E
Azaila 34 41.17 N 0.29 W
Azalea Park 220 28.32 N 81.18 W
Azama 174m 26.11 N 127.49 E
Azamatovo 80 53.18 N 53.28 E
Azambuja 34 39.04 N 8.52 W
Āzamgarh 124 26.04 N 83.11 E
Azamiga-dake ∧ 96 34.20 N 131.47 E
Azángaro 248 14.55 S 70.13 W
Azángaro ≃ 248 15.17 S 70.10 W
Azanka 86 58.02 N 64.48 E
Azao ∧ 148 25.12 N 8.08 E
Azaouâd ◆[1] 150 19.00 N 3.00 W
Azaouagh, Vallée de l' V 150 15.30 N 3.18 E
Azapa, Quebrada de ≃ 248 18.30 S 70.17 W
Azar V 150 16.02 N 4.04 E
Azara 150 8.21 N 9.12 E
Āzārbāyjān-e Gharbī □[4] 128 37.40 N 45.00 E
Āzārbāyjān-e Sharqī □[4] 128 38.00 N 47.00 E
Azare 150 11.40 N 10.11 E
Āzar Shahr 128 37.45 N 45.59 E
Azas ≃ 88 52.26 N 96.15 E
Azat, gora ∧[2] 86 46.55 N 69.00 E
Azay-le-Rideau 50 47.16 N 0.28 E
Azay-sur-Cher 50 47.21 N 0.51 E
Azay-sur-Indre 50 47.12 N 0.57 E
Aʻzāz 130 36.35 N 37.03 E
Azazga 148 36.44 N 4.22 E
Azcuénaga 258 34.23 S 59.21 W
Aždaak, gora ∧ 84 40.13 N 44.56 E
Azdavay 130 41.39 N 33.18 E
Azeffâl ⊥[8] 148 21.00 N 14.45 W
Azeffoun 148 36.53 N 4.25 E
Azejevo 80 54.41 N 42.02 E
Azemmour 148 33.20 N 8.25 W
Azenhas do Mar 266c 38.50 N 9.28 W
Azennezal, 'Erg V 148 22.50 N 0.25 E
Azerbaidzhan → Azerbaijan □[1] 22 40.30 N 47.30 E
Azerbaijan □[1], Asia 72 40.30 N 47.30 E
Azerbaijan □[1], Asia 84 40.30 N 47.30 E
Azerbajdžan → Azerbaijan □[1] 72 40.30 N 47.30 E
Azerbaydzan → Azerbaijan □[1] 72 40.30 N 47.30 E
Azergues ≃ 58 45.56 N 4.44 E
Azezo 144 12.35 N 37.28 E
Azgir 80 47.50 N 47.54 E
Azhikode 122 11.59 N 75.21 E
Azilal 148 31.58 N 6.34 W
Azilal □[4] 148 31.55 N 6.30 W
Azile 154 3.32 N 29.52 E
Azincourt 50 50.28 N 2.08 E
Azle 222 32.53 N 97.32 W
Aznakajevo 80 54.53 N 53.04 E
Aznapuquio 286d 11.59 S 77.04 W
Azogues 246 2.44 S 78.50 W
Azoia 266c 38.46 N 9.29 W
Azor 132 32.01 N 34.48 E
Azores → Açores II 148a 38.30 N 28.00 W
Azores-Gibraltar Ridge ✦[3] 10 37.00 N 16.00 W
Azores Plateau ✦[3] 10 39.00 N 30.00 W
Azoum, Bahr (Wādī ʻAẓūm) V 146 10.53 N 20.15 E
Azov 83 47.07 N 39.25 E
Azov, Sea of → Azovskoje more ⊤[2] 78 46.00 N 36.00 E
Azovo-Sivašskij zapovednik ◆[4] 78 46.08 N 35.08 E
Azovskij kanal ≋ 83 47.07 N 39.27 E
Azovskoje 78 45.34 N 34.34 E
Azovskoje more (Sea of Azov) ⊤[2] 78 46.00 N 36.00 E
Azoyú 234 16.43 N 98.44 W
Azpeitia 34 43.11 N 2.16 W
Azraq, Al-Bahr al- → Blue Nile ≃ 140 15.38 N 32.31 E
Azraq, Bahr ≃ 146 10.52 N 20.35 E
Azraq, Wādī al- V 140 10.33 N 28.40 E
Azraq ash-Shīshān 132 31.50 N 36.48 E
Azrou 148 33.27 N 5.14 W
Aztalan State Park ♦ 216 43.04 N 88.51 W
Aztec 200 36.49 N 107.59 W
Azteca, Estadio ♦ 286a 19.18 N 99.09 W
Aztec Peak ∧ 200 33.48 N 110.55 W
Aztec Ruins National Monument ♦ 200 36.51 N 108.10 W
Azua 238 18.27 N 70.44 W
Azuaga 34 38.16 N 5.41 W
Azuay □[4] 246 3.00 S 79.00 W
Azucena 252 37.29 S 59.18 W
Azuchi 94 35.09 N 136.08 E
Azuchi-jō ⊥ 94 35.10 N 136.08 E
Azuer ≃ 34 39.08 N 3.36 W
Azuero, Península de ›[1] 246 7.40 N 80.35 W
Azufre, Volcán ∧[1] 252 25.11 S 68.31 W
Azuga 38 45.27 N 25.33 E
Azul 252 36.47 S 59.51 W
Azul, Cerro ∧, C.R. 236 9.54 N 85.14 W
Azul, Cerro ∧, Ec. 246a 0.54 S 91.21 W
Azul, Cerro ∧, Hond. 236 14.32 N 88.23 W
Azul, Cordillera ⋏ 248 8.30 S 76.10 W
Azul Casa, Cerro ∧ 252 22.29 S 65.20 W
ʻAẓūm, Wādī (Bahr Azoum) V 146 10.53 N 20.15 E
Azuma, Nihon 94 36.31 N 139.19 E
Azuma, Nihon 94 36.33 N 138.54 E
Azuma, Nihon 94 35.56 N 140.28 E
Azuma, Nihon 94 36.36 N 138.20 E
Azumaya-san ∧ 94 36.32 N 138.25 E
Azumazaka 270 34.26 N 135.39 E
Azumi 94 36.11 N 137.47 E
Azur, Côte d' ⊥[2] 62 43.30 N 7.00 E
Azurduy 248 19.59 S 64.29 W
Azure Clouds, Temple of the ⱱ[1] 271a 40.00 N 116.11 E
Azure Lake ⊜ 182 52.23 N 120.00 W
Azusa 228 34.08 N 117.54 W
Azusa ≃ 94 36.17 N 137.56 E
Ažu-Tajga, gora ∧ 86 51.35 N 88.45 E
Az-Zabābidah 132 32.23 N 35.20 E
Az-Zabadānī 132 33.43 N 36.05 E
Az-Zāb al-Kabīr → Great Zab ≃ 128 36.00 N 43.21 E
Az-Zāb aṣ-Ṣaghīr → Little Zab ≃ 128 35.12 N 43.25 E
Aẓ-Ẓāhirīyah 132 31.25 N 34.58 E
Aẓ-Ẓahrān (Dhahran) 128 26.18 N 50.08 E
Az-Zamālik ◆[8] 273c 30.04 N 31.13 E
Azzanello 64 45.18 N 9.55 E
Az-Zankalūn 142 30.33 N 31.27 E
Azzano Decimo 64 45.53 N 12.43 E
Az-Zaqāzīq 142 30.35 N 31.31 E
Az-Zarbah 130 36.04 N 36.59 E
Az-Zarqāʼ 132 32.05 N 36.06 E
Az-Zarqāʼ □[8] 132 32.00 N 36.45 E
Az-Zawāmil 142 30.21 N 31.26 E
Az-Zāwiyah 146 32.45 N 12.44 E
Az-Zaydāb 140 17.26 N 33.53 E
Az-Zaydīyah 144 15.18 N 43.04 E
Az-Zaytīyah ◆[8] 142 29.58 N 32.31 E
Az-Zaytūn ◆[8] 273c 30.06 N 31.19 E
Azzel Matti, Sebkha ≍ 148 25.55 N 0.56 E
Az-Zilfī 128 26.18 N 44.48 E
Az-Zrārīyah 132 33.21 N 35.20 E
Az-Zubayr 128 30.23 N 47.43 E
ʻAzzūn 132 32.11 N 35.03 E
Azzurra, Grotta (Blue Grotto) ⊥[5] 68 40.35 N 14.14 E

B

Ba ≃, Viet 110 13.02 N 109.03 E
Ba ≃, Zhg. 100 30.25 N 115.02 E
Ba ≃, Zhg. 102 31.03 N 107.08 E
Ba ≃, Zhg. 271a 39.57 N 116.38 E
Ba, Loch ⊜ 46 56.36 N 4.44 W
Baa 112 10.43 S 123.03 E
Baaba, Île I 175f 20.03 S 163.59 E
Baacagaan 102 45.35 N 99.27 E
Baad 58 47.19 N 10.07 E
Baah 112 10.28 S 121.59 E
Baak 263 51.25 N 7.10 E
Baal 56 51.02 N 6.17 E
Baao 116 13.27 N 123.22 E
Baar 58 47.12 N 8.32 E
Baar ◆[1] 58 48.00 N 8.30 E
Baarbach ≃ 263 51.27 N 7.39 E
Baardheere (Bardera) 144 2.20 N 42.17 E
Baardskeerdersbos 158 34.34 S 19.35 E
Baargaal 144 11.17 N 51.04 E
Baarle-Hertog 56 51.27 N 4.56 E
Baarle-Nassau 52 51.27 N 4.53 E
Baarlo 52 51.20 N 6.05 E
Baarn 52 52.13 N 5.16 E
Baasrode 50 51.02 N 4.10 E
Baba 246 1.47 S 79.40 W
Baba ≃ 152 6.25 N 17.07 E
Baba Burnu ›, Tür. 130 39.29 N 26.04 E
Baba Burnu ›, Tür. 130 41.17 N 31.24 E
Babaçulândia 250 7.13 S 47.46 W
Babadag, Rom. 38 44.54 N 28.43 E
Babadağ, Tür. 130 37.48 N 28.52 E
Babadag, gora ∧ 84 41.02 N 48.19 E
Babaeski 130 41.26 N 27.06 E
Babahoyo 246 1.49 S 79.31 W
Babaī (Sarju) ≃ 124 27.42 N 81.16 E
Babailiqiao 100 32.26 N 118.57 E
Babajevo 76 59.23 N 35.56 E
Babajkovka 78 49.01 N 34.32 E
Babajurt 84 43.36 N 46.47 E
Babak 112 7.08 N 125.41 E
Babakin 162 32.07 S 118.01 E
Babana 150 10.26 N 3.50 E
Babanango 158 28.30 S 31.00 E
Babanka 78 48.43 N 30.26 E
Babanūsah 140 11.20 N 27.48 E
Babar, Kepulauan II 164 7.50 S 129.45 E
Babar, Pulau I 164 7.55 S 129.45 E
Bābarpur ◆[8] 272a 28.41 N 77.17 E
Babat, Indon. 112 2.45 S 103.38 E
Babat, Indon. 115a 7.06 S 112.10 E
Babatag, chrebet ⋏ 85 38.15 N 68.20 E
Babati 154 4.13 S 35.45 E
Bābā Valī Ṣāheb 120 31.40 N 65.40 E
Babb 182 48.51 N 113.26 W
Babbacombe Bay ⊂ 42 50.30 N 3.25 W
Babb Creek ≃ 210 41.33 N 77.23 W
Babbitt, Mn., U.S. 190 47.43 N 91.57 W
Babbitt, Nv., U.S. 204 38.32 N 118.38 W
Bʻabdā 132 33.50 N 35.32 E
Bʻabdāt 132 33.53 N 35.40 E
Babel, Mont de ∧ 186 51.27 N 68.42 W
Babelijamun 164 2.04 S 137.43 E
Bab el Mandeb → Mandeb, Bab el ᑌ 144 12.40 N 43.20 E
Babelsberg ◆[8] 264a 52.24 N 13.05 E
Babelsberg, Schloss ⊥ 264a 52.24 N 13.05 E
Babelthuap I 175b 7.30 N 134.36 E
Babenhausen, Dtsch. 56 49.57 N 8.56 E
Babenhausen, Dtsch. 58 48.09 N 10.15 E
Babenki 82 55.21 N 37.11 E
Babenkovo 83 49.15 N 37.21 E
Babeyru 154 1.52 N 27.27 E
Babi, Pulau I 114 2.05 N 96.39 E
Babia, Arroyo de la ≃ 196 28.25 N 101.45 W
Babian ≃ 102 22.58 N 101.44 E
Babiči 76 52.17 N 30.00 E
Bābil 142 30.41 N 31.00 E
Bābil □[4] 128 32.40 N 44.35 E
Bābil, Aṭlāl (Babylon) ⊥ 128 32.33 N 44.24 E
Babile 144 9.15 N 42.19 E
Babilônia 256 22.33 S 44.28 W
Babimost 30 52.10 N 15.51 E
Babīna 124 25.15 N 78.28 E
Babina Greda 38 45.07 N 18.33 E
Babinda 166 17.20 S 145.55 E
Babine 182 55.19 N 126.37 W
Babine ≃ 182 55.42 N 127.40 W
Babine Lake ⊜ 182 54.45 N 126.00 W
Babine Range ⋏ 182 55.00 N 126.25 W
Babino, Ross. 76 56.44 N 34.17 E
Babino, Ross. 76 59.14 N 31.26 E
Babino, Ross. 76 59.50 N 40.49 E
Babino, Ross. 80 57.22 N 48.45 E
Babiogórski Park Narodowy ♦ 30 49.35 N 19.30 E
Babo 164 2.33 S 133.25 E
Bābol 128 36.34 N 52.42 E
Bābol Sar 128 36.43 N 52.39 E
Baboon Point › 158 32.19 S 18.20 E
Baboquivari Mountains ⋏ 200 31.45 N 111.35 W
Baboquivari Peak ∧ 200 31.46 N 111.35 W
Babor, Djebel ∧ 34 36.30 N 5.28 E
Baborów 30 50.09 N 17.59 E
Babošino 82 54.13 N 37.08 E
Baboua 152 5.48 N 14.49 E
Babrongan Tower ∧[2] 162 18.36 S 123.33 E
Babson Park, Fl., U.S. 220 27.49 N 81.31 W
Babson Park, Ma., U.S. 283 42.18 N 71.23 W
Babson Reservoir ⊜[1] 283 42.38 N 70.40 W
Babstovo 89 48.07 N 132.27 E
Bab-Taza 148 35.03 N 5.14 W
Bābu Bheri 272b 22.51 N 88.14 E
Bābupur, India 126 24.01 N 87.10 E
Bābūpur, India 272a 28.30 N 76.59 E
Babura 150 12.46 N 9.01 E
Bābūsar Pass)(123 35.09 N 74.03 E
Babuškin 88 51.41 N 105.54 E
Babuškin ◆[8] 265b 55.52 N 37.42 E
Babuyan 116 10.00 N 118.54 E
Babuyan Channel ᑌ 116 18.44 N 121.40 E
Babuyan Island I 108 19.32 N 121.57 E
Babuyan Islands II 108 19.15 N 121.40 E
Babylon 210 40.41 N 73.19 W
Babylon → Bābil, Aṭlāl ⊥ 128 32.33 N 44.24 E
Babynino 76 54.23 N 35.43 E
Bača ≃ 64 46.09 N 13.48 E
Bacaadweeyn 144 7.12 N 47.32 E
Bacabal 250 4.14 S 44.47 W
Bacacay 116 13.18 N 123.47 E
Bacadéhuachi 232 29.44 N 109.10 W
Bacajaí ≃ 250 3.27 S 51.53 W
Bacalhau, Canal do ≋ 287a 23.03 S 43.35 W
Bacaligo 84 42.33 N 44.57 E
Bačalino 86 57.46 N 67.17 E
Bacan, Pulau I 164 0.35 S 127.30 E
Bacao 116 10.27 N 119.48 E
Bacarra 116 18.15 N 120.35 E
Bacatuba 250 5.40 S 43.42 W
Bacău 38 46.34 N 26.55 E
Bacău □[6] 38 46.30 N 26.45 E
Baccalieu Island I 186 48.08 N 52.48 W
Bac Can 110 22.08 N 105.50 E
Baccarat 58 48.27 N 6.45 E
Bacchiglione ≃ 64 45.11 N 12.14 E
Bacchus Marsh 169 37.41 S 144.27 E
Baceno 58 46.16 N 8.19 E
Bacerac 232 30.18 N 108.50 W
Bacevići 76 53.24 N 29.14 E
Bac Giang 110 21.16 N 106.12 E
Bach 58 47.16 N 10.24 E
Bachagou 98 40.36 N 122.54 E
Bachaquero 246 9.56 N 71.08 W
Bacharach 56 50.04 N 7.46 E
Bacharden 128 38.26 N 57.25 E
Bachardok 128 38.46 N 58.30 E
Bachauan 116 12.28 N 122.06 E
Bachčisaraj 78 44.45 N 33.51 E
Bache 106 31.05 N 120.40 E
Bacheng 106 31.27 N 120.52 E
Bachi 100 24.48 N 115.49 E
Bachiniva 232 28.45 N 107.15 W
Bach Ma 110 16.12 N 107.52 E
Bachmač 78 51.13 N 32.46 E
Bachmetjevka 80 51.06 N 44.46 E
Bachmut ≃ 83 48.56 N 38.03 E
Bachmutovka 83 48.52 N 39.03 E
Bachmutovo 76 56.22 N 34.03 E
Bacho 114 6.37 N 101.39 E
Bachok 114 6.04 N 102.24 E
Bacht 85 40.43 N 68.42 E
Bachta, Ross. 74 62.28 N 89.00 E
Bachta, Ross. 86 55.45 N 92.26 E
Bachtemir ≃ 80 45.43 N 47.38 E
Bachten-Berg ∧[2] 264a 52.20 N 12.54 E
Bachty 86 46.39 N 82.42 E
Bachu 90 39.50 N 78.20 E
Bachuma 144 6.48 N 35.53 E
Back ≃, N.T., Can. 176 67.15 N 95.15 W
Back ≃, Va., U.S. 208 37.06 N 76.17 W
Bačka ◆[1] 38 45.50 N 19.30 E
Bačka Palanka 38 45.15 N 19.24 E
Bačka Topola 38 45.49 N 19.38 E
Back Bay ◆[8] 283 42.21 N 71.05 W
Back Bay ⊂, India 272c 18.56 N 72.49 E
Back Bay ⊂, Va., U.S. 208 36.35 N 75.57 W
Backberg 40 60.37 N 16.37 E
Backbone Ranges ⋏ 180 63.30 N 129.00 W
Back Branch ≃ 284c 38.50 N 76.48 W
Back Brook ≃ 276 40.26 N 74.39 W
Back Channel ≃[1] 279b 40.30 N 80.05 W
Back Creek ≃ 188 38.02 N 79.54 W
Backe 26 63.49 N 16.24 E
Bäckefors 26 58.48 N 12.10 E
Bäckehagen 40 60.39 N 15.34 E
Backford 262 53.15 N 2.54 W
Bäckhammar 40 59.10 N 14.11 E
Bački Petrovac 38 45.22 N 19.35 E
Backnang 56 48.56 N 9.25 E
Back River ⊂ 208 39.16 N 76.27 W
Back River Neck ›[1] 284b 39.18 N 76.26 W
Backstairs Passage ᑌ 168b 35.42 S 138.05 E
Bac Lieu 110 9.17 N 105.44 E
Bacliff 222 29.31 N 94.59 W
Bac Ninh 110 21.11 N 106.03 E
Baco, Mount ∧ 116 12.49 N 121.10 E
Bacoachi 232 30.38 N 109.56 W
Bacoli 68 40.48 N 14.05 E
Bacolod 116 10.40 N 122.57 E
Bacon 116 13.03 N 124.03 E
Baconga ◆[8] 273b 4.18 S 15.16 E
Bacon Peak ∧ 224 48.39 N 121.31 W
Bacons Run ≃ 285 40.06 N 74.41 W
Baconton 192 31.22 N 84.09 W
Bacoor 116 14.28 N 120.56 E
Bacoor Bay ⊂ 269f 14.28 N 120.54 E
Bac Phan □[9] 110 22.00 N 105.00 E
Bac Quang 110 22.29 N 104.52 E
Bacqueville-en-Caux 50 49.47 N 1.00 E
Bácsalmás 30 46.08 N 19.20 E
Bács-Kiskun □[6] 30 46.30 N 19.25 E
Bacton 42 52.52 N 1.28 E
Bacuag 116 9.37 N 125.38 E
Bacuit Bay ⊂ 116 11.07 N 119.23 E
Bácum 232 27.33 N 110.05 W
Bacungan 116 9.56 N 118.42 E
Bacup 44 53.43 N 2.12 W
Bacuranao ≃ 286b 23.10 N 82.14 W
Bacuranao, Presa ⊜[1] 286b 23.07 N 82.13 W
Bacuri, Cachoeira do ∟ 250 5.29 S 54.18 W
Bacuri, Ilha do I 250 2.55 S 49.43 W
Bacuri, Lago do ⊜ 250 3.16 S 42.15 W
Bačurka 24 68.32 N 56.57 E
Bacuyangan 116 9.39 N 122.27 E
Bād 128 33.41 N 52.01 E
Bad ≃, Mi., U.S. 190 43.18 N 84.06 W
Bad ≃, S.D., U.S. 198 44.22 N 100.22 W
Bad ≃, Wi., U.S. 190 46.38 N 90.40 W
Badʻ, Wādī V 142 29.41 N 32.20 E
Bada 88 51.23 N 109.54 E
Bad Abbach 60 48.56 N 12.03 E
Badagara 122 11.36 N 75.35 E
Badagri 150 6.27 N 2.55 E
Badagri □[8] 273a 6.27 N 3.18 E
Badagri Creek ⊂ 273a 6.25 N 3.18 E
Badahl 142 28.56 N 30.54 E
Bad Aibling 64 47.52 N 12.00 E
Bada Jāmda 124 22.09 N 85.23 E
Badajia 100 33.57 N 120.17 E
Badajós ≃ 246 3.15 S 63.02 W
Badajós, Lago ⊜ 246 3.15 S 62.47 W
Badajoz 34 38.53 N 6.58 W
Badajoz □[4] 34 38.40 N 6.00 W
Badakani 152 4.46 S 14.52 E
Badakhshān □[4] 120 36.45 N 72.00 E
Badal Khān Goth 120 26.31 N 67.06 E
Badalona 34 41.27 N 2.15 E
Badalucco 62 43.55 N 7.51 E
Badam 85 42.23 N 69.15 E
Bādāmi 122 15.55 N 75.41 E
Bādāmpahār 124 22.06 N 86.06 E
Badana, Lach V 144 0.50 S 42.04 E
Badanah 128 30.59 N 41.02 E
Badanga 146 11.36 N 17.26 E
Badanganj 126 22.54 N 87.33 E
Badaohao 104 41.47 N 121.57 E
Badaohe, Zhg. 98 40.02 N 122.17 E
Badaohe, Zhg. 98 40.24 N 118.42 E
Badarīnāth 124 30.44 N 79.29 E
Badarma 88 57.46 N 102.36 E
Badas 112 4.36 N 114.27 E
Badas, Kepulauan II 112 0.35 N 107.06 E
Badata, gora ∧ 88 51.55 N 111.35 E
Bad Aussee 64 47.36 N 13.47 E
Bad Axe 190 43.48 N 83.00 W
Badaying 98 41.22 N 117.28 E
Badazhou 102 24.36 N 105.04 E
Bad Bentheim 52 52.19 N 7.10 E
Bad Bergzabern 56 49.07 N 8.00 E
Bad Berka 54 50.54 N 11.17 E
Bad Berleburg 56 51.03 N 8.23 E
Bad Berneck 60 50.03 N 11.40 E
Bad Bertrich 56 50.04 N 7.02 E
Bad Bibra 54 51.12 N 11.35 E
Bad Blankenburg 54 50.41 N 11.16 E
Bad Bramstedt 52 53.55 N 9.53 E
Bad Breisig 56 50.31 N 7.18 E
Bad Brückenau 56 50.18 N 9.47 E
Bad Buchau 58 48.03 N 9.36 E
Bad Camberg 56 50.18 N 8.16 E
Bad Creek ≃ 216 41.25 N 83.57 W
Baddā 132 33.41 N 36.26 E
Badda Rogghie ∧ 144 8.43 N 37.41 E
Baddeck 186 46.07 N 60.45 W
Bad Ditzenbach 56 48.35 N 9.41 E
Baddo ≃ 128 27.59 N 64.21 E
Bad Doberan 54 54.06 N 11.53 E
Baddomalhi 123 31.59 N 74.40 E
Bad Dreibergen 52 53.12 N 8.01 E
Bad Driburg 52 51.44 N 9.01 E
Bad Düben 54 51.36 N 12.34 E
Bad Dürkheim 56 49.28 N 8.10 E
Bad Dürrenberg 54 51.18 N 12.04 E
Bad Dürrheim 58 48.01 N 8.32 E
Badé, Centraf. 152 6.41 N 17.07 E
Bade, Indon. 164 7.10 S 139.35 E
Badeggi 150 9.05 N 6.08 E
Badéguichéri 150 14.31 N 5.22 E
Bad Eilsen 52 52.14 N 9.06 E
Badel 54 52.44 N 11.19 E
Bad Elster 54 50.17 N 12.14 E
Bad Ems 56 50.20 N 7.43 E
Baden, On., Can. 212 43.24 N 80.39 W
Baden, Dtsch. 52 53.00 N 9.04 E
Baden, Erit. 144 17.00 N 38.00 E
Baden, Öst. 61 48.00 N 16.14 E
Baden, Schw. 58 47.29 N 8.18 E
Baden, Pa., U.S. 214 40.38 N 80.13 W
Baden-Baden 56 48.46 N 8.14 E
Bad Endbach 56 50.45 N 8.32 E
Badenoch □[9] 46 56.57 N 4.19 W
Baden-Powell, Mount ∧ 228 34.21 N 117.46 W
Badenweiler 58 47.48 N 7.40 E
Baden-Württemberg □[3] 30 48.30 N 9.00 E
Badenyon 46 57.15 N 3.05 W
Baderna 64 45.12 N 13.46 E
Badersleben 54 51.59 N 10.53 E
Bad Essen 52 52.19 N 8.20 E
Bad Feilnbach 64 47.46 N 12.00 E
Badfish Creek ≃ 216 42.50 N 89.10 W
Bad Frankenhausen 54 51.21 N 11.06 E
Bad Freienwalde 54 52.47 N 14.01 E
Bad Friedrichshall 56 49.14 N 9.11 E
Bad Fusch 64 47.12 N 12.51 E
Badgam 123 34.01 N 74.43 E
Bad Gandersheim 52 51.52 N 10.01 E
Badgastein 64 47.07 N 13.08 E
Badger, Nf., Can. 186 48.59 N 56.02 W
Badger, Mn., U.S. 198 48.46 N 96.00 W
Badger Creek ≃, Co., U.S. 198 40.17 N 103.42 W
Badger Creek ≃, Co., U.S. 200 38.28 N 105.52 W
Badger Creek ≃, Or., U.S. 224 45.16 N 121.11 W
Badger Pass)(226 37.40 N 119.39 W
Badger's Mount 260 51.20 N 0.09 E
Badgery's Creek 274a 33.53 S 150.44 E
Badgerys Creek ≃ 274a 33.51 S 150.46 E
Bādghīs □[4] 128 35.00 N 63.45 E
Bad Gleichenberg 61 46.52 N 15.54 E
Bad Godesberg 56 50.41 N 7.10 E
Bad Goisern 64 47.38 N 13.37 E
Bad Gottleuba 54 50.51 N 13.56 E
Bad Griesbach 58 48.27 N 8.14 E
Bad Grund 52 51.48 N 10.14 E
Bad Hall 61 48.02 N 14.13 E
Bad Harzburg 54 51.53 N 10.33 E
Bad Heilbrunn 64 47.45 N 11.28 E
Badhela ◆[8] 272a 28.38 N 77.04 E
Bad Helmstedt 54 52.14 N 11.03 E
Bad Hersfeld 56 50.52 N 9.42 E
Badhoevedorp 52 52.21 N 4.46 E
Bad Hofgastein 64 47.10 N 13.06 E
Bad Homburg vor der Höhe 56 50.13 N 8.37 E
Bad Honnef 56 50.39 N 7.13 E
Bad Hönningen 56 50.31 N 7.19 E
Bādī ≃ 124 27.55 N 83.27 E
Badia (Abtei) 64 46.37 N 11.54 E
Badia, Val V 64 46.40 N 11.53 E
Badia Calavena 64 45.34 N 11.09 E
Badia Polesine 64 45.05 N 11.29 E
Badia Prataglia 66 43.47 N 11.52 E
Badia Tedalda 66 43.42 N 12.11 E
Badile Camuno, Pizzo ∧ 58 46.01 N 10.25 E
Badīn 120 24.39 N 68.50 E
Bādinan 272b 22.54 N 88.14 E
Badinko ≃ 150 13.42 N 9.35 W
Badin Lake ⊜[1] 192 35.27 N 80.06 W
Badiraguato 232 25.22 N 107.31 W
Bad Ischl 64 47.43 N 13.37 E
Bad Kissingen 56 50.12 N 10.04 E
Bad Kleinen 54 53.46 N 11.28 E
Bad Kleinkirchheim 64 46.49 N 13.49 E
Bad Klosterlausnitz 54 50.55 N 11.52 E
Bad Kohlgrub 64 47.40 N 11.03 E
Bad König 56 49.45 N 9.01 E
Bad Königshofen im Grabfeld 56 50.18 N 10.29 E
Bad Kösen 54 51.08 N 11.43 E
Bad Köstritz 54 50.56 N 12.01 E
Bad Kreuznach 56 49.52 N 7.51 E
Bad Krozingen 58 47.55 N 7.43 E
Bādkulla 126 23.17 N 88.32 E
Bad Laasphe 56 50.56 N 8.24 E
Badlands ⋏[2], U.S. 198 46.45 N 103.30 W
Badlands ⋏[2], S.D., U.S. 198 43.30 N 102.20 W
Badlands National Park ♦ 198 43.47 N 102.15 W
Bad Langensalza 56 51.06 N 10.38 E
Bad Lauchstädt 54 51.23 N 11.52 E
Bad Lausick 54 51.08 N 12.38 E
Bad Lauterberg [im Harz] 52 51.38 N 10.28 E
Bad Leonfelden 61 48.33 N 14.19 E
Bādli ◆[8] 272a 28.45 N 77.09 E
Bad Liebenstein 54 50.49 N 10.21 E
Bad Liebenwerda 54 51.31 N 13.23 E
Bad Liebenzell 56 48.46 N 8.44 E
Bad Lippspringe 52 51.46 N 8.49 E
Bad Meinberg 52 51.53 N 8.58 E
Bad Mergentheim 56 49.30 N 9.46 E
Bad Mitterndorf 60 47.33 N 13.55 E
Bad Mukran 54 54.26 N 13.35 E
Bad Münder 52 52.12 N 9.27 E
Bad Münster am Stein 56 49.49 N 7.51 E
Bad Münstereifel 56 50.33 N 6.46 E
Bad Muskau 54 51.32 N 14.43 E
Bad Nauheim 56 50.22 N 8.44 E
Bad Nenndorf 52 52.20 N 9.22 E
Badnera 122 20.52 N 77.44 E
Badner Lindkogel ∧ 264b 48.01 N 16.11 E
Bad Neuenahr-Ahrweiler 56 50.33 N 7.08 E
Bad Neustadt an der Saale 56 50.19 N 10.13 E
Bad Niedernau 58 48.27 N 8.53 E
Bad Oeynhausen 52 52.12 N 8.48 E
Badogo 150 11.02 N 8.13 W
Badolato 68 38.34 N 16.31 E
Bad Oldesloe 52 53.48 N 10.22 E
Ba Dong, Viet 110 9.40 N 106.34 E
Badong, Zhg. 102 31.02 N 110.20 E
Badonviller 58 48.30 N 6.54 E
Bad Orb 56 50.14 N 9.20 E
Badou, Togo 150 7.35 N 0.36 E
Badou, Zhg. 98 36.27 N 117.55 E
Badouling 100 32.10 N 117.36 E
Badoumbé 150 13.38 N 10.13 W
Bad Peterstal 58 48.26 N 8.12 E
Badplaas 158 25.57 S 30.35 E
Bad Pyrmont 52 51.59 N 9.15 E
Badr 142 30.33 N 30.43 E
Bad Radkersburg 61 46.41 N 15.59 E
Bad Ragaz 58 47.00 N 9.30 E
Bad Rappenau 56 49.14 N 9.06 E
Bad Rehburg 52 52.26 N 9.13 E
Bad Reichenhall 64 47.43 N 12.52 E
Badr Ḥunayn 128 23.44 N 38.46 E
Bad Rippoldsau 58 48.26 N 8.19 E
Bad River Indian Reservation ◆[4] 190 46.33 N 90.40 W
Bad Rothenfelde 52 52.06 N 8.09 E
Bad Saarow-Pieskow 54 52.17 N 14.03 E
Bad Sachsa 54 51.36 N 10.32 E
Bad Säckingen 58 47.33 N 7.56 E
Bad Salzdetfurth 52 52.03 N 10.01 E
Bad Salzig 56 50.12 N 7.38 E
Bad Salzschlirf 56 50.37 N 9.29 E
Bad Salzuflen 52 52.05 N 8.44 E
Bad Salzungen 56 50.48 N 10.13 E
Bad Sankt Leonhard im Lavanttal 61 46.58 N 14.48 E
Bad Sassendorf 52 51.35 N 8.10 E
Bad Schandau 54 50.55 N 14.10 E
Bad Schmiedeberg 54 51.41 N 12.44 E
Bad Schwalbach 56 50.08 N 8.04 E
Bad Schwartau 54 53.55 N 10.40 E
Bad Segeberg 52 53.56 N 10.17 E
Bādshāhpur 124 25.47 N 82.49 E
Bad Soden 56 50.08 N 8.30 E
Bad Soden-Salmünster 56 50.17 N 9.22 E
Bad Sooden-Allendorf 56 51.16 N 9.58 E
Bad Steben 54 50.22 N 11.38 E
Bad Stuer 54 53.22 N 12.19 E
Bad Suderode 54 51.44 N 11.07 E
Bad Sulza 54 51.05 N 11.37 E
Bad Sülze 54 54.06 N 12.38 E
Bad Tatzmannsdorf 61 47.20 N 16.13 E
Bad Teinach 56 48.41 N 8.41 E
Bad Tennstedt 54 51.09 N 10.50 E
Bad Tölz 64 47.46 N 11.34 E
Badu, Bra. 287a 22.54 S 43.04 W
Badu, Zhg. 100 26.51 N 119.35 E
Badu, Zhg. 100 28.32 N 117.57 E
Badu, Zhg. 102 24.15 N 105.41 E
Badu Island I 164 10.07 S 142.08 E
Badulla 122 6.59 N 81.03 E
Badung, Selat ᑌ 115b 8.40 S 115.22 E
Badupi 120 21.36 N 93.25 E
Bādura 126 22.16 N 90.21 E
Bad Urach 58 48.29 N 9.23 E
Bāduria 126 22.44 N 88.47 E
Badvel 122 14.45 N 79.03 E
Bad Vellach 61 46.26 N 14.33 E
Bad Vilbel 56 50.12 N 8.42 E
Bad Vöslau 61 47.57 N 16.16 E
Bad Waldsee 58 47.55 N 9.45 E
Badwater Creek ≃ 202 43.17 N 108.08 W
Bad Westernkotten 52 51.38 N 8.21 E
Bad Wiessee 64 47.43 N 11.43 E
Bad Wildungen 56 51.07 N 9.07 E
Bad Wilsnack 54 52.57 N 11.57 E
Bad Wimpfen 56 49.14 N 9.09 E
Bad Windsheim 56 49.31 N 10.25 E
Bad Wörishofen 58 48.00 N 10.36 E
Bad Wurzach 58 47.54 N 9.54 E
Badžalskij chrebet ⋏ 89 50.40 N 134.50 E
Bad Zwischenahn 52 53.11 N 8.00 E
Baediam 150 15.03 N 11.51 W
Bække 41 55.34 N 9.09 E
Baena 34 37.37 N 4.19 W
Baependi 256 21.57 S 44.53 W
Baependi ≃ 256 21.52 S 45.04 W
Baer Field ⊠ 216 40.59 N 85.11 W
Baerl ◆[8] 263 51.29 N 6.41 E
Baesweiler 56 50.54 N 6.11 E
Báez 240p 22.13 N 79.45 W
Baeza, Ec. 246 0.27 S 77.53 W
Baeza, Esp. 34 37.59 N 3.28 W
Baezaeko ≃ 182 53.09 N 123.48 W
Bafang 152 5.09 N 10.11 E
Bafatá 150 12.10 N 14.40 W
Bafelé 150 10.09 N 10.08 W
Baffa 123 34.26 N 73.13 E
Baffin Basin ✦[1] 16 73.15 N 67.00 W
Baffin Bay ⊂, N.A. 16 73.00 N 66.00 W
Baffin Bay ⊂, Tx., U.S. 196 27.15 N 97.33 W
Baffin Island I 176 68.00 N 70.00 W
Bafia 152 4.44 N 11.16 E
Bafilo 150 9.21 N 1.16 E
Bafing ≃, Afr. 150 13.49 N 10.50 W
Bafing ≃, Mali 150 12.27 N 7.07 W
Bafing Makana 150 12.33 N 10.15 W
Bafoulabé 150 13.48 N 10.50 W
Bafoussam 152 5.29 N 10.24 E
Bāfq 128 31.35 N 55.24 E
Bafra 130 41.34 N 35.56 E
Bafra Burnu › 130 41.44 N 35.58 E
Bāft 128 29.14 N 56.38 E
Bafuku 154 4.15 N 27.54 E
Bafwabaka 154 2.07 N 27.40 E
Bafwabalinga 154 0.51 N 27.04 E
Bafwaboli 154 0.39 N 26.10 E
Bafwangbe 154 1.39 N 26.51 E
Bafwapada 154 0.56 N 26.57 E
Bafwasende 154 1.05 N 27.16 E
Bafwasomboli 154 1.27 N 27.01 E
Baga 126 22.26 N 90.28 E
Bagabag 116 16.37 N 121.15 E
Bagabag Island I 164 4.50 S 146.15 E
Baga-Burul 80 46.00 N 44.36 E
Bagac 116 14.36 N 120.23 E
Bagacay Point › 116 8.58 N 124.48 E
Bagac Bay ⊂ 116 14.36 N 120.22 E
Bagaces 236 10.31 N 85.15 W
Baga Chentej nuruu ⋏ 88 48.30 N 107.30 E
Bagage ∧ 154 3.23 N 40.12 E
Bagagem ≃, Bra. 250 11.37 S 48.12 W
Bagagem ≃, Bra. 255 13.58 S 48.21 W
Bagaha 124 27.06 N 84.05 E
Bagahak ∧ 116 5.03 N 118.44 E
Bagajevskij 78 47.19 N 40.23 E
Bāgalkot 122 16.11 N 75.42 E
Bagamanoc 116 13.57 N 124.17 E
Bagamoyo 154 6.26 S 38.54 E
Bagan 86 54.06 N 77.40 E
Bagana 80 54.22 N 51.25 E
Bagana, Mount ∧ 175e 6.09 S 155.12 E
Bagan Datoh 114 3.59 N 100.47 E
Bagañga 116 7.35 N 126.34 E
Bagan Serai 114 5.01 N 100.32 E
Bagansiapiapi 114 2.09 N 100.49 E
Bagansinembah 114 1.46 N 100.29 E
Bagansitukang 114 2.38 N 100.15 E
Baganza ≃ 64 44.47 N 10.19 E
Bagara 85 40.55 N 68.26 E
Bağarası 130 37.42 N 27.33 E
Bagaroua 150 14.38 N 4.21 E
Bagasra 120 21.29 N 70.57 E
Bagata 152 3.44 S 17.57 E
Bāgātipāra 126 24.18 N 88.57 E
Bagawi 140 12.19 N 34.21 E
Bagband 52 53.21 N 7.36 E
Bagbe ≃ 150 8.42 N 11.15 W
Bagbele 154 4.21 N 29.17 E
Bāgda 126 23.13 N 86.41 E
Bagdad → Baghdād, ʻĪrāq 128 33.21 N 44.25 E
Bagdad, Az., U.S. 200 34.34 N 113.12 W
Bagdad, Fl., U.S. 194 30.35 N 87.01 W
Bagdad, Ky., U.S. 218 38.15 N 85.03 W
Bagdaha 126 23.13 N 88.53 E
Bagdanga 126 24.02 N 88.32 E
Bagdarin 88 54.26 N 113.36 E
Bagdati 84 42.06 N 42.48 E
Bağdere 130 38.07 N 40.44 E
Bagé 252 31.20 S 54.06 W
Bagehadu 120 35.25 N 84.50 E
Bâgé-le-Châtel 58 46.18 N 4.56 E
Bagenkop 41 54.45 N 10.41 E
Bāgerhāt 124 22.40 N 89.48 E
Bagerovo 78 45.23 N 36.17 E
Bages et de Sigean, Étang de ⊂ 32 43.05 N 3.03 E
Bāgevādi 122 16.35 N 75.58 E
Baggao 116 17.56 N 121.46 E
Baggeryd 24 57.30 N 14.07 E
Baggetorp 40 59.01 N 16.04 E
Baggio ◆[8] 266b 45.27 N 9.06 E
Bağgöze 130 37.43 N 41.55 E
Baggs 200 41.02 N 107.39 W
Baggy Point › 42 51.09 N 4.16 W
Bāgh 123 33.59 N 73.47 E
Baghdād 128 33.21 N 44.25 E
Baghdād □[4] 128 33.30 N 44.30 E
Baghdobā 126 22.08 N 87.54 E
Baghelkhand Plateau ⋏[1] 124 23.45 N 82.20 E
Bāgh-e Malek 128 31.32 N 49.55 E
Bagheria 70 38.05 N 13.30 E
Bāgherpāra 126 23.14 N 89.21 E
Bāghia 126 23.27 N 90.29 E
Baghia Bīl ≋ 126 23.07 N 90.03 E
Bāghīn 128 30.12 N 56.48 E
Baghlān 120 36.13 N 68.46 E
Baghlān □[4] 120 35.45 N 69.00 E
Bāghmundi 124 23.12 N 86.03 E
Bāghpat 124 28.57 N 77.13 E
Baghrān Khowleh 120 33.01 N 64.58 E
Bagillt 262 53.16 N 3.10 W
Bağırpaşa Dağı ∧ 130 39.30 N 40.06 E
Bağırsak (Sājūr) ≃ 130 36.40 N 38.05 E
Bağkonak 130 38.12 N 31.17 E
Bagley 198 47.31 N 95.23 W
Bāgli 124 22.39 N 76.21 E
Bağlıca 130 37.53 N 41.46 E
Bağlum 130 40.03 N 32.51 E
Bagmanl'ar 84 40.38 N 46.18 E
Bāgmāri ◆[8] 272b 22.34 N 88.25 E
Bāgmatī □[8] 124 27.45 N 85.30 E
Bāgmatī ≃ 124 25.31 N 86.44 E
Bagn 26 60.49 N 9.34 E
Bagnacavallo 66 44.25 N 12.00 E
Bagnaia 66 42.25 N 12.09 E
Bāgnān 126 22.28 N 87.59 E
Bagnara Calabra 68 38.18 N 15.49 E
Bagnara di Romagna 66 44.23 N 11.49 E
Bag Narin 102 38.57 N 94.08 E
Bagnasco 62 44.18 N 8.02 E
Bagnell Dam ◆[6] 194 38.11 N 92.39 W
Bagnères-de-Bigorre 32 43.04 N 0.09 E
Bagnères-de-Luchon 32 42.47 N 0.36 E
Bagnes, Vallée de V 58 46.03 N 7.18 E
Bagneux 261 48.48 N 2.18 E
Bagni Acque Albule 66 41.57 N 12.43 E
Bagni del Masino 58 46.15 N 9.36 E
Bagni di Lucca 66 44.01 N 10.35 E
Bagni di Rabbi 64 46.24 N 10.48 E
Bagno a Ripoli 66 43.45 N 11.19 E
Bagno di Romagna 66 43.50 N 11.57 E
Bagnolet 261 48.52 N 2.25 E
Bagnoli del Trigno 66 41.42 N 14.27 E
Bagnoli di Sopra 64 45.11 N 11.53 E
Bagnoli Irpino 68 40.50 N 15.04 E
Bagnolo in Piano 64 44.46 N 10.40 E
Bagnolo Mella 64 45.26 N 10.10 E
Bagnols-en-Forêt 62 43.32 N 6.42 E
Bagnols-les-Bains 62 44.30 N 3.40 E
Bagnols-sur-Cèze 62 44.10 N 4.37 E
Bagñon 116 13.44 N 122.50 E
Bagnone 64 44.19 N 10.00 E
Bagnoregio 66 42.37 N 12.05 E
Bagno Vignoni 66 43.02 N 11.39 E
Bago (Pegu) 110 17.20 N 96.29 E
Bago □[8] 110 18.00 N 96.00 E
Bågø I 41 55.18 N 9.49 E
Bago ≃ 116 10.33 N 122.50 E
Bagod 61 46.53 N 16.45 E
Bagodar 124 24.05 N 85.52 E
Bagodo 152 6.25 N 13.23 E
Bagoé ≃ 150 12.36 N 6.34 W
Bagolino 64 45.49 N 10.28 E
Bagoni 146 7.53 N 10.43 E
Bagot □[6] 206 45.40 N 72.45 W
Bagotville, Base des Forces canadiennes ■ 186 48.20 N 70.58 W
Bağpınar 130 37.35 N 38.19 E
Bagrationovsk 76 54.23 N 20.39 E
Bagraula ◆[8] 272a 28.34 N 77.04 E
Bagre 250 1.54 S 50.12 W
Bagrinovcy 78 49.17 N 27.56 E
Bagshot 42 51.22 N 0.42 W
Bag Tal 89 43.20 N 122.16 E

Symbols in the index entries represent the broad categories identified in the key at the right. Symbols with superior numbers (⋏[1]) identify subcategories (see complete key on page *I · 1).*

Symbole im Register stellen die rechts im Schlüssel erklärten Kategorien dar. Symbole mit hochgestellten Ziffern (⋏[1]) bezeichnen Unterabteilungen einer Kategorie (vgl. vollständiger Schlüssel auf Seite *I · 1).*

Los símbolos incluídos en el texto del índice representan las grandes categorías identificadas con la clave a la derecha. Los símbolos con numeros en su parte superior (⋏[1]) identifican las subcategorías (véase la clave completa en la página *I · 1).*

Les symboles de l'index représentent les catégories indiquées dans la légende à droite. Les symboles suivis d'un indice (⋏[1]) représentent des sous-catégories (voir légende complète à la page *I · 1).*

Os símbolos incluídos no texto do índice representam as grandes categorias identificadas com a chave à direita. Os símbolos com números em sua parte superior (⋏[1]) identificam as subcategorias (veja-se a chave completa à página *I · 1).*

∧ Mountain	Berg	Montaña	Montagne	Montanha
⋏ Mountains	Gebirge	Montañas	Montagnes	Montanhas
)(Pass	Paß	Paso	Col	Passo
V Valley, Canyon	Tal, Cañon	Valle, Cañón	Vallée, Canyon	Vale, Canhão
≍ Plain	Ebene	Llano	Plaine	Planície
› Cape	Kap	Cabo	Cap	Cabo
I Island	Insel	Isla	Île	Ilha
II Islands	Inseln	Islas	Îles	Ilhas
⊥ Other Topographic Features	Andere Topographische Objekte	Otros Elementos Topográficos	Autres données topographiques	Outros acidentes topográficos

ESPAÑOL Nombre	Página	Lat.°′	Long.°′ W=Oeste
Bāguiati	272b	22.36 N	88.26 E
Baguio	116	16.25 N	120.36 E
Bagula	126	23.19 N	88.39 E
Bagumbayan	269f	14.28 N	121.03 E
Bagyrlaj ≃	80	48.08 N	51.14 E
Bagzane ▲	150	17.43 N	8.45 E
Bāh	124	26.53 N	78.36 E
Bahādurābād Ghāt	124	25.09 N	88.42 E
Bahādurgarh	124	28.41 N	76.56 E
Bahādurpur	126	23.25 N	88.28 E
Bahaia, Monte ▲	144	11.20 N	49.45 E
Baha'i Temple ▪¹	278	42.05 N	87.41 W
Bahamas □¹, N.A.	230	24.15 N	76.00 W
Bahamas □¹, N.A.	238	24.15 N	76.00 W
Bahār	124	34.54 N	48.26 E
Baharāgora	126	22.17 N	86.43 E
Baharampur	124	24.06 N	88.15 E
Baharpur	126	23.41 N	89.34 E
Bahau	114	2.49 N	102.25 E
Bahau ≃	112	2.34 N	116.20 E
Bahāwalnagar	123	29.59 N	73.16 E
Bahāwalpur	123	29.24 N	71.41 E
Bahçe	124	37.14 N	36.34 E
Bahçeköy ▪⁸	267b	41.11 N	28.59 E
Bahçeköy su kemeri ≃¹	267b	41.03 N	28.59 E
Bahechuan	98	40.59 N	124.49 E
Baheri	124	28.47 N	79.30 E
Bahi, Pt.	116	13.53 N	123.38 E
Bahi, Tan.	154	5.59 S	35.19 E
Bahía	30	46.11 N	18.57 E
— Salvador	255	12.59 S	38.31 W
Bahía □³	250	11.00 S	42.00 W
Bahía, Islas de la II	236	16.20 N	86.30 W
Bahía Azul	236	9.11 N	81.54 W
Bahía Bustamante	254	45.08 S	66.32 W
Bahía Erasmo, Parque Nacional ♦	254	46.05 S	73.35 W
Bahía Honda	240p	22.54 N	83.10 W
Bahía Honda Key I	116	24.40 N	31.16 W
Bahía Honda Point ▸	116	9.24 N	118.07 E
Bahía Kino	232	28.50 N	111.55 W
Bahía Laura	254	48.24 S	66.29 W
Bahlj	142	30.56 N	29.35 E
Bahir Dar	144	11.35 N	37.28 E
Bahi Swamp ≋	154	6.05 S	35.10 E
Bahjoi	124	28.24 N	78.37 E
Bahoi	123	28.38 N	75.38 E
Bahlolpur	272a	28.37 N	77.24 E
Bahn	150	7.05 N	8.45 W
Bahnay	142	30.23 N	31.04 E
Bahnayā	142	30.41 N	31.23 E
Bahra	144	21.24 N	39.29 E
Bahraich	124	27.35 N	81.36 E
Bahrain (Al-Bahrayn) □¹, Asia	118	26.00 N	50.30 E
Bahrain (Al-Bahrayn) □¹, Asia	128	26.00 N	50.30 E
Bahr al-Ghazāl ≃	140	8.30 N	26.00 E
Bahrām Chāh	128	29.26 N	64.03 E
Bahrānī, Ḥālat al- I	128	24.23 N	54.14 E
Bahrayn, Khalīj al c	128	25.45 N	50.40 E
Bahrdorf	54	52.23 N	11.00 E
Bahrein — Bahrain □¹	128	26.00 N	50.30 E
Bahrīyah, Al-Wāḥāt al- ⨯⁴	140	28.15 N	28.57 E
Bahser	130	37.57 N	39.18 E
Bahtīm	142	30.08 N	31.17 E
Bahtīt	142	30.29 N	31.38 E
Bāhū Kalāt	128	25.43 N	61.25 E
Bāhū Kalāt ≃	128	25.11 N	61.31 E
Bahulu, Pulau I	112	3.33 S	122.18 E
Bahu-mbelu	142	2.13 S	121.41 E
Baï	142	31.10 N	31.19 E
Baï, Zhg.	150	13.38 N	3.22 W
Bai ≃, Zhg.	102	32.10 N	112.20 E
Bai ≃, Zhg.	106	40.43 N	116.33 E
Baia	68	40.49 N	14.04 E
Baia-de-Aramă	38	45.00 N	22.49 E
Baía dos Tigres	152	16.36 S	11.43 E
Baía Farta	152	12.40 S	13.11 E
Baia Mare	38	47.40 N	23.35 E
Baiano	68	40.57 N	14.37 E
Baião	250	2.41 S	49.41 W
Baiardo	62	43.54 N	7.43 E
Baía Rica ≃	248	12.40 S	63.04 W
Baia Sprie	38	47.40 N	23.42 E
Baibao	116	39.04 N	115.31 E
Baibokoum	146	7.46 N	15.43 E
Baibuting	106	30.33 N	120.46 E
Baicang	124	30.14 N	90.44 E
Baicao	102	41.13 N	116.07 E
Baicaocheng	102	32.08 N	103.59 E
Baicao Ling ⤨	100	26.40 N	99.30 E
Baicheng, Zhg.	89	45.38 N	122.46 E
Baicheng, Zhg.	100	41.46 N	81.52 E
Baidian	106	30.47 N	119.14 E
Baidiao	102	28.07 N	101.28 E
Baidoa — Baychabo	144	3.07 N	43.39 E
Baidunzi	102	43.11 N	95.19 E
Baidyabāti	126	22.47 N	88.20 E
Baidyanāth	124	24.29 N	86.42 E
Baidyer Bāzār	126	23.39 N	90.37 E
Baie-Comeau	186	49.13 N	68.10 W
Baie-Comeau-Hauterive, Réserve ♦	186	50.05 N	68.00 W
Baie-des-Ha! Ha!	186	50.56 N	59.10 W
Baie-de-Shawinigan	206	46.34 N	72.45 W
Baie-des-Moutons	186	50.47 N	59.02 W
Baie-du-Renard	186	49.17 N	61.50 W
Baie-d'Urfé	206	45.24 N	73.55 W
Baie-Johan-Beetz	186	50.17 N	62.48 W
Baie-Mahault	241o	16.16 N	61.35 W
Baienfurt	64	47.49 N	9.38 E
Baiersbronn	64	48.30 N	8.23 E
Baiersdorf	60	49.39 N	11.01 E
Baies, Lac des	190	47.17 N	77.40 W
Baie-Sainte-Claire	186	49.54 N	64.30 W
Baie-Saint-Paul	186	47.27 N	70.30 W
Baie-Trinité	186	49.25 N	67.18 W
Baie Verte	186	49.56 N	56.11 W
Baierkaupt	206	46.06 N	72.43 W
Baigezhuang	106	39.54 N	118.09 E
Baigneux-les-Juifs	58	47.36 N	4.38 E
Baigou	106	39.07 N	116.01 E
Baigou ≃	106	39.06 N	116.00 E
Baiguchu	100	33.10 N	93.05 E
Baihāli Jot ▲	123	32.51 N	76.32 E
Baihe, Zhg.	124	22.06 N	80.33 E
Baihe, Zhg.	102	32.49 N	110.06 E
Baihe, Zhg.	100	32.17 N	110.02 E
Baihebu	106	39.39 N	118.10 E
Baihegang	106	30.54 N	121.35 E
Baihou	105	24.18 N	116.48 E
Baihua	105	29.07 N	104.37 E
Baihua Shan ▲	106	39.50 N	115.35 E
Baijala	272b	22.51 N	88.28 E
Baijiang	105	24.59 N	107.04 E
Baijiang	105	28.51 N	105.21 E
Baijie	105	29.17 N	106.31 E
Baijietan	105	28.44 N	105.50 E
Baijnāth	124	29.55 N	79.37 E
Baikal, Lago	100	53.00 N	107.40 E
— Bajkal, ozero ⌀	88	53.00 N	107.40 E
Baikal, Lake — Bajkal, ozero ⌀	88	53.00 N	107.40 E
Baikal-See — Bajkal, ozero ⌀	88	53.00 N	107.40 E
Baikeshu	106	30.26 N	116.50 E

FRANÇAIS Nom	Page	Lat.°′	Long.°′ W=Ouest
Baikonur — Bajkonyr	86	47.50 N	66.03 E
Baikunthapur	272b	22.59 N	83.13 E
Baikunthpur	124	23.15 N	82.33 E
Bailadores	246	8.15 N	71.50 W
Bailaiqiao	100	32.40 N	113.23 E
Bailang	89	46.57 N	123.05 E
Baildon	44	53.52 N	1.46 W
Baile	105	39.55 N	114.51 E
Baile Átha Luain — Athlone	48	53.25 N	7.56 W
Bàile Govora	38	45.05 N	24.11 E
Bàile Herculane	38	44.54 N	22.25 E
Bailén	34	38.06 N	3.46 W
Bàile Olăneşti	38	45.11 N	24.16 E
Bailey	38	44.02 N	23.21 E
Bailey Lakes	192	35.46 N	78.07 W
Bailey Run ≃	214	40.57 N	82.21 W
Baileys Crossroads	279b	40.35 N	79.47 W
Bail Hongal	284c	38.51 N	77.08 W
Bailian	122	15.49 N	74.52 E
Bailicun	124	24.09 N	112.22 E
Bailieborough	102	25.45 N	110.33 E
Bailin, Zhg.	48	53.54 N	6.59 W
Bailin, Zhg.	100	27.12 N	120.10 E
Bailin, Zhg.	100	26.20 N	113.18 E
Bailingmiao	107	29.11 N	105.57 E
Bailique	107	28.45 N	106.26 E
Bailique, Ilha I	102	41.50 N	110.27 E
Bailleul	250	0.58 N	50.04 W
Bailleul-sous-Gallardon	250	1.02 N	49.58 W
Ba Illi	50	50.44 N	2.44 E
Baillie ≃	261	48.32 N	1.39 E
Baillie Islands II	146	10.30 N	16.34 E
Baïlif	176	65.10 N	104.24 W
Bailly-Romainvilliers	178	70.33 N	128.10 W
Bailong ≃	241o	16.01 N	61.45 W
Bailundo	261	48.50 N	2.49 E
Bailuchang	102	32.18 N	105.42 E
Bailu Hu ⌀	106	31.15 N	121.44 E
Bailundo	100	30.03 N	113.06 E
Bailuoji	152	12.12 S	15.52 E
Baima, Zhg.	100	29.37 N	113.15 E
Baima, Zhg.	107	31.35 N	119.10 E
Baimachang	107	30.03 N	103.44 E
Baimachang, Zhg.	102	29.18 N	107.30 E
Baimachang, Zhg.	105	41.59 N	122.30 E
Baimaguan	107	29.40 N	103.54 E
Baimakou	105	40.41 N	116.52 E
Baimamiao, Zhg.	102	25.55 N	102.06 E
Baimamiao, Zhg.	102	36.58 N	108.08 E
Baimao, Zhg.	106	31.39 N	120.52 E
Baimao, Zhg.	106	31.35 N	120.54 E
Baimazhai	100	27.12 N	110.32 E
Baimashi	100	29.15 N	118.42 E
Baimazhai	100	28.06 N	115.50 E
Baimiaozi, Zhg.	89	46.18 N	123.35 E
Baimiaozi, Zhg.	100	40.34 N	120.36 E
Baimiaozi, Zhg.	104	41.55 N	122.12 E
Baimugao	106	32.01 N	120.19 E
Baimuru	164	7.30 S	144.49 E
Bain ≃	44	53.05 N	0.12 W
Baiha Bondio	52	5.10 N	16.33 E
Bainang	124	29.11 N	89.12 E
Bainbridge, Ga., U.S.	192	30.54 N	84.34 W
Bainbridge, N.Y., U.S.	210	42.17 N	75.28 W
Bainbridge, Oh., U.S.	218	39.13 N	83.16 W
Bainbridge, Pa., U.S.	208	40.05 N	76.40 W
Bainbridge Island I	224	47.37 N	122.33 W
Bainchi	126	23.07 N	88.14 E
Bainchipota	272b	22.52 N	88.11 E
Bain-de-Bretagne	32	47.50 N	1.41 W
Bainiqiao	100	31.35 N	114.09 E
Bains-les-Bains	58	48.00 N	6.16 E
Bainville	198	48.08 N	104.13 W
Bainyik	164	3.40 S	143.00 E
Baipeng	102	24.09 N	109.25 E
Baipu	102	32.15 N	120.46 E
Baiqiao	100	31.15 N	114.27 E
Baiqu	100	32.44 N	112.18 E
Baiquan, Zhg.	89	47.36 N	126.07 E
Baiquan, Zhg.	100	30.06 N	122.08 E
Baiqueyuan	100	31.48 N	115.05 E
Baïr, Pa., U.S.	208	39.54 N	76.50 W
Baïr, Urd.	132	30.46 N	36.41 E
Baïr, Wādī V	132	31.16 N	37.10 E
Baird Co ⌀	197	35.00 N	83.00 E
Baird, Mount ▲	202	43.20 N	111.06 W
Bairdford	214	40.37 N	79.52 W
Baird Inlet c	180	60.45 N	164.00 W
Baird Mountains ⤨	180	67.35 N	161.30 W
Baire	240p	20.19 N	76.31 W
Bairiki	174t	1.20 N	173.01 E
Bairin Zuoqi	98	44.00 N	119.02 E
Bair Island I	282	37.32 N	122.13 W
Bairkum	85	42.05 N	68.35 E
Bairnsdale	166	37.50 S	147.33 E
Bairoil	200	42.14 N	107.34 W
Bairro Alto	256	22.36 S	47.06 W
Bairuopu	100	28.12 N	112.46 E
Bais, Fr.	32	48.15 N	0.22 W
Bais, Pil.	116	9.35 N	123.07 E
Baïse ≃	32	44.17 N	0.18 E
Baisha, Zhg.	100	25.40 N	118.59 E
Baishan	102	34.22 N	117.18 E
Baishanzhen	104	41.56 N	126.28 E
Baishidu	100	25.26 N	113.01 E
Baishizhai	100	24.49 N	110.49 E
Baishui, Zhg.	102	35.11 N	109.37 E
Baishui, Zhg.	105	28.42 N	103.58 E
Baishuijiang	102	33.13 N	106.01 E
Baishuijiang ≃	102	33.03 N	105.04 E
Baisogala	90	55.33 N	23.43 E
Baisrasi	272b	22.27 N	88.11 E
Baita, India	272b	22.27 N	88.41 E
Baitadi	124	29.33 N	80.33 E
Baitaji	106	32.57 N	117.42 E
Baitazi	98	42.28 N	120.19 E
Baitazibeigou	104	42.17 N	120.20 E
Bai Thuong	116	19.54 N	105.23 E
Baitings Reservoir ⌀¹	362	53.40 N	1.59 W
Baitou	107	30.37 N	103.36 E

PORTUGUÊS Nome	Página	Lat.°′	Long.°′ W=Oeste
Baitoutan	102	32.30 N	106.56 E
Baitu	106	31.59 N	119.21 E
Baitugang	100	33.28 N	112.22 E
Baiwang	102	24.14 N	108.32 E
Baiwen	102	38.15 N	111.06 E
Baixa da Banheira	266c	38.39 N	9.03 W
Baixa Grande	255	11.57 S	40.11 W
Baixi	107	29.39 N	106.28 E
Baixiang	98	37.32 N	114.34 E
Baixingt	89	43.08 N	121.03 E
Baixo	250	6.44 S	38.43 W
Baixo Longa	152	15.42 S	18.50 E
Baiyan, Zhg.	100	28.04 N	120.02 E
Baiyan, Zhg.	106	31.08 N	119.38 E
Baiyang	100	34.25 N	112.12 E
Baiyang Dian ⌀	106	38.53 N	116.00 E
Baiyanghe	86	43.13 N	88.28 E
Baiyan Shan ▲	106	26.05 N	118.25 E
Baiyer River	164	5.35 S	144.10 E
Baiyin	102	36.47 N	104.07 E
Baiyinheshuo	89	44.31 N	119.51 E
Baiyintaohai	98	43.12 N	120.23 E
Baiyü, Zhg.	102	31.18 N	98.49 E
Baiyu, Zhg.	105	40.01 N	115.37 E
Baiyundu	100	26.10 N	118.47 E
Baiyunguan	278	39.54 N	116.19 E
Baizhongpu	100	33.22 N	114.50 E
Baizi	107	30.06 N	105.43 E
Baja	30	46.11 N	18.57 E
Baja, Punta ▸	232	29.58 N	115.49 W
Baja California □³	232	32.18 N	115.12 W
Baja California □³	232	30.00 N	115.00 W
Baja California ▸¹	232	28.00 N	113.30 W
Baja California Seamount Province ⊹	16	26.00 N	124.00 W
Baja California Sur □³	232	26.00 N	112.00 W
Bajada del Agrio	254	38.23 S	70.02 W
Bajan, Azer.	84	40.34 N	46.09 E
Bajan, Méx.	196	26.32 N	101.15 W
Bajan Adraga	88	48.32 N	111.03 E
Bajanaul	86	50.47 N	75.42 E
Bajancagaan	102	45.00 N	98.59 E
Bajan Chajrchan	88	49.18 N	96.20 E
Bajanchongor	90	46.08 N	100.43 E
Bajanchongor □⁴	102	45.00 N	99.30 E
Bajancogt	88	45.54 N	106.10 E
Bajandaj	88	53.04 N	105.30 E
Bajandalaj	102	43.28 N	103.28 E
Bajandelger, Mong.	88	47.44 N	108.07 E
Bajan-Delger, Mong.	88	49.33 N	103.50 E
Bajan Dzan	88	49.13 N	113.23 E
Bandždargalan	88	45.40 N	107.59 E
Bajan Dzürch	88	50.12 N	98.58 E
Bajan-Enger	88	48.25 N	90.50 E
Bajangol, Ross.	88	48.55 N	106.06 E
Bajangol, Ross.	88	50.44 N	103.27 E
Bajan-Gol, Ross.	88	52.49 N	99.54 E
Bajan'gov'	88	44.33 N	100.50 E
Bajan Nuur	88	48.54 N	91.14 E
Bajanöǧij ⌀⁴	88	48.20 N	89.50 E
Bajan-Öndör	102	44.47 N	98.39 E
Bajan-Ovoo, Mong.	102	47.47 N	112.05 E
Bajan-Ovoo, Mong.	102	42.57 N	106.07 E
Bajánsenye	30	46.46 N	16.23 E
Bajan Tümen	88	48.04 N	114.24 E
Bajan Uul, Mong.	88	47.40 N	101.30 E
Bajan Uul, Mong.	88	49.10 N	112.50 E
Bajan Uul, Mong.	88	49.40 N	96.20 E
Bajawa	112	8.47 S	120.59 E
Bajčetau ⤨	85	41.12 N	75.15 E
Baj-Chak	88	51.31 N	94.34 E
Bajčunas	84	47.14 N	52.55 E
Bajdar	80	44.30 N	33.42 E
Bajdarackaja guba c	72	69.00 N	67.30 E
Bajdonovo	88	54.17 N	104.38 E
Bajdrag ≃	102	45.10 N	100.04 E
Bājgān, Kūh-e ▲	128	31.28 S	55.51 E
Bājgīran	128	37.36 N	58.24 E
Bājil	144	15.04 N	43.16 E
Bajimba, Mount ▲	166	29.18 S	152.07 E
Bajina Bašta	38	43.58 N	19.34 E
Bajkadam	85	43.44 N	69.55 E
Bajkal, Tür.	130	39.34 N	33.08 E
Bajkal, ozero (Lake Baikal) ⌀	88	53.00 N	107.40 E
Bajkalovo, Ross.	86	57.24 N	63.46 E
Bajkalovo, Ross.	86	57.45 N	67.40 E
Bajkal'sk	88	51.33 N	104.05 E
Bajkalovo, Ross.	86	55.00 N	108.00 E
Bajkal'skij chrebet ⤨	88	55.00 N	108.00 E
Bajkal'skij zapovednik ♦	88	51.25 N	105.10 E
Bajkal'skoje	88	55.21 N	109.12 E
Bajkit	74	61.41 N	96.25 E
Bajkonyr	86	47.50 N	66.03 E
Bajmak	72	52.36 N	58.19 E
Bajmok	38	45.58 N	19.25 E
Bajnazar	86	48.32 N	73.42 E
Bajo, Indon.	112	2.07 N	120.48 E
Bajo, Indon.	115b	8.35 S	119.53 E
Bajo Boquete	236	8.47 N	82.26 W
Bajool	166	23.39 S	150.39 E
Bajos de Haina	238	18.25 N	70.02 W
Bajos del Balsamar ▸	234	17.34 N	100.48 W
Bajram 'Ali	128	37.37 N	62.10 E
Bajram-Ali	82	37.37 N	62.10 E
Bajsa	72	53.58 N	113.33 E
Bajseit	85	43.35 N	78.20 E
Baj-Sot	88	51.42 N	95.20 E
Bajtak	88	48.14 N	91.20 E
Bajtik	100	44.52 N	83.36 E
Bajuk	85	40.11 N	69.58 E
Bak	61	46.43 N	16.51 E
Bakacak	130	40.12 N	27.06 E
Bakal	72	54.56 N	58.48 E
Bakala	146	5.42 N	20.19 E
Bakaldy	88	53.39 N	86.49 E
Bakali ≃	126	23.01 N	88.37 E
Bakalovo	72	55.03 N	53.47 E
Bakambe	152	5.39 S	23.57 E
Bakanas	86	44.48 N	76.16 E
Bakanas ≃	86	47.05 N	79.18 E
Bakar	30	45.18 N	14.32 E
Bakarganj	124	22.33 N	90.21 E
Bakau	271c	13.29 N	16.40 W
Bakaucil	115b	6.54 S	106.27 E
Bakbakty	86	44.59 N	76.01 E
Bakčar	88	57.01 N	82.05 E
Bakel	150	14.54 N	12.27 W
Bakeng	112	3.05 S	118.52 E
Baker, Ca., U.S.	204	35.15 N	116.04 W
Baker, Fl., U.S.	194	30.47 N	86.40 W
Baker, La., U.S.	194	30.35 N	91.10 W
Baker, Mt., U.S.	198	46.22 N	104.17 W
Baker, Or., U.S.	202	44.46 N	117.45 W
Baker, Chile	254	47.49 S	73.37 W
Baker ≃, Wa., U.S.	224	48.38 N	121.41 W
Baker, Canal ⋈	254	48.00 S	74.00 W
Baker, Mount ▲	224	48.47 N	121.45 W
Baker Butte ▲	200	34.27 N	111.22 W
Baker Canyon V	280	33.47 N	117.38 W
Baker Creek ≃, B.C., Can.	182	52.59 N	122.30 W
Baker Creek ≃, Oh., U.S.	279a	41.21 N	81.54 W
Baker Creek ≃, Or., U.S.	224	45.15 N	123.14 W
Baker Island I, Oc.	14	0.15 N	176.27 W
Baker Island I, Ak., U.S.	182	55.20 N	133.36 W
Baker Lake	116	64.15 N	96.00 W
Baker Lake ⌀, Austl.	162	26.54 S	126.05 E
Baker Lake ⌀¹, Can.	176	64.10 N	95.30 W
Baker Lake ⌀, U.S.	278	42.08 N	88.07 W
Baker Lake ⌀¹	224	48.43 N	121.37 W
Bakersfield	226	35.22 N	119.01 W
Bakersfield South	285	35.20 N	119.03 W
Bakers Hill	168a	31.45 S	116.27 E
Bakers Island I	283	42.32 N	70.47 W
Bakerstown	214	40.39 N	79.56 W
Baker Street	260	51.30 N	0.21 E
Bakersville, N.C., U.S.	192	36.00 N	82.09 W
Bakersville, Oh., U.S.	214	40.21 N	81.39 W
Bakerville	158	26.00 S	26.06 E
Bakeshu	98	42.26 N	124.37 E
Bā Kêv	110	13.42 N	107.12 E
Bakewell	44	53.13 N	1.40 W
Bakhra	126	22.24 N	88.11 E
Bākhrābād	126	23.43 N	90.53 E
Bakhri	124	25.35 N	86.16 E
Bākhtarān (Kermānshāh)	128	34.19 N	47.04 E
Bakhtarān □⁴	128	34.30 N	47.00 E
Bakhtegān, Daryācheh-ye ⌀	128	29.20 N	54.05 E
Bakhtiyārpur	124	25.28 N	85.31 E
Bakhuis	250	4.42 N	56.49 W
Bakile	154	13.58 S	35.15 E
Bakino	82	56.20 N	38.59 E
Bakinskaja	80	45.51 N	38.24 E
Bakinskij archipelag II	84	39.30 N	49.45 E
Baklan	130	38.55 N	27.00 E
Baklanka	76	58.43 N	40.06 E
Bakloh	123	32.28 N	75.55 E
Bakluši	80	52.07 N	43.22 E
Bako, C. Iv.	150	9.09 N	7.37 W
Bako, Ityo.	144	5.50 N	36.40 E
Bakool □⁴	144	4.15 N	44.00 E
Bakoondfontein	158	24.43 S	22.30 E
Bakori	150	11.34 N	7.27 E
Bakou — Baku	84	40.23 N	49.51 E
Bakouma	152	5.42 N	22.47 E
Bakovka	265b	55.41 N	37.20 E
Bakcy ≃	150	13.49 N	10.50 W
Baksan	84	43.40 N	43.32 E
Baksan ≃	84	43.42 N	43.32 E
Bakšejevo, Ross.	80	55.44 N	39.53 E
Bakšejevo, Ross.	82	57.26 N	73.00 E
Baker Chāndour	122	15.06 N	74.32 E
Bakšty	76	53.56 N	26.11 E
Baksuk ≃	86	51.50 N	69.30 E
Baku (Baky)	84	40.23 N	49.51 E
Bakulin Point ▸	116	8.33 N	126.22 E
Bakum	52	52.45 N	8.11 E
Bakumpai	112	1.26 S	113.05 E
Bakung, Pulau I	112	2.32 N	100.26 E
Bakuriani	114	41.46 N	43.32 E
Bakwa-Kenge	192	4.51 S	22.04 E
Bakwakwa — Mbuji-Mayi	152	6.09 S	23.38 E
Bakyrly	84	39.32 N	47.10 E
Bala, On., Can.	212	45.01 N	79.37 W
Bala, Sén.	150	14.02 N	13.10 W
Bala, Tür.	130	39.34 N	33.08 E
Bala, Wales, U.K.	44	52.54 N	3.35 W
Balabac	116	7.59 N	117.04 E
Balabac Island I	116	7.57 N	117.01 E
Balabac Strait ⋈	116	7.35 N	117.00 E
Bălă Bāgh	123	34.30 N	70.14 E
Ba'labakk	132	34.00 N	36.12 E
Balabalagan, Kepulauan II	112	2.20 S	117.25 E
Balabanovo	265b	55.11 N	36.40 E
Balabio, Île I	175f	20.07 S	164.11 E
Balačna	76	56.30 N	43.36 E
Balachta	88	55.24 N	91.35 E
Balachtison, gora ▲	88	54.36 N	93.50 E
Balad	128	34.01 N	44.09 E
Bala-Cynwyd	285	40.00 N	75.14 W
Baladabandh	272b	22.52 N	88.07 E
Balagansk	88	53.57 N	103.02 E
Bālāghāt	124	21.48 N	80.11 E
Balaghny Rangs ⤨	122	18.45 N	76.30 E
Balagny-sur-Thérain	261	49.17 N	2.24 E
Balaguer	34	41.47 N	0.49 E
Balaikarangan	112	0.50 N	110.26 E
Balaisepuah	112	0.04 S	109.40 E
Bālā	95	43.35 N	78.22 E
Balakété	152	4.51 N	19.57 E
Bālākot	123	34.23 N	73.21 E
Balakovo	72	52.02 N	47.47 E
Balal'ča	88	54.33 N	96.58 E
Bala Lake — Llyn Tegid ⌀	44	52.53 N	3.38 W
Balallan	46	58.05 N	6.35 W
Bal'ama, Urd.	132	32.14 N	35.42 E
Balamban	116	10.30 N	123.45 E
Balambangan, Pulau I	116	7.17 N	116.55 E
Bālā Morghāb	128	35.35 N	63.20 E
Balan	58	48.39 N	4.58 E
Balanda	272b	22.43 N	88.32 E

	Página	Lat.°′	Long.°′ W=Oeste
Bālāpur	122	20.40 N	76.46 E
Balaqs	273c	30.10 N	31.17 E
Balaqtar	142	31.05 N	30.13 E
Balaraja	115a	6.12 S	106.27 E
Balarāmbāti	272b	22.48 N	88.13 E
Balarāmpota	272b	22.31 N	88.08 E
Balarāmpur	126	23.07 N	86.13 E
Balaruc-le-Vieux	62	43.27 N	3.41 E
Balaši	80	51.24 N	49.55 E
Balašicha	82	55.49 N	37.58 E
Balašov	80	51.32 N	43.08 E
Balassagyarmat	30	48.05 N	19.18 E
Balāt	140	25.33 N	29.16 E
Balatan, Indon.	164	6.05 S	134.45 E
Balatan, Pil.	116	13.20 N	123.10 E
Balaton	198	44.14 N	95.52 W
Balaton ⌀	30	46.50 N	17.45 E
Balaurin	112	8.15 S	123.43 E
Balavé	150	12.23 N	4.09 W
Balayan	116	13.57 N	120.44 E
Balayan Bay c	116	13.51 N	120.47 E
Balazote	34	38.53 N	2.08 W
Balbi, Mount ▲¹	164	5.55 S	154.59 E
Balbieriškis	76	54.32 S	23.52 E
Balbigny	62	45.49 N	4.11 E
Balbina, Represa ⌀¹	250	1.20 S	59.40 W
Balboa	236	8.57 N	79.34 W
Balbriggan	48	53.37 N	6.11 W
Balcad	144	2.23 N	45.23 E
Balcanoona	166	30.33 S	139.18 E
Balcarce	252	37.50 S	58.15 W
Balcarres	184	50.48 N	103.33 W
Bălceşti	38	44.37 N	23.56 E
Balchaš	86	46.49 N	74.59 E
Balchaš, ozero (Lake Balkhash) ⌀	86	46.00 N	74.00 E
Balch Springs	222	32.43 N	96.37 W
Balci	130	43.25 N	28.10 E
Balcik	98	43.19 N	124.49 E
Bălcituța	172	46.14 S	169.44 E
Balcombe	42	51.04 N	0.08 W
Balcones Escarpment ⤨¹	196	29.30 N	99.15 W
Balde	252	33.20 S	66.38 W
Baldeador	287a	22.53 S	43.02 W
Bald Eagle	214	41.04 N	78.12 W
Bald Eagle Creek ≃	210	41.08 N	77.24 W
Bald Eagle Mountain ▲	214	41.00 N	77.45 W
Bald Eagle State Park ♦	214	41.00 N	77.40 W
Baldegger See ⌀	58	47.12 N	8.16 E
Baldeneysee ⌀	263	51.24 N	7.03 E
Balderschwang	58	47.26 N	10.06 E
Balderstone	262	53.47 N	2.34 W
Balderton	44	53.03 N	0.47 W
Bald Head ▸	162	35.07 S	118.01 E
Bald Hill ▲²	166	20.18 S	144.06 E
Bald Hill Branch ≃	284c	18.55 N	76.49 W
Baldhill Creek ≃	198	47.09 N	98.03 W
Baldim	255	19.17 S	43.57 W
Baldichieri d'Asti	62	44.54 N	8.07 E
Bald Knob	194	35.18 N	91.34 W
Bald Knob ▲, Ca., U.S.	280	37.25 N	122.21 W
Bald Knob ▲, Va., U.S.	192	37.56 N	79.51 W
Baldock Lake ⌀	184	56.33 N	97.57 W
Baldone	76	56.45 N	24.24 E
Baldovino, Arroyo ≃	288	34.46 S	58.07 W
Baldpate Pond ⌀	283	42.42 N	71.00 W
Baldur	184	49.23 N	99.15 W
Baldwin, Fl., U.S.	192	30.18 N	81.58 W
Baldwin, Mi., U.S.	194	43.54 N	85.51 W
Baldwin, N.Y., U.S.	210	40.39 N	73.36 W
Baldwin, Pa., U.S.	214	40.21 N	79.58 W
Baldwin ≃, U.S.	190	44.49 N	68.32 W
Baldwin City	198	38.46 N	95.13 W
Baldwin Hills ⤨²	280	33.59 N	118.23 W
Baldwin Park	280	34.05 N	117.58 W
Baldwin Peninsula ▸¹	180	66.40 N	162.15 W
Baldwinsville	210	43.09 N	76.19 W
Baldwinville	207	42.36 N	72.07 W
Baldwin-Wallace College ∪	279a	41.21 N	81.51 W
Baldwyn	194	34.31 N	88.38 W
Baldy Mountain ▲, Mb., Can.	184	51.28 N	100.44 W
Baldy Mountain ▲, B.C., Can.	182	53.12 N	120.02 W
Bale — Basel, Schw.	58	47.33 N	7.35 E
Baleares, Islas	34	39.30 N	3.00 E
Bale — Akiosi	273a	6.41 N	3.21 E
Baleares, Îles	34	39.30 N	3.00 E
Balearic Islands (Baleares, Islas) II	34	39.30 N	3.00 E
Baleares, Illes II	34	39.30 N	3.00 E
Baleares, Ilhas II	34	39.30 N	3.00 E
Balease, Gunung ▲	112	2.24 S	120.33 E
Baleine, Grande rivière de la ≃	176	55.16 N	77.47 W
Baleine, Petite rivière à la ≃	176	56.00 N	76.45 W
Baleine, Rivière à la ≃	176	58.15 N	67.40 W
Balej	88	51.35 N	116.38 E
Baleniki	76	58.20 N	25.01 E
Baler	116	15.46 N	121.34 E
Baler Bay c	116	15.46 N	121.40 E
Balestrand	26	61.12 N	6.32 E
Balezino	72	57.58 N	53.00 E
Balfate	236	15.48 N	86.25 W
Balfes Creek	166	20.13 S	145.55 E
Balfour, N.Z.	172	45.50 S	168.35 E
Balfour, S. Afr.	158	26.44 S	28.31 E
Balfour, Scot., U.K.	46	59.01 N	2.55 W
Balfour, N.C., U.S.	192	35.20 N	82.28 W
Balfour Downs	162	22.50 S	120.50 E
Balfour Park ♦	273d	26.08 S	28.06 E
Balfron	46	56.04 N	4.20 W
Balgach	58	47.25 N	9.35 E
Bālgarja □¹ — Bulgaria □¹	38	43.00 N	25.00 E
Balgazyn	88	51.08 N	95.00 E
Balgo	162	20.09 S	127.48 E
Balgowlah	274a	33.48 S	151.16 E
Balguerie, Cap ▸	174x	9.45 S	138.47 W
Balhannah	168b	35.00 S	138.50 E
Bāli	120	25.50 N	74.05 E
Balì	115b	8.20 S	115.00 E
Bali, Laut (Bali Sea) ⊤²	112	7.45 S	115.30 E
Bali, Selat ⋈	112	8.18 S	114.25 E
Bāliākāndi	126	23.38 N	89.33 E
Baliançao	116	8.40 N	123.36 E
Bāliāǧi	126	21.40 N	87.17 E
Bāliāti	126	23.59 N	90.03 E
Balibago	116	13.37 N	121.18 E
Bali Barat National Park ♦	115b	8.15 S	144.40 E
Baliceaux I	241h	12.57 N	61.08 W
Bāli Chak	126	22.22 N	87.33 E
Balicuatro Islands II	116	12.39 N	124.24 E
Balicuatro Point ▸	116	12.35 N	124.16 E
Balidianzi	98	43.19 N	124.49 E
Balidiha	126	21.58 N	86.38 E
Balige	114	2.20 N	99.04 E
Bāligha	126	21.57 N	87.35 E
Balihān	98	41.29 N	118.41 E
Bālīhāti	272b	22.44 N	88.19 E
Balikesir	130	39.39 N	27.53 E
Balikesir □⁴	130	39.30 N	28.00 E
Balik Gölü ⌀	84	39.44 N	43.34 E
Balīkh ≃	130	35.52 N	39.12 E
Balīkh ≃	130	36.00 N	38.55 E
Balikpapan	112	1.17 S	116.50 E
Balikumbat	152	5.54 N	10.24 E
Balimbing, Indon.	112	5.55 S	104.34 E
Balimbing, Pil.	116	5.05 N	119.58 E
Balimo	164	8.03 S	142.56 E
Balin, Ukr.	78	48.52 N	26.40 E
Balin, Ukr.	89	48.19 N	122.19 E
Balincol ig	48	51.53 N	8.35 W
Balindong (Watu)	116	7.55 N	124.12 E
Baling	114	5.40 N	100.55 E
Balingasag	116	8.45 N	124.47 E
Balingen	58	48.16 N	8.51 E
Balingsta	28	59.40 N	17.31 E
Balintang Channel ⋈	108	19.49 N	121.40 E
Balipu	100	39.53 N	117.48 E
Balışeyh	130	39.56 N	33.43 E
Baliung ≃	115a	6.50 S	106.52 E
Balingun Island I	164	5.09 S	120.12 E
Baliyingzi	104	41.59 N	121.14 E
Baliza	255	16.15 S	52.25 W
Balizhuang, Zhg.	105	39.16 N	116.28 E
Balk	52	52.54 N	5.34 E
Balkach, Lago — Balchaš, ozero ⌀	86	46.00 N	74.00 E
Balkan □⁸	128	39.30 N	55.00 E
Balkan Mountains — Stara Planina ⤨	38	42.45 N	25.00 E
Balkan Peninsula ▸¹	10	44.00 N	23.00 E
— Kabardino-Balkarja □³	84	43.30 N	43.30 E
Balkašino	86	52.31 N	68.46 E
Balkbrug	52	52.36 N	6.24 E
Balkh	120	36.46 N	66.54 E
Balkh □⁴	120	36.30 N	67.00 E
Balkhash, Lake — Balchaš, ozero ⌀	86	46.00 N	74.00 E
Balki	78	47.23 N	34.57 E
Balkwil	194	31.24 N	92.04 W
Balladonia	162	32.27 S	123.52 E
Ballaghaderreen	48	53.54 N	8.35 W
Ballan	168	37.36 S	144.14 E
Ballangen	26	68.20 N	16.50 E
Ballangeich	168	38.12 S	142.47 E
Ballantrae	46	55.06 N	5.00 W
Ballard, Mount ▲	224	48.06 N	120.38 W
Ballardvale	283	42.38 N	71.10 W
Ballater	46	57.05 N	3.03 W
Ballaugh	44	54.20 N	4.32 W
Ball Bay c	174c	29.03 S	167.59 E
Ball Ground	192	34.20 N	84.23 W
Balla Balla	154	20.26 S	29.02 E
Ballachulish	46	56.40 N	5.10 W
Ballaghderreen	158	22.27 S	30.51 E
Ballam	264	51.27 N	0.09 W
Ballantyne Strait ⋈	176	77.30 N	115.00 W
Ballao	66	39.42 N	9.20 E
Ballarat	166	37.34 S	143.52 E
Ballard, Lake ⌀	162	29.27 S	120.55 E
Ballaugh	44	54.19 N	4.32 W
Balle	150	15.18 N	8.43 W
Ballenas, Bahía de ⌀	232	26.45 N	113.26 W
Ballenas, Canal de ⋈	232	29.10 N	113.25 W
Ballenato, Punta ▸	286b	23.10 S	70.34 W
Ballendella	168	36.24 S	144.39 E
Ballenger Creek ≃	208	39.21 N	77.25 W
Ballenita, Punta ▸	252	25.45 S	70.44 W
Balleny Islands II	167	66.35 S	163.00 E
Ballesteros, Arg.	252	32.33 S	62.59 W
Ballesteros, Pil.	116	18.25 N	121.31 E
Balleza	232	26.57 N	106.21 W
Balleza ≃	232	27.31 N	105.09 W
Ballia	124	25.45 N	84.10 E
Ballidu	162	30.36 S	116.46 E
Ballina, Austl.	166	28.52 S	153.34 E
Ballina, Ire.	48	54.07 N	9.09 W
Ballinalack	48	53.37 N	7.28 W
Ballinasloe	48	53.20 N	8.13 W
Ballingarry	48	52.29 N	8.52 W
Ballinger	196	31.44 N	99.57 W

ENGLISH / DEUTSCH

Name	Page	Lat.°′	Long.°′
Ballon	50	48.10 N	0.14 E
Ballona Creek ≃	280	33.58 N	118.27 W
Ballouville	207	41.52 N	71.51 W
Ballsh	38	40.36 N	19.44 E
Balls Pyramid I	160	31.45 S	159.15 E
Ballston	224	45.04 N	123.19 W
Ballston Lake	210	42.54 N	73.52 W
Ballston Spa	210	43.00 N	73.50 W
Ballville	214	41.20 N	83.09 W
Ballwin	219	38.35 N	90.32 W
Bālly, India	272b	22.38 N	88.21 E
Bally, Pa., U.S.	208	40.24 N	75.35 W
Bālly ◆[8]	272b	22.39 N	88.21 E
Ballybay	48	54.08 N	6.54 W
Ballybofey	48	54.48 N	7.47 W
Ballybogy	48	55.07 N	6.34 W
Bālly Bridge ◆[5]	272b	22.39 N	88.21 E
Ballybunnion	48	52.31 N	9.40 W
Ballycanew	48	52.36 N	6.19 W
Ballycastle, Ire.	48	54.16 N	9.23 W
Ballycastle, N. Ire., U.K.	48	55.12 N	6.15 W
Ballyclare	48	54.45 N	6.00 W
Ballyconneely	48	53.26 N	10.02 W
Ballyconnell	48	54.07 N	7.35 W
Ballycotton	48	51.50 N	8.01 W
Ballycroy	48	54.01 N	9.51 W
Ballyduff, Ire.	48	52.27 N	9.40 W
Ballyduff, Ire.	48	52.09 N	8.03 W
Ballyferriter	48	52.09 N	10.26 W
Ballyfinboy ≃	48	53.02 N	8.15 W
Ballygar	48	53.32 N	8.20 W
Ballygawley	48	54.28 N	7.02 W
Ballygorman	48	55.22 N	7.21 W
Ballygowan	48	54.30 N	5.48 W
Ballygunge ◆[8]	272b	22.31 N	88.21 E
Ballyhaise	48	54.03 N	7.19 W
Ballyhalbert	48	54.30 N	5.28 W
Ballyhaunis	48	53.46 N	8.46 W
Ballyhoura Mountains ⋏	48	52.20 N	8.35 W
Ballyjamesduff	48	53.52 N	7.12 W
Ballylongford	48	52.33 N	9.28 W
Ballymacoda	48	51.57 N	7.54 W
Ballymahon	48	53.34 N	7.45 W
Ballymakeery (Ballyvourney)	48	51.55 N	9.09 W
Ballymena	48	54.52 N	6.17 W
Ballymoe	48	53.42 N	8.29 W
Ballymoney	48	55.04 N	6.31 W
Ballymote	48	54.06 N	8.31 W
Ballymurray	48	53.35 N	8.08 W
Ballynahinch	48	54.24 N	5.54 W
Ballyneety	48	52.35 N	8.33 W
Ballynoe	48	52.03 N	8.05 W
Ballyquintin Point ›	48	54.20 N	5.30 W
Ballyragget	48	52.47 N	7.20 W
Ballysadare	48	54.13 N	8.31 W
Ballyshannon	48	54.30 N	8.11 W
Ballyteige Bay c	48	52.11 N	6.39 W
Ballyvaghan	48	53.07 N	9.07 W
Ballyvoy	48	55.12 N	6.12 W
Ballywalter	48	54.33 N	5.30 W
Balm	220	27.45 N	82.15 W
Balmaceda	254	45.55 S	71.41 W
Balmaceda, Cerro ∧	254	51.25 S	73.11 W
Balmain	274a	33.51 S	151.11 E
Balme	62	45.18 N	7.13 E
Balmerino	46	56.24 N	3.02 W
Balmertown	184	51.04 N	93.44 W
Balmhorn ∧	58	46.25 N	7.43 E
Balmoral, Austl.	166	37.15 S	141.51 E
Balmoral, S. Afr.	158	25.52 S	28.59 E
Balmoral Castle ⊥	46	57.02 N	3.14 W
Balmorhea	196	30.59 N	103.45 W
Balmville	210	41.32 N	74.00 W
Balnacra	46	57.28 N	5.23 W
Balnearia	252	31.00 S	62.40 W
Balobanovo	82	55.51 N	38.14 E
Balobe	154	0.05 N	28.00 E
Baloda Bāzār	120	21.40 N	82.10 E
Balombo	152	12.21 S	14.46 E
Balong, Indon.	115a	7.57 S	111.26 E
Balong, Zhg.	102	36.17 N	97.20 E
Balonne ≃	166	28.47 S	147.56 E
Bālotra	120	25.50 N	72.14 E
Baloži	76	56.53 N	24.06 E
Balpahari Reservoir ⊜[1]	126	24.04 N	86.28 E
Balrāmpur	124	27.26 N	82.11 E
Balranald	166	34.38 S	143.33 E
Balș	38	44.21 N	24.06 E
Balsam Lake	190	45.27 N	92.27 W
Balsam Lake ⊜	212	44.35 N	78.50 W
Bálsamo	255	20.27 S	53.57 W
Balsas	250	7.31 S	46.02 W
Balsas ≃	234	17.55 N	102.10 W
Balsas, Rio das ≃, Bra.	250	7.14 S	44.33 W
Balsas, Rio das ≃, Bra.	250	9.58 S	47.52 W
Balsas Sur	234	17.59 N	99.47 W
Balseiro ≃	250	5.51 S	43.44 W
Balsham	42	52.08 N	0.20 E
Balsorano	66	41.49 N	13.34 E
Bålsta	40	59.35 N	17.30 E
Balsthal	58	47.19 N	7.42 E
Balta	78	47.55 N	29.37 E
Baltaj	80	52.28 N	46.38 E
Baltanás	34	41.56 N	4.15 W
Baltasar Brum	252	30.44 S	57.19 W
Baltasi	80	56.21 N	50.12 E
Baltasound	46a	60.45 N	0.52 W
Baltazar, Arroyo ≃	258	33.47 S	58.58 W
Bălți → Bel'c'	38	47.46 N	27.56 E
Baltic, Ct., U.S.	207	41.37 N	72.05 W
Baltic, Oh., U.S.	214	40.26 N	81.41 W
Baltic Bay c	190	48.22 N	83.43 W
Baltico, Mar → Baltic Sea ⊤[2]	24	57.00 N	19.00 E
Baltic Sea ⊤[2]	24	57.00 N	19.00 E
Baltic Station ◆[5]	265a	59.55 N	30.18 E
Baltijsk	76	54.39 N	19.55 E
Baltijskaja kosa ›[2]	30	54.25 N	19.35 E
Baltīm	142	31.33 N	31.05 E
Baltimore, Ire.	48	51.29 N	9.22 W
Baltimore, S. Afr.	156	23.15 S	28.20 E
Baltimore, Md., U.S.	208	39.17 N	76.36 W
Baltimore, Md., U.S.	284b	39.17 N	76.36 W
Baltimore, Oh., U.S.	188	39.50 N	82.36 W
Baltimore □[6]	208	39.22 N	76.36 W
Baltimore, University of ⊕[2]	284b	39.18 N	76.37 W
Baltimore Airpark ⊠	284b	39.24 N	76.25 W
Baltimore Highlands	284b	39.13 N	76.38 W
Baltimore-Washington International Airport ⊠	208	39.11 N	76.40 W
Baltinglass	48	52.55 N	6.41 W
Baltique, Mer → Baltic Sea ⊤[2]	24	57.00 N	19.00 E
Baltistān ◆[1]	123	35.18 N	75.37 E
Baltit	123	36.20 N	74.40 E
Baltoji-Vokė	76	54.28 N	25.06 E
Baltoro Glacier ⌂	123	35.42 N	76.10 E
Baltra, Isla I	246a	0.26 S	90.16 W
Baltrum I	52	53.44 N	7.23 E
Bālu ≃, Bngl.	126	23.44 N	90.30 E
Ba Lu ≃, Viet	110	14.18 N	107.52 E
Baluarte ≃	234	22.49 N	106.02 W
Baluarte, Arroyo V	196	27.09 N	98.07 W
Baluchistān □[4]	120	29.00 N	67.00 E
Baluchistan □[9]	128	28.00 N	63.00 E
Balud	116	12.02 N	123.12 E
Bālughāta	126	22.05 N	88.01 E
Bāluhāti	272b	22.39 N	88.16 E
Balui ≃	112	2.42 N	113.47 E
Balukbaluk Island I	116	6.40 N	121.43 E
Balupe ≃	76	56.57 N	26.55 E
Bālurghāt	124	25.13 N	88.46 E
Balut Island I	116	5.24 N	125.23 E
Balvano	68	40.39 N	15.31 E
Balve	56	51.20 N	7.51 E
Balvi	76	57.08 N	27.17 E
Balvicar	46	56.14 N	5.38 W
Balwina Aboriginal Reserve ◆[4]	162	20.30 S	128.00 E
Balwyn	274b	37.49 S	145.05 E
Balxuca, Arroyo de la ≃	266d	41.31 N	2.06 E
Balya	130	39.45 N	27.35 E
Balygyčan	74	63.56 N	154.12 E
Balykči	85	40.54 N	71.50 E
Balyksa	86	53.25 N	89.05 E
Balykši	80	47.05 N	51.54 E
Balyktyg-Chem ≃	88	51.15 N	96.54 E
Balzac	182	51.10 N	114.01 W
Balzar	246	1.22 S	79.54 W
Balzers	58	47.04 N	9.30 E
Bal'zino	88	51.03 N	113.35 E
Balzola	62	45.11 N	8.24 E
Bām, Īrān	128	36.58 N	57.59 E
Bam, Īrān	128	29.06 N	58.21 E
Bama, Nig.	146	11.30 N	13.41 E
Bama, Zhg.	102	24.21 N	107.08 E
Bamaga	164	10.52 S	142.24 E
Bamaji Lake ⊜	184	51.09 N	91.25 W
Bamako	150	12.39 N	8.00 W
Bāmangāchi	272b	22.46 N	88.31 E
Bāmangawān	126	24.14 N	86.49 E
Bāmanghāra	272b	22.31 N	88.28 E
Bāmanmura	272b	22.42 N	88.31 E
Bamao	100	29.26 N	120.59 E
Bamata	152	1.00 S	21.06 E
Bamba, Mali	150	17.02 N	1.24 W
Bamba, Zaïre	152	5.45 S	18.23 E
Bambamarca	248	6.41 S	78.32 W
Bambana ≃	236	13.27 N	83.50 W
Bambang	116	16.23 N	121.06 E
Bambannan Island I	116	5.37 N	120.17 E
Bambara Maoundé	150	15.51 N	2.47 W
Bambari	152	5.45 N	20.40 E
Bambaroo	166	18.52 S	146.12 E
Bambāvi	272c	18.58 N	73.03 E
Bamberg, Dtsch.	56	49.53 N	10.53 E
Bamberg, S.C., U.S.	192	33.17 N	81.02 W
Bamber Lake	208	39.54 N	74.19 W
Bamberton	224	48.35 N	123.31 W
Bambesa	154	3.28 N	25.43 E
Bambesi	144	9.45 N	34.38 E
Bambezi	154	20.00 S	28.56 E
Bambili	154	3.39 N	26.07 E
Bambinga	152	3.42 S	18.54 E
Bambio	152	3.54 N	16.59 E
Bamboesberg ⋏	158	31.30 S	26.10 E
Bamboi	150	8.10 N	2.02 W
Bamboo Creek	162	20.56 S	120.13 E
Bamboo Springs	162	22.04 S	119.38 E
Bambouti	154	5.24 N	27.12 E
Bambuí	255	20.01 S	45.58 W
Bambujka	88	55.47 N	115.48 E
Bambula	154	1.17 S	25.38 E
Bamburgh	44	55.36 N	1.42 W
Bamburral ≃	248	20.10 S	58.07 W
Bambuto ≃	200	30.51 N	110.52 W
Bam Co ⊜	120	31.30 N	91.05 E
Bamencheng	105	39.35 N	117.37 E
Bamenda	152	5.56 N	10.10 E
Bamendjou	152	5.24 N	10.19 E
Bamfield	182	48.50 N	125.08 W
Bamhā	142	29.35 N	31.14 E
Bami	128	38.44 N	56.48 E
Bāmīān	120	34.50 N	67.50 E
Bāmīān □[4]	120	34.45 N	67.15 E
Bamiancheng	89	43.13 N	124.02 E
Bamingui	152	7.34 N	20.11 E
Bamingui ≃	146	8.33 N	19.05 E
Bamingui-Bangoran □[5]	146	8.15 N	20.15 E
Bamingui-Bangoran, Parc National du ♦	146	8.00 N	19.40 E
Bam Island I	164	3.35 S	144.50 E
Bāmna	126	22.19 N	90.06 E
Bamndali ◆[8]	272a	28.33 N	77.03 E
Bamol	164	7.38 S	138.37 E
Bampton, Eng., U.K.	42	51.00 N	3.29 W
Bampton, Eng., U.K.	42	51.44 N	1.33 W
Bampūr	128	27.12 N	60.27 E
Bampūr ≃	128	27.18 N	59.06 E
Bāmra Hills ⋏[2]	120	21.30 N	84.30 E
Bamu ≃	164	8.01 S	143.33 E
Bamumo	120	32.30 N	93.15 E
Ban	150	14.05 N	2.27 W
Bana, Malaŵi	154	12.25 S	34.08 E
Ba Na, Viet	110	15.59 N	107.59 E
Banā, Wādī V	144	13.03 N	45.24 E
Banaba (Ocean Island) I	174d	0.52 S	169.35 E
Banabuiú ≃	250	5.07 S	38.06 W
Banabuiú, Açude ⊜[1]	250	5.20 S	39.05 W
Ban Aen	110	18.02 N	98.37 E
Banagher	48	53.11 N	7.59 W
Banagi	154	2.16 S	34.51 E
Banago	116	7.30 N	124.07 E
Banagrām	126	22.35 N	89.55 E
Banahao, Mount ∧	116	14.04 N	121.29 E
Banalia	154	1.33 N	25.20 E
Banamba	150	13.33 N	7.27 W
Banana, Austl.	166	24.28 S	150.07 E
Banana, Zaïre	152	6.01 S	12.24 E
Banana Creek ≃	220	28.36 N	80.38 W
Banana Islands II	150	8.07 N	13.13 W
Bananal	256	22.41 S	44.19 W
Bananal ≃, Bra.	250	8.33 S	49.26 W
Bananal ≃, Bra.	256	22.32 S	44.11 W
Bananal, Ilha do I	250	11.30 S	50.15 W
Banana River c	220	28.25 N	80.38 W
Bananeiras	250	6.45 S	35.37 W
Bananga	110	6.56 N	93.54 E
Banao, Loma de ∧	240p	21.51 N	79.36 W
Bānār ≃	124	24.04 N	90.38 E
Banaras → Vārānasi	124	25.20 N	83.00 E
Banari	71	40.34 N	8.42 E
Bānaripāra	126	22.47 N	90.10 E
Banarlı	130	41.04 N	27.20 E
Banās ≃	120	25.54 N	76.45 E
Banās, Ra's ›	140	23.54 N	35.48 E
Banat ◆[1]	38	45.20 N	20.40 E
Banate Bay c	116	10.58 N	122.48 E
Banaue	116	16.55 N	121.04 E
Banavie	46	56.47 N	5.07 W
Banay, Mount ∧	116	13.42 N	121.10 E
Banaz	130	38.46 N	29.46 E
Ban Baen Phichit	269a	13.50 N	100.40 E
Ban Ban	110	19.38 N	103.34 E
Ban Bang Chan	269a	13.49 N	100.42 E
Ban Bang O	269a	13.53 N	100.36 E
Ban Bang Phli Yai	269a	13.36 N	100.42 E
Ban Bang Phraek	269a	13.53 N	100.26 E
Ban Bang Pu	269a	13.31 N	100.39 E
Banbar	120	30.49 N	94.59 E
Ban Bat	110	13.13 N	108.39 E
Banbidian	271a	39.54 N	116.32 E
Ban Blech	110	13.12 N	108.13 E
Ban Bonèng	110	17.58 N	104.35 E
Ban Bouang-nom	110	15.47 N	106.47 E
Banbridge	48	54.21 N	6.16 W
Ban Bua Chum	110	15.15 N	101.12 E
Banbuji	100	33.34 N	116.44 E
Ban Bung Fang Nok	269a	13.48 N	100.43 E
Ban Bung Na Rang	110	16.11 N	100.09 E
Ban Bungxai	110	15.42 N	106.14 E
Banbury	42	52.04 N	1.20 W
Bancahsaga	114	0.49 N	101.07 E
Bancalan Island I	116	8.14 N	117.06 E
Banc d'Arguin, Parc National du ♦	150	20.00 N	16.20 W
Ban Chak	110	14.17 N	105.25 E
Ban Cha La	110	17.11 N	106.05 E
Bānchhārāmpur	126	23.46 N	90.48 E
Banchory	46	57.03 N	2.31 W
Banco, Punta ›	236	8.23 N	83.09 W
Bancos, Isla → Banks Island I	176	73.15 N	121.30 W
Bancroft, On., Can.	212	45.03 N	77.51 W
Bancroft, Id., U.S.	202	42.43 N	111.53 W
Bancroft, Ia., U.S.	190	43.17 N	94.13 W
Bancroft, Mi., U.S.	216	42.52 N	84.03 W
Bancroft, Ne., U.S.	198	42.00 N	96.34 W
Bancroft → Chililabombwe, Zam.	154	12.18 S	27.43 E
Bancun	106	30.53 N	118.48 E
Banda, India	124	24.03 N	78.57 E
Bānda, India	124	25.29 N	80.20 E
Banda, Zaïre	154	4.11 N	27.04 E
Banda, Kepulauan II	164	4.35 S	129.55 E
Banda, Laut (Banda Sea) ⊤[2]	108	5.00 S	128.00 E
Banda Aceh (Kuturaja)	114	5.34 N	95.20 E
Bandabe	157b	15.31 S	49.04 E
Banda Besar, Pulau I	164	4.34 S	129.55 E
Bānda Dāūd Shāh	123	33.16 N	71.11 E
Banda del Río Salí	252	26.50 S	65.10 W
Banda Elat	164	5.39 S	132.59 E
Bandahara, Gunung ∧	114	3.45 N	97.47 E
Bandai-Asahi-kokuritsu-kōen ♦	92	38.16 N	139.57 E
Bandai-san ∧	92	37.36 N	140.04 E
Bandak ⊜	26	59.24 N	8.15 E
Bandama ≃	150	5.10 N	5.00 W
Bandama Blanc ≃	150	6.54 N	5.31 W
Bandama Rouge ≃	150	6.54 N	5.31 W
Bandān, Īrān	128	31.23 N	60.44 E
Ban Dan, Thai	110	15.19 N	105.30 E
Bandanaira	164	4.32 S	129.54 E
Bandan'gou	105	39.08 N	115.11 E
Ban Dangtai	110	17.06 N	104.57 E
Ban Dan Lan Hoi	110	17.00 N	99.35 E
Bandar → Machilīpatnam, India	122	16.10 N	81.08 E
Bandar, Indon.	115a	7.02 S	109.47 E
Bandar Baharu	114	5.08 N	100.30 E
Bandar Beheshtī	128	25.18 N	60.37 E
Bandardurian	114	2.21 N	99.44 E
Bandar-e ʿAbbās	128	27.11 N	56.17 E
Bandar-e Anzalī (Bandar-e Pahlavī)	128	37.28 N	49.27 E
Bandar-e Būshehr	128	28.59 N	50.50 E
Bandar-e Chārak	128	26.43 N	54.16 E
Bandar-e Deylam	128	30.04 N	50.10 E
Bandar-e Gaz	128	36.47 N	53.59 E
Bandar-e Khomeynī (Bandar-e Shāhpūr)	128	30.25 N	49.05 E
Bandar-e Lengeh	128	26.33 N	54.53 E
Bandar-e Māh Shahr	128	30.33 N	49.12 E
Bandar-e Moghūyeh	128	26.35 N	54.31 E
Bandar-e Rīg	128	29.29 N	50.38 E
Bandar-e Torkeman	128	36.56 N	54.06 E
Bandar Penggaram → Batu Pahat	114	1.51 N	102.56 E
Bandarpulau	114	2.41 N	99.31 E
Bandar Seri Begawan	112	4.56 N	114.55 E
Bandawe	154	11.57 S	34.10 E
Bande	34	42.02 N	7.58 W
Banded Peak ∧	200	37.06 N	106.38 W
Bandeira, Pico da ∧	255	20.26 S	41.47 W
Bandeira do Sul	256	21.47 S	46.23 W
Bandeirantes, Bra.	255	13.41 S	50.48 W
Bandeirantes, Bra.	255	19.53 S	54.23 W
Bandeirantes, Bra.	255	23.06 S	50.21 W
Bandeirantes, Palácio dos ⊕	287b	23.36 S	46.43 W
Bandeirantes, Praia dos ⊥[2]	287a	23.01 S	43.25 W
Bandéko	152	1.56 N	17.28 E
Bāndel	272b	22.56 N	88.22 E
Bandeli	157a	12.55 S	45.13 E
Bandelier National Monument ♦	200	35.45 N	106.20 W
Bandera, Arg.	252	28.54 S	62.16 W
Bandera, Tx., U.S.	196	29.44 N	99.04 W
Bandera, Alto ∧	238	18.49 N	70.37 W
Banderas	200	31.01 N	105.35 W
Banderas, Bahía de c	234	20.40 N	105.25 W
Banderilla	234	19.36 N	96.56 W
Bāndhi	120	26.35 N	68.18 E
Bandholm	41	54.50 N	11.29 E
Bandiagara	150	14.21 N	3.37 W
Bandiantaolehai	102	41.41 N	104.06 E
Bāndīkūi	124	27.03 N	76.34 E
Bandipur, India	272b	22.44 N	88.26 E
Bandipur, India	272b	22.51 N	88.10 E
Bandipura	123	34.25 N	74.39 E
Bandırma	130	40.20 N	27.58 E
Bandırma Körfezi c	130	40.25 N	28.00 E
Bando	152	15.00 S	20.30 E
Bandol	62	43.08 N	5.45 E
Bandon, Ire.	48	51.45 N	8.45 W
Ban Don → Surat Thani, Thai	110	9.08 N	99.19 E
Bandon, Or., U.S.	202	43.07 N	124.24 W
Ban Don, Viet	110	12.53 N	107.48 E
Bandon ≃	48	51.42 N	8.30 W
Ban Don, Ao c	110	9.20 N	99.25 E
Ban Donhiang	110	18.05 N	101.48 E
Ban Dônko	110	16.12 N	106.17 E
Ban Don Muang	269a	13.55 N	100.36 E
B'andovan	84	39.46 N	49.23 E
Bāndra ◆[8]	272c	19.03 N	72.49 E
Bāndra Point ›	272c	19.03 N	72.49 E
Bānduān	126	22.53 N	86.31 E
Bandula	156	19.02 S	33.07 E
Ban Dulad V	144	8.26 N	45.54 E
Bandundu	152	3.18 S	17.20 E
Bandundu □[4]	152	4.30 S	18.30 E
Bandung	115a	6.54 S	107.36 E
Băneasa	38	44.04 N	27.42 E
Banegas	248	17.09 S	62.50 W
Bāneh	128	35.59 N	45.53 E
Banehra	272a	28.44 N	77.23 E
Banes	240p	20.58 N	75.43 W
Banff, Ab., Can.	182	51.10 N	115.34 W
Banff, Scot., U.K.	46	57.40 N	2.33 W
Banff National Park ♦	182	51.38 N	116.22 W
Banfield ◆[8]	258	34.44 S	58.23 W
Banfora	150	10.38 N	4.46 W
Banga, India	123	31.11 N	75.59 E
Banga, Pil.	116	11.38 N	122.20 E
Banga, Zaïre	152	5.27 S	20.28 E
Banga ≃	116	6.44 N	124.34 E
Bañgad	116	12.10 N	123.24 E
Bangaduni Island I	126	21.34 N	88.52 E
Bangala Dam ◆[6]	154	20.40 S	31.15 E
Bangall	210	41.53 N	73.42 W
Bangalore	122	12.58 N	77.36 E
Bangalur → Bangalore	122	12.58 N	77.36 E
Bangangté	152	5.09 N	10.31 E
Bangaon	126	23.04 N	88.49 E
Bangassou	152	4.50 N	23.07 E
Bangda	102	27.59 N	98.40 E
Bangdag Co ⊜	120	34.59 N	81.35 E
Bangeluo	120	32.27 N	90.35 E
Bangeswardi	126	23.29 N	89.44 E
Bangeta, Mount ∧	164	6.15 S	147.04 E
Banggai (Luwuk)	112	1.34 S	123.30 E
Banggai, Kepulauan II	112	1.30 S	123.15 E
Banggai, Pulau I	112	1.37 S	123.33 E
Banggi, Pulau I	116	7.17 N	117.12 E
Banggong Co ⊜	120	33.45 N	79.30 E
Banghāzī	146	32.07 N	20.04 E
Banghiang ≃	110	16.03 N	105.15 E
Bangholme	274b	38.02 S	145.11 E
Bangí → Bangui	152	4.22 N	18.35 E
Bangil	115a	7.36 S	112.47 E
Bangjang	140	11.23 N	32.42 E
Bangjun	105	39.59 N	117.16 E
Bangka, Pulau I, Indon.	112	2.15 S	106.00 E
Bangka, Pulau I, Indon.	112	1.48 N	125.09 E
Bangka, Selat ⊔	112	2.20 S	105.45 E
Bangkalan	115a	7.02 S	112.44 E
Bang Kapi	269a	13.46 N	100.39 E
Bang Kapi, Khlong ≋	269a	13.45 N	100.36 E
Bangkaru, Pulau I	114	2.04 N	97.07 E
Bang Khen	269a	13.52 N	100.36 E
Bang Khun Thian	269a	13.42 N	100.28 E
Bangkinang	112	0.21 N	101.02 E
Bangkir	112	0.48 N	120.14 E
Bangko	112	2.05 S	102.17 E
Bangkog Co ⊜	120	31.42 N	89.30 E
Bangkok → Krung Thep	110	13.45 N	100.31 E
Bangkok Station ◆[5]	269a	13.44 N	100.32 E
Bangkou	106	31.40 N	121.26 E
Bang Krathum	110	16.34 N	100.18 E
Bang Kruai	269a	13.48 N	100.29 E
Bangkulu, Pulau I	112	1.50 S	123.06 E
Bangkulua	115b	8.41 S	118.13 E
Bangladesch → Bangladesh □[1]	120	24.00 N	90.00 E
Bangladesh □[1], Asia	118	24.00 N	90.00 E
Bangladesh □[1], Asia	120	24.00 N	90.00 E
Bang Lamung	110	12.58 N	100.54 E
Bang Mun Nak	110	16.02 N	100.23 E
Ban Gnômmarat Kèo	110	17.36 N	105.10 E
Bangolo	150	7.01 N	7.29 W
Bangor, Ire.	48	54.09 N	9.45 W
Bangor, N. Ire., U.K.	44	54.40 N	5.40 W
Bangor, N. Ire., U.K.	48	54.40 N	5.40 W
Bangor, Wales, U.K.	44	53.13 N	4.08 W
Bangor, Ca., U.S.	226	39.23 N	121.24 W
Bangor, Me., U.S.	188	44.48 N	68.46 W
Bangor, Mi., U.S.	216	42.18 N	86.06 W
Bangor, Pa., U.S.	210	40.51 N	75.12 W
Bangoran ≃	146	8.42 N	19.06 E
Bang Pa In	110	14.14 N	100.35 E
Bāngra ≃	126	21.48 N	89.43 E
Bangriposi	126	22.10 N	86.32 E
Bangs	196	31.43 N	99.08 W
Bangs, Mount ∧	200	36.48 N	113.51 W
Bang Saphan	110	11.12 N	99.31 E
Bangshi	98	40.23 N	122.46 E
Bangs Lake ⊜	278	42.16 N	88.08 W
Bangsri	115a	6.30 S	110.45 E
Bangu ◆[8]	256	22.52 S	43.27 W
Bangué	152	3.01 N	15.07 E
Bangued	116	17.36 N	120.37 E
Bangui, Centraf.	152	4.22 N	18.35 E
Bangui, Pil.	116	18.32 N	120.46 E
Bangui Bay c	116	18.34 N	120.44 E
Bangunpurba	114	3.23 N	98.50 E
Banguru	154	0.27 N	27.17 E
Bangwei	102	23.46 N	107.34 E
Bangweulu, Lake ⊜	154	11.05 S	29.45 E
Bangweulu Swamps ≡	154	11.30 S	30.15 E
Bangzhen	106	31.39 N	121.29 E
Banhā	142	30.28 N	31.11 E
Ban Hatgnao	110	14.40 N	106.35 E
Ban Hatkiang	110	18.11 N	102.40 E
Ban Hat Yai → Hat Yai	110	7.01 N	100.28 E
Ban Ha Yaek Pak Kret	269a	13.54 N	100.31 E
Ban Hèt	110	14.44 N	107.29 E
Banhine, Parque Nacional de ♦	156	22.45 S	32.50 E
Ban Hin Heup	110	18.38 N	102.20 E
Ban Hom	110	15.33 N	98.46 E
Ban Hong	110	18.18 N	98.50 E
Ban Hong Muang	110	17.04 N	105.12 E
Ban Houayxay	110	20.18 N	100.26 E
Ban Huai Yang	110	11.36 N	99.40 E
Ban Hua Lamphu Thong	269a	13.32 N	100.38 E
Bani, Burkina	150	14.02 N	0.02 W
Bani, Centraf.	152	7.07 N	22.49 E
Bani, Pil.	116	16.11 N	119.52 E
Baní, Rep. Dom.	238	18.17 N	70.20 W
Bani ≃	150	14.30 N	4.12 W
Bani, Jbel ⋏	148	29.30 N	8.00 W
Bania	152	4.00 N	16.07 E
Baniachang	120	24.31 N	91.22 E
Banī ʿAdī al-Baḥrīyah	142	27.15 N	30.55 E
Banī ʿAdī al-Qiblīyah	142	27.15 N	30.56 E
Banī Aḥmad	142	28.03 N	30.46 E
Banī ʿAlī	142	28.29 N	30.43 E
Baniara, Indon.	114	2.31 N	98.39 E
Baniara, Pap. N. Gui.	164	9.46 S	149.53 E
Bānibaha	126	23.42 N	89.37 E
Bani Bangou	150	15.03 N	2.42 E
Banie	30	53.08 N	14.38 E
Banifing ≃	150	12.43 N	6.25 W
Banihāl Pass)(	123	33.31 N	75.13 E
Banī Ḥasan ash-Shurūq	142	27.54 N	30.51 E
Banī Khālid	142	27.50 N	30.44 E
Banikoara	150	11.18 N	2.26 E
Banima	152	5.26 N	23.54 E
Banī Majdūl	273c	30.02 N	31.07 E
Banī Mazār	142	28.30 N	30.48 E
Banī Muḥammadīyāt	142	27.17 N	31.05 E
Banī Mūsā	142	29.08 N	31.03 E
Banīnah	146	32.05 N	20.16 E
Banio, Lagune c	152	3.35 S	11.00 E
Baniou	34	35.25 N	4.21 E
Banī Rāfiʿ	142	27.22 N	30.53 E
Banī Salāmah	142	30.19 N	30.51 E
Banī Shaʿrān	142	27.19 N	30.51 E
Banī Shuqayr	142	27.23 N	30.59 E
Banister ≃	192	36.42 N	78.48 W
Banī Suhaylah	132	31.20 N	34.20 E
Banī Suwayf	142	29.05 N	31.05 E
Banī Suwayf □[4]	142	29.03 N	31.02 E
Banī ʿUbayd, Miṣr	142	31.01 N	31.39 E
Banī ʿUbayd, Miṣr	142	27.57 N	30.46 E
Banī Walīd	146	31.45 N	14.01 E
Bāniyās, Sūrīy.	130	35.11 N	35.57 E
Bāniyās, Sūrīy.	132	33.15 N	35.41 E
Banī Zayd	142	27.13 N	31.09 E
Banja Luka	36	44.46 N	17.11 E
Banjar	115a	7.22 S	108.32 E
Banjarmasin	112	3.20 S	114.35 E
Banjarnegara	115a	7.23 S	109.41 E
Banjin	106	32.19 N	120.24 E
Banjir Kanal ≋	269e	6.07 S	106.45 E
Banjita	104	41.11 N	120.52 E
Banjšćice ⋏[1]	64	46.04 N	13.42 E
Banjuangou	105	40.44 N	115.11 E
Banjul (Bathurst)	150	13.28 N	16.39 W
Bank	84	39.25 N	49.15 E
Bānka	124	24.53 N	86.55 E
Ban'ka ≃	265b	55.49 N	37.22 E
Banka Banka	162	18.48 S	134.01 E
Bānkādāba	126	22.58 N	87.21 E
Bankana	152	4.25 S	16.11 E
Bankas	150	14.04 N	3.31 W
Ban Katèp	110	16.48 N	105.52 E
Ban Kavak	110	17.18 N	105.37 E
Bankberg ⋏	158	32.22 S	25.26 E
Ban Kèngkabao	110	16.48 N	104.45 E
Ban Kèngkok	110	16.26 N	105.12 E
Ban Kèngtangan	110	16.05 N	105.22 E
Bankeryd	26	57.51 N	14.07 E
Bankfoot	46	56.30 N	3.30 W
Ban Khamphô	110	14.38 N	106.17 E
Ban Khan Na Yao	269a	13.47 N	100.41 E
Bankhari	126	23.44 N	90.03 E
Ban Kheun	110	20.13 N	101.07 E
Ban Khlong Bua Loi	269a	13.41 N	100.41 E
Ban Khlong Kua	110	6.57 N	100.08 E
Ban Khlong Samrong	269a	13.39 N	100.36 E
Ban Khlong Song	269a	13.51 N	100.43 E
Ban Khok Bao Sao	269a	13.52 N	100.39 E
Ban Khuan Mao	110	7.58 N	99.37 E
Bankilaré	150	14.35 N	0.44 E
Bankim	152	6.05 N	11.30 E
Bānkipur	272b	22.48 N	88.14 E
Ban Kota Baru	114	6.27 N	101.21 E
Ban Krang	110	12.52 N	99.18 E
Ban Kruat	110	14.25 N	103.07 E
Banks, Eng., U.K.	44	53.41 N	2.55 W
Banks, Al., U.S.	194	31.48 N	85.50 W
Banks, Or., U.S.	224	45.37 N	123.06 W
Banks, Cape ›	274a	34.00 S	151.15 E
Banks, Îles II	175f	13.50 S	167.30 E
Banks, Point ›	180	58.36 N	152.18 W
Banksian ≃	184	53.41 N	94.10 W
Banks Island I, B.C., Can.	182	53.25 N	130.10 W
Banks Island I, N.T., Can.	176	73.15 N	121.30 W
Banks Lake ⊜[1]	202	47.45 N	119.15 W
Banksmeadow	274a	33.58 S	151.13 E
Banks Peninsula ›[1]	172	43.45 S	173.00 E
Banks Strait ⊔	166	40.40 S	148.07 E
Banks / Torres □[8]	175f	13.50 S	167.20 E
Bankstown	170	33.55 S	151.02 E
Bankstown Aerodrome ⊠	274a	33.55 S	150.59 E
Banksville	276	41.09 N	73.38 W
Banksville ◆[8]	279b	40.24 N	80.03 W
Ban Kum Daeng	269a	13.53 N	100.36 E
Bankumuna	152	4.28 S	19.57 E
Bānkura	126	23.15 N	87.04 E
Ban Laem Sing	269a	13.30 N	100.34 E
Banlamen	104	41.51 N	122.27 E
Banlashanzi	104	41.26 N	123.28 E
Ban Lat Phrao	269a	13.47 N	100.36 E
Ban Le Kathe	110	15.49 N	98.53 E
Banliyuan	106	30.50 N	118.58 E
Ban Luk Kho	269a	13.34 N	100.27 E
Ban Mae La Luang	110	18.32 N	97.56 E
Ban Mae Mo	110	18.15 N	99.42 E
Bānmankhi Bazar	124	25.53 N	87.11 E
Banmauk	110	24.24 N	95.51 E
Ban M'diap	110	12.56 N	108.43 E
Ban M'drack	110	12.42 N	108.47 E
Banmian	100	26.02 N	118.06 E
Ban Mit	110	18.51 N	101.55 E
Ban Muangngat	110	19.05 N	104.04 E
Ban Muang Yot	110	19.22 N	100.34 E
Bann ≃	48	55.10 N	6.46 W
Banna ≃	62	45.11 N	7.51 E
Ban Nadou	110	15.51 N	105.38 E
Ban Nagnom	110	17.02 N	105.44 E
Ban Nahin	110	18.14 N	104.13 E
Bannaja	88	57.05 N	108.12 E
Ban Nakala	110	16.17 N	105.11 E
Ban Na Kha	110	9.26 N	98.28 E
Ban Nalan	110	15.50 N	106.04 E
Ban Nalè	110	18.42 N	101.34 E
Ban Namcha	110	19.09 N	102.53 E
Ban Nam Chan	110	18.01 N	103.53 E
Ban Namnga	110	20.22 N	102.19 E
Ban Nam Tao	110	17.50 N	101.15 E
Ban Nam Thaeng	110	15.34 N	105.30 E
Ban Naxon	110	18.12 N	103.05 E
Ban Naxouang	110	18.25 N	104.29 E
Bannay	50	47.23 N	2.53 E
Banner Elk	192	36.09 N	81.52 W
Bannerman, Mount ∧[2]	162	19.26 S	127.10 E
Banner Park ♦	284b	39.19 N	76.42 W
Bannertown	192	36.29 N	80.34 W
Bannesdorf	54	54.28 N	11.13 E
Bannewitz	54	51.00 N	13.43 E
Ban Ngam	110	20.11 N	104.53 E
Bannikovo	86	56.07 N	70.17 E
Banning	228	33.55 N	116.52 W
Banningville → Bandundu	152	3.18 S	17.20 E
Bannister	168a	32.40 S	116.33 E
Bannister ≃	168a	32.49 S	116.29 E
Bannister Ditch ≋	279a	41.18 N	82.01 W
Bannock	214	40.06 N	80.59 W
Bannockburn, Austl.	169	38.03 S	144.10 E
Bannockburn, Scot., U.K.	46	56.06 N	3.55 W
Bannockburn, Il., U.S.	278	42.12 N	87.52 W
Bannockburn, Zimb.	154	20.16 S	29.51 E
Bannockburn Battlesite ⊥	46	56.06 N	3.54 W
Bannock Creek ≃	202	42.53 N	112.40 W
Bannock Peak ∧	202	42.36 N	112.42 W
Ban Nong Lumphuk	110	14.40 N	102.43 E
Ban Nong Takhian	110	13.08 N	101.24 E
Bannovka	86	53.45 N	62.57 E
Bannovskij	83	49.02 N	37.35 E
Bannu	123	32.59 N	70.36 E
Bánokszentgyörgy	61	46.33 N	16.47 E
Banon	62	44.02 N	5.38 E
Ban O Pao	269a	13.50 N	100.38 E
Baños, Ec.	246	1.24 S	78.25 W
Baños, Perú	248	10.05 S	76.45 W
Baños de Cerrato	34	41.55 N	4.28 W
Banow	120	35.38 N	69.15 E
Ban Pak Bong	110	18.32 N	98.56 E
Ban Pak Chan	110	10.32 N	98.51 E
Ban Pakha	110	14.38 N	107.24 E
Ban Pakkhop	110	19.49 N	100.36 E
Ban Pak Nam	110	10.26 N	99.15 E
Ban Pakneun	110	19.14 N	101.50 E
Banpās	126	23.24 N	87.45 E
Ban Phai, Thai	110	16.04 N	102.44 E
Ban Phai, Thai	110	17.33 N	103.00 E
Ban Phe	110	12.38 N	101.26 E
Ban Pho	110	13.36 N	101.05 E
Ban Phon	110	15.25 N	106.42 E
Ban Phông Pho	110	14.36 N	105.52 E
Banphot Phisai	110	15.56 N	99.59 E
Ban Phraek Kasa	269a	13.34 N	100.38 E
Ban Phya	110	21.35 N	102.55 E
Ban Pong	110	13.49 N	99.53 E
Banpu	98	34.28 N	119.18 E
Banpura	126	22.27 N	87.22 E
Banqiao, Zhg.	100	30.06 N	120.27 E
Banqiao, Zhg.	100	31.46 N	112.31 E
Banqiao, Zhg.	100	33.21 N	116.41 E
Banqiao, Zhg.	105	39.56 N	115.51 E
Banqiao, Zhg.	106	31.55 N	118.39 E
Banqiao, Zhg.	107	29.31 N	105.59 E
Banqiaochang	107	29.54 N	104.21 E
Banqiaoji	100	32.19 N	116.37 E
Banqiaoxi	107	29.41 N	103.47 E
Banquan	98	35.07 N	118.42 E
Banraeaba	174t	1.20 N	173.02 E
Ban Ron Phibun	110	8.09 N	99.51 E
Ban Sa-ang	110	17.26 N	105.44 E
Ban Saen To	110	16.05 N	99.51 E
Ban Sakhla	269a	13.32 N	100.30 E
Bansalan	116	6.47 N	125.14 E
Ban Salik	110	18.30 N	100.45 E
Ban Samang	110	19.43 N	102.36 E
Ban Sam Phan	110	8.33 N	99.09 E
Ban Sam Pong	110	18.32 N	102.47 E
Ban Samrong	110	14.23 N	102.50 E
Bansang	150	13.26 N	14.39 W
Ban San Xieng La	110	19.27 N	102.26 E
Bansberia	126	22.58 N	88.24 E
Bānsda	120	20.45 N	73.22 E
Bansha	48	52.28 N	8.04 W
Banshadhāra ≃	122	18.21 N	84.08 E
Banshanpu	100	27.42 N	113.24 E
Banshi	100	25.20 N	115.23 E
Banshigou	104	41.09 N	120.58 E
Bānsi	124	27.11 N	82.56 E
Bansi ≃	126	23.50 N	90.15 E
Ban Signo	110	17.51 N	105.04 E
Banská Bystrica	30	48.44 N	19.07 E
Banská Štiavnica	30	48.28 N	18.56 E
Bansko	38	41.50 N	23.29 E
Bānskupi	126	24.10 N	86.41 E
Ban Songkhon	110	17.58 N	105.10 E
Ban Song Kong	269a	13.53 N	100.34 E
Ban Sop Huai Hai	110	19.33 N	98.05 E
Ban Sôppheung	110	18.33 N	104.17 E
Banstala	272b	22.32 N	88.25 E
Banstead	42	51.19 N	0.12 W
Bānswāra	120	23.33 N	74.27 E
Banta	226	37.45 N	121.22 W
Banta, Pulau I	115b	8.25 S	119.14 E
Bantaeng	112	5.32 S	119.56 E
Bantaian	114	1.56 N	100.54 E
Bantaji	100	32.41 N	118.35 E
Ban Takhlo	110	15.27 N	100.44 E
Bantam	207	41.43 N	73.14 W
Bantam Lake ⊜	207	41.42 N	73.13 W
Ban Tamru	269a	13.31 N	100.41 E
Ban Tao Pun	269a	13.53 N	100.41 E
Bantarkawung	115a	7.13 S	108.55 E
Bantayan	116	11.10 N	123.43 E
Bantayan Island I	116	11.13 N	123.44 E
Banteer	48	52.07 N	8.54 W
Banteln	52	52.04 N	9.44 E
Banten	115a	6.03 S	106.09 E
Banten, Teluk c	115a	6.00 S	106.10 E
Bantenan, Tanjung ›	115a	8.47 S	114.33 E
Ban Teung	110	17.54 N	105.29 E
Ban Thabôk	110	18.22 N	103.12 E
Ban Thanoun	110	19.50 N	101.29 E
Ban Thapayi	110	16.19 N	105.41 E
Bantheville	56	49.21 N	5.05 E
Ban Thieng	110	19.08 N	102.12 E
Ban Tian Sa	110	18.43 N	103.14 E
Bantigui Point ›	116	13.41 N	121.28 E
Banting	114	2.49 N	101.30 E
Banton (Jones)	116	12.57 N	122.05 E
Ban Tong Khop	110	17.04 N	104.16 E
Banton Island I	116	12.56 N	122.04 E
Bāntra	272b	22.35 N	88.19 E
Bantry	48	51.41 N	9.27 W
Bantry Bay c	48	51.38 N	9.48 W
Bantul	115a	7.54 S	110.20 E
Bāntva	120	21.29 N	70.05 E
Banūr	124	30.34 N	76.43 E
Ban Van Hom	110	18.44 N	104.01 E
Ban Vat	110	16.54 N	106.25 E
Banwell	42	51.20 N	2.52 W
Banwy ≃	42	52.42 N	3.16 W
Ban Xènkhalôk	110	19.42 N	101.54 E
Banxiancun	106	30.33 N	119.42 E
Ban Xot	110	18.11 N	104.05 E
Banya, Punta de la ›	34	40.34 N	0.38 E
Banyak, Kepulauan II	114	2.10 N	97.15 E
Ban Ya Plong	110	8.53 N	98.35 E
Banyo	152	6.45 N	11.49 E
Banyoles	34	42.07 N	2.46 E
Banyumas	115a	7.31 S	109.17 E
Banyuwangi	115a	8.12 S	114.21 E
Banyuwedang	115b	8.08 S	114.36 E
Banz	164	5.47 S	144.37 E
Banzare Coast ⊥[2]	9	67.00 S	126.00 E
Banzhuyuan	107	28.44 N	106.18 E
Banzi, It.	68	40.52 N	16.01 E
Banzi, Zhg.	100	24.18 N	117.19 E
Bao ≃, Zhg.	100	33.40 N	116.33 E
Bao ≃, Zhg.	105	39.02 N	115.39 E
Bao ≃, Zhg.	105	40.31 N	118.17 E
Bao, Ouadi V	146	16.36 N	23.55 E
Bao'an, Zhg.	100	30.11 N	114.43 E
Baoan → Zhuolu, Zhg.	105	40.22 N	115.12 E
Baoan, Zhg.	106	31.46 N	121.21 E
Baoancun	89	48.13 N	125.52 E
Baochang → Taibus Qi, Zhg.	98	41.56 N	115.22 E
Baochang, Zhg.	106	32.04 N	121.25 E
Baocheng	102	33.08 N	107.09 E
Baode	102	39.06 N	111.11 E
Baodi	105	39.44 N	117.17 E
Baoding	105	38.52 N	115.29 E
Baofeng	100	33.55 N	113.02 E
Baofu	106	30.31 N	119.29 E
Baoguosi	107	29.35 N	103.25 E
Bao Ha	110	22.11 N	104.21 E
Baohekou	105	40.32 N	118.15 E
Baoji, Zhg.	100	33.08 N	118.19 E
Baoji, Zhg.	102	34.23 N	107.09 E
Baojiagou	105	40.05 N	115.22 E
Baojiapu	104	40.51 N	122.14 E
Baojiatou	106	30.11 N	119.48 E
Baojiawazi	104	41.38 N	123.24 E
Baojing	102	28.43 N	109.25 E
Baokang → Horqin Zuoyi Zhongqi	89	44.07 N	123.18 E
Bao Lac, Viet	110	22.57 N	105.40 E
Bao Lac, Viet	110	11.32 N	107.48 E
Baolin	107	30.24 N	105.02 E
Baolizhen	89	42.56 N	123.46 E
Baolunyuan	102	32.22 N	105.40 E
Baomachang	107	29.58 N	104.12 E
Baon	116	6.47 N	126.05 E
Baonian	106	31.55 N	119.21 E
Baoning	102	23.31 N	106.24 E
Baoqing	89	46.21 N	132.14 E
Baoquan	98	36.16 N	119.04 E
Baoro	152	5.40 N	15.58 E
Baoshan, Zhg.	100	32.39 N	113.54 E
Baoshan, Zhg.	102	26.19 N	104.27 E
Baoshan, Zhg.	102	25.09 N	99.09 E
Baoshan, Zhg.	106	31.25 N	121.29 E
Baoting	110	18.42 N	109.45 E
Baotou (Paotow)	102	40.40 N	109.59 E
Baotun	104	42.29 N	122.52 E
Baoulé ≃	150	13.33 N	9.54 W
Baowei	102	22.39 N	106.50 E
Baoxikou	100	23.16 N	115.14 E
Baoxingchang	107	29.38 N	105.41 E
Baoxinji	100	32.35 N	115.00 E
Baoyi	100	32.13 N	116.42 E
Baoying	100	33.16 N	119.20 E
Baozhuchang	107	29.48 N	104.15 E
Baozidian	105	40.11 N	117.48 E
Bāp	120	27.23 N	72.21 E
Bapanling	104	40.58 N	123.08 E
Bāpatla	122	15.54 N	80.28 E
Bapaume	50	50.06 N	2.51 E
Bapchule	200	33.08 N	111.52 W
Bapsfontein	158	26.08 S	28.25 E
Baptiste Lake ⊜	212	45.07 N	78.02 W
Baptistown	208	40.31 N	75.00 W
Bāqa el Gharbīya	132	32.25 N	35.03 E
Baqar, Maṣrif Baḥr al- ≋	142	31.05 N	32.08 E
Baqar, Wādī al- V	146	27.49 N	18.37 E
Baqên	120	31.56 N	94.00 E
Baqing	120	32.15 N	93.30 E
Bʿaqlīn	132	33.41 N	35.33 E
Baʿqūbah	128	33.45 N	44.38 E
Baquedano	252	23.20 S	69.51 W
Ba Queo	269c	10.48 N	106.38 E
Bar, Jugo.	38	42.05 N	19.05 E
Bar, Ross.	88	51.17 N	107.33 E
Bar, Ukr.	78	49.04 N	27.40 E
Bar ≃	56	49.42 N	4.50 E
Bāra, India	124	25.13 N	87.22 E
Bara, India	272b	22.43 N	88.31 E
Bara, India	272b	22.46 N	88.17 E
Bara, Nig.	146	10.22 N	10.44 E
Baraawe	144	1.06 N	44.03 E
Barabai	112	2.35 S	115.23 E
Bara Bāngurda	126	22.57 N	86.24 E
Bāra Banki	124	26.55 N	81.12 E
Barabanovo	82	54.43 N	38.10 E
Barābhūm	126	23.02 N	86.22 E
Barabinsk	86	55.21 N	78.21 E
Barabinskaja step' ≚	86	55.00 N	79.00 E
Baraboo	190	43.28 N	89.44 W
Baraboo ≃	190	43.29 N	89.26 W
Baraboulé	150	14.12 N	1.51 W
Baracaju ≃	255	12.21 S	51.00 W
Baracaldo	34	43.18 N	2.59 W

Symbols in the index entries represent the broad categories identified in the key at the right. Symbols with superior numbers (⋏[1]) identify subcategories (see complete key on page *I · 1).*

Symbole im Register stellen die rechts im Schlüssel erklärten Kategorien dar. Symbole mit hochgestellten Ziffern (⋏[1]) bezeichnen Unterabteilungen einer Kategorie (vgl. vollständiger Schlüssel auf Seite *I · 1).*

Los símbolos incluídos en el texto del índice representan las grandes categorías identificadas con la clave a la derecha. Los símbolos con numeros en su parte superior (⋏[1]) identifican las subcategorías (véase la clave completa en la página *I · 1).*

Les symboles de l'index représentent les catégories indiquées dans la légende à droite. Les symboles suivis d'un indice (⋏[1]) représentent des sous-catégories (voir légende complète à la page *I · 1).*

Os símbolos incluídos no texto do índice representam as grandes categorias identificadas com a chave à direita. Os símbolos com números em sua parte superior (⋏[1]) identificam as subcategorias (veja-se a chave completa à página *I · 1).*

∧	Mountain	Berg	Montaña	Montagne	Montanha
⋏	Mountains	Gebirge	Montañas	Montagnes	Montanhas
)(	Pass	Paß	Paso	Col	Passo
V	Valley, Canyon	Tal, Cañon	Valle, Cañón	Vallée, Canyon	Vale, Canhão
≚	Plain	Ebene	Llano	Plaine	Planície
›	Cape	Kap	Cabo	Cap	Cabo
I	Island	Insel	Isla	Île	Ilha
II	Islands	Inseln	Islas	Îles	Ilhas
⊥	Other Topographic Features	Andere Topographische Objekte	Otros Elementos Topográficos	Autres données topographiques	Outros acidentes topográficos

ESPAÑOL

Nombre	Página	Lat.°′	Long.°′ W = Oeste
Barachit	144	14.39 N	39.27 E
Barachois Pond Provincial Park ♦	186	48.30 N	58.14 W
Baracoa, Cuba	240p	20.21 N	74.30 W
Baracoa, Hond.	236	15.43 N	87.52 W
Baradā ≃	132	33.30 N	36.28 E
Baradero	258	33.48 S	59.30 W
Baradero ≃	258	33.55 S	59.16 W
Baradili	71	39.43 N	8.54 E
Baradine	166	30.56 S	149.04 E
Bara Doāni	126	22.06 N	89.59 E
Baraga	190	46.46 N	88.29 W
Baragaon → Nālanda	124	25.07 N	85.25 E
Baragarh	120	21.20 N	83.37 E
Baragiano	68	40.41 N	15.35 E
Baragoi	154	1.47 N	36.47 E
Baraguá	240p	21.41 N	78.38 W
Baragwanath Aerodrome ⊠	273d	26.15 S	27.59 E
Baragwanath Military Hospital ᴗ	273d	26.16 S	27.56 E
Bārah	140	13.42 N	30.22 E
Barahānuddin	126	22.30 N	90.43 E
Barahona	238	18.12 N	71.06 W
Barāigrām	126	24.19 N	89.10 E
Bara Issa ≃	150	16.09 N	3.28 W
Barajas, Aeropuerto ⊠	266a	40.28 N	3.34 W
Barajas de Madrid ✢[8]	266a	40.28 N	3.35 E
Bara Jorda	126	23.10 N	86.50 E
Barak	130	36.51 N	37.59 E
Barāk ≃	120	24.52 N	92.30 E
Baraka	154	4.06 S	29.06 E
Baraka (Khawr Barakah) V	144	18.13 N	37.35 E
Barakah	140	10.58 N	27.59 E
Barakah, Khawr (Baraka) V	144	18.13 N	37.35 E
Barākar	126	24.07 N	86.14 E
Barākār ≃	126	23.42 N	86.48 E
Bara Khunta	126	21.43 N	86.38 E
Baraki	120	33.56 N	68.55 E
Barakkol'skij	86	52.12 N	67.49 E
Bārākpur, Bngl.	126	22.55 N	89.32 E
Bārākpur, India	126	22.46 N	88.21 E
Bārākpur Cantonment	272b	22.46 N	88.22 E
Barakula	166	26.26 S	150.31 E
Barāl	272b	22.27 N	88.22 E
Baral ≃	126	24.10 N	89.27 E
Baralaba	166	24.11 S	149.49 E
Barām	126	22.57 N	86.18 E
Baram ≃	112	4.36 N	113.59 E
Baram, Tanjong ›	112	4.35 N	113.59 E
Barama ≃	246	7.40 N	59.15 W
Barāmāria	126	21.42 N	87.04 E
Bārāmati	122	18.09 N	74.35 E
Bārāmūla	123	34.12 N	74.21 E
Baran', Bela.	76	54.29 N	30.18 E
Baran', Bela.	76	54.30 N	28.40 E
Bārān, India	124	25.06 N	76.31 E
Baranagar	126	22.38 N	88.22 E
Baranakovo	86	58.08 N	82.58 E
Barancevo	82	55.04 N	37.38 E
Baranello	66	41.32 N	14.34 E
Barangbarang	112	6.24 S	120.28 E
Barangeon ≃	50	47.12 N	2.10 E
Barani	150	13.10 N	3.53 W
Baraniki	80	46.31 N	41.50 E
Baranikovka	83	49.10 N	39.50 E
Baranoa	246	10.48 N	74.55 W
Barano d'Ischia	68	40.42 N	13.55 E
Baranof	180	57.05 N	134.50 W
Baranof Island I	180	57.00 N	135.00 W
Baranoviči	76	53.08 N	26.02 E
Baranovka	78	50.18 N	27.40 E
Baranovskoje	82	55.25 N	38.45 E
Barany, Ross.	76	57.20 N	29.09 E
Barany, Ross.	80	57.38 N	52.16 E
Baranya □[6]	30	46.05 N	18.15 E
Barão Ataliba Nogueira	256	22.24 S	46.45 W
Barão de Geraldo	256	22.49 S	47.06 W
Barão de Grajaú	250	6.45 S	43.01 W
Barão de Juparanã	256	22.21 S	43.41 W
Barão de Melgaço	248	16.13 S	55.58 W
Barão de Tromai	250	1.29 S	45.36 W
Baraolt	38	46.05 N	25.36 E
Baraque de Fraiture ∧	56	50.15 N	5.44 E
Baras	116	13.40 N	124.22 E
Barasāhi	126	21.43 N	86.44 E
Bārāsat, India	126	22.43 N	88.29 E
Bārāsat, India	272b	22.51 N	88.22 E
Baraševo	80	54.32 N	42.53 E
Baraši	78	50.43 N	28.01 E
Baraški	24	65.40 N	52.10 E
Barat, Lintasan ɥ	115a	7.08 S	112.40 E
Baratā	266c	38.48 N	9.19 W
Baratang Island I	110	12.13 N	92.45 E
Barataria	194	29.43 N	90.07 W
Barataria Bay ᴄ	194	29.22 N	89.57 W
Barat Daya, Kepulauan II	108	7.25 S	128.00 E
Barate	112	9.54 S	123.38 E
Bar'atino, Ross.	76	54.19 N	34.31 E
Bar'atino, Ross.	82	54.43 N	36.49 E
Baratolia	126	22.25 N	86.37 E
Baratta	166	31.59 S	139.06 E
Barauana ≃	246	1.14 N	60.41 W
Baraula	272a	28.34 N	77.22 E
Barauni	124	25.29 N	85.59 E
Baraut	124	29.06 N	77.16 E
Baraya	246	3.10 N	75.04 W
Barbacena	256	21.14 S	43.46 W
Barbacoas	246	1.41 N	78.09 W
Barbades → Barbados □[1]	241g	13.10 N	59.32 W
Barbadillo del Mercado	34	42.02 N	3.21 W
Barbadoes Island I	285	40.07 N	75.22 W
Barbados □[1], N.A.	230	13.10 N	59.32 W
Barbados □[1], N.A.	241g	13.10 N	59.32 W
Barbagia ✢[1]	71	39.55 N	9.12 E
Barbalha	250	7.19 S	39.17 W
Barbar	140	18.01 N	33.59 E
Barbarano Vicentino	64	45.24 N	11.32 E
Barbarasco	64	44.14 N	9.56 E
Barbareta, Isla I	236	16.26 N	86.09 W
Barbaria, Cap de ›	34	38.38 N	1.23 E
Barbaros	130	40.54 N	27.27 E
Barbas, Cap ›	148	22.18 N	16.41 W
Barbaši	76	57.42 N	28.24 E
Barbastro	34	42.02 N	0.08 E
Barbate ≃	34	36.11 N	5.55 W
Barbate de Franco	34	36.12 N	5.55 W
Barbeau Peak ∧	16	81.54 N	75.01 W
Barbentane	62	43.54 N	4.45 E
Barberà del Vallès	266d	41.31 N	2.08 E
Barber Booth	262	53.22 N	1.50 W
Barberena	236	14.18 N	90.22 W
Barberena ≃	234	22.34 N	97.52 W
Barberino di Mugello	66	44.00 N	11.15 E
Barberino Val d'Elsa	66	43.32 N	11.10 E
Barbers Point ›	229c	21.18 N	158.07 W
Barbers Point Naval Air Station ■	229c	21.19 N	158.04 W
Barberton, S. Afr.	156	25.48 S	31.03 E
Barberton, Oh., U.S.	214	41.00 N	81.36 W
Barbezieux	32	45.28 N	0.09 W
Bar Bigha	124	25.13 N	85.44 E
Barbil	124	22.06 N	85.20 E
Barbis	54	51.37 N	10.25 E
Barbizon	50	48.27 N	2.36 E
Barbosa, Col.	246	6.26 N	75.20 W
Barbosa, Col.	246	5.57 N	73.37 W
Barboursville	188	38.24 N	82.17 W
Barbourville	192	36.51 N	83.53 W

FRANÇAIS

Nom	Page	Lat.°′	Long.°′ W = Ouest
Barbuda I	238	17.38 N	61.48 W
Barbuise ≃	50	48.33 N	3.58 E
Barby	54	51.58 N	11.53 E
Barčadiv	85	38.19 N	72.29 E
Barca Grande ≃	258	34.09 S	58.23 W
Barcaldine	166	23.33 S	145.17 E
Barcarena	266c	38.44 N	9.17 W
Barcarena, Ribeira de ≃	266c	38.42 N	9.27 W
Barcarrota	34	38.31 N	6.51 W
Barcău (Berettyó) ≃	38	46.59 N	21.07 E
Barce → Al-Marj	146	32.30 N	20.54 E
Barcellona Pozzo di Gotto	70	38.09 N	15.13 E
Barcelona, Esp.	34	41.23 N	2.11 E
Barcelona, Esp.	266d	41.23 N	2.11 E
Barcelona, Méx.	232	26.12 N	103.25 W
Barcelona, Pil.	116	12.52 N	124.09 E
Barcelona, Ven.	246	10.08 N	64.42 W
Barcelona □[4]	34	41.40 N	2.00 E
Barcelona ✢[8]	266a	40.22 N	3.34 E
Barcelona, Aeropuerto Transoceánico de ⊠	266d	41.18 N	2.05 E
Barcelone → Barcelona	34	41.23 N	2.11 E
Barceloneta	240m	18.27 N	66.32 W
Barcelonnette	62	44.23 N	6.39 E
Barcelos, Bra.	246	0.58 S	62.57 W
Barcelos, Port.	34	41.32 N	8.37 W
Barchaticha	80	57.34 N	45.13 E
Barchyn ≃	88	48.43 N	110.17 E
Barcillonnette	62	44.26 N	5.55 E
Barcin	30	52.52 N	17.57 E
Barcis	64	46.11 N	12.33 E
Barclay	208	39.08 N	75.51 W
Barclay Brook ≃	276	40.19 N	74.22 W
Barcoo ≃	166	25.30 S	142.50 E
Barcroft, Lake ⊜[1]	284c	38.51 N	77.09 W
Barcs	30	45.58 N	17.28 E
Barcy	261	49.01 N	2.53 E
Barczewo	30	53.50 N	20.42 E
Bard	62	45.36 N	7.45 E
Barda, Azer.	84	40.23 N	47.08 E
Barda, Ross.	86	56.54 N	55.38 E
Barda del Medio	252	38.43 S	68.10 W
Bardagué, Enneri V	146	22.06 N	16.28 E
Bardai, Sūd.	140	12.43 N	21.53 E
Bardaï, Tchad	146	21.22 N	16.59 E
Bardawīl, Sabkhat al- ⩨	140	31.10 N	33.10 E
Barddhamān	126	23.15 N	87.51 E
Bardejov	30	49.18 N	21.16 E
Bardenas Reales ʌ[1]	34	42.10 N	1.25 W
Bardeskan	128	35.12 N	57.58 E
Bardi	62	44.38 N	9.44 E
Bardīyah	146	31.46 N	25.06 E
Bardız	130	40.26 N	42.20 E
Bardney	44	53.12 N	0.21 W
Bardo	36	36.50 N	10.06 E
Bardoc	162	30.20 S	121.17 E
Bārdoli	120	21.07 N	73.07 E
Bardolino	64	45.33 N	10.43 E
Bardonecchia	62	45.05 N	6.42 E
Bardonia	276	41.07 N	74.00 W
Bardoux, Lac ⊜	186	51.09 N	67.50 W
Bardowick	52	53.18 N	10.23 E
Bardsey Island I	42	52.45 N	4.45 W
Bardsey Sound ɥ	42	52.47 N	4.45 W
Bardstown	194	37.48 N	85.28 W
Bardu	24	68.52 N	18.21 E
Bardufoss	24	69.04 N	18.30 E
Bardwell, Ky., U.S.	194	36.52 N	89.00 W
Bardwell, Tx., U.S.	222	32.16 N	96.42 W
Bardwell Lake ⊜[1]	222	32.16 N	96.39 W
Bare	144	4.42 N	42.47 E
Bareggio	266b	45.29 N	9.00 E
Barei, Wādī V	140	13.27 N	23.57 E
Bareilly	124	28.21 N	79.25 E
Bareli	124	23.00 N	78.14 E
Barenburg	52	52.37 N	8.47 E
Barendrecht	52	51.51 N	4.32 E
Bärenklau	54	51.56 N	14.34 E
Bärenstein, Dtsch.	54	50.30 N	13.02 E
Bärenstein, Dtsch.	54	50.48 N	13.47 E
Barentin	50	49.33 N	0.57 E
Barents Sea ∓[2]	12	74.00 N	36.00 E
Barents Trough ✢[1]	12	75.00 N	29.00 E
Barentu	144	15.04 N	37.37 E
Bareo	112	3.45 N	115.27 E
Baresville	208	39.48 N	76.57 W
Bareta	123	29.52 N	75.42 E
Barfleur	32	49.40 N	1.15 W
Barfleur, Pointe de ›	32	49.42 N	1.16 W
Barga	64	44.04 N	10.29 E
Bargāchia, India	126	22.39 N	88.07 E
Bargāchia, India	272b	22.48 N	88.27 E
Bargagli	62	44.27 N	9.05 E
Bargaintown	208	39.22 N	70.35 W
Bargara	166	24.49 S	152.27 E
Bargas	34	39.56 N	4.03 W
Barge, It.	62	44.43 N	7.20 E
Barge, Ityo.	144	6.14 N	36.58 E
Barg-e Maṭāl	120	35.40 N	71.21 E
Bargemon	62	43.37 N	6.32 E
Bargen	58	47.48 N	8.37 E
Bargersville	218	39.31 N	86.10 W
Barghanak	128	33.56 N	62.26 E
Bargnop	140	9.30 N	28.28 E
Bargo	170	34.18 S	150.35 E
Bargoed	42	51.43 N	3.15 W
Bargteheide	52	53.44 N	10.16 E
Bārguna	126	22.09 N	90.07 E
Barguzin	88	53.37 N	109.37 E
Barguzin ≃	88	53.27 N	109.00 E
Barguzinskij chrebet ʌ	88	54.30 N	110.20 E
Barguzinskij zapovednik ♦	88	54.25 N	109.40 E
Bārh	124	25.29 N	85.43 E
Barhaj	124	26.17 N	83.44 E
Bar Harbor	188	44.23 N	68.12 W
Barharwa	124	24.52 N	87.47 E
Barhau	112	5.19 S	102.10 E
Barhi	124	24.18 N	85.25 E
Bar Hill	42	52.15 N	0.01 E
Barhiya	124	25.17 N	86.02 E
Bāri, India	124	23.03 N	78.05 E
Bāri, India	124	26.39 N	77.36 E
Bari, It.	68	41.07 N	16.52 E
Bari, Zaïre	152	3.19 N	19.23 E
Bari □[4], It.	68	40.56 N	16.40 E
Bari □[4], Som.	144	10.00 N	50.00 E
Baria ≃	246	1.56 N	66.35 W
Baricella	64	44.39 N	11.32 E
Barichara	246	6.38 N	73.14 W
Barīdī, Ra's ›	128	24.17 N	37.31 E
Bāri Doāb ʌ[1]	123	30.25 N	73.00 E
Barī Gāv	120	33.52 N	67.49 E
Barigazzo	64	44.16 N	10.39 E
Barigua, Salina de ⩨	241s	12.08 N	69.59 W
Barika	34	35.23 N	5.22 E
Barika, Oued ≃	34	35.22 N	5.18 E
Barikiwa	154	9.28 S	37.54 E
Barīkowṭ	120	35.18 N	71.32 E
Barile	68	40.57 N	15.40 E
Barillas	236	15.48 N	91.18 W
Bariloche → San Carlos de Bariloche	254	41.09 S	71.18 W
Barilo-Krepinskaja	83	47.45 N	39.32 E
Barīm (Perim) I	144	12.39 N	43.25 E
Barima ≃	246	8.33 N	60.25 W
Barima-Waini □[4]	246	7.45 N	59.30 W
Barin	84	39.13 N	44.28 E
Barinas, P.R.	240m	18.01 N	66.51 W
Barinas, Ven.	246	8.38 N	70.12 W
Barinas □[3]	246	8.10 N	69.50 W
Baring	224	47.46 N	121.29 W

PORTUGUÊS

Nome	Página	Lat.°′	Long.°′ W = Oeste
Baring, Cape ›	176	70.05 N	117.20 W
Baringa, Zaïre	152	6.17 S	16.55 E
Baringa, Zaïre	152	0.45 N	20.52 E
Baringo, Lake ⊜	154	0.38 N	36.05 E
Båring Vig ᴄ	41	55.32 N	9.56 E
Barinitas	246	8.45 N	70.25 W
Bāripada	126	21.56 N	86.43 E
Bariri	255	22.04 S	48.44 W
Bārīs	140	24.40 N	30.36 E
Barisacho	84	42.28 N	44.54 E
Bari Sādri	120	24.25 N	74.28 E
Barisāl	124	22.42 N	90.22 E
Barisan, Pegunungan ʌ	112	3.00 S	102.15 E
Bari Sardo	71	39.50 N	9.38 E
Barisciano	66	42.19 N	13.35 E
Bariti Bil ⊜	272b	22.48 N	88.26 E
Barito ≃	112	3.32 S	114.29 E
Baritú, Parque Nacional ♦	252	22.30 S	64.35 W
Barjā	132	33.39 N	35.26 E
Barjac	62	44.18 N	4.21 E
Barjols	62	43.33 N	6.00 E
Barjora	126	23.26 N	87.17 E
Barjūj, Wādī V	146	25.57 N	13.12 E
Bark ≃	216	42.55 N	88.50 W
Barka Kāna	124	23.37 N	85.29 E
Barkal	120	22.44 N	92.23 E
Barkam	102	31.50 N	102.40 E
Barkava	76	56.43 N	26.36 E
Barkelsby	41	54.30 N	9.50 E
Barker, N.Y., U.S.	210	43.19 N	78.33 W
Barker, Ur.	258	34.16 S	57.27 W
Barker Point ›	276	40.51 N	73.44 W
Barker Reservoir ⊜[1]	222	29.44 N	95.44 W
Barkers Brook ≃	285	40.03 N	74.45 W
Barkerville	182	53.04 N	121.31 W
Barkerville Historic Park ♦	182	53.04 N	121.30 W
Barkeyville	214	41.12 N	79.58 W
Barkhamsted Reservoir ⊜[1]	207	41.57 N	72.57 W
Bārkhān	120	29.54 N	69.31 E
Barkhanpur	126	23.50 N	89.33 E
Barking ✢[8]	42	51.33 N	0.06 E
Barkingside ✢[8]	260	51.36 N	0.05 E
Barki Saraiya	124	24.10 N	85.53 E
Barkisland	262	53.41 N	1.55 W
Bark Lake ⊜, On., Can.	190	46.54 N	82.28 W
Bark Lake ⊜, On., Can.	212	45.27 N	77.51 W
Barkley, Lake ⊜[1]	194	36.40 N	87.55 W
Barkley Sound ɥ	182	48.53 N	125.20 W
Barkly ≃	169	37.32 S	146.32 E
Barkly, Mount ∧[2]	162	21.34 S	132.28 E
Barkly East	158	30.58 S	27.33 E
Barkly Tableland ʌ[1]	162	18.00 S	136.00 E
Barkly West	158	28.05 S	24.31 E
Barkol	90	43.50 N	93.30 E
Barksdale	196	29.44 N	100.02 W
Barkuhi	124	22.13 N	78.42 E
Barla	130	38.01 N	30.47 E
Bârlad → Bîrlad	38	46.14 N	27.40 E
Barlassina	266b	45.39 N	9.08 E
Barlaston	42	52.57 N	2.10 W
Barlby	44	53.48 N	1.03 W
Barleben	54	52.12 N	11.37 E
Bar-le-Duc	56	48.47 N	5.10 E
Barlee, Lake ⊜	162	29.10 S	119.30 E
Barlee, Mount ∧[2]	162	24.37 S	128.06 E
Barlee Range ʌ	162	23.35 S	116.00 E
Barles	62	44.16 N	6.16 E
Barletta	68	41.19 N	16.17 E
Barlin	50	50.27 N	2.37 E
Barlinek	30	53.00 N	15.12 E
Barling	194	35.19 N	94.18 W
Barlow	194	37.03 N	89.02 W
Barluk	88	54.32 N	101.43 E
Barma	164	1.54 S	133.00 E
Barmancak, ozero ⊜	80	48.02 N	44.40 E
Barmašovo	78	47.07 N	32.26 E
Barmedman	166	34.09 S	147.23 E
Barmen ✢[8]	263	51.17 N	7.13 E
Bārmer	120	25.45 N	71.23 E
Barmera	166	34.15 S	140.28 E
Barmouth	42	52.43 N	4.03 W
Barmouth Bay ᴄ	42	52.42 N	4.08 W
Barmstedt	52	53.47 N	9.46 E
Barnaby Manor Oaks	284c	38.50 N	76.58 W
Barnagar	120	23.03 N	75.22 E
Barnāla	123	30.23 N	75.33 E
Barnard Castle	44	54.33 N	1.55 W
Barnasht	142	29.41 N	31.15 E
Bärnau	60	49.49 N	12.26 E
Barnaul	86	53.22 N	83.45 E
Bärnbach	61	47.05 N	15.06 E
Barn Bluff ∧	166	41.43 S	145.56 E
Barneberg	54	52.08 N	11.03 E
Barnegat	208	39.45 N	74.13 W
Barnegat Bay ᴄ	208	39.52 N	74.07 W
Barnegat Light	208	39.45 N	74.06 W
Barne Inlet ᴄ	9	80.15 S	160.15 E
Barnes	214	41.40 N	79.01 W
Barnes ✢[8]	260	51.28 N	0.15 W
Barnesboro	214	40.39 N	78.46 W
Barnes Corners	212	43.49 N	75.49 W
Barnes Ice Cap ⍓	176	70.00 N	73.15 W
Barnes Lake ⊜	184	56.23 N	98.06 W
Barnes Sound ɥ	220	25.14 N	80.23 W
Barnesville, Ga., U.S.	192	33.03 N	84.09 W
Barnesville, Mn., U.S.	198	46.39 N	96.25 W
Barnesville, Oh., U.S.	188	39.59 N	81.10 W
Barnet ✢[8]	42	51.40 N	0.13 W
Barnetby le Wold	44	53.35 N	0.25 W
Barnett	219	39.16 N	89.42 W
Barnetts	208	37.22 N	77.09 W
Barneveld, Ned.	52	52.08 N	5.35 E
Barneveld, N.Y., U.S.	210	43.16 N	75.12 W
Barneville-Carteret	32	49.23 N	1.47 W
Barnhart, Mo., U.S.	219	38.20 N	90.23 W
Barnhart, Tx., U.S.	196	31.08 N	101.10 W
Barnhill	214	40.27 N	81.21 W
Barnim ✢[1]	54	52.40 N	13.45 E
Barnoldswick	44	53.55 N	2.11 W
Barnówko	54	52.48 N	14.45 E
Barnsboro	285	39.46 N	75.09 W
Barnsdall	196	36.33 N	96.09 W
Barnsley	44	53.34 N	1.28 W
Barnstable	207	41.42 N	70.18 W
Barnstable □[6]	207	41.42 N	70.18 W
Barnstable Harbor ᴄ	207	41.43 N	70.18 W
Barnstaple	42	51.05 N	4.04 W
Barnstaple Bay ᴄ	42	51.05 N	4.20 W
Barnston	262	53.21 N	3.05 W
Barnstorf	52	52.42 N	8.30 E
Barnt Green	42	52.22 N	1.59 W
Barnton	262	53.16 N	2.33 W
Barntrup	52	51.59 N	9.06 E
Barnum Island	276	40.36 N	73.39 W
Barnwell, Ab., Can.	182	49.46 N	112.15 W
Barnwell, S.C., U.S.	192	33.14 N	81.21 W
Baro	150	8.37 N	6.25 E
Baro ≃	144	8.26 N	33.13 E
Barobo	116	8.33 N	126.07 E
Baroda → Vadodara, India	122	22.18 N	73.12 E
Baroda, India	124	25.30 N	76.39 E
Baroda, Mi., U.S.	216	41.57 N	86.29 W
Baroe	158	33.13 S	24.33 E
Barometer ∧	172	41.50 S	173.39 E
Baron Bluff ⊥[4]	241n	17.47 N	64.47 W
Baronissi	68	40.44 N	14.45 E
Barons	182	50.00 N	113.05 W
Barora Fa Island I	175e	7.30 S	158.20 E
Barora Ite Island I	175e	7.35 S	158.24 E
Barossa Reservoir ⊜[1]	168b	34.39 S	138.51 E
Barotac Nuevo	116	10.54 N	122.42 E
Barotac Viejo	116	11.03 N	122.51 E
Barouéli	150	13.04 N	6.50 W
Barpathār	120	26.17 N	93.53 E
Barpeta	120	26.19 N	91.00 E
Bar Point ›	214	42.03 N	83.06 W
Barqa	120	30.57 N	81.20 E
Barqah (Cyrenaica) □[9]	146	31.00 N	22.30 E
Barqah, Jabal al- ∧	132	30.25 N	34.18 E
Barq al-'Izz	142	31.01 N	31.26 E
Barque Canada Reef ✢[2]	108	8.12 N	113.19 E
Barques, Pointe aux ›	190	44.04 N	82.58 W
Barquisimeto	246	10.04 N	69.19 W
Barr	58	48.24 N	7.27 E
Barra, Bra.	250	11.05 S	43.10 W
Barra, Gam.	150	13.20 N	16.36 W
Barra I	46	56.58 N	7.29 W
Barra, Ponta da ›	156	23.47 S	35.32 E
Barra, Sound of ɥ	46	57.05 N	7.25 W
Barraba	166	30.22 S	150.36 E
Barracas ✢[8]	288	34.38 S	58.22 W
Barrackpore → Bārākpur	126	22.46 N	88.21 E
Barrackpore Airport ⊠	272b	22.47 N	88.22 E
Barrackville	188	39.30 N	80.10 W
Barracouta, Cape ›	158	34.26 S	21.22 E
Barra da Estiva	255	13.38 S	41.19 W
Barra de Santo Antônio	250	9.24 S	35.30 W
Barra de São Francisco	256	21.58 S	42.42 W
Barra do Bugres	248	15.05 S	57.11 W
Barra do Corda	250	5.30 S	45.15 W
Barra do Cuanza	152	9.09 S	13.00 E
Barra do Dande	152	8.28 S	13.22 E
Barra do Garças	255	15.53 S	52.15 W
Barra do Mendes	255	11.43 S	42.04 W
Barra do Pira	256	22.28 S	43.49 W
Barra do Ribeiro	252	30.18 S	51.18 W
Barra dos Coqueiros	250	10.54 S	37.03 W
Barra Falsa, Ponta da ›	156	22.55 S	35.37 E
Barrafranca	70	37.22 N	14.12 E
Barra Funda ✢[8]	287b	23.31 S	46.39 W
Barra Head ›	46	56.46 N	7.38 W
Barrali	71	39.28 N	9.06 E
Barra Mansa	256	22.32 S	44.11 W
Barranca, Perú	248	10.45 S	77.46 W
Barranca, Perú	248	4.50 S	76.42 W
Barrancabermeja	246	7.03 N	73.52 W
Barrancas, Col.	246	10.57 N	72.50 W
Barrancas, Ven.	246	8.46 N	70.06 W
Barrancas, Ven.	246	8.42 N	62.11 W
Barrancas ≃	252	36.52 S	69.45 W
Barranco	286d	12.09 S	77.02 W
Barranco Azul	196	29.21 N	104.17 W
Barranco de Guadalupe	196	30.02 N	104.44 W
Barranco do Velho	34	37.14 N	7.56 W
Barrancos	34	38.08 N	6.59 W
Barrânia	256	21.33 S	46.32 W
Barranqueras	252	27.29 S	58.56 W
Barranquilla	246	10.59 N	74.48 W
Barranquitas	240m	18.11 N	66.18 W
Barras	250	4.15 S	42.18 W
Barrax	34	39.03 N	2.12 W
Barre, Ma., U.S.	207	42.25 N	72.06 W
Barre, Vt., U.S.	188	44.11 N	72.30 W
Barrea	66	41.45 N	13.59 E
Barreal	252	31.38 S	69.28 W
Barree	214	40.35 N	78.06 W
Barre Falls Dam ✢[6]	207	42.26 N	72.02 W
Barreiras	255	12.08 S	45.00 W
Barreirinha	250	2.47 S	57.03 W
Barreirinhas	250	2.45 S	42.50 W
Barreiro	34	38.40 N	9.05 W
Barreiro ≃, Bra.	255	15.43 S	52.45 W
Barreiro ≃, Bra.	287a	22.52 S	43.34 W
Barreiros	250	8.49 S	35.12 W
Barrême	62	43.57 N	6.22 E
Barren ≃	194	37.11 N	86.37 W
Barren, Nosy II	157b	18.25 S	43.40 E
Barren Island I	110	12.16 N	93.51 E
Barren Islands II	180	58.55 N	152.15 W
Barrenjoey Head ›	170	33.34 S	151.20 E
Barren River Lake ⊜[1]	194	36.45 N	86.02 W
Barren Run ≃	279b	40.09 N	79.42 W
Barre Plains	207	42.22 N	72.06 W
Barret-le-Bas	62	44.16 N	5.44 E
Barretos	255	20.33 S	48.33 W
Barrett	222	29.53 N	95.04 W
Barrett, Mount ∧	162	18.10 S	127.33 E
Barrhead, Ab., Can.	182	54.08 N	114.24 W
Barrhead, Scot., U.K.	46	55.48 N	4.24 W
Barrhill	44	55.07 N	4.46 W
Barrie	212	44.24 N	79.40 W
Barriefield	212	44.14 N	76.28 W
Barrie Island I	190	45.55 N	82.40 W
Barrien	52	52.56 N	8.49 E
Barrier, Cape ›	172	36.21 S	175.31 E
Barrière	182	51.11 N	120.07 W
Barrier Range ʌ	166	31.25 S	141.25 E
Barrier Reef ✢[2]	164	11.36 S	153.00 E
Barrigada	174p	13.28 N	144.48 E
Barrilla Draw V	196	31.21 N	103.23 W
Barr Ilyās	132	33.46 N	35.54 E
Barrington, N.S., Can.	186	43.34 N	65.34 W
Barrington, Il., U.S.	216	42.09 N	88.08 W
Barrington, N.J., U.S.	285	39.51 N	75.03 W
Barrington, R.I., U.S.	207	41.44 N	71.18 W
Barrington Hills	216	42.07 N	88.09 W
Barrington Lake ⊜	184	56.55 N	100.15 W
Barrington Tops ∧	166	32.00 S	151.28 E
Barrington Woods	278	42.09 N	88.04 W
Barringun	166	29.01 S	145.43 E
Barrio de la Soledad	234	16.48 N	95.15 W
Barrita Vieja	236	13.55 N	90.54 W
Barrīyat al-Uṣayfir	142	31.18 N	30.40 E
Barro, Bra.	250	7.11 S	38.47 W
Barro, Gui.-B.	150	12.24 N	15.30 W
Barro Alto	255	15.04 S	48.58 W
Barron	190	45.24 N	91.50 W
Barron Creek ≃	282	37.27 N	122.05 W
Barron Lake	216	41.51 N	86.11 W
Barrouallie	241h	13.14 N	61.17 W
Barrow, Arg.	252	38.18 S	60.14 W
Barrow, Ak., U.S.	180	71.17 N	156.34 W
Barrow ≃	48	52.15 N	7.00 W
Barrow, Point ›	180	71.23 N	156.30 W
Barrow Bay ᴄ	212	44.58 N	81.13 W
Barrow Creek	162	21.33 S	133.53 E
Barrowford	44	53.52 N	2.13 W
Barrow-in-Furness	44	54.07 N	3.14 W
Barrow Island I	162	20.48 S	115.23 E
Barrows	184	52.49 N	101.27 W
Barrow Strait ɥ	176	74.21 N	94.10 W
Barrowsville	207	41.56 N	71.12 W
Barrow upon Humber	44	53.41 N	0.23 W
Barry, Wales, U.K.	42	51.24 N	3.18 W
Barry, Il., U.S.	219	39.41 N	91.02 W
Barry, Tx., U.S.	222	32.06 N	96.38 W
Barry □[6]	216	42.35 N	85.18 W
Barrydale	158	33.55 S	20.43 E
Barrys Bay	212	45.29 N	77.41 W
Barrys Bay ᴄ	212	45.28 N	77.42 W
Barryton	190	43.45 N	85.08 W
Barrytown	210	42.00 N	73.56 W
Barryville	210	41.28 N	74.54 W
Barsakel'mes, ostrov I	86	45.40 N	59.58 E
Barsalpur	120	28.10 N	72.15 E
Baršatas	86	48.13 N	78.21 E
Bårse	41	55.07 N	11.58 E
Bārsi	122	18.14 N	75.42 E
Baršin	86	49.45 N	69.36 E
Barsinghausen	52	52.18 N	9.27 E
Barskaun	85	42.10 N	77.37 E
Barsø I	41	55.07 N	9.34 E
Barssel	52	53.10 N	7.44 E
Barst	56	49.04 N	6.50 E
Barstow, Ca., U.S.	228	34.53 N	117.01 W
Barstow, Tx., U.S.	196	31.28 N	103.24 W
Barsuki	82	54.15 N	37.30 E
Bar-sur-Aube	58	48.14 N	4.43 E
Bar-sur-Seine	50	48.07 N	4.22 E
Bart	208	39.56 N	76.05 W
Bārta ≃	76	56.24 N	21.03 E
Bartala	272b	22.33 N	88.16 E
Bartang ≃	120	37.56 N	71.34 E
Bartazuga, Jabal ∧	140	21.44 N	33.33 E
Bartelso	219	38.32 N	89.28 W
Bartenheim	58	47.38 N	7.28 E
Bartenstein	56	49.21 N	9.53 E
Barter Island I	180	70.08 N	143.35 W
Barth	54	54.22 N	12.43 E
Barthe ≃	54	54.22 N	12.41 E
Barthélemy, Deo)(	110	19.26 N	104.06 E
Bartholomew □[6]	218	39.13 N	85.55 W
Bartholomew, Bayou ≃	194	32.43 N	92.04 W
Bartibougou	150	12.52 N	0.48 E
Bartica	246	6.24 N	58.37 W
Bartın	130	41.38 N	32.21 E
Bartle Frere ∧	166	17.23 S	145.49 E
Bartlesville	196	36.44 N	95.58 W
Bartlett, Il., U.S.	216	41.59 N	88.11 W
Bartlett, Ne., U.S.	198	41.53 N	98.33 W
Bartlett, N.H., U.S.	188	44.04 N	71.17 W
Bartlett, Tn., U.S.	194	35.12 N	89.52 W
Bartlett, Tx., U.S.	222	30.48 N	97.26 W
Bartlett Brook ≃	283	42.42 N	71.13 W
Bartlett Cove	180	58.27 N	135.55 W
Bartlett Reservoir ⊜[1]	200	33.52 N	111.37 W
Bartletts ∧[2]	168a	32.19 S	116.43 E
Bartletts Harbour	186	50.57 N	57.00 W
Bartley	198	40.14 N	100.18 W
Bartolomé Bavio → General Mansilla	258	35.05 S	57.45 W
Bartolomé de las Casas	252	25.24 S	59.34 W
Bartolomeu de Gusmão, Aeroporto ⊠	256	22.56 S	43.43 W
Bartolomeu Dias	156	21.10 S	35.09 E
Barton, Austl.	162	30.31 S	132.39 E
Barton, N.Y., U.S.	210	42.03 N	76.27 W
Barton, Oh., U.S.	214	40.06 N	80.50 W
Barton, Vt., U.S.	188	44.44 N	72.10 W
Barton Aerodrome ⊠	262	53.28 N	2.23 W
Barton Lake	216	42.06 N	85.35 W
Barton Lake ⊜	184	52.00 N	94.06 W
Barton-le-Clay	42	51.57 N	0.25 W
Barton Mills	42	52.20 N	0.31 E
Barton Park ♦	274a	33.57 S	151.09 E
Barton Run ≃	285	39.53 N	74.51 W
Barton-under-Needwood	42	52.45 N	1.43 W
Barton-upon-Humber	44	53.41 N	0.27 W
Bartonville	190	40.39 N	89.39 W
Barton Water Swing Bridge ✢[5]	262	53.28 N	2.21 W
Bartoszyce	30	54.16 N	20.49 E
Bartow, Fl., U.S.	220	27.53 N	81.50 W
Bartow, Ga., U.S.	192	32.52 N	82.28 W
Baru, Kali ≅	269e	6.10 S	106.51 E
Barú, Volcán ∧[1]	236	8.48 N	82.33 W
Barueri	256	23.31 S	46.53 W
Barugo	116	11.20 N	124.44 E
Bāruipāra	272b	22.46 N	88.14 E
Bāruipur	126	22.21 N	88.27 E
Bārūk, Jabal al- ∧	132	33.43 N	35.45 E
Barumini	71	39.42 N	9.00 E
Barumun ≃	114	2.30 N	100.09 E
Barun Bogd uul ∧	90	44.57 N	100.15 E
Barung, Nusa I	115a	8.28 S	113.20 E
Barun Su	102	42.27 N	111.01 E
Barun-Torej, ozero ⊜	88	50.10 N	115.30 E
Baruntse ∧	124	27.51 N	86.59 E
Barus	114	2.00 N	98.24 E
Baruta	286c	10.26 N	66.53 W
Baruth	54	52.03 N	13.30 E
Baruun Bajan-Ulaan	102	45.10 N	101.24 E
Baruun bogd uul ∧	102	44.57 N	100.15 E
Baruun-Urt	90	46.42 N	113.15 E
Barva, Volcán ∧[1]	236	10.08 N	84.06 W
Barvas	46	58.22 N	6.32 W
Barvenkovo	78	48.54 N	37.02 E
Barver	52	52.37 N	8.35 E
Barvicha	265b	55.44 N	37.16 E
Barview	202	43.21 N	124.18 W
Barwa	126	23.51 N	86.26 E
Barwāh	120	22.16 N	76.03 E
Barwāla ✢[8]	272a	28.46 N	77.04 E
Barwāni	120	22.02 N	74.54 E
Barwa Sāgar	124	25.23 N	78.44 E
Barwell	42	52.32 N	1.21 W
Barwice	30	53.45 N	16.22 E
Barwick	192	30.54 N	83.44 W
Barwidgee	162	27.02 S	120.54 E
Barwon ≃, Austl.	166	30.00 S	148.05 E
Barwon ≃, Austl.	169	38.13 S	144.25 E
Barwon Heads (South Barwon)	169	38.17 S	144.30 E
Barybino, Ross.	82	55.16 N	37.54 E
Barybino, Ross.	82	54.56 N	37.47 E
Barycz ≃	30	51.42 N	16.15 E
Barykino	83	49.17 N	38.24 E
Barykova, mys ›	180	63.02 N	179.29 E
Barykovo	82	54.38 N	38.48 E
Barynino	82	55.47 N	36.21 E
Baryš	80	53.39 N	47.08 E
Baryš ≃	80	54.35 N	46.48 E
Baryševka	78	50.22 N	31.19 E
Baryševo	86	54.58 N	83.11 E
Baryšniki	80	56.57 N	46.33 E
Barzah	132	33.34 N	36.19 E
Barzas	86	55.43 N	86.19 E
Barzio	58	45.57 N	9.27 E
Bas'a ≃	76	53.46 N	31.01 E
Basacato del Este	152	3.37 N	8.54 E
Basai Dārāpur ✢[8]	272a	28.40 N	77.08 E
Bāsa' Īdū	128	26.39 N	55.17 E
Basail, Arg.	252	27.52 S	59.18 W
Bāsāil, Bngl.	126	24.14 N	90.04 E
Basakin	80	48.11 N	42.18 E
Basāl	123	33.33 N	72.15 E
Basalt ≃	166	19.38 S	145.52 E
Basalt Island I	271d	22.19 N	114.22 E
Basaluzzo	62	44.46 N	8.42 E
Basandīlah	142	31.12 N	31.26 E
Basankusu	152	1.14 N	19.48 E
Bašanta	80	46.05 N	41.56 E
Basanti	126	22.12 N	88.42 E
Basarabi	38	44.10 N	28.24 E
Basatongwula Shan ∧	120	33.05 N	91.30 E
Basavakalyān	122	17.52 N	76.57 E
Basavilbaso	252	32.22 S	58.53 W
Baščelakskij chrebet ʌ	86	51.15 N	84.30 E
Baschi	66	42.40 N	12.13 E
Basco	108	20.27 N	121.58 E
Bascom	214	41.07 N	83.17 W
Bascuñán, Cabo ›	252	28.51 S	71.30 W
Basdahl	52	53.26 N	8.59 E
Basdorf, Dtsch.	54	52.44 N	13.26 E
Basdorf, Dtsch.	56	51.12 N	8.58 E
Basekpio	154	4.44 N	24.40 E
Basel (Bâle)	58	47.33 N	7.35 E
Baselga di Pinè	64	46.08 N	11.14 E
Baselice	68	41.24 N	14.58 E
Basel-Land □[3]	58	47.30 N	7.50 E
Basel-Stadt □[3]	58	47.38 N	7.40 E
Basen ≃	96	34.48 N	132.51 E
Bas-en-Basset	62	45.18 N	4.06 E
Basentello ≃	68	40.40 N	16.23 E
Basento ≃	68	40.21 N	16.50 E
Başeu ≃	38	47.44 N	27.15 E
Basey	116	11.17 N	125.04 E
Bashaw	182	52.35 N	112.58 W
Basher Kill ≃	210	41.27 N	74.35 W
Bashi Channel ɥ	108	22.00 N	121.00 E
Bashikejike	120	37.30 N	85.50 E
Bashiqiao	106	31.40 N	120.22 E
Bashkortostan → Baškirija □[3]	86	54.00 N	56.00 E
Bashtīl	273c	30.05 N	31.11 E
Basi, India	123	30.36 N	76.50 E
Basi, India	123	30.41 N	76.24 E
Basiad Bay ᴄ	116	14.16 N	122.19 E
Basiano	112	1.16 S	122.50 E
Basibasy	157b	22.10 S	43.40 E
Başıbüyük ✢[8]	267b	40.57 N	29.08 E
Basicò	70	38.04 N	15.04 E
Basid	85	38.07 N	72.09 E
Basilaki Island I	164	10.35 S	151.00 E
Basilan □[4]	116	6.35 N	121.55 E
Basilan Island I	116	6.34 N	122.03 E
Basilan Peak ∧	116	6.33 N	122.04 E
Basilan Strait ɥ	116	6.49 N	122.05 E
Basildon	42	51.35 N	0.25 E
Basildon □[8]	260	51.35 N	0.29 E
Basile	194	30.29 N	92.35 W
Basiliano	64	46.01 N	13.06 E
Basilicata □[4]	68	40.30 N	16.10 E
Basiluzzo, Isola I	70	38.39 N	15.07 E
Basin, Mt., U.S.	202	46.16 N	112.15 W
Basin, Wy., U.S.	202	44.22 N	108.02 W
Bäsingen ⊜	40	60.09 N	16.20 E
Basinger	220	27.24 N	81.01 W
Basingstoke	42	51.15 N	1.05 W
Basingstoke Canal ≅	260	51.21 N	0.29 W
Basingwerk Abbey ᴗ[1]	262	53.17 N	3.12 W
Basin Lake ⊜	184	52.38 N	105.18 W
Basīrhāt	126	22.40 N	88.53 E
Basīrpur	123	30.35 N	73.50 E
Basīṭ, Ra's al- ›	130	35.51 N	35.48 E
Basiyingzi	104	42.05 N	121.37 E
Basjanovskij	86	58.19 N	60.44 E
Baška	36	44.58 N	14.46 E
Baskahegan Lake ⊜	188	45.30 N	67.48 W
Baskakovka	76	54.36 N	34.19 E
Başkale	128	38.02 N	44.00 E
Baskatong, Réservoir ⊜[1]	190	46.48 N	75.50 W
Baškaus ≃	86	51.09 N	87.43 E
Basket Lake ⊜	184	49.43 N	92.00 W
Basking Ridge	276	40.42 N	74.32 W
Baškino	82	55.18 N	36.41 E
Baškirija □[3]	86	54.00 N	56.00 E
Baškirskij zapovednik ♦	86	53.30 N	57.58 E
Baskomutan Milli Parkı ♦	130	38.50 N	30.05 E
Başköy	84	39.53 N	44.32 E
Baskuduk	86	49.43 N	61.32 E
Baš-Kugandy	85	42.00 N	74.39 E
Baskunčak, ozero ⊜	80	48.12 N	46.54 E
Baslow	44	53.15 N	1.38 W
Başmakçı	130	37.54 N	30.01 E
Bašmakovo	80	53.12 N	43.02 E
Basmat	122	19.19 N	77.10 E
Bäsna	40	60.32 N	15.12 E
Bāsoda	124	23.51 N	77.56 E
Basoko	152	1.14 N	23.36 E
Basoko ≃	273b	4.19 S	15.16 E
Basoli	123	32.30 N	75.49 E
Basom	210	43.04 N	78.24 W
Basongo	152	4.20 S	20.24 E
Basora, Punt ›	241s	12.25 N	69.52 W
Basovizza	64	45.38 N	13.52 E
Başpınar	130	39.12 N	38.42 E
Basque Lands → Euskal Herriko □[4]	34	43.00 N	2.30 W
Basra → Al-Başrah	128	30.30 N	47.47 E
Bas-Rhin □[5]	32	48.35 N	7.40 E
Bass ≃	169	38.30 S	145.26 E
Bassano	182	50.47 N	112.28 W
Bassano del Grappa	64	45.46 N	11.44 E
Bassari	150	9.15 N	0.47 E
Bassas da India ✢[2]	138	21.25 S	39.42 E
Bass Creek ≃	216	42.37 N	89.04 W
Basse-Californie → Baja California ›[1]	232	28.00 N	113.30 W
Bassecourt	58	47.20 N	7.15 E
Bassein → Pathein	110	16.47 N	94.44 E
Bassein ≃[1]	110	15.56 N	94.18 E
Basse-Kotto □[5]	152	5.00 N	21.30 E
Bassella	34	42.01 N	1.18 E
Bassen	52	53.04 N	9.04 E
Bassendean	168a	31.55 S	115.56 E
Bassenthwaite	44	54.41 N	3.12 W
Bassenthwaite Lake ⊜	44	54.38 N	3.13 W
Basse-Pointe	240e	14.52 N	61.07 W
Basses, Pointe des ›	241o	15.52 N	61.17 W
Basse Santa Su	150	13.19 N	14.13 W
Basse-Terre, Guad.	241o	16.00 N	61.44 W
Basseterre, St. K.-N.	238	17.18 N	62.43 W
Basse Terre, Trin.	241r	10.08 N	61.18 W
Basse-Terre I	241o	16.10 N	61.40 W
Bassett, Ne., U.S.	198	42.35 N	99.32 W
Bassett, Va., U.S.	192	36.45 N	79.59 W
Bassett Creek ≃	194	31.25 N	87.56 W
Bassett Peak ∧	200	32.30 N	110.17 W
Bassfield	194	31.30 N	89.44 W
Bass Harbor	188	44.14 N	68.20 W
Bass Hill	274a	33.54 S	151.00 E
Bassignana	62	45.00 N	8.44 E
Bassikounou	150	15.52 N	5.57 W
Bassila	150	9.01 N	1.40 E
Bassin des Aghlabites ⊥	36	35.43 N	10.10 E
Bassingbourn	42	52.04 N	0.03 W
Bass Lake, Ca., U.S.	226	37.19 N	119.33 W
Bass Lake, In., U.S.	216	41.12 N	86.36 W
Bass Lake ⊜, On., Can.	212	44.49 N	76.08 W
Bass Lake ⊜, In., U.S.	216	41.13 N	86.36 W
Bass Lake ⊜[1]	226	37.19 N	119.34 W
Bass Point ›	170	34.36 S	150.54 E
Bass River	186	45.25 N	63.47 W
Bass Strait ɥ	166	39.20 S	145.30 E
Bassum	52	52.51 N	8.43 E
Basswood Lake ⊜, On., Can.	190	46.20 N	83.23 W
Basswood Lake ⊜, N.A.	190	48.06 N	91.40 W
Basta	126	21.41 N	87.03 E
Båstad	26	56.26 N	12.51 E
Basṭah	132	30.14 N	35.32 E
Bastak	128	27.14 N	54.22 E
Basṭām	128	36.29 N	55.04 E
Baštanka	78	47.24 N	32.25 E
Bastei ♦	54	50.58 N	14.04 E
Bastelica	36	42.00 N	9.02 E
Basti	124	26.48 N	82.43 E
Bastia, Fr.	36	42.42 N	9.27 E
Bastia, It.	66	43.04 N	12.33 E
Bastian	192	37.09 N	81.09 W
Bastiglia	64	44.43 N	11.00 E
Bastimentos	236	9.21 N	82.12 W
Bastimentos, Isla I	236	9.18 N	82.08 W
Bastogne	56	50.00 N	5.43 E
Bastrop, La., U.S.	194	32.46 N	91.54 W
Bastrop, Tx., U.S.	222	30.06 N	97.18 W
Bastrop □[6]	222	33.00 N	97.18 W
Bastrop, Lake ⊜[1]	222	30.09 N	97.18 W
Bastrop Bay ᴄ	222	29.06 N	95.11 W
Bastrop State Park ♦	222	30.07 N	97.17 W
Bastuträsk	26	64.47 N	20.02 E

≃	River	Fluß	Río	Rivière	Rio
≅	Canal	Kanal	Canal	Canal	Canal
ʟ	Waterfall, Rapids	Wasserfall, Stromschnellen	Cascada, Rápidos	Chute d'eau, Rapides	Cascata, Rápidos
ɥ	Strait	Meeresstraße	Estrecho	Détroit	Estreito
ᴄ	Bay, Gulf	Bucht, Golf	Bahía, Golfo	Baie, Golfe	Baía, Golfo
⊜	Lake, Lakes	See, Seen	Lago, Lagos	Lac, Lacs	Lago, Lagos
⩨	Swamp	Sumpf	Pantano	Marais	Pântano
⍓	Ice Features, Glacier	Eis- und Gletscherformen	Accidentes Glaciales	Formes glaciaires	Acidentes glaciares
∓	Other Hydrographic Features	Andere Hydrographische Objekte	Otros Elementos Hidrográficos	Autres données hydrographiques	Outros acidentes hidrográficos

✢	Submarine Features	Untermeerische Objekte	Accidentes Submarinos	Formes de relief sous-marin	Acidentes submarinos
□	Political Unit	Politische Einheit	Unidad Politica	Entité politique	Unidade política
ᴗ	Cultural Institution	Kulturelle Institution	Institución Cultural	Institution culturelle	Instituição cultural
⊥	Historical Site	Historische Stätte	Sitio Histórico	Site historique	Sitio histórico
♦	Recreational Site	Erholungs- und Ferienort	Sitio de Recreo	Centre de loisirs	Area de Lazer
⊠	Airport	Flughafen	Aeropuerto	Aéroport	Aeroporto
■	Military Installation	Militäranlage	Instalación Militar	Installation militaire	Instalação militar
✦	Miscellaneous	Verschiedenes	Misceláneo	Divers	Diversos

I · 16 Basu-Beav

ENGLISH Name Page Lat.°′ Long.°′ — DEUTSCH Name Seite Breite°′ Länge°′ E = Ost

Name	Page	Lat.	Long.
Basu, Pulau I	112	0.18 S	103.36 E
Basubāti	272b	22.47 N	88.12 E
Bāsudebpur, India	126	21.49 N	87.38 E
Bāsudebpur, India	272b	22.49 N	88.25 E
Basuo → Dongfang	110	19.05 N	108.39 E
Bāsūs	273c	30.08 N	31.13 E
Baswa	126	24.08 N	87.52 E
Basyūn	142	30.57 N	30.49 E
Bas-Zaïre □[4]	152	5.30 S	14.30 E
Bata	152	1.51 N	9.45 E
Bataan □[4]	116	14.40 N	120.25 E
Bataan, Mount ∧	116	14.31 N	120.28 E
Bataan Peninsula ›[1]	116	14.40 N	120.25 E
Batabanó	240p	22.43 N	82.17 W
Batabanó, Golfo de ⊂	240p	22.15 N	82.30 W
Batac	116	18.05 N	120.35 E
Batad	116	11.25 N	123.06 E
Batagaj	74	67.38 N	134.38 E
Batagaj-Alyta	74	67.48 N	130.25 E
Batag Island I	116	12.38 N	125.04 E
Batagol	88	52.22 N	100.45 E
Bataguassu	255	21.42 S	52.22 W
Bataiporã	255	22.20 S	53.17 W
Batajsk	83	47.10 N	39.44 E
Batak	38	41.57 N	24.13 E
Batak, jazovir ⊜[1]	38	41.59 N	24.11 E
Batakan	112	4.05 S	114.38 E
Batala	123	31.48 N	75.12 E
Batalha, Bra.	250	9.41 S	37.08 W
Batalha, Bra.	250	4.01 S	42.05 W
Batalha, Port.	34	39.39 N	8.50 W
Bataly	86	52.52 N	62.00 E
Batam, Pulau I	112	1.05 N	104.03 E
Batama, Ross.	88	53.53 N	101.36 E
Batama, Zaïre	154	0.56 N	26.39 E
Batamaj	74	63.31 N	129.27 E
Batamšinskij	86	50.36 N	58.16 E
Batan, Pil.	116	11.35 N	122.30 E
Batan, Zhg.	98	34.10 N	120.04 E
Batanagar	126	22.31 N	88.15 E
Batang, Indon.	115a	6.55 S	109.45 E
Batang, Zhg.	102	30.02 N	99.02 E
Batangafo	152	7.18 N	18.18 E
Batangas	116	13.45 N	121.03 E
Batangas □[4]	116	13.50 N	121.00 E
Batangas Bay ⊂	116	13.43 N	121.00 E
Batangbatangdaya	115a	6.56 S	113.59 E
Batang Berjuntai	114	3.23 N	101.25 E
Batang Kali	114	3.28 N	101.38 E
Batangtoru	114	1.29 N	99.03 E
Batan Island I, Pil.	108	20.26 N	121.58 E
Batan Island I, Pil.	116	13.15 N	124.00 E
Batan Islands II	108	20.30 N	121.50 E
Batanta, Pulau I	164	0.50 S	130.40 E
Batas ≃	287a	22.44 S	43.24 W
Batas Island I	116	11.10 N	119.36 E
Bátaszék	30	46.12 N	18.44 E
Batatais	255	20.53 S	47.37 W
Batatuba	256	23.04 S	46.25 W
Batavia, Arg.	252	34.47 S	65.41 W
Batavia, Il., U.S.	216	41.51 N	88.18 W
Batavia, Ia., U.S.	190	40.59 N	92.10 W
Batavia, Mi., U.S.	216	41.55 N	85.06 W
Batavia, N.Y., U.S.	210	42.59 N	78.11 W
Batavia, Oh., U.S.	218	39.04 N	84.10 W
Batawa	212	44.10 N	77.36 W
Batbatan Island I	116	11.28 N	121.55 E
Batcengel	88	47.47 N	101.58 E
Batchawana ≃	190	46.55 N	84.32 W
Batchawana Mountain ∧	190	47.04 N	84.24 W
Batchawanna Island I	190	46.53 N	84.30 W
Batchelor	164	13.04 S	131.01 E
Bătdâmbâng	110	13.06 N	103.12 E
Bate Bay ⊂	170	34.04 S	151.12 E
Bateckij	76	58.39 N	30.19 E
Bate Heath	262	53.19 N	2.28 W
Batéké, Plateaux ⋏[1]	152	3.30 S	15.45 E
Batemans Bay	166	35.43 S	150.11 E
Batenbrock ◆[8]	263	51.31 N	6.57 E
Batepito ≃	200	30.48 N	109.11 W
Bates, Mount ∧	174c	29.01 S	167.56 E
Batesburg	192	33.54 N	81.32 W
Bates Creek ≃	200	42.41 N	106.37 W
Bates Range ⋏	162	27.25 S	121.13 E
Batesville, Ar., U.S.	194	35.46 N	91.38 W
Batesville, In., U.S.	218	39.18 N	85.13 W
Batesville, Ms., U.S.	194	34.18 N	89.56 W
Batesville, Tx., U.S.	196	28.57 N	99.37 W
Bath, N.B., Can.	186	46.31 N	67.36 W
Bath, On., Can.	212	44.11 N	76.47 W
Bath, Eng., U.K.	42	51.23 N	2.22 W
Bath, Il., U.S.	219	40.11 N	90.08 W
Bath, Me., U.S.	188	43.54 N	69.49 W
Bath, Mi., U.S.	216	42.49 N	84.26 W
Bath, N.Y., U.S.	210	42.20 N	77.19 W
Bath, Oh., U.S.	214	41.11 N	81.38 W
Bath, Pa., U.S.	208	40.43 N	75.23 W
Bath □[6]	218	38.14 N	83.48 W
Batha □[5]	146	14.00 N	19.00 E
Batha ≃	146	12.47 N	17.34 E
Bath Addition	285	40.06 N	74.52 W
Bathgate, Scot., U.K.	46	55.55 N	3.39 W
Bathgate, N.D., U.S.	198	48.52 N	97.28 W
Bathinda	123	30.12 N	74.57 E
Bathsheba	241g	13.13 N	59.31 W
Bathurst, Austl.	166	33.25 S	149.35 E
Bathurst, N.B., Can.	186	47.36 N	65.39 W
Bathurst → Banjul, Gam.	150	13.28 N	16.39 W
Bathurst, S. Afr.	158	33.30 S	26.50 E
Bathurst, Cape ›	176	70.35 N	128.00 W
Bathurst, Lake ⊜	170	35.04 S	149.44 E
Bathurst Inlet	176	66.50 N	108.01 W
Bathurst Inlet ⊂	176	68.10 N	108.50 W
Bathurst Island I, Austl.	164	11.37 S	130.23 E
Bathurst Island I, N.T., Can.	16	76.00 N	100.30 W
Bathurst Island Aboriginal Reserve ◆[4]	164	11.37 S	130.23 E
Bati	144	11.10 N	40.02 E
Batia	150	10.54 N	1.29 E
Batiāgarh	124	24.07 N	79.21 E
Batié	150	9.53 N	2.55 W
Bāṭin, Wādī al- V	128	29.35 N	47.00 E
Batina	38	45.51 N	18.51 E
Batiquitos Lagoon ⊂	228	33.05 N	117.18 W
Batīr	132	31.16 N	35.42 E
Batiscan ≃	206	46.31 N	72.15 W
Batiste Creek ≃	222	30.04 N	94.28 W
Batkanu	150	9.05 N	12.25 W
Batken	85	40.03 N	70.50 E
Batley	44	53.44 N	1.37 W
Batlow	171b	35.31 S	148.09 E
Batman	130	37.52 N	41.07 E
Batman □[4]	130	38.00 N	41.15 E
Batna	148	35.34 N	6.11 E
Batna □[5]	148	35.30 N	6.10 E
Baṭn al-Ghūl	132	29.44 N	35.52 E
Batnorov	88	47.55 N	111.30 E
Batō, Nihon	94	36.44 N	140.10 E
Bato, Pil.	116	10.20 N	124.47 E
Ba To, Viet	110	14.46 N	108.44 E
Bato, Lake ⊜	116	13.19 N	123.21 E
Batoala	152	0.48 N	13.27 E
Batoche Rectory National Historic Site ⊥	184	52.41 N	106.02 W
Batoka	154	16.47 S	27.15 E
Baton Rouge	194	30.27 N	91.09 W
Bator	123	33.06 N	75.19 E
Batorampon Point ›	116	7.07 N	121.54 E
Batouri	152	4.26 N	14.22 E
Batovi	255	15.53 S	53.24 W
Batpajsagyr, peski ◆[2]	80	47.20 N	48.40 E
Baṭrā (Petra) ⊥	132	30.20 N	35.26 E
Batrā', Jibāl al- ⋏	132	29.53 N	35.38 E
Baṭrah	142	31.10 N	31.27 E
Ba Tri	110	10.02 N	106.36 E
Batsawul	120	34.15 N	70.52 E
Batson	222	30.15 N	94.37 W
Batsto ≃	285	39.39 N	74.39 W
Batsto, Skit Branch ≃	285	39.46 N	74.41 W
Batsto State Historic Site ⊥	208	39.39 N	74.39 W
Bat Sûmber	88	48.29 N	106.42 E
Battaglia Terme	64	45.17 N	11.47 E
Battambang → Bătdâmbâng	110	13.06 N	103.12 E
Battenberg	56	51.01 N	8.38 E
Batten Kill ≃	188	43.06 N	73.35 W
Batterie, Pointe de la ›	240e	14.44 N	60.54 W
Bätterkinden	58	47.08 N	7.32 E
Battersea ◆[8]	260	51.28 N	0.10 W
Battersea Park ♠	260	51.29 N	0.09 W
Batticaloa	122	7.43 N	81.42 E
Battice	56	50.39 N	5.49 E
Battin	224	45.29 N	122.34 W
Battipaglia	68	40.37 N	14.58 E
Battle	42	50.55 N	0.29 E
Battle ≃	176	52.43 N	108.15 W
Battle Creek, Ia., U.S.	198	42.18 N	95.35 W
Battle Creek, Mi., U.S.	216	42.19 N	85.10 W
Battle Creek, Ne., U.S.	198	41.59 N	97.35 W
Battle Creek ≃, N.A.	202	48.36 N	109.11 W
Battle Creek ≃, Ca., U.S.	204	40.21 N	122.11 W
Battle Creek ≃, Id., U.S.	202	42.14 N	116.32 W
Battle Creek ≃, Mi., U.S.	216	42.19 N	85.12 W
Battle Creek ≃, Tx., U.S.	196	32.50 N	98.58 W
Battle Creek, North Fork ≃	204	40.26 N	122.00 W
Battle Creek, South Fork ≃	204	40.26 N	122.00 W
Battlefields	154	18.31 S	29.52 E
Battle Green ⊥	283	42.27 N	71.14 W
Battle Ground, In., U.S.	216	40.30 N	86.50 W
Battle Ground, Wa., U.S.	224	45.46 N	122.31 W
Battle Harbour	176	52.16 N	55.35 W
Battle Lake	198	46.16 N	95.42 W
Battlement Mesa ∧	200	39.20 N	108.00 W
Battlemount	158	26.57 S	23.46 E
Battle Mountain	204	40.38 N	116.56 W
Battle Mountain ∧	200	41.02 N	107.16 W
Battlesbridge	260	51.37 N	0.34 E
Battonya	30	46.17 N	21.01 E
Battuello	266b	45.27 N	8.56 E
Batu	115a	7.52 S	112.31 E
Batu ∧	144	6.55 N	39.46 E
Batu, Bukit ∧	112	2.16 N	113.43 E
Batu, Kepulauan II	110	0.18 S	98.28 E
Batuan	116	12.25 N	123.47 E
Batu Arang	114	3.19 N	101.28 E
Batuata, Pulau I	112	6.12 S	122.42 E
Batuata, Tanjung ›	115b	9.37 S	120.29 E
Batu-Batu	112	4.09 S	119.52 E
Batu Berinchang, Gunong ∧	114	4.30 N	101.24 E
Batubetumpang	112	2.53 S	106.09 E
Batubrok, Bukit ∧	112	1.10 N	114.36 E
Batu Caves	114	3.14 N	101.40 E
Batudaka, Pulau I	112	0.28 S	121.48 E
Batu Enam	114	2.35 N	102.43 E
Batu Gajah	114	4.28 N	101.03 E
Batui	112	1.17 S	122.33 E
Batui, Pegunungan ⋏	112	1.15 S	122.10 E
Batuidu	112	10.38 S	123.25 E
Batukau, Bukit ∧	115b	8.20 S	115.05 E
Batukelau	112	0.48 N	115.01 E
Batu Laut	114	2.41 N	101.31 E
Batulicin	112	3.27 S	116.00 E
Batumata Point ›	164	10.17 S	148.57 E
Batumi	84	41.38 N	41.38 E
Batumundan	114	1.17 N	98.50 E
Batu Pahat (Bandar Penggaram)	114	1.51 N	102.56 E
Batupanjang	114	1.43 N	101.31 E
Batu Puteh, Gunong ∧	114	4.13 N	101.27 E
Batuputih	112	1.24 N	118.29 E
Baturaja	112	4.08 S	104.10 E
Batu Rakit	114	5.27 N	103.03 E
Baturetno	115a	7.59 S	110.56 E
Baturin	78	51.21 N	32.51 E
Baturino, Ross.	86	57.48 N	85.12 E
Baturino, Ross.	265b	55.35 N	37.31 E
Baturinskaja	78	45.47 N	39.22 E
Baturité	250	4.20 S	38.53 W
Baturotok	115b	8.42 S	117.10 E
Baturusa	112	2.02 S	106.07 E
Batusangkar	112	0.27 S	100.35 E
Batutinggi	112	1.55 S	113.19 E
Bat Yam	132	32.01 N	34.45 E
Batyrevo	80	55.04 N	47.38 E
Batyr-Mala, ozero ⊜	80	47.35 N	44.45 E
Bau	112	1.25 N	110.08 E
Baú ≃	250	7.26 S	54.47 W
Bauang	116	16.31 N	120.20 E
Baubašata, gory ⋏	85	41.20 N	72.45 E
Baubau	112	5.28 S	122.38 E
Bauchi	150	10.19 N	9.50 E
Bauchi □[3]	146	10.30 N	10.15 E
Baucina	70	37.55 N	13.32 E
Baud	32	47.52 N	3.01 W
Bauda	120	20.50 N	84.19 E
Baudette	190	48.42 N	94.35 W
Baudó ≃	246	4.57 N	77.22 W
Baudouin Stadium ♠	273b	4.20 S	15.20 E
Baudour	50	50.29 N	3.49 E
Bauernschaft	263	51.34 N	6.33 E
Bauerstown	279b	40.30 N	79.59 W
Baugo Creek ≃	216	41.40 N	86.04 W
Baukau	112	8.27 S	126.27 E
BAuland ◆[1]	56	49.31 N	9.29 E
Bauld, Cape ›	186	51.38 N	55.25 W
Baulkham Hills	274a	33.46 S	151.00 E
Baulmes	58	46.48 N	6.32 E
Bauma	58	47.23 N	8.53 E
Baumberg	263	51.07 N	6.54 E
Baume ≃	62	44.26 N	4.20 E
Baume-les-Dames	58	47.21 N	6.22 E
Baumholder	56	49.37 N	7.20 E
Baumschulenweg ◆[8]	264a	52.28 N	13.29 E
Baun	112	10.18 S	123.43 E
Baunach	56	49.59 N	10.50 E
Baunach ≃	56	49.59 N	10.51 E
Baunatal	56	51.16 N	9.25 E
Baunei	71	40.02 N	9.40 E
Baunt	88	55.16 N	113.08 E
Baunt, ozero ⊜	88	55.12 N	113.00 E
Bāuphal	126	22.25 N	90.33 E
Baure	150	12.50 N	8.45 E
Baures	248	13.35 S	63.35 W
Baures ≃	248	12.30 S	64.18 W
Bauru	255	22.19 S	49.04 W
Baús	255	18.19 S	53.10 W
Bausendorf	56	50.01 N	6.59 E
Bausenhagen	263	51.31 N	7.48 E
Bauska	76	56.24 N	24.14 E
Bauta	240p	22.59 N	82.33 W
Bauta □[7]	286b	22.59 N	82.33 W
Bautino	84	44.33 N	50.15 E
Bautzen	54	51.11 N	14.26 E
Bauxite	194	34.33 N	92.31 W
Bauya	150	8.11 N	12.34 W
Bavans	58	47.29 N	6.44 E
Bavari	62	44.26 N	9.01 E
Bavaria → Bayern □[3]	30	49.00 N	11.30 E
Bavarian Alps → Bayerische Alpen ⋏	64	47.30 N	11.00 E
Bavay	50	50.18 N	3.47 E
Båven ⊜	40	59.01 N	16.56 E
Baveno	58	45.55 N	8.30 E
Bavilliers	58	47.37 N	6.50 E
Bavispe	232	30.24 N	108.50 W
Bavispe ≃	232	29.15 N	109.11 W
Bavleny	80	56.24 N	39.34 E
Bavly	80	54.25 N	53.17 E
Bavnhöj ∧[2]	41	55.55 N	10.07 E
Bavtugaj	84	43.11 N	46.49 E
Baw	110	23.19 N	95.50 E
Bāwal	124	28.05 N	76.35 E
Bawal, Pulau I	112	2.44 S	110.06 E
Bāwāli	272b	22.25 N	88.12 E
Bawang	115a	7.06 S	109.55 E
Baw Baw, Mount ∧	169	37.50 S	146.17 E
Baw Baw National Park ♠	169	37.55 S	146.22 E
Baw Beese Lake ⊜	216	41.54 N	84.36 W
Bawdeswell	42	52.45 N	1.01 E
Bawdwin	110	23.06 N	97.18 E
Bawean, Pulau I	115a	5.46 S	112.40 E
Baweigang	106	31.57 N	120.14 E
Bawku	150	11.05 N	0.14 W
Bawlake	110	19.11 N	97.21 E
Bawmi	110	17.19 N	94.35 E
Bawria	126	22.29 N	88.10 E
Bawtry	44	53.26 N	1.01 W
Baxdo	144	5.46 N	47.15 E
Baxenden	262	53.44 N	2.20 W
Baxian, Zhg.	105	39.06 N	116.23 E
Baxian (Yudongxi), Zhg.	107	29.23 N	106.32 E
Baxley	192	31.46 N	82.20 W
Baxter, Ia., U.S.	190	41.49 N	93.09 W
Baxter, Mn., U.S.	190	46.20 N	94.17 W
Baxter, Tn., U.S.	194	36.09 N	85.38 W
Baxter Estates	276	40.50 N	73.42 W
Baxter Springs	198	37.02 N	94.44 W
Baxter State Park ♠	188	46.00 N	68.58 W
Baxterville	194	31.05 N	89.35 W
Bay	194	35.44 N	90.33 W
Bay □[4]	144	2.30 N	43.30 E
Bay, Laguna de ⊜	116	14.23 N	121.15 E
Baya, Zaïre	152	4.57 N	19.43 E
Baya, Zaïre	154	11.52 S	27.27 E
Bayāḍah, Wādī al- V	146	26.08 N	18.35 E
Bayāḍ an-Naṣārā	142	29.04 N	31.08 E
Bayag	116	18.16 N	121.02 E
Bayala	158	27.47 S	32.08 E
Bay al-Kabīr, Wādī V	146	31.15 N	15.57 E
Bayambang	116	15.49 N	120.27 E
Bayamo	240p	20.23 N	76.39 W
Bayamo ≃	240p	20.34 N	76.44 W
Bayamón	240m	18.24 N	66.09 W
Bayan, Indon.	115b	8.16 S	116.26 E
Bayan, Zhg.	89	46.05 N	127.24 E
Bāyan, Band-e ⋏	120	34.20 N	65.30 E
Bayāna	124	26.54 N	77.17 E
Bayanbayanan	269f	14.39 N	121.06 E
Bayanchagan	89	47.19 N	124.03 E
Bayang	116	7.48 N	124.12 E
Bayanga	152	2.53 N	16.19 E
Bayange	102	39.19 N	107.31 E
Bayan Har Shan ⋏	102	33.48 N	98.10 E
Bayanheshuomiao	89	48.51 N	119.46 E
Bayanjie	89	49.36 N	124.37 E
Bayanluke	89	50.52 N	119.33 E
Bayannaobao	102	39.44 N	107.40 E
Bayano, Lago ⊜[1]	246	9.10 N	78.40 W
Bayan Obo	102	41.58 N	110.02 E
Bayan Tal	89	43.44 N	123.16 E
Bayard, Ia., U.S.	198	41.51 N	94.33 W
Bayard, Ne., U.S.	198	41.45 N	103.19 W
Bayard, N.M., U.S.	200	32.45 N	108.07 W
Bayard, Oh., U.S.	214	40.46 N	81.04 W
Bayard, W.V., U.S.	188	39.16 N	79.21 W
Bayard, Col)(	62	44.37 N	6.05 E
Bayard Cutting Arboretum State Park ♠	276	40.45 N	73.10 W
Bayat, Indon.	112	2.06 S	103.38 E
Bayat, Tür.	130	38.59 N	30.56 E
Bayat, Tür.	130	40.39 N	34.15 E
Bayawan	116	9.22 N	122.48 E
Bayawan ≃	116	9.22 N	122.48 E
Baybay	116	10.41 N	124.48 E
Bayberry	210	43.08 N	76.13 W
Bayble	46	58.12 N	6.13 W
Bayboro	192	35.08 N	76.46 W
Bay Bulls	186	47.19 N	52.49 W
Bayburt	130	40.16 N	40.15 E
Bayburt □[4]	130	40.15 N	40.00 E
Bay Center	224	46.37 N	123.57 W
Bay City, Mi., U.S.	190	43.35 N	83.53 W
Bay City, Or., U.S.	224	45.31 N	123.53 W
Bay City, Tx., U.S.	222	28.58 N	95.58 W
Bay Creek ≃, Il., U.S.	194	37.16 N	88.31 W
Bay Creek ≃, Il., U.S.	219	39.20 N	90.46 W
Bayḍā', Bi'r ∓[4]	142	29.45 N	32.13 E
Bay de Verde	186	48.05 N	52.54 W
Baydhabo (Baidoa)	144	3.07 N	43.39 E
Bay du Nord ≃	186	47.44 N	55.25 W
Baye, Cap ›	175f	20.57 S	165.25 E
Bayel	58	48.12 N	4.47 E
Bayerische Alpen ⋏	64	47.30 N	11.00 E
Bayerisch Eisenstein	60	49.07 N	13.12 E
Bayerischer Wald ⋏	60	49.00 N	12.40 E
Bayerischer Wald, Nationalpark ♠	60	48.56 N	13.28 E
Bayern □[3]	30	49.00 N	11.30 E
Bayeuen	114	4.36 N	97.53 E
Bayeux, Bra.	250	7.08 S	34.56 W
Bayeux, Fr.	32	49.16 N	0.42 W
Bay Farm Island I	282	37.43 N	122.14 W
Bayfield, Co., U.S.	200	37.13 N	107.35 W
Bayfield, Wi., U.S.	190	46.48 N	90.49 W
Bayfield, Île I	186	51.13 N	58.23 W
Bayford	260	51.46 N	0.06 W
'Bayh	132	33.44 N	35.31 E
Bayḥān al-Qaṣād	144	14.48 N	45.43 E
Bay Harbor Islands	220	25.53 N	80.08 W
Bayhead, Scot., U.K.	46	57.33 N	7.24 W
Bay Head, N.J., U.S.	208	40.04 N	74.03 W
Bayiji	98	34.18 N	117.41 E
Bayındır	130	38.13 N	27.40 E
Bayingzi	104	41.28 N	120.46 E
Baykan	130	38.09 N	41.47 E
Baykonur → Bajkonyr	86	47.50 N	66.03 E
Bay Kurt	85	39.58 N	75.33 E
Bay L'Argent	186	47.33 N	54.54 W
Bayley Point ›	164	16.56 S	139.02 E
Baylis	219	39.44 N	90.54 W
Bay Meadows Race Track ♠	282	37.32 N	122.18 W
Bay Minette	194	30.52 N	87.46 W
Baynūnah ◆[1]	128	23.50 N	52.50 E
Bayo	34	43.09 N	8.58 W
Bayombong	116	16.29 N	121.09 E
Bayon	58	48.29 N	6.19 E
Bayona	34	42.07 N	8.51 W
Bayonne, Fr.	32	43.29 N	1.29 W
Bayonne, N.J., U.S.	210	40.40 N	74.06 W
Bayonne ≃	206	46.05 N	73.10 W
Bayonne Bridge ◆[5]	276	40.38 N	74.09 W
Bayons	62	44.20 N	6.10 E
Bayou Bodcau Reservoir ⊜[1]	194	32.45 N	93.30 W
Bayou Cane	194	29.37 N	90.45 W
Bayou D'Arbonne Lake ⊜[1]	194	32.45 N	92.25 W
Bayou La Batre	194	30.24 N	88.14 W
Bayovar	248	5.50 S	81.03 W
Bay Park	276	40.38 N	73.40 W
Bayport, Fl., U.S.	220	28.33 N	82.39 W
Bay Port, Mi., U.S.	190	43.50 N	83.22 W
Bayport, Mn., U.S.	190	45.01 N	92.46 W
Bayport, N.Y., U.S.	210	40.44 N	73.03 W
Bayramiç	130	39.48 N	26.37 E
Bayramören	130	40.57 N	33.12 E
Bayreuth	60	49.57 N	11.35 E
Bay Ridge	208	38.56 N	76.27 W
Bay Ridge ◆[8]	276	40.37 N	74.02 W
Bay Ridge Channel ʉ	276	40.39 N	74.02 W
Bayrischzell	64	47.40 N	12.00 E
Bay Roberts	186	47.36 N	53.16 W
Bayrūt (Beirut)	130	33.53 N	35.30 E
Bayrūt □[4]	132	33.56 N	35.30 E
Bays, Lake of ⊜	212	45.15 N	79.04 W
Bay Saint Louis	194	30.18 N	89.19 W
Bay Shore	210	40.43 N	73.14 W
Bayshore Gardens	220	27.25 N	82.35 W
Bayside, On., Can.	212	44.07 N	77.30 W
Bayside, Ma., U.S.	283	42.18 N	70.53 W
Bayside, Wi., U.S.	216	43.10 N	87.54 W
Bayside ◆[8]	276	40.46 N	73.46 W
Bay Springs	194	31.58 N	89.17 W
Bay Springs Lake ⊜[1]	194	34.35 N	88.20 W
Bayston Hill	42	52.40 N	2.45 W
Bayswater	274b	37.51 S	145.16 E
Bayswater North	274b	37.49 S	145.17 E
Bayt ad-Dīn	132	33.42 N	35.35 E
Bayt al-Faqīh	144	14.32 N	43.20 E
Bayt Ḥānūn	132	31.32 N	34.33 E
Bayt Jālā	132	31.43 N	35.11 E
Bayt Jinn	132	33.19 N	35.53 E
Bayt Laḥm (Bethlehem)	132	31.43 N	35.12 E
Bayt Mirī	132	33.52 N	35.36 E
Baytown	222	29.44 N	94.58 W
Bayt Sāḥūr	132	31.42 N	35.13 E
Bayt Sīrā	132	31.53 N	35.03 E
Bayunglencir	112	2.03 S	103.41 E
Bayview, Austl.	274a	33.40 S	151.18 E
Bay View, N.Z.	172	39.25 S	176.53 E
Bay View, N.Y., U.S.	210	42.47 N	78.51 W
Bay View, Oh., U.S.	214	41.28 N	82.50 W
Bayview ◆[8]	282	37.44 N	122.23 W
Bay Village	214	41.29 N	81.55 W
Bayville, N.J., U.S.	208	39.54 N	74.09 W
Bayville, N.Y., U.S.	210	40.54 N	73.33 W
Baywater	168a	31.55 S	115.56 E
Baywood Park	226	35.20 N	120.50 W
Bayyāḍah, Ra's al- ›	132	33.10 N	35.10 E
Bayyā'iyah al-Kabīrah	130	35.42 N	37.09 E
Bayyūḍah ∓[4]	140	17.32 N	32.07 E
Bayzo	150	13.52 N	4.45 E
Baza	34	37.29 N	2.46 W
Baza, Sierra de ⋏	34	37.15 N	2.45 W
Bazai	100	24.32 N	114.10 E
Bazainville	261	48.48 N	1.40 E
Bazalija	78	49.43 N	26.27 E
Bazar	88	53.58 N	116.05 E
Bazarčaj	84	39.40 N	45.48 E
Bazard'uz'u, gora ∧	84	41.13 N	47.51 E
Bāzār-e Panjvā'ī	120	31.32 N	65.28 E
Bazargic → Dobrič	38	43.34 N	27.50 E
Bazar-Kurgan	85	41.02 N	72.45 E
Bazarnyje Mataki	80	54.56 N	49.56 E
Bazarnyj Karabulak	80	52.16 N	46.25 E
Bazarnyj Syzgan	80	53.45 N	46.46 E
Bazarovo	82	54.47 N	38.10 E
Bazaršolan	80	49.04 N	51.56 E
Bazartobe	80	49.23 N	51.50 E
Bazaruto, Ilha do I	156	21.40 S	35.28 E
Bazas	32	44.26 N	0.13 W
Bazavluk ≃	78	47.34 N	34.04 E
Bazdār	120	26.21 N	65.03 E
Bazeilles	56	49.40 N	4.59 E
Bazemont	261	48.56 N	1.52 E
Bazetta	214	41.20 N	80.47 W
Bazhong	102	31.51 N	106.39 E
Bazi	100	24.46 N	113.10 E
Baziège	32	43.27 N	1.37 E
Bažigan	84	44.33 N	45.41 E
Bazine	198	38.26 N	99.41 W
Baziqiao	106	32.07 N	119.52 E
Bazkovskaja	80	49.36 N	41.43 E
Bazmān	128	27.49 N	60.12 E
Bazmān, Kūh-e ∧	128	28.04 N	60.00 E
Bazoches-les-Gallerandes	50	48.10 N	2.03 E
Bazoches-sur-Hoëne	50	48.33 N	0.28 E
Bazoj	86	55.45 N	83.22 E
Bazzano	64	44.30 N	11.05 E
Be ≃	110	11.06 N	106.58 E
Be, Nosy I	157b	13.20 S	48.15 E
Beach, Il., U.S.	216	42.26 N	87.50 W
Beach, N.D., U.S.	198	46.55 N	104.00 W
Beach, Tx., U.S.	222	30.20 N	95.29 W
Beach Channel ʉ	276	40.35 N	73.50 W
Beach City	214	40.39 N	81.34 W
Beach City Lake ⊜[1]	214	40.41 N	81.36 W
Beach Glen	276	40.56 N	74.29 W
Beach Haven, N.J., U.S.	208	39.33 N	74.14 W
Beach Haven, Pa., U.S.	210	41.04 N	76.11 W
Beach Haven Terrace	208	39.35 N	74.13 W
Beach Lake	210	41.36 N	75.09 W
Beach Lake ⊜	281	42.33 N	83.43 W
Beach Pond State Park ♠	207	41.35 N	71.45 W
Beachport	166	37.30 S	140.01 E
Beachville	212	43.05 N	80.49 W
Beachwood, N.J., U.S.	208	39.56 N	74.11 W
Beachwood, Oh., U.S.	214	41.27 N	81.30 W
Beachy Head ›	42	50.44 N	0.16 E
Beacon, Austl.	162	30.26 S	117.51 E
Beacon, N.Y., U.S.	210	41.30 N	73.58 W
Beacon Falls	207	41.26 N	73.03 W
Beacon Heights	284c	38.57 N	76.54 W
Beacon Hill, Austl.	274a	33.45 S	151.15 E
Beacon Hill, Wa., U.S.	224	46.08 N	122.57 W
Beacon Hill ∧[2], H.K.	271d	22.21 N	114.09 E
Beacon Hill ∧[2], Wales, U.K.	42	52.23 N	3.12 W
Beacon Rock State Park ♠	224	45.38 N	122.03 W
Beaconsfield, Austl.	166	41.12 S	146.48 E
Beaconsfield, Austl.	274b	38.03 S	145.22 E
Beaconsfield, P.Q., Can.	206	45.26 N	73.50 W
Beaconsfield, Eng., U.K.	42	51.37 N	0.39 W
Beaconsfield □[8]	260	51.34 N	0.35 W
Beadle Lake	216	42.18 N	85.12 W
Beagh, Slieve ∧[2]	48	54.21 N	7.12 W
Beagle, Canal ʉ	254	54.53 S	68.10 W
Beagle Bay	162	16.58 S	122.40 E
Beagle Gulf ⊂	164	12.00 S	130.20 E
Beagle Reef ✦[2]	160	15.20 S	123.29 E
Bealanana	157b	14.33 S	48.44 E
Beale, Cape ›	182	48.44 N	125.20 W
Beale, Lake ⊜	122	19.45 N	73.44 E
Beale Air Force Base ■	226	39.08 N	121.20 W
Bealiba	169	36.48 S	143.33 E
Bealiba, Mount ∧[2]	169	36.49 S	143.38 E
Beallsville	214	40.04 N	80.01 W
Beals Creek ≃	196	32.10 N	100.51 W
Beam ≃	260	51.31 N	0.10 E
Beaminster	42	50.49 N	2.45 W
Bean	260	51.25 N	0.17 E
Beanblossom Creek ≃	194	39.20 N	86.39 W
Bean Creek ≃	216	41.35 N	84.19 W
Bear ≃, Sk., Can.	184	54.33 N	103.58 W
Bear ≃, U.S.	200	41.30 N	112.08 W
Bear ≃, Ca., U.S.	226	38.57 N	121.35 W
Bear, Mount ∧	180	61.17 N	141.09 W
Beara	164	7.30 S	144.50 E
Bear Bay ⊂	176	75.47 N	87.00 W
Bear Branch	218	38.55 N	85.05 W
Bear Brook ≃, On., Can.	212	45.25 N	75.10 W
Bear Brook ≃, N.J., U.S.	276	41.02 N	74.03 W
Bear Brook State Park ♠	188	43.05 N	71.26 W
Bear Butte ∧	198	44.28 N	103.26 W
Bear Canyon V	280	34.14 N	118.07 W
Bear Cove	182	50.44 N	127.27 W
Bear Creek	210	41.11 N	75.45 W
Bear Creek ≃, On., Can.	214	42.44 N	82.23 W
Bear Creek ≃, U.S.	194	34.46 N	88.05 W
Bear Creek ≃, U.S.	196	37.45 N	101.23 W
Bear Creek ≃, U.S.	216	41.17 N	83.57 W
Bear Creek ≃, Al., U.S.	194	33.11 N	88.05 W
Bear Creek ≃, Ca., U.S.	226	38.56 N	122.20 W
Bear Creek ≃, Ca., U.S.	226	38.02 N	121.18 W
Bear Creek ≃, Ca., U.S.	226	37.17 N	120.50 W
Bear Creek ≃, Ca., U.S.	228	34.10 N	117.01 W
Bear Creek ≃, Ca., U.S.	280	34.14 N	117.53 W
Bear Creek ≃, Co., U.S.	200	39.40 N	105.00 W
Bear Creek ≃, Il., U.S.	219	39.33 N	89.23 W
Bear Creek ≃, Il., U.S.	219	40.07 N	91.29 W
Bear Creek ≃, Md., U.S.	284b	39.13 N	76.30 W
Bear Creek ≃, Mo., U.S.	219	39.03 N	91.14 W
Bear Creek ≃, N.D., U.S.	198	46.10 N	98.06 W
Bear Creek ≃, Oh., U.S.	218	39.39 N	84.17 W
Bear Creek ≃, Or., U.S.	202	44.06 N	120.46 W
Bear Creek ≃, Or., U.S.	202	42.26 N	122.58 W
Bear Creek ≃, Pa., U.S.	214	41.23 N	78.50 W
Bear Creek ≃, Wy., U.S.	198	41.41 N	104.13 W
Bear Creek, South Fork ≃	219	40.09 N	91.18 W
Bear Creek, West Fork ≃	280	34.16 N	117.53 W
Bearden	194	33.43 N	92.36 W
Beardmore	176	49.36 N	87.57 W
Beardmore Glacier ⊓	9	83.45 S	171.00 E
Beardsley Lake ⊜[1]	226	38.13 N	120.03 W
Beardstown, Il., U.S.	219	40.01 N	90.25 W
Beardstown, In., U.S.	216	41.08 N	86.36 W
Beardy and Okemasis Indian Reserves ◆[4]	184	52.48 N	106.20 W
Bearfort Mountain ∧	276	41.09 N	74.23 W
Bear Head Creek ≃	194	30.18 N	93.35 W
Bear Head Lake ⊜	184	55.33 N	96.10 W
Bear Head Lake State Park ♠	190	47.49 N	92.04 W
Bearhead Mountain ∧	224	47.02 N	121.53 W
Bear Hill ∧[2], Ct., U.S.	207	41.39 N	73.24 W
Bear Hill ∧[2], N.Y., U.S.	210	41.18 N	74.00 W
Bear-in-the-Lodge Creek ≃	198	43.41 N	101.50 W
Bear Island I, Ant.	9	74.30 S	110.45 W
Bear Island I, Mb., Can.	184	54.53 N	98.04 W
Bear Island I, Ire.	48	51.40 N	9.48 W
Bear Island → Bjørnøya I, Sval.	12	74.25 N	19.00 E
Bear Island I, Va., U.S.	284c	38.59 N	77.14 W
Bear Lake, B.C., Can.	182	56.11 N	126.51 W
Bear Lake, Pa., U.S.	214	42.00 N	79.30 W
Bear Lake ⊜, Ab., Can.	182	55.16 N	119.00 W
Bear Lake ⊜, B.C., Can.	182	56.06 N	126.45 W
Bear Lake ⊜, Mb., Can.	184	55.08 N	96.00 W
Bear Lake ⊜, On., Can.	212	45.26 N	79.35 W
Bear Lake ⊜, U.S.	200	42.00 N	111.20 W
Bear Mountain ∧, Ca., U.S.	228	35.12 N	118.38 W
Bear Mountain ∧, Ky., U.S.	192	37.32 N	84.16 W
Bear Mountain ∧, Or., U.S.	202	43.51 N	122.53 W
Bear Mountain ∧[2]	210	41.18 N	74.01 W
Bear Mountain State Park ♠	210	41.17 N	74.00 W
Béarn □[9]	32	43.20 N	0.45 W
Bear Pond ⊜	276	40.58 N	74.40 W
Bear River	186	44.34 N	65.39 W
Bear River Range ⋏	200	41.50 N	111.30 W
Bear Run ≃	279b	40.33 N	80.04 W
Bearsden	46	55.56 N	4.20 W
Bears Paw Mountains ⋏	202	48.15 N	109.30 W
Bearstead	260	51.16 N	0.35 E
Bearsville	210	42.02 N	74.09 W
Bear Swamp ≃	285	39.54 N	74.47 W
Bear Swamp ≡	285	39.53 N	74.45 W
Bear Swamp Brook ≃	276	41.04 N	74.13 W
Bear Swamp Lake ⊜	276	41.06 N	74.13 W
Beartooth Mountains ⋏	202	45.00 N	109.30 W
Beartooth Pass)(	202	44.58 N	109.28 W
Bear Town	194	31.13 N	90.27 W
Beās	123	31.31 N	75.17 E
Beās ≃	123	31.10 N	74.59 E
Beasain	34	43.03 N	2.11 W
Beas de Segura	34	38.15 N	2.53 W
Beasley	222	29.30 N	95.55 W
Beasley Bay ⊂	208	37.51 N	75.44 W
Beason	219	40.09 N	89.12 W
Beata, Cabo ›	238	17.36 N	71.25 W
Beata, Isla I	238	17.35 N	71.31 W
Beatenberg	58	46.42 N	7.48 E
Beato ◆[8]	266c	38.44 N	9.06 W
Beaton	182	50.44 N	117.44 W
Beatrice, Al., U.S.	194	31.44 N	87.12 W
Beatrice, Ne., U.S.	198	40.16 N	96.44 W
Beatrice, Zimb.	154	18.15 S	30.55 E
Beatrice, Cape ›	164	14.15 S	136.59 E
Beattie	198	39.51 N	96.25 W
Beattock	44	55.18 N	3.28 W
Beatton ≃	176	56.10 N	120.25 W
Beatty, Nv., U.S.	204	36.54 N	116.45 W
Beatty, Oh., U.S.	218	39.53 N	83.50 W
Beatty Saugeen ≃	212	44.08 N	81.02 W
Beattyville	192	37.34 N	83.42 W
Beaubru	56	49.46 N	5.05 E
Beaucaire	62	43.48 N	4.38 E
Beauce ◆[1]	50	48.22 N	1.50 E
Beauceville	188	46.12 N	70.46 W
Beauchamp	261	49.01 N	2.12 E
Beauchamp Roding	260	51.46 N	0.18 E
Beauchêne, Lac ⊜	190	46.39 N	78.55 W
Beauchêne Island I	254	52.55 S	59.12 W
Beaucoup Creek ≃, Il., U.S.	194	37.47 N	89.17 W
Beaucoup Creek ≃, Il., U.S.	219	38.13 N	89.20 W
Beaucourt	58	47.29 N	6.55 E
Beaudesert	171a	27.59 S	153.00 E
Beaudette ≃	206	45.12 N	74.19 W
Beaudry, Lac ⊜	190	47.44 N	78.55 W
Beauduc, Pointe de ›	62	43.22 N	4.34 E
Beaufays	56	50.34 N	5.38 E
Beaufort, Austl.	169	37.26 S	143.23 E
Beaufort, Fr.	58	46.34 N	5.26 E
Beaufort, Fr.	62	45.43 N	6.35 E
Beaufort, Lux.	56	49.51 N	6.18 E
Beaufort, Malay.	112	5.20 N	115.45 E
Beaufort, Mo., U.S.	219	38.26 N	91.12 W
Beaufort, N.C., U.S.	192	34.43 N	76.39 W
Beaufort, S.C., U.S.	192	32.25 N	80.40 W
Beaufort, Cape ›	162	34.26 S	115.32 E
Beaufort, Massif de ⋏[1]	62	45.44 N	6.35 E
Beaufort Castle → Qal'at ash-Shaqīf ⊥	132	33.19 N	35.32 E
Beaufort Island I	271d	22.11 N	114.15 E
Beaufort Marine Corps Air Station ■	192	32.30 N	80.44 W
Beaufort Sea ∓[2]	16	73.00 N	140.00 W
Beaufort West	158	32.18 S	22.36 E
Beaugency	50	47.47 N	1.38 E
Beauharnois	206	45.19 N	73.52 W
Beauharnois □[6]	206	45.15 N	74.00 W
Beauharnois, Barrage de ◆[6]	275a	45.19 N	73.55 W
Beauharnois, Canal de ≊	206	45.19 N	73.54 W
Beaujeu	58	46.09 N	4.36 E
Beaujolais □[9]	32	46.05 N	4.10 E
Beaulieu	42	50.49 N	1.27 W
Beaulieu-lès-Loches	50	47.07 N	1.01 E
Beaulieu-sur-Mer	62	43.42 N	7.20 E
Beauly	46	57.29 N	4.29 W
Beauly ≃	46	57.28 N	4.28 W
Beauly Firth ⊂[1]	46	57.30 N	4.23 W
Beaumaris, Austl.	274b	37.59 S	145.02 E
Beaumaris, Wales, U.K.	44	53.16 N	4.05 W
Beaumaris Bay ⊂	274b	38.00 S	145.03 E
Beaumes-de-Venise	62	44.07 N	5.02 E
Beaumesnil	50	49.01 N	0.43 E
Beaumetz-lès-Loges	50	50.14 N	2.39 E
Beaumont, Bel.	50	50.14 N	4.14 E
Beaumont, Nf., Can.	186	49.37 N	55.41 W
Beaumont, Fr.	32	49.40 N	1.51 W
Beaumont, N.Z.	172	45.49 S	169.32 E
Beaumont, Ca., U.S.	228	33.55 N	116.58 W
Beaumont, Ms., U.S.	194	31.10 N	88.55 W
Beaumont, Tx., U.S.	194	30.05 N	94.06 W
Beaumont-du-Gâtinais	50	48.08 N	2.29 E
Beaumont-en-Argonne	56	49.32 N	5.03 E
Beaumont Hill ∧[2]	166	31.33 S	145.13 E
Beaumont-la-Ronce	50	47.34 N	0.40 E
Beaumont-le-Roger	50	49.05 N	0.47 E
Beaumont Place	222	29.50 N	95.14 W
Beaumont-sur-Oise	50	49.08 N	2.17 E
Beaumont-sur-Sarthe	50	48.13 N	0.08 E
Beaune	58	47.02 N	4.50 E
Beaune-la-Rolande	50	48.04 N	2.26 E
Beauport	206	46.52 N	71.11 W
Beaupré	186	47.03 N	70.54 W
Beaupréau	32	47.12 N	1.00 W
Beaupre Island I	212	44.26 N	76.19 W
Beaupré Lake ⊜	184	54.30 N	107.10 W
Beauraing	56	50.07 N	4.58 E
Beaurepaire	62	45.20 N	5.03 E
Beaurepaire-en-Bresse	58	46.40 N	5.23 E
Beaurières	62	44.35 N	5.33 E
Beaurivage	206	46.25 N	71.14 W
Beaurivage ≃	206	46.42 N	71.16 W
Beauséjour, Mb., Can.	184	50.04 N	96.33 W
Beauséjour, Guad.	241o	16.18 N	61.04 W
Beausoleil	62	43.45 N	7.26 E
Beausoleil Island I	212	44.51 N	79.52 W
Beautor	50	49.39 N	3.20 E
Beauvais, Fr.	50	49.26 N	2.05 E
Beauvais, Fr.	261	48.32 N	2.03 E
Beauvais Creek ≃	202	45.29 N	107.45 W
Beauvais-Tillé, Aéroport ⊠	50	49.28 N	2.07 E
Beauval, Sk., Can.	184	55.09 N	107.37 W
Beauval, Fr.	50	50.06 N	2.20 E
Beauvezer	62	44.09 N	6.36 E
Beauville	32	44.17 N	0.52 E
Beauvoir	261	48.39 N	2.52 E
Beauvoir-sur-Mer	32	46.55 N	2.02 W
Beauvoir-sur-Niort	32	46.11 N	0.28 W
Beaux Arts	224	47.35 N	122.11 W
Beaver, Ak., U.S.	180	66.22 N	147.24 W
Beaver, Ok., U.S.	196	36.48 N	100.31 W
Beaver, Or., U.S.	224	45.16 N	123.49 W
Beaver, Pa., U.S.	214	40.41 N	80.18 W
Beaver, Ut., U.S.	200	38.16 N	112.38 W
Beaver, Wa., U.S.	224	48.03 N	124.19 W
Beaver, W.V., U.S.	192	37.44 N	81.08 W
Beaver □[6]	214	40.40 N	80.25 W
Beaver ≃, Can.	176	59.43 N	124.16 W
Beaver ≃, Can.	184	55.25 N	107.45 W
Beaver ≃, On., Can.	212	44.34 N	80.27 W
Beaver ≃, U.S.	196	36.35 N	99.30 W
Beaver ≃, N.Y., U.S.	188	43.54 N	75.30 W
Beaver ≃, Pa., U.S.	214	40.40 N	80.18 W
Beaver ≃, Ut., U.S.	200	39.10 N	112.57 W
Beaver Brook	210	40.55 N	75.59 W
Beaver Brook ≃, U.S.	207	42.40 N	71.19 W
Beaver Brook ≃, Ma., U.S.	283	42.03 N	70.58 W
Beaver Brook ≃, Ma., U.S.	283	42.36 N	71.21 W
Beaver Brook ≃, Ma., U.S.	283	42.23 N	71.14 W
Beaver Brook ≃, N.J., U.S.	276	40.54 N	74.30 W
Beaver Brook ≃, N.J., U.S.	276	40.58 N	74.35 W
Beaver City	198	40.08 N	99.49 W
Beaver Creek, Yk., Can.	180	62.22 N	140.52 W
Beavercreek, Oh., U.S.	218	39.43 N	84.03 W
Beavercreek, Or., U.S.	224	45.17 N	122.32 W
Beaver Creek ≃, On., Can.	212	44.30 N	77.42 W
Beaver Creek ≃, On., Can.	212	44.44 N	76.58 W
Beaver Creek ≃, On., Can.	275b	43.51 N	79.20 W
Beaver Creek ≃, On., Can.	284a	42.58 N	79.01 W
Beaver Creek ≃, U.S.	198	47.20 N	103.39 W
Beaver Creek ≃, U.S.	198	40.04 N	99.20 W
Beaver Creek ≃, U.S.	198	43.25 N	103.59 W
Beaver Creek ≃, U.S.	216	40.58 N	87.49 W
Beaver Creek ≃, Ak., U.S.	180	66.15 N	147.32 W
Beaver Creek ≃, Ca., U.S.	226	38.12 N	120.19 W
Beaver Creek ≃, Co., U.S.	198	40.20 N	103.33 W
Beaver Creek ≃, Co., U.S.	198	38.22 N	104.58 W
Beaver Creek ≃, Il., U.S.	216	42.16 N	88.56 W
Beaver Creek ≃, Il., U.S.	219	38.33 N	89.30 W

Symbols in the index entries represent the broad categories identified in the key at the right. Symbols with superior numbers (⋏[1]) identify subcategories (see complete key on page *I · 1).*

Symbole im Register stellen die rechts im Schlüssel erklärten Kategorien dar. Symbole mit hochgestellten Ziffern (⋏[1]) bezeichnen Unterabteilungen einer Kategorie (vgl. vollständiger Schlüssel auf Seite *I · 1).*

Los símbolos incluídos en el texto del índice representan las grandes categorías identificadas con la clave a la derecha. Los símbolos con numeros en su parte superior (⋏[1]) identifican las subcategorías (véase la clave completa en la página *I · 1).*

Les symboles de l'index représentent les catégories indiquées dans la légende à droite. Les symboles suivis d'un indice (⋏[1]) représentent des sous-catégories (voir légende complète à la page *I · 1).*

Os símbolos incluídos no texto do índice representam as grandes categorias identificadas com a chave à direita. Os símbolos com números em sua parte superior (⋏[1]) identificam as subcategorias (veja-se a chave completa à página *I · 1).*

∧ Mountain	Berg	Montaña	Montagne	Montanha
⋏ Mountains	Gebirge	Montañas	Montagnes	Montanhas
)(Pass	Paß	Paso	Col	Passo
V Valley, Canyon	Tal, Cañon	Valle, Cañón	Vallée, Canyon	Vale, Canhão
≃ Plain	Ebene	Llano	Plaine	Planície
› Cape	Kap	Cabo	Cap	Cabo
I Island	Insel	Isla	Île	Ilha
II Islands	Inseln	Islas	Îles	Ilhas
⊥ Other Topographic Features	Andere Topographische Objekte	Otros Elementos Topográficos	Autres données topographiques	Outros acidentes topográficos

ESPAÑOL Nombre	Página	Lat.	Long. W=Oeste	FRANÇAIS Nom	Page	Lat.	Long. W=Ouest	PORTUGUÊS Nome	Página	Lat.	Long. W=Oeste

ESPAÑOL

Nombre	Página	Lat.	Long. W=Oeste
Beaver Creek ≃, Ky., U.S.	218	38.31 N	84.11 W
Beaver Creek ≃, Md., U.S.	208	39.32 N	77.42 W
Beaver Creek ≃, Mo., U.S.	194	36.38 N	93.02 W
Beaver Creek ≃, Mt., U.S.	202	48.29 N	107.24 W
Beaver Creek ≃, Ne., U.S.	198	40.42 N	97.20 W
Beaver Creek ≃, Ne., U.S.	198	41.26 N	97.42 W
Beaver Creek ≃, N.J., U.S.	285	39.45 N	75.23 W
Beaver Creek ≃, N.Y., U.S.	212	44.36 N	75.22 W
Beaver Creek ≃, N.D., U.S.	198	46.15 N	100.29 W
Beaver Creek ≃, Oh., U.S.	216	41.25 N	83.51 W
Beaver Creek ≃, Oh., U.S.	216	40.34 N	84.45 W
Beaver Creek ≃, Oh., U.S.	218	39.57 N	93.46 W
Beaver Creek ≃, Ok., U.S.	196	34.00 N	97.57 W
Beaver Creek ≃, Or., U.S.	224	44.56 N	121.22 W
Beaver Creek ≃, Pa., U.S.	285	40.00 N	75.42 W
Beaver Creek ≃, Tx., U.S.	196	33.53 N	98.49 W
Beaver Creek ≃, Wy., U.S.	202	42.58 N	108.26 W
Beaver Creek State Park ↟	214	40.44 N	80.35 W
Beaver Crossing	198	40.46 N	97.16 W
Beaverdale	214	40.19 N	78.41 W
Beaver Dam, Ky., U.S.	194	37.24 N	86.52 W
Beaverdam, Oh., U.S.	216	40.50 N	83.59 W
Beaver Dam, Wi., U.S.	190	43.27 N	88.50 W
Beaverdam Brook ≃, U.S.	276	40.26 N	74.28 W
Beaverdam Creek ≃, U.S.	284c	38.55 N	76.57 W
Beaverdam Creek ≃, Md., U.S.	284	39.01 N	76.54 W
Beaverdam Creek ≃, N.J., U.S.	285	39.56 N	74.45 W
Beaver Dams Creek ≃	210	42.17 N	76.58 W
Beaver Dam Wash V	200	36.54 N	114.55 W
Beaverdell	182	49.26 N	119.05 W
Beaver Falls, N.Y., U.S.	212	43.53 N	75.25 W
Beaver Falls, Pa., U.S.	214	40.45 N	80.19 W
Beaverhead ≃	202	45.31 N	112.21 W
Beaverhead Mountains ↗	202	45.00 N	113.20 W
Beaverhill Lake ⌀, Ab., Can.	182	53.27 N	112.32 W
Beaver Hill Lake ⌀, Mb., Can.	184	54.16 N	94.53 W
Beaverhouse Lake ⌀	190	48.32 N	92.15 W
Beaver Island I	190	45.40 N	85.31 W
Beaver Island State Park ↟	210	42.58 N	78.57 W
Beaver Kill ≃	210	41.59 N	75.08 W
Beaver Lake ⌀, Ab., Can.	182	54.43 N	111.50 W
Beaver Lake ⌀, On., Can.	212	44.30 N	77.02 W
Beaver Lake ⌀, On., Can.	212	44.44 N	73.17 W
Beaver Lake ⌀, N.J., U.S.	276	41.05 N	74.33 W
Beaver Lake ⌀, N.Y., U.S.	276	40.53 N	73.34 W
Beaver Lake ⌀¹	194	36.20 N	93.55 W
Beaver Lake Indian Reserve ↯⁴	54	54.39 N	111.54 W
Beaverlodge	182	55.13 N	119.25 W
Beaver Meadow	210	42.40 N	75.41 W
Beaver Meadows	210	40.55 N	75.54 W
Beaver Mountains ↗	180	62.54 N	156.53 W
Beaver Run ≃, N.J., U.S.	276	41.11 N	74.35 W
Beaver Run ≃, Pa., U.S.	279b	40.34 N	79.33 W
Beaver Run ≃, Pa., U.S.	285	40.10 N	75.40 W
Beaver Run Reservoir ⌀¹	214	40.29 N	79.33 W
Beavers Bend State Park ↟	194	34.08 N	94.42 W
Beaver Springs	208	40.45 N	77.13 W
Beaver Swamp Brook ≃	276	40.57 N	73.43 W
Beaverton, On., Can.	212	44.26 N	79.09 W
Beaverton, Mi., U.S.	190	43.52 N	84.29 W
Beaverton, Or., U.S.	224	45.29 N	122.48 W
Beaverton ≃	212	44.26 N	79.10 W
Beavertown	210	40.45 N	77.10 W
Beaverville	216	40.57 N	87.39 W
Beáwar	120	26.06 N	74.19 E
Beazley	252	33.45 S	66.39 W
Bebao	157b	17.22 S	44.33 E
Bebar	114	3.07 N	103.27 E
Bebedouro	255	20.56 S	48.28 W
Bebeji	150	11.40 N	8.19 E
Bebek ≃⁶	267b	41.04 N	29.02 E
Bebelevo	82	54.32 N	36.02 E
Bebi	130	36.41 N	35.27 E
Beberibe	250	4.11 S	38.06 W
Bebertal	54	52.15 N	11.18 E
Bebington	44	53.23 N	3.01 W
Béboto	146	8.16 N	16.56 E
Bebra	56	50.58 N	9.47 E
Becal	232	20.27 N	90.02 W
Bécancour	206	46.20 N	72.26 W
Bécancour ≃	206	46.20 N	72.26 W
Beccar ≃⁸	288	34.28 S	58.31 W
Beccaria	214	40.46 N	78.27 W
Beccles	42	52.28 N	1.34 E
Becconsall	262	53.42 N	2.50 W
Bečej	38	45.37 N	20.03 E
Beceni	38	45.23 N	26.48 E
Becerra Creek ≃	196	28.05 N	98.55 W
Becerreá	34	42.51 N	7.10 W
Becerro, Cayos II	236	15.57 N	83.17 W
Béchar	148	31.37 N	2.13 W
Béchar □⁸	148	29.00 N	3.00 W
Becharof Lake ⌀	180	58.00 N	156.30 W
Bechem	150	7.05 N	2.02 W
Becher Bay c	224	48.19 N	123.37 W
Becher Point ›	158	32.23 S	115.44 E
Bechet	38	43.46 N	23.58 E
Bechevin Bay c	180	55.00 N	163.27 W
Bechhofen	56	49.09 N	10.33 E
Bechtelsville	208	40.22 N	75.37 W
Bechuanaland ⬦¹	148	27.10 S	22.10 E
Bechyně	30	49.18 N	14.29 E
Becke	263	33.24 N	9.11 W
Beckemeyer	219	38.36 N	89.26 W
Beckenham ↝⁸	263	51.24 N	0.02 W
Beckenried	58	46.58 N	8.29 E
Becket	210	42.20 N	73.05 W
Beckhausen ↝⁸	263	51.34 N	7.02 E
Beckington	56	51.16 N	2.18 W
Beck Lake	278	42.04 N	87.52 W
Beckler ≃	224	47.43 N	121.21 W
Beckley	188	37.46 N	81.11 W
Beck Pond ⌀	283	42.36 N	70.49 W

FRANÇAIS

Nom	Page	Lat.	Long. W=Ouest
Becks Creek ≃	219	39.08 N	88.56 W
Beckum	52	51.45 N	8.02 E
Beckville	222	32.14 N	94.27 W
Beckwith Island I	212	44.52 N	80.08 W
Becky Peak ⩘	204	39.58 N	114.36 W
Beclean	38	47.11 N	24.10 E
Bečov nad Teplou	54	50.02 N	12.19 E
Becsehely	61	46.27 N	16.48 E
Bedale	44	54.17 N	1.35 W
Bédarieux	32	43.37 N	3.09 E
Bédarrides	62	44.02 N	4.54 E
Bédaya	146	8.55 N	17.52 E
Bedburdyck	56	51.07 N	6.34 E
Bedburg	56	50.59 N	6.35 E
Bedburg-Hau	52	51.45 N	6.10 E
Beddgelert	44	53.01 N	4.06 W
Beddingestrand	41	55.21 N	13.29 E
Beddington ↝⁸	260	51.22 N	0.08 W
Beddome, Mount ⩘	162	25.50 S	134.22 E
Beddouza, Ras ›	148	32.34 N	9.19 W
Bedele	144	8.33 N	36.23 E
Beden Brook ≃	276	40.25 N	74.38 W
Bedeque Bay c	186	46.26 N	63.53 W
Bederesa	52	56.04 N	10.13 E
Bederkesa	52	53.38 N	8.50 E
Bederwanak	144	9.34 N	44.23 E
Bedesa	144	8.54 N	40.47 E
Bedford, P.Q., Can.	206	45.07 N	72.59 W
Bedford, S. Afr.	158	32.41 S	26.05 E
Bedford, Eng., U.K.	42	52.08 N	0.29 W
Bedford, In., U.S.	218	38.51 N	86.29 W
Bedford, Ia., U.S.	198	40.40 N	94.43 W
Bedford, Ky., U.S.	218	38.35 N	85.19 W
Bedford, Ma., U.S.	207	42.29 N	71.16 W
Bedford, Mi., U.S.	216	42.23 N	85.13 W
Bedford, N.Y., U.S.	210	41.12 N	73.39 W
Bedford, Oh., U.S.	214	41.23 N	81.32 W
Bedford, Pa., U.S.	188	40.01 N	78.30 W
Bedford, Tx., U.S.	222	32.50 N	97.08 W
Bedford, Va., U.S.	192	37.20 N	79.31 W
Bedford □⁶	214	40.09 N	78.30 W
Bedford, Cape ›	164	15.14 S	145.21 E
Bedfordale	168a	32.10 S	116.03 E
Bedford Harbour c	162	33.35 S	120.35 E
Bedford Heights	279a	41.25 N	81.31 W
Bedford Hills	210	41.14 N	73.42 W
Bedford Island I	126	21.51 N	88.05 E
Bedford Level ≈	42	52.27 N	0.02 W
Bedford Park	278	41.46 N	87.49 W
Bedford Park ↝⁸	276	40.52 N	73.53 W
Bedfordshire □⁶	42	52.05 N	0.30 W
Bedford-Stuyvesant ↝⁸	276	40.41 N	73.55 W
Bedi, India	120	22.30 N	70.02 E
Bédi, Tchad	146	11.06 N	18.33 E
Bedias	222	30.46 N	95.57 W
Bedias Creek ≃	222	30.54 N	95.37 W
Bedinggong	112	2.42 S	106.13 E
Bediondo	146	8.39 N	17.12 E
Bediri	130	39.35 N	36.38 E
Bedlington	44	55.08 N	1.35 W
Bedminster, N.J., U.S.	276	40.40 N	74.38 W
Bedminster, Pa., U.S.	208	40.26 N	75.11 W
Bednodemjanovsk	80	53.56 N	43.10 E
Bedoba	88	58.48 N	97.12 E
Bedok	271c	1.19 N	103.57 E
Bedonia	62	44.30 N	9.38 E
Bedourie	166	24.21 S	139.28 E
Bedum	52	53.17 N	6.36 E
Bedwas	42	51.35 N	3.13 W
Bedworth	42	52.28 N	1.29 W
Beeac	169	38.12 S	143.38 E
Beebe, P.Q., Can.	206	45.01 N	72.09 W
Beebe, Ar., U.S.	194	35.04 N	91.52 W
Beech ≃	194	35.37 N	88.10 W
Beechal Creek ≃	166	27.24 S	145.13 E
Beech Bottom	214	40.13 N	80.39 W
Beech Brook ≃	276	41.08 N	74.18 W
Beech Creek	194	37.01 N	87.03 W
Beech Creek ≃	214	41.04 N	77.34 W
Beechcrest	214	41.05 N	81.20 W
Beecher, Il., U.S.	216	41.20 N	87.37 W
Beecher, Mi., U.S.	216	43.05 N	83.42 W
Beecher City	219	39.11 N	88.47 W
Beecher Falls	206	45.00 N	71.30 W
Beechey Head ›	224	48.19 N	123.39 W
Beech Forest	169	38.38 S	143.34 E
Beech Fork ≃	194	37.46 N	85.41 W
Beech Grove	218	39.43 N	86.05 W
Beechmont	171a	28.07 S	153.11 E
Beechview ↝⁸	279b	40.25 N	80.02 W
Beechwood, Ky., U.S.	218	38.24 N	84.44 W
Beechwood, Ma., U.S.	283	42.12 N	70.49 W
Beechwood, Mi., U.S.	216	46.09 N	88.46 W
Beechworth	166	36.22 S	146.41 E
Beechy	184	50.51 N	107.25 W
Beeck ↝⁸	263	51.29 N	6.44 E
Beeckwerth ↝⁸	263	51.29 N	6.41 E
Beecroft	274a	33.45 S	151.04 E
Beecroft Head ›	170	35.01 S	150.51 E
Beecroft Peninsula ›¹	170	35.02 S	150.50 E
Beedenbostel	52	52.38 N	10.16 E
Beef Island I	240m	18.27 N	64.31 W
Beek, Ned.	52	51.51 N	5.54 E
Beek, Ned.	52	51.20 N	5.38 E
Beek, Ned.	56	50.56 N	5.49 E
Beelen	52	51.55 N	8.07 E
Beeleigh Abbey ⬦¹	260	51.44 N	0.40 E
Beelitz	54	52.14 N	12.58 E
Beemer	198	41.55 N	96.48 W
Beernem	52	51.08 N	3.20 E
Beerndorf	54	52.14 N	11.05 E
Beenleigh	171a	27.43 S	153.12 E
Beerburrum	171a	26.58 S	152.58 E
Beerfelden	56	49.34 N	8.58 E
Bee Ridge	220	27.17 N	82.28 W
Beesanjia ⁵	162	29.53 S	117.55 E
Beersheba	128	31.14 N	34.47 E
— Be'ér Sheva'	128	31.14 N	34.47 E
Beersheba Springs	194	35.28 N	85.39 W
Be'er Sheva' (Beersheba)	132	31.14 N	34.47 E
Be'er Sheva', Naḥal ≃	132	31.14 N	34.35 E
Beerta	52	53.10 N	7.06 E
Be'ér Toviyya	132	31.44 N	34.44 E
Beervlei Brak ›	158	29.58 S	23.12 E
Beerwah National Park ↟	171a	26.54 S	152.53 E
Be'er Ya'aqov	132	31.56 N	34.50 E
Beesenlaublingen	54	51.42 N	11.41 E
Beeskow	54	52.10 N	14.14 E
Beesten	52	52.25 N	7.28 E
Beetsterzwaag	52	53.03 N	6.04 E
Beeville	196	28.24 N	97.44 W
Beevor, Mount ⩘²	168b	34.56 S	139.02 E
Befale	152	0.28 N	20.58 E
Befandriana	157b	15.16 S	48.32 E
Befandriana Atsimo	157b	22.06 S	45.16 E
Befasy	157b	20.33 S	44.23 E
Befori	152	0.06 N	22.17 E
Befotaka, Madag.	157b	13.15 S	48.16 E
Befotaka, Madag.	157b	14.32 S	48.01 E
Befotaka, Madag.	157b	23.49 S	46.59 E
Befotaka, Madag.	157b	21.29 S	44.44 E
Befu ⩘⁸	106	34.40 N	135.02 E
Beg, Lough ⌀	48	54.47 N	6.28 W
Bega	166	36.40 S	149.50 E
Bega (Begej) ≃	38	45.13 N	20.19 E
Begamganj, Bngl.	124	22.49 N	91.07 E
Begamganj, India	124	23.36 N	78.20 E
Begampur ⩘⁸	272a	28.44 N	77.04 E
Begdeş	130	37.51 N	39.05 E
Begej (Bega) ≃	38	45.13 N	20.19 E
Beger	102	45.42 N	97.10 E
Beggs	196	35.44 N	96.04 W
Begičevskij	76	53.47 N	38.15 E
Beginsel	158	26.57 S	20.39 E
Beglickaja, kosa ›²	83	47.07 N	38.35 E
Begna ≃	26	60.10 N	10.16 E
Begoml'	76	54.44 N	28.04 E
Begonias, Presa ⌀¹	234	20.55 N	100.50 W
Begoro	150	6.23 N	0.23 W
Begovat	85	40.13 N	69.14 E
— Bekabad	85	40.13 N	69.14 E
Begun'	78	51.24 N	28.17 E
Begunicy	78	59.35 N	29.19 E
Begur, Cap de ›	34	41.57 N	3.14 E
Begusarai	124	25.25 N	86.08 E
Behäla	126	22.31 N	88.19 E
Behauge, Fointe ›	250	4.10 N	51.54 W
Behbahān	128	30.35 N	50.14 E
Behleg	120	36.47 N	91.41 E
Behm Canal ⌣	182	55.41 N	131.35 W
Behn	56	50.13 N	6.00 E
Béhoust	261	48.50 N	1.43 E
Behrämpur	124	34.31 N	52.32 E
Behren-lès-Forbach	56	49.10 N	6.57 E
Behring, Détroit de — Bering Strait ⌣	180	65.30 N	169.00 W
Behringen, Dtsch.	52	53.07 N	9.58 E
Behringen, Dtsch.	54	51.01 N	10.31 E
Behshahr	128	36.43 N	53.34 E
Beht, Oued ≃	148	34.25 N	6.26 W
Bei ≃	90	23.09 N	112.48 E
Bei'an	98	48.16 N	126.36 E
Beianhe ≃	105	40.04 N	116.06 E
Beibaihua	105	38.57 N	114.51 E
Beibaozhen	106	31.33 N	121.38 E
Beibei	107	29.49 N	106.26 E
Beicai	106	31.12 N	121.34 E
Beicang	105	39.13 N	117.07 E
— Al-Bayḍā'	146	32.46 N	21.43 E
Beida, Chott ⌀	34	35.56 N	5.49 E
Beidaihe	98	39.54 N	119.29 E
Beidaoqiao	86	44.12 N	89.38 E
Beidouzhen	107	30.02 N	104.26 E
Beier	100	26.42 N	118.57 E
Beierfeld	54	50.33 N	12.47 E
Beiersdorf	264a	52.42 N	13.47 E
Beifangcun	105	40.40 N	74.38 W
Beifangzi	105	41.22 N	121.03 E
Beigang	100	29.20 N	113.41 E
Beighton	44	53.20 N	1.20 W
Beiguan	105	40.17 N	119.50 E
Beiguan Dao I	100	27.10 N	120.32 E
Beiguo	106	31.47 N	120.33 E
Beihai	90	21.29 N	109.05 E
Bei Hai ⌀	271a	39.56 N	116.22 E
Beihedian	105	39.13 N	115.45 E
Beiheishang gou ⌀	105	39.16 N	117.33 E
Beihuaidian	105	41.08 N	124.02 E
Beijiang ≃	90	23.02 N	112.58 E
Beijiao	106	22.20 N	119.58 E
Beijiean	106	32.15 N	121.12 E
Beijiazhuang	105	40.01 N	114.51 E
Beijing (Peking) Zhg.	98	39.55 N	116.25 E
Beijing (Peking) Zhg.	271a	39.55 N	116.25 E
Beijing Ji Chang (Capitol Airport) ⬩	105	40.03 N	116.35 E
Beijing Shi (Peking Shih) □⁷	98	40.15 N	116.30 E
Beiji Shan I	100	27.38 N	121.12 E
Beijuma ≃	105	39.30 N	115.56 E
Beikan	100	32.52 N	121.21 E
Beili	110	19.10 N	108.43 E
Beilifang	104	41.59 N	121.57 E
Beiliu	110	22.43 N	110.22 E
Beiliuwangshui	105	38.57 N	115.03 E
Beilizigu	105	39.00 N	117.28 E
Beilrode	54	51.35 N	13.03 E
Beilstein, Dtsch.	56	49.02 N	9.18 E
Beilstein, Dtsch.	56	50.36 N	8.14 E
Beilstein, Dtsch.	56	50.06 N	7.14 E
Beimaizhu	100	39.31 N	117.44 E
Beiminjiatun	104	45.31 N	125.33 E
Beimuzhen	107	29.31 N	105.05 E
Beinamar	146	8.40 N	15.23 E
Beine-Nauroy	50	49.15 N	4.13 E
Beinette	64	44.22 N	7.39 E
Beinwil	58	47.22 N	7.35 E
Beinwil am See	58	47.16 N	8.13 E
Beipa	164	8.30 S	146.35 E
Beipan ≃	102	25.05 N	106.00 E
Beipanxiaozhen	108	25.05 N	106.07 E
Beipiao	98	41.49 N	120.45 E
Beipo	102	21.14 N	109.53 E
Beiqiao	106	31.03 N	121.24 E
Beiqiao	106	31.00 N	121.22 E
Beira Baixa ⬦⁹	34	39.45 N	7.30 W
Beira Litoral ⬦⁹	34	40.15 N	8.25 W
Beiru ≃	105	33.43 N	113.35 E
Beirut — Bayrūt	130	33.53 N	35.30 E
Beirut International Airport ⬩	132	33.49 N	35.30 E
Beisanjia	105	42.04 N	124.42 E
Beishan	100	39.21 N	113.32 W
Beishankou	105	39.08 N	116.07 E
Beishan	126	24.28 N	108.35 E
Bei Shan ⩘	102	41.30 N	96.00 E
Beishipan	105	39.28 N	116.58 E
Beishuiquan	98	40.32 N	117.24 E
Beishuiquan	102	34.50 N	95.07 E
Beisu	98	38.13 N	114.46 E
Beitang	98	39.07 N	117.42 E
Beitbridge	148	22.13 S	30.00 E
Beithan	105	35.44 N	110.44 E
Beitstadfjorden c²	24	63.53 N	11.00 E
Beiuş	38	46.40 N	22.21 E
Beiwei	105	32.05 N	121.12 E
Beiwenquan	107	29.51 N	106.24 E
Beiwu	105	40.04 N	116.48 E
Beixiadai	105	32.12 N	120.08 E
Beixin	105	39.38 N	116.21 E
Beixili	105	39.44 N	116.44 E
Beixindian	105	39.52 N	116.24 E
Beixinjing	106	31.13 N	121.22 E
Beixinzhen	104	45.18 N	131.02 E
Beiyan	105	36.33 N	118.42 E
Beiyi ⩘	105	39.59 N	115.39 E
Beiyindu	104	41.07 N	121.30 E
Beiyinfu	104	41.15 N	123.34 E
Beiyuan	105	40.01 N	116.24 E
Beizhaizhuang	105	40.11 N	113.50 E
Beizhaijiawopeng	104	41.14 N	122.41 E

PORTUGUÊS

Nome	Página	Lat.	Long. W=Oeste
Beizhen, Zhg.	98	37.22 N	118.01 E
Beizhen (Geoshanzi), Zhg.	104	41.36 N	121.47 E
Beizhouzhuang	106	31.52 N	120.24 E
Beizhu	98	42.09 N	120.29 E
Beja, Bra.	250	1.36 S	48.47 W
Beja, Port.	34	38.01 N	7.52 W
Beja, Ross.	86	53.03 N	90.54 E
Béja, Tun.	148	36.44 N	9.11 E
Beja □⁸	34	37.50 N	8.00 W
Bejaïa (Bougie)	148	36.45 N	5.05 E
Bejaïa □¹	148	36.35 N	9.20 E
Bejaïa, Golfe de c	148	36.45 N	5.25 E
Béjar	34	40.23 N	5.46 W
Bejhi ≃	120	29.47 N	67.58 E
Bejlagan	84	39.47 N	47.37 E
Bejneu	86	45.15 N	55.07 E
Bejsug ≃	78	45.54 N	38.56 E
Bejsugskij liman c	78	46.07 N	38.25 E
Bejtonovo	89	53.14 N	124.27 E
Bejucal	246	22.56 N	82.23 W
Bejucal □⁷	286b	22.56 N	82.23 W
Bejuco	236	8.36 N	79.53 W
Bejucos	234	18.36 N	100.40 W
Bejuma	246	10.11 N	68.16 W
Bek	152	2.29 N	15.15 E
Béka	146	9.04 N	12.53 E
Bekaa Valley — Al-Biqā' V	128	33.50 N	36.00 E
Bekabad	85	40.13 N	69.14 E
Bekancan	114	3.18 N	98.24 E
Bekasi	115a	6.14 S	106.59 E
Bekasi ≃	269e	6.10 S	107.02 E
Békásmegyer ⩘⁸	264c	47.36 N	19.03 E
Bekasovo	82	55.26 N	36.49 E
Bekdaš	72	41.34 N	52.32 E
Békés	30	46.46 N	21.08 E
Békés □⁶	30	46.41 N	21.08 E
Békéscsaba	30	46.41 N	21.06 E
Beketovo	89	53.13 N	125.01 E
Bekili	130	38.14 N	29.26 E
Bekily	157b	24.13 S	45.19 E
Bekirhan	130	38.10 N	41.19 E
Bekisopa	157b	21.40 S	45.54 E
Bekitro	157b	24.33 S	45.18 E
Bekkaria	36	35.22 N	8.15 E
Bekkersdal	273d	26.18 S	27.42 E
Bekkevoort	56	50.57 N	4.58 E
Beklemiševo Ross.	80	53.52 N	47.25 E
Beklemiševo Ross.	88	52.07 N	112.40 E
Bekodoka	157b	16.58 S	45.07 E
Bekojli	144	7.34 N	39.17 E
Bekok	114	2.18 N	103.08 E
Bekopaka	157b	19.09 S	44.48 E
Bekovo	80	52.28 N	43.43 E
Bektauata, gora ⩘	86	47.30 N	74.50 E
Bektyševo	82	56.34 N	39.14 E
Bekwai	150	6.27 N	1.35 W
Bela, India	124	25.56 N	81.59 E
Bela, Pāk.	120	26.14 N	66.19 E
Bela, Zaïre	154	0.38 N	29.14 E
Bēlabo	152	5.00 N	13.20 E
Belabolo	100	29.20 N	113.41 E
Bela Crkva	38	44.54 N	21.26 E
Bela Cruz	250	3.03 S	40.11 W
Belaga	108	2.42 N	113.47 E
Bel'agaš	86	50.48 N	80.44 E
Bel Air, Fr.	261	48.37 N	2.10 E
Bel Air, Md., U.S.	208	39.32 N	76.20 W
Bel Air, Va., U.S.	284c	38.52 N	77.10 W
Belaja ≃, Ross.	80	56.00 N	53.50 E
Belaja ≃, Ross.	78	55.37 N	73.48 W
Belaja ≃, Ross.	72	45.37 N	72.00 W
Belaja, Ross.	78	51.03 S	138.39 E
Belaja, Ross.	80	57.59 N	51.42 E
Belaja, Ross.	78	54.54 N	39.23 E
Belaja, Ross.	180	65.45 N	173.20 E
Belaja, gora ⩘, Ross.	88	53.10 N	119.50 E
Belaja, gora ⩘, Ross.	180	65.50 N	174.40 E
Belaja ≃, Ukr.	83	49.18 N	38.52 E
Belaja ≃, Ukr.	84	48.35 N	39.10 E
Belaja Bér'ozka	76	52.23 N	33.49 E
Belaja Cerkov'	84	49.49 N	30.07 E
Belaja Cholunica	80	58.50 N	50.48 E
Belaja Gora	76	58.31 N	31.45 E
Belaja Kalitva	84	48.11 N	40.46 E
Belaja Krinica Ukr.	78	47.21 N	33.10 E
Belaja Krinica Ukr.	78	50.38 N	29.29 E
Bel'ajevka, Ross.	86	51.24 N	56.26 E
Bel'ajevka, Ross.	78	51.24 N	56.26 E
Bel'ajevka, Ukr.	78	46.29 N	30.12 E
Bel'ajevo	76	53.51 N	31.06 E
Balalcázar	34	38.34 N	5.10 W
Bel Alton	208	38.27 N	76.58 W
Belambangnumpu	112	4.54 S	105.03 E
Belampalli	122	19.04 N	79.30 E
Bélá nad Radbuzou	54	49.34 N	12.46 E
Belang	112	0.57 N	124.47 E
Bélanger ≃	184	53.26 N	97.40 W
Bel'aninovo	265b	55.57 N	37.39 E
Bel'anskij	86	54.47 N	41.33 E
Bela Palanka	38	43.13 N	22.19 E
Belapurpáda	272c	19.01 N	73.02 E
Belarus ⬦¹, Europe	30	53.50 N	28.00 E
Belarus □¹, Europe	22	53.50 N	28.00 E
Belas	273d	25.47 S	37.35 E
Belau — Palau □²	14	5.00 N	137.00 E
Belavenona	157b	24.50 S	47.04 E
Belawan	114	3.47 N	98.41 E
Belayan ≃	111	0.14 S	116.36 E
Belaya Tserkov — Belaja Cerkov'	84	49.49 N	30.07 E
Belbo ≃	62	44.49 N	8.31 E
Belbunia	152	5.37 N	20.15 E
Bel'C (Bel'cy)	38	47.46 N	27.56 E
Belcamp	208	39.27 N	76.14 W
Belcastro	66	39.02 N	16.47 E
Belchatów	30	51.22 N	19.21 E
Belchen ⩘	58	47.49 N	7.50 E
Belcher ≃	194	33.44 N	93.49 W
Belcher Islands II	176	56.20 N	79.30 W
Belchertown	207	42.16 N	72.24 W
Bělčice	54	49.31 N	13.53 E
Belcoo	48	54.17 N	7.52 W
Belcovo	76	57.06 N	33.46 E
Beld ≃	56	48.53 N	10.03 E
Bel'd'aži	82	54.32 N	35.25 E
Beldanga	126	23.55 N	88.15 E
Beldibi	130	36.40 N	30.34 E
Bele, ozero ⌀	86	54.39 N	90.11 E
Belebej	80	54.07 N	54.07 E
Belecke ↝⁸	263	51.28 N	8.21 E
Beled	61	47.28 N	17.06 E
Beled Weyne	144	4.45 N	45.12 E
Beleko	150	11.48 N	6.53 W
Belel, Cam.	152	7.03 N	14.26 E
Belel, Ng.	146	9.01 N	11.13 E
Belém, Bra.	250	1.27 S	48.29 W
Belém, Moç.	156	13.36 S	33.58 E
Belém, Torre de ↳	266c	38.42 N	9.13 W
Belém de São Francisco	250	8.46 S	38.58 W
Belén, Arg.	252	27.39 S	67.02 W
Belén, Bol.	248	19.48 S	65.33 W
Belén, Chile	248	18.29 S	69.31 W
Belén, Col.	246	6.00 N	72.55 W
Belén, Nic.	236	11.30 N	85.53 W
Belén, Ross.	86	53.03 N	90.54 E
Belén, Tür.	130	36.32 N	36.10 E
Belén, N.M., U.S.	200	34.39 N	106.46 W
Belén, Ur.	252	30.47 S	57.47 W
Belén ≃	252	28.00 S	66.52 W
Belén de Escobar	258	34.21 S	58.47 W
Belén del Refugio	234	21.31 N	102.25 W
Belene	38	43.39 N	25.07 E
Belenichino	78	50.56 N	36.37 E
Belen'kaja ≃	83	48.33 N	38.29 E
Belen'koje, Ukr.	78	47.37 N	35.03 E
Belēnzinho ⩘⁸	287b	23.32 S	46.35 W
Beleriang II	144	10.15 S	163.40 E
Belesar, Embalse de ⌀¹	34	42.17 N	7.40 W
Belet Uen	144	4.45 N	45.12 E
Belews Lake ⌀¹	192	36.17 N	80.03 W
Belfair	224	47.27 N	122.48 E
Belfast, N.Z.	172	43.27 S	172.38 E
Belfast, S. Afr.	156	25.43 S	30.03 E
Belfast, N. Ire., U.K.	48	54.35 N	5.55 W
Belfast, Me., U.S.	188	44.25 N	69.00 W
Belfast, Oh., U.S.	210	42.20 N	78.06 W
Belfast (Aldergrove) Airport ⬩	48	54.39 N	6.12 W
Belfast Lough c	48	54.40 N	5.50 W
Belfeld	52	51.19 N	8.06 E
Belfield, N.D., U.S.	198	46.53 N	103.11 W
Belfiore	64	45.23 N	11.12 E
Belford, Eng., U.K.	44	55.36 N	1.49 W
Belford, N.J., U.S.	276	40.25 N	74.05 W
Belford Roxo	256	22.46 S	43.24 W
Belfort	58	47.38 N	6.52 E
Belfort □⁶	58	47.38 N	6.55 E
Belforte del Chienti	66	43.10 N	13.14 E
Belfry, Ky., U.S.	192	37.37 N	82.16 W
Belfry, Mt., U.S.	202	45.08 N	109.00 W
Belgaum	122	15.52 N	74.31 E
Belgern	54	51.29 N	13.07 E
Belgica Mountains ↗	9	72.35 S	31.10 E
— Belgium □¹	30	50.50 N	4.00 E
Belgien — Belgium □¹	30	50.50 N	4.00 E
Belgioioso	62	45.10 N	9.19 E
Belgique — Belgium □¹, Europe	22	50.50 N	4.00 E
Belgium □¹, Europe	30	50.50 N	4.00 E
Belgodère	36	42.35 N	9.01 E
Belgorod	78	50.36 N	36.35 E
Belgorod-Dnestrovskij	78	46.12 N	30.20 E
Belgorod Oblast' □⁴	78	50.45 N	37.30 E
Belgrad — Beograd	38	44.50 N	20.30 E
Belgrade — Beograd, Jugo.	38	44.50 N	20.30 E
Belgrade, Mn., U.S.	198	45.27 N	95.00 W
Belgrade, Mt., U.S.	202	45.46 N	111.10 W
Belgrade, Ne., U.S.	198	41.28 N	98.04 W
Belgrado — Beograd	38	44.50 N	20.30 E
Belgrad Ormanı ↝³	267b	41.10 N	28.55 E
Belgrano ≃⁸	288	34.34 S	58.28 W
Belgrano, Lago ⌀	254	48.15 S	71.14 W
Belgrano II ⁵	9	77.46 S	38.11 W
Belgrave	274b	37.55 S	145.21 E
Belhar	124	24.56 N	86.36 E
Belhaven	192	35.32 N	76.37 W
Belhus Park ↟	260	51.31 N	0.17 E
Beliäbera	126	22.17 N	86.57 E
Belica ≃	38	42.20 N	23.29 E
Belice ≃	36	37.35 N	12.55 E
Belichifor	140	6.33 N	33.16 E
Belida	86	52.14 N	61.00 E
Belīdži	84	41.46 N	48.23 E
Belim	82	54.09 N	36.16 E
Belimbing	112	0.50 S	100.14 E
Belin	32	44.30 N	0.47 W
Belinga	152	1.13 N	13.12 E
Belington	188	39.01 N	79.56 W
Belinskij	80	52.58 N	43.26 E
Belinyu	112	1.38 S	105.46 E
Belira ≃	236	9.04 N	79.31 W
Belitsa ≃	140	7.50 N	34.00 E
Belitung, Selat ⌣	112	3.00 S	107.40 E
Belitung, Pulau I	112	2.50 S	107.55 E
Belize — Belize City	232	17.30 N	88.12 W
Belize — Belize □¹	232	17.15 N	88.45 W
Belize ≃	232	17.33 N	88.14 W
Belize □¹	232	17.15 N	88.45 W
Belize City	232	17.30 N	88.12 W
Belize Inlet c	182	51.08 N	127.15 W
Belka	86	51.38 N	60.59 E
Belkina, mys ›	104	45.49 N	137.40 E
Bel'kovo	82	56.15 N	38.48 E
Bel'kovskij, Ostrov I	74	75.32 N	135.44 E
Bell, Austl.	274b	37.45 S	145.00 E
Bell, Ca., U.S.	282	33.59 N	118.11 W
Bell, Fl., U.S.	220	29.45 N	82.52 W
Bell ≃, Vt., U.S.	188	38.13 N	81.32 W
Bell ≃, Yk., Can.	180	67.17 N	137.46 W
Bella Bella	182	52.09 N	128.07 W
Bellac	32	46.07 N	1.02 E
Bella Coola	182	52.23 N	126.48 W
Bella Coola ≃	182	52.25 N	126.40 W
Bella Flor	248	11.09 S	67.49 W
Bellagio	62	45.59 N	9.15 E
Bellaire	210	40.01 N	80.44 W
Bellaire, Mi., U.S.	190	44.59 N	85.12 W
Bellaire, Oh., U.S.	214	40.00 N	80.45 W
Bellaire, Tx., U.S.	222	29.42 N	95.28 W
Bellamy ≃	188	43.11 N	70.52 W
Bellanew	274a	33.44 S	151.14 E
Bellair	220	27.58 N	82.48 W
Bellara	171a	26.48 S	153.08 E
Bellaria	64	44.09 N	12.28 E
Bellary	122	15.09 N	76.56 E
Bellas Artes, Museo de ⬦	286c	19.30 N	99.08 W
Bellas Artes, Palacio de ⬦	286a	19.26 N	99.08 W
Bellata	166	29.55 S	149.47 E
Bella Tola ⩘	46	46.15 N	7.39 E

Bella Unión	252	30.15 S	57.35 W
Bella Vista, Arg.	252	28.30 S	59.03 W
Bella Vista, Arg.	252	27.02 S	65.18 W
Bella Vista, Arg.	258	34.33 S	58.41 W
Bellavista, Chile	286e	33.31 S	70.37 W
Bella Vista, Para.	252	22.08 S	56.31 W
Bellavista, Perú	248	4.54 S	80.42 W
Bellavista, Perú	248	7.04 S	76.35 W
Bellavista, Perú	286d	12.04 S	77.08 W
Bellbird	170	32.51 S	151.21 E
Bellbrook, Austl.	166	30.49 S	152.31 E
Bellbrook, Oh., U.S.	218	39.38 N	84.04 W
Bell Brook ≃	168a	33.01 S	116.15 E
Bell Craigs ≃²	44	55.03 N	2.22 W
Bell Creek ≃, Ca., U.S.	280	34.12 N	118.36 W
Bell Creek ≃, In., U.S.	218	40.09 N	85.27 W
Bellé, Sén	150	14.25 N	12.18 W
Belle, Mo., U.S.	194	38.17 N	91.43 W
Belle ≃, Mi., U.S.	216	42.17 N	82.43 W
Belle ≃, Mi., U.S.	214	42.30 N	82.30 W
Belleair	220	27.55 N	82.48 W
Belleau	50	49.06 N	3.18 E
Belle Ayr Mountain ⩘	202	44.07 N	74.29 W
Belle Bay c	186	47.36 N	55.18 W
Belle Center	216	40.30 N	83.44 W
Belledonne, Chaîne ↗	62	45.18 N	6.08 E
Belle-Église	261	49.12 N	2.13 E
Belleek	48	54.28 N	8.06 W
Belle Farm Estates	208	39.23 N	76.45 W
Bellefontaine, Fr.	58	46.33 N	6.04 E
Bellefontaine, Fr.	261	49.06 N	2.22 E
Bellefontaine, Mart.	240e	14.40 N	61.10 W
Bellefontaine, Oh., U.S.	216	40.21 N	83.45 W
Bellefontaine Neighbors	219	38.44 N	90.13 W
Bellefonte, De., U.S.	208	39.45 N	75.30 W
Bellefonte, Md., U.S.	284c	38.47 N	76.52 W
Bellefonte, Pa., U.S.	208	40.54 N	77.46 W
Belle Fourche	198	44.40 N	103.51 W
Belle Fourche ≃	198	44.26 N	102.19 W
Belle Fourche Reservoir ⌀¹	198	44.44 N	103.42 W
Bellegarde, Fr.	58	46.06 N	5.49 E
Bellegarde, Fr.	62	43.45 N	4.31 E
Bellegarde-du-Loiret	47	47.59 N	2.26 E
Bellegrove	260	51.28 N	0.09 E
Belle Glade Camp	220	26.40 N	80.41 W
Belle Haven, Va., U.S.	208	37.33 N	75.49 W
Belle Haven, Va., U.S.	284c	38.47 N	77.04 W
Bellerbe	58	47.16 N	6.40 E
Belle Hôtesse ⩘	241o	16.16 N	61.46 W
Belle-Ile I	32	47.20 N	3.10 W
Belle Isle	220	28.27 N	81.21 W
Belle Isle I, Nf., Can.	281	51.55 N	55.20 W
Belle Isle I, Mi., U.S.	281	42.20 N	82.58 W
Belle Isle, Strait of ⌣	176	51.35 N	56.30 W
Belle Isle Park ‡	278	47.16 N	7.10 E
Belle Mead	208	40.28 N	74.39 W
Bellemoor	285	39.43 N	75.35 W
Bellencombre	50	49.42 N	1.14 E
Bellenden Ker National Park ↟	164	17.15 S	145.53 E
Belleoram	186	47.33 N	55.25 W
Belleplain	208	39.16 N	74.52 W
Belle-Plaine Sk., Can.	184	50.24 N	105.09 W
Belle Plaine, Ia., U.S.	190	41.53 N	92.16 W
Belle Plaine, Ks., U.S.	198	37.23 N	97.16 W
Belle Plaine, Mn. U.S.	190	44.37 N	93.46 W
Belle River	208	38.14 N	80.45 W
Bellerose	276	40.44 N	73.43 W
Bellerose Terrace	276	40.41 N	73.43 W
Belle Terre	210	40.58 N	73.04 W
Bellevaux-Ligneuville	56	50.24 N	6.06 E
Bellevesvre	58	46.50 N	5.22 E
Belleview, Fl., U.S.	220	29.03 N	82.03 W
Belleview, Mo., U.S.	194	37.40 N	90.41 W
Belleview, Oh., U.S.	212	44.10 N	77.23 W
Belleville, Fr.	58	46.49 N	6.06 E
Belleville, Il., U.S.	219	38.31 N	89.59 W
Belleville, Ks., U.S.	198	39.49 N	97.37 W
Belleville, N.J., U.S.	276	40.47 N	74.09 W
Belleville, N.Y., U.S.	212	43.47 N	76.07 W
Belleville, Pa., U.S.	207	40.36 N	77.43 W
Belleville, R.I., U.S.	207	41.36 N	71.26 W
Belle Vernon	214	40.08 N	79.52 W
Belle Vue, Maur.	269a	20.08 S	57.30 E
Bell Gardens	282	33.58 N	118.09 W
Bellheim	56	49.12 N	8.16 E
Bellin	176	60.01 N	70.01 W
Bellingen	41	55.20 N	8.58 E
Bellingham, Eng., U.K.	44	55.09 N	2.16 W
Bellingham, Mn., U.S.	198	45.08 N	96.17 W
Bellingham, Wa., U.S.	182	48.46 N	122.29 W
Bellingham Bay c	224	48.45 N	122.35 W
Bellinzona	58	46.11 N	9.02 E
Bell Island I, Nf., Can.	186	47.36 N	55.35 W
Bell Island Hot Springs	182	55.56 N	131.34 W
Bellmawr	208	39.51 N	75.05 W
Bellmead	222	31.36 N	97.06 W
Bell Mountain ⩘	200	38.21 N	120.22 W
Bellnhausen	56	50.42 N	8.43 E

Símbolo	ESPAÑOL	Deutsch	Nombre	Español	FRANÇAIS	Português
≃ River	Fluß	Río	Rivière	Rivière	Rio	
≋ Canal	Kanal	Canal	Canal	Canal	Canal	
ʟ Waterfall, Rapids	Wasserfall, Stromschnellen	Cascada, Rápidos	Cascada, Rápidos	Chute d'eau, Rapides	Cascata, Rápidos	
≍ Strait	Meeresstraße	Estrecho	Détroit	Estreito		
c Bay, Gulf	Bucht, Golf	Bahía, Golfo	Baie, Golfe	Baía, Golfo		
⌀ Lake, Lakes	See, Seen	Lago, Lagos	Lac, Lacs	Lago, Lagos		
≈ Swamp	Sumpf	Pantano	Marais	Pântano		
⬙ Ice Features, Glacier	Eis- und Gletscherformen	Accidentes Glaciares	Formes glaciaires	Accidentes glaciares	Hidrográficos	
⩶ Other Hydrographic Features	Andere Hydrographische Objekte	Otros Elementos Hidrográficos	Autres données hydrographiques	Outros acidentes hidrográficos		

↟ Submarine Features	Untermeerische Objekte	Accidentes Submarinos	Formes de relief sous-marin	Acidentes submarinos
↯ Political Unit	Politische Einheit	Unidad Política	Unité politique	Unidade política
⬦ Cultural Institution	Kulturelle Institution	Institución Cultural	Institution culturelle	Instituição cultural
↳ Historical Site	Historische Stätte	Sitio Histórico	Site historique	Sitio histórico
↟ Recreational Site	Erholungs- und Ferienort	Sitio de Recreo	Centre de loisirs	Area de Lazer
⬩ Airport	Flughafen	Aeropuerto	Aéroport	Aeroporto
◼ Military Installation	Militäranlage	Instalación Militar	Installation militaire	Instalação militar
⬥ Miscellaneous	Verschiedenes	Misceláneo	Divers	Diversos

ENGLISH — Name / Page / Lat.°′ / Long.°′ DEUTSCH — Name / Seite / Breite°′ / Länge°′ E = Ost

Bello, Col. 246 6.20 N 75.33 W
Bello, Cuba 286b 23.07 N 82.24 W
Bello Horizonte
→ Belo Horizonte 255 19.55 S 43.56 W
Bellona 210 42.46 N 77.01 W
Bellona, Récifs ✦[2] 160 21.30 S 159.00 E
Bellona Plateau ✦[3] 14 20.30 S 158.30 E
Bellone, Cap › 157b 16.14 S 49.51 E
Bellosguardo 68 40.25 N 15.19 E
Bellot Strait ʊ 176 71.58 N 94.45 W
Bellows Falls 188 43.08 N 72.26 W
Belloy-en-France 261 49.05 N 2.22 E
Bellpat 120 28.59 N 68.00 E
Bell Peninsula ›[1] 176 63.50 N 82.00 W
Bell Point 279b 40.33 N 79.33 W
Bells, Tn., U.S. 194 35.43 N 89.05 W
Bells, Tx., U.S. 196 33.37 N 96.25 W
Bellsbank 44 55.18 N 4.23 W
Bells Bay c 212 45.30 N 77.51 W
Bells Corners 212 45.19 N 75.50 W
Bellshill 46 55.49 N 4.01 W
Bells Lake 285 39.44 N 75.02 W
Bells Lake ⊜ 285 39.45 N 75.04 W
Belltown, De., U.S. 208 38.44 N 75.10 W
Belltown, Il., U.S. 219 39.23 N 90.25 W
Belluno 64 46.09 N 12.13 E
Belluno □[4] 64 46.15 N 12.08 E
Bellvale 210 41.15 N 74.18 W
Bell Ville, Arg. 252 32.37 S 62.42 W
Bellville, S. Afr. 158 33.53 S 18.36 E
Bellville, Oh., U.S. 214 40.37 N 82.30 W
Bellville, Tx., U.S. 222 29.57 N 96.15 W
Bellwood, Il., U.S. 278 41.52 N 87.52 W
Bellwood, Ne., U.S. 198 41.20 N 97.14 W
Bellwood, Pa., U.S. 214 40.36 N 78.19 W
Bellwood, Lake ⊜ 212 43.46 N 80.20 W
Belly ≃ 182 49.46 N 113.02 W
Bellyk 86 54.32 N 91.17 E
Belm 52 52.18 N 8.08 E
Belmar, Md., U.S. 284b 39.21 N 76.32 W
Belmar, N.J., U.S. 208 40.10 N 74.01 W
Bélmez 34 38.16 N 5.12 W
Belmiro Braga 256 21.57 S 43.25 W
Belmond 190 42.50 N 93.36 W
Belmont, Austl. 169 38.10 S 144.21 E
Belmont, Austl. 170 33.02 S 151.40 E
Belmont, Mb., Can. 184 49.24 N 99.27 W
Belmont, N.S., Can. 186 45.25 N 63.23 W
Belmont, On., Can. 212 42.53 N 81.05 W
Belmont, S. Afr. 158 29.28 S 24.22 E
Belmont, Eng., U.K. 262 53.38 N 2.30 W
Belmont, Ca., U.S. 226 37.31 N 122.16 W
Belmont, Ma., U.S. 283 42.23 N 71.10 W
Belmont, Mi., U.S. 216 43.05 N 85.37 W
Belmont, Ms., U.S. 194 34.30 N 88.12 W
Belmont, N.H., U.S. 188 43.26 N 71.28 W
Belmont, N.Y., U.S. 210 42.13 N 78.02 W
Belmont, Pa., U.S. 214 40.17 N 78.53 W
Belmont, S.C., U.S. 192 34.02 N 81.01 W
Belmont, Tx., U.S. 222 29.31 N 97.41 W
Belmont, Wi., U.S. 190 42.44 N 90.20 W
Belmont □[6] 214 40.05 N 80.54 W
Belmonte, Bra. 255 15.51 S 38.54 W
Belmonte, Esp. 34 43.17 N 6.14 W
Belmonte, Esp. 34 39.34 N 2.42 W
Belmonte, Port. 34 40.21 N 7.21 W
Belmonte Calabro 68 39.09 N 16.05 E
Belmonte Mezzagno 70 38.02 N 13.23 E
Belmont Harbor c 278 41.57 N 87.38 W
Belmont Lake ⊜, On., Can. 212 44.30 N 77.50 W
Belmont Lake ⊜, N.Y., U.S. 276 40.44 N 73.20 W
Belmont Lake State Park ♦ 276 40.43 N 73.20 W
Belmont Park 214 41.10 N 80.39 W
Belmont Park Race Track ♦ 276 40.43 N 73.43 W
Belmont Reservoir ⊜[1] 262 53.39 N 2.30 W
Belmont Slough ≃ 282 37.33 N 122.14 W
Belmopan 232 17.15 N 88.46 W
Belmore, Austl. 274a 33.55 S 151.05 E
Belmore, Oh., U.S. 216 41.09 N 83.56 W
Belmullet 48 54.14 N 10.00 W
Belmuri 272b 22.57 N 88.09 E
Belo 157b 19.42 S 44.33 E
Belœil, Bel. 50 50.33 N 3.43 E
Beloeil, P.Q., Can. 206 45.34 N 73.12 W
Belœil, Château de ʋ 50 50.35 N 3.44 E
Beloeil, Ruisseau ≃ 275a 45.39 N 73.12 W
Beloglazovo 86 56.05 N 72.40 E
Belogorje, Ross. 78 50.30 N 40.01 E
Belogorje, Ukr. 78 50.01 N 26.25 E
Belogorka 80 50.42 N 53.27 E
Belogornoje 80 52.25 N 47.35 E
Belogorode 82 54.23 N 38.31 E
Belogorodka 78 50.00 N 26.39 E
Belogorovka 83 48.55 N 38.15 E
Belogorsk, Ross. 86 55.05 N 88.28 E
Belogorsk, Ross. 89 50.57 N 128.25 E
Belogorsk, Ukr. 78 45.03 N 34.36 E
Belogorskij 86 49.27 N 83.10 E
Belogorskoje 80 53.35 N 48.12 E
Belogradčik 38 43.38 N 22.41 E
Beloguša 78 51.57 N 26.56 E
Beloha 157b 25.10 S 45.03 E
Belo Horizonte 255 19.55 S 43.56 W
Beloit, Ks., U.S. 198 39.27 N 98.06 W
Beloit, Oh., U.S. 214 40.55 N 80.59 W
Beloit, Wi., U.S. 216 42.30 N 89.01 W
Belo Jardim 250 8.20 S 36.26 W
Belojarsk 86 53.28 N 83.54 E
Beloje, Kaz. 86 48.55 N 82.58 E
Beloje, Ross. 80 58.23 N 39.24 E
Beloje, Ukr. 83 48.31 N 39.04 E
Beloje, ozero ⊜ 76 60.11 N 37.37 E
Beloje more (White Sea) ⩧[2] 24 65.30 N 38.00 E
Belokamenskoje ◆•[8] 83 48.41 N 38.06 E
Belokany 84 41.43 N 46.26 E
Belokurakino 83 49.33 N 38.44 E
Belokuricha 86 51.59 N 84.59 E
Beloluck 83 49.41 N 39.02 E
Belomestnaja 76 52.24 N 37.37 E
Belomestnaja Dvojn'a 80 52.42 N 41.03 E
Belomorsk 24 64.32 N 34.48 E
Belomorsko-Baltijskij kanal ≆ 24 62.48 N 34.48 E
Belondo 152 0.16 S 19.31 E
Belonge 152 2.06 S 19.32 E
Belonia 124 23.15 N 91.27 E
Beloomut 76 54.57 N 39.20 E
Beloozersk 76 52.28 N 25.11 E
Belopolje 78 51.09 N 34.18 E
Belorado 34 42.25 N 3.11 W
Belorečensk 78 44.46 N 39.52 E
Beloreck 86 53.58 N 58.24 E
Belören, Tür. 130 40.51 N 33.30 E
Belören, Tür. 130 37.39 N 37.34 E
Belören, Tür. 130 37.12 N 32.33 E
Belorussia
→ Belarus □[1] 22 53.35 N 28.00 E
Belorussija
→ Belarus □[1] 72 53.50 N 28.00 E
Belorussiya
→ Belarus □[1] 72 53.50 N 28.00 E
Belorusskaja gr'ada ∧ 76 53.40 N 27.00 E
Beloščelje 24 64.52 N 46.56 E
Belo-sur-mer 157b 20.44 S 44.00 E
Belot, Lac ⊜ 180 66.55 N 126.18 W
Belousovka, Kaz. 86 50.08 N 82.33 E
Belousovka, Ukr. 78 49.57 N 32.20 E
Belousovo 82 55.05 N 36.40 E
Bel'ov 76 53.48 N 36.08 E
Belo Vale 255 20.25 S 44.01 W
Beloveżskaja Pušča, zapovednik ♦ 76 52.40 N 23.50 E
Belovo, Ross. 86 52.57 N 82.16 E
Belovo, Ross. 86 54.25 N 86.18 E
Belovodsk 83 49.12 N 39.35 E
Belovodskoje 85 42.50 N 74.06 E
Beloz'orje, Ukr. 78 49.29 N 31.35 E
Beloz'orje, Ukr. 78 49.18 N 31.54 E
Beloz'orka 78 46.37 N 32.27 E
Beloz'orsk 76 60.02 N 37.48 E
Beloz'orskoje 78 48.33 N 37.04 E
Belp 58 46.53 N 7.30 E
Belpāda 272c 19.02 N 73.03 E
Belpasso 70 37.35 N 14.58 E
Belper 44 53.01 N 1.29 W
Belpre 188 39.16 N 81.34 W
Belrose 274a 33.44 S 151.13 E
Belsano 214 40.31 N 78.52 W
Belsele 50 51.09 N 4.05 E
Bel'skaja Vol'a 78 51.27 N 25.49 E
Bel'skoje, Ross. 80 54.44 N 40.22 E
Bel'skoje, Ross. 86 57.49 N 92.09 E
Belson Run ≃ 279b 40.12 N 79.37 W
Belspring 192 37.11 N 80.36 W
Belt 202 47.23 N 110.55 W
Beltana 166 30.48 S 138.25 E
Belt Creek ≃ 202 47.36 N 111.02 W
Belted Range ⋏ 204 37.25 N 116.10 W
Belterra 250 2.38 S 54.57 W
Belthorn 262 53.43 N 2.26 W
Beltinci 61 46.36 N 16.15 E
Belton, Eng., U.K. 42 52.34 N 1.41 E
Belton, Eng., U.K. 44 53.33 N 0.49 W
Belton, Mo., U.S. 194 38.48 N 94.31 W
Belton, S.C., U.S. 192 34.31 N 82.29 W
Belton, Tx., U.S. 222 31.03 N 97.27 W
Belton Lake ⊜[1] 222 31.08 N 97.32 W
Beltra 48 54.13 N 8.37 W
Beltrán 252 27.50 S 64.04 W
Beltsville, Md., U.S. 208 39.02 N 76.54 W
Beltsville, Md., U.S. 284c 39.02 N 76.54 W
Bel'tsy
→ Bel'c' 38 47.46 N 27.56 E
Belturbet 48 54.06 N 7.28 W
Beltway Plaza ◆•[9] 284c 39.00 N 76.54 W
Bel'tyrskij 86 53.02 N 90.16 E
Beltzville Lake ⊜[1] 210 40.52 N 75.37 W
Beltzville State Park ♦ 210 40.52 N 75.36 W
Belucha, gora ∧ 86 49.48 N 86.40 E
Belucha, ozero ⊜ 80 49.20 N 46.05 E
Belugino 82 54.47 N 37.54 E
Belumut, Gunong ∧ 114 2.02 N 103.34 E
Belūr, India 122 13.10 N 75.52 E
Belur, India 272b 22.38 N 88.18 E
Beluran 112 5.54 N 117.33 E
Belur Math ʋ[1] 272b 22.38 N 88.22 E
Belušje 24 66.54 N 47.31 E
Belvedere, It. 64 45.44 N 13.23 E
Belvedere, Ca., U.S. 226 37.52 N 122.28 W
Belvedere, Va., U.S. 284c 38.50 N 77.10 W
Belvedere ◆•[8] 260 51.29 N 0.09 E
Belvedere ʋ 264b 48.11 N 16.23 E
Belvedere di Spinello 68 39.12 N 16.53 E
Belvedere Homes 220 26.43 N 80.06 W
Belvedere Marittimo 68 39.37 N 15.52 E
Belvedere Ostrense 66 43.34 N 13.09 E
Belvès 32 44.47 N 1.00 E
Belvidere, De., U.S. 208 39.43 N 75.37 W
Belvidere, Il., U.S. 216 42.15 N 88.50 W
Belvidere, N.J., U.S. 210 40.49 N 75.04 W
Belview 198 44.36 N 95.19 W
Belvis 266a 40.33 N 3.33 W
Belvís de la Jara 34 39.45 N 4.57 W
Belvoir
→ Kokhav HaYarden ⊥ 132 32.36 N 35.31 E
Belvoir, Vale of V 42 52.57 N 0.53 W
Belyando ≃ 166 21.38 S 146.50 E
Belyj 76 55.50 N 32.56 E
Belyj, ostrov I 74 73.10 N 70.45 E
Belyje Berega 76 53.12 N 34.40 E
Belyje Kolodezi 82 54.55 N 38.42 E
Belyje Stolby 82 55.20 N 37.52 E
Belyje Vody 85 42.25 N 69.50 E
Belyj Gorodok 76 56.58 N 37.30 E
Belyj Jar, Ross. 80 53.57 N 48.58 E
Belyj Jar, Ross. 86 53.36 N 91.24 E
Belyj Jar, Ross. 86 58.26 N 85.01 E
Belyj Kalodez' 78 50.02 N 38.40 E
Belyj Kolodez' 78 50.12 N 37.08 E
Belyj Luch ≃ 80 57.43 N 43.42 E
Belyj Rast 82 56.08 N 37.26 E
Belyniči 76 53.59 N 29.42 E
Belynkoviči 76 53.15 N 32.08 E
Belz, Fr. 32 47.41 N 3.10 W
Belz, Ukr. 78 50.23 N 24.01 E
Bełżec 30 50.24 N 23.26 E
Belzig 54 52.08 N 12.35 E
Belzoni 194 33.11 N 90.29 W
Bełżyce 30 51.11 N 22.18 E
Bem 219 38.15 N 91.28 W
Bemaraha, Plateau du ⋏[1] 157b 19.15 S 45.00 E
Bemarivo, Madag. 157b 16.56 S 44.21 E
Bemarivo, Madag. 157b 21.45 S 44.45 E
Bemarivo ≃, Madag. 157b 15.27 S 47.40 E
Bemarivo ≃, Madag. 157b 14.09 S 50.09 E
Bemavo 157b 21.37 S 45.24 E
Bembe 152 7.02 S 14.18 E
Bembéréké 150 10.13 N 2.40 E
Bembézar ≃ 34 37.45 N 5.13 W
Bembezi ≃ 154 18.57 S 27.47 E
Bembou Sambayabé 150 10.55 N 13.44 W
Bembridge 42 50.41 N 1.05 W
Bement 194 39.55 N 88.34 W
Bemidji 190 47.28 N 94.52 W
Bemis 194 35.34 N 88.49 W
Bemmel 52 51.54 N 5.54 E
Bemolanga 157b 17.44 S 45.06 E
Bemposta 256 22.09 S 43.07 W
Bemus Point 214 42.09 N 79.23 W
Bemyž 80 56.08 N 51.44 E
Ben, Kinh ≆ 269c 10.43 N 106.37 E
Bena 150 11.18 N 5.55 E
Benaadir □[4] 144 2.07 N 45.24 E
Benāb 128 37.20 N 46.04 E
Benabarre 34 42.07 N 0.29 E
Bena-Dibele 152 4.07 S 22.50 E
Benagaria 126 24.11 N 87.37 E
Benagerie 166 31.25 S 140.24 E
Benahmed 148 33.07 N 7.17 W
Benain ≃ 112 9.39 S 124.59 E
Ben'akoni 76 54.15 N 25.22 E
Bena-Leka 152 5.08 S 22.10 E
Benalla 166 36.33 S 145.59 E
Benamejí 34 37.16 N 4.32 W
Benara ∧ 157a 12.53 S 45.10 E
Benares
→ Vārānasi 124 25.20 N 83.00 E
Bénat, Cap › 62 43.05 N 6.22 E
Benátky nad Jizerou 54 50.17 N 14.51 E
Bena-Tshadi 152 4.40 S 22.49 E
Benavente, Esp. 34 42.00 N 5.41 W
Benavente, Port. 34 38.59 N 8.48 W
Benavides 196 27.35 N 98.24 W
Benavidez 258 34.25 S 58.42 W
Ben Avon 279b 40.31 N 80.05 W
Ben Avon Heights 279b 40.31 N 80.04 W
Ben Badis 34 34.57 N 0.55 W
Benbane Head › 48 55.15 N 6.28 W
Benbecula I 46 57.26 N 7.21 W
Ben Bolt 196 27.39 N 98.05 W
Benbonyathe Hill ∧ 166 30.24 S 139.11 E
Benbrook 222 32.40 N 97.27 W
Benbrook Lake ⊜[1] 222 32.38 N 97.27 W
Ben Cat 110 11.09 N 106.36 E
Ben Cat, Rach ≃ 269c 10.50 N 106.42 E
Bencha, Khao Phanom ∧ 110 8.17 N 98.56 E
Ben-Chicao, Col de)(34 36.12 N 2.45 E
Bencubbin 162 30.48 S 117.52 E
Bend 202 44.03 N 121.18 W
Benda, Tanjung › 115a 6.37 S 111.29 E
Bendaja 150 7.10 N 11.15 W
Bende 150 5.36 N 7.39 E
Bendel □[3] 150 6.00 N 6.00 E
Bendela 152 3.18 S 17.36 E
Bendeleben, Mount ∧ 180 65.10 N 164.03 W
Bendemeer 166 30.53 S 151.10 E
Bender Beyla 144 9.29 N 50.49 E
Benderge ∧ 158 31.06 S 27.58 E
Bendersville 208 39.59 N 77.15 W
Bendery 38 46.48 N 29.29 E
Bendigo 169 36.46 S 144.17 E
Bendimahi ≃ 84 38.56 N 43.38 E
Bendorf 56 50.25 N 7.34 E
Bendugu 150 9.32 N 10.57 W
Bēne 76 56.29 N 23.04 E
Bene Beraq 132 32.05 N 34.50 E
Benedict 208 38.30 N 76.40 W
Benediktenwand ⦁[4] 64 47.39 N 11.28 E
Beneditinos 250 5.27 S 42.22 W
Benedito Leite 250 7.13 S 44.34 W
Bénéna 150 13.07 N 4.22 W
Benenitra 157b 23.27 S 45.05 E
Benepú, Rada ⩧[3] 174z 27.10 S 109.25 W
Beneraird ∧[2] 44 55.04 N 4.57 W
Benešov 30 49.47 N 14.43 E
Benešov nad Ploučnicí 54 50.45 N 14.22 E
Bénestroff 56 48.55 N 6.45 E
Benetutti 71 40.27 N 9.10 E
Beneuvre 58 47.42 N 4.57 E
Bene Vagienna 62 44.33 N 7.50 E
Bénévent-l'Abbaye 32 46.07 N 1.38 E
Benevento 68 41.08 N 14.45 E
Benevento □[4] 68 41.15 N 14.17 E
Benezett 214 41.19 N 78.23 W
Benfeld 58 48.22 N 7.36 E
Benfica ◆•[8], Bra. 287a 22.53 S 43.15 W
Benfica ◆•[8], Port. 266c 38.45 N 9.12 W
Benfica, Estádio ♦ 266c 38.45 N 9.11 W
Bèng ≃, Lao 110 19.53 N 101.08 E
Beng ≃, Zhg. 98 35.05 N 118.24 E
Benga 154 13.19 S 34.16 E
Bengābād 126 24.18 N 86.21 E
Bengal, Bay of c 12 15.00 N 90.00 E
Bengala, Golfo del
→ Bengal, Bay of c 12 15.00 N 90.00 E
Bengalen, Golf von
→ Bengal, Bay of c 12 15.00 N 90.00 E
Bengamisa 154 0.57 N 25.10 E
Bengara 112 3.11 N 117.12 E
Ben Gardane 148 33.08 N 11.13 E
Bengasi
→ Banghāzī 146 32.07 N 20.04 E
Bengbis 152 3.27 N 12.27 E
Bengbu 100 32.58 N 117.24 E
Benger 168a 33.11 S 115.52 E
Benghazi
→ Banghāzī 146 32.07 N 20.04 E
Ben Giang 110 15.41 N 107.47 E
Bengkalis 114 1.28 N 102.07 E
Bengkalis, Pulau I 114 1.30 N 102.15 E
Bengkalis, Selat ʊ 114 1.30 N 102.00 E
Bengkayang 112 0.50 N 109.29 E
Bengkoka ≃ 116 6.50 N 117.03 E
Bengkulu 112 3.48 S 102.16 E
Bengkulu □[4] 112 4.00 S 102.30 E
Bengo □[5] 152 8.30 S 13.20 E
Bengo ≃ 152 8.45 S 13.24 E
Bengo, Baía do c 152 8.43 S 13.21 E
Bengoi 164 3.01 S 130.12 E
Bengough 184 49.24 N 105.08 W
Bengtsfors 26 59.02 N 12.13 E
Benguela 152 12.35 S 13.25 E
Benguela □[5] 152 12.45 S 14.30 E
Benguerir 148 32.14 N 7.57 W
Benguet □[4] 116 16.30 N 120.40 E
Bengut, Cap › 34 36.55 N 3.54 E
Benha
→ Banhā 142 30.28 N 31.11 E
Benham 192 36.57 N 82.56 W
Ben Hur 222 31.30 N 96.44 W
Beni, Nig. 146 10.27 N 10.24 E
Beni, Zaïre 154 0.30 N 29.28 E
Beni □[5] 248 14.00 S 65.30 W
Beni ≃ 248 10.58 S 66.09 W
Béni Abbas 148 30.08 N 2.10 W
Benicarló 34 40.25 N 0.26 E
Benicia 226 38.02 N 122.09 W
Benicia Capitol State Historic Park ♦ 282 38.03 N 122.09 W
Benicia State Recreation Area ♦ 282 38.05 N 122.13 W
Benicito ≃ 248 11.32 S 65.47 W
Benidorm 34 38.32 N 0.08 W
Beni-Mellal 148 32.22 N 6.29 W
Beni-Mellal □[4] 148 32.22 N 6.27 W
Benin (Bénin) □[1], Afr. 134 9.30 N 2.15 E
Benin (Bénin) □[1], Afr. 150 9.30 N 2.15 E
Benin ≃ 150 5.45 N 5.04 E
Benin, Bight of c[3] 150 5.30 N 3.00 E
Benin City 150 6.19 N 5.41 E
Beni Saf 148 35.19 N 1.23 W
Benisheikh 146 11.49 N 12.29 E
Benissa 34 38.34 N 0.03 E
Beni Suef
→ Banī Suwayf 142 29.05 N 31.05 E
Benito 184 51.55 N 101.31 W
Benito Juárez, Arg. 252 37.40 S 59.48 W
Benito Juárez, Méx. 234 19.14 N 100.28 W
Benito Juárez, Méx. 234 17.50 N 92.32 W
Benito Juárez, Aeropuerto Internacional ⊠ 286a 19.26 N 99.04 W
Benito Juárez, Presa ⊜[1] 234 16.27 N 95.30 W
Benit Point › 116 9.54 N 125.17 E
Benjamim Constant 256 21.57 S 42.53 W
Benjamin 196 33.35 N 99.48 W
Benjamín, Isla I 254 44.40 S 74.08 W
Benjamín Aceval 252 24.58 S 57.34 W
Benjamin Constant 246 4.22 S 70.02 W
Benjamin Franklin Bridge ◆•[5] 285 39.57 N 75.08 W
Benjamín Hill 232 30.10 N 111.10 W
Benjamín Zorrilla 252 39.06 S 65.29 W
Benkelman 198 40.02 N 101.31 W
Benken 54 52.10 N 12.28 E
Benkovac 36 44.02 N 15.37 E
Benld 219 39.05 N 89.48 W
Benllech 44 53.19 N 4.13 W
Ben Lomond 226 37.05 N 122.05 W
Ben Lomond National Park ♦ 166 41.34 S 147.11 E
Ben Mehidi 36 36.46 N 7.54 E
Benmore, Lake ⊜[1] 172 44.25 S 170.15 E
Benndale 194 30.52 N 88.48 W
Benndorf 54 51.34 N 11.29 E
Benneckenstein 54 51.40 N 10.45 E
Bennekom 52 52.00 N 5.40 E
Bennet 198 40.40 N 96.30 W
Bennett, Lake ⊜ 162 22.55 S 130.57 E
Bennetta, ostrov I 74 76.21 N 148.56 E
Bennett Lake ⊜, Can. 180 60.05 N 134.50 W
Bennett Lake ⊜, Mb., Can. 184 53.28 N 96.05 W
Bennett Lake ⊜, On., Can. 212 44.55 N 76.27 W
Bennett Pass)(224 45.18 N 121.39 W
Bennettsbridge 48 52.36 N 7.12 W
Bennetts Creek ≃ 210 42.16 N 77.35 W
Bennettsville 192 34.37 N 79.41 W
Bennettswood 274b 37.51 S 145.07 E
Bennigsen 52 52.14 N 9.40 E
Benninghofen ◆•[8] 263 51.29 N 7.31 E
Bennington, In., U.S. 218 38.52 N 85.08 W
Bennington, Ks., U.S. 198 39.01 N 97.35 W
Bennington, Vt., U.S. 210 42.52 N 73.11 W
Bennington □[6] 207 42.50 N 73.08 W
Bennington Battle Monument ⊥ 210 42.53 N 73.13 W
Benniu 106 31.52 N 119.48 E
Beno 152 3.37 S 17.48 E
Benoa 115b 8.46 S 115.13 E
Ben Ohau Range ⋏ 172 44.00 S 170.00 E
Benoit 194 33.39 N 91.00 W
Benom, Gunong ∧ 114 3.49 N 102.04 E
Benoni 158 26.11 S 28.19 E
Benoni □[5] 273d 26.08 S 28.22 E
Benoni-Suid 273d 26.13 S 28.18 E
Bénoué (Benue) ≃ 134 7.48 N 6.46 E
Bénoué, Parc National de la ♦ 146 8.20 N 13.50 E
Benover 260 51.13 N 0.26 E
Bénoy 146 8.59 N 16.19 E
Benque Viejo del Carmen 232 17.05 N 89.08 W
Benrad ◆•[8] 263 51.20 N 6.30 E
Benrath ◆•[8] 56 51.10 N 6.51 E
Benrath, Schloss ⊥ 263 51.10 N 6.52 E
Bensalem 285 40.04 N 74.56 W
Bensbach ≃ 164 9.08 S 141.00 E
Bensberg 56 50.58 N 7.09 E
Bensdorf 54 52.24 N 12.20 E
Ben Sekka, Rass › 36 37.21 N 9.45 E
Bensenville 278 41.57 N 87.56 W
Bensersiel 52 53.40 N 7.34 E
Benshausen 54 50.38 N 10.35 E
Bensheim 56 49.41 N 8.37 E
Bensley 208 37.26 N 77.26 W
Ben-Slimane 148 33.41 N 7.10 W
Ben-Slimane □[4] 148 33.40 N 7.10 W
Ben Smih 36 36.23 N 7.31 E
Benson, Eng., U.K. 42 51.38 N 1.05 W
Benson, Az., U.S. 200 31.58 N 110.17 W
Benson, Md., U.S. 208 39.30 N 76.23 W
Benson, Mn., U.S. 198 45.18 N 95.35 W
Benson, N.C., U.S. 192 35.22 N 78.32 W
Bensonhurst ◆•[8] 276 40.35 N 73.59 W
Benson Point › 174o 1.56 N 157.29 W
Bens Run ≃ 284b 39.19 N 76.48 W
Bent 128 26.17 N 59.31 E
Benta 114 4.01 N 101.58 E
Benteng (Salayar) 112 6.08 S 120.27 E
Bentheim, Dtsch. 52 52.17 N 7.10 E
Bentheim, Mi., U.S. 216 42.42 N 85.55 W
Ben Thuy 110 18.39 N 105.42 E
Bentiaba 152 14.15 S 12.21 E
Bentiaba ≃ 152 14.29 S 12.50 E
Bentinck Island I, Austl. 164 17.04 S 139.30 E
Bentinck Island I, Mya. 110 11.45 N 98.03 E
Bentiu 140 9.14 N 29.50 E
Bentleigh 274b 37.55 S 145.02 E
Bentley, Ab., Can. 182 52.28 N 114.04 W
Bentley, Eng., U.K. 44 53.33 N 1.09 W
Bentley College ʋ[2] 283 42.23 N 71.13 W
Bentleyville, Oh., U.S. 279a 41.25 N 81.26 W
Bentleyville, Pa., U.S. 214 40.07 N 80.00 W
Bento Gomes ≃ 248 16.40 S 57.12 W
Bento Gonçalves 252 29.10 S 51.31 W
Bentol 150 6.26 N 10.36 W
Benton, Ar., U.S. 194 34.33 N 92.35 W
Benton, Il., U.S. 194 37.59 N 88.55 W
Benton, In., U.S. 216 41.30 N 85.45 W
Benton, Ky., U.S. 194 36.51 N 88.21 W
Benton, La., U.S. 194 32.41 N 93.44 W
Benton, Ms., U.S. 194 32.49 N 90.15 W
Benton, Mo., U.S. 194 37.05 N 89.33 W
Benton, Oh., U.S. 214 40.36 N 81.51 W
Benton, Pa., U.S. 210 41.11 N 76.23 W
Benton, Tn., U.S. 192 35.10 N 84.39 W
Benton, Wi., U.S. 190 42.34 N 90.22 W
Benton □[6] 216 40.37 N 87.19 W
Benton City, Mo., U.S. 219 39.08 N 91.45 W
Benton City, Wa., U.S. 202 46.15 N 119.29 W
Bentong 114 3.32 N 101.55 E
Benton Harbor 216 42.07 N 86.26 W
Benton Heights 216 42.07 N 86.24 W
Bentonia 194 32.38 N 90.21 W
Benton Lake ⊜ 202 47.40 N 111.20 W
Benton Ridge 216 41.00 N 83.47 W
Bentonville, Ar., U.S. 194 36.22 N 94.12 W
Bentonville, In., U.S. 218 39.45 N 85.15 W
Bentonville, Oh., U.S. 218 38.45 N 83.37 W
Ben Tre 110 10.14 N 106.23 E
Bent's Old Fort National Historic Site ⊥ 198 38.05 N 103.28 W
Benua, Pulau I 112 0.56 N 107.27 E
Benue □[3] 150 7.15 N 8.00 E
Benue (Bénoué) ≃ 134 7.48 N 6.46 E
Benut 114 1.38 N 103.16 E
Benwee ∧ 48 53.35 N 9.31 W
Benwee Head › 48 54.20 N 9.50 W
Ben Wheeler 222 32.27 N 95.42 W
Benxi (Penhsi), Zhg. 104 41.18 N 123.45 E
Benxi (Xiaoshi), Zhg. 104 41.17 N 124.07 E
Benza 152 6.16 S 12.57 E
Beograd (Belgrade) 38 44.50 N 20.30 E
Beohāri 124 24.03 N 81.23 E
Beonta 272b 22.31 N 88.31 E
Béoumi 150 7.40 N 5.34 W
Beowawe 204 40.35 N 116.28 W
Beppu 96 33.17 N 131.30 E
Beppu-wan c 96 33.18 N 131.35 E
Bequia I 241h 13.01 N 61.13 W
Bequimão 250 2.26 S 44.47 W
Bera 126 24.05 N 89.37 E
Berābāria 272b 22.52 N 88.34 E
Beraberi, India 272b 22.46 N 88.27 E
Berāberi, India 272b 22.51 N 88.12 E
Beraketa, Madag. 157b 24.11 S 45.42 E
Beraketa, Madag. 157b 23.07 S 44.25 E
Beramanja 157b 13.13 S 48.56 E
Bérandjoko 152 3.06 N 17.17 E
Berāsi 124 23.36 N 81.51 E
Berasia 124 23.38 N 77.26 E
Berat 38 40.42 N 19.57 E
Beratzhausen 60 49.06 N 11.48 E
Berau 58 47.42 N 8.15 E
Berau ≃ 112 2.10 N 117.42 E
Berau, Teluk c 164 2.30 S 132.30 E
Beravina 157b 18.10 S 45.14 E
Berazategui 258 34.46 S 58.13 W
Berazategui □[5] 288 34.50 S 58.10 W
Berbenno di Valtellina 64 46.10 N 9.44 E
Berbera 144 10.25 N 45.02 E
Berbérati 152 4.16 N 15.47 E
Berbice ≃ 246 6.17 N 57.32 W
Berceto 64 44.31 N 9.59 E
Berchem, Bel. 50 51.12 N 4.26 E
Berchem, Bel. 50 50.47 N 3.30 E
Berchem-Sainte-Agathe 56 50.52 N 4.17 E
Berchidda 71 40.47 N 9.10 E
Berching 60 49.07 N 11.27 E
Berchtesgaden 64 47.38 N 13.01 E
Berchtesgaden, Nationalpark ♦ 64 47.30 N 13.00 E
Berchum ◆•[8] 263 51.23 N 7.32 E
Berck 50 50.24 N 1.34 E
Berclair 196 28.32 N 97.36 W
Berčogur 86 48.25 N 58.44 E
Bercu 50 50.31 N 3.17 E
Berd 84 40.53 N 45.23 E
Berda ≃ 78 46.48 N 36.52 E
Berdaale 144 7.04 N 47.51 E
Berdale 144 4.56 N 45.02 E
Berd'ansk 78 46.45 N 36.49 E
Berd'anskaja kosa ›[2] 78 46.42 N 36.48 E
Berd'anskij zaliv c 78 46.42 N 36.35 E
Berd'auš 86 55.09 N 59.09 E
Berdičev 78 49.54 N 28.36 E
Berdigest'ach 74 62.06 N 126.40 E
Berdniki 80 57.25 N 46.33 E
Berdorf 56 49.50 N 6.21 E
Berdsk 86 54.47 N 83.02 E
Berd'užje 86 55.48 N 68.19 E
Berdyansk
→ Berd'ansk 78 46.45 N 36.49 E
Béré, Tchad 146 9.20 N 16.09 E
Bere, Turk. 128 39.47 N 58.06 E
Berea, Ky., U.S. 192 37.34 N 84.17 W
Berea, Oh., U.S. 214 41.21 N 81.51 W
Berea, S.C., U.S. 192 34.53 N 82.27 W
Bere Alston 42 50.29 N 4.11 W
Berebei 164 9.31 S 147.27 E
Beregajevo 86 57.10 N 87.32 E
Beregomet 78 48.12 N 25.21 E
Beregovo 78 48.13 N 22.39 E
Beregovoj 86 55.12 N 73.12 E
Bereguardo 62 45.15 N 9.01 E
Bereina 164 8.40 S 146.30 E
Bereka ≃ 78 49.12 N 36.59 E
Bereketli 130 40.31 N 37.18 E
Bereku 154 4.27 S 35.44 E
Berekua 240d 15.14 N 61.19 W
Berekum 150 7.27 N 2.37 W
Bérem 152 7.33 N 13.55 E
Beren, liman ⊜ 80 46.52 N 44.55 E
Berenda Slough ≃ 226 37.00 N 120.29 W
Berendejevo 82 56.36 N 39.01 E
Berens ≃ 184 52.21 N 97.02 W
Berens Island I 184 52.18 N 97.17 W
Berens River 184 52.22 N 97.02 W
Bere Regis 42 50.46 N 2.14 W
Beresford, N.B., Can. 186 47.42 N 65.42 W
Beresford, S.D., U.S. 198 43.04 N 96.46 W
Beresina
→ Berezina ≃ 76 52.33 N 30.14 E
Berestečko 78 50.23 N 25.07 E
Berești 38 46.06 N 27.53 E
Berettyó (Barcău) ≃ 38 46.59 N 21.07 E
Berettyóújfalu 30 47.14 N 21.32 E
Berevo, Madag. 157b 17.14 S 44.17 E
Berevo, Madag. 157b 19.44 S 44.58 E
Berezajka 76 57.59 N 33.54 E
Berezan' 78 50.19 N 31.30 E
Berezanskaja 78 45.43 N 39.34 E
Berezanskij liman c[1] 78 46.43 N 31.30 E
Berežany 78 49.27 N 24.56 E
Berezdov 78 50.27 N 27.05 E
Berezina ≃, Bela. 76 52.33 N 30.14 E
Berezina ≃, Bela. 76 53.48 N 25.59 E
Berezino, Bela. 76 53.49 N 28.59 E
Berezino, Bela. 76 54.54 N 28.12 E
Berezino, Kaz. 80 50.06 N 48.52 E
Berezino, Ukr. 78 46.14 N 29.12 E
Berezinskij zapovednik ♦ 76 54.40 N 28.15 E
Berezna 78 51.34 N 31.47 E
Berezn'agi 78 49.59 N 41.06 E
Berezn'aki, Ukr. 78 49.09 N 31.57 E
Berezn'aki, Ukr. 78 49.51 N 33.01 E
Bereznegovatoje 78 47.20 N 32.49 E
Berežnica 78 51.27 N 26.27 E
Bereznik 24 62.51 N 42.40 E
Berezniki 86 59.24 N 56.46 E
Berford Lake ⊜ 212 44.48 N 81.11 W
Berg, Dtsch. 64 47.58 N 11.21 E
Berg, Lux. 56 49.49 N 6.05 E
Berg, Nor. 24 69.26 N 17.15 E
Berg, Öst. 64 46.45 N 13.09 E
Berga, Dtsch. 54 50.45 N 12.10 E
Berga, Dtsch. 54 51.27 N 11.00 E
Berga, Esp. 34 42.06 N 1.51 E
Berga, Sve. 40 59.21 N 16.26 E
Bergama 130 39.07 N 27.11 E
Bergambacht 52 51.56 N 4.46 E
Bergamo 62 45.41 N 9.43 E
Bergamo □[4] 64 45.50 N 9.48 E
Bergan Point › 276 40.40 N 73.20 W
Bergantín 246 10.01 N 64.22 W
Bergantino 64 45.05 N 11.15 E
Bergara 34 43.07 N 2.25 W
Bergbau Museum ʋ 263 51.29 N 7.13 E
Bergby 26 60.56 N 17.02 E
Berge, Dtsch. 52 52.37 N 7.44 E
Berge, Dtsch. 54 53.15 N 11.50 E
Berge, Dtsch. 263 51.21 N 7.22 E
Bergedorf ◆•[8] 52 53.29 N 10.13 E
Bergei ∧[2] 263 51.13 N 7.46 E
Bergeijk 52 51.19 N 5.22 E
Bergen
→ Mons, Bel. 50 50.27 N 3.56 E
Bergen, Dtsch. 52 52.48 N 9.58 E
Bergen, Dtsch. 54 52.53 N 10.58 E
Bergen, Dtsch. 64 47.48 N 12.35 E
Bergen, Ned. 52 52.40 N 4.41 E
Bergen, Nor. 26 60.23 N 5.20 E
Bergen, N.Y., U.S. 210 43.05 N 77.56 W
Bergen □[6] 210 40.53 N 74.03 W
Bergen aan Zee 52 52.38 N 4.37 E
Bergen [auf Rügen] 54 54.25 N 13.26 E
Bergen Basin c 276 40.39 N 73.49 W
Bergen-Belsen-Denkmal ⊥ 52 52.46 N 9.55 E
Berg en Dal 250 5.09 N 55.04 W
Bergenfield 210 40.55 N 73.59 W
Bergen Mall ◆•[9] 276 40.55 N 74.04 W
Bergen op Zoom 52 51.30 N 4.17 E
Berger 219 38.40 N 91.20 W
Bergerac 32 44.51 N 0.29 E
Bergères-lès-Vertus 50 48.53 N 4.00 E
Bergerhof 263 51.12 N 7.21 E
Bergfelde 54 52.40 N 13.19 E
Berggiesshübel 54 50.52 N 13.57 E
Berghausen, Dtsch. 263 51.18 N 7.17 E
Berghausen, Dtsch. 263 51.07 N 6.55 E
Bergheim, Dtsch. 56 50.55 N 6.38 E
Bergheim, Fr. 58 48.12 N 7.22 E
Bergheim, Öst. 64 47.50 N 13.02 E
Berghem 52 51.46 N 5.34 E
Berghofen ◆•[8] 263 51.29 N 7.32 E
Bergholtz 210 43.06 N 78.53 W
Bergholtz Creek ≃ 284a 43.05 N 78.57 W
Bergholz 214 40.31 N 80.53 W
Bergholz-Rehbrücke 54 52.20 N 13.05 E
Bergisches Land ◆•[1] 56 51.00 N 7.30 E
Bergisch Gladbach 56 50.59 N 7.07 E
Bergkamen 52 51.38 N 7.38 E
Bergkvara 26 56.23 N 16.05 E
Bergland 190 46.35 N 89.34 W
Bergneustadt 56 51.01 N 7.39 E
Bergnicourt 50 49.25 N 4.15 E
Bergö I 26 62.58 N 21.11 E
Bergoo 188 38.29 N 80.18 W
Bergplaas 158 33.54 S 22.40 E
Bergrheinfeld 56 50.00 N 10.10 E
Bergsäng 40 60.06 N 13.33 E
Bergsbrunna 40 59.49 N 17.43 E
Bergsche Maas ≃ 52 51.45 N 5.08 E
Bergshamra 40 59.38 N 18.37 E
Bergsjö 26 61.59 N 17.04 E
Bergslagen ◆•[1] 40 59.55 N 15.00 E
Bergstrom Air Force Base ■ 222 30.12 N 97.40 W
Bergtheim 56 49.54 N 10.04 E
Berguent 148 34.03 N 2.02 W
Bergues 50 50.58 N 2.26 E
Bergum 52 53.11 N 5.59 E
Bergün 58 46.38 N 9.45 E
Bergville 158 28.52 S 29.18 E
Bergvreten 40 60.31 N 16.26 E
Bergwitz 54 51.48 N 12.35 E
Berhala, Selat ʊ 112 0.48 S 104.25 E
Beri 124 28.42 N 76.35 E
Berici, Monti ⋏ 64 45.26 N 11.31 E
Berikul'skij 86 55.32 N 88.08 E
Beringa, ostrov I 74 55.00 N 165.15 E
Beringen 56 51.03 N 5.13 E
Bering Glacier ⊓ 180 60.15 N 143.30 W
Beringhausen 56 51.24 N 8.46 E
Beringil 140 12.10 N 25.41 E
Beringin 112 3.41 S 104.18 E
Beringovskij 180 63.03 N 179.19 E
Bering Sea ⩧[2] 16 60.00 N 175.00 W
Bering Strait ʊ 180 65.30 N 169.00 W
Berinsfield 42 51.40 N 1.11 W
Berislav 78 46.51 N 33.26 E
Berisso 258 34.52 S 57.53 W
Berisso □[5] 288 34.55 S 57.53 W
Berja 34 36.51 N 2.57 W
Berkåk 26 62.50 N 10.00 E
Berkakit 74 56.34 N 124.48 E
Berkane 148 34.59 N 2.20 W
Berkel ≃ 52 52.09 N 6.12 E
Berkeley, Eng., U.K. 42 51.42 N 2.27 W
Berkeley, Ca., U.S. 226 37.52 N 122.16 W
Berkeley, Il., U.S. 278 41.53 N 87.54 W
Berkeley, Mo., U.S. 219 38.45 N 90.19 W
Berkeley, R.I., U.S. 207 41.55 N 71.25 W
Berkeley, Vale of V 42 51.43 N 2.25 W
Berkeley Heights 210 40.41 N 74.26 W
Berkeley Hills 279b 40.32 N 80.00 W
Berkeley Hills ⋏[2] 282 37.54 N 122.16 W
Berkeley Plantation ⊥ 208 37.19 N 77.10 W
Berkeley Springs 188 39.37 N 78.13 W
Berkhamsted 42 51.46 N 0.35 W
Berkheim 58 48.02 N 10.04 E
Berkley, Ma., U.S. 207 41.50 N 71.05 W
Berkley, Mi., U.S. 281 42.30 N 83.11 W
Berkner Island I 9 79.30 S 49.30 W
Berks □[6] 208 40.20 N 75.50 W
Berkshire, Ma., U.S. 207 42.30 N 73.11 W
Berkshire, N.Y., U.S. 210 42.18 N 76.11 W
Berkshire □[6], Eng., U.K. 42 51.30 N 1.20 W
Berkshire □[6], Ma., U.S. 207 42.27 N 73.15 W
Berkshire Downs ⋏[1] 42 51.33 N 1.24 W
Berkshire Hills ⋏[2] 207 42.20 N 73.10 W
Berlaar 56 51.07 N 4.39 E
Berlaimont 50 50.12 N 3.49 E
Berland ≃ 182 54.01 N 116.50 W
Berlanga de Duero 34 41.28 N 2.51 W
Berlenga I 34 39.25 N 9.30 W
Berlengas ≃ 250 5.39 S 42.19 W
Berlevåg 24 70.51 N 29.06 E
Berlicum 52 51.42 N 5.23 E
Berlikum 52 53.15 N 5.39 E
Berlin, Dtsch. 54 52.31 N 13.24 E
Berlin, Dtsch. 264a 52.31 N 13.24 E
Berlin, S. Afr. 158 32.54 S 27.35 E
Berlin, Ct., U.S. 207 41.37 N 72.44 W
Berlin, Md., U.S. 208 38.19 N 75.13 W
Berlin, Ma., U.S. 207 42.22 N 71.38 W
Berlin, N.H., U.S. 188 44.28 N 71.11 W
Berlin, N.J., U.S. 208 39.47 N 74.55 W
Berlin, N.Y., U.S. 210 42.42 N 73.23 W
Berlin, Oh., U.S. 214 40.34 N 81.48 W
Berlin, Pa., U.S. 188 39.55 N 78.57 W
Berlin, Wi., U.S. 190 43.58 N 88.56 W
Berlin □[3] 264a 52.33 N 13.30 E
Berlin, Mount ∧ 9 76.03 S 135.52 W
Berlin Center 214 41.01 N 80.57 W
Berlinchen 54 53.13 N 12.34 E
Berliner Brücke ◆•[5] 263 51.27 N 6.47 E
Berlinguet Inlet c 176 71.10 N 85.35 W
Berlin Heights 214 41.20 N 82.30 W
Berlin-Ichthyosaur State Park ♦ 204 38.51 N 117.35 W
Berlin Lake ⊜[1] 214 41.00 N 81.00 W
Berlin Mountain ∧ 210 42.42 N 73.17 W
Berlin Park ♦ 285 39.47 N 74.57 W
Berlin-Schönefeld, Flughafen ⊠ 54 52.23 N 13.31 E
Berlinsville 210 40.47 N 75.35 W
Berlin-Tegel, Flughafen ⊠ 54 52.34 N 13.18 E
Berlin-Tempelhof, Flughafen ⊠ 54 52.29 N 13.25 E
Bermagui 166 36.25 S 150.04 E
Bermamyt, gora ∧ 84 43.41 N 42.27 E
Bermejillo 232 25.53 N 103.37 W
Bermejito ≃ 252 25.39 S 60.11 W
Bermejo 252 31.37 S 67.39 W
Bermejo ≃, Arg. 252 31.52 S 67.22 W
Bermejo ≃, S.A. 252 26.51 S 58.23 W
Bermejo, Paso del)(252 32.50 S 70.05 W
Bermen, Lac ⊜ 176 53.35 N 68.55 W
Bermeo 34 43.26 N 2.43 W
Bermillo de Sayago 34 41.22 N 6.06 W
Bermo 124 23.47 N 85.57 E
Bermondsey ◆•[8] 260 51.30 N 0.04 W
Bermuda □[2], N.A. 230 32.20 N 64.45 W
Bermuda □[2], N.A. 240a 32.20 N 64.45 W
Bermuda Rise ✦[3] 16 32.30 N 65.00 W
Bermudes
→ Bermuda □[2] 240a 32.20 N 64.45 W
Bermudian Creek ≃ 208 40.01 N 76.55 W
Bern (Berne) 58 46.57 N 7.26 E
Bern (Berne) □[3] 58 46.55 N 7.35 E
Bern, Flughafen ⊠ 58 46.55 N 7.30 E
Berna
→ Bern 58 46.57 N 7.26 E
Bernabéu, Estadio ♦ 266a 40.27 N 3.41 W
Bernal ◆•[8] 258 34.42 S 58.17 W
Bernalda 68 40.24 N 16.41 E
Bernalillo 200 35.18 N 106.33 W
Bernam ≃ 114 3.48 N 100.57 E
Bernardo O'Higgins, Parque ♦ 286e 33.28 S 70.40 W
Bernardston 207 42.40 N 72.33 W
Bernardsville 210 40.43 N 74.34 W
Bernasconi 252 37.54 S 63.43 W
Bernate 266b 45.29 N 8.49 E
Bernau am Chiemsee 64 47.48 N 12.22 E
Bernau bei Berlin 54 52.40 N 13.35 E
Bernauer Heide ◆•[3] 264a 52.43 N 13.30 E
Bernaville 50 50.08 N 2.10 E
Bernay 50 49.06 N 0.36 E
Bernbeuren 58 47.44 N 10.46 E
Bernburg 54 51.48 N 11.44 E
Berndorf 61 47.57 N 16.08 E
Berne, Dtsch. 52 53.11 N 8.29 E
Berne
→ Bern, Schw. 58 46.57 N 7.26 E
Berne, In., U.S. 216 40.39 N 84.57 W
Berne, N.Y., U.S. 210 42.38 N 74.08 W
Berneburg 56 51.04 N 9.53 E
Berner Alpen ⋏ 58 46.30 N 7.30 E
Berneray I, Scot., U.K. 46 57.43 N 7.12 W
Berneray I, Scot., U.K. 46 56.47 N 7.38 W
Berneval-le-Grand 50 49.57 N 1.12 E
Berngardovka 265a 60.01 N 30.36 E
Bernhardina 158 27.53 S 28.40 E
Bernhards Bay 210 43.15 N 75.56 W
Bernhardsthal 61 48.41 N 16.52 E
Bernice 194 32.49 N 92.39 W
Bernie 194 36.40 N 89.58 W
Bernier Bay c 176 71.00 N 87.30 W
Bernier Island I 162 24.52 S 113.08 E
Bernina ⋏ 58 46.22 N 9.50 E
Bernina, Passo del)(58 46.24 N 10.03 E
Bernina, Piz ∧ 58 46.21 N 9.51 E
Bernisdale 46 57.27 N 6.24 W
Bernkastel-Kues 56 49.55 N 7.04 E
Bernried 64 47.52 N 11.17 E
Bernsbach 54 50.34 N 12.46 E
Bernsdorf 54 51.22 N 14.04 E
Bernsfelden 56 49.34 N 9.53 E
Bernstadt 54 51.03 N 14.50 E
Bernville 208 40.26 N 76.07 W
Bero ≃ 152 15.10 S 12.09 E
Beroga 114 2.56 N 101.55 E
Berolzheim 56 49.28 N 9.32 E
Beromünster 58 47.12 N 8.11 E
Berón de Astrada 252 27.33 S 57.32 W
Beror Ḥayil 132 31.33 N 34.38 E
Beroroha 157b 21.41 S 45.10 E
Ber'ostovica 76 53.07 N 23.58 E
Beroun 30 49.58 N 14.04 E
Berounka ≃ 30 50.00 N 14.24 E
Berovo 38 41.42 N 22.51 E
Berowra 170 33.37 S 151.09 E
Ber'oza, Bela. 76 52.32 N 24.59 E
Ber'oza, Ukr. 78 51.44 N 33.52 E

Symbols in the index entries represent the broad categories identified in the key at the right. Symbols with superior numbers (⋏[1]) identify subcategories (see complete key on page I · 1).

Symbole im Register stellen die rechts im Schlüssel erklärten Kategorien dar. Symbole mit hochgestellten Ziffern (⋏[1]) bezeichnen Unterabteilungen einer Kategorie (vgl. vollständiger Schlüssel auf Seite I · 1).

Los símbolos incluídos en el texto del índice representan las grandes categorías identificadas con la clave a la derecha. Los símbolos con numeros en su parte superior (⋏[1]) identifican las subcategorías (véase la clave completa en la página I · 1).

Les symboles de l'index représentent les catégories indiquées dans la légende à droite. Les symboles suivis d'un indice (⋏[1]) représentent des sous-catégories (voir légende complète à la page I · 1).

Os símbolos incluídos no texto do índice representam as grandes categorias identificadas com a chave à direita. Os símbolos com números em sua parte superior (⋏[1]) identificam as subcategorias (veja-se a chave completa à página I · 1).

	English	Deutsch	Español	Français	Português
∧	Mountain	Berg	Montaña	Montagne	Montanha
⋏	Mountains	Gebirge	Montañas	Montagnes	Montanhas
)(	Pass	Paß	Paso	Col	Passo
V	Valley, Canyon	Tal, Cañon	Valle, Cañón	Vallée, Canyon	Vale, Canhão
≃	Plain	Ebene	Llano	Plaine	Planície
›	Cape	Kap	Cabo	Cap	Cabo
I	Island	Insel	Isla	Île	Ilha
II	Islands	Inseln	Islas	Îles	Ilhas
⦁	Other Topographic Features	Andere Topographische Objekte	Otros Elementos Topográficos	Autres données topographiques	Outros acidentes topográficos

ESPAÑOL
Nombre | Página | Lat.°′ | Long.°′ W = Oeste

Ber'ozno 78 51.00 N 26.45 E
Ber'ožnoje 76 59.55 N 39.17 E
Ber'ozovaja ≐ 80 48.31 N 41.03 E
Ber'ozovaja Rudka 78 50.19 N 32.14 E
Ber'ozovka, Bela. 76 53.43 N 25.30 E
Ber'ozovka, Kaz. 80 51.11 N 53.16 E
Ber'ozovka, Ross. 24 65.00 N 56.26 E
Ber'ozovka, Ross. 76 53.26 N 38.53 E
Ber'ozovka, Ross. 80 52.06 N 45.07 E
Ber'ozovka, Ross. 86 51.51 N 82.58 E
Ber'ozovka, Ross. 86 56.03 N 93.07 E
Ber'ozovka, Ross. 86 54.02 N 76.35 E
Ber'ozovka, Ross. 86 59.24 N 82.38 E
Ber'ozovka, Ross. 86 59.35 N 56.02 E
Ber'ozovka, Ross. 86 57.37 N 57.18 E
Ber'ozovka, Ross. 88 57.46 N 116.09 E
Ber'ozovka, Ross. 89 50.35 N 127.52 E
Ber'ozovka, Ross. 265a 59.56 N 30.49 E
Ber'ozovka, Ukr. 78 47.49 N 32.28 E
Ber'ozovka, Ukr. 78 45.35 N 33.20 E
Ber'ozovka, Ukr. 78 47.12 N 30.55 E
Ber'ozovo, Ross. 74 63.56 N 65.02 E
Ber'ozovo, Ross. 80 51.56 N 48.28 E
Ber'ozovo, Ross. 82 54.03 N 36.24 E
Ber'ozovo, Ross. 82 54.19 N 38.17 E
Ber'ozovo, Ukr. 78 51.35 N 27.20 E
Ber'ozovskaja 80 50.16 N 43.59 E
Ber'ozovskij 86 55.39 N 86.16 E
Ber'ozovskij R'adok 76 58.06 N 34.29 E
Ber'ozovskoje 86 55.50 N 89.36 E
Berra 64 44.59 N 11.58 E
Berras, Arroyo los ≐ 288 34.34 S 58.40 W
Berre ≐ 62 44.24 N 4.40 E
Berre, Étang de c 62 43.27 N 5.08 E
Berrechid 148 33.17 N 7.35 W
Berre-des-Alpes 62 43.50 N 7.19 E
Berre-l'Étang 62 43.28 N 5.11 E
Ber Remad, Oued V 148 31.45 N 1.10 E
Berri 166 34.17 S 140.36 E
Berridale 171b 36.22 S 148.50 E
Berriedale 46 58.11 N 3.29 W
Berrien □[6] 216 41.59 N 86.30 W
Berrien Springs 216 41.56 N 86.20 W
Berrigan 166 35.40 S 145.49 E
Berrima 170 34.30 S 150.20 E
Berriozábal 234 16.48 N 93.16 W
Berriyyane 148 32.50 N 3.46 E
Berrouaghia 34 36.08 N 2.55 E
Berrugosa Point › 116 10.23 N 125.33 E
Berry, Austl. 170 34.47 S 150.42 E
Berry, Al., U.S. 194 33.39 N 87.36 W
Berry, Ky., U.S. 218 38.31 N 84.23 W
Berry □[9] 50 47.20 N 2.10 E
Berry, Canal du ≍ 50 47.17 N 1.25 E
Berry-au-Bac 50 49.24 N 3.54 E
Berry Creek ≐, Ab., Can. 182 50.50 N 111.36 W
Berry Creek ≐, Tx., U.S. 222 30.40 N 97.36 W
Berryessa, Lake ⊜[1] 226 38.35 N 122.14 W
Berryessa Creek ≐ 282 37.24 N 121.53 W
Berryessa Peak ∧ 226 38.40 N 122.11 W
Berry Islands II 238 25.34 N 77.45 W
Berry Mountain ∧ 208 40.31 N 77.02 W
Berrysburg 208 40.36 N 76.49 W
Berrys Creek ≐ 276 40.47 N 74.05 W
Berryville 194 36.21 N 93.34 W
Beršad' 78 48.23 N 29.30 E
Berseba 156 26.00 S 17.46 E
Bersenbrück 52 52.33 N 7.56 E
Bersut 80 55.32 N 50.54 E
Berta ≐ 130 41.09 N 41.53 E
Bertam 114 5.09 N 102.03 E
Berté, Lac ⊜ 186 50.48 N 68.30 W
Bertha 198 46.16 N 95.03 W
Berthåga 40 59.52 N 17.35 E
Berthelsdorf 54 51.05 N 14.13 E
Berthier □[6] 206 46.30 N 73.45 W
Berthierville 206 46.05 N 73.10 W
Berthold 198 48.18 N 101.44 W
Berthoud 200 40.18 N 105.04 W
Berthoud Pass)(200 39.45 N 105.45 W
Bertincourt 50 50.05 N 2.59 E
Bertinoro 66 44.09 N 12.08 E
Bertioga 256 23.51 S 46.09 W
Bertioga, Enseada da c 256 23.50 S 46.08 W
Bertkow 54 52.43 N 11.54 E
Bertlich 263 51.37 N 7.04 E
Bertogne 56 50.05 N 5.40 E
Bertolinia 250 7.38 S 43.57 W
Bertoua 152 4.35 N 13.41 E
Bertram 196 30.45 N 98.03 W
Bertrand, Mi., U.S. 216 41.46 N 86.15 W
Bertrand, Ne., U.S. 198 40.31 N 99.38 W
Bertrix 56 49.51 N 5.15 E
Bertry 50 50.05 N 3.27 E
Beru I 14 1.20 S 176.00 E
Beruas 114 4.30 N 100.47 E
Beruri 246 3.54 S 61.22 W
Berville 214 42.55 N 82.53 W
Berville-sur-Mer 50 49.26 N 0.22 E
Berwang 58 47.24 N 10.45 E
Berwick, Austl. 169 38.02 S 145.21 E
Berwick, N.S., Can. 186 45.03 N 64.44 W
Berwick, La., U.S. 194 29.41 N 91.13 W
Berwick, Me., U.S. 188 43.15 N 70.51 W
Berwick, Pa., U.S. 210 41.03 N 76.14 W
Berwick-upon-Tweed 44 55.46 N 2.00 W
Berwyn, Il., U.S. 216 41.51 N 87.47 W
Berwyn, Pa., U.S. 208 40.02 N 75.26 W
Berwyn ⋀ 42 52.53 N 3.24 W
Berwyn Heights 284c 38.59 N 76.54 W
Bērze ≐ 76 56.41 N 23.37 E
Berzé-la-Ville 58 46.22 N 4.42 E
Berz-Macomb Airport ⊠ 281 42.40 N 82.58 W
Bès ≐ 62 44.08 N 6.14 E
Besalampy 157b 16.45 S 44.30 E
Besana in Brianza 62 45.42 N 9.17 E
Besançon 58 47.15 N 6.02 E
Besani 124 24.08 N 80.17 E
Besar, Gunong ∧, Malay. 114 5.10 N 101.18 E
Besar, Gunong ∧, Malay. 114 2.30 N 103.10 E
Besar, Gunung ∧ 112 2.43 S 115.37 E
Besar, Pulau I 115b 8.28 S 122.22 E
Besar Hantu, Gunong ∧ 114 3.12 N 102.02 E
Besaya ≐ 34 43.21 N 4.04 W
Besbes 36 36.42 N 7.51 E
Besed' ≐ 76 52.38 N 31.09 E
Besedino 78 51.42 N 36.28 E
Besedy 265b 55.37 N 37.47 E
Besenfeld 56 48.35 N 8.25 E
Bešenkoviči 76 55.03 N 29.27 E
Beserah 114 3.52 N 103.22 E
Besigheim 56 49.00 N 9.08 E
Besikama 112 9.36 S 124.57 E
Beşiktaş ✦[8] 267b 41.03 N 29.01 E
Beşiri 130 37.55 N 41.18 E
Besitang 114 4.02 N 98.12 E
Beškent 128 38.49 N 65.39 E
Beskid Mountains ⋀ 30 49.40 N 20.00 E
Beşkonak 130 37.08 N 31.12 E
Beskra 148 34.51 N 5.44 E
Beskra □[5] 148 34.00 N 6.00 E
Beškube 85 39.50 N 68.18 E
Beskudnikovo ✦[8] 265b 55.52 N 37.34 E
Beslan 84 43.12 N 44.33 E
Beslenej 84 44.14 N 41.44 E
Besnard Lake ⊜ 184 55.24 N 106.05 W
Besni 130 37.41 N 37.52 E
Besor, Naḥal V 132 31.28 N 34.22 E
Besós ≐ 266d 41.25 N 2.04 E
Besozzo 62 45.51 N 8.39 E
Besp'atovo 82 54.45 N 38.54 E
Beşpınar, Tür. 130 41.09 N 35.14 E
Beşpınar, Tür. 130 37.51 N 41.36 E

FRANÇAIS
Nom | Page | Lat.°′ | Long.°′ W = Ouest

Besputa ≐ 82 54.50 N 37.58 E
Bessacarr 44 53.30 N 1.04 W
Bessancourt 261 49.02 N 2.13 E
Bessans 62 45.19 N 7.00 E
Bessarabia □[9] 38 47.00 N 28.30 E
Bessarabka, Mol. 78 46.20 N 28.58 E
Bessarabka, Ross. 86 53.37 N 73.17 E
Bessaz, gora ∧ 85 43.49 N 68.40 E
Bessbrook 48 54.12 N 6.25 W
Besse, Dtsch. 56 51.13 N 9.23 E
Besse, Nig. 150 11.15 N 4.30 E
Bessèges 62 44.17 N 4.06 E
Bessemer, Al., U.S. 194 33.24 N 86.57 W
Bessemer, Mi., U.S. 190 46.28 N 90.03 W
Bessemer, Pa., U.S. 214 40.58 N 80.29 W
Bessemer City 192 35.17 N 81.17 W
Besser 41 55.52 N 10.39 E
Bessé-sur-Braye 50 47.50 N 0.45 E
Bessheim 26 61.31 N 8.51 E
Besshiyama 96 33.50 N 133.23 E
Bessho 270 34.27 N 135.31 E
Bessonovka 80 53.18 N 45.03 E
Best 52 51.31 N 5.24 E
Best'ach 74 61.52 N 129.55 E
Bestamak, Kaz. 86 49.43 N 55.07 E
Bestamak, Kaz. 86 49.13 N 78.21 E
Beštau, gora ∧ 84 44.06 N 43.01 E
Besten 263 51.39 N 6.54 E
Bestensee 54 52.15 N 13.37 E
Bestfield 285 39.43 N 75.36 W
Bestobe 86 52.30 N 73.05 E
Beštor, gora ∧ 85 42.03 N 70.50 E
Bestuževo 24 61.37 N 43.58 E
Bestwig 52 51.22 N 8.24 E
Besuki 115a 7.45 S 113.41 E
Besut ≐ 114 5.48 N 102.35 E
Beswick Aboriginal Reserve ✦[4] 164 14.30 S 133.10 E
Betā 272b 22.55 N 88.14 E
Betafo 157b 19.50 S 46.51 E
Betāgi 126 22.25 N 90.11 E
Bet Alfa 132 32.31 N 35.26 E
Beta Main Canal ≍ 226 36.34 N 120.11 W
Betamba 152 2.13 S 21.23 E
Betang Melaka 114 2.28 N 102.25 E
Betano 112 9.10 S 125.43 E
Betanzos, Bol. 248 19.34 S 65.27 W
Betanzos, Esp. 34 43.17 N 8.12 W
Betanzos, Ría de c[1] 34 43.23 N 8.15 W
Betaré Oya 152 5.36 N 14.05 E
Betarsjön ⊜ 26 63.44 N 16.52 E
Bet Bet Creek ≐ 169 36.52 S 143.52 E
Betbetti 140 15.06 N 24.12 E
Betchworth 260 51.14 N 0.16 W
Bet Dagan 132 32.00 N 34.50 E
Bete Hor 144 11.37 N 39.02 E
Betém 256 22.52 S 44.17 W
Bétera 34 39.35 N 0.27 W
Bétérou 150 9.12 N 2.16 E
Bet Guvrin 132 31.36 N 34.54 E
Bet Ha'arava 132 31.48 N 35.32 E
Bethal 158 26.27 S 29.28 E
Bethalto 219 38.54 N 90.02 W
Bethanien 156 26.32 S 17.11 E
Bethanien □[5] 156 26.30 S 17.00 E
Bethany, Ct., U.S. 207 41.25 N 72.59 W
Bethany, Il., U.S. 219 39.38 N 88.44 W
Bethany, Mo., U.S. 194 40.16 N 94.01 W
Bethany, N.Y., U.S. 210 42.55 N 78.08 W
Bethany, Ok., U.S. 196 35.31 N 97.37 W
Bethany, Pa., U.S. 210 41.37 N 75.21 W
Bethany, W.V., U.S. 214 40.12 N 80.33 W
Bethany Reservoir ⊜[1] 226 37.47 N 121.37 W
Bet HaShitta 132 32.33 N 35.26 E
Bethel, Ak., U.S. 180 60.48 N 161.46 W
Bethel, Ct., U.S. 207 41.22 N 73.24 W
Bethel, De., U.S. 208 38.27 N 75.21 W
Bethel, Ky., U.S. 218 38.14 N 83.52 W
Bethel, Me., U.S. 188 44.24 N 70.47 W
Bethel, Mo., U.S. 219 39.52 N 92.01 W
Bethel, N.Y., U.S. 210 41.41 N 74.52 W
Bethel, N.C., U.S. 192 35.48 N 77.22 W
Bethel, Oh., U.S. 218 38.57 N 84.04 W
Bethel, Pa., U.S. 208 40.28 N 76.18 W
Bethel, Wa., U.S. 224 47.32 N 122.38 W
Bethel Acres 196 35.19 N 97.00 W
Bethel Island 226 38.01 N 121.39 W
Bethel Manor 208 37.06 N 76.25 W
Bethel Park 214 40.18 N 80.02 W
Bethelsdorp 158 33.52 S 25.34 E
Bethel Springs 194 35.14 N 88.36 W
Béthencourt-sur-Mer 50 50.05 N 1.30 E
Bethersden 42 51.08 N 0.48 E
Bethesda, Wales, U.K. 44 53.11 N 4.03 W
Bethesda, Md., U.S. 208 38.58 N 77.06 W
Bethesda, Oh., U.S. 188 40.00 N 81.04 W
Bethesdaweg 158 31.55 S 24.45 E
Bethford 284a 42.48 N 78.48 W
Bethgate 284b 39.18 N 76.51 W
Béthisy-Saint-Pierre 50 49.18 N 2.49 E
Bethlehem → Bayt Laḥm, Isr. Occ 132 31.43 N 35.12 E
Bethlehem, S. Afr. 158 28.15 S 28.15 E
Bethlehem, S. Afr. 158 27.10 S 24.00 E
Bethlehem, Ct., U.S. 207 41.38 N 73.12 W
Bethlehem, In., U.S. 218 38.32 N 85.25 W
Bethlehem, Ky., U.S. 218 38.24 N 85.04 W
Bethlehem, Pa., U.S. 210 40.37 N 75.22 W
Bethlehem, W.V., U.S. 188 40.02 N 80.41 W
Bethlehem Center 210 42.40 N 73.42 W
Bethlehem Steel Corporation ʊ[3], Md., U.S. 284b 39.13 N 76.29 W
Bethlehem Steel Corporation (Lackawanna Plant) ʊ[3], N.Y., U.S. 284a 42.49 N 78.52 W
Bethnal Green ✦[8] 260 51.32 N 0.03 W
Bethoncourt 58 47.32 N 6.48 E
Bethpage 210 40.44 N 73.28 W
Bethpage State Park ♦ 210 40.45 N 73.27 W
Bethulie 158 30.32 S 25.59 E
Bethune, Sk., Can. 184 50.43 N 105.08 W
Béthune, Fr. 50 50.32 N 2.38 E
Bethune, S.C., U.S. 192 34.24 N 80.20 W
Béthune ≐ 50 49.53 N 1.09 E
Beticos, Sistemas ⋀ 34 37.00 N 4.00 W
Betijoque 246 9.23 N 70.44 W
Betil 126 24.14 N 89.43 E
Betio 174t 1.21 N 172.56 E
Betioky 157b 23.42 S 44.22 E
Betis ≐ 114 4.53 N 101.48 E
Betlica 76 54.01 N 33.57 E
Betna ≐ 126 22.34 N 89.12 E
Bet Netofa, Biq'at ≡ 132 32.49 N 35.19 E
Betnoti 126 21.44 N 86.51 E
Beton-Bazoches 50 48.42 N 3.15 E
Betong, Malay. 112 1.24 N 111.31 E
Betong, Thai 110 5.45 N 101.05 E
Betoota 166 25.42 S 140.44 E
Bétou 152 3.03 N 18.31 E
Betpak-Dala ✦[2] 86 46.00 N 70.00 E
Betroka 157b 23.16 S 46.06 E
Betsham 260 51.25 N 0.19 E
Bet Sh'ean 132 32.30 N 35.30 E
Bet She'arim, Ḥorbat ⊥ 132 32.42 N 35.08 E
Bet Shemesh 132 31.45 N 35.00 E
Betsiamites 186 48.56 N 68.38 W
Betsiamites ≐ 186 48.56 N 68.38 W
Betsiamites, Barrage ✦[6] 186 49.22 N 69.47 W
Betsiamites, Pointe de › 186 48.55 N 68.37 W

PORTUGUÊS
Nome | Página | Lat.°′ | Long.°′ W = Oeste

Betsiamites, Réserve indienne de ✦[4] 186 49.05 N 68.37 W
Betsiboka ≐ 157b 16.03 S 46.36 E
Betsie, Point › 190 44.42 N 86.16 W
Betsioky 157b 21.31 S 44.28 E
Betsukai 92a 43.23 N 145.17 E
Betsy Layne 192 37.33 N 82.38 W
Betsy Ross Bridge ✦[5] 285 39.59 N 75.04 W
Bette ∧ 146 22.00 N 19.12 E
Bettembourg 56 49.32 N 6.02 E
Bettendorf 190 41.31 N 90.30 W
Betterton 208 39.21 N 76.03 W
Bettiah 124 26.48 N 84.30 E
Bettie 222 32.48 N 94.58 W
Bettles Field 180 66.55 N 151.30 W
Bettola 62 44.47 N 9.36 E
Bettona 66 43.01 N 12.29 E
Bettrath ✦[8] 263 51.13 N 6.26 E
Bettsville 214 41.14 N 83.14 W
Bettyhill 46 58.32 N 4.14 W
Betty's Bay 158 34.22 S 18.52 E
Betūl 124 21.55 N 77.54 E
Betumbe-Bongo 152 2.11 S 18.46 E
Betung, Indon. 112 1.52 S 103.16 E
Betung, Indon. 112 2.50 S 104.14 E
Betuwe ✦[1] 52 51.55 N 5.30 E
Betwa ≐ 124 25.55 N 80.12 E
Betws-y-Coed 44 53.05 N 3.48 W
Betz 50 49.09 N 2.57 E
Betz ≐ 50 48.09 N 2.45 E
Betzdorf 56 50.47 N 7.53 E
Betzenstein 60 49.41 N 11.25 E
Béu 152 6.14 S 15.28 E
Beucha 54 51.19 N 12.34 E
Beugneux 50 49.14 N 3.25 E
Beuil 62 44.06 N 6.59 E
Beulah, Austl. 166 35.56 S 142.26 E
Beulah, Co., U.S. 200 38.04 N 104.59 W
Beulah, Mi., U.S. 190 44.37 N 86.05 W
Beulah, Ms., U.S. 194 33.47 N 90.58 W
Beulah, N.D., U.S. 198 47.15 N 101.46 W
Beulah, Lake ⊜ 216 42.49 N 88.23 W
Beulah Beach 214 41.25 N 82.22 W
Beulah Reservoir ⊜[1] 202 43.56 N 118.09 W
Beulaville 192 34.55 N 77.46 W
Beult ≐ 42 51.14 N 0.25 E
Beure 58 47.12 N 6.00 E
Beureunun 114 5.18 N 95.59 E
Beuron 58 48.03 N 8.58 E
Beuthen → Bytom 30 50.22 N 18.54 E
Beuvron ≐, Fr. 50 47.28 N 3.31 E
Beuvron ≐, Fr. 50 47.29 N 1.15 E
Beuvronne ≐ 261 48.56 N 2.44 E
Beuvry 50 50.31 N 2.41 E
Beuzeville 50 49.20 N 0.21 E
Bevagna 66 42.56 N 12.36 E
Bevensen 52 53.05 N 10.34 E
Bever ≐ 52 52.01 N 7.46 E
Bevera ≐ 62 43.49 N 7.34 E
Beveren 50 51.13 N 4.15 E
B. Everett Jordan Lake ⊜[1] 192 35.45 N 79.00 W
Beverino 62 44.14 N 9.47 E
Beverley, Austl. 168a 32.06 S 116.56 E
Beverley, Eng., U.K. 44 53.52 N 0.26 W
Beverley Minster ʊ[1] 44 53.50 N 0.27 W
Beverley Springs 162 16.43 S 125.28 E
Beverlo 56 51.05 N 5.12 E
Beverly, Ma., U.S. 207 42.33 N 70.52 W
Beverly, N.J., U.S. 208 40.03 N 74.55 W
Beverly, Tx., U.S. 222 31.30 N 97.10 W
Beverly ✦[8] 278 41.43 N 87.41 W
Beverly Farms, Md., U.S. 284c 39.04 N 77.11 W
Beverly Farms, Ma., U.S. 283 42.34 N 70.49 W
Beverly Harbor c 283 42.32 N 70.53 W
Beverly Hills, Austl. 274a 33.57 S 151.05 E
Beverly Hills, Ca., U.S. 228 34.04 N 118.23 W
Beverly Hills, Fl., U.S. 220 28.56 N 82.28 W
Beverly Hills, Mi., U.S. 216 42.31 N 83.13 W
Beverly Lake ⊜ 176 64.36 N 100.30 W
Beverly Municipal Airport ⊠ 283 42.35 N 70.55 W
Beverly Run ≐ 208 37.55 N 77.11 W
Beverly Shores 216 41.41 N 86.58 W
Bevern 52 51.51 N 9.29 E
Beverstausee ⊜[1] 263 51.09 N 7.23 E
Beverstedt 52 53.26 N 8.49 E
Beverungen 52 51.39 N 9.22 E
Beverwijk 52 52.28 N 4.40 E
Bevier 194 39.45 N 92.34 W
Bevin, Lac ⊜ 206 45.57 N 74.35 W
Bevoalavo 157b 25.13 S 45.26 E
Bewani 164 3.02 S 141.10 E
Bewani Mountains ⋀ 164 3.10 S 141.25 E
Bewār 124 27.13 N 79.18 E
Bewdley, On., Can. 212 44.05 N 78.19 W
Bewdley, Eng., U.K. 42 52.22 N 2.19 W
Bewl Water ⊜[1] 42 51.04 N 0.24 E
Bex 58 46.15 N 7.01 E
Bexhill 42 50.50 N 0.29 E
Bexley, Austl. 274a 33.57 S 151.08 E
Bexley, Oh., U.S. 218 39.58 N 82.56 W
Bexley ✦[8] 42 51.26 N 0.10 E
Beyazköy 130 41.21 N 27.42 E
Beybach ≐ 56 50.13 N 7.23 E
Beyçayırı 130 40.15 N 26.55 E
Beycuma 130 41.19 N 31.59 E
Bey Dağları ⋀ 130 36.40 N 30.15 E
Beydagları Olimpos Milli Parkı ♦ 130 36.40 N 30.25 E
Beydili 130 40.10 N 31.01 E
Beyenburg ✦[8] 263 51.15 N 7.18 E
Beykoz ✦[8] 267b 41.08 N 29.05 E
Beyla 150 8.41 N 8.37 W
Beylerbeyi ✦[8] 267b 41.03 N 29.03 E
Beylikahır 130 39.42 N 31.13 E
Beylul 144 13.10 N 42.26 E
Beynes 261 48.51 N 1.53 E
Beynes-Thiverval, Aérodrome de ⊠ 261 48.51 N 1.54 E
Beyoğlu ✦[8] 267b 41.02 N 28.59 E
Beypazarı 130 40.10 N 31.56 E
Beypınarı 130 39.31 N 37.44 E
Beypore 122 11.11 N 75.49 E
Beyra 144 6.57 N 47.19 E
Beyrouth → Bayrūt 130 33.53 N 35.30 E
Beyşehir 130 37.41 N 31.43 E
Beyşehir Gölü ⊜ 130 37.40 N 31.30 E
Beytüşşebap 128 37.34 N 43.10 E
Bezaha 157b 23.30 S 44.31 E
Bežanickaja vozvyšennost' ⋀[1] 76 56.54 N 29.20 E
Bežanicy 76 56.58 N 29.53 E
Bezau 58 47.23 N 9.54 E
Bezavona ∧ 157b 15.02 S 49.52 E
Bezdež 76 52.19 N 25.18 E
Bezděz ∧ 54 50.32 N 14.43 E
Bezděz ⊥ 54 50.32 N 14.46 E
Bèze 58 47.28 N 5.16 E
Bežeck 76 57.47 N 36.39 E
Bežeckij Verch ⋀[1] 76 57.36 N 36.54 E
Bezenčuk 80 52.59 N 49.26 E
Bezerra ≐ 255 13.16 S 47.31 W
Bezerros 250 8.14 S 35.45 W
Bezet 132 33.05 N 35.08 E
Béziers 32 43.21 N 3.15 E
Bezmein 128 38.05 N 58.12 E
Bezmenšur 80 56.29 N 51.17 E
Bezno 54 50.22 N 14.48 E
Bezons 261 48.56 N 2.13 E
Bežta 84 42.08 N 46.08 E
Bezwada → Vijayawāda 122 16.31 N 80.37 E

Bezym'anka 80 49.56 N 43.15 E
Bezym'annaja 80 51.20 N 46.26 E
Bezymennoje 83 47.06 N 37.56 E
Bezzecca 64 45.55 N 10.43 E
Bezzubovo 82 55.27 N 38.55 E
Bhabānipur, India 272b 22.57 N 88.27 E
Bhabānipur, India 272b 22.56 N 88.13 E
Bhabhua 124 25.03 N 83.37 E
Bhābta 126 23.59 N 88.15 E
Bhadarwāh 123 32.59 N 75.43 E
Bhadaur 123 30.29 N 75.19 E
Bhādgāon → Bhaktapur 124 27.42 N 85.27 E
Bhadohi 124 25.25 N 82.34 E
Bhādra 123 29.07 N 75.10 E
Bhadra ≐[1] 126 22.19 N 89.31 E
Bhadrāchalam 122 17.40 N 80.53 E
Bhadrak 120 21.03 N 86.30 E
Bhadrapur 124 26.32 N 88.06 E
Bhadra Reservoir ⊜[1] 122 13.40 N 75.35 E
Bhadrāvati 122 13.52 N 75.43 E
Bhadreswar 126 22.50 N 88.21 E
Bhādua 272b 22.41 N 88.12 E
Bhāg 120 29.02 N 67.49 E
Bhagaiya 124 25.12 N 87.29 E
Bhāgalpur 124 25.15 N 87.00 E
Bhāgīrathi ≐, India 124 30.08 N 78.35 E
Bhāgīrathi ≐, India 126 23.25 N 88.23 E
Bhagirathpur 126 24.05 N 88.29 E
Bhagwānpur 126 22.07 N 87.45 E
Bhainsa 122 19.06 N 77.58 E
Bhāi Pheru 123 31.12 N 73.57 E
Bhairab ≐[1] 126 22.51 N 89.34 E
Bhairab Bāzār 120 24.04 N 90.58 E
Bhairhawā 124 27.31 N 83.24 E
Bhaironghāt 120 31.01 N 78.53 E
Bhakkar 123 31.38 N 71.04 E
Bhākra Dam ✦[6] 123 31.24 N 76.30 E
Bhaktapur 124 27.42 N 85.27 E
Bhal 272c 19.11 N 73.08 E
Bhālki 122 18.02 N 77.13 E
Bhalswa ✦[8] 272a 28.44 N 77.10 E
Bhalwāl 123 32.16 N 72.54 E
Bhamdūn 132 33.48 N 35.39 E
Bhamo 110 24.16 N 97.14 E
Bhandāra 120 21.10 N 79.39 E
Bhandārdaha 272b 22.37 N 88.13 E
Bhandāria 126 22.29 N 90.04 E
Bhānder 124 25.44 N 78.45 E
Bhander Plateau ⋀[1] 124 24.10 N 80.20 E
Bhāndup ✦[3] 272c 19.09 N 72.57 E
Bhānga 126 23.22 N 89.59 E
Bhāngar 126 22.31 N 88.37 E
Bhāngar Kāta Khāl ≐ 272b 22.31 N 88.33 E
Bhanvad 120 21.56 N 69.47 E
Bhārat → India □[1] 118 20.00 N 77.00 E
Bharatpur, India 124 27.13 N 77.29 E
Bharatpur, India 126 23.53 N 88.05 E
Bharatpur, Nepāl 124 27.14 N 84.21 E
Bharthana 124 26.45 N 79.14 E
Bharūch 120 21.42 N 72.58 E
Bhātai 126 23.36 N 89.11 E
Bhātāpāra 120 21.44 N 81.56 E
Bhātār 126 23.25 N 87.54 E
Bhatgaon → Bhaktapur 124 27.42 N 85.27 E
Bhātghar Lake ⊜[1] 122 18.12 N 73.49 E
Bhātiāpāra Ghāt 124 23.13 N 89.42 E
Bhatkal 122 13.58 N 74.34 E
Bhātpāra 126 22.52 N 88.24 E
Bhātpur 272b 22.43 N 88.25 E
Bhātsāla 126 22.33 N 90.30 E
Bhattapratāp 126 22.45 N 89.48 E
Bhattiprolu 122 16.06 N 80.47 E
Bhātua 272b 22.57 N 88.22 E
Bhaun 123 32.52 N 72.45 E
Bhaunja 272a 28.40 N 77.25 E
Bhavāni 122 11.27 N 77.41 E
Bhāvnagar 122 21.46 N 72.09 E
Bhawānīgarh 124 30.16 N 76.02 E
Bhawani Mandi 120 24.25 N 75.50 E
Bhawānipatna 122 19.54 N 83.10 E
Bhedia 126 23.36 N 87.42 E
Bheigeir, Beinn ∧[2] 46 55.44 N 6.05 W
Bhendkhal 272c 18.53 N 72.59 E
Bhera 123 32.29 N 72.55 E
Bheramara 126 24.02 N 88.58 E
Bherī □[8] 124 28.30 N 81.45 E
Bherī ≐ 124 28.44 N 81.16 E
Bheula, Beinn ∧ 46 56.08 N 4.58 W
Bhīkampur 272a 28.45 N 77.27 E
Bhīkangaon 120 21.52 N 75.57 E
Bhilai 120 21.13 N 81.26 E
Bhilainagar → Bhilai 120 21.13 N 81.26 E
Bhīlwāra 120 25.21 N 74.38 E
Bhīma ≐ 122 16.24 N 77.18 E
Bhīmavaram 122 16.32 N 81.32 E
Bhimbar 123 32.59 N 74.04 E
Bhīmphedī 124 27.32 N 85.07 E
Bhīmpur, India 126 22.37 N 87.08 E
Bhimpur, India 272b 22.46 N 88.08 E
Bhind 124 26.34 N 78.48 E
Bhinga 124 27.43 N 81.56 E
Bhīnmāl 120 25.00 N 72.15 E
Bhiwandi 122 19.18 N 73.04 E
Bhiwāni 124 28.47 N 76.08 E
Bhoāgāchi 272b 22.57 N 88.20 E
Bhojpur 124 27.10 N 87.03 E
Bhojudih 126 23.38 N 86.27 E
Bhokardan 122 20.16 N 75.46 E
Bhola 124 22.41 N 90.39 E
Bhola ≐[1] 126 22.04 N 89.49 E
Bhongaon 124 27.15 N 79.11 E
Bhongīr 122 17.31 N 78.53 E
Bhonrāsa 124 22.59 N 76.12 E
Bhopāl 124 23.16 N 77.24 E
Bhopar 272c 19.12 N 73.05 E
Bhopura 272a 28.42 N 77.20 E
Bhoutan → Bhutan □[1] 120 27.30 N 90.30 E
Bhowali 124 29.23 N 79.31 E
Bhuāpur 272a 28.43 N 77.26 E
Bhuban 120 20.53 N 85.50 E
Bhubaneshwar 120 20.14 N 85.50 E
Bhucho 123 30.13 N 75.06 E
Bhuj 120 23.16 N 69.40 E
Bhunarheri 124 30.13 N 76.27 E
Bhunya 158 26.32 S 31.01 E
Bhusāwal 120 21.03 N 75.46 E
Bhūshana 126 23.24 N 89.40 E
Bhutali 272c 19.07 N 73.04 E
Bhutan (Druk-Yul) □[1], Asia 118 27.30 N 90.30 E
Bhutan (Druk-Yul) □[1], Asia 120 27.30 N 90.30 E
Bia ≐, Afr. 150 5.21 N 3.11 W
Biá ≐, Bra. 246 3.28 S 67.23 W
Bia, Phou ∧ 110 18.59 N 103.09 E
Biābānak 128 32.11 N 64.11 E
Biabo ≐ 248 6.58 S 76.23 W
Biacesa 64 45.56 N 10.47 E
Biache-Saint-Vaast 50 50.18 N 2.57 E
Biadene 64 45.47 N 12.04 E
Biafra, Bight of c[3] 134 4.00 N 8.00 E
Biak I 164 1.00 S 136.00 E
Biała 30 50.23 N 17.40 E
Biała ≐ 30 50.03 N 20.55 E
Biała Piska 30 53.37 N 22.04 E
Biała Podlaska 30 52.02 N 23.06 E
Biała Podlaska □[4] 30 52.00 N 23.00 E
Biała Rawska 30 51.49 N 20.29 E
Białobrzegi 30 51.40 N 20.57 E
Białogard 30 54.01 N 16.00 E
Białowieski Park Narodowy ♦ 30 52.40 N 23.50 E
Biały Bór 30 53.54 N 16.51 E
Białystok 30 53.09 N 23.09 E
Białystok □[4] 30 53.00 N 23.00 E

Bian ≐ 164 8.07 S 139.56 E
Bian, Bidean nam ∧ 46 56.38 N 5.02 W
Biancavilla 70 37.38 N 14.52 E
Bianchi 68 39.06 N 16.24 E
Bianco 68 38.05 N 16.09 E
Bianco, Canale ≍ 64 45.02 N 12.05 E
Bianco, Capo › 70 37.23 N 13.16 E
Bianco, Monte (Mont Blanc) ∧ 62 45.50 N 6.52 E
Bian'er 102 31.14 N 101.28 E
Bianga 152 4.51 N 20.25 E
Bian'gezhuang 105 39.28 N 115.53 E
Biankouma 150 7.44 N 7.37 W
Bianlinzhen 98 37.26 N 116.32 E
Bianminchang 107 29.41 N 105.04 E
Bianniulupucun 104 41.30 N 123.42 E
Bianquanwopu 104 41.21 N 120.48 E
Bianzè 62 45.18 N 8.07 E
Biaora 124 23.55 N 76.54 E
Biaro, Pulau I 112 2.05 N 125.20 E
Biarritz 32 43.29 N 1.34 W
Biasca 58 46.22 N 8.58 E
Bias Fortes 256 21.36 S 43.46 W
Biassono 62 45.37 N 9.16 E
Biaza 86 56.38 N 78.18 E
Bibā 142 28.55 N 30.59 E
Bibai 92a 43.19 N 141.52 E
Bibala 152 14.46 S 13.21 E
Bībān 142 30.47 N 30.40 E
Bibane, Bahiret el c 148 33.16 N 11.19 E
Bibanga 152 6.15 S 23.56 E
Bibban, Khawr V 140 11.00 N 32.41 E
Bibb City 192 32.30 N 84.59 W
Bibbiano 64 44.40 N 10.28 E
Bibbiena 66 43.42 N 11.49 E
Bibbona 66 43.16 N 10.35 E
Bibémi 146 9.19 N 13.53 E
Biberach 58 48.20 N 8.02 E
Biberach an der Riss 58 48.06 N 9.47 E
Biberbach 56 48.31 N 10.48 E
Biberonne ≐ 261 48.59 N 2.41 E
Bibert ≐ 56 49.27 N 10.59 E
Bibey ≐ 34 42.24 N 7.13 W
Bibiani 150 6.28 N 2.20 W
Bībi Chīni 126 22.28 N 90.12 E
Bibione 64 45.38 N 13.00 E
Bibir'ovo 76 54.28 N 33.08 E
Biblián 246 2.42 S 78.52 W
Biblis 56 49.41 N 8.27 E
Bibo 102 29.02 N 99.20 E
Bic 186 48.22 N 68.42 W
Biča 86 57.53 N 70.37 E
Bicas 256 21.43 S 43.04 W
Bicaz 38 46.54 N 26.05 E
Biccari 68 41.24 N 15.11 E
Bicester 42 51.54 N 1.09 W
Bičevinka 76 59.44 N 37.40 E
Biche, Lac la ⊜ 182 54.50 N 112.03 W
Bichena 144 10.27 N 38.12 E
Bicheno 166 41.53 S 148.18 E
Bichhia 124 22.27 N 80.42 E
Bichl 64 47.43 N 11.24 E
Bichlbach 58 47.25 N 10.47 E
Bichota Canyon V 280 34.16 N 117.48 W
Biči ≐ 89 52.10 N 139.50 E
Bičigt 88 47.06 N 95.05 E
Bickerstaffe 262 53.32 N 2.50 W
Bickerton, Cape › 9 66.20 S 136.56 E
Bickerton Island I 164 13.45 S 136.12 E
Bickle Knob ∧ 188 38.56 N 79.44 W
Bickley ✦[8] 260 51.24 N 0.03 E
Bicknacre, Eng., U.K. 42 51.41 N 0.35 E
Bicknacre, Eng., U.K. 260 51.41 N 0.35 E
Bicknell, In., U.S. 194 38.46 N 87.18 W
Bicknell, Ut., U.S. 200 38.20 N 111.32 W
Bicknor 260 51.18 N 0.40 E
Bicol ≐ 116 13.44 N 123.07 E
Bicske 30 47.29 N 18.37 E
Bicudo ≐ 255 18.04 S 44.33 W
Bičura 88 50.36 N 107.35 E
Bičurina 86 56.51 N 55.25 E
Bīd 122 18.59 N 75.46 E
Bida, Nig. 146 12.20 N 13.25 E
Bida, Nig. 150 9.05 N 6.01 E
Bīdar 122 17.54 N 77.33 E
Bidde 144 0.58 N 42.37 E
Biddeford 188 43.29 N 70.27 W
Biddenden 42 51.07 N 0.39 E
Biddiyā 132 32.07 N 35.05 E
Biddulph 44 53.08 N 2.10 W
Bideford 42 51.01 N 4.13 W
Bidente ≐ 66 44.24 N 12.12 E
Bidford-on-Avon 42 52.10 N 1.51 W
Bidhūna 124 26.49 N 79.31 E
Bidian 100 32.38 N 113.03 E
Bīdokht 128 34.21 N 58.46 E
Bidoni 71 40.07 N 8.56 E
Bidor 114 4.07 N 101.17 E
Bidston 262 53.24 N 3.05 W
Bidwell 188 38.55 N 82.17 W
Bidwell, Mount ∧ 204 41.58 N 120.10 W
Bidya ≐[1] 126 21.56 N 88.42 E
Bidyādhari ≐ 272b 22.23 N 88.35 E
Bidyādharpur 272b 22.50 N 88.24 E
Bidžan 89 47.58 N 131.58 E
Bidžan ≐ 89 47.44 N 132.19 E
Bie 40 59.05 N 16.12 E
Bié □[5] 152 12.30 S 17.15 E
Biebelried 56 49.46 N 10.04 E
Bieber, Dtsch. 56 50.09 N 9.19 E
Bieber, Ca., U.S. 204 41.07 N 121.08 W
Biebrza ≐ 30 53.13 N 22.25 E
Biecz 30 49.44 N 21.14 E
Biedenkopf 56 50.55 N 8.32 E
Biederitz 54 52.09 N 11.43 E
Biedermannsdorf 264b 48.05 N 16.21 E
Bieguzhuang 105 39.19 N 116.39 E
Biei 92a 43.35 N 142.28 E
Biel (Bienne) 58 47.10 N 7.12 E
Bielawa 30 50.41 N 16.38 E
Bielawski, Mount ∧ 226 37.13 N 122.06 W
Bielefeld 52 52.01 N 8.31 E
Bieler Lake ⊜ 176 70.20 N 73.00 W
Bielersee ⊜ 58 47.05 N 7.10 E
Bielin 54 52.47 N 14.28 E
Biella 62 45.34 N 8.03 E
Bielsk 30 52.40 N 19.49 E
Bielsko-Biała 30 49.49 N 19.02 E
Bielsko-Biała □[4] 30 49.40 N 19.10 E
Bielsk Podlaski 30 52.47 N 23.12 E
Biemenhorst 52 51.49 N 6.36 E
Bienenbüttel 52 53.08 N 10.29 E
Bienfait 184 49.08 N 102.47 W
Bien Hoa 110 10.57 N 106.49 E
Bienne → Biel 58 47.10 N 7.12 E
Bienne ≐, Fr. 50 48.15 N 0.04 E
Bienne ≐, Fr. 58 46.20 N 5.38 E
Bienno 64 45.56 N 10.18 E
Bientina 66 43.42 N 10.37 E
Bienville 194 32.21 N 92.58 W
Bienville, Lac ⊜ 176 55.05 N 72.40 W
Biere, Dtsch. 54 51.58 N 11.39 E
Bière, Schw. 58 46.33 N 6.20 E
Bierné 28 47.49 N 0.32 W
Bieruń Stary 30 50.06 N 19.06 E
Bierutów 30 51.08 N 17.32 E
Bierwart 56 50.34 N 5.01 E
Biesbos ✦[1] 52 51.45 N 4.50 E
Biesdorf ✦[8] 264a 52.31 N 13.33 E
Biese ≐ 54 52.45 N 11.37 E
Biesel ✦[8] 263 51.10 N 6.29 E
Biesenthal 54 52.46 N 13.37 E
Bieshan 105 39.58 N 117.29 E
Biesiesvlei 158 26.22 S 25.55 E
Biesles 58 48.05 N 5.18 E
Bieszczadzki Park Narodowy ♦ 30 49.05 N 22.45 E
Bieteluobaoluosika 89 48.35 N 119.56 E
Bietigheim 56 48.54 N 8.14 E

Bietigheim-Bissingen 56 48.58 N 9.07 E
Bietschhorn ∧ 58 46.24 N 7.51 E
Bièvre 56 49.56 N 5.01 E
Bièvre ≐ 261 48.47 N 2.20 E
Bièvres 261 48.45 N 2.13 E
Biferno ≐ 66 41.59 N 15.02 E
Bifoun 152 0.22 S 10.23 E
Bifuka 92a 44.29 N 142.21 E
Bifurcación 258 34.19 S 56.48 W
Big ≐, Austl. 169 37.18 S 146.02 E
Big ≐, N.T., Can. 176 72.30 N 125.14 W
Big ≐, Sk., Can. 184 53.50 N 107.02 W
Big ≐, Ak., U.S. 180 63.00 N 154.56 W
Big ≐, Mo., U.S. 219 38.28 N 90.37 W
Biga 130 40.13 N 27.14 E
Bigadiç 130 39.23 N 28.08 E
Big A Mountain ∧ 192 37.03 N 82.02 W
Big Annemessex River c 208 38.03 N 75.50 W
Big Antelope Creek ≐ 202 42.28 N 117.13 W
Big Bald Mountain ∧, N.B., Can. 186 47.12 N 66.25 W
Big Bald Mountain ∧, Ga., U.S. 192 34.45 N 84.19 W
Big Baldy ∧ 202 44.47 N 115.13 W
Big Baldy Mountain ∧ 202 46.58 N 110.37 W
Big Bar Creek 182 51.12 N 122.06 W
Big Basin Redwoods State Park ♦ 226 37.09 N 122.17 W
Big Bay 190 46.49 N 87.44 W
Big Bay c, N.Z. 172 44.18 S 168.05 E
Big Bay c, Vanuatu 175f 15.06 S 166.54 E
Big Bay De Noc c 190 45.46 N 86.43 W
Big Bay Point › 212 44.24 N 79.31 W
Big Bear City 228 34.15 N 116.50 W
Big Bear Lake 228 34.15 N 116.53 W
Big Bear Lake ⊜ 228 34.15 N 116.55 W
Big Beaver, Sk., Can. 184 49.08 N 105.10 W
Big Beaver, Pa., U.S. 214 40.50 N 80.20 W
Big Beaver Airport ⊠ 281 42.33 N 83.06 W
Big Beaver Creek ≐, Mi., U.S. 281 42.32 N 83.01 W
Big Beaver Creek ≐, Oh., U.S. 218 39.01 N 83.03 W
Big Beaver Creek ≐, Wa., U.S. 224 48.40 N 121.08 W
Big Bell 162 27.21 S 117.40 E
Big Belt Mountains ⋀ 202 46.40 N 111.25 W
Big Bend, Swaz. 158 26.50 S 31.57 E
Big Bend, Wi., U.S. 216 42.52 N 88.12 W
Big Bend National Park ♦ 196 29.12 N 103.12 W
Big Bend Reservoir ⊜[1] 182 52.57 N 115.37 W
Big Black ≐ 194 32.00 N 91.05 W
Big Blue ≐, U.S. 198 39.11 N 96.32 W
Big Blue ≐, In., U.S. 218 39.20 N 85.59 W
Big Blue, West Fork ≐ 198 40.42 N 96.59 W
Big Bone Lick State Park ♦ 218 38.53 N 84.45 W
Big Bonito Creek ≐ 200 33.34 N 109.56 W
Big Brook ≐ 276 40.19 N 74.10 W
Big Brushy Creek ≐, Tx., U.S. 222 32.32 N 96.20 W
Big Brushy Creek ≐, Tx., U.S. 222 29.12 N 96.55 W
Big Bureau Creek ≐ 194 41.17 N 89.21 W
Bigbury Bay c 42 50.16 N 3.48 W
Big Cabin Creek ≐ 194 36.26 N 95.08 W
Big Canyon V 196 30.05 N 101.55 W
Big Carlos Pass c 220 26.24 N 81.52 W
Big Cedar Lake ⊜ 212 44.37 N 78.10 W
Big Chino Wash V 200 34.52 N 112.28 W
Big Clear Lake ⊜ 212 44.43 N 76.55 W
Big Clifty 194 37.32 N 86.09 W
Big Coulee Creek ≐ 202 46.17 N 108.56 W
Big Cow Creek ≐ 194 30.34 N 93.44 W
Big Creek, B.C., Can. 182 51.44 N 123.03 W
Big Creek, Ca., U.S. 226 37.12 N 119.14 W
Big Creek ≐, B.C., Can. 182 51.40 N 122.50 W
Big Creek ≐, On., Can. 214 42.19 N 82.27 W
Big Creek ≐, On., Can. 214 42.36 N 80.27 W
Big Creek ≐, Ar., U.S. 194 34.21 N 91.03 W
Big Creek ≐, Ca., U.S. 226 36.53 N 119.15 W
Big Creek ≐, Ca., U.S. 226 37.12 N 119.19 W
Big Creek ≐, Id., U.S. 202 45.06 N 114.44 W
Big Creek ≐, Il., U.S. 219 39.07 N 88.52 W
Big Creek ≐, In., U.S. 216 40.38 N 86.46 W
Big Creek ≐, In., U.S. 218 38.48 N 85.39 W
Big Creek ≐, Ks., U.S. 198 38.47 N 98.55 W
Big Creek ≐, La., U.S. 194 32.10 N 91.53 W
Big Creek ≐, Mo., U.S. 194 40.02 N 94.07 W
Big Creek ≐, Mo., U.S. 219 38.52 N 90.50 W
Big Creek ≐, Oh., U.S. 279a 41.27 N 81.41 W
Big Creek ≐, Or., U.S. 224 46.11 N 123.35 W
Big Creek ≐, Tx., U.S. 222 31.09 N 96.52 W
Big Creek ≐, Tx., U.S. 222 29.22 N 95.34 W
Big Creek ≐, Wa., U.S. 224 47.15 N 121.10 W
Big Creek, East Fork ≐ 194 40.16 N 94.03 W
Big Creek, West Fork ≐ 194 40.16 N 94.03 W
Big Creek Parkway ♦ 279a 41.24 N 81.45 W
Big Creek Peak ∧ 202 44.28 N 113.32 W
Big Crow Island I 276 40.37 N 73.33 W
Big Cypress Creek ≐ 222 33.00 N 94.51 W
Big Cypress Indian Reservation ✦[4] 220 26.14 N 80.49 W
Big Cypress National Preserve ♦ 220 25.55 N 81.10 W
Big Cypress Swamp ≡ 220 26.10 N 81.38 W
Big Dalton Canyon V 280 34.10 N 117.48 W
Big Dalton Wash V 280 34.04 N 117.58 W
Big Darby Creek ≐ 218 39.37 N 82.58 W
Big Delta 180 64.09 N 145.50 W
Big Desert ✦[2] 166 35.40 S 141.00 E
Big Diomede Island → Ratmanova, ostrov I 180 65.46 N 169.02 W
Big Ditch ≍ 216 40.13 N 88.22 W
Big Dry Creek ≐ 202 47.30 N 106.19 W
Big Dubbo Hill ∧ 171b 35.25 S 148.36 E
Big Eau Pleine ≐ 190 44.48 N 90.00 W
Big Elk Creek ≐ 208 39.35 N 75.52 W
Big Elkhart Creek ≐ 222 31.22 N 95.41 W
Big Elm Creek ≐ 222 30.53 N 96.56 W
Bigelow Bight c[3] 188 43.15 N 70.30 W
Big Escambia Creek ≐ 194 30.58 N 87.14 W
Big Falls 190 48.11 N 93.48 W
Big Flat 194 36.00 N 92.24 W
Big Flat Creek ≐ 194 31.33 N 87.31 W
Big Flats 210 42.08 N 76.56 W
Bigfork, Mn., U.S. 190 47.44 N 93.39 W
Bigfork, Mt., U.S. 202 48.04 N 114.04 W
Big Fork ≐ 190 48.31 N 93.43 W
Big Four Ditch ≍ 216 40.27 N 88.10 W
Big Frog Mountain ∧ 192 35.00 N 84.32 W
Biggar, Sk., Can. 184 52.04 N 108.00 W

Symbol	English	Deutsch	Español	Français	Português
≐	River	Fluß	Río	Rivière	Rio
≍	Canal	Kanal	Canal	Canal	Canal
⌊	Waterfall, Rapids	Wasserfall, Stromschnellen	Cascada, Rápidos	Chute d'eau, Rapides	Cascata, Rápidos
ʉ	Strait	Meeresstraße	Estrecho	Détroit	Estreito
c	Bay, Gulf	Bucht, Golf	Bahía, Golfo	Baie, Golfe	Baía, Golfo
⊜	Lake, Lakes	See, Seen	Lago, Lagos	Lac, Lacs	Lago, Lagos
≡	Swamp	Sumpf	Pantano	Marais	Pântano
⍓	Ice Features, Glacier	Eis- und Gletscherformen	Accidentes Glaciales	Formes glaciaires	Acidentes glaciares
⏚	Other Hydrographic Features	Andere Hydrographische Objekte	Otros Elementos Hidrográficos	Autres données hydrographiques	Outros acidentes hidrográficos
✣	Submarine Features	Untermeerische Objekte	Accidentes Submarinos	Formes de relief sous-marin	Acidentes submarinos
□	Political Unit	Politische Einheit	Unidad Politica	Entité politique	Unidade política
ʊ	Cultural Institution	Kulturelle Institution	Institución Cultural	Institution culturelle	Instituição cultural
⊥	Historical Site	Historische Stätte	Sitio Histórico	Site historique	Sitio histórico
♦	Recreational Site	Erholungs- und Ferienort	Sitio de Recreo	Centre de loisirs	Area de Lazer
⊠	Airport	Flughafen	Aeropuerto	Aéroport	Aeroporto
■	Military Installation	Militäranlage	Instalación Militar	Installation militaire	Instalação militar
✦	Miscellaneous	Verschiedenes	Misceláneo	Divers	Diversos

Symbols in the index entries represent the broad categories identified in the key at the right. Symbols with superscript numbers (↗¹) identify subcategories (see complete key on page I · 1).

Symbole im Register stellen die rechts im Schlüssel erklärten Kategorien ʼdarʼ. Symbole mit hochgestellten Ziffern (↗¹) bezeichnen Unterabteilungen einer Kategorie (vgl. vollständigen Schlüssel auf Seite I · 1).

Los símbolos incluidos en el texto del índice representan las grandes categorías identificadas con la clave a la derecha. Los símbolos con números en su parte superior (↗¹) identifican las subcategorías (véase la clave completa en la página I · 1).

Les symboles de lʼindex représentent les catégories indiquées dans la légende à droite. Les symboles suivis dʼun indice (↗¹) représentent des sous-catégories (voir légende complète à la page I · 1).

Os símbolos incluídos no texto do índice representam as grandes categorias identificadas com a chave à direita. Os símbolos com números em sua parte superior (↗¹) identificam as subcategorias (veja-se a chave completa à página I · 1).

ESPAÑOL — FRANÇAIS — PORTUGUÊS

Nombre / Nom / Nome	Página / Page / Página	Lat.°′	Long.°′ W = Oeste / W = Ouest / W = Oeste
Black ≃, On., Can.	190	48.42 N	80.38 W
Black ≃, On., Can.	190	48.36 N	86.16 W
Black ≃, On., Can.	212	44.32 N	77.22 W
Black ≃, On., Can.	212	44.20 N	79.20 W
Black ≃, On., Can.	212	44.42 N	79.19 W
Black ≃, U.S.	194	35.38 N	91.19 W
Black ≃, Ak., U.S.	180	66.39 N	144.50 W
Black ≃, Az., U.S.	200	33.44 N	110.13 W
Black ≃, La., U.S.	194	31.16 N	91.50 W
Black ≃, Mi., U.S.	190	46.40 N	90.03 W
Black ≃, Mi., U.S.	190	43.00 N	82.25 W
Black ≃, Mi., U.S.	190	45.39 N	84.29 W
Black ≃, Mi., U.S.	214	43.00 N	82.25 W
Black ≃, N.M., U.S.	196	32.14 N	104.03 W
Black ≃, N.Y., U.S.	188	43.59 N	76.04 W
Black ≃, N.C., U.S.	192	34.35 N	78.16 W
Black ≃, Oh., U.S.	214	41.28 N	82.11 W
Black ≃, S.C., U.S.	192	33.24 N	79.15 W
Black ≃, Vt., U.S.	188	43.16 N	72.27 W
Black ≃, Vt., U.S.	188	44.55 N	72.13 W
Black ≃, Wa., U.S.	224	46.49 N	123.13 W
Black ≃, Wi., U.S.	190	43.57 N	91.22 W
Black, East Branch ≃	214	41.22 N	82.07 W
Black, East Fork ≃	190	44.26 N	90.42 W
Black, Middle Branch ≃	216	42.25 N	86.14 W
Black, South Branch ≃	216	42.25 N	86.15 W
Black, West Branch ≃	214	41.22 N	82.07 W
Blackadder Water ≃	46	55.46 N	2.15 W
Blackall	166	24.25 S	145.28 E
Black Bay c	190	48.40 N	88.30 W
Black Bay Peninsula ›[1]	190	48.38 N	88.21 W
Black Bear Creek ≃	196	36.25 N	96.38 W
Black Bear Island Lake ⊜	184	55.38 N	105.40 W
Blackberry Creek ≃	216	41.38 N	88.27 W
Blackberry Heights	216	41.45 N	88.23 W
Black Birch Lake ⊜	184	56.54 N	107.45 W
Black Brook ≃, Ma., U.S.	283	41.59 N	71.03 W
Black Brook ≃, Ma., U.S.	283	42.38 N	71.21 W
Black Brook ≃, N.J., U.S.	276	40.42 N	74.31 W
Black Bullock Hill ∧[2]	168b	35.37 S	138.12 E
Blackburn, Austl.	274b	37.49 S	145.09 E
Blackburn, Eng., U.K.	44	53.45 N	2.29 W
Blackburn, Scot., U.K.	46	55.52 N	3.38 W
Blackburn □[8]	262	53.42 N	2.28 W
Blackburn, Mount ∧	180	61.44 N	143.26 W
Blackbutt	171a	26.53 S	152.06 E
Black Butte ∧, Ca., U.S.	228	34.33 N	117.43 W
Black Butte ∧, Mt., U.S.	202	44.54 N	111.51 W
Black Butte ∧, Mt., U.S.	202	46.47 N	110.56 W
Black Butte Lake ⊜[1]	204	39.45 N	122.20 W
Blackbutt Range ⩘	171a	27.00 S	152.00 E
Black Canyon of the Gunnison National Monument ♠	200	38.32 N	107.42 W
Blackcraig Hill ∧	44	55.20 N	4.08 W
Black Creek, B.C., Can.	182	49.50 N	125.08 W
Black Creek, On., Can.	284a	43.00 N	79.01 W
Black Creek, N.Y., U.S.	210	42.17 N	78.14 W
Black Creek ≃, On., Can.	214	42.43 N	82.21 W
Black Creek ≃, On., Can.	275b	43.41 N	79.32 W
Black Creek ≃, On., Can.	284a	42.59 N	79.01 W
Black Creek ≃, Az., U.S.	200	35.16 N	109.14 W
Black Creek ≃, Mi., U.S.	216	41.49 N	83.54 W
Black Creek ≃, Mi., U.S.	216	43.11 N	86.14 W
Black Creek ≃, Ms., U.S.	194	33.01 N	90.21 W
Black Creek ≃, Ms., U.S.	194	30.39 N	88.39 W
Black Creek ≃, Mo., U.S.	219	39.41 N	91.55 W
Black Creek ≃, N.Y., U.S.	210	43.06 N	77.41 W
Black Creek ≃, N.Y., U.S.	210	43.19 N	75.04 W
Black Creek ≃, N.Y., U.S.	284a	43.05 N	78.57 W
Black Creek ≃, N.Y., U.S.	284a	43.03 N	78.42 W
Black Creek ≃, Pa., U.S.	210	41.00 N	76.10 W
Black Creek ≃, S.C., U.S.	192	34.18 N	79.37 W
Black Creek Park ♠	275b	43.46 N	79.31 W
Black Creek Pioneer Village ♠	275b	43.47 N	79.32 W
Black Cypress Creek ≃	222	32.53 N	94.26 W
Blackden Heath	262	53.14 N	2.20 W
Black Devon ≃	46	56.06 N	3.47 W
Black Diamond, Ab., Can.	182	50.42 N	114.14 W
Black Diamond, Wa., U.S.	224	47.18 N	122.00 W
Black Donald Lake ⊜[1]	212	45.13 N	76.55 W
Black Down Hills ⩘[2]	42	50.57 N	3.09 W
Blackdown Tableland National Park ♠	166	23.43 S	149.05 E
Blackduck	190	47.43 N	94.32 W
Black Duck ≃	176	56.51 N	89.02 W
Black Eagle	202	47.31 N	111.16 W
Black Esk ≃	44	55.12 N	3.10 W
Blackfalds	182	52.23 N	113.47 W
Blackfeet Indian Reservation ◆[4]	202	48.40 N	113.00 W
Blackfoot, Id., U.S.	202	43.11 N	112.20 W
Blackfoot, Mt., U.S.	182	48.34 N	112.52 W
Blackfoot ≃, Id., U.S.	202	43.08 N	112.30 W
Blackfoot ≃, Mt., U.S.	202	46.52 N	113.53 W
Blackfoot, North Fork ≃	202	46.59 N	113.07 W
Blackfoot Indian Reserve ◆[4]	182	50.45 N	113.00 W
Blackfoot Reservoir ⊜[1]	202	42.55 N	111.35 W
Blackford	46	56.15 N	3.46 W
Blackford □[6]	216	40.27 N	85.22 W
Black Forest → Schwarzwald ⩘	58	48.00 N	8.15 E
Blackhall Colliery	44	54.44 N	1.14 W
Blackhall Mountain ∧	200	41.02 N	106.41 W
Black Hameldon ∧[2]	262	53.44 N	2.08 W
Black Hawk	184	48.48 N	93.59 W
Black Hawk Creek ≃	190	42.30 N	92.21 W
Black Head ›, Ire.	48	53.08 N	9.17 W
Black Head ›, Eng., U.K.	42	50.01 N	5.06 W
Blackhead Bay c	186	48.34 N	53.15 W
Blackheath, Austl.	170	33.38 S	150.17 E
Blackheath, S. Afr.	273d	26.08 S	27.58 E
Blackheath, Eng., U.K.	260	51.12 N	0.31 W
Black Hill ∧[2], Eng., U.K.	262	53.20 N	2.01 W
Black Hill ∧[2], Eng., U.K.	262	53.33 N	1.53 W
Black Hills ⩘	198	44.00 N	104.00 W
Black Hills ⩘[2]	282	37.50 N	121.52 W
Blackhope Scar ∧	46	55.44 N	3.05 W
Black Horse, Oh., U.S.	214	41.09 N	81.18 W
Black Horse, Pa., U.S.	285	40.06 N	75.19 W
Black Horse, Pa., U.S.	285	39.55 N	75.25 W
Black Horse Creek ≃	285	40.05 N	75.43 W
Black Island ɪ	184	51.10 N	96.30 W
Black Isle ›[1]	46	57.35 N	4.15 W
Black Jack	219	38.47 N	90.16 W
Black Jack Mountain ∧	228	33.23 N	118.24 W
Black-Lake	206	46.03 N	71.21 W
Black Lake ⊜, On., Can.	212	44.46 N	76.18 W
Black Lake ⊜, Sk., Can.	176	59.10 N	105.20 W
Black Lake ⊜, Mi., U.S.	190	45.28 N	84.15 W
Black Lake ⊜, N.Y., U.S.	212	44.31 N	75.35 W
Black Lake ⊜, Wa., U.S.	224	47.00 N	122.58 W
Black Lake Bayou ≃	194	32.01 N	93.09 W
Blacklegs Creek ≃	214	40.30 N	79.27 W
Blackley ◆[8]	262	53.31 N	2.13 W
Black Lick	214	40.28 N	79.11 W
Blacklick Creek ≃	214	40.28 N	79.13 W
Blacklick Creek, North Branch ≃	214	40.29 N	78.55 W
Blacklick Estates	218	39.54 N	83.22 W
Blacklog Mountain ∧	214	40.20 N	77.45 W
Blacklunans	46	56.44 N	3.22 W
Black Mesa ∧, U.S.	196	37.05 N	103.10 W
Black Mesa ∧, Az., U.S.	200	36.35 N	110.20 W
Blackmoor ⩘[1]	42	50.24 N	4.46 W
Blackmoorfoot Reservoir ⊜[1]	262	53.37 N	1.51 W
Blackmoor Vale V	42	50.56 N	2.25 W
Blackmore	260	51.41 N	0.19 E
Blackmore, Mount ∧	202	45.27 N	111.01 W
Black Moshannon State Park ♠	214	40.54 N	78.03 W
Black Mountain	192	35.37 N	82.19 W
Black Mountain ∧, D.Y.	124	27.17 N	90.23 E
Black Mountain ∧, Wales, U.K.	42	51.52 N	3.46 W
Black Mountain ∧, U.S.	192	36.54 N	82.54 W
Black Mountain ∧, Az., U.S.	200	32.46 N	110.57 W
Black Mountain ∧, Ca., U.S.	226	35.24 N	120.21 W
Black Mountain ∧, Ca., U.S.	228	35.08 N	117.14 W
Black Mountain ∧, Ca., U.S.	282	37.19 N	122.09 W
Black Mountain ∧, Id., U.S.	202	46.53 N	115.33 W
Black Mountain ∧, Mt., U.S.	202	46.44 N	112.31 W
Black Mountain ∧, Or., U.S.	202	45.13 N	119.17 W
Black Mountain ∧, Wy., U.S.	202	44.45 N	107.22 W
Black Mountain ∧[2], Austl.	166	21.08 S	139.41 E
Black Mountain ∧[2], Ca., U.S.	228	32.59 N	117.07 W
Black Mountain ∧[2], Tx., U.S.	222	31.09 N	97.44 W
Black Mountains ⩘, Wales, U.K.	42	51.57 N	3.08 W
Black Mountains ⩘, Az., U.S.	200	35.30 N	114.30 W
Black Nossob ≃	156	23.05 S	18.45 E
Black Oak	216	41.33 N	87.23 W
Black Peak ∧	200	34.08 N	114.13 W
Black Pine Peak ∧	202	42.08 N	113.08 W
Black Pipe Creek ≃	198	43.47 N	101.14 W
Black Point	226	38.07 N	122.31 W
Black Point ›, Austl.	168b	34.37 S	137.54 E
Black Point ›, Austl.	170	34.47 S	150.50 E
Black Point ›, Ak., U.S.	180	57.00 N	153.18 W
Blackpool	44	53.50 N	3.03 W
Blackpool □[8]	262	53.47 N	3.02 W
Blackpool (Squire's Gate) Airport ⊠	262	53.47 N	3.02 W
Blackpool Football Ground ♠	262	53.49 N	3.03 W
Blackpool Tower ʊ	262	53.49 N	3.03 W
Black Range ⩘	200	33.20 N	107.50 W
Black River, Jam.	241q	18.01 N	77.51 W
Black River, N.Y., U.S.	212	44.00 N	75.47 W
Black River Bay c	212	43.58 N	76.07 W
Black River Falls	190	44.17 N	90.51 W
Black Rock, Austl.	274b	37.59 S	145.01 E
Black Rock, Ar., U.S.	194	36.06 N	91.05 W
Black Rock, Ma., U.S.	283	42.14 N	70.49 W
Black Rock ɪ[2]	48	54.05 N	10.22 W
Black Rock ɪɪ[1]	244	53.39 S	41.48 W
Black Rock Desert ◆[2]	204	41.10 N	119.00 W
Blackrod	262	53.35 N	2.35 W
Blacksburg, S.C., U.S.	192	35.07 N	81.30 W
Blacksburg, Va., U.S.	192	37.13 N	80.24 W
Blacks Creek ≃	285	40.08 N	74.43 W
Black Sea ⊤[2]	22	43.00 N	35.00 E
Blacks Fork ≃	200	41.24 N	109.38 W
Blacks Harbour	186	45.03 N	66.47 W
Blackshear	192	31.18 N	82.14 W
Blackshear, Lake ⊜[1]	192	31.56 N	83.56 W
Blacksod Bay c	48	54.08 N	10.00 W
Black Springs, Austl.	170	33.52 S	149.42 E
Black Springs, Austl.	274b	37.46 S	145.19 E
Black Springs Hill ∧[2]	274b	37.46 S	145.19 E
Black Star Canyon V	280	33.47 N	117.39 W
Blackstone, Ma., U.S.	207	42.01 N	71.32 W
Blackstone, Va., U.S.	192	37.04 N	77.59 W
Blackstone ≃, Ab., Can.	182	52.50 N	116.07 W
Blackstone ≃, Yk., Can.	180	65.51 N	137.12 W
Blackstone Lake ⊜	212	45.14 N	79.53 W
Black Sugarloaf Mountain ∧	166	31.20 S	151.33 E
Black Thunder Creek ≃	198	43.33 N	104.41 W
Blacktown	170	33.46 S	150.55 E
Blackville	192	33.21 N	81.16 W
Black Volta (Volta Noire) ≃	150	8.41 N	1.33 W
Blackwall Tunnel ◆[5]	260	51.30 N	0.01 E
Blackwalnut Point ›	208	38.40 N	76.20 W
Black Warrior ≃	194	32.32 N	87.51 W
Blackwatch Hills	210	43.05 N	77.27 W
Blackwater, Austl.	166	23.35 S	148.53 E
Blackwater, Ire.	48	52.26 N	6.21 W
Blackwater ≃, Europe	48	54.31 N	6.34 W
Blackwater ≃, Ire.	48	51.51 N	7.50 W
Blackwater ≃, Ire.	48	53.39 N	6.43 W
Blackwater ≃, Eng., U.K.	42	51.45 N	1.00 E
Blackwater ≃, U.S.	194	30.36 N	87.02 W
Blackwater ≃, Md., U.S.	208	38.21 N	76.01 W
Blackwater ≃, Mo., U.S.	194	38.56 N	92.51 W
Blackwater ≃, Va., U.S.	208	36.33 N	76.55 W
Blackwater Creek ≃, Austl.	166	25.56 S	144.20 E
Black Water Creek ≃, Fl., U.S.	220	28.51 N	81.24 W
Blackwater Draw V	196	33.35 N	101.50 W
Blackwaterfoot	46	55.30 N	5.19 W
Blackwater Lake ⊜	180	64.00 N	123.05 W
Blackwater Reservoir ⊜[1], Scot., U.K.	46	56.44 N	3.14 W
Blackwater Reservoir ⊜[1], Scot., U.K.	46	56.41 N	4.46 W
Blackwater Sound ʉ	220	25.10 N	80.25 W
Blackwell, Ok., U.S.	196	36.48 N	97.16 W
Blackwell, Tx., U.S.	196	32.05 N	100.19 W
Blackwood, Austl.	168b	35.02 S	138.37 E
Blackwood, Austl.	169	37.29 S	144.19 E
Blackwood, N.J., U.S.	285	39.48 N	75.03 W
Blackwood ≃	162	34.19 S	115.11 E
Blackwood, Cape ›	164	7.50 S	144.30 E
Blackwood Terrace	285	39.48 N	75.05 W
Bladel	52	51.23 N	5.13 E
Bladenboro	192	34.32 N	78.47 W
Bladensburg, Md., U.S.	284c	38.56 N	76.56 W
Bladensburg, Oh., U.S.	214	40.17 N	82.17 W
Blades	208	38.38 N	75.36 W
Bladgrond	158	28.52 S	19.57 E
Bladnoch ≃	44	54.51 N	4.25 W
Bladworth	184	51.18 N	106.09 W
Blaenau Ffestiniog	42	52.59 N	3.56 W
Blaenavon	42	51.48 N	3.05 W
Bláfell ∧	24a	64.32 N	19.53 W
Blagaj	36	43.15 N	17.50 E
Blagdon	42	51.20 N	2.43 W
Blagodarnoje	86	47.03 N	82.10 E
Blagodarnyj	72	45.06 N	43.27 E
Blagodatnoje, Kaz.	86	51.18 N	72.49 E
Blagodatnoje, Ross.	78	51.32 N	34.54 E
Blagodatnoje, Ukr.	83	47.42 N	37.25 E
Blagodatnoje, Ukr.	83	47.53 N	38.29 E
Blagodatovka	80	52.14 N	50.27 E
Blagoevgrad	38	42.01 N	23.06 E
Blagoveščenka, Kaz.	86	54.22 N	66.58 E
Blagoveščenka, Ross.	80	51.19 N	44.03 E
Blagoveščenka, Ross.	86	52.50 N	79.52 E
Blagoveščensk, Ross.	86	55.01 N	55.59 E
Blagoveščensk, Ross.	89	50.17 N	127.32 E
Blagoveščenskoje, Kaz.	85	43.18 N	74.12 E
Blagoveščenskoje, Ross.	86	58.08 N	62.58 E
Blåhø ∧	26	62.45 N	9.19 E
Blåhøj	41	55.51 N	9.01 E
Blaichach	58	47.34 N	10.15 E
Blaikfjället ∧	26	64.33 N	16.12 E
Blain, Fr.	32	47.29 N	1.46 W
Blain, Pa., U.S.	208	40.20 N	77.31 W
Blaina	42	51.46 N	3.10 W
Blain City	214	40.45 N	78.34 W
Blaine, Mn., U.S.	190	45.09 N	93.14 W
Blaine, Wa., U.S.	224	48.59 N	122.44 W
Blaine Creek ≃	188	38.11 N	82.37 W
Blaine Hill	279b	40.16 N	79.53 W
Blaine Lake	184	52.50 N	106.54 W
Blaineys	224	48.53 N	123.47 W
Blainville	206	45.40 N	73.52 W
Blainville-sur-l'Eau	58	48.33 N	6.24 E
Blair, On., Can.	212	43.23 N	80.23 W
Blair, Ne., U.S.	198	41.32 N	96.07 W
Blair, Ok., U.S.	196	34.46 N	99.20 W
Blair, Wi., U.S.	190	44.18 N	91.14 W
Blair □[6]	214	40.30 N	78.25 W
Blair Athol	166	22.42 S	147.33 E
Blair Atholl	46	56.46 N	3.51 W
Blairgowrie	46	56.36 N	3.21 W
Blairs Mills	214	40.17 N	77.43 W
Blairstown, Ia., U.S.	190	41.54 N	92.05 W
Blairstown, N.J., U.S.	210	40.59 N	74.57 W
Blairsville, Ga., U.S.	192	34.52 N	83.57 W
Blairsville, Pa., U.S.	214	40.25 N	79.15 W
Blaise ≃, Fr.	50	48.46 N	1.25 E
Blaise ≃, Fr.	58	48.38 N	4.43 E
Blaisy-Bas	58	47.22 N	4.44 E
Blaj	38	46.11 N	23.55 E
Blakehurst	274a	33.59 S	151.07 E
Blakeley Canal ≊	226	36.09 N	119.48 W
Blakely, Ga., U.S.	192	31.22 N	84.56 W
Blakely, Pa., U.S.	210	41.28 N	75.35 W
Blakely Island ɪ	224	48.33 N	122.50 W
Blakeney, Eng., U.K.	42	52.58 N	1.00 E
Blakeney, Eng., U.K.	42	51.46 N	2.29 W
Blake Plateau ✣[4]	16	31.00 N	79.00 W
Blake Point ›	190	48.12 N	88.25 W
Blake Ridge ✣[3]	16	29.00 N	73.30 W
Blakes	208	37.30 N	76.22 W
Blakesburg	190	40.57 N	92.38 W
Blakeslee, Oh., U.S.	216	41.31 N	84.44 W
Blakeslee, Pa., U.S.	210	41.06 N	75.36 W
Blalock Island ɪ	202	45.53 N	119.41 W
Blâmont, Fr.	58	48.35 N	6.51 E
Blamont, Fr.	58	47.23 N	6.51 E
Blanc, Cap → Nouâdhibou, Râs ›, Afr.	148	20.46 N	17.03 W
Blanc, Cap ›, Tun.	36	37.20 N	9.51 E
Blanc, Mont ∧, P.Q., Can.	186	48.47 N	66.52 W
Blanc, Mont (Monte Bianco) ∧, Europe	62	45.50 N	6.52 E
Blanca	200	37.27 N	105.31 W
Blanca, Bahía c	252	38.55 S	62.10 W
Blanca, Isla ɪ	248	9.06 S	78.38 W
Blanca, Laguna ⊜	254	52.25 S	71.10 W
Blanca, Punta ›, Arg.	258	34.57 S	57.40 W
Blanca, Punta ›, Chile	252	25.06 S	70.30 W
Blanca, Sierra ∧	200	31.15 N	105.26 W
Blanca Lake ⊜	224	47.53 N	121.21 W
Blanca Peak ∧	200	37.35 N	105.29 W
Blancas, Peñas ⩘	236	13.15 N	85.41 W
Blanc du Cheilon, Mont ∧	58	45.59 N	7.25 E
Blanchard, Ok., U.S.	196	35.08 N	97.39 W
Blanchard, Pa., U.S.	210	41.04 N	77.36 W
Blanchard, Wa., U.S.	224	48.35 N	122.24 W
Blanchard ≃	216	41.02 N	84.18 W
Blanchardville	190	42.48 N	89.51 W
Blanche ≃, On., Can.	190	47.34 N	79.32 W
Blanche ≃, P.Q., Can.	206	46.40 N	72.08 W
Blanche, Cape ›	162	33.01 S	134.09 E
Blanche, Dent ∧	58	46.03 N	7.36 E
Blanche, Lake ⊜, Austl.	162	22.25 S	123.17 E
Blanche, Lake ⊜, Austl.	166	29.15 S	139.39 E
Blanche, Mer → Beloje more ⊤[2]	24	65.30 N	38.00 E
Blanche Channel ʉ	175e	8.30 S	157.30 E
Blancheface	261	48.32 N	2.06 E
Blanche Marie Val ⌊	250	4.44 N	56.53 W
Blanchester	218	39.17 N	83.59 W
Blanchisseuse	241r	10.47 N	61.18 W
Blanco, S. Afr.	158	33.57 S	22.24 E
Blanco, Tx., U.S.	196	30.06 N	98.25 W
Blanco ≃, Arg.	252	30.12 S	69.05 W
Blanco ≃, Arg.	254	47.22 S	71.12 W
Blanco ≃, Bol.	248	13.09 S	63.46 W
Blanco ≃, Ec.	246	0.28 N	79.25 W
Blanco ≃, Tx., U.S.	196	29.51 N	97.55 W
Blanco, Cabo → Nouâdhibou, Râs ›, Afr.	148	20.46 N	17.03 W
Blanco, Cabo ›, C.R.	236	9.34 N	85.07 W
Blanco, Cañon V	200	35.20 N	105.05 W
Blanco, Cape ›	202	42.50 N	124.34 W
Blanco, Lago ⊜	254	54.03 S	69.00 W
Blanco, Mar → Beloje more ⊤[2]	24	65.30 N	38.00 E
Blanco, Monte → Blanc, Mont ∧	62	45.50 N	6.52 E
Blanco, Rio ≃	200	37.07 N	107.03 W
Blanco Creek ≃	196	28.19 N	97.19 W
Blanc-Sablon	186	51.25 N	57.07 W
Bland, Mo., U.S.	219	38.18 N	91.37 W
Bland, Va., U.S.	192	37.06 N	81.06 W
Blanda ≃	24a	65.39 N	20.18 W
Blandburg	214	40.41 N	78.24 W
Blandford	207	42.10 N	72.55 W
Blandford Forum	42	50.52 N	2.11 W
Blanding	200	37.37 N	109.28 W
Blandinsville	190	40.33 N	90.51 W
Blandon	208	40.26 N	75.53 W
Blandy	261	48.34 N	2.47 E
Blanes	34	41.41 N	2.48 E
Blangkejeren	114	3.59 N	97.20 E
Blangpidie	114	3.45 N	96.51 E
Blangy-le-Château	50	49.14 N	0.17 E
Blangy-sur-Bresle	50	49.56 N	1.38 E
Blanice ≃	61	49.05 N	14.03 E
Blankenberg	56	50.45 N	7.22 E
Blankenberge	50	51.19 N	3.08 E
Blankenburg	54	51.48 N	10.58 E
Blankenburg ◆[8]	264a	52.35 N	13.28 E
Blankenese ◆[8]	52	53.33 N	9.48 E
Blankenfelde	54	52.20 N	13.23 E
Blankenfelde ◆[8]	264a	52.37 N	13.23 E
Blankenhain	54	50.51 N	11.21 E
Blankenheim, Dtsch.	54	51.31 N	11.25 E
Blankenheim, Dtsch.	56	50.26 N	6.39 E
Blankensee	54	52.14 N	13.08 E
Blankenstein	263	51.24 N	7.14 E
Blanket	196	31.49 N	98.47 W
Blanquilla, Isla ɪ	246	11.51 N	64.37 W
Blansko	30	49.22 N	16.39 E
Blanský Les ◆[3]	61	48.52 N	14.16 E
Blantyre	154	15.47 S	35.00 E
Blanzac	62	45.07 N	3.51 E
Blanzy	58	46.42 N	4.23 E
Blaricum	52	52.16 N	5.15 E
Blarney	48	51.56 N	8.34 W
Blarney Castle ⊥	48	51.56 N	8.34 W
Blasdell	210	42.47 N	78.49 W
Blasheim	52	52.18 N	8.34 E
Błaszki	30	51.39 N	18.27 E
Blatná	60	49.26 N	13.53 E
Blatnica	38	43.42 N	28.31 E
Blatten	58	46.25 N	7.50 E
Blatzheim	56	50.51 N	6.38 E
Blau ≃	58	48.23 N	9.49 E
Blaubeuren	58	48.24 N	9.47 E
Blauen ∧	58	47.47 N	7.42 E
Blauer Nil → Blue Nile ≃	140	15.38 N	32.31 E
Blaufelden	56	49.18 N	9.58 E
Blaustein	58	48.25 N	9.53 E
Blauvelt	276	41.03 N	73.57 W
Blauvelt State Park ♠	276	41.04 N	73.56 W
Blawenburg	276	40.24 N	74.42 W
Blawnox	279b	40.29 N	79.51 W
Blaxland	170	33.45 S	150.36 E
Blaxland Creek ≃	274a	33.48 S	150.46 E
Blaydon	44	54.58 N	1.42 W
Blaye-et-Sainte-Luce	32	45.08 N	0.39 W
Blayney	166	33.32 S	149.15 E
Blaze, Point ›	164	12.56 S	130.12 E
Błażowa	30	49.54 N	22.05 E
Bleaker Island ɪ	254	52.13 S	58.53 W
Bleaklow Head ∧	262	53.28 N	1.50 W
Blean	42	51.19 N	1.02 E
Bleckede	54	53.17 N	10.44 E
Bled	36	46.22 N	14.06 E
Bledsoe	196	33.38 N	103.01 W
Bleecker	210	43.07 N	74.22 W
Blefjell ∧	26	59.48 N	9.10 E
Blega	115a	7.08 S	113.03 E
Bleibach	58	48.07 N	8.01 E
Bleiberg ob Villach	64	46.37 N	13.41 E
Bleiburg	61	46.35 N	14.48 E
Bleicherode	54	51.26 N	10.34 E
Blekendorf	54	54.16 N	10.38 E
Blekinge □[9]	26	56.20 N	15.05 E
Blekinge Län □[6]	26	56.20 N	15.20 E
Bléneau	50	47.42 N	2.57 E
Blenheim, Austl.	171a	27.39 S	152.20 E
Blenheim, On., Can.	214	42.20 N	82.00 W
Blenheim, N.Z.	172	41.31 S	173.57 E
Blenheim, N.J., U.S.	285	39.48 N	75.05 W
Blenheim Palace ʊ	42	51.47 N	1.21 W
Blenio, Val V	58	46.27 N	8.58 E
Blénod-lès-Pont-à-Mousson	56	48.53 N	6.03 E
Blénod-lès-Toul	58	48.36 N	5.50 E
Bléone ≃	62	44.03 N	6.00 E
Blérancourt	50	49.31 N	3.09 E
Bléré	50	47.20 N	1.00 E
Blerick	52	51.23 N	6.10 E
Blériot-Plage	50	50.57 N	1.50 E
Blesbokspruit ≃	273d	26.14 S	28.29 E
Blessing	222	28.52 N	96.13 W
Blessington	48	53.10 N	6.32 W
Bletchingley	260	51.14 N	0.06 W
Bletchley	42	52.00 N	0.46 W
Bletterans	58	46.45 N	5.27 E
Bleu → Chang ≃	90	31.48 N	121.10 E
Bleue, Mer ≡	212	45.24 N	75.30 W
Bleury	261	48.31 N	1.45 E
Bleus, Monts ⩘	154	1.30 N	30.30 E
Blevio	62	45.50 N	9.05 E
Blewett Falls Lake ⊜[1]	192	35.03 N	79.54 W
Blexen	52	53.32 N	8.32 E
Blidö ɪ	40	59.37 N	18.54 E
Blidworth	44	53.06 N	1.07 W
Bliedinghausen ◆[8]	263	51.09 N	7.12 E
Bliersheim ◆[8]	263	51.23 N	6.43 E
Blies ≃	56	49.07 N	7.04 E
Blieskastel	56	49.14 N	7.16 E
Bligh Sound ʉ	172	44.50 S	167.32 E
Bligh Water ʉ	175g	17.00 S	178.00 E
Bligny	50	49.11 N	3.52 E
Bligny-sur-Ouche	58	47.06 N	4.40 E
Blik, Mount ∧	116	6.58 N	124.15 E
Blina	162	17.46 S	124.32 E
Blind ≃	276	40.57 N	73.42 W
Blind Creek ≃	274b	37.54 S	145.12 E
Blindley Heath	260	51.12 N	0.04 W
Blind River	190	46.10 N	82.58 W
Blinman	166	31.06 S	138.41 E
Blinnenhorn ∧	58	46.26 N	8.19 E
Blinovskij	80	49.23 N	42.19 E
Bliss	210	42.34 N	78.15 W
Blissfield, Mi., U.S.	216	41.49 N	83.51 W
Blissfield, Oh., U.S.	214	40.24 N	81.58 W
Blitar	115a	8.06 S	112.09 E
Blithe ≃	42	52.45 N	1.50 W
Blithfield Reservoir ⊜[1]	42	52.48 N	1.53 W
Blitta	150	8.19 N	0.59 E
Blizn'uki	78	48.52 N	36.33 E
Blocher	218	38.43 N	85.39 W
Block Dam ◆[6]	212	45.12 N	76.54 W
Block Island	207	41.10 N	71.33 W
Block Island ɪ	207	41.11 N	71.35 W
Block Island Sound ʉ	207	41.10 N	71.45 W
Blockley	42	52.01 N	1.45 W
Blockton	198	40.36 N	94.28 W
Blodgett Mills	210	42.34 N	76.08 W
Bloed ≃	158	28.15 S	30.30 E
Bloedel	182	50.07 N	125.23 W
Bloedrivier, S. Afr.	158	27.53 S	30.30 E
Bloedrivier, S. Afr.	158	28.06 S	30.33 E
Bloekomspruit	158	26.45 S	28.21 E
Bloemendaal	52	52.24 N	4.37 E
Bloemfontein	158	29.12 S	26.07 E
Bloemhof	158	27.38 S	25.32 E
Bloemhofdam ⊜[1]	158	27.40 S	25.40 E
Blois	50	47.35 N	1.20 E
Blokhus	26	57.15 N	9.35 E
Blokzijl	52	52.44 N	5.57 E
Blombacher Bach ◆[8]	263	51.15 N	7.14 E
Blombacka	40	59.37 N	13.47 E
Blomberg	52	51.56 N	9.05 E
Blomstermåla	26	56.59 N	16.20 E
Blonay	58	46.28 N	6.54 E
Blönduós	24a	65.39 N	20.15 W
Blongas	115b	8.53 S	116.02 E
Blonville-sur-Mer	50	49.19 N	0.02 E
Blood Indian Creek ≃	184	50.55 N	111.03 W
Blood Indian Reserve ◆[4]	182	49.30 N	113.10 W
Blood Mountain ∧	192	34.44 N	83.56 W
Blood River ⊥	158	28.20 S	30.35 E
Bloodsworth Island ɪ	208	38.10 N	76.03 W
Bloodvein ≃	184	51.45 N	96.44 W
Bloody Foreland ›	48	55.09 N	8.17 W
Bloomdale	216	41.10 N	83.33 W
Bloomer	190	45.06 N	91.29 W
Bloomfield, On., Can.	212	43.59 N	77.14 W
Bloomfield, Ct., U.S.	207	41.49 N	72.43 W
Bloomfield, In., U.S.	194	39.01 N	86.56 W
Bloomfield, Ia., U.S.	190	40.45 N	92.24 W
Bloomfield, Ky., U.S.	194	37.54 N	85.19 W
Bloomfield, Mo., U.S.	194	36.53 N	89.55 W
Bloomfield, Ne., U.S.	198	42.35 N	97.38 W
Bloomfield, N.J., U.S.	210	40.48 N	74.11 W
Bloomfield, N.M., U.S.	200	36.42 N	107.59 W
Bloomfield, Oh., U.S.	214	40.03 N	81.44 W
Bloomfield ◆[8]	279b	40.27 N	79.56 W
Bloomfield Glens	281	42.33 N	83.20 W
Bloomfield Highlands	281	42.36 N	83.16 W
Bloomfield Hills	216	42.35 N	83.14 W
Bloomfield Village	216	42.33 N	83.15 W
Bloomingburg, N.Y., U.S.	210	41.33 N	74.26 W
Bloomingburg, Oh., U.S.	218	39.36 N	83.23 W
Bloomingdale, Il., U.S.	216	41.57 N	88.04 W
Bloomingdale, Mi., U.S.	216	42.22 N	85.57 W
Bloomingdale, N.J., U.S.	210	41.00 N	74.19 W
Bloomingdale, Oh., U.S.	214	40.21 N	80.49 W
Blooming Glen	208	40.22 N	75.15 W
Blooming Grove, In., U.S.	218	39.30 N	85.04 W
Blooming Grove, N.Y., U.S.	210	41.25 N	74.11 W
Blooming Grove, Pa., U.S.	210	41.21 N	75.09 W
Blooming Grove, Tx., U.S.	222	32.06 N	96.43 W
Blooming Prairie	190	43.52 N	93.03 W
Bloomington, Ca., U.S.	228	34.04 N	117.23 W
Bloomington, Il., U.S.	216	40.29 N	88.59 W
Bloomington, In., U.S.	218	39.09 N	86.31 W
Bloomington, Mn., U.S.	190	44.50 N	93.17 W
Bloomington, N.Y., U.S.	210	41.53 N	74.03 W
Bloomington, Tx., U.S.	196	28.38 N	96.53 W
Bloomington, Wi., U.S.	190	42.53 N	90.55 W
Bloomington, Lake ⊜[1]	216	40.37 N	88.55 W
Blooming Valley	214	41.40 N	80.03 W
Bloomsburg	210	41.00 N	76.27 W
Bloomsbury, Austl.	166	20.43 S	148.35 E
Bloomsbury, N.J., U.S.	210	40.39 N	75.05 W
Bloomsdale Gardens	285	40.07 N	74.52 W
Bloomville, N.Y., U.S.	210	42.20 N	74.48 W
Bloomville, Oh., U.S.	214	41.03 N	83.00 W
Blora	115a	6.57 S	111.25 E
Bloserville	208	40.12 N	77.24 W
Blossburg	210	41.40 N	77.03 W
Blossom	196	33.39 N	95.23 W
Blossom Hill	208	40.05 N	76.19 W
Blötberget	40	60.07 N	15.04 E
Blotzheim	58	47.36 N	7.29 E
Blouberg	156	23.08 S	28.56 E
Blouberg ∧	156	23.01 S	28.59 E
Bloubergstrand	158	33.47 S	18.28 E
Blouin, Lac ⊜	190	48.10 N	77.44 W
Bloumet	148	23.27 N	6.06 E
Blountstown	192	30.26 N	85.02 W
Blountsville	194	34.04 N	86.35 W
Blountville	192	36.31 N	82.19 W
Blovice	60	49.35 N	13.33 E
Blovstrød	41	55.52 N	12.24 E
Blowering Reservoir ⊜[1]	171b	35.30 S	148.15 E
Blowing Rock	192	36.08 N	81.40 W
Bloxham	42	52.02 N	1.22 W
Bloxom	208	37.49 N	75.37 W
Blšanka ≃	54	50.10 N	13.34 E
Blšany	54	50.10 N	13.29 E
Bludenz	58	47.09 N	9.49 E
Bludnaja ≃	88	51.24 N	110.39 E
Blue ≃, Az., U.S.	200	33.13 N	109.11 W
Blue ≃, Co., U.S.	200	40.03 N	106.24 W
Blue ≃, In., U.S.	216	41.07 N	85.30 W
Blue ≃, In., U.S.	218	38.11 N	86.19 W
Blue ≃, Ok., U.S.	196	33.53 N	95.56 W
Blue, Middle Fork ≃	218	38.33 N	86.07 W
Blue, South Fork ≃	218	38.26 N	86.11 W
Blue, West Fork ≃	218	38.33 N	86.07 W
Blue Anchor	285	39.41 N	74.52 W
Blue Anchor Brook ≃	285	39.42 N	74.49 W
Blue Ash	218	39.13 N	84.22 W
Blue Ball	218	39.29 N	84.21 W
Blue Bell	208	40.09 N	75.16 W
Bluebell Hill	260	51.20 N	0.30 E
Blue Bonnets, Champ de Course ♠	275a	45.29 N	73.39 W
Blue Brook ≃	276	40.40 N	74.25 W
Blue Buck Knob ∧[2]	194	36.57 N	92.07 W
Bluebush Swamp ≡	162	20.30 S	137.25 E
Blue Creek, Oh., U.S.	218	38.47 N	83.20 W
Blue Creek, Wa., U.S.	182	48.19 N	117.49 W
Blue Creek, Wa., U.S.	202	48.19 N	117.49 W
Blue Creek ≃, Ca., U.S.	226	38.28 N	120.22 W
Blue Creek ≃, Id., U.S.	202	42.02 N	116.08 W
Blue Creek ≃, Ne., U.S.	198	41.19 N	102.10 W
Blue Creek ≃, Oh., U.S.	216	41.07 N	84.26 W
Blue Creek ≃, Ut., U.S.	200	41.31 N	112.24 W
Blue Cypress Lake ⊜	220	27.44 N	80.45 W
Blue Earth	190	43.38 N	94.06 W
Blue Earth ≃	190	44.09 N	94.02 W
Bluefield, Va., U.S.	192	37.15 N	81.16 W
Bluefield, W.V., U.S.	192	37.16 N	81.13 W
Bluefields	236	12.00 N	83.45 W
Bluefields, Bahía de c	236	12.02 N	83.44 W
Bluefields Bay c	241q	18.10 N	78.03 W
Blue Grass Airport ⊠	218	38.02 N	84.36 W
Blue Grotto → Azzurra, Grotta ⊥[5]	68	40.35 N	14.14 E
Blue Hill, Me., U.S.	188	44.24 N	68.35 W
Blue Hill, Ne., U.S.	198	40.19 N	98.26 W
Blue Hill Bay c	188	44.15 N	68.30 W
Blue Hills	207	41.40 N	72.56 W
Blue Hills of Couteau ⩘[2]	186	47.59 N	57.43 W
Blue Hills Reservation ♠	283	42.13 N	71.05 W
Blue Island	216	41.39 N	87.40 W
Blue Jay	228	34.15 N	117.13 W
Bluejoint Lake ⊜	202	42.35 N	119.40 W
Blue Knob ∧	214	40.17 N	78.34 W
Blue Knob State Park ♠	214	40.16 N	78.35 W
Blue Lagoon National Park ♠	154	15.30 S	27.25 E
Blue Lake National Park ♠	171a	27.31 S	153.29 E
Blue Licks Battlefield State Park ♠	218	38.26 N	84.00 W
Blue Marsh Lake ⊜[1]	208	40.25 N	76.05 W
Blue Mesa Reservoir ⊜[1]	200	38.27 N	107.10 W
Blue Mosque ʊ[1]	273c	30.02 N	31.15 E
Blue Mound, Il., U.S.	219	39.42 N	89.07 W
Blue Mound, Ks., U.S.	198	38.05 N	95.00 W
Blue Mound, Tx., U.S.	222	32.51 N	97.19 W
Blue Mountain, Ms., U.S.	194	34.40 N	89.01 W
Blue Mountain, N.Y., U.S.	210	42.07 N	74.01 W
Blue Mountain ∧, N.B., Can.	186	47.49 N	66.19 W
Blue Mountain ∧, Nf., Can.	186	50.24 N	57.10 W
Blue Mountain ∧, Ar., U.S.	194	34.41 N	94.03 W
Blue Mountain ∧, Mt., U.S.	198	47.16 N	104.10 W
Blue Mountain ∧, N.H., U.S.	188	44.47 N	71.28 W
Blue Mountain ∧, Pa., U.S.	188	40.15 N	77.30 W
Blue Mountain ∧[2], On., Can.	190	48.15 N	80.07 W
Blue Mountain ∧[2], On., Can.	212	44.40 N	77.58 W
Blue Mountain Peak ∧	241q	18.03 N	76.35 W
Blue Mountains ⩘, Austl.	170	33.37 S	150.17 E
Blue Mountains ⩘, Jam.	241q	18.06 N	76.40 W
Blue Mountains ⩘, U.S.	202	45.30 N	118.15 W
Blue Mountains ⩘, Me., U.S.	188	44.50 N	70.35 W
Blue Mountains National Park ♠	170	33.40 S	150.25 E
Blue Mud Bay c	164	13.26 S	135.56 E
Blue Nile (Al-Bahr al-Azraq) (Abay) ≃	140	15.38 N	32.31 E
Bluenose Lake ⊜	180	68.25 N	119.45 W
Blue Point	276	40.45 N	73.02 W
Blue Point ›	276	40.44 N	73.02 W
Blue Rapids	198	39.40 N	96.39 W
Blue Ridge, Ab., Can.	182	54.08 N	115.22 W
Blue Ridge, Ga., U.S.	192	34.51 N	84.19 W
Blue Ridge, Il., U.S.	216	40.17 N	88.29 W
Blue Ridge ⩘	178	37.00 N	82.00 W
Blue Ridge Summit	208	39.43 N	77.28 W
Blue River	182	52.05 N	119.17 W
Blue Rock Springs Park ♠	282	38.08 N	122.12 W
Bluesky	182	56.04 N	118.14 W
Blue Springs	198	40.08 N	96.39 W
Blue Stack Mountains ⩘	48	54.45 N	8.05 W
Bluestone ≃	192	37.34 N	80.59 W
Bluestone Dam ◆[6]	192	37.36 N	80.53 W
Bluestone Lake ⊜[1]	192	37.30 N	80.50 W
Bluestone State Park ♠	192	37.37 N	80.56 W
Bluewater	200	35.15 N	107.59 W
Blue Water Bridge ◆[5]	214	43.00 N	82.25 W
Bluff, N.Z.	172	46.36 S	168.20 E
Bluff, Ut., U.S.	200	37.17 N	109.33 W
Bluff Cape ›	110	18.00 N	94.26 E
Bluff City, Il., U.S.	219	38.57 N	89.02 W
Bluff City, Tn., U.S.	192	36.28 N	82.15 W
Bluff Cove c	280	33.48 N	118.24 W
Bluff Creek ≃, U.S.	196	36.58 N	97.26 W
Bluff Creek ≃, Ks., U.S.	198	37.02 N	99.29 W
Bluff Dale	196	32.21 N	98.01 W
Bluff Head ›	271d	22.11 N	114.12 E
Bluff Island ɪ	271d	22.19 N	114.21 E
Bluff Knoll ∧	162	34.23 S	118.20 E
Bluff Park	194	33.24 N	86.51 W
Bluff Point ›	162	27.50 S	114.06 E
Bluffs	219	39.45 N	90.32 W
Bluff Springs	219	39.59 N	90.21 W
Bluffton, In., U.S.	216	40.44 N	85.10 W
Bluffton, Oh., U.S.	216	40.53 N	83.53 W
Bluffton, S.C., U.S.	192	32.14 N	80.51 W
Bluffy Lake ⊜	184	50.47 N	92.55 W
Bluford	219	38.20 N	88.45 W
Blum	222	32.09 N	97.24 W
Blumberg, Dtsch.	54	52.36 N	13.37 E
Blumberg, Dtsch.	58	47.50 N	8.31 E
Blumenau	252	26.56 S	49.03 W
Blumenhof	184	50.01 N	107.41 W
Blümlisalp ∧	58	46.30 N	7.47 E
Blunt	198	44.30 N	99.59 W
Blup Blup Island ɪ	164	3.30 S	144.37 E
Bly	202	42.23 N	121.02 W
Blying Sound ʉ	180	59.50 N	149.15 W
Blyth, Austl.	168b	33.51 S	138.29 E
Blyth, On., Can.	190	43.44 N	81.26 W
Blyth, Eng., U.K.	44	55.07 N	1.30 W
Blyth ≃, Austl.	164	12.04 S	134.35 E
Blyth ≃, Eng., U.K.	42	52.18 N	1.40 E
Blyth ≃, Eng., U.K.	44	55.08 N	1.31 W
Blyth Bridge	46	55.42 N	3.24 W
Blythe	204	33.36 N	114.35 W
Blythedale	214	40.15 N	79.48 W
Blytheswood	214	42.07 N	82.36 W
Blytheville	194	35.55 N	89.55 W
Blytheville Air Force Base ■	194	35.57 N	89.57 W
Blyth Range ⩘	162	26.50 S	129.00 E
Bnei Braq → Bene Beraq	132	32.05 N	34.50 E
Bø, Nor.	24	68.37 N	14.33 E
Bø, Nor.	26	59.25 N	9.04 E
Bo, S.L.	150	7.56 N	11.21 W
Boa	154	10.32 S	28.06 E
Boac	116	13.27 N	121.50 E
Boaco	236	12.28 N	85.40 W
Boaco □[5]	236	12.30 N	85.30 W
Boadilla del Monte	266a	40.24 N	3.53 W
Boa Esperança, Bra.	255	21.05 S	45.34 W
Boa Esperança, Bra.	256	22.24 S	43.05 W
Boa Esperança, Bra.	256	22.48 S	42.34 W
Boa Esperança, Reprêsa ⊜[1]	250	6.50 S	44.00 W
Bo'ai	102	35.10 N	113.04 E
Boali	152	4.48 N	18.07 E
Boalia	126	23.35 N	88.57 E
Boalsburg	214	40.46 N	77.48 W
Boane	156	26.06 S	32.19 E
Boano, Pulau ɪ	164	2.56 S	127.56 E
Boa Nova	255	14.22 S	40.10 W
Bo'ao	110	19.14 N	110.34 E
Boara Pisani	64	45.08 N	11.47 E
Boara Polesine	64	45.07 N	11.48 E
Board Camp Mountain ∧	204	40.42 N	123.43 W

≃ River	Fluß	Río	Rivière	Rio
≊ Canal	Kanal	Canal	Canal	Canal
⌊ Waterfall, Rapids	Wasserfall, Stromschnellen	Cascada, Rápidos	Chute d'eau, Rapides	Cascata, Rápidos
ʉ Strait	Meeresstraße	Estrecho	Détroit	Estreito
c Bay, Gulf	Bucht, Golf	Bahía, Golfo	Baie, Golfe	Baía, Golfo
⊜ Lake, Lakes	See, Seen	Lago, Lagos	Lac, Lacs	Lago, Lagos
≡ Swamp	Sumpf	Pantano	Marais	Pântano
⍓ Ice Features, Glacier	Eis- und Gletscherformen	Accidentes Glaciales	Formes glaciaires	Acidentes glaciares
⊤ Other Hydrographic Features	Andere Hydrographische Objekte	Otros Elementos Hidrográficos	Autres données hydrographiques	Outros acidentes hidrográficos
✣ Submarine Features	Untermeerische Objekte	Accidentes Submarinos	Formes de relief sous-marin	Acidentes submarinos
□ Political Unit	Politische Einheit	Unidad Politica	Entité politique	Unidade política
ʊ Cultural Institution	Kulturelle Institution	Institución Cultural	Institution culturelle	Instituição cultural
⊥ Historical Site	Historische Stätte	Sitio Histórico	Site historique	Sitio histórico
♠ Recreational Site	Erholungs- und Ferienort	Sitio de Recreo	Centre de loisirs	Area de Lazer
⊠ Airport	Flughafen	Aeropuerto	Aéroport	Aeroporto
■ Military Installation	Militäranlage	Instalación Militar	Installation militaire	Instalação militar
◆ Miscellaneous	Verschiedenes	Misceláneo	Divers	Diversos

Boardman 214 41.01 N 80.39 W
Boardman ≃ 190 44.46 N 85.38 W
Boarhills 46 56.19 N 2.42 W
Boario Terme 64 45.54 N 10.10 E
Boat Basin 182 49.29 N 126.25 W
Boat Channel ʮ 212 44.10 N 76.31 W
Boath 46 57.44 N 4.23 W
Boat Lake ◎ 212 44.44 N 81.13 W
Boatman 166 27.16 S 146.55 E
Boat of Garten 46 57.20 N 3.44 W
Boa Viagem 250 5.07 S 39.44 W
Boa Vista, Bra. 246 2.49 N 60.40 W
Boa Vista, Bra. 256 21.25 S 45.35 W
Boa Vista I 150a 16.05 N 22.50 W
Boa Vista, Morro ʌ[2] 287a 22.53 S 43.06 W
Boavita 246 6.20 N 72.35 W
Boawai 115b 8.46 S 121.10 E
Boayan Island I 116 10.34 N 119.09 E
Boaz 194 34.12 N 86.09 W
Boba 115b 8.57 S 121.04 E
Bobai 102 22.12 N 109.52 E
Bobbau 54 51.41 N 12.16 E
Bobbili 122 18.34 N 83.22 E
Bobbing 260 51.21 N 0.43 E
Bobbingworth 260 51.44 N 0.13 E
Bobbin Head 274a 33.39 S 151.08 E
Bobbio 62 44.46 N 9.23 E
Bobbio Pellice 62 44.48 N 7.07 E
Bobbys Run ≃ 285 39.58 N 74.48 W
Bobcaygeon 212 44.33 N 78.33 W
Bobenheim-Roxheim 56 49.35 N 8.21 E
Bobigny 50 48.54 N 2.27 E
Böbingen, Dtsch. 56 48.49 N 9.54 E
Bobingen, Dtsch. 58 48.16 N 10.50 E
Bobitz 54 53.47 N 11.20 E
Bob Lake ◎ 212 44.55 N 78.47 W
Böblingen 56 48.41 N 9.01 E
Boblo Island
Amusement Park ♠ 281 42.06 N 83.07 W
Bobo Dioulasso 150 11.12 N 4.18 W
Boboiob, gora ʌ 85 40.52 N 70.21 E
Bobo Island I 164 9.08 S 143.14 E
Bobolice 30 53.57 N 16.36 E
Bobonaza ≃ 246 2.36 S 76.38 W
Bobonong 156 21.58 S 28.17 E
Bobos ≃ 234 20.15 N 96.47 W
Bobotsari 115a 7.18 S 109.22 E
Bobr 76 54.20 N 29.16 E
Bobr ≃, Bela. 76 54.03 N 28.51 E
Bóbr ≃, Pol. 30 52.04 N 15.04 E
Bobrik ≃ 76 52.08 N 26.46 E
Bobrikovo 83 47.56 N 39.13 E
Bobrinec 78 48.03 N 32.09 E
Bobrka 78 49.38 N 24.18 E
Bobrov 78 51.06 N 40.02 E
Bobrovica 78 50.44 N 31.22 E
Bobrujsk 76 53.09 N 29.14 E
Bobs Creek ≃ 219 38.57 N 90.42 W
Bobs Lake ◎ 212 44.40 N 76.35 W
Bobtown 188 39.45 N 79.58 W
Bobuk 140 11.30 N 34.05 E
Bobures 246 9.15 N 71.11 W
Boby, Pic ʌ 157b 22.12 S 46.55 E
Boca ◆[8] 288 34.38 S 58.21 W
Bôca, Cachoeira da ⌊ 250 5.27 S 54.24 W
Boca Brava, Isla I 236 8.13 N 82.16 W
Boca Chica 240m 17.59 N 66.32 W
Boca Chica Key I 220 24.34 N 81.42 W
Bôca da Mata 250 9.41 S 36.11 W
Boca del Monte 236 8.21 N 82.07 W
Boca del Río 234 19.06 N 96.06 W
Boca del Rosario 258 34.26 S 57.17 W
Boca de Pozo 246 11.00 N 64.23 W
Boca de Quadra ʮ 182 55.08 N 130.50 W
Boca do Acre 248 8.45 S 67.23 W
Bôca do Jari 250 1.07 S 51.58 W
Bocage, Cap › 175f 21.12 S 165.35 E
Boca Grande 220 26.44 N 82.15 W
Boca Grande
Channel ʮ 220 24.34 N 82.03 W
Boca Grande Key I 220 24.32 N 82.00 W
Bocaina ≃ 256 22.40 S 45.00 W
Bocaina, Parque
Nacional de ♠ 256 23.00 S 44.15 W
Bocaina, Serra da ʌʌ 256 22.43 S 44.40 W
Bocaina de Minas 256 22.10 S 44.24 W
Bocaiúva 255 17.07 S 43.49 W
Bocanda 150 7.04 N 4.30 W
Bocanegra 286d 12.01 S 77.07 W
Bocaranga 152 6.59 N 15.39 E
Boca Raton 220 26.21 N 80.05 W
Boca Reservoir ◎[1] 226 39.24 N 120.06 W
Bocas del Toro 236 9.20 N 82.15 W
Bocas del Toro □[4] 236 8.50 N 82.10 W
Bocas del Toro,
Archipiélago de II 236 9.20 N 82.10 W
Bocaue 116 14.48 N 120.55 E
Bocay 236 14.19 N 85.10 W
Bocay ≃ 236 14.20 N 85.10 W
Boccaleone 66 44.39 N 11.48 E
Boccea ◆[8] 267a 41.58 N 12.19 E
Bocchigliero 68 39.25 N 16.45 E
Bocconi 64 44.01 N 11.46 E
Bočejkovo 76 55.01 N 29.09 E
Bochan 88 53.09 N 103.48 E
Bochil 234 16.59 N 92.55 W
Böch Mörön 86 49.40 N 90.20 E
Bochnia 30 49.58 N 20.26 E
Bocholt, Bel. 56 51.10 N 5.35 E
Bocholt, Dtsch. 52 51.50 N 6.36 E
Bocholtz 56 50.49 N 6.00 E
Bochov 54 50.06 N 13.02 E
Bochum, Dtsch. 56 51.28 N 7.13 E
Bochum, Dtsch. 263 51.28 N 7.13 E
Bochum, S. Afr. 156 23.17 S 29.07 E
Bockel 52 53.12 N 9.17 E
Böckel ◆[8] 263 51.13 N 7.12 E
Bockenem 52 52.00 N 10.07 E
Bockhorn 52 53.23 N 8.01 E
Böckstein 64 47.05 N 13.07 E
Bockum ◆[8], Dtsch. 263 51.21 N 6.38 E
Bockum ◆[8], Dtsch. 263 51.20 N 6.44 E
Bockum-Hövel 52 51.42 N 7.46 E
Bocognano 36 42.05 N 9.03 E
Bocón, Caño ≃ 246 3.42 N 67.53 W
Boconó 246 9.15 N 70.16 W
Bocq ≃ 56 50.20 N 4.53 E
Bocșa 38 45.23 N 21.47 E
Boczów 54 52.19 N 14.58 E
Boda, Centraf. 152 4.19 N 17.28 E
Böda, Sve. 26 57.15 N 17.03 E
Boda, Sve. 26 61.01 N 15.13 E
Bodafors 26 57.30 N 14.42 E
Boda Glasbruk 26 56.44 N 15.40 E
Bodāi 272b 22.48 N 88.29 E
Bodajbo 88 57.51 N 114.10 E
Bodalangi 152 3.14 N 22.14 E
Bodalla 166 36.05 S 150.03 E
Bodallin 162 31.22 S 118.52 E
Bodåsgruvan 40 60.25 N 16.26 E
Bodcau Creek ≃ 194 33.01 N 93.31 W
Boddam, Scot., U.K. 46 57.28 N 1.47 W
Boddam, Scot., U.K. 46a 59.55 N 1.17 W
Boddington 168a 32.48 S 116.28 E
Bode 198 42.52 N 94.17 W
Bode ≃ 54 51.50 N 11.46 E
Bodega Bay c 204 38.15 N 123.00 W
Bodegraven 52 52.05 N 4.45 E
Bodélé ◆[1] 146 16.30 N 16.30 E
Bodelschwingh ◆[8] 263 51.33 N 7.22 E
Boden
→ Fleres, It. 64 46.58 N 11.21 E
Boden, Sve. 26 65.50 N 21.42 E
Bodenburg 52 52.01 N 10.01 E
Bodenfelde 52 51.38 N 9.33 E
Bodenheim 56 49.56 N 8.18 E
Bodenmais 60 49.04 N 13.06 E
Bodensee (Lake
Constance) ◎ 58 47.35 N 9.25 E
Bodenteich 54 52.50 N 10.41 E
Bodenwerder 52 51.59 N 9.31 E
Bodenwies ʌ 61 47.45 N 14.34 E
Bodenwöhr 60 49.16 N 12.19 E
Boderg, Lough ◎ 48 53.52 N 7.58 W
Bode Sadu 150 9.00 N 4.47 E
Bodhan 122 18.40 N 77.54 E
Bodh Gaya 124 24.42 N 84.59 E
Bodiam 42 51.00 N 0.33 E
Bodināyakkanūr 122 10.01 N 77.21 E
Bodine, Mount ʌ 182 55.37 N 125.49 W
Bodjoki 152 2.59 N 22.18 E
Bodjokola 152 3.54 N 20.17 E
Bodmin 42 50.29 N 4.43 W
Bodmin Moor ◆[3] 42 50.33 N 4.33 W
Bodø 24 67.17 N 14.23 E
Bodocó 250 7.47 S 39.55 W
Bodoquena, Serra da
ʌʌ[1] 248 21.00 S 56.50 W
Bodoukpa 152 5.43 N 17.36 E
Bodri ≃ 115a 6.52 S 110.10 E
Bodrog ≃ 30 48.07 N 21.25 E
Bodrum 130 37.02 N 27.26 E
Bodstedt 54 54.22 N 12.37 E
Bo Duc 110 11.58 N 106.48 E
Bodzentyn 30 50.56 N 20.57 E
Boè, Piz ʌ 64 46.31 N 11.48 E
Boëge 58 46.13 N 6.25 E
Boekelo 52 52.13 N 6.47 E
Boele ◆[8] 263 51.24 N 7.28 E
Boémbé 152 2.54 S 15.39 E
Boende 152 0.13 S 20.52 E
Bœng Lvea 110 12.36 N 105.34 E
Boeni 157a 12.55 S 45.06 E
Boën-sur-Lignon 62 45.44 N 3.59 E
Boeo, Capo › 70 37.48 N 12.25 E
Boerboonfontein 158 33.43 S 20.32 E
Boerne 196 29.47 N 98.43 W
Boeslunde 41 55.18 N 11.17 E
Boesmanland □[5] 156 19.30 S 20.00 E
Boesmans ≃, S. Afr. 158 33.42 S 26.39 E
Boesmans ≃, S. Afr. 158 28.46 S 30.09 E
Boesmansriviermond 158 33.42 S 26.39 E
Boetsap 158 27.59 S 24.30 E
Boeuf ≃ 194 31.52 N 91.47 W
Boeuf Creek ≃ 219 38.36 N 91.09 W
Boffa 150 10.10 N 14.02 W
Boffalora 266b 45.28 N 8.50 E
Boffzen 52 51.45 N 9.23 E
Bofoku 152 0.57 S 20.53 E
Bofors 40 59.20 N 14.32 E
Bofosso 150 8.40 N 9.42 W
Bōfu
→ Hōfu 96 34.03 N 131.34 E
Boga 154 1.03 N 29.56 E
Bogachiel ≃ 224 47.55 N 124.28 W
Bogadjim 164 5.25 S 145.45 E
Bogal, Lagh ≃ 154 0.45 N 40.50 E
Bogale 110 16.17 N 95.24 E
Bogalusa 194 30.47 N 89.50 W
Bogan ≃ 166 29.57 S 146.21 E
Bogandé 150 12.59 N 0.08 W
Bog and Vly
Meadows ≡ 276 40.56 N 74.19 W
Bogan Gate 166 33.07 S 147.48 E
Bogangolo 152 5.34 N 18.15 E
Bogantungan 166 23.39 S 147.18 E
Bogart, Mount ʌ 182 50.55 N 115.14 W
Bogastow Brook ≃ 283 42.12 N 71.22 W
Bogata 196 33.28 N 95.13 W
Bogataja Černeščina 78 48.59 N 35.35 E
Bogatiščevo-Jepišino 82 54.47 N 38.25 E
Bogatoje 80 53.04 N 51.24 E
Bogatyje Saby 80 56.01 N 50.27 E
Bogatynia 54 50.53 N 15.00 E
Bogatyr' 80 53.25 N 50.02 E
Bogatyrevo 80 50.22 N 48.46 E
Boğazkale 130 40.02 N 34.37 E
Boğazkaya 130 41.27 N 35.54 E
Boğazköy ◆[8] 267b 41.11 N 28.46 E
Boğazköy ≃ 267b 41.10 N 28.49 E
Boğazlıyan 130 39.12 N 35.15 E
Bogbonga 152 1.35 N 19.25 E
Bogcang ≃ 120 31.56 N 87.24 E
Bogd 102 45.11 N 100.43 E
Bogdanovič 86 56.47 N 62.01 E
Bogdanovka, Ross. 80 52.42 N 50.46 E
Bogdanovka, Ross. 80 52.10 N 52.37 E
Bogda Shan ʌʌ 90 43.30 N 89.45 E
Bogdo Ula ʌ 86 43.50 N 88.20 E
Bogel 56 50.11 N 7.48 E
Bogembaj 86 52.29 N 72.20 E
Bogen 60 48.55 N 12.43 E
Bogense 41 55.34 N 10.06 E
Boger City 192 35.29 N 81.12 W
Bogess Creek ≃ 282 37.18 N 122.19 W
Boget 80 49.40 N 47.59 E
Boggabilla 166 28.37 S 150.21 E
Boggabri 166 30.42 S 150.02 E
Boggeragh
Mountains ʌʌ 48 52.03 N 8.55 W
Boggola, Mount ʌ 162 23.48 S 117.40 E
Boggs Run ≃ 279b 40.32 N 80.14 W
Boggstown 218 39.34 N 85.55 W
Boggy Creek ≃ 222 31.07 N 95.46 W
Boggy Peak ʌ 240c 17.03 N 61.51 W
Bogia 164 4.15 S 144.55 E
Bogie Lake ◎ 281 42.37 N 83.31 W
Bogilima 152 3.34 N 19.16 E
Bogliasco 62 44.23 N 9.04 E
Bognanco Fonti 58 46.07 N 8.12 E
Bognes 24 68.10 N 16.00 E
Bognor Regis 42 50.47 N 0.41 W
Bogny-sur-Meuse 56 49.51 N 4.46 E
Bogo, Cam. 146 10.44 N 14.36 E
Bogo, Pil. 116 11.03 N 124.00 E
Bogø I 41 54.56 N 12.04 E
Bogo Bay c 116 11.05 N 124.01 E
Bogoduchov 78 50.10 N 35.30 E
Bogol Manyo 144 4.31 N 41.32 E
Bogol'ubovo, Ross. 76 55.32 N 32.57 E
Bogol'ubovo, Ross. 80 56.13 N 40.31 E
Bogomila 38 41.36 N 21.28 E
Bogong, Mount ʌ 166 36.45 S 147.18 E
Bogong Peaks ʌʌ 171b 35.34 S 148.28 E
Bogor 115a 6.35 S 106.47 E
Bogoria, Lake ◎ 154 0.15 N 36.06 E
Bogoro 154 1.24 N 30.17 E
Bogorodčany 78 48.48 N 24.32 E
Bogorodick 76 53.46 N 38.08 E
Bogorodickoje 80 46.20 N 41.10 E
Bogorodičnoje 83 49.01 N 37.30 E
Bogorodsk, Ross. 24 62.16 N 52.28 E
Bogorodsk, Ross. 80 56.06 N 43.31 E
Bogorodskoje, Ross. 80 57.51 N 50.45 E
Bogorodskoje, Ross. 80 46.20 N 43.53 E
Bogorodskoje, Ross. 82 55.02 N 38.29 E
Bogorodskoje, Ross. 82 55.26 N 36.14 E
Bogorodskoje, Ross. 89 52.22 N 140.30 E
Bogorodskoje ◆[8] 265b 55.49 N 37.44 E
Bogoso 150 5.34 N 2.01 W
Bogosskij chrebet ʌʌ 84 42.15 N 46.05 E
Bogotá
— Santa Fe de
Bogotá, Col. 246 4.36 N 74.05 W
Bogota, N.J., U.S. 276 40.52 N 74.01 W
Bogotol 86 56.12 N 89.33 E
Bogou 150 10.39 N 0.11 E
Bogovarovo 24 58.59 N 47.01 E
Bogra 124 24.51 N 89.22 E
Bograd 86 54.13 N 90.51 E
Bogrie Hill ʌ[2] 44 55.08 N 3.55 W
Bogučany 88 58.23 N 97.29 E
Bogučar 78 49.57 N 40.33 E
Bogučar ≃ 78 49.57 N 40.39 E
Bogué 150 16.35 N 14.16 W
Bogue Chitto 194 31.26 N 90.27 W
Bogue Chitto ≃ 194 30.35 N 89.49 W
Bogue Chitto Creek
≃ 194 32.10 N 87.14 W
Bogue Phalia ≃ 194 33.15 N 90.44 W
Bogues Bay c 208 37.52 N 75.29 W
Böğürtlen 130 37.10 N 38.04 E
Boguševsk 76 54.51 N 30.13 E
Boguslav 78 49.33 N 30.53 E
Bogustan 85 41.41 N 70.05 E
Bo Hai (Gulf of Chihli)
c 98 38.30 N 120.00 E
Bohai Haixia ʮ 98 38.15 N 121.00 E
Bohain-en-
Vermandois 50 49.59 N 3.27 E
Bohai Wan c 98 38.40 N 118.20 E
Bohan 56 49.52 N 4.53 E
Bohannon 208 37.24 N 76.22 W
Böheimkirchen 61 48.12 N 15.46 E
Bohemia 210 40.46 N 73.06 W
Bohemia
→ Čechy □[9] 30 49.50 N 14.00 E
Bohemia ≃ 208 39.29 N 75.55 W
Bohemia Downs 162 18.53 S 126.14 E
Bohemian Forest ʌʌ 30 49.15 N 12.45 E
Bohetai 104 42.01 N 123.13 E
Bohicon 150 7.12 N 2.04 E
Bohin 144 11.44 N 51.15 E
Bohinjska Bistrica 36 46.17 N 13.57 E
Bohinjsko Jezero ◎ 64 46.17 N 13.50 E
Böhlen 54 51.12 N 12.23 E
Böhlitz-Ehrenberg
◆[8] 54 51.21 N 12.17 E
Böhme ≃ 52 52.46 N 9.28 E
Böhmen
→ Čechy □[9] 30 49.50 N 14.00 E
Böhmenkirch 56 48.41 N 9.55 E
Böhmerwald
→ Bohemian
Forest ʌʌ 30 49.15 N 12.45 E
Bohmte 52 52.22 N 8.19 E
Bohners Lake 216 42.37 N 88.17 W
Böhnsdorf ◆[8] 264a 52.24 N 13.33 E
Bohodou 150 9.46 N 9.04 W
Bohol 144 5.45 N 46.09 E
Bohol □[4] 116 9.50 N 124.10 E
Bohol I 116 9.50 N 124.10 E
Bohol Sea ⊤[2] 116 9.10 N 124.25 E
Bohon 116 18.30 N 120.35 E
Bohongou 150 12.30 N 0.42 E
Bohorg 152 6.23 N 15.37 E
Bohorok 114 3.30 N 98.12 E
Bohsdorf 54 51.38 N 14.32 E
Bohuslän □[9] 26 58.15 N 11.50 E
Bohušovice nad Ohří 54 50.29 N 14.07 E
Bohutín 60 49.40 N 13.55 E
Boi 150 9.34 N 9.27 E
Boi, Ponta do › 256 23.58 S 45.15 W
Boiaçu 246 0.27 S 61.46 W
Boiano 66 41.29 N 14.29 E
Boiceville 210 41.59 N 74.15 W
Boiestown 186 46.27 N 66.25 W
Boigu Island I 164 9.16 S 142.12 E
Boila 154 16.10 S 39.50 E
Boiling Springs, N.C.,
U.S. 192 35.30 N 81.37 W
Boiling Springs, Pa.,
U.S. 208 40.08 N 77.07 W
Boim 250 2.49 S 55.10 W
Boinville-en-Mantois 261 48.56 N 1.46 E
Boinvilliers 261 48.55 N 1.40 E
Boipeba, Ilha de I 255 13.39 S 38.55 W
Boiro 34 42.39 N 8.54 W
Bois, Lac des ◎,
N.T., Can. 180 66.40 N 125.15 W
Bois, Lac des
→ Woods, Lake of
the ◎, N.A. 184 49.15 N 94.45 W
Bois, Rio dos ≃ 255 18.35 S 50.02 W
Bois Blanc Island I 190 45.45 N 84.28 W
Boisbriand 275a 45.37 N 73.51 W
Bois Brule ≃ 190 46.45 N 91.37 W
Boischâtel 206 46.54 N 71.08 W
Bois-Colombes 261 48.55 N 2.16 E
Boisdale, Loch c 46 57.08 N 7.19 W
Bois d'Arc Creek ≃ 196 33.50 N 95.50 W
Bois-d'Arcy 261 48.48 N 2.01 E
Bois-des-Filion 206 45.40 N 73.45 W
Bois de Sioux ≃ 198 46.16 N 96.36 W
Boise 202 43.36 N 116.12 W
Boise ≃ 202 43.49 N 117.01 W
Boise, Middle Fork ≃ 202 43.42 N 115.38 W
Boise, North Fork ≃ 202 43.42 N 115.38 W
Boise, South Fork ≃ 202 43.36 N 115.51 W
Boise City 196 36.43 N 102.30 W
Boisemont 261 49.01 N 2.00 E
Bois-Guillaume 50 49.28 N 1.08 E
Bois-le-Roi 50 48.28 N 2.42 E
Boissettes 261 48.31 N 2.37 E
Boissevain 184 49.14 N 100.03 W
Boissise-la-Bertrand 261 48.32 N 2.35 E
Boissy-l'Aillerie 261 49.05 N 2.02 E
Boissy-Saint-Léger 50 48.45 N 2.31 E
Boissy-sous-Saint-
Yon 261 48.34 N 2.13 E
Boistfort Peak ʌ 224 46.29 N 123.12 W
Boitzenburg 54 53.15 N 13.37 E
Boizenburg 54 53.22 N 10.43 E
Boja 115a 7.06 S 110.16 E
Bojadła 30 51.57 N 15.50 E
Bojarka 78 50.19 N 30.19 E
Bojarkino 82 54.57 N 38.31 E
Bojarsk 88 56.19 N 106.04 E
Bojayá ≃ 246 6.35 N 76.54 W
Bojeador, Cape › 116 18.30 N 120.34 E
Bojelebung 116 6.31 N 122.11 E
Bojevo 78 51.24 N 39.19 E
Boji Plain ≚ 154 1.30 N 39.45 E
Bojizhang 98 41.49 N 117.46 E
Bojnūrd 128 37.28 N 57.19 E
Bojonegoro 115a 7.09 S 111.52 E
Boju 150 7.25 N 7.52 E
Boju Ega 150 7.24 N 8.04 E
B'ojuk-Kirs, gora ʌ 84 39.41 N 46.44 E
Bojuru 252 31.38 S 51.26 W
Bokad 272c 18.53 N 72.58 E
Bokada 152 4.08 N 19.23 E
Bokal 168a 33.29 S 116.54 E
Bokala, Zaïre 152 3.07 S 17.02 E
Bokala, Zaïre 152 2.03 N 18.59 E
Bokani 150 9.26 N 5.13 E
Bokāro Steel City 124 23.45 N 86.07 E
Bokatola 152 0.38 S 18.46 E
Bokchito 196 34.01 N 96.08 W
Boké 150 10.56 N 14.18 W
Bokeelia 220 26.42 N 82.09 W
Bokel 52 53.23 N 8.46 E
Bokela 152 1.08 S 21.56 E
Bokes Creek ≃ 188 40.19 N 83.10 W
Bokfontein 158 32.48 S 19.16 E
Bokhara 158 27.57 S 20.30 E
Bokhara ≃ 166 29.55 S 146.42 E
Boki 146 8.48 N 13.32 E
Bokino 80 52.38 N 41.26 E
Bokkol ʌ 154 1.50 N 37.02 E
Bok Koŭ 110 10.37 N 104.03 E
Böklund 41 54.36 N 9.34 E
Boknafjorden c[2] 26 59.10 N 5.35 E
Boko, Congo 152 4.47 S 14.38 E
Boko, Kaz. 86 49.05 N 81.38 E
Bokod 116 16.30 N 120.50 E
Bokode 152 3.58 N 19.29 E
Bokolako 150 13.36 N 12.33 W
Bokonbajevskoje 85 42.07 N 77.00 E
Bokondji 152 2.22 N 18.42 E
Bokondo 152 0.15 N 22.32 E
Bokong 112 9.58 S 124.04 E
Bokoro 146 12.23 N 17.03 E
Boko Songo 152 4.26 S 13.37 E
Bokota 152 0.51 S 22.18 E
Bokote 152 0.05 S 20.08 E
Bokovo-Antratsit
→ Antracit 83 48.06 N 39.06 E
Bokovo Platovo 83 48.07 N 39.01 E
Bokovskaja 80 49.15 N 41.49 E
Bokpunt › 158 33.34 S 18.19 E
Bokpyin 110 11.16 N 98.46 E
Boksburg 158 26.12 S 28.14 E
Boksburg □[5] 273d 26.12 S 28.14 E
Boksburg-Noord 273d 26.12 S 28.15 E
Boksburg South 273d 26.14 S 28.15 E
Boksburg-West 273d 26.13 S 28.14 E
Boksitogorsk 76 59.28 N 33.51 E
Bokungu 152 0.41 S 22.19 E
Bol, Hrv. 36 43.16 N 16.40 E
Bol, Tchad 146 13.28 N 14.43 E
Bolaang Mongondow 112 0.56 N 124.10 E
Bolama, Gui.-B. 150 11.35 N 15.28 W
Bolama, Zaïre 152 1.57 N 22.58 E
Bolaman 130 41.03 N 37.37 E
Bolān ≃ 120 28.38 N 67.42 E
Bolanda, Jabal ʌ 140 7.44 N 25.28 E
Bol'andkiik ≃ 85 39.11 N 72.17 E
Bolangum 166 36.46 S 142.53 E
Bolaños 234 21.41 N 103.47 W
Bolaños ≃ 234 21.14 N 104.08 W
Bolaños de Calatrava 34 38.54 N 3.40 W
Bolān Pass)(120 29.45 N 67.35 E
Bolans 240c 17.02 N 61.53 W
Bolay I 152 4.20 N 17.21 E
Bolayır 130 40.31 N 26.45 E
Bolbec 50 49.34 N 0.29 E
Bolčary 86 59.49 N 68.48 E
Bolchov 76 53.27 N 36.01 E
Bolchuny 80 47.59 N 46.25 E
Bolda ≃ 80 46.10 N 48.14 E
Boldasevo 80 54.43 N 45.33 E
Boldekow 54 53.43 N 13.35 E
Bolderslev 41 54.59 N 9.18 E
Bold Heath 262 53.24 N 2.42 W
Boldon 44 54.57 N 1.27 W
Bol'džuan 85 38.19 N 69.40 E
Bole, Ghana 150 9.02 N 2.29 W
Bole, Zhg. 86 44.53 N 82.05 E
Bolechov 78 49.04 N 23.52 E
Boleko 152 1.31 S 19.53 E
Bolero 154 10.59 S 33.45 E
Boles 194 34.46 N 94.02 W
Bolesławiec 30 51.16 N 15.34 E
Boleszkowice 30 52.44 N 14.36 E
Boletice nad Labem 54 50.45 N 14.13 E
Boley 196 35.29 N 96.29 W
Bolgarčaj ≃ 84 39.28 N 48.36 E
Bolgart 162 31.16 S 116.30 E
Bolgatanga 150 10.46 N 0.52 W
Bolgrad 78 45.41 N 28.36 E
Boli, Sūd. 140 6.01 N 28.43 E
Boli, Tchad 146 10.50 N 18.43 E
Boli, Zhg. 89 45.46 N 130.31 E
Bolia 152 1.36 S 18.23 E
Boliden 26 64.52 N 20.23 E
Boligee 194 32.45 N 88.01 W
Boligeqiu 104 42.14 N 121.40 E
Bolíkov 61 49.02 N 15.22 E
Bolinao 116 16.23 N 119.54 E
Bolinas 226 37.54 N 122.42 W
Boling 222 29.15 N 95.56 W
Bolingbrook 216 41.41 N 88.04 W
Bolinger Creek ≃ 282 37.47 N 122.00 W
Bolingo 152 3.30 S 21.43 E
Bolishan 89 43.50 N 123.31 E
Bolivar, Austl. 168b 34.46 S 138.36 E
Bolívar, Col. 246 5.50 N 76.01 W
Bolívar, Col. 246 1.50 N 76.58 W
Bolívar, Col. 246 4.21 N 76.10 W
Bolívar, Perú 248 7.18 S 77.48 W
Bolivar, Mo., U.S. 194 37.36 N 93.24 W
Bolivar, N.Y., U.S. 210 42.04 N 78.10 W
Bolivar, Oh., U.S. 214 40.39 N 81.27 W
Bolivar, Pa., U.S. 214 40.23 N 79.09 W
Bolivar, Tn., U.S. 194 35.15 N 88.59 W
Bolívar □[3] 246 6.20 N 63.30 W
Bolívar □[4] 246 1.35 S 79.00 W
Bolívar □[5] 246 9.00 N 74.40 W
Bolívar, Cerro ʌ 246 7.28 N 63.25 W
Bolívar, Pico ʌ 246 8.30 N 71.02 W
Bolivar Peninsula ›[1] 196 29.27 N 94.39 W
Bolivar Run 214 41.59 N 78.39 W
Bolivia □[1], S.A. 242 17.00 S 65.00 W
Bolivia □[1], S.A. 248 17.00 S 65.00 W
Bolivie
→ Bolivia □[1] 248 17.00 S 65.00 W
Bolivien
→ Bolivia □[1] 248 17.00 S 65.00 W
Boljarovo 38 42.09 N 26.49 E
Boljoon 116 9.38 N 123.29 E
Bolkar Dağları ʌʌ 130 37.15 N 34.20 E
Bölkenbusch 263 51.21 N 7.06 E
Boll 56 48.38 N 9.37 E
Bolladello 266b 45.41 N 8.50 E
Bollate 62 45.33 N 9.07 E
Böllberg ʌ[2] 263 51.23 N 7.19 E
Bollendorf 56 49.51 N 6.22 E
Bollène 62 44.17 N 4.45 E
Bollensdorf 264a 52.31 N 13.43 E
Bolles Canal ≡ 220 26.38 N 80.34 W
Bolles Harbor 216 41.51 N 83.24 W
Bollin ≃ 44 53.23 N 2.28 W
Bolling Air Force
Base ■ 284c 38.51 N 77.02 W
Bollington, Eng., U.K. 44 53.18 N 2.06 W
Bollington, Eng., U.K. 262 53.22 N 2.25 W
Bollnäs 26 61.21 N 16.25 E
Bollon 166 28.05 S 147.15 E
Bollstabruk 26 63.00 N 17.39 E
Bollstanäs 40 59.30 N 17.56 E
Bollullos par del
Condado 34 37.20 N 6.32 W
Bollwerk 263 51.10 N 7.35 E
Bolmen ◎ 26 56.55 N 13.40 E
Bolnisi 84 41.28 N 44.33 E
Bolo 144 8.50 N 39.22 E
Bolobo 152 2.10 S 16.14 E
Bolochovo 82 54.05 N 37.50 E
Bologna 64 44.29 N 11.20 E
Bologna □[4] 64 44.28 N 11.26 E
Bologne, Fr. 58 48.12 N 5.08 E
Bologne
→ Bologna, It. 64 44.29 N 11.20 E
Bolognesi 248 6.35 S 73.10 W
Bolognetta 70 37.58 N 13.27 E
Bolognola 66 42.59 N 13.14 E
Bologoje 76 57.54 N 34.02 E
Bologovo 76 56.54 N 31.42 E
Bololo 152 3.50 S 21.08 E
Bolomba 152 0.29 N 19.12 E
Bolombo 152 3.59 S 21.22 E
Bolombo ≃ 152 1.32 N 21.14 E
Bolon' 89 49.55 N 136.07 E
Bolon', ozero ◎ 89 49.51 N 136.22 E
Bolonchén de Rejón 232 20.00 N 89.49 W
Bolondo 152 0.27 N 20.01 E
Bolondrón 240p 22.46 N 81.27 W
Bolong ≃ 170 34.15 S 149.36 E
Bolonia
→ Bologna 64 44.29 N 11.20 E
Bolótana 71 40.20 N 8.57 E
Bolotino 38 47.42 N 27.21 E
Bolotnoje 86 55.41 N 84.23 E
Boloto 82 54.10 N 36.20 E
Bolotovskoje 86 58.33 N 62.28 E
Bolovens, Plateau
des ʌʌ[1] 110 15.20 N 106.20 E
Bolpur 126 23.40 N 87.43 E
Bol'šaja 76 59.36 N 41.48 E
Bol'šaja ≃ 80 48.36 N 41.00 E
Bol'šaja Atn'a 80 56.15 N 49.27 E
Bol'šaja Balachn'a ≃ 74 73.37 N 107.05 E
Bol'šaja Ber'ostovica 76 53.11 N 24.01 E
Bol'šaja
Blagoveščenka 78 46.51 N 34.03 E
Bol'šaja Brembola 82 56.45 N 38.55 E
Bol'šaja Bukon' 86 48.53 N 82.43 E
Bol'šaja Čalykla ≃ 80 51.51 N 49.34 E
Bol'šaja Černigovka 80 52.07 N 50.52 E
Bol'šaja Chalan' 78 50.56 N 37.26 E
Bol'šaja Cheta ≃ 74 69.33 N 84.15 E
Bol'šaja Chobda ≃ 86 50.56 N 54.34 E
Bol'šaja Chundala 76 60.04 N 34.18 E

ENGLISH | DEUTSCH

Name	Page	Lat.°′	Long.°′	Name	Seite	Breite°′	Länge°′ E = Ost

Bol'šaja Čuja ≃ 88 58.56 N 112.13 E
Bol'šaja Čurakovka 86 53.03 N 64.20 E
Bol'šaja Damba 80 46.57 N 51.47 E
Bol'šaja Dmitrijevka 80 51.21 N 45.15 E
Bol'šaja Dora 76 59.05 N 37.38 E
Bol'šaja Džalga 80 45.59 N 42.41 E
Bol'šaja Glušica 80 52.24 N 50.28 E
Bol'šaja Ižora 76 59.56 N 29.34 E
Bol'šaja Ižorka ≃ 265a 59.48 N 30.36 E
Bol'šaja Kakša ≃ 80 57.53 N 45.28 E
Bol'šaja Kamenka 80 53.39 N 50.31 E
Bol'šaja Kamenka ≃ 83 48.22 N 40.04 E
Bol'šaja Kandala 80 54.32 N 49.22 E
Bol'šaja Kaskara 86 57.11 N 65.58 E
Bol'šaja Ket' 86 57.39 N 91.45 E
Bol'šaja Kinel' ≃ 80 53.14 N 50.30 E
Bol'šaja Kirsanovka 83 47.40 N 38.54 E
Bol'šaja Kokšaga ≃ 80 56.08 N 47.47 E
Bol'šaja Konkudera
≃ 88 57.34 N 112.30 E
Bol'šaja Kugul'ta ≃ 80 45.45 N 41.57 E
Bol'šaja Kuonamka
≃ 74 70.45 N 113.24 E
Bol'šaja Laba ≃ 84 44.16 N 40.53 E
Bol'šaja Lipovica 80 52.33 N 41.20 E
Bol'šaja Martynovka 80 47.17 N 41.40 E
Bol'šaja Mošanica 76 53.58 N 29.37 E
Bol'šaja Murta 86 56.55 N 93.07 E
Bol'šaja Neva ≃ 265a 59.58 N 30.13 E
Bol'šaja Norja 80 56.41 N 52.43 E
Bol'šaja Ochta ◆[8] 265a 59.57 N 30.25 E
Bol'šaja Ol'šanka 80 51.32 N 44.17 E
Bol'šaja Orlovka 80 47.20 N 41.16 E
Bol'šaja Osinovaja ≃ 180 66.30 N 174.00 E
Bol'šaja Pas'ma 80 58.38 N 43.53 E
Bol'šaja Rečka 88 51.57 N 104.44 E
Bol'šaja Ržaksa 80 52.08 N 42.13 E
Bol'šaja Sestra ≃ 82 56.16 N 35.56 E
Bol'šaja Smedva ≃ 82 54.50 N 38.34 E
Bol'šaja Sosnova 80 57.40 N 54.36 E
Bol'šaja Talovaja 78 46.58 N 40.37 E
Bol'šaja Tarel' 88 53.45 N 106.40 E
Bol'šaja Tavoložka 80 52.07 N 49.04 E
Bol'šaja Uča 80 56.37 N 52.05 E
Bol'šaja Usa 86 56.44 N 55.06 E
Bol'šaja Ussurka ≃ 89 45.57 N 133.42 E
Bol'šaja Višera 76 58.55 N 32.08 E
Bol'šaja Vladimirovka 86 50.53 N 79.31 E
Bol'šaja Vys' ≃ 78 48.45 N 30.54 E
Bolsa Knolls 226 36.44 N 121.38 W
Bol'šakovo, Ross. 76 54.53 N 21.40 E
Bol'šakovo, Ross. 265b 55.54 N 37.17 E
Bol'šečernigovka 83 48.57 N 39.25 E
Bol'šekrepinskaja 83 47.36 N 39.22 E
Bol'šelig 24 62.07 N 52.25 E
Bolsena 66 42.39 N 11.59 E
Bolsena, Lago di ◎ 66 42.36 N 11.56 E
Bol'šenarymskoje 86 49.16 N 84.32 E
Bol'šerečje 86 56.06 N 74.38 E
Bol'šereck 74 52.25 N 156.24 E
Bol'šetroickoje 78 50.33 N 37.17 E
Bol'šeustjikinskoje 86 55.57 N 58.16 E
Bol'ševik, Bela. 76 52.34 N 30.53 E
Bol'ševik, Ross. 74 62.44 N 147.30 E
Bol'ševik, Ross. 265a 59.49 N 30.30 E
Bol'ševik, ostrov I 74 78.40 N 102.30 E
Bol'šezemel'skaja
Tundra ◆[1] 72 67.30 N 56.00 E
Bolshoi Theatre ʋ 265b 55.46 N 37.37 E
Bol'šije Algaši 80 55.22 N 46.29 E
Bol'šije Avt'uki 78 52.04 N 29.32 E
Bol'šije Belyniči 82 54.38 N 38.50 E
Bol'šije Berezniki 80 54.11 N 45.58 E
Bol'šije Gorki, Ross. 82 56.28 N 35.51 E
Bol'šije Gorki, Ross. 265a 59.42 N 29.51 E
Bol'šije Kajbicy 80 55.25 N 48.13 E
Bol'šije Kizi, ozero ◎ 89 51.38 N 140.20 E
Bol'šije Kl'uči 80 55.59 N 48.47 E
Bol'šije Kl'učišči 80 54.08 N 48.14 E
Bol'šije Liachvi ≃ 84 41.58 N 44.06 E
Bol'šije Michalicyny 80 58.29 N 48.14 E
Bol'šije Ozerki 80 52.36 N 46.33 E
Bol'šije Pom'aly 80 56.42 N 46.40 E
Bol'šije Ručji 82 56.36 N 36.58 E
Bol'šije Saly 83 47.24 N 39.41 E
Bol'šije Tarchany 80 54.42 N 48.34 E
Bol'šije Ugli 88 57.47 N 112.51 E
Bol'šije Uki 86 56.57 N 72.37 E
Bol'šije Ždanovy 80 58.40 N 49.05 E
Bol'šoj 80 50.13 N 43.26 E
Bol'šoj An'uj ≃ 74 68.30 N 160.49 E
Bol'šoj Ažbulat,
ozero ◎ 86 53.17 N 77.25 E
Bol'šoj Begičev,
ostrov I 74 74.20 N 112.30 E
Bol'šoj Bogdo, gora
ʌ[2] 80 48.08 N 46.52 E
Bol'šoj Boktybaj,
gora ʌ 86 48.27 N 58.30 E
Bol'šoj Čeremšan ≃ 80 54.11 N 49.39 E
Bol'šoj Civil' ≃ 80 55.54 N 47.28 E
Bol'šoje, ozero ◎ 265a 60.04 N 30.39 E
Bol'šoje Aksu 86 43.20 N 79.35 E
Bol'šoje
Aleksejevskoje 82 55.14 N 38.12 E
Bol'šoje Boldino 80 54.59 N 45.19 E
Bol'šoje Bun'kovo 82 55.51 N 38.37 E
Bol'šoje Goloustnoje 88 52.01 N 105.25 E
Bol'šoje Gorodišče,
Ross. 76 57.17 N 30.31 E
Bol'šoje Gorodišče,
Ross. 78 50.37 N 37.06 E
Bol'šoje Ignatovo 80 55.02 N 45.34 E
Bol'šoje Jarovoje,
ozero ◎ 86 52.53 N 78.36 E
Bol'šoje
Jašaltinskoje,
ozero ◎ 80 46.17 N 42.27 E
Bol'šoje Kibejevo 80 56.55 N 47.05 E
Bol'šoje Korovino 82 54.30 N 39.02 E
Bol'šoje Manuškino 265a 59.53 N 30.49 E
Bol'šoje
Michajlovskoje 82 56.47 N 38.04 E
Bol'šoje Mikuškino 80 53.56 N 51.42 E
Bol'šoje Muraškino 80 55.47 N 44.46 E
Bol'šoje Nagatkino 80 54.31 N 47.58 E
Bol'šoje Nurkejevo 80 55.22 N 52.40 E
Bol'šoje Nyrsy 80 55.44 N 50.19 E
Bol'šoje Ogar'ovo 76 53.33 N 37.43 E
Bol'šoje Pikino 80 56.25 N 44.22 E
Bol'šoje Polpino 76 53.14 N 34.30 E
Bol'šoje Ramenje 76 58.21 N 36.40 E
Bol'šoje Rybuškino 80 55.25 N 45.48 E
Bol'šoje Sazonovo 80 58.06 N 53.21 E
Bol'šoje Selo 76 57.43 N 38.56 E
Bol'šoje Šem'akino 80 55.03 N 48.38 E
Bol'šoje Soldatskoje 78 51.21 N 35.31 E
Bol'šoje Sudačje 80 50.49 N 44.05 E
Bol'šoje Topol'noje,
ozero ◎ 86 53.20 N 78.00 E
Bol'šoje Uro 88 53.32 N 109.48 E
Bol'šoje Zagorje 76 57.51 N 28.57 E
Bol'šoje Žokovo 82 54.35 N 38.57 E
Bol'šoj Gašun ≃ 80 47.22 N 42.43 E
Bol'šoj Ginaldag,
gora ʌ 84 40.20 N 45.57 E
Bol'šoj Golec, gora ʌ 88 51.52 N 119.24 E
Bol'šoj Irgiz ≃ 80 52.01 N 47.24 E
Bol'šoj Jenisej (Bij-
Chem) ≃ 88 51.43 N 94.26 E
Bol'šoj Jugan ≃ 86 60.55 N 73.40 E
Bol'šoj Kamen' 89 43.06 N 132.21 E
Bol'šoj Kandarat' 80 54.25 N 47.00 E
Bol'šoj Kanym, gora
ʌ 86 54.13 N 88.20 E
Bol'šoj Karagaj 86 57.57 N 70.15 E
Bol'šoj Karaman ≃ 80 51.40 N 46.38 E
Bol'šoj Kavkaz
(Caucasus) ʌʌ 84 42.30 N 45.00 E
Bol'šoj Ketmen' 86 43.27 N 80.24 E
Bol'šoj Kujal'nik ≃ 78 46.46 N 30.36 E
Bol'šoj Kujaš 86 55.50 N 61.06 E
Bol'šoj Kundyš ≃ 80 56.32 N 47.23 E
Bol'šoj Kuvaj 80 54.37 N 47.05 E
Bol'šoj Kymynej,
gora ʌ 180 66.34 N 172.32 W
Bol'šoj L'achovskij,
ostrov I 74 73.35 N 142.00 E
Bol'šoj Lug 88 52.07 N 104.10 E
Bol'šoj Matačynaj,
gora ʌ 180 66.28 N 179.25 W
Bol'šoj Melik 80 51.38 N 43.18 E
Bol'šoj Nesvetaj ≃ 83 47.27 N 39.54 E
Bol'šoj Onguren 88 53.38 N 107.36 E
Bol'šoj Patom ≃ 88 59.15 N 113.56 E
Bol'šoj Pit ≃ 86 59.01 N 91.44 E
Bol'šoj Porog 86 52.35 N 92.18 E
Bol'šoj Šagan 80 50.57 N 51.08 E
Bol'šoj Sajan ʌʌ 88 52.00 N 99.30 E
Bol'šoj Salym ≃ 86 60.55 N 70.25 E
Bol'šoj Šantar, ostrov
I 89 55.00 N 137.42 E
Bol'šoj Šatan, gora ʌ 86 53.41 N 57.36 E
Bol'šoj Simonogont 265a 59.50 N 29.49 E
Bol'šoj Sorokino 86 56.38 N 69.53 E
Bol'šoj Suchodol 83 48.25 N 39.53 E
Bol'šoj Sundyr' 80 56.07 N 46.46 E
Bol'šoj Tal'cy 76 59.13 N 33.00 E
Bol'šoj Tolkaj 80 53.30 N 51.57 E
Bol'šoj T'uters,
ostrov I 76 59.51 N 27.13 E
Bol'šoj Uluj 86 56.39 N 90.36 E
Bol'šoj Uran ≃ 80 52.24 N 53.15 E
Bol'šoj Uvat, ozero ◎ 86 57.35 N 70.30 E
Bol'šoj Uzen' ≃ 80 48.50 N 49.40 E
Bol'šoj Uzigont 265a 59.48 N 29.53 E
Bol'šoj Vjass 80 53.48 N 45.30 E
Bol'šoj Vlasjevo 89 53.24 N 140.55 E
Bol'šoj Zelenčuk ≃ 84 44.36 N 41.56 E
Bol'šovcy 78 49.12 N 24.44 E
Bolsover 44 53.14 N 1.18 W
Bolsward 52 53.03 N 5.31 E
Boltaña 34 42.27 N 0.04 E
Boltigen 58 46.38 N 7.24 E
Boltino 265b 55.58 N 37.41 E
Bolton, On., Can. 212 43.53 N 79.44 W
Bolton, Eng., U.K. 44 53.35 N 2.26 W
Bolton, Ct., U.S. 207 41.46 N 72.26 W
Bolton, Ms., U.S. 194 32.20 N 90.27 W
Bolton, N.C., U.S. 192 34.19 N 78.24 W
Bolton □[8] 262 53.34 N 2.28 W
Bolton Abbey 44 53.59 N 1.53 W
Bolton Abbey ʋ[1] 44 53.59 N 1.54 W
Bolton Center 207 41.47 N 72.26 W
Bolton Creek ≃ 212 44.58 N 76.23 W
Bolton Lake ◎ 184 54.16 N 95.47 W
Bolton-le-Sands 44 54.06 N 2.47 W
Bolton upon Dearne 44 53.31 N 1.19 W
Bolton Wanderers
Football Ground ♠ 262 53.34 N 2.25 W
Bolu 130 40.44 N 31.37 E
Bolu □[4] 130 40.40 N 31.30 E
Bölükyazı 130 38.18 N 42.10 E
Boluntay 120 36.34 N 92.38 E
Boluo, Zhg. 100 23.11 N 114.17 E
Boluo, Zhg. 100 24.27 N 113.03 E
Boluochi 98 41.24 N 119.56 E
Boluokeng 100 24.05 N 113.22 E
Bolus Head › 48 51.46 N 10.21 W
Bolva ≃ 76 53.17 N 34.20 E
Bolvadin 130 38.42 N 31.04 E
Bolwarra 166 17.24 S 144.11 E
Bóly 30 45.58 N 18.32 E
Bolyčevo 82 55.46 N 35.43 E
Bolzaneto 62 44.27 N 8.54 E
Bolzano (Bozen) 64 46.31 N 11.22 E
Bolzano □[4] 64 46.43 N 11.30 E
Boma 152 5.51 S 13.03 E
Bomaderry 170 34.51 S 150.37 E
Bomal 56 50.23 N 5.32 E
Bomandjokou 152 0.34 N 14.23 E
Bomaneh 152 1.18 N 23.47 E
Bomarsund 26 60.13 N 20.15 E
Bomate 152 1.10 S 19.41 E
Bomba 66 42.02 N 14.22 E
Bombakabo 152 3.04 N 19.42 E
Bombala 166 36.54 S 149.14 E
Bombarral 34 39.16 N 9.09 W
Bombat 130 38.08 N 42.14 E
Bombay, India 122 18.58 N 72.50 E
Bombay, India 272c 18.58 N 72.50 E
Bombay, N.Y., U.S. 206 44.56 N 74.34 W
Bombay, University
of ʋ[2] 272c 18.57 N 72.50 E
Bombay Harbour c 272c 18.57 N 72.53 E
Bomberai,
Semenanjung ›[1] 164 3.00 S 133.00 E
Bombetoka, Baie de
c 157b 15.50 S 46.17 E
Bombimba 152 0.31 N 19.24 E
Bombo 154 0.35 N 32.32 E
Bombo ≃ 152 3.58 S 15.59 E
Bombo-Kasanji 152 5.54 S 21.51 E
Bomboma 152 2.25 N 18.54 E
Bombo-Makuka 152 5.26 S 16.19 E
Bombombwa 154 1.21 N 25.30 E
Bombon 261 48.34 N 2.52 E
Bomboyo 146 12.01 N 15.28 E
Bom Conselho 250 9.10 S 36.41 W
Bom Despacho 255 19.43 S 45.15 W
Bomdila 120 27.27 N 92.17 E
Bomei 100 22.57 N 115.46 E
Bömenzien 54 52.59 N 11.31 E
Bom Fim do Bom
Jesus 256 23.17 S 47.02 W
Bomhus 40 60.41 N 17.13 E
Bomili 154 1.40 N 27.01 E
Bom Jardim, Ilha do I 287a 23.02 S 43.35 W
Bom Jardim de Goiás 255 16.17 S 52.07 W
Bom Jardim de
Minas 256 21.57 S 44.11 W
Bom Jesus, Ang. 152 9.09 S 13.34 E
Bom Jesus, Bra. 250 9.04 S 44.22 W
Bom Jesus da Lapa 255 13.15 S 43.25 W
Bom Jesus de Goiás 255 18.12 S 49.44 W
Bom Jesus dos
Perdões 256 23.08 S 46.28 W
Bømlafjorden c[2] 26 59.39 N 5.20 E
Bomlitz 52 52.54 N 9.37 E
Bømlo I 26 59.46 N 5.12 E
Bommerholz 263 51.23 N 7.18 E
Bommern 263 51.25 N 7.20 E
Bomnak 89 54.46 N 128.51 E
Bomokandi ≃ 154 3.39 N 26.08 E
Bomongiri 152 1.57 S 21.13 E
Bomongo 152 1.22 N 18.21 E
Bompata 150 6.38 N 1.04 W
Bompensiere 70 37.28 N 13.47 E
Bompietro 70 37.44 N 14.06 E
Bomputu 152 0.20 S 20.06 E
Bom Repouso 256 22.28 S 46.09 W
Bom Retiro 252 27.48 S 49.31 W
Bom Retiro ◆[8] 287b 23.32 S 46.38 W
Bom Sucesso, Bra. 248 15.43 S 56.07 W
Bom Sucesso, Bra. 255 23.42 S 51.45 W
Bom Sucesso, Bra. 256 22.17 S 42.49 W
Bom Sucesso, Bra. 287b 23.25 S 46.24 W
Bomu (Mbomou) ≃ 136 4.08 N 22.26 E
Bon, Cap › 36 37.05 N 11.03 E
Bona 40 58.34 N 15.03 E
Bona Bona Island I 164 10.30 S 149.50 E
Bon Accord 158 25.38 S 28.11 E
Bonaduz 58 46.49 N 9.25 E
Bonaero Park 273d 26.07 S 28.16 E
Bonai 114 1.16 N 100.52 E
Bonaigarh 120 21.50 N 84.57 E
Bon Air 208 37.31 N 77.33 W
Bon Aire 214 40.54 N 79.55 W
Bonaire I 241s 12.10 N 68.15 W
Bonampak ⊥ 232 16.44 N 91.05 W
Bönan 40 60.44 N 17.18 E
Bonandolok 114 1.47 N 98.48 E

Symbols in the index entries represent the broad categories identified in the key at the right. Symbols with superior numbers (ʌʌ[1]) identify subcategories (see complete key on page *I · 1).*

Symbole im Register stellen die rechts im Schlüssel erklärten Kategorien dar. Symbole mit hochgestellten Ziffern (ʌʌ[1]) bezeichnen Unterabteilungen einer Kategorie (vgl. vollständiger Schlüssel auf Seite *I · 1).*

Los símbolos incluídos en el texto del índice representan las grandes categorías identificadas con la clave a la derecha. Los símbolos con numeros en su parte superior (ʌʌ[1]) identifican las subcategorías (véase la clave completa en la página *I · 1).*

Les symboles de l'index représentent les catégories indiquées dans la légende à droite. Les symboles suivis d'un indice (ʌʌ[1]) représentent des sous-catégories (voir légende complète à la page *I · 1).*

Os símbolos incluídos no texto do índice representam as grandes categorias identificadas com a chave à direita. Os símbolos com números em sua parte superior (ʌʌ[1]) identificam as subcategorias (veja-se a chave completa à página *I · 1).*

	English	Deutsch	Español	Français	Português
ʌ	Mountain	Berg	Montaña	Montagne	Montanha
ʌʌ	Mountains	Gebirge	Montañas	Montagnes	Montanhas
)(	Pass	Paß	Paso	Col	Passo
V	Valley, Canyon	Tal, Cañon	Valle, Cañón	Vallée, Canyon	Vale, Canhão
≚	Plain	Ebene	Llano	Plaine	Planície
›	Cape	Kap	Cabo	Cap	Cabo
I	Island	Insel	Isla	Île	Ilha
II	Islands	Inseln	Islas	Îles	Ilhas
⊥	Other Topographic Features	Andere Topographische Objekte	Otros Elementos Topográficos	Autres données topographiques	Outros acidentes topográficos

ESPAÑOL · FRANÇAIS · PORTUGUÊS

Nombre / Nom / Nome	Página / Page	Lat.°′	Long.°′ W = Oeste / W = Ouest
Bonanza, Nic.	236	14.01 N	84.35 W
Bonanza, Or., U.S.	202	42.11 N	121.24 W
Bonanza, Ut., U.S.	200	40.01 N	109.10 W
Bonanza Peak ∧	224	48.14 N	120.52 W
Bonao	238	18.56 N	70.25 W
Bonaparte	190	40.41 N	91.48 W
Bonaparte ≃	182	50.46 N	121.17 W
Bonaparte, Lake ⊜	212	44.09 N	75.23 W
Bonaparte, Mount ∧	202	48.45 N	119.08 W
Bonaparte Archipelago II	160	14.17 S	125.18 E
Bonaparte Lake ⊜	182	51.16 N	120.35 W
Bonar Bridge	46	57.53 N	4.21 W
Bonarcado	71	40.04 N	8.38 E
Bonasila Dome ∧	180	62.19 N	160.30 W
Bonasse	241r	10.05 N	61.52 W
Bonassola	62	44.11 N	9.35 E
Bonaventure	186	48.03 N	65.29 W
Bonaventure ≃	186	48.02 N	65.28 W
Bonaventure, Île I	186	48.30 N	64.10 W
Bonavista	186	48.39 N	53.07 W
Bonavista, Cape ›	186	48.42 N	53.05 W
Bonavista Bay c	186	48.45 N	53.20 W
Bonawe	46	56.26 N	5.13 W
Bonawon	116	9.08 N	122.55 E
Bonbeach	274b	38.04 S	145.08 E
Bonboillon	58	47.20 N	5.42 E
Bon Bon	162	30.26 S	135.28 E
Bonbonon Point ›	116	9.03 N	123.08 E
Bonchester Bridge	44	55.24 N	2.40 W
Boncourt	58	47.30 N	6.55 E
Boncuk Dağı ∧	130	36.53 N	29.17 E
Bond	194	30.54 N	89.10 W
Bond □[6]	219	38.53 N	89.25 W
Bondari	80	52.57 N	42.04 E
Bondar'ov	83	49.22 N	39.10 E
Bondar'ovka	83	49.23 N	39.37 E
Bondeno	64	44.53 N	11.25 E
Bondi	274a	33.53 S	151.17 E
Bondo, Zaïre	152	1.22 S	23.53 E
Bondo, Zaïre	152	3.49 N	23.40 E
Bondoc Peninsula ›[1]	116	13.30 N	122.30 E
Bondoc Point ›	116	13.10 N	122.36 E
Bondorf	58	48.31 N	8.49 E
Bondoufle	261	48.37 N	2.23 E
Bondoukou	150	8.02 N	2.48 W
Bondowoso	115a	7.55 S	113.49 E
Bondsville	207	42.12 N	72.20 W
Bonduel	190	44.44 N	88.26 W
Bondues	50	50.42 N	3.06 E
Bondy	261	48.54 N	2.28 E
Bondy, Forêt de ♠	261	48.55 N	2.35 E
Bône → Annaba, Alg.	148	36.54 N	7.46 E
Bone, Indon.	112	4.46 S	122.52 E
Bone → Watampone, Indon.	112	4.32 S	120.20 E
Bone, Indon.	112	5.09 S	122.37 E
Bone, Teluk c	112	4.00 S	120.40 E
Bonebone	112	2.36 S	120.33 E
Bon Echo Provincial Park ♠	212	44.52 N	77.15 W
Bonefro	66	41.42 N	14.56 E
Bone Island I	212	44.56 N	79.51 W
Bonelipu	112	4.50 S	123.11 E
Bonelohe	112	5.48 S	120.27 E
Bönen	52	51.36 N	7.44 E
Boneogeh	112	7.16 S	120.48 E
Bonerate, Pulau I	112	7.22 S	121.08 E
Bon Espérance, Cap de → Good Hope, Cape of ›	158	34.24 S	18.30 E
Bo'ness	46	56.01 N	3.37 W
Bonesteel	198	43.04 N	98.56 W
Bonete, Cerro ∧	252	27.51 S	68.47 W
Bonete Chico, Cerro ∧	252	28.01 S	68.45 W
Bonětice	60	49.41 N	12.49 E
Bonfield	216	41.09 N	88.03 W
Bonfinópolis de Minas	255	16.28 S	45.59 W
Bonfol	58	47.29 N	7.09 E
Bonga	144	7.17 N	36.15 E
Bongabon	116	15.38 N	121.08 E
Bongabon ≃	116	12.40 N	121.33 E
Bongabong	116	12.45 N	121.29 E
Bongaigaon	124	26.28 N	90.34 E
Bongak	140	7.27 N	33.14 E
Bongandanga	152	1.30 N	21.03 E
Bongao Island I	116	5.01 N	119.46 E
Bongaree	171a	27.05 S	153.10 E
Bonggaw	116	5.02 N	119.46 E
Bongka	112	0.58 S	121.27 E
Bongka ≃	112	0.59 S	121.05 E
Bong Mieu	110	15.25 N	108.24 E
Bongo, Ang.	152	8.48 S	17.49 E
Bongo, Gabon	152	2.10 S	10.12 E
Bongo, Massif des ⋏	146	8.40 N	22.25 E
Bongo I	152	3.01 N	20.06 E
Bongo II	152	1.47 S	17.41 E
Bongo Island I	116	7.20 N	124.02 E
Bongolu	152	2.48 N	22.29 E
Bongon	112	6.35 N	116.52 E
Bongor	146	10.17 N	15.22 E
Bongou ≃	140	6.42 N	22.04 E
Bongouanou	150	6.39 N	4.12 W
Bong Range ⋏	150	6.50 N	10.00 W
Bong Son	110	14.26 N	109.01 E
Bonham	196	33.34 N	96.10 W
Bonheiden	56	51.02 N	4.32 E
Bonhomme, Col du)(	58	48.10 N	7.06 E
Bonhomme, Morne ∧	238	19.05 N	72.18 W
Bonhomme Island I	219	38.42 N	90.36 W
Bonifacio, Fr.	36	41.23 N	9.10 E
Bonifacio, Pil.	116	8.03 N	123.37 E
Bonifacio, Strait of ⊔	36	41.20 N	9.15 E
Bonifacio Monument ⊥	269f	14.39 N	120.59 E
Bonifati	68	39.35 N	15.54 E
Bonifati, Capo ›	68	39.35 N	15.52 E
Bonifay	194	30.47 N	85.40 W
Bonifica del Volturno ≚	68	41.01 N	14.00 E
Bonilla Island I	182	53.29 N	130.36 W
Bonin Islands → Ogasawara-guntō II	14	27.00 N	142.10 E
Bonita	194	32.55 N	91.40 W
Bonita, Point ›	282	37.49 N	122.32 W
Bonita Springs	220	26.20 N	81.46 W
Bonito, Bra.	248	21.08 S	56.28 W
Bonito, Bra.	250	8.29 S	35.44 W
Bonito, It.	68	41.06 N	15.00 E
Bonito ≃, Bra.	255	16.31 S	51.23 W
Bonito ≃, Bra.	256	22.12 S	43.02 W
Bonito ≃, Bra.	256	22.09 S	43.40 W
Bonito, Pico ∧	236	15.38 N	86.55 W
Bonito, Rio ≃	200	33.23 N	105.15 W
Bonito de Santa Fé	250	7.19 S	38.31 W
Bonjol	112	0.01 S	100.13 E
Bonkoukou	150	14.01 N	3.13 E
Bon Meade	279b	40.33 N	80.14 W
Bonn	56	50.44 N	7.05 E
Bonnanaro	71	40.32 N	8.45 E
Bonndorf im Schwarzwald	58	47.49 N	8.20 E
Bonneauville	208	39.46 N	77.10 W
Bonne Bay (Woody Point)	186	49.30 N	57.56 W
Bonne Bay c	186	49.33 N	57.55 W
Bonnebosq	50	49.12 N	0.05 E
Bonnechere ≃	190	45.31 N	76.33 W
Bonneia	144	5.41 N	37.45 E
Bonnelles	261	48.37 N	2.02 E
Bonner	202	46.52 N	113.51 W
Bonners Ferry	202	48.41 N	116.18 W
Bonne-sur-Ménoge	58	46.10 N	6.20 E
Bonnet, Lac du ⊜	184	50.22 N	95.55 W
Bonnétable	50	48.11 N	0.26 E
Bonne Terre	194	37.55 N	90.33 W
Bonnet Plume ≃	180	65.55 N	134.58 W
Bonneuil-sur-Marne	261	48.46 N	2.29 E
Bonneval	50	48.11 N	1.24 E
Bonneval-sur-Arc	62	45.22 N	7.03 E
Bonnevaux	58	46.18 N	6.40 E
Bonneville, Fr.	58	46.05 N	6.25 E
Bonneville, Or., U.S.	224	45.38 N	121.57 W
Bonneville Dam ◆[6]	224	45.39 N	121.56 W
Bonneville Peak ∧	202	42.46 N	112.08 W
Bonneville Salt Flats ≚	200	40.45 N	113.52 W
Bonney, Lake ⊜	166	37.48 S	140.22 E
Bonney Lake	224	47.10 N	122.11 W
Bonnie Doone	192	35.05 N	78.57 W
Bonnières	50	49.02 N	1.35 E
Bonnie Rock	162	30.32 S	118.21 E
Bonnieux	62	43.49 N	5.18 E
Bonnievale	158	33.57 S	20.06 E
Bönninghardt	263	51.35 N	6.28 E
Bonnots Mill	219	38.34 N	91.58 W
Bonny	150	4.27 N	7.10 E
Bonny ≃[1]	150	4.20 N	7.10 E
Bonnyrigg, Austl.	274a	33.54 S	150.54 E
Bonnyrigg, Scot., U.K.	46	55.52 N	3.08 W
Bonny-sur-Loire	50	47.34 N	2.50 E
Bonnyville	182	54.16 N	110.44 W
Bono, It.	71	40.25 N	9.02 E
Bono, Ar., U.S.	194	35.54 N	90.48 W
Bono, Oh., U.S.	214	41.38 N	83.16 W
Bonoi	164	1.51 S	137.48 E
Bonorva	71	40.25 N	8.46 E
Bonoua	150	5.16 N	3.36 W
Bonpas Creek ≃	194	38.16 N	87.59 W
Bonriki	174t	1.23 N	173.09 E
Bonriki Airport ⊠	174t	1.22 N	173.10 E
Bons	58	46.16 N	6.23 E
Bonsall	228	33.17 N	117.13 W
Bonsari	272c	19.04 N	73.02 E
Bon Secour	194	30.18 N	87.43 W
Bon-Secours, Bel.	50	50.30 N	3.36 E
Bonsecours, Fr.	50	49.26 N	1.08 E
Bonshaw	186	46.12 N	63.21 W
Bonsucesso ◆[8]	287a	22.52 S	43.15 W
Bontang	112	0.08 N	117.30 E
Bontberg ∧	158	32.21 S	21.04 E
Bontebok National Park ♠	158	34.07 S	20.23 E
Bonthe	150	7.32 N	12.30 W
Bontoc	116	17.05 N	120.58 E
Bon Wier	194	30.44 N	93.39 W
Bonyhád	30	46.19 N	18.32 E
Boo, Kepulauan II	164	1.12 S	129.24 E
Booby Point ›	284b	39.17 N	76.23 W
Boock	54	53.29 N	14.15 E
Boody	219	39.46 N	89.03 W
Boogardie	162	28.02 S	117.47 E
Booischot	56	51.03 N	4.46 E
Bookabie	162	31.50 S	132.41 E
Bookaloo	166	31.55 S	137.22 E
Book Cliffs ⊥[4]	200	39.20 N	109.00 W
Booke	152	2.33 S	22.00 E
Booker	196	36.27 N	100.32 W
Booker T. Washington National Monument ♠	192	37.01 N	79.45 W
Bookwalter	218	39.42 N	83.32 W
Boola	150	8.22 N	8.43 W
Boolaloo	162	22.35 S	115.51 E
Booleroo Centre	166	32.53 S	138.21 E
Booligal	166	33.52 S	144.53 E
Boologooro	162	24.21 S	114.02 E
Boom	50	51.05 N	4.22 E
Boomarra	166	19.33 S	140.20 E
Boomer	188	38.09 N	81.17 W
Boomi	166	28.44 S	149.35 E
Boomrivier	158	29.33 S	20.27 E
Boonah	171a	28.00 S	152.41 E
Böön cagaan nuur ⊜	102	45.35 N	99.09 E
Boone, Ia., U.S.	190	42.03 N	93.52 W
Boone, N.C., U.S.	192	36.13 N	81.40 W
Boone □[6], Il., U.S.	216	42.15 N	88.50 W
Boone □[6], In., U.S.	218	40.03 N	86.28 W
Boone □[6], Ky., U.S.	218	38.57 N	84.45 W
Boone □[6], Mo., U.S.	219	38.55 N	92.15 W
Boone ≃	190	42.19 N	93.56 W
Boone Draw V	196	33.51 N	103.42 W
Boone Grove	216	41.21 N	87.08 W
Boone Lake ⊜[1]	192	36.25 N	82.25 W
Boone Reservoir ⊜[1]	279b	40.15 N	80.08 W
Boones Mill	192	37.06 N	79.57 W
Booneville, Ar., U.S.	194	35.08 N	93.55 W
Booneville, Ky., U.S.	192	37.28 N	83.40 W
Booneville, Ms., U.S.	194	34.39 N	88.34 W
Boon Point ›	240c	17.10 N	61.50 W
Boons	158	25.59 S	27.13 E
Boonsboro	208	39.30 N	77.39 W
Boonsville	222	33.04 N	97.52 W
Boonton	210	40.54 N	74.24 W
Boonton Reservoir ⊜[1]	276	40.53 N	74.25 W
Boonville, Ca., U.S.	204	39.00 N	123.21 W
Boonville, In., U.S.	194	38.02 N	87.16 W
Boonville, Mo., U.S.	194	38.58 N	92.44 W
Boonville, N.Y., U.S.	212	43.29 N	75.20 W
Boopi ≃	248	15.41 S	67.15 W
Boorabbin National Park ♠	162	31.13 S	120.10 E
Boorama	144	9.56 N	43.11 E
Boorindal	166	30.21 S	146.08 E
Booroorban	166	34.56 S	144.46 E
Boorowa	166	34.26 S	148.43 E
Boos	50	49.23 N	1.12 E
Boosaaso	144	11.17 N	49.11 E
Boossen	54	52.22 N	14.29 E
Boot	44	54.24 N	3.17 W
Bootahnie Indian Reserve ◆[4]	182	50.24 N	121.31 W
Booth	194	32.30 N	86.34 W
Booth, Lac ⊜	190	46.45 N	78.34 W
Boothbay Harbor	188	43.51 N	69.37 W
Boothby, Cape ›	9	66.34 S	57.16 E
Booth Corner	285	39.51 N	75.29 W
Boothia, Gulf of c	176	71.00 N	91.00 W
Boothia Peninsula ›[1]	176	70.30 N	95.00 W
Boothstown	262	53.30 N	2.25 W
Boothville	194	29.20 N	89.25 W
Booth Wood Reservoir ⊜[1]	262	53.38 N	1.58 W
Boothwyn	285	39.49 N	75.26 W
Bootle	44	53.28 N	3.00 W
Boot Reefs ✢[2]	164	10.00 S	144.40 E
Booué	152	0.06 S	11.56 E
Booysens ◆[8]	273d	26.14 S	28.01 E
Booze Creek ≃	284c	38.59 N	77.07 W
Bopfingen	56	48.51 N	10.21 E
Bo Phloi	110	14.19 N	99.31 E
Bophuthatswana □[1], Afr.	138	26.00 S	25.35 E
Bophuthatswana □[1], Afr.	156	26.00 S	25.35 E
Boping	98	36.36 N	116.07 E
Boping Ling ⋏	100	25.00 N	117.00 E
Bopo	150	7.37 N	7.52 E
Bopolu	150	7.03 N	10.32 W
Boppard	56	50.14 N	7.35 E
Boqér, Har ∧	132	30.52 N	34.43 E
Boqueirão, Ilha do I	287a	22.46 S	43.09 W
Boqueirão, Serra do ⋏[2]	250	11.30 S	43.45 W
Boquerón	236	8.30 N	82.34 W
Boquerón □[5]	252	21.30 S	60.00 W
Boquerón, Bahía de c	240m	18.01 N	67.12 W
Boquerón, Túnel ◆[5]	286c	10.34 N	67.00 W
Boquet	279b	40.23 N	79.36 W
Boquilla, Presa de la ⊜[1]	232	27.30 N	105.30 W
Boquilla del Refugio	196	25.33 N	102.28 W
Boquillas del Carmen	232	29.17 N	102.53 W
Boquim	250	11.09 S	37.37 W
Bor, Česká Rep.	60	49.43 N	12.47 E
Bor, Jugo.	38	44.05 N	22.07 E
Bor, Ross.	24	63.00 N	42.38 E
Bor, Ross.	80	56.22 N	44.05 E
Bor, Süd.	140	6.12 N	31.33 E
Bor, Tür.	130	37.54 N	34.34 E
Bor, Lak ≃	154	1.18 N	40.40 E
Bora-Bora I	14	16.30 S	151.45 W
Borabu	110	16.02 N	103.07 E
Boracay Island I	116	11.59 N	121.55 E
Boraha, Nosy I	157b	16.50 S	49.55 E
Borah Peak ∧	202	44.08 N	113.48 W
Boraldaj ≃	85	42.33 N	69.07 E
Borale	144	9.10 N	42.35 E
Borambola	171b	35.12 S	147.41 E
Borang, Tanjung ›	164	5.16 S	133.07 E
Borås	26	57.43 N	12.55 E
Borāzjān	128	29.16 N	51.12 E
Borba, Bra.	246	4.24 S	59.35 W
Borba, Port.	34	38.48 N	7.27 W
Borbeck ◆[8]	263	51.29 N	6.57 E
Borbera ≃	62	44.42 N	8.52 E
Borca di Cadore	64	46.26 N	12.13 E
Borcea, Braţul ≃	38	44.40 N	27.53 E
Borchen	52	51.39 N	8.44 E
Borçka	130	41.22 N	41.40 E
Borculo, Ned.	52	52.07 N	6.31 E
Borculo, Mi., U.S.	216	42.53 N	86.01 W
Borda, Cape ›	166	35.45 S	136.34 E
Borda da Mata	256	22.16 S	46.10 W
Bordeaux, Fr.	32	44.50 N	0.34 W
Bordeaux, S. Afr.	273d	26.06 S	28.01 E
Bordeaux ◆[8]	275a	45.33 N	73.41 W
Bordeaux Mountain ∧[2]	240m	18.20 N	64.44 W
Borden, Austl.	162	34.05 S	118.16 E
Borden, Sk., Can.	184	52.25 N	107.13 W
Borden, Eng., U.K.	260	51.20 N	0.42 E
Borden, In., U.S.	218	38.28 N	85.57 W
Borden, Canadian Forces Base ■	212	44.17 N	79.55 W
Borden Lake ⊜	190	47.50 N	83.18 W
Borden Peninsula ›[1]	176	73.00 N	83.00 W
Bordentown	208	40.08 N	74.42 W
Border Mountains ⋏	164	3.40 S	141.05 E
Borders □[4]	46	55.37 N	3.15 W
Bordertown	166	36.19 S	140.47 E
Bordesholm	30	54.11 N	10.01 E
Borđeyri	24a	65.15 N	21.10 W
Bordighera	62	43.46 N	7.39 E
Bording	41	56.12 N	9.17 E
Bording Kirkeby	41	56.10 N	9.15 E
Bordino, Fiume di ≃	70	37.53 N	12.37 E
Bordj Bou Arreridj	148	36.04 N	4.46 E
Bordj Bounaama	34	35.51 N	1.36 E
Bordj Menaïel	148	36.44 N	3.43 E
Bordj Omar Idriss	148	28.09 N	6.43 E
Bordj Sidi Toui	148	32.44 N	11.22 E
Bordunskij	85	42.40 N	75.37 E
Bore, It.	62	44.43 N	9.47 E
Bore, Ityo.	144	4.40 N	37.40 E
Boré, Mali	150	15.08 N	3.29 W
Boreda	144	6.32 N	37.48 E
Boreham	260	51.46 N	0.33 E
Borehamwood	42	51.40 N	0.16 W
Borel Hill ∧	282	37.19 N	122.12 W
Borello	66	44.03 N	12.11 E
Borensberg	26	58.34 N	15.17 E
Boreray I	46	57.42 N	7.18 W
Boretto	64	44.54 N	10.33 E
Borgå → Porvoo	26	60.24 N	25.40 E
Borgallo, Galleria del ◆[5]	62	44.25 N	9.53 E
Borgarnes	24a	64.35 N	21.53 W
Borgata Costiera	70	37.43 N	12.39 E
Børgefjell Nasjonalpark ♠	24	65.10 N	14.00 E
Borgentreich	52	51.34 N	9.14 E
Börger, Dtsch.	52	52.54 N	7.32 E
Borger, Ned.	52	52.55 N	6.46 E
Borger, Tx., U.S.	196	35.40 N	101.23 W
Borgerhout	50	51.13 N	4.26 E
Borgetto	70	38.03 N	13.08 E
Borggård	40	58.44 N	15.32 E
Borghetto	64	45.41 N	10.56 E
Borghetto di Vara	62	44.13 N	9.43 E
Borghetto Lodigiano	62	45.13 N	9.30 E
Borghetto Santo Spirito	62	44.06 N	8.14 E
Borgholm	26	56.53 N	16.39 E
Borghorst	52	52.07 N	7.23 E
Borgia	68	38.49 N	16.30 E
Borgio-Verezzi	62	44.10 N	8.18 E
Borgloon	56	50.48 N	5.20 E
Borg Mountain ∧	9	72.42 S	3.30 W
Borgne, Lake c	194	30.05 N	89.40 W
Borgnesse, Pointe ›	240e	14.27 N	60.54 W
Borgo	64	46.03 N	11.27 E
Borgo alla Collina	66	43.45 N	11.43 E
Borgo a Mozzano	66	43.59 N	10.33 E
Borgo Cerreto	66	42.49 N	12.54 E
Borgo d'Ale	62	45.21 N	8.03 E
Borgoforte	64	45.03 N	10.45 E
Borgofranco d'Ivrea	62	45.30 N	7.51 E
Borgolavezzaro	62	45.19 N	8.42 E
Borgomanero	62	45.42 N	8.28 E
Borgomaro	62	43.58 N	7.56 E
Borgonovo Val Tidone	62	45.01 N	9.26 E
Borgo Pace	66	43.39 N	12.17 E
Borgoricco	64	45.32 N	11.58 E
Borgorose	66	42.11 N	13.13 E
Borgo San Dalmazzo	62	44.20 N	7.30 E
Borgo San Giacomo	64	45.21 N	9.58 E
Borgo San Lorenzo	66	43.57 N	11.23 E
Borgosatollo	64	45.28 N	10.14 E
Borgosesia	62	45.43 N	8.16 E
Borgo Tossignano	66	44.16 N	11.35 E
Borgou □[5]	150	10.30 N	2.50 E
Borgo Val di Taro	62	44.29 N	9.46 E
Borgo Vercelli	62	45.21 N	8.28 E
Borgsdorf	54	52.42 N	13.14 E
Borgsdorf, Forst ◆[3]	264a	52.42 N	13.19 E
Borgu Game Reserve ◆[4]	150	10.15 N	4.10 E
Borgund v[1]	26	61.03 N	7.49 E
Bori	150	4.42 N	7.21 E
Borig Delijn els ◆[2]	88	50.00 N	94.00 E
Borikhan	110	18.33 N	103.43 E
Borilovo	76	53.22 N	35.58 E
Borinage □[9]	50	50.30 N	4.00 E
Boring, Md., U.S.	208	39.31 N	76.49 W
Boring, Or., U.S.	224	45.25 N	122.22 W
Borinskoje	76	52.27 N	39.22 E
Borislav	78	49.16 N	23.27 E
Borisoglebsk	80	51.23 N	42.06 E
Borisoglebskij	80	57.16 N	39.09 E
Borisov, Bela.	76	54.15 N	28.30 E
Borisov, Ukr.	78	50.11 N	26.31 E
Borisovka, Ross.	76	52.50 N	39.58 E
Borisovka, Ross.	78	50.36 N	36.01 E
Borisovo	82	55.25 N	36.03 E
Borisovo ◆[8]	265b	55.38 N	37.45 E
Borisovo-Sudskoje	76	59.54 N	36.01 E
Borisovskaja	76	60.12 N	39.48 E
Borispol'	78	50.21 N	30.57 E
Borja, Esp.	34	41.50 N	1.32 W
Borja, Perú	246	4.26 S	77.33 W
Bork	52	51.40 N	7.28 E
Borken, Dtsch.	52	51.51 N	6.51 E
Borken, Dtsch.	56	51.03 N	9.16 E
Borkenwirthe	52	51.53 N	6.50 E
Borki, Ross.	86	59.08 N	82.15 E
Borki, Ukr.	78	49.42 N	36.02 E
Borkoldoj, chrebet ⋏	85	41.25 N	77.50 E
Børkop	41	55.39 N	9.39 E
Borkou ◆[1]	146	18.15 N	18.50 E
Borkou-Ennedi-Tibesti □[5]	146	18.15 N	18.50 E
Borkoviči	76	55.40 N	28.20 E
Borkum	52	53.35 N	6.40 E
Borkum I	52	53.35 N	6.41 E
Borland Manor	279b	40.15 N	80.09 W
Borlänge	40	60.29 N	15.25 E
Borle ◆[8]	272c	19.02 N	72.55 E
Borlu	130	38.44 N	28.27 E
Bormes-les-Mimosas	62	43.09 N	6.20 E
Bormida ≃	62	44.56 N	8.40 E
Bormida di Millesimo ≃	62	44.40 N	8.20 E
Bormida di Spigno ≃	62	44.40 N	8.20 E
Bormio	64	46.28 N	10.22 E
Born, Dtsch.	54	52.22 N	11.28 E
Born, Dtsch.	54	54.23 N	12.32 E
Borna, Dtsch.	54	51.19 N	13.11 E
Borna, Dtsch.	54	51.07 N	12.30 E
Borndiep c	52	53.25 N	5.35 E
Borne	52	52.18 N	6.45 E
Borne ≃	62	45.03 N	3.54 E
Borneo (Kalimantan) I	112	0.30 N	114.00 E
Bornheim	56	50.46 N	6.59 E
Bornholm I	26	55.10 N	15.00 E
Bornholte	52	51.52 N	8.29 E
Bornhöved	54	54.04 N	10.16 E
Börnicke, Dtsch.	54	52.41 N	12.56 E
Börnicke, Dtsch.	264a	52.40 N	13.38 E
Börnig ◆[8]	263	51.33 N	7.16 E
Bornim ◆[8]	264a	52.26 N	13.00 E
Borno	64	45.56 N	10.12 E
Bornos, Embalse de ⊜[1]	34	36.50 N	5.30 W
Bornsdorf	54	51.46 N	13.41 E
Bornstedt ◆[8]	264a	52.25 N	13.02 E
Bornu □[3]	146	12.00 N	12.45 E
Boro ≃	140	8.52 N	26.11 E
Borobudur ⊥	115a	7.36 S	110.12 E
Borod'anka	78	50.39 N	29.56 E
Borodarou	150	10.59 N	2.53 E
Borodino, Ross.	82	55.32 N	35.50 E
Borodino, Ross.	82	56.53 N	37.00 E
Borodino, Ross.	88	55.55 N	94.55 E
Borodino, Ukr	78	46.18 N	29.13 E
Borodulicha	86	50.43 N	80.55 E
Borodulino	80	57.59 N	54.20 E
Borogoncy	74	62.42 N	131.08 E
Borohoro Shan ⋏	86	44.06 N	83.10 E
Boroko	112	0.55 N	123.16 E
Boroml'a	78	50.37 N	34.59 E
Boromo	150	11.45 N	2.56 W
Boron, Mali	150	14.01 N	7.30 W
Boron, Ca., U.S.	228	34.59 N	117.38 W
Boronga Islands II	110	19.58 N	93.06 E
Borongan	116	11.37 N	125.26 E
Boronia	274b	37.52 S	145.17 E
Boron'ki	76	53.09 N	32.08 E
Borore	71	40.13 N	8.48 E
Borotou	150	8.44 N	7.30 W
Boroughbridge	44	54.06 N	1.23 W
Borough Green	42	51.17 N	0.19 E
Borough Park ◆[8]	276	40.38 N	74.00 W
Borovaja, Ukr.	78	50.12 N	30.07 E
Borovaja, Ukr.	83	49.24 N	37.40 E
Borovaja ≃	83	48.58 N	38.24 E
Borovan	38	43.26 N	23.45 E
Borovany	61	48.54 N	14.39 E
Boroviči	76	58.24 N	33.55 E
Borovik ≃	83	49.11 N	38.33 E
Borovka ≃	80	52.54 N	52.00 E
Borovl'anka	86	52.38 N	84.29 E
Borovoj	24	59.55 N	51.38 E
Borovoje, Kaz.	86	53.04 N	70.19 E
Borovoje, Ukr.	78	51.06 N	27.13 E
Borovsk	82	55.12 N	36.30 E
Borovskaja	24	60.46 N	41.06 E
Borovskij	86	57.03 N	65.44 E
Borovskoj	86	53.48 N	64.12 E
Borovskoje, Ross.	86	52.39 N	82.08 E
Borovskoje, Ukr.	83	48.51 N	38.34 E
Borovucha	76	55.36 N	28.37 E
Borovy	60	49.33 N	13.18 E
Borozdino	82	54.07 N	38.22 E
Borraan	144	10.14 N	48.44 E
Borrachudo ≃	255	18.12 S	45.16 W
Borrazópolis	255	23.56 S	51.36 W
Borrby	26	55.27 N	14.10 E
Borre	41	55.00 N	12.28 E
Borre ⊥	26	59.23 N	10.28 E
Borreby	41	55.14 N	11.19 E
Borriana, Esp.	34	39.53 N	0.05 W
Borriana, It.	62	45.30 N	8.02 E
Borris	48	52.35 N	6.55 W
Borrisokane	48	52.59 N	8.07 W
Borrisoleigh	48	52.45 N	7.57 W
Borroloola	164	16.04 S	136.17 E
Borroloola Aboriginal Reserve ◆[4]	164	16.00 S	136.15 E
Borrowdale	44	54.31 N	3.10 W
Börry	52	52.01 N	9.27 E
Borş	38	47.07 N	21.49 E
Borşa, Rom.	38	47.39 N	24.40 E
Borşa, Rom.	38	46.56 N	23.40 E
Borsad	120	22.25 N	72.54 E
Borsano	266b	45.35 N	8.51 E
Borschemich	263	51.04 N	6.25 E
Borščov	78	48.48 N	26.03 E
Borščovo	82	56.30 N	36.51 E
Borščovočnyj chrebet ⋏	88	52.00 N	117.00 E
Borsdorf	54	51.21 N	12.32 E
Borskoje	80	53.02 N	51.43 E
Borsod-Abaúj-Zemplén □[6]	30	48.15 N	21.00 E
Börssum	54	52.04 N	10.35 E
Borstendorf	54	50.46 N	13.10 E
Bortala ≃	86	44.50 N	82.45 E
Borth, Dtsch.	52	51.36 N	6.33 E
Borth, Wales, U.K.	42	52.29 N	4.03 W
Borthwick Water ≃	44	55.24 N	2.50 W
Bortigali	71	40.17 N	8.50 E
Bortigiadas	71	40.53 N	9.02 E
Bort-les-Orgues	32	45.24 N	2.30 E
Bortniči	78	50.22 N	30.41 E
Borto	88	53.35 N	111.53 E
Bortondale	285	39.54 N	79.24 W
Boru	164	10.14 S	148.50 E
Boruca	236	9.00 N	83.20 W
Borūjen	128	31.59 N	51.18 E
Borūjerd	128	33.54 N	48.46 E
Bor Ul Shan ⋏	102	41.20 N	98.55 E
Borve	46	56.58 N	7.32 W
Borz'a	88	50.24 N	116.31 E
Borz'a ≃	88	50.38 N	115.38 E
Borzna	78	51.15 N	32.25 E
Boržomi	84	41.50 N	43.21 E
Boržomskij zapovednik ♠	84	41.50 N	43.10 E
Borzonasca	62	44.25 N	9.23 E
Borzyszkowy	30	54.03 N	17.22 E
Bosa	71	40.18 N	8.30 E
Bosaga	86	47.55 N	72.58 E
Bosambi	152	2.24 N	22.39 E
Bosanska Dubica	36	45.11 N	16.49 E
Bosanska Gradiška	36	45.09 N	17.15 E
Bosanska Krupa	36	44.53 N	16.10 E
Bosanski Novi	36	45.03 N	16.23 E
Bosanski Petrovac	36	44.33 N	16.22 E
Bosanski Šamac	38	45.03 N	18.28 E
Bosansko Grahovo	36	44.11 N	16.22 E
Bősárkány	61	47.41 N	17.14 E
Bosau	54	54.06 N	10.25 E
Bosavi, Mount ∧	164	6.35 S	142.50 E
Boscastle	42	50.41 N	4.42 W
Bosco, It.	66	44.53 N	12.14 E
Bosco, It.	66	43.08 N	12.28 E
Boscobel	190	43.08 N	90.42 W
Bosco Chiesanuova	64	45.37 N	11.02 E
Bosco Marengo	62	44.49 N	8.41 E
Boscoreale	68	40.46 N	14.28 E
Bose	102	23.54 N	106.37 E
Bösel	52	53.00 N	7.58 E
Bosencheve, Parque Nacional ♠	234	19.36 N	100.15 W
Bosenge	152	1.18 N	22.19 E
Bósforo, Estrecho del → İstanbul Boğazı ⊔	130	41.06 N	29.04 E
Bosham	42	50.49 N	0.52 W
Boshan	98	36.29 N	117.50 E
Boshkung Lake ⊜	212	45.04 N	78.44 W
Boshoek	156	25.30 S	27.09 E
Boshof	158	28.34 S	25.04 E
Boshrūyeh	128	33.53 N	57.26 E
Bosilegrad	38	42.29 N	22.28 E
Bösingen	58	48.14 N	8.34 E
Bosjökloster	41	55.54 N	13.31 E
Boškajnar	85	38.13 N	68.51 E
Boskop	158	26.34 S	27.08 E
Boskop ∧	273d	26.05 S	27.57 E
Boskovice	30	49.29 N	16.40 E
Boskuil	158	27.23 S	25.51 E
Bosman	164	4.10 S	144.40 E
Bosna	272b	22.37 N	88.30 E
Bosna ≃	36	45.04 N	18.29 E
Bosna-Hercegovina → Bosnia and Herzegovina □[1]	36	44.15 N	17.30 E
Bošn'akovo	89	49.38 N	142.10 E
Bosnia and Herzegovina □[1], Europe	22	44.15 N	17.30 E
Bosnia and Herzegovina (Bosna-Hercegovina) □[1], Europe	36	44.15 N	17.30 E
Bosnik	164	1.10 S	136.14 E
Boso	272b	22.58 N	88.08 E
Bosobolo	152	4.11 N	19.54 E
Boso-Djafo	152	1.06 N	19.14 E
Bosogo	85	41.09 N	76.25 E
Bōsō-hantō ›[1]	94	35.18 N	140.10 E
Bōsō-kyūryō ⋏[2]	268	35.08 N	139.56 E
Bososama	152	4.18 N	20.00 E
Bösperde	263	51.28 N	7.46 E
Bosphore, Détroit du → İstanbul Boğazı ⊔	130	41.06 N	29.04 E
Bosporus → İstanbul Boğazı ⊔	130	41.06 N	29.04 E
Bosque □[6]	222	31.55 N	97.35 W
Bosque, Paseo del ♠	288	34.55 S	57.56 W
Bosque Farms	200	34.53 N	106.40 W
Bosques	288	34.49 S	58.14 W
Bosques Petrificados, Monumento Natural ♠	254	47.39 S	68.07 W
Bosqueville	222	31.38 N	97.13 W
Bossangoa	152	6.29 N	17.27 E
Bossdorf	54	51.59 N	12.40 E
Bossé Bangou	150	13.21 N	1.18 E
Bossembélé	152	5.16 N	17.39 E
Bossentele	152	5.41 N	16.38 E
Bossert Estates	285	40.09 N	74.44 W
Bossier City	194	32.30 N	93.43 W
Bossley Park	274a	33.52 S	150.54 E
Bosso	146	13.42 N	13.19 E
Bosso, Dallol V	150	12.25 N	2.50 E
Bossolasco	62	44.32 N	8.02 E
Bossut, Cape ›	162	18.43 S	121.38 E
Bostān, Īrān	128	31.43 N	48.00 E
Bostān, Pāk.	120	30.26 N	67.02 E
Bostancı ◆[8]	267b	40.57 N	29.05 E
Bostandyk	80	49.38 N	48.54 E
Bosten Hu ⊜	90	42.00 N	87.00 E
Bostock Green	262	53.13 N	2.30 W
Boston, Pil.	116	7.52 N	126.22 E
Boston, Eng., U.K.	44	52.59 N	0.01 W
Boston, Ga., U.S.	192	30.47 N	83.47 W
Boston, In., U.S.	218	39.44 N	84.51 W
Boston, Ma., U.S.	207	42.21 N	71.03 W
Boston, Ma., U.S.	283	42.21 N	71.03 W
Boston, N.Y., U.S.	210	42.38 N	78.44 W
Boston, Pa., U.S.	279b	40.18 N	79.49 W
Boston Bar	182	49.52 N	121.26 W
Boston Bay c	283	42.22 N	70.54 W
Boston Brook ≃	283	42.37 N	71.00 W
Boston College v[2]	283	42.20 N	71.10 W
Boston Common ♠	283	42.21 N	71.05 W
Boston Corners	210	42.03 N	73.31 W
Boston Creek ≃	212	43.02 N	79.56 W
Boston Harbor	224	47.08 N	122.54 W
Boston Harbor c	283	42.20 N	70.58 W
Boston Heights	214	41.15 N	81.30 W
Boston Mill	214	41.16 N	81.34 W
Boston Mountains ⋏	194	35.50 N	93.20 W
Boston Spa	44	53.54 N	1.21 W
Boston University v[2]	283	42.21 N	71.07 W
Bosumtwi, Lake ⊜	150	6.30 N	1.25 W
Bosut ≃	38	44.57 N	19.22 E
Boswell, In., U.S.	216	40.31 N	87.22 W
Boswell, Ok., U.S.	196	34.01 N	95.52 W
Boswell, Pa., U.S.	214	40.09 N	79.01 W
Boswell Bay	180	60.24 N	146.08 W
Bosworth	194	39.28 N	93.20 W
Bosworth Airport ⊠	279a	41.26 N	82.00 W
Bosworth Field ⊥	42	52.36 N	1.25 W
Botād	120	22.10 N	71.40 E
Botafogo ◆[8]	287a	22.57 S	43.11 W
Botafogo, Enseada de c	287a	22.57 S	43.10 W
Botany	274a	33.57 S	151.12 E
Botany Bay ◆[8]	260	51.41 N	0.07 W
Botany Bay c	170	33.59 S	151.12 E
Botejevo	78	46.41 N	35.52 E
Botelhos	256	21.39 S	46.24 W
Botera	152	11.37 S	14.17 E
Botersleegte	158	30.35 S	21.22 E
Botesdale	42	52.20 N	1.01 E
Boteti ≃	156	20.08 S	23.23 E
Botev ∧	38	42.43 N	24.55 E
Botevgrad	38	42.54 N	23.47 E
Botha's Hill	158	29.45 S	30.45 E
Bothaville	158	27.27 S	26.36 E
Bothell	224	47.45 N	122.12 W
Bothe-Napa Valley State Park ♠	226	38.32 N	122.32 W
Bothnia, Gulf of c	26	63.00 N	20.00 E
Bothwell, Austl.	166	42.23 S	147.00 E
Bothwell, On., Can.	214	42.38 N	81.52 W
Boticas	34	41.41 N	7.40 W
Botija, Ilha da I	246	3.58 S	62.53 W
Botija, Isla I	258	33.52 S	59.02 W
Botkins	216	40.28 N	84.10 W
Botkul', ozero ⊜	80	48.46 N	46.40 E
Botkyrka	40	59.14 N	17.49 E
Botlich	84	42.39 N	46.14 E
Bot Makak	152	4.00 N	10.55 E
Botnia, Golfo de → Bothnia, Gulf of c	26	63.00 N	20.00 E
Botola	152	1.17 S	18.13 E
Botolan	116	15.17 N	120.01 E
Botoşani	38	47.45 N	26.40 E
Botoşani □[6]	38	48.00 N	26.45 E
Botoşaniţa	38	47.53 N	26.07 E
Botou	150	12.40 N	2.03 E
Botovo	82	56.03 N	38.26 E
Bo Trach	110	17.35 N	106.32 E
Botrange ∧	56	50.30 N	6.08 E
Botricello	68	38.56 N	16.51 E
Botro	150	7.51 N	5.19 W
Botsford	210	41.21 N	73.15 W
Botswana □[1], Afr.	138	22.00 S	24.00 E
Botswana □[1], Afr.	156	22.00 S	24.00 E
Botte Donato, Monte ∧	68	39.17 N	16.26 E
Bottenhavet (Selkämeri) c	26	62.00 N	20.00 E
Bottenviken (Perämeri) c	26	65.00 N	23.00 E
Bottesford	42	52.56 N	0.48 W
Bottineau	198	48.49 N	100.26 W
Bottisham	42	52.13 N	0.16 E
Bottnischer Meerbusen → Bothnia, Gulf of c	26	63.00 N	20.00 E
Bottoms Reservoir ⊜[1]	262	53.28 N	1.58 W
Bottrop	52	51.31 N	6.55 E
Botucatu	255	22.52 S	48.26 W
Botwood	186	49.09 N	55.21 W
Boty	88	52.24 N	118.32 E
Bötzingen	58	48.04 N	7.44 E
Bötzow	54	52.39 N	13.08 E
Bötzsee ⊜	264a	52.34 N	13.50 E
Bouaflé, C. Iv.	150	6.59 N	5.45 W
Bouafle, Fr.	261	48.58 N	1.54 E
Bou Ahmed	148	35.25 N	5.00 W
Bouaké	150	7.41 N	5.02 W
Bou Ali, Oued V	148	31.14 N	4.16 E
Bouânane	148	32.03 N	3.03 W
Bouandougou	150	8.13 N	5.40 W
Bouar	152	5.57 N	15.36 E
Bou Arada	36	36.20 N	9.38 E
Bou Areg, Sebkha c	34	35.10 N	2.45 W
Bouârfa	148	32.30 N	1.59 W
Bouaye	32	47.09 N	1.42 W
Boubandjidah, Parc National de ♠	146	8.45 N	14.45 E
Bou Bernous	148	27.18 N	2.59 W
Boubín ∧	60	48.59 N	13.51 E
Bouca	152	6.30 N	18.17 E
Bouchair	50	50.17 N	3.19 E
Bouchegouf	36	36.28 N	7.44 E
Boucher ≃	186	49.10 N	69.06 W
Boucher, Lac ⊜	186	51.07 N	59.35 W
Boucherville	206	45.36 N	73.27 W
Boucherville, Îles de II	275a	45.37 N	73.28 W
Bouches-du-Rhône □[5]	62	43.30 N	5.00 E
Bouchoir	50	49.45 N	2.41 E
Bouclans	58	47.14 N	6.15 E
Boucle du Baoulé, Parc National de la ♠	150	13.50 N	9.00 W
Bouddi National Park ♠	170	33.31 S	131.24 E
Boudjellil	34	36.20 N	4.21 E
Boudnib	148	31.57 N	4.38 W
Boudouaou	34	36.43 N	3.25 E
Boudry	58	46.57 N	6.50 E
Boué	50	50.01 N	3.42 E
Bouenza □[5]	152	4.00 S	13.45 E
Boufarik	148	36.34 N	2.55 E
Bouffémont	261	49.03 N	2.18 E
Bou Ficha	36	36.18 N	10.29 E
Bougaa	34	36.20 N	5.05 E
Bougainville □[5]	175e	6.00 S	155.00 E
Bougainville I	175e	6.00 S	155.00 E
Bougainville, Cape ›	164	13.54 S	126.06 E
Bougainville, Détroit de ⊔	175f	15.50 S	167.10 E
Bougainville Reef ✢[2]	164	15.30 S	147.06 E
Bougainville Strait ⊔	175e	6.40 S	156.10 E
Bougar'oûn, Cap ›	34	37.06 N	6.28 E
Bough Beech Reservoir ⊜[1]	260	51.13 N	0.08 E
Boughton	44	53.12 N	1.00 W
Boughton Green	260	51.14 N	0.32 E
Boughton Malherbe	260	51.13 N	0.42 E
Boughton Place v	260	51.13 N	0.32 E
Bougie → Bejaïa	148	36.45 N	5.05 E
Bougou	152	3.45 S	11.12 E
Bougouni	150	11.25 N	7.29 W
Bougouriba ≃	150	10.42 N	2.56 W
Bougzoul	34	35.42 N	2.51 E
Bou Hadjar	36	36.30 N	8.06 E
Bou Hajar	36	35.42 N	10.48 E
Bouillante	241o	16.06 N	61.45 W
Bouillon	56	49.48 N	5.04 E
Bouilly	50	48.12 N	4.00 E
Bouïra	148	36.23 N	3.54 E
Bouïra □[5]	148	36.00 N	4.00 E
Bouisy, Ru de ≃	261	48.34 N	2.45 E
Bou Izakarn	148	29.09 N	9.44 W
Boujad	148	32.48 N	6.26 W
Boujailles	58	46.53 N	6.05 E
Boujdour, Cap ›	148	26.08 N	14.30 W
Bouka ≃	150	11.00 N	10.50 W
Bou Kadir	148	36.04 N	1.07 E
Bou Khadra	36	35.45 N	8.02 E
Boukiéro	273b	4.12 S	15.18 E
Boukiéro, Mont ∧[2]	273b	4.11 S	15.17 E
Boukombé	150	10.11 N	1.06 E
Boula Ibib	146	9.34 N	13.46 E
Boulaide	56	49.54 N	5.49 E
Boularderie Island I	186	46.15 N	60.30 W
Boulay-Moselle	56	49.11 N	6.30 E
Boulbon	62	43.52 N	4.41 E
Boulder, Co., U.S.	200	40.00 N	105.16 W
Boulder, Mt., U.S.	202	46.14 N	112.07 W
Boulder ≃	202	45.52 N	111.57 W
Boulder City	204	35.58 N	114.49 W
Boulder Creek	226	37.07 N	122.07 W
Boulder Creek ≃	200	37.47 N	111.22 W
Boulder Hill	216	41.41 N	88.25 W
Bouleaux, Lac des ⊜	275a	45.33 N	73.19 W
Bouli ≃	150	13.15 N	0.03 E
Boulia	166	22.54 S	139.54 E
Bouligny	56	49.17 N	5.45 E
Boullay-les-Troux	261	48.41 N	2.03 E
Boulmane	148	33.22 N	4.45 E
Boulmane □[4]	148	33.00 N	4.00 W
Boulogne ◆[8]	258	34.31 S	58.34 W
Boulogne, Bois de ♠	261	48.50 N	2.15 E
Boulogne-Billancourt	50	48.50 N	2.15 E
Boulogne-sur-Gesse	32	43.18 N	0.39 E
Boulogne-sur-Mer	50	50.43 N	1.37 E
Bouloire	50	47.58 N	0.33 E
Boulouli	150	15.34 N	9.21 W
Bouloupari	175f	21.52 S	166.04 E
Boulouris-sur-Mer	62	43.25 N	6.48 E
Boulsa	150	12.39 N	0.34 W
Boulsworth Hill ∧	44	53.48 N	2.06 W
Bouly	150	15.19 N	11.48 W
Bou Maad, Djebel ∧	34	36.26 N	2.08 E
Boumalne	148	31.32 N	5.27 W
Boumba ≃	152	2.02 N	15.12 E
Boumbé I ≃	152	4.04 N	15.23 E
Boumbé II ≃	152	4.08 N	15.08 E
Boumboum	150	15.01 N	1.42 W
Boûmdeïd	150	17.26 N	9.50 W
Bou Medfaa	34	36.22 N	2.28 E
Boumentana	152	6.59 N	16.56 E
Boumnyebe	152	3.52 N	10.49 E
Boumou	146	9.02 N	16.26 E
Bouna	150	9.16 N	3.00 W
Boundary	180	64.04 N	141.06 W
Boundary Bay c	224	49.00 N	122.58 W
Boundary Peak ∧	204	37.51 N	118.21 W
Boundary Ranges ⋏	180	59.00 N	134.00 W
Bound Brook	210	40.34 N	74.32 W
Bound Brook ≃, Ma., U.S.	283	42.13 N	70.47 W
Bound Brook ≃, N.J., U.S.	276	40.35 N	74.30 W
Boundiali	150	9.31 N	6.29 W
Boun Nua	110	21.38 N	101.54 E
Bountiful	200	40.53 N	111.52 W
Bounty Bay c	174e	25.04 S	130.05 W
Bounty Islands II	14	47.42 S	179.04 E

Symbol	English	Deutsch	Español	Français	Português
≃	River	Fluß	Río	Rivière	Rio
≍	Canal	Kanal	Canal	Canal	Canal
∟	Waterfall, Rapids	Wasserfall, Stromschnellen	Cascada, Rápidos	Chute d'eau, Rapides	Cascata, Rápidos
⊔	Strait	Meeresstraße	Estrecho	Détroit	Estreito
c	Bay, Gulf	Bucht, Golf	Bahía, Golfo	Baie, Golfe	Baía, Golfo
⊜	Lake, Lakes	See, Seen	Lago, Lagos	Lac, Lacs	Lago, Lagos
≚	Swamp	Sumpf	Pantano	Marais	Pântano
⊓	Ice Features, Glacier	Eis- und Gletscherformen	Accidentes Glaciales	Formes glaciaires	Acidentes glaciares
⊤	Other Hydrographic Features	Andere Hydrographische Objekte	Otros Elementos Hidrográficos	Autres données hydrographiques	Outros acidentes hidrográficos
✢	Submarine Features	Untermeerische Objekte	Accidentes Submarinos	Formes de relief sous-marin	Acidentes submarinos
□	Political Unit	Politische Einheit	Unidad Política	Entité politique	Unidade política
v	Cultural Institution	Kulturelle Institution	Institución Cultural	Institution culturelle	Instituição cultural
⊥	Historical Site	Historische Stätte	Sitio Histórico	Site historique	Sitio histórico
♠	Recreational Site	Erholungs- und Ferienort	Sitio de Recreo	Centre de loisirs	Area de Lazer
⊠	Airport	Flughafen	Aeropuerto	Aéroport	Aeroporto
■	Military Installation	Militäranlage	Instalación Militar	Installation militaire	Instalação militar
◆	Miscellaneous	Verschiedenes	Misceláneo	Divers	Diversos

	ENGLISH	DEUTSCH	ESPAÑOL	FRANÇAIS	PORTUGUÊS
∧	Mountain	Berg	Montaña	Montagne	Montanha
⋀	Mountains	Gebirge	Montañas	Montagnes	Montanhas
⋊	Pass	Paß	Paso	Col	Passo
V	Valley, Canyon	Tal, Cañon	Valle, Cañón	Vallée, Cañon	Vale, Canhão
≂	Plain	Ebene	Llano	Plaine	Planície
⌁	Cape	Kap	Cabo	Cap	Cabo
⌁	Island	Insel	Isla	Île	Ilha
⌁⌁	Islands	Inseln	Islas	Îles	Ilhas
⌁	Other Topographic Features	Andere Topographische Objekte	Otros Elementos Topográficos	Autres données topographiques	Outros acidentes topográficos

ESPAÑOL — Nombre / Página / Lat.°' / Long.°' W = Oeste
FRANÇAIS — Nom / Page / Lat.°' / Long.°' W = Ouest
PORTUGUÊS — Nome / Página / Lat.°' / Long.°' W = Oeste

Brennero, Passo del → Brenner Pass)(64 47.00 N 11.30 E
Brenner Pass)(64 47.00 N 11.30 E
Brenc, It. 64 45.57 N 10.18 E
Brenc, Schw. 58 46.02 N 8.53 E
Bréncd 58 46.04 N 5.36 E
Brent, Al., U.S. 194 32.56 N 87.09 W
Brent, Fl., U.S. 194 30.28 N 87.14 W
Brent ✦[8] 42 51.34 N 0.17 W
Brent ≐ 260 51.28 N 0.18 W
Brenta ≐ 64 45.11 N 12.18 E
Brenta, Gruppo di ⋏ 64 46.11 N 10.54 E
Brentford ✦[8] 260 51.29 N 0.18 W
Brenthurst 273d 26.16 S 28.23 E
Brentino 64 45.40 N 10.55 E
Brentonico 64 45.49 N 10.57 E
Brent Reservoir ⊜[1] 260 51.35 N 0.15 W
Brentwood, Eng., U.K. 42 51.38 N 0.18 E
Brentwood, Eng., U.K. 260 51.38 N 0.18 E
Brentwood, Ca., U.S. 226 37.55 N 121.41 W
Brentwood, Md., U.S. 208 38.56 N 76.57 W
Brentwood, N.Y., U.S. 210 40.46 N 73.14 W
Brentwood, Oh., U.S. 218 39.13 N 84.31 W
Brentwood, Pa., U.S. 214 40.22 N 79.58 W
Brentwood, Tn., U.S. 194 36.01 N 86.46 W
Brentwood □[8] 260 51.37 N 0.20 E
Brentwood Bay 224 48.35 N 123.28 W
Brentwood Estates 214 40.25 N 80.45 W
Brentwood Heights ✦[8] 280 34.04 N 118.30 W
Brentwood Lake 214 41.19 N 82.05 W
Brentwood Park 273d 26.08 S 28.18 E
Brenz ≐ 56 48.34 N 10.24 E
Breo 62 44.23 N 7.49 E
Bréon, Ruisseu du ≐ 261 48.40 N 2.49 E
Brera, Palazzo di ✪ 266b 45.28 N 9.11 E
Brereton Park 158 26.55 S 30.30 E
Brescello 64 44.54 N 10.31 E
Brescia 64 45.33 N 10.15 E
Brescia □[4] 64 45.38 N 10.18 E
Bresewitz 54 54.24 N 12.40 E
Brésil → Brazil □[1] 242 10.00 S 55.00 W
Breskens 52 51.24 N 3.34 E
Breslau, On., Can. 212 43.28 N 80.25 W
Breslau → Wrocław, Pol. 30 51.06 N 17.00 E
Breslau, Tx., U.S. 222 29.31 N 97.00 W
Bresle ≐ 50 50.04 N 1.22 E
Bresles 50 49.25 N 2.15 E
Bresnahan, Mount ʌ 162 23.50 S 117.55 E
Bressanone (Brixen) 64 46.43 N 11.39 E
Bressay I 46a 60.08 N 1.05 W
Bressay Sound ʉ 46a 60.07 N 1.09 W
Bresse ✦[1] 58 46.30 N 5.15 E
Bresso 266b 45.32 N 9.11 E
Bressuire 32 46.51 N 0.30 W
Brest, Blg. 38 43.38 N 24.35 E
Brest, Bela. 76 52.06 N 23.42 E
Brest, Fr. 32 48.24 N 4.29 W
Brest □[8] 76 52.30 N 25.30 E
Brestanica 36 45.59 N 15.29 E
Bretagne (Brittany) □[9] 32 48.00 N 3.00 W
Bretenoux 32 44.55 N 1.50 E
Breteuil 50 49.38 N 2.18 E
Breteuil-sur-Iton 50 48.50 N 0.55 E
Brethercourt 261 48.30 N 1.55 E
Bretherton 262 53.41 N 2.48 W
Brétigny ■ 261 48.35 N 2.20 E
Brétigny-sur-Orge 50 48.37 N 2.19 E
Bretnig 54 51.08 N 14.04 E
Breton 182 53.07 N 114.28 W
Bretón, Canal de ʉ 240p 21.10 N 79.30 W
Breton, Pertuis ʉ 32 46.25 N 1.20 W
Breton Bay c 208 38.16 N 76.39 W
Breton Islands II 194 29.28 N 89.11 W
Breton Sound ʉ 194 29.30 N 89.30 W
Breton Woods 208 40.02 N 74.06 W
Brett ≐ 42 51.58 N 0.58 E
Brett, Cape › 172 35.10 S 174.20 E
Bretten 56 49.02 N 8.42 E
Breu, Rio do ≐ 246 3.29 S 66.20 W
Breueh, Pulau I 110 5.41 N 95.05 E
Breuil-Bois-Robert 261 48.57 N 1.43 E
Breuil-Cervinia 58 45.56 N 7.38 E
Breuillet 261 48.34 N 2.10 E
Breuilpont 50 48.58 N 1.26 E
Breukelen 52 52.10 N 5.00 E
Breux 261 48.34 N 2.11 E
Brevard 192 35.14 N 82.44 W
Brevard □[6] 220 28.18 N 80.42 W
Brévenne ≐ 62 45.51 N 4.40 E
Brevens bruk 40 59.01 N 15.35 E
Breves 250 1.40 S 50.29 W
Brevig Mission 180 65.20 N 166.29 W
Brevik, Nor. 26 59.04 N 9.42 E
Brevik, Sve. 40 59.21 N 18.12 E
Brevoort Island I 176 63.30 N 64.20 W
Brewarrina 166 29.57 S 146.52 E
Brewer 188 44.47 N 68.45 W
Brewer Island I 282 37.33 N 122.16 W
Brewersville 218 39.05 N 85.37 W
Brewerton 210 43.14 N 76.08 W
Brewerville 150 6.26 N 10.47 W
Brewongle 170 33.29 S 149.43 E
Brewood 42 52.41 N 2.10 W
Brewster, Ks., U.S. 198 39.22 N 101.22 W
Brewster, Ma., U.S. 207 41.45 N 70.05 W
Brewster, Mn., U.S. 198 43.41 N 95.28 W
Brewster, Ne., U.S. 198 41.56 N 99.51 W
Brewster, N.Y., U.S. 210 41.23 N 73.37 W
Brewster, Oh., U.S. 214 40.42 N 81.35 W
Brewster, Wa., U.S. 202 48.05 N 119.46 W
Brewster, Kap › 16 70.19 N 22.05 W
Brewster, Lake ⊜ 166 33.28 S 146.00 E
Brewster, Mount ʌ 172 44.04 S 169.27 E
Brewton 194 31.06 N 87.04 W
Breyten 158 26.16 S 30.00 E
Břežany 61 48.52 N 16.20 E
Brežice 36 45.54 N 15.36 E
Brézina 148 33.04 N 1.14 E
Brézins 62 45.21 N 5.19 E
Březnice 60 49.33 N 13.57 E
Breznik 38 42.44 N 22.54 E
Březno, Česká Rep. 54 50.24 N 13.26 E
Brezno, Slvk. 30 48.50 N 19.39 E
Brézolles 50 48.41 N 1.04 E
Březová 54 50.06 N 12.39 E
Březové Hory 60 49.41 N 13.58 E
Bria 152 6.32 N 21.59 E
Brian Boru Peak ʌ 182 55.05 N 127.35 W
Briançon 62 44.54 N 6.39 E
Brian Head ʌ 200 37.41 N 112.50 W
Brianza □[9] 62 45.40 N 9.10 E
Briar 222 33.00 N 97.34 W
Briarcliff Manor 210 41.08 N 73.49 W
Briar Creek 210 40.10 N 76.46 W
Briar Creek ≐ 222 32.06 N 96.22 W
Briare 50 47.38 N 2.44 E
Briare, Canal de ≋ 50 48.02 N 2.43 E
Briarres-sur-Essonne 50 48.14 N 2.25 E
Briarwood Beach 214 41.06 N 81.54 W
Briarwood Center ✦[9] 281 42.14 N 83.45 W
Briatico 68 38.43 N 16.02 E
Bribano 64 46.06 N 12.05 E
Bribie Island I 171a 27.00 S 153.07 E
Bričany 38 48.22 N 27.04 E
Bricelyn 190 43.33 N 93.48 W
Brice Run ≐ 284b 39.19 N 76.50 W
Brices Cross Roads National Battlefield Site ⊥ 194 34.31 N 88.41 W
Briceville 192 36.10 N 84.11 W
Bricherasio 62 44.49 N 7.18 E
Bricht 263 51.41 N 6.51 E
Brickebacken 40 59.15 N 15.15 E
Brick Lake ⊜ 220 28.10 N 81.12 W
Brick Township 208 40.04 N 74.08 W
Briçonnet, Lac ⊜ 186 51.27 N 60.11 W
Bricquebec 32 49.28 N 1.38 W
Bridal Veil 224 45.33 N 122.10 W
Bridalveil Fall L 226 37.43 N 119.39 W
Bride 44 54.22 N 4.22 W
Bride ≐ 48 52.04 N 7.52 W
Bridesburg ✦[8] 285 40.00 N 75.04 W
Brides-les-Bains 62 45.27 N 6.34 E
Bridge 42 51.14 N 1.07 E
Bridge ≐ 182 50.45 N 121.55 W
Bridge City 194 30.01 N 93.50 W
Bridge Creek ≐ 224 48.26 N 120.52 W
Bridgehampton 207 40.56 N 72.18 W
Bridge Lake 182 51.29 N 120.43 W
Bridgend, Scot., U.K. 46 55.48 N 6.16 W
Bridgend, Scot., U.K. 46 56.48 N 2.45 W
Bridgend, Wales, U.K. 42 51.31 N 3.35 W
Bridgenorth 212 44.23 N 78.23 W
Bridge of Allan 46 56.09 N 3.57 W
Bridge of Gaur 46 56.41 N 4.27 W
Bridge of Orchy 46 56.30 N 4.46 W
Bridge of Weir 46 55.52 N 4.35 W
Bridgeport, On., Can. 212 43.29 N 80.29 W
Bridgeport, Al., U.S. 194 34.56 N 85.42 W
Bridgeport, Ca., U.S. 226 38.10 N 119.13 W
Bridgeport, Ct., U.S. 207 41.10 N 73.12 W
Bridgeport, Il., U.S. 194 38.42 N 87.45 W
Bridgeport, Mi., U.S. 190 43.21 N 83.52 W
Bridgeport, Ne., U.S. 198 41.39 N 103.05 W
Bridgeport, N.J., U.S. 285 39.48 N 75.20 W
Bridgeport, N.Y., U.S. 210 43.09 N 75.58 W
Bridgeport, Oh., U.S. 214 40.04 N 80.44 W
Bridgeport, Pa., U.S. 285 40.06 N 75.21 W
Bridgeport, Tx., U.S. 222 33.12 N 97.45 W
Bridgeport, Wa., U.S. 202 48.00 N 119.40 W
Bridgeport, W.V., U.S. 188 39.17 N 80.15 W
Bridgeport ✦[8] 278 41.51 N 87.39 W
Bridgeport, Lake ⊜[1] 222 33.13 N 97.48 W
Bridgeport, University of ✪[2] 276 41.10 N 73.12 W
Bridgeport Airport ⊠ 285 39.47 N 75.20 W
Bridgeport Harbor c 276 41.10 N 73.11 W
Bridgeport Municipal Airport ⊠ 276 41.10 N 73.08 W
Bridgeport Reservoir ⊜[1] 226 38.22 N 119.14 W
Bridger 202 45.17 N 108.54 W
Bridge River Indian Reserve ✦[4] 182 50.45 N 122.00 W
Bridger Peak ʌ 200 41.12 N 107.02 W
Bridges Point › 174o 1.58 N 157.28 W
Bridgeton, Mo., U.S. 219 38.44 N 90.24 W
Bridgeton, N.J., U.S. 208 39.25 N 75.14 W
Bridgetown, Austl. 162 33.57 S 116.08 E
Bridgetown, Barb. 241g 13.06 N 59.37 W
Bridgetown, N.S., Can. 186 44.51 N 65.18 W
Bridgetown, Oh., U.S. 218 39.09 N 84.38 W
Bridge Trafford 262 53.14 N 2.49 W
Bridgeview 278 41.45 N 87.48 W
Bridgeville, De., U.S. 208 38.44 N 75.36 W
Bridgeville, Pa., U.S. 214 40.21 N 80.06 W
Bridgewater, Austl. 166 42.44 S 147.14 E
Bridgewater, Austl. 168b 35.02 S 138.47 E
Bridgewater, N.S., Can. 186 44.23 N 64.31 W
Bridgewater, Ct., U.S. 210 41.32 N 73.22 W
Bridgewater, Me., U.S. 186 46.25 N 67.50 W
Bridgewater, Ma., U.S. 207 41.59 N 70.58 W
Bridgewater, N.Y., U.S. 210 42.58 N 75.15 W
Bridgewater, Pa., U.S. 285 40.05 N 74.55 W
Bridgewater, S.D., U.S. 198 43.33 N 97.30 W
Bridgewater, Va., U.S. 188 38.22 N 78.58 W
Bridgewater Canal ≋ 262 53.20 N 2.45 W
Bridgewater State College ✪[2] 283 41.59 N 70.58 W
Bridgman 216 41.57 N 86.33 W
Bridgnorth 42 52.33 N 2.25 W
Bridgton 188 44.03 N 70.42 W
Bridgwater 42 51.08 N 3.00 W
Bridgwater Bay c 42 51.16 N 3.12 W
Bridlington 44 54.05 N 0.12 W
Bridlington Bay c 44 54.04 N 0.08 W
Bridport 42 50.44 N 2.46 W
Brie ✦[1] 50 48.40 N 3.20 E
Briec 32 48.06 N 4.00 W
Brie-Comte-Robert 50 48.41 N 2.37 E
Brie Française ✦[1] 261 48.48 N 2.46 E
Brieg → Brzeg 30 50.52 N 17.27 E
Brielle, Ned. 52 51.54 N 4.10 E
Brielle, N.J., U.S. 208 40.06 N 74.03 W
Brienne-le-Château 58 48.24 N 4.32 E
Brienne-sur-Aisne 50 49.26 N 4.03 E
Brienno 58 45.55 N 9.07 E
Brienon-sur-Armançon 50 48.00 N 3.37 E
Brien Run ≐ 284b 39.20 N 76.28 W
Brienz 58 46.46 N 8.03 E
Brienza 68 40.29 N 15.37 E
Brienzer Rothorn ʌ 58 46.48 N 8.04 E
Brienzersee ⊜ 58 46.43 N 7.57 E
Brier Creek ≐ 192 32.47 N 81.26 W
Brierfield 44 53.50 N 2.14 W
Brier Hill 212 44.32 N 75.40 W
Brier Island I 186 44.16 N 66.22 W
Brierley Hill 42 52.29 N 2.07 W
Brier Mountain ʌ 210 41.37 N 77.02 W
Briese 264a 52.42 N 13.18 E
Briese ≐ 264a 52.41 N 13.15 E
Brieselang 54 52.35 N 13.00 E
Briesen 54 52.20 N 14.16 E
Brieske 54 51.29 N 13.57 E
Brieskow-Finkenheerd 54 52.16 N 14.35 E
Briest 54 52.31 N 12.08 E
Briey 56 49.15 N 5.56 E
Brig 58 46.19 N 8.00 E
Brigach ≐ 58 47.58 N 8.30 E
Brigantine 208 39.24 N 74.21 W
Brig Bay 186 51.04 N 56.55 W
Brigden 214 42.49 N 82.17 W
Brigg 44 53.34 N 0.30 W
Briggs 196 30.53 N 97.56 W
Brigham City 200 41.30 N 112.00 W
Brighouse 44 53.42 N 1.47 W
Brighstone 42 50.38 N 1.24 W
Bright 166 36.44 S 146.58 E
Brightlingsea 42 51.49 N 1.02 E
Brightmoor ✦[8] 281 42.24 N 83.14 W
Brighton, Austl. 168b 35.01 S 138.31 E
Brighton, Austl. 169 37.55 S 145.00 E
Brighton, On., Can. 212 44.02 N 77.44 W
Brighton, N.Z. 172 45.57 S 170.20 E
Brighton, Eng., U.K. 42 50.50 N 0.08 W
Brighton, Co., U.S. 200 39.59 N 104.49 W
Brighton, Fl., U.S. 220 27.14 N 81.06 W
Brighton, Il., U.S. 219 39.02 N 90.08 W
Brighton, Ia., U.S. 190 41.10 N 91.49 W
Brighton, Md., U.S. 284b 39.21 N 76.43 W
Brighton, Mi., U.S. 216 42.31 N 83.46 W
Brighton, N.Y., U.S. 210 43.08 N 77.33 W
Brighton ✦[8] 283 42.21 N 71.08 W
Brighton Airport ⊠ 281 42.34 N 83.47 W
Brighton Downs 166 23.22 S 141.34 E
Brighton Indian Reservation ✦[4] 220 27.04 N 81.05 W
Brighton-Le-Sands 274a 33.58 S 151.09 E
Brighton Park ✦[8] 278 41.49 N 87.42 W
Brighton State Recreation Area ♦ 216 42.30 N 83.48 W
Brightsand Lake ⊜ 184 53.36 N 108.52 W
Brightwater 172 41.23 S 173.07 E
Brightwaters 276 40.43 N 73.16 W
Brightwood 224 45.23 N 122.01 W
Brightwood ✦[8] 284c 38.58 N 77.02 W
Brigittenau ✦[8] 264b 48.14 N 16.22 E
Brignoles 62 43.24 N 6.04 E
Brignoud 62 45.15 N 5.54 E
Brig o'Turk 46 56.13 N 4.22 W
Brigstock 42 52.27 N 0.36 W
Brigus 186 47.32 N 53.13 W
Brihuega 34 40.45 N 2.52 W
Briis-sous-Forges 261 48.38 N 2.07 E
Brijuni (Brioni) 64 44.55 N 13.46 E
Brijuni I 64 44.55 N 13.46 E
Brikama 150 13.15 N 16.39 W
Brilhante ≐ 255 21.58 S 54.18 W
Brill 42 51.49 N 1.03 W
Brilliant, B.C., Can. 182 49.19 N 117.38 W
Brilliant, Al., U.S. 194 34.01 N 87.45 W
Brilliant, Oh., U.S. 214 40.15 N 80.37 W
Brillion 190 44.10 N 88.03 W
Brilon 56 51.24 N 8.34 E
Brilyn Park 284c 38.54 N 77.10 W
Brimfield, Eng., U.K. 42 52.18 N 2.42 W
Brimfield, In., U.S. 216 41.27 N 85.24 W
Brimfield, Ma., U.S. 207 42.07 N 72.12 W
Brimfield, Oh., U.S. 214 41.06 N 81.21 W
Brimington 44 53.16 N 1.23 W
Brindabella 171b 35.23 S 148.45 E
Brindisi 68 40.38 N 17.56 E
Brindisi □[4] 68 40.35 N 17.40 E
Brindisi Montagna 68 40.37 N 15.57 E
Brindle 262 53.43 N 2.36 W
Bringelly 170 33.56 S 150.44 E
Bringelly Creek ≐ 274a 33.58 S 150.38 E
Brinje 36 45.00 N 15.08 E
Brinkerton 279b 40.13 N 79.32 W
Brinkhaven 214 40.28 N 82.12 W
Brinkleigh 284b 39.18 N 76.50 W
Brinkley, Austl. 168b 35.14 S 139.13 E
Brinkley, Ar., U.S. 194 34.53 N 91.11 W
Brinkum 52 53.00 N 8.47 E
Brinkworth 166 33.42 S 138.24 E
Brinnon 224 47.40 N 122.53 W
Brinon-sur-Beuvron 50 47.17 N 3.30 E
Brins, Ābār al- ⊤[4] 142 30.29 N 30.05 E
Brinscall 262 53.41 N 2.34 W
Brinyan 46 59.07 N 2.59 W
Brion, Île I 186 47.48 N 61.28 W
Brione 58 46.18 N 8.47 E
Briones Hills ⋏[2] 282 37.56 N 122.08 W
Briones Regional Park ♦ 282 37.56 N 122.08 W
Briones Reservoir ⊜[1] 282 37.55 N 122.12 W
Brionne 50 49.12 N 0.43 E
Brion-sur-Ource 58 47.55 N 4.39 E
Brioude 32 45.18 N 3.23 E
Briouze 32 48.42 N 0.22 W
Brisbane, Austl. 171a 27.28 S 153.02 E
Brisbane, Ca., U.S. 226 37.41 N 122.24 W
Brisbane ≐ 171a 27.24 S 153.09 E
Brisbane, Mount ʌ 171a 27.05 S 152.32 E
Brisbane International Airport ⊠ 171a 27.27 S 153.11 E
Brisbane Ranges National Park ♦ 169 37.52 S 144.14 E
Brisbane Water c 170 33.28 S 151.20 E
Brisbane Water National Park ♦ 170 33.30 S 151.15 E
Brisben 210 42.22 N 75.41 W
Brisbin 214 40.50 N 78.21 W
Briseñas 234 20.16 N 102.33 W
Brisighella 66 44.13 N 11.46 E
Brissac 62 43.52 N 3.42 E
Brissago 58 46.07 N 8.43 E
Bristol, Eng., U.K. 42 51.27 N 2.35 W
Bristol, Ct., U.S. 207 41.41 N 72.57 W
Bristol, Fl., U.S. 192 30.25 N 84.58 W
Bristol, Il., U.S. 216 41.39 N 88.27 W
Bristol, In., U.S. 216 41.43 N 85.49 W
Bristol, N.H., U.S. 188 43.35 N 71.44 W
Bristol, Pa., U.S. 208 40.06 N 74.51 W
Bristol, R.I., U.S. 207 41.40 N 71.16 W
Bristol, S.D., U.S. 198 45.20 N 97.44 W
Bristol, Tn., U.S. 192 36.35 N 82.11 W
Bristol, Vt., U.S. 188 44.08 N 73.04 W
Bristol, Va., U.S. 192 36.35 N 82.11 W
Bristol, Wi., U.S. 216 42.33 N 88.02 W
Bristol □[6], Ma., U.S. 207 41.54 N 71.06 W
Bristol □[6], R.I., U.S. 207 41.42 N 71.18 W
Bristol (Lulsgate) Airport ⊠ 42 51.23 N 2.43 W
Bristol Bay c 180 58.00 N 159.00 W
Bristol-Blake Reservation ♦ 283 42.06 N 71.19 W
Bristol Center 210 42.49 N 77.23 W
Bristol Channel ʉ 42 51.20 N 4.00 W
Bristol Lake ⊜ 204 34.28 N 115.41 W
Bristolville 214 41.23 N 80.52 W
Bristow 196 35.49 N 96.23 W
Britânia 255 15.14 S 51.09 W
Británicas, Islas → British Isles II 4 54.00 N 4.00 W
Britannia, On., Can. 275b 43.37 N 79.41 W
Britannia, Eng., U.K. 262 53.41 N 2.11 W
Britannia Beach 182 49.38 N 123.12 W
Britische Jungfern-Inseln → British Virgin Islands □[2] 240m 18.30 N 64.30 W
Britisches Antarktis-Territorium → British Antarctic Territory □[2] 9 60.00 S 45.00 W
British Antarctic Territory □[2] 9 60.00 S 45.00 W
British Columbia □[4], Can. 176 54.00 N 125.00 W
British Columbia □[4], Can. 182 54.00 N 125.00 W
British Honduras → Belize □[1] 232 17.15 N 88.45 W
British Indian Ocean Territory □[2] 12 7.00 S 72.00 E
British Isles II 4 54.00 N 4.00 W
British Mountains ⋏ 180 69.00 N 140.20 W
British Museum ✪ 260 51.31 N 0.08 W
British Solomon Islands → Solomon Islands □[1] 175e 8.00 S 159.00 E
British Virgin Islands □[2], N.A. 230 18.30 N 64.30 W
British Virgin Islands □[2], N.A. 240m 18.30 N 64.30 W
Britland Edge Hill ʌ[2] 262 53.31 N 1.50 W
Briton Ferry 42 51.38 N 3.49 W
Brits 158 25.42 S 27.45 E
Britstown 158 30.37 S 23.30 E
Britt 190 43.05 N 93.48 W
Brittany → Bretagne □[9] 32 48.00 N 3.00 W
Brittas 48 53.14 N 6.27 W
Britten 158 27.42 S 25.17 E
Brittingham 196 25.45 N 103.24 W
Britton, Mi., U.S. 216 41.59 N 83.49 W
Britton, S.D., U.S. 198 45.47 N 97.45 W
Britton, Tx., U.S. 222 32.33 N 97.04 W
Britton, Mount ʌ[2] 162 26.31 S 134.43 E
Britz 54 52.53 N 13.49 E
Britz ✦[8] 264a 52.27 N 13.26 E
Brive-la-Gaillarde 32 45.10 N 1.32 E
Brives-Charensac 62 45.03 N 3.56 E
Briviesca 34 42.33 N 3.19 W
Brivio 62 45.44 N 9.27 E
Brixen im Thale 64 47.27 N 12.15 E
Brixham 42 50.24 N 3.30 W
Brixlegg 64 47.25 N 11.53 E
Brixton 166 23.32 S 144.57 E
Brixworth 42 52.20 N 0.54 W
Brlik 85 43.40 N 73.49 E
Brloh 61 48.56 N 14.13 E
Brno 30 49.12 N 16.37 E
Bro 40 59.31 N 17.38 E
Broa, Ensenada de la c 240p 22.35 N 82.00 W
Broad ≐, U.S. 192 34.00 N 81.04 W
Broad ≐, Fl., U.S. 220 25.28 N 81.09 W
Broad ≐, Ga., U.S. 192 33.59 N 82.39 W
Broadalbin 210 43.03 N 74.11 W
Broad Arrow 162 30.20 S 121.27 E
Broad Axe 285 40.10 N 75.15 W
Broadback ≐ 176 51.21 N 78.52 W
Broad Bay c 46 58.15 N 6.15 W
Broadbottom 262 53.26 N 2.01 W
Broad Brook 207 41.54 N 72.32 W
Broad Chalke 42 51.02 N 1.57 W
Broadclyst 42 50.46 N 3.26 W
Broad Creek c 208 38.45 N 76.15 W
Broad Creek ≐ 208 39.42 N 76.14 W
Broadford, Austl. 169 37.13 S 145.03 E
Broadford, Scot., U.K. 46 57.14 N 5.54 W
Broad Haven c 48 54.18 N 9.55 W
Broadheath 262 53.24 N 2.21 W
Broadhurst Range ⋏ 162 22.23 S 122.09 E
Broadkill ≐ 208 38.47 N 75.10 W
Broad Law ʌ 46 55.30 N 3.22 W
Broadley Common 260 51.45 N 0.04 E
Broadmeadows 169 37.40 S 144.54 E
Broadmoor 226 37.41 N 122.29 W
Broad Neck ›[1] 208 39.03 N 76.27 W
Broad Oak 42 50.57 N 0.36 E
Broad Pass)(180 63.18 N 149.09 W
Broad Run ≐, Pa., U.S. 285 39.56 N 75.41 W
Broad Run ≐, Pa., U.S. 285 39.59 N 75.40 W
Broad Run ≐, Va., U.S. 208 38.41 N 77.29 W
Broad Sound ʉ, Austl. 166 22.10 S 149.45 E
Broad Sound ʉ, Ma., U.S. 283 42.25 N 70.58 W
Broad Sound Channel ʉ 166 22.05 S 150.20 E
Broadstairs 42 51.22 N 1.27 E
Broad Street 260 51.17 N 0.38 E
Broad Top 214 40.12 N 78.08 W
Broadus 198 45.26 N 105.24 W
Broadview, Sk., Can. 184 50.20 N 102.30 W
Broadview, Il., U.S. 216 41.51 N 87.51 W
Broadview, In., U.S. 218 39.10 N 87.33 W
Broadview Heights 214 41.18 N 81.41 W
Broadwater 198 41.35 N 102.51 W
Broadway, Eng., U.K. 42 52.02 N 1.51 W
Broadway, Oh., U.S. 214 40.20 N 83.24 W
Broadway, Va., U.S. 188 38.38 N 78.46 W
Broadwell 219 40.04 N 89.27 W
Broadwindsor 42 50.49 N 2.48 W
Broadwood 172 35.16 S 173.23 E
Broager 41 54.53 N 9.41 E
Brobo 150 7.43 N 4.42 W
Broby 26 56.15 N 14.05 E
Brobyværk 41 55.14 N 10.15 E
Broc 58 46.36 N 7.06 E
Brocēni 76 56.42 N 22.35 E
Brochel 46 57.26 N 6.01 W
Brochet 176 57.53 N 101.40 W
Brochet, Lac au ⊜ 186 49.40 N 69.37 W
Brochterbeck 52 52.13 N 7.44 E
Brock 184 51.27 N 108.42 W
Brock ≐ 44 53.52 N 2.47 W
Brock Creek ≐ 285 40.15 N 74.50 W
Brocken ʌ 54 51.48 N 10.36 E
Brockenhurst 42 50.49 N 1.34 W
Brockenscheidt 263 51.38 N 7.25 E
Brockhagen 52 51.59 N 8.20 E
Brockham 260 51.14 N 0.17 W
Brockman ≐ 168a 31.41 S 116.07 E
Brockman, Mount ʌ 162 22.28 S 117.18 E
Brock Monument ⊥ 284a 43.09 N 79.04 W
Brockport, N.Y., U.S. 210 43.12 N 77.56 W
Brockport, Pa., U.S. 214 41.16 N 78.44 W
Brocks Beach 212 44.27 N 80.06 W
Brocks Creek 164 13.28 S 131.25 E
Brockton, Ma., U.S. 207 42.05 N 71.01 W
Brockton, Mt., U.S. 198 48.09 N 104.54 W
Brockton, Pa., U.S. 208 40.45 N 76.04 W
Brockton Reservoir ⊜[1] 283 42.07 N 71.03 W
Brock University ✪[2] 284a 43.07 N 79.15 W
Brockville 212 44.35 N 75.41 W
Brockway 214 41.15 N 78.47 W
Brockworth 42 51.51 N 2.09 W
Brocoió, Ilha de I 287a 22.45 S 43.07 W
Brocton 214 42.23 N 79.26 W
Brod, Česká Rep. 60 49.51 N 12.45 E
Brod, Mak. 38 41.31 N 21.12 E
Broddbo 40 59.59 N 16.28 E
Brodenbach 56 50.14 N 7.26 E
Broderick 226 38.35 N 121.30 W
Brodeur Peninsula ›[1] 176 73.00 N 88.00 W
Brodhead, Ky., U.S. 192 37.24 N 84.24 W
Brodhead, Wi., U.S. 190 42.37 N 89.22 W
Brodhead Creek ≐ 210 40.59 N 75.08 W
Brodheadsville 210 40.55 N 75.24 W
Brodick 46 55.35 N 5.09 W
Brodnax 192 36.42 N 78.01 W
Brodnica 30 53.16 N 19.23 E
Brodokalmak 86 55.35 N 62.06 E
Brody, Pol. 30 51.45 N 14.45 E
Brody, Ukr. 78 50.06 N 25.10 E
Broedersput 158 26.49 S 25.08 E
Broek [op Langendijk] 52 52.40 N 4.48 E
Brogan 202 44.14 N 117.30 W
Broglie 50 49.01 N 0.32 E
Brohlbach ≐ 56 50.29 N 7.20 E
Broich ✦[8] 263 51.25 N 6.51 E
Broichweiden 56 50.49 N 6.09 E
Brok 30 52.43 N 21.52 E
Brok ʌ 123 34.32 N 76.35 E
Brokdorf 52 53.52 N 9.19 E
Broke 170 32.45 S 151.06 E
Broke Inlet c 162 34.55 S 116.25 E
Broken ≐ 169 36.41 S 146.00 E
Broken Arrow 196 36.03 N 95.47 W
Broken Bay c 170 33.34 S 151.18 E
Broken Bow, Ne., U.S. 198 41.24 N 99.38 W
Broken Bow, Ok., U.S. 194 34.01 N 94.44 W
Broken Bow Lake ⊜[1] 194 34.10 N 94.40 W
Broken Cross, Eng., U.K. 262 53.15 N 2.29 W
Broken Cross, Eng., U.K. 262 53.15 N 2.10 W
Brokenhead ≐ 184 50.25 N 96.40 W
Broken Hill, Austl. 166 31.57 S 141.27 E
Broken Hill → Kabwe, Zam. 154 14.27 S 28.27 E
Broken Ridge ✣[3] 12 31.30 S 95.00 E
Brokenstraw Creek ≐ 214 41.51 N 79.09 W
Broken Sword Creek ≐ 214 40.46 N 83.11 W
Brokopondo 250 5.04 N 54.58 W
Brokopondo □[5] 250 4.40 N 55.00 W
Brokopondo Stuwmeer ⊜[1] 250 4.45 N 55.00 W
Brölbach ≐ 56 50.47 N 7.18 E
Brolo 70 38.09 N 14.50 E
Bromberg → Bydgoszcz 30 53.08 N 18.00 E
Bromborough 262 53.19 N 2.59 W
Brome, P.Q., Can. 206 45.12 N 72.34 W
Brome, Dtsch. 54 52.36 N 10.56 E
Brome □[6] 206 45.10 N 72.30 W
Brome, Lac ⊜ 206 45.15 N 72.30 W
Brome, Mont ʌ 206 45.17 N 72.38 W
Bromham 42 52.09 N 0.31 W
Bromley ✦[8] 42 51.24 N 0.02 E
Bromley Common ✦[8] 260 51.22 N 0.03 E
Bromley Plateau ✣[3] 18 32.00 S 35.00 W
Bromma ✦[8] 40 59.21 N 17.55 E
Bromma flygplats ⊠ 40 59.21 N 17.55 E
Brommö I 40 58.50 N 13.41 E
Bromo, Gunung ʌ 115a 7.57 S 112.57 E
Bromölla 26 56.04 N 14.28 E
Brompton, Eng., U.K. 44 54.22 N 1.25 W
Brompton, Eng., U.K. 260 51.23 N 0.33 E
Brompton, Lac ⊜ 206 45.27 N 72.09 W
Bromptonville 206 45.28 N 71.57 W
Bromsgrove 42 52.20 N 2.03 W
Bromyard 42 52.11 N 2.30 W
Bron 62 45.44 N 4.55 E
Brønderslev 26 57.16 N 9.58 E
Bronevskaja 24 61.43 N 39.10 E
Brong-Ahafo □[4] 150 7.45 N 1.30 W
Broni 62 45.04 N 9.16 E
Bronickaja Guta 78 50.56 N 27.19 E
Bronkhorstspruit 158 25.48 S 28.44 E
Bronkhorstspruitdam ⊜[1] 158 25.55 S 28.42 E
Bronkow 54 51.40 N 13.55 E
Bronllys 42 52.01 N 3.16 W
Bronlund Peak ʌ 176 57.26 N 126.38 W
Bronn 60 49.44 N 11.28 E
Bronnicy 82 55.25 N 38.16 E
Bronnikovo 86 58.32 N 68.25 E
Bronnoje 76 52.19 N 30.29 E
Brønnøysund 24 65.30 N 12.10 E
Bronnzell 56 50.31 N 9.41 E
Brøns 41 55.11 N 8.44 E
Bronson, Fl., U.S. 192 29.26 N 82.38 W
Bronson, Ks., U.S. 198 37.54 N 95.04 W
Bronson, Mi., U.S. 216 41.52 N 85.11 W
Bronson, Tx., U.S. 194 31.21 N 94.01 W
Bronson Lake ⊜ 184 53.52 N 109.43 W
Bronte, It. 70 37.47 N 14.50 E
Bronte, Tx., U.S. 196 31.53 N 100.18 W
Bronte Creek ≐ 212 43.23 N 79.43 W
Bronwood 192 31.49 N 84.21 W
Bronx □[6] 210 40.49 N 73.56 W
Bronx ✦[8] 276 40.49 N 73.56 W
Bronx ≐ 276 40.49 N 73.52 W
Bronx Park ♦ 276 40.52 N 73.53 W
Bronxville 276 40.56 N 73.49 W
Bronx-Whitestone Bridge ✦[5] 276 40.48 N 73.50 W
Bronx Zoo ♦ 276 40.51 N 73.53 W
Bronzolo (Branzoll) 64 46.24 N 11.19 E
Brooch, Lac ⊜ 186 50.44 N 67.58 W
Broodsnyersplaas 158 26.03 S 29.29 E
Brook 216 40.51 N 87.21 W
Brookdale 226 37.06 N 122.06 W
Brooke 208 38.23 N 77.22 W
Brooke □[6] 214 40.18 N 80.33 W
Brookeborough 48 54.19 N 7.24 W
Brookeland 194 31.09 N 94.00 W
Brooker 192 29.53 N 82.19 W
Brooke's Point 116 8.47 N 117.50 E
Brookfield, N.S., Can. 186 45.15 N 63.17 W
Brookfield, Ct., U.S. 207 41.28 N 73.24 W
Brookfield, Il., U.S. 216 41.49 N 87.51 W
Brookfield, Ma., U.S. 207 42.12 N 72.06 W
Brookfield, Mi., U.S. 216 42.27 N 84.47 W
Brookfield, Mo., U.S. 194 39.47 N 93.04 W
Brookfield, N.Y., U.S. 210 42.48 N 75.19 W
Brookfield, Oh., U.S. 214 41.14 N 80.34 W
Brookfield, Wi., U.S. 216 43.03 N 88.06 W
Brookfield Center 207 41.27 N 73.23 W
Brookfield Zoo ♦ 278 41.50 N 87.50 W
Brookford 192 35.42 N 81.20 W
Brookhaven, De., U.S. 285 39.42 N 75.41 W
Brookhaven, Ms., U.S. 194 31.34 N 90.26 W
Brookhaven, Pa., U.S. 285 39.52 N 75.22 W
Brookhaven National Laboratory ✪[3] 207 40.54 N 72.52 W
Brookings, Or., U.S. 202 42.03 N 124.16 W
Brookings, S.D., U.S. 198 44.18 N 96.47 W
Brookland, Eng., U.K. 42 50.59 N 0.50 E
Brookland, Ar., U.S. 194 35.54 N 90.34 W
Brookland ✦[8] 284c 38.56 N 76.59 W
Brooklands 214 42.38 N 83.06 W
Brookland Terrace 285 39.44 N 75.37 W
Brooklandville 284b 39.25 N 76.40 W
Brooklawn 285 39.52 N 75.07 W
Brooklet 192 32.22 N 81.39 W
Brooklin 212 43.57 N 78.57 W
Brookline, Ma., U.S. 207 42.21 N 71.07 W
Brookline, N.H., U.S. 207 42.44 N 71.39 W
Brooklyn, N.S., Can. 186 44.03 N 64.42 W
Brooklyn, Ct., U.S. 207 41.47 N 71.57 W
Brooklyn, Il., U.S. 219 40.14 N 90.46 W
Brooklyn, In., U.S. 218 39.32 N 86.22 W
Brooklyn, Ia., U.S. 190 41.44 N 92.26 W
Brooklyn, Mi., U.S. 216 42.06 N 84.14 W
Brooklyn, Ms., U.S. 194 31.03 N 89.11 W
Brooklyn, Oh., U.S. 214 41.26 N 81.44 W
Brooklyn, Pa., U.S. 210 41.45 N 75.48 W
Brooklyn, Wa., U.S. 224 46.47 N 123.31 W
Brooklyn, Wi., U.S. 216 42.51 N 89.22 W
Brooklyn ✦[8], Md., U.S. 284b 39.14 N 76.36 W
Brooklyn ✦[8], N.Y., U.S. 210 40.42 N 74.00 W
Brooklyn Battery Tunnel ✦[5] 276 40.42 N 74.01 W
Brooklyn Bridge ✦[5] 276 40.42 N 74.00 W
Brooklyn Center 190 45.04 N 93.19 W
Brooklyn Heights 279a 41.24 N 81.40 W
Brooklyn Marine Park ♦ 276 40.35 N 73.55 W
Brooklyn Museum ✪ 276 40.40 N 73.58 W
Brookmans Park 260 51.43 N 0.12 W
Brookmere 182 49.49 N 120.53 W
Brookmont 284c 38.57 N 77.07 W
Brookneal 192 37.03 N 78.56 W
Brook Park 214 41.23 N 81.48 W
Brookport 194 37.07 N 88.37 W
Brooks, Ab., Can. 182 50.35 N 111.53 W
Brooks, Ca., U.S. 226 38.45 N 122.09 W
Brooks, Me., U.S. 188 44.33 N 69.07 W
Brooks, Or., U.S. 224 45.02 N 122.57 W
Brooks, Mount ʌ 180 63.11 N 150.40 W
Brooks Air Force Base ■ 196 29.21 N 98.25 W
Brooks Bay c 182 50.13 N 127.55 W
Brooksburg 218 38.44 N 85.15 W
Brookshire 222 29.47 N 95.57 W
Brookside, De., U.S. 285 39.40 N 75.43 W
Brookside, N.J., U.S. 276 40.48 N 74.34 W
Brookside, Pa., U.S. 214 42.08 N 80.00 W
Brookside, Tx., U.S. 222 29.35 N 95.18 W
Brookside Park ♦ 279a 41.27 N 81.43 W
Brooks Island I 282 37.54 N 122.21 W
Brooks Mountain ʌ 180 65.33 N 167.09 W
Brooks Place 283 42.02 N 71.01 W
Brooks Range ⋏ 180 68.00 N 154.00 W
Brookston 216 40.36 N 86.52 W
Brook Street 260 51.37 N 0.17 E
Brooksville, Fl., U.S. 220 28.33 N 82.23 W
Brooksville, Ky., U.S. 218 38.40 N 84.03 W
Brooksville, Ms., U.S. 194 33.14 N 88.34 W
Brookton 162 32.22 S 117.01 E
Brooktondale 210 42.23 N 76.24 W
Brookvale 274a 33.46 S 151.17 E
Brookview 210 42.32 N 73.43 W
Brookville, In., U.S. 218 39.25 N 85.00 W
Brookville, Ma., U.S. 207 42.07 N 71.00 W
Brookville, N.Y., U.S. 276 40.48 N 73.34 W
Brookville, Oh., U.S. 218 39.50 N 84.24 W
Brookville, Pa., U.S. 214 41.09 N 79.05 W
Brookville Lake ⊜[1] 218 39.30 N 85.00 W
Brookwood 260 51.18 N 0.38 W
Brooloo 166 26.29 S 152.42 E
Broom, Little Loch c 46 57.54 N 5.22 W
Broom, Loch c 46 57.52 N 5.08 W
Broomall 285 39.58 N 75.21 W
Broome 162 17.58 S 122.14 E
Broome □[6] 210 42.08 N 75.54 W
Broome County Airport ⊠ 210 42.13 N 75.59 W
Broomes Island 208 38.25 N 76.32 W
Broomfield, Eng., U.K. 260 51.46 N 0.28 E
Broomfield, Eng., U.K. 260 51.14 N 0.38 E
Broomfield, Co., U.S. 200 39.55 N 105.05 W
Broons 32 48.19 N 2.16 W
Brooten 198 45.30 N 95.07 W
Brophy, Mount ʌ[2] 162 19.11 S 128.51 E
Brora 46 58.01 N 3.51 W
Brora ≐ 46 58.01 N 3.52 W
Brørup 41 55.29 N 9.01 E
Broseley 42 52.37 N 2.29 W
Brosewere Bay c 276 40.37 N 73.42 W
Brosna ≐ 48 53.13 N 7.58 W
Brošnev-Osada 78 49.00 N 24.13 E
Brossac 32 45.20 N 0.03 W
Brossard 206 45.26 N 73.29 W
Brossasco 62 44.34 N 7.21 E
Brosso 62 45.30 N 7.48 E
Brotas de Macaúbas 255 12.00 S 42.38 W
Brothers Brook ≐ 276 41.02 N 73.36 W
Brötjärna 40 60.30 N 15.01 E
Broto 34 42.36 N 0.06 W
Brotterode 54 50.49 N 10.26 E
Brotton 44 54.34 N 0.56 W
Brou 50 48.13 N 1.11 E
Brough, Eng., U.K. 44 54.32 N 2.19 W
Brough, Eng., U.K. 44 53.44 N 0.35 W
Brough, Scot., U.K. 46 58.39 N 3.20 W
Brougham 212 43.55 N 79.06 W
Brough Head › 46 59.08 N 3.17 W
Broughshane 48 54.54 N 6.12 W
Broughton, Eng., U.K. 42 52.23 N 0.46 W
Broughton, Eng., U.K. 44 53.34 N 0.33 W
Broughton, Eng., U.K. 44 53.49 N 2.44 W
Broughton, Eng., U.K. 262 53.49 N 2.44 W
Broughton, Scot., U.K. 46 55.37 N 3.25 W
Broughton, Wales, U.K. 44 53.10 N 2.59 W
Broughton, Pa. U.S. 214 40.21 N 79.59 W
Broughton in Furness 44 54.17 N 3.12 W
Broughton Island I 176 67.35 N 63.50 W
Broughtown 46 59.15 N 2.36 W
Broughty Ferry 46 56.28 N 2.53 W
Broumov 30 50.35 N 16.20 E
Brousseval 58 48.29 N 4.58 E
Brou-sur-Chantereine 261 48.53 N 2.38 E
Brouvelieures 58 48.14 N 6.44 E
Brouwersdam ✦[6] 52 51.46 N 3.51 E
Brouwershaven 52 51.44 N 3.54 E
Brovary 78 50.31 N 30.46 E
Brovst 26 57.06 N 9.32 E
Broward □[6] 220 26.09 N 80.29 W
Browerville 198 46.05 N 94.51 W
Brown □[6], Il., U.S. 219 39.59 N 90.45 W
Brown □[6], In., U.S. 218 39.12 N 86.15 W
Brown □[6], Oh., U.S. 218 38.52 N 83.54 W
Brown, Mount ʌ 202 48.52 N 111.09 W
Brown, Point › 224 46.56 N 124.10 W
Brownbacks 285 40.11 N 75.37 W
Brown City 190 43.12 N 82.59 W
Brown Clee Hill ʌ[2] 42 52.28 N 2.35 W
Brown County State Park ♦ 218 39.09 N 86.14 W
Brown Creek ≐ 276 40.43 N 73.04 W
Browndale 210 41.40 N 75.27 W
Brown Deer 216 43.09 N 87.57 W
Browne Bay c 176 73.08 N 97.30 W
Brownfield 196 33.10 N 102.16 W
Brown Gelly ʌ[2] 42 50.32 N 4.32 W
Brownhills 42 52.39 N 1.55 W
Browning, Il., U.S. 219 40.08 N 90.22 W
Browning, Mo., U.S. 194 40.02 N 93.09 W
Browning, Mt., U.S. 202 48.33 N 113.00 W
Browning Entrance c 182 53.41 N 130.30 W
Browning Island I 212 45.00 N 79.25 W
Brown Lake ⊜ 176 65.55 N 91.15 W
Brownlee Park 216 42.18 N 85.05 W
Brownlee Reservoir ⊜[1] 202 44.40 N 117.05 W
Brown Mountain ʌ, Ca., U.S. 204 35.41 N 117.01 W
Brown Mountain ʌ, Ca., U.S. 280 34.14 N 118.08 W
Brown Mountain ʌ[2] 222 31.51 N 97.39 W
Brown Point › 276 40.43 N 73.04 W
Brownsberg, Natuurpark ♦ 250 4.50 N 55.10 W
Brownsboro 222 32.18 N 95.37 W
Browns Brook ≐ 276 41.09 N 73.17 W
Brownsburg, P.Q., Can. 206 45.41 N 74.25 W
Brownsburg, In., U.S. 218 39.50 N 86.23 W
Browns Canyon V 280 34.18 N 118.35 W
Brownsdale 190 43.44 N 92.52 W
Browns Island I 282 38.02 N 121.52 W
Browns Lake 216 42.42 N 88.14 W
Brownsmead 224 46.13 N 123.32 W
Browns Mills 208 39.58 N 74.35 W
Browns Point 224 47.18 N 122.21 W
Browns Town, Jam. 241q 18.24 N 77.22 W
Brownstown, Il., U.S. 219 38.59 N 88.57 W
Brownstown, In., U.S. 218 38.52 N 86.02 W
Brownstown, Pa., U.S. 208 40.08 N 76.13 W
Brownstown Creek ≐ 281 42.06 N 83.13 W
Browns Valley, Ca., U.S. 226 39.15 N 121.23 W
Browns Valley, Mn., U.S. 198 45.35 N 96.49 W
Brownsville, On., Can. 212 42.52 N 80.50 W
Brownsville, Ca., U.S. 226 39.28 N 121.16 W
Brownsville, Fl., U.S. 220 25.50 N 80.17 W
Brownsville, In., U.S. 218 39.39 N 85.00 W
Brownsville, Ky., U.S. 194 37.11 N 86.16 W
Brownsville, La., U.S. 194 32.30 N 92.10 W
Brownsville, Or., U.S. 202 44.23 N 122.59 W
Brownsville, Pa., U.S. 188 40.01 N 79.53 W
Brownsville, Tn., U.S. 194 35.35 N 89.15 W
Brownsville, Tx., U.S. 196 25.54 N 97.29 W
Brownton 190 44.43 N 94.21 W
Browntown 276 40.24 N 74.19 W
Brownvale 182 56.08 N 117.53 W
Brownville, Al., U.S. 194 33.23 N 87.45 W
Brownville, Me., U.S. 188 45.18 N 69.02 W
Brownville, Ne., U.S. 198 40.23 N 95.39 W
Brownville, N.Y., U.S. 212 44.00 N 75.59 W
Brownville Junction 188 45.21 N 69.03 W
Brown Willy ʌ[2] 42 50.35 N 4.36 W
Brownwood 196 31.42 N 98.59 W
Brownwood, Lake ⊜[1] 196 31.51 N 99.02 W
Browse Island I 160 14.07 S 123.33 E
Broxbourne 260 51.45 N 0.01 W
Broxbourne □[8] 260 51.44 N 0.04 W
Broxton 192 31.37 N 82.53 W
Broye ≐ 58 46.55 N 7.02 E
Broyhill Park 284c 38.51 N 77.11 W

	English	Deutsch	Español	Français	Português
≐	River	Fluß	Río	Rivière	Rio
≋	Canal	Kanal	Canal	Canal	Canal
L	Waterfall, Rapids	Wasserfall, Stromschnellen	Cascada, Rápidos	Chute d'eau, Rapides	Cascata, Rápicos
ʉ	Strait	Meeresstraße	Estrecho	Détroit	Estreito
c	Bay, Gulf	Bucht, Golf	Bahía, Golfo	Baie, Golfe	Baía, Golfo
⊜	Lake, Lakes	See, Seen	Lago, Lagos	Lac, Lacs	Lago, Lagos
※	Swamp	Sumpf	Pantano	Marais	Pântano
▨	Ice Features, Glacier	Eis- und Gletscherformen	Accidentes Glaciales	Formes glaciaires	Acidentes glaciares
⊤	Other Hydrographic Features	Andere Hydrographische Objekte	Otros Elementos Hidrográficos	Autres données hydrographiques	Outros acidentes hidrográficos
✣	Submarine Features	Untermeerische Objekte	Accidentes Submarinos	Formes de relief sous-marin	Acidentes submarinos
□	Political Unit	Politische Einheit	Unidad Política	Entité politique	Unidade política
✪	Cultural Institution	Kulturelle Institution	Institución Cultural	Institution culturelle	Instituição cultural
⊥	Historical Site	Historische Stätte	Sitio Histórico	Site historique	Sítio histórico
♦	Recreational Site	Erholungs- und Ferienort	Sitio de Recreo	Centre de loisirs	Área de Lazer
⊠	Airport	Flughafen	Aeropuerto	Aéroport	Aeroporto
■	Military Installation	Militäranlage	Instalación Militar	Installation militaire	Instalação militar
✦	Miscellaneous	Verschiedenes	Misceláneo	Divers	Diversos

Name	Page	Lat. °′	Long. °′
Broža	76	52.57 N	29.07 E
Brozas	34	39.37 N	6.46 W
Brozzo	64	45.43 N	10.14 E
Brtonigla	64	45.23 N	13.38 E
Brû	58	48.21 N	6.41 E
Bruay-en-Artois	50	50.29 N	2.33 E
Bruay-sur-l'Escaut	50	50.23 N	3.32 E
Bruce, Ms., U.S.	194	33.59 N	89.20 W
Bruce, S.D., U.S.	198	44.26 N	96.53 W
Bruce, Wi., U.S.	190	45.27 N	91.16 W
Bruce □[6]	212	44.30 N	81.15 W
Bruce, Mount ʌ	162	22.36 S	118.08 E
Bruce Bay	172	43.35 S	169.41 E
Bruce Creek ≃	275b	43.52 N	79.18 W
Bruce Lake	184	50.48 N	93.24 W
Bruce Lake ⊜	184	50.49 N	93.20 W
Bruce Mines	190	46.18 N	83.48 W
Bruce Museum ♥	276	41.01 N	73.37 W
Bruce Peninsula ›[1]	190	44.50 N	81.20 W
Bruce Peninsula National Park ♦	190	45.12 N	81.40 W
Bruce Rock	162	31.53 S	118.09 E
Bruceville	222	31.19 N	97.14 W
Bruchberg ʌ	54	51.47 N	10.29 E
Bruche ≃	58	48.34 N	7.43 E
Bruchhausen	56	51.26 N	8.01 E
Bruchhausen-Vilsen	52	52.50 N	9.00 E
Bruchmühlbach-Miesau	56	49.24 N	7.26 E
Bruchmühle	264a	52.33 N	13.47 E
Br'uchoveckaja	78	45.48 N	38.59 E
Bruchsal	56	49.07 N	8.35 E
Brück, Dtsch.	54	52.12 N	12.46 E
Bruck, Öst.	64	47.17 N	12.49 E
Bruck an der Leitha	61	48.02 N	16.47 E
Bruck an der Mur	61	47.25 N	15.16 E
Bruckhausen ➛[8]	263	51.29 N	6.44 E
Bruck in der Oberpfalz	60	49.15 N	12.18 E
Brückl	61	46.45 N	14.32 E
Bruckmühl	64	47.53 N	11.54 E
Brucoli ➛[8]	70	37.17 N	15.11 E
Brudager	41	55.07 N	10.41 E
Bruderheim	182	53.47 N	112.56 W
Brue ≃	42	51.13 N	3.00 W
Brue-Auriac	62	43.32 N	5.57 E
Brueil-en-Vexin	261	49.02 N	1.49 E
Brüel	54	53.44 N	11.43 E
Bruff	48	52.29 N	8.33 W
Bruges → Brugge	50	51.13 N	3.14 E
Brugg	58	47.29 N	8.12 E
Brugge (Bruges), Bel.	50	51.13 N	3.14 E
Brügge, Dtsch.	263	51.13 N	7.34 E
Brüggen	56	51.14 N	6.11 E
Brugherio	62	45.33 N	9.18 E
Brugnato	62	44.14 N	9.43 E
Brühl	56	50.48 N	6.54 E
Bruin, Ky., U.S.	218	38.11 N	83.01 W
Bruin, Pa., U.S.	214	41.04 N	79.44 W
Bruinisse	52	51.40 N	4.06 E
Bruin Point ʌ	200	39.39 N	110.22 W
Bruit, Pulau I	112	2.35 N	111.20 E
Bruja, Cerro ʌ	236	9.29 N	79.34 W
Brule	198	41.05 N	101.53 W
Brule ≃	190	45.57 N	88.12 W
Brûlé, Lac ⊜, Can.	176	52.17 N	63.52 W
Brûlé, Lac ⊜, P.Q., Can.	190	46.57 N	77.12 W
Brule Lake ⊜	212	45.03 N	77.04 W
Brûly	50	49.58 N	4.31 E
Brumadinho	255	20.08 S	44.13 W
Brumado	255	14.13 S	41.40 W
Brumath	56	48.44 N	7.43 E
Brumby Creek ≃	162	24.09 S	118.39 E
Brummen	52	52.05 N	6.09 E
Brumunddal	26	60.53 N	10.56 E
Bruna ≃	66	42.45 N	10.53 E
Brunate	62	45.49 N	9.06 E
Brunau	54	52.45 N	11.28 E
Brundall	42	52.37 N	1.26 E
Brundby	41	55.49 N	10.37 E
Brundidge	194	31.43 N	85.48 W
Brune ≃	50	49.45 N	3.47 E
Bruneau	202	42.52 N	115.47 W
Bruneau ≃	202	42.57 N	115.58 W
Brunei → Bandar Seri Begawan	112	4.56 N	114.55 E
Brunei □[1], Asia	108	4.30 N	114.40 E
Brunei □[1], Asia	112	4.30 N	114.40 E
Brunei, Teluk ⊂	112	5.05 N	115.18 E
Brünen	52	51.43 N	6.39 E
Brunette Creek ≃	162	18.47 S	135.41 E
Brunette Downs	162	18.38 S	135.57 E
Brunette Island I	186	47.16 N	55.54 W
Brunflo	26	63.05 N	14.49 E
Brungle	171b	35.10 S	148.14 E
Brunico (Bruneck)	64	46.48 N	11.56 E
Brünigpass)(	58	46.46 N	8.09 E
Brüninghausen	263	51.13 N	7.41 E
Brunkeberg	26	59.26 N	8.29 E
Brünn → Brno, Česká Rep.	30	49.12 N	16.37 E
Brünn, Dtsch.	54	50.27 N	10.51 E
Brunn, Dtsch.	54	53.40 N	13.22 E
Brunna	40	59.51 N	17.26 E
Brunn am Gebirge	61	48.07 N	16.17 E
Brunnen, Dtsch.	60	48.38 N	11.18 E
Brunnen, Schw.	58	47.00 N	8.36 E
Brunner, Lake ⊜	172	42.37 S	171.27 E
Brunnerville	208	40.11 N	76.17 W
Brunni	58	47.03 N	8.42 E
Brunnsvik	40	60.12 N	15.08 E
Bruno	184	52.15 N	105.30 W
Brunot Island I	279b	40.28 N	80.03 W
Brunow	264a	52.44 N	13.52 E
Brunoy	50	48.42 N	2.30 E
Brunsbüttel	52	53.54 N	9.07 E
Brunsbüttelkoog	52	53.54 N	9.08 E
Brunson	192	32.55 N	81.11 W
Brunssum	56	50.56 N	5.59 E
Brunswick, Austl.	274b	37.46 S	144.58 E
Brunswick → Braunschweig, Dtsch.	52	52.16 N	10.31 E
Brunswick, Ga., U.S.	192	31.08 N	81.29 W
Brunswick, Me., U.S.	188	43.54 N	69.57 W
Brunswick, Md., U.S.	208	39.18 N	77.37 W
Brunswick, Mo., U.S.	194	39.25 N	93.07 W
Brunswick, Oh., U.S.	214	41.14 N	81.50 W
Brunswick ≃	168a	33.15 S	115.45 E
Brunswick, Península ›[1]	254	53.30 S	71.25 W
Brunswick Junction	168a	33.15 S	115.51 E
Brunswick Lake ⊜	190	49.00 N	83.23 W
Brunswick Naval Air Station ■	188	43.54 N	69.56 W
Brunswick Square ➛[9]	276	40.25 N	74.23 W
Bruntál	30	49.59 N	17.28 E
Bruree	48	52.26 N	8.36 W
Brus, Laguna de ⊂	236	15.50 N	84.35 W
Brus'any	80	53.13 N	49.24 E
Brusasco	62	45.09 N	8.04 E
Bruselas → Bruxelles	50	50.50 N	4.20 E
Brusendorf	264a	52.19 N	13.31 E
Brush	198	40.15 N	103.37 W
Brush Creek ≃, Oh., U.S.	216	41.26 N	84.24 W
Brush Creek ≃, Pa., U.S.	279b	40.23 N	79.46 W
Brush Run ≃, Pa., U.S.	279b	40.18 N	80.07 W
Brush Run ≃, Pa., U.S.	279b	40.16 N	80.10 W
Brush Valley	214	40.32 N	79.04 W
Brushy Creek ≃, Austl.	274b	37.43 S	145.17 E
Brushy Creek ≃, Ok., U.S.	196	34.55 N	95.34 W
Brushy Creek ≃, Tx., U.S.	222	32.59 N	96.12 W
Brushy Creek ≃, Tx., U.S.	222	30.48 N	95.09 W
Brushy Creek ≃, Tx., U.S.	222	31.55 N	95.26 W
Brushy Creek ≃, Tx., U.S.	222	30.43 N	97.03 W
Brushy Creek ≃, Tx., U.S.	222	29.04 N	96.34 W
Brusilov	78	50.17 N	29.32 E
Brusio	58	46.14 N	10.07 E
Brus Laguna	236	15.47 N	84.35 W
Brusovo	76	57.51 N	35.24 E
Brusque	252	27.06 S	48.56 W
Brussel → Bruxelles	50	50.50 N	4.20 E
Brussels → Bruxelles, Bel.	50	50.50 N	4.20 E
Brussels, On., Can.	212	43.44 N	81.15 W
Brussels, Il., U.S.	219	38.57 N	90.36 W
Brusson	62	45.45 N	7.44 E
Brüssow	54	53.24 N	14.07 E
Brusy	30	53.53 N	17.45 E
Brutelles	50	50.08 N	1.31 E
Bruthen	166	37.43 S	147.48 E
Bruton	42	51.07 N	2.27 W
Brüx → Most	54	50.32 N	13.39 E
Bruxelles (Brussels) (Brussel)	56	50.50 N	4.20 E
Bruxelles National, Aéroport ⊠	50	50.54 N	4.30 E
Bruyères	58	48.12 N	6.43 E
Bruyères-le-Châtel	261	48.36 N	2.11 E
Bruzual	246	8.03 N	69.19 W
Bruzzano Zeffirio	68	38.02 N	16.05 E
Brwinów	30	52.09 N	20.43 E
Bryan, Oh., U.S.	216	41.28 N	84.33 W
Bryan, Tx., U.S.	222	30.40 N	96.22 W
Bryan, Mount ʌ	166	33.26 S	138.59 E
Bryan Coast ⏊[2]	9	73.45 S	82.00 W
Bryansk → Br'ansk	76	53.15 N	34.22 E
Bryans Road	208	38.37 N	77.04 W
Bryant, Ar., U.S.	194	34.35 N	92.29 W
Bryant, In., U.S.	216	40.32 N	84.58 W
Bryant, S.D., U.S.	198	44.35 N	97.28 W
Bryant Creek ≃	194	36.36 N	92.17 W
Bryant Mountain ʌ	207	42.28 N	72.58 W
Bryantville	207	42.02 N	70.50 W
Bryas, Lac ⊜	206	46.44 N	73.05 W
Bryce Canyon National Park ♦	200	37.29 N	112.12 W
Bryher I	42a	49.57 N	6.20 W
Brykalansk	24	65.30 N	54.12 E
Brykovka	80	52.32 N	48.35 E
Bryli	76	53.54 N	30.33 E
Brymbo	44	53.06 N	3.04 W
Bryn	262	53.30 N	2.39 W
Brynamman	42	51.49 N	3.52 W
Bryn Athyn	285	40.08 N	75.04 W
Bryn Brawd ʌ[2]	42	52.09 N	3.54 W
Bryncethin	42	51.33 N	3.34 W
Bryne	26	58.44 N	5.39 E
Brynford	262	53.16 N	3.14 W
Bryn Gates	262	53.30 N	2.37 W
Bryn'kovskaja	78	46.02 N	38.35 E
Brynmawr, Wales, U.K.	42	51.49 N	3.11 W
Bryn Mawr, Ca., U.S.	228	34.03 N	117.14 W
Bryn Mawr, Pa., U.S.	208	40.01 N	75.18 W
Bryn Mawr College ♥[2]	285	40.02 N	75.19 W
Bryrup	41	56.01 N	9.31 E
Bryson, P.Q., Can.	188	45.41 N	76.37 W
Bryson, Tx., U.S.	196	33.10 N	98.23 W
Bryson City	192	35.25 N	83.26 W
Bryte	226	38.36 N	121.33 W
Brza Palanka	38	44.28 N	22.27 E
Brzeg	30	50.52 N	17.27 E
Brześć Kujawski	30	52.37 N	18.55 E
Brześć nad Bugiem → Brest	76	52.06 N	23.42 E
Brzesko	30	49.59 N	20.36 E
Brzeszcze	30	49.59 N	19.08 E
Brzeziny	30	51.48 N	19.46 E
Brzozów	30	49.42 N	22.02 E
Bsharrī	130	34.15 N	36.01 E
Bua ≃	154	12.42 S	34.13 E
Bu'aale	144	1.05 N	42.35 E
Buada Lagoon ⊂	174b	0.31 S	166.55 E
Buad Island I	116	11.40 N	124.51 E
Buagan ≃	269e	6.17 S	106.55 E
Buala	175e	8.08 S	159.35 E
Bū al-Ḥīdān, Wādī V	146	27.25 N	19.22 E
Buangor, Mount ʌ	169	37.18 S	143.13 E
Buapinang	112	4.46 S	121.34 E
Buariki	174t	1.36 N	172.58 E
Buatan	114	0.44 N	101.51 E
Bua Yai	110	15.35 N	102.25 E
Buayan ≃	116	6.06 N	125.14 E
Bu'ayrāt al-Ḥasūn	146	31.24 N	15.44 E
Buba	150	11.36 N	14.55 W
Bubai	268	35.40 N	139.29 E
Bū Bānī, Jabal ʌ	140	22.38 N	25.00 E
Bubanza	154	3.06 S	29.23 E
Bubaque	150	11.17 N	15.50 W
Bubendorf	58	47.27 N	7.44 E
Bubia	164	6.40 S	146.55 E
Būbiyān I	128	29.45 N	48.15 E
Bubu ≃	154	6.03 S	35.19 E
Bubu, Gunong ʌ	114	4.42 N	100.47 E
Bubuan Island I, Pil.	116	6.21 N	121.58 E
Bubuan Island I, Pil.	116	6.11 N	120.58 E
Bubuduo	120	30.06 N	84.38 E
Buburu	152	1.26 N	18.03 E
Bubye ≃	154	22.20 S	31.07 E
Buc	261	48.46 N	2.08 E
Bučač	78	49.04 N	25.23 E
Bucak	130	37.28 N	30.36 E
Bucakkışla	130	36.57 N	33.02 E
Bucaramanga	246	7.08 N	73.09 W
Bucarest → București	38	44.26 N	26.06 E
Bucas Grande Island I	116	9.40 N	125.57 E
Buccaneer Archipelago II	160	16.17 S	123.20 E
Buccheri	70	37.08 N	14.51 E
Bucchianico	66	42.18 N	14.11 E
Buccinasco	266b	45.24 N	9.07 E
Buccino	68	40.37 N	15.23 E
Buccurale	144	4.31 N	42.01 E
Bucelas	266c	38.54 N	9.07 W
Bucelas ʌ[2]	266c	38.53 N	9.07 W
Buch ➛[8]	264a	52.38 N	13.30 E
Buchanan, Arg.	258	34.58 S	58.13 W
Buchanan, Sk., Can.	184	51.43 N	102.45 W
Buchanan, Liber.	150	5.57 N	10.02 W
Buchanan, Ga., U.S.	192	33.48 N	85.11 W
Buchanan, Mi., U.S.	216	41.49 N	86.21 W
Buchanan, N.Y., U.S.	210	41.16 N	73.56 W
Buchanan, Va., U.S.	192	37.31 N	79.40 W
Buchanan, Lake ⊜	166	21.28 S	145.52 E
Buchanan, Lake ⊜[1]	196	30.48 N	98.25 W
Buchanan Creek ≃	162	19.11 S	136.16 E
Buchanan Field ⊠	282	37.59 N	122.03 W
Buchanan Hills ⋏[2]	162	18.53 S	131.02 E
Buchan Ness ›	46	57.28 N	1.45 W
Buchans	186	48.49 N	56.52 W
Buchara	128	39.48 N	64.25 E
Buchara □[8]	128	40.00 N	64.00 E
Bucharest → București	38	44.26 N	26.06 E
Buchbach	60	48.19 N	12.17 E
Buchelay	261	48.59 N	1.40 E
Büchen, Dtsch.	52	53.29 N	10.36 E
Buchen, Dtsch.	56	49.32 N	9.17 E
Buchenberg	58	47.42 N	10.14 E
Büchenbeuren	56	49.55 N	7.16 E
Buchenwald-Denkmal ⊥	54	51.01 N	11.15 E
Buchholz, Dtsch.	54	52.10 N	12.55 E
Buchholz, Dtsch.	56	50.41 N	7.23 E
Buchholz, Dtsch.	263	51.23 N	7.15 E
Buchholz, Dtsch.	264a	52.35 N	13.47 E
Buchholz ➛[8], Dtsch.	263	51.23 N	6.46 E
Buchholz ➛[8], Dtsch.	264a	52.36 N	13.26 E
Buchholz in der Nordheide	52	53.20 N	9.52 E
Büchlberg	60	48.40 N	13.30 E
Buchloe	58	48.02 N	10.44 E
Bucholt	263	51.39 N	6.43 E
Buchon, Point ›	226	35.15 N	120.54 W
Buchow-Karpzow	264a	52.31 N	12.57 E
Buchs, Schw.	58	47.23 N	8.04 E
Buchs, Schw.	58	47.10 N	9.28 E
Buchufontein	158	30.18 S	19.36 E
Buchy	50	49.35 N	1.22 E
Bučina	60	48.58 N	13.36 E
Bucine	66	43.29 N	11.37 E
Buck, Lake ⊜	162	19.38 S	130.21 E
Buckatunna	194	31.32 N	88.31 W
Buckatunna Creek ≃	194	31.30 N	88.32 W
Buck Branch ≃	284b	39.01 N	77.10 W
Buck Creek	216	40.29 N	86.46 W
Buck Creek ≃, U.S.	196	34.35 N	99.58 W
Buck Creek ≃, In., U.S.	218	39.37 N	85.56 W
Buck Creek ≃, In., U.S.	218	40.11 N	85.30 W
Buck Creek ≃, Ky., U.S.	192	36.59 N	84.29 W
Buck Creek ≃, Oh., U.S.	218	39.56 N	83.51 W
Buck Creek ≃, Pa., U.S.	285	40.15 N	74.50 W
Buckden, Eng., U.K.	42	52.17 N	0.16 W
Buckden, Eng., U.K.	44	54.12 N	2.05 W
Bückeburg	52	52.16 N	9.02 E
Bücken	52	52.46 N	9.07 E
Buckeye	200	33.22 N	112.34 W
Buckeye Creek ≃	226	38.54 N	121.55 W
Buckeye Lake	188	39.56 N	82.28 W
Buckeystown	208	39.20 N	77.25 W
Buckfastleigh	42	50.29 N	3.46 W
Buckhannon	188	38.59 N	80.13 W
Buckhaven	46	56.11 N	3.03 W
Buck Hill Falls	210	41.11 N	75.15 W
Buck Hollow ≃	224	45.10 N	120.50 W
Buckholts	222	30.52 N	97.08 W
Buckhorn ≃	180	66.13 N	161.10 W
Buckhorn Draw V	196	30.39 N	100.52 W
Buckhorn Island State Park ♦	284a	43.03 N	78.59 W
Buckhorn Lake ⊜, On., Can.	212	44.28 N	78.23 W
Buckhorn Lake ⊜, Ca., U.S.	228	34.50 N	117.59 W
Buckie	46	57.40 N	2.58 W
Buckingham, Austl.	168a	33.24 S	116.19 E
Buckingham, P.Q., Can.	188	45.35 N	75.25 W
Buckingham, Eng., U.K.	42	52.00 N	1.00 W
Buckingham, Pa., U.S.	208	40.18 N	75.01 W
Buckingham, Va., U.S.	192	37.32 N	78.37 W
Buckingham Bay ⊂	164	12.10 S	135.46 E
Buckingham Palace ♥	260	51.30 N	0.08 W
Buckinghamshire □[6]	42	51.45 N	0.48 W
Buck Island I	241n	17.48 N	64.37 W
Buck Island Reef National Monument ♦	241n	17.48 N	64.37 W
Buck Lake ⊜, Ab., Can.	182	53.00 N	114.45 W
Buck Lake ⊜, On., Can.	212	45.25 N	79.24 W
Buckland, Austl.	166	42.37 S	147.43 E
Buckland, Eng., U.K.	260	51.15 N	0.15 W
Buckland, Ak., U.S.	180	65.59 N	161.07 W
Buckland, Ma., U.S.	207	42.35 N	72.47 W
Buckland, Oh., U.S.	216	40.37 N	84.16 W
Buckland Brewer	42	50.57 N	4.14 W
Buckland Common	260	51.45 N	0.39 W
Bucklands	158	29.03 S	23.44 E
Buckleboo	166	32.55 S	136.12 E
Buckley, Wales, U.K.	44	53.09 N	3.04 W
Buckley, Il., U.S.	216	40.36 N	88.02 W
Buckley, Wa., U.S.	224	47.09 N	122.01 W
Buckley ≃	166	20.22 S	137.57 E
Buckley Bay ⊂	9	68.16 S	148.12 E
Bucklin, Ks., U.S.	198	37.32 N	99.38 W
Bucklin, Mo., U.S.	194	39.46 N	92.53 W
Buck Lodge	284c	39.01 N	76.58 W
Buck Mountain ʌ, Va., U.S.	192	36.40 N	81.15 W
Buck Mountain ʌ, Wa., U.S.	202	48.26 N	119.50 W
Bucknell Heights	284c	38.46 N	77.04 W
Bucknell Manor	208	38.46 N	77.04 W
Buckner	218	38.23 N	85.26 W
Buckner Creek ≃	198	38.11 N	99.34 W
Buckners Creek ≃	222	29.53 N	96.53 W
Buckow	54	52.34 N	14.04 E
Buckow ➛[8]	264a	52.25 N	13.26 E
Bucks □[6]	208	40.19 N	75.08 W
Bucksburn	46	57.12 N	2.18 W
Buckshot Lake ⊜	212	45.00 N	77.04 W
Buckskin Creek ≃	218	39.14 N	83.17 W
Buckskin Gulch V	200	37.01 N	111.52 W
Bucks Knob ʌ	224	46.41 N	123.20 W
Bucksport	188	44.34 N	68.47 W
Bucktown	285	40.10 N	75.43 W
Bückwitz	54	52.52 N	12.29 E
Buc-Louis-Blériot, Aérodrome de ⊠	261	48.45 N	2.05 E
Bučmany	78	51.04 N	28.04 E
Bucoda	224	46.47 N	122.52 W
Buco Zau	152	4.46 S	12.33 E
Bucquoy	50	50.08 N	2.42 E
Buctouche	186	46.28 N	64.43 W
Bucun	98	36.37 N	117.27 E
București (Bucharest)	38	44.26 N	26.06 E
Bucutua Island I	116	6.09 N	121.49 E
Bucy-lès-Pierrepont	50	49.39 N	3.54 E
Bucyrus	214	40.48 N	82.58 W
Bud	26	62.55 N	6.55 E
Buda, Il., U.S.	190	41.19 N	89.40 W
Buda, Tx., U.S.	196	30.05 N	97.51 W
Buda ➛[8]	264c	47.30 N	19.02 E
Buda Castle ⊥	264c	47.30 N	19.02 E
Budafok ➛[8]	264c	47.26 N	19.02 E
Budagovo	88	54.38 N	100.08 E
Budai-hegység ⋏	264c	47.31 N	18.58 E
Budakalász	264c	47.37 N	19.03 E
Budakeszi	264c	47.31 N	18.56 E
Buda-Kosel'ovo	76	52.43 N	30.34 E
Budalin	110	22.22 N	95.08 E
Budaörs	264c	47.27 N	18.58 E
Budapest, Magy.	30	47.30 N	19.05 E
Budapest, Magy.	264c	47.30 N	19.05 E
Budapest □[7]	264c	47.30 N	19.05 E
Búđardalur	24a	65.10 N	21.42 W
Budarin	80	47.54 N	42.36 E
Budarino	80	50.31 N	51.04 E
Budatétény ➛[8]	264c	47.25 N	19.01 E
Budaun	124	28.03 N	79.07 E
Budawang National Park ♦	170	35.26 S	150.02 E
Budawang Range ⋏	170	35.20 S	150.03 E
Budayuan	98	40.56 N	125.19 E
Budberg	263	51.32 N	6.38 E
Budbud	144	4.11 N	46.28 E
Budd Coast ⏊[2]	9	66.30 S	113.00 E
Buddh Gaya → Bodh Gaya	124	24.42 N	84.59 E
Budd Inlet ⊂	224	47.06 N	122.54 W
Budd Lake	210	40.52 N	74.44 W
Buddtown	285	39.56 N	74.42 W
Buddu	140	11.54 N	24.08 E
Buddusò	71	40.35 N	9.15 E
Bude, Eng., U.K.	42	50.50 N	4.33 W
Bude, Ms., U.S.	194	31.27 N	90.51 W
Bude Bay ⊂	42	50.50 N	4.37 W
Budel	52	51.17 N	5.35 E
Budelli, Isola I	71	41.17 N	9.21 E
Büdelsdorf	41	54.18 N	9.40 E
Büderich	52	51.37 N	6.34 E
Budești	38	44.14 N	26.28 E
Budge Budge	126	22.27 N	88.10 E
Budhāthum	124	28.04 N	84.50 E
Budhhāta	126	22.36 N	89.10 E
Budhī Gaṇḍakī ≃	124	27.48 N	84.45 E
Budhlāda	123	29.56 N	75.34 E
Budi	152	3.04 S	23.56 E
Büdingen	56	50.17 N	9.07 E
Búđir	24a	64.56 N	13.58 W
Budišov nad Budišovkou	30	49.47 N	17.38 E
Budjala	152	2.39 N	19.42 E
Budkov	61	49.03 N	15.39 E
Budleigh Salterton	42	50.38 N	3.20 W
Budogošč'	76	59.17 N	32.27 E
Budogovišči	76	53.36 N	36.18 E
Budoni	71	40.43 N	9.42 E
Bud'onnovka	80	50.52 N	52.48 E
Bud'onnovsk	84	44.46 N	44.09 E
Bud'onnovskaja	80	46.56 N	41.33 E
Bud'onnyj, Kyrg.	85	42.30 N	72.35 E
Bud'onnyj, Ross.	83	47.27 N	39.46 E
Budrio	64	44.32 N	11.32 E
Budslav	76	54.47 N	27.27 E
Budweis → České Budějovice	30	48.59 N	14.28 E
Budworth Mere ⊜	262	53.17 N	2.31 W
Budy	78	49.53 N	36.02 E
Budylka	78	50.30 N	34.26 E
Budyně nad Ohří	54	50.22 N	14.09 E
Budžak ⋏[1]	78	46.10 N	29.00 E
Buea	152	4.09 N	9.14 E
Buëch ≃	62	44.12 N	5.57 E
Buechel	218	38.11 N	85.39 W
Buehl Airport ⊠	285	40.11 N	74.54 W
Bueil	50	48.56 N	1.27 E
Buela	152	5.55 S	14.33 E
Buell	219	39.02 N	91.27 W
Bue Marino, Grotta del ⏊[5]	71	40.15 N	9.38 E
Buena	208	39.30 N	74.55 W
Buena Esperanza	252	34.45 S	65.15 W
Buena Esperanza, Cabo de → Good Hope, Cape of ›	158	34.24 S	18.30 E
Buena Park, Ca., U.S.	228	33.52 N	117.59 W
Buena Park, Wi., U.S.	216	42.48 N	88.14 W
Buenaventura, Col.	246	3.53 N	77.04 W
Buenaventura, Méx.	232	29.51 N	107.29 W
Buena Vista, Bol.	248	17.27 S	63.40 W
Buena Vista, Méx.	204	32.32 N	116.44 W
Buenavista, Méx.	234	22.36 N	100.09 W
Buena Vista, Para.	252	26.08 S	56.03 W
Buenavista, Pil.	116	8.59 N	125.24 E
Buenavista, Pil.	116	13.15 N	121.57 E
Buenavista, Pil.	116	10.04 N	118.49 E
Buenavista, Pil.	116	7.15 N	122.16 E
Buena Vista, Co., U.S.	200	38.50 N	106.07 W
Buena Vista, Fl., U.S.	220	28.11 N	82.44 W
Buena Vista, Ga., U.S.	192	32.19 N	84.31 W
Buena Vista, Md., U.S.	284c	38.57 N	76.50 W
Buena Vista, Ms., U.S.	194	33.53 N	88.50 W
Buena Vista, Pa., U.S.	279b	40.17 N	79.48 W
Buena Vista, Va., U.S.	192	37.44 N	79.21 W
Buena Vista, Bahía de ⊂	240p	22.30 N	79.08 W
Buena Vista Canal ≖	228	35.21 N	119.06 W
Buenavista de Cuéllar	234	18.27 N	99.25 W
Buena Vista Lake Bed ⊜	204	35.11 N	119.17 W
Buenavista Tomatlán	234	19.12 N	102.36 W
Buen Día	196	26.21 N	104.32 W
Buendia, Embalse de ⊜[1]	34	40.25 N	2.43 W
Buenga ≃	152	6.07 S	15.58 E
Bueno ≃	254	40.13 S	73.43 W
Bueno Brandão	256	22.27 S	46.21 W
Buenópolis	255	17.54 S	44.11 W
Buenos Aires, Arg.	258	34.36 S	58.27 W
Buenos Aires, Arg.	288	34.36 S	58.27 W
Buenos Aires, Col.	246	3.02 N	76.38 W
Buenos Aires, C.R.	236	9.10 N	83.20 W
Buenos Aires □[4]	252	36.00 S	60.00 W
Buenos Aires, Lago (Lago General Carrera) ⊜	254	46.35 S	72.00 W
Buen Pasto	254	45.05 S	69.28 W
Buer ➛[8]	263	51.36 N	7.03 E
Buerarema	255	14.57 S	39.19 W
Buerāt, Bi'r ⫪[4]	142	28.59 N	32.10 E
Buertuokai	85	39.35 N	74.58 E
Buesaco	246	1.23 N	77.09 W
Buescher State Park ♦	222	30.02 N	97.09 W
Buet, Le ʌ	58	46.02 N	6.52 E
Buey ≃	240p	20.28 N	77.05 W
Bufalotta, Fosso della ≃	267a	41.59 N	12.30 E
Buffalo, Il., U.S.	219	39.51 N	89.25 W
Buffalo, In., U.S.	216	40.53 N	86.45 W
Buffalo, Ks., U.S.	198	37.42 N	95.41 W
Buffalo, Mn., U.S.	190	45.10 N	93.52 W
Buffalo, Mo., U.S.	194	37.38 N	93.05 W
Buffalo, N.Y., U.S.	210	42.53 N	78.52 W
Buffalo, N.Y., U.S.	284a	42.53 N	78.52 W
Buffalo, Oh., U.S.	188	39.54 N	81.31 W
Buffalo, Ok., U.S.	196	36.50 N	99.37 W
Buffalo, S.C., U.S.	192	34.43 N	81.41 W
Buffalo, S.D., U.S.	198	45.35 N	103.32 W
Buffalo, Tx., U.S.	222	31.28 N	96.04 W
Buffalo, Wy., U.S.	202	44.20 N	106.41 W
Buffalo ≃, Can.	176	60.55 N	115.00 W
Buffalo ≃, S. Afr.	158	28.43 S	30.37 E
Buffalo ≃, Ar., U.S.	194	36.10 N	92.26 W
Buffalo ≃, Mn., U.S.	198	47.06 N	96.49 W
Buffalo ≃, Ms., U.S.	194	31.04 N	91.34 W
Buffalo ≃, N.Y., U.S.	284a	42.53 N	78.53 W
Buffalo ≃, Tn., U.S.	194	36.00 N	87.50 W
Buffalo ≃, Wi., U.S.	190	44.22 N	91.55 W
Buffalo, State University College at ♥[2]	284a	42.56 N	78.53 W
Buffalo Airpark ⊠	284a	42.52 N	78.43 W
Buffalo Bayou ≃	222	29.46 N	95.05 W
Buffalo Bill Ranch State Historical Park ♦	198	41.10 N	100.48 W
Buffalo Bill Reservoir ⊜[1]	202	44.29 N	109.13 W
Buffalo Bill State Park ♦	202	44.30 N	109.14 W
Buffalo Center	190	43.23 N	93.56 W
Buffalo Coast Guard Base ■	284a	42.52 N	78.54 W
Buffalo Creek ≃, U.S.	198	45.57 N	102.56 W
Buffalo Creek ≃, U.S.	214	40.16 N	80.37 W
Buffalo Creek ≃, Il., U.S.	278	42.08 N	87.55 W
Buffalo Creek ≃, Ia., U.S.	190	42.06 N	91.18 W
Buffalo Creek ≃, Ks., U.S.	198	39.35 N	97.43 W
Buffalo Creek ≃, Ky., U.S.	218	38.28 N	83.03 W
Buffalo Creek ≃, Mn., U.S.	198	44.51 N	94.00 W
Buffalo Creek ≃, N.Y., U.S.	210	42.52 N	78.47 W
Buffalo Creek ≃, Ok., U.S.	196	36.47 N	99.15 W
Buffalo Creek ≃, Pa., U.S.	208	40.29 N	77.08 W
Buffalo Creek ≃, Pa., U.S.	210	40.58 N	76.53 W
Buffalo Creek ≃, Pa., U.S.	214	40.40 N	79.41 W
Buffalo Grove	216	42.09 N	87.57 W
Buffalo Harbor ⊂	284a	42.51 N	78.52 W
Buffalo Lake	198	44.44 N	94.37 W
Buffalo Lake ⊜, Ab., Can.	182	52.27 N	112.54 W
Buffalo Lake ⊜, N.T., Can.	176	60.10 N	115.30 W
Buffalo Lake ⊜[1]	196	34.54 N	102.07 W
Buffalo Museum of Science ♥	284a	42.54 N	78.51 W
Buffalo Narrows	184	55.51 N	108.30 W
Buffalo National River ♦	194	35.58 N	92.53 W
Buffalo Pound Lake ⊜	184	50.39 N	105.30 W
Buffalo Pound Provincial Park ♦	184	50.36 N	105.30 W
Buffalo Run ≃	279b	40.12 N	79.37 W
Buffalo Zoo ♦	284a	42.56 N	78.51 W
Buffels ≃, S. Afr.	156	29.41 S	17.03 E
Buffels ≃, S. Afr.	158	33.45 S	21.11 E
Buffington Harbor ⊂	278	41.38 N	87.25 W
Buffum, Lake ⊜	220	27.48 N	81.40 W
Buford, Ga., U.S.	192	34.07 N	84.00 W
Buford, Oh., U.S.	218	39.04 N	83.50 W
Buford Dam ➛[6]	192	34.11 N	84.03 W
Buftea	38	44.34 N	25.57 E
Bug ≃	22	52.31 N	21.05 E
Buga, Col.	246	3.54 N	76.17 W
Buga, Nig.	150	8.30 N	7.21 E
Bugajevka, Ross.	83	49.39 N	39.42 E
Bugajevka, Ukr.	83	49.28 N	37.23 E
Bugajevka, Ukr.	83	48.25 N	38.53 E
Bugalagrande	246	4.11 N	76.09 W
Bugala Island I	154	0.40 S	32.20 E
Bugallon	116	15.57 N	120.13 E
Buganga	154	0.03 S	31.59 E
Bugasong	116	11.03 N	122.04 E
Bugat, Mong.	86	48.59 N	90.10 E
Bugat, Mong.	88	47.55 N	101.16 E
Bugbrooke	42	52.12 N	1.01 W
Bug Catooti	144	10.44 N	50.35 E
Buğdaylı	130	40.13 N	27.46 E
Bugeat	32	45.35 N	1.59 E
Bugel, Ujung ›	115a	6.26 S	111.03 E
Bugene	154	1.35 S	31.08 E
Bugey ➛[1]	58	45.55 N	5.30 E
Buggenhout	50	51.01 N	4.12 E
Buggerru	71	39.24 N	8.24 E
Bugio I	266c	38.39 N	9.18 W
Bugiri	154	0.34 N	33.45 E
Bugle	42	50.24 N	4.47 W
Bug Méridional → Južnyj Bug ≃	78	46.59 N	31.58 E
Bugojno	36	44.03 N	17.27 E
Bugøynes	24	69.58 N	29.39 E
Bugrino	24	68.48 N	49.09 E
Bugry, Ross.	76	58.46 N	35.15 E
Bugry, Ross.	265a	60.04 N	30.24 E
Bugsanga ≃	116	12.26 N	120.59 E
Bugsuk Island I	116	8.15 N	117.18 E
Bugt, Zhg.	89	48.46 N	121.57 E
Bugt, Zhg.	98	42.20 N	120.43 E
Buguba	164	3.41 S	137.30 E
Buguey	116	18.17 N	121.50 E
Bugui Point ›	116	12.36 N	123.14 E
Bugul'dejka	88	52.33 N	106.05 E
Bugul'ma	80	54.33 N	52.48 E
Bugul'minsko-Belebejevskaja vozvyšennost' ⋏[1]	80	54.54 N	52.42 E
Bugun' ≃	85	42.58 N	68.35 E
Bugun'skoje vodochranilišče ⊜[1]	85	42.45 N	69.05 E
Buguruslan	80	53.39 N	52.26 E
Buh ≃	102	36.58 N	99.48 E
Buhanhua	104	42.39 N	122.46 E
Bū Ḥashīshah, Thamad ⫪[4]	146	26.23 N	18.47 E
Buḥayrah, Rayyāḥ al- ≖	142	30.43 N	30.45 E
Buḥaythān, Jabal al- ʌ	132	30.55 N	35.53 E
Buhera	154	19.18 S	31.29 E
Buhi	116	13.26 N	123.31 E
Buhi, Lake ⊜	116	13.26 N	123.31 E
Bühl, Dtsch.	56	48.42 N	8.08 E
Buhl, Fr.	58	47.56 N	7.11 E
Buhl, Id., U.S.	202	42.35 N	114.45 W
Buhl, Mn., U.S.	190	47.29 N	92.46 W
Buhler	198	38.08 N	97.46 W
Bühler ≃	56	49.10 N	9.47 E
Bühlertal	56	48.41 N	8.10 E
Buhuai	120	33.22 N	80.36 E
Buhuși	38	46.43 N	26.41 E
Bui Dam ➛[6]	150	8.22 N	2.10 W
Buie, Loch ⊂	46	56.20 N	5.52 W
Buile Hill Park ♦	262	53.29 N	2.18 W
Builth Wells	42	52.09 N	3.24 W
Buin, Chile	252	33.44 S	70.45 W
Buin, Pap. N. Gui.	175e	6.50 S	155.44 E
Buin, Piz ʌ	58	46.50 N	10.08 E
Buinen	52	52.55 N	6.50 E
Buinsk, Ross.	80	55.12 N	47.03 E
Buinsk, Ross.	80	54.57 N	48.17 E
Buíque	250	8.37 S	37.09 W
Buis-les-Baronnies	62	44.16 N	5.16 E
Buitenpost	52	53.15 N	6.09 E
Buj	80	58.30 N	41.30 E
Buj ≃	80	56.13 N	54.12 E
Bujaki	24	59.03 N	48.40 E
Bujalance	34	37.54 N	4.22 W
Bujant, Mong.	86	48.33 N	89.34 E
Bujant, Mong.	86	48.10 N	91.55 E
Bujant ≃	88	47.08 N	97.38 E
Bujant-Ovoo	102	44.58 N	107.05 E
Bujaraloz	34	41.30 N	0.09 W
Buje	36	45.24 N	13.40 E
Buji	102	33.58 N	95.22 E
Bujnaksk	84	42.49 N	47.07 E
Bujnoviči	78	51.52 N	28.33 E
Bujr nuur ⊜	88	47.48 N	117.42 E
Bujukly	89	49.30 N	142.47 E
Bujumbura	154	3.23 S	29.22 E
Bük, Magy.	61	47.23 N	16.45 E
Buk, Pol.	30	52.22 N	16.31 E
Buka	85	40.48 N	69.11 E
Bukačača	88	52.59 N	116.55 E
Bukačevcy	78	49.15 N	24.29 E
Buka Island I	175e	5.15 S	154.35 E
Bukama	154	9.12 S	25.51 E
Būkān, Īrān	128	36.31 N	46.12 E
Bukan', Ross.	76	53.55 N	34.42 E
Bukanovskaja	80	49.42 N	42.18 E
Buka Passage ⩌	175e	5.25 S	154.41 E
Bukarest → București	38	44.26 N	26.06 E
Bukarevo	82	55.57 N	36.44 E
Bukavu	154	2.30 S	28.52 E
Bukene	154	4.14 S	32.53 E
Bukhara → Buchara	128	39.48 N	64.25 E
Bukhayt, Bi'r ⫪[4]	142	29.13 N	32.17 E
Bukide, Pulau I	112	3.47 N	125.36 E
Bukidnon □[4]	116	8.00 N	125.00 E
Bukima	154	1.48 S	33.25 E
Bukit Baharu	114	2.13 N	102.16 E
Bukitbatu	114	1.27 N	102.00 E
Bukit Betong	114	4.15 N	101.56 E
Bukit Fraser	114	3.43 N	101.45 E
Bukit Kachi	114	6.24 N	100.32 E
Bukit Mandai	271c	1.25 N	103.45 E
Bukit Mertajam	114	5.22 N	100.28 E
Bukit Panjang	271c	1.23 N	103.46 E
Bukit Serok	114	2.55 N	102.50 E
Bukit Timah	271c	1.20 N	103.47 E
Bukit Timah Race Course ♦	271c	1.20 N	103.48 E
Bukittinggi	112	0.19 S	100.22 E
Bükk ⋏	30	48.05 N	20.30 E
Bukoba	154	1.20 S	31.49 E
Bukombe	154	3.31 S	32.03 E
Bukovica ➛[1]	36	44.10 N	15.40 E
Bukovina □[9]	78	48.00 N	25.30 E
Bukrino	82	54.48 N	36.14 E
Bukuka	88	51.11 N	116.39 E
Bukukun	88	49.27 N	111.08 E
Bukum, Pulau I	271c	1.14 N	103.47 E
Bukumbirwa	154	0.46 S	28.44 E
Bukum Kechil, Pulau I	271c	1.14 N	103.46 E
Bukunga	154	7.41 S	25.56 E
Bukuru	150	9.48 N	8.51 E
Bukuya	154	0.41 N	31.50 E
Bula	164	3.06 S	130.30 E
Bula ≃	80	55.12 N	48.23 E
Bula Atumba	152	8.40 S	14.48 E
Bulacan □[4]	116	15.00 N	121.05 E
Bulacaue Point ›	116	11.36 N	123.09 E
Bülach	58	47.31 N	8.32 E
Bulajevo	86	54.54 N	70.26 E
Bulak	88	51.02 N	115.21 E
Bulaka ≃	164	8.06 S	139.12 E
Bulak Gölü ⊜	130	38.32 N	32.55 E
Bulalacao	116	12.20 N	121.20 E
Bulalacao Island I	116	11.45 N	120.10 E
Bulalaqui Point ›	116	11.17 N	124.03 E
Bulan, Pil.	116	12.40 N	123.52 E
Bulan, Pil.	116	6.44 N	124.47 E
Bulan, Ky., U.S.	192	37.18 N	83.09 W
Bulanaš	86	57.16 N	62.00 E
Bulancak	130	40.57 N	38.14 E
Bulandshahr	124	28.24 N	77.51 E
Bulanicha	86	52.48 N	84.57 E
Bulanık	130	39.05 N	42.15 E
Bulan Island I	116	6.08 N	121.50 E
Bulanovo	86	52.27 N	55.10 E
Būlāq	140	25.12 N	30.32 E
Būlāq ➛[8]	273c	30.04 N	31.14 E
Būlāq ad-Dakrūr	273c	30.02 N	31.11 E
Bulava	89	51.55 N	140.25 E
Bulavinovka	83	49.25 N	38.58 E
Bulawa, Gunung ʌ	112	0.30 N	123.34 E
Bulawayo	154	20.09 S	28.36 E
Bulbjerg ʌ[2]	26	57.09 N	9.02 E
Bulbul	130	36.46 N	36.49 E
Bulbul, Wādī V	140	10.59 N	24.33 E
Bulcherry Island I	126	21.33 N	88.31 E
Buldan	130	38.03 N	28.51 E
Buldāna	122	20.32 N	76.11 E
Buldern	52	51.52 N	7.22 E
Buldibuyo	248	8.07 S	77.22 W
Buldir Island I	181a	52.21 N	175.54 E
Buldon	116	7.33 N	124.25 E
Buldurtinskij	80	50.05 N	53.11 E
Buldyrty ≃	80	49.48 N	52.34 E
Bulembu	158	25.56 S	31.06 E
Bulga	170	32.39 S	151.01 E
Bulgakovka	83	49.11 N	38.33 E
Bulgakovo	76	55.14 N	32.08 E
Bulgan, Mong.	86	46.53 N	91.05 E
Bulgan, Mong.	88	48.45 N	103.34 E
Bulgan, Mong.	102	44.05 N	103.32 E
Bulgan □[4]	88	49.00 N	103.30 E
Bulgar	80	54.57 N	49.05 E
Bulgaria (Bâlgarija) □[1], Europe	22	43.00 N	25.00 E
Bulgaria (Bâlgarija) □[1], Europe	38	43.00 N	25.00 E
Bulgarie → Bulgaria □[1]	38	43.00 N	25.00 E
Bulgarien → Bulgaria □[1]	38	43.00 N	25.00 E
Bulger	214	40.23 N	80.20 W
Bulgnéville	58	48.13 N	5.50 E
Bulgroo	166	25.48 S	143.59 E
Bulhale	144	5.20 N	46.29 E
Buliluyan	116	8.20 N	117.12 E
Buliluyan, Cape ›	116	8.20 N	117.11 E
Bulim	271c	1.22 N	103.43 E
Bulimba	171a	27.25 S	153.04 E
Bulki	144	6.10 N	36.40 E
Bulkington	42	52.29 N	1.25 W
Bulkley ≃	182	55.13 N	127.40 W
Bulkley Ranges ⋏	182	54.30 N	127.30 W
Bull ≃	182	49.28 N	115.26 W
Bullabulling	162	31.01 S	120.32 E
Bullaque ≃	34	38.59 N	4.17 W
Bullara	162	22.40 S	114.03 E
Bullard	222	32.08 N	95.19 W
Bulla Regia ⊥	36	36.34 N	8.46 E
Bullas	34	38.03 N	1.40 W
Bullaxaar	144	10.23 N	44.25 E
Bullay	56	50.03 N	7.08 E
Bull Creek ≃, Nv., U.S.	204	38.43 N	115.34 W
Bull Creek ≃, N.Y., U.S.	284a	43.03 N	78.50 W
Bull Creek ≃, Oh., U.S.	214	40.42 N	80.32 W
Bull Creek ≃, S.D., U.S.	198	43.41 N	99.28 W
Bull Creek ≃, S.D., U.S.	198	45.40 N	103.18 W
Bull Creek ≃, Tx., U.S.	196	32.36 N	101.10 W
Bulldog	164	7.45 S	146.25 E
Bulle	58	46.37 N	7.04 E
Buller ≃	172	41.44 S	171.35 E
Buller, Mount ʌ	169	37.09 S	146.26 E
Bullfinch	162	30.59 S	119.06 E
Bullfrog Creek ≃	200	37.19 N	110.44 W
Bull Harbour	182	50.54 N	127.55 W
Bullhead	198	45.45 N	101.04 W
Bullhead City	204	35.08 N	114.34 W
Bull Hide Creek ≃	222	31.23 N	97.01 W
Bull Hill ʌ[2]	262	53.40 N	2.21 W
Bulli	170	34.20 S	150.55 E
Bullicame ⊥	66	42.22 N	12.04 E
Büllingen	56	50.25 N	6.16 E
Bullioh	171b	36.12 S	147.20 E
Bullion	261	48.37 N	2.00 E
Bull Lake ⊜[1]	202	43.11 N	109.07 W
Bull Lake Creek ≃	202	43.14 N	109.02 W
Bull Mountain ʌ	202	46.05 N	112.04 W
Bullock	192	36.30 N	78.33 W
Bullock Creek	166	17.43 S	144.31 E
Bullock Creek ≃	166	21.40 S	145.09 E
Bulloo ≃	166	28.43 S	142.30 E
Bulloo Downs	166	28.31 S	142.57 E
Bulloo Lake ⊜	166	28.43 S	142.25 E
Bulloo River Overflow ≚	166	28.50 S	142.40 E
Bullpound Creek ≃	182	51.05 N	111.58 W
Bull Run ≃, Or., U.S.	224	45.26 N	122.15 W
Bull Run ≃, Va., U.S.	208	38.43 N	77.23 W
Bull Run Lake ⊜	224	45.27 N	121.50 W
Bull Run Reservoir Number 2 ⊜[1], Or., U.S.	224	45.28 N	122.10 W

ENGLISH: Name, Page, Lat. °′, Long. °′ — DEUTSCH: Name, Seite, Breite °′, Länge °′ E = Ost

Symbols in the index entries represent the broad categories identified in the key at the right. Symbols with superior numbers (⋏[1]) identify subcategories (see complete key on page *I · 1*).

Symbole im Register stellen die rechts im Schlüssel erklärten Kategorien dar. Symbole mit hochgestellten Ziffern (⋏[1]) bezeichnen Unterabteilungen einer Kategorie (vgl. vollständiger Schlüssel auf Seite *I · 1*).

Los símbolos incluídos en el texto del índice representan las grandes categorías identificadas con la clave a la derecha. Los símbolos con numeros en su parte superior (⋏[1]) identifican las subcategorías (véase la clave completa en la página *I · 1*).

Les symboles de l'index représentent les catégories indiquées dans la légende à droite. Les symboles suivis d'un indice (⋏[1]) représentent des sous-catégories (voir légende complète à la page *I · 1*).

Os símbolos incluídos no texto do índice representam as grandes categorias identificadas com a chave à direita. Os símbolos com números em sua parte superior (⋏[1]) identificam as subcategorias (veja-se a chave completa à página *I · 1*).

Symbol	English	Deutsch	Español	Français	Português
ʌ	Mountain	Berg	Montaña	Montagne	Montanha
⋏	Mountains	Gebirge	Montañas	Montagnes	Montanhas
)(	Pass	Paß	Paso	Col	Passo
V	Valley, Canyon	Tal, Cañon	Valle, Cañón	Vallée, Canyon	Vale, Canhão
≚	Plain	Ebene	Llano	Plaine	Planície
›	Cape	Kap	Cabo	Cap	Cabo
I	Island	Insel	Isla	Île	Ilha
II	Islands	Inseln	Islas	Îles	Ilhas
⏊	Other Topographic Features	Andere Topographische Objekte	Otros Elementos Topográficos	Autres données topographiques	Outros acidentes topográficos

ESPAÑOL Nombre	Página	Lat.°′	Long.°′ W = Oeste
Bull Run Reservoir Number 1⊜[1], Or., U.S.	224	45.30 N	122.04 W
Bullrun Rock ʌ	202	44.21 N	118.17 W
Bulls	172	40.10 S	175.23 E
Bulls Bay ɕ	192	32.59 N	79.33 W
Bullsbrook	168a	31.40 S	116.01 E
Bulls Gap	192	36.15 N	83.05 W
Bull Shoals	194	36.23 N	92.34 W
Bull Shoals Lake ⊜[1]	194	36.30 N	92.50 W
Bullskin Creek ≃	218	38.10 N	85.19 W
Bullville	210	41.33 N	74.22 W
Bully Creek ≃	202	43.58 N	117.15 W
Bully Hill	214	41.22 N	79.50 W
Bully-les-Mines	50	50.26 N	2.43 E
Bulmke-Hüllen ✦[8]	263	51.31 N	7.06 E
Bulnaj nuruu ✗	88	49.05 N	93.30 E
Bulnes	252	36.44 S	72.18 W
Bulo Ghedudo	144	2.52 N	43.01 E
Bulolo	164	7.10 S	146.40 E
Bulpham	260	51.33 N	0.22 E
Bulpitt	219	39.35 N	89.26 W
Bulsār	122	20.38 N	72.56 E
Bulstrode ≃	206	46.02 N	72.15 W
Bultei	71	40.27 N	9.03 E
Bultfontein	158	28.20 S	26.05 E
Buluan	116	6.44 N	124.47 E
Buluan ≃	116	6.47 N	124.47 E
Buluan, Lake ⊜	116	6.40 N	124.49 E
Bulududu	114	2.20 N	98.14 E
Bulugansk	83	52.24 N	110.23 E
Bulukumba	112	5.33 S	120.11 E
Bulukuto	152	0.12 S	21.42 E
Bululawang	115a	8.05 S	112.38 E
Bulungu, Zaïre	152	6.04 S	21.54 E
Bulungu, Zaïre	152	4.33 S	18.36 E
Bulupayung	114	1.38 N	99.11 E
Bulusan	116	12.45 N	124.08 E
Bulusan Volcano ʌ	116	12.46 N	124.03 E
Bulwater	158	32.29 S	21.48 E
Bulwer	158	29.46 S	29.47 E
Bulyčevo	82	55.06 N	37.15 E
Bulyee	162	32.22 S	117.31 E
Bumba	152	2.11 N	22.28 E
Bumban, Khalīj al- ɕ	146	32.20 N	23.10 E
Bumbire Island I	154	1.40 S	31.53 E
Bumbles Green	260	51.44 N	0.02 E
Bumbo	152	6.55 S	19.16 E
Bumbu ≃	273b	4.23 S	15.18 E
Bumbulan	112	0.29 N	122.04 E
Bumbun, Pulau I	112	4.27 N	118.40 E
Bumbuna	150	9.03 N	11.44 W
Bumbunga Lake ⊜	168b	33.54 S	138.11 E
Bumiayu	115a	7.15 S	109.00 E
Bumijawa	115a	7.10 S	109.07 E
Bumkin Island I	283	42.17 N	70.54 W
Bumping ≃	224	46.59 N	121.06 W
Bumping Lake ⊜	224	46.52 N	121.19 W
Bumpus, Mount ʌ[2]	176	69.33 N	112.40 W
Bumtang ≃	124	26.56 N	90.51 E
Bumu Hu ⊜	120	31.15 N	91.10 E
Buna, Kenya	154	2.47 N	39.31 E
Buna, Pap. N. Gui.	164	8.40 S	148.25 E
Buna, Tx., U.S.	194	30.26 N	93.58 W
Buna, Zaïre	152	3.15 S	18.59 E
Bunagāti	126	23.19 N	89.25 E
Bunai	164	2.11 S	147.14 E
Bunaj	85	38.26 N	71.32 E
Bun'atino	82	56.24 N	37.15 E
Bunavista	196	35.39 N	101.28 W
Bunawan	116	8.12 N	125.57 E
Bunazi	154	1.13 S	31.24 E
Bunbeg	48	55.03 N	8.18 W
Bunbury	168a	33.19 S	115.38 E
Bunceton	194	38.47 N	92.47 W
Bunclody	48	52.38 N	6.40 W
Buncrana	48	55.08 N	7.27 W
Bundaberg	166	24.52 S	152.21 E
Bundanoon	170	34.39 S	150.18 E
Bundarra	166	30.10 S	151.05 E
Bunde, Dtsch.	52	53.11 N	7.16 E
Bünde, Dtsch.	52	52.12 N	8.35 E
Bunde, Ned.	56	50.54 N	5.45 E
Bundeena	274a	34.05 S	151.09 E
Bundenthal	56	49.06 N	7.48 E
Bundey ≃	162	21.46 S	135.37 E
Bündheim	54	51.53 N	10.32 E
Būndi, India	120	25.27 N	75.39 E
Bundi, Pap. N. Gui.	164	5.40 S	145.15 E
Bundick Creek ≃	194	30.36 N	92.57 W
Bundoora	274b	37.42 S	145.04 E
Bundoran	48	54.28 N	8.17 W
Būndu, India	124	23.11 N	85.35 E
Bundu, S. Afr.	158	29.45 S	22.02 E
Bunduqiyah	154	5.06 N	30.53 E
Bund'ur	86	57.32 N	82.01 E
Buner ▫[9]	123	34.35 N	72.35 E
Bunessan	46	56.19 N	6.14 W
Bunga	150	11.04 N	9.38 E
Bunga ≃	150	11.23 N	9.56 E
Bungamas	112	3.42 S	102.23 E
Bungay	42	52.28 N	1.26 E
Bungbulang	115a	7.27 S	107.35 E
Bunge	26	57.51 N	19.01 E
Bungegep	164	7.48 S	139.52 E
Bungendore	171b	35.15 S	149.27 E
Bunger Hills ✗[2]	9	66.17 S	100.47 E
Bung Kan	110	18.23 N	103.37 E
Bungku	112	2.33 S	121.58 E
Bungo	152	7.26 S	15.23 E
Bungoma	154	0.34 N	34.34 E
Bungonia	170	34.51 S	149.57 E
Bungo-suidō ⵡ	92	33.00 N	132.13 E
Bungo-takada	96	33.33 N	131.27 E
Bungsberg ʌ[2]	54	54.12 N	10.43 E
Bungtlang	120	22.20 N	92.46 E
Bungu	154	7.38 S	39.03 E
Buni ≃	115a	7.26 S	106.47 E
Bunia	154	1.34 N	30.15 E
Bunianga	152	3.34 S	20.06 E
Būnīken, Kūh-e ʌ	128	26.46 N	58.12 E
Buninyong	169	37.39 S	143.53 E
Buninyong, Mount ʌ	169	37.39 S	143.56 E
Bunji	123	35.40 N	74.36 E
Bunkeflo strand	41	55.33 N	12.57 E
Bunker	194	37.27 N	91.12 W
Bunker Group II	166	23.48 S	152.20 E
Bunker Hill, Il., U.S.	219	39.02 N	89.57 W
Bunker Hill, In., U.S.	216	40.40 N	86.06 W
Bunker Hill, Or., U.S.	202	43.21 N	124.12 W
Bunker Hill, Tx., U.S.	222	29.46 N	95.32 W
Bunker Hill ʌ	204	39.15 N	117.08 W
Bunker Hill Monument ⊥	283	42.22 N	71.04 W
Bunkeya	154	10.07 S	27.17 E
Bunkie	194	30.57 N	92.10 W
Bunkyō ✦[8]	268	35.43 N	139.45 E
Bunnahowen	48	54.11 N	9.54 W
Bunnell	192	29.27 N	81.15 W
Bunnik	52	52.04 N	5.12 E
Bünningstedt	52	53.41 N	10.13 E
Bunola	214	40.14 N	79.56 W
Bun Plains ≚	154	0.44 N	40.42 E
Bunratty Castle ⊥	48	52.42 N	8.43 W
Bunschoten	52	52.14 N	5.22 E
Bunsuru ≃	150	13.21 N	6.23 E
Bunta	112	0.48 S	122.10 E
Buntine	162	29.59 S	116.34 E
Buntingford	42	51.57 N	0.01 W
Buntok	112	1.42 S	114.48 E
Bununu Dass	150	10.00 N	9.31 E
Bunut	112	0.46 N	112.30 E
Bunyambili	154	2.21 S	29.25 E
Bünyan	130	38.51 N	35.52 E
Bunyip	169	38.06 S	145.43 E
Bunyip ≃	169	38.13 S	145.27 E
Bunyolo	34	39.25 N	0.47 W
Bunyrevo	82	54.34 N	37.09 E
Bunyu, Pulau I	112	3.30 N	117.50 E
Bunza	150	12.08 N	4.00 E
FRANÇAIS Nom	Page	Lat.°′	Long.°′ W = Ouest
Buochs	58	46.58 N	8.22 E
Buol	112	1.10 N	121.26 E
Buolkalach	74	72.56 N	119.50 E
Buonalbergo	68	41.13 N	14.59 E
Buona Vista	271c	1.16 N	103.47 E
Buon Bu N'jang	110	12.06 N	107.40 E
Buonconvento	66	43.08 N	11.29 E
Buon Me Thuot	110	12.40 N	108.03 E
Buon Mrong	110	12.48 N	108.28 E
Buon Ngo	110	12.30 N	108.28 E
Buon Thach Hom	110	12.17 N	108.48 E
Buon Ya Soup	110	13.05 N	107.52 E
Buor-Chaja, guba ɕ	74	71.30 N	131.00 E
Buor-Chaja, mys ⟩	74	71.56 N	132.40 E
Bupul	164	7.31 S	140.52 E
Buqay'āwīyah, Qā' al- ≚	132	32.03 N	37.07 E
Buqayq	128	25.56 N	49.40 E
Buqda Koosaar	144	4.31 N	44.49 E
Buqde Caqable	144	4.04 N	45.15 E
Buquira ≃	256	23.10 S	45.54 W
Buquirivu ≃	287b	23.28 S	46.28 W
Buqūm, Harrat al- ⊥[9]	144	20.54 N	42.00 E
Bur	88	58.47 N	107.01 E
Bura, Kenya	154	3.30 S	38.18 E
Bura, Kenya	154	1.06 S	39.57 E
Bura Gaurānga ≃[1]	126	22.00 N	90.33 E
Burakin	162	30.31 S	117.10 E
Buraly	80	55.04 N	52.52 E
Buram	140	10.49 N	25.10 E
Buran	86	48.04 N	85.15 E
Burangulovo	86	53.26 N	58.23 E
Buranhém ≃	255	16.27 S	39.04 W
Burankol'	86	46.14 N	54.12 E
Burannoje	86	50.59 N	54.28 E
Burano ≃	66	43.37 N	12.40 E
Burao Kibir	144	8.42 N	45.29 E
Burāq	132	33.10 N	36.29 E
Burāri ✦[8]	272a	28.46 N	77.12 E
Buras	194	29.21 N	89.31 W
Buraševo	82	56.44 N	35.52 E
Burauen	116	10.58 N	124.53 E
Burayd, Bi'r ⊤[4]	142	29.08 N	32.07 E
Buraydah	128	26.20 N	43.59 E
Burayk	146	26.33 N	13.08 E
Buraykah	132	32.50 N	36.34 E
Burbach	56	50.45 N	8.05 E
Burbage, Eng., U.K.	42	51.20 N	1.40 W
Burbage, Eng., U.K.	262	53.15 N	1.56 W
Burbank, Ca., U.S.	226	37.19 N	121.55 W
Burbank, Ca., U.S.	228	34.10 N	118.18 W
Burbank, Il., U.S.	216	41.45 N	87.45 W
Burbank, Il., U.S.	278	41.45 N	87.46 W
Burbank, Oh., U.S.	214	40.59 N	81.59 W
Burbank, Wa., U.S.	202	46.12 N	119.00 W
Burbank Studios ✪[3]	280	34.09 N	118.21 W
Burbure	50	50.32 N	2.28 E
Burç	130	37.02 N	37.10 E
Burcei	71	39.21 N	9.21 E
Burcevo	82	55.02 N	38.09 E
Burcher	166	33.32 S	147.18 E
Burcin	62	45.26 N	5.26 E
Burco	144	9.31 N	45.34 E
Burda	124	25.50 N	77.35 E
Burdalyk	128	38.25 N	64.20 E
Burdekin ≃	166	19.39 S	147.30 E
Burdekin Falls ⌊	166	20.39 S	147.09 E
Burden	198	37.18 N	96.45 W
Burdeos → Bordeaux, Fr.	32	44.50 N	0.34 W
Burdeos, Pil.	116	14.51 N	121.58 E
Burdeos Bay ɕ	116	14.44 N	122.06 E
Burdett, Ab., Can.	182	49.50 N	111.32 W
Burdett, Ks., U.S.	198	38.11 N	99.31 W
Burdett, N.Y., U.S.	210	42.25 N	76.50 W
Burdul	272c	19.07 N	73.07 E
Burdur	130	37.43 N	30.17 E
Burdur ▫[4]	130	37.30 N	30.00 E
Burdur Gölü ⊜	130	37.44 N	30.12 E
Burdwood Bank ✤[3]	18	54.15 S	59.00 W
Bure, Ityo.	144	10.47 N	37.06 E
Bure, Ityo.	144	8.15 N	35.09 E
Bure ≃	42	52.37 N	1.43 E
Bure, Pic de ʌ	62	44.38 N	5.56 E
Bureå	26	64.37 N	21.12 E
Bureälven ≃	26	64.37 N	21.13 E
Bureg Changaj	88	48.14 N	103.57 E
Bureinskij chrebet ✗	89	50.35 N	133.35 E
Bureja	89	49.52 N	129.48 E
Bureja ≃	89	49.25 N	129.35 E
Burekup	168a	33.19 S	115.49 E
Büren, Dtsch.	52	51.33 N	8.33 E
Büren, Mong.	88	47.13 N	95.54 E
Büren an der Aare	58	47.08 N	7.23 E
Büren Chaan	88	49.29 N	99.14 E
Bürengijn nuruu ✗	88	49.15 N	104.30 E
Bures	261	48.57 N	1.58 E
Bures-sur-Yvette	261	48.42 N	2.10 E
Burey-en-Vaux	58	48.34 N	5.40 E
Burfjord	24	69.56 N	22.00 E
Burford, On., Can.	212	43.06 N	80.26 W
Burford, Eng., U.K.	42	51.49 N	1.38 W
Būr Fu'ād ✦[8]	142	31.15 N	32.19 E
Burg, Dtsch.	54	51.49 N	14.08 E
Burg, Dtsch.	54	52.16 N	11.51 E
Burg, Dtsch.	56	50.42 N	8.19 E
Burg ✦[8]	263	51.08 N	7.09 E
Burg, Schloss ⊥	263	51.08 N	7.10 E
Burga	76	58.45 N	32.29 E
Burgas	38	42.30 N	27.28 E
Burgas ▫[4]	130	42.10 N	27.00 E
Burgaski zaliv ɕ	38	42.30 N	27.33 E
Burgau	58	48.26 N	10.25 E
Burg [auf Fehmarn]	54	54.26 N	11.12 E
Burgaw	192	34.33 N	77.55 W
Burgaz ✦[8]	267b	40.53 N	29.03 E
Burgaz Adası I	267b	40.53 N	29.04 E
Burgbernheim	56	49.27 N	10.19 E
Burgdorf, Dtsch.	52	52.27 N	10.00 E
Burgdorf, Schw.	58	47.04 N	7.37 E
Burgebrach	56	49.50 N	10.44 E
Bürgel	54	50.56 N	11.45 E
Burgenland ▫[3]	61	47.30 N	16.20 E
Burgeo	186	47.37 N	57.37 W
Burgersdorp	158	31.00 S	26.20 E
Burger Township	273d	26.05 S	27.46 E
Burges, Mount ʌ[2]	162	30.50 S	121.06 E
Burgess	208	37.53 N	76.21 W
Burgess Hill	42	50.57 N	0.07 W
Burgessville	212	43.01 N	80.39 W
Burgettstown	214	40.22 N	80.23 W
Burggrafenberg ʌ[2]	263	51.13 N	7.07 E
Burghausen	60	48.09 N	12.49 E
Burghead	46	57.42 N	3.30 W
Burgheim	60	48.42 N	11.01 E
Burgh Heath	260	51.18 N	0.13 W
Burghill	214	41.22 N	80.34 W
Burgh le Marsh	44	53.09 N	0.15 E
Burghūth, Sabkhat al- ⊜	130	34.58 N	41.06 E
Burgin	194	37.45 N	84.46 W
Burgio	70	37.36 N	13.17 E
Burgjoss	56	50.12 N	9.29 E
Burgkirchen	60	48.12 N	13.06 E
Burgkunstadt	54	50.08 N	11.14 E
Bürglen, Schw.	58	46.53 N	8.40 E
Bürglen, Schw.	58	47.33 N	9.09 E
Burglengenfeld	60	49.13 N	12.03 E
Burgoon	214	41.16 N	83.15 W
Burgos, Esp.	34	42.21 N	3.42 W
Burgos, It.	71	40.23 N	8.59 E
Burgos, Méx.	232	24.57 N	98.47 W
Burgos, Pil.	116	16.04 N	119.52 E
Burgos, Pil.	116	15.30 N	120.24 E
Burgos ▫[4]	34	42.20 N	3.40 W
Burgsinn	56	50.09 N	9.38 E
Burgstädt	54	50.55 N	12.49 E
Burgstall, Dtsch.	54	52.24 N	11.41 E
Burgstall → Postal, It.	64	46.36 N	11.11 E
PORTUGUÊS Nome	Página	Lat.°′	Long.°′ W = Oeste
Burg Stargard	54	53.29 N	13.18 E
Burgsvik	26	57.03 N	18.16 E
Burgueño, Arroyo ≃	288	34.24 S	58.47 W
Burgund → Bourgogne ▫[9]	32	47.00 N	4.30 E
Burgundy → Bourgogne ▫[9]	32	47.00 N	4.30 E
Burgusio (Burgeis)	64	46.42 N	10.31 E
Burgwedel	52	52.29 N	9.51 E
Burgwindheim	56	49.49 N	10.35 E
Burhābalang ≃	126	21.28 N	87.04 E
Burham	260	51.20 N	0.29 E
Burhan Budai Shan ✗	102	36.00 N	96.00 E
Burhaniye, Tür.	130	37.57 N	28.45 E
Burhaniye, Tür.	130	39.30 N	26.58 E
Burhānpur	120	21.18 N	76.14 E
Burhar	124	23.13 N	81.32 E
Burhave	52	53.34 N	8.21 E
Burholme ✦[8]	285	40.03 N	75.05 W
Buri	255	23.48 S	48.35 W
Burias Island I	116	12.57 N	123.08 E
Burias Pass ⵡ	116	13.00 N	123.15 E
Buribaj	86	51.57 N	58.11 E
Būr Ibrāhīm ✦[8]	142	29.57 N	32.34 E
Burica, Punta ⟩	236	8.03 N	82.53 W
Burien	224	47.28 N	122.20 W
Burigi, Lake ⊜	154	2.05 S	31.15 E
Burila Mare	38	44.27 N	22.34 E
Burin	186	47.02 N	55.10 W
Burin Peninsula ⟩[1]	186	47.00 N	55.40 W
Buri Ram	110	15.00 N	103.07 E
Buriswar ≃[1]	126	21.58 N	90.02 E
Buritama	255	21.03 S	50.08 W
Buriti, Bra.	250	3.55 S	42.57 W
Buriti, Bra.	255	16.27 S	53.27 W
Buriti ≃	248	12.50 S	58.28 W
Buriti Alegre	255	18.09 S	49.03 W
Buriti Bravo	250	5.50 S	43.50 W
Buriticupu ≃	250	4.13 S	46.33 W
Buriti dos Lopes	250	3.10 S	41.52 W
Buritizeiro	255	17.21 S	44.58 W
Būriya	124	30.09 N	77.21 E
Burj al-'Arab	140	30.55 N	29.32 E
Burjassot	34	39.31 N	0.25 W
Burjatija ▫[3]	88	53.00 N	109.00 E
Burji	144	5.20 N	37.57 E
Burj Islām	130	35.41 N	35.48 E
Burj Mughayzil	142	31.27 N	30.23 E
Burkan ≃	85	41.43 N	76.46 E
Burkau	54	51.10 N	14.10 E
Burkburnett	196	34.05 N	98.34 W
Burke, S.D., U.S.	198	43.10 N	99.17 W
Burke, Tx., U.S.	222	31.14 N	94.46 W
Burke, Va., U.S.	284c	38.47 N	77.16 W
Burke ≃	166	23.12 S	139.33 E
Burke Channel ⵡ	182	52.07 N	127.38 W
Burke Island I	9	73.15 S	104.35 W
Burke Lake ⊜[1]	284c	38.46 N	77.18 W
Burke Lake County Park ♦	284c	38.45 N	77.18 W
Burke Lakefront Airport ⊠	279a	41.31 N	81.41 W
Burkesville	194	36.47 N	85.22 W
Burket	216	41.09 N	85.58 W
Burketown	166	17.43 S	139.34 E
Burkett Gardens	226	37.57 N	121.15 W
Burkettsville	216	40.21 N	84.39 W
Burkhardtsdorf	54	50.44 N	12.55 E
Burkina Faso ▫[1], Afr.	134	13.00 N	1.30 W
Burkina Faso ▫[1], Afr.	150	13.00 N	1.30 W
Burkit	80	47.03 N	50.42 E
Burksville	219	38.16 N	90.09 W
Burla	86	53.19 N	78.21 E
Burla ≃	86	53.20 N	78.02 E
Burladingen	58	48.17 N	9.07 E
Burleigh	208	39.02 N	74.51 W
Burleigh Falls	212	44.34 N	78.13 W
Burleigh Heads	171a	28.06 S	153.27 E
Burleson	222	32.32 N	97.19 W
Burleson ▫[6]	222	30.30 N	96.43 W
Burley, Id., U.S.	202	42.32 N	113.47 W
Burley, Wa., U.S.	224	47.25 N	122.37 W
Burley Griffin, Lake ⊜	171b	35.13 S	149.05 E
Burli, Kaz.	80	51.25 N	52.44 E
Burli, Kaz.	86	53.36 N	61.55 E
Burlingame, Ca., U.S.	226	37.35 N	122.21 W
Burlingame, Ks., U.S.	198	38.45 N	95.00 W
Burlingame State Park ♦	207	41.22 N	71.43 W
Burlington, Nf., Can.	186	49.45 N	56.02 W
Burlington, On., Can.	212	43.19 N	79.47 W
Burlington, Co., U.S.	198	39.18 N	102.16 W
Burlington, Ct., U.S.	207	41.46 N	72.57 W
Burlington, Il., U.S.	216	42.03 N	88.33 W
Burlington, In., U.S.	216	40.29 N	86.24 W
Burlington, Ia., U.S.	190	40.48 N	91.06 W
Burlington, Ks., U.S.	198	38.11 N	95.44 W
Burlington, Ky., U.S.	218	39.01 N	84.43 W
Burlington, Ma., U.S.	207	42.30 N	71.11 W
Burlington, Mi., U.S.	216	42.06 N	85.05 W
Burlington, N.J., U.S.	208	40.04 N	74.51 W
Burlington, N.C., U.S.	192	36.05 N	79.26 W
Burlington, N.D., U.S.	198	48.16 N	101.25 W
Burlington, Pa., U.S.	210	41.47 N	76.37 W
Burlington, Tx., U.S.	222	31.01 N	96.60 W
Burlington, Vt., U.S.	188	44.28 N	73.12 W
Burlington, Wa., U.S.	224	48.28 N	122.19 W
Burlington, Wi., U.S.	216	42.40 N	88.16 W
Burlington, Wy., U.S.	202	44.26 N	108.25 W
Burlington ▫[6]	208	39.50 N	74.47 W
Burlington Beach	216	41.30 N	87.03 W
Burlington County Airpark ⊠	285	39.56 N	74.50 W
Burlington Island I	285	40.05 N	74.51 W
Burlington Junction	194	40.26 N	95.03 W
Burlington Mall ✦[9]	283	42.29 N	71.13 W
Burlit	89	46.33 N	134.14 E
Burluk	80	50.34 N	44.33 E
Burma → Myanmar ▫[1]	110	22.00 N	98.00 E
Burmā, Tall ʌ	132	30.38 N	35.50 E
Burmakino	80	57.27 N	40.20 E
Burn ≃	44	54.12 N	1.38 W
Burnaby	224	49.15 N	122.57 W
Burnaby Island I	182	52.24 N	131.20 W
Burnage	262	53.26 N	2.12 W
Burnas, ozero ⊜	78	45.52 N	30.08 E
Burnet	196	30.45 N	98.13 W
Burnett ≃	166	24.46 S	152.25 E
Burnett Bay ɕ	176	73.53 N	124.00 W
Burnett Brook ≃	276	40.46 N	74.38 W
Burnett Heads	166	24.46 S	152.25 E
Burnettsville	216	40.46 N	86.36 W
Burney, Ca., U.S.	204	40.52 N	121.39 W
Burney, In., U.S.	218	39.19 N	85.38 W
Burnham, Eng., U.K.	42	51.33 N	0.39 W
Burnham, Il., U.S.	278	41.39 N	87.34 W
Burnham, Pa., U.S.	208	40.38 N	77.34 W
Burnham Beeches ✦[3]	260	51.34 N	0.38 W
Burnham Market	42	52.57 N	0.44 E
Burnham-on-Crouch	42	51.38 N	0.49 E
Burnham-on-Sea	42	51.15 N	3.00 W
Burnhamthorpe	275b	43.37 N	79.36 W
Burnhaven	46	57.29 N	1.47 W
Burnie	166	41.04 S	145.54 E
Burning Tree Estates	284c	39.01 N	77.12 W
Burnips	216	42.44 N	85.50 W
Burniston	44	54.19 N	0.26 W
Burnley	44	53.48 N	2.14 W
Burnley ▫[8]	262	53.46 N	2.15 W
Burnley Creek ≃	212	44.13 N	77.51 W
Burnley Football Ground ♦	262	53.48 N	2.14 W
Burnmouth	46	55.50 N	2.04 W
Burnoje	85	42.37 N	70.46 E
Burno-Okt'abr'skoje	85	42.42 N	70.49 E
Burnpur	126	23.40 N	86.57 E
Burns, Ks., U.S.	198	38.05 N	96.53 W
Burns, Or., U.S.	202	43.35 N	119.03 W
Burns, Tn., U.S.	194	36.03 N	87.18 W
Burns, Wy., U.S.	198	41.11 N	104.21 W
Burns Creek ≃	198	47.22 N	104.25 W
Burns Flat	196	35.20 N	99.10 W
Burns Harbor	216	41.37 N	87.10 W
Burnside, Austl.	168b	34.57 S	138.40 E
Burnside, Ky., U.S.	192	36.59 N	84.36 W
Burnside, Pa., U.S.	214	40.49 N	78.47 W
Burnside ≃	176	66.51 N	108.04 W
Burnside, Lake ⊜	162	25.33 S	123.02 E
Burns Lake	182	54.14 N	125.46 W
Burnsville, Al., U.S.	194	32.28 N	86.53 W
Burnsville, Ms., U.S.	194	34.50 N	88.18 W
Burnsville, N.C., U.S.	192	35.55 N	82.18 W
Burnsville, W.V., U.S.	188	38.51 N	80.39 W
Burnt ≃, On., Can.	212	44.35 N	78.46 W
Burnt ≃, Or., U.S.	202	44.22 N	117.14 W
Burnt Cabins	214	40.05 N	77.54 W
Burnt Corn Creek ≃	194	31.06 N	87.04 W
Burnt Hills	210	42.54 N	73.53 W
Burnt Island, Nf., Can.	186	47.36 N	58.53 W
Burntisland, Scot., U.K.	46	56.03 N	3.15 W
Burnt Meadow Brook ≃	276	41.05 N	74.18 W
Burnt Mills, Lake ⊜	208	36.50 N	76.38 W
Burnt Mills Hills	284c	39.02 N	77.00 W
Burnt Mills Manor	284c	39.02 N	77.00 W
Burnt Mountain ʌ	228	33.12 N	117.04 W
Burntop	158	26.49 S	30.54 E
Burnt Pine	174c	29.02 S	167.56 E
Burnt Pond ⊜	186	48.11 N	57.24 W
Burntwick Island I	260	51.25 N	0.41 E
Burntwood	42	52.41 N	1.56 W
Burntwood ≃	184	56.08 N	96.30 W
Burntwood Lake ⊜	184	55.29 N	100.07 W
Burnyj, porog ⌊	86	57.43 N	95.18 E
Buro	144	11.28 N	49.41 E
Buron	84	42.48 N	44.03 E
Buronzo	62	45.29 N	8.16 E
Burow	54	53.46 N	13.16 E
Burpengary	171a	27.10 S	152.57 E
Burpham	260	51.15 N	0.33 W
Burqin	86	47.43 N	86.53 E
Burqin ≃	86	47.40 N	86.55 E
Burra	166	33.40 S	138.56 E
Burra Burra Creek ≃	170	34.10 S	149.38 E
Burracoppin	162	31.23 S	118.29 E
Burra Creek ≃	168b	33.51 S	139.18 E
Burrage	283	42.02 N	70.51 W
Burrage Pond ⊜	283	42.01 N	70.52 W
Burragorang, Lake ⊜[1]	170	33.57 S	150.26 E
Burramurra	166	20.30 S	137.20 E
Burravoe	46a	60.32 N	1.28 W
Burrawang	170	34.36 S	150.31 E
Burray I	46	58.51 N	2.54 W
Burrel, Shq.	38	41.37 N	20.00 E
Burrel, Ca., U.S.	226	36.30 N	119.59 W
Burrendong Reservoir ⊜[1]	166	32.39 S	149.15 E
Burren Junction	166	30.06 S	148.58 E
Burrill Lake ɕ	170	35.23 S	150.27 E
Burrinjuck Reservoir ⊜[1]	166	35.00 S	148.45 E
Burro, Serranías del ✗	196	29.10 N	102.05 W
Burr Oak, In., U.S.	216	41.15 N	86.25 W
Burr Oak, Ks., U.S.	198	39.51 N	98.18 W
Burr Oak, Mi., U.S.	216	41.50 N	85.19 W
Burro Burro ≃	246	4.48 N	58.51 W
Burro Creek ≃	200	34.32 N	113.35 W
Burro Peak ʌ	200	32.35 N	108.26 W
Burrowa, Mount ʌ	171b	36.05 S	147.42 E
Burrowa-Pine Mountain National Park ♦	171b	36.06 S	147.44 E
Burrow Head ⟩	44	54.41 N	4.24 W
Burrowhill	260	51.21 N	0.36 W
Burrows	216	40.40 N	86.30 W
Burrows Island I	224	48.29 N	122.42 W
Burr Ridge	278	41.46 N	87.55 W
Burrs Mill Brook ≃	285	39.53 N	74.42 W
Burrton	198	38.01 N	97.40 W
Burrumbeet, Lake ⊜	169	37.30 S	143.39 E
Burrundie	164	13.32 S	131.42 E
Burruyacú	252	26.30 S	64.45 W
Burrwood	194	28.58 N	89.22 W
Burry Holms I	42	51.37 N	4.18 W
Burry Port	42	51.42 N	4.15 W
Bürs	58	47.09 N	9.48 E
Bursa	130	40.11 N	29.04 E
Bursa ▫[4]	130	40.10 N	29.00 E
Būr Safājah	140	26.44 N	33.56 E
Būr Sa'īd (Port Said)	142	31.16 N	32.18 E
Būr Sa'īd ▫[4]	142	30.36 N	32.15 E
Burscheid	56	51.05 N	7.06 E
Burscough	262	53.35 N	2.51 W
Burscough Bridge	44	53.36 N	2.52 W
Bursey, Mount ʌ	9	76.00 S	132.40 W
Bursol'	86	53.11 N	78.27 E
Bürstadt	56	49.38 N	8.27 E
Burstall	184	50.40 N	109.54 W
Burštyn	78	49.17 N	24.37 E
Būr Sūdān (Port Sudan)	140	19.37 N	37.14 E
Burt, Ia., U.S.	190	43.11 N	94.13 W
Burt, N.Y., U.S.	210	43.19 N	78.43 W
Būr Tawfīq ✦[8]	128	29.57 N	32.34 E
Burtenbach	58	48.20 N	10.26 E
Burt Lake ⊜	190	45.27 N	84.40 W
Burtnieks ezers ⊜	76	57.45 N	25.16 E
Burton, B.C., Can.	182	49.59 N	117.54 W
Burton, Eng., U.K.	42	50.44 N	1.45 W
Burton, Eng., U.K.	262	53.16 N	3.01 W
Burton, Il., U.S.	219	39.55 N	91.15 W
Burton, Mi., U.S.	216	43.01 N	84.16 W
Burton, Mi., U.S.	216	43.02 N	83.36 W
Burton, Oh., U.S.	214	41.28 N	81.08 W
Burton, Tx., U.S.	222	30.11 N	96.36 W
Burton, Wa., U.S.	224	47.23 N	122.27 W
Burton, Lake ⊜[1]	192	34.50 N	83.33 W
Burton Fleming	44	54.08 N	0.20 W
Burton Latimer	42	52.23 N	0.41 W
Burtons Bridge	216	42.17 N	88.14 W
Burton Seamount ✤[3]	14	32.00 S	171.45 W
Burtonsville	208	39.07 N	76.56 W
Burton upon Stather	44	53.39 N	0.41 W
Burton upon Trent	42	52.49 N	1.36 W
Burtonwood	262	53.26 N	2.39 W
Burtonwood Airfield ⊠	262	53.24 N	2.39 W
Burträsk	26	64.31 N	20.39 E
Burtundy	166	33.44 S	142.16 E
Burṭus	142	30.09 N	31.08 E
Buru I	108	3.24 S	126.40 E
Buruanga	116	11.51 N	121.53 E
Burukan	89	53.02 N	136.03 E
Buruldaj	85	42.48 N	75.52 E
Burullus, Buḥayrat al- ⊜	142	31.30 N	30.50 E
Burūm	144	14.22 N	48.57 E
Burundaj	85	43.23 N	76.51 E
Burundi ▫[1], Afr.	138	3.15 S	30.00 E
Burundi ▫[1], Afr.	154	3.15 S	30.00 E
Burundučicha	80	58.21 N	46.07 E
Burun-Šibertuj, gora ʌ	88	49.42 N	109.59 E
Bururi	154	3.57 S	29.37 E
Burutu	150	5.21 N	5.31 E
Buruz Bāgān	126	23.03 N	89.00 E
Burwash	190	46.19 N	80.48 W
Burwash Landing	180	61.21 N	139.00 W
Burwell, Eng., U.K.	42	52.16 N	0.19 E
Burwell, Ne., U.S.	198	41.46 N	99.07 W
Burwell Bay ɕ	208	37.04 N	76.38 W
Burwick	46	58.44 N	2.57 W
Burwood, Austl.	274a	33.53 S	151.06 E
Burwood, Austl.	274b	37.51 S	145.06 E
Bury, P.Q., Can.	206	45.28 N	71.30 W
Bury, Eng., U.K.	42	50.54 N	0.34 W
Bury, Eng., U.K.	44	53.36 N	2.17 W
Bury ▫[8]	262	53.35 N	2.19 W
Buryatia → Burjatija ▫[3]	88	53.00 N	109.00 E
Buryn'	78	51.13 N	33.49 E
Bury Saint Edmunds	42	52.15 N	0.43 E
Burzaco	258	34.49 S	58.24 W
Burzet	62	44.44 N	4.15 E
Burzil	123	34.52 N	75.07 E
Burzil Pass)(	123	34.54 N	75.06 E
Būṣ, Ghubbat al- ɕ	142	29.36 N	32.22 E
Busa, Mount ʌ	116	6.08 N	124.39 E
Busachi	71	40.02 N	8.54 E
Busalla	62	44.34 N	8.57 E
Busambra, Rocca ʌ	70	37.51 N	13.24 E
Busan → Pusan	98	35.06 N	129.03 E
Busana	64	44.22 N	10.19 E
Busanga	152	0.51 S	22.04 E
Busanga Swamp ≡	154	14.10 S	25.50 E
Busangu	154	8.32 S	25.31 E
Buṣayrah	130	35.09 N	40.26 E
Busby, Austl.	274a	33.54 S	150.53 E
Busby, Mt., U.S.	202	45.32 N	106.57 W
Busca	62	44.31 N	7.29 E
Buscate	266b	45.32 N	8.49 E
Buscbusc ≃	144	1.08 S	41.49 E
Buschberg ʌ[2]	61	48.34 N	16.23 E
Busche	64	46.02 N	11.59 E
Busch Gardens ♦	280	34.13 N	118.28 W
Buschhausen ✦[8]	263	51.30 N	6.51 E
Busdorf	41	54.29 N	9.32 E
Buseck	56	50.36 N	8.47 E
Buseto Palizzolo	70	38.01 N	12.43 E
Būsh	142	29.09 N	31.08 E
Bush ≃, N. Ire., U.K.	44	55.13 N	6.32 W
Bush ≃, S.C., U.S.	192	34.08 N	81.36 W
Būshehr ▫[4]	128	28.50 N	51.20 E
Bushenyi	154	0.32 S	30.11 E
Bushey	42	51.39 N	0.22 W
Bushey Heath	260	51.38 N	0.20 W
Bushi	268	35.50 N	139.22 E
Bushimaie ≃	152	6.02 S	23.45 E
Bushiribana	241s	12.33 N	69.58 W
Bushkill	210	41.06 N	75.00 W
Bush Kill ≃	210	41.05 N	74.59 W
Bushkill Falls ⌊	210	41.09 N	75.01 W
Bushland	196	35.11 N	102.04 W
Bush Lot	246	6.12 N	57.16 W
Bushman Land ▫[9]	158	29.15 S	20.00 E
Bushmills	48	55.12 N	6.32 W
Bushnell, Fl., U.S.	220	28.39 N	82.06 W
Bushnell, Il., U.S.	190	40.33 N	90.30 W
Bush River ≃	208	39.21 N	76.14 W
Bushton	198	38.30 N	98.23 W
Bū Shubayrim, Wādī V	146	27.07 N	19.30 E
Bushwick ✦[8]	276	40.42 N	73.55 W
Bushy Park	166	21.16 S	139.43 E
Bushy Park ♦	260	51.25 N	0.20 W
Bushy Run ≃	279b	40.20 N	79.40 W
Bushy Run Battlefield ⊥	279b	40.21 N	79.38 W
Busia	154	0.28 N	34.05 E
Busigny	50	50.02 N	3.28 E
Busing, Pulau I	271c	1.14 N	103.45 E
Businga	152	3.20 N	20.53 E
Büsingen	58	47.42 N	8.41 E
Busira ≃	152	0.15 S	18.59 E
Busjön ⊜, Sve.	40	60.06 N	13.28 E
Busjön ⊜, Sve.	40	60.31 N	13.58 E
Busk	78	49.58 N	24.37 E
Buskerud ▫[6]	26	60.25 N	9.12 E
Buskhyttan	40	58.40 N	16.56 E
Busko Zdrój	30	50.28 N	20.44 E
Buskul'	86	53.45 N	61.12 E
Busle	144	5.28 N	44.25 E
Busoga ▫[5]	154	0.40 N	33.30 E
Busovača	36	44.06 N	17.53 E
Buṣrā al-Ḥarīrī (Bosor)	132	32.50 N	36.20 E
Buṣrá ash-Shām	132	32.31 N	36.29 E
Bussana	62	43.49 N	7.51 E
Bussang	58	47.53 N	6.51 E
Bussang, Col de)(	58	47.54 N	6.54 E
Busselton	162	33.39 S	115.20 E
Busseri ≃	140	7.41 N	28.03 E
Busseto	64	44.59 N	10.02 E
Bussey	190	41.12 N	92.52 W
Bussières	62	45.50 N	4.16 E
Bussi sul Tirino	66	42.12 N	13.49 E
Busskoje	84	43.50 N	44.37 E
Bussolengo	64	45.28 N	10.51 E
Bussoleno	62	45.08 N	7.09 E
Bussum	52	52.16 N	5.10 E
Bussy-Rabutin, Château de ⊥	58	47.35 N	4.31 E
Bussy-Saint-Georges	261	48.51 N	2.42 E
Bustamante, Méx.	232	26.33 N	100.30 W
Bustamante, Méx.	234	23.26 N	99.47 W
Bustān, Wādī al- V	142	28.24 N	30.49 E
Buštěhrad	54	50.09 N	14.10 E
Buşteni	38	45.25 N	25.32 E
Busti	214	42.02 N	79.17 W
Bustleton ✦[8]	285	40.05 N	75.02 W
Busto Arsizio	62	45.37 N	8.51 E
Busto Garolfo	62	45.33 N	8.53 E
Buston, Taj.	85	40.31 N	69.19 E
Buston, Uzb.	128	40.04 N	64.49 E
Buštyna	78	48.04 N	23.27 E
Busu-Adula	152	2.05 N	21.40 E
Busuanga	116	12.10 N	119.55 E
Busuanga Island I	116	12.05 N	120.05 E
Busu-Djanoa	152	1.43 N	21.23 E
Bušuicha	76	59.02 N	40.26 E
Bušulej	88	52.45 N	117.13 E
Büsum	30	54.08 N	8.51 E
Busu-Melo	152	1.48 N	20.15 E
Bū Sunbul, Jabal ✗[2]	146	23.10 N	22.21 E
Buta, Ross.	80	55.02 N	51.57 E
Buta, Zaïre	154	2.48 N	24.44 E
Butag	116	12.38 N	123.56 E
Butajira	144	8.07 N	38.22 E
Butala	164	6.42 S	147.37 E
Butan	38	43.39 N	23.45 E
Bután → Bhutan ▫[1]	120	27.30 N	90.30 E
Butand State Park ♦	226	37.13 N	122.20 W
Butantã ✦[8]	287b	23.34 S	46.43 W
Butantã, Instituto ✪[3]	287b	23.34 S	46.43 W
Buta Ranquil	252	37.03 S	69.50 W
Butare	154	2.36 S	29.44 E
Butaritari I[1]	14	3.07 N	172.48 E
Butarque, Arroyo de ≃	266a	40.19 N	3.39 W
Butauanan Island I	116	14.07 N	123.17 E
Butchart Gardens ♦	224	48.33 N	123.28 W
Butcher Island (Dia Deva) I	272c	18.58 N	72.54 E
Bute	168b	33.52 S	138.01 E
Bute, Island of I	46	55.50 N	5.06 W
Bute, Kyles of ⵡ	46	55.53 N	5.13 W
Bute, Sound of ⵡ	46	55.44 N	5.12 W
Büteelijn nuruu ✗	88	50.00 N	104.50 E
Bute Giarti	144	4.33 N	37.45 E
Bute Inlet ɕ	182	50.37 N	124.53 W
Butemba	154	1.09 N	31.36 E
Butembo	154	0.09 N	29.17 E
Butera	70	37.11 N	14.11 E
Butere	154	0.13 N	34.30 E
Bütgenbach	56	50.26 N	6.12 E
Butha Buthe	158	28.45 S	28.15 E
Butha Qi (Zalantun)	89	48.02 N	122.43 E
Buthidaung	110	20.52 N	92.32 E
Buthier ≃	62	45.44 N	7.22 E
Buthroton ⊥	38	39.46 N	20.00 E
Buti	66	43.44 N	10.35 E
Butiá	252	30.07 S	51.58 W
Butiaba	154	1.49 N	31.19 E
Butig Mountains ✗	116	7.39 N	124.20 E
Butka	86	56.47 N	63.47 E
Butler, Al., U.S.	194	32.05 N	88.13 W
Butler, Ga., U.S.	192	32.33 N	84.14 W
Butler, Il., U.S.	219	39.12 N	89.32 W
Butler, In., U.S.	216	41.25 N	84.52 W
Butler, Ky., U.S.	218	38.47 N	84.22 W
Butler, Mo., U.S.	194	38.15 N	94.19 W
Butler, N.J., U.S.	210	41.00 N	74.20 W
Butler, Oh., U.S.	214	40.35 N	82.25 W
Butler, Ok., U.S.	196	35.38 N	99.11 W
Butler, Pa., U.S.	214	40.51 N	79.53 W
Butler, Tx., U.S.	222	30.19 N	97.18 W
Butler, Wi., U.S.	216	43.06 N	88.04 W
Butler ▫[6], Oh., U.S.	218	39.26 N	84.30 W
Butler ▫[6], Pa., U.S.	214	40.52 N	79.54 W
Butler, Lake ⊜	220	28.28 N	81.33 W
Butler Lake ⊜	278	42.17 N	87.58 W
Butler Point ⟩	207	41.40 N	70.43 W
Butler Reservoir ⊜[1]	276	40.59 N	74.23 W
Butlers Bridge	48	54.02 N	7.22 W
Butlerville	218	39.02 N	85.30 W
Butmīyah	132	32.56 N	35.53 E
Butnau Lake ⊜	184	56.13 N	95.20 W
Butner	192	36.07 N	78.45 W
Buto	152	15.46 S	15.09 E
Buton, Pulau I	112	5.00 S	122.55 E
Butong	112	1.06 S	114.50 E
Butru	166	21.30 S	139.43 E
Butsha	154	0.57 N	29.13 E
Buttapietra	64	45.20 N	11.00 E
Butte, Mt., U.S.	202	46.00 N	112.32 W
Butte, Ne., U.S.	198	42.54 N	98.50 W
Butte ▫[6]	226	39.27 N	121.30 W
Butte City	226	39.28 N	121.59 W
Butte Creek ≃, Ca., U.S.	204	39.12 N	121.56 W
Butte Creek ≃, Or., U.S.	224	45.09 N	122.46 W
Butte du Lion ⊥	50	50.40 N	4.24 E
Butte Falls	202	42.32 N	122.33 W
Buttelstedt	54	51.05 N	11.20 E
Butte Mountains ✗	204	39.50 N	115.05 W
Butten	56	48.58 N	7.13 E
Butter Brook ≃	283	42.31 N	71.24 W
Butter Creek ≃	202	45.52 N	119.19 W
Butterfield, Il., U.S.	278	41.50 N	88.02 W
Butterfield, Mn., U.S.	198	43.57 N	94.47 W
Butterfield Creek ≃	278	41.33 N	87.37 W
Butterfield Lake ⊜	212	44.19 N	75.46 W
Butterley Reservoir ⊜[1]	262	53.35 N	1.56 W
Buttermere	44	54.33 N	3.17 W
Butternut	190	46.00 N	90.29 W
Butternut Creek ≃, N.Y., U.S.	210	42.25 N	75.22 W
Butternut Creek ≃, N.Y., U.S.	210	43.06 N	76.00 W
Butterwick	44	52.59 N	0.05 E
Butterworth, Malay.	114	5.25 N	100.24 E
Butterworth, Transkei	158	32.23 S	28.04 E
Buttevant	48	52.14 N	8.40 W
Büttgen	56	51.12 N	6.36 E
Buttlar	56	50.45 N	9.57 E
Buttle Lake ⊜	182	49.46 N	125.36 W
Button Islands II	176	60.35 N	64.45 W
Buttonville	275b	43.52 N	79.22 W
Buttonville Airfield ⊠	275b	43.52 N	79.23 W
Buttonwillow	226	35.24 N	119.28 W
Buttrio	64	46.01 N	13.20 E
Buttstädt	54	51.07 N	11.25 E
Butty Head ⟩	162	33.54 S	121.38 E
Buttzville	210	40.49 N	75.00 W
Butuan	116	8.57 N	125.33 E
Butuan Bay ɕ	116	9.06 N	125.20 E
Butuj	88	53.27 N	112.22 E
Bū Tumayyim, Wādī V	146	26.56 N	19.13 E
Buṭūris	142	31.00 N	30.15 E
Buturlino, Ross.	80	55.34 N	44.55 E
Buturlino, Ross.	82	54.55 N	37.29 E
Buturlinovka	78	50.50 N	40.36 E
Butwal	124	27.42 N	83.27 E
Butylicy	80	55.32 N	41.31 E
Butzbach	56	50.26 N	8.40 E
Bützfleth	52	53.39 N	9.28 E
Bützow	54	53.50 N	11.59 E
Bützsee ⊜	54	52.49 N	12.53 E
Butztown	208	40.39 N	75.22 W
Buuhoodle	144	8.15 N	46.20 E
Buulo Berde	144	3.51 N	45.34 E
Buur Gaabo	144	1.12 S	41.51 E
Buurgplaatz ʌ	56	50.10 N	6.01 E
Buur Hakaba	144	2.47 N	44.05 E
Buur Haybe	144	3.57 N	45.07 E
Buwaraḥ, Sabkhat al- ≡	130	35.09 N	41.12 E
Buwayḍān	132	33.12 N	36.26 E
Buxar	124	25.35 N	83.59 E
Buxtehude	52	53.28 N	9.41 E
Buxton, Boph.	158	27.38 S	24.42 E
Buxton, Guy.	246	6.47 N	58.02 W
Buxton, Eng., U.K.	44	53.15 N	1.55 W
Buxton, N.C., U.S.	192	35.16 N	75.32 W
Buxton, N.D., U.S.	198	47.36 N	97.05 W
Buxton, Or., U.S	224	45.41 N	123.11 W
Buxton, Mount ʌ	182	51.35 N	127.55 W
Buxy	58	46.43 N	4.41 E
Buye	154	4.38 N	27.30 E
Buyiqiao	106	31.47 N	119.48 E
Buyo	150	6.16 N	7.03 W
Buyo, Barrage de ✦[6]	150	6.15 N	7.05 W
Buyuan ≃	102	21.51 N	101.13 E
Büyükada	130	40.52 N	29.07 E
Büyükada I	267b	40.52 N	29.07 E
Büyükarmutlu	130	39.35 N	38.26 E
Büyükbakkal ✦[8]	267b	40.59 N	29.11 E
Büyükçeçeli	130	39.43 N	33.52 E
Büyükçekmece	130	41.01 N	28.34 E
Büyükdere ✦[8]	267b	41.09 N	29.02 E
Büyükeceli	130	36.11 N	33.40 E
Büyükkale	130	38.01 N	27.34 E
Büyükkarıştıran	130	41.18 N	27.32 E
Büyükkemikli Burnu ⟩	130	40.18 N	26.14 E
Büyükmenderes ≃	130	37.28 N	27.11 E
Büyükzap → Great Zab ≃	128	36.00 N	43.21 E
Buyun Shan ʌ	98	40.06 N	122.42 E
Buyun Uzun	128	39.13 N	63.19 E
Buzan ≃	80	46.18 N	49.06 E
Buzanaj, peski ✦[2]	80	47.30 N	49.50 E
Buzançais	32	46.53 N	1.25 E
Buzancy	56	49.25 N	4.57 E
Bužaninovo	82	56.23 N	38.18 E
Bužarovo	82	55.59 N	36.47 E
Buzău	38	45.09 N	26.49 E
Buzău ▫[6]	38	45.15 N	26.45 E
Buzău ≃	38	45.26 N	27.44 E
Buzen	96	33.37 N	131.08 E
Búzi ≃	156	19.50 S	34.43 E
Buziaş	38	45.39 N	21.36 E
Buziji	100	33.49 N	118.14 E
Buzinovka	80	48.32 N	43.53 E
Búzios, Ilha dos I	256	23.48 S	45.08 W
Búzios, Ponta dos ⟩	255	22.44 S	41.53 W
Buzlanovo	265b	55.46 N	37.13 E
Buzovna	84	40.31 N	50.04 E
Buzuluk, Kaz.	86	51.55 N	66.16 E
Buzuluk, Ross.	80	52.47 N	52.15 E
Buzuluk ≃, Ross.	80	50.13 N	42.12 E
Buzuluk ≃, Ross.	80	52.47 N	52.16 E
Buzzards Bay	207	41.44 N	70.37 W
Buzzards Bay ɕ	207	41.33 N	70.47 W
Bwana Mkubwa	154	13.01 S	28.42 E
Bwasa	152	3.53 S	18.25 E
Bwendi	154	4.01 N	26.41 E
Bwlch	42	51.54 N	3.15 W
By	40	60.12 N	16.28 E
Byādgi	122	14.41 N	75.29 E

Symbol	English	Deutsch	Español	Français	Português
≃	River	Fluß	Río	Rivière	Rio
≍	Canal	Kanal	Canal	Canal	Canal
⌊	Waterfall, Rapids	Wasserfall, Stromschnellen	Cascada, Rápidos	Chute d'eau, Rapides	Cascata, Rápidos
ⵡ	Strait	Meeresstraße	Estrecho	Détroit	Estreito
ɕ	Bay, Gulf	Bucht, Golf	Bahía, Golfo	Baie, Golfe	Baía, Golfo
⊜	Lake, Lakes	See, Seen	Lago, Lagos	Lac, Lacs	Lago, Lagos
≡	Swamp	Sumpf	Pantano	Marais	Pântano
⍓	Ice Features, Glacier	Eis- und Gletscherformen	Accidentes Glaciales	Formes glaciaires	Acidentes glaciares
⊤	Other Hydrographic Features	Andere Hydrographische Objekte	Otros Elementos Hidrográficos	Autres données hydrographiques	Outros acidentes hidrográficos
✤	Submarine Features	Untermeerische Objekte	Accidentes Submarinos	Formes de relief sous-marin	Acidentes submarinos
▫	Political Unit	Politische Einheit	Unidad Politica	Entité politique	Unidade política
✪	Cultural Institution	Kulturelle Institution	Institución Cultural	Institution culturelle	Institução cultural
⊥	Historical Site	Historische Stätte	Sitio Histórico	Site historique	Sitio histórico
♦	Recreational Site	Erholungs- und Ferienort	Sitio de Recreo	Centre de loisirs	Area de Lazer
⊠	Airport	Flughafen	Aeropuerto	Aéroport	Aeroporto
■	Military Installation	Militäranlage	Instalación Militar	Installation militaire	Instalação militar
✦	Miscellaneous	Verschiedenes	Misceláneo	Divers	Diversos

Name	Page	Lat.	Long.
Byam Channel ʊ	176	75.20 N	105.20 W
Byam Martin Channel ʊ	176	75.45 N	104.00 W
Byam Martin Island ı	176	75.15 N	104.00 W
Byberry Creek ≃	285	40.04 N	74.59 W
Byblos			
— Jubayl	130	34.07 N	35.39 E
Byček ≃	83	48.26 N	37.47 E
Bychawa	30	51.01 N	22.32 E
Bychov	76	53.32 N	30.12 E
Byčicha	76	55.41 N	29.58 E
Byčki, Ross.	76	54.15 N	34.39 E
Byčki, Ross.	80	53.38 N	40.54 E
Byculla ← 8	272c	18.58 N	72.49 E
Byczyna	30	51.07 N	18.11 E
Bydalen	26	63.06 N	13.47 E
Bydgoszcz	30	53.08 N	18.00 E
Bydgoszcz ⌂ 4	30	53.15 N	18.00 E
Byelorussia			
— Belarus ⌐ 1	72	53.50 N	28.00 E
Byers, Pa., U.S.	285	40.05 N	75.41 W
Byers, Tx., U.S.	196	34.04 N	98.11 W
Byersdale	279b	40.37 N	80.13 W
Byers Run ≃	279b	40.24 N	79.42 W
Byesville	188	39.58 N	81.32 W
Byfang ← 8	263	51.24 N	7.06 E
Byfield, Eng., U.K.	42	52.11 N	1.14 W
Byfield, Ma., U.S.	207	42.45 N	70.56 W
Byfleet	42	51.20 N	0.29 W
Byford	168a	32.13 S	116.00 E
Byforde	284c	39.01 N	77.05 W
Bygdeå	26	64.04 N	20.51 E
Bygdeträsket ⌀	26	64.26 N	20.32 E
Bygdin	26	61.20 N	8.48 E
Bygdin ⌀	26	61.21 N	8.36 E
Bygi	80	57.13 N	53.44 E
Byglandsfjord	26	58.41 N	7.48 E
Byglandsfjorden ⌀	26	58.48 N	7.50 E
Byhalia	194	34.52 N	89.41 W
Byk ≃	38	46.55 N	29.28 E
Bykle	26	59.21 N	7.20 E
Bykov	89	47.21 N	142.32 E
Bykovec	38	47.13 N	28.27 E
Bykovka, Ross.	82	55.29 N	37.40 E
Bykovka, Ukr.	78	50.17 N	27.58 E
Bykovo, Ross.	80	49.47 N	45.22 E
Bykovo, Ross.	82	54.01 N	37.54 E
Bykovo, Ross.	82	55.37 N	38.04 E
Bykovo Airport ⌖	265b	55.36 N	38.05 E
Bylas	200	33.08 N	110.07 W
Bylbasovka	83	48.51 N	37.30 E
Bylderup	41	54.57 N	9.07 E
Byley	262	53.13 N	2.25 W
Bylkyldak	86	48.38 N	75.16 E
Bylot Island ı	30	49.04 N	18.01 E
Bylot Island ı	176	73.13 N	78.34 W
Byng Inlet	190	45.46 N	80.33 W
Bynum, Mt., U.S.	182	47.58 N	112.18 W
Bynum, N.C., U.S.	192	35.46 N	79.08 W
Bynum, Tx., U.S.	222	31.58 N	97.00 W
Byödön Temple ✦ 1	270	34.53 N	135.48 E
Byram ≃	276	40.59 N	73.39 W
Byramgore Reef ⌖	122	11.54 N	71.49 E
Byram Lake Reservoir ⌀ 1	276	41.10 N	73.41 W
Byrd, Lac ⌀	190	47.01 N	76.56 W
Byrdstown	194	36.34 N	85.07 W
Byrka	88	50.39 N	118.31 E
Byrne Arena ✦	276	40.49 N	74.05 W
Byrnedale	214	41.17 N	78.30 W
Byro	166	26.05 S	116.09 E
Byrock	166	30.40 S	146.24 E
Byron, Ca., U.S.	226	37.52 N	121.38 W
Byron, Ga., U.S.	192	32.39 N	83.45 W
Byron, Il., U.S.	190	42.07 N	89.15 W
Byron, Mi., U.S.	216	42.49 N	83.57 W
Byron, N.Y., U.S.	210	43.04 N	78.03 W
Byron, Wy., U.S.	202	44.47 N	108.30 W
Byron, Cape ⋗	166	28.39 S	153.38 E
Byron, Isla ı	254	47.47 S	75.12 W
Byron Bay	166	28.39 S	153.37 E
Byron Center	216	42.49 N	85.42 W
Byrranga, gory ☒	74	75.00 N	104.00 E
Byšice-Liblice	54	50.19 N	14.38 E
Bysjön ⌀	40	60.23 N	14.30 E
Byske	26	64.57 N	21.12 E
Byskeälven ≃	26	64.57 N	21.13 E
Bystraja ≃	80	47.58 N	41.00 E
Bystřany	54	50.33 N	13.51 E
Bystřice ≃	80	58.38 N	49.05 E
Bystřice	30	49.45 N	14.41 E
Bystřice pod Hostýnem	30	49.24 N	17.40 E
Bystrovka	85	55.46 N	54.35 E
Bystryj	86	57.50 N	73.58 E
Bystryj Istok	86	52.23 N	84.24 E
Bystrzyca Kłodzka	30	50.18 N	16.38 E
Bytantaj ≃	88	68.46 N	134.20 E
Bytča, Bela.	76	54.18 N	28.24 E
Bytča, Slvk.	30	49.14 N	18.36 E
Byten'	76	52.54 N	25.29 E
Bytkov	78	48.38 N	24.26 E
Bytom (Beuthen)	30	50.22 N	18.54 E
Bytoš	76	53.50 N	34.06 E
Bytôš	54	54.11 N	17.30 E
Byumba	154	1.35 S	30.04 E
Byvalki	76	51.50 N	30.37 E
Byxelkrok	26	57.20 N	17.00 E
Bzyb' ≃	84	43.12 N	40.18 E
Bzybski chrebet ☒	84	43.18 N	40.15 E

C

Name	Page	Lat.	Long.
Ca ≃	110	18.46 N	105.47 E
Čaa-Chol'	88	51.32 N	92.23 E
Čaacupé	252	25.23 S	57.09 W
Čaadajevka	83	53.09 N	45.56 E
Čaadajevo	85	55.40 N	42.02 E
Čaaguazú	252	25.26 S	56.00 W
Čaaguazú ⌐ 5	252	25.00 S	55.45 W
Čaála	152	12.51 S	15.33 E
Caamaño Sound ʊ	182	52.49 N	129.28 W
Caapiranga	246	3.18 S	61.13 W
Caapucú	252	26.13 S	57.12 W
Caarapó	255	22.38 S	54.48 W
Caazapá	252	26.09 S	56.24 W
Caazapá ⌐ 5	252	26.10 S	56.00 W
Cabaçal ≃	248	16.00 S	57.42 W
Cabadbaran	116	9.10 N	125.38 E
Cabadiangan Plateau			
☒	116	9.50 N	122.36 E
Cabagan	116	17.26 N	121.46 E
Cabaguán	240	22.05 N	79.30 W
Cabalete Island ı	116	14.11 N	121.50 E
Cabalian	116	10.16 N	125.10 E
Cabaliana, Lago ⌀	246	3.20 S	60.50 W
Cabalian Bay c	116	10.13 N	125.10 E
Cabalian Point ⋗	116	12.06 N	122.01 E
Caballo ≃ 1	116	12.34 N	124.50 E
Caballo Mountains ☒	198	33.00 N	107.15 W
Caballones, Cayo ı	240	20.58 N	79.00 W
Caballo Reservoir ⌀ 1	200	32.58 N	107.18 W
Cabana	248	8.28 S	78.10 W
Cabanaconde	248	15.37 S	71.59 W
Cabañas	240p	22.58 N	82.55 W
Cabanatuan	116	15.29 N	120.58 E
Cabangan	116	15.10 N	120.03 E
Cabano	186	47.41 N	68.53 W
Čabanovka	83	49.02 N	38.46 E
Cabarroguis	116	16.33 N	121.32 E
Cabarruyan Island ı	116	16.18 N	119.59 E
Cabcallero Creek ≃	116	12.34 N	124.50 E
Cabeceiras	255	15.48 S	46.59 W
Cabeço de Montachique	266c	38.54 N	9.11 W

Name	Page	Lat.	Long.
Cabellera, Sierra de la ☒	200	30.55 N	109.07 W
Cabery	216	41.00 N	88.12 W
Cabeza del Buey	34	38.43 N	5.13 W
Cabeza de Tigre	286c	10.28 N	66.46 W
Cabezas	248	18.46 S	63.24 W
Cabiao	116	15.15 N	120.51 E
Cabiate	266b	40.45 N	9.10 E
Cabildo, Arg.	252	38.29 S	61.54 W
Cabildo, Chile	252	32.26 S	71.05 W
Cabimas	246	10.23 N	71.28 W
Cabin Branch ≃, Md., U.S.	284b	39.13 N	76.35 W
Cabin Branch ≃, Md., U.S.	284c	38.51 N	76.48 W
Cabin Creek ≃	198	46.55 N	104.52 W
Cabinda	152	5.33 S	12.12 E
Cabinda ⌐ 5	152	5.00 S	12.30 E
Cabinet Mountains ☒	202	48.20 N	116.00 W
Cabingaan Island ı	116	5.41 N	121.03 E
Cabin John	208	38.58 N	77.09 W
Cabin John Creek ≃	284b	38.58 N	77.09 W
Cabin John Creek Park ✦	284c	38.59 N	77.09 W
Cabin John Regional Park ✦	284c	39.02 N	77.09 W
Cabiri	152	8.52 S	13.39 E
Cabixi ≃	248	13.41 S	60.44 W
Cable	190	46.12 N	91.17 W
Cable Airport ⌖	280	34.08 N	117.41 W
Cables	162	27.59 S	123.23 E
Cabo	250	8.17 S	35.02 W
Cabo Blanco	254	47.12 S	65.45 W
Cabo de Hornos, Parque Nacional ✦	254	55.45 S	67.25 W
Cabo Delgado ⌐ 5	154	12.35 S	39.00 E
Cabo Frio	255	22.53 S	42.01 W
Cabo Gracias a Dios	236	14.59 N	83.10 W
Cabo Ledo	152	9.39 S	13.17 E
Cabonga, Réservoir ⌀ 1	190	47.20 N	76.35 W
Cabool	194	37.07 N	92.06 W
Caboolture	166	27.05 S	152.57 E
Cabo Orange, Parque Nacional do ✦	250	3.00 N	51.00 W
Cabora Bassa	154	15.35 S	32.48 E
Cabora Bassa Dam ✦ 6	154	15.35 S	32.42 E
Cabo Raso	254	44.21 S	65.14 W
Caborca	232	30.37 N	112.06 W
Cabo Rojo	240m	18.05 N	67.09 W
Cabot, Ar., U.S.	194	34.58 N	92.00 W
Cabot, Pa., U.S.	214	40.46 N	79.46 W
Cabot, Vt., U.S.	184	44.31 N	71.24 W
Cabot Head ⋗	212	45.14 N	81.17 W
Cabot Strait ʊ	186	47.20 N	59.30 W
Cabo Verde	255	21.28 S	46.24 W
Cabo Verde			
— Cape Verde ⌐ 1	150a	16.00 N	24.00 W
Cabo Verde ≃	255	21.28 S	46.17 W
Cabra	34	37.28 N	4.27 W
Cabra Corral, Embalse ⌀ 1	252	25.15 S	65.25 W
Cabra Island ı	116	13.53 N	120.02 E
Cabramatta	274a	33.54 S	150.56 E
Cabramatta Creek ≃	274a	33.54 S	150.57 E
Cabramurra	171b	35.58 S	148.23 E
Cabras	71	39.56 N	8.32 E
Cabras, Stagno di ⌀	71	39.57 N	8.29 E
Cabras Island ı	174p	13.27 N	144.40 E
Cabrera, ⌐, Col.	246	4.25 N	74.29 W
Cabrera ≃, Esp.	34	42.25 N	6.49 W
Cabrera, Illa de ı	34	39.09 N	2.56 E
Cabrera, Sierra de la ☒	34	42.12 N	6.40 W
Cabrera de Mar	266d	41.32 N	2.24 E
Cabreúva	255	23.18 S	47.08 W
Cabri	184	50.37 N	108.28 W
Cabria	64	45.54 N	13.35 E
Cabriel ≃	34	39.14 N	1.03 W
Cabrillo National Monument ✦	228	32.41 N	117.15 W
Cabrils	266d	41.32 N	2.22 E
Cabrobó	250	8.31 S	39.19 W
Cabruta	246	7.38 N	66.15 W
Cabucgayan	116	11.29 N	124.34 E
Cabuçu ≃, Bra.	256	22.50 S	42.55 W
Cabuçu ≃, Bra.	287a	22.59 S	43.37 W
Cabuçu ≃, Bra.	287a	22.48 S	43.37 W
Cabuçu de Cima ≃	287b	23.31 S	46.33 W
Cabugao	116	17.48 N	120.27 E
Cabuluan Island ı	116	11.23 N	120.06 E
Cabullones, Punta ⋗	240m	17.58 N	66.35 W
Cabulo	152	10.15 S	16.40 E
Cabure	246	11.08 N	69.38 W
Cabuta	152	9.50 S	14.48 E
Cabuya	236	9.36 N	85.06 W
Cabuyal ≃	240	21.49 N	76.34 W
Caca	80	48.11 N	44.40 E
Caçador	252	26.47 S	51.00 W
Čačak	38	43.53 N	20.21 E
Cacaohatán	236	14.59 N	92.10 W
Cacaoui, Lac ⌀	186	50.53 N	66.58 W
Caçapava	255	23.06 S	45.42 W
Caçapava do Sul	252	30.30 S	53.30 W
Caçapava Velha	256	23.07 S	45.39 W
Capacon ≃	188	39.37 N	78.16 W
Capacon State Park ✦	188	39.32 N	78.23 W
Cacas	130	38.23 N	41.17 E
Caccamo	70	37.56 N	13.40 E
Caccia, Capo ⋗	71	40.34 N	8.09 E
Caccuri	68	39.14 N	16.47 E
Čačenka ⌀	265b	55.46 N	37.18 E
Cacequi	252	29.53 S	54.49 W
Cáceres, Bra.	248	16.04 S	57.41 W
Cáceres, Col.	246	7.35 N	75.20 W
Cáceres, Esp.	34	39.29 N	6.22 W
Cáceres ⌐ 4	34	39.45 N	6.05 E
Cachan	261	48.48 N	2.20 E
Cachari	252	36.24 S	59.32 W
Cache ≃, Ar., U.S.	194	34.42 N	91.20 W
Cache ≃, Il., U.S.	194	37.04 N	89.10 W
Caché, Lac ⌀	206	46.21 N	74.39 W
Cache Creek	182	50.48 N	121.19 W
Cache Creek ≃, Ca., U.S.	226	38.42 N	121.42 W
Cache Creek ≃, Ok., U.S.	228	35.06 N	117.58 W
Cache Creek, North Fork ≃	226	38.59 N	122.30 W
Cache la Poudre ≃	200	40.25 N	104.36 W
Cache la Poudre, North Fork ≃	198	40.54 N	105.22 W
Cache Peak ⋀, Ca., U.S.	180	65.31 N	147.20 W
Cache Peak ⋀, Ca., U.S.	228	35.33 N	118.15 W
Cache Slough ≃	226	38.15 N	121.40 W
Cachéu	150	12.16 N	16.10 W
Cachi ≃	255	25.06 S	66.11 W
Cachimbo, Serra do ☒	250	8.30 S	55.50 W
Cachito	152	8.21 S	21.20 E
Cachoeira, Bra.	152	13.05 S	16.43 E
Cachir	130	36.36 N	98.52 E
Cachkadzor	84	40.33 N	44.43 E
Cachoeira ≃, Bra.	286c	10.28 N	66.46 W
Cachoeira, Reservatório ⌀ 1	287a	23.03 S	46.15 W
Cachoeira, Rio de ≃	255	18.48 S	50.38 W
Cachoeira Alta	255	18.48 S	50.58 W
Cachoeira de Goiás	255	16.44 S	50.38 W

Name	Page	Lat.	Long.
Cachoeira de Manteiga	255	16.39 S	45.16 W
Cachoeira de Minas	256	22.21 S	45.47 W
Cachoeira do Arari	250	1.01 S	48.58 W
Cachoeira do Sul	252	30.02 S	52.54 W
Cachoeira Grande, Alto da ⋀	256	21.54 S	44.06 W
Cachoeira Paulista	256	22.40 S	45.01 W
Cachoeiras	287a	22.39 S	43.28 W
Cachoeiras de Macacu	256	22.28 S	42.39 W
Cachoeirinha	250	8.29 S	36.14 W
Cachoeiro de Itapemirim	255	20.51 S	41.06 W
Cachos, Punta ⋗	252	27.39 S	71.02 W
Cachos, Rio dos ≃	287b	23.36 S	46.26 W
Cachrov	60	49.16 N	13.18 E
Cachuela Esperanza	248	10.32 S	65.38 W
Cachuma, Lake ⌀ 1	204	34.35 N	119.55 W
Cacilhas	266c	38.41 N	9.09 W
Cacine	150	11.08 N	14.57 W
Caciporé ≃	250	3.51 N	51.08 W
Caciporé, Cabo ⋗	250	3.55 N	51.07 W
Cáciulaţi	38	44.38 N	26.10 E
Cacnipa Island ı	116	10.30 N	119.04 E
Cacócum	240p	20.44 N	76.23 W
Cacólo	152	10.07 S	19.17 E
Cacoconda	152	13.43 S	15.06 E
Caconde	256	21.33 S	46.38 W
Cacra	248	12.48 S	75.48 W
Cactus	196	36.04 N	102.00 W
Cactus Flat ≃	204	37.45 N	116.45 W
Cactus Peak ⋀	204	37.47 N	116.53 W
Caçu	255	18.37 S	51.04 W
Cacuaco	152	8.47 S	13.22 E
Cacula	152	14.29 S	14.05 E
Caculé	255	14.30 S	42.13 W
Caculuvar ≃	152	16.46 S	14.36 E
Cacuri, Ang.	152	8.14 S	18.20 E
Cacuri, Ven.	246	4.48 N	65.21 W
Cacuso	152	9.26 S	15.43 E
Cadale	144	2.45 N	46.19 E
Cadaqués	34	42.17 N	3.17 E
Cadarini ≃	248	6.20 N	59.45 W
Čadca	30	49.26 N	18.48 E
Caddington	42	51.51 N	0.27 W
Caddo, Ok., U.S.	196	34.07 N	96.15 W
Caddo, Tx., U.S.	196	32.38 N	98.40 W
Caddo ≃	194	34.10 N	93.03 W
Caddo Creek ≃	196	34.14 N	96.59 W
Caddo Lake ⌀ 1	194	32.42 N	94.01 W
Caddo Mills	222	33.04 N	96.14 W
Caddo Peak ⋀	222	32.29 N	97.24 W
Caddy Vista	216	42.50 N	87.54 W
Cadell ≃	162	22.51 S	141.55 E
Cadena, Arroyo de la ≃	196	26.17 N	104.00 W
Cadena, Cerro ⋀	200	26.50 N	104.04 W
Cadena, Punta ⋗	240m	18.18 N	67.14 W
Cadenberge	52	53.46 N	9.04 E
Cadenet	62	43.44 N	5.22 E
Cadeo	62	44.58 N	9.48 E
Cadereyta de Jiménez	232	25.36 N	100.00 W
Cader Idris ⋀	42	52.42 N	3.54 W
Cadibarrawirracanna, Lake ⌀	162	28.52 S	135.27 E
Cadig, Mount ⋀	116	14.09 N	122.27 E
Cadillac, Sk., Can.	184	49.44 N	107.43 W
Cadillac, Fr.	62	44.38 N	0.19 W
Cadillac, Mi., U.S.	216	44.15 N	85.24 W
Cadipietra (Steinhaus)	64	46.59 N	11.59 E
Cadishead	262	53.25 N	2.26 W
Cadix			
— Cádiz ⌐	34	36.32 N	6.18 W
Cádiz, Esp.	34	36.32 N	6.18 W
Cádiz, Pil.	116	10.57 N	123.18 E
Cadiz, In., U.S.	218	39.55 N	85.29 W
Cadiz, Ky., U.S.	194	36.51 N	87.50 W
Cadiz, Oh., U.S.	214	40.16 N	80.59 W
Cádiz, Bahía de c	34	36.35 N	6.50 W
Cádiz, Golfo de c	34	36.50 N	7.10 W
Cadiz Lake ⌀	204	34.18 N	115.24 W
Cadlao Island ı	116	11.13 N	119.21 E
Cadnam	42	50.55 N	1.35 W
Cadobec ≃	88	58.40 N	98.51 E
Cadobec ≃	88	58.40 N	98.51 E
Cadogan	214	40.49 N	79.34 W
Cadomin	182	53.02 N	117.20 W
Cadoneghe	64	45.26 N	11.55 E
Cadore ≃ 1	64	46.30 N	12.20 E
Cadosia	210	41.58 N	75.18 W
Cadott	190	44.56 N	91.09 W
Cadoux	168a	30.47 S	117.08 E
Caduruan Point ⋗	116	11.45 N	124.05 E
Caduta, Fosso delle ≃	267a	41.56 N	12.12 E
Cadwell	192	32.20 N	83.02 W
Cady Marsh Ditch ≃	278	41.33 N	87.29 W
Cady Mountain ⋀ 2	228	34.48 N	116.27 W
Čadyr-Lunga	38	46.03 N	28.49 E
Cadzand	52	51.22 N	3.25 E
Caen	62	49.11 N	0.21 W
Caengo (Kwenge) ≃	152	4.50 S	18.42 E
Caerano di San Marco	64	45.47 N	12.04 E
Caere ≃ 1	66	42.00 N	12.07 E
Caergwrie	44	53.07 N	3.03 W
Caerleon	42	51.37 N	2.57 W
Caernarfon	44	53.08 N	4.16 W
Caernarfon Bay c	44	53.05 N	4.30 W
Caernarvon Castle ⌂	44	53.08 N	4.16 W
Caerphilly	42	51.35 N	3.14 W
Caerphilly Castle ⌂	42	51.34 N	3.14 W
Caersws	42	52.31 N	3.25 W
Caesar Creek ≃	218	39.29 N	84.06 W
Caesar Creek, Anderson Fork ≃	218	39.33 N	83.58 W
Caesar Creek Lake ⌀ 1	218	39.30 N	84.00 W
Cæsarea			
— Qesari, Ḥorbat ⌂ 1	132	32.30 N	34.53 E
Caetanópolis	255	19.18 S	44.24 W
Caeté	255	19.54 S	43.40 W
Caeté ≃	246	3.03 S	68.39 W
Caeté, Morro ⋀ 2	287a	23.03 S	43.39 W
Caetité	255	14.04 S	42.29 W
Cafayate	252	26.05 S	65.58 W
Cafelândia do Leste	255	16.40 S	53.25 W
Cafima	152	16.39 S	16.27 E
Cafu	152	16.27 S	15.14 E
Cafuini ≃	246	1.17 N	57.11 W
Cagaan Chajrchan	88	49.25 N	94.15 E
Cagaan Gol	86	48.57 N	89.07 E
Cagaan Nuur, Mong.	86	49.32 N	89.42 E
Cagaannuur, Mong.	100	49.00 N	105.03 E
Cagaan-Ovoo	102	45.51 N	105.17 E
Cagaan-Üür	88	49.28 N	98.30 E
Cágado ≃	256	50.32 N	101.30 E
Cagayan ≃	116	18.22 N	121.37 E
Cagayan ⌐ 3	116	17.55 N	121.50 E
Cagayancillo	116	9.35 N	121.15 E
Cagayan de Tawi-Tawi ı	116	7.01 N	118.30 E
Cagayan Island ı	116	9.36 N	121.14 E
Cagayan Islands ıı	116	9.40 N	121.16 E
Cagayan Sulu Island ı	116	7.01 N	118.30 E
Çagda	75	58.45 N	130.37 E
Caggiano	68	40.34 N	15.33 E
Çağış	130	39.30 N	28.01 E

Name	Page	Lat.	Long.
Çağlarca	130	39.05 N	39.10 E
Čagli	66	43.33 N	12.39 E
Cagliari	71	39.13 N	9.07 E
Cagliari ⌐ 4	71	39.30 N	8.45 E
Cagliari, Golfo di c	71	39.08 N	9.11 E
Cagliari, Stagno di ⌀	71	39.13 N	9.02 E
Caglinica ≃	86	53.59 N	69.47 E
Cagnano Varano	68	41.49 N	15.47 E
Cagnes-sur-Mer	62	43.40 N	7.09 E
Čagoda	76	59.10 N	35.17 E
Čagoda ≃	76	59.05 N	35.18 E
Čagodošča ≃	76	58.57 N	36.35 E
Cagojan	89	52.08 N	128.15 E
Cagra ≃	80	52.37 N	48.15 E
Cagraray Island ı	116	13.18 N	123.52 E
Cagua	246	10.11 N	67.27 W
Caguán ≃	246	0.08 S	74.18 W
Caguas	240m	18.14 N	66.02 W
Çaveri	84	41.48 N	43.29 E
Cagwait	116	8.55 N	126.18 E
Cahaba ≃	194	32.20 N	87.05 W
Cahabón	236	15.34 N	89.49 W
Cahabón ≃	236	15.35 N	89.36 W
Caha Mountains ☒	48	51.45 N	9.45 W
Caher	48	52.21 N	7.56 W
Caherdaniel	48	51.45 N	10.05 W
Cahersiveen	48	51.57 N	10.13 W
Cahokia	190	38.34 N	90.11 W
Cahokia Creek ≃	219	38.47 N	90.01 W
Cahokia Mounds State Park ✦	219	38.39 N	90.03 W
Cahoon Creek ≃	279a	41.29 N	81.55 W
Cahoon Park ✦	279a	41.29 N	81.56 W
Cahoonzie	210	41.23 N	74.48 W
Cahore Point ⋗	48	52.34 N	6.11 W
Cahors	62	44.27 N	1.26 E
Cahto Peak ⋀	204	39.41 N	123.35 W
Cahuilla Indian Reservation ← 4	204	33.30 N	116.43 W
Cahuinari ≃	246	1.21 S	70.44 W
Cahuita, Punta ⋗	236	9.44 N	82.45 W
Cai ≃	34	38.50 N	7.05 W
Caianda	152	11.02 S	23.31 E
Caiapó ≃, Bra.	250	8.52 S	49.36 W
Caiapó ≃, Bra.	255	15.49 S	51.53 W
Caiapó, Serra do ☒	255	17.00 S	52.00 W
Caiapônia	255	16.57 S	51.49 W
Caiazzo	68	41.11 N	14.22 E
Caibarién	240p	22.31 N	79.28 W
Cai Bau, Dao ı	110	21.10 N	107.27 E
Caibirán	116	11.34 N	124.35 E
Caiçara, Bra.	255	6.36 S	35.29 W
Caiçara, Bra.	255	15.34 S	50.12 W
Caicara de Maturín	246	9.49 N	63.36 W
Caicara de Orinoco	246	7.37 N	66.10 W
Caicedonia	246	4.20 N	75.50 W
Caicó	250	6.27 S	37.06 W
Caicos Bank ⌖ 1	238	21.35 N	71.55 W
Caicos Islands ıı	238	21.56 N	71.58 W
Caicos Passage ʊ	238	22.00 N	72.30 W
Caieiras	256	23.22 S	46.44 W
Caieiras ≃ 7	287b	23.23 S	46.44 W
Caigou	100	33.16 N	114.32 E
Caiguna	162	32.17 S	125.25 E
Caihuaping	100	26.54 N	113.23 E
Caijiachong	107	24.39 N	106.29 E
Caijialou	104	34.17 N	107.39 E
Caijiazhuang	105	40.48 N	114.44 E
Caiku	102	40.48 N	114.47 E
Cailloma	248	15.12 S	71.46 W
Caillou Bay c	194	29.06 N	90.56 W
Caima Bay c	116	13.42 N	122.48 E
Caimán, Islas			
— Cayman Islands	238	19.30 N	80.40 W
Caimanera	240p	19.59 N	75.09 W
Caimanes			
— Cayman Islands	238	19.30 N	80.40 W
Caiman Point ⋗	116	15.55 N	119.46 E
Caimbambo	152	12.58 S	14.01 E
Caine ≃	42	52.46 N	3.08 W
Cain Creek ≃	194	34.19 N	98.10 W
Caine ≃	248	18.23 S	65.21 W
Cainhoy	192	32.57 N	79.51 W
Cainsville	194	40.28 N	93.59 W
Cainsdorf	54	50.41 N	12.29 E
Cai Nuoc	109	8.56 N	105.01 E
Cairano	68	40.54 N	15.22 E
Cairari	250	2.33 S	49.07 W
Caird Coast ± 2	9	76.00 S	24.30 W
Caire, Le			
— Al-Qāhirah	142	30.03 N	31.15 E
Cairn Curran Reservoir ⌀ 1	169	37.04 S	143.59 E
Cairngorm Mountains ☒	46	57.06 N	3.50 W
Cairn Mountain ⋀	180	61.10 N	155.20 W
Cairnryan	46	54.58 N	5.02 W
Cairns	166	16.55 S	145.46 E
Cairns Lake ⌀	184	51.42 N	94.30 W
Cairnsmore of Carsphairn ⋀	46	55.15 N	4.12 W
Cairnsmore of Fleet ⋀			
Cairo, Ga., U.S.	192	30.52 N	84.12 W
Cairo, Ne., U.S.	198	41.00 N	98.36 W
Cairo, N.Y., U.S.	210	42.17 N	73.59 W
Cairo, Oh., U.S.	216	40.49 N	84.05 W
Cairo, W.V., U.S.	188	39.11 N	81.09 W
Cairo (Almaza)			
Airport ⌖, Miṣr	273c	30.06 N	31.22 E
Cairo (Imbābah)			
Airport ⌖, Miṣr	273c	30.04 N	31.12 E
Cairo, University of			
Cairoca, Pico do ⋀	256	23.18 S	44.36 W
Cairofa	152	14.05 S	12.54 E
Cairo International			
Airport ⌖	142	30.08 N	31.24 E
Cairo Main Station	273c	30.04 N	31.15 E
Cairo Montenotte	62	44.24 N	8.16 E
Cairu	255	13.30 S	39.03 W
Caister-on-Sea	44	52.39 N	1.44 E
Caistor	44	53.30 N	0.20 W
Caitingqiao	100	39.54 N	117.39 E
Caivano	68	40.57 N	14.18 E
Caiwu	102	35.46 N	117.28 E
Caiyan	102	25.15 N	116.28 E
Caiyu	105	39.42 N	116.37 E
Caizi Hu ⌀	100	30.48 N	117.05 E
Caja ≃, Ross.	85	56.18 N	52.56 E
Caja ≃, Ross.	88	52.28 N	122.35 E
Cajamaru, Ec.	246	1.42 S	78.46 W
Cajamarca, Perú	248	7.37 S	78.31 W
Cajamarca ⌐ 5	248	7.00 S	78.30 W
Cajamarquilla ⌂ 1	248	11.53 S	76.50 W
Cajari ≃	250	0.52 S	51.49 W
Cajatambo	248	10.28 S	77.02 W
Cajatyn, chrebet ☒	89	52.25 N	138.25 E
Čajek	85	41.56 N	74.30 E
Čajkovskij	80	56.47 N	54.09 E
Čajniče	38	43.33 N	19.04 E
Cajones, Cayos ıı 2	236	16.05 N	83.12 W
Cajon Mountain ⋀	228	34.16 N	117.25 W
Cajon Pass ≋	228	34.19 N	117.26 W
Cajon Summit ⋋	228	34.21 N	117.27 W
Cajuru	255	21.17 S	47.18 W
Caka	102	36.48 N	99.19 E
Caka Yanhu	102	36.40 N	99.20 E
Čakar, chrebet ☒	85	38.35 N	67.28 E
Čakeni	152	17.48 S	19.27 E
Çakir	88	50.27 N	103.35 E
Čakiran	130	41.10 N	35.47 E
Çakmak	130	40.34 N	39.42 E
Çakmak Daği ⋀	130	40.36 N	42.12 E
Cakovec	61	46.23 N	16.26 E
Cakovice ← 8	54	50.08 N	14.31 E
Čakung ⌀	269e	6.06 S	106.56 E
Čal	130	38.05 N	29.24 E
Cala, Transkei	158	31.30 S	27.37 E
Cala, Tür.	84	41.05 N	43.21 E
Cala, Embalse de ⌀ 1	34	37.50 N	6.00 W
Calabacillas ≃	234	23.13 N	99.45 W
Calabanga	116	13.42 N	123.12 E
Calabar	150	4.57 N	8.19 E
Calabasas, Arroyo ≃	280	34.12 N	118.36 W
Calabazar ← 8	286b	23.01 N	82.22 W
Calabazas Creek ≃	282	37.25 N	121.58 W
Calabernardo	70	36.52 N	15.08 E
Calabogie	206	45.18 N	76.43 W
Calabogie Lake ⌀	212	45.16 N	76.45 W
Calabozo	246	8.56 N	67.26 W
Calabozo, Ensenada de c	246	11.30 N	71.45 W
Calabria ⌐ 4	68	39.00 N	16.30 E
Calabria, Parco Nazionale di ✦	68	38.09 N	15.54 E
Calabugdong Island ı	116	11.06 N	119.41 E
Calacuccia	71	42.20 N	9.03 E
Caladang, Mount ⋀	116	14.49 N	121.21 E
Caladesi Island State Park ✦	208	28.02 N	82.49 W
Cala d'Oliva	71	41.05 N	8.20 E
Calafat	38	43.59 N	22.56 E
Calafquén, Lago ⌀	254	39.31 S	72.10 W
Calagand Island ı	116	11.29 N	123.13 E
Cala Gonone	71	40.18 N	9.38 E
Calaguas Islands ıı	116	14.27 N	122.55 E
Calahorra	34	42.18 N	1.58 W
Calais, Fr.	62	50.57 N	1.50 E
Calais, Me., U.S.	188	45.11 N	67.16 W
Calais, Canal de ≃	52	50.57 N	1.51 E
Calais, Pas de (Strait of Dover) ʊ			
Calako	152	12.59 S	23.30 E
Calalaste, Sierra de ☒	252	25.50 S	67.30 W
Calalzo di Cadore	64	46.27 N	12.23 E
Calama	252	22.28 S	68.56 W
Calamar, Col.	246	10.15 N	74.55 W
Calamar, Col.	246	1.58 N	72.41 W
Calamarca	248	16.55 S	68.09 W
Calamba, Pil.	116	14.13 N	121.10 E
Calamba, Pil.	116	8.35 N	123.39 E
Calamian Group ıı	116	12.00 N	120.00 E
Calamity Creek ≃	196	29.41 N	103.42 W
Calamocha	34	40.55 N	1.18 W
Calamonaci	70	37.31 N	13.17 E
Calañas	34	37.39 N	6.53 W
Calanca, Val V	64	46.16 N	9.07 E
Calandula	152	9.07 S	16.00 E
Calangianus	71	40.56 N	9.11 E
Calanna	68	38.11 N	15.43 E
Calapan	116	13.25 N	121.10 E
Calapooia ≃	202	44.38 N	123.08 W
Calapooya Mountains ☒			
Calarca	246	4.31 N	75.38 W
Calascibetta	70	37.35 N	14.16 E
Calasetta	71	39.07 N	8.23 E
Calatafimi	70	37.55 N	12.52 E
Calatayud	34	41.21 N	1.38 W
Calau	54	51.44 N	13.57 E
Calauag Bay c	116	13.55 N	122.17 E
Calavá, Capo ⋗	70	38.09 N	14.54 E
Calaveras ≃ 6	226	37.54 N	122.02 W
Calaveras, North Fork ≃	226	38.12 N	120.43 W
Calaveras Big Trees State Park ✦	226	38.16 N	120.19 W
Calaveras Point ⋗	282	37.29 N	122.02 W
Calaveras Reservoir ⌀			
Calaveritas Creek ≃	226	38.06 N	120.38 W
Calavino	64	46.03 N	10.59 E
Calavite, Cape ⋗	116	13.27 N	120.18 E
Calavite, Mount ⋀	116	13.26 N	120.20 E
Calavite Passage ʊ	116	13.30 N	120.25 E
Calbayog	116	12.04 N	124.36 E
Calbe	54	51.54 N	11.46 E
Calbuco	254	41.46 S	73.08 W
Calca	248	13.19 S	71.57 W
Calçado	250	8.44 S	36.22 W
Calcasieu ≃	194	30.00 N	93.20 W
Calcasieu Lake ⌀	194	29.55 N	93.17 W
Calceta	246	0.51 S	80.10 W
Calcha	248	20.53 S	66.09 W
Calchaquí	252	29.53 S	60.18 W
Calchaquí ≃	252	25.46 S	65.30 W
Calcinaia	66	43.41 N	10.37 E
Calcio	62	45.31 N	9.51 E
Calçoene	250	2.30 N	50.57 W
Calcutta, India	118	22.32 N	88.22 E
Calcutta, India	272b	22.32 N	88.22 E
Calcutta, Oh., U.S.	214	40.40 N	80.34 W
Calcutta University			

Name	Page	Lat.	Long.
Caldas da Rainha	34	39.24 N	9.08 W
Caldas de Reyes	34	42.36 N	8.38 W
Caldas Novas	255	17.45 S	48.38 W
Caldè	58	45.57 N	8.38 E
Caldecott Tunnel ← 5	282	37.52 N	122.12 W
Calden, Eng., U.K.	44	53.43 N	1.21 W
Calder, Eng., U.K.	262	53.49 N	2.24 W
Calder, Loch ⌀	46	58.31 N	3.36 W
Caldera	252	27.04 S	70.50 W
Caldera de Taburiente, Parque Nacional de la ✦	148	28.48 N	17.52 W
Calder and Hebble Navigation Canal ≃	262	53.43 N	1.54 W
Calder Bridge	44	54.27 N	3.29 W
Calderbrook	262	53.39 N	2.05 W
Calderdale ← 8	262	53.44 N	2.00 W
Calderstones Park ✦	262	53.23 N	2.54 W
Caldes	266d	41.37 N	10.56 E
Caldew ≃	44	54.54 N	2.56 W
Caldey Island ı	42	51.38 N	4.41 W
Caldicot	42	51.36 N	2.45 W
Caldiero	64	45.22 N	11.11 E
Caldiran	84	39.09 N	43.55 E
Caldonazzo	64	46.01 N	11.15 E
Caldonazzo, Lago di ⌀	88	53.47 N	119.12 E
Caldonka	88	53.47 N	119.12 E
Caldwell, Id., U.S.	202	43.39 N	116.41 W
Caldwell, Ks., U.S.	196	37.01 N	97.36 W
Caldwell, N.J., U.S.	276	40.51 N	74.17 W
Caldwell, Oh., U.S.	188	39.44 N	81.31 W
Caldwell, Tx., U.S.	222	30.31 N	96.41 W
Caldwell, Tx., U.S.	222	29.50 N	97.40 W
Caldwell Creek ≃	214	41.37 N	79.37 W
Caldwell-Wright Airport ⌖	276	40.53 N	74.17 W
Caldy	262	53.21 N	3.10 W
Cale ≃	42	50.59 N	2.20 W
Caledon, On., Can.	212	43.52 N	80.00 W
Caledon, S. Afr.	158	34.12 S	19.23 E
Caledon (Mohokare) ≃			
Caledon East	212	43.52 N	79.52 W
Caledon East	158		
Caledon East	232		
Caledonia, Belize	232	18.14 N	88.29 W
Caledonia, N.S., Can.	186	44.22 N	65.02 W
Caledonia, On., Can.	212	43.04 N	79.56 W
Caledonia, Mi., U.S.	216	42.47 N	85.31 W
Caledonia, Mn., U.S.	190	43.38 N	91.29 W
Caledonia, Ms., U.S.	194	33.40 N	88.19 W
Caledonia, N.Y., U.S.	214	42.58 N	77.51 W
Caledonia, Oh., U.S.	214	40.38 N	82.58 W
Caledonia, Wi., U.S.	216	41.17 N	78.27 W
Caledonian Canal ≃	46	56.50 N	5.06 W
Caledonia State Park ✦	208	39.56 N	77.29 W
Calego	152	12.10 S	23.36 E
Calella	34	41.37 N	2.40 E
Calemba	152	16.04 S	15.44 E
Calendzicha	84	42.37 N	42.04 E
Calenzano	66	43.51 N	11.09 E
Calera, Al., U.S.	194	33.06 N	86.45 W
Calera, Ok., U.S.	196	33.56 N	96.25 W
Calera Creek ≃	282	37.27 N	121.54 W
Caleta Olivia	254	46.26 S	67.32 W
Caleufú	252	35.35 S	64.33 W
Calexico	204	32.40 N	115.29 W
Calf Island ı	283	42.20 N	70.54 W
Calf Islands ıı	278	40.59 N	73.38 W
Calfkiller ≃	188	35.49 N	85.28 W
Calf of Man ı	44	54.03 N	4.48 W
Calfpasture ≃	188	37.58 N	79.28 W
Calf Pasture Point ⋗	276	41.05 N	73.24 W
Calgary	182	51.03 N	114.05 W
Calhan	198	39.02 N	104.17 W
Calhern ≃	266c	38.44 N	9.12 W
Calhoun, Al., U.S.	194	32.46 N	86.30 W
Calhoun, Ga., U.S.	192	34.30 N	84.57 W
Calhoun, Ky., U.S.	194	37.32 N	87.16 W
Calhoun, Mo., U.S.	194	38.28 N	93.37 W
Calhoun Falls	192	34.05 N	82.36 W
Cali, Col.	246	3.27 N	76.31 W
Cali, Tür.	130	40.10 N	28.54 E
Calian Point ⋗	116	6.07 N	125.42 E
Calicoan Island ı	116	10.59 N	125.48 E
Calico Ghost Town ı	204	34.57 N	116.52 W
Calico Rock	196	36.07 N	92.08 W
Calicut	122	11.15 N	75.46 E
California, Mo., U.S.	194	38.37 N	92.33 W
California, Pa., U.S.	214	40.04 N	79.54 W
California ⌐ 3, Ca., U.S.	180	37.30 N	119.30 W
California ⌐ 3, Méx.	232	30.00 N	115.00 W
California, Gulf of c	232	28.00 N	112.00 W
California, University of ⌂ 2			
California Aqueduct ≃	204	33.52 N	117.12 W
California City	204	35.08 N	117.55 W
California Creek ≃	196	35.59 N	99.33 W
California Institute of Technology ⌂ 2	280	34.08 N	118.08 W
California Institution for Men ⌂ 2	280	33.59 N	117.40 W
California Institution for Women ⌂ 2	280	33.57 N	117.38 W
California-Los Angeles, University of (U.C.L.A.) ⌂ 2	280	34.04 N	118.26 W
California State Polytechnic University ⌂ 2	280	34.04 N	117.49 W
California State University (Long Beach) ⌂ 2	280	33.47 N	118.06 W
California State University (Los Angeles) ⌂ 2	280	34.04 N	118.10 W
California State University (Dominguez Hills) ⌂ 2	280	33.52 N	118.17 W
California State University (Fullerton), Ca., U.S. ⌂ 2	280	33.53 N	117.53 W
California State University (Northridge), Ca., U.S. ⌂ 2	280	34.14 N	118.32 W
California State University (Hayward) ⌂ 2, Ca.			
Calilegua, Parque Nacional ✦	252	23.40 S	64.50 W
Calimere, Point ⋗	122	10.18 N	79.52 E
Calindó	248	5.33 S	43.51 W
Calimesa	228	34.00 N	117.03 W
Cálinești	38	45.18 N	23.33 E

Symbol	English	Berg/Deutsch	Español	Français	Português
⋀	Mountain	Berg	Montaña	Montagne	Montanha
☒	Mountains	Gebirge	Montañas	Montagnes	Montanhas
≋	Pass	Paß	Paso	Col	Passo
V	Valley, Canyon	Tal, Cañon	Valle, Cañón	Vallée, Canyon	Vale, Canhão
≃	Plain	Ebene	Llano	Plaine	Planície
⋗	Cape	Kap	Cabo	Cap	Cabo
ı	Island	Insel	Isla	Île	Ilha
ıı	Islands	Inseln	Islas	Îles	Ilhas
±	Other Topographic Features	Andere Topographische Objekte	Otros Elementos Topográficos	Autres données topographiques	Outros acidentes topográficos

ESPAÑOL

Nombre	Página	Lat.°′	Long.°′ W = Oeste
Calion	194	33.19 N	92.32 W
Calipatria	204	33.07 N	115.30 W
Calispell Peak ʌ	202	48.26 N	117.30 W
Calistoga	226	38.34 N	122.34 W
Calitri	68	40.54 N	15.27 E
Calitzdorp	158	33.33 S	21.42 E
Calizzano	62	44.14 N	8.07 E
Calka	84	41.37 N	44.05 E
Calkinskoje vodochranilišče ⊜[1]	84	41.38 N	44.03 E
Čalkojdy	85	40.44 N	73.39 E
Calla	226	37.46 N	121.11 W
Callabonna, Lake ⊜	166	29.45 S	140.04 E
Callabonna Creek ≃	166	29.38 S	140.08 E
Callac	32	48.24 N	3.26 W
Callaghan, Mount ʌ	204	39.42 N	116.57 W
Callahan	192	30.33 N	81.49 W
Callahan, Mount ʌ	200	39.26 N	108.07 W
Callahans	276	40.53 N	74.37 W
Callan	48	52.33 N	7.23 W
Callander, On., Can.	190	46.13 N	79.23 W
Callander, Scot., U.K.	46	56.15 N	4.14 W
Callang	116	17.02 N	121.38 E
Callanish	46	58.12 N	6.43 W
Callanmarca	248	12.52 S	74.38 W
Callanna	166	29.38 S	137.55 E
Callantsoog	52	52.49 N	4.41 E
Callao, Perú	248	12.04 S	77.09 W
Callao, Va., U.S.	208	37.58 N	76.33 W
Callao □[4]	286d	12.04 S	77.09 W
Callaquén, Volcán ʌ[1]	252	37.54 S	71.26 W
Callas	62	43.35 N	6.32 E
Callaway	198	41.17 N	99.55 W
Callaway □[6]	219	38.50 N	91.52 W
Callaway Gardens ♦	192	32.51 N	84.52 W
Calle	56	51.20 N	8.13 E
Callensburg	214	41.08 N	79.33 W
Callery	214	40.45 N	80.02 W
Call Hill ʌ[2]	210	42.13 N	77.40 W
Calliano, It.	62	45.00 N	8.15 E
Calliano, It.	64	45.56 N	11.05 E
Calliaqua	241h	13.08 N	61.12 W
Callicoon	210	41.46 N	75.03 W
Callicoon Center	210	41.50 N	74.57 W
Calliham	196	28.29 N	98.21 W
Calling Lake	182	55.15 N	113.12 W
Calling Lake ⊜	182	55.13 N	113.15 W
Callington, Austl.	168b	35.07 S	139.02 E
Callington, Eng., U.K.	42	50.30 N	4.18 W
Calliope	166	24.00 S	151.12 E
Callosa d'En Sarrià	34	38.39 N	0.07 W
Callosa de Segura	34	38.08 N	0.52 W
Calloway Canal ≊	226	35.24 N	119.01 W
Calmar, Ab., Can.	182	53.16 N	113.49 W
Calmar → Kalmar, Sve.	26	56.40 N	16.22 E
Calmar, Ia., U.S.	190	43.11 N	91.51 W
Călmăţui ≃	38	44.50 N	27.50 E
Calmazzo	66	43.40 N	12.46 E
Calmbach	56	48.46 N	8.35 E
Calm Lake ⊜	190	48.46 N	92.04 W
Čal'mny-Varre	24	67.10 N	37.33 E
Čalna	24	61.55 N	34.01 E
Calnali	234	20.55 N	98.35 W
Calne	42	51.27 N	2.00 W
Calobre	236	8.19 N	80.51 W
Calola	152	16.30 S	17.51 E
Calolbon	116	13.36 N	124.06 E
Calólo	152	10.00 S	14.53 E
Calolziocorte	62	45.48 N	9.26 E
Calonne-Ricouart	50	50.29 N	2.29 E
Caloocan	116	14.39 N	120.58 E
Caloosahatchee ≃	220	26.31 N	82.01 W
Caloosahatchee Canal ≊	220	26.46 N	81.27 W
Caloote	168b	34.58 S	139.16 E
Calore ≃, It.	68	41.11 N	14.28 E
Calore ≃, It.	68	40.31 N	15.01 E
Caloundra	166	26.48 S	153.09 E
Calouste-Gulbenkian, Museu de ⊎	266c	38.44 N	9.08 W
Caloveto	68	39.30 N	16.45 E
Calp	34	38.39 N	0.03 E
Calpulalpan	234	19.35 N	98.35 W
Čalpy	80	55.05 N	53.06 E
Calshot	42	50.49 N	1.19 W
Calstock	42	50.30 N	4.12 W
Caltabellotta	70	37.34 N	13.13 E
Caltagirone	70	37.14 N	14.31 E
Caltagirone ≃	70	37.21 N	14.42 E
Caltanissetta	70	37.29 N	14.04 E
Caltanissetta □[4]	70	37.29 N	14.04 E
Caltavuturo	70	37.49 N	13.53 E
Çaltılıbük	130	39.57 N	28.36 E
Caltra	48	53.26 N	8.25 W
Čaltyr'	83	47.17 N	39.30 E
Caluango	152	8.21 S	19.40 E
Calubian	116	11.27 N	124.26 E
Calucinga	152	11.18 S	16.12 E
Călugăreni	38	44.07 N	26.01 E
Caluire-et-Cuire	62	45.48 N	4.51 E
Calumbolaca	152	9.09 S	13.48 E
Calumet, Mi., U.S.	190	47.14 N	88.27 W
Calumet, Mn., U.S.	190	47.19 N	93.16 W
Calumet, Pa., U.S.	214	40.13 N	79.28 W
Calumet ≃	278	41.44 N	87.32 W
Calumet, Lake ⊜	216	41.41 N	87.35 W
Calumet City	216	41.36 N	87.31 W
Calumet Harbor ⊂	278	41.44 N	87.32 W
Calumet Park	278	41.39 N	87.39 W
Calumet Park ♦	278	41.43 N	87.32 W
Calumet Sag Channel ≊	278	41.42 N	87.57 W
Calumpit	116	14.55 N	120.46 E
Calunda	152	12.06 S	23.23 E
Caluquembe	152	13.47 S	14.44 E
Calusa Island I	116	9.37 N	121.01 E
Caluso	62	45.18 N	7.53 E
Caluula	144	11.58 N	50.45 E
Caluula, Raasiga ›	144	11.59 N	50.47 E
Caluya Island I	116	11.55 N	121.34 E
Calvados □[5]	32	49.10 N	0.30 W
Calvello	68	40.28 N	15.51 E
Calver	44	53.16 N	1.38 W
Calvera	68	40.09 N	16.09 E
Calvert, Al., U.S.	194	31.09 N	88.01 W
Calvert, Tx., U.S.	222	30.58 N	96.40 W
Calvert □[6]	208	38.33 N	76.35 W
Calvert ≃	164	16.17 S	137.44 E
Calvert, Lough ⊜	169	38.11 S	143.42 E
Calvert City	194	37.02 N	88.21 W
Calvert Hills	166	17.15 S	137.20 E
Calvert Island I	182	51.35 N	128.00 W
Calverton, Eng., U.K.	44	53.02 N	1.05 W
Calverton, Md., U.S.	284c	39.03 N	76.56 W
Calverton, N.Y., U.S.	207	40.55 N	72.45 W
Calvi	36	42.34 N	8.45 E
Calvi, Monte ʌ	66	43.05 N	10.37 E
Calvia	34	39.34 N	2.31 E
Calvi dell'Umbria	66	42.24 N	12.34 E
Calvillo	234	21.51 N	102.43 W
Calvin, Ok., U.S.	196	34.58 N	96.14 W
Calvin, Pa., U.S.	214	40.20 N	78.02 W
Calvinia	158	31.25 S	19.45 E
Calvisano	64	45.20 N	10.20 E
Calvo, Monte ʌ	68	41.44 N	15.46 E
Calvörde	54	52.23 N	11.17 E
Calw	56	48.43 N	8.44 E
Calwa	226	36.42 N	119.45 W
Calypso	192	35.09 N	78.06 W
Calzada	248	6.02 S	77.02 W
Cam ≃	42	52.21 N	0.15 E
Camabatela	152	8.11 S	15.22 E
Camaçã ≃	248	6.35 S	66.27 W
Camaçari	255	12.41 S	38.18 W
Camachigama, Lac ⊜	190	47.50 N	76.19 W
Camacupa	152	12.03 S	17.30 E
Camaguán	246	8.06 N	67.36 W
Camagüey	240p	21.23 N	77.55 W
Camagüey □[4]	240p	21.30 N	78.00 W
Camagüey, Archipiélago de II	240p	22.30 N	78.10 W
Camaiore	64	43.56 N	10.18 E
Camaiú ≃	248	5.30 S	59.42 W
Camajuaní	240p	22.28 N	79.44 W
Camaldoli, Eremo di ⊎[1]	66	43.46 N	11.47 E
Camamu	255	13.57 S	39.07 W
Camaná	248	16.37 S	72.42 W
Camaná ≃	248	16.39 S	72.46 W
Camanaú ≃	246	1.51 S	61.14 W
Camanche	190	41.47 N	90.15 W
Camanche Reservoir ⊜[1]	226	38.13 N	120.58 W
Camandag Island I	116	11.59 N	124.25 E
Camanducaia	256	22.46 S	46.09 W
Camanducaia ≃, Bra.	256	22.39 S	46.58 W
Camanducaia ≃, Bra.	256	22.55 S	46.25 W
Camano Island I	224	48.10 N	122.30 W
Camaoí ≃	250	3.12 S	48.04 W
Camapuã	255	19.30 S	54.05 W
Camaquã	252	30.51 S	51.49 W
Camaquã ≃	252	31.17 S	51.47 W
Camará	246	3.55 S	62.44 W
Camarajibe	250	8.01 S	34.58 W
Camararé ≃	248	12.15 S	58.55 W
Camarat, Cap ›	62	43.12 N	6.41 E
Camarda	66	42.23 N	13.29 E
Çamardı	130	37.50 N	35.00 E
Camarès	32	43.49 N	2.53 E
Camargo, Bol.	248	20.39 S	65.13 W
Camargo, Méx.	232	27.40 N	105.10 W
Camargos, Represa de ⊜[1]	256	21.25 S	44.30 W
Camargue ◆[1]	62	43.34 N	4.34 E
Camargue, Parc Naturel Regional de ♦	62	43.30 N	4.28 E
Camarillo	228	34.12 N	119.02 W
Camarillo Heights	228	34.14 N	119.02 W
Camarina ⊥	70	36.52 N	14.27 E
Camariñas	34	43.07 N	9.10 W
Camarines Norte □[4]	116	14.10 N	122.40 E
Camarines Sur □[4]	116	13.35 N	123.20 E
Camarón, Arroyo ≃	196	27.08 N	100.00 W
Camarón, Cabo ›	236	15.00 N	85.05 W
Camarones	254	44.48 S	65.42 W
Camarones, Bahía ⊂	254	44.45 S	65.34 W
Camas, Esp.	34	37.24 N	6.02 W
Çamaş, Tür.	130	40.55 N	37.32 E
Camas, Wa., U.S.	224	45.35 N	122.23 W
Camas Creek ≃, Id., U.S.	202	43.20 N	114.24 W
Camas Creek ≃, Id., U.S.	202	44.53 N	114.44 W
Camas Creek ≃, Id., U.S.	202	43.53 N	112.21 W
Camas Creek ≃, Or., U.S.	202	45.01 N	118.59 W
Camastra	70	37.15 N	13.47 E
Camatagua, Embalse de ⊜[1]	246	9.50 N	67.00 W
Camatambo	152	6.30 S	15.18 E
Ca Mau	110	9.11 N	105.08 E
Ca Mau, Mui ›	110	8.38 N	104.44 E
Camaxilo	152	8.21 S	18.56 E
Camba	112	4.54 S	119.50 E
Camba Cassai	152	9.40 S	19.18 E
Cambados	34	42.30 N	8.48 W
Cambará	255	23.03 S	50.05 W
Čambarak	84	40.36 N	45.21 E
Camberley	42	51.21 N	0.45 W
Camberwell	169	37.50 S	145.04 E
Camberwell ◆[8]	260	51.28 N	0.05 W
Cambiano	62	44.58 N	7.47 E
Cambo	44	55.10 N	1.57 W
Cambo ≃	152	7.40 S	17.17 E
Cambodia (Kâmpŭchéa) □[1], Asia	108	13.00 N	105.00 E
Cambodia (Kâmpŭchéa) □[1], Asia	110	13.00 N	105.00 E
Cambois	44	55.10 N	1.31 W
Cambonda, Serra ⋏	152	12.06 S	14.00 E
Camboon	166	25.03 S	150.26 E
Cambooya	171a	27.42 S	151.52 E
Camboriú	252	27.01 S	48.38 W
Camborne	42	50.12 N	5.19 W
Cambra	210	41.11 N	76.18 W
Cambrai, Austl.	168b	34.39 S	139.17 E
Cambrai, Fr.	50	50.10 N	3.14 E
Cambremer	50	49.09 N	0.03 E
Cambria, Ca., U.S.	226	35.33 N	121.04 W
Cambria, In., U.S.	216	40.22 N	86.33 W
Cambria, Mi., U.S.	216	41.49 N	84.39 W
Cambria, Wi., U.S.	190	43.32 N	89.06 W
Cambria □[6]	214	40.29 N	79.16 W
Cambria Ice Field ⊓	182	55.55 N	129.30 W
Cambrian Mountains ⋏	28	52.35 N	3.35 W
Cambrian Park	226	37.15 N	121.55 W
Cambridge (Galt), On., Can.	212	43.22 N	80.19 W
Cambridge, N.Z.	172	37.53 S	175.28 E
Cambridge, Eng., U.K.	42	52.13 N	0.08 E
Cambridge, Id., U.S.	202	44.34 N	116.41 W
Cambridge, Il., U.S.	190	41.18 N	90.11 W
Cambridge, Ia., U.S.	190	41.53 N	93.31 W
Cambridge, Md., U.S.	208	38.33 N	76.04 W
Cambridge, Ma., U.S.	207	42.22 N	71.06 W
Cambridge, Mn., U.S.	190	45.34 N	93.13 W
Cambridge, Ne., U.S.	198	40.16 N	100.09 W
Cambridge, N.Y., U.S.	210	43.01 N	73.22 W
Cambridge, Oh., U.S.	188	40.02 N	81.35 W
Cambridge, Wi., U.S.	216	43.00 N	89.01 W
Cambridge Bay	176	69.03 N	105.05 W
Cambridge City	218	39.48 N	85.10 W
Cambridge Fiord ⊂[2]	176	71.20 N	74.44 W
Cambridge Gulf ⊂	164	14.55 S	128.15 E
Cambridge Park	274a	33.45 S	150.43 E
Cambridge Reservoir ⊜[1]	283	42.24 N	71.16 W
Cambridgeshire □[6]	42	52.20 N	0.05 E
Cambridge Springs	214	41.48 N	80.03 W
Cambrils	34	41.04 N	1.03 E
Cambriú, Ponta de ›	252	25.10 S	47.55 W
Cambuci ◆[8]	287b	23.34 S	46.37 W
Cambuí	256	22.37 S	46.04 W
Cambulo	152	7.48 S	21.14 E
Cambundi-Catembo	152	10.09 S	17.31 E
Cambuquira	256	21.51 S	45.18 W
Cambural	286c	10.26 N	66.59 W
Camburg	54	51.03 N	11.42 E
Camburú ≃	256	23.41 S	45.28 W
Camby	218	39.40 N	86.19 W
Čamčakly	128	37.56 N	63.06 E
Camden, Austl.	170	34.03 S	150.42 E
Camden, S. Afr.	158	26.38 S	30.07 E
Camden, Al., U.S.	194	31.59 N	87.17 W
Camden, Ar., U.S.	194	33.35 N	92.50 W
Camden, De., U.S.	208	39.06 N	75.32 W
Camden, Il., U.S.	219	40.09 N	90.46 W
Camden, In., U.S.	216	40.36 N	86.32 W
Camden, Me., U.S.	188	44.12 N	69.03 W
Camden, Mi., U.S.	216	41.45 N	84.45 W
Camden, Ms., U.S.	194	32.46 N	89.50 W
Camden, N.J., U.S.	208	39.55 N	75.07 W
Camden, N.Y., U.S.	210	43.20 N	75.44 W
Camden, N.C., U.S.	192	36.19 N	76.10 W
Camden, Oh., U.S.	218	39.37 N	84.38 W
Camden, S.C., U.S.	192	34.14 N	80.36 W
Camden, Tn., U.S.	194	36.03 N	88.05 W
Camden, Tx., U.S.	222	30.55 N	94.44 W
Camden □[6], N.J., U.S.	208	39.57 N	75.07 W
Camden □[6], N.C., U.S.	208	36.28 N	76.21 W

FRANÇAIS

Nom	Page	Lat.°′	Long.°′ W = Ouest
Camden ◆[8]	260	51.33 N	0.10 W
Camden, Grupo II	254	54.40 S	71.58 W
Camden Aerodrome ⊠	274a	34.03 S	150.41 E
Camden Bay ⊂	180	70.00 N	145.00 W
Camden Hills State Park ♦	188	44.17 N	69.05 W
Camden Lake ⊜	212	44.25 N	76.52 W
Camden Station ◆[5]	284b	39.17 N	76.37 W
Camdenton	194	38.00 N	92.44 W
Camedo	58	46.09 N	8.37 E
Cameia, Parque Nacional da ♦	152	11.45 S	21.20 E
Camel ≃	42	50.33 N	4.55 W
Camel, Mount ʌ[2]	169	36.45 S	144.43 E
Camelback Mountain ʌ, Ak., U.S.	180	62.33 N	157.20 W
Camelback Mountain ʌ, Pa., U.S.	210	41.03 N	75.21 W
Camelford	42	50.37 N	4.41 W
Çameli	130	37.05 N	29.20 E
Camels Hump ʌ	188	44.19 N	72.53 W
Cameo Acres	282	37.51 N	121.58 W
Camerano	66	43.32 N	13.33 E
Cameri	62	45.30 N	8.39 E
Cameri, Aeroporto di ⊠	266b	45.32 N	8.40 E
Camerino	66	43.08 N	13.04 E
Cameron, Ca., U.S.	226	38.39 N	120.56 W
Cameron, La., U.S.	194	29.47 N	93.19 W
Cameron, Mo., U.S.	194	39.44 N	94.14 W
Cameron, N.Y., U.S.	210	42.12 N	77.24 W
Cameron, Pa., U.S.	214	41.27 N	78.10 W
Cameron, S.C., U.S.	192	33.33 N	80.42 W
Cameron, Tx., U.S.	222	30.51 N	96.58 W
Cameron, W.V., U.S.	188	39.49 N	80.34 W
Cameron, Wi., U.S.	190	45.24 N	91.44 W
Cameron □[6]	214	41.31 N	78.14 W
Cameron ≃	224	49.17 N	124.38 W
Cameron, Lac ⊜	206	46.06 N	74.50 W
Cameron Highlands	114	4.29 N	101.27 E
Cameron Hills ⋏[2]	176	59.48 N	118.00 W
Cameron Lake ⊜, B.C., Can.	224	49.17 N	124.37 W
Cameron Lake ⊜, On., Can.	212	44.34 N	78.45 W
Cameron Mills	210	42.11 N	77.22 W
Cameron Mountains ⋏	172	46.00 S	167.00 E
Cameron Run ≃	284c	38.48 N	77.04 W
Cameroon (Cameroun) □[1]	134	6.00 N	12.00 E
Cameroon Mountain ʌ	152	4.12 N	9.11 E
Camerota	68	40.02 N	15.23 E
Cameroun → Cameroon □[1]	134	6.00 N	12.00 E
Camerún → Cameroon □[1]	134	6.00 N	12.00 E
Cametá	250	2.15 S	49.30 W
Camfield	164	17.09 S	131.21 E
Çamiçi Gölü ⊜	130	37.30 N	27.25 E
Camiguin □[4]	116	9.15 N	124.40 E
Camiguin Island I, Pil.	116	18.56 N	121.55 E
Camiguin Island I, Pil.	116	9.11 N	124.42 E
Camiling	116	15.42 N	120.24 E
Camilla	192	31.13 N	84.12 W
Camillus	210	43.02 N	76.19 W
Camin	54	53.27 N	10.58 E
Camiña	248	19.18 S	69.26 W
Caminha	34	41.52 N	8.50 W
Camino	226	38.44 N	120.40 W
Camiranga	250	1.48 S	46.17 W
Camiri	248	20.03 S	63.31 W
Camisano Vicentino	64	45.31 N	11.43 E
Camisea ≃	248	11.35 S	72.58 W
Camissombo	152	8.10 S	20.39 E
Camlad ≃	42	52.36 N	3.10 W
Çamlıbel	130	40.05 N	36.29 E
Çamlıdere, Tür.	130	37.08 N	39.03 E
Çamlıdere, Tür.	130	40.30 N	32.29 E
Çamlıyayla	130	37.09 N	34.36 E
Cam Lo	110	16.49 N	106.59 E
Čamlyk ≃	84	44.45 N	40.45 E
Cammal	210	41.24 N	77.28 W
Cammarata	70	37.38 N	13.38 E
Cammarta, Monte ʌ	70	37.37 N	13.36 E
Camoapa	236	12.23 N	85.31 W
Camocim	250	2.54 S	40.50 W
Camogli	62	44.21 N	9.09 E
Çamoluk	130	40.08 N	38.45 E
Camonica, Val V	64	46.00 N	10.20 E
Camooweal	166	19.55 S	138.07 E
Camopi ≃	250	3.11 N	52.20 W
Camorim ≃	287a	22.59 S	43.25 W
Camorim, Represa do ⊜[1]	287a	22.58 S	43.27 W
Camorta Island I	110	8.08 N	93.30 E
Camote, Cerro ʌ	286d	11.57 S	77.06 W
Camotes Islands II	116	10.40 N	124.24 E
Camotes Sea ⊤[2]	116	10.30 N	124.15 E
Camotlán ≃	234	22.01 N	104.15 W
Camowen ≃	48	54.36 N	7.18 W
Camp □[6]	222	33.00 N	94.58 W
Campagna	68	40.40 N	15.08 E
Campagna di Roma ◆[1]	66	41.50 N	12.35 E
Campagna Lupia	64	45.21 N	12.06 E
Campagnano di Roma	66	42.08 N	12.23 E
Campagnatico	66	42.53 N	11.16 E
Campagne-lès-Hesdin	50	50.24 N	1.52 E
Campaign	194	35.46 N	85.37 W
Campamento	236	14.33 N	86.42 W
Campana, Arg.	258	34.10 S	58.57 W
Campana, It.	68	39.24 N	16.50 E
Campana, Isla I	254	48.20 S	75.15 W
Campanario	34	38.52 N	5.37 W
Campanario, Cerro de ʌ	248	5.57 S	77.31 W
Campanella, Punta ›	68	40.34 N	14.19 E
Campanero, Cerro ʌ	246	5.54 N	65.12 W
Campanha	256	21.50 S	45.24 W
Campania □[4]	68	40.55 N	14.50 E
Campania Island I	182	53.05 N	129.30 W
Camparada	266b	45.39 N	9.19 E
Campaspe ≃, Austl.	166	21.00 S	146.24 E
Campaspe ≃, Austl.	169	36.41 S	144.31 E
Campbell, S. Afr.	158	28.48 S	23.44 E
Campbell, Ca., U.S.	226	37.17 N	121.56 W
Campbell, Mn., U.S.	198	46.05 N	96.24 W
Campbell, Mo., U.S.	194	36.29 N	90.04 W
Campbell, Ne., U.S.	198	40.18 N	98.44 W
Campbell, N.Y., U.S.	210	42.13 N	77.11 W
Campbell, Oh., U.S.	214	41.04 N	80.35 W
Campbell, Tx., U.S.	222	33.09 N	95.57 W
Campbell □[6]	218	38.55 N	84.20 W
Campbell, Cape ›	172	41.44 S	174.17 E
Campbell Airport ⊠	279b	40.21 N	80.11 W
Campbellfield	274b	37.41 S	144.57 E
Campbellford	212	44.18 N	77.48 W
Campbell Hall	210	41.27 N	74.16 W
Campbell Hill ʌ[2]	216	40.22 N	83.43 W
Campbell Island	182	52.10 N	128.09 W
Campbell Island I	9	52.30 S	169.05 E
Campbell Lake ⊜	182	50.01 N	125.27 W
Campbell Plateau ✢[3]	9	51.00 S	170.00 E
Campbell Point ›	171a	27.22 S	153.55 E
Campbellpore	123	33.46 N	72.22 E
Campbell Range ⋏	180	61.08 N	129.45 W
Campbell River	182	50.01 N	125.15 W
Campbells ≃	170	33.42 S	149.37 E
Campbell's Airport ⊠	278	42.20 N	88.04 W
Campbell's-Bay	188	45.44 N	76.36 W
Campbellsburg, In., U.S.	218	38.39 N	86.15 W
Campbellsburg, Ky., U.S.	218	38.31 N	85.12 W
Campbell Slough ≃	226	39.22 N	121.51 W
Campbellsport	190	43.35 N	88.16 W

PORTUGUÊS

Nome	Página	Lat.°′	Long.°′ W = Oeste
Campbells River	170	33.54 S	149.37 E
Campbells Run ≃	279b	40.24 N	80.05 W
Campbellsville	194	37.20 N	85.20 W
Campbellton, N.B., Can.	186	48.00 N	66.40 W
Campbellton, Nf., Can.	186	49.17 N	54.56 W
Campbellton, P.E., Can.	186	46.47 N	64.18 W
Campbellton, Fl., U.S.	192	30.56 N	85.24 W
Campbell Town, Austl.	166	41.56 S	147.29 E
Campbelltown, Austl.	168b	34.53 S	138.40 E
Campbelltown, Austl.	170	34.04 S	150.49 E
Campbelltown, Pa., U.S.	208	40.17 N	76.35 W
Campbellville	212	43.29 N	79.59 W
Campbeltown	46	55.26 N	5.36 W
Camp Creek ≃, Ca., U.S.	226	38.38 N	120.40 W
Camp Creek ≃, Mo., U.S.	219	39.02 N	91.12 W
Camp Creek Lake ⊜[1]	222	31.03 N	96.19 W
Camp David ⊎	208	39.38 N	77.28 W
Camp de Frileuse ■	261	48.52 N	1.55 E
Camp de Satory ■	261	48.47 N	2.06 E
Camp Dix	218	38.29 N	83.17 W
Camp Douglas	190	43.55 N	90.16 W
Campeche	232	19.51 N	90.32 W
Campeche □[3], Méx.	232	19.00 N	90.30 W
Campeche □[3], Méx.	232	19.00 N	90.30 W
Campeche, Bahía de ⊂	232	20.00 N	94.00 W
Campeche Bank ✢[4]	16	22.00 N	90.00 W
Campechuela	240p	20.14 N	77.17 W
Campegine	64	44.45 N	10.32 E
Campello Monti	58	45.56 N	8.15 E
Camperdown, Austl.	169	38.14 S	143.09 E
Camperdown, S. Afr.	158	29.42 S	30.33 E
Camperville	184	51.59 N	100.09 W
Campestre	256	21.43 S	46.15 W
Cam Pha	110	21.01 N	107.19 E
Camp Hill, Al., U.S.	194	32.48 N	85.39 W
Camp Hill, Pa., U.S.	208	40.14 N	76.55 W
Campi Bisenzio	66	43.49 N	11.08 E
Campidano ◆[1]	71	39.30 N	8.47 E
Campiglia dei Fosci	66	43.27 N	11.03 E
Campiglia Marittima	66	43.03 N	10.37 E
Campillo de Llerena	34	38.30 N	5.50 W
Campillos	34	37.03 N	4.51 W
Campina ◆[1]	34	37.45 N	4.45 W
Campina Grande	250	7.13 S	35.53 W
Campinas	256	22.54 S	47.05 W
Campina Verde	255	19.31 S	49.28 W
Campinho, Rio do ≃	287a	22.52 S	43.37 W
Campione	58	45.58 N	8.58 E
Campione del Garda	64	45.45 N	10.45 E
Campi Salentina	68	40.24 N	18.01 E
Campitello	64	46.28 N	11.44 E
Camp King	150	4.55 N	7.58 W
Camp Lake	216	42.32 N	88.09 W
Camp Lake ⊜	212	45.27 N	78.54 W
Camp Leger ■	261	48.34 N	2.34 E
Camp Lejeune Marine Corps Base ■	192	34.40 N	77.21 W
Campli	66	42.43 N	13.41 E
Camplong	112	10.02 S	123.55 E
Campo, Cam.	152	2.22 N	9.49 E
Campo, Moç.	156	17.44 S	36.21 E
Campo, Co., U.S.	198	37.06 N	102.34 W
Campo, Réserve de ◆[4]	152	2.35 N	9.57 E
Campoalegre	246	2.41 N	75.20 W
Campo Alegre ≃	250	9.19 S	50.06 W
Campo Alegre de Goiás	255	17.39 S	47.45 W
Campobasso	66	41.34 N	14.39 E
Campobasso □[4]	66	41.38 N	14.35 E
Campobello di Licata	70	37.15 N	13.55 E
Campobello di Mazara	70	37.38 N	12.45 E
Campobello Island I	186	44.53 N	66.55 W
Campo Belo	255	20.53 S	45.16 W
Campo Blenio	58	46.34 N	8.56 E
Campocologno	58	46.13 N	10.08 E
Campodarsego	64	45.30 N	11.54 E
Campo de Criptana	34	39.24 N	3.07 W
Campo de la Cruz	246	10.23 N	74.53 W
Campo de Marte ♦	286d	12.04 S	77.03 W
Campo de Marte ■	287b	23.30 S	46.37 W
Campo de Mayo ■	288	34.32 S	58.38 W
Campo di Giove	66	42.01 N	14.03 E
Campo di Trens (Trens)	64	46.52 N	11.29 E
Campo do Coelho	256	22.15 S	42.39 W
Campodolcino	58	46.24 N	9.21 E
Campo Erê	252	26.23 S	53.03 W
Campofelice di Fitalia	70	37.50 N	13.29 E
Campofelice di Roccella	70	37.59 N	13.53 E
Campofiorito	70	37.45 N	13.16 E
Campo Florido	255	19.47 S	48.35 W
Campoformido	64	46.01 N	13.09 E
Campo Formoso	250	10.31 S	40.20 W
Campofranco	70	37.30 N	13.43 E
Campogalliano	64	44.41 N	10.50 E
Campo Gallo	252	26.35 S	62.51 W
Campo Grande, Arg.	252	27.13 S	54.58 W
Campo Grande, Bra.	255	20.27 S	54.37 W
Campo Grande ◆[8], Bra.	256	22.54 S	43.34 W
Campo Grande ◆[8], Port.	266c	38.45 N	9.09 W
Campo Indian Reservation ◆[4]	204	32.40 N	116.20 W
Campo Largo, Arg.	252	26.48 S	60.50 W
Campo Largo, Bra.	252	25.26 S	49.32 W
Campolaro	64	45.55 N	10.20 E
Campolasta (Astfeld)	64	46.40 N	11.22 E
Campolato, Capo ›	70	37.17 N	15.12 E
Campo Libertad ■	286b	23.05 N	82.26 W
Campolide	256	21.36 S	43.53 W
Campolieto	66	41.38 N	14.46 E
Campo Ligure	62	44.32 N	8.42 E
Campo Limpo Paulista	256	23.12 S	46.48 W
Campo Maior, Bra.	250	4.49 S	42.10 W
Campo Maior, Port.	34	39.01 N	7.04 W
Campomarino	66	41.57 N	15.02 E
Campo Militar Número Uno ■	286a	19.27 N	99.14 W
Campomorone	62	44.30 N	8.53 E
Campo Mourão	255	24.03 S	52.22 W
Campo Novo	252	27.42 S	53.48 W
Campo Pequeno ♦	266c	38.44 N	9.08 W
Campo Quijano	252	24.55 S	65.39 W
Campora	68	40.19 N	15.17 E
Camporeale	70	37.54 N	13.06 E
Camporgiano	64	44.09 N	10.20 E
Camporredondo	248	6.07 S	78.21 W
Campos	255	21.45 S	41.18 W
Campos Altos	255	19.41 S	46.10 W
Camposampiero	64	45.34 N	11.56 E
Campo Santo, Arg.	252	24.40 S	65.06 W
Camposanto, It.	64	44.47 N	11.08 E
Campos Belos	255	13.03 S	46.53 W
Campos de Cunha	256	22.55 S	44.49 W
Campos do Jordão	256	22.44 S	45.35 W
Campos Elisios	256	22.42 S	43.17 W
Campos Gerais	256	21.14 S	45.46 W
Campos Novos	252	27.24 S	51.12 W
Campos Sales	250	7.04 S	40.23 W
Campo Tencia, Pizzo ʌ	58	46.26 N	8.43 E
Campotosto	66	42.33 N	13.22 E
Campotosto, Lago di ⊜	66	42.32 N	13.22 E
Campo Tures (Sand in Taufers)	64	46.55 N	11.57 E
Campovalano	66	42.44 N	13.40 E
Camp Parks Communications Annex ■	282	37.44 N	121.54 W
Camp Pendleton Marine Corps Base ■	228	33.19 N	117.18 W
Camp Point	219	40.02 N	91.04 W
Camp Ruby	222	30.42 N	94.45 W
Campsie	274a	33.55 S	151.06 E
Campsie Fells ⋏[2]	46	56.02 N	4.12 W
Camp Springs	208	38.48 N	76.54 W
Campti	194	31.53 N	93.07 W
Campton	192	37.44 N	83.32 W
Camptonville	226	39.27 N	121.03 W
Camptown	210	41.43 N	76.14 W
Campus	216	41.01 N	88.18 W
Campuya ≃	246	1.43 S	73.30 W
Camp Verde	200	34.33 N	111.51 W
Campville	210	42.06 N	76.09 W
Camp Wood	196	29.40 N	100.01 W
Cam Ranh	110	11.54 N	109.09 E
Cam Ranh, Vinh ⊂	110	11.53 N	109.10 E
Camrose, Ab., Can.	182	53.01 N	112.50 W
Camrose, Wales, U.K.	42	51.51 N	5.01 W
Camsell ≃	176	65.40 N	118.07 W
Camu ≃	250	1.15 N	57.09 W
Camucia	66	43.16 N	11.58 E
Camucuio	152	14.12 S	13.20 E
Camurí Chiquito, Quebrada ≃	286c	10.37 N	66.52 W
Çamurlu Dağ ʌ	130	40.21 N	42.26 E
Camuy	240m	18.29 N	66.51 W
Çam Xuyen	110	18.15 N	106.00 E
Čamyndy	85	41.37 N	74.20 E
Čamzinka	80	54.24 N	45.47 E
Çan, Tür.	130	40.02 N	27.03 E
Çan, Tür.	130	39.09 N	40.13 E
Can ≃	42	51.44 N	0.28 E
Canaan, Ct., U.S.	207	42.01 N	73.19 W
Canaan, Fl., U.S.	220	28.48 N	81.14 W
Canaan, In., U.S.	218	38.52 N	85.25 W
Canaan, N.Y., U.S.	210	42.25 N	73.27 W
Canaan, Vt., U.S.	206	44.59 N	71.32 W
Canaan ≃	186	45.55 N	65.47 W
Canaan Lake ⊜	276	40.47 N	73.01 W
Canaan Valley State Park ♦	188	39.02 N	79.32 W
Cana-brava ≃, Bra.	255	13.11 S	48.11 W
Cana-brava ≃, Bra.	255	12.12 S	48.40 W
Cañacao Bay ⊂	269f	14.29 N	120.55 E
Canaçari, Lago ⊜	250	2.57 S	58.15 W
Canada □[1]	176	60.00 N	95.00 W
Cañada, Loma la ʌ[2]	240p	21.41 N	82.57 W
Canada Bay ⊂	186	50.43 N	56.10 W
Cañada de Caracheo	234	20.22 N	100.57 W
Cañada de Gómez	252	32.49 S	61.24 W
Cañada Honda	252	31.59 S	68.33 W
Canada Lake ⊜	210	43.10 N	74.32 W
Cañada Nieto	258	33.43 S	58.05 W
Canadarago Lake ⊜	210	42.48 N	75.01 W
Canada's Wonderland ♦	275b	43.51 N	79.33 W
Cañada Verde → Villa Huidobro	252	34.50 S	64.35 W
Canadaway Creek ≃	214	42.28 N	79.22 W
Canadensis	210	41.11 N	75.15 W
Canadian	196	35.54 N	100.22 W
Canadian ≃, U.S.	196	35.27 N	95.03 W
Canadian ≃, Co., U.S.	200	40.53 N	106.20 W
Canadian, Deep Fork ≃	196	35.28 N	95.50 W
Canadian Forces Base Trenton ■	212	44.07 N	77.33 W
Canadice Lake ⊜	210	42.43 N	77.34 W
Cañadón Seco	254	46.33 S	67.35 W
Canaguá ≃	246	7.57 N	69.36 W
Canaima	246	6.14 N	62.52 W
Canaima, Parque Nacional ♦	246	4.27 N	62.00 W
Canajoharie	210	42.54 N	74.34 W
Çanakkale	130	40.09 N	26.24 E
Çanakkale □[4]	130	40.10 N	26.45 E
Çanakkale Boğazı (Dardanelles) ʮ	130	40.15 N	26.25 E
Canal, Islas del → Channel Islands II	28	49.20 N	2.20 W
Canala	175f	21.32 S	165.57 E
Canale	62	44.48 N	8.00 E
Canale, Val V	64	46.29 N	13.30 E
Canalejas	234	19.57 N	99.39 W
Canal Flats	182	50.09 N	115.48 W
Canal Fulton	214	40.53 N	81.35 W
Canal Lake ⊜	212	44.34 N	79.03 W
Canal Lewisville	214	40.18 N	81.50 W
Canal Point	220	26.51 N	80.38 W
Canals	252	33.33 S	62.53 W
Canal Winchester	188	39.51 N	82.48 W
Canamã ≃	248	8.45 S	59.15 W
Canandaigua	210	42.52 N	77.20 W
Canandaigua Lake ⊜	210	42.49 N	77.16 W
Canandaigua Outlet ≃	210	43.04 N	77.00 W
Cananea	232	30.57 N	110.18 W
Cananéia	252	25.01 S	47.57 W
Canan Station	214	40.28 N	78.26 W
Canapine, Forca)(	66	42.45 N	13.12 E
Canápolis	255	18.44 S	49.13 W
Canapville	50	49.19 N	0.08 E
Cañar	246	2.33 S	78.56 W
Cañar □[4]	246	2.30 S	79.00 W
Canard ≃	214	42.09 N	83.06 W
Canard, Lac au ⊜	206	45.48 N	71.31 W
Canarias, Islas (Canary Islands) II	148	28.00 N	15.30 W
Canaries	241f	13.55 N	61.04 W
Canaro	64	44.56 N	11.40 E
Canarreos, Archipiélago de los II	240p	21.50 N	82.30 W
Canarsie ◆[8]	276	40.38 N	73.53 W
Canarsie Park ♦	276	40.38 N	73.53 W
Canarsie Polder I	276	40.37 N	73.52 W
Canary Basin ✢[1]	10	30.00 N	25.00 W
Canary Islands → Canarias, Islas II	148	28.00 N	15.30 W
Cañas	236	10.25 N	85.07 W
Canaseraga	210	42.27 N	77.46 W
Canaseraga Creek ≃	210	42.45 N	77.50 W
Cañasgordas	246	6.45 N	76.01 W
Canastota	210	43.04 N	75.45 W
Canatlán	232	24.31 N	104.47 W
Canaveral, Cape ›	220	28.27 N	80.32 W
Canaveral Bight ⊂[3]	220	28.26 N	80.33 W
Canaveral National Seashore ♦	220	28.45 N	80.45 W
Canaveral Peninsula ›[1]	220	28.28 N	80.34 W
Cañaveras	34	40.22 N	2.24 W
Canavese □[9]	62	45.20 N	7.40 E
Canavieiras	255	15.39 S	38.57 W
Cañazas	236	8.19 N	81.13 W
Canazei	64	46.28 N	11.46 E
Canbelego	166	31.33 S	146.19 E
Canberra	171b	35.17 S	149.08 E
Canberra Wildlife Gardens ♦	171b	35.20 S	149.09 E
Canby, Ca., U.S.	204	41.26 N	120.52 W
Canby, Mn., U.S.	198	44.42 N	96.16 W
Canby, Or., U.S.	224	45.15 N	122.41 W
Cancajanang, Mount ʌ	116	11.04 N	124.47 E
Cancale	32	48.41 N	1.51 W
Cancano, Lago di ⊜	64	46.31 N	10.18 E
Cance ≃	62	45.12 N	4.48 E
Cancellara	68	40.44 N	15.56 E
Cancello e Arnone	68	41.04 N	14.03 E
Canchaque	248	5.24 S	79.36 W
Canche ≃	50	50.31 N	1.39 E
Cancon	32	44.32 N	0.38 E
Cancún	232	21.05 N	86.46 W
Čančur	88	53.49 N	106.59 E
Canda	64	45.03 N	11.30 E
Candala → Qandala	144	11.28 N	49.52 E
Candarave	248	17.16 S	70.15 W
Çandarlı	130	38.56 N	26.56 E
Çandarlı Körfezi ⊂	130	38.52 N	26.55 E
Candás	34	43.35 N	5.46 W
Candé	32	47.34 N	1.02 W
Candeias, Bra.	255	12.40 S	38.33 W
Candeias, Bra.	255	20.47 S	45.16 W
Candeias ≃	248	8.39 S	63.31 W
Candela, It.	68	41.08 N	15.31 E
Candela, Méx.	232	26.50 N	100.40 W
Candela, Río de ≃	196	27.16 N	100.18 W
Candelaria, Arg.	252	27.28 S	55.44 W
Candelaria, Arg.	252	32.04 S	65.49 W
Candelária, Bra.	252	29.40 S	52.48 W
Candelaria, Col.	246	3.25 N	76.20 W
Candelaria, Cuba	240p	22.44 N	82.58 W
Candelaria, Pil.	116	15.38 N	119.56 E
Candelaria ≃	232	18.37 N	91.14 W
Candelaria Loxicha	234	15.54 N	96.31 W
Candelaro ≃	68	41.34 N	15.53 E
Candeleda	34	40.09 N	5.14 W
Candelo, Austl.	166	36.46 S	149.42 E
Candelo, It.	62	45.33 N	8.07 E
Candia → Iráklion	38	35.20 N	25.09 E
Candiac	206	45.23 N	73.31 W
Candia Canavese	62	45.20 N	7.53 E
Candia Lomellina	62	45.11 N	8.36 E
Cándido Aguilar	232	25.30 N	98.02 W
Cândido de Abreu	252	24.35 S	51.20 W
Cândido Mendes	250	1.27 S	45.43 W
Candies Creek ≃	192	35.18 N	84.51 W
Candijay	116	9.49 N	124.30 E
Çandır, Tür.	130	40.16 N	33.29 E
Çandır, Tür.	130	39.15 N	35.32 E
Candle	180	65.55 N	161.56 W
Candle Lake ⊜	184	53.50 N	105.18 W
Candlemas Islands II	18	57.03 S	26.40 W
Candlestick	194	32.15 N	90.20 W
Candlestick Park ♦	282	37.43 N	122.23 W
Candlewood, Lake ⊜	207	41.32 N	73.27 W
Candlewood Isle	207	41.28 N	73.27 W
Candlewood Knolls	207	41.28 N	73.27 W
Candlewood Shores	207	41.28 N	73.26 W
Čandman', Mong.	86	50.02 N	92.03 E
Čandman', Mong.	102	45.20 N	97.59 E
Cando, Ang.	152	16.30 S	18.19 E
Cando, Sk., Can.	184	52.23 N	108.14 W
Cando, N.D., U.S.	198	48.29 N	99.12 W
Candombé ≃	152	16.54 S	21.52 E
Candon	116	17.12 N	120.27 E
Candon Point ›	116	17.13 N	120.24 E
Candor, N.Y., U.S.	210	42.13 N	76.20 W
Candor, N.C., U.S.	192	35.17 N	79.44 W
Candover	158	27.28 S	31.57 E
Cane ≃, Austl.	162	21.33 S	115.23 E
Cane ≃, La., U.S.	194	31.31 N	92.43 W
Cane ≃, N.C., U.S.	192	36.00 N	82.16 W
Canea → Khaniá	38	35.31 N	24.02 E
Caneadea	210	42.23 N	78.09 W
Caneças	266c	38.49 N	9.14 W
Cane Creek ≃	194	36.29 N	90.28 W
Canegrate	266b	45.34 N	8.56 E
Canela	252	29.22 S	50.50 W
Canelas	232	25.06 N	106.34 W
Canelles, Embalse de ⊜[1]	34	42.10 N	0.30 E
Canelli	62	44.43 N	8.17 E
Canelones	258	34.32 S	56.17 W
Canelones □[5]	258	34.35 S	56.15 W
Canelón Grande, Arroyo ≃	258	34.30 S	56.24 W
Cane Run ≃	218	38.13 N	84.37 W
Cañete, Chile	252	37.48 S	73.24 W
Cañete, Esp.	34	40.03 N	1.35 W
Caneva	64	45.58 N	12.26 E
Caney	198	37.00 N	95.56 W
Caney ≃	196	36.20 N	95.42 W
Caney Brook ≃	276	41.07 N	73.50 W
Caney Creek ≃, Ar., U.S.	194	33.46 N	93.07 W
Caney Creek ≃, Tx., U.S.	196	28.46 N	95.39 W
Caney Creek ≃, Tx., U.S.	222	32.48 N	95.33 W
Caney Creek ≃, Tx., U.S.	222	30.28 N	95.38 W
Caney Creek ≃, Tx., U.S.	222	30.04 N	96.08 W
Caney Creek ≃, Tx., U.S.	222	31.52 N	96.13 W
Caney Creek ≃, Tx., U.S.	222	31.03 N	94.33 W
Caney Creek ≃, Tx., U.S.	222	30.53 N	95.48 W
Caney Creek ≃, Tx., U.S.	222	30.07 N	95.10 W
Canfield	214	41.01 N	80.45 W
Canfield Island I	276	41.06 N	73.23 W
Canfranc	34	42.43 N	0.31 W
Cangaíba ◆[8]	287b	23.30 S	46.31 W
Cangallo	248	13.33 S	74.12 W
Cangamba	152	13.40 S	19.54 E
Cangandala	152	9.45 S	16.33 E
Cangandala, Parque Nacional da ♦	152	9.45 S	16.50 E
Cangas, Bra.	248	16.05 S	56.33 W
Cangas, Esp.	34	42.16 N	8.47 W
Cangas de Narcea	34	43.11 N	6.33 W
Cangas de Onís	34	43.21 N	5.07 W
Cangbu	100	30.49 N	114.35 E
Can Gioc ≃	269c	10.42 N	106.37 E
Cangkuang, Tanjung ›	115a	6.51 S	105.15 E
Cangniutun	105	39.23 N	115.54 E
Cango Caves ⊥[5]	158	33.23 S	22.14 E
Cangola	152	7.58 S	15.52 E
Cangombe	152	14.24 S	19.59 E
Cangongo	152	9.24 S	17.30 E
Cangqian, Zhg	106	30.18 N	120.00 E
Cangqian, Zhg	106	30.17 N	120.25 E
Cangshangtun	105	40.03 N	117.32 E
Canguaretama	250	6.24 S	35.08 W
Canguçu	252	31.24 S	52.41 W
Canguera	256	23.36 S	47.09 W
Cangumbe	152	12.00 S	19.17 E
Cangwu	102	23.22 N	111.13 E
Cangxi	102	31.48 N	105.57 E
Čangyrtas	85	40.53 N	72.50 E
Cangyuan	102	23.12 N	99.16 E
Cangzhou	98	38.19 N	116.51 E
Canhoca	152	9.15 S	14.41 E
Canhotinho	250	8.53 S	36.12 W
Caniapiscau ≃	176	57.40 N	69.30 W
Caniapiscau, Lac ⊜	176	54.10 N	69.55 W
Canicanian	116	14.46 N	122.01 E
Canicattì	70	37.21 N	13.51 E
Canicattini Bagni	70	37.02 N	15.04 E
Canigao Channel ʮ	116	10.15 N	124.42 E
Canigou, Pic du ʌ	32	42.31 N	2.27 E
Canillas ◆[8]	266a	40.28 N	3.38 W
Canillejas ◆[8]	266a	40.27 N	3.37 W
Canim Lake	182	51.46 N	120.54 W
Canim Lake ⊜	182	51.52 N	120.45 W
Canim Lake Indian Reserve ◆[4]	182	51.47 N	121.00 W
Canindé	250	4.22 S	39.19 W
Canindé ≃	250	6.15 S	42.52 W
Canindeyú □[5]	252	24.15 S	55.15 W

≃ River	Fluß	Río	Rivière	Rio
≊ Canal	Kanal	Canal	Canal	Canal
∟ Waterfall, Rapids	Wasserfall, Stromschnellen	Cascada, Rápidos	Chute d'eau, Rapides	Cascata, Rápidos
ʮ Strait	Meeresstraße	Estrecho	Détroit	Estreito
⊂ Bay, Gulf	Bucht, Golf	Bahía, Golfo	Baie, Golfe	Baía, Golfo
⊜ Lake, Lakes	See, Seen	Lago, Lagos	Lac, Lacs	Lago, Lagos
⩦ Swamp	Sumpf	Pantano	Marais	Pântano
⊓ Ice Features, Glacier	Eis- und Gletscherformen	Accidentes Glaciales	Formes glaciaires	Acidentes glaciares
⊤ Other Hydrographic Features	Andere Hydrographische Objekte	Otros Elementos Hidrográficos	Autres données hydrographiques	Outros acidentes hidrográficos

✢ Submarine Features	Untermeerische Objekte	Accidentes Submarinos	Formes de relief sous-marin	Acidentes submarinos
□ Political Unit	Politische Einheit	Unidad Politica	Entité politique	Unidade política
⊎ Cultural Institution	Kulturelle Institution	Institución Cultural	Institution culturelle	Instituição cultural
⊥ Historical Site	Historische Stätte	Sitio Histórico	Site historique	Sitio histórico
♦ Recreational Site	Erholungs- und Ferienort	Sitio de Recreo	Centre de loisirs	Area de Lazer
⊠ Airport	Flughafen	Aeropuerto	Aéroport	Aeroporto
■ Military Installation	Militäranlage	Instalación Militar	Installation militaire	Instalação militar
◆ Miscellaneous	Verschiedenes	Misceláneo	Divers	Diversos

Column 1

Canino 66 42.28 N 11.45 E
Canipaan 116 8.35 N 117.16 E
Canipo Island I 116 10.59 N 120.57 E
Canisius College ◡² 284a 42.55 N 78.52 W
Canisp ⋏ 46 58.07 N 5.03 W
Canistear Reservoir @¹ 276 41.08 N 74.29 W
Canisteo 210 42.16 N 77.36 W
Canisteo ≃ 210 42.07 N 77.08 W
Canistota 198 43.35 N 97.17 W
Cañitas de Felipe Pescador 234 23.36 N 102.43 W
Canjáyar 34 37.00 N 2.44 W
Canjinge 152 10.12 S 21.17 E
Cankhor 144 10.46 N 46.13 E
Çankırı 130 40.36 N 33.37 E
Çankırı ◻⁴ 130 40.40 N 34.00 E
Canlanan 116 10.22 N 123.12 E
Canlaon Volcano ⋏¹ 116 10.25 N 123.08 E
Canley Vale 274a 33.53 S 150.57 E
Canmore 182 51.05 N 115.21 W
Canna 68 40.05 N 16.30 E
Canna I 46 57.04 N 6.34 W
Canna, Sound of ⊔ 46 57.03 N 6.25 W
Cannanore 122 11.51 N 75.22 E
Cannara 66 43.00 N 12.35 E
Canne I 68 41.18 N 16.08 E
Cannel City 192 37.47 N 83.16 W
Cannelton 194 37.54 N 86.44 W
Canner ≃ 56 49.24 N 6.16 E
Cannero-Riviera 56 46.01 N 8.41 E
Cannes 62 43.33 N 7.01 E
Cannes, Bayou des ≃ 194 30.12 N 92.35 W
Canneto, It. 66 43.12 N 10.44 E
Canneto, It. 70 38.29 N 14.58 E
Canneto sull'Oglio 64 45.09 N 10.25 E
Cannich 46 57.21 N 4.44 W
Cannich ≃ 46 57.21 N 4.44 W
Cannifton 212 44.12 N 77.23 W
Canning, Arg. 288 34.53 S 58.30 W
Canning, Austl. 168a 32.02 S 115.56 E
Canning, N.S., Can. 186 45.09 N 64.25 W
Canning ≃, Austl. 168a 32.01 S 115.51 E
Canning ≃, Ak., U.S. 180 70.05 N 145.30 W
Canning Hill ⋏ 162 28.50 S 117.49 E
Canning Lake 212 44.56 N 78.38 W
Canning Reservoir @¹ 168a 32.10 S 116.09 E
Cannington, On., Can. 212 44.21 N 79.02 W
Cannington, Eng., U.K. 42 51.09 N 3.04 W
Cannobio 58 46.04 N 8.42 E
Cannock 42 52.42 N 2.09 W
Cannock Chase ◄¹ 42 52.43 N 2.00 W
Cannon ≃ 190 44.35 N 92.33 W
Cannon Air Force Base ◼ 196 34.23 N 103.18 W
Cannon Ball 198 46.23 N 100.35 W
Cannonball ≃ 198 46.26 N 100.38 W
Cannon Beach 224 45.53 N 123.57 W
Cannondale 207 41.12 N 73.25 W
Cannon Falls 190 44.30 N 92.54 W
Cannonsburg 216 43.03 N 85.28 W
Cannonsville Reservoir @¹ 210 42.08 N 75.19 W
Cannonvale 166 20.17 S 148.42 E
Cann River 166 37.34 S 149.10 E
Caño, Isla del I 236 8.44 N 83.53 W
Canoas 252 29.56 N 51.55 W
Canoas ≃, Bra. 252 27.36 S 51.25 W
Canoas ≃, Bra. 256 21.30 S 47.09 W
Canobie Lake 283 42.48 N 71.14 W
Canobie Lake ⊝ 283 42.48 N 71.15 W
Canobie Lake Park ♦ 283 42.48 N 71.15 W
Canoe ≃ 182 50.45 N 119.13 W
Canoe ≃, B.C., Can. 182 52.09 N 118.87 W
Canoe ≃, Ma., U.S. 283 41.58 N 71.08 W
Canoe Brook ≃ 276 40.45 N 74.22 W
Canoe Brook Reservoirs @¹ 276 40.45 N 74.21 W
Canoe Creek Indian Reserve ◄⁴ 182 51.32 N 122.15 W
Canoe Lake ⊝ 184 55.11 N 108.15 W
Canoe Lake Indian Reserve ◄⁴
Canoga Park ◼⁸ 280 34.12 N 118.35 W
Canoinhas 252 26.10 S 50.24 W
Canol 180 65.14 N 126.56 W
Canon 231 34.21 N 83.07 W
Canon ≃ 224 46.36 N 123.53 W
Canonbie 44 55.05 N 2.57 W
Canon City 200 38.24 N 105.13 W
Cañon del Sumidero, Parque Nacional ♦ 234 16.45 N 93.05 W
Caño Negro 236 10.54 N 84.44 W
Canonsburg 204 40.16 N 80.11 W
Canonsburg Lake ⊝ 279b 40.16 N 80.07 W
Canoochee ≃ 192 31.59 N 81.18 W
Canoole Cise 144 2.02 N 42.19 E
Canopus ⊥ 142 31.18 N 30.03 E
Canora 184 51.37 N 102.26 W
Canosa di Puglia 68 41.13 N 16.04 E
Canosino 64 44.35 N 10.27 E
Canot, Pointe ▸ 241o 16.12 N 61.28 W
Canouan I 238 12.43 N 61.20 W
Canova 198 43.52 N 97.30 W
Canova Beach 220 28.08 N 80.34 W
Cañovanas 240m 18.23 N 65.54 W
Cánoves ≃ 266d 41.37 N 2.22 E
Canova 54 53.12 N 12.54 E
Canowindra 166 33.34 S 148.38 E
Can Quer, Torrente de ≃ 266d 41.31 N 2.11 E
Cansado 148 20.51 N 17.02 W
Cansançõn 250 10.41 S 39.31 W
Canso 186 45.20 N 61.00 W
Canso, Strait of ⊔ 186 45.39 N 61.25 W
Canta 248 11.25 S 76.38 W
Cantabria 234 19.50 N 101.44 W
Cantabria (Santander) ◻⁴, Esp. 34 44.15 N 4.00 W
Cantábria ◻⁴, Esp. 34 43.15 N 4.00 W
Cantábrica, Cordillera ⋏ 34 43.00 N 5.00 W
Cantabriques — Cantábrica, Cordillera ⋏ 34 43.00 N 5.00 W
Cantagalo 255 21.58 S 42.22 W
Cantagalo, Cachoeira ⌐ 250 7.18 S 54.52 W
Cantal ◻⁵ 32 45.05 N 2.46 E
Cantalejo 34 41.15 N 3.55 W
Cantalupo in Sabina 66 42.18 N 12.39 E
Cantalupo nel Sannio 66 41.31 N 14.24 E
Cantal'vejergyn ≃ 180 67.38 N 179.22 W
Cantanhede, Bra. 250 3.39 S 44.24 W
Cantanhede, Port. 34 40.21 N 8.36 W
Cantareira ◄⁸ 287b 23.27 S 46.37 W
Cantareira, Serra da ⋏ 287b 23.25 S 46.39 W
Cantaura 246 9.19 N 64.21 W
Cant Clough Reservoir @¹ 262 53.46 N 2.09 W
Canteleu 50 49.27 N 1.02 E
Canterbury, Austl. 274a 33.55 S 151.07 E
Canterbury, Austl. 274b 37.49 S 145.05 E
Canterbury, N.B., Can. 186 45.53 N 67.29 W
Canterbury, Eng., U.K. 42 51.17 N 1.05 E
Canterbury Bight c³ 172 44.15 S 171.38 E
Canterbury Cathedral ⌂¹ 42 51.17 N 1.05 E
Canterbury Park Racecourse ⋏ 274a 33.54 S 151.07 E
Canterbury Plains ≃ 172 44.04 N 171.45 E
Canterbury Woods 284c 38.49 N 77.16 W
Can Tho 110 10.02 N 105.47 E
Cantiano 66 43.28 N 12.38 E

Column 2

Cantil 228 35.18 N 117.58 W
Cantiles, Cayo I 240p 21.36 N 82.02 W
Cantin Lake ⊝ 184 53.27 N 95.10 W
Canto do Buriti 250 8.07 S 42.58 W
Canto do Pontes 287a 22.58 S 43.04 W
Canto Grande, Quebrada V 286d 11.59 S 77.01 W
Cantoira 62 45.21 N 7.23 E
Canton, Ct., U.S. 207 41.49 N 72.53 W
Canton, Ga., U.S. 192 34.14 N 84.29 W
Canton, Il., U.S. 190 40.33 N 90.02 W
Canton, Ks., U.S. 198 38.23 N 97.25 W
Canton, Ma., U.S. 207 42.09 N 71.08 W
Canton, Mn., U.S. 190 43.31 N 91.55 W
Canton, Mo., U.S. 194 32.36 N 90.02 W
Canton, Mo., U.S. 219 40.07 N 91.37 W
Canton, N.J., U.S. 208 39.28 N 75.24 W
Canton, N.C., U.S. 188 44.35 N 75.10 W
Canton, N.Y., U.S. 192 35.31 N 82.50 W
Canton, Oh., U.S. 204 40.47 N 81.22 W
Canton, Ok., U.S. 196 36.03 N 98.35 W
Canton, Pa., U.S. 210 41.39 N 76.51 W
Canton, S.D., U.S. 198 43.18 N 96.35 W
Canton, Tx., U.S. 222 32.33 N 95.51 W
Canton — Guangzhou, Zhg. 100 23.06 N 113.16 E
Canton — Kanton I 174h 2.50 S 171.40 W
Canton Airport ◼ 174h 2.46 S 171.43 W
Canton Lake @¹ 196 36.08 N 98.36 W
Canton Lake State Recreational Area 196 36.08 N 98.39 W
Cantonment 194 30.36 N 87.20 W
Cantonbéry — Canterbury 42 51.17 N 1.05 E
Cantral 219 39.56 N 89.41 W
Cantribana 266c 38.53 N 9.25 W
Cantù 62 45.44 N 9.08 E
Cantua Creek 226 36.30 N 120.19 W
Cantua Creek ≃ 226 36.28 N 120.17 W
Cantwell 180 63.23 N 148.57 W
Cañuelas 258 35.03 S 58.44 W
Cañuelas ≃ 288 34.56 S 58.41 W
Cañuelas, Arroyo ≃ 258 34.55 S 58.38 W
Canumã 246 4.02 S 59.04 W
Canumã ≃ 246 3.55 S 59.10 W
Canunga 171a 28.01 S 153.12 E
Canungra 171a 28.05 S 153.10 E
Canungra Creek ≃ 171a 27.55 S 153.06 E
Canungra Jungle Training Ground ◼ 171a 28.02 S 153.10 E
Canutama 248 6.32 S 64.20 W
Canutillo 200 31.54 N 106.35 W
Canvasstown 172 44.18 S 173.40 E
Canvey Island 42 51.32 N 0.36 E
Canvey Island I 42 51.33 N 0.34 E
Çany 86 55.19 N 76.46 E
Çany, ozero ⊝ 86 54.50 N 77.30 E
Cany-Barville 50 49.47 N 0.38 E
Canyon, Yk., Can. 182 60.52 N 137.02 W
Canyon ≃, U.S. 282 37.19 N 122.09 W
Canyon, Tx., U.S. 196 34.58 N 101.55 W
Canyon City 202 44.23 N 118.56 W
Canyon Country 228 34.25 N 118.28 W
Canyon Creek ≃, Az., U.S. 200 33.49 N 110.40 W
Canyon Creek ≃, Ca., U.S. 226 39.22 N 120.45 W
Canyon Creek ≃, Id., U.S. 202 42.59 N 115.59 W
Canyon Creek ≃, Wa., U.S. 224 45.57 N 122.22 W
Canyon Creek ≃, Wa., U.S. 224 48.43 N 120.55 W
Canyon de Chelly National Monument ♦ 200 36.01 N 109.26 W
Canyon Ferry Lake @¹ 202 46.33 N 111.37 W
Canyonlands National Park ♦ 200 38.10 N 110.00 W
Canyonville 202 42.56 N 123.16 W
Canzar 152 7.38 S 21.32 E
Canzo 62 45.51 N 9.16 E
Cao ≃, Zhg. 98 40.29 N 124.08 E
Cao ≃, Zhg. 105 38.52 N 115.46 E
Cao Bang 110 22.40 N 106.15 E
Caochi 107 30.19 N 104.24 E
Caocun 100 31.42 N 118.56 E
Caodian, Zhg. 108 28.39 N 120.23 E
Caodian, Zhg. 100 33.21 N 112.39 E
Caodian, Zhg. 102 32.32 N 111.11 E
Cao'e 100 30.01 N 120.52 E
Cao'e ≃ 100 30.01 N 120.40 E
Caofang 100 26.04 N 116.35 E
Caogezhai 105 40.09 N 117.50 E
Caochezhang 104 40.54 N 123.53 E
Caojian 100 25.38 N 99.07 E
Caojiawopeng 104 42.40 N 122.12 E
Caojiawopu 104 42.37 N 122.19 E
Caojiawu 105 39.24 N 116.31 E
Caojiazhen 106 31.55 N 121.38 E
Caojiezi 107 29.53 N 106.24 E
Caojing 100 30.47 N 121.24 E
Caojun 100 29.41 N 116.17 E
Cao Lanh 110 10.27 N 105.38 E
Caclaoji 110 33.06 N 117.22 E
Caclisport, Loch c 46 55.54 N 5.37 W
Cacmaji 98 34.52 N 116.17 E
Caombo 152 8.43 S 16.51 E
Caonao ≃ 240p 22.05 N 78.05 W
Caonian 100 32.56 N 120.20 E
Caopeng 104 31.44 N 121.17 E
Caoping 106 28.48 N 118.22 E
Caoqiao 106 31.55 N 121.38 E
Caoqu 107 29.53 N 106.24 E
Caoshi, Zhg. 98 42.17 N 125.16 E
Caoshi, Zhg. 100 33.32 N 116.29 E
Caota 100 29.42 N 120.08 E
Caotang 104 31.16 N 118.59 E
Caoxi 100 31.48 N 117.18 E
Caoxian 98 34.53 N 115.33 E
Caoyangzi 100 26.34 N 118.47 E
Cap, Pointe du ▸ 241l 14.07 N 60.57 W
Capac 190 43.01 N 82.55 W
Capaccio 68 40.25 N 15.05 E
Capacciotti, Lago di ⊝¹ 68 41.10 N 15.47 E
Capage 70 38.10 N 13.14 E
Çapajev 152 13.21 S 21.05 E
Çapajev ≃ 80 50.12 N 51.10 E
Çapajevka, Ross. 82 54.38 N 35.50 E
Çapajevka, Ukr. 78 47.29 N 36.20 E
Çapajevo 80 49.21 N 35.54 E
Çapajevsk 80 52.58 N 49.41 E
Capalbio 66 42.27 N 11.25 E
Capalonga 116 14.20 N 122.30 E
Capanaparo ≃ 246 7.01 N 67.07 W
Capanema, Bra. 250 1.12 S 47.11 W
Capanema, Bra. 252 25.40 S 53.48 W
Capanne, Monte ⋏ 66 42.46 N 10.10 E
Capannoli 66 43.35 N 10.41 E

Column 3

Capão Bonito 255 24.01 S 48.20 W
Capão Doce, Morro ⋏ 252 26.43 S 51.25 W
Capão Redondo ◄⁸ 287b 23.40 S 46.46 W
Capaotigamau, Lac ⊝ 186 50.18 N 68.14 W
Caparaó, Parque Nacional do ♦ 255 20.33 S 41.45 W
Caparica 266c 38.40 N 9.12 W
Caparo Viejo ≃ 246 7.46 N 70.23 W
Capas 116 15.20 N 120.35 E
Capatárida 246 11.11 N 70.37 W
Cap-aux-Meules (Grindstone Island) 186 47.23 N 61.52 W
Cap aux Meules, Île du I 186 47.23 N 61.54 W
Capay 226 38.32 N 122.03 W
Cap-Chat 186 49.06 N 66.42 W
Cap-de-la-Madeleine 206 46.22 N 72.31 W
Cape (Kaap) ◻⁴ 156 31.00 S 23.00 E
Cape ≃ 206 20.49 S 146.51 E
Cape Arid National Park ♦ 162 33.40 S 123.25 E
Cape Barren Island I 166 40.25 S 148.12 E
Cape Bougainville Aboriginal Reserve ◄⁴ 164 14.10 S 126.30 E
Cape Breton Highlands National Park ♦ 186 46.45 N 60.45 W
Cape Breton Island I 196 46.00 N 60.30 W
Cape Broyle 186 47.06 N 52.57 W
Cape Canaveral 220 28.24 N 80.36 W
Cape Canaveral Air Force Station ◼ 220 28.29 N 80.35 W
Cape Charles 208 37.16 N 76.01 W
Cape Coast 150 5.05 N 1.15 W
Cape Cod Bay c 207 41.52 N 70.22 W
Cape Cod Canal ⊠ 207 41.47 N 70.30 W
Cape Cod National Seashore ♦ 207 41.56 N 70.00 W
Cape Comorin — Kanniyākumari 122 8.05 N 77.34 E
Cape Coral 220 26.33 N 81.56 W
Cape Croker Indian Reserve ◄⁴ 212 44.55 N 81.01 W
Cape Dorset 178 64.14 N 76.32 W
Cape Elizabeth 188 43.30 N 70.12 W
Cape Fear ≃ 192 33.53 N 78.00 W
Cape Girardeau 194 37.18 N 89.31 W
Cape Hatteras National Seashore ♦ 192 35.30 N 76.35 W
Cape Henlopen State Park ♦ 208 38.45 N 75.06 W
Cape Jervis 168b 35.36 S 138.06 E
Cape Johnson Tablemount ◄³ 17 17.08 N 177.15 W
Cape Krusenstern National Monument ♦ 180 67.30 N 163.40 W
Capela 250 10.30 S 37.04 W
Cape LaHave Island I 186 44.12 N 64.22 W
Cape la Hune 186 47.33 N 56.52 W
Capel Curig 44 53.06 N 3.54 W
Capelengue 152 9.12 S 19.43 E
Capelinha 255 17.42 S 42.31 W
Capelinha do Embirazal 256 22.02 S 45.26 W
Cape Lisburne 180 68.52 N 166.05 W
Capel'ka 76 58.03 N 28.59 E
Capella 166 23.05 S 148.02 E
Capella I 164 5.00 S 141.05 E
Capella [aan de IJssel] 56 51.55 N 4.35 E
Capellen 56 49.38 N 5.59 E
Capelongo 152 14.54 S 15.08 E
Cape Lookout National Seashore ♦ 192 34.40 N 76.23 W
Cape Lookout State Park ♦ 224 45.21 N 123.59 W
Cape Saint Mary 42 52.00 N 1.04 E
Cape May, N.J. 208 38.56 N 74.54 W
Cape May ◻⁶ 208 38.56 N 74.55 W
Cape May Coast Guard Air Station ◼ 208 38.57 N 74.53 W
Cape May Court House 208 39.04 N 74.49 W
Cape May Point 208 39.09 N 74.46 W
Capel'ka ≃ 152 16.10 S 21.00 E
Cape Melville National Park ♦ 164 14.20 S 144.30 E
Capenda Camulemba 152 9.24 S 18.27 E
Capenga ≃ 287a 22.49 S 43.37 W
Capenhurst 262 53.15 N 2.57 W
Cape of Good Hope Nature Reserve ♦ 158 34.18 S 18.26 E
Cape Pole 180 55.58 N 133.48 W
Cape Pond 226 42.38 N 70.38 W
Cape Porpoise 188 43.22 N 70.26 W
Cape Range National Park ♦ 162 22.10 S 113.55 E
Cape Rise ◄³ 8 42.00 S 15.00 E
Capemaum — Kefar Naḥum ⊥ 132 32.53 N 35.34 E
Cape Romanzof 180 61.49 N 165.56 W
Capertee 170 33.09 S 149.59 E
Cape Sable Island I 186 43.25 N 65.37 W
Cape Scott Provincial Park ♦ 182 50.45 N 128.20 W
Capesterre, Pointe de la ▸ 241o 16.03 N 61.33 W
Capesterre-Belle-Eau 241o 16.03 N 61.34 W
Capesthorne Hall ⌂¹ 262 53.15 N 2.14 W
Capestrano 66 42.16 N 13.46 E
Capetinga ≃ 256 22.04 S 47.14 W
Cape Tormentine 186 46.08 N 63.47 W
Cape Town (Kaapstad) 158 33.55 S 18.22 E
Cape Verde (Cabo Verde) ◻¹, Afr. 134 16.00 N 24.00 W
Cape Verde (Cabo Verde) ◻¹, Afr. 150a 16.00 N 24.00 W
Cape Verde Islands — Cape Verde ◻¹ 150a 16.00 N 24.00 W
Cape Verde Terrace
Cape Vincent 208 37.12 N 75.57 W
Cape Yakataga 180 60.04 N 142.26 W

Column 4

Capitan 200 33.32 N 105.34 W
Capitán Aracena, Isla I 254 54.10 S 71.20 W
Capitán Arturo Prat ◄³ 9 62.30 S 59.41 W
Capitán Bado 255 23.16 S 55.32 W
Capitán Bermúdez 252 32.49 S 60.43 W
Capitán Meza 252 26.55 S 55.15 W
Capitan Peak ⋏ 200 33.36 N 105.16 W
Capitán Sarmiento 252 34.10 S 59.48 W
Capitão de Campos 250 4.28 S 41.57 W
Capitão Enéas 255 16.21 S 43.43 W
Capitola 226 36.58 N 121.57 W
Capitol Heights 208 38.53 N 76.54 W
Capitol Park 208 39.08 N 75.30 W
Capitol Peak ⋏ 204 41.50 N 117.18 W
Capitol Reef National Park ♦ 200 38.11 N 111.20 W
Capitol View 192 33.57 N 80.56 W
Capivara ≃, Bra. 255 19.16 S 57.10 W
Capivari, Bra. 255 12.30 S 39.55 W
Capivari ≃, Bra. 256 22.14 S 44.57 W
Capivari ≃, Bra. 256 21.53 S 46.15 W
Capivari ≃, Bra. 256 22.26 S 45.47 W
Capivari ≃, Bra. 256 22.56 S 47.16 W
Capivari ≃, Bra. 256 21.30 S 44.20 W
Capivari ≃, Bra. 256 21.55 S 41.00 W
Capivari ≃, Bra. 256 24.09 S 46.48 W
Capivari, Canal ⊠ 287a 22.42 S 43.21 W
Capiz — Roxas 116 11.35 N 122.45 E
Capiz ◻⁴ 116 11.30 N 122.30 E
Capizzi 70 37.51 N 14.29 E
Caplan 186 48.06 N 65.41 W
Çaplejevka 78 51.43 N 33.12 E
Caplen 222 29.29 N 94.33 W
Caples Lake @¹ 226 38.42 N 120.03 W
Caplina ≃ 248 18.14 S 70.33 W
Çaplino, Ross. 180 64.25 N 172.15 W
Çaplino, Ukr. 78 48.09 N 36.14 E
Çapljina 36 43.07 N 17.42 E
Caplone, Monte ⋏ 64 45.50 N 10.38 E
Caplygin 76 53.14 N 39.58 E
Capnoyan Island I 116 10.44 N 120.54 E
Capoche ≃ 154 15.23 S 32.53 E
Capodichino, Aeroporto di ◼ 68 40.50 N 14.17 E
Capodimonte 66 42.33 N 11.55 E
Capo di Ponte 64 46.02 N 10.21 E
Capo d'Orlando 70 38.10 N 14.53 E
Capologo 58 45.55 N 8.59 E
Capoliveri 66 42.45 N 10.22 E
Caporolo ≃ 152 12.56 S 13.00 E
Caposele 68 40.49 N 15.13 E
Capostrada 66 43.57 N 10.54 E
Capot ≃ 240e 14.51 N 61.07 W
Capoterra 72 39.11 N 8.58 E
Capoti-an, Mount ⋏ 116 11.45 N 125.15 E
Capotoan, Mount ⋏ 116 12.09 N 124.57 E
Cappadocia ◻⁹ 130 38.30 N 36.00 E
Cappamore 68 52.37 N 8.20 W
Cap-Pelé 186 46.13 N 64.18 W
Capple Islands II 240m 18.17 N 64.54 W
Cappeln 52 52.48 N 8.07 E
Cappenberg 263 51.39 N 7.32 E
Cappenberg, Schloss ⌂ 263 51.39 N 7.32 E
Cappercleuch 44 55.29 N 3.12 W
Cappoquin 68 52.08 N 7.50 W
Cappricia ≃ 66 41.50 N 14.16 E
Capraia 66 43.03 N 9.50 E
Capraia, Isola ◻ 66 42.08 N 15.31 E
Capraia, Isola di I 66 43.02 N 9.49 E
Capranica 66 42.15 N 12.11 E
Caprara, Punta ▸ 71 41.07 N 8.19 E
Capreol 190 46.43 N 80.56 W
Capreol ≃ 71 41.12 N 9.28 E
Caprese Michelangelo 66 43.39 N 11.59 E
Capri 68 40.33 N 14.14 E
Capri, Isola di I 68 40.33 N 14.13 E
Capricorn, Cape ▸ 166 23.30 S 151.13 E
Capricorn Channel ⊔ 166 23.00 S 152.00 E
Capricorn Group II 166 23.28 S 152.00 E
Capri Leone 70 38.05 N 14.44 E
Caprivi Oss ◻⁵ 156 17.45 S 24.00 E
Caprivi Zipfel (Caprivi Strip) ◄⁵ 156 17.59 S 23.00 E
Caprock, Lago di ◻ 116 41.21 N 12.58 E
Capron, Il., U.S. 216 42.24 N 88.44 W
Capron, Va., U.S. 208 36.42 N 77.12 W
Cap Saint Jacques — Vung Tau 110 10.21 N 107.04 E
Cap-Santé 206 46.40 N 71.47 W
Capsoine 260 51.21 N 0.34 E
Captain Anthony Meldahl Dam ◄⁶ 192 39.43 N 84.15 W
Captain Cook 229d 19.29 N 155.55 W
Captain Cook Bridge ◄ 274a 34.00 S 151.08 E
Captain Cook Landing Place Park ♦ 274a 34.00 S 151.14 E
Captain Cook Monument ⊥ 174c 29.00 S 167.56 E
Captain Daniel Wright Woods ♦ 278 42.13 N 87.56 W
Captain Harbor c 207 41.00 N 73.35 W
Captain Pond ⊝ 283 42.48 N 71.10 W
Captains Flat 171b 35.35 S 149.27 E
Captieux 32 44.18 N 0.16 W
Captiva 220 26.31 N 82.11 W
Captiva Island I 220 26.31 N 82.11 W
Captree State Park ♦ 276 40.39 N 73.16 W
Capua 68 41.06 N 14.13 E
Capuá Island I 116 6.20 N 121.24 E
Capuáva 287b 23.39 S 46.29 W
Capuça ◄⁸ 152 17.22 S 21.18 E
Capuçapu ≃ 246 1.45 S 58.35 W
Capucin ▸ 240d 15.38 N 61.28 W
Çapul 180 65.37 N 128.43 W
Çapul Island I 116 12.26 N 124.11 E
Capulin Mountain National Monument ♦ 196 36.48 N 103.55 W
Capunda 152 15.38 S 19.43 E
Capurso 68 41.04 N 16.55 E
Caputh 54 52.21 N 12.26 E
Cap-Vert — Cape Verde ◻¹ 150a 16.00 N 24.00 W
Caquaenda 256 21.20 S 44.30 W
Caquetá ◻⁵ 248 1.00 N 74.00 W
Caquetá (Japurá) ≃ 248 1.30 S 69.20 W
Çar 72 50.22 N 80.55 E
Çara, Ityo. 144 5.52 S 30.10 E
Çara, Ross. 86 56.54 N 118.12 E
Cará, Ilha do I 250 0.01 S 50.50 W
Caraballeda 246 10.37 N 66.50 W
Carabanchel Alto ◄⁸ 266b 40.23 N 3.45 W
Carabanchel Bajo ◄⁸ 266b 40.23 N 3.47 W
Carabao Island I 116 12.04 N 121.56 E
Cardeña 248 14.43 N 70.17 W

Column 5

Carabaya, Cordillera de ⋏ 248 13.50 S 70.45 W
Carabayllo 248 11.52 S 77.02 W
Carabelas Grande ≃ 258 34.15 S 58.43 W
Carabiani ≃ 246 1.58 S 61.31 W
Caraboho ◻³ 246 10.10 N 68.05 W
Carabost 171b 35.36 S 147.44 E
Caracal 38 44.07 N 24.21 E
Caracalla, Terme di ⊥ 267a 41.53 N 12.29 E
Caracaraí 246 1.50 N 61.08 W
Caracas, Ven. 246 10.30 N 66.56 W
Caracas, Ven. 246 10.30 N 66.56 W
Carach 86 59.03 N 62.15 E
Carache 246 9.38 N 70.14 W
Caracol, Bra. 250 9.17 S 43.20 W
Caracol, Bra. 252 22.01 S 57.02 W
Caracollo 248 17.39 S 67.10 W
Caracorum — Karakoram Range ⋏ 120 35.30 N 77.00 E
Carácuaro de Morelos 234 18.46 N 101.02 W
Caradoc Indian Reserve ◄⁴ 214 42.59 N 81.29 W
Caraffa di Catanzaro 68 38.53 N 16.29 E
Caraga 116 7.20 N 126.34 E
Caragh, Lough ⊝ 48 52.03 N 9.52 W
Caraghnan Mountain ⋏ 166 31.20 S 149.03 E
Caraglio 62 44.25 N 7.26 E
Caraguata, Arroyo ≃ 288 34.24 S 58.38 W
Caraguatatuba 256 23.37 S 45.25 W
Caraguatatuba, Enseada de c 256 23.40 S 45.20 W
Caraguatay 252 25.16 S 56.52 W
Caraí 255 17.12 S 41.42 W
Caraíbamba 248 14.24 S 73.09 W
Caraíbas, Îles des — West Indies II 230 19.00 N 70.00 W
Caraïbes, Mer des — Caribbean Sea ⊤² 230 15.00 N 73.00 W
Caraigres, Cerro ⋏ 236 9.43 N 84.05 W
Caraíva ≃ 255 16.48 S 39.08 W
Carajari ≃ 250 4.45 S 54.20 W
Carajás 250 6.06 S 50.23 W
Carajás, Serra dos ⋏ 250 5.50 S 51.20 W
Carajás Bluff ⋏² 166 33.26 S 136.16 E
Caramagna-Piemonte 62 44.46 N 7.44 E
Caramánico Terme 66 42.09 N 14.00 E
Caramay 110 11.10 N 119.14 E
Caramanta ≃ 246 4.02 N 74.08 W
Caramanta Peninsula 116 13.46 N 123.52 E
Caramoran 116 13.59 N 124.08 E
Caramy ≃ 62 43.26 N 6.12 E
Caranavi 248 15.46 S 67.36 W
Carandaí 255 20.57 S 43.48 W
Carandayti 248 20.45 S 63.04 W
Carangola 255 20.44 S 42.02 W
Carano ≃ 64 46.16 N 11.27 E
Caranesbes 38 45.25 N 22.13 E
Carapá ≃ 252 24.30 S 54.20 W
Carapachay ≃¹ 288 34.25 S 58.35 W
Carapajó 250 2.16 S 49.22 W
Cara-Paraná ≃ 246 1.45 S 73.13 W
Carapeguá 252 25.48 S 57.14 W
Carapelle ≃ 68 41.30 N 15.55 E
Carapicuíba 256 23.31 S 46.50 W
Carapicuiba ◄⁷ 287b 23.31 S 46.50 W
Carapo ≃ 246 7.30 N 64.02 W
Caraquet 186 47.48 N 64.57 W
Caráquez 246 0.36 S 80.25 W
Carare ≃ 246 8.48 N 74.06 W
Carasco 62 44.21 N 9.21 E
Caras-Severin ◻⁶ 38 45.20 N 22.00 E
Carasca, Laguna ⊝ 236 15.23 N 83.55 W
Carate Brianza 62 45.41 N 9.14 E
Caratinga 255 19.47 S 42.08 W
Carauari 246 4.52 S 66.54 W
Caraúbas 250 5.47 S 37.34 W
Caravaca 34 38.06 N 1.51 W
Caravaggio 62 45.30 N 9.38 E
Caravelas 255 17.45 S 39.15 W
Caravelí 248 15.46 S 73.22 W
Caravelle, Presqu'île de la ▸ 240e 14.45 N 60.55 W
Caravius, Monte is ⋏ 72 39.01 N 8.55 E
Caraway 194 35.45 N 90.19 W
Carayaó 252 25.10 S 56.26 W
Carazinho 252 28.18 S 52.48 W
Carazo ◻⁵ 236 11.45 N 86.15 W
Carballino 34 42.26 N 8.05 W
Carballo 34 43.13 N 8.41 W
Carbet, Pitons du ⋏ 240e 14.42 N 61.07 W
Carbo 232 29.42 N 110.58 W
Carbol ≃ 70 37.32 N 12.59 E
Carbon, Ab., Can. 182 51.29 N 113.09 W
Carbon, Pa., U.S. 279b 40.17 N 79.52 W
Carbon, Tx., U.S. 222 32.16 N 98.50 W
Carbón ≃ 258 40.52 S 75.45 W
Carbon, Cap ▸ 36 36.47 N 5.06 E
Carbonado 224 47.04 N 122.03 W
Carbonara, Capo ▸ 71 39.06 N 9.31 E
Carbonara, Pizzo ⋏ 70 37.55 N 14.02 E
Carbonate 226 45.41 N 8.56 E
Carbon-Blanc 32 44.53 N 0.31 W
Carbon Canyon Dam ◄⁶ 280 33.55 N 117.50 W
Carbon Creek ≃ 280 33.49 N 118.04 W
Carbondale, Co., U.S. 200 39.24 N 107.12 W
Carbondale, Il., U.S. 194 37.43 N 89.13 W
Carbondale, Ks., U.S. 198 38.49 N 95.41 W
Carbondale, Pa., U.S. 210 41.34 N 75.30 W
Carbonear 186 47.45 N 53.13 W
Carboneras de Guadazaon 34 39.53 N 1.48 W
Carbon Hill 192 33.53 N 87.31 W
Carbonia 72 39.10 N 8.31 E
Carbonin (Schluderbach) 64 46.37 N 12.13 E
Carbost 46 57.18 N 6.22 W
Carcaixent 34 39.08 N 0.27 W
Carcajou ≃ 180 65.37 N 128.43 W
Carcans, Lac de c 32 45.08 N 1.08 W
Carcar 116 10.06 N 123.38 E
Carcarañá 252 32.51 S 61.09 W
Carcarañá ≃ 252 32.27 S 60.48 W
Carcar Point ≃ 116 10.05 N 123.41 E
Carcassonne 32 43.13 N 2.21 E
Carcavelos, Port. 266c 38.41 N 9.20 W
Carceri, Eremo delle ⊥ 66 43.05 N 12.42 E
Carcès 62 43.28 N 6.11 E
Carcross 180 60.10 N 134.42 W
Çardak, Tür. 130 38.06 N 36.49 E
Çardak, Uzb. 85 41.37 N 69.56 E
Cardal 266d 41.23 N 2.11 E

Column 6 (DEUTSCH)

Cárdenas, Cuba 240p 23.02 N 81.12 W
Cárdenas, Méx. 234 22.00 N 99.40 W
Cárdenas, Méx. 234 17.59 N 93.22 W
Cárdenas, Nic. 236 11.12 N 85.31 W
Cárdenas, Bahía de c 240p 23.05 N 81.10 W
Cardener ≃ 34 41.41 N 1.51 E
Carderock Springs 284a 38.59 N 77.10 W
Cardiel, Lago ⊝ 254 48.55 S 71.15 W
Cardiff, Austl. 170 32.57 S 151.41 E
Cardiff, Wales, U.K. 42 51.29 N 3.13 W
Cardiff ◻⁴, Wales, U.K. 208 39.43 N 76.20 W
Cardiff, N.J., U.S. 208 39.24 N 74.35 W
Cardiff by the Sea 228 33.01 N 117.16 W
Cardigan, P.E., Can. 186 46.14 N 62.37 W
Cardigan, Wales, U.K. 42 52.06 N 4.40 W
Cardigan Bay c, P.E., Can. 186 46.10 N 62.30 W
Cardigan Bay c, Wales, U.K. 42 52.30 N 4.20 W
Cardigan Island I 42 52.08 N 4.41 W
Cardigan State Park ♦ 188 43.38 N 71.54 W
Cardinal 212 44.47 N 75.23 W
Cardinale 68 38.38 N 16.23 E
Cardinal Heights 212 45.27 N 74.53 W
Cardinal Lake ⊝ 56 56.14 N 117.44 W
Cardington, Boph. 158 27.11 S 23.02 E
Cardington, Oh., U.S. 214 40.30 N 82.53 W
Cardinia Creek ≃ 274b 38.12 S 145.23 E
Cardona 169 37.58 S 145.25 E
Cardona 258 33.53 S 57.23 W
Cardonal, Punta ▸ 232 28.28 N 111.45 W
Cardoso 255 20.04 S 49.54 W
Cardozo 252 32.38 S 56.21 W
Card Sound ⊔ 220 25.20 N 80.18 W
Cardston 182 49.12 N 113.18 W
Cardwell, Austl. 166 18.16 S 146.02 E
Cardwell, Mo., U.S. 194 36.02 N 90.17 W
Cardwell Mountain ⋏ 194 35.41 N 85.41 W
Cardżou 128 39.06 N 63.34 E
Cardżou ◻⁴ 128 38.51 N 63.34 E
Careaçu 256 22.02 S 45.42 W
Careen Lake ⊝ 184 57.00 N 108.10 W
Carega, Cima ⋏ 64 45.41 N 11.08 E
Carei 38 47.42 N 22.28 E
Careiro 246 3.12 S 59.45 W
Careiro, Ilha do I 246 3.10 S 59.50 W
Carén 252 30.51 S 70.47 W
Çarencavan 84 40.24 N 44.38 E
Carencro 194 30.19 N 92.02 W
Carentan 32 49.18 N 1.14 W
Careri 68 38.18 N 16.07 E
Cares ≃ 34 43.19 N 4.36 W
Caresana 62 45.13 N 8.32 E
Caretta 192 37.20 N 81.40 W
Carevičšina 80 52.27 N 46.43 E
Carey, Lake ⊝ 162 29.05 S 122.15 E
Carey Downs 162 25.38 S 115.27 E
Careysburg 150 6.30 N 10.32 W
Cargados Carajos Shoals II 12 16.38 S 59.38 E
Cargill 32 56.33 N 3.22 W
Carhaix-Plouguer 32 48.17 N 3.35 W
Carhuamayo 248 10.55 S 76.02 W
Carhuanca 248 13.45 S 73.48 W
Carhuaz 248 9.16 S 77.38 W
Carhué 252 37.10 S 62.44 W
Caria ≃¹ 130 37.30 N 28.00 E
Cariaciaca 255 20.16 S 40.25 W
Cariaco 246 10.29 N 63.33 W
Cariaco, Golfo de c 246 10.30 N 64.00 W
Cariamanga 246 4.20 S 79.35 W
Cariati 68 39.30 N 16.56 E
Cariba, Punta ▸ 246 11.37 N 70.52 W
Caribbean Sea ⊤² 230 15.00 N 73.00 W
Caribe, Mar — Caribbean Sea ⊤² 230 15.00 N 73.00 W
Caribou ≃ 176 59.20 N 94.44 W
Caribou, N.S., Can. 186 45.46 N 62.42 W
Caribou, Me., U.S. 186 46.51 N 68.00 W
Caribou Island I 190 47.22 N 85.49 W
Caribou Mountain ⋏ 202 43.06 N 111.18 W
Caribou Mountains ⋏ 188 45.26 N 70.38 W
Caribou Range ⋏ 202 43.05 N 111.15 W
Caricin — Volgograd 80 48.44 N 44.25 E
Caridad, Pil. 269f 14.29 N 120.53 E
Caridade 250 4.15 S 39.15 W
Carife 68 41.01 N 15.12 E
Carignan 50 49.38 N 5.10 E
Carigara Bay c 116 11.24 N 124.40 E
Carignan, P.Q., Can. 214 45.27 N 73.18 W
Carignano 62 44.54 N 7.40 E
Carinaro 112 13.02 N 120.46 E
Carinda 166 30.28 S 147.41 E
Caringbah 274a 34.03 S 151.08 E
Carinhanha 255 14.18 S 43.47 W
Carinhanha ≃ 255 14.20 S 43.47 W
Carini 70 38.08 N 13.11 E
Carinhall ⊥ 54 52.59 N 13.22 E
Carini, Golfo di c 70 38.08 N 13.11 E
Carinish 46 57.31 N 7.18 W
Carinola 68 41.11 N 13.58 E
Carini ≃ 246 3.14 S 59.34 W
Carioca, Serra da ⋏ 226 22.47 S 43.18 W
Caripi ≃ 250 10.12 S 63.29 W
Caripito 246 10.08 N 63.06 W
Caripore 122 10.30 N 72.10 E
Caririaçú 250 7.02 S 39.17 W
Carirá 250 10.22 S 37.42 W
Caririé 3 0.57 S 40.27 W
Carisbrook 169 37.02 S 143.49 E
Carisbrooke ⌂ 260 50.41 N 1.19 W
Carisolo 64 46.10 N 10.45 E
Caritianas 248 9.25 S 63.06 W
Çarkari 85 41.41 N 69.54 E
Carkeek 283 41.08 N 74.18 W
Carków 54 52.52 N 14.44 E
Carlentini 70 37.16 N 15.01 E
Carle Place 276 40.44 N 73.36 W
Carleton, Méx. 234 25.44 N 103.44 W
Carleton, P.Q., Can. 186 48.06 N 66.08 W
Carleton, Mi., U.S. 216 42.03 N 83.23 W
Carleton, Ne., U.S. 198 40.18 N 97.40 W
Carleton, Mount ⋏ 186 47.23 N 66.53 W
Carleton Place 198 45.08 N 76.09 W

Carl-Cast I · 31

ESPAÑOL: Nombre · Página · Lat.°′ · Long.°′ W = Oeste
FRANÇAIS: Nom · Page · Lat.°′ · Long.°′ W = Ouest
PORTUGUÊS: Nome · Página · Lat.°′ · Long.°′ W = Oeste

Nombre / Nom / Nome	Página / Page	Lat.°′	Long.°′
Carlisle, Oh., U.S.	218	39.35 N	84.20 W
Carlisle, Pa., U.S.	208	40.12 N	77.11 W
Carlisle Barracks ■	208	40.13 N	77.11 W
Carlisle Bay c	241g	13.05 N	59.37 W
Carlisle Gardens	210	43.11 N	78.39 W
Carlisle Island I	180	52.52 N	170.02 W
Carlisle Springs	208	40.16 N	77.10 W
Carl Junction	194	37.10 N	94.33 W
Carlls ≐	276	40.41 N	73.20 W
Carloforte	71	39.08 N	8.18 E
Carlopoli	68	39.03 N	16.27 E
Carlópolis	255	23.25 S	49.41 W
Carlos, Isla I	254	54.03 S	73.20 W
Carlos Alves	256	21.37 S	43.07 W
Carlos Barbosa	252	29.18 S	51.30 W
Carlos Beguerie	258	35.29 S	59.06 W
Carlos Casares	252	35.38 S	61.21 W
Carlos Chagas	255	17.43 S	40.45 W
Carlos City	218	40.02 N	85.02 W
Carlos Forseca Amador	236	11.59 N	86.31 W
Carlos Keen	258	34.29 S	59.14 W
Carlos Manuel de Céspedes	240p	21.35 N	78.17 W
Carlos Pellegrini	252	32.03 S	61.48 W
Carlos Reyles	252	33.03 S	56.29 W
Carlos Sampaio	287a	22.42 S	43.31 W
Carlos Tejedor	252	35.23 S	62.25 W
Carlow	48	52.50 N	6.55 W
Carlow □6	48	52.40 N	6.50 W
Carloway	46	58.17 N	6.48 W
Carl Sandburg Home National Historic Site ⊥	192	35.16 N	82.27 W
Carlsbad → Karlovy Vary, Česká Rep.	54	50.11 N	12.52 E
Carlsbad, Ca., U.S.	228	33.09 N	117.20 W
Carlsbad, N.M., U.S.	196	32.25 N	104.13 W
Carlsbad, Tx., U.S.	196	31.36 N	100.38 W
Carlsbad Caverns National Park ♦	196	32.08 N	104.35 W
Carlsberg Ridge ✣3	12	6.00 N	61.00 E
Carlsborg	224	48.05 N	123.10 W
Carlsfeld	54	50.26 N	12.35 E
Carlstadt	276	40.50 N	74.05 W
Carlton, Austl.	274a	33.58 S	151.09 E
Carlton, Eng., U.K.	42	52.58 N	1.05 W
Carlton, Eng., U.K.	44	53.42 N	1.01 W
Carlton, Mn., U.S.	190	46.39 N	92.25 W
Carlton, Or., U.S.	224	45.18 N	123.11 W
Carlton, Tx., U.S.	196	31.55 N	98.10 W
Carlton Gardens ♦	274b	37.48 S	144.59 E
Carlton Lake ⊜	224	45.18 N	123.11 W
Carluke	46	55.45 N	3.51 W
Carlyle, Sk., Can.	184	49.38 N	102.16 W
Carlyle, Il., U.S.	219	38.36 N	89.22 W
Carlyle Lake ⊜1	219	38.40 N	89.18 W
Carmacks	180	62.05 N	136.18 W
Carmagnola	62	44.51 N	7.43 E
Carman	184	49.32 N	98.00 W
Carmanah Creek ≐	224	48.37 N	124.44 W
Carmangay	182	50.08 N	113.07 W
Carmanville	186	49.24 N	54.17 W
Carmarthen	42	51.52 N	4.19 W
Carmarthen Bay c	42	51.40 N	4.30 W
Carmaux	32	44.03 N	2.09 E
Carmel, Wales, U.K.	262	53.17 N	3.15 W
Carmel, Ca., U.S.	226	36.33 N	121.55 W
Carmel, In., U.S.	218	39.58 N	86.07 W
Carmel, N.J., U.S.	208	39.26 N	75.07 W
Carmel, N.Y., U.S.	210	41.26 N	73.41 W
Carmel ≐	226	36.32 N	121.56 W
Carmel, Mount ∧, Ca., U.S.	226	36.23 N	121.47 W
Carmel, Mount → Karmel, Har ∧, Yis.	132	32.44 N	35.02 E
Carmel Bay c	226	36.33 N	121.57 W
Carmel Head >	44	53.24 N	4.34 W
Carmel Highlands	226	36.30 N	121.56 W
Carmel Hills	226	36.32 N	121.53 W
Carmel Mountain ∧2	228	32.55 N	117.13 W
Carmelo	258	34.00 S	58.17 W
Carmel Point	226	36.31 N	122.55 W
Carmel Valley	226	36.29 N	121.43 W
Carmel Woods	226	36.34 N	121.54 W
Carmen → Ciudad del Carmen, Méx.	232	18.38 N	91.50 W
Carmen, Pil.	116	8.59 N	125.17 E
Carmen, Pil.	116	9.50 N	124.12 E
Carmen, Pil.	116	10.35 N	124.01 E
Carmen, Pil.	116	12.37 N	122.07 E
Carmen, Ok., U.S.	196	36.34 N	98.27 W
Carmen, Ur.	252	33.15 S	56.01 W
Carmen, Isla I	232	25.57 N	111.12 W
Carmen, Isla del I	232	13.42 N	91.40 W
Carmen, Río del ≐	252	23.45 S	70.30 W
Carmen Alto	252	23.11 S	69.40 W
Carmen de Apicalá	246	4.09 N	74.44 W
Carmen de Areco	252	34.22 S	59.49 W
Carmen de Huechuraba	286e	33.21 S	70.40 W
Carmen de Patagones	254	40.48 S	62.59 W
Carmer Hill ∧2	214	41.54 N	77.59 W
Carmi	194	38.05 N	88.03 W
Carmi, Lake ⊜	206	44.58 N	72.53 W
Carmiano	68	40.21 N	18.03 E
Carmichael	226	38.37 N	121.19 W
Carmignano di Brenta	64	45.38 N	11.42 E
Carmila	166	21.55 S	149.25 E
Carmine	222	30.09 N	96.41 W
Carmo	256	21.56 S	42.37 W
Carmo, Monte ∧	62	44.11 N	8.11 E
Carmo, Ribeirão do ≐	256	21.20 S	45.10 W
Carmo, Rio do ≐	250	5.02 S	37.12 W
Carmo da Cachoeira	256	21.28 S	45.13 W
Carmo de Minas	256	22.07 S	45.06 W
Carmo do Paranaíba	255	18.59 S	46.21 W
Carmo do Rio Verde	255	15.21 S	49.42 W
Carmody Hills	284c	38.54 N	76.54 W
Carmona, Esp.	34	37.28 N	5.38 W
Carmona, Pil.	116	14.19 N	121.03 E
Carmópolis de Minas	255	20.33 S	44.38 W
Carmzow	54	53.23 N	14.02 E
Carnaíba	250	7.48 S	37.49 W
Carnamah	162	29.42 S	115.53 E
Carnarvon, Austl.	162	24.53 S	113.40 E
Carnarvon, S. Afr.	158	30.56 S	22.08 E
Carnarvon → Caernarfon, Wales, U.K.	44	53.08 N	4.16 W
Carnarvon National Park ♦	166	25.00 S	148.00 E
Carnatic □9	118	12.30 N	78.15 E
Carnation	224	47.38 N	121.54 W
Carnaval, Arroyo ≐	288	34.52 S	58.02 W
Carnaxide	266c	38.43 N	9.15 W
Carncastle	48	54.54 N	5.53 W
Carndonagh	48	55.15 N	7.15 W
Carnduff	184	49.10 N	101.50 W
Carnedd Llewelyn ∧	44	53.10 N	3.58 W
Carnedd Wen ∧	42	52.41 N	3.35 W
Carnegie, Austl.	162	25.43 S	122.59 E
Carnegie, N.Y., U.S.	210	42.45 N	78.51 W
Carnegie, Ok., U.S.	196	35.06 N	98.36 W
Carnegie, Pa., U.S.	214	40.24 N	80.05 W
Carnegie, Lake ⊜	162	26.10 S	122.30 E
Carnegie Institute ✪2	279b	40.27 N	79.57 W
Carnegie-Mellon University ✪2	279b	40.27 N	79.57 W
Carnegie Ridge ✣3	18	1.00 S	85.00 W
Carnelian Bay	226	39.14 N	120.05 W
Carnetin	261	48.54 N	2.42 E
Carnew	48	52.43 N	6.30 W
Carneys Point	208	39.42 N	75.28 W
Carnforth	44	54.03 N	2.46 W
Carnia	64	46.22 N	13.08 E
Carnia ◆1	64	46.25 N	13.00 E
Carniche, Alpi (Karnische Alpen) ∧	64	46.40 N	13.00 E
Car Nicobar Island I	110	9.10 N	92.47 E
Carnide ◆8	266c	38.46 N	9.11 W
Carnières	50	50.10 N	3.21 E
Carniques → Karnische Alpen ∧	64	46.40 N	13.00 E
Carnlough	48	54.59 N	6.00 W
Carno	42	52.33 N	3.31 W
Carnon-Plage	62	43.32 N	3.59 E
Carnot, Centraf.	152	4.56 N	15.52 E
Carnot, Pa., U.S.	214	40.31 N	80.13 W
Carnot, Cape >	166	34.57 S	135.38 E
Carnoules	62	43.18 N	6.11 E
Carnoustie	46	56.30 N	2.44 W
Carnsore Point >	48	52.10 N	6.22 W
Carnwath	46	55.43 N	3.38 W
Carnwath ≐	180	68.26 N	128.50 W
Caro	190	43.29 N	83.23 W
Caroga Creek ≐	210	42.58 N	74.38 W
Caroga Lake	210	43.08 N	74.29 W
Carol Beach Estates	216	42.31 N	87.49 W
Carol City	220	25.56 N	80.14 W
Carole Acres	284c	39.04 N	77.00 W
Caroleen	192	35.16 N	81.47 W
Carole Highlands	284c	38.58 N	76.59 W
Carolei	68	39.15 N	16.13 E
Carolina, Bra.	250	7.20 S	47.28 W
Carolina, Col.	246	6.43 N	75.17 W
Carolina, El Sal.	236	13.51 N	88.19 W
Carolina, P.R.	240m	18.23 N	65.57 W
Carolina, S. Afr.	158	26.05 S	30.06 E
Carolina, R.I., U.S.	207	41.27 N	71.39 W
Carolina Beach	192	34.02 N	77.53 W
Carolinas, Puntan >	174n	14.55 N	145.38 E
Caroline □6, Md., U.S.	208	38.53 N	75.50 W
Caroline □6, Va., U.S.	208	38.00 N	77.20 W
Caroline I1	14	9.58 S	150.13 W
Caroline du Nord → North Carolina □3	192	35.30 N	80.00 W
Caroline du Sud → South Carolina □3	192	34.00 N	81.00 W
Caroline Islands II	14	8.00 N	147.00 E
Caroline Livermore, Mount ∧2	282	37.52 N	122.26 W
Caroline Peak ∧	172	45.56 S	167.13 E
Carol Stream	278	41.54 N	88.08 W
Caron	184	50.28 N	105.52 W
Caron, Lac ⊜	190	48.00 N	78.53 W
Carona	64	46.01 N	9.47 E
Čaronda	76	60.34 N	38.59 E
Caroní ≐	246	8.21 N	62.43 W
Caronia	70	38.01 N	14.26 E
Caronia ≐	70	38.03 N	14.26 E
Carono Pertusella	266b	45.36 N	9.03 E
Carora	246	10.11 N	70.05 W
Carosino	68	40.27 N	17.23 E
Carouge	58	46.11 N	6.09 E
Car'ov	80	48.40 N	45.22 E
Carovigno	68	40.42 N	17.39 E
Carovilli	66	41.43 N	14.17 E
Car'ovščina	80	53.37 N	44.15 E
Carozero	76	60.28 N	38.39 E
Carp	212	45.21 N	76.02 W
Carp ≐, On., Can.	212	45.29 N	76.14 W
Carp ≐, Mi., U.S.	190	46.02 N	84.42 W
Carpaneto Piacentino	62	44.55 N	9.47 E
Carpanzano	68	39.09 N	16.18 E
Carpates → Carpathian Mountains ∧	22	48.00 N	24.00 E
Carpathian Mountains ∧	22	48.00 N	24.00 E
Carpații Meridionali ∧	38	45.30 N	24.15 E
Cárpatos → Carpathian Mountains ∧	22	48.00 N	24.00 E
Carpegna	66	43.47 N	12.20 E
Carpenedolo	64	45.22 N	10.26 E
Carpentaria, Gulf of c	164	14.00 S	139.00 E
Carpenter	198	41.02 N	104.21 W
Carpenter Creek ≐	216	40.54 N	87.12 W
Carpenter Lake ⊜	182	50.50 N	122.30 W
Carpentersville	216	42.07 N	88.15 W
Carpentertown	279b	40.11 N	79.31 W
Carpentras	62	44.03 N	5.03 E
Carpet Museum ✪	267d	35.43 N	51.24 E
Carpi	64	44.47 N	10.53 E
Carpignano Sesia	62	45.32 N	8.25 E
Carpina	250	7.51 S	35.15 W
Carpineti	64	44.28 N	10.31 E
Carpineto Romano	66	41.36 N	13.05 E
Carpino	68	41.51 N	15.51 E
Carpinone	66	41.35 N	14.19 E
Carpinteria	204	34.23 N	119.31 W
Carpio	198	48.26 N	101.42 W
Carp Lake ⊜	182	54.45 N	123.17 W
Carpolac	166	36.44 S	141.19 E
Carquefou	32	47.18 N	1.30 W
Carqueiranne	62	43.05 N	6.05 E
Carquinez Bridge ◆5	282	38.04 N	122.14 W
Carquinez Strait ⊔	282	38.02 N	122.12 W
Carra, Lough ⊜	48	53.42 N	9.16 W
Carrabelle	192	29.51 N	84.39 W
Carradale	46	55.35 N	5.28 W
Carramar	274a	33.53 S	150.58 E
Carrancas	256	21.30 S	44.39 W
Carr and Craggs Moor ◆3	262	53.43 N	2.09 W
Carranglan	116	15.58 N	121.04 E
Carranza, Cabo >	252	35.36 S	72.38 W
Carrara	64	44.05 N	10.06 E
Carrascal	116	9.22 N	125.56 E
Carrasco ◆8	258	34.54 S	56.05 W
Carrasco, Aeropuerto Nacional de ⊠	258	34.52 S	56.02 W
Carrathool	166	34.24 S	145.26 E
Carrauntoohil ∧	48	51.59 N	9.45 W
Carrazedo	250	1.36 S	51.54 W
Carrboro	192	35.54 N	79.04 W
Carr Bridge	46	57.17 N	3.49 W
Carrcroft	285	39.47 N	75.30 W
Carrcroft Crest	285	39.47 N	75.30 W
Carrefour Pompadour ◆	261	48.46 N	2.26 E
Carregueira, Serra da ∧	266c	38.48 N	9.15 W
Carreria	252	21.59 S	58.35 W
Carreta, Punta >	248	14.13 S	76.18 W
Carreta Quemada, Arroyo ≐	288	34.21 S	56.41 W
Carriacou I	238	12.30 N	61.27 W
Carrick ◆8	279b	40.23 N	79.59 W
Carrick ◆1	44	55.12 N	4.38 W
Carrickart	48	55.10 N	7.47 W
Carrickfergus	48	54.43 N	5.49 W
Carrickmacross	48	53.58 N	6.43 W
Carrick on Shannon	48	53.57 N	8.05 W
Carrick on Suir	48	52.21 N	7.25 W
Carrie, Mount ∧	224	47.53 N	123.39 W
Carriere	194	30.37 N	89.39 W
Carrière, Lac ⊜	190	47.14 N	77.12 W
Carrières-sous-Bois	261	48.57 N	2.07 E
Carrières-sous-Poissy	261	48.57 N	2.03 E
Carrières-sur-Seine	261	48.55 N	2.11 E
Carriers Mills	194	37.41 N	88.38 W
Carrieton	166	32.26 S	138.32 E
Carrigahorig	48	53.04 N	8.09 W
Carrigaline	48	51.48 N	8.24 W
Carrigallen	48	53.59 N	7.39 W
Carrillo, C.R.	236	9.52 N	85.30 W
Carrillo, Méx.	232	26.54 N	103.55 W
Carrington, Eng., U.K.	262	53.26 N	2.24 W
Carrington, N.D., U.S.	198	47.26 N	99.07 W
Carrington Island I	202	41.00 N	112.37 W
Carrington Moss ◆3	262	53.25 N	2.23 W
Carr Inlet c	224	47.17 N	122.42 W
Carrión ≐	34	41.53 N	4.32 W
Carrión de los Condes	34	42.20 N	4.36 W
Carrizal ≐	234	23.03 N	97.46 W
Carrizal, Cerro ∧	196	26.43 N	100.36 W
Carrizal Bajo	252	28.05 S	71.10 W
Carrizo	34	42.35 N	5.50 W
Carrizo Creek ≐, U.S.	196	36.05 N	102.36 W
Carrizo Creek ≐, N.M., U.S.	196	35.40 N	103.43 W
Carrizo Mountain ∧	200	33.41 N	105.42 W
Carrizo Mountains ∧	200	36.45 N	109.10 W
Carrizo Plain ≚	226	35.25 N	120.00 W
Carrizo Springs	196	28.31 N	99.51 W
Carrizo Wash V, U.S.	200	34.36 N	109.26 W
Carrizo Wash V, Ca., U.S.	204	33.05 N	115.56 W
Carrizozo	200	33.38 N	105.52 W
Carro	62	43.20 N	5.02 E
Carrodano	62	44.14 N	9.39 E
Carroll, Ia., U.S.	198	42.03 N	94.52 W
Carroll, Ne., U.S.	198	42.16 N	97.11 W
Carroll □6, In., U.S.	216	40.36 N	86.41 W
Carroll □6, Ky., U.S.	218	38.39 N	85.06 W
Carroll □6, Md., U.S.	208	39.35 N	77.00 W
Carroll □6, Oh., U.S.	214	40.34 N	81.05 W
Carroll Lake ⊜	184	51.07 N	95.05 W
Carroll Park ♦	284b	39.17 N	76.39 W
Carrolls	224	46.05 N	122.52 W
Carrollton, Al., U.S.	194	33.10 N	88.06 W
Carrollton, Ga., U.S.	192	33.35 N	85.05 W
Carrollton, Il., U.S.	219	39.18 N	90.24 W
Carrollton, Ky., U.S.	218	38.40 N	85.10 W
Carrollton, Mi., U.S.	190	43.27 N	83.55 W
Carrollton, Ms., U.S.	194	33.30 N	89.55 W
Carrollton, Mo., U.S.	194	39.21 N	93.29 W
Carrollton, Oh., U.S.	214	40.34 N	81.05 W
Carrollton, Tx., U.S.	222	32.57 N	96.53 W
Carrollton Manor	208	39.05 N	76.35 W
Carrolltown	214	40.36 N	78.43 W
Carrollwood	284b	39.20 N	76.23 W
Carron ≐, Austl.	166	17.45 S	141.06 E
Carron ≐, Scot., U.K.	46	56.02 N	4.21 W
Carron ≐, Scot., U.K.	46	57.25 N	5.27 W
Carron ≐, Scot., U.K.	46	57.53 N	4.21 W
Carron, Loch c	46	57.22 N	5.31 W
Carronbridge	44	55.16 N	3.48 W
Carron Valley Reservoir ⊜1	46	56.02 N	4.05 W
Carros	62	43.48 N	7.11 E
Carrot ≐	184	53.50 N	101.17 W
Carrot River	184	53.17 N	103.35 W
Carrouges	28	48.34 N	0.09 W
Carrowmore Lake ⊜	48	54.12 N	9.47 W
Carrsville	208	36.43 N	76.50 W
Carrù	62	44.29 N	7.52 E
Carrum	169	38.05 S	145.08 E
Carrum Downs	274b	38.06 S	145.11 E
Carrum North	274b	38.03 S	145.09 E
Carrville	194	32.32 N	85.52 W
Carryduff	48	54.31 N	5.53 W
Carry Falls Reservoir ⊜1	188	44.25 N	74.45 W
Carry-le-Rouet	62	43.20 N	5.09 E
Carsaig	46	56.17 N	6.00 W
Čaršamba	130	41.12 N	36.44 E
Čaršanga	128	37.30 N	66.01 E
Carseland	182	50.51 N	113.28 W
Carshalton ◆8	260	51.22 N	0.10 W
Čarsk	86	49.35 N	81.05 E
Carsoli	66	42.06 N	13.05 E
Carson, Ca., U.S.	228	33.49 N	118.16 W
Carson, N.D., U.S.	198	46.25 N	101.33 W
Carson, Va., U.S.	208	37.02 N	77.23 W
Carson, Wa., U.S.	224	45.43 N	121.49 W
Carson ≐	204	39.45 N	118.40 W
Carson, East Fork ≐	226	38.59 N	119.49 W
Carson, West Fork ≐	226	38.59 N	119.49 W
Carson City, Mi., U.S.	190	43.10 N	84.50 W
Carson City, Nv., U.S.	226	39.10 N	119.46 W
Carsondale	284c	38.57 N	76.50 W
Carson Lake ⊜, On., Can.	212	45.31 N	77.46 W
Carson Lake ⊜, Nv., U.S.	204	39.19 N	118.43 W
Carson Range ∧	226	39.15 N	119.50 W
Carson Sink ⊜	204	39.45 N	118.30 W
Carson Valley V	226	39.00 N	119.48 W
Carstairs, Ab., Can.	182	51.34 N	114.06 W
Carstairs, Scot., U.K.	46	55.42 N	3.42 W
Carstensz-Toppen → Jaya, Puncak ∧	164	4.05 S	137.11 E
Carswell Air Force Base ■	222	32.47 N	97.26 W
Cartagena, Chile	252	33.33 S	71.37 W
Cartagena, Col.	246	10.25 N	75.32 W
Cartagena, Esp.	34	37.36 N	0.59 W
Cartago, Col.	246	4.45 N	75.55 W
Cartago, C.R.	236	9.52 N	83.55 W
Cartago □4	236	9.50 N	83.45 W
Čartak	85	41.05 N	71.50 E
Cartaxo	34	39.09 N	8.47 W
Cartaxos ∧2	266c	38.54 N	9.20 W
Cartaya	34	37.17 N	7.09 W
Carter	196	35.13 N	99.30 W
Carter □6	218	38.20 N	83.05 W
Carter Bridge ◆5	273a	6.28 N	3.23 E
Carter Caves State Resort Park ♦	218	38.22 N	83.10 W
Carteret	210	40.34 N	74.13 W
Carter Lake	198	41.17 N	95.55 W
Carter Mountain ∧	202	44.12 N	109.25 W
Carters Lake ⊜1	192	34.35 N	84.35 W
Cartersville	192	34.09 N	84.48 W
Carterton, N.Z.	172	41.02 S	175.31 E
Carterton, Eng., U.K.	42	51.45 N	1.35 W
Carterville	194	37.45 N	89.04 W
Carthage, Tun.	148	36.51 N	10.21 E
Carthage, Ar., U.S.	194	34.04 N	92.33 W
Carthage, Il., U.S.	190	40.24 N	91.08 W
Carthage, In., U.S.	218	39.44 N	85.34 W
Carthage, Ms., U.S.	194	32.43 N	89.32 W
Carthage, Mo., U.S.	194	37.10 N	94.18 W
Carthage, N.Y., U.S.	212	43.58 N	75.36 W
Carthage, N.C., U.S.	192	35.20 N	79.25 W
Carthage, S.D., U.S.	198	44.10 N	97.42 W
Carthage, Tn., U.S.	194	36.15 N	85.57 W
Carthage, Tx., U.S.	194	32.09 N	94.20 W
Carthage ⊥	36	36.52 N	10.20 E
Cartier Islands II	160	12.32 S	123.32 E
Cartierville ◆8	275a	45.32 N	73.42 W
Cartierville, Aéroport de ⊠	275a	45.31 N	73.43 W
Cartridge Hill ∧2	262	53.41 N	2.30 W
Cartura	64	45.16 N	11.50 E
Cartwright, Mb., Can.	184	49.06 N	99.20 W
Cartwright, Nf., Can.	176	53.42 N	57.01 W
Caruaru	250	8.17 S	35.58 W
Caruban	115a	7.33 S	111.39 E
Carumas	248	16.49 S	70.43 W
Čarüngol	88	49.14 N	106.29 E
Carunjamba ≐	152	13.57 S	12.25 E
Carúpano	246	10.40 N	63.14 W
Caruray	116	10.20 N	119.00 E
Carutapera	250	1.13 S	46.01 W
Caruthers	226	36.32 N	119.50 W
Caruthersville	194	36.11 N	89.39 W
Carutu ≐	246	5.05 N	63.28 W
Carvalhopolis	256	21.47 S	46.51 W
Carvalhos	256	22.00 S	44.28 W
Carver	207	41.53 N	70.45 W
Carversville	208	40.23 N	75.04 W
Carvin	50	50.29 N	2.58 E
Carvoeiro	246	1.24 S	61.59 W
Carvoeiro, Cabo >	34	39.21 N	9.24 W
Carwitzer See ⊜	54	53.18 N	13.28 E
Cary, Il., U.S.	216	42.12 N	88.14 W
Cary, Ms., U.S.	194	32.48 N	90.55 W
Cary, N.C., U.S.	192	35.47 N	78.46 W
Cary ≐	42	51.09 N	2.59 W
Caryčelekskij zapovednik ♦	85	41.50 N	71.55 E
Čaryk, ozero ⊜	80	46.13 N	42.43 E
Čarymovo	86	58.31 N	77.42 E
Čaryn	86	43.46 N	79.24 E
Čaryš ≐	86	52.22 N	83.45 E
Čaryšskoje	86	51.24 N	83.35 E
Caryville, Fl., U.S.	194	30.46 N	85.48 W
Caryville, Tn., U.S.	192	36.17 N	84.13 W
Casablanca (Dar-el-Beida)	148	33.39 N	7.35 W
Casablanca □4	148	33.35 N	7.30 W
Casablanca ◆8	286b	23.09 N	82.20 W
Casabona	68	39.15 N	16.57 E
Casa Branca	256	21.46 S	47.04 W
Casacalenda	68	41.44 N	14.51 E
Casa de la Torrecilla	266a	40.19 N	3.37 W
Casa del Campo ♦	266a	40.32 N	3.47 W
Casa de Piedra, Embalse ⊜1	252	38.15 S	67.20 W
Casa Grande	200	32.52 N	111.45 W
Casa Grande National Monument ♦	200	32.59 N	111.32 W
Casainhos	266c	38.53 N	9.10 W
Casalanguida	66	42.03 N	14.30 E
Casalattico	66	41.37 N	13.43 E
Casalbordino	66	42.09 N	14.35 E
Casalbuono	68	40.13 N	15.41 E
Casalbuttano	64	45.15 N	9.58 E
Casal di Principe	68	41.00 N	14.08 E
Casale Abbruciato ◆8	267a	41.44 N	12.33 E
Casalecchio di Reno	64	44.28 N	11.16 E
Casale Monferrato	62	45.08 N	8.27 E
Casale sul Sile	64	45.36 N	12.19 E
Casaletto Spartano	68	40.09 N	15.37 E
Casalmaggiore	64	44.59 N	10.26 E
Casalmorano	62	45.17 N	9.54 E
Casalnuovo Monterotaro	68	41.37 N	15.06 E
Casa Loma ✪	275b	43.41 N	79.25 W
Casalone ◆8	267a	41.56 N	12.41 E
Casalotti ◆8	267a	41.55 N	12.22 E
Casalpusterlengo	62	45.11 N	9.39 E
Casal Velino	68	40.11 N	15.06 E
Casalvieri	66	41.38 N	13.43 E
Casamance ≐	150	12.33 N	16.46 W
Casamari, Abbazia di ✪1	66	41.41 N	13.29 E
Casamassima	68	40.57 N	16.55 E
Casamicciola Terme	68	40.45 N	13.54 E
Casanare □3	246	5.45 N	72.00 W
Casanare ≐	246	6.02 N	69.51 W
Casanay	246	10.30 N	63.25 W
Casa Nova	250	9.07 S	40.58 W
Casarano	68	40.00 N	18.10 E
Casar de Cáceres	34	39.34 N	6.25 W
Casarsa della Delizia	64	45.57 N	12.50 E
Casas	234	23.44 N	98.45 W
Casas Adobes	200	32.19 N	110.59 W
Casas Grandes ≐	232	31.22 N	107.31 W
Casas Ibáñez	34	39.17 N	1.28 W
Casasimarro	34	39.22 N	2.02 W
Casauman ≐	116	7.16 N	126.31 E
Casa Verde ◆8	287b	23.30 S	46.39 W
Casavieja	34	40.17 N	4.46 W
Casbas	252	36.45 S	62.30 W
Casca	252	28.34 S	51.59 W
Casca, Rio da ≐	248	14.52 S	55.52 W
Cascadas Basaseachic, Parque Nacional ♦	232	28.10 N	108.22 W
Cascade, B.C., Can.	182	49.01 N	118.13 W
Cascade, Id., U.S.	202	44.30 N	116.02 W
Cascade, Ia., U.S.	190	42.17 N	91.00 W
Cascade, Mi., U.S.	216	42.55 N	85.30 W
Cascade, Mt., U.S.	202	47.16 N	111.41 W
Cascade, Wi., U.S.	190	43.39 N	88.00 W
Cascade ≐, N.Z.	172	44.02 S	168.22 E
Cascade ≐, Wa., U.S.	224	48.32 N	121.26 W
Cascade Bay c	174c	29.01 S	167.58 E
Cascade Locks	224	45.40 N	121.53 W
Cascade Mountains (Cascade Range) ∧	202	45.00 N	121.30 W
Cascade Park ♦	279a	41.23 N	82.06 W
Cascade Point >	172	44.00 S	168.22 E
Cascade Range ∧	178	45.00 N	121.30 W
Cascade Reservoir ⊜1	202	44.35 N	116.06 W
Cascade Tunnel ◆5	224	47.40 N	121.03 W
Cascadura ◆8	287a	22.53 S	43.20 W
Cascais	34	38.42 N	9.25 W
Cascalho Rico	255	18.34 S	47.52 W
Cascapédia ≐	186	48.11 N	65.54 W
Cascatinha	256	22.29 S	43.09 W
Cascavel, Bra.	250	4.07 S	38.14 W
Cascavel, Bra.	252	24.57 S	53.28 W
Cascia	66	42.43 N	13.01 E
Casciana Terme	66	43.31 N	10.32 E
Cascina	66	43.41 N	10.33 E
Casco Bay c	188	43.40 N	70.00 W
Cascumpec Bay c	186	46.45 N	64.03 W
Čascy	82	55.37 N	36.52 E
Casei Gerola	62	45.00 N	8.55 E
Case Inlet c	224	47.19 N	122.53 W
Casekow	54	53.12 N	14.12 E
Casella	62	44.32 N	9.00 E
Caselle, Aeroporto di ⊠	62	45.13 N	7.40 E
Caselle in Pittari	68	40.10 N	15.33 E
Caselle Torinese	62	45.10 N	7.39 E
Cà Selva, Lago di ⊜1	64	46.16 N	12.40 E
Casenove	66	42.58 N	12.50 E
Casentino V	66	43.40 N	11.50 E
Casenuove	266b	45.38 N	8.42 E
Case-Pilote	240e	14.38 N	61.08 W
Caseros	258	34.36 S	58.33 W
Caserta	68	41.04 N	14.20 E
Caserta □4	68	41.14 N	14.10 E
Caseville	190	43.56 N	83.16 W
Case Western Reserve University ✪2	279a	41.30 N	81.36 W
Casey, Il., U.S.	194	39.17 N	87.59 W
Casey, Ia., U.S.	198	41.30 N	94.31 W
Casey ✪3	9	66.17 S	110.32 E
Casey, Mount ∧	202	48.26 N	116.42 W
Casey Bay c	9	67.20 S	48.00 E
Casey Key I	220	27.10 N	82.29 W
Caseyr >	144	11.49 N	51.15 E
Caseyville	219	38.38 N	90.02 W
Cash	222	32.59 N	96.07 W
Cashel, Ire.	48	53.25 N	9.48 W
Cashel, Ire.	48	52.31 N	7.53 W
Cashie ≐	192	35.53 N	76.49 W
Cashiers	192	35.06 N	83.05 W
Cashmere	202	47.31 N	120.28 W
Cashmere Downs	162	28.58 S	119.35 E
Cashton	190	43.44 N	90.46 W
Cashtown	208	39.53 N	77.22 W
Casigua	246	8.46 N	72.30 W
Casiguran, Pil.	116	16.17 N	122.07 E
Casiguran, Pil.	116	12.52 N	124.00 E
Casiguran Sound ⊔	116	16.06 N	121.58 E
Casilda, Arg.	252	33.03 S	61.10 W
Casilda, Cuba	240p	21.46 N	79.59 W
Casimcea	38	44.43 N	28.23 E
Casimiro Castillo	234	19.38 N	104.28 W
Casina	64	44.30 N	10.30 E
Casino	166	28.52 S	153.03 E
Casiquiare ≐	246	2.01 N	67.07 W
Casita	200	31.00 N	110.53 W
Casitas Springs	228	34.22 N	119.18 W
Čáslav	30	49.54 N	15.23 E
Casma	248	9.28 S	78.19 W
Čašniki	76	54.52 N	29.08 E
Čašnikovo	265b	55.59 N	37.25 E
Časnočor, gora ∧	24	67.45 N	33.25 E
Casola in Lunigiana	64	44.14 N	10.10 E
Casola Valsenio	66	44.13 N	11.37 E
Casole d'Elsa	66	43.20 N	11.02 E
Casoli	66	42.07 N	14.18 E
Cason	222	33.02 N	94.49 W
Casorate Primo	62	45.19 N	9.01 E
Casorate Sempione	62	45.40 N	8.44 E
Casorezzo	266b	45.31 N	8.54 E
Casoria	68	40.54 N	14.17 E
Časov Jar	83	48.35 N	37.50 E
Časovo	24	62.01 N	50.36 E
Caspe	34	41.14 N	0.02 W
Casper	200	42.52 N	106.18 W
Casper Creek, Middle Fork ≐	200	43.01 N	106.29 W
Caspian	190	46.03 N	88.37 W
Caspian Sea ₸2	72	42.00 N	50.30 E
Caspienne, Mer → Caspian Sea ₸2	72	42.00 N	50.30 E
Caspio, Depresión del → Prikaspijskaja nizmennost' ≚	80	48.00 N	52.00 E
Caspio, Mar → Caspian Sea ₸2	72	42.00 N	50.30 E
Caspoggio	64	46.16 N	9.52 E
Cass □6, Il., U.S.	219	39.57 N	90.13 W
Cass □6, In., U.S.	216	40.45 N	86.21 W
Cass □6, Mi., U.S.	216	41.55 N	86.01 W
Cass □6, Tx., U.S.	222	33.05 N	94.32 W
Cass ≐	190	43.23 N	83.59 W
Cassadaga	214	42.20 N	79.18 W
Cassadaga Creek ≐	214	42.05 N	79.08 W
Cassadaga Lakes ⊜	214	42.21 N	79.19 W
Cassaday Point >	284a	42.52 N	79.13 W
Cassagnas	62	44.16 N	3.45 E
Cassai	152	10.33 S	21.59 E
Cassai (Kasai) ≐	152	3.02 S	16.57 E
Cassamba	152	13.06 S	20.18 E
Cassandra	214	40.24 N	78.38 W
Cassanje ≐	248	17.06 S	57.23 W
Cassano allo Ionio	68	39.47 N	16.20 E
Cassano d'Adda	62	45.32 N	9.31 E
Cassano delle Murge	68	40.53 N	16.46 E
Cassano Magnago	62	45.41 N	8.50 E
Cassaro	70	37.07 N	14.56 E
Cass Benton Parkway ♦	281	42.25 N	83.28 W
Cass City	190	43.36 N	83.10 W
Cassel	50	50.48 N	2.29 E
Casselberry	220	28.40 N	81.19 W
Cassella	216	40.25 N	84.34 W
Casselman	206	45.19 N	75.05 W
Casselton	198	46.54 N	97.12 W
Cássia, Bra.	255	20.36 S	46.56 W
Cassia, Fl., U.S.	220	28.53 N	81.28 W
Cássia dos Coqueiros	256	21.17 S	47.10 W
Cassiar	180	59.16 N	129.40 W
Cassiar Mountains ∧	176	59.00 N	129.00 W
Cassibile ≐	70	36.57 N	15.11 E
Cassidy	224	49.04 N	123.53 W
Cassidy Airfield ⊠	174o	1.57 N	157.18 W
Cassilândia	255	19.09 S	51.45 W
Cassimbazar	126	24.07 N	88.16 E
Cassine	62	44.45 N	8.31 E
Cassinetta di Lugagnano	266b	45.25 N	8.54 E
Cassinga	152	15.08 S	16.05 E
Cassino, Bra.	252	32.11 S	52.10 W
Cassino, It.	66	41.30 N	13.49 E
Cassio	64	44.35 N	10.02 E
Cassipore ◆8	272b	22.37 N	88.22 E
Cassis	62	43.13 N	5.32 E
Cass Lake	190	47.22 N	94.36 W
Cass Lake ⊜, Mi., U.S.	281	42.36 N	83.22 W
Cass Lake ⊜, Mn., U.S.	190	47.25 N	94.32 W
Cassley ≐	46	57.58 N	4.35 W
Cassoalala	152	9.30 S	14.22 E
Cassoango	152	13.42 S	20.56 E
Cassolnovo	62	45.22 N	8.48 E
Cassone	64	45.44 N	10.46 E
Cassongue	152	11.51 S	15.03 E
Cassopolis	216	41.54 N	86.00 W
Casstown	218	40.03 N	84.07 W
Cassumba, Ilha I	255	17.46 S	39.17 W
Cassunda	152	10.57 S	21.03 E
Cassununga	255	16.03 S	53.38 W
Cassville, In., U.S.	216	40.33 N	86.08 W
Cassville, Mo., U.S.	194	36.40 N	93.52 W
Cassville, N.Y., U.S.	210	42.57 N	75.15 W
Cassville, Pa., U.S.	214	40.18 N	78.02 W
Cassville, Wi., U.S.	190	42.42 N	90.59 W
Castac Lake ⊜	228	34.50 N	118.51 W
Castagnaro	64	45.07 N	11.24 E
Castagneto Carducci	66	43.10 N	10.36 E
Castaic	228	34.30 N	118.37 W
Castaic Creek ≐	228	34.25 N	118.37 W
Castaic Lake ⊜1	228	34.32 N	118.37 W
Castalia	214	41.24 N	82.48 W
Castanea	210	41.07 N	77.25 W
Castanhal	250	1.18 S	47.55 W
Castanheira de Pêra	34	40.00 N	8.13 W
Castaños	196	26.47 N	101.25 W
Castañones, Punta >	236	12.28 N	87.11 W
Castano Primo	62	45.33 N	8.47 E
Casteggio	62	45.00 N	9.07 E
Castel	43b	49.28 N	2.34 W
Castelar	258	34.40 S	58.40 W
Castel Baronia	68	41.03 N	15.11 E
Castel Bolognese	66	44.19 N	11.48 E
Castelbuono	70	37.56 N	14.05 E
Castelcivita	68	40.30 N	15.15 E
Casteldaccia	70	38.03 N	13.32 E
Castel d'Ario	64	45.11 N	10.58 E
Casteldarne (Ehrenburg)	64	46.48 N	11.50 E
Casteldelfino	62	44.35 N	7.04 E
Castel del Monte	66	42.22 N	13.43 E
Castel del Piano	66	42.53 N	11.32 E
Castel del Rio	66	44.12 N	11.30 E
Castel di Decima ◆8	267a	41.45 N	12.26 E
Castel di Guido ◆8	267a	41.54 N	12.17 E
Castel di Ieri	66	42.06 N	13.44 E
Castel di Iudica	70	37.30 N	14.38 E
Castel di Leva ◆8	267a	41.47 N	12.32 E
Castel di Lucio	70	37.53 N	14.19 E
Castel di Sangro	66	41.47 N	14.06 E
Castel di Tora	66	42.13 N	12.58 E
Castelfidardo	66	43.28 N	13.33 E
Castelfiorentino	66	43.36 N	10.58 E
Castelfondo	64	46.27 N	11.07 E
Castelforte	66	41.18 N	13.49 E
Castelfranco Emilia	64	44.37 N	11.03 E
Castelfranco in Miscano	68	41.18 N	15.05 E
Castelfranco Veneto	64	45.40 N	11.55 E
Castel Frentano	66	42.12 N	14.22 E
Castel Fusano ◆8	267a	41.44 N	12.19 E
Castel Gandolfo	66	41.45 N	12.39 E
Castel Giorgio	66	42.42 N	11.59 E
Castelgrande	68	40.47 N	15.26 E
Castelhanos, Baía de c	256	23.51 S	45.15 W
Castelhanos, Ponta dos >	256	23.10 S	44.06 W
Castellabate	68	40.17 N	14.57 E
Castell'Alfero	62	44.59 N	8.13 E
Castellalto	66	42.40 N	13.49 E
Castellammare, Golfo di c	70	38.08 N	12.54 E
Castellammare del Golfo	70	38.01 N	12.53 E
Castellammare di Stabia	68	40.42 N	14.29 E
Castellamonte	62	45.23 N	7.42 E
Castellana, Grotte di ♦5	68	40.53 N	17.07 E
Castellana Grotte	68	40.53 N	17.11 E
Castellana Sicula	70	37.47 N	14.02 E
Castellane	62	43.51 N	6.31 E
Castellaneta	68	40.37 N	16.57 E
Castellanza	62	45.37 N	8.54 E
Castellarano	64	44.30 N	10.44 E
Castell'Arquato	62	44.51 N	9.52 E
Castell'Azzara	66	42.46 N	11.42 E
Castellazzo Bormida	62	44.51 N	8.34 E
Castellbisbal	266d	41.29 N	1.59 E
Castellcefels	266d	41.17 N	1.59 E
Castelleone	62	45.18 N	9.46 E
Castelletto	266b	45.30 N	8.48 E
Castelletto di Brenzone	64	45.41 N	10.45 E
Castelli, Arg.	252	36.06 S	57.47 W
Castelli, It.	66	42.29 N	13.43 E
Castellina in Chianti	66	43.28 N	11.17 E
Castellina Marittima	66	43.25 N	10.35 E
Castelli Romani ◆1	267a	41.48 N	12.42 E
Castelló □4	34	40.10 N	0.10 W
Castello, Monte ∧2	66	43.03 N	9.49 E
Castello d'Annone	62	44.53 N	8.19 E
Castelló de la Plana	34	39.59 N	0.02 W
Castello di Fiemme	64	46.17 N	11.26 E
Castello Lavazzo	64	46.17 N	12.18 E
Castellote	34	40.48 N	0.19 W
Castello Tesino	64	46.04 N	11.38 E
Castellucchio	64	45.09 N	10.39 E
Castelluccio	68	40.00 N	15.58 E
Castell'Umberto	70	38.05 N	14.48 E
Castelluzzo	70	38.06 N	12.44 E
Castel Madama	66	41.58 N	12.52 E
Castel Maggiore	64	44.34 N	11.22 E
Castelmagno	62	44.24 N	7.13 E
Castelmassa	64	45.01 N	11.18 E
Castelmauro	66	41.50 N	14.43 E
Castelmezzano	68	40.32 N	16.03 E
Castelmoron-sur-Lot	32	44.24 N	0.30 E
Castelnaudary	32	43.19 N	1.57 E
Castelnau-Montratier	32	44.16 N	1.21 E
Castelnovo di Sotto	64	44.49 N	10.34 E
Castelnovo ne'Monti	64	44.26 N	10.24 E
Castelnuovo	64	45.26 N	10.47 E
Castelnuovo Berardenga	66	43.21 N	11.30 E
Castelnuovo dell'Abate	66	43.00 N	11.31 E
Castelnuovo della Daunia	68	41.35 N	15.07 E
Castelnuovo di Garfagnana	64	44.06 N	10.24 E
Castelnuovo di Porto	66	42.07 N	12.30 E
Castelnuovo di Val di Cecina	66	43.12 N	10.59 E
Castelnuovo Don Bosco	62	45.03 N	7.58 E
Castelnuovo Nigra	62	45.26 N	7.41 E
Castelnuovo Rangone	64	44.33 N	10.56 E
Castelnuovo Scrivia	62	44.59 N	8.53 E
Castelo	255	20.36 S	41.12 W
Castelo Branco	34	39.49 N	7.30 W
Castelo do Piauí	250	5.20 S	41.33 W
Castel Pagano	68	41.24 N	14.48 E
Castel Porziano ◆8	267a	41.44 N	12.24 E
Castelraimondo	66	43.12 N	13.04 E
Castel Romano ◆8	267a	41.44 N	12.27 E
Castel San Gimignano	66	43.24 N	11.00 E
Castel San Giorgio	68	40.47 N	14.42 E
Castel San Giovanni	62	45.04 N	9.26 E
Castel San Lorenzo	68	40.25 N	15.14 E
Castel San Pietro Terme	66	44.24 N	11.35 E
Castel Sant'Elia	66	42.15 N	12.22 E
Castelsaraceno	68	40.10 N	16.00 E
Castelsardo	71	40.55 N	8.43 E
Castelsarrasin	32	44.02 N	1.06 E
Castelsilano	68	39.16 N	16.46 E
Casteltermini	70	37.32 N	13.39 E
Castelvecchio Subequo	66	42.08 N	13.44 E
Castelvetere in Val Fortore	68	41.27 N	14.56 E
Castelvetrano	70	37.41 N	12.47 E
Castelvetro di Modena	64	44.30 N	10.57 E
Castelvetro Piacentino	64	45.05 N	9.59 E
Castel Viscardo	66	42.45 N	12.00 E
Castel Volturno	68	41.02 N	13.56 E
Castenaso	64	44.30 N	11.28 E
Castenedolo	64	45.28 N	10.18 E
Casterton	166	37.35 S	141.24 E
Castets	32	43.53 N	1.09 W
Castiglioncello	66	43.24 N	10.24 E
Castiglione Chiavarese	62	44.16 N	9.21 E
Castiglione d'Adda	62	45.13 N	9.41 E
Castiglione dei Pepoli	66	44.08 N	11.09 E
Castiglione del Lago	66	43.07 N	12.03 E
Castiglione della Pescaia	66	42.46 N	10.53 E
Castiglione delle Stiviere	64	45.23 N	10.29 E
Castiglione di Sicilia	70	37.53 N	15.07 E
Castiglione d'Orcia	66	43.00 N	11.37 E
Castiglione d'Ossola	58	46.03 N	8.13 E
Castiglione Messer Marino	66	41.52 N	14.27 E
Castiglione Olona	62	45.46 N	8.52 E
Castiglion Fibocchi	66	43.32 N	11.46 E
Castiglion Fiorentino	66	43.20 N	11.55 E
Castile	210	42.37 N	78.03 W
Castilho	255	20.52 S	51.29 W
Castilla	248	5.12 S	80.38 W
Castilla, Playa de ♦2	34	37.00 N	6.33 W
Castilla-La Mancha □4	34	39.30 N	3.00 W
Castilla la Nueva □9	34	40.00 N	3.45 W
Castilla la Vieja □9	34	41.30 N	4.00 W
Castilla-León □4	34	41.30 N	5.00 W
Castillo	258	33.53 S	57.40 W
Castillo, Cerro ∧	254	43.03 S	71.57 W
Castillo, Pampa del ≚	254	45.58 S	68.24 W
Castillo de San Marcos National Monument ♦	192	29.44 N	81.20 W
Castillo Incaico de Ingapirca ⊥	246	2.34 S	78.50 W
Castillon-la-Bataille	32	44.51 N	0.03 W
Castillos	252	34.12 S	53.50 W
Castillos, Laguna de ⊜	252	34.20 S	53.54 W
Castine	188	44.23 N	68.48 W
Castione della Presolana	64	45.54 N	10.04 E
Castions di Strada	64	45.54 N	13.11 E
Castle Acre	42	52.42 N	0.41 E
Castle Air Force Base ■	226	37.22 N	120.34 W
Castlebar	48	53.52 N	9.17 W
Castlebay	46	56.57 N	7.28 W
Castlebellingham	48	53.54 N	6.23 W
Castleberry	194	31.17 N	87.01 W

Symbol	English	Deutsch	Español	Français	Português
≐	River	Fluß	Río	Rivière	Rio
≡	Canal	Kanal	Canal	Canal	Canal
⌞	Waterfall, Rapids	Wasserfall, Stromschnellen	Cascada, Rápidos	Chute d'eau, Rapides	Cascata, Rápidos
⊔	Strait	Meeresstraße	Estrecho	Détroit	Estreito
c	Bay, Gulf	Bucht, Golf	Bahía, Golfo	Baie, Golfe	Baía, Golfo
⊜	Lake, Lakes	See, Seen	Lago, Lagos	Lac, Lacs	Lago, Lagos
≚	Swamp	Sumpf	Pantano	Marais	Pântano
⊞	Ice Features, Glacier	Eis- und Gletscherformen	Accidentes Glaciales	Formes glaciaires	Acidentes glaciares
₸	Other Hydrographic Features	Andere Hydrographische Objekte	Otros Elementos Hidrográficos	Autres données hydrographiques	Outros acidentes hidrográficos
✣	Submarine Features	Untermeerische Objekte	Accidentes Submarinos	Formes de relief sous-marin	Acidentes submarinos
□	Political Unit	Politische Einheit	Unidad Política	Entité politique	Unidade política
✪	Cultural Institution	Kulturelle Institution	Institución Cultural	Institution culturelle	Instituição cultural
⊥	Historical Site	Historische Stätte	Sitio Histórico	Site historique	Sitio histórico
♦	Recreational Site	Erholungs- und Ferienort	Sitio de Recreo	Centre de loisirs	Area de Lazer
⊠	Airport	Flughafen	Aeropuerto	Aéroport	Aeroporto
■	Military Installation	Militäranlage	Instalación Militar	Installation militaire	Instalação militar
◆	Miscellaneous	Verschiedenes	Misceláneo	Divers	Diversos

ENGLISH — Name Page Lat.°′ Long.°′ / DEUTSCH — Name Seite Breite°′ Länge°′ E = Ost

Castleblayney 48 54.07 N 6.44 W
Castle Bruce 240d 15.26 N 61.16 W
Castle Cape › 180 56.15 N 158.06 W
Castle Cary 42 51.06 N 2.31 W
Castlecliff 172 39.57 S 174.59 E
Castlecomer 48 52.48 N 7.12 W
Castleconnell 48 52.43 N 8.30 W
Castlecrag 274a 33.48 S 151.13 E
Castle Crags State Park ♠ 204 41.10 N 122.20 W
Castle Creek 210 42.14 N 75.55 W
Castle Creek ≃, Austl. 169 36.41 S 145.29 E
Castle Creek ≃, Id., U.S. 202 43.06 N 116.16 W
Castle Dale 200 39.23 N 110.27 W
Castledawson 48 54.47 N 6.33 W
Castlederg 48 54.42 N 7.36 W
Castledermot 48 52.55 N 6.50 W
Castle Dome Peak ʌ 200 33.05 N 114.08 W
Castle Donington 42 52.51 N 1.19 W
Castle Douglas 44 54.57 N 3.56 W
Castlefinn 48 54.47 N 7.35 W
Castleford 44 53.44 N 1.21 W
Castlegar 182 49.19 N 117.40 W
Castle Harbour ⊂ 240a 32.21 N 64.40 W
Castle Hill 274a 33.44 S 151.00 E
Castle Hills, De., U.S. 208 39.41 N 75.33 W
Castle Hills, Tx., U.S. 196 29.32 N 98.31 W
Castleisland 48 52.14 N 9.27 W
Castlemaine, Austl. 169 37.04 S 144.13 E
Castlemaine, Ire. 48 52.09 N 9.43 W
Castlemartyr 48 51.55 N 8.03 W
Castlemore 275b 43.47 N 79.41 W
Castle Mountain ʌ, Ab., Can. 182 51.18 N 115.55 W
Castle Mountain ʌ, Yk., Can. 180 64.32 N 135.25 W
Castle Mountain ʌ, Ca., U.S. 226 35.56 N 120.20 W
Castle Neck ›[1] 283 42.41 N 70.45 W
Castle Neck ≃ 283 42.40 N 70.44 W
Castle Park 228 32.36 N 117.04 W
Castle Peak ʌ, Co., U.S. 200 39.01 N 106.52 W
Castle Peak ʌ, Id., U.S. 202 44.02 N 114.35 W
Castle Peak ʌ, Wa., U.S. 224 48.58 N 120.51 W
Castlepoint 172 40.54 S 176.13 E
Castle Point □[8] 260 51.33 N 0.35 E
Castlepollard 48 53.40 N 7.17 W
Castlerea 48 53.46 N 8.29 W
Castlereagh ≃ 166 30.12 S 147.32 E
Castle Rock, Co., U.S. 200 39.22 N 104.51 W
Castle Rock, Pa., U.S. 285 39.58 N 75.26 W
Castle Rock, Wa., U.S. 224 46.16 N 122.54 W
Castle Rock ʌ, Or., U.S. 202 44.02 N 118.11 W
Castle Rock ʌ, Va., U.S. 192 37.57 N 78.44 W
Castle Rock Butte ʌ 198 45.00 N 103.27 W
Castle Rock Lake ⊜[1] 190 43.56 N 89.58 W
Castle Shannon 279b 40.21 N 80.01 W
Castleshaw Moor ◆[3] 262 53.36 N 2.00 W
Castleside 44 54.50 N 1.52 W
Castleton, Eng., U.K. 44 53.21 N 1.46 W
Castleton, Eng., U.K. 44 54.28 N 0.56 W
Castleton, Eng., U.K. 262 53.35 N 2.11 W
Castleton, In., U.S. 218 39.54 N 86.03 W
Castleton, Vt., U.S. 188 43.36 N 73.10 W
Castleton on Hudson 210 42.32 N 73.45 W
Castletown, I. of Man 44 54.04 N 4.40 W
Castletown, Scot., U.K. 46 58.35 N 3.23 W
Castletown Bearhaven (Castletown Bere) 48 51.39 N 9.55 W
Castletown Bere → Castletown Bearhaven 48 51.39 N 9.55 W
Castletown Geoghegan 48 53.26 N 7.38 W
Castletownroche 48 52.10 N 8.28 W
Castletownshend 48 51.32 N 9.11 W
Castlewellan 48 54.16 N 5.57 W
Castlewood, Ky., U.S. 218 38.04 N 84.27 W
Castlewood, S.D., U.S. 198 44.43 N 97.01 W
Castlewood, Va., U.S. 192 36.53 N 82.16 W
Častoje 82 54.11 N 37.47 E
Častooz'ornoje 86 55.34 N 67.53 E
Castor 182 52.13 N 111.53 W
Castor ≃, On., Can. 212 45.18 N 75.10 W
Castor ≃, Mo., U.S. 194 36.51 N 89.44 W
Castorano 66 42.54 N 13.43 E
Castor Creek ≃ 194 31.47 N 92.22 W
Castorland 212 43.53 N 75.30 W
Castra Vetera ⊥ 263 51.39 N 6.28 E
Castres 32 43.36 N 2.15 E
Castricum 52 52.33 N 4.39 E
Castries, Fr. 62 43.40 N 3.59 E
Castries, St. Luc. 241f 14.01 N 61.00 W
Castries, Port ⊂ 241f 14.01 N 61.01 W
Castro, Bra. 252 24.47 S 50.00 W
Castro, Chile 254 42.29 S 73.46 W
Castro, It. 64 45.48 N 10.04 E
Castro, Arroyo de ≃ 258 33.37 S 56.10 W
Castro, Punta › 254 43.22 S 65.03 W
Castro Barros 252 30.35 S 65.44 W
Castrocaro Terme 66 44.10 N 11.57 E
Castrocielo 66 41.32 N 13.42 E
Castro Daire 34 40.54 N 7.56 W
Castro dei Volsci 66 41.30 N 13.24 E
Castro del Río 34 37.41 N 4.28 W
Castrofilippo 70 37.21 N 13.46 E
Castrojeriz 34 42.17 N 4.08 W
Castro Marim 34 37.13 N 7.26 W
Castronuño 34 41.23 N 5.16 W
Castronuovo di Sant'Andrea 68 40.11 N 16.11 E
Castronuovo di Sicilia 70 37.41 N 13.36 E
Castropol 34 43.32 N 7.02 W
Castrop-Rauxel 52 51.34 N 7.18 E
Castroreale 70 38.06 N 15.12 E
Castro-Urdiales 34 43.23 N 3.13 W
Castro Valley 226 37.41 N 122.05 W
Castro Verde 34 37.42 N 8.05 W
Castrovillari 68 39.49 N 16.13 E
Castroville, Ca., U.S. 226 36.45 N 121.45 W
Castroville, Tx., U.S. 196 29.21 N 98.52 W
Castrovirreyna 248 13.16 S 75.19 W
Castuera 34 38.43 N 5.33 W
Čast uul ʌ 86 48.40 N 90.45 E
Častyje 80 57.19 N 54.59 E
Casummit Lake 184 51.28 N 92.24 W
Casupá 252 34.07 S 55.39 W
Caswell Sound ʊ 172 45.00 S 167.10 E
Çat 130 39.40 N 41.00 E
Čat ≃ 184 51.07 N 91.25 W
Catabola 152 12.09 S 17.16 E
Cataby 162 30.43 S 115.31 E
Catacamas 236 14.48 N 85.54 W
Catacaos 248 5.16 S 80.41 W
Catacocha 246 4.04 S 79.38 W
Cataguarino 256 21.18 S 42.43 W
Cataguases 256 21.24 S 42.41 W
Catahoula Lake ⊜ 194 31.30 N 92.06 W
Çatak 128 38.01 N 43.07 E
Çatakköprü 130 38.09 N 41.12 E
Catalaban Island I 116 11.51 N 125.28 E
Çatalan 130 37.14 N 35.16 E
Catalão 255 18.10 S 47.57 W
Catalão, Ponta do › 287a 22.51 S 43.13 W
Çatalca 130 41.09 N 28.27 E
Çatalçam 130 40.00 N 38.51 E
Catalfaro ≃ 70 37.22 N 14.43 E
Catalina, Nf., Can. 186 48.31 N 53.05 W
Catalina, Chile 252 25.13 S 69.43 W
Catalina → Santa Catalina Island I 228 33.23 N 118.24 W
Catalina, Punta › 254 52.32 S 68.47 W
Catalonia → Catalunya □[4] 34 41.40 N 1.30 E
Catalunya □[4] 34 41.40 N 1.30 E
Catalzeytin 130 41.57 N 34.13 E
Catamarca □[4] 252 27.00 S 67.00 W
Catamare 286c 10.36 N 67.02 W
Catamayo 246 3.59 S 79.21 W
Catamayo ≃ 246 4.18 S 80.09 W
Catanauan 116 13.36 N 122.19 E
Catanduanes □[4] 116 13.47 N 124.16 E
Catanduanes Island I 116 13.45 N 124.15 E
Catanduva 255 21.08 S 48.58 W
Catane → Catania 70 37.30 N 15.06 E
Catania 70 37.30 N 15.06 E
Catania □[4] 70 37.23 N 14.40 E
Catania, Golfo di ⊂ 70 37.24 N 15.09 E
Catania, Piana di ≚ 70 37.25 N 14.51 E
Cataño 240m 18.27 N 66.07 W
Catanzaro 68 38.54 N 16.36 E
Catanzaro □[4] 68 38.54 N 16.36 E
Catanzaro Lido 68 38.49 N 16.36 E
Cataonia □[9] 130 38.00 N 35.00 E
Catára ≃ 152 13.34 S 12.35 E
Cataract Canyon V 200 36.03 N 112.35 W
Cataract Reservoir ⊜[1] 170 34.16 S 150.48 E
Catarama 246 1.35 S 79.28 W
Cataraqui 212 44.16 N 76.32 W
Cataraqui ≃ 212 44.13 N 76.28 W
Catarina 250 6.12 S 39.54 W
Catarman, Pil. 116 9.08 N 124.40 E
Catarman, Pil. 116 12.30 N 124.38 E
Catarroja 34 39.24 N 0.24 W
Catasauqua 208 40.39 N 75.29 W
Catatumbo ≃ 246 9.22 N 71.45 W
Catawba 218 40.00 N 83.37 W
Catawba ≃ 192 34.36 N 80.54 W
Catawba Island 214 41.35 N 82.50 W
Catawissa, Mo., U.S. 219 38.25 N 90.47 W
Catawissa, Pa., U.S. 210 40.57 N 76.27 W
Catawissa Creek ≃ 210 40.57 N 76.28 W
Cataxa 154 15.58 S 33.12 E
Cat Ba, Dao I 110 20.50 N 107.00 E
Catbalogan 116 11.46 N 124.53 E
Catchabutan, Punta › 236 15.50 N 86.32 W
Catchacoma Lake ⊜ 212 44.45 N 78.20 W
Cateco Cangola 152 8.27 S 15.48 E
Catedral, Cerro ʌ[2] 252 34.23 S 54.40 W
Cateel 116 7.48 N 126.27 E
Cateel ≃ 116 7.47 N 126.27 E
Cateel Bay ⊂ 116 7.54 N 126.25 E
Catemaco 234 18.25 N 95.07 W
Catemaco, Laguna ⊜ 234 18.25 N 95.05 W
Catembe 156 26.00 S 32.33 E
Catenanuova 70 37.34 N 14.41 E
Caterham 42 51.17 N 0.04 W
Caterino Rodriguez 232 24.51 N 100.19 W
Catete 152 9.06 S 13.43 E
Catete ◆[8] 287a 22.55 S 43.10 W
Catete ≃ 250 6.04 S 54.09 W
Catfish Creek ≃, On., Can. 212 42.39 N 81.01 W
Catfish Creek ≃, N.Y., U.S. 212 43.31 N 76.19 W
Catfish Creek ≃, Tx., U.S. 222 31.47 N 95.56 W
Catford ◆[8] 260 51.27 N 0.01 W
Catharine Creek ≃ 210 42.21 N 76.51 W
Cathcart 158 32.18 S 27.09 E
Cathead Mountain ʌ 210 43.17 N 74.17 W
Cathedral City 204 33.46 N 116.27 W
Cathedral Gorge State Park ♠ 204 37.50 N 114.30 W
Cathedral Mountain ʌ 196 30.10 N 103.40 W
Cathedral of the Pines ʋ[1] 207 42.47 N 71.58 W
Cathedral Provincial Park ♠ 202 49.05 N 120.10 W
Cathedral Range ⩘ 226 37.47 N 119.21 W
Catherines Peak ʌ 241q 18.04 N 76.42 W
Catheys Valley 226 37.25 N 120.06 W
Cathlamet 224 46.12 N 123.22 W
Catholic University ʋ[2] 284c 38.56 N 77.00 W
Catia ◆[8] 286c 10.31 N 66.57 W
Catia La Mar 286c 10.36 N 67.02 W
Ca' Tiepolo 66 44.56 N 12.22 E
Catignano 66 42.21 N 13.57 E
Catió 150 11.13 N 15.10 W
Catirina, Punta ʌ 71 40.29 N 9.32 E
Cat Island I, Ba. 238 24.27 N 75.30 W
Cat Island I, Ma., U.S. 283 42.31 N 70.49 W
Cat Island I, Ms., U.S. 194 30.13 N 89.06 W
Čatkal ≃ 85 41.38 N 70.01 E
Čatkal'skij chrebet ⩘ 85 41.40 N 71.05 E
Cat Lake ⊜ 184 51.40 N 91.50 W
Catlettsburg 188 38.24 N 82.36 W
Catlin 194 40.03 N 87.42 W
Catlins ≃ 172 46.29 S 169.43 E
Catlodge 46 57.00 N 4.15 W
Catnip Mountain ʌ 204 41.52 N 119.23 W
Cato 210 43.10 N 76.34 W
Catoche, Cabo › 232 21.35 N 87.05 W
Catoctin Creek ≃ 208 39.18 N 77.33 W
Catoctin Mountain ʌ 208 39.26 N 77.31 W
Cato Island I 166 23.15 S 155.32 E
Catolé do Rocha 250 6.21 S 37.45 W
Católica, Universidad ʋ[2], Chile 286e 33.27 S 70.39 W
Católica, Universidad ʋ[2], Perú 286d 12.04 S 77.05 W
Caton 44 54.04 N 2.43 W
Catonsville 208 39.16 N 76.43 W
Catonsville Manor 284b 39.18 N 76.44 W
Catoosa 196 36.11 N 95.44 W
Catorce 234 23.42 N 100.54 W
Catorce, Sierra de ⩘ 234 23.36 N 100.52 W
Catota 152 13.52 S 17.15 E
Catria, Monte ʌ 66 43.28 N 12.42 E
Catriló 252 36.26 S 63.24 W
Catrimani ≃ 246 0.28 N 61.44 W
Catrine 46 55.30 N 4.20 W
Cats, Mont des ʌ[2] 50 50.47 N 2.40 E
Catshill 42 52.22 N 2.03 W
Catskill 210 42.13 N 73.51 W
Catskill Aqueduct ≃ 276 41.11 N 73.48 W
Catskill Creek ≃ 210 42.12 N 73.51 W
Catskill Game Farm ♠ 210 42.15 N 74.01 W
Catskill Mountains ⩘ 210 42.10 N 74.30 W
Catskill Park ♠ 210 42.00 N 74.30 W
Cat Spring 222 29.51 N 96.20 W
Catt, Mount ʌ 182 54.21 N 128.47 W
Cattai Creek ≃ 274a 33.40 S 150.56 E
Cattaraugus 210 42.19 N 78.52 W
Cattaraugus □[6] 214 42.15 N 78.45 W
Cattaraugus Creek ≃ 214 42.35 N 79.10 W
Cattaraugus Creek, South Branch ≃ 214 42.26 N 78.53 W
Cattaraugus Indian Reservation ◆[4] 210 42.33 N 78.56 W
Cattenom 56 49.25 N 6.15 E
Catterick 44 54.22 N 1.38 W
Catterick Garrison 44 54.22 N 1.43 W
Cattle Canyon V 280 34.14 N 117.46 W
Cattolica 66 43.58 N 12.44 E
Cattolica del Sacro Cuore, Università ʋ[2] 266b 45.27 N 9.11 E
Cattolica Eraclea 70 37.26 N 13.24 E
Catton 44 54.55 N 2.15 W
Catu 255 12.21 S 38.23 W
Catuala 152 16.29 S 19.03 E
Catuane 156 26.48 S 32.18 E
Catubig 116 12.24 N 125.03 E
Catubig ≃ 116 12.34 N 125.01 E
Catuçaba 256 23.15 S 45.12 W
Catumbela 152 12.25 S 13.34 E
Catumbela ≃ 152 12.27 S 13.29 E
Catur 154 13.45 S 35.30 E
Catus 32 44.34 N 1.20 E
Catwick, Îles II 110 10.00 N 109.00 E
Čatyrk'ol', ozero ⊜ 85 40.38 N 75.17 E
Čatyrtaš 85 40.55 N 76.26 E
Cau ≃ 110 21.07 N 106.18 E
Cau, Rach ≃ 269c 10.51 N 106.49 E
Cauaburi ≃ 246 0.17 S 65.56 W
Cauayan, Pil. 116 16.56 N 121.46 E
Cauayan, Pil. 116 9.58 N 122.37 E
Caubvick, Mount (Mont d'Iberville) ʌ 176 58.53 N 63.43 W
Cauca □[5] 246 2.30 N 76.50 W
Cauca ≃ 246 8.54 N 74.28 W
Caucaia 250 3.42 S 38.39 W
Caucaia do Alto 256 23.41 S 47.02 W
Caucase, Monts du → Bol'šoj Kavkaz ⩘ 84 42.30 N 45.00 E
Caucasia 246 8.00 N 75.12 W
Caucaso → Bol'šoj Kavkaz ⩘ 84 42.30 N 45.00 E
Caucasus → Bol'šoj Kavkaz ⩘ 84 42.30 N 45.00 E
Caucete 252 31.39 S 68.17 W
Cauchari, Salar de ≚ 252 23.50 S 66.50 W
Cauchon Lake ⊜ 184 55.25 N 96.30 W
Caudebec-en-Caux 50 49.32 N 0.44 E
Caudebec-lés-Elbeuf 50 49.17 N 1.02 E
Caudry 50 50.08 N 3.25 E
Caughdenoy 210 43.16 N 76.12 W
Caughnawaga 275a 45.25 N 73.41 W
Caughnawaga Indian Reserve ◆[4] 206 45.23 N 73.41 W
Cauitan, Mount ʌ 116 17.16 N 121.00 E
Cauit Point ›, Pil. 116 12.16 N 122.38 E
Cauit Point ›, Pil. 116 9.18 N 126.12 E
Cauldcleuch Head ʌ 44 55.18 N 2.51 W
Caulfield 169 37.53 S 145.03 E
Caulfield Racecourse ♠ 274b 37.53 S 145.02 E
Caulkerbush 44 54.54 N 3.40 W
Caulonia 68 38.23 N 16.25 E
Caumont-sur-Durance 62 43.54 N 4.57 E
Caumsett State Park ♠ 276 40.55 N 73.28 W
Caúngula 152 8.25 S 18.40 E
Čaunskaja guba ⊂ 74 69.20 N 170.00 E
Cauquenes 252 35.58 S 72.21 W
Caura ≃ 246 7.38 N 64.53 W
Caurés ≃ 246 1.21 S 62.20 W
Caurimare ≃ 286c 10.28 N 66.48 W
Causapscal 186 48.22 N 67.14 W
Čausovo 82 54.49 N 36.55 E
Caussade 32 44.10 N 1.32 E
Čausy 76 53.48 N 30.58 E
Cautário ≃ 248 12.13 S 64.34 W
Caution, Cape › 182 51.10 N 127.47 W
Cauto ≃ 240p 20.33 N 77.14 W
Čauvaj 85 40.08 N 72.13 E
Caux, Pays de ◆[1] 50 49.40 N 0.40 E
Cava 256 22.41 S 43.26 W
Cava de' Tirreni 68 40.42 N 14.42 E
Cávado ≃ 34 41.32 N 8.48 W
Cavaglià 62 45.24 N 8.05 E
Cavaillon 62 43.50 N 5.02 E
Cavalaire-sur-Mer 62 43.10 N 6.32 E
Cavalcante 255 13.48 S 47.30 W
Cavalese 64 46.17 N 11.27 E
Cavalheiro 255 17.15 S 48.02 W
Cavalier 198 48.47 N 97.37 W
Cavalière 62 43.09 N 6.26 E
Cavalla (Cavally) ≃ 150 4.22 N 7.32 W
Cavalleria, Cap de › 34 40.05 N 4.05 E
Cavallermaggiore 62 44.43 N 7.41 E
Cavalli Islands II 172 35.02 S 173.58 E
Cavallino, Litorale di ⊥[2] 64 45.27 N 12.30 E
Cavallo, Île I 71 41.21 N 9.16 E
Cavallo, Monte ʌ 64 46.08 N 12.30 E
Cavally (Cavalla) ≃ 150 4.22 N 7.32 W
Cavalos, Ribeirão dos ≃ 256 21.29 S 44.13 W
Cava Manara 62 45.08 N 9.07 E
Cavan 48 54.00 N 7.21 W
Cavan □[6] 48 53.55 N 7.15 W
Cavanaugh, Lake ⊜ 224 48.23 N 122.00 W
Čavan'ga 24 66.06 N 37.47 E
Cavarzere 64 45.08 N 12.05 E
Cavaso del Tomba 64 45.51 N 11.52 E
Çavdır 130 37.09 N 29.42 E
Cave, It. 66 41.49 N 12.56 E
Cave, N.Z. 172 44.19 S 170.57 E
Cave City, Ar., U.S. 194 35.56 N 91.32 W
Cave City, Ky., U.S. 194 37.08 N 85.57 W
Cave Creek ≃ 200 33.34 N 112.07 W
Cave del Predil 64 46.26 N 13.34 E
Cavedine 64 45.59 N 10.59 E
Cave In Rock 194 37.29 N 88.10 W
Caveiras ≃ 252 27.35 S 50.56 W
Cavelo 152 17.33 S 19.21 E
Cavendish 166 37.31 S 142.02 E
Cavernago 62 45.38 N 9.46 E
Cavertitz 54 51.23 N 13.08 E
Cave Run Lake ⊜[1] 188 38.03 N 83.30 W
Cave Spring 192 34.14 N 85.20 W
Cavettsville 279b 40.22 N 79.46 W
Cavezzo 64 44.50 N 11.02 E
Cavi 62 44.17 N 9.22 E
Caviana de Fora, Ilha I 250 0.10 N 50.10 W
Cavili Island I 116 9.17 N 120.50 E
Cavinzas, Isla I 286d 12.07 S 77.13 W
Cavite 116 14.29 N 120.55 E
Cavite □[4] 116 14.15 N 120.50 E
Čavka 84 41.44 N 41.45 E
Čavlisaj 85 41.08 N 69.44 E
Cavo, Monte ʌ 267a 41.45 N 12.42 E
Cavoli, Isola dei I 71 39.05 N 9.33 E
Cavonne ≃ 68 40.17 N 16.47 E
Cavour 62 44.47 N 7.22 E
Cavour, Canale ≊ 62 45.11 N 7.54 E
Cavriago 64 44.42 N 10.31 E
Cavriana 64 45.21 N 10.36 E
Cavtat 38 42.35 N 18.13 E
Çavuş 130 37.36 N 31.56 E
Çavuşbaşı ≃ 267b 40.58 N 28.51 E
Çavuşçu Gölü ⊜ 130 38.25 N 31.53 E
Cawatose, Lac ⊜ 190 47.20 N 77.07 W
Cawayan 116 11.56 N 123.46 E
Cawdor 46 57.31 N 3.56 W
Cawker City 198 39.30 N 98.26 W
Cawnpore → Kānpur 124 26.28 N 80.21 E
Cawood, Eng., U.K. 44 53.50 N 1.07 W
Cawood, Ky., U.S. 192 36.47 N 83.13 W
Cawston, B.C., Can. 182 49.11 N 119.45 W
Cawston, Eng., U.K. 42 52.46 N 1.10 E
Cawthon 222 30.25 N 96.14 W
Caxambu 256 21.59 S 44.56 W
Caxias, Bra. 250 4.50 S 43.21 W
Caxias, Port. 266c 38.42 N 9.16 W
Caxias do Sul 252 29.10 S 51.11 W
Caxinas, Punta › 236 16.01 N 86.02 W
Caxito 152 8.33 S 13.36 E
Caxiuana, Baía de ⊂ 250 1.45 S 51.20 W
Caxopa 152 11.52 S 20.52 E
Çay 130 38.35 N 31.02 E
Cayacal, Punta › 234 17.56 N 102.11 W
Çayağzı ◆[8] 267b 41.13 N 29.12 E
Çayağzı ≃ 267b 41.14 N 29.12 E
Cayambe 246 0.03 N 78.08 W
Cayambe ʌ[1] 246 0.00 77.59 W
Cayapoñga 116 5.48 N 125.33 E
Çaybaşı 130 41.02 N 37.06 E
Cayce 192 33.57 N 81.04 W
Çaycuma 130 41.25 N 32.05 E
Caycuse 224 48.53 N 124.22 W
Caycuse ≃ 224 48.48 N 124.41 W
Cay Duong, Vinh ⊂ 110 10.10 N 104.45 E
Cayenne 250 4.56 N 52.20 W
Cayenne □[8] 250 4.00 N 52.30 W
Cayes → Les Cayes 238 18.12 N 73.45 W
Cayeux-sur-Mer 50 50.11 N 1.29 E
Cayey 240m 18.07 N 66.10 W
Cayey, Sierra de ⩘ 240m 18.07 N 66.02 W
Çayıralan 130 39.18 N 35.40 E
Çayırbaşı 130 40.53 N 42.36 E
Çayırhan 130 40.06 N 31.37 E
Çayırlı 130 39.48 N 40.01 E
Çaylarbası 130 37.41 N 39.00 E
Caylus 32 44.14 N 1.46 E
Cayman Brac I 238 19.43 N 79.49 W
Cayman Islands □[2], N.A. 230 19.30 N 80.40 W
Cayman Islands □[2], N.A. 238 19.30 N 80.40 W
Cayman Trench ✢[1] 16 19.00 N 80.00 W
Cayna 248 10.11 S 76.20 W
Caynabo 144 8.57 N 46.26 E
Cayo Agua, Isla I 236 9.09 N 82.02 W
Çayözü 130 39.36 N 38.11 E
Cay Point › 240b 24.59 N 77.25 W
Çayra 130 40.41 N 39.06 E
Cayres 62 44.55 N 3.48 E
Cay Sal Bank ✢[2] 238 23.45 N 80.00 W
Çaytepe 130 38.48 N 40.41 E
Cayucos 226 35.27 N 120.54 W
Cayuga, In., U.S. 194 39.56 N 87.27 W
Cayuga, N.Y., U.S. 210 42.55 N 76.44 W
Cayuga, N.D., U.S. 198 46.04 N 97.23 W
Cayuga, Tx., U.S. 222 31.57 N 95.57 W
Cayuga □[6] 210 42.56 N 76.34 W
Cayuga and Seneca Canal ≊ 210 42.56 N 76.44 W
Cayuga Creek ≃, N.Y., U.S. 210 42.52 N 78.47 W
Cayuga Creek ≃, N.Y., U.S. 284a 43.04 N 78.57 W
Cayuga Heights 210 42.27 N 76.29 W
Cayuga Lake ⊜ 210 42.45 N 76.45 W
Cayuta 210 42.17 N 76.42 W
Cayuta Creek ≃ 210 41.59 N 76.30 W
Cazage 152 11.02 S 20.45 E
Cazalla de la Sierra 34 37.56 N 5.45 W
Căzănești 38 44.37 N 27.01 E
Cazaux et de Sanguinet, Lac de ⊂ 32 44.30 N 1.10 W
Cazenovia 210 42.55 N 75.51 W
Cazenovia Creek ≃ 210 42.52 N 78.50 W
Cazenovia Creek, East Branch ≃ 210 42.46 N 78.38 W
Cazenovia Creek, West Branch ≃ 210 42.46 N 78.39 W
Cazenovia Lake ⊜ 210 42.57 N 75.53 W
Cazenovia Park ♠ 284a 42.51 N 78.48 W
Cazères 32 43.13 N 1.05 E
Cazhai 269b 31.12 N 121.34 E
Cazin 36 44.58 N 15.57 E
Čazis 58 46.43 N 9.25 E
Čazma 36 45.45 N 16.37 E
Cazombo 152 11.54 S 22.52 E
Cazones ≃ 234 20.44 N 97.12 W
Cazones, Golfo de ⊂ 240p 21.55 N 81.20 W
Cazorla, Esp. 34 37.55 N 3.00 W
Cazorla, Ven. 246 8.01 N 67.00 W
Cazula 154 15.25 S 33.40 E
Ccapi 248 13.52 S 72.05 W
Cchaltubo 84 42.20 N 42.35 E
Cchenisckali ≃ 84 42.07 N 42.18 E
Cchinvali 84 42.13 N 43.56 E
Čchorocku 84 42.32 N 42.07 E
Cchunkuri 84 42.23 N 42.34 E
Cea ≃ 34 42.00 N 5.36 W
Ceanannus Mór (Kells) 48 53.44 N 6.53 W
Ceará → Fortaleza 250 3.43 S 38.30 W
Ceará □[3] 250 5.00 S 40.00 W
Ceará-Mirim 250 5.38 S 35.26 W
Ceará-Mirim ≃ 250 5.40 S 35.13 W
Ceatharlach → Carlow 48 52.50 N 6.55 W
Cebaco, Isla De I 246 7.32 N 81.09 W
Čeballos 232 26.32 N 104.09 W
Čebarkul' 86 54.58 N 60.25 E
Čebeci ◆[8] 267b 41.07 N 28.52 E
Čeboksarskoje vodochranilišče ⊜[1] 24 56.10 N 46.00 E
Čeboksary 80 56.09 N 47.15 E
Cebolla Creek ≃ 200 38.29 N 107.13 W
Cebollar 252 29.06 S 66.33 W
Cebollas 234 23.23 N 104.50 W
Cebollatí 252 33.16 S 53.47 W
Cebollatí ≃ 252 33.09 S 53.38 W
Cebollita Peak ʌ 200 34.43 N 107.51 W
Céboruco, Volcán ʌ[1] 234 21.09 N 104.30 W
Čebotovka, Ross. 83 48.42 N 39.51 E
Čebotovka, Ross. 83 48.41 N 40.00 E
Cebreros 34 40.27 N 4.28 W
Čebrikovo 78 47.09 N 30.06 E
Čebsara 76 59.12 N 38.50 E
Cebu 116 10.18 N 123.54 E
Cebu □[4] 116 10.20 N 123.45 E
Cebu I 116 10.20 N 123.45 E
Čeburgol' 78 45.34 N 38.07 E
Cebu Strait ʊ 116 9.45 N 123.40 E
Ceccano 66 41.34 N 13.20 E
Cecchignola ◆[8] 267a 41.49 N 12.29 E
Ceceda 196 26.04 N 103.25 W
Čečel'nik 78 48.14 N 29.21 E
Čečen', ostrov I 84 43.58 N 47.45 E
Cecer Chaan → Öndörchaan 88 47.19 N 110.39 E
Cecerleg, Mong. 88 47.30 N 101.27 E
Cecerleg, Mong. 88 49.30 N 97.36 E
Cecerleg, Mong. 88 48.52 N 101.14 E
Čečersk 76 52.55 N 30.55 E
Čečeviči 76 53.31 N 29.51 E
Cecheng 105 39.06 N 116.48 E
Čechov, Ross. 82 55.09 N 37.27 E
Čechov, Ross. 89 47.28 N 141.59 E
Čechova, gora ʌ 89 47.03 N 142.50 E
Čechtice 30 49.37 N 15.03 E
Čechy □[9] 30 49.50 N 14.00 E
Cecil, Ga., U.S. 192 31.02 N 83.23 W
Cecil, Oh., U.S. 216 41.13 N 84.35 W
Cecil, Pa., U.S. 214 40.19 N 80.10 W
Cecil □[6] 208 39.36 N 75.50 W
Cecil Field Naval Air Station ■ 192 30.12 N 81.52 W
Cecilia 194 37.39 N 85.57 W
Cecilia, Mount ʌ[2] 162 20.45 S 120.55 E
Cecil Park 274a 33.52 S 150.51 E
Cecil Plains 166 27.32 S 151.12 E
Cecil Rhodes, Mount ʌ 162 25.26 S 121.26 E
Cecilton 208 39.24 N 75.52 W
Cecina 66 43.19 N 10.31 E
Cecina ≃ 66 43.18 N 10.29 E
Cecita, Lago di ⊜ 68 39.24 N 16.30 E
Čečnja-Ingušetija □[3] 84 43.15 N 45.40 E
Čečuj ≃ 88 58.12 N 109.18 E
Čečujsk 88 58.05 N 108.42 E
Cedar ≃, U.S. 190 41.17 N 91.21 W
Cedar ≃, Mi., U.S. 190 45.25 N 87.21 W
Cedar ≃, Mi., U.S. 190 43.53 N 84.29 W
Cedar ≃, Ne., U.S. 198 41.22 N 97.57 W
Cedar ≃, N.Y., U.S. 188 43.51 N 74.11 W
Cedar ≃, Wa., U.S. 224 47.30 N 122.12 W
Cedar, Middle Branch ≃ 216 42.38 N 84.05 W
Cedar, West Branch ≃ 216 42.41 N 84.09 W
Cedar, West Fork ≃ 190 42.37 N 92.29 W
Cedar Bayou ≃ 222 29.41 N 94.56 W
Cedar Beach 284b 39.17 N 76.25 W
Cedar Bluff Reservoir ⊜[1] 198 38.47 N 99.47 W
Cedar Bluffs 198 41.23 N 96.36 W
Cedar Breaks National Monument ♠ 200 37.29 N 112.53 W
Cedar Brook 208 39.42 N 74.54 W
Cedar Brook ≃, N.J., U.S. 276 40.19 N 74.33 W
Cedar Brook ≃, N.J., U.S. 276 40.23 N 74.23 W
Cedar Brook ≃, N.J., U.S. 285 39.40 N 74.43 W
Cedar Brook Park ♠ 275b 43.45 N 79.14 W
Cedarburg 190 43.17 N 87.59 W
Cedar City, Mo., U.S. 219 38.35 N 92.10 W
Cedar City, Ut,. U.S. 200 37.40 N 113.03 W
Cedar Creek 222 30.05 N 97.30 W
Cedar Creek ≃, Al., U.S. 194 32.13 N 87.06 W
Cedar Creek ≃, Az., U.S. 200 33.48 N 110.18 W
Cedar Creek ≃, Ct., U.S. 276 41.09 N 73.13 W
Cedar Creek ≃, De., U.S. 208 38.55 N 75.20 W
Cedar Creek ≃, Ga., U.S. 194 34.08 N 85.19 W
Cedar Creek ≃, Id., U.S. 202 42.24 N 114.49 W
Cedar Creek ≃, In., U.S. 216 41.12 N 85.02 W
Cedar Creek ≃, Ia., U.S. 190 40.58 N 91.40 W
Cedar Creek ≃, Ia., U.S. 198 42.24 N 94.59 W
Cedar Creek ≃, Ky., U.S. 218 38.25 N 84.53 W
Cedar Creek ≃, Mo., U.S. 219 38.38 N 92.13 W
Cedar Creek ≃, N.D., U.S. 198 46.07 N 101.18 W
Cedar Creek ≃, Oh., U.S. 214 41.38 N 83.17 W
Cedar Creek ≃, Pa., U.S. 279b 40.10 N 79.47 W
Cedar Creek ≃, Tx., U.S. 196 32.53 N 98.37 W
Cedar Creek ≃, Tx., U.S. 222 30.51 N 96.12 W
Cedar Creek ≃, Tx., U.S. 222 32.04 N 96.05 W
Cedar Creek ≃, Tx., U.S. 222 30.02 N 97.17 W
Cedar Creek ≃, Wa., U.S. 224 45.56 N 122.37 W
Cedar Creek Reservoir ⊜[1] 222 32.20 N 96.10 W
Cedar Crest Manor 285 39.41 N 75.28 W
Cedaredge 200 38.54 N 107.55 W
Cedar Falls 190 42.31 N 92.26 W
Cedar Grove, On., Can. 275b 43.52 N 79.12 W
Cedar Grove, In., U.S. 218 39.21 N 84.56 W
Cedar Grove, N.J., U.S. 276 40.51 N 74.13 W
Cedar Grove, W.V., U.S. 188 38.13 N 81.25 W
Cedar Grove, Wi., U.S. 190 43.34 N 87.49 W
Cedar Grove Reservoir ⊜[1] 276 40.52 N 74.13 W
Cedar Heights, Md., U.S. 284c 38.54 N 76.54 W
Cedar Heights, Pa., U.S. 285 40.05 N 75.17 W
Cedar Hill, Mo., U.S. 219 38.21 N 90.39 W
Cedar Hill, N.Y., U.S. 210 42.33 N 73.47 W
Cedar Hill, Tn., U.S. 194 36.33 N 86.59 W
Cedar Hill, Tx., U.S. 222 32.35 N 96.57 W
Cedar Hills 224 45.30 N 122.47 W
Cedar Hollow 285 40.04 N 75.31 W
Cedarhurst, Md., U.S. 208 39.07 N 76.41 W
Cedarhurst, N.Y., U.S. 276 40.37 N 73.43 W
Cedar Island I, Md., U.S. 208 37.56 N 75.52 W
Cedar Island I, N.Y., U.S. 276 40.38 N 73.21 W
Cedar Island I, Va., U.S. 208 37.39 N 75.36 W
Cedar Island Lake ⊜ 281 42.38 N 83.28 W
Cedar Key 192 29.08 N 83.02 W
Cedar Knolls 276 40.49 N 74.26 W
Cedar Lake, In., U.S. 216 41.21 N 87.26 W
Cedar Lake, Tx., U.S. 222 28.54 N 95.35 W
Cedar Lake ⊜, On., Can. 190 46.02 N 78.30 W
Cedar Lake ⊜, In., U.S. 216 41.22 N 87.26 W
Cedar Lake ⊜, N.J., U.S. 276 40.55 N 74.28 W
Cedar Lake ⊜, Tx., U.S. 196 32.49 N 102.17 W
Cedar Lake ⊜[1] 184 53.15 N 100.10 W
Cedar Lake Creek ≃ 222 28.50 N 95.35 W
Cedar Lane 222 28.54 N 95.38 W
Cedar Mill 224 45.32 N 122.51 W
Cedarmont 158 26.50 S 29.01 E
Cedar Mountain ʌ 204 41.36 N 120.16 W
Cedar Point 216 41.16 N 89.08 W
Cedar Point ›, Ct., U.S. 276 41.06 N 73.22 W
Cedar Point ›, Oh., U.S. 214 41.42 N 83.20 W
Cedar Point ›, Oh., U.S. 214 41.30 N 82.41 W
Cedar Pond ⊜ 276 41.07 N 74.06 W
Cedar Rapids, Ia., U.S. 190 41.59 N 91.40 W
Cedar Rapids, Ne., U.S. 198 41.34 N 98.09 W
Cedar Ridge 226 39.12 N 121.01 W
Cedar Run ≃ 208 38.41 N 77.29 W
Cedars 285 40.13 N 75.22 W
Cedars of Lebanon → Arz Lubnān ◆[3] 130 34.14 N 36.03 E
Cedar Springs, On., Can. 214 42.17 N 82.02 W
Cedar Springs, Mi., U.S. 190 43.13 N 85.33 W
Cedar Swamp ≡, Ma., U.S. 283 42.33 N 71.05 W
Cedar Swamp ≡, N.J., U.S. 285 39.48 N 75.20 W
Cedartown 192 34.03 N 85.15 W
Cedarvale, B.C., Can. 182 55.01 N 128.20 W
Cedar Vale, Ks., U.S. 198 37.06 N 96.30 W
Cedarville, S. Afr. 158 30.23 S 29.03 E
Cedarville, Ca., U.S. 204 41.31 N 120.10 W
Cedarville, In., U.S. 216 41.12 N 85.01 W
Cedarville, Ma., U.S. 207 41.48 N 70.33 W
Cedarville, Mi., U.S. 190 46.00 N 84.22 W
Cedarville, N.J., U.S. 208 39.19 N 75.12 W
Cedarville, N.Y., U.S. 210 42.56 N 75.07 W
Cedarville, Oh., U.S. 218 39.44 N 83.48 W
Cedarville, Pa., U.S. 285 40.14 N 75.40 W
Cedarville Reservoir ⊜[1] 216 41.12 N 85.01 W
Cedar Wash V 200 35.53 N 111.25 W
Cedarwood Park 208 40.03 N 74.08 W
Cedegolo 64 46.05 N 10.21 E
Çedeira 34 43.39 N 8.03 W
Čeder 88 51.25 N 94.45 E
Cedillo, Embalse de ⊜[1] 34 39.40 N 7.25 W
Cedral 234 23.48 N 100.44 W
Cedrino ≃ 71 40.23 N 9.44 E
Cedro 250 6.36 S 39.03 W
Cedro, Cerro ʌ 234 18.35 N 99.42 W
Cedros, Hond. 236 14.35 N 87.08 W
Cedros, Méx. 232 24.41 N 101.47 W
Cedros, Isla I 232 28.12 N 115.15 W
Ceduna 162 32.07 S 133.40 E
Cedynia 30 52.50 N 14.14 E
Ceel 102 45.36 N 95.51 E
Ceelaayo 144 11.15 N 48.54 E
Ceel Afweyne 144 9.55 N 47.15 E
Ceel Berdaale 144 3.14 N 43.11 E
Ceel Berde 144 4.50 N 43.39 E
Ceel Buur 144 4.40 N 46.37 E
Ceel Dhaab 144 8.56 N 46.30 E
Ceel Dheere, Som. 144 3.51 N 47.12 E
Ceeldheere, Som. 144 5.22 N 46.11 E
Ceel Doofaar 144 10.38 N 49.02 E
Ceel Waaq 144 2.44 N 41.01 E
Ceel Xamurre 144 7.13 N 48.54 E
Ceemadle 144 5.14 N 46.56 E
Ceepeecee 182 49.52 N 126.43 W
Ceerigaabo 144 10.37 N 47.22 E
Cefalà Diana 70 37.54 N 13.28 E
Cefalonia → Kefallinía I 38 38.15 N 20.35 E
Cefalù 70 38.02 N 14.01 E
Cefni ≃ 44 53.12 N 4.23 W
Cefn-mawr 42 52.58 N 3.04 W
Ceg 144 8.58 N 45.20 E
Çega ≃ 34 41.33 N 4.46 W
Čeganly 80 53.54 N 53.34 E
Čegdomyn 89 51.07 N 133.05 E
Čegem ≃ 84 43.38 N 43.48 E
Čegem Pervyj 84 43.34 N 43.35 E
Čegitun' 180 66.34 N 171.06 W
Cegléd 30 47.10 N 19.48 E
Ceglie Messapico 68 40.39 N 17.31 E
Cehegín 34 38.06 N 1.48 W
Ceheng 102 25.10 N 105.48 E
Cehnice 60 49.12 N 14.02 E
Cehu-Silvaniei 38 47.25 N 23.11 E
Ceiba 240m 18.16 N 65.39 W
Ceibo ≃ 258 33.57 S 58.27 W
Ceilán → Sri Lanka □[1] 122 7.00 N 81.00 E
Čeil'dag 84 40.17 N 49.18 E
Ceiriog ≃ 42 52.57 N 3.02 W
Ceirw ≃ 44 52.59 N 3.27 W
Čejč 61 48.57 N 16.57 E
Čekalin 82 54.06 N 36.15 E
Čekan 80 54.51 N 53.34 E
Čekanovskij 88 56.13 N 101.25 E
Çekerek 130 40.04 N 35.31 E
Çekerek ≃ 130 40.34 N 35.46 E
Čekmaguš 86 55.08 N 54.40 E
Çekme ◆[8] 267b 41.03 N 29.10 E
Čekšino 76 59.39 N 40.33 E
Čekujevo 24 63.34 N 38.56 E
Čekunda 89 50.48 N 132.10 E
Čel'abinsk 86 55.10 N 61.24 E
Čel'abinsk Oblast' □[4] 86 54.30 N 60.30 E
Čelákovice 54 50.10 N 14.46 E
Celâlli 130 39.42 N 37.26 E
Celano 66 42.05 N 13.33 E
Celanova 34 42.09 N 7.58 W
Celaya 234 20.31 N 100.49 W
Čelbas ≃ 78 46.06 N 38.59 E
Čelbasskaja 78 45.59 N 39.22 E
Celbridge 48 53.20 N 6.33 W
Celebes → Sulawesi I 112 2.00 S 121.00 E
Celebes Basin ✢[1] 14 4.00 N 122.00 E
Celebes Sea ⊤[2] 112 3.00 N 122.00 E
Čeleken 128 39.26 N 53.07 E
Celendín 248 6.52 S 78.09 W
Celenza sul Trigno 66 41.52 N 14.35 E
Celenza Valfortore 68 41.34 N 14.58 E
Celerina 58 46.31 N 9.51 E
Celeryville 214 41.02 N 82.45 W
Celeste 196 33.18 N 96.12 W
Celestún 232 20.52 N 90.24 W
Celica 246 4.07 S 79.59 W
Celico 68 39.19 N 16.20 E
Çelikhan 130 38.02 N 38.15 E
Čelina, Ross. 80 46.32 N 41.02 E
Celina, Oh., U.S. 216 40.32 N 84.34 W
Celina, Tn., U.S. 194 36.33 N 85.30 W
Celina, Tx., U.S. 196 33.19 N 96.47 W
Celinnoje, Ross. 86 53.04 N 85.40 E
Celinnoje, Ross. 86 54.31 N 63.39 E
Celinnyj 80 46.40 N 44.32 E
Celinograd 86 51.10 N 71.30 E
Celinograd □[8] 86 51.00 N 70.00 E
Celje 36 46.14 N 15.16 E
Čelkar 86 47.50 N 59.36 E
Cellar Head › 46 58.26 N 6.10 W
Celldömölk 30 47.16 N 17.09 E
Celle 52 52.37 N 10.05 E
Celle, Ruisseau la ≃ 261 48.35 N 2.01 E
Celle Ligure 62 44.20 N 8.33 E
Celles 56 50.14 N 5.01 E
Celles-sur-Plaine 58 48.28 N 6.57 E
Cellettes 50 47.32 N 1.23 E
Cellina ≃ 64 46.02 N 12.47 E
Cellino Attanasio 66 42.36 N 13.52 E
Cellino San Marco 68 40.28 N 17.58 E
Čelmozero 24 64.18 N 31.48 E
Čelno-Veršiny 80 54.26 N 51.06 E
Čelobitjevo 265b 55.55 N 37.40 E
Celone ≃ 68 41.36 N 15.41 E
Celorico da Beira 34 40.38 N 7.23 W
Celoron 214 42.06 N 79.17 W
Celtic Sea ⊤[2] 28 51.00 N 6.30 W
Celtic Shelf ✢[4] 10 49.15 N 7.00 W
Çeltikçi, Tür. 130 40.20 N 32.28 E
Çeltikçi, Tür. 130 37.32 N 30.29 E
Čel'uš 86 51.32 N 87.46 E
Čel'uskin, mys › 74 77.45 N 104.20 E
Čel'uskincev park ♠ 265a 60.01 N 30.19 E
Cemaes Head › 42 52.07 N 4.44 W
Čemal 86 51.25 N 86.01 E
Čembilej 80 55.19 N 45.43 E
Cembra 64 46.10 N 11.13 E
Cembra, Val di V 64 46.10 N 11.13 E
Cement 196 34.55 N 98.08 W
Cement City 216 42.04 N 84.19 W
Cementon, N.Y., U.S. 210 42.09 N 73.55 W
Cementon, Pa., U.S. 208 40.41 N 75.30 W
Čemer 78 51.07 N 31.13 E
Čemerisy 78 51.42 N 30.24 E
Čemerno 36 43.11 N 18.37 E
Čemerovcy 78 49.01 N 26.21 E
Cemesskaja buchta ⊂ 78 44.40 N 37.50 E
Cemilbey 130 40.21 N 35.04 E
Çemişkezek 130 39.04 N 38.55 E
Cemmaes 42 52.37 N 3.42 W
Čemolgan 85 43.23 N 76.37 E
Cempi, Teluk ⊂ 115b 8.44 S 118.25 E
Čenča 88 55.57 N 110.59 E
Cencenighe 64 46.21 N 11.58 E
Čenchermandal 88 47.37 N 109.05 E
Čency 82 56.03 N 36.01 E
Cenderawasih, Teluk ⊂ 164 2.30 S 135.20 E
Cendras 62 44.09 N 4.04 E
Cene 62 45.47 N 9.49 E
Cenepa ≃ 246 4.35 S 78.12 W
Čengel 86 48.56 N 89.10 E
Čengel'dy, Kaz. 85 43.59 N 77.26 E
Čengel'dy, Kaz. 85 41.51 N 68.59 E
Çengelköy ◆[8] 267b 41.03 N 29.03 E
Çengerli 130 39.48 N 38.52 E
Cengles, Croda di ʌ 64 46.34 N 10.38 E
Ceno ≃ 36 44.41 N 10.05 E

Symbols in the index entries represent the broad categories identified in the key at the right. Symbols with superior numbers (⩘[1]) identify subcategories (see complete key on page *I · 1)*.

Symbole im Register stellen die rechts im Schlüssel erklärten Kategorien dar. Symbole mit hochgestellten Ziffern (⩘[1]) bezeichnen Unterabteilungen einer Kategorie (vgl. vollständiger Schlüssel auf Seite *I · 1)*.

Los símbolos incluídos en el texto del índice representan las grandes categorías identificadas con la clave a la derecha. Los símbolos con numeros en su parte superior (⩘[1]) identifican las subcategorías (véase la clave completa en la página *I · 1)*.

Les symboles de l'index représentent les catégories indiquées dans la légende à droite. Les symboles suivis d'un indice (⩘[1]) représentent des sous-catégories (voir légende complète à la page *I · 1)*.

Os símbolos incluídos no texto do índice representam as grandes categorias identificadas com a chave à direita. Os símbolos com números em sua parte superior (⩘[1]) identificam as subcategorias (veja-se a chave completa à página *I · 1)*.

	English	Deutsch	Español	Français	Português
ʌ	Mountain	Berg	Montaña	Montagne	Montanha
⩘	Mountains	Gebirge	Montañas	Montagnes	Montanhas
)(	Pass	Paß	Paso	Col	Passo
V	Valley, Canyon	Tal, Cañon	Valle, Cañón	Vallée, Canyon	Vale, Canhão
≚	Plain	Ebene	Llano	Plaine	Planície
›	Cape	Kap	Cabo	Cap	Cabo
I	Island	Insel	Isla	Île	Ilha
II	Islands	Inseln	Islas	Îles	Ilhas
⊥	Other Topographic Features	Andere Topographische Objekte	Otros Elementos Topográficos	Autres données topographiques	Outros acidentes topográficos

ESPAÑOL — Nombre / Página / Lat.°′ / Long.°′ W = Oeste
FRANÇAIS — Nom / Page / Lat.°′ / Long.°′ W = Ouest
PORTUGUÊS — Nome / Página / Lat.°′ / Long.°′ W = Oeste

Cenovo 38 43.32 N 25.39 E
Cenrana 112 3.18 S 118.50 E
Censeau 58 46.49 N 6.04 E
Centallo 62 44.30 N 7.35 E
Centenario 252 38.48 S 68.08 W
Centenário do Sul 255 22.48 S 51.37 W
Centennial Lake ⊜ 285 39.50 N 74.51 W
Centennial Lake ⊜[1] 212 45.10 N 72.05 W
Centennial Mountains ⋏ 202 44.35 N 111.55 W
Centennial Park ♠, Austl. 274a 33.54 S 151.14 E
Centennial Park ♠, On., Can. 275b 43.39 N 79.35 W
Centennial Wash V 200 33.14 N 112.46 W
Centeno 66 42.48 N 11.49 E
Center, Co., U.S. 200 37.45 N 106.06 W
Center, In., U.S. 216 40.26 N 86.04 W
Center, Mo., U.S. 219 39.30 N 91.31 W
Center, Ne., U.S. 198 42.36 N 97.52 W
Center, N.D., U.S. 198 47.06 N 101.17 W
Center, Tx., U.S. 194 31.47 N 94.10 W
Centerbrook 207 41.21 N 72.24 W
Center Brunswick 210 42.45 N 73.37 W
Centerburg 214 40.18 N 82.41 W
Center City 190 45.23 N 92.48 W
Center Cross 208 37.48 N 76.46 W
Centereach 210 40.51 N 73.06 W
Centerfield 218 38.21 N 83.24 W
Center Hill 220 28.38 N 81.59 W
Center Hill Lake ⊜[1] 194 36.00 N 85.45 W
Center Line 214 42.29 N 83.01 W
Center Moriches 188 40.48 N 72.47 W
Center Mountain ∧ 202 45.06 N 115.13 W
Center Point, Al., U.S. 194 33.37 N 86.41 W
Center Point, Ia., U.S. 190 42.11 N 91.47 W
Center Point, Tx., U.S. 196 29.57 N 99.02 W
Centerport, N.Y., U.S. 210 40.54 N 73.22 W
Centerport, Pa., U.S. 208 40.29 N 76.01 W
Center Square, N.J., U.S. 285 39.46 N 75.23 W
Center Square, Pa., U.S. 208 40.10 N 75.18 W
Centerton, In., U.S. 218 39.30 N 86.23 W
Centerton, N.J., U.S. 285 39.31 N 75.10 W
Center Valley 208 40.32 N 75.24 W
Centerville, De., U.S. 285 39.49 N 75.37 W
Centerville, In., U.S. 218 39.49 N 84.59 W
Centerville, Ia., U.S. 190 40.43 N 92.52 W
Centerville, Ma., U.S. 207 41.38 N 70.20 W
Centerville, Mo., U.S. 194 37.26 N 90.57 W
Centerville, N.Y., U.S. 210 42.29 N 78.15 W
Centerville, Oh., U.S. 218 39.37 N 84.09 W
Centerville, Pa., U.S. 188 40.02 N 79.58 W
Centerville, S.D., U.S. 198 43.07 N 96.57 W
Centerville, Tn., U.S. 194 35.46 N 87.28 W
Centerville, Tx., U.S. 222 31.15 N 95.58 W
Centerville, Ut., U.S. 200 40.55 N 111.52 W
Centerville, Wa., U.S. 224 45.45 N 120.54 W
Centinela 196 28.47 N 100.34 W
Cento 64 44.43 N 11.17 E
Centocelle ◆[8] 267a 41.53 N 12.34 E
Cento Croci, Passo di)(62 44.25 N 9.37 E
Centola 68 40.04 N 15.19 E
Central, Bra. 250 11.08 S 42.08 W
Central, Ak., U.S. 180 65.34 N 144.48 W
Central, Az., U.S. 200 32.52 N 109.47 W
Central, N.M., U.S. 200 32.46 N 108.08 W
Central, S.C., U.S. 192 34.43 N 82.46 W
Central, Tx., U.S. 222 31.26 N 94.49 W
Central □[4], Ghana 150 5.30 N 1.00 W
Central □[4], Kenya 154 0.45 S 37.00 E
Central □[4], Malaŵi 154 13.00 S 34.00 E
Central □[4], Sol.Is. 175e 9.10 S 159.50 E
Central □[4], Scot., U.K. 46 56.05 N 4.20 W
Central □[4], Zam. 154 14.30 S 29.00 E
Central □[5], Bots. 156 21.30 S 26.00 E
Central □[5], Pap. N. Gui. 164 9.00 S 147.00 E
Central □[5], Para. 252 25.30 S 57.30 W
Central □[5], Ug. 154 0.10 N 32.00 E
Central, Cordillera ⋏, Col. 246 5.00 N 75.00 W
Central, Cordillera ⋏, C.R. 236 10.10 N 84.05 W
Central, Cordillera ⋏, Pan. 236 8.30 N 81.30 W
Central, Cordillera ⋏, Perú 248 8.00 S 77.00 W
Central, Cordillera ⋏, Pil. 116 17.20 N 120.57 E
Central, Cordillera ⋏, P.R. 240m 18.10 N 66.35 W
Central, Macizo → Central, Massif ⋏ 32 45.00 N 3.10 E
Central, Massif ⋏ 32 45.00 N 3.10 E
Central, Planalto ⋏[1] 242 18.00 S 47.00 W
Central, Sistema ⋏ 34 40.30 N 5.00 W
Central African Republic □[1] 136 7.00 N 21.00 E
Central Aguirre 240m 17.57 N 66.13 W
Central Barren 218 38.22 N 86.06 W
Central Brāhui Range ⋏ 120 29.20 N 66.55 E
Central Bridge 210 42.42 N 74.20 W
Central Butte 184 50.47 N 106.30 W
Central City, Il., U.S. 219 38.32 N 89.07 W
Central City, Ia., U.S. 190 42.12 N 91.31 W
Central City, Ky., U.S. 194 37.17 N 87.07 W
Central City, Ne., U.S. 198 41.06 N 98.00 W
Central City, Pa., U.S. 214 40.06 N 78.48 W
Central Division □[5] 175g 18.05 S 178.30 E
Centrale, Stazione ◆[5] 266b 45.29 N 9.12 E
Central Falls 207 41.53 N 71.23 W
Central Heights 200 33.24 N 110.48 W
Central Highlands 279b 40.16 N 79.50 W
Centralia, Il., U.S. 219 38.31 N 89.08 W
Centralia, Ks., U.S. 198 39.43 N 96.07 W
Centralia, Mo., U.S. 219 39.12 N 92.03 W
Centralia, Tx., U.S. 222 31.16 N 95.02 W
Centralia, Wa., U.S. 224 46.42 N 122.57 W
Centralia, Lake ⊜ 219 38.32 N 88.59 W
Centralia Draw V 196 31.27 N 101.16 W
Centralia Reservoir ⊜[1] 219 38.32 N 89.08 W
Centralina 255 18.34 S 49.13 W
Central Intelligence Agency ʋ 284c 38.57 N 77.09 W
Central Island I 154 3.30 N 36.03 E
Central Islip 210 40.47 N 73.12 W
Central Kalahari Game Reserve ◆[4] 156 22.15 S 23.45 E
Central Lake 190 45.04 N 85.15 W
Central Makrān Range ⋏ 128 26.40 N 64.30 E
Central'no-Bokovskoj ◆[8] 83 48.11 N 39.03 E
Central'nolesnoj zapovednik ◆[4] 76 56.32 N 32.50 E
Central Nyack 276 41.06 N 73.57 W
Central'nyj, Ross. 76 53.41 N 39.38 E
Central'nyj, Ross. 86 55.12 N 87.40 E
Central'nyj, Ross. 86 58.45 N 84.28 E
Central'nyj, Ross. 86 57.41 N 80.57 E
Central'nyj, Ross. 265b 55.53 N 37.52 E
Central'nyje Karakumy ◆[2] 128 39.00 N 60.00 E
Central Pacific Basin ✤[1] 14 5.00 N 175.00 W
Central Park, N.J., U.S. 276 40.26 N 74.18 W
Central Park, Wa., U.S. 224 46.58 N 123.41 W
Central Park ♠ 276 40.47 N 73.58 W
Central Point 202 42.22 N 122.54 W
Central Railroad Station ◆[5] 272c 18.58 N 72.50 E
Central Range ⋏, Leso. 158 29.35 S 28.35 E
Central Range ⋏, Pap. N. Gui. 164 5.00 S 142.30 E
Central Square 210 43.17 N 76.08 W
Central Utah Canal ≍ 200 39.35 N 112.12 W
Central Valley, Ca., U.S. 204 40.40 N 122.22 W
Central Valley, N.Y., U.S. 210 41.19 N 74.07 W
Central Village 207 41.43 N 71.54 W
Centre 194 34.09 N 85.40 W
Centre □[6] 210 40.55 N 77.47 W
Centre, Canal du ≍ 32 46.27 N 4.07 E
Centre Atomique de Marcoule ʋ[3] 62 44.08 N 4.42 E
Centre City 285 39.46 N 75.10 W
Centre d'Énergie de Pierrelatte ʋ[3] 62 44.21 N 4.44 E
Centre Hall 214 40.50 N 77.41 W
Centre Island 276 40.54 N 73.32 W
Centre Island I 172 46.28 S 167.51 E
Centre Island Park ♠ 275b 43.37 N 79.23 W
Centre Lake ⊜ 212 44.36 N 75.51 W
Centre Peak ∧ 182 55.41 N 126.26 W
Centre-Sud □[4] 152 4.10 N 12.00 E
Centreville, Al., U.S. 194 32.56 N 87.08 W
Centreville, Il., U.S. 219 38.35 N 90.07 W
Centreville, Ky., U.S. 218 38.13 N 84.24 W
Centreville, Md., U.S. 208 39.02 N 76.04 W
Centreville, Mi., U.S. 216 41.55 N 85.31 W
Centreville, Ms., U.S. 194 31.05 N 91.04 W
Centreville, Va., U.S. 208 38.50 N 77.25 W
Centro Puntas 240m 18.22 N 67.16 W
Centro Simón Bolívar ◆[9] 286c 10.30 N 66.55 W
Centuripe 70 37.37 N 14.44 E
Century, Fl., U.S. 194 30.58 N 87.15 W
Century, W.V., U.S. 188 39.05 N 80.11 W
Century City ◆[8] 280 34.03 N 118.26 W
Century III Mall ◆[9] 279b 40.21 N 79.57 W
Century Village 220 26.42 N 80.05 W
Cenxi 102 22.59 N 111.00 E
Čepca 80 57.54 N 53.25 E
Čepca ≃ 80 58.36 N 50.04 E
Čepeckij 80 58.29 N 51.12 E
Čepel' 78 49.19 N 36.55 E
Čepelare 38 41.44 N 24.41 E
Čepel'ovo 82 55.11 N 37.30 E
Čepovan 64 46.03 N 13.47 E
Cepoy 50 48.03 N 2.44 E
Ceprano 66 41.33 N 13.31 E
Čepřovice 60 49.10 N 13.59 E
Ceptia 152 12.56 S 17.35 E
Cepu 115a 7.09 S 111.35 E
Ceraino 64 45.35 N 10.50 E
Ceram → Seram I 164 3.00 S 129.00 E
Cerami 70 37.49 N 14.30 E
Cerami ≃ 70 37.42 N 14.29 E
Ceram Sea → Seram, Laut ⊤[2] 108 2.30 S 128.00 E
Cerano, It. 62 45.25 N 8.47 E
Cerano, Méx. 234 20.07 N 101.23 W
Ceraso 68 40.11 N 15.15 E
Cerbicale, Îles II 71 41.34 N 9.24 E
Čerčany 30 49.51 N 14.43 E
Cerchiara di Calabria 68 39.51 N 16.23 E
Čerchov ∧ 60 49.23 N 12.47 E
Cercié 58 46.07 N 4.40 E
Cerco, Alto do ∧ 256 22.38 S 45.22 W
Cerda 70 37.54 N 13.49 E
Čerdakly 80 54.23 N 48.51 E
Cerdanyola del Vallès 266d 41.30 N 2.09 E
Cerdas 248 20.48 S 66.29 W
Cerdeña, Isla de → Sardegna I 71 40.00 N 9.00 E
Čerdojak 86 48.48 N 84.00 E
Cerdon, Fr. 50 47.38 N 2.22 E
Cerdon, Fr. 58 46.05 N 5.28 E
Čerdyn' 24 60.23 N 56.24 E
Cère ≃ 32 44.55 N 1.53 E
Cerea 64 45.12 N 11.13 E
Cereal 184 51.25 N 110.48 W
Cereales 252 36.49 S 63.51 W
Čerecha ≃ 76 57.46 N 28.21 E
Cereglio 64 44.18 N 11.04 E
Čereja 76 54.37 N 29.17 E
Čerek ≃ 84 43.42 N 44.03 E
Čeremchovo 88 53.09 N 103.05 E
Čeremisinovo 78 51.54 N 37.15 E
Čeremoš ≃ 78 48.23 N 25.37 E
Čeremšan, Ross. 80 55.15 N 48.07 E
Čeremšan, Ross. 80 54.40 N 51.30 E
Čeremšanka, Ross. 86 59.10 N 76.51 E
Čeremšanka, Ross. 86 56.07 N 60.19 E
Čeremšany 89 44.42 N 135.43 E
Cerenti 112 0.30 S 101.52 E
Čerepanovka 80 57.07 N 54.10 E
Čerepanovo 86 54.13 N 83.22 E
Čerepaška, ostrov I 83 47.11 N 38.59 E
Čerepet' 82 54.07 N 36.23 E
Čerepkovo ◆[8] 265b 55.46 N 37.23 E
Čerepovec 76 59.08 N 37.54 E
Ceres, Arg. 252 29.53 S 61.57 W
Ceres, Bra. 255 15.17 S 49.35 W
Ceres, It. 62 45.19 N 7.23 E
Ceres, S. Afr. 158 33.21 S 19.18 E
Ceres, Ca., U.S. 226 37.35 N 120.57 W
Ceres, N.Y., U.S. 210 42.00 N 78.16 W
Ceresco, Mi., U.S. 216 42.16 N 85.04 W
Ceresco, Ne., U.S. 198 41.03 N 96.38 W
Ceresole Reale 62 45.26 N 7.15 E
Céreste 62 43.51 N 5.35 E
Céret 32 42.29 N 2.45 E
Cereté 246 8.53 N 75.48 W
Čerevkovka 78 48.50 N 37.40 E
Čerevkovka ◆[8] 83 48.50 N 37.40 E
Čerevkovo 24 61.46 N 45.12 E
Cereweh 115b 8.52 S 116.51 E
Cerf Island I 138 9.32 S 50.59 E
Čerga 86 51.35 N 85.38 E
Cergy 261 49.02 N 2.04 E
Ceri ≃ 42 52.03 N 4.29 W
Ceriale 62 44.06 N 8.14 E
Ceriana 62 43.53 N 7.46 E
Ceriano 266b 45.38 N 9.05 E
Cerignola 68 41.16 N 15.54 E
Čerikov 76 53.34 N 31.23 E
Cérilly 32 46.37 N 2.49 E
Cerisano 68 39.16 N 16.11 E
Cerisiers 50 48.08 N 3.29 E
Čerkašina 88 58.37 N 108.30 E
Čerkasovo 82 54.33 N 36.48 E
Čerkasskoje, Ross. 80 52.26 N 47.13 E
Čerkasskoje, Ukr. 78 48.44 N 35.22 E
Čerkasskoje, Ukr. 83 48.50 N 37.23 E
Čerkassy, Ross. 76 52.41 N 38.43 E
Čerkassy, Ukr. 78 49.26 N 32.04 E
Čerkassy □[4] 78 49.30 N 31.30 E
Çerkeş 130 40.50 N 32.54 E
Čerkesovskij 80 50.41 N 42.34 E
Čerkessk 84 44.14 N 42.04 E
Çerkezköy 130 41.17 N 28.00 E
Čerkizovo, Ross. 82 55.12 N 38.45 E
Čerkizovo, Ross. 265b 55.58 N 37.48 E
Čerkizovo, Ross. 265b 55.57 N 37.22 E
Cerknica 36 45.48 N 14.22 E
Čerkovišče 76 55.54 N 30.51 E
Čerlak 86 54.09 N 74.48 E
Čerlakskij 86 53.47 N 74.31 E
Cermei 38 46.33 N 21.51 E
Čermen 84 43.11 N 44.42 E
Cermignano 66 42.35 N 13.47 E
Çermik 130 38.09 N 39.27 E
Čermoz 86 58.53 N 56.08 E
Čern' 76 53.27 N 36.55 E
Cerna, Hrv. 38 45.11 N 18.42 E
Cerna, Rom. 38 45.04 N 28.18 E
Čern'achov 78 50.27 N 28.39 E
Čern'achovsk (Insterburg) 76 54.38 N 21.49 E
Černá hora ∧ 60 48.58 N 13.48 E
Čern'ajevo 89 52.45 N 126.00 E
Černak 85 43.24 N 68.02 E
Čern'anka 78 50.55 N 37.49 E
Cernăuți → Černovcy 78 48.18 N 25.56 E
Černava 76 53.37 N 39.09 E
Černavčicy 76 52.13 N 23.44 E
Černavka, Ross. 80 52.18 N 47.14 E
Černavka, Ross. 80 52.11 N 42.25 E
Cernavodă 38 44.21 N 28.01 E
Černá v Pošumaví 61 48.44 N 14.07 E
Cernay 58 47.49 N 7.10 E
Cernay-la-Ville 50 48.40 N 1.58 E
Cerne Abbas 42 50.49 N 2.29 W
Černeckoje 82 55.15 N 37.20 E
Cernei, Munții ⋏ 38 45.02 N 22.31 E
Černelica 78 48.48 N 25.26 E
Černevcy 78 48.33 N 28.09 E
Černigov 78 51.30 N 31.18 E
Černigov □[4] 78 51.15 N 32.00 E
Černigovka, Kaz. 86 50.28 N 71.27 E
Černigovka, Ross. 89 49.37 N 129.57 E
Černigovka, Ross. 89 44.21 N 132.33 E
Černigovka, Ukr. 78 47.13 N 36.14 E
Černigovskaja 78 44.41 N 39.40 E
Černi vrăh ∧ 38 42.34 N 23.17 E
Černobaj 78 49.41 N 32.19 E
Cernobbio 62 45.50 N 9.04 E
Černobyl' 78 51.16 N 30.14 E
Černogolovka 82 56.00 N 38.22 E
Černogorsk 86 53.49 N 91.18 E
Černokol'skaja 86 56.42 N 72.49 E
Černomorskij zapovednik ◆[4] 78 46.10 N 32.00 E
Černorečenskoje 85 43.00 N 74.55 E
Černorečje 84 43.15 N 45.41 E
Černošín 60 49.49 N 12.53 E
Černovcy 78 48.18 N 25.56 E
Černovcy □[8] 78 43.30 N 26.00 E
Černovice 60 49.49 N 13.06 E
Černovka, Ross. 86 56.47 N 76.28 E
Černovka, Ross. 89 51.43 N 128.12 E
Čern'ovo, Ross. 76 58.39 N 28.14 E
Čern'ovo, Ross. 82 54.43 N 38.36 E
Čern'ovo, Ross. 265b 55.50 N 37.18 E
Černovskije Kopi 88 52.00 N 113.15 E
Černovskoje, Ross. 80 58.42 N 47.23 E
Černovskoje, Ross. 80 57.29 N 54.36 E
Černucha 80 55.36 N 43.46 E
Černuchi 78 50.16 N 32.57 E
Černuchino 83 48.19 N 38.30 E
Cernusco sul Naviglio 62 45.31 N 9.19 E
Černuška, Ross. 86 56.29 N 56.03 E
Černuška, Ross. 88 52.58 N 101.55 E
Cerny-en-Laonnois 50 49.27 N 3.40 E
Černyševsk 88 52.35 N 117.00 E
Černyševskij 74 63.00 N 112.15 E
Černyškovskij 80 48.27 N 42.14 E
Černyšova, gr'ada ⋏ 24 66.30 N 59.00 E
Čer'omuchova 80 54.57 N 51.09 E
Čer'omuski ◆[8] 265b 55.41 N 37.35 E
Cerralvo 232 26.06 N 99.37 W
Cerralvo, Isla I 232 24.15 N 109.55 W
Cerreto, Passo del)(64 44.18 N 10.13 E
Cerreto d'Esi 66 43.19 N 12.59 E
Cerreto Guidi 66 43.45 N 10.53 E
Cerreto Sannita 68 41.17 N 14.33 E
Cerrigydrudion 44 53.02 N 3.33 W
Cërrik 38 41.02 N 19.57 E
Cerrillos, Arg 252 24.54 S 65.29 W
Cerrillos, Chile 286e 33.30 S 70.43 W
Cerrillos, N.M., U.S. 200 35.26 N 106.07 W
Cerrina 62 45.07 N 8.13 E
Cerritos, Méx. 234 22.26 N 100.17 W
Cerritos, Ca., U.S. 280 33.52 N 118.05 W
Cerro 58 45.54 N 8.36 E
Cerro, Forca di)(66 42.45 N 12.47 E
Cerro Azul, Arg. 252 27.38 S 55.29 W
Cerro Azul, Bra. 252 24.50 S 49.15 W
Cerro Azul, Méx. 234 21.12 N 97.44 W
Cerro Azul, Perú 248 13.02 S 76.30 W
Cerro Chato 252 33.06 S 55.08 W
Cerro Colorado 252 33.52 S 55.33 W
Cerro Corá 250 6.03 S 36.21 W
Cerro de las Mesas ⊥ 234 18.47 N 96.05 W
Cerro de los Angeles ʋ[1] 266a 40.19 N 3.41 W
Cerro de Pasco 248 10.41 S 76.16 W
Cerro Gordo 219 39.53 N 88.43 W
Cerro Grande ≃ 286c 10.37 N 66.49 W
Cerro Largo 252 28.09 S 54.45 W
Cerro Maggiore 266b 45.36 N 8.58 E
Cerro Moreno 252 23.28 S 70.25 W
Cerrón, Cerro ∧ 246 10.19 N 70.39 W
Cerro Navia 286e 33.25 S 70.43 W
Cerrón Grande, Embalse ⊜[1] 236 14.00 N 89.00 W
Cerro Prieto 204 32.27 N 115.17 W
Cerros Colorados Embalse ⊜[1] 252 38.35 S 68.40 W
Cerros de Amotape, Parque Nacional ♠ 246 4.10 S 80.30 W
Cerro Tololo, Observatorio ʋ[3] 252 30.05 S 71.00 W
Cerro Vera 252 33.11 S 57.28 W
Čerskij 74 68.45 N 161.45 E
Čerskogo, chrebet ⋏, Ross. 74 65.00 N 144.00 E
Čerskogo, chrebet ⋏, Ross. 88 52.00 N 114.00 E
Čerskogo, gora ∧ 88 55.05 N 108.40 E
Cersosimo 68 40.03 N 16.21 E
Certaldo 66 43.33 N 11.02 E
Čertanovka ≃ 265b 55.38 N 37.47 E
Čertanovo ◆[8] 265b 55.38 N 37.37 E
Čertkovo 83 49.23 N 40.10 E
Čertolino 76 56.12 N 33.54 E
Čertomlyk 78 47.37 N 34.09 E
Certosa (Karthaus) 64 46.42 N 10.54 E
Certosa di Pavia 62 45.15 N 9.09 E
Čerusti 76 55.33 N 40.01 E
Červ'anka 88 57.41 N 99.33 E
Cervantes, Austl. 162 30.30 S 115.04 E
Cervantes, Pil. 116 16.59 N 120.44 E
Cervarezza 64 44.23 N 10.20 E
Cervaro 66 41.29 N 13.54 E
Cervaro ≃ 68 41.30 N 15.52 E
Cervati, Monte ∧ 68 40.17 N 15.29 E
Cervelló 266d 41.24 N 1.57 E
Cervello, Cozzo ∧ 68 39.24 N 16.05 E
Cervelló, Riera de ≃ 266d 41.24 N 2.01 E
Červen' 76 53.42 N 28.26 E
Červen Brjag 38 43.16 N 24.06 E
Červený Kostelec 30 50.29 N 16.06 E
Cervera 34 41.40 N 1.17 E
Cervera del Río Alhama 34 42.01 N 1.57 W
Cervera de Pisuerga 34 42.52 N 4.30 W
Cerveteri 66 42.00 N 12.06 E
Cervi, Monte dei ∧ 70 37.53 N 13.58 E
Cervia 66 44.15 N 12.22 E
Cervialto, Monte ∧ 68 40.47 N 15.08 E
Cervignano del Friuli 64 45.49 N 13.20 E
Cervin, Mont → Matterhorn ∧ 58 45.59 N 7.43 E
Cervinara 68 41.01 N 14.37 E
Cervino (Matterhorn) ∧ 58 45.59 N 7.43 E
Cervione 36 42.20 N 9.31 E
Červl'onnaja 84 43.30 N 45.54 E
Cervo, Esp. 34 43.40 N 7.25 W
Cervo, It. 62 43.55 N 8.07 E
Cervo ≃ 62 45.22 N 8.24 E
Cervo, Capo › 62 43.55 N 8.08 E
Cervo, Rio do ≃, Bra. 256 22.07 S 45.49 W
Cervo, Rio do ≃, Bra. 256 21.12 S 45.10 W
Cervo, Serra do ∧ 256 22.06 S 46.07 W
Červonaja Kamenka 78 48.38 N 33.26 E
Červonoarmejsk, Ukr. 78 50.08 N 25.16 E
Červonoarmejsk, Ukr. 78 50.28 N 28.14 E
Červonoarmejskoje, Ukr. 78 45.47 N 28.44 E
Červonoarmejskoje, Ukr. 78 47.57 N 35.27 E
Červonograd 78 50.24 N 24.14 E
Červonogranitnoje 78 50.34 N 28.33 E
Červonoje, Ukr. 78 51.46 N 34.04 E
Červonoje, Ukr. 78 49.57 N 28.53 E
Červonoje, ozero ⊜ 76 52.24 N 27.57 E
Červonopartizansk 83 48.04 N 39.50 E
Červonyj Donec 78 49.29 N 36.34 E
Cesana Torinese 62 44.57 N 6.47 E
Cesano, It. 66 43.45 N 13.10 E
Cesano, It. 66 42.07 N 12.21 E
Cesano ≃ 66 43.45 N 13.10 E
Cesano Boscone 266b 45.27 N 9.06 E
Cesano Maderno 62 45.38 N 9.08 E
Cesar □[5] 246 9.20 N 73.30 W
Cesar ≃ 246 9.00 N 73.58 W
Cesarò 70 37.50 N 14.43 E
Cesate 266b 45.36 N 9.05 E
Cesena 66 44.08 N 12.15 E
Cesenatico 66 44.12 N 12.24 E
Cesi, Poggio ∧[2] 267a 42.02 N 12.44 E
Cesiomaggiore 64 46.05 N 11.59 E
Cēsis 76 57.18 N 25.15 E
Česká Kamenice 54 50.47 N 14.26 E
Česká Kublice 60 49.22 N 12.52 E
Česká Lípa 54 50.42 N 14.32 E
Česká Třebová 30 49.54 N 16.27 E
České Budějovice 61 48.59 N 14.28 E
České středohoří ⋏ 54 50.35 N 14.09 E
Českomoravská vrchovina ⋏[1] 30 49.20 N 15.30 E
Český Brod 54 50.02 N 14.58 E
Český Krumlov 61 48.49 N 14.19 E
Česma 86 53.50 N 60.40 E
Çeşme 130 38.18 N 26.19 E
Cessalto 64 45.42 N 12.36 E
Češskaja guba c 24 67.30 N 46.30 E
Cessnock 170 32.50 S 151.21 E
Cesson 261 48.34 N 2.36 E
Cestos ≃ 150 5.40 N 9.10 W
Cesvaine 76 56.58 N 26.19 E
Čet' ≃ 86 56.51 N 86.48 E
Cetara 68 40.39 N 14.42 E
Cetate 38 44.06 N 23.03 E
Cetatea Albă → Belgorod-Dnestrovskij 78 46.12 N 30.20 E
Četbulak 85 41.17 N 73.58 E
Cetian 100 25.44 N 116.22 E
Cetina ≃ 36 43.26 N 16.42 E
Cetinje 38 42.23 N 18.55 E
Çetinkaya 130 39.15 N 37.38 E
Cetona 66 42.58 N 11.54 E
Cetona, Monte ∧ 66 42.56 N 11.52 E
Cetraro 68 39.31 N 15.56 E
Cetronia 208 40.35 N 75.31 W
Četyrboki 78 50.02 N 27.01 E
Céüse, Montagne de ∧ 62 44.31 N 5.57 E
Ceuta 34 35.53 N 5.19 W
Ceva 62 44.23 N 8.02 E
Cevedale, Monte (Zufallspitze) ∧ 64 46.27 N 10.37 E
Cevennen → Cévennes ◆[1] 32 44.00 N 3.30 E
Cévennes ◆[1] 32 44.00 N 3.30 E
Cévennes, Parc National des ♠ 32 44.15 N 3.40 E
Cevins 62 45.35 N 6.28 E
Cevio 58 46.19 N 8.36 E
Cevizli 130 37.12 N 31.45 E
Ceyhan 130 37.04 N 35.47 E
Ceyhan ≃ 130 36.45 N 35.41 E
Ceylanpınar 130 36.51 N 40.02 E
Ceylon, Sk., Can. 184 49.28 N 104.36 W
Ceylon, Mn., U.S. 198 43.32 N 94.37 W
Ceylon → Sri Lanka □[1] 122 7.00 N 81.00 E
Ceyzériat 58 46.10 N 5.19 E
Cèze ≃ 62 44.06 N 4.42 E
Chaam, Ned. 52 51.31 N 4.52 E
Cha-am, Thai 110 12.48 N 99.58 E
Chaanling 100 29.39 N 113.49 E
Chaatl Island I 182 53.00 N 132.25 W
Chabanais 32 45.52 N 0.43 E
Chabang Tiga 114 5.19 N 103.08 E
Chabaricha 24 65.50 N 52.16 E
Chabařovice 54 50.40 N 13.56 E
Chabarovo 72 69.39 N 60.24 E
Chabarovsk 89 48.27 N 135.06 E
Chabarovsk Kraj □[8] 89 52.00 N 138.00 E
Chabarowsk → Chabarovsk 89 48.27 N 135.06 E
Chabary 86 53.37 N 79.33 E
Chabás 252 33.15 S 61.22 W
Chabeuil 62 44.54 N 5.01 E
Chabez 84 44.02 N 41.47 E
Chābi 124 22.49 N 80.41 E
Chabjuwardoo Bay c 162 22.57 S 113.48 E
Chablais ◆[1] 58 46.18 N 6.39 E
Chablis 50 47.49 N 3.48 E
Chabogongba 120 31.47 N 81.14 E
Chaboje 265a 59.53 N 30.46 E
Chabot, Lake ⊜, Ca., U.S. 282 38.08 N 122.14 W
Chabot, Lake ⊜, Ca., U.S. 282 37.43 N 122.07 W
Chabris 50 47.15 N 1.39 E
Chabuchaer 86 43.42 N 81.04 E
Chabu-Rabot, pereval)(85 38.40 N 70.43 E
Chacabuco 252 34.38 S 60.29 W
Chacaito, Quebrada ≃ 286c 10.29 N 66.52 W
Chacaltianguis 234 18.20 N 95.50 W
Chacao 286c 10.30 N 66.51 W
Chácara 256 21.41 S 43.13 W
Chacarita, Cementerio de la ◆ 288 34.33 S 58.28 W
Chacarrão, Cachoeira do ʟ 250 6.32 S 58.12 W
Chacayán 248 10.24 S 76.25 W
Chachani, Nevado ∧ 248 16.12 S 71.33 W
Chachapoyas, Perú 242 6.13 S 77.51 W
Chachapoyas, Perú 248 6.13 S 77.51 W
Chachas 248 15.30 S 72.16 W
Chachoengsao 110 13.42 N 101.05 E
Chāchora 124 24.10 N 76.59 E
Chāchro 120 25.07 N 70.15 E
Chachu 120 33.16 N 81.41 E
Chačinčaj ≃ 84 40.13 N 47.18 E
Chaclacayo 248 11.59 S 76.46 W
Chačmas 84 41.28 N 48.48 E
Chaco □[4] 252 26.25 S 60.30 W
Chaco □[5] 248 20.00 S 60.30 W
Chaco ≃ 200 36.46 N 108.39 W
Chaco Austral ◆[1] 252 26.30 S 61.30 W
Chaco Boreal ◆[1] 252 23.00 S 60.00 W
Chaco Central ◆[1] 252 25.00 S 59.45 W
Chaco Culture National Historical Park ♠ 200 36.06 N 108.00 W
Chaco Mesa ∧ 200 35.47 N 107.35 W
Chacón, Arroyo ≃ 288 34.53 S 58.39 W
Chacon, Cape › 182 54.42 N 132.00 W
Chacra Cerro 286d 11.55 S 77.04 W
Chacuaco Creek ≃ 196 37.34 N 103.38 W
Chad (Tchad) □[1], Afr. 136 15.00 N 19.00 E
Chad (Tchad) □[1], Afr. 146 15.00 N 19.00 E
Chad, Lake (Lac Tchad) ⊜ 146 13.20 N 14.00 E
Chada-Bulak 88 50.38 N 116.18 E
Chadbourn 192 34.19 N 78.49 W
Chadderton 44 53.33 N 2.08 W
Chadds Ford 285 39.52 N 75.35 W
Chādegān 128 32.46 N 50.39 E
Chadian, Zhg. 102 26.48 N 105.48 E
Chadian, Zhg. 105 39.14 N 117.45 E
Chadian, Zhg. 107 30.14 N 105.56 E
Chadianzi 107 30.31 N 104.22 E
Chadiza 154 14.05 S 32.28 E
Chadron 198 42.49 N 103.00 W
Chadstone 274b 37.53 S 145.05 E
Chadwell Saint Mary 260 51.29 N 0.22 E
Chadwick 190 42.01 N 89.53 W
Chadwick Manor 284b 39.19 N 76.46 W
Chadwick Pond ⊜ 283 42.44 N 71.05 W
Chadwicks 210 43.01 N 75.16 W
Chadyženk 78 44.25 N 39.33 E
Chadžalmachi 84 42.26 N 47.13 E
Chadžibejskij liman ⊜ 78 46.39 N 30.33 E
Chae Hom 110 18.43 N 99.35 E
Chaem ≃ 110 18.11 N 98.38 E
Chaersen 89 46.19 N 121.54 E
Chaeryŏng 98 38.24 N 125.36 E
Chafarinas, Islas II 34 35.11 N 2.26 W
Chafe 150 11.56 N 6.55 E
Chaffee 194 37.10 N 89.39 W
Chaffins 207 42.21 N 71.51 W
Chāgai 128 29.18 N 64.42 E
Chāgai Hills ⋏[2] 128 29.30 N 64.15 E
Chagandianlisu 102 41.47 N 103.29 E
Chagang Do □[4] 98 40.50 N 126.30 E
'Chaghcharān 120 34.32 N 65.15 E
Chagny 58 46.55 N 4.45 E
Chagos Archipelago II 12 6.00 S 72.00 E
Chagos-Laccadive Plateau ✤[3] 12 3.00 N 73.00 E
Chagrin ≃ 214 41.40 N 81.27 W
Chagrin, Aurora Branch ≃ 279a 41.25 N 81.25 W
Chagrin Falls 214 41.26 N 81.24 W
Chagrin Falls Park 214 41.21 N 81.32 W
Chagrin Valley Parkway ♠ 279a 41.26 N 81.25 W
Chaguanas 241r 10.31 N 61.25 W
Chaguaramas 246 9.20 N 66.16 W
Chahaignes 50 47.44 N 0.31 E
Chāhak 128 33.17 N 58.54 E
Chahal 236 15.45 N 89.34 W
Chahancheluo 98 41.39 N 114.22 E
Chahanwusu → Dulan 102 36.16 N 98.28 E
Chahār Borjak 128 30.17 N 62.03 E
Chahār Deh-ye Ghowrband 120 34.59 N 68.44 E
Chahār Maḩāl va Bakhtīārī □[4] 128 32.00 N 51.00 E
Chahayang 89 48.24 N 124.15 E
Chahe, Zhg. 100 33.16 N 119.02 E
Chahe, Zhg. 102 33.48 N 97.22 E
Chahe, Zhg. 105 39.50 N 115.21 E
Chāh Gheybī, Hāmūn-e ≡ 128 28.06 N 60.50 E
Chahuamiao 100 33.00 N 115.56 E
Chahuites 234 16.17 N 94.11 W
Chai ≃ 104 42.20 N 123.52 E
Chai Badan 110 15.04 N 101.05 E
Chāībāsa 124 22.34 N 85.49 E
Chaigou 98 36.15 N 119.36 E
Chaihe 89 44.47 N 129.42 E
Chaijiawan 100 29.10 N 113.06 E
Chaillé-les-Marais 32 46.24 N 1.01 W
Chailley 50 48.05 N 3.42 E
Chailly-en-Bière 50 48.28 N 2.35 E
Chai Nat 110 15.11 N 100.08 E
Chainhurst 260 51.12 N 0.29 E
Chain O'Lakes State Park ♠, Il., U.S. 216 42.27 N 88.11 W
Chain O'Lakes State Park ♠, In., U.S. 216 41.20 N 85.26 W
Chainpur 124 23.08 N 84.15 E
Chaipudyrskaja guba c 24 68.30 N 59.30 E
Chaiqiao 100 29.51 N 121.56 E
Chairel, Laguna de c 234 22.17 N 97.57 W
Chaishudian 105 40.46 N 116.30 E
Chaiši 84 42.57 N 42.12 E
Chait 85 39.11 N 70.53 E
Chaital 126 22.31 N 88.47 E
Chaitén 254 42.55 S 72.43 W
Chaiwopu 86 43.33 N 87.59 E
Chaiya 110 9.23 N 99.14 E
Chaiyaphum 110 15.48 N 102.02 E
Chajarí 252 30.46 S 57.59 W
Chajdarken 85 39.57 N 71.21 E
Chajia 107 29.37 N 104.27 E
Chajian 100 32.40 N 118.46 E
Chajianling 98 39.14 N 114.36 E
Chajiaqiao 100 34.00 N 120.07 E
Chajrchan 88 48.35 N 101.56 E
Chajrchandulaan 102 45.57 N 102.03 E
Chajul 236 15.30 N 91.02 W
Chaka 154 4.49 N 31.14 E
Chakachamna Lake ⊜ 180 61.13 N 152.35 W
Chakāltor 126 23.14 N 86.22 E
Chak Amru 123 32.22 N 75.11 E
Chakari 154 18.05 S 29.51 E
Chakaria 120 21.45 N 92.05 E
Chakamaba 146 14.13 N 20.51 E
Chakasija □[3] 86 53.00 N 90.00 E
Chākdaha, India 126 23.05 N 88.31 E
Chakdaha, India 272b 22.20 N 88.20 E
Chake Chake 154 5.15 S 39.46 E
Chakhānsūr 128 31.10 N 62.04 E
Chākia 124 25.25 N 85.03 E
Chakkarat 110 15.00 N 102.16 E
Chakou, Zhg. 98 38.03 N 113.36 E
Chakou, Zhg. 105 38.53 N 116.41 E
Chakradharpur 124 22.42 N 85.38 E
Chakrāta 120 30.42 N 77.51 E
Chākṣu 120 26.36 N 75.57 E
Chākulia 126 22.29 N 86.43 E
Chakwadām 102 27.29 N 98.31 E
Chakwāl 123 32.56 N 72.52 E
Chal 272c 19.06 N 73.08 E
Chala 248 15.52 S 74.16 W
Chalabesa 154 11.22 S 31.01 E
Chalais 32 45.16 N 0.02 E
Chālakuda 122 10.18 N 76.20 E
Chalamont 58 46.00 N 5.10 E
Chalampé 58 47.49 N 7.33 E
Chalan Kanoa 174n 15.08 N 145.43 E
Chalatenango 236 14.03 N 88.56 W
Chalaua 154 16.06 S 39.11 E
Chalaux ≃ 50 47.23 N 3.54 E
Chalaxung 102 34.10 N 97.44 E
Chalbi Desert ◆[2] 154 3.00 N 37.20 E
Chalchgol 88 48.11 N 114.54 E
Chalchihuites 234 23.29 N 103.53 W
Chalchis Terara ∧ 144 9.08 N 36.44 E
Chalchuapa 236 13.59 N 89.41 W
Chalchyn ≃ 88 47.55 N 117.47 E
Chalcis → Khalkís 38 38.28 N 23.36 E
Chalco ≃ 286a 19.19 N 99.08 W
Chaldan 84 40.43 N 47.15 E
Chaldon 260 51.17 N 0.07 W
Chaleine 261 48.36 N 1.43 E
Chalengkou 120 38.02 N 93.54 E
Châlette-sur-Loing 50 48.01 N 2.44 E
Chaleur Bay c 186 48.00 N 65.45 W
Chalfant 279b 40.25 N 79.52 W
Chalfant Run ≃ 279b 40.25 N 79.48 W
Chalfont 208 40.17 N 75.13 W
Chalfont Common 260 51.38 N 0.33 W
Chalfonte 285 39.49 N 75.32 W
Chalfont Saint Giles 260 51.38 N 0.34 W
Chalfont Saint Peter 42 51.37 N 0.33 W
Chalford 42 51.45 N 2.09 W
Chalhuanca 248 14.17 S 73.15 W
Chalía ≃ 254 49.35 S 69.34 W
Chalifert 261 48.53 N 2.46 E
Chalilovo 86 51.24 N 58.04 E
Chalindrey 58 47.48 N 5.26 E
Chaling 100 26.47 N 113.33 E
Chālisgaon 122 20.28 N 75.01 E
Chalisi 102 32.55 N 102.04 E
Chaliun 88 48.50 N 103.59 E
Chalk 260 51.26 N 0.25 E
Chalkabad 86 42.42 N 59.43 E
Chalk Draw V 196 29.36 N 103.15 W
Chalk River 190 46.01 N 77.27 W
Chalkyitsik 180 66.39 N 143.43 W
Challakere 122 14.19 N 76.39 E
Challans 32 46.51 N 1.53 W
Challapata 248 18.54 S 66.47 W
Challenge 226 39.29 N 121.13 W
Challenger, Mount ∧ 224 48.50 N 121.20 W
Challenger Deep ✤[1] 14 11.21 N 142.12 E
Challes-les-Eaux 62 45.33 N 5.59 E
Challis 202 44.30 N 114.13 W
Challviri, Salar de ≡ 248 22.32 S 67.34 W
Chal'mer-Ju 24 67.58 N 64.50 E
Chalmers 216 40.39 N 86.52 W
Chalmette 194 29.56 N 89.57 W
Chalone Creek ≃ 226 36.21 N 121.14 W
Chalonnes-sur-Loire 32 47.21 N 0.46 W
Châlons-sur-Marne 50 48.57 N 4.22 E
Chalon-sur-Saône 58 46.47 N 4.51 E
Chalosse ◆[1] 32 43.45 N 0.30 W
Chalt 123 36.15 N 74.20 E
Chaltel, Cerro (Monte Fitzroy) ∧ 254 49.17 S 73.05 W
Chalturino 78 49.31 N 35.17 E
Chaluhe 89 43.43 N 126.00 E
Châlus, Fr. 32 45.39 N 0.59 E
Chālūs, Īrān 128 36.38 N 51.26 E
Cham, Dtsch. 60 49.13 N 12.41 E
Cham, Schw. 58 47.11 N 8.28 E
Chama 200 36.54 N 106.34 W
Chama ≃ 246 9.03 N 71.40 W
Chama, Rio ≃ 200 36.03 N 106.05 W
Chamah, Gunong ∧ 114 5.13 N 101.33 E
Chamaicó 252 35.03 S 64.58 W
Chamama 154 12.55 S 33.43 E
Chamamat'urt 84 43.36 N 46.30 E
Chaman 120 30.55 N 66.27 E
Chamangonge 152 11.16 S 20.24 E
Chamao, Khao ∧ 110 12.57 N 101.45 E
Chamarande 261 48.31 N 2.13 E
Chamar-Daban, chrebet ⋏ 88 51.15 N 105.00 E
Chāmārpāra 272b 22.35 N 88.08 E
Chamaya ≃ 248 5.44 S 78.39 W
Chamb ≃ 60 49.13 N 12.42 E
Chamba, India 123 32.34 N 76.08 E
Chamba, Moç. 154 12.07 S 36.57 E
Chamba, Tan. 154 11.35 S 36.58 E
Chambal ≃ 120 26.30 N 79.15 E
Chambaran, Plateau de ⋏[1] 62 45.15 N 5.15 E
Chambas 240p 22.12 N 78.55 W
Chamberlain, Sk., Can. 184 50.50 N 105.34 W
Chamberlain, S.D., U.S. 198 43.48 N 99.19 W
Chamberlain ≃ 164 15.08 S 128.06 E
Chamberlain Lake ⊜ 186 46.17 N 69.20 W
Chamberlin, Mount ∧ 180 69.16 N 144.55 W
Chamberry, Ruisseau ≃ 275a 45.20 N 73.58 W
Chambers, Az., U.S. 200 35.11 N 109.25 W
Chambers, Ne., U.S. 198 42.12 N 98.44 W
Chambers, N.Y., U.S. 210 42.16 N 76.57 W
Chambers □[6] 222 29.42 N 94.40 W
Chambers Brook ≃ 276 40.35 N 74.41 W
Chambersburg, Il., U.S. 219 39.49 N 90.39 W
Chambersburg, In., U.S. 218 38.31 N 86.24 W
Chambersburg, Pa., U.S. 208 39.56 N 77.39 W
Chambers Corner 285 40.01 N 74.44 W
Chambers Creek ≃ 222 31.58 N 96.10 W
Chambers Creek, North Fork ≃ 222 32.16 N 96.58 W
Chambers Creek, South Fork ≃ 222 32.16 N 96.58 W
Chambers Island I 190 45.11 N 87.21 W
Chambéry 62 45.34 N 5.56 E
Chambeshi ≃ 154 11.21 S 30.37 E
Chambi, Jebel ∧ 148 35.11 N 8.42 E
Chambira ≃, Perú 246 4.28 S 74.50 W
Chambira ≃, Perú 246 3.55 S 73.45 W
Chamblee 192 33.53 N 84.17 W
Chambley-Bussières 56 49.03 N 5.54 E
Chambly, P.Q., Can. 206 45.27 N 73.17 W
Chambly, Fr. 50 49.10 N 2.15 E
Chambly □[6] 206 45.30 N 73.20 W
Chambly, Bassin de ⊜ 206 45.27 N 73.17 W
Chambly, Canal de ≍ 275a 45.25 N 73.15 W
Chambois 50 48.48 N 0.07 E
Chambon-sur-Dolore 62 45.30 N 3.37 E
Chambon-sur-Voueize 32 46.11 N 2.25 E
Chambord, Château de ⊥ 50 47.37 N 1.31 E
Chambourcy 261 48.54 N 2.03 E
Chambri Lake ⊜ 164 4.16 S 143.08 E
Chambry 261 49.00 N 2.54 E
Chamburi Kalāt 128 26.09 N 64.43 E
Chamdo → Qamdo 102 31.11 N 97.15 E
Chāme, Nepāl 124 28.33 N 84.15 E
Chame, Pan. 236 8.35 N 79.53 W
Chame, Punta › 236 8.39 N 79.42 W
Chamela 234 19.32 N 105.05 W
Chamelecón 236 15.24 N 88.01 W
Chamelecón ≃ 236 15.51 N 87.49 W
Chamical 252 30.21 S 66.19 W
Chamizo 258 34.10 S 56.41 W
Chamizo, Arroyo ≃ 258 34.15 S 56.44 W
Chamkanī 120 33.48 N 69.49 E
Chāmlūjā ≃ 124 29.38 N 80.24 E
Chamo, Lake ⊜ 144 5.50 N 37.33 E
Chamois, It 62 45.50 N 7.37 E
Chamois, Mo., U.S. 219 38.40 N 91.46 W
Chamojie 89 49.25 N 124.45 E
Chamoli 124 30.24 N 79.21 E
Chamonix-Mont-Blanc 58 45.55 N 6.52 E
Chamousset 62 45.33 N 6.12 E
Chamoux-sur-Gelon 62 45.32 N 6.13 E
Chāmpa 124 22.03 N 82.39 E
Champagne, Yk., Can. 180 60.47 N 136.29 W
Champagne, Fr. 62 45.16 N 4.48 E
Champagne □[9] 32 49.00 N 4.30 E
Champagne Castle ∧ 158 29.06 S 29.20 E
Champagne-en-Valromay 58 45.54 N 5.41 E
Champagner-Berg ∧[2] 264a 52.31 N 13.05 E
Champagne-sur-Seine 50 48.24 N 2.48 E
Champagney 58 47.42 N 6.41 E
Champagnole 58 46.45 N 5.55 E
Champagny 62 45.27 N 6.42 E
Chāmpāhāti 126 22.23 N 88.29 E
Champaign 194 40.06 N 88.14 W

Symbol	English	Deutsch	Español	Français	Português
≃	River	Fluß	Río	Rivière	Rio
≍	Canal	Kanal	Canal	Canal	Canal
ʟ	Waterfall, Rapids	Wasserfall, Stromschnellen	Cascada, Rápidos	Chute d'eau, Rapides	Cascata, Rápidos
ų	Strait	Meeresstraße	Estrecho	Détroit	Estreito
c	Bay, Gulf	Bucht, Golf	Bahía, Golfo	Baie, Golfe	Baía, Golfo
⊜	Lake, Lakes	See, Seen	Lago, Lagos	Lac, Lacs	Lago, Lagos
≡	Swamp	Sumpf	Pantano	Marais	Pântano
⍓	Ice Features, Glacier	Eis- und Gletscherformen	Accidentes Glaciales	Formes glaciaires	Acidentes glaciares
⊤	Other Hydrographic Features	Andere Hydrographische Objekte	Otros Elementos Hidrográficos	Autres données hydrographiques	Outros acidentes hidrográficos
✤	Submarine Features	Untermeerische Objekte	Accidentes Submarinos	Formes de relief sous-marin	Acidentes submarinos
□	Political Unit	Politische Einheit	Unidad Política	Entité politique	Unidade política
ʋ	Cultural Institution	Kulturelle Institution	Institución Cultural	Institution culturelle	Instituição cultural
⊥	Historical Site	Historische Stätte	Sitio Histórico	Site historique	Sitio histórico
♠	Recreational Site	Erholungs- und Ferienort	Sitio de Recreo	Centre de loisirs	Área de Lazer
⊠	Airport	Flughafen	Aeropuerto	Aéroport	Aeroporto
■	Military Installation	Militäranlage	Instalación Militar	Installation militaire	Instalação militar
◆	Miscellaneous	Verschiedenes	Misceláneo	Divers	Diversos

ENGLISH — Name / Page / Lat.°′ / Long.°′
DEUTSCH — Name / Seite / Breite°′ / Länge°′ E = Ost

Champaign □6, Il., U.S. 216 40.07 N 88.12 W
Champaign □6, Oh., U.S. 218 40.07 N 83.45 W
Champapur 126 24.02 N 86.31 E
Champaquí, Cerro ʌ 252 31.59 S 64.56 W
Champasak 110 14.53 N 105.52 E
Champāwat 124 29.20 N 80.06 E
Champcueil 261 48.31 N 2.27 E
Champdāni 126 22.48 N 88.21 E
Champdeniers 32 46.29 N 0.24 W
Champdepraz 62 45.41 N 7.39 E
Champdeuil 261 48.37 N 2.44 E
Champdor 58 46.01 N 5.36 E
Champdoré, Lac ⊜ 176 55.55 N 65.49 W
Champeaux 50 48.35 N 2.48 E
Champeix 32 45.36 N 3.08 E
Champerico 236 14.18 N 91.55 W
Champéry 58 46.10 N 6.52 E
Champex 58 46.02 N 7.07 E
Champier 62 45.27 N 5.17 E
Champigneulles 56 48.44 N 6.10 E
Champigny-sur-Marne 261 48.49 N 2.31 E
Champion, Ab., Can. 182 50.14 N 113.09 W
Champion, Mi., U.S. 190 46.30 N 87.57 W
Champion, Oh., U.S. 214 41.17 N 80.51 W
Champion, Pa., U.S. 214 40.05 N 79.21 W
Champions 222 29.59 N 95.31 W
Champlain 206 44.59 N 73.26 W
Champlain □6 206 46.45 N 72.35 W
Champlain ≃ 206 46.27 N 72.17 W
Champlain, Lake ⊜ 188 44.45 N 73.15 W
Champlain, Pont ➔5 206 45.28 N 73.32 W
Champlain Canal ≅ 210 43.20 N 73.34 W
Champlan 261 48.43 N 2.16 E
Champlin Creek ≃ 276 40.43 N 73.12 W
Champlitte-et-le-Prélot 58 47.37 N 5.31 E
Champlon 56 50.07 N 5.28 E
Champoluc 62 45.50 N 7.44 E
Champotón 232 19.21 N 90.43 W
Champrond-en-Gâtine 50 48.24 N 1.05 E
Champs 50 47.44 N 3.36 E
Champs-sur-Marne 261 48.51 N 2.36 E
Chāmpua 124 22.05 N 85.40 E
Champvans 58 47.06 N 5.26 E
Chāmrāil 272b 22.38 N 88.18 E
Chāmrājnagar Rāmasamudram 122 11.55 N 76.57 E
Chamrousse 62 45.08 N 5.52 E
Chamsara ≃ 88 52.42 N 95.46 E
Chamusca 34 39.21 N 8.29 W
Chamza Chakimzada 85 40.26 N 71.30 E
Chana 110 6.55 N 100.44 E
Chanabadskij 85 40.49 N 72.58 E
Chanakyapuri □9 272a 28.36 N 77.11 E
Chañar 252 30.32 S 65.58 W
Chañaral 252 26.21 S 70.37 W
Chañaral, Isla I 252 29.02 S 71.35 W
Chanas 62 45.18 N 4.49 E
Chānasma 120 23.43 N 72.07 E
Chanbogd 102 43.12 N 107.10 E
Chancay 248 11.35 S 77.16 W
Chancay ≃ 248 11.37 S 77.15 W
Chance 208 38.10 N 75.56 W
Chanceaux 58 47.31 N 4.42 E
Chanceaux-sur-Choisille 50 47.28 N 0.42 E
Chanch 88 51.30 N 100.40 E
Chanchelulla Peak ʌ 204 40.28 N 122.59 W
Chanchiang → Zhanjiang 102 21.16 N 110.28 E
Chanchŏchij uul ⋏ 88 49.30 N 94.30 E
Chanchongor 102 43.50 N 104.25 E
Chanco 252 35.44 S 72.32 W
Chancy 58 46.08 N 6.00 E
Chanda → Chandrapur, India 122 19.57 N 79.18 E
Chanda, Ross. 88 55.00 N 107.14 E
Chanda ≃ 88 55.00 N 107.14 E
Chāndābila 126 22.05 N 87.00 E
Chandagajty 86 50.44 N 92.03 E
Chandalar 180 67.30 N 148.30 W
Chandalar ≃ 180 66.36 N 145.48 W
Chandalar, East Fork ≃ 180 67.05 N 147.16 W
Chandalar, Middle Fork ≃ 180 67.10 N 148.19 W
Chandalar, North Fork ≃ 180 67.10 N 148.19 W
Chandan Chauki 124 28.33 N 80.47 E
Chandankiāri 126 23.34 N 86.22 E
Chandannagar 126 22.51 N 88.21 E
Chandanpratāp 126 23.33 N 89.24 E
Chāndar 126 23.54 N 89.58 E
Chandausi 124 28.27 N 78.46 E
Chāndbāli 120 20.47 N 86.46 E
Chandeleur Islands II 194 29.48 N 88.51 W
Chandeleur Sound ⊔ 194 29.55 N 89.10 W
Chanderi 124 24.43 N 78.08 E
Chandernagore → Chandannagar 126 22.51 N 88.21 E
Chandīgarh 123 30.44 N 76.55 E
Chandīgarh □8 123 30.45 N 76.50 E
Chāndil 124 22.58 N 86.03 E
Chandīpur 126 23.59 N 89.01 E
Chanditala 272b 22.41 N 88.16 E
Chandla 124 25.05 N 80.12 E
Chandler, P.Q., Can. 186 48.21 N 64.41 W
Chandler, Az., U.S. 200 33.18 N 111.50 W
Chandler, In., U.S. 194 38.02 N 87.22 W
Chandler, Ok., U.S. 196 35.42 N 96.52 W
Chandler, Tx., U.S. 222 32.18 N 95.29 W
Chandler ≃ 180 69.27 N 151.30 W
Chandler, Mount ʌ2 162 27.00 S 133.20 E
Chandler Lake ⊜ 180 68.15 N 152.43 W
Chandler Park ◆ 281 42.24 N 82.58 W
Chandler's Cross 260 51.40 N 0.27 W
Chandler's Ford 42 50.59 N 1.23 W
Chandlers Valley 214 41.56 N 79.18 W
Chandlerville 219 40.02 N 90.09 W
Chandless ≃ 248 9.08 S 69.51 W
Chāndor Hills ⋏2 122 20.30 N 74.00 E
Chandos Lake ⊜ 212 44.49 N 78.00 W
Chāndpara 126 22.58 N 88.47 E
Chāndpur, Bngl. 120 22.08 N 91.55 E
Chāndpur, Bngl. 124 23.13 N 90.39 E
Chāndpur, India 124 29.09 N 78.16 E
Chāndpur ➔8 272a 28.45 N 77.01 E
Chāndra 126 22.28 N 87.09 E
Chandrabhāga ≃ 123 32.59 N 76.25 E
Chandra Dighalia 126 23.04 N 89.46 E
Chandrakona 126 22.44 N 87.31 E
Chandrakona Road 126 22.44 N 87.21 E
Chandrapur 122 19.57 N 79.18 E
Chāndvad 122 20.20 N 74.15 E
Chandyga 74 62.40 N 135.36 E
Chanfang 105 39.56 N 115.55 E
Chang (Yangtze) ≃, Zhg. 90 31.48 N 121.10 E
Chang ≃, Zhg. 100 26.53 N 119.41 E
Chang ≃, Zhg. 100 28.59 N 116.42 E
Chang, Ko I 110 12.05 N 102.20 E
Changa 84 44.27 N 50.36 E
Changaj 88 47.52 N 99.28 E
Changajn nuruu ⋏ 90 47.30 N 100.00 E
Changal 88 49.19 N 104.24 E
Changalane 156 26.17 S 32.11 E
Changan → Xi'an, Zhg. 102 34.15 N 108.52 E
Chang'an, Zhg. 102 26.00 N 109.34 E
Changanācheri 122 9.28 N 76.33 E
Changane ≃ 156 24.43 S 33.32 E
Chang'anzhen 106 30.28 N 120.27 E
Changara 154 16.54 S 33.14 E
Changarul'skij chrebet ⋏ 88 51.10 N 103.00 E
Changbai 98 41.26 N 128.11 E
Changbai Shan ⋏ 98 41.40 N 128.00 E
Changbu 100 23.48 N 115.26 E
Changcaocun 105 39.49 N 115.47 E
Changchaoling 106 31.00 N 119.40 E
Changcheng, Zhg. 100 31.49 N 116.54 E
Changcheng, Zhg. 110 19.24 N 108.42 E
Chang Cheng (Great Wall) ⊥ 98 40.30 N 116.30 E
Chang Chenmo ≃ 120 34.17 N 78.19 E
Changchiak'ou → Zhangjiakou 105 40.50 N 114.53 E
Ch'angchih → Changzhi 102 36.11 N 113.08 E
Changchou → Zhangzhou 100 24.33 N 117.39 E
Changchow → Changzhou 106 31.47 N 119.57 E
Changchun 89 43.53 N 125.19 E
Changchunling 89 45.22 N 125.28 E
Changdan 98 37.56 N 126.45 E
Changdang Hu ⊜ 106 31.35 N 119.35 E
Changdao (Sihou) 98 37.56 N 120.42 E
Changde 102 29.02 N 111.41 E
Changdian 105 40.01 N 116.32 E
Ch'angdo 98 38.30 N 127.40 E
Ch'ang-dong 98 39.03 N 126.34 E
Change Islands 186 49.40 N 54.25 W
Changeon ≃ 50 47.16 N 0.05 E
Changfeng 100 32.27 N 117.09 E
Changgang 100 24.38 N 113.05 E
Changgangzi 104 41.26 N 122.41 E
Changge 100 34.15 N 113.50 E
Changgi-ap › 98 36.05 N 129.34 E
Changgi-li 271b 37.35 N 126.44 E
Changgi-ri 271b 37.38 N 126.41 E
Changgou 105 39.34 N 115.53 E
Changgouyu 105 39.44 N 115.52 E
Changguandian 100 32.58 N 115.16 E
Changguowei 100 29.15 N 121.56 E
Changgye-ri 98 34.33 N 126.49 E
Changgyong Palace ʋ 271b 37.36 N 127.00 E
Changhai, Zhg. 98 39.18 N 122.35 E
Chang-hai → Shanghai, Zhg. 106 31.14 N 121.28 E
Changhang 98 36.01 N 126.40 E
Changhe 106 30.11 N 120.11 E
Changhowŏn 98 37.08 N 127.39 E
Chang Hu ⊜ 100 30.15 N 112.35 E
Changhua, T'aiwan 100 24.05 N 120.32 E
Changhua, Zhg. 100 30.11 N 119.13 E
Changhŭng 98 34.41 N 126.52 E
Changhŭng-ni 98 40.24 N 128.19 E
Changi 271c 1.23 N 103.59 E
Changi, Tanjong › 271c 1.23 N 104.00 E
Changi International Airport ⊠ 271c 1.22 N 103.59 E
Changi Prison ʋ 271c 1.22 N 103.58 E
Changji 86 44.01 N 87.19 E
Changjiang, Zhg. 100 25.19 N 113.56 E
Changjiang, Zhg. 110 19.17 N 109.02 E
Changjiangbu 100 30.52 N 113.43 E
Changjiapuzi 104 40.51 N 123.43 E
Changjiazhuang 105 40.35 N 115.24 E
Changjie 100 29.16 N 121.40 E
Changjing 106 31.45 N 120.29 E
Changjin-gang ≃ 98 41.24 N 127.45 E
Changjin-ŭp 98 40.23 N 127.15 E
Changkai 100 28.04 N 116.18 E
Changkalajier 85 40.09 N 76.59 E
Changkeng 106 30.19 N 121.57 E
Changkiakow → Zhangjiakou 105 40.50 N 114.53 E
Changlapod Pass)(124 30.08 N 87.06 E
Changle, Zhg. 98 36.42 N 118.49 E
Changle, Zhg. 100 29.25 N 120.37 E
Changle, Zhg. 100 26.00 N 119.31 E
Changlejie 100 28.52 N 113.19 E
Changleqiao 106 30.21 N 119.51 E
Changlezhen 106 31.56 N 121.15 E
Changli, Zhg. 98 39.43 N 119.11 E
Changli, Zhg. 98 36.57 N 119.45 E
Changling 89 44.15 N 123.58 E
Changlingfeng 105 40.11 N 118.24 E
Changlingji 100 32.30 N 114.54 E
Changlingzi, Zhg. 98 39.47 N 122.43 E
Changlingzi, Zhg. 98 39.33 N 121.19 E
Changlinhe 100 31.40 N 117.29 E
Changlun 114 6.26 N 100.26 E
Changmar 120 34.15 N 79.45 E
Changmong-ni 98 34.58 N 128.41 E
Changning, Zhg. 102 26.19 N 112.21 E
Changning, Zhg. 102 24.55 N 99.35 E
Changning (Anningqiao), Zhg. 102 28.21 N 104.53 E
Changning, Zhg. 105 39.59 N 114.55 E
Ch'angnyŏng 98 35.33 N 128.29 E
Changnyŏn-ni 98 38.37 N 125.16 E
Changokurt 72 61.58 N 64.18 E
Ch'angpin 100 23.19 N 121.27 E
Changping 105 40.14 N 116.14 E
Changputong 102 28.05 N 98.29 E
Ch'angp'yŏng-dong 98 41.27 N 127.31 E
Changqiao, Zhg. 100 24.15 N 117.39 E
Changqiao, Zhg. 100 26.49 N 118.50 E
Changqing 98 36.34 N 116.43 E
Changsa 102 19.51 N 110.53 E
Changsan-got › 98 38.08 N 124.39 E
Changsha, Zhg. 100 28.12 N 112.58 E
Changsha, Zhg. 100 24.13 N 116.07 E
Changshaba Shuiku ⊜1 107 29.42 N 104.40 E
Changshageng 107 30.00 N 104.35 E
Changshan, Zhg. 98 36.54 N 117.50 E
Changshan, Zhg. 100 28.55 N 118.30 E
Changshan, Zhg. 107 29.30 N 104.13 E
Changshan ≃ 100 28.57 N 118.50 E
Changshan Qundao II 98 39.00 N 122.45 E
Changsheng 100 26.16 N 116.01 E
Changshengqiao 107 29.31 N 106.39 E
Changshitai 104 42.33 N 120.43 E
Changshitou 102 35.03 N 99.11 E
Changshou 102 29.51 N 107.06 E
Changshoudian 100 31.26 N 112.35 E
Changshoujie 100 28.44 N 113.57 E
Changshu 106 31.39 N 120.45 E
Changshui 102 34.21 N 111.29 E
Changsŏng 98 35.20 N 126.49 E
Changsŏng-ni 98 40.58 N 127.04 E
Changsu 98 35.40 N 127.32 E
Changtai, Zhg. 100 24.40 N 117.46 E
Changtai, Zhg. 100 28.34 N 118.37 E
Changtai, Zhg. 104 41.34 N 122.00 E
Changtancun 104 41.33 N 123.02 E
Ch'angte → Changde 102 29.02 N 111.41 E
Changteh → Anyang 98 36.06 N 114.21 E
Changting, Zhg. 89 44.32 N 128.47 E
Changting, Zhg. 100 25.52 N 116.20 E
Changtumiao 102 43.30 N 114.34 E
Changuinola 236 9.25 N 82.32 W
Changuinola ≃ 236 9.28 N 82.27 W
Changwu, Zhg. 89 46.00 N 125.36 E
Changwu, Zhg. 102 35.09 N 107.42 E
Changxindianzhen 105 39.49 N 116.12 E
Changxing 106 31.01 N 119.54 E
Changxing Dao I, Zhg. 98 39.34 N 121.23 E
Changxing Dao I, Zhg. 106 31.24 N 121.42 E
Changxingdian, Zhg. 104 41.27 N 121.44 E
Changxingdian, Zhg. 104 41.33 N 123.23 E
Changxingzhen 104 41.40 N 122.14 E
Changxuanling 100 31.08 N 114.20 E
Changyi 98 36.51 N 119.23 E
Changyŏn 98 38.15 N 125.06 E
Changyuan 98 35.13 N 114.39 E
Changyukou 105 40.46 N 115.08 E
Changzhi 102 36.11 N 113.08 E
Changzhou (Changchow) 106 31.47 N 119.57 E
Chanhanga 152 16.04 S 14.07 E
Chanh Hung 269c 10.44 N 106.41 E
Chani 88 57.05 N 120.58 E
Chani ≃ 88 57.02 N 120.59 E
Chanino 76 54.13 N 36.37 E
Chanka, ozero (Xingkai Hu) ⊜ 89 45.00 N 132.24 E
Chankiang → Zhanjiang 102 21.16 N 110.28 E
Chankou 102 35.52 N 104.27 E
Chanlar 84 40.34 N 46.20 E
Channagiri 122 14.02 N 75.56 E
Channahon 216 41.26 N 88.14 W
Channapatna 122 12.39 N 77.13 E
Channel Country ➔1 166 24.45 S 141.00 E
Channel Islands II, Europe 43b 49.20 N 2.20 W
Channel Islands II, Ca., U.S. 204 33.30 N 119.15 W
Channel Islands National Park ◆ 204 33.28 N 119.02 W
Channel Lake 216 42.29 N 88.08 W
Channel-Port-aux-Basques 186 47.34 N 59.09 W
Channel Tunnel ➔5 50 51.00 N 1.35 E
Channelview 222 29.46 N 95.06 W
Channing, Mi., U.S. 190 46.08 N 88.05 W
Channing, Tx., U.S. 196 35.41 N 102.20 W
Chānpādānga 126 22.50 N 87.58 E
Chantada 34 42.37 N 7.46 W
Chantajskoje, ozero ⊜ 74 68.20 N 91.00 E
Chantajskoje vodochranilišče ⊜1 72 68.00 N 88.00 E
Chantang 100 33.41 N 117.37 E
Chantau 86 44.13 N 73.51 E
Chanteloup 261 48.51 N 2.44 E
Chanteloup-les-Vignes 261 48.59 N 2.02 E
Chanthaburi 110 12.36 N 102.09 E
Chantilly 50 49.12 N 2.28 E
Chantraine 58 48.10 N 6.26 E
Chantrans 58 47.03 N 6.09 E
Chantrey Inlet ⊂ 176 67.48 N 96.20 W
Chanty-Mansijsk 74 61.00 N 69.06 E
Chanty-Mansijskij Avtonomnyj Okrug □8 86 60.15 N 70.45 E
Chanujn ≃ 88 49.22 N 102.22 E
Chanumla 110 8.19 N 93.05 E
Chanute 198 37.40 N 95.27 W
Chanute Air Force Base ■ 216 40.18 N 88.09 W
Chanuwāla 123 32.44 N 73.08 E
Chanžonkovo 83 48.06 N 38.06 E
Chao ≃ 105 40.36 N 117.08 E
Chao, Isla I 248 8.45 S 78.47 W
Chao'an 100 23.41 N 116.38 E
Chaobai ≃ 105 39.48 N 117.08 E
Chaobai Xinhe ≃ 105 39.37 N 117.26 E
Chaocheng 98 36.05 N 115.35 E
Ch'aochou, T'aiwan 100 22.33 N 120.32 E
Ch'aochou → Chao'an, Zhg. 100 23.41 N 116.38 E
Chao Hu ⊜ 100 31.31 N 117.33 E
Chaomidian 105 39.04 N 117.01 E
Chao Phraya ≃ 110 13.32 N 100.36 E
Chaor ≃ 89 46.48 N 123.37 E
Chaoshui, Zhg. 89 49.44 N 127.21 E
Chaoshui, Zhg. 98 37.42 N 120.55 E
Chaouen 148 35.10 N 5.16 W
Chaouen □4 148 35.15 N 5.00 W
Chaource 50 48.04 N 4.08 E
Chaoxian 100 31.36 N 117.52 E
Chaoyang, Zhg. 89 44.34 N 126.20 E
Chaoyang, Zhg. 100 23.17 N 116.37 E
Chaoyang, Zhg. 104 41.35 N 120.28 E
Chaoyangchuan 98 42.54 N 129.21 E
Chaoyangcun 89 50.02 N 124.16 E
Chaoyanggou 104 42.07 N 121.04 E
Chaoyangpo 89 43.37 N 124.42 E
Chaoyangshan 89 43.02 N 125.40 E
Chaozhuang 98 34.18 N 114.56 E
Chapada dos Guimarães 248 15.26 S 55.45 W
Chapada dos Veadeiros, Parque Nacional da ◆ 255 13.58 S 47.30 W
Chapadinha 250 3.44 S 43.21 W
Chapala 234 20.18 N 103.12 W
Chapala, Laguna de ⊜ 234 20.15 N 103.00 W
Chapare ≃, Bol. 248 15.58 S 64.42 W
Chapare ≃, Bol. 248 16.25 S 64.35 W
Chapareillan 62 45.28 N 5.58 E
Chāparmukh 120 26.12 N 92.32 E
Chaparra, Bahía de ⊂ 240p 21.13 N 76.31 W
Chaparral 246 3.43 N 75.28 W
Chapčeranga 88 49.42 N 112.24 E
Chapeauroux 62 44.50 N 3.44 E
Chapecó 252 27.06 S 52.36 W
Chapel-en-le-Frith 44 53.20 N 1.54 W
Chapelfell Top ʌ 44 54.41 N 2.13 W
Chapelhall 46 55.50 N 3.56 W
Chapel Hill, De., U.S. 285 39.42 N 75.44 W
Chapel Hill, N.C., U.S. 192 35.54 N 79.03 W
Chapel Hill, Tn., U.S. 194 35.37 N 86.41 W
Chapel Hill Channel ⊔ 276 40.32 N 74.02 W
Chapelle Creek ≃ 198 44.16 N 99.55 W
Chapellerie 261 49.02 N 2.26 E
Chapel Oaks 284c 38.54 N 76.55 W
Chapel Point › 42 50.16 N 4.46 W
Chapel Saint Leonards 44 53.13 N 0.19 E
Chapelton 241q 18.05 N 77.16 W
Chapeltown, Eng., U.K. 44 53.28 N 1.28 W
Chapeltown, Eng., U.K. 262 53.38 N 2.24 W
Chapet 261 48.58 N 1.56 E
Chapéu, Morro do ʌ 255 14.55 S 42.31 W
Chapéu, Ribeirão do ≃ 256 23.14 S 45.18 W
Chapicuy 252 31.39 S 57.54 W
Chapimarca 248 13.58 S 73.04 W
Chapin 219 39.46 N 90.24 W
Chapin, Lake ⊜ 216 41.56 N 86.21 W
Chaplain, Lake ⊜1 224 47.57 N 121.51 W
Chapleau 190 47.50 N 83.24 W
Chapleau ≃ 190 48.29 N 82.57 W
Chapleau, Lac ⊜ 206 46.14 N 74.57 W
Chaplin, Sk., Can. 184 50.28 N 106.40 W
Chaplin, Ct., U.S. 207 41.47 N 72.07 W
Chaplin ≃ 194 37.50 N 85.11 W
Chaplin Lake ⊜ 184 50.18 N 106.35 W
Chapman, Ks., U.S. 198 38.58 N 97.01 W
Chapman, Ne., U.S. 198 41.01 N 98.09 W
Chapman, Pa., U.S. 208 40.46 N 75.24 W
Chapman, Cape › 176 69.12 N 88.59 W
Chapman, Mount ʌ 182 51.50 N 118.20 W
Chapman College ʋ2 280 33.47 N 117.51 W
Chapman Creek ≃ 198 38.58 N 97.00 W
Chapman Lake ⊜ 184 56.58 N 98.12 W
Chapman's (Okwa) ≃ 156 22.30 S 23.00 E
Chapmanville 188 37.58 N 82.01 W
Chapman Woods 280 34.08 N 118.05 W
Chapo 196 29.17 N 104.20 W
Chaponval 261 49.04 N 2.09 E
Chappaqua 210 41.09 N 73.45 W
Chappell 198 41.05 N 102.28 W
Chappell Hill 222 30.09 N 96.16 W
Chāpra 126 23.32 N 88.33 E
Chapry 83 47.14 N 39.31 E
Chaptico Bay ⊂ 208 38.21 N 76.49 W
Chapultepec, Méx. 204 31.50 N 116.38 W
Chapultepec, Méx. 204 32.22 N 115.05 W
Chapultepec, Bosque de ◆ 286a 19.25 N 99.12 W
Chapultepec, Castillo de ⊥ 286a 19.25 N 99.11 W
Chá Pungana 152 13.44 S 18.39 E
Chaqui 248 19.36 S 65.32 W
Chaquiago 252 27.32 S 66.21 W
Char ≃ 42 50.44 N 2.53 W
Char ⊤4 148 21.31 N 12.51 W
Charaa ≃ 88 49.38 N 105.49 E
Charabali 80 47.24 N 47.16 E
Chara-Chužar 88 52.30 N 99.39 E
Charadai 252 27.38 S 59.54 W
Charagauli 84 42.01 N 43.12 E
Charagua 248 19.48 S 63.13 W
Charagun 88 51.36 N 111.05 E
Char-Ajrag 102 45.49 N 109.17 E
Charal 88 51.58 N 96.39 E
Charalá 246 6.17 N 73.10 W
Charām 128 30.45 N 50.44 E
Charaña 248 17.36 S 69.28 W
Charanor 88 50.05 N 116.40 E
Charanpur 126 23.45 N 87.02 E
Charapán 234 19.41 N 102.06 W
Charapucu, Ilha I 250 0.18 S 50.48 W
Charata 252 27.13 S 61.12 W
Charauz 88 52.16 N 106.17 E
Charavines-les-Bains 62 45.26 N 5.31 E
Charazani → Amarete 248 15.14 S 68.58 W
Charazargaj 88 52.57 N 104.41 E
Charbala 74 64.07 N 120.19 E
Char Bansi 126 22.59 N 90.43 E
Charbatovo 88 53.46 N 106.00 E
Charbon 170 32.54 S 149.58 E
Charcana 248 15.15 S 73.04 W
Charcas 234 23.08 N 101.07 W
Charco Azul, Bahía de ⊂ 236 8.15 N 82.45 W
Charco Hondo 240m 18.25 N 66.43 W
Charcos de Figueroa 232 27.45 N 102.11 W
Charcos de Risa 232 26.15 N 103.10 W
Charcot Island I 9 69.45 S 75.15 W
Charcyzsk 83 48.02 N 38.09 E
Chard 42 50.53 N 2.58 W
Chardon 214 41.36 N 81.08 W
Charduār 120 26.52 N 92.46 E
Chardzhou → Čardžou 128 39.06 N 63.34 E
Charef, Oued V 148 34.07 N 2.05 W
Charente □5 32 45.40 N 0.10 E
Charente ≃ 32 45.57 N 1.05 W
Charente-Maritime □5 32 45.30 N 0.45 W
Charenton-du-Cher 32 46.44 N 2.38 E
Charenton-le-Pont 261 48.49 N 2.25 E
Charentonne ≃ 50 49.07 N 0.44 E
Charest ≃ 206 46.36 N 72.14 W
Chārghāt 126 24.17 N 88.45 E
Char Hāim 126 23.04 N 90.38 E
Chari ≃ 146 12.58 N 14.31 E
Chariāl Canal ≅ 272b 22.28 N 88.11 E
Chari-Baguirmi □5 146 11.30 N 16.30 E
Charik 88 54.15 N 101.39 E
Chārīkār 120 35.01 N 69.11 E
Charing 42 51.13 N 0.48 E
Charing Cross 214 42.20 N 82.06 W
Charino, Ross. 76 59.57 N 43.44 E
Charino, Ross. 82 54.33 N 37.52 E
Charistvala 84 42.26 N 43.02 E
Chariton 190 41.00 N 93.18 W
Chariton ≃ 194 39.19 N 92.57 W
Chariton, Mussel Fork ≃ 194 39.24 N 92.55 W
Charitonovo, Ross. 24 61.27 N 47.28 E
Charitonovo, Ross. 82 56.52 N 36.44 E
Charity 246 7.24 N 58.36 W
Charkhāri 124 25.24 N 79.45 E
Charkhi Dādri 124 28.37 N 76.16 E
Char'kin 80 48.46 N 51.49 E
Charkop ➔8 272c 19.13 N 72.49 E
Char'kov (Kharkov) 78 50.00 N 36.15 E
Char'kov □4 78 49.30 N 36.30 E
Charkow → Char'kov 78 50.00 N 36.15 E
Char Lākhpur 126 24.04 N 90.40 E
Charland, Lac ⊜ 206 46.52 N 74.11 W
Charlbury 42 51.53 N 1.29 W
Charl Cilliers 158 26.39 S 29.12 E
Charlemagne 206 45.43 N 73.29 W
Charlemont 207 42.37 N 72.52 W
Charleroi, Bel. 50 50.25 N 4.26 E
Charleroi, Pa., U.S. 214 40.08 N 79.53 W
Charleroi à Bruxelles, Canal de ≅ 50 50.51 N 4.19 E
Charles □6 208 38.32 N 76.59 W
Charles ≃ 207 42.22 N 71.03 W
Charles, Cape › 208 37.08 N 75.58 W
Charles, Lake ⊜ 278 42.15 N 87.58 W
Charles, Peak ʌ 162 32.52 S 121.11 E
Charlesbourg 206 46.51 N 71.16 W
Charles Branch ≃ 284c 38.47 N 76.48 W
Charles City, Ia., U.S. 190 43.03 N 92.40 W
Charles City, Va., U.S. 208 37.20 N 77.04 W
Charles City □6 208 37.20 N 77.02 W
Charles de Gaulle, Aéroport ⊠ 50 49.01 N 2.33 E
Charles Island I 176 62.40 N 74.15 W
Charles Lee Tilden Regional Park ◆ 282 37.54 N 122.15 W
Charles Mill Lake ⊜1 214 40.45 N 82.22 W
Charles Mound ʌ2 190 42.30 N 90.14 W
Charles Point › 164 12.23 S 130.36 E
Charles Sound ⊔ 172 45.02 S 167.04 E
Charleston, Austl. 168b 34.55 S 138.54 E
Charleston, N.Z. 172 41.54 S 171.26 E
Charleston, Ar., U.S. 194 35.17 N 94.02 W
Charleston, Il., U.S. 194 39.29 N 88.10 W
Charleston, Ms., U.S. 194 34.00 N 90.03 W
Charleston, Mo., U.S. 194 36.55 N 89.21 W
Charleston, S.C., U.S. 192 32.46 N 79.55 W
Charleston, W.V., U.S. 188 38.20 N 81.37 W
Charleston Air Force Base ■ 192 32.55 N 80.03 W
Charleston Lake ⊜ 212 44.32 N 76.00 W
Charleston Peak ʌ 204 36.16 N 115.42 W
Charlestown, Austl. 170 32.58 S 151.42 E
Charlestown, Ire. 48 53.57 N 8.49 W
Charlestown, St. K.-N. 238 17.08 N 62.37 W
Charlestown, S. Afr. 158 27.30 S 29.55 E
Charlestown, In., U.S. 218 38.27 N 85.40 W
Charlestown, Md., U.S. 208 39.34 N 75.58 W
Charlestown, N.H., U.S. 188 43.14 N 72.25 W
Charlestown, Pa., U.S. 285 40.06 N 75.33 W
Charlestown, R.I., U.S. 207 41.22 N 71.38 W
Charles Town, W.V., U.S. 188 39.17 N 77.51 W
Charlestown ➔8 283 42.23 N 71.04 W
Charlestown of Aberlour 46 57.28 N 3.14 W
Charlesworth 262 53.26 N 1.59 W
Charleville, Austl. 166 26.24 S 146.15 E
Charleville → Ráth Luirc, Ire. 48 52.21 N 8.41 W
Charleville-Mézières 56 49.46 N 4.43 E
Charlevoix 190 45.19 N 85.15 W
Charlevoix, Lake ⊜ 190 45.15 N 85.08 W
Charley ≃ 180 65.20 N 142.49 W
Charlie Bluff 216 42.50 N 88.58 W
Charlie Creek ≃ 220 27.21 N 81.49 W
Charlie Lake 182 56.16 N 120.57 W
Charlieu 32 46.10 N 4.10 E
Charlotte, Mi., U.S. 216 42.33 N 84.50 W
Charlotte, N.C., U.S. 192 35.13 N 80.50 W
Charlotte, Tn., U.S. 194 36.10 N 87.20 W
Charlotte, Tx., U.S. 196 28.51 N 98.42 W
Charlotte □6 220 26.54 N 81.58 W
Charlotte Amalie 240m 18.21 N 64.56 W
Charlotte Court House 192 37.03 N 78.39 W
Charlotte Creek ≃ 210 42.27 N 75.01 W
Charlotte Harbor 220 26.57 N 82.04 W
Charlotte Harbor ⊂ 220 26.45 N 82.12 W
Charlotte Lake ⊜ 182 52.11 N 125.20 W
Charlottenberg 26 59.53 N 12.17 E
Charlottenburg ➔8 264a 52.31 N 13.16 E
Charlottenburg, Schloss ⊥ 264a 52.31 N 13.14 E
Charlottesburg Reservoir ⊜1 276 41.02 N 74.26 W
Charlottes Pass ◆ 171b 36.25 S 145.20 E
Charlottesville, In., U.S. 218 39.47 N 85.36 W
Charlottesville, Va., U.S. 192 38.01 N 78.28 W
Charlottetown 186 46.14 N 63.08 W
Charlotteville 210 42.33 N 74.40 W
Charlovka 24 68.47 N 37.15 E
Charlton, Austl. 166 36.16 S 143.21 E
Charlton, Ma., U.S. 207 42.08 N 71.58 W
Charlton ➔8 260 51.29 N 0.02 E
Charlton City 207 42.08 N 71.59 W
Charlton Island I 176 52.00 N 79.30 W
Charlton Kings 42 51.53 N 2.03 W
Charlu 24 61.48 N 30.52 E
Charly-sur-Marne 50 48.58 N 3.17 E
Charm 214 40.30 N 81.47 W
Charmentray 261 48.57 N 2.47 E
Charmes 58 48.22 N 6.17 E
Charmes-sur-Rhône 62 44.52 N 4.50 E
Charmey 58 46.38 N 7.10 E
Charminster 42 50.43 N 2.28 W
Charmois-l'Orgueilleux 58 48.06 N 6.16 E
Charmont-en-Beauce 50 48.14 N 2.06 E
Charmouth 42 50.45 N 2.55 W
Charnay-lès-Mâcon 58 46.18 N 4.47 E
Charneca 266c 38.44 N 9.27 W
Charneca ➔8 266c 38.47 N 9.08 W
Charnley ≃ 164 16.25 S 124.57 E
Charnock Richard 262 53.38 N 2.41 W
Char nuur ⊜, Mong. 88 48.20 N 96.05 E
Char nuur ⊜, Mong. 88 48.06 N 93.12 E
Charnwood Forest ➔3 42 52.43 N 1.15 W
Charny, P.Q., Can. 206 46.43 N 71.16 W
Charny, Fr. 50 47.53 N 3.06 E
Charny, Fr. 261 48.58 N 2.46 E
Charny-sur-Meuse 56 49.12 N 5.22 E
Charo 234 19.45 N 101.03 W
Charolles 32 46.26 N 4.17 E
Charouine 148 29.01 N 0.16 W
Charovsk 76 59.59 N 40.11 E
Charpi ≃ 89 49.40 N 136.10 E
Charquemont 58 47.13 N 6.49 E
Charred Oak Estates 284c 39.00 N 77.10 W
Charrette Creek ≃ 219 38.37 N 91.03 W
Charron Lake ⊜ 184 52.45 N 95.15 W
Charroux 32 46.09 N 0.24 E
Chars 50 49.10 N 1.56 E
Chārsadda 123 34.09 N 71.44 E
Charter Oak, Ca., U.S. 280 34.06 N 117.52 W
Charter Oak, Ia., U.S. 198 42.04 N 95.35 W
Charters Towers 166 20.05 S 146.16 E
Charterwood 279b 40.33 N 80.00 W
Chartiers Creek ≃ 214 40.28 N 80.03 W
Chartiers Run ≃, Pa., U.S. 279b 40.36 N 79.43 W
Chartiers Run ≃, Pa., U.S. 279b 40.15 N 80.12 W
Chartley 207 41.56 N 71.13 W
Chartres 50 48.27 N 1.30 E
Chartrettes 50 48.29 N 2.42 E
Chartridge 260 51.44 N 0.39 W
Chart Sutton 260 51.13 N 0.35 E
Chartwell ⊥ 260 51.14 N 0.05 E
Char Us nuur ⊜ 90 48.00 N 92.10 E
Charutajuvom 24 66.49 N 59.30 E
Chās 126 23.38 N 86.10 E
Chasav'urt 84 43.15 N 46.37 E
Chascomús 258 35.34 S 58.01 W
Chascomús, Laguna ⊜ 258 35.36 S 58.01 W
Chašdala 85 39.42 N 67.07 E
Chase, B.C., Can. 182 50.49 N 119.41 W
Chase, Ak., U.S. 180 62.27 N 150.07 W
Chase, Ks., U.S. 198 38.21 N 98.20 W
Chase, Md., U.S. 208 39.21 N 76.22 W
Chase, Mount ʌ 188 46.07 N 68.29 W
Chase Brook ≃ 283 42.48 N 71.27 W
Chase City 192 36.47 N 78.27 W
Chase Field Naval Air Station ■ 196 28.21 N 97.40 W
Chasefu 154 11.55 S 33.08 E
Chase Lake 212 43.46 N 75.19 W
Chase River 224 49.08 N 123.55 W
Chashma Barrage ➔6 123 32.26 N 71.23 E
Chasicó 254 40.18 S 68.58 W
Chasidaba 104 42.19 N 121.19 E
Chaska 190 44.47 N 93.36 W
Chaslands Mistake › 172 46.38 S 169.22 E
Chasŏng 98 41.27 N 126.37 E
Chasŏngganggu 98 41.34 N 126.36 E
Chassahowitzka 220 28.43 N 82.34 W
Chassahowitzka Bay ⊂ 220 28.41 N 82.40 W
Chassahowitzka Swamp ≡ 220 28.38 N 82.37 W
Chasseron, Mont ʌ 58 46.51 N 6.33 E
Chasse-sur-Rhône 62 45.34 N 4.49 E
Chassezac ≃ 62 44.26 N 4.19 E
Chašuri 84 42.00 N 43.36 E
Chasurta 88 52.17 N 108.52 E
Chasuta 248 6.35 S 76.11 W
Chāt 128 37.59 N 55.16 E
Chatanbulag 102 43.09 N 109.08 E
Chatanga 74 71.58 N 102.30 E
Chatanga ≃ 74 72.55 N 106.00 E
Chatangskij zaliv ⊂ 74 73.30 N 109.00 E
Chatanika 180 65.07 N 147.31 W
Chatanika ≃ 180 65.04 N 149.18 W
Château-Arnoux 62 44.06 N 6.00 E
Chateaubelair 241h 13.17 N 61.15 W
Châteaubriant 32 47.43 N 1.23 W
Château-Chinon 32 47.04 N 3.56 E
Château d'Oex 58 46.28 N 7.08 E
Château-du-Loir 50 47.42 N 0.25 E
Châteaudun 50 48.05 N 1.20 E
Châteaufort 261 48.44 N 2.06 E
Chateaugay 206 44.55 N 74.04 W
Château-Gontier 32 47.50 N 0.42 W
Châteauguay 206 45.23 N 73.45 W
Châteauguay □6 206 45.15 N 73.45 W
Châteauguay ≃ 188 45.24 N 73.45 W
Châteauguay-Centre 206 45.21 N 73.45 W
Châteauguay Heights 275a 45.23 N 73.44 W
Château-Landon 50 48.09 N 2.42 E
Château-la-Vallière 50 47.33 N 0.19 E
Châteaulin 32 48.12 N 4.05 W
Châteaumeillant 32 46.34 N 2.12 E
Châteauneuf 62 43.23 N 5.10 E
Châteauneuf-de-Randon 62 44.39 N 3.40 E
Châteauneuf-du-Pape 62 44.03 N 4.50 E
Châteauneuf-du-Rhône 62 44.29 N 4.43 E
Châteauneuf-en-Thymerais 50 48.35 N 1.15 E
Châteauneuf-sur-Charente 32 45.36 N 0.03 W
Châteauneuf-sur-Loire 50 47.52 N 2.14 E
Châteauneuf-sur-Sarthe 32 47.41 N 0.30 W
Châteauneuf-Val-de-Bargis 50 47.17 N 3.14 E
Château-Porcien 50 49.32 N 4.15 E
Château-Queyras 62 44.45 N 6.47 E
Châteauredon 62 44.01 N 6.13 E
Châteaurenard, Fr. 50 47.56 N 2.56 E
Châteaurenard, Fr. 62 43.53 N 4.51 E
Château-Renault 50 47.35 N 0.55 E
Château-Richer 186 46.58 N 71.01 W
Châteauroux 32 46.49 N 1.42 E
Château-Salins 56 48.49 N 6.30 E
Château-Thierry 50 49.03 N 3.24 E
Châteauvillain 58 48.02 N 4.55 E
Châtel 58 46.17 N 6.50 E
Châtel-Censoir 50 47.31 N 3.38 E
Châtelet 50 50.24 N 4.31 E
Châtelineau 56 50.25 N 4.31 E
Châtellerault 32 46.49 N 0.33 E
Châtel-Saint-Denis 58 46.32 N 6.54 E
Châtel-sur-Moselle 58 48.18 N 6.24 E
Châtelus-Malvaleix 32 46.18 N 2.01 E
Châtenay-en-France 261 49.04 N 2.27 E
Châtenay-Malabry 261 48.46 N 2.17 E
Châtenois, Fr. 58 48.18 N 5.50 E
Châtenois, Fr. 58 48.16 N 7.24 E
Châtenois-les-Forges 58 47.34 N 6.51 E
Chater ≃ 42 52.38 N 0.32 W
Chatfield, Mn., U.S. 190 43.50 N 92.11 W
Chatfield, Oh., U.S. 214 40.57 N 82.56 W
Chatgal 88 50.26 N 100.09 E
Chatham, N.B., Can. 186 47.02 N 65.28 W
Chatham, On., Can. 214 42.24 N 82.11 W
Chatham, Eng., U.K. 42 51.23 N 0.32 E
Chatham, Il., U.S. 219 39.40 N 89.42 W
Chatham, La., U.S. 194 32.18 N 92.27 W
Chatham, Ma., U.S. 207 41.40 N 69.57 W
Chatham, N.J., U.S. 210 40.44 N 74.23 W
Chatham, N.Y., U.S. 210 42.21 N 73.35 W
Chatham, Oh., U.S. 214 41.06 N 82.01 W
Chatham, Pa., U.S. 208 39.51 N 75.49 W
Chatham, Va., U.S. 192 36.49 N 79.23 W
Chatham ➔8 278 41.45 N 87.37 W
Chatham ≃ 220 25.42 N 81.17 W
Chatham, Isla I 254 50.40 S 74.20 W
Chatham Head 186 47.00 N 65.33 W
Chatham Islands II 14 43.55 S 176.30 W
Chatham Rise ➔3 14 43.30 S 178.00 W
Chatham Sound ⊔ 182 54.32 N 130.35 W
Chatham Strait ⊔ 180 57.30 N 134.45 W
Chatian 100 27.54 N 118.58 E
Châtillon, Fr. 261 48.48 N 2.17 E
Châtillon, It. 62 45.45 N 7.37 E
Châtillon-Coligny 50 47.50 N 2.51 E
Châtillon-en-Bazois 32 47.03 N 3.40 E
Châtillon-en-Diois 62 44.41 N 5.28 E
Châtillon-la-Borde 261 48.33 N 2.49 E
Châtillon-sur-Chalaronne 58 46.07 N 4.58 E
Châtillon-sur-Indre 32 46.59 N 1.11 E
Châtillon-sur-Loire 50 47.35 N 2.45 E
Châtillon-sur-Marne 50 49.06 N 3.45 E
Châtillon-sur-Seine 58 47.51 N 4.33 E
Chating 106 31.21 N 119.25 E
Chātmohar 126 24.13 N 89.15 E
Chat Moss ➔3 262 53.27 N 2.27 W
Chato, Cerro ʌ 254 42.29 S 72.01 W
Chatom 194 31.27 N 88.15 W
Chatonville 261 48.33 N 1.52 E
Chatou 261 48.54 N 2.09 E
Chatpur ➔8 272b 22.36 N 88.22 E
Chatra, India 124 24.13 N 84.52 E
Chatra, India 272b 22.46 N 88.20 E
Châtres 261 48.43 N 2.49 E
Chats, Lac des ⊜ 212 45.28 N 76.23 W
Chatsquot Mountain ʌ 182 53.08 N 127.30 W
Chatswood 274a 33.48 S 151.12 E
Chatsworth, Austl. 166 21.58 S 140.19 E
Chatsworth, On., Can. 212 44.27 N 80.54 W
Chatsworth, Ga., U.S. 192 34.45 N 84.46 W
Chatsworth, Il., U.S. 216 40.45 N 88.17 W
Chatsworth, N.J., U.S. 208 39.49 N 74.32 W
Chatsworth, Zimb. 154 19.38 S 31.13 E
Chatsworth ➔8 280 34.15 N 118.36 W
Chatsworth House ʋ 44 53.13 N 1.36 W
Chatsworth Reservoir ⊜1 228 34.14 N 118.37 W
Chattahoochee 192 30.42 N 84.50 W
Chattahoochee ≃ 192 30.52 N 84.57 W
Chattanooga, Oh., U.S. 216 40.38 N 84.47 W
Chattanooga, Tn., U.S. 194 35.02 N 85.18 W
Chattaroy 192 37.42 N 82.16 W
Chattenden 260 51.25 N 0.32 E
Chatteris 42 52.27 N 0.03 E
Châttillon-de-Michaille 58 46.08 N 5.47 E
Chattolanee 284b 39.24 N 76.45 W
Chatton 44 55.33 N 1.55 W
Chatun' 82 55.00 N 37.50 E
Chaturat 110 15.34 N 101.51 E
Chatwood 208 39.58 N 75.35 W
Chatyrka 74 62.03 N 175.15 E
Chaubaria 126 22.59 N 88.40 E
Chaubourg, Mount ʌ2 241f 14.02 N 60.57 W
Chauconin 261 48.58 N 2.51 E
Chaudes-Aigues 32 44.51 N 3.00 E
Chaudfontaine 56 50.35 N 5.38 E
Chaudière ≃ 186 46.45 N 71.17 W
Chau Doc 110 10.42 N 105.07 E
Chauekuktuli, Lake ⊜ 180 60.03 N 158.45 W
Chauffayer 62 44.45 N 6.01 E
Chaugācha, Bngl. 126 23.16 N 89.01 E
Chaugācha, Bngl. 126 23.16 N 89.01 E
Chauhtan 120 25.29 N 71.04 E
Chauk 110 20.54 N 94.50 E
Chaukhandi 272a 28.37 N 77.24 E
Chaullay 248 12.57 S 72.39 W
Chaulnes 50 49.49 N 2.48 E
Chaumergy 58 46.51 N 5.29 E
Chaumes-en-Brie 261 48.40 N 2.51 E
Chaumont, Fr. 58 48.07 N 5.08 E
Chaumont, N.Y., U.S. 212 44.04 N 76.07 W
Chaumont ≃ 212 44.04 N 76.08 W
Chaumont Bay ⊂ 212 44.02 N 76.13 W
Chaumont-en-Vexin 50 49.16 N 1.53 E
Chaumont-Porcien 50 49.39 N 4.15 E
Chaumont-sur-Aire 56 48.56 N 5.15 E
Chaumont-sur-Loire 50 47.29 N 1.11 E
Chaumont-sur-Tharonne 50 47.37 N 1.54 E
Chaumua 272b 22.39 N 88.33 E
Chauncey 188 39.23 N 82.07 W
Chaŭn-do I 98 34.53 N 126.03 E
Chaungwabyin 110 13.41 N 98.22 E
Chaungzon 110 16.22 N 97.32 E
Chauny 50 49.37 N 3.13 E
Chaupāran 124 24.23 N 85.15 E
Chaussin 58 46.58 N 5.25 E
Chausu-yama ʌ 94 35.14 N 137.39 E
Chausuyama-kofun ⊥ 94 36.25 N 139.50 E
Chautārā 124 27.46 N 85.42 E
Chautauqua 214 42.12 N 79.28 W
Chautauqua □6 214 42.15 N 79.30 W
Chautauqua Creek ≃ 214 42.20 N 79.36 W
Chautauqua Lake ⊜ 214 42.12 N 79.27 W
Chautengo, Laguna ⊂ 234 16.37 N 99.07 W
Chauvigny 32 46.34 N 0.39 E
Chauvin, Ab., Can. 184 52.42 N 110.07 W
Chauvin, La., U.S. 194 29.26 N 90.35 W
Chauvirey-le-Châtel 58 47.47 N 5.45 E
Chauvry 261 49.03 N 2.16 E
Chavakkad 122 10.32 N 76.06 E
Chaval 250 3.02 S 41.15 W
Chavanges 58 48.31 N 4.34 E
Chavannes, Lac ⊜ 190 46.51 N 77.10 W
Chavarría, Arg. 252 28.57 S 58.35 W
Chavarría, Perú 286d 12.01 S 77.05 W
Chavast 85 40.13 N 68.50 E
Chavenay 261 48.51 N 1.59 E

Symbols in the index entries represent the broad categories identified in the key at the right. Symbols with superior numbers (⋏1) identify subcategories (see complete key on page *I · 1).*

Symbole im Register stellen die rechts im Schlüssel erklärten Kategorien dar. Symbole mit hochgestellten Ziffern (⋏1) bezeichnen Unterabteilungen einer Kategorie (vgl. vollständiger Schlüssel auf Seite *I · 1).*

Los símbolos incluídos en el texto del índice representan las grandes categorías identificadas con la clave a la derecha. Los símbolos con numeros en su parte superior (⋏1) identifican las subcategorías (véase la clave completa en la página *I · 1).*

Les symboles de l'index représentent les catégories indiquées dans la légende à droite. Les symboles suivis d'un indice (⋏1) représentent des sous-catégories (voir légende complète à la page *I · 1).*

Os símbolos incluídos no texto do índice representam as grandes categorias identificadas com a chave à direita. Os símbolos com números em sua parte superior (⋏1) identificam as subcategorias (veja-se a chave completa à página *I · 1).*

	English	Deutsch	Español	Français	Português
ʌ	Mountain	Berg	Montaña	Montagne	Montanha
⋏	Mountains	Gebirge	Montañas	Montagnes	Montanhas
)(	Pass	Paß	Paso	Col	Passo
V	Valley, Canyon	Tal, Cañon	Valle, Cañón	Vallée, Canyon	Vale, Canhão
≃	Plain	Ebene	Llano	Plaine	Planície
›	Cape	Kap	Cabo	Cap	Cabo
I	Island	Insel	Isla	Île	Ilha
II	Islands	Inseln	Islas	Îles	Ilhas
⊥	Other Topographic Features	Andere Topographische Objekte	Otros Elementos Topográficos	Autres données topographiques	Outros acidentes topográficos

ESPAÑOL

Nombre	Página	Lat.°′	Long.°′ W = Oeste
Chavenay-Villepreux, Aérodrome de ⊠	261	48.51 N	1.58 E
Chavertovo	82	54.17 N	39.12 E
Chaves, Bra.	250	0.10 S	49.55 W
Chaves, Port.	34	41.44 N	7.28 W
Chaville	261	48.48 N	2.10 E
Chaviña	248	14.59 S	73.50 W
Cháviva	246	4.22 N	72.20 W
Chavki	82	54.20 N	38.13 E
Chavornay	58	46.43 N	6.34 E
Chavuma	152	13.05 S	22.40 E
Chawa'nanake	120	31.36 N	89.41 E
Chawang	110	8.25 N	99.30 E
Chawinda	123	32.21 N	74.42 E
Chay ≏	110	21.39 N	105.12 E
Chayanta	248	18.27 S	66.30 W
Chayuan, Zhg.	100	29.20 N	121.34 E
Chayuan, Zhg.	100	27.40 N	112.57 E
Chayue	106	30.49 N	119.21 E
Chazay-d'Azergues	62	45.53 N	4.37 E
Chazelles-sur-Lyon	62	45.38 N	4.23 E
Chazratišoch, chrebet ⋀	85	38.30 N	70.15 E
Chazy	188	44.53 N	73.26 W
Chbar ≏	110	13.19 N	107.05 E
Cheadle, Eng., U.K.	42	52.59 N	1.59 W
Cheadle, Eng., U.K.	44	53.24 N	2.13 W
Cheadle Hulme	262	53.22 N	2.12 W
Cheaha Mountain ∧	194	33.30 N	85.47 W
Cheakamus Indian Reserve ◆[4]	182	49.48 N	123.11 W
Cheam ◆[8]	260	51.21 N	0.13 W
Cheam View	224	49.15 N	121.41 W
Cheapside	222	29.17 N	97.24 W
Cheat ≏	188	39.45 N	79.54 W
Cheat, Shavers Fork ≏	188	39.06 N	79.33 W
Cheb	54	50.01 N	12.25 E
Chebacco Lake ⊜	283	42.37 N	70.48 W
Chebanse	216	41.00 N	87.54 W
Chebba	148	35.14 N	10.02 E
Chebeigou	89	43.28 N	127.04 E
Chebogue Point ›	186	43.45 N	66.07 W
Cheboksary → Čeboksary	80	56.09 N	47.15 E
Cheboygan	190	45.38 N	84.28 W
Chech, Erg ◆[2]	148	25.00 N	2.15 W
Ch'ech'eng	100	22.05 N	120.42 E
Chechnia → Čečnja-Ingušetija □[3]	84	43.15 N	45.40 E
Chech'on	98	37.08 N	128.12 E
Chęciny	30	50.48 N	20.28 E
Checleset Bay ⊂	182	50.03 N	127.40 W
Checotah	196	35.28 N	95.31 W
Chedabucto Bay ⊂	186	45.23 N	61.10 W
Chedaoyu	105	40.22 N	117.57 E
Cheddar	42	51.17 N	2.46 W
Cheddleton	44	53.04 N	2.02 W
Cheduba Island I	110	18.48 N	93.38 E
Cheduba Strait ≍	110	18.56 N	93.45 E
Chedun	100	24.09 N	117.19 E
Chée ≏	56	48.45 N	4.39 E
Cheektowaga	210	42.55 N	78.46 W
Cheepie	166	26.39 S	145.01 E
Cheesequake	276	40.25 N	74.17 W
Cheesequake Creek ≏	276	40.28 N	74.16 W
Cheesequake State Park ♠	276	40.26 N	74.16 W
Cheetham Hill ◆[8]	262	53.31 N	2.15 W
Chefang, Zhg.	104	41.35 N	121.26 E
Chefang, Zhg.	106	31.15 N	120.45 E
Chef-Boutonne	32	46.07 N	0.04 W
Chefoo → Yantai	98	37.33 N	121.20 E
Chefornak	180	60.13 N	164.12 W
Chefumage ≏	152	12.15 S	22.19 E
Chefuzwe	156	17.38 S	24.30 E
Chegar Perah	114	4.25 N	101.56 E
Chegga ⍑[4]	148	25.30 N	5.46 W
Chegutu	154	18.10 S	30.14 E
Chehalis	224	46.39 N	122.57 W
Chehalis ≏	224	46.57 N	123.50 W
Chehalis, South Fork ≏	224	46.40 N	123.15 W
Chehalis Indian Reservation ◆[4]	224	46.49 N	123.13 W
Chehe	102	25.00 N	107.38 E
Chehel Dokhtarān	128	35.06 N	62.19 E
Cheheqiao	105	40.21 N	118.16 E
Cheil, Ras el ›	144	7.44 N	49.50 E
Cheine	54	52.52 N	11.04 E
Cheiron, Cime du ∧	62	43.49 N	6.58 E
Chejiatun	104	41.57 N	123.01 E
Chejiawopeng	104	42.29 N	123.07 E
Cheju	90	33.31 N	126.32 E
Cheju-do I	90	33.20 N	126.30 E
Chekiang → Zhejiang □[4]	100	29.00 N	120.00 E
Chek Jawa, Tanjong ›	271c	1.24 N	104.00 E
Chek Kang	271d	22.26 N	114.21 E
Chela, Serra da ∧	152	16.00 S	13.10 E
Chelan	202	47.50 N	120.00 W
Chelan □[6]	224	47.56 N	120.52 W
Chelan, Lake ⊜	202	48.05 N	120.30 W
Chelas ◆[8]	266c	38.45 N	9.07 W
Cheleiros	266c	38.53 N	9.20 W
Cheleiros, Ribeira de ≏	266c	38.54 N	9.22 W
Chelelektu	144	6.00 N	38.09 E
Chelford	262	53.16 N	2.16 W
Chelforó	252	39.04 S	66.32 W
Chelghoum el Aïd	148	36.10 N	6.10 E
Chéliff, Oued ≏	148	36.01 N	0.07 E
Chelīk-e Yās Khān	120	37.05 N	66.14 E
Chellaston	42	52.53 N	1.27 W
Chelles	50	48.53 N	2.36 E
Chelles-le-Pin, Aérodrome de ⊠	261	48.55 N	2.35 E
Chełm	30	51.10 N	23.28 E
Chełm □[4]	30	51.20 N	23.20 E
Chelmer ≏	42	51.44 N	0.42 E
Chelmer and Blackwater Navigation ≊	260	51.44 N	0.43 E
Chełmno	30	53.22 N	18.26 E
Chelmorton	262	53.13 N	1.50 W
Chelmsford, On., Can.	190	46.35 N	81.12 W
Chelmsford, Eng., U.K.	42	51.44 N	0.28 E
Chelmsford, Ma., U.S.	207	42.35 N	71.21 W
Chelmsford □[8]	260	51.44 N	0.30 E
Chelmsford Dam ⊜[1]	158	28.02 S	29.52 E
Chełmża	30	53.12 N	18.37 E
Chelsea, Austl.	169	38.03 S	145.07 E
Chelsea, Ia., U.S.	190	41.55 N	92.23 W
Chelsea, Ma., U.S.	207	42.23 N	71.02 W
Chelsea, Mi., U.S.	216	42.19 N	84.01 W
Chelsea, Ok., U.S.	196	36.32 N	95.25 W
Chelsea, Pa., U.S.	285	39.52 N	75.28 W
Chelsea, Vt., U.S.	188	43.59 N	72.26 W
Chelsea Estates	208	39.41 N	75.36 W
Chelsea Park	224	47.28 N	122.21 W
Chelsfield ◆[8]	260	51.21 N	0.08 E
Cheltenham, Austl.	274a	33.46 S	151.05 E
Cheltenham, Austl.	274b	37.58 S	145.03 E
Cheltenham, Eng., U.K.	42	51.54 N	2.04 W
Cheltenham, Md., U.S.	208	38.44 N	76.49 W
Cheltenham, Pa., U.S.	208	40.03 N	75.05 W
Chel'ul'ja	26	51.44 N	30.41 E
Chelvand	128	38.18 N	48.50 E
Chelyabinsk → Čel'abinsk	86	55.10 N	61.24 E

FRANÇAIS

Nom	Page	Lat.°′	Long.°′ W = Ouest
Chelyāma	126	23.37 N	86.33 E
Chelyan	188	38.11 N	81.29 W
Chemaïa	148	32.05 N	8.37 W
Chemainus	224	48.55 N	123.43 W
Chemainus ⊜	224	48.53 N	123.41 W
Chemaogang	106	31.33 N	121.52 E
Chemax	232	20.39 N	87.56 W
Chemba	154	17.08 S	34.52 E
Chembūr ◆[8]	272c	19.04 N	72.54 E
Chemchâm, Sebkhet ⊜	148	21.05 N	12.05 W
Chemčik ≏	86	51.47 N	92.00 E
Chemehuevi Indian Reservation ◆[4]	204	34.30 N	114.23 W
Chemillé	32	47.13 N	0.44 W
Chemin	58	46.59 N	5.19 E
Cheminis, Colline ∧[2]	190	48.08 N	79.31 W
Chemnitz	54	50.50 N	12.55 E
Chemnitz ≏	54	50.59 N	12.47 E
Chemor	114	4.43 N	101.07 E
Chemulpo → Inch'ŏn	98	37.28 N	126.38 E
Chemult	202	43.13 N	121.46 W
Chemung, Il., U.S.	216	42.25 N	88.40 W
Chemung, N.Y., U.S.	210	42.01 N	76.37 W
Chemung □[6]	210	42.06 N	76.49 W
Chemung ≏	210	41.55 N	76.31 W
Chemung County Airport ⊠	210	42.10 N	76.53 W
Chemung Lake ⊜	212	44.25 N	78.22 W
Chena, Cerro ∧	286e	33.36 N	70.45 W
Chenāb ≏	123	29.23 N	71.02 E
Chenachane	148	26.00 N	4.15 W
Chenail Ecarté ≏[1]	214	42.28 N	82.29 W
Chenango □[6]	210	42.32 N	75.31 W
Chenango ≏	210	42.05 N	75.55 W
Chenango Bridge	210	42.10 N	75.51 W
Chenango Forks	210	42.14 N	75.50 W
Chenango Valley State Park ♠	210	42.14 N	75.50 W
Chenārān	128	36.39 N	59.06 E
Chenaut	258	34.15 S	59.13 W
Chen Barag Qi	89	49.21 N	119.31 E
Chenbofang	98	37.27 N	115.18 E
Chencai	100	29.37 N	120.22 E
Chenchiang → Zhenjiang	106	32.13 N	119.26 E
Chencun	100	22.58 N	113.13 E
Chendai	100	23.48 N	117.24 E
Chendauli ◆[8]	272c	19.07 N	72.54 E
Chenderiang	114	4.16 N	101.14 E
Chenderoh, Tasek ⊜	114	4.58 N	100.57 E
Chêne, Rivière du ≏, P.Q., Can.	206	46.34 N	72.00 W
Chêne, Rivière du ≏, P.Q., Can.	206	45.33 N	73.54 W
Chenele	152	12.54 S	23.54 E
Chenequa	216	43.06 N	88.23 W
Chénéville	206	45.53 N	75.03 W
Cheney, Ks., U.S.	198	37.37 N	97.46 W
Cheney, Wa., U.S.	202	47.29 N	117.34 W
Cheney Reservoir ⊜[1]	198	37.45 N	97.50 W
Cheneys Point	214	42.08 N	79.24 W
Cheneyville	194	31.00 N	92.17 W
Chenfang	100	28.01 N	117.32 E
Cheng'an	98	36.27 N	114.41 E
Chengannūr	122	9.20 N	76.38 E
Chengbu	102	26.18 N	110.13 E
Chengchow → Zhengzhou	102	34.48 N	113.39 E
Chengde, Zhg.	105	40.58 N	117.53 E
Chengde (Xiabancheng), Zhg.	105	40.47 N	118.08 E
Chengdu (Chengtu)	107	30.39 N	104.04 E
Chengele	120	28.47 N	96.16 E
Chenggang	100	26.32 N	115.26 E
Chenggu	102	33.10 N	107.22 E
Chenghai	100	23.30 N	116.46 E
Cheng Hu ⊜	106	31.13 N	120.49 E
Chenghuang	102	22.32 N	109.39 E
Chengjia	100	24.50 N	112.50 E
Chengjiahe	100	32.18 N	112.27 E
Chengjiang	102	24.45 N	102.54 E
Chengjiangzhen	107	29.52 N	106.23 E
Chengjiazhen	107	29.24 N	104.36 E
Chengkou	102	31.54 N	108.41 E
Chenglingji	100	29.26 N	113.09 E
Chenglong	100	24.51 N	114.41 E
Chengmai	110	19.48 N	110.02 E
Chengmao	106	31.10 N	120.53 E
Chengpu	100	25.46 N	118.48 E
Chengqian	98	35.21 N	117.21 E
Chengqianwei	100	28.09 N	116.13 E
Chengshan Jiao ›	98	37.24 N	122.42 E
Chengteh → Chengde	105	40.58 N	117.53 E
Chengtu → Chengdu	107	30.39 N	104.04 E
Ch'engtzuliao	269d	25.06 N	121.27 E
Chengwu	98	34.58 N	115.52 E
Chengxian	102	33.43 N	105.41 E
Chengxi Hu ⊜	100	32.24 N	116.15 E
Chengyang, Zhg.	98	36.18 N	120.22 E
Chengyang, Zhg.	100	29.59 N	119.44 E
Chengzi, Zhg.	98	41.57 N	117.16 E
Chengzi, Zhg.	105	39.58 N	116.02 E
Chengzitan	98	39.30 N	122.30 E
Ch'enhsien → Chenxian	100	25.48 N	112.59 E
Chen Hu ⊜	100	30.29 N	113.22 E
Chenies	260	51.41 N	0.32 W
Chenil, Lac ⊜	186	51.51 N	59.41 W
Cheniménil	58	48.08 N	6.36 E
Chenji	100	33.50 N	119.11 E
Chenjiachang, Zhg.	107	29.35 N	104.52 E
Chenjiachang, Zhg.	107	30.04 N	105.15 E
Chenjiagang	98	34.25 N	119.49 E
Chenjiahe	102	29.28 N	109.59 E
Chenjiaji	100	30.42 N	114.21 E
Chenjiapang	106	31.14 N	119.42 E
Chenjiapu	105	40.31 N	115.37 E
Chenjiaqiao	106	31.27 N	121.16 E
Chenjiatun, Zhg.	104	42.20 N	124.06 E
Chenjiatun, Zhg.	104	40.57 N	121.01 E
Chenjiawan	106	31.02 N	120.35 E
Chenjiaxiang	100	31.29 N	113.45 E
Chenjiazhen	106	31.30 N	121.48 E
Chenjiazui	105	39.17 N	116.59 E
Chenkeng	100	25.06 N	116.15 E
Chenlingjiao	106	30.23 N	118.47 E
Chenliu	98	34.43 N	114.31 E
Chenlong	269b	31.17 N	121.25 E
Chennevières	261	49.00 N	2.07 E
Chennevières-lès-Louvres	261	49.03 N	2.33 E
Chenoa	216	40.44 N	88.43 W
Chenonceaux	50	47.20 N	1.04 E
Chenonceaux, Château de ⊥	50	47.20 N	1.04 E
Chenôve	58	47.17 N	5.00 E
Chenoweth	224	45.37 N	121.13 W
Chenqiao	98	34.58 N	114.32 E
Chenquingqiao	89	49.08 N	127.16 E
Chenshanzhuang	105	39.43 N	117.30 E
Chenshichang	107	29.17 N	106.00 E
Chens-sur-Léman	58	46.20 N	6.16 E
Chentang	102	23.54 N	110.39 E
Chentejn nuruu ⋀	88	48.30 N	108.30 E
Chentij	88	48.05 N	109.45 E
Chentij □[4]	88	48.00 N	110.30 E
Chenxi	102	27.51 N	109.59 E
Chenxian	100	25.48 N	112.59 E
Chenxiangtun	104	41.36 N	123.30 E
Chenyang, Zhg.	100	33.47 N	120.10 E
Chenyang → Shenyang, Zhg.	104	41.48 N	123.27 E
Cheonan → Ch'ŏnan	98	36.48 N	127.09 E

PORTUGUÊS

Nome	Página	Lat.°′	Long.°′ W = Oeste
Cheongju → Ch'ŏngju	98	36.39 N	127.31 E
Cheo Reo	110	13.24 N	108.27 E
Chepachet	207	41.54 N	71.40 W
Chepaúa	152	12.58 S	22.43 E
Chepén	248	7.13 S	79.27 W
Chépénéhé	175f	20.47 S	167.09 E
Chepes	252	31.21 S	66.36 W
Chepkotet ∧	154	1.15 N	35.26 E
Chepo	246	9.10 N	79.06 W
Chepstow	42	51.39 N	2.41 W
Cheptainville	261	48.33 N	2.16 E
Cher □[5]	32	47.05 N	2.30 E
Cher ≏	32	47.21 N	0.29 E
Cheradi, Isole II	68	40.27 N	17.10 E
Cherain	56	50.11 N	5.52 E
Cherán	234	19.41 N	101.57 W
Chéran ≏	62	45.53 N	5.56 E
Cheranchi	150	12.40 N	7.42 E
Cherangany Hills ⋀[2]	154	1.15 N	35.27 E
Cherasco	62	44.39 N	7.51 E
Cherāt	123	33.49 N	71.53 E
Cheraw	192	34.41 N	79.53 W
Cheraw State Park ♠	192	34.36 N	79.55 W
Cherbaniani Reef ✣[2]	122	12.18 N	71.53 E
Cherbourg	32	49.39 N	1.39 W
Cherchell	148	36.36 N	2.12 E
Cheremkhovo → Čeremchovo	88	53.09 N	103.05 E
Chérence	261	49.05 N	1.41 E
Chereponi	150	10.09 N	0.17 E
Cherepovets → Čerepovec	76	59.08 N	37.54 E
Chergui, Chott ech ⊜	148	34.21 N	0.30 E
Chergui, Île I	148	34.44 N	11.14 E
Chergui, Zahrez ⊜	148	35.12 N	3.32 E
Cheribon → Cirebon	115a	6.44 S	108.34 E
Cherio ≏	64	45.34 N	9.51 E
Cherita, Sebkhet ⊜	36	35.21 N	10.19 E
Cheriton	208	37.17 N	75.58 W
Cheriyam Island I	122	10.09 N	73.40 E
Cherkassy → Čerkassy	78	49.26 N	32.04 E
Cherkessia → Karačajevo-Čerkesija □[3]	84	44.00 N	42.00 E
Cherkessk → Čerkessk	84	44.14 N	42.04 E
Cherlen → Kerulen ≏	90	48.48 N	117.00 E
Chermside	171a	27.23 S	153.02 E
Chernigov → Černigov	78	51.30 N	31.18 E
Chernobyl → Černobyl'	78	51.16 N	30.14 E
Chernofski	180	53.24 N	167.33 W
Chernogorsk → Černogorsk	86	53.49 N	91.18 E
Chernovtsy → Černovcy	78	48.18 N	25.56 E
Chero ≏	62	45.03 N	9.51 E
Cherokee, Al., U.S.	194	34.45 N	87.58 W
Cherokee, Ia., U.S.	198	42.44 N	95.33 W
Cherokee, Ks., U.S.	198	37.20 N	94.48 W
Cherokee, Ok., U.S.	196	36.45 N	98.21 W
Cherokee, Tx., U.S.	196	30.59 N	98.43 W
Cherokee □[6]	222	31.48 N	95.10 W
Cherokee, Lake ⊜[1]	222	32.21 N	94.39 W
Cherokee Canal ≊	226	39.18 N	121.55 W
Cherokee Lake ⊜[1]	192	36.16 N	83.20 W
Cherokee Point ›	192	26.16 N	77.03 W
Cherokee Ranch	208	40.25 N	75.55 W
Cherokees, Lake O' The ⊜[1]	194	36.39 N	94.49 W
Cherokee Village	194	36.17 N	91.30 W
Chéroy	50	48.12 N	3.00 E
Cherpuči	89	53.01 N	138.52 E
Cherquenco	252	38.41 S	72.00 W
Cherrabun	162	18.29 S	125.19 E
Cherrapunji	120	25.18 N	91.42 E
Cherry Brook ≏, Ma., U.S.	283	42.23 N	71.17 W
Cherry Brook ≏, N.J., U.S.	276	41.01 N	74.00 W
Cherry City	279b	40.29 N	79.58 W
Cherry Creek, B.C., Can.	224	49.17 N	124.47 W
Cherry Creek, N.Y., U.S.	214	42.17 N	79.06 W
Cherry Creek ≏, Az., U.S.	200	33.41 N	110.49 W
Cherry Creek ≏, Ca., U.S.	226	37.53 N	119.58 W
Cherry Creek ≏, Co., U.S.	198	39.45 N	105.01 W
Cherry Creek ≏, Mt., U.S.	198	46.48 N	105.15 W
Cherry Creek ≏, N.D., U.S.	198	47.41 N	103.02 W
Cherry Creek ≏, S.D., U.S.	198	44.36 N	101.30 W
Cherry Creek ≏, Tx., U.S.	196	31.13 N	103.34 W
Cherry Creek, East Fork ≏	226	38.06 N	119.47 W
Cherry Creek, West Fork ≏	226	38.04 N	119.54 W
Cherry Fork	218	38.53 N	83.37 W
Cherry Grove, N.Y., U.S.	210	40.39 N	73.06 W
Cherry Grove, Cr., U.S.	224	45.26 N	123.14 W
Cherry Hill, Il., U.S.	278	41.32 N	88.02 W
Cherry Hill, N.J., U.S.	208	39.56 N	75.01 W
Cherry Hill ◆[8]	284b	39.15 N	76.38 W
Cherry Hill Mall ◆[9]	285	39.56 N	75.02 W
Cherry Island I	285	39.43 N	75.31 W
Cherry Lake ⊜[1]	226	38.00 N	119.54 W
Cherryland	226	37.41 N	122.06 W
Cherry Lane	279b	40.34 N	79.33 W
Cherryplain	210	42.38 N	73.22 W
Cherry Point Marine Corps Air Station ■	192	34.54 N	76.54 W
Cherryvale	198	37.16 N	95.33 W
Cherry Valley, Ar., U.S.	194	35.24 N	90.45 W
Cherry Valley, Ca., U.S.	228	33.57 N	116.53 W
Cherry Valley, Il., U.S.	216	42.14 N	88.56 W
Cherry Valley, Ma., U.S.	207	42.14 N	71.52 W
Cherry Valley, N.Y., U.S.	210	42.47 N	74.45 W
Cherry Valley, Pa., U.S.	214	41.10 N	79.48 W
Cherry Valley Creek ≏	210	42.35 N	74.56 W
Cherryville, N.C., U.S.	192	35.22 N	81.22 W
Cherryville, Pa., U.S.	208	40.45 N	75.33 W
Cherrywood	275b	43.52 N	79.08 W
Cherson	78	46.38 N	32.35 E
Cherson □[4]	78	46.45 N	33.30 E
Chersonesskij, mys ›	78	44.35 N	33.23 E
Chertsey	42	51.24 N	0.30 W
Cherwell ≏	42	51.44 N	1.15 W
Chesaco Park	284b	39.19 N	76.30 W
Chesaning	190	43.11 N	84.06 W
Chesapeake	208	36.49 N	76.16 W
Chesapeake and Delaware Canal ≊	208	39.32 N	75.51 W
Chesapeake and Ohio Canal National Historical Park ♠	208	39.03 N	77.16 W
Chesapeake Bay ⊂	208	38.40 N	76.25 W
Chesapeake Bay Bridge-Tunnel ◆[5]	208	37.00 N	76.02 W
Chesapeake Beach	208	38.41 N	76.32 W
Chesaw	182	48.56 N	119.03 W
Chesdin, Lake ⊜[1]	208	37.15 N	77.33 W
Cheseaux	58	46.35 N	6.36 E
Chesham	42	51.43 N	0.38 W
Chesham Bois	260	51.41 N	0.37 W
Cheshire, Ct., U.S.	207	41.29 N	72.54 W
Cheshire, Ma., U.S.	207	42.33 N	73.09 W
Cheshire, N.Y., U.S.	210	42.49 N	77.20 W
Cheshire □[6], Eng., U.K.	44	53.23 N	2.30 W
Cheshire □[6], N.H., U.S.	207	42.50 N	72.15 W
Cheshire Plain ≚	44	53.17 N	2.40 W
Cheshire Reservoir ⊜[1]	207	42.32 N	73.11 W
Chesht-e Sharīf	128	34.21 N	63.44 E
Cheshunt	42	51.43 N	0.02 W
Chesil Beach ⩲[2]	42	50.38 N	2.33 W
Chesilhurst	285	39.43 N	74.52 W
Cheslatta Lake ⊜	182	53.44 N	125.18 W
Chesley	212	44.17 N	81.05 W
Chesnee	192	35.08 N	81.51 W
Chess ≏	260	51.38 N	0.27 W
Chessington ◆[8]	260	51.21 N	0.18 W
Chessy	261	48.53 N	2.46 E
Chest Creek ≏	214	40.53 N	78.44 W
Chester, Eng., U.K.	44	53.12 N	2.54 W
Chester, Ca., U.S.	204	40.18 N	121.13 W
Chester, Ct., U.S.	207	41.24 N	72.27 W
Chester, Il., U.S.	194	37.54 N	89.49 W
Chester, Md., U.S.	208	38.58 N	76.17 W
Chester, Ma., U.S.	207	42.16 N	72.58 W
Chester, Mt., U.S.	202	48.30 N	110.58 W
Chester, Ne., U.S.	198	40.00 N	97.37 W
Chester, N.J., U.S.	210	40.47 N	74.41 W
Chester, Ok., U.S.	196	36.12 N	98.55 W
Chester, Pa., U.S.	208	39.50 N	75.21 W
Chester, S.C., U.S.	192	34.42 N	81.12 W
Chester, Tx., U.S.	222	30.55 N	94.36 W
Chester, Vt., U.S.	188	43.15 N	72.35 W
Chester, Va., U.S.	208	37.21 N	77.26 W
Chester, W.V., U.S.	214	40.36 N	80.33 W
Chester □[6]	208	39.58 N	75.36 W
Chester □[8]	262	53.16 N	2.52 W
Chester ≏	208	39.00 N	76.10 W
Chester Basin	186	44.34 N	64.19 W
Chesterbrook	284c	38.55 N	77.09 W
Chester Brook ≏	283	42.23 N	71.14 W
Chesterbrook Woods	284c	38.56 N	77.08 W
Chester Creek ≏	208	39.50 N	75.22 W
Chester Creek, East Branch ≏	285	39.56 N	75.32 W
Chester Creek, West Branch ≏	285	39.54 N	75.27 W
Chesterfield, Eng., U.K.	44	53.15 N	1.25 W
Chesterfield, Ct., U.S.	207	41.24 N	72.11 W
Chesterfield, Il., U.S.	219	39.15 N	90.04 W
Chesterfield, In., U.S.	218	40.06 N	85.35 W
Chesterfield, Ma., U.S.	207	42.23 N	72.50 W
Chesterfield, S.C., U.S.	192	34.44 N	80.05 W
Chesterfield, Va., U.S.	192	37.22 N	77.30 W
Chesterfield □[6]	208	37.20 N	77.25 W
Chesterfield, Îles II	160	19.30 S	158.00 E
Chesterfield, Nosy I	157b	16.20 S	43.58 E
Chesterfield Inlet	176	63.21 N	90.42 W
Chesterfield Inlet ⊂	176	63.25 N	90.45 W
Chester Heights	285	39.53 N	75.28 W
Chester Hill, Austl.	274a	33.53 S	151.00 E
Chesterhill, Oh., U.S.	188	39.29 N	81.51 W
Chester Hill, Pa., U.S.	214	40.53 N	78.14 W
Chester Island I	285	39.50 N	75.21 W
Chesterland	214	41.31 N	81.21 W
Chester-le-Street	44	54.52 N	1.34 W
Chester Morse Lake ⊜[1]	224	47.23 N	121.42 W
Chesters	44	55.23 N	2.36 W
Chester Springs	285	40.06 N	75.37 W
Chesterton	216	41.36 N	87.03 W
Chesterton Range ⋀	166	25.30 S	147.27 E
Chestertown	208	39.12 N	76.04 W
Chesterville, On., Can.	212	45.06 N	75.14 W
Chesterville, Oh., U.S.	214	40.29 N	82.41 W
Chestnut	219	40.03 N	89.11 W
Chestnut Hill, Ma., U.S.	283	42.20 N	71.10 W
Chestnut Hill, Pa., U.S.	210	40.04 N	75.12 W
Chestnut Hill ◆[8]	285	40.04 N	75.13 W
Chestnut Hill ∧[2]	285	40.13 N	75.45 W
Chestnut Hill Estates	285	39.41 N	75.42 W
Chestnut Hill Reservoir ⊜[1]	283	42.20 N	71.10 W
Chestnut Ridge ∧	214	40.09 N	79.24 W
Chestnut Ridge Park ♠	284a	42.43 N	78.46 W
Chest Peak ∧	172	43.06 S	172.01 E
Chesuncook Lake ⊜	188	46.00 N	69.20 W
Cheswick	214	40.32 N	79.47 W
Cheswold	208	39.13 N	75.35 W
Chet ≏	42	52.33 N	1.32 E
Cheta ≏	74	71.54 N	102.06 E
Chetaibi	36	37.04 N	7.23 E
Chetco ≏	202	42.03 N	124.16 W
Chetek	190	45.18 N	91.39 W
Chéticamp	186	46.38 N	61.01 W
Chet Iter, Oued V	148	21.39 N	2.30 E
Chetopa	198	37.02 N	95.05 W
Chettlatt Island I	122	11.42 N	72.42 E
Chetumal	232	18.30 N	88.18 W
Chetumal, Bahía ⊂	232	18.20 N	88.05 W
Chetwynd	182	55.42 N	121.40 W
Cheung Chau I	271d	22.12 N	114.01 E
Cheung Shue Tan	271d	22.26 N	114.12 E
Chevak	180	61.39 N	165.17 W
Cheval Blanc, Sommet du ∧	62	44.07 N	6.26 E
Chevannes	261	48.32 N	2.27 E
Chevelon Creek ≏	200	34.57 N	110.31 W
Chevening	260	51.18 N	0.08 E
Chevenoz	58	46.20 N	6.39 E
Cheverly	284c	38.55 N	76.54 W
Cheverny	50	47.30 N	1.28 E
Chevillon	58	48.32 N	5.08 E
Chevilly-Larue	261	48.46 N	2.21 E
Cheviot, N.Z.	172	42.49 S	173.16 E
Cheviot, Oh., U.S.	218	39.09 N	84.36 W
Cheviot Hills ⋀[2]	44	55.22 N	2.22 W
Chevreuse	50	48.42 N	2.03 E
Chèvreville	261	49.07 N	2.51 E
Chevril, Lac du ⊜	62	45.29 N	6.56 E
Chevry-Cossigny	261	48.43 N	2.40 E
Chevy Chase	284c	38.58 N	77.04 W
Chevy Chase Heights	214	40.36 N	79.08 W
Chevy Chase View	284c	39.01 N	77.05 W
Chewaucan ≏	202	42.30 N	120.18 W
Chew Bahir (Lake Stefanie) ⊜	144	4.40 N	36.50 E
Chewelah	202	48.16 N	117.42 W
Chew Magna	42	51.22 N	2.35 W
Chew Reservoir ⊜[1]	262	53.31 N	1.56 W
Chews Landing	285	39.50 N	75.04 W
Chewton, Austl.	169	37.05 S	144.16 E
Chewton, Pa., U.S.	214	40.53 N	80.20 W
Chexbres	58	46.29 N	6.47 E
Cheyenne, Ok., U.S.	196	35.36 N	99.40 W
Cheyenne, Wy., U.S.	200	41.08 N	104.49 W
Cheyenne ≏	198	44.40 N	101.15 W
Cheyenne, Dry Fork ≏	198	43.25 N	105.23 W
Cheyenne River Indian Reservation ◆[4]	198	45.00 N	100.40 W
Cheyenne Wells	198	38.49 N	102.21 W
Cheyne Bay ⊂	162	34.35 S	118.50 E
Cheyne Point ›	162	33.58 S	122.34 E
Cheyney	285	39.56 N	75.31 W
Cheyney University of Pennsylvania ⊍[2]	285	39.56 N	75.32 W
Chezhen	98	37.54 N	117.37 E
Chhabra	124	24.40 N	76.50 E
Chhachhrauli	124	30.15 N	77.22 E
Chhajārsi	272a	28.38 N	77.23 E
Chhalera Bāngar	272a	28.33 N	77.20 E
Chhanka	126	23.59 N	89.55 E
Chhapra	124	25.46 N	84.45 E
Chhātak	120	25.02 N	91.40 E
Chhatarpur, India	124	24.23 N	84.11 E
Chhatarpur, India	124	24.55 N	79.36 E
Chhātna	126	23.18 N	86.58 E
Chhatrapur	122	19.21 N	84.59 E
Chhattīsgarh ≚	122	21.15 N	82.00 E
Chhay Arêng ≏	110	11.31 N	103.25 E
Chhêb Kândal	110	13.45 N	105.24 E
Chhibrāmau	124	27.09 N	79.31 E
Chhināmor	272b	22.48 N	88.18 E
Chhindwāra	124	22.04 N	78.56 E
Chhiruti	126	24.01 N	88.11 E
Chhitauni	124	27.09 N	83.58 E
Chhlong ≏	110	12.15 N	105.58 E
Chhota Bāisdia	126	22.00 N	90.27 E
Chhota-Chhindwāra	124	23.03 N	79.29 E
Chhota Udepur	120	22.19 N	74.01 E
Chhukha Dzong	124	27.09 N	89.36 E
Chi ≏, Thai	110	15.11 N	104.43 E
Chi ≏, Thai	110	15.18 N	103.31 E
Chi ≏, Zhg.	100	32.51 N	117.59 E
Chía	246	4.52 N	74.04 W
Chia, Laguna ⊜	234	22.10 N	98.02 W
Chiador	256	22.01 S	43.03 W
Chiahsien	100	23.05 N	120.35 E
Chiahsing → Jiaxing	106	30.46 N	120.45 E
Chiai	100	23.29 N	120.27 E
Chialamberto	62	45.22 N	7.21 E
Chiali	100	23.10 N	120.10 E
Chiambala ≏	152	16.22 S	11.49 E
Chiampo	64	45.33 N	11.17 E
Chiampo ≏	64	45.20 N	11.16 E
Chiamussu → Jiamusi	89	46.50 N	130.21 E
Chian → Ji'an	100	27.07 N	114.58 E
Chiana, Val di V	66	43.15 N	11.50 E
Chianciano Terme	66	43.03 N	11.50 E
Chiang Dao	110	19.22 N	98.58 E
Chiange	152	15.45 S	13.48 E
Chiang Kham	110	19.32 N	100.18 E
Chiang Khan	110	17.52 N	101.36 E
Chiang Khian	110	19.37 N	100.00 E
Chiang Mai	110	18.47 N	98.59 E
Chiangmen → Jiangmen	100	22.35 N	113.05 E
Chiang Rai	110	19.54 N	99.50 E
Chiang Saen	110	20.16 N	100.05 E
Chiangtu → Yangzhou	100	32.24 N	119.26 E
Chiangyin → Jiangyin	106	31.55 N	120.16 E
Chiani ≏	66	42.44 N	12.07 E
Chianni	66	43.29 N	10.38 E
Chianti □[9]	66	43.25 N	11.20 E
Chianti, Monti del ⋀	66	43.32 N	11.25 E
Chiachsi	100	24.49 N	121.46 E
Chiachsien → Jiaoxian	98	36.18 N	119.58 E
Chiaopan	100	24.50 N	121.21 E
Chiaotso → Jiaozuo	102	35.15 N	113.13 E
Chiao-Tung Normal University ⊍[2]	269b	31.14 N	121.24 E
Chiapa	248	19.32 S	69.13 W
Chiapa de Corzo	234	16.42 N	93.00 W
Chiapaot'ai	100	24.11 N	121.00 E
Chiapas □[3]	232	16.30 N	92.30 W
Chiaramonte Gulfi	70	37.02 N	14.42 E
Chiaramonti	71	40.45 N	8.49 E
Chiaravalle	66	43.36 N	13.19 E
Chiaravalle Centrale	68	38.41 N	16.25 E
Chiareggio	64	46.19 N	9.47 E
Chiari	62	45.32 N	9.56 E
Chiaromonte	68	40.07 N	16.13 E
Chiasso	58	45.50 N	9.01 E
Chiautla de Tapia	234	18.17 N	98.36 W
Chiavari	62	44.19 N	9.19 E
Chiavenna	58	46.19 N	9.24 E
Chiawelo	273d	26.17 S	27.52 E
Chiba	94	35.36 N	140.07 E
Chiba □[5]	94	35.30 N	140.20 E
Chibabava	156	20.19 S	33.39 E
Chiba-kō ⊂	268	35.35 N	140.06 E
Chibakou	100	29.36 N	113.01 E
Chibango	152	13.38 S	21.56 E
Chiba University ⊍[2]	268	35.38 N	140.06 E
Chibemba	152	15.45 S	14.05 E
Chibi	154	20.19 S	30.30 E
Chibia	152	15.11 S	13.41 E
Chibouet ≏	206	45.47 N	72.52 W
Chibougamau	176	49.55 N	74.22 W
Chibuto	156	24.44 S	33.33 E
Chibuzhangchu Hu ⊜	120	33.25 N	90.15 E
Chibwe	154	14.12 S	28.31 E
Chicago, Il., U.S.	216	41.51 N	87.39 W
Chicago, Il., U.S.	278	41.51 N	87.39 W
Chicago, North Branch ≏	216	41.53 N	87.38 W
Chicago, North Branch, West Fork ≏	278	42.03 N	87.54 W
Chicago, South Branch ≏	278	41.53 N	87.38 W
Chicago, University of ⊍[2]	278	41.47 N	87.36 W
Chicago Botanic Garden ♠	278	42.09 N	87.47 W
Chicago Harbor ⊂	278	41.53 N	87.37 W
Chicago Heights	216	41.30 N	87.38 W
Chicago-Hinsdale Airport ⊠	278	41.46 N	87.56 W
Chicago Lawn ◆[8]	278	41.47 N	87.41 W
Chicago-Midway Airport ⊠	216	41.47 N	87.45 W
Chicago-O'Hare International Airport ⊠	278	41.59 N	87.54 W
Chicago Park	226	39.09 N	120.58 W
Chicago Portage National Historic Site ⊥	278	41.48 N	87.49 W
Chicago Ridge	216	41.42 N	87.46 W
Chicago Sanitary and Ship Canal ≊	216	41.32 N	88.05 W
Chicago Stadium ♠	278	41.53 N	87.40 W
Chicama ≏	248	7.56 S	79.17 W
Chicamacomico ≏	208	38.26 N	75.59 W
Chicamba, Barragem de ◆[6]	156	19.08 S	33.00 E
Chicapa ≏	152	6.26 S	20.47 E
Chicayán ≏	234	21.59 N	94.06 W
Chic-Chocs, Monts ⋀	186	48.55 N	66.00 W
Chichagof Island I	180	57.30 N	135.30 W
Chichas, Cordillera de ⋀	248	21.00 S	66.20 W
Chīchāwatni	123	30.32 N	72.42 E
Chiché ≏	250	8.15 S	53.30 W
Chicheng	98	40.54 N	115.46 E
Chichén Itzá ⊥	232	20.40 N	88.35 W
Chichester, Eng., U.K.	42	50.50 N	0.48 W
Chichester, N.Y., U.S.	210	42.06 N	74.19 W
Chichester Range ⋀	162	22.00 S	118.50 E
Chichi	100	23.50 N	120.47 E
Chichibu	94	35.59 N	139.05 E
Chichibu-Tama-kokuritsu-kōen ♠	94	35.52 N	139.00 E
Chichica	236	8.22 N	81.40 W
Chichicastenango	236	14.56 N	91.07 W
Chichigalpa	236	12.34 N	87.02 W
Chichigapa	234	17.47 N	94.25 W
Ch'ich'ihaerh → Qiqihar	89	47.19 N	123.55 E
Chichihualco	234	17.41 N	99.39 W
Chichijima-rettō II	14	27.06 N	142.12 E
Chichimilá	232	20.37 N	88.13 W
Chichiriviche	246	10.56 N	68.16 W
Chicholi	124	22.01 N	77.40 E
Chichra	126	22.19 N	86.53 E
Chickahominy ≏	208	37.14 N	76.53 W
Chickaloon	180	61.48 N	148.28 W
Chickamauga	192	34.52 N	85.17 W
Chickamauga Lake ⊜[1]	192	35.22 N	85.02 W
Chickamin ≏	182	55.47 N	130.58 W
Chickasaw, Al., U.S.	194	30.45 N	88.04 W
Chickasaw, Oh., U.S.	216	40.26 N	84.30 W
Chickasaw Bogue ≏	194	32.17 N	87.55 W
Chickasawhatchie Creek ≏	192	31.19 N	84.29 W
Chickasawhay ≏	194	31.00 N	88.45 W
Chickasaw National Recreation Area ♠	196	34.25 N	96.59 W
Chickasha	196	35.03 N	97.56 W
Chicken	180	64.04 N	141.56 W
Chicken Brook ≏	283	42.08 N	71.25 W
Chickerell	42	50.37 N	2.30 W
Chickies Creek ≏	208	40.03 N	76.32 W
Chiclana de la Frontera	34	36.25 N	6.08 W
Chiclayo	248	6.46 S	79.51 W
Chico, Ca., U.S.	204	39.43 N	121.50 W
Chico, Tx., U.S.	196	33.17 N	97.47 W
Chico, Wa., U.S.	224	47.36 N	122.42 W
Chico ≏, Arg.	254	43.48 S	66.25 W
Chico ≏, Arg.	254	42.25 S	70.30 W
Chico ≏, Arg.	254	49.56 S	68.32 W
Chico ≏, Cuba	286b	23.02 N	82.17 W
Chico ≏, Pan.	236	8.20 N	80.28 W
Chico ≏, Pil.	116	17.58 N	121.36 E
Chico ≏, S.A.	254	51.40 S	69.09 W
Chicoasén, Presa ⊜[1]	234	16.55 N	93.05 W
Chicobi, Lac ⊜	190	48.53 N	78.30 W
Chico Creek ≏	198	38.15 N	104.20 W
Chicolete Creek ≏	222	29.05 N	96.49 W
Chicomba	152	14.09 S	14.57 E
Chicomo	156	24.31 S	34.17 E
Chicomuselo	232	15.46 N	92.16 W
Chiconautla, Cerro ∧	286a	19.39 N	98.58 W
Chiconono	154	12.56 S	35.43 E
Chicontepec de Tejeda	234	20.58 N	98.10 W
Chicopee, Ga., U.S.	192	34.15 N	83.50 W
Chicopee, Ma., U.S.	207	42.08 N	72.36 W
Chicopee ≏	207	42.09 N	72.37 W
Chicora	214	40.56 N	79.44 W
Chicot, Lake ⊜	194	33.20 N	91.14 W
Chicot, Rivière du ≏	275a	45.35 N	73.51 W
Chicot State Park ♠	194	30.47 N	92.19 W
Chicoutimi	186	48.26 N	71.04 W
Chicoutimi ≏	186	48.26 N	71.05 W
Chicoutimi, Réserve ♠	186	48.30 N	70.15 W
Chicú, Cerro ∧	236	8.35 N	80.51 W
Chicualoque	234	20.23 N	97.39 W
Chicuma	152	13.23 S	14.51 E
Chicxulub	232	21.08 N	89.31 W
Chidambaram	122	11.24 N	79.42 E
Chiddingfold	42	51.06 N	0.37 W
Chiddingstone Causeway	260	51.12 N	0.10 E
Chidenguele	156	24.54 S	34.13 E
Chidlow	168a	31.52 S	116.14 E
Chi-do I	98	35.04 N	126.13 E
Chidralada Palace ⊍	269a	13.46 N	100.32 E
Chief	222	32.33 N	96.10 W
Chief Justice William Cushing Memorial State Park ♠	283	42.10 N	70.45 W
Chiefland	192	29.28 N	82.51 W
Chiefs Point ›	212	44.42 N	81.18 W
Chief's Point Indian Reserve ◆[4]	212	44.41 N	81.17 W
Chiehyang → Jieyang	100	23.35 N	116.21 E
Chiemgauer Alpen ⋀	64	47.40 N	12.30 E
Chiemsee ⊜	64	47.54 N	12.29 E
Chien, Bayou de ≏	194	36.35 N	89.11 W
Chienes (Kiens)	64	46.48 N	11.50 E
Chiengi	154	8.39 S	29.10 E
Chiengo	152	13.20 S	21.55 E
Chiens, Rivière aux ≏	275a	45.39 N	73.46 W
Chienti ≏	66	43.18 N	13.45 E
Chieo Lan Reservoir ⊜[1]	110	9.00 N	98.45 E
Chieri	62	45.01 N	7.49 E
Chiers ≏	56	49.39 N	5.00 E
Chiesa in Valmalenco	64	46.16 N	9.51 E
Chiese ≏	64	45.08 N	10.25 E
Chieti	66	42.21 N	14.10 E
Chieti □[4]	66	42.07 N	14.21 E
Chietla	234	18.31 N	98.35 W
Chieuti	68	41.51 N	15.10 E
Chieveley	42	51.27 N	1.19 W
Chièvres	50	50.35 N	3.48 E
Chifeng (Ulanhad)	98	42.18 N	119.00 E
Chigasaki	94	35.19 N	139.24 E
Chiginagak, Mount ∧	180	57.08 N	156.59 W
Chigmit Mountains ⋀	180	60.00 N	153.00 W
Chignahuapan	234	19.50 N	98.02 W
Chignall Saint James	260	51.46 N	0.25 E
Chignall Smealy	260	51.47 N	0.25 E
Chignecto, Cape ›	186	45.20 N	64.57 W
Chignecto Bay ⊂	186	45.35 N	64.45 W
Chignik	180	56.18 N	158.23 W
Chignik Bay ⊂	180	56.22 N	158.15 W
Chignik Lagoon	180	56.21 N	158.31 W
Chignik Lake	180	56.15 N	158.45 W
Chignolo Po	62	45.09 N	9.29 E
Chigombe ≏	156	23.26 S	33.19 E
Chigorodó	246	7.41 N	76.42 W
Chigu	100	27.34 N	114.40 E
Chigubo	156	22.50 S	33.34 E
Chigu Co ⊜	120	28.40 N	91.45 E
Chigwell	42	51.38 N	0.05 E
Chigwell Row	260	51.37 N	0.07 E
Chigyŏng	98	39.51 N	127.26 E
Chihaya-akasaka	270	34.24 N	135.38 E
Chihaya Castle ⊥	270	34.24 N	135.40 E
Chihe	100	32.32 N	117.58 E
Ch'ihfeng → Chifeng	98	42.18 N	119.00 E
Chihli, Gulf of → Bo Hai ⊂	98	38.30 N	120.00 E
Chihpen	100	22.42 N	121.02 E
Ch'ihshang	100	23.07 N	121.12 E
Chihsi → Jixi	89	45.17 N	130.59 E
Ch'ihsing Shan ∧, T'aiwan	100	25.10 N	121.33 E
Ch'ihsing Shan ∧, T'aiwan	269d	25.10 N	121.33 E
Ch'ihsing Yen I	100	21.46 N	120.49 E
Chihtungtsun	100	22.44 N	120.14 E
Chihu	100	24.07 N	117.51 E
Chihuahua	232	28.38 N	106.05 W
Chihuahua □[3]	232	28.30 N	106.00 W
Chihuahuan Desert ◆[2]	16	35.00 N	106.00 W
Chii-san ∧	98	35.20 N	127.44 E
Chii-san Kukrip Kongwŏn ♠	98	35.20 N	127.39 E
Chiitola	26	61.16 N	29.38 E
Chikaskia ≏	196	36.37 N	97.15 W
Chik Ballāpur	122	13.28 N	77.44 E

≏	River	Fluß	Río	Rivière	Rio
≊	Canal	Kanal	Canal	Canal	Canal
∟	Waterfall, Rapids	Wasserfall, Stromschnellen	Cascada, Rápidos	Chute d'eau, Rapides	Cascata, Rápidos
≍	Strait	Meeresstraße	Estrecho	Détroit	Estreito
⊂	Bay, Gulf	Bucht, Golf	Bahía, Golfo	Baie, Golfe	Baía, Golfo
⊜	Lake, Lakes	See, Seen	Lago, Lagos	Lac, Lacs	Lago, Lagos
⩩	Swamp	Sumpf	Pantano	Marais	Pântano
⍓	Ice Features, Glacier	Eis- und Gletscherformen	Accidentes Glaciales	Formes glaciaires	Acidentes glaciares
⍑	Other Hydrographic Features	Andere Hydrographische Objekte	Otros Elementos Hidrográficos	Autres données hydrographiques	Outros acidentes hidrográficos
✣	Submarine Features	Untermeerische Objekte	Accidentes Submarinos	Formes de relief sous-marin	Acidentes submarinos
□	Political Unit	Politische Einheit	Unidad Politica	Entité politique	Unidade política
⊍	Cultural Institution	Kulturelle Institution	Institución Cultural	Institution culturelle	Instituição cultural
⊥	Historical Site	Historische Stätte	Sitio Histórico	Site historique	Sítio histórico
♠	Recreational Site	Erholungs- und Ferienort	Sitio de Recreo	Centre de loisirs	Area de Lazer
⊠	Airport	Flughafen	Aeropuerto	Aéroport	Aeroporto
■	Military Installation	Militäranlage	Instalación Militar	Installation militaire	Instalação militar
◆	Miscellaneous	Verschiedenes	Misceláneo	Divers	Diversos

Chikhli 122 20.21 N 76.15 E
Chikindzonot 232 20.20 N 88.29 W
Chikmagalūr 122 13.19 N 75.47 E
Chiknai ≐ 126 24.06 N 89.17 E
Chiknāyakanhalli 122 13.26 N 76.37 E
Chikoa 154 13.24 S 32.07 E
Chikodi 122 16.26 N 74.36 E
Chikou 100 30.44 N 117.32 E
Chikrêng ≐ 110 12.51 N 104.14 E
Ch'iku 100 23.08 N 120.07 E
Chikugo 96 33.12 N 130.30 E
Chikugo ≐ 92 33.09 N 130.21 E
Chikujō-kichi, Kōkū-jieitai- ■ 96 33.41 N 131.03 E
Chikuma ≐ 94 36.59 N 138.35 E
Chikuminuk Lake ◎ 180 60.14 N 159.00 W
Chikura 94 34.57 N 139.57 E
Chikusa 96 35.09 N 134.26 E
Chikusa ≐ 96 34.44 N 134.24 E
Chikushino 96 33.29 N 130.31 E
Chikwawa 154 16.03 S 34.48 E
Chi-kyaw 110 20.17 N 93.54 E
Chikyu-misaki › 92a 42.18 N 141.00 E
Chila 152 12.04 S 14.29 E
Chilacachapa 234 18.17 N 99.43 W
Chilakalūrupet 122 16.05 N 80.10 E
Chilako ≐ 182 53.54 N 122.59 W
Chilam Chauki 123 35.03 N 75.07 E
Chilanga 154 15.34 S 28.17 E
Chilanko Forks 182 52.06 N 124.10 W
Chilapa de Álvarez 234 17.36 N 99.10 W
Chilās 123 35.26 N 74.05 E
Chilaw 122 7.34 N 79.47 E
Chilca, Perú 248 12.32 S 76.44 W
Chilca, Perú 248 12.09 S 75.11 W
Chilca, Punta › 248 12.27 S 76.48 W
Chilchota 234 19.51 N 102.08 W
Chilcotin ≐ 182 51.45 N 122.24 W
Chilcott Island I 166 16.58 S 149.58 E
Childers 166 25.14 S 152.17 E
Childersburg 194 33.16 N 86.21 W
Childer Thornton 262 53.17 N 2.57 W
Childress 196 34.25 N 100.12 W
Childs 210 41.34 N 75.32 W
Chile □1 244 30.00 S 71.00 W
Chile, Hipódromo ♦ 286e 33.24 S 70.41 W
Chile, Universidad de ✿2 286e 33.27 S 70.40 W
Chile Basin ✢1 18 33.00 S 80.00 W
Chile Chico 254 46.33 S 71.44 W
Chilecito, Arg. 252 29.10 S 67.30 W
Chilecito, Arg. 252 33.53 S 69.03 W
Chilengue, Serra do ⋏ 152 13.10 S 15.18 E
Chileno, Arroyo ≐, Ur. 258 33.55 S 58.08 W
Chileno, Arroyo ≐, Ur. 288 34.22 S 57.54 W
Chile Rise ✢3 18 40.00 S 90.00 W
Chilete 248 7.14 S 78.51 W
Chilham 42 51.15 N 0.57 E
Chilhowie 192 36.47 N 81.40 W
Chili 216 40.52 N 86.02 W
Chili → Chile □1 244 30.00 S 71.00 W
Chili ≐ 248 16.23 S 71.46 W
Chili, Ouadi V 146 16.44 N 20.53 E
Chilia, Braţul ≐1 78 45.18 N 29.40 E
Chili Center 210 43.06 N 77.44 W
Chilika Lake ◎ 122 19.45 N 85.25 E
Chililabombwe (Bancroft) 154 12.18 S 27.43 E
Chilin → Jilin 89 43.51 N 126.33 E
Chilingchang 107 28.58 N 105.31 E
Chilivani 71 40.36 N 8.56 E
Chilkat Pass)(180 59.43 N 136.35 W
Chilko ≐ 182 52.08 N 123.30 W
Chilko Lake ◎ 182 51.20 N 124.05 W
Chilko Lake Indian Reserve ✦4 182 51.25 N 124.07 W
Chillagoe 166 17.09 S 144.32 E
Chillán 252 36.36 S 72.07 W
Chillar 252 37.18 S 59.59 W
Chilla Saroda ✦8 272a 28.36 N 77.18 E
Chillicothe, Il., U.S. 190 40.55 N 89.29 W
Chillicothe, Mo., U.S. 194 39.47 N 93.33 W
Chillicothe, Oh., U.S. 218 39.19 N 82.58 W
Chillicothe, Tx., U.S. 196 34.15 N 99.30 W
Chilliwack 224 49.10 N 121.57 W
Chilliwack ≐ 224 49.05 N 121.57 W
Chilliwack Lake ◎ 224 49.03 N 121.25 W
Chillón 286d 11.55 S 77.05 W
Chillón ≐ 248 11.57 S 77.09 W
Chillon, Château de ⊥ 58 46.25 N 6.56 E
Chillum 284c 38.58 N 76.59 W
Chilly 84 39.25 N 49.05 E
Chilly-Mazarin 261 48.42 N 2.19 E
Chilmāri 124 25.33 N 89.43 E
Chilmark 207 41.20 N 70.44 W
Chilo 218 38.48 N 84.08 W
Chiloane, Ilha I 156 20.40 S 34.55 E
Chiloé, Isla Grande de I 254 42.30 S 73.55 W
Chilok 88 51.21 N 110.28 E
Chilok ≐ 88 51.19 N 106.59 E
Chilón 232 17.14 N 92.25 W
Chilonga 154 12.03 S 31.21 E
Chilongo 152 13.55 S 16.35 E
Chiloquin 202 42.34 N 121.51 W
Chilovo 76 57.46 N 29.23 E
Chilpancingo de los Bravo 234 17.33 N 99.30 W
Chilpi 124 22.15 N 81.33 E
Chilston Park ♦ 260 51.12 N 0.42 E
Chiltern □8 260 51.40 N 0.37 W
Chiltern Hills ⋏2 42 51.42 N 0.48 W
Chilton, Eng., U.K. 44 54.39 N 1.33 W
Chilton, Tx., U.S. 222 31.16 N 97.03 W
Chilton, Wi., U.S. 190 44.01 N 88.09 W
Chiluage 152 9.30 S 21.47 E
Chilubula Mission 154 10.09 S 31.00 E
Chilumba 154 10.28 S 34.12 E
Chilung 100 25.08 N 121.44 E
Chilung ≐ 269d 25.07 N 121.27 E
Chilung Kang ⊂ 269d 25.09 N 121.45 E
Chilung Shih □7 269d 25.08 N 121.45 E
Chiluvya 154 12.18 S 34.01 E
Chilwa, Lake ◎ 154 15.12 S 35.50 E
Chilwell 169 38.10 S 144.21 E
Chimaco 152 15.12 S 21.56 E
Chimacum 224 48.00 N 122.46 W
Chimacum Creek ≐ 224 48.03 N 122.45 W
Chimakela 152 15.24 S 16.58 E
Chimaltenango 236 14.40 N 90.49 W
Chimaltenango □5 236 14.40 N 90.55 W
Chimaltitán 234 21.46 N 103.50 W
Chimán 246 8.42 N 78.37 W
Chimanimani National Park ♦ 154 19.48 S 33.56 E
Chimay 50 50.03 N 4.19 E
Chimayo 200 36.00 N 105.55 W
Chimbarongo 252 34.42 S 71.03 W
Chimbas 252 31.29 S 68.32 W
Chimborazo □4 246 2.00 S 78.40 W
Chimborazo ∧ 236 13.05 N 85.58 W
Chimborazo ∧1 246 1.28 S 78.48 W
Chimbote 248 9.05 S 78.36 W
Chimbu □5 164 6.05 S 145.00 E
Chimbua 152 16.32 S 15.08 E
Ch'imei Yü I 100 23.13 N 119.26 E
Chimichagua 246 9.15 N 73.49 W
Chimkent → Čimkent 85 42.18 N 69.36 E
Chimki 82 55.54 N 37.26 E
Chimki-Chovrino ✦8 265b 55.51 N 37.30 E
Chimkinskoje vodochranilišče ◎1 265b 55.51 N 37.28 E
Chimney Reservoir ◎1 204 41.25 N 117.10 W
Chimney Rock National Historic Site ⊥ 198 41.39 N 103.20 W
Chimoio 156 19.08 S 33.29 E
Chimon Island I 276 41.04 N 73.23 W
Chimpay 252 39.10 S 66.09 W
Chimpembe 154 9.31 S 29.33 E
Chimpôro ≐ 152 17.20 S 17.17 E
Chin □8 110 22.00 N 93.30 E
China, Méx. 232 25.42 N 99.14 W
Chinā, Nihon 174m 26.24 N 127.46 E
China (Zhongguo) □1 90 35.00 N 105.00 E
China, Tanjong › 271c 1.14 N 103.51 E
Chinácota 246 7.37 N 72.36 W
China Grove 192 35.34 N 80.34 W
China Lake ◎ 204 35.46 N 117.39 W
China Lake Naval Weapons Center ■ 204 35.35 N 117.10 W
Chinameca 236 13.30 N 88.21 W
China Meridional, Mar de → South China Sea ⊤2 108 10.00 N 113.00 E
Chinan, Taehan 98 35.48 N 127.25 E
Chinan → Jinan, Zhg. 98 36.40 N 116.57 E
Chinandega 236 12.37 N 87.09 W
Chinandega □5 236 12.45 N 87.05 W
China Spring 222 31.39 N 97.18 W
Chinati Peak ∧ 196 29.57 N 104.29 W
Chinatown ✦8 282 37.48 N 122.26 W
Chincha Alta 248 13.27 S 76.08 W
Chinchaga ≐ 176 58.50 N 118.20 W
Chincheros 248 13.27 S 73.44 W
Chinchiang → Quanzhou 100 24.54 N 118.35 E
Chinchilla, Austl. 166 26.45 S 150.38 E
Chinchilla, Pa., U.S. 210 41.28 N 75.41 W
Chinchiná 246 4.58 N 75.36 W
Chincholi 272c 19.10 N 73.08 E
Chinchón, Esp. 34 40.08 N 3.25 W
Chinch'ŏn, Taehan 98 36.52 N 127.26 E
Chinchorro, Banco ✢4 232 18.35 N 87.22 W
Chinchou → Jinzhou 104 41.07 N 121.08 E
Chincilla de Monte Aragón 34 38.55 N 1.43 W
Chincolco 252 32.13 S 70.50 W
Chincoteague 208 37.55 N 75.22 W
Chincoteague Bay ⊂ 208 38.06 N 75.15 W
Chincoteague Inlet ⊂ 208 37.53 N 75.25 W
Chinde 156 18.37 S 36.24 E
Chindo 98 34.28 N 126.15 E
Chin-do I 98 34.25 N 126.15 E
Chindong 98 35.07 N 128.29 E
Chindwinn ≐ 110 21.26 N 95.15 E
Chine (la République populaire de) → China □1, Asia 90 35.00 N 105.00 E
Chine (nationaliste) → Taiwan □1, Asia 100 23.30 N 121.00 E
Chinen 174m 26.09 N 127.49 E
Chineni 123 33.02 N 75.17 E
Chine Orientale, Mer de → East China Sea ⊤2 90 30.00 N 126.00 E
Chinese Camp 226 37.52 N 120.26 W
Chinese Cemetery ✦ 269f 14.38 N 120.59 E
Chinese University ✿2 271d 22.26 N 114.12 E
Chingamba 152 12.49 S 18.20 E
Chingansk 89 49.07 N 131.11 E
Chingarora Creek ≐ 276 40.27 N 74.12 W
Ch'ingchiang → Qingjiang 100 33.35 N 119.02 E
Chingford ✦8 260 51.38 N 0.01 E
Chingleput 122 12.42 N 79.59 E
Chingmei ✦8 269d 24.59 N 121.32 E
Chingola 154 12.32 S 27.52 E
Chingoni 157a 12.48 S 45.08 E
Chingoroi 152 13.37 S 14.01 E
Chingshih → Jinshi 102 29.39 N 111.52 E
Ch'ingtao → Qingdao 98 36.06 N 120.19 E
Chingtechen → Jingdezhen 100 29.16 N 117.11 E
Ch'ingt'ung 269d 25.02 N 121.43 E
Chinguar 152 12.36 S 16.20 E
Chinguetti 150 20.27 N 12.22 W
Chingune 156 20.38 S 34.55 E
Chinhae 98 35.09 N 128.40 E
Chinhae-man ⊂ 98 35.01 N 128.34 E
Chin Hills ⋏2 110 22.30 N 93.30 E
Chinhoyi 154 17.22 S 30.12 E
Chinhsien → Jinxian 98 39.04 N 121.40 E
Chinhua → Jinhua 100 29.07 N 119.39 E
Ch'inhuangtao → Qinhuangdao 98 39.56 N 119.36 E
Chīni 120 31.32 N 78.15 E
Chiniak, Cape › 180 57.36 N 152.08 W
Chining → Jining, Zhg. 98 35.25 N 116.36 E
Chining → Jining, Zhg. 102 40.57 N 113.02 E
Chiniot 123 31.43 N 72.59 E
Chinit ≐ 110 12.55 N 105.35 E
Chinitna Point › 180 59.43 N 153.02 W
Chinizíua 156 19.00 S 35.09 E
Chinjan 120 30.34 N 67.58 E
Chinju 98 35.11 N 128.05 E
Chinkiang → Zhenjiang 106 32.13 N 119.26 E
Chinko ≐ 136 4.50 N 23.53 E
Chinkuashih 100 25.07 N 121.51 E
Chin Lakes ◎ 182 49.37 N 112.13 W
Chinle 200 36.09 N 109.33 W
Chinle Creek ≐ 200 37.12 N 109.43 W
Chinle Wash V 200 36.54 N 109.45 W
Chinley 262 53.20 N 1.56 W
Chinley Churn ∧2 262 53.21 N 1.57 W
Chinmen 100 24.27 N 118.21 E
Chinmen Tao I 100 24.27 N 118.23 E
Chinnampo → Namp'o 98 38.45 N 125.23 E
Chinnor 42 51.43 N 0.56 W
Chino, Nihon 94 35.59 N 138.09 E
Chino, Ca., U.S. 228 34.00 N 117.41 W
Chino Airport ⊠ 280 33.59 N 117.38 W
Chino Creek ≐ 280 33.53 N 117.38 W
Chino Hills ⋏2 280 33.56 N 117.45 W
Chinon 50 47.10 N 0.15 E
Chinook, Ab., Can. 184 51.27 N 110.56 W
Chinook, Mt., U.S. 202 48.35 N 109.13 W
Chinook, Wa., U.S. 224 46.16 N 123.56 W
Chinook Cove 182 51.14 N 120.10 W
Chino Valley 200 34.45 N 112.27 W
Chinowths Corner 226 36.20 N 119.19 W
Chinpāi 126 23.50 N 87.28 E
Chinquapin 192 34.49 N 77.49 W
Chinsali 154 10.34 S 32.03 E
Chinshan 100 25.13 N 121.38 E
Chinshui 100 24.36 N 120.53 E
Chintāmani 122 13.24 N 78.04 E
Chintembwe 154 13.25 S 33.59 E
Chintheche 154 11.52 S 34.09 E
Chinú 246 9.06 N 75.24 W
Chinunje 154 11.19 S 37.19 E
Chinwangtao → Qinhuangdao 98 39.56 N 119.36 E
Chiny 56 49.44 N 5.20 E
Chinyama Litapi 152 13.31 S 22.21 E
Chioco 154 16.25 S 32.50 E
Chioggia 64 45.13 N 12.17 E
Chiomonte 62 45.07 N 6.59 E
Chios → Khíos 38 38.22 N 26.08 E
Chios → Khíos I 38 38.22 N 26.00 E
Chipamanu (Xipamanu) ≐ 248 10.43 S 67.50 W
Chipao 248 14.15 S 73.57 W
Chipata (Fort Jameson) 154 13.39 S 32.40 E
Chipei Tao I 100 23.45 N 119.37 E
Chipera 154 15.28 S 32.30 E
Chiperone ∧ 154 16.28 S 35.12 E
Chipili 154 10.44 S 29.04 E
Chiping 98 36.37 N 116.16 E
Chipinge 154 20.12 S 32.38 E
Chip Lake ◎ 182 53.40 N 115.20 W
Chipley 194 30.46 N 85.32 W
Chiplūn 122 17.32 N 73.31 E
Chipman 186 46.11 N 65.53 W
Chipogolo 154 6.52 S 36.02 E
Chipoka 154 14.00 S 34.31 E
Chipola ≐ 192 30.01 N 85.05 W
Chippawa ✦8 284a 43.04 N 79.03 W
Chippawa Channel ≐1 284a 43.04 N 79.01 W
Chippego Lake ◎ 212 44.34 N 76.49 W
Chippenham 42 51.28 N 2.07 W
Chipperfield 260 51.42 N 0.29 W
Chippewa ≐, Mi., U.S. 190 43.35 N 84.17 W
Chippewa ≐, Mn., U.S. 198 44.56 N 95.44 W
Chippewa ≐, Wi., U.S. 190 44.25 N 92.10 W
Chippewa, East Branch ≐ 198 45.20 N 95.36 W
Chippewa, East Fork ≐ 190 45.53 N 91.05 W
Chippewa, Lake ◎ 190 45.56 N 91.13 W
Chippewa Bay ⊂ 212 44.27 N 75.47 W
Chippewa Creek ≐ 212 44.27 N 75.46 W
Chippewa Falls 190 44.56 N 91.23 W
Chippewa Lake 214 41.04 N 81.54 W
Chippewanuck Creek ≐ 216 41.07 N 86.12 W
Chipping Campden 42 52.03 N 1.46 W
Chipping Norton 42 51.56 N 1.32 W
Chipping Ongar 42 51.43 N 0.15 E
Chipping Sodbury 42 51.33 N 2.24 W
Chippis 58 46.17 N 7.33 E
Chippokes Plantation State Park ♦ 208 37.08 N 76.44 W
Chipps Island I 282 38.03 N 121.55 W
Chipre → Cyprus □1 130 35.00 N 33.00 E
Chipstead, Eng., U.K. 260 51.17 N 0.09 E
Chipstead, Eng., U.K. 260 51.18 N 0.10 W
Chipuriro 154 16.39 S 30.42 E
Chiquelequele 152 16.40 S 19.06 E
Chiquián 248 10.09 S 77.11 W
Chiquihuitlán 234 17.59 N 96.48 W
Chiquimula 236 14.48 N 89.33 W
Chiquimula □5 236 14.40 N 89.25 W
Chiquimulilla 236 14.05 N 90.23 W
Chiquinquirá 246 5.37 N 73.50 W
Chiquintirca 248 13.09 S 73.41 W
Chiquita 152 8.38 S 17.05 E
Chiquito ≐ 234 18.29 N 101.07 W
Chiquito Creek ≐ 226 37.20 N 119.20 W
Chira ≐ 246 4.54 S 81.08 W
Chira, Isla I 236 10.06 N 85.09 W
Chirad 272c 19.09 N 73.07 E
Chiradzulu 154 15.42 S 35.10 E
Chirāgh Delhi ✦8 272a 28.32 N 77.14 E
Chīrāla 122 15.49 N 80.21 E
Chiramba 154 16.55 S 34.39 E
Chirape 156 21.18 S 33.33 E
Chirāwa 120 28.15 N 75.38 E
Chirchik → Čirčik 85 41.29 N 69.35 E
Chire (Shire) ≐ 154 17.42 S 35.19 E
Chiredzi 154 21.03 S 31.45 E
Chireno 194 31.30 N 94.21 W
Chirens 62 45.25 N 5.33 E
Chirfa 146 20.57 N 12.21 E
Chīrgaon 124 25.35 N 78.49 E
Chiriaco ≐ 248 5.05 S 78.19 W
Chiricahua Mountains ⋏ 200 31.50 N 109.15 W
Chiricahua National Monument ♦ 200 32.02 N 109.19 W
Chiricahua Peak ∧ 200 31.52 N 109.20 W
Chiriguaná 246 9.22 N 73.36 W
Chirikof Island I 180 55.50 N 155.35 W
Chirilagua 236 13.13 N 88.08 W
Chirinos 248 5.16 S 78.52 W
Chiriquí 236 8.24 N 82.19 W
Chiriquí □4 236 8.30 N 82.00 W
Chiriquí, Golfo de ⊂ 246 8.00 N 82.20 W
Chiriquí, Laguna de ⊂ 236 9.03 N 82.00 W
Chiriquí Grande 236 8.57 N 82.07 W
Chiriquí Viejo ≐ 236 8.20 N 82.41 W
Chirk 42 52.56 N 3.03 W
Chirki 126 24.03 N 86.09 E
Chirle 272c 18.56 N 73.02 E
Chirmiri 124 23.12 N 82.21 E
Chirnside 46 55.48 N 2.13 W
Chiromo 154 16.33 S 35.08 E
Chirovo 76 58.56 N 33.24 E
Chirripó ≐ 236 10.41 N 83.41 W
Chirripó, Cerro ∧ 236 9.29 N 83.30 W
Chirripó, Parque Nacional ♦ 236 9.30 N 83.30 W
Chirsa 84 41.31 N 46.06 E
Chirundu 154 15.59 S 28.54 E
Chirvosti 265a 59.57 N 30.37 E
Chiryū 94 35.00 N 137.02 E
Chisago City 190 45.22 N 92.53 W
Chisamba 154 14.58 S 28.23 E
Chisana 180 62.09 N 142.10 W
Chisasibi 176 53.50 N 79.00 W
Chiscas 246 6.33 N 72.29 W
Chisec 236 15.49 N 90.17 W
Chiseldon 42 51.31 N 1.44 W
Chisenga 154 9.56 S 33.26 E
Chisep'o 98 34.50 N 128.42 E
Ch'ishan 100 22.53 N 120.28 E
Chishanji 98 36.56 N 122.23 E
Chishi 100 27.42 N 117.58 E
Chishisi 100 25.32 N 113.11 E
Chisholm, Al., U.S. 194 32.25 N 86.15 W
Chisholm, Me., U.S. 188 44.28 N 70.12 W
Chisholm, Mn., U.S. 190 47.29 N 92.53 W
Chisholm, Tx., U.S. 222 32.51 N 96.22 W
Chisholm Mills 182 54.55 N 114.08 W
Chishtiān Mandi 123 29.48 N 72.52 E
Chishui 102 28.29 N 105.38 E
Chishui ≐, Zhg. 102 28.53 N 105.48 E
Chishui ≐, Zhg. 107 28.49 N 105.50 E
Chishuihe 102 27.50 N 105.32 E
Chišig-Öndör 88 48.19 N 103.25 E
Chisimaio → Kismaayo 144 0.22 N 42.32 E
Chişinău → Kišin'ov 38 47.00 N 28.50 E
Chişineu-Criş 38 46.31 N 21.31 E
Chislaviči 76 54.11 N 32.10 E
Chislehurst ✦8 260 51.25 N 0.04 E
Chisone ≐ 62 44.49 N 7.25 E
Chisone, Valle del V 62 45.01 N 7.07 E
Chisos Mountains ⋏ 196 29.15 N 103.20 W
Chisseaux 50 47.20 N 1.05 E
Chissengue 152 9.14 S 20.42 E
Chissilo 152 13.34 S 16.30 E
Chistochina 180 62.34 N 144.40 W
Chistopol → Čistopol' 80 55.21 N 50.37 E
Chiswellgreen 260 51.44 N 0.22 W
Chiswick ✦8 260 51.29 N 0.16 W
Chita, Bol. 248 20.06 S 66.57 W
Chita, Col. 246 6.11 N 72.28 W
Chita, Nihon 94 35.00 N 136.51 E
Chita → Čita, Ross. 88 52.03 N 113.30 E
Chitado 152 17.20 S 13.54 E
Chitagá 246 7.09 N 72.40 W
Chita-hantō ›1 94 34.50 N 136.53 E
Chitambo 154 12.55 S 30.39 E
Chitanda ≐ 152 16.01 S 15.12 E
Chitarda 126 21.50 N 86.57 E
Chitata 152 13.47 S 15.43 E
Chitato 152 7.20 S 20.47 E
Chita-wan ⊂ 94 34.47 N 136.58 E
Chitek ≐ 184 54.06 N 108.16 W
Chitek Lake ◎, Mb., Can. 184 52.26 N 99.25 W
Chitek Lake ◎, Sk., Can. 184 53.44 N 107.47 W
Chitembo 152 13.34 S 16.40 E
Chitina 180 61.31 N 144.27 W
Chitina ≐ 180 61.30 N 144.28 W
Chitipa 154 9.43 S 33.16 E
Chitokoloki 152 13.50 S 23.13 E
Chitose 92a 42.49 N 141.39 E
Chitose-chūtonchi, Rikujō-jieitai- ■ 92a 42.46 N 141.40 E
Chitou Shan I 100 27.40 N 120.50 E
Chitra ≐1 126 22.53 N 89.40 E
Chitradurga 122 14.14 N 76.24 E
Chitrakūt Dham 124 25.11 N 80.52 E
Chitrāl 123 35.51 N 71.47 E
Chitrasāli 272b 22.52 N 88.09 E
Chitrāvati ≐ 122 14.48 N 78.14 E
Chitré 236 7.58 N 80.26 W
Chittagong 120 22.20 N 91.50 E
Chittagong □5 120 23.00 N 91.00 E
Chīttāpur 122 17.07 N 77.05 E
Chittaranjan 126 23.52 N 86.52 E
Chittaurgarh 120 24.53 N 74.38 E
Chittenango 210 43.02 N 75.52 W
Chittenango Creek ≐ 210 43.11 N 76.00 W
Chittenango Falls 210 42.59 N 75.50 W
Chittering 162 31.29 S 116.06 E
Chittoor 122 13.12 N 79.07 E
Chittūr 122 10.42 N 76.45 E
Chitu, Ityo. 144 8.36 N 37.59 E
Ch'itu, T'aiwan 269d 25.06 N 121.43 E
Chitungwiza 154 17.45 S 31.16 E
Chiuchiang → Jiujiang 100 29.44 N 115.59 E
Chíuchíu 252 22.21 S 68.39 W
Chiuduno 62 45.40 N 9.51 E
Chiumbe 152 12.29 S 16.08 E
Chiumbe ≐ 152 7.00 S 21.12 E
Chiúme 152 15.03 S 21.14 E
Chiuppano 64 45.46 N 11.28 E
Chiuro 64 46.10 N 9.59 E
Chiusa (Klausen) 64 46.38 N 11.34 E
Chiusa di Pesio 62 44.19 N 7.40 E
Chiusa di San Michele 62 45.06 N 7.19 E
Chiusaforte 64 46.24 N 13.18 E
Chiusa Sclafani 70 37.41 N 13.16 E
Chiusella ≐ 62 45.24 N 7.55 E
Chiusi 66 43.01 N 11.57 E
Chiusi, Lago di ◎ 66 43.03 N 11.58 E
Chiúta 154 15.34 S 33.17 E
Chiuta, Lake ◎ 154 14.55 S 35.50 E
Chiv 84 41.46 N 47.54 E
Chiva 72 41.24 N 60.22 E
Chivacoa 246 10.10 N 68.54 W
Chivasso 62 45.11 N 7.53 E
Chivato, Punta › 232 27.05 N 111.59 W
Chivay 248 15.40 S 71.35 W
Chivhu 154 19.01 S 30.53 E
Chivilcoy 252 34.53 S 60.01 W
Chivirira Falls ∟ 154 21.14 S 32.20 E
Chiwanda 154 11.22 S 34.54 E
Chiwawa ≐ 224 47.47 N 120.40 W
Chixi 100 28.22 N 116.22 E
Chixoy (Salinas) ≐ 232 16.28 N 90.33 W
Chixoy, Embalse ◎1 236 15.15 N 90.30 W
Chiyoda, Nihon 94 36.12 N 139.26 E
Chiyoda, Nihon 94 36.11 N 140.14 E
Chiyoda, Nihon 96 34.41 N 132.32 E
Chiyoda ✦8 268 35.41 N 139.44 E
Chizarira National Park ♦ 154 17.45 S 28.00 E
Chizhen 100 31.55 N 118.12 E
Chizizhen 100 32.22 N 115.11 E
Chizu 96 35.16 N 134.14 E
Chjargas 88 49.32 N 93.48 E
Chjargas nuur ◎ 88 49.12 N 93.24 E
Chkalov → Orenburg 86 51.54 N 55.06 E
Chlebnikovo, Ross. 80 56.38 N 49.56 E
Chlebnikovo, Ross. 265b 55.58 N 37.31 E
Chlebodarnyj 80 46.41 N 40.50 E
Chlebodarovka 83 47.29 N 37.23 E
Chlevnoje 76 52.12 N 39.05 E
Chloride 200 35.24 N 114.11 W
Chlum 60 48.52 N 13.55 E
Chlum ∧ 61 48.42 N 14.04 E
Chmelevicy 80 57.45 N 46.22 E
Chmelevo 82 56.09 N 39.08 E
Chmelevoje 78 48.34 N 31.24 E
Chmelita 76 55.25 N 33.53 E
Chmel'nickij 78 49.25 N 27.00 E
Chmel'nickij □4 78 49.30 N 27.00 E
Chmel'nik 78 49.33 N 27.57 E
Chmel'niki, Ross. 82 56.52 N 38.13 E
Chmel'niki, Ross. 82 56.53 N 38.39 E
Chmielnik 30 50.37 N 20.46 E
Chmost' ≐ 76 54.45 N 32.34 E
Choa Chu Kang 271c 1.22 N 103.41 E
Choāli 272b 22.24 N 88.24 E
Chŏâm Khsant 110 14.13 N 104.56 E
Choba 154 2.26 N 38.03 E
Chobe □5 156 18.30 S 25.00 E
Chobe ≐ 156 17.50 S 25.05 E
Chobeju 24 64.53 N 60.10 E
Chobe National Park ♦ 156 18.45 S 24.15 E
Chobham 260 51.21 N 0.36 W
Chobham Common ♦ 260 51.23 N 0.37 W
Chobi 84 42.21 N 41.53 E
Chocamán 234 18.59 N 97.01 W
Choccolocco Creek ≐ 194 33.33 N 86.11 W
Choceň 30 50.00 N 16.13 E
Chocenice 60 49.33 N 13.31 E
Chochis, Cerro ∧ 248 18.04 S 60.03 W
Choch'iwŏn 98 36.37 N 127.18 E
Chochloma 80 56.58 N 43.54 E
Chöchmor't 88 47.21 N 94.33 E
Chochol'skij 78 51.34 N 38.45 E
Cho Chu 110 21.54 N 105.39 E
Chocianów 30 51.25 N 15.55 E
Chociwel 30 53.28 N 15.19 E
Chocó □5 246 6.00 N 77.00 W
Chocolate Bay ⊂ 222 29.11 N 95.09 W
Chocolate Bayou ≐ 222 29.13 N 95.13 W
Chocolate Mountains ⋏ 204 33.20 N 115.15 W
Chocontá 246 5.09 N 73.41 W
Chocope 248 7.47 S 79.13 W
Choctawhatchee, East Fork ≐ 194 31.21 N 85.33 W
Choctawhatchee, West Fork ≐ 194 31.21 N 85.33 W
Choctawhatchee Bay ⊂ 194 30.25 N 86.21 W
Choctaw Lake ◎1 218 39.58 N 83.29 W
Chodarus 88 52.36 N 99.19 E
Chodavaram 122 17.50 N 82.57 E
Chodecz 30 52.24 N 19.01 E
Ch'o-do I, C.M.I.K. 98 38.32 N 124.50 E
Ch'o-do I, Taehan 98 34.14 N 127.15 E
Chodoi 114 2.50 N 101.27 E
Chodorov 78 49.24 N 24.17 E
Chodosy 76 53.56 N 31.29 E
Chodov 54 50.11 N 12.43 E
Chodovaja Griva 80 57.08 N 50.16 E

ENGLISH

Name Page Lat.°′ Long.°′
Chodovaricha 24 68.57 N 53.40 E
Chodz' ≐ 84 44.43 N 40.45 E
Chodžaimetk 85 39.37 N 69.14 E
Chodžakala 128 38.43 N 56.20 E
Chodžejli 72 42.48 N 59.25 E
Chodzież 30 52.59 N 16.56 E
Choele-Choel 252 39.16 S 65.41 W
Chofombo 154 14.35 S 31.50 E
Chōfu 94 35.39 N 139.33 E
Chofu Airport ⊠ 268 35.40 N 139.32 E
Chogo Lungma Glacier ⊓ 123 35.52 N 75.19 E
Chogot 88 53.15 N 105.52 E
Choiceland 184 53.27 N 104.25 W
Choichuff, Laga ≐ 154 1.34 N 39.24 E
Choire, Loch ◎ 46 58.13 N 4.21 W
Choisel 261 48.41 N 2.01 E
Choiseul 241f 13.47 N 61.03 W
Choiseul I 175e 7.05 S 157.00 E
Choiseul Sound ʮ 254 51.57 S 58.35 W
Choisy 58 45.59 N 6.03 E
Choisy-le-Roi 261 48.46 N 2.25 E
Choix 232 26.43 N 108.17 W
Chojna 30 52.58 N 14.28 E
Chojnice 30 53.42 N 17.34 E
Chojniki 78 51.53 N 29.56 E
Chojnów 30 51.17 N 15.56 E
Chōkai-san ∧ 92 39.06 N 140.03 E
Choke ⋏ 144 10.45 N 37.35 E
Choke Canyon Lake ◎1 196 28.30 N 98.20 W
Chokio 198 45.34 N 96.10 W
Chokoloskee 220 25.48 N 81.21 W
Chokwé 156 24.36 S 33.00 E
Cholame 226 35.43 N 120.17 W
Cholame Creek ≐ 226 35.39 N 120.22 W
Cholame Hills ⋏2 226 35.45 N 120.30 W
Cholbon 88 51.53 N 116.15 E
Choldarkipčak 85 39.51 N 68.52 E
Cholet 32 47.04 N 0.53 W
Cholila 254 42.31 S 71.27 W
Chŏlla Namdo □4 98 34.45 N 127.00 E
Chŏlla Pukdo □4 98 35.45 N 127.15 E
Cholm 76 57.09 N 31.11 E
Cholmeč', Bela. 78 52.09 N 30.37 E
Cholmec, Ross. 76 56.21 N 33.21 E
Cholmogorovka 86 44.25 N 78.31 E
Cholmogorskaja 24 63.49 N 40.39 E
Cholmogory 24 64.15 N 41.40 E
Cholmsk 89 47.03 N 142.03 E
Cholmskij 78 44.52 N 38.24 E
Cholmy, Ross. 82 54.56 N 38.33 E
Cholmy, Ukr. 78 51.52 N 32.36 E
Cholm-Žirkovskij 76 55.31 N 33.29 E
Cholodnaja Balka 83 48.02 N 38.04 E
Choloj ≐ 88 53.12 N 112.47 E
Choloma 236 15.34 N 87.56 W
Chölönbujr 88 47.55 N 112.57 E
Cholopeniči 76 54.31 N 28.58 E
Ch'ŏlsan 98 39.46 N 124.40 E
Cholsey 42 51.34 N 1.10 W
Choltobino 82 54.11 N 38.28 E
Choltoson 88 50.20 N 103.20 E
Choluj, Ross. 80 56.34 N 41.53 E
Choluj, Ross. 80 56.04 N 42.08 E
Cholula [de Rivadabia] 234 19.04 N 98.18 W
Choluteca 236 13.18 N 87.12 W
Choluteca □5 236 13.20 N 87.10 W
Choluteca ≐ 236 13.07 N 87.19 W
Choma 154 16.48 S 26.59 E
Chomedey ✦8 275a 45.32 N 73.44 W
Chomen Swamp ≋ 144 9.25 N 37.20 E
Chomérac 62 44.42 N 4.39 E
Chomičev 80 48.11 N 45.01 E
Chomiomo ∧ 124 28.01 N 88.31 E
Cho Moi, Viet 110 10.33 N 105.24 E
Cho Moi, Viet 269c 10.51 N 106.38 E
Chomo Lhāri ∧ 124 27.50 N 89.15 E
Chom Thong 110 18.25 N 98.41 E
Chomūm 120 27.10 N 75.44 E
Chomutec 78 50.06 N 33.44 E
Chomutov 54 50.28 N 13.26 E
Chomutovka 78 51.56 N 34.33 E
Chomutovka ≐ 54 50.11 N 13.37 E
Chomutovo, Ross. 76 52.51 N 37.27 E
Chomutovo, Ross. 88 52.28 N 104.25 E
Chomutovskaja 83 47.03 N 40.04 E
Chomutovskaja Step', zapovednik ♦ 83 47.17 N 38.11 E
Chōnan, Nihon 94 35.24 N 140.14 E
Ch'ŏnan, Taehan 98 36.48 N 127.09 E
Chon'atino 82 55.11 N 38.07 E
Chon Buri 110 13.22 N 100.59 E
Chonchi 254 42.38 S 73.47 W
Choncholoj 88 51.08 N 108.14 E
Chon Daen 110 16.11 N 100.51 E
Chone 246 0.41 S 80.06 W
Chone ≐ 246 0.35 S 80.25 W
Chong'an 100 27.45 N 118.02 E
Ch'ŏngch'ŏn-gang ≐ 98 39.35 N 125.28 E
Ch'ŏngdan 98 37.58 N 125.56 E
Chongde 106 30.32 N 120.26 E
Ch'ŏngdo 98 35.38 N 128.43 E
Chonggu 106 31.12 N 121.10 E
Ch'ŏngha 98 36.13 N 129.20 E
Ch'onghak-ni 271b 37.43 N 127.05 E
Chonghe 89 44.43 N 127.45 E
Ch'ŏngjin 98 41.47 N 129.50 E
Chŏngju, C.M.I.K. 98 39.41 N 125.13 E
Ch'ŏngju, Taehan 98 36.39 N 127.31 E
Chŏng Kal 110 13.57 N 103.35 E
Chongkanzhen 107 30.09 N 105.37 E
Chongli (Xiwanzi) 98 40.54 N 115.16 E
Chongming 106 31.37 N 121.24 E
Chongming Dao I 106 31.36 N 121.33 E
Chongoene 156 25.00 S 33.47 E
Chongor 102 45.59 N 112.45 E
Chongos Bajo 248 12.07 S 75.16 W
Chongoyape 248 6.39 S 79.24 W
Chong Pang 271c 1.26 N 103.50 E
Chŏngp'yŏng-chŏsuji ◎1 98 37.40 N 127.30 E
Chongqing, Zhg. 107 30.39 N 103.41 E
Chongqing (Chungking), Zhg. 107 29.34 N 106.35 E
Chongren, Zhg. 100 29.37 N 120.43 E
Chongren, Zhg. 100 27.46 N 116.01 E
Chongru 100 27.01 N 120.10 E
Ch'ŏngsan 98 36.22 N 127.46 E
Ch'ŏngsan-do I 98 34.11 N 126.54 E
Chongshi 100 25.24 N 115.28 E
Chŏngsŏn 98 37.22 N 128.38 E
Ch'ŏngsong 98 41.47 N 129.48 E
Chŏngŭp 98 35.36 N 126.51 E
Chongwe ≐ 154 15.43 S 29.20 E
Chongwu 100 24.53 N 118.55 E
Chongxi 98 42.07 N 128.59 E
Chongxin 102 35.13 N 107.29 E
Ch'ŏngyang, Taehan 98 36.27 N 126.48 E
Chongyang, Zhg. 100 29.33 N 114.00 E
Chongyang ≐ 100 27.18 N 118.08 E
Chongyi 100 25.44 N 114.18 E
Chongzuo 102 22.21 N 107.26 E
Choni 84 42.20 N 42.25 E
Chŏnju 98 35.49 N 127.08 E
Chonkham 120 27.48 N 96.02 E
Ch'ŏnma 98 40.03 N 125.01 E
Chonobad 85 40.48 N 72.58 E
Chonos, Archipiélago de los II 254 45.00 S 74.00 W
Ch'ŏnsu-ri 98 41.43 N 128.45 E
Chontaleña, Cordillera ⋏ 236 11.50 N 84.50 W
Chontales □5 236 12.05 N 85.10 W
Chon Thanh 110 11.24 N 106.36 E
Chŏnŭi 98 36.42 N 127.11 E
Chonuu 74 66.27 N 143.06 E
Chonzie, Ben ∧ 46 56.27 N 3.59 W

DEUTSCH

Name Seite Breite°′ Länge°′ E = Ost
Cho Oyu → Chopu ∧ 124 28.06 N 86.39 E
Chopda 120 21.15 N 75.18 E
Cho Phuoc Hai 110 10.26 N 107.18 E
Chopim ≐ 252 25.35 S 53.05 W
Chopinzinho 252 25.51 S 52.30 W
Chopon 124 24.31 N 83.02 E
Chop'or ≐ 80 49.36 N 42.19 E
Chop'orskij zapovednik ✦4 80 51.15 N 41.48 E
Choptank ≐ 208 38.38 N 76.13 W
Chopu ∧ 124 28.06 N 86.39 E
Chopwell 44 54.55 N 1.49 W
Chor 89 47.53 N 134.58 E
Chor ≐ 89 47.48 N 134.43 E
Chora Saādatpur 272a 28.36 N 77.21 E
Chordil sar'dag ⋏ 88 50.50 N 99.40 E
Chorejver 24 67.25 N 58.03 E
Chorges 62 44.33 N 6.17 E
Chorin ⊥ 54 52.54 N 13.52 E
Chorina ≐ 83 49.23 N 38.13 E
Chorinsk 88 52.10 N 109.46 E
Chorley 44 53.39 N 2.39 W
Chorley □8 262 53.38 N 2.38 W
Chorleywood 260 51.39 N 0.31 W
Chorlovo 82 55.20 N 38.49 E
Chorlton-cum-Hardy ✦8 262 53.27 N 2.17 W
Chorog 120 37.31 N 71.33 E
Chorol', Ross. 89 44.25 N 132.04 E
Chorol, Ukr. 78 49.47 N 33.17 E
Chorol ≐ 78 49.28 N 33.47 E
Chorolque, Cerro ∧ 248 20.56 S 66.01 W
Choros, Isla I 252 29.16 S 71.33 W
Chorošovo 82 55.08 N 38.47 E
Chorošovo ✦8 265b 55.47 N 37.28 E
Chorostkov 78 49.13 N 25.55 E
Choroszcz 30 53.09 N 22.59 E
Chorreras 232 28.50 N 105.18 W
Chorrillos 286d 12.10 S 77.02 W
Chorrochó 250 8.59 S 39.06 W
Chorro Creek ≐ 226 35.20 N 120.50 W
Chort'ak, gora ∧ 88 53.15 N 110.45 E
Ch'ŏrwŏn 98 38.16 N 127.12 E
Chorzele 30 53.16 N 20.55 E
Ch'osan 98 40.50 N 125.47 E
Chosanch'am 98 40.22 N 126.11 E
Chosedachard 24 67.02 N 59.22 E
Chosen 220 26.42 N 80.41 W
Chošeutovo 80 47.02 N 47.50 E
Chōshi 94 35.44 N 140.50 E
Choshi-ōhashi ✦5 94 35.44 N 140.50 E
Chōshi-zuka-kofun ⊥ 94 34.42 N 137.50 E
Choshui ≐ 100 24.03 N 120.24 E
Chosica 248 11.54 S 76.42 W
Chos Malal 252 37.23 S 70.16 W
Chosŏn Minjujuŭi In'min Konghwaguk → Korea, North □1 98 40.00 N 127.00 E
Chosrech 84 41.59 N 47.18 E
Chosta 84 43.33 N 39.53 E
Choszczno 30 53.10 N 15.26 E
Chota 248 6.33 S 78.39 W
Chotanāgpur Plateau ⋏1 124 23.30 N 84.30 E
Chotča ≐ 82 56.54 N 37.35 E
Choteau 202 47.48 N 112.10 W
Choteau Creek ≐ 198 42.51 N 98.09 W
Chotěboř 30 49.43 N 15.40 E
Choten' 78 51.07 N 34.46 E
Chotěšov, Česká Rep. 60 49.39 N 13.12 E
Chotešov, Ukr. 78 51.43 N 24.47 E
Chotila 120 22.25 N 71.11 E
Chotilovo 76 57.44 N 34.05 E
Chotimsk 76 53.26 N 32.35 E
Chotin 78 48.29 N 26.30 E
Chotisino 82 54.24 N 36.33 E
Chot'kovo, Ross. 76 53.46 N 35.14 E
Chot'kovo, Ross. 76 52.56 N 35.23 E
Chot'kovo, Ross. 82 56.15 N 38.00 E
Chotovn'a 76 53.17 N 30.32 E
Chotuš' 82 54.32 N 37.44 E
Chotynec 76 53.08 N 35.24 E
Chotyniči 76 52.38 N 26.18 E
Chouchiak'ou → Shangshui 100 33.33 N 114.34 E
Chouk'ou → Shangshui 100 33.33 N 114.34 E
Choûm 148 21.18 N 13.01 W
Chouteau 196 36.11 N 95.20 W
Chovaling 85 38.21 N 69.58 E
Chovd, Mong. 86 49.16 N 90.55 E
Chovd, Mong. 86 48.08 N 91.23 E
Chovd, Mong. 86 48.01 N 91.38 E
Chovd, Mong. 102 44.42 N 102.24 E
Chovd □4 86 48.00 N 91.30 E
Chovd ≐ 90 48.06 N 92.11 E
Chövsgöl 102 43.36 N 109.39 E
Chövsgöl □4 88 50.00 N 100.00 E
Chövsgöl nuur ◎ 88 51.00 N 100.30 E
Chovu-Aksy 88 51.11 N 93.53 E
Chowan ≐ 192 36.00 N 76.40 W
Chowchilla 226 37.07 N 120.15 W
Chowchilla ≐ 226 37.07 N 120.32 W
Chowchilla, East Fork ≐ 226 37.20 N 119.50 W
Chowchilla, West Fork ≐ 226 37.20 N 119.50 W
Chowkay 123 34.41 N 70.56 E
Chown, Mount ∧ 182 53.24 N 119.22 W
Ch'owŏn-ni 98 39.40 N 127.17 E
Choya 252 28.30 S 64.52 W
Choyak-to I 98 34.22 N 126.54 E
Chrapun' 78 51.42 N 27.29 E
Chr'aščevka 80 53.48 N 49.06 E
Chrást 60 49.48 N 13.29 E
Chrebtovo 82 56.35 N 38.16 E
Chrenovoje 80 51.07 N 40.17 E
Chreščatij 83 49.37 N 39.42 E
Chřibská 54 50.50 N 14.29 E
Chříč 60 49.57 N 13.39 E
Chriesman 222 30.36 N 96.46 W
Chrisman 194 39.48 N 87.40 W
Chrissiesmeer 158 26.16 S 30.13 E
Chrissiesmeer ◎ 158 26.19 S 30.13 E
Christanshåb (Qasigiannguit) 176 68.50 N 51.12 W
Christchurch, N.Z. 172 43.32 S 172.38 E
Christchurch, Eng., U.K. 42 50.44 N 1.45 W
Christ Church Cathedral ✿1 273a 6.27 N 3.23 E
Christian □6 219 39.33 N 89.18 W
Christian ≐ 180 66.36 N 145.49 W
Christian, Cape › 176 70.31 N 68.18 W
Christian, Point › 174e 25.04 S 130.07 W
Christiana, Jam. 241q 18.10 N 77.29 W
Christiana, S. Afr. 158 27.52 S 25.08 E
Christiana, De., U.S. 285 39.39 N 75.39 W
Christiana, Pa., U.S. 208 39.57 N 75.59 W
Christiana Creek ≐ 216 41.41 N 85.59 W
Christianburg 218 38.17 N 85.06 W
Christian Channel ʮ 212 44.47 N 80.08 W
Christian Island I 212 44.50 N 80.13 W
Christian Island Indian Reserve ✦4 212 44.50 N 80.10 W
Christiansburg, Oh., U.S. 218 40.03 N 84.01 W
Christiansburg, Va., U.S. 192 37.07 N 80.24 W
Christiansfeld 41 55.21 N 9.29 E
Christiansø I 26 55.19 N 15.12 E
Christian Sound ʮ 180 55.56 N 134.40 W
Christiansted 241n 17.45 N 64.42 W
Christie, Mount ∧ 180 63.01 N 129.40 W
Christie, Mount ∧2 216 42.53 N 83.20 W
Christie Bay ⊂ 176 62.32 N 111.10 W
Christie Lake ◎, Mb., Can. 184 56.54 N 96.56 W

Symbols in the index entries represent the broad categories identified in the key at the right. Symbols with superior numbers (⋏1) identify subcategories (see complete key on page *I · 1).*

Symbole im Register stellen die rechts im Schlüssel erklärten Kategorien dar. Symbole mit hochgestellten Ziffern (⋏1) bezeichnen Unterabteilungen einer Kategorie (vgl. vollständiger Schlüssel auf Seite *I · 1).*

Los símbolos incluídos en el texto del índice representan las grandes categorías identificadas con la clave a la derecha. Los símbolos con numeros en su parte superior (⋏1) identifican las subcategorías (véase la clave completa en la página *I · 1).*

Les symboles de l'index représentent les catégories indiquées dans la légende à droite. Les symboles suivis d'un indice (⋏1) représentent des sous-catégories (voir légende complète à la page *I · 1).*

Os símbolos incluídos no texto do índice representam as grandes categorias identificadas com a chave à direita. Os símbolos com números em sua parte superior (⋏1) identificam as subcategorias (veja-se a chave completa à página *I · 1).*

∧ Mountain	Berg	Montaña	Montagne	Montanha
⋏ Mountains	Gebirge	Montañas	Montagnes	Montanhas
)(Pass	Paß	Paso	Col	Passo
V Valley, Canyon	Tal, Cañon	Valle, Cañón	Vallée, Canyon	Vale, Canhão
≃ Plain	Ebene	Llano	Plaine	Planície
› Cape	Kap	Cabo	Cap	Cabo
I Island	Insel	Isla	Île	Ilha
II Islands	Inseln	Islas	Îles	Ilhas
± Other Topographic Features	Andere Topographische Objekte	Otros Elementos Topográficos	Autres données topographiques	Outros acidentes topográficos

Chri-Clar I · 37

ESPAÑOL Nombre	Página	Lat.°′	Long.°′ W = Oeste
Christie Lake ⊜, On., Can.	212	44.48 N	76.26 W
Christina ≃, Ab., Can.	184	56.40 N	111.03 W
Christina ≃, De., U.S.	285	39.43 N	75.31 W
Christina Lake ⊜, Ab., Can.	182	55.38 N	110.55 W
Christina Lake ⊜, B.C., Can.	182	49.05 N	118.14 W
Christinovka	78	48.49 N	29.58 E
Christišče	83	48.55 N	37.30 E
Christmas	220	28.32 N	81.01 W
Christmas Bay ⊂	222	29.03 N	95.11 W
Christmas Creek	162	18.53 S	125.55 E
Christmas Creek ≃	162	18.29 S	125.23 E
Christmas Island □[2], Oc.	108	10.30 S	105.40 E
Christmas Island □[2], Oc.	112	10.30 S	105.40 E
Christmas Island → Kiritimati I[1]	174o	1.52 N	157.20 W
Christmas Mountain ∧	180	64.34 N	160.34 W
Christmas Ridge ✦[3]	14	5.00 N	160.00 W
Christoforovka	78	47.59 N	33.05 E
Christoforovo	24	60.53 N	47.13 E
Christ of the Andes → Cristo Redentor ⊥	252	32.50 S	70.05 W
Christoph Columbus-Spitze → Cristóbal Colón, Pico ∧	246	10.50 N	73.41 W
Christopher	194	37.58 N	89.03 W
Christopher, Lake ⊜	162	24.49 S	127.42 E
Christoval	196	31.12 N	100.30 W
Chroma ≃	74	71.36 N	144.49 E
Chromtau	86	50.17 N	58.27 E
Chrudim	30	49.57 N	15.48 E
Chrustal'nyj	89	44.24 N	135.06 E
Chrzanów	30	50.09 N	19.24 E
Chu (Xam) ≃, Asia	110	19.53 N	105.45 E
Chu ≃, Zhg.	100	32.08 N	118.43 E
Chu ≃, Zhg.	106	32.15 N	119.03 E
Chuādanga	124	23.38 N	88.51 E
Chualar	226	36.34 N	121.31 W
Chuanbu	106	31.17 N	119.49 E
Chuanchang ≅	100	33.46 N	119.51 E
Chuanergu	105	39.20 N	117.43 E
Chuan'gang	106	31.57 N	121.04 E
Chuangjiaozi	104	40.50 N	124.06 E
Chuanliao	100	28.17 N	120.13 E
Chuansha	106	31.12 N	121.42 E
Chuanshan	100	29.53 N	121.57 E
Chuanxindian	104	41.25 N	120.30 E
Chuanyao Gang ⊂	106	32.12 N	121.25 E
Chuathbaluk	180	61.40 N	159.15 W
Chubbuck	202	42.55 N	112.27 W
Chūbu-Sangaku-kokuritsu-kōen ♠	94	36.30 N	137.41 E
Chubut □[4]	254	44.00 S	69.00 W
Chubut ≃	254	43.20 S	65.03 W
Ch'üchiang → Shaoguan	100	24.50 N	113.37 E
Chuchi Lake ⊜	182	55.10 N	124.33 W
Chuchou → Zhuzhou	100	27.50 N	113.09 E
Chuchra	78	50.13 N	34.49 E
Chu Chua	182	51.21 N	120.10 W
Chuchuwayha Indian Reserve ➛[4]	182	49.21 N	120.06 W
Chuckatuck	208	36.52 N	76.35 W
Chučni	84	41.57 N	47.55 E
Chucuito	248	15.53 S	69.53 W
Chucun	100	33.04 N	116.32 E
Chucunaque ≃	246	8.09 N	77.44 W
Chudan ≃	88	52.08 N	109.40 E
Chudanskij chrebet ⋀	88	52.00 N	110.00 E
Chudat	84	41.38 N	48.42 E
Chudeč	60	49.58 N	13.05 E
Chudleigh	42	50.36 N	3.38 W
Chudojelan'	88	54.42 N	99.37 E
Chudžand (Leninabad)	85	40.17 N	69.37 E
Chudžand □[4]	85	39.15 N	69.30 E
Chudzirt	86	47.05 N	91.10 E
Chuen Lung	271d	22.24 N	114.06 E
Chugach Islands II	180	59.06 N	151.42 W
Chugach Mountains ⋀	180	61.00 N	145.00 W
Chuginadak Island I	180	52.49 N	169.50 W
Chūgoku-sanchi ⋀	96	34.58 N	132.57 E
Chugwater	200	41.45 N	104.49 W
Chugwater Creek ≃	198	42.07 N	104.51 W
Chugyn-ri	271b	37.39 N	126.50 E
Chūhar Kāna	123	31.45 N	73.48 E
Chuhe	100	34.03 N	113.35 E
Chuhuichupa	232	29.38 N	108.22 W
Chuí	252	33.41 S	53.27 W
Chuius Mountain ∧	182	54.51 N	124.30 W
Chukai	114	4.15 N	103.25 E
Chukchi Sea ⫪[2]	16	69.00 N	171.00 W
Chuke Hu ⊜	120	31.40 N	88.00 E
Chukou	100	25.44 N	113.22 E
Chulalongkorn University ʊ[2]	269a	13.44 N	100.33 E
Chula Vista	228	32.38 N	117.05 W
Chuld	102	45.04 N	105.35 E
Chulga ≃	24	64.20 N	61.00 E
Chullora	274a	33.54 S	151.04 E
Chulmleigh	42	50.55 N	3.52 W
Chulo	84	41.41 N	42.18 E
Chulp'o	98	35.37 N	126.40 E
Chulucanas	248	5.06 S	80.10 W
Chulumani	248	16.24 S	67.31 W
Chuluota	220	28.38 N	81.10 W
Chuma	248	15.24 S	68.56 W
Chumalag	84	43.14 N	44.28 E
Chumbicha	252	28.52 S	66.14 W
Chummi, ozero ⊜	89	50.18 N	137.17 E
Chum Phae	110	16.32 N	102.06 E
Chumphon	110	10.30 N	99.10 E
Chumphon Buri	110	15.21 N	103.24 E
Chumpi	248	15.06 S	73.46 W
Chum Saeng	110	15.54 N	100.19 E
Chumunjin	98	37.54 N	128.49 E
Chunal	262	53.25 N	1.57 W
Chunan, T'aiwan	100	24.41 N	120.52 E
Chun'an, Zhg.	100	29.35 N	118.58 E
Chunār	124	25.08 N	82.54 E
Chuncheon → Ch'unch'ŏn	98	37.52 N	127.43 E
Chunchi, Ec.	246	2.17 S	78.55 W
Chunchi, Zhg.	100	27.22 N	119.20 E
Ch'unch'ŏn	98	37.52 N	127.43 E
Chunchula	194	30.55 N	88.12 W
Chūnd	123	31.26 N	72.16 E
Chung-ang University ʊ[2]	271b	37.30 N	126.58 E
Chungari ≃	89	50.04 N	136.55 E
Ch'ungch'ŏng Namdo □[4]	98	36.30 N	127.00 E
Ch'ungch'ŏng Pukdo □[4]	98	36.45 N	128.00 E
Chunggang-ni	98	40.52 N	127.20 E
Chung Hau	271d	22.16 N	114.00 E
Chungho	269d	25.00 N	121.30 E
Chung Hsing Bridge ➛[5]	269d	25.03 N	121.29 E
Chunghwa	98	38.52 N	125.47 E
Ch'ungju	98	36.58 N	127.58 E
Chungking → Chongqing	107	29.34 N	106.35 E
Chungli	100	24.57 N	121.13 E
Chungliao	100	22.41 N	121.28 E
Ch'ungmu	98	34.51 N	128.25 E
Chungp'u	100	23.25 N	120.31 E
Chungp'yŏngjang	98	41.11 N	128.03 E
Chungsam-ni	98	38.34 N	127.09 E
Chŭngsan	98	39.06 N	125.22 E

FRANÇAIS Nom	Page	Lat.°′	Long.°′ W = Ouest
Chŭngsanha-ri ➛[8]	271b	37.35 N	126.54 E
Chungshan → Zhongshan	100	22.31 N	113.22 E
Chungshan Bridge ➛[5]	269d	25.05 N	121.31 E
Chunguj ≃	88	48.51 N	93.32 E
Chungyang Shanmo ⋀	100	23.30 N	121.00 E
Chunheji	100	32.12 N	115.22 E
Chunhua, Zhg.	102	34.50 N	108.31 E
Chunhua, Zhg.	106	31.56 N	118.56 E
Chunhuhux	232	19.12 N	88.55 W
Chūniān	123	30.58 N	73.59 E
Chuntuquí	232	17.31 N	90.09 W
Chünüj ≃	88	48.48 N	102.00 E
Chunya	154	8.32 S	33.25 E
Ch'unyang, Taehan	98	36.56 N	128.54 E
Chunyang, Zhg.	89	43.43 N	129.28 E
Chunzach	84	42.33 N	46.43 E
Chūō	96	35.00 N	133.58 E
Chūō ➛[8], Nihon	268	35.40 N	139.47 E
Chūō ➛[8], Nihon	270	34.42 N	135.11 E
Chuŏr Phnum Krâvanh ⋀	110	12.00 N	103.15 E
Chuosijia	102	31.53 N	101.59 E
Chupaca	248	12.04 S	75.19 W
Chupadera Arroyo V	200	33.47 N	106.37 W
Chupadero, Cerro ∧	200	31.01 N	111.37 W
Chupara Point ›	241r	10.48 N	61.22 W
Chuquibamba	248	15.50 S	72.39 W
Chuquibambilla	248	14.07 S	72.43 W
Chuquicamata	252	22.19 S	68.56 W
Chuquisaca □[5]	248	20.00 S	64.20 W
Chuquitanta	286d	11.58 S	77.06 W
Chur	58	46.51 N	9.32 E
Churach ≃	88	48.37 N	110.42 E
Churāchāndpur	120	24.20 N	93.40 E
Churāmankāti	126	23.14 N	89.09 E
Churcampa	248	12.42 S	74.24 W
Church	262	53.45 N	2.24 W
Churchdown	42	51.53 N	2.10 W
Church Hill	192	36.31 N	82.42 W
Churchill, Mb., Can.	176	58.46 N	94.10 W
Churchill, Oh., U.S.	214	41.09 N	80.39 W
Churchill, Pa., U.S.	279b	40.27 N	79.51 W
Churchill, Va., U.S.	284c	38.54 N	77.10 W
Churchill ≃, Can.	176	58.47 N	94.12 W
Churchill ≃, Nf., Can.	176	53.30 N	60.10 W
Churchill, Cape ›	176	58.46 N	93.12 W
Churchill, Mount ∧, B.C., Can.	182	49.58 N	123.51 W
Churchill, Mount ∧, Ak., U.S.	180	61.25 N	141.43 W
Churchill Downs ♠	218	38.12 N	85.46 W
Churchill Falls ∟	176	53.35 N	64.27 W
Churchill Lake ⊜	184	55.55 N	108.20 W
Churchill National Park ♠	169	37.58 S	145.17 E
Church Point	194	30.24 N	92.12 W
Church Rock	200	35.32 N	108.35 W
Church Street	260	51.26 N	0.28 E
Church Stretton	42	52.32 N	2.49 W
Churchton	208	38.48 N	76.32 W
Churchtown, Eng., U.K.	262	53.40 N	2.58 W
Churchtown, Pa., U.S.	208	40.08 N	75.58 W
Church View	208	37.41 N	76.41 W
Churchville, On., Can.	275b	43.38 N	79.45 W
Churchville, Md., U.S.	208	39.33 N	76.14 W
Churchville, N.Y., U.S.	210	43.06 N	77.53 W
Churchville, Pa., U.S.	285	40.11 N	75.01 W
Churdan	198	42.09 N	94.28 W
Churen Himāl ∧	124	28.44 N	83.12 E
Chure Śringklā ⋀	124	27.40 N	83.40 E
Churfirsten ⋀	58	47.08 N	9.17 E
Chürmen	102	43.20 N	104.05 E
Churmuli	89	51.00 N	136.50 E
Churn ≃	42	51.38 N	1.53 W
Churn Creek ≃	182	51.30 N	122.17 W
Churnet ≃	44	52.55 N	1.50 W
Churni ≃[1]	126	23.08 N	88.30 E
Chursdorf	54	50.46 N	12.15 E
Chūru	120	28.18 N	74.57 E
Churubusco, In., U.S.	216	41.13 N	85.19 W
Churubusco, N.Y., U.S.	206	44.57 N	73.56 W
Churuguara	246	10.49 N	69.32 W
Churumuco de Morelos	234	18.37 N	101.38 W
Churwalden	58	46.47 N	9.33 E
Chušenga	88	51.27 N	110.55 E
Chushan	100	23.45 N	120.40 E
Chushul	120	33.36 N	78.39 E
Chuska Mountains ⋀	200	36.15 N	108.50 W
Chuska Peak ∧	200	35.53 N	108.50 W
Chusovoy → Čusovoj	86	58.17 N	57.49 E
Chust	78	48.10 N	23.18 E
Chusuut uul ∧	88	47.45 N	105.45 E
Chūta	174m	26.32 N	127.58 E
Chutag	88	49.23 N	102.43 E
Chutag Uul	102	43.23 N	110.13 E
Chute-à-Blondeau	206	45.35 N	74.29 W
Chute-Panet	206	46.51 N	71.51 W
Chutorskoj	80	46.52 N	42.59 E
Chutu ≃	89	49.27 N	140.02 E
Chutung	100	24.44 N	121.05 E
Chuŭl	98	41.33 N	129.34 E
Chuvashia → Čuvašija □[3]	80	55.30 N	47.00 E
Chuwang	98	36.02 N	114.52 E
Chuwang-san Kukrip Kongwŏn ♠	98	36.26 N	129.10 E
Chuwei	269d	25.08 N	121.27 E
Chuxian	100	32.19 N	118.17 E
Chuxiong	102	25.02 N	101.30 E
Chuy	252	33.41 S	53.27 W
Chuzenji-ko ⊜	94	36.44 N	139.29 E
Chuzhai	100	33.22 N	113.37 E
Chužir	88	53.11 N	107.20 E
Chūzu	94	35.06 N	136.00 E
Chvalynsk	80	52.30 N	48.07 E
Chvančkara	84	42.34 N	43.01 E
Chvastoviči	76	53.28 N	35.06 E
Chvatovka	80	52.21 N	46.34 E
Chvojnaja	76	58.54 N	34.32 E
Chvorost'anka	80	52.36 N	48.59 E
Chvostovo	92a	46.08 N	142.14 E
Chwefru ≃	42	52.09 N	3.25 W
Ch'wiya-ri	98	38.03 N	125.32 E
Chynčešt' (Kotovsk)	38	46.49 N	28.34 E
Chypre → Cyprus □[1]	130	35.00 N	33.00 E
Chyrov	78	49.33 N	22.49 E
Ci ≃, Zhg.	98	38.19 N	115.23 E
Ci ≃, Zhg.	100	33.27 N	115.31 E
Ciago	64	46.12 N	12.46 E
Ciagola, Monte ∧	68	39.54 N	15.53 E
Ciales	240m	18.20 N	66.28 W
Ciamis	115a	7.20 S	108.21 E
Ciampino	66	41.48 N	12.36 E
Ciampino, Aeroporto di ⊠	267a	41.48 N	12.36 E
Cianciana	70	37.31 N	13.26 E
Ciandur	115a	6.24 S	105.59 E
Cianjur	115a	6.49 S	107.08 E
Ciano d'Enza	64	44.36 N	10.24 E
Cianorte	255	23.37 S	52.37 W
Çians, Gorges du V	62	43.57 N	6.59 E
Čiatura	84	42.17 N	43.17 E
Ciavolo	70	37.46 N	12.33 E
Ciawi, Indon.	115a	7.10 S	108.09 E
Ciawi, Indon.	115a	6.40 S	106.50 E
Ciawigebang	115a	6.58 S	108.34 E
Ciba	107	29.07 N	105.55 E
Cibadak	115a	6.53 S	106.46 E
Cibaliung	115a	6.46 S	105.51 E
Čibargata	85	41.08 N	69.48 E

PORTUGUÊS Nome	Página	Lat.°′	Long.°′ W = Oeste
Cibatu	115a	7.06 S	107.59 E
Cibeber	115a	6.56 S	107.07 E
Cibecue	200	34.02 N	110.29 W
Cibiana	64	46.23 N	12.17 E
Cibinong	115a	6.27 S	106.51 E
Čibisovka	78	50.47 N	40.05 E
Čibižek	86	54.27 N	93.40 E
Cibolo Creek ≃, Tx., U.S.	196	28.57 N	97.53 W
Cibolo Creek ≃, Tx., U.S.	196	29.34 N	104.24 W
Cibolo Creek ≃, Tx., U.S.	196	28.27 N	98.54 W
Cibuta	200	31.04 N	110.54 W
Cicagna	62	44.25 N	9.14 E
Cicala	68	39.01 N	16.29 E
Cicalengka	115a	6.59 S	107.50 E
Ćićarija ⋀	36	45.30 N	13.54 E
Čičatka	89	54.03 N	121.18 E
Cicciano	68	40.58 N	14.32 E
Cicero, Il., U.S.	216	41.50 N	87.45 W
Cicero, In., U.S.	218	40.07 N	86.00 W
Cicero, N.Y., U.S.	210	43.10 N	76.07 W
Cicero Creek ≃	194	40.01 N	86.01 W
Cícero Dantas	250	10.36 S	38.23 W
Čichačovo, Ross.	76	57.17 N	29.54 E
Čichačovo, Ross.	89	51.50 N	141.07 E
Čichareši	84	42.48 N	43.03 E
Ciche, Sgurr na ∧	46	57.01 N	5.27 W
Cicheng	100	30.00 N	121.22 E
Čičikleja ≃	78	47.23 N	31.34 E
Čičkajul ≃	86	57.34 N	85.44 E
Cicladas, Islas → Kikládhes II	38	37.30 N	25.00 E
Cicolano ➛[1]	66	42.12 N	13.12 E
Cicurug	115a	6.47 S	106.47 E
Cidacos ≃	34	42.19 N	1.55 W
Cidade, Rio da ≃	256	22.25 S	43.09 W
Cidade Universitária ʊ[2], Bra.	287a	22.52 S	43.14 W
Cidade Universitária ʊ[2], Bra.	287b	23.33 S	46.43 W
Cide	130	41.54 N	33.00 E
Cidra	240m	18.11 N	66.10 W
Cidra, Lago de ⊜[1]	240m	18.12 N	66.08 W
Ciechanów	30	52.53 N	20.38 E
Ciechanów □[4]	30	53.00 N	20.20 E
Ciechanowiec	30	52.42 N	22.31 E
Ciechocinek	30	52.52 N	18.49 E
Ciego de Ávila	240p	21.51 N	78.46 W
Ciego de Ávila □[4]	240p	22.00 N	78.40 W
Ciempozuelos	34	40.10 N	3.37 W
Ciénaga	246	11.01 N	74.15 W
Ciénaga de Oro	246	8.53 N	75.37 W
Ciénega de Flores	196	25.57 N	100.11 W
Cienfuegos	240p	22.09 N	80.27 W
Cienfuegos □[4]	240p	22.10 N	80.25 W
Cienfuegos, Bahía de ⊂	240p	22.07 N	80.29 W
Čierna [nad Tiscu]	30	48.25 N	22.05 E
Čierny Balog	30	48.45 N	19.40 E
Cíes, Islas II	34	42.13 N	8.54 W
Cieszanów	30	50.16 N	23.08 E
Cieszyn	30	49.45 N	18.38 E
Cieza	34	38.14 N	1.25 W
Çiftalan ➛[8]	267b	41.15 N	28.54 E
Çiftehan	130	37.31 N	34.46 E
Çifteler	130	39.22 N	31.03 E
Çiftlik	130	38.11 N	34.30 E
Cifuentes, Cuba	240p	22.39 N	80.03 W
Cifuentes, Esp.	34	40.47 N	2.37 W
Čiganak, Kaz.	86	45.06 N	73.58 E
Čiganak, Ross.	80	51.47 N	43.18 E
Čiganaki	80	47.57 N	43.05 E
Čigirin	78	49.04 N	32.40 E
Cigliano	62	45.18 N	8.01 E
Čigorak	80	51.26 N	42.09 E
Cigou	100	33.51 N	113.35 E
Cigüela ≃	34	39.08 N	3.44 W
Cihanbeyli	130	38.40 N	32.56 E
Cihara	115a	6.52 S	106.06 E
Cihuatlán	234	19.14 N	104.35 W
Čiili	86	44.10 N	66.45 E
Cijara, Embalse de ⊜[1]	34	39.18 N	4.52 W
Čijen	85	43.08 N	75.55 E
Cijiawu	105	39.48 N	115.59 E
Čijirčik, pereval)(	85	40.15 N	73.20 E
Čijli ≃	85	40.17 N	72.38 E
Cijulang	115a	7.44 S	108.27 E
Čik	86	55.01 N	82.27 E
Cikajang	115a	7.22 S	107.47 E
Cikalong-kulon	115a	6.42 S	107.12 E
Cikampek	115a	6.24 S	107.27 E
Čikan	88	54.54 N	105.39 E
Cikarang	115a	6.15 S	107.09 E
Cikatomas	115a	7.37 S	108.15 E
Čikišl'ar	128	37.34 N	53.55 E
Čikoj	88	50.16 N	106.54 E
Čikoj ≃	88	51.02 N	106.39 E
Čikola	84	43.12 N	43.55 E
Cikou	100	29.42 N	114.46 E
Cıksı	130	38.30 N	40.55 E
Cilacap	115a	7.44 S	109.00 E
Cilamaya	115a	6.15 S	107.35 E
Cilavegna	62	45.19 N	8.44 E
Çıldır	84	41.08 N	43.07 E
Çıldır Gölü ⊜	84	41.04 N	43.15 E
Ciledug	115a	6.54 S	108.44 E
Cilegon	115a	6.01 S	106.03 E
Čilekovo	80	47.50 N	43.30 E
Cilento ➛[1]	68	40.15 N	15.15 E
Čil'gazi	85	40.10 N	70.39 E
Cili	102	29.17 N	111.00 E
Cilicia □[9]	130	36.40 N	34.20 E
Čilik, Kaz.	85	43.36 N	78.15 E
Čilik, Kaz.	86	51.07 N	54.07 E
Čilik ≃	85	43.05 N	78.28 E
Cililin	115a	6.56 S	107.26 E
Cilimus	115a	6.52 S	108.29 E
Cilincing ➛[8]	269e	6.06 S	106.56 E
Cill Airne → Killarney	48	52.03 N	9.30 W
Cill Chainnigh → Kilkenny	48	52.39 N	7.15 W
Cilleruelo de Bezana	34	42.58 N	3.51 W
Cil'ma ≃	24	65.27 N	52.06 E
Cimabanche (Schluderbach)	64	46.37 N	12.11 E
Cima Gogna	64	46.31 N	12.28 E
Cimahi	115a	6.53 S	107.32 E
Cimalaka	115a	6.49 S	107.56 E
Cimalmotto	58	46.17 N	8.29 E
Cimarron, Ks., U.S.	198	37.48 N	100.20 W
Cimarron, N.M., U.S.	200	36.30 N	104.54 W
Cimarron ≃, U.S.	196	36.10 N	96.17 W
Cimarron ≃, N.M., U.S.	196	36.20 N	104.31 W
Cimarron, North Fork ≃	196	37.25 N	101.13 W
Čimbaj	86	42.57 N	59.47 E
Čimčinej, gora ∧[2]	180	63.37 N	178.04 E
Cimini, Monti ⋀	66	42.20 N	12.10 E
Ciminna	70	37.54 N	13.34 E
Cimino, Monte ∧	66	42.24 N	12.12 E
Čimion	85	40.16 N	71.31 E
Čimišlija	38	46.32 N	28.44 E
Cimitile	68	40.56 N	14.31 E
Čimkent	85	42.18 N	69.36 E
Čimkent □[4]	85	42.30 N	68.30 E
Čimkorgon	85	42.50 N	75.30 E
Cimla ≃	80	48.01 N	42.24 E
Ciml'ansk	80	47.38 N	42.04 E
Ciml'anskoje vodochranilišče ⊜[1]	80	48.00 N	43.00 E
Cimolais	64	46.17 N	12.26 E
Cimone, Monte ∧	64	44.12 N	10.42 E
Cîmpeni	38	46.22 N	23.03 E
Cîmpia Turzii	38	46.33 N	23.54 E
Cîmpina	38	45.08 N	25.44 E

Cimpu	112	3.25 S	120.22 E
Cîmpulung	38	45.16 N	25.03 E
Cîmpulung Moldovenesc	38	47.31 N	25.34 E
Čimtarga, gora ∧	85	39.12 N	68.10 E
Čina ≃	88	54.20 N	112.24 E
Cina, Tanjung ›	112	5.56 S	104.45 E
Činabad	85	40.52 N	71.58 E
Činadijevo	78	48.30 N	22.50 E
Cinandali	84	41.53 N	45.34 E
Çınar	130	37.44 N	40.25 E
Çınarcık	130	40.39 N	29.06 E
Cinaruco ≃	246	6.41 N	67.07 W
Činaz	85	40.56 N	68.45 E
Cinca ≃	34	41.26 N	0.21 E
Cincar ∧	36	43.54 N	17.04 E
Cincinnati, Ia., U.S.	190	40.37 N	92.55 W
Cincinnati, Oh., U.S.	218	39.09 N	84.27 W
Cincinnatus	210	42.32 N	75.53 W
Cinco, Canal Numero ≅	252	37.35 S	57.20 W
Cinco Balas, Cayos II	240p	21.06 N	79.20 W
Cinco de Mayo	196	25.46 N	104.19 W
Cinco Pinos	236	13.14 N	86.52 W
Cinco Saltos	252	38.49 S	68.04 W
Cinderella	273d	26.15 S	28.16 E
Cinderella Dam ⊜[1]	273d	26.15 S	28.14 E
Cinderford	42	51.50 N	2.29 W
Cinder Island I	276	40.36 N	73.36 W
Çine	130	37.36 N	28.04 E
Činebar	224	46.36 N	122.32 W
Cinecittà ʊ[3]	267a	41.51 N	12.34 E
Cinema	182	53.14 N	122.27 W
Ciney	56	50.18 N	5.06 E
Cinfães	34	41.04 N	8.05 W
Čingaly	86	60.13 N	69.45 E
Čingis	86	54.08 N	81.41 E
Čingistaj	86	49.13 N	85.55 E
Cingoli	66	43.22 N	13.13 E
Cinigiano	66	42.53 N	11.24 E
Cinisello Balsamo	62	45.33 N	9.13 E
Činišeucy	38	47.42 N	28.52 E
Cinisi	70	38.09 N	13.06 E
Činja-Voryk	24	63.13 N	52.38 E
Cinkota ➛[8]	264c	47.31 N	19.14 E
Cinnaminson	285	40.00 N	74.59 W
Cínovec	54	50.43 N	13.45 E
Cinq, Lac des ⊜	206	46.51 N	72.59 W
Cinq Doigts, Lac ⊜	206	46.36 N	74.32 W
Cinquefrondi	68	38.25 N	16.06 E
Cinquemiglia, Piano delle ≃	66	41.50 N	14.00 E
Cinqueterre □[9]	62	44.10 N	9.45 E
Cintalapa	234	16.44 N	93.43 W
Cinto, Monte ∧	36	42.23 N	8.56 E
Cinto Euganeo	64	45.16 N	11.40 E
Cintra → Sintra	34	38.48 N	9.23 W
Cintra, Golfe de ⊂	148	23.00 N	16.20 W
Ciocăneşti	38	44.12 N	27.04 E
Ciociaria ➛[1]	66	41.45 N	13.15 E
Ciomas	115a	6.12 S	106.01 E
Čiovo, Otok I	36	43.30 N	16.20 E
Cipa ≃	88	55.23 N	115.55 E
Ciparay	115a	7.03 S	107.43 E
Cipatujah	115a	7.45 S	108.00 E
Cipikan	88	54.55 N	113.21 E
Cipikan ≃	88	55.14 N	113.05 E
Cipó	250	11.06 S	38.31 W
Cipó ≃	255	18.40 S	43.59 W
Cipolândia	255	20.08 S	55.24 W
Cipolletti	252	38.56 S	67.59 W
Ciqikou	107	29.35 N	106.26 E
Čir	80	48.29 N	43.10 E
Čir ≃	80	48.35 N	42.51 E
Ciraadhame	144	10.30 N	49.22 E
Čirachčaj ≃	84	41.40 N	48.11 E
Čiragidzor	84	40.27 N	46.19 E
Ciranjang	115a	6.49 S	107.14 E
Circeo, Monte ∧	66	41.14 N	13.03 E
Circeo, Parco Nazionale del ♠	66	41.17 N	13.05 E
Čirčik	85	41.29 N	69.35 E
Čirčik ≃	85	40.54 N	68.41 E
Çırçır	130	40.04 N	36.48 E
Circle, Ak., U.S.	180	65.50 N	144.04 W
Circle, Mt., U.S.	202	47.20 N	105.35 W
Circle Hot Springs	180	65.28 N	144.39 W
Circleville, N.Y., U.S.	210	41.31 N	75.23 W
Circleville, Oh., U.S.	218	39.36 N	82.56 W
Circleville, Pa., U.S.	279b	40.20 N	79.44 W
Circleville, Ut., U.S.	200	38.10 N	112.16 W
Circleville Mountain ∧	200	38.12 N	112.24 W
Circular Reef ✦[2]	164	3.25 S	147.47 E
Circus World ♠	220	28.14 N	81.38 W
Cirebon	115a	6.44 S	108.34 E
Cireglio	66	43.59 N	10.51 E
Ciremay, Gunung ∧	115a	6.54 S	108.24 E
Cirencester	42	51.44 N	1.59 W
Cirey-sur-Vezouze	58	48.35 N	6.57 E
Čirgalandy	88	50.36 N	97.20 E
Ciriè	62	45.14 N	7.36 E
Cirigliano	68	40.24 N	16.10 E
Čirikovo	82	55.23 N	37.14 E
Ciriquiri ≃	248	8.05 S	65.18 W
Čirk, gora ∧	180	64.33 N	175.25 E
Cîrlibaba	38	47.35 N	25.07 E
Cirò	68	39.23 N	17.04 E
Cirò Marina	68	39.22 N	17.08 E
Ciro Redondo	240p	22.01 N	78.43 W
Čirpan	38	42.12 N	25.20 E
Ciruas	115a	6.06 S	106.13 E
Cisa, Passo della)(	64	44.28 N	9.55 E
Cisano	64	45.32 N	10.43 E
Cisarua	115a	6.40 S	106.59 E
Cisco, Il., U.S.	219	40.01 N	88.43 W
Cisco, Tx., U.S.	196	32.23 N	98.58 W
Cishan	98	36.37 N	114.07 E
Cishangang	106	30.55 N	119.31 E
Ciskei □[1], Afr.	138	32.50 S	27.00 E
Ciskei □[1], Afr.	158	32.50 S	27.00 E
Cislago	62	45.39 N	8.58 E
Cisliano	266b	45.27 N	8.59 E
Cismar	54	54.11 N	10.59 E
Čismena	82	56.02 N	36.13 E
Cismon ≃	64	45.55 N	11.43 E
Cismon del Grappa	64	45.55 N	11.44 E
Čišmy	86	54.35 N	55.20 E
Cisnădie	38	45.43 N	24.09 E
Cisne	194	38.31 N	88.26 W
Cisneros	246	6.33 N	75.04 W
Cisnes ≃	254	44.45 S	72.42 W
Cisolok	115a	6.57 S	106.26 E
Cison di Valmarino	64	45.58 N	12.10 E
Cispus ≃	224	46.25 N	122.10 W
Cisse ≃	50	47.25 N	0.47 E
Cissna Park	216	40.33 N	87.53 W
Čistá, Česká Rep.	54	50.06 N	12.44 E
Čistá, Česká Rep.	60	50.02 N	13.35 E
Cisterna di Latina	66	41.35 N	12.49 E
Cisternino	68	40.44 N	17.25 E
Cistern Point ›	238	23.43 N	77.35 W
Cistierna	34	42.48 N	5.07 W
Čistoje	80	56.32 N	43.02 E
Čistooz'ornoje	86	54.43 N	76.33 E
Čistopol'	80	55.21 N	50.37 E
Čistopolje, Kaz.	86	52.34 N	67.15 E
Čistopolje, Ross.	83	47.31 N	39.27 E
Čistovodovka	83	49.24 N	37.20 E
Čita	88	52.03 N	113.30 E
Čita ≃	88	52.00 N	113.30 E
Citac, Nevado ∧	248	12.48 S	75.14 W
Čita Oblast' □[4]	88	52.00 N	117.00 E
Citaré ≃	250	1.11 N	54.41 W
Cité Universitaire ʊ[2]	261	48.49 N	2.20 E
Citlaltépetl, Volcán → Orizaba, Pico de ∧[1]	234	19.01 N	97.16 E
Citra	192	29.24 N	82.06 W
Citronelle	194	31.05 N	88.13 W

Citrus □[6]	220	28.52 N	82.28 W
Citrusdal	158	32.36 S	19.00 E
Citrus Heights	226	38.42 N	121.16 W
Citrus Springs	220	29.00 N	82.27 W
Citrus Tower ʊ	220	28.33 N	81.44 W
Cittadella	64	45.39 N	11.47 E
Città della Pieve	66	42.57 N	12.00 E
Città del Vaticano → Vatican City □[1]	66	41.54 N	12.27 E
Città di Castello	66	43.27 N	12.14 E
Cittaducale	66	42.23 N	12.57 E
Cittanova	68	38.21 N	16.05 E
Cittareale	66	42.37 N	13.10 E
Città Sant'Angelo	66	42.31 N	14.03 E
Città Universitaria ʊ[2]	267a	41.55 N	12.31 E
City Beach	168a	31.56 S	115.45 E
City Bell ➛[8]	258	34.52 S	58.05 W
City Island ➛[8]	276	40.51 N	73.47 W
City Mills	283	42.06 N	71.21 W
City of Hope National Medical Center ʊ	280	34.08 N	117.58 W
City Of Industry	280	34.01 N	117.57 W
City of London ➛[8]	260	51.31 N	0.05 W
City of Refuge → Pu'uhonua o Honaunau National Historic Site ⊥	229d	19.25 N	155.54 W
City of Sunrise	220	26.08 N	80.14 W
City Point	220	28.24 N	80.45 W
City University of New York Brooklyn College ʊ[2]	276	40.38 N	73.57 W
City University of New York City College ʊ[2]	276	40.49 N	73.57 W
City University of New York Queens College ʊ[2]	276	40.44 N	73.49 W
City University of New York York College ʊ[2]	276	40.42 N	73.48 W
Ciucaş, Vîrful ∧	38	45.31 N	25.55 E
Ciudad Acuña	232	29.18 N	100.55 W
Ciudad Altamirano	234	18.20 N	100.40 W
Ciudad Barrios	236	13.46 N	88.16 W
Ciudad Bolívar	246	8.08 N	63.33 W
Ciudad Bolivia	246	8.21 N	70.34 W
Ciudad Camargo	232	26.19 N	98.50 W
Ciudad Constitución	232	24.59 N	111.39 W
Ciudad Cortés	236	8.58 N	83.32 W
Ciudad Cuauhtémoc	234	22.28 N	102.20 W
Ciudad Darío	236	12.43 N	86.08 W
Ciudad de Carangas	248	17.53 S	66.11 W
Ciudad de Guayana → Ciudad Guayana	246	8.22 N	62.40 W
Ciudad de la Habana □[4]	240p	23.08 N	82.22 W
Ciudad del Cabo → Cape Town	158	33.55 S	18.22 E
Ciudad del Carmen	232	18.38 N	91.50 W
Ciudad del Este	252	25.30 S	54.36 W
Ciudad del Maíz	234	22.24 N	99.36 W
Ciudad de los Deportes ♠	286a	19.23 N	99.11 W
Ciudad del Vaticano → Vatican City □[1]	66	41.54 N	12.27 E
Ciudad de México (Mexico City), Méx.	234	19.24 N	99.09 W
Ciudad de México (Mexico City), Méx.	286a	19.24 N	99.09 W
Ciudad de Nutrias	246	8.05 N	69.18 W
Ciudad Deportiva ♠, Cuba	286b	23.07 N	82.22 W
Ciudad Deportiva ♠, Méx.	286a	19.24 N	99.06 W
Ciudadela, Parque de la ♠	266d	41.23 N	2.11 E
Ciudad General Belgrano	288	34.43 S	58.32 W
Ciudad Guayana	246	8.22 N	62.40 W
Ciudad Guzmán	234	19.41 N	103.29 W
Ciudad Hidalgo, Méx.	234	19.41 N	100.34 W
Ciudad Hidalgo, Méx.	236	14.41 N	92.09 W
Ciudad Juárez	232	31.44 N	106.29 W
Ciudad Lerdo	196	25.32 N	103.32 W
Ciudad Lerdo de Tejada	234	18.37 N	95.31 W
Ciudad Lineal ➛[8]	266a	40.27 N	3.40 W
Ciudad López Mateos	286a	19.33 N	99.15 W
Ciudad Madero	234	22.16 N	97.50 W
Ciudad Mante	234	22.44 N	98.57 W
Ciudad Manuel Doblado	234	20.44 N	101.56 W
Ciudad Mendoza	234	18.48 N	97.11 W
Ciudad Miguel Alemán	232	26.23 N	99.01 W
Ciudad Morelos	232	32.38 N	114.52 W
Ciudad Obregón	232	27.29 N	109.56 W
Ciudad Ojeda (Lagunillas)	246	10.12 N	71.19 W
Ciudad Piar	246	7.27 N	63.19 W
Ciudad Real	34	38.59 N	3.56 W
Ciudad Real □[4]	34	38.50 N	3.45 W
Ciudad Rodrigo	34	40.36 N	6.32 W
Ciudad Sahagún	234	19.47 N	98.33 W
Ciudad Sandino	236	13.43 N	86.08 W
Ciudad Serdán	234	18.59 N	97.27 W
Ciudad Tecún Umán	236	14.40 N	92.09 W
Ciudad Trujillo → Santo Domingo	238	18.28 N	69.54 W
Ciudad Universitaria ➛[8]	266a	40.27 N	3.44 W
Ciudad Universitaria ʊ[2], Esp.	266a	40.27 N	3.43 W
Ciudad Universitaria ʊ[2], Méx.	286a	19.20 N	99.11 W
Ciudad Universitaria ʊ[2], Ven.	286c	10.29 N	66.53 W
Ciudad Valles	234	21.59 N	99.01 W
Ciudad Victoria, Méx.	204	32.20 N	115.06 W
Ciudad Victoria, Méx.	234	23.44 N	99.08 W
Ciudad Vieja	236	14.31 N	90.46 W
Ciuma	152	13.14 S	15.40 E
Ciutadella	34	40.02 N	3.50 E
Civa Burnu ›	130	41.22 N	36.35 E
Civate	62	45.50 N	9.21 E
Civenna	58	45.56 N	9.16 E
Civetta, Monte ∧	64	46.23 N	12.03 E
Civezzano	64	46.05 N	11.11 E
Cividale del Friuli	64	46.06 N	13.25 E
Cividate al Piano	62	45.33 N	9.50 E
Cividate Camuno	64	45.57 N	10.17 E
Civil' ≃	80	56.08 N	47.35 E
Civil'sk	80	55.53 N	47.29 E
Civita	68	39.49 N	16.18 E
Civitacampomarano	66	41.47 N	14.41 E
Civita Castellana	66	42.17 N	12.25 E
Civita di Bagno	66	42.18 N	13.26 E
Civitanova Alta	66	43.19 N	13.40 E
Civitanova del Sannio	66	41.40 N	14.24 E
Civitanova Marche	66	43.18 N	13.44 E
Civitaquana	66	42.19 N	13.54 E
Civitavecchia	66	42.06 N	11.48 E
Civitella del Tronto	66	42.46 N	13.40 E
Civitella di Romagna	66	44.00 N	11.56 E
Civitella in Val di Chiana	66	43.25 N	11.43 E
Civitella Marittima	66	43.00 N	11.17 E
Civitella Roveto	66	41.54 N	13.25 E
Civray	32	46.09 N	0.18 E
Çivril	130	38.18 N	29.45 E
Ciwidey	115a	7.06 S	107.27 E
Cixerri ≃	71	39.17 N	8.59 E
Cixi	100	30.11 N	121.15 E
Cixian	98	36.22 N	114.23 E
Ciyutuo	104	41.31 N	122.53 E
Čiža	24	67.06 N	44.19 E
Čižapka ≃	86	59.01 N	79.36 E
Čiža Vtoraja	80	50.52 N	49.40 E

Cize	58	46.12 N	5.26 E
Cizhuping	107	29.11 N	103.36 E
Čižinskije razlivy ≡	80	50.25 N	49.40 E
Cizre	130	37.20 N	42.12 E
C.J. Strike Reservoir ⊜[1]	202	42.57 N	115.53 W
Čkalov → Orenburg	86	51.54 N	55.06 E
Čkalovo, Kaz.	86	53.38 N	70.24 E
Čkalovo, Ukr.	78	46.28 N	34.11 E
Čkalovsk, Kaz.	85	41.15 N	68.00 E
Čkalovsk, Ross.	80	56.46 N	43.16 E
Čkalovsk, Taj.	85	40.13 N	69.50 E
Čkalovskij	265b	55.54 N	38.04 E
C K Creek ≃	202	47.36 N	108.29 W
Čkyně	60	49.07 N	13.49 E
Čl'a, ozero ⊜	89	53.27 N	140.03 E
Clachan	46	55.45 N	5.34 W
Clackamas	224	45.24 N	122.34 W
Clackamas □[6]	224	45.10 N	122.16 W
Clackamas ≃	224	45.22 N	122.36 W
Clackamas, Oak Grove Fork ≃	224	45.05 N	122.03 W
Clackamas Heights	224	45.23 N	122.34 W
Clackline	168a	31.43 S	116.31 E
Clackmannan	46	56.06 N	3.46 W
Clacton-on-Sea	42	51.48 N	1.09 E
Cladich	46	56.21 N	5.05 W
Claerwen ≃	42	52.16 N	3.35 W
Claerwen Reservoir ⊜[1]	42	52.17 N	3.43 W
Claflin	198	38.31 N	98.32 W
Claiborne	194	31.32 N	87.31 W
Clain ≃	32	46.47 N	0.32 E
Claire, Lake ⊜	176	58.35 N	112.05 W
Claire, Pointe ›	275a	45.25 N	73.50 W
Clairefontaine-en-Yvelines	50	48.37 N	1.55 E
Clair Engle Lake ⊜[1]	204	40.52 N	122.43 W
Claireville	275b	43.45 N	79.38 W
Claireville Reservoir ⊜[1]	275b	43.44 N	79.39 W
Clairis ≃	50	48.07 N	2.45 E
Clairmarais	50	50.46 N	2.18 E
Clairmont	182	55.16 N	118.47 W
Clairton	214	40.17 N	79.52 W
Clairvaux-les-Lacs	58	46.34 N	5.45 E
Claix	62	45.07 N	5.40 E
Clallam □[6]	224	48.10 N	123.49 W
Clallam Bay	224	48.15 N	124.15 W
Clam ≃, Mi., U.S.	190	44.05 N	85.00 W
Clam ≃, Wi., U.S.	190	45.57 N	92.33 W
Clam, North Fork ≃	190	45.46 N	92.18 W
Clamart	261	48.48 N	2.16 E
Clamecy	50	47.27 N	3.31 E
Clam Gulch	180	60.15 N	151.22 W
Clam Lake ⊜	184	55.19 N	105.43 W
Clampton	162	29.56 S	119.06 E
Clan Alpine Mountains ⋀	204	39.40 N	117.55 W
Clandonald	182	53.34 N	110.44 W
Clandon Park ♠	260	51.15 N	0.30 W
Clandulla	170	32.55 S	149.57 E
Clane	48	53.18 N	6.41 W
Clans	62	44.00 N	7.09 E
Clanton	194	32.50 N	86.37 W
Clanwilliam	158	32.11 S	18.54 E
Claonaig	46	55.46 N	5.22 W
Clapham	42	52.09 N	0.29 W
Clapier, Mont ∧	62	44.07 N	7.25 E
Clapperton Island I	190	46.02 N	82.13 W
Clapp Farm	214	41.24 N	79.32 W
Clàr, Loch nan ⊜	46	58.17 N	4.08 W
Clara, Arg.	252	31.50 S	58.49 W
Clara, Ire	48	53.20 N	7.36 W
Clara, Ms., U.S.	194	31.34 N	88.41 W
Clara ≃	166	18.30 S	141.18 E
Clara City	198	44.57 N	95.21 W
Clara Island I	110	10.54 N	97.55 E
Claraz	252	37.54 S	59.17 W
Clare, Austl.	166	33.25 S	143.55 E
Clare, Austl.	168b	33.50 S	138.36 E
Clare, Eng., U.K.	42	52.05 N	0.35 E
Clare, Mi., U.S.	190	43.49 N	84.46 W
Clare □[6]	48	52.50 N	9.00 W
Clare ≃, On., Can.	212	44.28 N	77.17 W
Clare ≃, Ire.	48	53.20 N	9.03 W
Clarecastle	48	52.49 N	8.57 W
Claregalway	48	53.21 N	8.57 W
Clare Island I	48	53.48 N	10.00 W
Claremont, On., Can.	212	43.58 N	79.07 W
Claremont, Eng., U.K.	260	51.21 N	0.22 W
Claremont, Ca., U.S.	228	34.05 N	117.43 W
Claremont, N.H., U.S.	188	43.22 N	72.20 W
Claremont, S.D., U.S.	198	45.40 N	98.00 W
Claremont, Va., U.S.	208	37.13 N	76.57 W
Claremont ∧	204	39.53 N	120.57 W
Claremore	196	36.18 N	95.36 W
Claremorris	48	53.44 N	9.00 W
Clarence, N.Z.	172	42.10 S	173.56 E
Clarence, Il., U.S.	216	40.28 N	87.58 W
Clarence, Ia., U.S.	190	41.53 N	91.03 W
Clarence, Mo., U.S.	219	39.44 N	92.15 W
Clarence, N.Y., U.S.	210	42.59 N	78.35 W
Clarence, Pa., U.S.	214	41.03 N	77.56 W
Clarence ≃, Austl.	166	29.25 S	153.22 E
Clarence ≃, N.Z.	172	42.10 S	173.57 E
Clarence, Isla I	254	54.10 S	71.50 W
Clarence, Port ⊂	180	65.15 N	166.40 W
Clarence Cannon Dam ➛[6]	219	39.31 N	91.39 W
Clarence Center	210	43.00 N	78.35 W
Clarence Creek	206	45.30 N	75.13 W
Clarence Fahnestock Memorial State Park ♠	210	41.26 N	73.50 W
Clarence Island I	9	61.09 S	54.06 W
Clarence J. Brown Reservoir ⊜[1]	218	39.58 N	83.44 W
Clarence Strait ⊔, Austl.	164	12.00 S	131.00 E
Clarence Strait ⊔, Ak., U.S.	180	55.25 N	132.00 W
Clarence Town, Austl.	170	32.35 S	151.47 E
Clarence Town, Ba	238	23.06 N	74.59 W
Clarenceville, P.Q., Can.	206	45.04 N	73.15 W
Clarenceville, Mi., U.S.	281	42.27 N	83.19 W
Clarendon, Austl.	168b	35.07 S	138.38 E
Clarendon, Ar., U.S.	194	34.41 N	91.18 W
Clarendon, N.Y., U.S.	210	43.11 N	78.04 W
Clarendon, Pa., U.S.	214	41.46 N	79.05 W
Clarendon, Tx., U.S.	196	34.56 N	100.53 W
Clarendon Hills	278	41.47 N	87.57 W
Clarens	158	28.30 S	28.29 E
Clarenville	186	48.10 N	53.58 W
Claresholm	182	50.02 N	113.35 W
Claret	62	43.52 N	3.54 E
Clarholz	52	51.54 N	8.11 E
Claridge	214	40.21 N	79.37 W
Clarie Coast ⊥[2]	9	66.30 S	133.00 E
Clarin	116	9.58 N	124.01 E
Clarinda	198	40.44 N	95.02 W
Clarines	246	9.56 N	65.10 W
Clarington	214	41.20 N	79.07 W
Clarion, Ia., U.S.	190	42.43 N	93.43 W
Clarion, Pa., U.S.	214	41.12 N	79.23 W
Clarion □[6]	214	41.13 N	79.24 W
Clarion ≃	214	41.07 N	79.41 W
Clarión, Isla I	232	18.22 N	114.44 W
Clarion, West Branch ≃	214	41.29 N	78.41 W
Clarion Fracture Zone ✦	16	18.00 N	122.00 W
Clarissa	198	46.07 N	94.56 W
Clark, N.J., U.S.	276	40.38 N	74.18 W
Clark, Oh., U.S.	214	40.27 N	81.54 W
Clark, S.D., U.S.	198	44.52 N	97.43 W

≃ River	Fluß	Río	Rivière	Rio
≅ Canal	Kanal	Canal	Canal	Canal
∟ Waterfall, Rapids	Wasserfall, Stromschnellen	Cascada, Rápidos	Chute d'eau, Rapides	Cascata, Rápidos
⊔ Strait	Meeresstraße	Estrecho	Détroit	Estreito
⊂ Bay, Gulf	Bucht, Golf	Bahía, Golfo	Baie, Golfe	Baía, Golfo
⊜ Lake, Lakes	See, Seen	Lago, Lagos	Lac, Lacs	Lago, Lagos
≡ Swamp	Sumpf	Pantano	Marais	Pântano
⊓ Ice Features, Glacier	Eis- und Gletscherformen	Accidentes Glaciales	Formes glaciaires	Acidentes glaciares
⫪ Other Hydrographic Features	Andere Hydrographische Objekte	Otros Elementos Hidrográficos	Autres données hydrographiques	Outros acidentes hidrográficos

✦ Submarine Features	Untermeerische Objekte	Accidentes Submarinos	Formes de relief sous-marin	Acidentes submarinos
□ Political Unit	Politische Einheit	Unidad Política	Entité politique	Unidade política
ʊ Cultural Institution	Kulturelle Institution	Institución Cultural	Institution culturelle	Instituição cultural
⊥ Historical Site	Historische Stätte	Sitio Histórico	Site historique	Sítio histórico
♠ Recreational Site	Erholungs- und Ferienort	Sitio de Recreo	Centre de loisirs	Área de Lazer
⊠ Airport	Flughafen	Aeropuerto	Aéroport	Aeroporto
■ Military Installation	Militäranlage	Instalación Militar	Installation militaire	Instalação militar
➛ Miscellaneous	Verschiedenes	Misceláneo	Divers	Diversos

Clark, Tx., U.S.	222	30.23 N 94.46 W
Clark □⁶, In., U.S.	218	38.17 N 85.44 W
Clark □⁶, Oh., U.S.	218	39.56 N 83.49 W
Clark □⁶, Wa., U.S.	224	45.48 N 122.31 W
Clark, Lake ∅	180	60.15 N 154.15 W
Clark, Mount ʌ	180	64.25 N 124.12 W
Clark, Point ›	190	44.04 N 81.45 W
Clark Air Base (U.S.)		
▪	116	15.11 N 120.32 E
Clark Branch ≃	285	39.43 N 74.45 W
Clark Canyon Reservoir ∅¹	202	44.58 N 112.51 W
Clark Creek ≃	208	40.22 N 76.58 W
Clarkdale	200	34.46 N 112.03 W
Clarke ≃	166	19.12 S 145.30 E
Clarke City	186	50.12 N 66.38 W
Clarke Island I	166	40.33 S 148.10 E
Clarke Lake ∅	184	54.25 N 106.51 W
Clarke Range ʌ	166	20.50 S 148.33 E
Clarkesville	192	34.36 N 83.31 W
Clarkfield	198	44.47 N 95.48 W
Clark Fork	202	48.08 N 116.10 W
Clark Fork ≃	202	48.09 N 116.15 W
Clark Hill	218	38.18 N 83.12 W
Clarklake	216	42.04 N 84.21 W
Clark Lake ∅	216	42.07 N 84.19 W
Clark Mills	210	43.06 N 75.22 W
Clark Mountain ʌ, Ca., U.S.	204	35.32 N 115.35 W
Clark Mountain ʌ, Wa., U.S.	224	48.03 N 120.57 W
Clarks, La., U.S.	194	32.01 N 92.08 W
Clarks, Ne., U.S.	198	41.12 N 97.50 W
Clarks ≃	194	37.03 N 88.33 W
Clarks, West Fork ≃	194	36.59 N 88.31 W
Clarksboro	285	39.47 N 75.13 W
Clarksburg, On., Can.	212	44.43 N 80.27 W
Clarksburg, Ca., U.S.	226	38.25 N 121.32 W
Clarksburg, Il., U.S.	219	39.20 N 88.44 W
Clarksburg, In., U.S.	218	39.26 N 85.20 W
Clarksburg, Md., U.S.	208	39.14 N 77.16 W
Clarksburg, N.J., U.S.		40.11 N 74.26 W
Clarksburg, W.V., U.S.	218	39.30 N 83.09 W
Clarksburg State Park ♦	207	42.43 N 73.06 W
Clarks Creek ≃, Ks., U.S.		
Clarks Creek ≃, Ky., U.S.	198	39.05 N 96.42 W
Clarksdale	218	38.40 N 84.44 W
Clarks Green	194	34.12 N 90.34 W
Clark's Harbour	210	41.30 N 75.42 W
Clarks Hill	186	43.26 N 65.38 W
Clarks Hill Lake ∅¹	216	40.14 N 86.43 W
Clarks Island I	192	33.50 N 82.20 W
Clarks Mills	283	42.01 N 70.38 W
Clarkson, On., Can.	214	41.24 N 80.11 W
Clarkson, Ky., U.S.	275b	43.31 N 79.37 W
Clarkson, Ne., U.S.	194	37.29 N 86.13 W
Clarkson, N.Y., U.S.	198	41.43 N 97.07 W
Clarks Summit	210	43.14 N 77.56 W
Clarkston, Mi., U.S.	210	41.29 N 75.42 W
Clarkston, Wa., U.S.	216	42.44 N 83.25 W
Clark's Town	202	46.24 N 117.02 W
Clarksville, Ar., U.S.	241q	18.25 N 77.34 W
Clarksville, De., U.S.	194	35.28 N 93.27 W
Clarksville, In., U.S.	208	38.32 N 75.08 W
Clarksville, Ia., U.S.	218	38.15 N 85.47 W
Clarksville, Md., U.S.	190	42.47 N 92.40 W
Clarksville, Mo., U.S.	208	39.12 N 76.56 W
Clarksville, N.Y., U.S.	216	42.00 N 85.14 W
Clarksville, Oh., U.S.	219	39.22 N 90.54 W
Clarksville, Tn., U.S.	210	42.35 N 73.58 W
Clarksville, Tx., U.S.	218	39.24 N 83.58 W
Clarksville City	196	36.31 N 87.21 W
Clarkton, Mo., U.S.	196	36.37 N 78.33 W
Clarkton, N.C., U.S.	222	32.32 N 94.34 W
Claro ≃, Bra.	194	36.27 N 89.58 W
Claro ≃, Bra.	192	34.29 N 78.39 W
Claro ≃, Bra.	248	13.25 S 56.35 W
Claro, Arroyo ≃	255	15.28 S 51.43 W
Claro, Ribeirão ≃	255	19.06 S 47.52 W
Clary	255	19.08 S 50.40 W
Claryville	288	34.25 S 58.41 W
Clashmore	287b	23.40 S 46.17 W
Claskanie ≃	50	50.05 N 3.24 E
Classkanie	210	41.55 N 74.34 W
Clastsop Spit ›²	48	52.00 N 7.48 W
Clatteringshaws Lake ∅	224	46.06 N 123.12 W
Claude	224	46.08 N 123.14 W
Claudy	224	46.01 N 123.41 W
Claughton	224	46.13 N 124.01 W
Claussnitz		
Clausthal-Zellerfeld	44	55.05 N 4.17 W
Claver	198	35.07 N 101.22 W
Claverack	48	54.54 N 7.09 W
Claveria, Pil.	44	54.06 N 2.40 W
Claveria, Pil.	54	50.56 N 12.53 E
Clavet	52	51.48 N 10.20 E
Clavey ≃	116	9.35 N 125.44 E
Clawat, Mount ʌ	210	42.13 N 73.44 W
Clawson, Mi., U.S.	116	18.37 N 121.05 E
Clawson, Tx., U.S.	116	8.38 N 124.55 E
Claxton	184	52.00 N 106.23 W
Clay, Ky., U.S.	226	37.52 N 120.07 W
Clay, Tx., U.S.	116	16.58 N 120.58 E
Clay, W.V., U.S.	281	42.32 N 83.08 W
Clay □⁶	222	31.24 N 94.47 W
Claybank Creek ≃	182	32.09 N 81.54 W
Clay Center, Ks., U.S.	194	32.59 N 87.36 W
	182	30.23 N 96.21 W
Clay Center, Ne., U.S.	188	38.27 N 81.05 W
	219	38.45 N 88.40 W
Clay City, Il., U.S.	194	31.10 N 85.44 W
Clay City, In., U.S.	198	39.22 N 97.07 W
Clay City, Ky., U.S.	198	40.31 N 98.03 W
Clay Cross	214	41.33 N 83.21 W
Claydon	194	38.49 N 88.21 W
Claye-Souilly	219	39.16 N 87.06 W
Claygate	192	37.51 N 83.55 W
Claygate Cross	44	53.10 N 1.24 W
Clayhole Wash V	42	52.06 N 1.07 E
Clayhurst	260	51.22 N 0.20 W
Claymont	182	56.15 N 120.07 W
Clayoquot Sound ʊ	200	36.59 N 113.17 W
Claypole	208	39.48 N 75.27 W
Claypool, Az., U.S.	182	49.11 N 126.08 W
Claypool, In., U.S.	288	34.48 S 58.20 W
Claysburg	200	33.24 N 110.50 W
Clay Springs	218	41.08 N 85.52 W
Claysville	214	40.17 N 78.27 W
Clayton, Austl.	200	34.21 N 110.17 W
Clayton, Eng., U.K.	274b	37.56 S 145.07 E
Clayton, De., U.S.	262	53.47 N 1.50 W
Clayton, Ga., U.S.	212	31.32 N 125.44 E
Clayton, Il., U.S.	219	37.57 N 75.38 W
Clayton, In., U.S.	192	34.53 N 83.24 W
Clayton, La., U.S.	219	40.01 N 90.57 W
Clayton, Mi., U.S.	216	41.52 N 84.14 W
Clayton, Mo., U.S.	194	31.43 N 91.32 W
Clayton, N.J., U.S.	216	41.52 N 84.14 W
Clayton, N.M., U.S.	196	36.27 N 103.11 W
Clayton, N.Y., U.S.	212	44.14 N 76.05 W
Clayton, N.C., U.S.	192	35.39 N 78.27 W
Clayton, Ok., U.S.	196	34.35 N 95.21 W
Clayton, Tx., U.S.	222	32.06 N 94.28 W
Clayton, Wa., U.S.	202	48.00 N 117.33 W

Clayton ≃	166	29.06 S 138.05 E
Claytonia	214	41.00 N 79.58 W
Clayton-le-Moors	262	53.47 N 2.23 W
Clayton-le-Woods	262	53.41 N 2.38 W
Clayton Park ♦	285	39.52 N 75.29 W
Clayton Valley V	282	37.58 N 121.58 W
Claytonville	216	40.34 N 87.49 W
Clay Village	218	38.11 N 85.07 W
Clayville	210	42.59 N 75.15 W
Clear ≃	182	56.11 N 119.42 W
Clear, Cape ›, Ire.	48	51.24 N 9.30 W
Clear, Cape ›, Ak.,		
Clear, Lake ∅	180	59.48 N 147.54 W
Clear, Mount ʌ	212	45.26 N 77.12 W
Clear Boggy Creek ≃	171b	35.52 S 149.04 E
Clearbrook, B.C.,	196	34.03 N 95.47 W
Can.	224	49.08 N 122.26 W
Clearbrook, Mn., U.S.	198	47.41 N 95.25 W
Clear Creek ≃, Al.,	218	39.07 N 86.32 W
U.S.	194	34.00 N 87.19 W
Clear Creek ≃, Az.,		
U.S.	200	34.59 N 110.38 W
Clear Creek ≃, Ca.,		
U.S.	200	40.31 N 122.22 W
Clear Creek ≃, Ca.,		
U.S.	280	34.17 N 118.12 W
Clear Creek ≃, Co.,		
U.S.	282	37.20 N 122.21 W
Clear Creek ≃, Id.,	218	38.10 N 85.17 W
U.S.		
Clear Creek ≃, Mo.,	194	38.00 N 93.56 W
U.S.		
Clear Creek ≃, Mt.,	202	48.46 N 109.25 W
U.S.		
Clear Creek ≃, Ne.,	198	41.08 N 99.06 W
U.S.		
Clear Creek ≃, Oh.,	218	39.33 N 84.20 W
U.S.		
Clear Creek ≃, Or.,	224	45.23 N 122.29 W
U.S.		
Clear Creek ≃, Or.,	224	45.09 N 121.31 W
U.S.		
Clear Creek ≃, Tn.,	192	36.05 N 84.42 W
U.S.		
Clear Creek ≃, Tx.,	196	33.16 N 97.03 W
U.S.		
Clear Creek ≃, Tx.,	222	29.33 N 95.05 W
U.S.		
Clear Creek ≃, Tx.,	222	29.09 N 97.23 W
U.S.		
Clear Creek ≃, Wa.,		
U.S.	224	46.07 N 122.00 W
Clear Creek ≃, Wy.,		
U.S.	194	44.53 N 106.04 W
Clear Creek State		
Park ♦	214	41.20 N 79.05 W
Clearco	214	40.48 N 94.28 W
Clearfield, Ia., U.S.	218	38.09 N 83.25 W
Clearfield, Ky., U.S.	214	41.01 N 78.26 W
Clearfield, Pa., U.S.	200	41.06 N 112.01 W
Clearfield, Ut., U.S.	214	41.02 N 78.27 W
Clearfield Creek ≃	214	41.02 N 78.24 W
Clear Fork Reservoir		
∅¹	214	40.42 N 82.38 W
Clearing	278	41.47 N 87.47 W
Clear Island I	48	51.26 N 9.30 W
Clearlake, Ca., U.S.	226	38.57 N 122.38 W
Clear Lake, Ia., U.S.	190	43.08 N 93.22 W
Clear Lake, S.D.,		
U.S.	198	44.44 N 96.40 W
Clear Lake, Wa., U.S.	224	48.28 N 122.14 W
Clear Lake, Wi., U.S.	190	45.15 N 92.16 W
Clear Lake ∅, Mb.,		
Can.	184	50.42 N 100.00 W
Clear Lake ∅, On.,		
Can.	212	44.59 N 79.33 W
Clear Lake ∅, On.,		
Can.	212	44.30 N 78.13 W
Clear Lake ∅, On.,		
Can.	212	45.14 N 79.57 W
Clear Lake ∅, Ca.,		
U.S.	226	39.02 N 122.50 W
Clear Lake ∅, La.,		
U.S.	194	31.55 N 93.05 W
Clearlake Oaks	226	39.07 N 122.40 W
Clearlake Park	226	38.58 N 122.39 W
Clear Lake Reservoir		
∅¹	226	41.52 N 121.08 W
Clear Lake Shores	222	29.33 N 95.02 W
Clearmont	202	44.38 N 106.22 W
Clear Run	285	39.40 N 80.16 W
Clear Site	180	64.19 N 149.11 W
Clearview, Oh., U.S.	279a	41.25 N 82.01 W
Clearview, W.A., U.S.	224	47.45 N 122.06 W
Clearview Estates	279b	40.34 N 80.16 W
Clearwater, B.C.,		
Can.	182	51.38 N 120.02 W
Clearwater, Mb.,		
Can.	184	49.08 N 99.01 W
Clearwater, Fl., U.S.	192	27.57 N 82.48 W
Clearwater, Ks., U.S.	198	37.30 N 97.30 W
Clearwater, Ne., U.S.	198	42.10 N 98.11 W
Clearwater, S.C.,		
U.S.	192	33.29 N 81.53 W
Clearwater, Wa., U.S.	224	47.34 N 124.17 W
Clearwater ≃, Can.	184	56.44 N 111.23 W
Clearwater ≃, B.C.,		
Can.	182	52.23 N 114.50 W
Clearwater ≃, Id.,	202	46.25 N 117.02 W
U.S.		
Clearwater ≃, Mn.,		
U.S.	198	47.54 N 96.16 W
Clearwater ≃, Mt.,		
U.S.	202	46.58 N 113.23 W
Clearwater ≃, Wa.,		
U.S.	224	47.33 N 124.21 W
Clearwater, Middle		
Fork ≃	202	46.09 N 115.59 W
Clearwater, North		
Fork ≃	202	46.30 N 116.19 W
Clearwater, South		
Fork ≃	202	46.09 N 115.59 W
Clear Water Bay c	271d	22.17 N 114.18 E
Clearwater Beach		
Island I	220	27.59 N 82.49 W
Clearwater Lake ∅,		
B.C., Can.	182	52.15 N 120.13 W
Clearwater Lake ∅,		
Mb., Can.	184	54.05 N 101.00 W
Clearwater Lake		
Provincial Park ♦	184	54.03 N 101.10 W
Clearwater		
Mountains ʌ	202	46.30 N 115.30 W
Cleator Moor	44	54.31 N 3.30 W
Clebit	196	34.21 N 94.52 W
Cleburne	222	32.20 N 97.23 W
Cleckheaton	44	53.43 N 1.43 W
Cle Elum	224	47.11 N 120.56 W
Cle Elum ≃	224	47.11 N 121.01 W
Cle Elum Lake ∅¹	224	47.18 N 121.06 W
Cleethorpes	44	53.34 N 0.02 W
Cleeve Cloud ʌ²	42	51.54 N 2.00 W
Cleggan	48	53.06 N 10.08 W
Cleland Conservation		
Park ♦	168b	34.59 S 138.44 E
Cleland Heights	285	39.44 N 75.34 W
Clelles	62	44.50 N 5.37 E
Clementon	285	39.48 N 74.58 W
Clemmons	192	36.01 N 80.23 W
Clemson	192	34.41 N 82.50 W
Clenchwarton	44	52.45 N 0.24 E
Clendenin	188	38.29 N 81.20 W
Clendening Lake ∅¹	214	40.17 N 81.13 W

Clenze	54	52.56 N 10.58 E
Cleobury Mortimer	42	52.23 N 2.29 W
Cleona	208	40.20 N 76.28 W
Cléon-d'Andran	62	44.37 N 4.56 E
Cleopatra Needle ʌ	116	10.07 N 118.58 E
Clères	50	49.36 N 1.07 E
Clerke Rocks II¹	244	55.01 S 34.41 W
Clermont, Austl.	166	22.49 S 147.39 E
Clermont, P.Q., Can.	186	47.41 N 70.14 W
Clermont, Fr.	50	49.23 N 2.24 E
Clermont, Fl., U.S.	220	28.32 N 81.46 W
Clermont, N.J., U.S.	285	39.59 N 74.48 W
Clermont, Pa., U.S.	214	41.41 N 78.29 W
Clermont □⁶	218	39.05 N 84.11 W
Clermont-en-Argonne	56	49.06 N 5.04 E
Clermont-Ferrand	32	45.47 N 3.05 E
Clermont State Park		
♦	210	42.05 N 73.55 W
Clerval	58	47.24 N 6.30 E
Clervaux	56	50.04 N 6.01 E
Cléry-Saint-André	50	47.49 N 1.45 E
Cles	64	46.22 N 11.02 E
Cleve	166	33.42 S 136.30 E
Clevedon	42	51.27 N 2.51 W
Cleveland, Austl.	171a	27.32 S 153.17 E
Cleveland, Al., U.S.	194	33.59 N 86.34 W
Cleveland, Ga., U.S.	220	26.57 N 80.34 W
Cleveland, Ga., U.S.	192	34.35 N 83.45 W
Cleveland, Ms., U.S.	194	33.44 N 90.43 W
Cleveland, N.Y., U.S.	210	43.14 N 75.53 W
Cleveland, N.C., U.S.	192	35.43 N 80.40 W
Cleveland, Oh., U.S.	214	41.29 N 81.41 W
Cleveland, Oh., U.S.	279a	41.29 N 81.41 W
Cleveland, Ok., U.S.	196	36.18 N 96.27 W
Cleveland, Tn., U.S.	194	35.09 N 84.52 W
Cleveland, Tx., U.S.	222	30.20 N 95.05 W
Cleveland, Va., U.S.	192	36.56 N 82.09 W
Cleveland □⁶	46	54.35 N 1.15 W
Cleveland, Cape ›	166	19.11 S 147.01 E
Cleveland, Mount ʌ,		
Austl.	166	41.25 S 145.23 E
Cleveland, Mount ʌ,		
Mt., U.S.	202	48.56 N 113.51 W
Cleveland Heights	214	41.31 N 81.33 W
Cleveland Hills ʌ²	44	54.23 N 1.05 W
Cleveland-Hopkins		
International		
Airport ⊞	279a	41.25 N 81.51 W
Clevelândia	252	26.24 S 52.21 W
Clevelândia do Norte	250	3.49 N 51.52 W
Cleveland Museum of		
Art ⊡	279a	41.31 N 81.37 W
Cleveland National		
Forest ♦	280	33.47 N 117.38 W
Cleveland Park ⊶ᴮ	284c	38.56 N 77.04 W
Cleveland Peninsula		
⊁¹	182	55.45 N 132.00 W
Cleveland Pond ⊙	283	42.07 N 70.58 W
Cleveland State		
University ⊡²	279a	41.30 N 81.40 W
Cleveland Zoo ♦	279a	41.27 N 81.43 W
Cleveleys	44	53.53 N 3.03 W
Cleversburg	208	40.02 N 77.28 W
Cleves	52	51.48 N 6.09 E
— Kleve, Dtsch.	52	51.48 N 6.09 E
Cleves, Oh., U.S.	218	39.10 N 84.45 W
Clew Bay c	48	53.50 N 9.50 W
Clewer	158	25.55 S 29.07 E
Clewiston	220	26.45 N 80.56 W
Cley next the Sea	42	52.58 N 1.03 E
Clichy	50	48.54 N 2.18 E
Clichy-sous-Bois	261	48.55 N 2.33 E
Cliffden	48	53.29 N 10.01 W
Cliffden Bay c	48	53.28 N 10.05 W
Cliffdale Creek ≃	166	16.56 S 138.48 E
Cliffdell	224	46.44 N 120.42 W
Cliffe	42	51.28 N 0.30 E
Cliffe Marshes ⊞	42	51.28 N 0.30 E
Cliffe Woods	260	51.26 N 0.30 E
Clifford, On., Can.	212	43.58 N 80.58 W
Clifford, S. Afr.	158	31.04 S 27.28 E
Clifford, In., U.S.	218	39.16 N 85.52 W
Clifford, Pa., U.S.	210	41.39 N 75.36 W
Clifford Park ♦	274b	37.43 S 145.16 E
Cliffside	210	42.31 N 74.59 W
Cliffside Park	276	40.49 N 74.00 W
Cliffwood	276	40.26 N 74.14 W
Cliffwood Beach	276	40.26 N 74.13 W
Clifton, Austl.	171a	27.56 S 151.54 E
Clifton, Eng., U.K.	262	53.46 N 2.49 W
Clifton, Az., U.S.	200	33.03 N 109.17 W
Clifton, Il., U.S.	216	40.56 N 87.56 W
Clifton, Ks., U.S.	198	39.34 N 97.17 W
Clifton, N.J., U.S.	210	40.51 N 74.09 W
Clifton, N.Y., U.S.	210	44.13 N 77.49 W
Clifton, Or., U.S.	224	46.12 N 123.27 W
Clifton, Tx., U.S.	194	35.23 N 87.59 W
Clifton, Tx., U.S.	222	31.46 N 97.34 W
Clifton, Lake ∅	168a	32.49 S 115.41 E
Clifton Court Forebay		
∅	226	37.50 N 121.35 W
Clifton Forge	192	37.48 N 79.49 W
Clifton Gorge V²	42	51.28 N 2.37 W
Clifton Heights, N.Y.,		
U.S.	284a	42.44 N 78.56 W
Clifton Heights, Pa.,		
U.S.	285	39.55 N 75.17 W
Clifton Hills	166	26.52 S 138.50 E
Clifton Knolls	210	42.52 N 73.46 W
Clifton Park ♦	279a	39.19 N 76.35 W
Clifton Point ›	240b	25.01 N 77.34 W
Clifton Springs	210	42.57 N 77.08 W
Clifty, Mount ʌ	224	47.07 N 121.10 W
Clifty Creek ≃	218	39.09 N 85.54 W
Clifty Falls State Park		
♦	218	38.45 N 85.26 W
Clignon ≃	50	49.07 N 3.04 E
Climax, Sk., Can.	184	49.13 S 108.23 W
Climax, Co., U.S.	200	39.22 N 106.10 W
Climax, Ga., U.S.	192	30.52 N 84.25 W
Climax, Mi., U.S.	216	42.14 N 85.20 W
Climax, N.Y., U.S.	214	40.59 N 79.23 W
Climax ≃	192	35.53 N 84.29 W
Clinch ≃	192	37.09 N 82.21 W
Clingen	54	51.14 N 10.55 E
Clingmans Dome ʌ	192	35.35 N 83.30 W
Clinton, B.C., Can.	182	51.05 N 121.35 W
Clinton, On., Can.	212	43.37 N 81.32 W
Clinton, N.Z.	172	46.13 S 169.22 E
Clinton, Ar., U.S.	194	35.35 N 92.27 W
Clinton, Ct., U.S.	210	41.16 N 72.31 W
Clinton, In., U.S.	219	40.09 N 87.57 W
Clinton, In., U.S.	218	39.40 N 87.24 W
Clinton, Ia., U.S.	190	41.50 N 90.11 W
Clinton, La., U.S.	194	30.52 N 91.01 W
Clinton, Ma., U.S.	210	42.25 N 71.41 W
Clinton, Md., U.S.	285	38.45 N 76.54 W
Clinton, Mi., U.S.	216	42.04 N 83.58 W
Clinton, Mo., U.S.	194	38.22 N 93.46 W
Clinton, N.J., U.S.	210	40.38 N 74.54 W
Clinton, N.Y., U.S.	210	43.03 N 75.23 W
Clinton, N.C., U.S.	192	35.00 N 78.19 W
Clinton, Oh., U.S.	214	40.56 N 81.38 W
Clinton, Ok., U.S.	196	35.30 N 98.58 W
Clinton, S.C., U.S.	192	34.28 N 81.52 W
Clinton, Tn., U.S.	192	36.06 N 84.07 W
Clinton, Wi., U.S.	216	42.33 N 88.51 W
Clinton ≃	214	42.38 N 82.43 W
Clinton ≃	166	22.31 S 150.45 E
Clinton, Cape ›	166	22.32 S 150.47 E
Clinton, Lake ∅¹	194	40.10 N 88.50 W
Clinton, Middle		
Branch ≃	281	42.36 N 82.54 W
Clinton, North Branch		
≃	214	42.36 N 82.54 W
Clinton-Colden Lake		
∅	176	63.58 N 107.27 W
Clintondale	210	41.01 N 77.29 W
Clinton Lake ∅¹	210	42.36 N 73.43 W
Clinton Park	276	41.05 N 74.27 W
Clinton Reservoir ∅¹	276	41.06 N 74.27 W
Clinton Township	214	42.33 N 82.53 W
Clintonville, Mi., U.S.	281	42.43 N 83.22 W
Clintonville, Pa., U.S.	214	41.12 N 79.53 W
Clintonville, Wi., U.S.	190	44.37 N 88.45 W
Clintwood	192	37.09 N 82.27 W
Clio, Al., U.S.	194	31.42 N 85.36 W
Clio, Mi., U.S.	190	43.10 N 83.44 W
Clio, S.C., U.S.	192	34.34 N 79.32 W
Clipperton, Île I¹	123	10.17 N 109.13 W
Clipperton Fracture		
Zone ✦	16	10.00 N 115.00 W
Clisham ʌ	46	57.57 N 6.49 W
Clisson	32	47.05 N 1.17 W
Clitheroe	44	53.53 N 2.23 W
Clitunno ≃	64	42.56 N 12.37 E
Clive	172	39.35 S 176.55 E
Cloates, Point ›	162	22.43 S 113.40 E
Clock Face	262	53.25 N 2.43 W
Clocolan	158	29.00 S 27.30 E
Clodomira	252	27.35 S 64.08 W
Cloe	214	40.56 N 78.56 W
Cloete	196	27.55 N 101.10 W
Cloghan, Ire.	48	54.51 N 7.56 W
Cloghan, Ire.	48	53.13 N 7.53 W
Cloghan, Ire.	48	52.13 N 10.12 W
Cloghboola	48	52.16 N 8.00 W
Clogher	48	54.25 N 7.12 W
Clogher Head ›	48	53.48 N 6.12 W
Clogherjordan	48	52.57 N 8.02 W
Clonakilty	48	51.37 N 8.54 W
Clonakilty Bay c	48	51.35 N 8.50 W
Cloncurry	166	20.42 S 140.30 E
Cloncurry ≃	166	18.37 S 140.40 E
Clondalkin	48	53.19 N 6.24 W
Clonee	48	53.25 N 6.26 W
Clones	48	54.11 N 7.15 W
Clonfert	48	53.14 N 8.05 W
Clonmacnois ⊥	48	53.20 N 7.59 W
Clonmany	48	55.14 N 7.25 W
Clonmel	48	52.21 N 7.42 W
Clonroche	48	52.27 N 6.43 W
Cloo-close	224	48.40 N 124.49 W
Cloppenburg	52	52.50 N 8.02 E
Cloqualum Creek ≃	224	46.58 S 123.24 W
Cloquet	190	46.43 N 92.27 W
Cloquet ≃	190	46.52 N 92.35 W
Clorinda	252	25.17 S 57.43 W
Closter	276	40.58 N 73.57 W
Cloudcroft	200	32.57 N 105.44 W
Cloud Peak ʌ, Ak.,		
U.S.	180	68.24 N 148.26 W
Cloud Peak ʌ, Wy.,		
U.S.	202	44.25 N 107.10 W
Cloudy Bay c	172	41.27 S 174.10 E
Cloudy Mountain ʌ	180	63.11 S 156.05 W
Clough	48	54.18 N 5.50 W
Cloughy Foot ʌ	262	53.43 N 2.08 W
Clova	46	56.50 N 3.06 W
Clova, Glen V	46	56.49 N 3.04 W
Clove Lakes Park ♦	276	40.37 N 74.06 W
Clovelly, Austl.	274a	33.55 S 151.16 E
Clovelly, Eng., U.K.	42	51.00 N 4.24 W
Clover	192	35.06 N 81.13 W
Clover Bank	210	42.45 N 78.53 W
Clover Creek ≃, Id.,		
U.S.	202	42.34 N 115.38 W
Clover Creek ≃, Id.,		
U.S.	202	42.34 N 115.38 W
Cloverdale, B.C.,		
Can.	224	49.06 N 122.44 W
Cloverdale, Al., U.S.	194	34.56 N 87.46 W
Cloverdale, Ca., U.S.	204	38.48 N 123.00 W
Cloverdale, Il., U.S.	278	41.56 N 88.07 W
Cloverdale, In., U.S.	194	39.30 N 86.47 W
Cloverdale, Ky., U.S.	218	38.10 N 84.53 W
Cloverdale, Mi., U.S.	216	42.32 N 85.23 W
Cloverdale Mall ⊶⁹	275d	43.38 N 79.34 W
Cloverdene	275d	26.09 S 28.22 E
Cloverleaf	222	29.46 N 95.10 W
Clover Pass	182	55.28 N 131.47 W
Cloverport	194	37.50 N 86.37 W
Cloverville	281	43.11 N 86.10 W
Clovis, Ca., U.S.	226	36.49 N 119.42 W
Clovis, N.M., U.S.	196	34.24 N 103.12 W
Clowbridge Reservoir		
∅¹	262	53.45 N 2.16 W
Clowne	44	53.18 N 1.16 W
Cloyes-sur-le-Loir	50	48.00 N 1.14 E
Cloyne	48	51.51 N 8.08 W
— Clonmel	48	52.21 N 7.42 W
Cluanie, Loch ∅¹	46	57.07 N 5.05 W
Cluj □⁴	38	46.45 N 23.45 E
Cluj-Napoca	38	46.47 N 23.36 E
Clun	42	52.26 N 3.02 W
Clun ≃	42	52.25 N 2.53 W
Clune	214	40.34 N 79.18 W
Clunes	169	37.18 S 143.47 E
Clun Forest ⊶³	42	52.28 N 3.07 W
Clunie Water ≃	46	57.00 N 3.24 W
Cluny, Austl.	166	24.31 S 139.35 E
Cluny, Fr.	58	46.26 N 4.39 E
Cluses	58	46.04 N 6.36 E
Clusone	64	45.53 N 9.57 E
Clute	222	29.01 N 95.23 W
Clutha ≃	172	46.21 S 169.48 E
Clutha □⁵	192	37.09 N 82.21 W
Clwyd □⁶	44	53.05 N 3.20 W
Clwyd, Vale of V	44	53.15 N 3.30 W
Clwydian Range ʌ	44	53.10 N 3.20 W
Clydach	42	51.42 N 3.54 W
Clyde, N.Z.	172	45.11 S 169.19 E
Clyde, Ab., Can.	182	54.09 N 113.39 W
Clyde, Ca., U.S.	282	38.01 N 122.03 W
Clyde, Ks., U.S.	198	39.35 N 97.24 W
Clyde, Mi., U.S.	281	42.41 N 83.37 W
Clyde, N.C., U.S.	192	35.32 N 82.55 W
Clyde, N.Y., U.S.	210	43.05 N 76.52 W
Clyde, Oh., U.S.	214	41.18 N 82.59 W
Clyde, Tx., U.S.	196	32.24 N 99.30 W
Clyde ≃, N.S., Can.	186	43.23 N 65.28 W
Clyde ≃, Scot., U.K.	46	55.56 N 4.29 W
Clyde, Firth of c¹	46	55.42 N 5.00 W
Clydebank	46	55.54 N 4.24 W
Clydedale Lake ∅	182	55.18 N 111.28 W
Clyde Park	202	45.53 N 110.36 W
Clyde Ports ⊶		

Cna ≃, Ross.	76	57.33 N 34.36 E	Coburn Mountain ʌ	188	45.28 N 70.06 W
Cna ≃, Ross.	80	54.32 N 42.05 E	Coca ≃	246	0.29 S 76.58 W
Cna ≃, Ross.	82	55.03 N 39.09 E	Coca, Laguna ∅	286b	22.57 N 82.27 W
Cnori	84	41.37 N 45.59 E	Coca, Pizzo di ʌ	64	46.04 N 10.01 E
Cnossus			Cocachacra	248	17.06 S 71.46 W
— Knossós ⊥	38	35.20 N 25.10 E	Cocais, Ribeirão dos		
Côa ≃	34	41.05 N 7.06 W	≃	256	21.59 S 47.15 W
Coacalco	286a	19.37 N 99.05 W	Cocal	250	3.28 S 41.34 W
Coachella	204	33.40 N 116.10 W	Cocalico Creek ≃	208	40.07 N 76.14 W
Coachella Canal ≖	204	33.34 N 116.00 W	Coccaglio	64	45.34 N 9.58 E
Coachford	48	51.53 N 8.48 W	Cocconato	62	45.05 N 8.02 E
Coacoyole	232	24.31 N 106.34 W	Cocentaina	34	38.45 N 0.26 W
Coaculco	234	21.07 N 98.35 W	Cochabamba	248	17.24 S 66.09 W
Coahoma	196	32.18 N 101.18 W	Cochabamba □⁵	248	17.30 S 65.40 W
Coahuayana	234	18.44 N 103.41 W	Cochatauri	84	42.01 N 42.15 E
Coahuayutla de			Cochato ≃	283	42.10 N 71.01 W
Guerrero	234	18.19 N 101.49 W	Coche, Isla I	246	10.45 N 63.55 W
Coahuila	200	32.12 N 114.59 W	Cochem	56	50.11 N 7.09 E
Coahuila □³	232	27.20 N 102.00 W	Cochesett	283	42.01 N 71.02 W
Coalbrook	180	59.39 N 126.57 W	Cochetopa Creek ≃	200	38.31 N 106.47 W
Coalbrookdale	158	26.51 S 27.53 E	Cochichewick, Lake		
Coalburg	42	52.38 N 2.30 W	∅	283	42.42 N 71.06 W
Coalburn	214	41.11 N 80.36 W	Cochin	122	9.58 N 76.14 E
Coal City	46	55.36 N 3.54 W	Cochin China		
Coalcomán ≃	216	41.17 N 88.17 W	— Nam Phan □⁹	110	11.00 N 107.00 E
Coalcomán de	234	18.11 N 103.08 W	Cochinos, Bahía de		
Matamoros	234	18.47 N 103.09 W	(Bay of Pigs) c	286b	22.07 N 81.10 W
Coaldale, Ab., Can.	182	49.43 N 112.37 W	Cochinos, Cayos II	236	15.57 N 86.33 W
Coaldale, Pa., U.S.	208	40.49 N 75.54 W	Cochise Head ʌ	200	32.03 N 109.18 W
Coal Fire Creek ≃	194	33.15 N 88.18 W	Cochiti Indian		
Coalfork	188	38.19 N 81.32 W	Reservation □⁴	200	35.37 N 106.20 W
Coalgate	196	34.32 N 96.13 W	Cochituate	207	42.19 N 71.21 W
Coalgate, Ok., U.S.	196	34.30 N 96.12 W	Cochituate, Lake ∅	283	42.17 N 71.22 W
Coal Grove	188	38.30 N 82.38 W	Cochituate State		
Coal Harbour	182	50.36 N 127.35 W	Park ♦	207	42.19 N 71.22 W
Coal Hill	194	35.26 N 93.40 W	Cochran	192	32.23 N 83.21 W
Coal Hill Park ♦	271a	39.56 N 116.23 E	Cochrane, Ab., Can.	182	51.11 N 114.28 W
Coalhurst	182	49.45 N 112.56 W	Cochrane, On., Can.	186	49.04 N 81.01 W
Coalinga	226	36.08 N 120.21 W	Cochrane, Chile	254	47.16 S 72.33 W
Coalisland	48	54.11 N 7.15 W	Cochrane, Wi., U.S.	190	44.13 N 91.50 W
Coal Island ∅	172	46.07 S 166.38 E	Cochrane ≃	176	57.52 N 101.38 W
Coalmont	182	49.31 N 120.41 W	Cochrane, Cerro		
Coalpit Heath	42	51.32 N 2.28 W	(Monte San		
Coalport	214	40.44 N 78.32 W	Lorenzo) ʌ	254	47.37 S 72.19 W
Coal River	180	59.45 N 126.55 W	Cochrane, Lago		
Coal Run	279b	40.20 N 80.07 W	(Lago Pueyrredón)		
Coalspur	182	53.11 N 117.01 W	∅	254	47.20 S 72.00 W
Coalton	219	39.17 N 89.19 W	Cochranton	214	41.31 N 80.02 W
Coaltown	214	41.02 N 80.20 W	Cochranville	208	39.53 N 75.55 W
Coal Valley V	204	38.00 N 115.05 W	Cockatoo ≃	54	51.53 N 11.24 E
Coalville, S. Afr.	158	26.01 S 29.10 E	Cockatoo-Inseln		
Coalville, Eng., U.K.	42	52.44 N 1.20 W	— Buccaneer		
Coalville, Ut., U.S.	200	40.55 N 111.23 W	Archipelago II	160	16.17 S 123.20 E
Coamo	240m	18.05 N 66.22 W	Cock Bridge	46	57.09 N 3.14 W
Coamo, Lago ∅¹	240m	18.08 N 66.23 W	Cockburn	166	32.05 S 141.00 E
Coapilla	234	17.08 N 93.10 W	Cockburn, Canal ≖	254	54.20 S 71.30 W
Coaraci	255	14.38 S 39.32 W	Cockburn, Cape ›	164	11.20 S 132.52 E
Coari	246	4.05 S 63.08 W	Cockburn, Mount ʌ	164	23.46 S 130.36 E
Coari ≃	246	4.30 S 63.33 W	Cockburn Island I	190	45.55 N 83.22 W
Coari, Lago de ∅	246	4.15 S 63.22 W	Cockburn Sound ⊔	168a	32.12 S 115.42 E
Coarsegold	226	37.16 N 119.42 W	Cockburnspath	46	55.56 N 2.21 W
Coast □⁴	154	3.00 S 39.30 E	Cock Clarks	260	51.42 N 0.37 E
Coast Mountains ↗	176	55.00 N 129.00 W	Cockenoe Island I	276	41.05 N 73.21 W
Coast Ranges ↗	178	41.00 N 123.30 W	Cockerel	46	55.58 N 2.59 W
Coatán ≃	236	14.48 N 92.31 W	Cockermouth	44	54.40 N 3.21 W
Coatbridge	46	55.52 N 4.01 W	Cockeysville	208	39.28 N 76.38 W
Coatepec	234	19.27 N 96.58 W	Cockfield	44	54.37 N 1.48 W
Coatepec Harinas	234	18.54 N 99.43 W	Cockfosters ⊶⁸	260	51.39 N 0.09 W
Coatepeque	236	14.42 N 91.52 W	Cocklebiddy	162	32.02 S 126.06 E
Coatesville	208	39.59 N 75.49 W	Cockpit Country ⊶¹	241q	18.18 N 77.43 W
Coaticook	206	45.08 N 71.48 W	Cockrell Hill	222	32.44 N 96.53 W
Coats Island I	176	62.30 N 83.00 W	Cockroach Island I	240m	18.24 N 65.04 W
Coats Land ⊶¹	197	77.00 S 28.00 W	Cockscomb Point ›	174u	14.14 S 170.40 W
Coatzacoalcos	234	18.09 N 94.25 W	Cocle □⁴	236	8.30 N 80.15 W
Coatzacoalcos ≃	234	18.10 N 94.27 W	Coclé del Norte ≃	236	9.05 N 80.35 W
Coatzintla	234	20.29 N 97.27 W	Coclois	50	48.25 N 4.15 E
Coayllo	248	12.44 S 76.28 W	Coco ≃	236	14.58 N 83.15 W
Coazze	62	45.03 N 7.18 E	Coco, Cayo I	230	22.30 N 78.24 W
Coba ⊥	234	20.30 N 87.35 W	Coco, Isla del I	230	5.32 N 87.04 W
Cobadin	38	44.04 N 28.13 E	Côco, Rio do ≃	250	9.27 S 50.02 W
Cobalt, On., Can.	186	47.24 N 79.41 W	Cocoa	220	28.21 N 80.44 W
Cobalt, Ct., U.S.	207	41.33 N 72.33 W	Cocoa Beach	220	28.19 N 80.36 W
Cobán	236	15.29 N 90.19 W	Cocobeach	152	0.59 N 9.36 E
Çobanlar	130	38.43 N 30.47 E	Coco Channel ⋓	110	14.00 N 93.30 E
Cobar	166	31.30 S 145.49 E	Cococi	250	6.25 S 40.30 W
Cobargo	166	36.23 S 149.53 E	Coco Channel ⋓	250	30.58 N 92.25 W
Cobb ≃	172	40.53 S 172.38 E	Cocodrie Lake ∅¹	194	30.58 N 92.25 W
Cobb, Mount ʌ	166	36.52 S 148.10 E	Coco Islands II	110	14.05 N 93.18 E
Cobbetts Pond ∅	283	42.48 N 71.17 W	Cocos (Keeling)		
Cobbin's Brook ≃	260	51.41 N 0.01 W	Islands ⊡²	14	12.10 S 96.55 E
Cobb Island I, Md.,			Cocos Island I	241r	10.27 N 61.00 W
U.S.	208	38.16 N 76.51 W	Cocos Island I	174p	13.14 N 144.39 E
Cobb Island I, Va.,			Cocos Lagoon c	174p	13.14 N 144.38 E
U.S.	208	37.20 N 75.44 W	Cocos Ridge ↗⁴	16	5.30 N 86.00 W
Cobbitty	274a	34.01 S 150.41 E	Cocui ≃	248	10.59 N 71.17 W
Cobbitty ʌ²	166	34.30 S 149.21 E	Cocuiza ≃	248	10.59 N 71.17 W
Cobble Hill	283	33.59 S 150.32 E	Cocula, Méx.	234	18.14 N 99.40 W
Cobble Mountain			Cocula, Méx.	234	20.23 N 103.50 W
Reservoir ∅¹	207	42.08 N 72.55 W	Cod ≃	44	54.10 N 1.22 W
Cobblestone	44	57.00 N 3.24 W	Cod, Cape › I	207	41.42 N 70.15 W
Cobbs Creek ≃	285	39.54 N 75.15 W	Codajás	246	3.50 S 62.05 W
Cobbs Creek Park ♦	285	39.56 N 75.15 W	Codaru	71	40.56 N 9.28 E
Cobb Seamount ↝³	16	46.46 N 130.49 W	Coddenham	42	52.09 N 1.07 E
Cobden, Austl.	169	38.20 S 143.05 E	Codera, Cabo ›	246	10.35 N 66.05 W
Cobden, On., Can.	212	45.37 N 76.53 W	Coderre	184	50.12 N 106.23 W
Cobden, Il., U.S.	208	37.32 N 89.15 W	Coderre, Ruisseau ≃	275	45.43 N 73.19 W
Cobh	48	51.51 N 8.17 W	Codera	182	46.13 N 167.38 W
Cobham, Eng., U.K.	42	51.20 N 0.24 E	Codfish Island I	172	46.43 S 167.38 E
Cobham, Eng., U.K.	260	51.25 N 0.25 E	Cod Island I	176	57.45 N 61.50 W
Cobham Hall ⊥	260	51.24 N 0.24 E	Codlea	38	45.43 N 25.27 E
Cobija, Bol.	248	11.02 S 68.44 W	Codó	250	4.28 S 43.53 W
Cobija, Chile	254	22.33 S 70.16 W	Cod, Wy., U.S.	202	44.31 N 109.04 W
Coblenz			Cody, Ne., U.S.	198	42.56 N 101.14 W
— Koblenz, Dtsch.	56	50.21 N 7.35 E	Cody, Wy., U.S.	202	44.31 N 109.04 W
Coboconk	212	44.39 N 78.48 W	Coeburn	192	36.57 N 82.27 W
Cobos ≃, Austl.	166	38.52 S 145.28 E	Coelemu	252	36.29 S 72.42 W
Cobos ≃, Austl.	166	13.56 S 143.42 E	Coelho da Rocha	256	22.47 S 43.23 W
Coboconk, gora ʌ	88	46.44 N 130.49 W	Coelho Neto	250	4.15 S 43.00 W
Coboto, Cerro ʌ	200	31.29 N 112.05 W	Coemba	152	12.08 S 18.05 E
Cobourg	212	43.58 N 78.10 W	Coen, Austl.	166	13.56 S 143.12 E
Cobourg Peninsula			Coen ≃	166	13.52 S 142.06 E
⊁¹	164	11.20 S 132.15 E	Coesfeld	52	51.56 N 7.10 E
Cobram	169	35.56 S 145.39 E	Coëtivy Island I	138	7.08 S 56.16 E
Cobre, Barranca del			Coeur d'Alene	202	47.41 N 116.45 W
≃	232	27.20 N 107.50 W	Coeur d'Alene Indian		
Cobre ≃	232	8.01 N 81.18 W	Reservation □⁴	202	47.18 N 116.45 W
Cobre, Barranca del			Coeur d'Alene Lake		
≃	232	27.20 N 107.50 W	∅	202	47.32 N 116.45 W
Côbué	159	12.08 S 34.45 E	Coeur d'Alene		
Coburg, Austl.	169	37.45 S 144.58 E	Mountains ʌ	202	47.30 N 116.05 W
Coburg, Dtsch.	54	50.15 N 10.58 E	Coevorden	52	52.40 N 6.45 E
Coburg Island I	176	76.00 N 79.25 W	Coffee ≃	219	39.05 N 89.38 W
Coburn	210	40.54 N 77.28 W	Coffee Lake ∅¹	194	33.58 N 89.40 W
			Coffeeville	194	31.45 N 88.06 W

Symbols in the index entries represent the broad categories identified in the key at the right. Symbols with superior numbers (ʌ¹) identify subcategories (see complete key on page I · 1).

Symbole im Register stellen die rechts im Schlüssel erklärten Kategorien dar. Symbole mit hochgestellten Ziffern (ʌ¹) bezeichnen Unterabteilungen einer Kategorie (vgl. vollständiger Schlüssel auf Seite I · 1).

Los símbolos incluídos en el texto del índice representan las grandes categorías identificadas con la clave a la derecha. Los símbolos con números en su parte superior (ʌ¹) identifican las subcategorías (véase la clave completa a página I · 1).

Os símbolos incluídos no texto do índice representam as grandes categorias identificadas com a chave à direita. Os símbolos com números em sua parte superior (ʌ¹) identificam as subcategorias (veja-se a chave completa à página I · 1).

Les symboles de l'index représentent les catégories indiquées dans la légende à droite. Les symboles suivis d'un indice (ʌ¹) représentent des sous-catégories (voir légende complète à la page I · 1).

ʌ Mountain	Berg	Montaña	Montaña	Montanha
↗ Mountains	Gebirge	Montañas	Montagnes	Montanhas
⊀ Pass	Paß	Paso	Col	Passo
V Valley, Canyon	Tal, Cañon	Valle, Cañón	Vallée, Canyon	Vale, Canhão
⊳ Plain	Ebene	Llano	Plaine	Planície
› Cape	Kap	Cabo	Cap	Cabo
I Island	Insel	Isla	Île	Ilha
II Islands	Inseln	Islas	Îles	Ilhas
♦ Other Topographic Features	Andere Topographische Objekte	Otros Elementos Topográficos	Autres données topographiques	Outros acidentes topográficos

ESPAÑOL: Nombre · Página · Lat.°′ · Long.°′ W = Oeste — FRANÇAIS: Nom · Page · Lat.°′ · Long.°′ W = Ouest — PORTUGUÊS: Nome · Página · Lat.°′ · Long.°′ W = Oeste

Nombre / Nom / Nome	Página / Page	Lat.°′	Long.°′
Coffeyville	198	37.02 N	95.36 W
Coffin Bay	162	34.37 S	135.29 E
Coffin Bay c	162	34.27 S	135.19 E
Coffin Bay Peninsula ≻[1]	162	34.32 S	135.15 E
Coffs Harbour	166	30.18 S	153.08 E
Cofimvaba	158	32.00 S	27.35 E
Cofradía	236	15.24 N	88.09 W
Cofre de Perote, Cerro ∧	234	19.29 N	97.08 W
Cofre de Perote, Parque Nacional ♠	234	19.32 N	97.10 W
Cofrents	34	39.14 N	1.04 W
Coggeshall	42	51.52 N	0.41 E
Coggiola	62	45.41 N	8.11 E
Coggon	190	42.16 N	91.31 W
Coghill, Mount ∧	170	35.10 S	149.44 E
Coghinas ≃	71	40.56 N	8.48 E
Coghinas, Lago del ⊜	71	40.45 N	9.02 E
Coglians, Monte (Hohe Warte) ∧	64	46.37 N	12.53 E
Cogliate	266b	45.39 N	9.05 E
Cognac	32	45.42 N	0.20 W
Cogne	62	45.37 N	7.21 E
Cognin	62	45.34 N	5.54 E
Cogo	152	1.05 N	9.42 E
Cogoleto	62	44.23 N	8.39 E
Cogolin	62	43.15 N	6.32 E
Cogollo del Cengio	64	45.47 N	11.25 E
Cogolludo	34	40.57 N	3.05 W
Cogolo	64	46.21 N	10.41 E
Cogoon ≃	166	27.19 S	143.50 E
Čograjuskoje vodochranilišče ⊜[1]	80	45.30 N	44.25 E
Cogswell	198	46.06 N	97.46 W
Cogswell Reservoir ⊜[1]	280	34.14 N	117.58 W
Cogt	102	45.20 N	96.33 E
Cogtoandman'	102	45.50 N	104.23 E
Cogton Bay c	116	9.51 N	124.33 E
Cogt-Ovoo	102	44.25 N	105.20 E
Çoğun	130	39.20 N	34.03 E
Cohansey ≃	208	39.21 N	75.22 W
Cohasset	207	42.14 N	70.48 W
Cohasset Harbor c	283	42.15 N	70.47 W
Cohengu ≃	248	10.17 S	73.57 W
Cohoctah	216	42.46 N	83.57 W
Cohocton	210	42.30 N	77.30 W
Cohocton ≃	210	42.09 N	77.05 W
Cohoe	180	60.23 N	151.18 W
Cohoes	210	42.46 N	73.42 W
Cohoon, Lake ⊜[1]	208	36.45 N	76.38 W
Cohuna	166	35.49 S	144.13 E
Coiba, Isla de I	246	7.27 N	81.45 W
Coig ≃	254	50.58 S	69.11 W
Coigeach, Rubha ≻	46	58.06 N	5.26 W
Coignières	261	48.45 N	1.55 E
Coihaique	254	45.34 S	72.04 W
Coils Creek ≃	204	39.32 N	116.16 W
Coimbatore	122	11.00 N	76.58 E
Coimbra, Bra.	248	19.55 S	57.47 W
Coimbra, Bra.	255	20.52 S	42.48 W
Coimbra, Port.	34	40.12 N	8.25 W
Coín, Esp.	34	36.40 N	4.45 W
Coin, Ia., U.S.	198	40.39 N	95.13 W
Coina ≃	266c	38.38 N	9.03 W
Coipasa, Lago ⊜	248	19.12 S	68.07 W
Coipasa, Salar de ≚	248	19.26 S	68.09 W
Coire → Chur	58	46.51 N	9.32 E
Čojbalsan, Mong.	88	48.25 N	114.52 E
Čojbalsan, Mong.	88	48.04 N	114.30 E
Čojbalsan uul ∧	88	47.49 N	107.00 E
Cojedes	246	9.37 N	68.55 W
Cojedes □[3]	246	9.20 N	68.20 W
Cojímar ◆[8]	286b	23.10 N	82.18 W
Cojímar ≃	286b	23.10 N	82.17 W
Cojudo Blanco, Cerro ∧	254	47.05 S	69.20 W
Cojumatlán de Régules	234	20.07 N	102.50 W
Cojutepeque	236	13.43 N	88.56 W
Çokak	130	37.45 N	36.19 E
Cokato	190	45.04 N	94.11 W
Cokeburg	214	40.06 N	80.04 W
Coker	273a	6.29 N	3.20 E
Cokeville	200	42.04 N	110.57 W
Čoktal	85	42.36 N	76.44 E
Čokurdach	74	70.38 N	147.55 E
Colāba ◆[8]	272c	18.54 N	72.48 E
Colāba Point ≻	272c	18.53 N	72.48 E
Colac	169	38.20 S	143.35 E
Colac, Lake ⊜	169	38.18 S	143.35 E
Çolaklı	130	38.22 N	38.33 E
Colalao del Valle	252	26.22 S	65.57 W
Colapsin Point ≻	116	6.38 N	125.25 E
Colares, Bra.	250	0.56 S	48.17 W
Colares, Port.	266c	38.48 N	9.27 W
Colares, Ribeira de ≃	266c	38.49 N	9.28 W
Colatina	255	19.32 S	40.37 W
Cölbe	56	50.51 N	8.48 E
Colbeck, Cape ≻	9	77.06 S	157.48 W
Colberry Park	281	42.36 N	83.16 W
Colbert	196	33.51 N	96.30 W
Colbinabbin	166	36.35 S	144.49 E
Colbitz	54	52.19 N	11.36 E
Colbitz-Letzlinger Heide ◆[3]	54	52.27 N	11.35 E
Colborne, On., Can.	212	42.51 N	80.19 W
Colborne, On., Can.	212	44.00 N	77.53 W
Colbún	252	35.42 S	71.25 W
Colbún, Embalse ⊜[1]	252	35.40 S	71.20 W
Colburn, Eng., U.K.	44	54.23 N	1.41 W
Colburn, In., U.S.	216	40.31 N	86.42 W
Colby, Ks., U.S.	198	39.23 N	101.03 W
Colby, Wi., U.S.	190	44.54 N	90.18 W
Colca	248	12.18 S	75.13 W
Colca ≃	248	15.51 S	72.26 W
Colcamar	248	6.16 S	77.55 W
Colchester, On., Can.	214	41.59 N	82.56 W
Colchester, Eng., U.K.	42	51.54 N	0.54 E
Colchester, Ct., U.S.	207	41.34 N	72.19 W
Colchester, Il., U.S.	190	40.25 N	90.47 W
Coldbackie	46	58.31 N	4.23 W
Cold Bay	180	55.11 N	162.30 W
Cold Bay c	180	55.13 N	162.33 W
Coldblow ◆[8]	260	51.26 N	0.10 E
Cold Brook	210	43.15 N	75.03 W
Cold Creek ≃	212	44.12 N	77.36 W
Colden	210	42.39 N	78.41 W
Cold Fell ∧	44	54.54 N	2.36 W
Cold Harbor Battlefield ⊥	208	37.36 N	77.20 W
Coldingham	46	55.53 N	2.10 W
Colditz	54	51.07 N	12.48 E
Cold Lake	184	54.27 N	110.10 W
Cold Lake ⊜	184	54.33 N	110.05 W
Cold Lake, Canadian Forces Base ■	184	54.25 N	110.17 W
Cold Lake Indian Reserve ◆[4]	184	54.33 N	110.10 W
Cold Norton	260	51.40 N	0.40 E
Coldrano	64	46.38 N	10.50 E
Cold Spring, Ky., U.S.	218	39.01 N	84.26 W
Cold Spring, Mn., U.S.	190	45.27 N	94.25 W
Cold Spring, N.J., U.S.	208	38.58 N	74.55 W
Cold Spring, N.Y., U.S.	210	41.25 N	73.57 W
Coldspring, Tx., U.S.	222	30.36 N	95.08 W
Cold Spring Harbor	276	40.52 N	73.27 W
Cold Spring Harbor c	276	40.53 N	73.28 W
Coldsprings, On., Can.	212	44.17 N	78.18 W
Cold Springs, N.Y., U.S.	210	43.08 N	76.15 W
Cold Spring Terrace	276	40.50 N	73.25 W
Coldstream, Austl.	169	37.44 S	145.23 E
Coldstream, Scot., U.K.	46	55.39 N	2.15 W
Cold Stream ≃	226	39.35 N	120.22 W
Coldwater, On., Can.	212	44.42 N	79.40 W
Coldwater, Ks., U.S.	198	37.16 N	99.19 W
Coldwater, Mi., U.S.	216	41.56 N	85.00 W
Coldwater, Ms., U.S.	194	34.41 N	89.58 W
Coldwater, Oh., U.S.	216	40.28 N	84.37 W
Coldwater ≃, On., Can.	212	44.44 N	79.39 W
Coldwater ≃, Mi., U.S.	216	42.04 N	85.08 W
Coldwater ≃, Ms., U.S.	194	34.11 N	90.13 W
Coldwater Canyon V	280	34.14 N	117.44 W
Coldwater Creek ≃	196	36.40 N	101.08 W
Coldwater Indian Reserve ◆[4]	182	50.04 N	120.48 W
Coldwater Lake ⊜	216	41.49 N	84.58 W
Cole □[6]	219	38.30 N	92.13 W
Cole ≃, Ang.	152	9.07 S	15.50 E
Cole ≃, Eng., U.K.	42	51.42 N	1.42 W
Coleambally	166	34.49 S	145.52 E
Colebrook, N.H., U.S.	188	44.53 N	71.29 W
Colebrook, Oh., U.S.	214	41.32 N	80.46 W
Colebrook River Lake ⊜[1]	207	42.03 N	73.04 W
Cole Camp	194	38.27 N	93.12 W
Coledale	170	34.17 S	150.57 E
Coleen ≃	180	67.05 N	142.31 W
Coleford, Eng., U.K.	42	51.48 N	2.36 W
Coleford, Eng., U.K.	42	51.14 N	2.27 W
Colégio, Morro do ∧	287b	23.38 S	46.21 W
Coleman, Ab., Can.	182	49.38 N	114.30 W
Coleman, Fl., U.S.	220	28.47 N	82.04 W
Coleman, Md., U.S.	208	39.20 N	76.04 W
Coleman, Mi., U.S.	190	43.45 N	84.35 W
Coleman, Tx., U.S.	196	31.49 N	99.25 W
Coleman, Wi., U.S.	190	45.03 N	88.02 W
Coleman ≃	164	15.06 S	141.38 E
Coleman, Lake ⊜[1]	196	32.02 N	99.30 W
Colembert	50	50.45 N	1.50 E
Colen Lakes ⊜	184	54.33 N	95.25 W
Colenso	158	28.50 S	29.44 E
Colerain	214	40.07 N	80.49 W
Coleraine, Austl.	166	37.36 S	141.42 E
Coleraine, N. Ire., U.K.	48	55.08 N	6.40 W
Coleraine, Mn., U.S.	190	47.17 N	93.25 W
Coleridge	198	42.30 N	97.12 W
Coleridge, Lake ⊜	172	43.17 S	171.30 E
Coles	194	31.16 N	91.01 W
Coles, Punta ≻	248	17.42 S	71.23 W
Colesberg	158	30.45 S	25.05 E
Coles Brook ≃	276	40.55 N	74.02 W
Coleshill, Eng., U.K.	42	52.30 N	1.42 W
Coleshill, Eng., U.K.	260	51.39 N	0.38 W
Coles Point	208	38.09 N	76.38 W
Colesville, Md., U.S.	284c	39.05 N	77.00 W
Colesville, N.J., U.S.	210	41.15 N	74.39 W
Coleto Creek ≃	196	28.41 N	97.01 W
Coleville, Sk., Can.	184	51.43 N	109.16 W
Coleville, Ca., U.S.	226	38.33 N	119.30 W
Colfax, Ca., U.S.	226	39.06 N	120.57 W
Colfax, Il., U.S.	216	40.34 N	88.36 W
Colfax, In., U.S.	194	40.11 N	86.40 W
Colfax, Ia., U.S.	190	41.40 N	93.14 W
Colfax, La., U.S.	194	31.31 N	92.42 W
Colfax, Wa., U.S.	202	46.52 N	117.21 W
Colfax, Wi., U.S.	190	44.59 N	91.43 W
Colfiorito	66	43.02 N	12.55 E
Colgate	216	43.12 N	88.12 W
Colgate Creek ≃	284b	39.15 N	76.32 W
Colgong	124	25.16 N	87.13 E
Colgrave Sound ⊔	46a	60.37 N	0.58 W
Colhué Huapi, Lago ⊜	254	45.30 S	68.48 W
Coliban ≃	169	36.56 S	144.33 E
Colibris, Pointe des ≻, Guad.	241o	16.15 N	61.11 W
Colibris, Pointe des ≻, Guad.	241o	16.17 N	61.06 W
Colico	58	46.08 N	9.22 E
Coligny, Fr.	58	46.23 N	5.21 E
Coligny, S. Afr.	158	26.17 S	26.15 E
Colijnsplaat	52	51.46 N	3.51 E
Colima, Méx.	200	32.25 N	115.05 W
Colima, Méx.	234	19.14 N	103.43 W
Colima □[3]	234	19.10 N	104.00 W
Colima, Nevado de ∧	234	19.33 N	103.38 W
Colimes ≃	246	1.32 S	80.00 W
Colin ≃	50	47.08 N	2.32 E
Colina	252	33.12 S	70.41 W
Colinas, Bra.	250	6.02 S	44.14 W
Colinas, Bra.	255	14.12 S	48.03 W
Colinet	186	47.13 N	53.33 W
Colinton, Austl.	171b	35.51 S	149.09 E
Colinton, Ab., Can.	182	54.37 N	113.15 W
Coliseum → Colosseo ⊥	267a	41.54 N	12.29 E
Coll I	46	56.38 N	6.34 W
Colla	258	34.04 S	57.21 W
Colla, Arroyo ≃	258	34.19 S	57.20 W
Collagna	64	44.21 N	10.16 E
Collalbo (Klobenstein)	64	46.32 N	11.28 E
Collalto Sabino	66	42.08 N	13.02 E
Collamer	210	43.06 N	76.04 W
Collarenebri	166	29.33 S	148.35 E
Collarmele	66	42.03 N	13.38 E
Collaroy	274a	33.44 S	151.18 E
Collazzone	66	42.54 N	12.26 E
Collbran	200	39.14 N	107.57 W
Collecchio	64	44.45 N	10.13 E
Collecorvino	66	42.27 N	14.01 E
Colle di Tora	66	42.13 N	12.57 E
Colle di Val d'Elsa	66	43.25 N	11.07 E
Colleen Bawn	154	21.00 S	29.13 E
Colleferro	66	41.44 N	12.59 E
College	180	64.51 N	147.47 W
College City	226	39.00 N	122.00 W
College Corner	218	39.30 N	84.36 W
Collegedale	194	35.04 N	85.03 W
College Meadows	218	39.56 N	86.07 W
College Park, Ga., U.S.	192	33.39 N	84.26 W
College Park, Md., U.S.	208	38.58 N	76.56 W
College Park Airport ⊠	284c	38.58 N	76.55 W
College Place	202	46.02 N	118.23 W
College Point ◆[8]	276	40.47 N	73.51 W
College Station, Ar., U.S.	194	34.43 N	92.13 W
College Station, Tx., U.S.	222	30.37 N	96.20 W
Collegeville, In., U.S.	216	40.54 N	87.09 W
Collegeville, Pa., U.S.	208	40.11 N	75.27 W
Collégien	261	48.50 N	2.40 E
Collegno	62	45.05 N	7.34 E
Colle Isarco (Gossensass)	64	46.56 N	11.26 E
Collepardo	66	41.46 N	13.22 E
Collepasso	68	40.04 N	18.10 E
Collepietro	66	42.13 N	13.46 E
Collerina	166	29.41 S	146.38 E
Collesalvetti	66	43.35 N	10.28 E
Colle Sannita	68	41.22 N	14.50 E
Collesano	70	37.55 N	13.56 E
Colletorto	66	41.40 N	14.58 E
Colleymount	182	54.01 N	126.09 W
Colleyville	222	32.52 N	97.09 W
Colliano	68	40.43 N	15.17 E
Colli a Volturno	66	41.36 N	14.06 E
Colli del Tronto	66	42.52 N	13.44 E
Colli di Monte Bove	66	42.06 N	13.09 E
Collie	168a	33.21 S	116.09 E
Collie East ≃	168a	33.16 S	116.10 E
Collier □[6]	220	26.10 N	81.22 W
Collier Bay c	160	16.10 S	124.15 E
Collier Bridge ◆[5]	220	26.57 N	82.04 W
Collier City	220	26.14 N	80.09 W
Collier Law ∧[2]	44	54.46 N	1.58 W
Collier Range ⋏	162	24.43 S	119.12 E
Collier Range National Park ♠	162	24.40 S	119.15 E
Collier Row ◆[8]	260	51.36 N	0.10 E
Colliers	214	40.22 N	80.32 W
Collier-Seminole State Park ♠	220	25.59 N	81.36 W
Colliersville	210	42.29 N	74.59 W
Collierville	194	35.02 N	89.39 W
Collie South ≃	168a	33.18 S	116.10 E
Collieston	46	57.21 N	1.56 W
Colliford Lake Reservoir ⊜[1]	42	50.32 N	4.33 W
Colligan ≃	48	52.06 N	7.38 W
Collin □[6]	222	33.07 N	96.35 W
Collingbourne Kingston	42	51.18 N	1.40 W
Collingdale	208	39.54 N	75.16 W
Collingham	44	53.54 N	1.24 W
Collingswood	285	39.55 N	75.04 W
Collingwood, Austl.	274b	37.48 S	145.00 E
Collingwood, On., Can.	212	44.29 N	80.13 W
Collingwood, N.Z.	172	40.40 S	172.41 E
Collingwood Bay c	164	9.20 S	149.30 E
Collins, Ga., U.S.	192	32.10 N	82.06 W
Collins, Ia., U.S.	190	41.54 N	93.18 W
Collins, Ms., U.S.	194	31.38 N	89.33 W
Collins, N.Y., U.S.	210	42.30 N	78.55 W
Collins, Oh., U.S.	214	41.16 N	82.30 W
Collins ≃	194	35.48 N	85.37 W
Collins, Mount ∧[2]	190	47.51 N	80.59 W
Collins Bay	212	44.15 N	76.36 W
Collinsburg	214	40.13 N	79.46 W
Collins Center	210	42.30 N	78.51 W
Collins Lake ⊜	212	44.22 N	76.27 W
Collins Park	208	39.41 N	75.33 W
Collinston	194	32.41 N	91.52 W
Collinsville, Austl.	166	20.34 S	147.51 E
Collinsville, Al., U.S.	194	34.15 N	85.51 W
Collinsville, Ca., U.S.	282	38.05 N	121.51 W
Collinsville, Ct., U.S.	207	41.48 N	72.55 W
Collinsville, Il., U.S.	219	38.40 N	89.59 W
Collinsville, Ms., U.S.	194	32.29 N	88.50 W
Collinsville, N.J., U.S.	276	40.49 N	74.28 W
Collinsville, Ok., U.S.	196	36.21 N	95.50 W
Collinsville, Tx., U.S.	196	33.32 N	96.54 W
Collinwood	194	35.10 N	87.44 W
Collio	64	45.48 N	10.20 E
Collipulli	252	37.57 S	72.26 W
Collister	202	43.38 N	116.15 W
Collobrières	62	43.14 N	6.18 E
Collombey	58	46.16 N	6.57 E
Collomsville	210	41.09 N	77.09 W
Collon	48	53.47 N	6.29 W
Collonges	58	46.08 N	5.54 E
Collooney	48	54.11 N	8.29 W
Collserola, Serra de ⋏	266d	41.26 N	2.07 E
Colma	226	37.41 N	122.28 W
Colma Creek ≃	282	37.38 N	122.23 W
Colman	198	43.58 N	96.48 W
Colmar	58	48.05 N	7.22 E
Colmar Manor	284c	38.55 N	76.56 W
Colmars	62	44.11 N	6.38 E
Colmenar	34	36.54 N	4.20 W
Colmenar de Oreja	34	40.06 N	3.23 W
Colmenar Viejo	34	40.40 N	3.46 W
Colmeneros	234	18.06 N	101.40 W
Colmesneil	194	30.54 N	94.25 W
Colmnitz	54	50.54 N	13.31 E
Colmonell	44	55.08 N	4.55 W
Coln ≃	42	51.42 N	1.42 W
Colnbrook	260	51.29 N	0.31 W
Colne	44	53.52 N	2.09 W
Colne ≃, Eng., U.K.	42	51.48 N	1.01 E
Colne ≃, Eng., U.K.	260	51.26 N	0.30 W
Colney Heath	260	51.44 N	0.15 W
Colney Street	260	51.42 N	0.20 W
Colo	190	42.01 N	93.18 W
Colo ≃	170	33.26 S	150.53 E
Colobraro	68	40.11 N	16.25 E
Cologna Veneta	64	45.18 N	11.23 E
Cologne → Köln, Dtsch.	56	50.56 N	6.59 E
Cologne, Mn., U.S.	190	44.46 N	93.46 W
Cologne, N.J., U.S.	208	39.30 N	74.36 W
Cologno al Serio	62	45.37 N	9.42 E
Cologno Monzese	266b	45.32 N	9.17 E
Cololo, Nevado ∧	248	14.53 S	69.06 W
Coloma, Ca., U.S.	226	38.48 N	120.53 W
Coloma, Mi., U.S.	216	42.11 N	86.18 W
Coloma, Wi., U.S.	190	44.02 N	89.31 W
Colomb-Béchar → Béchar	148	31.37 N	2.13 W
Colombes	50	48.55 N	2.15 E
Colombey-les-Belles	58	48.32 N	5.54 E
Colombey-les-Deux-Églises	58	48.13 N	4.53 E
Colômbia, Bra.	255	20.30 S	48.37 W
Colombia, Col.	246	3.24 N	74.49 W
Colombia, Cuba	240p	20.59 N	77.25 W
Colombia, Méx.	196	27.42 N	99.45 W
Colombia □[1], S.A.	242	4.00 N	72.00 W
Colombia □[1], S.A.	246	4.00 N	72.00 W
Colombian Basin ✢[1]	16	13.00 N	76.00 W
Colombie → Colombia □[1]	246	4.00 N	72.00 W
Colombie-Britannique → British Columbia □[4]	182	54.00 N	125.00 W
Colombier	58	46.58 N	6.52 E
Colombo, Bra.	252	25.17 S	49.14 W
Colombo, S. Lan.	122	6.56 N	79.51 E
Colome	198	43.15 N	99.42 W
Colomiers	32	43.37 N	1.20 E
Colón, Arg.	252	33.53 S	61.07 W
Colón, Arg.	252	32.13 S	58.08 W
Colón, Cuba	240p	22.43 N	80.54 W
Colón, Méx.	234	20.48 N	100.03 W
Colón, Pan.	236	9.22 N	79.54 W
Colon, Mi., U.S.	216	41.57 N	85.19 W
Colón, Ur.	252	33.53 S	54.43 W
Colón, Ur.	258	34.48 S	56.14 W
Colón □[4]	236	9.00 N	80.20 W
Colón □[5]	236	15.40 N	85.30 W
Colón, Archipiélago de (Galapagos Islands) II	246a	0.30 S	90.30 W
Colón, Cementerio ◆	286b	23.08 N	82.23 W
Colón, Isla I	236	9.24 N	82.17 W
Colón, Montañas de ⋏	236	14.55 N	84.45 W
Colón, Teatro ♠	288	34.36 S	58.23 W
Colona	162	31.38 S	132.05 E
Colonard-Corubert	50	48.25 N	0.39 E
Colonarie ≃	241h	13.14 N	61.06 W
Colonel Danforth Park ♠	275b	43.47 N	79.10 W
Colonelganj	124	27.08 N	81.42 E
Coloneşti	38	46.34 N	27.18 E
Colonet	204	31.05 N	116.10 W
Colonet, Cabo ≻	204	30.58 N	116.19 W
Colongulac, Lake ⊜	169	38.10 S	143.11 E
Colonia → Köln, Dtsch.	56	50.56 N	6.59 E
Colonia, Micron.	174q	9.31 N	138.08 E
Colonia, N.J., U.S.	210	40.34 N	74.18 W
Colonia □[5]	258	34.10 S	57.30 W
Colônia ≃	255	15.11 S	39.45 W
Colonia, Aeropuerto ⊠	258	34.28 S	57.49 W
Colonia, Cuchilla de la ⋏[2]	258	34.15 S	57.35 W
Colonia Alvear	252	35.00 S	67.40 W
Colonia Caroya	252	31.02 S	64.05 W
Colonia del Sacramento	258	34.28 S	57.51 W
Colonia Dora	252	28.36 S	62.57 W
Colonia Elisa	252	26.56 S	59.32 W
Colonia Guadalupe	204	32.04 N	116.37 W
Colonia Hogar Ricardo Gutiérrez	288	34.51 S	58.51 W
Colonia José Mármol	252	26.59 S	60.44 W
Colonial Acres	208	39.31 N	76.20 W
Colonia Lavalleja	252	31.06 S	57.01 W
Colonial Beach	208	38.15 N	76.57 W
Colonial Crest	208	40.20 N	76.50 W
Colônia Leopoldina	250	8.57 S	35.39 W
Colonial Heights	208	37.14 N	77.24 W
Colonial Manor	285	39.51 N	75.09 W
Colonial National Historical Park ♠	208	37.12 N	76.45 W
Colonial Park	208	40.18 N	76.48 W
Colonial Village, N.Y., U.S.	210	43.08 N	78.58 W
Colonial Village, Pa., U.S.	285	40.04 N	75.24 W
Colonial Village Airport ⊠	284a	43.08 N	78.58 W
Colonial Williamsburg ⊥	208	37.16 N	76.42 W
Colonia Morelos	200	30.50 N	109.10 W
Colonia Nicolich	258	34.50 S	56.02 W
Colonia Progreso	204	32.35 N	115.37 W
Colonia Providencia	240m	17.59 N	66.00 W
Colonias Unicas	252	26.42 S	59.38 W
Colonia Valdense	258	34.20 S	57.14 W
Colonia Vicente Guerrero	232	30.45 N	116.00 W
Colonia Villafañe	252	26.12 S	59.05 W
Colonie	210	42.43 N	73.50 W
Colon Koret	152	0.34 N	23.28 E
Colonna	267a	41.50 N	12.45 E
Colonna, Capo ≻	68	39.02 N	17.11 E
Colonnata	64	44.05 N	10.10 E
Colón Ridge ✢[3]	18	2.00 N	96.00 W
Colonsay	184	51.59 N	105.53 W
Colonsay I	46	56.04 N	6.13 W
Colony	198	38.04 N	95.21 W
Colora	208	39.40 N	76.06 W
Colorada, Laguna ≚	254	44.50 S	68.15 W
Colorada, Punta ≻	288	34.45 S	58.06 W
Coloradas, Lomas ⋏[2]	254	43.24 S	67.24 W
Colorado, C.R.	236	10.46 N	83.35 W
Colorado, Hond.	236	15.47 N	87.19 W
Colorado, Ak., U.S.	180	63.09 N	149.26 W
Colorado □[6]	222	29.40 N	96.30 W
Colorado □[3]	178	39.00 N	105.30 W
Colorado ≃, Arg.	244	39.50 S	62.08 W
Colorado ≃, Bra.	248	13.03 S	62.20 W
Colorado ≃, Méx.	234	16.30 N	97.31 W
Colorado ≃, N.A.	200	31.54 N	114.57 W
Colorado ≃, Tx., U.S.	196	28.36 N	95.58 W
Colorado, Canal do ≊	287a	23.00 S	43.25 W
Colorado, Cerro ∧, Arg.	254	45.02 S	69.38 W
Colorado, Cerro ∧, Chile	286e	33.24 S	70.45 W
Colorado, Cerro ∧, Perú	286d	12.07 S	76.55 W
Colorado, Williams Fork ≃	200	40.03 N	106.11 W
Colorado City, Az., U.S.	200	36.59 N	112.58 W
Colorado City, Co., U.S.	200	37.56 N	104.50 W
Colorado City, Tx., U.S.	196	32.23 N	100.51 W
Colorado de Abajo	196	26.28 N	99.54 W
Colorado Grande, Salina ≚	252	38.15 S	63.47 W
Colorado National Monument ♠	200	39.04 N	108.25 W
Colorado Plateau ⋏[1]	200	36.30 N	108.00 W
Colorado River Aqueduct ≊[1]	204	33.50 N	117.23 W
Colorado River Indian Reservation ◆[4]	200	34.00 N	114.25 W
Colorados, Archipiélago de los II	240p	22.36 N	84.20 W
Colorado Springs	200	38.50 N	104.49 W
Colorines	234	19.07 N	100.12 W
Colorno	64	44.56 N	10.23 E
Colosimi	68	39.07 N	16.24 E
Colosseo ⊥	267a	41.54 N	12.29 E
Colotepec ≃	234	15.47 N	97.03 W
Colotlán	234	22.06 N	103.16 W
Colotlán ≃	234	22.06 N	103.42 W
Colotlipa	234	17.25 N	99.09 W
Colo Vale	170	34.24 S	150.29 E
Čolpon	85	42.12 N	75.28 E
Čolpon-Ata	85	42.40 N	77.06 E
Colpoys Bay c	212	44.47 N	81.05 W
Colquechaca	248	18.40 S	66.01 W
Colquencha	248	17.00 S	68.17 W
Colquiri	248	17.25 S	67.08 W
Colquitt	192	31.10 N	84.44 W
Colsterworth	42	52.48 N	0.37 W
Colstrip	202	45.53 N	106.37 W
Colt	194	35.07 N	90.48 W
Colta	248	15.10 S	73.18 W
Coltauco	252	34.18 S	71.06 W
Coltishall	42	52.44 N	1.22 E
Colton, Austl.	162	33.29 S	134.56 E
Colton, Ca., U.S.	228	34.04 N	117.18 W
Colton, Oh., U.S.	216	41.28 N	83.57 W
Colton, Or., U.S.	224	45.10 N	122.26 W
Colton, S.D., U.S.	198	43.47 N	96.55 W
Coltons Point	208	38.13 N	76.45 W
Colts Neck	208	40.17 N	74.10 W
Coltsville Center	214	41.05 N	80.34 W
Columbia, Al., U.S.	192	31.17 N	85.06 W
Columbia, Ca., U.S.	226	38.02 N	120.24 W
Columbia, Ct., U.S.	207	41.42 N	72.18 W
Columbia, Il., U.S.	219	38.26 N	90.12 W
Columbia, In., U.S.	218	39.35 N	85.12 W
Columbia, Ky., U.S.	194	37.06 N	85.18 W
Columbia, La., U.S.	194	32.06 N	92.04 W
Columbia, Md., U.S.	208	39.14 N	76.50 W
Columbia, Ms., U.S.	194	31.15 N	89.50 W
Columbia, Mo., U.S.	219	38.57 N	92.20 W
Columbia, N.J., U.S.	210	40.55 N	75.05 W
Columbia, N.C., U.S.	192	35.55 N	76.15 W
Columbia, Pa., U.S.	208	40.02 N	76.30 W
Columbia, S.C., U.S.	192	34.00 N	81.02 W
Columbia, Tn., U.S.	194	35.36 N	87.02 W
Columbia □[6], N.Y., U.S.	210	42.15 N	73.47 W
Columbia □[6], Or., U.S.	224	45.57 N	123.03 W
Columbia □[6], Pa., U.S.	210	41.00 N	76.28 W
Columbia ≃	176	46.15 N	124.05 W
Columbia, Cape ≻	16	83.08 N	70.35 W
Columbia, Lake ⊜[1]	216	42.05 N	84.18 W
Columbia, Mount ∧	182	52.09 N	117.25 W
Columbia Airport ⊠	279a	41.19 N	81.58 W
Columbia Basin ≚[1]	202	46.45 N	119.05 W
Columbia Center	279a	41.19 N	81.56 W
Columbia City, In., U.S.	216	41.09 N	85.29 W
Columbia City, Or., U.S.	224	45.53 N	122.48 W
Columbia Cross Roads	210	41.50 N	76.48 W
Columbia Falls, Me., U.S.	188	44.39 N	67.43 W
Columbia Falls, Mt., U.S.	202	48.22 N	114.10 W
Columbia Heights	224	46.09 N	122.58 W
Columbia Hills	284b	39.15 N	76.50 W
Columbia Icefield ⍓	182	52.10 N	117.30 W
Columbia Lake ⊜	182	50.15 N	115.52 W
Columbia Lake Indian Reserve ◆[4]	182	50.25 N	115.57 W
Columbia Mountains ⋏	182	52.00 N	119.00 W
Columbiana, Al., U.S.	194	33.10 N	86.36 W
Columbiana, Oh., U.S.	214	40.53 N	80.41 W
Columbiana □[6]	214	40.47 N	80.46 W
Columbia Plateau ⋏[1]	202	44.00 N	117.30 W
Columbia Regional Airport ⊠	219	38.50 N	92.13 W
Columbia Road Reservoir ⊜[1]	198	45.45 N	98.15 W
Columbia State Historical Park ♠	226	38.02 N	120.25 W
Columbia Station	214	41.20 N	81.57 W
Columbia University ʊ[2]	276	40.48 N	73.58 W
Columbiaville, Mi., U.S.	190	43.09 N	83.24 W
Columbiaville, N.Y., U.S.	210	42.19 N	73.45 W
Columbine, Cape ≻	158	32.47 S	17.52 E
Columbrets, Illes II	34	39.52 N	0.40 E
Columbus, Ga., U.S.	192	32.29 N	84.59 W
Columbus, In., U.S.	218	39.12 N	85.55 W
Columbus, Ks., U.S.	198	37.10 N	94.50 W
Columbus, Ms., U.S.	194	33.29 N	88.25 W
Columbus, Mt., U.S.	202	45.38 N	109.15 W
Columbus, Ne., U.S.	198	41.25 N	97.22 W
Columbus, N.J., U.S.	208	40.04 N	74.43 W
Columbus, N.M., U.S.	200	31.49 N	107.38 W
Columbus, N.C., U.S.	192	35.15 N	82.11 W
Columbus, N.D., U.S.	198	48.54 N	102.46 W
Columbus, Oh., U.S.	214	39.57 N	82.59 W
Columbus, Pa., U.S.	214	41.56 N	79.35 W
Columbus, Tx., U.S.	222	29.42 N	96.32 W
Columbus, Wi., U.S.	190	43.20 N	89.00 W
Columbus Air Force Base ■	194	33.38 N	88.26 W
Columbus Grove	216	40.55 N	84.03 W
Columbus Junction	190	41.16 N	91.21 W
Columbus Lake ⊜[1]	194	33.35 N	88.30 W
Columbus Park ♠	278	41.53 N	87.47 W
Columbus Point ≻, Ba.	238	24.08 N	75.16 W
Columbus Point ≻, Trin.	241r	11.08 N	60.48 W
Columbus Salt Marsh ≚	204	38.04 N	117.58 W
Coluna	255	18.14 S	42.50 W
Colusa	226	39.12 N	122.00 W
Colusa □[6]	226	39.13 N	122.01 W
Colusa Trough ≊	226	39.02 N	121.59 W
Colver	214	40.32 N	78.47 W
Colville, N.Z.	172	36.38 S	175.28 E
Colville, Wa., U.S.	202	48.32 N	117.54 W
Colville ≃, Ak., U.S.	180	70.25 N	150.30 W
Colville ≃, Wa., U.S.	202	48.37 N	118.05 W
Colville, Cape ≻	172	36.28 S	175.21 E
Colville Channel ⊔	172	36.23 S	175.24 E
Colville Indian Reservation ◆[4]	202	48.15 N	119.00 W
Colville Lake ⊜	180	67.10 N	126.00 W
Colvin Run	284c	38.58 N	77.18 W
Colwell	44	55.04 N	2.04 W
Colwood	224	48.26 N	123.29 W
Colwyn	285	39.55 N	75.15 W
Colwyn Bay	44	53.18 N	3.43 W
Colyton, Austl.	274a	33.47 S	150.48 E
Colyton, Eng., U.K.	42	50.44 N	3.04 W
Comacchio	66	44.42 N	12.11 E
Comacchio, Valli di c	66	44.38 N	12.06 E
Comal	115a	6.55 S	109.31 E
Comala	234	19.19 N	103.45 W
Comalapa, Guat.	236	14.44 N	90.53 W
Comalapa, Nic.	236	12.17 N	85.31 W
Comalcalco	234	18.16 N	93.13 W
Comallo, Arroyo ≃	254	40.29 S	70.12 W
Coman, Mount ∧	9	74.02 S	65.04 W
Comana	38	43.54 N	28.19 E
Comanche, Ok., U.S.	196	34.22 N	97.57 W
Comanche, Tx., U.S.	196	31.53 N	98.36 W
Comanche Creek ≃, Co., U.S.	198	39.53 N	104.19 W
Comanche Creek ≃, Tx., U.S.	196	31.06 N	102.24 W
Comandante Ferraz ʊ[3]	9	62.05 S	58.23 W
Comandante Fontana	252	25.20 S	59.41 W
Comandante Leal	252	30.53 S	65.47 W
Comandante Luis Piedrabuena	254	49.59 S	68.54 W
Comandante Nicanor Otamendi	252	38.07 S	57.51 W
Comănești	38	46.25 N	26.26 E
Comanjá de Corona	234	21.19 N	101.42 W
Comarapa	248	17.54 S	64.29 W
Comar Gambon	144	3.10 N	45.47 E
Comas, Perú	248	11.46 S	75.02 W
Comas, Perú	286d	11.57 S	77.04 W
Comayagua	236	14.25 N	87.37 W
Comayagua □[5]	236	14.30 N	87.40 W
Comayagua, Montañas de ⋏	236	14.23 N	87.26 W
Combahee ≃	192	32.30 N	80.31 W
Combarbalá	252	31.11 S	71.02 W
Combault	261	48.48 N	2.36 E
Combeaufontaine	58	47.43 N	5.53 E
Combe Bank ✢[3]	14	12.32 S	177.35 W
Combe Martin	42	51.13 N	4.02 W
Comber, On., Can.	214	42.14 N	82.33 W
Comber, N. Ire., U.K.	48	54.33 N	5.45 W
Comberbach	262	53.17 N	2.32 W
Combermere Bay c	110	19.37 N	93.34 E
Comberton	42	52.11 N	0.02 E
Combie, Lake ⊜[1]	226	39.01 N	121.02 W
Comblain-au-Pont	56	50.28 N	5.35 E
Combles	50	50.01 N	2.52 E
Combloux	62	45.54 N	6.39 E
Combourg	32	48.25 N	1.45 W
Comboyne	166	31.36 S	152.29 E
Comboyuro Point ≻	171a	27.04 S	153.24 E
Combres	50	48.19 N	1.04 E
Combronde	32	45.59 N	3.05 E
Combs	262	53.18 N	1.57 W
Combs-la-Ville	50	48.40 N	2.34 E
Combs Reservoir ⊜[1]	262	53.19 N	1.57 W
Comburg ʊ[1]	56	49.06 N	9.44 E
Comb Wash V	200	37.13 N	109.42 W
Come by Chance	186	47.51 N	53.58 W
Comeglians	64	46.31 N	12.52 E
Comelico Superiore	64	46.35 N	12.30 E
Comendado Levy Gasparain	256	22.01 S	43.12 W
Comendador	238	18.53 N	71.42 W
Comendador Gomes	255	19.41 S	49.05 W
Comer	192	34.03 N	83.07 W
Comercinho	255	16.19 S	41.47 W
Comerío	240m	18.13 N	66.14 W
Comet	166	23.37 S	148.33 E
Comet ≃	166	23.34 S	148.32 E
Cometela	156	21.51 S	34.29 E
Comfort, N.C., U.S.	192	35.00 N	77.30 W
Comfort, Tx., U.S.	196	29.58 N	98.54 W
Comfort, Cape ≻	176	65.08 N	83.21 W
Comfort, Point ≻	276	40.27 N	74.08 W
Comfrey	198	44.06 N	94.54 W
Comilla	124	23.27 N	91.12 E
Comines	50	50.46 N	3.01 E
Comino → Kemmuna I	36	36.00 N	14.20 E
Comino, Capo ≻	71	40.32 N	9.49 E
Comiskey Park ♠	278	41.50 N	87.38 W
Comiso	70	36.56 N	14.36 E
Comitan de Dominguez	232	16.15 N	92.08 W
Comitini	70	37.24 N	13.39 E
Comloşu Mare	38	45.54 N	20.38 E
Commack	210	40.50 N	73.17 W
Commagene □[9]	130	37.50 N	38.00 E
Commencement Bay c	224	47.17 N	122.28 W
Commentry	32	46.17 N	2.44 E
Commerce, Ca., U.S.	280	34.00 N	118.09 W
Commerce, Ga., U.S.	192	34.12 N	83.27 W
Commerce, Mi., U.S.	216	42.34 N	83.30 W
Commerce, Ok., U.S.	196	36.56 N	94.52 W
Commerce, Tx., U.S.	196	33.14 N	95.53 W
Commerce City	198	39.49 N	104.56 W
Commerciale Luigi Bocconi, Università ʊ[2]	266b	45.26 N	9.11 E
Commercial Point	218	39.46 N	83.04 W
Commercy	56	48.45 N	5.35 E
Commewijne □[5]	250	5.50 N	55.00 W
Comminges ◆[1]	32	43.15 N	0.45 E
Committee Bay c	176	68.30 N	86.30 W
Commodore	214	40.43 N	78.57 W
Commodore Barry Bridge ◆[5]	285	39.49 N	75.22 W
Commondale	158	27.20 S	30.56 E
Common Edge	262	53.47 N	3.02 W
Commonwealth Bay c	9	66.54 S	142.40 E
Commonwealth Range ⋏	9	84.15 S	172.20 E
Commoron Creek ≃	166	28.22 S	150.08 E
Community Center	228	34.16 N	118.44 W
Como, Austl.	274a	34.00 S	151.04 E
Como, It.	62	45.47 N	9.05 E
Como, Ms., U.S.	194	34.30 N	89.56 W
Como, N.C., U.S.	208	36.30 N	77.00 W
Como, Tx., U.S.	222	33.03 N	95.28 W
Como, Wi., U.S.	216	42.37 N	88.28 W
Como □[4]	58	45.59 N	9.13 E
Como, Lago di ⊜	58	46.00 N	9.20 E
Como, Lake ⊜	216	42.36 N	88.29 W
Como, Mount ∧	226	39.02 N	119.28 W
Comodoro Rivadavia	254	45.52 S	67.30 W
Como Lake ⊜	190	47.55 N	83.30 W
Comologno	58	46.12 N	8.34 E
Comonfort	234	20.43 N	100.46 W
Comoras → Comoros □[1]	157a	12.10 S	44.15 E
Comores → Comoros □[1]	157a	12.10 S	44.15 E
Comores, Archipel des II	157a	12.10 S	44.15 E
Comorin, Cape ≻	122	8.06 N	77.33 E
Comoros (Comores) □[1], Afr.	138	12.10 S	44.15 E
Comoros (Comores) □[1], Afr.	157a	12.10 S	44.15 E
Comox	182	49.40 N	124.55 W
Comox, Canadian Forces Base ■	182	49.43 N	124.54 W
Companhia Siderúrgica Nacional ʊ[3]	256	22.31 S	44.07 W
Compans	261	49.00 N	2.40 E
Compatsch	58	46.58 N	10.25 E
Compiègne	50	49.25 N	2.50 E
Compo Cove c	276	41.07 N	73.21 W
Compostela, Méx.	234	21.15 N	104.53 W
Compostela, Pil.	116	7.40 N	126.02 E
Comprida, Ilha I, Bra.	252	24.50 S	47.42 W
Comprida, Ilha I, Bra.	287a	23.02 S	43.12 W
Comps-sur-Artuby	62	43.43 N	6.30 E
Compstall	262	53.25 N	2.03 W
Compton, Eng., U.K.	260	51.13 N	0.38 W
Compton, Ca., U.S.	228	33.53 N	118.13 W
Compton, Il., U.S.	216	41.42 N	89.05 W
Compton □[6]	206	45.20 N	71.25 W
Compton Airport ⊠	280	33.53 N	118.15 W
Compton Creek ≃, Ca., U.S.	280	33.50 N	118.12 W
Compton Creek ≃, N.J., U.S.	276	40.26 N	74.05 W
Comptonville	273d	26.17 S	27.58 E
Comrie	46	56.22 N	4.00 W
Comstock, Mi., U.S.	216	42.17 N	85.30 W
Comstock, Ne., U.S.	198	41.33 N	99.15 W
Comstock, Tx., U.S.	196	29.41 N	101.11 W
Comstock Park	216	43.02 N	85.40 W
Comunanza	66	42.57 N	13.25 E
Con ≃, Ross.	76	52.54 N	36.00 E
Con ≃, Viet	110	19.02 N	104.58 E
Čona ≃, Ross.	74	62.54 N	111.06 E
Cona ≃, Scot., U.K.	46	56.46 N	5.14 W
Co Nag ⊜	120	32.00 N	91.15 E
Conakry	150	9.31 N	13.43 W
Conambo ≃	246	2.07 S	76.03 W
Conanicut Island I	207	41.32 N	71.21 W
Cona Niyeo	254	41.53 S	67.00 W
Conara Junction	166	41.50 S	147.26 E
Conasauga ≃	192	34.33 N	84.55 W
Conaskonk Point ≻	276	40.27 N	74.11 W
Conca ≃	66	43.58 N	12.43 E
Concarán	252	32.34 S	65.15 W
Concarneau	32	47.52 N	3.55 W
Conceição, Bra.	248	7.24 S	58.05 W
Conceição, Bra.	250	7.33 S	38.31 W
Conceição, Moç.	156	18.45 S	36.10 E
Conceição, Cachoeira ∟	248	9.34 S	64.22 W
Conceição, Ilha da I	287a	22.52 S	43.07 W
Conceição da Barra	255	18.35 S	39.45 W
Conceição da Pedra	256	22.09 S	45.27 W
Conceição das Alagoas	255	19.55 S	48.23 W
Conceição de Ipanema	255	19.55 S	41.41 W
Conceição de Jacareí	256	23.02 S	44.09 W
Conceição do Almeida	255	12.48 S	39.12 W
Conceição do Araguaia	250	8.15 S	49.17 W
Conceição do Canindé	250	7.54 S	41.34 W
Conceição do Coité	250	11.33 S	39.16 W
Conceição do Formoso	256	21.25 S	43.21 W
Conceição do Mato Dentro	255	19.01 S	43.25 W
Conceição do Maú	246	3.35 N	59.53 W
Conceição do Norte	255	12.13 S	47.18 W
Conceição do Rio Verde	256	21.53 S	45.05 W
Conceição dos Ouros	256	22.25 S	45.47 W
Concepción, Arg.	252	28.23 S	57.53 W
Concepción, Arg.	252	27.20 S	65.35 W
Concepción, Bol.	248	11.29 S	66.31 W
Concepción, Bol.	248	16.15 S	62.04 W
Concepción, Chile	252	36.50 S	73.03 W
Concepción, Col.	246	6.46 N	72.42 W
Concepción, Para.	252	23.25 S	57.17 W
Concepción, Perú	248	11.55 S	75.17 W
Concepcion, Fil.	116	11.13 N	123.06 E
Concepcion, Fil.	116	10.42 N	123.03 E
Concepcion, Fil.	116	12.24 N	122.06 E
Concepcion, Fil.	116	15.19 N	120.39 E
Concepción □[5]	252	23.00 S	57.00 W
Concepción, Bahía c	232	26.39 N	111.48 W
Concepción, Canal ⊔	254	50.30 S	74.55 W
Concepción, Laguna ⊜	248	17.29 S	61.25 W
Concepción, Volcán ∧[1]	236	11.34 N	85.37 W
Concepcion Bay c	116	11.15 N	123.07 E
Concepción de Ataco	236	13.52 N	89.51 W
Concepción de Buenos Aires	234	19.58 N	103.16 W
Concepción de la Sierra	252	27.59 S	55.31 W
Concepción del Oro	232	24.38 N	101.25 W
Concepción del Uruguay	252	32.29 S	58.14 W
Concepción Huista	236	15.37 N	91.41 W
Concepción Quezaltepeque	236	14.06 N	88.58 W

Symbol	English	Deutsch	Español	Français	Português
≃	River	Fluß	Río	Rivière	Rio
≊	Canal	Kanal	Canal	Canal	Canal
∟	Waterfall, Rapids	Wasserfall, Stromschnellen	Cascada, Rápidos	Chute d'eau, Rapides	Cascata, Rápidos
⊔	Strait	Meeresstraße	Estrecho	Détroit	Estreito
c	Bay, Gulf	Bucht, Golf	Bahía, Golfo	Baie, Golfe	Baía, Golfo
⊜	Lake, Lakes	See, Seen	Lago, Lagos	Lac, Lacs	Lago, Lagos
≚	Swamp	Sumpf	Pantano	Marais	Pântano
⍓	Ice Features, Glacier	Eis- und Gletscherformen	Accidentes Glaciales	Formes glaciaires	Acidentes glaciares
⊤	Other Hydrographic Features	Andere Hydrographische Objekte	Otros Elementos Hidrográficos	Autres données hydrographiques	Outros acidentes hidrográficos
✢	Submarine Features	Untermeerische Objekte	Accidentes Submarinos	Formes de relief sous-marin	Acidentes submarinos
□	Political Unit	Politische Einheit	Unidad Política	Entité politique	Unidade política
ʊ	Cultural Institution	Kulturelle Institution	Institución Cultural	Institution culturelle	Instituição cultural
⊥	Historical Site	Historische Stätte	Sitio Histórico	Site historique	Sítio histórico
♠	Recreational Site	Erholungs- und Ferienort	Sitio de Recreo	Centre de loisirs	Area de Lazer
⊠	Airport	Flughafen	Aeropuerto	Aéroport	Aeroporto
■	Military Installation	Militäranlage	Instalación Militar	Installation militaire	Instalação militar
◆	Miscellaneous	Verschiedenes	Misceláneo	Divers	Diversos

I · 40 **Conc-Coro**

ENGLISH			DEUTSCH		
Name	Page	Lat.°ʳ Long.°ʳ	Name	Seite	Breite°ʳ Länge°ʳ E = Ost

Symbols in the index entries represent the broad categories identified in the key at the right. Symbols with superior numbers (⌃¹) identify subcategories (see complete key on page I · 1).

Symbole im Register stellen die rechts im Schlüssel erklärten Kategorien dar. Symbole mit hochgestellten Ziffern (⌃¹) bezeichnen Unterabteilungen einer Kategorie (vgl. vollständiger Schlüssel auf Seite I · 1).

Los símbolos incluidos en el texto del índice representan las grandes categorías identificadas con la clave a la derecha. Los símbolos con números en su parte superior (⌃¹) identifican las subcategorías (véase la clave completa en la página I · 1).

Les symboles de l'index représentent les catégories indiquées dans la légende à droite. Les symboles suivis d'un indice (⌃¹) représentent les sous-catégories (voir légende complète à la page I · 1).

Os símbolos incluídos no texto do índice representam as grandes categorias identificadas com a chave à direita. Os símbolos com números em sua parte superior (⌃¹) identificam as subcategorias (veja-se a chave completa à página I · 1).

	Berg	Montaña	Montagne	Montanha
⌃ Mountains	Gebirge	Montañas	Montagnes	Montanhas
⌄ Pass	Paß	Paso	Col	Paso
✓ Valley, Canyon	Tal, Cañon	Valle, Cañón	Vallée, Canyon	Vale, Canhão
≃ Plain	Ebene	Llano	Plaine	Planície
➤ Cape	Kap	Cabo	Cap	Cabo
⇥ Island	Insel	Isla	Île	Ilha
⇥⇥ Islands	Inseln	Islas	Îles	Ilhas
⌅ Other Topographic Features	Andere Topographische Objekte	Otros Elementos Topográficos	Autres données topographiques	Outros acidentes topográficos

ESPAÑOL Nombre Página Lat.°′ Long.°′ W = Oeste | FRANÇAIS Nom Page Lat.°′ Long.°′ W = Ouest | PORTUGUÊS Nome Página Lat.°′ Long.°′ W = Oeste
Coro-Creq I · 41

Coronel Vidal 252 37.27 S 57.43 W
Coronel Vivida 252 25.58 S 52.34 W
Corongo 248 8.35 S 77.55 W
Corongoros 234 19.17 N 102.48 W
Coronie ▫[5] 250 5.50 N 56.20 W
Coron Island I 116 11.55 N 120.14 E
Coronita 228 33.52 N 117.36 W
Coropuna, Nevado ▲ 248 15.31 S 72.42 W
Çorovodë 38 40.30 N 20.13 E
Corowa 166 36.02 S 146.23 E
Corozal, Belize 232 18.24 N 88.24 W
Corozal, Col. 246 9.19 N 75.18 W
Corozal, Hond. 236 15.48 N 86.43 W
Corozal, P.R. 240m 18.21 N 66.17 W
Corps 62 44.49 N 5.57 E
Corpus 252 27.07 S 55.31 W
Corpus Christi 196 27.48 N 97.23 W
Corpus Christi, Lake ⊜[1] 196 28.10 N 97.53 W
Corpus Christi Bay ⊂ 196 27.48 N 97.20 W
Corpus Christi Naval Air Station ■ 196 27.42 N 97.16 W
Corque 248 18.21 S 67.42 W
Corquín 236 14.34 N 88.52 W
Corral 254 39.52 S 73.26 W
Corral de Almaguer 34 39.46 N 3.11 W
Corral de Bustos 252 33.17 S 62.12 W
Corralero, Laguna ⊂ 234 16.12 N 98.07 W
Corralillo 240p 22.59 N 80.35 W
Corralito 252 32.03 S 64.12 W
Corralito, Arroyo del ≃ 258 33.39 S 58.03 W
Corralito, Cuchilla del ⊼[2] 258 33.40 S 57.44 W
Corralitos, Méx. 196 26.57 N 104.39 W
Corralitos, Ca., U.S. 226 36.59 N 121.48 W
Corran 46 56.43 N 5.14 W
Corraun Peninsula >[1] 48 53.54 N 9.53 W
Correas, Arroyo ≃ 288 34.24 S 58.32 W
Correboi, Arcu ⅹ 71 40.05 N 9.21 E
Correctionville 198 42.28 N 95.47 W
Corredor 287b 23.27 S 46.19 W
Correggio 64 44.46 N 10.47 E
Corregidor Island I 116 14.23 N 120.35 E
Corrego do Bom Jesus 256 22.38 S 46.02 W
Córrego do Ouro 256 21.22 S 45.47 W
Córrego Rico 255 15.14 S 47.48 W
Correia de Almeida 256 21.17 S 43.38 W
Corrente 250 10.27 S 45.10 W
Corrente ≃, Bra. 255 19.19 S 50.50 W
Corrente ≃, Bra. 255 13.08 S 43.28 W
Correntes 250 9.08 S 33.19 W
Correntes ≃ 248 17.21 S 55.37 W
Correntes, Cabo das > 156 24.11 S 35.34 E
Correnti, Isola delle I 70 36.38 N 15.05 E
Correntina 255 13.20 S 44.39 W
Corrèze ▫[5] 32 45.20 N 1.50 E
Correzzana 266b 45.40 N 9.18 E
Corrib, Lough ⊜ 48 53.26 N 9.14 W
Corridonia 66 43.15 N 13.30 E
Corrientes 252 27.28 S 58.50 W
Corrientes ▫[4] 252 29.00 S 58.00 W
Corrientes ≃, Arg. 252 30.21 S 59.33 W
Corrientes ≃, S.A. 246 3.43 S 74.35 W
Corrientes, Bahía de ⊂ 240p 21.51 N 84.36 W
Corrientes, Cabo >, Arg. 252 38.01 S 57.32 W
Corrientes, Cabo >, Col. 246 5.30 N 77.34 W
Corrientes, Cabo >, Cuba 240p 21.45 N 84.31 W
Corrientes, Cabo >, Méx. 234 20.25 N 105.42 W
Corrigan 222 30.59 N 94.49 W
Corrigin 162 32.21 S 117.52 E
Corrimal 170 34.22 S 150.54 E
Corringham 260 51.31 N 0.28 E
Corriverton 246 5.53 N 57.08 W
Corrofin 48 52.56 N 9.03 W
Corroios 266c 38.38 N 9.09 W
Corropoli 66 42.49 N 13.50 E
Corrumpa Creek ≃ 196 36.36 N 102.52 W
Corry 214 41.55 N 79.38 W
Corryong 171b 36.12 S 147.54 E
Corryong Creek ≃ 171b 36.06 S 147.59 E
Corryvreckan, Gulf of Џ 46 56.09 N 5.44 W
Corsano 68 39.53 N 18.22 E
Corse (Corsica) I 36 42.00 N 9.00 E
Corse, Cap > 36 43.00 N 9.25 E
Corse-du-Sud ▫[5] 36 41.50 N 9.00 E
Corserine ▲ 44 55.09 N 4.22 W
Corsham 42 51.26 N 2.11 W
Corsica, Pa., U.S. 214 41.10 N 79.12 W
Corsica, S.D., U.S. 198 43.25 N 98.24 W
Corsica — Corse I 36 42.00 N 9.00 E
Corsicana 222 32.05 N 96.28 W
Corsica River ⊂ 208 39.05 N 76.08 W
Corsico 62 45.26 N 9.07 E
Corsock 44 55.04 N 3.57 W
Corson Inlet ⊂ 208 39.12 N 74.39 W
Cortaccia (Kurtatsch) 64 46.19 N 11.13 E
Cortachy 46 56.43 N 2.58 W
Cort Adelaer, Kap > 176 62.00 N 42.00 W
Cortale 68 38.50 N 16.25 E
Cortazar 234 20.29 N 100.56 W
Corte 36 42.18 N 9.08 E
Corte Alto 254 40.57 S 73.10 W
Cortegana 34 37.55 N 6.49 W
Corte Madera 226 37.55 N 122.31 W
Corte Madera Creek ≃ 282 37.23 N 122.14 W
Cortemaggiore 64 44.59 N 9.55 E
Cortemilia 62 44.35 N 8.12 E
Corteno Golgi 64 46.10 N 10.15 E
Cortes 116 9.17 N 126.11 E
Cortés ▫[5] 236 15.30 N 88.00 W
Cortes ⊍ 266a 40.25 N 3.41 W
Cortés, Bahía de ⊂ 240p 22.05 N 83.52 W
Cortez, Co., U.S. 200 37.20 N 108.35 W
Cortez, Fl., U.S. 220 27.28 N 82.41 W
Cortez, Sea of — California, Golfo de ⊂ 232 28.00 N 112.00 W
Cortez Mountains ⊼ 204 40.20 N 116.20 W
Cortina Creek ≃ 226 39.06 N 122.02 W
Cortina d'Ampezzo 64 46.32 N 12.08 E
Cortines 258 34.34 S 59.13 W
Cortkov 78 49.01 N 25.48 E
Cortland, Il., U.S. 216 41.55 N 88.41 W
Cortland, In., U.S. 218 38.58 N 85.58 W
Cortland, Ne., U.S. 198 40.30 N 96.42 W
Cortland, N.Y., U.S. 210 42.36 N 76.10 W
Cortland, Oh., U.S. 214 41.19 N 80.43 W
Cortland ▫[6] 210 42.36 N 76.11 W
Corton 42 52.32 N 1.44 E
Cortona 66 43.16 N 11.59 E
Çorubal (Koliba) ≃ 150 11.57 N 15.06 W
Čoruch-Dajron 85 40.24 N 69.40 E
Coruche 34 38.57 N 8.31 W
Çoruh (Čoroch) ≃ 130 41.36 N 41.35 E
Çorum, Tür. 130 39.14 N 28.27 E
Çorum, Tür. 130 40.33 N 34.58 E
Çorum ▫[4] 130 40.30 N 34.40 E
Corumbá 248 19.01 S 57.39 W
Corumbá ≃ 255 18.19 S 48.55 W
Corumbá de Goiás 255 15.55 S 48.48 W
Corumbaíba 255 18.09 S 48.34 W
Corumbataí ≃ 252 23.55 S 51.57 W
Corumbaú, Ponta do > 255 16.53 S 39.06 W
Corumbiara ≃ 248 13.13 S 62.06 W
Corumo ≃ 64 6.49 S 60.52 W
Corund 38 46.28 N 25.11 E
Corunna, On., Can. 214 42.53 N 82.26 W
Corunna — La Coruña, Esp. 34 43.22 N 8.23 W
Corunna, In., U.S. 216 41.26 N 85.08 W
Corunna, Mi., U.S. 216 42.58 N 84.07 W
Corunna Downs 162 21.28 S 119.51 E
Coruripe 250 10.08 S 36.10 W
Corvallis, Mt., U.S. 202 46.18 N 114.06 W
Corvallis, Or., U.S. 202 44.33 N 123.15 W
Corvara in Badia 64 46.33 N 11.52 E
Corve Dale ∨ 42 52.30 N 2.40 W
Corvey, Kloster ⊍[1] 52 51.46 N 9.25 E
Corviale ✈[8] 267a 41.52 N 12.25 E
Corvo I 148a 39.42 N 31.06 W
Corwen 42 52.59 N 3.22 W
Corwin, Cape > 180 59.54 N 165.41 W
Corwith 190 42.59 N 93.57 W
Corydon, In., U.S. 218 38.12 N 86.07 W
Corydon, Ia., U.S. 190 40.45 N 93.19 W
Corydon, Ky., U.S. 194 37.44 N 87.42 W
Coryell 222 31.33 N 97.37 W
Coryell ▫[6] 222 31.25 N 97.40 W
Coryell Creek ≃ 222 31.23 N 97.35 W
Coryton 260 51.31 N 0.31 E
Coryville 214 41.53 N 78.24 W
Corzu 38 44.28 N 23.10 E
Corzuela 252 26.57 S 60.58 W
Cos — Kos I 38 36.50 N 27.10 E
Cosa (Ansedonia) ⊥ 66 42.25 N 11.18 E
Cosamaloapan [de Carpio] 232 18.22 N 95.48 W
Cosapa 248 18.11 S 68.40 W
Coscile ≃ 68 39.42 N 16.28 E
Cos Cob 276 41.02 N 73.36 W
Cos Cob Harbor ⊂ 276 41.01 N 73.36 W
Coscomatepec [de Bravo] 234 19.04 N 97.02 W
Coseley 42 52.33 N 2.06 W
Cosenza 68 39.17 N 16.15 E
Cosenza ▫[4] 68 39.28 N 16.25 E
Cosgroves Creek ≃ 274a 33.50 S 150.46 E
Coshocton 214 40.16 N 81.51 W
Coshocton ▫[6] 214 40.16 N 81.51 W
Cosigüina, Punta > 236 12.54 N 87.41 W
Cosigüina, Volcán ▲[1] 236 12.59 N 87.34 W
Coslada 266a 40.26 N 3.34 W
Cosmo ✈[8] 256 22.54 S 43.37 W
Cosmoledo Island I 138 9.43 S 47.35 E
Cosmópolis, Bra. 256 22.38 S 47.12 W
Cosmopolis, Wa., U.S. 224 46.57 N 123.46 W
Cosmos 198 44.56 N 94.41 W
Cosmos ✈[8] 287a 22.55 S 44.37 W
Cosne-Cours-sur-Loire 50 47.24 N 2.55 E
Cosoleacaque 234 18.00 N 94.37 W
Cospán 248 7.26 S 78.33 W
Cosquín 252 31.15 S 64.29 W
Cossato 62 45.34 N 8.10 E
Cossatot ≃ 194 33.48 N 94.09 W
Cossayuna 210 43.11 N 73.26 W
Cossayuna Lake ⊜ 210 43.12 N 73.25 W
Cossebaude 54 51.05 N 13.38 E
Cossé-le-Vivien 28 47.57 N 0.55 W
Cossoine 71 40.27 N 8.43 E
Cosson ≃ 50 47.30 N 1.15 E
Cossonay 58 46.37 N 6.31 E
Cost 222 29.26 N 97.32 W
Costa, Cayo I 220 26.41 N 82.15 W
Costa, Cordillera de la ⊼ 286c 10.33 N 66.52 W
Costa, Sierra de la — Coast Ranges ⊼ 178 41.00 N 123.30 W
Costacciaro 66 43.21 N 12.42 E
Costa de Caparica 266c 38.38 N 9.14 W
Costa del Marfil — Cote d'Ivoire ▫[1] 150 8.00 N 5.00 W
Costa de San José 258 33.51 S 56.53 W
Costa di Rovigo 64 45.03 N 11.42 E
Costa Mesa 228 33.38 N 117.55 W
Costanera, Cadena — Coast Mountains ⊼ 176 55.00 N 129.00 W
Costanera Sur, Parque Natural ♦ 288 34.37 S 58.21 W
Costanero, Canal de ≃ 288 34.28 S 58.28 W
Costa Rica 232 24.32 N 107.18 W
Costa Rica ▫[1], N.A. 230 10.00 N 84.00 W
Costa Rica ▫[1], N.A. 236 10.00 N 84.00 W
Costaros 62 44.54 N 3.50 E
Costas 256 22.39 S 45.56 W
Costello 214 41.36 N 78.03 W
Costelloe 48 53.17 N 9.32 W
Costermansville — Bukavu 154 2.30 S 28.52 E
Costesey 42 52.40 N 1.11 E
Costeşti 38 44.40 N 24.53 E
Costiera, Catena ⊼ 68 39.20 N 16.05 E
Costigan Lake ⊜ 184 56.56 N 105.55 W
Costigliole d'Asti 62 44.47 N 8.11 E
Costigliole Saluzzo 62 44.34 N 7.29 E
Costilla 200 36.58 N 105.31 W
Costilla Creek ≃ 200 36.59 N 105.43 W
Cosumnes ≃ 226 38.16 N 121.26 W
Cosumnes, Middle Fork ≃ 226 38.33 N 120.51 W
Cosumnes, North Fork ≃ 226 38.33 N 120.51 W
Cosumnes, South Fork ≃ 226 38.33 N 120.49 W
Coswig, Dtsch. 54 51.07 N 13.34 E
Coswig, Dtsch. 54 51.53 N 12.26 E
Cotabambas 248 13.45 S 72.21 W
Cotabato 116 7.13 N 124.15 E
Cotacajes ≃ 248 16.00 S 67.01 W
Cotagaita 248 20.50 S 65.41 W
Cotagaita ≃ 248 21.01 S 65.23 W
Cotahuasi 248 15.12 S 72.56 W
Cotão ⊼[2] 266c 38.45 N 9.18 W
Cotati 226 38.20 N 122.42 W
Coteau-Landing 206 45.15 N 74.13 W
Coteau-Station 206 45.17 N 74.14 W
Coteaux 238 18.12 N 74.02 W
Cote d'Ivoire (Ivory Coast) ▫[1], Afr. 134 8.00 N 5.00 W
Cote d'Ivoire ▫[1], Afr. 150 8.00 N 5.00 W
Côte-d'Or ▫[5] 32 47.30 N 4.50 E
Cotegipe 255 12.02 S 44.15 W
Cote Indian Reserve ♦[4] 184 51.38 N 101.53 W
Cotentin > 32 49.30 N 1.30 W
Côte-Saint-Luc 275a 45.28 N 73.40 W
Côtes-d'Armor ▫[5] 32 48.25 N 2.40 W
Côte Visitation ✈[8] 275a 45.33 N 73.36 W
Cothi ≃ 42 51.52 N 4.10 W
Coti ≃ 248 8.36 S 65.33 W
Cotia 256 23.37 S 46.56 W
Cotia ▫[7] 287b 23.43 S 46.55 W
Cotia ≃ 256 23.31 S 46.51 W
Cotia, Represa de ⊜[1] 287b 23.44 S 46.57 W
Cotignac 62 43.32 N 6.09 E
Cotignola 64 44.23 N 11.56 E
Cotija de la Paz 234 19.49 N 102.43 W
Cotingo ≃ 246 3.55 N 60.30 W
Cotis, Laguna ⊜ 248 12.33 S 68.47 W
Cotmeana ≃ 38 44.24 N 24.45 E
Cotoca 248 17.49 S 63.03 W
Cotonou 150 6.21 N 2.26 E
Cotopaxi ▫[4] 246 0.55 S 78.55 W
Cotopaxi ▲[1] 246 0.40 S 78.26 W
Cotopaxi, Parque Nacional ♦ 246 0.15 S 78.25 W
Cotorra, Isla I 241r 10.02 N 62.16 W
Cotorro ✈[8] 286b 23.03 N 82.16 W
Cotronei 68 39.09 N 16.47 E
Cotswold Hills ⊼[2] 42 51.45 N 2.10 W
Cottage Grove, In., U.S. 218 39.36 N 84.52 W
Cottage Grove, Or., U.S. 202 43.47 N 123.03 W
Cottage Grove, Wi., U.S. 216 43.05 N 89.12 W
Cottage Hills 219 38.55 N 90.04 W
Cottageville 192 32.56 N 80.28 W
Cottam, On., Can. 214 42.08 N 82.45 W
Cottam, Eng., U.K. 262 53.47 N 2.46 W
Cottanello 66 42.24 N 12.41 E
Cottbus 54 51.45 N 14.19 E
Cottekill 210 41.51 N 74.06 W
Cottel Island I 186 48.51 N 53.42 W
Cottenham 42 52.18 N 0.09 E
Cotter 194 36.16 N 92.32 W
Cotter ≃ 171b 35.19 S 148.57 E
Cottesloe 168a 31.59 S 115.45 E
Cottiennes, Alpes (Alpi Cozie) ⊼ 62 44.45 N 7.00 E
Cottingham 44 53.47 N 0.24 W
Cottleville 219 38.44 N 90.39 W
Cottondale, Al., U.S. 194 33.11 N 87.27 W
Cottondale, Fl., U.S. 192 30.47 N 85.22 W
Cotton Lake ⊜, Mb., Can. 184 55.05 N 96.50 W
Cotton Lake ⊜, Tx., U.S. 222 29.48 N 94.48 W
Cotton Plant 194 35.00 N 91.15 W
Cottonport 194 30.59 N 92.03 W
Cotton Valley 194 32.49 N 93.25 W
Cottonwood, Az., U.S. 200 34.44 N 112.00 W
Cottonwood, Ca., U.S. 204 40.23 N 122.16 W
Cottonwood, Id., U.S. 202 46.02 N 116.20 W
Cottonwood, Mn., U.S. 198 44.36 N 95.40 W
Cottonwood ≃, Ks., U.S. 198 38.23 N 96.03 W
Cottonwood ≃, Mn., U.S. 198 44.17 N 94.25 W
Cottonwood Creek ≃, Ca., U.S. 226 36.52 N 120.12 W
Cottonwood Creek ≃, Ca., U.S. 226 36.27 N 119.20 W
Cottonwood Creek ≃, Mt., U.S. 202 48.33 N 107.45 W
Cottonwood Creek ≃, N.D., U.S. 198 46.16 N 98.15 W
Cottonwood Creek ≃, Ok., U.S. 196 35.54 N 97.27 W
Cottonwood Creek ≃, Or., U.S. 202 43.53 N 117.43 W
Cottonwood Creek ≃, Tx., U.S. 196 31.23 N 103.46 W
Cottonwood Creek ≃, Tx., U.S. 196 32.48 N 100.21 W
Cottonwood Creek ≃, Ut., U.S. 200 39.09 N 110.55 W
Cottonwood Creek ≃, Wy., U.S. 202 43.51 N 108.09 W
Cottonwood Creek, Middle Fork ≃ 204 40.23 N 122.20 W
Cottonwood Creek, South Fork ≃ 204 40.23 N 122.20 W
Cottonwood Falls 198 38.22 N 96.32 W
Cottonwood Wash ∨, Az., U.S. 200 36.19 N 113.59 W
Cottonwood Wash ∨, Az., U.S. 200 35.00 N 110.39 W
Cotubanamá 287a 22.51 S 43.01 W
Cotuhé ≃ 246 2.53 S 69.44 W
Cotui 238 19.03 N 70.09 W
Cotuit 207 41.37 N 70.26 W
Cotulla 196 28.26 N 99.14 W
Cotunduba, Ilha de I 287a 22.58 S 43.09 W
Coubert 261 48.40 N 2.42 E
Coubre, Pointe de la > 32 45.41 N 1.13 W
Coubron 261 48.55 N 2.35 E
Couches-les-Mines 58 46.52 N 4.34 E
Couchiching, Lake ⊜ 212 44.40 N 79.23 W
Coucouron 62 44.48 N 3.58 E
Coucy-le-Château-Auffrique 50 49.31 N 3.19 E
Coudekerque-Branche 50 51.02 N 2.24 E
Couderspsort 214 41.46 N 78.01 W
Coudres, Île aux I 186 47.24 N 70.23 W
Couesnon ≃ 32 48.37 N 1.31 W
Cougar 224 46.03 N 122.17 W
Cougar Reservoir ⊜[1] 202 44.06 N 122.12 W
Couhé 32 46.18 N 0.11 E
Couillet 50 50.23 N 4.27 E
Couilly-Pont-aux-Dames 261 48.53 N 2.52 E
Coulanges-la-Vineuse 50 47.42 N 3.35 E
Coulanges-sur-Yonne 50 47.31 N 3.32 E
Coulee City 202 47.36 N 119.17 W
Coulee Dam 202 47.57 N 118.58 W
Coulee Dam National Recreation Area ♦ 202 48.10 N 118.15 W
Coulihaut 240d 15.30 N 61.29 W
Coulman Island I 9 73.27 S 169.40 E
Coulmier-le-Sec 58 47.45 N 4.29 E
Coulogne 50 50.55 N 1.53 E
Coulomby 50 50.42 N 2.00 E
Coulommiers 50 48.49 N 3.05 E
Coulon ≃ 62 43.51 N 5.00 E
Coulonge ≃ 190 45.51 N 76.44 W
Coulonge Est ≃ 190 46.06 N 76.44 W
Coulsdon ✈[8] 260 51.19 N 0.08 W
Coulta 166 34.23 S 135.29 E
Coulters 279b 40.18 N 79.48 W
Coulterville, Ca., U.S. 226 37.42 N 120.11 W
Coulterville, Il., U.S. 194 38.11 N 89.36 W
Counce 194 35.02 N 88.16 W
Council 202 44.44 N 116.26 W
Council Bluffs 198 41.15 N 95.51 W
Council Grove 198 38.39 N 96.29 W
Council Grove Lake ⊜[1] 198 38.42 N 96.31 W
Coundon 44 54.40 N 1.39 W
Countegany 171b 36.11 S 149.27 E
Countesthorpe 42 52.33 N 1.08 W
Country Campus 222 30.49 N 95.26 W
Country Club Estates 220 28.03 N 81.57 W
Country Club Hills 278 41.34 N 87.43 W
Country Club View 284c 38.49 N 77.19 W
Country Hills 279b 40.19 N 79.42 W
Country Homes 202 47.44 N 117.24 W
Country Ridge Estates 276 41.02 N 73.41 W
Countryside 278 41.47 N 87.52 W
Countryside Lake ⊜ 278 42.15 N 88.03 W
Countryside Manor 278 42.18 N 87.56 W
Coupar Angus 46 56.33 N 3.17 W
Coupeville 224 48.13 N 122.41 W
Coupland 222 30.28 N 97.24 W
Coupon 214 40.32 N 78.31 W
Coupvray 261 48.53 N 2.48 E
Courbevoie 50 48.54 N 2.15 E
Courbons 62 44.06 N 6.12 E
Courçay 50 47.15 N 0.52 E
Courcelle 261 48.42 N 2.06 E
Courcelles, Bel. 50 50.28 N 4.22 E
Courcelles, Fr. 261 49.07 N 2.18 E
Courcelles-Chaussy 56 49.07 N 6.24 E
Courcelles-sur-Nied 56 49.04 N 6.18 E
Courchevel 62 45.25 N 6.38 E
Cour-Cheverny 50 47.30 N 1.27 E
Courcôme 32 46.00 N 0.13 E
Courçon 32 46.15 N 0.49 W
Courcouronnes 261 48.37 N 2.25 E
Courdimanche 261 49.02 N 2.00 E
Cour-et-Buis 62 45.26 N 5.00 E
Courgent, Fr. 261 48.54 N 1.40 E
Courgent, Fr. 261 49.04 N 1.35 E
Courland — Kurzeme ▫[9] 76 56.50 N 22.30 E
Courmayeur 62 45.47 N 6.58 E
Couronne, Cap > 62 43.19 N 5.03 E
Couronnement, Île du — Coronation Island I 9 60.37 S 45.30 W
Courpière 62 45.45 N 3.33 E
Courquetaine 261 48.41 N 2.45 E
Course Brook ≃ 283 42.17 N 71.22 W
Courseulles 28 49.20 N 0.27 W
Courson-les-Carrières 50 47.36 N 3.30 E
Court 58 47.14 N 7.20 E
Courtacon 50 48.42 N 3.17 E
Courtalain 50 48.05 N 1.09 E
Courteilles 50 48.58 N 0.29 E
Courtenay, B.C., Can. 182 49.41 N 125.00 W
Courtenay, Fr. 50 48.02 N 3.03 E
Courthézon 62 44.05 N 4.53 E
Courtice 212 43.55 N 78.46 W
Courtisols 56 48.59 N 4.31 E
Courtland, On., Can. 212 42.51 N 80.38 W
Courtland, Al., U.S. 194 34.40 N 87.18 W
Courtland, Ca., U.S. 226 38.20 N 121.34 W
Courtland, Va., U.S. 208 36.42 N 77.04 W
Courtleigh 284b 39.22 N 76.46 W
Courtmacsherry 48 51.38 N 8.43 W
Courtmacsherry Bay ⊂ 48 51.35 N 8.40 W
Courtney, Pa., U.S. 279b 40.13 N 79.58 W
Courtney, Tx., U.S. 222 30.16 N 96.04 W
Courtney Creek ≃ 196 31.16 N 102.50 W
Courtomer, Fr. 50 48.38 N 0.22 E
Courtomer, Fr. 261 48.39 N 2.54 E
Courtown 48 52.38 N 6.13 W
Courtrai — Kortrijk 50 50.50 N 3.16 E
Courtright 214 42.49 N 82.28 W
Courtry, Fr. 261 48.33 N 2.46 E
Courtry, Fr. 261 48.55 N 2.36 E
Court-Saint-Étienne 50 50.39 N 4.34 E
Courville-sur-Eure 50 48.27 N 1.15 E
Coushatta 194 32.00 N 93.20 W
Cousin ≃ 50 47.32 N 3.46 E
Cousiño Macul, Parque ♦ 286e 33.30 S 70.35 W
Cousolre 50 50.15 N 4.09 E
Coussegrey 50 47.57 N 4.01 E
Coussey 58 48.25 N 5.41 E
Coustellet 62 43.53 N 5.11 E
Coutances 32 49.03 N 1.26 W
Coutevroult 261 48.52 N 2.51 E
Couto do Magalhães 250 8.17 S 49.16 W
Couto Magalhães ≃ 255 13.37 S 53.09 W
Coutras 32 45.02 N 0.08 W
Coutts 182 49.00 N 111.57 W
Couture, Lac ⊜ 176 60.07 N 75.20 W
Couture-sur-Loir 50 47.45 N 0.41 E
Couves, Ilha das I 256 23.25 S 44.52 W
Couvet 58 46.56 N 6.38 E
Couvin 50 50.03 N 4.29 E
Cova da Piedade 266c 38.40 N 9.10 W
Covanne 156 21.22 S 33.56 E
Covasna 38 45.51 N 26.11 E
Covasna ▫[6] 38 46.00 N 26.00 E
Cove, Scot., U.K. 46 57.51 N 5.42 W
Cove, Or., U.S. 202 45.17 N 117.48 W
Cove Bay 46 57.06 N 2.04 W
Covedale 218 39.07 N 84.36 W
Cove Harbor ⊂ 276 41.03 N 73.30 W
Cove Island I 190 45.17 N 81.44 W
Covelo, Ang. 152 12.06 S 13.55 E
Covelo, Ca., U.S. 204 39.47 N 123.14 W
Cove Neck 276 40.53 N 73.31 W
Cove Neck >[1] 276 40.53 N 73.30 W
Coventry, Eng., U.K. 42 52.25 N 1.30 W
Coventry, Ct., U.S. 207 41.46 N 72.18 W
Coventry, De., U.S. 285 39.40 N 75.38 W
Coventry, R.I., U.S. 207 41.41 N 71.34 W
Coventry Cathedral ⊍[1] 42 52.25 N 1.30 W
Coventryville 285 40.10 N 75.41 W
Cove Palisades State Park ♦ 202 44.34 N 121.15 W
Cove Point 208 38.22 N 76.20 W
Cove Point > 208 38.23 N 76.23 W
Cover ≃ 44 54.17 N 1.46 W
Covered Wells 200 31.48 N 111.59 W
Covert 216 42.17 N 86.15 W
Coviglaio 66 44.08 N 11.18 E
Covilhã 34 40.17 N 7.30 W
Covina 228 34.05 N 117.53 W
Covington, Ga., U.S. 192 33.35 N 83.51 W
Covington, In., U.S. 194 40.08 N 87.23 W
Covington, Ky., U.S. 218 39.05 N 84.30 W
Covington, La., U.S. 194 30.28 N 90.06 W
Covington, Oh., U.S. 218 40.07 N 84.21 W
Covington, Ok., U.S. 196 36.18 N 97.35 W
Covington, Pa., U.S. 210 41.45 N 77.05 W
Covington, Tn., U.S. 194 35.33 N 89.38 W
Covington, Tx., U.S. 222 32.11 N 97.16 W
Covington, Va., U.S. 192 37.47 N 79.59 W
Covões 266c 38.50 N 9.20 W
Covunco, Arroyo ≃ 252 38.29 S 69.32 W
Cow ≃ 190 47.23 N 83.59 W
Cowal > 46 56.05 N 5.08 W
Cowan, Lake ⊜ 162 31.50 S 121.50 E
Cowan, Ky., U.S. 218 38.24 N 83.54 W
Cowan, Tn., U.S. 194 35.09 N 86.00 W
Cowan, Lake ⊜ 162 31.50 S 121.50 E
Cowan Creek ≃ 274a 33.40 S 151.10 E
Cowanesque 210 41.56 N 77.30 W
Cowanesque ≃ 210 42.00 N 77.07 W
Cowan Heights 280 33.47 N 117.47 W
Cowan Lake ⊜, Sk., Can. 184 54.00 N 107.15 W
Cowan Lake ⊜, Oh., U.S. 218 39.23 N 83.54 W
Cowan Lake State Park ♦ 218 39.23 N 83.53 W
Cowansburg 279b 40.15 N 79.46 W
Cowanshannock Creek ≃ 214 40.51 N 79.30 W
Cowansville, P.Q., Can. 206 45.12 N 72.45 W
Cowansville, Pa., U.S. 214 40.53 N 79.36 W
Cowaramup 162 33.52 S 115.05 E
Coward 192 33.58 N 79.44 W
Coward Springs 166 29.24 S 136.49 E
Cowarie 166 27.43 S 138.20 E
Cow Bayou ≃ 222 31.19 N 97.00 W
Cowbridge 42 51.28 N 3.27 W
Cowburn Tunnel ✈[5] 262 53.21 N 1.52 W
Cow Canyon ∨ 200 34.01 N 120.06 W
Cowcowing Lakes ⊜ 162 31.01 S 117.18 E
Cow Creek ≃, Ks., U.S. 198 38.02 N 97.56 W
Cow Creek ≃, Mt., U.S. 202 47.47 N 108.56 W
Cow Creek ≃, Ok., U.S. 196 34.10 N 98.20 W
Cow Creek ≃, Or., U.S. 202 42.57 N 123.20 W
Cow Creek ≃, Wa., U.S. 202 46.45 N 118.09 W
Cowden, Il., U.S. 219 39.15 N 88.52 W
Cowden, Pa., U.S. 279b 40.19 N 80.13 W
Cowdenbeath 46 56.07 N 3.21 W
Coweeman ≃ 224 46.06 N 122.52 W
Cowell 166 33.41 S 136.55 E
Cowen 188 38.24 N 80.33 W
Cowen, Mount ▲ 202 45.23 N 110.29 W
Cowes, Austl. 169 38.27 S 145.14 E
Cowes, Eng., U.K. 42 50.45 N 1.18 W
Cowessess Indian Reserve ♦[4] 184 50.31 N 102.42 W
Coweta 196 35.57 N 95.39 W
Cow Green Reservoir ⊜[1] 44 54.40 N 2.18 W
Cow Gulch ≃ 202 46.02 N 107.52 W
Cow Head 186 49.55 N 57.48 W
Cowhouse Creek ≃ 222 31.10 N 97.35 W
Cowichan ≃ 224 48.46 N 123.38 W
Cowichan Bay 224 48.44 N 123.40 W
Cowichan Lake ⊜ 224 48.54 N 124.20 W
Cowiche Creek, North Fork ≃ 224 46.38 N 120.41 W
Cowiche Creek, South Fork ≃ 224 46.38 N 120.41 W
Cowie Water ≃ 46 56.58 N 2.12 W
Cowles Dam ⊜[1] 273d 26.13 S 28.28 E
Cowlesville 210 42.51 N 78.28 W
Cowley, Austl. 166 26.54 S 144.49 E
Cowley, Ab., Can. 182 49.34 N 114.05 W
Cowley, Eng., U.K. 42 51.43 N 1.12 W
Cowley, Wy., U.S. 202 44.53 N 108.28 W
Cowley ✈[8] 260 51.32 N 0.29 W
Cowley, Mount ▲ 169 38.33 S 143.52 E
Cowlitz ▫[6] 224 46.07 N 122.43 W
Cowlitz ≃ 224 46.05 N 122.53 W
Cowm Reservoir ⊜[1] 262 53.40 N 2.11 W
Cow Palace ⊍ 282 37.42 N 122.25 W
Cowpasture ≃ 188 37.48 N 79.45 W
Cowpens 192 35.01 N 81.48 W
Cowpens National Battlefield ♦ 192 35.06 N 81.46 W
Cowra 166 33.50 S 148.41 E
Cox 164 15.19 S 135.25 E
Cox, Mount ▲[2] 162 24.55 S 125.36 E
Coxá ≃ 255 14.16 S 44.11 W
Cox Creek ≃ 212 43.35 N 80.29 W
Coxheath 42 51.14 N 0.30 E
Coxim 255 18.30 S 54.45 W
Coxim ≃ 255 18.34 S 54.45 W
Coxipi, Lac ⊜ 186 51.33 N 58.25 W
Coxquihui 234 20.11 N 97.35 W
Cox River Aboriginal Reserve ♦[4] 164 15.40 S 134.45 E
Coxs ≃ 170 33.57 S 150.25 E
Coxsackie 210 42.21 N 73.48 W
Cox's Bāzār 120 21.26 N 91.59 E
Cox's Cove 186 49.07 N 58.05 W
Coyaguaima, Cerro ▲ 252 22.55 S 66.35 W
Coyah 150 9.43 N 13.23 W
Coyame 232 29.28 N 105.06 W
Coyanosa Draw ∨ 196 31.18 N 103.06 W
Coya Sur 252 22.25 S 69.38 W
Coyle, Water of ≃ 44 55.28 N 4.32 W
Coyoacán ✈[8] 286a 19.20 N 99.10 W
Coyote 226 37.13 N 121.44 W
Coyote Creek ≃, Ca., U.S. 204 33.13 N 116.13 W
Coyote Creek ≃, Ca., U.S. 226 37.28 N 122.03 W
Coyote Creek ≃, Ca., U.S. 280 33.47 N 118.05 W
Coyote Creek, East Fork ≃ 226 37.10 N 121.30 W
Coyote Creek, Middle Fork ≃ 226 37.10 N 121.30 W
Coyote Hills ⊼[2] 282 37.33 N 122.05 W
Coyote Hills Regional Park ♦ 282 37.33 N 122.06 W
Coyote Lake ⊜ 204 35.04 N 116.45 W
Coyote Lake ⊜[1] 226 37.06 N 121.32 W
Coyotepec 234 19.46 N 99.12 W
Coyote Point > 282 37.35 N 122.19 W
Coyote Wash ∨, Az., U.S. 200 32.40 N 114.08 W
Coyote Wash ∨, N.M., U.S. 200 36.11 N 108.33 W
Coy Pond ⊜ 283 42.36 N 70.49 W
Coyuca de Benítez 234 17.02 N 100.04 W
Coyuca de Catalán 234 18.20 N 100.39 W
Coyutla 234 20.15 N 97.39 W
Cozad 198 40.51 N 99.59 W
Cozes 32 45.35 N 0.50 W
Cozie, Alpi (Alpes Cottiennes) ⊼ 62 44.45 N 7.00 E
Cozoyoapan 234 16.46 N 98.15 W
Cozumel 232 20.31 N 86.55 W
Cozumel, Isla I 232 20.25 N 86.55 W
Cozy Lake 276 41.01 N 74.30 W
Crab Alley Bay ⊂ 208 38.55 N 76.17 W
Crab Creek ≃ 202 46.49 N 119.55 W
Crab Meadow ⊞ 276 40.55 N 73.20 W
Crab Orchard, Ky., U.S. 192 37.27 N 84.30 W
Crab Orchard, Tn., U.S. 192 35.54 N 84.52 W
Crab Orchard Lake ⊜[1] 194 37.43 N 89.05 W
Crabtree 214 40.21 N 79.28 W
Crabtree Creek ≃ 279b 40.21 N 79.30 W
Crabtree Mills 206 45.58 N 73.28 W
Craches 261 48.34 N 1.49 E
Crackenback ≃ 171b 36.21 S 148.36 E
Craco 68 40.23 N 16.26 E
Cracovie — Kraków 30 50.03 N 19.58 E
Cradle Mountain-Lake Saint Clair National Park ♦ 166 42.00 S 146.00 E
Cradock, Austl. 166 32.04 S 138.30 E
Cradock, S. Afr. 158 32.08 S 25.36 E
Cradock Channel Џ 172 36.11 S 175.15 E
Crafers 168b 35.01 S 138.47 E
Crafton 214 40.26 N 80.03 W
Crafts Creek ≃ 285 40.07 N 74.46 W
Cragg Vale 262 53.42 N 2.00 W
Cragsmoor 210 41.40 N 74.23 W
Crai 42 51.55 N 3.36 W
Craig, B.C., Can. 224 49.18 N 124.15 W
Craig, Ak., U.S. 182 55.29 N 133.09 W
Craig, Co., U.S. 200 40.30 N 107.32 W
Craig, Mo., U.S. 194 40.11 N 95.22 W
Craig, Ne., U.S. 198 41.47 N 96.21 W
Craig, Point ▲ 162 26.51 S 126.19 E
Craigavon 48 54.27 N 6.24 W
Craig Beach 214 41.07 N 81.01 W
Craig Creek ≃ 192 37.39 N 79.49 W
Craigellachie 182 50.59 N 118.43 W
Craighall ✈[8] 273d 26.07 S 28.02 E
Craighall Park ✈[8] 273d 26.08 S 28.01 E
Craighouse 46 55.51 N 5.57 W
Craigmont 202 46.14 N 116.27 W
Craigmyle 182 51.40 N 112.15 W
Craigmish Point > 46 56.07 N 5.37 W
Craignure 46 56.28 N 5.42 W
Craigsville, Pa., U.S. 214 40.51 N 79.39 W
Craigsville, Va., U.S. 192 38.04 N 79.23 W
Craigville 216 40.47 N 85.06 W
Craik 184 51.03 N 105.49 W
Crail 46 56.16 N 2.38 W
Crailsheim 56 49.08 N 10.04 E
Craiova 38 44.19 N 23.48 E
Crake ≃ 44 54.14 N 3.03 W
Craley 208 39.57 N 76.31 W
Cramant 50 48.59 N 3.59 E
Cramlington 44 55.05 N 1.36 W
Cranage 262 53.12 N 2.22 W
Cranberry 214 41.21 N 79.43 W
Cranberry Brook ≃ 283 42.11 N 71.01 W
Cranberry Creek 210 43.09 N 74.14 W
Cranberry Island I 212 44.44 N 81.18 W
Cranberry Lake 210 40.57 N 74.44 W
Cranberry Lake ⊜, On., Can. 212 44.26 N 76.19 W
Cranberry Lake ⊜, On., Can. 212 44.47 N 75.50 W
Cranberry Lake ⊜, N.Y., U.S. 188 44.10 N 74.50 W
Cranberry Lake ⊜, Wa., U.S. 224 47.17 N 123.05 W
Cranberry Mountain ▲ 182 50.42 N 118.12 W
Cranberry Pond ⊜ 276 41.08 N 74.12 W
Cranberry Portage 184 54.35 N 101.23 W
Cranborne Chase ⊼[3] 42 50.55 N 2.05 W
Cranbourne 169 38.06 S 145.17 E
Cranbrook, Austl. 162 34.18 S 117.32 E
Cranbrook, B.C., Can 182 49.31 N 115.46 W
Cranbrook, Eng., U.K. 42 51.06 N 0.33 E
Cranbrook Academy of Art ⊍ 281 42.34 N 83.14 W
Cranbury 276 40.18 N 74.30 W
Cranbury Brook ≃ 276 40.19 N 74.37 W
Crandall 222 32.37 N 96.27 W
Crandon 190 45.34 N 88.54 W
Crandon Lakes 210 41.07 N 74.50 W
Crane, Az., U.S. 204 32.42 N 114.40 W
Crane, In., U.S. 194 38.53 N 86.54 W
Crane, Mo., U.S. 194 36.54 N 93.34 W
Crane, Tx., U.S. 196 31.23 N 102.20 W
Crane Beach ⊼[2] 283 42.41 N 70.46 W
Cranebrook 274a 33.43 S 150.42 E
Crane Creek ≃ 190 43.01 N 91.58 W
Crane Lake ⊜, On., Can. 212 45.13 N 79.57 W
Crane Lake ⊜, Sk., Can. 184 50.06 N 109.06 W
Crane Mountain ▲ 202 42.04 N 120.13 W
Crane Neck Point > 210 40.58 N 73.10 W
Crane River Indian Reserve ♦[4] 184 51.30 N 99.14 W
Cranesville 214 41.54 N 80.21 W
Cranfield 42 52.05 N 0.35 W
Cranfills Gap 222 31.46 N 97.50 W
Cranford 210 40.39 N 74.19 W
Crange ✈[8] 263 51.32 N 7.11 E
Cran-Gévrier 58 45.54 N 6.06 E
Crank 262 53.29 N 2.45 W
Cranleigh 42 51.09 N 0.30 W
Crans 58 46.19 N 7.28 E
Cranston 207 41.46 N 71.26 W
Cranston Heights 285 39.38 N 75.38 W
Craon 32 47.51 N 0.57 W
Craonne 50 49.26 N 3.47 E
Craponne, Fr. 62 45.44 N 4.43 E
Craponne, Fr. 62 45.20 N 3.51 E
Craponne, Canal de ≃ 62 43.40 N 4.39 E
Craryville 210 42.11 N 73.35 W
Crasna, Rom. 38 46.31 N 27.51 E
Crasna, Rom. 38 45.36 N 26.08 E
Crasna (Kraszna) ≃ 38 48.09 N 22.20 E
Crassier 58 46.22 N 6.11 E
Crater Lake ⊜ 202 42.56 N 122.06 W
Crater Lake National Park ♦ 202 42.49 N 122.08 W
Crater Mount ▲ 164 6.30 S 145.10 E
Crater Point > 164 5.22 S 152.09 E
Craters of the Moon National Monument ♦ 202 43.20 N 113.35 W
Crateús 250 5.10 S 40.40 W
Crathie 46 57.02 N 3.12 W
Crati ≃ 68 39.43 N 16.31 E
Crato 250 7.14 S 39.23 W
Crau ⊼[1] 62 43.36 N 4.50 E
Crawford, Cape > 176 73.44 N 84.50 W
Craughwell 48 53.13 N 8.43 W
Cravant 50 47.41 N 3.41 E
Cravari ≃ 248 12.06 S 58.03 W
Cravat 219 38.25 N 89.06 W
Craven 184 50.39 N 104.50 W
Craven Arms 42 52.26 N 2.50 W
Cravensville 171b 36.24 S 147.34 E
Cravo Norte 246 6.18 N 70.12 W
Cravo Norte ≃ 246 6.18 N 70.12 W
Cravo Sur ≃ 246 4.42 N 71.36 W
Crawfish ≃ 216 43.00 N 88.49 W
Crawford, Scot., U.K. 44 55.28 N 3.40 W
Crawford, Co., U.S. 200 38.42 N 107.36 W
Crawford, Ms., U.S. 194 33.18 N 88.36 W
Crawford, Ne., U.S. 198 42.40 N 103.24 W
Crawford, Tx., U.S. 222 31.32 N 97.27 W
Crawford ▫[6], In., U.S. 218 38.20 N 86.28 W
Crawford ▫[6], Oh., U.S. 214 40.48 N 82.58 W
Crawford ▫[6], Pa., U.S. 214 41.39 N 80.10 W
Crawford Bay 182 49.42 N 116.48 W
Crawford Countryside 278 41.32 N 87.43 W
Crawford Notch State Park ♦ 188 44.13 N 71.25 W
Crawfordsville, Ar., U.S. 194 35.13 N 90.19 W
Crawfordsville, In., U.S. 194 40.02 N 86.52 W
Crawfordville, Fl., U.S. 192 30.10 N 84.22 W
Crawfordville, Ga., U.S. 192 33.33 N 82.53 W
Crawinkel 54 50.47 N 10.47 E
Crawley 42 51.07 N 0.12 W
Crawshawbooth 262 53.43 N 2.17 W
Crayford ✈[8] 260 51.27 N 0.11 E
Crays Hill 260 51.36 N 0.28 E
Crazy Mountains ⊼ 202 46.08 N 110.20 W
Crazy Peak ▲ 202 46.01 N 110.16 W
Crazy Woman Creek ≃ 202 44.29 N 106.08 W
Creagan 46 56.33 N 5.17 W
Creagorry 46 57.26 N 7.19 W
Creal Springs 194 37.37 N 88.50 W
Creamery 285 40.13 N 75.25 W
Crean Lake ⊜ 184 54.05 N 106.10 W
Crêches-sur-Saône 58 46.15 N 4.47 E
Crécy, Forêt de ♦ 261 48.48 N 2.53 E
Crécy-en-Brie 50 48.51 N 2.55 E
Crécy-en-Ponthieu 50 50.15 N 1.53 E
Crécy-sur-Serre 50 49.42 N 3.37 E
Credenhill 42 52.06 N 2.48 W
Credit ≃ 212 43.33 N 79.35 W
Crediton 42 50.47 N 3.39 W
Cree ≃, Sk., Can. 176 59.00 N 105.47 W
Cree ≃, Scot., U.K. 44 54.52 N 4.20 W
Creede 200 37.50 N 106.55 W
Creedmoor 192 36.07 N 78.41 W
Creedmoor 222 30.12 N 97.43 W
Creegh 48 52.44 N 9.26 W
Creek Brook ≃ 283 42.47 N 71.02 W
Creek Locks 210 41.52 N 74.03 W
Creekmouth ✈[8] 260 51.31 N 0.06 E
Creekside 214 40.40 N 79.11 W
Creekwood 278 41.39 N 87.59 W
Creel 232 27.45 N 107.38 W
Cree Lake ⊜ 176 57.30 N 106.30 W
Creemore 212 44.19 N 80.06 W
Creetown 44 54.54 N 4.23 W
Cregganbaun 48 53.42 N 9.51 W
Creglingen 56 49.28 N 10.01 E
Crégy-lès-Meaux 261 48.58 N 2.52 E
Créhange 56 49.03 N 6.35 E
Creighton, Sk., Can. 184 54.45 N 101.54 W
Creighton, S. Afr. 158 30.01 S 29.51 E
Creighton, Ne., U.S. 198 42.28 N 97.54 W
Creighton, Pa., U.S. 214 40.35 N 79.46 W
Creighton Mine 190 46.28 N 81.11 W
Creightons Creek ≃ 169 36.43 S 145.22 E
Creil, Fr. 50 49.16 N 2.29 E
Creil, Ned. 52 52.45 N 5.40 E
Crema 62 45.22 N 9.41 E
Cremia 58 46.05 N 9.16 E
Crémieu 62 45.43 N 5.15 E
Cremlingen 54 52.15 N 10.39 E
Cremona 62 45.07 N 10.02 E
Cremona, Ab., Can. 182 51.33 N 114.29 W
Cremona, It. 64 45.07 N 10.02 E
Cremona ▫[4] 64 45.12 N 10.00 E
Crenshaw, Ms., U.S. 194 34.30 N 90.12 W
Crenshaw, Pa., U.S. 214 41.15 N 78.56 W
Crep Nudo ▲ 64 46.13 N 12.24 E
Crepori ≃ 250 5.42 S 57.08 W
Crépy-en-Laonnois 50 49.36 N 3.31 E
Crépy-en-Valois 50 49.14 N 2.54 E
Créquy 50 50.29 N 2.03 E

≃ River / Fluß / Río / Rivière / Rio
≃ Canal / Kanal / Canal / Canal / Canal
⌊ Waterfall, Rapids / Wasserfall, Stromschnellen / Cascada, Rápidos / Chute d'eau, Rapides / Cascata, Rápidos
Џ Strait / Meeresstraße / Estrecho / Détroit / Estreito
⊂ Bay, Gulf / Bucht, Golf / Bahía, Golfo / Baie, Golfe / Baía, Golfo
⊜ Lake, Lakes / See, Seen / Lago, Lagos / Lac, Lacs / Lago, Lagos
⊞ Swamp / Sumpf / Pantano / Marais / Pântano
☒ Ice Features, Glacier / Eis- und Gletscherformen / Accidentes Glaciales / Formes glaciaires / Acidentes glaciares
☂ Other Hydrographic Features / Andere Hydrographische Objekte / Otros Elementos Hidrográficos / Autres données hydrographiques / Outros acidentes hidrográficos

✈ Submarine Features / Untermeerische Objekte / Accidentes Submarinos / Formes de relief sous-marin / Acidentes submarinos
▫ Political Unit / Politische Einheit / Unidad Política / Entité politique / Unidade política
⊍ Cultural Institution / Kulturelle Institution / Institución Cultural / Institution culturelle / Instituição cultural
⊥ Historical Site / Historische Stätte / Sitio Histórico / Site historique / Sitio histórico
♦ Recreational Site / Erholungs- und Ferienort / Sitio de Recreo / Centre de loisirs / Area de Lazer
⊠ Airport / Flughafen / Aeropuerto / Aéroport / Aeroporto
■ Military Installation / Militäranlage / Instalación Militar / Installation militaire / Instalação militar
✈ Miscellaneous / Verschiedenes / Misceláneo / Divers / Diversos

Name	Page	Lat. °′	Long. °′
Creran, Loch ⊜	46	56.31 N	5.20 W
Cres	36	44.58 N	14.25 E
Cres, Otok I	36	44.50 N	14.25 E
Cresaptown	188	39.35 N	78.50 W
Crescent, N.Y., U.S.	210	42.49 N	73.43 W
Crescent, Ok., U.S.	196	35.57 N	97.35 W
Crescent, Or., U.S.	202	43.27 N	121.41 W
Crescent, Lake ⊜	224	48.05 N	123.50 W
Crescent Beach, B.C., Can.	224	49.04 N	122.53 W
Crescent Beach, Fl., U.S.	220	27.15 N	82.32 W
Crescent City, Ca., U.S.	204	41.45 N	124.12 W
Crescent City, Fl., U.S.	192	29.25 N	81.30 W
Crescent City, Il., U.S.	216	40.46 N	87.51 W
Crescent Ditch ≋	226	36.29 N	120.07 W
Crescent Heights, N.J., U.S.	285	39.58 N	74.43 W
Crescent Heights, Tx., U.S.	222	32.11 N	95.56 W
Crescent Lake ⊜, Fl., U.S.	192	29.28 N	81.30 W
Crescent Lake ⊜, Or., U.S.	202	43.29 N	121.59 W
Crescent Lake Estates	281	42.38 N	83.25 W
Crescent Spur	182	53.35 N	120.41 W
Crescentville ◆[8]	285	40.02 N	75.05 W
Crescenzago ◆[8]	266b	45.30 N	9.15 E
Cresco, Ia., U.S.	190	43.22 N	92.06 W
Cresco, Pa., U.S.	210	41.09 N	75.17 W
Crespano del Grappa	64	45.49 N	11.50 E
Crespian	62	43.53 N	4.06 E
Crespières	261	48.53 N	1.55 E
Crespin	50	50.25 N	3.39 E
Crespino	64	44.59 N	11.53 E
Crespo	252	32.02 S	60.19 W
Cressbrook Creek ≃	171a	27.05 S	152.27 E
Cressely	261	48.43 N	2.05 E
Cressey	226	37.25 N	120.40 W
Cresskill	276	40.56 N	73.57 W
Cresskill Brook ≃	276	40.57 N	73.58 W
Cresson, Pa., U.S.	214	40.27 N	78.35 W
Cresson, Tx., U.S.	222	32.32 N	97.37 W
Cressona	208	40.37 N	76.11 W
Cressy	169	38.02 S	143.38 E
Crest	62	44.44 N	5.02 E
Cresta	58	46.28 N	9.31 E
Crested Butte	200	38.52 N	106.59 W
Cresthaven	220	26.03 N	80.08 W
Crest Hill	216	41.33 N	88.05 W
Crestline, Ca., U.S.	228	34.14 N	117.17 W
Crestline, Oh., U.S.	214	40.47 N	82.44 W
Creston, B.C., Can.	182	49.06 N	116.31 W
Creston, Nf., Can.	186	47.09 N	55.11 W
Creston, Ca., U.S.	226	35.31 N	120.31 W
Creston, Il., U.S.	216	41.56 N	88.58 W
Creston, Ia., U.S.	198	41.03 N	94.21 W
Creston, Oh., U.S.	214	40.59 N	81.53 W
Crestone Peak ∧	200	37.58 N	105.36 W
Crestview, Fl., U.S.	194	30.45 N	86.34 W
Crestview, Wi., U.S.	216	42.49 N	87.49 W
Crestview Heights	210	42.05 N	76.07 W
Crestwood, Il., U.S.	278	41.39 N	87.45 W
Crestwood, Ky., U.S.	218	38.19 N	85.28 W
Crestwood, Mo., U.S.	219	38.33 N	90.22 W
Crestwood Hills	192	35.56 N	84.05 W
Creswell, Eng., U.K.	44	53.16 N	1.12 W
Creswell, Or., U.S.	202	43.55 N	123.01 W
Creswell Bay ⊂	176	72.35 N	93.25 W
Creswell Creek ≃	162	18.10 S	135.11 E
Creswell Downs	162	17.57 S	135.55 E
Creswick	169	37.26 S	143.54 E
Creta → Kríti I	38	35.15 N	25.00 E
Crete, Il., U.S.	216	41.27 N	87.38 W
Crete, Ne., U.S.	198	40.37 N	96.57 W
Crete → Kríti I	38	35.15 N	25.00 E
Crete, Sea of → Kritikón Pélagos ▿[2]	38	35.46 N	23.54 E
Créteil	50	48.48 N	2.28 E
Crétéville	36	36.40 N	10.20 E
Cretin, Cape ›	164	6.40 S	147.52 E
Creus, Cap de ›	34	42.19 N	3.19 E
Creuse □[5]	32	46.05 N	2.00 E
Creuse ≃	32	47.00 N	0.34 E
Creussen	60	49.51 N	11.37 E
Creutzwald	56	49.12 N	6.41 E
Creuzburg	56	51.03 N	10.15 E
Crevacuore	62	45.41 N	8.15 E
Crevalcore	64	44.43 N	11.09 E
Creve Coeur, Il., U.S.	190	40.38 N	89.35 W
Creve Coeur, Mo., U.S.	219	38.39 N	90.25 W
Crèvecœur-en-Auge	50	49.07 N	0.01 E
Crèvecœur-en-Brie	261	48.45 N	2.55 E
Crèvecœur-le-Grand	50	49.36 N	2.05 E
Crevillent	34	38.15 N	0.48 W
Crevoladossola	58	46.09 N	8.18 E
Crewe, Eng., U.K.	44	53.05 N	2.27 W
Crewe, Va., U.S.	192	37.10 N	78.07 W
Crewkerne	42	50.53 N	2.48 W
Crews Lake ⊜	220	28.23 N	82.31 W
Crewsville	220	27.16 N	81.36 W
Crianlarich	46	56.23 N	4.36 W
Crib Point	169	38.22 S	145.12 E
Cricamola ≃	236	8.59 N	81.54 W
Cricaré ≃	255	18.37 S	40.05 W
Criccieth	42	52.55 N	4.14 W
Crichi	68	38.57 N	16.38 E
Criciúma	252	28.40 S	49.23 W
Crick	42	52.21 N	1.07 W
Cricket	192	36.10 N	81.11 W
Crickhowell	42	51.53 N	3.07 W
Cricklade	42	51.39 N	1.51 W
Cridersville	216	40.39 N	84.09 W
Crieff	46	56.23 N	3.52 W
Criel-sur-Mer	50	50.01 N	1.19 E
Criffell ∧	44	54.57 N	3.38 W
Crikvenica	36	45.11 N	14.42 E
Crillon, Mount ∧	180	58.40 N	137.10 W
Crimea → Krymskij poluostrov ›[1]	78	45.00 N	34.00 E
Crimmitschau	54	50.49 N	12.23 E
Crimond	46	57.36 N	1.54 W
Crinan	46	56.05 N	5.35 W
Crîngeni	38	44.01 N	24.47 E
Cringila	170	34.28 S	150.53 E
Cripple Creek	200	38.44 N	105.10 W
Criquetot l'Esneval	50	49.39 N	0.16 E
Crirninoso, Monte ∧	256	21.32 S	43.25 W
Crisenoy	261	48.36 N	2.45 E
Crisfield	208	37.59 N	75.51 W
Crisólia	256	22.15 S	46.25 W
Crisóstomo, Ribeirão ≃	250	10.19 S	50.26 W
Crispiano	68	40.36 N	17.14 E
Criss Creek	182	51.03 N	120.44 W
Crissiumal	252	27.30 S	54.07 W
Cristal, Monts de ⋏	152	0.30 N	10.30 E
Cristal, Sierra del ⋏	240p	20.33 N	75.31 W
Cristalândia	250	10.36 S	49.11 W
Cristália	255	16.43 S	42.52 W
Cristalina	255	16.45 S	47.36 W
Cristalino ≃	255	12.38 S	50.40 W
Cristallo ∧	64	46.34 N	12.12 E
Cristianópolis	255	17.13 S	48.45 W
Cristina	256	22.13 S	45.16 W
Cristinápolis	250	11.29 S	37.46 W
Cristino Castro	250	8.49 S	44.13 W
Cristóbal	236	9.21 N	79.55 W
Cristóbal Colón, Pico ∧	246	10.50 N	73.41 W
Cristóbal Obregón	234	16.20 N	93.30 W
Cristoforo Colombo, Aeroporto di ⊠	62	44.25 N	8.49 E
Cristo Redentor ⊥	252	32.50 S	70.05 W
Cristo Redentor, Estatua do ⊕[1]	287a	22.57 S	43.13 W
Cristuru-Secuiesc	38	46.17 N	25.02 E
Crişul Alb ≃	38	46.42 N	21.17 E
Crişul Negru ≃	38	46.42 N	21.16 E
Crişul Repede (Sebes Körös) ≃	38	46.55 N	20.59 E
Crittenden	218	38.46 N	84.36 W
Crivitz, Dtsch.	54	53.35 N	11.38 E
Crivitz, Wi., U.S.	190	45.13 N	88.00 W
Crixalândia	255	15.18 S	47.15 W
Crixás	255	14.27 S	49.58 W
Crixás ≃	250	11.02 S	48.34 W
Crixás-Açu ≃	255	13.19 S	50.36 W
Crixás-Mirim ≃	255	13.30 S	50.30 W
Črna	61	46.28 N	14.51 E
Crna ≃	38	41.35 N	21.59 E
Crna Gora □[3]	38	42.30 N	19.18 E
Črni vrh ∧	61	46.29 N	15.14 E
Črnomelj	36	45.34 N	15.11 E
Croachy	46	57.19 N	4.14 W
Croagh Patrick ∧	48	53.46 N	9.40 W
Croajingolong National Park ♠	166	37.40 S	149.30 E
Croal ≃	262	53.33 N	2.23 W
Croatia □[1], Europe	22	45.10 N	15.30 E
Croatia (Hrvatska) □[1], Europe	36	45.10 N	15.30 E
Croce dello Scrivano, Passo ⋈	68	40.34 N	15.50 E
Croce Domini, Passo di ⋈	64	45.54 N	10.24 E
Crocefieschi	62	44.35 N	9.01 E
Crocetta del Montello	64	45.50 N	12.02 E
Crocheron	208	38.14 N	76.03 W
Crockenhill	260	51.23 N	0.10 E
Crocker	194	37.56 N	92.15 W
Crocker, Banjaran ⋏	112	5.40 N	116.14 E
Crockery Creek ≃	216	43.02 N	86.05 W
Crocketford	44	55.02 N	3.50 W
Crockett, Ca., U.S.	226	38.03 N	122.12 W
Crockett, Tx., U.S.	222	31.19 N	95.27 W
Crockham Hill	260	51.14 N	0.04 E
Crocus Hill → The Valley	238	18.13 N	63.04 W
Croft	262	53.26 N	2.33 W
Crofton, B.C., Can.	224	48.52 N	123.38 W
Crofton, Ky., U.S.	194	37.02 N	87.29 W
Crofton, Md., U.S.	208	39.00 N	76.41 W
Crofton, Ne., U.S.	198	42.43 N	97.29 W
Croft State Park ♠	192	34.49 N	81.52 W
Croggan	46	56.22 N	5.42 W
Croghan	212	43.53 N	75.23 W
Croglin	44	54.49 N	2.39 W
Croick	46	57.53 N	4.35 W
Croil Islands II	206	44.58 N	74.58 W
Croisette, Cap ›	62	43.13 N	5.20 E
Croisilles	50	50.12 N	2.53 E
Croissy-Beaubourg	261	48.50 N	2.40 E
Croissy-sur-Seine	261	48.53 N	2.09 E
Croix	50	50.40 N	3.09 E
Croix, Lac à la ⊜	186	51.16 N	70.13 W
Croix, Lac la ⊜	190	48.21 N	92.05 W
Croker, Cape ›, Austl.	164	10.58 S	132.35 E
Croker, Cape ›, On., Can.	212	44.58 N	80.59 W
Croker Island I	164	11.12 S	132.32 E
Crolles	62	45.17 N	5.53 E
Cromarty	46	57.40 N	4.02 W
Cromarty Firth ⊂[1]	46	57.41 N	4.07 W
Cromby	285	40.09 N	75.32 W
Cromer, Austl.	274a	33.44 S	151.17 E
Cromer, Eng., U.K.	42	52.56 N	1.18 E
Cromford	44	53.06 N	1.34 W
Cromínia	255	17.17 S	49.21 W
Cromore	46	58.09 N	6.29 W
Crompton Point ›	240d	15.35 N	61.19 W
Cromwell, N.Z.	172	45.03 S	169.12 E
Cromwell, Al., U.S.	194	32.13 N	88.16 W
Cromwell, Ct., U.S.	207	41.35 N	72.38 W
Cromwell, In., U.S.	216	41.24 N	85.36 W
Cromwell Park ♠	279a	41.28 N	82.08 W
Cronadun	172	42.02 S	171.52 E
Cronenberg ◆[8]	263	51.12 N	7.08 E
Cronin, Mount ∧	182	54.54 N	126.52 W
Cronton	262	53.23 N	2.46 W
Cronulla	170	34.03 S	151.09 E
Cronulla Beach ⊥[2]	274a	34.02 S	151.11 E
Croob, Slieve ∧[2]	48	54.20 N	5.58 W
Crook, Eng., U.K.	44	54.43 N	1.44 W
Crook, Co., U.S.	198	40.51 N	102.48 W
Crooked ≃, B.C., Can.	182	54.50 N	122.54 W
Crooked ≃, Mo., U.S.	194	39.13 N	93.49 W
Crooked ≃, Or., U.S.	202	44.34 N	121.16 W
Crooked Creek	180	61.52 N	158.08 W
Crooked Creek ≃, U.S.	196	36.57 N	100.06 W
Crooked Creek ≃, Ar., U.S.	194	36.14 N	92.29 W
Crooked Creek ≃, Il., U.S.	219	38.30 N	89.25 W
Crooked Creek ≃, In., U.S.	216	40.45 N	86.30 W
Crooked Creek ≃, Mo., U.S.	219	39.34 N	91.55 W
Crooked Creek ≃, Pa., U.S.	210	41.55 N	77.08 W
Crooked Creek ≃, Pa., U.S.	214	40.45 N	79.33 W
Crooked Creek Lake ⊜[1]	214	40.42 N	79.30 W
Crooked Island I	238	22.45 N	74.13 W
Crooked Island Passage ⊔	238	22.55 N	74.35 W
Crooked Lake, In., U.S.	216	41.41 N	85.02 W
Crooked Lake, Mi., U.S.	216	42.29 N	85.25 W
Crooked Lake ⊜, Nf., Can.	186	48.24 N	56.17 W
Crooked Lake ⊜, Sk., Can.	184	50.36 N	102.45 W
Crooked Lake ⊜, N.A.	190	48.13 N	91.50 W
Crooked Lake ⊜, Fl., U.S.	220	27.48 N	81.35 W
Crooked Lake ⊜, In., U.S.	216	41.40 N	85.03 W
Crooked River	184	52.51 N	103.44 W
Crookes Point ›	276	40.32 N	74.08 W
Crookham	279b	40.12 N	79.59 W
Crookston	198	47.46 N	96.36 W
Crookstown	48	51.50 N	8.50 W
Crooksville	188	39.46 N	82.05 W
Crookwell	166	34.28 S	149.28 E
Croom	48	52.31 N	8.42 W
Cropalati	68	39.31 N	16.43 E
Cropani	68	38.58 N	16.47 E
Cropper	218	38.18 N	85.06 W
Crosby, Eng., U.K.	44	53.30 N	3.02 W
Crosby, Mn., U.S.	190	46.28 N	93.57 W
Crosby, Ms., U.S.	194	31.17 N	91.03 W
Crosby, N.D., U.S.	198	48.54 N	103.17 W
Crosby, Pa., U.S.	214	41.45 N	78.24 W
Crosby, Tx., U.S.	222	29.55 N	95.04 W
Crosby, Mount ∧	202	43.53 N	109.20 W
Crosby Lake ⊜	212	44.45 N	76.26 W
Crosbyton	196	33.39 N	101.14 W
Crosia	68	39.34 N	16.46 E
Crosne	261	48.43 N	2.28 E
Cross ≃	152	4.42 N	8.21 E
Cross Banks II	283	42.43 N	70.49 W
Cross Bay ⊂	184	53.15 N	99.25 W
Cross Bay Bridge ◆[5]	276	40.35 N	73.49 W
Crossbost	46	58.08 N	6.23 W
Cross City	192	29.38 N	83.07 W
Cross County Center ◆[9]	276	40.56 N	73.51 W
Cross Creek ≃, Ca., U.S.	226	36.08 N	119.38 W
Cross Creek ≃, Oh., U.S.	214	40.18 N	80.36 W
Crossen	54	50.45 N	12.29 E
Crossens	262	53.41 N	2.57 W
Crossett	194	33.07 N	91.57 W
Cross Fell ∧	44	54.42 N	2.29 W
Crossfield	182	51.26 N	114.02 W
Crossgar	48	54.24 N	5.45 W
Cross Hands	42	51.48 N	4.04 W
Crosshaven	48	51.48 N	8.17 W
Crosshill	44	55.19 N	4.39 W
Crossinsee ⊜	264a	52.22 N	13.41 E
Cross Island I	272c	18.57 N	72.51 E
Cross Keys	285	39.42 N	75.01 W
Cross Keys Airfield ⊠	285	39.42 N	75.02 W
Cross Lake	184	54.37 N	97.47 W
Cross Lake ⊜, Mb., Can.	184	54.45 N	97.30 W
Cross Lake ⊜, On., Can.	190	46.53 N	79.57 W
Cross Lake ⊜, N.Y., U.S.	210	43.08 N	76.29 W
Crossley, Mount ∧	172	42.50 S	172.04 E
Crossmaglen	48	54.05 N	6.37 W
Crossman	168a	32.47 S	116.36 E
Crossman ≃	168a	32.47 S	116.32 E
Crossman Peak ∧	200	34.32 N	114.07 W
Crossmolina	48	54.06 N	9.20 W
Cross Plains, In., U.S.	218	38.57 N	85.12 W
Cross Plains, Tx., U.S.	196	32.08 N	99.11 W
Cross Plains, Wi., U.S.	190	43.06 N	89.39 W
Cross River □[3]	150	5.50 N	8.30 E
Cross Roads	222	32.03 N	95.58 W
Cross Sound ⊔	180	58.10 N	136.30 W
Crossville, Il., U.S.	194	38.09 N	88.03 W
Crossville, Tn., U.S.	194	35.56 N	85.01 W
Crosswicks	285	40.09 N	74.38 W
Crosswicks Creek ≃	208	40.09 N	74.43 W
Crostolo ≃	64	44.55 N	10.38 E
Croston	44	53.39 N	2.46 W
Croswell	190	43.16 N	82.37 W
Crotch Lake ⊜	212	44.55 N	76.48 W
Crotenay	58	46.45 N	5.49 E
Crothersville	218	38.48 N	85.50 W
Croton	214	40.14 N	82.41 W
Crotona Park ♠	276	40.50 N	73.54 W
Croton Creek ≃	196	33.18 N	100.25 W
Crotone	68	39.05 N	17.07 E
Croton Falls	210	41.21 N	73.40 W
Croton-on-Hudson	210	41.12 N	73.53 W
Croton Point ›	276	41.10 N	73.54 W
Crottendorf	54	50.30 N	12.56 E
Crouch ≃	42	51.37 N	0.57 E
Crouse Run ≃	279b	40.35 N	79.58 W
Crouy	50	49.24 N	3.22 E
Crow ≃	190	45.15 N	93.31 W
Crow, North Fork ≃	190	45.05 N	93.45 W
Crow, South Fork ≃	190	45.05 N	93.45 W
Crow Agency	202	45.36 N	107.27 W
Crowborough	42	51.03 N	0.09 E
Crow Creek ≃, U.S.	198	40.23 N	104.29 W
Crow Creek ≃, Ca., U.S.	282	37.42 N	122.03 W
Crow Creek ≃, Il., U.S.	194	40.56 N	89.27 W
Crow Creek ≃, Mt., U.S.	198	45.45 N	105.06 W
Crow Creek ≃, Mt., U.S.	202	46.11 N	111.29 W
Crow Creek ≃, S.D., U.S.	198	43.57 N	99.15 W
Crow Creek ≃, Wy., U.S.	202	43.19 N	109.09 W
Crow Creek Indian Reservation ◆[4]	198	44.11 N	99.30 W
Crowder, Ms., U.S.	194	34.10 N	90.08 W
Crowder, Ok., U.S.	196	35.07 N	95.40 W
Crowduck Lake ⊜	184	50.08 N	95.15 W
Crowdy Head ›	166	31.50 S	152.45 E
Crowe ≃	212	44.22 N	77.46 W
Crowe Lake ⊜	212	44.29 N	77.46 W
Crowell	196	33.59 N	99.43 W
Crowfoot, Mount ∧	172	45.33 S	167.03 E
Crow Hill ∧[2]	262	53.42 N	1.58 W
Crowhurst	260	51.12 N	0.01 W
Crow Indian Reservation ◆[4]	202	45.27 N	108.00 W
Crow Lake	184	49.12 N	93.57 W
Crow Lake ⊜	212	44.43 N	76.37 W
Crowland	42	52.41 N	0.11 W
Crowle	44	53.37 N	0.49 W
Crowley, Ca., U.S.	226	36.21 N	119.17 W
Crowley, La., U.S.	194	30.12 N	92.22 W
Crowley, Tx., U.S.	222	32.34 N	97.21 W
Crowley, Lake ⊜[1]	204	37.37 N	118.44 W
Crowleys Ridge ∧	194	35.45 N	90.45 W
Crowlin Islands II	46	57.20 N	5.44 W
Crown	214	41.23 N	79.16 W
Crown Hill	212	44.26 N	79.39 W
Crown Island I	164	5.05 S	146.55 E
Crown Memorial Beach ♠	282	37.46 N	122.16 W
Crown Mines ◆[7]	273d	26.13 S	28.00 E
Crown Mountain ∧	240m	18.21 N	64.58 W
Crown Point, In., U.S.	216	41.25 N	87.21 W
Crownpoint, N.M., U.S.	200	35.40 N	108.09 W
Crown Point, N.Y., U.S.	188	43.57 N	73.26 W
Crown Point State Park ♠	224	45.32 N	122.15 W
Crown Prince Frederik Island I	176	70.02 N	86.50 W
Crown Village	276	40.40 N	73.27 W
Crow Peak ∧	202	46.18 N	111.54 W
Crow Rock Creek ≃	202	47.06 N	106.15 W
Crows Fork Creek ≃	219	38.47 N	91.52 W
Crows Landing	226	37.24 N	121.04 W
Crows Nest, Austl.	171a	27.16 S	152.03 E
Crows Nest, Austl.	274a	33.50 S	151.12 E
Crowsnest, Ab., Can.	182	49.38 N	114.41 W
Crows Nest Falls National Park ♠	171a	27.16 S	152.08 E
Crowsnest Pass	182	49.36 N	114.26 W
Crowsnest Pass ⋈	182	49.39 N	114.45 W
Crows Nest Peak ∧	198	44.03 N	103.58 W
Crowthorne	42	51.23 N	0.49 W
Crowton	262	53.16 N	2.38 W
Crow Wing ≃	198	46.19 N	94.20 W
Croxley Green	42	51.39 N	0.27 W
Croxteth Park ♠	262	53.26 N	2.53 W
Croy	46	57.31 N	4.02 W
Croyde	42	51.07 N	4.13 W
Croydon, Austl.	166	18.12 S	142.14 E
Croydon, Austl.	169	37.48 S	145.17 E
Croydon, Austl.	274a	33.53 S	151.07 E
Croydon, Pa., U.S.	208	40.05 N	74.54 W
Croydon ◆[8]	42	51.23 N	0.06 W
Croydon Park	274a	33.54 S	151.07 E
Croydon Peak ∧	188	43.28 N	72.13 W
Croydon Station	182	53.05 N	119.44 W
Crozet	192	38.04 N	78.42 W
Crozet, Archipel II	6	46.00 S	52.00 E
Crozet Basin ✣[1]	6	39.00 S	60.00 E
Crozon	32	48.15 N	4.29 W
Cruachan, Ben ∧	46	56.25 N	5.08 W
Cruas	62	44.39 N	4.46 E
Crucea	38	44.32 N	28.14 E
Crucero	248	14.21 S	70.00 W
Cruces, Cuba	240p	22.21 N	80.16 W
Cruces, Méx.	232	29.26 N	107.24 W
Crucoli	68	39.25 N	17.00 E
Cruden Bay	46	57.25 N	1.50 W
Crudgington	42	52.46 N	2.33 W
Crudine Creek ≃	170	33.05 S	149.40 E
Cruger	194	33.19 N	90.13 W
Cruillas	232	24.45 N	98.31 W
Crum Creek ≃	285	39.51 N	75.19 W
Crumhorn Mountain ∧	210	42.33 N	74.55 W
Crumlin, On., Can.	212	43.01 N	81.09 W
Crumlin, N. Ire., U.K.	48	54.37 N	6.14 W
Crum Lynne	285	39.52 N	75.20 W
Crummock Water ⊜	44	54.34 N	3.18 W
Crump Lake ⊜	202	42.17 N	119.50 W
Crumpton	208	39.14 N	75.55 W
Crumstown	216	41.38 N	86.25 W
Crupet	56	50.21 N	4.48 E
Cruseilles	58	46.02 N	6.07 E
Cruser Brook ≃	276	40.27 N	74.39 W
Crusheen	48	52.58 N	8.53 W
Crusnes	56	49.26 N	5.55 E
Crusnes ≃	56	49.27 N	5.36 E
Crustepec, Cerro ∧	234	21.15 N	97.53 W
Cruz, Arroyo de la ≃, Ca., U.S.	226	35.42 N	121.09 W
Cruz, Arroyo de la ≃, Ur.	258	34.00 S	56.08 W
Cruz, Cabo ›	240p	19.51 N	77.44 W
Cruz, Cañada de la ≃	258	34.09 S	58.58 W
Cruz, Cayo I	240p	22.15 N	77.49 W
Cruz, Pico de la ∧	148	28.44 N	17.52 W
Cruz Alta, Arg.	252	33.01 S	61.49 W
Cruz Alta, Bra.	252	28.39 S	53.36 W
Cruz Bay	240m	18.20 N	64.48 W
Cruz de Elorza	234	23.49 N	100.29 W
Cruz del Eje	252	30.44 S	64.48 W
Cruz del Marquez, Cerro ∧	286a	19.12 N	99.15 W
Cruzeiro	256	22.34 S	44.58 W
Cruzeiro do Oeste	255	23.46 S	53.04 W
Cruzeiro do Sul	248	7.38 S	72.36 W
Cruzeta	250	6.25 S	36.47 W
Cruz Grande, Chile	252	29.25 S	71.18 W
Cruz Grande, Méx.	234	16.44 N	99.08 W
Cruzília	256	21.50 S	44.48 W
Cruz Machado	252	26.01 S	51.21 W
Cruzy-le-Châtel	50	47.51 N	4.12 E
Crvenka	38	45.39 N	19.28 E
Crymych	42	51.59 N	4.40 W
Crynant	42	51.43 N	3.45 W
Crysler	188	45.13 N	75.09 W
Crystal, Mn., U.S.	190	45.01 N	93.21 W
Crystal, N.D., U.S.	198	48.35 N	97.40 W
Crystal ≃	200	39.25 N	107.14 W
Crystal Bay	226	39.13 N	120.00 W
Crystal Bay ⊂	220	28.55 N	82.43 W
Crystal Beach, On., Can.	284a	42.52 N	79.04 W
Crystal Beach, Fl., U.S.	220	28.05 N	82.46 W
Crystal Beach, Tx., U.S.	222	29.27 N	94.38 W
Crystal Brook	166	33.21 S	138.13 E
Crystal Cave ⊥[5]	208	40.32 N	75.51 W
Crystal City, Mb., Can.	184	49.09 N	98.56 W
Crystal City, Mo., U.S.	219	38.13 N	90.22 W
Crystal City, Tx., U.S.	196	28.40 N	99.49 W
Crystal Creek ≃	278	41.58 N	87.51 W
Crystal Falls	190	46.05 N	88.20 W
Crystal Gardens	216	42.14 N	88.23 W
Crystal Lake, Il., U.S.	216	42.14 N	88.18 W
Crystal Lake, N.Y., U.S.	210	42.31 N	74.12 W
Crystal Lake, N.Y., U.S.	210	42.28 N	78.20 W
Crystal Lake ⊜, On., Can.	212	44.45 N	78.30 W
Crystal Lake ⊜, Ma., U.S.	283	42.48 N	71.09 W
Crystal Lake ⊜, Ma., U.S.	283	42.29 N	71.05 W
Crystal Lake ⊜, Mi., U.S.	190	44.40 N	86.10 W
Crystal Lake ⊜, N.J., U.S.	276	41.02 N	74.15 W
Crystal Lakes	218	39.52 N	84.04 W
Crystal Lawns	216	41.34 N	88.09 W
Crystal Manor	216	42.14 N	88.17 W
Crystal Palace Stadium and Motor Race Track ♠	260	51.25 N	0.04 W
Crystal River	192	28.54 N	82.35 W
Crystal Spring Lake ⊜	285	39.43 N	75.01 W
Crystal Springs, Fl., U.S.	220	28.10 N	82.09 W
Crystal Springs, Ms., U.S.	194	31.59 N	90.21 W
Crystal Springs Dam ◆[6]	282	37.32 N	122.22 W
Crystal Vista	216	42.14 N	88.24 W
Csepel ◆[8]	264c	47.24 N	19.14 E
Csepel-sziget I	30	47.15 N	18.57 E
Csepreg	61	47.24 N	16.43 E
Cserhát ⋏	30	47.55 N	19.30 E
Cserta ≃	61	46.35 N	16.36 E
Csesznek ⊥	30	47.16 N	17.53 E
Csesztreg	61	46.43 N	16.31 E
Csobánka	264c	47.38 N	18.58 E
Csomád	264c	47.40 N	19.15 E
Csömodér	61	46.37 N	16.39 E
Csömör	264c	47.33 N	19.14 E
Csömöri-patak ≃	264c	47.36 N	19.07 E
Csongrád	30	46.43 N	20.09 E
Csongrád □[6]	30	46.25 N	20.15 E
Csorna	30	47.37 N	17.16 E
Csurgó	30	46.16 N	17.06 E
Ču	85	43.36 N	73.45 E
Ču □[4]	85	42.30 N	74.30 E
Ču ≃	86	45.00 N	67.44 E
Cúa	246	10.10 N	66.54 W
Cuacnopalan	234	18.49 N	97.30 W
Cuácua ≃	154	17.54 S	36.48 E
Cuajimalpa ◆[8]	286a	19.21 N	99.18 W
Cuajinicuilapa	234	16.28 N	98.25 W
Cuajone	248	17.00 S	70.43 W
Cuále	152	8.06 S	16.03 E
Cua Lo	110	18.49 N	105.43 E
Cuamato	152	17.05 S	15.09 E
Cuamba	154	14.49 S	36.33 E
Cuambog	116	7.20 N	125.52 E
Cuanavale ≃	152	15.07 S	19.14 E
Cuando	152	16.32 S	22.07 E
Cuando (Kwando) ≃	152	18.27 S	23.32 E
Cuando Cubango □[5]	152	16.00 S	20.00 E
Cuangar	152	17.36 S	18.39 E
Cuango, Ang.	152	14.30 S	18.59 E
Cuango, Ang.	152	9.10 S	17.58 E
Cuango, Ang.	152	6.17 S	16.41 E
Cuango (Kwango) ≃	152	3.14 S	17.23 E
Cuanza ≃	152	9.19 S	13.08 E
Cuanza Norte □[5]	152	8.50 S	14.30 E
Cuanza Sul □[5]	152	10.50 S	14.50 E
Cuao ≃	246	4.55 N	67.40 W
Cuapiaxtla	234	19.18 N	97.46 W
Cuareim (Quaraí) ≃	252	30.12 S	57.36 W
Cuaró	252	30.37 S	56.54 W
Cuartillo, Arroyo ≃	258	33.45 S	59.06 W
Cuarto ≃	252	33.25 S	62.56 W
Cuatir ≃	152	17.01 S	18.09 E
Cuatro Caminos	286b	22.54 N	82.23 W
Cuatro Ciénegas [de Carranza]	196	26.59 N	102.05 W
Cuatro Islands II	116	10.31 N	124.39 E
Cuauhtémoc, Méx.	232	28.25 N	106.52 W
Cuauhtémoc, Méx.	234	19.20 N	103.36 W
Cuauhtémoc, Méx.	234	22.38 N	98.08 W
Cuautepec el Alto ◆[8]	286a	19.34 N	99.08 W
Cuautitlán	234	19.26 N	104.23 W
Cuautitlán ≃	286a	19.41 N	99.13 W
Cuautitlán [de Romero Rubio]	234	19.40 N	99.11 W
Cuautitlán Izcalli	286a	19.39 N	99.13 W
Cuautla, Méx.	234	20.11 N	104.21 W
Cuautla, Méx.	234	18.48 N	98.57 W
Cuautzin, Volcán ∧[1]	286a	19.09 N	99.06 W
Cuba, Port.	34	38.10 N	7.53 W
Cuba, Al., U.S.	194	32.25 N	88.22 W
Cuba, Il., U.S.	190	40.29 N	90.11 W
Cuba, Ks., U.S.	198	39.48 N	97.27 W
Cuba, Mo., U.S.	194	38.03 N	91.24 W
Cuba, N.M., U.S.	200	36.01 N	106.57 W
Cuba, N.Y., U.S.	210	42.13 N	78.16 W
Cuba □[1], N.A.	230	21.30 N	80.00 W
Cuba □[1], N.A.	240p	21.30 N	80.00 W
Cubabi, Cerro ∧	200	31.42 N	112.46 W
Cubadak	112	0.19 N	100.00 E
Cubagua, Isla I	246	10.48 N	64.10 W
Cuba Island I	276	40.38 N	73.32 W
Cubal	152	13.02 S	14.19 E
Cubal ≃, Ang.	152	15.22 S	12.39 E
Cubal ≃, Ang.	152	12.42 S	13.56 E
Cubal ≃, Ang.	152	11.19 S	13.48 E
Cuba Lake ⊜	210	42.15 N	78.18 W
Cubanea	254	41.02 S	70.16 W
Cubango (Okavango) ≃	138	18.50 S	22.25 E
Cubangui ≃	152	14.22 S	19.58 E
Čubaricha	86	57.37 N	68.22 E
Čubarovo	82	55.12 N	36.56 E
Cubatão	256	23.53 S	46.25 W
Cubatão, Serra do ⊥[4]	256	23.52 S	46.28 W
Cubati	250	6.51 S	36.21 W
Cub Hills ⋏[2]	184	54.20 N	104.30 W
Cubia ≃	152	16.01 S	21.50 E
Čublas	24	64.44 N	45.00 E
Cub Run ≃	208	38.48 N	77.28 W
Çubuk	130	40.15 N	33.02 E
Cuc ≃	250	1.22 N	53.33 W
Cucamonga	228	34.06 N	117.35 W
Cucamonga Creek ≃	280	33.57 N	117.37 W
Cucamonga Peak ∧	228	34.14 N	117.36 W
Cuccaro Vetere	68	40.09 N	15.18 E
Cucco, Monte ∧	66	43.22 N	12.45 E
Čučeviči	76	52.35 N	26.52 E
Cucharas ≃	198	37.55 N	104.32 W
Cucharas, Sierra ⋏	234	22.20 N	98.55 W
Cuchi	152	14.36 S	16.58 E
Cuchi ≃	152	15.28 S	17.21 E
Cuchibi ≃	152	15.00 S	20.45 E
Cuchilla Alta, Cerro ∧	236	15.10 N	88.12 W
Cuchillo-Có	252	38.20 S	64.37 W
Cuchillo Negro Creek ≃	200	33.08 N	107.14 W
Cuchivero ≃	246	7.40 N	65.57 W
Čuchloma	76	58.45 N	42.41 E
Čuchlomskoje, ozero ⊜	76	58.46 N	42.35 E
Cuchumatanes, Sierra los ⋏	236	15.35 N	91.25 W
Cuckels Brook ≃	276	40.33 N	74.33 W
Cuckfield	42	51.00 N	0.09 W
Cuckney	44	53.15 N	1.08 W
Cuckold Point ›	284b	39.14 N	76.24 W
Čučkovo, Ross.	76	59.36 N	41.14 E
Čučkovo, Ross.	80	54.17 N	41.26 E
Cucuí	246	1.12 N	66.50 W
Čučuleny	38	47.02 N	28.22 E
Cucumbi	152	10.17 S	19.05 E
Cucuron	62	43.47 N	5.26 E
Cucurpe	232	30.20 N	110.43 W
Cúcuta	246	7.54 N	72.31 W
Cudachar	84	42.21 N	47.11 E
Cudahy, Ca., U.S.	280	33.57 N	118.11 W
Cudahy, Wi., U.S.	216	42.57 N	87.51 W
Cuddalore	122	11.45 N	79.45 E
Cuddapah	122	14.28 N	78.49 E
Cuddeback Lake ⊜	228	35.18 N	117.28 W
Cuddebackville	210	41.28 N	74.36 W
Cuddia ≃	70	37.53 N	12.37 E
Cuddington	44	53.14 N	2.36 W
Cuddle Lake ⊜	184	55.25 N	95.47 W
Cuddy	279b	40.21 N	80.09 W
Cuddy Mountain ∧	202	44.46 N	116.47 W
Cudgegong	170	32.48 S	149.49 E
Cudgegong ≃	170	32.37 S	149.43 E
Cudgewa	171b	36.12 S	147.46 E
Cudgewa Creek ≃	171b	36.03 S	147.55 E
Cudham ◆[8]	260	51.19 N	0.05 E
Cudia Park ♠	275b	43.43 N	79.13 W
Čudin	76	52.44 N	26.59 E
Cudjoe Key I	220	24.40 N	81.30 W
Čudnov	78	50.04 N	28.06 E
Čudovo	76	59.07 N	31.41 E
Čudskoje ozero (Peipsi järv) ⊜	76	58.45 N	27.30 E
Cudworth, Sk., Can.	184	52.30 N	105.45 W
Cudworth, Eng., U.K.	44	53.35 N	1.25 W
Cue	162	27.25 S	117.54 E
Cuebe ≃	152	15.48 S	17.30 E
Cueio ≃, Ang.	152	15.27 S	21.21 E
Cueio ≃, Ang.	152	16.17 S	17.46 E
Cuelei ≃	152	15.33 S	17.21 E
Cuéllar	34	41.24 N	4.19 W
Cuenca, Ec.	246	2.53 S	78.59 W
Cuenca, Esp.	34	40.04 N	2.08 W
Cuenca □[4]	34	39.55 N	2.10 W
Cuencamé [de Ceniceros]	232	24.53 N	103.42 W
Cuerámaro	234	20.37 N	101.43 W
Cuernavaca	234	18.55 N	99.15 W
Cuero	222	29.05 N	97.17 W
Cuers	62	43.14 N	6.04 E
Cuervos	204	32.38 N	114.52 W
Cuesmes	50	50.26 N	3.55 E
Cuesta Pass ⋈	226	35.21 N	120.38 W
Cueto	240p	20.39 N	75.56 W
Cuetzala del Progreso	234	18.07 N	99.50 W
Cuetzalan del Progreso	234	20.02 N	97.31 W
Cuevas del Almanzora	34	37.18 N	1.53 W
Cuevo	248	20.27 S	63.32 W
Čufarovo	80	54.06 N	47.19 E
Cuffley	42	51.42 N	0.07 W
Cufra → Al-Kufrah ▿[4]	146	24.20 N	23.15 E
Cufré	258	34.12 S	57.06 W
Cufré, Arroyo ≃	258	34.27 S	57.09 W
Cuggiono	62	45.31 N	8.49 E
Cugir	38	45.50 N	23.22 E
Cuglieri	71	40.11 N	8.34 E
Cugo ≃	152	7.18 S	16.39 E
Čugujev	78	49.50 N	36.41 E
Čugujevka	89	44.08 N	133.53 E
Čugunaš	86	52.52 N	87.46 E
Čuguš, gora ∧	84	43.47 N	40.16 E
Cuiabá	248	15.35 S	56.05 W
Cuiabá ≃	248	17.53 S	57.27 W
Cuiari	246	1.30 N	68.11 W
Cuiari ≃	246	1.30 N	68.11 W
Cuicatlán	234	17.48 N	96.58 W
Cuichapa	234	17.59 N	94.15 W
Cuieiras ≃	246	2.50 S	60.31 W
Cuigezhuang, Zhg.	105	40.01 N	116.28 E
Cuigezhuang, Zhg.	105	40.02 N	117.54 E
Cuihuangkou	105	39.32 N	117.11 E
Cuijiatun	104	40.57 N	121.09 E
Cuijiazhuang	104	40.57 N	122.44 E
Cuilapa	236	14.17 N	90.18 W
Cuilcagh ∧	48	54.10 N	7.48 W
Cuilco	236	15.24 N	91.58 W
Cuillin Hills ⋏[2]	46	57.15 N	6.15 W
Cuilo (Kwilu) ≃, Afr.	152	3.22 S	17.22 E
Cuilo ≃, Afr.	152	5.52 S	16.35 E
Cuilo Futa	152	6.25 S	15.44 E
Cuimba	152	6.08 S	14.38 E
Cuio	152	12.58 S	12.58 E
Cuiqiao	98	34.12 N	114.36 E
Cuiseaux	58	46.30 N	5.24 E
Cuisery	58	46.33 N	5.00 E
Cuisy	261	49.01 N	2.46 E
Cuité	250	6.29 S	36.09 W
Cuitláhuac	234	18.49 N	96.43 W
Cuíto ≃	152	18.01 S	20.48 E
Cuíto-Cuanavale	152	15.10 S	19.10 E
Cuitzeo, Laguna de ⊜	234	19.55 N	101.05 W
Cuitzeo del Porvenir	234	19.59 N	101.09 W
Cuiuni ≃	246	0.45 S	63.07 W
Cuivre ≃	219	38.56 N	90.42 W
Cuivre, North Fork ≃	219	39.02 N	90.59 W
Cuivre, West Fork ≃	219	39.02 N	90.59 W
Cuivre River State Park ♠	219	39.02 N	90.57 W
Čuja	88	59.12 N	112.25 E
Čuja ≃, Ross.	86	50.24 N	86.39 E
Čuja ≃, Ross.	88	59.17 N	112.24 E
Cují	286c	10.28 N	67.02 W
Cukas	112	0.25 S	104.18 E
Čukčagirskoje ozero ⊜	89	52.00 N	136.36 E
Čukotskaja Avtonomnaja Oblast' □[8]	180	66.00 N	178.00 E
Čukotskij, mys ›	180	64.14 N	173.10 W
Čukotskij poluostrov ›[1]	180	66.00 N	175.00 W
Çukurca	128	37.15 N	43.37 E
Čukurčak	85	41.47 N	71.07 E
Cukurino	83	48.05 N	37.18 E
Culaba	116	11.40 N	124.32 E
Čulak-Kurgan	85	43.46 N	69.12 E
Culaman	116	5.58 N	125.40 E
Culari ≃	250	1.27 N	53.42 W
Culasi, Pil.	116	11.26 N	122.03 E
Culasi, Pil.	116	10.43 N	125.43 E
Culasian	116	8.51 N	117.29 E
Culasi Point ›	116	11.37 N	122.42 E
Culbertson, Mt., U.S.	198	48.08 N	104.30 W
Culbertson, Ne., U.S.	198	40.13 N	100.50 W
Culbertson Run ≃	285	40.03 N	75.45 W
Culbin	168a	33.10 S	116.50 E
Culburra	170	34.57 S	150.47 E
Culcairn	166	35.40 S	147.03 E
Culcheth	262	53.27 N	2.32 W
Culdaff	48	55.18 N	7.11 W
Culdaff Bay ⊂	48	55.17 N	7.10 W
Culebra	240m	18.18 N	65.18 W
Culebra, Isla de I	240m	18.19 N	65.17 W
Culebra, Sierra de la ⋏	34	41.54 N	6.20 W
Culebra Peak ∧	200	37.07 N	105.11 W
Culebrinas ≃	240m	18.24 N	67.11 W
Culebrita, Isla I	240m	18.19 N	65.14 W
Culebro, Arroyo del ≃	266a	40.19 N	3.34 W
Culemborg	52	51.56 N	5.13 E
Culgoa ≃	166	29.56 S	146.20 E
Culham Inlet ⊂	162	33.55 S	120.04 E
Culiacán, Méx.	232	24.04 N	107.05 W
Culiacán, Méx.	232	24.48 N	107.24 W
Culiacán, Cerro ∧	234	20.20 N	100.58 W
Culiacancito	232	24.50 N	107.32 W
Culijón, Nevado ∧	248	14.38 S	69.14 W
Culion	116	11.53 N	120.01 E
Culion Island I	116	11.50 N	119.55 E
Cúllar de Baza	34	37.35 N	2.34 W
Cull Creek ≃	282	37.42 N	122.03 W
Cullen, Scot., U.K.	46	57.41 N	2.49 W
Cullen, La., U.S.	194	32.58 N	93.27 W
Cullen Bullen	170	33.18 S	150.01 E
Cullen Point ›	164	11.57 S	141.54 E
Culleoka, Tn., U.S.	194	35.28 N	86.58 W
Culleoka, Tx., U.S.	222	33.08 N	96.29 W
Cullera	34	39.10 N	0.15 W
Cullicudden	46	57.39 N	4.13 W
Cullin, Lough ⊜	48	53.57 N	9.12 W
Cullinan	158	25.40 S	28.31 E
Cullman	194	34.10 N	86.50 W
Culloden Battlesite ⊥	46	57.28 N	4.05 W
Cullom	216	40.53 N	88.16 W
Cullompton	42	50.52 N	3.24 W
Cullowhee	192	35.18 N	83.10 W
Cully	58	46.29 N	6.44 E
Cullybackey	48	54.53 N	6.21 W
Culm ≃	42	50.46 N	3.31 W
Čul'man	74	56.52 N	124.52 E
Cülmen	130	37.19 N	38.48 E
Culmore	284c	38.51 N	77.08 W
Culoz	62	45.51 N	5.47 E
Culpeper	188	38.28 N	77.59 W
Culpina	248	20.50 S	64.58 W
Culrain	46	57.55 N	4.24 W
Cults	46	57.07 N	2.10 W
Cultus Lake	224	49.04 N	121.58 W
Cultus Lake ⊜	224	49.03 N	121.58 W
Cultus Lake Provincial Park ♠	224	49.03 N	121.58 W
Culú-Culú, Arroyo ≃	258	35.19 S	58.57 W
Culú-Culú, Laguna ⊜	258	35.20 S	58.59 W
Culuene ≃	255	12.56 S	52.51 W
Čuluunchoroot	88	49.41 N	114.15 E
Čuluut	102	45.48 N	107.05 E
Čuluutyn ≃	88	49.11 N	100.41 E
Culvain ∧	46	56.56 N	5.17 W
Culver, In., U.S.	216	41.13 N	86.25 W
Culver, Or., U.S.	202	44.31 N	121.12 W
Culver, Point ›	162	32.54 S	124.43 E
Culver City	228	34.01 N	118.23 W
Culverden	172	42.46 S	172.51 E
Culvers Lake	210	41.10 N	74.48 W
Culverstone Green	260	51.20 N	0.21 E
Čulym	86	55.06 N	80.58 E
Čulym ≃, Ross.	86	54.38 N	78.16 E
Čulym ≃, Ross.	86	57.43 N	83.51 E
Čulyšman ≃	86	51.20 N	87.45 E
Čum	24	67.06 N	63.07 E
Cuma	152	12.52 S	15.05 E
Cuma (Cumae) ⊥	68	40.50 N	14.06 E
Čumakovo	86	55.41 N	79.02 E
Cumalı	130	36.42 N	27.27 E
Cuman'	78	50.49 N	25.53 E
Cumaná	246	10.28 N	64.10 W
Cumanacoa	246	10.15 N	63.55 W
Cumanayagua	240p	22.09 N	80.12 W
Cumaovası	130	38.15 N	27.09 E
Cumare, Cerro ∧[2]	246	0.28 N	73.52 W
Cumari	255	18.16 S	48.11 W
Cumbal	246	0.54 N	77.47 W
Cumbal, Nevado ∧	246	0.57 N	77.52 W
Cumbe	250	10.21 S	37.14 W
Cumbee	220	28.04 N	81.55 W
Cumberland, B.C., Can.	182	49.37 N	125.01 W
Cumberland, Ia., U.S.	198	41.16 N	94.52 W
Cumberland, Ky., U.S.	192	36.58 N	82.59 W
Cumberland, Md., U.S.	188	39.39 N	78.45 W
Cumberland, Va., U.S.	192	37.29 N	78.14 W
Cumberland, Wa., U.S.	224	47.16 N	121.55 W
Cumberland, Wi., U.S.	190	45.31 N	92.01 W
Cumberland □[6], N.J., U.S.	208	39.26 N	75.14 W
Cumberland □[6], Pa., U.S.	208	40.12 N	77.12 W
Cumberland ≃	178	37.09 N	88.25 W
Cumberland, Lake ⊜[1]	194	36.57 N	84.55 W
Cumberland, South Fork ≃	192	36.58 N	84.36 W
Cumberland City	194	36.23 N	87.38 W

Symbols in the index entries represent the broad categories identified in the key at the right. Symbols with superior numbers (⋏[1]) identify subcategories (see complete key on page *I · 1).*

Symbole im Register stellen die rechts im Schlüssel erklärten Kategorien dar. Symbole mit hochgestellten Ziffern (⋏[1]) bezeichnen Unterabteilungen einer Kategorie (vgl. vollständiger Schlüssel auf Seite *I · 1).*

Los símbolos incluídos en el texto del índice representan las grandes categorías identificadas con la clave a la derecha. Los símbolos con numeros en su parte superior (⋏[1]) identifican las subcategorías (véase la clave completa en la página *I · 1).*

Les symboles de l'index représentent les catégories indiquées dans la légende à droite. Les symboles suivis d'un indice (⋏[1]) représentent des sous-catégories (voir légende complète à la page *I · 1).*

Os símbolos incluídos no texto do índice representam as grandes categorias identificadas com a chave à direita. Os símbolos com números em sua parte superior (⋏[1]) identificam as subcategorias (veja-se a chave completa à página *I · 1).*

	ENGLISH	DEUTSCH	ESPAÑOL	FRANÇAIS	PORTUGUÊS
∧	Mountain	Berg	Montaña	Montagne	Montanha
⋏	Mountains	Gebirge	Montañas	Montagnes	Montanhas
⋈	Pass	Paß	Paso	Col	Passo
∨	Valley, Canyon	Tal, Cañon	Valle, Cañón	Vallée, Canyon	Vale, Canhão
≃	Plain	Ebene	Llano	Plaine	Planície
›	Cape	Kap	Cabo	Cap	Cabo
I	Island	Insel	Isla	Île	Ilha
II	Islands	Inseln	Islas	Îles	Ilhas
⊥	Other Topographic Features	Andere Topographische Objekte	Otros Elementos Topográficos	Autres données topographiques	Outros acidentes topográficos

ESPAÑOL · FRANÇAIS · PORTUGUÊS

Nombre / Nom / Nome	Página / Page / Página	Lat.°′	Long.°′ W = Oeste / W = Ouest / W = Oeste
Cumberland Falls State Resort Park ♠	192	36.50 N	84.20 W
Cumberland Gap)(	192	36.36 N	83.41 W
Cumberland Gap National Historical Park ♠	192	36.36 N	83.40 W
Cumberland Hill	207	41.58 N	71.27 W
Cumberland House	184	53.58 N	102.16 W
Cumberland Indian Reserve ◆[4]	184	53.04 N	104.50 W
Cumberland Island National Seashore ♠	192	30.50 N	81.27 W
Cumberland Islands II	166	20.40 S	149.09 E
Cumberland Lake ⊜	184	54.02 N	102.17 W
Cumberland Peninsula ≻[1]	176	66.50 N	64.00 W
Cumberland Plateau ⋏[1]	192	36.20 N	84.30 W
Cumberland Sound ⊔	176	65.10 N	65.30 W
Cumbernauld	46	55.58 N	3.59 W
Cumborah	166	29.44 S	147.46 E
Cumbria □[6]	44	54.30 N	3.00 W
Cumbrian Mountains ⋏	44	54.30 N	3.05 W
Čumbur-Kosa	83	46.57 N	38.53 E
Cumby	222	33.08 N	95.50 W
Cumeral Nuevo	200	30.54 N	110.51 W
Cumiana	62	44.59 N	7.22 E
Čumikan	89	54.42 N	135.19 E
Cuminá → Paru de Oeste ≃	250	1.30 S	56.00 W
Cuminapanema ≃	250	1.09 S	54.54 W
Cuminestown	46	57.32 N	2.20 W
Cumming	192	34.12 N	84.08 W
Cummings Mountain ∧	228	35.03 N	118.34 W
Cummington	207	42.27 N	72.53 W
Cummins	166	34.16 S	135.44 E
Cummins, Mount ∧	182	52.03 N	118.15 W
Cummins Creek ≃	222	29.43 N	96.31 W
Cummins Range ⋏	162	19.05 S	127.10 E
Cumnock	44	55.27 N	4.16 W
Cumnor	42	51.44 N	1.20 W
Cumpas	232	30.02 N	109.48 W
Çumra	130	37.34 N	32.48 E
Cumshewa Inlet ⊂	182	53.03 N	131.45 W
Cumuripa	232	28.08 N	109.53 W
Cumwhinton	44	54.52 N	2.51 W
Čumyš ≃	86	53.31 N	83.10 E
Čun'a ≃, Ross.	74	61.36 N	96.30 E
Čuna ≃, Ross.	88	57.47 N	95.26 E
Cunani	250	2.52 N	51.06 W
Cunauaru ≃	246	3.10 S	63.01 W
Cunaviche	246	7.22 N	67.25 W
Cunco	252	38.55 S	72.02 W
Cuncumén	252	31.53 S	70.38 W
Cundeelee Reserve ◆[4]	162	30.30 S	123.25 E
Cunderdin	162	31.39 S	117.15 E
Cundinamarca □[5]	246	5.00 N	74.00 W
Cunduacán	234	18.04 N	93.10 W
Čundža	86	43.32 N	79.28 E
Cunene □[5]	152	16.30 S	15.30 E
Cunene (Kunene) ≃	152	17.20 S	11.50 E
Cuneo	62	44.23 N	7.32 E
Cuneo □[4]	62	44.31 N	7.34 E
Cunewalde	54	51.06 N	14.30 E
Cuney	222	32.02 N	95.25 W
Cung Hau, Cua ≃[1]	110	9.46 N	106.34 E
Cung Son	110	13.02 N	108.58 E
Çüngüş	130	38.13 N	39.17 E
Cunha	256	23.05 S	44.58 W
Cunhambebe	256	23.00 S	44.20 W
Cunha Porã	252	26.54 S	53.09 W
Cunhinga	152	12.11 S	16.47 E
Cunhinga ≃	152	10.38 S	16.48 E
Cunhuã, Igarapé ≃	248	5.46 S	64.36 W
Cunlhat	62	45.38 N	3.35 E
Cunliffe	168b	34.05 S	137.45 E
Cunnamulla	166	28.04 S	145.41 E
Cunningham, Austl.	171a	28.09 S	151.51 E
Cunningham, Ks., U.S.	198	37.38 N	98.25 W
Cunningham, Lake ⊜	240b	25.04 N	77.26 W
Cunninghame □[9]	46	55.40 N	4.30 W
Cunningham Falls State Park ♠	208	39.35 N	77.27 W
Cunningham Park ♠, Ma., U.S.	283	42.15 N	71.03 W
Cunningham Park ♠, N.Y., U.S.	276	40.44 N	73.46 W
Čunojar	88	57.27 N	97.18 E
Cunqian	100	28.30 N	115.10 E
Čunskij, Ross.	88	56.05 N	99.41 E
Čunskij, Ross.	88	57.26 N	97.31 E
Cuntan	107	29.37 N	106.36 E
Cunucunuma ≃	246	3.13 N	65.58 W
Čuny	76	59.39 N	33.04 E
Čuokkaraš'ša ∧	24	69.57 N	24.32 E
Cuorgnè	62	45.23 N	7.39 E
Čupa	24	66.16 N	33.00 E
Čupachovka	78	50.23 N	34.36 E
Čupalejka	80	55.11 N	42.33 E
Cupar, Sk., Can.	184	50.57 N	104.12 W
Cupar, Scot., U.K.	46	56.19 N	3.01 W
Cupecê, Ribeirão ≃	287b	23.37 S	46.42 W
Cupello	66	42.04 N	14.40 E
Cuperly	50	49.04 N	4.26 E
Cupertino	226	37.19 N	122.01 W
Cupica, Golfo de ⊂	246	6.35 N	77.25 W
Cupins	255	19.51 S	51.03 W
Cupra Marittima	66	43.01 N	13.51 E
Cupramontana	66	43.27 N	13.07 E
Ćuprija	38	43.56 N	21.23 E
Čuprovo	24	64.14 N	46.36 E
Cupsaw Lake ⊜	276	41.07 N	74.15 W
Cuqiao	107	30.36 N	103.59 E
Cuquema ≃	152	12.03 S	17.40 E
Cuquenán ≃	246	4.45 N	61.30 W
Cuquío	234	20.55 N	103.02 W
Čur	80	57.07 N	52.58 E
Curaçá	250	8.59 S	39.54 W
Curaçao I	241s	12.11 N	69.00 W
Curacautín	252	38.26 S	71.53 W
Curacaví	252	33.24 S	71.09 W
Čuračiki	80	55.44 N	47.26 E
Curaglia	58	46.41 N	8.51 E
Cural Novo, Ribeirão ≃	256	21.17 S	43.51 W
Curanilahue	252	37.28 S	73.21 W
Curanipe	252	35.50 S	72.38 W
Curanja ≃	248	9.58 S	70.58 W
Čurapča	74	62.00 N	132.24 E
Curapi ≃	250	1.25 N	53.49 W
Curaray ≃	246	2.20 S	74.05 W
Čurbek	85	39.59 N	69.56 E
Curcani	38	44.12 N	26.35 E
Curdies ≃	169	38.30 S	142.55 E
Cure ≃	50	47.40 N	3.41 E
Curecanti National Recreation Area ♠	200	38.24 N	107.25 W
Curepipe	157c	20.19 S	57.31 E
Curepto	252	35.05 S	72.01 W
Curequetê ≃	248	8.20 S	65.40 W
Čureški prohod)(	38	42.47 N	23.49 E
Curiapo	246	8.33 N	61.00 W
Curib	84	42.14 N	46.49 E
Curiche Grande (Corixo Grande) ≃	248	17.43 S	57.43 W
Curicó	252	34.59 S	71.14 W
Curicuriari ≃	246	0.14 S	66.48 W
Curières, Lac ⊜	206	46.41 N	74.51 W
Curimatá	250	10.02 S	44.17 W
Curimeo	234	20.01 N	101.42 W
Curinga	68	38.49 N	16.19 E
Curious, Mount ∧	162	27.28 S	114.20 E
Curisevo ≃	255	12.14 S	53.17 W
Curitiba	252	25.25 S	49.15 W
Curitibanos	252	27.18 S	50.36 W
Curiuaú ≃	246	1.51 S	61.14 W
Curiúva	255	24.02 S	50.27 W
Curl Curl	274a	33.46 S	151.18 E
Curlew	182	48.53 N	118.35 W
Curlewis	166	31.07 S	150.16 E
Curnamona	166	31.39 S	139.32 E
Curoca Norte	152	16.18 S	12.58 E
Curone ≃	62	45.03 N	8.54 E
Curon Venosta (Graun)	64	46.49 N	10.32 E
Čurovići	78	52.10 N	32.01 E
Currais Novos	250	6.15 S	36.31 W
Curralinho	250	1.48 S	49.47 W
Curramulka	168b	34.42 S	137.42 E
Curran	219	39.44 N	89.46 W
Currant Creek ≃, Co., U.S.	200	38.29 N	105.24 W
Currant Creek ≃, Mt., U.S.	202	46.22 N	108.39 W
Currant Mountain ∧	204	38.55 N	115.25 W
Currarong	170	35.01 S	150.49 E
Currency Creek	168b	35.28 S	138.46 E
Current ≃, On., Can.	190	48.27 N	89.11 W
Current ≃, U.S.	194	36.16 N	90.57 W
Current Islands II	192	25.22 N	76.49 W
Currie, Austl.	166	39.56 S	143.52 E
Currie, Scot., U.K.	46	55.54 N	3.20 W
Currie, Mn., U.S.	198	44.04 N	95.39 W
Currituck	192	36.26 N	76.00 W
Currituck □[6]	208	36.28 N	76.03 W
Currituck Seamount ✦[3]	14	30.00 S	173.30 W
Currituck Sound ⊔	192	36.20 N	75.52 W
Curry	180	62.37 N	150.01 W
Curry, Lake ⊜[1]	226	38.22 N	122.08 W
Curry Rivel	42	51.02 N	2.52 W
Curryville, Mo., U.S.	219	39.20 N	91.20 W
Curryville, Pa., U.S.	214	40.17 N	78.20 W
Cursi	68	40.09 N	18.18 E
Curslack ◆[8]	52	53.27 N	10.13 E
Curtarolo	64	45.31 N	11.50 E
Curtea de Argeș	38	45.08 N	24.41 E
Curtice	214	41.29 N	82.49 W
Curtina	252	32.09 S	56.07 W
Curtin Springs	162	25.20 S	131.45 E
Curtis, Esp.	34	43.07 N	8.03 W
Curtis, Ar., U.S.	194	33.59 N	93.06 W
Curtis, Ne., U.S.	198	40.37 N	100.30 W
Curtis, Port ⊤[3]	166	24.00 S	151.30 E
Curtis Bay ⊂	284b	39.13 N	76.35 W
Curtis Channel ⊔	166	23.30 S	151.45 E
Curtis Creek ⊂	284b	39.12 N	76.35 W
Curtis Island I, Austl.	166	23.38 S	151.09 E
Curtis Island I, N.Z.	14	30.30 S	178.34 W
Curtis Lake ⊜	176	66.38 N	89.02 W
Curtisville	214	40.38 N	79.51 W
Curu ≃	250	3.22 S	39.04 W
Curuá ≃, Bra.	250	5.23 S	54.22 W
Curuá ≃, Bra.	250	1.55 S	55.07 W
Curuá ≃, Bra.	255	13.51 S	51.38 W
Curuá, Ilha do I	250	0.48 N	50.10 W
Curuaés ≃	250	7.30 S	54.45 W
Curuan	116	7.13 N	122.14 E
Curuá-Una ≃	250	2.24 S	54.05 W
Curubandé	236	10.43 N	85.26 W
Curuçá	250	0.43 S	47.50 W
Curuçá ◆[8]	287b	23.30 S	46.25 W
Curuçá ≃	246	4.27 S	71.23 W
Curuçambaba	250	2.08 S	49.18 W
Curug, Indon.	115a	6.15 S	106.33 E
Čurug, Jugo.	38	45.29 N	20.04 E
Curuguaty	252	24.31 S	55.42 W
Curumo	286c	10.27 N	66.52 W
Curumu	250	1.01 S	51.03 W
Curunga	152	12.51 S	21.12 E
Curup	112	3.28 S	102.32 E
Curupá	250	9.54 S	45.54 W
Curupayty, Riacho ≃	248	22.03 S	58.00 W
C'urupinsk	78	46.37 N	32.43 E
Cururu ≃, Bra.	248	7.12 S	58.03 W
Cururu ≃, Bra.	250	0.39 S	50.11 W
Cururu-Açu ≃	250	8.58 S	57.13 W
Cururupu	250	1.50 S	44.52 W
Curuzú Cuatiá	252	29.47 S	58.03 W
Curva Grande	250	2.37 S	45.27 W
Curvelo	255	18.45 S	44.25 W
Curwensville	214	40.58 N	78.31 W
Curwensville Lake ⊜[1]	214	40.55 N	78.37 W
Curwensville State Park ♠	214	40.55 N	78.34 W
Cusago	266b	45.27 N	9.02 E
Cusano Milanino	62	45.33 N	9.11 E
Cusano Mutri	68	41.20 N	14.30 E
Cusco	248	13.31 S	71.59 W
Cusco □[5]	248	12.30 S	72.30 W
Cuscuzeiro, Pico do ∧	256	23.18 S	44.47 W
Cushabatay ≃	248	7.09 S	75.08 W
Cushendall	48	55.06 N	6.04 W
Cushendun	48	55.07 N	6.03 W
Cushina ≃	48	53.11 N	7.05 W
Cushing, Ok., U.S.	196	35.59 N	96.46 W
Cushing, Tx., U.S.	222	31.43 N	94.50 W
Cushing Memorial State Park ♠	283	42.10 N	70.45 W
Cushman	194	35.52 N	91.45 W
Cushman, Lake ⊜[1]	224	47.28 N	123.14 W
Cusiana ≃	246	4.33 N	71.51 W
Cusick	202	48.20 N	117.17 W
Cusihuiriáchic	232	28.14 N	106.50 W
Cusna, Monte ∧	64	44.17 N	10.23 E
Čusovaja ≃	86	58.13 N	56.22 E
Čusovoj	86	58.17 N	57.49 E
Cusset	32	46.08 N	3.28 E
Cusseta	192	32.18 N	84.46 W
Cussewago Creek ≃	214	41.38 N	80.11 W
Cussey-sur-l'Ognon	58	47.20 N	5.56 E
Cusso ≃	152	14.16 S	15.36 E
Cust, N.Z.	172	43.19 S	172.22 E
Čust, Uzb.	85	41.00 N	71.15 E
Custar	216	41.17 N	83.51 W
Custer, Mi., U.S.	190	43.57 N	86.13 W
Custer, Mt., U.S.	202	46.07 N	107.33 W
Custer, Ok., U.S.	196	35.40 N	98.53 W
Custer, S.D., U.S.	198	43.46 N	103.35 W
Custer, Wa., U.S.	224	48.55 N	122.38 W
Custer Battlefield National Monument ♠	202	45.32 N	107.20 W
Custer City	214	41.54 N	78.39 W
Custer Creek ≃	198	46.42 N	105.29 W
Custer State Park ♠	198	43.43 N	103.23 W
Custines	56	48.48 N	6.09 E
Custódia	250	8.07 S	37.39 W
Custonaci	70	38.04 N	12.41 E
Cut, Nuhu I	164	5.35 S	133.00 E
Cut and Shoot	222	30.19 N	95.25 W
Cutato ≃	152	10.33 S	16.48 E
Cut Bank	202	48.37 N	112.19 W
Cutbank ≃	182	54.44 N	118.31 W
Cut Bank Creek ≃, N.A.	198	48.35 N	100.52 W
Cut Bank Creek ≃, Mt., U.S.	202	48.29 N	112.14 W
Cut Beaver Lake ⊜	184	53.47 N	102.38 W
Čutejevo	80	55.16 N	47.47 E
Cutervo	248	6.22 S	78.51 W
Cutervo, Parque Nacional ♠	248	6.10 S	78.45 W
Cuthand Creek ≃	194	33.23 N	94.57 W
Cuthbert	192	31.46 N	84.47 W
Cut Knife	184	52.44 N	109.01 W
Cutler, Ca., U.S.	226	36.31 N	119.17 W
Cutler, Me., U.S.	188	44.39 N	67.12 W
Cutler Ridge	220	25.34 N	80.20 W
Cutlerville	216	42.50 N	85.39 W
Čutovo	78	49.43 N	35.10 E
Cutral-Có	252	38.56 S	69.14 W
Cutro	68	39.02 N	16.59 E
Cutrofiano	68	40.07 N	18.12 E
Cuttack	120	20.30 N	85.50 E
Cuttyhunk Island I	207	41.25 N	70.56 W
Čutyr'	80	57.24 N	53.17 E
Cutzamala ≃	234	18.22 N	100.39 W
Cutzamala de Pinzón	234	18.28 N	100.34 W
Cutzio	234	18.39 N	100.54 W
Čuvašija □[3]	80	55.30 N	47.00 E
Cuvette □[5]	152	0.30 S	16.00 E
Cuvier, Cape ≻	162	24.05 S	113.22 E
Cuvilly	50	49.33 N	2.42 E
Cuvo ≃	152	10.50 S	13.47 E
Cuxhaven	52	53.52 N	8.42 E
Cuxton	260	51.22 N	0.27 E
Cuyabá → Cuiabá	248	15.35 S	56.05 W
Cuyaguateje ≃	240p	22.05 N	83.58 W
Cuyahoga □[6]	214	41.30 N	81.41 W
Cuyahoga ≃	214	41.30 N	81.42 W
Cuyahoga County Airport ⊠	279a	41.34 N	81.29 W
Cuyahoga Falls	214	41.08 N	81.29 W
Cuyahoga Heights	279a	41.26 N	81.39 W
Cuyahoga Valley National Recreation Area ♠	214	41.20 N	81.35 W
Cuyama ≃	204	34.54 N	120.18 W
Cuyamaca Peak ∧	204	32.57 N	116.36 W
Cuyamaca Rancho State Park ♠	204	32.58 N	116.32 W
Cuyamel	236	15.38 N	88.12 W
Cuyapo	116	15.46 N	120.40 E
Cuyk	52	51.44 N	5.52 E
Cuyler	210	42.44 N	75.57 W
Cuylerville	210	42.47 N	77.52 W
Cuyo	116	10.51 N	121.00 E
Cuyo East Pass ⊔	116	11.00 N	121.28 E
Cuyo Island I	116	10.51 N	121.02 E
Cuyo Islands II	116	11.04 N	120.57 E
Cuyo West Pass ⊔	116	11.00 N	120.30 E
Cuyubini ≃	246	8.20 N	60.20 W
Cuyuni ≃	246	6.23 N	58.41 W
Cuyuni-Mazaruni □[4]	246	6.00 N	60.00 W
Cuyutlán, Laguna ⊂	234	19.00 N	104.10 W
Cuzco → Cusco	248	13.31 S	71.59 W
Čuzik ≃	86	58.03 N	80.37 E
Cuzna ≃	34	38.04 N	4.41 W
Cuzzago	58	46.00 N	8.22 E
Cvetkovo	78	49.11 N	31.33 E
Cvetnogorsk	86	54.14 N	90.27 E
Cvetnoje	78	48.57 N	32.29 E
Cvikov	54	50.48 N	14.40 E
Cwmbran	42	51.39 N	3.00 W
Cyangugu	154	2.29 S	28.54 E
Cybinka	30	52.12 N	14.48 E
Cybulev	78	49.06 N	29.50 E
Cyclades → Kikládhes II	38	37.30 N	25.00 E
Cyclone	214	41.50 N	78.35 W
Cygnet	216	41.14 N	83.38 W
Cygnet Bay ⊂	162	16.35 S	123.05 E
Cygnet Lake ⊜	184	56.47 N	94.54 W
Cygnet River	168b	35.42 S	137.31 E
Cylburn Park ♠	284b	39.21 N	76.39 W
Cynin ≃	42	51.48 N	4.29 W
Cynthiana, Ky., U.S.	218	38.23 N	84.17 W
Cynthiana, Oh., U.S.	218	39.10 N	83.21 W
Cynwyl Elfed	42	51.55 N	4.22 W
Cypern → Cyprus □[1]	130	35.00 N	33.00 E
Cypress, Ca., U.S.	280	33.49 N	118.02 W
Cypress, La., U.S.	194	31.36 N	93.02 W
Cypress, Tx., U.S.	222	29.58 N	95.42 W
Cypress Bayou ≃	194	35.03 N	91.42 W
Cypress Creek ≃, Fl., U.S.	220	28.05 N	82.24 W
Cypress Creek ≃, Tx., U.S.	194	30.19 N	93.45 W
Cypress Creek ≃, Tx., U.S.	222	30.02 N	95.19 W
Cypress Gardens ♠	220	28.00 N	81.42 W
Cypress Hills ⋏[2]	184	49.40 N	109.30 W
Cypress Hills Provincial Park ♠, Ab., Can.	184	49.39 N	110.10 W
Cypress Hills Provincial Park ♠, Sk., Can.	184	49.39 N	109.30 W
Cypress Island I	224	48.35 N	122.42 W
Cypress Lake ⊜, Sk., Can.	184	49.28 N	109.29 W
Cypress Lake ⊜, Fl., U.S.	220	28.05 N	81.19 W
Cypress Point ≻	226	36.35 N	121.59 W
Cypress Quarters	220	27.15 N	80.48 W
Cypress River	184	49.34 N	99.05 W
Cypress Swamp ≃	208	37.02 N	76.53 W
Cypress Swamp ≡	208	38.30 N	75.17 W
Cyprus □[1], Asia	22	35.00 N	33.00 E
Cyprus □[1], Asia	130	35.00 N	33.00 E
Cyprus, North (Kuzey Kıbrıs) □[1], Asia	22	35.15 N	33.40 E
Cyprus, North (Kuzey Kıbrıs) □[1], Asia	130	35.15 N	33.40 E
Cyrenaica → Barqah □[9]	146	31.00 N	22.30 E
Cyrene	219	39.17 N	91.06 W
Cyrene ⊥	146	32.49 N	21.52 E
Cyril	196	34.53 N	98.12 W
Cyrildene ◆[8]	273d	26.11 S	28.06 E
Cyrus Field Bay ⊂	176	62.50 N	64.55 W
Cysoing	50	50.34 N	3.13 E
Cythera → Kíthira I	38	36.20 N	22.58 E
Czaplinek	30	53.34 N	16.14 E
Czarna Białostocka	30	53.19 N	23.16 E
Czarna Woda	30	53.51 N	18.06 E
Czarne	30	53.42 N	16.57 E
Czarnków	30	52.55 N	16.34 E
Czech Republic (Česká Republika) □[1], Europe	22	49.40 N	15.10 E
Czech Republic (Česká Republika) □[1], Europe	30	49.40 N	15.10 E
Czempiń	30	52.10 N	16.47 E
Czerniejewo	30	52.26 N	17.30 E
Czernowitz → Černovcy	78	48.18 N	25.56 E
Czersk	30	53.48 N	18.00 E
Czerwieńsk	30	52.01 N	15.25 E
Częstochowa	30	50.49 N	19.06 E
Częstochowa □[4]	30	50.40 N	19.15 E
Człopa	30	53.06 N	16.08 E
Człuchów	30	53.41 N	17.21 E
Czudec	30	49.57 N	21.50 E
D			
Da → Black ≃ Asia	110	21.15 N	105.20 E
Da ≃, Zhg.	100	28.10 N	120.14 E
Daaden	56	50.44 N	7.58 E
Da'an, Zhg.	89	45.28 N	124.18 E
Da'an, Zhg.	100	23.05 N	115.37 E
Da'an, Zhg.	107	29.23 N	106.01 E
Da'an, Zhg.	110	23.19 N	110.34 E
Daanbantayan	116	11.14 N	124.00 E
Daba	104	42.06 N	122.00 E
Ḍabāb, Jabal aḍ- ∧	132	31.02 N	35.38 E
Dabagou	104	42.27 N	122.00 E
Ḍab'ah, Ra's aḍ- ≻	140	31.05 N	28.26 E
Dabai	150	11.31 N	5.11 E
Dabaizhuang	105	39.27 N	117.23 E
Dabajuro	246	11.02 N	70.40 W
Dabakala	150	8.22 N	4.26 W
Dabali	104	41.51 N	120.37 E
Daba Ling ∧	100	24.28 N	113.17 E
Dabancheng	86	43.21 N	88.19 E
Dabangdian	100	31.37 N	113.41 E
Dabaojiagangzi	104	42.09 N	123.33 E
Dabaozhuang	105	40.18 N	116.58 E
Dabaozi	105	40.11 N	115.10 E
Daba Shan ⋏	102	31.55 N	109.05 E
Dabasi	107	28.55 N	105.09 E
Dabat	144	12.58 N	37.48 E
Dabayingzi	104	42.11 N	121.35 E
Dabbāgh, Jabal ∧	128	27.52 N	35.45 E
Dabbūriya	132	32.41 N	35.22 E
Dabegabis	158	28.07 S	18.36 E
Dabeiba	246	7.01 N	76.16 W
Dabeiwa	105	40.48 N	117.31 E
Dabeiyingzi	104	42.05 N	122.08 E
Dabendorf	54	52.14 N	13.26 E
Daberas	156	25.38 S	18.29 E
Daberg ◆[8]	263	51.40 N	7.47 E
Dabhoi	120	22.11 N	73.26 E
Dābhol	122	17.36 N	73.10 E
Dab'ī, Wādī aḍ- V	132	31.42 N	36.42 E
Dąbie	30	52.06 N	18.49 E
Dąbie ◆[3]	54	53.24 N	14.40 E
Dąbie, Jezioro ⊜	54	53.27 N	14.40 E
Dabie Shan ⋏	100	31.00 N	115.40 E
Dabilda	146	12.46 N	14.34 E
Dablān	130	34.52 N	40.34 E
Ďáblice ◆[8]	54	50.08 N	14.29 E
Dabnou	150	14.09 N	5.22 E
Dabo	58	48.39 N	7.14 E
Dabob Bay ⊂	224	47.47 N	122.50 W
Dabobeizhuang	105	39.18 N	117.59 E
Dabola	150	10.45 N	11.07 W
Dabong	114	5.23 N	102.01 E
Daborow	144	6.21 N	48.43 E
Dabou	150	5.19 N	4.23 W
Daboya	150	9.32 N	1.23 W
Dabra	124	25.54 N	78.20 E
Dābri ◆[8]	272a	28.37 N	77.05 E
Dabringhausen	52	51.05 N	7.11 E
Dąbrowa Białostocka	30	53.39 N	23.20 E
Dąbrowa Tarnowska	30	50.11 N	21.00 E
Dabsan Hu ⊜	102	36.58 N	94.55 E
Dabu, Zhg.	100	24.19 N	116.43 E
Dabu, Zhg.	100	23.52 N	116.54 E
Dabu, Zhg.	100	24.20 N	114.35 E
Dabus ≃	144	10.48 N	35.10 E
Dabusutu-Ula, gora ∧	86	50.44 N	92.40 E
Dacaitun	104	41.38 N	121.18 E
Dacangzigou	104	40.59 N	121.01 E
Dacaocun	105	40.34 N	117.07 E
Dacca → Dhaka	126	23.43 N	90.25 E
Dachakou	100	29.38 N	118.18 E
Dachang, Zhg.	105	39.53 N	116.59 E
Dachang, Zhg.	106	32.12 N	118.45 E
Dachang, Zhg.	106	31.18 N	121.25 E
Dachang Airport ⊠	269b	31.18 N	121.25 E
Dachangshan Dao I	98	39.10 N	122.34 E
Dachau	60	48.15 N	11.27 E
Dachauer Moos ≡	60	48.12 N	11.25 E
Dacheng	100	28.34 N	115.31 E
Dachengji	100	33.52 N	119.26 E
Dachenjiabao	106	32.11 N	120.22 E
Dachen Shan I	106	30.21 N	121.52 E
Dachixu	100	25.10 N	116.46 E
Dachongyu	105	40.23 N	117.41 E
Dachsberg ∧[2]	263	51.30 N	6.30 E
Dachsteinhöhlen ±[5]	64	47.32 N	13.43 E
Dačice	61	49.05 N	15.26 E
Dac Lac, Cao Nguyen ⋏[1]	110	12.50 N	108.05 E
Dačnoje ◆[8]	265a	59.50 N	30.16 E
Dacoma	196	36.39 N	98.33 W
Dacorum □[8]	260	51.45 N	0.30 W
Dac To	110	14.42 N	107.51 E
Dacun, Zhg.	102	27.55 N	101.08 E
Dacun, Zhg.	106	31.12 N	119.40 E
Dadal	88	49.01 N	111.37 E
Dadanawa	246	2.50 N	59.30 W
Dadaolizhuang	105	39.59 N	116.59 E
Dadaotun	104	41.46 N	122.13 E
Dadar ◆[8]	272c	19.01 N	72.50 E
Daday	130	41.28 N	33.28 E
Dadayungou	104	41.23 N	123.25 E
Daddys Creek ≃	192	36.05 N	84.47 W
Dade □[6]	220	25.33 N	80.32 W
Dade Battlefield Historic Memorial ⊥	220	28.38 N	82.09 W
Dade City	220	28.21 N	82.11 W
Dadeldhurā	124	29.18 N	80.35 E
Dadès, Oued ≃	148	30.55 N	6.47 W
Dadeville	194	32.49 N	85.45 W
Dādhar	120	29.28 N	67.39 E
Dadian	100	33.36 N	117.16 E
Dadiangas → General Santos	116	6.07 N	125.11 E
Dadianzi	104	42.11 N	124.02 E
Dadingjiawopu	104	41.13 N	122.16 E
D'adino	88	55.44 N	105.45 E
Dadiya	146	9.37 N	11.26 E
Dadle	144	5.20 N	46.58 E
Ḍadnah	128	25.33 N	56.21 E
Dadonggejiang	105	39.51 N	116.48 E
Dadongzhou	104	41.44 N	124.00 E
Dadou ≃	32	43.44 N	1.49 E
Dādpur, India	272b	22.42 N	88.33 E
Dādpur, India	272b	22.54 N	88.31 E
Dādra and Nagar Haveli □[8]	122	20.05 N	73.00 E
Dādu	120	26.44 N	67.47 E
Dadu ≃	102	29.33 N	103.45 E
Dadugang	102	22.23 N	100.55 E
Dadukou, Zhg.	100	25.44 N	119.05 E
Dadukou, Zhg.	107	28.45 N	105.13 E
Dadukou, Zhg.	107	29.28 N	106.29 E
Daegu → Taegu	98	35.52 N	128.35 E
Daejeon → Taejŏn	98	36.20 N	127.26 E
Daerhanwangfu	89	44.19 N	122.15 E
Da'erhao	98	41.45 N	116.01 E
Daet	116	14.05 N	122.55 E
Daf'	146	28.03 N	19.57 E
Dafan, Zhg.	100	29.41 N	114.40 E
Dafan, Zhg.	104	42.38 N	122.11 E
Dafang	102	27.04 N	105.31 E
Dafangshen, Zhg.	104	42.25 N	123.14 E
Dafangshen, Zhg.	104	42.34 N	123.28 E
Dafangshen, Zhg.	104	42.36 N	123.04 E
Dafanhe	104	42.13 N	123.43 E
Dafanpuzi	104	41.37 N	122.50 E
Dafeng	100	33.12 N	120.30 E
Dafna	132	33.14 N	35.38 E
Dafoe	184	51.46 N	104.32 W
Dafoe ≃	184	55.55 N	94.48 W
Dafoe Lake ⊜	184	55.43 N	96.15 W
Da Fo Si (Great Buddha Temple) ʊ[1]	106	30.16 N	120.09 E
Dafoutuo	105	40.24 N	115.58 E
Dafu	100	29.55 N	118.35 E
Dafu ≃	100	30.52 N	113.32 E
Dāfūr al-Janūbīyah □[4]	140	11.45 N	25.25 E
Dagā ≃	110	16.56 N	94.45 E
Daga Medo	144	7.59 N	43.01 E
Dagana	150	16.31 N	15.30 W
Dagang, Zhg.	100	33.12 N	120.07 E
Dagang, Zhg.	100	22.49 N	113.23 E
Dagang, Zhg.	106	32.12 N	119.39 E
Dagangtou	100	28.18 N	119.44 E
Daganwangzhai	104	40.49 N	122.33 E
Daganzo de Arriba	266a	40.33 N	3.27 W
Dagaokan	104	40.46 N	122.22 E
Dagaolifangzun	104	41.10 N	122.28 E
Dagaolitun	104	42.26 N	123.53 E
Dagaoyang	106	30.35 N	120.26 E
Daga Post	140	9.12 N	33.58 E
Dağardı	130	39.26 N	29.00 E
Dagash	140	19.22 N	33.24 E
Dağbeli	130	37.12 N	30.31 E
Dagcanglhamo	102	34.02 N	102.30 E
Dagda	76	56.06 N	27.32 E
Dageløkke	41	55.04 N	10.53 E
Dagenham ◆[8]	260	51.32 N	0.10 E
Dagestan □[3], Ross.	72	43.00 N	47.00 E
Dagestan → Altaj □[3], Ross.	86	51.00 N	86.00 E
Dagestanskije Ogni	84	42.07 N	48.12 E
Daggafontein	273d	26.18 S	28.28 E
Daggafontein Mines ◆[7]	273d	26.18 S	28.29 E
Daggett	228	34.51 N	116.53 W
Dagg Sound ⊔	172	45.23 S	166.46 E
Daghfalī	140	19.17 N	32.30 E
Dağkızılca	130	38.18 N	27.24 E
Daglung	120	28.54 N	90.33 E
Dagmersellen	58	47.13 N	7.59 E
Dagö → Hiiumaa I	76	58.52 N	22.40 E
Dagomys	84	43.40 N	39.41 E
Dagongtun	89	42.48 N	121.58 E
Dagoretti	154	1.18 S	36.46 E
Dagsboro	208	38.32 N	75.14 W
Dagshai	123	30.53 N	77.03 E
Dagu	105	38.59 N	117.41 E
Dagu ≃	98	36.15 N	120.06 E
Dagua	164	3.25 S	143.20 E
Daguan, Zhg.	100	31.14 N	117.01 E
Daguan, Zhg.	102	27.44 N	104.16 E
Daguan Hu ⊜	100	30.00 N	116.24 E
Daguao	240m	18.14 N	65.41 W
Dagufen'gou	105	40.41 N	116.20 E
D'Aguilar, Cape ≻	271d	22.14 N	114.15 E
D'Aguilar, Mount ∧	171a	27.19 S	152.47 E
D'Aguilar Range ⋏	171a	27.10 S	152.45 E
Dagujia	98	42.22 N	124.52 E
Dagujiazi	104	42.20 N	123.20 E
Da Guokui Shan ∧	89	45.17 N	129.30 E
Dagupan	116	16.03 N	120.20 E
Daguragu Aboriginal Reserve ◆[4]	162	17.35 S	130.30 E
Dagushan	104	41.03 N	123.02 E
Dagus Mines	214	41.21 N	78.36 W
Dagutang	100	29.38 N	116.06 E
Dagwin	110	18.04 N	97.41 E
Dagzê Co ⊜	120	31.55 N	87.35 E
Dahabān	144	21.55 N	39.04 E
Dahalac National Park ♠	144	15.40 N	40.05 E
Dahanchang	105	39.29 N	117.05 E
Dahaneh-ye Ghowrī	120	35.54 N	68.30 E
Dahaneh-ye Kāshār	120	35.09 N	66.14 E
Dahan-e Qowmghī	120	34.28 N	66.31 E
Dahantun	104	42.10 N	122.41 E
Dahasah, Wādī V	142	28.08 N	31.00 E
Dahḍāḥ, Tall ∧[2]	132	32.36 N	36.03 E
Dahe	106	31.42 N	120.37 E
Dahebei	105	39.10 N	117.39 E
Dahei	120	21.42 N	72.35 E
Daheiding Shan ∧	89	47.58 N	129.07 E
Daheiyugou	104	41.21 N	121.55 E
Dahekou	106	32.16 N	119.05 E
Dahengdu	100	29.03 N	121.30 E
Dahenqin Dao I	100	22.06 N	113.30 E
Daheqiao	100	29.25 N	115.16 E
Dahijuri	126	22.31 N	86.59 E
Da Hinggan Ling ⋏	90	49.00 N	122.00 E
Dahīrpur ◆[8]	272a	28.43 N	77.12 E
Dahl	56	51.18 N	7.31 E
Dahlak Archipelago II	144	15.45 N	40.30 E
Dahle	263	51.18 N	7.45 E
Dahlem	56	50.23 N	6.33 E
Dahlem ◆[8]	264a	52.28 N	13.17 E
Dahlem, Museum ʊ	264a	52.27 N	13.18 E
Dahlen	54	51.22 N	12.59 E
Dahlenburg	54	53.11 N	10.44 E
Dahlerau	263	51.13 N	7.19 E
Dahlewitz	54	52.19 N	13.26 E
Dahlgren, Il., U.S.	194	38.12 N	88.41 W
Dahlgren, Va., U.S.	208	38.19 N	77.03 W
Dahlhausen	54	53.03 N	12.20 E
Dahlia	154	18.35 S	27.08 E
Dahlonega	192	34.31 N	83.59 W
Dahlonega Plateau ⋏[1]	192	34.10 N	84.20 W
Dahlwitz	264a	52.30 N	13.38 E
Dahlwitz-Hoppegarten	54	52.30 N	13.38 E
Dahmani	36	35.57 N	8.50 E
Dahmarū	142	28.41 N	30.49 E
Dahme, Dtsch.	54	51.52 N	13.25 E
Dahme, Dtsch.	54	54.13 N	11.04 E
Dahme ≃	54	52.25 N	13.35 E
Dahn	56	49.09 N	7.47 E
Dāhod	120	22.50 N	74.16 E
Dahomey → Benin □[1]	150	9.30 N	2.15 E
Dahong	106	31.53 N	121.17 E
Dahongmen	105	39.50 N	116.25 E
Dahongqi	104	41.52 N	122.36 E
Dahong Shan ⋏	100	31.30 N	113.00 E
Dahongtaizi	104	41.41 N	121.23 E
Dahoucun	105	38.51 N	115.37 E
Dahra	146	29.34 N	17.50 E
Dahra ⋏	34	36.25 N	1.00 E
Dähre	54	52.48 N	10.54 E
Dahsah, Wādī ad- V	142	27.19 N	31.26 E
Dahshūr	142	29.45 N	31.14 E
Dahu, Zhg.	100	26.22 N	119.06 E
Dahu, Zhg.	100	26.04 N	117.19 E
Dahua	102	23.44 N	107.59 E
Dahuan	100	22.33 N	113.29 E
Dahuangdi	104	42.08 N	122.27 E
Dahuangji	98	35.06 N	115.15 E
Dahuangpu	105	39.26 N	117.16 E
Dahuangshanpu	104	41.16 N	121.23 E
Dahuashan	105	40.17 N	117.04 E
Dahuasi	107	30.05 N	104.08 E
Dahujiang	100	26.10 N	114.57 E
Dahūk	128	36.52 N	43.00 E
Dahūk □[4]	128	37.00 N	43.00 E
Dahuni	164	10.31 S	149.55 E
Dahuofang Shuiku ⊜[1]	98	41.55 N	124.15 E
Dahushan	104	41.37 N	122.09 E
Dahy, Nafūd ad- ◆[2]	118	22.20 N	45.35 E
Dai I	175e	7.57 S	160.37 E
Dai ≃	100	26.14 N	119.40 E
Dai, Pulau I	164	7.33 S	129.41 E
Daia	38	44.00 N	25.59 E
Daian	94	35.05 N	136.33 E
Daibosatsu-rei ∧	94	35.45 N	138.51 E
Daibu, Zhg.	100	32.19 N	117.12 E
Daibu, Zhg.	106	31.18 N	119.30 E
Daibutsu ʊ[1]	94	35.19 N	139.32 E
Daiei	96	35.29 N	133.45 E
Daifang	100	27.32 N	115.41 E
Daigo	94	36.46 N	140.21 E
Daigo ◆[8]	270	34.57 N	135.50 E
Daiguantun	105	39.57 N	117.50 E
Dai Hai ⊜	102	40.31 N	112.43 E
Daihaiyingzi	104	42.30 N	121.26 E
Daiji	100	33.48 N	115.03 E
Daijiagou	107	30.00 N	106.33 E
Daijiayao	100	32.56 N	120.19 E
Daikanbō ∧	96	33.00 N	131.04 E
Daik-u	110	17.47 N	96.40 E
Dā'il	132	32.45 N	36.08 E
Dailekh	124	28.50 N	81.44 E
Dailing	89	47.01 N	129.02 E
Dailly	44	55.16 N	4.43 W
Daimanji-san ∧	92	36.15 N	133.19 E
Daimiel	34	39.04 N	3.37 W
Daimon, Nihon	94	36.44 N	137.03 E
Daimon, Nihon	268	35.53 N	139.44 E
Daimuken-zan ∧	94	35.15 N	138.10 E
Dainan	100	32.43 N	120.06 E
Daingean	48	53.18 N	7.17 W
Daingerfield	222	33.01 N	94.43 W
Dainhāt	126	23.37 N	88.04 E
Dainichiga-take ∧	94	36.00 N	136.50 E
Dainkog	102	32.31 N	97.59 E
Daintree	164	16.15 S	145.19 E
Daintree National Park ♠	164	16.15 S	145.10 E
Daiō-zaki ≻	92	34.17 N	136.54 E
Dāira Dīn Panāh	123	30.34 N	70.56 E
Dairago	266b	45.34 N	8.52 E
Daireaux	252	36.36 S	61.45 W
Dairen → Dalian	98	38.53 N	121.35 E
Dairsie	46	56.20 N	2.56 W
Dairy City → Cypress	280	33.50 N	118.01 W
Dairy Creek, East Fork ≃	224	45.34 N	123.09 W
Dairy Creek, West Fork ≃	224	45.34 N	123.09 W
Dairyland → La Palma, Ca., U.S.	280	33.51 N	118.02 W
Dairyland, N.Y., U.S.	210	41.45 N	74.33 W
Dairyland Reservoir ⊜[1]	190	45.30 N	91.00 W
Dairy Valley → Cerritos	280	33.51 N	118.05 W
Dai-sen ∧	96	35.22 N	133.33 E
Daisen-oki-kokuritsu-kōen ♠	96	35.20 N	133.35 E
Daisen-zan ∧	96	34.07 N	133.56 E
Daisetsu-zan-kokuritsu-kōen ♠	92a	43.30 N	142.57 E
Daisetta	222	30.06 N	94.38 W
Daishan	100	30.14 N	122.12 E
Daishin	94	37.12 N	140.15 E
Daishōji ≃	94	36.18 N	136.15 E
Daisizhen	107	29.14 N	105.09 E
Daitō, Nihon	96	34.42 N	135.38 E
Daitō, Nihon	96	35.19 N	132.58 E
Daiwa, Nihon	96	34.32 N	132.57 E
Daiwa, Nihon	96	34.57 N	132.39 E
Daixi	106	30.40 N	120.01 E
Daixian	102	39.08 N	113.01 E
Daixiqiao	106	31.36 N	120.04 E
Daiya ≃	94	36.45 N	139.46 E
Daiyun Shan ⋏	100	25.46 N	118.16 E
Dajabón	238	19.33 N	71.42 W
Dājal	120	29.33 N	70.23 E
Da'jānīyah, Jabal ad- ∧	132	30.34 N	35.43 E
Dajarra	166	21.41 S	139.31 E
Dajian Shan ∧	102	26.42 N	103.34 E
Dajidian	105	38.50 N	115.26 E
Dajindian	100	34.24 N	112.58 E
Dajing, Zhg.	100	28.24 N	121.07 E
Dajing, Zhg.	100	28.59 N	113.19 E
Dajin Shan II	106	30.41 N	121.26 E
Dajishan	100	24.38 N	114.26 E
Dajitai	104	42.20 N	121.11 E
Dajiuba	120	36.50 N	89.35 E
Daji Yang ⊔	100	30.54 N	122.18 E
Daju	105	39.12 N	115.31 E
Da Juh	102	36.36 N	94.04 E
Dak ⊜	128	32.48 N	61.14 E
Daka ≃	150	8.19 N	0.13 W
Dakangpu	104	41.32 N	121.06 E
Dakanzi	104	40.52 N	122.53 E
Dakar	150	14.40 N	17.26 W
Dakar □[4]	150	14.45 N	17.25 W
Dākātia ≃[1]	126	22.57 N	90.42 E
Dakeng	100	26.18 N	115.32 E
Dakengkou	100	24.33 N	113.37 E
Daketa ≃	144	7.16 N	42.13 E
Dak Gle	110	15.11 N	107.48 E
Dakhal, Bi'r ad- ⊤[4]	142	28.40 N	32.24 E
Dakhal, Wādī ad- V	142	28.49 N	32.45 E
Dākhilah, Al-Wāḥāt ad- ⊤[4]	140	25.30 N	29.05 E
Dakhin Shāhbāzpur Island I	126	22.30 N	90.45 E
Dakhla	148	23.43 N	15.57 W
Dakhlet Nouâdhibou □[4]	148	20.40 N	16.00 W
Dakingari	150	11.37 N	4.01 E
Dakka → Dhaka	124	23.43 N	90.25 E
Dākoānk	110	7.02 N	93.43 E
Dakongcheng	105	39.30 N	117.09 E
Dakongwan	104	40.51 N	122.19 E
Dakoro	150	14.31 N	6.46 E
Dakota City, Ia., U.S.	190	42.43 N	94.12 W
Dakota City, Ne., U.S.	198	42.24 N	96.25 W
Dakou	100	34.27 N	112.44 E
Dakoutun	105	39.35 N	117.14 E
Đakovica	38	42.23 N	20.25 E
Đakovo	38	45.19 N	18.25 E
Dakshin Gangotri ʊ[3]	9	70.05 S	12.00 E
Dakshingram	126	24.03 N	87.48 E
Dakumu	89	48.51 N	124.18 E
Dakunlun	98	36.34 N	117.52 E
Dakwa	154	4.00 N	26.26 E
Dakwah, Tall ad- ∧[2]	132	33.25 N	36.56 E
Dala, Ang.	152	11.03 S	20.17 E
Dala, Ang.	152	8.05 S	15.50 E
Dala, Sol.Is.	175e	8.35 S	160.40 E
Dalaas	58	47.07 N	10.00 E
Dalaba	150	10.42 N	12.15 W
Dalabani	150	10.28 N	9.27 W
Dala Cachibo	152	10.28 S	14.39 E
Dalad Qi	102	40.28 N	110.02 E
Dala-Floda	40	60.31 N	14.47 E
Dalaguete	116	9.46 N	123.32 E
Dalahan (Shiqizhan)	89	52.06 N	125.46 E
Dala-Husby	40	60.21 N	16.00 E
Dala-Järna	26	60.33 N	14.21 E
Dalajchöl	86	47.59 N	90.47 E
Dalaji	89	51.38 N	120.06 E
Dalälven ≃	40	60.38 N	17.27 E
Dalama	130	37.48 N	28.04 E
Dalaman ≃	130	36.40 N	28.45 E
Dalāmī	140	11.52 N	30.28 E
Dalan	100	23.19 N	114.47 E
Dalan Dzadgad	102	43.37 N	104.29 E
Dalandžargalan	102	45.55 N	109.05 E
Dalane ◆[1]	26	58.35 N	6.20 E
Dalang	100	22.57 N	113.56 E
Dalantuozi	104	41.28 N	122.47 E
Dalao	150	11.29 N	13.40 W
Dalarna □[9]	26	61.01 N	14.04 E
Dalarö	40	59.08 N	18.24 E
Dalat, Malay.	112	2.44 N	111.56 E
Da Lat, Viet	110	11.56 N	108.25 E
Dalayaozi	105	40.49 N	117.41 E
Dālbandin	128	28.53 N	64.25 E
Dalbeattie	44	54.56 N	3.49 W
D'Albertis Dome ∧	164	5.00 S	142.05 E
Dalbosjön ⊂	26	58.45 N	12.48 E
Dalby, Austl.	166	27.11 S	151.16 E
Dalby, Sve.	41	55.40 N	13.20 E
Dalby Söderskogs Nationalpark ♠	41	55.43 N	13.17 E
Dalcahue	254	42.23 S	73.40 W
Dalch ≃	42	50.52 N	3.47 W
Dale, Nor.	26	60.35 N	5.49 E
Dale, Nor.	26	61.22 N	5.25 E
Dale, Wales, U.K.	42	51.43 N	5.11 W
Dale, In., U.S.	194	38.10 N	86.59 W
Dale, Pa., U.S.	214	40.18 N	78.54 W
Dale, Tx., U.S.	222	29.56 N	97.34 W
Dale ≃	168a	32.10 S	116.49 E
Dale, Mount ∧	168a	32.08 S	116.18 E
Dale Bridge	168a	32.05 S	116.49 E
Dalecarlia → Dalarna □[9]	26	61.01 N	14.04 E
Dale City	208	38.38 N	77.18 W
Dale Hollow Lake ⊜[1]	192	36.36 N	85.19 W

≃	River	Fluß	Río	Rivière	Rio
≊	Canal	Kanal	Canal	Canal	Canal
ʟ	Waterfall, Rapids	Wasserfall, Stromschnellen	Cascada, Rápidos	Chute d'eau, Rapides	Cascata, Rápidos
⊔	Strait	Meeresstraße	Estrecho	Détroit	Estreito
⊂	Bay, Gulf	Bucht, Golf	Bahía, Golfo	Baie, Golfe	Baía, Golfo
⊜	Lake, Lakes	See, Seen	Lago, Lagos	Lac, Lacs	Lago, Lagos
≡	Swamp	Sumpf	Pantano	Marais	Pântano
⊓	Ice Features, Glacier	Eis- und Gletscherformen	Accidentes Glaciales	Formes glaciaires	Acidentes glaciares
⊤	Other Hydrographic Features	Andere Hydrographische Objekte	Otros Elementos Hidrográficos	Autres données hydrographiques	Outros acidentes hidrográficos

✦	Submarine Features	Untermeerische Objekte	Accidentes Submarinos	Formes de relief sous-marin	Acidentes submarinos
□	Political Unit	Politische Einheit	Unidad Politica	Entité politique	Unidade política
ʊ	Cultural Institution	Kulturelle Institution	Institución Cultural	Institution culturelle	Instituição cultural
⊥	Historical Site	Historische Stätte	Sitio Histórico	Site historique	Sitio histórico
♠	Recreational Site	Erholungs- und Ferienort	Sitio de Recreo	Centre de loisirs	Area de Lazer
⊠	Airport	Flughafen	Aeropuerto	Aéroport	Aeroporto
±	Military Installation	Militäranlage	Instalación Militar	Installation militaire	Instalação militar
◆	Miscellaneous	Verschiedenes	Misceláneo	Divers	Diversos

Dale Lake ◎ 204 34.08 N 115.42 W
Dalen 26 59.27 N 8.00 E
Dalengtu 98 41.11 N 113.45 E
Dalešice, údolní nádrž ◎[1] 61 49.09 N 16.05 E
Daleside 158 26.30 S 28.04 E
Dale South ≃ 168a 32.16 S 116.47 E
Dalesville 206 45.42 N 74.24 W
Dalesville ≃ 206 45.40 N 74.24 W
Daleszyce 30 50.48 N 20.48 E
Dalet 110 19.59 N 93.51 E
Daleville, Al., U.S. 194 31.18 N 85.42 W
Daleville, In., U.S. 218 40.07 N 85.33 W
Daleville, Pa., U.S. 210 41.18 N 75.31 W
Dalfsen 52 52.30 N 6.16 E
Dalgaranga 162 27.46 S 117.02 E
Dalgaranger ∧ 162 27.51 S 117.06 E
Dalgety 171b 36.30 S 148.50 E
Dalgety Bay 46 56.02 N 3.20 W
Dalgety Brook ≃ 162 25.07 S 115.47 E
Dalgety Downs 162 25.17 S 116.15 E
Dalgomai 124 26.06 N 90.47 E
Dalhalvaig 46 58.28 N 3.54 W
Dalhart 196 36.03 N 102.30 W
Dalhausen 52 51.37 N 9.17 E
Dalhousie, N.B., Can. 186 48.04 N 66.23 W
Dalhousie, India 123 32.32 N 75.59 E
Dalhousie, Cape › 180 70.14 N 129.42 W
Dalhousie Island I 126 21.35 N 88.45 E
Dalhousie Lake ◎ 212 44.58 N 76.35 W
Dalhousie Square ♦ 272b 22.33 N 88.22 E
Dali, Zhg. 102 34.47 N 109.57 E
Dali, Zhg. 102 25.38 N 100.09 E
Dalian (Dairen) 98 38.53 N 121.35 E
Dalian Dao I 100 25.40 N 119.42 E
Daliangdi 98 41.54 N 115.45 E
Daliang Shan ⋏ 102 28.00 N 103.00 E
Dalianhe 104 40.57 N 123.15 E
Daliankeng 105 40.54 N 117.45 E
Dalian Wan ⊂ 98 38.57 N 121.45 E
Dalianwukou 106 30.17 N 119.00 E
Daliao ≃ 104 40.42 N 122.08 E
Dalías 34 36.49 N 2.52 W
Dalikou 100 26.52 N 118.00 E
Dalin, Zhg. 89 43.43 N 122.45 E
Dalin, Zhg. 107 30.17 N 104.07 E
Daling 104 41.27 N 121.15 E
Daling ≃ 98 40.56 N 121.43 E
Dalingbeigou 104 40.42 N 123.08 E
Dalipe Point › 116 10.46 N 121.55 E
Daliushugou 104 40.46 N 122.14 E
Daliutai 104 41.25 N 121.55 E
Daliutun 104 42.14 N 122.46 E
Daliuzhen 105 38.51 N 116.19 E
Daliuzhuang 100 33.04 N 114.03 E
Daliyat et Karmil 132 32.42 N 35.03 E
Daliyya 132 32.35 N 35.04 E
Dalizi 98 41.45 N 126.49 E
Dalj 38 45.29 N 18.59 E
Daljā' 142 27.39 N 30.42 E
Dalkarlsberg 40 59.26 N 14.51 E
Dalkeith 46 55.54 N 3.04 W
Dālkola 124 25.52 N 87.51 E
Dall, Mount ∧ 180 62.35 N 152.18 W
Dāllah, 'Ayn ⍑[4] 140 27.19 N 27.20 E
Dallardsville 222 30.38 N 94.38 W
Dallas, Scot., U.K. 46 57.33 N 3.28 W
Dallas, Al., U.S. 194 33.50 N 86.39 W
Dallas, Ga., U.S. 192 33.55 N 84.50 W
Dallas, N.C., U.S. 192 35.18 N 81.10 W
Dallas, Or., U.S. 202 44.55 N 123.18 W
Dallas, Pa., U.S. 210 41.20 N 75.57 W
Dallas, Tx., U.S. 222 32.46 N 96.47 W
Dallas, Wi., U.S. 190 45.15 N 91.48 W
Dallas □[6] 222 32.17 N 96.47 W
Dallas Center 190 41.41 N 93.57 W
Dallas City 190 40.38 N 91.10 W
Dallas-Fort Worth Regional Airport ⊠ 222 32.54 N 97.01 W
Dallas Naval Air Station ■ 222 32.44 N 96.59 W
Dallastown 208 39.53 N 76.38 W
Dallgow 54 52.32 N 13.05 E
Dallıbahçe 130 39.09 N 39.53 E
Dalli Rājhara 122 20.35 N 81.04 E
Dall Island I 182 54.50 N 132.55 W
Dall Lake ◎ 180 60.18 N 163.35 W
Dalmā I 128 24.30 N 52.20 E
Dalmacija □[9] 36 43.00 N 17.00 E
Dalmacio Vélez Sarsfield 252 32.36 S 63.35 W
Dalmally 46 56.24 N 4.58 W
Dal'mamedli 84 40.42 N 46.34 E
Dalmatia 208 40.39 N 76.54 W
Dalmatia → Dalmacija □[9] 36 43.00 N 17.00 E
Dalmatovo 86 56.16 N 62.56 E
Dalmau 124 26.04 N 81.02 E
Dalmellington 44 55.19 N 4.24 W
Dalmeny 184 52.20 N 106.46 W
Dalmine 62 45.39 N 9.36 E
Dalmose 41 55.18 N 11.26 E
Dal'n'aja 89 45.56 N 142.04 E
Dal'n'aja Muja 88 54.21 N 103.37 E
Dalnaspidal 46 56.50 N 4.14 W
Dal'negorsk 89 44.35 N 135.35 E
Dal'neje-Konstantinovo 80 55.49 N 44.06 E
Dal'nerečensk 89 45.55 N 133.43 E
Dal'ne-Rusanovo 82 54.15 N 36.45 E
Dal'nik 78 46.28 N 30.34 E
Daloa 150 6.53 N 6.27 W
Dalongchang 105 39.50 N 116.06 E
Dalonghua 105 39.18 N 115.18 E
Dalongtian 100 24.14 N 115.44 E
Dalovice 54 50.11 N 12.55 E
Dalqū 140 20.07 N 30.37 E
Dalroy 182 51.07 N 113.39 W
Dalry, Scot., U.K. 44 55.07 N 4.10 W
Dalry, Scot., U.K. 46 55.43 N 4.44 W
Dalrymple 44 55.23 N 4.35 W
Dalrymple, Mount ∧ 166 21.02 S 148.38 E
Dalrymple Creek ≃ 171a 27.59 S 151.46 E
Dalrymple Lake ◎ 212 44.38 N 79.07 W
Dalsbruk (Taalintehdas) 26 60.02 N 22.31 E
Dalsingpara 124 26.47 N 89.22 E
Dalsing Sarai 124 25.40 N 85.50 E
Dalsjöfors 26 57.43 N 13.05 E
Dalsland □[9] 26 58.30 N 12.50 E
Dals-Långed 26 58.55 N 12.18 E
Dal'stroja 180 68.19 N 177.39 W
Dāltenganj 124 24.02 N 84.04 E
Dalton, S. Afr. 158 29.20 S 30.40 E
Dalton, Eng., U.K. 262 53.34 N 2.46 W
Dalton, Ga., U.S. 192 34.47 N 84.58 W
Dalton, Ma., U.S. 207 42.28 N 73.10 W
Dalton, Ne., U.S. 198 41.24 N 102.58 W
Dalton, N.Y., U.S. 210 42.32 N 77.57 W
Dalton, Oh., U.S. 214 40.47 N 81.41 W
Dalton, Pa., U.S. 210 41.32 N 75.44 W
Dalton City 219 39.43 N 88.48 W
Dalton Gardens 202 47.43 N 116.46 W
Dalton-in-Furness 44 54.09 N 3.11 W
Dalu 104 41.27 N 123.19 E
Dalubeikou 105 38.59 N 117.12 E
Daludalu 114 1.05 N 100.15 E
Dalu Dao I 98 39.44 N 123.45 E
Daluis, Gorges de V 62 44.04 N 6.49 E
Dalum, Dan. 41 55.22 N 10.22 E
Dalum, Dtsch. 52 52.35 N 7.14 E
Daluojiazhuang 106 32.09 N 120.08 E
Daluotaozi 104 41.17 N 122.52 E
Daluoxi 100 25.14 N 118.36 E
Daluping 100 26.11 N 114.30 E
Dalupiri Island I, Pil. 116 19.05 N 121.14 E
Dalupiri Island I, Pil. 116 12.25 N 124.16 E
Daluxi 100 24.28 N 117.01 E
Dalview 273d 26.15 S 28.21 E
Dalvík 24a 65.59 N 18.32 W
Dalwallinu 162 30.17 S 116.40 E
Dalwhinnie 46 56.56 N 4.14 W
Dalworthington Gardens 222 32.42 N 97.10 W
Daly ≃ 164 13.20 S 130.19 E
Daly Bay ⊂ 176 64.00 N 89.40 W
Daly City 226 37.43 N 122.31 W
Daly Lake ◎ 184 56.33 N 105.40 W
Daly Point › 212 44.53 N 80.14 W
Daly River 164 13.45 S 130.50 E
Daly River Aboriginal Reserve ◈[4] 164 14.20 S 130.00 E
Daly Waters 164 16.15 S 133.22 E
Dam ≃ 120 33.56 N 92.41 E
Dāmā, Sūrīy. 132 32.57 N 36.25 E
Dama, Zhg. 100 32.03 N 118.02 E
Damagum 146 11.41 N 11.20 E
Damān 122 20.25 N 72.51 E
Damān □[8] 122 20.10 N 73.00 E
Damanhār Shubra 273c 30.07 N 31.14 E
Damanhūr 142 31.02 N 30.28 E
Damanling 105 40.36 N 115.08 E
Damaopu 104 41.16 N 121.07 E
Damar 130 41.15 N 41.34 E
Damar, Pulau I, Indon. 164 1.00 S 128.24 E
Damar, Pulau I, Indon. 164 7.09 S 128.40 E
Damara 152 4.58 N 18.42 E
Damaraland □[5] 156 21.00 S 14.20 E
Damaraland □[9] 156 22.34 S 17.06 E
Damāṣ, Miṣr 142 30.48 N 31.20 E
Damas → Dimashq, Sūrīy. 132 33.30 N 36.18 E
Damasco → Dimashq 132 33.30 N 36.18 E
Damascus → Dimashq, Sūrīy. 132 33.30 N 36.18 E
Damascus, Ar., U.S. 194 35.22 N 92.24 W
Damascus, Ga., U.S. 192 34.33 N 84.56 W
Damascus, Md., U.S. 208 39.17 N 77.12 W
Damascus, Oh., U.S. 214 40.54 N 80.58 W
Damascus, Pa., U.S. 210 41.42 N 75.04 W
Damascus, Va., U.S. 192 36.38 N 81.47 W
Damascus International Airport ⊠ 132 33.29 N 36.13 E
Damaskus → Dimashq 132 33.30 N 36.18 E
Damāṭ 142 30.57 N 30.57 E
Damaturu 146 11.45 N 11.58 E
Damāvand 128 35.43 N 52.04 E
Damāvand, Qolleh-ye ∧ 128 35.56 N 52.08 E
Damba 152 6.41 S 15.08 E
Dambach-la-Ville 58 48.20 N 7.26 E
Dambarta 150 12.26 N 8.31 E
Dambeck 54 52.48 N 11.09 E
Dambuki 89 54.21 N 127.38 E
Dam Doi 110 8.50 N 105.15 E
Damelevières 58 48.33 N 6.23 E
Damen Dao I 100 27.58 N 121.06 E
Damengjialazi 104 41.04 N 120.53 E
Damengzhuang 105 39.32 N 116.59 E
Damergou ◈[1] 150 15.00 N 8.55 E
Damerham 42 50.57 N 1.52 W
Dämeritzsee ◎ 264a 52.25 N 13.45 E
Damery 50 49.04 N 3.53 E
Dames Quarter 208 38.11 N 75.53 W
Dam Gamad 140 13.17 N 27.28 E
Dāmghān 128 36.09 N 54.22 E
Damianópolis 255 14.33 S 46.10 W
Damianzhen 107 30.36 N 104.10 E
Damiao, Zhg. 98 42.26 N 118.22 E
Damiao, Zhg. 98 34.20 N 117.23 E
Damiao, Zhg. 102 37.18 N 104.39 E
Damiao, Zhg. 104 42.33 N 122.18 E
Damiaochang 107 29.39 N 106.05 E
Damiaogou 104 41.06 N 123.52 E
Damiaojiang 106 31.00 N 120.28 E
Damiaoshang 105 39.56 N 115.12 E
Dămienești 38 46.44 N 26.59 E
Damietta → Dumyāṭ 142 31.25 N 31.48 E
Damietta Branch → Dumyāṭ, Far' ≃ 142 31.32 N 31.51 E
Damietta Mouth → Dumyāṭ, Maṣabb ≃[1] 142 31.32 N 31.51 E
Damin 100 28.56 N 120.29 E
Daming 98 36.19 N 115.06 E
Damingzhen 104 42.34 N 123.36 E
Damintun 104 41.52 N 122.56 E
Dāmiyā 132 32.06 N 35.33 E
Damlacık 130 37.56 N 38.39 E
Damm 263 51.40 N 6.48 E
Dammai Island I 116 5.47 N 120.25 E
Dammarie 50 48.21 N 1.30 E
Dammarie-lès-Lys 50 48.31 N 2.39 E
Dammartin-en-Goële 50 49.03 N 2.41 E
Dammartin-en-Serve 50 48.54 N 1.37 E
Dammastock ∧ 58 46.39 N 8.25 E
Damme, Bel. 50 51.15 N 3.17 E
Damme, Dtsch. 54 53.17 N 14.01 E
Dammer Berge ⋏[2] 52 52.32 N 8.10 E
Dāmodar ≃ 124 22.17 N 88.05 E
Dāmodar Main Canal ≍ 126 23.01 N 87.53 E
Damoh, India 118 23.50 N 79.27 E
Damoh, India 124 23.50 N 79.27 E
Damon 222 29.17 N 95.45 W
Damongo 150 9.05 N 1.49 W
Damotapāda 272c 19.03 N 73.04 E
Damous 34 36.33 N 1.42 E
Damozhuang 105 39.53 N 115.40 E
Dampar, Tasek ◎ 114 3.02 N 102.43 E
Dampelas → Sabang 112 0.11 N 119.51 E
Dampier 162 20.39 S 116.45 E
Dampier, Cape › 164 6.02 S 151.02 E
Dampier, Selat ʯ 164 0.40 S 130.40 E
Dampier Archipelago II 162 20.35 S 116.35 E
Dampier Land ›[1] 162 17.30 S 122.55 E
Dampierre, Fr. 50 48.42 N 1.59 E
Dampierre, Fr. 58 47.09 N 5.45 E
Dampierre, Château de ⊥ 261 48.42 N 1.59 E
Dampierre-en-Burly 50 47.46 N 2.31 E
Dampierre-sur-Linotte 58 47.31 N 6.14 E
Dampierre-sur-Salon 58 47.33 N 5.41 E
Dampier Strait ʯ 164 5.36 S 148.12 E
Dampit 115a 8.13 S 112.45 E
Dampmart 261 48.53 N 2.44 E
Damprichard 58 47.15 N 6.53 E
Dâmrei, Chuŏr Phnum ⋏ 110 11.00 N 104.05 E
Damují ≃ 240p 22.11 N 80.33 W
Damüls 58 47.17 N 9.53 E
Dāmurhuda 126 23.36 N 88.47 E
Damutougou 98 42.28 N 118.56 E
Damville 50 48.52 N 1.04 E
Damvillers 56 49.20 N 5.24 E
Damxung 120 30.31 N 91.08 E
Dan 132 33.14 N 35.39 E
Dan ≃, U.S. 192 36.42 N 78.45 W
Dan ≃, Zhg. 102 33.02 N 111.20 E
Dana, Cam. 146 10.14 N 15.18 E
Dana, In., U.S. 194 39.48 N 87.29 W
Dana, Mount ∧ 226 37.54 N 119.13 W
Dana, Pulau I 112 10.50 S 121.16 E
Danahu 102 42.28 N 93.32 E
Danai 112 0.29 N 103.26 E
Danajon Bank ✥[4] 116 10.16 N 124.17 E
Danakil → Denakil ◈[1] 144 13.00 N 41.00 E
Danakil National Park ♦ 144 10.50 N 40.45 E
Danané 150 7.16 N 8.09 W
Da Nang 110 16.04 N 108.13 E
Danan'gou 105 40.32 N 117.49 E
Danao, Pil. 116 10.32 N 124.02 E
Danao, Pil. 116 12.29 N 122.39 E
Dana Point 228 33.29 N 117.44 W
Dana Point › 228 33.28 N 117.43 W
Dānāpur 124 25.38 N 85.03 E
Danba 102 31.00 N 101.50 E
Danboro 208 40.21 N 75.08 W
Danbury, Eng., U.K. 42 51.44 N 0.33 E
Danbury, Ct., U.S. 207 41.23 N 73.27 W
Danbury, Ia., U.S. 198 42.14 N 95.43 W
Danbury, Ne., U.S. 198 40.02 N 100.24 W
Danbury, N.C., U.S. 192 36.24 N 80.12 W
Danbury, Tx., U.S. 222 29.14 N 95.21 W
Danby Lake ◎ 204 34.14 N 115.07 W
Dancheng 100 33.39 N 115.11 E
Danchengji 100 33.47 N 116.17 E
Dancug 144 10.58 N 49.04 E
Dand 120 31.37 N 65.41 E
Dandaragan 162 30.40 S 115.42 E
Dande ≃ 152 8.28 S 13.21 E
Dandeli 122 15.15 N 74.37 E
Dandenong 169 37.59 S 145.12 E
Dandenong, Mount ∧ 274b 37.50 S 145.21 E
Dandenong Creek ≃ 274b 38.01 S 145.05 E
Dandenong Ranges National Park ♦ 169 37.53 S 145.20 E
Danderyd 40 59.25 N 18.01 E
Dandīl 142 29.10 N 31.02 E
Dandong 98 40.08 N 124.20 E
Dandot 123 32.39 N 72.58 E
Dandridge 192 36.00 N 83.24 W
Dan Dume 150 11.27 N 7.10 E
Dane □[6] 216 43.04 N 89.15 W
Dane ≃ 44 53.15 N 2.31 W
Dane County Regional Airport-Truax Field ⊠ 216 43.08 N 89.20 W
Dänemark → Denmark □[1] 26 56.00 N 10.00 E
Dänemark-Strasse → Denmark Strait ʯ 10 67.00 N 25.00 W
Danevang 222 29.03 N 96.13 W
Danewitz 264a 52.44 N 13.40 E
Danfeng 102 33.40 N 110.17 E
Danfengzhen 102 24.50 N 103.56 E
Danforth, Il., U.S. 216 40.49 N 87.59 W
Danforth, Me., U.S. 188 45.39 N 67.52 W
Danforth Hills ⋏ 200 40.15 N 108.00 W
Dang ≃ 102 40.30 N 94.42 E
Dānga, Bngl. 126 23.54 N 90.36 E
Dānga, India 272b 22.47 N 88.28 E
Danga ≃ 271c 1.27 N 103.43 E
Dangādiha 126 21.30 N 86.19 E
Dangan Liedao II 100 22.00 N 114.14 E
Dangara, Taj. 85 38.06 N 69.22 E
Dangara, Uzb. 85 40.35 N 70.54 E
Dangba 98 40.46 N 118.32 E
Dangchang 102 34.03 N 104.23 E
Dangcheng 98 38.46 N 114.34 E
Dange, Ang. 152 8.09 S 14.46 E
Dange, Ang. 152 7.56 S 15.02 E
Dange, Nig. 150 12.52 N 5.21 E
Dange-Iá-Menha 152 9.32 S 14.39 E
Danger, Point › 171a 28.10 S 153.33 E
Danger Point › 158 34.40 S 19.17 E
Danggali Conservation Park ♦ 166 33.20 S 140.40 E
Danghe Nanshan ⋏ 102 38.53 N 96.11 E
Danghui 105 40.03 N 117.04 E
Dangila 144 11.16 N 36.50 E
Dangkou 106 31.32 N 120.34 E
Dango 140 10.00 N 24.45 E
Dan Gora 150 11.30 N 8.09 E
Dāngori 120 27.40 N 95.32 E
Dangriga 232 16.58 N 88.13 W
Dangshan 98 34.26 N 116.21 E
Dangtu 100 31.34 N 118.30 E
Dan Gulbi 150 11.38 N 6.16 E
Dangyang 102 30.50 N 111.38 E
Dangyu 105 40.00 N 118.01 E
Dani 150 13.43 N 0.10 W
Dania 220 26.03 N 80.08 W
Daniel 200 42.51 N 110.04 W
Daniel, Mount ∧ 224 47.34 N 121.11 W
Daniel Boone Home ⊥ 219 38.39 N 90.52 W
Daniel Boone Homestead State Historic Site ⊥ 208 40.21 N 75.49 W
Daniel-Johnson, Barrage ◈[6] 186 50.39 N 68.44 W
Daniels 284b 39.26 N 77.03 W
Daniel's Harbour 186 50.14 N 57.35 W
Danielskuil 158 28.11 S 23.33 E
Danielson 207 41.48 N 71.53 W
Daniels Pass)(200 40.18 N 111.15 W
Daniels Run ≃ 284c 38.51 N 77.17 W
Danielsville, Ga., U.S. 192 34.07 N 83.13 W
Danielsville, Pa., U.S. 208 40.48 N 75.32 W
Danilov 80 58.12 N 40.12 E
Danilovka, Kaz. 86 52.23 N 70.39 E
Danilovka, Ross. 80 52.33 N 45.23 E
Danilovka, Ross. 80 50.21 N 44.06 E
Danilovo 82 55.40 N 38.46 E
Danilovskaja vozvyšennost' ⋏[1] 80 58.12 N 40.16 E
Danilovskoje 82 56.48 N 35.45 E
Daning, Zhg. 102 24.39 N 111.51 E
Daning, Zhg. 102 36.33 N 110.38 E
Daningbashi 85 38.45 N 75.04 E
Dänisch Nienhof 54 54.28 N 10.07 E
Daniupucun 104 41.23 N 122.37 E
Danja 150 11.21 N 7.31 E
Danjiangkou Shuiku ◎[1] 102 32.37 N 111.30 E
Danjo-guntō II 92 32.02 N 128.23 E
Danjoutin 58 47.37 N 6.52 E
Dank 128 23.33 N 56.17 E
Dankama 150 13.20 N 7.44 E
Dankersen 52 52.17 N 8.58 E
Danki 82 54.55 N 37.34 E
Dankov 76 53.15 N 39.08 E
Dankova, Pik ∧ 85 41.05 N 77.38 E
Danleng, Zhg. 102 29.58 N 103.31 E
Danleng, Zhg. 102 29.18 N 103.10 E
Danleng, Zhg. 107 30.01 N 103.30 E
Danlí 236 14.00 N 86.35 W
Danmark → Denmark □[1] 26 56.00 N 10.00 E
Dannebrog 198 41.07 N 98.32 W
Dannemare 41 54.45 N 11.12 E
Dannemarie 58 47.38 N 7.08 E
Dannemora, Sve. 40 60.11 N 17.49 E
Dannemora, N.Y., U.S. 188 44.43 N 73.43 W
Dannenberg 54 53.06 N 11.05 E
Dannenreich 264a 52.19 N 13.45 E
Dannenwalde 54 53.04 N 13.11 E
Dannevirke 172 40.12 S 176.07 E
Dannewerk 41 54.29 N 9.31 E
Dannhauser 158 28.04 S 30.04 E
Dano 150 11.09 N 3.04 W
Danompari 112 0.09 N 115.02 E
Dañoso, Cabo › 254 48.50 S 67.13 W
Dan Ryan Woods ♦ 278 41.45 N 87.39 W
Dan Sai 110 17.17 N 101.09 E
Danshan 107 30.06 N 104.54 E
Danshui 100 22.49 N 114.27 E
Dansville, Mi., U.S. 216 42.34 N 84.18 W
Dansville, N.Y., U.S. 210 42.33 N 77.41 W
Dāntan 126 21.57 N 87.16 E
Dante 192 36.58 N 82.17 W
Dantewāra 122 18.54 N 81.21 E
Dantuzhen 106 32.12 N 119.31 E
Danube ≃ 22 45.20 N 29.40 E
Danube, Mouths of the ≃[1] 38 45.10 N 29.50 E
Danubio → Danube ≃ 22 45.20 N 29.40 E
Danubyu 110 17.15 N 95.35 E
Danvers, Il., U.S. 190 40.31 N 89.10 W
Danvers, Ma., U.S. 207 42.34 N 70.55 W
Danvers ≃ 283 42.32 N 70.53 W
Danville, P.Q., Can. 206 45.47 N 72.01 W
Danville, Ar., U.S. 194 35.03 N 93.23 W
Danville, Ca., U.S. 226 37.49 N 121.59 W
Danville, Ga., U.S. 192 32.36 N 83.14 W
Danville, Il., U.S. 194 40.07 N 87.37 W
Danville, In., U.S. 218 39.45 N 86.31 W
Danville, Ky., U.S. 194 37.42 N 84.46 W
Danville, Mo., U.S. 219 38.54 N 91.32 W
Danville, Oh., U.S. 214 40.26 N 82.15 W
Danville, Pa., U.S. 210 40.57 N 76.36 W
Danville, Vt., U.S. 188 44.25 N 72.07 W
Danville, Va., U.S. 192 36.35 N 79.23 W
Danville, Wa., U.S. 182 48.59 N 118.30 W
Danxian (Nada) 110 19.35 N 109.17 E
Danyang, Zhg. 100 26.22 N 119.30 E
Danyang, Zhg. 106 32.00 N 119.35 E
Danzig → Gdańsk 30 54.23 N 18.40 E
Dao 116 10.31 N 121.57 E
Dâo ≃, Port. 34 40.20 N 8.11 W
Dao ≃, Zhg. 100 30.44 N 114.39 E
Daocheng 102 29.06 N 100.38 E
Daodemiao 89 43.41 N 120.19 E
Daodi 105 39.32 N 118.11 E
Daoguanhe 100 30.54 N 114.57 E
Daohu 100 29.42 N 117.29 E
Daolazui 105 40.06 N 115.06 E
Daoliban 104 41.52 N 121.37 E
Daolin 100 27.59 N 112.42 E
Daolinggang 98 34.02 N 114.34 E
Daoliupu 107 30.12 N 105.09 E
Daomaguan 98 39.07 N 114.38 E
Daosa 124 26.53 N 76.20 E
Daoshiwu 106 30.18 N 118.57 E
Daoshuqiao 106 31.51 N 119.41 E
Daotiandi 89 48.53 N 130.03 E
Dao Timmi 146 20.32 N 13.33 E
Daotou 98 37.14 N 120.20 E
Daoukro 150 7.03 N 3.58 W
Daoulas 32 48.22 N 4.15 W
Daoura, Oued V 148 28.15 N 3.30 W
Daoxian 102 25.35 N 111.27 E
Daozhen 102 28.42 N 107.56 E
Daozi 89 45.00 N 123.43 E
Dapa 116 9.46 N 126.03 E
Dapango 150 10.52 N 0.12 E
Dapanzhuang 98 37.20 N 115.28 E
Dapaozi 89 45.27 N 122.07 E
Dapchi 146 12.28 N 11.32 E
Dapdap 116 14.14 N 122.15 E
Dapeng 100 22.34 N 114.29 E
Daphne 194 30.36 N 87.54 W
Dapiak, Mount ∧ 116 8.15 N 123.28 E
Daping, Zhg. 100 23.11 N 115.49 E
Daping, Zhg. 100 24.24 N 115.58 E
Dapingshan 102 25.30 N 109.39 E
Dapishi 100 26.30 N 112.54 E
Dapitan 116 8.39 N 123.25 E
Dapitan ≃ 116 8.38 N 123.25 E
Dapitan Bay ⊂ 116 8.40 N 123.23 E
Dapto 170 34.30 S 150.47 E
Dapu, Zhg. 98 40.34 N 124.12 E
Dapu, Zhg. 100 23.16 N 113.32 E
Dapu, Zhg. 106 31.19 N 119.56 E
Dapujie 100 27.01 N 112.46 E
Da Qaidam 102 37.53 N 95.07 E
Da Qaidam Hu ◎ 102 37.50 N 95.00 E
Daqian 106 30.55 N 120.11 E
Daqiangmen 106 31.29 N 120.27 E
Daqiangzi 104 42.21 N 120.29 E
Daqiao, Zhg. 100 29.39 N 121.26 E
Daqiao, Zhg. 100 26.38 N 118.54 E
Daqiao, Zhg. 100 28.11 N 114.16 E
Daqiao, Zhg. 100 32.21 N 119.41 E
Daqiao, Zhg. 100 24.56 N 113.09 E
Daqiao, Zhg. 106 30.59 N 121.14 E
Daqiao, Zhg. 107 28.52 N 105.40 E
Daqiaojie 106 30.46 N 119.14 E
Daqiaokou 100 27.06 N 113.38 E
Daqiaotou 106 30.47 N 120.52 E
Daqiaozhai 102 25.21 N 106.15 E
Daqing 98 39.13 N 118.51 E
Daqing ≃ 105 39.04 N 116.55 E
Daqinggou, Zhg. 98 41.16 N 114.10 E
Daqinggou, Zhg. 98 41.12 N 125.07 E
Daqing Shan ∧, Zhg. 89 45.35 N 127.51 E
Daqing Shan ∧, Zhg. 104 42.03 N 123.45 E
Daqing Shan ∧, Zhg. 104 41.47 N 121.15 E
Daqiu 100 25.24 N 119.39 E
Daqqāq 140 12.56 N 26.58 E
Daquan 102 41.21 N 95.17 E
Daquanshan 98 40.14 N 113.47 E
Daquantou 105 39.31 N 114.46 E
Daquanyan 104 42.37 N 123.32 E
Dāqūf 142 28.24 N 30.38 E
Daqu Shan I 100 30.27 N 122.20 E
Dara, Sén. 150 15.21 N 15.29 W
Dar'ā, Sūrīy. 132 32.37 N 36.06 E
Dar'ā □[8] 132 33.00 N 36.10 E
Dārāb 128 28.45 N 54.34 E
Darāban 120 31.44 N 70.20 E
Darabani 38 48.11 N 26.35 E
Darāfisah 140 13.23 N 31.59 E
Daraga 116 11.54 N 123.52 E
Daragodleh 144 10.10 N 44.51 E
Daraina 157b 13.12 S 49.40 E
Darājīl 142 30.39 N 30.52 E
Daram Island I 116 11.38 N 124.47 E
Dārān 128 32.59 N 50.24 E
Daraoli ◈[8] 272c 19.11 N 72.48 E
Darap 112 1.13 S 112.03 E
Dār as-Salām 273c 29.59 N 31.13 E
Darasun 88 51.40 N 114.00 E
Daraut-Kurgan 85 39.33 N 72.13 E
Darave 272c 19.02 N 73.01 E
Darāw 140 24.25 N 32.56 E
Darawah 142 30.13 N 31.06 E
Dārayyā 132 33.27 N 36.15 E
Darazo 146 11.00 N 10.24 E
Darb Al-Ḥājj 142 30.10 N 31.33 E
Darb al-Ḥajj, Jabal ∧ 132 30.05 N 35.26 E
Darband 123 34.20 N 72.52 E
Darbāsīyah 130 37.04 N 40.39 E
Darbaza 85 41.35 N 69.02 E
Darbėnai 76 56.01 N 21.15 E
Dar-Beni-Kriche-Bahri 34 35.30 N 5.20 W
Darbhanga 124 26.10 N 85.54 E
Darbod (Taikang) 89 46.52 N 124.27 E
D'Arbonne, Bayou ≃ 194 32.34 N 92.09 W
Darburruk 144 9.44 N 44.31 E
Darby, Mt., U.S. 202 46.01 N 114.10 W
Darby, Pa., U.S. 208 39.55 N 75.15 W
Darby, Cape › 180 64.20 N 162.22 W
Darby Creek ≃ 285 39.52 N 75.18 W
Darbydale 218 39.51 N 83.11 W
Darčeli 84 42.27 N 41.42 E
Darchan 88 49.29 N 105.55 E
D'Archiac, Mount ∧ 172 43.28 S 170.35 E
D'Arcy 182 50.33 N 122.29 W
D'Arcy Island I 224 48.34 N 123.17 W
Darda 38 45.37 N 18.41 E
Dardadine 168a 33.14 S 116.50 E
Dardanelle, Ar., U.S. 194 35.13 N 93.09 W
Dardanelle, Ca., U.S. 226 38.20 N 119.50 W
Dardanelle Lake ◎[1] 194 35.25 N 93.20 W
Dardanelles → Çanakkale Boğazı ʯ 130 40.15 N 26.25 E
Dardanup 168a 33.24 S 115.45 E
Dardara 34 35.08 N 5.15 W
Dardenelles Cone ∧ 226 38.25 N 119.53 W
Dardenne Creek ≃ 219 38.52 N 90.32 W
Dardesheim 54 51.59 N 10.49 E
Dardistān □[9] 123 35.30 N 74.00 E
Dare 208 37.10 N 76.26 W
Darebin Creek ≃ 274b 37.47 S 145.02 E
Dareda 154 4.13 S 35.33 E
Dar-el-Beida → Casablanca 148 33.39 N 7.35 W
Darende 130 38.34 N 37.30 E
Darent ≃ 42 51.28 N 0.13 E
Daresbury 262 53.21 N 2.38 W
Dar es Salaam 154 6.48 S 39.17 E
Dar es Salaam □[4] 154 6.30 S 39.25 E
Daressalam → Dar es Salaam 154 6.48 S 39.17 E
Darfeld 52 52.01 N 7.16 E
Darfo 64 45.53 N 10.11 E
Dārfūr ash-Shamālīyah □[4] 140 16.00 N 25.25 E
Dargai 123 34.30 N 71.54 E
Dargan-Ata 72 40.29 N 62.10 E
Dargaville 172 35.56 S 173.53 E
Dargeçit 130 37.33 N 41.44 E
Dargol 150 13.55 N 1.15 E
Dargol ≃ 150 13.53 N 1.33 E
Dargun 54 53.54 N 12.51 E
Darhan Muminggan Lianheqi 102 41.50 N 110.27 E
Dari 140 5.48 N 30.21 E
Dāriāpur 126 23.36 N 89.27 E
Darıca 130 40.45 N 29.23 E
Darie Hills ⋏ 144 8.21 N 47.16 E
Darién, Col. 246 3.56 N 76.31 W
Darien, Ct., U.S. 207 41.04 N 73.28 W
Darien, Ga., U.S. 192 31.22 N 81.26 W
Darien, Il., U.S. 278 41.45 N 87.58 W
Darien, N.Y., U.S. 210 42.54 N 78.21 W
Darien, Wi., U.S. 216 42.36 N 88.42 W
Darien, Parque Nacional ♦ 246 7.40 N 77.40 W
Darién, Serranía del ⋏ 246 8.20 N 77.22 W
Darien Center 210 42.54 N 78.23 W
Darien Lakes State Park ♦ 210 42.55 N 78.25 W
Dariense, Cordillera ⋏ 236 12.55 N 85.30 W
Dariganga 102 45.18 N 113.52 E
Darigayos Point › 116 16.50 N 120.20 E
Dariv 88 46.57 N 93.38 E
Darjevka 83 47.42 N 39.41 E
Dārjiling 124 27.02 N 88.16 E
Darjinskij 86 49.04 N 72.56 E
Darjinskoje 80 51.20 N 51.44 E
Darkan 168a 33.20 S 116.44 E
Darke □[6] 218 40.06 N 84.38 W
Darke Peak 166 33.28 S 136.12 E
Darkhāna 123 30.39 N 72.11 E
Dar Khazīneh 128 31.54 N 48.59 E
Dark Head › 241h 13.17 N 61.16 W
Darkin ≃ 168a 32.00 S 116.14 E
Darkūsh 130 35.59 N 36.23 E
Darlag 102 33.48 N 99.52 E
Darley Woods 285 39.49 N 75.28 W
Darling, S. Afr. 158 33.23 S 18.23 E
Darling, Ms., U.S. 194 34.21 N 90.16 W
Darling ≃ 166 34.07 S 141.55 E
Darling, Lake ◎[1] 198 48.35 N 101.40 W
Darling Downs ◈[1] 166 27.30 S 150.30 E
Darlingford 184 49.12 N 98.22 W
Darling Range ⋏ 162 31.25 S 116.00 E
Darlington, Austl. 169 38.00 S 143.03 E
Darlington, Eng., U.K. 44 54.31 N 1.34 W
Darlington, Md., U.S. 208 39.38 N 76.12 W
Darlington, Pa., U.S. 214 40.49 N 80.26 W
Darlington, Pa., U.S. 285 39.54 N 75.28 W
Darlington, S.C., U.S. 192 34.17 N 79.52 W
Darlington, Wi., U.S. 190 42.40 N 90.07 W
Darlington Brook ≃ 276 41.05 N 74.11 W
Darlington Corners 285 39.55 N 75.34 W
Darlington Range ⋏ 171a 27.50 S 153.15 E
Darlot, Lake ◎ 162 27.48 S 121.35 E
Darłowo 30 54.26 N 16.23 E
Darmagī, Kūh-e ∧ 128 26.35 N 58.54 E
Darmstadt 56 49.53 N 8.40 E
Darmstadt □[5] 56 49.45 N 8.40 E
Darnah 146 32.46 N 22.39 E
Darnall 158 29.23 S 31.18 E
Darnétal 50 49.27 N 1.09 E
Darney 58 48.05 N 6.03 E
Darnick 166 32.51 S 143.37 E
Darnley, Cape › 9 67.43 S 69.30 E
Darnley Bay ⊂ 176 69.35 N 123.30 W
Daroca 34 41.07 N 1.25 W
Darodih 126 23.14 N 86.27 E
Daror 144 8.14 N 44.42 E
Dar-Ould-Zidouh 148 32.22 N 6.49 W
Darou Mousti 150 15.03 N 16.03 W
Darovoje 82 54.34 N 38.22 E
Darr ≃ 166 23.39 S 143.50 E
Darra 171a 27.34 S 152.58 E
Darragh 279b 40.16 N 79.41 W
Darrah, Mount ∧ 182 49.28 N 114.35 W
Darregueira 252 37.42 S 63.10 W
Darreh Gaz 128 37.27 N 59.07 E
Darrington 224 48.15 N 121.36 W
Darrouzett 196 36.27 N 100.20 W
Darryl Gardens 284b 39.25 N 76.25 W
Dārsana 126 23.32 N 88.52 E
Darscheid 56 50.12 N 6.53 E
Darss ›[1] 54 54.25 N 12.31 E
Darsser Ort › 54 54.29 N 12.31 E
Dart ≃ 42 50.20 N 3.33 W
Dart, Cape › 9 73.06 S 126.20 W
Dār Ta'izzah 130 36.17 N 36.51 E
Dartford 42 51.27 N 0.14 E
Dartford □[8] 260 51.26 N 0.15 E
Dartford Tunnel ◈[5] 260 51.28 N 0.16 E
Dartmoor 166 37.55 S 141.17 E
Dartmoor ◈[3] 42 50.35 N 3.55 W
Dartmoor National Park ♦ 42 50.37 N 3.52 W
Dartmouth, N.S., Can. 186 44.40 N 63.34 W
Dartmouth, Eng., U.K. 42 50.21 N 3.35 W
Dartmouth ≃ 186 48.53 N 64.34 W
Dartmouth, Lake ◎ 166 26.04 S 145.18 E
Dartmouth Woods 285 39.50 N 75.31 W
Darton 44 53.36 N 1.32 W
Daru, Pap. N. Gui. 164 9.04 S 143.21 E
Daru, S.L. 150 7.59 N 10.50 W
Daruvar 36 45.36 N 17.13 E
Darvaza 128 40.11 N 58.24 E
Darvazskij chrebet ⋏ 85 38.30 N 71.15 E
Darvel 46 55.37 N 4.18 W
Darvinskij zapovednik ◈[4] 76 58.50 N 37.40 E
Darwāzahgêy 120 31.48 N 67.44 E
Darwen 44 53.42 N 2.28 W
Darwen ≃ 262 53.45 N 2.41 W
Darwendale 154 17.43 S 30.33 E
Dārwha 122 20.19 N 77.46 E
Darwin, Arg. 254 39.12 S 65.46 W
Darwin, Austl. 164 12.28 S 130.50 E
Darwin, Bahía ⊂ 254 45.27 S 74.40 W
Darwin, Cordillera ⋏ 254 54.40 S 70.00 W
Darwin, Isla I 246a 1.39 N 92.00 W
Darwin, Volcán ∧[1] 246a 0.10 S 91.18 W
Darwin River 164 12.49 S 130.58 E
Daryābād 124 26.53 N 81.33 E
Darya Khān 123 31.48 N 71.06 E
Daryāpur 120 20.56 N 77.20 E
Darzāb 120 35.58 N 65.22 E
Darzo 64 45.51 N 10.33 E
Dār Zubi 140 13.07 N 23.40 E
Dās 123 35.05 N 75.05 E
Dās I 128 25.09 N 52.53 E
Dasanjiazi 104 42.31 N 122.54 E
Dašava 78 49.16 N 24.01 E
Daš Balbar 88 49.31 N 114.21 E
Dasburg 56 50.03 N 6.07 E
Dase → Dese 144 11.05 N 39.41 E
Dašev 78 49.00 N 29.26 E
Dasha ≃ 98 38.20 N 115.22 E
Dashafa 105 39.19 N 116.19 E
Dashalitu 104 42.31 N 122.30 E
Dashan 98 38.02 N 117.39 E
Dashankou 105 40.17 N 115.49 E
Dashanpu 107 29.25 N 104.49 E
Dashaping 100 29.24 N 113.51 E
Dashengfenchang 106 31.53 N 121.34 E
Dashengpu 104 41.13 N 121.02 E
Dashentang 105 39.13 N 117.56 E
Dashetai 102 40.58 N 109.19 E
Dashi 107 30.39 N 105.37 E
Dashi ≃ 105 39.35 N 116.05 E
Dashields Dam ◈[6] 214 40.33 N 80.12 W
Dashiqiao, Zhg. 100 33.57 N 113.53 E
Dashiqiao, Zhg. 104 41.52 N 123.17 E
Dashiqiao, Zhg. 107 30.07 N 106.12 E
Dashiqiao, Zhg. 107 30.28 N 106.29 E
Dashitou, Zhg. 89 43.19 N 128.28 E
Dashitou, Zhg. 102 42.49 N 95.19 E
Dashizhai 89 46.16 N 121.25 E
Dashlūṭ 142 27.34 N 30.42 E
Dash Point 224 47.19 N 122.26 W
Dasht ≃ 128 25.10 N 61.40 E
Dashu 106 31.13 N 120.56 E
Dashun 100 28.06 N 119.52 E
Dashutang 102 23.00 N 103.55 E
Dashuwan 105 40.37 N 117.19 E
Dasi (Huangfansi) 102 38.15 N 100.22 E
Dasiji 100 33.48 N 115.55 E
Dašinčilen 88 47.51 N 104.03 E
Dasing 60 48.23 N 11.03 E
Dasizhan 89 45.53 N 130.24 E
Daska 123 32.20 N 74.21 E
Daškesan 84 40.30 N 46.04 E
Daskop 158 33.44 S 22.43 E
Daškovka 76 53.44 N 30.13 E
Dasmina 126 22.17 N 90.35 E
Dasol 116 15.59 N 119.52 E
Dasol Bay ⊂ 116 15.53 N 119.51 E
Dassalan Island I 116 6.45 N 121.28 E
Dassel, Dtsch. 52 51.48 N 9.41 E
Dassel, Mn., U.S. 190 45.04 N 94.18 W
Dasseneiland I 158 33.26 S 18.04 E
Dasserat, Lac ◎ 190 48.16 N 79.25 W
Dassiefontein 158 31.35 S 24.25 E
Dassow 54 53.50 N 10.59 E
Dasswang 60 49.09 N 11.40 E
Dastakert 84 39.23 N 46.02 E
Dastgardān 128 34.19 N 56.51 E
Daštidžum 85 38.01 N 70.12 E
Daštioburdon 85 39.24 N 69.04 E
Dastjerd 128 34.33 N 50.15 E
Dasūa 123 31.49 N 75.38 E
Dāsuria 126 24.07 N 89.08 E
Datachang 107 28.55 N 104.21 E
Datagenoyang 112 2.03 N 115.10 E
Datai 105 39.58 N 115.54 E
Dataizi 104 41.17 N 121.46 E
Datan, Zhg. 98 41.35 N 116.00 E
Datan, Zhg. 98 39.31 N 122.11 E
Datang, Zhg. 100 24.47 N 113.43 E
Datang, Zhg. 100 25.17 N 114.56 E
Datang, Zhg. 102 22.23 N 108.23 E
Datang, Zhg. 102 24.11 N 109.00 E
Datça 130 36.45 N 27.40 E
Datchet 260 51.29 N 0.34 W
Datchet Reservoir ◎[1] 260 51.29 N 0.33 W
Date 92a 42.27 N 140.51 E
Date Creek ≃ 200 34.13 N 113.29 W
Datia 124 25.40 N 78.28 E
Datian, Zhg. 100 25.42 N 117.49 E
Datian, Zhg. 100 24.06 N 116.19 E
Datian Ding ∧ 102 22.17 N 111.13 E
Datianwei 100 25.54 N 115.10 E
Dativli 272c 19.11 N 73.03 E
D'at'kovo 76 53.36 N 34.20 E
D'atlovići 76 52.20 N 26.50 E
D'atlovo, Bela. 76 53.28 N 25.24 E
D'atlovo, Ross. 82 56.14 N 36.16 E
Datong, Zhg. 89 46.03 N 124.50 E
Datong, Zhg. 100 30.48 N 117.45 E
Datong, Zhg. 100 32.50 N 118.52 E
Datong, Zhg. 102 37.03 N 101.45 E
Datong, Zhg. 102 40.05 N 113.18 E
Datong ≃ 102 36.20 N 102.55 E
Datong Shan ⋏ 102 38.00 N 99.30 E
Datongzhen 106 32.12 N 121.19 E
Datoushan 98 41.50 N 117.08 E
Dātra 272b 22.58 N 88.16 E
Datta 89 49.18 N 140.22 E
Dattapāra 126 23.01 N 90.53 E
Dattapukur 126 22.45 N 88.33 E
Dattapulia 126 23.14 N 88.43 E
Datteln 52 51.40 N 7.23 E
Datteln-Hamm-Kanal ≍ 263 51.39 N 7.21 E
Dattilo 70 37.58 N 12.39 E
Datu, Tanjung › 112 2.05 N 109.39 E
Datuan 106 30.58 N 121.44 E
Datumakuta 112 2.32 N 117.51 E
Datun, Zhg. 89 43.49 N 125.12 E
Datun, Zhg. 98 40.37 N 119.57 E
Datun, Zhg. 104 40.59 N 122.55 E
Datuopu 100 28.03 N 112.58 E
Datu Piang 116 7.01 N 124.30 E
Daua (Dawa) ≃ 144 4.11 N 42.06 E
Daudkāndi 126 23.32 N 90.43 E
Dāud Khel 123 32.53 N 71.34 E
Daudnagar 124 25.02 N 84.24 E
Daugai 76 54.22 N 24.20 E
Daugård 41 55.44 N 9.43 E
Daugava (Zapadnaja Dvina) ≃ 76 57.04 N 24.03 E
Daugavpils 76 55.53 N 26.32 E
Dauin 116 9.12 N 123.16 E
Daulatabad 126 24.08 N 88.22 E
Daulatkhān 126 22.38 N 90.49 E
Daulatpur, Bngl. 126 24.00 N 88.52 E
Daulatpur, Bngl. 126 22.53 N 89.31 E
Daulatpur, Bngl. 126 23.58 N 89.50 E
Daulatpur, India 272b 22.26 N 88.18 E
Daulatpur, Pāk. 120 26.30 N 67.58 E
Daulatpur ◈[8] 272a 28.44 N 77.06 E
Daule, Ec. 246 0.24 N 80.00 W
Daule, Ec. 246 1.50 S 79.56 W
Daule, India 272c 19.10 N 73.03 E
Daule ≃ 246 2.10 S 79.52 W
Daultāla 123 33.12 N 73.09 E
Daulton Creek ≃ 226 37.04 N 119.59 W
Daun 56 50.11 N 6.50 E
Daund 122 18.28 N 74.36 E
Daung Kyun I 110 12.14 N 98.05 E
Dauphin, Mb., Can. 184 51.09 N 100.03 W
Dauphin, Pa., U.S. 208 40.22 N 76.55 W
Dauphin □[6] 208 40.15 N 76.52 W
Dauphin ≃ 184 51.58 N 98.04 W
Dauphiné □[9] 62 44.50 N 6.00 E
Dauphin Island 194 30.15 N 88.07 W
Dauphin Island I 194 30.14 N 88.12 W
Dauphin Lake ◎ 184 51.17 N 99.48 W
Daura 150 13.02 N 8.21 E
Daurija 88 49.56 N 116.52 E
Daurskoje 86 55.14 N 92.05 E
Dausenau 56 50.20 N 7.45 E
D'Auteuil, Lac ◎ 186 50.38 N 61.17 W
Dautphetal 56 50.51 N 8.32 E
Dāvangere 122 14.28 N 75.55 E
Davant 194 29.37 N 89.51 W
Davao 116 7.04 N 125.36 E
Davao □[4] 116 7.40 N 125.50 E
Davao ≃ 116 7.04 N 125.37 E
Davao del Sur □[4] 116 6.50 N 125.20 E
Davao Gulf ⊂ 116 6.40 N 125.55 E
Davao Oriental □[4] 116 7.30 N 126.30 E
Dāvar Panāh 128 27.21 N 62.21 E
Dāvarzan 128 36.23 N 56.50 E
Davegoriale 144 8.45 N 44.50 E
Davel 158 26.24 S 29.40 E
Daveluyville 206 46.12 N 72.08 W
Davenda 88 53.33 N 119.18 E
Davenham 262 53.14 N 2.31 W
Davenport, Ca., U.S. 226 37.00 N 122.11 W
Davenport, Fl., U.S. 220 28.09 N 81.36 W
Davenport, Ia., U.S. 190 41.31 N 90.34 W

Symbols in the index entries represent the broad categories identified in the key at the right. Symbols with superior numbers (⋏[1]) identify subcategories (see complete key on page *I · 1)*.

Symbole im Register stellen die rechts im Schlüssel erklärten Kategorien dar. Symbole mit hochgestellten Ziffern (⋏[1]) bezeichnen Unterabteilungen einer Kategorie (vgl. vollständiger Schlüssel auf Seite *I · 1)*.

Los símbolos incluídos en el texto del índice representan las grandes categorías identificadas con la clave a la derecha. Los símbolos con numeros en su parte superior (⋏[1]) identifican las subcategorías (véase la clave completa en la página *I · 1)*.

Les symboles de l'index représentent les catégories indiquées dans la légende à droite. Les symboles suivis d'un indice (⋏[1]) représentent des sous-catégories (voir légende complète à la page *I · 1)*.

Os símbolos incluídos no texto do índice representam as grandes categorias identificadas com a chave à direita. Os símbolos com números em sua parte superior (⋏[1]) identificam as subcategorias (veja-se a chave completa à página *I · 1)*.

Symbol	English	Deutsch	Español	Français	Português
∧	Mountain	Berg	Montaña	Montagne	Montanha
⋏	Mountains	Gebirge	Montañas	Montagnes	Montanhas
)(	Pass	Paß	Paso	Col	Passo
V	Valley, Canyon	Tal, Cañon	Valle, Cañón	Vallée, Canyon	Vale, Canhão
≚	Plain	Ebene	Llano	Plaine	Planície
›	Cape	Kap	Cabo	Cap	Cabo
I	Island	Insel	Isla	Île	Ilha
II	Islands	Inseln	Islas	Îles	Ilhas
⊥	Other Topographic Features	Andere Topographische Objekte	Otros Elementos Topográficos	Autres données topographiques	Outros acidentes topográficos

Nombre / Nom / Nome	Página/Page	Lat.°'	Long.°' W=Oeste/Ouest
Davenport, Ne., U.S.	198	40.18 N	97.48 W
Davenport, N.Y., U.S.	210	42.28 N	74.51 W
Davenport, Ok., U.S.	196	35.42 N	96.45 W
Davenport, Wa., U.S.	202	47.39 N	118.08 W
Davenport, Mount ▲	162	22.23 S	130.51 E
Davenport Downs	166	24.08 S	141.07 E
Davenport Range ✹	162	20.47 S	134.48 E
Daventry	42	52.16 N	1.09 W
Davey, Port ☰	166	43.19 S	145.55 E
Daveyton	273d	26.09 S	28.25 E
David	236	8.26 N	82.26 W
David City	198	41.15 N	97.07 W
Davido-Nikol'skoje	78	52.03 N	27.14 E
Davidov ⊚	83	48.30 N	39.50 E
Davids Island ☰	276	40.53 N	73.46 W
Davidson, Sk., Can.	184	51.16 N	105.59 W
Davidson, N.C., U.S.	192	35.29 N	80.50 W
Davidson, Ok., U.S.	196	34.14 N	99.04 W
Davidson, Mount ▲	170	33.09 S	150.07 E
Davidson Creek ☰	222	30.21 N	96.27 W
Davidson Heights	214	40.35 N	80.15 W
Davidson Lake ⊚	184	53.47 N	99.37 W
Davidson Mountains ✹	180	68.45 N	142.10 W
Davidson Park ✦	274a	33.45 S	151.12 E
Davidsville	214	40.14 N	78.56 W
Davie	220	26.03 N	80.13 W
Davies, Mount ▲	162	26.14 S	129.16 E
Davignab	158	27.32 S	19.48 E
Davila	116	18.29 N	120.35 E
Davilla	222	30.47 N	97.17 W
Davington	46	55.18 N	3.12 W
Davin Lake ⊚	184	56.50 N	103.40 W
Davinópolis	255	15.58 S	50.08 W
Daviot	46	57.25 N	4.08 W
Davis, Ca., U.S.	226	38.32 N	121.44 W
Davis, N.C., U.S.	192	34.47 N	76.27 W
Davis, Ok., U.S.	196	34.30 N	97.07 W
Davis, W.V., U.S.	188	39.07 N	79.27 W
Davis ☰	162	21.42 S	121.05 E
Davis ꞏ³	9	68.35 S	77.58 E
Davis, Mount ▲	188	39.47 N	79.10 W
Davisboro	192	32.58 N	82.36 W
Davisburg	218	42.45 N	83.33 W
Davis City	190	40.38 N	93.48 W
Davis Cove	186	47.40 N	54.18 W
Davis Creek ☰, Mi., U.S.	281	42.27 N	83.43 W
Davis Creek ☰, Mo., U.S.	219	39.12 N	91.53 W
Davis Dam	200	35.10 N	114.33 W
Davis Dam ✦⁶	200	35.11 N	114.21 W
Davis Island ☰	189	40.29 N	80.05 W
Davis Lake ⊚	278	42.16 N	88.05 W
Davis-Monthan Air Force Base ✈	200	32.11 N	110.53 W
Davis Mountains ✹	196	30.35 N	104.00 W
Davison	216	43.02 N	83.31 W
Davis Park	210	40.42 N	72.59 W
Davis Point ▸	282	38.02 N	122.15 W
Davis Sea ꞏ²	9	66.00 S	92.00 E
Davis Strait ⊔	176	67.00 N	57.00 W
Davlekanovo	86	54.13 N	55.03 E
Davo ☰	150	5.00 N	6.08 W
Davoli	58	38.39 N	16.29 E
Davron	210	42.29 N	73.45 W
Davst	86	50.36 N	92.28 E
Davulga	130	38.58 N	31.23 E
Davutlar	130	37.43 N	27.17 E
Davy	192	37.28 N	81.39 W
Davydkovo, Ross.	82	56.17 N	36.49 E
Davydkovo, Ross.	265b	55.51 N	37.12 E
Davydov, gora ▲	88	52.34 N	107.25 E
Davydov Brod	78	46.14 N	33.12 E
Davydovka	78	51.10 N	39.25 E
Davydovo	82	55.37 N	38.52 E
Davydovskoje	82	55.52 N	36.48 E
Dawa, Zhg.	104	41.00 N	122.03 E
Dawa, Zhg.	104	41.54 N	123.32 E
Dawaki	150	12.06 N	8.20 E
Dawan	102	23.52 N	109.29 E
Dawang	98	38.58 N	118.31 E
Dawangcun	108	30.45 N	118.59 E
Dawangdian	105	30.45 N	115.26 E
Dawangdong	105	38.53 N	116.21 E
Dawangjia Dao ☰	98	39.27 N	123.07 E
Dawangsangou	104	41.33 N	121.36 E
Dawangzhai	269b	31.22 N	121.26 E
Dawangzhuang, Zhg.	105	39.23 N	116.28 E
Dawangzhuang, Zhg.	105	38.59 N	115.56 E
Dawāsir, Wādī ad- V	144	20.24 N	45.29 E
Dawatun	144	41.05 N	121.01 E
Dawei (Tavoy)	110	14.05 N	98.12 E
Daweizhuang	105	39.34 N	116.53 E
Daweizigou	104	42.38 N	123.09 E
Dawen ☰	98	35.38 N	116.24 E
Dawenkou	98	35.59 N	117.07 E
Dawera, Pulau ☰	164	7.44 S	130.00 E
Dawes Park ✦	278	42.03 N	87.40 W
Dawlan	110	16.44 N	98.01 E
Dawlish	42	50.35 N	3.28 W
Dawn	208	37.50 N	77.22 W
Dawna Range ✹	110	16.50 N	98.15 E
Dawqah	144	19.36 N	40.54 E
Dawrah	140	12.24 N	44.19 E
Daws Heath	260	51.34 N	0.37 E
Dawson, Yk., Can.	180	64.04 N	139.25 W
Dawson, Ga., U.S.	192	31.46 N	84.26 W
Dawson, Il., U.S.	219	39.51 N	89.28 W
Dawson, Mn., U.S.	198	44.55 N	96.03 W
Dawson, Ne., U.S.	198	40.07 N	95.49 W
Dawson, Tx., U.S.	222	31.53 N	96.42 W
Dawson ☰	166	23.38 S	149.46 E
Dawson, Isla ☰	254	53.55 S	70.45 W
Dawson, Mount ▲	184	51.09 N	117.25 W
Dawson Bay ☰	184	52.55 N	100.50 W
Dawson Creek	184	55.46 N	120.14 W
Dawson Inlet ☰	176	61.50 N	93.25 W
Dawson Range ✹, Austl.	166	24.20 S	149.45 E
Dawson Range ✹, Yk., Can.	180	62.40 N	139.00 W
Dawson Ridge	214	40.42 N	80.22 W
Dawson Springs	194	37.10 N	87.41 W
Dawsonville	192	34.22 N	84.07 W
Dawu, Zhg.	102	31.34 N	114.06 E
Dawu, Zhg.	102	31.07 N	101.08 E
Dawudapu	104	41.36 N	121.05 E
Dawuji	271a	36.11 N	116.30 E
Dawujiawopeng	104	41.55 N	122.29 E
Dawujiazi	104	42.16 N	121.55 E
Dawulah	104	42.13 N	122.23 E
Dawulah	104	42.16 N	121.05 E
Dax	32	43.43 N	1.03 W
Daxian, Zhg.	102	31.18 N	107.30 E
Daxin, Zhg.	102	33.54 N	118.30 E
Daxin, Zhg.	102	22.50 N	107.26 E
Daxing, Zhg.	98	39.44 N	116.20 E
Daxing (Huangcun), Zhg.	105	39.44 N	116.20 E
Daxincun	104	31.50 N	121.40 E
Daxinggou	107	30.17 N	103.26 E
Daxingzhai	102	23.13 N	102.21 E
Daxinji	100	34.03 N	119.28 E
Daxinzhuang, Zhg.	105	40.23 N	116.44 E
Daxinzhuang, Zhg.	105	39.26 N	116.28 E
Daxiyang	108	29.11 N	121.58 E
Daxu, Zhg.	102	29.32 N	121.52 E
Daxu, Zhg.	100	25.09 N	110.21 E
Daxue Shan ✹	102	32.10 N	101.50 E
Daxujia	98	34.18 N	117.34 E
Dayakou	102	22.46 N	100.18 E
Dayang, Zhg.	100	27.41 N	109.55 E
Dayang, Zhg.	98	36.04 N	116.31 E
Dayang, Zhg.	100	31.18 N	118.48 E

Nom	Page	Lat.°'	Long.°'
Dayang ≈	98	39.54 N	123.40 E
Dayang Bunting, Pulau ☰	114	6.14 N	99.48 E
Dayangcha	98	42.04 N	126.43 E
Dayanggou	104	41.14 N	123.51 E
Dayang Shan ☰	106	30.35 N	122.00 E
Dayang, Zhg.	89	49.45 N	124.35 E
Dayao, Zhg.	100	27.59 N	113.42 E
Dayao, Zhg.	102	25.43 N	131.13 E
Dayaoshan	102	24.05 N	110.17 E
Dayboro	171a	27.11 S	152.50 E
Daye	100	30.06 N	114.57 E
Dayghar	272c	19.09 N	73.03 E
Day Heights	218	39.11 N	34.14 W
Dayi	107	30.37 N	103.31 E
Dayiji	100	32.32 N	119.14 E
Daying, Zhg.	98	34.27 N	113.59 E
Daying, Zhg.	98	37.19 N	115.43 E
Daying, Zhg.	98	39.53 N	123.07 E
Daying, Zhg.	98	39.11 N	113.46 E
Daying, Zhg.	100	39.53 N	112.51 E
Daying, Zhg.	105	39.05 N	116.06 E
Daying (Taping), Zhg.	102	24.17 N	97.14 E
Dayingzi, Zhg.	98	41.19 N	118.19 E
Dayingzi, Zhg.	98	41.28 N	120.21 E
Dayingzi, Zhg.	104	41.08 N	122.50 E
Dayiqiao	106	31.44 N	120.45 E
Day Island	224	47.15 N	122.33 W
Day Lake ⊚	224	48.23 N	121.58 W
Daylesford	169	37.21 S	144.09 E
Daymán ☰	252	31.30 S	58.02 W
Daym Zubayr	140	7.43 N	26.13 E
Dayong, Zhg.	100	22.28 N	113.16 E
Dayong, Zhg.	102	29.06 N	110.29 E
Dayou	98	34.12 N	119.52 E
Dayr, Jabal ad- ▲	140	12.27 N	30.42 E
Dayr Abū Sa'īd	132	32.30 N	35.41 E
Dayr al-Balah	132	31.25 N	34.21 E
Dayr al-Ghuṣūn	132	32.21 N	35.05 E
Dayr 'Alī	132	33.17 N	36.18 E
Dayr 'Allā	132	32.12 N	35.37 E
Dayr Birhān	132	34.06 N	36.46 E
Dayr az-Zawr	130	35.20 N	40.09 E
Dayr az-Zawr ꞏ⁸	130	35.00 N	40.39 E
Dayr Dibwān	132	31.55 N	35.16 E
Dayr Ḥāfir	130	36.09 N	37.42 E
Dayr Jabal Aṭ-Ṭayr	142	28.17 N	30.45 E
Dayr Mawās	142	27.38 N	30.51 E
Dayr Qānūn	132	33.36 N	36.08 E
Dayr Sharaf	132	32.15 N	35.11 E
Dayrūṭ, Miṣr	142	27.33 N	30.49 E
Dayrūṭ, Miṣr	142	31.13 N	30.30 E
Dayrūṭ ash-Sharīf	142	27.35 N	30.49 E
Dayr Sulṭān ▸	284b	39.24 N	76.22 W
Daysland	182	52.52 N	112.15 W
Day Star Indian Reserve ◄⁴	182	51.43 N	104.14 W
Dayton, Il., U.S.	216	41.23 N	68.47 W
Dayton, In., U.S.	216	40.22 N	86.46 W
Dayton, Ia., U.S.	190	42.15 N	94.04 W
Dayton, Ky., U.S.	216	39.06 N	84.28 W
Dayton, Nv., U.S.	226	39.14 N	119.35 W
Dayton, N.J., U.S.	276	40.22 N	74.30 W
Dayton, Oh., U.S.	216	39.45 N	84.11 W
Dayton, Or., U.S.	224	45.13 N	123.04 W
Dayton, Pa., U.S.	214	40.52 N	79.14 W
Dayton, Tn., U.S.	194	35.29 N	85.00 W
Dayton, Tx., U.S.	222	30.03 N	94.53 W
Dayton, Va., U.S.	188	38.24 N	78.56 W
Dayton, Wa., U.S.	202	46.19 N	117.58 W
Dayton, Wy., U.S.	202	44.53 N	107.15 W
Daytona Beach	192	29.12 N	81.01 W
Dayton Municipal Airport ✈	218	39.54 N	84.13 W
Dayu, Indon.	112	1.59 S	115.04 E
Dayu, Zhg.	100	25.24 N	114.22 E
Dayu, Zhg.	100	29.15 N	103.34 E
Dayu Ling ✹	100	25.22 N	114.16 E
Da Yunhe (Grand Canal) ☰	90	32.12 N	119.31 E
Dayu Shan ☰, Zhg.	100	26.57 N	120.21 E
Dayu Shan ☰, Zhg.	100	31.21 N	121.58 E
Dayville, Ct., U.S.	207	41.50 N	71.53 W
Dayville, Or., U.S.	202	44.28 N	119.32 W
Dazaifu ☰	96	33.31 N	130.31 E
Dazaoliyingzi	104	42.07 N	121.20 E
Dazaomiao	106	31.20 N	121.29 E
Dazhang ≈	108	25.56 N	119.12 E
Dazhangzi	104	41.14 N	123.03 E
Dazhengjiatun	98	39.37 N	122.52 E
Dazhengzhuangzi	105	39.16 N	116.46 E
Dazhi	98	34.29 N	113.17 E
Dazhou	100	27.09 N	99.52 E
Dazhou ☰	100	28.53 N	118.58 E
Dazhuangke	105	40.48 N	107.12 E
Dazhubao	107	28.59 N	103.48 E
Dazhuyuan	105	23.43 N	115.57 E
Dazifangshen	104	42.11 N	124.12 E
Daziling	104	41.21 N	121.26 E
Daziying	104	41.42 N	123.36 E
Dazu	107	29.53 N	29.52 E
Dazu	107	29.43 N	105.42 E
Dazuo	100	10.16 N	114.02 E
De Aar	158	30.39 S	24.00 E
Dead ☰, Me., U.S.	188	45.20 N	69.58 W
Dead ☰, Mi., U.S.	216	46.20 N	87.24 W
Deadhorse	180	70.11 N	148.27 W
Dead Horse Point State Park ✦	200	38.28 N	109.44 W
Deadman ☰	182	50.45 N	120.55 W
Deadman Brook ☰	276	41.28 N	73.22 W
Deadman Creek ☰	226	37.12 N	120.42 W
Deadman Hill ▲	162	23.48 S	119.25 E
Deadman's Cay	238	23.14 N	75.14 W
Deadmans Creek ◄⁴	182	50.49 N	121.00 W
Deadman's Creek Indian Reserve ◄⁴	182	50.49 N	121.00 W
Dead Sea (Al-Baḥr al-Mayyit) (Yam HaMelaḥ) ⊚	132	31.30 N	35.30 E
Deadwood	198	44.22 N	103.43 W
Deagan Island ☰	116	5.15 N	123.51 E
Deakin	162	30.46 S	128.58 E
Deakin, Mount ▲²	167	17.38 S	130.48 E
Deal	42	51.13 N	1.24 E
Deal, Eng., U.K.	42	68.23 S	150.17 E
Deal, N.J., U.S.	208	40.15 N	74.00 W
Deale	208	38.46 N	76.33 W
Dealesville	158	28.40 S	25.45 E
Deal Island	208	38.09 N	75.56 W
Deal Island ☰	208	38.09 N	75.56 W
Deal Island ⊚¹	169	39.29 S	147.20 E
De'an	99	29.20 N	115.46 E
Dean ☰, B.C., Can.	182	52.50 N	126.57 W
Dean, Eng., U.K.	262	53.13 N	2.11 W
Deansboro	210	43.05 N	75.24 W
Deans Dundas Bay ☰	176	72.15 N	118.25 W
Deanville	222	30.26 N	96.46 W
Dearborn	216	42.19 N	83.11 W
Dearborn ☰	218	39.06 N	84.51 W
Dearborn Heights	218	42.20 N	83.16 W
Dearg, Beinn ▲	46	57.47 N	4.56 W
Dearham	44	54.42 N	3.26 W

Nom	Page	Lat.°'	Long.°'
Dearne ≈	44	53.30 N	1.16 W
Dear Reservoir ⊚¹	44	55.20 N	3.37 W
Dease ≈	180	59.54 N	128.30 W
Dease Arm ☰	180	66.52 N	119.37 W
Dease Lake ⊚	180	58.35 N	130.02 W
Dease Strait ⊔	176	68.40 N	108.00 W
Death Valley	200	36.18 N	116.25 W
Death Valley ✦	204	36.30 N	117.00 W
Death Valley National Monument ✦	204	36.30 N	117.00 W
Deatsville	194	32.36 N	86.23 W
Deauville	50	49.22 N	0.04 E
Deba	146	10.20 N	11.54 E
Debagrām	124	23.41 N	88.18 E
Debal'cevo	83	48.20 N	38.24 E
Debandandapur	272b	22.56 N	88.22 E
Debao	102	23.21 N	106.31 E
Debar	38	41.31 N	20.30 E
De Bary	220	28.53 N	81.18 W
Debauch Mountain ▲	180	64.31 N	159.52 W
Débé	241r	10.12 N	61.27 W
Debed ≈	84	41.22 N	44.58 E
Debenham	42	52.13 N	1.11 E
De Beque	200	39.20 N	108.12 W
De Berry	194	32.36 N	94.10 W
Debesy	80	57.39 N	53.49 E
Debhāta	124	22.33 N	88.58 E
Debica	30	50.04 N	21.24 E
De Bilt	52	52.06 N	5.10 E
Debipur	126	24.14 N	88.38 E
Debir Char	126	22.24 N	90.41 E
Deblin	30	51.35 N	21.50 E
Debno	30	52.45 N	14.40 E
Débo, Lac ⊚	150	15.18 N	4.09 W
Deborah, Mount ▲	180	63.38 N	147.15 W
Deborah West, Lake ⊚	162	30.45 S	119.07 E
Deboyne Islands II	164	10.45 S	152.25 E
Debra	126	22.24 N	87.33 E
Debra Sina	144	9.51 N	39.50 E
Debre Birhan	144	9.40 N	39.33 E
Debrecen	30	47.32 N	21.38 E
Debre Markos	144	10.20 N	37.45 E
Debre May	144	11.19 N	37.30 E
Debre Tabor	144	11.50 N	38.05 E
Debre Zeoit	144	11.50 N	38.40 E
Debre Zeyit	144	8.45 N	38.59 E
Debrzno	30	53.33 N	17.14 E
Debstedt	52	53.37 N	8.38 E
Decatur, Al., U.S.	194	34.36 N	86.59 W
Decatur, Ga., U.S.	192	33.46 N	84.17 W
Decatur, Il., U.S.	219	39.50 N	88.57 W
Decatur, In., U.S.	216	40.50 N	84.56 W
Decatur, Mi., U.S.	216	42.06 N	85.58 W
Decatur, Ms., U.S.	194	32.26 N	89.06 W
Decatur, Ne., U.S.	198	42.00 N	96.14 W
Decatur, Tn., U.S.	193	35.30 N	84.47 W
Decatur, Tx., U.S.	222	33.14 N	97.35 W
Decatur ☰	219	39.50 N	88.52 W
Decatur Island ☰	224	48.31 N	122.50 W
Decatur Municipal Airport ✈	219	39.50 N	88.52 W
Decaturville	194	35.35 N	88.07 W
Deccan ꞏ²	122	17.00 N	78.00 E
Decelles, Réservoir ⊚¹	190	47.42 N	78.08 W
Deception ≈	156	21.04 S	24.25 E
Deception, Mount ▲	224	47.49 N	123.14 W
Deception Bay ☰	171a	27.07 S	153.05 E
Deception Island ☰	184	56.33 N	104.15 W
Deception Pass ☰	224	48.24 N	122.38 W
Deception Pass State Park ✦	224	48.24 N	122.39 W
Dechang	102	27.24 N	102.10 E
Dechäne, La ≈	186	51.15 N	57.51 W
Dechenhönle ± ⁵	263	51.22 N	7.39 E
Decherd	194	35.12 N	86.04 W
Dechhu	120	26.47 N	72.20 E
Déchy	50	50.21 N	3.07 E
Decimomannu	71	39.19 N	8.58 E
Decimoputzu	71	39.20 N	8.55 E
Děčín	54	50.48 N	14.13 E
Decize	32	46.50 N	3.27 E
Decker Lake	182	54.17 N	125.50 W
Decker Lake ⊚¹	222	30.18 N	97.36 W
Deckers Point ▲	214	40.46 N	78.59 W
Deckerville	190	43.31 N	82.44 W
De Cocksdorp	52	53.08 N	4.52 E
Decollatura	58	39.03 N	16.21 E
Decorah	190	43.19 N	91.47 W
Decs	30	46.17 N	18.46 E
Deda	30	46.57 N	24.53 E
Dedaye	110	16.24 N	95.53 E
Deddington	42	51.59 N	1.19 W
Dedegöl Dağlan ✹	130	37.47 N	31.13 E
Dedegöl Tapesi ▲	130	37.39 N	31.17 E
Dedeleben	54	52.02 N	10.54 E
Dedeli	84	39.11 N	43.05 E
Dedelow	52	53.22 N	13.48 E
Dedemsvaart	52	52.36 N	6.28 E
Dederevo	82	56.15 N	37.31 E
Dedesdorf	52	53.30 N	8.30 E
Dedham	207	42.14 N	71.10 W
Dedilovskaja Vyselki	82	54.02 N	38.03 E
Dedinovo	82	55.03 N	39.07 E
Dedo, Cerro ▲	254	45.53 S	71.52 W
Dedo de Deus, Pico ▲	256	22.30 S	43.03 W
De Doorns	158	33.28 S	19.41 E
Dedoplis-Ckaro	84	41.28 N	46.07 E
Dédougou	150	12.28 N	3.28 W
Dedovići	76	57.32 N	29.56 E
Dedovsk	82	55.52 N	37.07 E
Dedza	154	14.22 S	34.20 E
Deduru ≈	122	7.36 N	79.48 E
Dee ≈, Ire.	48	53.52 N	6.21 W
Dee ≈, Eng., U.K.	44	54.18 N	2.32 W
Dee ≈, Scot., U.K.	44	54.50 N	4.03 W
Dee ≈, Scot., U.K.	46	57.08 N	2.04 W
Dee, Loch ⊚	44	55.05 N	4.24 W
Deedsville	216	40.45 N	86.06 W
De Efteling ✦	52	51.39 N	5.02 E
Deeg	124	27.28 N	77.20 E
Deelfontein	158	30.59 S	23.48 E
Deelpan	158	26.19 S	25.36 E
Deenwood	192	31.16 N	82.22 W
Deep ≈, In., U.S.	216	41.34 N	87.17 W
Deep ≈, N.C., U.S.	192	35.36 N	79.03 W
Deepavaal Brook ≈	276	40.53 N	74.16 W
Deep Bay ☰	184	56.25 N	103.00 W
Deep Brook ≈, Ma., U.S.	184	52.30 N	104.04 W
Deep Brook ≈, N.J., U.S.	276	40.58 N	74.09 W
Deep Creek ≈, Austl.	169	37.35 S	144.48 E
Deep Creek ≈, Id., U.S.	202	42.15 N	116.40 W
Deep Creek ≈, Md., U.S.	284b	39.17 N	76.28 W

Nom / Nome	Page	Lat.°'	Long.°'
Deep Creek ≈, Tx., U.S.	222	32.33 N	100.30 W
Deep Creek ≈, Tx., U.S.	196	32.31 N	100.00 W
Deep Creek ≈, Ut., U.S.	200	41.36 N	113.50 W
Deep Creek Conservation Park ✦	168d	35.39 S	138.12 E
Deep Creek Indian Reserve ◄⁴	182	52.16 N	122.07 W
Deeping Fen ≈	42	52.44 N	0.13 W
Deep Red Creek ≈	196	34.17 N	98.39 W
Deep River, On., Can.	190	46.06 N	77.30 W
Deep River, Ct., U.S.	207	41.23 N	72.26 W
Deep River, Ia., U.S.	190	41.34 N	92.22 W
Deep River, Wa., U.S.	224	46.21 N	123.41 W
Deep Run ≈, Md., U.S.	284b	39.13 N	76.42 W
Deep Run ≈, Md., U.S.	284b	39.25 N	76.40 W
Deep Run ≈, N.J., U.S.	276	40.26 N	74.22 W
Deep Run ≈, N.J., U.S.	285	39.44 N	74.41 W
Deepwater, Austl.	166	29.27 S	151.51 E
Deepwater, Mo., U.S.	194	38.15 N	93.46 W
Deep Water, N.J., U.S.	208	39.41 N	75.29 W
Deep Well	162	24.25 S	134.05 E
Deer ≈, N.Y., U.S.	212	43.56 N	74.43 W
Deer Creek, In., U.S.	216	40.37 N	86.23 W
Deer Creek ≈, Mn., U.S.	198	46.23 N	95.19 W
Deer Creek ≈, Ca., U.S.	208	39.37 N	76.09 W
Deer Creek ≈, Ca., U.S.	204	39.56 N	122.04 W
Deer Creek ≈, Il., U.S.	226	39.13 N	121.17 W
Deer Creek ≈, In., U.S.	216	40.34 N	86.41 W
Deer Creek ≈, Ks., U.S.	198	39.40 N	99.06 W
Deer Creek ≈, Ms., U.S.	194	32.33 N	90.47 W
Deer Creek ≈, Ne., U.S.	198	40.28 N	100.00 W
Deer Creek ≈, Oh., U.S.	216	39.27 N	83.00 W
Deer Creek ≈, Ok., U.S.	196	35.38 N	98.28 W
Deer Creek ≈, Or., U.S.	224	45.58 N	123.15 W
Deer Creek ≈, Pa., U.S.	279b	40.32 N	79.51 W
Deer Creek ≈, Wa., U.S.	224	48.16 N	121.55 W
Deer Creek ≈, Wy., U.S.	200	42.52 N	105.52 W
Deer Creek Indian Reservation ◄⁴	192	57.50 N	93.25 W
Deer Creek Lake ⊚	218	39.40 N	83.15 W
Deerfield, Il., U.S.	216	42.10 N	87.50 W
Deerfield, Ks., U.S.	198	37.58 N	101.07 W
Deerfield, Ma., U.S.	207	42.32 N	72.37 W
Deerfield, Mi., U.S.	216	41.53 N	83.46 W
Deerfield, Oh., U.S.	216	41.01 N	81.03 W
Deerfield, Wi., U.S.	216	43.03 N	89.04 W
Deerfield ≈	207	42.35 N	72.35 W
Deerfield Beach	220	26.19 N	80.06 W
Deerfield Street	208	39.31 N	75.14 W
Deer Harbor	224	48.37 N	123.00 W
Deering, Mount ▲²	162	24.53 S	129.04 E
Deer Island ꞏ³	283	42.21 N	70.58 W
Deer Island, N.B., Can.	188	45.00 N	66.57 W
Deer Island ☰, Ak., U.S.	180	54.53 N	162.25 W
Deer Isle	188	44.13 N	68.40 W
Deer Lake, Nf., Can.	186	49.10 N	57.26 W
Deer Lake ≈, Nf., Can.	186	49.10 N	57.26 W
Deer Lakes Regional Park ✦	279b	40.38 N	79.49 W
Deerlijk	50	50.51 N	3.21 E
Deer Lodge	202	46.24 N	112.44 W
Deer Mountain ▲	188	45.10 N	70.56 W
Deer Park, Austl.	174b	37.47 S	144.47 E
Deer Park, Ca., U.S.	226	38.32 N	122.28 W
Deer Park, Il., U.S.	278	42.10 N	88.04 W
Deer Park, N.Y., U.S.	276	40.45 N	73.19 W
Deer Park, Tx., U.S.	222	29.42 N	95.07 W
Deer Park, Wa., U.S.	202	47.57 N	117.28 W
Deer Park Airport ✈	279a	28.33 N	77.11 E
Deerpass Bay ☰	182	65.56 N	122.25 W
Deer Pond ≈, Nf., Can.	186	48.30 N	54.45 W
Deer Pond ≈, N.Y., U.S.	210	42.17 N	74.55 W
Deer Ridge ≈	278	42.50 N	88.24 W
Deer Sound ☰	46	58.58 N	2.48 W
Deersville	214	40.17 N	81.11 W
Deer Trail	198	39.36 N	104.02 W
Deerwood	190	46.28 N	93.53 W
Dee Why	170	33.45 S	151.17 E
Dee Why Head ▸	274a	33.45 S	151.18 E
Deex Nugaaleed V	148	7.48 N	49.51 E
Defengzhuang	105	40.55 N	122.25 E
Defereggen Alpen ✹	60	46.55 N	12.15 E
Deferiet	212	44.02 N	75.41 W
Defiance, Ia., U.S.	198	41.49 N	95.20 W
Defiance, Oh., U.S.	216	41.17 N	84.21 W
Defiance, Pa., U.S.	214	40.10 N	78.14 W
Defiance, Mount ▲	224	45.38 N	121.43 W
Defiance Plateau ꞏ¹	200	36.00 N	109.15 W
De Forest	190	43.14 N	89.20 W
Deer Creek Lake ⊚	276	41.06 N	73.22 W
Defu	271c	1.21 N	103.54 E
De Funiak Springs	194	30.43 N	86.06 W
Deganga	272b	22.41 N	88.41 E
Deganwy	44	53.17 N	3.50 W
Dêgê	102	31.50 N	98.40 E
Degeberga	26	55.50 N	14.05 E
Degeh Bur	144	8.13 N	43.34 E
Dégelis (Sainte-Rose-du-Dégelis)	186	47.33 N	68.39 W
Degerfors	24	59.14 N	14.26 E
Degerhamn	26	56.21 N	16.24 E
Deggendorf	64	48.51 N	12.59 E
Deggingen	64	48.34 N	9.45 E

Nome	Página	Lat.°'	Long.°'
Değirmenlik	130	35.15 N	33.29 E
Deglunden ⊚	40	60.05 N	13.49 E
Dego	62	44.27 N	8.19 E
Degollado	234	20.28 N	102.09 W
Degoma ≈	144	12.28 N	37.37 E
Degong	114	4.05 N	101.08 E
De Graafschap ◄¹	52	52.00 N	6.30 E
De Graff	216	40.18 N	83.54 W
De Gray Lake ⊚¹	194	34.15 N	93.15 W
De Grey	162	20.10 S	119.12 E
De Grey ≈	162	20.12 S	119.11 E
Degt'ari	78	50.35 N	32.45 E
Degt'arka ≈	265a	59.57 N	30.52 E
Degunino ꞏ⁸	265b	55.52 N	37.33 E
De Haan	50	51.16 N	3.02 E
Dehak ≈	128	32.01 N	58.35 E
Dehalak Deset ☰	144	15.45 N	40.05 E
Deharda	126	21.40 N	87.25 E
De Hart Reservoir ⊚¹	208	40.58 N	74.35 W
Deh Bālā	123	34.04 N	70.29 E
Deh Bīd	128	30.38 N	53.13 E
Dehdez	128	31.43 N	50.17 E
Deh-e Salm	128	31.12 N	59.19 E
Dehgolān	128	35.17 N	47.25 E
Dehibat	148	32.01 N	10.42 E
Dehiwala-Mount Lavinia	122	6.51 N	79.52 E
Deh Kord	128	32.49 N	49.53 E
Dehlorān	128	32.41 N	47.16 E
De Hoek	158	32.57 S	18.45 E
Dehpehk ☰	174r	6.57 N	158.18 E
Dehra Dūn	124	30.19 N	78.02 E
Dehri	124	24.52 N	84.11 E
Dehu	122	18.35 N	73.10 E
Dehua	98	25.32 N	118.15 E
Dehuang	98	35.12 N	114.25 E
Dehui	89	44.34 N	125.43 E
Deidesheim	56	49.24 N	8.11 E
Deilbach ≈	263	51.23 N	7.05 E
Deilinghofen	56	51.22 N	7.47 E
Deining	60	49.13 N	11.32 E
Deinze	50	50.59 N	3.32 E
Deir el Asad	132	32.56 N	35.16 E
Deister ✹	52	52.15 N	9.30 E
Deiva Marina	62	44.13 N	9.30 E
Dej	38	47.09 N	23.52 E
Dejima	94	36.05 N	140.20 E
Dejnau	128	39.13 N	63.11 E
Deka ≈	154	18.04 S	26.42 E
De Kalb, Il., U.S.	216	41.55 N	88.45 W
De Kalb, Ms., U.S.	194	32.46 N	88.39 W
De Kalb, Tx., U.S.	194	33.30 N	94.36 W
De Kalb ꞏ⁶, In., U.S.	216	41.59 N	85.41 W
De Kalb Junction	212	44.30 N	75.16 W
Dekan, Hochland von — Deccan ꞏ²	122	17.00 N	78.00 E
De-Kastri	89	51.28 N	140.47 E
Dekehtik ☰	174r	7.00 N	158.12 E
Dekemhare	144	15.05 N	39.02 E
Dekese	152	3.27 S	21.24 E
Deke Sokehs ☰	174r	6.59 N	158.11 E
Dekhgila Military Base ≈	142	31.08 N	29.48 E
Dexina	150	7.39 N	7.02 E
Dékoa	152	6.19 N	19.04 E
De Koog	52	53.05 N	4.45 E
De Krim	52	52.38 N	6.38 E
De La Blanche, Lac ⊚	186	50.05 N	69.29 W
Delabole	42	50.38 N	4.42 W
Delafield	216	43.03 N	88.24 W
Del Aire	280	33.55 N	118.21 W

Nome	Página	Lat.°'	Long.°'
Delburne	182	52.12 N	113.14 W
Delcambre	194	29.57 N	91.59 W
Del Campillo	252	34.22 S	64.29 W
Del Carril	258	35.31 S	59.30 W
Del Dios	280	33.04 N	117.08 W
Delegate	166	37.03 S	148.58 E
Délembé	146	9.53 N	22.37 E
Delémont	58	47.22 N	7.21 E
De Leon	196	32.06 N	98.32 W
De Leon Springs	192	29.07 N	81.21 W
Delet	26	60.15 N	20.35 E
Delfin Moreira	256	22.30 S	45.17 E
Delfinópolis	256	20.20 S	46.51 W
Delft	52	52.00 N	4.21 E
Delft Island ☰	122	9.30 N	79.42 E
Delfzijl	52	53.19 N	6.46 E
Delgada, Punta ▸	254	46.46 S	63.38 W
Delgado, Cabo ▸	154	10.40 S	40.35 E
Delgerhaan	88	45.50 N	101.00 E
Delgerchangai	102	45.15 N	104.50 E
Delgerhet	102	45.52 N	110.26 E
Delgereogt	102	46.08 N	106.23 E
Delger nuur ⊚	88	49.18 N	111.12 E
Delger Haven	208	39.03 N	74.56 W
Delhi, On., Can.	212	42.51 N	80.30 W
Delhi, India	124	28.40 N	77.13 E
Delhi, India	272a	28.40 N	77.13 E
Delhi, Il., U.S.	219	39.03 N	90.15 W
Delhi, La., U.S.	190	32.27 N	91.29 W
Delhi, N.Y., U.S.	210	42.16 N	74.54 W
Delhi Cantonment	272a	28.36 N	77.08 E
Delhi Hills	218	39.05 N	84.36 W
Delhi Railroad Station	272a	28.40 N	77.13 E
Delhi Tai Distributary ≈	272a	28.41 N	77.10 E
Delhi University ꞏ²	272a	28.42 N	77.13 E
Deli, Pulau ☰	115a	7.00 S	105.32 E
Delia, Ab., Can.	182	51.38 N	112.23 W
Delia, It.	70	37.21 N	13.55 E
Delice	130	37.38 N	12.37 E
Delice ≈	88	38.14 N	15.55 E
Deliblato	38	44.50 N	21.03 E
Delicias, Cuba	232	21.16 N	76.34 W
Delicias, Méx.	230	28.13 N	105.28 W
De Lier	52	51.57 N	4.15 E
Delight	214	34.01 N	93.30 W
Delitzsch	54	51.32 N	12.20 E
Dell City	200	31.56 N	105.12 W
Delle	58	47.30 N	7.00 E
Dellenbaugh, Mount ▲	200	36.07 N	113.32 W

Symbol	ESPAÑOL	Fluß/FRANÇAIS	Río	Rivière	Rio
≈	River	Fluß	Río	Rivière	Rio
≈	Canal	Kanal	Canal	Canal	Canal
⌄	Waterfall, Rapids	Wasserfall, Stromschnellen	Cascada, Rápidos	Chute d'eau, Rapides	Cascata, Rápidos
⊔	Strait	Meeresstraße	Estrecho	Détroit	Estreito
c	Bay, Gulf	Bucht, Golf	Bahía, Golfo	Baie, Golfe	Baía, Golfo
≤	Lake, Lakes	See, Seen	Lago, Lagos	Lac, Lacs	Lago, Lagos
⧖	Swamp	Sumpf	Pantano	Marais	Pântano
⧉	Ice Features, Glacier	Eis- und Glatscherformen	Accidentes Glaciares	Formes glaciaires	Acidentes glaciares
▽	Other Hydrographic Features	Andere Hydrographische Objekte	Otros Elementos Hidrográficos	Autres données hydrographiques	Outros acidentes hidrográficos
►	Submarine Features	Untermeerische Objekte	Accidentes Submarinos	Formes de relief sous-marin	Acidentes submarinos
□	Political Unit	Politische Einheit	Unidad Política	Entité politique	Unidade política
⌂	Historical Site	Historische Stätte	Institución Cultural	Institution culturelle	Sítio histórico
★	Recreational Site	Erholungs- und Ferienort	Sitio de Recreo	Centre de loisirs	Área de Lazer
✈	Airport	Flughafen	Aeropuerto	Aéroport	Aeroporto
⊩	Military Installation	Militäranlage	Instalación Militar	Installation militaire	Instalação militar
►	Miscellaneous	Verschiedenes	Misceláneo	Divers	Diversos

ENGLISH / DEUTSCH

Name	Page	Lat.°′	Long.°′
Delta City	194	33.04 N	90.47 W
Delta Downs	166	17.00 S	141.18 E
Delta Junction	180	64.02 N	145.41 W
Delta Mendota Canal ≊	226	37.49 N	121.34 W
Delta Peak ∧	180	56.39 N	129.34 W
Delta Reservoir ⊜[1]	210	43.17 N	75.26 W
Deltaville	208	37.33 N	76.20 W
Delton	216	42.29 N	85.24 W
Deltona	220	28.54 N	81.15 W
Delungra	166	29.39 S	150.50 E
Del'un-Uranskij chrebet ⋀	88	56.30 N	114.00 E
Delüün	86	47.42 N	90.59 E
De Luz Creek ≃	228	33.22 N	117.19 W
Del Valle	222	30.12 N	97.40 W
Del Valle, Lake ⊜[1]	226	37.35 N	121.43 W
Del Verme Falls ∟	144	5.27 N	40.17 E
Delvin	48	53.36 N	7.05 W
Delvinë	38	39.57 N	20.06 E
Del Viso	258	34.27 S	58.48 W
Delyn □[8]	262	53.16 N	3.11 W
Demak	115a	6.53 S	110.38 E
Demaki	80	58.26 N	51.43 E
Dem'ansk	76	57.38 N	32.28 E
Demarcation Point ≻	180	69.40 N	141.15 W
Demarest	276	40.57 N	73.57 W
Demarest Brook ≃	276	40.57 N	73.58 W
Demavend, Mount → Damāvand, Qolleh-ye ∧	128	35.56 N	52.08 E
Demba	152	5.30 S	22.16 E
Demba Chio	152	9.41 S	13.41 E
Dembecha	144	10.35 N	37.30 E
Dembéni	157a	11.50 S	43.24 E
Dembi	144	8.05 N	36.27 E
Dembia, Centraf.	154	5.07 N	24.25 E
Dembia, Zaïre	154	3.31 N	25.50 E
Dembi Dolo	144	8.32 N	34.48 E
Dembo	152	3.56 S	12.35 E
Dême ≃	50	47.43 N	0.29 E
Demer ≃	56	50.58 N	4.42 E
Demerara ≃	246	6.48 N	58.10 W
Demerara-Mahaica □[4]	246	6.40 N	58.00 W
Demerthin	54	52.58 N	12.17 E
Demidov	76	55.16 N	31.31 E
Demidovka	78	50.25 N	25.20 E
Demidovo	76	59.17 N	38.17 E
Deming, N.M., U.S.	200	32.16 N	107.45 W
Deming, Wa., U.S.	224	48.49 N	122.12 W
Demini ≃	246	0.46 S	62.56 W
Demirci	130	39.03 N	28.40 E
Demirköprü Barajı ⊜[1]	130	38.40 N	28.20 E
Demirköy	130	41.49 N	27.45 E
Demirtaş	130	40.16 N	29.06 E
Demitz-Thumitz	54	51.09 N	14.14 E
Demjanka ≃	86	59.34 N	69.20 E
Demjanovo	24	60.22 N	47.03 E
Demjanskoje	86	59.36 N	69.18 E
Demjas	80	51.13 N	49.08 E
Demmeltrath -◆-[8]	263	51.11 N	7.03 E
Demmin	54	53.54 N	13.02 E
Demmitt	182	55.26 N	119.54 W
Demnate	148	31.44 N	6.59 W
Democracy Monument ⊥	269a	13.45 N	100.30 E
Democrat Point ≻	276	40.37 N	73.18 W
Demoiselles, Grotte des ⊥[5]	62	43.55 N	3.45 E
Demone, Val -◆-[1]	70	37.58 N	14.35 E
Demonte	62	44.19 N	7.17 E
De Montigny, Lac ⊜	190	48.08 N	77.54 W
Demopolis	194	32.31 N	87.50 W
Demorest	192	34.33 N	83.32 W
De Mossville	218	38.48 N	84.25 W
Demotte	216	41.12 N	87.12 W
Dempo, Gunung ∧	112	4.02 S	103.09 E
Dempster, Point ≻	162	33.39 S	123.52 E
Demsa	146	9.32 N	13.14 E
Demta	164	2.20 S	140.08 E
Demurino	78	48.10 N	36.29 E
De Naauwte	158	30.08 S	21.42 E
Denain	50	50.20 N	3.23 E
Denair	226	37.32 N	120.47 W
Denakil -◆-[1]	144	13.00 N	41.00 E
Denali	180	63.11 N	147.28 W
Denali National Park	180	63.44 N	148.54 W
Denali National Park ♠	180	63.15 N	150.30 W
Denan	144	6.30 N	43.30 E
Denare Beach	184	54.40 N	102.05 W
Denau	85	38.16 N	67.54 E
Denbigh, On., Can.	212	45.08 N	77.16 W
Denbigh, Wales, U.K.	44	53.11 N	3.25 W
Denbigh, Cape ≻	180	64.23 N	161.31 W
Den Burg	52	53.03 N	4.48 E
Denby Dale	44	53.35 N	1.38 W
Den Chai	110	17.59 N	100.04 E
Dendang	112	3.05 S	107.54 E
Dender (Dendre) ≃	50	51.02 N	4.06 E
Denderleeuw	50	50.53 N	4.04 E
Dendermonde	50	51.02 N	4.07 E
Dendre (Dender) ≃	50	51.02 N	4.06 E
Dendron, S. Afr.	156	23.25 S	29.11 E
Dendron, Va., U.S.	208	37.02 N	76.56 W
Dendy Park ♠	274b	37.56 S	145.00 E
Deneba	144	9.50 N	39.09 E
Denekamp	52	52.23 N	7.00 E
Denenchōfu -◆-[8]	268	35.35 N	139.41 E
Deneysville	158	26.53 S	28.06 E
Denežnikovo, Ross.	82	55.26 N	38.07 E
Denežnikovo, Ukr.	83	49.02 N	38.57 E
Dengcheng	100	33.41 N	114.27 E
Deng Deng	152	5.12 N	13.31 E
Denge	154	3.34 N	28.14 E
Denge Marsh ≡	42	50.57 N	0.55 E
Dengfeng	100	34.29 N	113.04 E
Denggongchang	107	30.24 N	103.49 E
Dengguanzhen	107	29.10 N	104.56 E
Dengkou	102	40.20 N	106.59 E
Denglongshu	98	41.20 N	115.15 E
Dengmingsi	98	37.53 N	116.42 E
Dêngqên	102	31.32 N	95.27 E
Dengshahe	98	39.13 N	122.04 E
Dengta	100	24.01 N	114.49 E
Denguiro	152	5.38 N	23.02 E
Dengxian	102	32.42 N	112.01 E
Dengyoufang	98	41.34 N	114.32 E
Den Haag → 's-Gravenhage	52	52.06 N	4.18 E
Denham, Austl.	162	25.55 S	113.32 E
Denham, Eng., U.K.	260	51.34 N	0.30 W
Denham, In., U.S.	216	41.09 N	86.43 W
Denham, Mount ∧	241q	18.13 N	77.32 W
Denham Aerodrome ⊠	260	51.36 N	0.31 W
Denham Island I	166	16.43 S	139.09 E
Denham Place υ	260	51.34 N	0.30 W
Denham Range ⋀	166	21.55 S	147.46 E
Denham Sound ʉ	162	25.40 S	113.15 E
Denham Springs	194	30.29 N	90.57 W
Den Helder	52	52.54 N	4.45 E
Denholme	262	53.48 N	1.54 W
Dénia	34	38.51 N	0.07 E
Denial Bay	162	32.06 S	133.32 E
Dénié	150	11.14 N	7.29 W
Deniliquin	166	35.32 S	144.58 E
Deniskoviči, Bela.	76	52.44 N	26.41 E
Deniskoviči, Ross.	76	52.19 N	31.43 E
Denison, Ia., U.S.	198	42.01 N	95.21 W
Denison, Tx., U.S.	196	33.45 N	96.32 W
Denison, Mount ∧	180	58.25 N	154.27 W
Denison Dam -◆-[6]	196	33.50 N	96.34 W
Denisovka	24	66.14 N	55.20 E
Denisōvo	82	54.28 N	37.51 E
Denisy	261	48.33 N	1.56 E
Denizli	130	37.46 N	29.06 E
Denizli □[4]	130	37.40 N	29.15 E
Denkanikota	122	12.32 N	77.48 E
Denkendorf	60	48.56 N	11.27 E
Denkingen	58	47.53 N	9.19 E
Denklingen, Dtsch.	56	50.55 N	7.39 E
Denklingen, Dtsch.	58	47.55 N	10.51 E
Den'kovo	82	56.01 N	36.21 E
Denmark, Austl.	162	34.57 S	117.21 E
Denmark, S.C., U.S.	192	33.19 N	81.08 W
Denmark, Wi., U.S.	190	44.20 N	87.49 W
Denmark (Danmark) □[1], Europe	22	56.00 N	10.00 E
Denmark (Danmark) □[1], Europe	26	56.00 N	10.00 E
Denmark, Lake ⊜	276	40.58 N	74.31 W
Denmark Bay ⊂	176	70.33 N	103.20 W
Denmark Strait ʉ	10	67.00 N	25.00 W
Denmead	42	50.54 N	1.04 W
Dennemont	261	49.01 N	1.42 E
Dennery	241f	13.55 N	60.54 W
Dennis	207	41.44 N	70.11 W
Dennis Head ≻	46	59.23 N	2.23 W
Dennison	214	40.23 N	81.20 W
Dennis Port	207	41.39 N	70.07 W
Denniston	172	41.44 S	171.48 E
Denniston Creek ≃	282	37.30 N	122.28 W
Dennisville	208	39.11 N	74.49 W
Denny	46	56.02 N	3.55 W
Den Oever	52	52.56 N	5.02 E
Denouval	261	48.58 N	2.03 E
Denpasar	115b	8.39 S	115.13 E
Denshaw	262	53.35 N	2.02 W
Dent Ditch ≊	279a	41.18 N	82.08 W
Denton, Eng., U.K.	44	53.27 N	2.07 W
Denton, Md., U.S.	208	38.53 N	75.49 W
Denton, Mi., U.S.	281	42.20 N	83.03 W
Denton, Mt., U.S.	202	47.19 N	109.56 W
Denton, N.C., U.S.	192	35.38 N	80.06 W
Denton, Tx., U.S.	222	33.12 N	97.07 W
Denton □[6]	222	33.07 N	97.10 W
Denton Creek ≃	196	32.58 N	96.57 W
Dentonia Park ♠	275b	43.42 N	79.17 W
D'Entrecasteaux, Point ≻	162	34.50 S	116.00 E
D'Entrecasteaux Islands II	164	9.30 S	150.40 E
D'Entrecasteaux National Park ♠	162	34.41 S	115.58 E
Dents du Midi ⋀	58	46.10 N	6.56 E
Denver, Co., U.S.	200	39.44 N	104.59 W
Denver, In., U.S.	216	40.51 N	86.04 W
Denver, Ia., U.S.	190	42.40 N	92.20 W
Denver, Pa., U.S.	208	40.13 N	76.08 W
Denver City	196	32.57 N	102.49 W
Denville	210	40.53 N	74.28 W
Denzlingen	58	48.04 N	7.52 E
Deoband	124	29.42 N	77.41 E
Deocha	126	24.03 N	87.35 E
Deodoro -◆-[8]	287a	22.51 S	43.23 W
Deogarh, India	120	25.32 N	73.54 E
Deogarh, India	122	21.32 N	84.44 E
Deogarh, India	124	24.33 N	78.15 E
Deogarh ∧	124	23.32 N	82.16 E
Deogarh Hills ⋀[2]	124	23.35 N	82.30 E
Deoghar	124	24.29 N	86.42 E
Deogsu Palace υ	271b	37.35 N	126.58 E
Deolāli	122	19.57 N	73.50 E
Deoli	126	22.03 N	86.49 E
Deoli -◆-[8]	272a	28.30 N	77.14 E
Deongwar, Mount ∧	171a	27.12 S	152.16 E
Deopāra	126	22.55 N	90.15 E
Deori, India	124	23.08 N	78.41 E
Deori, India	124	23.24 N	79.01 E
Deoria	124	26.31 N	83.47 E
Deosai Mountains ⋀	123	35.20 N	75.12 E
Deosil	124	23.42 N	82.15 E
Dep ≃	89	52.54 N	127.45 E
Depāl	126	21.44 N	87.33 E
De Panne	50	51.06 N	2.35 E
Depāra	272b	22.53 N	88.34 E
Departure Bay	224	49.12 N	123.58 W
DePaul University υ[2]	278	41.56 N	87.39 W
Depauville	212	44.08 N	76.04 W
Depauw	218	38.20 N	86.13 W
De Peel ≡	52	51.25 N	6.00 E
De Pere	190	44.26 N	88.03 W
Depew, N.Y., U.S.	210	42.54 N	78.41 W
Depew, Ok., U.S.	196	35.48 N	96.30 W
Deping	98	37.28 N	116.57 E
De Pinte	50	51.00 N	3.39 E
Depoe Bay	202	44.48 N	124.03 W
Depok	115a	6.24 S	106.50 E
Deport	196	33.32 N	95.19 W
Deposit	210	42.03 N	75.25 W
Deptford	285	39.50 N	75.07 W
Deptford -◆-[8]	260	51.28 N	0.02 W
Deptford Mall -◆-[9]	285	39.50 N	75.06 W
Deptford Terrace	285	39.48 N	75.09 W
Depuch Island I	162	20.38 S	117.43 E
Depue	190	41.19 N	89.18 W
Deputy	218	38.48 N	85.39 W
Dêqên	102	28.38 N	98.52 E
Deqing, Zhg.	102	23.09 N	111.45 E
Deqing, Zhg.	106	30.33 N	120.05 E
De Queen	194	34.02 N	94.20 W
De Quincy	194	30.27 N	93.25 W
Dera ≃	264c	47.39 N	19.05 E
Dera, Lach (Lak Dera) V	144	0.35 N	41.50 E
Dera Bugti	120	29.02 N	69.09 E
Dera Ghāzi Khān	123	30.03 N	70.38 E
Dera Gopipur	123	31.54 N	76.13 E
Dera Ismāīl Khān	123	31.50 N	70.54 E
Derakht-e Yaḥyá	120	31.50 N	68.08 E
Dera Nānak	123	32.02 N	75.01 E
Dera Nawāb	123	29.06 N	71.16 E
Derāwar Fort	123	28.46 N	71.20 E
Deražn'a	78	49.16 N	27.26 E
Derbent	84	42.03 N	48.18 E
Derbeškinskij	80	55.52 N	53.30 E
Derbetovka	80	45.48 N	43.05 E
Der Bodden ʉ	54	54.16 N	13.12 E
Derby, Austl.	162	17.18 S	123.38 E
Derby, Austl.	166	41.09 S	147.47 E
Derby, S. Afr.	158	25.55 S	27.02 E
Derby, Eng., U.K.	42	52.55 N	1.29 W
Derby, Ct., U.S.	207	41.19 N	73.05 W
Derby, Ks., U.S.	198	37.32 N	97.16 W
Derby, Me., U.S.	188	45.14 N	68.58 W
Derby, N.Y., U.S.	210	42.40 N	78.58 W
Derby, Oh., U.S.	218	39.46 N	83.12 W
Derby, Vt., U.S.	206	44.57 N	72.08 W
Derby Acres	226	35.15 N	119.35 W
Derby Line	206	45.00 N	72.05 W
Derbyshire □[6]	44	53.00 N	1.33 W
Der-Chantecoq, Lac du ⊜[1]	58	48.35 N	4.46 E
Derdepoort	156	24.42 S	26.20 E
Dere	130	39.00 N	39.18 E
Derečin	76	53.15 N	24.55 E
Derecske	30	47.21 N	21.34 E
Dereköy, Tür.	130	41.56 N	27.21 E
Dereköy, Tür.	130	39.16 N	27.19 E
Dereköy, Tür.	130	40.08 N	37.47 E
Dereli	130	40.45 N	38.27 E
Derenburg	54	51.52 N	10.54 E
Derendorf -◆-[8]	263	51.15 N	6.48 E
Derenwu	105	39.40 N	116.46 E
Dereseki -◆-[8]	267b	41.08 N	29.08 E
Derev'anka	24	61.34 N	34.27 E
Derg ≃	48	54.44 N	7.25 W
Derg, Lough ⊜, Ire.	48	52.57 N	8.19 W
Derg, Lough ⊜, Ire.	48	54.36 N	7.53 W
Dergači, Ross.	80	51.14 N	48.46 E
Dergači, Ukr.	78	50.07 N	36.07 E
Dergaon	120	26.42 N	93.58 E
Der Grabow ⊂	54	54.23 N	12.50 E
De Ridder	194	30.50 N	93.17 W
De Rijp	52	52.34 N	4.50 E
Derik	130	37.22 N	40.17 E
Derinkuyu	130	38.23 N	34.45 E
Der Kanal → English Channel ʉ	28	50.20 N	1.00 W
Derkul	80	51.16 N	51.18 E
Derkul ≃	83	48.35 N	39.41 E
Dermbach	56	50.43 N	10.06 E
Dermott	194	33.31 N	91.26 W
Dermulo	64	46.20 N	11.04 E
Derne	263	51.35 N	7.41 E
Derne -◆-[8]	263	51.34 N	7.31 E
Dernieres, Isles II	194	29.02 N	90.47 W
Dernoviči	78	51.36 N	29.43 E
Deroche	224	49.11 N	122.04 W
Dero Eri	144	9.01 N	46.43 E
Dêrong	102	28.47 N	99.14 E
Déroute, Passage de la ʉ	32	49.25 N	2.00 W
Derrame	196	26.19 N	104.23 W
Derravaragh, Lough ⊜	48	53.40 N	7.24 W
Derre	154	16.56 S	36.11 E
Derrick City	214	41.58 N	78.34 W
Derrinallum	169	37.57 S	143.13 E
Derry → Londonderry, N. Ire., U.K.	48	54.59 N	7.20 W
Derry, N.H., U.S.	188	42.52 N	71.19 W
Derry, Pa., U.S.	214	40.20 N	79.18 W
Derrybrien	48	53.04 N	8.36 W
Derrykeighan	48	55.08 N	6.29 W
Derryveagh Mountains ⋀	48	55.00 N	8.05 W
Derry West	275b	43.39 N	79.42 W
Der Sārāi -◆-[8]	272a	28.33 N	77.11 E
Dersau	54	54.07 N	10.20 E
Dersingham	42	52.51 N	0.30 E
Derudeb	140	17.32 N	36.06 E
De Rust	158	33.30 S	22.32 E
Deruta	66	42.59 N	12.25 E
De Ruyter	210	42.45 N	75.53 W
DeRuyter Reservoir ⊜[1]	210	42.49 N	75.53 W
Der'uzino	82	56.18 N	38.16 E
Derval	32	47.40 N	1.40 W
Derventa	38	44.58 N	17.55 E
Derwent	182	53.39 N	110.58 W
Derwent ≃, Austl.	166	43.03 S	147.22 E
Derwent ≃, Eng., U.K.	44	52.53 N	1.17 W
Derwent ≃, Eng., U.K.	44	53.45 N	0.57 W
Derwent ≃, Eng., U.K.	44	54.57 N	1.41 W
Derwent ≃, Eng., U.K.	44	54.38 N	3.34 W
Derwent Bridge	166	42.08 S	146.13 E
Derwent Reservoir ⊜[1]	44	54.50 N	2.00 W
Derwent Water ⊜	44	54.34 N	3.08 W
Deržavino	80	53.13 N	52.22 E
Deržavinsk	86	51.03 N	66.19 E
Desaguadero ≃, Arg.	252	34.13 S	66.47 W
Desaguadero ≃, Bol.	248	18.24 S	67.05 W
Desagüe, Canal de ≊	286a	19.29 N	99.05 W
Des Allemands	194	29.49 N	90.28 W
Desamparados	236	9.54 N	84.04 W
Désappointement, Îles du II	14	14.10 S	141.20 W
Des Arc	194	34.58 N	91.29 W
Desborough	42	52.27 N	0.49 W
Descabezado Grande, Volcán ∧[1]	252	35.36 S	70.45 W
Descanso, Bra.	252	26.50 S	53.35 W
Descanso, Ca., U.S.	204	32.51 N	116.37 W
Descanso, Punta ≻	204	32.16 N	117.03 W
Descanso Gardens ♠	280	34.12 N	118.13 W
Descartes	32	46.58 N	0.42 E
Deschaillons	206	46.32 N	72.07 W
Deschambault	206	46.39 N	71.56 W
Deschambault Lake	184	54.55 N	103.22 W
Deschambault Lake ⊜	184	54.40 N	103.35 W
Descharme Lake ⊜	184	57.05 N	109.13 W
Deschênes	212	45.23 N	75.48 W
Deschênes, Lac ⊜	212	45.22 N	75.51 W
Deschutes ≃, Or., U.S.	202	45.38 N	120.54 W
Deschutes ≃, Wa., U.S.	224	47.02 N	122.54 W
Descoberto	256	21.27 S	42.58 W
Desdunes	238	19.17 N	72.39 W
Dese	144	11.05 N	39.41 E
Deseado ≃	254	47.45 S	65.54 W
Deseado, Cabo ≻	254	52.44 S	74.44 W
Desembarco de los 0303 Orientales, Monumento ⊥	258	33.48 S	58.25 W
Desengaño, Punta ≻	254	49.15 S	67.37 W
Desenzano del Garda	64	45.28 N	10.32 E
Deseret Peak ∧	200	40.28 N	112.38 W
Deseronto	212	44.12 N	77.03 W
Désert ≃	190	46.23 N	75.58 W
Désert, Lac ⊜	190	46.35 N	76.19 W
Desertas, Ilhas II	148	32.30 N	16.30 W
Desert Creek ≃	226	38.48 N	119.19 W
Desert Hot Springs	204	33.57 N	116.30 W
Desert Lake ⊜, On., Can.	212	44.32 N	76.35 W
Desert Lake ⊜, Nv., U.S.	204	36.58 N	115.05 W
Desert Mountains ⋀	226	39.16 N	119.00 W
Desert Peak ∧	200	41.11 N	113.22 W
Desert Valley V	204	41.15 N	118.20 W
Desert View Highlands	228	34.37 N	118.13 W
Desford	42	52.39 N	1.17 W
Desha	194	35.44 N	91.40 W
Deshaies	241o	16.18 N	61.48 W
Desheng	102	24.45 N	108.28 E
Deshengchang	107	29.06 N	105.25 E
Deshengpo	102	26.58 N	103.59 E
Deshengtai	104	42.14 N	123.45 E
Deshengyingzi	104	41.44 N	123.14 E
Deshler, Ne., U.S.	198	40.08 N	97.43 W
Deshler, Oh., U.S.	216	41.12 N	83.53 W
Deshnok	120	27.48 N	73.21 E
Deshon Manor	214	40.52 N	79.57 W
Deshu	128	30.26 N	63.19 E
Deshun	106	31.58 N	120.29 E
Desiderio Tello	252	31.13 S	66.19 W
Desio	62	45.37 N	9.13 E
Des Lacs ≃	198	48.17 N	101.25 W
Deslinde, Arroyo ≃	258	33.44 S	58.52 W
Desloge	194	37.52 N	90.31 W
Desmarais	182	55.56 N	113.49 W
De Smet	198	44.23 N	97.33 W
De Smet, Lake ⊜[1]	202	44.29 N	106.45 W
Des Moines, Ia., U.S.	190	41.36 N	93.36 W
Des Moines, N.M., U.S.	196	36.45 N	103.50 W
Des Moines, Wa., U.S.	224	47.24 N	122.19 W
Des Moines ≃	178	40.22 N	91.26 W
Des Moines, East Fork ≃	198	42.41 N	94.12 W
Dešná, Česká Rep.	61	48.58 N	15.33 E
Desna, Ukr.	78	50.56 N	30.46 E
Desna ≃, Europe	78	50.33 N	30.32 E
Desna ≃, Ross.	82	55.26 N	37.30 E
Desolación, Isla I	254	53.00 S	74.10 W
Désolation, Cap de la → Disappointment, Cape ≻	244	54.53 S	36.07 W
Desolation Point ≻	116	10.28 N	125.39 E
Desor, Mount ∧[2]	190	47.58 N	89.01 W
De Soto, Il., U.S.	194	37.49 N	89.13 W
De Soto, In., U.S.	216	40.15 N	85.17 W
De Soto, Mo., U.S.	194	38.08 N	90.33 W
De Soto, Tx., U.S.	222	32.35 N	96.51 W
De Soto □[6]	220	27.11 N	81.48 W
De Soto City	220	27.26 N	81.24 W
De Soto National Memorial ⊥	220	27.31 N	82.40 W
De Soto State Park ♠	194	34.28 N	85.36 W
Despatch	158	33.46 S	25.30 E
Despeñaperros, Desfiladero de)(	34	38.24 N	3.30 W
Des Plaines	216	42.02 N	87.53 W
Des Plaines ≃	216	41.24 N	88.16 W
Despotovac	38	44.05 N	21.33 E
Despujols	116	12.31 N	122.01 E
Desroches, Île I	138	5.41 S	53.41 E
Desruisseaux	241f	13.47 N	60.56 W
Dessau	54	51.50 N	12.14 E
Dessel	56	51.14 N	5.07 E
Deşt	130	39.10 N	39.22 E
Destacado Island I	116	12.16 N	124.06 E
De Steeg	52	52.02 N	6.04 E
Destek	130	40.51 N	36.12 E
Destelbergen	50	51.03 N	3.48 E
Desterro	250	7.17 S	37.06 W
Destin	194	30.23 N	86.29 W
Destruction, Mount ∧[2]	162	24.35 S	127.59 E
Destruction Bay	180	61.15 N	138.48 W
Destruction Island I	224	47.40 N	124.30 W
Desulo	71	40.01 N	9.14 E
Desvres	50	50.40 N	1.50 E
Deta	38	45.24 N	21.13 E
Detčino	82	54.49 N	36.19 E
Dete	154	18.38 S	26.50 E
Dethlingen	52	52.57 N	10.07 E
Detling	260	51.18 N	0.34 E
Detmold	52	51.56 N	8.52 E
Detmold □[5]	52	52.00 N	8.45 E
Detour, Point ≻	190	45.36 N	86.37 W
De Tour Village	190	46.00 N	83.54 W
Detrital Wash V	200	36.02 N	114.28 W
Detroit, Il., U.S.	219	39.37 N	90.40 W
Detroit, Mi., U.S.	216	42.20 N	83.03 W
Detroit, Mi., U.S.	281	42.20 N	83.03 W
Detroit, Or., U.S.	202	44.44 N	122.08 W
Detroit, Tx., U.S.	196	33.40 N	95.16 W
Detroit ≃	214	42.06 N	83.08 W
Detroit Beach	216	41.55 N	83.20 W
Detroit City Airport ⊠	281	42.25 N	83.01 W
Detroit Institute of Arts υ	281	42.22 N	83.04 W
Detroit Lake ⊜[1]	202	44.42 N	122.10 W
Detroit Lakes	198	46.48 N	95.50 W
Detroit Mercy, University Of υ[2]	281	42.25 N	83.08 W
Detroit Metropolitan-Wayne County Airport ⊠	281	42.13 N	83.22 W
Detroit Race Course ♠	281	42.23 N	83.19 W
Detroit-Windsor Tunnel -◆-[5]	281	42.20 N	83.02 W
Detroit Zoological Park ♠	281	42.29 N	83.09 W
Detskosel'skij	265a	59.44 N	30.28 E
Dettelbach	56	49.48 N	10.09 E
Dettifoss ∟	24a	65.50 N	16.20 W
Dettingen an der Erms	56	48.32 N	9.20 E
Dettwiller	56	48.45 N	7.28 E
Det Udom	110	14.54 N	105.05 E
Detva	30	48.31 N	19.28 E
Deua National Park ♠	166	36.00 S	149.45 E
Deuben	54	51.06 N	12.04 E
Deuels Corners	284a	42.45 N	78.45 W
Deuil-la-Barre	261	48.59 N	2.20 E
Deūlgaon Rāja	122	20.01 N	76.02 E
Deulpur	272b	22.36 N	88.10 E
Deulti	126	22.26 N	87.56 E
Deurne, Bel.	50	51.13 N	4.28 E
Deurne, Ned.	52	51.28 N	5.47 E
Deusen -◆-[8]	263	51.33 N	7.26 E
Deutsche Bucht ⊂	30	54.30 N	7.30 E
Deutsch Eylau → Iława	30	53.37 N	19.33 E
Deutschfeistritz	61	47.11 N	15.20 E
Deutschkreutz	61	47.36 N	16.38 E
Deutsch Krone → Wałcz	30	53.17 N	16.28 E
Deutschland → Germany □[1]	30	51.00 N	10.00 E
Deutschlandsberg	61	46.49 N	15.13 E
Deutsch-Neudorf	54	50.38 N	13.27 E
Deutsch Wagram	61	48.18 N	16.34 E
Deutsch Wusterhausen	264a	52.18 N	13.35 E
Deutzen	54	51.06 N	12.26 E
Deux-Montagnes	206	45.32 N	73.53 W
Deux-Montagnes □[6]	206	45.35 N	74.05 W
Deux Montagnes, Lac des ⊜	206	45.28 N	73.59 W
Deux-Sèvres □[5]	32	46.30 N	0.20 W
Deva	38	45.53 N	22.55 E
Devakottai	122	9.57 N	78.49 E
De Valls Bluff	194	34.47 N	91.27 W
Devaprayāg	124	30.09 N	78.37 E
Dev'atern'a	80	56.12 N	53.24 E
Dev'atiny	24	60.56 N	36.46 E
Devault	285	40.05 N	75.32 W
Dévaványa	30	47.02 N	20.58 E
Devecikonağı	130	39.55 N	28.34 E
Devecser	30	47.06 N	17.26 E
Devedağı Tepesi ∧	130	40.34 N	41.21 E
Devegeçidi Barajı ⊜[1]	130	38.05 N	39.55 E
Develi	130	38.23 N	35.30 E
Deventer	52	52.15 N	6.10 E
Deveron ≃	46	57.40 N	2.31 W
Devers	222	30.02 N	94.36 W
Devers Canal, West Branch ≊	222	29.57 N	94.46 W
Deversoir Military Base ■	142	30.25 N	32.20 E
Devès, Monts du ⋀	32	45.00 N	3.45 E
Devgadh Bāriva	120	22.42 N	73.54 E
De View, Bayou ≃	194	34.48 N	91.18 W
Devīkot	120	26.42 N	71.12 E
Devil Lake ⊜	212	44.35 N	76.27 W
Deville	56	49.53 N	4.42 E
Déville-lès-Rouen	50	49.28 N	1.02 E
Devil Peak ∧	226	37.32 N	119.44 W
Devil River Peak ∧	172	40.58 S	172.39 E
Devils ≃	196	29.39 N	100.58 W
Devil's Bridge	42	52.23 N	3.51 W
Devils Brook ≃	276	40.20 N	74.37 W
Devils Canyon V	280	34.16 N	117.58 W
Devil's Den State Park ♠	194	35.46 N	94.16 W
Devils Hole Rapids ∟	284a	43.08 N	79.03 W
Devils Hopyard State Park ♠	207	41.28 N	72.22 W
Devils Island → Diable, Île du I	250	5.17 N	52.35 W
Devils Lake	198	48.06 N	98.51 W
Devils Lake ⊜, Mi., U.S.	216	41.58 N	84.17 W
Devils Lake ⊜, N.D., U.S.	198	48.01 N	98.52 W
Devils Lake State Park ♠	190	43.24 N	89.44 W
Devils Marbles ♠	162	20.30 S	134.14 E
Devils Paw ∧	180	58.44 N	133.50 W
Devils Postpile National Monument ♠	226	37.37 N	119.05 W
Devils Tower ∧	198	44.31 N	104.57 W
Devils Tower National Monument ♠	198	44.31 N	104.57 W
Devil's Water ≃	44	54.58 N	2.02 W
Devin	38	41.45 N	24.24 E
Devine, B.C., Can.	182	50.32 N	122.30 W
Devine, Tx., U.S.	196	29.08 N	98.54 W
Devizes	42	51.22 N	1.59 W
Devladovo	78	48.07 N	33.45 E
Devli	120	25.45 N	75.23 E
De Voe Lake ⊜	276	40.23 N	74.23 W
Devoll ≃	38	40.49 N	19.51 E
Dévoluy ⋀	62	44.39 N	5.53 E
Devon, Ab., Can.	182	53.22 N	113.44 W
Devon, S. Afr.	158	26.21 S	28.48 E
Devon, Pa., U.S.	285	40.02 N	75.25 W
Devon □[6]	42	50.45 N	3.50 W
Devon ≃, Eng., U.K.	42	53.04 N	0.43 W
Devon ≃, Scot., U.K.	46	56.07 N	3.51 W
Devon Island I	16	75.00 N	87.00 W
Devonport, Austl.	166	41.11 S	146.21 E
Devonport, N.Z.	172	36.49 S	174.48 E
Devonport, Eng., U.K.	42	50.22 N	4.10 W
Devonshire	285	39.49 N	75.32 W
Devonshire Plaza -◆-[9]	281	42.17 N	83.00 W
Devore	228	34.13 N	117.25 W
Devoto	252	31.24 S	62.19 W
Devrek	130	41.13 N	31.57 E
Devrekâni	130	41.36 N	33.51 E
Devres ≃	130	41.06 N	34.25 E
Devure ≃	154	20.00 S	32.20 E
Dewa, Ujung ≻	114	2.55 N	95.48 E
Dewakang-lompo, Pulau I	112	5.24 S	118.25 E
Dewar	196	35.27 N	95.56 W
Dewart	210	41.07 N	76.53 W
Dewart Lake ⊜	216	41.22 N	85.47 W
Dewās	120	22.58 N	76.04 E
Dewa-sanchi ⋀[2]	92	39.05 N	140.10 E
Dewdney	224	49.10 N	122.12 W
Dewetsdorp	158	29.33 S	26.34 E
Dewey, Il., U.S.	216	40.19 N	88.17 W
Dewey, Ok., U.S.	196	36.47 N	95.56 W
Dewey, Wa., U.S.	224	48.25 N	122.37 W
Dewey Beach	208	38.41 N	75.04 W
Deweyville	194	30.18 N	93.45 W
De Witt, Ar., U.S.	194	34.17 N	91.20 W
Dewitt, Il., U.S.	219	40.11 N	88.47 W
De Witt, Ia., U.S.	190	41.49 N	90.32 W
De Witt, Mi., U.S.	216	42.50 N	84.34 W
De Witt, Ne., U.S.	198	40.23 N	96.55 W
De Witt, N.Y., U.S.	210	43.02 N	76.03 W
De Witt □[6], Il., U.S.	216	40.12 N	88.55 W
De Witt □[6], Tx., U.S.	222	29.07 N	97.20 W
Dewittville	214	42.14 N	79.27 W
Dewsbury	44	53.42 N	1.37 W
Dexing	100	28.54 N	117.36 E
Dexingjie	98	39.54 N	122.50 E
Dexter, Me., U.S.	188	45.01 N	69.17 W
Dexter, Mi., U.S.	216	42.20 N	83.53 W
Dexter, Mo., U.S.	194	36.47 N	89.57 W
Dexter, N.M., U.S.	196	33.11 N	104.22 W
Dexter, N.Y., U.S.	212	44.00 N	76.02 W
Dexterity Fiord ⊂[2]	176	71.11 N	73.03 W
Deyang	102	31.14 N	104.22 E
Dey-Dey, Lake ⊜	162	29.12 S	131.04 E
Deyhūk	128	33.17 N	57.30 E
Deyyer	128	27.50 N	51.55 E
Dez ≃	128	31.39 N	48.52 E
Dezfūl	128	32.23 N	48.24 E
Dez Gerd	128	30.45 N	51.57 E
Dezhou	98	37.27 N	116.18 E
Dežneva, mys ≻	180	66.06 N	169.45 W
Dezong	120	32.09 N	90.20 E
Dezzo di Scalve	64	45.59 N	10.05 E
Dgâmcha, Sebkhet te-n- ⊜	150	18.45 N	15.48 W
Dhabān Singh	123	31.44 N	73.34 E
Dhāding	124	27.52 N	84.55 E
Dhādkā	126	22.47 N	86.30 E
Dháfna ∧	267c	38.07 N	23.38 E
Dháfni, Ellás	38	37.48 N	22.01 E
Dháfni, Ellás	267c	38.01 N	23.38 E
Dhafnion Monastery υ[1]	267c	38.01 N	23.38 E
Dhahab	140	28.29 N	34.32 E
Dhahab, Wādī adh- V	132	32.44 N	35.54 E
Dhahran → Az-Zahrān	128	26.18 N	50.08 E
Dhaka (Dacca), Bngl.	126	23.43 N	90.25 E
Dhāka, India	124	26.41 N	85.10 E
Dhaka □[5]	120	24.15 N	90.15 E
Dhākauli	124	24.45 N	77.51 E
Dhakuria Lake ⊜	272b	22.31 N	88.22 E
Dhaleswari ≃	126	23.32 N	90.34 E
Dháli	130	35.01 N	33.25 E
Dhamār	144	14.46 N	44.23 E
Dhāmpur	124	29.19 N	78.31 E
Dhāmrai	126	23.55 N	90.13 E
Dhamtari	122	20.41 N	81.34 E
Dhāmura	126	22.53 N	90.12 E
Dhanaula	123	30.17 N	75.35 E
Dhanaura	124	28.58 N	78.15 E
Dhanbād	126	23.48 N	86.27 E
Dhandhuka	120	22.22 N	71.59 E
Dhanera	126	23.25 N	86.39 E
Dhaneswargāti	126	23.25 N	89.20 E
Dhangadhī	124	28.41 N	80.36 E
Dhaniakhāli	126	22.58 N	88.06 E
D'Hanis	196	29.20 N	99.17 W
Dhankuṭa	124	26.59 N	87.20 E
Dhansar	272c	19.07 N	73.05 E
Dhānyahānā	272b	22.48 N	88.11 E
Dhār	120	22.36 N	75.18 E
Dharampur	122	20.32 N	73.11 E
Dharān	124	26.49 N	87.17 E
Dharangaon	120	21.01 N	75.16 E
Dhārāpuram	122	10.44 N	77.31 E
Dhāri	120	21.20 N	71.01 E
Dhārīwāl	123	31.57 N	75.19 E
Dharmābād	122	18.54 N	77.51 E
Dharmapuri	122	12.08 N	78.10 E
Dharmavaram	122	14.26 N	77.43 E
Dharmjaygarh	124	22.28 N	83.13 E
Dharmkot	123	30.57 N	75.14 E
Dharmshāla	123	32.13 N	76.19 E
Dharoor, Tog V	144	10.20 N	50.30 E
Dharug National Park ♠	170	33.25 S	151.05 E
Dhasān ≃	124	25.48 N	79.24 E
Dhātrigrām	126	23.15 N	88.20 E
Dhaulpur	124	26.42 N	77.54 E
Dhawalāgiri □[8]	124	28.30 N	83.30 E
Dhawalāgiri ∧	124	28.42 N	83.30 E
Dhebar Lake ⊜	120	24.16 N	74.00 E
Dhelfoí ⊥	38	38.30 N	22.29 E
Dhenkānāl	120	20.40 N	85.36 E
Dhenoúsa I	38	37.06 N	25.49 E
Dherínia	130	35.03 N	33.57 E
Dhërmiu υ[1]	38	40.08 N	19.42 E
Dherue, Loch an ⊜	46	58.25 N	4.27 W
Dheskáti	38	39.55 N	21.49 E
Dheune ≃	58	46.54 N	5.00 E
Dhiavolítsion	38	37.18 N	21.58 E
Dhībān	132	31.30 N	35.47 E
Dhidhimótikhon	38	41.21 N	26.30 E
Dhiinsoor	144	2.24 N	42.59 E
Dhíkti ∧	38	35.08 N	25.30 E
Dhílos ⊥	38	37.26 N	25.16 E
Dhimitsána	38	37.37 N	22.03 E
Dhiónisos	267c	38.06 N	23.53 E
Dhī Qār □[4]	128	31.00 N	46.15 E
Dhirāsrām	126	23.57 N	90.25 E
Dhirwah, Wādī adh- V	132	31.18 N	36.56 E
Dhodhekánisos (Dodecanese) II	38	36.30 N	27.00 E
Dhodhóni ⊥	38	39.34 N	20.47 E
Dhofar → Ẓufār -◆-[1]	118	17.00 N	54.10 E
Dhokra	272b	22.40 N	88.34 E
Dholka	120	22.43 N	72.28 E
Dhomhnuill, Sgurr ∧	46	56.45 N	5.27 W
Dhone	122	15.25 N	77.53 E
Dhopākhola	126	23.08 N	89.10 E
Dhorāji	120	21.44 N	70.27 E
Dhosha	126	22.15 N	88.33 E
Dhowa	126	24.03 N	86.54 E
Dhoxáton	38	41.05 N	24.14 E
Dhrāngadhra	120	22.59 N	71.28 E
Dhrapetsóna	267c	37.57 N	23.37 E
Dhrol	120	22.34 N	70.25 E
Dhron ≃	56	49.52 N	6.54 E
Dhubāb	144	12.56 N	43.25 E
Dhuburi	124	26.01 N	89.59 E
Dhudiāl	123	33.04 N	72.58 E
Dhulāgarh	272b	22.35 N	88.11 E
Dhule	120	20.54 N	74.47 E
Dhulia → Dhule	120	20.54 N	74.47 E
Dhuliān	124	24.41 N	87.58 E
Dhulikhel	124	27.37 N	85.33 E
Dhūlsīrās -◆-[8]	272a	28.33 N	77.02 E
Dhünn	56	51.06 N	7.16 E
Dhünn-Stausee ⊜[1]	263	51.05 N	7.16 E
Dhupgāri	124	26.36 N	89.01 E
Dhurbo	144	11.37 N	50.20 E
Dhūri	124	30.22 N	75.52 E
Dhutumkhar ≃	272c	18.54 N	73.00 E
Dhuudo	144	9.20 N	50.12 E
Dhuudo V	144	9.14 N	50.39 E
Dhuusa Mareeb	144	5.31 N	46.24 E
Día I	38	35.27 N	25.13 E
Diabaig	46	57.34 N	5.40 W
Diabakania	150	10.38 N	10.58 W
Diable, Île du (Devils Island) I	250	5.17 N	52.35 W
Diable, Lac du ⊜	206	46.31 N	74.20 W
Diable, Pointe du ≻	240e	14.47 N	60.54 W
Diable, Rivière du ≃	206	46.03 N	74.38 W
Diables, Morne aux ∧	240d	15.37 N	61.27 W
Diablo, Ca., U.S.	226	37.50 N	121.58 W
Diablo, Wa., U.S.	224	48.43 N	121.09 W
Diablo, Canyon V	200	35.18 N	110.59 W
Diablo, Isla del → Diable, Île du I	250	5.17 N	52.35 W
Diablo, Mount ∧	226	37.53 N	121.55 W
Diablo, Pico del ∧	232	30.59 N	115.45 W
Diablo, Sierra del ⋀	196	27.20 N	104.05 W
Diablo Lake ⊜[1]	224	48.43 N	121.08 W
Diablo Plateau ⋀[1]	200	31.30 N	105.30 W
Diablo Range ⋀	226	37.00 N	121.20 W
Diablotins, Morne ∧	240d	15.30 N	61.24 W
Diabo	150	7.47 N	5.11 W
Diaca	154	11.30 S	39.59 E
Diadema	256	23.42 S	46.37 W
Diadema □[7]	287b	23.42 S	46.36 W
Diafarabé	150	14.09 N	5.01 W
Diagonal	198	40.48 N	94.20 W
Diaka ≃[1]	150	15.13 N	4.14 W
Dialakoto	150	13.19 N	13.18 W
Dialassagou	150	13.45 N	3.37 W
Diamant, Pointe du ≻	240e	14.27 N	61.03 W
Diamante, Arg.	252	32.04 S	60.39 W
Diamante, It.	68	39.41 N	15.49 E
Diamante ≃	252	34.31 S	66.56 W
Diamante, Punta ≻	234	16.47 N	99.52 W
Diamante de Ubá	256	21.12 S	42.55 W
Diamantina	255	18.15 S	43.36 W
Diamantina ≃	166	26.45 S	139.10 E
Diamantina Fracture Zone ✦	14	36.00 S	105.00 E
Diamantina Lakes	166	23.46 S	141.09 E
Diamantino	248	14.25 S	56.27 W
Diamantino ≃	255	16.08 S	52.28 W
Diamond, Il., U.S.	216	41.17 N	88.15 W
Diamond, Mo., U.S.	194	37.00 N	94.19 W
Diamond, Oh., U.S.	214	41.06 N	81.01 W
Diamond Bar	228	34.01 N	117.48 W
Diamond Brook ≃	276	40.56 N	74.08 W
Diamond Creek	274b	37.41 S	145.09 E
Diamond Creek ≃	169	37.44 S	145.09 E
Diamond Harbour	126	22.12 N	88.12 E
Diamond Head ⊥[6]	229c	21.16 N	157.49 W
Diamond Hill	207	41.59 N	71.24 W
Diamond Hill Reservoir ⊜[1]	283	42.00 N	71.24 W
Diamond Hill State Park ♠	283	42.00 N	71.26 W
Diamond Islets II	166	17.25 S	150.58 E
Diamond Lake	216	42.15 N	88.00 W
Diamond Lake ⊜, On., Can.	212	45.04 N	78.02 W
Diamond Lake ⊜, Il., U.S.	278	42.15 N	88.00 W
Diamond Lake ⊜, Mi., U.S.	216	41.54 N	85.59 W
Diamond Lake ⊜, Or., U.S.	202	43.10 N	122.09 W
Diamond Peak ∧, Id., U.S.	202	44.09 N	113.05 W
Diamond Peak ∧, Or., U.S.	202	43.33 N	122.09 W
Diamond Peak ∧, Wa., U.S.	202	46.07 N	117.32 W
Diamond Springs	226	38.41 N	120.48 W
Diamondville	200	41.46 N	110.32 W
Diana	222	32.43 N	94.45 W
Diana Bay ⊂	176	60.50 N	69.50 W
Dianalund	41	55.32 N	11.30 E
Dianbai	102	21.30 N	111.01 E
Dian Chi ⊜	102	24.50 N	102.42 E
Diancun	105	39.55 N	116.14 E
Dianfangba	102	32.54 N	103.35 E
Diangounté Kamara	150	14.33 N	9.31 W
Dianhu	100	33.58 N	119.38 E
Dianji	98	36.32 N	120.27 E
Dianjiang	102	30.21 N	107.23 E
Diano, Vallo di V	68	40.21 N	15.36 E
Diano Marina	62	43.54 N	8.05 E
Dianópolis	250	11.38 S	46.50 W
Dianqianhe	100	30.44 N	116.02 E
Dianra	150	8.45 N	6.14 W
Dianshang	106	31.10 N	118.51 E
Dianshan Hu ⊜	106	31.08 N	120.55 E
Diantou	100	27.18 N	120.11 E
Dianzi	104	41.37 N	122.05 E
Diaobingshan	104	42.28 N	123.33 E
Diao'ecun	105	40.43 N	115.49 E
Diaohetou	105	39.17 N	116.41 E
Diaopu	100	32.22 N	119.54 E
Diaoshuilouzi	104	40.59 N	122.22 E
Diaotai	100	29.40 N	119.39 E
Diaowo	105	39.30 N	116.04 E
Diapaga	150	12.04 N	1.47 E
Diapangou	150	12.07 N	0.11 E
Diapblo, Puntan ≻	174n	15.00 N	145.35 E
Dias	256	22.28 S	45.34 W
Diascund Creek Reservoir ⊜[1]	208	37.27 N	76.54 W
Diawala	150	10.07 N	5.28 W
Diaz	194	35.38 N	91.15 W
Diaz Point ≻	156	26.38 S	15.05 E
Dibai	124	28.13 N	78.15 E
Dibāng ≃	120	27.50 N	95.32 E
Dibay → Dubayy	128	25.18 N	55.18 E
Dibaya	152	6.30 S	22.57 E
Dibbīn	132	32.26 N	36.34 E
Dibeng	158	27.35 S	22.54 E
D'Iberville	194	30.25 N	88.53 W
Dibete	156	23.45 S	26.26 E
Dibi	144	4.13 N	41.56 E
Dibo	144	6.31 N	41.52 E
Diboll	222	31.11 N	94.46 W
Dibrugarh	120	27.29 N	94.54 E
Dibs	140	12.34 N	24.14 E
Dibs, Bi'r ⊤[4]	140	22.12 N	29.32 E
Dichāon Kalān -◆-[8]	272a	28.39 N	76.59 E
Dick, Mount ∧[2]	168a	31.35 S	116.42 E
Dickelsbach ≃	263	51.24 N	6.45 E
Dickens	196	33.37 N	100.50 W
Dickerson	208	39.13 N	77.25 W
Dickey ≃	224	47.55 N	124.37 W
Dickey Lake ⊜, On., Can.	212	44.47 N	77.44 W
Dickey Lake ⊜, Wa., U.S.	224	48.06 N	124.31 W
Dickinson, N.D., U.S.	198	46.52 N	102.47 W
Dickinson, Pa., U.S.	208	40.07 N	77.20 W
Dickinson, Tx., U.S.	222	29.27 N	95.03 W
Dickinson Bayou ≃	222	29.28 N	94.58 W
Dickinson Island I	281	42.37 N	82.38 W
Dickins Seamount ✦[3]	16	54.30 N	137.00 W

Symbols in the index entries represent the broad categories identified in the key at the right. Symbols with superior numbers (⋀[1]) identify subcategories (see complete key on page *I · 1).*

Symbole im Register stellen die rechts im Schlüssel erklärten Kategorien dar. Symbole mit hochgestellten Ziffern (⋀[1]) bezeichnen Unterabteilungen einer Kategorie (vgl. vollständiger Schlüssel auf Seite *I · 1).*

Los símbolos incluídos en el texto del índice representan las grandes categorías identificadas con la clave a la derecha. Los símbolos con numeros en su parte superior (⋀[1]) identifican las subcategorías (véase la clave completa en la página *I · 1).*

Les symboles de l'index représentent les catégories indiquées dans la légende à droite. Les symboles suivis d'un indice (⋀[1]) représentent des sous-catégories (voir légende complète à la page *I · 1).*

Os símbolos incluídos no texto do índice representam as grandes categorias identificadas com a chave à direita. Os símbolos com números em sua parte superior (⋀[1]) identificam as subcategorias (veja-se a chave completa à página *I · 1).*

∧ Mountain	Berg	Montaña	Montagne	Montanha
⋀ Mountains	Gebirge	Montañas	Montagnes	Montanhas
)(Pass	Paß	Paso	Col	Passo
V Valley, Canyon	Tal, Cañon	Valle, Cañón	Vallée, Canyon	Vale, Canhão
≚ Plain	Ebene	Llano	Plaine	Planície
≻ Cape	Kap	Cabo	Cap	Cabo
I Island	Insel	Isla	Île	Ilha
II Islands	Inseln	Islas	Îles	Ilhas
⊥ Other Topographic Features	Andere Topographische Objekte	Otros Elementos Topográficos	Autres données topographiques	Outros acidentes topográficos

ESPAÑOL — Nombre · Página · Lat.°′ · Long.°′ W = Oeste

Dicks 158 27.43 S 30.10 E
Dickson, Ok., U.S. 196 34.11 N 96.59 W
Dickson, Tn., U.S. 194 36.04 N 87.23 W
Dickson City 210 41.28 N 75.36 W
Dicle, Tür. 130 37.18 N 42.04 E
Dicle, Tür. 130 38.22 N 40.04 E
Dicle → Tigris ≃ 128 31.00 N 47.25 E
Dicomano 66 43.53 N 11.31 E
Diculom 116 7.54 N 122.14 E
Dicun 100 33.46 N 117.32 E
Didam 52 51.56 N 6.08 E
Didao 89 45.22 N 130.51 E
Didbiran 89 51.58 N 139.20 E
Didcot 42 51.37 N 1.15 W
Didesa ≃ 144 9.56 N 35.45 E
Didiéni 150 13.53 N 8.06 W
Didimbo 152 17.30 S 21.45 E
Didinga Hills ⋏ 154 4.20 N 33.35 E
Didsbury 182 51.40 N 114.08 W
Didsbury ●[8] 262 53.25 N 2.14 W
Diduyon ≃ 116 16.36 N 121.42 E
Dīdwāna 120 27.24 N 74.34 E
Didy 157b 18.07 S 48.32 E
Die 62 44.45 N 5.22 E
Die Aue ●[1] 263 51.40 N 6.35 E
Die Berg ∧ 156 25.12 S 30.09 E
Die Boss 158 31.59 S 19.44 E
Diébougou 150 10.58 N 3.15 W
Dieburg 56 49.54 N 8.50 E
Dieciocho de Julio 252 33.41 S 53.33 W
Diecke 150 7.21 N 8.58 W
Diedenhofen → Thionville 56 49.22 N 6.10 E
Diedersdorf 264a 52.20 N 13.21 E
Die Erpe ≃ 264a 52.27 N 13.38 E
Diefenbaker, Lake ⊜[1] 184 51.00 N 106.55 W
Diego de Almagro 252 26.23 S 70.03 W
Diego de Almagro, Isla I 254 51.25 S 75.10 W
Diego de Ocampo, Pico ∧ 238 19.35 N 70.45 W
Diego Garcia I 12 7.20 S 72.25 E
Diego Gaynor 258 34.17 S 59.14 W
Diego Pérez, Cayería de II 240p 22.05 N 81.40 W
Diego Ramírez, Islas II 244 56.30 S 68.44 W
Die Haard ●[1] 263 51.41 N 7.15 E
Diekirch 56 49.53 N 6.10 E
Dieksee ⊜ 54 54.10 N 10.30 E
Dieleemu 86 46.22 N 88.43 E
Dielingen 52 52.26 N 8.20 E
Dielsdorf 58 47.29 N 8.27 E
Diéma 150 14.32 N 9.12 W
Diemansputs 158 29.54 S 21.33 E
Diembéring 150 12.28 N 16.47 W
Diemel ≃ 52 51.39 N 9.27 E
Diemel-Talsperre ●[6] 56 51.22 N 8.43 E
Diemen 52 52.20 N 4.58 E
Diemuchuoke 120 32.42 N 79.29 E
Dien Bien Phu 110 21.23 N 103.01 E
Dien Khanh 110 12.15 N 109.06 E
Diepenau 52 52.25 N 8.44 E
Diepenbeek 56 50.54 N 5.24 E
Diepenheim 52 52.12 N 6.33 E
Diepensee 264a 52.22 N 13.31 E
Diepenveen 52 52.18 N 6.08 E
Diepholz 52 52.35 N 8.21 E
Diepoldsau 58 47.23 N 9.38 E
Dieppe, N.B., Can. 186 46.06 N 64.45 W
Dieppe, Fr. 50 49.56 N 1.05 E
Dierbao 98 40.20 N 114.32 E
Dierdorf 56 50.33 N 7.39 E
Dieren 52 52.03 N 6.06 E
Dierks 194 34.07 N 94.00 W
Diersbach 60 48.25 N 13.34 E
Di'er Songhua ≃ 89 45.26 N 124.39 E
Diesdorf 54 52.45 N 10.52 E
Dieskau 54 51.26 N 12.02 E
Diessem ●[8] 263 51.20 N 6.35 E
Diessen 64 47.56 N 11.06 E
Diessenhofen 58 47.41 N 8.45 E
Diest 56 50.59 N 5.03 E
Dietenheim 58 48.12 N 10.04 E
Dietersburg 60 48.30 N 12.55 E
Dietersdorf 56 50.13 N 10.49 E
Dietfurt 56 48.57 N 10.56 E
Dietfurt an der Altmühl 60 49.02 N 11.35 E
Dietikon 58 47.24 N 8.24 E
Dietmannsried 58 47.49 N 10.17 E
Dietrich 202 42.54 N 114.15 W
Dietzenbach 56 50.01 N 8.47 E
Dietzhölztal 56 50.50 N 8.19 E
Dieue-sur-Meuse 56 49.04 N 5.25 E
Dieulefit 62 44.31 N 5.04 E
Dieulouard 56 48.51 N 6.04 E
Dieuze 56 48.49 N 6.43 E
Dieveniškės 76 54.12 N 25.37 E
Diever 52 52.52 N 6.19 E
Die Ville ⋏[2] 56 50.40 N 6.55 E
Die Wurzen (Koren))(64 46.31 N 13.45 E
Diez 56 50.22 N 8.01 E
Diez de Octubre 232 24.44 N 104.39 W
Dif 144 0.59 N 40.57 E
Difang 98 35.23 N 117.52 E
Diffa 146 13.19 N 12.37 E
Diffa □[5] 146 16.00 N 13.30 E
Differdange 56 49.32 N 5.52 E
Difficult Run ≃ 284c 38.58 N 77.14 W
Diffun 116 16.34 N 121.33 E
Difuri I 122 5.24 N 73.38 E
Digambar Jain Temple ♥[1] 272b 22.36 N 88.23 E
Digambarpur 126 21.57 N 88.22 E
Digba 154 4.24 N 25.47 E
Digboi 120 27.23 N 95.38 E
Digby 186 44.37 N 65.46 W
Digby Neck ›[1] 186 44.30 N 66.10 W
Dige 98 34.22 N 114.28 E
Digerberget ∧[2] 40 60.35 N 13.25 E
Digges Islands II 176 62.35 N 77.50 W
Diggle 262 53.34 N 1.59 W
Dighalia 126 23.07 N 89.39 E
Dighipāra 126 21.58 N 88.17 E
Dighode 272c 18.54 N 73.02 E
Dighra 272b 22.47 N 88.32 E
Dighton, Ks., U.S. 198 38.28 N 100.28 W
Dighton, Ma., U.S. 207 41.48 N 71.07 W
Di Giorgio 228 35.15 N 118.51 W
Dīglūr 122 18.33 N 77.36 E
Digmoor 262 53.32 N 2.45 W
Dīgnagar 126 23.27 N 87.41 E
Dignano 64 46.05 N 12.56 E
Digne 62 44.06 N 6.14 E
Digoin 32 46.29 N 3.59 E
Digomi 84 41.47 N 44.44 E
Digong 104 42.11 N 122.03 E
Digor 84 40.23 N 43.24 E
Digora 84 43.10 N 44.09 E
Digos 116 6.45 N 125.20 E
Digra 272b 22.50 N 88.20 E
Digras 122 20.07 N 77.43 E
Digri 120 25.10 N 69.07 E
Digui 152 5.28 N 20.50 E
Digul ≃ 164 7.07 S 138.42 E
Dihaer 86 42.35 N 89.49 E
Dihun 144 7.18 N 42.42 E
Diirmentobe 86 45.44 N 63.37 E
Dijag 24 65.48 N 57.39 E
Dijlah → Tigris ≃ 128 31.00 N 47.25 E
Dijlah, Wādī V 142 29.58 N 31.13 E
Dijle (Dyle) ≃ 56 51.04 N 4.25 E
Dijohan Point › 116 16.19 N 122.14 E
Dijon 58 47.19 N 5.01 E
Dik 146 9.58 N 17.31 E
Dikaja 76 59.15 N 39.30 E
Dikala 154 4.41 N 31.23 E

FRANÇAIS — Nom · Page · Lat.°′ · Long.°′ W = Ouest

Dikan'ka 78 49.49 N 34.32 E
Dikbıyık 130 41.13 N 36.38 E
Dike 190 42.27 N 92.37 W
Dikhil 144 11.06 N 42.22 E
Dikili 130 39.04 N 26.53 E
Dikirnis 142 31.05 N 31.35 E
Dikli 76 57.35 N 25.06 E
Diklosmta, gora ∧ 84 42.29 N 45.47 E
Dikmen 130 39.53 N 32.50 E
Dikodougou 150 9.04 N 5.46 W
Diksmuide (Dixmude) 50 51.02 N 2.52 E
Dikson 74 73.30 N 80.35 E
Dikwa 146 12.02 N 13.56 E
Dila 144 6.21 N 38.17 E
Dilektepe 130 38.04 N 41.49 E
Dile Point › 116 17.34 N 120.20 E
Dilerpur 272b 22.51 N 88.10 E
Dili 112 8.33 S 125.35 E
Dilia V 146 16.53 N 11.00 E
Diligent Strait ʯ 110 12.11 N 92.57 E
Di Linh 110 11.35 N 108.04 E
Diližan 84 40.45 N 44.52 E
Diližanskij zapovednik ♠ 84 40.40 N 45.00 E
Dill ≃ 56 50.33 N 8.29 E
Dill City 196 35.16 N 99.08 W
Dillenburg 56 50.44 N 8.17 E
Diller 198 40.06 N 96.56 W
Dilley, Or., U.S. 224 45.29 N 123.07 W
Dilley, Tx., U.S. 196 28.40 N 99.10 W
Dilling 140 12.03 N 29.39 E
Dillingen 56 49.21 N 6.44 E
Dillingen an der Donau 56 48.34 N 10.29 E
Dillingham 180 59.02 N 158.29 W
Dillon, Co., U.S. 200 39.37 N 106.02 W
Dillon, Mt., U.S. 202 45.12 N 112.38 W
Dillon, S.C., U.S. 192 34.24 N 79.22 W
Dillon ≃ 184 55.56 N 108.57 W
Dillon Cone ∧ 172 42.16 S 173.13 E
Dillon Lake ⊜ 184 55.45 N 109.30 W
Dillon Lake ⊜[1] 188 40.02 N 82.10 W
Dillon Mountain ∧ 200 33.51 N 108.48 W
Dillon Reservoir ⊜[1] 200 39.35 N 106.02 W
Dillon State Park ♠ 188 40.03 N 82.08 W
Dillonvale 214 40.11 N 80.46 W
Dillsboro 218 39.01 N 85.03 W
Dillsburg 208 40.06 N 77.02 W
Dilltown 214 40.29 N 79.00 W
Dillwyn 192 37.32 N 78.27 W
Dilly 150 15.01 N 7.40 W
Dilolo 152 10.42 S 22.20 E
Dilsen 56 51.02 N 5.44 E
Dilworth 198 46.52 N 96.42 W
Dilworthtown 285 39.54 N 75.34 W
Dima, Ang. 152 15.27 S 20.10 E
Dima, Indon. 114 1.20 N 97.20 E
Dimāpur 120 25.54 N 93.44 E
Dimaro 64 46.20 N 10.52 E
Dimasalang 116 12.12 N 123.51 E
Dimashq (Damascus) 132 33.30 N 36.18 E
Dimashq □[8] 132 33.30 N 37.00 E
Dimass, Rass › 36 35.37 N 11.03 E
Dimataling 116 7.32 N 123.22 E
Dimbelenge 152 5.33 S 23.07 E
Dimbokro 150 6.39 N 4.42 W
Dimboola 166 36.27 S 142.02 E
Dîmbovița □[6] 38 45.00 N 25.30 E
Dîmbovița ≃ 38 44.14 N 26.27 E
Dimbulah 166 17.09 S 145.07 E
Dime 144 6.16 N 36.20 E
Dime Box 222 30.21 N 96.50 W
Dimitrov 83 48.15 N 37.18 E
Dimitrovgrad, Blg. 38 42.03 N 25.36 E
Dimitrovgrad, Jugo. 38 43.01 N 22.47 E
Dimitrovgrad, Ross. 80 54.14 N 49.39 E
Dimitrovo → Pernik, Blg. 38 42.36 N 23.02 E
Dimitrovo, Ukr. 78 48.36 N 33.01 E
Dimitrovskoje 85 40.16 N 69.03 E
Dimlang ∧ 146 8.24 N 11.47 E
Dimmitt 196 34.33 N 102.18 W
Dimo 154 5.19 N 29.10 E
Dimock 210 41.45 N 75.32 W
Dimona 132 31.04 N 35.02 E
Dimondale 216 42.38 N 84.38 W
Dina 123 33.02 N 73.36 E
Dinach 144 9.15 N 50.37 E
Dinagat 116 9.59 N 125.35 E
Dinagat Island I 116 10.12 N 125.35 E
Dinagat Sound ʯ 116 9.59 N 125.50 E
Dinahican Point › 116 14.42 N 121.44 E
Dinājpur 124 25.38 N 88.38 E
Dinalupihan 116 14.52 N 120.28 E
Dinamarca → Denmark □[1] 26 56.00 N 10.00 E
Dinamarca, Estrecho de → Denmark Strait ʯ 10 67.00 N 25.00 W
Dinami 68 38.31 N 16.09 E
Dinamita 196 25.43 N 103.38 W
Dinamo 80 50.15 N 41.38 E
Dinan 32 48.27 N 2.02 W
Dīnānagar 123 32.09 N 75.28 E
Dinant 56 50.16 N 4.55 E
Dinar 130 38.04 N 30.10 E
Dinara (Dinaric Alps) ⋏ 36 43.50 N 16.35 E
Dinard 32 48.38 N 2.04 W
Dinaric Alps → Dinara ⋏ 36 43.50 N 16.35 E
Dinarische Alpen → Dinara ⋏ 36 43.50 N 16.35 E
Dinas, Pil. 116 7.38 N 123.20 E
Dinas, Wales, U.K. 42 52.00 N 4.54 W
Dinas Head › 42 52.02 N 4.55 W
Dinas Powys 42 51.26 N 3.14 W
Dindanko 150 14.08 N 9.30 W
Dindar, Nahr ad- (Dinder) ≃ 140 14.06 N 33.40 E
Dīndārpur ●[8] 272a 28.36 N 76.59 E
Dinde 152 14.12 S 13.44 E
Dinder (Nahr ad-Dindar) ≃ 140 14.06 N 33.40 E
Dinder National Park ♠ 140 12.40 N 35.20 E
Dindi ≃ 122 16.21 N 79.13 E
Dindigul 122 10.21 N 77.57 E
Dindima 150 10.18 N 10.12 E
Dindori 124 22.57 N 81.05 E
Dineksaray 130 37.23 N 32.37 E
Dinga, Pāk. 120 25.26 N 67.10 E
Dinga, Pāk. 123 32.38 N 73.43 E
Dinga, Zaïre 152 5.19 S 16.34 E
Dingalan Bay ⊂ 116 15.18 N 121.25 E
Ding'an 110 19.44 N 110.21 E
Dingba 154 3.24 N 27.55 E
Dingbian 102 37.40 N 107.41 E
Dingbianji 102 36.37 N 108.41 E
Dingbu 106 31.18 N 119.10 E
Dingden 52 51.46 N 6.37 E
Dinge 152 4.58 S 12.22 E
Dingelsdorf 58 47.44 N 9.09 E
Dingelstädt 54 51.18 N 10.19 E
Dingelstedt 54 51.58 N 10.58 E
Dingeryu 105 39.37 N 114.55 E
Dingfeng 106 31.20 N 121.45 E
Dinggou 100 32.34 N 119.39 E
Dinggyê 124 28.29 N 88.06 E
Dinghai 100 30.02 N 122.06 E
Dingila 154 3.39 N 26.22 E
Dingjia 107 29.24 N 106.09 E
Dingjiagou 104 40.40 N 122.35 E
Dingjiandian 106 32.06 N 120.52 E
Dingjiasuo 100 32.32 N 120.40 E
Dingjiazhuang 106 32.11 N 120.16 E
Dingkouzhen 102 39.55 N 106.40 E
Dingle 48 52.08 N 10.15 W
Dingle ●[8] 262 53.23 N 2.57 W

PORTUGUÊS — Nome · Página · Lat.°′ · Long.°′ W = Oeste

Dingle Bay ⊂ 48 52.05 N 10.15 W
Dingley 274b 37.58 S 145.07 E
Dinglingen 58 48.20 N 7.50 E
Dingman Creek ≃ 212 42.55 N 81.25 W
Dingmans Ferry 210 41.14 N 74.53 W
Dingnan 100 24.48 N 114.59 E
Dingnan ≃ 100 24.28 N 115.26 E
Dingo 166 23.39 S 149.20 E
Dingolfing 60 48.38 N 12.31 E
Dingras 116 18.06 N 120.42 E
Dingshuzhen 106 31.17 N 119.50 E
Dingtao 98 35.04 N 115.34 E
Dingtuna 40 59.34 N 16.22 E
Dinguira 150 14.11 N 11.16 W
Dinguiraye 150 11.18 N 10.43 W
Dingwall, N.S., Can. 186 46.54 N 60.28 W
Dingwall, Scot., U.K. 46 57.35 N 4.29 W
Dingxi 102 35.33 N 104.32 E
Dingxian 98 38.32 N 114.59 E
Dingxiang 102 38.30 N 113.00 E
Dingxiao 102 25.13 N 105.07 E
Dingxing 105 39.17 N 115.46 E
Dingyan 100 32.23 N 120.45 E
Dingyuan 100 32.32 N 117.40 E
Dingzhouying 105 40.20 N 115.43 E
Dingzichang 107 28.54 N 106.08 E
Dingzi Gang ⊂ 98 36.37 N 120.50 E
Dinh, Mui › 110 11.22 N 109.01 E
Dinhāta 124 26.08 N 89.28 E
Dinh Ca 110 21.45 N 106.03 E
Dinh Lap 110 21.33 N 107.06 E
Dinin ≃ 48 52.43 N 7.18 W
Dinkel ≃ 52 52.30 N 6.58 E
Dinkelsbühl 56 49.04 N 10.19 E
Dinkelscherben 58 48.21 N 10.35 E
Dinkey Creek ≃ 226 36.54 N 119.07 W
Dinklage 52 52.40 N 8.07 E
Dinnebito Wash V 200 35.29 N 111.14 W
Dinner Point › 220 28.28 N 82.41 W
Dinnet 46 57.03 N 2.54 W
Dinnington 44 53.22 N 1.12 W
Dinokwe 156 23.24 S 26.40 E
Dinorwic 184 49.41 N 92.30 W
Dinorwic Lake ⊜ 184 49.37 N 92.33 W
Dinosaur 200 40.14 N 109.00 W
Dinosaur Lake ⊜[1] 182 55.57 N 122.07 W
Dinosaur National Monument ♠ 200 40.32 N 108.58 W
Dinosaur Provincial Park ♠ 182 50.45 N 111.30 W
Dinskaja 78 45.13 N 39.14 E
Dinslaken 52 51.34 N 6.44 E
Dinslakener Bruch 263 51.35 N 6.43 E
Dinslaken-Schwarze Heide, Flughafen ⊠ 263 51.37 N 6.51 E
Dinsmore 184 51.20 N 107.26 W
Dintel ≃ 52 51.39 N 4.22 E
Dinteloord 52 51.37 N 4.22 E
Dinuba 226 36.32 N 119.23 W
Dinwiddie, S. Afr. 273d 26.16 S 28.10 E
Dinwiddie, Va., U.S. 208 37.04 N 77.35 W
Dinwiddie □[6] 208 37.10 N 77.20 W
Dinxperlo 52 51.52 N 6.29 E
Diö 26 56.38 N 14.13 E
Diobo 152 2.16 N 20.29 E
Dioïla 150 12.29 N 6.48 W
Diois ●[1] 62 44.40 N 5.20 E
Diomede 180 65.47 N 169.00 W
Dion ≃ 150 10.12 N 8.39 W
Dionísio 255 19.49 S 42.45 W
Dionísio Cerqueira 252 26.15 S 53.38 W
Dionne, Lac ⊜ 186 49.26 N 67.55 W
Dions 62 43.56 N 4.19 E
Diorama 255 16.21 S 51.14 W
Dios 175e 5.33 S 154.58 E
Dios, Cayos de II 240p 21.39 N 81.09 W
Diósd 264c 47.25 N 18.57 E
Diouloulou 150 13.03 N 16.36 W
Dioumanténé 150 10.32 N 5.55 W
Dioundiou 150 12.37 N 3.33 E
Dioungani 150 14.19 N 2.44 W
Dioura 150 14.50 N 5.15 W
Diourbel 150 14.40 N 16.15 W
Diourbel □[4] 150 14.45 N 16.30 W
Dipaculao 116 15.51 N 121.32 E
Dipai 100 23.50 N 114.06 E
Dīpālpur 123 30.40 N 73.39 E
Dipignano 68 39.15 N 16.15 E
Dipilo, Pizzo ∧ 70 37.57 N 13.59 E
Dipkarpaz 130 35.36 N 34.23 E
Diplo 120 24.28 N 69.35 E
Dipolog 116 8.35 N 123.20 E
Dippoldiswalde 54 50.54 N 13.40 E
Dipton 172 45.54 S 168.22 E
Dipu 106 30.38 N 119.41 E
Diqiyingzi 104 42.11 N 121.29 E
Dique Florentino Ameghino 254 43.40 S 66.25 W
Dīr 123 35.12 N 71.53 E
Dira, Djebel ∧ 34 36.05 N 3.38 E
Diré 150 16.16 N 3.24 W
Direction, Cape › 164 12.51 S 143.32 E
Dire Dawa 144 9.37 N 41.52 E
Direkli 130 39.43 N 36.40 E
Diriamba 236 11.51 N 86.14 W
Dirico 152 17.58 S 20.47 E
Dirillo, Lago ⊜ 70 37.08 N 14.42 E
Diriomo 236 11.52 N 86.03 W
Dirj 146 30.09 N 10.26 E
Dirk Hartog Island I 162 25.48 S 113.00 E
Dirkiesdorp 158 27.10 S 30.25 E
Dirkou 146 19.01 N 12.53 E
Dirkshorn 52 52.45 N 4.45 E
Dirksland 52 51.44 N 4.06 E
Dirnaich 60 48.27 N 12.30 E
Dirrah 140 13.37 N 26.06 E
Dirranbandi 166 28.35 S 148.14 E
Dirri 144 4.20 N 46.37 E
Dirs 144 18.32 N 42.05 E
Dirschau → Tczew 30 54.06 N 18.47 E
Dirty Devil ≃ 200 37.53 N 110.24 W
Dīsa 120 24.15 N 72.10 E
Dīsah 140 12.02 N 34.19 E
Disappointment, Cape ›, S. Geor. 244 54.53 S 36.07 W
Disappointment, Cape ›, Wa., U.S. 224 46.18 N 124.03 W
Disappointment, Lake ⊜ 162 23.30 S 122.50 E
Disappointment, Mount ∧ 169 37.25 S 145.18 E
Disappointment Creek ≃ 200 38.01 N 108.51 W
Disaster Bay ⊂ 166 37.17 S 150.00 E
Disautel 182 48.22 N 119.14 W
Disbrow Drain ≊ 281 42.06 N 83.27 W
Disco 214 42.41 N 83.02 W
Discovery 273d 26.10 S 27.54 E
Discovery Bay ⊂, Austl. 166 38.12 S 141.07 E
Discovery Bay ⊂, H.K. 271d 22.18 N 114.01 E
Discovery Bay ⊂, Wa., U.S. 224 48.05 N 122.52 W
Discovery Island I 224 48.25 N 123.15 W
Discovery Passage ʯ 182 50.00 N 125.15 W
Discovery Tablemount ✦[3] 8 42.00 S 0.10 E
Disentis 58 46.43 N 8.51 E
Dishāshah 142 28.59 N 30.51 E
Dishergarh 126 23.41 N 86.50 E
Dishman 202 47.39 N 117.16 W
Dishnā 140 26.07 N 32.28 E
Dishna ≃ 180 63.37 N 157.18 W
Disihao 89 50.28 N 124.35 E
Disko 216 41.00 N 85.57 W
Disko I 176 69.50 N 53.30 W
Disko Bugt ⊂ 176 69.15 N 52.00 W
Disley 262 53.21 N 2.02 W

Disley Tunnel ●[5] 262 53.22 N 2.03 W
Dismal ≃ 198 41.50 N 100.05 W
Dismal Lakes ⊜ 176 67.26 N 117.07 W
Dismal Swamp Canal ≊ 208 36.45 N 76.20 W
Disna 76 55.33 N 28.10 E
Disna ≃ 76 55.34 N 28.12 E
Disney 196 36.28 N 95.00 W
Disneyland ♠ 228 33.48 N 117.55 W
Disneyworld ♠ 220 28.27 N 81.28 W
Diso 68 40.00 N 18.23 E
Dispur 120 26.08 N 91.47 E
Disputanta 208 37.07 N 77.13 W
Disraeli 206 45.54 N 71.21 W
Diss 42 52.23 N 1.07 E
Dissen 52 52.07 N 8.12 E
Dissimieux, Lac ⊜ 186 49.51 N 69.48 W
Distant 214 40.58 N 79.21 W
Disteghil Sār ∧ 123 36.19 N 75.12 E
Disteln 263 51.36 N 7.09 E
Distington 44 54.36 N 3.32 W
District Heights 284c 38.51 N 76.53 W
District of Columbia □[3] 208 38.54 N 77.01 W
Distrito Especial □[5] 246 4.15 N 74.15 W
Distrito Federal □[5], Arg. 258 34.36 S 58.26 W
Distrito Federal □[5], Bra. 255 15.45 S 47.45 W
Distrito Federal □[5], Méx. 234 19.15 N 99.10 W
Distrito Federal □[5], Ven. 246 10.30 N 66.55 W
Distroff 56 49.20 N 6.16 E
Disūq 142 31.08 N 30.39 E
Ditfurt 54 51.50 N 11.11 E
Dithmarschen ●[1] 30 54.05 N 9.00 E
Dit Island I 116 11.15 N 120.56 E
Dittáino ≃ 70 37.25 N 15.00 E
Ditton, Eng., U.K. 260 51.18 N 0.27 E
Ditton, Eng., U.K. 262 53.22 N 2.45 W
Ditton ≃ 206 45.23 N 71.12 W
Ditton Priors 42 52.30 N 2.35 W
Ditzingen 56 48.49 N 9.03 E
Ditzum 52 53.18 N 7.16 E
Diu 120 20.42 N 70.59 E
Diu □[8] 120 20.42 N 70.59 E
Diuata Mountains ⋏ 116 9.10 N 125.47 E
Diuata Point › 116 9.05 N 125.12 E
Dīva 272c 19.09 N 72.59 E
Divalá 236 8.25 N 82.43 W
Dīvāndarreh 128 35.55 N 47.02 E
Dívčice 61 49.06 N 14.19 E
Dive 272c 19.11 N 73.02 E
Divejevo 80 55.03 N 43.15 E
Divenié 152 2.41 S 12.05 E
Divenskaja 76 59.12 N 30.01 E
Diveria ≃ 58 46.09 N 8.19 E
Divernon 219 39.33 N 89.39 W
Dives ≃ 32 49.19 N 0.05 W
Diviči 84 41.12 N 48.59 E
Dividing Creek 208 39.16 N 75.06 W
Dividing Creek ≃ 208 38.05 N 75.32 W
Dividing Ridge ∧ 219 39.07 N 90.39 W
Divignano 266b 45.40 N 8.36 E
Divilacan Bay ⊂ 116 17.25 N 122.19 E
Divin 76 51.58 N 24.35 E
Divine Corners 210 41.48 N 74.40 W
Divinhe 156 20.40 S 34.49 E
Divino 255 20.37 S 42.09 W
Divinolândia 256 21.40 S 46.45 W
Divinópolis 255 20.09 S 44.54 W
Divi Point › 122 15.58 N 81.09 E
Divis ∧[2] 48 54.37 N 6.01 W
Divisa Nova 256 21.31 S 46.12 W
Divisor, Serra do (Cordillera Ultraoriental) ⋏[1] 248 8.20 S 73.30 W
Divizija 78 45.57 N 29.59 E
Divnogorsk 86 55.58 N 92.22 E
Divnoje 80 45.55 N 43.22 E
Divo 150 5.50 N 5.22 W
Divodar 120 24.06 N 71.47 E
Divonne-les-Bains 58 46.22 N 6.08 E
Divriği 130 39.23 N 38.07 E
Dīwāl Qol 120 34.19 N 67.54 E
Dix, Il., U.S. 219 38.27 N 88.56 W
Dix, Ne., U.S. 198 41.14 N 103.29 W
Dix ≃ 192 37.49 N 84.43 W
Dix, Lac des ⊜ 58 46.03 N 7.24 E
Dixboro 216 42.19 N 83.39 W
Dixfield 188 44.32 N 70.27 W
Dix Hills 276 40.49 N 73.22 W
Dixie 275b 43.36 N 79.36 W
Dixie Valley V 204 39.50 N 117.55 W
Dix Milles, Lac ⊜ 190 46.46 N 77.45 W
Dixmoor 278 41.38 N 87.40 W
Dixmude → Diksmuide 50 51.02 N 2.52 E
Dixon, Ca., U.S. 226 38.19 N 121.49 W
Dixon, Il., U.S. 190 41.50 N 89.28 W
Dixon, Ky., U.S. 194 37.31 N 87.41 W
Dixon, Mo., U.S. 194 37.59 N 92.05 W
Dixon, N.M., U.S. 200 36.11 N 105.53 W
Dixon, Oh., U.S. 216 40.57 N 84.48 W
Dixon Entrance ʯ 182 54.25 N 132.30 W
Dixons Mills 194 32.04 N 87.47 W
Dixons Pond ⊜ 276 40.56 N 74.27 W
Dixonville 214 40.42 N 79.00 W
Dixville 206 45.04 N 71.46 W
Diyā al-Kawm 142 30.38 N 31.05 E
Diyadin 84 39.33 N 43.41 E
Diyālā □[4] 128 34.00 N 45.00 E
Diyālā (Sīrvān) ≃ 128 33.14 N 44.31 E
Diyanga 152 1.29 S 11.52 E
Diyarbakır 130 37.55 N 40.14 E
Diyarbakır □[4] 130 38.05 N 40.15 E
Diyarb Najm 142 30.45 N 31.26 E
Diyu al-Wasta 142 30.54 N 31.30 E
Dizangsi 104 41.26 N 120.57 E
Dizhou 102 23.00 N 106.20 E
Dizy 50 49.04 N 3.58 E
Dizzard Point › 42 50.45 N 4.38 W
Dja ≃ 152 2.02 N 15.12 E
Dja, Réserve du ●[4] 152 3.05 N 13.00 E
Djabalpur → Jabalpur 124 23.10 N 79.57 E
Djabir 152 0.32 N 24.05 E
Djadié ≃ 152 0.46 N 12.58 E
Djado 146 21.01 N 12.18 E
Djado, Plateau du ⋏[1] 146 21.45 N 12.50 E
Djaipur → Jaipur 120 26.55 N 75.49 E
Djakarta → Jakarta 269e 6.10 S 106.48 E
Djakonovo 82 54.34 N 38.20 E
Djakovka 80 50.43 N 46.46 E
Djakovo 83 47.57 N 39.09 E
Djakovo ●[8] 265b 55.39 N 37.40 E
Djamâa 148 33.32 N 6.00 E
Djamba, Ang. 152 16.46 S 13.59 E
Djamba, Zaïre 152 9.49 S 22.07 E
Djambala 152 2.33 S 14.45 E
Djamschedpur → Jamshedpur 126 22.48 N 86.11 E
Djanet 148 24.34 N 9.29 E
Djaouro Mbali 152 5.52 N 13.29 E
Djaret, Oued V 148 26.32 N 1.30 E
Djebobo ∧ 150 8.20 N 0.35 E
Djébrène 146 11.14 N 19.01 E
Djédaa 146 13.31 N 18.34 E
Djedda → Jiddah 144 21.30 N 39.12 E
Djedi, Oued V 148 34.28 N 6.05 E
Djéké Djéké 146 8.25 N 18.12 E
Djelo-Binza 273b 4.23 S 15.16 E
Djema 140 6.03 N 25.19 E
Djember → Jember, Incon. 115a 8.10 S 113.42 E
Djember, Tchad 146 10.25 N 17.50 E

Djemila ⊥ 34 36.25 N 5.44 E
Djénné 150 13.54 N 4.33 W
Djenoun, Garet el ∧ 148 25.05 N 5.25 E
Djérem ≃ 152 5.20 N 13.24 E
Djibasso 150 13.07 N 4.10 W
Djibo 150 14.06 N 1.38 W
Djibouti 144 11.36 N 43.09 E
Djibouti □[1], Afr. 136 11.30 N 43.00 E
Djibouti □[1], Afr. 144 11.30 N 43.00 E
Djibrouïa 150 13.13 N 11.14 W
Djiri 273b 4.08 S 15.19 E
Djiri ≃ 273b 4.11 S 15.20 E
Djchong 152 6.50 N 14.42 E
Djokjakarta → Yogyakarta 115a 7.48 S 110.22 E
Djokoumatombi 152 0.47 N 15.22 E
Djokupunda 152 5.27 S 20.58 E
Djolu 152 0.37 N 22.21 E
Djombo 152 1.21 N 20.22 E
Djoua ≃ 152 1.13 N 13.12 E
Djouari ≃ 273b 4.13 S 15.08 E
Djoubissi 152 6.12 N 20.45 E
Djoué ≃ 273b 4.19 S 15.14 E
Djougou 150 9.42 N 1.40 E
Djoum 152 2.40 N 12.40 E
Djouna 146 10.27 N 20.04 E
Djourab, Erg du ⛬[8] 146 16.40 N 18.50 E
Djugu 154 1.55 N 30.30 E
Djúpivogur 24a 64.40 N 14.10 W
Djura 40 60.37 N 15.00 E
Djurås 40 60.33 N 15.08 E
Djurmo 40 60.33 N 15.10 E
Djurö 40 59.19 N 18.41 E
Djurö I 26 58.52 N 13.28 E
Djursholm 40 59.24 N 18.05 E
Dlouhá Ves 60 49.12 N 13.31 E
Dmanisi 84 41.22 N 44.12 E
Dmitr'ašovka 76 52.09 N 39.04 E
Dmitrija Lapteva, proliv ʯ 74 73.00 N 142.00 E
Dmitrijevka, Kaz. 85 43.30 N 77.02 E
Dmitrijevka, Ross. 76 52.53 N 40.47 E
Dmitrijevka, Ross. 86 55.10 N 75.36 E
Dmitrijevka, Ukr. 78 50.56 N 32.58 E
Dmitrijevka, Ukr. 83 48.55 N 39.10 E
Dmitrijevka, Ukr. 83 47.56 N 38.56 E
Dmitrijev-L'govskij 78 52.08 N 35.05 E
Dmitrijevskij 86 49.08 N 57.50 E
Dmitrijevskoje, Ross. 80 45.48 N 41.54 E
Dmitrijevskoje, Ross. 82 54.40 N 37.38 E
Dmitrijev Usad, Ross. 76 54.08 N 43.08 E
Dmitrijev Usad, Ross. 80 54.14 N 43.18 E
Dmitrijevy Gory 80 55.12 N 41.47 E
Dmitrov 82 56.21 N 37.31 E
Dmitrovcy 82 55.16 N 38.55 E
Dmitroviči 76 53.59 N 29.06 E
Dmitrovka, Ukr. 78 48.48 N 32.44 E
Dmitrovka, Ukr. 78 45.29 N 35.04 E
Dmitrovka, Ukr. 78 46.51 N 36.35 E
Dmitrovskij Pogost 76 55.19 N 39.49 E
Dmitrovsk-Orlovskij 76 52.30 N 35.09 E
Dmuchajlovka 78 49.03 N 34.46 E
Dnepr ≃ 78 46.30 N 32.18 E
Dnepr'any 78 46.44 N 33.16 E
Dneprodzeržinsk 78 48.30 N 34.37 E
Dneprodzeržinskoje vodochranilišče ⊜[1] 78 48.45 N 34.00 E
Dnepropetrovsk 78 48.27 N 34.59 E
Dnepropetrovsk □[4] 78 48.30 N 35.00 E
Dneprovka 78 47.26 N 34.38 E
Dneprovskij liman ⊂[1] 78 46.35 N 31.55 E
Dneprovsko-Bugskij kanal ≊ 76 52.03 N 25.35 E
Dneprovskoje 76 55.40 N 33.55 E
Dnestr ≃ 78 46.18 N 30.17 E
Dnestrovskij liman ⊜ 78 46.15 N 30.17 E
Dnieper → Dnepr ≃ 78 46.30 N 32.18 E
Dniepropetrovsk → Dnepropetrovsk 78 48.27 N 34.59 E
Dniester → Dnestr ≃ 78 46.18 N 30.17 E
Dno 76 57.50 N 29.59 E
Do, Lac ⊜ 150 15.54 N 2.45 W
Doa 154 16.44 S 34.32 E
Do Āb-e Mīkh-e Zarrīn 120 35.16 N 68.00 E
Doaktown 186 46.33 N 66.08 W
Doangdoangan-Besar, Pulau I 112 5.24 S 117.55 E
Doany 157b 14.22 S 49.31 E
Doba 146 8.39 N 16.51 E
Dobane 140 6.24 N 24.42 E
Dobbertin 54 53.37 N 12.04 E
Dobbiaco (Toblach) 64 46.44 N 12.14 E
Dobbin 222 30.22 N 95.46 W
Dobbins 226 39.22 N 121.12 W
Dobbins Air Force Base ■ 192 33.54 N 84.31 W
Dobbs Ferry 210 41.00 N 73.52 W
Dobczyce 30 49.54 N 20.06 E
Dobel 56 48.48 N 8.29 E
Dobele 76 56.37 N 23.16 E
Döbeln 54 51.07 N 13.07 E
Doberai, Jazirah (Vogelkop) ›[1] 164 1.30 S 132.30 E
Döberitz 264a 52.33 N 13.03 E
Doberlug-Kirchhain 54 51.38 N 13.34 E
Döbern 54 51.37 N 14.36 E
Dobiegniew 30 52.59 N 15.47 E
Döbling ●[8] 264b 48.15 N 16.22 E
Dobo 164 5.46 S 134.13 E
Doboj 38 44.44 N 18.06 E
Dobra, Pol. 30 51.54 N 18.37 E
Dobra, Pol. 30 53.35 N 15.18 E
Dobra ≃ 36 45.33 N 15.31 E
Dobr'anka, Ross. 86 58.27 N 56.24 E
Dobr'anka, Ukr. 78 52.04 N 31.11 E
Dobr'ankka 78 48.21 N 30.54 E
Dobřany 60 49.40 N 13.18 E
Dobra Stausee ⊜[1] 61 48.35 N 15.20 E
Dobre Miasto 30 53.59 N 20.25 E
Döbriach 64 46.47 N 13.39 E
Dobrič 38 43.34 N 27.50 E
Dobrich → Dobrič 38 43.34 N 27.50 E
Dobrinka, Ross. 80 52.09 N 40.29 E
Dobrinka, Ross. 80 48.49 N 42.58 E
Dobrinka, Ross. 80 50.49 N 41.51 E
Dobříš 30 49.47 N 14.11 E
Dobritz 54 52.01 N 12.13 E
Dobrodzień 30 50.44 N 18.27 E
Dobroje, Ross. 76 57.06 N 32.02 E
Dobroje, Ross. 76 52.52 N 39.48 E
Dobroměřice 54 50.23 N 13.46 E
Dobromil' 78 49.34 N 22.47 E
Dobropolje 78 48.28 N 37.05 E
Dobroslavka 76 52.24 N 26.15 E
Dobroteasa 38 44.47 N 24.23 E
Dobrotvor 78 50.14 N 24.22 E
Dobroveličkovka 78 48.23 N 31.11 E
Dobrovolje 78 48.41 N 36.37 E
Dobrovol'sk 76 54.46 N 22.31 E
Dobrudžansko plato ⋏[1] 38 43.32 N 27.50 E
Dobruja ●[1] 38 44.00 N 28.00 E
Dobruš 76 52.25 N 31.19 E
Dobruška 30 50.17 N 16.10 E
Dobryn' 78 51.46 N 29.12 E
Dobrzany 30 53.22 N 15.25 E
Dobrzyń nad Wisłą 30 52.38 N 19.20 E
Dobšiná 30 48.49 N 20.23 E
Dobson 192 36.23 N 80.43 W
Dobzha 120 28.28 N 88.14 E
Doce ≃, Bra. 255 19.37 S 39.49 W
Doce ≃, Bra. 255 18.28 S 51.05 W
Doce de Octubre 196 25.38 N 97.47 W
Dochart ≃ 46 56.28 N 4.20 W
Döčin ≃ 88 49.39 N 114.48 E
Docker River 162 24.52 S 129.05 E

Docking 42 52.55 N 0.38 E
Dock Junction 192 31.11 N 81.31 W
Dockton 224 47.22 N 122.27 W
Dockweiler 56 50.15 N 6.46 E
Dockweiler Beach State Park ♠ 280 33.55 N 118.26 W
Doctor Arroyo 234 23.40 N 100.11 W
Doctor Cecilio Báez 252 25.03 S 56.19 W
Doctor Coss 196 25.55 N 99.11 W
Doctor Edmund A. Babler Memorial State Park ♠ 219 38.36 N 90.43 W
Doctor Hicks Range ⋏ 162 28.40 S 124.20 E
Doctor Pedro P. Peña 252 22.26 S 62.22 W
Doctors Creek ≃ 208 40.11 N 74.41 W
Doda 123 33.08 N 75.34 E
Dod Ballāpur 122 13.18 N 77.32 E
Doddinghurst 42 51.40 N 0.18 E
Doddridge 194 33.05 N 93.54 W
Dodds Island I 219 38.35 N 91.59 W
Doddsville 194 33.39 N 90.31 W
Dodecanese → Dhodhekánisos II 38 36.30 N 27.00 E
Dodéo 152 7.29 N 12.04 E
Dodge, Ne., U.S. 198 41.43 N 96.52 W
Dodge, Tx., U.S. 222 30.45 N 95.24 W
Dodge □[6] 216 43.14 N 88.40 W
Dodge Brothers State Park Number 4♠, Mi., U.S. 281 42.37 N 83.22 W
Dodge Brothers State Park Number 8♠, Mi., U.S. 281 42.36 N 83.01 W
Dodge Center 190 44.01 N 92.51 W
Dodge City 198 37.45 N 100.01 W
Dodge Park 284c 38.56 N 76.53 W
Dodger Stadium ♠ 280 34.04 N 118.14 W
Dodgeville 190 42.57 N 90.07 W
Dodman Point › 42 50.13 N 4.48 W
Dodo Goei 140 5.57 N 29.26 E
Dodola 144 7.02 N 39.07 E
Dodoma 154 6.11 S 35.45 E
Dodoma □[4] 154 6.00 S 36.00 E
Dodori ≃ 154 1.52 S 41.02 E
Dodsland 184 51.48 N 108.49 W
Dodson, La., U.S. 194 32.04 N 92.39 W
Dodson, Mt., U.S. 202 48.23 N 108.14 W
Dodson, Tx., U.S. 196 34.46 N 100.02 W
Dodurga 130 39.48 N 29.55 E
Doe Lake ⊜ 212 45.32 N 79.25 W
Doe River 182 56.00 N 120.05 W
Doerun 192 31.19 N 83.55 W
Doesburg 52 52.01 N 6.09 E
Doetinchem 52 51.58 N 6.17 E
Dog ≃ 190 48.51 N 89.37 W
Dogācha 272b 22.58 N 88.31 E
Dogai Coring ⊜ 120 34.30 N 89.15 E
Dōga-mori ∧ 96 33.09 N 132.53 E
Doğanbey, Tür. 130 37.37 N 27.11 E
Doğanbey, Tür. 130 38.04 N 26.53 E
Doğanbey, Tür. 130 37.48 N 31.54 E
Doğanca 130 37.49 N 42.20 E
Doğançay 130 40.37 N 30.20 E
Doganella 66 41.34 N 12.56 E
Doğanhisar 130 38.09 N 31.41 E
Doğankent, Tür. 130 40.48 N 38.56 E
Doğankent, Tür. 130 36.52 N 35.18 E
Doğanşehir 130 38.06 N 37.53 E
Doğanyol 130 38.19 N 39.03 E
Doğanyurt, Tür. 130 42.00 N 33.27 E
Doğanyurt, Tür. 130 40.41 N 36.43 E
Dog Creek 182 51.35 N 122.15 W
Dog Creek ≃, B.C., Can. 182 51.35 N 122.17 W
Dog Creek ≃, Mt., U.S. 202 47.44 N 109.36 W
Dog Creek ≃, Oh., U.S. 216 41.03 N 84.23 W
Dog Ear Creek ≃ 198 43.42 N 99.59 W
Dog Island I, Anguilla 238 18.17 N 63.16 W
Dog Island I, Fl., U.S. 192 29.48 N 84.35 W
Dog Islands II 240m 18.29 N 64.28 W
Dog Lake ⊜, Mb., Can. 184 51.02 N 98.30 W
Dog Lake ⊜, On., Can. 190 48.46 N 89.32 W
Dog Lake ⊜, On., Can. 190 48.18 N 84.10 W
Dog Lake ⊜, On., Can. 212 44.27 N 76.20 W
Dogliani 62 44.32 N 7.56 E
Dogna 64 46.27 N 13.19 E
Dōgo I 92 36.15 N 133.16 E
Do Gonbadān 128 30.21 N 50.48 E
Dogondoutchi 150 13.38 N 4.02 E
Doğonşar 130 40.14 N 37.33 E
Dōgo-yama ∧ 96 35.04 N 133.14 E
Dogpound Creek ≃ 182 51.50 N 114.24 W
Dogs, Isle of I 260 51.29 N 0.01 W
D'ogtevo, Ross. 78 49.10 N 40.39 E
D'ogtevo, Ross. 80 49.11 N 40.39 E
Doğubayazıt 84 39.32 N 44.08 E
Doguéraoua 150 13.58 N 5.35 E
Doğu Karadeniz Dağları ⋏ 130 40.30 N 40.30 E
Dogura 164 10.05 S 150.05 E
Doha → Ad-Dawḥah 128 25.17 N 51.32 E
Dohār 126 23.35 N 90.09 E
Dohhi 124 24.32 N 84.54 E
Dohna 54 50.57 N 13.51 E
Dohrgaul 263 51.06 N 7.27 E
Dohrīghāt 124 26.16 N 83.31 E
Doi 96 33.57 N 133.26 E
Doi, Kinh ≊ 269c 10.43 N 106.37 E
Doilungdêqên 124 29.48 N 90.47 E
Doiran, Lake ⊜ 38 41.13 N 22.44 E
Doiras, Embalse de ⊜[1] 34 43.10 N 6.45 W
Dois de Novembro, Cachoeira ᒐ 248 8.52 S 62.16 W
Dois Irmãos, Pico ∧ 287a 22.59 S 43.14 W
Dois Irmãos de Goiás 250 9.16 S 49.05 W
Doi Suthep-Pui National Park ♠ 110 18.50 N 98.50 E
Dōjō 268 35.51 N 139.37 E
Dōjō ●[8] 270 34.52 N 135.14 E
Doka, Indon. 164 6.39 S 134.15 E
Doka, Sūd. 140 13.31 N 35.46 E
Doki ≃ 96 34.18 N 133.48 E
Dokka 26 60.50 N 10.05 E
Dokkum 52 53.19 N 6.00 E
Dökmetepe 130 40.19 N 36.18 E
Dokri 120 27.23 N 68.06 E
Dokšicy 76 54.54 N 27.46 E
Dokská pahorkatina ⋏[2] 54 50.30 N 14.45 E
Doksy 54 50.35 N 14.38 E
Dokučajevsk 83 47.44 N 37.40 E
Dol'a, Ukr. 83 47.53 N 37.41 E
Dola, Oh., U.S. 216 40.47 N 83.42 W
Dolak ≃ 164 7.48 S 139.00 E
Doland 198 44.53 N 98.06 W
Dolany 60 49.27 N 13.15 E
Dolavon 254 43.18 S 65.42 W
Dolayoba 267b 40.54 N 29.15 E
Dolbeau 176 48.53 N 72.14 W
Dolberg 52 51.42 N 7.55 E
Dolceacqua 62 43.51 N 7.37 E
Dolcedorme, Serra ∧ 68 39.53 N 16.13 E
Dol-de-Bretagne 32 48.33 N 1.45 W
Dole 58 47.06 N 5.30 E
Dolega 236 8.34 N 82.25 W
Dolen 222 30.26 N 94.54 W
Dolgaja 86 55.49 N 64.15 E
Dolgaja, kosa ›[2] 78 46.43 N 37.41 E
Dolgarrog 44 53.11 N 3.51 W

Symbol	English	Deutsch	Español	Français	Português
≃	River	Fluß	Río	Rivière	Rio
≊	Canal	Kanal	Canal	Canal	Canal
ᒐ	Waterfall, Rapids	Wasserfall, Stromschnellen	Cascada, Rápidos	Chute d'eau, Rapides	Cascata, Rápidos
ʯ	Strait	Meeresstraße	Estrecho	Détroit	Estreito
⊂	Bay, Gulf	Bucht, Golf	Bahía, Golfo	Baie, Golfe	Baía, Golfo
⊜	Lake, Lakes	See, Seen	Lago, Lagos	Lac, Lacs	Lago, Lagos
≡	Swamp	Sumpf	Pantano	Marais	Pântano
⛬	Ice Features, Glacier	Eis- und Gletscherformen	Accidentes Glaciales	Formes glaciaires	Acidentes glaciares
⊤	Other Hydrographic Features	Andere Hydrographische Objekte	Otros Elementos Hidrográficos	Autres données hydrographiques	Outros acidentes hidrográficos
✦	Submarine Features	Untermeerische Objekte	Accidentes Submarinos	Formes de relief sous-marin	Acidentes submarinos
□	Political Unit	Politische Einheit	Unidad Política	Entité politique	Unidade política
♥	Cultural Institution	Kulturelle Institution	Institución Cultural	Institution culturelle	Instituição cultural
⊥	Historical Site	Historische Stätte	Sitio Histórico	Site historique	Sítio histórico
♠	Recreational Site	Erholungs- und Ferienort	Sitio de Recreo	Centre de loisirs	Área de Lazer
⊠	Airport	Flughafen	Aeropuerto	Aéroport	Aeroporto
■	Military Installation	Militäranlage	Instalación Militar	Installation militaire	Instalação militar
●	Miscellaneous	Verschiedenes	Misceláneo	Divers	Diversos

Symbols in the index entries represent the broad categories identified in the key at the right. Symbols with superior numbers (⋖¹) identify subcategories (see complete key on page I · 1).

Symbole im Register stellen die rechts im Schlüssel erklärten Kategorien dar. Symbole mit hochgestellten Ziffern (⋖¹) bezeichnen Unterteilungen einer Kategorie (vgl. vollständiger Schlüssel auf Seite I · 1).

Los símbolos incluidos en el texto del índice representan las grandes categorías identificadas con la clave a la derecha. Los símbolos con números en su parte superior (⋖¹) identifican las subcategorías (véase la clave completa en la página I · 1).

Les symboles de l'index représentent les catégories indiquées dans la légende à droite. Les symboles suivis d'un indice (⋖¹) représentent des sous-catégories (voir légende complète à la page I · 1).

Os símbolos incluídos no texto do índice representam as grandes categorias identificadas com a chave à direita. Os símbolos com números em sua parte superior (⋖¹) identificam as subcategorias (veja-se a chave completa à página I · 1).

Symbol	English	Deutsch	Español	Français	Português
⋏	Mountain	Berg	Montaña	Montagne	Montanha
⋰	Mountains	Gebirge	Montañas	Montagnes	Montanhas
⌓	Pass	Paß	Paso	Col	Paso
∨	Valley, Canyon	Tal, Cañon	Valle, Cañón	Vallée, Canyon	Vale, Canhão
≃	Plain	Ebene	Llano	Plaine	Planície
⊳	Cape	Kap	Cabo	Cap	Cabo
I	Island	Insel	Isla	Île	Ilha
II	Islands	Inseln	Islas	Îles	Ilhas
⍩	Other Topographic Features	Andere Topographische Objekte	Otros Elementos Topográficos	Autres données topographiques	Outros acidentes topográficos

ESPAÑOL Nombre	Página	Lat.°′	Long.°′ W = Oeste
Downham, Eng., U.K.	260	51.38 N	0.30 E
Downham Market	42	52.36 N	0.23 E
Down House ⊥	260	51.20 N	0.03 E
Downieville	226	39.33 N	120.49 W
Downing	194	40.29 N	92.22 W
Downingtown	208	40.00 N	75.42 W
Downingtown Airport ⊠	285	39.59 N	75.45 W
Downpatrick	48	54.20 N	5.43 W
Downpatrick Head >	48	54.20 N	9.20 W
Downs, Il., U.S.	216	40.24 N	88.52 W
Downs, Ks., U.S.	198	39.30 N	98.32 W
Downs Mountain ∧	200	43.18 N	109.40 W
Downsview Dells Park ♠	275b	43.44 N	79.30 W
Downsville	210	42.04 N	74.59 W
Downsville Dam ◆[6]	210	42.05 N	74.58 W
Downton	42	51.00 N	1.44 W
Downton, Mount ∧	182	52.42 N	124.51 W
Downton Lake ⊜	182	50.51 N	123.00 W
Downwind Acres Airfield ⊠	281	42.09 N	83.34 W
Dows	190	42.39 N	93.30 W
Dowshī	120	35.37 N	68.41 E
Doygaab	144	0.59 N	43.32 E
Doyle	204	40.01 N	120.06 W
Doyles	186	47.50 N	59.12 W
Doylesburg	214	40.13 N	77.42 W
Doylestown, Oh., U.S.	214	40.58 N	81.41 W
Doylestown, Pa., U.S.	208	40.18 N	75.07 W
Doyline	194	32.32 N	93.25 W
Dōzan ≃	96	33.58 N	133.47 E
Dōzen II	92	36.05 N	133.05 E
Dozier	194	31.29 N	86.21 W
Dozois, Réservoir ⊜[1]	190	47.30 N	77.05 W
Dozza	66	44.22 N	11.37 E
Drâa, Cap >	148	28.44 N	11.08 W
Dra'a, Hamada du ◆[2]	148	29.00 N	6.45 W
Drâa, Oued V	148	28.43 N	11.09 W
Draa el Mizan	34	36.32 N	3.50 E
Drabble → José Enrique Rodó	258	33.41 S	57.34 W
Drabenderhöhe	56	50.57 N	7.27 E
Drabov	78	49.58 N	32.08 E
Drac ≃	62	45.13 N	5.41 E
Dracena	255	21.32 S	51.29 W
Drachenfels ⊥	56	50.40 N	7.12 E
Drachten	52	53.06 N	6.05 E
Dracut	207	42.40 N	71.18 W
Dragalina	38	44.26 N	27.20 E
Drăgănești-Olt	38	44.10 N	24.32 E
Drăgănești-Vlașca	38	44.06 N	25.36 E
Drăgășani	38	44.40 N	24.16 E
Drag Lake ⊜	212	45.05 N	78.24 W
Dragone ≃	64	44.23 N	10.37 E
Dragonera I	34	39.35 N	2.19 E
Dragoni	68	41.16 N	14.18 E
Dragonja ≃	64	45.28 N	13.37 E
Dragons Mouths ⋃	241r	10.45 N	61.46 W
Dragon Swamp ≃	208	37.33 N	76.34 W
Dragoon	200	32.01 N	110.02 W
Dragør	41	55.36 N	12.41 E
Draguignan	62	43.32 N	6.28 E
Drain	202	43.39 N	123.19 W
Drake, Mo., U.S.	219	38.28 N	91.28 W
Drake, N.D., U.S.	198	47.55 N	100.22 W
Drakenburg	52	52.41 N	9.13 E
Drakensberg ʌ	156	27.00 S	30.00 E
Drake Passage ⋃	18	58.00 S	70.00 W
Drake Peak ∧	202	42.19 N	120.07 W
Drakesboro	194	37.13 N	87.02 W
Drakes Branch	192	36.59 N	78.36 W
Drakes Brook ≃	276	40.49 N	74.43 W
Drake Well Museum ʊ	214	41.36 N	79.39 W
Drakino	82	54.52 N	37.17 E
Dráma	38	41.09 N	24.08 E
Drammen	26	59.44 N	10.15 E
Dran	110	11.51 N	108.35 E
Drancy	50	48.56 N	2.27 E
Dranda	84	42.53 N	41.09 E
Drang ≃	110	13.19 N	107.21 E
Drangajökull ⊓	24a	66.11 N	22.15 W
Drangstedt	52	53.36 N	8.44 E
Dranov, Ostrovul I	38	44.52 N	29.15 E
Dransfeld	52	51.30 N	9.45 E
Dranske	54	54.38 N	13.14 E
Drap	62	43.45 N	7.19 E
Draper, N.C., U.S.	192	36.31 N	79.41 W
Draper, Ut,. U.S.	200	40.31 N	111.51 W
Draperstown	48	54.48 N	6.47 W
Drās	123	34.27 N	75.46 E
Drās ≃	123	34.37 N	75.59 E
Drau (Drava) (Dráva) ≃	36	45.33 N	18.55 E
Drava (Drau) (Dráva) ≃	36	45.33 N	18.55 E
Draveil	50	48.41 N	2.25 E
Dravinja ≃	36	46.22 N	15.57 E
Dravograd	61	46.35 N	15.02 E
Dravosburg	279b	40.21 N	79.51 W
Drawno	30	53.13 N	15.45 E
Drawsko Pomorskie	30	53.32 N	15.48 E
Drayton, On., Can.	212	43.46 N	80.40 W
Drayton, Eng., U.K.	42	51.38 N	1.18 W
Drayton, N.D., U.S.	198	48.34 N	97.10 W
Drayton, S.C., U.S.	192	34.58 N	81.54 W
Drayton Plains	216	42.41 N	83.22 W
Drayton Valley	182	53.13 N	114.59 W
Draženov	60	49.28 N	12.52 E
Drean	36	36.41 N	7.46 E
Drebkau	54	51.39 N	14.13 E
Dreieich	56	50.01 N	8.41 E
Dreifelder Weiher ⊜	56	50.36 N	7.49 E
Dreihausen	56	50.43 N	8.50 E
Dreiherrnspitze (Picco dei Tre Signori) ∧	64	47.04 N	12.15 E
Dreikikir	164	3.35 S	142.45 E
Drejø I	41	54.58 N	10.25 E
Dremsel, Mount ∧	164	2.10 S	146.55 E
Drena	64	45.58 N	10.56 E
Drenovec	38	43.42 N	22.59 E
Drensteinfurt	52	51.48 N	7.44 E
Drenthe □[4]	52	52.45 N	6.30 E
Dresde → Dresden	54	51.03 N	13.44 E
Dresden, On., Can.	214	42.35 N	82.11 W
Dresden, Dtsch.	54	51.03 N	13.44 E
Dresden, N.Y., U.S.	210	42.41 N	76.58 W
Dresden, Oh., U.S.	214	40.07 N	82.00 W
Dresden, Tn., U.S.	194	36.17 N	88.42 W
Dresher	285	40.08 N	75.10 W
Dretun	76	55.41 N	29.13 E
Dreux	50	48.44 N	1.22 E
Drevenack	263	51.40 N	6.45 E
Drew	194	33.48 N	90.31 W
Drewer	263	51.40 N	7.07 E
Drewitz, Dtsch.	54	52.22 N	13.07 E
Drewitz, Dtsch.	54	52.12 N	12.10 E
Drewitz ◆[8]	264a	52.22 N	13.08 E
Drewryville	208	36.42 N	77.18 W
Drews Reservoir ⊜[1]	202	42.10 N	120.40 W
Drew University ʊ[2]	276	40.46 N	74.25 W
Drexel	218	39.44 N	84.17 W
Drexel Gardens	218	39.44 N	86.15 W
Drexel Hill	285	39.56 N	75.17 W
Drexel University ʊ[2]	285	39.57 N	75.11 W
Drezdenko	30	52.51 N	15.50 E
Drezna	82	55.44 N	38.51 E
Dribin	76	54.08 N	31.06 E
Driebergen	52	52.03 N	5.16 E
Drienov	30	48.53 N	21.17 E
Drifton	210	41.00 N	75.54 W
Driftpile ≃	182	55.23 N	115.40 W
Drift Pile River Indian Reserve ◆[4]	182	55.18 N	115.45 W

FRANÇAIS Nom	Page	Lat.°′	Long.°′ W = Ouest
Driftwood, B.C., Can.	182	55.49 N	126.25 W
Driftwood, Pa., U.S.	214	41.20 N	78.08 W
Driftwood ≃, B.C., Can.	182	55.43 N	126.15 W
Driftwood ≃, In., U.S.	218	39.12 N	85.56 W
Driftwood Creek ≃	198	40.11 N	100.39 W
Driggs	202	43.43 N	111.06 W
Drimnin	46	56.36 N	6.00 W
Drimoleague	48	51.38 N	9.14 W
Drin ≃	38	41.45 N	19.34 E
Drina ≃	38	44.53 N	19.21 E
Dringenberg	52	51.40 N	9.02 E
Drinit, Gjiri i c	38	41.45 N	19.28 E
Driorejo	115a	7.21 S	112.37 E
Driscoll	196	27.40 N	97.45 W
Driskill Mountain ∧[2]	194	32.25 N	92.54 W
Drissa ≃	76	55.47 N	27.55 E
Drisv'aty, ozero ⊜	76	55.38 N	26.35 E
Driver	208	36.49 N	76.30 W
Drizzle Lake ⊜	212	45.20 N	78.10 W
Drjanovo	38	42.58 N	25.27 E
Drnholec	61	48.52 N	16.29 E
Drniš	36	43.51 N	16.09 E
Dro	64	45.58 N	10.54 E
Drøbak	26	59.39 N	10.39 E
Drobeta-Turnu Severin	38	44.38 N	22.39 E
Drobylevo	82	55.44 N	35.53 E
Drobyšovo, Ross.	86	53.58 N	74.40 E
Drobyš'ovo, Ukr.	83	49.02 N	37.44 E
Drochtersen	52	53.42 N	9.23 E
Drocourt	261	49.03 N	1.46 E
Droë Harts ≃	158	27.35 S	24.41 E
Drogheda (Droichead Átha)	48	53.43 N	6.21 W
Drogičin	76	52.11 N	25.09 E
Drogobyč	78	49.21 N	23.30 E
Drohiczyn	30	52.24 N	22.41 E
Drohobycz → Drogobyč	78	49.21 N	23.30 E
Droichead Átha → Drogheda	48	53.43 N	6.21 W
Droichead Nua	48	53.11 N	6.48 W
Droitwich	42	52.16 N	2.09 W
Drokija	38	48.03 N	27.48 E
Drolshagen	56	51.01 N	7.46 E
Dromahair	48	54.14 N	8.19 W
Dromana	169	38.21 S	144.58 E
Dromara	48	54.23 N	6.01 W
Dromcolliher	48	52.20 N	8.54 W
Drôme □[5]	62	44.35 N	5.10 E
Drôme ≃	62	44.46 N	4.46 E
Drömling ◆[1]	54	52.29 N	11.04 E
Dromod	48	53.51 N	7.55 W
Dromore, N. Ire., U.K.	48	54.31 N	7.28 W
Dromore, N. Ire., U.K.	48	54.25 N	6.09 W
Dromore West	48	54.15 N	8.53 W
Dronero	62	44.28 N	7.22 E
Dronfield	44	53.19 N	1.27 W
Drongan	44	55.26 N	4.27 W
Drongen	50	51.03 N	3.40 E
Dronne ≃	32	45.02 N	0.09 W
Dronninglund	26	57.09 N	10.18 E
Dronrijp	52	53.11 N	5.38 E
Dröschede	263	51.22 N	7.39 E
Drosendorf Stadt	61	48.52 N	15.37 E
Drosiá	267c	38.07 N	23.52 E
Drösing	61	48.32 N	16.54 E
Droskovo	76	52.31 N	37.05 E
Drottningholm slott ⊥	40	59.19 N	17.53 E
Droué	50	48.02 N	1.05 E
Droue-sur-Drouette	261	48.36 N	1.42 E
Drouette ≃	261	48.37 N	1.37 E
Drouin	169	38.08 S	145.51 E
Drov'anaja	88	51.35 N	113.02 E
Droylsden	262	53.29 N	2.10 W
Droyssig	54	51.02 N	12.01 E
Dr. Petru Groza	38	46.32 N	22.28 E
Druid Hill Park ♠	284b	39.19 N	76.39 W
Druja	76	55.47 N	27.27 E
Druk-Yul → Bhutan □[1]	120	27.30 N	90.30 E
Drulingen	56	48.52 N	7.11 E
Drum, Mount ∧	180	62.07 N	144.35 W
Drumbeg	46	58.14 N	5.12 W
Drumbo	212	43.14 N	80.33 W
Drumcliff	48	54.20 N	8.30 W
Drumheller	182	51.28 N	112.42 W
Drumlish	48	53.48 N	7.46 W
Drummond, N.Z.	172	46.09 S	168.09 E
Drummond, Mt., U.S.	202	46.40 N	113.08 W
Drummond, Wi., U.S.	190	46.20 N	91.15 W
Drummond □[6]	206	45.50 N	72.20 W
Drummond, Lake ⊜	208	36.36 N	76.28 W
Drummond Island I	190	46.00 N	83.40 W
Drummond Range ʌ	166	23.30 S	147.15 E
Drummondville	206	45.53 N	72.29 W
Drummore	44	54.42 N	4.54 W
Drummoyne	274a	33.51 S	151.09 E
Drumquin	48	54.37 N	7.30 W
Drumright	196	35.59 N	96.36 W
Drumshanbo	48	54.02 N	8.02 W
Drunen	52	51.42 N	5.08 E
Drusenheim	56	48.46 N	7.57 E
Druskininkai	76	54.01 N	23.58 E
Drut' ≃	76	53.03 N	30.42 E
Druten	52	51.54 N	5.36 E
Druyes-les-Belles-Fontaines	50	47.33 N	3.25 E
Družba, Kaz.	86	45.15 N	82.26 E
Družba, Ross.	265b	55.53 N	37.45 E
Družba, Ukr.	78	52.03 N	33.56 E
Družina	74	68.14 N	145.18 E
Družkovka	83	48.37 N	37.33 E
Družnaja Gorka	76	59.17 N	30.08 E
Drvar	36	44.22 N	16.24 E
Drwęca ≃	30	53.00 N	18.42 E
Dry ≃	164	14.54 S	132.24 E
Dry Arm c	202	47.45 N	106.20 W
Dry Bay c	180	59.08 N	138.25 W
Dryberry Lake ⊜	184	49.33 N	93.53 W
Dryburgh Abbey ʊ[1]	46	55.34 N	2.40 W
Dry Cimarron ≃	196	36.54 N	102.59 W
Dry Creek ≃, Ca., U.S.	204	38.35 N	122.51 W
Dry Creek ≃, Ca., U.S.	226	37.27 N	120.37 W
Dry Creek ≃, Ca., U.S.	226	38.39 N	121.28 W
Dry Creek ≃, Ca., U.S.	226	38.22 N	122.18 W
Dry Creek ≃, Ca., U.S.	226	38.58 N	121.32 W
Dry Creek ≃, Ca., U.S.	226	39.13 N	121.25 W
Dry Creek ≃, Ca., U.S.	226	38.14 N	121.24 W
Dry Creek ≃, Ca., U.S.	226	36.58 N	120.13 W
Dry Creek ≃, Ca., U.S.	226	36.47 N	119.46 W
Dry Creek ≃, Ca., U.S.	282	37.22 N	122.23 W
Dry Creek ≃, Or., U.S.	202	43.34 N	117.21 W
Dry Creek ≃, Or., U.S.	224	45.30 N	121.03 W
Dry Creek ≃, Tx., U.S.	222	32.46 N	95.28 W
Dry Creek ≃, Wy., U.S.	202	43.13 N	108.54 W
Dry Creek ≃, Wy., U.S.	202	44.30 N	108.03 W
Dry Creek Mountain ∧	204	41.22 N	116.22 W
Dryden, On., Can.	184	49.47 N	92.50 W
Dryden, N.Y., U.S.	210	42.29 N	76.17 W

PORTUGUÊS Nome	Página	Lat.°′	Long.°′ W = Oeste
Dryden, Wa., U.S.	224	47.32 N	120.33 W
Dry Devils ≃, Tx., U.S.	196	30.20 N	100.57 W
Dry Devils ≃, Tx., U.S.	196	29.47 N	100.59 W
Dryfe Water ≃	44	55.08 N	3.26 W
Dry Fork ≃	194	37.58 N	91.31 W
Dry Frio ≃	196	29.17 N	99.39 W
Drygalski Island I	9	65.45 S	92.30 E
Dry Lake ⊜	198	48.15 N	98.58 W
Drymen	46	56.04 N	4.27 W
Dry Prong	194	31.34 N	92.31 W
Dry Ridge	218	38.40 N	84.35 W
Dry Run	214	40.10 N	77.45 W
Drysdale	169	38.11 S	144.34 E
Drysdale ≃	164	13.59 S	126.51 E
Drysdale River National Park ♠	164	15.00 S	127.00 E
Dry Tortugas II	220	24.38 N	82.55 W
Drzewica	30	51.27 N	20.28 E
Drzewice	54	52.38 N	14.38 E
Dschang	152	5.27 N	10.04 E
Dschidda → Jiddah	144	21.30 N	39.12 E
Dschuba → Jubba ≃	144	0.15 S	42.38 E
Du	150	10.30 N	0.59 W
Du ≃	102	32.48 N	110.38 E
Dua ≃	152	3.20 N	20.53 E
Duabo	150	5.40 N	8.05 W
Duāigaon	126	24.14 N	90.51 E
Duala → Douala	152	4.03 N	9.42 E
Dualchi	71	40.13 N	8.54 E
Du'an	102	24.06 N	108.10 E
Duancun	105	38.52 N	115.56 E
Duane L. Bliss State Park ♠	226	38.59 N	120.06 W
Duanesburg	210	42.46 N	74.08 W
Duanjialing	105	39.59 N	117.09 E
Duaringa	166	23.43 S	149.40 E
Duarte	228	34.08 N	117.58 W
Duarte, Pico ∧	238	19.02 N	70.59 W
Duartina	255	22.24 S	49.25 W
Duas Barras	256	22.02 S	42.32 W
Duayaw Nkwanta	150	7.10 N	2.06 W
Dubā, Ar. Su.	128	27.21 N	35.40 E
Dubá, Česká Rep.	54	50.34 N	14.33 E
Dubach	194	32.41 N	92.39 W
Dubai → Dubayy	128	25.18 N	55.18 E
Dubawnt ≃	176	64.33 N	100.06 W
Dubawnt Lake ⊜	176	63.08 N	101.30 W
Dubayy	128	25.18 N	55.18 E
Dubbeldam	52	51.47 N	4.42 E
Dubbo	166	32.15 S	148.36 E
Dube ≃	150	5.45 N	8.00 W
Dubele	154	2.54 N	29.33 E
Dübendorf	58	47.25 N	8.38 E
Dübener Heide ◆[3]	54	51.40 N	12.40 E
Dubenskij	86	51.27 N	56.38 E
Dubesar' (Dubossary)	38	47.16 N	29.08 E
Dubh Artach II[1]	46	56.08 N	6.40 W
Dubí	54	50.42 N	13.45 E
Dubi Bheri	272b	22.53 N	88.17 E
Dubica	36	45.11 N	16.48 E
Dubie	154	8.33 S	28.32 E
Dubinino	82	56.09 N	37.01 E
Dubino	58	46.09 N	9.27 E
Dubjazy	80	56.08 N	49.13 E
Dubki, Ross.	265a	60.00 N	30.00 E
Dubki, Ross.	265b	55.41 N	37.14 E
Dublin, Austl.	168b	34.27 S	138.21 E
Dublin, On., Can	212	43.31 N	81.17 W
Dublin (Baile Átha Cliath), Ire.	48	53.20 N	6.15 W
Dublin, Ca., U.S.	226	37.42 N	121.56 W
Dublin, Ga., U.S.	192	32.32 N	82.54 W
Dublin, In., U.S.	218	39.48 N	85.12 W
Dublin, Md., U.S.	208	39.39 N	76.16 W
Dublin, Oh., U.S.	214	40.06 N	83.07 W
Dublin, Pa., U.S.	208	40.22 N	75.12 W
Dublin, Tx., U.S.	196	32.05 N	98.20 W
Dublin, Va., U.S.	192	37.06 N	80.41 W
Dublin □[6]	48	53.20 N	6.15 W
Dublin (Collinstown) Airport ⊠	48	53.26 N	6.15 W
Dublin Bay c	48	53.20 N	6.06 W
Dublin Canyon V	282	37.42 N	121.59 W
Dublon I	175c	7.23 N	151.53 E
Dubna, Ross.	82	54.09 N	36.58 E
Dubna, Ross.	82	56.44 N	37.10 E
Dubna ≃, Lat.	76	56.22 N	26.10 E
Dubna ≃, Ross.	82	56.47 N	37.15 E
Dubňany	30	48.55 N	17.06 E
Dubnevo	82	55.06 N	38.08 E
Dubnica nad Váhom	30	48.58 N	18.09 E
Dubno	78	50.26 N	25.44 E
Dubois, Id., U.S.	202	44.10 N	112.13 W
Dubois, Il., U.S.	219	38.13 N	89.13 W
Dubois, In., U.S.	194	38.26 N	86.48 W
Du Bois, Ne., U.S.	198	40.02 N	96.02 W
Du Bois, Pa., U.S.	214	41.07 N	78.45 W
Dubois, Wy., U.S.	200	43.32 N	109.37 W
Du Bois Reservoir ⊜[1]	214	41.06 N	78.38 W
Duboistown	210	41.13 N	77.02 W
Dub'onki	80	54.27 N	46.18 E
Dubossarskoje vodochranilišče ⊜[1]	38	47.35 N	29.00 E
Dubovaja Rošča	76	53.11 N	36.04 E
Dubov'azovka	78	51.08 N	33.22 E
Dubovići	78	51.38 N	33.35 E
Dubovka, Ross.	78	51.26 N	41.25 E
Dubovka, Ross.	80	49.03 N	44.50 E
Dubovoje	76	53.08 N	40.05 E
Dubovskij	80	56.21 N	46.48 E
Dubovskoje	80	47.25 N	42.46 E
Dubovyj Ovrag	80	48.20 N	44.37 E
Dubovyj Umet	80	52.59 N	50.17 E
Duboweitun	89	50.42 N	120.14 E
Dubra	126	23.32 N	86.31 E
Dubrājpur	126	23.48 N	87.23 E
Dubréka	150	9.48 N	13.31 W
Dubrova, Bela.	76	52.25 N	29.58 E
Dubrova, Bela.	78	51.47 N	28.13 E
Dubrova, Ross.	80	56.59 N	54.33 E
Dubrova, Ross.	80	57.42 N	55.01 E
Dubrovica	78	51.34 N	26.34 E
Dubroviči	80	54.39 N	39.56 E
Dubrovicy	82	56.46 N	39.10 E
Dubrovino	86	55.28 N	83.17 E
Dubrovka, Ross.	76	59.13 N	36.13 E
Dubrovka, Ross.	76	53.42 N	33.30 E
Dubrovka, Ross.	76	59.51 N	30.56 E
Dubrovka, Ross.	82	54.44 N	36.21 E
Dubrovka, Ukr.	83	47.54 N	39.02 E
Dubrovki	80	53.49 N	43.19 E
Dubrovnik	38	42.38 N	18.07 E
Dubrovno	76	54.35 N	30.41 E
Dubrovnoje, Kaz.	86	54.49 N	68.06 E
Dubrovnoje, Ross.	86	57.58 N	69.25 E
Dubrovo	76	59.51 N	33.34 E
Dubrovskoje	88	58.45 N	111.10 E
Dubunskaja	86	43.46 N	80.13 E
Dubuque	190	42.30 N	90.39 W
Dubysa ≃	76	55.05 N	23.26 E
Duchana	85	38.02 N	68.13 E
Duchang	100	29.15 N	116.13 E
Duchcov	54	50.37 N	13.45 E
Ducherow	54	53.46 N	13.46 E
Duchesne	200	40.09 N	110.24 W
Duchesne ≃	200	40.05 N	109.41 W
Duchess	166	21.22 S	139.52 E
Duchovnickoje	80	52.28 N	48.15 E
Duchovščina	76	55.12 N	32.25 E
Duck ≃, Austl.	274a	33.50 S	151.02 E
Duck ≃, Tn., U.S.	194	36.02 N	87.52 W
Duckabush ≃	224	47.38 N	122.56 W
Duck Bay	184	52.10 N	100.09 W
Duck Creek ≃, On., Can.	281	42.18 N	82.41 W
Duck Creek ≃, Ca., U.S.	226	37.55 N	121.16 W
Duck Creek ≃, In., U.S.	218	40.08 N	85.57 W
Duck Creek ≃, Nv., U.S.	204	40.06 N	114.43 W
Duck Creek ≃, N.D., U.S.	198	46.03 N	102.14 W
Duck Creek ≃, Tx., U.S.	196	33.14 N	100.42 W
Duck Creek ≃, Tx., U.S.	222	32.48 N	96.31 W
Duck Creék ≃, Tx., U.S.	222	31.06 N	96.17 W
Duck Creek ≃, Wi., U.S.	190	44.33 N	88.02 W
Duck Hill	194	33.37 N	89.42 W
Duck Island Harbor c	276	40.55 N	73.23 W
Duck Key I	220	24.46 N	80.56 W
Duck Lake, Sk., Can.	184	52.47 N	106.13 W
Duck Lake, Mi., U.S.	216	42.24 N	84.47 W
Duck Lake ⊜, Mb., Can.	184	54.52 N	98.11 W
Duck Lake ⊜, Mi., U.S.	216	42.23 N	84.47 W
Duck Lake ⊜, Mi., U.S.	281	42.40 N	83.35 W
Duck Mountain ∧	184	51.35 N	101.00 W
Duck Mountain Provincial Park ♠, Mb., Can.	184	51.36 N	100.55 W
Duck Mountain Provincial Park ♠, Sk., Can.	184	51.38 N	101.53 W
Duck Valley Indian Reservation ◆[4]	204	42.00 N	116.10 W
Duckwall Mountain ∧	226	37.58 N	120.07 W
Duclair	50	49.29 N	0.53 E
Ducos	240e	14.34 N	60.58 W
Du Couedic, Cape >	166	36.04 S	136.42 E
Ducun	106	31.07 N	120.27 E
Duda ≃	246	2.33 N	74.02 W
Dudačkino	76	59.57 N	32.53 E
Dudčany	78	47.12 N	33.46 E
Duddington	42	52.36 N	0.32 W
Duddon ≃	44	54.15 N	3.13 W
Dudelange	56	49.28 N	6.05 E
Dudergofka ≃	265a	59.52 N	30.12 E
Duderstadt	52	51.31 N	10.16 E
Dūdhi	124	24.13 N	83.15 E
Dudhkośī ≃	124	27.08 N	86.26 E
Dudhnai	124	25.59 N	90.44 E
Dudinka	74	69.25 N	86.15 E
Dudkin	78	47.53 N	40.32 E
Dudley, Eng., U.K.	42	52.30 N	2.05 W
Dudley, Eng., U.K.	44	55.03 N	1.35 W
Dudley, Ma., U.S.	207	42.02 N	71.55 W
Dudley, Pa., U.S.	214	40.12 N	78.10 W
Dudley Pond ⊜	283	42.20 N	71.22 W
Dudleyville	200	32.58 N	110.47 W
Dudna ≃	122	19.07 N	76.54 E
Dudorovskij	76	53.40 N	35.22 E
Dūḍuwā Śringklā ʌ	124	27.45 N	82.30 E
Dudwa National Park ♠	124	28.30 N	80.40 E
Dudweiler	56	49.17 N	7.02 E
Dudzele	50	51.17 N	3.14 E
Due	89	50.50 N	142.06 E
Duékoué	150	6.45 N	7.21 W
Dueré	250	11.20 S	49.17 W
Dueré ≃	250	10.59 S	49.48 W
Duerji	89	45.39 N	121.49 E
Duerna ≃	34	42.19 N	5.54 W
Duero (Douro) ≃	34	41.08 N	8.40 W
Dueville	64	45.38 N	11.32 E
Due West	192	34.20 N	82.23 W
Dufault, Lac ⊜	190	48.19 N	79.00 W
Duff Dunbar	123	32.15 N	77.12 E
Duffel	50	51.06 N	4.31 E
Dufferin □[6]	212	44.05 N	80.15 W
Duffer Peak ∧	204	41.40 N	118.44 W
Duffield, Austl.	162	25.50 S	134.40 E
Duffield, Eng., U.K.	44	52.58 N	1.29 W
Duffins Creek ≃	212	43.49 N	79.02 W
Dufftown	46	57.26 N	3.08 W
Dufourspitze ∧	58	45.55 N	7.52 E
Dufresne ≃	206	46.16 N	73.59 W
Dufur	224	45.27 N	121.07 W
Dugadda	124	29.48 N	78.37 E
Duga Resa	36	45.27 N	15.30 E
Duga-Zapadnaja, mys >	74	59.09 N	145.59 E
Dugdemona ≃	194	31.47 N	92.22 W
Dugede	120	30.54 N	90.48 E
Dugger	194	39.04 N	87.16 W
Dugino	83	47.09 N	39.27 E
Dugi Otok I	36	44.00 N	15.04 E
Dugna	82	54.25 N	36.51 E
Dugny-sur-Meuse	56	49.06 N	5.23 E
Dug Pond ⊜	283	42.17 N	71.22 W
Du Gué ≃	176	57.21 N	70.45 W
Dugui Qarag	102	39.38 N	108.40 E
Dugway Proving Ground ■	200	40.10 N	113.15 W
Duhernal Lake ⊜	276	40.24 N	74.22 W
Duhi	140	7.07 N	28.45 E
Duhnen	52	53.53 N	8.38 E
Duhu	100	22.04 N	112.56 E
Duhūr ash-Shuwayr	132	33.55 N	35.43 E
Duich, Loch c	46	57.14 N	5.30 W
Duida, Cerro ∧	246	3.25 N	65.40 W
Duifken Point >	164	12.33 S	141.38 E
Duingen	52	52.00 N	9.42 E
Duingt	62	45.50 N	6.12 E
Duino	64	45.46 N	13.36 E
Duirinish	46	57.19 N	5.41 W
Duisburg, Dtsch.	56	51.25 N	6.46 E
Duisburg, Dtsch.	263	51.25 N	6.46 E
Duissern ◆[8]	263	51.26 N	6.47 E
Duitama	246	5.50 N	73.02 W
Duitsland → Germany □[1]	30	51.00 N	10.00 E
Duiveland I	52	51.38 N	4.00 E
Duiwelskloof	156	23.42 S	30.06 E
Duji, Zhg.	98	37.44 N	116.50 E
Duji, Zhg.	98	34.11 N	115.48 E
Dujiahang	106	31.03 N	121.29 E
Dujuuma	144	1.15 N	42.34 E
Dukambiya	144	14.47 N	37.28 E
Dukana ⊤[4]	154	3.59 N	37.16 E
Dukazi	120	30.54 N	92.52 E
Duke	196	34.39 N	99.34 W
Duke Center	214	41.57 N	78.28 W
Duke Island I	182	54.56 N	131.20 W
Duke of York Bay c	176	65.25 N	84.50 W
Duke of York Island I	164	4.10 S	152.26 E
Dukes □[6]	207	41.23 N	70.31 W
Dukes Brook ≃	276	40.33 N	74.37 W
Duk Fadiat	140	7.45 N	31.25 E
Duk Faiwil	140	7.30 N	31.29 E
Dukhān	128	25.25 N	50.48 E
Dukhmays	142	31.07 N	31.04 E
Duki	120	30.09 N	68.34 E
Dukinfield	262	53.29 N	2.05 W
Dukla	30	49.34 N	21.41 E
Dukla Pass)(	30	49.25 N	21.43 E
Dukou	102	26.40 N	101.39 E
Dūkštas	76	55.32 N	26.20 E
Duku, Nig.	146	10.49 N	10.46 E
Duku, Nig.	150	11.10 N	4.55 E
Dula	152	4.41 N	20.22 E
Dūlāb ◆[8]	267d	35.39 N	51.27 E
Dulag	116	10.57 N	125.02 E
Dulāi	124	23.57 N	89.31 E
Dulais ≃	42	51.41 N	3.47 W
Dulan (Chahanwusu)	102	36.16 N	98.28 E
Dul'apino	80	57.15 N	40.49 E
Dulas ≃	42	52.36 N	3.50 W
Dulas Bay c	44	53.23 N	4.15 W
Dulata	86	43.26 N	80.50 E
Dulayb, Khawr V	140	11.45 N	32.47 E
Dulaym	146	25.58 N	14.03 E
Dulce	200	36.56 N	106.59 W
Dulce ≃	252	30.31 S	62.32 W
Dulce, Arroyo ≃	258	35.28 S	57.41 W
Dulce, Golfo c	236	8.32 N	83.14 W
Dulce Grande	234	22.59 N	102.14 W
Dulce Nombre de Culmí	236	15.09 N	85.37 W
Dul'durga	88	50.41 N	113.36 E
Duleek	48	53.39 N	6.25 W
Dulgalach ≃	74	67.44 N	133.12 E
Dulin	98	38.22 N	116.43 E
Duliu, Zhg.	105	39.13 N	116.16 E
Duliu, Zhg.	105	39.01 N	116.54 E
Duliu Jianhe ≃	105	38.51 N	117.20 E
Duljo Point >	116	9.35 N	123.43 E
Dulkaninna	166	29.01 S	138.27 E
Dülken	56	51.15 N	6.20 E
Dulles International Airport ⊠	208	38.58 N	77.28 W
Dullstroom	156	25.27 S	30.07 E
Dülmen	52	51.51 N	7.16 E
Dulnain Bridge	46	57.16 N	3.41 W
Dulnan ≃	46	57.18 N	3.40 W
Dulovka	76	57.32 N	28.20 E
Dulovo	38	43.49 N	27.09 E
Dulq Maghār	130	36.22 N	38.39 E
D'ul'tydag, gora ∧	84	41.58 N	46.56 E
Dulung ≃	126	22.08 N	87.05 E
Dulunguin Point >	116	7.45 N	122.05 E
Duluth, Ga., U.S.	192	34.00 N	84.08 W
Duluth, Mn., U.S.	190	46.45 N	92.07 W
Dulverton	42	51.03 N	3.33 W
Dulwich ◆[8]	260	51.26 N	0.05 W
Duma, Bots.	156	18.45 S	22.46 E
Dūmā, Lubnān	130	34.12 N	35.50 E
Dūmā, Sūrīy.	132	33.35 N	36.24 E
Duma, Zaïre	154	4.57 N	27.19 E
Dumaguete	116	9.18 N	123.18 E
Dumai	114	1.41 N	101.27 E
Dumalag	116	11.18 N	122.37 E
Dumalinao	116	7.49 N	123.23 E
Dumali Point >	116	13.07 N	121.33 E
Dumanjug	116	10.04 N	123.26 E
Dumanlıdağ ∧	84	40.31 N	43.25 E
Dumanquilas Bay c	116	7.34 N	123.04 E
Dumaran Channel ⋃	116	10.25 N	119.45 E
Dumaran Island I	116	10.33 N	119.51 E
Dumaresq ≃	166	28.40 S	150.28 E
Dumaring	112	1.36 N	118.12 E
Dumas, Ar., U.S.	194	33.53 N	91.29 W
Dumas, Tx., U.S.	196	35.51 N	101.58 W
Ḍumayr	132	33.38 N	36.40 E
Dumbarton	46	55.57 N	4.35 W
Dumbarton Bridge ◆[5]	282	37.31 N	122.07 W
Dumbarton Point >	282	37.30 N	122.06 W
Ďumbier ∧	30	48.57 N	19.37 E
Dumbleyung	162	33.19 S	117.44 E
Dumbo	152	14.06 S	17.24 E
Dumboa	146	11.10 N	12.45 E
Dumbrăveni	38	46.14 N	24.35 E
Dum Dum	126	22.35 N	88.24 E
Dum Dum International Airport ⊠	126	22.38 N	88.25 E
Dume, Point >	228	34.00 N	118.48 W
Dumei	100	24.47 N	117.21 E
Dumfries, Scot., U.K.	44	55.04 N	3.37 W
Dumfries, Va., U.S.	208	38.34 N	77.19 W
Dumfries and Galloway □[4]	44	55.00 N	4.00 W
Duminiči	76	53.55 N	35.06 E
Dumjor	272b	22.38 N	88.13 E
Dumka	126	24.16 N	87.15 E
Dumlupınar	130	38.52 N	30.00 E
Dummar	132	33.32 N	36.14 E
Dümmer ⊜	52	52.31 N	8.19 E
Dummer Range ʌ	162	20.11 S	125.59 E
Dumoga-Bone National Park ♠	112	0.30 N	123.25 E
Dumoga Kecil	112	0.31 N	123.55 E
Dumoine ≃	190	46.13 N	77.51 W
Dumoine, Lac ⊜	190	46.53 N	77.54 W
Dumont, Ia., U.S.	190	42.45 N	92.58 W
Dumont, N.J., U.S.	210	40.56 N	73.59 W
Dumont, Lac ⊜	190	46.04 N	76.27 W
Dumont d'Urville ʊ[3]	9	66.35 S	140.00 E
Dümpelfeld	56	50.27 N	6.56 E
Dümpten ◆[8]	263	51.27 N	6.54 E
Dumpu	164	5.50 S	145.45 E
Dumra	124	26.34 N	85.31 E
Dumraon	124	25.33 N	84.09 E
Dumuria, Bngl.	126	22.47 N	89.26 E
Dumuriā, India	126	22.11 N	86.20 E
Dumyāṭ (Damietta)	142	31.25 N	31.48 E
Dumyāṭ □[4]	142	31.20 N	31.45 E
Dumyāṭ, Far' (Damietta Branch) ≃	142	31.32 N	31.51 E
Dumyāṭ, Maṣabb (Damietta Mouth) ≃[1]	142	31.32 N	31.51 E
Dün ∧	54	51.21 N	10.30 E
Duna → Danube ≃	22	45.20 N	29.40 E
Dünaburg → Daugavpils	76	55.53 N	26.32 E
Dunaff Head >	48	55.17 N	7.33 W
Dunaföldvár	30	46.48 N	18.55 E
Dunaharaszti	30	47.21 N	19.05 E
Dunaj, Ross.	89	42.52 N	132.22 E
Dunaj, Ross.	265a	59.58 N	30.56 E
Dunaj → Danube ≃	22	45.20 N	29.40 E
Dunaj, ostrova II	74	73.52 N	124.29 E
Dunajec ≃	30	50.14 N	20.44 E
Dunajevcy	78	48.54 N	26.51 E
Dunajevo	88	52.05 N	117.02 E
Dunajská Streda	30	48.01 N	17.35 E
Dunakeszi	30	47.38 N	19.08 E
Dunany Point >	48	53.52 N	6.14 W
Dunărea → Danube ≃	22	45.20 N	29.40 E
Dunărea Veche, Brațul ≃	38	45.17 N	28.02 E
Duna-Tisza-csatorna ≊	264c	47.21 N	19.05 E
Dunaújváros	30	46.58 N	18.57 E
Dunav → Danube ≃	22	45.20 N	29.40 E
Dunavățu-de-Sus	38	44.59 N	29.13 E
Duna-Völgyi-főcsatorna ≊	30	46.12 N	18.56 E
Dunback	172	45.23 S	170.38 E
Dunbar, Scot., U.K.	46	56.00 N	2.31 W
Dunbar, W.V., U.S.	188	38.21 N	81.44 W
Dunbarton	275b	43.49 N	79.06 W
Dunbeath	46	58.15 N	3.25 W
Dunblane, Sk., Can.	184	51.11 N	106.52 W
Dunblane, Scot., U.K.	46	56.12 N	3.59 W
Dunboyne	48	53.24 N	6.28 W
Duncan, B.C., Can.	224	48.47 N	123.42 W
Duncan, Az., U.S.	200	32.43 N	109.06 W
Duncan, Ms., U.S.	194	34.02 N	90.44 W
Duncan, Ok., U.S.	196	34.30 N	97.57 W
Duncan ≃	182	50.11 N	116.57 W
Duncan Lake ⊜[1]	182	50.20 N	117.00 W
Duncannon	208	40.23 N	77.01 W
Duncan Passage ⋃	110	11.00 N	92.30 E
Duncans	241q	18.28 N	77.32 W
Duncansby Head >	46	58.39 N	3.02 W
Duncans Creek ≃	274a	33.53 S	150.39 E
Duncansville	214	40.25 N	78.26 W
Duncanville	222	32.39 N	96.54 W
Dunchurch	42	52.20 N	1.16 W
Duncormick	48	52.14 N	6.39 W
Dundaga	76	57.31 N	22.21 E
Dundāhera	272a	28.38 N	77.26 E
Dundalk, On., Can.	212	44.10 N	80.24 W
Dundalk (Dún Dealgan), Ire.	48	54.01 N	6.25 W
Dundalk, Md., U.S.	208	39.15 N	76.31 W
Dundalk Bay c	48	53.57 N	6.17 W
Dundas, Austl.	274a	33.48 S	151.02 E
Dundas, On., Can.	212	43.16 N	79.58 W
Dundas, Mn., U.S.	190	44.25 N	93.12 W
Dundas, Cape >	212	44.57 N	81.07 W
Dundas, Lake ⊜	162	32.35 S	121.50 E
Dundas Island I	182	54.33 N	130.55 W
Dundas Peninsula >[1]	176	74.50 N	111.30 W
Dundas Strait ⋃	164	11.20 S	131.35 E
Dún Dealgan → Dundalk	48	54.01 N	6.25 W
Dundee, S. Afr.	158	28.12 S	30.16 E
Dundee, Scot., U.K.	46	56.28 N	2.58 W
Dundee, Fl., U.S.	220	28.01 N	81.37 W
Dundee, Il., U.S.	216	42.06 N	88.17 W
Dundee, Mi., U.S.	216	41.57 N	83.39 W
Dundee, Ms., U.S.	194	34.31 N	90.27 W
Dundee, N.Y., U.S.	210	42.31 N	76.58 W
Dundee, Oh., U.S.	214	40.35 N	81.37 W
Dundee, Or., U.S.	224	45.16 N	123.00 W
Dundee Creek c	284b	39.21 N	76.22 W
Dundgov' □[4]	102	45.30 N	106.30 E
Dundīṭ	142	30.41 N	31.18 E
Dundonald	46	55.34 N	4.35 W
Dundoo	166	27.39 S	144.39 E
Dundrum, Ire.	48	52.33 N	8.03 W
Dundrum, N. Ire., U.K.	48	54.16 N	5.51 W
Dundrum Bay c	48	54.13 N	5.45 W
Dundurn	184	51.49 N	106.30 W
Duneaton Water ≃	46	55.32 N	3.42 W
Dunedin, N.Z.	172	45.52 S	170.30 E
Dunedin, Fl., U.S.	220	28.01 N	82.46 W
Dunedoo	166	32.01 S	149.24 E
Duneland Beach	216	41.35 N	86.50 W
Duneller	276	40.35 N	74.28 W
Dunewood	276	40.38 N	73.11 W
Dunfanaghy	48	55.11 N	7.59 W
Dunfermline	46	56.04 N	3.29 W
Du Ngae, Khao ∧	110	15.10 N	98.47 E
Dungannon, N. Ire., U.K.	48	54.31 N	6.46 W
Dungannon, Va., U.S.	192	36.49 N	82.28 W
Dūngarpur	120	23.50 N	73.43 E
Dungarvan	48	52.05 N	7.37 W
Dungarvan Harbour c	48	52.10 N	7.35 W
Dungas	150	13.04 N	9.20 E
Dungau ◆[1]	60	48.50 N	12.40 E
Dungeness >	42	50.55 N	0.58 E
Dungeness ≃	224	48.08 N	123.06 W
Dungeness, Punta >	254	52.23 S	68.25 W
Dungeness Bay c	224	48.10 N	123.07 W
Dungeness Spit >[2]	224	48.10 N	123.09 W
Dungiven	48	54.55 N	6.55 W
Dunglow	48	54.57 N	8.22 W
Dungo, Lagoa do ⊜	152	17.20 S	18.58 E
Dungog	166	32.24 S	151.46 E
Dungu	154	3.37 N	28.34 E
Dungu ≃	154	3.37 N	28.34 E
Dungun	114	4.47 N	103.26 E
Dungun ≃	114	4.47 N	103.23 E
Dunham	206	45.08 N	72.48 W
Dunham Lake ⊜	281	42.39 N	83.41 W
Dunham-on-the-Hill	262	53.15 N	2.47 W
Dunham Park ♠	262	53.23 N	2.24 W
Dunham Town	262	53.23 N	2.24 W
Dunhevec, Austl.	274a	33.45 S	150.47 E
Dunhevec → Launceston, Eng., U.K.	42	50.38 N	4.21 W
Dunholme	44	53.18 N	0.28 W
Dunhou	100	27.02 N	114.58 E
Dunhua	89	43.21 N	128.13 E
Dunhuang	102	40.12 N	94.41 E
Dunières	62	45.13 N	4.20 E
Dunilovo, Ross.	76	57.46 N	38.55 E
Dunilovo, Ross.	80	57.00 N	41.27 E
Dunkeld	46	56.34 N	3.35 W
Dunkeld ◆[8]	273d	26.09 S	28.03 E
Dunkellin ≃	48	53.12 N	8.54 W
Dunkelsteinerwald ◆[3]	61	48.15 N	15.29 E
Dunkern ⊜	40	59.09 N	16.52 E
Dunkerque	50	51.03 N	2.22 E
Dunkerrin	48	52.55 N	7.55 W
Dunkery Hill ∧[2]	42	51.11 N	3.35 W
Dunkineely	48	54.38 N	8.23 W
Dunkinsville	218	38.51 N	83.30 W
Dunkirk → Dunkerque, Fr.	50	51.03 N	2.22 E
Dunkirk, Eng., U.K.	42	51.17 N	0.59 E
Dunkirk, In., U.S.	216	40.22 N	85.12 W
Dunkirk, N.Y., U.S.	214	42.28 N	79.20 W
Dunkirk, Oh., U.S.	216	40.47 N	83.38 W
Dunk's Green	260	51.15 N	0.19 E
Dunkuj	140	12.50 N	32.49 E
Dunkwa, Ghana	150	5.58 N	1.46 W
Dunkwa, Ghana	150	5.22 N	1.12 W
Dún Laoghaire	48	53.17 N	6.08 W
Dunlap, In., U.S.	216	41.38 N	85.55 W
Dunlap, Ia., U.S.	198	41.51 N	95.36 W
Dunlap, Tn., U.S.	194	35.22 N	85.23 W
Dunlap Acres	228	34.03 N	117.06 W
Dunlavin	48	53.02 N	6.41 W
Dunleary → Dún Laoghaire	48	53.17 N	6.08 W
Dunleer	48	53.50 N	6.24 W
Dunleith	285	39.42 N	75.33 W
Dun-le-Palestel	32	46.18 N	1.40 E
Dunlo	214	40.17 N	78.43 W
Dunlop	46	55.43 N	4.32 W
Dunloy	48	55.01 N	6.25 W
Dunmanus Bay c	48	51.35 N	9.45 W
Dunmanway	48	51.43 N	9.06 W
Dunmarra	164	16.42 S	133.25 E
Dunmore, Ire.	48	53.36 N	8.46 W
Dunmore, Pa., U.S.	210	41.25 N	75.37 W
Dunmore Cave ⊥[5]	48	52.44 N	7.15 W
Dunmore East	48	52.09 N	7.00 W
Dunmore Town	238	25.30 N	76.39 W
Dunmurry	48	54.33 N	6.01 W
Dunn	192	35.18 N	78.36 W
Dunnamanagh	48	54.52 N	7.18 W
Dünnbach ≃	56	50.10 N	7.18 E
Dunnellon	220	29.02 N	82.27 W
Dunnet	46	58.37 N	3.20 W
Dunnet Bay c	46	58.37 N	3.24 W
Dunnet Head >	46	58.40 N	3.24 W
Dunnigan	226	38.53 N	121.58 W
Dunning	198	41.49 N	100.06 W
Dunning Creek ≃	214	40.02 N	78.28 W
Dunnington	44	53.57 N	0.59 W
Dunningtown	279b	40.25 N	79.35 W
Dunn Loring	284c	38.53 N	77.14 W
Dunn Loring Woods	284c	38.52 N	77.14 W
Dunnockshaw	262	53.45 N	2.17 W
Dunnottar Castle ⊥	46	56.57 N	2.11 W
Dunns Bridge	216	41.13 N	86.59 W
Dunnville	212	42.54 N	79.36 W
Dunolly	169	36.52 S	143.44 E
Dunoon	46	55.57 N	4.56 W
Dunqul ⊤[4]	140	23.26 N	31.37 E
Dunqulah	140	19.10 N	30.29 E
Dunqulah al-Qadīmah	140	18.13 N	30.45 E
Dunqunāb	140	21.06 N	37.05 E
Dunqunāb, Khalīj c	140	21.05 N	37.08 E
Dunrea	184	49.25 N	99.44 W
Dun Rig ∧	46	55.34 N	3.10 W
Duns	46	55.47 N	2.20 W
Dunsandel	172	43.40 S	172.11 E
Dunsborough	162	33.36 S	115.06 E
Dunseith	198	48.48 N	100.03 W
Dunsford	42	50.41 N	3.40 W
Dunsmuir	204	41.13 N	122.16 W

≃	River	Fluß	Río	Rivière	Rio
≊	Canal	Kanal	Canal	Canal	Canal
∟	Waterfall, Rapids	Wasserfall, Stromschnellen	Cascada, Rápidos	Chute d'eau, Rapides	Cascata, Rápidos
⋃	Strait	Meeresstraße	Estrecho	Détroit	Estreito
c	Bay, Gulf	Bucht, Golf	Bahía, Golfo	Baie, Golfe	Baía, Golfo
⊜	Lake, Lakes	See, Seen	Lago, Lagos	Lac, Lacs	Lago, Lagos
≡	Swamp	Sumpf	Pantano	Marais	Pântano
⊓	Ice Features, Glacier	Eis- und Gletscherformen	Accidentes Glaciales	Formes glaciaires	Acidentes glaciares
⊤	Other Hydrographic Features	Andere Hydrographische Objekte	Otros Elementos Hidrográficos	Autres données hydrographiques	Outros acidentes hidrográficos

✦	Submarine Features	Untermeerische Objekte	Accidentes Submarinos	Formes de relief sous-marin	Acidentes submarinos
□	Political Unit	Politische Einheit	Unidad Politica	Entité politique	Unidade política
ʊ	Cultural Institution	Kulturelle Institution	Institución Cultural	Institution culturelle	Instituição cultural
⊥	Historical Site	Historische Stätte	Sitio Histórico	Site historique	Sitio histórico
♠	Recreational Site	Erholungs- und Ferienort	Sitio de Recreo	Centre de loisirs	Area de Lazer
⊠	Airport	Flughafen	Aeropuerto	Aéroport	Aeroporto
■	Military Installation	Militäranlage	Instalación Militar	Installation militaire	Instalação militar
◆	Miscellaneous	Verschiedenes	Misceláneo	Divers	Diversos

ENGLISH				DEUTSCH		Länge[0']
Name	Page	Lat.[0']	Long.[0']	Name	Seite	Breite[0'] E = Ost

Symbols in the index entries represent the broad categories identified in the key at the right. Symbols with superscript numbers (⋏¹) identify subcategories (see complete key on page I · 1).

Symbole im Register stellen die rechts im Schlüssel erklärten Kategorien dar. Symbole mit hochgestellten Ziffern (⋏¹) bezeichnen Unterteilungen einer Kategorie (vgl. vollständiger Schlüssel auf Seite I · 1).

Los símbolos incluidos en el texto del índice representan las grandes categorías identificadas con la clave a la derecha. Los símbolos con números en su parte superior (⋏¹) identifican las subcategorías (véase la clave completa en página I · 1).

Les symboles de l'index représentent les catégories indiquées dans la légende à droite. Les symboles suivis d'un indice (⋏¹) représentent des sous-catégories (voir légende complète à la page I · 1).

Os símbolos incluídos no texto do índice representam as grandes categorias identificadas com a chave à direita. Os símbolos com números em sua parte superior (⋏¹) identificam as subcategorias (veja-se a chave completa à página I · 1).

⋀ Mountain	Berg	Montaña	Montagne	Montanha
⋆ Mountains	Gebirge	Montañas	Montagnes	Montanhas
⤬ Pass	Paß	Paso	Col	Passo
V Valley, Canyon	Tal, Cañon	Valle, Cañón	Vallée, Canyon	Vale, Canhão
⊵ Plain	Ebene	Llano	Plaine	Planície
⊁ Cape	Kap	Cabo	Cap	Cabo
I Island	Insel	Isla	Île	Ilha
II Islands	Inseln	Islas	Îles	Ilhas
⊷ Other Topographic Features	Andere Topographische Objekte	Otros Elementos Topográficos	Autres données topographiques	Outros acidentes topográficos

East-Ekal *I* · 51

ESPAÑOL — FRANÇAIS — PORTUGUÊS

Nombre / Nom / Nome	Página / Page / Página	Lat.°′	Long.°′ W = Oeste / W = Ouest / W = Oeste
Easton, Tx., U.S.	222	32.23 N	94.35 W
Easton, Wa., U.S.	224	47.14 N	121.10 W
Eastondale	283	42.02 N	71.04 W
Easton Reservoir ⊜[1]	207	41.16 N	73.16 W
East Orange	210	40.46 N	74.12 W
East Orleans	207	41.47 N	69.58 W
East Otto	210	42.23 N	78.45 W
Eastover	192	33.52 N	80.41 W
East Pacific Rise ✦[3]	6	20.00 S	115.00 W
East Pakistan → Bangladesh □[1]	118	24.00 N	90.00 E
East Palatka	192	29.39 N	81.35 W
East Palestine	214	40.50 N	80.32 W
East Palo Alto	226	37.28 N	122.08 W
East Park Reservoir ⊜[1]	226	39.21 N	122.30 W
East Parkrose	224	45.33 N	122.32 W
East Peak ∧	116	11.13 N	119.29 E
East Peckham	42	51.15 N	0.23 E
East Pecos	200	35.34 N	105.39 W
East Pembroke, Ma., U.S.	283	42.05 N	70.46 W
East Pembroke, N.Y., U.S.	210	42.59 N	78.18 W
East Peoria	190	40.39 N	89.34 W
East Pepperell	207	42.39 N	71.34 W
East Petersburg	208	40.06 N	76.21 W
East Pharsalia	210	42.34 N	75.43 W
East Pine	182	55.43 N	121.13 W
East Pines	284c	38.57 N	76.55 W
East Pittsburgh	279b	40.23 N	79.50 W
Eastpoint, Fl., U.S.	192	29.44 N	84.52 W
East Point, Ga., U.S.	192	33.40 N	84.26 W
East Point >, P.E., Can.	186	46.27 N	61.58 W
East Point >, Ma., U.S.	207	42.25 N	70.54 W
East Point >, Vir. Is., U.S.	241n	17.45 N	64.34 W
Eastpoint ◆[9]	284b	39.18 N	76.31 W
Eastport, Nf., Can.	186	48.39 N	53.45 W
Eastport, Id., U.S.	202	49.00 N	116.10 W
Eastport, Me., U.S.	188	44.54 N	66.59 W
Eastport, N.Y., U.S.	207	40.49 N	72.44 W
East Porterville	204	36.04 N	118.56 W
East Potomac Park ♠	284c	38.52 N	77.01 W
East Prairie	194	36.46 N	89.23 W
East Prairie ≃	182	55.34 N	116.25 W
East Prospect	208	39.58 N	76.31 W
East Providence	207	41.48 N	71.22 W
East Pryor Mountain ∧	202	45.11 N	108.20 W
East Quogue	207	40.51 N	72.35 W
East Rājasthān Uplands ⩘[1]	124	26.40 N	76.35 E
East Randolph	210	42.10 N	78.56 W
East Retford	44	53.19 N	0.56 W
East Richmond	226	37.57 N	122.19 W
Eastridge Center ◆[9]	282	37.20 N	121.49 W
East Rigaud ≃	206	45.27 N	74.22 W
Eastriggs	44	54.59 N	3.10 W
East River ⊂	208	37.24 N	76.21 W
East Rochester, N.Y., U.S.	210	43.06 N	77.29 W
East Rochester, Oh., U.S.	214	40.45 N	81.02 W
East Rockaway	276	40.38 N	73.40 W
East Rockingham	192	34.55 N	79.45 W
East Rockwood	216	42.03 N	83.13 W
East Rosebud Creek ≃	202	45.29 N	109.27 W
East Rudolf National Park ♠	154	3.55 N	36.20 E
East Rutherford	276	40.50 N	74.05 W
Eastry	42	51.15 N	1.18 E
East Saint Louis	219	38.38 N	90.09 W
East Salem	208	40.37 N	77.14 W
East Salt Creek ≃	200	39.13 N	108.54 W
East Sandwich	207	41.44 N	70.27 W
East Sandy Creek ≃	214	41.22 N	79.51 W
East Schodack	210	42.34 N	73.38 W
East Scotia Basin ✦[1]	9	57.00 S	35.00 W
East Sepik □[5]	164	4.00 S	143.30 E
East Setauket	210	40.57 N	73.06 W
East Shoal Lake ⊜	184	50.23 N	97.37 W
East Siberian Sea → Vostočno-Sibirskoje more ⍑[2]	12	74.00 N	166.00 E
East Side	210	41.04 N	75.46 W
Eastside Bypass ≊	226	37.05 N	120.28 W
East Side Canal ≊, Ca., U.S.	226	37.21 N	120.55 W
East Side Canal ≊, Ca., U.S.	226	35.33 N	119.33 W
East Sixteen Mile Creek ≃	275b	43.28 N	79.48 W
East Smethport	214	41.49 N	78.26 W
East Smithfield	210	41.52 N	76.38 W
East Sooke	224	48.22 N	123.43 W
Eastsound	224	48.41 N	122.54 W
East Sound ʯ	224	48.39 N	122.53 W
East Sparta	214	40.40 N	81.21 W
East Spencer	192	35.40 N	80.25 W
East Springbrook	284c	39.04 N	77.00 W
East Springfield, Oh., U.S.	214	40.27 N	80.52 W
East Springfield, Pa., U.S.	214	41.57 N	80.28 W
East Stony Creek ≃	210	43.15 N	74.12 W
East Stour ≃	42	51.08 N	0.53 E
East Stroudsburg	210	40.59 N	75.10 W
East Sudbury	283	42.24 N	71.24 W
East Sussex □[6]	42	50.55 N	0.15 E
East Syracuse	210	43.04 N	76.05 W
East Tawas	190	44.16 N	83.29 W
East Templeton	207	42.33 N	72.02 W
East Texas	210	40.33 N	75.33 W
East Thompson	207	42.00 N	71.43 W
East Tilbury	260	51.28 N	0.25 E
East Troy	216	42.47 N	88.24 W
East Tustin	280	33.46 N	117.49 W
Eastvale	214	40.46 N	80.19 W
East Vandergrift	214	40.36 N	79.34 W
Eastview	218	40.19 N	80.38 W
Eastville	208	37.21 N	75.56 W
East Walker ≃	204	38.53 N	119.10 W
East Walpole	207	42.09 N	71.12 W
East Wareham	207	41.45 N	70.40 W
East Washington	214	40.10 N	80.14 W
East Waterford	208	40.22 N	77.36 W
East Wemyss	46	56.09 N	3.04 W
East Wenatchee	202	47.24 N	120.17 W
East Wenonah	285	39.47 N	75.08 W
East White Plains	276	41.03 N	73.47 W
Eastwick ◆[8]	285	39.55 N	75.14 W
East Wickham ◆[8]	260	51.28 N	0.07 E
East Williamson	210	43.14 N	77.09 W
East Williston	276	40.46 N	73.38 W
East Wilmington	192	34.13 N	77.53 W
East Wittering	42	50.41 N	0.53 W
Eastwood, Austl.	274a	33.48 S	151.05 E
Eastwood, Eng., U.K.	44	53.01 N	1.18 W
Eastwood, Eng., U.K.	260	51.34 N	0.40 E
Eastwood, Eng., U.K.	262	53.43 N	2.03 W
Eastwood, Mi., U.S.	216	42.18 N	85.33 W
Eastwood, Pa., U.S.	279b	40.17 N	79.31 W
East Worcester	210	42.37 N	74.40 W
East Yegua Creek ≃	222	30.19 N	96.45 W
East Yellow Creek ≃	194	39.38 N	93.04 W
East York, On., Can.	212	43.41 N	79.20 W
East York, Pa., U.S.	208	39.58 N	76.43 W
Eaton, Austl.	168a	33.19 S	115.43 E
Eaton, Co., U.S.	200	40.31 N	104.42 W
Eaton, In., U.S.	216	40.20 N	85.21 W
Eaton, N.Y., U.S.	210	42.51 N	75.37 W
Eaton, Oh., U.S.	218	39.44 N	84.38 W
Eaton ≃	206	45.28 N	71.39 W
Eaton Estates	214	41.19 N	82.01 W
Eatonia	184	51.13 N	109.23 W
Eaton Nord ≃	206	45.24 N	71.35 W
Eaton Park	220	28.00 N	81.54 W
Eaton Rapids	216	42.30 N	84.39 W
Eatons Neck	276	40.56 N	73.24 W
Eatons Neck >[1]	276	40.57 N	73.23 W
Eatons Neck Point >	210	40.57 N	73.24 W
Eaton Socon	42	52.13 N	0.18 W
Eatonton	192	33.19 N	83.23 W
Eatontown	208	40.17 N	74.03 W
Eatonville	224	46.52 N	122.15 W
Eaton Wash V	280	34.04 N	118.03 W
Eaton Wash Dam ◆[6]	280	34.10 N	118.06 W
Eau ≃	44	53.31 N	0.44 W
Eaubonne	261	49.00 N	2.17 E
Eau Claire, Mi., U.S.	216	41.59 N	86.17 W
Eau Claire, Pa., U.S.	214	41.08 N	79.48 W
Eau Claire, Wi., U.S.	190	44.48 N	91.29 W
Eau Claire ≃, Wi., U.S.	190	44.49 N	91.31 W
Eau Claire ≃, Wi., U.S.	190	44.55 N	89.37 W
Eau Claire, Lac à l' ⊜, P.Q., Can.	176	56.10 N	74.25 W
Eau Claire, Lac à l' ⊜, P.Q., Can.	206	46.33 N	73.04 W
Eau d'Heure ≃	56	50.18 N	4.24 E
Eau Galle ≃	190	44.37 N	92.00 W
Eau Gallie	220	28.08 N	80.38 W
Eaulne ≃	50	49.54 N	1.07 E
Eauripik I[1]	108	6.42 N	143.03 E
Eauripik Rise ✦[3]	14	3.00 N	142.00 E
Eauze	32	43.52 N	0.06 E
Ebabaka	152	2.30 S	18.19 E
Eban	150	9.44 N	4.56 E
Ebanga	152	12.44 S	14.44 E
Ebangalakata	152	0.29 S	21.29 E
Ebano	234	22.13 N	98.22 W
Ebb and Flow Indian Reserve ◆[4]	184	51.05 N	99.05 W
Ebb and Flow Lake ⊜	184	51.05 N	98.56 W
Ebbegebirge ⩘	56	51.08 N	7.46 E
Ebben Creek ≃	283	42.38 N	70.45 W
Ebberup	41	55.15 N	9.59 E
Ebbetts Pass)(	226	38.33 N	119.48 W
Ebbs	64	47.38 N	12.13 E
Ebbw ≃	42	51.33 N	2.59 W
Ebbw Vale	42	51.47 N	3.12 W
Ebebiyín	152	2.09 N	11.20 E
Ebeji (El Beïd) ≃	146	12.32 N	14.11 E
Ebejty, ozero ⊜	86	54.38 N	71.44 E
Ebeleben	54	51.17 N	10.43 E
Ebeltoft	41	56.12 N	10.41 E
Ebeltoft Vig ⊂	41	56.10 N	10.36 E
Ebenau	64	47.47 N	13.11 E
Ebendorf	54	52.11 N	11.34 E
Ebene Reichenau	64	46.51 N	13.54 E
Ebenezer	275b	43.46 N	79.40 W
Ebenezer Ridge ∧	218	39.06 N	84.55 W
Eben Junction	190	46.21 N	86.58 W
Ebensburg	214	40.29 N	78.43 W
Ebensee	64	47.48 N	13.46 E
Ebensfeld	56	50.04 N	10.58 E
Eberbach	56	49.28 N	8.59 E
Ebergassing	264b	48.03 N	16.31 E
Eber Gölü ⊜	130	38.38 N	31.12 E
Ebergötzen	52	51.34 N	10.06 E
Ebermannstadt	60	49.43 N	11.13 E
Ebern	56	50.05 N	10.47 E
Eberndorf	61	46.35 N	14.38 E
Ebersbach, Dtsch.	54	51.00 N	14.35 E
Ebersbach, Dtsch.	56	48.43 N	9.31 E
Ebersberg	60	48.05 N	11.58 E
Eberschwang	60	48.09 N	13.34 E
Ebersdorf	52	53.31 N	9.03 E
Ebersdorf bei Coburg	56	50.13 N	11.04 E
Eberstein	61	46.48 N	14.34 E
Eberswalde	54	52.50 N	13.49 E
Ebetsu	92a	43.07 N	141.34 E
Ebian	102	29.10 N	103.20 E
Ebina	94	35.26 N	139.25 E
Ebino	92	32.03 N	130.50 E
Ebinur Hu ⊜	86	44.55 N	82.55 E
Ebi-Sekigahara-Yōrō-kokutei-kōen ♠	94	35.30 N	136.30 E
Ebnat	58	47.15 N	9.08 E
Ebo	152	11.02 S	14.41 E
Ebola ≃	152	3.20 N	20.57 E
Eboli	68	40.37 N	15.04 E
Ebolowa	152	2.54 N	11.09 E
Ebon I[1]	14	4.35 N	168.44 E
Ebonda	152	2.12 N	22.21 E
Ebony	156	22.05 S	15.15 E
Eboshi-yama ∧	96	35.04 N	133.04 E
Eboué Stadium ♠	273b	4.17 S	15.18 E
Ebrach	56	49.50 N	10.29 E
Ebre, Delta de l' ≚[2]	34	40.43 N	0.54 E
Ebreichsdorf	61	47.58 N	16.24 E
Ébrié, Lagune ⊂	150	5.14 N	4.26 W
Ebro (Ebre) ≃	34	40.43 N	0.54 E
Ebro, Embalse del ⊜[1]	34	43.00 N	3.58 W
Ebstorf	52	53.01 N	10.25 E
Ebute-Ikorodu	273a	6.37 N	3.30 E
Ebute-Metta ◆[8]	273a	6.29 N	3.23 E
Ecatepec	286a	19.35 N	99.04 W
Écaussinnes-d'Enghen	50	50.34 N	4.10 E
Ecclefechan	44	55.03 N	3.17 W
Eccles, Eng., U.K.	44	53.29 N	2.21 W
Eccles, Eng., U.K.	260	51.19 N	0.29 E
Eccles, W.V., U.S.	192	37.46 N	81.15 W
Eccleshall	42	52.52 N	2.15 W
Eccleston, Eng., U.K.	44	53.38 N	2.43 W
Eccleston, Eng., U.K.	262	53.27 N	2.47 W
Eccleston, Md., U.S.	284b	39.24 N	76.44 W
Eceabat	130	40.11 N	26.21 E
Echabi	89	53.30 N	142.59 E
Echague	116	16.42 N	121.40 E
Echallens	58	46.38 N	6.38 E
Echaporã	255	22.26 S	50.12 W
Echarcon	261	48.34 N	2.24 E
Échauffour	50	48.44 N	0.23 E
Ech Cheliff (Orléansville)	148	36.10 N	1.20 E
Ech Cheliff □[5]	148	36.20 N	1.50 E
Echeconnee Creek ≃	192	32.39 N	83.36 W
Echelon Mall ◆[9]	285	39.51 N	75.00 W
Echeng	100	30.24 N	114.51 E
Échenoz-la-Méline	58	47.36 N	6.08 E
Echi ≃	94	35.13 N	136.07 E
Echigawa	94	35.10 N	136.12 E
Echigo-sammyaku ⩘	92	37.50 N	139.50 E
Echimamish ≃	184	54.20 N	97.27 W
Eching	60	48.18 N	11.37 E
Echizen	94	35.54 N	136.00 E
Echizen-Kaga-kaigan-kokutei-kōen ♠	94	36.08 N	136.05 E
Echizen-misaki >	94	35.59 N	135.57 E
Echo	198	44.37 N	95.25 W
Echo Bay	176	66.05 N	118.02 W
Echo Bay ⊂	276	40.54 N	73.46 W
Echoing ≃	184	55.51 N	92.05 W
Echoing Lake ⊜	184	54.31 N	92.15 W
Echo Lake ⊜, Il., U.S.	278	42.13 N	88.05 W
Echo Lake ⊜, N.J., U.S.	276	41.04 N	74.25 W
Echo Summit ∧	226	38.50 N	120.02 W
Echouani, Lac ⊜	190	47.46 N	75.42 W
Echt, Ned.	52	51.06 N	5.52 E
Echt, Scot., U.K.	46	57.08 N	2.26 W
Echternach	56	49.48 N	6.26 E
Echternacherbrück	56	49.49 N	6.25 E
Echuca	166	36.08 S	144.46 E
Echunga	168b	35.07 S	138.48 E
Écija	34	37.32 N	5.05 W
Ecilda Paullier	258	34.22 S	57.04 W
Eck, Loch ⊜	46	56.05 N	5.00 W
Eckartsberga	54	51.07 N	11.34 E
Eckbolsheim	58	48.35 N	7.41 E
Eckernförde	41	54.28 N	9.50 E
Eckernförder Bucht ⊂	41	54.30 N	10.02 E
Eckerö I	26	60.14 N	19.35 E
Eckington	44	53.19 N	1.21 W
Eckley	210	40.59 N	75.51 W
Eckville	182	52.21 N	114.22 W
Eckwarderhörne	52	53.31 N	8.14 E
Eclectic	194	32.38 N	86.02 W
Ecleto	222	29.03 N	97.45 W
Ecleto Creek ≃	196	28.52 N	97.45 W
Eclipse Sound ʯ	176	72.38 N	79.00 W
Ečmiadzin	84	40.10 N	44.18 E
Ecola State Park ♠	224	45.57 N	123.58 W
Ècole ≃	261	48.32 N	2.33 E
École Militaire (Saint-Cyr) ■	261	48.48 N	2.04 E
Écommoy	50	47.50 N	0.16 E
Econfina ≃	192	30.02 N	83.55 W
Econlockhatchee ≃	220	28.42 N	81.02 W
Economy, In., U.S.	218	39.58 N	85.05 W
Economy, Pa., U.S.	214	40.39 N	80.14 W
Economy Park ♠	279b	40.37 N	80.12 W
Ecoporanga	255	18.23 S	40.50 W
Écorce, Lac de l' ⊜[1]	190	47.05 N	76.24 W
Écorces, Lac des ⊜	206	46.00 N	74.32 W
Ecorse	216	42.14 N	83.08 W
Ecorse ≃	281	42.14 N	83.09 W
Ecorse, South Branch ≃	281	42.14 N	83.09 W
Écos	50	49.10 N	1.39 E
Écosse → Scotland □[8]	28	57.00 N	4.00 W
Écouen	50	49.01 N	2.23 E
Écouen, Château d' ⊥	261	49.01 N	2.23 E
Écouis	50	49.19 N	1.26 E
Ecoute, Ru d' ≃	261	48.39 N	2.26 E
Ecquevilly	261	48.57 N	1.55 E
Écrins, Barre des ∧	62	44.55 N	6.22 E
Écrins, Massif des ⩘[1]	62	44.55 N	6.20 E
Écrins, Parc National des ♠	62	44.50 N	6.15 E
Écrosnes	261	48.33 N	1.44 E
Ecru	194	34.21 N	89.01 W
Ecser	264c	47.27 N	19.20 E
Ecstall ≃	182	54.09 N	129.56 W
Ecuador □[1], S.A.	242	2.00 S	77.30 W
Ecuador □[1], S.A.	246	2.00 S	77.30 W
Ecuandureo	234	20.10 N	102.11 W
Écueillé	32	47.05 N	1.21 E
Écuisses	58	46.45 N	4.32 E
Ecum Secum	186	44.58 N	62.08 W
Écury-sur-Coole	50	48.54 N	4.20 E
Ed, Erit.	144	13.52 N	41.40 E
Ed, Sve.	26	58.55 N	11.55 E
Eda ◆[8]	268	35.34 N	139.34 E
Edah	162	28.17 S	117.10 E
Edam, Sk., Can.	184	53.12 N	108.46 W
Edam, Ned.	52	52.31 N	5.03 E
Eday I	46	59.11 N	2.47 W
Edderton	46	57.50 N	4.10 W
Eddington Gardens	285	40.06 N	74.57 W
Eddleston	46	55.43 N	3.13 W
Eddrachillis Bay ⊂	46	58.18 N	5.15 W
Eddy	222	31.18 N	97.15 W
Eddystone	208	39.51 N	75.20 W
Eddystone Point >	166	41.00 S	148.21 E
Eddystone Rocks II[1]	42	50.12 N	4.15 W
Eddyville, Ia., U.S.	190	41.09 N	92.38 W
Eddyville, Ky., U.S.	194	37.05 N	88.04 W
Eddyville, N.Y., U.S.	210	41.54 N	74.02 W
Ede, Ned.	52	52.03 N	5.40 E
Ede, Nig.	150	7.44 N	4.27 E
Edéa	152	3.48 N	10.08 E
Edebäck	40	60.04 N	13.33 E
Edebo	40	60.01 N	18.34 E
Edegem	52	51.09 N	4.27 E
Edehon Lake ⊜	176	60.25 N	97.15 W
Edéia	255	17.18 S	49.55 W
Edelény	30	48.18 N	20.44 E
Edelsfeld	60	49.34 N	11.42 E
Edelshausen	60	48.37 N	11.17 E
Edelweiss	273d	26.16 S	28.28 E
Edelweiss Spitze ∧	64	47.07 N	12.50 E
Edemissen	52	52.23 N	10.16 E
Eden, Austl.	166	37.04 S	149.54 E
Éden, Bra.	287a	22.48 S	43.24 W
Eden, N. Ire., U.K.	48	54.44 N	5.47 W
Eden, Mi., U.S.	216	42.32 N	84.26 W
Eden, Ms., U.S.	194	32.59 N	90.19 W
Eden, N.Y., U.S.	210	42.39 N	78.53 W
Eden, Tx., U.S	196	31.12 N	99.50 W
Eden, Wy., U.S.	200	42.03 N	109.26 W
Eden ≃, Eng., U.K.	42	51.10 N	0.11 E
Eden ≃, Eng., U.K.	44	54.57 N	3.01 W
Eden ≃, Scot., U.K.	46	56.22 N	2.50 W
Eden ≃, Wales, U.K.	42	52.48 N	3.53 W
Edenbridge	42	51.12 N	0.04 E
Edenburg	158	29.45 S	25.56 E
Eden Canyon V	282	37.42 N	122.01 W
Edendale, N.Z.	172	46.19 S	168.47 E
Edendale, S. Afr.	158	29.39 S	30.18 E
Edendale, S. Afr.	273d	26.09 S	28.09 E
Edenderry	48	53.20 N	7.03 W
Edenfield	262	53.40 N	2.18 W
Eden Hill ∧[2]	207	41.20 N	73.19 W
Edenkoben	56	49.17 N	8.07 E
Eden Lake ⊜	184	56.38 N	100.15 W
Eden Mills	212	43.35 N	80.09 W
Eden Park ◆[8]	260	51.23 N	0.02 W
Edenside V	44	54.40 N	2.35 W
Edenton	192	36.03 N	76.36 W
Edenvale	273d	26.08 S	28.09 E
Eden Valley, Austl.	168b	34.39 S	139.06 E
Eden Valley, Mn., U.S.	190	45.19 N	94.32 W
Edenville	158	27.37 S	27.34 E
Edeowie	166	31.27 S	138.27 E
Eder ≃	56	51.13 N	9.27 E
Ederkopf ∧	56	50.56 N	8.12 E
Ederny	48	54.32 N	7.39 W
Edersee ⊜[1]	56	51.11 N	9.00 E
Eder-Talsperre ◆[6]	56	51.11 N	9.02 E
Edesheim	56	49.16 N	8.08 E
Edessa → Édhessa	38	40.48 N	22.03 E
Edewecht	52	53.07 N	8.02 E
Edfu → Idfū	140	24.58 N	32.52 E
Edgar, Ne., U.S	198	40.22 N	97.58 W
Edgar, Wi., U.S.	190	44.55 N	89.57 W
Edgard	194	30.03 N	90.34 W
Edgar Ranges ⩘	162	18.43 S	123.25 E
Edgars Creek ≃	274b	37.44 S	144.58 E
Edgartown	207	41.23 N	70.30 W
Edgartown Harbor ⊂	207	41.24 N	70.30 W
Edgecliff	222	32.39 N	97.22 W
Edgecumbe	172	37.59 S	176.50 E
Edgefield	192	33.47 N	81.55 W
Edge Hill ◆[8]	262	53.24 N	2.57 W
Edge Hill ∧	42	52.08 N	1.27 W
Edgeley, On., Can.	275b	43.48 N	79.31 W
Edgeley, N.D., U.S.	198	46.21 N	98.42 W
Edgely	285	40.07 N	74.50 W
Edgemere	208	39.14 N	76.26 W
Edgemont, Ca., U.S.	228	33.53 N	117.18 W
Edgemont, Pa., U.S.	285	39.57 N	75.27 W
Edgemont, S.D., U.S.	198	43.18 N	103.49 W
Edgemont Park	216	42.44 N	84.36 W
Edgemoor	285	39.45 N	75.30 W
Edge Mountain ∧	180	58.12 N	152.06 W
Edgeøya I	12	77.45 N	22.30 E
Edgeroi	166	30.07 S	149.48 E
Edgerton, Ab., Can.	184	52.45 N	110.27 W
Edgerton, In., U.S.	216	41.05 N	84.49 W
Edgerton, Mn., U.S.	198	43.52 N	96.07 W
Edgerton, Oh., U.S.	216	41.26 N	84.44 W
Edgerton, Wi., U.S.	216	42.50 N	89.04 W
Edgerton, Wy., U.S.	200	43.24 N	106.14 W
Edgewater, Al., U.S.	194	33.31 N	86.57 W
Edgewater, Fl., U.S.	220	28.59 N	80.54 W
Edgewater, N.J., U.S.	276	40.50 N	73.58 W
Edgewater Park	285	40.04 N	74.54 W
Edgewater Park ♠	279a	41.29 N	81.43 W
Edgewater Point >	276	40.55 N	73.44 W
Edgewood, B.C., Can.	182	49.47 N	118.08 W
Edgewood, Fl., U.S.	220	28.29 N	81.22 W
Edgewood, Il., U.S.	219	38.55 N	88.40 W
Edgewood, In., U.S.	218	40.06 N	85.44 W
Edgewood, Ia., U.S.	190	42.38 N	91.24 W
Edgewood, Md., U.S.	208	39.25 N	76.17 W
Edgewood, Oh., U.S.	214	41.52 N	80.46 W
Edgewood, Pa., U.S.	279b	40.25 N	79.52 W
Edgewood, Tx., U.S.	222	32.42 N	95.53 W
Edgeworth	214	40.33 N	80.11 W
Edgeworthstown → Mostrim	48	53.42 N	7.36 W
Edgware ◆[8]	260	51.37 N	0.17 W
Edgworth	262	53.39 N	2.24 W
Édhessa	38	40.48 N	22.03 E
Ediger	56	50.06 N	7.09 E
Edimbourg → Edinburgh	46	55.57 N	3.13 W
Edimburgo → Edinburgh	46	55.57 N	3.13 W
Edina, Liber.	150	6.01 N	10.10 W
Edina, Mn., U.S.	190	44.53 N	93.20 W
Edina, Mo., U.S.	219	40.10 N	92.10 W
Edinboro	214	41.52 N	80.07 W
Edinboro Lake ⊜	214	41.53 N	80.08 W
Edinburg, Il., U.S.	219	39.39 N	89.23 W
Edinburg, In., U.S.	218	39.21 N	85.58 W
Edinburg, Ms., U.S.	194	32.47 N	89.20 W
Edinburg, N.Y., U.S.	210	43.13 N	74.07 W
Edinburg, N.D., U.S.	198	48.29 N	97.51 W
Edinburg, Oh., U.S.	214	41.06 N	81.09 W
Edinburg, Tx., U.S.	196	26.18 N	98.09 W
Edinburg, Va., U.S.	188	38.49 N	78.33 W
Edinburgh	46	55.57 N	3.13 W
Edinburgh (Turnhouse) Airport ⊠	46	55.57 N	3.21 W
Edinburgh, Arrecife ✦[2]	236	14.50 N	82.39 W
Edinburgh Castle ⊥	46	55.56 N	3.14 W
Edinburgh Channel ʯ	236	14.45 N	82.40 W
Edinburgh Mountain ∧	224	48.38 N	124.24 W
Edincik	130	40.20 N	27.51 E
Edingen → Enghien	50	50.42 N	4.02 E
Edirne	130	41.40 N	26.34 E
Edirne □[4]	130	41.20 N	26.40 E
Edison, Ga., U.S.	192	31.33 N	84.44 W
Edison, N.J., U.S.	210	40.27 N	74.18 W
Edison, Oh., U.S.	214	40.33 N	82.51 W
Edison, Pa., U.S.	208	40.17 N	75.07 W
Edison Bridge ◆[5]	214	41.27 N	82.49 W
Edison National Historic Site ⊥	276	40.47 N	74.14 W
Edison Park ◆[8]	278	42.01 N	87.49 W
Edisseja	84	44.03 N	44.33 E
Edisto ≃	192	32.39 N	80.24 W
Edisto, North Fork ≃	192	33.16 N	80.53 W
Edisto, South Fork ≃	192	33.16 N	80.53 W
Edisto Island I	192	32.35 N	80.20 W
Edith	170	33.48 S	149.55 E
Edith, Mount ∧	202	46.26 N	111.11 W
Edithburgh	168b	35.06 S	137.44 E
Edith Cavell, Mount ∧	182	52.40 N	118.03 W
Edith River	164	14.11 S	132.02 E
Edithvale	274b	38.02 S	145.07 E
Edith Weston	42	52.37 N	0.37 W
Edjejou, Oued i-n- V	148	22.46 N	4.05 E
Edjeleh	148	27.38 N	9.50 E
Edjerir ≃	150	18.06 N	0.50 E
Edjudina	162	29.48 S	122.23 E
Edmeston	210	42.41 N	75.14 W
Edmond	196	35.39 N	97.28 W
Edmondbyers	44	54.51 N	1.58 W
Edmonds	224	47.48 N	122.22 W
Edmondson Heights	284b	39.18 N	76.43 W
Edmonston	284c	38.57 N	76.56 W
Edmonton, Austl.	166	17.01 S	145.45 E
Edmonton, Ab., Can.	182	53.33 N	113.28 W
Edmonton, Ky., U.S.	194	36.58 N	85.36 W
Edmonton ◆[8]	260	51.37 N	0.04 W
Edmore, Mi., U.S.	190	43.24 N	85.02 W
Edmore, N.D., U.S.	198	48.24 N	98.27 W
Edmund	162	23.46 S	116.02 E
Edmund Lake ⊜	184	54.45 N	93.15 W
Edmundson Acres	228	35.14 N	118.49 W
Edmundston	186	47.22 N	68.20 W
Edna, Ks., U.S.	198	37.03 N	95.21 W
Edna, Pa., U.S.	279b	40.19 N	79.39 W
Edna, Tx., U.S.	222	28.58 N	96.38 W
Edna Bay	180	55.57 N	133.40 W
Ednor	208	39.09 N	76.59 W
Edo ≃	94	35.37 N	139.53 E
Edogawa ◆[8]	268	35.42 N	139.52 E
Edolo	64	46.11 N	10.20 E
Edom	222	32.22 N	95.37 W
Edon	216	41.33 N	84.46 W
Edosaki	94	35.57 N	140.19 E
Edremit	130	39.35 N	27.01 E
Edremit Körfezi ⊂	130	39.30 N	26.45 E
Edrengijn nuruu ⩘	102	44.15 N	97.45 E
Edsall Park	284c	38.48 N	77.11 W
Edsbro	40	59.54 N	18.29 E
Edsbruk	26	58.02 N	16.28 E
Edsbyn	26	61.23 N	15.49 E
Edsgatan	40	59.26 N	13.33 E
Edson	182	53.35 N	116.26 W
Edson Butte ∧	202	42.52 N	124.20 W
Eduardo Castex	252	35.54 S	64.18 W
Eduardo VII, Península → Edward VII Peninsula >[1]	9	77.40 S	155.00 W
Eduni, Mount ∧	180	64.15 N	128.04 W
Edward ≃, Austl.	164	14.44 S	141.35 E
Edward ≃, Austl.	166	35.33 S	144.58 E
Edward, Lake ⊜	154	0.25 S	29.30 E
Edward, Mount ∧	162	23.22 S	131.55 E
Edwardes Park ♠	274b	37.43 S	145.00 E
Edward Island I	190	48.24 N	88.36 W
Edward River Aboriginal Reserve ◆[4]	164	14.30 S	141.45 E
Edwards, Ca., U.S.	228	34.54 N	117.53 W
Edwards, Ms. U.S.	194	32.19 N	90.36 W
Edwards, N.Y., U.S.	212	44.19 N	75.15 W
Edwards ≃	190	41.09 N	90.59 W
Edwards Air Force Base ■	228	34.54 N	117.52 W
Edwards Airport ⊠	276	40.45 N	73.03 W
Edwardsburg	216	41.47 N	86.04 W
Edwards Butte ∧	224	45.23 N	123.41 W
Edwards Gardens ♠	275b	43.44 N	79.22 W
Edwards Plateau ⩘[1]	196	31.20 N	101.00 W
Edwards Point >	169	38.13 S	144.42 E
Edwards Run ≃	285	39.48 N	75.12 W
Edwardsville, Il., U.S.	219	38.48 N	89.57 W
Edwardsville, In., U.S.	218	38.16 N	85.55 W
Edwardsville, Pa., U.S.	210	41.16 N	75.55 W
Edward VIII Bay ⊂	9	66.50 S	57.00 E
Edward VII Peninsula >[1]	9	77.40 S	155.00 W
Edwinstowe	44	53.12 N	1.04 W
Edzell	46	56.48 N	2.39 W
Edziza, Mount ∧	180	57.40 N	130.36 W
Eede	52	51.15 N	3.28 E
Eefde	52	52.10 N	6.14 E
Eek	180	60.12 N	162.15 W
Eek ≃	180	60.12 N	162.15 W
Eeklo	50	51.11 N	3.34 E
Eel ≃, Ca., U.S.	204	40.40 N	124.20 W
Eel ≃, In., U.S	194	39.07 N	86.57 W
Eel ≃, In., U.S	216	40.45 N	86.22 W
Eel, Middle Fork ≃	204	39.42 N	123.21 W
Eel, North Fork ≃	204	39.57 N	123.26 W
Eel, South Fork ≃	204	40.22 N	123.55 W
Eel Bay ⊂	212	44.19 N	76.02 W
Eelde	52	53.07 N	6.35 E
Eels Creek ≃	212	44.35 N	78.03 W
Eels Lake ⊜	212	44.54 N	78.08 W
Eemskanaal ≊	52	53.15 N	6.45 E
Eerbeek	52	52.07 N	6.04 E
Eersel	52	51.22 N	5.19 E
Eesti → Estonia □[1]	22	59.00 N	26.00 E
Eexta	52	53.10 N	6.59 E
Efate □[8]	175f	17.45 S	168.20 E
Éfaté I	175f	17.40 S	168.25 E
Eferding	61	48.18 N	14.02 E
Efes (Ephesus) ⊥	130	37.55 N	27.17 E
Effigy Mounds National Monument ♠	190	43.06 N	91.13 W
Effingham, Eng., U.K.	260	51.16 N	0.24 W
Effingham, Il., U.S.	194	39.07 N	88.32 W
Effingham, Ks., U.S.	198	39.31 N	95.24 W
Effingham □[6]	219	39.07 N	88.33 W
Effingham Lake ⊜	212	44.59 N	77.22 W
Effort	210	40.56 N	75.26 W
Efiduasi	150	6.51 N	1.24 W
Efkere	130	38.47 N	35.40 E
Eflâni	130	41.26 N	32.57 E
Eforie Nord	38	44.06 N	28.38 E
Eforie Sud	38	44.03 N	28.38 E
Efringen-Kirchen	58	47.39 N	7.34 E
Ega ≃	34	42.19 N	1.55 W
Egadi, Isole II	70	37.58 N	12.16 E
Egan	222	32.28 N	97.17 W
Egaña	252	36.59 S	59.06 W
Egan Range ⩘	204	39.10 N	114.55 W
Eganville	190	45.32 N	77.06 W
Egau ≃	56	48.36 N	10.34 E
Egba □[8]	273a	6.41 N	3.23 E
Egbe, Nig.	150	8.16 N	5.31 E
Egbe, Nig.	273a	6.33 N	3.17 E
Egbunda	154	2.44 N	27.12 E
Egedesminde (Aasiaat)	176	68.42 N	52.45 W
Égée, Mer → Aegean Sea ⍑[2]	38	38.30 N	25.00 E
Egegik	180	58.13 N	157.22 W
Egeln	54	51.56 N	11.25 E
Egeo, Mar → Aegean Sea ⍑[2]	38	38.30 N	25.00 E
Eger → Cheb, Česká Rep.	54	50.01 N	12.25 E
Eger, Magy.	30	47.54 N	20.23 E
Eger ≃, Dtsch.	56	48.50 N	10.37 E
Eger (Ohře) ≃, Europe	54	50.32 N	14.08 E
Egeria Mountain ∧	182	53.55 N	130.22 W
Egernsund	41	54.54 N	9.37 E
Egerpohl	263	51.07 N	7.27 E
Egersund	26	58.27 N	6.00 E
Egerton	262	53.38 N	2.26 W
Egerton, Mount ∧	9	80.50 S	158.50 E
Egeskov ⊥	41	55.10 N	10.30 E
Egestorf	52	53.11 N	10.04 E
Egestorf [am Süntel]	52	52.17 N	9.31 E
Egg	58	47.26 N	9.54 E
Egg Creek ≃	198	48.22 N	100.47 W
Egge ⩘	52	51.40 N	8.55 E
Eggebek	41	54.37 N	9.22 E
Eggelsberg	60	48.05 N	13.00 E
Eggenberg, Schloss ⊥	61	47.05 N	15.25 E
Eggenburg	61	48.39 N	15.50 E
Eggenfelden	60	48.25 N	12.46 E
Eggenstein-Leopoldshafen	56	49.04 N	8.23 E
Eggerscheid	263	51.19 N	6.53 E
Eggersdorf	54	52.32 N	13.49 E
Eggesin	54	53.41 N	14.05 E
Egg Harbor City	208	39.31 N	74.38 W
Egg Island Point >	208	39.11 N	75.08 W
Egg Lagoon	166	39.39 S	143.58 E
Egg Lake ⊜, Mb., Can.	184	54.21 N	101.26 W
Egg Lake ⊜, Sk., Can.	184	55.05 N	105.30 W
Egglestone Abbey ʊ[1]	44	54.32 N	1.54 W
Egglham	60	48.32 N	13.04 E
Egglkofen	60	48.24 N	12.27 E
Eggmühl	60	48.51 N	12.11 E
Egham	42	51.26 N	0.34 W
Egherta	144	2.04 N	43.11 E
Éghezée	56	50.36 N	4.54 E
Egijn ≃	88	49.24 N	103.36 E
Eğil	130	38.15 N	40.05 E
Egilsay I	46	59.09 N	2.56 W
Egilsstaðir	24a	65.16 N	14.18 W
Eging	60	48.43 N	13.16 E
Egipto → Egypt □[1]	140	27.00 N	30.00 E
Égletons	32	45.24 N	2.03 E
Eglin Air Force Base ■	194	30.29 N	86.30 W
Eglinton	48	55.02 N	7.11 W
Eglisau	58	47.34 N	8.32 E
Egloskerry	42	50.39 N	4.27 W
Égly	261	48.35 N	2.13 E
Egmond aan Zee	52	52.36 N	4.37 E
Egmond-Binnen	52	52.35 N	4.39 E
Egmont, Cape >	172	39.17 S	173.45 E
Egmont, Mount → Taranaki, Mount ∧	172	39.18 S	174.04 E
Egmont Bay ⊂	186	46.35 N	64.12 W
Egmont Channel ʯ	220	27.36 N	82.45 W
Egmont Key I	220	27.35 N	82.46 W
Egmont National Park ♠	172	39.15 S	174.05 E
Egna (Neumarkt)	64	46.19 N	11.16 E
Egnach	58	47.33 N	9.23 E
Egnazia ⊥	68	40.53 N	17.24 E
Egoryevsk → Jegorjevsk	82	55.23 N	39.02 E
Egota ◆[8]	268	35.43 N	139.40 E
Egra	126	21.54 N	87.32 E
Egremont, Ab., Can.	182	54.02 N	113.08 W
Egremont, Eng., U.K.	44	54.29 N	3.33 W
Égreville	50	48.10 N	2.52 E
Eğridir	130	37.52 N	30.51 E
Eğridir Gölü ⊜	130	38.02 N	30.53 E
Eğriköy	130	38.44 N	27.21 E
Egrisskij chrebet ⩘	84	42.49 N	42.24 E
Egton	44	54.26 N	0.45 W
Egtved	41	55.37 N	9.18 E
Éguas, Rio das ≃	255	13.26 S	44.14 W
Éguilles	62	43.34 N	5.22 E
Eguisheim	58	48.03 N	7.18 E
Egum Atoll I[1]	164	9.25 S	151.55 E
Egvekinot	180	66.19 N	179.10 W
Egyházasrádóc	61	47.05 N	16.37 E
Egypt, Ma., U.S.	207	42.12 N	70.45 W
Egypt, Pa., U.S.	208	40.41 N	75.32 W
Egypt, Tx., U.S.	222	29.24 N	96.14 W
Egypt (Mişr) □[1], Afr.	136	27.00 N	30.00 E
Egypt (Mişr) □[1], Afr.	140	27.00 N	30.00 E
Egypt, Lake of ⊜[1]	194	37.35 N	88.55 W
Égypte → Egypt □[1]	140	27.00 N	30.00 E
Egyptian Museum ʊ	273c	30.03 N	31.14 E
Eha-Amufu	150	6.40 N	7.46 E
Ehekirchen	60	48.38 N	11.06 E
Ehen ≃	44	54.25 N	3.30 W
Ehime □[5]	96	33.40 N	132.50 E
Ehingen	58	48.17 N	9.43 E
Ehingen ◆[8]	263	51.22 N	6.42 E
Ehle ≃	54	52.12 N	11.44 E
Ehmen	54	52.24 N	10.41 E
Ehra-Lessien	54	52.34 N	10.46 E
Ehrang	56	49.49 N	6.41 E
Ehrenberg	200	33.36 N	114.31 W
Ehrenberg Range ⩘	162	23.18 S	130.20 E
Ehrenbreitstein, Feste ⊥	56	50.21 N	7.37 E
Ehrenburg ⊥	56	50.12 N	7.27 E
Ehrenfeld	214	40.22 N	78.46 W
Ehrenfriedersdorf	54	50.38 N	12.58 E
Ehrenhausen	61	46.43 N	15.35 E
Ehreshoven	56	50.58 N	7.20 E
Ehrhardt	192	33.05 N	81.00 W
Ehrhorn	52	53.10 N	9.53 E
Ehringhausen	263	51.11 N	7.33 E
Ehringhausen ◆[8]	263	51.09 N	7.11 E
Ehrwald	64	47.24 N	10.55 E
Ehwa Women's University ʊ[2]	271b	37.34 N	126.56 E
Ei	92	31.12 N	130.30 E
Eibar	34	43.11 N	2.28 W
Eibau	54	50.58 N	14.40 E
Eibelstadt	56	49.43 N	10.00 E
Eibenstock	54	50.29 N	12.35 E
Eibergen	52	52.06 N	6.39 E
Eibiswald	61	46.41 N	15.15 E
Eibsee ⊜	64	47.27 N	10.58 E
Eicha	54	50.21 N	10.34 E
Eich-Berg ∧[2]	264a	52.39 N	13.50 E
Eiche, Dtsch.	264a	52.34 N	13.36 E
Eiche, Dtsch.	264a	52.25 N	12.58 E
Eichenbarleben	54	52.10 N	11.24 E
Eichenbrandt	264a	52.38 N	13.51 E
Eichendorf	60	48.38 N	12.51 E
Eichgraben	61	48.10 N	15.59 E
Eichlinghofen ◆[8]	263	51.29 N	7.24 E
Eichsfeld ◆[1]	56	51.20 N	10.10 E
Eichstädt	264a	52.42 N	13.07 E
Eichstätt	60	48.54 N	11.12 E
Eichstetten	58	48.05 N	7.44 E
Eichtersheim	56	49.14 N	8.46 E
Eichwalde	54	52.22 N	13.37 E
Eickelborn	52	51.39 N	8.13 E
Eicken ◆[3]	263	51.13 N	6.26 E
Eickerend	263	51.13 N	6.34 E
Eickerkopf ∧[2]	263	51.21 N	7.42 E
Eicklingen	52	52.33 N	10.10 E
Eide	26	62.55 N	7.26 E
Eidelstedt ◆[8]	52	53.36 N	9.53 E
Eider ≃	41	54.19 N	8.58 E
Eiderstedt >[1]	41	54.22 N	8.50 E
Eidfjord	26	60.28 N	7.05 E
Eidsvåg, Nor.	26	60.27 N	5.21 E
Eidsvåg, Nor.	26	62.47 N	8.03 E
Eidsvold	166	25.22 S	151.07 E
Eidsvoll	26	60.19 N	11.14 E
Eifa	56	50.58 N	8.34 E
Eifel ⩘	56	50.15 N	6.45 E
Eiffel, Tour ⊥	261	48.51 N	2.18 E
Eiffel Flats	154	18.15 S	29.59 E
Eifgenbach ≃	263	51.05 N	7.09 E
Eige, Carn ∧	46	57.17 N	5.07 W
Eigen ◆[8]	263	51.33 N	6.57 E
Eigenji	94	35.04 N	136.18 E
Eigenrieden	54	51.11 N	10.22 E
Eiger ∧	58	46.35 N	8.00 E
Eigg I	46	56.54 N	6.10 W
Eigg, Sound of ʯ	46	56.51 N	6.13 W
Eight Degree Channel ʯ	122	8.00 N	73.00 E
Eighteenmile Creek ≃, N.Y., U.S.	210	42.43 N	78.58 W
Eighteenmile Creek ≃, N.Y., U.S.	210	43.21 N	78.43 W
Eight Mile Creek ≃, On., Can.	284a	43.14 N	79.11 W
Eightmile Creek ≃, In., U.S.	216	40.57 N	85.22 W
Eightmile Creek ≃, Or., U.S.	224	45.36 N	121.05 W
Eights Coast ⩡[2]	9	73.30 S	93.00 W
Eighty Four	279b	40.11 N	80.08 W
Eighty Mile Beach ⩡[2]	162	19.45 S	121.00 E
Eiheiji	94	36.05 N	136.20 E
Eijerlandsche Gat ⊂	52	53.12 N	4.50 E
Eijsden	56	50.47 N	5.43 E
Eikeren ⊜	26	59.38 N	9.58 E
Eikisdalsvatnet ⊜	26	62.34 N	8.11 E
Eildon	169	37.14 S	145.56 E
Eildon, Lake ⊜[1]	169	37.11 S	145.55 E
Eilean Gowan Island I	212	45.02 N	79.25 W
Eileen	216	41.17 N	88.15 W
Eilenburg	54	51.27 N	12.37 E
Eil Malk I	175b	7.09 N	134.22 E
Eilsleben	54	52.09 N	11.13 E
Eimbeckhausen	52	52.14 N	9.25 E
Eimke	52	52.58 N	10.19 E
Eina	26	60.38 N	10.36 E
Einasleigh	166	18.31 S	144.05 E
Einasleigh ≃	166	17.30 S	142.17 E
Einbeck	52	51.49 N	9.52 E
Eindhoven	52	51.26 N	5.28 E
Eine	50	50.52 N	3.37 E
Einme	110	16.54 N	95.11 E
Einöd	56	49.16 N	7.19 E
Einödriegel ∧	60	48.56 N	13.02 E
Einruhr	56	50.35 N	6.22 E
Einsiedel	54	50.46 N	12.58 E
Einsiedeln	58	47.08 N	8.45 E
Einville-au-Jard	58	48.39 N	6.30 E
Eirauli	272c	19.10 N	72.59 E
Éire → Ireland □[1]	48	53.00 N	8.00 W
Eiru ≃	248	6.42 S	69.52 W
Eirunepé	248	6.40 S	69.52 W
Eisbach ≃	56	49.38 N	8.22 E
Eisch ≃	56	49.45 N	6.07 E
Eiseb ≃	156	20.33 S	20.59 E
Eisenach	54	50.59 N	10.19 E
Eisenberg, Dtsch.	54	50.58 N	11.53 E
Eisenberg, Dtsch.	56	49.38 N	8.05 E
Eisenberg ∧[2]	61	47.12 N	16.24 E
Eisenerz	61	47.33 N	14.53 E
Eisenerzer Alpen ⩘	61	47.28 N	14.45 E
Eisenhower Center ʊ	198	38.54 N	97.12 W
Eisenhower Memorial Park ♠	276	40.44 N	73.34 W
Eisenhüttenstadt	54	52.10 N	14.39 E
Eisenkappel	61	46.29 N	14.35 E
Eisenschmitt	56	50.03 N	6.43 E
Eisenstadt	61	47.51 N	16.32 E
Eisfeld	54	50.26 N	10.54 E
Eisgarn	61	48.54 N	15.06 E
Eishken	46	58.01 N	6.32 W
Eishort, Loch ⊂	46	57.10 N	5.59 W
Eišiškės	76	54.10 N	25.00 E
Eisk → Jejsk	78	46.42 N	38.16 E
Eisleben	54	51.31 N	11.32 E
Eislingen	56	48.42 N	9.42 E
Eisriesenwelt ⩡[5]	64	47.32 N	13.10 E
Eita	174t	1.21 N	173.05 E
Eitorf	56	50.46 N	7.26 E
Eivissa	34	38.54 N	1.26 E
Eivissa (Ibiza) I	34	39.00 N	1.25 E
Ejasi → Eyasi, Lake ⊜	154	3.40 S	35.05 E
Ejby, Dan.	41	55.30 N	12.07 E
Ejby, Dan.	41	55.26 N	9.57 E
Ejea de los Caballeros	34	42.08 N	1.08 W
Ejeda	157b	24.20 S	44.31 E
Ejército Rebelde, Presa ⊜[1]	286b	23.01 N	82.20 W
Ejido	246	8.33 N	71.14 W
Ejido Jaboncillos	232	28.57 N	102.39 W
Ejigbo	273a	6.33 N	3.18 E
Ejin Horo Qi	102	39.27 N	109.40 E
Ejin Qi	102	41.50 N	100.50 E
Ejstrup	41	55.59 N	9.17 E
Ejura	150	7.23 N	1.22 W
Ejutla de Crespo	234	16.34 N	96.44 W
Ekalaka	198	45.53 N	104.33 W

Symbol	English	Deutsch	Español	Français	Português
≃	River	Fluß	Río	Rivière	Rio
≊	Canal	Kanal	Canal	Canal	Canal
∟	Waterfall, Rapids	Wasserfall, Stromschnellen	Cascada, Rápidos	Chute d'eau, Rapides	Cascata, Rápidos
ʯ	Strait	Meeresstraße	Estrecho	Détroit	Estreito
⊂	Bay, Gulf	Bucht, Golf	Bahía, Golfo	Baie, Golfe	Baía, Golfo
⊜	Lake, Lakes	See, Seen	Lago, Lagos	Lac, Lacs	Lago, Lagos
≡	Swamp	Sumpf	Pantano	Marais	Pântano
⊓	Ice Features, Glacier	Eis- und Gletscherformen	Accidentes Glaciales	Formes glaciaires	Acidentes glaciares
⍑	Other Hydrographic Features	Andere Hydrographische Objekte	Otros Elementos Hidrográficos	Autres données hydrographiques	Outros acidentes hidrográficos
✦	Submarine Features	Untermeerische Objekte	Accidentes Submarinos	Formes de relief sous-marin	Acidentes submarinos
□	Political Unit	Politische Einheit	Unidad Política	Entité politique	Unidade política
ʊ	Cultural Institution	Kulturelle Institution	Institución Cultural	Institution culturelle	Instituição cultural
⊥	Historical Site	Historische Stätte	Sitio Histórico	Site historique	Sitio histórico
♠	Recreational Site	Erholungs- und Ferienort	Sitio de Recreo	Centre de loisirs	Area de Lazer
⊠	Airport	Flughafen	Aeropuerto	Aéroport	Aeroporto
■	Military Installation	Militäranlage	Instalación Militar	Installation militaire	Instalação militar
◆	Miscellaneous	Verschiedenes	Misceláneo	Divers	Diversos

The legend at the foot of the page reads:

Symbols in the index entries represent the broad categories identified in the key at the right. Symbols with superior numbers (ᴀ¹) identify subcategories (see complete key on page I · 1).

Symbole im Register stellen die rechts im Schlüssel erklärten Kategorien dar. Symbole mit hochgestellten Ziffern (ᴀ¹) bezeichnen Unterabteilungen einer Kategorie (vgl. vollständiger Schlüssel auf Seite I · 1).

Los símbolos incluídos en el texto del índice representan las grandes categorías identificadas con la clave a la derecha. Los símbolos con numeros en su parte superior (ᴀ¹) identifican las subcategorías (ver clave completa en página I · 1).

Les symboles de l'index représentent les catégories indiquées dans la légende à droite. Les symboles suivis d'un indice (ᴀ¹) représentent les sous-catégories (voir légende complète à la page I · 1).

Os símbolos incluídos no texto do índice representam as grandes categorias identificadas com a chave à direita. Os símbolos suivis d'un índice (ᴀ¹) identificam as subcategorias (veja-se a chave completa à página I · 1).

Symbol	English	Deutsch	Español	Français	Português
ᴀ	Mountain	Berg	Montaña	Montagne	Montanha
ᴀ	Mountains	Gebirge	Montañas	Montagnes	Montanhas
)(	Pass	Paß	Paso	Col	Passo
⋁	Valley, Canyon	Tal, Cañon	Valle, Cañón	Vallée, Canyon	Vale, Canhão
≊	Plain	Ebene	Llano	Plaine	Planície
⋿	Cape	Kap	Cabo	Cap	Cabo
I	Island	Insel	Isla	Île	Ilha
II	Islands	Inseln	Islas	Îles	Ilhas
⋆	Other Topographic Features	Andere Topographische Objekte	Otros Elementos Topográficos	Autres données topographiques	Outros acidentes topográficos

Elpo-Erie I · 53

ESPAÑOL — Nombre, Página, Lat.°′, Long.°′ W = Oeste
FRANÇAIS — Nom, Page, Lat.°′, Long.°′ W = Ouest
PORTUGUÊS — Nome, Página, Lat.°′, Long.°′ W = Oeste

Nombre / Nom / Nome	Página / Page	Lat.°′	Long.°′ W = Oeste / Ouest
El Porvenir, Perú	248	8.05 S	79.00 W
El Potosí, Punta ≻	234	17.32 N	101.28 W
El Potrero	196	26.23 N	100.27 W
El Prat de Llobregat	34	41.20 N	2.06 E
El Progreso, Ec.	246a	0.54 S	89.33 W
El Progreso, Guat.	236	14.21 N	89.51 W
El Progreso, Hond.	236	15.21 N	87.49 W
El Progreso □[5]	236	14.50 N	90.00 W
El Puente del Arzobispo	34	39.48 N	5.10 W
El Puerto de Santa María	34	36.36 N	6.13 W
El Puesto	252	27.57 S	67.38 W
El Qala	148	36.50 N	8.30 E
El Qoll	148	37.00 N	6.34 E
El Quebrachal	252	25.17 S	64.04 W
El Quelite	234	23.32 N	106.28 W
Elquera Bushland ♦	274a	33.42 S	151.04 E
Elqui ≃	252	29.54 S	71.17 W
Elrama	214	40.15 N	79.55 W
El Ranchito	234	18.40 N	103.41 W
El Rastro	246	9.03 N	67.27 W
El Real de Santa María	246	8.08 N	77.43 W
El Recreo ◆[8]	286c	10.30 N	66.53 W
El Refugio	234	21.57 N	100.02 W
El Remolino	196	28.44 N	101.07 W
El Reno	196	35.31 N	97.57 W
El Rey, Parque Nacional ♦	252	25.00 S	64.40 W
El Rio	228	34.13 N	119.10 W
El Rito	200	36.20 N	106.11 W
El Rito ≃	200	36.12 N	106.14 W
El Roba	154	3.57 N	40.01 E
El Roble, Mesa ∧	232	31.31 N	115.31 W
El Rom	132	33.11 N	35.46 E
El Rosario, Laguna ⊜	234	17.52 N	93.48 W
El Rosarito	232	28.38 N	114.04 W
Elrose	184	51.13 N	108.01 W
Elroy	190	43.44 N	90.16 W
El Rucio	234	23.23 N	102.05 W
Elsa, Yk., Can.	180	63.55 N	135.28 W
Elsa, Tx., U.S.	196	26.17 N	97.59 W
Elsa ≃	66	43.43 N	10.52 E
Elsah	219	38.57 N	90.22 W
El Sahuaro	200	31.05 N	112.55 W
El Salado	252	26.25 S	70.19 W
El Salado, Parque Nacional ♦	246	2.12 S	80.00 W
El Salitre	246	1.50 S	79.48 W
El Salto, Méx.	234	23.47 N	105.22 W
El Salto, Méx.	234	20.32 N	103.11 W
El Salvador, Chile	252	26.17 S	69.43 W
El Salvador, Pil.	116	8.34 N	124.32 E
El Salvador □[1], N.A.	230	13.50 N	88.55 W
El Salvador □[1], N.A.	236	13.50 N	88.55 W
El Samán de Apure	246	7.55 N	68.44 W
El Santo	240p	22.42 N	79.41 W
Elsass → Alsace □[9]	32	48.30 N	7.30 E
El Sauce, Laguna ⊜	258	35.20 S	58.16 W
El Sauz	232	29.02 N	106.16 W
El Sauzal	232	31.54 N	116.41 W
Elsberry	219	39.10 N	90.46 W
Elsbethen	64	47.45 N	13.05 E
Elsburg	273d	26.15 S	28.12 E
Elsdorf, Dtsch.	52	53.14 N	9.20 E
Elsdorf, Dtsch.	56	50.54 N	6.34 E
El Seco, Laguna ⊜	258	35.31 S	58.42 W
El Segundo	228	33.55 N	118.24 W
El Seibo	238	18.46 N	69.02 W
Elsen	52	51.44 N	8.39 E
Elsenham	42	51.55 N	0.14 E
Elsen Nur ⊜	120	35.11 N	92.15 E
Elsenz ≃	56	49.24 N	8.48 E
Elsfleth	52	53.14 N	8.28 E
El Siasgo, Arroyo ≃	258	35.33 S	58.33 W
Elsie, Mi., U.S.	216	43.05 N	84.23 W
Elsie, Or., U.S.	224	45.52 N	123.35 W
Elsinore → Helsingør, Dan.	41	56.02 N	12.37 E
Elsinore, Ut,. U.S.	200	38.40 N	112.08 W
Elsinore, Lake ⊜[1]	228	33.39 N	117.21 W
El Sitio	286c	10.28 N	66.46 W
Elsmere, De., U.S.	208	39.44 N	75.35 W
Elsmere, Ky., U.S.	218	39.00 N	84.36 W
Elsmere, N.Y., U.S.	210	42.37 N	73.49 W
El Sobrante	226	37.58 N	122.17 W
El Socorro	246	8.59 N	65.44 W
El Sombrero	246	9.23 N	67.03 W
Elspark	273d	26.16 S	28.14 E
Elspeet	52	52.17 N	5.46 E
Elst	52	51.55 N	5.50 E
Elstal	54	52.32 N	12.59 E
Elstead	42	51.11 N	0.43 W
Elster	54	51.50 N	12.49 E
Elsterberg	54	50.36 N	12.10 E
Elstergebirge ⩕	54	50.15 N	12.20 E
Elsterwerda	54	51.28 N	13.31 E
Elston, In., U.S.	216	40.22 N	86.55 W
Elston, Mo., U.S.	219	38.37 N	92.19 W
Elstra	54	51.13 N	14.08 E
Elstree	42	51.39 N	0.16 W
Elstree Aerodrome ⊠	260	51.39 N	0.19 W
El Sueco	232	29.54 N	106.24 W
El Tagarete, Cerro ∧	232	26.31 N	105.56 W
El Tajín ⊥	234	20.27 N	97.23 W
El Tala	252	26.07 S	65.17 W
El Talar	258	34.27 S	58.39 W
El Tamarindo	236	13.11 N	87.54 W
El Tambo, Col.	246	1.26 N	77.23 W
El Tambo, Perú	248	12.04 S	75.13 W
El Tanque	196	26.28 N	99.38 W
El Tapextle	234	23.52 N	105.33 W
El Tarf	36	36.45 N	8.20 E
El Tecuán	232	25.29 N	107.00 W
El Tejocote, Cerro ∧	234	18.48 N	103.03 W
Elten	52	51.52 N	6.10 E
El Terrero	234	18.58 N	102.28 W
Eltham, Austl.	169	37.44 S	145.09 E
Eltham, N.Z.	172	39.26 S	174.18 E
Eltham ◆[8]	260	51.27 N	0.04 E
Eltham Palace ʋ	260	51.27 N	0.03 E
El Tigre	246	8.55 N	64.15 W
El Tigre, Isla I	236	13.16 N	87.38 W
El Tigrito → San José de Guanipa	246	8.54 N	64.09 W
El Timbiriche	234	18.38 N	101.31 W
Eltmann	56	49.58 N	10.40 E
El Tocuyo	246	9.47 N	69.48 W
El Tofo	252	29.27 S	71.15 W
El'ton, Ross.	80	49.08 N	46.50 E
Elton, Eng., U.K.	262	53.16 N	2.49 W
Elton, La., U.S.	194	30.28 N	92.41 W
Elton, Pa., U.S.	214	40.17 N	78.48 W
El'ton, ozero ⊜	80	49.16 N	46.35 E
El Toreo ♦	286a	19.27 N	99.13 W
El Toro	228	33.37 N	117.41 W
El Toro ∧	240m	18.16 N	65.49 W
El Toro, Isla I	234	21.26 N	97.31 W
El Toro Marine Corps Air Station ■	228	33.41 N	117.44 W
El Tranco, Embalse de ⊜[1]	34	38.10 N	2.45 W
El Tránsito, Chile	252	28.52 S	70.17 W
El Tránsito, El Sal.	236	13.22 N	88.21 W
El Trébol	252	32.12 S	61.42 W
El Triunfo, Hond.	236	13.06 N	87.00 W
El Triunfo, Méx.	232	23.47 N	110.08 W
El Triunfo, Cerro ∧	234	15.40 N	92.49 W
El Triunfo de la Cruz	236	15.46 N	87.26 W
El Tuito	234	20.19 N	105.22 W
El Tulillo	234	22.30 N	104.05 W
El Tunal	252	25.15 S	64.27 W
El Turbio	254	51.41 S	72.05 W
Eltville	56	50.02 N	8.07 E
Eltz, Burg ⊥	56	50.12 N	7.20 E
El-Uarre	144	3.41 N	45.20 E
Elura → Ellora	122	20.01 N	75.10 E
Elūru	122	16.42 N	81.06 E
Elva	76	58.13 N	26.25 E
El Valle	236	8.36 N	80.08 W
El Valle ◆[8]	286c	10.27 N	66.55 W
Elvas	34	38.53 N	7.10 W
Elvas ≃	256	21.12 S	44.08 W
Elven	32	47.44 N	2.35 W
El Vendrell	34	41.13 N	1.32 E
El Verano	226	38.18 N	122.29 W
El Verde	234	23.21 N	106.09 W
Elverdissen	52	52.05 N	8.38 E
Elverlingsen	263	51.17 N	7.42 E
Elverta	226	38.43 N	121.28 W
Elverum	26	60.53 N	11.34 E
El Viejo	236	12.40 N	87.10 W
El Vigía	246	8.38 N	71.39 W
El Vigía, Cerro ∧	234	21.19 N	104.03 W
Elvins	194	37.50 N	90.31 W
Elvira	258	35.14 S	59.29 W
Elvo ≃	62	45.23 N	8.21 E
El Volcán	252	33.49 S	70.11 W
El Wad	148	33.20 N	6.58 E
El Wak	154	2.49 N	40.56 E
El Walamo	234	23.07 N	106.15 W
El Wanza	148	35.57 N	8.04 E
Elwell, Lake ⊜[1]	202	48.22 N	111.17 W
Elwha ≃	224	48.10 N	123.35 W
Elwood, Austl.	274b	37.53 S	144.59 E
Elwood, Il., U.S.	216	41.24 N	88.07 W
Elwood, In., U.S.	216	40.16 N	85.50 W
Elwood, Ks., U.S.	198	39.45 N	94.52 W
Elwood, Ne., U.S.	198	40.35 N	99.51 W
Elwood, N.J., U.S.	208	39.35 N	74.43 W
Elwood, N.Y., U.S.	207	40.50 N	73.20 W
Elwood Park, Fl., U.S.	220	27.28 N	82.30 W
Elwood Park, Pa., U.S.	279b	40.10 N	80.17 W
Elwy ≃	44	53.16 N	3.26 W
Elwyn	285	39.54 N	75.24 W
Elx	34	38.15 N	0.42 W
Elxleben	54	51.02 N	10.56 E
Ely, Eng., U.K.	42	52.24 N	0.16 E
Ely, Mn., U.S.	190	47.54 N	91.52 W
Ely, Mo., U.S.	219	39.41 N	91.39 W
Ely, Nv., U.S.	204	39.14 N	114.53 W
Ely, Isle of ◆[1]	42	52.24 N	0.10 E
El Yagual	246	7.29 N	68.25 W
Ely Cathedral ʋ[1]	42	52.24 N	0.16 E
Elyria	214	41.22 N	82.06 W
Elyria Airport ⊠	279a	41.20 N	82.06 W
Elysburg	210	40.51 N	76.33 W
Elysian Park ♦	280	34.05 N	118.14 W
El Yunque ∧	240m	18.19 N	65.48 W
Elywood Park ♦	279a	41.23 N	82.06 W
Elz	56	50.25 N	8.02 E
Elz ≃	58	48.21 N	7.45 E
Elzach	58	48.10 N	8.04 E
El Zamural	286c	10.27 N	67.00 W
El Zapotal	234	15.27 N	93.10 W
Elzbach ≃	56	50.12 N	7.22 E
Elze, Dtsch.	52	52.35 N	9.44 E
Elze, Dtsch.	52	52.07 N	9.44 E
El Zig-Zag	286c	10.33 N	66.58 W
Émaé I	175f	17.04 S	168.24 E
Emajõgi ≃	76	58.26 N	27.15 E
Emali	154	2.05 S	37.38 E
Emam Khomeyni Mosque ʋ[1]	267d	35.40 N	51.25 E
Emāmshahr (Shāhrūd)	128	36.25 N	55.01 E
Emån ≃	26	57.08 N	16.30 E
Émancé	261	48.35 N	1.44 E
Emas, Parque Nacional das ♦	255	18.08 S	52.48 W
Emba	86	48.50 N	58.08 E
Emba ≃	80	46.38 N	53.14 E
Embarcación	252	23.13 S	64.06 W
Embarras ≃, Ab., Can.	182	53.27 N	116.37 W
Embarras ≃, Il., U.S.	194	38.39 N	87.37 W
Embarras, North Fork ≃	194	38.55 N	87.59 W
Embarrass	190	44.39 N	88.42 W
Embarrass ≃, Mn., U.S.	190	47.24 N	92.25 W
Embarrass ≃, Wi., U.S.	190	44.23 N	88.45 W
Embetsu	92a	44.44 N	141.47 E
Embid	34	40.58 N	1.43 W
Embleton	44	55.30 N	1.37 W
Embo	46	57.54 N	3.59 W
Emboabas	256	21.18 S	44.08 W
Embondo	152	0.15 N	19.38 E
Emborcação, Reprêsa ⊜[1]	255	18.30 S	47.50 W
Embrach	58	47.30 N	8.36 E
Embreeville, Pa., U.S.	285	39.56 N	75.44 W
Embreeville, Tn., U.S.	192	36.10 N	82.27 W
Embro	212	43.09 N	80.54 W
Embrun, On., Can.	212	45.16 N	75.17 W
Embrun, Fr.	62	44.34 N	6.30 E
Embry	50	50.29 N	1.58 E
Embsay	44	53.58 N	1.59 W
Embu, Bra.	256	23.39 S	46.51 W
Embu, Kenya	154	0.32 S	37.27 E
Embu □[7]	287b	23.40 S	46.50 W
Embu-Guaçu	256	23.49 S	46.48 W
Embu-Guaçu □[7]	287b	23.48 S	46.48 W
Embu-mirim ≃	287b	23.39 S	46.51 W
Emden, Dtsch.	52	53.22 N	7.12 E
Emden, Il., U.S.	194	40.18 N	89.29 W
Emden, Mo., U.S.	219	39.48 N	91.52 W
Emei	107	29.36 N	103.31 E
Emeigh	214	40.42 N	78.47 W
Emel' (Emin) ≃	86	46.20 N	81.46 E
Emelle	194	32.43 N	88.18 W
Emerado	198	47.55 N	97.21 W
Émerainville	261	48.49 N	2.37 E
Emerald, Austl.	166	23.32 S	148.10 E
Emerald, Austl.	169	37.56 S	145.26 E
Emerald Bay State Park ♦	226	38.57 N	120.05 W
Emerald Lake	226	37.28 N	122.16 W
Emerson, Mb., Can.	184	49.00 N	97.12 W
Emerson, Ar., U.S.	194	33.05 N	93.11 W
Emerson, Ga., U.S.	192	34.07 N	84.45 W
Emerson, Ia., U.S.	198	41.01 N	95.24 W
Emerson, Mo., U.S.	219	39.53 N	91.42 W
Emerson, Ne., U.S.	198	42.17 N	96.44 W
Emerson, N.J., U.S.	276	40.58 N	74.01 W
Emery, S.D., U.S.	198	43.36 N	97.37 W
Emery, Ut,. U.S.	200	38.55 N	111.14 W
Emeryville, On., Can.	214	42.18 N	82.45 W
Emeryville, Ca., U.S.	226	37.50 N	122.17 W
Emet	130	39.20 N	29.15 E
Emgayet	146	29.04 N	12.58 E
Emhouse	222	32.09 N	96.35 W
Emi	88	50.36 N	97.49 E
Emigrant Gap	226	39.17 N	120.40 W
Emigrant Gap)(	226	39.18 N	120.40 W
Emigsville	208	40.01 N	76.44 W
Emiliano Mitre, Canal ʮ	288	34.36 S	58.18 W
Emiliano Zapata, Méx.	232	17.45 N	91.46 W
Emiliano Zapata, Méx.	234	16.10 N	94.01 W
Emiliano Zapata, Bahía ᴄ	232	19.40 N	87.30 W
Emilia-Romagna □[4]	36	44.35 N	11.00 E
Emílio de Carvalho	152	5.55 S	12.57 E
Emily Provincial Park ♦	212	44.21 N	78.31 W
Emin	86	46.32 N	83.39 E
Emin (Emel') ≃	86	46.20 N	81.46 E
Eminābād	123	32.02 N	74.16 E
Emine, nos ≻	38	42.42 N	27.51 E
Eminence, Ky., U.S.	218	38.22 N	85.10 W
Eminence, Mo., U.S.	194	37.09 N	91.21 W
Emiralem	130	38.36 N	27.09 E
Emiratos Arabes Unidos → United Arab Emirates □[1]	128	24.00 N	54.00 E
Emirau Island I	164	1.40 S	150.00 E
Emirdağ	130	39.01 N	31.10 E
Emır Dağları ⩕	130	38.50 N	31.15 E
Emirhan	130	39.42 N	37.46 E
Emir Pasha Gulf ᴄ	154	2.32 S	31.52 E
Emissi, Tarso ∧	146	21.13 N	18.32 E
Emita	166	40.00 S	147.54 E
Emlembe ∧	158	25.57 S	31.11 E
Emlenton	214	41.11 N	79.43 W
Emlichheim	52	52.36 N	6.50 E
Emmaån ≃	40	58.44 N	15.35 E
Emmaboda	26	56.38 N	15.32 E
Emmaste	76	58.42 N	22.36 E
Emmaus, Ross.	82	56.47 N	36.07 E
Emmaus, Pa., U.S.	208	40.32 N	75.29 W
Emmaville	166	29.26 S	151.36 E
Emme ≃	58	47.13 N	7.34 E
Emmeline Lake ⊜	184	55.00 N	106.22 W
Emmeloord	52	52.43 N	5.45 E
Emmen	52	52.47 N	6.54 E
Emmenbrücke	58	47.04 N	8.17 E
Emmendingen	58	48.07 N	7.50 E
Emmental V	58	46.56 N	7.45 E
Emmer ≃	52	52.03 N	9.23 E
Emmer-Compascuum	52	52.48 N	7.02 E
Emmer-Erfscheidenveen	52	52.48 N	7.01 E
Emmerich	52	51.50 N	6.15 E
Emmerstedt	54	52.15 N	10.58 E
Emmerthal	52	52.03 N	9.23 E
Emmet, Austl.	166	24.40 S	144.28 E
Emmet, Ar., U.S.	194	33.43 N	93.28 W
Emmetsburg	198	43.06 N	94.40 W
Emmett, Id., U.S.	202	43.52 N	116.29 W
Emmett, Mi., U.S.	214	42.59 N	82.45 W
Emmiganūru	122	15.44 N	77.29 E
Emmitsburg	208	39.42 N	77.20 W
Emmonak	180	62.46 N	164.30 W
Emneth	42	52.38 N	0.11 E
Emo	190	48.38 N	93.50 W
Emőd	30	47.56 N	20.49 E
Emory	222	32.52 N	95.46 W
Emory ≃	192	35.56 N	84.29 W
Emory Peak ∧	196	29.13 N	103.17 W
Empalme	232	27.58 N	110.51 W
Empalme Escobedo	234	20.41 N	100.44 W
Empalme Purísima	234	23.55 N	105.05 W
Empalme San Vicente	258	34.58 S	58.22 W
Empangeni	158	28.50 S	31.48 E
Empedrado, Arg.	252	27.57 S	58.48 W
Empedrado, Chile	252	35.36 S	72.17 W
Emperor Jimmu, Tomb of ⊥	270	34.29 N	135.47 E
Emperor Nintoku, Tomb of ⊥	270	34.34 N	135.29 E
Emperor Range ⩕	175e	5.45 S	154.55 E
Emperor Seamounts ✦[3]	6	42.00 N	170.00 E
Emperor Tenchi, Tomb of ⊥	270	34.59 N	135.48 E
Empfingen	58	48.24 N	8.42 E
Empire, Ca., U.S.	226	37.38 N	120.54 W
Empire, La., U.S.	194	29.23 N	89.35 W
Empire, Nv., U.S.	204	40.34 N	119.20 W
Empire, Oh., U.S.	214	40.30 N	80.37 W
Empoli	66	43.43 N	10.57 E
Emporia, Ks., U.S.	198	38.24 N	96.10 W
Emporia, Va., U.S.	208	36.41 N	77.32 W
Emporium	214	41.30 N	78.14 W
Empress	184	50.57 N	110.00 W
Empress Augusta Bay ᴄ	175e	6.25 S	155.05 E
Emptinne	56	50.19 N	5.07 E
Empty Quarter → Ar-Rub' al-Khālī ◆[2]	118	20.00 N	51.00 E
Ems ≃	52	53.20 N	7.06 E
Emscher ≃	263	51.34 N	6.42 E
Emscherbruch ◆[1]	263	51.34 N	7.09 E
Emsdetten	52	52.10 N	7.31 E
Ems-Jade-Kanal ≊	52	53.19 N	7.10 E
Emskirchen	56	49.33 N	10.43 E
Emsland ◆[1]	52	52.50 N	7.20 E
Emst ◆[8]	263	51.21 N	7.30 E
Emstek	52	52.50 N	8.09 E
Emsworth, Eng., U.K.	42	50.51 N	0.56 W
Emsworth, Pa., U.S.	214	40.30 N	80.05 W
Emsworth Dam ◆[6]	279b	40.30 N	80.05 W
Emu	89	43.45 N	128.10 E
Emu, Mount ∧[2]	169	37.35 S	143.27 E
Emu Creek ≃	171a	26.56 S	152.19 E
Emu Downs	168b	33.54 S	138.59 E
Emukae	92	33.18 N	129.38 E
Emu Park	166	23.15 S	150.50 E
Emu Plains	274a	33.45 S	150.41 E
Emur ≃	89	53.24 N	124.00 E
Emuren	273a	6.40 N	3.31 E
Emyvale	48	54.20 N	6.59 W
En (Inn) ≃, Europe	32	48.35 N	13.28 E
En ≃, Zhg.	100	27.12 N	115.08 E
Ena	94	35.27 N	137.25 E
Enana	156	17.29 S	16.19 E
Enånger	26	61.32 N	17.00 E
Enard Bay ᴄ	46	58.05 N	5.20 W
Enarotali	164	3.55 S	136.21 E
Ena-san ∧	94	35.26 N	137.36 E
Ena-san Tunnel ◆[5]	94	35.30 N	137.40 E
Enbacka	40	60.25 N	15.36 E
Enborne ≃	42	51.24 N	1.06 W
Encampment	200	41.12 N	106.47 W
Encampment ≃	200	41.18 N	106.43 W
Encantado	252	29.15 S	51.53 W
Encantado ◆[8]	287a	22.54 S	43.18 W
Encanto, Cape ≻	116	15.44 N	121.37 E
Encarnação ◆[8]	266c	38.47 N	9.06 W
Encarnación	252	27.20 S	55.54 W
Encarnación de Díaz	234	21.31 N	102.14 W
Encha	98	37.25 N	115.42 E
Enchenberg	56	49.01 N	7.20 E
Enchi	150	5.49 N	2.49 W
Enchilayas	200	30.50 N	112.50 W
Enchovas, Enseada das ᴄ	256	23.57 S	45.18 W
Enciastraia, Monte ∧	62	44.22 N	6.53 E
Encinal	196	28.02 N	99.21 W
Encinitas	228	33.02 N	117.17 W
Encino, N.M., U.S.	200	34.39 N	105.27 W
Encino, Tx., U.S	196	26.57 N	98.08 W
Encino ◆[8]	280	34.09 N	118.30 W
Encino Reservoir ⊜[1]	280	34.05 N	118.31 W
Encontrados	246	9.03 N	72.14 W
Encounter Bay ᴄ	168b	35.35 S	138.44 E
Encrucijada, Cuba	240p	22.37 N	79.52 W
Encrucijada, Méx.	234	18.18 N	93.29 W
Encruzilhada	255	15.31 S	40.54 W
Encruzilhada do Sul	252	30.32 S	52.31 W
Encs	30	48.20 N	21.08 E
Endako	182	54.05 N	125.02 W
Endako ≃	182	54.05 N	124.55 W
Endau ≃	114	2.39 N	103.38 E
Ende	115b	8.50 S	121.39 E
Ende, Pulau I	115b	8.53 S	121.32 E
Ende, Teluk ᴄ	115b	8.52 S	121.30 E
Endeavor, Pa., U.S.	214	41.35 N	79.23 W
Endeavor, Wi., U.S.	190	43.42 N	89.27 W
Endeavour	184	52.08 N	102.40 W
Endeavour Strait ʮ	164	10.50 S	142.15 E
Endelave I	41	55.46 N	10.17 E
Enderbury I[1]	14	3.08 S	171.05 W
Enderby, B.C., Can.	182	50.33 N	119.08 W
Enderby, Eng., U.K.	42	52.36 N	1.12 W
Enderby Land ◆[1]	9	67.30 S	53.00 E
Enderlin	198	46.37 N	97.36 W
Endicott, N.Y., U.S.	210	42.05 N	76.02 W
Endicott, Wa., U.S.	202	46.55 N	117.40 W
Endicott Mountains ⩕	180	67.50 N	152.00 W
Endimari ≃	248	8.46 S	66.07 W
Endine	64	45.46 N	9.59 E
Endine Gaiano	64	45.48 N	9.59 E
Endingen	58	48.09 N	7.42 E
Endja, Oued ≃	34	36.31 N	6.15 E
Endō	268	35.23 N	139.27 E
Endola	156	17.37 S	15.50 E
'En Dor	132	32.39 N	35.25 E
Endorf in Oberbayern	64	47.54 N	12.18 E
Endre ≃	62	43.28 N	6.36 E
Endrick ∧	170	35.12 S	150.12 E
Endrick ≃	170	35.01 S	150.03 E
Endwell	210	42.06 N	76.01 W
Ene ≃	248	11.09 S	74.19 W
Eneabba	162	29.50 S	115.20 E
Enemonzo	64	46.25 N	12.53 E
Enewetak I[1]	14	11.30 N	162.15 E
Enez	130	40.44 N	26.04 E
Enfida	36	36.07 N	10.23 E
Enfield, Austl.	168b	34.53 S	138.35 E
Enfield, Austl.	274a	33.53 S	151.06 E
Enfield, N.Z.	172	45.03 S	170.52 E
Enfield, Ct., U.S.	207	41.58 N	72.35 W
Enfield, N.H., U.S.	188	43.38 N	72.08 W
Enfield, N.C., U.S.	192	36.10 N	77.40 W
Enfield, Va., U.S.	208	37.43 N	77.12 W
Enfield ◆[8]	42	51.40 N	0.05 W
Enga □[5]	164	5.30 S	143.30 E
Engadine	170	34.04 S	151.01 E
Engaño, Cabo ≻	238	18.37 N	68.20 W
Engaru	92a	44.03 N	143.31 E
Engažimo	88	57.51 N	114.56 E
Engcobo	158	31.37 S	28.00 E
'En Gedi	132	31.27 N	35.23 E
Engelberg	58	46.49 N	8.25 E
Engelhard	192	35.30 N	75.59 W
Engelhartszell	60	48.31 N	13.44 E
Engel's	80	51.30 N	46.07 E
Engelsdorf	54	51.20 N	12.29 E
Engelskirchen	56	50.59 N	7.24 E
Engelsmanplaat I	52	53.28 N	6.02 E
Engel's'ovo	83	48.22 N	39.23 E
Engen, B.C. Can.	182	54.02 N	124.18 W
Engen, Dtsch.	58	47.51 N	8.46 E
Engenheiro Navarro	255	17.17 S	43.57 W
Engenheiro Passos	256	22.30 S	44.41 W
Engenheiro Paulo de Frontin	256	22.33 S	43.41 W
Engenho	248	15.10 S	56.25 W
Engenho, Ilha do I	287a	22.50 S	43.07 W
Engenho de Dentro ◆[8]	287a	22.54 S	43.18 W
Engenho do Mato	287a	22.52 S	43.01 W
Éngenho Novo	256	21.49 S	43.00 W
Engenho Nôvo ◆[8]	287a	22.55 S	43.17 W
Enger	52	52.08 N	8.34 E
Engestofte	41	54.46 N	11.34 E
Engesvang	41	56.10 N	9.21 E
'En Gev	132	32.47 N	35.38 E
Enggano, Pulau I	112	5.24 S	102.16 E
Enghershatu ∧	144	16.40 N	38.20 E
Enghien (Edingen)	50	50.42 N	4.02 E
Enghien-les-Bains	261	48.58 N	2.19 E
Enghien-Moisselles, Aéroport d' ⊠	261	49.02 N	2.21 E
Engiadina Bassa V	58	46.50 N	10.20 E
Engis	56	50.35 N	5.25 E
Engizek Dağ ∧	130	37.50 N	37.10 E
Engjan	26	63.09 N	8.32 E
England	194	34.32 N	91.58 W
England □[8]	28	52.30 N	1.30 W
England Air Force Base ■	194	31.20 N	92.33 W
Englebright Lake ⊜[1]	226	39.15 N	121.15 W
Englee	186	50.44 N	56.06 W
Englefield, Cape ≻	176	69.51 N	85.39 W
Englefield Green	260	51.26 N	0.35 W
Englefontaine	50	50.11 N	3.39 E
Englehart	190	47.49 N	79.52 W
Englehart ≃	190	47.51 N	79.50 W
Engleside	208	38.43 N	77.05 W
Englewood, B.C., Can.	182	50.33 N	126.53 W
Englewood, Co., U.S.	200	39.38 N	104.59 W
Englewood, Fl., U.S.	220	26.57 N	82.21 W
Englewood, In., U.S.	218	38.50 N	86.31 W
Englewood, Ks., U.S.	198	37.02 N	99.58 W
Englewood, N.J., U.S.	210	40.53 N	73.58 W
Englewood, Oh., U.S.	218	39.52 N	84.18 W
Englewood, Tn., U.S.	192	35.25 N	84.29 W
Englewood ◆[8]	278	41.47 N	87.39 W
Englewood Cliffs	276	40.53 N	73.57 W
Englewood Dam ◆[6]	218	39.52 N	84.17 W
English, In., U.S.	218	38.20 N	86.27 W
English, Ky., U.S.	218	38.37 N	85.08 W
English ≃, On., Can.	176	50.12 N	95.00 W
English (Rivière des Anglais) ≃, N.A.	206	45.13 N	73.50 W
English ≃, Ia., U.S.	190	41.29 N	91.30 W
English Bay	180	59.22 N	151.55 W
English Bāzār → Ingrāj Bāzār	124	25.00 N	88.09 E
English Center	210	41.26 N	77.17 W
English Channel (La Manche) ʮ	28	50.20 N	1.00 W
English Coast ⩡[2]	9	73.45 S	73.00 W
English Harbour West	186	47.28 N	55.29 W
Englishman ≃	224	49.22 N	124.18 W
Englishtown	208	40.17 N	74.21 W
Engong	152	0.36 N	10.06 E
Engter	52	52.23 N	8.04 E
Énguera	34	38.59 N	0.41 W
Engum	41	55.44 N	9.40 E
Engure	76	57.10 N	23.13 E
Engures ezers ⊜	76	57.16 N	23.06 E
Engwilen	58	47.37 N	9.05 E
'En Harod	132	32.33 N	35.23 E
'En HaShofét	132	32.35 N	35.06 E
Enid	196	36.23 N	97.52 W
Enid Lake ⊜[1]	194	34.10 N	89.50 W
Enilda	182	55.25 N	116.18 W
Eningen unter Achalm	58	48.29 N	9.16 E
Eniwa	92a	42.45 N	141.33 E
Eniwetok → Enewetak I[1]	14	11.30 N	162.15 E
eNjesuthi ∧	158	29.09 S	29.23 E
Enka	192	35.32 N	82.39 W
Enkenbach	56	49.29 N	7.54 E
Enkhuizen	52	52.42 N	5.17 E
Enkirch	56	49.59 N	7.07 E
Enköping	40	59.38 N	17.04 E
Enle	102	24.00 N	101.07 E
Enmedio	196	29.04 N	103.29 W
Enmedio, Cerro de ∧	234	19.48 N	100.36 W
Enmelen	180	65.01 N	175.54 W
Enna	70	37.34 N	14.16 E
Enna □[4]	70	37.35 N	14.26 E
Ennadai Lake ⊜	176	60.53 N	101.15 W
Enné, Ouadi V	146	14.24 N	18.45 E
Ennedi ⩕[1]	146	17.15 N	22.00 E
Ennell, Lough ⊜	48	53.28 N	7.24 W
Ennenda	58	47.01 N	9.05 E
Ennepe ≃	263	51.22 N	7.27 E
Ennepestausee ⊜[1]	263	51.14 N	7.25 E
Ennepetal	56	51.18 N	7.22 E
Ennerdale Water ⊜	44	54.31 N	3.23 W
Ennery	261	49.05 N	2.06 E
Enngonia	166	29.19 S	145.51 E
Enniger	52	51.50 N	7.56 E
Ennigerloh	52	51.50 N	8.02 E
Ennigloh	52	52.12 N	8.34 E
Ennis, Ire.	48	52.50 N	8.59 W
Ennis, Mt., U.S	202	45.20 N	111.43 W
Ennis, Tx., U.S.	222	32.19 N	96.37 W
Enniscorthy	48	52.30 N	6.34 W
Enniskillen	48	54.21 N	7.38 W
Ennis Lake ⊜[1]	202	45.26 N	111.41 W
Ennistimon	48	52.57 N	9.15 W
Enns	61	48.13 N	14.29 E
Enns ≃	61	48.14 N	14.32 E
Ennstaler Alpen ⩕	61	47.37 N	14.35 E
Eno	26	62.48 N	30.09 E
Enø I	41	55.10 N	11.40 E
Eno ≃	96	34.53 N	132.41 E
Enochs	196	33.52 N	102.46 W
Enogera Military Camp ■	171a	27.25 S	152.58 E
Enola	208	40.17 N	76.56 W
Enon	218	39.53 N	83.56 W
Enontekiö	24	68.23 N	23.38 E
Enon Valley	214	40.51 N	80.28 W
Enoree ≃	192	34.26 N	81.25 W
Enosburg Falls	188	44.54 N	72.48 W
Eno-shima I	94	35.18 N	139.29 E
Enping	102	22.11 N	112.17 E
Enrekang	112	3.34 S	119.47 E
Enrile	116	17.34 N	121.42 E
Enrique Fynn	258	34.50 S	59.08 W
Enrique Urien	252	27.34 S	60.32 W
Enriquillo	238	17.54 N	71.14 W
Enriquillo, Lago ⊜	238	18.27 N	71.39 W
Ens	52	52.38 N	5.50 E
Ensay I	46	57.46 N	7.05 W
Enschede	52	52.12 N	6.53 E
Ensdorf	60	49.21 N	11.56 E
Ensenada, Arg.	258	34.51 S	57.55 W
Ensenada, Méx.	232	31.52 N	116.37 W
Ensenada, P.R.	240m	17.58 N	66.56 W
Ensenada □[5]	288	34.50 S	58.00 W
Enshi	102	30.17 N	109.19 E
Enshū-nada ⊤[2]	92	34.27 N	137.38 E
Ensisheim	58	47.52 N	7.21 E
Enstaberga	40	58.45 N	16.51 E
Entebbe	154	0.04 N	32.28 E
Entenbühl ∧	60	49.46 N	12.24 E
Enter	52	52.18 N	6.34 E
Enterprise, Guy.	246	6.56 N	58.24 W
Enterprise, Al., U.S.	194	31.18 N	85.51 W
Enterprise, Ca., U.S.	204	39.32 N	121.22 W
Enterprise, Ks., U.S.	198	38.54 N	97.07 W
Enterprise, Ms., U.S.	194	32.10 N	88.49 W
Enterprise, Or., U.S.	202	45.25 N	117.16 W
Enterprise, Ut,. U.S.	200	37.34 N	113.43 W
Entiat ≃	202	47.40 N	120.14 W
Entiat, Lake ⊜[1]	202	47.40 N	120.12 W
Entiat Mountains ⩕	224	48.00 N	120.42 W
Entinas, Punta de las ≻	34	36.41 N	2.46 W
Entlebuch	58	47.00 N	8.04 E
Entlebuch V	58	46.58 N	8.00 E
Entracque	62	44.14 N	7.24 E
Entraigues-sur-Sorgue	62	44.00 N	4.55 E
Entrains-sur-Nohain	50	47.27 N	3.15 E
Entrance, Cape ≻	164	2.21 S	150.12 E
Entraunes	62	44.11 N	6.45 E
Entraygues	32	44.39 N	2.34 E
Entrechaux	62	44.13 N	5.08 E
Entrée, Île d' I	186	47.17 N	61.42 W
Entremont-le-Vieux	62	45.26 N	5.53 E
Entrepeñas, Embalse de ⊜[1]	34	40.34 N	2.42 W
Entre Rios, Bol.	248	21.32 S	64.12 W
Entre Rios, Bra.	255	11.56 S	38.05 W
Entre Ríos □[4]	252	32.00 S	59.00 W
Entre Ríos, Cordillera ⩕	236	14.05 N	85.37 W
Entre-Rios de Minas	255	20.41 S	44.04 W
Entrevaux	62	43.57 N	6.49 E
Entrèves	62	45.49 N	6.57 E
Entriken	214	40.20 N	78.12 W
Entroncamento	34	39.28 N	8.28 W
Entupido	256	22.30 S	44.51 W
Entwistle	182	53.36 N	115.00 W
Enu, Pulau I	164	7.05 S	134.30 E
Enugu	150	6.27 N	7.27 E
Enumclaw	224	47.12 N	121.59 W
Enurmino	180	66.57 N	171.49 W
Envalira, Port d')(	34	42.35 N	1.45 E
Envermeu	50	49.54 N	1.16 E
Envies, Rivière des ≃	206	46.37 N	72.24 W
Envigado	246	6.10 N	75.35 W
Envira	248	7.18 S	70.13 W
Envira ≃	248	6.42 S	69.46 W
'En Yahav	132	30.38 N	35.11 E
Enyamba	154	3.40 S	24.58 E
Enyang	102	31.48 N	106.31 E
Enyellé	152	2.49 N	18.06 E
Enys, Mount ∧	172	43.14 S	171.38 E
Enz ≃	56	49.01 N	9.07 E
Enza ≃	64	44.54 N	10.31 E
Enzan	94	35.42 N	138.44 E
Enzbach ≃	56	49.54 N	6.25 E
Enzenkirchen	60	48.23 N	13.39 E
Enzesfeld	61	47.55 N	16.10 E
Enzklösterle	56	48.40 N	8.28 E
Eo ≃	34	43.28 N	7.03 W
Eolia	219	39.14 N	91.00 W
Eolie o Lipari, Isole II	70	38.30 N	14.50 E
Epanomí	38	40.26 N	22.56 E
Épars, Bois de l' ♦	261	48.45 N	1.45 E
Epe, Dtsch.	52	52.11 N	7.02 E
Epe, Ned.	52	52.21 N	6.00 E
Epe, Nig.	150	6.37 N	3.59 E
Epecuén, Lago ⊜	252	37.10 S	62.54 W
Épéhy	50	50.02 N	3.10 E
Epéna	152	1.22 N	17.29 E
Épernay	50	49.03 N	3.57 E
Épernon	50	48.37 N	1.41 E
Epes	194	32.41 N	88.07 W
Ephesus → Efes ⊥	130	37.55 N	27.17 E
Ephraim	200	39.21 N	111.35 W
Ephrata, Pa., U.S.	208	40.10 N	76.10 W
Ephrata, Wa., U.S.	202	47.19 N	119.33 W
Ephrata Cloister ⊥	208	40.12 N	76.09 W
Ephratah	210	43.00 N	74.32 W
Epi □[8]	175f	16.42 S	168.15 E
Épi I	175f	16.43 S	168.15 E
Épiais-lès-Louvres	261	49.02 N	2.33 E
Épila	34	41.36 N	1.17 W
Épinac-les-Mines	58	46.59 N	4.31 E
Épinal	58	48.11 N	6.27 E
Épinay-sous-Sénart	261	48.42 N	2.31 E
Épinay-sur-Orge	261	48.40 N	2.20 E
Épinay-sur-Seine	261	48.57 N	2.19 E
Epirus → Ípeiros □[9]	38	39.40 N	20.50 E
Episcopia	68	40.04 N	16.06 E
Episkopí	130	34.40 N	32.54 E
Époisses	50	47.30 N	4.10 E
Epokiro	156	21.41 S	19.08 E
Epomeo, Monte ∧	68	40.44 N	13.54 E
Épône	261	48.57 N	1.49 E
Eport, Loch ᴄ	46	57.33 N	7.11 W
Eppalock, Lake ⊜[1]	169	36.52 S	144.31 E
Eppelborn	56	49.24 N	6.58 E
Eppendorf ◆[8]	263	51.27 N	7.11 E
Eppenhausen ◆[8]	263	51.21 N	7.31 E
Eppeville	50	49.44 N	3.03 E
Epping, Austl.	169	37.39 S	145.02 E
Epping, Austl.	274a	33.46 S	151.05 E
Epping, Eng., U.K.	42	51.43 N	0.07 E
Epping, N.H., U.S.	188	43.02 N	71.04 W
Eppingen	56	49.08 N	8.54 E
Epping Forest □[8]	260	51.43 N	0.10 E
Epping Forest ◆[3]	42	51.40 N	0.03 E
Epping Green, Eng., U.K.	260	51.44 N	0.05 E
Epping Green, Eng., U.K.	260	51.45 N	0.07 W
Epping Upland	260	51.43 N	0.06 E
Epsom	42	51.20 N	0.16 W
Epsom and Ewell □[8]	260	51.20 N	0.16 W
Epsom Downs Race Course ♦	260	51.19 N	0.15 W
Epte ≃	50	49.04 N	1.37 E
Épuisay	50	47.54 N	0.56 E
Epukiro ≃	156	20.45 S	21.05 E
Epupa Falls ʟ	152	16.55 S	13.10 E
Epuyén	254	42.14 S	71.21 W
Epworth	44	53.32 N	0.49 W
Eqlīd	128	30.55 N	52.39 E
Equality	194	37.44 N	88.20 W
Équateur □[4]	152	1.00 N	20.30 E
Équateur → Ecuador □[1]	246	2.00 S	77.30 W
Equatorial Guinea (Guinea Ecuatorial) □[1]	152	2.00 N	9.00 E
Équihen-Plage	50	50.41 N	1.34 E
Equimina ≃	152	13.11 S	12.47 E
Equinox Mountain ∧	210	43.10 N	73.08 W
Equinunk	210	41.51 N	75.14 W
Equi Terme	64	44.09 N	10.10 E
Era ≃, It.	66	43.40 N	10.38 E
Era ≃, Pap. N. Gui.	164	7.35 S	144.41 E
Erac Creek ≃	166	26.56 S	145.48 E
Eraclea	64	45.35 N	12.40 E
Eraclea ⊥	68	40.13 N	16.40 E
Eraclea Minoa ⊥	70	37.23 N	13.17 E
Eradu	162	28.41 S	115.02 E
Éragny	261	49.01 N	2.06 E
Eramosa ≃	212	43.32 N	80.14 W
Eran Bay ᴄ	116	9.06 N	117.43 E
Eranga	152	1.52 S	18.56 E
Erangal ◆[8]	272c	19.10 N	72.47 E
Erap	164	6.35 S	146.40 E
Erath	194	29.57 N	92.02 W
Erave	164	6.40 S	143.50 E
Erave ≃	164	6.40 S	143.55 E
Erba	62	45.48 N	9.15 E
Erba, Jabal ∧, Sūd.	140	19.04 N	36.46 E
Erba, Jabal ∧, Sūd.	140	20.45 N	36.50 E
Erbaa	130	40.42 N	36.36 E
Erbach, Dtsch.	56	49.40 N	8.59 E
Erbach, Dtsch.	58	48.20 N	9.53 E
Erbendorf	60	49.50 N	12.03 E
Erbeskopf ∧	56	49.44 N	7.05 E
Erchie	68	40.26 N	17.44 E
Erciş	84	39.02 N	43.22 E
Erciyes Dağı ∧	130	38.32 N	35.28 E
Ercolano	68	40.48 N	14.21 E
Ercolano (Herculaneum) ⊥	68	40.46 N	14.20 E
Érd	30	47.23 N	18.56 E
Erdao ≃, Zhg.	98	42.39 N	127.35 E
Erdao ≃, Zhg.	104	42.16 N	122.20 E
Erdao Bai ≃	98	42.34 N	128.08 E
Erdaobaihe	98	42.22 N	128.07 E
Erdaofang, Zhg.	104	41.54 N	123.57 E
Erdaofang, Zhg.	104	41.37 N	122.34 E
Erdaofangshen	104	42.09 N	123.17 E
Erdaogangzi, Zhg.	104	41.57 N	122.09 E
Erdaogangzi, Zhg.	104	42.04 N	123.06 E
Erdaohe	89	43.37 N	127.35 E
Erdaohezi, Zhg.	89	45.07 N	127.16 E
Erdaohezi, Zhg.	89	45.08 N	129.39 E
Erdaojingzi	104	41.49 N	122.20 E
Erdaoliangzi, Zhg.	98	40.50 N	119.04 E
Erdaoliangzi, Zhg.	105	40.31 N	118.03 E
Erdaowan	89	47.58 N	124.33 E
Erdek	130	40.24 N	27.48 E
Erdemli	130	36.37 N	34.18 E
Erdene, Mong.	88	47.48 N	107.55 E
Erdene, Mong.	102	45.08 N	97.45 E
Erdene, Mong.	102	44.15 N	111.14 E
Erdene Bulgan	88	50.07 N	101.35 E
Erdene-Büren	86	48.26 N	91.27 E
Erdenedala	102	46.02 N	104.55 E
Erdene Mandal	88	48.30 N	101.21 E
Erdenheim	285	40.05 N	75.12 W
Erdevik	38	45.07 N	19.25 E
Erdiao	106	32.12 N	121.12 E
Erding	60	48.18 N	11.54 E
Erdinger Moos ≡	60	48.22 N	11.52 E
Erdnijevskij	80	46.52 N	46.17 E
Erebato ≃	246	5.54 N	64.16 W
Erebus, Mount ∧	9	77.32 S	167.09 E
Ereğli, Tür.	130	37.31 N	34.04 E
Ereğli, Tür.	130	41.17 N	31.25 E
Eregun	273a	6.36 N	3.22 E
Erei, Monti ⩕	70	37.27 N	14.19 E
Erenas	116	12.25 N	124.19 E
Erenhot	102	43.46 N	112.05 E
Erenköy ◆[8]	267b	40.58 N	29.04 E
Erepecuru, Lago do ⊜	250	1.20 S	56.35 W
Eresma ≃	34	41.26 N	4.45 W
Eressós	38	39.10 N	25.56 E
Erétria	38	38.24 N	23.48 E
Erexim	252	27.38 S	52.17 W
Erez	132	31.34 N	34.34 E
Érezée	56	50.18 N	5.33 E
Erfa ≃	56	49.43 N	9.15 E
Erfde	41	54.19 N	9.19 E
Erfelek	130	41.53 N	34.55 E
Erfenisdam ⊜[1]	158	28.33 S	26.50 E
Erfoud	148	31.28 N	4.10 W
Erft ≃	56	51.11 N	6.44 E
Erftstadt	56	50.48 N	6.46 E
Erfurt	54	50.58 N	11.01 E
Ergak-Targak-Tajga, chrebet ⩕	88	53.25 N	95.30 E
Ergani	130	38.17 N	39.46 E
Ergene ≃	130	41.01 N	26.22 E
Ergenzingen	58	48.29 N	8.48 E
Erges (Erjas) ≃	34	39.40 N	7.01 W
Ērgļi	76	56.54 N	25.38 E
Ergolding	60	48.35 N	12.10 E
Ergoldsbach	60	48.41 N	12.12 E
Ergste	56	51.25 N	7.34 E
Erguig, Bahr ≃	146	11.22 N	15.24 E
Ergun (Argun') ≃	74	53.20 N	121.28 E
Ergun Youqi	89	50.14 N	120.10 E
Ergun Zuoqi	89	50.47 N	121.31 E
Erguvejem ≃	180	65.20 N	176.00 W
Er Hai ⊜	102	25.48 N	100.11 E
Erhlin	100	23.54 N	120.22 E
Erhshui	100	23.49 N	120.36 E
Erhulai	98	41.23 N	125.08 E
Eria ≃	34	42.03 N	5.44 W
Erial	208	39.46 N	75.00 W
Eriba	140	16.37 N	36.04 E
Eriboll	46	58.28 N	4.41 W
Eriboll, Loch ᴄ	46	58.31 N	4.41 W
Erica, Austl.	169	37.59 S	146.22 E
Erica, Ned.	52	52.43 N	6.55 E
Erice	70	38.02 N	12.35 E
Ericeira	34	38.59 N	9.25 W
Erichsen Lake ⊜	176	70.38 N	80.21 W
Erichshagen	52	52.40 N	9.14 E
Ericht, Loch ⊜	46	56.48 N	4.24 W
Erick	196	35.12 N	99.51 W
Erickson, B.C., Can.	182	49.05 N	116.28 W
Erickson, Mb., Can.	184	50.30 N	99.55 W
Ericson	198	41.46 N	98.40 W
Erie, Co., U.S.	200	40.03 N	105.03 W
Erie, Il., U.S.	190	41.39 N	90.04 W
Erie, Ks., U.S.	198	37.34 N	95.14 W
Erie, Mi., U.S.	216	41.47 N	83.29 W
Erie, Pa., U.S.	214	42.07 N	80.05 W
Erie □[6], N.Y., U.S.	210	42.54 N	78.53 W
Erie □[6], Oh., U.S.	214	41.27 N	82.42 W
Erie □[6], Pa., U.S.	214	42.08 N	80.04 W
Erie, Lake ⊜	214	42.15 N	81.00 W
Erieau	214	42.16 N	81.56 W
Erie Basin ᴄ	276	40.40 N	74.01 W
Erie Beach, On., Can.	214	42.16 N	82.00 W
Erie Beach, On., Can.	284a	42.53 N	78.57 W
Erie Canal → New York State Barge Canal ≊	210	43.05 N	78.43 W

	English	Deutsch	Español	Français	Português
≃	River	Fluß	Río	Rivière	Rio
≊	Canal	Kanal	Canal	Canal	Canal
ʟ	Waterfall, Rapids	Wasserfall, Stromschnellen	Cascada, Rápidos	Chute d'eau, Rapides	Cascata, Rápidos
ʮ	Strait	Meeresstraße	Estrecho	Détroit	Estreito
ᴄ	Bay, Gulf	Bucht, Golf	Bahía, Golfo	Baie, Golfe	Baía, Golfo
⊜	Lake, Lakes	See, Seen	Lago, Lagos	Lac, Lacs	Lago, Lagos
≡	Swamp	Sumpf	Pantano	Marais	Pântano
⊼	Ice Features, Glacier	Eis- und Gletscherformen	Accidentes Glaciales	Formes glaciaires	Acidentes glaciares
⊤	Other Hydrographic Features	Andere Hydrographische Objekte	Otros Elementos Hidrográficos	Autres données hydrographiques	Outros acidentes hidrográficos

	English	Deutsch	Español	Français	Português
✦	Submarine Features	Untermeerische Objekte	Accidentes Submarinos	Formes de relief sous-marin	Acidentes submarinos
□	Political Unit	Politische Einheit	Unidad Politica	Entité politique	Unidade política
ʋ	Cultural Institution	Kulturelle Institution	Institución Cultural	Institution culturelle	Instituição cultural
⊥	Historical Site	Historische Stätte	Sitio Histórico	Site historique	Sitio histórico
♦	Recreational Site	Erholungs- und Ferienort	Sitio de Recreo	Centre de loisirs	Area de Lazer
⊠	Airport	Flughafen	Aeropuerto	Aéroport	Aeroporto
■	Military Installation	Militäranlage	Instalación Militar	Installation militaire	Instalação militar
◆	Miscellaneous	Verschiedenes	Misceláneo	Divers	Diversos

I · 54 **Erie-Exet**

ENGLISH / DEUTSCH

Name	Page	Lat.°′	Long.°′
Erie County Fairgrounds ♦	284a	42.45 N	78.49 W
Erie International Airport ⊠	214	42.05 N	80.11 W
Eriksberg ⊥	40	58.56 N	16.22 E
Eriksdale	184	50.52 N	98.06 W
Erímanthos ∧	38	37.59 N	21.51 E
Erimo	92a	42.01 N	143.09 E
Erimo-misaki ›	92a	41.55 N	143.15 E
Erin, On., Can.	212	43.45 N	80.07 W
Erin, N.Y., U.S.	210	42.11 N	76.40 W
Erin, Tn., U.S.	194	36.19 N	87.41 W
Erindale	275b	43.32 N	79.39 W
Ering	60	48.18 N	13.09 E
Eriskay I	46	57.04 N	7.18 W
Erisort, Loch c	46	58.07 N	6.24 W
Eriswil	58	47.05 N	7.51 E
Erith ◆[8]	260	51.29 N	0.10 E
Erithraí	38	38.13 N	23.19 E
Eritrea □[1], Afr.	144	15.20 N	39.00 E
Erivan → Jerevan	84	40.11 N	44.30 E
Erjas (Erges) ≃	34	39.40 N	7.01 W
Erjiazhen	106	32.02 N	121.13 E
Erkelenz	56	51.05 N	6.19 E
Erken ⊜	40	59.51 N	18.34 E
Erken-Jurt	84	44.27 N	41.54 E
Erkheim	58	48.02 N	10.20 E
Erkilet	130	38.49 N	35.27 E
Erkina ≃	48	52.51 N	7.23 W
Erkner	54	52.25 N	13.45 E
Erkner, Forst ◆[3]	264a	52.22 N	13.47 E
Erkowit	140	18.46 N	37.07 E
Erkrath	56	51.13 N	6.55 E
Erl	64	47.41 N	12.11 E
Erlach, Öst.	61	47.43 N	16.13 E
Erlach, Schw.	58	47.03 N	7.06 E
Erlands Point	224	47.36 N	122.42 W
Erlangen	60	49.36 N	11.01 E
Erlanger	218	39.01 N	84.36 W
Erlanghe	100	30.19 N	116.04 E
Erlangmiao	100	33.46 N	112.23 E
Erlau ≃	60	48.34 N	13.36 E
Erlauf ≃	61	48.12 N	15.11 E
Erlbach	54	50.18 N	12.22 E
Erldunda	162	25.14 S	133.12 E
Erle ◆[8]	263	51.33 N	7.05 E
Erli	62	44.08 N	8.06 E
Erling	106	31.53 N	119.36 E
Erling, Lake ⊜[1]	194	33.05 N	93.35 W
Erlistoun	162	28.20 S	122.08 E
Erlongshan, Zhg.	89	47.20 N	132.28 E
Erlongshan, Zhg.	89	50.04 N	126.47 E
Erlongshantun	89	48.28 N	126.31 E
Erlsbach	64	46.55 N	12.15 E
Erma	208	38.58 N	74.54 W
Ermana, chrebet ⋏	88	50.00 N	113.30 E
Ermatingen	58	47.41 N	9.06 E
Erme ≃	42	50.18 N	3.56 W
Ermelindo Matarazo ◆[8]	287b	23.29 S	46.29 W
Ermelo, Ned.	52	52.17 N	5.37 E
Ermelo, S. Afr.	158	26.34 S	29.58 E
Ermendegou	104	42.02 N	121.56 E
Ermenek	130	36.38 N	32.54 E
Ermenek ≃	130	36.35 N	33.23 E
Ermenonville	50	49.08 N	2.42 E
Ermidas	34	38.00 N	8.23 W
Ermil Post	140	13.37 N	27.36 E
Ermineskin Indian Reserve ◆[4]	182	52.52 N	113.30 W
Ermington	274a	33.48 S	151.04 E
Ermita de Guadalupe	234	22.36 N	103.03 W
Ermita de los Correas	234	22.54 N	103.01 W
Ermont	50	48.59 N	2.16 E
Ermoúpolis	38	37.26 N	24.56 E
Ermsleben	54	51.44 N	11.21 E
Ernaballa	162	26.17 S	132.07 E
Erndtebrück	56	50.59 N	8.15 E
Erne ≃	48	54.30 N	8.16 W
Erne, Lower Lough ⊜	48	54.26 N	7.46 W
Erne, Upper Lough ⊜	48	54.14 N	7.32 W
Ernée	32	48.18 N	0.56 W
Ernest	214	40.41 N	79.10 W
Ernestina	258	35.16 S	59.34 W
Ernest Sound ɥ	182	55.52 N	132.10 W
Ernici, Monti ⋏	66	41.48 N	13.22 E
Ernstbrunn	61	48.32 N	16.22 E
Ernst Thälmann, Pioneerpark ♦	264a	52.28 N	13.33 E
Ernst-Thälmann-Stadion ♦	264a	52.23 N	13.05 E
Ernz Blanche ≃	56	49.52 N	6.16 E
Erode	122	11.21 N	77.44 E
Eromanga	166	26.40 S	143.16 E
Erongo	156	21.44 S	15.53 E
Erongo ⋏	156	21.45 S	15.37 E
Erota	144	16.14 N	37.55 E
Erp	56	50.46 N	6.43 E
Erpuzi	105	40.29 N	115.33 E
Erquelinnes	50	50.18 N	4.07 E
Err, Piz d' ∧	58	46.33 N	9.41 E
Errabiddy	162	25.28 S	117.07 E
Er-Rachidia	148	31.58 N	4.25 W
Er-Rachidia □[4]	148	31.15 N	4.05 W
Errego	154	16.02 S	37.14 E
Errer ≃	144	7.32 N	42.05 E
Er-Riad → Ar-Riyāḑ	128	24.38 N	46.43 E
Errigal Mountain ∧	48	55.02 N	8.07 W
Errington	224	49.17 N	124.22 W
Erris Head ›	48	54.19 N	10.00 W
Errochty, Loch ⊜	46	56.45 N	4.12 W
Errogie	46	57.16 N	4.22 W
Errol Heights	224	45.28 N	122.36 W
Erromango I	175f	18.45 S	169.05 E
Ersekë	38	40.20 N	20.41 E
Ershijiazi	104	41.17 N	120.32 E
Ershilipu	105	40.07 N	117.24 E
Ershiqizhan	89	53.23 N	123.16 E
Ershiwuzhan	89	53.22 N	123.55 E
Erskine	198	47.40 N	96.00 W
Erskine, Lake ⊜	276	41.06 N	74.15 W
Erskine Inlet c	176	76.15 N	102.20 W
Erskine Park	274a	33.49 S	150.47 E
Erstein	58	48.26 N	7.40 E
Erste Wiener Hochquellenleitung ≖[1]	61	48.10 N	16.17 E
Erstfeld	58	46.49 N	8.39 E
Ertai, Zhg.	86	46.07 N	90.06 E
Ertai, Zhg.	86	44.14 N	80.52 E
Ertaizi, Zhg.	104	41.52 N	121.56 E
Ertaizi, Zhg.	104	42.05 N	123.35 E
Ertaizi, Zhg.	104	42.35 N	124.00 E
Ertaizi, Zhg.	104	40.47 N	120.54 E
Ertil'	78	51.51 N	40.49 E
Ertingen	58	48.06 N	9.28 E
Ertix (Irtyš) ≃	74	61.04 N	68.52 E
Erto	64	46.16 N	12.22 E
Ertuğrul	130	39.34 N	27.43 E
Ertvelde	50	51.11 N	3.45 E
Eruar	126	23.28 N	87.52 E
Erudina	166	31.28 S	139.23 E
Eruh	130	37.46 N	42.11 E
Erundu	156	20.36 S	16.25 E
Erunkan	273a	6.37 N	3.24 E
Erva, Ponta da ›	266c	38.50 N	8.58 W
Erval	252	32.02 S	53.24 W
Erval d'Oeste	252	27.13 S	51.34 W
Ervalla	40	59.22 N	15.15 E
Erving	207	42.36 N	72.23 W
Ervy-le-Châtel	50	48.02 N	3.55 E
Erwin, N.C., U.S.	192	35.19 N	78.40 W
Erwin, Tn., U.S.	192	36.08 N	82.25 W
Erwitte	52	51.37 N	8.20 E
Erwood	184	52.50 N	102.10 W
Erxleben	54	52.13 N	11.14 E
Érythrée → Eritrea □[1]	144	15.20 N	39.00 E
Eryuan	102	26.06 N	99.55 E
Erzaohang	106	31.05 N	121.49 E
Erzberg ◆[7]	61	47.32 N	14.54 E
Erzgebirge (Krušné hory) ⋏	54	50.30 N	13.10 E
Erzhan	89	43.58 N	128.44 E
Erzhuang	105	39.24 N	117.22 E
Erzin	88	50.15 N	95.10 E
Erzincan	130	39.44 N	39.29 E
Erzincan □[4]	130	39.40 N	39.30 E
Erzingen	58	47.39 N	8.25 E
Erzurum	130	39.55 N	41.17 E
Erzurum □[4]	130	40.00 N	41.30 E
Esa'ala	164	9.44 S	150.49 E
Esambo	152	3.40 S	23.24 E
Esan-misaki ›	92a	41.49 N	141.11 E
Esashi, Nihon	92	41.52 N	140.07 E
Esashi, Nihon	92	39.12 N	141.09 E
Esashi, Nihon	92a	44.56 N	142.35 E
Esbiye	130	40.57 N	38.44 E
Esbjerg	26	55.28 N	8.27 E
Esbly	261	48.54 N	2.49 E
Esbo → Espoo	26	60.13 N	24.40 E
Esborn	263	51.23 N	7.20 E
Esca ≃	34	42.37 N	1.03 W
Escada	250	8.22 S	35.14 W
Escalada	258	34.10 S	59.07 W
Escalante, Pil.	116	10.50 N	123.33 E
Escalante, Ut,. U.S.	200	37.46 N	111.36 W
Escalante ≃, Ut,. U.S.	200	37.17 N	110.53 W
Escalante ≃, Ven.	246	9.15 N	71.50 W
Escalante Desert ◆[2]	200	37.50 N	113.30 W
Escalaplano	71	39.37 N	9.21 E
Escalón, Méx.	232	26.45 N	104.20 W
Escalon, Ca., U.S.	226	37.47 N	120.59 W
Escalona	34	40.10 N	4.24 W
Escambia ≃	194	30.32 N	87.11 W
Escanaba	190	45.44 N	87.04 W
Escanaba ≃	190	45.47 N	87.04 W
Escandón, Puerto)(	34	40.17 N	1.00 W
Escárcega	232	18.37 N	90.43 W
Escarpada Point ›	116	18.31 N	122.13 E
Escarpado Peak ∧	116	8.36 N	117.22 E
Escarpment	284a	43.10 N	79.00 W
Escatawpa ≃	194	30.25 N	88.35 W
Escaudain	50	50.20 N	3.21 E
Escaut (Schelde) ≃	50	51.22 N	4.15 E
Eschach	58	47.44 N	9.36 E
Eschau	58	48.29 N	7.43 E
Esche ≃	56	48.54 N	6.04 E
Eschebrügge	52	52.37 N	6.46 E
Eschede	52	52.44 N	10.14 E
Eschen	58	47.13 N	9.31 E
Eschenau	60	49.34 N	11.12 E
Eschenbach	60	49.45 N	11.49 E
Eschenburg	56	50.49 N	8.20 E
Eschenlohe	64	47.36 N	11.11 E
Eschershausen	52	51.56 N	9.38 E
Eschlkam	60	49.18 N	12.55 E
Escholzmatt	58	46.55 N	7.56 E
Eschscholtz Bay c	180	66.18 N	161.25 W
Esch-sur-Alzette	56	49.30 N	5.59 E
Esch-sur-Sûre	56	49.55 N	5.55 E
Eschwege	56	51.11 N	10.04 E
Eschweiler	56	50.49 N	6.16 E
Esclave, Grand Lac de l' → Great Slave Lake ⊜	176	61.30 N	114.00 W
Esclavo, Gran Lago del → Great Slave Lake ⊜	176	61.30 N	114.00 W
Escobal	236	9.09 N	79.58 W
Escobar □[5]	288	34.23 S	58.46 W
Escobar, Arroyo ≃	288	34.21 S	58.44 W
Escobedo, Méx.	196	27.13 N	101.21 W
Escobedo, Méx.	232	29.05 N	102.19 W
Escocesa, Bahía c	238	19.25 N	69.45 W
Escoheag	207	41.36 N	71.45 W
Escondido	228	33.07 N	117.05 W
Escondido ≃, Méx.	196	28.39 N	100.34 W
Escondido ≃, Nic.	236	12.04 N	83.45 W
Escondido Creek ≃	228	33.01 N	117.15 W
Escorial → San Lorenzo de El Escorial	34	40.35 N	4.09 W
Escoutay ≃	62	44.29 N	4.42 E
Escravos ≃[1]	150	5.35 N	5.10 E
Escrick	44	53.53 N	1.02 W
Escuadrón 201 ◆[8]	286a	19.22 N	99.06 W
Escudero, Arroyo ≃	258	34.20 S	57.05 W
Escudo de Veraguas, Isla I	236	9.06 N	81.33 W
Escuinapa de Hidalgo	234	22.51 N	105.48 W
Escuintla, Guat.	236	14.18 N	90.47 W
Escuintla, Méx.	232	15.20 N	92.38 W
Escuintla □[5]	236	14.10 N	91.00 W
Escuminac, Point ›	186	47.04 N	64.46 W
Esebi	154	2.57 N	30.39 E
Eséka	152	3.39 N	10.46 E
Eşen	130	36.27 N	29.16 E
Eşen ≃	130	36.16 N	29.15 E
Esenler ◆[8]	267b	41.02 N	28.51 E
Esens	52	53.39 N	7.37 E
Esera ≃	34	42.06 N	0.15 E
Esesi	130	39.49 N	39.19 E
Eşfahān (Isfahan)	128	32.40 N	51.38 E
Eşfahān □[4]	128	33.00 N	52.00 E
Esfandaqeh	128	28.38 N	57.12 E
Esfarāyen	128	37.02 N	57.27 E
Esgueva ≃	34	41.40 N	4.43 W
Eshan	102	24.11 N	102.22 E
Esher ◆[8]	42	51.23 N	0.22 W
Eshkāshem	123	36.42 N	71.34 E
Eshowe	158	28.58 S	31.29 E
Esh-Sham → Dimashq	132	33.30 N	36.18 E
Eshta'ol	132	31.47 N	35.00 E
Esh Winning	44	54.47 N	1.43 W
Esiama	150	4.56 N	2.21 W
Esigodini	154	20.18 S	28.56 E
Esine	64	45.55 N	10.15 E
Esino ≃	66	43.39 N	13.22 E
Esira	157b	24.20 S	46.42 E
Esk	171a	27.15 S	152.25 E
Esk ≃, N.Z.	172	43.06 S	171.57 E
Esk ≃, U.K.	44	54.58 N	3.04 W
Esk ≃, Eng., U.K.	44	54.21 N	3.23 W
Esk ≃, Eng., U.K.	44	54.29 N	0.37 W
Esk ≃, Scot., U.K.	46	55.57 N	3.03 W
Eskdale, N.Z.	172	39.24 S	176.50 E
Eskdale, W.V., U.S.	188	38.05 N	81.26 W
Eskdale V	44	55.10 N	3.00 W
Eske, Lough ⊜	48	54.41 N	8.03 W
Eski Dzhumaya → Târgovište	38	43.15 N	26.34 E
Eskifjörður	24a	65.04 N	13.59 W
Eskiikan	85	43.12 N	68.31 E
Eskilstrup	41	54.51 N	11.54 E
Eskilstuna	40	59.22 N	16.30 E
Eskimalatya	130	38.26 N	38.23 E
Eskimo Lakes ⊜	180	69.15 N	132.17 W
Eskimo Point	176	61.07 N	94.03 W
Eskipazar	130	40.58 N	32.33 E
Eskişehir	130	39.46 N	30.32 E
Eskişehir □[4]	130	39.35 N	31.10 E
Eskridge	198	38.51 N	96.06 W
Esla ≃	34	41.29 N	6.03 W
Eslāmābād	128	34.06 N	46.31 E
Eslām Qal'eh	128	34.40 N	61.04 E
Eslāmshahr	128	35.40 N	51.10 E
Eslarn	60	49.35 N	12.32 E
Eslohe	56	51.15 N	8.09 E
Eslöv	41	55.50 N	13.20 E
Eşme	130	38.24 N	28.59 E
Esmeralda, Austl.	166	18.50 S	142.34 E
Esmeralda, Cuba	240p	21.51 N	78.07 W
Esmeralda, Méx.	196	25.40 N	103.30 W
Esmeralda, Isla I	254	48.57 S	75.25 W
Esmeraldas	246	0.59 N	79.42 W
Esmeraldas □[4]	246	0.40 N	79.30 W
Esmeraldas ≃	246	0.58 N	79.38 W
Esmirna → İzmir	130	38.25 N	27.09 E
Esmond, N.D., U.S.	198	48.02 N	99.45 W
Esmond, R.I., U.S.	207	41.52 N	71.29 W
Esnagi Lake ⊜	190	48.38 N	84.32 W
Esneux	56	50.32 N	5.34 E
Esong	152	2.09 N	10.58 E
Esopus Creek ≃	210	42.04 N	73.56 W
Espada, Punta ›	246	12.05 N	71.07 W
Espagne → Spain □[1]	34	40.00 N	4.00 W
Espalion	32	44.31 N	2.46 E
Espaly-Saint-Marcel	62	45.03 N	3.52 E
España → Spain □[1]	34	40.00 N	4.00 W
Espanola, On., Can.	190	46.15 N	81.46 W
Espanola, N.M., U.S.	200	35.59 N	106.04 W
Española, Isla I	246a	1.25 S	89.42 W
Esparto	226	38.41 N	122.00 W
Esparza	236	9.59 N	84.40 W
Espasingen	58	47.49 N	9.00 E
Espe, Dan.	41	55.12 N	10.25 E
Espe, Kaz.	85	43.52 N	74.10 E
Espejo	34	37.41 N	4.33 W
Espelkamp	52	52.25 N	8.36 E
Espenberg, Cape ›	180	66.33 N	163.36 W
Espenhain	54	51.11 N	12.29 E
Espera, Arroyo ≃[1]	288	34.24 S	58.36 W
Espera Feliz	255	20.39 S	41.55 W
Esperança, Bra.	246	4.24 S	69.52 W
Esperança, Bra.	250	7.01 S	35.51 W
Esperance, Austl.	162	33.51 S	121.53 E
Esperance, N.Y., U.S.	210	42.46 N	74.15 W
Esperance Bay c	162	33.51 S	121.53 E
Esperantina	250	3.54 S	42.14 W
Esperantinópolis	250	4.53 S	44.53 W
Esperanza, Arg.	252	31.27 S	60.56 W
Esperanza, Cuba	240p	22.27 N	80.06 W
Esperanza, Méx.	232	27.35 N	109.56 W
Esperanza, Méx.	234	18.52 N	97.24 W
Esperanza, Pil.	116	8.43 N	125.36 E
Esperanza, Pil.	116	11.44 N	124.03 E
Esperanza, P.R.	240m	18.06 N	65.28 W
Esperanza, S. Afr.	158	30.21 S	30.40 E
Esperanza ʋ[3]	9	63.24 S	56.59 W
Esperanza Inlet c	182	49.48 N	126.50 W
Espergærde	41	56.00 N	12.34 E
Esperia	66	41.23 N	13.41 E
Esperito, Arroyo ≃[1]	288	34.23 S	58.36 W
Espevær	26	59.36 N	5.10 E
Espichel, Cabo ›	34	38.25 N	9.13 W
Espinal	246	4.09 N	74.53 W
Espinazo	196	26.16 N	101.06 W
Espinazo, Sierra del → Espinhaço, Serra do ⋏	255	17.30 S	43.30 W
Espingarda ≃	250	10.03 S	47.13 W
Espinhaço, Serra do ⋏	255	17.30 S	43.30 W
Espinho	34	41.00 N	8.39 W
Espinillo	252	24.58 S	58.34 W
Espinillo, Arroyo ≃	258	34.59 S	57.36 W
Espinillo, Punta del ›	258	34.50 S	56.26 W
Espino	246	8.34 N	66.01 W
Espinosa	255	14.56 S	42.50 W
Espírito Santo → Vila Velha	250	3.13 N	51.13 W
Espírito Santo □[3]	255	19.30 S	40.30 W
Espírito Santo do Dourado	256	22.03 S	45.58 W
Espiritu Santo I	175f	15.15 S	166.50 E
Espíritu Santo, Isla I	232	24.30 N	110.22 W
Espita	232	21.01 N	88.19 W
Espoir, Bay d' c	186	47.50 N	55.51 W
Espoo (Esbo)	26	60.13 N	24.40 E
Esposende	34	41.32 N	8.47 W
Esposizione Universale di Roma ♦	267a	41.50 N	12.28 E
Espugues de Llobregat	266d	41.22 N	2.05 E
Espumoso	252	28.44 S	52.51 W
Espungabera	156	20.29 S	32.48 E
Espy	210	41.00 N	76.24 W
Espyville Station	214	41.36 N	80.29 W
Esquatzel Coulee V	202	46.17 N	119.07 W
Esquel	254	42.54 S	71.19 W
Esquimalt	224	48.26 N	123.24 W
Esquina	252	30.01 S	59.32 W
Esquina Negra	258	35.02 S	58.03 W
Esquipulas, Guat.	236	14.34 N	89.21 W
Esquipulas, Nic.	236	12.40 N	85.47 W
Esquiú	252	29.23 S	65.17 W
Esrum Sø ⊜	41	56.00 N	12.24 E
Essa ≃	76	54.53 N	28.40 E
Essaoui Mellene, Oued V	148	27.26 N	6.40 E
Essaouira (Mogador)	148	31.30 N	9.47 W
Essaouira □[4]	148	31.25 N	9.30 W
Essarts	261	48.30 N	1.46 E
Essé	152	4.05 N	11.53 E
Esse ≃	66	43.16 N	11.54 E
Esseg → Osijek	38	45.33 N	18.41 E
Es-Sekhira	148	34.17 N	10.06 E
Essen, Bel.	50	51.28 N	4.28 E
Essen, Dtsch.	52	52.43 N	7.57 E
Essen, Dtsch.	56	51.28 N	7.01 E
Essen, Dtsch.	263	51.28 N	7.01 E
Essenbach	60	48.37 N	12.13 E
Essenberg ◆[8]	263	51.26 N	6.42 E
Essendon, Austl.	169	37.46 S	144.55 E
Essendon, Eng., U.K.	260	51.46 N	0.09 W
Essendon, Mount ∧	162	24.59 S	120.28 E
Essendon Airport ⊠	169	37.43 S	144.53 E
Essen-Mülheim, Flughafen ⊠	263	51.24 N	6.58 E
Essentuki → Jessentuki	84	44.03 N	42.51 E
Essequibo ≃	246	6.59 N	58.23 W
Essequibo Islands-West Demerara □[4]	246	6.40 N	58.30 W
Es Sers	36	36.04 N	9.02 E
Essex, On., Can.	214	42.10 N	82.49 W
Essex, Ct., U.S.	207	41.21 N	72.23 W
Essex, Il., U.S.	216	41.11 N	88.11 W
Essex, Ia., U.S.	198	40.50 N	95.18 W
Essex, Md., U.S.	208	39.18 N	76.28 W
Essex, Ma., U.S.	207	42.37 N	70.47 W
Essex, Mo., U.S.	194	36.48 N	89.51 W
Essex, Mt., U.S.	182	48.16 N	113.36 W
Essex □[6], On., Can.	214	42.10 N	82.50 W
Essex □[6], Eng., U.K.	42	51.48 N	0.40 E
Essex □[6], Ma., U.S.	207	42.40 N	70.55 W
Essex □[6], N.J., U.S.	210	40.48 N	74.12 W
Essex □[6], Vt., U.S.	206	44.57 N	71.43 W
Essex □[6], Va., U.S.	208	37.55 N	76.55 W
Essex ≃	283	42.39 N	70.46 W
Essex Bay c	283	42.39 N	70.44 W
Essex Fells	276	40.49 N	74.17 W
Essex Junction	188	44.29 N	73.06 W
Essex Skypark ⊠	284b	39.18 N	76.28 W
Essexville	190	43.36 N	83.50 W
Essing	60	48.56 N	11.47 E
Essington	285	39.52 N	75.18 W
Essling ◆[8]	264b	48.13 N	16.32 E
Esslingen	56	48.45 N	9.16 E
Es Smala es Souassi	36	35.21 N	10.33 E
Esson Lake ⊜	212	45.02 N	78.16 W
Essonne □[5]	50	48.36 N	2.20 E
Essonne ≃	50	48.37 N	2.29 E
Essoyes	58	48.04 N	4.32 E
Es-Suki	140	13.20 N	33.54 E
Essvik	26	62.19 N	17.24 E
Est □[4]	152	4.00 N	14.00 E
Est, Canal de l' ≖	56	48.45 N	5.35 E
Est, Cap ›	157b	15.16 S	50.29 E
Est, Gare ◆[5]	261	48.53 N	2.22 E
Est, Île de l' I	186	47.37 N	61.26 W
Est, Pointe de l' ›	186	49.08 N	61.41 W
Estacada	224	45.17 N	122.19 W
Estaca de Bares, Punta de la ›	34	43.46 N	7.42 W
Estacado, Llano ≚	196	33.30 N	102.40 W
Estación La Colorado	234	23.52 N	102.26 W
Estado, Parque do ♦	287b	23.39 S	46.37 W
Estados, Isla de los (Staten Island) I	254	54.47 S	64.15 W
Estados Unidos → United States □[1]	178	38.00 N	97.00 W
Eşţahbān	128	29.08 N	54.04 E
Estaires	50	50.38 N	2.43 E
Estambul → İstanbul	130	41.01 N	28.58 E
Estância, Bra.	250	11.16 S	37.26 W
Estancia, Pil.	116	11.28 N	123.09 E
Estancia, S. Afr.	158	26.17 S	29.52 E
Estancia, N.M., U.S.	200	34.45 N	106.03 W
Estancia Los López	234	20.53 N	104.31 W
Estanislao del Campo	252	25.03 S	60.06 W
Estanzuelas	236	13.38 N	88.30 W
Estarreja	34	40.45 N	8.34 W
Estats, Pique d' ∧	34	42.40 N	1.24 E
Estavayer-le-Lac	58	46.51 N	6.50 E
Estcourt	158	29.01 S	29.52 E
Este	64	45.14 N	11.39 E
Este ≃	52	53.32 N	9.47 E
Este, Parque Nacional del ♦	286c	10.30 N	66.50 W
Este, Punta ›	240m	18.08 N	65.16 W
Esteban Echeverría	258	34.50 S	58.28 W
Esteban Echeverría □[5]	288	34.51 S	58.32 W
Estefanía, Lago → Stefanie, Lake ⊜	144	4.40 N	36.50 E
Esteio	252	29.51 S	51.10 W
Estelí	236	13.05 N	86.23 W
Estelí □[5]	236	13.10 N	86.20 W
Estella	34	42.40 N	2.02 W
Estelline, S.D., U.S.	198	44.34 N	96.54 W
Estelline, Tx., U.S.	196	34.33 N	100.26 W
Estell Manor	208	39.24 N	74.44 W
Estèng	62	44.14 N	6.45 E
Estepa	34	37.18 N	4.54 W
Estepas de Kirguises → Kirgizskij chrebet ⋏	85	42.30 N	74.00 E
Estepona	34	36.26 N	5.08 W
Ester	180	64.51 N	148.01 W
Esterel ⋏	62	43.30 N	6.50 E
Esterhazy	184	50.40 N	102.08 W
Esterhazy, Schloss ⊥	61	47.51 N	16.32 E
Estérias, Cap ›	152	0.37 N	9.20 E
Esternay	50	48.44 N	3.34 E
Estero	220	26.26 N	81.49 W
Estero Bay c, Ca., U.S.	226	35.24 N	120.53 W
Estero Bay c, Fl., U.S.	220	26.25 N	81.52 W
Estero Island I	220	26.26 N	81.56 W
Estéron ≃	62	43.49 N	7.11 E
Esteros	252	26.37 S	63.39 W
Esterwegen	52	52.59 N	7.38 E
Estes Park	200	40.22 N	105.31 W
Este Sudeste, Cayos del II	236	12.26 N	81.27 W
Estevan	184	49.08 N	102.59 W
Estevan Group II	182	53.05 N	129.40 W
Estevan Point	182	49.23 N	126.33 W
Esther Island I	180	60.50 N	148.05 W
Estherville	198	43.24 N	94.49 W
Estill	192	32.45 N	81.14 W
Estissac	50	48.16 N	3.49 E
Estiva	256	22.28 S	46.02 W
Estiva, Ribeirão da ≃	287b	23.44 S	46.23 W
Estiva, Rio da ≃	255	12.23 S	45.05 W
Estling, Lake ⊜	276	40.53 N	74.30 W
Estocolmo → Stockholm	40	59.20 N	18.03 E
Eston, Sk., Can.	184	51.10 N	108.46 W
Eston, Eng., U.K.	44	54.34 N	1.07 W
Estonia (Eesti) □[1], Europe	22	59.00 N	26.00 E
Estonia (Eesti) □[1], Europe	76	59.00 N	26.00 E
Estoril	34	38.42 N	9.23 W
Estrasburgo → Strasbourg	58	48.35 N	7.45 E
Estrées-Saint-Denis	50	49.26 N	2.39 E
Estrela	252	29.29 S	51.58 W
Estrela ∧	34	40.19 N	7.37 W
Estrela ≃	287a	22.43 S	43.13 W
Estrela, Serra da ⋏	34	40.20 N	7.38 W
Estrela do Norte	255	13.49 S	49.04 W
Estrela do Sul	255	18.46 S	47.42 W
Estrella ≃	226	35.45 N	120.41 W
Estremadura □[9]	34	39.15 N	9.10 W
Estremoz	34	38.51 N	7.35 W
Estribo	234	22.26 N	99.17 W
Estrondo, Serra do ⋏[1]	250	9.00 S	48.45 W
Estuaire □[4]	152	0.15 N	10.00 E
Estuary	184	50.56 N	109.46 W
Esumba, Île I	152	2.00 N	21.12 E
Eszék → Osijek	38	45.33 N	18.41 E
Esztergom	30	47.48 N	18.45 E
Étables	32	48.38 N	2.50 W
Etadunna	166	28.43 S	138.38 E
Etah, India	124	27.38 N	78.40 E
Etah, Kal. Nun.	16	78.19 N	72.38 W
Étain	56	49.13 N	5.38 E
Etajima	96	34.15 N	132.30 E
Eta-jima I	96	34.15 N	132.28 E
Étalle	56	49.41 N	5.36 E
Étamaniou ≃	186	50.17 N	59.58 W
Étampes	50	48.26 N	2.09 E
Etamunbanie, Lake ⊜	166	26.15 S	139.44 E
Étaples	50	50.31 N	1.39 E
États-Unis → United States □[1]	178	38.00 N	97.00 W
Etāwah	124	26.46 N	79.02 E
Etchemin ≃	186	46.46 N	71.14 W
Etchojoa	232	26.55 N	109.38 W
Etéké	152	1.29 S	11.35 E
Etembue	152	1.17 N	9.25 E
Etendard, Pic de l' ∧	62	45.09 N	6.09 E
Ethan	198	43.32 N	97.59 W
Ethel	194	33.07 N	89.27 W
Ethel ≃	162	24.09 S	118.26 E
Ethel, Mount ∧	200	40.39 N	106.41 W
Ethelbert	184	51.31 N	100.22 W
Ethel Creek	162	22.54 S	120.09 E
Ethel Lake ⊜	180	63.21 N	136.00 W
Etherow ≃	262	53.24 N	2.03 W
Ethiopia (Ityopiya) □[1], Afr.	136	9.00 N	39.00 E
Ethiopia (Ityopiya) □[1], Afr.	144	9.00 N	39.00 E
Ethiopian Plateau ⋏[1]	144	9.00 N	38.00 E
Ethiopie → Ethiopia □[1]	144	9.00 N	39.00 E
Ethridge, Mt., U.S.	202	48.33 N	112.07 W
Ethridge, Tn., U.S.	194	35.19 N	87.18 W
Eticoga	150	11.09 N	16.08 W
Eticuera Creek ≃	226	38.41 N	122.16 W
Etigo-heiya ≚	92	37.45 N	139.00 E
Etili	130	39.59 N	26.54 E
Étiolles	261	48.38 N	2.29 E
Etiopía → Ethiopia □[1]	144	9.00 N	39.00 E
Etive, Loch ⊜	46	56.29 N	5.09 W
Etiwanda	228	34.08 N	117.31 W
Etjo ∧	156	21.09 S	16.30 E
Etna, Ca., U.S.	204	41.27 N	122.53 W
Etna, N.Y., U.S.	210	42.29 N	76.23 W
Etna, Pa., U.S.	214	40.30 N	79.56 W
Etna, Wy., U.S.	200	43.02 N	111.00 W
Etna, Monte (Mongibello) ∧[1]	70	37.46 N	15.00 E
Etna Green	216	41.17 N	86.03 W
Etne	26	59.40 N	5.56 E
Etobicoke	212	43.42 N	79.32 W
Etobicoke Creek ≃	212	43.35 N	79.32 W
Etoile	154	11.38 S	27.34 E
Étoile, Chaîne de l' ⋏	62	43.22 N	5.30 E
Etoka	152	0.10 N	23.23 E
Etolin Island I	180	56.08 N	132.26 W
Etolin Strait ɥ	180	60.20 N	165.15 W
Etomami ≃	184	52.48 N	102.33 W
Eton, Austl.	166	21.16 S	148.58 E
Eton, Eng., U.K.	42	51.30 N	0.36 W
Eton College ʋ[2]	260	51.30 N	0.36 W
Etondo	152	7.46 S	23.36 E
Etorofu-tō → Iturup, ostrov I	92a	44.54 N	147.30 E
Etosha National Park ♦	156	19.00 S	15.50 E
Etosha Pan ≚	156	18.45 S	16.15 E
Etoumbi	152	0.01 S	14.57 E
Etowah	192	35.19 N	84.31 W
Etowah ≃	192	34.15 N	85.11 W
Étréchy	50	48.30 N	2.12 E
Étrépagny	50	49.18 N	1.37 E
Étretat	50	49.42 N	0.12 E
Etrotroka	157b	22.53 S	47.36 E
Etroubles	62	45.49 N	7.14 E
Etrusca, Necropoli ⊥	66	42.15 N	11.47 E
Etsch → Adige ≃	64	45.10 N	12.20 E
Ettal	64	47.34 N	11.05 E
Ettalong	170	33.31 S	151.21 E
Ettelbruck	56	49.52 N	6.05 E
Ettenheim	58	48.15 N	7.49 E
Etten-Leur	52	51.34 N	4.38 E
Etterbeek	56	50.50 N	4.23 E
Etters	208	40.09 N	76.45 W
Et Tîdra I	150	19.44 N	16.24 W
Ettington	42	52.09 N	1.36 W
Ettlingen	56	48.56 N	8.24 E
Ettrema Creek ≃	170	34.50 S	150.22 E
Ettrick	208	37.14 N	77.25 W
Ettrick Forest ◆[3]	46	55.30 N	3.00 W
Ettrick Pen ∧	44	55.22 N	3.16 W
Ettrick Water ≃	46	55.31 N	2.55 W
Ettringen, Dtsch.	56	50.21 N	7.13 E
Ettringen, Dtsch.	58	48.06 N	10.39 E
Etuku	154	3.43 S	25.44 E
Etyka	88	51.00 N	116.50 E
Etzatlán	234	20.46 N	104.05 W
Etzikom Coulee ≃	184	49.25 N	111.10 W
Etzná ⊥	232	19.35 N	90.15 W
Eu	50	50.03 N	1.25 E
Eua I	14	21.22 S	174.56 W
Eua Iki I	174w	21.07 S	174.59 W
Eubank Acres	222	30.23 N	97.42 W
Euboea → Évvoia I	38	38.34 N	23.50 E
Eucalyptus Hills	228	32.56 N	116.56 W
Euchiniko ≃	182	53.14 N	123.30 W
Eucla	162	31.43 S	128.52 E
Euclid, Oh., U.S.	214	41.35 N	81.31 W
Euclid, Pa., U.S.	214	41.00 N	79.56 W
Euclid Center	216	42.08 N	86.24 W
Euclid Creek ≃	279a	41.35 N	81.35 W
Euclid Creek Reservation ♦	279a	41.33 N	81.32 W
Euclides da Cunha	250	10.31 S	39.01 W
Eucumbene	171b	36.07 S	148.38 E
Eucumbene ≃	171b	36.21 S	148.38 E
Eucumbene, Lake ⊜[1]	171b	36.05 S	148.45 E
Eudistes, Lac des ⊜	186	50.30 N	65.15 W
Eudora, Ar., U.S.	194	33.06 N	91.15 W
Eudora, Ks., U.S.	198	38.56 N	95.05 W
Eudunda	168b	34.11 S	139.04 E
Eufaula, Al., U.S.	194	31.53 N	85.08 W
Eufaula, Ok., U.S.	196	35.17 N	95.34 W
Eufaula Lake ⊜[1]	196	35.17 N	95.31 W
Eufrates → Euphrates ≃	128	31.00 N	47.25 E
Euganei, Colli ⋏[2]	64	45.19 N	11.40 E
Eugendorf	64	47.52 N	13.07 E
Eugene	202	44.03 N	123.05 W
Eugenia, Punta ›	232	27.50 N	115.05 W
Eugenia Lake ⊜	212	44.20 N	80.30 W
Eugenio Bustos	252	33.46 S	69.04 W
Eugênio de Melo	256	23.09 S	45.47 W
Eugmo I	26	63.49 N	22.45 E
Eugowra	166	33.26 S	148.23 E
Euijeongbu → Ŭijŏngbu	98	37.44 N	127.03 E
Euless	222	32.50 N	97.04 W
Eulo	166	28.10 S	145.03 E
Eume ≃	34	43.25 N	8.08 W
Eumemmerring Creek ≃	274b	38.03 S	145.10 E
Eumungerie	166	31.57 S	148.37 E
Eunápolis	255	16.22 S	39.35 W
Eungella National Park ♦	166	21.00 S	148.30 E
Eunice, La., U.S.	194	30.29 N	92.25 W
Eunice, N.M., U.S.	196	32.26 N	103.09 W
Eupen	56	50.38 N	6.02 E
Euphrat → Euphrates ≃	128	31.00 N	47.25 E
Euphrates (Fırat) (Nahr al-Furāt) ≃	128	31.00 N	47.25 E
Eupora	194	33.32 N	89.16 W
Eure	208	36.25 N	76.51 W
Eure □[5]	50	49.10 N	1.00 E
Eure ≃	50	49.18 N	1.12 E
Eure-et-Loir □[5]	50	48.30 N	1.30 E
Eureka, Ak., U.S.	180	61.56 N	147.10 W
Eureka, Ca., U.S.	204	40.48 N	124.09 W
Eureka, Il., U.S.	190	40.43 N	89.16 W
Eureka, Ks., U.S.	198	37.49 N	96.17 W
Eureka, Mo., U.S.	219	38.30 N	90.37 W
Eureka, Mt., U.S.	202	48.52 N	115.03 W
Eureka, Nv., U.S.	204	39.30 N	115.57 W
Eureka, Pa., U.S.	214	40.15 N	78.46 W
Eureka, S.C., U.S.	192	34.42 N	81.11 W
Eureka, S.D., U.S.	198	45.46 N	99.37 W
Eureka, Tx., U.S.	222	32.01 N	96.18 W
Eureka, Ut,. U.S.	200	39.57 N	112.07 W
Eureka, Mount ∧	162	26.34 S	121.32 E
Eureka Springs	194	36.24 N	93.44 W
Eurialo, Castello ⊥	70	37.06 N	15.14 E
Eurinilla Creek ≃	166	30.50 S	140.01 E
Euroa	169	36.45 S	145.35 E
Euro Disney, Parc ♦	261	48.51 N	2.47 E
Europa, Île I	138	22.20 S	40.22 E
Europa, Picos de ⋏	34	43.12 N	4.48 W
Europabrücke ◆[5]	64	47.11 N	11.23 E
Europa Point ›	34	36.10 N	5.22 W
Europe ⊻[1]	4	50.00 N	28.00 E
Europe ⊻[1]	10	50.00 N	28.00 E
Europoort ◆[5]	52	51.57 N	4.07 E
Eursinge	52	52.46 N	6.28 E
Eurville	58	48.35 N	5.02 E
Euseigne	58	46.10 N	7.25 E
Euskal Herriko □[4]	34	43.00 N	2.30 W
Euskirchen	56	50.39 N	6.47 E
Eustace	222	32.18 N	96.01 W
Eustis, Fl., U.S.	220	28.51 N	81.41 W
Eustis, Ne., U.S.	198	40.39 N	100.09 W
Eustis, Lake ⊜	220	28.50 N	81.44 W
Euston	166	34.35 S	142.44 E
Euston Station ◆[5]	260	51.32 N	0.08 W
Eutaw	194	32.50 N	87.53 W
Eutin	54	54.08 N	10.37 E
Eutingen	56	48.55 N	8.45 E
Eutsuk Lake ⊜	182	53.20 N	126.44 W
Eutzsch	54	51.49 N	12.38 E
Euxton	44	53.39 N	2.40 W
Euzet-les-Bains	62	44.04 N	4.14 E

Name	Seite	Breite°′	Länge°′ E = Ost
Eva	194	34.20 N	86.46 W
Evadale	194	30.21 N	94.04 W
Eva Downs	162	18.01 S	134.52 E
Evale	152	16.33 S	15.44 E
Evällen ⊜	40	60.03 N	18.20 E
Evançon ≃	62	45.40 N	7.41 E
Evandale	166	41.34 S	147.14 E
Evans	200	40.22 N	104.41 W
Evans, Lac ⊜	176	50.55 N	77.00 W
Evans, Mount ∧	200	39.35 N	105.38 W
Evansburg, Ab., Can.	182	53.36 N	115.01 W
Evansburg, Pa., U.S.	285	40.11 N	75.26 W
Evans Center	210	42.39 N	79.02 W
Evans City	214	40.46 N	80.03 W
Evans Creek ≃	202	42.25 N	123.11 W
Evansdale	190	42.28 N	92.16 W
Evans Head ›	166	29.07 S	153.26 E
Evans Mills	212	44.05 N	75.48 W
Evansport	216	41.25 N	84.24 W
Evans Strait ɥ	176	63.15 N	82.00 W
Evanston, Il., U.S.	216	42.02 N	87.41 W
Evanston, Pa., U.S.	279b	40.16 N	79.41 W
Evanston, Wy., U.S.	200	41.16 N	110.57 W
Evansville, Il., U.S.	194	38.05 N	89.56 W
Evansville, In., U.S.	194	37.58 N	87.33 W
Evansville, Mn., U.S.	198	46.00 N	95.40 W
Evansville, Wi., U.S.	216	42.46 N	89.17 W
Evansville, Wy., U.S.	200	42.51 N	106.16 W
Evant	196	31.29 N	98.09 W
Evanton	46	57.40 N	4.20 W
Eva Perón → La Plata	258	34.55 S	57.57 W
Evart	190	43.54 N	85.15 W
Evarts	192	36.51 N	83.11 W
Evaz	128	27.46 N	53.59 E
Ève	261	49.05 N	2.42 E
Evecquemont	261	49.02 N	1.57 E
Eveking	263	51.14 N	7.44 E
Eveleth	190	47.27 N	92.32 W
Evelyn, Mount ∧[2]	164	13.36 S	132.53 E
Evening Shade	194	36.04 N	91.37 W
Evenkamp	263	51.40 N	7.39 E
Evenlode ≃	42	51.47 N	1.21 W
Evensk	74	61.57 N	159.14 E
Evenwood	44	54.37 N	1.46 W
Even Yehuda	132	32.16 N	34.53 E
Everard, Lake ⊜	162	31.25 S	135.05 E
Everard, Mount ∧, Austl.	162	26.16 S	132.04 E
Everard, Mount ∧, B.C., Can.	182	51.05 N	125.45 W
Everard Ranges ⋏	162	27.05 S	132.28 E
Evercreech	42	51.09 N	2.30 W
Evere	56	50.52 N	4.24 E
Everest	198	39.40 N	95.25 W
Everest, Mount (Qomolangma Feng) ∧	124	27.59 N	86.56 E
Everett, On., Can.	212	44.11 N	79.57 W
Everett, Ma., U.S.	207	42.24 N	71.03 W
Everett, N.J., U.S.	276	40.21 N	74.09 W
Everett, Pa., U.S.	188	40.00 N	78.22 W
Everett, Wa., U.S.	224	47.58 N	122.12 W
Everett, Mount ∧	207	42.06 N	73.25 W
Evergem	50	51.07 N	3.42 E
Everglades City	220	25.52 N	81.23 W
Everglades National Park ♦	220	25.27 N	80.53 W
Evergreen, Al., U.S.	194	31.26 N	86.57 W
Evergreen, Ca., U.S.	204	35.54 N	120.26 W
Evergreen, Mt., U.S.	202	48.13 N	114.18 W
Evergreen, Tx., U.S.	222	30.33 N	95.14 W
Evergreen Lake ⊜[1]	216	40.40 N	89.02 W
Evergreen Park	216	41.43 N	87.42 W
Evergreen Plaza ◆[9]	278	41.43 N	87.41 W
Everly	198	43.09 N	95.19 W
Everman	222	32.37 N	97.17 W
Everman, Volcán ∧[1]	232	18.48 N	110.59 W
Everöd	26	55.54 N	14.06 E
Eversael	263	51.33 N	6.39 E
Eversberg	56	51.21 N	8.20 E
Eversen	52	52.45 N	10.02 E
Everson, Pa., U.S.	214	40.05 N	79.35 W
Everson, Wa., U.S.	224	48.55 N	122.20 W
Everswinkel	52	51.55 N	7.50 E
Everton	218	39.34 N	85.05 W
Everton ◆[8]	262	53.25 N	2.58 W
Everton Football Ground ♦	262	53.26 N	2.58 W
Evesen	52	52.17 N	8.59 E
Evesham, Sk., Can.	184	52.24 N	109.50 W
Evesham, Eng., U.K.	42	52.06 N	1.56 W
Evesham, Vale of V	42	52.06 N	1.50 W
Évian-les-Bains	58	46.23 N	6.35 E
Evijärvi	26	63.22 N	23.29 E
Evinayong	152	1.27 N	10.34 E
Eving ◆[8]	263	51.33 N	7.29 E
Evingsen	263	51.18 N	7.44 E
Evionnaz	58	46.11 N	7.01 E
Evisa	36	42.15 N	8.47 E
Evje	26	58.36 N	7.51 E
Evolène	58	46.07 N	7.30 E
Évora	34	38.34 N	7.54 W
Evoron, ozero ⊜	89	51.28 N	136.30 E
Evpatoria → Jevpatorija	78	45.12 N	33.22 E
Évrange	56	49.30 N	6.12 E
Évreux	50	49.01 N	1.09 E
Evrieu	62	45.35 N	5.34 E
'Evron	132	32.59 N	35.06 E
Évros (Marica) (Meriç) ≃	38	40.52 N	26.12 E
Evrótas ≃	38	36.48 N	22.40 E
Évry	50	48.38 N	2.27 E
Évry-les-Châteaux	261	48.39 N	2.38 E
E. V. Spence Reservoir ⊜[1]	196	31.55 N	100.35 W
Evungu	154	4.27 S	25.12 E
Évvoia I	38	38.34 N	23.50 E
Évzonos ∧	267c	37.57 N	23.49 E
Ewa	229c	21.20 N	158.02 W
Ewa Beach	229c	21.18 N	158.00 W
Ewan	285	39.42 N	75.11 W
Ewaninga	162	23.58 S	133.58 E
Ewan Lake ⊜	285	39.42 N	75.11 W
Ewansville	285	39.59 N	74.44 W
Ewbank	158	26.14 S	23.35 E
Ewbank da Câmara	256	21.31 S	43.33 W
Ewe, Loch c	46	57.48 N	5.40 W
Ewell, Eng., U.K.	260	51.21 N	0.15 W
Ewell, Md., U.S.	208	37.59 N	76.02 W
Ewen	190	46.32 N	89.16 W
Ewenkiku Zizhiqi	89	49.07 N	119.40 E
Ewes Water ≃	44	55.08 N	3.00 W
Ewing, Ky., U.S.	218	38.25 N	83.51 W
Ewing, Mo., U.S.	219	40.00 N	91.42 W
Ewing, Ne., U.S.	198	42.15 N	98.20 W
Ewing, Va., U.S.	192	36.38 N	83.25 W
Ewingsville	279b	40.24 N	80.06 W
Ewing Township	208	40.16 N	74.46 W
Ewo	152	0.53 S	14.49 E
Ewu	273a	6.33 N	3.19 E
Exaltación	248	13.16 S	65.15 W
Excelda	158	32.16 S	22.08 E
Excello	218	39.29 N	84.25 W
Excelsior	158	28.56 S	27.06 E
Excelsior Mountain ∧	226	38.02 N	119.18 W
Excelsior Park ♦	274a	33.45 S	151.01 E
Excelsior Springs	194	39.20 N	94.13 W
Excenevex	58	46.21 N	6.21 E
Exchange	210	41.07 N	76.41 W
Exchange Station ◆[5]	262	53.25 N	2.59 W
Excursion Inlet	180	58.25 N	135.27 W
Exe ≃	42	50.37 N	3.25 W
Executive Committee Range ⋏	9	76.50 S	126.00 W
Exeter, Austl.	170	34.38 S	150.19 E
Exeter, On., Can.	190	43.21 N	81.29 W
Exeter, Eng., U.K.	42	50.43 N	3.31 W
Exeter, Ca., U.S.	226	36.17 N	119.08 W
Exeter, Ne., U.S.	198	40.38 N	97.27 W

Symbols in the index entries represent the broad categories identified in the key at the right. Symbols with superior numbers (⋏[1]) identify subcategories (see complete key on page *I* · *1)*.

Symbole im Register stellen die rechts im Schlüssel erklärten Kategorien dar. Symbole mit hochgestellten Ziffern (⋏[1]) bezeichnen Unterabteilungen einer Kategorie (vgl. vollständiger Schlüssel auf Seite *I* · *1)*.

Los símbolos incluídos en el texto del índice representan las grandes categorías identificadas con la clave a la derecha. Los símbolos con numeros en su parte superior (⋏[1]) identifican las subcategorías (véase la clave completa en la página *I* · *1)*.

Les symboles de l'index représentent les catégories indiquées dans la légende à droite. Les symboles suivis d'un indice (⋏[1]) représentent des sous-catégories (voir légende complète à la page *I* · *1)*.

Os símbolos incluídos no texto do índice representam as grandes categorias identificadas com a chave à direita. Os símbolos com números em sua parte superior (⋏[1]) identificam as subcategorias (veja-se a chave completa à página *I* · *1)*.

∧ Mountain	Berg	Montaña	Montagne	Montanha
⋏ Mountains	Gebirge	Montañas	Montagnes	Montanhas
)(Pass	Paß	Paso	Col	Passo
V Valley, Canyon	Tal, Cañon	Valle, Cañón	Vallée, Canyon	Vale, Canhão
≚ Plain	Ebene	Llano	Plaine	Planície
› Cape	Kap	Cabo	Cap	Cabo
I Island	Insel	Isla	Île	Ilha
II Islands	Inseln	Islas	Îles	Ilhas
⊻ Other Topographic Features	Andere Topographische Objekte	Otros Elementos Topográficos	Autres données topographiques	Outros acidentes topográficos

ESPAÑOL	FRANÇAIS	PORTUGUÊS
Nombre / Página / Lat.⁰ʳ / Long.⁰ʳ W = Oeste	Nom / Page / Lat.⁰ʳ / Long.⁰ʳ W = Ouest	Nome / Página / Lat.⁰ʳ / Long.⁰ʳ W = Oeste

Column 1

Nombre	Página	Lat.	Long.
Exeter, N.H., U.S.	188	42.58 N	70.56 W
Exeter, Pa., U.S.	210	41.19 N	75.49 W
Exeter, R.I., U.S.	207	41.34 N	71.32 W
Exeter ≈	188	43.02 N	70.55 W
Exeter Sound ⊍	176	66.14 N	62.00 W
Exford	42	51.08 N	3.38 W
Exhibition of Economic Achievements ⍟	265b	55.50 N	37.37 E
Exhibition Park ♦	275b	43.38 N	79.25 W
Exhibition Stadium ♦	275b	43.38 N	79.25 W
Exincourt	58	47.30 N	6.50 E
Exira	198	41.35 N	34.52 W
Exline Slough ≈	216	41.35 N	37.47 W
Exmes	50	48.46 N	0.11 E
Exminster	42	50.41 N	3.29 W
Exmoor ⍈[1]	42	51.10 N	3.45 W
Exmoor National Park ♦	42	51.12 N	3.46 W
Exmore	208	37.31 N	75.49 W
Exmouth, Austl.	162	21.56 S	114.07 E
Exmouth, Eng., U.K.	42	50.37 N	3.25 W
Exmouth Gulf c	162	22.00 S	114.20 E
Exmouth Plateau ♦[3]	14	19.00 S	114.00 E
Exning	42	52.16 N	0.21 E
Expedition Range ⍅	166	24.30 S	149.05 E
Experiment	192	33.15 N	84.16 W
Exploits ≈	186	49.05 N	55.20 W
Exploits, Bay of c	186	49.24 N	55.00 W
Exploits Dam ♦[6]	186	48.45 N	56.30 W
Expo Memorial Park ♦	270	34.48 N	135.32 E
Export	214	40.25 N	79.37 W
Exposition Park ♦	280	34.01 N	118.17 W
Exshaw	182	51.03 N	115.09 W
Extension	224	49.06 N	123.57 W
Exter	52	52.08 N	8.46 E
Externsteine ⍓	52	51.52 N	8.55 E
Extertal	52	52.04 N	9.07 E
Exton	208	40.02 N	75.37 W
Extoraz ≈	234	21.06 N	99.23 W
Extrema	256	22.51 S	46.19 W
Extremadura ⍁[4]	34	39.15 N	6.15 W
Exu	250	7.31 S	39.43 W
Exuma Cays II	238	24.15 N	76.30 W
Exuma Sound ⊍	238	24.15 N	76.00 W
Eyak	180	60.32 N	145.36 W
Eyam	44	53.17 N	1.41 W
Eyasi, Lake ⍟	154	3.40 S	35.05 E
Eydehavn	26	58.31 N	8.53 E
Eye, Eng., U.K.	42	52.19 N	1.09 E
Eye, Eng., U.K.	42	52.35 N	0.10 W
Eyebrow	184	50.47 N	106.09 W
Eyehill Creek ≈	184	52.40 N	109.09 W
Eyemouth	46	55.52 N	2.06 W
Eye Peninsula ⍈[1]	46	58.13 N	6.13 W
Eyers Grove	210	41.05 N	76.31 W
Eye Water ≈	46	55.53 N	2.06 W
Eygalières	62	43.45 N	4.57 E
Eyguières	62	43.42 N	5.02 E
Eyhorne Street	260	51.16 N	0.38 E
Eyjafjörður c	24a	65.54 N	18.15 W
Eyl	144	7.59 N	49.49 E
Eylar Mountain ⍐	204	37.28 N	121.33 W
Eymet	32	44.40 N	0.24 E
Eymir	130	40.02 N	35.14 E
Eymoutiers	32	45.44 N	1.44 E
Eynesil	130	41.03 N	39.08 E
Eynhallow Sound ⊍	46	59.08 N	3.06 W
Eynort, Loch c	46	57.13 N	7.18 W
Eynsford	260	51.22 N	0.13 E
Eynsham	42	51.48 N	1.22 W
Eyota	190	43.59 N	92.13 W
Eyrarbakki	24a	63.53 N	21.05 W
Eyre	162	32.15 S	126.18 E
Eyrecourt	48	53.11 N	3.07 W
Eyre Creek ≈	166	26.40 S	139.00 E
Eyre Mountains ⍅	172	45.20 S	168.30 E
Eyre North, Lake ⍟	166	28.40 S	137.10 E
Eyre Peninsula ⍈[1]	166	34.00 S	135.45 E
Eyre South, Lake ⍟	166	29.30 S	137.20 E
Eyrieux ≈	62	44.48 N	4.43 E
Eyrstrup	52	52.46 N	9.13 E
Eythorne	42	51.11 N	1.17 E
Eythra	54	51.14 N	12.17 E
Eyüp ♦[8]	267b	41.03 N	28.55 E
Eyvánekey	128	35.20 N	52.04 E
Eyzaguirre, Canal ≈	286e	33.36 S	70.41 W
Ezanville	261	49.02 N	2.22 E
Ezbekîyah ♦[8]	273c	30.03 N	31.15 E
Ezeiza, Aeropuerto Internacional de ≈	288	34.49 S	58.32 W
Ezequiel Ramos Mexía, Embalse ⍟[1]	254	39.30 S	69.00 W
Ezere	76	56.26 N	22.22 E
Eželis	66	54.53 N	23.37 E
Ezeriş	38	45.24 N	21.53 E
Ezine	130	39.47 N	26.20 E
Ezinepazan	130	40.34 N	36.09 E
Ezop, chrebet ⍅	89	52.36 N	133.37 E
Ežva	24	61.47 N	50.40 E
Ézy-sur-Eure	50	48.52 N	1.25 E
Ezzell	222	29.17 N	96.58 W

F

Nombre	Página	Lat.	Long.
Faaa Airport ≈	174s	17.33 S	149.36 W
Faafaxdhuun	144	2.13 N	41.37 E
Faal	174q	9.37 N	138.10 E
Faaone	174q	17.40 S	149.16 W
Fabala	150	9.44 N	9.05 W
Fabbrico	64	44.52 N	10.50 E
Fabens	200	31.30 N	106.09 W
Fåberg	26	61.10 N	10.23 E
Faber Lake ⍟	176	63.56 N	117.15 W
Fabert Seamount ♦[3]	14	24.07 S	158.33 W
Fåborg	52	55.06 N	10.15 E
Fábrega, Cerro ⍐	236	9.07 N	82.52 W
Fabrègues	62	43.33 N	3.46 E
Fabreville ♦[6]	275a	45.34 N	73.50 W
Fabriano	66	43.20 N	12.18 E
Fábrica di Roma	66	42.20 N	12.18 E
Fabrício	85	43.11 N	76.24 E
Fabrizia	68	38.29 N	16.18 E
Facatativá	246	4.49 N	74.22 W
Facha	146	29.27 N	17.18 E
Faches-Thumesnil	50	50.34 N	3.04 E
Fachi	146	18.06 N	11.34 E
Facpi Point: ⍈	174p	13.20 N	144.38 E
Factoryville	210	41.34 N	75.46 W
Facundo	254	45.18 S	69.58 W
Fada	146	17.14 N	21.33 E
Fada, Lochan ⍟	46	57.38 N	5.18 W
Fadalto	64	46.05 N	12.20 E
Fada Ngourma	150	12.04 N	0.21 E
Faddeja, zaliv c	74	76.40 N	107.20 E
Faddejevskij, ostrov I	74	75.30 N	144.00 E
Faddoi	140	8.07 N	32.07 E
Fadian Point ⍈	174p	13.26 N	144.49 E
Fadiffolu Atoll I[1]	122	5.25 N	73.30 E
Fadit	140	9.58 N	33.13 E
Faedis	64	46.10 N	13.21 E
Faenza	66	44.17 N	11.53 E
Faena I	41	55.29 N	9.42 E
Faeroe Islands ⍁[2]	22	62.00 N	7.00 W
Faeröerne — Faeroe Islands ⍁[2]	22	62.00 N	7.00 W
Faete, Monte ⍐	267a	41.45 N	12.44 E
Fafa	150	15.20 N	0.43 E
Fafa I	174f	7.18 N	18.16 E
Fafakourou	150	13.04 N	14.34 W
Fafe	34	41.27 N	8.10 W
Fafen ≈	144	5.59 N	44.25 E
Faga	150	13.15 N	0.55 E

Column 2

Nom	Page	Lat.	Long.
Fagaitua	174u	14.16 S	170.37 W
Fagamalo	175a	13.25 S	172.21 W
Fâgâraş	38	45.51 N	24.58 E
Fâgâraşului, Munţii ⍅	38	45.35 N	25.00 E
Fagasa	174u	14.17 S	170.43 W
Fagatogo	174u	14.17 S	170.41 W
Fagernes	26	60.59 N	9.15 E
Fagersta	40	60.00 N	15.47 E
Fagertärn ♦[4]	40	58.46 N	14.42 E
Fagerviken	40	60.33 N	17.45 E
Fäget	38	45.51 N	22.10 E
Faggen Bach ≈	64	47.05 N	10.40 E
Faggo	150	11.23 N	9.57 E
Fagnano, Lago ⍟	254	54.35 S	68.00 W
Fagnano Castello	68	39.34 N	16.03 E
Fagnano Olona	62	45.40 N	8.52 E
Fagnières	50	48.58 N	4.19 E
Fagubine, Lac ⍟	150	16.45 N	3.54 W
Fagundes, Rio do ≈	256	22.12 S	43.31 W
Fagundsmýri	24a	63.54 N	16.38 W
Fagwir	140	9.33 N	30.25 E
Fahan	48	55.05 N	7.28 W
Fahl, Oued el V	148	31.15 N	4.41 E
Fahraj	128	28.58 N	58.52 E
Fähridorf	54	53.58 N	11.28 W
Fahrland	54	52.28 N	13.01 E
Fahrlander See ⍟	264a	52.27 N	13.01 E
Fahrnau	58	47.39 N	7.50 E
Fahuaqiao	106	30.52 N	121.25 E
Faial I	148a	38.34 N	28.42 W
Faichuk II	175c	7.23 N	151.40 E
Fä'id	142	30.20 N	32.16 E
Fä'id Military Base ≈	142	30.20 N	32.16 E
Faido	58	46.29 N	8.48 E
Faillon, Lac ⍟	190	48.21 N	76.38 W
Failsworth	44	53.31 N	2.09 W
Fains-les-Sources	44	48.47 N	5.08 E
Fairbairn Airport ≈	171b	35.18 S	149.15 E
Fairbairn Park ♦	284c	37.47 S	144.55 E
Fairbairn Reservoir ⍟	166	23.45 S	148.00 E
Fairbank	190	42.38 N	92.02 W
Fairbanks, Ak., U.S.	180	64.51 N	147.43 W
Fairbanks, La., U.S.	194	30.00 N	92.02 W
Fair Bluff	192	34.18 N	79.02 W
Fairborn	218	39.49 N	84.01 W
Fairbourne	42	52.41 N	4.03 W
Fairbury, Il., U.S.	216	40.44 N	88.30 W
Fairbury, Ne., U.S.	198	40.08 N	97.10 W
Fairchance	210	39.49 N	79.45 W
Fairchild	190	44.36 N	90.57 W
Fairchild Air Force Base ≈	202	47.38 N	117.38 W
Fairchild Creek ≈	212	43.07 N	80.07 W
Fairdale	216	42.06 N	88.56 W
Faire	116	17.53 N	121.34 E
Fairfax, Al., U.S.	194	32.47 N	85.11 W
Fairfax, Ca., U.S.	226	37.59 N	122.35 W
Fairfax, De., U.S.	285	39.47 N	75.32 W
Fairfax, Mn., U.S.	198	44.31 N	94.43 W
Fairfax, Mo., U.S.	194	40.20 N	95.23 W
Fairfax, Ok., U.S.	196	36.34 N	96.42 W
Fairfax, S.C., U.S.	192	32.57 N	81.14 W
Fairfax, S.D., U.S.	198	43.01 N	98.53 W
Fairfax, Vt., U.S.	188	44.39 N	73.00 W
Fairfax, Va., U.S.	208	38.50 N	77.18 W
Fairfax ⍁[6]	208	38.45 N	77.15 W
Fairfax Forest	284c	38.52 N	77.15 W
Fairfax Park	284c	38.47 N	77.14 W
Fairfax State Recreation Area ♦	218	39.02 N	86.29 W
Fairfax Station	284c	38.48 N	77.19 W
Fairfield, Austl.	170	33.52 S	150.57 E
Fairfield, Ca., U.S.	226	38.14 N	122.02 W
Fairfield, Ct., U.S.	208	41.08 N	73.15 W
Fairfield, Id., U.S.	202	43.00 N	114.47 W
Fairfield, Il., U.S.	194	38.22 N	88.21 W
Fairfield, Ia., U.S.	190	41.00 N	91.57 W
Fairfield, Me., U.S.	188	44.35 N	69.35 W
Fairfield, Mt., U.S.	202	47.36 N	111.58 W
Fairfield, Ne., U.S.	198	40.25 N	98.06 W
Fairfield, N.C., U.S.	192	35.33 N	76.12 W
Fairfield, N.Y., U.S.	210	43.08 N	74.55 W
Fairfield, Oh., U.S.	218	39.20 N	84.33 W
Fairfield, Pa., U.S.	214	39.47 N	77.22 W
Fairfield, Tx., U.S.	222	31.43 N	96.09 W
Fairfield ♦[6]	207	41.15 N	73.20 W
Fairfield Lake ⍟[1]	222	31.50 N	96.05 W
Fairfield University ⍌[2]	276	41.09 N	73.15 W

Column 3

Nome	Página	Lat.	Long.
Fair Oaks, Ga., U.S.	192	33.54 N	84.32 W
Fair Oaks, In., U.S.	216	41.05 N	87.16 W
Fairoaks, Pa., U.S.	279b	40.34 N	80.13 W
Fairoaks Airport ≈	260	51.21 N	0.32 W
Fair Plain	216	42.05 N	86.27 W
Fairplains	192	36.13 N	81.10 W
Fairplay	200	39.13 N	106.00 W
Fairpoint	214	40.07 N	80.55 W
Fairport, On., Can.	275b	43.49 N	79.05 W
Fairport, N.Y., U.S.	210	43.05 N	77.26 W
Fairport Beach	275b	43.48 N	79.06 W
Fairport Harbor	214	41.44 N	81.16 W
Fairseat	260	51.20 N	0.20 E
Fairton	208	39.22 N	75.13 W
Fairview, Aust.	164	15.33 S	144.19 E
Fairview, Ab., Can.	182	56.04 N	118.23 W
Fairview, Ga., U.S.	192	34.56 N	85.17 W
Fairview, Il., U.S.	190	40.38 N	90.10 W
Fairview, In., U.S.	216	40.18 N	85.11 W
Fairview, Ks., U.S.	198	39.50 N	95.43 W
Fairview, Md., U.S.	208	39.09 N	76.29 W
Fairview, Mi., U.S.	190	44.43 N	84.03 W
Fairview, Mt., U.S.	198	47.51 N	104.02 W
Fairview, N.J., U.S.	276	40.51 N	73.58 W
Fairview, N.Y., U.S.	210	41.43 N	73.55 W
Fairview, Oh., U.S.	214	40.03 N	81.14 W
Fairview, Ok., U.S.	196	36.16 N	98.28 W
Fairview, Pa., U.S.	214	42.01 N	80.15 W
Fairview, Tn., U.S.	194	35.58 N	87.07 W
Fairview, Ut., U.S.	200	39.37 N	111.26 W
Fairview, W.V. U.S.	188	39.35 N	80.14 W
Fairview Heights	219	38.10 N	90.00 W
Fairview Lanes	214	41.23 N	82.40 W
Fairview Mall ♦[9]	275b	43.47 N	79.21 W
Fairview Park, In., U.S.	194	39.40 N	87.25 W
Fairview Park, Oh., U.S.	214	41.26 N	81.51 W
Fairview Park, Pa., U.S.	210	41.10 N	75.53 W
Fairview Peak ⍐, Nv., U.S.	204	39.14 N	118.08 W
Fairview Peak ⍐, Or., U.S.	202	43.35 N	122.39 W
Fairview Pointe Claire Centre ♦[9]	275a	45.28 N	73.50 W
Fairview Shores	220	28.35 N	81.23 W
Fairview Village	285	40.10 N	75.23 W
Fairvilla	220	28.35 N	81.24 W
Fairville	285	39.51 N	75.38 W
Fairweather Mountain ⍐	180	58.54 N	137.32 W
Fairy Lake ⍟	212	45.20 N	79.11 W
Fairy Meadow	170	34.23 S	150.54 E
Fairy Stone State Park ♦	192	36.48 N	80.06 W
Fairy Water ≈	48	54.37 N	7.20 W
Faisalabad (Lyallpur)	124	31.25 N	73.05 E
Faisleberg	108	8.36 N	144.33 E
Faistós ⍓	132	35.06 N	78.08 W
Faith	198	45.01 N	102.02 W
Fayum — Al-Fayyūm	142	29.19 N	30.50 E
Faizābād ⍁[1]	124	26.47 N	82.08 E
Fajanosvyj	76	54.04 N	34.24 E
Fajardo	240m	18.20 N	65.39 W
Fajou, îlet à I	241o	16.21 N	61.35 W
Fajr, Wādī V	128	30.06 N	38.18 E
Fajzabad	85	38.34 N	69.19 E
Fakahatchee Strand ♦	220	39.35 N	89.25 W
Fakaofo I[1]	14	9.22 S	171.14 W
Fakarava I[1]	14	16.20 S	145.37 W
Fakejev	80	48.57 N	49.56 E
Fakenham	42	52.50 N	0.51 E
Fakfak	164	2.55 S	132.18 E
Fakiragram	124	26.14 N	89.53 E
Fakiraj	106	47.50 N	127.26 E
Fakirganj	124	25.58 N	90.02 E
Fakel Šädiq	140	12.08 N	23.55 E
Fakrinkotti	128	18.01 N	31.20 E
Fakse	41	55.15 N	12.08 E
Fakse Bugt c	41	55.10 N	12.15 E
Fakse Ladeplads	41	55.13 N	12.11 E
Faku	114	42.30 N	123.24 E
Fal ≈	42	50.08 N	5.02 W
Faladyé	150	9.51 N	11.19 W
Falâkâta	124	26.32 N	89.12 E
Falam	110	22.55 N	93.40 E
Falâvarjân	128	32.33 N	51.30 E
Falcade	64	46.21 N	11.51 E
Falcão	256	22.17 S	44.16 W
Falciu	38	46.18 N	28.08 E
Falck	56	49.14 N	6.38 E
Falcognana di Sotto	267a	41.45 N	12.33 E
Falcon, Cap ⍈	34	35.46 N	0.48 W
Falcon, Cape ⍈	224	45.46 N	123.59 W
Falcón, Presa (Falcon Reservoir) ⍟[1]	196	26.37 N	99.11 W
Falconara Albanese	68	39.16 N	16.05 E
Falconara Alta	66	43.37 N	13.24 E
Falconara Marittima	66	43.37 N	13.24 E
Falconbridge	190	46.35 N	80.48 W
Falconcrest	285	39.58 N	75.33 W
Falcone	70	38.07 N	15.05 E
Falcone, Capo del ⍈	71	40.58 N	8.12 E
Falconer	214	42.07 N	79.11 W
Falcon Heights	202	42.08 N	121.45 W
Falconwood ♦[1]	196	26.37 N	99.11 W
Faldsled	41	55.09 N	10.09 E
Faleasao	174y	14.13 S	169.32 W
Falelatai	175a	13.55 S	171.59 W
Falelima	175a	13.32 S	172.41 W
Falémé ≈	150	14.46 N	12.14 W
Falenki	80	58.22 N	51.35 E
Falerii Novi ⍓	66	42.16 N	12.20 E
Falerone	66	43.07 N	13.27 E
Falfurrias	196	27.13 N	98.08 W
Falher	182	55.44 N	117.12 W
Falíraki	132	36.20 N	28.13 E
Fálirou, Órmos c	267c	37.56 N	23.40 E
Falkenberg, Dtsch.	54	52.48 N	13.58 E
Falkenberg, Dtsch.	54	51.35 N	13.14 E
Falkenberg, Sve.	26	56.54 N	12.28 E
Falkenhagen, Dtsch.	54	53.12 N	12.12 E
Falkenhagen, Dtsch.	54	52.28 N	14.15 E
Falkenhagener See ⍟	275a	52.33 N	13.10 E
Falkensee	54	52.34 N	13.04 E
Falkenstein	54	50.29 N	12.22 E
Falkenthal	54	52.54 N	13.17 E
Falkirk	46	56.00 N	3.48 W
Falkland, B.C., Can.	182	50.30 N	119.33 W
Falkland, Scot., U.K.	46	56.15 N	3.12 W
Falkland-Inseln — Falkland Islands ⍁[2]	254	51.45 S	59.00 W
Falkland Islands ⍁[2] S.A.	244	51.45 S	59.00 W
Falkland Islands ⍁[2], S.A.	254	51.45 S	59.00 W
Falkland Plateau ♦[1]	18	51.00 S	50.00 W
Falkland Sound ⊍	254	51.45 S	59.25 W
Falköping	26	58.10 N	13.31 E
Falkville	194	34.22 N	86.54 W
Fall, On., Can.	212	44.59 N	76.22 W
Fall, Ks., U.S.	198	37.24 N	95.40 W

Column 4

Nom	Page	Lat.	Long.
Fall ≈, Wa., U.S.	224	46.47 N	123.30 W
Falla	40	58.41 N	15.45 E
Fallbach	56	50.37 N	5.10 E
Fallbach	61	48.39 N	16.25 E
Fallbrook	228	33.22 N	117.15 W
Fallbrook Square ♦[9]	280	34.12 N	118.38 W
Fall City	224	47.34 N	121.53 W
Fall Creek	190	44.45 N	91.16 W
Fall Creek ≈, In., U.S.	218	39.47 N	86.11 W
Fall Creek ≈, N.Y., U.S.	210	42.28 N	76.31 W
Fall Creek Falls State Park ♦, Tn., U.S.	194	35.39 N	85.25 W
Fall Creek Falls State Park ♦, Tn., U.S.	194	35.35 N	85.25 W
Fallen Jerusalem I	240m	18.25 N	64.27 W
Fallen Leaf	226	38.53 N	120.04 W
Fallen Leaf Reservoir ⍟[1]	226	38.54 N	120.03 W
Fallentimber	214	40.41 N	78.30 W
Fallentimber Creek ≈	182	51.45 N	114.39 W
Fallen Timbers State Memorial ⍓	216	41.33 N	83.42 W
Fallersleben	54	52.25 N	10.43 E
Falli	46	56.06 N	3.52 W
Falling ≈	192	37.01 N	78.55 W
Fallingbostel	52	52.52 N	9.41 E
Falling Creek	208	37.26 N	77.26 W
Fallon, Mt., U.S.	198	46.50 N	105.07 W
Fallon, Nv., U.S.	204	39.28 N	118.46 W
Fall River, Ks., U.S.	198	37.36 N	96.01 W
Fall River, Ma., U.S.	207	41.42 N	71.09 W
Fall River, Wi., U.S.	190	43.23 N	89.02 W
Fall River Lake ⍟[1]	198	37.42 N	96.08 W
Fall River Mills	204	41.00 N	121.26 W
Falls	210	41.28 N	75.51 W
Falls ≈[6]	192	31.17 N	96.55 W
Fallsburg	210	41.44 N	74.36 W
Falls Church	208	38.53 N	77.11 W
Falls City, Ne., U.S.	198	40.03 N	95.36 W
Falls City, Or., U.S.	202	44.51 N	123.26 W
Falls Creek, Austl.	134	34.59 S	150.36 E
Falls Creek, Pa., U.S.	214	41.09 N	78.48 W
Falls Creek ≈	228	37.57 N	119.46 W
Fallsington	285	40.12 N	74.48 W
Falls Lake ⍟[1]	208	36.00 N	78.45 W
Falls Pond ⍟	283	41.58 N	71.20 W
Falls Run ≈	284b	39.22 N	76.52 W
Fallston	208	39.31 N	76.25 W
Falls Village	207	41.57 N	73.21 W
Falmer	260	50.51 N	0.04 W
Falmouth, Jam.	241q	18.30 N	77.39 W
Falmouth, Eng., U.K.	42	50.08 N	5.04 W
Falmouth, Ky., U.S.	218	38.40 N	84.19 W
Falmouth, Me., U.S.	188	43.43 N	70.14 W
Falmouth, Va., U.S.	208	38.19 N	77.28 W
Falmouth Bay c	42	50.05 N	5.01 W
Falmouth Heights	207	41.33 N	70.36 W
Falo I	174f	7.22 S	149.59 W
False Cape ⍈	208	36.39 N	76.51 W
False Divi Point ⍈	122	15.43 N	80.49 E
False Ducks Islands II	212	43.57 N	76.49 W
False Pass	180	54.52 N	163.24 W
Falset	34	41.08 N	0.49 E
Falsino ≈	250	0.56 N	51.35 W
Fal'sivyj Gelendžik	78	44.31 N	38.09 E
Falso, Cabo ⍈, Hond.	236	15.12 N	83.20 W
Falso, Cabo ⍈, Rep. Dom.	238	17.47 N	71.41 W
Falso Cabo de Hornos ⍈	254	55.43 S	68.05 W
Falster I	41	54.48 N	11.58 E
Falsterbo	41	55.24 N	12.50 E
Falticeni	38	47.28 N	26.18 E
Falun, Sve.	40	60.36 N	15.38 E
Falun, Zhg.	107	29.58 N	104.29 E
Falzarego, Passo di ⍊	64	46.31 N	12.00 E
Fam, Kepulauan II	164	0.40 S	130.15 E
Fama	256	21.25 S	46.51 W
Fama, Ouadi V	146	15.22 N	20.34 E
Famagusta — Gazimağusa	130	35.07 N	33.57 E
Famaillá	252	27.03 S	65.24 W
Famatina	252	28.55 S	67.31 W
Famatina, Sierra de ⍅	252	29.00 S	67.51 W
Fambach	54	50.44 N	10.22 E
Fameck	56	49.18 N	6.07 E
Famenne ⍈[1]	56	50.10 N	5.15 E
Familieureux	56	50.31 N	4.12 E
Family Lake ⍟	184	51.54 N	95.30 W
Family Tree ≈	220	28.53 N	81.55 W
Famjin	22	61.30 N	6.52 W
Fana ≈	66	43.57 N	6.22 W
Fanaco, Lago ⍟	70	37.40 N	13.33 E
Fanad Head ⍈	48	55.16 N	7.38 W
Fanambana	157b	13.34 S	50.00 E
Fanan I	175c	7.11 N	151.59 E
Fanaro	64	44.24 N	10.47 E
Fanârah	142	30.17 N	32.21 E
Fancrang	105	31.07 N	118.12 E
Fanch'eng	102	32.03 N	112.01 E
Fancher, Il., U.S.	210	43.16 N	78.04 W
Fanchon, Pointe ⍈	238	18.26 N	74.29 W
Fanchuan	241h	22.08 N	121.45 E
Fancy	241h	13.22 N	61.11 W
Fancy Creek ≈	198	39.28 N	96.45 W
Fancy Prairie	216	40.02 N	89.39 W
Fandriana	157b	20.14 S	47.23 E
Fane ≈	64	53.57 N	6.22 W
Fanepura	123	31.29 N	72.54 E
Faneromeni Monastery ⍓	267c	37.59 N	23.26 E
Fang	110	19.55 N	99.13 E
Fangaga ≈	140	17.30 N	36.01 E
Fangak	140	9.04 N	30.53 E
Fangcheng, Zhg.	100	31.42 N	119.06 E
Fangcheng, Zhg.	102	33.18 N	113.00 E
Fangdao	100	27.01 N	118.06 E
Fängesee ⍟	264a	52.44 N	13.50 E
Fangfu	100	28.45 N	119.03 E
Fanggang	105	31.54 N	115.35 E
Fangjiazhuang	100	34.24 N	120.26 E
Fangliao	114	22.22 N	120.35 E
Fangniu	106	32.13 N	118.11 E
Fangshan, Zhg.	100	34.55 N	111.10 E
Fang Shan ⍐[2]	106	31.29 N	119.09 E
Fangshen	106	31.54 N	122.05 E
Fangshengbu	100	30.20 N	104.54 E
Fangtai	100	31.19 N	120.47 E
Fangxian	102	32.03 N	110.45 E
Fangxincun	100	30.41 N	113.37 E
Fangzheng	106	45.50 N	128.50 E
Fanhões	266c	38.53 N	9.09 W
Fanipol	76	53.45 N	27.20 E
Fanjakana	157b	20.45 S	46.33 E
Fanjiadian	104	41.41 N	121.15 W
Fanjiatun	100	43.40 N	125.12 E
Fanjiazhuang	100	39.12 N	117.20 E

Column 5

Nom	Page	Lat.	Long.
Fannaråki ⍐	26	61.31 N	7.55 E
Fannettsburg	214	40.04 N	77.50 W
Fannich, Loch ⍟	46	57.38 N	5.00 W
Fanrem	26	63.16 N	9.50 E
Fanny, Mount ⍐	202	45.20 N	117.41 W
Fanny Bay	182	49.30 N	124.50 W
Fano	66	43.50 N	13.01 E
Fanø I	26	55.25 N	8.25 E
Fanning, Col des ⍊	100	28.48 N	121.10 E
Fans, Col dos ⍊	62	44.56 N	4.47 E
Fanshan, Zhg.	100	27.21 N	120.24 E
Fanshan, Zhg.	105	40.13 N	115.25 E
Fanshang	106	31.40 N	120.01 E
Fanshawe Lake ⍟	212	43.05 N	81.10 W
Fansher Creek ≈	214	42.37 N	82.01 W
Fanshui	100	33.07 N	119.25 E
Fan Si Pan ⍐	110	22.15 N	103.46 E
Fantasy Island ♦	284a	43.02 N	78.58 W
Fanthyttan	40	59.40 N	15.06 E
Fanwood	276	40.38 N	74.23 W
Fanxian	102	35.57 N	115.38 E
Fanzhen	98	36.14 N	117.21 E
Faoïleann, Bàgh nam c	46	57.23 N	7.17 W
Faradofay	157b	25.02 S	47.00 E
Farafangana	157b	22.49 S	47.50 E
Farâfirah, Al-Wāhat al- ⍈	140	27.15 N	28.10 E
Farâh	128	32.22 N	62.07 E
Farâh ⍁[1]	128	33.00 N	62.30 E
Farâh ≈	128	31.29 N	61.24 E
Farahābād	267d	35.41 N	51.25 E
Farahâlana	157b	14.26 S	50.10 E
Farā id, Jabal al- ⍐	140	23.31 N	35.20 E
Fara in Sabina	66	42.12 N	12.43 E
Farallón, Paso del ⍈	288	34.41 S	57.57 W
Farallón de Medinilla I	108	16.01 N	146.04 E
Farallón de Pajaros I	108	20.32 N	144.54 E
Farallón Islands II	204	37.43 N	123.03 W
Farânah	150	12.03 N	4.40 W
Farângi Samariás (Samaria Gorge) V	38	35.18 N	24.00 E
Fara Novarese	62	45.33 N	8.27 E
Farasān, Jazā ir I	144	16.48 N	41.54 E
Farasān al-Kabīr I	144	16.48 N	41.54 E
Faratsiho	157b	19.24 S	46.57 E
Faraulep I[1]	108	8.36 N	144.33 E
Farber	219	39.16 N	91.34 W
Farbovano	78	50.09 N	31.51 E
Farcău, Vîrful ⍐	38	47.56 N	24.27 E
Farchant	64	47.32 N	11.06 E
Farcy	261	48.31 N	2.37 E
Fardes ≈	34	37.35 N	3.00 W
Fareham	42	50.51 N	1.10 W
Fåreveile	41	55.48 N	11.27 E
Farewell	180	62.31 N	153.53 W
Farewell, Cape ⍈	172	40.30 S	172.40 E
Farewell Spit ⍈[2]	172	40.31 S	172.52 E
Färgelanda	26	58.56 N	12.02 E
Farginiers	50	43.39 N	3.19 E
Fargo	198	46.52 N	96.47 W
Faria ≈	266c	38.40 N	9.20 W
Färi ah, Wādī al- V	132	32.06 N	35.31 E
Faribault	190	44.17 N	93.16 W
Faribault, Lac ⍟	176	59.00 N	72.00 W
Faridābad	124	28.26 N	77.19 E
Farīdkot	124	30.40 N	74.45 E
Farīdnagar	267e	28.46 N	77.37 E
Faridpur, Bngl.	124	23.36 N	89.50 E
Faridpur, Bngl.	124	23.36 N	89.50 E
Faridpur, India	124	28.13 N	79.33 E
Färila	40	61.48 N	15.51 E
Farilhões II	34	39.28 N	9.34 W
Farîm	150	35.43 N	59.53 E
Farina	166	30.04 S	138.17 E
Farington	42	53.43 N	2.40 W
Farinha ≈	250	6.51 S	47.30 W
Farini d'Olmo	64	44.51 N	9.44 E
Fariş	85	40.35 N	66.52 E
Fariskūr	142	31.20 N	31.46 E
Farit, Amba ⍐	140	11.45 N	38.00 E
Fariza	34	41.33 N	6.18 W
Farjestaden	26	56.39 N	16.27 E
Farkasréti Temető ♦	265a	47.29 N	19.00 E
Farkhor	85	37.30 N	69.24 E
Farleigh	42	51.19 N	0.02 W
Farley Green	260	51.11 N	0.28 W
Farley, Il., U.S.	219	38.51 N	89.51 W
Farlington	42	53.14 N	1.15 W
Farmers	218	38.07 N	83.33 W
Farmer City	216	40.14 N	88.39 W
Farmers Branch	222	32.55 N	96.53 W
Farmersburg	216	39.15 N	87.23 W
Farmers Fork ≈	198	38.02 N	76.45 W
Farmer's Museum ⍓	210	42.42 N	74.55 W
Farmer's Retreat	218	38.58 N	85.06 W
Farmersville, Il., U.S.	216	36.17 N	119.12 W
Farmersville, Pa., U.S.	219	39.26 N	89.39 W
Farmersville Station	210	42.26 N	78.22 W
Farmerville	194	32.46 N	92.24 W
Farmingdale, N.J., U.S.	285	40.11 N	74.10 W
Farmingdale, N.Y., U.S.	276	40.43 N	73.26 W
Farmington, Ca., U.S.	226	37.56 N	120.59 W
Farmington, Ct., U.S.	207	41.43 N	72.49 W
Farmington, De., U.S.	208	38.52 N	75.34 W
Farmington, Il., U.S.	190	40.41 N	90.00 W
Farmington, Mi., U.S.	216	42.27 N	83.23 W
Farmington, Mo., U.S.	190	44.38 N	93.08 W
Farmington, N.H., U.S.	188	43.23 N	71.03 W
Farmington, Ut., U.S.	200	40.58 N	111.53 W
Farmington, West Branch ≈	207	41.54 N	72.38 W
Farmington Flood Control Basin ♦[1]	226	37.55 N	120.55 W
Farmington Hills	216	42.29 N	83.24 W
Far Mountain ⍐	182	52.46 N	125.17 W
Farm Pond ⍟, Ma., U.S.	283	42.17 N	71.26 W
Farm Pond ⍟, Ma., U.S.	283	42.17 N	71.26 W
Farmville, N.C., U.S.	192	35.35 N	77.35 W
Farmville, Va., U.S.	192	37.18 N	78.23 W
Färna	40	59.47 N	15.51 E
Farnam	198	40.42 N	100.12 W
Farnaẉā ≈	142	30.59 N	30.39 E

Column 6

Nom	Page	Lat.	Long.
Farnborough ♦[3]	260	51.21 N	0.04 E
Farncombe	260	51.12 N	0.36 W
Farncombe	44	53.05 N	0.51 W
Färneboljärden ⍟	40	60.14 N	16.47 E
Farne Islands II	44	55.38 N	1.38 W
Farnham, P.Q., Can.	206	45.17 N	72.59 W
Farnham, Eng., U.K.	42	51.13 N	0.49 W
Farnham, N.Y., U.S.	214	42.36 N	79.05 W
Farnham, Ya., U.S.	208	37.53 N	76.37 W
Farnham, Mount ⍐	182	50.29 N	116.30 W
Farnham Common	260	51.33 N	0.37 W
Farnham Royal	260	51.32 N	0.37 W
Farnhamville	198	42.16 N	94.24 W
Farningham	261	51.23 N	0.13 E
Farnroda	54	50.56 N	10.23 E
Farnworth, Eng., U.K.	44	53.33 N	2.24 W
Farnworth, Eng., U.K.	262	53.23 N	2.44 W
Faro, Bra.	250	2.11 S	56.44 W
Faro, Port.	34	37.01 N	7.56 W
Faro ⍈[5]	34	37.15 N	8.00 W
Faro ≈	146	9.21 N	12.55 E
Faro, Punta del ⍈	70	38.16 N	15.39 E
Faro, Réserve du ♦[4]	146	8.10 N	12.35 E
Färöar — Faeroe Islands ⍁[2]	22	62.00 N	7.00 W
Fårö I	26	57.56 N	19.08 E
Fårösund	26	57.52 N	19.03 E
Farquhar, Cape ⍈	162	23.37 S	113.37 E
Farquhar Group I[1]	138	10.10 S	51.10 E
Farr	46	57.21 N	4.12 W
Farra d'Isonzo	64	45.56 N	13.31 E
Farragut	198	40.43 N	95.28 W
Farragut State Recreation Area ♦	202	47.55 N	116.35 W
Farrandsville	210	41.10 N	77.31 W
Farrar ≈	46	57.24 N	4.50 W
Farrar Pond ⍟	283	42.25 N	71.21 W
Farrars Creek ≈	166	25.35 S	140.43 E
Farrarsband	128	28.53 N	52.06 E
Farrell	214	41.12 N	80.29 W
Farrell Flat	168b	33.50 S	138.47 E
Farrer Park ♦	271c	1.19 N	103.51 E
Farrington Lake ⍟	276	40.26 N	74.28 W
Farrington Lake ⍟	276	40.26 N	74.27 W
Far Rockaway ♦[9]	276	40.36 N	73.45 W
Farrukhābād	124	27.24 N	79.34 E
Farrukhnagar, India	124	28.27 N	76.49 E
Farrukhnagar, India	272a	28.43 N	77.23 E
Färs ⍁[4]	128	29.00 N	53.00 E
Fârsala	132	39.18 N	22.23 E
Farschviller	56	49.06 N	6.54 E
Fârsî	128	27.58 N	50.11 E
Fârsî, Jazîreh-ye I	128	27.58 N	50.11 E
Farsis	142	30.40 N	31.14 E
Farsø	26	56.47 N	9.21 E
Farsta	40	59.14 N	18.04 E
Farsund	26	58.05 N	6.48 E
Fartak, Ra's ⍈	118	15.38 N	52.15 E
Farukolu I	122	6.12 N	73.16 E
Farum	41	55.49 N	12.22 E
Fårvang	41	56.16 N	9.44 E
Farvel, Kap ⍈	176	59.45 N	44.00 W
Farwell, Mi., U.S.	190	43.50 N	84.52 W
Farwell, Tx., U.S.	196	30.15 N	103.15 W
Färyāb ⍁[4]	128	36.00 N	65.00 E
Fasā	128	28.56 N	53.42 E
Fašková	61	48.56 N	18.40 E
Fashkeh, 'Ayn ⍇[4]	132	31.43 N	35.27 E
Fāsjön ⍟	40	59.36 N	14.58 E
Faskrudhsfjördhur	24a	64.55 N	14.01 W
Fassa	150	13.26 N	8.15 W
Fassberg	52	52.54 N	10.10 E
Fasterholt	41	56.01 N	9.07 E
Fastnet Rock I[2]	48	51.24 N	9.35 W
Fasto	78	50.06 N	29.55 E
Fastoveckaja	75	54.44 N	40.09 E
Fatagar Tuting, Tanjung ⍈	164	2.46 S	131.57 E
Fataki	154	4.46 S	28.11 E
Fatala ≈	150	10.13 N	14.00 W
Fatatá	140	8.05 N	31.48 E
Fathom Five National Marine Park ♦	190	45.15 N	81.40 W
Fatick	150	14.20 N	16.25 W
Fatick ⍈[1]	150	14.30 N	16.40 W
Fatigue, Mount ⍐	168	34.33 S	146.18 E
Fatima, Arg.	258	34.26 S	59.04 W
Fátima, Cór.	34	39.37 N	8.39 W
Fatima do Sul	250	22.16 S	54.25 W
Fatima do Sul	250	22.16 S	54.25 W
Fāṭimah, Wādī V	144	21.27 N	39.10 E
Fatoʼz	76	52.07 N	35.52 E
Fatsa	130	41.02 N	37.31 E
Fatu — Foshan	100	23.03 N	113.09 E
Fat Tong Point ⍈	271d	22.16 N	114.15 E
Fatu-Berlo	58	8.56 S	125.52 E
Fatula	250	7.36 S	39.29 W
Fatumu	174w	21.13 S	175.07 W
Fatwā	152	4.08 S	17.13 E
Fauabu	175e	8.34 S	160.43 E
Faucigny	58	46.11 N	6.27 E
Faucille, Col de la ⍊	58	46.22 N	6.02 E
Faucogney-et- la-Mer	58	47.51 N	6.34 E
Faucon- Barcelonnette	62	44.24 N	6.41 E
Faulhorn ⍐	58	46.40 N	8.05 E
Faulkton	198	45.01 N	99.07 W
Fauquembergues	50	50.36 N	2.05 E
Faure Island I	162	25.51 S	113.53 E
Fauresmith	156	29.42 S	25.21 E
Fauro Island I	175e	6.55 S	156.05 E
Fauske	26	67.15 N	15.24 E
Faustovo	265b	55.22 N	38.29 E
Fauville-en-Caux	50	49.39 N	0.34 E
Faux-Cap	157b	25.35 S	45.32 E
Fauville	157b	25.37 S	45.32 E
Fåvang	26	61.27 N	10.11 E
Favara	70	37.19 N	13.39 E
Favara ≈	44	47.46 N	0.06 E
Faverges	58	45.45 N	6.18 E
Faversham	42	51.20 N	0.54 E
Favignana	70	37.56 N	12.20 E
Favignana, Isola I	70	37.56 N	12.19 E
Favoriten ♦[8]	266b	48.11 N	16.23 E
Favourable Lake ⍟	184	52.53 N	93.56 W
Favrieux	261	48.58 N	1.39 E
Fawcett	182	54.32 N	114.05 W
Fawcett Lake ⍟	182	54.19 N	113.05 W
Fawkham Green	261	51.19 N	0.17 E
Fawkner	274b	37.43 S	144.58 E
Fawkner Park ♦	274b	37.50 S	144.59 E
Fawley	42	50.49 N	1.20 W

ENGLISH / DEUTSCH

Name	Page / Seite	Lat.°′ / Breite°′	Long.°′ / Länge°′ E = Ost
Fawn ≃, On., Can.	**176**	55.22 N	88.20 W
Fawn ≃, U.S.	**216**	41.51 N	85.40 W
Fawn Grove	**208**	39.44 N	76.27 W
Fawnie Nose ∧	**182**	53.16 N	125.08 W
Fawnie Range ⋀	**182**	53.10 N	125.00 W
Fawsett Farms	**284c**	38.59 N	77.14 W
Faxaflói ⊂	**24a**	64.25 N	23.00 W
Faxälven ≃	**26**	63.13 N	17.13 E
Faxinal	**255**	23.59 S	51.22 W
Faxinal do Soturno	**252**	29.37 S	53.26 W
Faxon	**210**	41.15 N	76.58 W
Faya	**146**	17.55 N	19.07 E
Fayd	**128**	27.07 N	42.27 E
Fayence	**62**	43.37 N	6.41 E
Fayerweather Island I	**276**	41.08 N	73.13 W
Fayette, Al., U.S.	**194**	33.41 N	87.49 W
Fayette, Ia., U.S.	**190**	42.50 N	91.48 W
Fayette, Ms., U.S.	**194**	31.42 N	91.03 W
Fayette, Mo., U.S.	**194**	39.08 N	92.41 W
Fayette, N.Y., U.S.	**210**	42.49 N	76.49 W
Fayette, Oh., U.S.	**216**	41.40 N	84.19 W
Fayette □[6], Il., U.S.	**219**	38.58 N	89.06 W
Fayette □[6], In., U.S.	**218**	39.39 N	85.08 W
Fayette □[6], Ky., U.S.	**218**	38.07 N	84.30 W
Fayette □[6], Oh., U.S.	**218**	39.32 N	83.26 W
Fayette □[6], Pa., U.S.	**214**	40.05 N	79.39 W
Fayette □[6], Tx., U.S.	**222**	29.50 N	96.57 W
Fayette, Lake ⊜[1]	**222**	29.56 N	96.44 W
Fayette City	**214**	40.06 N	79.50 W
Fayetteville, Ar., U.S.	**194**	36.03 N	94.09 W
Fayetteville, Ga., U.S.	**192**	33.26 N	84.27 W
Fayetteville, Il., U.S.	**219**	38.22 N	89.48 W
Fayetteville, N.Y., U.S.	**210**	43.02 N	76.00 W
Fayetteville, N.C., U.S.	**192**	35.03 N	78.52 W
Fayetteville, Oh., U.S.	**218**	39.11 N	83.55 W
Fayetteville, Pa., U.S.	**208**	39.54 N	77.33 W
Fayetteville, Tn., U.S.	**194**	35.09 N	86.34 W
Fayetteville, Tx., U.S.	**222**	29.54 N	96.41 W
Fayetteville, W.V., U.S.	**188**	38.03 N	81.06 W
Faylakah I	**128**	29.27 N	48.20 E
Fayl-Billot	**58**	47.47 N	5.36 E
Fayrā	**144**	13.17 N	43.25 E
Fay-sur-Lignon	**62**	44.59 N	4.14 E
Fayville	**207**	42.17 N	71.30 W
Fayyum → Al-Fayyūm	**142**	29.19 N	30.50 E
Fažana	**64**	44.55 N	13.49 E
Fazao	**150**	8.42 N	0.46 E
Fazao, Parc National du ♦	**150**	8.40 N	0.42 E
Fazeley	**42**	52.37 N	1.42 W
Fazenda de Cima	**248**	15.56 S	56.37 W
Fazenda Libongo	**152**	8.24 S	13.24 E
Fazenda Nova	**255**	16.11 S	50.48 W
Fāzilka	**123**	30.24 N	74.02 E
Fāzilpur	**120**	29.18 N	70.27 E
Fazzān (Fezzan) □[9]	**146**	26.00 N	14.00 E
Fdérik	**148**	22.41 N	12.43 W
Feale ≃	**48**	52.28 N	9.40 W
Fear, Cape ›	**192**	33.50 N	77.58 W
Fearnhead	**262**	53.25 N	2.33 W
Feasterville	**208**	40.08 N	75.00 W
Feather ≃	**204**	38.47 N	121.36 W
Feather, Middle Fork ≃	**204**	39.34 N	121.26 W
Feather, North Fork ≃	**204**	39.34 N	121.28 W
Feather, North Fork, East Branch ≃	**204**	40.01 N	121.13 W
Feather, South Fork ≃	**204**	39.33 N	121.28 W
Featherbed Top ∧	**262**	53.26 N	1.52 W
Featherly Regional Park ♦	**280**	33.52 N	117.42 W
Featherston	**172**	41.07 S	175.20 E
Featherstone, Eng., U.K.	**44**	53.41 N	1.21 W
Featherstone, Zimb.	**154**	18.42 S	30.49 E
Feathertop, Mount ∧	**166**	36.54 S	147.08 E
Fécamp	**50**	49.45 N	0.22 E
Fedala → Mohammedia	**148**	33.44 N	7.24 W
Fedderwardergroden	**52**	53.35 N	8.05 E
Feddet ›[1]	**41**	55.09 N	12.07 E
Federación	**252**	31.00 S	57.54 W
Federal, Arg.	**252**	30.57 S	58.48 W
Federal, Pa., U.S.	**279b**	40.23 N	80.09 W
Federal Capital Territory □[3]	**150**	9.00 N	7.15 E
Federalsburg	**208**	38.41 N	75.46 W
Federal Territory □[8]	**273a**	6.29 N	3.25 E
Federal Way	**224**	47.19 N	122.18 W
Federation Forest State Park ♦	**224**	47.09 N	121.40 W
Federsee ⊜	**58**	48.05 N	9.38 E
Fedeshk	**128**	32.45 N	58.50 E
Fedje	**26**	60.47 N	4.42 E
Fedorino	**82**	55.08 N	36.06 E
Fedosejevka	**80**	46.53 N	44.00 E
Fedosejevskaja	**24**	62.07 N	40.42 E
Fedosicha	**86**	54.47 N	81.54 E
Fedosjino	**82**	55.08 N	38.30 E
Fedotovo	**82**	55.41 N	39.12 E
Feeagh, Lough ⊜	**48**	53.55 N	9.36 W
Feeding Hills	**207**	42.04 N	72.40 W
Feerfeer	**144**	8.30 N	47.55 E
Feesburg	**218**	38.52 N	83.58 W
Fefan I	**175c**	7.21 N	151.51 E
Fehérgyarmat	**30**	47.58 N	22.32 E
Fehmarn I	**54**	54.28 N	11.08 E
Fehmarnbelt (Femer Bælt) ɥ	**41**	54.35 N	11.15 E
Fehmarnsund ɥ	**54**	54.24 N	11.07 E
Fehrbellin	**54**	52.49 N	12.46 E
Fehring	**61**	46.56 N	16.01 E
Feia, Lagoa ⊂	**255**	22.00 S	41.20 W
Feicheng	**98**	36.15 N	116.46 E
Feichten	**58**	47.02 N	10.44 E
Feidong	**100**	31.52 N	117.29 E
Feignies	**50**	50.18 N	3.55 E
Feigumfossen ∟	**26**	61.23 N	7.26 E
Feiheji	**100**	33.36 N	115.36 E
Fei Huang ≃	**100**	33.35 N	119.02 E
Feijó	**248**	8.09 S	70.21 W
Feiketu	**89**	45.46 N	127.09 E
Feilding	**172**	40.13 S	175.34 E
Feiler ∧	**64**	47.07 N	10.52 E
Feiliqiao	**106**	31.05 N	119.05 E
Feilitzsch	**54**	50.22 N	11.56 E
Feilong, Zhg.	**107**	30.25 N	106.20 E
Feilong, Zhg.	**107**	30.36 N	105.54 E
Feilongguan	**107**	28.57 N	105.05 E
Feiluan	**100**	26.35 N	119.35 E
Feira	**154**	15.37 S	30.25 E
Feira de Santana	**255**	12.15 S	38.57 W
Feistritz ≃	**61**	47.01 N	16.08 E
Feistritz an der Gail	**64**	46.34 N	13.36 E
Feistritzer Spitze ∧	**61**	46.31 N	14.45 E
Feixi	**100**	31.42 N	117.10 E
Feixian	**98**	35.18 N	117.57 E
Feixiang	**98**	36.34 N	114.49 E
Feiyun ≃	**100**	27.48 N	120.36 E
Fejaj, Chott ≡	**148**	33.55 N	9.10 E
Fejér □[6]	**30**	47.10 N	18.35 E
Fejø I	**41**	54.57 N	11.26 E
Feke	**130**	37.53 N	35.58 E
Feklistova, ostrov I	**89**	55.02 N	136.55 E
Felâhiye	**130**	39.06 N	35.35 E
Felanitx	**34**	39.28 N	3.08 E
Felbertauerntunnel ◆[5]	**64**	47.08 N	12.31 E
Felda	**220**	26.33 N	81.26 W
Felda ≃, Dtsch.	**56**	50.42 N	9.03 E
Felda ≃, Dtsch.	**56**	50.51 N	10.05 E
Feldafing	**64**	47.57 N	11.17 E
Feldaist ≃	**61**	48.19 N	14.34 E
Feld am See	**64**	46.47 N	13.45 E
Feldbach	**61**	46.57 N	15.54 E
Feldberg, Dtsch.	**54**	53.20 N	13.26 E
Feldberg, Dtsch.	**58**	47.51 N	8.02 E
Feldberg ∧	**58**	47.52 N	8.00 E
Felderbach ≃	**263**	51.22 N	7.08 E
Feldhausen ◆[8]	**263**	51.37 N	6.59 E
Feldis	**58**	46.48 N	9.26 E
Feldkirch	**58**	47.14 N	9.36 E
Feldkirchen an der Donau	**61**	48.21 N	14.03 E
Feldkirchen bei Graz	**61**	47.01 N	15.27 E
Feldkirchen in Kärnten	**61**	46.43 N	14.05 E
Feldmark	**263**	51.41 N	6.38 E
Feldstetten	**58**	48.28 N	9.37 E
Felhit	**144**	16.43 N	38.02 E
Feliciano, Méx.	**234**	18.01 N	101.58 W
Feliciano, P.R.	**240m**	18.28 N	67.08 W
Feliciano, Arroyo ≃	**252**	31.06 S	59.54 W
Felicity	**218**	38.50 N	84.05 W
Felina	**64**	44.27 N	10.27 E
Felino	**64**	44.42 N	10.15 E
Felipe Carrillo Puerto, Méx.	**234**	21.09 N	104.52 W
Felipe Carrillo Puerto, Méx.	**234**	19.08 N	102.42 W
Felix, Cape ›	**176**	69.54 N	97.50 W
Felix, Rio ≃	**196**	33.08 N	104.19 W
Felixburg	**154**	19.29 S	30.51 E
Felixdorf	**61**	47.53 N	16.15 E
Felixlândia	**255**	18.47 S	44.55 W
Felixstowe	**42**	51.58 N	1.20 E
Felixton	**158**	28.50 S	31.53 E
Félix U. Gómez	**232**	29.50 N	111.30 W
Felizzano	**62**	44.54 N	8.26 E
Fella ≃	**64**	46.21 N	13.07 E
Fellbach	**56**	48.48 N	9.15 E
Felletin	**32**	45.53 N	2.10 E
Felling	**44**	54.57 N	1.33 W
Fellingsbro	**40**	59.26 N	15.35 E
Fellows	**226**	35.11 N	119.32 W
Fellows Creek ≃	**281**	42.17 N	83.26 W
Fellowship	**285**	39.55 N	74.58 W
Fellsburg	**214**	40.11 N	79.49 W
Fellsmere	**220**	27.46 N	80.36 W
Fellwick	**285**	40.08 N	75.11 W
Felpham	**42**	50.47 N	0.39 W
Felsberg	**56**	51.08 N	9.25 E
Felső-Válicka ≃	**61**	46.52 N	16.53 E
Feltham ◆[8]	**260**	51.27 N	0.24 W
Felt Lake ⊜	**282**	37.23 N	122.11 W
Felton, Ca., U.S.	**226**	37.03 N	122.04 W
Felton, De., U.S.	**208**	39.00 N	75.34 W
Felton, Pa., U.S.	**208**	39.51 N	76.34 W
Feltre	**64**	46.01 N	11.54 E
Felts Mills	**212**	44.01 N	75.46 W
Feltwell	**42**	52.29 N	0.32 E
Femer Bælt (Fehmarnbelt) ɥ	**41**	54.35 N	11.15 E
Femme Osage Creek ≃	**219**	38.39 N	90.44 W
Femmøller	**41**	56.14 N	10.35 E
Femø I	**41**	54.58 N	11.33 E
Femund ⊜	**26**	62.12 N	11.52 E
Femundsenden	**26**	61.55 N	11.55 E
Femundsmarka Nasjonalpark ♦	**26**	62.20 N	12.07 E
Fen ≃	**102**	35.36 N	110.42 E
Fena Valley Reservoir ⊜[1]	**174p**	13.21 N	144.42 E
Fendaozi	**104**	41.35 N	120.51 E
Fenelon Falls	**212**	44.32 N	78.45 W
Fenelton	**214**	40.52 N	79.44 W
Fener ◆[8]	**267b**	41.02 N	28.56 E
Fenerbahce Stadium ♦	**267b**	40.59 N	29.02 E
Fener Burnu ›	**130**	41.07 N	39.25 E
Fener Tepesi ∧[2]	**267b**	41.09 N	28.47 E
Fenestrelle	**62**	45.02 N	7.03 E
Fénétrange	**56**	48.51 N	7.01 E
Feng ≃	**105**	39.25 N	116.57 E
Fengcheng, Zhg.	**98**	40.27 N	124.02 E
Fengcheng, Zhg.	**100**	28.10 N	115.46 E
Fengcheng, Zhg.	**102**	38.32 N	101.50 E
Fengcheng, Zhg.	**106**	30.55 N	121.38 E
Fengdengwu	**105**	39.42 N	117.55 E
Fengdian	**107**	30.41 N	104.51 E
Fengdu	**102**	29.58 N	107.41 E
Fengfeng	**98**	36.28 N	114.14 E
Fenggang, Zhg.	**100**	28.34 N	116.34 E
Fenggang, Zhg.	**102**	27.58 N	107.47 E
Fenggaopu	**107**	29.24 N	105.41 E
Fenghua	**100**	29.40 N	121.24 E
Fenghuang, Zhg.	**100**	23.58 N	116.44 E
Fenghuang, Zhg.	**102**	24.25 N	107.17 E
Fenghuang, Zhg.	**102**	27.58 N	109.19 E
Fenghuang, Zhg.	**106**	31.21 N	121.44 E
Fenghuangchang	**107**	29.44 N	106.19 E
Fenghuang Shan ∧	**107**	28.54 N	106.35 E
Fenghuanjing	**100**	31.11 N	117.49 E
Fenghui	**100**	29.56 N	120.58 E
Fengjia, Zhg.	**98**	37.03 N	121.42 E
Fengjia, Zhg.	**104**	42.35 N	122.30 E
Fengjiabao	**102**	36.12 N	104.49 E
Fengjiakou	**98**	38.11 N	116.44 E
Fengjianjiao	**106**	30.41 N	120.51 E
Fengjiatun	**104**	41.14 N	122.00 E
Fengjiawopeng	**104**	42.19 N	123.40 E
Fengjiaxiang	**106**	30.56 N	121.06 E
Fengjie	**102**	31.03 N	109.31 E
Fengjing	**106**	30.53 N	121.01 E
Fengkou	**100**	30.05 N	113.18 E
Fengle, Zhg.	**89**	45.47 N	125.26 E
Fengle, Zhg.	**100**	27.13 N	118.11 E
Fenglezhen	**98**	36.14 N	114.18 E
Fengliang	**100**	23.59 N	116.14 E
Fenglin, T'aiwan	**100**	23.45 N	121.26 E
Fenglin, Zhg.	**100**	28.19 N	120.46 E
Fengling Guan)(	**100**	28.14 N	118.29 E
Fenglingtou	**100**	28.26 N	117.50 E
Fengman	**89**	43.46 N	126.41 E
Fengnan (Xugezhuang)	**105**	39.34 N	118.06 E
Fengning (Dagezhen)	**98**	41.12 N	116.32 E
Fengpin	**100**	23.36 N	121.31 E
Fengpingzi	**102**	32.46 N	105.12 E
Fengqiao, Zhg.	**100**	29.46 N	120.26 E
Fengqiao, Zhg.	**106**	31.19 N	120.33 E
Fengqing	**102**	24.46 N	99.52 E
Fengqiu	**98**	35.05 N	114.25 E
Fengrun	**105**	39.50 N	118.07 E
Fengshan, Zhg.	**89**	46.22 N	128.30 E
Fengshan, Zhg.	**98**	41.14 N	117.05 E
Fengshan, Zhg.	**102**	22.01 N	109.59 E
Fengshi	**100**	24.42 N	116.34 E
Fengshun	**100**	23.48 N	116.11 E
Fengtai, Zhg.	**100**	32.44 N	116.43 E
Fengtai, Zhg.	**105**	39.51 N	116.16 E
Fengtian, Zhg.	**100**	27.24 N	114.43 E
Fengtian, Zhg.	**100**	25.46 N	115.30 E
Fengtien → Shenyang	**104**	41.48 N	123.27 E
Fengting	**100**	25.16 N	118.54 E
Fengwan	**100**	24.48 N	113.50 E
Fengxi	**102**	31.48 N	109.50 E
Fengxian, Zhg.	**98**	34.42 N	116.34 E
Fengxian, Zhg.	**102**	33.57 N	106.44 E
Fengxian, Zhg.	**106**	30.55 N	121.27 E
Fengxiang	**102**	34.29 N	107.29 E
Fengxin	**100**	28.43 N	115.23 E
Fengyang, Zhg.	**100**	32.52 N	117.34 E
Fengyang, Zhg.	**100**	24.49 N	117.53 E
Fengyi	**102**	31.44 N	103.53 E
Fengyu	**100**	26.31 N	119.18 E
Fengyüan	**100**	24.15 N	120.43 E
Fengzhen	**102**	40.24 N	113.09 E
Fengzhou	**100**	25.41 N	113.52 E
Fengzhuangtou	**106**	31.00 N	118.39 E
Fenholloway ≃	**192**	29.59 N	83.47 W
Fen Hu ⊜	**106**	31.00 N	120.47 E
Feni	**124**	23.00 N	91.24 E
Fenicia Moncata ⏊	**70**	37.33 N	14.57 E
Feni Islands II	**14**	4.05 S	153.42 E
Fenimore Pass ɥ	**180**	52.00 N	175.35 W
Fenino	**265b**	55.44 N	37.57 E
Fenis	**62**	45.44 N	7.29 E
Feniscowles	**262**	53.43 N	2.32 W
Fenjie	**106**	32.17 N	120.20 E
Fennimore	**190**	42.59 N	90.39 W
Fennville	**216**	42.35 N	86.06 W
Fenny Compton	**42**	52.09 N	1.20 W
Fenny Stratford	**42**	52.00 N	0.43 W
Feno, Capo di ›, Fr.	**36**	41.57 N	8.36 E
Feno, Capo di ›, Fr.	**71**	41.23 N	9.06 E
Fenoarivo, Madag.	**157b**	18.26 S	46.34 E
Fenoarivo, Madag.	**157b**	21.43 S	46.24 E
Fenoarivo, Madag.	**157b**	20.52 S	46.53 E
Fenoarivo Atsinanana	**157b**	17.22 S	49.25 E
Fensfjorden ⊂[2]	**26**	60.51 N	4.50 E
Fenshui	**104**	40.41 N	122.32 E
Fenshui ≃	**100**	29.49 N	119.41 E
Fenshui'ao	**100**	25.20 N	114.43 E
Fenshuidunshen	**106**	31.30 N	120.01 E
Fenshuiling, Zhg.	**107**	28.51 N	105.35 E
Fenshuiling, Zhg.	**107**	30.20 N	105.15 E
Fenshuipu	**107**	30.05 N	104.05 E
Fenshuizhen	**107**	29.44 N	103.55 E
Fenshuizui	**100**	30.35 N	113.38 E
Fensmark	**41**	55.17 N	11.49 E
Fenstanton	**42**	52.18 N	0.04 W
Fenton, Mi., U.S.	**216**	42.47 N	83.42 W
Fenton, Mo., U.S.	**219**	38.32 N	90.22 W
Fenton, Lake ⊜	**216**	42.50 N	83.43 W
Fentou	**105**	38.53 N	116.32 E
Fentress	**222**	29.45 N	97.47 W
Fenway Park ♦	**283**	42.21 N	71.06 W
Fenwick	**188**	38.13 N	80.34 W
Fenwick Island ›[1]	**208**	38.25 N	75.03 W
Fenyang	**102**	37.17 N	111.48 E
Fenyi	**100**	27.47 N	114.42 E
Feodosija	**78**	45.02 N	35.23 E
Feodosijskij zaliv ⊂	**78**	45.05 N	35.35 E
Fépin	**56**	50.01 N	4.44 E
Fer, Cap de ›	**148**	37.05 N	7.10 E
Ferbane	**48**	53.15 N	7.49 W
Ferbitz	**264a**	52.30 N	13.01 E
Ferch	**264a**	52.19 N	12.56 E
Fercher Berge ∧[2]	**264a**	52.19 N	12.57 E
Ferchland	**54**	52.26 N	12.00 E
Ferdig	**182**	48.45 N	111.46 W
Ferdinand	**194**	38.13 N	86.51 W
Ferdinandshof	**54**	53.39 N	13.53 E
Ferdows	**128**	34.00 N	58.09 E
Fère-Champenoise	**50**	48.45 N	3.59 E
Fère-en-Tardenois	**50**	49.12 N	3.31 E
Ferencváros ◆[8]	**264c**	47.28 N	19.06 E
Ferentillo	**66**	42.37 N	12.47 E
Ferentino	**66**	41.42 N	13.15 E
Fergana	**85**	40.23 N	71.46 E
Fergana □[4]	**85**	40.30 N	71.20 E
Ferganskaja dolina V	**85**	40.50 N	71.30 E
Ferganskij chrebet ⋀	**85**	41.00 N	74.00 E
Fergus	**212**	43.42 N	80.22 W
Fergus Falls	**198**	46.16 N	96.04 W
Ferguson, Austl.	**168a**	33.26 S	115.51 E
Ferguson, B.C., Can.	**182**	50.41 N	117.28 W
Ferguson, Ky., U.S.	**192**	37.04 N	84.36 W
Ferguson, Mo., U.S.	**219**	38.44 N	90.18 W
Ferguson ≃	**168a**	33.21 S	115.40 E
Fergusonville	**285**	40.07 N	74.54 W
Fergusson Island I	**164**	9.30 S	150.40 E
Fériana	**148**	34.57 N	8.34 E
Ferihegyi Airport ⊠	**264c**	47.26 N	19.15 E
Ferkéssédougou	**150**	9.36 N	5.12 W
Ferla	**70**	37.07 N	14.56 E
Ferlach	**61**	46.31 N	14.18 E
Ferleiten	**64**	47.10 N	12.49 E
Ferlo ◆[1]	**150**	0.15 N	0.14 W
Ferlo, Vallée du V	**150**	15.42 N	15.30 W
Fermiers, Île aux I	**275a**	45.40 N	73.27 W
Fermignano	**66**	43.40 N	12.39 E
Fermin, Point ›	**228**	33.42 N	118.18 W
Fermi National Accelerator Laboratory ʊ[3]	**216**	41.50 N	88.15 W
Fermo	**66**	43.09 N	13.43 E
Fermont	**176**	52.47 N	67.05 W
Fermoselle	**34**	41.19 N	6.23 W
Fermoy	**48**	52.08 N	8.16 W
Fernández	**252**	27.55 S	63.54 W
Fernández Leal	**200**	30.51 N	108.17 W
Fernandina, Isla I	**246a**	0.25 S	91.30 W
Fernandina Beach	**192**	30.40 N	81.27 W
Fernando de la Mora	**252**	25.19 S	57.36 W
Fernando de Noronha, Ilha I	**250**	3.51 S	32.25 W
Fernandópolis	**255**	20.16 S	50.14 W
Fernando Póo → Bioko I	**152**	3.30 N	8.40 E
Fernán-Núñez	**34**	37.40 N	4.43 W
Fernão Veloso, Baía de ⊂	**154**	14.20 S	40.45 E
Ferndale, S. Afr.	**273d**	26.05 S	27.59 E
Ferndale, Ca., U.S.	**204**	40.34 N	124.15 W
Ferndale, Fl., U.S.	**220**	28.37 N	81.42 W
Ferndale, Md., U.S.	**208**	39.10 N	76.38 W
Ferndale, Mi., U.S.	**216**	42.27 N	83.08 W
Ferndale, N.Y., U.S.	**210**	41.46 N	74.44 W
Ferndale, Pa., U.S.	**214**	40.17 N	78.54 W
Ferndale, Wa., U.S.	**202**	48.50 N	122.35 W
Ferndale Lake ⊜	**222**	32.57 N	95.05 W
Ferndown	**42**	50.48 N	1.55 W
Ferney-Voltaire	**58**	46.15 N	6.07 E
Fern Glen	**210**	40.57 N	76.10 W
Fernhill Heath	**42**	52.14 N	2.12 W
Fernie	**182**	49.30 N	115.03 W
Fernilee	**262**	53.18 N	1.58 W
Fernilee Reservoir ⊜[1]	**262**	53.17 N	1.59 W
Fernley	**204**	39.36 N	119.15 W
Ferno	**266b**	45.37 N	8.45 E
Fernow, Mount ∧	**224**	47.45 N	121.14 W
Fern Park	**220**	28.41 N	81.20 W
Fernpass)(	**58**	47.22 N	10.50 E
Fern Ridge Lake ⊜[1]	**202**	44.05 N	123.18 W
Ferns	**48**	52.35 N	6.31 W
Fernvale	**171a**	27.27 S	152.39 E
Fernway	**214**	40.41 N	80.07 W
Fernwood, Id., U.S.	**202**	47.06 N	116.23 W
Fernwood, N.Y., U.S.	**210**	43.16 N	73.40 W
Fernwood, Pa., U.S.	**285**	39.57 N	75.15 W
Ferny Creek	**274b**	37.53 S	145.21 E
Feroé, Islas → Faeroe Islands □[2]	**22**	62.00 N	7.00 W
Feroës → Faeroe Islands □[2]	**22**	62.00 N	7.00 W
Ferokh	**122**	11.11 N	75.51 E
Feroleto Antico	**68**	38.58 N	16.23 E
Feroleto della Chiesa	**68**	38.28 N	16.04 E
Ferolle Point ›	**186**	51.05 N	57.07 W
Ferozepore → Fīrozpur	**123**	30.55 N	74.36 E
Ferrandina	**68**	40.29 N	16.28 E
Ferrara	**64**	44.50 N	11.35 E
Ferrara □[4]	**64**	44.48 N	11.50 E
Ferrat, Cap ›	**34**	35.54 N	0.23 W
Ferrato, Capo ›	**71**	39.18 N	9.38 E
Ferraz de Vasconcelos	**256**	23.32 S	46.22 W
Ferraz de Vasconcelos □[7]	**287b**	23.33 S	46.21 W
Ferrazzano	**66**	41.32 N	14.40 E
Ferré, Cap ›	**240e**	14.28 N	60.49 W
Ferreira, Ang.	**152**	12.53 S	22.48 E
Ferreira, S. Afr.	**158**	29.13 S	26.10 E
Ferreira do Alentejo	**34**	38.03 N	8.07 W
Ferreira Gomes	**250**	0.48 N	51.08 W
Ferreiros	**256**	22.25 S	43.34 W
Ferrell	**285**	39.41 N	75.12 W
Ferrell's Bridge Dam ◆[6]	**222**	32.45 N	94.30 W
Ferreñafe	**248**	6.38 S	79.45 W
Ferrera Erbognone	**62**	45.07 N	8.52 E
Ferret	**58**	45.55 N	7.06 E
Ferret, Cap ›	**32**	44.37 N	1.15 W
Ferreyra	**252**	31.28 S	64.08 W
Ferriday	**194**	31.37 N	91.33 W
Ferriere	**62**	44.38 N	9.30 E
Ferrière-la-Grande	**50**	50.15 N	4.00 E
Ferrières	**50**	48.05 N	2.47 E
Ferrières-en-Brie	**50**	48.49 N	2.43 E
Ferris	**222**	32.32 N	96.39 W
Ferritslev	**41**	55.18 N	10.36 E
Ferro ≃	**255**	12.27 S	54.31 W
Ferro, Canale del V	**64**	46.21 N	13.07 E
Ferrol → El Ferrol del Caudillo	**34**	43.29 N	8.14 W
Ferrol, Península de ›[1]	**248**	9.10 S	78.37 W
Ferron	**200**	39.05 N	111.08 W
Ferron Creek ≃	**200**	39.09 N	110.55 W
Ferros	**255**	19.14 S	43.02 W
Ferru, Monte ∧, It.	**71**	40.08 N	8.36 E
Ferru, Monte ∧, It.	**71**	39.44 N	9.38 E
Ferruzzano	**68**	38.02 N	16.05 E
Ferry, Pointe ›	**241o**	16.17 N	61.49 W
Ferryhill	**44**	54.41 N	1.33 W
Ferryland	**186**	47.02 N	52.53 W
Ferry Point Park ♦	**276**	40.49 N	73.50 W
Ferrysburg	**216**	43.05 N	86.13 W
Ferry Village	**284a**	43.58 N	78.57 W
Ferryville → Menzel Bourguiba	**148**	37.10 N	9.48 E
Feršampenuaz	**86**	53.32 N	59.51 E
Fertile	**198**	47.32 N	96.16 W
Fertilia, Aeroporto di ⊠	**71**	40.37 N	8.15 E
Fertő (Neusiedler See) ⊜	**61**	47.50 N	16.45 E
Fertőd ⏊	**61**	47.37 N	16.53 E
Fertőrákos	**61**	47.43 N	16.39 E
Fertőújlak	**61**	47.40 N	16.51 E
Ferulargiu, Monte ∧	**71**	40.31 N	9.34 E
Ferzikovo	**82**	54.32 N	36.45 E
Fès	**148**	34.05 N	4.57 W
Fès □[4]	**148**	33.55 N	4.57 W
Feshi	**152**	6.07 S	18.10 E
Feshie ≃	**46**	57.08 N	3.55 W
Fessenden	**198**	47.38 N	99.37 W
Festus	**219**	38.13 N	90.23 W
Fetcham	**42**	51.17 N	0.22 W
Fet Dom, Tanjung ›	**164**	1.53 S	129.43 E
Fété Bowé	**150**	14.56 N	13.30 W
Fetești	**38**	44.23 N	27.50 E
Fethaland, Point of ›	**46a**	60.38 N	1.18 W
Fethard	**48**	52.27 N	7.41 W
Fethiye	**130**	36.37 N	29.07 E
Fethiye Körfezi ⊂	**130**	36.40 N	29.00 E
Fetisovo	**72**	42.46 N	52.38 E
Fetlar I	**46a**	60.37 N	0.52 W
Fetsund	**26**	59.56 N	11.10 E
Fetterangus	**46**	57.33 N	2.01 W
Fettercairn	**46**	56.51 N	2.34 W
Feucherolles	**261**	48.52 N	1.58 E
Feucht	**60**	49.22 N	11.13 E
Feuchtwangen	**56**	49.10 N	10.20 E
Feudingen	**56**	50.56 N	8.19 E
Feuerland → Tierra del Fuego, Isla Grande de I	**254**	54.00 S	69.00 W
Feuet	**146**	24.57 N	10.04 E
Feuilles, Baie aux ⊂	**176**	58.55 N	69.20 W
Feuilles, Rivière aux ≃	**176**	58.47 N	70.04 W
Feuquières-en-Vimeu	**50**	50.04 N	1.36 E
Feura Bush	**210**	42.35 N	73.53 W
Feurs	**62**	45.45 N	4.14 E
Fevik	**26**	58.23 N	8.42 E
Fevzipaşa	**130**	37.07 N	36.37 E
Féy	**56**	49.02 N	6.06 E
Feyẕābād, Afg.	**120**	37.06 N	70.34 E
Feyẕābād, Īrān	**128**	35.01 N	58.46 E
Feyzin	**62**	45.40 N	4.51 E
Fez → Fès	**148**	34.05 N	4.57 W
Fezzan → Fazzān □[9]	**146**	26.00 N	14.00 E
Ffestiniog	**42**	52.58 N	3.55 W
Fforest Fawr ◆[1]	**42**	51.52 N	3.36 W
F. Gilbert Hills State Forest ♦	**283**	42.03 N	71.17 W
Fhada, Beinn ∧	**46**	57.13 N	5.18 W
Fiambalá	**252**	27.41 S	67.38 W
Fiamignano	**66**	42.16 N	13.07 E
Fian	**150**	10.23 N	2.29 W
Fianarantsoa	**157b**	21.26 S	47.05 E
Fianarantsoa □[4]	**157b**	22.00 S	47.00 E
Fianga	**146**	9.55 N	15.09 E
Fiano	**62**	45.13 N	7.31 E
Fiantsonana	**157b**	19.09 S	46.12 E
Fiastra, Abbazia di ʊ[1]	**66**	43.13 N	13.25 E
Fiavè	**64**	46.00 N	10.50 E
Ficarazzi	**70**	38.05 N	13.28 E
Ficarolo	**64**	44.57 N	11.26 E
Ficarra	**70**	38.06 N	14.50 E
Fiche	**144**	9.52 N	38.46 E
Fichtelberg	**60**	50.01 N	11.51 E
Fichtelberg ∧	**54**	50.26 N	12.57 E
Fichtelgebirge ⋀	**30**	50.00 N	11.55 E
Fichtenau	**264a**	52.27 N	13.42 E
Ficksburg	**158**	28.57 S	27.50 E
Ficulle	**66**	42.50 N	12.04 E
Ficuzza ≃	**70**	37.00 N	14.20 E
Fidalgo ≃	**250**	7.28 S	42.32 W
Fidalgo Island I	**224**	48.25 N	122.35 W
Fidān, Wādī al- V	**132**	30.46 N	35.18 E
Fiddlers Hamlet	**260**	51.41 N	0.08 E
Fiddletown	**226**	38.30 N	120.46 W
Fiddyment Creek ≃	**278**	41.36 N	88.03 W
Fidelity	**219**	39.09 N	90.10 W
Fidenza	**64**	44.52 N	10.03 E
Fidīmīn	**142**	29.23 N	30.46 E
Fiditi	**150**	7.45 N	3.53 E
Fidji → Fiji □[1]	**175g**	18.00 S	178.00 E
Fidler Lake ⊜	**184**	57.11 N	96.57 W
Fidschi → Fiji □[1]	**175g**	18.00 S	178.00 E
Fiè (Völs)	**64**	46.31 N	11.30 E
Fieberbrunn	**64**	47.29 N	12.33 E
Field	**182**	51.24 N	116.29 W
Fieldale	**192**	36.42 N	79.56 W
Field Museum ʊ	**278**	41.53 N	87.37 W
Fieldon	**219**	39.07 N	90.30 W
Fieldsboro	**285**	40.08 N	74.43 W
Fieldstone	**276**	40.44 N	74.33 W
Fiemme, Val di V	**64**	46.20 N	11.35 E
Fiener Bruch ≡	**54**	52.19 N	12.10 E
Fienvillers	**50**	50.07 N	2.14 E
Fier	**38**	40.43 N	19.34 E
Fier ≃	**58**	45.56 N	5.50 E
Fiéra Campionaria ♦	**266b**	45.28 N	9.09 E
Fiera di Primiero	**64**	46.10 N	11.49 E
Fierenana	**157b**	18.29 S	48.24 E
Fiery Creek ≃, Austl.	**166**	18.23 S	139.52 E
Fiery Creek ≃, Austl.	**169**	37.44 S	142.56 E
Fiery Range ⋀	**171b**	35.30 S	148.40 E
Fierzës, Liqeni i ⊜[1]	**38**	42.10 N	20.15 E
Fiesch	**58**	46.20 N	8.10 E
Fiesole	**66**	43.48 N	11.17 E
Fiesso d'Artico	**64**	45.24 N	12.02 E
Fiesso Umbertiano	**64**	44.56 N	11.36 E
Fife	**224**	47.14 N	122.22 W
Fife □[4]	**46**	56.13 N	3.02 W
Fife Lake, Sk., Can.	**184**	49.12 N	105.43 W
Fife Lake, Mi., U.S.	**190**	44.34 N	85.21 W
Fife Lake ⊜	**184**	49.14 N	105.53 W
Fife Ness ›	**46**	56.17 N	2.36 W
Fifield	**190**	45.52 N	90.25 W
Fifteenmile Creek ≃, Or., U.S.	**224**	45.37 N	121.07 W
Fifteenmile Creek ≃, Wy., U.S.	**202**	44.01 N	108.01 W
Fifth Cataract → Khāmis, Ash-Shallāl al- ∟	**140**	18.23 N	33.47 E
Fifth Depot Lake ⊜	**212**	44.36 N	76.52 W
Figeac	**32**	44.37 N	2.02 E
Figeholm	**26**	57.22 N	16.33 E
Fig Garden	**226**	36.48 N	119.47 W
Fighting Island I	**281**	42.13 N	83.07 W
Figline Valdarno	**66**	43.37 N	11.28 E
Figtree	**154**	20.24 S	28.21 E
Figueira → Governador Valadares, Bra.	**255**	18.51 S	41.56 W
Figueira, Bra.	**287a**	22.42 S	43.27 W
Figueira, Cachoeira ∟	**250**	9.49 S	58.13 W
Figueira da Foz	**34**	40.09 N	8.52 W
Figueres	**34**	42.16 N	2.58 E
Figuig	**148**	32.10 N	1.15 W
Figuig □[4]	**148**	32.40 N	2.15 W
Fihaonana	**157b**	18.36 S	47.12 E
Fiherenana ≃	**157b**	23.19 S	43.37 E
Fiji □[1], Oc.	**14**	18.00 S	178.00 E
Fiji □[1], Oc.	**175g**	18.00 S	178.00 E
Fiji Islands II	**14**	18.00 S	178.00 E
Fijnaart	**52**	51.37 N	4.31 E
Fik	**144**	8.10 N	42.18 E
Fika	**146**	11.17 N	11.18 E
Fiktūriyā, Bi'r ⍑[4]	**142**	30.24 N	30.36 E
Filabusi	**154**	20.34 S	29.20 E
Filadélfia, Bra.	**250**	7.21 S	47.30 W
Filadelfia, C.R.	**236**	10.26 N	85.34 W
Filadelfia, It.	**68**	38.48 N	16.18 E
Filadelfia → Philadelphia, Pa., U.S.	**208**	39.57 N	75.07 W
Fil'akovo	**30**	48.17 N	19.51 E
Filandari	**68**	38.37 N	16.02 E
Filatova Gora	**76**	57.40 N	28.10 E
Filchner Ice Shelf ⊓	**9**	79.00 S	40.00 W
Filderstadt	**56**	48.41 N	9.13 E
File Lake ⊜	**184**	54.53 N	100.20 W
Filettino	**66**	41.53 N	13.19 E
Filey	**44**	54.12 N	0.17 W
Filey Bay ⊂	**44**	54.12 N	0.16 W
Fili ◆[8]	**265b**	55.45 N	37.31 E
Filí ⏊	**38**	38.06 N	23.40 E
Filiano	**68**	40.49 N	15.42 E
Filiași	**38**	44.33 N	23.31 E
Filiatrá	**38**	37.10 N	21.35 E
Filicudi, Isola I	**70**	38.34 N	14.34 E
Filimonovo	**86**	56.12 N	95.28 E
Filingué	**150**	14.21 N	3.19 E
Filipinas → Philippines □[1]	**116**	13.00 N	122.00 E
Filipinas, Mar de → Philippine Sea ⍑[2]	**14**	20.00 N	135.00 E
Filipino Cemetery and Memorial ◆	**269f**	14.31 N	121.02 E
Fílippoi ⏊	**38**	41.00 N	24.16 E
Filippovka	**80**	53.59 N	49.46 E
Filippovo	**80**	58.18 N	50.30 E
Filippovskoje, Ross.	**82**	56.06 N	38.37 E
Filippovskoje, Ross.	**82**	56.48 N	39.07 E
Filipstad	**40**	59.43 N	14.10 E
Filisola	**234**	17.50 N	94.19 W
Fillmore, Sk., Can.	**184**	49.50 N	103.25 W
Fillmore, Ca., U.S.	**228**	34.23 N	118.55 W
Fillmore, Il., U.S.	**219**	39.07 N	89.17 W
Fillmore, N.Y., U.S.	**210**	42.27 N	78.06 W
Fillmore, Ut,. U.S.	**200**	38.58 N	112.19 W
Fillmore Glen State Park ♦	**210**	42.42 N	76.20 W
Filogaso	**68**	38.41 N	16.14 E
Filomeno Mata	**234**	20.12 N	97.42 W
Filonovskaja	**80**	50.34 N	42.46 E
Filottrano	**66**	43.26 N	13.21 E
Fils ≃	**56**	48.42 N	9.25 E
Filskov	**41**	55.48 N	9.02 E
Filton	**42**	51.31 N	2.35 W
Filtu	**144**	5.07 N	40.39 E
Filzbach	**58**	47.07 N	9.08 E
Fimi ≃	**152**	3.01 S	16.58 E
Fina, Réserve de ◆[4]	**150**	12.50 N	8.30 W
Finale Emilia	**64**	44.50 N	11.17 E
Finale Ligure	**62**	44.10 N	8.20 E
Finarwa	**144**	13.06 N	39.01 E
Fincastle	**192**	37.29 N	79.52 W
Finch	**206**	45.11 N	75.07 W
Fincham	**42**	52.37 N	0.30 E
Finchley ◆[8]	**260**	51.36 N	0.10 W
Finderne	**276**	40.34 N	74.35 W
Findhorn	**46**	57.39 N	3.36 W
Findhorn ≃	**46**	57.38 N	3.38 W
Fındık	**130**	37.31 N	41.58 E
Findlay, Il., U.S.	**219**	39.31 N	88.45 W
Findlay, Oh., U.S.	**216**	41.02 N	83.39 W
Findlay, Mount ∧	**182**	50.04 N	116.28 W
Findley Lake	**214**	42.07 N	79.44 W
Findley Lake ⊜	**214**	42.06 N	79.43 W
Findochty	**46**	57.41 N	2.54 W
Fine Arts, Museum of ʊ	**283**	42.20 N	71.06 W
Finedon	**42**	52.20 N	0.39 W
Finejevo	**82**	56.02 N	38.53 E
Finesville	**210**	40.36 N	75.10 W
Fingal, On., Can.	**214**	42.43 N	81.19 W
Fingal, N.D., U.S.	**198**	46.45 N	97.47 W
Finger Lake ⊜	**184**	53.09 N	93.30 W
Fíngoè	**154**	15.12 S	31.50 E
Finike	**130**	36.18 N	30.09 E
Finike Körfezi ⊂	**130**	36.17 N	30.16 E
Finisk ≃	**48**	52.07 N	7.50 W
Finistère □[5]	**32**	48.20 N	4.00 W
Finisterre	**196**	25.59 N	103.15 W
Finisterre → Land's End ›	**42**	50.03 N	5.44 W
Finisterre, Cabo de ›	**34**	42.53 N	9.16 W
Finisterre Range ⋀	**164**	5.50 S	146.05 E
Finja	**41**	56.10 N	13.41 E
Finjasjön ⊜	**41**	56.08 N	13.42 E
Finke	**162**	25.34 S	134.35 E
Finke ≃	**162**	26.20 S	136.00 E
Finke, Mount ∧[2]	**162**	30.55 S	134.02 E
Finke Gorge National Park ♦	**162**	24.15 S	132.50 E
Finkenkrug	**264a**	52.34 N	13.03 E
Finkenwerder ◆[8]	**52**	53.31 N	9.52 E
Finksburg	**208**	39.29 N	76.53 W
Finland (Suomi) □[1], Europe	**22**	64.00 N	26.00 E
Finland (Suomi) □[1], Europe	**24**	64.00 N	26.00 E
Finland, Gulf of (Suomenlahti) (Finskij zaliv) ⊂	**26**	60.00 N	27.00 E
Finlande → Finland □[1]	**24**	64.00 N	26.00 E
Finlandia → Finland □[1]	**24**	64.00 N	26.00 E
Finlandia, Golfo de → Finland, Gulf of ⊂	**26**	60.00 N	27.00 E
Finland Station ◆[5]	**265a**	59.57 N	30.22 E
Finlas, Loch ⊜	**44**	55.15 N	4.25 W
Finlay ≃	**176**	56.54 N	124.57 W
Finley, Austl.	**166**	35.39 S	145.35 E
Finley, N.D., U.S.	**198**	47.30 N	97.50 W
Finley Creek ≃	**194**	36.58 N	93.22 W
Finleyville, Pa., U.S.	**214**	40.09 N	78.11 W
Finleyville, Pa., U.S.	**214**	40.15 N	80.00 W
Finleyville Airport ⊠	**279b**	40.15 N	80.01 W
Finmoore	**182**	53.59 N	123.37 W
Finn ≃	**48**	54.50 N	7.29 W
Finne ◆[1]	**54**	51.13 N	11.19 E
Finnegan	**182**	51.07 N	112.04 W
Finnentrop	**56**	51.09 N	7.58 E
Finnerödja	**40**	58.56 N	14.26 E
Finney Creek ≃	**224**	48.31 N	121.51 W
Finnhamn	**40**	59.28 N	18.50 E
Finnigan, Mount ∧	**164**	15.49 S	145.17 E
Finnis, Cape ›	**162**	33.38 S	134.51 E
Finnischer Meerbusen → Finland, Gulf of ⊂	**26**	60.00 N	27.00 E
Finniss	**168b**	35.24 S	138.49 E
Finniss ≃	**168b**	35.30 S	138.53 E
Finnland → Finland □[1]	**24**	64.00 N	26.00 E
Finnmark □[6]	**24**	70.00 N	25.00 E
Finn Mountain ∧	**180**	60.37 N	157.11 W
Finno ∧[2]	**154**	3.27 N	41.32 E
Finnskogen ◆[3]	**26**	60.40 N	12.40 E
Finnsnes	**24**	69.14 N	17.59 E
Finocchio ◆[8]	**267a**	41.53 N	12.41 E
Finow	**54**	52.50 N	13.43 E
Finowfurt	**54**	52.51 N	13.41 E
Finowkanal ≅	**54**	52.51 N	13.24 E
Fins, Fr.	**50**	50.02 N	3.03 E
Fins, 'Umān	**128**	22.56 N	59.13 E
Finsbury	**273d**	26.13 S	27.39 E
Finschhafen	**164**	6.35 S	147.50 E
Finse	**26**	60.36 N	7.30 E
Finskij zaliv → Finland, Gulf of ⊂	**26**	60.00 N	27.00 E
Finspång	**40**	58.43 N	15.47 E
Finsta	**40**	59.44 N	18.30 E
Finsteraarhorn ∧	**58**	46.32 N	8.08 E
Finsterwalde	**54**	51.38 N	13.42 E
Finsterwolde	**52**	53.12 N	7.04 E
Fintel	**52**	53.10 N	9.40 E
Fintona	**48**	54.30 N	7.19 W
Fintown	**48**	54.52 N	8.08 W
Finvoy	**48**	55.00 N	6.30 W
Fionn Loch ⊜	**46**	57.46 N	5.29 W
Fiora ≃	**66**	42.20 N	11.34 E
Fiorano Modenese	**64**	44.32 N	10.49 E
Fiordland National Park ♦	**172**	45.30 S	167.20 E
Fiorenzuola d'Arda	**62**	44.56 N	9.55 E
Fiorenzuola di Focara	**66**	43.57 N	12.48 E
Fiorito ◆[8]	**288**	34.42 S	58.27 W
Fīq	**132**	32.47 N	35.42 E
Fırat → Euphrates ≃	**128**	31.00 N	47.25 E
Firavitoba	**246**	5.40 N	73.00 W
Fircrest	**224**	47.14 N	122.30 W
Fire ≃	**190**	48.52 N	83.21 W
Firebaugh	**226**	36.51 N	120.27 W
Firebrick	**218**	38.41 N	83.03 W
Fire Island I	**210**	40.42 N	73.00 W
Fire Island Inlet ⊂	**276**	40.38 N	73.16 W
Fire Island National Seashore ♦	**188**	40.38 N	73.08 W
Fire Island Pines	**276**	40.40 N	73.04 W
Fire Islands II	**276**	40.40 N	73.11 W
Firenze (Florence)	**66**	43.46 N	11.15 E
Firenze □[4]	**66**	43.50 N	11.20 E
Firenzuola	**66**	44.07 N	11.23 E
Firesteel Creek ≃	**198**	43.43 N	97.58 W
Firgrove	**262**	53.37 N	2.08 W
Firmat	**252**	33.27 S	61.29 W
Firminópolis	**255**	16.40 S	50.19 W
Firminy	**62**	45.23 N	4.18 E
Firmo	**68**	39.43 N	16.10 E
Firovo	**76**	57.29 N	33.40 E
Fīrozābād	**124**	27.09 N	78.25 E
Fīrozpur	**123**	30.55 N	74.36 E
Firozpur Jhirka	**124**	27.48 N	76.57 E
Firsanovka	**265b**	55.57 N	37.15 E
Firsovo	**88**	52.20 N	118.06 E
First Broad ≃	**192**	35.11 N	81.37 W
First Cataract → Awwal, Ash-Shallāl al- ∟	**140**	24.01 N	32.52 E
First Cliff ⍊[4]	**283**	42.12 N	70.43 W
First Connecticut Lake ⊜	**206**	45.05 N	71.15 W
First Han-gang Bridge ◆[5]	**271b**	37.32 N	126.56 E
First Herring Brook ≃	**283**	42.11 N	70.45 W
First Watchung Mountain ∧	**276**	40.55 N	74.10 W
Firth	**198**	40.31 N	96.36 W
Firth ≃	**180**	69.32 N	139.22 W
Fir'uza	**128**	37.56 N	58.04 E
Fīrūzābād	**128**	28.50 N	52.36 E
Fīrūz Kūh	**128**	35.45 N	52.47 E
Fischa ≃	**61**	48.07 N	16.41 E
Fischamend	**61**	48.07 N	16.37 E
Fischbach, Dtsch.	**56**	49.44 N	7.23 E
Fischbach, Dtsch.	**60**	49.25 N	11.12 E
Fischbachau	**64**	47.43 N	11.57 E
Fischbacher Alpen ⋀	**61**	47.28 N	15.30 E
Fischbeck, Dtsch.	**52**	52.09 N	9.17 E
Fischbeck, Dtsch.	**54**	52.32 N	12.01 E
Fischeln ◆[8]	**263**	51.18 N	6.35 E
Fischen	**58**	47.28 N	10.16 E
Fischhausen → Primorsk	**76**	54.44 N	20.01 E
Fischland ⍊[2]	**54**	54.22 N	12.25 E
Fish ≃, Austl.	**170**	33.29 S	149.37 E
Fish (Vis) ≃, Namibia	**156**	28.07 S	17.45 E
Fish ≃, Al., U.S.	**194**	30.25 N	87.50 W
Fish ≃, Me., U.S.	**186**	47.15 N	68.36 W
Fishbourne	**42**	50.44 N	1.12 W
Fish Brook ≃, Ma., U.S.	**283**	42.38 N	70.58 W
Fish Brook ≃, Ma., U.S.	**283**	42.42 N	71.13 W
Fish Camp	**226**	37.29 N	119.38 W
Fish Canyon V	**280**	34.11 N	117.55 W
Fish Creek ≃, On., Can.	**212**	43.13 N	81.13 W
Fish Creek ≃, U.S.	**216**	41.28 N	84.45 W
Fish Creek ≃, Mi., U.S.	**190**	43.04 N	84.51 W
Fish Creek ≃, Mt., U.S.	**202**	46.17 N	109.13 W
Fish Creek ≃, N.Y., U.S.	**212**	43.12 N	75.43 W
Fish Creek ≃, Or., U.S.	**224**	45.09 N	122.09 W
Fish Creek, East Branch ≃	**212**	43.16 N	75.38 W
Fish Creek, West Branch ≃	**212**	43.16 N	75.38 W
Fish Creek Mountain ∧	**224**	45.05 N	122.08 W
Fisheating Creek ≃	**220**	26.57 N	81.07 W
Fisher, Austl.	**162**	30.33 S	130.58 E
Fisher, Ar., U.S.	**194**	35.29 N	90.58 W
Fisher, Il., U.S.	**216**	40.18 N	88.21 W
Fisher, La., U.S.	**194**	31.29 N	93.27 W
Fisher, Pa., U.S.	**214**	41.16 N	79.15 W
Fisher ≃, Mb., Can.	**184**	51.26 N	97.18 W
Fisher ≃, Mt., U.S.	**202**	48.22 N	115.19 W
Fisher Bay ⊂, Mb., Can.	**184**	51.30 N	97.16 W
Fisher Bay ⊂, Mi., U.S.	**281**	42.36 N	82.39 W
Fisher Branch	**184**	51.05 N	97.37 W
Fisher Channel ɥ	**182**	52.10 N	127.42 W
Fisher Heights	**279b**	40.10 N	79.54 W
Fishermans Island I	**208**	37.06 N	75.58 W
Fisherman's Wharf ⏊	**282**	37.48 N	122.25 W
Fisher Peak ∧	**192**	36.33 N	80.50 W
Fisher River Indian Reserve ◆[4]	**184**	51.26 N	97.20 W
Fishers, In., U.S.	**218**	39.57 N	86.00 W
Fishers, N.Y., U.S.	**210**	43.00 N	77.28 W
Fishers Island I	**207**	41.16 N	72.02 W
Fishers Peak ∧	**196**	37.06 N	104.28 W
Fisher Strait ɥ	**176**	63.15 N	83.30 W
Fishertown	**214**	40.08 N	78.35 W
Fisherville	**275b**	43.47 N	79.28 W

Symbols in the index entries represent the broad categories identified in the key at the right. Symbols with superior numbers (⋀[1]) identify subcategories (see complete key on page *I* · *1*).

Symbole im Register stellen die rechts im Schlüssel erklärten Kategorien dar. Symbole mit hochgestellten Ziffern (⋀[1]) bezeichnen Unterabteilungen einer Kategorie (vgl. vollständiger Schlüssel auf Seite *I* · *1*).

Los símbolos incluídos en el texto del índice representan las grandes categorías identificadas con la clave a la derecha. Los símbolos con numeros en su parte superior (⋀[1]) identifican las subcategorías (véase la clave completa en la página *I* · *1*).

Les symboles de l'index représentent les catégories indiquées dans la légende à droite. Les symboles suivis d'un indice (⋀[1]) représentent des sous-catégories (voir légende complète à la page *I* · *1*).

Os símbolos incluídos no texto do índice representam as grandes categorias identificadas com a chave à direita. Os símbolos com números em sua parte superior (⋀[1]) identificam as subcategorias (veja-se a chave completa à página *I* · *1*).

∧ Mountain	Berg	Montaña	Montagne	Montanha
⋀ Mountains	Gebirge	Montañas	Montagnes	Montanhas
)(Pass	Paß	Paso	Col	Passo
V Valley, Canyon	Tal, Cañon	Valle, Cañón	Vallée, Canyon	Vale, Canhão
≚ Plain	Ebene	Llano	Plaine	Planície
› Cape	Kap	Cabo	Cap	Cabo
I Island	Insel	Isla	Île	Ilha
II Islands	Inseln	Islas	Îles	Ilhas
⍊ Other Topographic Features	Andere Topographische Objekte	Otros Elementos Topográficos	Autres données topographiques	Outros acidentes topográficos

ESPAÑOL Nombre Página Lat.°′ Long.°′ W = Oeste — FRANÇAIS Nom Page Lat.°′ Long.°′ W = Ouest — PORTUGUÊS Nome Página Lat.°′ Long.°′ W = Oeste

Fish-Form I · 57

Nombre	Página	Lat.°′	Long.°′ W = Oeste
Fishguard	42	51.59 N	4.59 W
Fishhook	219	39.48 N	90.53 W
Fish House	210	43.08 N	74.08 W
Fishing Bay ⊂	208	38.18 N	76.01 W
Fishing Creek	208	38.20 N	76.14 W
Fishing Creek ≃, Ky., U.S.	192	37.06 N	84.41 W
Fishing Creek ≃, N.C., U.S.	192	35.57 N	77.31 W
Fishing Creek ≃, Pa., U.S.	210	40.58 N	76.28 W
Fishing Creek ≃, Pa., U.S.	210	41.07 N	77.29 W
Fishing Creek ≃, S.C., U.S.	192	34.36 N	80.54 W
Fishing Islands II	212	44.45 N	81.20 W
Fishing Lake ⊜, Mb., Can.	184	52.07 N	95.25 W
Fishing Lake ⊜, Sk., Can.	184	51.50 N	103.32 W
Fishkill	210	41.32 N	73.53 W
Fishkill Creek ≃	210	41.29 N	73.59 W
Fish Lake	216	41.34 N	86.33 W
Fish Lake ⊜, On., Can.	212	44.06 N	77.11 W
Fish Lake ⊜, Mi., U.S.	216	42.03 N	85.52 W
Fish Lake ⊜, Wa., U.S.	224	47.50 N	120.42 W
Fishmoor Reservoir ⊜[1]	262	53.44 N	2.28 W
Fish Point ›	214	41.43 N	82.40 W
Fishpool	262	53.35 N	2.17 W
Fish River	166	17.55 S	137.45 E
Fishs Eddy	210	41.58 N	75.10 W
Fisk	194	36.46 N	90.12 W
Fiskárdhon	38	38.27 N	20.35 E
Fiskdale	207	42.06 N	72.06 W
Fiskebäckskil	26	58.15 N	11.27 E
Fismes	50	49.18 N	3.41 E
Fišt, gora ∧	84	43.58 N	39.54 E
Fitchburg, Ma., U.S.	207	42.35 N	71.48 W
Fitchburg, Wi., U.S.	216	42.57 N	89.28 W
Fitchville, Ct., U.S.	207	41.33 N	72.09 W
Fitchville, Oh., U.S.	214	41.06 N	82.29 W
Fitful Head ›	46a	59.54 N	1.23 W
Fitiuta	174y	14.13 S	169.27 W
Fito, Mount ∧	175a	13.55 S	171.44 W
Fitri, Lac ⊜	146	12.50 N	17.28 E
Fittja	40	59.15 N	17.52 E
Fittleworth	42	50.58 N	0.35 W
Fitzgerald	192	31.42 N	83.15 W
Fitzgerald River National Park ♦	162	34.00 S	119.30 E
Fitz Henry	279b	40.10 N	79.45 W
Fitz Hugh Sound ⊔	182	51.40 N	127.57 W
Fitzmaurice ≃	164	14.50 S	129.44 E
Fitz Roy, Arg.	254	47.02 S	67.15 W
Fitzroy, Austl.	274b	37.48 S	144.59 E
Fitzroy ≃, Austl.	162	17.31 S	123.35 E
Fitzroy ≃, Austl.	166	23.32 S	150.52 E
Fitzroy, Monte (Cerro Chaltel) ∧	254	49.17 S	73.05 W
Fitzroy Crossing	162	18.11 S	125.35 E
Fitzroy Falls Reservoir ⊜[1]	170	34.38 S	150.30 E
Fitzwilliam	207	42.46 N	72.08 W
Fitzwilliam Island I	190	45.30 N	81.45 W
Fiuggi	66	41.48 N	13.13 E
Fiumalbo	64	44.11 N	10.39 E
Fiume → Rijeka	36	45.20 N	14.27 E
Fiumecinisi	70	38.02 N	15.23 E
Fiumefreddo Bruzio	68	39.14 N	16.04 E
Fiumefreddo di Sicilia	70	37.47 N	15.12 E
Fiumesino	66	43.38 N	13.22 E
Fiume Veneto	64	45.56 N	12.44 E
Fiumicino ◆[8]	66	41.46 N	12.14 E
Five Corners	283	42.01 N	71.07 W
Five Cowrie Creek ≃[1]	273a	6.27 N	3.27 E
Five Dock	274a	33.52 S	151.08 E
Five Forks	284c	38.47 N	77.16 W
Five Islands	186	45.25 N	64.02 W
Five Islands Harbour ⊂	240c	17.06 N	61.54 W
Fivemile ≃	276	41.03 N	73.27 W
Fivemile Creek ≃, N.Y., U.S.	210	42.22 N	77.22 W
Fivemile Creek ≃, Or., U.S.	224	45.36 N	121.05 W
Fivemile Creek ≃, Wy., U.S.	202	43.14 N	108.12 W
Fivemile Point	210	42.06 N	75.48 W
Fivemiletown	48	54.23 N	7.18 W
Five Penny Borve	46	58.25 N	6.25 W
Five Points, Ca., U.S.	226	36.26 N	120.06 W
Five Points, In., U.S.	218	39.35 N	86.20 W
Five Points, N.M., U.S.	200	35.03 N	106.39 W
Five Points, Oh., U.S.	218	39.41 N	83.12 W
Five Points, Pa., U.S.	214	40.34 N	80.15 W
Five Points, Pa., U.S.	285	39.50 N	75.42 W
Fivizzano	64	44.14 N	10.08 E
Fiwila Mission	154	13.58 S	29.36 E
Fixin	58	47.15 N	4.58 E
Fix-Saint-Geneys	62	45.08 N	3.40 E
Fizi	154	4.18 S	28.57 E
Fizuli	84	39.37 N	47.08 E
Fjællebroen	41	55.03 N	10.24 E
Fjærlandsfjorden ⊂[2]	26	61.17 N	6.40 E
Fjällåsen	24	67.29 N	20.10 E
Fjällbacka	26	58.36 N	11.17 E
Fjällsjöälven ≃	26	63.29 N	16.50 E
Fjärdhundra	40	59.47 N	16.56 E
Fjärdhundra □[9]	40	59.47 N	16.55 E
Fjenneslev	41	55.26 N	11.40 E
Fjerritslev	26	57.05 N	9.16 E
Fjugesta	40	59.10 N	14.52 E
Fkih-Ben-Salah	148	32.32 N	6.40 W
Flacksta	40	59.23 N	16.27 E
Fladnitz im Raabtal	61	46.59 N	15.47 E
Fladså ≃	41	55.19 N	8.54 E
Fladungen	56	50.31 N	10.08 E
Flag Creek ≃	278	41.43 N	87.55 W
Flagler	198	39.17 N	103.04 W
Flagler Beach	192	29.28 N	81.07 W
Flagstaff, Transkei	158	31.05 S	29.29 E
Flagstaff, Az., U.S.	200	35.11 N	111.39 W
Flagstaff Lake ⊜[1]	188	45.10 N	70.15 W
Flagtown	276	40.31 N	74.41 W
Flaken-See ⊜	264a	52.25 N	13.46 E
Flåm	26	60.50 N	7.07 E
Flambeau ≃	190	45.18 N	91.15 W
Flambeau, South Fork ≃	190	45.39 N	90.48 W
Flamborough, On., Can.	212	43.20 N	79.53 W
Flamborough, Eng., U.K.	44	54.06 N	0.07 W
Flamborough Head ›	44	54.07 N	0.04 W
Fläming ◆[1]	54	52.00 N	12.30 E
Flaming Gorge National Recreation Area ♦	200	41.30 N	109.30 W
Flaming Gorge Reservoir ⊜[1]	200	41.15 N	109.30 W
Flamingo	220	25.09 N	80.56 W
Flamingo, Teluk ⊂	164	5.33 S	138.00 E
Flanagan	216	40.52 N	88.51 W
Flanagan ≃	184	52.50 N	93.28 W
Flanagan Passage ⊔	240m	18.18 N	64.39 W
Flanders, On., Can.	190	48.44 N	92.05 W
Flanders, N.J., U.S.	276	40.50 N	74.41 W
Flanders, N.Y., U.S.	207	40.49 N	72.36 W
Flanders (Flandre) □[9]	50	51.00 N	3.00 E
Flanders Airport ⊠	276	40.50 N	74.41 W
Flandes	246	4.18 N	74.49 W
Flandorf	264b	48.21 N	16.23 E
Flandre → Flanders □[9]	50	51.00 N	3.00 E
Flandreau	198	44.02 N	96.35 W
Flannan Islands II	46	58.18 N	7.36 W
Flåren ⊜	26	57.02 N	14.06 E
Flasher	198	46.27 N	101.13 W
Flåsjön ⊜	26	64.06 N	15.51 E
Flat, Ak., U.S.	180	62.27 N	158.01 W
Flat, Tx., U.S.	222	31.19 N	97.38 W
Flat ≃, N.T., Can.	180	61.33 N	125.18 W
Flat ≃, Mi., U.S.	190	42.56 N	85.20 W
Flat ≃, N.C., U.S.	192	36.05 N	78.49 W
Flat Bay	186	48.24 N	58.36 W
Flat Branch ≃	219	39.33 N	89.16 W
Flatbush ◆[8]	276	40.39 N	73.56 W
Flat Creek ≃, Ky., U.S.	218	38.17 N	83.48 W
Flat Creek ≃, Mo., U.S.	194	36.45 N	93.31 W
Flat Creek ≃, Mt., U.S.	202	47.43 N	109.50 W
Flat Creek ≃, N.J., U.S.	276	40.27 N	74.10 W
Flat Creek Reservoir ⊜[1]	222	32.14 N	95.45 W
Flatey	24a	65.19 N	23.07 W
Flateyri	24a	65.59 N	23.42 W
Flathead ≃	202	47.22 N	114.47 W
Flathead, Middle Fork ≃	202	48.28 N	114.04 W
Flathead, North Fork ≃	202	48.28 N	114.04 W
Flathead, South Fork ≃	202	48.23 N	114.04 W
Flathead Indian Reservation ◆[4]	202	47.30 N	114.25 W
Flathead Lake ⊜	202	47.52 N	114.08 W
Flat Holm I	42	51.23 N	3.08 W
Flat Lake ⊜	182	54.39 N	112.55 W
Flat Lick	192	36.49 N	83.46 W
Flatonia	222	29.41 N	97.06 W
Flatow	264a	52.44 N	12.57 E
Flat River, P.E., Can.	186	46.01 N	62.52 W
Flat River, Mo., U.S.	194	37.51 N	90.31 W
Flat River Reservoir ⊜[1]	207	41.42 N	71.37 W
Flat Rock, Al., U.S.	194	34.46 N	85.42 W
Flat Rock, Il., U.S.	194	38.54 N	87.40 W
Flat Rock, In., U.S.	218	39.22 N	85.50 W
Flat Rock, Mi., U.S.	216	42.05 N	83.17 W
Flat Rock, Oh., U.S.	214	41.14 N	82.51 W
Flatrock ≃	218	39.12 N	85.56 W
Flatrock Creek ≃	216	41.10 N	84.27 W
Flatrock Lake ⊜	184	55.37 N	100.47 W
Flatruet ⋀[2]	26	62.45 N	12.50 E
Flats	222	32.50 N	95.53 W
Flattery, Cape ›, Austl.	164	14.58 S	145.21 E
Flattery, Cape ›, Wa., U.S.	224	48.23 N	124.43 W
Flatts	240a	32.19 N	64.44 W
Flatwillow Creek ≃	202	46.56 N	107.55 W
Flatwood	194	32.27 N	86.15 W
Flatwoods	188	38.31 N	82.43 W
Flaugherty Run ≃	279b	40.33 N	80.13 W
Flaunden	260	51.42 N	0.32 W
Flavigny-sur-Moselle	58	48.34 N	6.11 E
Flavigny-sur-Ozerain	58	47.30 N	4.32 E
Flavy-le-Martel	50	49.43 N	3.12 E
Flawil	58	47.24 N	9.12 E
Flaxcombe	184	51.29 N	109.36 W
Flaxman Island I	180	70.13 N	146.00 W
Flax Pond ⊜, Ma., U.S.	283	42.29 N	70.57 W
Flax Pond ⊜, N.Y., U.S.	276	40.58 N	73.08 W
Flaxton	198	48.53 N	102.23 W
Flaxville	198	48.48 N	105.10 W
Flechas Point ›	116	10.22 N	119.34 E
Flechtingen	54	52.20 N	11.14 E
Fleckeby	41	54.29 N	9.41 E
Flecken Zechlin	54	53.09 N	12.46 E
Fleesensee ⊜	54	53.30 N	12.29 E
Fleet	42	51.16 N	0.50 W
Fleet ≃	46	57.57 N	4.05 W
Fleets Bay ⊂	208	37.40 N	76.19 W
Fleetville	210	41.36 N	75.43 W
Fleetwing Estates	285	40.07 N	74.51 W
Fleetwood, Eng., U.K.	44	53.56 N	3.01 W
Fleetwood, Pa., U.S.	208	40.27 N	75.49 W
Flehe ◆[8]	263	51.12 N	6.47 E
Flehingen	56	49.05 N	8.46 E
Fleischmanns	210	42.09 N	74.31 W
Fleischman Village	284c	38.51 N	76.57 W
Flekkefjord	26	58.17 N	6.41 E
Fleming, Co., U.S.	198	40.40 N	102.50 W
Fleming, Pa., U.S.	214	40.55 N	77.52 W
Fleming □[6]	218	38.21 N	83.42 W
Fleming Creek ≃, On., Can.	214	42.38 N	81.47 W
Fleming Creek ≃, Ky., U.S.	218	38.22 N	83.57 W
Fleming Creek ≃, Mi., U.S.	281	42.16 N	83.40 W
Fleming-Neon	192	37.11 N	82.42 W
Flemingsburg	218	38.25 N	83.44 W
Flemington, N.J., U.S.	210	40.30 N	74.51 W
Flemington, Pa., U.S.	210	41.07 N	77.28 W
Flemington Racecourse ♦	274b	37.47 S	144.55 E
Flemish Cap ✢[4]	16	47.00 N	45.00 W
Flemsdorf	54	53.02 N	14.10 E
Flen	40	59.04 N	16.35 E
Flensburg	41	54.47 N	9.26 E
Flensburger Förde ⊂	41	54.49 N	9.45 E
Fleres (Boden)	64	46.58 N	11.21 E
Flers	32	48.45 N	0.34 W
Flers-sur-Noye	50	49.44 N	2.15 E
Flesherton	212	44.16 N	80.33 W
Flesko, Tanjung ›	112	0.29 N	124.30 E
Fletcher, On., Can.	214	42.18 N	82.18 W
Fletcher, N.C., U.S.	192	35.25 N	82.30 W
Fletcher, Oh., U.S.	218	40.08 N	84.06 W
Fletcher, Ok., U.S.	196	34.49 N	98.14 W
Fletcher Islands II	9	72.40 S	94.10 W
Fletcher Moss Museum ʊ	262	53.25 N	2.14 W
Fletcher Pond ⊜[1]	190	44.58 N	83.52 W
Fletchers Creek ≃	275b	43.38 N	79.42 W
Fleurance	32	43.50 N	0.40 E
Fleur-de-Lys	186	50.07 N	56.08 W
Fleurier	58	46.54 N	6.35 E
Fleurieu Peninsula ›[1]	168b	35.30 S	138.30 E
Fleurus	56	50.29 N	4.33 E
Fleurville	58	46.27 N	4.53 E
Fleury-les-Aubrais	50	47.56 N	1.55 E
Fleury-Mérogis	261	48.38 N	2.22 E
Fleury-sur-Andelle	50	49.22 N	1.22 E
Fleuth ≃	263	51.32 N	6.26 E
Flevoland □[4]	52	52.30 N	5.30 E
Flexanville	261	48.51 N	1.44 E
Flexenpass)(	58	47.09 N	10.10 E
Fley ◆[8]	263	51.23 N	7.30 E
Flieden	56	50.25 N	9.33 E
Flierich	263	51.35 N	7.48 E
Flight Locks ʊ[3]	284a	43.08 N	79.12 W
Flimby	44	54.41 N	3.31 W
Flims	58	46.50 N	9.17 E
Flinders	169	38.28 S	145.01 E
Flinders ≃	166	17.36 S	140.36 E
Flinders Bay ⊂	162	34.23 S	115.19 E
Flinders Chase National Park ♦	166	36.00 S	136.45 E
Flinders Island I, Austl.	162	33.44 S	134.31 E
Flinders Island I, Austl.	166	40.00 S	148.00 E
Flinders Peak ∧	171a	27.49 S	152.49 E
Flinders Peak ∧[2]	169	37.51 S	144.24 E
Flinders Ranges National Park ♦	166	31.20 S	138.45 E
Flinders Reefs ✢[2]	166	17.37 S	148.31 E
Flinders Street Station ◆[5]	274b	37.49 S	144.58 E
Flinesjön ⊜	40	60.23 N	16.06 E
Flines-lèz-Râches	50	50.25 N	3.11 E
Flin Flon	184	54.46 N	101.53 W
Flingern ◆[8]	263	51.14 N	6.49 E
Flins-sur-Seine	261	48.58 N	1.52 E
Flint, Wales, U.K.	44	53.15 N	3.07 W
Flint, Mi., U.S.	216	43.00 N	83.41 W
Flint, Tx., U.S.	222	32.12 N	95.21 W
Flint I	14	11.26 S	151.48 W
Flint ≃, U.S.	194	34.30 N	86.31 W
Flint ≃, Ga., U.S.	192	30.52 N	84.38 W
Flint ≃, Mi., U.S.	190	43.21 N	84.03 W
Flint, South Branch ≃	216	43.10 N	83.23 W
Flint Castle ⊥	262	53.16 N	3.07 W
Flint Creek ≃, Al., U.S.	194	34.30 N	86.57 W
Flint Creek ≃, Mt., U.S.	202	46.39 N	113.08 W
Flint Creek ≃, N.Y., U.S.	210	42.57 N	77.03 W
Flint Creek Range ⋀	202	46.20 N	113.05 W
Flinthill	219	38.53 N	90.52 W
Flint Hills ⋀[2]	198	37.50 N	96.40 W
Flint Lake ⊜, N.T., Can.	176	69.10 N	74.20 W
Flint Lake ⊜, In., U.S.	216	41.31 N	87.03 W
Flinton, Austl.	166	27.54 S	149.34 E
Flinton, Pa., U.S.	214	40.43 N	78.31 W
Flint Peak ∧	280	34.10 N	118.12 W
Flint Pond ⊜	283	42.40 N	71.26 W
Flintrännan ⊔	41	55.34 N	12.50 E
Flintridge	228	34.11 N	118.11 W
Flints Pond ⊜	283	42.26 N	71.19 W
Flintville	194	35.03 N	86.25 W
Flipper Point ›	174a	19.18 N	166.35 E
Flippin	194	36.16 N	92.35 W
Flirey	56	48.53 N	5.50 E
Flirsch	58	47.09 N	10.24 E
Flisa	26	60.34 N	12.06 E
Flitwick	42	52.00 N	0.29 W
Flix, Pantà de ⊜[1]	34	41.15 N	0.25 E
Flixecourt	50	50.01 N	2.05 E
Flize	56	49.42 N	4.46 E
Flobecq (Vloesberg)	50	50.44 N	3.44 E
Floby	26	58.08 N	13.20 E
Floda, Sve.	26	57.48 N	12.22 E
Floda, Sve.	40	59.04 N	16.21 E
Flodden	44	55.38 N	2.10 W
Flodden Field Battlesite ⊥	44	55.38 N	2.13 W
Flogny	50	47.57 N	3.52 E
Flöha	54	50.51 N	13.04 E
Flöha ≃	54	50.51 N	13.04 E
Floing	56	49.43 N	4.56 E
Flomaton	194	31.00 N	87.15 W
Flomborn	56	49.41 N	8.08 E
Flomot	196	34.14 N	100.59 W
Floodwood	190	46.55 N	92.55 W
Flora, Il., U.S.	194	38.40 N	88.29 W
Flora, In., U.S.	216	40.32 N	86.31 W
Flora, Ms., U.S.	194	32.32 N	90.18 W
Florac	32	44.19 N	3.36 E
Florala	194	31.00 N	86.19 W
Floral City	220	28.45 N	82.17 W
Floral Park, Mt., U.S.	202	45.57 N	112.26 W
Floral Park, N.Y., U.S.	210	40.43 N	73.42 W
Florange	56	49.20 N	6.07 E
Florânia	250	6.08 S	36.49 W
Flora Vista	200	36.47 N	108.04 W
Flore, Piton ∧	241f	13.58 N	60.57 W
Floreffe	56	50.26 N	4.45 E
Florence → Firenze, It.	66	43.46 N	11.15 E
Florence, Al., U.S.	194	34.47 N	87.40 W
Florence, Az. U.S.	200	33.02 N	111.23 W
Florence, Ca. U.S.	228	33.58 N	118.14 W
Florence, Co. U.S.	200	38.23 N	105.07 W
Florence, Ks., U.S.	198	38.14 N	96.55 W
Florence, Ky., U.S.	218	38.59 N	84.37 W
Florence, N.J., U.S.	285	40.07 N	74.49 W
Florence, Or., U.S.	202	43.58 N	124.05 W
Florence, Pa., U.S.	214	40.26 N	80.26 W
Florence, S.C., U.S.	192	34.11 N	79.45 W
Florence, Tx., U.S.	222	30.51 N	97.48 W
Florence, Wi., U.S.	190	45.55 N	88.15 W
Florencia, Col	246	1.36 N	75.36 W
Florencia → Firenze, It.	66	43.46 N	11.15 E
Florencio Sánchez	258	33.53 S	57.24 W
Florencio Varela	258	34.49 S	58.17 W
Florencio Varela □[5]	288	34.52 S	58.15 W
Florennes	56	50.15 N	4.37 E
Florentia	273d	26.16 S	28.08 E
Florentino Ameghino, Embalse ⊜[1]	254	43.55 S	66.20 W
Florenville	56	49.42 N	5.18 E
Florenz → Firenze	66	43.46 N	11.15 E
Flores	250	7.51 S	37.59 W
Flores □[5]	258	33.48 S	56.50 W
Flores ◆[8]	288	34.38 S	58.28 W
Flores I, Indon.	115b	8.30 S	121.00 E
Flores I, Port.	148a	39.26 N	31.13 W
Flores, Laut (Flores Sea) ⊤[2]	112	8.00 S	120.00 E
Flores, Rio das ≃	256	22.05 S	43.34 W
Flores, Selat ⊔	115b	8.25 S	122.55 E
Flores da Cunha	252	29.02 S	51.11 W
Flores de Goiás	255	14.34 S	47.04 W
Flores Island I	182	49.20 N	126.10 W
Flores Sea → Flores, Laut ⊤[2]	112	8.00 S	120.00 E
Floresta, Bra.	250	8.36 S	38.34 W
Floresta, It.	70	37.59 N	14.55 E
Floresta ◆[8]	288	34.38 S	58.29 W
Floresta Azul	255	14.51 S	39.41 W
Florestal de Monsanto, Parque ♦	266c	38.43 N	9.11 W
Floreşty	38	47.53 N	28.17 E
Floresville	196	29.08 N	98.09 W
Florham Park	210	40.47 N	74.23 W
Floriano, Bra.	250	6.47 S	43.01 W
Floriano, Bra.	256	22.27 S	44.18 W
Floriano Peixoto	248	9.03 S	67.24 W
Florianópolis	252	27.35 S	48.34 W
Florida, Col.	246	3.21 N	76.15 W
Florida, Cuba	240p	21.32 N	78.14 W
Florida, Hond.	236	15.01 N	88.50 W
Florida, Perú	248	5.50 S	77.55 W
Florida, P.R.	240m	18.22 N	66.34 W
Florida, P.R.	240m	18.14 N	65.47 W
Florida, S. Afr.	273d	26.11 S	27.55 E
Florida, In., U.S.	218	40.10 N	85.42 W
Florida, N.Y., U.S.	210	41.19 N	74.21 W
Florida, Oh., U.S.	216	41.20 N	84.12 W
Florida, Ur.	258	34.06 S	56.13 W
Florida □[5]	258	34.00 S	56.15 W
Florida ◆[8]	288	34.31 S	58.30 W
Florida □[3], U.S.	178	28.00 N	82.00 W
Florida □[3], U.S.	192	28.00 N	82.00 W
Florida ≃	200	37.03 N	107.52 W
Florida, Cape ›	220	25.40 N	80.09 W
Florida, Straits of ⊔	238	25.00 N	79.45 W
Florida Bay ⊂	220	25.00 N	80.45 W
Floridablanca	246	7.04 N	73.06 W
Florida Caverns State Park ♦	192	30.50 N	85.18 W
Florida City	220	25.26 N	80.28 W
Florida Islands II	175e	9.00 S	160.10 E
Florida Keys II	220	24.45 N	81.00 W
Florida Lake ⊜[1]	273d	26.11 S	27.54 E
Florida Ridge	220	27.35 N	80.23 W
Floridia	70	37.05 N	15.09 E
Florido ≃	232	27.43 N	105.10 W
Floridsdorf ◆[8]	264b	48.16 N	16.24 E
Floridsdorfer Brücke ◆[5]	264b	48.14 N	16.23 E
Florien	194	31.26 N	93.27 W
Florin	226	38.29 N	121.24 W
Flórina	38	40.47 N	21.24 E
Florisbad	158	28.46 S	26.06 E
Florissant	219	38.47 N	90.19 W
Florissant Fossil Beds National Monument ♦	200	38.54 N	105.16 W
Floriston	226	39.24 N	120.01 W
Florø	26	61.36 N	5.00 E
Flörsheim	56	50.01 N	8.26 E
Florvåg	26	60.25 N	5.14 E
Flosaille	62	45.39 N	5.18 E
Floss	60	49.44 N	12.17 E
Flossach ≃	58	48.24 N	10.25 E
Flossenbürg	60	49.44 N	12.21 E
Flossmoor	216	41.32 N	87.41 W
Flotantes, Jardínes ♦	286a	19.16 N	99.06 W
Flöthbach ≃	263	51.17 N	6.26 E
Flotta I	46	58.50 N	3.07 W
Flotte, Cap de ›	175f	21.10 S	167.25 E
Flotten Lake ⊜	184	54.38 N	108.30 W
Flourtown	285	40.06 N	75.12 W
Flower Hill	276	40.48 N	73.40 W
Flower Mound	222	33.02 N	97.04 W
Flower's Cove	186	51.18 N	56.44 W
Flowery Branch	192	34.11 N	83.55 W
Floyd, N.M., U.S.	196	34.13 N	103.35 W
Floyd, Tx., U.S.	222	33.09 N	96.15 W
Floyd, Va., U.S.	192	36.54 N	80.19 W
Floyd □[6]	218	38.18 N	85.49 W
Floyd ≃	198	42.29 N	96.23 W
Floydada	196	33.59 N	101.20 W
Floyds Fork ≃	194	38.00 N	85.41 W
Fluchthorn ∧	58	46.53 N	10.13 E
Flüela Pass)(	58	46.45 N	9.57 E
Flüelen	58	46.54 N	8.38 E
Fluessen ⊜	52	52.57 N	5.30 E
Flühli	58	46.53 N	8.01 E
Flumen ≃	34	41.43 N	0.09 W
Flumendosa ≃	71	39.26 N	9.37 E
Flumendosa, Lago Alto del ⊜	71	39.56 N	9.26 E
Flumendosa, Lago del ⊜[1]	71	39.40 N	9.17 E
Flumeri	68	41.05 N	15.09 E
Flumet	62	45.49 N	6.30 E
Fluminimaggiore	71	39.26 N	8.30 E
Flums	58	47.05 N	9.20 E
Flüren	263	51.41 N	6.33 E
Flushing → Vlissingen, Ned.	52	51.26 N	3.35 E
Flushing, Mi., U.S.	216	43.03 N	83.51 W
Flushing, Oh., U.S.	214	40.08 N	81.03 W
Flushing ◆[8]	276	40.45 N	73.49 W
Flushing Airport ⊠	276	40.47 N	73.50 W
Flushing Bay ⊂	276	40.47 N	73.51 W
Flushing Meadow-Corona Park ♦	276	40.45 N	73.51 W
Fluvanna, N.Y., U.S.	214	42.07 N	79.18 W
Fluvanna, Tx., U.S.	196	32.53 N	101.09 W
Fluvià ≃	34	42.12 N	3.07 E
Fly ≃	164	8.30 S	143.41 E
Fly Creek	210	42.43 N	74.59 W
Fly Creek ≃	202	45.59 N	107.59 W
Flyinge	41	55.45 N	13.21 E
Flying Fish Cove	112	10.25 S	105.43 E
Flynn	222	31.09 N	96.08 W
Foam Lake	184	51.39 N	103.33 W
Fobbing	260	51.32 N	0.29 E
Fobello	62	45.53 N	8.10 E
Foča, Bos.	38	43.31 N	18.46 E
Foça, Tür.	130	38.39 N	26.46 E
Focene ◆[8]	267a	41.48 N	12.14 E
Fochabers	46	57.37 N	3.05 W
Fochville	158	26.30 S	27.30 E
Fockbek	41	54.18 N	9.36 E
Focşani	38	45.41 N	27.11 E
Fodda, Oued ≃	34	35.14 N	1.28 E
Fodé	152	5.29 N	23.18 E
Fodécontea	150	10.50 N	14.22 W
Foding Shan ∧	102	27.08 N	108.02 E
F'odorovka, Kaz.	80	51.09 N	51.59 E
F'odorovka, Kaz.	86	53.22 N	76.18 E
F'odorovka, Kaz.	86	53.38 N	62.42 E
F'odorovka, Ross.	80	53.28 N	49.38 E
F'odorovka, Ross.	80	52.21 N	52.55 E
F'odorovka, Ross.	82	56.15 N	37.14 E
F'odorovka, Ross.	83	47.20 N	38.23 E
F'odorovka, Ross.	86	56.05 N	78.49 E
F'odorovka, Ross.	86	53.11 N	55.11 E
F'odorovka, Ukr.	78	49.23 N	35.07 E
F'odorovka, Ukr.	78	47.33 N	36.33 E
F'odorovskoje, Ross.	82	56.44 N	36.58 E
F'odorovskoje, Ross.	82	56.08 N	38.04 E
F'odorovskoje, Ross.	82	56.07 N	38.52 E
Foëcy	50	47.10 N	2.10 E
Foelsche ≃	164	16.03 S	136.50 E
Foeni	38	45.30 N	20.53 E
Fogang (Shijiao)	100	23.52 N	113.32 E
Fogdön ›[1]	40	59.25 N	16.52 E
Fogelevo	85	42.03 N	69.32 E
Fogelsville	208	40.35 N	75.38 W
Foggaret el Arab	148	27.03 N	2.59 E
Foggaret ez Zoua	148	27.20 N	3.00 E
Foggia	68	41.27 N	15.34 E
Foggia □[4]	68	41.30 N	15.30 E
Foggy Island Bay ⊂	180	70.15 N	147.30 W
Foglia ≃	66	43.55 N	12.54 E
Foglianise	68	41.10 N	14.40 E
Fogliano, Lago di ⊂	66	41.24 N	12.54 E
Foglizzo	62	45.16 N	7.49 E
Fogo	186	49.43 N	54.17 W
Fogo I	150a	14.55 N	24.25 W
Fogo, Cape ›	186	49.39 N	54.00 W
Fogo Island I	186	49.40 N	54.13 W
Fogolawa	150	12.19 N	8.41 E
Fogueteiro	266c	38.37 N	9.07 W
Fohnsdorf	61	47.13 N	14.41 E
Föhr I	30	54.43 N	8.30 E
Foia ∧	34	37.19 N	8.36 W
Foiano della Chiana	66	43.15 N	11.49 E
Foiano di Val Fortore	68	41.21 N	14.59 E
Foinaven ∧	46	58.25 N	4.53 W
Foins, Lac aux ⊜	190	47.05 N	78.11 W
Foivre ≃	56	49.30 N	4.32 E
Foix	32	42.58 N	1.36 E
Foix □[9]	32	43.00 N	1.40 E
Fojnica	36	43.58 N	17.54 E
Foki	80	56.42 N	54.21 E
Fokino	76	53.27 N	34.24 E
Fokku	150	11.40 N	4.31 E
Folakara	157b	18.20 S	45.02 E
Folamasi	104	41.56 N	121.27 E
Folarskardnuten ∧	26	60.37 N	7.45 E
Folcroft	208	39.53 N	75.17 W
Folda ⊂[2]	24	67.36 N	14.50 E
Foldingbro	41	55.26 N	9.01 E
Folégandros I	38	36.38 N	24.54 E
Folembray	50	49.33 N	3.17 E
Foley, Al., U.S.	194	30.24 N	87.41 W
Foley, Mn., U.S.	190	45.39 N	93.54 W
Foley, Mo., U.S.	219	39.02 N	90.44 W
Foleyet	190	48.15 N	82.27 W
Foley Island I	176	68.35 N	75.10 W
Folgaria	64	45.55 N	11.10 E
Folgefonni ⊓	26	60.00 N	6.20 E
Folger Hill ∧[2]	207	41.17 N	70.01 W
Foligno	66	42.57 N	12.42 E
Folk	219	38.26 N	92.06 W
Folkärna	40	60.09 N	16.19 E
Folkestone	42	51.05 N	1.11 E
Folkingham	42	52.54 N	0.24 W
Folkston	192	30.49 N	82.00 W
Folkwangmuseum ʊ	263	51.27 N	7.00 E
Follafoss	26	63.59 N	11.06 E
Follainville-Dennemont	261	49.01 N	1.43 E
Follansbee	214	40.19 N	80.35 W
Folldal	26	62.08 N	10.03 E
Folle Anse, Pointe de ›	241o	15.57 N	61.20 W
Follebu	26	61.14 N	10.17 E
Follets Island I	222	29.02 N	95.10 W
Follett	196	36.26 N	100.08 W
Follina	64	45.57 N	12.07 E
Föllinge	26	63.40 N	14.37 E
Follonica	66	42.55 N	10.45 E
Follonica, Golfo di ⊂	66	42.54 N	10.43 E
Folly Branch ≃	284b	38.56 N	76.49 W
Folmhusen	52	53.10 N	7.28 E
Folschviller	56	49.04 N	6.41 E
Folsom, Ca., U.S.	226	38.40 N	121.10 W
Folsom, N.J., U.S.	208	39.36 N	74.50 W
Folsom, Pa., U.S.	285	39.53 N	75.19 W
Folsom Lake ⊜[1]	226	38.43 N	121.08 W
Folsom Lake State Recreation Area ♦	226	38.46 N	121.06 W
Fomboni	157a	12.16 S	43.45 E
Fomento, Cuba	240p	22.06 N	79.43 W
Fomento, Ur.	258	34.26 S	57.14 W
Fomin	80	46.58 N	43.38 E
Fominiči	76	54.07 N	34.41 E
Fominki	80	55.57 N	42.22 E
Fominskaja	24	61.17 N	48.40 E
Fominskoje, Ross.	24	59.43 N	42.05 E
Fominskoje, Ross.	76	58.59 N	39.06 E
Fomkino	80	54.25 N	50.30 E
Foncine-le-Bas	58	46.38 N	6.03 E
Fonda, Ia., U.S.	198	42.34 N	94.50 W
Fonda, N.Y., U.S.	210	42.57 N	74.22 W
Fondachelli	70	37.58 N	15.11 E
Fond du Lac, Sk., Can.	176	59.19 N	107.10 W
Fond du Lac, Wi., U.S.	190	43.46 N	88.26 W
Fond du Lac ≃	176	59.17 N	106.00 W
Fond du Lac Indian Reservation ◆[4]	190	46.45 N	92.37 W
Fondi	66	41.21 N	13.25 E
Fondi, Lago di ⊂	66	41.19 N	13.20 E
Fondo	64	46.26 N	11.08 E
Fondouk el Aouareb	36	35.34 N	9.46 E
Fongfong	140	12.56 N	23.14 E
Fonni	71	40.07 N	9.15 E
Fonsagrada	34	43.08 N	7.04 W
Fonseca	246	10.54 N	72.51 W
Fonseca, Golfo de ⊂	236	13.10 N	87.40 W
Fons-Outre-Gardon	62	43.54 N	4.11 E
Font ≃	44	55.10 N	1.44 W
Fontaine, Fr.	58	47.40 N	7.00 E
Fontaine, Fr.	62	45.11 N	5.40 E
Fontainebleau, Fr.	50	48.24 N	2.42 E
Fontainebleau, S. Afr.	273d	26.07 S	27.59 E
Fontaine-Française	58	47.31 N	5.22 E
Fontaine-le-Dun	50	49.49 N	0.51 E
Fontaine-lès-Dijon	58	47.21 N	5.01 E
Fontaine-lès-Grès	50	48.25 N	3.54 E
Fontaine-lès-Luxeuil	58	47.51 N	6.20 E
Fontaines	58	46.51 N	4.46 E
Fontaines-sur-Saône	62	45.50 N	4.51 E
Fontan	62	44.00 N	7.33 E
Fontana, Arg.	252	27.25 S	59.02 W
Fontana, Ca., U.S.	228	34.05 N	117.26 W
Fontana, Wi., U.S.	216	42.33 N	88.34 W
Fontana, Lago ⊜	254	44.56 S	71.30 W
Fontanafredda	64	45.58 N	12.34 E
Fontana Lake ⊜[1]	192	35.26 N	83.38 W
Fontanarosa	68	41.01 N	15.01 E
Fontanarossa, Aeroporto di ⊠	70	37.29 N	15.03 E
Fontanelas	266c	38.51 N	9.26 W
Fontanelice	66	44.15 N	11.33 E
Fontanella	64	45.27 N	9.48 E
Fontanellato	64	44.53 N	10.10 E
Fontanelle	198	41.17 N	94.33 W
Fontanetto Po	62	45.12 N	8.11 E
Fontanigorda	62	44.33 N	9.19 E
Fontarabie, Lac ⊜	186	51.10 N	66.25 W
Fontas ≃	176	58.20 N	121.50 W
Fonte, Bra.	287b	23.25 S	46.21 W
Fonte, It.	64	45.47 N	11.53 E
Fonte, It.	66	41.46 N	13.13 E
Fonte Avellana, Monastero di ʊ[1]	66	43.29 N	12.45 E
Fonte Blanda	66	42.34 N	11.10 E
Fonte Boa	246	2.32 S	66.01 W
Fonte Colombo, Convento di ʊ[1]	66	42.23 N	12.50 E
Fontenay, Abbaye de ʊ[1]	50	47.39 N	4.24 E
Fontenay-aux-Roses	261	48.47 N	2.17 E
Fontenay-en-Parisis	261	49.03 N	2.27 E
Fontenay-le-Comte	32	46.28 N	0.48 W
Fontenay-le-Fleury	261	48.49 N	2.03 E
Fontenay-lès-Briis	261	48.37 N	2.09 E
Fontenay-le-Vicomte	261	48.33 N	2.24 E
Fontenay-Saint-Père	261	49.02 N	1.45 E
Fontenay-sous-Bois	261	48.51 N	2.29 E
Fontenay-Trésigny	50	48.42 N	2.52 E
Fonteneau, Lac ⊜	186	51.55 N	61.30 W
Fontenelle	186	48.53 N	64.33 W
Fontenelle Creek ≃	200	42.05 N	110.08 W
Fontenelle Reservoir ⊜[1]	200	42.05 N	110.06 W
Fontespina	66	43.17 N	13.45 E
Fontevivo	64	44.51 N	10.10 E
Font Hill Manor	284b	39.17 N	76.52 W
Fonti del Clitunno ⊤[4]	66	42.49 N	12.46 E
Fontoy	56	49.21 N	6.00 E
Fontur ›	24a	66.23 N	14.30 W
Fontvieille	62	43.43 N	4.43 E
Fonyód	30	46.44 N	17.34 E
Fonzaso	64	46.01 N	11.48 E
Foochow → Fuzhou	100	26.06 N	119.17 E
Foot Creek ≃	198	45.26 N	98.29 W
Foothill Farms	226	38.40 N	121.20 W
Foothills	182	53.04 N	116.48 W
Footprint Lake ⊜	184	55.47 N	98.53 W
Footscray	169	37.48 S	144.54 E
Footville	216	42.40 N	89.12 W
Foping	102	33.21 N	107.59 E
Foppolo	64	46.03 N	9.45 E
Fora, Ponta de ›	287a	22.57 S	43.07 W
Foraker, Mount ∧	180	62.56 N	151.26 W
Forari	175f	17.39 S	168.32 E
Forbach, Dtsch.	56	48.41 N	8.21 E
Forbach, Fr.	56	49.11 N	6.54 E
Forbes	166	33.23 S	148.01 E
Forbes, Lac ⊜	206	46.31 N	74.12 W
Forbes, Mount ∧	182	51.52 N	116.56 W
Forbes Field ♦	279b	40.27 N	79.57 W
Forbesganj	124	26.18 N	87.15 E
Forbes Reef	158	26.10 S	31.05 E
Forbes Road	214	40.21 N	79.32 W
Forbestown	226	39.31 N	121.16 W
Forcados	150	5.22 N	5.24 E
Forcados ≃[1]	150	5.25 N	5.19 E
Forcalquier	62	43.58 N	5.47 E
Force	214	41.15 N	78.30 W
Forchheim, Dtsch.	54	50.43 N	13.16 E
Forchheim, Dtsch.	60	49.43 N	11.04 E
Forclaz, Col de la)(	58	46.04 N	7.00 E
Ford, Scot., U.K.	46	56.10 N	5.26 W
Ford, Ks., U.S.	198	37.38 N	99.45 W
Ford □[6]	216	40.27 N	88.06 W
Ford ≃	190	45.40 N	87.09 W
Ford, Cape ›	164	13.26 S	129.52 E
Ford City, Ca., U.S.	226	35.09 N	119.27 W
Ford City, Pa., U.S.	214	40.46 N	79.31 W
Ford City ◆[9]	278	41.46 N	87.44 W
Ford Cliff	214	40.45 N	79.32 W
Ford Dam ◆[6]	281	42.13 N	83.33 W
Ford Dry Lake ⊜	204	33.38 N	115.00 W
Førde, Nor.	26	59.36 N	5.29 E
Førde, Nor.	26	61.27 N	5.52 E
Førdefjorden ⊂[2]	26	61.28 N	5.39 E
Forden	42	52.36 N	3.08 W
Förderstedt	54	51.54 N	11.38 E
Fordham University ʊ[2]	276	40.51 N	73.53 W
Fordingbridge	42	50.56 N	1.47 W
Ford Lake ⊜	281	42.13 N	83.36 W
Ford Mansion ⊥	276	40.48 N	74.28 W
Ford Motor Company (River Rouge Plant) ʊ[3]	281	42.18 N	83.10 W
Ford Museum ʊ	281	42.18 N	83.14 W
Fordongianus	71	39.59 N	8.48 E
Ford Ranges ⋀	9	77.00 S	145.00 W
Fords	276	40.31 N	74.18 W
Fords Bridge	166	29.45 S	145.26 E
Fordsburg ◆[8]	273d	26.13 S	28.02 E
Fords Prairie	224	46.44 N	122.59 W
Fordsville	194	37.38 N	86.43 W
Fordville	198	48.13 N	97.47 W
Fordyce	194	33.48 N	92.24 W
Fordyce Lake ⊜[1]	226	39.23 N	120.28 W
Foré	150	13.08 N	10.42 W
Forécariah	150	9.26 N	13.06 W
Forel, Mont ∧	176	67.00 N	37.00 W
Foreland Point ›	42	51.16 N	3.47 W
Foreman	194	33.43 N	94.23 W
Foremost	184	49.29 N	111.25 W
Forenza	68	40.51 N	15.51 E
Forepaugh Airport ⊠	279a	41.21 N	81.30 W
Foresman	216	40.52 N	87.18 W
Forest, Bel.	50	50.48 N	4.19 E
Forest, On., Can.	190	43.06 N	82.00 W
Forest, In., U.S.	216	40.22 N	86.19 W
Forest, Ms., U.S.	194	32.21 N	89.28 W
Forest, Oh., U.S.	216	40.48 N	83.30 W
Forest □[6]	214	41.29 N	79.27 W
Forest, Middle Branch ≃	198	48.13 N	97.48 W
Forest Acres	192	34.01 N	80.59 W
Forestburg	182	52.35 N	112.04 W
Forest City, Ia., U.S.	190	43.15 N	93.38 W
Forest City, N.C., U.S.	192	35.20 N	81.51 W
Forest City, Pa., U.S.	210	41.39 N	75.28 W
Forest Creek ≃	226	38.23 N	120.28 W
Forest Gate ◆[8]	260	51.33 N	0.02 E
Forest Glade	222	31.39 N	96.31 W
Forest Grove, B.C., Can.	182	51.46 N	121.06 W
Forest Grove, Or., U.S.	224	45.31 N	123.06 W
Forest Grove, Pa., U.S.	279b	40.18 N	75.04 W
Forest Heights	284c	38.49 N	77.00 W
Forest Hill, Austl.	171a	27.35 S	152.22 E
Forest Hill, Austl.	171b	35.09 S	147.27 E
Forest Hill, Austl.	274b	37.50 S	145.11 E
Foresthill, Ca., U.S.	226	39.01 N	120.49 W
Forest Hill, Md., U.S.	208	39.35 N	76.23 W
Forest Hill, Tx., U.S.	222	32.40 N	97.16 W
Forest Hill ◆[8]	275b	43.42 N	79.24 W
Forest Hill Park ♦	279a	41.31 N	81.35 W
Forest Hill Parkway ♦	279a	41.33 N	81.36 W
Forest Hills	279b	40.25 N	79.51 W
Forest Hills ◆[8]	276	40.42 N	73.51 W
Forest Home	194	31.52 N	86.50 W
Forestier Peninsula ›[1]	166	42.57 S	147.55 E
Forest Knolls	284c	39.02 N	77.01 W
Forest Lake, Il., U.S.	216	42.13 N	88.03 W
Forest Lake, Mn., U.S.	190	45.16 N	92.59 W
Forest Lake ⊜, Il., U.S.	278	42.13 N	88.03 W
Forest Lake ⊜, Ma., U.S.	283	42.43 N	71.15 W
Forest Lawn Memorial Park ◆	280	34.09 N	118.19 W
Forest Manor	284c	38.50 N	76.53 W
Forest Park, Ga., U.S.	192	33.37 N	84.22 W
Forest Park, Il., U.S.	278	41.52 N	87.48 W
Forest Park, Oh., U.S.	218	39.16 N	84.34 W
Forest Park ◆[8]	284b	39.19 N	76.41 W
Forest Park ♦	276	40.42 N	73.51 W
Forest River	278	42.05 N	87.54 W
Forest Row	42	51.06 N	0.02 E
Forest View	278	41.49 N	87.47 W
Forestville, Austl.	274a	33.46 S	151.13 E
Forestville, P.Q., Can.	186	48.45 N	69.06 W
Forestville, Md., U.S.	284c	38.50 N	76.52 W
Forestville, N.Y., U.S.	214	42.28 N	79.10 W
Forestville, Pa., U.S.	214	41.06 N	80.00 W
Forestville, Wi., U.S.	190	44.41 N	87.28 W
Forêt l'Orient, Lac de la ⊜[1]	50	48.17 N	4.20 E
Forêt-Noire → Schwarzwald ⋀	58	48.00 N	8.15 E
Forez, Monts du ⋀	32	45.35 N	3.48 E
Forfar	46	56.38 N	2.54 W
Forfry	261	49.03 N	2.51 E
Forgan	196	36.54 N	100.32 W
Forgaria	64	46.13 N	12.58 E
Forge Acres	284b	39.25 N	76.27 W
Forge Heights	284b	39.25 N	76.25 W
Forges-les-Bains	261	48.38 N	2.06 E
Forges-les-Eaux	50	49.37 N	1.33 E
Forget, Pointe ›	275a	45.27 N	73.58 W
Forge Village	207	42.34 N	71.29 W
Forggensee ⊜	58	47.36 N	10.44 E
Forillon, Parc National de ♦	186	48.55 N	64.12 W
Forino	68	40.52 N	14.44 E
Foristell	219	38.49 N	90.57 W
Fork	208	39.28 N	76.27 W
Forked Creek ≃	216	41.19 N	88.09 W
Forked Deer ≃	194	35.56 N	89.35 W
Forked Deer, Middle Fork ≃	194	36.01 N	89.13 W
Forked Deer, North Fork ≃	194	36.00 N	89.26 W
Forked Deer, South Fork ≃	194	36.00 N	89.26 W
Forked River	208	39.50 N	74.11 W
Forks	224	47.57 N	124.23 W
Forkston	210	41.31 N	76.07 W
Forksville	210	41.29 N	76.36 W
Forleti, Arroyo ≃	288	34.35 S	58.41 W
Forlì	66	44.13 N	12.03 E
Forlì □[4]	64	44.05 N	12.02 E
Forlimpopoli	66	44.11 N	12.07 E
Forman	198	46.06 N	97.38 W
Formazza	58	46.22 N	8.26 E
Formby	44	53.34 N	3.05 W
Formby Hills ⋀[2]	262	53.34 N	3.06 W
Formby Point ›	44	53.33 N	3.06 W
Formentera I	34	38.42 N	1.28 E
Formentor, Cap de ›	34	39.58 N	3.12 E
Formerie	50	49.39 N	1.44 E
Formia	66	41.15 N	13.37 E
Formiga	255	20.27 S	45.25 W
Formiga ≃	250	11.15 S	48.27 W
Formigine	64	44.34 N	10.51 E
Formignana	64	44.50 N	11.51 E
Formosa, Arg.	252	26.11 S	58.11 W
Formosa, Bra.	255	15.32 S	47.20 W
Formosa □[4]	252	25.00 S	60.00 W
Formosa → Taiwan □[1]	100	23.30 N	121.00 E
Formosa, Ilha I	150	11.29 N	15.58 W
Formosa, Serra ⋀[1]	250	12.00 S	55.00 W
Formosa Strait → Taiwan Strait ⊔	100	24.00 N	119.00 E
Formoso ≃, Bra.	250	10.34 S	49.56 W
Formoso ≃, Bra.	255	13.26 S	44.14 W

≃ River	Fluß	Río	Rivière	Rio
≍ Canal	Kanal	Canal	Canal	Canal
⌊ Waterfall, Rapids	Wasserfall, Stromschnellen	Cascada, Rápidos	Chute d'eau, Rapides	Cascata, Rápidos
⊔ Strait	Meeresstraße	Estrecho	Détroit	Estreito
⊂ Bay, Gulf	Bucht, Golf	Bahía, Golfo	Baie, Golfe	Baía, Golfo
⊜ Lake, Lakes	See, Seen	Lago, Lagos	Lac, Lacs	Lago, Lagos
≡ Swamp	Sumpf	Pantano	Marais	Pântano
⊓ Ice Features, Glacier	Eis- und Gletscherformen	Accidentes Glaciales	Formes glaciaires	Acidentes glaciares
⊤ Other Hydrographic Features	Andere Hydrographische Objekte	Otros Elementos Hidrográficos	Autres données hydrographiques	Outros acidentes hidrográficos
✢ Submarine Features	Untermeerische Objekte	Accidentes Submarinos	Formes de relief sous-marin	Acidentes submarinos
□ Political Unit	Politische Einheit	Unidad Politica	Entité politique	Unidade política
ʊ Cultural Institution	Kulturelle Institution	Institución Cultural	Institution culturelle	Instituição cultural
⊥ Historical Site	Historische Stätte	Sitio Histórico	Site historique	Sitio histórico
♦ Recreational Site	Erholungs- und Ferienort	Sitio de Recreo	Centre de loisirs	Area de Lazer
⊠ Airport	Flughafen	Aeropuerto	Aéroport	Aeroporto
■ Military Installation	Militäranlage	Instalación Militar	Installation militaire	Instalação militar
◆ Miscellaneous	Verschiedenes	Misceláneo	Divers	Diversos

Formoso ≐, Bra. 255 18.25 S 52.28 W
Formoso ≐, Bra. 256 21.20 S 43.10 W
Fornæs ≻ 26 56.27 N 10.58 E
Forncelle 66 43.55 N 11.06 E
Fornelli 71 41.00 N 8.14 E
Forney 222 32.44 N 96.28 W
Forni Avoltri 64 46.35 N 12.46 E
Forni di sopra 64 46.25 N 12.35 E
Forni di sotto 64 46.23 N 12.40 E
Forni di Val d'Astico 64 45.51 N 11.22 E
Forno 64 46.21 N 8.50 E
Forno Alpi Graie 62 45.22 N 7.13 E
Forno di Zoldo 64 46.21 N 12.11 E
Fornosovo 76 59.35 N 30.35 E
Fornovo di Taro 64 44.42 N 10.06 E
Foro Romano ⊥ 267a 41.54 N 12.29 E
Føroyar → Faeroe Islands □2 22 62.00 N 7.00 W
Forpost 86 56.47 N 72.10 E
Forres, Arg. 252 27.53 S 63.58 W
Forres, Scot., U.K. 46 57.37 N 3.38 W
Forrest, Austl. 162 30.51 S 128.06 E
Forrest, Austl. 169 38.31 S 143.43 E
Forrest, Il., U.S. 216 40.45 N 88.24 W
Forrest ≐ 164 15.18 S 128.04 E
Forrest, Mount ▲ 162 24.48 S 127.45 E
Forrestal Research Center ☣3 276 40.21 N 74.37 W
Forrest City 194 35.00 N 90.47 W
Forrester Island I 182 54.48 N 133.32 W
Forrest Lakes ⊜ 162 29.12 S 128.46 E
Forreston, Il., U.S. 190 42.07 N 89.34 W
Forreston, Tx., U.S. 222 32.16 N 96.52 W
Forrest River Aboriginal Reserve ◆4 164 15.00 S 127.40 E
Fors 40 60.13 N 16.18 E
Forsan 196 32.07 N 101.22 W
Forsayth 166 18.35 S 143.36 E
Forsbacka 40 60.37 N 16.53 E
Forsby 26 60.30 N 25.56 E
Forserum 26 57.42 N 14.28 E
Forshaga 40 59.32 N 13.28 E
Forsmark 40 60.22 N 18.09 E
Forssa 26 60.49 N 23.38 E
Forst 54 51.44 N 14.39 E
Förste 52 51.44 N 10.10 E
Forster 166 32.11 S 152.31 E
Forstwald ◆8 263 51.18 N 6.30 E
Forsyth, Ga., U.S. 192 33.02 N 83.56 W
Forsyth, Il., U.S. 219 39.56 N 88.57 W
Forsyth, Mo., U.S. 194 36.41 N 93.07 W
Forsyth, Mt., U.S. 202 46.15 N 106.40 W
Forsyth Island I 164 16.50 S 139.06 E
Forsyth Range ⛰ 166 22.45 S 143.15 E
Fort ◆8 272c 18.56 N 72.50 E
Fort Abbās 123 29.12 N 72.52 E
Fort Adams 194 31.05 N 91.32 W
Fort Albany 176 52.15 N 81.37 W
Fort Alexander Indian Reserve ◆4 184 50.27 N 96.15 W
Fortaleza 250 3.43 S 38.30 W
Fortaleza ≐ 248 10.40 S 77.52 W
Fortaleza de Santa Teresa ⊥ 252 33.59 S 53.32 W
Fortaleza do Ituxi 248 7.29 S 66.20 W
Fortaleza dos Nogueiras 250 6.54 S 46.09 W
Fort Amherst National Historic Park ♦ 186 46.12 N 63.09 W
Fort Ancient State Memorial ⊥ 218 39.24 N 84.06 W
Fort Anne National Historic Park ♦ 186 44.44 N 65.26 W
Fort Apache Indian Reservation ◆4 200 34.01 N 110.28 W
Fort-Archambault → Sarh 146 9.09 N 18.23 E
Fort Assiniboine 182 54.20 N 114.46 W
Fort Atkinson 216 42.55 N 88.50 W
Fort Augusta ⊥ 210 40.53 N 76.46 W
Fort Augustus 46 57.09 N 4.41 W
Fort Baker ■ 282 37.50 N 122.29 W
Fort Battleford National Historic Park ♦ 184 52.42 N 108.15 W
Fort Bayard → Zhanjiang 102 21.16 N 110.28 E
Fort Beaufort 158 32.46 S 26.40 E
Fort Beauséjour National Historic Park ♦ 186 45.51 N 64.18 W
Fort Belknap Agency 202 48.28 N 108.45 W
Fort Belknap Indian Reservation ◆4 202 48.16 N 108.38 W
Fort Belvoir ■ 208 38.44 N 77.10 W
Fort Bend □6 222 29.32 N 95.47 W
Fort Benjamin Harrison ■ 218 39.52 N 86.01 W
Fort Benning ■ 192 32.22 N 84.50 W
Fort Benton 202 47.49 N 110.40 W
Fort Berthold Indian Reservation ◆4 198 47.40 N 102.25 W
Fort Bidwell 204 41.51 N 120.09 W
Fort Bliss ■ 200 32.15 N 106.00 W
Fort Bowie National Historic Site ⊥ 200 32.09 N 109.24 W
Fort Bragg 204 39.26 N 123.48 W
Fort Bragg ■ 192 35.09 N 78.59 W
Fort Branch 194 38.15 N 87.34 W
Fort Bridger 200 41.19 N 110.23 W
Fort Calhoun 198 41.27 N 96.01 W
Fort Campbell ■ 194 36.39 N 87.29 W
Fort Canby State Park ♦ 224 46.17 N 124.04 W
Fort-Carnot 157b 21.53 S 47.28 E
Fort Caroline National Memorial ⊥ 192 30.20 N 81.30 W
Fort Carson ■ 200 38.44 N 104.48 W
Fort Casey Historical State Park ♦ 224 48.10 N 122.40 W
Fort Chambly National Historic Park ♦ 206 45.27 N 73.17 W
Fort Chipewyan 176 58.42 N 111.08 W
Fort Churchill Historic State Monument ⊥ 226 39.18 N 119.17 W
Fort Clatsop National Memorial ⊥ 224 46.08 N 123.54 W
Fort Cobb 196 35.05 N 98.26 W
Fort Cobb Reservoir ⊜1 196 35.12 N 98.29 W
Fort Collins 200 40.35 N 105.05 W
Fort Columbia Historical State Park ♦ 224 46.15 N 123.56 W
Fort Constantine 166 20.28 S 140.37 E
Fort-Coulonge 188 45.51 N 76.44 W
Fort Covington 206 44.59 N 74.29 W
Fort Custer State Recreation Area ♦ 216 42.18 N 85.20 W
Fort Davis, Al., U.S. 194 32.14 N 85.42 W
Fort Davis, Tx., U.S. 196 30.35 N 103.53 W
Fort Davis National Historic Site ⊥ 196 30.33 N 103.53 W
Fort de Douaumont ⊥ 56 49.13 N 5.25 E
Fort Defiance 200 35.44 N 109.04 W
Fort-de-France 240e 14.36 N 61.05 W
Fort-de-France, Baie de c 240e 14.34 N 61.04 W
Fort-de-France-Lamentin, Aérodrome de ⊠ 240e 14.35 N 61.00 W
Fort Deposit 194 31.59 N 86.34 W
Fort Detrick ■ 208 39.27 N 77.26 W
Fort de Vaux ⊥ 56 49.12 N 5.28 E
Fort Devens ■ 207 42.32 N 71.37 W
Fort Dix ■ 208 40.00 N 74.33 W
Fort Dodge 190 42.29 N 94.10 W
Fort Donelson National Military Park ♦ 194 36.26 N 87.49 W
Fort Duchesne 200 40.17 N 109.51 W
Fort Dupont Park ♦ 284c 38.53 N 76.57 W
Forte, Monte ▲2 71 40.43 N 8.15 E
Forteau 186 51.28 N 56.58 W
Forte dei Marmi 64 43.57 N 10.10 E
Forte de Magoito 266c 38.52 N 9.27 W
Fort Edward 210 43.16 N 73.35 W
Forte República 152 7.45 S 16.23 E
Fort Erie 212 42.54 N 78.56 W
Fort Erie Race Track ♦ 284a 42.55 N 78.56 W
Fortescue ≐ 162 21.00 S 116.06 E
Fort Eustis ■ 208 37.09 N 76.35 W
Fortevoit 46 56.20 N 3.32 W
Fortezza (Franzensfeste) 64 46.47 N 11.37 E
Fort Fairfield 186 46.46 N 67.50 W
Fort Fitzgerald 176 59.53 N 111.37 W
Fort Foote Village 284c 38.46 N 77.01 W
Fort Foureau 146 12.05 N 15.02 E
Fort Frances 190 48.36 N 93.24 W
Fort Franklin 180 65.11 N 123.46 W
Fort Fraser 182 54.04 N 124.33 W
Fort Frederica National Monument ♦ 192 31.12 N 81.26 W
Fort Gaines 192 31.36 N 85.02 W
Fort Garland 200 37.25 N 105.26 W
Fort Gay 188 38.06 N 82.35 W
Fort George ⊥ 284a 43.15 N 79.04 W
Fort George G. Meade ■ 208 39.05 N 76.50 W
Fort Gibson 196 35.47 N 95.15 W
Fort Gibson Lake ⊜1 196 36.00 N 95.18 W
Fort Good Hope 180 66.15 N 128.38 W
Fort Gordon ■ 192 33.25 N 82.11 W
Fort-Gouraud → Fdérik 148 22.41 N 12.43 W
Fort Green 220 27.36 N 81.56 W
Forth 46 55.47 N 3.41 W
Forth ≐ 46 56.03 N 3.44 W
Forth, Carse of V 46 56.08 N 4.05 W
Forth, Firth of c 46 56.10 N 2.45 W
Förtha 56 50.56 N 10.14 E
Fort Hall 202 43.02 N 112.26 W
Fort Hall Indian Reservation ◆4 202 43.10 N 112.10 W
Fort Hamilton ■ 276 40.37 N 74.02 W
Forth Bridge ◆5 46 56.00 N 3.25 W
Fort Hertz → Putao 102 27.21 N 97.24 E
Fort Hill → Chitipa 154 9.43 S 33.16 E
Fort Hill ■ 188 38.04 N 77.19 W
Fort Hill State Memorial ⊥ 218 39.07 N 83.25 W
Fort Hood ■ 222 31.08 N 97.46 W
Fort Howard 208 39.12 N 76.27 W
Fort Huachuca ■ 200 31.33 N 110.20 W
Fort Hunter 210 42.57 N 74.17 W
Fort Hunter Liggett ■ 226 35.55 N 121.15 W
Fortierville 206 46.29 N 72.02 W
Fortín 234 18.54 N 97.00 W
Fortín, Lac ⊜ 186 50.50 N 67.46 W
Fortín Ayacucho 248 19.58 S 59.47 W
Fortín Coroneles Sanchez 248 19.20 S 59.58 W
Fortine 182 48.45 N 114.54 W
Fortín Florida 248 20.45 S 59.17 W
Fortín Garrapatal 248 21.27 S 61.30 W
Fortín Teniente Montanía 252 22.04 S 59.57 W
Fortín Uno 252 38.51 S 65.17 W
Fort Jackson ■ 192 34.01 N 80.57 W
Fort Jameson → Chipata 154 13.39 S 32.40 E
Fort Jefferson National Monument ♦ 220 24.37 N 82.54 W
Fort Jennings 216 40.54 N 84.17 W
Fort Jeudy, Point of ≻ 241k 12.00 N 61.42 W
Fort Johnson 210 42.57 N 74.14 W
Fort Johnston → Mangochi 154 14.28 S 35.16 E
Fort Jones 204 41.36 N 122.50 W
Fort Kent 186 47.15 N 68.35 W
Fort Klamath 202 42.42 N 121.59 W
Fort Knox ■ 194 37.54 N 85.57 W
Fort-Lamy → N'Djamena 146 12.07 N 15.03 E
Fort Langley 224 49.10 N 122.35 W
Fort Langley National Historic Park ♦ 224 49.10 N 122.35 W
Fort Laramie 200 42.12 N 104.31 W
Fort Laramie National Historic Site ⊥ 198 42.09 N 104.41 W
Fort Larned National Historic Site ⊥ 198 38.10 N 99.12 W
Fort Lauderdale 220 26.07 N 80.08 W
Fort Lauderdale-Hollywood International Airport ⊠ 220 26.04 N 80.09 W
Fort Laurens State Memorial ⊥ 214 40.38 N 81.27 W
Fort Leavenworth ■ 198 39.21 N 94.55 W
Fort Le Boeuf ⊥ 214 41.56 N 79.59 W
Fort Lee 210 40.51 N 73.58 W
Fort Lee ■ 208 37.14 N 77.20 W
Fort Lennox National Historic Park ♦ 206 45.06 N 73.16 W
Fort Leonard Wood ■ 194 37.45 N 92.07 W
Fort Lewis ■ 224 47.05 N 122.37 W
Fort Liard 176 60.15 N 123.28 W
Fort-Liberté 238 19.39 N 71.49 W
Fort Lincoln State Park ♦ 198 46.45 N 100.52 W
Fort Littleton 210 40.04 N 77.58 W
Fort Loramie 216 40.21 N 84.22 W
Fort Loudoun Lake ⊜1 192 35.45 N 84.10 W
Fort Lupton 200 40.05 N 104.48 W
Fort Lyon Canal ≅ 198 38.11 N 102.31 W
Fort Macleod 182 49.43 N 113.25 W
Fort Madison 190 40.37 N 91.18 W
Fort-Mahon-Plage 50 50.21 N 1.34 E
Fort Malden National Historic Park ♦ 281 42.06 N 83.07 W
Fort Matanzas National Monument ♦ 192 29.40 N 81.18 W
Fort McClellan ■ 194 33.43 N 85.47 W
Fort McDermitt Indian Reservation ◆4 202 42.00 N 117.32 W
Fort McDowell Indian Reservation ◆4 200 33.38 N 111.41 W
Fort McHenry National Monument and Historic Shrine ♦ 208 39.16 N 76.35 W
Fort Mckinley 218 39.47 N 84.15 W
Fort McMurray 184 56.44 N 111.23 W
Fort McNair ■ 284c 38.52 N 77.04 W
Fort McPherson 180 67.27 N 134.53 W
Fort Meade 220 27.45 N 81.48 W
Fort Mill 192 35.00 N 80.56 W
Fort Miller 210 43.10 N 73.35 W
Fort Mitchell, Al., U.S. 192 32.21 N 85.01 W
Fort Mitchell, Ky., U.S. 218 39.03 N 84.32 W
Fort Mojave Indian Reservation ◆4 200 34.55 N 114.35 W
Fort Monmouth ■ 208 40.19 N 74.02 W
Fort Monroe ■ 208 37.00 N 76.18 W
Fort Montgomery 210 41.20 N 73.59 W
Fort Morgan 198 40.15 N 103.47 W
Fort Myer ■ 284c 38.53 N 77.05 W
Fort Myers 220 26.38 N 81.52 W
Fort Myers Beach 220 26.27 N 81.56 W
Fort Myers Shores 220 26.43 N 81.45 W
Fort Myers Villas 220 26.34 N 81.52 W
Fort Necessity National Battlefield ⊥ 188 39.47 N 79.39 W
Fort Neck ≻1 276 40.39 N 73.28 W
Fort Nelson 176 58.49 N 122.43 W
Fort Nelson ≐ 176 59.30 N 124.00 W
Fort Niagara Beach 284a 43.16 N 79.03 W
Fort Niagara State Park ♦, N.Y., U.S. 210 43.16 N 79.03 W
Fort Niagara State Park ♦, N.Y., U.S. 284a 43.16 N 79.03 W
Fort Nonsense ⊥ 276 40.48 N 74.29 W
Fort Norman 180 64.54 N 125.34 W
Fort Nottingham 158 29.25 S 29.55 E
Fort Ogden 220 27.05 N 81.57 W
Fort Ord ■ 226 36.40 N 121.48 W
Fortore ≐ 68 41.55 N 15.17 E
Fort Parker State Park ♦ 222 31.36 N 96.33 W
Fort Payne 194 34.26 N 85.43 W
Fort Peck 202 48.00 N 106.26 W
Fort Peck Dam ◆6 202 47.52 N 106.38 W
Fort Peck Indian Reservation ◆4 202 48.22 N 105.40 W
Fort Peck Lake ⊜1 202 47.45 N 106.50 W
Fort Pierce 220 27.26 N 80.19 W
Fort Pierce Inlet c 220 27.28 N 80.18 W
Fort Pierre 198 44.21 N 100.22 W
Fort Pitt Tunnels ◆5 279b 40.25 N 80.00 W
Fort Plain 210 42.55 N 74.37 W
Fort Point National Historic Site ⊥ 282 37.48 N 122.28 W
Fort Polk ■ 194 31.04 N 93.11 W
Fort Portal 154 0.40 N 30.17 E
Fort Providence 176 61.21 N 117.39 W
Fort Pulaski National Monument ♦ 192 32.01 N 80.59 W
Fort Qu'Appelle 184 50.46 N 103.48 W
Fort Raleigh National Historic Site ⊥ 192 35.55 N 75.40 W
Fort Randall Dam ◆6 198 42.48 N 98.35 W
Fort Recovery 216 40.24 N 84.46 W
Fort Resolution 176 61.10 N 113.40 W
Fortress Mountain ▲ 202 44.20 N 109.47 W
Fortress of Louisbourg National Historic Park ♦ 186 45.56 N 59.57 W
Fort Riley ■ 198 39.04 N 96.47 W
Fort Ritchie ■ 208 39.43 N 77.30 W
Fort Rixon 154 20.01 S 29.18 E
Fort Robinson State Park ♦ 198 42.41 N 103.30 W
Fort Rodd Hill National Historic Park ♦ 224 48.26 N 123.28 W
Fortrose, N.Z. 172 46.34 S 168.48 E
Fortrose, Scot., U.K. 46 57.34 N 4.09 W
Fort Rosebery → Mansa 154 11.12 S 28.53 E
Fort Rucker ■ 194 31.20 N 85.42 W
Fort Saint James 182 54.26 N 124.15 W
Fort Saint John 182 56.15 N 120.51 W
Fort Salonga 276 40.55 N 73.18 W
Fort Sam Houston ■ 196 29.27 N 98.27 W
Fort Saskatchewan 182 53.43 N 113.13 W
Fort Scott 198 37.50 N 94.42 W
Fort Seneca 214 41.13 N 83.10 W
Fort-Ševčenko 84 44.31 N 50.16 E
Fort Severn 176 56.00 N 87.38 W
Fort Shawnee 216 40.41 N 84.08 W
Fort Sheridan ■ 216 42.13 N 87.48 W
Fort Sill ■ 196 34.40 N 98.25 W
Fort Simcoe Historical State Park ♦ 224 46.21 N 120.50 W
Fort Simpson 176 61.52 N 121.23 W
Fort Sisseton State Park ♦ 198 45.39 N 97.32 W
Fort Smith, N.T., Can. 176 60.00 N 111.53 W
Fort Smith, Ar., U.S. 194 35.23 N 94.23 W
Fort Steele 182 49.37 N 115.38 W
Fort Stevens State Park ♦ 224 46.10 N 124.00 W
Fort Stewart ■ 192 31.52 N 81.37 W
Fort Stockton 196 30.53 N 102.52 W
Fort Sumner 196 34.28 N 104.14 W
Fort Sumter National Monument ♦ 192 32.44 N 79.46 W
Fort Supply 196 36.34 N 99.34 W
Fort Tejon State Historical Park ♦ 228 34.52 N 118.53 W
Fort Thomas, Az., U.S. 200 33.02 N 109.57 W
Fort Thomas, Ky., U.S. 218 39.04 N 84.26 W
Fort Thompson 198 44.04 N 99.26 W
Fort Tilden ■ 276 40.33 N 73.53 W
Fort Totten 198 47.58 N 98.59 W
Fort Totten Indian Reservation ◆4 198 47.53 N 98.50 W
Fort Totten Park ♦ 284c 38.57 N 77.00 W
Fort Towson 196 34.01 N 95.15 W
Fort-Trinquet → Bîr Mogreïn 148 25.14 N 11.35 W
Fortuna, Arg. 252 35.07 S 65.23 W
Fortuna, C.R. 236 10.30 N 84.35 W
Fortuna, Ca., U.S. 204 40.35 N 124.09 W
Fortuna, Río de la ≐ 248 16.36 S 58.46 W
Fortuna Ledge (Marshall) 180 61.53 N 162.05 W
Fortune 186 47.04 N 55.50 W
Fortune Bay c 186 47.25 N 55.25 W
Fortune Ditch ≅ 279a 41.20 N 82.03 W
Fortune Harbour 186 49.31 N 55.15 W
Fortuneswell 42 50.34 N 2.27 W
Fort Union National Monument ♦ 200 35.55 N 105.01 W
Fort Union Trading Post National Historic Site ⊥ 198 48.00 N 104.03 W
Fort Valley 192 32.33 N 83.53 W
Fort Vancouver National Historic Site ⊥ 224 45.38 N 122.37 W
Fort Vermilion 176 58.24 N 116.00 W
Fortville 218 39.55 N 85.50 W
Fort Walton Beach 194 30.24 N 86.37 W
Fort Washakie 200 43.00 N 108.52 W
Fort Washington 208 40.08 N 75.12 W
Fort Washington Forest 208 38.43 N 76.59 W
Fort Washington State Park ♦ 285 40.07 N 75.14 W
Fort Wayne 216 41.07 N 85.07 W
Fort Wayne Military Museum ☣ 281 42.18 N 83.06 W
Fort Wellington 246 6.24 N 57.36 W
Fort Wellington National Historic Park ♦ 212 44.44 N 75.31 W
Fort White 192 29.55 N 82.42 W
Fort William → Thunder Bay, On., Can. 190 48.23 N 89.15 W
Fort William, Scot., U.K. 46 56.49 N 5.07 W
Fort Worth 222 32.43 N 97.19 W
Fort Yates 198 46.05 N 100.37 W
Forty Foot Drain ≅ 42 52.28 N 0.05 W
Forty Fort 210 41.16 N 75.52 W
Fortymile ≐ 180 64.26 N 140.32 W
Fort Yukon 180 66.34 N 145.17 W
Fort Yuma Indian Reservation ◆4 204 32.48 N 114.34 W
Forum ♦ 275a 45.29 N 73.35 W
Forūr, Jazīreh-ye I 128 26.17 N 54.32 E
Forza d'Agrò 70 37.55 N 15.20 E
Foscagno, Passo di ⋈ 64 46.30 N 10.08 E
Fosdinovo 64 44.08 N 10.01 E
Fosforescente, Bahía c 240m 17.59 N 67.01 W
Fosforitnyj 82 55.19 N 38.54 E
Foshan 100 23.03 N 113.09 E
Fosna ≻1, Nor. 24 64.00 N 10.30 E
Fosna ≻1, Nor. 26 63.45 N 10.25 E
Fosnavåg 26 62.21 N 5.39 E
Foso 150 5.42 N 1.17 W
Foss 46 56.41 N 3.58 W
Foss ≐, Eng., U.K. 44 53.57 N 1.06 W
Foss ≐, Wa., U.S. 224 47.43 N 121.18 W
Fossacesia 66 42.15 N 14.29 E
Fossacesia Marina 66 42.15 N 14.30 E
Fossa Eugeniana ≅ 263 51.33 N 6.36 E
Fossano 62 44.33 N 7.43 E
Fossato, Colle di ⋈ 66 43.19 N 12.47 E
Fossé 56 49.27 N 5.00 E
Fosse-Martin 261 49.05 N 2.54 E
Fosses 261 49.06 N 2.29 E
Fosses-la-Ville 56 50.24 N 4.42 E
Fossil 202 44.59 N 120.12 W
Fossil Butte National Monument ♦ 202 41.50 N 110.40 W
Fossil Downs 162 18.08 S 125.38 E
Fossil Lake ⊜ 202 43.18 N 120.25 W
Fossombrone 66 43.41 N 12.48 E
Fosston 198 47.34 N 95.45 W
Fos-sur-Mer 62 43.26 N 4.57 E
Foster, Austl. 169 38.39 S 146.12 E
Foster, Ky., U.S. 218 38.47 N 84.12 W
Foster, R.I., U.S. 207 41.51 N 71.45 W
Foster ≐ 184 55.47 N 105.49 W
Foster, Mount ▲ 180 59.48 N 135.29 W
Foster Brook 214 41.59 N 78.37 W
Foster City 226 37.33 N 122.16 W
Foster Creek ≐ 198 44.34 N 98.12 W
Fosterdale 210 41.42 N 74.58 W
Foster Joseph Sayers Reservoir ⊜1 214 41.02 N 77.40 W
Foster Park 228 34.21 N 119.18 W
Fosters 194 33.05 N 87.41 W
Fosters Pond ⊜ 283 42.37 N 71.08 W
Foster Street 260 51.46 N 0.09 E
Foster Village 229c 21.21 N 157.55 W
Fostoria 214 41.09 N 83.25 W
Fót 264c 47.37 N 19.12 E
Fotadrevo 157b 24.03 S 45.01 E
Fotan 100 24.12 N 117.53 E
Fóti-Somlyó ▲2 264c 47.38 N 19.13 E
Foucarmont 50 49.51 N 1.34 E
Fou-Chouen → Fushun 104 41.52 N 123.53 E
Fouesnant 32 47.54 N 4.01 W
Foug 56 48.41 N 5.47 E
Fougamou 152 1.13 S 10.36 E
Fougères 32 48.21 N 1.12 W
Fougères-sur-Bièvre 50 47.27 N 1.21 E
Fougerolles 58 47.53 N 6.24 E
Fouhsin → Fuxin 104 42.03 N 121.46 E
Fouju 261 48.35 N 2.47 E
Fouke 194 33.16 N 93.53 W
Foula I 46a 60.08 N 2.05 W
Foulain 58 48.02 N 5.13 E
Foulalaba 150 10.41 N 7.22 W
Foula Mori 150 12.10 N 13.51 W
Foulatari 146 13.41 N 12.03 E
Foul Bay c 140 23.30 N 35.39 E
Fouling → Fuling 102 29.42 N 107.21 E
Foulness ≐ 44 53.47 N 0.43 W
Foulness Island I 42 51.36 N 0.55 E
Foulness Point ≻ 42 51.38 N 0.58 E
Foulpointe 157b 17.41 S 49.31 E
Foulsham 42 52.48 N 1.01 E
Foulwind, Cape ≻ 172 41.45 S 171.28 E
Foumban 152 5.43 N 10.55 E
Foumbot 152 5.30 N 10.38 E
Foumbouni 157a 11.50 S 43.30 E
Foum-el-Hisn 148 28.55 N 8.55 W
Foum-Zguid 148 30.04 N 6.52 W
Foundiougne 150 14.08 N 16.28 W
Fountain, Co., U.S. 198 38.40 N 104.42 W
Fountain, Fl., U.S. 192 30.09 N 85.38 W
Fountain □6 216 40.17 N 87.13 W
Fountain City, In., U.S. 218 39.57 N 84.55 W
Fountain City, Wi., U.S. 190 44.07 N 91.43 W
Fountain Creek ≐, Co., U.S. 198 38.15 N 104.35 W
Fountain Creek ≐, Il., U.S. 219 38.20 N 90.22 W
Fountain Green 200 39.37 N 111.38 W
Fountain Hill 208 40.36 N 75.23 W
Fountain Inn 192 34.41 N 82.11 W
Fountain Park 216 41.50 N 84.32 W
Fountain Peak ▲ 204 34.57 N 115.32 W
Fountain Place 194 30.31 N 91.09 W
Fountains Abbey ☣1 44 54.07 N 1.34 W
Fountains Creek ≐ 208 36.33 N 77.21 W
Fountaintown 218 39.41 N 85.47 W
Fountain Valley 228 33.42 N 117.57 W
Fourche LaFave ≐ 194 34.58 N 92.35 W
Fourche Maline ≐ 196 34.55 N 94.55 W
Fourchu 186 45.43 N 60.15 W
Four Corners 202 44.55 N 122.58 W
Four Elms 260 51.13 N 0.06 E
Four Hole Swamp ≐ 192 33.03 N 80.24 W
Fouriesburg 158 28.38 S 28.14 E
Fourmies 50 50.00 N 4.03 E
Four Mile Creek ≐, On., Can. 284a 43.15 N 79.08 W
Fourmile Creek ≐, N.Y., U.S. 284a 43.17 N 79.00 W
Four Mile Creek ≐, Oh., U.S. 218 39.26 N 84.32 W
Four Mile Creek State Park ♦ 284a 43.16 N 79.00 W
Fourmile Draw V 196 32.40 N 104.18 W
Fourmile Lake ⊜ 212 44.40 N 78.44 W
Four Mile Run ≐ 284c 38.50 N 77.02 W
Four Mountains, Islands of II 180 52.50 N 170.00 W
Fournaise, Piton de la ▲ 157c 21.14 S 55.43 E
Fourneau, Pointe à ≻ 275a 45.22 N 73.51 W
Fourneaux, Fr. 50 47.53 N 1.48 E
Fourneaux, Fr. 62 45.11 N 6.39 E
Fournier, Lac ⊜ 186 51.33 N 65.25 W
Fournière, Lac ⊜ 190 48.04 N 78.03 W
Fournoi I 38 37.34 N 26.30 E
Four Oaks 192 35.26 N 78.25 W
Fourqueux 261 48.53 N 2.04 E
Fours 32 46.49 N 3.43 E
Fourteenmile Creek ≐ 218 38.26 N 85.37 W
Fourth Cataract → Rābi', Ash-Shallāl ar- ↳ 140 18.47 N 32.03 E
Fourth Cliff ≻4 283 42.09 N 70.42 W
Four Towns 281 42.37 N 83.25 W
Fous, Pointe des ≻ 240d 15.12 N 61.20 W
Foussard ≐ 50 48.16 N 1.17 E
Fouta Djalon ◆1 150 11.30 N 12.30 W
Fou-Tcheou → Fuzhou 100 26.06 N 119.17 E
Foux, Cap à ≻ 238 19.41 N 73.27 W
Fouyang → Fuyang 100 32.54 N 115.49 E
Fouzon ≐ 50 47.16 N 1.27 E
Foveaux Strait ⊔ 172 46.35 S 168.00 E
Foveran 46 57.18 N 2.02 W
Fowey 42 50.20 N 4.38 W
Fowler, Ca., U.S. 226 36.37 N 119.40 W
Fowler, Co., U.S. 198 38.07 N 104.01 W
Fowler, In., U.S. 216 40.37 N 87.19 W
Fowler, Ks., U.S. 198 37.23 N 100.11 W
Fowler, Mi., U.S. 216 43.00 N 84.44 W
Fowler, Oh., U.S. 214 41.19 N 80.40 W
Fowler, Lake ⊜ 168b 35.06 S 137.37 E
Fowler, Point ≻ 162 32.02 S 132.29 E
Fowler Creek ≐ 281 42.17 N 83.30 W
Fowlers Bay 162 31.59 S 132.27 E
Fowlerton 196 28.28 N 98.48 W
Fowlerville 216 42.39 N 84.04 W
Fowliang → Jingdezhen 100 29.16 N 117.11 E
Fowman 128 37.13 N 49.19 E
Fox 180 64.51 N 147.46 W
Fox ≐, Mb., Can. 184 56.03 N 93.18 W
Fox ≐, U.S. 190 40.18 N 91.30 W
Fox ≐, U.S. 216 41.21 N 88.50 W
Fox ≐, Il., U.S. 194 38.32 N 88.08 W
Fox ≐, Wi., U.S. 190 44.32 N 88.01 W
Fox, Cape ≻ 182 54.47 N 130.51 W
Foxboro, On., Can. 212 44.15 N 77.26 W
Foxboro, Ma., U.S. 207 42.03 N 71.15 W
Foxboro Raceway ♦ 283 42.06 N 71.16 W
Foxboro Stadium ♦ 283 42.05 N 71.16 W
Fox Brook ≐ 276 41.03 N 74.13 W
Foxburg 214 41.09 N 79.41 W
Fox Chapel 279b 40.30 N 79.55 W
Fox Chase ◆8 285 40.04 N 75.05 W
Fox Chase Manor 285 40.05 N 75.06 W
Fox Creek ≐, Ky., U.S. 218 38.16 N 83.41 W
Fox Creek ≐, N.Y., U.S. 210 42.41 N 74.18 W
Foxe Basin c 176 68.25 N 77.00 W
Foxe-Becken → Foxe Basin c 176 68.25 N 77.00 W
Foxe Channel ⊔ 176 64.30 N 80.00 W
Foxen ⊜ 26 59.23 N 11.52 E
Foxe Peninsula ≻1 176 65.00 N 76.00 W
Foxford 48 53.58 N 9.08 W
Fox Glacier 172 43.28 S 170.00 E
Foxhall 284c 39.04 N 77.03 W
Fox Harbour 186 47.19 N 53.55 W
Fox Hills 284c 39.02 N 77.11 W
Foxhole 42 50.21 N 4.52 W
Foxholes 44 54.08 N 0.28 W
Fox Hollow Lake ⊜ 276 41.02 N 74.40 W
Fox Island I, On., Can. 212 44.28 N 78.24 W
Fox Island I, Wa., U.S. 224 47.16 N 122.37 W
Fox Islands II 180 53.30 N 168.00 W
Fox Lake, Il., U.S. 216 42.23 N 88.11 W
Fox Lake, Wi., U.S. 190 43.33 N 88.54 W
Fox Lake ⊜ 216 42.25 N 88.09 W
Fox Mountain ▲ 180 61.55 N 133.22 W
Foxpark 200 41.05 N 106.09 W
Fox Point 216 43.09 N 87.54 W
Fox Point ≻ 276 40.54 N 73.35 W
Fox River Estates 216 41.58 N 88.20 W
Fox River Grove 216 42.12 N 88.12 W
Foxton 172 40.28 S 175.18 E
Foxton Beach 172 40.28 S 175.14 E
Foxvale 283 42.02 N 71.14 W
Fox Valley, Austl. 274a 33.45 S 151.06 E
Fox Valley, Sk., Can. 184 50.29 N 109.28 W
Foxwells 208 37.38 N 76.18 W
Foxwist Green 262 53.12 N 2.34 W
Foxworth 194 31.14 N 89.52 W
Foyedong 98 40.41 N 119.12 E
Foyers 46 57.14 N 4.29 W
Foyle ≐ 48 54.59 N 7.18 W
Foyle, Lough c 48 55.06 N 7.08 W
Foynes 48 52.37 N 9.06 W
Foza 64 45.54 N 11.38 E
Foz do Areia, Represa de ⊜1 252 26.00 S 51.35 W
Foz do Cunene 152 17.16 S 11.50 E
Foz do Iguaçu 252 25.33 S 54.35 W
Foz do Jordão 248 9.23 S 71.56 W
Foz Giraldo 34 40.00 N 7.43 W
Fozilíng 100 31.20 N 116.17 E
Frabosa Soprana 62 44.17 N 7.48 E
Frackville 208 40.47 N 76.13 W
Fraction Run ≐ 277 41.34 N 80.04 W
Fraga, Arg. 252 33.30 S 65.48 W
Fraga, Esp. 34 41.31 N 0.21 E
Fragagnano 68 40.26 N 17.28 E
Fragneto Monforte 68 41.15 N 14.46 E
Fragoso, Cayo I 240p 22.44 N 79.30 W
Fragrant Hills Park ♦ 271a 39.59 N 116.11 E
Fragua, Sierra de la ⛰ 196 26.41 N 102.13 W
Fraile Muerto 252 32.31 S 54.32 W
Fraïn, Chott el ⊜ 34 35.57 N 5.38 E
Fraire 50 50.16 N 4.30 E
Fraisans 58 47.09 N 5.46 E
Fraisse 62 45.23 N 4.15 E
Fraize 58 48.11 N 7.00 E
Fram 61 46.27 N 15.38 E
Frameries 50 50.24 N 3.54 E
Framingham 207 42.16 N 71.25 W
Framingham State College ☣2 283 42.18 N 71.26 W
Framlingham 42 52.13 N 1.21 E
Frammersbach 56 50.04 N 9.28 E
Framnes Mountains ⛰ 9 67.50 S 62.35 E
Frampol 30 50.41 N 22.40 E
Frampton Cotterell 42 51.32 N 2.29 W
Frampton on Severn 42 51.46 N 2.22 W
França, Bra. 250 11.34 S 40.36 W
Franca, Bra. 255 20.32 S 47.24 W
Franca-Iosifa, Zemľa (Franz Josef Land) II 12 81.00 N 55.00 E
Français, Récif des ◆2 175f 19.40 S 163.20 E
Francavilla al Mare 66 42.25 N 14.17 E
Francavilla Angitola 68 38.46 N 16.16 E
Francavilla d'Ete 66 43.11 N 13.32 E
Francavilla di Sicilia 70 37.54 N 15.08 E
Francavilla Fontana 68 40.31 N 17.35 E
Francavilla in Sinni 68 40.05 N 16.12 E
Francavilla Marittima 68 39.49 N 16.23 E
France □1, Europe 22 46.00 N 2.00 E
France □1, Europe 32 46.00 N 2.00 E
Frances ≐ 180 60.12 N 129.02 W
Francés, Cabo ≻, Cuba 240p 21.54 N 84.02 W
Francés, Cabo ≻, Cuba 240p 21.38 N 83.12 W
Frances Creek 164 13.35 S 131.52 E
Francés dos Carvalhos 256 22.05 S 44.29 W
Frances Lake ⊜ 180 61.25 N 129.30 W
Francés Viejo, Cabo ≻ 238 19.39 N 69.55 W
Francesville 216 40.59 N 86.52 W
Franceville 152 1.38 S 13.35 E
Francfort-sur-Main → Frankfurt am Main 56 50.07 N 8.40 E
Franche-Comté □9 58 47.00 N 6.00 E
Franchère, Lac ⊜ 206 46.47 N 74.58 W
Franches-Montagnes ⛰ 58 47.12 N 7.00 E
Francia 252 32.33 S 56.37 W
Francia → France □1 32 46.00 N 2.00 E
Francia, Estación de ◆5 266d 41.23 N 2.11 E
Francia, Peña de ▲ 34 42.35 N 8.02 W
Francis 184 50.05 N 103.55 W
Francis, Lake ⊜ 206 45.02 N 71.20 W
Francis Case, Lake ⊜1 198 43.15 N 99.00 W
Francisco A. Berra 258 35.23 S 58.51 W
Francisco Álvarez 258 34.38 S 58.52 W
Francisco Beltrão 252 26.05 S 53.04 W
Francisco I. Madero, Méx. 232 25.45 N 103.21 W
Francisco I. Madero, Méx. 232 24.32 N 104.22 W
Francisco I. Madero, Méx. 234 21.36 N 104.49 W
Francisco José, Tierra → Franca-Iosifa, Zemľa II 12 81.00 N 55.00 E
Francisco Morato 256 23.16 S 46.45 W
Francisco Morazán □5 236 14.15 N 87.15 W
Francisco Murguía 234 24.00 N 103.01 W
Francisco Perito Moreno, Parque Nacional ♦ 254 47.50 S 72.08 W
Francisco Sá 255 16.28 S 43.30 W
Francisco Zarco 204 32.06 N 116.30 W
Francis E. Warren Air Force Base ■ 198 41.09 N 104.52 W
Francistown 156 21.11 S 27.32 E
Francitas 222 28.52 N 96.20 W
Franco da Rocha 256 23.20 S 46.43 W
Francofonte 70 37.14 N 14.53 E
François 186 47.35 N 56.45 W
François, Lacs à ⊜ 186 51.40 N 65.49 W
François-Joseph, Îles du → Franca-Iosifa, Zemľa II 12 81.00 N 55.00 E
François Lake 182 54.04 N 125.44 W
François Lake ⊜ 182 54.00 N 125.40 W
Francolise 68 41.11 N 14.03 E
Franconia Notch State Park ♦ 188 44.06 N 71.43 W
Franconville 261 48.59 N 2.14 E
Francs Peak ▲ 202 43.58 N 109.20 W
Francueil 50 47.19 N 1.05 E
Franeker 52 53.11 N 5.32 E
Frangy 58 46.01 N 5.56 E
Frank 279b 40.16 N 79.48 W
Frank and Poet Drain ≅ 281 42.06 N 83.12 W
Frankby 262 53.22 N 3.08 W
Frankel City 196 32.23 N 102.47 W
Franken □9 30 50.00 N 10.00 E
Frankenau 56 51.05 N 8.56 E
Frankenbach 56 50.40 N 8.34 E
Frankenberg 54 50.54 N 13.01 E
Frankenberg-Eder 56 51.03 N 8.48 E
Frankenburg 60 48.05 N 13.30 E
Frankenheim 56 50.32 N 10.04 E
Frankenhöhe ⛰ 56 49.15 N 10.15 E
Frankenmarkt 64 47.59 N 13.25 E
Frankenmuth 190 43.19 N 83.44 W
Frankenstein 56 49.26 N 7.58 E
Frankenthal 56 49.32 N 8.21 E
Frankenwald ⛰ 54 50.18 N 11.36 E
Frankfield 241q 18.09 N 77.22 W
Frankford, On., Can. 212 44.12 N 77.36 W
Frankford, De., U.S. 208 38.31 N 75.14 W
Frankford, Mo., U.S. 219 39.29 N 91.19 W
Frankford ◆8 285 40.01 N 75.05 W
Frankford Arsenal ■ 285 40.00 N 75.04 W
Frankfort, S. Afr. 158 32.44 S 27.28 E
Frankfort, S. Afr. 158 27.15 S 28.30 E
Frankfort, Il., U.S. 216 41.29 N 87.50 W
Frankfort, In., U.S. 216 40.16 N 86.30 W
Frankfort, Ks., U.S. 198 39.42 N 96.25 W
Frankfort, Ky., U.S. 218 38.12 N 84.52 W
Frankfort, Mi., U.S. 190 44.38 N 86.14 W
Frankfort, N.Y., U.S. 210 43.02 N 75.04 W
Frankfort, Oh., U.S. 218 39.24 N 83.10 W
Frankfort, S.D., U.S. 198 44.52 N 98.18 W
Frankfort Springs 214 40.30 N 80.25 W
Frankfurt am Main 56 50.07 N 8.40 E
Frankfurt am Main, Flughafen ⊠ 56 50.02 N 8.33 E
Frankfurt an der Oder 54 52.20 N 14.33 E
Frank G. Bonelli Regional County Park ♦ 280 34.05 N 117.49 W
Frank Hann National Park ♦ 162 32.50 S 120.25 E
Fränkische Alb ⛰2 60 49.20 N 11.30 E
Fränkische Rezat ≐ 56 49.11 N 11.01 E
Fränkische Saale ≐ 56 50.03 N 9.42 E
Fränkische Schweiz ◆1 60 49.45 N 11.25 E
Frank Key I 220 25.07 N 80.54 W
Frankland ≐ 162 34.58 S 116.49 E
Frankleben 54 51.18 N 11.56 E
Franklin, S. Afr. 158 30.18 S 29.30 E
Franklin, Az., U.S. 200 32.40 N 109.04 W
Franklin, Ga., U.S. 192 33.16 N 85.05 W
Franklin, Id., U.S. 202 42.00 N 111.48 W
Franklin, Il., U.S. 219 39.37 N 90.03 W
Franklin, In., U.S. 218 39.28 N 86.03 W
Franklin, Ky., U.S. 194 36.43 N 86.34 W
Franklin, La., U.S. 194 29.47 N 91.30 W
Franklin, Me., U.S. 188 44.35 N 68.13 W
Franklin, Ma., U.S. 207 42.05 N 71.23 W
Franklin, Mi., U.S. 281 42.31 N 83.18 W
Franklin, Mn., U.S. 198 44.31 N 94.52 W
Franklin, Ne., U.S. 198 40.05 N 98.57 W
Franklin, N.H., U.S. 188 43.26 N 71.38 W
Franklin, N.J., U.S. 210 41.07 N 74.34 W
Franklin, N.Y., U.S. 210 42.20 N 75.09 W
Franklin, N.C., U.S. 192 35.10 N 83.22 W
Franklin, Oh., U.S. 218 39.33 N 84.18 W
Franklin, Pa., U.S. 214 41.24 N 79.50 W
Franklin, Tn., U.S. 194 35.55 N 86.52 W
Franklin, Tx., U.S. 222 31.01 N 96.29 W
Franklin, Vt., U.S. 206 44.58 N 72.55 W
Franklin, Va., U.S. 208 36.40 N 76.55 W
Franklin, W.V., U.S. 188 38.39 N 79.20 W
Franklin, Wi., U.S. 216 42.54 N 88.03 W
Franklin □6, In., U.S. 218 39.25 N 85.01 W
Franklin □6, Ky., U.S. 218 38.14 N 84.52 W
Franklin □6, Ma., U.S. 207 42.36 N 72.36 W
Franklin □6, Mo., U.S. 219 38.25 N 91.03 W
Franklin □6, N.Y., U.S. 206 44.57 N 74.18 W
Franklin □6, Oh., U.S. 218 39.57 N 83.00 W
Franklin □6, Pa., U.S. 208 39.56 N 77.40 W
Franklin □6, Tx., U.S. 222 33.07 N 95.13 W
Franklin □6, Vt., U.S. 206 44.57 N 72.52 W
Franklin, Mount ▲ 171b 35.29 S 148.47 E
Franklin, Point ≻ 180 70.54 N 158.48 W
Franklin Bay c 176 69.45 N 126.00 W
Franklin Canyon Reservoir ⊜1 280 34.06 N 118.25 W
Franklin Delano Roosevelt National Historic Site ⊥ 210 41.46 N 73.56 W
Franklin Delano Roosevelt Park ♦ 285 39.54 N 75.11 W
Franklin D. Roosevelt Lake ⊜1 202 48.20 N 118.10 W
Franklin Farms 279b 40.10 N 80.16 W
Franklin Grove 190 41.50 N 89.18 W
Franklin Harbor c 168a 33.42 S 136.56 E
Franklin Institute ☣ 285 39.57 N 75.11 W
Franklin Island I 281 42.24 N 80.20 W
Franklin Lake ⊜, N.T., Can. 176 66.56 N 96.03 W
Franklin Lake ⊜, Nv., U.S. 204 40.24 N 115.12 W
Franklin Lake ⊜, N.J., U.S. 276 40.59 N 74.13 W
Franklin Lakes 276 41.01 N 74.12 W
Franklin-Lower Gordon Wild Rivers National Park ♦ 166 42.46 S 145.45 E
Franklin Mountains ⛰, N.T., Can. 180 63.00 N 123.50 W
Franklin Mountains ⛰, N.Z. 172 44.55 S 167.45 E
Franklin Park, Il., U.S. 216 41.56 N 87.51 W

Symbols in the index entries represent the broad categories identified in the key at the right. Symbols with superior numbers (⛰1) identify subcategories (see complete key on page I · 1).

Symbole im Register stellen die rechts im Schlüssel erklärten Kategorien dar. Symbole mit hochgestellten Ziffern (⛰1) bezeichnen Unterabteilungen einer Kategorie (vgl. vollständiger Schlüssel auf Seite I · 1).

Los símbolos incluídos en el texto del índice representan las grandes categorías identificadas con la clave a la derecha. Los símbolos con numeros en su parte superior (⛰1) identifican las subcategorías (véase la clave completa en la página I · 1).

Les symboles de l'index représentent les catégories indiquées dans la légende à droite. Les symboles suivis d'un indice (⛰1) représentent des sous-catégories (voir légende complète à la page I · 1).

Os símbolos incluídos no texto do índice representam as grandes categorias identificadas com a chave à direita. Os símbolos com números em sua parte superior (⛰1) identificam as subcategorias (veja-se a chave completa à página I · 1).

▲	Mountain	Berg	Montaña	Montagne	Montanha
⛰	Mountains	Gebirge	Montañas	Montagnes	Montanhas
⋈	Pass	Paß	Paso	Col	Passo
V	Valley, Canyon	Tal, Cañon	Valle, Cañón	Vallée, Canyon	Vale, Canhão
≍	Plain	Ebene	Llano	Plaine	Planície
≻	Cape	Kap	Cabo	Cap	Cabo
I	Island	Insel	Isla	Île	Ilha
II	Islands	Inseln	Islas	Îles	Ilhas
⊥	Other Topographic Features	Andere Topographische Objekte	Otros Elementos Topográficos	Autres données topographiques	Outros acidentes topográficos

ESPAÑOL / FRANÇAIS / PORTUGUÊS

Nombre / Nom / Nome	Página / Page / Página	Lat.°′	Long.°′ W = Oeste / W = Ouest / W = Oeste
Franklin Park, Md., U.S.	284c	39.03 N	77.06 W
Franklin Park, N.J., U.S.	276	40.26 N	74.32 W
Franklin Park, N.Y., U.S.	210	43.05 N	76.05 W
Franklin Park, Pa., U.S.	279b	40.35 N	80.06 W
Franklin Park, Va., U.S.	284c	38.55 N	77.09 W
Franklin Park ♠	283	42.18 N	71.06 W
Franklin Pond ⊜	276	41.06 N	74.35 W
Franklin Ridge ∧	282	38.00 N	122.10 W
Franklin River	224	49.06 N	124.49 W
Franklin Roosevelt Park ◆[8]	273d	26.09 S	27.59 E
Franklin Springs	210	43.02 N	75.24 W
Franklin Square	210	40.42 N	73.40 W
Franklin State Forest ♠	283	42.04 N	71.26 W
Franklin Strait ɰ	176	72.00 N	96.00 W
Franklinton, La., U.S.	194	30.50 N	90.09 W
Franklinton, N.C., U.S.	192	36.06 N	78.27 W
Franklintown	208	40.05 N	77.02 W
Franklinville, N.J., U.S.	208	39.37 N	75.04 W
Franklinville, N.Y., U.S.	210	42.20 N	78.27 W
Frankreich → France □[1]	32	46.00 N	2.00 E
Frankston, Austl.	169	38.08 S	145.07 E
Frankston, Tx., U.S.	222	32.03 N	95.30 W
Franksville	216	42.45 N	87.54 W
Frankton	216	40.13 N	85.46 W
Frankville	194	31.38 N	88.08 W
Frånö	26	62.54 N	17.50 E
Fr'anovo	82	56.08 N	38.27 E
Franschhoek	158	33.55 S	19.09 E
Fransfontein	156	20.12 S	15.01 E
Fränsta	26	62.30 N	16.09 E
Františkovy Lázně	54	50.04 N	12.21 E
Franvillers	50	49.58 N	2.30 E
Franzburg	54	54.11 N	12.52 E
Franzensburg ⊥	264b	48.04 N	16.22 E
Franzensfeste → Fortezza	64	46.47 N	11.37 E
Franz Josef	172	43.24 S	170.11 E
Franz Josef Land → Franca Iosifa, Zeml'a II	12	81.00 N	55.00 E
Franz-Josefs-Bahnhof ◆[5]	264b	48.13 N	16.21 E
Franz-Josefs-Höhe ♠	64	47.04 N	12.45 E
Französische Süd- und Antarktis-Gebiete → French Southern and Antarctic Ter □[2]	6	49.30 S	69.30 E
Französisch-Polynesien → French Polynesia □[2]	14	15.00 S	140.00 W
Frasca, Capo della ›	71	39.46 N	8.27 E
Frascati	66	41.48 N	12.41 E
Frascineto	68	39.50 N	16.16 E
Frasdorf	64	47.48 N	12.16 E
Fraser, Co., U.S.	200	39.56 N	105.49 W
Fraser, Mi., U.S.	281	42.32 N	82.56 W
Fraser ≏, B.C., Can.	182	49.09 N	123.12 W
Fraser ≏, Nf., Can.	176	56.35 N	61.55 W
Fraser ≏, Co., U.S.	200	40.06 N	105.58 W
Fraser, Mount ∧	162	25.39 S	118.23 E
Fraserburg	158	31.55 S	21.30 E
Fraserburgh	46	57.42 N	2.00 W
Fraser Island I	166	25.15 S	153.10 E
Fraser Lake	182	54.04 N	124.51 W
Fraser Lake ⊜	182	54.05 N	124.35 W
Fraser Mills	224	49.14 N	122.52 W
Fraser National Park ♠	169	37.10 S	145.50 E
Fraser Plateau ⋏[1]	182	52.00 N	123.00 W
Fraser Range	162	32.03 S	122.48 E
Frasertown	172	38.58 S	177.24 E
Frasne	58	46.51 N	6.10 E
Frasnes-lez-Anvaing	50	50.40 N	3.36 E
Frassine ≏	64	45.18 N	11.37 E
Frassinoro	64	44.18 N	10.34 E
Frati, Monte dei ∧	66	43.40 N	12.10 E
Fratres	61	48.59 N	15.21 E
Frattamaggiore	68	40.57 N	14.16 E
Frattócchie	267a	41.46 N	12.37 E
Frauenfeld	58	47.34 N	8.54 E
Frauenkirchen	61	47.50 N	16.56 E
Frauenstein	54	50.48 N	13.32 E
Frauental an der Lassnitz	61	46.48 N	15.14 E
Frauenwald	54	50.35 N	10.51 E
Fray Bentos	252	33.08 S	58.18 W
Fray Jorge, Parque Nacional ♠	252	30.40 S	71.45 W
Fray Luis Beltrán	252	39.19 S	65.46 W
Fray Marcos	252	34.11 S	55.44 W
Frazee	198	46.43 N	95.42 W
Frazer, Mt., U.S.	202	48.03 N	106.02 W
Frazer, Pa., U.S.	208	40.02 N	75.33 W
Frazeysburg	214	40.07 N	82.07 W
Frazier Mountain ∧	228	34.47 N	118.58 W
Frazier Park	228	34.49 N	118.56 W
Fr'azino	82	55.58 N	38.04 E
Frazzanò	70	38.04 N	14.44 E
Frechen	56	50.54 N	6.49 E
Frechilla	34	42.08 N	4.50 W
Freckenhorst	52	51.55 N	7.58 E
Freckleton	262	53.45 N	2.52 W
Freddo ≏	70	38.01 N	12.54 E
Fredeburg	56	51.11 N	8.18 E
Freden	52	51.56 N	9.54 E
Fredensborg	41	55.58 N	12.24 E
Fredensborg ⊥	41	55.58 N	12.23 E
Frederic	190	45.39 N	92.28 W
Frederica	208	39.00 N	75.27 W
Fredericia	41	55.35 N	9.46 E
Frederick, Il., U.S.	219	40.04 N	90.26 W
Frederick, Md., U.S.	208	39.24 N	77.24 W
Frederick, Ok., U.S.	196	34.23 N	99.01 W
Frederick, S.D., U.S.	198	45.49 N	98.30 W
Frederick □[6]	208	39.25 N	77.25 W
Frederick Hills ⋏[2]	164	12.41 S	136.00 E
Frederick House ≏	190	49.06 N	81.10 W
Frederick House Lake ⊜	190	48.40 N	80.55 W
Frederick Island I	162	34.04 S	122.00 E
Frederick Reef ✦[2]	166	20.58 S	154.23 E
Fredericksburg, In., U.S.	218	38.26 N	86.11 W
Fredericksburg, Ia., U.S.	190	42.57 N	92.11 W
Fredericksburg, Oh., U.S.	214	40.40 N	81.52 W
Fredericksburg, Pa., U.S.	214	40.27 N	76.26 W
Fredericksburg, Tx., U.S.	196	30.16 N	98.52 W
Fredericksburg, Va., U.S.	208	38.18 N	77.27 W
Fredericksburg Battlefield ⊥	208	38.17 N	77.28 W
Frederick Sound ɰ	180	57.00 N	133.00 W
Fredericktown, Mo., U.S.	194	37.33 N	90.17 W
Fredericktown, Oh., U.S.	214	40.28 N	82.32 W
Frederico Westphalen	252	27.22 S	53.24 W
Fredericton	186	45.58 N	66.39 W
Fredericton Junction	186	45.40 N	66.37 W
Frederik Hendrikeiland → Yos Sudarso, Pulau I	164	7.50 S	138.30 E
Frederiksberg, Dan.	41	55.25 N	11.34 E
Frederiksberg, Dan.	41	55.41 N	12.32 E
Frederiksborg □[6]	41	55.56 N	12.18 E
Frederiksborg ⊥	41	55.56 N	12.19 E
Frederikshåb (Paamiut)	176	62.00 N	49.43 W
Frederikshavn	26	57.26 N	10.32 E
Frederikssund	41	55.50 N	12.04 E
Frederiksted	241n	17.43 N	64.53 W
Frederiksværk	41	55.58 N	12.02 E
Frederik Willem IV Vallen ∟	250	3.28 N	57.37 W
Fredersdorf bei Berlin	54	52.31 N	13.44 E
Fredonia, Col.	246	5.55 N	75.41 W
Fredonia, Az., U.S.	200	36.03 N	112.08 W
Fredonia, Ks., U.S.	198	37.32 N	95.49 W
Fredonia, N.Y., U.S.	214	42.26 N	79.19 W
Fredonia, N.D., U.S.	198	46.19 N	99.05 W
Fredonia, Pa., U.S.	214	41.20 N	80.14 W
Fredrika	26	64.05 N	18.24 E
Fredriksberg	40	60.08 N	14.23 E
Fredrikstad	26	59.13 N	10.57 E
Freeburg, Il., U.S.	219	38.25 N	89.54 W
Freeburg, Mo., U.S.	219	38.18 N	91.55 W
Freeburg, Pa., U.S.	208	40.46 N	76.57 W
Freedom, Ca., U.S.	226	36.56 N	121.46 W
Freedom, Pa., U.S.	214	40.40 N	80.14 W
Freehold, N.J., U.S.	208	40.15 N	74.16 W
Freehold, N.Y., U.S.	210	42.22 N	74.03 W
Freeland, Mi., U.S.	190	43.31 N	84.07 W
Freeland, Pa., U.S.	210	41.01 N	75.53 W
Freeland, Wa., U.S.	224	48.01 N	122.32 W
Freeland Park	216	40.37 N	87.30 W
Freeling, Mount ∧	162	22.35 S	133.06 E
Freel Peak ∧	226	38.52 N	119.54 W
Freels, Cape ›, Nf., Can.	186	49.15 N	53.28 W
Freels, Cape ›, Nf., Can.	186	46.37 N	53.33 W
Freeman	198	43.21 N	97.26 W
Freeman ≏	182	54.20 N	114.47 W
Freeman, Lake ⊜	216	40.42 N	86.45 W
Freemansburg	210	40.37 N	75.20 W
Freemount	48	52.16 N	8.53 W
Freeport, Ba.	238	26.30 N	78.45 W
Freeport, N.S., Can.	186	44.17 N	66.19 W
Freeport, On., Can.	212	43.25 N	80.25 W
Freeport, Fl., U.S.	194	30.29 N	86.08 W
Freeport, Il., U.S.	190	42.17 N	89.37 W
Freeport, Me., U.S.	188	43.51 N	70.06 W
Freeport, Mi., U.S.	216	42.45 N	85.18 W
Freeport, N.Y., U.S.	210	40.39 N	73.35 W
Freeport, Oh., U.S.	214	40.12 N	81.15 W
Freeport, Pa., U.S.	210	40.40 N	79.41 W
Freeport, Tx., U.S.	222	28.57 N	95.21 W
Freer	196	27.52 N	98.37 W
Freest	54	54.08 N	13.43 E
Freeston	222	31.32 N	96.15 W
Freestone	171a	28.08 S	152.08 E
Freestone □[6]	222	31.44 N	96.10 W
Freetown, Antig.	240c	17.03 N	61.42 W
Freetown, S.L.	150	8.30 N	13.15 W
Freetown, In., U.S.	218	38.58 N	86.07 W
Freetown, N.Y., U.S.	207	40.58 N	72.11 W
Freeville	210	42.30 N	76.20 W
Freewood Acres	208	40.10 N	74.15 W
Freezeout Lake ⊜	202	47.40 N	112.03 W
Fregenal de la Sierra	34	38.10 N	6.39 W
Fregene ◆[8]	66	41.51 N	12.12 E
Freiberg	54	50.54 N	13.20 E
Freiberger Mulde ≏	54	51.10 N	12.48 E
Freiburg → Fribourg	58	46.48 N	7.09 E
Freiburg □[5]	58	48.00 N	8.25 E
Freiburg an der Elbe	52	53.49 N	9.17 E
Freiburg im Breisgau	58	47.59 N	7.51 E
Freienbach	58	47.12 N	8.45 E
Freienhufen	54	51.35 N	13.58 E
Freie Universität ɷ[2]	264a	52.26 N	13.16 E
Freigericht	56	50.08 N	9.07 E
Freihung	60	49.37 N	11.55 E
Freiland	61	47.58 N	15.34 E
Freilassing	64	47.50 N	12.59 E
Freilingen	56	50.33 N	7.50 E
Freinberg	60	48.34 N	13.31 E
Freinsheim	56	49.30 N	8.13 E
Freirina	252	28.30 S	71.06 W
Freisen	56	49.33 N	7.14 E
Freisenbruch ◆[8]	263	51.27 N	7.06 E
Freising	60	48.23 N	11.44 E
Freistadt	61	48.31 N	14.31 E
Freital	54	51.00 N	13.39 E
Freiwalde	54	51.58 N	13.44 E
Freixial	266c	38.54 N	9.09 W
Fréjus	62	43.26 N	6.44 E
Fréjus, Tunnel du ◆[5]	62	45.08 N	6.40 E
Frémainville	261	49.04 N	1.52 E
Fremantle	168a	32.03 S	115.45 E
Fremdingen	56	48.58 N	10.27 E
Fremington	42	51.04 N	4.07 W
Fremont, Ca., U.S.	226	37.32 N	121.59 W
Fremont, In., U.S.	216	41.43 N	84.55 W
Fremont, Ia., U.S.	190	41.12 N	92.26 W
Fremont, Mi., U.S.	190	43.28 N	85.56 W
Fremont, Ne., U.S.	198	41.26 N	96.29 W
Fremont, N.C., U.S.	192	35.32 N	77.58 W
Fremont, Oh., U.S.	214	41.21 N	83.07 W
Fremont, Wi., U.S.	190	44.15 N	88.51 W
Fremont ≏	200	38.24 N	110.42 W
Fremont Canyon ∨	280	33.48 N	117.42 W
Fremont Island I	200	41.09 N	112.20 W
Fremont Lake ⊜	202	42.57 N	109.49 W
Fremont Peak ∧, Ca., U.S.	226	36.46 N	121.30 W
Fremont Peak ∧, Ca., U.S.	228	35.12 N	117.27 W
Fremont Valley ∨	228	35.10 N	118.00 W
French ≏	190	45.56 N	80.54 W
French Broad ≏	192	35.57 N	83.51 W
Frenchburg	192	37.57 N	83.37 W
French Camp	226	37.53 N	121.16 W
Frenchcap Cay I	240m	18.14 N	64.51 W
French Creek ≏, Mb., Can.	184	57.02 N	92.12 W
French Creek ≏, U.S.	214	41.25 N	79.50 W
French Creek ≏, Oh., U.S.	279a	41.27 N	82.07 W
French Creek ≏, Pa., U.S.	208	40.08 N	75.31 W
French Creek ≏, S.D., U.S.	198	43.38 N	102.55 W
French Creek, South Branch ≏, Pa., U.S.	214	41.54 N	79.54 W
French Creek, South Branch ≏, Pa., U.S.	285	40.10 N	75.42 W
French Creek, West Branch ≏	214	41.58 N	79.52 W
French Creek State Park ♠	208	40.13 N	75.47 W
French Frigate Shoals ✦[2]	14	23.45 N	166.10 W
French Guiana (Guyane français) □[2], S.A.	242	4.00 N	53.00 W
French Guiana (Guyane français) □[2], S.A.	250	4.00 N	53.00 W
French Island I	169	38.21 S	145.21 E
French Lick	194	38.32 N	86.37 W
Frenchman (Frenchman Creek) ≏	202	48.24 N	107.05 W
Frenchman Bay ⊂	188	44.25 N	68.10 W
Frenchman Butte	184	53.35 N	109.38 W
Frenchman Creek (Frenchman) ≏, N.A.	202	48.24 N	107.05 W
Frenchman Creek ≏, U.S.	198	40.13 N	100.50 W
Frenchman Lake ⊜	204	36.48 N	116.56 W
Frenchman Point ›	212	44.35 N	81.18 W
Frenchman's Bay ⊂	275b	43.49 N	79.05 W
Frenchmans Cap ∧	166	42.16 S	145.50 E
Frenchman's Creek ≏, On., Can.	284a	42.56 N	78.56 W
Frenchmans Creek ≏, Ca., U.S.	282	37.29 N	122.27 W
French Meadows Reservoir ⊜[1]	226	39.07 N	120.25 W
Frenchpark	48	53.52 N	8.26 W
French Pass	172	40.56 S	173.50 E
French Polynesia □[2]	14	15.00 S	140.00 W
Frenchs Forest	274a	33.45 S	151.14 E
French Southern and Antarctic Territories □[2]	6	49.30 S	69.30 E
French Stream ≏	283	42.07 N	70.53 W
Frenchtown	210	40.31 N	75.03 W
Frenda	148	35.02 N	1.01 E
Freneuse	261	49.03 N	1.36 E
Frensdorferhaar	52	52.25 N	7.03 E
Frenštát pod Radhoštěm	30	49.33 N	18.14 E
Frentani, Monti dei ⋏	66	41.54 N	14.37 E
Frépillon	261	49.03 N	2.12 E
Frere	158	28.52 S	29.47 E
Freren	52	52.29 N	7.32 E
Fresco	150	5.05 N	5.34 W
Fresco ≏	250	6.39 S	51.59 W
Freshfield	262	53.34 N	3.04 W
Freshfield, Mount ∧	182	51.44 N	116.57 W
Freshford	48	52.43 N	7.24 W
Fresh Meadows ◆[8]	276	40.44 N	73.48 W
Fresh Pond ⊜, Ma., U.S.	283	42.23 N	71.09 W
Fresh Pond ⊜, N.Y., U.S.	276	40.55 N	73.18 W
Freshwater	42	50.40 N	1.30 W
Freshwater Creek ≏	226	39.12 N	122.04 W
Fresia	254	41.09 S	73.27 W
Fresnes	261	48.45 N	2.19 E
Fresne-Saint-Mamès	58	47.33 N	5.52 E
Fresnes-en-Woëvre	56	49.08 N	5.39 E
Fresnes-sur-Escaut	50	50.26 N	3.35 E
Fresnes-sur-Marne	261	48.56 N	2.45 E
Fresnillo	234	23.10 N	102.53 W
Fresno, Col.	246	5.09 N	75.01 W
Fresno, Ca., U.S.	226	36.44 N	119.46 W
Fresno, Oh., U.S.	214	40.20 N	81.44 W
Fresno, Tx., U.S.	222	29.32 N	95.27 W
Fresno □[6]	226	36.38 N	119.45 W
Fresno ≏	226	37.05 N	120.33 W
Fresno, Lewis Fork ≏	226	37.20 N	119.39 W
Fresno Air Terminal ⊠	226	36.46 N	119.43 W
Fresno Reservoir ⊜[1]	202	48.41 N	109.57 W
Fresno Slough ≏	226	36.47 N	120.22 W
Fresnoy-Folny	50	49.53 N	1.26 E
Fresnoy-le-Grand	50	49.57 N	3.25 E
Fressenneville	50	50.04 N	1.34 E
Fressin	50	50.27 N	2.03 E
Freswick	46	58.35 N	3.05 W
Fréteval	50	47.53 N	1.13 E
Frétigney-et-Velloreille	58	47.29 N	5.56 E
Fretin	50	50.33 N	3.08 E
Frettes	58	47.41 N	5.34 E
Freu, Cap des ›	34	39.45 N	3.27 E
Freudenberg, Dtsch.	56	49.44 N	9.19 E
Freudenberg, Dtsch.	56	50.54 N	7.52 E
Freudenberg, Dtsch.	264a	52.42 N	13.49 E
Freudenstadt	58	48.28 N	8.25 E
Frévent	50	50.16 N	2.17 E
Frew ≏	162	20.00 S	135.38 E
Frewena	162	19.25 S	135.25 E
Frewsburg	214	42.03 N	79.09 W
Freyburg	54	51.13 N	11.46 E
Freycinet, Cape ›	162	34.06 S	114.59 E
Freycinet Estuary ⊂[1]	162	26.25 S	113.45 E
Freycinet National Park ♠	166	42.10 S	148.20 E
Freycinet Peninsula ›[1]	166	42.13 S	148.18 E
Freyenstein	54	53.17 N	12.20 E
Freyming-Merlebach	56	49.09 N	6.48 E
Freyre	252	31.10 S	62.06 W
Freystadt	60	49.12 N	11.20 E
Freyung	60	48.48 N	13.33 E
Fria	150	10.05 N	13.32 W
Fria, Cape ›	152	18.30 S	12.01 E
Friant	226	36.59 N	119.42 W
Friant Dam ◆[6]	226	37.00 N	119.43 W
Friant-Kern Canal ≊	226	35.22 N	119.06 W
Friars Point	194	34.22 N	90.38 W
Frías, Arg.	252	28.39 S	65.09 W
Frías, Perú	248	4.52 S	79.57 W
Fribourg (Freiburg)	58	46.48 N	7.09 E
Fribourg (Freiburg) □[3]	58	46.45 N	7.05 E
Frick	58	47.31 N	8.01 E
Frick Park ♠	279b	40.26 N	79.54 W
Friday	222	31.07 N	95.15 W
Friday Harbor	224	48.32 N	123.00 W
Fridaythorpe	44	54.01 N	0.40 W
Fridingen an der Donau	58	48.01 N	8.56 E
Fridley	190	45.05 N	93.15 W
Fridolfing	60	48.00 N	12.49 E
Fridtjof Nansen, Mount ∧	9	85.21 S	167.33 W
Friedberg, Dtsch.	56	50.20 N	8.45 E
Friedberg, Dtsch.	58	48.21 N	10.58 E
Friedberg, Öst.	61	47.27 N	16.03 E
Friedeburg [/Saale]	54	51.37 N	11.44 E
Friedenau ◆[8]	264a	52.28 N	13.20 E
Friedens	214	40.03 N	79.00 W
Friedensburg	208	40.36 N	76.14 W
Friedersdorf, Dtsch.	54	52.17 N	13.47 E
Friedersdorf, Dtsch.	54	51.01 N	14.34 E
Friedersdorf, Dtsch.	54	51.39 N	12.21 E
Friedesheim	158	27.55 S	26.43 E
Friedland, Dtsch.	54	52.06 N	14.16 E
Friedland, Dtsch.	54	53.40 N	13.33 E
Friedland, Dtsch.	56	51.25 N	9.55 E
Friedrich-Ebert-Brücke ◆[5]	263	51.28 N	6.43 E
Friedrich Krupp-Aktiengesellschaft ɷ[3]	263	51.28 N	7.00 E
Friedrichroda	54	50.52 N	10.34 E
Friedrichsbrunn	54	51.41 N	11.02 E
Friedrichsdorf	56	50.15 N	8.38 E
Friedrichsfeld	263	51.38 N	6.39 E
Friedrichsfelde ◆[8]	264a	52.31 N	13.31 E
Friedrichshafen	58	47.39 N	9.28 E
Friedrichshagen ◆[8]	264a	52.27 N	13.38 E
Friedrichshain ◆[8]	264a	52.31 N	13.25 E
Friedrichshof	264a	52.19 N	13.46 E
Friedrichsort ◆[8]	54	54.24 N	10.11 E
Friedrichsruh, Schloss ⊥	52	53.32 N	10.20 E
Friedrichsruhe	54	53.31 N	11.45 E
Friedrichstadt	41	54.22 N	9.05 E
Friedrichsthal, Dtsch.	54	52.48 N	13.16 E
Friedrichsthal, Dtsch.	56	49.19 N	7.06 E
Friedrichstrasse, Bahnhof ◆[5]	264a	52.31 N	13.24 E
Friedrichswalde	54	53.02 N	13.42 E
Frielas	266c	38.49 N	9.09 W
Frielendorf	56	50.58 N	9.19 E
Friemersheim ◆[8]	263	51.23 N	6.42 E
Friend, Ne., U.S.	198	40.39 N	97.17 W
Friend, Or., U.S.	224	45.21 N	121.16 W
Friends Colony ◆[8]	272a	28.34 N	77.16 E
Friendship, N.Y., U.S.	210	42.12 N	78.08 W
Friendship, Tn., U.S.	194	35.54 N	89.14 W
Friendship, Wi., U.S.	190	43.58 N	89.49 W
Friendship Creek ≏	285	39.55 N	74.43 W
Friendship Shoal ✦[2]	112	5.58 N	112.31 E
Friends Meeting House State Memorial ⊥	214	40.09 N	80.47 W
Friendswood	222	29.31 N	95.12 W
Friern Barnet ◆[8]	260	51.37 N	0.10 W
Fries	192	36.42 N	80.58 W
Friesach	61	46.57 N	14.24 E
Friesack	54	52.44 N	12.34 E
Friesenheim	58	48.22 N	7.53 E
Friesenhofen	58	47.45 N	10.04 E
Friesenried	58	47.52 N	10.31 E
Friesland □[4]	52	53.03 N	5.45 E
Friesland □[9]	30	53.00 N	5.40 E
Fries Mills	285	39.39 N	75.03 W
Friesoythe	52	53.01 N	7.51 E
Frigate Point ›	174g	28.11 N	177.24 W
Frigento	68	41.01 N	15.06 E
Frignano	68	41.00 N	14.10 E
Frignano ◆[1]	64	44.20 N	10.51 E
Friguia	150	12.03 N	10.56 W
Fritala	26	61.26 N	21.52 E
Frillendorf ◆[8]	263	51.28 N	7.05 E
Frindsbury	260	51.24 N	0.30 E
Frinsted	260	51.17 N	0.43 E
Frinton-on-Sea	42	51.50 N	1.14 E
Frintrop ◆[8]	263	51.29 N	6.55 E
Frío ≏, N.A.	236	11.08 N	84.46 W
Frio ≏, Tx., U.S.	196	28.30 N	98.10 W
Frio, Cabo ›	255	22.53 S	42.00 W
Friockheim	46	56.38 N	2.38 W
Frio Draw ∨	196	34.50 N	102.19 W
Friona	196	34.38 N	102.43 W
Frisa, Loch ⊜	46	56.34 N	6.05 W
Frisange	56	49.32 N	6.12 E
Frisches Haff → Vislinskij zaliv ⊂	30	54.27 N	19.40 E
Frisco, Pa., U.S.	214	40.51 N	80.16 W
Frisco, Tx., U.S.	222	33.09 N	96.49 W
Frisco City	194	31.26 N	87.24 W
Frisco Creek ≏	196	36.34 N	101.23 W
Frisian Islands II	30	53.35 N	6.40 E
Friskney	44	53.04 N	0.11 E
Fristad	26	57.50 N	13.01 E
Fritch	196	35.38 N	101.36 W
Fritsla	26	57.33 N	12.47 E
Fritzlar	56	51.08 N	9.16 E
Friuli □[9]	64	46.00 N	13.00 E
Friuli-Venezia Giulia □[4]	64	46.00 N	13.00 E
Friza, proliv ɰ	74	45.30 N	149.10 E
Frizington	44	54.32 N	3.30 W
Frobisher	184	49.12 N	102.26 W
Frobisher Bay ⊂	176	62.30 N	66.00 W
Frobisher Lake ⊜	184	56.25 N	108.20 W
Frodsham, Eng., U.K.	44	53.18 N	2.44 W
Frodsham, Eng., U.K.	262	53.18 N	2.44 W
Frog Lake ⊜	184	53.55 N	110.18 W
Frohavet ɰ	24	63.52 N	9.26 E
Frohburg	54	51.03 N	12.33 E
Frohlinde ◆[8]	263	51.32 N	7.21 E
Frohnau ◆[8]	264a	52.38 N	13.18 E
Frohnhausen	263	51.29 N	7.48 E
Frohnhausen ◆[8]	263	51.27 N	6.58 E
Frohnleiten	61	47.16 N	15.20 E
Frohse	54	52.02 N	11.43 E
Froid	198	48.20 N	104.30 W
Froid, Lac ⊜	206	46.40 N	74.32 W
Froid, Ruisseau ≏	206	46.23 N	74.46 W
Froidmont-Cohartille	50	49.41 N	3.42 E
Froidos	56	49.03 N	5.07 E
Froissy	50	49.34 N	2.13 E
Froitzheim	56	50.42 N	6.34 E
Frolišči, Ross.	80	56.25 N	42.39 E
Frolišči, Ross.	82	56.18 N	39.13 E
Frolovo	80	49.47 N	43.39 E
Froman Run ≏	279b	40.12 N	80.00 W
Fromberg	202	45.23 N	108.54 W
Frombork	30	54.22 N	19.41 E
Frome	42	51.14 N	2.20 W
Frome ≏, Austl.	166	29.06 S	137.52 E
Frome ≏, Eng., U.K.	42	52.03 N	2.38 W
Frome ≏, Eng., U.K.	42	50.41 N	2.04 W
Frome, Lake ⊜	166	30.48 S	139.48 E
Frome Downs	166	31.13 S	139.46 E
Fromelennes	56	50.08 N	4.52 E
Fromentières	50	48.54 N	3.43 E
Frömern	263	51.30 N	7.44 E
Frommern	58	48.15 N	8.52 E
Fröndenberg	56	51.28 N	7.46 E
Frönsberg	263	51.21 N	7.46 E
Fronteiras	250	7.05 S	40.37 W
Frontenac, Fl., U.S.	220	28.27 N	80.46 W
Frontenac, Ks., U.S.	198	37.27 N	94.41 W
Frontenac □[6], On., Can.	212	44.40 N	76.45 W
Frontenac □[6], P.Q., Can.	206	45.42 N	71.15 W
Frontenard	58	46.55 N	5.10 E
Frontenex-Villard-Rosset	62	45.38 N	6.19 E
Frontera, Méx.	232	26.56 N	101.27 W
Frontera, Méx.	234	18.32 N	92.38 W
Fronteras	200	30.56 N	109.31 W
Frontier, Sk., Can.	184	49.12 N	108.34 W
Frontier, Mi., U.S.	216	41.47 N	84.36 W
Frontier, Wy., U.S.	200	41.48 N	110.32 W
Frontignan	62	43.27 N	3.45 E
Frontino	246	6.46 N	76.08 W
Frontino, Páramo ∧	246	6.28 N	76.04 W
Frontón, Isla I	286d	12.07 S	77.11 W
Front Range ⋏, Leso.	158	29.05 S	28.20 E
Front Range ⋏, Co., U.S.	200	39.45 N	105.45 W
Front Royal	188	38.55 N	78.11 W
Frose	54	51.48 N	11.23 E
Frosinone	66	41.38 N	13.19 E
Frosinone □[4]	66	41.37 N	13.27 E
Frosolone	66	41.36 N	14.27 E
Frösön	26	63.11 N	14.32 E
Frost	222	32.05 N	96.48 W
Frostavallen	41	55.58 N	13.30 E
Frostburg	188	39.39 N	78.55 W
Frostproof	220	27.44 N	81.31 W
Frotheim	52	52.21 N	8.40 E
Frouard	56	48.46 N	6.08 E
Frövi	40	59.28 N	15.22 E
Frøya I	24	63.43 N	8.42 E
Fruges	50	50.31 N	2.08 E
Fruita	200	39.09 N	108.43 W
Fruitdale, Al., U.S.	194	31.20 N	88.24 W
Fruitdale, Or., U.S.	202	42.24 N	123.20 W
Fruithurst	194	33.43 N	85.26 W
Fruitland, Id., U.S.	202	44.00 N	116.54 W
Fruitland, Md., U.S.	208	38.19 N	75.37 W
Fruitland Park	220	28.51 N	81.54 W
Fruitport	216	43.07 N	86.09 W
Fruitvale, B.C., Can.	182	49.07 N	117.33 W
Fruitvale, Tx., U.S.	222	32.41 N	95.48 W
Fruitvale, Wa., U.S.	202	46.37 N	120.33 W
Fruitville	192	27.19 N	82.27 W
Frumușița	38	45.40 N	28.04 E
Frunze → Biškek, Kyrg.	85	42.54 N	74.36 E
Frunze, Kyrg.	85	40.07 N	71.44 E
Frunze, Ukr.	78	46.16 N	34.52 E
Frunze, Ukr.	83	48.40 N	38.45 E
Frunzovka	78	47.20 N	29.44 E
Frutal	255	20.02 S	48.55 W
Frutigen	58	46.35 N	7.39 E
Frutillar	254	41.07 S	73.03 W
Fryburg	214	41.21 N	79.26 W
Frýdek-Místek	30	49.41 N	18.22 E
Frýdlant	30	50.56 N	15.05 E
Frye	279b	40.11 N	79.56 W
Fryeburg	188	44.00 N	70.58 W
Fryerning	260	51.41 N	0.22 E
Fryingpan ≏	200	39.22 N	107.02 W
Fu ≏, Zhg.	100	29.52 N	115.28 E
Fu ≏, Zhg.	100	28.36 N	116.04 E
Fu ≏, Zhg.	102	29.59 N	106.16 E
Fua'amotu	174w	21.16 S	175.08 W
Fua'amotu International Airport ⊠	174w	21.17 S	175.08 W
Fu'an, Zhg.	100	27.08 N	119.40 E
Fu'an, Zhg.	100	32.41 N	120.41 E
Fuanjie	100	25.29 N	117.53 E
Fubao	107	28.47 N	106.05 E
Fubine	62	44.58 N	8.26 E
Fucecchio	66	43.44 N	10.48 E
Fuchang	100	30.06 N	113.08 E
Fucheng	98	37.52 N	116.07 E
Fuchikou	100	29.51 N	115.27 E
Fuchow → Fuzhou	100	28.01 N	116.20 E
Fuchs-Berg ∧[2]	264a	52.27 N	13.51 E
Fuchskaute ∧	56	50.40 N	8.06 E
Füchtorf	52	52.03 N	8.02 E
Fuchū, Nihon	94	35.40 N	139.29 E
Fuchū, Nihon	94	36.39 N	137.10 E
Fuchū, Nihon	96	34.24 N	132.30 E
Fuchū, Nihon	96	34.34 N	133.14 E
Fuchun ≏	106	30.10 N	120.09 E
Fucine	64	46.18 N	10.44 E
Fucino, Conca del ≚	66	42.01 N	13.31 E
Fudan University ɷ[2]	269b	31.17 N	121.29 E
Fuday I	46	57.03 N	7.23 W
Fuding	100	27.21 N	120.12 E
Fudu ≏	107	29.52 N	106.10 E
Fuefuki ≏	94	35.33 N	138.28 E
Fuego, Volcán de ∧[1]	236	14.29 N	90.53 W
Fuelbeckestausee ⊜[1]	263	51.15 N	7.40 E
Fuencaliente	34	38.24 N	4.18 W
Fuencarral ◆[8]	266a	40.30 N	3.41 W
Fuenlabrada	266a	40.17 N	3.48 W
Fuensalida	34	40.03 N	4.12 W
Fuensanta, Embalse de ⊜[1]	34	38.23 N	2.13 W
Fuente	196	28.40 N	100.32 W
Fuente de Cantos	34	38.15 N	6.18 W
Fuente de Oro	246	3.28 N	73.37 W
Fuenteobejuna	34	38.16 N	5.25 W
Fuentesaúco	34	41.14 N	5.30 W
Fuentes de Ebro	34	41.31 N	0.38 W
Fuerli	105	39.40 N	116.41 E
Fuerte ≏	232	25.54 N	109.22 W
Fuerte Olimpo	248	21.02 S	57.54 W
Fuerteventura I	148	28.20 N	14.00 W
Fuerza, Castillo de la ⊥	286b	23.09 N	82.21 W
Fufeng	102	34.20 N	107.51 E
Fuga Island I	116	18.52 N	121.22 E
Fugama, Wādī ∨	140	14.43 N	24.36 E
Fügen	64	47.21 N	11.51 E
Fuglebjerg	41	55.18 N	11.34 E
Fugløysund ɰ	24	70.12 N	20.20 E
Fugong	102	27.09 N	98.52 E
Fugou	98	34.04 N	114.24 E
Fuhai	86	47.06 N	87.23 E
Fuhe	100	23.22 N	113.37 E
Fuhlenbrock ◆[8]	263	51.32 N	6.54 E
Fuhrberg	52	52.34 N	9.50 E
Fuhse ≏	52	52.37 N	10.03 E
Fuhsien → Fuxian	98	39.37 N	122.01 E
Fuhu	100	29.11 N	118.04 E
Fuji, Nihon	94	35.09 N	138.39 E
Fuji, Zhg.	98	34.24 N	114.48 E
Fuji, Zhg.	107	29.09 N	105.23 E
Fuji ≏	94	35.07 N	138.39 E
Fuji, Mount → Fuji-san ∧[1]	94	35.22 N	138.44 E
Fujiafeng	105	39.11 N	117.32 E
Fujian (Fukien) □[4]	100	26.00 N	118.00 E
Fujiatun	104	41.42 N	123.44 E
Fujiawopu	104	40.58 N	122.14 E
Fujiazhen	107	29.57 N	104.18 E
Fujiazhuangcun	104	41.15 N	122.20 E
Fujie	106	31.09 N	119.27 E
Fujieda	94	34.52 N	138.16 E
Fuji-Hakone-Izu-kokuritsu-kōen ♠	94	35.21 N	138.44 E
Fujiidera	96	34.34 N	135.36 E
Fujikawa	94	35.08 N	138.37 E
Fujikubo	268	35.50 N	139.32 E
Fujimi, Nihon	94	36.27 N	139.05 E
Fujimi, Nihon	94	35.55 N	138.15 E
Fujimi, Nihon	94	35.51 N	139.33 E
Fujin	89	47.14 N	132.00 E
Fujino	94	35.37 N	139.10 E
Fujinomiya	94	35.12 N	138.38 E
Fujioka, Nihon	94	35.12 N	137.12 E
Fujioka, Nihon	94	36.15 N	139.05 E
Fujioka, Nihon	94	36.15 N	139.39 E
Fuji-san ∧[1]	94	35.22 N	138.44 E
Fujisawa	94	35.21 N	139.29 E
Fujishiro	94	35.55 N	140.07 E
Fujiwara, Nihon	94	35.09 N	136.30 E
Fujiwara, Nihon	94	36.51 N	139.44 E
Fujiwara-dam ◆[6]	94	36.49 N	139.02 E
Fujiyama → Fuji-san ∧[1]	94	35.22 N	138.44 E
Fuji-yoshida	94	35.29 N	138.48 E
Fukagawa	92a	43.43 N	142.03 E
Fukagawa ◆[8]	268	35.40 N	139.48 E
Fukami	268	35.28 N	139.28 E
Fukane I	174w	21.05 S	175.02 W
Fukang	86	44.10 N	87.59 E
Fukasaka-tunnel ◆[5]	94	35.35 N	136.10 E
Fuka Shan ∧	89	47.55 N	120.53 E
Fukaya	94	36.12 N	139.17 E
Fukiage	94	36.06 N	139.27 E
Fukiai ◆[8]	270	34.42 N	135.12 E
Fukien → Fujian □[4]	100	26.00 N	118.00 E
Fukou, Zhg.	100	25.45 N	118.28 E
Fukou, Zhg.	100	26.28 N	117.40 E
Fukube	96	35.33 N	134.18 E
Fukuchiyama	96	35.18 N	135.07 E
Fukude	94	34.40 N	137.53 E
Fukue	92	32.41 N	128.50 E
Fukuei Chiao ›	100	25.18 N	121.32 E
Fukue-jima I	92	32.40 N	128.45 E
Fukui, Nihon	94	36.04 N	136.13 E
Fukui, Nihon	270	34.51 N	135.34 E
Fukui □[5]	92	36.00 N	136.15 E
Fukuma	96	33.46 N	130.28 E
Fukumitsu	94	36.33 N	136.52 E
Fukuno	94	36.35 N	136.55 E
Fukuoka, Nihon	94	35.34 N	137.27 E
Fukuoka, Nihon	94	36.42 N	136.56 E
Fukuoka, Nihon	96	33.35 N	130.24 E
Fukuoka □[5]	96	33.45 N	130.30 E
Fukuoka-chūtonchi, Rikujō-jieitai- ■	96	33.32 N	130.28 E
Fukuroda-no-taki ∟	94	36.46 N	140.25 E
Fukuroi	94	34.45 N	137.55 E
Fukushima, Nihon	92	37.45 N	140.28 E
Fukushima, Nihon	92a	41.29 N	140.15 E
Fukushima □[5]	94	37.08 N	140.00 E
Fukushima ◆[8]	270	34.42 N	135.29 E
Fukusumi	270	34.37 N	135.56 E
Fukutani ◆[8]	270	34.43 N	135.02 E
Fukuyama	96	34.29 N	133.22 E
Fukuzaki	96	34.57 N	134.45 E
Fulacunda	150	11.44 N	15.03 W
Fūlādī, Kūh-e ∧	120	34.38 N	67.32 E
Fūlād Maḥalleh	128	36.02 N	53.44 E
Fulanga Island I	175g	19.08 S	178.34 W
Fulanga Passage ɰ	175g	19.00 S	178.40 W
Fulbourn	42	52.11 N	0.13 E
Fulda, Dtsch.	56	50.33 N	9.41 E
Fulda, Mn., U.S.	198	43.52 N	95.36 W
Fulda ≏	30	51.25 N	9.39 E
Fuldatal	56	51.22 N	9.31 E
Fuldera	58	46.37 N	10.22 E
Fule	102	25.27 N	104.19 E
Fulerum ◆[8]	263	51.26 N	6.57 E
Fulford Harbour	224	48.46 N	123.27 W
Fulgatore	70	37.57 N	12.42 E
Fulham ◆[8]	260	51.29 N	0.12 W
Fuli	100	23.11 N	121.14 E
Fuliji	100	33.46 N	116.58 E
Fuling	102	29.42 N	107.21 E
Fulitun	89	46.42 N	131.10 E
Fullarton ≏	166	20.15 S	141.10 E
Fullen ⊜	40	60.31 N	16.09 E
Fuller Springs	222	31.18 N	94.41 W
Fullerton, Ca., U.S.	228	33.52 N	117.55 W
Fullerton, Ky., U.S.	218	38.43 N	82.58 W
Fullerton, Md., U.S.	284b	39.22 N	76.31 W
Fullerton, Ne., U.S.	198	41.21 N	97.58 W
Fullerton, Pa., U.S.	208	40.38 N	75.28 W
Fullerton Municipal Airport ⊠	280	33.52 N	117.59 W
Fullerton Point ›	240c	17.06 N	61.54 W
Fulmer	260	51.33 N	0.34 W
Fulong	102	22.57 N	107.41 E
Fulongchang	107	30.03 N	103.38 E
Fulongquan	89	44.22 N	124.36 E
Fulpmes	64	47.10 N	11.21 E
Fulshear	222	29.41 N	95.54 W
Fulton, Al., U.S.	194	31.47 N	87.43 W
Fulton, Ar., U.S.	194	33.36 N	93.48 W
Fulton, Il., U.S.	190	41.52 N	90.09 W
Fulton, In., U.S.	216	40.56 N	86.15 W
Fulton, Ks., U.S.	198	38.00 N	94.43 W
Fulton, Ky., U.S.	194	36.30 N	88.52 W
Fulton, Md., U.S.	208	39.09 N	76.55 W
Fulton, Mi., U.S.	216	47.17 N	88.21 W
Fulton, Ms., U.S.	194	34.16 N	88.24 W
Fulton, Mo., U.S.	219	38.50 N	91.56 W
Fulton, N.Y., U.S.	210	43.19 N	76.25 W
Fulton, Oh., U.S.	214	40.27 N	82.49 W
Fulton, Tx., U.S.	196	28.04 N	97.02 W
Fulton □[6], Il., U.S.	219	40.13 N	90.17 W
Fulton □[6], In., U.S.	216	41.04 N	86.13 W
Fulton □[6], N.Y., U.S.	210	43.00 N	74.22 W
Fulton □[6], Oh., U.S.	216	41.33 N	84.09 W
Fulton □[6], Pa., U.S.	214	40.06 N	78.04 W
Fulton ≏	182	54.48 N	126.07 W
Fultondale	194	33.36 N	86.47 W
Fultonham	210	42.31 N	75.03 W
Fultonville	210	42.57 N	74.22 W
Fuluchang	107	29.38 N	106.08 E
Fulufjället ∧	26	61.33 N	12.43 E
Fuluzhen	107	29.18 N	103.40 E
Fulwood	44	53.47 N	2.41 W
Fumaça	256	22.17 S	44.19 W
Fumahashi	94	36.42 N	137.19 E
Fumane	156	24.29 S	33.58 E
Fumay	56	49.59 N	4.42 E
Fumel	32	44.29 N	0.57 E
Fumin, Zhg.	102	25.16 N	102.26 E
Fumin, Zhg.	106	31.54 N	121.10 E
Fumintun	98	42.29 N	126.22 E
Fuminzhen	106	31.37 N	121.39 E
Funa ≏	273b	4.23 S	15.19 E
Funabashi	94	35.42 N	139.59 E
Funafuti I	14	8.31 S	179.13 E
Funagawa → Oga	92	39.53 N	139.51 E
Funakuyā	175d	24.30 N	124.17 E
Funan	100	32.39 N	115.32 E
Funan Gaba	144	4.25 N	37.57 E
Funaoka	96	35.23 N	134.14 E
Funasaka	270	34.48 N	135.17 E
Funäsdalen	26	62.32 N	12.33 E
Funchal	148	32.38 N	16.54 W
Funchal □[5]	148	32.40 N	16.55 W
Fundación	246	10.31 N	74.11 W
Fundão	34	40.08 N	7.30 W
Fundão, Ilha do I	287a	22.51 S	43.14 W
Funde	272c	18.54 N	72.58 E
Fundo ≏	250	10.12 S	44.39 W
Fundo, Arroio ≏	287a	22.58 S	43.22 W
Fundy, Bay of ⊂	186	45.00 N	66.00 W
Fundy National Park ♠	186	45.38 N	65.00 W
Fünfkirchen → Pécs	30	46.05 N	18.13 E
Funhalouro	156	23.03 S	34.25 E
Funil, Reprêsa do ⊜[1]	256	22.33 S	44.35 W
Funil, Ribeirão do ≏	256	22.02 S	43.46 W
Funil, Rio do ≏	256	22.58 S	44.34 W
Funing, Zhg.	98	39.54 N	119.14 E
Funing, Zhg.	100	33.47 N	119.48 E
Funing, Zhg.	102	23.33 N	105.35 E
Funiuchang	107	29.03 N	106.33 E
Funiu Shan ⋏	100	33.40 N	112.30 E
Funk Island I	186	49.46 N	53.10 W
Funks Creek ≏	226	39.19 N	122.11 W
Funkturm ɷ	264a	52.31 N	13.16 E
Funne ≏	263	51.42 N	7.36 E
Funnel Creek ≏	166	22.18 S	148.57 E
Funnel Hill ∧[2]	272c	18.54 N	73.07 E
Funo	96	34.53 N	132.47 E
Funshinagh, Lough ⊜	48	53.31 N	8.07 W
Funsi	150	10.17 N	1.58 W
Funtana Coberta ⊥	71	39.34 N	9.21 E
Funtua	150	11.31 N	7.17 E
Funza	246	4.40 N	74.09 W
Fuorn, Pass dal (Ofenpass) ⟩⟨	58	46.37 N	10.15 E
Fuping	102	34.47 N	109.07 E
Fuqiao	106	31.36 N	121.12 E
Fuqikou	100	29.44 N	117.48 E
Fuqing	100	25.44 N	119.22 E
Fuquay-Varina	192	35.35 N	78.48 W
Füramoos	58	48.00 N	9.53 E
Furancungo	154	14.55 S	33.35 E
Furano	92a	43.21 N	142.24 E
Furāt, Nahr al- → Euphrates ≏	128	31.00 N	47.25 E
Furci Siculo	70	37.57 N	15.23 E
Furculești	38	43.52 N	25.09 E
Fures	62	45.19 N	5.30 E
Fūrg	128	28.18 N	55.13 E
Furkapass ⟩⟨	58	46.34 N	8.25 E
Furka-Tunnel ◆[5]	58	46.33 N	8.26 E
Furlong	208	40.18 N	75.05 W
Furmanov	80	57.15 N	41.07 E
Furmanovka	86	44.17 N	72.57 E
Furmanovo	80	49.42 N	49.28 E
Furn, Wādī al- ∨	142	30.13 N	31.40 E
Furnace	46	56.09 N	5.10 W
Furnace Brook ≏	283	42.06 N	70.43 W
Furnace Creek ≏	284b	39.11 N	76.35 W
Furnace Pond ⊜	283	42.03 N	70.49 W
Furnari	70	38.07 N	15.08 E
Furnas, Reprêsa de ⊜[1]	255	20.45 S	46.00 W
Furn ash-Shubbāk	132	33.52 N	35.31 E
Furneaux Group II	166	40.10 S	148.05 E
Furnes → Veurne	50	51.04 N	2.40 E
Furness Abbey ɷ[1]	44	54.07 N	3.12 W
Furness Fells ⋏[2]	44	54.18 N	3.07 W
Furong Shan ∧	100	27.30 N	115.52 E
Furqlus	130	34.36 N	37.05 E
Fürstenau, Dtsch.	52	52.31 N	7.40 E
Fürstenau, Dtsch.	52	51.50 N	9.19 E
Fürstenberg, Dtsch.	52	51.44 N	9.24 E
Fürstenberg, Dtsch.	54	52.09 N	14.40 E
Fürstenberg/Havel	54	53.11 N	13.08 E
Fürstenfeld	61	47.03 N	16.05 E
Fürstenfeldbruck	60	48.10 N	11.15 E
Fürstenhagen	56	51.12 N	9.41 E
Fürstenstein	60	48.43 N	13.20 E
Fürstenwalde	54	52.21 N	14.04 E
Fürstenwerder	54	53.24 N	13.34 E
Fürstenzell	60	48.32 N	13.19 E
Furtei	71	39.34 N	8.57 E
Fürth, Dtsch.	56	49.28 N	10.59 E
Fürth, Dtsch.	56	49.39 N	8.47 E
Furth im Wald	60	49.18 N	12.51 E

	English	Deutsch	Español	Français	Português
≏	River	Fluß	Río	Rivière	Rio
≊	Canal	Kanal	Canal	Canal	Canal
∟	Waterfall, Rapids	Wasserfall, Stromschnellen	Cascada, Rápidos	Chute d'eau, Rapides	Cascata, Rápidos
ɰ	Strait	Meeresstraße	Estrecho	Détroit	Estreito
⊂	Bay, Gulf	Bucht, Golf	Bahía, Golfo	Baie, Golfe	Baía, Golfo
⊜	Lake, Lakes	See, Seen	Lago, Lagos	Lac, Lacs	Lago, Lagos
≚	Swamp	Sumpf	Pantano	Marais	Pântano
⊞	Ice Features, Glacier	Eis- und Gletscherformen	Accidentes Glaciales	Formes glaciaires	Acidentes glaciares
⫪	Other Hydrographic Features	Andere Hydrographische Objekte	Otros Elementos Hidrográficos	Autres données hydrographiques	Outros acidentes hidrográficos
✦	Submarine Features	Untermeerische Objekte	Accidentes Submarinos	Formes de relief sous-marin	Acidentes submarinos
□	Political Unit	Politische Einheit	Unidad Política	Entité politique	Unidade política
ɷ	Cultural Institution	Kulturelle Institution	Institución Cultural	Institution culturelle	Instituição cultural
⊥	Historical Site	Historische Stätte	Sitio Histórico	Site historique	Sitio histórico
♠	Recreational Site	Erholungs- und Ferienort	Sitio de Recreo	Centre de loisirs	Área de Lazer
⊠	Airport	Flughafen	Aeropuerto	Aéroport	Aeroporto
■	Military Installation	Militäranlage	Instalación Militar	Installation militaire	Instalação militar
◆	Miscellaneous	Verschiedenes	Misceláneo	Divers	Diversos

Furtwangen 58 48.03 N 8.12 E
Furuba ≃ 256 23.21 S 44.57 W
Furubō-san ∧² 270 34.53 N 135.19 E
Furudal 26 61.10 N 15.08 E
Furudono 94 37.05 N 140.34 E
Furukawa, Nihon 92 38.34 N 140.58 E
Furukawa, Nihon 94 36.14 N 137.11 E
Furulund 41 55.46 N 13.04 E
Furusund 40 59.40 N 18.55 E
Furu-tone ≃ 94 35.48 N 139.51 E
Furuvik 40 60.39 N 17.20 E
Furuyakami 268 35.55 N 139.32 E
Fürwiggestausee ⊜¹ 263 51.09 N 7.41 E
Fury and Hecla Strait ꓤ 176 69.56 N 84.00 W
Fusagasugá 246 4.21 N 74.22 W
Fusain ≃ 50 48.09 N 2.45 E
Fusan → Pusan 98 35.06 N 129.03 E
Fuscaldo 68 39.25 N 16.02 E
Fusch 64 47.13 N 12.49 E
Fuschl am See 64 47.48 N 13.18 E
Fuschun → Fushun 104 41.52 N 123.53 E
Fuse → Higashiōsaka, Nihon 96 34.39 N 135.35 E
Fuse, Nihon 268 35.53 N 140.00 E
Fushan, Zhg. 98 37.29 N 121.16 E
Fushan, Zhg. 102 35.58 N 111.51 E
Fushan, Zhg. 106 31.49 N 120.46 E
Fushimi ✦⁸ 270 34.55 N 135.46 E
Fushino ≃ 96 34.03 N 131.24 E
Fushuigang 100 31.21 N 113.40 E
Fushun (Funan), Zhg. 104 41.52 N 123.53 E
Fushun, Zhg. 107 29.11 N 105.00 E
Fushuncheng 104 41.53 N 123.51 E
Fusignano 66 44.28 N 11.57 E
Fusilier 184 51.51 N 109.46 W
Fusin → Fuxin 104 42.03 N 121.46 E
Fusine in Valromana 64 46.30 N 13.39 E
Fusio 58 46.27 N 8.40 E
Fusō 94 35.21 N 136.55 E
Fusong 98 42.18 N 127.20 E
Fussa 94 35.45 N 139.20 E
Füssen 64 47.34 N 10.42 E
Fuste, Picacho del ∧ 196 27.35 N 102.47 W
Fusui 102 22.32 N 107.56 E
Futa, Passo della)(66 44.05 N 11.17 E
Futaba 94 35.41 N 138.30 E
Futago-san ∧ 96 33.35 N 131.36 E
Futamata → Tenryū 94 34.52 N 137.49 E
Futamatagawa ✦⁸ 268 35.28 N 139.33 E
Futami, Nihon 94 34.30 N 136.47 E
Futami, Nihon 96 33.41 N 132.38 E
Futang, Zhg. 102 24.26 N 112.09 E
Futang, Zhg. 106 30.40 N 119.35 E
Futaoi-jima I 96 34.06 N 130.47 E
Futatabi-yama ∧ 270 34.43 N 135.11 E
Futatsubashi ✦⁸ 268 35.28 N 139.30 E
Futatsu-ne I² 174f 24.46 N 141.18 E
Fu Tau Pun Chau I 271d 22.21 N 114.22 E
Futian 100 27.26 N 114.56 E
Futianhe 100 31.30 N 115.05 E
Futianpu 100 27.22 N 112.47 E
Futjāni ≃ 126 24.06 N 90.09 E
Futschou → Fuzhou 100 26.06 N 119.17 E
Futtsu, Nihon 94 35.19 N 139.49 E
Futtsu, Nihon 94 35.13 N 139.52 E
Futtsu-misaki > 268 35.19 N 139.46 E
Futun ≃ 100 26.51 N 117.46 E
Futuna I 175f 19.32 S 170.14 E
Futuna, Île I 14 14.15 S 178.09 W
Futuyu 105 39.18 N 114.50 E
Fuveau 62 43.27 N 5.34 E
Fuwah 142 31.12 N 30.33 E
Fuwen 86 47.13 N 89.39 E
Fuxi, Zhg. 100 27.14 N 119.50 E
Fuxi, Zhg. 100 25.14 N 113.52 E
Fuxi ≃ 107 29.09 N 104.57 E
Fuxian (Wafangdian), Zhg. 98 39.37 N 122.01 E
Fuxian, Zhg. 102 36.02 N 109.13 E
Fuxian Hu ⊜ 102 24.30 N 102.55 E
Fuxin, Zhg. 104 42.08 N 121.45 E
Fuxin, Zhg. 104 42.03 N 121.46 E
Fuxing, Zhg. 107 30.27 N 106.04 E
Fuxing, Zhg. 107 30.24 N 104.53 E
Fuxing, Zhg. 107 29.54 N 105.43 E
Fuxingchang 107 29.40 N 105.13 E
Fuxing Dao I 269b 31.17 N 121.23 E
Fuxinghao 104 42.35 N 120.32 E
Fuyang, Zhg. 100 32.54 N 115.49 E
Fuyang, Zhg. 100 30.03 N 119.57 E
Fuyang, Zhg. 100 23.36 N 116.37 E
Fuyang ≃ 98 38.14 N 116.05 E
Fuyouertuo Shan ∧ 89 45.52 N 119.48 E
Fuyu, Zhg. 89 47.49 N 124.27 E
Fuyu, Zhg. 89 45.10 N 124.50 E
Fuyuan, Zhg. 89 48.21 N 134.18 E
Fuyuan, Zhg. 102 25.39 N 104.12 E
Fuzhai 100 29.32 N 120.02 E
Fuzhong 102 24.28 N 111.22 E
Fuzhou, Zhg. 100 28.01 N 116.20 E
Fuzhou (Foochow), Zhg. 100 26.06 N 119.17 E
Fuzhoucheng 98 39.45 N 121.47 E
Fuzhuang 98 34.57 N 118.17 E
Fuzhuangyi 98 38.02 N 116.08 E
Fyfield 42 51.45 N 0.16 E
Fylde □⁸ 262 53.46 N 2.53 W
Fylde >¹ 44 53.47 N 2.56 W
Fyn □⁶ 41 55.20 N 10.25 E
Fyn I 41 55.20 N 10.30 E
Fyne, Loch c 46 56.00 N 5.24 W
Fyns Hoved > 41 55.37 N 10.36 E
Fyresvatn ⊜ 26 59.06 N 8.12 E
Fyrisån ≃ 40 59.47 N 17.39 E
Fysingen ⊜ 40 59.34 N 17.55 E
Fyvie 46 57.25 N 2.23 W
Fzâra, Gara'et ⊜ 36 36.47 N 7.30 E

G

Ga 150 9.47 N 2.30 W
Gaaden 264b 48.03 N 16.12 E
Gaalkacyo 144 6.47 N 47.26 E
Gaanderen 52 51.56 N 6.21 E
Gabah 144 8.08 N 50.02 E
Gabai 146 11.05 N 11.39 E
Gabaldon 116 15.28 N 121.19 E
Gabare 38 43.19 N 23.55 E
Gabarus 186 45.50 N 60.09 W
Gabarus Bay c 186 45.51 N 60.07 W
Gabas ≃ 32 43.46 N 0.42 W
Gabbs 204 38.52 N 117.55 W
Gabby Heights 214 40.09 N 80.15 W
Gabela, Ang. 152 10.48 S 14.20 E
Gabel'a, Azer. 84 40.59 N 47.50 E
Gaberones → Gaborone 156 24.45 S 25.55 E
Gabès 148 33.53 N 10.07 E
Gabès □⁸ 148 33.15 N 9.00 E
Gabès, Golfe de c 148 34.00 N 10.25 E
Gabia 152 4.34 S 17.07 E
Gabiarra 255 16.15 S 39.41 W
Gabicce Mare 66 43.58 N 12.46 E
Gabii ⊥ 267a 41.54 N 12.43 E
Gabil 146 11.09 N 18.12 E
Gabilan Creek ≃ 226 36.41 N 121.38 W
Gabilan Range ⩘ 226 36.30 N 121.15 W
Gabin 30 52.25 N 19.44 E
Gabir 140 8.35 N 24.40 E
Gable Mountain ∧ 182 54.30 N 121.40 W
Gablenz 54 51.41 N 14.31 E
Gablingen 58 48.27 N 10.49 E
Gablitz 61 48.14 N 16.09 E
Gablonz → Jablonec nad Nisou 30 50.44 N 15.10 E
Gabon □¹, Afr. 138 1.00 S 11.45 E
Gabon □¹, Afr. 152 1.00 S 11.45 E
Gabon, Estuaire du c¹ 152 0.25 N 9.20 E
Gaborone 156 24.45 S 25.55 E
Gabras 140 10.16 N 26.14 E
Gabria 64 45.52 N 13.34 E
Gabriel 250 11.14 S 41.53 W
Gabriel Strait ꓤ 176 61.45 N 65.30 W
Gabriel y Galan, Embalse de ⊜¹ 34 40.15 N 6.15 W
Gabriel Zamora 234 19.05 N 102.05 W
Gābrīk 128 25.44 N 58.28 E
Gabriola 224 49.12 N 123.50 W
Gabriola Island I 224 49.10 N 123.47 W
Gabrovo 38 42.52 N 25.19 E
Gabun → Gabon □¹ 152 1.00 S 11.45 E
Gaby 62 45.43 N 7.53 E
Gacé 50 48.48 N 0.18 E
Gachetá 246 4.49 N 73.36 W
Gachpar 174q 9.33 N 138.10 E
Gachsārān 128 30.12 N 50.47 E
Gackle 198 46.37 N 99.08 W
Gacko 38 43.10 N 18.32 E
Gad'ač 78 50.22 N 34.00 E
Gadag 122 15.25 N 75.37 E
Gadamai 140 17.09 N 36.06 E
Gādarwāra 124 22.55 N 78.47 E
Gadbjerg 41 55.46 N 9.20 E
Gäddede 26 64.30 N 14.09 E
Gadderbaum 52 52.00 N 8.31 E
Gade ≃ 260 51.38 N 0.28 W
Gadebusch 54 53.42 N 11.07 E
Gadein 140 8.11 N 28.44 E
Gadera ≃ 64 46.47 N 11.54 E
Gadevang 41 55.58 N 12.18 E
Gadiloviči 76 53.05 N 30.16 E
Gadis ≃ 114 1.03 N 98.55 E
Gadmen 58 46.44 N 8.21 E
Gado Bravo, Ilha do I 250 10.54 S 42.52 W
Gádor 34 36.57 N 2.29 W
Gadra 120 25.40 N 70.37 E
Gadrut 84 39.32 N 47.02 E
Gadsden, Al., U.S. 194 34.00 N 86.00 W
Gadsden, Az., U.S. 200 32.33 N 114.47 W
Gadwāl 122 16.14 N 77.48 E
Gadzi 152 4.47 N 16.42 E
Gaerwen 44 53.13 N 4.16 W
Găești 38 44.43 N 25.19 E
Gaeta 66 41.12 N 13.35 E
Gaeta, Golfo di c 66 41.06 N 13.30 E
Gaferut I 108 9.14 N 145.23 E
Gaffney 192 35.04 N 81.39 W
Gafour 36 36.18 N 9.19 E
Gafsa 148 34.25 N 8.48 E
Gafsa □⁸ 148 34.15 N 8.25 E
Gafurov 85 40.14 N 69.44 E
Gag, Pulau I 164 0.27 S 129.52 E
Gagal 146 9.01 N 15.08 E
Gagarawa 150 12.25 N 9.32 E
Gagarin 76 55.33 N 35.00 E
Gage 196 36.18 N 99.45 W
Gagere ≃ 150 13.21 N 6.23 E
Gages Lake 278 42.21 N 87.59 W
Gages Lake ⊜ 278 42.21 N 88.00 W
Gagetown 186 45.47 N 66.09 W
Gagetown, Canadian Forces Base ■ 186 45.43 N 66.15 W
Gaggenau 56 48.48 N 8.19 E
Gaggi 70 37.51 N 15.13 E
Gaggiano 62 45.24 N 9.02 E
Gaghamni 140 11.41 N 28.19 E
Gagil Tamil I 174q 9.32 N 138.10 E
Gagino 80 55.14 N 45.02 E
Gagliano Castelferrato 70 37.43 N 14.32 E
Gagliano del Capo 68 39.50 N 18.22 E
Gagnef 40 60.35 N 15.04 E
Gagnia 152 1.28 S 16.02 E
Gagnoa 150 6.08 N 5.56 W
Gagnon 176 51.53 N 68.10 W
Gagnon, Lac ⊜ 206 46.07 N 75.07 W
Gagny 261 48.53 N 2.32 E
Gagra 84 43.20 N 40.15 E
Gagret 123 31.40 N 76.04 E
Gahanna 218 40.01 N 82.52 W
Gahlen 52 51.40 N 6.52 E
Gaiarine 64 45.52 N 12.29 E
Gaibandha 124 25.19 N 89.33 E
Gaichtpass)(58 47.27 N 10.37 E
Gaigalava 76 56.40 N 27.18 E
Gaighāta 126 22.56 N 88.44 E
Gaijiatun 104 40.50 N 122.37 E
Gail 196 32.46 N 101.27 W
Gail ≃ 64 46.36 N 13.53 E
Gailberg Sattel)(64 46.43 N 12.58 E
Gail Creek ≃ 222 31.07 N 95.23 W
Gaildorf 56 49.00 N 9.46 E
Gaillac 32 43.54 N 1.55 E
Gaillard, Château ⊥ 50 49.13 N 1.25 E
Gaillard, Lac ⊜ 186 50.06 N 68.47 W
Gaillard, Lake ⊜ 207 41.21 N 72.46 W
Gaillefontaine 50 49.39 N 1.37 E
Gaillimh → Galway 48 53.16 N 9.03 W
Gaillon, Fr. 50 49.10 N 1.20 E
Gaillon, Fr. 261 49.02 N 1.54 E
Gailtaler Alpen ⩘ 64 46.42 N 13.00 E
Gaima 164 8.20 S 142.55 E
Gaimán 254 43.17 S 65.29 W
Gaimersheim 60 48.49 N 11.22 E
Gaines, Mi., U.S. 216 42.52 N 83.54 W
Gaines, Pa., U.S. 210 41.45 N 77.34 W
Gainesboro 194 36.21 N 85.39 W
Gainesville, Fl., U.S. 192 29.39 N 82.19 W
Gainesville, Ga., U.S. 192 34.17 N 83.49 W
Gainesville, Mo., U.S. 194 36.36 N 92.25 W
Gainesville, N.Y., U.S. 210 42.38 N 78.08 W
Gainesville, Tx., U.S. 196 33.37 N 97.07 W
Gainford 44 54.32 N 1.44 W
Gainsborough, Sk., Can. 184 49.10 N 101.26 W
Gainsborough, Eng., U.K. 44 53.24 N 0.46 W
Gainsborough Creek ≃ 184 49.10 N 101.02 W
Gaiole in Chianti 66 43.28 N 11.26 E
Gairatganj 124 23.24 N 78.13 E
Gairdner ≃ 162 34.17 S 119.28 E
Gairdner, Lake ⊜ 162 31.35 S 136.00 E
Gairloch 46 57.42 N 5.40 W
Gairloch, Loch c 46 57.44 N 5.44 W
Gairn ≃ 46 57.03 N 3.05 W
Gais, It. 64 46.50 N 11.57 E
Gais, Schw. 58 47.22 N 9.27 E
Gaisberg ∧ 64 47.48 N 13.07 E
Gaisbeuren 58 47.54 N 9.43 E
Gaital, Cerro ∧ 236 8.37 N 80.07 W
Gaither 208 39.21 N 76.59 W
Gaithersburg 208 39.08 N 77.12 W
Gaixian 98 40.24 N 122.22 E
Gaizina Kalns ∧² 76 56.52 N 25.57 E
Gaj, Hrv. 36 45.29 N 17.02 E
Gaj, Ross. 86 51.27 N 58.27 E
Gajā 272b 22.52 N 88.10 E
Gajahmungkur, Waduk ⊜¹ 115a 7.55 S 110.55 E
Gajčur ≃ 78 47.57 N 36.11 E
Gajendragarh 122 15.44 N 75.59 E
Gajiram 146 12.30 N 13.12 E
Gajny 24 60.15 N 54.15 E
Gājol 126 25.13 N 88.14 E
Gajsin 78 48.48 N 29.24 E
Gajsinghpur 123 29.40 N 73.27 E
Gajuapara ≃ 250 4.17 S 47.25 W
Gajutino 76 58.42 N 38.32 E
Gajvoron 78 48.22 N 29.52 E
Gakarosa ∧ 158 27.54 S 23.33 E
Gakona 180 62.18 N 145.18 W
Gākuch 123 36.10 N 73.45 E
Gakugsa 24 61.34 N 36.26 E
Gāla, Bngl. 126 24.18 N 89.54 E
Gala, Zhg. 124 28.16 N 89.23 E
Galaassija 128 39.52 N 64.27 E
Galāchipa 126 22.10 N 90.25 E
Galahad 182 52.31 N 111.56 W
Galamares 266c 38.48 N 9.25 W
Galán, Cerro ∧ 252 25.55 S 66.52 W
Galana ≃ 154 3.09 S 40.08 E
Galangue 152 13.48 S 16.09 E
Galanovo 80 56.09 N 54.07 E
Galanta 30 48.12 N 17.43 E
Galápagos □⁴ 246a 0.30 S 90.30 W
Galápagos, Parque Nacional de ◆ 246a 0.15 S 90.15 W
Galapagos Islands → Colón, Archipiélago de II 246a 0.30 S 90.30 W
Galaroza 34 37.55 N 6.42 W
Galas ≃ 114 5.31 N 102.12 E
Galashiels 46 55.37 N 2.49 W
Galata ✦⁸ 267b 41.01 N 28.58 E
Galata Köprüsü ✦⁵ 267b 41.00 N 28.57 E
Galata Tower ⊥ 267b 41.01 N 28.58 E
Galatea 172 38.25 S 176.45 E
Galați 38 45.26 N 28.03 E
Galați □⁶ 38 45.45 N 27.45 E
Galatia 194 37.50 N 88.36 W
Galatia □⁹ 130 39.30 N 32.40 E
Galatina 68 40.10 N 18.10 E
Galatone 68 40.09 N 18.04 E
Galatro 68 38.28 N 16.06 E
Galátsion 267c 38.01 N 23.45 E
Galatz → Galați 38 45.26 N 28.03 E
Galaure ≃ 62 45.11 N 4.49 E
Gala Water ≃ 46 55.37 N 2.48 W
Galax 192 36.39 N 80.55 W
Galaxídhion 38 38.22 N 22.23 E
Galbyn gov' ✦² 102 42.30 N 107.00 E
Galdhøpiggen ∧ 26 61.37 N 8.17 E
Gale, Lac ⊜ 190 46.46 N 76.51 W
Galeairy Lake ⊜ 212 45.29 N 78.17 W
Galeana, Méx. 232 30.07 N 107.38 W
Galeana, Méx. 232 24.50 N 100.04 W
Galeão, Aeroporto do ✈ 256 22.50 S 43.15 W
Galeata 66 44.00 N 11.55 E
Galegu 140 12.36 N 35.02 E
Galeh Dār 128 27.38 N 52.42 E
Galela 108 1.50 N 127.50 E
Galena, Austl. 162 27.50 S 114.41 E
Galena, Ak., U.S. 180 64.44 N 156.57 W
Galena, Il., U.S. 190 42.25 N 90.25 W
Galena, In., U.S. 218 38.21 N 85.56 W
Galena, Ks., U.S. 198 37.04 N 94.38 W
Galena, Md., U.S. 208 39.20 N 75.52 W
Galena, Mo., U.S. 194 36.48 N 93.27 W
Galena, Oh., U.S. 214 40.12 N 82.52 W
Galena Park 222 29.43 N 95.13 W
Galenbecker See ⊜ 54 53.38 N 13.43 E
Galeota Point > 241r 10.08 N 60.59 W
Galera ≃ 248 14.25 S 60.07 W
Galera, Punta >, Chile 254 39.59 S 73.43 W
Galera, Punta >, Ec. 246 0.49 N 80.03 W
Galera, Punta de > 34 39.10 N 1.05 E
Galera Point > 241r 10.49 N 60.55 W
Galeras, Volcán ∧¹ 246 1.13 N 77.22 W
Galeria ⊥ 267a 42.02 N 12.18 E
Galeria, Fosso la ≃ 267a 41.48 N 12.21 E
Galesburg, Il., U.S. 190 40.56 N 90.22 W
Galesburg, Mi., U.S. 216 42.17 N 85.25 W
Gales Creek 224 45.35 N 123.12 W
Gales Creek ≃ 224 45.29 N 123.06 W
Gales Ferry 207 41.25 N 72.04 W
Gales Point > 283 42.33 N 70.47 W
Galesville, Md., U.S. 208 38.50 N 76.32 W
Galesville, Wi., U.S. 190 44.04 N 91.20 W
Galeton 214 41.43 N 77.38 W
Galeville 210 43.05 N 76.10 W
Galgasc 144 0.11 N 41.38 E
Galgate 44 54.00 N 2.47 W
Galguduud □⁴ 144 5.00 N 46.30 E
Galheiros 255 13.18 S 46.25 W
Gali 84 42.38 N 41.44 E
Gali, Torrente de ≃ 266d 41.28 N 2.00 E
Galiano 224 48.52 N 123.21 W
Galiano Island I 224 48.56 N 123.29 W
Galibier, Col du)(62 45.04 N 6.24 E
Galič, Ross. 80 58.23 N 42.21 E
Galič, Ukr. 78 49.08 N 24.43 E
Galicia □⁴ 34 42.45 N 8.00 W
Galicia □⁹ 22 49.00 N 22.00 E
Galičskaja vozvyšennost' ⩘² 24 58.25 N 42.20 E
Galičskoje, ozero ⊜ 80 58.24 N 42.18 E
Galien 216 41.47 N 86.29 W
Galien ≃ 216 41.48 N 86.45 W
Galilee 207 41.22 N 71.30 W
Galilee → HaGalil □⁹ 132 32.54 N 35.20 E
Galilee, Lake ⊜ 166 22.21 S 145.48 E
Galilee, Sea of → Kinneret, Yam ⊜ 132 32.48 N 35.35 E
Galiléia 255 19.00 S 41.33 W
Galim 152 7.06 N 12.29 E
Galina Point > 241q 18.24 N 76.53 W
Galindo Creek ≃ 282 37.58 N 122.02 W
Galion 214 40.44 N 82.47 W
Galion, Baie du c 240e 14.44 N 60.57 W
Galis 115a 7.08 S 113.33 E
Galisteo Creek ≃ 200 35.31 N 106.22 W
Galite, Canal de la ꓤ 36 37.20 N 9.00 E
Galiuro Mountains ⩘ 200 32.40 N 110.20 W
Galiwinku 164 12.02 S 135.34 E
Galižana 64 44.56 N 13.52 E
Galka'yo 144 6.47 N 47.26 E
Galkhausen 263 51.05 N 6.58 E
Galkino, Kaz. 86 52.14 N 78.20 E
Galkino, Ross. 82 54.46 N 35.49 E
Galkino, Ross. 86 55.36 N 62.55 E
Gall'aaral 85 40.02 N 67.35 E
Gallan Head > 46 58.14 N 7.03 W
Gallarate 62 45.40 N 8.47 E
Gallardon 50 48.32 N 1.42 E
Gallatin, Mo., U.S. 194 39.54 N 93.57 W
Gallatin, Pa., U.S. 279b 40.12 N 79.53 W
Gallatin, Tn., U.S. 194 36.23 N 86.26 W
Gallatin, Tx., U.S. 222 31.54 N 95.09 W
Gallatin □⁶ 218 38.45 N 84.51 W
Gallatin ≃ 202 45.56 N 111.29 W
Gallatin Range ⩘ 202 45.15 N 111.05 W
Galle 122 6.02 N 80.13 E
Gállego ≃ 34 41.39 N 0.51 W
Gallegos ≃ 254 51.36 S 68.59 W
Galles → Wales □⁸ 28 52.30 N 3.30 W
Galleyend 260 51.42 N 0.29 E
Galley Head > 48 51.30 N 8.57 W
Galleywood 260 51.42 N 0.28 E
Galliano 194 29.26 N 90.17 W
Galliate 62 45.29 N 8.42 E
Gallicano 64 44.04 N 10.26 E
Gallicano nel Lazio 267a 41.52 N 12.49 E
Gallicchio 68 40.17 N 16.08 E
Gallico 68 38.10 N 15.41 E
Galliera Veneta 64 45.39 N 11.49 E
Gallinara I 62 44.02 N 8.14 E
Gallinas ≃ 196 35.10 N 104.55 W
Gallinas, Punta > 246 12.28 N 71.40 W
Gallinas Creek ≃ 282 38.01 N 122.30 W
Gallinas Peak ∧ 200 34.13 N 105.45 W
Gallio 64 45.53 N 11.33 E
Gallipoli, Austl. 166 19.10 S 137.55 E
Gallipoli, It. 68 40.03 N 17.58 E
Gallipoli → Gelibolu, Tür. 130 40.24 N 26.40 E
Gallipoli Peninsula → Gelibolu Yarımadası >¹ 130 40.20 N 26.30 E
Gallipolis 188 38.48 N 82.12 W
Gallitzin 214 40.28 N 78.33 W
Gallivaggio 58 46.21 N 9.21 E
Gällivare 24 67.07 N 20.45 E
Gallneukirchen 61 48.21 N 14.25 E
Gällö 26 62.55 N 15.14 E
Gallo, Capo > 70 38.13 N 13.19 E
Gallo, Lago del ⊜¹ 64 46.37 N 10.10 E
Gallo, Lago di ⊜¹ 58 46.37 N 10.10 E
Gallo, Laguna ⊜ 258 35.30 S 58.28 W
Gallo Arroyo V 200 33.55 N 105.00 W
Galloo Island I 212 43.54 N 76.25 W
Galloupes Point > 283 42.28 N 70.53 W
Galloway □⁹ 44 55.00 N 4.25 W
Galloway, Mull of > 44 54.38 N 4.50 W
Galloway Creek ≃, Md., U.S. 284b 39.18 N 76.23 W
Galloway Creek ≃, Mi., U.S. 281 42.39 N 83.12 W
Galluis 261 48.48 N 1.48 E
Gallup 200 35.31 N 108.44 W
Gallupville 210 42.40 N 74.14 W
Gallur 34 41.52 N 1.19 W
Gallura ✦¹ 71 41.00 N 9.13 E
Gally, Ru de ≃ 261 48.53 N 1.53 E
Gälnan ꓤ 40 59.31 N 18.45 E
Gålö I 40 59.05 N 18.17 E
Galop Island I 212 44.46 N 75.24 W
Galoppo, Ippodromo del ◆ 266b 45.28 N 9.07 E
Galougo 150 13.50 N 11.04 W
Galsi 126 23.20 N 87.42 E
Galston 46 55.36 N 4.24 W
Galt, Mong. 88 48.46 N 99.53 E
Galt, Ca., U.S. 226 38.15 N 121.17 W
Gal Tardo 144 3.34 N 45.58 E
Galtat Zemmour 148 25.15 N 12.20 W
Galtelli 71 40.23 N 9.37 E
Galten 41 56.09 N 9.55 E
Galten c 40 59.27 N 16.09 E
Galtür 58 46.58 N 10.11 E
Galtymore Mountain ∧ 48 52.22 N 8.10 W
Galty Mountains ⩘ 48 52.25 N 8.10 W
Galūgāh-e Āsīyeh 128 34.01 N 59.55 E
Galugur 114 2.34 N 99.39 E
Galula 154 8.36 S 33.02 E
Galunggung, Gunung ∧ 115a 7.15 S 108.03 E
Galuut 88 48.33 N 113.12 E
Galva, Il., U.S. 190 41.10 N 90.02 W
Galva, Ia., U.S. 198 42.30 N 95.25 W
Galva, Ks., U.S. 198 38.22 N 97.32 W
Galvarino 252 38.24 S 72.47 W
Galveston, In., U.S. 216 40.34 N 86.11 W
Galveston, Tx., U.S. 222 29.17 N 94.47 W
Galveston □⁶ 222 29.20 N 94.53 W
Galveston Bay c 222 29.36 N 94.57 W
Galveston Island I 222 29.13 N 94.55 W
Gálvez 252 32.02 S 61.13 W
Gálvez ≃ 248 5.12 S 72.53 W
Galvin, Austl. 274b 37.51 S 144.49 E
Galvin, Wa., U.S. 224 46.44 N 123.01 W
Galway (Gaillimh), Ire. 48 53.16 N 9.03 W
Galway, N.Y., U.S. 210 43.01 N 74.02 W
Galway □⁶ 48 53.20 N 9.00 W
Galway Bay c 48 53.10 N 9.15 W
Gam (Jin) ≃ 110 21.55 N 105.12 E
Gam, Pulau I 164 0.27 S 130.36 E
Gama, Isla I 254 40.29 S 62.12 W
Gamaches 50 49.59 N 1.33 E
Gamagōri 94 34.50 N 137.14 E
Gamalejevka 80 52.16 N 53.26 E
Gamaliel 194 36.38 N 85.47 W
Ga-Mankoeng 156 23.57 S 29.42 E
Gamare, Lake ⊜ 144 11.30 N 41.40 E
Gamarra 246 8.20 N 73.45 W
Gamawa 146 12.08 N 10.32 E
Gamay 116 12.23 N 125.18 E
Gamay Bay c 116 12.21 N 125.21 E
Gamba 120 28.17 N 88.32 E
Gambach 56 50.28 N 8.44 E
Gambaga 150 10.32 N 0.26 W
Gambais 261 48.46 N 1.40 E
Gambaiseuil 261 48.45 N 1.44 E
Gambang 114 3.43 N 103.06 E
Gambara, It. 64 45.15 N 10.18 E
Gámbara, Méx. 234 18.55 N 102.05 W
Gambarie 68 38.10 N 15.50 E
Gambassi 66 43.32 N 10.57 E
Gambatesa 66 41.30 N 14.54 E
Gambela 144 8.18 N 34.37 E
Gambell 180 63.46 N 171.46 W
Gambellara 64 45.28 N 11.20 E
Gamber 208 39.27 N 76.56 W
Gambia □¹, Afr. 134 13.30 N 15.30 W
Gambia □¹, Afr. 150 13.30 N 15.30 W
Gambia (Gambie) ≃ 150 13.28 N 16.34 W
Gambi Aṭrash 140 10.03 N 33.47 E
Gambie → Gambia □¹ 150 13.30 N 15.30 W
Gambie (Gambia) ≃ 150 13.28 N 16.34 W
Gambier 214 40.22 N 82.23 W
Gambier, Îles II 6 21.20 S 136.30 W
Gamble Mansion State Historic Site ⊥ 220 27.32 N 82.32 W
Gambo, Nf., Can. 186 48.46 N 54.14 W
Gambo, Centraf. 152 4.39 N 22.16 E
Gamboa 236 9.07 N 79.42 W
Gamboli 120 29.50 N 68.26 E
Gambolò 62 45.15 N 8.51 E
Gamboma 152 1.53 S 15.51 E
Gamboula 152 4.08 N 15.09 E
Gambrill State Park ◆ 208 39.30 N 77.30 W
Gamchab ≃ 156 28.15 S 17.26 E
Gamé 150 6.44 N 1.11 E
Game Creek ≃ 285 39.41 N 75.28 W
Gamensee ⊜ 264a 52.40 N 13.51 E
Gaming 61 47.56 N 15.06 E
Gamka ≃ 158 33.18 S 21.39 E
Gamlakarleby → Kokkola 26 63.50 N 23.07 E
Gamla Uppsala 40 59.54 N 17.38 E
Gamleby 26 57.54 N 16.24 E
Gamlitz 61 46.43 N 15.33 E
Gammel Estrup ⊥ 26 56.26 N 10.21 E
Gammelstad ⊥¹ 26 65.38 N 22.01 E
Gammertingen 58 48.15 N 9.13 E
Gammon ≃ 184 51.07 N 95.09 W
Gammon, Point > 207 41.36 N 70.16 W
Gammon Ranges National Park ◆ 166 30.29 S 139.10 E
Gamō, Nihon 94 35.03 N 136.11 E
Gamō, Nihon 268 35.52 N 139.48 E
Gamoep 158 29.55 S 18.25 E
Ga-Mogara ≃ 158 27.07 S 22.57 E
Gamo Gofa □⁴ 144 5.45 N 37.00 E
Gamon 150 13.20 N 12.55 W
Gamova, mys > 89 42.35 N 131.12 E
Gamph, Slieve ⩘ 48 54.05 N 9.00 W
Gampoko 273b 4.16 S 15.10 E
Gampola 122 7.10 N 80.34 E
Gampongbatak 114 4.48 N 97.39 E
Gampoui 273b 4.08 S 15.22 E
Gams 58 47.12 N 9.28 E
Gamsfeld ∧ 64 47.37 N 13.29 E
Gamtoos ≃ 158 33.58 S 25.01 E
Gamud ∧ 144 4.05 N 38.03 E
G'amyš, gora ∧ 84 40.18 N 46.23 E
Gan ≃, Zhg. 89 49.12 N 125.14 E
Gan ≃, Zhg. 100 29.12 N 116.00 E
Ganado, Az., U.S. 200 35.42 N 109.33 W
Ganado, Tx., U.S. 222 29.02 N 96.31 W
Ganano ≃ 116 16.45 N 121.44 E
Gananoque 212 44.20 N 76.10 W
Gananoque ≃ 212 44.19 N 76.09 W
Gananoque Lake ⊜ 212 44.27 N 76.09 W
Ganaraska ≃ 212 43.57 N 78.18 W
Ganargua Creek ≃ 210 43.04 N 77.00 W
Ganassi 116 7.49 N 124.06 E
Ganāveh 128 29.34 N 50.31 E
Gancevići 76 52.45 N 26.26 E
Ganchangba 107 28.52 N 103.41 E
Ganči 85 39.58 N 69.08 E
Gand → Gent 50 51.03 N 3.43 E
Ganda, Ang. 152 13.02 S 14.40 E
Ganda, Zaïre 152 4.05 N 23.32 E
Gandadiwata, Bulu ∧ 112 2.42 S 119.27 E
Gandajika 152 6.45 S 23.57 E
Gandak (Nārāyaṇi) ≃ 124 25.39 N 85.13 E
Gaṇḍakī □⁸ 124 28.15 N 84.15 E
Gandara 258 35.26 S 58.06 W
Ganda Singhwāla 123 31.02 N 74.31 E
Gandāva 120 28.37 N 67.29 E
Gandavaroyi Falls ∟ 154 17.17 S 29.07 E
Gānde 126 24.10 N 86.26 E
Gander 186 48.57 N 54.37 W
Gander ≃ 186 49.15 N 54.30 W
Gander Bay 186 49.18 N 54.29 W
Gander Bay c 186 49.25 N 54.28 W
Ganderkesee 52 53.02 N 8.32 E
Gander Lake ⊜ 186 48.55 N 54.40 W
Gandesa 34 41.03 N 0.26 E
Gandevi 120 20.49 N 72.59 E
Gāndhinagar 120 23.12 N 72.40 E
Gāndhi Sāgar ⊜¹ 120 24.18 N 75.21 E
Gandi 150 12.55 N 5.49 E
Gandi, Wādī V 140 11.23 N 24.31 E
Gandia 34 38.58 N 0.11 W
Gandino 62 45.49 N 9.54 E
Gando 152 12.30 S 17.25 E
Gandole 146 8.26 N 11.34 E
Gandou 152 2.24 N 17.27 E
Gandrange 56 49.16 N 6.08 E
Gandria 58 46.01 N 9.00 E
Gandu 255 13.45 S 39.30 W
Gandy Bridge ✦⁵ 220 27.53 N 82.34 W
G'andžačaj ≃ 84 40.54 N 46.28 E
Ganfang 100 28.40 N 114.51 E
Ganfosi 107 29.36 N 104.03 E
Ganga → Ganges ≃ 124 23.22 N 90.32 E
Gangādharpur 272b 22.36 N 88.11 E
Gangafani 150 14.23 N 2.24 W
Gangājalghāti 126 23.25 N 87.07 E
Gangala-Na-Bodio 154 3.41 N 29.08 E
Gangalingolo 273b 4.20 S 15.09 E
Gan Gan 254 42.30 S 68.16 W
Gangānagar 123 29.55 N 73.53 E
Gangāpur, India 120 25.13 N 74.16 E
Gangāpur, India 122 19.41 N 75.01 E
Gangāpur, India 124 26.29 N 76.43 E
Gangara, Niger 150 14.36 N 8.30 E
Gangara, Niger 150 13.33 N 7.14 E
Gāngārāmpur 124 25.24 N 88.31 E
Ganga Sāgar 126 21.38 N 88.05 E
Gangaw 110 22.11 N 94.07 E
Gangāwati 122 15.26 N 76.32 E
Gangaw Range ⩘ 110 24.50 N 96.40 E
Ganga-Yamuna Doāb ⩘¹ 124 26.40 N 79.30 E
Gangcheng 98 35.52 N 116.52 E
Gangdaba, Tchabal ∧ 152 7.44 N 12.45 E
Gangdhār 120 23.57 N 75.37 E
Gangdisê Shan ⩘ 120 31.00 N 82.00 E
Gangelt 56 50.59 N 5.59 E
Ganges, B.C., Can. 224 48.51 N 123.30 W
Ganges, Fr. 62 43.56 N 3.42 E
Ganges (Ganga) (Padma) ≃ 124 23.22 N 90.32 E
Ganges, Mouths of the ≃¹ 120 22.00 N 89.00 E
Ganges Delta ≃² 124 23.00 N 89.00 E
Ganghu 120 32.05 N 86.45 E
Gangi 70 37.49 N 14.13 E
Gangkofen 60 48.26 N 12.34 E
Gangkou, Zhg. 100 29.45 N 115.44 E
Gangkou, Zhg. 100 29.21 N 117.58 E
Gangkou, Zhg. 100 22.38 N 113.22 E
Gangkou, Zhg. 100 22.36 N 114.54 E
Gangkou, Zhg. 100 29.12 N 113.19 E
Gangkou, Zhg. 106 30.44 N 118.54 E
Gangkouzhen 106 31.45 N 120.40 E
Gangmar Co ⊜ 120 33.46 N 84.15 E
Gang Mills 210 42.08 N 77.06 W
Gāngnāpur 126 23.09 N 88.38 E
Gangneung → Kangnŭng 98 37.45 N 128.54 E
Gango ≃ 152 9.48 S 15.40 E
Gangoa 102 37.15 N 100.28 E
Gangoh 124 29.46 N 77.15 E
Gangotri, India 120 30.56 N 79.02 E
Gangotri, India 120 31.01 N 78.27 E
Gangou 98 40.30 N 119.27 E
Gangoumen 98 41.40 N 116.35 E
Gangouyi 102 36.01 N 105.03 E
Gangqiao 107 30.13 N 105.22 E
Gang Ranch 182 51.33 N 122.20 W
Gangshangji 100 28.06 N 116.30 E
Gangtok 124 27.20 N 88.37 E
Gangtou 98 38.04 N 113.56 E
Gangtouli 106 31.42 N 119.02 E
Gangu 102 34.45 N 105.20 E
Gangwa, Zaïre 152 3.30 S 20.55 E
Gangwa, Zhg. 105 39.48 N 116.10 E
Gangwei 100 24.20 N 118.01 E
Ganhezi 86 44.08 N 88.32 E
Ganhu 102 44.33 N 94.09 E
Gani 164 0.47 S 128.13 E
Ganišob 85 39.03 N 70.47 E
Ganj Dundwara 124 27.44 N 78.57 E
Ganjiang 107 29.42 N 103.38 E
Ganlan Shan ∧ 124 29.54 N 90.02 E
Ganlu 106 31.32 N 120.35 E
Ganluchang 107 29.54 N 104.47 E
Ganluo 102 29.03 N 102.59 E
Gannahoek 158 26.44 S 24.08 E
Gannan 89 47.54 N 123.30 E
Gannano, Lago di ⊜ 68 40.19 N 16.26 E
Gannapan 158 30.23 S 22.12 E
Gannat 32 46.06 N 3.12 E
Gannett Peak ∧ 200 43.11 N 109.39 W
Gannovka 83 48.33 N 38.35 E
Gannvalley 198 44.02 N 98.59 W
Ganpingsi 102 35.13 N 102.30 E
Ganpu 106 30.24 N 120.53 E
Ganq 120 37.25 N 92.15 E
Ganquan 102 36.25 N 109.16 E
Gansbaai 158 34.35 S 19.22 E
Gänsbrunnen 58 47.16 N 7.28 E
Gänserndorf 61 48.20 N 16.43 E
Gansevoort 210 43.12 N 73.39 W
Ganshoren 56 50.52 N 4.18 E
Ganspan 158 27.57 S 24.47 E
Gansu (Kansu) □⁴ 102 37.00 N 103.00 E
Ganta 150 7.15 N 8.59 W
Gantan 100 29.37 N 119.34 E
Gantang, Zhg. 100 26.56 N 119.40 E
Gantang, Zhg. 102 22.58 N 109.00 E
Gantao ≃ 98 38.01 N 114.07 E
Gante → Gent 50 51.03 N 3.43 E
Gantheaume, Cape > 166 36.05 S 137.27 E
Gantheaume Bay c 162 27.44 S 114.07 E
Gantheaume Point > 162 17.59 S 122.10 E
Gantiadi 84 43.24 N 40.06 E
Gantian 100 27.30 N 113.10 E
Gantt 194 31.24 N 86.29 W
Gantung 112 2.58 S 108.09 E
Gantung, Mount ∧ 116 8.57 N 117.48 E
Gan Uškino 80 46.36 N 49.16 E
Ganwo 150 11.13 N 4.42 E
Ganxi, Zhg. 100 28.08 N 118.06 E
Ganxi, Zhg. 102 29.02 N 109.32 E
Ganyanchi 102 36.39 N 105.18 E
Ganyesa 158 26.35 S 24.10 E
Ganyu (Qing Kou) 98 34.52 N 119.10 E
Ganzê 102 31.40 N 100.01 E
Ganzhenyi 100 30.33 N 113.21 E
Ganzhou, Zhg. 100 25.54 N 114.55 E
Ganzhou, Zhg. 100 28.49 N 115.25 E
Ganzhou → Zhangye, Zhg. 102 38.56 N 100.27 E
Ganzhuermiao 88 48.24 N 118.08 E
Ganzlin 54 53.23 N 12.15 E
Ganzo Azul 248 8.51 S 74.44 W
Gao 150 16.16 N 0.03 W
Gao □⁴ 150 18.00 N 1.30 E
Gao'an 100 28.25 N 115.22 E
Gaobaita 271a 39.53 N 116.30 E
Gaobei 100 26.37 N 114.38 E
Gaobeidian 271a 39.54 N 116.33 E
Gaobu 100 27.48 N 117.01 E
Gaochang 107 28.49 N 104.24 E
Gaocheng, Zhg. 98 38.04 N 114.49 E
Gaocheng, Zhg. 100 31.57 N 113.25 E
Gaocheng, Zhg. 106 31.28 N 119.48 E
Gaochengzhai 104 41.24 N 123.43 E
Gaochun 106 31.20 N 118.52 E
Gaocun 98 37.05 N 122.12 E
Gaodianzi 102 30.40 N 110.01 E
Gao Feng ∧ 106 30.34 N 118.40 E
Gaogongmiao 100 33.25 N 115.53 E
Gaogou 100 34.03 N 119.15 E
Gaohe 100 22.47 N 112.57 E
Gaohebu 100 30.44 N 116.50 E
Gaoil, Sliabh ∧ 46 55.55 N 5.28 W
Gaojiabu 102 38.30 N 110.11 E
Gaojiadi 98 41.33 N 114.58 E
Gaojiadian 98 42.40 N 124.28 E
Gaojian 100 29.04 N 121.14 E
Gaojiapuzi 104 41.22 N 123.36 E
Gaojiaqiao 106 30.43 N 120.38 E
Gaojiatun 104 41.06 N 121.19 E
Gaojiawopeng 104 41.28 N 122.10 E
Gaojiawopu 104 41.50 N 122.47 E
Gaojiazhai 269b 31.23 N 121.33 E
Gaojiazhen 102 30.05 N 107.51 E
Gaokan 104 40.46 N 122.23 E
Gaokeng 100 27.40 N 113.58 E
Gaolan 102 36.25 N 103.56 E
Gaolan Dao I 100 21.55 N 113.15 E
Gaolao 104 41.54 N 120.59 E
Gaoli 105 39.17 N 115.38 E
Gaoliang 107 29.45 N 105.15 E
Gaoliban 104 41.39 N 121.58 E
Gaolifangshen 104 42.27 N 123.21 E
Gaolimen 98 40.22 N 124.02 E
Gaoling 105 40.32 N 117.01 E
Gaolinying 105 39.06 N 115.38 E
Gaoliying 105 40.10 N 116.29 E
Gaoliyingzi 104 41.56 N 124.17 E
Gaolong 100 26.56 N 113.45 E
Gaolou 105 39.59 N 116.50 E
Gaolouchang, Zhg. 107 29.51 N 104.41 E
Gaolouchang, Zhg. 107 30.03 N 105.58 E
Gaoluo 98 37.27 N 113.55 E
Gaomi 98 36.23 N 119.44 E
Gaona 252 25.12 S 64.05 W
Gaopi 100 24.14 N 116.39 E
Gaoping, Zhg. 102 35.48 N 112.52 E
Gaoping, Zhg. 107 30.28 N 105.45 E
Gaopingba 107 30.47 N 106.06 E
Gaoqiao, Zhg. 100 30.08 N 119.56 E
Gaoqiao, Zhg. 100 26.36 N 117.46 E
Gaoqiao, Zhg. 102 28.06 N 106.36 E
Gaoqiao, Zhg. 106 32.14 N 119.38 E
Gaoqiao, Zhg. 106 31.21 N 121.34 E
Gaoqiaomen 106 32.01 N 118.51 E
Gaoqiaozhen 104 40.55 N 121.00 E
Gaoqing (Tianzhen) 98 37.11 N 117.47 E
Gaoqipu 104 41.32 N 121.40 E
Gaosha 100 26.27 N 117.56 E
Gaoshaling 105 38.51 N 117.36 E
Gaoshan, Zhg. 100 25.29 N 119.34 E
Gaoshan, Zhg. 107 29.26 N 104.28 E
Gaoshanbao 105 40.40 N 117.29 E
Gaoshangbao 98 39.11 N 118.30 E
Gaoshanpu 102 27.10 N 105.14 E
Gaoshantai 104 42.22 N 122.28 E
Gaoshanzi 104 41.34 N 122.02 E
Gaoshengchang 107 29.59 N 105.31 E
Gaoshengzhen 104 41.20 N 122.12 E
Gaoshi 107 29.36 N 104.44 E
Gaoshikan 107 29.12 N 105.04 E
Gaosichang 107 30.17 N 104.52 E
Gaotai 102 39.20 N 99.58 E
Gaotaishan 104 42.02 N 122.52 E
Gaotan, Zhg. 100 30.23 N 117.23 E
Gaotan, Zhg. 100 23.12 N 115.22 E
Gaotan, Zhg. 102 32.22 N 108.36 E
Gaotang 98 36.54 N 116.14 E
Gaotangji 100 32.24 N 116.01 E
Gaotingsi 100 26.05 N 112.53 E
Gaotuozi 104 41.08 N 122.40 E
Gaoua 150 10.20 N 3.11 W
Gaoual 150 11.45 N 13.12 W
Gaoxian 102 28.20 N 104.38 E
Gaoxingru 100 26.28 N 115.14 E
Gaoxinji 98 34.11 N 115.33 E
Gaoya 98 36.22 N 118.49 E
Gaoyang 98 34.30 N 114.40 E
Gaoyapu 107 29.14 N 106.19 E
Gaoyi 98 37.36 N 114.36 E
Gaoyou, Zhg. 100 32.47 N 119.27 E
Gaoyou, Zhg. 100 28.25 N 115.31 E
Gaoyou Hu ⊜ 100 32.50 N 119.20 E
Gaozhangjia 102 36.06 N 107.18 E
Gaozhou 102 21.55 N 110.50 E
Gaozi 106 32.11 N 119.18 E
Gaoziba 107 29.01 N 106.00 E
Gaozuo 100 33.57 N 118.03 E
Gap, Fr. 62 44.34 N 6.05 E
Gap, Pa., U.S. 208 39.59 N 76.01 W
Gapālnagar 272b 22.49 N 88.08 E
Gapan 116 15.19 N 120.57 E
Gapeau ≃ 62 43.07 N 6.11 E
Gapern ⊜ 40 59.31 N 13.40 E
Gar 120 32.11 N 79.59 E
Gar ≃ 120 32.28 N 79.44 E
Gara, Lough ⊜ 48 53.55 N 8.25 W
Garacad 144 6.57 N 49.19 E
Garachiné 246 8.04 N 78.22 W
Garadag 144 9.26 N 46.52 E
Gārādāha 126 24.14 N 89.34 E
Garagoa 246 5.05 N 73.21 W
Garaguso 68 40.33 N 16.14 E
Garah 166 29.04 S 149.38 E
Garai ≃¹ 126 23.32 N 89.31 E
Garaina 164 7.50 S 147.10 E
Gārākhola → Madhukhāli 126 23.33 N 89.38 E
Garamba ≃ 154 3.53 N 29.12 E
Garamba, Parc National de la ◆ 154 4.10 N 29.30 E
Gara Muleta ∧ 144 9.17 N 41.47 E
Garānberia 272b 22.24 N 88.34 E
Garancières 261 48.49 N 1.45 E
Garango 150 11.48 N 0.34 W
Garanhuns 250 8.54 S 36.29 W
Garapan 174n 15.12 N 145.43 E
Garara 164 8.37 S 148.17 E
Garautha 124 25.34 N 79.18 E
Garba 146 9.12 N 20.30 E
Garbagna 62 44.47 N 9.00 E
Garbagnate Milanese 266b 45.35 N 9.05 E
Garbahaarrey 144 3.19 N 42.13 E
Garbatella ✦⁸ 267a 41.52 N 12.29 E
Garba Tula 154 0.32 N 38.31 E
Garber 196 36.26 N 97.35 W
Garberville 204 40.06 N 123.47 W
Garbokaraj 88 54.09 N 92.52 E
Garboldisham 42 52.24 N 0.56 E
Garbsen 52 52.25 N 9.36 E
Garça 255 22.14 S 49.37 W
Garças, Rio das ≃ 255 15.54 S 52.16 W

Symbols in the index entries represent the broad categories identified in the key at the right. Symbols with superior numbers (⩘¹) identify subcategories (see complete key on page *I · 1*).

Symbole im Register stellen die rechts im Schlüssel erklärten Kategorien dar. Symbole mit hochgestellten Ziffern (⩘¹) bezeichnen Unterabteilungen einer Kategorie (vgl. vollständiger Schlüssel auf Seite *I · 1*).

Los símbolos incluidos en el texto del índice representan las grandes categorías identificadas con la clave a la derecha. Los símbolos con números en su parte superior (⩘¹) identifican las subcategorías (véase la clave completa en la página *I · 1*).

Les symboles de l'index représentent les catégories indiquées dans la légende à droite. Les symboles suivis d'un indice (⩘¹) représentent des sous-catégories (voir légende complète à la page *I · 1*).

Os símbolos incluídos no texto do índice representam as grandes categorias identificadas com a chave à direita. Os símbolos com números em sua parte superior (⩘¹) identificam as subcategorias (veja-se a chave completa à página *I · 1*).

English	Deutsch	Español	Français	Português
∧ Mountain	Berg	Montaña	Montagne	Montanha
⩘ Mountains	Gebirge	Montañas	Montagnes	Montanhas
)(Pass	Paß	Paso	Col	Passo
V Valley, Canyon	Tal, Cañon	Valle, Cañón	Vallée, Canyon	Vale, Canhão
≃ Plain	Ebene	Llano	Plaine	Planície
> Cape	Kap	Cabo	Cap	Cabo
I Island	Insel	Isla	Île	Ilha
II Islands	Inseln	Islas	Îles	Ilhas
⊥ Other Topographic Features	Andere Topographische Objekte	Otros Elementos Topográficos	Autres données topographiques	Outros acidentes topográficos

ESPAÑOL — Nombre / Página / Lat.°′ / Long.°′ W = Oeste
FRANÇAIS — Nom / Page / Lat.°′ / Long.°′ W = Ouest
PORTUGUÊS — Nome / Página / Lat.°′ / Long.°′ W = Oeste

Garcevo 76 52.45 N 32.59 E
Garches 261 48.51 N 2.11 E
Garching 60 48.15 N 11.39 E
Garching an der Alz 60 48.08 N 12.34 E
Garchitorena 116 13.52 N 123.40 E
García 232 29.59 N 108.20 W
García, Laguna ⊜ 288 34.58 S 58.09 W
García de la Cadena 234 21.09 N 103.28 W
García de Sola, Embalse de ⊜[1] 34 39.15 N 5.05 W
Garcia Hernandez 116 9.37 N 124.18 E
Garcias 255 20.34 S 52.13 W
Garcitas Creek ≃ 222 28.51 N 96.46 W
Gard □[5] 32 44.00 N 4.00 E
Gard ≃ 62 43.51 N 4.37 E
Gard, Pont du -◆[5] 62 43.56 N 4.36 E
Garda 64 45.34 N 10.42 E
Garda, Lago di ⊜ 64 45.40 N 10.41 E
Gardabani 84 41.28 N 45.06 E
Gardanne 62 43.27 N 5.28 E
Garde, Lac la ⊜ 190 46.46 N 78.14 W
Gardelegen 54 52.31 N 11.23 E
Garden ≃ 190 46.32 N 84.09 W
Gardena 228 33.53 N 118.18 W
Gardena, Val V 64 46.35 N 11.35 E
Garden Acres 226 37.58 N 121.13 W
Garden City, Ga., U.S. 192 32.06 N 81.09 W
Garden City, Ks., U.S. 198 37.58 N 100.52 W
Garden City, Mi., U.S. 216 42.19 N 83.19 W
Garden City, Mo., U.S. 194 38.33 N 94.11 W
Garden City, N.Y., U.S. 210 40.43 N 73.38 W
Garden City, Tx., U.S. 196 31.52 N 101.29 W
Garden City → Qasr al-Dubārā -◆[8] 273c 30.02 N 31.14 E
Garden City Park 276 40.44 N 73.39 W
Garden City Raceway ♦ 284a 43.09 N 79.11 W
Gardendale 194 33.39 N 86.48 W
Garden Farms 226 35.24 N 120.07 W
Garden Gate Village 282 37.20 N 122.02 W
Garden Grove, Ca., U.S. 228 33.46 N 117.56 W
Garden Grove, Ia., U.S. 190 40.50 N 93.36 W
Garden Home 224 45.27 N 122.45 W
Garden Island I, Austl. 168a 32.13 S 115.41 E
Garden Island I, Mi., U.S. 190 45.49 N 85.30 W
Garden Lakes 192 34.17 N 85.16 W
Garden Peninsula ›[1] 190 45.45 N 86.35 W
Garden Plain 198 37.39 N 97.41 W
Garden Prairie 216 42.15 N 88.44 W
Garden Reach 126 22.33 N 88.17 E
Gardenside 218 38.03 N 84.33 W
Garden State Arts Center ʊ 276 40.24 N 74.11 W
Garden State Park Race Track ♦, N.J., U.S. 285 39.55 N 75.02 W
Garden State Park Race Track ♦, Pa., U.S. 285 39.55 N 75.02 W
Garden State Plaza -◆[9] 276 40.55 N 74.05 W
Gardenton 184 49.05 N 96.40 W
Garden Valley 226 38.51 N 120.51 W
Garden View 210 41.16 N 77.03 W
Gardenville 208 40.22 N 75.07 W
Gardermoen 26 60.13 N 11.06 E
Gardey 252 37.17 S 59.21 W
Gardeyz 120 33.37 N 69.07 E
Gardinas → Grodno 76 53.41 N 23.50 E
Gardiner, Me., U.S. 188 44.13 N 69.46 W
Gardiner, Mt., U.S. 202 45.01 N 110.42 W
Gardiner, N.Y., U.S. 210 41.41 N 74.09 W
Gardiner, Or., U.S. 202 43.43 N 124.06 W
Gardiner, Wa., U.S. 224 48.03 N 122.55 W
Gardiner Dam -◆[6] 184 51.17 N 106.51 W
Gardiner Range ⋏ 162 23.50 S 131.46 E
Gardiners Bay c 207 41.08 N 72.10 W
Gardiners Creek ≃ 274b 37.50 S 145.02 E
Gardiners Island I 207 41.05 N 72.07 W
Garding 41 54.20 N 8.46 E
Gardner, Il., U.S. 216 41.11 N 88.18 W
Gardner, Ks., U.S. 198 38.48 N 94.55 W
Gardner, Ma., U.S. 207 42.34 N 71.59 W
Gardner Canal c 182 53.28 N 128.15 W
Gardner Lake ⊜ 207 41.31 N 72.13 W
Gardner Pinnacles II[1] 14 25.00 N 167.55 W
Gardnersville 218 38.46 N 84.30 W
Gardnertown 210 41.32 N 74.04 W
Gardnerville 226 38.56 N 119.44 W
Gardno 54 53.15 N 14.38 E
Gardolo 64 46.07 N 11.05 E
Gardon d'Alès ≃ 62 44.02 N 4.08 E
Gardon d'Anduze ≃ 62 44.02 N 4.08 E
Gardone Riviera 64 45.37 N 10.34 E
Gardone Val Trompia 64 45.41 N 10.11 E
Gårdsjö 40 58.52 N 14.19 E
Gårdskär 40 60.37 N 17.35 E
Gare Loch c 46 56.01 N 4.48 W
Garelochhead 46 56.05 N 4.50 W
Gareloi Island I 181a 51.47 N 178.48 W
Garenfeld -◆[8] 263 51.24 N 7.31 E
Garenin 46 58.21 N 6.50 W
Gare Simon 273b 4.15 S 15.11 E
Garešnica 36 45.35 N 16.56 E
Garessio 62 44.12 N 8.02 E
Garet, Mont ʌ[1] 175f 14.16 S 167.30 E
Garfield, Ks., U.S. 198 38.04 N 99.14 W
Garfield, N.J., U.S. 210 40.52 N 74.06 W
Garfield, N.M., U.S. 200 32.45 N 107.15 W
Garfield, Wa., U.S. 202 47.00 N 117.08 W
Garfield Heights 214 41.25 N 81.36 W
Garfield Mountain ʌ 202 44.31 N 112.37 W
Garfield Park 285 39.42 N 75.33 W
Garfield Park ♦, Il., U.S. 278 41.53 N 87.43 W
Garfield Park ♦, Oh., U.S. 279a 41.26 N 81.36 W
Garfield Peak ʌ 200 42.47 N 107.18 W
Garforth 44 53.48 N 1.22 W
Garga 88 54.26 N 110.33 E
Gargaliánoi 38 37.04 N 21.39 E
Gargano, Promontorio del › 68 41.50 N 16.00 E
Gargano, Testa del › 68 41.49 N 16.12 E
Gargantua, Cape › 190 47.36 N 85.02 W
Garga Sarali 152 5.11 N 14.00 E
Gargazzone (Gargazon) 64 46.35 N 11.12 E
Gargellen 58 46.58 N 9.56 E
Gargenville 261 49.00 N 1.49 E
Garges-lès-Gonesse 261 48.58 N 2.25 E
Gargnano 64 45.41 N 10.40 E
Gargouna 150 15.56 N 0.13 E
Gargrave 44 53.59 N 2.06 W
Gargždai 76 55.43 N 21.24 E
Garhākota 124 23.46 N 79.09 E
Garhbeta 126 22.51 N 87.19 E
Garhdīwāla 123 31.44 N 75.45 E
Garhi Habībullāh Khān 123 34.24 N 73.23 E
Garhi Jasaya 272a 28.46 N 77.16 E
Garhi Katiya 272a 28.45 N 77.16 E
Garhi Khairo 120 28.04 N 67.59 E
Garhi Malehra 124 25.02 N 79.40 E
Garhjāt Hills ⋏[2] 126 21.47 N 86.20 E
Garhmuktesar 124 28.48 N 78.06 E
Garhshankar 123 31.13 N 76.08 E
Garhwa 124 24.11 N 83.49 E

Gari 86 59.26 N 62.21 E
Garibaldi, Bra. 252 29.15 S 51.32 W
Garibaldi, B.C., Can. 182 49.58 N 123.09 W
Garibaldi, Or., U.S. 224 45.34 N 123.55 W
Garibaldi, Casa di ⊥ 71 41.13 N 9.27 E
Garibaldi, Mount ʌ 182 49.51 N 123.01 W
Garibaldi Provincial Park ♦ 182 50.00 N 122.50 W
Garies 158 30.30 S 18.00 E
Garigliano ≃ 66 41.13 N 13.45 E
Gariglione, Monte ʌ 68 39.09 N 16.41 E
Garín 258 34.26 S 58.44 W
Garín, Arroyo ≃ 288 34.23 S 58.43 W
Garin Regional Park ♦ 282 37.38 N 122.03 W
Garipçe Burnu › 267b 41.13 N 29.07 E
Garissa 154 0.28 S 39.38 E
Garita Palmera 236 13.44 N 90.05 W
Gariya 272b 22.28 N 88.23 E
Gārji 272b 22.51 N 88.19 E
Garkida 146 10.25 N 12.36 E
Garko 150 11.38 N 8.48 E
Garland, Al., U.S. 194 31.33 N 86.49 W
Garland, Md., U.S. 284b 39.11 N 76.39 W
Garland, Pa., U.S. 214 41.49 N 79.27 W
Garland, Tx., U.S. 222 32.54 N 96.38 W
Garland, Ut., U.S. 200 41.44 N 112.09 W
Garland Park ♦ 275b 43.44 N 79.35 W
Garland Peak ʌ 224 48.01 N 120.43 W
Garlasco 62 45.12 N 8.55 E
Garlate 62 45.49 N 9.23 E
Garlate, Lago di ⊜ 58 45.49 N 9.24 E
Garliava 76 54.49 N 23.52 E
Garlieston 44 54.48 N 4.22 W
Garlin 32 43.34 N 0.15 W
Garm 85 39.02 N 70 22 E
Garm Āb 120 32.14 N 65.01 E
Garmal 144 8.35 N 50.19 E
Gärmersdorf 60 49.26 N 11.54 E
Garmī 128 39.01 N 48.03 E
Garmisch-Partenkirchen 64 47.29 N 11.05 E
Garmouth 46 57.40 N 3.07 W
Garmsār 128 35.20 N 52.13 E
Garnavillo 190 42.52 N 91.14 W
Garne 261 48.41 N 1.58 E
Garner, Ia., U.S. 190 43.06 N 93.36 W
Garner, N.C., U.S. 192 35.42 N 78.36 W
Garnet Range ⋏ 202 46.45 N 113.15 W
Garnett 198 38.16 N 95.14 W
Garnijskij zapovednik ♦ 84 40.00 N 44.55 E
Garnish 186 47.14 N 55.22 W
Garnock ≃ 46 55.38 N 4.42 W
Garnpung, Lake ⊜ 166 33.30 S 143.12 E
Gāro Hills ⋏[2] 124 25.30 N 90.30 E
Garona → Garonne ≃ 32 45.02 N 0.36 W
Garonne ≃ 32 45.02 N 0.36 W
Garoowe 144 8.24 N 48.29 E
Garou, Lac ⊜ 150 16.04 N 2.45 W
Garoua, Cam. 146 9.18 N 13.24 E
Garoua, Niger 146 13.53 N 13.11 E
Garoua Boulaï 152 5.53 N 14.33 E
Garove Island I 164 4.40 S 149.30 E
Garpenberg 40 60.19 N 16.12 E
Garphyttan 40 59.19 N 14.56 E
Garphyttans Nationalpark ♦ 40 59.17 N 14.51 E
Garqu Yan, Zhg. 118 34.29 N 92.35 E
Garqu Yan, Zhg. 120 33.50 N 92.28 E
Garraf, Costa de ⊤[2] 266d 41.16 N 2.02 E
Garrattsville 210 42.39 N 75.10 W
Garrel 52 52.57 N 8.01 E
Garret Mountain Reservation ♦ 276 40.54 N 74.11 W
Garretson 198 43.43 N 96.30 W
Garrett, In., U.S. 216 41.20 N 85.08 W
Garrett, Ky., U.S. 192 37.28 N 82.49 W
Garrett Creek ≃ 222 32.57 N 95.44 W
Garrett Park 208 39.02 N 77.05 W
Garrett Park Estates 284c 39.02 N 77.06 W
Garrettsville 214 41.17 N 81.06 W
Garrison, N. Ire., U.K. 48 54.25 N 8.05 W
Garrison, Ky., U.S. 218 38.36 N 83.10 W
Garrison, Md., U.S. 208 39.24 N 76.45 W
Garrison, Mt., U.S. 202 46.31 N 112.48 W
Garrison, N.Y., U.S. 210 41.23 N 73.56 W
Garrison, N.D., U.S. 198 47.39 N 101.24 W
Garrison, Tx., U.S. 222 31.49 N 94.30 W
Garrison Dam -◆[6] 198 47.22 N 101.25 W
Garron Point › 48 55.03 N 5.57 W
Garros 46 57.37 N 6.11 W
Garrovillas 34 39.43 N 6.33 W
Garry ≃ 46 56.43 N 3.47 W
Garry, Loch ⊜ 206 45.15 N 74.43 W
Garry Bay c 176 68.55 N 85.05 W
Garry Lake ⊜ 176 66.00 N 100.00 W
Gars am Kamp 61 48.36 N 15.40 E
Garsdale Head 44 54.19 N 2.20 W
Garsen 154 2.16 S 40.07 E
Garskolk 158 30.41 S 22.02 E
Gårslev 41 55.38 N 9.43 E
Garson 190 46.34 N 80.52 W
Garson Lake ⊜ 184 56.19 N 110.02 W
Garstang 44 53.55 N 2.47 W
Garstedt 52 53.41 N 9.58 E
Garstedterheide -◆[3] 52 53.17 N 8.43 E
Garsten 61 48.01 N 14.24 E
Garston 260 51.41 N 0.23 W
Garston -◆[8] 262 53.21 N 2.53 W
Garswood 262 53.29 N 2.40 W
Gartempe ≃ 32 46.48 N 0.50 E
Gartenstadt -◆[8] 263 51.30 N 7.26 E
Garthby Station (Beaulac) 206 45.50 N 71.23 W
Gartow 54 53.02 N 11.29 E
Gartrop-Bühl 263 51.40 N 6.49 E
Gartz 54 53.12 N 14.23 E
Garu 150 10.51 N 0.11 W
Garub 156 26.33 S 16.00 E
Garubhāsa 124 26.33 N 90.22 E
Gārulia 126 22.49 N 88.22 E
Garut 115a 7.13 S 107.54 E
Garve 46 57.37 N 4.42 W
Garvellachs II 46 56.14 N 5.47 W
Garvey Reservoir ⊜[1] 280 34.13 N 118.07 W
Garvie Mountains ⋏ 172 45.30 S 168.50 E
Garwin 190 42.05 N 92.40 W
Garwolin 30 51.54 N 21.37 E
Garwood, N.J., U.S. 276 40.39 N 74.19 W
Garwood, Tx., U.S. 222 29.27 N 96.24 W
Gary, In., U.S. 216 41.35 N 87.20 W
Gary, S.D., U.S. 198 44.47 N 96.27 W
Gary, Tx., U.S. 194 32.07 N 94.22 W
Gary, W.V., U.S. 192 37.21 N 81.33 W
Garyarsa 120 31.44 N 80.21 E
Gary Harbor c 278 41.38 N 87.20 W
Garyi 102 30.54 N 98.56 E
Gary Municipal Airport ⊠ 278 41.37 N 87.25 W
Garysburg 208 36.27 N 77.33 W
Garz 54 54.19 N 13.20 E
Garza 252 28.09 S 63.32 W
Garza Ayala 196 26.29 N 100.02 W
Garza García 196 25.40 N 100.24 W
Garzas Creek ≃ 226 37.13 N 120.57 W
Garzeno 58 46.08 N 9.15 E
Garzón, Col. 246 2.12 N 75.38 W
Garzón, Ur. 252 34.36 S 54.33 W
Gas 261 48.34 N 1.40 E
Gasan 116 13.19 N 121.51 E
Gasan-Kuli 128 37.27 N 53.59 E
Gas City 216 40.29 N 85.36 W
Gascogne □[9] 32 44.00 N 0.05 E
Gascogne, Golfe de → Biscay, Bay of c 32 44.00 N 4.00 W
Gasconade 219 38.40 N 91.33 W
Gasconade □[6] 219 38.27 N 91.30 W

Gasconade ≃ 194 38.40 N 91.33 W
Gasconade, Osage Fork ≃ 194 37.45 N 92.26 W
Gascoyne ≃ 162 24.52 S 113.37 E
Gascoyne, Mount ʌ 162 24.58 S 116.38 E
Gascoyne Junction 162 25.03 S 115.12 E
Gash (Nahr al-Qāsh) ≃ 140 16.48 N 35.51 E
Gashaka 146 7.21 N 11.27 E
Gasherbrum I ʌ 123 35.43 N 76.43 E
Gas Hu ⊜ 120 38.10 N 90.42 E
Gashua 146 12.54 N 11.00 E
Gasline 284a 42.53 N 79.11 W
Gasny 50 49.05 N 1.36 E
Gaspar 252 26.56 S 48.58 W
Gaspard Creek ≃ 182 51.34 N 122.17 W
Gasparilla Island I 220 26.46 N 82.16 W
Gasparilla Sound ɥ 220 26.48 N 82.15 W
Gaspé 186 48.50 N 64.29 W
Gaspé, Baie de c 186 48.46 N 64.17 W
Gaspé, Cap › 186 48.45 N 64.10 W
Gaspé Peninsula → Gaspésie, Péninsule de la ›[1] 186 48.30 N 65.00 W
Gaspereau Lake ⊜ 186 44.57 N 64.34 W
Gasperina 68 38.44 N 16.30 E
Gaspésie, Parc Provincial de la ♦ 186 48.55 N 66.00 W
Gaspésie, Péninsule de la ›[1] 186 48.30 N 65.00 W
Gaspoltshofen 60 48.08 N 13.46 E
Gasport 210 43.11 N 78.34 W
Gaspra 78 44.27 N 34.07 E
Gassan 150 12.49 N 3.12 W
Gas-san ʌ 92 38.32 N 140.01 E
Gassaway 188 38.40 N 80.46 W
Gasse 64 47.23 N 11.09 E
Gasselte 52 52.57 N 6.46 E
Gassin 62 43.13 N 6.35 E
Gassino Torinese 62 45.08 N 7.49 E
Gassol 146 8.32 N 10.28 E
Gastein → Badgastein 64 47.07 N 13.08 E
Gasteiner Tal V 64 47.11 N 13.06 E
Gasteiz → Vitoria 34 42.51 N 2.40 W
Gastello 89 49.07 N 142.58 E
Gaston, In., U.S. 216 40.18 N 85.30 W
Gaston, N.C., U.S. 192 36.30 N 77.38 W
Gaston, Or., U.S. 224 45.26 N 123.08 W
Gaston, Lake ⊜[1] 192 36.35 N 78.00 W
Gastonia, N.C., U.S. 192 35.15 N 81.11 W
Gastonia, Tx., U.S. 222 32.37 N 96.24 W
Gastonville 279b 40.15 N 79.59 W
Gastoúni 38 37.51 N 21.16 E
Gastre 254 42.17 S 69.14 W
Gästrikland □[9] 40 60.30 N 16.27 E
Gat 132 31.37 N 34.47 E
Gata, Cabo de › 34 36.43 N 2.12 W
Gata, Sierra de ⋏ 34 40.14 N 6.45 W
Gătaia 38 45.26 N 21.26 E
Gátas, Akrotírion › 130 34.34 N 33.02 E
Gatčina 76 59.34 N 30.08 E
Gate 196 36.51 N 100.03 W
Gateacre -◆[8] 262 53.23 N 2.51 W
Gate City 192 36.38 N 82.34 W
Gatehouse of Fleet 44 54.53 N 4.11 W
Gatersleben 54 51.49 N 11.17 E
Gates, N.Y., U.S. 210 43.09 N 77.41 W
Gates, N.C., U.S. 208 36.30 N 76.46 W
Gates □[6] 208 36.28 N 76.43 W
Gateshead 44 54.58 N 1.37 W
Gateshead Island I 176 70.22 N 100.27 W
Gates Mills 279a 41.31 N 81.24 W
Gates of the Arctic National Park ♦ 180 67.45 N 153.30 W
Gatesville, N.C., U.S. 192 36.24 N 76.45 W
Gatesville, Tx., U.S. 222 31.26 N 97.44 W
Gateway 200 38.40 N 108.58 W
Gateway Arch ʊ 219 38.37 N 90.12 W
Gateway National Recreation Area ♦ 276 40.34 N 74.06 W
Gateway of India ⊥ 272c 18.55 N 72.50 E
Gateway Stadium ♦ 279a 41.30 N 81.41 W
Gaths Mine 154 20.00 S 30.31 E
Gathurst 262 53.34 N 2.42 W
Gatié Loumo 150 15.28 N 4.37 W
Gatineau 212 45.29 N 75.38 W
Gatineau □[6] 212 45.25 N 75.45 W
Gatineau ≃ 176 45.27 N 75.40 W
Gatineau, Parc de la ♦ 188 45.30 N 76.05 W
Gatley 262 53.23 N 2.14 W
Gatlinburg 192 35.42 N 83.30 W
Gato, Arroyo del ≃, Arg. 288 34.51 S 57.56 W
Gato, Arroyo del ≃, Arg. 288 34.55 S 58.37 W
Ga'ton 132 33.00 N 35.13 E
Gato Negro 286c 10.33 N 66.57 W
Gatow -◆[8] 54 52.29 N 13.11 E
Gatow, Flugplatz ⊠ 264a 52.28 N 13.08 E
Gattendorf 61 48.01 N 16.59 E
Gattières 62 43.46 N 7.11 E
Gattinara 62 45.37 N 8.22 E
Gatton 171a 27.33 S 152.17 E
Gattorna 62 44.26 N 9.11 E
Gatún, Esclusas de -◆[5] 236 9.16 N 79.55 W
Gatún, Lago ⊜[1] 236 9.12 N 79.55 W
Gatvand 128 32.15 N 48.50 E
Gau-Algesheim 56 49.57 N 8.01 E
Gauchy 50 49.49 N 3.16 E
Gaucín 34 36.31 N 5.19 W
Gauer Lake ⊜ 184 57.00 N 97.50 W
Gauguin, Musée ʊ 174s 17.45 S 149.23 W
Gauja ≃ 76 57.09 N 24.16 E
Gaujiena 76 57.30 N 26.40 E
Gaukler Point › 281 42.27 N 82.52 W
Gaula ≃ 26 63.21 N 10.14 E
Gauley ≃ 188 38.10 N 81.12 W
Gauley Bridge 188 38.10 N 81.11 W
Gaultois 186 47.36 N 55.54 W
Gaunless ≃ 44 54.40 N 1.41 W
Gau-Odernheim 56 49.47 N 8.11 E
Gaur 124 26.46 N 85.17 E
Gaurain-Ramecroix 50 50.35 N 3.29 E
Gaurambha 126 22.39 N 89.34 E
Gaurela 124 22.45 N 81.54 E
Gaurhāti 126 22.46 N 87.48 E
Gauribaradia 126 23.45 N 89.52 E
Gauribidanūr 122 13.37 N 77.31 E
Gauri Phānta 124 28.41 N 80.33 E
Gauripur 124 26.05 N 89.58 E
Gaurīśaṅgkar ʌ 124 27.57 N 86.21 E
Gaurnadi 126 22.58 N 90.14 E
Gause 222 30.47 N 96.43 W
Gausta ʌ 26 59.50 N 8.35 E
Gauthiot, Chutes ᒪ 146 9.43 N 14.34 E
Gauting 60 48.04 N 11.23 E
Gavà 34 41.18 N 2.01 E
Gāvanpāda 272c 18.57 N 73.01 E
Gavardo 64 45.35 N 10.26 E
Gávdhos I 38 34.50 N 24.06 E
Gávea -◆[8] 287a 22.58 S 43.14 W
Gávea, Hipódromo da ♦ 287a 22.58 S 43.13 W
Gávea, Pedra da ʌ 287a 23.00 S 43.17 W
Gavel-Långsjön ⊜ 40 59.50 N 18.18 E
Gavello 64 45.01 N 11.55 E
Gavet 62 45.04 N 5.52 E
Gavi 62 44.41 N 8.49 E
Gavia, Arroyo de la ≃ 266a 40.21 N 3.40 W
Gavião ≃ 255 14.06 S 41.01 W
Gavião, Pico do ʌ 256 21.37 S 44.50 W
Gavien 164 3.54 S 144.07 E
Gavilán 286c 10.24 N 66.51 W
Gavinana 66 44.05 N 10.45 E

Gavins Point Dam -◆[6] 198 42.48 N 97.40 W
Gaviões 256 22.34 S 42.33 W
Gavirate 62 45.50 N 8.43 E
Gavja ≃ 76 53.49 N 25.35 E
Gāv Khūnī, Bāṭlāq-e ≡ 128 32.10 N 52.50 E
Gävle 40 60.40 N 17.10 E
Gävleborgs Län □[6] 26 61.30 N 16.15 E
Gävlebukten c 40 60.42 N 17.20 E
Gavnø 41 55.11 N 11.44 E
Gavoi 71 40.10 N 9.12 E
Gavorrano 66 42.55 N 10.54 E
Gavrilov-Jam 80 57.18 N 39.51 E
Gavrilovka 83 48.37 N 37.31 E
Gavrilovka Vtoraja 80 52.53 N 42.46 E
Gavrilov Posad 80 56.33 N 40.07 E
Gávrion 38 37.52 N 24.46 E
Gavry 76 56.55 N 27.53 E
Gawachab 156 27.03 S 17.50 E
Gāwān 124 24.37 N 85.55 E
Gaweinstal 61 48.28 N 16.35 E
Gāwīlgarh Hills ⋏[2] 122 21.20 N 77.00 E
Gawler 168b 34.37 S 138.44 E
Gawler ≃ 168b 34.41 S 138.27 E
Gawler Ranges ⋏ 162 32.30 S 136.00 E
Gawso 150 6.48 N 2.31 W
Gawsworth 262 53.13 N 2.10 W
Gawthorpe Hall ⊥ 262 53.48 N 2.18 W
Gaxun Nur (Juyanhai) ⊜ 102 42.22 N 100.34 E
Gaya, India 124 24.47 N 85.00 E
Gaya, Niger 150 11.53 N 3.27 E
Gaya, Nig. 150 11.53 N 9.02 E
Gay City State Park ♦ 207 41.42 N 72.28 W
Gayéri 150 12.39 N 0.29 E
Gay Head 207 41.20 N 70.48 W
Gay Hill 222 30.16 N 96.30 W
Gaylord, Mi., U.S. 190 45.01 N 84.40 W
Gaylord, Mn., U.S. 190 44.33 N 94.13 W
Gaylordsville 207 41.38 N 73.29 W
Gayndah 166 25.37 S 151.36 E
Gays Mills 190 43.19 N 90.50 W
Gayton, Eng., U.K. 42 52.45 N 0.34 E
Gayton, Eng., U.K. 262 53.19 N 3.06 W
Gaza → Ghazzah 132 31.30 N 34.28 E
Gaza □[5] 156 23.30 S 32.45 E
Gazalkent 85 41.33 N 69.47 E
Gazaoua 150 13.32 N 7.55 E
Gaza Strip □[9] 132 31.25 N 34.20 E
Gazelle Channel ɥ 164 2.50 S 150.55 E
Gazelle Peninsula ›[1] 164 4.40 S 152.00 E
Gazeran 261 48.38 N 1.46 E
Gazeran, Bois de ♦ 261 48.40 N 1.45 E
Gazi, Kenya 154 4.25 S 39.30 E
Gazi, Zaïre 154 1.04 N 24.31 E
Gaziantep 130 37.05 N 37.22 E
Gaziantep □[4] 130 37.00 N 37.20 E
Gazimağusa (Famagusta) 130 35.07 N 33.57 E
Gazimağusa Körfezi c 130 35.15 N 34.10 E
Gazimur ≃ 88 52.57 N 120.22 E
Gazimurskij Zavod 88 51.33 N 118.22 E
Gazipaşa 130 36.17 N 32.20 E
Gazira Sporting Club ♦ 273c 30.04 N 31.13 E
Gazivoda Jezero ⊜[1] 38 42.55 N 20.40 E
Gaznau 85 40.10 N 71.02 E
Gazoldo degli Ippoliti 64 45.12 N 10.35 E
Gazos Creek ≃ 226 37.10 N 122.22 W
Gazzada 62 45.47 N 8.51 E
Gazzaniga 62 45.48 N 9.50 E
Gazzuolo 64 45.04 N 10.35 E
Gbangbatok 150 7.48 N 12.23 W
Gbanhala ≃ 150 10.14 N 8.38 W
Gbaoui Bodanga 152 5.33 N 16.45 E
Gbarnga 150 7.00 N 9.29 W
Gbogbo 273a 6.36 N 3.31 E
Gboko 150 7.20 N 8.57 E
Gbon 150 9.50 N 6.27 W
Gbwado 152 3.54 N 20.46 E
Gcoverega 156 19.08 S 24.15 E
Gdańsk (Danzig) 30 54.23 N 18.40 E
Gdańsk □[4] 30 54.15 N 18.25 E
Gdansk, Gulf of c 30 54.40 N 19.15 E
Gden' 78 51.20 N 30.25 E
Gdov 76 58.44 N 27.48 E
Gdyel 34 35.48 N 0.26 W
Gdynia 30 54.32 N 18.33 E
Gearhart 224 46.01 N 123.54 W
Gearhart Mountain ʌ 202 42.30 N 120.53 W
Gearhartville 214 40.53 N 78.15 W
Geary, N.B., Can. 186 45.46 N 66.29 W
Geary, Ok., U.S. 196 35.43 N 98.22 W
Geauga □[6] 214 41.35 N 81.12 W
Geauga Lake Park ♦ 279a 41.21 N 81.23 W
Geba ≃ 150 11.46 N 15.36 W
Gebaberg ʌ 56 50.36 N 10.16 E
Gebe, Pulau I 164 0.05 S 129.20 E
Gebeit Mine 140 21.03 N 36.19 E
Gebenbach 60 49.32 N 11.53 E
Gebesee 54 51.07 N 10.56 E
Gebi 84 42.46 N 43.30 E
Gebilu 144 10.35 N 41.28 E
Gebiz 130 37.06 N 30.56 E
Gebra 54 51.24 N 10.35 E
Gebweiler → Guebwiller 58 47.55 N 7.12 E
Gebze 130 40.48 N 29.25 E
Gecha 144 7.31 N 35.22 E
Gechang 106 31.05 N 119.27 E
Geçitkale 130 35.15 N 33.45 E
Gecun 106 32.10 N 119.37 E
Geddes, Mi., U.S. 281 42.16 N 83.40 W
Geddes, S.D., U.S. 198 43.15 N 98.41 W
Gede, Gunung ʌ 115a 6.47 S 106.59 E
Gedera 132 31.49 N 34.46 E
Gedern 56 50.25 N 9.12 E
Gedian 100 30.32 N 114.38 E
Gedikler 130 39.06 N 38.49 E
Gediksaray 130 40.27 N 35.38 E
Gedi National Monument ♦ 154 3.19 S 40.03 E
Gedinne 56 49.59 N 4.56 E
Gediz 130 39.02 N 29.25 E
Gediz ≃ 130 38.35 N 26.48 E
Geclegube 144 6.52 N 45.02 E
Geco 144 8.58 N 37.27 E
Geco □[4] 144 3.00 N 42.00 E
Gedongdalem 112 5.04 S 105.25 E
Gedongtataan 115a 5.23 S 105.05 E
Gedser 41 54.35 N 11.57 E
Gedser Odde › 41 54.34 N 11.59 E
Geduld 273d 26.15 S 28.25 E
Gedun 100 27.39 N 118.26 E
Geebung 171a 27.22 S 153.03 E
Gee Cross 262 53.26 N 2.04 W
Geehi 171b 36.24 S 148.11 E
Geehi ≃ 171b 36.11 S 148.02 E
Geel 56 51.10 N 5.00 E
Geelong 169 38.08 S 144.21 E
Geelong West 169 38.08 S 144.20 E
Geelvink Channel ɥ 162 28.30 S 114.10 E
Geer ≃ 56 50.51 N 5.42 E
Geeste ≃ 52 53.32 N 8.35 E
Geesthacht 52 53.26 N 10.22 E
Geeveston 166 43.10 S 146.55 E
Gefell 54 50.26 N 11.52 E
Gefle → Gävle 40 60.40 N 17.10 E
Gefrees 54 50.06 N 11.44 E
Gegang 100 30.04 N 117.38 E
Gegenmiao 89 45.58 N 122.15 E
Gegong 100 30.05 N 117.11 E
Gegou 98 35.24 N 118.32 E
Gegu 105 38.59 N 117.30 E
Gehackte Berge ⋏[2] 264a 52.41 N 13.30 E

Gehrden 52 52.18 N 9.36 E
Gehren 54 50.39 N 10.59 E
Gehu 100 27.46 N 119.16 E
Ge Hu ⊜ 106 31.36 N 119.51 E
Gehua 164 10.20 S 150.25 E
Geidam 146 12.57 N 11.57 E
Geiger 194 32.52 N 88.18 W
Geigertown 208 40.13 N 75.50 W
Geihoku 96 34.44 N 132.17 E
Geikie ≃ 176 57.45 N 103.52 W
Geilenkirchen 56 50.57 N 6.07 E
Geilo 26 60.31 N 8.12 E
Geinō 94 34.48 N 136.25 E
Geiranger 26 62.06 N 7.12 E
Geisa 56 50.43 N 9.57 E
Geisberg ʌ 60 49.53 N 11.03 E
Geisecke 263 51.27 N 7.37 E
Geisei 96 33.31 N 133.49 E
Geiselhöring 60 48.50 N 12.23 E
Geisenfeld 60 48.41 N 11.37 E
Geisenhausen 60 48.28 N 12.15 E
Geisenheim 56 49.59 N 7.58 E
Geisingen 58 47.55 N 8.38 E
Geislingen an der Steige 56 48.36 N 9.50 E
Geismar 52 51.31 N 9.57 E
Geispolsheim 58 48.31 N 7.39 E
Geisstein ʌ 64 47.20 N 12.30 E
Geistenbeck -◆[3] 263 51.09 N 6.27 E
Geistown 214 40.17 N 78.52 W
Geist Reservoir ⊜[1], In., U.S. 218 39.56 N 85.56 W
Geist Reservoir ⊜[1], Pa., U.S. 285 39.57 N 75.24 W
Geisweid 56 50.55 N 8.01 E
Geita 154 2.52 S 32.10 E
Geithain 54 51.03 N 12.41 E
Geiyō-shotō II 96 34.10 N 132.45 E
Gejah 272a 28.31 N 77.23 E
Gejiatun 98 40.27 N 119.55 E
Gejiu (Kokiu) 102 23.22 N 103.06 E
Geka, mys › 180 64.26 N 178.10 E
Gela 70 37.04 N 14.15 E
Gela ≃ 70 37.03 N 14.15 E
Gela, Golfo di c 70 37.03 N 14.10 E
Geladandong ʌ 120 33.16 N 91.27 E
Geladi 144 6.57 N 46.25 E
Gelai ʌ[1] 154 2.33 S 36.05 E
Gelan 102 30.03 N 107.04 E
Gelang, Tanjong › 114 3.58 N 103.26 E
Gelaochang 107 29.36 N 103.39 E
Gelasa, Selat ɥ 112 2.40 S 107.15 E
Gelber Fluss → Huang ≃ 90 37.32 N 118.19 E
Gelbes Meer → Yellow Sea ⊤[2] 90 36.00 N 123.00 E
Gelderland □[4] 52 52.10 N 5.50 E
Geldermalsen 52 51.53 N 5.17 E
Geldern 52 51.31 N 6.20 E
Geldrop 52 51.25 N 5.33 E
Geleen 56 50.58 N 5.52 E
Gelembe 130 39.10 N 27.50 E
Gelemso 144 8.48 N 40.35 E
Gelenau 54 50.42 N 12.58 E
Gelendost 130 38.07 N 31.01 E
Gelendžik 78 44.33 N 38.06 E
Gelfingen 58 47.13 N 8.16 E
Gelgaudiškis 76 55.05 N 23.00 E
Gelib → Jilib 144 0.29 N 42.46 E
Gelibolu 130 40.24 N 26.40 E
Gelibolu Yarımadası (Gallipoli Peninsula) ›[1] 130 40.20 N 26.30 E
Gelibolu Yarımadası Milli Parkı ♦ 130 40.05 N 26.10 E
Gelinden 56 50.46 N 5.15 E
Gélise ≃ 32 44.11 N 0.17 E
Geliting 115b 8.39 S 122.18 E
Geliting, Teluk c 115b 8.36 S 122.17 E
Gellénháza 61 46.46 N 16.47 E
Gellenstrom ɥ 54 54.28 N 13.03 E
Gellep-Stratum -◆[8] 263 51.20 N 6.41 E
Gellibrand ≃ 169 38.41 S 143.09 E
Gellibrand, Mount ʌ[2] 169 38.14 S 143.48 E
Gellibrand, Point › 274b 37.52 S 144.54 E
Gellibrand River 169 38.32 S 143.32 E
Gellingen → Ghislenghien 50 50.39 N 3.52 E
Gellinsoor 144 6.26 N 46.42 E
Gel'm'azov 78 49.49 N 31.49 E
Gelnhausen 56 50.11 N 9.11 E
Gelså ≃ 41 55.19 N 8.54 E
Gelsdorf 56 50.35 N 7.02 E
Gelsenkirchen 52 51.31 N 7.07 E
Gelsenkirchen-Horst, Galopprennbahn ♦ 263 51.32 N 7.02 E
Gelsted 41 55.24 N 9.59 E
Gelt ≃ 44 54.56 N 2.47 W
Geltendorf 60 48.07 N 11.01 E
Gelterkinden 58 47.28 N 7.51 E
Gelting 41 54.45 N 9.53 E
Geltow 54 52.22 N 12.58 E
Geltsa 144 6.14 N 37.05 E
Geluji 98 37.08 N 121.50 E
Geluksburg 158 28.30 S 29.33 E
Geluwe 50 50.48 N 3.04 E
Gemas 114 2.35 N 102.37 E
Gembloux 56 50.34 N 4.41 E
Gembrook 169 37.57 S 145.33 E
Gemen 52 51.51 N 6.52 E
Gemena 152 3.15 N 19.46 E
Gémenos 62 43.18 N 5.38 E
Gemerek 130 39.11 N 36.05 E
Gemert 52 51.34 N 5.40 E
Gemla 26 56.52 N 14.38 E
Gemlik 130 40.26 N 29.09 E
Gemlik Körfezi c 130 40.25 N 28.55 E
Gemolong 115a 7.24 S 110.50 E
Gemona del Friuli 64 46.16 N 13.09 E
Gemonio 62 45.53 N 8.40 E
Gemsbok National Park ♦ 156 25.15 S 21.10 E
Gemünd 56 50.34 N 6.30 E
Gemünden, Dtsch. 56 50.03 N 9.41 E
Gemünden, Dtsch. 56 50.58 N 8.58 E
Gemünden, Dtsch. 56 49.54 N 7.28 E
Gen ≃ 89 50.16 N 119.22 E
Genadendal 158 34.02 S 19.33 E
Genaibashi 268 35.21 N 140.04 E
Genale (Jubba) ≃ 144 0.15 S 42.38 E
Genappe 50 50.36 N 4.27 E
Genarp 41 55.36 N 13.23 E
Genazzano 66 41.50 N 12.58 E
Genç 130 38.46 N 40.35 E
Gençay 32 46.23 N 0.24 E
Gencek 130 37.27 N 31.33 E
Gencsapáti 61 47.17 N 16.36 E
Gending 115a 7.48 S 113.18 E
Gendrey 58 47.12 N 5.41 E
Gendringen 52 51.52 N 6.22 E
Gendt 52 51.53 N 5.59 E
Genegantslet Creek ≃ 210 42.18 N 75.48 W
Genemuiden 52 52.37 N 6.07 E
General ≃ 236 8.59 N 83.11 W
General Acha 252 37.23 S 64.36 W
General Alvear, Arg. 252 36.03 S 60.01 W
General Alvear, Arg. 252 34.58 S 67.42 W
General Aquino 252 24.26 S 56.42 W
General Arenales 252 34.18 S 61.18 W
General Belgrano 252 35.46 S 58.30 W
General Bernardo O'Higgins ʊ[3] 9 63.19 S 57.54 W
General Bravo 232 25.48 N 99.10 W
General Butler State Resort Park ♦ 218 38.40 N 85.10 W
General Cabrera 252 32.48 S 63.52 W
General Campos 252 31.32 S 58.24 W
General Carneiro 255 15.42 S 52.45 W

General Carrera, Lago (Lago Buenos Aires) ⊜ 254 46.35 S 72.00 W
General Cepeda 232 25.23 N 101.27 W
General Conesa, Arg. 252 36.30 S 57.20 W
General Conesa, Arg. 254 40.06 S 64.26 W
General Daniel Cerri 252 38.42 S 62.24 W
General del Sur, Cementerio -◆ 286c 10.28 N 66.55 W
General Elizardo Aquino 252 26.53 S 56.17 W
General Enrique Martínez 252 33.12 S 53.48 W
General Enrique Mosconi 252 22.36 S 63.49 W
General Escobedo, Méx. 196 25.49 N 100.20 W
General Escobedo, Méx. 232 25.30 N 105.15 W
General Eugenio A. Garay, Para. 248 20.31 S 62.08 W
General Eugenio A. Garay, Para. 252 25.55 S 56.11 W
General Galarza 252 32.43 S 59.24 W
General Güemes 252 24.40 S 65.03 W
General Guido 252 36.40 S 57.46 W
General Hornos 258 34.53 S 58.56 W
General Island I 116 9.25 N 126.00 E
General José de San Martín 252 26.33 S 59.21 W
General Juan José Ríos 232 25.40 N 108.40 W
General Juan Madariaga 252 37.00 S 57.09 W
General La Madrid 252 37.16 S 61.17 W
General Las Heras 258 34.56 S 58.57 W
General Las Heras □[5] 288 34.56 S 58.51 W
General Lavalle 252 36.24 S 56.58 W
General Leonidas Plaza Gutiérrez 246 2.58 S 78.25 W
General Levalle 252 34.01 S 63.56 W
General Lorenzo Vintter 254 40.44 S 64.29 W
General Luna 116 9.47 N 126.09 E
General MacArthur (Pambuhan Sur) 116 11.15 N 125.32 E
General Mansilla (Bartolomé Bavio) 258 35.05 S 57.45 W
General Manuel Belgrano, Cerro ʌ 252 29.01 S 67.49 W
General Mitchell Field ⊠ 216 42.57 N 87.54 W
General Motors Corporation (Pontiac Division) ʊ[3] 281 42.49 N 83.17 W
General Motors Proving Grounds ʊ[3] 281 42.35 N 83.41 W
General Motors Technical Center ʊ[3] 281 42.31 N 83.02 W
General'nyj ≃ 265a 60.00 N 30.32 E
General O'Brien 252 34.54 S 60.45 W
General Pacheco 288 34.28 S 58.38 W
General Pánfilo Natera 234 22.40 N 102.06 W
General Paz 258 35.31 S 58.19 W
General Pico 252 35.40 S 63.44 W
General Pinedo 252 27.19 S 61.17 W
General Pinto 252 34.46 S 61.53 W
General Pizarro 252 24.13 S 64.01 W
General Roca 252 39.02 S 67.35 W
General Rodríguez 258 34.36 S 58.57 W
General San Martín, Arg. 252 37.59 S 63.34 W
General San Martín, Arg. 258 34.34 S 58.32 W
General San Martín □[5] 288 34.34 S 58.34 W
General Santos (Dadiangas) 116 6.07 N 125.11 E
General Sarmiento 258 34.33 S 58.43 W
General Sarmiento □[5] 288 34.32 S 58.43 W
General'skoje 83 47.28 N 39.35 E
General Terán 232 25.16 N 99.41 W
General Tinio 116 15.21 N 121.03 E
General Toševo 38 43.42 N 28.02 E
General Treviño 196 26.14 N 99.29 W
General Viamonte (Los Toldos) 252 35.01 S 61.01 W
General Villegas 252 35.02 S 63.01 W
General Vintter, Lago (Lago Palena) ⊜ 254 43.55 S 71.40 W
General Warren Village 285 40.02 N 75.32 W
General Zuazua 196 25.54 N 100.07 W
Gênes → Genova 62 44.25 N 8.57 E
Genesee, Id., U.S. 202 46.33 N 116.55 W
Genesee, Pa., U.S. 214 41.59 N 77.52 W
Genesee, Wi., U.S. 216 42.58 N 88.21 W
Genesee □[6], Mi., U.S. 216 42.56 N 83.41 W
Genesee □[6], N.Y., U.S. 210 43.00 N 78.11 W
Genesee ≃ 210 43.16 N 77.36 W
Geneseo, Il., U.S. 190 41.26 N 90.09 W
Geneseo, Ks., U.S. 198 38.30 N 98.09 W
Geneseo, N.Y., U.S. 210 42.47 N 77.49 W
Geneva → Genève, Schw. 58 46.12 N 6.09 E
Geneva, S. Afr. 158 27.50 S 27.08 E
Geneva, Al., U.S. 194 31.01 N 85.51 W
Geneva, Fl., U.S. 220 28.44 N 81.07 W
Geneva, Il., U.S. 216 41.53 N 88.18 W
Geneva, In., U.S. 216 40.35 N 84.57 W
Geneva, Ne., U.S. 198 40.31 N 97.35 W
Geneva, N.Y., U.S. 210 42.52 N 77.00 W
Geneva, Oh., U.S. 214 41.48 N 80.56 W
Geneva, Pa., U.S. 214 41.35 N 80.14 W
Geneva, Wa., U.S. 224 48.45 N 122.24 W
Geneva, Lake (Lac Léman) (Lac de Genève) ⊜, Europe 58 46.25 N 6.30 E
Geneva, Lake ⊜, Wi., U.S. 216 42.34 N 88.30 W
Geneva-on-the-Lake 214 41.52 N 80.57 W
Genève (Geneva) 58 46.12 N 6.09 E
Genève □[3] 58 46.15 N 6.10 E
Genève, Lac de → Geneva, Lake ⊜ 58 46.25 N 6.30 E
Genève-Cointrin, Aéroport ⊠ 58 46.14 N 6.06 E
Genevois -◆[1] 58 46.03 N 6.14 E
Genévriers, Île des I 186 51.15 N 58.26 W
Genf → Genève 58 46.12 N 6.09 E
Genga 66 43.26 N 12.56 E
Gengenbach 58 48.24 N 8.01 E
Genghis Khan, Wall of ⊥, Asia 88 49.00 N 115.00 E
Genghis Khan, Wall of ⊥, Mong. 88 49.00 N 116.00 E
Gengji 100 33.47 N 112.47 E
Gengma 102 23.34 N 99.06 E
Gengputou 106 31.12 N 119.55 E
Gengzhuang 104 40.59 N 122.42 E
Geničesk 78 46.11 N 34.48 E
Génicourt 261 49.05 N 2.04 E
Génicourt-sur-Meuse 56 49.02 N 5.26 E
Genil ≃ 34 37.42 N 5.19 W
Génissiat 58 46.03 N 5.47 E
Genk 56 50.58 N 5.30 E
Genkai 96 33.51 N 130.30 E
Genkai-kokutei-kōen ♦ 96 33.54 N 130.31 E
Genkai-nada ⊤[2] 92 34.00 N 130.00 E
Genkanyj, chrebet ⋏ 180 66.15 N 172.20 W
Genlis 58 47.14 N 5.13 E

Symbol	English	Deutsch	Español	Français	Português
≃	River	Fluß	Río	Rivière	Rio
≊	Canal	Kanal	Canal	Canal	Canal
ᒪ	Waterfall, Rapids	Wasserfall, Stromschnellen	Cascada, Rápidos	Chute d'eau, Rapides	Cascata, Rápidos
ɥ	Strait	Meeresstraße	Estrecho	Détroit	Estreito
c	Bay, Gulf	Bucht, Golf	Bahía, Golfo	Baie, Golfe	Baía, Golfo
⊜	Lake, Lakes	See, Seen	Lago, Lagos	Lac, Lacs	Lago, Lagos
≡	Swamp	Sumpf	Pantano	Marais	Pântano
⊓	Ice Features, Glacier	Eis- und Gletscherformen	Accidentes Glaciales	Formes glaciaires	Acidentes glaciares
⊤	Other Hydrographic Features	Andere Hydrographische Objekte	Otros Elementos Hidrográficos	Autres données hydrographiques	Outros acidentes hidrográficos

Symbol	English	Deutsch	Español	Français	Português
✢	Submarine Features	Untermeerische Objekte	Accidentes Submarinos	Formes de relief sous-marin	Acidentes submarinos
□	Political Unit	Politische Einheit	Unidad Politica	Entité politique	Unidade política
ʊ	Cultural Institution	Kulturelle Institution	Institución Cultural	Institution culturelle	Institução cultural
⊥	Historical Site	Historische Stätte	Sitio Histórico	Site historique	Sitio histórico
♦	Recreational Site	Erholungs- und Ferienort	Sitio de Recreo	Centre de loisirs	Area de Lazer
⊠	Airport	Flughafen	Aeropuerto	Aéroport	Aeroporto
■	Military Installation	Militäranlage	Instalación Militar	Installation militaire	Instalação militar
-◆	Miscellaneous	Verschiedenes	Misceláneo	Divers	Diversos

I · 62 Genn-Glac

ENGLISH: Name Page Lat.°′ Long.°′ — DEUTSCH: Name Seite Breite°′ Länge°′ E = Ost

Gennach ≃ 58 48.10 N 10.43 E
Gennargentu, Monti del ⋏ 71 40.01 N 9.19 E
Gennebreck 263 51.19 N 7.12 E
Gennep 52 51.42 N 5.58 E
Genner 41 55.07 N 9.26 E
Gennes 32 47.20 N 0.14 W
Gennevilliers 261 48.56 N 2.18 E
Genoa, Austl. 166 37.29 S 149.35 E
Genoa → Genova, It. 62 44.25 N 8.57 E
Genoa, Il., U.S. 216 42.05 N 88.41 W
Genoa, Ne., U.S. 198 41.26 N 97.43 W
Genoa, Nv., U.S. 226 39.00 N 119.50 W
Genoa, N.Y., U.S. 210 42.40 N 76.32 W
Genoa, Oh., U.S. 214 41.31 N 83.21 W
Genoa, Wi., U.S. 190 43.34 N 91.13 W
Genoa, Arroyo ≃ 254 44.58 S 70.06 W
Genoa City 216 42.29 N 88.19 W
Genoa Peak ∧ 226 39.03 N 119.53 W
Genola 62 44.35 N 7.39 E
Génolhac 62 44.21 N 3.57 E
Genova (Genoa) 62 44.25 N 8.57 E
Genova □[4] 62 44.30 N 9.04 E
Genova, Golfo di c 62 44.10 N 8.55 E
Genova, Val V 64 46.11 N 10.40 E
Genovesa, Isla I 246a 0.20 N 89.58 W
Genrijetty, ostrov I 74 77.06 N 156.30 E
Gensan → Wŏnsan 98 39.09 N 127.25 E
Gens de Terre ≃ 190 46.53 N 76.00 W
Genshagen 264a 52.19 N 13.19 E
Genshagener Heide ◆[3] 264a 52.20 N 13.18 E
Genshiryoku-kenkyūsho ʊ[3] 94 36.27 N 140.36 E
Gensingen 56 49.53 N 7.55 E
Gensungen 56 51.08 N 9.26 E
Gent (Gand) 50 51.03 N 3.43 E
Gentbrugge 50 51.03 N 3.45 E
Gent-Brugge, Kanaal ≋ 50 51.03 N 3.43 E
Genteng 115a 8.22 S 114.09 E
Genteng, Gili I 115a 7.12 S 113.54 E
Genteng, Tanjung › 115a 7.23 S 106.24 E
Genthin 54 52.24 N 12.09 E
Gentilly 261 48.49 N 2.21 E
Gentilly ≃ 206 46.24 N 72.21 W
Genting 114 3.42 N 98.10 E
Gentio do Ouro 250 11.25 S 42.30 W
Gentioux 32 45.47 N 1.59 E
Gentofte 41 55.45 N 12.33 E
Gentry 194 36.16 N 94.29 W
Gentry, Lake ⊜ 220 28.08 N 81.15 W
Genua → Genova 62 44.25 N 8.57 E
Genuang 114 2.29 N 102.53 E
Genval 50 50.43 N 4.29 E
Genyem 164 2.46 S 140.12 E
Genzano di Lucania 68 40.51 N 16.02 E
Genzano di Roma 66 41.42 N 12.41 E
Geographe Bay c 162 33.35 S 115.15 E
Geographe Channel U 162 24.40 S 113.20 E
Geokčaj 84 40.39 N 47.44 E
Geokčaj ≃ 84 40.39 N 47.45 E
Geok-Tepe 128 38.09 N 57.58 E
Geonkhāli 126 22.12 N 88.03 E
George, S. Afr. 158 33.58 S 22.24 E
George, Ia., U.S. 198 43.20 N 96.00 W
George, Tx., U.S. 222 30.59 N 96.07 W
George ≃, Austl. 162 20.50 S 117.28 E
George ≃, P.Q., Can. 176 58.49 N 66.10 W
George, Cape › 186 45.53 N 61.53 W
George, Lake ⊜, Austl. 162 22.37 S 123.38 E
George, Lake ⊜, Austl. 166 35.05 S 149.25 E
George, Lake ⊜, N.A. 190 46.28 N 84.10 W
George, Lake ⊜, Ug. 154 0.02 N 30.12 E
George, Lake ⊜, U.S. 216 41.45 N 85.00 W
George, Lake ⊜, Fl., U.S. 192 29.17 N 81.36 W
George, Lake ⊜, In., U.S. 216 41.40 N 87.30 W
George, Lake ⊜, N.Y., U.S. 188 43.35 N 73.35 W
George Air Force Base ■ 228 34.35 N 117.22 W
George B. Stevenson Dam ◆[6] 214 41.25 N 78.01 W
George Gill Range ⋏ 162 24.15 S 131.36 E
George H. Crosby Manitou State Park ♦ 190 47.29 N 91.10 W
George Island I 254 52.19 S 59.45 W
George Mason University ʊ[2] 284c 38.50 N 77.17 W
Georgensgmünd 56 49.11 N 11.00 E
Georgenthal 54 50.49 N 10.40 E
Georges ≃ 170 33.57 S 150.58 E
Georges Bank ✢[4] 16 41.15 N 67.30 W
Georges Island I 283 42.19 N 70.56 W
George Sound U 172 44.50 S 167.23 E
Georges River Bridge ◆[5] 274a 34.00 S 151.07 E
Georges Run 214 40.21 N 80.37 W
Georges Run ≃ 279b 40.23 N 80.06 W
Georgetown, Austl. 166 18.18 S 143.33 E
George Town, Austl. 166 41.06 S 146.50 E
Georgetown → Halton Hills, On., Can. 190 43.37 N 79.56 W
Georgetown, P.E., Can. 186 46.11 N 62.32 W
George Town, Cay. Is. 238 19.18 N 81.23 W
Georgetown, Gam. 150 13.30 N 14.47 W
Georgetown, Guy. 246 6.48 N 58.10 W
George Town (Pinang), Malay. 114 5.25 N 100.20 E
Georgetown, St. Vin. 241h 13.16 N 61.08 W
Georgetown, Ca., U.S. 226 38.54 N 120.50 W
Georgetown, Co., U.S. 200 39.42 N 105.41 W
Georgetown, Ct., U.S. 207 41.15 N 73.26 W
Georgetown, De., U.S. 208 38.41 N 75.23 W
Georgetown, Fl., U.S. 192 29.23 N 81.38 W
Georgetown, Ga., U.S. 192 31.53 N 85.06 W
Georgetown, Id., U.S. 202 42.29 N 111.22 W
Georgetown, Il., U.S. 194 39.58 N 87.38 W
Georgetown, In., U.S. 218 38.17 N 85.58 W
Georgetown, Ky., U.S. 218 38.12 N 84.33 W
Georgetown, Ma., U.S. 207 42.43 N 70.59 W
Georgetown, Ms., U.S. 194 31.52 N 90.09 W
Georgetown, N.J., U.S. 285 40.04 N 74.39 W
Georgetown, N.Y., U.S. 210 42.46 N 75.44 W
Georgetown, Oh., U.S. 218 38.51 N 83.54 W
Georgetown, Pa., U.S. 214 40.39 N 80.30 W
Georgetown, S.C., U.S. 192 33.22 N 79.17 W
Georgetown, Tx., U.S. 222 30.37 N 97.40 W
Georgetown ◆[8] 284c 38.54 N 77.03 W
Georgetown, Lake ⊜[1] 222 30.40 N 97.45 W
Georgetown Lake ⊜ 202 46.11 N 113.17 W
Georgetown Rowley State Forest ♦ 283 42.42 N 70.58 W
Georgetown University ʊ[2] 284c 38.54 N 77.04 W
George V Coast ⊥[2] 9 68.30 S 147.30 E
George VI Sound U 9 71.00 S 68.00 W
George Washington Birthplace National Monument ♦ 208 38.11 N 76.56 W
George Washington Bridge ◆[5] 276 40.51 N 73.57 W
George Washington Carver National Monument ♦ 194 37.00 N 94.19 W
George West 196 28.19 N 98.07 W
Georg Forster ʊ[3] 9 70.47 S 11.51 E
Georgia □[1], Asia 72 42.00 N 44.00 E
Georgia □[1], Asia 84 42.00 N 44.00 E
Georgia □[3], U.S. 178 32.50 N 83.15 W
Georgia □[3], U.S. 192 32.50 N 83.15 W
Georgia, Strait of U 182 49.20 N 124.00 W
Georgia del Sur, Isla de → South Georgia I 244 54.15 S 36.45 W
Georgiana 194 31.38 N 86.44 W
Georgian Bay c 190 45.15 N 80.50 W
Georgian Bay Islands National Park ♦ 190 44.54 N 79.52 W
Géorgie du Sud → South Georgia I 244 54.15 S 36.45 W
Georgijevka, Kaz. 85 43.03 N 74.43 E
Georgijevka, Kaz. 85 42.11 N 70.00 E
Georgijevka, Kaz. 86 49.19 N 81.35 E
Georgijevka, Ross. 80 53.18 N 51.01 E
Georgijevka, Ukr. 83 48.26 N 39.17 E
Georgijevsk 84 44.09 N 43.28 E
Georgina ≃ 166 23.30 S 139.47 E
Georgina Island I 212 44.23 N 79.17 W
Georgina Island Indian Reserve ◆[4] 212 44.22 N 79.19 W
Georgsmarienhütte 52 52.12 N 8.02 E
Georg von Neumayer ʊ[3] 9 70.37 S 8.22 W
Gera 54 50.52 N 12.04 E
Gera ≃ 54 51.08 N 10.56 E
Geraardsbergen 50 50.46 N 3.52 E
Geraberg 54 50.43 N 10.50 E
Gerabronn 56 49.15 N 9.55 E
Gerace 68 38.16 N 16.13 E
Geraci Siculo 70 37.51 N 14.09 E
Geral, Serra ⊥[4], Bra. 250 11.15 S 46.30 W
Geral, Serra ⊥[4], Bra. 252 26.30 S 50.30 W
Gerald 219 38.23 N 91.19 W
Geral de Goiás, Serra ⊥[4] 242 13.00 S 46.15 W
Geraldine, N.Z. 172 44.05 S 171.14 E
Geraldine, Mt., U.S. 202 47.36 N 110.15 W
Geraldton, Austl. 162 28.46 S 114.36 E
Geraldton, On., Can. 176 49.44 N 86.57 W
Gerar, Naḥal V 132 31.24 N 34.26 E
Gerard, Lake ⊜ 276 41.06 N 74.33 W
Gerard, Mount ∧ 162 27.13 S 122.41 E
Gérardmer 58 48.04 N 6.53 E
Geras 61 48.48 N 15.40 E
Gerasa ⊥ 132 32.17 N 35.53 E
Gerasdorf 61 48.18 N 16.28 E
Gerasimovka 86 58.37 N 71.53 E
Gerber 204 40.03 N 122.08 W
Gerber Reservoir ⊜[1] 202 42.12 N 121.06 W
Gerbéviller 58 48.30 N 6.31 E
Gerblingerode 52 51.29 N 10.15 E
Gerbstedt 54 51.38 N 11.37 E
Gerca 78 48.09 N 26.16 E
Gerchsheim 56 49.42 N 9.47 E
Gercüş 130 37.34 N 41.23 E
Gerdau 158 26.28 S 26.06 E
Gerdine, Mount ∧ 180 61.35 N 152.26 W
Gerdview 273d 26.10 S 28.11 E
Gère ≃ 62 45.32 N 4.54 E
Gerede 130 40.48 N 32.12 E
Gereja Cathedral ʊ[1] 269e 6.10 S 106.49 E
Gerenzano 266b 45.38 N 9.00 E
Gereshk 120 31.48 N 64.34 E
Geretsried 64 47.51 N 11.28 E
Gérgal 34 37.07 N 2.33 W
Gerge'bil 84 42.31 N 47.05 E
Gerger 130 37.57 N 39.01 E
Geria Nij 126 23.56 N 86.55 E
Gerik 114 5.25 N 101.08 E
Gering 198 41.49 N 103.39 W
Geringswalde 54 51.04 N 12.54 E
Geriş 130 36.58 N 31.44 E
Gerlachovský štít ∧ 30 49.12 N 20.08 E
Gerlafingen 58 47.10 N 7.34 E
Gerli ◆[8] 288 34.41 S 58.23 W
Gerlingen 56 48.48 N 9.03 E
Gerlos 64 47.14 N 12.02 E
Gerlospass)(64 47.14 N 12.08 E
Gerlova Hut' 60 49.10 N 13.17 E
Germa (Jarmah) ⊥ 146 26.33 N 13.04 E
Germagnano 62 45.15 N 7.28 E
Germain, Grand lac ⊜ 186 51.12 N 66.41 W
Germania 214 41.39 N 77.40 W
Germano 214 40.25 N 80.57 W
Germanoviči 76 55.25 N 27.44 E
Germansen, Mount ∧ 182 55.37 N 124.50 W
Germansen Lake ⊜ 182 55.41 N 124.53 W
Germansen Landing 182 55.47 N 124.43 W
Germansville 208 40.42 N 75.42 W
Germantown, Il., U.S. 219 38.33 N 89.32 W
Germantown, Ky., U.S. 218 38.39 N 83.57 W
Germantown, N.Y., U.S. 210 42.08 N 73.54 W
Germantown, Oh., U.S. 218 39.37 N 84.22 W
Germantown, Tn., U.S. 194 35.05 N 89.48 W
Germantown, Wi., U.S. 216 43.13 N 88.06 W
Germantown ◆[8] 285 40.03 N 75.11 W
Germantown Dam ◆[6] 218 39.38 N 84.24 W
Germany (Deutschland) □[1], Europe 22 51.00 N 10.00 E
Germany (Deutschland) □[1], Europe 30 51.00 N 10.00 E
Germany Flats ≚ 276 41.05 N 74.39 W
Germay 58 48.25 N 5.21 E
Germencik 130 37.51 N 27.37 E
Germendorf 54 52.45 N 13.10 E
Germering 60 48.08 N 11.22 E
Germersheim 56 49.13 N 8.22 E
Germfask 190 46.14 N 85.55 W
Germiston 158 26.13 S 28.11 E
Germiston □[5] 273d 26.15 S 28.10 E
Germiston South 273d 26.15 S 28.10 E
Gernika-Lumo (Guernica y Luno) 34 43.19 N 2.41 W
Gernrode 54 51.43 N 11.08 E
Gernsbach 56 48.46 N 8.19 E
Gernsheim 56 49.44 N 8.29 E
Gero 94 35.48 N 137.14 E
Geroda 56 50.17 N 9.53 E
Gerola Alta 58 46.03 N 9.32 E
Geroldsgrün 54 50.20 N 11.35 E
Geroldstein 56 50.06 N 7.56 E
Gerolsbach 60 48.30 N 11.22 E
Gerolstein 56 50.13 N 6.40 E
Gerolzhofen 56 49.54 N 10.21 E
Gerona → Girona, Esp. 34 41.59 N 2.49 E
Gerona, Pil. 116 15.36 N 120.36 E
Geronimo 196 34.28 N 98.22 W
Gerpinnes 50 50.20 N 4.31 E
Gerrards Cross 260 51.35 N 0.34 W
Gerrei ◆[1] 71 39.28 N 9.17 E
Gerresheim ◆[8] 263 51.14 N 6.52 E
Gerringong 170 34.45 S 150.50 E
Gerry 214 42.12 N 79.15 W
Gers □[5] 32 43.40 N 0.30 E
Gers ≃ 32 44.09 N 0.39 E
Gersau 58 47.00 N 8.32 E
Gersdorf 54 50.45 N 12.42 E
Gersfeld 56 50.27 N 9.55 E
Gershøj 41 55.43 N 11.59 E
Gersprenz ≃ 56 49.59 N 9.04 E
Gerstetten 56 48.37 N 10.01 E
Gersthofen 58 48.25 N 10.53 E
Gerstungen 56 50.58 N 10.04 E
Gertak Sanggul, Tanjong › 114 5.15 N 100.11 E
Gerthe ◆[8] 263 51.31 N 7.17 E
Gerufa 156 19.17 S 26.02 E
Gervais 224 45.06 N 122.53 W
Gerwisch 54 52.10 N 11.44 E
Gerza 142 29.26 N 31.11 E
Gerze, Tür. 130 41.48 N 35.12 E
Gêrzê, Zhg. 120 32.16 N 84.12 E
Gerzen 60 48.31 N 12.25 E
Gerzensee 58 46.51 N 7.33 E
Gescher 52 51.57 N 6.59 E
Geschriebenstein (Írottkő) ∧ 61 47.21 N 16.26 E
Geschwenda 54 50.44 N 10.49 E
Gesees 60 49.54 N 11.32 E
Geseke 52 51.38 N 8.31 E
Geser 164 3.53 S 130.54 E
Gesher HaZiw 132 33.02 N 35.06 E
Gesi 115a 7.20 S 111.01 E
Gesoa 164 8.25 S 143.35 E
Gespunsart 56 49.49 N 4.50 E
Gessertshausen 58 48.20 N 10.44 E
Gesso ≃ 62 44.24 N 7.33 E
Gessopalena 66 42.03 N 14.16 E
Gesten 41 55.31 N 9.12 E
Gesualdo 68 41.00 N 15.04 E
Geta 26 60.23 N 19.50 E
Getafe 34 40.18 N 3.43 W
Getafe, Aeropuerto ⊠ 266a 40.18 N 3.43 W
Gete ≃ 56 50.57 N 5.07 E
Gethaoli 272c 19.08 N 73.01 E
Geti 154 1.13 N 30.12 E
Getinge 26 56.49 N 12.44 E
Gettorf 41 54.24 N 9.58 E
Gettysburg, Oh., U.S. 218 40.06 N 84.29 W
Gettysburg, Pa., U.S. 208 39.49 N 77.13 W
Gettysburg, S.D., U.S. 198 45.00 N 99.57 W
Gettysburg National Military Park ♦ 208 39.49 N 77.15 W
Getulândia 256 22.40 S 44.06 W
Getulina 255 21.49 S 49.55 W
Getulio 116 10.45 N 122.40 E
Getúlio Vargas 252 27.50 S 52.16 W
Getz Ice Shelf ⊓ 9 75.00 S 129.00 W
Getzville 210 43.01 N 78.46 W
Geumpang 114 4.48 N 96.09 E
Geureudong, Gunung ∧ 114 4.48 N 96.48 E
Gevān 128 26.03 N 57.17 E
Gevaş 128 38.16 N 43.07 E
Gevelsberg 56 51.19 N 7.20 E
Gevgelija 38 41.08 N 22.30 E
Gévora ≃ 34 38.53 N 6.57 W
Gevrey-Chambertin 58 47.14 N 4.57 E
Gewane 144 10.10 N 40.39 E
Geweke ◆[8] 263 51.22 N 7.25 E
Gex 58 46.20 N 6.04 E
Geyer 54 50.37 N 12.55 E
Geyer Ditch ≋ 216 41.36 N 86.25 W
Geyikli 130 39.48 N 26.12 E
Geysdorp 158 26.32 S 25.18 E
Geyser 202 47.15 N 110.29 W
Geyserville 204 38.42 N 122.54 W
Geyshtasar, Kūh-e ∧ 84 38.51 N 47.14 E
Geyuan 100 28.31 N 117.44 E
Geyve 130 40.30 N 30.18 E
Gézenti 146 21.41 N 18.18 E
Gezer 132 31.52 N 34.55 E
Gföhl 61 48.31 N 15.30 E
Ghaapplato ⋏[1] 158 27.30 S 24.00 E
Ghabāghib 132 33.10 N 36.13 E
Ghābat al-ʻArab 140 9.02 N 29.29 E
Ghadaf, Wādī al- V 132 31.46 N 36.50 E
Ghadāmis 146 30.08 N 9.30 E
Ghaddūwah 146 26.26 N 14.18 E
Ghafe 272c 19.05 N 73.07 E
Ghagghar ≃ 123 29.30 N 74.53 E
Ghāghara ≃ 124 25.47 N 84.37 E
Ghaghar Reservoir ⊜[1] 124 24.38 N 83.11 E
Ghāghra 124 23.17 N 84.33 E
Ghakhar 123 32.18 N 74.09 E
Ghallah, Wādī al- V 140 10.25 N 27.32 E
Ghammāzah al-Kubrā 142 29.43 N 31.18 E
Ghamrīn 142 30.30 N 30.55 E
Ghana □[1], Afr. 134 8.00 N 1.00 W
Ghana □[1], Afr. 150 8.00 N 1.00 W
Ghansoli 272c 19.08 N 72.59 E
Ghanzi 156 21.38 S 21.45 E
Ghanzi □[5] 156 22.00 S 23.00 E
Ghārāpuri 272c 18.54 N 72.56 E
Gharaunda 124 29.33 N 76.58 E
Gharbah, Wādī V 142 29.40 N 31.58 E
Gharbi, Chott ⊜ 148 33.50 N 1.30 W
Gharbi, Oued el V 148 31.50 N 0.51 E
Gharbīyah, Aṣ-Ṣaḥrā' al- (Western Desert) ◆[2] 140 27.00 N 27.00 E
Ghardaïa 148 32.31 N 3.37 E
Ghardimaou 36 36.26 N 8.27 E
Gharghoda 124 22.10 N 83.21 E
Gharībwāl 123 32.41 N 73.10 E
Gharīfah 132 33.38 N 35.33 E
Gharig 140 10.47 N 27.33 E
Ghārīyat al-Gharbīyah 132 32.41 N 36.13 E
Ghārīyat ash-Sharqīyah 132 32.40 N 36.16 E
Gharo 120 24.44 N 67.35 E
Gharrāf, Shaṭṭ al- ≃ 128 32.30 N 45.48 E
Gharroli ◆[8] 272a 28.37 N 77.20 E
Gharsa, Chott el ⊜ 148 34.06 N 7.50 E
Gharw, Jazīrat I 142 31.21 N 30.06 E
Gharyān 146 32.10 N 13.01 E
Ghaṣm 132 32.33 N 36.22 E
Ghāt 146 24.58 N 10.11 E
Ghātāl 126 22.40 N 87.43 E
Ghatampur 272b 22.54 N 88.10 E
Ghatere, Mount ∧ 175e 7.49 S 158.54 E
Ghates Occidentales → Western Ghāts ⋏ 122 14.00 N 75.00 E
Ghates Orientales → Eastern Ghāts ⋏ 122 14.00 N 78.50 E
Ghātkopar ◆[8] 272c 19.05 N 72.54 E
Ghātprabha ≃ 122 16.20 N 75.48 E
Ghātsīla 126 22.36 N 86.29 E
Għawdex (Gozo) I 36 36.03 N 14.15 E
Ghawr ash-Sharqīyah, Qanāt al- (East Ghor Canal) ≋ 132 32.41 N 35.38 E
Ghaylah ∧[1] 132 33.11 N 37.05 E
Ghayl Bā Wazīr 144 14.48 N 49.21 E
Ghayl Bin Yumayn ╤[4] 144 15.33 N 49.23 E
Ghayth, Wādī V 132 30.59 N 36.00 E
Ghazāl, Baḥr al- ≃ 140 9.31 N 30.25 E
Ghazal, Bahr el V 146 13.01 N 15.28 E
Ghazālat al-Khīs 142 30.34 N 31.34 E
Ghāziābād 123 28.40 N 77.26 E
Ghāzīpur, India 124 25.35 N 83.34 E
Ghazipur, India 272b 22.36 N 88.34 E
Ghāzīpur ◆[8] 272a 28.38 N 77.19 E
Ghazīr 130 34.01 N 35.40 E
Ghazlūna 120 31.24 N 67.49 E
Ghaznī 120 33.33 N 68.26 E
Ghaznī □[4] 120 33.15 N 67.45 E
Ghaznī ≃ 120 32.35 N 67.58 E
Ghazni Khel 123 32.33 N 70.44 E
Ghazzah (Gaza), Isr. Occ 132 31.30 N 34.28 E
Ghazzah, Lubnān 132 33.40 N 35.49 E
Gheā ≃ 272b 22.52 N 88.19 E
Ghedi 64 45.24 N 10.16 E
Ghemme 62 45.37 N 8.25 E
Ghennes Heights 279b 40.09 N 79.56 W
Ghent → Gent, Bel. 50 51.03 N 3.43 E
Ghent, Ky., U.S. 218 38.44 N 85.03 W
Ghent, N.Y., U.S. 210 42.19 N 73.36 W
Ghent, Oh., U.S. 214 41.09 N 81.38 W
Gheora ◆[8] 272a 28.42 N 77.01 E
Gheorghe Gheorghiu-Dej 38 46.14 N 26.44 E
Gheorgheni 38 46.43 N 25.36 E
Gherla 38 47.02 N 23.55 E
Ghesar 272c 19.09 N 73.05 E
Ghigo 62 44.53 N 7.03 E
Ghilarza 71 40.07 N 8.50 E
Ghilizane 148 35.44 N 0.30 E
Ghīn, Tall ∧ 132 32.39 N 36.43 E
Ghior 126 23.54 N 89.53 E
Ghislenghien (Gellingen) 50 50.39 N 3.52 E
Ghisonaccia 36 42.00 N 9.25 E
Ghizar ≃ 123 36.15 N 73.25 E
Ghizunabeana Islands II 175e 7.31 S 158.42 E
Ghlin 50 50.28 N 3.53 E
Ghlò, Beinn a' ∧ 46 56.50 N 3.43 W
Ghogha 120 21.41 N 72.17 E
Gholson 222 31.43 N 97.12 W
Ghonda ◆[8] 272a 28.41 N 77.16 E
Ghondi ◆[8] 272a 28.42 N 77.16 E
Ghorāsahan 124 26.50 N 85.08 E
Ghoshpur, Bngl. 126 23.27 N 89.39 E
Ghoshpur, India 272b 22.23 N 88.29 E
Ghotki 120 28.01 N 69.19 E
Ghowr □[4] 128 34.00 N 65.00 E
Ghubaysh 140 12.09 N 27.21 E
Ghudāf, Wādī al- V 128 32.56 N 43.30 E
Ghulayfiqah 144 14.27 N 43.02 E
Ghunthur 130 34.23 N 37.09 E
Ghurāb, Jabal ∧[2] 142 28.58 N 31.16 E
Ghurayrah 144 18.37 N 42.41 E
Ghūrīān 128 34.21 N 61.30 E
Ghushuri 272b 22.37 N 88.22 E
Ghuwaybah, Wādī V 142 29.36 N 32.20 E
Ghuwayr, ʻAyn al- ╤[4] 132 31.37 N 35.25 E
Ghuzzayil, Sabkhat ⊜ 146 29.50 N 19.35 E
Giaginskaja 78 44.53 N 40.05 E
Gianh ≃ 110 17.40 N 106.30 E
Giannutri, Isola di I 66 42.15 N 11.06 E
Giano, Monte ∧ 66 42.25 N 13.06 E
Giano dell'Umbria 66 42.50 N 12.35 E
Giant City State Park ♦ 194 37.39 N 89.12 W
Giant Mountain ∧ 188 44.10 N 73.44 W
Giant's Castle ∧ 158 29.21 S 29.27 E
Giant's Castle Game Reserve ◆[4] 158 29.16 S 29.30 E
Giant's Causeway ♦ 48 55.14 N 6.30 W
Giants Neck 207 41.18 N 72.13 W
Giants Stadium ♦ 276 40.49 N 74.05 W
Giants Tomb Island I 212 44.55 N 80.00 W
Gianyar 115b 8.32 S 115.20 E
Gia Rai 110 9.14 N 105.28 E
Giardinello 70 38.05 N 13.09 E
Giardinetto 68 41.19 N 15.24 E
Giardini 70 37.50 N 15.17 E
Giarratana 70 37.03 N 14.48 E
Giarre 70 37.43 N 15.11 E
Giaveno 62 45.02 N 7.21 E
Giazza 64 45.39 N 11.07 E
Giba 71 39.04 N 8.38 E
Gibara 240p 21.07 N 76.08 W
Gibbon, Mn., U.S. 190 44.32 N 94.31 W
Gibbon, Ne., U.S. 198 40.44 N 98.50 W
Gibbons 182 53.50 N 113.20 W
Gibbonsville 202 45.33 N 113.55 W
Gibb River 164 16.25 S 126.22 E
Gibbs, Mount ∧ 162 32.55 S 120.00 E
Gibbsboro 285 39.50 N 74.58 W
Gibbstown 208 39.49 N 75.17 W
Gibellina 70 37.47 N 12.58 E
Gibeon 156 25.09 S 17.43 E
Gibilmanna, Santuario di ʊ[1] 70 37.59 N 14.02 E
Gibraleón 34 37.23 N 6.58 W
Gibraltar, Gib. 34 36.08 N 5.21 W
Gibraltar, Mi., U.S. 216 42.06 N 83.12 W
Gibraltar, Pa., U.S. 208 40.17 N 75.52 W
Gibraltar □[2], Europe 22 36.08 N 5.21 W
Gibraltar □[2], Europe 34 36.08 N 5.21 W
Gibraltar, Strait of (Estrecho de Gibraltar) U 34 35.57 N 5.36 W
Gibraltar Point ›, On., Can. 275b 43.36 N 79.23 W
Gibraltar Point ›, Eng., U.K. 44 53.05 N 0.19 E
Gibsland 194 32.32 N 93.03 W
Gibson, Austl. 162 33.39 S 121.48 E
Gibson, Ga., U.S. 192 33.14 N 82.35 W
Gibson, N.Y., U.S. 210 42.08 N 76.59 W
Gibson, Pa., U.S. 210 41.44 N 75.38 W
Gibson ≃ 212 44.58 N 79.51 W
Gibson, Lake ⊜[1] 284a 43.06 N 79.14 W
Gibsonburg 214 41.23 N 83.19 W
Gibson City 216 40.27 N 88.22 W
Gibson Desert ◆[2] 162 24.30 S 126.00 E
Gibson Hill ∧[2] 214 41.51 N 80.10 W
Gibsonia, Fl., U.S. 220 28.06 N 81.58 W
Gibsonia, Pa., U.S. 214 40.38 N 79.59 W
Gibson Indian Reserve ◆[4] 212 45.01 N 79.44 W
Gibson Island I 208 39.05 N 76.26 W
Gibsons 182 49.24 N 123.30 W
Gibsonton 220 27.51 N 82.22 W
Gidajevo 24 59.57 N 52.22 E
Gidami 144 9.58 N 34.37 E
Gidda 144 9.34 N 35.23 E
Giddalūr 122 15.21 N 78.55 E
Giddarbāha 123 30.12 N 74.40 E
Giddings 222 30.10 N 96.56 W
Gideälven ≃ 26 63.20 N 19.08 E
Gidea Park ◆[8] 260 51.35 N 0.12 E
Gideåvallen 26 63.29 N 18.58 E
Gideon 194 36.27 N 89.55 W
Gidgee 162 27.16 S 119.22 E
Gidgi, Lake ⊜ 162 29.16 S 126.03 E
Gidhni 126 22.29 N 86.51 E
Gidole 144 5.38 N 37.30 E
Gidrotorf 80 56.28 N 43.33 E
Gidžaki, gora ∧ 84 40.25 N 49.01 E
Giebelstadt 56 49.39 N 9.56 E
Gieboldehausen 52 51.36 N 10.13 E
Giedraičiai 76 55.05 N 25.15 E
Gielow 54 53.42 N 12.44 E
Gielsdorf 264a 52.36 N 13.52 E
Gien 50 47.42 N 2.38 E
Giengen 56 48.37 N 10.14 E
Giens 62 43.02 N 6.08 E
Gier ≃ 62 45.35 N 4.46 E
Gierath 263 51.07 N 6.33 E
Gierle 56 51.16 N 4.51 E
Gieselwerder 52 51.36 N 9.33 E
Giesenkirchen ◆[8] 263 51.09 N 6.30 E
Giessbachfälle ⌊ 58 46.42 N 8.03 E
Giessen 56 50.35 N 8.40 E
Giessen □[5] 56 50.40 N 8.40 E
Gieten 52 53.00 N 6.46 E
Giethoorn 52 52.43 N 6.05 E
Gièvres 50 47.16 N 1.40 E
Giez 62 45.45 N 6.15 E
Giffone 68 38.27 N 16.10 E
Gifford, Scot., U.K. 46 55.54 N 2.45 W
Gifford, Fl., U.S. 220 27.40 N 80.24 W
Gifford, Il., U.S. 216 40.18 N 88.01 W
Gifford, In., U.S. 216 41.06 N 87.01 W
Gifford, Pa., U.S. 214 41.51 N 78.36 W
Gifford ≃ 176 70.21 N 83.05 W
Gifford Creek 162 24.05 S 116.11 E
Gifford Pinchot State Park ♦ 208 40.04 N 76.53 W
Giffre ≃ 58 46.05 N 6.30 E
Gifhorn 52 52.29 N 10.33 E
Giflitz 56 51.09 N 9.07 E
Gif-sur-Yvette 261 48.42 N 2.08 E
Gifu 94 35.25 N 136.45 E
Gifu □[5] 94 35.45 N 137.00 E
Gigant 80 46.30 N 41.20 E
Giganta, Sierra de la ⋏ 232 26.00 N 111.30 W
Gigante 246 2.23 N 75.33 W
Gigante Islands II 116 11.36 N 123.20 E
Gigen 38 43.42 N 24.29 E
Gigena → Alcira 252 32.45 S 64.20 W
Giggleswick 44 54.04 N 2.17 W
Gigha, Sound of U 46 55.41 N 5.42 W
Gigha Island I 46 55.41 N 5.46 W
Gig Harbor 224 47.19 N 122.34 W
Giglio, Isola del I 66 42.21 N 10.54 E
Giglio Castello 66 42.22 N 10.54 E
Gigliola 66 44.51 N 12.14 E
Giglio Porto 66 42.22 N 10.55 E
Gigmoto 116 13.47 N 124.23 E
Gignod 62 45.46 N 7.17 E
Gihu → Gifu 94 35.25 N 136.45 E
Gijón 34 43.32 N 5.40 W
Gikongoro 154 2.29 S 29.34 E
Gila ≃ 200 32.43 N 114.33 W
Gila, Middle Fork ≃ 200 33.14 N 108.14 W
Gila Bend 200 32.56 N 112.42 W
Gila Bend Indian Reservation ◆[4] 200 33.00 N 112.46 W
Gila Bend Mountains ⋏ 200 33.10 N 113.10 W
Gila Cliff Dwellings National Monument ♦ 200 33.02 N 108.16 W
Gila Mountains ⋏ 200 33.05 N 109.50 W
Gīlān □[4] 128 37.15 N 49.30 E
Gīlān-e Gharb 128 34.08 N 45.55 E
Gila River Indian Reservation ◆[4] 200 33.12 N 112.00 W
Gilātala 126 22.36 N 89.41 E
Gilberdyke 44 53.45 N 0.44 W
Gilbert, La., U.S. 194 32.02 N 91.39 W
Gilbert, Mn., U.S. 190 47.29 N 92.27 W
Gilbert ≃, Austl. 166 16.35 S 141.15 E
Gilbert ≃, Austl. 168b 34.22 S 138.40 E
Gilbert, Mount ∧ 182 50.51 N 124.20 W
Gilbert Airport ⊠ 279a 41.22 N 81.58 W
Gilbert Island I 219 39.35 N 91.11 W
Gilbert Islands → Kiribati □[1] 14 5.00 S 170.00 W
Gilbert Lake ⊜ 281 42.34 N 83.17 W
Gilbert Lake State Park ♦ 210 42.36 N 75.08 W
Gilberton 210 40.48 N 76.13 W
Gilbertown 194 31.52 N 88.19 W
Gilbert Peak ∧ 224 46.30 N 121.25 W
Gilbert Plains 184 51.09 N 100.29 W
Gilbert River 166 18.09 S 142.52 E
Gilberts 216 42.06 N 88.23 W
Gilbert Seamount ✢[3] 16 52.50 N 150.10 W
Gilbertsville, N.Y., U.S. 210 42.28 N 75.19 W
Gilbertsville, Pa., U.S. 208 40.19 N 75.37 W
Gilbertville 207 42.18 N 72.12 W
Gilbjerg Hoved › 41 56.08 N 12.17 E
Gilboa 216 41.01 N 83.55 W
Gilboaʻ, Haré ⋏[2] 132 32.30 N 35.23 E
Gilbués 250 9.50 S 45.21 W
Gilching 60 48.07 N 11.17 E
Gildehaus 52 52.18 N 7.06 E
Gildford 202 48.34 N 110.17 W
Gilead 216 41.48 N 85.09 W
Giles, Arroyo de ≃ 258 34.20 S 59.23 W
Giles Meteorological Station ʊ[3] 162 25.02 S 128.18 E
Giles Point › 168b 35.03 S 137.45 E
Gilette 62 43.51 N 7.10 E
Gilford 48 54.23 N 6.22 W
Gilford Island I 182 50.45 N 126.25 W
Gilford Park 208 39.58 N 74.08 W
Gilgai 162 31.15 S 119.56 E
Gilgandra 166 31.42 S 148.39 E
Gilgil 154 0.30 S 36.19 E
Gil Gil Creek ≃ 166 29.10 S 148.51 E
Gilgit 123 35.55 N 74.18 E
Gilgit ≃ 123 35.44 N 74.38 E
Gilgo Island I 276 40.38 N 73.25 W
Gilgo State Park ♦ 276 40.38 N 73.22 W
Gilima 154 3.55 N 28.22 E
Gilimanuk 115a 8.10 S 114.26 E
Gilirang 112 3.55 S 120.09 E
Gil Island I 182 53.13 N 129.15 W
Gill, Lough ⊜ 48 54.16 N 8.24 W
Gillam 184 56.21 N 94.43 W
Gilleland Creek ≃ 222 30.13 N 97.32 W
Gilleleje 41 56.07 N 12.19 E
Gillen, Lake ⊜ 162 26.11 S 124.38 E
Gilles, Lake ⊜ 166 32.50 S 136.45 E
Gillespie 219 39.07 N 89.49 W
Gillespies Point › 172 43.24 S 169.50 E
Gillett, Ar., U.S. 194 34.07 N 91.22 W
Gillett, Pa., U.S. 210 41.57 N 76.48 W
Gillett, Wi., U.S. 190 44.53 N 88.18 W
Gillette, N.J., U.S. 276 40.41 N 74.28 W
Gillette, Wy., U.S. 198 44.17 N 105.30 W
Gillette Castle State Park ♦ 207 41.26 N 72.25 W
Gillian, Lake ⊜ 176 69.32 N 75.23 W
Gillingham, Eng., U.K. 42 51.24 N 0.33 E
Gillingham, Eng., U.K. 42 51.02 N 2.17 W
Gillingham □[8] 260 51.22 N 0.35 E
Gills Rock 190 45.17 N 87.01 W
Gilman, Ct., U.S. 207 41.34 N 72.11 W
Gilman, Il., U.S. 216 40.46 N 87.59 W
Gilman, Ia., U.S. 190 41.52 N 92.47 W
Gilman, Wi., U.S. 190 45.10 N 90.48 W
Gilman Hot Springs 228 33.50 N 116.59 W
Gilman Lake 285 39.41 N 75.11 W
Gilmer, Il., U.S. 278 42.14 N 88.02 W
Gilmer, Tx., U.S. 222 32.43 N 94.56 W
Gilmer Park 216 41.36 N 86.15 W
Gilmore 171b 35.20 S 148.11 E
Gilmore City 198 42.44 N 94.27 W
Gilmore Creek ≃ 171b 35.18 S 148.13 E
Gilo ≃ 144 8.10 N 33.15 E
Gilroy 226 37.00 N 121.34 W
Gilserberg 56 50.57 N 9.04 E
Gilsizer Slough ≃ 226 38.58 N 121.44 W
Gilston Park ♦ 260 51.48 N 0.04 E
Giltner 198 40.46 N 98.09 W
Gil'uj ≃ 89 53.58 N 127.30 E
Giluwe, Mount ∧ 164 6.05 S 143.50 E
Gilwern 42 51.51 N 3.06 W
Gilze 52 51.33 N 4.57 E
Gimån ≃ 26 62.28 N 16.20 E
Gimbi 144 9.10 N 35.42 E
Gimborn 52 51.03 N 7.28 E
Gimcheon → Kimch'ŏn 98 36.07 N 128.05 E
Gimie, Mount ∧ 241f 13.52 N 61.01 W
Gimigliano 68 38.58 N 16.32 E
Gimlet 218 38.13 N 83.09 W
Gimli 184 50.38 N 96.59 W
Gimo 40 60.11 N 18.11 E
Gimoly 24 63.03 N 32.19 E
Gimone ≃ 32 44.00 N 1.06 E
Gimont 32 43.38 N 0.53 E
Gimpu 112 1.36 S 120.02 E
Ginderich 263 51.39 N 6.32 E
Ginebra → Genève 58 46.12 N 6.09 E
Gineste, Col de la)(62 43.15 N 5.27 E
Gingell 216 42.43 N 83.17 W
Gingera, Mount ∧ 171b 35.35 S 148.47 E
Ginger Hill 279b 40.12 N 80.00 W
Ginger Island I 240m 18.24 N 64.28 W
Gingin, Austl. 162 31.21 S 115.42 E
Gin Gin, Austl. 166 25.00 S 151.58 E
Gingindlovu 158 29.02 S 31.30 E
Gingoog 116 8.50 N 125.07 E
Gingoog Bay c 116 8.59 N 125.05 E
Gingst 54 54.27 N 13.16 E
Ginir 144 7.07 N 40.46 E
Ginkakuji Temple ʊ[1] 270 35.03 N 135.47 E
Ginkgo State Park ♦ 202 46.59 N 120.01 W
Ginnosar 132 32.51 N 35.31 E
Ginosa 68 40.35 N 16.46 E
Ginostra 70 38.47 N 15.11 E
Ginowan 174m 26.17 N 127.46 E
Ginoza 174m 26.28 N 127.57 E
Ginter 214 40.46 N 78.23 W
Ginza ◆[8] 268 35.40 N 139.47 E
Gioi 68 40.17 N 15.13 E
Gioia, Golfo di c 68 38.30 N 15.45 E
Gioia dei Marsi 66 41.57 N 13.42 E
Gioia del Colle 68 40.48 N 16.56 E
Gioia Tauro 68 38.26 N 15.54 E
Gioia Vecchio 66 41.54 N 13.44 E
Gioiosa Ionica 68 38.20 N 16.18 E
Gioiosa Marea 70 38.10 N 14.54 E
Giong Rieng 110 9.55 N 105.19 E
Giornico 58 46.24 N 8.52 E
Giovi, Passo dei)(62 44.33 N 8.57 E
Giovinazzo 68 41.11 N 16.40 E
Giporlos 116 11.07 N 125.27 E
Gipping ≃ 42 52.04 N 1.10 E
Gipsy 214 40.48 N 78.53 W
Gipuzkoako □[4] 34 43.10 N 2.10 W
Giraglia, Île de la I 62 43.02 N 9.24 E
Giralia 162 22.41 S 114.21 E
Giraltovce 30 49.07 N 21.31 E
Girard, Il., U.S. 219 39.26 N 89.46 W
Girard, Ks., U.S. 198 37.30 N 94.50 W
Girard, Mi., U.S. 216 42.02 N 85.00 W
Girard, Oh., U.S. 214 41.09 N 80.42 W
Girard, Pa., U.S. 214 42.00 N 80.19 W
Girard, Tx., U.S. 196 33.22 N 100.40 W
Girardot 246 4.18 N 74.48 W
Girardville 208 40.47 N 76.17 W
Giraud, Pointe › 240d 15.19 N 61.15 W
Giraul ≃ 152 15.04 S 12.08 E
Giraumont 56 49.10 N 5.55 E
Girbovu 38 44.44 N 23.21 E
Girdletree 208 38.05 N 75.23 W
Giresun 130 40.55 N 38.24 E
Giresun □[4] 130 40.30 N 38.30 E
Giresun Dağları ⋏ 130 40.30 N 39.00 E
Girgarre 166 36.24 S 144.59 E
Girgaum ◆[8] 272c 18.57 N 72.48 E
Girgenti → Agrigento 70 37.18 N 13.35 E
Girgir, Cape › 164 3.50 S 144.34 E
Giri ≃ 152 0.28 N 17.59 E
Girīdīh 126 24.11 N 86.18 E
Girifalco 68 38.49 N 16.25 E
Girilambone 166 31.15 S 146.54 E
Girmeli 130 37.07 N 41.26 E
Girna ≃ 122 21.08 N 75.19 E
Gir National Park ♦ 120 21.00 N 70.50 E
Girne (Kyrenia) 130 35.20 N 33.19 E
Giro, Nig. 150 11.06 N 4.46 E
Giro, Zaïre 154 3.08 N 29.15 E
Giromagny 58 47.45 N 6.50 E
Girón, Ec. 246 3.10 S 79.08 W
Giron, Fr. 58 46.14 N 5.46 E
Girona 34 41.59 N 2.49 E
Girona □[4] 34 42.00 N 2.40 E
Gironde □[5] 32 44.45 N 0.35 W
Gironde c[1] 32 45.20 N 0.45 W
Gironville-sous-les-Côtes 56 48.48 N 5.40 E
Girou ≃ 32 43.46 N 1.23 E
Girouxville 182 55.45 N 117.20 W
Gīr Range ⋏ 120 21.18 N 71.00 E
Girton 42 52.14 N 0.05 E
Girtys Run ≃ 279b 40.28 N 79.58 W
Giru 166 19.31 S 147.06 E
Giruá 252 28.02 S 54.21 W
Girvan 44 55.15 N 4.51 W
Girvan, Water of ≃ 44 55.15 N 4.51 W
Girvas 24 62.30 N 33.40 E
Gisborne, Austl. 169 37.29 S 144.35 E
Gisborne, N.Z. 172 38.40 S 178.01 E
Gisborne Lake ⊜ 186 47.48 N 54.50 W
Giscome 182 54.04 N 122.22 W
Gisenyi 154 1.42 S 29.15 E
Gishyita 154 2.11 S 29.18 E
Gislaved 26 57.18 N 13.32 E
Gislev 41 55.13 N 10.37 E
Gislinge 41 55.44 N 11.33 E
Gislövs läge 41 55.21 N 13.14 E
Gisors 50 49.17 N 1.47 E
Gissar 85 38.33 N 68.35 E
Gissarskij chrebet ⋏ 85 39.00 N 68.40 E
Gisselfeld 41 55.18 N 11.59 E
Gissi 66 42.01 N 14.33 E
Gisslarbo 40 59.38 N 15.49 E
Gistel 50 51.10 N 2.57 E
Giswil 58 46.50 N 8.11 E
Gitambo 154 4.21 S 24.45 E
Gitarama 154 2.07 S 29.45 E
Gitega 154 3.26 S 29.56 E
Gittelde 52 51.48 N 10.10 E
Giuba, Isole II 144 0.45 S 42.19 E
Giudicarie, Valli V 64 45.58 N 10.45 E
Giugliano in Campania 68 40.56 N 14.12 E
Giuliana 70 37.40 N 13.14 E
Giulianova 66 42.45 N 13.57 E
Giulie, Alpi → Julian Alps ⋏ 36 46.00 N 14.00 E
Giumbo → Jumboo 144 0.15 S 42.38 E
Giurgiu 38 43.53 N 25.57 E
Giurgiu □[6] 38 44.10 N 26.00 E
Giussano 62 45.42 N 9.14 E
Giuvala, Pasul)(38 45.26 N 25.17 E
Givʻatayim 132 32.04 N 34.48 E
Givʻat Brenner 132 31.52 N 34.48 E
Give 41 55.51 N 9.15 E
Giverny 50 49.04 N 1.32 E
Givet 56 50.08 N 4.50 E
Givors 62 45.35 N 4.46 E
Givrine, Col de la)(58 46.27 N 6.05 E
Givry 58 46.47 N 4.45 E
Givry-en-Argonne 56 48.57 N 4.53 E
Givry Island I 175c 7.07 N 151.53 E
Giyon 144 8.30 N 38.00 E
Giza → Al-Jīzah 142 30.01 N 31.13 E
Gīzāb 120 33.23 N 66.16 E
Gižduvan 128 40.06 N 64.41 E
Gizen 140 10.49 N 34.48 E
Gizeux 50 47.24 N 0.12 E
Gižiga 74 62.03 N 160.30 E
Gižiginskaja guba c 74 61.30 N 158.00 E
Gizo 175e 8.06 S 156.51 E
Gizo Island I 175e 8.04 S 156.48 E
Giżycko 30 54.03 N 21.47 E
Gizzeria 68 38.59 N 16.12 E
Gjandža 84 40.40 N 46.22 E
Gjedved 41 55.56 N 9.51 E
Gjern 41 56.14 N 9.45 E
Gjirokastër 38 40.05 N 20.10 E
Gjoa Haven 176 68.38 N 95.57 W
Gjøvik 26 60.48 N 10.42 E
Gjuesevo 38 42.14 N 22.28 E
Gjuhëzës, Kep i › 38 40.25 N 19.18 E
Glace Bay 186 46.12 N 59.57 W
Glacier, B.C., Can. 182 51.16 N 117.31 W
Glacier, Wa., U.S. 224 48.53 N 121.56 W
Glacier Bay c 180 58.40 N 136.00 W

Symbols in the index entries represent the broad categories identified in the key at the right. Symbols with superior numbers (⋏[1]) identify subcategories (see complete key on page I · 1).

Symbole im Register stellen die rechts im Schlüssel erklärten Kategorien dar. Symbole mit hochgestellten Ziffern (⋏[1]) bezeichnen Unterabteilungen einer Kategorie (vgl. vollständiger Schlüssel auf Seite I · 1).

Los símbolos incluídos en el texto del índice representan las grandes categorías identificadas con la clave a la derecha. Los símbolos con numeros en su parte superior (⋏[1]) identifican las subcategorías (véase la clave completa en la página I · 1).

Les symboles de l'index représentent les catégories indiquées dans la légende à droite. Les symboles suivis d'un indice (⋏[1]) représentent des sous-catégories (voir légende complète à la page I · 1).

Os símbolos incluídos no texto do índice representam as grandes categorias identificadas com a chave à direita. Os símbolos com números em sua parte superior (⋏[1]) identificam as subcategorias (veja-se a chave completa à página I · 1).

	English	Deutsch	Español	Français	Português
∧	Mountain	Berg	Montaña	Montagne	Montanha
⋏	Mountains	Gebirge	Montañas	Montagnes	Montanhas
)(	Pass	Paß	Paso	Col	Passo
V	Valley, Canyon	Tal, Cañon	Valle, Cañón	Vallée, Canyon	Vale, Canhão
≚	Plain	Ebene	Llano	Plaine	Planície
›	Cape	Kap	Cabo	Cap	Cabo
I	Island	Insel	Isla	Île	Ilha
II	Islands	Inseln	Islas	Îles	Ilhas
⊥	Other Topographic Features	Andere Topographische Objekte	Otros Elementos Topográficos	Autres données topographiques	Outros acidentes topográficos

ENGLISH — Name | Page | Lat.°′ | Long.°′
DEUTSCH — Name | Seite | Breite°′ | Länge°′ E = Ost

Gondarbal 123 34.14 N 74.47 E
Gonder 144 12.40 N 37.30 E
Gonder □[4] 144 13.10 N 37.00 E
Gondey 146 9.09 N 19.19 E
Gondia 120 21.27 N 80.12 E
Gondola 156 19.10 S 33.40 E
Gondomar 34 41.09 N 8.32 W
Gondrecourt-le-Château 58 48.31 N 5.30 E
Gondreville 58 48.42 N 5.58 E
Gondrexange, Étang de ⊜ 56 48.42 N 6.54 E
Goneāna 123 30.19 N 74.54 E
Gönen, Tür. 130 40.06 N 27.39 E
Gonén, Yis. 132 33.08 N 35.39 E
Gonesse 50 48.59 N 2.27 E
Gonfaron 62 43.19 N 6.17 E
Gong ≃ 100 26.00 N 115.22 E
Gong'an 102 30.02 N 112.04 E
Gonganbao 86 44.59 N 86.18 E
Gonganpucun 104 41.19 N 123.27 E
Gongbuchang 105 40.17 N 116.15 E
Gongchangling 104 41.06 N 123.30 E
Gongcheng 102 24.49 N 110.46 E
Gongchenqiao 106 30.20 N 120.08 E
Gongchuan, Zhg. 100 26.06 N 117.24 E
Gongchuan, Zhg. 102 23.40 N 107.50 E
Gongcun 105 39.28 N 116.10 E
Gongdaoqiao 100 32.36 N 119.22 E
Gongdian 100 28.06 N 116.56 E
Gongen-yama ∧ 94 35.40 N 139.01 E
Gongfang 100 27.36 N 115.34 E
Gonggar 120 29.17 N 90.46 E
Gongga Shan (Minya Konka) ∧ 102 29.35 N 101.51 E
Gonghe 102 36.20 N 100.48 E
Gonghui 98 41.12 N 114.37 E
Gongjialu 106 31.17 N 121.40 E
Gongjiatun 104 40.55 N 120.37 E
Gongjiazhai 104 41.57 N 124.01 E
Gongjing 107 29.21 N 104.43 E
Gongjingying 105 39.12 N 116.11 E
Gongkou 98 35.38 N 119.47 E
Gongli 98 35.55 N 117.24 E
Gongling 100 26.18 N 119.40 E
Gongliu 86 43.30 N 82.15 E
Gonglu Shan ∧ 106 30.39 N 119.18 E
Gongo 146 9.00 N 18.56 E
Gongola □[3] 146 9.00 N 11.40 E
Gongola ≃ 146 9.30 N 12.04 E
Gongoué 152 0.32 S 9.12 E
Gongo-Yembe 152 1.58 S 18.40 E
Gongpengzi 89 45.09 N 125.39 E
Gongping 100 23.05 N 115.24 E
Gongpingxu 100 26.12 N 112.51 E
Gongshan 102 25.50 N 103.13 E
Gongshiya 120 31.25 N 84.37 E
Gongsizhen 106 31.41 N 121.48 E
Gongtangtou 106 31.48 N 118.42 E
Gongxi 100 27.38 N 115.52 E
Gongxian 102 34.48 N 113.03 E
Gongyefu 98 42.16 N 118.32 E
Gongyemiao 89 43.40 N 121.06 E
Gongyingzi 98 40.54 N 119.41 E
Gongzhutun 104 42.10 N 123.00 E
Gongzui 107 29.19 N 103.28 E
Goni, It. 71 39.34 N 9.17 E
Goñi, Ur. 252 33.31 S 56.24 W
Goniądz 30 53.30 N 22.45 E
Gonini ≃ 250 4.10 N 54.24 W
Goniri 146 11.30 N 12.20 E
Gonjo 102 30.43 N 98.19 E
Gonnesa 71 39.16 N 8.28 E
Gonnesa, Golfo di ⊂ 71 39.17 N 8.23 E
Gonnosfanadiga 71 39.29 N 8.39 E
Gonnostramatza 71 39.41 N 8.50 E
Gonochovo 86 52.57 N 81.20 E
Gōnoura 92 33.45 N 129.41 E
Gonubie Mouth 158 32.57 S 28.01 E
Gonža 89 53.36 N 125.19 E
Gonzaga, It. 64 44.57 N 10.49 E
Gonzaga, Pil. 116 18.16 N 122.00 E
Gonzales, Ca., U.S. 226 36.30 N 121.26 W
Gonzales, La., U.S. 194 30.14 N 90.55 W
Gonzales, Tx., U.S. 222 29.30 N 97.27 W
Gonzales □[6] 222 29.28 N 97.30 W
González, Méx. 234 22.50 N 98.27 W
González, Ur. 258 34.14 S 56.52 W
González, Riacho ≃ 252 22.48 S 57.54 W
González Catán 258 34.46 S 58.39 W
González Chaves 252 38.02 S 60.06 W
González Moreno 252 35.33 S 63.22 W
González Ortega, Méx. 204 32.40 N 115.23 W
González Ortega, Méx. 234 23.59 N 103.27 W
González Ortega, Méx. 234 23.11 N 102.29 W
González Risos 258 34.52 S 59.13 W
Gonzanamá 246 4.15 S 79.27 W
Goobarragandra ≃ 171b 35.20 S 148.15 E
Goochland 192 37.41 N 77.53 W
Good Easter 260 51.47 N 0.21 E
Goodells 214 42.59 N 82.40 W
Goode Mountain ∧ 224 48.29 N 120.55 W
Goodenough, Mount ∧ 180 67.56 N 135.31 W
Goodenough Bay ⊂ 164 9.55 S 150.00 E
Goodenough Island I 164 9.20 S 150.15 E
Gooderham 212 44.54 N 78.23 W
Goodeve 184 51.04 N 103.10 W
Goodfellow Air Force Base ■ 196 31.26 N 100.25 W
Good Hope, S. Afr. 158 31.51 S 21.55 E
Good Hope, Oh., U.S. 218 39.26 N 83.21 W
Good Hope, Cape of (Kaap die Gooie Hoop) › 158 34.24 S 18.30 E
Goodhope Bay ⊂ 180 66.10 N 163.45 W
Good Hope Mountain ∧ 182 51.09 N 124.10 W
Goodhouse 158 28.57 S 18.13 E
Goodhue 190 44.24 N 92.37 W
Gooding 202 42.56 N 114.42 W
Goodison 214 42.44 N 83.10 W
Goodland, Fl., U.S. 220 25.55 N 81.38 W
Goodland, In., U.S. 216 40.45 N 87.17 W
Goodland, Ks., U.S. 198 39.21 N 101.42 W
Goodlands 184 49.05 N 100.35 W
Goodlow Park 222 32.07 N 96.14 W
Goodman, Ms., U.S. 194 32.58 N 89.54 W
Goodman, Wi., U.S. 190 45.37 N 88.21 W
Goodna 171a 27.37 S 152.54 E
Goodnews Bay 180 59.07 N 161.35 W
Goodnight 200 38.14 N 104.43 W
Goodooga 166 29.07 S 147.27 E
Goodradigbee ≃ 171b 35.08 S 148.41 E
Goodrich, Mi., U.S. 216 42.55 N 83.30 W
Goodrich, N.D., U.S. 198 47.28 N 100.07 W
Goodrich, Tx., U.S. 222 30.36 N 94.57 W
Good Spirit Lake ⊜ 184 51.34 N 102.40 W
Good Spirit Lake Provincial Park ♦ 184 51.36 N 102.45 W
Good Thunder 190 44.00 N 94.03 W
Goodview 190 44.03 N 91.41 W
Goodville 208 40.08 N 76.00 W
Goodwater 194 33.03 N 86.03 W
Goodwell 196 36.35 N 101.38 W
Goodwick 42 52.00 N 5.00 W
Goodwin, Lake ⊜ 224 48.08 N 122.18 W
Goodwives ≃ 276 41.04 N 73.28 W
Goodwood 212 44.02 N 79.12 W
Goodyear 200 33.26 N 112.21 W
Goof, Webi ≃ 144 1.10 N 43.43 E
Googong Reservoir ⊜[1] 171b 35.27 S 149.16 E
Gooie Hoop, Kaap die → Good Hope, Cape of › 158 34.24 S 18.30 E
Goole 44 53.42 N 0.52 W
Goolgowi 166 33.59 S 145.42 E
Goolwa 168b 35.31 S 138.47 E
Goomalling 162 31.19 S 116.49 E
Goombalie 166 29.59 S 145.23 E
Goombungee 171a 27.18 S 151.51 E
Goomburra 171a 28.03 S 152.07 E
Goonda 156 19.51 S 34.00 E
Goondiwindi 166 28.32 S 150.19 E
Goongarrie 162 30.03 S 121.09 E
Goongarrie National Park ♦ 162 29.58 S 121.34 E
Goonyella 166 21.45 S 147.55 E
Goor 52 52.14 N 6.35 E
Goose ≃, Ab., Can. 182 54.58 N 117.11 W
Goose ≃, N.D., U.S. 198 47.28 N 96.52 W
Goose Bay → Happy Valley-Goose Bay 176 53.20 N 60.25 W
Goose Bay ⊂ 281 42.35 N 82.41 W
Gooseberry Creek ≃ 202 43.55 N 108.04 W
Goose Creek 192 32.58 N 80.01 W
Goose Creek ≃, U.S. 202 42.33 N 113.46 W
Goose Creek ≃, Ne., U.S. 198 42.02 N 100.03 W
Goose Creek ≃, N.Y., U.S. 214 42.06 N 79.22 W
Goose Creek ≃, Va., U.S. 208 39.06 N 77.29 W
Goose Island I 182 51.55 N 128.25 W
Goose Lake ⊜, Mb., Can. 184 54.26 N 101.30 W
Goose Lake ⊜, On., Can. 184 51.46 N 93.00 W
Goose Lake ⊜, On., Can. 212 44.25 N 78.52 W
Goose Lake ⊜, On., Can. 214 42.31 N 82.31 W
Goose Lake ⊜, Sk., Can. 184 51.45 N 107.23 W
Goose Lake ⊜, U.S. 204 41.57 N 120.25 W
Goose Lake Canal ≅ 226 35.50 N 119.37 W
Goose Lake Prairie State Park ♦ 216 41.21 N 88.18 W
Gooseprairie 224 46.54 N 121.15 W
Goostrey 262 53.13 N 2.20 W
Gooty 122 15.07 N 77.38 E
Gopālganj, Bngl. 124 23.01 N 89.50 E
Gopālganj, India 124 26.28 N 84.26 E
Gopālnagar, India 126 23.03 N 88.45 E
Gopālnagar, India 272b 22.50 N 88.14 E
Gopālpur, Bngl. 124 24.33 N 89.56 E
Gopālpur, India 272b 22.38 N 88.27 E
Gopeng 114 4.28 N 101.10 E
Göpfritz an der Wild 61 48.43 N 15.24 E
Gopiballabhpur 126 22.13 N 86.54 E
Gopichettipālaiyam 122 11.28 N 77.27 E
Gopinagar 272b 22.50 N 88.07 E
Goppenstein 58 46.22 N 7.45 E
Göppingen 56 48.42 N 9.40 E
Goqên 102 29.15 N 96.59 E
Go Quao 110 9.43 N 105.17 E
Gor 123 35.32 N 74.31 E
Góra, Pol. 30 51.40 N 16.33 E
Gora, Ross. 76 60.02 N 41.43 E
Gor'ačegorsk 86 55.24 N 88.55 E
Gor'ačij Kl'uč 84 44.37 N 39.07 E
Gor'ačinsk 88 52.59 N 108.18 E
Goradit 144 11.25 N 38.25 E
Goradiz 84 39.27 N 47.20 E
Góra Kalwaria 30 51.59 N 21.12 E
Gorakhpur 124 26.45 N 83.22 E
Gor'any 76 55.25 N 29.02 E
Goras 124 25.32 N 76.56 E
Goražde 38 43.40 N 18.56 E
Gorbačevo Michajlovka 83 47.50 N 38.00 E
Gorbatov 80 56.08 N 43.04 E
Gorbatovka 80 56.15 N 43.45 E
Gorbica 88 53.06 N 119.13 E
Gorboviči 76 53.49 N 30.41 E
Gorčucha 80 57.43 N 43.43 E
Gorda, Punta ›, Chile 248 19.18 S 70.18 W
Gorda, Punta ›, Cuba 240p 22.24 N 82.10 W
Gorda, Punta ›, Nic. 236 11.26 N 83.48 W
Gorda, Punta ›, Nic. 236 14.21 N 83.12 W
Gorda, Punta ›, Ca., U.S. 204 40.16 N 124.22 W
Gordejevka 76 52.59 N 31.58 E
Gordes, Fr. 62 43.54 N 5.12 E
Gördes, Tür. 130 38.54 N 28.18 E
Gordil 146 9.44 N 21.35 E
Gørding 41 55.29 N 8.48 E
Gordion ⊥ 130 39.41 N 32.01 E
Gordo 194 33.19 N 87.54 W
Gordo, Cerro ∧ 234 20.46 N 102.35 W
Gordola 58 46.11 N 8.52 E
Gordon, Scot., U.K. 46 55.41 N 2.34 W
Gordon, Ga., U.S. 192 32.52 N 83.19 W
Gordon, Ne., U.S. 198 42.48 N 102.12 W
Gordon, Oh., U.S. 218 39.56 N 84.31 W
Gordon, Pa., U.S. 208 40.45 N 76.21 W
Gordon, Wi., U.S. 190 46.14 N 91.47 W
Gordon ≃ 224 48.35 N 124.24 W
Gordon, Isla I 254 54.58 S 69.35 W
Gordon, Lake ⊜[1] 166 42.42 S 146.12 E
Gordon Creek ≃ 198 42.49 N 100.40 W
Gordon Downs 162 18.44 S 128.35 E
Gordon Heights 207 40.51 N 72.58 W
Gordon Horne Peak ∧ 182 51.46 N 118.50 W
Gordon Indian Reserve ◆[4] 184 51.16 N 104.16 W
Gordon Lake ⊜, Ab., Can. 184 56.30 N 110.25 W
Gordon Lake ⊜, Sk., Can. 184 55.50 N 106.26 W
Gordon Lakes 276 41.03 N 74.22 W
Gordon Pass ⊂ 220 26.06 N 81.48 W
Gordon River 224 48.47 N 124.21 W
Gordon's Bay 158 34.10 S 18.52 E
Gordonsville 188 38.08 N 78.11 W
Gordonton 172 37.40 S 175.18 E
Gordonvale 166 17.05 S 145.47 E
Gordonville 220 27.57 N 81.49 W
Gore, Austl. 166 28.17 S 151.29 E
Gore, N.S., Can. 186 45.07 N 63.43 W
Gore, Ityo. 144 8.08 N 35.33 E
Gore, N.Z. 172 46.06 S 168.58 E
Goré, Tchad 146 7.53 N 16.40 E
Gore Bay 190 45.55 N 82.28 W
Gorebridge 46 55.51 N 3.02 W
Goreda 164 3.39 S 134.58 E
Goree 196 33.28 N 99.31 W
Gore Hill 274a 33.49 S 151.11 E
Görele 130 41.02 N 39.00 E
Gorelki 82 54.15 N 37.37 E
Goreloje 80 52.57 N 41.28 E
Gorelovo 265a 59.47 N 30.08 E
Gorelovo Airport ⊠ 265a 59.47 N 30.05 E
Gorelyj ≃ 265a 59.58 N 30.28 E
Göreme Milli Parkı ♦ 130 38.26 N 34.54 E
Gore Mountain ∧ 188 44.55 N 71.48 W
Gorenki 265b 55.48 N 37.55 E
Gore Point ›, Austl. 166 17.38 S 139.56 E
Gore Point ›, Ak., U.S. 180 59.12 N 151.00 W
Gore Range ⋏ 200 40.00 N 106.30 W
Goretovka ≃ 265b 55.56 N 37.20 E
Goreville 194 37.33 N 88.58 W
Gorey, Ire. 48 52.40 N 6.18 W
Gorey, Jersey 43b 49.12 N 2.02 W
Gorfoundurei 144 4.30 N 46.41 E
Gorgān 128 36.50 N 54.29 E
Gorgān ≃ 128 36.59 N 54.00 E
Gorgany ⋏ 78 48.30 N 24.00 E
Gorge Lake ⊜[1] 224 48.42 N 121.13 W
Görgeshausen 56 50.24 N 7.56 E
Gorgoglione 68 40.23 N 16.09 E
Gorgol □[4] 150 16.00 N 13.00 W
Gorgol el Abioḍ ≃ 150 16.14 N 12.58 W
Gorgol el Akhḍar ≃ 150 16.13 N 12.58 W
Gorgona, Isla I 246 2.59 N 78.12 W
Gorgona, Isola di I 36 43.26 N 9.54 E
Gorgonzola 62 45.32 N 9.24 E
Gorgor 248 10.35 S 77.02 W
Gorgora 144 12.13 N 37.16 E
Gorgoram 146 12.38 N 10.43 E
Gorgota 38 44.47 N 26.05 E
Gorgova 38 45.11 N 29.10 E
Gorham, Me., U.S. 188 43.40 N 70.26 W
Gorham, N.H., U.S. 188 44.23 N 71.10 W
Gorham, N.Y., U.S. 210 42.47 N 77.07 W
Gorhambury House ⊥ 260 51.47 N 0.24 W
Gori 84 41.58 N 44.07 E
Goria 272b 22.24 N 88.29 E
Gorica → Gorizia 64 45.57 N 13.38 E
Goričan 61 46.23 N 16.41 E
Goricy 76 57.09 N 36.44 E
Gorinchem 52 51.50 N 5.00 E
Goring 42 51.32 N 1.09 W
Goring-by-Sea 42 50.49 N 0.25 W
Goring Gap V 42 51.32 N 1.08 W
Goris 84 39.31 N 46.23 E
Göritz 54 53.24 N 13.54 E
Göritzhain 54 50.58 N 12.47 E
Gorizia 64 45.57 N 13.38 E
Gorizia □[4] 64 45.55 N 13.30 E
Gorj □[6] 38 45.00 N 23.20 E
Gorjani 38 45.24 N 18.21 E
Gor'kaja Balka 84 44.17 N 43.59 E
Gor'kaja balka ≃ 84 44.38 N 45.00 E
Görke 54 53.51 N 13.38 E
Gorkhā 124 28.00 N 84.37 E
Gorki, Bela. 76 54.17 N 30.59 E
Gorki, Ross. 80 57.38 N 45.05 E
Gorki → Nižnij Novgorod, Ross. 80 56.20 N 44.00 E
Gorki, Ross. 82 54.18 N 36.08 E
Gorki, Ross. 82 55.32 N 37.45 E
Gorki, Ross. 82 56.54 N 38.51 E
Gorki, Ross. 265b 55.57 N 37.55 E
Gor'kij → Nižnij Novgorod 80 56.20 N 44.00 E
Gorki Vtoryje 265b 55.44 N 37.11 E
Gor'koje, ozero ⊜ 86 52.30 N 81.20 E
Gor'kovskoje 86 55.22 N 74.24 E
Gor'kovskoje vodochranilišče ⊜[1] 80 57.00 N 43.10 E
Gorky → Nižnij Novgorod 80 56.20 N 44.00 E
Gorky Park ♦ 265b 55.44 N 37.36 E
Gorlago 62 45.40 N 9.49 E
Gorla Maggiore 266b 45.40 N 8.53 E
Gorla Minore 266b 45.39 N 8.54 E
Gorleston on Sea 42 52.36 N 1.43 E
Gørlev 41 55.32 N 11.14 E
Gorlice 30 49.40 N 21.10 E
Görlitz 54 51.09 N 14.59 E
Gorlosen 54 53.11 N 11.27 E
Gorlovka, Sak. 84 41.14 N 43.42 E
Gorlovka, Ukr. 83 48.18 N 38.03 E
Gorlovo 76 53.50 N 39.02 E
Gorm, Loch ⊜ 46 55.48 N 6.25 W
Gorman, Ca., U.S. 228 34.48 N 118.51 W
Gorman, Tx., U.S. 196 32.12 N 98.40 W
Gorman Creek ≃ 228 34.38 N 118.45 W
Görmin 54 53.59 N 13.16 E
Gorn'ackij, Ross. 24 67.32 N 64.03 E
Gorn'ackij, Ross. 78 48.17 N 40.55 E
Gorn'ackoje 78 47.42 N 34.08 E
Gorna Dzhumaya → Blagoevgrad 38 42.01 N 23.06 E
Gornaja Prolejka 80 49.24 N 44.59 E
Gorn'ak, Ross. 76 53.36 N 39.29 E
Gorn'ak, Ross. 86 51.00 N 81.29 E
Gorn'ak, Ukr. 78 50.20 N 24.10 E
Gorn'ak, Ukr. 83 48.04 N 37.24 E
Gornalunga ≃ 70 37.24 N 15.03 E
Gorna Orjahovica 38 43.07 N 25.41 E
Gornergrat ♦ 58 45.59 N 7.47 E
Gornja Radgona 36 46.41 N 16.00 E
Gornji Grad 36 46.18 N 14.49 E
Gornji Milanovac 38 44.01 N 20.27 E
Gornji Vakuf 36 43.56 N 17.35 E
Gorno-Altajsk 86 51.58 N 85.58 E
Gorno-Altay → Altaj □[3] 86 51.00 N 86.00 E
Gorno-Badachšanskaja Avtonomnaja Respublika □[3] 85 38.30 N 73.00 E
Gornoje 86 48.29 N 85.00 E
Gorno-Lesnoj zapovednik ♦ 85 41.10 N 69.55 E
Gornopravdinsk 86 60.07 N 69.54 E
Gornostajevka 78 47.01 N 33.44 E
Gorno-Vod'anoje 80 49.16 N 44.56 E
Gornovodnoje 89 43.42 N 134.44 E
Gornozavodsk, Ross. 86 58.20 N 58.32 E
Gornozavodsk, Ross. 89 46.34 N 141.49 E
Gornyj, Ross. 80 51.46 N 48.34 E
Gornyj, Ross. 89 50.48 N 136.29 E
Gornyj, Ross. 89 44.57 N 133.59 E
Gornyj Balyklej 80 49.34 N 45.04 E
Gornyje Kl'uči 89 45.12 N 133.31 E
Gornyj Tikič ≃ 78 48.47 N 30.53 E
Goro, Ityo. 144 6.56 N 40.32 E
Goro, N. Cal. 175f 22.16 S 167.02 E
Gorochan ∧ 144 9.22 N 37.04 E
Gorochov 78 50.30 N 24.45 E
Gorochovatka 83 49.21 N 37.31 E
Gorochovec 80 56.12 N 42.40 E
Gorochovje 76 56.31 N 30.29 E
Gorodec, Bela. 76 52.58 N 30.21 E
Gorodec, Bela. 76 53.33 N 30.02 E
Gorodec, Bela. 76 52.12 N 24.40 E
Gorodec, Ross. 76 58.32 N 29.47 E
Gorodec, Ross. 80 56.38 N 43.30 E
Gorodec, Ukr. 78 51.17 N 26.19 E
Gorodeja 76 53.19 N 26.32 E
Gorodenka 38 48.41 N 25.29 E
Gorodišče, Bela. 76 53.19 N 26.00 E
Gorodišče, Bela. 76 53.44 N 29.48 E
Gorodišče, Ross. 76 59.38 N 32.08 E
Gorodišče, Ross. 78 51.09 N 38.04 E
Gorodišče, Ross. 80 53.17 N 45.42 E
Gorodišče, Ross. 80 48.48 N 44.29 E
Gorodišče, Ross. 82 54.53 N 38.13 E
Gorodišče, Ross. 82 56.47 N 38.52 E
Gorodišče, Ukr. 78 49.17 N 31.27 E
Gorodišče, Ukr. 83 48.19 N 38.39 E
Gorodišče, Ukr. 83 49.03 N 39.38 E
Gorodišči 82 55.52 N 39.05 E
Gorodkovka 78 48.23 N 28.42 E
Gorodn'a, Ross. 82 54.57 N 38.49 E
Gorodn'a, Ross. 82 56.43 N 36.19 E
Gorodn'a, Ukr. 78 51.53 N 31.36 E
Gorodn'a ≃ 265b 55.38 N 37.48 E
Gorodnica 78 50.48 N 27.20 E
Gorodno 76 57.32 N 29.35 E
Gorodok, Bela. 76 55.28 N 29.59 E
Gorodok, Ukr. 78 49.10 N 26.34 E
Gorodok, Ukr. 78 49.47 N 23.39 E
Gorod'onka 78 48.41 N 25.29 E
Goroka 164 6.05 S 145.25 E
Gorokan 170 33.16 S 151.30 E
Gorom-Gorom 150 14.26 N 0.14 W
Gorong, Pulau I 164 3.59 S 131.25 E
Gorongosa, Parque Nacional da ♦ 156 18.45 S 34.15 E
Gorongosa, Serra da ∧ 154 18.30 S 34.03 E
Gorongose ≃ 156 20.30 S 34.40 E
Gorontalo 112 0.33 N 123.03 E
Goronyo 150 13.29 N 5.39 E
Goroubi ≃ 150 12.54 N 2.23 E
Gorouol ≃ 150 14.42 N 0.53 E
Górowo Iławeckie 30 54.17 N 20.30 E
Gorple Reservoirs ⊜[1] 262 53.47 N 2.06 W
Gorran ⊜ 40 59.43 N 17.32 E
Gorredijk 52 53.00 N 6.05 E
Gorron 28 48.25 N 0.49 W
Görsdorf 54 51.54 N 13.29 E
Goršečnoje 78 51.32 N 38.02 E
Gorsedd 262 53.17 N 3.16 W
Gorseinon 42 51.40 N 4.02 W
Gorskaja 265a 60.03 N 29.59 E
Gorskoje 83 48.46 N 38.30 E
Gorškovo 82 54.26 N 37.59 E
Gorst 224 47.32 N 122.42 W
Gort 48 53.04 N 8.50 W
Gortahork 48 55.08 N 8.09 W
Gorton ◆[8] 262 53.27 N 2.10 W
Görtschitz ≃ 61 46.45 N 14.32 E
Goru, Vîrful ∧ 38 45.48 N 26.25 E
Görükle 130 40.14 N 28.50 E
Gorumna Island I 48 53.14 N 9.40 W
Gor'un ≃ 89 50.45 N 137.50 E
Gorutuba ≃ 255 14.57 S 43.33 W
Görwihl 58 47.39 N 8.04 E
Gory, Bela. 76 54.16 N 31.13 E
Gory, Kaz. 80 48.38 N 51.46 E
Goryn' ≃ 78 52.08 N 27.17 E
Görz → Gorizia 64 45.57 N 13.38 E
Gorzano, Monte ∧ 66 42.37 N 13.24 E
Gorze 56 49.03 N 6.00 E
Görzig 54 51.40 N 12.00 E
Görzke 54 52.10 N 12.22 E
Górzno 30 53.13 N 19.38 E
Gorzów Śląski 30 51.02 N 18.24 E
Gorzów Wielkopolski (Landsberg an der Warthe) 30 52.44 N 15.15 E
Gorzów Wielkopolski □[4] 30 52.45 N 15.20 E
Górzyca 54 52.29 N 14.40 E
Gosāba 126 22.10 N 88.48 E
Gosairhāt 126 23.05 N 90.26 E
Gosaldo 64 46.13 N 11.58 E
Gosau 64 47.34 N 13.31 E
Gosauseen ⊜ 64 47.32 N 13.31 E
Gosberton 42 52.51 N 0.09 W
Gošča 78 50.36 N 26.41 E
Göschenen 58 46.40 N 8.35 E
Goschen Strait ⊔ 164 10.09 S 150.56 E
Gose 96 34.27 N 135.44 E
Gosen, Dtsch. 264a 52.24 N 13.43 E
Gosen, Nihon 92 37.44 N 139.11 E
Gosford 170 33.26 S 151.21 E
Gosforth, Eng., U.K. 44 55.01 N 1.37 W
Gosforth, Eng., U.K. 44 54.26 N 3.27 W
Gosforth Park ♦ 273d 26.14 S 28.10 E
Gosforth Park Race Course ♦ 273d 26.14 S 28.08 E
Goshabi 140 17.58 N 31.06 E
Goshen, N.S., Can. 186 45.23 N 61.59 W
Goshen, Ca., U.S. 226 36.21 N 119.25 W
Goshen, Ct., U.S. 207 41.49 N 73.13 W
Goshen, In., U.S. 216 41.34 N 85.50 W
Goshen, Ma., U.S. 207 42.26 N 72.48 W
Goshen, N.J., U.S. 208 39.08 N 74.51 W
Goshen, N.Y., U.S. 210 41.24 N 74.19 W
Goshen, Oh., U.S. 218 39.14 N 84.10 W
Goshiki 96 34.24 N 134.47 E
Goshogawara 92 40.48 N 140.27 E
Goshute Indian Reservation ◆[4] 200 39.53 N 114.08 W
Goshute Lake ⊜ 204 40.08 N 114.38 W
Goshute Valley V 204 40.40 N 114.30 W
Goslar 52 51.54 N 10.25 E
Gosnells 168a 32.04 S 116.00 E
Gospić 36 44.33 N 15.23 E
Gosport, Eng., U.K. 42 50.48 N 1.08 W
Gosport, In., U.S. 194 39.21 N 86.40 W
Gossa 54 51.40 N 12.26 E
Gossas 150 14.30 N 16.04 W
Gossau 58 47.25 N 9.15 E
Gosse ◆[8] 263 51.08 N 7.01 E
Gosse Bluff ∧ 162 23.49 S 132.19 E
Gosselies 56 50.28 N 4.25 E
Gössenheim 56 50.01 N 9.46 E
Gossensass → Colle Isarco 64 46.56 N 11.26 E
Gosser Hill 279b 40.37 N 79.37 W
Gossi 150 15.49 N 1.17 W
Gossinga 140 8.39 N 25.59 E
Gössnitz 54 50.53 N 12.26 E
Gossolengo 62 44.59 N 9.37 E
Gössweinstein 60 49.46 N 11.20 E
Gostagajevskaja 78 45.01 N 37.30 E
Gostilovo 82 55.18 N 38.36 E
Gostiščevo 78 50.47 N 36.39 E
Gostivar 38 41.47 N 20.54 E
Göstling an der Ybbs 61 47.48 N 14.55 E
Gostyń 30 51.53 N 17.00 E
Gostynin 30 52.26 N 19.29 E
Gosudarev Bajrak 83 48.21 N 38.08 E
Göta älv ≃ 26 57.42 N 11.52 E
Göta kanal ≅ 40 58.50 N 13.58 E
Gotchen Creek ≃ 224 46.00 N 121.30 W
Got Creek ≃ 284a 43.03 N 78.42 W
Gotebo 196 35.04 N 98.52 W
Göteborg (Gothenburg) 26 57.43 N 11.58 E
Göteborgs och Bohus län □[6] 26 58.30 N 11.30 E
Gotel Mountains ⋏ 152 6.55 N 11.15 E
Gotemba 94 35.18 N 138.56 E
Götene 26 58.32 N 13.29 E
Gotešty 38 46.09 N 28.10 E
Gotha, Dtsch. 54 50.57 N 10.41 E
Gotha, Fl., U.S. 220 28.32 N 81.31 W
Gothem 26 57.35 N 18.43 E
Gothenburg → Göteborg, Sve. 26 57.43 N 11.58 E
Gothenburg, Ne., U.S. 198 40.55 N 100.09 W
Gothèye 150 13.52 N 1.34 E
Gotland I 26 57.30 N 18.33 E
Gotlands Län □[6] 26 57.30 N 18.30 E
Gotoputovo 86 56.46 N 70.10 E
Gotō-rettō II 92 32.50 N 129.00 E
Gotska Sandön I 26 58.23 N 19.16 E
Gōtsu 96 35.00 N 132.14 E
Gottenheim 58 48.03 N 7.44 E
Götterswickerhamm 263 51.35 N 6.40 E
Gottesbrücke 264a 52.25 N 13.49 E
Gotthard Tunnel ◆[5] 58 46.35 N 8.35 E
Göttin 264a 52.27 N 12.54 E
Göttingen, Dtsch. 52 51.32 N 9.55 E
Göttingen, Dtsch. 56 50.52 N 8.46 E
Göttin See ⊜ 264a 52.28 N 12.54 E
Gottmadingen 58 47.44 N 8.47 E
Gottolengo 64 45.17 N 10.16 E
Gottorf, Schloss ⊥ 41 54.30 N 9.32 E
Gottsbüren 52 51.35 N 9.30 E
Gottvaterkapelle ʋ[1] 60 49.42 N 11.41 E
Götzendorf 264b 48.01 N 16.35 E
Gőtzis 58 47.20 N 9.38 E
Gouarec 32 48.13 N 3.11 W
Goubangzi 104 41.22 N 121.46 E
Goubone 146 20.43 N 17.08 E
Gouda, Ned. 52 52.01 N 4.43 E
Gouda, S. Afr. 158 33.19 S 19.04 E
Goudet 62 44.53 N 3.55 E
Goudge 252 34.40 S 68.08 W
Goudhurst 42 51.07 N 0.28 E
Goudiry 150 14.11 N 12.43 W
Goudoumaria 146 13.42 N 11.10 E
Goudswaard 52 51.47 N 4.16 E
Gouéké 150 8.02 N 8.43 W
Goûfi, Djebel el ∧ 34 36.57 N 6.27 E
Gougezhuang 105 38.53 N 116.11 E
Gough Island I 10 40.20 S 10.00 W
Gough Lake ⊜ 182 52.02 N 112.28 W
Gouin, Réservoir ⊜[1] 176 48.38 N 74.54 W
Goujiaozhen 107 30.36 N 106.33 E
Goukou 89 48.39 N 122.06 E
Goulais ≃ 190 46.43 N 84.27 W
Goulburn 170 34.45 S 149.43 E
Goulburn ≃ 169 36.41 S 145.12 E
Goulburn Islands II 164 11.33 S 133.26 E
Goulburn Weir ⊜[1] 169 36.45 S 145.08 E
Gould 194 33.59 N 91.33 W
Gould City 190 46.05 N 85.41 W
Gould Park 214 40.04 N 82.53 W
Goulds 220 25.33 N 80.22 W
Gouldsboro 210 41.44 N 75.28 W
Gouldsboro State Park ♦ 210 41.13 N 75.28 W
Goulet Lake ⊜ 184 55.23 N 96.18 W
Goulia 150 10.01 N 7.11 W
Goulicun 106 31.40 N 120.00 E
Goulimime 148 28.56 N 10.04 W
Goulimine □[4] 148 28.30 N 9.45 W
Goulmima 148 31.02 N 5.00 W
Goumbati ∧[2] 150 13.08 N 12.06 W
Goumbou 150 14.59 N 7.27 W
Gouménissa 38 40.57 N 22.27 E
Goumois 58 47.16 N 6.57 E
Gouna 146 8.32 N 13.34 E
Gounda ≃ 146 9.25 N 20.57 E
Goundam 150 16.25 N 3.40 W
Goundi 146 9.22 N 17.22 E
Gounou-Gaya 146 9.38 N 15.31 E
Gouougang, Mount ∧ 170 33.53 S 150.07 E
Goupillières 261 48.53 N 1.46 E
Gouraya 34 36.34 N 1.55 E
Gourbassi 150 13.24 N 11.38 W
Gourbeyre 241o 16.00 N 61.42 W
Gourcy 150 13.13 N 2.21 W
Gourdhead Run ≃ 279b 40.33 N 79.57 W
Gourdon, Fr. 32 44.44 N 1.23 E
Gourdon, Fr. 62 43.43 N 6.59 E
Gouré 150 13.58 N 10.18 E
Gouri ⊥ 124 24.53 N 88.07 E
Gourin 32 48.08 N 3.36 W
Gouripur 124 24.46 N 90.34 E
Gourits ≃ 158 34.21 S 21.52 E
Gourlay Lake ⊜ 190 48.52 N 84.54 W
Gourma Rharous 150 16.53 N 1.55 W
Gournay-en-Bray 50 49.29 N 1.44 E
Gournay-sur-Marne 261 48.52 N 2.34 E
Gouro 146 19.33 N 19.33 E
Gourock 46 55.58 N 4.49 W
Goussainville 50 49.01 N 2.28 E
Goussonville 261 48.55 N 1.46 E
Goutou 105 39.49 N 117.11 E
Gouveia, Bra. 255 18.27 S 43.44 W
Gouveia, Port. 266c 38.50 N 9.26 W
Gouverneur 212 44.20 N 75.27 W
Gouyadong 100 25.10 N 112.55 E
Gouyave 241k 12.10 N 61.44 W
Gov'altaj □[4] 102 45.30 N 96.00 E
Govan 184 51.18 N 105.00 W
Go Vap 269c 10.49 N 106.41 E
Govardhan 124 27.30 N 77.28 E
Gove 198 38.57 N 100.29 W
Govea ≃ 286b 22.56 N 82.30 W
Govena, mys › 74 59.48 N 166.06 E
Govenlock 184 49.15 N 109.48 W
Gove Peninsula ›[1] 164 12.20 S 136.50 E
Goverla, gora ∧ 78 48.10 N 24.32 E
Governador, Ilha do I 287a 22.48 S 43.12 W
Governador Portela 256 22.29 S 43.30 W
Governador Valadares 255 18.51 S 41.56 W
Government Camp 224 45.18 N 121.45 W
Governor Bond Lake ⊜[1] 219 38.56 N 89.23 W
Governor Dodge State Park ♦ 190 43.00 N 90.07 W
Governor Generoso 116 6.39 N 126.05 E
Governor Head › 170 35.07 S 150.46 E
Governor Nice Memorial Bridge ◆[5] 208 38.22 N 77.00 W
Governor Printz Park ♦ 285 39.52 N 75.18 W
Governor's Harbour 238 25.10 N 76.14 W
Governors Island I 276 40.41 N 74.01 W
Govind Ballabh Pant Sāgar ⊜[1] 124 24.05 N 82.50 E
Govindgarh 124 24.23 N 81.18 E
Govind Sāgar ⊜[1] 123 31.20 N 76.45 E
Gov'-Ugtaal 102 46.04 N 107.30 E
Gowan ≃ 184 55.49 N 94.08 W
Gowanda 210 42.27 N 78.56 W
Gowan Range ⋏ 166 25.00 S 145.00 E
Gowen City 208 40.45 N 76.32 W
Gower 194 39.36 N 94.35 W
Gower ›[1] 42 51.36 N 4.10 W
Gowerton 42 51.39 N 4.01 W
Gowienica ≃ 54 53.40 N 14.38 E
Gowmal (Gumal) ≃ 120 31.56 N 70.22 E
Gowmal Kalay 120 32.29 N 68.55 E
Gowna, Lough ⊜ 48 53.51 N 7.34 W
Gowrie 198 42.16 N 94.17 W
Gowy ≃ 44 53.17 N 2.51 W
Goya 252 29.08 S 59.16 W
Goyania → Goiânia 255 16.40 S 49.16 W
Goyatz 54 52.01 N 14.09 E
Goyave 241o 16.08 N 61.34 W
Goyaves, Grande Rivière à ≃ 241o 16.18 N 61.37 W
Goyaves, Îlets à II 241o 16.10 N 61.48 W
Goyder ≃ 164 12.38 S 135.11 E
Goyder Creek ≃ 162 25.39 S 134.47 E
Goyelle, Lac ⊜ 186 50.47 N 60.45 W
Goyeneche 258 35.20 S 58.43 W
Goyer, Île I 275a 45.29 N 73.17 W
Goyerkāta 124 26.42 N 89.02 E
Göynücek 130 40.24 N 35.32 E
Göynük, Tür. 130 40.24 N 30.47 E
Göynük, Tür. 130 39.08 N 40.53 E
Göynük ≃, Tür. 130 40.20 N 30.05 E
Göynük ≃, Tür. 130 38.53 N 40.34 E
Goyt ≃ 262 53.24 N 2.09 W
Goz-Beïda 146 12.13 N 21.25 E
Gozdnica 30 51.26 N 15.06 E
Gozdowice 54 52.45 N 14.18 E
Göze Dağı ∧ 130 41.24 N 42.30 E
Gözeli 130 38.25 N 39.04 E
Gozen-yama 94 36.32 N 140.20 E
Gozha Co ⊜ 120 34.59 N 81.06 E
Gözne 130 36.59 N 34.34 E
Gozo → Għawdex I 36 36.03 N 14.15 E
Göz Tepe ∧[2] 267b 41.06 N 29.06 E
Gozzano 62 45.45 N 8.26 E
Graaff-Reinet 158 32.14 S 24.32 E
Graafwater 158 32.00 S 18.37 E
Graauw 52 51.20 N 4.05 E
Grabc'ovo 82 54.34 N 36.22 E
Graben-Neudorf 56 49.09 N 8.29 E
Grabenstätt 64 47.51 N 12.32 E
Grabill 216 41.12 N 84.58 W
Grabo 150 4.55 N 7.30 W
Grabouw 158 34.09 S 19.02 E
Grabovaja Balka, les ♦ 83 48.09 N 38.37 E
Grabovo 86 53.07 N 74.52 E
Grabow 54 53.16 N 11.34 E
Grabowiec 30 50.50 N 23.33 E
Grabów nad Prosną 30 51.31 N 18.06 E
Gračac 36 44.18 N 15.51 E
Gračanica 38 44.42 N 18.19 E
Gračanica, Manastir ʋ[1] 38 42.36 N 21.09 E
Graçay 50 47.08 N 1.51 E
Grace 202 42.34 N 111.43 W
Gracefield 188 46.06 N 76.03 W
Graceham 208 39.36 N 77.22 W
Graceton 214 40.30 N 79.10 W
Graceville, Fl., U.S. 192 30.57 N 85.31 W
Graceville, Mn., U.S. 198 45.34 N 96.26 W
Gračevka 82 55.06 N 36.49 E
Grächen 58 46.12 N 7.50 E
Grachovo 80 56.04 N 51.58 E
Grači 80 49.49 N 43.33 E
Gracia ◆[8] 266d 41.23 N 2.09 E
Gracias 236 14.35 N 88.35 W
Gracias a Dios □[5] 236 15.10 N 84.20 W
Gracias a Dios, Cabo › 236 15.00 N 83.10 W
Gračiki ≃ 83 48.30 N 39.52 E
Graciosa I 148a 39.04 N 28.00 W
Graciosa, Isla I 148 29.15 N 13.30 W
Gračov 80 49.26 N 41.32 E
Gračovka, Ross. 80 52.07 N 40.01 E
Gračovka, Ross. 80 52.57 N 52.52 E
Gračov Kust 80 51.59 N 49.50 E
Gradačac 38 44.53 N 18.26 E
Gradara 66 43.57 N 12.46 E
Gradaús 250 7.43 S 51.11 W
Gr'adcy 76 56.24 N 31.55 E
Gräddö 40 59.46 N 19.02 E
Gradisca d'Isonzo 64 45.53 N 13.30 E
Gradižsk 78 49.13 N 33.07 E
Grado, Esp. 34 43.23 N 6.04 W
Grado, It. 64 45.40 N 13.23 E
Grado, Laguna di ⊂ 64 45.43 N 13.20 E
Gradoli 66 42.39 N 11.51 E
Grady, Ar., U.S. 194 34.04 N 91.42 W
Grady, N.M., U.S. 196 34.49 N 103.19 W
Gradyville 285 39.57 N 75.28 W
Graemsay I 46 58.56 N 3.17 W
Græsted 41 56.04 N 12.17 E
Graettinger 198 43.14 N 94.45 W
Gräfelfing 60 48.07 N 11.25 E
Grafenau 60 48.52 N 13.25 E
Gräfenberg 60 49.39 N 11.15 E
Grafenberg ◆[8] 263 51.14 N 6.50 E
Gräfenhainichen 54 51.44 N 12.27 E
Gräfenroda 54 50.45 N 10.48 E
Gräfenthal 54 50.31 N 11.18 E
Gräfentonna 54 51.05 N 10.44 E
Grafenwöhr 60 49.43 N 11.54 E
Graffignano 66 42.34 N 12.12 E
Grafham Water ⊜ 42 52.17 N 0.20 W
Gräfinau-Angstedt 54 50.42 N 11.01 E
Grafing bei München 60 48.02 N 11.59 E
Gråfjell ∧ 26 60.16 N 9.29 E
Graford 196 32.56 N 98.14 W
Gräfrath ◆[8] 263 51.13 N 7.04 E
Grafschaft Bentheim □[9] 52 52.30 N 7.00 E
Grafton, Austl. 166 29.41 S 152.56 E
Grafton, On., Can. 212 44.00 N 78.01 W
Grafton, Il., U.S. 219 38.58 N 90.25 W
Grafton, Ma., U.S. 207 42.12 N 71.41 W
Grafton, N.Y., U.S. 210 42.46 N 73.27 W
Grafton, N.D., U.S. 198 48.24 N 97.24 W
Grafton, Oh., U.S. 214 41.16 N 82.03 W
Grafton, W.V., U.S. 188 39.20 N 80.01 W
Grafton, Wi., U.S. 190 43.19 N 87.57 W
Grafton, Cape › 164 16.52 S 145.55 E
Grafton Lakes State Park ♦ 210 42.48 N 73.28 W
Grafty Green 260 51.12 N 0.41 E
Graglia 62 45.33 N 7.59 E
Gragnano 68 40.41 N 14.31 E
Gragnano Trebbiense 62 45.01 N 9.34 E
Graham, Ca., U.S. 280 34.15 N 118.31 W
Graham, N.C., U.S. 192 36.04 N 79.24 W
Graham, Tx., U.S. 196 33.06 N 98.35 W
Graham, Wa., U.S. 224 47.03 N 122.17 W
Graham, Mount ∧ 200 32.42 N 109.52 W
Graham Cave State Park ♦ 219 38.55 N 91.32 W
Graham Creek ≃ 218 38.49 N 85.39 W
Graham Hill County Park ♦ 276 41.07 N 73.48 W
Graham Island I 182 53.40 N 132.30 W
Graham Lake ⊜, On., Can. 212 44.34 N 75.53 W
Graham Lake ⊜, Me., U.S. 188 44.40 N 68.25 W
Graham Land ◆[1] 9 66.00 S 63.30 W
Graham Memorial Park ♦ 284b 39.25 N 76.30 W
Graham Moore, Cape › 176 72.52 N 76.04 W
Graham Moore Bay ⊂ 176 75.26 N 101.25 W
Grahamstad → Grahamstown 158 33.19 S 26.31 E
Grahamstown 158 33.19 S 26.31 E
Grahamsville 210 41.51 N 74.33 W
Grahn 218 38.17 N 83.04 W
Graie, Alpi (Alpes Grées) ⋏ 62 45.30 N 7.10 E
Graiguenarmanagh 48 52.32 N 6.57 W
Grain 42 51.28 N 0.43 E
Grain, Isle of I 42 51.27 N 0.41 E
Grain Coast ⊥[2] 150 5.00 N 9.00 W
Grainfield 198 39.06 N 100.27 W
Grajagan 115a 8.35 S 114.13 E
Grajagan, Teluk ⊂ 115a 8.40 S 114.18 E
Grajaú 250 5.49 S 46.08 W
Grajaú ≃ 250 3.41 S 44.48 W
Grajewo 30 53.39 N 22.27 E
Grajvoron 78 50.28 N 35.39 E
Gram 41 55.17 N 9.04 E
Gramacho 287a 22.44 S 43.18 W
Gramada 38 43.50 N 22.39 E
Gramado 252 29.24 S 50.54 W
Gramalote 246 7.53 N 72.48 W
Gramastetten 61 48.23 N 14.12 E
Gramat 32 44.47 N 1.43 E
Gramatneusiedl 264b 48.02 N 16.29 E
Grambling 194 32.31 N 92.42 W
Gramilla 252 27.18 S 64.37 W
Gramínea 256 22.10 S 46.38 W
Graminha, Represa ⊜[1] 256 21.40 S 46.35 W
Grammer 218 39.09 N 85.43 W
Grammichele 70 37.13 N 14.38 E
Grammont → Geraardsbergen 50 50.46 N 3.52 E
Gramoteino 86 54.31 N 86.22 E
Grampian 214 40.57 N 78.36 W
Grampian □[4] 46 57.15 N 2.45 W
Grampian Mountains ⋏ 46 56.55 N 4.00 W
Grampians National Park ♦ 166 37.20 S 142.30 E
Gramschatz 56 49.56 N 9.58 E
Gramsh 38 40.52 N 20.11 E
Gramzow 54 53.12 N 14.00 E
Gran → Esztergom 30 47.48 N 18.45 E
Grana ≃ 62 44.25 N 7.27 E
Granaatboskolk 158 30.02 S 19.51 E
Granada, Col. 246 3.34 N 73.45 W
Granada, Esp. 34 37.13 N 3.41 W
Granada, Nic. 236 11.56 N 85.57 W
Granada, Pil. 116 10.40 N 123.02 E
Granada, Co., U.S. 198 38.03 N 102.18 W
Granada, Mn., U.S. 190 43.41 N 94.20 W
Granada □[4] 34 37.15 N 3.15 W
Granada □[5] 236 11.50 N 86.00 W
Granada → Grenada □[1] 241k 12.07 N 61.40 W
Granada Hills ◆[8] 280 34.16 N 118.31 W
Granado 286d 12.04 S 76.57 W
Granaglione 66 44.07 N 10.58 E
Gran Altiplanicie Central ⋏[1] 254 48.55 S 69.45 W
Granard 48 53.47 N 7.30 W
Granarolo dell'Emilia 64 44.33 N 11.27 E
Granatello 70 37.53 N 12.32 E
Gran Bahía Australiana → Great Australian Bight ⊂[3] 162 35.00 S 135.00 E
Gran Bajo de San Julián V 254 49.30 S 68.30 W

Symbols in the index entries represent the broad categories identified in the key at the right. Symbols with superior numbers (⋏[1]) identify subcategories (see complete key on page *I · 1).*

Symbole im Register stellen die rechts im Schlüssel erklärten Kategorien dar. Symbole mit hochgestellten Ziffern (⋏[1]) bezeichnen Unterabteilungen einer Kategorie (vgl. vollständiger Schlüssel auf Seite *I · 1).*

Los símbolos incluídos en el texto del índice representan las grandes categorías identificadas con la clave a la derecha. Los símbolos con numeros en su parte superior (⋏[1]) identifican las subcategorías (véase la clave completa en la página *I · 1).*

Les symboles de l'index représentent les catégories indiquées dans la légende à droite. Les symboles suivis d'un indice (⋏[1]) représentent des sous-catégories (voir légende complète à la page *I · 1).*

Os símbolos incluídos no texto do índice representam as grandes categorias identificadas com a chave à direita. Os símbolos com números em sua parte superior (⋏[1]) identificam as subcategorias (veja-se a chave completa à página *I · 1).*

	English	Deutsch	Español	Français	Português
∧	Mountain	Berg	Montaña	Montagne	Montanha
⋏	Mountains	Gebirge	Montañas	Montagnes	Montanhas
)(	Pass	Paß	Paso	Col	Passo
V	Valley, Canyon	Tal, Cañon	Valle, Cañón	Vallée, Canyon	Vale, Canhão
⩡	Plain	Ebene	Llano	Plaine	Planície
›	Cape	Kap	Cabo	Cap	Cabo
I	Island	Insel	Isla	Île	Ilha
II	Islands	Inseln	Islas	Îles	Ilhas
⊥	Other Topographic Features	Andere Topographische Objekte	Otros Elementos Topográficos	Autres données topographiques	Outros acidentes topográficos

Gran-Grea I · 65

ESPAÑOL

Nombre	Página	Lat.°′	Long.°′ W = Oeste
Gran Barrera de Arrecifes → Great Barrier Reef ✢[2]	160	18.00 S	145.50 E
Granbergsdal	40	59.24 N	14.35 E
Granbury	222	32.26 N	97.47 W
Granbury, Lake ⊜[1]	222	32.25 N	97.45 W
Granby, P.Q., Can.	206	45.24 N	72.44 W
Granby, Co., U.S.	200	40.05 N	105.56 W
Granby, Ct., U.S.	207	41.57 N	72.47 W
Granby, Ma., U.S.	207	42.15 N	72.31 W
Granby, Mo., U.S.	194	36.55 N	94.15 W
Granby ≃	182	49.03 N	118.25 W
Granby, Lake ⊜[1]	200	40.09 N	105.50 W
Gran Canaria I	148	28.00 N	15.36 W
Grancey-le-Château	58	47.40 N	5.02 E
Gran Chaco ≚	18	23.00 S	60.00 W
Grand	58	48.23 N	5.29 E
Grand ≃, On., Can.	212	42.51 N	79.34 W
Grand ≃, U.S.	194	39.23 N	93.06 W
Grand ≃, Mi., U.S.	216	43.04 N	86.15 W
Grand ≃, Oh., U.S.	214	41.46 N	81.17 W
Grand ≃, S.D., U.S.	198	45.40 N	100.32 W
Grand ≃, Wi., U.S.	190	43.45 N	89.16 W
Grand, East Fork ≃	194	40.12 N	94.21 W
Grand, Lac ⊜	190	47.10 N	76.57 W
Grand, North Fork ≃	198	45.47 N	102.16 W
Grand, South Fork ≃	198	45.43 N	102.17 W
Grandas	34	43.13 N	6.52 W
Grand Bahama I	238	26.38 N	78.25 W
Grand Ballon ∧	58	47.55 N	7.08 E
Grand Bank	186	47.06 N	55.46 W
Grand Banks of Newfoundland ✢[4]	16	45.00 N	53.00 W
Grand-Bassam	150	5.12 N	3.44 W
Grand Bay, N.B., Can.	186	45.18 N	66.12 W
Grand Bay, Al., U.S.	194	30.28 N	88.20 W
Grand Beach	184	50.35 N	96.40 W
Grand Bend	190	43.15 N	81.45 W
Grand Béréby	150	4.38 N	6.55 W
Grand Blanc	216	42.55 N	83.37 W
Grand-Bourg	241o	15.53 N	61.19 W
Grand Bruit	186	47.41 N	58.13 W
Grand Caille Point ›	241f	13.52 N	61.05 W
Grand Calumet ≃	278	41.38 N	87.34 W
Grand Calumet, Île du I	190	45.44 N	76.41 W
Grand Canal ≍, Ire.	48	53.21 N	6.14 W
Grand Canal → Da Yunhe ≍, Zhg.	90	32.12 N	119.31 E
Grand Cane	194	32.05 N	93.48 W
Grand Cañon du Verdon ♠	62	43.47 N	6.27 E
Grand Canyon	200	36.03 N	112.08 W
Grand Canyon ∨	200	36.10 N	112.45 W
Grand Canyon National Park ♠	200	36.15 N	112.58 W
Grand Canyon of Pennsylvania ♠	210	41.43 N	77.28 W
Grand Cayman I	238	19.20 N	81.15 W
Grand Central Terminal ⬥[5]	276	40.45 N	73.59 W
Grand Centre	184	54.25 N	110.13 W
Grand Cess	150	4.36 N	8.10 W
Grandchamp, Fr.	58	47.43 N	5.27 E
Grandchamp, Fr.	261	48.43 N	1.37 E
Grand-Charmont	58	47.32 N	6.50 E
Grand Chenier	194	29.46 N	92.58 W
Grand Combin ∧	58	45.56 N	7.18 E
Grand Coulee	202	47.56 N	119.00 W
Grand Coulee ∨	202	47.45 N	119.15 W
Grand Coulee Dam ⬥[6]	202	47.57 N	118.59 W
Grand-Couronne	50	49.21 N	1.00 E
Grand Cul-de-Sac Marin c	241o	16.20 N	61.35 W
Grande ≃, Arg.	252	24.12 S	64.42 W
Grande ≃, Arg.	252	36.52 S	69.45 W
Grande ≃, Bol.	248	15.51 S	64.39 W
Grande ≃, Bra.	242	11.05 S	43.09 W
Grande ≃, Bra.	255	20.06 S	51.04 W
Grande ≃, Bra.	287a	22.55 S	43.25 W
Grande ≃, Bra.	287b	23.45 S	46.22 W
Grande ≃, Chile	252	30.35 S	71.11 W
Grande ≃, Esp.	34	39.07 N	0.44 W
Grande ≃, It.	70	37.55 N	13.13 E
Grande ≃, Méx.	234	17.43 N	96.56 W
Grande ≃, Méx.	234	18.50 N	102.05 W
Grande ≃, Nic.	236	12.28 N	86.21 W
Grande ≃, Pan.	236	8.18 N	80.24 W
Grande ≃, Perú	248	14.59 S	75.29 W
Grande ≃, S.A.	254	53.48 S	67.40 W
Grande ≃, Ven.	246	8.39 N	60.59 W
Grande, Arroyo ≃, Arg.	258	34.37 S	59.25 W
Grande, Arroyo ≃, Arg.	288	34.45 S	58.08 W
Grande, Arroyo ≃, Méx.	234	23.55 N	98.44 W
Grande, Arroyo ≃, Ur.	252	33.08 S	57.09 W
Grande, Arroyo ≃, Ur.	258	33.37 S	57.09 W
Grande, Bahía c[3]	254	50.45 S	68.45 W
Grande, Boca c	220	26.43 N	82.16 W
Grande, Boca ≃[1]	246	8.38 N	60.30 W
Grande, Cañada ≃, Arg.	258	35.15 S	59.23 W
Grande, Cañada ≃, Arg.	258	35.19 S	57.48 W
Grande, Cayo I	240p	20.59 N	79.09 W
Grande, Cerro ∧, Méx.	232	28.46 N	107.32 W
Grande, Cerro ∧, Méx.	234	21.45 N	103.05 W
Grande, Cerro ∧, Méx.	234	20.43 N	101.12 W
Grande, Cerro ∧, Méx.	234	23.39 N	100.51 W
Grande, Cerro ∧, Méx.	234	23.22 N	103.35 W
Grande, Corixa (Curiche Grande) ≡	248	17.10 S	58.20 W
Grande, Cuchilla ∧	252	33.15 S	55.07 W
Grande, Curiche (Corixa Grande) ≃	248	17.10 S	58.20 W
Grande, Igarapé ≃	250	3.37 S	48.53 W
Grande, Ilha I, Bra.	252	23.45 S	54.03 W
Grande, Ilha I, Bra.	256	23.09 S	44.14 W
Grande, Isola I	70	37.53 N	12.26 E
Grande, Lago ⊜, Arg.	254	47.44 S	68.04 W
Grande, Lago ⊜, Bra.	250	2.16 S	54.17 W
Grande, Laguna ⊜, Arg.	258	34.14 S	58.53 W
Grande, Laguna ⊜, Méx.	234	20.06 N	96.40 W
Grande, Mare c	68	40.27 N	17.12 E
Grande, Naviglio ≍	266b	45.35 N	8.42 E
Grande, Ponta ›	255	16.22 S	39.01 W
Grande, Praia ♠[2]	256	24.05 S	46.30 W
Grande, Punta ›	252	21.54 S	70.12 W
Grande, Ribeirão ≃	256	21.24 S	44.29 W
Grande, Rio (Bravo del Norte) ≃	178	25.55 N	97.09 W
Grande, Salina ≡	68	40.26 N	17.18 E
Grande, Serra ⋀	250	6.00 S	40.52 W
Grande, Sierra ⋀	196	29.40 N	104.55 W
Grande-Anse	186	47.48 N	65.11 W
Grande Anse, La c	275a	45.23 N	73.53 W
Grande Anse Bay c	241k	12.02 N	61.45 W
Grande Baie, La c	275a	45.29 N	74.00 W
Grande Cache	182	53.53 N	119.08 W
Grande Casse, Pointe de la ∧	62	45.24 N	6.50 E
Grande Cayemite I	238	18.37 N	73.45 W
Grande Chartreuse, Couvent de la ʊ[1]	62	45.22 N	5.50 E
Grande de Añasco ≃	240m	18.16 N	67.11 W

FRANÇAIS

Nom	Page	Lat.°′	Long.°′ W = Ouest
Grande de Arecibo ≃	240m	18.29 N	66.42 W
Grande de Jutaí, Ilha I	250	3.15 S	49.37 W
Grande de Lipez ≃	248	20.47 S	67.14 W
Grande de Loíza ≃	240m	18.27 N	65.53 W
Grande de Manacapuru, Lago ⊜	246	3.04 S	61.25 W
Grande de Manatí ≃	240m	18.29 N	66.32 W
Grande de Matagalpa ≃	236	12.54 N	83.32 W
Grande de Santiago ≃	234	21.36 N	105.26 W
Grande de Tarija ≃	248	22.53 S	64.21 W
Grande de Térraba ≃	236	8.59 N	83.37 W
Grande do Curuaí, Lago ⊜	250	2.15 S	55.20 W
Grande do Gurupá, Ilha I	250	1.00 S	51.30 W
Grande do Tapará, Ilha I	250	2.14 S	54.39 W
Grande Île de Criques I	273b	4.20 S	15.25 E
Grande Inferior, Cuchilla ⋀[2]	258	33.50 S	56.27 W
Grand-Entrée	186	47.33 N	61.34 W
Grande-Prairie	182	55.10 N	118.48 W
Grand Erg de Bilma ⬥[2]	146	18.30 N	14.00 E
Grand Erg Occidental ⬥[2]	148	30.30 N	0.30 E
Grand Erg Oriental ⬥[2]	148	30.30 N	7.00 E
Grande-Rivière	186	48.24 N	64.30 W
Grande Rivière, La ≃	176	53.50 N	79.00 W
Grande Ronde ≃	202	46.05 N	116.59 W
Grandes, Salinas ≚, Arg.	252	30.05 S	65.05 W
Grandes, Salinas ≚, Arg.	252	23.43 S	66.00 W
Grandes Antillas, Islas → Greater Antilles II	238	20.00 N	74.00 W
Grandes Antilles, Îles → Greater Antilles II	238	20.00 N	74.00 W
Grande Sassière, Aiguille de la ∧	62	45.30 N	7.00 E
Grande Sauldre ≃	50	47.26 N	2.05 E
Gran Desierto de Arena → Great Sandy Desert ⬥[2]	162	21.30 S	125.00 E
Gran Desierto Victoria → Great Victoria Desert ⬥[2]	162	28.30 S	127.45 E
Grandes-Piles	206	46.41 N	72.44 W
Grande-Synthe	50	51.01 N	2.19 E
Grand-Étang	186	46.33 N	61.02 W
Grande-Terre I	241o	16.20 N	61.25 W
Grande Vigie, Pointe de la ›	241o	16.31 N	61.28 W
Grand Eyvia ≃	62	45.42 N	7.14 E
Grand Falls, N.B., Can.	186	47.03 N	67.44 W
Grand Falls, Nf., Can.	186	48.56 N	55.40 W
Grandfalls, Tx., U.S.	196	31.20 N	102.51 W
Grandfather Mountain ∧	192	36.07 N	81.48 W
Grandfield	196	34.13 N	98.41 W
Grand Forks, B.C., Can.	182	49.02 N	118.27 W
Grand Forks, N.D., U.S.	198	47.55 N	97.01 W
Grand Forks Air Force Base ■	198	47.57 N	97.25 W
Grand-Fort-Philippe	50	51.00 N	2.06 E
Grand-Fougeray	32	47.44 N	1.44 W
Grand-Gallargues	62	43.43 N	4.10 E
Grand Gorge	210	42.21 N	74.29 W
Grand-Halleux	56	50.19 N	5.54 E
Grand Haven	216	43.03 N	86.13 W
Grand Haven State Park ♠	216	43.02 N	86.13 W
Grand Hers ≃	32	43.47 N	1.20 E
Grandiči	76	53.43 N	23.49 E
Grandin, Lac ⊜	176	63.59 N	119.00 W
Grandioznyj, pik ∧	88	53.50 N	96.11 E
Grand Island, Fl., U.S.	220	28.53 N	81.44 W
Grand Island, Ne., U.S.	198	40.55 N	98.20 W
Grand Island, N.Y., U.S.	212	43.01 N	78.58 W
Grand Island I, On., Can.	212	44.34 N	78.50 W
Grand Island I, Mi., U.S.	190	46.30 N	86.40 W
Grand Island I, N.Y., U.S.	210	43.02 N	78.58 W
Grand Isle	194	29.14 N	89.59 W
Grand Isle □[6]	206	44.57 N	73.17 W
Grand Junction, Co., U.S.	200	39.03 N	108.33 W
Grand Junction, Ia., U.S.	198	42.01 N	94.14 W
Grand Junction, Mi., U.S.	216	42.24 N	86.04 W
Grand Junction, Tn., U.S.	194	35.02 N	89.11 W
Grand Lac Salé → Great Salt Lake ⊜	200	41.10 N	112.30 W
Grand lac Victoria ⊜	190	47.31 N	77.30 W
Grand-Lahou	150	5.08 N	5.01 W
Grand Lake	200	40.15 N	105.49 W
Grand Lake ⊜, N.B., Can.	186	45.55 N	66.05 W
Grand Lake ⊜, Nf., Can.	186	49.00 N	57.25 W
Grand Lake ⊜, N.A.	186	45.43 N	67.50 W
Grand Lake ⊜, La., U.S.	194	29.55 N	92.47 W
Grand Lake ⊜, La., U.S.	194	29.55 N	91.25 W
Grand Lake ⊜, Mi., U.S.	190	45.18 N	83.30 W
Grand Lake ⊜, Oh., U.S.	216	40.30 N	84.32 W
Grand Lake Saint Marys State Park ♠	216	40.33 N	84.27 W
Grand Ledge	216	42.45 N	84.44 W
Grand Lieu, Lac de ⊜	32	47.06 N	1.40 W
Grand'Maison, Barrage de ⬥[6]	62	45.12 N	6.07 E
Grand Manan Channel ʮ	186	44.45 N	66.52 W
Grand Manan Island I	186	44.40 N	66.50 W
Grand Marais, Mi., U.S.	190	46.40 N	85.59 W
Grand Marais, Mn., U.S.	190	47.45 N	90.20 W
Grand Meadow	190	43.42 N	92.34 W
Grand-Mère	206	46.37 N	72.41 W
Grand Mesa ∧	200	39.00 N	108.00 W
Grandmesnil, Lac ⊜	186	51.19 N	67.33 W
Grand Morin ≃	50	48.54 N	2.50 E
Grand Muveran ∧	58	46.14 N	7.08 E
Grandola, It.	58	46.02 N	9.13 E
Grândola, Port.	34	38.10 N	8.34 W
Grand Pabos, Rivière du ≃	186	48.21 N	64.43 W
Grand Palace ʊ	269a	13.45 N	100.30 E
Grand Passage ʮ	175f	18.45 S	163.10 E
Grand-Popo	150	6.17 N	1.50 E
Grand Portage	190	47.57 N	89.41 W
Grand Portage Indian Reservation ⬥[4]	190	47.55 N	89.45 W

PORTUGUÊS

Nome	Página	Lat.°′	Long.°′ W = Oeste
Grand Portage National Monument ♠	190	48.02 N	89.38 W
Grand Prairie	222	32.44 N	96.59 W
Grandpré	56	49.20 N	4.52 E
Grand Pré National Historic Park ♠	186	45.08 N	64.18 W
Grand Prix Airport ⊠	281	42.33 N	83.11 W
Grand Rapids, Mb., Can.	184	53.08 N	99.20 W
Grand Rapids, Mi., U.S.	216	42.58 N	85.40 W
Grand Rapids, Mn., U.S.	190	47.14 N	93.31 W
Grand Rapids, Oh., U.S.	216	41.24 N	83.51 W
Grand Rhône ≃	62	43.20 N	4.50 E
Grand Ridge	216	41.14 N	88.50 W
Grandrieu, Bel.	50	50.12 N	4.10 E
Grandrieu, Fr.	62	44.47 N	3.38 E
Grand River	214	41.44 N	81.17 W
Grand' Rivière	240e	14.52 N	61.11 W
Grand Ronde	224	45.03 N	123.36 W
Grand Roy	241k	12.08 N	61.45 W
Grand Ruisseau, Le ≃	275a	45.39 N	73.12 W
Grand-Saint-Bernard, Col du)(	58	45.50 N	7.10 E
Grand-Saint-Bernard, Tunnel du ⬥[5]	58	45.51 N	7.11 E
Grand Saline	222	32.40 N	95.42 W
Grand Saline Creek ≃	222	32.41 N	95.36 W
Grand-Santi	250	4.19 N	54.24 W
Grandson	58	46.49 N	6.38 E
Grand Terrace	228	34.02 N	117.18 W
Grand Teton ∧	202	43.44 N	110.48 W
Grand Teton National Park ♠	202	43.30 N	110.45 W
Grand Tower	194	37.37 N	89.29 W
Grand Traverse Bay c	190	45.02 N	85.30 W
Grand Traverse Bay, East Arm c	190	44.52 N	85.28 W
Grand Traverse Bay, West Arm c	190	44.52 N	85.35 W
Grandtully	46	56.39 N	3.46 W
Grand Turk	238	21.28 N	71.08 W
Grand Union Canal ≍	260	51.30 N	0.02 W
Grand Valley, On., Can.	212	43.54 N	80.19 W
Grand Valley, Pa., U.S.	214	41.43 N	79.32 W
Grandview, Mb., Can.	184	51.10 N	100.42 W
Grandview, Il., U.S.	219	42.06 N	89.50 W
Grandview, Mo., U.S.	194	38.53 N	94.31 W
Grandview, Pa., U.S.	279b	40.10 N	79.52 W
Grandview, Tx., U.S.	222	32.16 N	97.11 W
Grandview, Wa., U.S.	202	46.15 N	119.54 W
Grand View, Wi., U.S.	190	46.22 N	91.06 W
Grandview Beach	216	41.50 N	83.24 W
Grandview Heights, Oh., U.S.	218	39.58 N	83.02 W
Grandview Heights, Pa., U.S.	208	40.03 N	76.17 W
Grandview Homes	216	40.44 N	84.04 W
Grand View-on-Hudson	276	41.44 N	73.55 W
Grandvillars	58	47.33 N	6.58 E
Grandville	216	42.54 N	85.45 W
Grandvilliers	50	49.40 N	1.56 E
Grand Wash Cliffs ♠[4]	200	35.40 N	113.50 W
Grandyle Village	210	43.00 N	78.57 W
Grâne	62	44.44 N	4.55 E
Grañén	34	41.56 N	0.22 W
Graneros	252	34.04 S	70.44 W
Granetalsperre ⬥[6]	52	51.48 N	10.27 E
Graney, Lough ⊜	48	52.59 N	8.40 W
Grangärde	40	60.16 N	14.59 E
Grange, Austl.	168b	34.54 S	138.30 E
Grange, Eng., U.K.	262	53.23 N	3.09 W
Grange, Bois de la ♠	261	48.45 N	2.30 E
Grange-Bléneau, Château de la ⊥	50	48.41 N	2.55 E
Grange Hill	260	51.37 N	0.05 E
Grangemouth	46	56.02 N	3.45 W
Grängen ⊜	40	59.45 N	14.47 E
Grangent, Lac de ⊜[1]	62	45.25 N	4.15 E
Grange-over-Sands	44	54.12 N	2.55 W
Granger, Tx., U.S.	222	30.43 N	97.26 W
Granger, Wa., U.S.	202	46.20 N	120.11 W
Granger, Wy., U.S.	200	41.35 N	109.58 W
Granger Draw ∨	196	30.20 N	100.57 W
Granger Lake ⊜[1]	222	30.42 N	97.22 W
Granges → Grenchen	58	47.11 N	7.24 E
Grängesberg	40	60.05 N	14.59 E
Granges-sur-Vologne	58	48.09 N	6.47 E
Grangeville, Id., U.S.	202	45.55 N	116.07 W
Grangeville, Pa., U.S.	208	39.47 N	76.58 W
Grangousier Hill ∧[2]	190	47.35 N	84.56 W
Gran Guardia	252	25.52 S	58.53 W
Granite, Md., U.S.	284b	39.21 N	76.51 W
Granite, Ok., U.S.	196	34.57 N	99.22 W
Granite City	219	38.42 N	90.08 W
Granite Creek ≃	224	48.43 N	120.55 W
Granite Dome ∧	226	38.13 N	119.44 W
Granite Downs	162	26.57 S	133.30 E
Granite Falls, Mn., U.S.	198	44.48 N	95.32 W
Granite Falls, N.C., U.S.	192	35.47 N	81.25 W
Granite Falls, Wa., U.S.	224	48.05 N	121.58 W
Granite Lake ⊜[1]	186	48.08 N	57.05 W
Granite Mountain ∧, Austl.	171b	35.44 S	148.13 E
Granite Mountain ∧, Ak., U.S.	180	65.26 N	161.14 W
Granite Mountain ∧, Ak., U.S.	182	55.30 N	132.35 W
Granite Mountains ⋀	202	42.35 N	107.30 W
Granite Pass)(	202	44.38 N	107.30 W
Granite Peak	162	25.38 S	121.21 E
Granite Peak ∧, Mt., U.S.	202	45.10 N	109.48 W
Granite Peak ∧, Mt., U.S.	202	45.34 N	112.02 W
Granite Peak ∧, Nv., U.S.	204	41.40 N	117.35 W
Granite Peak ∧, Nv., U.S.	204	40.48 N	119.25 W
Granite Range ⋀	204	41.00 N	119.35 W
Graniteville, Ma., U.S.	207	42.35 N	71.27 W
Graniteville, S.C., U.S.	192	33.33 N	81.48 W
Graniteville, Vt., U.S.	188	44.09 N	72.29 W
Graniti	70	37.53 N	15.14 E
Granitnoje	83	47.27 N	37.52 E
Granitogorsk	85	42.44 N	73.27 E
Granitola, Capo ›	70	37.34 N	12.41 E
Granitola Torretta	70	37.34 N	12.40 E
Granity	172	41.38 S	171.51 E
Granitzenbach ≃	61	47.11 N	14.46 E
Granja, Bra.	250	3.06 S	40.50 W
Granja, Port.	266c	38.51 N	9.06 W
Gran Khingan → Da Hinggan Ling ⋀	90	49.00 N	122.00 E
Granki	76	54.51 N	31.27 E
Grankulla (Kauniainen)	26	60.13 N	24.45 E
Gran Lago Salado → Great Salt Lake ⊜	200	41.10 N	112.30 W
Gran Laguna Salada ⊜	254	44.24 S	67.23 W
Granma □[4]	240p	21.20 N	76.50 W

Gränna	26	58.01 N	14.28 E
Grannoch, Loch ⊜	44	55.00 N	4.17 W
Granollers	34	41.37 N	2.18 E
Granön	26	64.15 N	19.19 E
Granov	78	48.52 N	29.34 E
Gran Pajonal ⋀	248	10.45 S	74.30 W
Gran Paradiso ∧	62	45.32 N	7.16 E
Gran Paradiso, Parco Nazionale del ♠	62	45.34 N	7.18 E
Gran Pilastro (Hochfeiler) ∧	64	46.58 N	11.44 E
Gran Rio ≃	250	4.01 N	55.31 W
Gran Sasso d'Italia ⋀	66	42.27 N	13.42 E
Gransee	54	53.00 N	13.09 E
Grant, Fl., U.S.	220	27.55 N	80.31 W
Grant, Mi., U.S.	190	43.20 N	85.48 W
Grant, Ne., U.S.	198	40.50 N	101.43 W
Grant □[6], In., U.S.	216	40.33 N	85.40 W
Grant □[6], Ky., U.S.	218	38.39 N	84.39 W
Grant ≃	190	42.40 N	90.45 W
Grant, Lake ⊜	218	39.00 N	83.53 W
Grant, Mount ∧	204	38.34 N	118.48 W
Grant, Point ›	169	38.31 S	145.07 E
Granta ≃	42	52.10 N	0.06 E
Grant Birthplace ⊥	218	38.54 N	84.14 W
Grant City	194	40.29 N	94.24 W
Grantham, Austl.	171a	27.34 S	152.12 E
Grantham, Eng., U.K.	42	52.55 N	0.39 W
Grantham, Pa., U.S.	208	40.09 N	77.00 W
Grant-Kohrs Ranch National Historic Site ⊥	202	46.25 N	112.40 W
Grant Lake ⊜[1]	226	37.50 N	119.07 W
Grantley Adams International Airport ⊠	241g	13.04 N	59.29 W
Grant Mills	283	41.57 N	71.26 W
Granton	46	55.59 N	3.14 W
Grantorto	64	45.36 N	11.43 E
Grantown-on-Spey	46	57.19 N	3.37 W
Grant Park	216	41.14 N	87.39 W
Grant Park ♠	278	41.52 N	87.37 W
Grant Point ›	176	68.19 N	98.53 W
Grant Range ⋀	204	38.25 N	115.30 W
Grants	200	35.09 N	107.50 W
Grantsburg, In., U.S.	218	38.17 N	86.28 W
Grantsburg, Wi., U.S.	190	45.46 N	92.40 W
Grantshouse	46	55.53 N	2.19 W
Grants Pass	202	42.26 N	123.19 W
Grants Patch	162	30.27 S	121.07 E
Grant-Suttie Bay c	176	69.47 N	77.15 W
Grantsville, Ut., U.S.	200	40.36 N	112.27 W
Grantsville, W.V., U.S.	188	38.55 N	81.05 W
Grantville, Ga., U.S.	192	33.14 N	84.50 W
Grantville, Pa., U.S.	208	40.23 N	76.39 W
Granum	182	49.52 N	113.30 W
Granville, Austl.	274a	33.50 S	151.01 E
Granville, Fr.	32	48.50 N	1.36 W
Granville, Il., U.S.	190	41.15 N	89.13 W
Granville, Ma., U.S.	207	42.04 N	72.51 W
Granville, Mo., U.S.	219	39.34 N	92.06 W
Granville, N.Y., U.S.	188	43.24 N	73.15 W
Granville, N.D., U.S.	198	48.16 N	100.50 W
Granville, Oh., U.S.	214	40.04 N	82.31 W
Granville, Pa., U.S.	208	40.33 N	77.38 W
Granville, W.V., U.S.	188	39.38 N	79.59 W
Granville Lake ⊜	184	56.18 N	100.30 W
Granvin	26	60.33 N	6.43 E
Granzin, Dtsch.	54	53.25 N	12.53 E
Granzin, Dtsch.	54	53.30 N	11.56 E
Grão Mogol	255	16.34 S	42.54 W
Grão-Mogol ≃	256	21.46 S	43.40 W
Grape Creek ≃	200	38.26 N	105.16 W
Grape Island I	283	42.16 N	70.55 W
Grapeland	222	31.29 N	95.28 W
Grapeview	224	47.19 N	122.50 W
Grapeville	214	40.19 N	79.36 W
Grapevine	222	32.56 N	97.04 W
Grapevine Lake ⊜[1]	222	32.59 N	97.06 W
Grapevine Peak ∧	204	36.57 N	117.09 W
Grappa, Monte ∧	64	45.52 N	11.48 E
Grappenhall	262	53.22 N	2.32 W
Grarem	34	36.31 N	6.19 E
Gras, Lac de ⊜	176	64.30 N	110.30 W
Grasbult	158	30.52 S	21.47 E
Grasdorf	52	52.06 N	10.09 E
Graskop	156	24.58 S	30.49 E
Grasleben	54	52.18 N	11.01 E
Grasmere, S. Afr.	158	26.26 S	27.52 E
Grasmere, Eng., U.K.	44	54.28 N	3.02 W
Grasmere Lake ⊜	276	40.36 N	74.05 W
Gräsö	40	60.21 N	18.28 E
Gräsö I	40	60.24 N	18.25 E
Grasonville	208	38.57 N	76.12 W
Grass ≃, Mb., Can.	184	56.03 N	96.33 W
Grass ≃, N.Y., U.S.	188	44.59 N	74.46 W
Grass, North Branch ≃	188	44.25 N	75.06 W
Grass, South Branch ≃	188	44.22 N	75.05 W
Grassano	68	40.38 N	16.18 E
Grassau	64	47.47 N	12.27 E
Grass Creek	202	43.56 N	108.39 W
Grass Creek ≃	202	43.52 N	108.22 W
Grasscroft	262	53.32 N	2.02 W
Grasse	62	43.40 N	6.55 E
Grassendale ⬥[8]	262	53.21 N	2.54 W
Grassflat	214	41.00 N	78.07 W
Grass Hassock Channel ʮ	276	40.36 N	73.48 W
Grasshopper Creek ≃	202	45.06 N	112.47 W
Grassington	44	54.04 N	2.00 W
Grass Island I	276	40.39 N	73.18 W
Grässjön ⊜	40	59.52 N	13.43 E
Grass Lake	216	42.15 N	84.13 W
Grass Lake ⊜	216	42.27 N	88.10 W
Grassmere, Lake ⊜	172	41.44 S	174.10 E
Grass Patch	162	33.14 S	121.43 E
Grass Range	202	47.01 N	108.48 W
Grassridge Dam ⊜[1]	158	31.45 S	25.29 E
Grass River Provincial Park ♠	184	54.40 N	100.50 W
Grass Valley, Austl.	168a	31.38 S	116.48 E
Grass Valley, Ca., U.S.	226	39.13 N	121.03 W
Grass Valley, Or., U.S.	224	45.21 N	120.47 W
Grassy	166	40.03 S	144.04 E
Grassy ≃	190	48.22 N	81.27 W
Grassy Bay c	276	40.38 N	73.48 W
Grassy Brook ≃	284a	43.03 N	79.07 W
Grassy Creek ≃, In., U.S.	216	40.55 N	86.30 W
Grassy Creek ≃, Mo., U.S.	219	39.54 N	91.37 W
Grassy Hill ∧	271d	22.25 N	114.09 E
Grassy Island I	276	41.04 N	73.23 W
Grassy Island Lake ⊜	184	51.50 N	110.20 W
Grassy Key I	220	24.46 N	80.57 W
Grassy Lake	182	49.49 N	111.43 W
Grassy Lake ⊜	220	27.13 N	81.20 W
Grassy Plains	182	53.57 N	125.54 W
Grassy Sprain Reservoir ⊜[1]	276	40.58 N	73.51 W
Gråsten	41	54.55 N	9.36 E
Grästorp	26	58.20 N	12.40 E
Graterford	285	40.13 N	75.27 W
Graterford State Correctional Institution ʊ	285	40.14 N	75.26 W
Grates Point ›	186	48.10 N	52.57 W
Gratis	218	39.38 N	84.31 W
Gratitunon	115a	7.43 S	113.00 E
Gratkorn	61	47.08 N	15.21 E
Gratwein	61	47.07 N	15.19 E
Gratz, Ky., U.S.	218	38.28 N	84.57 W
Gratz, Pa., U.S.	208	40.37 N	76.43 W
Gratztown	279b	40.14 N	79.47 W

Graubünden (Grischun) □[3]	58	46.45 N	9.30 E
Graudenz → Grudziądz	30	53.29 N	18.45 E
Graue Hörner ∧	58	46.57 N	9.23 E
Graukogel ∧	64	47.06 N	13.10 E
Graulhet	32	43.46 N	2.00 E
Graulinster	56	49.45 N	6.18 E
Graun → Curon Venosta	64	46.49 N	10.32 E
Graupa	54	51.00 N	13.54 E
Gravatá	250	8.12 S	35.34 W
Gravatá ≃	255	16.53 S	42.10 W
Grave	52	51.45 N	5.44 E
Grave Creek ≃	202	42.39 N	123.35 W
Gravedona	58	46.09 N	9.18 E
Gravelbourg	184	49.53 N	106.34 W
Gravelines	50	50.59 N	2.07 E
Gravellona-Toce	58	45.55 N	8.26 E
Gravell Point ›	176	67.10 N	76.43 W
Gravelly Bay c	284a	42.52 N	79.15 W
Gravelly Brook ≃	276	40.25 N	74.13 W
Gravelly Pond ⊜	283	42.36 N	70.48 W
Gravelotte, Fr.	56	49.07 N	6.01 E
Gravelotte, S. Afr.	156	23.56 S	30.34 E
Gravenhurst	212	44.55 N	79.22 W
Grävenwiesbach	56	50.23 N	8.27 E
Grave Peak ∧	202	46.24 N	114.44 W
Gravesend, Austl.	166	29.35 S	150.19 E
Gravesend, Eng., U.K.	42	51.27 N	0.24 E
Gravesend Bay c	276	40.36 N	74.01 W
Gravesham □[8]	260	51.25 N	0.24 E
Gravette	194	36.25 N	94.27 W
Gravigny	50	49.03 N	1.10 E
Gravina	70	37.34 N	15.03 E
Gravina di Matera ≃	68	40.29 N	16.43 E
Gravina in Puglia	68	40.49 N	16.25 E
Gravina Island I	182	55.17 N	131.45 W
Gray, Fr.	58	47.27 N	5.35 E
Gray, Ga., U.S.	192	33.00 N	83.32 W
Gray, Ky., U.S.	192	36.56 N	84.00 W
Gray, Pa., U.S.	214	40.08 N	79.05 W
Grayback Mountain ∧, Ak., U.S.	180	57.08 N	153.54 W
Grayback Mountain ∧, Or., U.S.	202	42.07 N	123.18 W
Grayland	224	46.48 N	124.05 W
Grayling, Ak., U.S.	180	62.57 N	160.03 W
Grayling, Mi., U.S.	190	44.39 N	84.42 W
Graylyn Crest	285	39.48 N	75.31 W
Grays	42	51.29 N	0.20 E
Grays ≃	224	46.18 N	123.41 W
Grays Harbor □[6]	224	47.09 N	123.45 W
Grays Harbor c	224	46.56 N	124.05 W
Grayshott	42	51.11 N	0.45 W
Grayslake	216	42.21 N	88.03 W
Grays Lake ⊜	278	42.21 N	88.03 W
Grays Lake ≡	202	43.04 N	111.26 W
Grays Lake Outlet ≃	202	43.22 N	111.46 W
Grayson, Sk., Can.	184	50.44 N	102.40 W
Grayson, Al., U.S.	194	34.16 N	87.19 W
Grayson, Ca., U.S.	226	37.33 N	121.10 W
Grayson, Ky., U.S.	218	38.19 N	82.56 W
Grayson, La., U.S.	194	32.02 N	92.06 W
Grayson Lake ⊜[1]	218	38.13 N	83.00 W
Grayson Lake State Park ♠	218	38.13 N	83.02 W
Grays Peak ∧	200	39.37 N	105.45 W
Grays Point	274a	34.04 S	151.05 E
Grays River	224	46.21 N	123.36 W
Gray Summit	219	38.29 N	90.49 W
Graysville	194	35.26 N	85.05 W
Graytown	214	41.33 N	83.16 W
Grayville	194	37.57 N	88.10 W
Gray Wolf ≃	224	47.55 N	123.07 W
Graz	61	47.05 N	15.27 E
Grazalema	34	36.46 N	5.22 W
Graždanka ⬥[8]	265a	60.00 N	30.24 E
Gr'azeva ≃	265b	55.51 N	37.08 E
Gr'azi	80	52.29 N	39.57 E
Grazierville	214	40.40 N	78.16 W
Gr'aznoje	82	54.02 N	39.07 E
Gr'aznovo, Ross.	82	54.18 N	36.49 E
Gr'aznovo, Ross.	265b	55.57 N	37.34 E
Gr'aznyj Irtek	80	51.56 N	53.11 E
Gr'azovec	76	58.53 N	40.14 E
Grdelica	38	42.54 N	22.04 E
Greåker	26	59.16 N	11.02 E
Greasby	262	53.23 N	3.07 W
Great ≃	241k	12.08 N	61.36 W
Great Adventure ♠	208	40.09 N	74.27 W
Great Altcar	262	53.33 N	3.01 W
Great America ♠	282	37.24 N	121.59 W
Great Amwell	260	51.48 N	0.01 W
Great Artesian Basin ≚[1]	166	25.00 S	143.00 E
Great Australian Bight c[3]	162	35.00 S	130.00 E
Great Ayton	44	54.30 N	1.08 W
Great Baddow	42	51.43 N	0.29 E
Great Bahama Bank ✢[4]	238	23.15 N	78.00 W
Great Barford	42	52.09 N	0.21 W
Great Barrier Island I	172	36.10 S	175.25 E
Great Barrier Reef ✢[2]	160	18.00 S	146.50 E
Great Barrier Reef Marine Park ♠	166	21.00 S	151.00 E
Great Barrington	207	42.11 N	73.21 W
Great Barrow	262	53.12 N	2.48 W
Great Basin ≚[1]	178	40.00 N	117.00 W
Great Basin National Park ♠	204	38.55 N	114.14 W
Great Bay c	208	39.30 N	74.23 W
Great Bear ≃	180	64.54 N	125.35 W
Great Bear Lake ⊜	176	66.00 N	120.00 W
Great Beaver Lake ⊜	182	54.25 N	123.45 W
Great Belt → Storebælt ʮ	41	55.30 N	11.00 E
Great Bend, Ks., U.S.	198	38.21 N	98.45 W
Great Bend, N.Y., U.S.	212	44.02 N	75.43 W
Great Bend, Pa., U.S.	210	41.58 N	75.44 W
Great Bernera I	46	58.13 N	6.49 W
Great Bitter Lake → Murrah al-Kubrā, Al-Buḥayrah al- ⊜	142	30.20 N	32.23 E
Great Blasket Island I	48	52.05 N	10.32 W
Great Blue Hill ∧[2]	207	42.13 N	71.07 W
Great Bookham	260	51.16 N	0.22 W
Great Braxted	260	51.48 N	0.42 E
Great Brewster Island I	283	42.20 N	70.53 W
Great Britain I	22	54.00 N	2.00 W
Great Brook ≃	276	40.42 N	74.31 W
Great Buddha ʊ[1]	268	35.19 N	139.32 E
Great Budworth	262	53.18 N	2.30 W
Great Burnt Lake ⊜	186	48.20 N	56.13 W
Great Burstead	260	51.36 N	0.25 E
Great Camanoe I	240m	18.29 N	64.32 W
Great Captain Island I	276	40.59 N	73.38 W
Great Central	182	49.19 N	124.59 W
Great Central Lake ⊜	182	49.27 N	125.12 W
Great Channel ʮ	110	6.25 N	94.20 E
Great Chazy ≃	188	44.56 N	73.23 W
Great Clifton	44	54.39 N	3.29 W
Great Coco Island I	110	14.05 N	93.24 E
Great Coharie Creek ≃	192	34.50 N	78.22 W
Great Cove c	276	40.43 N	73.14 W
Great Crosby	262	53.29 N	3.01 W
Great Crossing	218	38.08 N	84.38 W
Great Cumbrae Island I	46	55.46 N	4.55 W
Great Dismal Swamp ≡	192	36.30 N	76.30 W
Great Ditch ≍	276	40.24 N	74.31 W

Great Divide Basin ≚[1]	202	42.00 N	108.10 W
Great Dividing Range ⋀	160	25.00 S	147.00 E
Great Driffield	44	54.00 N	0.27 W
Great Duck Island I	190	45.40 N	82.58 W
Great Dunmow	42	51.53 N	0.22 E
Great Eau ≃	44	53.25 N	0.13 E
Great Egg Harbor ≃	208	39.18 N	74.40 W
Great Egg Harbor Bay c	208	39.18 N	74.37 W
Great Egg Harbor Inlet c	208	39.20 N	74.34 W
Greater Antilles II	238	20.00 N	74.00 W
Greater Buffalo International Airport ⊠	210	42.56 N	78.44 W
Greater Cincinnati Airport ⊠	218	39.03 N	84.40 W
Greater Khingan Range → Da Hinggan Ling ⋀	90	49.00 N	122.00 E
Greater London □[6]	42	51.30 N	0.10 W
Greater Manchester □[6]	44	53.30 N	2.20 W
Greater Pittsburgh International Airport ⊠	214	40.29 N	80.14 W
Greater Sunda Islands II	108	2.00 S	110.00 E
Greater Wilmington Airport ⊠	208	39.41 N	75.36 W
Greater Wollongong → Wollongong	170	34.25 S	150.54 E
Great Escape ♠	210	43.22 N	73.42 W
Great Exuma I	238	23.32 N	75.50 W
Great Falls, Mb., Can.	184	50.27 N	96.02 W
Great Falls, Mt., U.S.	202	47.30 N	111.17 W
Great Falls, S.C., U.S.	192	34.34 N	80.54 W
Great Falls, Va., U.S.	284c	39.00 N	77.17 W
Great Falls ⌊	284c	39.00 N	77.16 W
Great Falls Park ♠	284c	39.00 N	77.15 W
Great Fish Point ›	158	33.30 S	27.10 E
Great Gable ∧	44	54.28 N	3.12 W
Great Gaddesden	260	51.47 N	0.30 W
Great Grimsby → Grimsby	44	53.35 N	0.05 W
Great Guana Cay I	238	24.00 N	76.20 W
Great Hameldon ∧[2]	262	53.45 N	2.19 W
Great Harwood	44	53.48 N	2.24 W
Great Haywood	42	52.48 N	2.00 W
Great Himalaya Range ⋀	120	29.00 N	83.00 E
Greathouse Peak ∧	202	46.46 N	109.21 W
Great Inagua I	238	21.05 N	73.18 W
Great Indian Desert (Thar Desert) ⬥[2]	120	27.00 N	71.00 E
Great Island I, Ire.	48	51.52 N	8.17 W
Great Island I, N.Y., U.S.	276	40.38 N	73.30 W
Great Island I, N.Y., U.S.	276	41.05 N	73.44 W
Great Karroo (Groot Karroo) ⋀[1]	158	32.25 S	22.40 E
Great Kills ⬥[8]	276	40.33 N	74.10 W
Great Kills Harbor c	276	40.32 N	74.08 W
Great Kills Park ♠	276	40.33 N	74.08 W
Great La Cloche Island I	190	46.01 N	81.52 W
Great Lake ⊜	166	41.52 S	146.45 E
Great Lakes Naval Training Center ■	216	42.18 N	87.50 W
Great Lakes Steel Works ʊ[3]	281	42.15 N	83.08 W
Great Machipongo Inlet c	208	37.22 N	75.43 W
Great Malvern	42	52.07 N	2.19 W
Great Marsh ≡	208	36.32 N	75.57 W
Great Marton	262	53.48 N	3.02 W
Great Massingham	42	52.46 N	0.40 E
Great Meadows	210	40.52 N	74.54 W
Great Meadows National Wildlife Refuge ⬥[4]	283	42.29 N	71.20 W
Great Mercury Island I	172	36.37 S	175.48 E
Great Meteor Tablemount ✢[3]	18	30.00 N	28.30 W
Great Miami ≃	188	39.06 N	84.49 W
Great Mills	208	38.14 N	76.30 W
Great Misery Island I	283	42.33 N	70.48 W
Great Missenden	42	51.43 N	0.43 W
Great Mis Tor ∧	42	50.34 N	4.01 W
Great Mosque ʊ[1]	146	32.46 N	22.40 E
Great Namaqualand □[9]	156	25.00 S	17.00 E
Great Neck	276	40.48 N	73.43 W
Great Neck ›[1], Ma., U.S.	283	42.42 N	70.48 W
Great Neck ›[1], N.Y., U.S.	276	40.50 N	73.45 W
Great Neck Estates	276	40.47 N	73.44 W
Great Nicobar I	110	7.00 N	93.50 E
Great North East Channel ʮ	164	9.30 S	143.25 E
Great Notch Reservoir ⊜[1]	276	40.53 N	74.12 W
Great Ormes Head ›	44	53.21 N	3.52 W
Great Ouse ≃	42	52.47 N	0.22 E
Great Oxney Green	260	51.44 N	0.25 E
Great Palm Island I	166	18.43 S	146.37 E
Great Parndon	260	51.45 N	0.05 E
Great Patchogue Lake ⊜	276	40.46 N	73.01 W
Great Peconic Bay c	207	40.56 N	72.30 W
Great Pee Dee ≃	192	33.21 N	79.16 W
Great Piece Meadows ≡	276	40.54 N	74.19 W
Great Plain of the Koukdjuak ≚	176	66.00 N	73.00 W
Great Plains ≚	16	42.00 N	100.00 W
Great Point ›	207	41.23 N	70.03 W
Great Pubnico Lake ⊜	186	43.42 N	65.43 W
Great Quittacas Pond ⊜	207	41.48 N	70.54 W
Great River	276	40.45 N	73.10 W
Great Ruaha ≃	154	7.56 S	37.52 E
Great Sacandaga Lake ⊜	210	43.08 N	74.10 W
Great Saint Bernard Pass → Grand-Saint-Bernard, Col du)(	58	45.50 N	7.10 E
Great Sale Cay I	192	27.00 N	78.12 W
Great Salt Lake ⊜	200	41.10 N	112.30 W
Great Salt Lake Desert ⬥[2]	200	40.40 N	113.30 W
Great Salt Plains Lake ⊜[1]	196	36.44 N	98.12 W
Great Sand Dunes National Monument ♠	200	37.43 N	105.36 W
Great Sand Hills ⋀[2]	184	50.35 N	109.05 W
Great Sandy Desert ⬥[2]	162	21.30 S	125.00 E
Great Sandy National Park ♠	166	24.59 S	153.17 E
Great Sankey	44	53.23 N	2.37 W
Great Santa Cruz Island I	116	6.52 N	122.03 E
Great Scarcies (Kolenté) ≃	150	8.55 N	13.08 W
Great Sea Reef ✢[2]	175g	16.15 S	179.00 E
Great Seneca Creek ≃	208	39.08 N	77.20 W
Great Shelford	42	52.09 N	0.09 E

≃ River	Fluß	Río	Rivière	Rio	✢ Submarine Features	Untermeerische Objekte	Accidentes Submarinos	Formes de relief sous-marin	Acidentes submarinos
≍ Canal	Kanal	Canal	Canal	Canal	□ Political Unit	Politische Einheit	Unidad Politica	Entité politique	Unidade política
⌊ Waterfall, Rapids	Wasserfall, Stromschnellen	Cascada, Rápidos	Chute d'eau, Rapides	Cascata, Rápidos	ʊ Cultural Institution	Kulturelle Institution	Institución Cultural	Institution culturelle	Instituição cultural
ʮ Strait	Meeresstraße	Estrecho	Détroit	Estreito	⊥ Historical Site	Historische Stätte	Sitio Histórico	Site historique	Sitio histórico
c Bay, Gulf	Bucht, Golf	Bahía, Golfo	Baie, Golfe	Baía, Golfo	♠ Recreational Site	Erholungs- und Ferienort	Sitio de Recreo	Centre de loisirs	Area de Lazer
⊜ Lake, Lakes	See, Seen	Lago, Lagos	Lac, Lacs	Lago, Lagos	⊠ Airport	Flughafen	Aeropuerto	Aéroport	Aeroporto
≡ Swamp	Sumpf	Pantano	Marais	Pântano	■ Military Installation	Militäranlage	Instalación Militar	Installation militaire	Instalação militar
⊠ Ice Features, Glacier	Eis- und Gletscherformen	Accidentes Glaciales	Formes glaciaires	Acidentes glaciares	⬥ Miscellaneous	Verschiedenes	Misceláneo	Divers	Diversos
⊤ Other Hydrographic Features	Andere Hydrographische Objekte	Otros Elementos Hidrográficos	Autres données hydrographiques	Outros acidentes hidrográficos					

ENGLISH				DEUTSCH			
Name	Page	Lat.°ᴵ	Long.°ᴵ	Name	Seite	Breite°ᴵ	Länge°ᴵ E=Ost

Great Sitkin Island ⅼ 180 52.03 N 176.07 W
Great Slave Lake ⌀ 176 61.30 N 114.00 W
Great Smoky Mountains ⋏ 192 35.35 N 83.30 W
Great Smoky Mountains National Park ♦ 192 35.39 N 83.30 W
Great Sound ᴹ, Ber. 240a 32.17 N 64.51 W
Great Sound ᴹ, N.J., U.S. 208 39.06 N 74.47 W
Great South Bay ᴄ 210 40.40 N 73.17 W
Great Stour ≃ 42 51.19 N 1.15 E
Great Sutton 262 53.17 N 2.56 W
Great Swamp ≃ 276 40.43 N 74.28 W
Great Swamp National Wildlife Refuge ♦⁴ 276 40.43 N 74.28 W
Great Tenasserim ≃ 110 12.24 N 98.37 E
Great Tobago ⅼ 240m 18.27 N 64.48 W
Great Torrington 42 50.57 N 4.08 W
Great Totham 260 51.47 N 0.43 E
Great Usutu (Maputo) (Lusutfu) ≃ 158 26.11 S 32.42 E
Great Valley 210 42.13 N 78.38 W
Great Victoria Desert ◦² 162 28.30 S 127.45 E
Great Wall ʋ³ 9 62.13 S 58.58 W
— Chang Cheng ⅼ 98 40.30 N 116.32 E
Great Waltham 260 51.48 N 0.28 E
Great Warley 260 51.35 N 0.17 E
Great Western Forum ♦ 280 33.57 N 118.20 W
Great Whernside ⋏ 44 54.09 N 1.59 W
Great Wicomico ≃ 208 37.48 N 76.18 W
Great Wyrley 42 52.41 N 2.01 W
Great Yarmouth 42 52.37 N 1.44 E
Great Zab (Büyükzap) (Az-Zāb al-Kabīr) ≃ 128 36.00 N 43.21 E
Great Zimbabwe Ruins National Park ♦ 154 20.17 S 30.57 E
Grebbestad 26 58.42 N 11.15 E
Grebenhain 56 50.29 N 9.19 E
Grebenka 78 50.07 N 32.25 E
Grebenstein 56 51.26 N 9.24 E
Grebnevo 265b 55.58 N 38.05 E
Greb'onki 78 49.57 N 30.12 E
Grèboun ⋏ 150 20.00 N 8.35 E
Grèce
— Greece ◦¹ 38 39.00 N 22.00 E
Grecia 236 10.05 N 84.18 W
Grecia
— Greece ◦¹ 38 39.00 N 22.00 E
Grečíkino 83 48.52 N 38.54 E
Grecken ⌀ 40 59.35 N 14.44 E
Greco 252 32.48 S 57.03 W
Greco ◦⁸ 266b 45.30 N 9.13 E
Greco, Monte ⋏ 66 41.48 N 14.00 E
Greco Island ♦ 284 37.31 N 122.11 W
Greding 60 49.03 N 11.21 E
Gredos, Sierra de ⋏ 34 40.18 N 5.05 W
Gredstedbro 41 55.24 N 8.45 E
Greece 210 43.12 N 77.41 W
Greece (Ellás) ◦¹, Europe 22 39.00 N 22.00 E
Greece (Ellás) ◦¹, Europe 38 39.00 N 22.00 E
Greeley, Co., U.S. 200 40.25 N 104.42 W
Greeley, Ks., U.S. 198 38.19 N 95.26 W
Greeley, Ne., U.S. 198 41.33 N 98.32 W
Greeley, Pa., U.S. 210 41.25 N 75.00 W
Greeleyville 192 33.34 N 79.59 W
Green ◦⁶ 194 22.48 N 89.25 W
Green ≃, N.B., Can. 198 47.18 N 68.09 W
Green ≃, U.S. 200 38.11 N 109.53 W
Green ≃, U.S. 192 42.35 N 73.36 W
Green ≃, U.S. 207 42.10 N 73.22 W
Green ≃, II., U.S. 190 41.28 N 90.23 W
Green ≃, II., U.S. 216 41.46 N 89.10 W
Green ≃, Ky., U.S. 194 37.55 N 87.30 W
Green ≃, N.D., U.S. 198 46.52 N 102.35 W
Green ≃, Ut., U.S. 210 43.06 N 73.19 W
Green ≃, Wa., U.S. 224 47.33 N 122.20 W
Green ≃, Wa., U.S. 224 46.20 N 123.00 W
Greenacres, Ca., U.S. 226 35.23 N 119.07 W
Green Acres, De., U.S. 285 39.47 N 75.30 W
Greenacres, Wa., U.S. 224 47.39 N 117.06 W
Green Acres ♦⁹ 276 40.40 N 73.43 W
Greenacres City 220 26.37 N 80.07 W
Greenbackville 208 38.00 N 75.23 W
Greenbank 214 48.06 N 122.34 W
Green Bay 190 44.31 N 88.01 W
Green Bay ᴄ, Nf., Can. 186 49.43 N 55.58 W
Green Bay ᴄ, On., Can. 212 44.38 N 76.36 W
Green Bay ᴄ, U.S. 190 45.00 N 87.30 W
Greenbelt 284c 39.00 N 76.52 W
Greenbelt Park ♦ 284c 38.59 N 76.54 W
Greenbo Lake ⌀ 208 38.29 N 82.54 W
Greenbo Lake State Resort Park ♦ 218 38.29 N 82.54 W
Greenbooth Reservoir ⌀¹ 262 53.38 N 2.13 W
Greenbrae 226 37.57 N 122.31 W
Greenbrier, Ar., U.S. 194 35.14 N 92.23 W
Greenbrier, Tn., U.S. 194 36.26 N 86.48 W
Greenbrier ≃ 192 37.49 N 80.53 W
Greenbrier State Park ♦ 208 39.33 N 77.38 W
Green Brook 276 40.36 N 74.27 W
Green Brook ≃ 276 40.33 N 74.32 W
Greenburg 194 30.51 N 90.40 W
Greenbush, Ma., U.S. 207 42.11 N 70.45 W
Greenbush, Mn., U.S. 198 48.42 N 96.10 W
Greenbush, Va., U.S. 208 37.45 N 75.41 W
Greenbushes 162 33.51 S 116.03 E
Green Camp 214 40.31 N 83.12 W
Green Cape ⊳ 166 37.15 S 150.03 E
Greencastle, Ire. 48 55.12 N 6.59 W
Greencastle, In., U.S. 190 39.38 N 86.51 W
Greencastle, Pa., U.S. 188 39.47 N 77.43 W
Green City 190 40.16 N 92.57 W
Green Cove Springs 192 29.59 N 81.40 W
Green Creek 198 39.02 N 74.54 W
Green Creek, Oh., U.S. 214 40.16 N 83.01 W
Green Creek ≃, Pa., U.S. 285 39.53 N 75.28 W
Greencrest Park 214 41.03 N 80.24 W
Greendale, Austl. 274a 33.55 S 150.39 E
Greendale, In., U.S. 218 39.06 N 84.51 W
Greendale, Wi., U.S. 218 42.56 N 87.59 W
Greene, Dtsch. 56 51.52 N 9.56 E
Greene, Ia., U.S. 190 42.53 N 92.48 W
Greene, N.Y., U.S. 210 42.17 N 75.46 W
Greene, R.I., U.S. 207 41.41 N 71.43 W
Greene ◦⁶, II., U.S. 218 39.18 N 90.24 W
Greene ◦⁶, Oh., U.S. 218 40.23 N 73.52 W
Greene ◦⁸ 218 39.41 N 83.56 W
Greenebaum 56 52.32 N 11.06 E
Greenfield, Enq., U.K. 262 53.32 N 2.01 W
Greenfield, Wales, U.K. 42 53.17 N 3.13 W
Greenfield, Ca., U.S. 226 36.19 N 121.14 W
Greenfield, In., U.S. 190 39.47 N 85.46 W
Greenfield, Ia., U.S. 198 41.18 N 94.27 W
Greenfield, Ma., U.S. 207 42.35 N 72.35 W
Greenfield, Mo., U.S. 190 37.24 N 93.50 W
Greenfield, Tn., U.S. 194 36.09 N 88.48 W
Greenfield, Wi., U.S. 218 42.58 N 88.02 W
Greenfield-Park, P.Q., Can. 275a 45.29 N 73.29 W

Greenfield Park, N.Y., U.S. 210 41.44 N 74.29 W
Greenfields Village 285 75.10 N 39.49 W
Greenfield Village ⊥ 281 42.18 N 83.14 W
Greenford ⊗ 260 51.32 N 0.21 W
Green Forest 194 36.20 N 93.26 W
Green Harbor 207 42.04 N 70.39 W
Green Harbor 283 42.05 N 70.39 W
Green Head ⊳ 162 30.05 S 114.58 E
Green Hill 283 39.59 N 75.36 W
Greenhill ◦⁸ 260 51.35 N 0.20 W
Greenhills, S. Afr. 273d 26.10 S 27.40 E
Greenhills, Oh., U.S. 218 39.16 N 84.31 W
Greenhithe 260 51.27 N 0.17 E
Greenhorn Creek ≃ 198 38.08 N 104.38 W
Greenhurst 214 42.07 N 79.19 W
Green Hut Park 276 40.50 N 74.39 W
Green Island, N.Z. 172 45.54 S 170.26 E
Greenland, N. Ire., U.K. 48 54.42 N 5.52 W
Green Island, N.Y., U.S. 210 42.44 N 73.41 W
Green Island Bay ᴄ 116 10.12 N 119.22 E
Green Islands ⅼⅼ 14 4.30 S 154.10 E
Green Knoll 276 40.36 N 74.36 W
Green Lake, Sk., Can. 184 54.17 N 107.47 W
Green Lake, Wi., U.S. 190 43.50 N 88.57 W
Green Lake ⌀, B.C., Can. 182 51.24 N 121.15 W
Green Lake ⌀, Sk., Can. 184 54.10 N 107.43 W
Green Lake ⌀, Mi., U.S. 218 42.55 N 83.25 W
Green Lake ⌀, N.Y., U.S. 284a 42.45 N 76.45 W
Green Lake ⌀, Wi., U.S. 190 43.41 N 88.57 W
Green Lakes State Park ♦ 212 43.03 N 75.58 W
Greenlal (Saint-Grégoire-de-Greenlay) 206 45.34 N 72.01 W
Green Lane 208 40.20 N 75.28 W
Green Lane Reservoir ⌀¹ 208 40.22 N 75.29 W
Greenlaw 46 55.43 N 2.28 W
Greenlawn 276 40.52 N 73.21 W
Greenlawn Park 285 40.07 N 74.51 W
Greenleaf 198 39.43 N 96.58 W
Green Lookout Mountain ⋏ 224 45.52 N 122.08 W
Green Manorville 207 42.00 N 72.32 W
Green Meadows 284c 38.58 N 76.57 W
Greenmount, Austl. 171a 27.47 S 151.54 E
Greenmount, Enq., U.K. 262 53.37 N 2.20 W
Greenmount, Md., U.S. 208 39.37 N 76.51 W
Green Mountains ⋏ 188 43.45 N 72.45 W
Green Oak Lake ⌀ 281 42.27 N 83.43 W
Green Oaks 278 42.18 N 87.55 W
Greenock, Austl. 168b 34.27 S 138.55 E
Greenock, Scot., U.K. 46 55.57 N 4.45 W
Greenock, Pa., U.S. 279b 40.19 N 79.48 W
Greenod 44 54.14 N 3.04 W
Greenore Point ⊳ 48 52.15 N 6.18 W
Greenough 162 28.57 S 114.44 E
Greenough ≃ 162 28.51 S 114.38 E
Greenough, Mount ⋏ 180 69.10 N 141.35 W
Green Park 208 44.28 N 122.30 W
Green Peter Lake ⌀¹ 224 44.28 N 122.30 W
Green Point ⊳ 276 40.43 N 73.06 W
Green Pond, Al., U.S. 194 33.13 N 87.07 W
Green Pond, N.J., U.S. 276 41.01 N 74.29 W
Green Pond ⌀ 276 41.00 N 74.30 W
Green Pond Brook ≃ 276 41.00 N 74.34 W
Greenport 207 41.06 N 72.21 W
Green Ridge 285 39.51 N 75.25 W
Green River, Pap. N. Gui. 164 3.55 S 141.10 E
Green River, Ut., U.S. 200 38.59 N 110.09 W
Green River, Wy., U.S. 200 41.31 N 109.27 W
Green River Lake ⌀¹ 194 37.15 N 85.15 W
Greensboro, Fl., U.S. 194 30.34 N 84.44 W
Greensboro, Md., U.S. 208 33.34 N 81.04 W
Greensboro, N.C., U.S. 192 36.04 N 79.47 W
Greensborough 274b 37.42 S 145.06 E
Greensburg, In., U.S. 218 39.20 N 85.29 W
Greensburg, Ks., U.S. 198 37.36 N 99.17 W
Greensburg, Oh., U.S. 214 40.56 N 81.28 W
Greensburg, Pa., U.S. 214 40.18 N 79.32 W
Greens Farms 276 41.07 N 73.19 W
Greens Fork 218 39.53 N 85.02 W
Greens Fork ≃ 218 39.45 N 85.07 W
Green Tree 279d 26.09 S 28.01 E
Greens Lake ⌀ 222 29.16 N 94.59 W
Greens Peak ⋏ 200 34.07 N 109.35 W
Greenspond 186 49.04 N 53.34 W
Green Springs 214 41.15 N 83.03 W
Greensted 260 51.39 N 0.13 E
Greenstone 298 39.45 N 77.27 W
Greenstone Point ⊳ 46 57.55 N 5.38 W
Green Street 260 51.40 N 0.16 W
Green Street Green 260 51.21 N 0.06 E
Greensville ◦⁶ 208 36.40 N 77.30 W
Green Swamp ⅁, Fl., U.S. 220 28.20 N 81.48 W
Green Swamp ≃, N.C., U.S. 192 34.10 N 78.20 W
Greentown, In., U.S. 216 40.28 N 85.58 W
Greentown, Oh., U.S. 214 40.56 N 81.28 W
Greentown, Pa., U.S. 210 41.19 N 75.18 W
Greenup, Il., U.S. 194 39.14 N 88.09 W
Greenup, Ky., U.S. 218 38.34 N 82.49 W
Greenup ◦⁶ 218 38.39 N 82.52 W
Greenup Dam ⊹ 218 38.39 N 82.52 W
Greenvale, Austl. 166 18.59 S 145.07 E
Greenvale, N.Y., U.S. 276 40.49 N 73.38 W
Green Valley, Austl. 274a 45.16 N 74.36 W
Green Valley, Az., U.S. 200 31.52 N 110.59 W
Green Valley, Il., U.S. 190 40.24 N 89.38 W
Green Valley Creek ≃ 226 38.13 N 122.08 W
Greenview, Ill., U.S. 190 40.05 N 89.44 W
Green Village, N.J., U.S. 276 40.44 N 74.27 W
Greenvillage, Pa., U.S. 188 40.00 N 77.36 W
Greenville, Al., U.S. 194 31.49 N 86.37 W
Greenville, Ca., U.S. 226 40.08 N 120.57 W

Greenville, Fl., U.S. 192 30.28 N 83.37 W
Greenville, Ga., U.S. 192 33.01 N 84.42 W
Greenville, Il., U.S. 219 38.53 N 89.24 W
Greenville, In., U.S. 218 38.22 N 85.59 W
Greenville, Ky., U.S. 194 37.12 N 87.10 W
Greenville, Me., U.S. 188 45.28 N 69.35 W
Greenville, Mi., U.S. 190 43.10 N 85.15 W
Greenville, Ms., U.S. 194 33.24 N 91.03 W
Greenville, Mo., U.S. 194 37.08 N 90.27 W
Greenville, N.H., U.S. 207 42.46 N 71.48 W
Greenville, N.Y., U.S. 210 40.59 N 73.49 W
Greenville, N.Y., U.S. 276 40.59 N 73.49 W
Greenville, N.C., U.S. 192 35.36 N 77.22 W
Greenville, Oh., U.S. 218 40.06 N 84.37 W
Greenville, Pa., U.S. 214 41.24 N 80.23 W
Greenville, R.I., U.S. 207 41.52 N 71.33 W
Greenville, S.C., U.S. 192 34.51 N 82.23 W
Greenville, Tx., U.S. 222 33.08 N 96.06 W
Greenville Creek ≃ 218 40.07 N 84.22 W
Greenville Place 285 39.46 N 75.36 W
Greenwater 224 47.09 N 121.39 W
Greenwater Lake ⌀ 190 48.34 N 91.20 W
Greenwater Lake Provincial Park ♦ 184 52.33 N 103.33 W
Greenwell Point 170 34.55 S 150.44 E
Greenwich, Austl. 274a 33.50 S 151.11 E
Greenwich, Ct., U.S. 207 41.01 N 73.37 W
Greenwich, N.J., U.S. 208 39.23 N 75.20 W
Greenwich, N.Y., U.S. 210 43.05 N 73.29 W
Greenwich, Oh., U.S. 214 41.01 N 82.30 W
Greenwich ◦⁴ 42 51.28 N 0.02 E
Greenwich Cove ᴄ 276 41.01 N 73.36 W
Greenwich Creek ≃ 276 41.02 N 73.37 W
Greenwich Observatory ♦ 260 51.28 N 0.00
Greenwich Point ⊳ 276 41.00 N 73.34 W
Greenwich Village ♦⁸ 276 40.44 N 74.00 W
Greenwood, B.C., Can. 182 49.05 N 118.41 W
Greenwood, Ar., U.S. 194 35.12 N 94.15 W
Greenwood, Ca., U.S. 226 38.54 N 120.55 W
Greenwood, De., U.S. 208 38.48 N 75.35 W
Greenwood, In., U.S. 218 39.36 N 86.06 W
Greenwood, Ma., U.S. 283 42.29 N 71.04 W
Greenwood, Ms., U.S. 194 33.30 N 90.10 W
Greenwood, Ne., U.S. 198 40.57 N 96.26 W
Greenwood, N.Y., U.S. 210 42.08 N 77.38 W
Greenwood, Pa., U.S. 214 40.32 N 78.21 W
Greenwood, S.C. 192 34.11 N 82.09 W
Greenwood, Wi., U.S. 190 44.46 N 90.35 W
Greenwood, Lake ⌀ 192 34.15 N 82.00 W
Greenwood Cemetery ♦ 276 40.39 N 73.59 W
Greenwood Lake 210 41.13 N 74.17 W
Greenwood Lake ⌀, U.S. 210 41.14 N 74.19 W
Greenwood Lake ⌀, Ma., U.S. 283 42.00 N 71.17 W
Greenwood Race Track ♦ 275b 43.39 N 79.19 W
Greer, Oh., U.S. 214 40.31 N 82.13 W
Greer, S.C., U.S. 192 34.56 N 82.13 W
Greers Ferry Lake ⌀¹ 194 35.30 N 92.10 W
Greerton 172 37.43 S 176.08 E
Grées, Alpes (Alpi Graie) ⋏ 62 45.31 N 7.10 E
Greeson, Lake ⌀¹ 194 34.10 N 93.45 W
Greetland 44 53.03 N 0.53 W
Greetland 48 53.03 N 1.52 W
Greetsiel 52 53.41 N 7.05 E
Greffiers 261 48.37 N 1.51 E
Grefrath, Dtsch. 56 51.20 N 6.20 E
Grefrath, Dtsch. 263 51.10 N 6.38 E
Gregadoo 171b 35.14 S 147.27 E
Gregg 150 8.48 N 6.43 W
Gregg 279b 40.24 N 80.10 W
Gregg ≃ 222 32.30 N 94.50 W
Greggio 62 45.27 N 8.23 E
Greg Greg 171b 36.03 S 148.02 E
Gregoire Lake Indian Reserve ♦⁴ 184 56.28 N 111.10 W
Gregório ≃ 248 6.50 S 70.46 W
Gregory, Mi., U.S. 216 42.27 N 84.05 W
Gregory, S.D., U.S. 198 43.13 N 99.25 W
Gregory, Tx., U.S. 196 27.55 N 97.17 W
Gregory ≃ 166 17.53 S 139.17 E
Gregory, Lake ⌀, Austl. 162 20.10 S 127.20 E
Gregory, Lake ⌀, Austl. 162 25.38 S 119.58 E
Gregory, Lake ⌀, Austl. 166 28.55 S 139.00 E
Gregory National Park ♦ 164 16.30 S 130.30 E
Gregory Range ⋏ 166 19.00 S 143.05 E
Grégy-sur-Yerre 261 48.40 N 2.37 E
Greifenburg 54 46.45 N 13.11 E
Greifendorf 54 51.01 N 13.06 E
Greifensee 58 47.22 N 8.41 E
Greifensee ⌀ 58 47.21 N 8.41 E
Greifenstein 264b 48.11 N 16.15 E
Greiffenberg 54 53.05 N 13.58 E
Greifenhagen 263 51.20 N 6.38 E
Greifswald 54 54.05 N 13.23 E
Greifswalder Bodden ᴄ 54 54.15 N 13.35 E
Greifswalder Oie ⅼ 54 54.14 N 13.55 E
Grein 61 48.14 N 14.09 E
Greiz 54 50.39 N 12.12 E
Grejdermoje 80 46.53 N 45.01 E
Grejsdal 41 55.45 N 9.32 E
Grekov 80 47.24 N 43.41 E
Grekovo 83 48.58 N 40.14 E
Grem'ačevo 82 54.14 N 36.15 E
Grem'ačij 88 57.01 N 108.12 E
Grem'ačinsk, Ross. 88 52.48 N 107.57 E
Grem'ačinsk, Ross. 78 58.34 N 57.51 E
Grem'ačje 78 52.19 N 39.00 E
Gremersdorf 54 54.18 N 11.02 E
Gremicha 24 68.03 N 39.27 E
Grenå 41 56.25 N 10.53 E
Grenada 194 33.46 N 89.48 W
Grenada ◦¹, N.A. 230 12.07 N 61.40 W
Grenada Lake ⌀ 194 33.50 N 89.40 W
Grenada ◦¹, N.A. 241k 12.07 N 61.40 W
— Grenada ◦¹ 241k 12.07 N 61.40 W
Grenadier Island ⅼ 212 44.12 N 76.22 W
Grenadier Pond 275b 43.38 N 79.28 W
Grenadines ⅼⅼ 238 12.40 N 61.15 W
Grenagh 48 52.00 N 8.37 W
Grenay 50 50.27 N 2.44 E
Grenchen 58 47.11 N 7.24 E
Grenell 212 44.16 N 76.04 W
Grenfell, Austl. 166 33.54 S 148.10 E
Grenfell, Sk., Can. 184 50.25 N 102.56 W
Grenô 78 59.47 N 75.03 W
Grenoble 62 45.10 N 5.43 E
Grenora 198 37.20 N 96.27 W
Grenville, Gren. 241k 12.07 N 61.37 W
Grenville, Cape ⊳ 166 11.58 S 143.14 E
Grenville Bay 206 45.38 N 74.36 W
Grenville Channel ᴹ 182 53.40 N 129.40 W
Grenzau ≃ 52 52.59 N 6.45 E
Grenz-Berge ⋏² 264 52.27 N 13.41 E
Grenzlandring ⊥ 56 51.11 N 6.17 E
Grenzland ♦ 54 53.47 N 13.47 E

Gréoux-les-Bains 62 43.45 N 5.53 E
Greppin 54 51.39 N 12.18 E
Gresenhorst 54 54.09 N 12.26 E
Gresham 224 45.29 N 122.25 W
Gresham Park 192 33.42 N 84.19 W
Gresik, Indon. 112 2.18 S 103.57 E
Gresik, Indon. 115a 7.09 S 112.38 E
Gressåmoen Nasjonalpark ♦ 26 64.15 N 13.08 E
Gresse-en-Vercors 261 48.50 N 5.34 E
Gressey 261 48.50 N 1.37 E
Gressitt 208 37.29 N 76.43 W
Gresk 261 51.13 N 27.29 E
Gressoney, Val di ◡ 62 45.47 N 7.49 E
Gressoney-la-Trinité 62 45.50 N 7.49 E
Gressoney-Saint-Jean 62 45.47 N 7.49 E
Gressy 261 48.58 N 2.41 E
Gresten 61 48.00 N 15.02 E
Grésy-sur-Aix 62 45.43 N 5.55 E
Grésy-sur-Isère 62 45.36 N 6.15 E
Greta 170 32.41 S 151.24 E
Greta ≃, Eng., U.K. 44 54.09 N 2.36 W
Greta ≃, Eng., U.K. 44 54.32 N 1.53 W
Greta ≃, Eng., U.K. 44 54.36 N 3.10 W
Gretna, Scot., U.K. 44 55.00 N 3.04 W
Gretna, Mb., Can. 184 49.02 N 97.35 W
Gretna, La., U.S. 194 29.54 N 90.03 W
Gretna, Va., U.S. 192 36.57 N 79.21 W
Gretz-Armainvilliers 50 48.44 N 2.44 E
Greussen 54 51.14 N 10.57 E
Greve, Dan. 41 55.36 N 12.15 E
Greve, It. 66 43.35 N 11.19 E
Greve ≃ 263 51.34 N 7.33 E
Grevelingen ᴹ 52 51.45 N 4.00 E
Grevelingendam ⊹⁵ 52 51.40 N 4.10 E
Greven 52 52.05 N 7.36 E
Grevená 38 40.05 N 21.25 E
Grevenbroich 56 51.05 N 6.35 E
Greven-Granzin 54 53.29 N 10.48 E
Grevenmachen 56 49.42 N 6.20 E
Grevesmühlen 54 53.51 N 11.10 E
Greve Strand 41 55.35 N 12.14 E
Greville Bay ᴄ 186 45.22 N 64.38 W
Grevinge 41 55.48 N 11.34 E
Grey ≃, Nf., Can. 186 47.38 N 57.05 W
Grey ≃, N.Z. 172 42.57 S 171.12 E
Grey, Cape ⊳ 164 13.00 S 136.40 E
Grey, Point ⊳, Austl. 169 38.34 S 143.59 E
Grey, Point ⊳, B.C., Can. 224 49.16 N 123.16 W
Greyabbey 48 54.32 N 5.33 W
Greybull 198 44.29 N 108.03 W
Greybull ≃ 198 44.28 N 108.03 W
Grey Eagle 190 45.49 N 94.45 W
Grey Islands ⅼⅼ 186 50.50 N 55.37 W
Greylingstad 158 26.44 S 28.45 E
Greylock, Mount ⋏ 207 42.38 N 73.10 W
Greymouth 172 42.28 S 171.12 E
Grey Range ⋏ 166 27.00 S 143.35 E
Grey River 186 47.35 N 57.06 W
Greystanes 274a 33.49 S 150.55 E
Greystoke 44 54.40 N 2.52 W
Greystones 48 53.09 N 6.04 W
Greyton 158 34.04 S 19.38 E
Greytown, N.Z. 172 41.05 S 175.27 E
Greytown
— San Juan del Norte, Nic. 236 10.55 N 83.42 W
Greytown, S. Afr. 158 29.07 S 30.30 E
Grez-Doiceau 52 50.44 N 4.42 E
Grez-sur-Loing 50 48.19 N 2.42 E
Grezzana 62 45.31 N 11.01 E
Gribanovskij 80 51.27 N 41.58 E
Gribbel Island ⅼ 182 53.25 N 129.00 W
Gribbin Head ⊳ 42 50.19 N 4.40 W
Gribingui ≃ 152 7.00 N 19.15 E
Gribingui-Bamingui, Réserve de Faune du ♦⁴ 146 8.00 N 19.10 E
Gribova 30 50.12 N 22.32 E
Gricev 92 49.58 N 27.14 E
Gridley, Ca., U.S. 226 39.21 N 121.41 W
Gridley, Il., U.S. 216 40.44 N 88.52 W
Griebnitz See ⌀ 264a 52.24 N 13.06 E
Griechenland
— Greece ◦¹ 38 39.00 N 22.00 E
Griekwastad 158 28.49 S 23.15 E
Grier City 210 40.50 N 76.04 W
Gries am Brenner 60 47.03 N 11.29 E
Griesbach im Rottal 60 48.28 N 13.11 E
Griesen 64 47.29 N 10.56 E
Griesheim 56 49.52 N 8.34 E
Gries im Sellrain 60 48.14 N 13.50 E
Grieskirchen 60 48.14 N 13.50 E
Griesspitzen ⋏ 54 52.00 N 9.12 E
Griffin 278 46.42 N 144.44 E
Griffin, Sk., Can. 184 49.40 N 103.26 W
Griffin, Ga., U.S. 192 33.14 N 84.15 W
Griffin, Lake ⌀ 220 28.52 N 81.51 W
Griffin Bay ᴄ 224 48.30 N 122.58 W
Griffiss Air Force Base ♦ 210 43.14 N 75.26 W
Griffith, Austl. 168 34.17 S 146.03 E
Griffith, In., U.S. 216 41.32 N 87.25 W
Griffith Airport ♦ 278 41.31 N 87.23 W
Griffith Island ⅼ, N.T., Can. 178 74.35 N 95.30 W
Griffith Island ⅼ, On., Can. 212 44.51 N 80.54 W
Griffith Park ♦ 280 34.09 N 118.17 W
Grifton 192 35.22 N 77.26 W
Griggs Drain ≃ 281 42.21 N 83.26 W
Griggs Reservoir ⌀¹ 214 40.03 N 83.06 W
Griggsville 216 39.42 N 90.43 W
Grignan 62 44.25 N 4.54 E
Grignasco 62 45.42 N 13.43 E
Grignols 62 44.46 N 0.03 E
Grigny, Fr. 261 48.42 N 1.27 E
Grigny, Fr. 261 48.40 N 2.24 E
Grigoriopol' 92 47.10 N 29.18 E
Grigorjevka, Kyrg. 88 42.43 N 77.10 E
Grigorjevka, Ross. 83 47.25 N 40.04 E
Grigorjevka, Ross. 82 54.49 N 37.59 E
Grigorjevskoje, Ross. 82 55.43 N 38.19 E
Grigorovka, Ross. 82 54.13 N 36.20 E
Grigorovka, Ukr. 93 50.03 N 30.39 E
Grigorovka, Ukr. 92 50.13 N 31.10 E
Grijalva ≃, Méx. 232 18.36 N 92.39 W
Grijalva (Guico) ≃ 232 17.01 N 93.22 W
Grijota 34 42.05 N 4.26 W
Grillby 41 59.37 N 17.16 E
Grillenburg 54 50.58 N 13.31 E
Grim, Cape ⊳ 166 40.41 S 144.41 E
Grimaila 31 54.44 N 25.08 E
Grimaldi 68 39.00 N 16.14 E
Grimaud 62 43.16 N 6.31 E
Grimeford Village 262 53.36 N 2.34 W
Grimes, Col. 62 50.56 N 4.25 E
Grimingham 263 51.50 N 6.50 E
Grimma 54 51.14 N 12.43 E
Grimmen 54 54.07 N 13.03 E
Grimmenstein 61 47.34 N 16.06 E
Grimmialp 58 46.34 N 7.29 E
Grimsby, On., Can. 212 43.12 N 79.34 W
Grimsby, Eng., U.K. 44 53.35 N 0.05 W
Grimselpass ⏆ 58 46.34 N 8.21 E
Grimselsee ⌀ 58 46.34 N 8.18 E
Grimsey ⅼ 24a 66.34 N 18.00 W
Grimshaw 182 56.11 N 117.36 W
Grimstad 26 58.20 N 8.36 E
Grimstad 208 37.30 N 76.18 W
Grímsvötn ⋏ 24a 64.24 N 17.22 W
Grindavík 24a 63.52 N 22.27 W
Grindelwald 58 46.37 N 8.02 E
Grindsted 41 55.45 N 8.56 E
Grindstone Island
— Cap-aux-Meules 186 47.23 N 61.52 W
Grindstone Island ⅼ 212 44.16 N 76.07 W
Grinnell 190 41.44 N 92.43 W
Grinnell, Lake ⌀ 276 41.06 N 74.38 W
Grinnell Peninsula ⊳¹ 176 76.40 N 95.00 W
Grin'ovo 78 76.40 N 33.04 E
Grintavec ⋏ 61 46.21 N 14.32 E
Grinzing ◦⁸ 264b 48.15 N 16.21 E
Grip 26 63.14 N 7.37 E
Gripsholm slott ⅼ 40 59.15 N 17.13 E
Gripsholmsviken ᴄ 40 59.17 N 17.20 E
Griqualand East ◦⁹ 158 30.30 S 29.00 E
Griqualand West ◦⁹ 158 28.20 S 23.30 E
Grisdale 224 47.22 N 123.37 W
Grisee 64 55.56 N 12.15 E
— Gresik 115a 7.09 S 112.38 E
Grišino 82 56.13 N 37.40 E
Griškovcy 92 49.56 N 28.36 E
Gris-Nez, Cap ⊳ 50 50.52 N 1.35 E
Grisolia 68 39.43 N 15.51 E
Grisons
— Graubünden ◦³ 58 46.45 N 9.30 E
Grisslehamn 40 60.06 N 18.50 E
Grissom Air Force Base ♦ 216 40.40 N 86.08 W
Gristow 54 54.10 N 13.20 E
Griswold, Ia., U.S. 198 41.14 N 95.08 W
Griswold Creek ≃ 279a 41.21 N 81.23 W
Griswoldville 207 42.39 N 72.42 W
Grisy-Suisnes 261 48.41 N 2.40 E
Grival Pamia 152 7.27 N 17.12 E
Grivenskaja ≃ 75 48.33 N 38.09 E
Grizim ≃ 75 46.40 N 66.45 E
Grizzana 64 44.15 N 11.09 E
Grizzly Bay ᴄ 226 38.07 N 122.01 W
Grizzly Bear Mountain ⋏ 176 65.22 N 121.00 W
Grizzly Bear's Head and Lead Man Indian Reserve ♦⁴ 184 52.33 N 108.16 W
Grizzly Creek ≃ 282 52.32 N 122.06 W
Grizzly Flats 226 38.38 N 120.31 W
Grizzly Island ⅼ 282 38.08 N 121.58 W
Grizzly Mountain ⋏, Id., U.S. 202 47.43 N 116.06 W
Grizzly Mountain ⋏, Or., U.S. 202 44.26 N 120.57 W
Grizzly Mountain ⋏, Wa., U.S. 224 48.25 N 118.30 W
Grizzly Slough ≃ 282 38.06 N 121.53 W
Grmeč ⋏ 36 44.40 N 16.30 E
Groairas 250 3.53 S 40.23 W
Groais Island ⅼ 186 50.57 N 55.35 W
Groebondonk 56 50.57 N 55.35 W
Gröben 264a 52.17 N 13.10 E
Gröbener-See ⌀ 264a 52.17 N 13.11 E
Gröbenzell 60 48.11 N 11.22 E
Grobina 76 56.33 N 21.10 E
Groblershoop 158 28.55 S 20.59 E
Gröbzig 54 51.42 N 11.52 E
Grodekovo 85 42.49 N 71.29 E
Gródig 54 52.03 N 13.59 E
Gröditz 54 51.24 N 13.27 E
Grodków 30 50.43 N 17.22 E
Grodno 76 53.41 N 23.50 E
Grodno ◦⁸ 76 53.30 N 25.00 E
Grodovka 76 48.13 N 37.23 E
Grodz'anka 76 53.33 N 28.45 E
Grodzisk Mazowiecki 30 52.07 N 20.37 E
Grodzisk [Wielkopolski] 30 52.14 N 16.22 E
Groß 54 54.09 N 13.20 E
Groen ≃, S. Afr. 158 30.40 S 23.17 E
Groen ≃, S. Afr. 158 29.00 S 22.10 E
Groenland
— Greenland ◦² 16 70.00 N 40.00 W
Groenlandia
— Greenland ◦² 16 70.00 N 40.00 W
Groenlo 52 52.02 N 6.36 E
Groenvlei 158 27.27 S 30.13 E
Groesbeck, Oh., U.S. 218 39.13 N 84.35 W
Groesbeck, Tx., U.S. 222 31.31 N 96.32 W
Groesbeek 52 51.47 N 5.56 E
Grofa, gora ⋏ 30 48.41 N 24.02 E
Grófaszög ≃ 31 46.20 N 16.59 E
Grögelhofen 60 49.05 N 11.44 E
Grogan 214 41.21 N 82.54 W
Grögló, Kali ≃ 269e 6.13 S 106.47 E
Grogol-hilir ◦⁸ 269e 6.10 S 106.45 E
Grohnde 56 52.01 N 9.25 E
Groitzsch 54 51.09 N 12.16 E
Groix 62 47.38 N 3.28 W
Groix, Île de ⅼ 62 47.38 N 3.28 W
Grójec 30 51.52 N 20.52 E
Grokgak 115a 8.11 S 114.47 E
Grolley 58 46.48 N 7.04 E
Grombalia 148 36.36 N 10.30 E
Grömitz 54 54.09 N 10.57 E
Gromo 62 45.58 N 9.56 E
Gromokleja ≃ 92 47.42 N 31.54 E
Gromoslavka 80 48.24 N 43.26 E
Gromovka 92 48.19 N 35.53 E
Gronau, Dtsch. 52 52.13 N 7.01 E
Gronau, Dtsch. 56 52.05 N 9.46 E
Grønbjerg 41 56.04 N 8.29 E
Grønborg 41 54.53 N 12.08 E
Grönenbach 60 47.52 N 10.22 E
Grønhøj 41 56.18 N 9.12 E
Grönhøgen 40 56.16 N 16.26 E
Groningen, Ned. 52 53.13 N 6.34 E
Groningen, Sur. 250 5.48 N 55.28 W
Groningen ◦⁸ 52 53.16 N 6.45 E
Grønland
— Greenland ◦² 16 70.00 N 40.00 W
Grønlid 184 53.06 N 104.28 W
Grønnedal 16 61.14 N 48.06 W
Grönsinka 40 60.19 N 16.43 E
Grönskåra 40 57.07 N 15.56 E
Grooplaats 158 28.46 S 24.36 E
Groot ≃, S. Afr. 158 33.45 S 24.58 E
Groot-Berg ≃, S. Afr. 158 32.47 S 18.08 E
Groot-Brakrivier 158 34.02 S 22.14 E
Groot-Drakrivier 158 34.02 S 22.14 E
Grootdraaidam ♦¹ 158 26.55 S 29.18 E
Grootdrink 158 28.28 S 21.49 E
Groote Eylandt ⅼ 164 14.00 S 136.40 E
Grim, Cape ⊳ 166 40.41 S 144.41 E
Grootfontein 158 19.32 S 18.05 E
Groot Karasberge ⋏ 158 27.20 S 18.40 E
Groot Karroo
— Great Karroo ◦¹ 158 32.25 S 22.40 E
Grimes, Col. 216 40.06 N 80.39 W
Groote-S. Afr. 158 30.55 S 18.01 E
Groote-Letaba ≃ 158 23.58 S 31.09 E
Groot-Marico 158 25.37 S 26.26 E
Groot-Swartberge ⋏ 158 33.20 S 22.00 E
Grootvlei 158 26.47 S 28.30 E
Grootvloer ≃ 158 30.00 S 20.40 E
Gröpelingen ◦⁸ 52 53.07 N 8.46 E
Gropello Cairoli 62 45.11 N 9.00 E
Gropeni 38 45.04 N 27.53 E
Großbliederstorff 56 49.09 N 7.01 E
Gros Bois, Parc de ♦ 261 48.44 N 2.32 E
Groscavallo 62 45.22 N 7.15 E
Grose ≃ 170 33.36 S 150.41 E
Grosio 64 46.18 N 10.16 E
Gros Islet 241f 14.05 N 60.58 W
Groslay 261 48.59 N 2.21 E
Gros Mécatina, Cap du ⊳ 186 50.45 N 59.00 W
Gros-Morne 240e 14.43 N 61.01 W
Gros Morne ⋏ 186 49.36 N 57.48 W
Gros Morne National Park ♦ 186 49.40 N 57.45 W
Grosne ≃ 58 46.42 N 4.56 E
Gromez Point ⊳ 43b 49.16 N 2.15 W
Grosotto 64 46.17 N 10.15 E
Gros Piton ⋏ 241f 13.49 N 61.04 W
Grosvenore 261 48.47 N 1.46 E
Grossa, Ponta ⊳, Bra. 256 23.35 S 45.13 W
Grossa, Ponta ⊳, Bra. 287a 22.47 S 43.11 W
Grossache (Tiroler Ache) ≃ 60 47.51 N 12.30 E
Grossalmerode 56 51.15 N 9.48 E
Grossalsleben 54 51.59 N 11.13 E
Gross Ammensleben 54 52.14 N 11.31 E
Grossarl 64 47.14 N 13.12 E
Gross-Beeren 54 52.21 N 13.18 E
Gross Berkel 52 52.04 N 9.19 E
Grossbodungen 54 51.28 N 10.28 E
Grossbottwar 56 49.00 N 9.17 E
Grossbreitenbach 54 50.35 N 11.02 E
Grossdeuben 54 51.14 N 12.23 E
Grossdubrau 54 51.15 N 14.28 E
Gross Düngen 52 52.06 N 10.01 E
Gross Antillen
— Greater Antilles ⅼⅼ 238 20.00 N 74.00 W
Grosse Aue ≃ 52 52.37 N 9.10 E
Grosse Australische Bucht
— Great Australian Bight ᴄ³ 162 35.00 S 135.00 E
Grossefehn 52 53.24 N 7.36 E
Grosse Herrenwiese 264a 52.17 N 13.20 E
Grosse Ile 216 42.08 N 83.09 W
Grosse Île, La ⅼ 186 47.37 N 61.31 W
Grosse Laber ≃ 60 48.52 N 12.30 E
Grosse Mühl ≃ 61 48.25 N 13.59 E
Grossenbrode 54 54.22 N 11.05 E
Grossenbrode 263 51.22 N 6.47 E
Grossengottern 54 51.06 N 10.34 E
Grossengstingen 54 48.23 N 9.17 E
Grossenhain 54 51.17 N 13.33 E
Grossen-Linden 56 50.31 N 8.39 E
Grossenlüder 56 50.35 N 9.32 E
Grossenwiehe 41 54.42 N 9.11 E
Grossen-Enzersdorf 61 48.12 N 16.33 E
Grosse Pointe 214 42.23 N 82.54 W
Grosse Pointe ⊳ 241e 16.01 N 61.16 W
Grosse Pointe Farms 214 42.25 N 82.53 W
Grosse Pointe Park 214 42.22 N 82.56 W
Grosse Pointe Woods 214 42.26 N 82.54 W
Grosser Arber ⋏ 60 49.07 N 13.07 E
Grosser Bären-See
— Great Bear Lake ⌀ 176 66.00 N 120.00 W
Grosser Beerberg ⋏ 56 50.37 N 10.44 E
Grosser Bösenstein ⋏ 61 47.26 N 14.24 E
Grosser Buchstein ⋏ 61 47.36 N 14.35 E
Grosser Chingan Ling
— Da Hinggan Ling ⋏ 90 49.00 N 122.00 E
Grosser Feldberg ⋏ 56 50.14 N 8.26 E
Grosser Gattenberg ⋏ 61 47.30 N 11.58 E
Grosser Gleichberg ⋏ 54 50.23 N 10.35 E
Grosser Heuberg ⋏¹ 56 48.14 N 8.55 E
Grosser Inselsberg ⋏ 54 50.52 N 10.28 E
Grosser Jasmunder Bodden ᴄ 54 54.31 N 13.29 E
Grosser Knallstein ⋏ 61 47.19 N 13.58 E
Gross Köningstuhl ⋏ 64 46.57 N 13.47 E
Grosser Müggelsee ᴄ 264a 52.26 N 13.40 E
Grosser Plöner See ⌀ 54 54.09 N 10.26 E
Grosser Rachel ⋏ 60 48.59 N 13.24 E
Grosser Ravens-Berg ⋏² 264a 52.21 N 13.04 E
Grosser Salzsee
— Great Salt Lake ⌀ 200 41.10 N 112.30 W
Grosser Seddiner See ⌀ 264a 52.17 N 13.02 E
Grosser Selchower See ⌀ 54 52.14 N 13.53 E
Grosser Sklaven-See
— Great Slave Lake ⌀ 176 61.30 N 114.00 W
Grosser Speikkogel ⋏ 61 46.47 N 14.58 E
Grosser Walfisch-Fluss
— Baleine, Grande rivière de la ≃ 176 55.16 N 77.47 W
Grosser Wannsee ⌀ 264a 52.26 N 13.11 E
Grosser Winterberg ⋏ 54 50.54 N 14.16 E
Grosser Zern-See ⌀ 264a 52.12 N 12.56 E
Grosse Santow ⌀ 264a 46.46 N 12.49 E
Grosse Sandwüste
— Great Sandy Desert ◦² 162 21.30 S 125.00 E
Grosses Barriere-Riff
— Great Barrier Reef ♦² 160 18.00 S 145.50 E
Grosses Moor ◦⁸ 52 53.26 N 7.17 E
Grosses Moor ⊹³, Dtsch. 54 53.08 N 8.45 E
Grosses Moor ⊹³, Dtsch. 52 52.30 N 8.20 E
Grosses Schulerloch ⋏ 60 48.55 N 11.48 E
Grosse Sundainseln
— Greater Sunda Islands ⅼⅼ 108 2.00 S 110.00 E
Grosse Walsertal ◡ 58 47.14 N 9.56 E
Grosse Syrte
— Surt, Khalij ᴄ 146 31.30 N 18.00 E
Grosseto 64 42.46 N 11.08 E
Grosseto, Formiche di ⅼⅼ 64 42.35 N 10.53 E
Gross-Gerau 56 49.55 N 8.29 E
Grossglockner ⋏ 54 47.04 N 12.42 E
Grossharras 61 48.41 N 16.23 E
Grossharthau 54 51.08 N 14.13 E
Grosshartmannsdorf 54 50.52 N 13.21 E
Grossheringen 54 51.06 N 11.35 E

⋏ Mountain	Berg	Montaña	Montagne	Montanha
⋏ Mountains	Gebirge	Montañas	Montagnes	Montanhas
⏆ Pass	Paß	Paso	Col	Passo
◡ Valley, Canyon	Tal, Cañon	Vale, Cañón	Vallée, Canyon	Vale, Canhão
⊳ Plain	Ebene	Llano	Plaine	Planície
⊳ Cape	Kap	Cabo	Cap	Cabo
ⅼ Island	Insel	Isla	Île	Ilha
ⅼⅼ Islands	Inseln	Islas	Îles	Ilhas
⋏ Other Topographic Features	Andere Topographische Objekte	Otros Elementos Topográficos	Autres données topographiques	Outros acidentes topográficos

Gros-Guir I · 67

ESPAÑOL — Nombre | Página | Lat.°' | Long.°' W = Oeste
FRANÇAIS — Nom | Page | Lat.°' | Long.°' W = Ouest
PORTUGUÊS — Nome | Página | Lat.°' | Long.°' W = Oeste

Gross Gleidingen 54 52.14 N 10.25 E
Gross Glienicke 264a 52.28 N 13.07 E
Gross-Glienicker See ⊜ 264a 52.28 N 13.06 E
Grossglockner ∧ 64 47.04 N 12.42 E
Grossgmain 64 47.43 N 12.55 E
Grossgörschen 54 51.13 N 12.11 E
Gross Grönau 54 53.46 N 10.44 E
Grosshansdorf 52 53.40 N 10.17 E
Grosshartmannsdorf 54 50.48 N 13.19 E
Gross-Hehlen 52 52.39 N 10.03 E
Grossheide 52 53.35 N 7.20 E
Grosshennersdorf 54 50.59 N 14.47 E
Grosshöchstetten 58 46.55 N 7.38 E
Grossholzleute 58 47.41 N 10.05 E
Grossjedlersdorf ✦[8] 264b 48.17 N 16.25 E
Grosskayna 54 51.17 N 11.56 E
Gross Kienitz 264a 52.19 N 13.28 E
Gross-Kollmar 52 53.44 N 9.30 E
Grosskorbetha 54 51.16 N 12.01 E
Gross Kreutz 54 52.24 N 12.46 E
Grosskrut 61 48.38 N 16.43 E
Grosslehna 54 51.18 N 12.10 E
Gross Leine 54 52.00 N 14.03 E
Grosslittgen 56 50.02 N 6.47 E
Gross-Machnow 264a 52.16 N 13.28 E
Grossmehring 60 48.46 N 11.32 E
Grossmont 228 32.47 N 116.59 W
Gross Muckrow 54 52.04 N 14.26 E
Gross Oesingen 52 52.38 N 10.29 E
Grossörner 54 51.37 N 11.29 E
Grossos 250 4.59 S 37.09 W
Grossostheim 56 49.55 N 9.04 E
Grosspetersdorf 61 47.14 N 16.19 E
Grosspostwitz 54 51.07 N 14.26 E
Grossquenstedt 54 51.56 N 11.07 E
Grossraming 61 47.53 N 14.33 E
Grossräschen 54 51.35 N 14.00 E
Gross Rhüden 52 51.56 N 10.07 E
Grossrinderfeld 56 49.39 N 9.44 E
Gross Rodensleben 54 52.08 N 11.25 E
Grossröhrsdorf 54 51.08 N 14.01 E
Gross Rosenburg 54 51.55 N 11.53 E
Grossrückerswalde 54 50.38 N 13.07 E
Grossrudestedt 54 51.05 N 11.06 E
Gross Sankt Florian 61 46.49 N 15.19 E
Gross-Sarau 54 53.45 N 10.44 E
Grossschirma 54 50.58 N 13.17 E
Grossschönau 54 50.54 N 14.40 E
Gross Schönebeck 54 52.54 N 13.32 E
Gross-Schulzendorf 264a 52.16 N 13.21 E
Gross-Siegharts 61 48.48 N 15.24 E
Grosssölk 64 47.25 N 13.58 E
Gross-Umstadt 56 49.52 N 8.55 E
Grossvenediger ∧ 64 47.06 N 12.21 E
Grosswardein → Oradea 38 47.03 N 21.57 E
Grossweil 64 47.41 N 11.18 E
Grossweissenbach 61 48.33 N 15.10 E
Gross Wittensee 41 54.24 N 9.46 E
Gross Ziethen, Dtsch. 264a 52.24 N 13.27 E
Gross Ziethen, Dtsch. 264a 52.44 N 13.01 E
Gross-Zimmern 56 49.52 N 8.50 E
Grostenquin 56 48.59 N 6.44 E
Grosvenor, Lake ⊜ 180 58.40 N 155.15 W
Grosvenor Dale 207 41.58 N 71.53 W
Gros Ventre ≃ 202 43.33 N 110.46 W
Groswater Bay ᑕ 176 54.20 N 57.30 W
Grote Nete ≃ 56 51.07 N 4.34 E
Groton, Ct., U.S. 207 41.21 N 72.04 W
Groton, Ma., U.S. 207 42.36 N 71.34 W
Groton, N.Y., U.S. 210 42.35 N 76.22 W
Groton, S.D., U.S. 198 45.26 N 98.05 W
Grottaferrata 66 41.47 N 12.40 E
Grottaglie 68 40.32 N 17.26 E
Grottaminarda 68 41.04 N 15.02 E
Grottammare 66 42.59 N 13.52 E
Grotte 70 37.24 N 13.42 E
Grotte di Castro 66 42.40 N 11.52 E
Grotteria 68 38.22 N 16.17 E
Grottoes 188 38.16 N 78.49 W
Grottole 68 40.36 N 16.23 E
Grou, Oued V 148 33.56 N 6.45 W
Grouard Mission 182 55.31 N 116.09 W
Groundbirch 182 55.47 N 120.55 W
Groundhog ≃ 176 49.43 N 81.58 W
Grouse Creek ≃, Ks., U.S. 198 37.00 N 96.55 W
Grouse Creek ≃, Ut., U.S. 200 41.22 N 113.55 W
Grouse Creek Mountain ∧ 202 44.22 N 113.54 W
Grouw 52 53.05 N 5.45 E
Grove, Eng., U.K. 42 51.36 N 1.25 W
Grove, Ok., U.S. 196 36.35 N 94.46 W
Grove, Pa., U.S. 285 40.01 N 75.38 W
Grove City, Fl., U.S. 220 26.54 N 82.19 W
Grove City, Mn., U.S. 198 45.09 N 94.40 W
Grove City, Oh., U.S. 218 39.52 N 83.05 W
Grove City, Pa., U.S. 214 41.09 N 80.05 W
Grove Hill 194 31.42 N 87.46 W
Groveland, Ca., U.S. 226 37.50 N 120.13 W
Groveland, Fl., U.S. 220 28.33 N 81.51 W
Groveland, Ma., U.S. 207 42.45 N 71.01 W
Groveland, N.Y., U.S. 210 42.39 N 77.46 W
Grovely Ridge ∧ 42 51.08 N 2.04 W
Grove Mountains ⩘ 9 72.53 S 74.53 E
Grove Park ✦[8] 260 51.26 N 0.01 E
Groveport 218 39.52 N 82.53 W
Grover 210 41.37 N 76.52 W
Grover City 204 35.07 N 120.37 W
Grover Cleveland Birthplace ⊥ 276 40.50 N 74.16 W
Grover Cleveland Park ♦ 284a 42.57 N 78.49 W
Grover Hill 216 41.01 N 84.28 W
Grovers Mills 276 40.19 N 74.37 W
Groves 194 29.56 N 93.55 W
Groveton, N.H., U.S. 188 44.35 N 71.30 W
Groveton, Pa., U.S. 279b 40.30 N 80.06 W
Groveton, Tx., U.S. 222 31.03 N 95.07 W
Groveton, Va., U.S. 284c 38.46 N 77.05 W
Grovetown 192 33.27 N 82.11 W
Groveville 208 40.10 N 74.40 W
Growa Point ≻ 150 4.21 N 7.37 W
Growler Peak ∧ 200 32.24 N 113.07 W
Growler Wash V 200 32.35 N 113.30 W
Groznoje 85 42.36 N 71.12 E
Groznyj 84 43.20 N 45.42 E
Groznyy → Groznyj 84 43.20 N 45.42 E
Grube, Dtsch. 54 54.14 N 11.01 E
Grube, Dtsch. 264a 52.26 N 12.57 E
Grubišno Polje 36 45.42 N 17.10 E
Grubweg 60 48.35 N 13.29 E
Grudovo 38 42.21 N 27.10 E
Grudziądz 30 53.29 N 18.45 E
Gruesa, Punta ≻ 248 20.22 S 70.11 W
Gruetli-Laager 194 35.22 N 85.40 W
Grugapark ♦ 263 51.26 N 7.00 E
Grugliasco 62 45.04 N 7.35 E
Gruia 38 44.16 N 22.42 E
Gruinard Bay ᑕ 46 57.53 N 5.31 W
Gruinart, Loch ᑕ 46 55.52 N 6.20 W
Gruiten 56 51.14 N 7.01 E
Gruitrode 56 51.05 N 5.35 E
Grulla 196 26.16 N 98.39 W
Grumello del Monte 62 45.38 N 9.52 E
Grumento Nova 68 40.17 N 15.53 E
Grumentum ⊥ 68 40.17 N 15.55 E
Grumman-Bethpage Airport ⊠ 276 40.45 N 73.29 W
Grumman Corporation ⊍[3] 276 40.45 N 73.30 W
Grumme ✦[8] 263 51.30 N 7.14 E
Grumo Appula 68 41.01 N 16.42 E
Grums 26 59.21 N 13.06 E
Grun' 78 50.16 N 34.36 E

Grüna 54 50.49 N 12.47 E
Grünau 156 27.44 S 18.23 E
Grünau ✦[8] 264a 52.25 N 13.34 E
Grünau im Almtal 64 47.51 N 13.57 E
Grunavat, Loch ⊜ 46 58.10 N 6.55 W
Grünbach 54 50.26 N 12.22 E
Grünberg, Dtsch. 56 50.35 N 8.58 E
Grünberg → Zielona Góra, Pol. 30 51.56 N 15.31 E
Grünburg 61 47.57 N 14.15 E
Grundlsee ⊜ 64 47.38 N 13.52 E
Grundy 192 37.16 N 82.05 W
Grundy □[6] 216 41.22 N 88.26 W
Grundy Center 190 42.21 N 92.46 W
Grundy Lake Provincial Park ♦ 190 45.48 N 80.34 W
Grünefeld 264a 52.41 N 12.58 E
Grünenplan 52 51.57 N 9.44 E
Grünewald, Dtsch. 54 51.24 N 14.00 E
Grünewald, Dtsch. 263 51.13 N 7.37 E
Grunewald ✦[8] 264a 52.30 N 13.17 E
Grunewald, Berliner Forst ✦[3] 264a 52.28 N 13.13 E
Grunewald, Jagdschloss ⊥ 264a 52.28 N 13.16 E
Grünhain 54 50.35 N 12.48 E
Grünhainichen 54 50.46 N 13.08 E
Grünheide 54 52.25 N 13.49 E
Grünsfeld 56 49.36 N 9.44 E
Grünstadt 56 49.34 N 8.10 E
Grüntal 264a 52.45 N 13.44 E
Grunthal 184 49.25 N 96.52 W
Grünwald 60 48.02 N 11.31 E
Gruševka 78 47.55 N 40.40 E
Gruševka ≃ 83 47.26 N 40.00 E
Gruševskaja 83 47.26 N 39.57 E
Grušino 76 59.27 N 44.09 E
Gruting 46a 60.14 N 1.30 W
Gruver 196 36.16 N 101.24 W
Gruyère, Lac de la ⊜ 58 46.38 N 7.06 E
Gruyères 58 46.35 N 7.05 E
Gruzdžiai 76 56.06 N 23.16 E
Gruzija → Georgia □[1] 72 42.00 N 44.00 E
Gruziya → Georgia □[1] 72 42.00 N 44.00 E
Gruznovka 88 55.09 N 105.12 E
Gruzskaja Balka 78 46.25 N 40.19 E
Gruzskij Jelančik ≃ 83 47.07 N 38.04 E
Gruzskoje 83 48.33 N 37.18 E
Gruzsko-Zor'anskoje 83 47.56 N 38.06 E
Grybów 30 49.38 N 20.56 E
Grycken ⊜ 40 60.27 N 16.13 E
Gryfice 30 53.56 N 15.12 E
Gryfino 30 53.12 N 14.30 E
Grytgöl 40 58.48 N 15.33 E
Grythyttan 40 59.42 N 14.32 E
Gschnitz 64 47.03 N 11.22 E
Gschütt, Pass)(64 47.35 N 13.30 E
Gschwend 56 48.56 N 9.44 E
Gstaad 58 46.28 N 7.17 E
Gsteig 58 46.23 N 7.16 E
Gu ≃ 100 27.02 N 115.03 E
Gua 124 22.12 N 85.23 E
Guabaria ≃[1] 126 22.10 N 90.30 E
Guabito 236 9.30 N 82.37 W
Guabu 106 32.16 N 118.53 E
Guacanayabo, Golfo de ᑕ 240p 20.28 N 77.30 W
Guacara 246 10.14 N 67.53 W
Guacarí 246 3.46 N 76.20 W
Gu Achi 200 32.19 N 112.02 W
Guachinango 234 20.32 N 104.24 W
Guachiría ≃ 246 5.27 N 70.36 W
Guachochi 232 26.51 N 107.05 W
Guaçuí 255 20.46 S 41.41 W
Guadajira ≃ 34 38.52 N 6.41 W
Guadajoz ≃ 34 37.50 N 4.51 W
Guadalajara, Esp. 34 40.38 N 3.10 W
Guadalajara, Méx. 234 20.40 N 103.20 W
Guadalajara □[4] 34 40.50 N 2.30 W
Guadalaviar ≃ 34 40.21 N 1.08 W
Guadalcanal 34 38.06 N 5.49 W
Guadalcanal □[4] 175e 9.50 S 160.00 E
Guadalcanal I 175e 9.32 S 160.12 E
Guadalcázar 234 22.37 N 100.24 W
Guadalén ≃ 34 38.05 N 3.32 W
Guadalén, Embalse de ⊜[1] 34 38.25 N 3.15 W
Guadalentin ≃ 34 37.59 N 1.04 W
Guadalete ≃ 34 36.35 N 6.13 W
Guadalhorce ≃ 34 36.41 N 4.27 W
Guadalimar ≃ 34 38.05 N 3.06 W
Guadalmena ≃ 34 38.19 N 2.56 W
Guadalmez ≃ 34 38.46 N 5.04 W
Guadalope ≃ 34 41.15 N 0.03 W
Guadalquivir ≃ 34 36.47 N 6.22 W
Guadalupe, Bol. 248 18.33 S 64.05 W
Guadalupe, Col. 246 2.01 N 75.45 W
Guadalupe, C.R. 236 9.57 N 84.03 W
Guadalupe, Méx. 196 28.09 N 100.36 W
Guadalupe, Méx. 232 25.41 N 100.15 W
Guadalupe, Méx. 234 22.45 N 102.31 W
Guadalupe, Perú 248 7.15 S 79.29 W
Guadalupe, Ca., U.S. 204 34.58 N 120.34 W
Guadalupe □[6] 222 29.37 N 97.45 W
Guadalupe ✦[8] 287a 22.50 S 43.23 W
Guadalupe → Guadeloupe □[2] 241o 16.15 N 61.35 W
Guadalupe ≃, Méx. 204 32.05 N 116.53 W
Guadalupe ≃, Ca., U.S. 282 37.25 N 121.58 W
Guadalupe ≃, Tx., U.S. 196 28.30 N 96.53 W
Guadalupe, Basílica de ⊍[1] 286a 19.29 N 99.07 W
Guadalupe, Isla I 178 29.00 N 118.16 W
Guadalupe, Presa de ⊜[1] 286a 19.37 N 99.16 W
Guadalupe, Sierra de ⩘, Esp. 34 39.26 N 5.25 W
Guadalupe, Sierra de ⩘, Méx. 286a 19.35 N 99.08 W
Guadalupe [Bravos] 232 31.23 N 106.07 W
Guadalupe del Norte ≊ 286a 19.34 N 99.01 W
Guadalupe de Ramírez 234 17.45 N 98.10 W
Guadalupe Mountains ⩘ 196 32.20 N 105.00 W
Guadalupe Mountains National Park ♦ 196 31.55 N 104.55 W
Guadalupe Peak ∧ 196 31.50 N 104.52 W
Guadalupe Seamount ✢[3] 14 27.50 N 168.45 E
Guadalupe Slough ≃ 282 37.27 N 122.02 W
Guadalupe Victoria, Méx. 196 27.47 N 101.04 W
Guadalupe Victoria, Méx. 232 24.27 N 104.07 W
Guadalupe Victoria, Méx. 234 19.17 N 97.21 W
Guadalupe Victoria, Presa ⊜[1] 234 23.50 N 104.46 W
Guadalupita 200 36.08 N 105.14 W
Guadarrama, Puerto de)(34 40.43 N 4.10 W
Guadarrama, Sierra de ⩘ 34 40.55 N 4.00 W
Guadazaón ≃ 34 39.42 N 1.36 W
Guadeloupe □[2], N.A. 230 16.15 N 61.35 W
Guadeloupe □[2], N.A. 241o 16.15 N 61.35 W
Guadeloupe Passage ⊻ 238 16.45 N 61.30 W
Guadiana ≃ 34 37.14 N 7.22 W
Guadiana, Bahía de ᑕ 240p 22.05 N 84.24 W
Guadiana Menor ≃ 34 37.56 N 3.15 W
Guadiaro ≃ 34 36.17 N 5.17 W
Guadiato ≃ 34 38.20 N 5.22 W

Guadiela ≃ 34 40.22 N 2.49 W
Guadix 34 37.18 N 3.08 W
Guafo, Isla I 254 43.36 S 74.43 W
Guagnano 68 40.24 N 17.57 E
Guagua 116 14.58 N 120.38 E
Guahe 105 39.12 N 115.00 E
Guaianases ✦[8] 287b 23.33 S 46.25 W
Guaíba 252 30.06 S 51.19 W
Guaíba ᑕ[1] 252 30.15 S 51.12 W
Guaicaipuro □[5] 286c 10.25 N 66.57 W
Guaihe 100 33.28 N 112.59 E
Guaimaca 236 14.32 N 86.51 W
Guáimaro 240p 21.03 N 77.21 W
Guaimoreto, Laguna de ᑕ 236 15.58 N 85.55 W
Guaimozi 98 41.31 N 125.26 E
Guainía □[5] 246 2.30 N 69.00 W
Guainía ≃ 246 2.01 N 67.07 W
Guaió ≃ 287b 23.31 S 46.19 W
Guaipava 256 21.40 S 45.43 W
Guaiquinima, Cerro ∧ 246 5.49 N 63.40 W
Guaíra, Bra. 252 24.04 S 54.15 W
Guaíra, Bra. 255 20.19 S 48.18 W
Guairá □[5] 252 25.45 S 56.30 W
Guaire ≃ 286c 10.25 N 66.46 W
Guáitara ≃ 246 1.34 N 77.27 W
Guaitecas, Archipiélago de las II 254 43.57 S 73.50 W
Guajaba, Cayo I 240p 21.50 N 77.30 W
Guajará ≃ 250 1.48 S 53.02 W
Guajará-Açu 250 1.38 S 48.07 W
Guajará-Miri 250 1.29 S 48.17 W
Guajará-Mirim 248 10.48 S 65.22 W
Guajataca ≃ 240m 18.29 N 66.57 W
Guajataca, Lago de ⊜[1] 240m 18.23 N 66.55 W
Guajiasi 104 41.15 N 120.54 E
Gualaca 236 8.32 N 82.18 W
Gualaceo 246 2.54 S 78.47 W
Gualala 204 38.45 N 123.31 W
Gualán 236 15.08 N 89.22 W
Gualaquiza 246 3.24 S 78.33 W
Gualdo Tadino 66 43.14 N 12.47 E
Gualeguay 252 33.09 S 59.20 W
Gualeguay ≃ 252 33.19 S 59.39 W
Gualeguaychú 252 33.01 S 58.31 W
Gualicho, Salina del ≊ 254 40.24 S 65.15 W
Gualjaina 254 42.42 S 70.30 W
Gualtieri 64 44.54 N 10.38 E
Guam □[2], Oc. 14 13.28 N 144.47 E
Guam □[2], Oc. 174p 13.28 N 144.47 E
Guamá ≃, Bra. 250 1.29 S 48.30 W
Guamá ≃, Cuba 240p 22.11 N 83.41 W
Guamal, Col. 246 9.09 N 74.14 W
Guamal, Col. 246 3.52 N 73.44 W
Guamal, Quebrada ≃ 286c 10.31 N 66.59 W
Guamblín, Isla I 254 44.51 S 75.05 W
Guaminí 252 37.02 S 62.25 W
Guam International Airport ⊠ 174p 13.29 N 144.48 E
Guamo 246 4.02 N 74.58 W
Guamo Embarcadero 240p 20.37 N 76.58 W
Guamote 246 1.56 S 78.43 W
Guamúchil, Méx. 232 25.28 N 108.06 W
Guamúchil, Méx. 234 25.28 N 108.06 W
Guamués ≃ 246 0.32 N 76.33 W
Gua Musang 114 4.53 N 101.58 E
Gu'an 105 39.26 N 116.18 E
Guan ≃, Zhg. 100 32.16 N 115.42 E
Guan ≃, Zhg. 100 34.29 N 119.49 E
Guanábana 240m 18.01 N 67.07 W
Guanabara, Baía de ᑕ 287a 22.50 S 43.10 W
Guanabara, Palácio ⊍ 287a 22.56 S 43.11 W
Guanacaste □[4] 236 10.30 N 85.15 W
Guanacaste, Cordillera de ⩘ 236 10.45 N 85.05 W
Guanacaste, Parque Nacional ♦ 236 10.50 N 85.30 W
Guanacaure, Cerro ∧ 236 13.14 N 87.07 W
Guanaceví 232 25.56 N 105.57 W
Guanache ≃ 248 5.53 S 74.21 W
Guanahacabibes, Golfo de ᑕ 240p 22.08 N 84.35 W
Guanahacabibes, Península de ≻[1] 240p 21.57 N 84.35 W
Guana Island I 240m 18.29 N 64.34 W
Guanaja 236 16.27 N 85.54 W
Guanaja, Isla de I 236 16.30 N 85.55 W
Guanajay 240p 22.55 N 82.42 W
Guanajibo ≃ 240m 18.10 N 67.11 W
Guanajibo, Punta ≻ 240m 18.10 N 67.11 W
Guanajuato 234 21.01 N 101.15 W
Guanajuato □[3] 234 21.00 N 101.00 W
Guanambi 255 14.13 S 42.47 W
Guanaparo, Caño ≃ 246 8.19 N 68.10 W
Guañape, Islas II 248 8.33 S 78.57 W
Guanare 246 9.03 N 69.45 W
Guanare ≃ 246 8.13 N 67.46 W
Guanarito 246 8.42 N 69.12 W
Guanay 248 15.28 S 67.52 W
Guanay, Cerro ∧ 246 5.51 N 66.18 W
Guanay, Cerro ∧[2] 286d 12.07 S 77.13 W
Guanbuqiao 100 29.56 N 114.21 E
Guanchao 100 26.41 N 114.58 E
Guancheng, Zhg. 100 30.11 N 121.25 E
Guancheng, Zhg. 107 30.01 N 103.54 E
Guancun 106 31.30 N 119.43 E
Guandacol 252 29.31 S 68.32 W
Guandanghu 100 30.06 N 113.37 E
Guandi, Zhg. 98 41.48 N 116.52 E
Guandi, Zhg. 98 42.37 N 118.27 E
Guandian 100 32.40 N 118.04 E
Guandu, Zhg. 100 24.17 N 113.53 E
Guandu, Zhg. 107 30.04 N 106.25 E
Guane 240p 22.12 N 84.05 W
Guang'an 107 30.28 N 106.39 E
Guang'anmen Station ✦[5] 271a 39.53 N 116.20 E
Guangchang 100 26.50 N 116.14 E
Guangde 106 30.54 N 119.26 E
Guangdong (Kwangtung) □[4] 90 23.00 N 113.00 E
Guangfeng 100 28.25 N 118.11 E
Guangfu, Zhg. 106 31.18 N 120.23 E
Guangfu, Zhg. 107 30.13 N 104.41 E
Guangfu, Zhg. 269b 31.21 N 121.19 E
Guangfuyingzi 104 42.14 N 120.58 E
Guanghua 102 32.25 N 111.36 E
Guangji 100 29.52 N 115.34 E
Guangling, Zhg. 98 39.47 N 114.17 E
Guangling, Zhg. 106 32.06 N 120.13 E
Guanglu Dao I 98 39.09 N 122.21 E
Guangmao Shan ∧ 102 27.02 N 100.58 E
Guangming Ding ∧ 100 30.07 N 118.10 E
Guangnan 102 24.10 N 105.06 E
Guangningsi, Zhg. 98 39.08 N 121.45 E
Guangningsi, Zhg. 98 40.27 N 118.31 E
Guangping 98 36.30 N 114.57 E
Guangrao 98 37.02 N 118.25 E
Guangsbunchang 107 29.22 N 105.31 E
Guangshan 100 32.02 N 114.52 E
Guangshui 100 31.40 N 114.00 E
Guangxing 107 29.04 N 106.33 E
Guangxi Zhuangzu Zizhiqu (Kwangsi Chuang) □[4] 102 24.00 N 109.00 E
Guangyuan 102 32.26 N 105.52 E
Guangyuanzhen 107 30.37 N 104.47 E
Guangze 100 27.32 N 117.20 E
Guangzhen 106 30.45 N 121.07 E
Guangzhou (Canton) 100 23.06 N 113.16 E
Guangzong 98 37.06 N 115.08 E
Guanhães 255 18.46 S 42.53 W
Guanhu 98 34.26 N 117.59 E
Guánica 240m 17.58 N 66.55 W
Guánica, Laguna de ⊜ 240m 18.00 N 66.56 W

Guaniguanico, Cordillera de ⩘ 240p 22.35 N 83.45 W
Guanipa ≃ 246 9.56 N 62.26 W
Guanjian 107 29.59 N 105.59 E
Guanjian ≃ 107 30.00 N 106.01 E
Guankou, Zhg. 100 30.35 N 115.20 E
Guankou, Zhg. 107 30.39 N 103.26 E
Guanlin 106 31.32 N 119.42 E
Guanling 102 25.57 N 105.29 E
Guanlipu 104 41.37 N 123.18 E
Guanmenshan 89 47.23 N 122.20 E
Guannan (Xin'anzhen) 98 34.07 N 119.23 E
Guano 246 1.35 S 78.38 W
Guano Creek ≃ 202 42.12 N 119.31 W
Guanputou 105 38.58 N 117.04 E
Guanqian, Zhg. 100 30.42 N 117.39 E
Guanqian, Zhg. 100 27.48 N 118.31 E
Guanqian, Zhg. 100 25.57 N 116.33 E
Guanqian, Zhg. 100 26.12 N 117.57 E
Guanqiao, Zhg. 98 34.58 N 117.14 E
Guanqiao, Zhg. 100 25.03 N 118.06 E
Guanqiaopu 100 31.08 N 112.54 E
Guanshanchang 107 28.46 N 103.42 E
Guanshi 100 26.43 N 112.53 E
Guanshui 98 40.55 N 124.33 E
Guanta 246 10.14 N 64.36 W
Guantánamo 240p 20.08 N 75.12 W
Guantánamo □[4] 240p 20.20 N 75.00 W
Guantánamo ≃ 240p 19.55 N 75.12 W
Guantánamo, Bahía de ᑕ 240p 20.00 N 75.08 W
Guantanamo Bay Naval Station ■ 240p 19.55 N 75.10 W
Guantang 106 31.37 N 119.06 E
Guantangqiao 106 32.09 N 119.27 E
Guantao (Nanguantao) 98 36.35 N 115.19 E
Guanting, Zhg. 100 34.19 N 113.47 E
Guanting, Zhg. 105 40.13 N 115.37 E
Guanting Shuiku ⊜[1] 105 40.20 N 115.38 E
Guantou, Zhg. 100 28.03 N 120.41 E
Guantou, Zhg. 100 26.08 N 119.33 E
Guantunpu 98 40.28 N 113.24 E
Guanxian, Zhg. 98 36.30 N 115.27 E
Guanxian, Zhg. 102 31.00 N 103.40 E
Guanxun 100 24.19 N 117.45 E
Guanyin 107 30.16 N 103.51 E
Guanyinchang, Zhg. 107 29.15 N 104.02 E
Guanyinchang, Zhg. 107 30.28 N 105.16 E
Guanyingzicun 104 41.52 N 121.53 E
Guanyinpu 107 28.58 N 104.53 E
Guanyinqiao, Zhg. 107 29.05 N 104.46 E
Guanyinqiao, Zhg. 107 29.46 N 104.12 E
Guanyinshan 106 32.01 N 120.58 E
Guanyinsi 106 31.48 N 118.57 E
Guanyintan 107 29.35 N 105.14 E
Guanyintang, Zhg. 100 31.01 N 112.35 E
Guanyintang, Zhg. 105 39.52 N 116.31 E
Guanyintang, Zhg. 106 32.09 N 121.09 E
Guanyinzhen 107 29.06 N 104.24 E
Guanyinzhou 100 29.30 N 113.09 E
Guanyun (Dayishan) 98 34.20 N 119.17 E
Guanzhuang, Zhg. 98 37.12 N 114.30 E
Guanzhuang, Zhg. 100 32.49 N 114.16 E
Guanzhuang, Zhg. 100 28.58 N 117.24 E
Guapí 246 2.36 N 77.54 W
Guapiaçu ≃ 256 22.40 S 42.55 W
Guapiara 255 24.10 S 48.32 W
Guápiles 236 10.13 N 83.46 W
Guapimirim 256 22.32 S 42.59 W
Guapimirim ≃ 256 22.40 S 42.58 W
Guapo Bay ᑕ 241r 10.12 N 61.40 W
Guaporé 252 28.51 S 51.54 W
Guaporé (Itenes) ≃ 248 11.54 S 65.01 W
Guaqui 248 16.35 S 68.51 W
Guará ≃ 255 12.59 S 44.49 W
Guara, Sierra de ⩘ 34 42.17 N 0.10 W
Guarabira 250 6.51 S 35.29 W
Guaraçaí 255 21.02 S 51.11 W
Guaracarumbo 286c 10.34 N 66.59 W
Guaraci 255 20.29 S 48.57 W
Guaraciaba do Norte 250 4.10 S 40.46 W
Guaraciana 255 17.03 S 43.41 W
Guaraguara, Punta ≻ 241r 10.31 N 62.19 W
Guaraí ≃ 287a 22.42 S 43.02 W
Guaramirim 252 26.27 S 49.00 W
Guaranda 246 1.36 S 79.00 W
Guaranésia 256 21.18 S 46.48 W
Guarani 256 21.22 S 43.03 W
Guaraniaçu 252 25.06 S 52.52 W
Guarani das Missões 252 28.08 S 54.34 W
Guarani de Goiás 255 13.59 S 46.31 W
Guarapari 255 20.40 S 40.30 W
Guarapiranga, Reprêsa ⊜[1] 256 23.44 S 46.44 W
Guarapuava 252 25.23 S 51.27 W
Guaraqueçaba 252 25.17 S 48.21 W
Guarará 256 21.43 S 43.02 W
Guarará ≃ 287b 23.39 S 46.30 W
Guararé 246 7.49 N 80.17 W
Guararema 256 23.25 S 46.02 W
Guaratiba, Morro de ∧ 287a 23.04 S 43.33 W
Guaratinga 255 16.34 S 39.34 W
Guaratinguetá 256 22.49 S 45.13 W
Guaratinguetá ≃ 256 22.49 S 45.13 W
Guaratuba 252 25.54 S 48.34 W
Guar Chempedak 114 5.52 N 100.28 E
Guarcino 66 41.48 N 13.19 E
Guarda 34 40.32 N 7.16 W
Guardado de Abajo 196 26.22 N 98.57 W
Guardafui, Cape → Caseyr ≻ 144 11.49 N 51.15 E
Guardavalle 68 38.30 N 16.30 E
Guardea 66 42.37 N 12.18 E
Guardia Escolta 252 28.59 S 62.08 W
Guardiagrele 66 42.11 N 14.13 E
Guardia Lombardi 68 40.57 N 15.12 E
Guardia Mitre 254 40.26 S 63.41 W
Guardia Sanframondi 68 41.15 N 14.36 E
Guardo 34 42.47 N 4.50 W
Guareña 34 38.51 N 6.06 W
Guareña ≃ 34 41.29 N 5.23 W
Guarenas 246 10.28 N 66.37 W
Guarenas ≃ 286c 10.30 N 66.45 W
Guariba ≃ 248 7.41 S 60.18 W
Guarico 246 9.32 N 69.48 W
Guárico □[3] 246 8.40 N 66.35 W
Guárico ≃ 246 7.55 N 67.23 W
Guárico, Embalse del ⊜[1] 246 9.05 N 67.25 W
Guarico, Punta ≻ 240p 20.37 N 74.44 W
Guariquito ≃ 246 7.40 N 66.18 W
Guarizama 236 14.55 N 86.20 W
Guarujá 256 24.00 S 46.16 W
Guarulhos 256 23.28 S 46.32 W
Guarulhos □[7] 287b 23.26 S 46.29 W
Guasare ≃ 246 11.03 N 72.02 W
Guasave 232 25.34 N 108.27 W
Guasdualito 246 7.15 N 70.44 W
Guasila 71 39.34 N 9.03 E
Guasipati 246 7.28 N 61.54 W
Guastalla 64 44.55 N 10.39 E
Guastatoya 236 14.51 N 90.04 W
Guāsuba ≃[1] 126 21.38 N 88.53 E
Guatajiagua 236 13.40 N 88.13 W
Guatemala, Cuba 240p 20.46 N 75.39 W
Guatemala, Guat. 236 14.38 N 90.31 W
Guatemala □[5] 236 14.40 N 90.30 W
Guatemala □[1], N.A. 230 15.30 N 90.15 W
Guatemala □[1], N.A. 236 15.30 N 90.15 W
Guatemala Basin ✢[1] 16 11.00 N 95.00 W
Guateque 246 5.00 N 73.28 W
Guatimozín 252 33.27 S 62.27 W
Guatopo, Parque Nacional ♦ 246 10.05 N 66.25 W
Guatraché 252 37.40 S 63.32 W
Guatuaro Point ≻ 241r 10.20 N 60.59 W
Guaugurina 164 10.37 S 150.28 E
Guavi ≃ 164 7.49 S 143.15 E

Guaviare □[8] 246 2.00 N 72.00 W
Guaviare ≃ 246 4.03 N 67.44 W
Guaxindiba ≃ 287a 22.44 S 43.02 W
Guaxupé 256 21.18 S 46.42 W
Guayabal, Cuba 240p 20.42 N 77.36 W
Guayabal, Ven. 246 8.00 N 67.24 W
Guayabal, Lago ⊜[1] 240m 18.06 N 66.30 W
Guayabero ≃ 246 2.36 N 72.47 W
Guayacán 252 29.58 S 71.22 W
Guayaguayare 241r 10.08 N 61.02 W
Guayalejo ≃ 234 22.27 N 98.29 W
Guayama 240m 17.59 N 66.07 W
Guayambre ≃ 236 14.26 N 86.02 W
Guayameo 234 18.12 N 101.19 W
Guayana → Ciudad Guayana 246 8.22 N 62.40 W
Guayana → Guyana □[1] 246 5.00 N 59.00 W
Guayaneco, Archipiélago II 254 47.45 S 75.10 W
Guayanés, Punta ≻ 240m 18.04 N 65.48 W
Guayanilla 240m 18.01 N 66.47 W
Guayanilla, Bahía de ᑕ 240m 18.00 N 66.46 W
Guayape 236 14.45 N 86.52 W
Guayape ≃ 236 14.26 N 85.58 W
Guayapo ≃ 246 4.30 N 67.35 W
Guayaquil 246 2.10 S 79.50 W
Guayaquil, Golfo de ᑕ 246 3.00 S 80.30 W
Guayaramerín 248 10.48 S 65.23 W
Guayas □[4] 246 2.00 S 80.00 W
Guayas ≃, Col. 246 1.23 N 74.50 W
Guayas ≃, Ec. 246 2.36 S 79.52 W
Guayatayoc, Laguna de ⊜ 252 23.25 S 65.51 W
Guaycora 232 28.50 N 109.21 W
Guaycurú, Arroyo ≃ 258 34.00 S 56.50 W
Guaymas 232 27.56 N 110.54 W
Guaynabo 240m 18.22 N 66.07 W
Guayquiraró ≃ 252 30.10 S 58.34 W
Guayuriba ≃ 246 3.55 N 73.05 W
Guazacapán 236 14.04 N 90.25 W
Guazapares 232 27.22 N 108.15 W
Guazárachi 232 26.57 N 106.43 W
Guazhou 106 32.15 N 119.23 E
Guazunamby, Arroyo ≃ 288 34.24 S 58.38 W
Guba, Ityo. 144 10.16 N 35.17 E
Guba, Zaïre 154 10.40 S 26.26 E
Gubacha 86 58.52 N 57.36 E
Gubam 164 8.40 S 141.55 E
Gubany 76 56.37 N 30.40 E
Gubari 80 51.32 N 42.33 E
Gubat 116 12.55 N 124.07 E
Gubavica ∟ 36 43.26 N 16.54 E
Gubbi 122 13.19 N 76.56 E
Gubbio 66 43.21 N 12.35 E
Gubeikou 105 40.42 N 117.09 E
Guben 54 51.57 N 14.43 E
Gubentaoligai 104 42.16 N 122.13 E
Gubin 30 51.56 N 14.45 E
Gubinicha 78 48.48 N 35.15 E
Gubino, Ross. 80 53.19 N 48.44 E
Gubino, Ross. 82 55.42 N 39.07 E
Gubio 146 12.29 N 12.48 E
Gubkin 78 51.18 N 37.32 E
Gubug 115a 7.03 S 110.40 E
Gucheng (Zhengjiakou), Zhg. 98 37.22 N 115.56 E
Gucheng, Zhg. 100 33.59 N 117.29 E
Gucheng, Zhg. 100 25.53 N 116.11 E
Gucheng, Zhg. 100 32.46 N 118.32 E
Gucheng, Zhg. 102 32.18 N 111.35 E
Gucheng, Zhg. 105 40.32 N 116.02 E
Gucheng, Zhg. 105 39.08 N 115.42 E
Gucheng, Zhg. 106 30.29 N 119.46 E
Guchengcang 100 32.34 N 115.20 E
Gucheng Hu ⊜ 106 31.17 N 118.54 E
Guchengzi, Zhg. 104 42.33 N 123.45 E
Guchengzi, Zhg. 104 40.58 N 122.36 E
Guchengzi, Zhg. 104 40.40 N 120.31 E
Guchengzi, Zhg. 104 41.44 N 123.35 E
Gučin-Us 102 45.27 N 102.25 E
Gücük 130 38.12 N 37.29 E
Gūdalūr 122 9.41 N 77.16 E
Gúdar, Sierra de ⩘ 34 40.27 N 0.42 W
Gudauta 84 43.06 N 40.37 E
Gudbrandsdalen V 26 61.30 N 10.00 E
Gudenå ≃ 26 56.29 N 10.13 E
Gudensberg 56 51.10 N 9.22 E
Gudermes 84 43.20 N 46.08 E
Guderup 41 54.59 N 9.53 E
Gudgenby ≃ 171b 35.39 S 149.04 E
Gudhjem 26 55.13 N 14.59 E
Gudianzi 100 31.49 N 116.05 E
Gudivāda 122 16.27 N 80.59 E
Gudiyāttam 122 12.57 N 78.52 E
Gudme 41 55.09 N 10.43 E
Gudow 54 53.33 N 10.46 E
Güdül 130 40.13 N 32.15 E
Gūdūr 122 14.08 N 79.51 E
Gudvangen 26 60.52 N 6.50 E
Guebwiller (Gebweiler) 58 47.55 N 7.12 E
Guéckédou 150 8.33 N 10.09 W
Gué-de-Longroi 261 48.30 N 1.43 E
Gué-d'Hossus 50 49.57 N 4.32 E
Guédi, Mont ∧ 146 12.14 N 18.58 E
Guéguen, Lac ⊜ 190 48.06 N 77.13 W
Guéherville 261 48.32 N 1.53 E
Güejar ≃ 246 2.55 N 73.14 W
Guélendeng 146 10.56 N 15.32 E
Guelma 148 36.28 N 7.26 E
Guelma □[5] 148 36.10 N 7.50 E
Guelph 212 43.33 N 80.15 W
Guémené-sur-Scorff 32 48.04 N 3.12 W
Güemes 234 23.56 N 99.00 W
Guemes Island I 224 48.33 N 122.37 W
Guené 150 11.44 N 3.13 E
Guenguel ≃ 254 45.41 S 70.20 W
Guer 32 47.54 N 2.07 W
Guéra □[5] 146 11.30 N 18.30 E
Guéra, Massif de ∧ 146 11.55 N 18.12 E
Guérande 32 47.20 N 2.26 W
Guercif 148 34.15 N 3.21 W
Guerdjoumane, Djebel ∧ 34 36.25 N 2.51 E
Güere ≃ 246 9.50 N 65.08 W
Guéréda 146 14.31 N 22.05 E
Guéret 32 46.10 N 1.52 E
Guérin Kouka 150 9.41 N 0.37 E
Guerla Mandata Shan ∧ 120 30.26 N 81.20 E
Guermantes 261 48.51 N 2.42 E
Guerne 214 40.46 N 81.54 W
Guernes 261 49.01 N 1.38 E
Guerneville 204 38.30 N 123.00 W
Guernica, Arg. 258 34.56 S 58.25 W
Guernica → Gernika-Lumo, Esp. 34 43.19 N 2.41 W
Guernsey 200 42.16 N 104.44 W
Guernsey □[6] 214 40.08 N 81.30 W
Guernsey □[2], Europe 22 49.28 N 2.35 W
Guernsey □[2], Europe 43b 49.28 N 2.35 W
Guernsey Reservoir ⊜[1] 198 42.19 N 104.48 W
Guernsey State Park ♦ 198 42.20 N 104.50 W
Guerrero, Méx. 196 28.20 N 100.23 W
Guerrero, Méx. 232 28.33 N 107.30 W
Guerrero □[3] 234 17.40 N 100.00 W
Guerrero Negro 232 27.56 N 114.08 W
Guerville 261 48.57 N 1.44 E
Guerzim 148 29.45 N 1.47 W
Guesle ≃ 261 48.36 N 1.40 E
Guessou-Sud 150 10.03 N 2.38 E
Guest Peninsula ≻[1] 9 76.18 S 148.00 W
Gueydan 194 30.01 N 92.30 W

Guéyo 150 5.49 N 6.36 W
Gufang 100 29.04 N 119.32 E
Guffin Bay ᑕ 212 44.01 N 76.09 W
Guga 89 52.43 N 137.35 E
Gugang 100 28.17 N 113.46 E
Guge ∧ 144 6.10 N 37.26 E
Gugera 123 30.58 N 73.19 E
Gugging 264b 48.19 N 16.15 E
Güglia, Pass dal)(58 46.28 N 9.44 E
Güglingen 56 49.04 N 9.00 E
Guglionesi 66 41.55 N 14.55 E
Gugu ∧ 144 8.12 N 39.58 E
Guguan 102 40.27 N 99.13 E
Guguan I 108 17.19 N 145.51 E
Guhe 100 31.54 N 117.58 E
Gui ≃ 102 23.28 N 111.18 E
Guia 248 15.22 S 56.14 W
Guia de Pacobaíba 256 22.43 S 43.10 W
Guia Lopes da Laguna 248 21.26 S 56.07 W
Guiana Basin ✢[1] 18 11.00 N 52.00 W
Guiana Island I 240c 17.07 N 61.44 W
Guibércua 150 6.14 N 6.10 W
Guibes 156 26.41 S 16.42 E
Güicán 246 6.28 N 72.25 W
Guicher 32 47.58 N 1.48 W
Guichi 100 30.40 N 117.28 E
Guichón 252 32.21 S 57.12 W
Guicun 100 33.37 N 114.11 E
Guidan Roumji 150 13.40 N 6.42 E
Guidari 146 9.17 N 16.40 E
Guide 102 36.03 N 101.28 E
Guide, Mount ∧[2] 162 22.36 S 136.54 E
Guide Post 44 55.10 N 1.35 W
Guider 146 9.56 N 13.57 E
Guide Rock 198 40.04 N 98.19 W
Guidexiang 107 29.51 N 104.47 E
Guidigri 146 13.40 N 9.51 E
Guidimaka □[4] 150 15.30 N 12.10 W
Guidimouni 150 13.42 N 9.30 E
Guiding 102 26.34 N 107.14 E
Guidizzolo 64 45.19 N 10.35 E
Guidong 100 26.05 N 113.57 E
Guidonia 66 42.01 N 12.45 E
Guidouma 152 1.37 S 10.41 E
Guiers ≃ 62 45.37 N 5.37 E
Guiers, Lac de ⊜ 150 16.12 N 15.50 W
Guifujie 100 27.20 N 120.01 E
Guiglia 64 44.26 N 10.58 E
Guiglo 150 6.33 N 7.29 W
Guignes-Rabutin 50 48.38 N 2.48 E
Guihuayuan 107 30.37 N 105.25 E
Guihulngan 116 10.07 N 123.16 E
Güija, Lago de ⊜ 236 14.17 N 89.31 W
Guijalo 116 13.44 N 123.52 E
Guiji 100 32.51 N 116.33 E
Guijingqiao 106 31.21 N 119.40 E
Guijuelo 34 40.33 N 5.40 W
Guil ≃ 62 44.40 N 6.36 E
Guilarte, Monte ∧ 240m 18.09 N 66.46 W
Guilderland 210 42.42 N 73.54 W
Guildford, Austl. 274a 33.51 S 150.59 E
Guildford, Eng., U.K. 42 51.14 N 0.35 W
Guildford □[8] 260 51.16 N 0.32 W
Guildford Cathedral ⊍[1] 260 51.14 N 0.35 W
Guildhall 188 44.33 N 71.33 W
Guildtown 46 56.28 N 3.24 W
Guiler 89 46.11 N 121.45 E
Guilford, Ct., U.S. 207 41.17 N 72.40 W
Guilford, In., U.S. 218 39.10 N 84.55 W
Guilford, Me., U.S. 188 45.10 N 69.23 W
Guilford, N.Y., U.S. 210 42.24 N 75.29 W
Guilford Courthouse National Military Park ♦ 192 36.01 N 79.45 W
Guilherand 62 44.56 N 4.52 E
Guilin (Kweilin) 102 25.17 N 110.17 E
Guilinchang 107 30.13 N 105.50 E
Guilinzhen 107 30.15 N 104.53 E
Guillaume-Delisle, Lac ⊜ 176 56.15 N 76.17 W
Guillaumes 62 44.05 N 6.51 E
Guillermo E. Hudson 288 34.47 S 58.10 W
Guillestre 62 44.40 N 6.39 E
Guillon 50 47.31 N 4.06 E
Guilsfield 42 52.42 N 3.09 W
Guilvinec 32 47.47 N 4.17 W
Guimarães, Bra. 250 2.08 S 44.36 W
Guimarães, Port. 34 41.27 N 8.18 W
Guimaras Island I 116 10.35 N 122.37 E
Guimaras Strait ⊻ 116 10.30 N 122.44 E
Guimba 116 15.40 N 120.46 E
Guimbal 116 10.40 N 122.19 E
Guimeishan 100 24.44 N 114.52 E
Guimu Zhang ∧ 100 24.40 N 116.48 E
Guin 194 33.57 N 87.54 W
Guinan 102 35.24 N 100.57 E
Guinayang 269f 14.42 N 121.08 E
Guinayangan 116 13.54 N 122.27 E
Guinda 226 38.50 N 122.12 W
Guindulman 116 9.46 N 124.29 E
Guindulman Bay ᑕ 116 9.44 N 124.29 E
Guiné → Guinea-Bissau □[1] 150 12.00 N 15.00 W
Guinea 208 38.08 N 77.26 W
Guinea (Guinée) □[1], Afr. 134 11.00 N 10.00 W
Guinea (Guinée) □[1], Afr. 150 11.00 N 10.00 W
Guinea, Gulf of ᑕ 10 2.00 N 2.30 E
Guinea Basin ✢[1] 10 0.00 5.00 W
Guinea-Bissau (Guiné-Bissau) □[1], Afr. 134 12.00 N 15.00 W
Guinea-Bissau (Guiné-Bissau) □[1], Afr. 150 12.00 N 15.00 W
Guineacor Creek ≃ 170 34.21 S 150.05 E
Guinea Ecuatorial → Equatorial Guinea □[1] 152 2.00 N 9.00 E
Guinea Rise ✢[3] 10 8.00 S 0.00
Guiné-Bissau → Guinea-Bissau □[1] 150 12.00 N 15.00 W
Guinecourt, Lac ⊜ 186 50.55 N 69.16 W
Guinée → Guinea □[1] 150 11.00 N 10.00 W
Guinée-Bissau → Guinea-Bissau □[1] 150 12.00 N 15.00 W
Guinée équitoriale → Equatorial Guinea □[1] 152 2.00 N 9.00 E
Güines, Cuba 240p 22.50 N 82.02 W
Guînes, Fr. 50 50.52 N 1.52 E
Guingamp 32 48.33 N 3.11 W
Guinguinéo 150 14.16 N 15.57 W
Guinobatan 116 13.11 N 123.36 E
Güinope 236 13.51 N 86.55 W
Guintacan Island I 116 11.19 N 123.54 E
Guintinguintin, Mount ∧ 116 12.25 N 122.24 E
Guintinua Island I 116 14.26 N 122.51 E
Guiones, Punta ≻ 236 9.54 N 85.41 W
Guiong 116 6.25 N 122.01 E
Guiperreux 261 48.40 N 1.42 E
Guiperreux, Étang de ⊜ 261 48.40 N 1.43 E
Guiping 102 23.20 N 110.09 E
Guir, Hammada du ✦[2] 148 30.45 N 3.15 W
Guir, Oued V 148 30.29 N 2.17 W
Güira de Melena 240p 22.48 N 82.30 W
Guiraí ≃ 255 22.40 S 53.34 W
Guiratinga 255 16.21 S 53.45 W
Guiren 100 33.42 N 118.12 E
Güiria 246 10.34 N 62.18 W

≃ River	Fluß	Río	Rivière	Rio
≊ Canal	Kanal	Canal	Canal	Canal
∟ Waterfall, Rapids	Wasserfall, Stromschnellen	Cascada, Rápidos	Chute d'eau, Rapides	Cascata, Rápidos
⊻ Strait	Meeresstraße	Estrecho	Détroit	Estreito
ᑕ Bay, Gulf	Bucht, Golf	Bahía, Golfo	Baie, Golfe	Baía, Golfo
⊜ Lake, Lakes	See, Seen	Lago, Lagos	Lac, Lacs	Lago, Lagos
≡ Swamp	Sumpf	Pantano	Marais	Pântano
⊓ Ice Features, Glacier	Eis- und Gletscherformen	Accidentes Glaciales	Formes glaciaires	Acidentes glaciares
⊤ Other Hydrographic Features	Andere Hydrographische Objekte	Otros Elementos Hidrográficos	Autres données hydrographiques	Outros acidentes hidrográficos
✢ Submarine Features	Untermeerische Objekte	Accidentes Submarinos	Formes de relief sous-marin	Acidentes submarinos
□ Political Unit	Politische Einheit	Unidad Politica	Entité politique	Unidade política
⊍ Cultural Institution	Kulturelle Institution	Institución Cultural	Institution culturelle	Instituição cultural
⊥ Historical Site	Historische Stätte	Sitio Histórico	Site historique	Sitio histórico
♦ Recreational Site	Erholungs- und Ferienort	Sitio de Recreo	Centre de loisirs	Area de Lazer
⊠ Airport	Flughafen	Aeropuerto	Aéroport	Aeroporto
■ Military Installation	Militäranlage	Instalación Militar	Installation militaire	Instalação militar
✦ Miscellaneous	Verschiedenes	Misceláneo	Divers	Diversos

ENGLISH | DEUTSCH

Name	Page	Lat.°′	Long.°′
Guiricema	255	21.00 S	42.43 W
Guisachan Forest •[3]	46	57.17 N	4.55 W
Guisanbourg	250	4.25 N	51.56 W
Guisborough	44	54.32 N	1.04 W
Guiscard	50	49.39 N	3.03 E
Guise	50	49.54 N	3.38 E
Guiseley	44	53.53 N	1.42 W
Guisijan	116	11.05 N	122.03 E
Güisisil ∧	236	12.37 N	86.13 W
Guist Creek ≃	218	38.09 N	85.13 W
Guitiriz	34	43.11 N	7.54 W
Guitou	100	24.58 N	113.25 E
Guitrancourt	261	49.01 N	1.47 E
Guîtres	32	45.03 N	0.11 W
Guitry	150	5.31 N	5.14 W
Guiuan	116	11.02 N	125.43 E
Guixi	100	28.16 N	117.10 E
Guixian	102	23.06 N	109.39 E
Guiyang, Zhg.	100	25.46 N	112.43 E
Guiyang (Kweiyang), Zhg.	102	26.35 N	106.43 E
Güiza ≃	246	1.22 N	78.36 W
Guizhou (Kweichow) □[4]	102	27.00 N	107.00 E
Gujarāt □[3]	118	22.00 N	72.00 E
Gūjar Khān	123	33.16 N	73.19 E
Gujba	146	11.30 N	11.55 E
Gujiabeng	106	30.45 N	120.59 E
Gujiang	100	27.11 N	114.49 E
Gujiatun	104	40.39 N	124.08 E
Gujiatuo	107	29.14 N	106.12 E
Gujiazhai	269b	31.22 N	121.28 E
Gujiazi, Zhg.	104	42.02 N	123.01 E
Gujiazi, Zhg.	104	41.44 N	124.11 E
Gujrānwāla	123	32.09 N	74.11 E
Gujrāt	123	32.34 N	74.05 E
Gukas'an	84	41.03 N	43.52 E
Gukou	100	26.27 N	118.38 E
Gukovo	83	48.03 N	39.56 E
Gul, Tanjong ›	271c	1.17 N	103.39 E
Gul'a	88	54.41 N	121.01 E
Gul'aj-Borisovka	78	46.38 N	40.13 E
Gul'ajevskije Koški, ostrova II	24	68.55 N	55.10 E
Gul'ajpole	78	47.38 N	36.16 E
Gulang	102	37.36 N	102.58 E
Gulaothi	124	28.36 N	77.47 E
Gulargambone	166	31.20 S	148.28 E
Gulbarga	122	17.20 N	76.50 E
Gulbene	76	57.11 N	26.45 E
Gul'ča	85	40.19 N	73.26 E
Gul'ča ≃	85	40.20 N	73.26 E
Guldasteh	267d	35.36 N	51.16 E
Guldborg	41	54.52 N	11.45 E
Guldborg Sund ʮ	41	54.48 N	11.48 E
Guldsmedshyttan	40	59.42 N	15.06 E
Güldüzü	130	36.52 N	37.07 E
Gülebağdı	130	39.52 N	39.50 E
Guledagudda	122	16.03 N	75.48 E
Guleitou	100	23.47 N	117.36 E
Gülek Boğazı)(	130	37.16 N	34.48 E
Gulf □[5]	164	7.00 S	145.00 E
Gulf Gate Estates	220	27.15 N	82.31 W
Gulf Hammock	192	29.15 N	82.43 W
Gulf Harbors	220	28.14 N	82.45 W
Gulf Islands National Seashore ♦	194	30.14 N	88.42 W
Gulf of Alaska Seamount Province ✢	16	56.00 N	147.00 W
Gulfport, Fl., U.S.	220	27.45 N	82.40 W
Gulfport, Ms., U.S.	194	30.22 N	89.05 W
Gulf Shores	194	30.14 N	87.42 W
Gulf State Park ♦	194	30.16 N	87.40 W
Gulf Stream ≃	212	43.51 N	75.56 W
Gulgong	166	32.22 S	149.32 E
Guli	106	31.38 N	120.50 E
Gulian	89	52.55 N	122.19 E
Gulicun	106	31.52 N	118.41 E
Gul Imām	123	32.16 N	70.32 E
Gulistān, Pāk.	120	30.36 N	66.35 E
Gulistan, Uzb.	85	40.30 N	68.46 E
Guliya Shan ∧	89	49.48 N	122.25 E
Guljanci	38	43.38 N	24.42 E
Gulkana	180	62.16 N	145.23 W
Gull ≃	212	44.37 N	78.49 W
Gulland Rock II[1]	42	50.34 N	4.59 W
Gullane	46	56.02 N	2.50 W
Gullfoss ⌞	24a	64.24 N	20.08 W
Gullholmen	26	58.11 N	11.24 E
Gullion, Slieve ∧[2]	48	54.08 N	6.27 W
Gull Island I	281	42.32 N	82.41 W
Gullivan Bay c	220	25.52 N	81.38 W
Gull Lake	184	50.08 N	108.27 W
Gull Lake ⊜, Ab., Can.	182	52.35 N	114.00 W
Gull Lake ⊜, On., Can.	184	51.18 N	91.58 W
Gull Lake ⊜, On., Can.	212	44.51 N	78.47 W
Gull Lake ⊜, Mi., U.S.	216	42.24 N	85.25 W
Gull Lake ⊜, Mn., U.S.	190	46.25 N	94.20 W
Gullrock Lake ⊜	184	50.58 N	93.40 W
Gullspång	40	58.59 N	14.06 E
Güllük	130	37.14 N	27.36 E
Güllük Körfezi c	130	37.12 N	27.20 E
Gulmarg	123	34.03 N	74.23 E
Gulnam	140	6.55 N	29.30 E
Gülnar	130	36.20 N	33.25 E
Gulong	89	45.51 N	124.14 E
Gulpen	56	50.48 N	5.54 E
Gülper See ⊜	54	52.44 N	12.14 E
Gulph Mills	285	40.04 N	75.21 W
Gülpınar	130	39.32 N	26.07 E
Gul'ripš	84	42.57 N	41.06 E
Gul'šad	86	46.39 N	74.24 E
Gülşehir	130	38.45 N	34.38 E
Gulshan	126	23.49 N	90.27 E
Gulsvik	26	60.23 N	9.35 E
Gulu, Ug.	154	2.47 N	32.18 E
Gulu, Zhg.	120	28.06 N	89.17 E
Gulukguluk	115a	7.04 S	113.40 E
Guluogongba	120	34.20 N	84.50 E
Guluy	144	14.44 N	36.43 E
Gulwe	154	6.30 S	36.29 E
Gumaca	116	13.55 N	122.06 E
Gumahang	116	12.35 N	123.16 E
Gumal (Gowmal) ≃	120	31.56 N	70.22 E
Gumare	156	19.21 S	22.12 E
Gumba, Ang.	152	11.40 S	16.34 E
Gumba, Zaïre	152	2.57 N	21.26 E
Gumbinnen → Gusev	76	54.36 N	22.12 E
Gumbiro	154	10.16 S	35.39 E
Gumel	150	12.39 N	9.22 E
Gumeracha	168b	34.49 S	138.53 E
Gumiao	100	32.26 N	113.16 E
Gumieńce •[8]	54	53.25 N	14.30 E
Gumistskij zapovednik ♦	84	43.15 N	41.05 E
Gumla	124	23.03 N	84.33 E
Gumma □[5]	94	36.30 N	139.00 E
Gummersbach	56	51.02 N	7.34 E
Gummi	150	12.09 N	5.09 E
Gumpas Pond ⊜	283	42.44 N	71.22 W
Gumpas Pond Brook ≃	283	42.42 N	71.21 W
Gumpoldskirchen	264b	48.03 N	16.17 E
Gum Swamp Creek ≃	192	32.08 N	82.55 W
Gumti ≃	126	23.32 N	90.43 E
Gümüşçay	130	40.16 N	27.17 E
Gümüşhacıköy	130	40.53 N	35.14 E
Gümüşhane	130	40.27 N	39.29 E
Gümüşhane □[4]	130	40.15 N	39.45 E
Gümüşkent	130	38.50 N	34.32 E
Gümüşköy •[8]	267b	41.14 N	28.58 E
Gümüşova	130	40.51 N	30.57 E
Gümüşsü	130	38.14 N	30.01 E
Gun ≃	216	42.28 N	85.40 W
Guna, India	124	24.39 N	77.19 E
Guna, Ityo.	144	8.19 N	39.51 E
Guna ∧	144	11.42 N	38.12 E
Gunbar	166	34.01 S	145.25 E
Gun Barrel City	222	32.20 N	96.10 W
Gun Creek ≃	284a	43.03 N	78.55 W
Gunda	88	52.47 N	111.44 E
Gundagai	166	35.04 S	148.07 E
Gundelfingen	56	48.33 N	10.22 E
Gundelsheim	56	49.17 N	9.09 E
Gundik	115a	7.12 S	110.54 E
Gundji	152	2.05 N	21.27 E
Gundlakamma ≃	122	15.32 N	80.14 E
Gundlupet	122	11.48 N	76.41 E
Gündoğdu	130	40.15 N	27.07 E
Gündoğmuş	130	36.48 N	32.01 E
Guneh Ghar ∧	123	35.19 N	71.47 E
Güney	130	38.09 N	29.05 E
Gungartan ∧	171b	36.18 S	148.24 E
Gungi	152	6.21 S	19.15 E
Gungo	152	11.48 S	14.08 E
Güngören •[8]	267b	41.01 N	28.53 E
Gungu	152	5.44 S	19.19 E
Gunib	84	42.25 N	46.57 E
Gunisao ≃	184	53.54 N	97.58 W
Gunisao Lake ⊜	184	53.33 N	96.15 W
Gunjrauliya	124	26.35 N	84.34 E
Gun Lake ⊜	216	42.37 N	85.32 W
Gunma	94	36.24 N	139.00 E
Gunnar	176	59.23 N	108.53 W
Günnarijn	102	45.38 N	102.01 E
Gunnarn	26	65.00 N	17.40 E
Gunnbjørn Fjeld ∧	16	68.55 N	29.53 W
Gunnebo	26	57.43 N	16.32 E
Gunnedah	166	30.59 S	150.15 E
Gunning Island I	276	40.22 N	73.59 W
Gunnislake	42	50.31 N	4.12 W
Gunnison, Co., U.S.	200	38.32 N	106.55 W
Gunnison, Ut., U.S.	200	39.09 N	111.49 W
Gunnison ≃	200	39.03 N	108.35 W
Gunnison, Lake Fork ≃	200	38.28 N	107.19 W
Gunnison, North Fork ≃	200	38.47 N	107.50 W
Gunn Peak ∧	224	47.49 N	121.27 W
Gunong Mulu National Park ♦	112	4.10 N	114.55 E
Gunpowder Creek ≃, Austl.	166	19.14 S	139.58 E
Gunpowder Creek ≃, Ky., U.S.	218	38.53 N	84.47 W
Gunpowder Falls ≃	208	39.24 N	76.22 W
Gunpowder Falls State Park ♦	208	39.37 N	76.40 W
Gunpowder River c	208	39.22 N	76.22 W
Gunsan → Kunsan	98	35.58 N	126.41 E
Gunskirchen	60	48.08 N	13.57 E
Gunston Cove c	208	38.40 N	77.09 W
Guntakal	122	15.10 N	77.23 E
Güntersberge	54	51.38 N	10.59 E
Guntersblum	56	49.47 N	8.21 E
Guntersdorf	61	48.39 N	16.03 E
Guntersville	194	34.21 N	86.17 W
Guntersville Dam •[6]	194	34.13 N	86.23 W
Guntersville Lake ⊜[1]	194	34.45 N	86.03 W
Guntingsaga	114	2.33 N	99.39 E
Guntramsdorf	61	48.03 N	16.19 E
Guntung	114	1.38 N	101.34 E
Guntūr	122	16.18 N	80.27 E
Gunungkencana	115a	6.34 S	106.04 E
Gunungmegang	112	3.27 S	103.52 E
Gunungsahilan	112	0.06 N	101.18 E
Gunungsitoli	114	1.17 N	97.37 E
Gunungtua	114	1.30 N	99.37 E
Gunupur	122	19.05 N	83.49 E
Gunyidi	162	30.08 S	116.04 E
Günyüzü	130	39.24 N	31.50 E
Günz ≃	58	48.27 N	10.16 E
Gunza ≃	152	11.10 S	13.50 E
Günzburg	58	48.27 N	10.16 E
Gunzenhausen	56	49.07 N	10.45 E
Gunzigou	104	41.31 N	123.58 E
Guo ≃	100	32.57 N	117.14 E
Guobei	107	29.33 N	105.08 E
Guodian	106	30.27 N	120.33 E
Guoji	100	32.59 N	113.06 E
Guojiadian	104	41.51 N	121.30 E
Guojiajiang	106	32.17 N	120.50 E
Guojiatun, Zhg.	98	41.31 N	117.02 E
Guojiatun, Zhg.	104	42.00 N	122.51 E
Guojiatun, Zhg.	104	40.52 N	122.04 E
Guojiawopeng	104	42.03 N	122.46 E
Guojiayao	105	40.37 N	115.39 E
Guojiayuan	106	32.10 N	120.35 E
Guojiga	86	43.47 N	80.48 E
Guoleizhuang	98	40.44 N	114.36 E
Guolutan	100	32.04 N	115.40 E
Guosu	98	38.24 N	114.00 E
Guoyang	100	33.32 N	116.12 E
Guoyangzhen	102	38.54 N	112.50 E
Guozhuang	98	35.25 N	117.10 E
Guozhuangmiao	106	31.49 N	119.01 E
Gupei	98	34.09 N	117.54 E
Gupis	123	36.14 N	73.26 E
Gura	80	57.18 N	51.25 E
Gura, Wādī V	140	17.28 N	35.10 E
Gurabo	240m	18.16 N	65.58 W
Guraferda	144	6.51 N	35.04 E
Gura-Galbena	38	46.43 N	28.42 E
Gurage ∧	144	8.24 N	38.24 E
Gurahonț	38	46.16 N	22.21 E
Gura Humorului	38	47.33 N	25.54 E
Gurais	123	34.38 N	74.50 E
Guran	88	54.46 N	100.38 E
Gurara ≃	150	8.12 N	6.41 E
Gurban Anggir	102	37.45 N	97.30 E
Gurban Obo	102	43.14 N	112.28 E
Gurdāspur	123	32.02 N	75.31 E
Gurdon	194	33.55 N	93.09 W
Gurdžaani	84	41.43 N	45.48 E
Güre	130	38.39 N	29.10 E
Gurejev	80	47.21 N	43.16 E
G'urg'an	84	40.23 N	50.19 E
Gurgaon	124	28.28 N	77.02 E
Gurgei, Jabal ∧	140	13.50 N	24.19 E
Gurghiului, Munții ⋏	38	46.41 N	25.12 E
Gurgó ∧[2]	61	46.31 N	16.50 E
Gurgueia ≃	250	6.50 S	43.24 W
Gurgur	144	7.48 N	41.32 E
Gurha	120	25.11 N	71.40 E
Guri	144	7.27 N	40.36 E
Guri, Embalse de ⊜[1]	246	7.30 N	62.50 W
Gurig National Park ♦	164	11.25 S	132.15 E
Gurjevo	82	54.42 N	36.28 E
Gurjevsk, Ross.	76	54.47 N	20.38 E
Gurjevsk, Ross.	86	54.17 N	85.56 E
Gurk	61	46.52 N	14.18 E
Gurk ≃	61	46.36 N	14.31 E
Gurk ⚲[1]	61	46.52 N	14.15 E
Gurktaler Alpen ⋏	64	46.55 N	14.00 E
Gūr Kūh ∧	128	26.06 N	58.28 E
Gurla Mandhata → Guerla Mandata Shan ∧	120	30.26 N	81.20 E
Gurlevo	76	59.28 N	28.54 E
Gurnee	216	42.22 N	87.54 W
Gurnet Point ›	283	42.01 N	70.34 W
Gürpınar	128	38.18 N	43.25 E
Gurror	174q	9.27 N	138.04 E
Gursarai	124	25.37 N	79.11 E
Gurskoje	89	50.21 N	138.12 E
Gurskøy I	26	62.15 N	5.41 E
Gürsu	130	40.13 N	29.12 E
Gurué	154	15.25 S	36.58 E
Guru Har Sahāi	123	30.43 N	74.25 E
Gurumeti ≃	154	2.05 S	33.57 E
Gurun, Malay.	114	5.49 N	100.29 E
Gürün, Tür.	130	38.43 N	37.17 E
Gurupá	250	1.25 S	51.39 W
Gurupi	250	11.43 S	49.04 W
Gurupi ≃	250	1.13 S	46.06 W
Guru Sikhar ∧	120	24.39 N	72.46 E
Gurvanbulag	88	47.38 N	103.31 E
Gurvansajchan	102	45.32 N	107.00 E
Gurvan Sajchan uul ⋏	102	43.50 N	103.30 E
Gurvantes	102	43.26 N	101.36 E
Gurzuf	78	44.33 N	34.17 E
Gus' ≃	80	55.00 N	41.11 E
Gusar	85	39.28 N	67.50 E
Gušari	85	38.55 N	68.51 E
Gusarka	78	47.23 N	36.31 E
Gus'atin	78	49.05 N	26.11 E
Gusau	150	12.12 N	6.40 E
Gus'-Chrustal'nyj	80	55.37 N	40.40 E
Guselka	80	50.27 N	45.09 E
Güsen	54	52.21 N	11.59 E
Gusen ≃	61	48.15 N	14.30 E
Gusev, Ross.	76	54.36 N	22.12 E
Gusev, Ross.	78	48.27 N	40.32 E
Gusevo	76	56.06 N	33.21 E
Gusevskij	80	55.40 N	40.34 E
Gushan, Zhg.	98	39.53 N	123.36 E
Gushan, Zhg.	98	36.30 N	116.53 E
Gushan, Zhg.	106	31.44 N	120.33 E
Gu Shan ∧, Zhg.	100	26.05 N	119.22 E
Gu Shan ∧, Zhg.	104	41.18 N	120.35 E
Gushanbeizifu	104	42.10 N	120.30 E
Gushankou	105	39.38 N	115.49 E
Gushantun	89	48.18 N	123.47 E
Gushanzi, Zhg.	98	40.22 N	120.03 E
Gushanzi, Zhg.	104	41.03 N	123.03 E
Gushi, Zhg.	100	28.34 N	119.24 E
Gushi, Zhg.	100	32.12 N	115.41 E
Gushiago	150	9.55 N	0.12 W
Gushikami	174m	26.07 N	127.45 E
Gushikawa	174m	26.21 N	127.52 E
Gushu, Zhg.	104	42.36 N	123.26 E
Gushu, Zhg.	105	39.55 N	117.35 E
Gushuji	98	34.15 N	115.48 E
Gusi	112	6.07 N	117.08 E
Gusino	76	54.44 N	31.22 E
Gusinoje, ozero ⊜	88	51.12 N	106.24 E
Gusinoje Ozero	88	51.09 N	106.10 E
Gusinoozersk	88	51.17 N	106.30 E
Guskef	85	39.02 N	69.20 E
Guskhara	126	23.30 N	87.45 E
Gus'-Khrustal'nyy → Gus'-Chrustal'nyj	80	55.37 N	40.40 E
Guskube	175d	24.45 N	125.26 E
Gusong	102	28.18 N	105.14 E
Guspini	71	39.32 N	8.37 E
Gussago	64	45.35 N	10.09 E
Gusselby	40	59.39 N	15.14 E
Güssing	61	47.04 N	16.20 E
Gussola	64	45.00 N	10.20 E
Gusswerk	61	47.45 N	15.18 E
Gustav Holm, Kap ›	176	67.00 N	34.00 W
Gustavo A. Madero •[8]	286a	19.29 N	99.07 W
Gustavo Díaz Ordaz	234	17.44 N	94.23 W
Gustavsberg	40	59.19 N	18.23 E
Gustavus	180	58.25 N	135.44 W
Güsten	54	51.49 N	11.35 E
Gustia	272b	22.59 N	88.26 E
Gustine, Ca., U.S.	226	37.15 N	120.59 W
Gustine, Tx., U.S.	196	31.51 N	98.24 W
Gustorf	56	51.04 N	6.34 E
Güstrow	54	53.48 N	12.10 E
Gusum	26	58.16 N	16.29 E
Gus'-Železnyj	80	55.03 N	41.10 E
Gutach	58	48.15 N	8.13 E
Gutaj	88	49.59 N	108.12 E
Gutanggou	104	42.02 N	124.10 E
Gutara ≃	88	54.50 N	97.23 E
Gutarskij chrebet ⋏	88	54.30 N	97.40 E
Gutau	61	48.25 N	14.37 E
Gutcher	46a	60.40 N	1.00 W
Gutenfels, Burg ⊥	56	50.07 N	7.46 E
Guten Hoffnung, Kap der → Good Hope, Cape of ›	158	34.24 S	18.30 E
Güterfelde	264a	52.22 N	13.12 E
Gütersloh	52	51.54 N	8.23 E
Guthrie, In., U.S.	218	38.59 N	86.31 W
Guthrie, Ky., U.S.	194	36.38 N	87.09 W
Guthrie, Ok., U.S.	196	35.52 N	97.25 W
Guthrie, Tx., U.S.	196	33.37 N	100.19 W
Guthrie Center	198	41.40 N	94.30 W
Guthrie Lake ⊜	184	55.17 N	100.38 W
Gutian, Zhg.	100	26.36 N	118.46 E
Gutian, Zhg.	100	25.15 N	116.46 E
Gutian, Zhg.	100	25.43 N	116.57 E
Gutian ≃	100	26.22 N	118.42 E
Gutierrez	248	19.25 S	63.34 W
Gutiérrez Zamora	234	20.27 N	97.05 W
Gutland •[1]	56	49.40 N	6.10 E
Gutob Bay c	116	12.09 N	119.54 E
Guton, gora ∧	84	41.51 N	46.45 E
Gutorfölde	61	46.39 N	16.44 E
Guttannen	58	46.39 N	8.18 E
Guttau	54	51.15 N	14.34 E
Guttenberg, Ia., U.S.	190	42.47 N	91.05 W
Guttenberg, N.J., U.S.	276	40.47 N	74.00 W
Gutu	154	19.38 S	31.10 E
Gutujevskij, ostrov I	265a	59.54 N	30.14 E
Gutulia Nasjonalpark ♦	26	62.02 N	12.12 E
Guty	78	50.08 N	35.21 E
Gützkow	54	53.56 N	13.24 E
Güvem	130	40.36 N	32.40 E
Guwāhāti	120	26.10 N	91.45 E
Guxhagen	56	51.12 N	9.28 E
Guxi	107	30.18 N	105.52 E
Guxian, Zhg.	98	37.35 N	121.09 E
Guxian, Zhg.	100	32.26 N	113.37 E
Guxian, Zhg.	100	27.09 N	115.31 E
Guxiandu	100	29.06 N	116.50 E
Guxiansi	100	32.01 N	116.20 E
Guxiong	106	31.55 N	118.38 E
Guy	222	29.21 N	95.47 W
Guyana □[1], S.A.	242	5.00 N	59.00 W
Guyana □[1], S.A.	246	5.00 N	59.00 W
Guyancourt	261	48.46 N	2.04 E
Guyancourt, Aéroport de ⊠	261	48.45 N	2.05 E
Guyandotte ≃	188	38.26 N	82.23 W
Guyane → Guyana □[1]	246	5.00 N	59.00 W
Guyane française → French Guiana □[2]	250	4.00 N	53.00 W
Guyang, Zhg.	98	34.58 N	114.58 E
Guyang, Zhg.	102	41.03 N	110.03 E
Guye	105	39.44 N	118.25 E
Guy Fawkes River National Park ♦	166	30.02 S	152.18 E
Guyi, Zhg.	100	25.38 N	118.47 E
Guyi, Zhg.	107	30.22 N	103.33 E
Guyin	102	23.58 N	105.47 E
Guymon	196	36.40 N	101.28 W
Guyonne, Ruisseau la ≃	261	48.49 N	1.52 E
Guyot, Mount ∧	192	35.42 N	83.15 W
Guyra	166	30.14 S	151.40 E
Guysborough	186	45.23 N	61.30 W
Guys Mills	214	41.38 N	79.59 W
Guyton	192	32.20 N	81.23 W
Guyuan (Pingdingbu), Zhg.	98	41.40 N	115.41 E
Guyuan, Zhg.	102	36.01 N	106.17 E
Guzar	72	38.36 N	66.15 E
Güzel ≃	84	39.44 N	43.01 E
Güzelbahçe	130	38.21 N	26.54 E
Güzelsu	130	36.54 N	31.53 E
Güzelyurt, Kıbrıs	130	35.12 N	32.59 E
Güzelyurt, Tür.	130	38.17 N	34.23 E
Güzelyurt Körfezi c	130	35.10 N	32.50 E
Guzhang	102	28.31 N	109.57 E
Guzhen, Zhg.	100	22.37 N	113.11 E
Guzhen, Zhg.	100	33.19 N	117.21 E
Guzhu	100	26.58 N	116.16 E
Guzmán, Méx.	232	31.13 N	107.27 W
Guzmán → Ciudad Guzmán, Méx.	234	19.41 N	103.29 W
Guzmán, Laguna de ⊜	200	31.20 N	107.30 W
Gvardejsk	76	54.39 N	21.05 E
Gvardejskoje, Ukr.	78	45.07 N	34.01 E
Gvardejskoje, Ukr.	78	48.44 N	35.19 E
Gvardejskoje, Ukr.	78	49.20 N	26.42 E
Gvazda	78	50.44 N	40.30 E
Gvozdec	78	48.34 N	25.17 E
Gwa	110	17.36 N	94.35 E
Gwabegar	166	30.36 S	148.58 E
Gwadabawa	150	13.20 N	5.15 E
Gwādar	128	25.07 N	62.19 E
Gwagwada	150	10.14 N	7.14 E
Gwai	154	19.15 S	27.42 E
Gwai ≃	154	17.59 S	26.52 E
Gwalangu	152	2.19 N	18.11 E
Gwalchmai	44	53.15 N	4.25 W
Gwāl Haidarzai	120	30.44 N	68.48 E
Gwalia	162	28.55 S	121.20 E
Gwalior	124	26.13 N	78.10 E
Gwambygine	168a	31.59 S	116.48 E
Gwanda	154	20.57 S	29.01 E
Gwandu	150	12.30 N	4.41 E
Gwane	154	4.43 N	25.50 E
Gwangjang Bridge •[5]	271b	37.33 N	127.05 E
Gwangju → Kwangju	98	35.09 N	126.54 E
Gwarzo	150	11.56 N	7.56 E
Gwasero	150	9.29 N	3.30 E
Gwash ≃	42	52.39 N	0.27 W
Gwātar Bay c	128	25.04 N	61.36 E
Gwatt	58	46.43 N	7.38 E
Gwaun ≃	42	52.00 N	4.58 W
Gwda ≃	30	53.04 N	16.44 E
Gweebarra ≃	48	54.50 N	8.20 W
Gweebarra Bay c	48	54.52 N	8.20 W
Gweedore	48	55.03 N	8.14 W
Gweesalia	48	54.07 N	9.54 W
Gwelo ≃	154	18.45 S	28.36 E
Gwembe	154	16.30 S	27.35 E
Gwendraeth Fâch ≃	42	51.44 N	4.18 W
Gwendraeth Fawr ≃	42	51.43 N	4.18 W
Gwent □[6]	42	51.43 N	2.57 W
Gweru	154	19.27 S	29.49 E
Gweta	156	20.10 S	25.18 E
Gwinhurst	285	39.47 N	75.29 W
Gwinn	190	46.16 N	87.26 W
Gwinner	198	46.13 N	97.39 W
Gwobu	154	2.37 N	26.13 E
Gwongorella National Park ♦	171a	28.10 S	153.17 E
Gwydir ≃	166	29.27 S	149.48 E
Gwynedd	285	40.12 N	75.15 W
Gwynedd □[6]	28	53.00 N	4.00 W
Gwynedd Square	285	40.13 N	75.18 W
Gwynedd Valley	285	40.11 N	75.15 W
Gwynn	208	37.30 N	76.17 W
Gwynneville	218	39.39 N	85.38 W
Gwynn Island I	208	37.30 N	76.17 W
Gwynns Falls ≃	284b	39.16 N	76.37 W
Gwynns Falls Park ♦	284b	39.18 N	76.41 W
Gy	58	47.24 N	5.49 E
Gyál	264c	47.23 N	19.14 E
Gya La)(	124	28.44 N	84.40 E
Gyáli-patak ≃	264c	47.24 N	19.07 E
Gyangtse → Gyangzê	120	28.57 N	89.35 E
Gyangzê	120	28.57 N	89.35 E
Gyaring Co ⊜	120	31.10 N	88.15 E
Gyaring Hu ⊜	102	34.53 N	97.58 E
Gybdan	80	56.33 N	51.39 E
Gyda	74	70.52 N	78.30 E
Gydanskaja guba c	74	71.20 N	76.30 E
Gydanskij poluostrov ›[1]	74	70.50 N	79.00 E
Gyebu	164	3.03 S	133.51 E
Gyemo Chen ∧	124	27.20 N	88.52 E
Gyeongbog Palace ⚲	271b	37.36 N	126.57 E
Gyeongju → Kyŏngju	98	35.51 N	129.14 E
Gyirong, Zhg.	120	28.29 N	85.20 E
Gyirong, Zhg.	120	28.57 N	85.15 E
Gyldenløves Fjord c[2]	176	64.30 N	41.30 W
Gyldenløveshøj ∧[2]	41	55.33 N	11.52 E
Gylling	41	55.53 N	10.11 E
Gymea Bay	274a	34.02 S	151.05 E
Gym Peak ∧	200	32.04 N	107.35 W
Gympie	166	26.11 S	152.40 E
Gyobingauk	110	18.13 N	95.39 E
Gyōda	94	36.08 N	139.28 E
Gyoma	30	46.56 N	20.50 E
Gyöngyös	30	47.47 N	19.56 E
Gyöngyös ≃	61	47.14 N	16.55 E
Győr	30	47.42 N	17.38 E
Győr-Moson-Sopron □[6]	30	47.35 N	17.15 E
Gypsey Race ≃	44	54.05 N	0.12 W
Gypsum, Co., U.S.	200	39.38 N	106.57 W
Gypsum, Ks., U.S.	198	38.42 N	97.25 W
Gypsum, Oh., U.S.	214	41.29 N	82.52 W
Gypsum Creek ≃, U.S.	200	37.09 N	109.52 W
Gypsum Creek ≃, Ks., U.S.	198	38.51 N	97.25 W
Gypsum Hills ⋏[2]	196	36.25 N	99.20 W
Gypsum Point ›	176	61.53 N	114.35 W
Gypsumville	184	51.45 N	98.35 W
Gyrbovec	38	46.50 N	29.21 E
Gysinge	40	60.17 N	16.53 E
Gyttorp	40	59.31 N	14.58 E
Gyula	30	46.39 N	21.17 E
Gyulafehérvár → Alba Iulia	38	46.04 N	23.35 E
Gžat' ≃	76	55.56 N	34.33 E
Gžatsk	86	55.42 N	78.11 E
Gžel'	82	55.36 N	38.24 E
Gzhatsk → Gagarin	76	55.33 N	35.00 E
H			
Haag → 's-Gravenhage, Ned.	52	52.06 N	4.18 E
Haag, Öst.	61	48.07 N	14.34 E
Haag am Hausruck	60	48.11 N	13.38 E
Haagen	58	47.38 N	7.40 E
Haag in Oberbayern	60	48.10 N	12.11 E
Haaksbergen	52	52.09 N	6.44 E
Haalenberg	156	26.52 S	15.30 E
Haaltert	50	50.54 N	4.00 E
Haamstede	52	51.43 N	3.45 E
Haan	56	51.11 N	7.00 E
Haapajärvi	26	63.45 N	25.20 E
Haapajärvi ⊜	26	63.33 N	27.00 E
Haapamäki	26	62.15 N	24.28 E
Haapavesi	26	64.08 N	25.22 E
Haapiti	174s	17.34 S	149.52 W
Haapsalu	76	58.56 N	23.33 E
Haar	60	48.06 N	11.44 E
Haar •[8]	263	51.26 N	7.13 E
Ha'Arava (Wādī al-'Arabah) V, Asia	132	30.10 N	35.10 E
Ha'Arava (Wādī al-Jayb) V, Asia	132	30.58 N	35.24 E
Haardt ⋏	56	49.15 N	8.00 E
Haaren, Dtsch.	52	51.34 N	8.44 E
Haaren, Ned.	52	51.36 N	5.12 E
Haarlem, Ned.	52	52.23 N	4.38 E
Haarlem, S. Afr.	158	33.44 S	23.20 E
Haarlemmermeer •[1]	52	52.15 N	4.38 E
Haarstrang ∧	52	51.35 N	8.10 E
Haarzopf •[8]	263	51.25 N	6.58 E
Haast	172	43.53 S	169.03 E
Haast ≃	172	43.50 S	169.02 E
Haast Bluff	162	23.30 S	131.50 E
Haast Pass)(	172	44.06 S	169.21 E
Haasts Bluff Reserve •[4]	162	23.30 S	130.30 E
Haatinao, Pointe ›	174x	9.47 S	138.51 W
Haava, Canal ʮ	174x	9.53 S	139.04 W
Hab ≃	120	24.53 N	66.41 E
Habahe	86	47.53 N	86.12 E
Habana, Bahía de la c	286b	23.08 N	82.20 W
Habaqi, Zhg.	104	42.38 N	122.02 E
Habaqi, Zhg.	104	42.36 N	122.52 E
Habaqila	102	42.01 N	106.02 E
Habartov	54	50.08 N	12.33 E
Ḥabashīyah, Jabal ⋏	144	16.40 N	49.40 E
Habaswein	154	1.01 N	39.29 E
Ḥabawnah, Wādī V	144	17.51 N	44.59 E
Habay-la-Neuve	56	49.44 N	5.39 E
Ḥabbān	144	14.21 N	47.05 E
Ḥabbānīyah, Hawr al- ⊜	128	33.17 N	43.29 E
Ḥabbūsh	132	33.24 N	35.29 E
Hab Chauki	120	25.01 N	66.53 E
Habère-Poche	58	46.15 N	6.29 E
Haberfield	274a	33.53 S	151.08 E
Haberli	130	37.19 N	41.38 E
Habermehl Peak ∧	9	71.49 S	6.38 E
Ḥabīb, Wādī V	142	27.20 N	31.30 E
Habiganj	120	24.23 N	91.25 E
Habikino	96	34.33 N	135.37 E
Habīlah	140	12.41 N	22.33 E
Habinghorst	263	51.35 N	7.18 E
Habo	26	57.55 N	14.04 E
Habob, Wādī V	140	18.07 N	35.01 E
Habomai-shotō → Malaja Kuril'skaja Gr'ada II	92a	43.30 N	146.10 E
Haboro	92a	44.22 N	141.42 E
Hābra	126	22.50 N	88.38 E
Habsburg ⊥	58	47.28 N	8.13 E
Habsheim	58	47.44 N	7.25 E
Habu	270	34.27 N	135.24 E
Habur (Nahr al-Khābūr) ≃	130	35.08 N	40.26 E
Habutaki	270	34.25 N	135.26 E
Hache, Lac la ⊜	182	51.50 N	121.30 W
Hachen	56	51.22 N	7.59 E
Hachenburg	56	50.39 N	7.50 E
Hachi	120	27.46 N	94.01 E
Hachijō	270	34.37 N	135.48 E
Hachijō-jima I	90	33.05 N	139.48 E
Hachiman → Ōmi-hachiman, Nihon	94	35.08 N	136.06 E
Hachiman, Nihon	94	35.45 N	136.57 E
Hachiman-misaki ›	94	35.08 N	140.19 E
Hachinohe	92	40.30 N	141.29 E
Hachiōji	94	35.39 N	139.20 E
Hachmühlen	52	52.10 N	9.28 E
Hacıbektaş	130	38.57 N	34.35 E
Hacienda Heights	228	34.00 N	117.57 W
Hacienda Miravalles	236	10.41 N	85.14 W
Hacienda Murciélago	236	10.55 N	85.44 W
Hacıhamza	130	41.05 N	34.28 E
Hacılar	130	38.39 N	35.27 E
Hack, Mount ∧	166	30.46 S	138.48 E
Hackås	26	62.55 N	14.31 E
Hackberry, Az., U.S.	200	35.22 N	113.43 W
Hackberry, La., U.S.	194	29.59 N	93.20 W
Hackberry Creek ≃, Ks., U.S.	198	38.48 N	100.03 W
Hackberry Creek ≃, Tx., U.S.	222	31.53 N	97.12 W
Hackensack	210	40.53 N	74.02 W
Hackensack ≃	276	40.43 N	74.06 W
Hacketstown	48	52.52 N	6.33 W
Hackett, Ar., U.S.	194	35.11 N	94.24 W
Hackett, Pa., U.S.	279b	40.15 N	80.01 W
Hacketts	260	51.45 N	0.05 W
Hackettstown	210	40.52 N	74.48 W
Hacking ≃	274a	34.04 S	151.06 E
Hacking, Port c	274a	34.05 S	151.09 E
Hackleburg	194	34.16 N	87.49 W
Hackney •[8]	260	51.33 N	0.03 W
Hack Point	208	39.27 N	75.52 W
Håckren ⊜	26	63.11 N	13.35 E
Haco	152	10.12 S	15.44 E
Hacreş Dağları ⋏	130	38.38 N	41.37 E
Hadāli	123	32.18 N	72.12 E
Hadalīya	140	16.10 N	36.06 E
Hadamar	56	50.27 N	8.02 E
Ḥaḍan, Ḥarrat ⊥[9]	144	21.30 N	41.23 E
Hadano	94	35.22 N	139.14 E
Ḥadāribah, Ra's al- ›	140	22.04 N	36.54 E
HaDarom □[5]	132	30.40 N	34.50 E
Hadat	89	49.40 N	119.40 E
Hadayingzi	104	42.22 N	121.40 E
Ḥadd, Ra's al- ›	118	22.32 N	59.48 E
Haddad, Ouadi V	146	14.40 N	18.46 E
Ḥaddādīn, Qārat al- ∧[2]	142	30.04 N	30.58 E
Haddam, Ct., U.S.	207	41.28 N	72.30 W
Haddam, Ks., U.S.	198	39.51 N	97.18 W
Haddenham, Eng., U.K.	42	51.46 N	0.56 W
Haddenham, Eng., U.K.	42	52.22 N	0.09 E
Haddington	46	55.58 N	2.47 W
Haddock	192	33.01 N	83.25 W
Haddon Downs	166	26.21 S	140.50 E
Haddonfield	208	39.53 N	75.02 W
Haddon Heights	208	39.52 N	75.03 W
Haddon Hills	285	39.54 N	75.03 W
Hadejia	150	12.30 N	9.59 E
Hadejia ≃	134	12.50 N	10.51 E
Hadeln, Land •[1]	52	53.45 N	8.45 E
Haden	171a	27.14 S	151.53 E
Ḥadera	132	32.26 N	34.55 E
Ḥadera ≃	132	32.27 N	34.53 E
Hadersdorf •[8]	264b	48.13 N	16.14 E
Hadersfeld	264b	48.20 N	16.15 E
Haderslev	41	55.15 N	9.30 E
Haderslev Fjord c	41	55.17 N	9.40 E
Hadfield, Austl.	274b	37.42 S	144.56 E
Hadfield, Eng., U.K.	262	53.28 N	1.58 W
Hadībū	118	12.38 N	54.02 E
Ḥadīd, Jabal ∧[2]	142	30.20 N	30.06 E
Ḥadīd, Jabal al- ∧[2]	142	28.47 N	31.04 E
Hadım	130	36.59 N	32.28 E
Hadjout	34	36.31 N	2.25 E
Hadleigh, Eng., U.K.	42	52.03 N	0.58 E
Hadleigh, Eng., U.K.	260	51.33 N	0.37 E
Hadleigh Castle ⊥	260	51.33 N	0.36 E
Hadley, Eng., U.K.	42	52.42 N	2.29 W
Hadley, Ma., U.S.	207	42.20 N	72.35 W
Hadley, Mi., U.S.	216	42.57 N	83.24 W
Hadley, N.Y., U.S.	210	43.19 N	73.50 W
Hadley, Pa., U.S.	214	41.25 N	80.14 W
Hadley Bay c	176	72.30 N	107.45 W
Hadley Creek ≃	219	39.37 N	91.12 W
Hadlock	224	48.01 N	122.45 W
Hadlow	42	51.14 N	0.20 E
Hadlyme	207	41.25 N	72.24 W
Hadmersleben	54	51.59 N	11.18 E
Hadong, Taehan	98	35.05 N	127.44 E
Ha Dong, Viet	110	20.58 N	105.46 E
Ḥaḍramawt •[1]	144	15.00 N	50.00 E
Hadrian's Wall ⊥	44	54.59 N	2.26 W
Hadsten	41	56.20 N	10.03 E
Hadsund	26	56.43 N	10.07 E
Hadyai → Hat Yai	110	7.01 N	100.28 E
Haeju	98	38.02 N	125.42 E
Haemgon-ni •[8]	271b	37.35 N	126.49 E
Haena	229b	22.14 N	159.34 W
Haenam	98	34.34 N	126.35 E

Name	Seite	Breite°′	Länge°′ E = Ost
Haena Point ›	229b	22.14 N	159.34 W
Haenertsburg	156	24.00 S	29.50 E
Haengyŏng-ni	98	42.33 N	129.56 E
Haernao	104	41.46 N	120.28 E
Hafeïra, Oued el V	148	25.18 N	10.48 W
Hafelekarspitze ∧	64	47.19 N	11.23 E
Haffen-Mehr	52	51.44 N	6.28 E
Hafford	184	52.43 N	107.21 W
Haffouz	36	35.38 N	9.41 E
Hafik	130	39.52 N	37.24 E
Ḥafīra, Qā' al- ≚	132	31.06 N	36.14 E
Ḥafīrat al-'Ayda	128	26.26 N	39.10 E
Ḥafīt, Jabal ∧	128	24.03 N	55.46 E
Ḥāfiẓ, Bi'r ⊤[4]	142	30.51 N	29.40 E
Hāfizābād	123	32.04 N	73.41 E
Hāflong	120	25.11 N	93.02 E
Hafnarfjörður	24a	64.03 N	21.56 W
Haft Gel	128	31.27 N	49.27 E
Hafun, Ras ›	144	10.27 N	51.24 E
Haga, Nihon	94	36.32 N	140.04 E
Haga, Nihon	96	35.09 N	134.33 E
Hagachi-zaki ›	94	34.41 N	138.45 E
HaGadol, HaMakhtésh ⊥[7]	132	30.56 N	34.59 E
Haga-Haga	158	32.46 S	28.14 E
Hagal	98	40.23 N	127.15 E
HaGalil (Galilee) □[9]	132	32.54 N	35.20 E
Hagaman	210	42.59 N	74.09 W
Hagan	192	32.09 N	81.56 W
Hagari ≃	122	15.45 N	76.56 E
Hagar Shores	216	42.13 N	86.22 W
Hagarstown	219	38.57 N	89.10 W
Hage	52	53.36 N	7.17 E
Hagelberg ∧[2]	54	52.08 N	12.32 E
Hagemeister Island I	180	58.40 N	161.00 W
Hagen, Dtsch.	52	52.34 N	9.26 E
Hagen, Dtsch.	52	52.12 N	7.59 E
Hagen, Dtsch.	56	51.22 N	7.28 E
Hagenbrunn	264b	48.20 N	16.25 E
Hagengebirge ⋏	64	47.32 N	13.07 E
Hagenow	54	53.26 N	11.11 E
Hagensborg	182	52.23 N	126.33 W
Hagenwerder	54	51.04 N	14.58 E
Hagere Hiywet	144	8.59 N	37.51 E
Hagere Selam	144	6.29 N	38.31 E
Hagerman, Id., U.S.	202	42.48 N	114.53 W
Hagerman, N.M., U.S.	196	33.06 N	104.19 W
Hagerman Corners	275b	43.50 N	79.18 W
Hagerstown, In., U.S.	218	39.54 N	85.09 W
Hagerstown, Md., U.S.	188	39.38 N	77.43 W
Hagersville	212	42.58 N	80.03 W
Hagetmau	32	43.40 N	0.35 W
Hagfors	40	60.02 N	13.42 E
Haggen ⊜	40	60.06 N	15.13 E
Haggetts Pond ⊜	283	42.39 N	71.12 W
Haggin, Mount ∧	202	46.05 N	113.05 W
Hagi	96	34.24 N	131.25 E
Ha Giang	110	22.50 N	104.59 E
Hagitani	270	34.54 N	135.35 E
Hagiwara	94	35.52 N	137.12 E
Hagley	42	52.26 N	2.08 W
Hagley Museum ⚲	285	39.46 N	75.35 W
Hagondange	56	49.15 N	6.10 E
HaGosherim	132	33.13 N	35.37 E
Hags Head ›	48	52.57 N	9.30 W
Hague, Sk., Can.	184	52.30 N	106.25 W
Hague, N.D., U.S.	198	46.01 N	99.59 W
Hague, Cap de la ›	32	49.43 N	1.57 W
Haguenau	56	48.49 N	7.47 E
Hagues Peak ∧	200	40.29 N	105.38 W
Hahaïa	157a	11.33 S	43.17 E
Hahajima-rettō II	14	26.37 N	142.10 E
Haharro, Uebi ≃	144	1.37 N	44.13 E
Hāhipur	272b	22.47 N	88.10 E
Hahira	192	30.59 N	83.22 W
Hahlen	52	52.18 N	8.50 E
Hahn am See	56	50.31 N	7.53 E
Hahnbach	60	49.32 N	11.48 E
Hahndorf	168b	35.03 S	138.49 E
Hahnenberg	263	51.12 N	7.24 E
Hahnenkamm ∧	64	47.25 N	12.22 E
Hahnenklee-Bockswiese	52	51.51 N	10.20 E
Hahnerberg •[8]	263	51.13 N	7.09 E
Hahnstätten	56	50.18 N	8.04 E
Hahntown	279b	40.19 N	79.44 W
Haho ≃	150	6.17 N	1.23 E
Hahyŏn-ni	98	38.33 N	127.57 E
Hai ≃	105	39.00 N	117.43 E
Hai'an	100	32.34 N	120.28 E
Haian Shanmo ⋏	100	23.25 N	121.25 E
Haibara, Nihon	94	34.32 N	135.57 E
Haibara, Nihon	94	34.44 N	138.13 E
Haibatpur	272a	28.37 N	77.26 E
Haibei	89	47.39 N	126.51 E
Haicheng, Zhg.	100	24.25 N	117.51 E
Haicheng, Zhg.	104	40.52 N	122.45 E
Haicheng ≃	104	40.56 N	122.21 E
Haidargarh	124	26.37 N	81.22 E
Haidārpur •[8]	272a	28.43 N	77.09 E
Haidenaab ≃	60	49.36 N	12.08 E
Haiderabad → Hyderābād, India	122	17.23 N	78.29 E
Haiderabad → Hyderābād, Pāk.	120	25.22 N	68.22 E
Haidershofen	61	48.05 N	14.28 E
Haidian	105	39.59 N	116.18 E
Haiding	60	48.13 N	13.58 E
Haidmühle	60	48.50 N	13.46 E
Haïdra	36	35.34 N	8.27 E
Haidstein ∧	60	49.13 N	12.48 E
Haidun	100	29.36 N	121.49 E
Hai Duong	110	20.56 N	106.19 E
Haifa → Ḥefa	132	32.50 N	35.00 E
Haifa, Bay of → Ḥefa, Mifraẕ c	132	32.52 N	35.03 E
Haifeng	100	22.59 N	115.21 E
Haifengzheng	106	31.53 N	121.46 E
Haifuzhen	106	31.59 N	121.42 E
Haig	162	31.01 S	126.05 E
Haig, Mount ∧	182	49.17 N	114.29 W
Haiger	56	50.44 N	8.13 E
Haigerloch	58	48.22 N	8.48 E
Haigh	262	53.35 N	2.36 W
Haigler	198	40.00 N	101.56 W
Haihezhen	100	33.44 N	120.02 E
Haijima	268	35.42 N	139.21 E
Haikang	102	20.56 N	110.04 E
Haikou, Zhg.	100	28.20 N	120.06 E
Haikou, Zhg.	100	25.43 N	119.28 E
Haikou, Zhg.	100	29.04 N	117.46 E
Haikou, Zhg.	102	20.03 N	110.19 E
Haiku	229a	20.55 N	156.19 W
Ḥā'il	128	27.33 N	41.42 E
Hailākāndi	120	24.41 N	92.34 E
Hailar	89	49.12 N	119.42 E
Hailar ≃	90	49.35 N	117.55 E
Hailasen	89	46.13 N	121.00 E
Hailesboro	212	44.18 N	75.27 W
Hailey, Eng., U.K.	260	51.46 N	0.01 W
Hailey, Id., U.S.	202	43.31 N	114.18 W
Haileybury	190	47.27 N	79.38 W
Haileyville	196	34.51 N	95.34 W
Hailin	89	44.35 N	129.22 E
Hailing Dao I	102	21.37 N	111.55 E
Haillicourt	50	50.28 N	2.35 E
Hailong (Meihekou)	98	42.32 N	125.38 E
Hailsham	42	50.52 N	0.16 E
Hailun	89	47.28 N	126.58 E
Hailuoto	26	65.00 N	24.43 E
Hailuoto I	26	65.02 N	24.42 E
Haiman Tepesi ∧[2]	267b	41.12 N	29.15 E
Haimen, Zhg.	100	28.41 N	121.27 E
Haimen, Zhg.	100	23.14 N	116.38 E
Haimen, Zhg.	106	31.55 N	121.10 E
Haimen Wan c	100	23.09 N	116.34 E

Symbols in the index entries represent the broad categories identified in the key at the right. Symbols with superior numbers (⋏[1]) identify subcategories (see complete key on page *I · 1).*

Symbole im Register stellen die rechts im Schlüssel erklärten Kategorien dar. Symbole mit hochgestellten Ziffern (⋏[1]) bezeichnen Unterabteilungen einer Kategorie (vgl. vollständiger Schlüssel auf Seite *I · 1).*

Los símbolos incluídos en el texto del índice representan las grandes categorías identificadas con la clave a la derecha. Los símbolos con numeros en su parte superior (⋏[1]) identifican las subcategorías (véase la clave completa en la página *I · 1).*

Les symboles de l'index représentent les catégories indiquées dans la légende à droite. Les symboles suivis d'un indice (⋏[1]) représentent des souscatégories (voir légende complète à la page *I · 1).*

Os símbolos incluídos no texto do índice representam as grandes categorias identificadas com a chave à direita. Os símbolos com números em sua parte superior (⋏[1]) identificam as subcategorias (vejase a chave completa à página *I · 1).*

∧	Mountain	Berg	Montaña	Montagne	Montanha
⋏	Mountains	Gebirge	Montañas	Montagnes	Montanhas
)(	Pass	Paß	Paso	Col	Passo
V	Valley, Canyon	Tal, Cañon	Valle, Cañón	Vallée, Canyon	Vale, Canhão
≚	Plain	Ebene	Llano	Plaine	Planície
›	Cape	Kap	Cabo	Cap	Cabo
I	Island	Insel	Isla	Île	Ilha
II	Islands	Inseln	Islas	Îles	Ilhas
⊥	Other Topographic Features	Andere Topographische Objekte	Otros Elementos Topográficos	Autres données topographiques	Outros acidentes topográficos

ESPAÑOL / FRANÇAIS / PORTUGUÊS

Nombre / Nom / Nome	Página / Page	Lat.°′	Long.°′ W = Oeste / W = Ouest
Haimhausen	60	48.19 N	11.34 E
Haimiao	98	37.13 N	119.51 E
Haiming	64	47.15 N	10.53 E
Haina	56	51.02 N	8.58 E
Hainan □[4]	110	19.00 N	109.30 E
Hainan → Hainan Dao I	110	19.00 N	109.30 E
Hainan Dao I	110	19.00 N	109.30 E
Hainault •[8]	260	51.36 N	0.06 E
Hainaut □[4]	50	50.30 N	3.50 E
Hainaut □[9]	50	50.30 N	3.50 E
Hainburg an der Donau	61	48.09 N	16.57 E
Hainchen	56	50.51 N	8.12 E
Haines, Ak., U.S.	180	59.14 N	135.27 W
Haines, Or., U.S.	202	44.54 N	117.56 W
Haines City	220	28.06 N	81.37 W
Haines Falls	210	42.11 N	74.05 W
Haines Junction	180	60.45 N	137.30 W
Hainesport	208	39.59 N	74.49 W
Hainesville	278	42.21 N	88.04 W
Hainewalde	54	50.54 N	14.41 E
Hainfeld	61	48.02 N	15.46 E
Hainich ⋏	54	51.05 N	10.27 E
Hainichen	54	50.58 N	13.07 E
Haining (Xiashi)	106	30.32 N	120.41 E
Hainleite ⋏	54	51.20 N	10.48 E
Hainsberg	54	50.59 N	13.38 E
Hainzenberg	64	47.13 N	11.54 E
Hai Phong	110	20.52 N	106.41 E
Haiqiao	106	31.47 N	121.19 E
Haiqing	89	47.53 N	134.40 E
Haitangxi	107	29.33 N	106.35 E
Haitan Xia ▬	100	25.27 N	119.38 E
Haiti (Haïti) □[1], N.A.	230	19.00 N	72.25 W
Haiti (Haïti) □[1], N.A.	238	19.00 N	72.25 W
Haitou, Zhg.	98	34.56 N	119.10 E
Haitou, Zhg.	110	19.34 N	108.58 E
Haitouji	98	35.23 N	115.19 E
Haitun	102	38.50 N	96.41 E
Haiwee Reservoirs ⊜[1]	204	36.10 N	117.57 W
Haiyan, Zhg.	102	36.54 N	101.12 E
Haiyan, Zhg.	106	30.31 N	120.57 E
Haiyang (Dongcun)	98	36.46 N	121.10 E
Haiyang Dao I	98	39.02 N	123.14 E
Haiyuan	102	36.35 N	105.40 E
Haizhou, Zhg.	98	34.34 N	119.11 E
Haizhou, Zhg.	100	22.40 N	113.10 E
Haizhoumiao	104	42.00 N	121.39 E
Haizhou Wan c	98	35.00 N	119.30 E
Haizhouyingzi	104	42.07 N	121.46 E
Ḥajar, Tall al- ∧[2]	132	33.21 N	37.03 E
Ḥajar Banga	140	11.30 N	23.00 E
Hajdú-Bihar □[6]	30	47.25 N	21.30 E
Hajdúböszörmény	30	47.41 N	21.30 E
Hajdúnánás	30	47.51 N	21.26 E
Hajdúszoboszló	30	47.27 N	21.24 E
Hajeb el Ayoun	36	35.24 N	9.33 E
Hajiadian	98	41.32 N	117.10 E
Hājīganj	126	23.15 N	90.50 E
Hajiki-saki ›	92	38.19 N	138.31 E
Haji Langar	120	35.52 N	79.21 E
Hājīpur, India	124	25.41 N	85.13 E
Hājīpur, India	126	22.49 N	87.38 E
Hajipur, India	272b	22.57 N	88.19 E
Ḥājj, Wādī al- V	142	30.03 N	32.45 E
Hajnówka	30	52.45 N	23.36 E
Hajo-do I	98	34.17 N	126.03 E
Ḥajr, Wādī V	144	14.04 N	48.40 E
Ḥajūl, Wādī V	142	29.42 N	32.22 E
Hakata	96	34.12 N	133.07 E
Hakata-jima I	96	34.13 N	133.05 E
Hakataramea ≃	172	44.44 S	170.29 E
Hakendover	56	50.48 N	4.59 E
Hakha	110	22.39 N	93.37 E
Haki	96	33.20 N	130.50 E
Ḥakīm, Abyār al- ⫪[4]	146	31.36 N	23.29 E
Hakkâri	128	37.34 N	43.45 E
Hakkâri □[4]	128	37.20 N	43.45 E
Hakken-san ∧	92	34.10 N	135.54 E
Hakkōda-san ∧	92	40.40 N	140.53 E
Hako-dake ∧	92a	44.40 N	142.25 E
Hakodate	92a	41.45 N	140.43 E
Hakone	94	35.12 N	139.06 E
Hakone-no-seki-ato ⊥	94	35.10 N	139.02 E
Hakone-tōge)(	94	35.11 N	139.01 E
Hakone-yama ∧	94	35.14 N	139.02 E
Håksberg	40	60.11 N	15.12 E
Hakskeenpan ≚	158	26.48 S	20.12 E
Haktanır	130	36.51 N	38.50 E
Hakuba	94	36.42 N	137.52 E
Hakui	94	36.53 N	136.47 E
Hakupu	174v	19.06 S	169.50 W
Hakusan	94	34.38 N	136.21 E
Haku-san ∧	94	36.09 N	136.46 E
Haku-san-kokuritsu-kōen ♦	94	36.12 N	136.47 E
Hakushū	94	35.48 N	138.20 E
Hakuta	96	35.21 N	133.17 E
Hakuta ≃	96	35.26 N	133.15 E
Hāla	120	25.49 N	68.25 E
Halaaobao	102	42.11 N	107.20 E
Ḥalab (Aleppo)	130	36.12 N	37.10 E
Ḥalab □[8]	130	36.00 N	37.30 E
Ḥalabjah	128	35.10 N	45.59 E
Halachó	232	20.29 N	90.05 W
Halaerjige	104	42.24 N	122.11 E
Halagetu	104	42.34 N	122.40 E
Halahai	89	44.39 N	125.07 E
Halahushao	104	42.11 N	121.44 E
Halā'ib	140	22.13 N	36.38 E
Halalii Lake ⊜	229b	21.52 N	160.11 W
Halamutai	86	46.10 N	84.52 E
Halangingie Point ›	174v	19.03 S	169.57 W
Halasa	140	14.26 N	30.39 E
Halas-patak ≃	264c	47.24 N	19.20 E
Halataojie	104	42.30 N	122.06 E
Halatieke Shan ⋏	85	40.30 N	77.05 E
Halaula	229d	20.14 N	155.48 W
Hålaveden ⋏[2]	26	58.05 N	14.45 E
Halawa, Cape ›	229a	21.10 N	156.43 W
Halawa Bay c	229a	21.10 N	156.44 W
Halawa Heights	229c	21.22 N	157.55 W
Halawotelake	120	37.17 N	90.20 E
Halbach •[8]	263	51.12 N	7.12 E
Halba Deset I	144	12.56 N	42.55 E
Halbe	54	52.06 N	13.42 E
Halberstadt	54	51.54 N	11.02 E
Halbert, Lake ⊜[1]	222	32.04 N	96.25 W
Halberton	42	50.55 N	3.25 W
Halbrite	184	49.30 N	103.33 W
Ḥalbūn	132	33.40 N	36.15 E
Halbury	168b	34.05 S	138.31 E
Halcombe	172	40.09 S	175.30 E
Halcon, Mount ∧	116	13.16 N	121.00 E
Halcottsville	210	42.12 N	74.36 W
Haldeman	218	38.15 N	83.19 W
Halden	26	59.09 N	11.23 E
Halden •[8]	263	51.23 N	7.31 E
Haldensleben	54	52.18 N	11.26 E
Haldern	52	51.46 N	6.27 E
Haldī	126	22.03 N	88.05 E
Haldī ≃	126	22.01 N	88.03 E
Haldībāri	124	26.20 N	88.46 E
Haldībunia	126	22.26 N	89.38 E
Haldimand	212	42.56 N	79.51 W
Haldimand-Norfolk □[6]	212	42.48 N	80.10 W
Haldwāni	124	29.13 N	79.31 E
Hale, Eng., U.K.	44	53.23 N	2.21 W
Hale, Eng., U.K.	262	53.20 N	2.48 W
Hale, Mo., U.S.	194	39.36 N	93.20 W
Hale ≃	162	24.56 S	135.53 E
Haleakala Crater ⩟[6]	229a	20.43 N	156.13 W
Haleakala National Park ♦	229a	20.44 N	156.13 W
Haleb → Ḥalab	130	36.12 N	37.10 E
Halebarns	262	53.22 N	2.19 W
Hale Center	196	34.03 N	101.50 W
Hale Creek ≃	282	37.23 N	122.06 W
Haledon	276	40.56 N	74.11 W
Haledon Reservoir ⊜[1]	276	40.59 N	74.12 W
Hale Eddy	210	42.00 N	75.23 W
Hale Head ›	262	53.19 N	2.48 W
Haleiwa	229c	21.35 N	158.06 W
Halekii-Pihana Heiaus State Monument ⊥	229a	20.54 N	156.29 W
Halenkov	30	49.19 N	18.08 E
Hales Corners	216	42.56 N	88.02 W
Halesite	207	40.52 N	73.25 W
Halesowen	42	52.26 N	2.05 W
Hale Street	260	51.13 N	0.24 E
Halesworth	42	52.21 N	1.30 E
Halewood	262	53.22 N	2.49 W
Haleyville	194	34.13 N	87.37 W
Half Assini	150	5.03 N	2.53 W
Ḥalfāyah, Naqb al- (Halfaya Pass))(	140	31.30 N	25.11 E
Halfaya Pass → Ḥalfāyah, Naqb al-)(	140	31.30 N	25.11 E
Half Day	278	42.12 N	87.56 W
Halfeti	130	37.15 N	37.52 E
Half Hollow Hills	276	40.48 N	73.21 W
Halfing	64	47.57 N	12.16 E
Halfmoon Bay, B.C., Can.	182	49.31 N	123.54 W
Halfmoon Bay, N.Z.	172	46.54 S	168.08 E
Half Moon Bay, Ca., U.S.	226	37.27 N	122.25 W
Halfmoon Bay c, Austl.	274b	37.58 S	145.00 E
Half Moon Bay c, Ca., U.S.	282	37.29 N	122.28 W
Half Moon Bay Airport ⊠	282	37.31 N	122.30 W
Half Moon Bay State Beach ♦	282	37.29 N	122.27 W
Halfway, Md., U.S.	188	39.37 N	77.45 W
Halfway, Or., U.S.	202	44.52 N	117.06 W
Halfway ≃	176	56.10 N	121.35 W
Halfway Lake ⊜	184	55.03 N	98.24 W
Halgån ≃	40	60.16 N	13.27 E
Ḥalḥūl	132	31.35 N	35.07 E
Ḥalī ⫪[4]	144	18.42 N	41.20 E
Haliburton	212	45.03 N	78.31 W
Haliburton □[6]	212	44.10 N	78.30 W
Haliburton Lake ⊜	212	45.12 N	78.24 W
Halibut Point ›	283	42.42 N	70.38 W
Haliç (Golden Horn) c	267b	41.02 N	28.58 E
Halicarnassus ⊥	130	37.03 N	27.23 E
Halifax, Austl.	166	18.35 S	146.18 E
Halifax, N.S., Can.	186	44.39 N	63.36 W
Halifax, Eng., U.K.	44	53.44 N	1.52 W
Halifax, Ma., U.S.	207	41.59 N	70.51 W
Halifax, N.C., U.S.	192	36.19 N	77.35 W
Halifax, Pa., U.S.	208	40.28 N	76.55 W
Halifax, Va., U.S.	192	36.45 N	78.55 W
Halifax, Canadian Forces Base ■	186	44.43 N	63.38 W
Halifax Bay c	166	18.50 S	146.30 E
Halifax Citadel National Historic Park ♦	186	44.36 N	63.39 W
Halifax Harbour c	186	44.35 N	63.31 W
Haliimaile	229a	20.52 N	156.20 W
Halīl ≃	128	27.28 N	58.44 E
Halimatazi	104	42.37 N	122.35 E
Halim Perdanakusuma Airport ■	269e	6.16 S	106.54 E
Halimun, Gunung ∧	115a	6.42 S	106.26 E
Halingen	263	51.27 N	7.44 E
Hālisahar	126	22.56 N	88.25 E
Haliyāl	122	15.20 N	74.46 E
Haljala	76	59.26 N	26.16 E
Halkalı •[8]	267b	41.02 N	28.47 E
Halkapınar	130	37.25 N	34.13 E
Halkett, Cape ›	180	70.49 N	152.12 W
Halkirk	46	58.30 N	3.30 W
Halkyn	262	53.14 N	3.11 W
Halkyn Mountain ∧	262	53.14 N	3.13 W
Hall, Austl.	171b	35.10 S	149.04 E
Hall, In., U.S.	218	39.33 N	86.32 W
Hall, N.Y., U.S.	210	42.48 N	77.04 W
Hällabrottet	40	59.07 N	15.12 E
Halladale ≃	46	58.33 N	3.55 W
Hallam	274b	38.01 S	145.06 E
Hallam Peak ∧	182	52.11 N	118.46 W
Halland □[9]	26	57.00 N	12.40 E
Hallandale	220	25.58 N	80.08 W
Hallands Län □[6]	26	56.45 N	13.00 E
Hallands Väderö I	26	56.26 N	12.33 E
Halla-san ∧	90	33.22 N	126.32 E
Hallau	58	47.42 N	8.27 E
Hällberga	40	59.19 N	16.36 E
Hällbybrunn	40	59.24 N	16.25 E
Hällbymagasinet ⊜[1]	26	63.56 N	17.13 E
Halle, Bel.	50	50.44 N	4.13 E
Halle, Dtsch.	52	52.04 N	8.22 E
Halle, Dtsch.	52	51.59 N	9.33 E
Halle, Dtsch.	54	51.29 N	11.58 E
Halleberg ∧[2]	26	58.23 N	12.27 E
Hällefors	40	59.47 N	14.30 E
Hälleforsnäs	40	59.10 N	16.30 E
Hallein	64	47.41 N	13.06 E
Hällekis	26	58.38 N	13.25 E
Hallen	26	63.11 N	14.05 E
Hallenberg	56	51.06 N	8.37 E
Hallencourt	50	49.59 N	1.53 E
Halle-Neustadt	54	51.29 N	11.56 E
Hallertau •[1]	60	48.35 N	11.45 E
Hällestad	40	58.44 N	15.34 E
Hallett, Cape ›	9	72.19 S	170.18 E
Hallettsville	222	29.26 N	96.56 W
Halley ʊ[3]	9	75.36 S	26.46 W
Halliday	198	47.21 N	102.20 W
Halligen II	30	54.35 N	8.35 E
Halling	260	51.21 N	0.27 E
Hallingdalselvi ≃	26	60.24 N	9.35 E
Hällingsåfallet ⌊	26	64.20 N	14.20 E
Hall in Tirol	64	47.17 N	11.31 E
Hall Island I	180	60.40 N	173.05 W
Hall Islands II	14	8.37 N	152.00 E
Halliste ≃	76	58.31 N	25.03 E
Hall-i'-th'-Wood ♦	262	53.36 N	2.26 W
Hall Lake ⊜	176	68.41 N	82.17 W
Hall Meadow Brook Reservoir ⊜[1]	207	41.52 N	73.10 W
Hall Mountain ∧	202	48.49 N	117.15 W
Hällnäs	26	64.19 N	19.38 E
Hallock	198	48.46 N	96.56 W
Hallowell	188	44.17 N	69.47 W
Hall Peninsula ›[1]	176	63.30 N	66.00 W
Halls	194	35.52 N	89.23 W
Halls Bayou ≃	222	29.12 N	95.07 W
Hallsberg	40	59.04 N	15.07 E
Halls Brook ≃	283	42.00 N	70.43 W
Halls Creek	162	18.16 S	127.46 E
Halls Creek ≃	200	37.18 N	110.45 W
Halls Gap	166	37.08 S	142.31 E
Halls Lake ⊜	212	45.07 N	78.45 W
Halls Stream ≃	206	45.01 N	71.30 W
Hållsta	40	59.18 N	16.27 E
Hallstadt	56	49.55 N	10.52 E
Hallstahammar	40	59.37 N	16.13 E
Hallstatt	64	47.33 N	13.39 E
Hallstätter See ⊜	64	47.35 N	13.39 E
Hallstavik	40	60.03 N	18.36 E
Hallstead	210	41.57 N	75.44 W
Hallsville, Mo., U.S.	219	39.07 N	92.13 W
Hallsville, Tx., U.S.	222	32.30 N	94.34 W
Halluin	50	50.47 N	3.08 E
Hallwiler See ⊜	58	47.18 N	8.13 E
Hallwood	208	37.52 N	75.35 W
Halma	56	50.05 N	5.08 E
Halmahera I	108	1.00 N	128.00 E
Halmahera, Laut (Halmahera Sea) ⫪[2]	108	1.00 S	129.00 E
Halmstad	26	56.39 N	12.50 E
Halpine Village	284c	39.04 N	77.07 W
Hals	26	57.00 N	10.19 E
Halsafjorden c[2]	26	63.03 N	8.11 E
Halsall	262	53.35 N	2.57 W
Halsbrücke	54	50.57 N	13.21 E
Halsey, Ne., U.S.	198	41.54 N	100.16 W
Halsey, Or., U.S.	202	44.23 N	123.06 W
Halsey Harbor c	116	11.45 N	119.56 E
Halsey Valley	210	42.08 N	76.27 W
Hälsingborg → Helsingborg	41	56.03 N	12.42 E
Hälsingland □[9]	26	61.30 N	17.00 E
Halstad	198	47.21 N	96.49 W
Halstead, Eng., U.K.	42	51.57 N	0.38 E
Halstead, Eng., U.K.	260	51.20 N	0.08 E
Halstead, Ks., U.S.	198	38.00 N	97.30 W
Halstenbek	52	53.38 N	9.50 E
Halsteren	52	51.32 N	4.16 E
Halstow Marshes ≚	260	51.29 N	0.33 E
Haltang ≃	102	39.00 N	94.40 E
Haltern	52	51.46 N	7.10 E
Haltiatunturi ∧	24	69.18 N	21.16 E
Haltom City	222	32.47 N	97.16 W
Halton, Eng., U.K.	44	54.05 N	2.46 W
Halton, Eng., U.K.	262	53.20 N	2.42 W
Halton □[6]	212	43.30 N	79.53 W
Halton □[8]	262	53.20 N	2.44 W
Halton Hills	212	43.39 N	79.55 W
Haltwhistle	44	54.58 N	2.27 W
Halura, Pulau I	115b	10.19 S	120.11 E
Ḥaluẓa, Ḥolot ⩟[8]	132	31.05 N	34.28 E
Halūzonī, Wādī al- V	273c	30.05 N	31.24 E
Halvarsgårdarna	40	60.24 N	15.23 E
Halvarsnoren ⊜	40	59.35 N	14.36 E
Halver	56	51.11 N	7.30 E
Halvorson, Mount ∧	182	53.15 N	120.33 W
Halwell	42	50.22 N	3.43 W
Ham, Fr.	50	49.45 N	3.04 E
Ham, Tchad	146	10.00 N	15.41 E
Ham •[8]	260	51.26 N	0.19 W
Ham ≃	158	28.32 S	19.34 E
Ham, Oued el ≃	34	35.42 N	4.52 E
Ḥamad	140	15.19 N	33.43 E
Hamada	96	34.53 N	132.05 E
Hamadān	128	34.48 N	48.30 E
Hamadān □[4]	128	35.00 N	48.40 E
Ḥamāh	130	35.08 N	36.45 E
Ḥamāh □[8]	130	35.10 N	37.00 E
Hamahika-jima I	174m	26.19 N	127.57 E
Hamakeza	89	47.05 N	120.52 E
Hamakita	94	34.48 N	137.47 E
Hamale	150	10.59 N	2.44 W
Hamamatsu	94	34.42 N	137.44 E
Hamamatsukita-kichi, Kōkū-jieitai- ■	94	34.45 N	137.42 E
Hamamözü	130	40.48 N	35.02 E
Haman	98	35.15 N	128.24 E
Hamanaka	92a	43.05 N	145.10 E
Hamana-ko ⊜	94	34.45 N	137.34 E
Hamano	268	35.33 N	140.08 E
Hamaoka	94	34.39 N	138.08 E
Hamar	26	60.48 N	11.06 E
Hamasaka	96	35.37 N	134.27 E
Hamāṭah, Jabal ∧	140	24.12 N	35.00 E
Hamatang	98	40.12 N	124.20 E
Hama-tombetsu	92a	45.07 N	142.23 E
Hambach	56	49.04 N	7.02 E
Hambaek-san ∧	98	37.09 N	128.55 E
Hambantota	122	6.07 N	81.07 E
Hambergen	52	53.18 N	8.49 E
Hamber Provincial Park ♦	182	52.25 N	117.40 W
Hamble	42	50.52 N	1.19 W
Hambledon	42	50.56 N	1.04 W
Hambleton	44	53.52 N	2.57 W
Hambleton Hills ⋏[2]	44	54.16 N	1.12 W
Hamborn •[8]	263	51.29 N	6.46 E
Hambourg → Hamburg	52	53.33 N	9.59 E
Hamburg, Ciskei	158	33.17 S	27.28 E
Hamburg, Dtsch.	52	53.33 N	9.59 E
Hamburg, Ar., U.S.	194	33.13 N	91.47 W
Hamburg, Ct., U.S.	207	41.23 N	72.21 W
Hamburg, Il., U.S.	219	39.14 N	90.43 W
Hamburg, Ia., U.S.	198	40.36 N	95.39 W
Hamburg, Mi., U.S.	216	42.27 N	83.48 W
Hamburg, N.J., U.S.	210	41.09 N	74.34 W
Hamburg, N.Y., U.S.	210	42.42 N	78.49 W
Hamburg, Pa., U.S.	208	40.33 N	75.58 W
Hamburg □[3]	52	53.35 N	10.00 E
Hamburg, Flughafen ⊠	52	53.38 N	10.00 E
Hamburg Airport ⊠	284a	42.42 N	78.55 W
Hamburg Ditch ≡	208	36.31 N	76.33 W
Hamburger Hallig ›[1]	41	54.36 N	8.49 E
Hamburg Mountains ⋏	276	41.08 N	74.32 W
Hamburgo → Hamburg	52	53.33 N	9.59 E
Hamburgsund	26	58.33 N	11.16 E
Ḥamḍ, Wādī al- V	128	25.54 N	36.38 E
Ḥamḍah	144	19.02 N	43.36 E
Hamdallay Timbou	150	12.03 N	10.37 W
Hamdam Āb, Dasht-e ≚	128	34.45 N	61.30 E
Ḥamdānah	144	19.58 N	40.35 E
Hamden, Ct., U.S.	207	41.23 N	72.53 W
Hamden, N.Y., U.S.	210	42.12 N	75.00 W
Hamden, Oh., U.S.	188	39.09 N	82.31 W
Hamdibey	130	39.50 N	27.15 E
Häme •[1]	26	61.45 N	25.10 E
Hämeenkangas •[3]	26	61.45 N	22.40 E
Hämeenkylä	26	60.16 N	24.47 E
Hämeen lääni □[4]	26	61.30 N	24.30 E
Hämeenlinna	26	61.00 N	24.27 E
Hamel	168a	32.52 S	115.55 E
HaMelah, Yam → Dead Sea ⊜	132	31.30 N	35.30 E
Hämelerwald	52	52.22 N	10.05 E
Hamelin	162	26.26 S	114.11 E
Hamelin Pool c	162	26.15 S	114.05 E
Hameln	52	52.06 N	9.21 E
HaMerkaz □[5]	132	32.05 N	34.55 E
Hamer Koke	144	5.12 N	36.45 E
Hamero Hadad	144	7.34 N	42.18 E
Hamersleben	54	52.04 N	11.05 E
Hamersley Range ⋏	162	21.53 S	116.46 E
Hamersley Range National Park ♦	162	22.40 S	118.15 E
Hamersville	218	38.55 N	83.59 W
Hames Creek ≃	226	35.53 N	120.50 W
Hamgyŏng Namdo □[4]	98	40.00 N	127.30 E
Hamgyŏng Pukdo □[4]	98	41.45 N	129.50 E
Hamgyŏng-sanmaek ⋏	98	41.00 N	128.30 E
Ham House ⊥	260	51.27 N	0.19 W
Hamhŭng	98	39.54 N	127.32 E
Hami (Kumul)	102	42.48 N	93.27 E
Hamidiye	130	41.09 N	26.40 E
Hamiguitan, Mount ∧	116	6.44 N	126.11 E
Hamilton, Austl.	166	37.45 S	142.02 E
Hamilton, Ber.	240a	32.17 N	64.46 W
Hamilton, On., Can.	212	43.15 N	79.51 W
Hamilton, N.Z.	172	37.47 S	175.17 E
Hamilton, Scot., U.K.	46	55.47 N	4.03 W
Hamilton, Al., U.S.	194	34.08 N	87.59 W
Hamilton, Ak., U.S.	180	62.54 N	163.53 W
Hamilton, Ga., U.S.	192	32.45 N	84.52 W
Hamilton, Il., U.S.	190	40.23 N	91.20 W
Hamilton, In., U.S.	216	41.32 N	84.54 W
Hamilton, Ks., U.S.	198	37.58 N	96.09 W
Hamilton, Ma., U.S.	207	42.37 N	70.52 W
Hamilton, Mi., U.S.	216	42.40 N	86.00 W
Hamilton, Mo., U.S.	194	39.44 N	93.59 W
Hamilton, Mt., U.S.	202	46.14 N	114.09 W
Hamilton, N.Y., U.S.	210	42.49 N	75.32 W
Hamilton, N.C., U.S.	192	35.56 N	77.12 W
Hamilton, Oh., U.S.	218	39.23 N	84.33 W
Hamilton, R.I., U.S.	207	41.32 N	71.26 W
Hamilton, Tx., U.S.	196	31.42 N	98.07 W
Hamilton, Wa., U.S.	224	48.31 N	121.59 W
Hamilton □[6], In., U.S.	218	40.03 N	86.01 W
Hamilton □[6], N.Y., U.S.	210	43.24 N	74.25 W
Hamilton □[6], Oh., U.S.	218	39.06 N	84.31 W
Hamilton •[8]	284b	39.21 N	76.33 W
Hamilton ≃	166	23.30 S	139.47 E
Hamilton, Lake ⊜	220	28.03 N	81.39 W
Hamilton, Lake ⊜[1]	194	34.30 N	93.05 W
Hamilton, Mount ∧, Ak., U.S.	180	61.10 N	159.46 W
Hamilton, Mount ∧, Ca., U.S.	226	37.21 N	121.38 W
Hamilton, Mount ∧, Nv., U.S.	204	39.14 N	115.32 W
Hamilton Acres	180	64.51 N	147.40 W
Hamilton Air Force Base ■	282	38.03 N	122.31 W
Hamilton City	204	39.44 N	122.00 W
Hamilton Creek ≃	162	26.40 S	135.19 E
Hamilton Creek Indian Reserve •[4]	182	50.11 N	120.30 W
Hamilton Dome	200	43.46 N	108.34 W
Hamilton Harbour c	212	43.17 N	79.50 W
Hamilton Hill	168a	32.05 S	115.46 E
Hamilton Hotel	166	22.50 S	140.35 E
Hamilton Inlet c	176	54.00 N	57.30 W
Hamilton Lake ⊜	216	41.33 N	84.55 W
Hamilton Mountain ∧	188	43.25 N	74.22 W
Hamilton Park, In., U.S.	216	40.17 N	85.19 W
Hamilton Park, Pa., U.S.	208	40.02 N	76.20 W
Hamilton Sound ▬	186	49.30 N	54.30 W
Hamilton Square	285	40.13 N	74.39 W
Hamilton-Wentworth □[6]	212	43.15 N	80.00 W
Hamīm, Wādī al- V	146	30.10 N	21.32 E
Hamina	26	60.34 N	27.12 E
Hamiota	184	50.11 N	100.36 W
Ḥāmir, Wādī V	128	31.37 N	42.12 E
Hamīrpur, India	123	31.41 N	76.31 E
Hamīrpur, India	124	25.57 N	80.09 E
Hamjong-ni	98	38.59 N	125.17 E
Hamler	216	41.13 N	84.02 W
Hamlet, In., U.S.	216	41.32 N	86.34 W
Hamlet, N.C., U.S.	192	34.53 N	79.41 W
Hamlet, Oh., U.S.	218	39.01 N	84.12 W
Hamlet, Mount ∧	180	68.47 N	165.57 W
Hamley Bridge	168b	34.21 S	138.41 E
Hamlin, N.Y., U.S.	210	43.18 N	77.55 W
Hamlin, Pa., U.S.	210	41.24 N	75.24 W
Hamlin, Tx., U.S.	196	32.53 N	100.08 W
Hamlin, W.V., U.S.	188	38.16 N	82.06 W
Hamlin Beach State Park ♦	210	43.22 N	77.58 W
Hamlin Lake ⊜	190	44.03 N	86.27 W
Hamlin Valley Wash V	200	38.53 N	114.01 W
Hamm	52	51.41 N	7.49 E
Hamm •[8], Dtsch.	263	51.12 N	6.44 E
Hamm •[8], Dtsch.	263	51.23 N	7.03 E
Ḥammād, Wādī V	142	29.45 N	32.24 E
Hamma Hamma ≃	224	47.33 N	123.03 W
Hammålfjell ∧	26	62.27 N	11.17 E
Ḥammām at-Turkumān	130	36.32 N	39.03 E
Hammamet, Alg.	36	35.27 N	7.58 E
Hammamet, Tun.	148	36.24 N	10.37 E
Hammamet, Golfe de c	36	36.05 N	10.40 E
Hammam Lif	148	36.44 N	10.20 E
Ḥammānā	132	33.49 N	35.44 E
Hammar	40	58.49 N	14.57 E
Ḥammār, Hawr al- ⊜	128	30.50 N	47.10 E
Hammarby	40	60.33 N	16.34 E
Hammarn	40	59.45 N	14.30 E
Hammarö	40	59.20 N	13.31 E
Hammarön I	40	59.19 N	13.31 E
Hammarstrand	26	63.06 N	16.21 E
Hamme	50	51.06 N	4.08 E
Hamme ≃	52	53.10 N	8.44 E
Hammel	41	56.15 N	9.52 E
Hammelburg	56	50.07 N	9.53 E
Hamme-Mille	56	50.47 N	4.43 E
Hammerdal	26	63.36 N	15.21 E
Hammerfest	24	70.40 N	23.42 E
Hämmern	263	51.08 N	7.21 E
Hammershus ⊥	26	55.16 N	14.45 E
Hammersley Inlet c	224	47.12 N	123.00 W
Hammersmith •[8]	260	51.30 N	0.14 W
Hammerum	41	56.08 N	9.04 E
Hamminkeln	52	51.44 N	6.35 E
Hammon	196	35.37 N	99.22 W
Hammonasset ≃	207	41.16 N	72.33 W
Hammond, In., U.S.	216	41.35 N	87.30 W
Hammond, La., U.S.	194	30.30 N	90.27 W
Hammond, N.Y., U.S.	212	44.26 N	75.41 W
Hammond, Or., U.S.	224	46.12 N	123.57 W
Hammond, Wi., U.S.	190	44.58 N	92.26 W
Hammond Island I, Austl.	164	10.35 S	142.13 E
Hammond Island I, Ca., U.S.	282	38.06 N	121.57 W
Hammond Pond Park ♦	283	42.19 N	71.11 W
Hammondsport	210	42.24 N	77.13 W
Hammondsville	214	40.33 N	80.43 W
Hammondville	274a	33.57 S	150.57 E
Hammonia	158	28.43 S	27.49 E
Hammonton	208	39.38 N	74.48 W
Hamningberg	24	70.31 N	30.37 E
Ham-Nord	206	45.54 N	71.39 W
Hamoir	56	50.26 N	5.32 E
Hamont	56	51.15 N	5.33 E
HaMore, Giv'at ∧	132	32.37 N	35.21 E
Hamorton	285	39.52 N	75.39 W
Hamoyet, Jabal ∧	144	17.33 N	38.02 E
Hampden, Austl.	168b	34.09 S	139.03 E
Hampden, Nf., Can.	186	49.33 N	56.51 W
Hampden, N.Z.	172	45.19 S	170.49 E
Hampden, Me., U.S.	188	44.44 N	68.50 W
Hampden, Ma., U.S.	207	42.03 N	72.24 W
Hampden, N.D., U.S.	198	48.32 N	98.39 W
Hampden □[6]	207	42.07 N	72.36 W
Hampden Sydney	192	37.15 N	78.29 W
Hampetorp	40	59.09 N	15.40 E
Hampi	122	15.24 N	76.37 E
Hampshire	216	42.05 N	88.31 W
Hampshire □[6], Eng., U.K.	42	51.05 N	1.15 W
Hampshire □[6], Ma., U.S.	207	42.19 N	72.38 W
Hampshire Downs ⋏[1]	42	51.15 N	1.17 W
Hampshire Heights	279b	40.20 N	79.33 W
Hampstead, P.Q., Can.	275a	45.29 N	73.38 W
Hampstead, Md., U.S.	208	39.36 N	76.51 W
Hampstead, N.C., U.S.	192	34.22 N	77.42 W
Hampstead •[8]	260	51.33 N	0.11 W
Hampstead Heath ♦	260	51.34 N	0.10 W
Hampton, Austl.	274b	37.56 S	145.00 E
Hampton, N.B., Can.	186	45.32 N	65.51 W
Hampton, On., Can.	212	43.58 N	78.45 W
Hampton, Ar., U.S.	194	33.32 N	92.28 W
Hampton, Ct., U.S.	207	41.47 N	72.03 W
Hampton, Fl., U.S.	192	29.51 N	82.07 W
Hampton, Ga., U.S.	192	33.23 N	84.16 W
Hampton, Ia., U.S.	190	42.44 N	93.12 W
Hampton, Ne., U.S.	198	40.52 N	97.53 W
Hampton, N.H., U.S.	188	42.56 N	70.50 W
Hampton, N.J., U.S.	210	40.42 N	74.57 W
Hampton, Pa., U.S.	208	39.56 N	77.04 W
Hampton, S.C., U.S.	192	32.52 N	81.06 W
Hampton, Tn., U.S.	192	36.17 N	82.10 W
Hampton, Va., U.S.	208	37.01 N	76.20 W
Hampton •[8]	260	51.25 N	0.22 W
Hampton, Mount ∧	9	76.29 S	125.48 W
Hampton Bays	207	40.52 N	72.31 W
Hampton Butte ∧	202	43.46 N	120.17 W
Hampton Court Palace ʊ	42	51.24 N	0.20 W
Hampton Harbour c	162	20.40 S	116.30 E
Hampton National Historic Site ⊥	284b	39.25 N	76.35 W
Hampton Park	274b	38.02 S	145.15 E
Hampton Roads ⫪[3]	208	36.58 N	76.20 W
Hampton Roads Bridge-Tunnel •[5]	208	37.00 N	76.18 W
Hampton Tableland ⋏[1]	162	32.10 S	126.10 E
Hamp'yŏng	98	35.05 N	126.30 E
Hamr	54	50.35 N	13.35 E
Hamra	26	61.39 N	15.00 E
Ḥamrā', Al-Ḥamādah al- •[2]	146	30.00 N	12.00 E
Hamra, As Saquia al V	148	27.15 N	13.21 W
Hamra, Ouadi V	146	12.52 N	21.15 E
Ḥamrah, Jabal al- ∧	132	29.39 N	34.47 E
Ḥamran, Har ∧	132	30.41 N	34.34 E
Hamra Nationalpark ♦	26	61.45 N	14.55 E
Ḥamrat ash-Shaykh	140	14.35 N	27.58 E
Hams Bluff ⩟[4]	241n	17.46 N	64.52 W
Hams Fork ≃	200	41.35 N	109.59 W
Hamstreet	42	51.04 N	0.51 E
Ham-Sud	206	45.46 N	71.36 W
Ham Tan	110	10.40 N	107.46 E
Hamtramck	216	42.23 N	83.02 W
Hāmūn, Daryācheh-ye ⊜	128	30.50 N	61.07 E
Hamur	84	39.36 N	42.59 E
Hamura	94	35.45 N	139.19 E
Hamyang	98	35.32 N	127.42 E
Hamzalı	130	38.19 N	41.09 E
Han	150	10.41 N	2.27 W
Han ≃, Zhg.	100	23.41 N	116.38 E
Han ≃, Zhg.	102	30.35 N	114.17 E
Han, Grottes de ⩟[5]	56	50.08 N	5.15 E
Han, Nong ⊜	110	17.12 N	104.11 E
Hana	229a	20.45 N	155.59 W
Hanábana ≃	240p	22.23 N	80.58 W
Hanahan	192	32.55 N	80.01 W
Hanailike	85	39.16 N	76.26 E
Ḥanak	128	25.33 N	36.56 E
Hanakaoo Point ›	229a	20.55 N	156.42 W
Hanalei	229b	22.12 N	159.30 W
Hanalei Bay c	229b	22.13 N	159.31 W
Hanamaki	92	39.23 N	141.07 E
Hanamaulu	229b	21.59 N	159.21 W
Hanamenu, Baie c	174x	9.46 S	139.08 W
Hanam-ni	98	38.23 N	126.43 E
Hanang ∧	154	4.26 S	35.24 E
Hanapepe	229b	21.54 N	159.35 W
Hānār Char	126	23.08 N	90.38 E
Hanataka-sen ∧	96	35.24 N	132.45 E
Hanateio	174x	9.59 S	139.06 W
Hanatetena	174x	9.58 S	139.04 W
Hanau	56	50.08 N	8.55 E
Hanaui	174x	9.45 S	139.05 W
Hanawa, Nihon	94	36.57 N	140.25 E
Hanawa, Nihon	268	35.13 N	139.53 E
Hanbury ≃	176	63.37 N	104.33 W
Hanceville, B.C., Can.	182	51.55 N	123.03 W
Hanceville, Al., U.S.	194	34.03 N	86.46 W
Hanchang	107	30.26 N	103.43 E
Hancheng, Zhg.	102	35.28 N	110.29 E
Hancheng, Zhg.	105	39.39 N	118.02 E
Hanches	261	48.36 N	1.39 E
Hanchō	270	34.49 N	135.27 E
Han-ch'ŏn ≃	271b	37.33 N	127.02 E
Hanchuan	100	30.39 N	113.48 E
Hanchung → Hanzhong	102	33.08 N	107.02 E
Hancock, Md., U.S.	188	39.41 N	78.10 W
Hancock, Mi., U.S.	190	47.07 N	88.34 W
Hancock, Mn., U.S.	198	45.29 N	95.47 W
Hancock, N.Y., U.S.	210	41.57 N	75.17 W
Hancock, Wi., U.S.	190	44.08 N	89.31 W
Hancock □[6], Il., U.S.	219	40.13 N	91.15 W
Hancock □[6], In., U.S.	218	39.47 N	85.46 W
Hancock □[6], Oh., U.S.	216	41.02 N	83.39 W
Hancock □[6], W.V., U.S.	214	40.30 N	80.33 W
Hancock, Lake ⊜	220	27.58 N	81.50 W
Hancocks Bridge	208	39.30 N	75.27 W
Hancun	105	39.24 N	116.36 E
Handa, Nihon	94	34.53 N	136.56 E
Handa, Nihon	96	34.02 N	134.02 E
Handa, Som.	144	10.40 N	51.07 E
Handa I	46	58.22 N	5.12 W
Handan	98	36.37 N	114.29 E
Handaokou	98	34.16 N	116.24 E
Handawor	123	34.24 N	74.17 E
Handen	40	59.10 N	18.08 E
Handeni	154	5.26 S	38.01 E
Handforth	262	53.21 N	2.13 W
Handlová	30	48.44 N	18.46 E
Handöl	26	63.16 N	12.26 E
Handorf	52	51.59 N	7.41 E
Handsworth	184	49.48 N	103.00 W
Handub	140	19.14 N	37.16 E
Handzame	50	51.02 N	3.00 E
Haneda Airport ⊠	268	35.33 N	139.46 E
HaNegev (Negev Desert) •[1]	132	30.30 N	34.55 E
Haney	224	49.13 N	122.36 W
Hane-yama ∧	96	33.14 N	131.08 E
Hane-zaki ›	96	33.22 N	134.02 E
Hanford	226	36.19 N	119.38 W
Hanford Site ʊ[3]	202	46.35 N	119.30 W
Han'gang	98	34.39 N	114.38 E
Han-gang ≃	98	37.45 N	126.11 E
Hanga Roa	174z	27.09 S	109.26 W
Hangatiki	172	38.15 S	175.10 E
Hangbu	100	28.53 N	118.49 E
Hangchow → Hangzhou	106	30.15 N	120.10 E
Hangchow Bay → Hangzhou Wan c	100	30.25 N	121.00 E
Hanger ≃	144	9.35 N	36.02 E
Hanggai	106	30.35 N	119.23 E
Hanggin Houqi	102	40.55 N	107.15 E
Hanggin Qi	102	39.56 N	108.54 E
Hang Hau Town	271d	22.19 N	114.16 E
Hanging Gardens ♦	272c	18.58 N	72.48 E
Hanging Rock State Park ♦	192	36.25 N	80.15 W
Hangingstone Hill ∧[2]	42	50.39 N	3.57 W
Hanging Woman Creek ≃	202	45.19 N	106.31 W
Hangklip, Kaap ›	158	34.26 S	18.48 E
Hangkou	100	29.03 N	114.27 E
Hangman Creek ≃	202	47.38 N	117.27 W
Hangö (Hanko)	26	59.50 N	22.57 E
Hangou	105	39.18 N	117.07 E
Hang-Tcheou → Hangzhou	106	30.15 N	120.10 E
Hangtou	106	31.01 N	121.35 E
Hangtschou → Hangzhou	106	30.15 N	120.10 E
Hangu, Pāk.	123	33.32 N	71.04 E
Hangu, Zhg.	105	39.15 N	117.47 E
Hangu, Zhg.	107	28.58 N	104.30 E
Hanguang	100	24.16 N	113.08 E
Hanguchang	107	29.32 N	106.21 E
Hangugang	105	39.15 N	116.56 E
Hangzhou (Hangchow)	106	30.15 N	120.10 E
Hangzhou Wan (Hangchow Bay) c	100	30.25 N	121.00 E
Hani	130	38.24 N	40.24 E
Hänigsen	52	52.29 N	10.05 E
Hanimadu I	122	6.45 N	73.09 E
Ḥanīsh II	144	13.45 N	42.45 E
Ḥanīsh al-Kabīr, Jazīrat al- I	144	13.43 N	42.45 E
Ḥanita	132	33.05 N	35.10 E
Hanjalipan	112	2.15 S	112.47 E
Hanjiagou	104	40.42 N	120.47 E
Hanjiang	100	25.30 N	119.06 E
Hanjiapuzi	104	40.48 N	123.14 E
Hanjiashu	105	39.11 N	117.04 E
Hanjiawa	106	31.16 N	119.18 E
Hankamer	222	29.51 N	94.38 W
Hankasalmi	26	62.23 N	26.26 E
Hanke	26	59.12 N	10.47 E
Hankendi	130	38.35 N	39.04 E
Hankensbüttel	54	52.44 N	10.36 E
Hankey	158	33.50 S	24.53 E
Hankins	210	41.49 N	75.05 W
Hankinson	198	46.04 N	96.54 W
Hanko → Hangö	26	59.50 N	22.57 E
Hankow → Wuhan	100	30.36 N	114.17 E
Hanks Pond ⊜	276	41.05 N	74.26 W
Hanku → Hangu	105	39.15 N	117.47 E
Hānle	120	32.48 N	79.00 E
Hanley	184	51.37 N	106.27 W
Hanmer	190	46.39 N	80.56 W
Hanmer Springs	172	42.31 S	172.49 E
Hanmiao	89	44.33 N	119.59 E
Hann ≃	164	17.10 S	126.10 E
Hann, Mount ∧	164	15.51 S	125.48 E
Hanna, Ab., Can.	182	51.38 N	111.54 W
Hanna, In., U.S.	216	41.24 N	86.46 W
Hanna, Ok., U.S.	196	35.12 N	95.53 W
Hanna, Wy., U.S.	200	41.52 N	106.33 W
Hanna City	190	40.41 N	89.47 W
Hannaford	198	47.18 N	98.11 W
Hannah	198	48.58 N	98.41 W
Hannah Bay c	176	51.05 N	79.45 W
Hannastown	214	40.21 N	79.30 W
Hannibal, Mo., U.S.	219	39.42 N	91.21 W
Hannibal, N.Y., U.S.	210	43.19 N	76.34 W
Hanningfield Reservoir ⊜[1]	260	51.39 N	0.31 E
Hannō	94	35.51 N	139.19 E
Hannover	52	52.24 N	9.44 E
Hannover □[5]	52	52.30 N	9.15 E
Hannover, Flughafen ⊠	52	52.27 N	9.42 E
Hannut	56	50.40 N	5.05 E
Hanö I	26	56.00 N	14.50 E
Hanobası	130	38.35 N	33.50 E
Hanöbukten c	26	55.45 N	14.30 E
Ha Noi	110	21.02 N	105.51 E
Hanönü	130	41.38 N	34.28 E
Hanoura	96	33.57 N	134.38 E
Hanover, On., Can.	212	44.09 N	81.02 W
Hanover → Hannover, Dtsch.	52	52.24 N	9.44 E
Hanover, S. Afr.	158	31.04 S	24.29 E
Hanover, Ct., U.S.	207	41.38 N	72.03 W
Hanover, Il., U.S.	190	42.15 N	90.16 W
Hanover, In., U.S.	218	38.42 N	85.28 W
Hanover, Ks., U.S.	198	39.53 N	96.52 W
Hanover, Ma., U.S.	207	42.06 N	70.48 W
Hanover, Mi., U.S.	216	42.06 N	84.33 W
Hanover, N.H., U.S.	188	43.42 N	72.17 W
Hanover, N.M., U.S.	200	32.48 N	108.05 W
Hanover, Oh., U.S.	214	40.04 N	82.15 W
Hanover, Pa., U.S.	208	39.48 N	76.59 W
Hanover, Va., U.S.	208	37.45 N	77.22 W
Hanover, Wi., U.S.	216	42.38 N	89.10 W
Hanover □[6]	208	37.42 N	77.20 W
Hanover, Isla I	254	51.00 S	74.40 W
Hanover Airport ⊠	276	40.50 N	74.21 W
Hanover Center	283	42.07 N	70.50 W
Hanover Park	216	42.00 N	88.09 W
Hanover Road	158	30.58 S	24.33 E
Hanoverton	214	40.45 N	80.56 W
Hanovre → Hannover	52	52.24 N	9.44 E
Hanpan, Cape ›	175e	5.01 S	154.37 E
Hanryeosudo Kukrip Kongwŏn ♦	98	34.46 N	128.30 E
Hansanjiazi	104	41.44 N	122.57 E
Hansard	182	54.05 N	121.52 W
Hanscom Air Force Base ■	207	42.28 N	71.17 W
Hans Creek ≃	210	43.06 N	74.08 W
Hansdiha	124	24.36 N	87.05 E
Hansen Dam •[6]	280	34.16 N	118.23 W
Hansen Flood Control Basin ⊜[1]	228	34.16 N	118.23 W
Hanshan	100	31.44 N	118.08 E
Hansharo ⊥	94	35.02 N	138.56 E
Hansi, India	120	32.27 N	77.50 E
Hānsi, India	123	29.06 N	75.58 E
Hansia	272b	22.48 N	88.24 E
Hanska	198	44.08 N	94.29 W
Hānskhāli	126	23.21 N	88.37 E
Hans Lollik Island I	240m	18.24 N	64.55 W
Hanslope	42	52.06 N	0.49 W
Hans Meyer Range ⋏	164	4.20 S	152.55 E
Hanson	207	42.04 N	70.52 W
Hanson ≃	162	20.15 S	133.25 E
Hanson Lake ⊜	184	54.42 N	102.49 W
Hanstholm	26	57.07 N	8.38 E
Han-sur-Lesse	56	50.08 N	5.11 E
Han-sur-Nied	56	48.59 N	6.26 E
Hansville	224	47.55 N	122.33 W
Hansweert	52	51.26 N	4.00 E
Hantaj	88	49.31 N	103.13 E
Hāntālbunia	126	22.44 N	89.31 E
Hantamsberg ⋏	158	31.22 S	19.45 E
Hantan → Handan	98	36.37 N	114.29 E
Hantes ≃	50	50.19 N	4.11 E
Hant's Harbour	186	48.01 N	53.16 W
Hantsport	186	45.04 N	64.11 W
Hantu, Pulau I	271c	1.14 N	103.45 E
Hantu, Tanjong ›	114	4.18 S	100.34 E
Hantzsch ≃	176	67.32 N	72.25 W
Hanumangarh	123	29.35 N	74.19 E
Hanumān Nagar	124	26.30 N	86.51 E
Hanušovce nad Topľou	30	49.02 N	21.30 E
Hanušovice	30	50.05 N	16.55 E
Hanveden ⋏[2]	40	59.07 N	18.00 E
Hanwood	166	34.20 S	146.03 E
Hanworth •[8]	260	51.26 N	0.23 W
Hanxinzhuang	105	40.16 N	116.44 E
Hanyang	107	29.44 N	103.44 E
Hanyangping	102	32.41 N	108.34 E
Hanyin	102	32.42 N	108.50 E
Hanyū	94	36.10 N	139.32 E
Hanyuan	102	29.22 N	102.38 E
Hanyuangai	102	29.30 N	102.31 E
Hanzan	96	34.16 N	133.51 E
Hanzhong	102	33.08 N	107.02 E
Hanzhuang	98	34.38 N	117.24 E
Hao I[1]	14	18.15 S	140.54 W
Hao ≃	100	28.27 N	119.56 E
Haohekou	100	28.38 N	112.49 E
Haojiadian	100	31.47 N	113.44 E
Haoli → Hegang	89	47.24 N	130.17 E
Haoluqi	106	30.38 N	119.34 E
HaOn	132	32.43 N	35.38 E
Hāora	126	22.35 N	88.20 E
Hāora Bridge •[5]	272b	22.35 N	88.21 E
Hāora Railroad Station •[5]	272b	22.35 N	88.21 E
Haouach, Ouadi V	146	16.45 N	19.35 E
Haoxue	102	30.00 N	112.20 E
Haozhikou	107	29.36 N	105.02 E

≃	River	Fluß	Río	Rivière	Rio
≡	Canal	Kanal	Canal	Canal	Canal
⌊	Waterfall, Rapids	Wasserfall, Stromschnellen	Cascada, Rápidos	Chute d'eau, Rapides	Cascata, Rápidos
▬	Strait	Meeresstraße	Estrecho	Détroit	Estreito
c	Bay, Gulf	Bucht, Golf	Bahía, Golfo	Baie, Golfe	Baía, Golfo
⊜	Lake, Lakes	See, Seen	Lago, Lagos	Lac, Lacs	Lago, Lagos
≚	Swamp	Sumpf	Pantano	Marais	Pântano
⊏	Ice Features, Glacier	Eis- und Gletscherformen	Accidentes Glaciales	Formes glaciaires	Acidentes glaciares
⫪	Other Hydrographic Features	Andere Hydrographische Objekte	Otros Elementos Hidrográficos	Autres données hydrographiques	Outros acidentes hidrográficos
✣	Submarine Features	Untermeerische Objekte	Accidentes Submarinos	Formes de relief sous-marin	Acidentes submarinos
□	Political Unit	Politische Einheit	Unidad Politica	Entité politique	Unidade política
ʊ	Cultural Institution	Kulturelle Institution	Institución Cultural	Institution culturelle	Instituição cultural
⊥	Historical Site	Historische Stätte	Sitio Histórico	Site historique	Sitio histórico
♦	Recreational Site	Erholungs- und Ferienort	Sitio de Recreo	Centre de loisirs	Area de Lazer
⊠	Airport	Flughafen	Aeropuerto	Aéroport	Aeroporto
■	Military Installation	Militäranlage	Instalación Militar	Installation militaire	Instalação militar
•	Miscellaneous	Verschiedenes	Misceláneo	Divers	Diversos

ENGLISH — Name / Page / Lat.°′ / Long.°′
DEUTSCH — Name / Seite / Breite°′ / Länge°′ E = Ost

Name	Page	Lat.°′	Long.°′
Haparanda	26	65.50 N	24.10 E
Hapatoni, Baie ⊂	174x	9.58 S	139.07 W
Hapert	52	51.23 N	5.15 E
Hapeville	192	33.39 N	84.24 W
Happ'o-ri	98	40.40 N	127.49 E
Happy	196	34.45 N	101.52 W
Happy Camp	204	41.47 N	123.22 W
Happy Jack	200	34.45 N	111.11 W
Happy Valley-Goose Bay	176	53.20 N	60.25 W
Happy Valley Race Course ♦	271d	22.16 N	114.10 E
Hapsford	262	53.16 N	2.48 W
Hapsu	98	41.13 N	128.51 E
Hapton	262	53.47 N	2.19 W
Hāpur	124	28.43 N	77.47 E
Ḥaql	128	29.18 N	34.57 E
Haquira	248	14.13 S	72.11 W
Har	164	5.20 S	133.10 E
Har, Laga ≃	154	1.40 N	39.36 E
Hara, Nihon	94	35.58 N	138.14 E
Hara, Nihon	268	35.50 N	139.46 E
Ḥaraḍ, Ar. Su.	128	24.08 N	49.05 E
Härad, Sve.	40	59.23 N	16.55 E
Ḥaraḍ, Yaman	144	16.28 N	43.04 E
Ḥaraḍ, Jabal al- ∧	132	29.40 N	35.49 E
Haraiki I[1]	14	17.28 S	143.27 W
Harajuku	268	35.54 N	139.21 E
Haraldsted	41	55.30 N	11.47 E
Haramachi	92	37.38 N	140.58 E
Haramachida	268	35.33 N	139.27 E
Haramosh ∧	123	35.50 N	74.54 E
Haramosh Range ⋏	123	35.40 N	75.22 E
Harappa	123	30.38 N	72.52 E
Harappa Road	123	30.36 N	72.55 E
Harar → Harer	144	9.18 N	42.08 E
Harare (Salisbury)	154	17.50 S	31.03 E
Ḥarash, Bi'r al- ⊤[4]	146	25.30 N	22.12 E
Ḥarastā al-Baṣal	132	33.34 N	36.22 E
Hārāt	272b	22.53 N	88.11 E
Haraz-Djombo	146	13.57 N	19.26 E
Haraze-Mangueigne	146	9.55 N	20.48 E
Harbāti	272b	22.55 N	88.33 E
Harbert	216	41.52 N	86.38 W
Harbeson	208	38.43 N	75.17 W
Harbin	89	45.45 N	126.41 E
Harbiye	130	36.11 N	36.05 E
Harbke	54	52.12 N	11.03 E
Harbo	40	60.06 N	17.12 E
Harbonnières	50	49.51 N	2.40 E
Harboør	26	56.37 N	8.12 E
Harbor	202	42.03 N	124.15 W
Harbor Beach	190	43.50 N	82.39 W
Harbor City ◆[8]	280	33.48 N	118.17 W
Harborcreek	214	42.10 N	79.57 W
Harbord	170	33.47 S	151.17 E
Harbor Isle	276	40.36 N	73.40 W
Harbor Side	228	32.37 N	117.05 W
Harbor Springs	190	45.25 N	84.59 W
Harborton	208	37.39 N	75.49 W
Harbor Tunnel ◆[5]	284b	39.15 N	76.34 W
Harbor View	214	41.42 N	83.27 W
Harbour Breton	186	47.29 N	55.48 W
Harbour Buffett	186	47.31 N	54.05 W
Harbour Deep	186	50.22 N	56.31 W
Harbour Grace	186	47.42 N	53.13 W
Harbours, Bay of ⊂	254	52.15 S	59.15 W
Harbourville	186	45.09 N	64.49 W
Harburg	56	48.47 N	10.41 E
Harburg ◆[8]	52	53.28 N	9.59 E
Hårby	41	55.13 N	10.07 E
Harchies	50	50.29 N	3.41 E
Harcourt, Austl.	169	37.00 S	144.15 E
Harcourt, Fr.	50	49.10 N	0.48 E
Harcuvar Mountains ⋏	200	34.00 N	113.30 W
Hard	58	47.29 N	9.41 E
Harda	124	22.20 N	77.06 E
Hardangerfjorden ⊂[2]	26	60.10 N	6.00 E
Hardangerjøkulen ⍓	26	60.33 N	7.26 E
Hardangervidda ⋏[1]	26	60.20 N	7.30 E
Hardangervidda Nasjonalpark ♦	26	60.15 N	7.05 E
Hardapdam ⊜[1]	156	24.28 S	17.48 E
Hardee □[6]	220	27.29 N	81.48 W
Hardeeville	192	32.17 N	81.04 W
Hardegarijp	52	53.13 N	5.56 E
Hardegsen	52	51.39 N	9.49 E
Hardelot-Plage	50	50.38 N	1.35 E
Hardenberg	52	52.34 N	6.37 E
Harderwijk	52	52.21 N	5.36 E
Hardesty	196	36.36 N	101.11 W
Hardey ≃	162	22.45 S	116.07 E
Hardgrave, Mount ∧[2]	171a	27.30 S	153.29 E
Hardheim	56	49.36 N	9.28 E
Hardin, Il., U.S.	219	39.09 N	90.37 W
Hardin, Mt., U.S.	202	45.43 N	107.36 W
Hardin, Tx., U.S.	222	30.09 N	94.44 W
Hardin □[6], Oh., U.S.	216	40.39 N	83.36 W
Hardin □[6], Tx., U.S.	222	30.20 N	94.35 W
Harding, S. Afr.	158	30.34 S	29.58 E
Harding, Il., U.S.	216	41.31 N	88.51 W
Harding, Ma., U.S.	283	42.12 N	71.27 W
Harding, Lake ⊜[1]	192	32.40 N	85.06 W
Harding Lake ⊜	184	56.13 N	98.23 W
Harding Lakes	208	39.27 N	74.45 W
Hardinsburg, In., U.S.	218	38.27 N	86.16 W
Hardinsburg, Ky., U.S.	194	37.46 N	86.27 W
Hardisty	182	52.40 N	111.18 W
Hardisty Lake ⊜	176	64.30 N	117.45 W
Hardoi	124	27.25 N	80.07 E
Hardoi Branch ≋	124	28.41 N	80.08 E
Hardricourt	261	49.01 N	1.54 E
Hardscrabble Wash V	200	34.39 N	109.28 W
Hardt	263	51.07 N	6.58 E
Hardtner	198	37.00 N	98.38 W
Hardwick, Ga., U.S.	192	33.04 N	83.13 W
Hardwick, Ma., U.S.	207	42.21 N	72.12 W
Hardwick, Vt., U.S.	188	44.30 N	72.22 W
Hardwood	194	30.49 N	91.23 W
Hardwood Ridge ∧	210	41.15 N	75.23 W
Hardy, Ar., U.S.	194	36.18 N	91.28 W
Hardy, Ne., U.S.	198	40.00 N	97.55 W
Hardy, Península ≻[1]	254	55.25 S	68.30 W
Hardy Bay ⊂	176	75.02 N	115.16 W
Hardy Creek ≃	214	42.52 N	81.52 W
Hardy Lake ⊜[1]	218	38.47 N	85.42 W
Hardy Lake State Recreation Area ♦	218	38.44 N	86.26 W
Hardys Pond ⊜	283	42.25 N	71.15 W
Hare, Mount ∧	180	66.38 N	136.12 W
Hare Bay	186	48.51 N	54.01 W
Hare Bay ⊂	186	51.18 N	55.50 W
Harefield ◆[8]	260	51.36 N	0.29 W
Hareid	26	62.22 N	6.02 E
Hare Indian ≃	180	66.18 N	128.38 W
Harelbeke	50	50.51 N	3.18 E
Haren, Dtsch.	52	52.47 N	7.14 E
Haren, Ned.	52	53.10 N	6.35 E
Hareøen I	176	70.25 N	54.50 W
Harer	144	9.18 N	42.08 E
Harerge □[4]	144	8.00 N	43.00 E
Hareskov	41	55.46 N	12.25 E
Hareto	144	9.20 N	37.06 E
Harewa	144	9.55 N	41.59 E
Harewood	172	43.29 S	172.35 E
Harewood Park	284b	39.23 N	76.22 W
Harfaz	130	38.01 N	41.19 E
Harfleur	50	49.30 N	0.12 E
Harford, N.Y., U.S.	210	42.26 N	76.14 W
Harford, Pa., U.S.	210	41.47 N	75.42 W
Harford □[6]	208	39.32 N	76.21 W
Harford Heights	279b	40.22 N	79.46 W
Harford Mills	210	42.25 N	76.12 W
Harg, Sve.	40	59.49 N	18.57 E
Harg, Sve.	40	60.11 N	18.24 E
Hargele	144	5.20 N	42.05 E
Hargeville	261	48.53 N	1.45 E
Hargeysa	144	9.35 N	44.04 E
Harghita □[6]	38	46.35 N	25.30 E
Harghita, Munţii ⋏	38	46.15 N	25.45 E
Hargrave ≃	184	54.24 N	98.48 W
Hargrave Lake ⊜	184	54.29 N	99.40 W
Hargshamn	40	60.10 N	18.28 E
Har Hu (Heihai) ⊜	102	38.15 N	97.40 E
Hāriabhānga ≃[1]	126	21.43 N	89.05 E
Hariāna	123	31.38 N	75.51 E
Hariarapitu	114	2.33 N	98.35 E
Ḥarīb	144	14.57 N	45.30 E
Haribes	156	24.20 S	17.40 E
Ḥaricha, Ḥamâda el ◆[2]	148	22.36 N	3.31 W
Haridwār	124	29.58 N	78.10 E
Harigabessho	270	34.37 N	135.58 E
Harihar	122	14.31 N	75.48 E
Harihari	172	43.09 S	170.33 E
Hariharpāra	126	24.02 N	88.27 E
Harīke	123	31.10 N	74.57 E
Ḥārim	130	36.12 N	36.31 E
Ḥarim, Jabal al- ∧	128	25.58 N	56.14 E
Harima	96	34.42 N	134.53 E
Harima-nada ⊤[2]	96	34.29 N	134.35 E
Harinagar	124	27.09 N	84.19 E
Harinākunda	126	23.39 N	89.03 E
Haringey ◆[8]	42	51.35 N	0.07 W
Hāringhāta ≃[1]	126	21.54 N	89.57 E
Haringvliet ų	52	51.47 N	4.10 E
Haringvlietbrug ◆[5]	52	51.43 N	4.20 E
Haringvlietdam ◆[5]	52	51.50 N	4.03 E
Haripāl	272b	22.49 N	88.07 E
Haripur, India	126	24.18 N	87.05 E
Haripur, India	272b	22.56 N	88.14 E
Harīpur, Pāk.	123	33.59 N	72.56 E
Harirāmpur	126	23.42 N	89.57 E
Harīrūd (Tedžen) ≃	128	37.24 N	60.38 E
Harischandra Range ⋏	122	19.15 N	74.05 E
Ḥārithān	130	36.16 N	37.05 E
Hariyo	144	5.00 N	47.23 E
Harjavalta	26	61.19 N	22.08 E
Härjedalen □[9]	26	62.20 N	13.00 E
Harkaway	274b	38.00 S	145.21 E
Härkeberga	40	59.42 N	17.11 E
Harkema-Opeinde	52	53.11 N	6.08 E
Harker Heights	222	31.05 N	97.40 W
Harkers Island	192	34.41 N	76.33 W
Harker Village	285	39.51 N	75.09 W
Harkness Memorial State Park ♦	207	41.18 N	72.07 W
Harkortsee ⊜	263	51.24 N	7.25 E
Harlaching ◆[8]	60	48.06 N	11.33 E
Harlan, In., U.S.	216	41.11 N	84.55 W
Harlan, Ia., U.S.	198	41.39 N	95.19 W
Harlan, Ky., U.S.	192	36.50 N	83.19 W
Harlan County Lake ⊜[1]	198	40.04 N	99.16 W
Harlech	42	52.52 N	4.07 W
Harlem, Fl., U.S.	220	26.44 N	80.57 W
Harlem, Ga., U.S.	192	33.24 N	82.18 W
Harlem, Mt., U.S.	202	48.32 N	108.47 W
Harlem ◆[8]	276	40.49 N	73.56 W
Harlem River ų	276	40.48 N	73.54 W
Harlem Springs	214	40.31 N	81.02 W
Harlesden ◆[8]	260	51.32 N	0.15 W
Harlesiel	52	53.43 N	7.49 E
Harleston	42	52.24 N	1.18 E
Harleton	222	32.41 N	94.35 W
Hårlev	41	55.21 N	12.15 E
Harleysville	208	40.17 N	75.23 W
Harlin	171a	26.59 S	152.22 E
Harlingen, Ned.	52	53.10 N	5.24 E
Harlingen, Tx., U.S.	196	26.11 N	97.41 W
Harlinger Land ◆[1]	52	53.40 N	7.30 E
Harlingerode	54	51.54 N	10.31 E
Harlington ◆[8]	260	51.29 N	0.26 W
Harlösa	41	55.43 N	13.32 E
Harlow	42	51.47 N	0.08 E
Harlow □[8]	260	51.44 N	0.07 E
Harlowton	202	46.26 N	109.50 W
Harlpur	272b	22.42 N	88.10 E
Harman	188	38.55 N	79.31 W
Harmancık	130	39.41 N	29.10 E
Harmånger	26	61.56 N	17.13 E
Harmanli, Blg.	38	41.56 N	25.54 E
Harmanlı, Tür.	130	37.51 N	37.45 E
Harmanschlag	61	48.39 N	14.47 E
Harmar Heights	279b	40.33 N	79.49 W
Harmarville	279b	40.32 N	79.51 W
Hármashatár-hegy ∧	264c	47.33 N	19.00 E
Harmelen	52	52.05 N	4.58 E
Harmil I	144	16.31 N	40.09 E
Harmonsburg	214	41.40 N	80.19 W
Harmonville	285	40.06 N	75.17 W
Harmony, Ca., U.S.	226	35.35 N	121.01 W
Harmony, In., U.S.	194	39.32 N	87.06 W
Harmony, Mn., U.S.	190	43.33 N	92.00 W
Harmony, N.J., U.S.	210	40.44 N	75.08 W
Harmony, Pa., U.S.	214	40.48 N	80.07 W
Harmony, R.I., U.S.	207	41.53 N	71.35 W
Harmony Brook ≃	276	40.48 N	74.34 W
Harmony Heights	220	27.29 N	80.21 W
Harmony Hills	285	39.42 N	75.41 W
Harmonyville	285	40.11 N	75.43 W
Harnai, India	122	17.48 N	73.06 E
Harnai, Pāk.	120	30.06 N	67.56 E
Harnäs	40	60.39 N	17.22 E
Harnātānr	124	27.19 N	84.01 E
Harndrup	41	55.28 N	10.02 E
Harnes	50	50.27 N	2.54 E
Härnevi	40	59.44 N	17.05 E
Harney ≃	220	25.25 N	81.10 W
Harney, Lake ⊜	220	28.45 N	81.03 W
Harney Basin ≚[1]	202	43.15 N	119.00 W
Harney Lake ⊜	202	43.14 N	119.07 W
Harney Peak ∧	198	43.51 N	103.31 W
Harney Pond Canal ≋	220	27.00 N	81.04 W
Härnösand	26	62.38 N	17.56 E
Haro, Esp.	34	42.35 N	2.51 W
Haro, Ityo.	144	8.28 N	38.37 E
Haro, Cabo ≻	232	27.52 N	110.54 W
Ḥarod ≃	132	32.31 N	35.33 E
Harola	272a	28.36 N	77.19 E
Harold Hill ◆[8]	260	51.36 N	0.13 E
Harold Parker State Forest ♦	283	42.37 N	71.05 W
Haroldswick	46a	60.41 N	0.50 W
Harold Wood ◆[8]	260	51.36 N	0.14 E
Haro Strait ų	224	48.30 N	123.15 W
Haroué	58	48.28 N	6.11 E
Harpālpur	124	25.17 N	79.20 E
Harpanahalli	122	14.48 N	75.59 E
Harpen ◆[8]	263	51.29 N	7.16 E
Harpenden	42	51.49 N	0.22 W
Harper, Liber.	150	4.25 N	7.43 W
Harper, Ks., U.S.	198	37.17 N	98.01 W
Harper, Tx., U.S.	196	30.18 N	99.15 W
Harper, Wa., U.S.	224	47.31 N	122.31 W
Harper, Mount ∧	180	64.14 N	143.50 W
Harper Lake ⊜	228	35.02 N	117.17 W
Harpers Ferry National Historical Park ♦	188	39.13 N	77.45 W
Harpersfield	210	42.26 N	74.41 W
Harper Town	44	54.55 N	2.31 W
Harper Woods	214	42.25 N	82.55 W
Harpille ∧	62	43.50 N	6.48 E
Harpstedt	52	52.54 N	8.35 E
Harpster	214	40.44 N	83.15 W
Harpsund ʊ	40	59.06 N	16.29 E
Harpurhey ◆[8]	262	53.31 N	2.13 W
Harpur Hill	262	53.14 N	1.54 W
Harpursville	210	42.11 N	75.38 W
Harqin	98	41.08 N	119.38 E
Harqin Qi (Jinshan)	98	41.56 N	118.36 E
Harquahala Mountain ∧	200	33.49 N	113.21 W
Ḥarrah	144	14.57 N	50.19 E
Ḥārrah, Jabal al- ∧	132	33.04 N	35.59 E
Harrai	124	22.37 N	79.13 E
Harran	130	36.51 N	39.00 E
Ḥarrān al-ʿAwāmīd	132	33.27 N	36.34 E
Harray, Loch of ⊜	46	59.01 N	3.13 W
Harrell	194	33.30 N	92.23 W
Harricana ≃	176	51.15 N	79.45 W
Harrietfield	46	56.25 N	3.39 W
Harrietsham	42	51.15 N	0.41 E
Harriman, N.Y., U.S.	210	41.18 N	74.09 W
Harriman, Tn., U.S.	192	35.56 N	84.33 W
Harriman Reservoir ⊜[1]	207	42.50 N	72.53 W
Harriman State Park ♦	210	41.14 N	74.09 W
Harrington, Eng., U.K.	44	54.37 N	3.34 W
Harrington, De., U.S.	208	38.55 N	75.34 W
Harrington, Me., U.S.	188	44.37 N	67.48 W
Harrington, Wa., U.S.	202	47.28 N	118.15 W
Harrington Creek ≃	282	37.19 N	122.18 W
Harrington Drain ≋	281	42.36 N	82.54 W
Harrington Park	276	40.59 N	73.58 W
Harris, Sk., Can.	184	51.44 N	107.35 W
Harris, Scot., U.K.	46	56.59 N	6.20 W
Harris, Mn., U.S.	190	45.35 N	92.58 W
Harris, N.Y., U.S.	210	41.43 N	74.44 W
Harris, R.I., U.S.	207	41.43 N	71.31 W
Harris □[6]	222	29.50 N	95.22 W
Harris ≃	168a	33.18 S	116.09 E
Harris ◆[1]	46	57.55 N	6.50 W
Harris, Lake ⊜, Austl.	162	31.08 S	135.14 E
Harris, Lake ⊜, Fl., U.S.	220	28.46 N	81.49 W
Harris, Sound of ų	46	57.45 N	7.10 W
Harris Bay ⊂	212	45.23 N	77.50 W
Harris Brook ≃	283	42.44 N	71.13 W
Harrisburg, Ar., U.S.	194	35.33 N	90.43 W
Harrisburg, Il., U.S.	194	37.44 N	88.32 W
Harrisburg, In., U.S.	218	39.41 N	85.11 W
Harrisburg, Ne., U.S.	198	41.33 N	103.44 W
Harrisburg, Oh., U.S.	214	40.53 N	81.13 W
Harrisburg, Or., U.S.	202	44.16 N	123.10 W
Harrisburg, Pa., U.S.	208	40.16 N	76.53 W
Harrisburg International Airport ⊠	208	40.12 N	76.45 W
Harris Creek ⊂	208	38.45 N	76.18 W
Harris Creek ≃, Austl.	274a	33.57 S	150.57 E
Harris Creek ≃, Tx., U.S.	222	32.33 N	95.08 W
Harrisfield	274b	37.57 S	145.11 E
Harris Hill	210	42.58 N	78.40 W
Harrislee	41	54.48 N	9.22 E
Harrismith, Austl.	162	32.56 S	117.52 E
Harrismith, S. Afr.	158	28.18 S	29.03 E
Harrison, Ar., U.S.	194	36.13 N	93.06 W
Harrison, Id., U.S.	202	47.27 N	116.47 W
Harrison, Il., U.S.	216	42.25 N	89.11 W
Harrison, Mi., U.S.	190	44.01 N	84.47 W
Harrison, Ne., U.S.	198	42.41 N	103.53 W
Harrison, N.J., U.S.	276	40.44 N	74.09 W
Harrison, N.Y., U.S.	210	40.58 N	73.43 W
Harrison, Oh., U.S.	218	39.15 N	84.49 W
Harrison □[6], In., U.S.	218	38.17 N	86.07 W
Harrison □[6], Ky., U.S.	218	38.25 N	84.19 W
Harrison □[6], Oh., U.S.	214	40.16 N	81.05 W
Harrison □[6], Tx., U.S.	222	32.35 N	94.35 W
Harrison ≃	224	49.14 N	121.57 W
Harrison, Cape ≻	176	54.55 N	57.55 W
Harrison Bay ⊂	180	70.30 N	151.30 W
Harrisonburg, La., U.S.	194	31.46 N	91.49 W
Harrisonburg, Va., U.S.	188	38.26 N	78.52 W
Harrison City	279b	40.21 N	79.39 W
Harrison Hot Springs	224	49.18 N	121.47 W
Harrison Islands II	176	69.13 N	90.30 W
Harrison Lake ⊜	182	49.30 N	121.50 W
Harrison Mills	224	49.14 N	121.57 W
Harrisons Brook ≃	276	40.38 N	74.34 W
Harrison Tomb State Memorial ⊥	218	39.09 N	84.46 W
Harrison Valley	214	41.57 N	77.39 W
Harrisonville, Md., U.S.	284b	39.23 N	77.50 W
Harrisonville, Mo., U.S.	194	38.39 N	94.20 W
Harrisonville, N.J., U.S.	285	39.41 N	75.15 W
Harris Park	274a	33.49 S	151.01 E
Harris Pond ⊜	283	42.45 N	71.16 W
Harris Reservoir ⊜[1]	222	29.14 N	95.33 W
Harriston, On., Can.	212	43.54 N	80.53 W
Harriston, Ms., U.S.	194	31.43 N	91.01 W
Harristown	219	39.51 N	89.05 W
Harrisville, Austl.	171a	27.49 S	152.40 E
Harrisville, Mi., U.S.	190	44.39 N	83.17 W
Harrisville, N.Y., U.S.	212	44.09 N	75.19 W
Harrisville, Oh., U.S.	214	40.11 N	80.53 W
Harrisville, Pa., U.S.	214	41.08 N	80.00 W
Harrisville, R.I., U.S.	207	41.57 N	71.40 W
Harrisville, W.V., U.S.	188	39.12 N	81.03 W
Harrod	216	40.42 N	83.55 W
Harrodsburg	194	37.45 N	84.50 W
Harrods Creek ≃	218	38.20 N	85.38 W
Harrogate	44	54.00 N	1.33 W
Harrold	196	34.05 N	99.02 W
Harrop Lake ⊜	184	52.38 N	95.58 W
Harrow	214	42.02 N	82.55 W
Harrow ◆[8]	42	51.35 N	0.21 W
Harrow on the Hill ◆[8]	260	51.34 N	0.20 W
Harrow School ʊ[2]	260	51.34 N	0.20 W
Harrowsmith	212	44.24 N	76.40 W
Harry S. Truman Airport ⊠	240m	18.21 N	64.59 W
Harry S. Truman Reservoir ⊜[1]	194	38.10 N	93.45 W
Har Sai Shan ∧	102	35.28 N	97.55 E
Harsefeld	52	53.27 N	9.30 E
Harsens Island	214	42.34 N	82.34 W
Harsens Island I	281	42.35 N	82.38 W
Harsewinkel	52	51.58 N	8.13 E
Harsīn	128	34.16 N	47.35 E
Harşit ≃	130	41.01 N	38.52 E
Harskamp	52	52.07 N	5.45 E
Harsleben	54	51.52 N	11.05 E
Harstad	24	68.46 N	16.30 E
Harstena	26	58.16 N	17.01 E
Har Su	89	48.09 N	122.25 E
Harsūd	124	22.06 N	76.44 E
Harsum	52	52.12 N	9.57 E
Hart, Mi., U.S.	190	43.41 N	86.21 W
Hart, Tx., U.S.	196	34.23 N	102.07 W
Hart ≃	180	65.51 N	136.22 W
Hart, Lake ⊜, Austl.	166	31.08 S	136.24 E
Hart, Lake ⊜, Fl., U.S.	220	28.22 N	81.13 W
Ḥartā	132	32.42 N	35.51 E
Hartbees ≃	158	28.45 S	20.32 E
Hartbeesfontein	158	26.42 S	26.26 E
Hartbeespoort	158	25.44 S	27.52 E
Hartberg	61	47.17 N	15.59 E
Hartenholm	52	53.54 N	10.03 E
Hartenstein	54	50.39 N	12.40 E
Hart Fell ∧	44	55.25 N	3.25 W
Hartfield	208	37.34 N	76.30 W
Hartford, Eng., U.K.	262	53.15 N	2.33 W
Hartford, Al., U.S.	194	31.06 N	85.41 W
Hartford, Ar., U.S.	194	35.01 N	94.22 W
Hartford, Ct., U.S.	207	41.46 N	72.41 W
Hartford, Il., U.S.	219	38.50 N	90.05 W
Hartford, In., U.S.	218	38.59 N	84.57 W
Hartford, Ks., U.S.	198	38.18 N	95.57 W
Hartford, Ky., U.S.	194	37.27 N	86.54 W
Hartford, Mi., U.S.	216	42.12 N	86.10 W
Hartford, N.J., U.S.	285	39.58 N	74.53 W
Hartford, N.Y., U.S.	210	43.21 N	73.22 W
Hartford, Oh., U.S.	214	41.19 N	80.34 W
Hartford, S.D., U.S.	198	43.37 N	96.56 W
Hartford, Wi., U.S.	190	43.19 N	88.22 W
Hartford □[6]	207	41.46 N	72.41 W
Hartford City	216	40.27 N	85.22 W
Hartha	54	51.05 N	12.58 E
Hartington	198	42.37 N	97.15 W
Hart Island I	276	40.51 N	73.46 W
Hart Lake ⊜	202	42.24 N	119.51 W
Hartland, N.B., Can.	186	46.18 N	67.32 W
Hartland, Eng., U.K.	42	50.59 N	4.29 W
Hartland, Il., U.S.	216	42.22 N	88.31 W
Hartland, Me., U.S.	188	44.53 N	69.26 W
Hartland, Mi., U.S.	216	42.39 N	83.45 W
Hartland, N.Y., U.S.	210	43.14 N	78.35 W
Hartland, Wi., U.S.	216	43.06 N	88.20 W
Hartland Point ≻	42	51.02 N	4.31 W
Hartlepool	44	54.42 N	1.11 W
Hartleton	210	40.54 N	77.10 W
Hartley, Austl.	170	33.33 S	150.11 E
Hartley, Eng., U.K.	260	51.23 N	0.19 E
Hartley, Ia., U.S.	198	43.10 N	95.28 W
Hartley, Tx., U.S.	196	35.53 N	102.24 W
Hartley Bay	182	53.25 N	129.15 W
Hartlip	260	51.21 N	0.39 E
Hart Lot	210	43.01 N	76.28 W
Hartly	208	39.10 N	75.42 W
Hartmannsdorf	54	50.53 N	12.48 E
Hartmannshain	56	50.28 N	9.16 E
Hart-Miller Island I	208	39.15 N	76.23 W
Hart Mountain ∧	184	52.29 N	101.25 W
Hartney	184	49.28 N	100.30 W
Hartola	26	61.35 N	26.01 E
Harts ≃	158	28.24 S	24.17 E
Hartsburg	219	38.41 N	92.18 W
Hartsdale	210	41.01 N	73.47 W
Hartselle	194	34.26 N	86.56 W
Härtsfeld ◆[1]	56	48.50 N	10.15 E
Hartshill	42	52.32 N	1.32 W
Hartshorne	196	34.50 N	95.33 W
Harts Range	162	23.00 S	134.55 E
Hartstene Island I	224	47.14 N	122.53 W
Hartstown	214	41.33 N	80.23 W
Hartsville, In., U.S.	218	39.16 N	85.41 W
Hartsville, Pa., U.S.	285	40.14 N	75.05 W
Hartsville, S.C., U.S.	192	34.22 N	80.04 W
Hartsville, Tn., U.S.	194	36.23 N	86.10 W
Hartswater	158	27.34 S	24.43 E
Hartville, Mo., U.S.	194	37.15 N	92.30 W
Hartville, Oh., U.S.	214	40.57 N	81.19 W
Hartwell	192	34.21 N	82.55 W
Hartwell Lake ⊜[1]	192	34.30 N	82.55 W
Hartwick	210	42.39 N	75.02 W
Hartwick Pines State Park ♦	190	44.47 N	84.41 W
Hartz Mountains National Park ♦	166	43.15 S	146.50 E
Harue	94	36.08 N	136.14 E
Haruki	270	34.29 N	135.23 E
Haruku, Pulau I	164	3.34 S	128.29 E
Hārūn	140	11.20 N	25.43 E
Haruna	94	36.23 N	138.53 E
Hārūnābād	123	29.37 N	73.08 E
Haruna-san ∧	94	36.28 N	138.52 E
Haruniye	130	37.17 N	36.27 E
Haruno, Nihon	94	34.57 N	137.53 E
Haruno, Nihon	96	33.30 N	133.30 E
Harūr	122	12.04 N	78.30 E
Hārūt ≃	128	31.35 N	61.18 E
Harvard, Il., U.S.	216	42.25 N	88.36 W
Harvard, Ma., U.S.	207	42.30 N	71.35 W
Harvard, Ne., U.S.	198	40.37 N	98.05 W
Harvard University ʊ[2]	283	42.22 N	71.07 W
Harvel, Eng., U.K.	260	51.21 N	0.22 E
Harvel, Il., U.S.	219	39.21 N	89.32 W
Harvest, Mount ∧[2]	162	25.54 S	126.28 E
Harvey, Austl.	168a	33.05 S	115.54 E
Harvey, N.B., Can.	186	45.43 N	64.43 W
Harvey, Il., U.S.	216	41.36 N	87.38 W
Harvey, N.D., U.S.	198	47.46 N	99.56 W
Harvey ≃	168a	32.46 S	115.43 E
Harvey Estuary ⊂[1]	168a	32.43 S	115.42 E
Harvey Mountain ∧	207	42.18 N	73.25 W
Harvey Reservoir ⊜[1]	168a	33.05 S	115.58 E
Harveysburg	218	39.30 N	84.00 W
Harveys Lake	210	41.23 N	76.02 W
Harwell	42	51.37 N	1.18 W
Harwich, Eng., U.K.	42	51.57 N	1.17 E
Harwich, Ma., U.S.	207	41.41 N	70.04 W
Harwich Port	207	41.40 N	70.04 W
Harwick	279b	40.34 N	79.48 W
Harwinton	207	41.46 N	73.03 W
Harwood, Eng., U.K.	262	53.35 N	2.23 W
Harwood, Tx., U.S.	222	29.40 N	97.30 W
Harwood Heights	278	41.58 N	87.48 W
Harwood Mines	210	40.57 N	76.01 W
Harwood Park	284b	39.12 N	76.44 W
Haryāna □[3]	120	29.20 N	76.20 E
Harz ⋏	54	51.45 N	10.30 E
Harzgerode	54	51.38 N	11.08 E
Ḥaṣā, Bi'r al- ⊤[4]	140	22.58 N	35.40 E
Ḥasā, Wādī al- V	132	31.05 N	35.27 E
Hasafen	86	45.14 N	90.20 E
Ḥaṣāh, Wādī al- V	132	30.38 N	37.09 E
Hasaki	94	35.44 N	140.50 E
Hasalbag	120	37.54 N	76.44 E
Ḥasanābād	267d	35.44 N	51.19 E
Ḥasanābād-e Khāleṣeh	267d	35.37 N	51.12 E
Hasan Abdāl	123	33.49 N	72.41 E
Hasançelebi	130	38.58 N	37.54 E
Hasan Dağı ∧	130	38.08 N	34.12 E
Hasankale → Pasinler	130	39.59 N	41.41 E
Hasankeyf	130	37.43 N	41.25 E
Ḥasan Kīādeh	128	37.24 N	49.58 E
Hasanpur	124	28.43 N	78.17 E
Hasayaz	130	40.15 N	33.20 E
Ḥāṣbānī, Nahr al- ≃	132	33.11 N	35.37 E
Ḥāṣbayyā	132	33.24 N	35.41 E
Hasbek	130	39.33 N	35.33 E
Hasbergen, Dtsch.	52	52.14 N	7.57 E
Hasbergen, Dtsch.	52	53.05 N	8.40 E
Hasbrouck Heights	276	40.51 N	74.04 W
Hascosay I	46a	60.37 N	0.59 W
Hasdo ≃	120	21.44 N	82.44 E
Hasdo-Rāmpur Basin ≚[1]	124	22.50 N	82.35 E
Hase, Nihon	94	35.47 N	138.06 E
Hase, Nihon	270	34.32 N	135.54 E
Hase ≃, Dtsch.	52	52.41 N	7.18 E
Hase ≃, Nihon	270	34.34 N	135.38 E
Hasel ≃	54	50.32 N	10.27 E
Häselgehr	58	47.19 N	10.30 E
Haselhorst ◆[8]	264a	52.33 N	13.15 E
Haselünne	52	52.40 N	7.29 E
Hasenkamp	252	31.31 S	59.51 W
Ḥashā', Jabal al- ∧	144	13.45 N	44.30 E
HaShefela ◆[1]	132	31.40 N	34.55 E
Hashima	94	35.19 N	136.42 E
Hashimoto, Nihon	96	34.19 N	135.37 E
Hashimoto, Nihon	270	34.26 N	135.23 E
Hashira-jima I	96	34.01 N	132.25 E
Hashiri-jima I	96	34.21 N	133.27 E
Hashitai	89	49.24 N	125.18 E
Hasht Sāl ◆[8]	272a	28.38 N	77.03 E
Hasil, Pulau I	164	1.06 S	128.24 E
Hāsilpur	123	29.43 N	72.33 E
Ḥāsīn-e Bozorg	84	39.23 N	44.42 E
Haskayne	262	53.34 N	2.58 W
Haskeir Islands II	46	57.42 N	7.41 W
Haskell, Ok., U.S.	196	35.49 N	95.40 W
Haskell, Tx., U.S.	196	33.09 N	99.44 W
Haskell Pond ⊜	283	42.37 N	70.44 W
Hasketh Bank	262	53.43 N	2.51 W
Haskins	216	41.27 N	83.42 W
Haskovo	38	41.56 N	25.33 E
Haskovo □[4]	130	41.50 N	25.50 E
Hasköy, Tür.	130	40.59 N	42.52 E
Hasköy, Tür.	130	41.38 N	26.41 E
Hasköy ◆[8]	267b	41.02 N	28.58 E
Haslach im Kinzigtal	58	48.16 N	8.06 E
Hasle, Dan.	41	55.10 N	10.10 E
Hasle, Schw.	58	47.01 N	7.39 E
Haslemere	42	51.06 N	0.43 W
Haslett	216	42.44 N	84.24 W
Haslev	41	55.20 N	11.58 E
Haslingden	44	53.43 N	2.18 W
Haslingden Grane	262	53.42 N	2.21 W
Haslington	44	53.06 N	2.24 W
Haslital V	58	46.42 N	8.10 E
Haslum	26	59.50 N	10.22 E
Hasmark	41	55.33 N	10.28 E
Ḥasmat ʿUmar, Bi'r ⊤[4]	140	21.46 N	34.00 E
Hāsnābād	126	22.35 N	88.55 E
Hasnācha	272b	22.26 N	88.09 E
Haspe ◆[8]	263	51.21 N	7.26 E
Hasperos Canyon V	200	33.50 N	105.02 W
Hasper-Stausee ⊜[1]	263	51.18 N	7.25 E
Haspres	50	50.15 N	3.25 E
Ḥaṣṣ, Jabal al- ∧[2]	130	35.52 N	37.22 E
Hassa	130	36.50 N	36.29 E
Hassan	122	13.00 N	76.05 E
Hassard	219	39.39 N	91.40 W
Hassayampa ≃	200	33.20 N	112.43 W
Hassberge ⋏[2]	56	50.12 N	10.29 E
Hassbergen	52	52.44 N	9.13 E
Hassel, Dtsch.	52	52.48 N	9.11 E
Hassel, Dtsch.	263	51.39 N	7.30 E
Hassel ◆[8]	263	51.36 N	7.03 E
Hasselbeck-Schwarzbach	263	51.16 N	6.53 E
Hasselfelde	54	51.41 N	10.51 E
Hasselfors	40	59.05 N	14.39 E
Hassels ◆[8]	263	51.10 N	6.53 E
Hasselt, Bel.	56	50.56 N	5.20 E
Hasselt, Ned.	52	52.35 N	6.05 E
Hassfurt	56	50.02 N	10.31 E
Hassi Bel Guebbour	148	28.46 N	6.27 E
Hassi el Ghella	34	35.28 N	1.03 W
Hassi Mameche	34	35.52 N	0.04 E
Hassi Messaoud	148	31.43 N	5.59 E
Hassi Zehana	34	35.01 N	0.53 W
Hassleben	54	53.13 N	13.41 E
Hässleholm	41	56.09 N	13.46 E
Hasslinghausen	56	51.20 N	7.17 E
Hassloch	56	49.22 N	8.16 E
Hasson Heights	214	41.26 N	79.41 W
Hästbo	40	60.27 N	16.27 E
Hasten ◆[8], Dtsch.	263	51.12 N	7.09 E
Hästen ◆[8], Dtsch.	263	51.09 N	7.06 E
Hastière-Lavaux	56	50.13 N	4.50 E
Hastings, Austl.	169	38.18 S	145.11 E
Hastings, Barb.	241g	13.04 N	59.35 W
Hastings, On., Can.	212	44.18 N	77.57 W
Hastings, N.Z.	172	39.38 S	176.51 E
Hastings, Eng., U.K.	42	50.51 N	0.36 E
Hastings, Fl., U.S.	192	29.43 N	81.30 W
Hastings, Il., U.S.	278	41.41 N	87.58 W
Hastings, Mi., U.S.	216	42.39 N	85.17 W
Hastings, Mn., U.S.	190	44.44 N	92.51 W
Hastings, Ne., U.S.	198	40.35 N	98.23 W
Hastings, N.Y., U.S.	210	43.22 N	76.09 W
Hastings, Pa., U.S.	214	40.39 N	78.42 W
Hastings □[6]	212	44.45 N	77.40 W
Hastings Battlesite ⊥	42	50.53 N	0.31 E
Hastings-on-Hudson	276	40.59 N	73.52 W
Hastingwood	260	51.45 N	0.09 E
Hastrup	41	55.26 N	12.11 E
Hasty	198	38.06 N	102.57 W
Hasuda	94	35.59 N	139.40 E
Hasumi	96	34.52 N	132.37 E
Haswell	198	38.27 N	103.09 W
Hata	94	36.11 N	137.51 E
Hat'ae-do I	98	34.32 N	126.03 E
Ha Tan	110	18.30 N	105.20 E
Hatanagi-dam ◆[6]	94	35.18 N	138.12 E
Hatashō	94	35.10 N	136.15 E
Hatay □[4]	130	36.30 N	36.15 E
Hatboro	208	40.10 N	75.06 W
Hatch, N.M., U.S.	200	32.39 N	107.09 W
Hatch, Ut,. U.S.	200	37.38 N	112.26 W
Hat Chao Mai National Park ♦	110	7.40 N	99.35 E
Hatches Creek	162	20.56 S	135.12 E
Hatchet Creek ≃	194	32.52 N	86.20 W
Hatchet Lake	186	44.35 N	63.40 W
Hatchie ≃	194	35.35 N	89.53 W
Hatchineha, Lake ⊜	220	28.02 N	81.25 W
Hatchlands ⊥	260	51.15 N	0.28 W
Hatchmere	262	53.15 N	2.40 W
Hatchville	207	41.37 N	70.33 W
Hatch Wash V	200	38.32 N	109.36 W
Hat Creek ≃, U.S.	198	43.16 N	103.36 W
Hat Creek ≃, Ca., U.S.	204	40.59 N	121.33 W
Hațeg	38	45.37 N	22.57 E
Hateruma-shima I	175d	24.03 N	123.47 E
Hatfield, Austl.	166	33.52 S	143.45 E
Hatfield, Eng., U.K.	42	51.46 N	0.13 W
Hatfield, Eng., U.K.	44	53.34 N	1.00 W
Hatfield, Ar., U.S.	194	34.29 N	94.22 W
Hatfield, Ma., U.S.	207	42.22 N	72.35 W
Hatfield Aerodrome ⊠	260	51.46 N	0.16 W
Hatfield House ⊥	260	51.46 N	0.13 W
Hatfield Peverel	42	51.47 N	0.35 E
Hatfield Swamp ≡	276	40.50 N	74.20 W
Hathāla	123	32.03 N	70.34 E
Hathaway Pines	226	38.07 N	120.28 W
Hatherleigh	42	50.49 N	4.04 W
Hathersage	44	53.19 N	1.38 W
Hāthras	124	27.36 N	78.03 E
Hātia ų	124	22.30 N	91.15 E
Ḥāṭibah, Ra's ≻	144	21.55 N	38.58 E
Ha Tien	110	10.23 N	104.29 E
Hatillo	240m	18.29 N	66.49 W
Ha Tinh	110	18.20 N	105.54 E
Hatinoe → Hachinohe	92	40.30 N	141.29 E
Hatiozi → Hachiōji	94	35.39 N	139.20 E
Hatip	130	37.46 N	32.25 E
Hātisāla	272b	22.33 N	88.32 E
Hato, Bocht van ⊂	241s	12.13 N	68.58 W
Hatogaya	94	35.50 N	139.44 E
Hato Mayor [del Rey]	238	18.46 N	69.15 W
Hato Rey	240m	18.25 N	66.03 W
Hatoyama	94	35.59 N	139.20 E
Hāt Pīplia	124	22.46 N	76.18 E
Hatsukaichi	96	34.21 N	132.20 E
Hatsu-shima I	94	35.02 N	139.10 E
Hatsutomi	268	35.46 N	140.01 E
Hatta	124	24.07 N	79.36 E
Hattab, Oued el V	36	35.23 N	9.32 E
Hattah-Kulkyne National Park ♦	166	34.40 S	142.30 E
Hattem	52	52.28 N	6.04 E
Hatten, Dtsch.	52	53.02 N	8.22 E
Hatten, Fr.	56	48.54 N	7.59 E
Hattenhofen	60	48.13 N	11.07 E
Hatteras	192	35.13 N	75.41 W
Hatteras, Cape ≻	192	35.13 N	75.32 W
Hatteras Island I	192	35.25 N	75.30 W
Hattiesburg	194	31.19 N	89.17 W
Hatting	41	55.51 N	9.46 E
Hattingen	56	51.23 N	7.10 E
Hattingspruit	158	28.09 S	30.11 E
Hatton, Eng., U.K.	262	53.20 N	2.36 W
Hatton, Scot., U.K.	46	57.25 N	1.54 W
Hatton, Al., U.S.	194	34.33 N	87.24 W
Hatton, N.D., U.S.	198	47.38 N	97.27 W
Hatton ◆[8]	260	51.28 N	0.25 W
Hatton Fields	226	36.33 N	121.54 W
Hattorf [am Harz]	52	51.39 N	10.14 E
Hattori, Nihon	270	34.46 N	135.27 E
Hattori, Nihon	270	34.52 N	135.36 E
Hattstatt	58	48.01 N	7.17 E
Hattstedt	41	54.31 N	9.01 E
Hatunsaray	130	37.35 N	32.21 E
Hatvan	30	47.40 N	19.41 E
Hat Yai	110	7.01 N	100.28 E
Hatzfeld ◆[8]	263	51.17 N	7.11 E
Hatzic	224	49.09 N	122.15 W
Hatzic Lake ⊜	224	49.10 N	122.14 W
Haubstadt	194	38.12 N	87.34 W
Hāudullāpur	272b	22.25 N	88.33 E
Hauge	26	58.18 N	6.15 E
Haugesund	26	59.25 N	5.18 E
Haugh of Urr	44	54.58 N	3.52 W
Haughton Green	262	53.27 N	2.06 W
Haugsdorf	61	48.42 N	16.05 E
Hau Hoi Wan ⊂	100	22.28 N	113.56 E
Hauhungaroa Range ⋏	172	38.50 S	175.34 E
Haukeligrend	26	59.45 N	7.31 E
Haukipudas	26	65.11 N	25.21 E
Haukivesi ⊜	26	62.06 N	28.28 E
Haukivuori	26	62.01 N	27.13 E
Hauldres, Ru des ≃	261	48.37 N	2.28 E
Haulerwijk	52	53.04 N	6.20 E
Haultain ≃	184	55.51 N	106.46 W
Haune ≃	56	50.52 N	9.43 E
Haunersdorf	60	48.36 N	12.43 E
Haunstetten	58	48.18 N	10.54 E
Haunts Creek ų	276	40.37 N	73.31 W
Hauppauge	210	40.49 N	73.12 W
Hauptsrus	158	26.33 S	26.18 E
Hauraki Gulf ⊂	172	36.20 S	175.05 E
Hauroko, Lake ⊜	172	46.00 S	167.20 E
Hauru, Pointe ≻	174s	17.29 S	149.55 W
Haus	64	47.25 N	13.49 E
Hausa	273a	6.37 N	3.21 E
Hausach	58	48.17 N	8.10 E
Hausham	64	47.45 N	11.50 E
Hausruck ⋏	60	48.07 N	13.35 E
Haussee ⊜	264a	52.38 N	13.41 E
Haussömmern	54	51.11 N	10.49 E
Haut, Isle au I	188	44.03 N	68.38 W
Haut Atlas ⋏	148	31.30 N	6.00 W
Haut-Bout	261	48.32 N	1.55 E
Haute Colme, Canal de la ≋	50	50.50 N	2.12 E
Hautecombe, Abbaye de ʊ[1]	62	45.45 N	5.50 E
Haute-Corse □[5]	36	42.30 N	9.00 E
Haute-Garonne □[5]	32	43.25 N	1.30 E
Haute-Kotto □[5]	152	7.00 N	23.00 E
Haute-Loire □[5]	32	45.05 N	3.50 E
Hauteluce	62	45.45 N	6.35 E
Haute-Marne □[5]	58	48.05 N	5.10 E
Hauterive	186	49.12 N	68.16 W
Hauterives	62	45.15 N	5.02 E
Hautes-Alpes □[5]	62	44.40 N	6.30 E
Haute-Sangha □[5]	152	4.30 N	16.00 E
Haute-Saône □[5]	58	47.40 N	6.10 E
Haute-Savoie □[5]	32	46.00 N	6.20 E
Haute Seine, Canal de la ≋	50	48.34 N	3.43 E
Hautes Fagnes ⋏	56	50.30 N	6.05 E
Hautes-Pyrénées □[5]	32	43.00 N	0.10 E
Haute Sûre, Lac de la ⊜[1]	56	49.52 N	5.52 E
Haute-Vienne □[5]	32	45.50 N	1.15 E
Hauteville-Lompnes	58	45.58 N	5.36 E
Haute Volta → Burkina Faso □[1]	150	13.00 N	1.30 W
Haut-Folin ∧	32	47.00 N	4.02 E
Haut-Kœnigsbourg, Château du ⊥	58	48.14 N	7.22 E
Haut-Mbomou □[5]	140	6.00 N	26.00 E
Hautmont	50	50.15 N	3.56 E
Haut-Ogooué □[4]	152	1.00 S	13.50 E
Haut-Rhin □[5]	58	47.53 N	7.13 E
Hauts-de-Seine □[5]	261	48.50 N	2.11 E
Hautvillers	50	49.05 N	3.57 E
Haut-Zaïre □[4]	154	2.20 N	27.00 E
Hauula	229c	21.36 N	157.54 W
Hauzenberg	60	48.39 N	13.38 E
Hauz Rāni ◆[8]	272a	28.32 N	77.13 E
Havana → La Habana, Cuba	240p	23.08 N	82.22 W
Havana, Ar., U.S.	194	35.06 N	93.31 W
Havana, Fl., U.S.	192	30.37 N	84.24 W
Havana, Il., U.S.	194	40.18 N	90.03 W
Havana, N.D., U.S.	198	45.57 N	97.37 W
Havane, La → La Habana	240p	23.08 N	82.22 W
Havannah, Canal de la ų	175f	22.22 S	167.01 E
Havant	42	50.51 N	0.59 W
Havasu, Lake ⊜[1]	200	34.30 N	114.20 W
Havasu Creek ≃	200	36.19 N	112.46 W
Havasupai Indian Reservation ◆[4]	200	36.13 N	112.40 W
Havdrup	41	55.32 N	12.08 E
Havel ≃	54	52.53 N	11.58 E
Havelange	56	50.23 N	5.14 E
Havelberg	54	52.50 N	12.04 E
Havelberg ∧[2]	264a	52.28 N	13.12 E
Haveli	123	30.27 N	73.42 E
Haveliān	123	34.03 N	73.10 E
Havel-Kanal ≋	264a	52.36 N	13.12 E
Havelland ◆[1]	54	52.25 N	12.45 E
Havelländischer Grosser Hauptkanal ≋	264a	52.37 N	13.03 E
Havelländisches Luch ≡	54	52.40 N	12.40 E
Havelock, On., Can.	212	44.26 N	77.53 W
Havelock, N.Z.	172	41.17 S	173.46 E
Havelock, N.C., U.S.	192	34.52 N	76.54 W
Havelock Island I	110	11.58 N	93.00 E
Havelock North	172	39.40 S	176.53 E
Haven	198	37.53 N	97.46 W
Haverford	285	40.00 N	75.17 W
Haverford College ʊ[2]	285	40.00 N	75.18 W
Haverfordwest	42	51.49 N	4.58 W
Haverhill, Eng., U.K.	42	52.05 N	0.26 E
Haverhill, Ma., U.S.	207	42.46 N	71.04 W
Haverhill Airport ⊠	283	42.48 N	71.04 W
Haverhill-Riverside Airport ⊠	283	42.46 N	71.02 W
Hāveri	122	14.48 N	75.24 E
Haverigg	44	54.11 N	3.17 W
Havering ◆[8]	42	51.34 N	0.14 E
Havering-atte-Bower ◆[8]	260	51.37 N	0.11 E
Havering's Grove	260	51.38 N	0.23 E
Havern ⊜	26	62.17 N	15.07 E
Haverö	26	62.24 N	15.05 E
Haverstraw	210	41.11 N	73.57 W
Havertown	208	39.58 N	75.18 W
Haviland, Ks., U.S.	198	37.37 N	99.06 W
Haviland, Oh., U.S.	216	41.01 N	84.35 W
Haviland Brook ≃	276	41.07 N	73.33 W
Ḥavīq	128	38.10 N	48.54 E
Havířov	30	49.47 N	18.27 E
Havixbeck	52	51.58 N	7.25 E
Hävla	40	58.55 N	15.52 E
Havlíčkův Brod	30	49.36 N	15.35 E
Havnbjerg	41	55.02 N	9.48 E
Havnsø	41	55.45 N	11.20 E
Havran	130	39.33 N	27.06 E
Havré, Bel.	50	50.28 N	4.02 E
Havre → Le Havre, Fr.	50	49.30 N	0.08 E
Havre, Mt., U.S.	202	48.32 N	109.40 W
Havre-Aubert	186	47.14 N	61.51 W
Havre Aubert, Île du I	186	47.14 N	61.57 W
Havre aux Maisons, Île du I	186	47.25 N	61.47 W
Havre de Grace	208	39.32 N	76.05 W
Havre de Grace Heights	208	39.35 N	76.07 W
Havre North	202	48.36 N	109.41 W
Havre-Saint-Pierre	186	50.14 N	63.36 W
Havsa	130	41.33 N	26.49 E
Havza	130	40.58 N	35.41 E
Haw ≃	192	35.36 N	79.03 W
Hawaii □[3]	229d	20.00 N	157.45 W
Hawaii I	229d	19.30 N	155.30 W
Hawaiian Gardens	280	33.49 N	118.04 W
Hawaiian Islands II	229d	20.30 N	157.30 W

Symbols in the index entries represent the broad categories identified in the key at the right. Symbols with superior numbers (⋏[1]) identify subcategories (see complete key on page *I · 1*).

Symbole im Register stellen die rechts im Schlüssel erklärten Kategorien dar. Symbole mit hochgestellten Ziffern (⋏[1]) bezeichnen Unterabteilungen einer Kategorie (vgl. vollständiger Schlüssel auf Seite *I · 1*).

Los símbolos incluídos en el texto del índice representan las grandes categorías identificadas con la clave a la derecha. Los símbolos con numeros en su parte superior (⋏[1]) identifican las subcategorías (véase la clave completa en la página *I · 1*).

Les symboles de l'index représentent les catégories indiquées dans la légende à droite. Les symboles suivis d'un indice (⋏[1]) représentent des sous-catégories (voir légende complète à la page *I · 1*).

Os símbolos incluídos no texto do índice representam as grandes categorias identificadas com a chave à direita. Os símbolos com números em sua parte superior (⋏[1]) identificam as subcategorias (veja-se a chave completa à página *I · 1*).

	English	Deutsch	Español	Français	Português
∧	Mountain	Berg	Montaña	Montagne	Montanha
⋏	Mountains	Gebirge	Montañas	Montagnes	Montanhas
)(	Pass	Paß	Paso	Col	Passo
V	Valley, Canyon	Tal, Cañon	Valle, Cañón	Vallée, Canyon	Vale, Canhão
≚	Plain	Ebene	Llano	Plaine	Planície
≻	Cape	Kap	Cabo	Cap	Cabo
I	Island	Insel	Isla	Île	Ilha
II	Islands	Inseln	Islas	Îles	Ilhas
⊥	Other Topographic Features	Andere Topographische Objekte	Otros Elementos Topográficos	Autres données topographiques	Outros acidentes topográficos

ESPAÑOL / FRANÇAIS / PORTUGUÊS

Nombre / Nom / Nome	Página / Page / Página	Lat.°′	Long.°′ W = Oeste / W = Ouest / W = Oeste
Hawaiian Ridge ✣[3]	14	24.00 N	165.00 W
Hawaii Volcanoes National Park ♠	229d	19.23 N	155.17 W
Hawal ≃	146	10.00 N	12.05 E
Hawarden, Sk., Can.	184	51.23 N	106.36 W
Hawarden, N.Z.	172	42.56 S	172.38 E
Hawarden, Wales, U.K.	44	53.11 N	3.02 W
Hawarden, Ia., U.S.	198	42.59 N	96.29 W
Ḥawashīyah, Wādī ∨	140	28.31 N	32.58 E
Haw Creek ≃	218	39.11 N	85.55 W
Hawea, Lake ⊜	172	44.30 S	169.17 E
Hawera	172	39.35 S	174.17 E
Hawes	44	54.18 N	2.12 W
Hawesville	194	37.54 N	86.45 W
Haweswater Reservoir ⊜	44	54.32 N	2.48 W
Ḥawf, Jabal ⋏[2]	273c	29.55 N	31.21 E
Ḥawf, Wādī ∨	142	29.53 N	31.18 E
Hawi	229d	20.14 N	155.50 W
Hawick	44	55.25 N	2.47 W
Hawk Creek ≃	198	44.44 N	95.25 W
Hawkdun Range ⋏	172	44.46 S	170.00 E
Hawke, Cape ≻	166	32.13 S	152.34 E
Hawke Bay ⊂	172	39.20 S	177.30 E
Hawker	166	31.53 S	138.25 E
Hawkes, Mount ∧	9	83.56 S	55.45 W
Hawkes Brook ≃	283	42.45 N	71.08 W
Hawkesbury	206	45.36 N	74.37 W
Hawkesbury ≃	170	33.30 S	151.10 E
Hawkesbury Island I	182	53.38 N	129.00 W
Hawkes Pond ⊜	283	42.30 N	71.02 W
Hawkeye	190	42.56 N	91.57 W
Hawkhurst	42	51.02 N	0.30 E
Hawking	42	51.06 N	1.10 E
Hawkins, Tx., U.S.	222	32.35 N	95.12 W
Hawkins, Wi., U.S.	190	45.30 N	90.43 W
Hawkins, Lake ⊜[1]	222	32.38 N	95.15 W
Hawkins Island I	180	60.30 N	146.00 W
Hawkinsville	192	32.17 N	83.28 W
Hawk Junction	190	48.05 N	84.34 W
Hawk Lake	184	49.48 N	93.59 W
Haw Knob ∧	192	35.19 N	84.02 W
Hawk Point	219	38.58 N	91.07 W
Hawk Run	214	40.55 N	78.12 W
Hawksbill ∧	188	38.33 N	78.23 W
Hawksbill Creek ⊂	192	26.32 N	78.43 W
Hawks Nest Point ≻	238	24.09 N	75.32 W
Hawkwell	260	51.36 N	0.40 E
Hawkwood	166	25.47 S	150.50 E
Hawley, Eng., U.K.	260	51.25 N	0.14 E
Hawley, Mn., U.S.	198	46.52 N	96.18 W
Hawley, Pa., U.S.	210	41.28 N	75.10 W
Hawleyton	210	42.01 N	75.55 W
Hawleyville	207	41.25 N	73.21 W
Haworth, Eng., U.K.	44	53.49 N	1.57 W
Haworth, N.J., U.S.	276	40.57 N	73.59 W
Haw Par Villa ʊ	271c	1.16 N	103.47 E
Hawr	142	27.52 N	30.44 E
Ḥawrān, Wādī ∨	128	33.58 N	42.34 E
Ḥawsh ʻĪsā	142	30.55 N	30.17 E
Hawthorn, Austl.	274b	37.49 S	145.02 E
Hawthorn, Pa., U.S.	214	41.01 N	79.17 W
Hawthorne, Ca., U.S.	228	33.54 N	118.21 W
Hawthorne, Fl., U.S.	192	29.35 N	82.05 W
Hawthorne, Nv., U.S.	204	38.31 N	118.37 W
Hawthorne, N.J., U.S.	210	40.56 N	74.09 W
Hawthorne, N.Y., U.S.	210	41.06 N	73.47 W
Hawthorne Lake ⊜	276	41.03 N	74.35 W
Hawthorne Municipal Airport ⊠	280	33.55 N	118.20 W
Hawthorne Race Course ♠	278	41.50 N	87.45 W
Hawthorn Woods	278	42.13 N	88.03 W
Ḥawwārah	132	32.32 N	35.54 E
Hawwārat ʻAdlān	142	29.12 N	30.58 E
Hawwārat al-Maqṭaʻ	142	29.15 N	30.54 E
Hawza	148	27.06 N	10.55 W
Hawzen	144	13.56 N	39.28 E
Haxby	44	54.01 N	1.04 W
Haxey	44	53.29 N	0.50 W
Haxtun	198	40.38 N	102.37 W
Hay	166	34.30 S	144.51 E
Hay ≃, Austl.	166	25.14 S	138.00 E
Hay ≃, Can.	176	60.52 N	115.44 W
Hay ≃, Wi., U.S.	190	44.59 N	91.51 W
Hay, Cape ≻	176	74.25 N	113.00 W
Hay, Mount ∧, Austl.	162	23.28 S	133.05 E
Hay, Mount ∧, Austl.	170	33.37 S	150.26 E
Hay, Mount ∧, N.A.	180	59.15 N	137.37 W
Hay, South Fork ≃	190	45.03 N	91.57 W
Haya	164	3.27 S	129.33 E
Haya ≃, Nihon	94	35.14 N	139.09 E
Haya ≃, Nihon	94	35.25 N	138.27 E
Hayachine-san ∧	92	39.34 N	141.29 E
Hayakawa	94	35.25 N	138.22 E
Hayama, Nihon	94	35.16 N	139.35 E
Hayama, Nihon	96	33.26 N	133.13 E
Hayang	98	35.55 N	128.47 E
Hayange	56	49.20 N	6.03 E
HaYarden → Jordan ≃	132	31.46 N	35.33 E
Hayashima	96	34.36 N	133.50 E
Hayastan → Armenia □[1]	22	40.00 N	45.00 E
Hayasui-seto Џ	96	33.18 N	131.59 E
Haybān	140	11.13 N	30.31 E
Haybān, Jabal ∧	140	11.15 N	30.31 E
Hay Bay ⊂	212	44.10 N	76.55 W
Haybes	56	50.00 N	4.43 E
Haydān, Wādī al- ∨	132	31.27 N	35.36 E
Haydarlı	130	38.16 N	30.23 E
Hayden, Az., U.S.	200	33.00 N	110.47 W
Hayden, Co., U.S.	200	40.29 N	107.15 W
Hayden, In., U.S.	218	38.58 N	85.44 W
Hayden Peak ∧	202	42.59 N	116.39 W
Haydenville, Ma., U.S.	207	42.22 N	72.42 W
Haydenville, Oh., U.S.	188	39.28 N	82.19 W
Haydock	44	53.28 N	2.39 W
Haydock Park Race Course ♠	262	53.29 N	2.37 W
Haydon Bridge	44	54.58 N	2.14 W
Haye, La → 's-Gravenhage	52	52.06 N	4.18 E
Hayes	194	30.06 N	92.55 W
Hayes ◆[8], Eng., U.K.	260	51.31 N	0.25 W
Hayes ◆[8], Eng., U.K.	260	51.23 N	0.01 E
Hayes ≃, Mb., Can.	184	57.03 N	92.09 W
Hayes ≃, N.T., Can.	176	67.18 N	95.02 W
Hayes, Mount ∧	180	63.37 N	146.43 W
Hayes Center	198	40.30 N	101.01 W
Hayes State Memorial ⊥	214	41.21 N	83.08 W
Hayesville, N.C., U.S.	192	35.02 N	83.49 W
Hayesville, Oh., U.S.	214	40.46 N	82.15 W
Hayesville, Or., U.S.	224	44.59 N	122.58 W
Hayfield, Eng., U.K.	262	53.23 N	1.57 W
Hayfield, Mn., U.S.	190	43.53 N	92.50 W
Hayford Peak ∧	204	36.40 N	115.11 W
Hayfork	204	40.33 N	123.10 W
Hayfork Bally ∧	204	40.39 N	123.13 W
Hayfork Creek ≃	204	40.37 N	123.26 W
Hay Island I	212	44.53 N	80.58 W
Hayk, Lake ⊜	144	11.21 N	39.43 E
Haykota	144	15.10 N	37.03 E
Hay Lake ⊜	212	45.23 N	78.11 W
Hay Lakes	182	53.13 N	113.03 W
Hayle	42	50.11 N	5.23 W
Haymakers Run ≃	279b	40.25 N	79.43 W
Haymana	130	39.27 N	32.30 E
Haynes	194	34.53 N	90.47 W
Haynes Creek ≃	285	39.53 N	74.50 W
Haynesville, La., U.S.	194	32.57 N	93.08 W
Haynesville, Va., U.S.	208	37.57 N	76.40 W
Hayneville	194	32.11 N	86.34 W
Haynin	144	15.50 N	48.19 E
Hay-on-Wye	42	52.04 N	3.07 W
Hay Point ≻	166	21.17 S	149.18 E
Hayrabolu	130	41.12 N	27.06 E
Hay River	176	60.51 N	115.40 W
Hays, Ab., Can.	182	50.06 N	111.48 W
Hays, Ks., U.S.	198	38.52 N	99.19 W
Hays, Mt., U.S.	202	47.59 N	108.41 W
Hays □[6]	222	30.02 N	97.45 W
Hays ◆[8]	279b	40.23 N	79.56 W
Hayshah, Sabkhat al- ≡	146	31.45 N	15.20 E
Hays Mill Creek ≃	285	39.44 N	74.50 W
Hay Springs	198	42.41 N	102.41 W
Haystack Mountain ∧	204	41.39 N	115.38 W
Haysville, Ks., U.S.	198	37.33 N	97.21 W
Haysville, Pa., U.S.	279b	40.32 N	80.09 W
Hayti, Mo., U.S.	194	36.14 N	89.44 W
Hayti, Pa., U.S.	208	39.59 N	75.51 W
Hayti, S.D., U.S.	198	44.39 N	97.12 W
Hayward, Ca., U.S.	226	37.40 N	122.04 W
Hayward, Wi., U.S.	190	46.00 N	91.29 W
Hayward Brook ≃	283	42.22 N	71.20 W
Hayward Municipal Airport ⊠	282	37.40 N	122.08 W
Haywards Heath	42	51.00 N	0.06 W
Haywood	184	49.40 N	98.12 W
Ḥayy, Jabal al- ∧	142	29.43 N	31.35 E
HaẔafon □[5]	132	32.50 N	35.20 E
Hazār, Kūh-e ∧	128	29.30 N	57.18 E
Hazard	192	37.14 N	83.11 W
Hazardville	207	41.59 N	72.32 W
Hazar Gölü ⊜	130	38.30 N	39.25 E
Hazārībāg	124	23.59 N	85.21 E
Hazārībāg Plateau ⋏[1]	124	24.00 N	85.10 E
Haze, Cape ≻	220	26.46 N	82.10 W
Hazebrouck	50	50.43 N	2.32 E
Hazel ≃	188	38.33 N	77.51 W
Hazelbrook	170	33.44 S	150.27 E
Hazel Crest	278	41.34 N	87.41 W
Hazel Dell	224	45.40 N	122.39 W
Hazel Green	190	42.31 N	90.26 W
Hazelgrove, Austl.	170	33.40 S	149.52 E
Hazel Grove, Eng., U.K.	44	53.23 N	2.08 W
Hazel Hurst	214	41.42 N	78.35 W
Hazel Kirk	279b	40.11 N	79.57 W
Hazel Park	216	42.27 N	83.06 W
Hazel Park Raceway ♠	281	42.29 N	83.05 W
Hazelton, B.C., Can.	182	55.15 N	127.40 W
Hazelton, Id., U.S.	202	42.35 N	114.08 W
Hazelton, N.D., U.S.	198	46.29 N	100.16 W
Hazelton Mountains ⋏	182	54.30 N	128.20 W
Hazelton Peak ∧	202	44.06 N	107.03 W
Hazelwood, Mo., U.S.	219	38.46 N	90.22 W
Hazelwood, N.C., U.S.	192	35.28 N	83.00 W
Hazelwood ◆[8]	279b	40.25 N	79.56 W
Hazen, Ar., U.S.	194	34.46 N	91.34 W
Hazen, Nv., U.S.	226	39.33 N	119.02 W
Hazen, N.D., U.S.	198	47.17 N	101.37 W
Hazen, Pa., U.S.	214	41.12 N	78.58 W
Hazen Bay ⊂	180	61.00 N	165.10 W
Ḥazerim	132	31.14 N	34.43 E
Hazlehurst, Ga., U.S.	192	31.52 N	82.35 W
Hazlehurst, Ms., U.S.	194	31.51 N	90.23 W
Hazlet, Sk., Can.	184	50.25 N	108.36 W
Hazlet, N.J., U.S.	208	40.26 N	74.13 W
Hazleton, Ia., U.S.	190	42.37 N	91.54 W
Hazleton, Pa., U.S.	210	40.57 N	75.58 W
Hazlett, Lake ⊜	162	21.30 S	128.48 E
Ḥazor HaGelilit	132	32.59 N	35.33 E
Hazro, Pāk.	123	33.54 N	72.29 E
Hazro, Tür.	130	38.15 N	40.47 E
Hazu	94	34.47 N	137.08 E
He ≃, Zhg.	100	27.05 N	114.59 E
He ≃, Zhg.	102	23.26 N	111.30 E
Heacham	42	52.55 N	0.30 E
Head ≃	212	44.44 N	79.15 W
Head Bay d'Espoir	186	47.56 N	55.45 W
Headcorn	42	51.11 N	0.37 E
Headford	48	53.28 N	9.05 W
Head Lake ⊜	212	44.45 N	78.55 W
Headland	194	31.21 N	85.20 W
Headlands	154	18.14 S	32.03 E
Headley, Eng., U.K.	42	51.07 N	0.50 W
Headley, Eng., U.K.	260	51.17 N	0.16 W
Headley, Mount ∧	202	47.44 N	115.15 W
Head of the Harbor	276	40.54 N	73.10 W
Heald Green	262	53.22 N	2.14 W
Heald Moor ◆[3]	262	53.44 N	2.10 W
Healdsburg	204	38.36 N	122.52 W
Healdton	196	34.13 N	97.29 W
Healesville	169	37.40 S	145.31 E
Healing	44	53.34 N	0.10 W
Healy, Ak., U.S.	180	63.52 N	148.58 W
Healy, Ks., U.S.	198	38.36 N	100.37 W
Healy, Mount ∧	180	63.46 N	149.01 W
Healy Lake ⊜	212	45.10 N	79.55 W
Heani, Mont ∧	174x	9.47 S	139.04 W
Heanna	174m	26.19 N	127.54 E
Heanor	44	53.01 N	1.22 W
Heany Junction	154	20.06 S	28.54 E
Heard Island I	6	53.06 S	73.30 E
Heard Pond ⊜	283	42.21 N	71.22 W
Hearne	222	30.52 N	96.35 W
Hearst	176	49.41 N	83.40 W
Hearst Island I	9	69.25 S	62.10 W
Hearst San Simeon State Historical Park ♠	226	35.42 N	121.10 W
Heart ≃, Ab., Can.	182	56.14 N	117.17 W
Heart ≃, N.D., U.S.	198	46.47 N	100.51 W
Heart Lake ⊜, Ab., Can.	182	55.02 N	111.30 W
Heart Lake ⊜, On., Can.	275b	43.44 N	79.48 W
Heart Lake Indian Reserve ◆[4]	182	55.02 N	111.30 W
Heart Pond ⊜	283	42.34 N	71.23 W
Heart's Content	186	47.53 N	53.22 W
Heath, Ma., U.S.	207	42.40 N	72.49 W
Heath, Oh., U.S.	214	40.02 N	82.28 W
Heath, Tx., U.S.	222	32.50 N	96.29 W
Heath ≃	248	12.31 S	68.38 W
Heath, Pointe ≻	186	49.05 N	61.42 W
Heathcote, Austl.	169	36.55 S	144.42 E
Heathcote, Austl.	274a	34.05 S	151.01 E
Heathcote Brook ≃	276	40.23 N	74.37 W
Heath End	42	51.22 N	1.09 W
Heatherton	274b	37.58 S	145.06 E
Heathfield	42	50.59 N	0.17 E
Heathmont	274b	37.49 S	145.15 E
Heath Springs	192	34.35 N	80.40 W
Heathsville	208	37.55 N	76.28 W
Heatley	262	53.24 N	2.27 W
Heaton Hall ⊥	262	53.32 N	2.15 W
Heaton Moor	262	53.25 N	2.11 W
Heaven, Temple of ʊ[1]	271a	39.53 N	116.25 E
Heavener	194	34.53 N	94.36 W
Heaverham	260	51.18 N	0.15 E
Heaviley	262	53.24 N	2.09 W
Hebaochang	107	29.33 N	105.32 E
Hebao Dao I	100	21.52 N	113.09 E
Hebbronville	196	27.18 N	98.40 W
Hebburn	44	54.59 N	1.30 W
Hebbville	284b	39.20 N	77.46 W
Hebden Bridge	44	53.45 N	2.00 W
Hebden Water ≃	262	53.44 N	2.00 W
Hebei, Zhg.	104	40.43 N	122.12 E
Hebei, Zhg.	104	41.01 N	123.51 E
Hebei (Hopeh) □[4]	98	38.00 N	116.00 E
Hebeitun	105	39.35 N	117.07 E
Hebel	166	28.59 S	147.48 E
Heber, Az., U.S.	200	34.25 N	110.35 W
Heber, Ca., U.S.	204	32.44 N	115.32 W
Heber City	200	40.30 N	111.24 W
Heber Springs	194	35.29 N	92.01 W
Hebgen Lake ⊜[1]	202	44.47 N	111.14 W
Hebi	98	35.59 N	114.11 E
Hebian	107	30.29 N	105.08 E
Hebo, Or., U.S.	224	45.13 N	123.51 W
Hebo, Zhg.	102	31.29 N	98.58 E
Hebo, Mount ∧	224	45.12 N	123.45 W
Hébridas, Islas → Hebrides II	46	57.00 N	6.30 W
Hebrides II	22	57.00 N	6.30 W
Hebrides, Sea of the ╤[2]	46	57.07 N	6.55 W
Hebron, Nf., Can.	176	58.12 N	62.38 W
Hebron → Al-Khalīl, Isr. Occ	132	31.32 N	35.06 E
Hebron, Ct., U.S.	207	41.39 N	72.21 W
Hebron, Il., U.S.	216	42.28 N	88.25 W
Hebron, In., U.S.	216	41.19 N	87.12 W
Hebron, Ky., U.S.	218	39.03 N	84.42 W
Hebron, Md., U.S.	208	38.25 N	75.41 W
Hebron, Ne., U.S.	198	40.09 N	97.35 W
Hebron, N.D., U.S.	198	46.54 N	102.02 W
Hebron, Pa., U.S.	208	40.21 N	76.24 W
Hebron, Tx., U.S.	222	33.01 N	96.52 W
Hebron, Wi., U.S.	216	42.56 N	88.42 W
Hebu	100	27.50 N	115.22 E
Hebutu	104	42.19 N	122.20 E
Heby	40	59.56 N	16.53 E
Hecao	105	40.21 N	116.47 E
Hecate Strait Џ	182	53.00 N	131.00 W
Hecelchakán	232	20.10 N	90.08 W
Heceta Island I	180	55.45 N	133.35 W
Hechi	102	24.42 N	108.02 E
Hechiceros	196	28.33 N	103.38 W
Hechingen	58	48.21 N	8.58 E
Hechtel	56	51.08 N	5.21 E
Hechthausen	52	53.38 N	9.14 E
Hechuan	107	30.00 N	106.16 E
Heckelberg	54	52.44 N	13.50 E
Hecker	219	38.18 N	90.00 W
Heckington	42	52.59 N	0.18 W
Hecklingen	54	51.51 N	11.32 E
Heckscher State Park ♠	210	40.43 N	73.10 W
Hecla, Mb., Can.	184	51.08 N	96.40 W
Hecla, S.D., U.S.	198	45.52 N	98.09 W
Hecla Island I	184	51.08 N	96.45 W
Hecla Provincial Park ♠	184	51.12 N	96.35 W
Hectanooga	186	44.06 N	66.02 W
Hector, N.Z.	172	41.36 S	171.53 E
Hector, Mn., U.S.	198	44.44 N	94.42 W
Hector, Mount ∧	172	40.57 S	175.17 E
Heda	94	34.58 N	138.46 E
Hedal	26	60.37 N	9.42 E
Hedaru	154	4.30 S	37.54 E
Heddal ʊ[1]	26	59.35 N	9.11 E
Hedding	285	40.06 N	74.44 W
Hédé, Fr.	32	48.18 N	1.48 W
Hede, Sve.	26	62.25 N	13.30 E
Hedehusene	41	55.39 N	12.12 E
Hedel	52	51.45 N	5.15 E
Hedemora	40	60.17 N	15.59 E
Hedemünden	56	51.23 N	9.46 E
Hedensted	41	55.46 N	9.42 E
Hedersleben	54	51.51 N	11.15 E
Hedesunda	40	60.24 N	16.59 E
Hedesundafjärdarna ⊜	40	60.20 N	17.00 E
He Devil ∧	202	45.21 N	116.33 W
Hedge End	42	50.54 N	1.18 W
Hedgerley	260	51.35 N	0.36 W
Hedian	100	32.45 N	114.18 E
Hedley, B.C., Can.	182	49.21 N	120.04 W
Hedley, Tx., U.S.	196	34.52 N	100.39 W
Hedmark □[6]	26	61.30 N	11.45 E
Hednesford	42	52.43 N	2.00 W
Hedo	174m	26.51 N	128.16 E
Hedo-misaki ≻	174m	26.52 N	128.16 E
Hedon	44	53.44 N	0.12 W
Hedrick	190	41.10 N	92.18 W
Hedströmmen ≃	40	59.28 N	16.04 E
Hedutne	272c	19.10 N	73.06 E
Hedwig Village	222	29.47 N	95.27 W
Heek	52	52.07 N	7.06 E
Heel	52	51.11 N	5.53 E
Heel Point ≻	174a	19.19 N	166.37 E
Heemskerk	52	52.31 N	4.40 E
Heemstede	52	52.21 N	4.37 E
Heepen	52	52.01 N	8.35 E
Heer, Bel.	56	50.10 N	4.50 E
Heer, Ned.	56	50.50 N	5.44 E
Heerde	52	52.23 N	6.03 E
Heerdt ◆[8]	263	51.13 N	6.43 E
Heerenveen	52	52.57 N	5.55 E
Heeren-Werve	52	51.35 N	7.43 E
Heerhugowaard	52	52.40 N	4.50 E
Heerkan	107	29.32 N	103.56 E
Heerlen	56	50.54 N	5.59 E
Heesch	52	51.44 N	5.32 E
Heeslingen	52	53.19 N	9.20 E
Heessen	52	51.42 N	7.50 E
Heeze	52	51.24 N	5.35 E
Ḥefa (Haifa)	132	32.50 N	35.00 E
Ḥefa □[5]	132	32.35 N	35.00 E
Ḥefa, Mifraẕ ⊂	132	32.52 N	35.03 E
Ḥefa, Sede-Teʻufa ⊠	132	32.49 N	35.02 E
Hefei	100	31.51 N	117.17 E
Hefengchang	107	30.26 N	104.43 E
Heffron Park ♠	274a	33.57 S	151.15 E
Heflin	194	33.38 N	85.35 W
Hegang	89	47.24 N	130.22 E
Hegau ◆[1]	58	47.50 N	8.45 E
Hégenheim	58	47.34 N	7.32 E
Hegewisch ◆[8]	278	41.40 N	87.33 W
Hegins	208	40.39 N	76.29 W
Hegra	26	63.28 N	11.07 E
Hegura-jima I	92	37.51 N	136.55 E
Heguri	270	34.38 N	135.42 E
Hegyeshalom	61	47.55 N	17.10 E
Hehlen	52	51.59 N	9.28 E
Heho	110	20.43 N	96.49 E
Hehou	100	28.40 N	114.28 E
Hei ≃, Zhg.	102	40.18 N	99.26 E
Hei ≃, Zhg.	105	40.44 N	116.27 E
Heicheng (Karakhoto) ⊥	102	41.47 N	101.03 E
Heichengzhen	102	36.16 N	106.06 E
Heichengzi	104	42.10 N	121.01 E
Heidayingzi	98	40.52 N	116.12 E
Heidberg ∧[2]	263	51.15 N	7.21 E
Heide	30	54.12 N	9.06 E
Heide ◆[8], Dtsch.	263	51.26 N	7.01 E
Heide ◆[8], Dtsch.	263	51.31 N	6.52 E
Heideck	60	49.08 N	11.07 E
Heidelberg, Austl.	169	37.45 S	145.04 E
Heidelberg, On., Can.	212	43.31 N	80.37 W
Heidelberg, Dtsch.	56	49.25 N	8.43 E
Heidelberg, S. Afr.	158	34.06 S	20.59 E
Heidelberg, S. Afr.	158	26.32 S	28.18 E
Heidelberg, Ms., U.S.	194	31.53 N	88.59 W
Heidelberg, Pa., U.S.	279b	40.23 N	80.05 W
Heidelberg □[5]	273d	26.19 S	28.16 E
Heidelberg, Schloss ⊥	56	49.24 N	8.42 E
Heidelsheim	56	49.06 N	8.38 E
Heiden, Dtsch.	52	51.59 N	8.50 E
Heiden, Schw.	58	47.27 N	9.33 E
Heiden, Port ⊂	180	56.55 N	158.45 W
Heidenau, Dtsch.	52	53.19 N	9.39 E
Heidenau, Dtsch.	54	50.59 N	13.52 E
Heidenheim	56	49.01 N	10.44 E
Heidenheim an der Brenz	56	48.40 N	10.08 E
Heidenheimer	222	31.01 N	97.18 W
Heidenoldendorf	52	51.57 N	8.50 E
Heidenreichstein	61	48.52 N	15.07 E
Heider Ditch ≍	279a	41.31 N	82.01 W
Heiderscheid	56	49.53 N	5.54 E
Heidhausen ◆[8]	263	51.23 N	7.01 E
Heidhof ◆[8]	263	51.11 N	7.11 E
Heidlersburg	208	39.57 N	77.09 W
Heidouwo	105	39.42 N	117.15 E
Heigenbrücken	56	50.02 N	9.23 E
Heigoutaicun	104	41.30 N	123.01 E
Heigun-tō I	96	33.47 N	132.14 E
Heihai → Har Hu ⊜	102	38.15 N	97.40 E
Heihe → Aihui	89	50.16 N	127.28 E
Heijō → P'yŏngyang	98	39.01 N	125.45 E
Heikega-dake ∧	96	34.19 N	131.54 E
Heikendorf	54	54.22 N	10.12 E
Heil	263	51.38 N	7.35 E
Heilangkou	105	39.37 N	117.24 E
Heilbron	158	27.21 S	27.58 E
Heilbronn	56	49.08 N	9.13 E
Heilenbecker-Stausee ⊜[1]	263	51.15 N	7.22 E
Heiligenberg	58	47.49 N	9.19 E
Heiligenblut	64	47.02 N	12.50 E
Heiligendamm	54	54.08 N	11.50 E
Heiligenhafen	54	54.22 N	10.58 E
Heiligenhaus	56	51.19 N	6.59 E
Heiligensee ◆[8]	264a	52.36 N	13.13 E
Heiligenstadt, Dtsch.	56	51.23 N	10.09 E
Heiligenstadt, Dtsch.	60	49.51 N	11.10 E
Heilin	98	35.01 N	118.58 E
Hei Ling Chau I	271d	22.15 N	114.02 E
Heilong (Amur) ≃	89	52.56 N	141.10 E
Heilongguan	102	36.19 N	111.11 E
Heilongjiang □[4]	89	48.00 N	128.00 E
Heilongtan, Zhg.	105	40.44 N	116.31 E
Heilongtan, Zhg.	105	40.02 N	116.11 E
Heilongtan Shuiku ⊜[1]	107	30.03 N	104.02 E
Heiloo	52	52.36 N	4.43 E
Heilsbronn	56	49.20 N	10.47 E
Heiltz-le-Maurupt	56	48.48 N	4.49 E
Heilungkiang → Heilongjiang □[4]	89	48.00 N	128.00 E
Heilwood	214	40.37 N	78.54 W
Heimaey I	24a	63.26 N	20.17 W
Heimbach	56	50.38 N	6.28 E
Heimbuchenthal	56	49.53 N	9.17 E
Heimburg	54	51.49 N	10.54 E
Heimdal	26	63.21 N	10.22 E
Heimenkirch	58	47.37 N	9.53 E
Heimsheim	56	48.48 N	8.51 E
Heinävesi	26	62.26 N	28.36 E
Heinersdorf, Dtsch.	54	52.27 N	14.13 E
Heinersdorf, Dtsch.	264a	52.23 N	13.20 E
Heinersdorf ◆[8]	264a	52.34 N	13.27 E
Heiniuyingzi	98	41.07 N	120.19 E
Heino	52	52.26 N	6.14 E
Heinola	26	61.13 N	26.02 E
Heinrichshorst	54	52.20 N	11.42 E
Heinsberg	56	51.03 N	6.05 E
Heiquan	102	39.32 N	99.42 E
Heirnkut	110	25.14 N	94.45 E
Heisfelde	52	53.15 N	7.26 E
Heishan	104	41.41 N	122.07 E
Heishanguan	98	38.33 N	113.41 E
Heishantou, Zhg.	89	50.13 N	119.28 E
Heishantou, Zhg.	98	42.28 N	125.33 E
Heishui	98	42.09 N	119.28 E
Heishuisi	102	36.08 N	108.42 E
Heisingen ◆[8]	263	51.25 N	7.04 E
Heisler	182	52.41 N	112.13 W
Heislerville	208	39.13 N	74.59 W
Heissen ◆[8]	263	51.26 N	6.56 E
Heist-aan-Zee	50	51.21 N	3.15 E
Heist-op-den-Berg	56	51.05 N	4.43 E
Heitang	102	26.29 N	105.09 E
Heitersheim	58	47.53 N	7.40 E
Heiwa	94	35.12 N	136.44 E
Heiyanghebao	105	39.07 N	118.15 E
Heiyantang	102	27.28 N	101.11 E
Heiyanzi	105	39.13 N	118.08 E
Hejaz → Al-Ḥijāz ◆[1]	118	24.30 N	38.30 E
Hejiachang	107	29.24 N	104.56 E
Hejian, Zhg.	98	38.26 N	116.05 E
Hejian, Zhg.	105	39.25 N	116.25 E
Hejiang	107	28.49 N	105.50 E
Hejiangzhen	107	29.16 N	104.16 E
Hejiaqiao	100	27.24 N	113.21 E
Hejiawopeng	104	41.32 N	122.07 E
Hejiaying	105	39.55 N	118.19 E
Hejiazhen	107	29.52 N	104.26 E
Hejin	102	35.39 N	110.40 E
Hejlsminde	41	55.22 N	9.37 E
Hejnsvig	41	55.41 N	8.59 E
Hekelgem	50	50.54 N	4.06 E
Hekili Point ≻	229a	20.48 N	156.37 W
Hekimhan	130	38.49 N	37.56 E
Hekinan	94	34.51 N	136.58 E
Hekla ∧[1]	24a	64.00 N	19.39 W
Hekou, Zhg.	100	31.22 N	114.26 E
Hekou, Zhg.	102	36.09 N	103.22 E
Hekou, Zhg.	102	28.22 N	108.14 E
Hekou, Zhg.	102	29.57 N	111.04 E
Hekou, Zhg.	102	22.38 N	103.56 E
Hekouchang	107	29.21 N	104.21 E
Hekouji	100	32.09 N	116.04 E
Hekoujie	102	26.31 N	100.39 E
Hekpoort	158	25.55 S	27.38 E
Hel	30	54.37 N	18.48 E
Helagsfjället ∧	26	62.55 N	12.27 E
Helaluo	102	33.56 N	102.10 E
Helangou	104	41.00 N	123.25 E
Helan Shan ⋏	102	38.40 N	105.57 E
Helbe ≃	54	51.13 N	11.06 E
Helbra	54	51.33 N	11.29 E
Helchteren	56	51.03 N	5.22 E
Helcburg	54	50.17 N	10.44 E
Helden	56	51.07 N	7.56 E
Heldra	56	51.07 N	10.11 E
Heldrungen	54	51.18 N	11.13 E
Helechos, Cañada de los ≃	286a	19.22 N	99.12 W
Helemano Stream ≃	229c	21.35 N	158.06 W
Helen, Mount ∧	166	21.34 S	141.13 E
Helena, Ar., U.S.	194	34.31 N	90.35 W
Helena, Mt., U.S.	202	46.35 N	112.02 W
Helena, N.Y., U.S.	206	44.55 N	74.44 W
Helena, Oh., U.S.	214	41.21 N	83.18 W
Helena, Ok., U.S.	196	36.32 N	98.16 W
Helena ≃	168a	31.54 S	116.00 E
Helena River Reservoir ⊜[1]	168a	31.59 S	116.13 E
Helendale	228	34.45 N	117.18 W
Helenenberg	56	49.51 N	6.32 E
Helenental ∨	264b	48.01 N	16.11 E
Helen Island I	108	2.58 N	131.49 E
Helensburgh, Austl.	170	34.11 S	150.59 E
Helensburgh, Scot., U.K.	46	56.01 N	4.44 W
Helen Springs	162	18.26 S	133.52 E
Helensville	172	36.40 S	174.28 E
Helenville	216	43.01 N	88.41 W
Helenwood	192	36.25 N	84.32 W
Ḥelez	132	31.35 N	34.40 E
Helfenberg	61	48.32 N	14.08 E
Helfenstein	208	40.45 N	76.27 W
Helfta	54	51.30 N	11.34 E
Helgaå ≃	26	55.53 N	14.08 E
Helgenæs ≻[1]	41	56.08 N	10.32 E
Helgoland I	30	54.12 N	7.53 E
Helgoländer Bucht ⊂	30	54.10 N	8.04 E
Heli	89	47.05 N	130.16 E
Helicoide ◆[9]	286c	10.29 N	66.55 W
Helidon	171a	27.33 S	152.08 E
Heliodora	256	22.04 S	45.32 W
Heliópolis	287a	22.45 S	43.25 W
Heliopolis → Miṣr al-Jadīdah ◆[8]	273c	30.06 N	31.20 E
Heliopolis ⊥	142	30.08 N	31.17 E
Heliopolis Aerodrome ⊠	273c	30.04 N	31.19 E
Heliopolis Racing Club ♠	273c	30.06 N	31.19 E
Heliuji	100	33.02 N	116.57 E
Helixi	106	30.40 N	118.59 E
Hell	26	63.26 N	10.54 E
Hellam	208	40.00 N	76.36 W
Hellberge ∧[2]	54	52.34 N	11.17 E
Hellbrunn, Schloss ⊥	64	47.46 N	13.04 E
Hellebæk	41	56.04 N	12.34 E
Helleh ≃	128	29.10 N	50.40 E
Hellen Blazes, Lake ⊜	220	28.01 N	80.47 W
Hellendoorn	52	52.24 N	6.26 E
Hellenthal	56	50.29 N	6.26 E
Hellerau ◆[8]	54	51.07 N	13.44 E
Hellern	52	52.15 N	7.58 E
Hellersen	263	51.12 N	7.39 E
Hellertown	208	40.34 N	75.20 W
Hellesylt	26	62.05 N	6.54 E
Hellevad	41	55.05 N	9.13 E
Hellevoetsluis	52	51.49 N	4.08 E
Hell Gate Џ	276	40.47 N	73.56 W
Hell Hole Reservoir ⊜[1]	226	39.04 N	120.22 W
Hellifield	44	54.01 N	2.12 W
Hellín	34	38.31 N	1.41 W
Helli Ness ≻	46a	60.02 N	1.10 W
Hellmonsödt	61	48.26 N	14.18 E
Hell Point ≻	186	44.16 N	64.15 W
Hells Canyon ∨	202	45.20 N	116.45 W
Hellsee ⊜	264a	52.45 N	13.35 E
Hells Gate ∨	182	49.47 N	121.27 W
Hell-Ville	157b	13.25 S	48.16 E
Hellweg ◆[1]	52	51.36 N	8.32 E
Helm	226	36.31 N	120.05 W
Helmand □[4]	128	31.00 N	64.00 E
Helmand ≃	128	31.12 N	61.34 E
Helmbrechts	54	50.14 N	11.43 E
Helmcken Falls ∟	182	51.57 N	120.11 W
Helme ≃	54	51.20 N	11.20 E
Helmeringhausen	156	25.54 S	16.57 E
Helmetta	276	40.22 N	74.25 W
Helmetta Pond ⊜	276	40.23 N	74.26 W
Helmond	52	51.29 N	5.40 E
Helmsburg	218	39.16 N	86.18 W
Helmsdale	46	58.07 N	3.40 W
Helmsdale ≃	46	58.07 N	3.40 W
Helmshore	262	53.41 N	2.20 W
Helmsley	44	54.14 N	1.04 W
Helmstedt	54	52.13 N	11.00 E
Helnæs I	41	55.08 N	10.02 E
Helong	98	42.32 N	128.59 E
Helper	200	39.41 N	110.51 W
Helpmekaar	158	28.29 S	30.29 E
Helpter Berg ∧[2]	54	53.30 N	13.36 E
Helsby	44	53.16 N	2.46 W
Helsby Hill ∧[2]	262	53.16 N	2.46 W
Helsingborg	41	56.03 N	12.42 E
Helsinge	41	56.01 N	12.12 E
Helsingfors → Helsinki	26	60.10 N	24.58 E
Helsingør (Elsinore)	41	56.02 N	12.37 E
Helsinki (Helsingfors)	26	60.10 N	24.58 E
Helska, Mierzeja ≻[2]	30	54.45 N	18.39 E
Helston	42	50.05 N	5.16 W
Heltonville	218	38.55 N	86.22 W
Helvecia	252	31.06 S	60.05 W
Helvellyn ∧	44	54.31 N	3.01 W
Helvick Head ≻	48	52.03 N	7.33 W
Helvoirt	52	51.38 N	5.13 E
Hem ≃	50	50.51 N	2.06 E
Ḥemar, Naḥal ∨	132	31.08 N	35.22 E
Hemau	60	49.03 N	11.47 E
Hemāvati ≃	122	12.31 N	76.27 E
Hembe	152	1.54 N	22.42 E
Hemel Hempstead	42	51.46 N	0.28 W
Hemelingen ◆[8]	52	53.03 N	8.53 E
Hemeln	52	51.30 N	9.36 E
Hemer	56	51.23 N	7.46 E
Hemet	228	33.44 N	116.58 W
Hemfjärden ⊂	40	59.17 N	15.20 E
Hemford	186	44.30 N	64.47 W
Hemfurth-Edersee	56	51.10 N	9.02 E
Hemiksem	50	51.09 N	4.21 E
Héming	58	48.42 N	6.57 E
Hemingford	198	42.19 N	103.04 W
Hemingway	192	33.45 N	79.26 W
Hemlock, In., U.S.	216	40.25 N	86.03 W
Hemlock, N.Y., U.S.	210	42.47 N	77.36 W
Hemlock Lake ⊜	210	42.43 N	77.37 W
Hemmerde	52	51.33 N	7.48 E
Hemmerden	263	51.07 N	6.36 E
Hemmingen-Westerfeld	52	52.19 N	9.45 E
Hemmoor	52	53.41 N	9.08 E
Hemphill	194	31.20 N	93.50 W
Hempnall	42	52.30 N	1.19 E
Hempstead, N.Y., U.S.	210	40.42 N	73.37 W
Hempstead, Tx., U.S.	222	30.05 N	96.04 W
Hempstead Harbor ⊂	276	40.50 N	73.39 W
Hempstead Lake ⊜	276	40.41 N	73.38 W
Hempstead Lake State Park ♠	276	40.41 N	73.38 W
Hemsby	42	52.41 N	1.42 E
Hemse	26	57.14 N	18.22 E
Hemsedal	26	60.52 N	8.34 E
Hemsön I	26	62.43 N	18.05 E
Hemstreet Park	210	42.54 N	73.41 W
Hemsworth	44	53.38 N	1.21 W
Hemujing	98	37.54 N	115.22 E
Henan	102	34.35 N	101.34 E
Henan (Honan) □[4]	90	34.00 N	114.00 E
Hen and Chickens II	172	35.55 S	174.45 E
Henares ≃	34	40.24 N	3.30 W
Henbury, Austl.	162	24.35 S	133.15 E
Henbury, Eng., U.K.	262	53.15 N	2.11 W
Hendek	130	40.48 N	30.45 E
Henderson, Arg.	252	36.18 S	61.43 W
Henderson, In., U.S.	218	39.40 N	85.31 W
Henderson, Ky., U.S.	194	37.50 N	87.35 W
Henderson, Mn., U.S.	190	44.31 N	93.54 W
Henderson, Ne., U.S.	198	40.46 N	97.48 W
Henderson, Nv., U.S.	204	36.02 N	114.58 W
Henderson, N.Y., U.S.	212	43.51 N	76.11 W
Henderson, N.C., U.S.	192	36.19 N	78.23 W
Henderson, Tn., U.S.	194	35.26 N	88.38 W
Henderson, Tx., U.S.	222	32.09 N	94.47 W
Henderson □[6]	222	32.13 N	95.50 W
Henderson Bay ⊂, N.Y., U.S.	212	43.54 N	76.10 W
Henderson Bay ⊂, Wa., U.S.	224	47.18 N	122.42 W
Henderson Creek ≃	190	40.52 N	91.02 W
Henderson Island I	6	24.22 S	128.19 W
Hendersonville, N.C., U.S.	192	35.19 N	82.27 W
Hendersonville, Pa., U.S.	214	40.18 N	80.09 W
Hendersonville, Tn., U.S.	194	36.18 N	86.37 W
Hendījān	128	30.14 N	49.43 E
Hendon ◆[8]	260	51.35 N	0.14 W
Hendorābī, Jazīreh-ye I	128	26.40 N	53.37 E
Hendricks, Mn., U.S.	198	44.30 N	96.25 W
Hendricks, W.V., U.S.	188	39.04 N	79.37 W
Hendricks □[6]	218	39.46 N	86.26 W
Hendrik Verwoerddam ⊜[1]	158	30.40 S	25.40 E
Hendrina	158	26.11 S	29.45 E
Hendry □[6]	220	26.36 N	81.13 W
Hendrysburg	214	40.04 N	81.10 W
Hendy	42	51.43 N	4.04 W
Henefer	200	41.01 N	111.29 W
Henfield	42	50.56 N	0.17 W
Heng ≃, Zhg.	102	28.40 N	104.25 E
Heng ≃, Zhg.	107	28.57 N	105.22 E
Hengām, Jazīreh-ye I	128	26.39 N	55.53 E
Henganofi	164	6.15 S	145.35 E
Hengchow → Hengyang	102	26.54 N	112.36 E
Hengdaochuan	98	41.15 N	125.31 E
Hengdaohe	104	42.02 N	123.51 E
Hengdaohezi	89	43.13 N	126.44 E
Hengdaozi	89	43.18 N	127.18 E
Hengdong	100	27.03 N	112.57 E
Hengelo	52	52.15 N	6.45 E
Hengersberg	60	48.47 N	13.03 E
Hengfan	106	30.20 N	119.45 E
Hengfeng	100	28.24 N	117.34 E
Henggang	100	29.32 N	115.27 E
Henggouzi	89	43.12 N	124.47 E
Henghutou	104	42.05 N	124.00 E
Hengjie	106	31.13 N	119.30 E
Hengjing	106	31.11 N	120.32 E
Hengjinghong	106	30.34 N	120.59 E
Hengli	100	23.12 N	114.37 E
Henglin	106	31.42 N	120.06 E
Henglu	98	41.26 N	126.04 E
Henglutou	106	30.19 N	119.19 E
Hengmian	106	31.09 N	121.38 E
Hengoed	42	51.39 N	3.10 W
Hengsen	263	51.29 N	7.38 E
Heng Sha I	106	31.20 N	121.50 E
Hengshan, Zhg.	100	27.15 N	112.51 E
Hengshan, Zhg.	102	37.56 N	108.53 E
Hengshan, Zhg.	106	31.01 N	120.32 E
Heng Shan ∧	100	27.16 N	112.35 E
Heng Shan ⋏	102	39.30 N	113.45 E
Hengshanchang	107	30.33 N	105.24 E
Hengshanqiao	106	31.46 N	120.07 E
Hengshanxia	106	30.18 N	118.44 E
Hengshi, Zhg.	100	26.05 N	114.38 E
Hengshi, Zhg.	100	23.52 N	113.15 E
Hengshi, Zhg.	100	29.32 N	114.41 E
Hengshui	98	37.43 N	115.40 E
Hengsteysee ⊜[1]	263	51.25 N	7.28 E
Hengtangshi	106	31.41 N	121.02 E
Hengtianchi	107	29.07 N	105.01 E
Hengtianxi	107	29.05 N	105.03 E
Hengxi, Zhg.	100	29.42 N	121.35 E
Hengxi, Zhg.	100	28.46 N	120.29 E
Hengxi, Zhg.	106	31.43 N	118.46 E
Hengxian	102	22.42 N	109.13 E
Hengxiang	106	32.12 N	120.15 E
Hengxikou	100	29.26 N	121.26 E
Hengyang	102	26.54 N	112.36 E
Hénin-Beaumont	50	50.25 N	2.56 E
Henley Beach	168b	34.55 S	138.30 E
Henley-in-Arden	42	52.17 N	1.46 W
Henley-on-Thames	42	51.32 N	0.56 W
Henlopen, Cape ≻	208	38.48 N	75.05 W
Henlow	42	52.02 N	0.18 W
Hennan ⊜	26	62.06 N	15.46 E
Hennaya	34	34.58 N	1.22 W
Henneberg	54	50.29 N	10.21 E
Hennebont	32	47.48 N	3.17 W
Hennef	56	50.46 N	7.16 E
Hennen	56	51.27 N	7.39 E
Hennenman	158	27.59 S	27.01 E
Hennepin	190	41.15 N	89.21 W
Hennepin, Point ≻	281	42.12 N	83.09 W
Hennersdorf	264b	48.07 N	16.22 E
Hennessey	196	36.06 N	97.53 W
Hennessey Lake ⊜[1]	226	38.29 N	122.22 W
Hennickendorf	54	52.30 N	13.51 E
Henniez	58	46.44 N	6.54 E
Hennigsdorf	54	52.38 N	13.12 E
Henniker	188	43.10 N	71.49 W
Henning, Il., U.S.	216	40.18 N	87.42 W
Henning, Mn., U.S.	198	46.19 N	95.26 W
Henning, Tn., U.S.	194	35.40 N	89.34 W
Henri ≃	206	46.30 N	71.47 W
Henri, Cap ≻	186	49.48 N	64.23 W
Henri-Chapelle	56	50.40 N	5.56 E
Henrichemont	50	47.18 N	2.32 E
Henrichenburg	263	51.35 N	7.19 E
Henrico □[6]	208	37.30 N	77.20 W
Henrietta, N.Y., U.S.	210	43.03 N	77.36 W
Henrietta, N.C., U.S.	192	35.15 N	81.47 W
Henrietta, Tx., U.S.	196	33.49 N	98.11 W
Henrietta Maria Cape ≻	176	55.09 N	82.20 W
Henri Pittier, Parque Nacional ♠	246	10.25 N	67.43 W
Henry, Il., U.S.	190	41.06 N	89.21 W
Henry, S.D., U.S.	198	44.52 N	97.27 W
Henry □[6], In., U.S.	218	39.55 N	85.22 W
Henry □[6], Ky., U.S.	218	38.26 N	85.09 W
Henry □[6], Oh., U.S.	216	41.20 N	84.04 W
Henry ≃	162	22.40 S	115.40 E
Henry, Cape ≻	208	36.55 N	76.01 W
Henry, Mount ∧	202	48.53 N	115.31 W
Henry, Mount ∧[2]	274a	33.50 S	150.38 E
Henry, Point ≻	162	34.29 S	119.23 E
Henry Cowell Redwoods State Park ♠	226	37.02 N	122.03 W
Henryetta	196	35.26 N	95.58 W
Henry Island I	224	48.35 N	123.11 W
Henry Kater, Cape ≻	176	69.05 N	66.44 W
Henry Mountains ⋏	200	38.00 N	110.50 W
Henrys Bend	214	41.28 N	79.37 W
Henrys Fork ≃, U.S.	200	41.00 N	109.39 W
Henrys Fork ≃, Id., U.S.	202	43.45 N	111.56 W
Henryville, P.Q., Can.	206	45.08 N	73.11 W
Henryville, In., U.S.	218	38.32 N	85.46 W
Henry W. Coe State Park ♠	226	37.12 N	121.30 W
Hensall	190	43.26 N	81.30 W
Henshaw, Lake ⊜[1]	204	33.15 N	116.45 W
Hensley	194	34.30 N	92.12 W
Hensley Lake ⊜[1]	226	37.07 N	119.53 W
Henslow, Cape ≻	175e	9.56 S	160.38 E
Henson Creek ≃	284b	38.46 N	77.00 W
Hensonville	210	42.17 N	74.13 W
Henstedt-Ulzburg	52	53.47 N	9.58 E
Henstridge	42	50.59 N	2.24 W
Hentiesbaai	156	22.08 S	14.18 E
Henty	166	35.31 S	147.02 E
Henzada	110	17.38 N	95.28 E
Hepburn	184	52.31 N	106.43 W
Hepburn Springs	169	37.19 S	144.09 E
Hephzibah	192	33.18 N	82.05 W
Heping, Zhg.	100	27.10 N	117.18 E
Heping, Zhg.	100	22.01 N	112.59 E
Heping, Zhg.	100	23.17 N	116.29 E
Heping, Zhg.	100	24.28 N	114.58 E
Heping, Zhg.	106	30.50 N	119.54 E
Heppenheim	56	49.39 N	8.38 E
Heppner	202	45.21 N	119.33 W
Heptonstall	262	53.45 N	2.01 W
Heptonstall Moor ≃	262	53.46 N	2.05 W
Hepu (Lianzhou)	102	21.39 N	109.11 E
Hepworth	212	44.37 N	81.09 W
Heqiao, Zhg.	100	32.55 N	118.22 E
Heqiao, Zhg.	105	31.30 N	119.53 E
Heqing	102	26.34 N	100.12 E
Hequ	102	39.26 N	111.08 E
Héraðsflói ⊂	24a	65.45 N	14.10 W
Hera Lacinia, Tempio di ⊥	68	39.01 N	17.13 E
Herāt	128	34.20 N	62.12 E
Herāt □[4]	128	34.30 N	62.00 E
Hérault □[5]	32	43.40 N	3.30 E
Hérault ≃	32	43.17 N	3.26 E
Herbasse ≃	62	45.02 N	4.57 E
Herbault	50	47.36 N	1.08 E
Herbede	56	51.25 N	7.16 E
Herbern	52	51.44 N	7.39 E
Herbert, Sk., Can.	184	50.26 N	107.12 W
Herbert, N.Z.	172	45.14 S	170.47 E
Herbert ≃	166	18.32 S	146.17 E
Herbert, Mount ⋏	172	43.41 S	172.44 E

Symbol	English	Deutsch	Español	Français	Português
≃	River	Fluß	Río	Rivière	Rio
≍	Canal	Kanal	Canal	Canal	Canal
∟	Waterfall, Rapids	Wasserfall, Stromschnellen	Cascada, Rápidos	Chute d'eau, Rapides	Cascata, Rápidos
Џ	Strait	Meeresstraße	Estrecho	Détroit	Estreito
⊂	Bay, Gulf	Bucht, Golf	Bahía, Golfo	Baie, Golfe	Baía, Golfo
⊜	Lake, Lakes	See, Seen	Lago, Lagos	Lac, Lacs	Lago, Lagos
≡	Swamp	Sumpf	Pantano	Marais	Pântano
⩀	Ice Features, Glacier	Eis- und Gletscherformen	Accidentes Glaciales	Formes glaciaires	Acidentes glaciares
╤	Other Hydrographic Features	Andere Hydrographische Objekte	Otros Elementos Hidrográficos	Autres données hydrographiques	Outros acidentes hidrográficos
✣	Submarine Features	Untermeerische Objekte	Accidentes Submarinos	Formes de relief sous-marin	Acidentes submarinos
□	Political Unit	Politische Einheit	Unidad Politica	Entité politique	Unidade política
ʊ	Cultural Institution	Kulturelle Institution	Institución Cultural	Institution culturelle	Instituição cultural
⊥	Historical Site	Historische Stätte	Sitio Histórico	Site historique	Sitio histórico
♠	Recreational Site	Erholungs- und Ferienort	Sitio de Recreo	Centre de loisirs	Area de Lazer
⊠	Airport	Flughafen	Aeropuerto	Aéroport	Aeroporto
■	Military Installation	Militäranlage	Instalación Militar	Installation militaire	Instalação militar
◆	Miscellaneous	Verschiedenes	Misceláneo	Divers	Diversos

Herbertabad 110 11.43 N 92.37 E
Herbert Hoover National Historic Site ⊥ 190 41.38 N 91.23 W
Herbertingen 58 48.04 N 9.26 E
Herbert Island ı 180 52.45 N 170.10 W
Herberton 166 17.23 S 145.23 E
Herbertsdale 158 34.01 S 21.46 E
Herbeumont 56 49.47 N 5.14 E
Herbignac 32 47.27 N 2.19 W
Herb Lake 184 54.47 N 99.47 W
Herblay 50 49.00 N 2.10 E
Herblet Lake ⊜ 184 54.56 N 99.54 W
Herbolzheim 58 48.13 N 7.47 E
Herborn 56 50.40 N 8.17 E
Herbrechtingen 56 48.37 N 10.10 E
Herbringhauser-Stausee ⊜¹ 263 51.14 N 7.16 E
Herbsleben 54 51.07 N 10.50 E
Herbstein 56 50.34 N 9.20 E
Herceg-Novi 38 42.27 N 18.32 E
Herculaneum 219 38.16 N 90.22 W
Hercules, Méx. 232 28.02 N 103.48 W
Hercules, Ca., U.S. 282 38.01 N 122.17 W
Herdecke 56 51.24 N 7.26 E
Herdorf 56 50.46 N 7.56 E
Herdringen 52 51.25 N 7.58 E
Herdubreid ∧ 24a 65.13 N 16.18 W
Heredia 236 10.00 N 84.07 W
Heredia □⁴ 236 10.30 N 84.00 W
Hereford, Eng., U.K. 42 52.04 N 2.43 W
Hereford, Az., U.S. 200 31.26 N 110.05 W
Hereford, Md., U.S. 208 39.35 N 76.39 W
Hereford, Tx., U.S. 196 34.48 N 102.23 W
Hereford and Worcester □⁶ 42 52.10 N 2.30 W
Hereford Cathedral ⊕¹ 42 52.04 N 2.43 W
Hereford Mountain ∧ 206 45.05 N 71.36 W
Hereke 130 40.48 N 29.39 E
Herekino 172 35.15 S 173.13 E
Herencia 34 39.21 N 3.22 W
Herent 56 50.54 N 4.40 E
Herentals 56 51.11 N 4.50 E
Hereroland Oos □⁵ 156 21.00 S 20.00 E
Hereroland Wes □⁵ 156 20.30 S 18.15 E
Herfølge 41 55.25 N 12.10 E
Herford 52 52.06 N 8.40 E
Hergatz 58 47.39 N 9.50 E
Hergisdorf 54 51.32 N 11.28 E
Hergla 36 36.02 N 10.31 E
Herhahn 56 50.33 N 6.26 E
Héricourt 58 47.35 N 6.45 E
Hérimoncourt 58 47.26 N 6.53 E
Heringen 54 51.27 N 10.52 E
Heringsdorf 54 54.18 N 11.00 E
Herington 198 38.40 N 96.56 W
Heriot 172 45.50 S 169.16 E
Herisau 58 47.23 N 9.17 E
Heritage Range ∧ 9 79.30 S 84.00 W
Herk ≃ 56 50.58 N 5.07 E
Herk-de-Stad 56 50.56 N 5.10 E
Herkimer 210 43.01 N 74.59 W
Herkimer □⁶ 210 43.02 N 74.59 W
Herlen — Kerulen ≃ 90 48.48 N 117.00 E
Herleshausen 56 51.00 N 10.09 E
Herlev 41 55.43 N 12.27 E
Herlong 204 40.09 N 120.08 W
Herlufmagle 41 55.19 N 11.46 E
Herlufsholm 41 55.15 N 11.46 E
Hermagor 64 46.37 N 13.22 E
Herman, Mn., U.S. 198 45.48 N 96.08 W
Herman, Ne., U.S. 198 41.40 N 96.13 W
Herman, Pa., U.S. 214 40.50 N 79.49 W
Herman, Lake ⊜ 282 38.05 N 122.09 W
Hermana Mayor Island ı 116 15.48 N 119.48 E
Hermanas 196 27.13 N 101.14 W
Herman Eksteen Park ♦ 273d 26.10 S 28.02 E
Herma Ness ≻ 46a 60.50 N 0.55 W
Hermann 219 38.42 N 91.26 W
Hermannsburg, Austl. 162 23.57 S 132.45 E
Hermannsburg, Dtsch. 52 52.50 N 10.05 E
Hermannsburg Aboriginal Reserve ♦⁴ 162 24.00 S 132.45 E
Hermanns-Denkmal ⊥ 52 51.55 N 8.50 E
Hermannskogel ∧ 264b 48.16 N 16.18 E
Hermannstadt — Sibiu 38 45.48 N 24.09 E
Hermano Peak ∧ 200 37.13 N 108.48 W
Hermansverk 26 61.11 N 6.51 E
Hermansville 190 45.42 N 87.36 W
Hermanus 158 34.25 S 19.16 E
Hermanville 194 31.57 N 90.50 W
Hermeray 261 48.38 N 1.41 E
Hermes 50 49.22 N 2.15 E
Hermeskeil 56 49.39 N 6.56 E
Hermidale 166 31.33 S 146.43 E
Hermies 50 50.07 N 3.02 E
Herminie 214 40.15 N 79.43 W
Hermiston 202 45.50 N 119.17 W
Hermitage, Nf., Can. 186 47.33 N 55.56 W
Hermitage, Eng., U.K. 42 51.27 N 1.16 W
Hermitage, Ar., U.S. 194 33.26 N 92.10 W
Hermitage, Mo., U.S. 194 37.56 N 93.18 W
Hermitage Bay c 186 47.35 N 56.05 W
Hermitage Park 284c 39.05 N 77.04 W
Hermite, Isla ı 254 55.52 S 67.20 W
Hermit Islands ıı 164 1.30 S 145.05 E
Hermleigh 196 32.38 N 100.46 W
Hermon, S. Afr. 158 33.27 S 18.59 E
Hermon, N.Y., U.S. 212 44.28 N 75.13 W
Hermon, Mount — Shaykh, Jabal ash- ∧ 132 33.26 N 35.51 E
Hermosa Beach 280 33.51 N 118.23 W
Hermosillo, Méx. 200 32.30 N 114.59 W
Hermosillo, Méx. 232 29.04 N 110.58 W
Hermoso, Cerro ∧ 246 1.10 S 78.12 W
Hermsdorf 54 50.54 N 11.52 E
Hermsdorf ◆⁸ 54 52.37 N 13.18 E
Hermyingyi 110 14.15 N 98.21 E
Hernád ≃ 30 47.56 N 21.08 E
Hernals ◆⁸ 264b 48.13 N 16.20 E
Hernandarias 252 25.22 S 54.45 W
Hernández 234 23.01 N 102.01 W
Hernandez Reservoir ⊜¹ 226 36.22 N 120.49 W
Hernando, Arg. 252 32.25 S 63.44 W
Hernando, Fl., U.S. 220 28.54 N 82.22 W
Hernando, Ms., U.S. 194 34.49 N 89.59 W
Hernando □⁶ 220 28.34 N 82.22 W
Hernando de Magallanes, Parque Nacional ♦ 254 54.15 S 72.00 W
Hernani 116 11.20 N 125.37 E
Herndon, Ca., U.S. 226 36.49 N 119.54 W
Herndon, Ks., U.S. 198 39.54 N 100.47 W
Herndon, Pa., U.S. 210 40.42 N 76.50 W
Herndon, Va., U.S. 208 38.58 N 77.23 W
Herndon Canal ≅ 226 36.46 N 119.46 W
Herne 52 51.32 N 7.13 E
Herne Bay 42 51.23 N 1.08 E
Herne Hill 168a 31.50 S 116.01 E
Herning 41 56.08 N 8.59 E
Hernwood Heights 284b 39.22 N 77.50 W
Heroica Zitácuaro 234 19.24 N 100.22 W
Herongate 260 51.36 N 0.21 E
Herongen 56 51.24 N 6.15 E
Heron Island ı 166 23.26 S 151.55 E
Heron Lake 198 43.47 N 95.19 W
Hérons, Île aux ı 275a 45.25 N 73.35 W
Heronsgate 260 51.38 N 0.31 W
Hérouville 261 49.06 N 2.08 E
Hérouville-Saint-Clair 32 49.12 N 0.21 W
Herpf 54 50.34 N 10.20 E
Herradura 252 26.29 S 58.18 W
Herräng 40 60.08 N 18.39 E
Herreid 198 45.50 N 100.04 W
Herrenalb 56 48.48 N 8.26 E
Herrenberg 56 48.35 N 8.52 E
Herrenchiemsee, Schloss ⊥ 64 47.52 N 12.23 E
Herrera 252 28.29 S 63.04 W
Herrera □⁴ 236 7.54 N 80.38 W
Herrera del Duque 34 39.10 N 5.03 W
Herrera de Pisuerga 34 42.36 N 4.20 W
Herrick, Austl. 166 41.06 S 147.52 E
Herrick, Il., U.S. 219 39.13 N 88.59 W
Herrick Creek ≃ 182 54.20 N 121.30 W
Herrick Grove 212 44.04 N 76.12 W
Herricks 276 40.45 N 73.40 W
Herrieden 56 49.14 N 10.30 E
Herrin 194 37.48 N 89.01 W
Herring Bay c 208 38.44 N 76.33 W
Herring Brook ≃ 283 42.10 N 70.44 W
Herring Cove, N.S., Can. 186 44.34 N 63.34 W
Herring Cove, Ak., U.S. 182 55.21 N 131.41 W
Herring Creek ≃ 208 37.49 N 77.07 W
Herringen 52 51.40 N 7.44 E
Herring Run ≃ 284b 39.18 N 76.31 W
Herring Run Park ♦ 284b 39.19 N 76.33 W
Herritslev 41 54.42 N 11.41 E
Herrljunga 26 58.05 N 13.02 E
Herrnburg 54 53.47 N 10.46 E
Herrnhut 54 51.01 N 14.44 E
Herrsching am Ammersee 60 48.00 N 11.10 E
Hers Island ı 279b 40.28 N 79.58 W
Herrskogen 40 59.32 N 16.15 E
Herry 50 47.13 N 2.57 E
Hersbruck 60 49.30 N 11.26 E
Herschbach 56 50.34 N 7.44 E
Herscheid 56 51.10 N 7.44 E
Herschel, Sk., Can. 184 51.38 N 108.21 W
Herschel, Transkei 158 30.37 S 27.12 E
Herschel Island ı 180 69.35 N 139.05 W
Herscher 216 41.03 N 88.06 W
Herselt 56 51.03 N 4.53 E
Herserange 56 49.31 N 5.47 E
Hersham 260 51.22 N 0.23 W
Hershey, Ne., U.S. 198 41.09 N 101.00 W
Hershey, Pa., U.S. 208 40.17 N 76.39 W
Hersman 219 39.57 N 90.44 W
Herstadberg 40 58.38 N 16.10 E
Herstal 56 50.40 N 5.38 E
Herstmonceux 42 50.53 N 0.20 E
Herten 52 51.35 N 7.07 E
Hertford, Eng., U.K. 42 51.48 N 0.05 W
Hertford, N.C., U.S. 192 36.11 N 76.27 W
Hertford □⁶ 208 36.28 N 77.01 W
Hertfordshire □⁶ 42 51.50 N 0.10 W
Hertingfordbury 260 51.48 N 0.06 W
Hertsmere □⁸ 260 51.41 N 0.17 W
Hertzogville 158 28.08 S 25.33 E
Heruncun 104 40.58 N 123.27 E
Hervás 34 40.16 N 5.51 W
Herve 56 50.38 N 5.48 E
Hervest 263 51.40 N 7.01 E
Hervey Bay c 166 25.00 S 153.00 E
Herxheim 56 49.09 N 8.13 E
Héry, Fr. 50 47.54 N 3.38 E
Héry, Fr. 62 45.46 N 6.28 E
Herzberg, Dtsch. 54 52.54 N 12.58 E
Herzberg, Dtsch. 54 51.41 N 13.14 E
Herzberg am Harz 52 51.39 N 10.20 E
Herzebrock 52 51.53 N 8.14 E
Herzfelde 54 52.29 N 13.50 E
Herzhausen 56 51.11 N 8.53 E
Herzliyya 132 32.10 N 34.51 E
Herznach 58 47.28 N 8.03 E
Herzogenaurach 56 49.34 N 10.53 E
Herzogenbuchsee 58 47.12 N 7.41 E
Herzogenburg 61 48.17 N 15.42 E
Herzogenrath 56 50.52 N 6.06 E
Herzsprung 54 53.04 N 12.28 E
Heṣār, Kūh-e ∧ 120 34.50 N 66.30 E
Hesarak 267d 35.47 N 51.19 E
Hesdin 50 50.22 N 2.02 E
Hesel 52 53.18 N 7.35 E
Hesepe 52 52.26 N 7.58 E
Heshachang 107 30.37 N 105.40 E
Heshan 110 23.52 N 108.52 E
Heshangqiao 100 34.15 N 113.47 E
Heshengqiao 100 30.00 N 114.22 E
Heshi, Zhg. 100 25.04 N 118.37 E
Heshi, Zhg. 107 29.10 N 104.22 E
Heshui, Zhg. 100 24.24 N 114.56 E
Heshui, Zhg. 102 22.48 N 112.29 E
Heshuijian 100 30.33 N 116.05 E
Heshun, Zhg. 100 27.30 N 117.24 E
Heshun, Zhg. 102 37.21 N 113.35 E
Heshuo 86 42.15 N 86.53 E
Hesketh Bank 262 53.42 N 2.51 W
Hesketh Out Marsh ≡ 262 53.43 N 2.55 W
Heskin Green 262 53.38 N 2.42 W
Hesler 218 38.28 N 84.47 W
Hesperange 56 49.34 N 6.09 E
Hesperia, Ca., U.S. 228 34.25 N 117.18 W
Hesperia, Mi., U.S. 190 43.34 N 86.02 W
Hesperus Mountain ∧ 200 37.27 N 108.05 W
Hess ≃ 180 63.34 N 133.57 W
Hesselager 41 55.10 N 10.45 E
Hesselberg ∧ 56 49.04 N 10.32 E
Hesselø ı 41 56.12 N 11.43 E
Hesselte 52 52.25 N 7.22 E
Hessen 54 52.01 N 10.47 E
Hessen □³ 30 50.30 N 9.15 E
Hessen Cassal 216 41.00 N 85.05 W
Hessenthal 56 49.55 N 9.17 E
Hessisch Lichtenau 56 51.12 N 9.43 E
Hessisch Oldendorf 52 52.10 N 9.15 E
Hessle 44 53.44 N 0.26 W
Hesso 166 32.08 S 137.27 E
Hess Tablemount ✦³ 14 17.50 N 174.15 W
Hesston, Ks., U.S. 198 38.08 N 97.25 W
Hesston, Pa., U.S. 214 40.26 N 78.07 W
Heston ◆⁸ 260 51.29 N 0.22 W
Heswall 44 53.20 N 3.06 W
Het ≃ 110 20.49 N 104.01 E
Hetai 102 23.22 N 112.19 E
Hetanbu 100 28.21 N 117.11 E
Hetang, Zhg. 100 26.40 N 119.09 E
Hetang, Zhg. 106 31.43 N 120.27 E
Hetang, Zhg. 107 28.58 N 106.03 E
Heṭauṇḍā 124 27.26 N 85.02 E
Hetch Hetchy Aqueduct ≅¹ 226 37.29 N 122.19 W
Hetch Hetchy Reservoir ⊜¹ 226 37.57 N 119.43 W
Hethersett 42 52.36 N 1.11 E
Hetian, Zhg. 100 25.41 N 116.26 E
Hetian, Zhg. 100 23.19 N 115.38 E
Het Loo, Paleis ⊕ 52 52.14 N 5.56 E
Hetou 100 24.18 N 113.29 E
Hetoudian 98 37.02 N 120.35 E
Hettange-Grande 56 49.24 N 6.09 E
Hettenleidelheim 56 49.32 N 8.04 E
Hettick 219 39.21 N 90.02 W
Hettingen 58 48.13 N 9.14 E
Hettinger 198 46.00 N 102.38 W
Hetton-le-Hole 44 54.50 N 1.27 W
Hettstedt 54 51.38 N 11.30 E
Hetupu 100 30.50 N 116.03 E
Hetzendorf ◆⁸ 264b 48.10 N 16.18 E
Hetzerath 56 49.52 N 6.49 E
Het Zoute 50 51.21 N 3.18 E
Heuchin 50 50.28 N 2.16 E
Heudeber 54 51.54 N 10.50 E
Heule 50 50.50 N 3.14 E
Heuningspruit 158 27.26 S 27.28 E
Heusden, Bel. 50 51.02 N 3.48 E
Heusden, Bel. 56 51.02 N 5.16 E
Heustreu 56 50.21 N 10.15 E
Heusweiler 56 49.20 N 6.55 E
Heuvelton 212 44.37 N 75.24 W
Hève, Cap de la ≻ 50 49.31 N 0.04 E
Heven 263 51.26 N 7.17 E
Heverlee 56 50.52 N 4.42 E
Heves 30 47.36 N 20.17 E
Heves □⁶ 30 47.50 N 20.15 E
Hevlín 61 48.45 N 16.23 E
Ḥevron, Naḥal V 132 31.15 N 34.50 E
Hewanorra International Airport ⊠ 241f 13.45 N 60.56 W
Hewitt, N.J., U.S. 210 41.08 N 74.18 W
Hewitt, Tx., U.S. 222 31.27 N 97.11 W
Hewittsville 219 39.32 N 89.19 W
Hewlett, N.Y., U.S. 276 40.38 N 73.41 W
Hewlett, Va., U.S. 208 37.55 N 77.35 W
Hewlett Bay Park 276 40.38 N 73.42 W
Hewlett Harbor 276 40.38 N 73.41 W
Hewlett Neck 276 40.37 N 73.42 W
Hewlett Point ≻ 276 40.50 N 73.45 W
Hewopu 104 41.14 N 122.24 E
Hewu 100 26.41 N 113.40 E
Hexen Kopf ∧ 58 47.01 N 10.28 E
Hexham 44 54.58 N 2.06 W
Hexi, Zhg. 100 24.52 N 117.15 E
Hexi, Zhg. 102 24.09 N 102.39 E
Hexi, Zhg. 106 31.03 N 119.49 E
Hexian, Zhg. 100 31.43 N 118.22 E
Hexian, Zhg. 102 24.15 N 111.43 E
Hexibao 102 38.34 N 102.11 E
Hexingchang 107 30.05 N 104.45 E
Hexingjie 106 31.55 N 120.36 E
Hexiwu 105 39.38 N 116.58 E
Hex Rivierberge ∧ 158 33.25 S 19.37 E
Hextable 260 51.25 N 0.11 E
Hexton 172 38.37 S 177.58 E
Heyan 104 42.30 N 120.29 E
Heyang, Zhg. 98 35.27 N 118.33 E
Heyang, Zhg. 102 35.15 N 110.06 E
Heybeli ◆⁸ 267b 40.53 N 29.05 E
Heybeli Ada ı 267b 40.53 N 29.05 E
Heybridge, Eng., U.K. 260 51.44 N 0.41 E
Heybridge, Eng., U.K. 260 51.40 N 0.22 E
Heyburn 202 42.33 N 113.45 W
Heyerode 54 51.10 N 10.25 E
Heyrieux 62 45.38 N 5.03 E
Heysham 44 54.02 N 2.54 W
Heyuan 100 23.44 N 114.41 E
Heywood, Austl. 166 38.08 S 141.38 E
Heywood, Eng., U.K. 44 53.36 N 2.13 W
Heyworth 216 40.18 N 88.58 W
Heze (Caozhou) 98 35.17 N 115.27 E
Hezhang 102 27.08 N 104.37 E
Hezhao 98 37.08 N 115.17 E
Hezhen 100 29.56 N 120.10 E
Hezheng 102 35.25 N 103.10 E
Hezijiang 105 40.13 N 116.03 E
Hezixu 100 24.54 N 115.14 E
Hezuo 102 34.58 N 102.57 E
Hiale 110 15.55 N 107.34 E
Hialeah 220 25.51 N 80.16 W
Hialeah Park Race Track ♦ 220 25.51 N 80.17 W
Hiaohei 100 31.21 N 114.02 E
Hiawassee 192 34.56 N 83.45 W
Hiawatha, Ks., U.S. 198 39.51 N 95.32 W
Hiawatha, Ut., U.S. 200 39.29 N 111.00 W
Hiba-Dōgo-Taishaku-kokutei-kōen ♦ 96 35.07 N 133.08 E
Hibaldstow 44 53.31 N 0.32 W
Hibbing 190 47.25 N 92.56 W
Hibbs, Point ≻ 166 42.38 S 145.15 E
Hibernia 276 40.57 N 74.30 W
Hibernia Reef ✦² 160 12.00 S 123.23 E
Hibiki-nada ▾² 96 34.00 N 130.30 E
Hiburi-shima ı 96 33.10 N 132.17 E
Hibuson Island ı 116 10.27 N 125.29 E
Hickam Air Force Base ■ 229c 21.20 N 157.57 W
Hickey, Mount ∧ 169 37.22 S 145.19 E
Hickman, Ca., U.S. 226 37.37 N 120.45 W
Hickman, Ky., U.S. 194 36.34 N 89.11 W
Hickman, Ne., U.S. 198 40.37 N 96.37 W
Hickman, Pa., U.S. 279b 40.23 N 80.09 W
Hickman's Harbour 186 48.06 N 53.44 W
Hickory, Ms., U.S. 194 32.19 N 89.01 W
Hickory, N.C., U.S. 192 35.43 N 81.20 W
Hickory, Pa., U.S. 214 40.18 N 80.18 W
Hickory Corners 216 42.26 N 85.22 W
Hickory Creek ≃, Il., U.S. 278 41.30 N 88.06 W
Hickory Creek ≃, Mi., U.S. 216 42.05 N 86.29 W
Hickory Creek ≃, Tx., U.S. 222 31.29 N 95.07 W
Hickory Flat 194 34.36 N 89.11 W
Hickory Hills 216 41.43 N 87.49 W
Hickory Run State Park ♦ 210 41.02 N 75.41 W
Hickory Township 214 41.15 N 80.27 W
Hicks, Point ≻ 166 37.48 S 149.17 E
Hicks Bay 172 37.36 S 178.18 E
Hickson Lake ⊜ 184 56.17 N 104.25 W
Hicksville, N.Y., U.S. 210 40.46 N 73.31 W
Hicksville, Oh., U.S. 216 41.17 N 84.45 W
Hico 196 31.58 N 98.02 W
Hicpochee, Lake ⊜ 220 26.50 N 81.10 W
Hida — Hita 96 33.19 N 130.56 E
Hida ≃ 94 35.26 N 137.03 E
Hidaka, Nihon 94 35.54 N 139.21 E
Hidaka, Nihon 96 35.28 N 134.47 E
Hidaka, Nihon 96 33.55 N 135.09 E
Hidaka ≃ 96 33.52 N 135.09 E
Hidaka-sammyaku ∧ 92a 42.35 N 142.45 E
Hida-Kiso-gawa-kokutei-kōen ♦ 94 35.37 N 137.15 E
Hida-kōchi ∧¹ 94 36.16 N 137.25 E
Hidalgo, Méx. 232 27.47 N 99.52 W
Hidalgo, Méx. 232 25.59 N 100.27 W
Hidalgo, Méx. 232 24.15 N 99.26 W
Hidalgo □³ 234 20.30 N 99.00 W
Hidalgo del Parral 232 26.56 N 105.40 W
Hida-sammyaku ∧ 94 36.25 N 137.40 E
Hiddenhausen 52 52.08 N 8.38 E
Hidden Hills 228 34.09 N 118.43 W
Hiddensee ı 54 54.33 N 13.07 E
Hidden Valley, Ca., U.S. 226 38.46 N 121.09 W
Hidden Valley, Tx., U.S. 222 29.54 N 95.25 W
Hiddesen 52 51.55 N 8.50 E
Hiddinghausen 263 51.22 N 7.17 E
Hıdırbaba 130 38.47 N 39.00 E
Hidrolândia 255 16.58 S 49.14 W
Hidrolina 255 14.37 S 49.25 W
Hieflau 61 47.36 N 14.44 E
Hienghène 175f 20.41 S 164.56 E
Hierapolis — Pamukkale ⊥ 130 37.58 N 29.19 E
Hierges 56 50.06 N 4.44 E
Hierro (Ferro) ı 148 27.45 N 18.00 W
Hiesfeld 263 51.33 N 6.46 E
Hietzing ◆⁸ 264b 48.11 N 16.18 E
Higashi 174m 26.38 N 128.09 E
Higashi ◆⁸ 270 34.41 N 135.31 E
Higashibetsuin 270 34.55 N 135.34 E
Higashi-enshūjō ■ 94 35.17 N 138.51 E
Higashihiroshima 96 34.26 N 132.42 E
Higashiichiki 92 31.40 N 130.20 E
Higashiiyayama 96 33.52 N 133.54 E
Higashiizu 94 34.48 N 139.04 E
Higashi-jima ı 174f 24.47 N 141.23 E
Higashikurume 268 35.45 N 139.32 E
Higashimatsuyama 94 36.02 N 139.24 E
Higashimonzen 268 35.56 N 139.40 E
Higashimurayama 94 35.46 N 139.29 E
Higashinada ◆⁸ 270 34.43 N 135.16 E
Higashinakano 268 35.38 N 139.25 E
Higashinari ◆⁸ 270 34.40 N 135.33 E
Higashine 92 38.26 N 140.24 E
Higashinose 270 34.55 N 135.30 E
Higashiōizumi ◆⁸ 268 35.45 N 139.36 E
Higashiōsaka 96 34.39 N 135.35 E
Higashishirakawa 94 35.39 N 137.19 E
Higashisumiyoshi ◆⁸ 270 34.37 N 135.32 E
Higashitokonoo-san ∧ 96 35.25 N 134.55 E
Higashitsuno 96 33.23 N 133.02 E
Higashiura, Nihon 94 34.59 N 136.58 E
Higashiura, Nihon 270 34.33 N 135.00 E
Higashiyama ◆⁸ 270 35.00 N 135.48 E
Higashiyamato 268 35.44 N 139.26 E
Higashiyodogawa ◆⁸ 270 34.44 N 135.31 E
Higashiyoshino 94 34.24 N 135.58 E
Higbee 194 39.18 N 92.30 W
Higganum 207 41.29 N 72.33 W
Higgins 196 36.07 N 100.02 W
Higgins, Mount ∧ 224 48.19 N 121.45 W
Higgins Lake ⊜ 190 44.30 N 84.45 W
Higginsport 218 38.47 N 83.58 W
Higginsville, Austl. 162 31.45 S 121.43 E
Higginsville, Mo., U.S. 194 39.04 N 93.43 W
Higgs' Hope 158 29.19 S 23.16 E
Higham Ferrers 42 52.18 N 0.36 W
Higham Upshire 260 51.26 N 0.28 E
Highbank 222 31.10 N 96.50 W
High Bank Creek ≃ 216 42.37 N 85.11 W
High Bar Indian Reserve ◆⁴ 182 51.06 N 122.00 W
High Beach 260 51.39 N 0.02 E
High Bentham 44 54.08 N 2.30 W
High Bluff Island ı 212 43.58 N 77.45 W
Highbridge, Eng., U.K. 42 51.13 N 2.49 W
High Bridge, N.J., U.S. 210 40.40 N 74.53 W
Highbury 164 16.25 S 143.09 E
Highcliff 279b 40.32 N 80.03 W
Higher Ballam 262 53.46 N 2.59 W
Higher Broughton ◆⁸ 262 53.30 N 2.15 W
Higher Hogshead ∧² 262 53.42 N 2.09 W
Higher Penwortham 262 53.45 N 2.44 W
Higher Walton, Eng., U.K. 44 53.44 N 2.39 W
Higher Walton, Eng., U.K. 262 53.22 N 2.37 W
Higher Whitley 262 53.19 N 2.35 W
Highett 274b 37.57 S 145.03 E
High Falls 210 41.50 N 74.08 W
High Falls ∟ 212 43.56 N 75.23 W
High Force ∟ 44 54.38 N 2.13 W
Highgate 214 42.30 N 81.49 W
Highgate Center 206 44.56 N 73.02 W
Highgate Springs 206 44.58 N 73.06 W
Highgrove 228 34.01 N 117.20 W
High Halstow 260 51.27 N 0.34 E
High Hesket 44 54.48 N 2.48 W
High Hill 219 38.52 N 91.23 W
High Hill ∧² 276 40.49 N 73.25 W
High Hill ≃, Can. 184 56.45 N 110.30 W
High Hill ≃, Mb., Can. 184 55.52 N 94.42 W
High Hill Lake ⊜ 184 55.34 N 95.40 W
High Island ı, H.K. 271d 22.22 N 114.21 E
High Island ı, Mi., U.S. 190 45.42 N 85.40 W
High Island Creek ≃ 190 44.35 N 93.54 W
High Island Reservoir ⊜¹ 271d 22.23 N 114.21 W
Highland, Ca., U.S. 228 34.07 N 117.12 W
Highland, Il., U.S. 219 38.44 N 89.40 W
Highland, In., U.S. 216 41.33 N 87.27 W
Highland, Ks., U.S. 198 39.51 N 95.16 W
Highland, Md., U.S. 208 39.11 N 76.57 W
Highland, Mi., U.S. 281 42.38 N 83.37 W
Highland, N.Y., U.S. 210 41.43 N 73.57 W
Highland, Oh., U.S. 218 39.21 N 83.36 W
Highland, Pa., U.S. 279b 40.33 N 80.04 W
Highland □⁴ 46 57.40 N 5.00 W
Highland □⁶ 218 39.12 N 83.37 W
Highland Beach 220 26.25 N 80.04 W
Highland City 220 27.58 N 81.53 W
Highland Creek ≃, On., Can. 275b 43.46 N 79.08 W
Highland Creek ≃, Ca., U.S. 226 38.24 N 121.14 W
Highland Falls 210 41.22 N 73.58 W
Highland Heights, Ky., U.S. 218 39.04 N 84.27 W
Highland Heights, Oh., U.S. 214 41.33 N 81.28 W
Highland Hills 278 41.52 N 88.01 W
Highland Home 194 31.57 N 86.18 W
Highland Lake, Il., U.S. 278 42.21 N 88.04 W
Highland Lake, Ma., U.S. 283 42.41 N 72.37 W
Highland Lake, N.Y., U.S. 210 41.32 N 74.51 W
Highland Lake ⊜, Ct., U.S. 207 41.54 N 73.06 W
Highland Lake ⊜, Il., U.S. 278 42.22 N 88.04 W
Highland Lake ⊜, N.J., U.S. 276 41.10 N 74.28 W
Highland Lakes 210 41.10 N 74.28 W
Highland-on-the-Lake 284a 42.42 N 79.59 W
Highland Park, Il., U.S. 216 42.10 N 87.48 W
Highland Park, Md., U.S. 284c 38.54 N 76.54 W
Highland Park, Mi., U.S. 216 42.24 N 83.05 W
Highland Park, N.J., U.S. 210 40.29 N 74.25 W
Highland Park, Pa., U.S. 210 40.38 N 77.35 W
Highland Park, Tx., U.S. 222 32.50 N 96.48 W
Highland Park ◆⁸ 280 34.07 N 118.13 W
Highland Park ♦, Ma., U.S. 283 42.30 N 70.55 W
Highland Park ♦, Pa., U.S. 279b 40.29 N 79.55 W
Highland Peak ∧ 226 38.33 N 119.45 W
Highland Point ≻ 220 25.30 N 81.12 W
Highlands, N.J., U.S. 208 40.24 N 73.59 W
Highlands, N.C., U.S. 192 35.03 N 83.11 W
Highlands, Tx., U.S. 222 29.49 N 95.03 W
Highlands □⁶ 220 27.20 N 81.16 W
Highlands Hammock State Park ♦ 220 27.28 N 81.33 W
Highland Silver Lake ⊜¹ 219 38.47 N 89.39 W
Highlands North ◆⁸ 273d 26.09 S 28.05 E
Highland Springs 208 37.32 N 77.19 W
Highlands Reservoir ⊜¹ 222 29.50 N 95.02 W
Highland State Recreation Area ♦ 216 42.39 N 83.33 W
Highlandtown ◆⁸ 284b 39.17 N 76.33 W
High Laver 260 51.45 N 0.13 E
High Legh 262 53.21 N 2.27 W
Highley 42 52.27 N 2.23 W
Highmore 198 44.31 N 99.26 W
High Ongar 260 51.43 N 0.16 E
High Park ♦ 275b 43.39 N 79.28 W
High Peak □⁸ 262 53.23 N 1.55 W
High Peak ∧, Pil. 116 15.29 N 120.07 E
High Peak ∧, N.Y., U.S. 210 42.09 N 74.05 W
High Peak ◆¹ 44 53.22 N 1.50 W
High Point, Fl., U.S. 220 27.55 N 82.42 W
High Point, N.C., U.S. 192 35.57 N 80.00 W
Highpoint, Oh., U.S. 218 39.14 N 84.24 W
High Point ∧, N.J., U.S. 210 41.19 N 74.40 W
High Point ∧, Wy., U.S. 202 41.37 N 107.47 W
High Point State Park ♦ 210 41.18 N 74.41 W

ENGLISH — Name / Page / Lat.°′ / Long.°′

High Prairie 182 55.26 N 116.29 W
High Ridge 219 38.27 N 90.32 W
High River 182 50.35 N 113.52 W
High Rock 192 26.36 N 76.18 W
High Rock ∧ 188 39.33 N 79.06 W
Highrock Indian Reserve ◆⁴ 184 55.54 N 100.30 W
Highrock Lake ⊜, Mb., Can. 184 55.45 N 100.30 W
Highrock Lake ⊜, Sk., Can. 184 57.04 N 105.30 W
High Rock Lake ⊜¹ 192 35.40 N 80.17 W
High Seat ∧ 44 54.24 N 2.18 W
High Spire 208 40.12 N 76.47 W
High Springs 192 29.49 N 82.35 W
High Street ∧ 44 54.29 N 2.52 W
Hightown 44 53.31 N 3.03 W
Hightstown 208 40.16 N 74.31 W
High View 210 41.33 N 74.27 W
Highwater 206 45.01 N 72.26 W
Highway City 226 36.49 N 119.54 W
High Willhays ∧ 42 50.41 N 3.59 W
Highwood, Il., U.S. 216 42.11 N 87.48 W
Highwood, Mt., U.S. 202 47.35 N 110.47 W
Highwood ≃ 182 50.49 N 113.47 W
Highwood Baldy ∧ 202 47.27 N 110.37 W
Highwood Creek ≃ 202 47.40 N 111.00 W
Highwood Mountains ∧ 202 47.25 N 110.30 W
Highworth 42 51.38 N 1.43 W
High Wycombe 42 51.38 N 0.46 W
Higlet 154 1.04 S 40.19 E
Higuera Blanca 234 19.42 N 105.10 W
Higuera de Abuya 232 24.16 N 107.04 W
Higuera de Zaragoza 232 25.59 N 109.16 W
Higueras 196 25.58 N 100.01 W
Higüero, Punta ≻ 240m 18.22 N 67.16 W
Higüey 238 18.37 N 68.42 W
Higuito ≃ 236 14.43 N 88.40 W
Hihétro 150 7.32 N 1.06 E
Hihyā 142 30.40 N 31.36 E
Hii ≃ 96 35.26 N 132.54 E
Hiidenportin kansallispuisto ♦ 26 63.50 N 28.59 E
Hiiraan □⁴ 144 4.00 N 45.30 E
Hiiumaa ı 76 58.52 N 22.40 E
Hījānah, Buḥayrat al- ⊜ 132 33.18 N 36.36 E
Híjar 34 41.10 N 0.27 W
Hiji 96 33.22 N 131.32 E
Hiji ≃ 96 33.36 N 132.29 E
Hijikawa 96 33.27 N 132.41 E
Hijiri-dake ∧ 94 35.26 N 138.10 E
Hikami 96 35.10 N 135.02 E
Hikari, Nihon 94 35.39 N 140.30 E
Hikari, Nihon 96 33.58 N 131.56 E
Hikarigaoka 268 35.50 N 139.58 E
Hikawa 96 35.25 N 132.50 E
Hikawa Shrine ⊕¹ 268 35.54 N 139.38 E
Hiketa 96 34.13 N 134.24 E
Hiki ≃ 96 33.33 N 135.27 E
Hikigawa 96 33.34 N 135.27 E
Hikimi 96 34.34 N 132.01 E
Hikimi ≃ 96 34.37 N 131.48 E
Hikiura 270 34.33 N 134.58 E
Hikone 94 35.15 N 136.15 E
Hikone-jō ⊥ 94 35.15 N 136.14 E
Hiko-san ∧ 96 33.27 N 130.54 E
Hikueru ı¹ 14 17.36 S 142.37 W
Hikurangi 172 35.36 S 174.18 E
Hikurangi ∧ 172 37.55 S 178.04 E
Hikutaia 172 37.17 S 175.39 E
Hikutivake 174v 18.56 S 169.53 W
Hila 112 7.35 S 127.24 E
Hilaban Island ı 116 12.03 N 125.34 E
Hilāl, Jabal ∧ 132 30.40 N 34.00 E
Hilāl, Ra's al- ≻ 146 32.57 N 22.10 E
Hilbersdorf 54 50.55 N 13.23 E
Hilbert 190 44.08 N 88.09 W
Hilbre Islands ıı 262 53.23 N 3.13 W
Hilbre Point ≻ 262 53.23 N 3.12 W
Hilchenbach 56 51.00 N 8.06 E
Hilda 184 50.28 N 110.03 W
Hildburghausen 54 50.25 N 10.44 E
Hilden 56 51.10 N 6.56 E
Hildenborough 260 51.13 N 0.15 E
Hilders 56 50.34 N 10.00 E
Hildesheim 52 52.09 N 9.57 E
Hildreth 198 40.20 N 99.02 W
Hilgen 263 51.06 N 7.09 E
Hilialawa 114 0.41 N 97.53 E
Hiligeo 114 1.22 N 97.10 E
Hiliotaluwa 114 0.44 N 97.53 E
Hill □⁶ 222 32.02 N 97.10 W
Hillaby, Mount ∧ 241g 13.12 N 59.35 W
Hill Air Force Base ■ 202 41.05 N 111.58 W
Hillandale, S. Afr. 158 33.06 S 20.36 E
Hillandale, Md., U.S. 284c 39.01 N 76.58 W
Hillandale Heights 284c 39.01 N 76.59 W
Hill Bank 232 17.35 N 88.42 W
Hillburn 210 41.08 N 74.10 W
Hill City, Ks., U.S. 198 39.21 N 99.50 W
Hill City, Mn., U.S. 190 46.59 N 93.35 W
Hill City, S.D., U.S. 198 43.55 N 103.34 W
Hill Creek ≃ 200 39.55 N 109.40 W
Hillcrest, Il., U.S. 216 41.57 N 89.04 W
Hillcrest, N.Y., U.S. 210 41.07 N 74.02 W
Hillcrest, N.Y., U.S. 210 42.09 N 75.53 W
Hillcrest Center 228 35.23 N 118.57 W
Hillcrest Heights 284c 38.49 N 76.57 W
Hillcrest Mines 182 49.34 N 114.23 W
Hillcrest Orchard 216 41.51 N 83.29 W
Hillcrest Park 226 38.07 N 122.16 W
Hill Cumorah ⊥ 210 43.01 N 77.15 W
Hille, Dtsch. 52 52.20 N 8.44 E
Hille, Sve. 40 60.44 N 17.11 E
Hillegom 52 52.18 N 4.35 E
Hillegossen 52 51.59 N 8.37 E
Hillerød 41 55.56 N 12.19 E
Hillers Creek ≃ 219 38.38 N 91.54 W
Hillesheim 56 50.18 N 6.38 E
Hilli 124 25.17 N 89.01 E
Hilliard, Fl., U.S. 192 30.41 N 81.55 W
Hilliard, Oh., U.S. 218 40.02 N 83.09 W
Hilliards 214 41.05 N 79.50 W
Hillingdon ◆⁸ 42 51.32 N 0.27 W
Hillisburg 216 40.17 N 86.20 W
Hill Island Lake ⊜ 176 60.29 N 109.50 W
Hillister 194 30.40 N 94.23 W
Hillman 190 45.03 N 83.54 W
Hillman ≃ 168a 33.26 S 116.48 E
Hillmersdorf 54 51.42 N 13.29 E
Hill of Fearn 46 57.45 N 3.56 W
Hills 198 43.31 N 96.21 W
Hills and Dales 214 39.42 N 84.13 W
Hillsboro, Il., U.S. 219 39.09 N 89.29 W
Hillsboro, Ks., U.S. 198 38.21 N 97.12 W
Hillsboro, Ky., U.S. 218 38.18 N 83.40 W
Hillsboro, Md., U.S. 208 38.55 N 75.56 W
Hillsboro, Mo., U.S. 219 38.13 N 90.33 W
Hillsboro, N.H., U.S. 188 43.06 N 71.53 W
Hillsboro, N.M., U.S. 200 32.55 N 107.33 W
Hillsboro, N.D., U.S. 198 47.24 N 97.03 W
Hillsboro, Oh., U.S. 218 39.12 N 83.36 W
Hillsboro, Or., U.S. 224 45.31 N 122.59 W
Hillsboro, Tx., U.S. 222 32.00 N 97.07 W
Hillsboro, Wi., U.S. 190 43.39 N 90.20 W
Hillsboro Beach 220 26.18 N 80.05 W
Hillsboro Canal ≅ 220 26.19 N 80.05 W
Hillsborough, N.B., Can. 186 45.56 N 64.39 W
Hillsborough, N. Ire., U.K. 48 54.28 N 6.05 W
Hillsborough, Ca., U.S. 226 37.34 N 122.22 W
Hillsborough, N.C., U.S. 192 36.04 N 79.06 W
Hillsborough □⁶, Fl., U.S. 220 27.55 N 82.15 W
Hillsborough □⁶, N.H., U.S. 207 42.49 N 71.41 W

DEUTSCH — Name / Seite / Breite°′ / Länge°′ E = Ost

Hillsborough ≃ 220 27.56 N 82.27 W
Hillsborough, Cape ≻ 166 20.54 S 149.03 E
Hillsborough Bay c, P.E., Can. 186 46.10 N 63.05 W
Hillsborough Bay c, Fl., U.S. 220 27.52 N 82.27 W
Hillsborough River State Park ♦ 220 28.09 N 82.14 W
Hillsburgh 212 43.47 N 80.09 W
Hills Creek Lake ⊜¹ 202 43.40 N 122.26 W
Hillsdale, Mi., U.S. 216 41.55 N 84.37 W
Hillsdale, N.J., U.S. 276 41.00 N 74.02 W
Hillsdale, N.Y., U.S. 210 42.10 N 73.31 W
Hillsdale, Pa., U.S. 214 40.45 N 78.53 W
Hillsdale □⁶ 216 41.53 N 84.36 W
Hillsdale ◆⁹ 282 37.32 N 122.18 W
Hillsdale Lake ⊜¹ 198 38.40 N 94.55 W
Hills Flat 226 39.14 N 121.03 W
Hillsgrove 210 41.27 N 76.42 W
Hillside, Austl. 162 21.44 S 119.23 E
Hillside, Scot., U.K. 46 56.44 N 2.29 W
Hillside, Il., U.S. 278 41.52 N 87.54 W
Hillside, N.J., U.S. 276 40.42 N 74.13 W
Hillside ◆⁸ 276 40.42 N 73.47 W
Hillside Gardens 216 42.16 N 84.27 W
Hillside Heights 285 39.41 N 75.41 W
Hillside Lake 210 41.36 N 73.50 W
Hillston 166 33.29 S 145.32 E
Hillsville, Pa., U.S. 214 41.00 N 80.29 W
Hillsville, Va., U.S. 192 36.45 N 80.44 W
Hillswick 46a 60.28 N 1.30 W
Hilltop 208 39.49 N 75.04 W
Hilltop Center ◆⁹ 282 37.59 N 122.19 W
Hilltown, N. Ire., U.K. 48 54.12 N 6.09 W
Hilltown, Pa., U.S. 208 40.20 N 75.14 W
Hillview 219 39.27 N 90.33 W
Hillview Reservoir ⊜¹ 276 40.55 N 73.52 W
Hillwood 284c 38.52 N 77.10 W
Hilmar 226 37.25 N 120.51 W
Hilo 229d 19.43 N 155.05 W
Hilo Bay c 229d 19.44 N 155.05 W
Hilonghilong, Mount ∧ 116 9.06 N 125.44 E
Hilongos 116 10.23 N 124.45 E
Hilpotstein 60 49.12 N 11.12 E
Hilpsford Point ≻ 44 54.03 N 3.12 W
Hils ∧ 52 51.55 N 9.40 E
Hilshire Village 222 29.49 N 95.26 W
Hiltaba, Mount ∧ 162 32.09 S 135.03 E
Hilter 52 52.08 N 8.08 E
Hilton, N.Y., U.S. 210 43.17 N 77.47 W
Hilton, Pa., U.S. 208 40.00 N 76.49 W
Hilton Head Island ı 192 32.12 N 80.45 W
Hiltpoltstein 60 49.40 N 11.19 E
Hiltrop ◆⁸ 263 51.30 N 7.15 E
Hiltrup 52 51.54 N 7.38 E
Hilvan 130 37.35 N 38.57 E
Hilvarenbeek 52 51.29 N 5.09 E
Hilversum 52 52.14 N 5.10 E
Hima 192 37.07 N 83.46 W
Himāchal Pradesh □³ 120 32.00 N 77.00 E
Himalayas ∧ 120 28.00 N 84.00 E
Himāl Chulī ∧ 124 28.25 N 84.39 E
Himamaylan 116 10.06 N 122.52 E
Himanka 26 64.04 N 23.39 E
Himarë 38 40.07 N 19.44 E
Himatnagar 120 23.36 N 72.57 E
Himberg 61 48.05 N 16.26 E
Hime ≃ 94 37.02 N 137.49 E
Himeji 96 34.49 N 134.42 E
Hime-shima ı 96 33.43 N 131.40 E
Himeville 158 29.44 S 29.31 E
Himi 94 36.51 N 136.59 E
Himmelbjerget ∧² 41 56.06 N 9.42 E
Himmelgeist ◆⁸ 263 51.10 N 6.49 E
Himmelpforten 52 53.36 N 9.18 E
Himmelsthür 52 52.09 N 9.55 E
Himmerfjärden c² 40 59.00 N 17.43 E
Himmerland ◆¹ 26 56.50 N 9.45 E
Himmetdede 130 38.55 N 35.07 E
Himrod 210 42.35 N 76.57 W
Ḥimṣ (Homs) 130 34.44 N 36.43 E
Ḥimṣ □⁸ 130 34.15 N 38.00 E
Hinabangan 116 11.42 N 125.04 E
Hīnah 132 33.21 N 35.56 E
Hinako, Kepulauan ıı 114 0.52 N 97.21 E
Hinase 96 34.44 N 134.16 E
Hinatuan 116 8.23 N 126.20 E
Hinatuan Island ı 116 9.47 N 125.43 E
Hinatuan Passage ꞷ 116 9.45 N 125.47 E
Hinche 238 19.09 N 72.01 W
Hinchinbrook Entrance ꞷ 180 60.25 N 146.50 W
Hinchinbrook Island ı, Austl. 166 18.23 S 146.17 E
Hinchinbrook Island ı, Ak., U.S. 180 60.22 N 146.30 W
Hinchinbrook Island National Park ♦ 166 18.20 S 146.20 E
Hinckley, Eng., U.K. 42 52.33 N 1.21 W
Hinckley, Il., U.S. 216 41.46 N 88.38 W
Hinckley, Mn., U.S. 190 46.00 N 92.56 W
Hinckley, Oh., U.S. 214 41.14 N 81.45 W
Hinckley, Ut,. U.S. 200 39.19 N 112.40 W
Hinckley Reservoir ⊜¹ 210 43.20 N 75.05 W
Hindan ≃ 272a 28.30 N 77.27 E
Hindang 116 10.26 N 124.44 E
Hindaun 124 26.43 N 77.01 E
Hindelang 58 47.30 N 10.22 E
Hindelbank 58 47.03 N 7.32 E
Hindeloopen 52 52.56 N 5.24 E
Hindenburg — Zabrze 30 50.18 N 18.46 E
Hindhead 42 51.07 N 0.44 W
Hindley 44 53.32 N 2.35 W
Hindley Green 262 53.31 N 2.32 W
Hindman 192 37.20 N 82.58 W
Hindmarsh, Lake ⊜ 166 36.03 S 141.55 E
Hindmarsh Island ı 168b 35.32 S 138.52 E
Hindmarsh Valley 168b 35.30 S 138.38 E
Hindon 42 51.06 N 2.08 W
Hinds 172 44.00 S 171.34 E
Hindsholm ≻¹ 41 55.33 N 10.40 E
Hinds Lake ⊜ 186 48.57 N 57.00 W
Hindu Kush ∧ 120 36.00 N 71.30 E
Hindūmalkot 123 30.09 N 73.55 E
Hindupur 122 13.49 N 77.29 E
Hi-Nella 285 39.50 N 75.01 W
Hines 202 43.33 N 119.04 W
Hines Creek 182 56.15 N 118.36 W
Hines Creek ≃ 182 55.54 N 118.37 W
Hines Peak ∧ 228 34.31 N 119.05 W
Hinesville 192 31.50 N 81.35 W
Hinganghāt 122 20.34 N 78.50 E
Hingatungan 116 10.35 N 125.11 E
Hingham, Eng., U.K. 42 52.35 N 0.59 E
Hingham, Ma., U.S. 207 42.14 N 70.53 W
Hingham Bay c 207 42.17 N 70.55 W
Hingham Harbor c 283 42.15 N 70.53 W
Hingol ≃ 128 25.23 N 65.28 E
Hingoli 122 19.43 N 77.09 E
Hinigaran 116 10.17 N 122.51 E
Hınıs 130 39.22 N 41.44 E
Hınıs ≃ 130 39.18 N 42.12 E
Hinkley 228 34.56 N 117.11 W
Hinkson Creek ≃ 219 38.56 N 92.23 W
Hinkston Creek ≃ 188 38.18 N 84.14 W
Hinnerjoki 26 61.00 N 22.00 E
Hinnerup 41 56.16 N 10.04 E
Hinnøya ı 24 68.30 N 16.00 E
Hino, Nihon 94 35.00 N 136.15 E
Hino, Nihon 94 35.41 N 139.24 E
Hino, Nihon 96 35.14 N 133.27 E
Hino ≃, Nihon 94 35.09 N 136.02 E
Hino ≃, Nihon 94 36.04 N 136.11 E
Hino ≃, Nihon 96 35.27 N 133.23 E
Hinoba-an 116 9.35 N 122.28 E
Hinode 94 35.45 N 139.14 E
Hinoemata 94 37.01 N 139.23 E
Hinohara 94 35.43 N 139.09 E

Symbols in the index entries represent the broad categories identified in the key at the right. Symbols with superior numbers (∧¹) identify subcategories (see complete key on page I · 1).

Symbole im Register stellen die rechts im Schlüssel erklärten Kategorien dar. Symbole mit hochgestellten Ziffern (∧¹) bezeichnen Unterabteilungen einer Kategorie (vgl. vollständiger Schlüssel auf Seite I · 1).

Los símbolos incluídos en el texto del índice representan las grandes categorías identificadas con la clave a la derecha. Los símbolos con numeros en su parte superior (∧¹) identifican las subcategorías (véase la clave completa en la página I · 1).

Les symboles de l'index représentent les catégories indiquées dans la légende à droite. Les symboles suivis d'un indice (∧¹) représentent des sous-catégories (voir légende complète à la page I · 1).

Os símbolos incluídos no texto do índice representam as grandes categorias identificadas com a chave à direita. Os símbolos com números em sua parte superior (∧¹) identificam as subcategorias (veja-se a chave completa à página I · 1).

∧ Mountain	Berg	Montaña	Montagne	Montanha
∧ Mountains	Gebirge	Montañas	Montagnes	Montanhas
⨯ Pass	Paß	Paso	Col	Passo
V Valley, Canyon	Tal, Cañon	Valle, Cañón	Vallée, Canyon	Vale, Canhão
≡ Plain	Ebene	Llano	Plaine	Planície
≻ Cape	Kap	Cabo	Cap	Cabo
ı Island	Insel	Isla	Île	Ilha
ıı Islands	Inseln	Islas	Îles	Ilhas
⊥ Other Topographic Features	Andere Topographische Objekte	Otros Elementos Topográficos	Autres données topographiques	Outros acidentes topográficos

ESPAÑOL — Nombre, Página, Lat.°′, Long.°′ W = Oeste
FRANÇAIS — Nom, Page, Lat.°′, Long.°′ W = Ouest
PORTUGUÊS — Nome, Página, Lat.°′, Long.°′ W = Oeste

Nombre / Nom / Nome	Página / Page	Lat.°′	Long.°′
Hinojosa del Duque	34	38.30 N	5.09 W
Hinokage	92	32.39 N	131.24 E
Hinomi-saki ›, Nihon	96	33.53 N	135.04 E
Hinomi-saki ›, Nihon	96	35.26 N	132.38 E
Hinsbeck	56	51.21 N	6.17 E
Hinsdale, Il., U.S.	216	41.48 N	87.56 W
Hinsdale, Ma., U.S.	207	42.26 N	73.07 W
Hinsdale, Mt., U.S.	202	48.23 N	107.05 W
Hinsdale, N.H., U.S.	207	42.47 N	72.29 W
Hinsdale, N.Y., U.S.	210	42.10 N	78.23 W
Hinsel ◆[8]	263	51.26 N	7.05 E
Hinsen ⊜	40	60.39 N	16.05 E
Hinte	52	53.25 N	7.11 E
Hinterbichl	64	47.01 N	12.20 E
Hinterbrühl	61	48.05 N	16.15 E
Hinterhermsdorf	54	50.55 N	14.22 E
Hinterrhein	58	46.32 N	9.12 E
Hinterrhein ≃	58	46.49 N	9.25 E
Hintersdorf	264b	48.18 N	16.13 E
Hintersee	54	53.37 N	14.16 E
Hinterstoder	61	47.41 N	14.09 E
Hintertux	64	47.07 N	11.41 E
Hinterweidenthal	56	49.12 N	7.45 E
Hinterzarten	58	47.54 N	8.06 E
Hinton, Ab., Can.	182	53.25 N	117.34 W
Hinton, Mo., U.S.	219	39.03 N	92.21 W
Hinton, Ok., U.S.	196	35.28 N	98.21 W
Hinton, W.V., U.S.	192	37.40 N	80.53 W
Hi-numa ⊜	94	36.16 N	140.30 E
Hinuma ≃	94	36.16 N	140.28 E
Hinundayan	116	10.21 N	125.15 E
Hinwil	58	47.18 N	8.51 E
Hinzik	84	40.08 N	40.58 E
Hípico, Club ♠	286e	33.28 S	70.41 W
Hipólito	232	25.41 N	101.26 W
Hipólito Yrigoyen	252	32.55 S	66.20 W
Hippolytushoef	52	52.54 N	4.57 E
Hirado	92	33.22 N	129.33 E
Hirado-shima I	92	33.20 N	129.30 E
Hiraiwa-hana ›	174f	24.48 N	141.18 E
Hiraizumi	92	38.59 N	141.07 E
Hirakata, Nihon	96	34.48 N	135.38 E
Hirakata, Nihon	268	35.56 N	139.33 E
Hirakawa	270	34.52 N	135.47 E
Hīrākud	122	21.31 N	83.57 E
Hīrākud Reservoir ⊜[1]	120	21.35 N	83.50 E
Hiram, Me., U.S.	188	43.52 N	70.48 W
Hiram, Oh., U.S.	214	41.18 N	81.08 W
Hiraman ≃	154	1.07 S	39.55 E
Hirano	175d	24.35 N	124.19 E
Hirano ◆[8]	270	34.36 N	135.34 E
Hirao	96	33.56 N	132.04 E
Hirao-dai ♠	96	33.45 N	130.52 E
Hiraoka → Higashiōsaka	96	34.39 N	135.35 E
Hīrāpur	124	24.22 N	79.13 E
Hirara	175d	24.48 N	125.17 E
Hirata, Nihon	94	35.15 N	136.38 E
Hirata, Nihon	96	35.26 N	132.49 E
Hiratsuka	94	35.19 N	139.21 E
Hiraya	94	35.19 N	137.37 E
Hirfanlı Barajı ⊜[1]	130	39.10 N	33.35 E
Hirhafok	148	23.49 N	5.45 E
Hiriyūr	122	13.58 N	76.36 E
Hirjillah	132	33.22 N	36.18 E
Hîrlău	38	47.25 N	26.54 E
Hirokawa, Nihon	96	33.15 N	130.32 E
Hirokawa, Nihon	96	34.01 N	135.11 E
Hirok Sāmi	128	26.02 N	63.25 E
Hiromi	96	33.15 N	132.41 E
Hiroo	92a	42.17 N	143.19 E
Hirooka	268	35.15 N	140.04 E
Hirosaki	92	40.35 N	140.28 E
Hiroschima → Hiroshima	96	34.24 N	132.27 E
Hirose	96	35.22 N	133.10 E
Hiroshima	96	34.24 N	132.27 E
Hiroshima □[5]	96	34.30 N	133.00 E
Hiro-shima I	96	34.22 N	133.43 E
Hiroshima-wan c	96	34.06 N	132.20 E
Hirosima → Hiroshima	96	34.24 N	132.27 E
Hirota	270	34.45 N	135.21 E
Hirsau	56	48.44 N	8.44 E
Hirschaid	56	49.49 N	10.59 E
Hirschau	60	49.33 N	11.57 E
Hirschbach	54	50.33 N	10.44 E
Hirschberg, Dtsch.	54	50.24 N	11.49 E
Hirschberg → Jelenia Góra, Pol.	30	50.55 N	15.46 E
Hirschfeld	54	51.23 N	13.37 E
Hirschfelde, Dtsch.	54	50.57 N	14.53 E
Hirschfelde, Dtsch.	264a	52.38 N	13.48 E
Hirschhorn	56	49.27 N	8.53 E
Hirschstetten ◆[8]	264b	48.14 N	16.29 E
Hirshfeld Brook ≃	276	40.57 N	74.02 W
Hirsingue	58	47.35 N	7.15 E
Hirson	50	49.55 N	4.05 E
Hîrşova	38	44.41 N	27.57 E
Hirsts Hill ∧	171a	27.13 S	152.06 E
Hirtshals	26	57.35 N	9.58 E
Hirtzfelden	58	47.55 N	7.27 E
Hirukawa	94	35.31 N	137.23 E
Hiru-zen ∧	96	35.19 N	133.40 E
Hirwaun	42	51.45 N	3.30 W
Hisābpur	272b	22.51 N	88.32 E
Hisai, Nihon	94	34.40 N	136.28 E
Hisai, Nihon	270	34.25 N	135.28 E
Hisār	123	29.10 N	75.43 E
Hisarönü	130	41.33 N	32.02 E
Ḥisbān	132	31.48 N	35.48 E
Hisiu	164	9.05 S	146.45 E
Hisn al-ʿAbr	144	16.05 N	47.22 E
Ḥiṣn al-Qarn	144	15.11 N	49.05 E
Hispaniola I	238	19.00 N	71.00 W
Hispar Glacier ⊓	123	36.05 N	75.20 E
Histon	42	52.15 N	0.06 E
Hisua	124	24.50 N	85.25 E
Ḥisyah	130	34.24 N	36.45 E
Hīt	128	33.38 N	42.49 E
Hita	96	33.19 N	130.56 E
Hitachi	94	36.36 N	140.39 E
Hitachi-ōta	94	36.32 N	140.31 E
Hitati → Hitachi	94	36.36 N	140.39 E
Hitchcock	222	29.20 N	95.00 W
Hitchin	42	51.57 N	0.17 W
Hitchins	218	38.16 N	82.55 W
Hither Green ◆[8]	260	51.27 N	0.01 W
Hither Hills State Park ♠	207	41.01 N	72.01 W
Hitiaa	174s	17.36 S	149.18 W
Hitokura	270	34.55 N	135.25 E
Hitotsubashi University υ[2]	268	35.42 N	139.27 E
Hitoyoshi	92	32.13 N	130.45 E
Hitra I	26	63.33 N	8.45 E
Hittarp	41	56.06 N	12.38 E
Hittisau	58	47.27 N	9.57 E
Hitzacker	54	53.09 N	11.02 E
Hitze-Berge ∧[2]	264a	52.35 N	13.07 E
Hiu I	175f	13.10 S	166.35 E
Hiuchiga-take ∧	94	36.57 N	139.17 E
Hiuchi-nada ⊤[2]	96	34.05 N	133.20 E
Hiūnchuli Pātan ∧	124	28.50 N	82.37 E
Hiva Oa I	174x	9.45 S	139.00 W
Hi Vista	228	34.44 N	117.47 W
Hiwa	96	34.59 N	132.59 E
Hiwannee	194	31.48 N	88.41 W
Hiwasa	96	33.44 N	134.32 E
Hiwassee ≃	192	35.19 N	84.47 W
Hiwassee Lake ⊜[1]	192	35.10 N	84.05 W
Hixon	182	53.27 N	122.36 W
Hixson	192	35.09 N	85.14 W
Hiyoshi, Nihon	94	35.53 N	137.45 E
Hiyoshi, Nihon	96	33.20 N	132.48 E
Hiyoshi, Nihon	96	35.09 N	135.31 E
Hiyoshi ◆[8]	268	35.33 N	139.39 E
Ḫiyyon, Naḥal V	132	30.12 N	35.07 E
Hizaonna	174m	26.24 N	127.50 E
Hjälmare kanal ≍	40	59.24 N	15.56 E
Hjälmaren ⊜	40	59.15 N	15.45 E
Hjälmaresund ⊔	40	59.15 N	16.06 E
Hjarnø I	41	55.50 N	10.05 E
Hjelm I	41	56.08 N	10.48 E
Hjelmelandsvågen	26	59.14 N	6.11 E
Hjeltefjorden c[2]	26	60.40 N	4.55 E
Hjembæk	41	55.42 N	11.25 E
Hjo	26	58.18 N	14.17 E
Hjøllund	41	56.05 N	9.25 E
Hjordkær	41	55.01 N	9.19 E
Hjørring	26	57.28 N	9.59 E
Hjortkvarn	40	58.53 N	15.25 E
Hjørundfjorden c[2]	26	62.21 N	6.23 E
Hkakabo Razi ∧	102	28.20 N	97.32 E
Hkok (Kok) ≃	110	20.14 N	100.09 E
Hlabisa	158	28.08 S	31.52 E
Hlaingbwe	110	17.08 N	97.50 E
Hlatikulu	158	27.00 S	31.25 E
Hlegu	110	17.06 N	96.14 E
Hlinsko	30	49.45 N	15.55 E
Hlobane	158	27.42 S	31.00 E
Hlohovec	30	48.25 N	17.47 E
Hluboká ⊥	61	49.05 N	14.25 E
Hluboká nad Vltavou	61	49.03 N	14.27 E
Hluboš	60	49.45 N	14.02 E
Hlučín	30	49.54 N	18.12 E
Hluhluwe	158	28.01 S	32.15 E
Hluhluwe Game Reserve ◆[4]	158	28.05 S	32.04 E
Hluti	158	27.13 S	31.35 E
Hmawbi	110	17.06 N	96.02 E
H. Neely Henry Lake ⊜[1]	194	33.55 N	86.05 W
Ho	150	6.35 N	0.30 E
Hoa Binh	110	20.50 N	105.20 E
Hoa Da	110	11.11 N	108.33 E
Hoagland	216	40.56 N	84.59 W
Hoagland Ditch ≍	216	40.48 N	86.48 W
Hoanib ≃	156	19.27 S	12.46 E
Hoare Bay c	176	65.20 N	62.30 W
Hoarusib ≃	156	19.03 S	12.36 E
Hoa Thoi	269c	10.44 N	106.35 E
Hoback ≃	202	43.19 N	110.44 W
Hobart, Austl.	166	42.53 S	147.19 E
Hobart, In., U.S.	216	41.31 N	87.15 W
Hobart, N.Y., U.S.	210	42.22 N	74.40 W
Hobart, Ok., U.S.	196	35.01 N	99.05 W
Hobart, Wa., U.S.	224	47.25 N	121.58 W
Hobbs, In., U.S.	216	40.17 N	85.57 W
Hobbs, N.M., U.S.	196	32.42 N	103.08 W
Hobbs Coast ⏊[2]	9	74.45 S	131.00 W
Hobe Sound	220	27.03 N	80.08 W
Hobgood	192	36.01 N	77.23 W
Hobhole Drain ≍	44	52.59 N	0.02 E
Hobhouse	158	29.31 S	27.08 E
Hobo	246	2.35 N	75.27 W
Hoboken, Bel.	50	51.10 N	4.21 E
Hoboken, N.J., U.S.	210	40.44 N	74.01 W
Hoboksar	86	46.47 N	85.43 E
Hobq Shamo ◆[2]	102	40.30 N	107.55 E
Hobro	26	56.38 N	9.48 E
Hobson	202	47.00 N	109.52 W
Hobson Lake ⊜	182	52.30 N	120.20 W
Hobsons Bay c	274b	37.51 S	144.56 E
Hoburgen ›	26	56.55 N	18.07 E
Hobyo	144	5.21 N	48.32 E
Hocaköy	130	41.03 N	30.17 E
Hocalar	130	38.34 N	30.00 E
Hocalı	130	38.41 N	27.41 E
Hochalmspitze ∧	64	47.01 N	13.19 E
Hochandochtla Mountain ∧	180	65.32 N	154.50 W
Höchberg	56	49.49 N	9.51 E
Hochburg	60	48.07 N	12.52 E
Hochdahl	56	51.13 N	6.56 E
Hochdorf	58	47.10 N	8.17 E
Höchenschwand	58	47.44 N	8.10 E
Hochfeiler (Gran Pilastro) ∧	64	46.58 N	11.44 E
Hochfeld	156	21.28 S	17.58 E
Hochfeld ◆[8]	263	51.25 N	6.46 E
Hochfelden	56	48.45 N	7.34 E
Hochfilzen	64	47.28 N	12.37 E
Hochfinstermünz	58	46.56 N	10.29 E
Hochgern ∧	64	47.45 N	12.30 E
Hochgolling ∧	64	47.16 N	13.45 E
Hochheide ◆[8]	263	51.27 N	6.41 E
Hochheim, Dtsch.	56	50.01 N	8.20 E
Hochheim, Tx., U.S.	222	29.19 N	97.17 W
Hochiss ∧	64	47.27 N	11.46 E
Hochkirch	54	51.09 N	14.34 E
Hochkönig ∧	64	47.25 N	13.04 E
Hochkreuz ∧	64	46.49 N	13.04 E
Hochlantsch ∧	61	47.21 N	15.25 E
Hochlar	263	51.36 N	7.10 E
Hochneukirch	56	51.06 N	6.26 E
Hochobir ∧	61	46.30 N	14.29 E
Hochreichhart ∧	61	47.22 N	14.41 E
Hochries ∧	64	47.45 N	12.14 E
Hochschwab ∧	61	47.37 N	15.09 E
Hochschwab ⋏	61	47.36 N	15.05 E
Hochsimmer ∧	56	50.21 N	7.12 E
Hochspeyer	56	49.26 N	7.54 E
Höchst, Dtsch.	56	49.48 N	8.59 E
Höchst, Öst.	58	47.28 N	9.38 E
Höchst ◆[8]	56	50.07 N	8.33 E
Höchstadt an der Aisch	56	49.42 N	10.44 E
Höchstädt an der Donau	56	48.36 N	10.34 E
Höchsten ◆[8]	263	51.27 N	7.29 E
Höchstenbach	56	50.38 N	7.44 E
Hochstuhl (Veliki Stol) ∧	61	46.26 N	14.10 E
Hochtor)(	64	47.05 N	12.51 E
Hoch'uan → Hechuan	107	30.00 N	106.16 E
Ho Chung	271d	22.22 N	114.14 E
Hochvogel ∧	58	47.23 N	10.26 E
Hochwildstelle ∧	64	47.20 N	13.50 E
Hockenheim	56	49.19 N	8.33 E
Hockeroda	54	50.35 N	11.26 E
Hockessin	285	39.47 N	75.41 W
Hocking ≃	188	39.12 N	81.45 W
Hocking Hills State Park ♠	188	39.30 N	82.32 W
Hockley, Eng., U.K.	42	51.37 N	0.40 E
Hockley, Tx., U.S.	222	30.02 N	95.51 W
Hockomock Swamp ≡	283	41.59 N	71.05 W
Hôḍ ◆[1]	150	16.10 N	8.40 W
Hodal	124	27.54 N	77.22 E
Hōdatsu-zan ∧	94	36.47 N	136.49 E
Hodder ≃	44	53.50 N	2.25 W
Hoddesdon	42	51.46 N	0.01 W
Hoddlesden	262	53.42 N	2.26 W
Hodeida → Al-Ḥudaydah	144	14.48 N	42.57 E
Hodenhagen	52	52.46 N	9.35 E
Hodge	194	32.16 N	92.43 W
Hodgenville	194	37.34 N	85.44 W
Hodges, Lake ⊜[1]	228	33.03 N	117.05 W
Hodges Brook ≃	283	41.58 N	71.14 W
Hodges Hill ∧[2]	186	49.04 N	55.53 W
Hodgeville	184	50.08 N	106.58 W
Hodgkins	278	41.46 N	87.51 W
Hodgson	184	51.13 N	97.34 W
Hodgson ≃	164	14.48 S	134.35 E
Hodgson, Mount ∧[2]	162	22.26 S	121.10 E
Hod HaSharon	132	32.09 N	34.53 E
Hodh ech Chargui □[4]	150	18.10 N	7.15 W
Hodh el Gharbi □[4]	150	16.30 N	10.00 W
Hódmezővásárhely	30	46.25 N	20.20 E
Hodmo V	144	10.41 N	46.13 E
Hodna, Chott el ⊜	148	35.25 N	4.45 E
Hodna, Monts du ⋏	34	35.50 N	4.50 E
Hodna, Plaine du ≚	34	35.38 N	4.30 E
Hodnet	42	52.51 N	2.35 W
Hodogaya ◆[8]	268	35.27 N	139.36 E
Hodogaya Baseball Ground ♠	268	35.27 N	139.35 E
Hodonín	30	48.51 N	17.08 E
Hodoš	61	46.50 N	16.20 E
Hodzana ≃	180	66.15 N	147.48 W
Hoed	41	56.19 N	10.49 E
Hoedekenskerke	52	51.25 N	3.55 E
Hoehne	198	37.16 N	104.22 W
Hoeksche Waard I	52	51.45 N	4.30 E
Hoek van Holland	52	51.59 N	4.09 E
Hoeningen	263	51.05 N	6.41 E
Hoensbroek	56	50.55 N	5.55 E
Hœrdt	58	48.42 N	7.47 E
Hoerstgen	263	51.30 N	6.27 E
Hoeryŏng	98	42.27 N	129.44 E
Hoeyang	98	38.43 N	127.36 E
Hof, Dtsch.	54	50.18 N	11.55 E
Hof, Ísland	24a	64.34 N	14.39 W
Hofburg υ	264b	48.12 N	16.22 E
Höfðakaupstaður	24a	65.50 N	20.19 W
Hofei → Hefei	100	31.51 N	117.17 E
Höfen, Dtsch.	56	50.32 N	6.15 E
Höfen, Dtsch.	60	49.08 N	11.21 E
Hoffman, Il., U.S.	219	38.32 N	89.16 W
Hoffman, Mn., U.S.	198	45.49 N	95.47 W
Hoffman Estates	216	42.02 N	88.04 W
Hoffman Island I	276	40.35 N	74.03 W
Hoffmans	210	42.54 N	74.05 W
Hoffman Station	284a	43.04 N	78.50 W
Hoffnung	263	51.07 N	7.13 E
Hofgeismar	52	51.30 N	9.22 E
Hofheim	56	50.07 N	8.26 E
Hofheim in Unterfranken	56	50.08 N	10.31 E
Hofkirchen an der Trattnach	60	48.13 N	13.44 E
Höflein an der Donau	264b	48.21 N	16.17 E
Hofmeyr	158	31.39 S	25.50 E
Höfn	24a	64.17 N	15.10 W
Hofors	40	60.33 N	16.17 E
Hofsjökull ⊓	24a	64.48 N	18.50 W
Hofstade	50	50.58 N	4.02 E
Hofstede ◆[3]	263	51.30 N	7.12 E
Hofstra University υ[2]	276	40.43 N	73.36 W
Hōfu	96	34.03 N	131.34 E
Hofuf → Al-Hufūf	128	25.22 N	49.34 E
Hofweier	58	48.25 N	7.55 E
Hog, Tanjong ›	116	5.18 N	119.16 E
Hogalbāria	126	23.53 N	88.51 E
Höganäs	41	56.12 N	12.33 E
Hogan Lake ⊜	190	45.52 N	78.30 W
Hogansburg	206	44.58 N	74.39 W
Hogansville	192	33.10 N	84.54 W
Hogatza ≃	180	66.00 N	155.29 W
Hogback Mountain ∧, U.S.	207	42.43 N	72.25 W
Hogback Mountain ∧, Mt., U.S.	202	44.54 N	112.07 W
Hogback Mountain ∧, Ne., U.S.	198	41.40 N	103.44 W
Hogback Mountain ∧, S.C., U.S.	192	35.10 N	82.17 W
Högbo	40	60.40 N	16.48 E
Hog Canyon V	226	35.42 N	120.35 W
Hog Creek ≃	222	31.32 N	97.18 W
Hoge Veluwe, Nationale Park de ♠	52	52.02 N	5.55 E
Högfors	40	59.59 N	15.01 E
Hoggar → Ahaggar ⋏	148	23.00 N	6.30 E
Hoghton	262	53.44 N	2.35 W
Hoghton Tower ⊥	262	53.44 N	2.34 W
Hog Island I, Ma., U.S.	283	42.40 N	70.46 W
Hog Island I, Mi., U.S.	190	45.48 N	85.22 W
Hog Island I, Vt., U.S.	206	44.57 N	73.13 W
Hog Island I, Va., U.S.	208	37.25 N	75.41 W
Hog Island Bay c	208	37.27 N	75.46 W
Hogoro	154	5.57 S	36.27 E
Hog Point ›	208	37.12 N	76.41 W
Hogs Back ⏊[4]	42	51.13 N	0.40 W
Högsby	26	57.10 N	16.02 E
Högsjö	40	59.02 N	15.41 E
Hoh ≃	224	47.45 N	124.29 W
Hoh, South Fork ≃	224	47.46 N	124.01 W
Hohe Acht ∧	56	50.23 N	7.00 E
Hohebach	56	49.22 N	9.44 E
Hohe Eifel ⋏	56	50.15 N	6.45 E
Hohegeiss	54	51.40 N	10.40 E
Hohenau	252	27.05 S	55.45 W
Hohenau an der March	61	48.36 N	16.55 E
Höhenberg	61	48.46 N	14.53 E
Hohenbrunn	60	48.03 N	11.42 E
Hohenbucko	54	51.46 N	13.28 E
Hohenbudberg ◆[8]	263	51.23 N	6.40 E
Hohenburg	60	49.18 N	11.48 E
Hohendorf	54	54.01 N	13.44 E
Hohenebra	54	51.18 N	10.49 E
Hohenems	58	47.22 N	9.41 E
Hohenfels	60	49.12 N	11.51 E
Hohenfurch	58	47.51 N	10.54 E
Hohengüstow	54	53.14 N	13.59 E
Hohenhameln	52	52.15 N	10.03 E
Hohenheide	263	51.29 N	7.47 E
Hohenkammer	60	48.25 N	11.32 E
Hohenkirchen, Dtsch.	52	53.39 N	7.55 E
Hohenkirchen, Dtsch.	54	50.51 N	10.41 E
Hohenkirchen, Dtsch.	54	53.51 N	11.17 E
Hohenkirchen, Dtsch.	56	51.23 N	9.29 E
Hohenleipisch	54	51.30 N	13.34 E
Hohenleuben	54	50.43 N	12.03 E
Hohenlimburg	56	51.21 N	7.35 E
Hohenlimburg, Schloss ⊥	263	51.21 N	7.34 E
Hohenlinden	60	48.09 N	12.00 E
Hohenmölsen	54	51.09 N	12.06 E
Hohen Neuendorf	54	52.40 N	13.16 E
Hohenpolding	60	48.23 N	12.08 E
Hohensalza → Inowrocław	30	52.48 N	18.15 E
Hohenschönhausen ◆[8]	264a	52.33 N	13.30 E
Hohenseeden	54	52.19 N	12.01 E
Hohenseefeld	54	51.53 N	13.18 E
Hohenstaufen	56	48.44 N	9.43 E
Hohenstein-Ernstthal	54	50.48 N	12.42 E
Hohensyburg ⊥	56	51.25 N	7.29 E
Hohentauern	61	47.26 N	14.29 E
Hohenthurm	54	51.31 N	12.05 E
Hohenthurn	64	46.33 N	13.40 E
Hohentwiel ∧	58	47.46 N	8.49 E
Hohenwald	194	35.32 N	87.33 W
Hohenwart	60	48.36 N	11.23 E
Hohenwarte-Stausee ⊜[1]	54	50.32 N	11.30 E
Hohenwarthe	54	52.13 N	11.42 E
Hohenwutzen	54	52.51 N	14.07 E
Hohenzethen	54	53.03 N	10.49 E
Hohenzollern, Burg ⊥	58	48.19 N	8.58 E
Hohenzollernkanal ≍	264a	52.32 N	13.20 E
Hoher Bogen ∧	60	49.15 N	12.55 E
Hoher Dachstein ∧	64	47.28 N	13.35 E
Hoher Freschen ∧	58	47.18 N	9.46 E
Hohe Rhön ⋏	56	50.30 N	10.00 E
Hoher Ifen ∧	58	47.21 N	10.05 E
Hoherlehme	264a	52.19 N	13.37 E
Hoher Mechtin ∧[2]	54	53.03 N	10.55 E
Hoher Riffler ∧	58	47.07 N	10.22 E
Hoher Sonnblick ∧	64	47.03 N	12.57 E
Hoher Zinken ∧	64	47.40 N	13.20 E
Hohe Tauern ⋏	64	47.10 N	12.45 E
Hohe Warte (Monte Coglians) ∧	64	46.37 N	12.53 E
Hoh Head ›	224	47.46 N	124.29 W
Hohhot	102	40.51 N	111.40 E
Höhn	56	50.37 N	8.00 E
Hohndorf	54	50.45 N	12.40 E
Hohne	52	52.35 N	10.22 E
Hohneck, Le ∧	58	48.02 N	7.01 E
Hohnstein	54	50.59 N	14.10 E
Hohoe	150	7.09 N	0.28 E
Hōhoku	96	34.17 N	130.57 E
Ho-Ho-Kus	276	40.59 N	74.06 W
Hohokus Brook ≃	276	40.57 N	74.06 W
Hoholitna ≃	180	61.31 N	157.00 W
Hoh Sai Hu ⊜	120	35.43 N	92.45 E
Höhscheid ◆[8]	263	51.09 N	7.04 E
Hohultslätt	26	56.58 N	15.39 E
Hohwacht	54	54.19 N	10.41 E
Hohwachter Bucht c	54	54.20 N	10.45 E
Hoh Xil Hu ⊜	120	35.35 N	91.06 E
Hoh Xil Shan ⋏	120	35.20 N	90.00 E
Hoi An	110	15.52 N	108.19 E
Hoihow → Haikou	102	20.03 N	110.19 E
Hoima	154	1.26 N	31.21 E
Hoisdorf	52	53.39 N	10.20 E
Hoisington	198	38.31 N	98.46 W
Hoisten	263	51.08 N	6.42 E
Hoi Xuan	110	20.22 N	105.07 E
Hojāi	120	26.00 N	92.51 E
Højby, Dan.	41	55.55 N	11.37 E
Højby, Dan.	41	55.20 N	10.27 E
Höje	40	59.54 N	13.33 E
Højer	26	54.58 N	8.43 E
Højerup	41	55.17 N	12.27 E
Hōjō, Nihon	96	34.54 N	134.56 E
Hōjō, Nihon	96	33.58 N	132.46 E
Hōjō → Kasai, Nihon	96	34.56 N	134.50 E
Hokah	190	43.45 N	91.20 W
Hokang → Hegang	89	47.24 N	130.17 E
Hökåsen	40	59.40 N	16.35 E
Hokendauqua	208	40.39 N	75.29 W
Hökensås ⋏[2]	26	58.11 N	14.08 E
Hokes Bluff	194	33.59 N	85.51 W
Hōki ≃	94	36.47 N	140.08 E
Hokianga Harbour c	172	35.32 S	173.22 E
Hokitika	172	42.43 S	170.58 E
Hokkaidō □[5]	92a	44.00 N	143.00 E
Hokkaidō I	92a	44.00 N	143.00 E
Hokksund	26	59.47 N	9.59 E
Hoko ≃	224	48.17 N	124.22 W
Hōkōji	270	34.52 N	135.07 E
Hököpinge	41	55.30 N	13.00 E
Hokota	94	36.09 N	140.31 E
Hok So Wan	271d	22.13 N	114.14 E
Hokubo	96	34.57 N	133.38 E
Hokudan	96	34.32 N	134.56 E
Hokura ≃	94	37.10 N	138.16 E
Hokuriku-tunnel ◆[5]	94	35.42 N	136.10 E
Hokusei	94	35.09 N	136.31 E
Hola	154	1.29 S	40.02 E
Holalkere	122	14.02 N	76.11 E
Holanda → Netherlands □[1]	30	52.15 N	5.30 E
Holbæk	41	55.43 N	11.43 E
Holbeach	42	52.49 N	0.01 E
Holbeach Marsh ≡	42	52.52 N	0.05 E
Holberg	182	50.39 N	128.00 W
Holborn ◆[8]	260	51.31 N	0.07 W
Holbrook, Austl.	171b	35.44 S	147.19 E
Holbrook, Az., U.S.	200	34.54 N	110.09 W
Holbrook, Il., U.S.	278	41.32 N	87.38 W
Holbrook, Md., U.S.	284b	39.24 N	76.51 W
Holbrook, Ma., U.S.	207	42.09 N	71.00 W
Holbrook, Ne., U.S.	198	40.18 N	100.00 W
Holbrook, N.Y., U.S.	210	40.48 N	73.04 W
Holbrook, Lake ⊜[1]	222	32.42 N	95.33 W
Holbrook Mountain ∧[2]	212	44.25 N	77.51 W
Holckenhavn	41	55.17 N	10.47 E
Holcomb, Il., U.S.	216	42.04 N	89.06 W
Holcomb, N.Y., U.S.	210	42.54 N	77.25 W
Holcomb Creek ≃	228	34.17 N	117.08 W
Holden, Ab., Can.	182	53.14 N	112.14 W
Holden, Ma., U.S.	207	42.21 N	71.51 W
Holden, Mo., U.S.	194	38.42 N	93.59 W
Holden, Ut,. U.S.	200	39.05 N	112.16 W
Holden, W.V., U.S.	188	37.49 N	82.03 W
Holden, Mount ∧[2]	216	41.40 N	87.03 W
Holdenstedt	52	52.55 N	10.31 E
Holden Village	224	48.12 N	120.47 W
Holdenville	196	35.04 N	96.23 W
Holder	220	28.58 N	82.25 W
Holderness ›[1]	44	53.47 N	0.10 W
Holdfast	184	50.58 N	105.25 W
Holdich	254	45.57 S	68.13 W
Holdingford	190	45.43 N	94.28 W
Holdorf	52	52.35 N	8.07 E
Holdrege	198	40.26 N	99.22 W
Holeby	41	54.43 N	11.28 E
Hole in the Mountain Peak ∧	204	40.55 N	115.05 W
Hole Narsipur	122	12.47 N	76.15 E
Holešov	30	49.20 N	17.35 E
Holetown	241g	13.11 N	59.39 W
Holgate, S. Afr.	158	33.59 S	22.21 E
Holgate, Oh., U.S.	216	41.14 N	84.07 W
Holguín	240p	20.53 N	76.15 W
Holguín □[4]	240p	20.55 N	75.50 W
Hol-Hol	144	11.19 N	42.57 E
Holíč	30	48.49 N	17.10 E
Holiday Beach Provincial Park ♠	214	42.02 N	83.05 W
Holiday Hills	216	42.18 N	88.13 W
Holiday Lake Amusement Park ♠	285	40.02 N	74.56 W
Holiday Shores	219	38.55 N	89.56 W
Holitna ≃	180	61.40 N	157.12 W
Höljes	26	60.54 N	12.36 E
Hollabrunn	61	48.34 N	16.05 E
Holladay	200	40.40 N	111.49 W
Holland, Mb., Can.	184	49.36 N	98.53 W
Holland, Mi., U.S.	216	42.47 N	86.06 W
Holland, N.Y., U.S.	210	42.38 N	78.32 W
Holland, Oh., U.S.	216	41.37 N	83.42 W
Holland, Pa., U.S.	285	40.10 N	74.59 W
Holland, Tx., U.S.	222	30.53 N	97.24 W
Holland, Va., U.S.	208	36.41 N	76.47 W
Holland □[9]	52	52.20 N	4.45 E
Holland → Netherlands □[1]	30	52.15 N	5.30 E
Holland ≃	212	44.12 N	79.31 W
Holland, Mount ∧[2]	162	32.12 S	119.44 E
Hollandale	194	33.10 N	90.51 W
Holland Creek ≃	169	36.43 S	146.06 E
Hollande, Étangs de ⊜	261	48.44 N	1.48 E
Holland Fen ≡	44	53.00 N	0.10 W
Hollandia → Jayapura	164	2.32 S	140.42 E
Holland Landing	212	44.06 N	79.29 W
Holland Park	171a	27.31 S	153.03 E
Holland Patent	210	43.14 N	75.15 W
Holland Point ›	208	38.43 N	76.32 W
Holland Pond State Park ♠	207	42.04 N	72.09 W
Hollandsbird Island I	156	24.45 S	14.34 E
Hollandsch Diep ⊔	52	51.42 N	4.30 E
Hollandstoun	46	59.21 N	2.26 W
Holland Straits ⊔	208	38.08 N	76.02 W
Holland Tunnel ◆[5]	276	40.44 N	74.02 W
Hollansburg	218	39.59 N	84.47 W
Holleben	54	51.26 N	11.53 E
Hollenfels, Château ⊥	56	49.43 N	6.03 E
Höllengebirge ⋏	64	47.48 N	13.39 E
Hollenstedt	52	53.22 N	9.43 E
Hollenstein an der Ybbs	61	47.48 N	14.46 E
Höllensteinberg ∧	264b	48.06 N	16.11 E
Höllental V	61	47.45 N	15.47 E
Hollern	52	53.36 N	9.32 E
Holleton	162	31.57 S	119.02 E
Holley	210	43.13 N	78.01 W
Hollfeld	60	49.56 N	11.18 E
Hollick-Kenyon Plateau ⋏[1]	9	79.00 S	97.00 W
Holliday, Mo., U.S.	219	39.29 N	92.07 W
Holliday, Tx., U.S.	196	33.49 N	98.42 W
Holliday Creek ≃	196	33.55 N	98.28 W
Holliday Park ♠	281	42.21 N	83.24 W
Hollidaysburg	214	40.25 N	78.23 W
Hollingbourne	260	51.16 N	0.38 E
Hollingstedt	41	54.27 N	9.19 E
Hollingworth	262	53.28 N	1.59 W
Hollingworth Lake ⊜	262	53.38 N	2.06 W
Hollins, Eng., U.K.	262	53.34 N	2.17 W
Hollins, Va., U.S.	192	37.20 N	79.56 W
Hollins Green	262	53.25 N	2.27 W
Hollinswood	284c	38.55 N	77.13 W
Hollis, N.H., U.S.	207	42.44 N	71.35 W
Hollis, Ok., U.S.	196	34.41 N	99.54 W
Hollis ◆[8]	276	40.43 N	73.46 W
Hollister	226	36.51 N	121.24 W
Hollister, Mount ∧[2]	162	22.08 S	114.01 E
Holliston	207	42.12 N	71.25 W
Hollman, Cape ›	164	4.59 S	150.06 E
Holloman Air Force Base ■	200	32.51 N	106.05 W
Holloway	214	40.10 N	81.08 W
Holloway Terrace	285	39.42 N	75.32 W
Hollow Rock	194	36.02 N	88.16 W
Hollowville	210	42.12 N	73.42 W
Hollsopple	214	40.13 N	78.56 W
Hollum	52	53.26 N	5.37 E
Höllviken c	41	55.26 N	12.54 E
Höllviksnäs	41	55.25 N	12.57 E
Holly, Co., U.S.	198	38.03 N	102.07 W
Holly, Mi., U.S.	216	42.47 N	83.37 W
Holly, Wa., U.S.	224	47.34 N	122.58 W
Holly, Mount ∧[2]	285	40.00 N	74.47 W
Holly Brook	285	39.59 N	74.48 W
Holly Grove	194	34.35 N	91.11 W
Holly Hill, Fl., U.S.	192	29.14 N	81.02 W
Holly Hill, S.C., U.S.	192	33.19 N	80.24 W
Holly Park, N.J., U.S.	208	39.53 N	74.10 W
Holly Park, Va., U.S.	284c	38.50 N	77.17 W
Holly Pond ⊜	276	41.03 N	73.30 W
Holly River State Park ♠	188	38.40 N	80.21 W
Holly Run ≃	285	39.47 N	75.03 W
Holly Springs	194	34.46 N	89.26 W
Holly State Recreation Area ♠	216	42.49 N	83.32 W
Hollywood, Ire.	48	53.06 N	6.35 W
Hollywood, Fl., U.S.	220	26.00 N	80.08 W
Hollywood, Md., U.S.	208	38.20 N	76.34 W
Hollywood, Pa., U.S.	285	40.05 N	75.06 W
Hollywood ◆[8]	228	34.06 N	118.21 W
Hollywood, Mount ∧	280	34.08 N	118.18 W
Hollywood Bowl ♠	280	34.07 N	118.20 W
Hollywood-Burbank Airport ⊠	228	34.12 N	118.21 W
Hollywood Heights	219	38.39 N	89.59 W
Hollywood Indian Reservation ◆[4]	220	26.02 N	80.13 W
Hollywood Park Race Track ♠	280	33.57 N	118.20 W
Hollywood Reservoir ⊜[1]	280	34.07 N	118.20 W
Holman	176	70.43 N	117.43 W
Hólmavík	24a	65.43 N	21.43 W
Holmdel	208	40.20 N	74.11 W
Holme, Dan.	41	56.07 N	10.11 E
Holme, Eng., U.K.	262	53.33 N	1.50 W
Holme ≃	44	53.41 N	1.43 W
Holme Chapel	262	53.45 N	2.11 W
Holmen, Nor.	26	60.40 N	10.22 E
Holmen, Wi., U.S.	190	43.57 N	91.15 W
Holme-on-Spaulding-Moor	44	53.50 N	0.46 W
Holmes, N.Y., U.S.	210	41.31 N	73.39 W
Holmes, Pa., U.S.	285	39.54 N	75.19 W
Holmes □[6]	214	40.33 N	81.55 W
Holmes, Mount ∧	202	44.49 N	110.51 W
Holmes Beach	220	27.31 N	82.43 W
Holmesburg ◆[8]	285	40.02 N	75.03 W
Holmes Chapel	44	53.12 N	2.22 W
Holmes Creek ≃	194	30.30 N	85.47 W
Holmesglen	274b	37.53 S	145.06 E
Holmes Harbor c	224	48.04 N	122.32 W
Holmes Lake ⊜	184	57.05 N	96.45 W
Holmes Reef ✢[2]	164	16.27 S	148.00 E
Holmes Run ≃	284c	38.48 N	77.07 W
Holmes Run Acres	284c	38.51 N	77.13 W
Holmestrand	26	59.29 N	10.18 E
Holmesville, N.Y., U.S.	210	42.31 N	75.24 W
Holmesville, Oh., U.S.	214	40.37 N	81.55 W
Holmeswood	262	53.39 N	2.52 W
Holmfirth	44	53.35 N	1.46 W
Holmia	246	4.58 N	59.35 W
Holmön I	26	63.47 N	20.53 E
Holmsbu	26	59.33 N	10.27 E
Holmsjön ⊜, Sve.	26	62.41 N	16.33 E
Holmsjön ⊜, Sve.	26	62.25 N	15.20 E
Holmsund	26	63.42 N	20.21 E
Hölö	40	59.01 N	17.35 E
Holod	38	46.47 N	22.08 E
Holoit, Punta ›	232	21.37 N	88.08 W
Ḥolon	132	32.01 N	34.46 E
Holoog	156	27.22 S	17.55 E
Holopaw	220	28.08 N	81.04 W
Holroyd	274a	33.50 S	150.58 E
Holroyd ≃	164	14.10 S	141.36 E
Holsloot	52	52.44 N	6.48 E
Holstebro	26	56.21 N	8.38 E
Holsted	41	55.30 N	8.55 E
Holstein	198	42.29 N	95.32 W
Holsteinborg ⊥	41	55.13 N	11.28 E
Holsteinische Schweiz ◆[1]	54	54.11 N	10.36 E
Holsteinsborg (Sisimiut)	176	66.55 N	53.40 W
Holsterhausen	263	51.41 N	6.57 E
Holston ≃	192	35.57 N	83.51 W
Holston, North Fork ≃	192	36.33 N	82.36 W
Holston High Knob ∧	192	36.27 N	82.05 W
Holsworthy	42	50.49 N	4.21 W
Holt, Eng., U.K.	42	52.55 N	1.05 E
Holt, Wales, U.K.	44	53.05 N	2.53 W
Holt, Al., U.S.	194	33.14 N	87.29 W
Holt, Ca., U.S.	226	37.56 N	121.26 W
Holt, Fl., U.S.	194	30.42 N	86.44 W
Holt, Mi., U.S.	216	42.38 N	84.30 W
Holt Creek ≃	198	42.28 N	98.50 W
Holte	41	55.49 N	12.28 E
Holtemme ≃	54	51.57 N	11.10 E
Holten	52	52.17 N	6.25 E
Holten ◆[8]	263	51.31 N	6.48 E
Holtenau ◆[8]	54	54.22 N	10.08 E
Holter Lake ⊜[1]	202	46.55 N	111.57 W
Holthausen, Dtsch.	52	52.33 N	7.17 E
Holthausen, Dtsch.	263	51.12 N	7.01 E
Holthausen, Dtsch.	263	51.23 N	7.13 E
Holthausen ◆[8]	263	51.34 N	7.26 E
Holthusen	52	53.08 N	7.18 E
Holton, In., U.S.	218	39.04 N	85.23 W
Holton, Ks., U.S.	198	39.27 N	95.44 W
Holtorf	52	52.40 N	9.13 E
Holts Summit	219	38.39 N	92.07 W
Holtsville	210	40.49 N	73.02 W
Holtug	41	55.21 N	12.25 E
Holtville	204	32.48 N	115.22 W
Holtwick	52	52.00 N	7.05 E
Holtwood	208	39.50 N	76.19 W
Holwerd	52	53.22 N	5.54 E
Holycross, Ire.	48	52.38 N	7.52 W
Holy Cross, Ak., U.S.	180	62.12 N	159.47 W
Holy Cross Mountain ∧	182	53.47 N	120.47 W
Holyhead	44	53.19 N	4.38 W
Holyhead Bay c	44	53.23 N	4.37 W
Holy Island I, Eng., U.K.	44	55.41 N	1.48 W
Holy Island I, Scot., U.K.	46	55.32 N	5.04 W
Holy Island I, Wales, U.K.	44	53.18 N	4.37 W
Holy Island I, Ma., U.S.	283	42.43 N	70.50 W
Holyoke, Co., U.S.	198	40.35 N	102.18 W
Holyoke, Ma., U.S.	207	42.12 N	72.37 W
Holyrood	198	38.35 N	98.24 W
Holyrood Palace υ	46	55.56 N	3.12 W
Holýšov	60	49.36 N	13.05 E
Holywell	44	53.17 N	3.13 W
Holywell Green	262	53.41 N	1.52 W
Holywood	48	54.38 N	5.50 W
Holzbüttgen	263	51.12 N	6.37 E
Holzen	56	51.26 N	7.31 E
Holzgau	58	47.16 N	10.21 E
Holzgerlingen	56	48.38 N	9.00 E
Holzhausen, Dtsch.	52	52.17 N	8.32 E
Holzhausen, Dtsch.	52	52.13 N	8.01 E
Holzhausen, Dtsch.	52	52.01 N	8.44 E
Holzhausen, Dtsch.	54	51.18 N	12.28 E
Holzhausen an der Haide	56	50.13 N	7.55 E
Holzheim	56	51.09 N	6.39 E
Holzkirchen	64	47.52 N	11.42 E
Holzminden	52	51.50 N	9.27 E
Holzweissig	54	51.36 N	12.18 E
Holzwickede	52	51.30 N	7.36 E
Hom ≃	158	28.51 S	18.37 E
Homa Bay	154	0.31 S	34.27 E
Homalin	110	24.52 N	94.55 E
Homathko ≃	182	50.55 N	124.50 W
Homathko Icefield ⊓	182	51.05 N	124.30 W
Homberg, Dtsch.	56	50.43 N	8.59 E
Homberg, Dtsch.	56	51.02 N	9.24 E
Homberg, Dtsch.	56	51.28 N	6.43 E
Homberg, Dtsch.	263	51.18 N	6.56 E
Hombori	150	15.17 N	1.42 W
Hombori Tondo ∧	150	15.16 N	1.40 W
Hombourg-Haut	56	49.08 N	6.46 E
Hombre Muerto, Salar del ≚	252	25.23 S	67.06 W
Hombruch ◆[8]	263	51.29 N	7.26 E
Homburg, Dtsch.	56	49.19 N	7.20 E
Homburg → Bad Homburg vor der Höhe, Dtsch.	56	50.13 N	8.37 E
Home, Pa., U.S.	214	40.44 N	79.06 W
Home, Wa., U.S.	224	47.17 N	122.46 W
Homeacre	214	40.51 N	79.55 W
Home Bay c, N.T., Can.	176	68.45 N	67.10 W
Home Bay c, Kiribati	174d	0.53 S	169.35 E
Homebush Bay c	274a	33.50 S	151.05 E
Home Corner	216	40.31 N	85.38 W
Homécourt	56	49.14 N	5.59 E
Home Creek ≃	196	31.29 N	99.14 W
Homedale, Id., U.S.	202	43.37 N	116.55 W
Homedale, Oh., U.S.	214	40.04 N	83.02 W
Home Gardens	228	33.52 N	117.31 W
Home Hill	166	19.40 S	147.25 E
Homeland, Ca., U.S.	228	33.44 N	117.07 W
Homeland, Fl., U.S.	220	27.49 N	81.49 W
Homeland Canal ≍	226	35.57 N	119.27 W
Homeland Park	192	34.27 N	82.41 W
Home Place	218	39.56 N	86.08 W
Homer, Ak., U.S.	180	59.39 N	151.33 W
Homer, Ga., U.S.	192	34.20 N	83.29 W
Homer, La., U.S.	194	32.47 N	93.03 W
Homer, Mi., U.S.	216	42.08 N	84.48 W
Homer, Ne., U.S.	198	42.19 N	96.29 W
Homer, N.Y., U.S.	210	42.38 N	76.10 W
Homer, Oh., U.S.	214	40.15 N	82.31 W
Homer, Tx., U.S.	222	31.18 N	94.36 W
Homer City	214	40.32 N	79.09 W
Homert ∧[2]	263	51.11 N	7.39 E
Homer Tunnel ◆[5]	172	44.45 S	168.00 E
Homerville, Ga., U.S.	192	31.02 N	82.44 W
Homerville, Oh., U.S.	214	41.02 N	82.08 W
Homer Wash V	204	34.20 N	115.02 W
Homer Youngs Peak ∧	202	45.19 N	113.41 W
Home Seamount ✢[3]	14	12.55 S	175.37 W
Homestead, Austl.	166	20.22 S	145.39 E
Homestead, Fl., U.S.	220	25.28 N	80.28 W
Homestead, Pa., U.S.	279b	40.24 N	79.54 W
Homestead Air Force Base ■	220	25.29 N	80.23 W
Homestead National Monument of America ♠	198	40.14 N	96.54 W
Homestead Valley	282	37.54 N	122.32 W
Hometown, Il., U.S.	278	41.44 N	87.43 W
Hometown, Pa., U.S.	210	40.49 N	75.59 W
Homewood, Al., U.S.	194	33.28 N	86.48 W
Homewood, Ca., U.S.	226	39.05 N	120.09 W
Homewood, Il., U.S.	216	41.33 N	87.39 W
Homewood, Oh., U.S.	218	39.23 N	84.33 W
Homewood ◆[8]	279b	40.27 N	79.54 W
Homewood Acres	278	41.34 N	87.43 W
Homeworth	214	40.50 N	81.03 W
Hominy	196	36.24 N	96.23 W
Hominy Creek ≃	196	36.20 N	96.00 W
Hommersåk	26	58.58 N	5.42 E
Hommura	92	34.22 N	139.15 E
Homnābād	122	17.46 N	77.08 E
Homochitto ≃	194	31.09 N	91.31 W
Homoine	156	23.52 S	35.09 E
Homonhon Island I	116	10.44 N	125.43 E
Homosassa	220	28.46 N	82.36 W
Homosassa Bay c	220	28.45 N	82.43 W
Homosassa Springs	220	28.48 N	82.35 W
Homs → Al-Khums, Lībiyā	146	32.39 N	14.16 E
Homs → Ḥimṣ, Sūrīy.	130	34.44 N	36.43 E
Honai	96	33.30 N	132.25 E
Honaker	192	37.00 N	81.58 W
Honami	96	33.36 N	130.42 E
Honan → Luoyang	102	34.41 N	112.28 E
Honan → Henan □[4]	90	34.00 N	114.00 E
Honāvar	122	14.17 N	74.27 E
Honaz	130	37.45 N	29.17 E
Honbetsu	92a	43.07 N	143.37 E
Hon Chong	110	10.10 N	104.37 E
Honda	246	5.12 N	74.45 W
Honda, Bahía c, Col.	246	12.21 N	71.47 W
Honda, Bahía c, Cuba	240p	22.57 N	83.10 W
Honda, Cañada ≃	258	33.57 S	59.21 W
Honda Bay c	116	9.53 N	118.49 E
Honddu ≃, U.K.	42	51.54 N	2.58 W
Honddu ≃, Wales, U.K.	42	51.57 N	3.23 W
Hondeklipbaai	156	30.20 S	17.18 E
Honderfontein	158	32.12 S	21.22 E
Hon Dien, Nui ∧	110	11.33 N	108.38 E
Hondo, Ab., Can.	182	55.04 N	114.02 W
Hondo, Nihon	92	32.27 N	130.12 E
Hondo, N.M., U.S.	200	33.23 N	105.16 W
Hondo, Tx., U.S.	196	29.20 N	99.08 W
Hondo ≃, Méx.	286a	19.26 N	99.15 W
Hondo ≃, N.A.	232	18.29 N	88.19 W
Hondo, Arroyo ≃	226	37.28 N	121.47 W
Hondo, Rio ≃, Ca., U.S.	280	33.55 N	118.10 W

≃	River	Fluß	Río	Rivière	Rio
≍	Canal	Kanal	Canal	Canal	Canal
∟	Waterfall, Rapids	Wasserfall, Stromschnellen	Cascada, Rápidos	Chute d'eau, Rapides	Cascata, Rápidos
⊔	Strait	Meeresstraße	Estrecho	Détroit	Estreito
c	Bay, Gulf	Bucht, Golf	Bahía, Golfo	Baie, Golfe	Baía, Golfo
⊜	Lake, Lakes	See, Seen	Lago, Lagos	Lac, Lacs	Lago, Lagos
≡	Swamp	Sumpf	Pantano	Marais	Pântano
⊓	Ice Features, Glacier	Eis- und Gletscherformen	Accidentes Glaciales	Formes glaciaires	Acidentes glaciares
⊤	Other Hydrographic Features	Andere Hydrographische Objekte	Otros Elementos Hidrográficos	Autres données hydrographiques	Outros acidentes hidrográficos
✢	Submarine Features	Untermeerische Objekte	Accidentes Submarinos	Formes de relief sous-marin	Acidentes submarinos
□	Political Unit	Politische Einheit	Unidad Politica	Entité politique	Unidade política
υ	Cultural Institution	Kulturelle Institution	Institución Cultural	Institution culturelle	Institução cultural
⊥	Historical Site	Historische Stätte	Sitio Histórico	Site historique	Sitio histórico
♠	Recreational Site	Erholungs- und Ferienort	Sitio de Recreo	Centre de loisirs	Area de Lazer
⊠	Airport	Flughafen	Aeropuerto	Aéroport	Aeroporto
■	Military Installation	Militäranlage	Instalación Militar	Installation militaire	Instalação militar
◆	Miscellaneous	Verschiedenes	Misceláneo	Divers	Diversos

Symbols in the index entries represent the broad categories identified in the key at the right. Symbols with superior numbers (⋀¹) identify subcategories (see complete key on page I · 1).

Symbole im Register stellen die rechts im Schlüssel erklärten Kategorien dar. Symbole mit hochgestellten Ziffern (⋀¹) bezeichnen Unterabteilungen einer Kategorie (vgl. vollständiger Schlüssel auf Seite I · 1).

Los símbolos incluídos en el texto del índice representan las grandes categorías identificadas con la clave a la derecha. Los símbolos con números en su parte superior (⋀¹) identifican las subcategorías (véase la clave completa en la página I · 1).

Les symboles de l'index représentent les catégories indiquées dans la légende à droite. Les symboles suivis d'un indice (⋀¹) représentent des sous-catégories (voir légende complète à la page I · 1).

Os símbolos incluídos no texto do índice representam as grandes categorias identificadas com a chave à direita. Os símbolos com números em sua parte superior (⋀¹) identificam as subcategorias (veja-se a chave completa à página I · 1).

⋀ Mountain	Berg	Montaña	Montagne	Montanha
⋀ Mountains	Gebirge	Montañas	Montagnes	Montanhas
⋎ Pass	Paß	Paso	Col	Passo
⌄ Valley, Canyon	Tal, Cañon	Valle, Cañón	Vallée, Canyon	Vale, Canhão
⋀¹ Plain	Ebene	Llano	Plaine	Planície
› Cape	Kap	Cabo	Cap	Cabo
I Island	Insel	Isla	Île	Ilha
II Islands	Inseln	Islas	Îles	Ilhas
≃ Other Topographic Features	Andere Topographische Objekte	Otros Elementos Topográficos	Autres données topographiques	Outros acidentes topográficos

---

Huisne ⇇	50	47.59 N	0.11 E	Humenné	30	48.56 N	21.55 E	Huntington, N.Y., U.S.	210	40.51 N	73.25 W

I · 76 **Hurs-Ilka**

Hurstville 170 33.58 S 151.06 E
Hurstwood Reservoir ⊜[1] 262 53.47 N 2.10 W
Hurt 192 37.05 N 79.17 W
Hurtado ≃ 252 30.35 S 71.11 W
Hurtaut ≃ 50 49.42 N 4.01 E
Hürth 56 50.52 N 6.51 E
Hurtsboro 194 32.14 N 85.24 W
Hurunui ≃ 172 42.55 S 173.17 E
Hurup 26 56.45 N 8.25 E
Hurworth-on-Tees 44 54.29 N 1.31 W
Husainābād 124 24.32 N 84.01 E
Husainīwāla 123 30.59 N 74.34 E
Husainpur 124 24.25 N 90.40 E
Húsavík 24a 66.04 N 17.18 W
Husby-Långhundra 40 59.45 N 18.01 E
Huse
→ Higashiōsaka 96 34.39 N 135.35 E
Husen ◆[8] 263 51.33 N 7.36 E
Hushan, Zhg. 89 45.35 N 130.35 E
Hushan, Zhg. 100 28.36 N 118.59 E
Hushan, Zhg. 100 22.09 N 113.10 E
Husheib 140 14.54 N 35.07 E
Hushi 107 28.57 N 105.22 E
Hushiha 98 40.52 N 116.59 E
Hushitai 104 41.57 N 123.30 E
Hushu, Zhg. 106 31.52 N 118.59 E
Hushu, Zhg. 106 30.18 N 120.08 E
Huși 38 46.40 N 28.04 E
Husinec 60 49.03 N 13.58 E
Huskisson 170 35.02 S 150.40 E
Huskvarna 26 57.48 N 14.16 E
Huslia 180 65.42 N 156.25 W
Hussar 182 51.03 N 112.41 W
Hussigny-Godbrange 56 49.29 N 5.52 E
Hustisford 190 43.21 N 88.36 W
Huston ≃ 220 25.42 N 81.17 W
Hustontown 214 40.03 N 78.02 W
Hustopeče 61 48.57 N 16.44 E
Husum, Dtsch. 41 54.28 N 9.03 E
Husum, Sve. 26 63.20 N 19.10 E
Husum, Wa., U.S. 224 45.47 N 121.29 W
Hutaimbaru 114 1.34 N 99.44 E
Hutangqiao 106 31.46 N 119.57 E
Hutan Melintang 114 3.53 N 100.56 E
Hutanopan 114 0.41 N 99.42 E
Hutaym, Harrat ⊥[9] 128 26.15 N 40.20 E
Hutberg ∧[2] 54 52.09 N 14.33 E
Hutchins 222 32.39 N 96.43 W
Hutchinson, S. Afr. 158 31.30 S 23.09 E
Hutchinson, Ks., U.S. 198 38.03 N 97.55 W
Hutchinson, Mn., U.S. 190 44.53 N 94.22 W
Hutchinson, Pa., U.S. 214 40.13 N 79.44 W
Hutchinson ≃ 276 40.52 N 73.50 W
Hutchinson Island I 220 27.25 N 80.17 W
Hutch Mountain ∧ 200 34.47 N 111.22 W
Hutou, Zhg. 100 25.15 N 118.03 E
Hutou, Zhg. 100 26.04 N 118.46 E
Hutou, Zhg. 106 31.37 N 119.37 E
Hutou, Zhg. 106 32.14 N 120.17 E
Hutouya 98 37.13 N 119.46 E
Hutsonville 194 39.06 N 87.39 W
Hüttau 64 47.25 N 13.18 E
Hütteldorf ◆[8] 264b 48.12 N 16.16 E
Hüttener Berge ⋏[2] 41 54.26 N 9.40 E
Hüttenheim ◆[8] 263 51.22 N 6.43 E
Hüttental 56 50.54 N 8.02 E
Hutte Sauvage, Lac de la ⊜ 176 56.15 N 64.45 W
Huttig 194 33.02 N 92.10 W
Hütting 60 48.48 N 11.07 E
Hutto 222 30.33 N 97.33 W
Hutton, Eng., U.K. 260 51.38 N 0.22 E
Hutton, Eng., U.K. 262 53.44 N 2.46 W
Hutton, Mount ∧ 166 25.51 S 148.20 E
Hutton Rudby 44 54.27 N 1.17 W
Huttonsville 212 43.38 N 79.48 W
Huttrop ◆[8] 263 51.27 N 7.03 E
Hüttschlag 64 47.10 N 13.14 E
Huttwil 58 47.07 N 7.51 E
Hutubi 86 44.07 N 86.57 E
Hutuo ≃ 98 38.14 N 116.05 E
Hutwisch ∧ 61 47.28 N 16.13 E
Huu 115b 8.48 S 118.25 E
Huvalu Forest ◆[3] 174v 19.03 S 169.51 W
Huveaune ≃ 62 43.15 N 5.23 E
Huvudskär I 40 58.57 N 18.34 E
Huwan 100 31.41 N 114.53 E
Huwei 100 23.43 N 120.26 E
Huwun 144 4.23 N 40.08 E
Ḥuwwārah 132 32.09 N 35.15 E
Huxford 194 31.13 N 87.28 W
Huxi 100 26.12 N 114.44 E
Huxian 102 34.09 N 108.32 E
Huxley 182 51.56 N 113.14 W
Huy 56 50.31 N 5.14 E
Huy ∧ 54 51.57 N 10.57 E
Huyangzhen 100 32.25 N 112.45 E
Huyton-with-Roby 262 53.25 N 2.52 W
Huyuesi 106 30.23 N 118.45 E
Hüyük 130 37.57 N 31.37 E
Huyutou 100 26.44 N 119.49 E
Hūzgān 128 31.27 N 48.04 E
Huzhen 100 28.50 N 120.15 E
Huzhou 106 30.52 N 120.06 E
Huzhu 102 37.00 N 102.00 E
Huzhuangtun 104 40.43 N 122.33 E
Huzi 100 30.56 N 113.42 E
Huzisawa
→ Fujisawa 94 35.21 N 139.29 E
Hvalsø 41 55.36 N 11.50 E
Hvannadalshnúkur ∧ 24a 64.01 N 16.41 W
Hvar 36 43.10 N 16.27 E
Hvar, Otok I 36 43.09 N 16.45 E
Hvarski Kanal ʊ 36 43.15 N 16.37 E
Hveragerði 24a 64.03 N 21.10 W
Hvide Sande 26 55.59 N 8.08 E
Hvidovre 41 55.39 N 12.29 E
Hvittingfoss 26 59.29 N 10.01 E
Hvolsvöllur 24a 63.45 N 20.10 W
Hwach'ŏn 98 38.06 N 127.41 E
Hwach'ŏn-chŏsuji ⊜[1] 98 38.07 N 127.52 E
Hwach'ŏn-ni 98 39.01 N 126.02 E
Hwainan
→ Huainan 100 32.40 N 117.00 E
Hwaining
→ Anqing 100 30.31 N 117.02 E
Hwange 154 18.22 S 26.29 E
Hwange National Park ♦ 154 19.00 S 26.35 E
Hwanggong-ni 98 40.03 N 129.27 E
Hwanghae Namdo □[4] 98 38.15 N 125.30 E
Hwanghae Pukdo □[4] 98 38.30 N 126.25 E
Hwang Ho
→ Huang ≃ 90 37.32 N 118.19 E
Hwangju 98 38.42 N 125.46 E
Hwangshih
→ Huangshi 100 30.13 N 115.05 E
Hyak 224 47.23 N 121.23 W
Hyakuna 174m 26.08 N 127.48 E
Hyakuri-ga-dake ∧ 94 35.23 N 135.49 E
Hyakuri-kichi, Kōkū-jieitai- ■ 94 36.11 N 140.25 E
Hyannis, Ma., U.S. 207 41.39 N 70.17 W
Hyannis, Ne., U.S. 198 42.00 N 101.45 W
Hyannis Port 207 41.38 N 70.18 W
Hyattsville 208 38.57 N 76.56 W
Hyattville 202 44.14 N 107.36 W
Hybla Valley 208 38.44 N 77.05 W
Hyco ≃ 192 36.40 N 78.45 W
Hyco Lake ⊜[1] 192 36.30 N 79.05 W
Hydaburg 182 55.12 N 132.49 W
Hyde, N.Z. 172 45.18 S 170.15 E
Hyde, Eng., U.K. 44 53.27 N 2.04 W
Hyde, Pa., U.S. 214 41.00 N 78.28 W
Hyden, Austl. 162 32.27 S 118.53 E
Hyden, Ky., U.S. 192 37.10 N 83.22 W
Hyde Park, Guy. 246 6.30 N 58.16 W
Hyde Park, N.Y., U.S. 210 41.47 N 73.56 W
Hyde Park, Vt., U.S. 188 44.35 N 72.37 W
Hyde Park ◆[8], Il., U.S. 278 41.48 N 87.36 W
Hyde Park ◆[8], Ma., U.S. 283 42.15 N 71.08 W
Hyde Park ♦, Austl. 274a 33.53 S 151.13 E
Hyde Park ♦, Eng., U.K. 260 51.30 N 0.10 W
Hyde Park ♦, N.Y., U.S. 284a 43.06 N 79.01 W
Hyder 182 55.55 N 130.01 W
Hyderābād, India 122 17.23 N 78.29 E
Hyderābād, Pāk. 120 25.22 N 68.22 E
Hydetown 214 41.40 N 79.44 W
Hydra
→ Ídhra I 38 37.20 N 23.32 E
Hydraulic 182 52.36 N 121.42 W
Hydro 196 35.21 N 98.22 W
Hydrographers Passage ʊ 166 20.45 S 150.15 E
Hyen ⊜ 40 60.36 N 16.12 E
Hyères 62 43.07 N 6.07 E
Hyères, Îles d' II 62 43.00 N 6.20 E
Hyères-Plage 62 43.06 N 6.10 E
Hyesan 98 41.23 N 128.12 E
Hyland ≃ 180 59.50 N 128.10 W
Hylestad 26 59.05 N 7.32 E
Hyllekrog I 41 54.36 N 11.30 E
Hyllinge, Dan. 41 55.16 N 11.37 E
Hyllinge, Sve. 41 56.06 N 12.51 E
Hyllstofta 41 56.08 N 13.16 E
Hyltebruk 26 57.00 N 13.14 E
Hymaya ≃ 232 24.31 N 107.41 W
Hymera 194 39.11 N 87.18 W
Hyndburn □[8] 262 53.45 N 2.23 W
Hyndman 188 39.49 N 78.43 W
Hyndman Peak ∧ 202 43.45 N 114.08 W
Hynish Bay c 46 56.28 N 6.50 W
Hyōgo □[5] 96 35.00 N 135.00 E
Hyōgo ◆[8] 270 34.39 N 135.10 E
Hyŏn-ni 98 37.57 N 128.20 E
Hyōno-sen ∧ 96 35.21 N 134.31 E
Hyōnosen-Ushiroyama-Nagisan-kokutei-kōen ♦ 96 35.15 N 134.30 E
Hyŏpch'ŏn 98 35.35 N 128.08 E
Hyrum 200 41.38 N 111.51 W
Hyrynsalmi 26 64.40 N 28.32 E
Hysham 202 46.17 N 107.14 W
Hythe, Ab., Can. 182 55.20 N 119.33 W
Hythe, Eng., U.K. 42 51.05 N 1.05 E
Hythe, Eng., U.K. 42 50.51 N 1.24 W
Hythe End 260 51.27 N 0.32 W
Hyūga 92 32.25 N 131.38 E
Hyūga-nada ⊤[2] 92 32.00 N 131.35 E
Hyvinge
→ Hyvinkää 26 60.38 N 24.52 E
Hyvinkää 26 60.38 N 24.52 E

I

Iacanga 255 21.54 S 49.01 W
Iaciara 255 14.09 S 46.40 W
Iaco (Yaco) ≃ 248 9.03 S 68.34 W
Iaçu 255 12.45 S 40.13 W
Iaeger 192 37.27 N 81.48 W
Iago 222 29.17 N 95.58 W
Iakora 157b 23.06 S 46.40 E
Ialomița □[6] 38 44.40 N 27.20 E
Ialomița ≃ 38 44.42 N 27.51 E
Ialomiței, Balta ≡ 38 44.30 N 28.00 E
Iamonia, Lake ⊜ 192 30.38 N 84.14 W
Ianaivo ≃ 157b 22.56 S 46.54 E
Ianakafy 157b 23.21 S 45.28 E
Ianga 146 9.07 N 18.11 E
Iango 152 9.11 S 17.39 E
Iano, Monte ∧ 267a 41.46 N 12.44 E
Iapó ≃ 252 24.30 S 50.24 W
Iapu 255 19.26 S 42.13 W
Iași 38 47.10 N 27.35 E
Iași □[6] 38 47.15 N 27.15 E
Iato 70 37.58 N 13.07 E
Iato ≃ 70 38.04 N 13.02 E
Iatt, Lake ⊜[1] 194 31.35 N 92.40 W
Iauaretê 246 0.36 N 69.12 W
Iazu 38 44.44 N 27.25 E
Ib ≃ 120 21.34 N 83.48 E
Iba, Pil. 116 15.20 N 119.58 E
Iba, Zaïre 152 3.05 S 17.38 E
'Ibādah, Wādī V 142 27.49 N 30.54 E
Ibadan 150 7.17 N 3.30 E
Ibagué 246 4.27 N 75.14 W
Ibaiti 255 23.50 S 50.10 W
Ibajay 116 11.49 N 122.10 E
Ibajay ≃ 116 11.49 N 122.10 E
Ibaka 152 4.16 S 23.12 E
Ibambi 154 2.22 N 27.37 E
Ibanda 154 0.08 S 30.29 E
Ibănești 38 48.04 N 26.22 E
Ibans, Laguna de c 236 15.53 N 84.52 W
Ibanshe 152 4.58 S 21.30 E
Ibapah Peak ∧ 200 39.50 N 113.55 W
Ibar ≃ 38 43.44 N 20.45 E
Ibara 96 34.36 N 133.28 E
Ibaraki, Nihon 94 36.17 N 140.26 E
Ibaraki, Nihon 96 34.49 N 135.34 E
Ibaraki □[5] 94 36.30 N 140.30 E
Ibarra 246 0.21 N 78.07 W
Ibarreta 252 25.13 S 59.51 W
Ibb 144 14.01 N 44.10 E
Ibba 154 4.48 N 29.06 E
Ibba ≃ 140 7.09 N 28.41 E
Ibbenbüren 52 52.16 N 7.43 E
Ibeke Gembo 152 1.24 S 18.51 E
Ibembo 152 2.38 N 23.37 E
Ibenga ≃ 152 2.20 N 18.08 E
Iberá, Esteros del ≡ 252 28.05 S 57.05 W
Iberia, Mo., U.S. 194 38.05 N 92.17 W
Iberia, Oh., U.S. 214 40.40 N 82.51 W
Ibérica, Península >[1] 10 40.00 N 5.00 W
Ibérico, Sistema ⋏ 34 41.00 N 2.30 W
Ibertioga 256 21.25 S 43.58 W
Iberville 206 45.18 N 73.14 W
Iberville □[6] 206 45.15 N 73.10 W
Iberville, Mont d' (Mount Caubvick) ∧ 176 58.53 N 63.43 W
Ibese 273a 6.33 N 3.29 E
Ibeto 150 10.29 N 5.09 E
Ibi 150 8.12 N 9.45 E
Ibi ≃ 94 35.03 N 136.42 E
Ibiá 255 19.29 S 46.32 W
Ibiapina 250 3.55 S 40.54 W
Ibicaraí 255 14.51 S 39.36 W
Ibicuí 255 14.51 S 39.59 W
Ibicuí ≃ 252 29.25 S 56.47 W
Ibicuicito, Arroyo ≃ 258 33.49 S 58.49 W
Ibicuy 258 33.44 S 59.10 W
Ibicuy ≃[1] 258 33.48 S 59.10 W
Ibigawa 94 35.29 N 136.34 E
Ibipira 250 6.31 S 44.38 W
Ibiquera 255 12.38 S 40.57 W
Ibiraci 255 20.28 S 47.08 W
Ibiraçu 255 19.50 S 40.22 W
Ibirama 252 27.04 S 49.31 W
Ibirapuã 255 17.39 S 40.07 W
Ibirapuera ◆[8] 287b 23.37 S 46.40 W
Ibirapuera, Parque ♦ 287b 23.35 S 46.39 W
Ibirapuitã ≃ 252 29.22 S 55.57 W
Ibirataia 255 14.04 S 39.38 W
Ibiri 154 4.56 S 32.33 E
Ibirubá 252 28.38 S 53.06 W
Ibitiara 255 12.39 S 42.13 W
Ibitinga 255 21.45 S 48.49 W
Ibitiúra De Minas 256 22.04 S 46.26 W
Ibiúna 256 23.39 S 47.13 W
Ibiza
→ Eivissa I 34 39.00 N 1.25 E
Iblei, Monti ⋏ 70 37.10 N 14.50 E
Ibnahs 142 30.34 N 31.07 E
Ibn Hāni', Ra's > 130 35.35 N 35.43 E
Ibn Sarrār, Bi'r ⊤[4] 144 19.30 N 42.41 E
Ibo 154 12.20 S 40.35 E
Ibo ≃ 96 34.46 N 134.35 E
Ibondo 154 2.38 S 32.40 E
Ibonma 164 3.28 S 133.28 E
Ibor ≃ 34 39.49 N 5.33 W
Ibotirama 255 12.11 S 43.13 W
Iboundji, Mont ∧ 152 1.08 S 11.48 E
Ibrah, Wādī V 140 10.36 N 24.58 E
Ibrāhīmīyah, Qārah al- ≚ 142 29.10 N 31.10 E
Ibresi 80 55.18 N 47.03 E
'Ibrī 128 23.14 N 56.30 E
İbriktepe 130 41.00 N 26.30 E
Ibshān 142 31.10 N 31.10 E
Ibshawāy 142 29.22 N 30.41 E
Ibstock 42 52.42 N 1.23 W
Ibta' 132 32.47 N 36.09 E
Ibu 174m 26.45 N 128.19 E
Ibuki 94 35.24 N 136.23 E
Ibuki-jima I 96 34.08 N 133.32 E
Ibuki-sanchi ⋏ 94 35.35 N 136.18 E
Ibuki-yama ∧ 94 35.25 N 136.24 E
Iburg 52 52.09 N 8.02 E
Ibusuki 92 31.16 N 130.39 E
Ibwe Munyama 154 16.09 S 28.34 E
Ibychen, gora ∧ 88 51.36 N 109.45 E
Ica 248 14.04 S 75.42 W
Ica □[5] 248 14.20 S 75.30 W
Ića ≃, Lat. 76 56.52 N 26.59 E
Ica ≃, Perú 248 14.54 S 75.34 W
Ića ≃, Ross. 86 55.30 N 77.13 E
Içá (Putumayo) ≃, S.A. 246 3.07 S 67.58 W
Icabarú ≃ 246 4.45 N 62.15 W
Icacos Point > 241r 10.03 N 61.56 W
Icadambanauan Island I 116 10.49 N 119.38 E
Icamaquã ≃ 252 28.34 S 56.00 W
Icamole 196 25.55 N 100.43 W
Içana 246 0.21 N 67.19 W
Içana (Isana) ≃ 246 0.26 N 67.19 W
Icaño, Arg. 252 28.54 S 65.19 W
Icaño, Arg. 252 28.41 S 62.54 W
Icatu 250 2.46 S 44.04 W
Iceberg Pass)(200 40.25 N 105.45 W
Ice House Reservoir ⊜[1] 226 38.49 N 120.23 W
İçel (Mersin) 130 36.48 N 34.38 E
İçel □[4] 130 36.45 N 34.00 E
Iceland (Ísland) □[1], Europe 22 65.00 N 18.00 W
Iceland (Ísland) □[1], Europe 24a 65.00 N 18.00 W
Iceland Basin ◆[1] 10 59.00 N 23.00 W
Icém 255 20.21 S 49.12 W
Ice Mountain ∧ 182 54.25 N 121.08 W
Ičera 88 58.32 N 109.47 E
Ichaikaronji 122 16.42 N 74.28 E
Ichāmati ≃, Asia 126 22.35 N 88.57 E
Ichāmati ≃, Bngl. 126 24.00 N 89.15 E
Ichang
→ Yichang 102 30.42 N 111.17 E
Ichawaynochaway Creek ≃ 192 31.10 N 84.28 W
Ich Bajan Ajrag uul ∧ 88 47.55 N 95.02 E
Ichbulag 102 45.21 N 113.10 E
Ich Buural uul ∧ 88 48.00 N 94.30 E
Ichchāpuram 122 19.07 N 84.42 E
Ichdžargalan 102 45.31 N 108.48 E
Ichenhausen 58 48.22 N 10.18 E
Ichenheim 58 48.26 N 7.49 E
Ichhapur 126 22.50 N 88.24 E
Ichhāwar 124 23.01 N 77.01 E
Ichi ≃ 96 34.46 N 134.41 E
Ichiba 96 34.05 N 134.17 E
Ichihara 94 35.31 N 140.05 E
Ichikai 94 36.32 N 140.06 E
Ichikawa, Nihon 94 35.44 N 139.55 E
Ichikawa, Nihon 96 34.59 N 134.46 E
Ichikawa-daimon 94 35.34 N 138.30 E
Ichilo ≃ 248 15.57 S 64.42 W
Ichinohe 92 40.13 N 141.17 E
Ichinomiya, Nihon 94 34.41 N 137.26 E
Ichinomiya, Nihon 94 35.18 N 136.48 E
Ichinomiya, Nihon 94 35.22 N 140.22 E
Ichinomiya, Nihon 94 35.39 N 138.41 E
Ichinomiya, Nihon 96 34.28 N 134.51 E
Ichinomiya, Nihon 96 32.57 N 131.07 E
Ichinomiya, Nihon 96 35.07 N 134.34 E
Ichinomoto 270 34.37 N 135.50 E
Ichinose 270 34.53 N 135.10 E
Ichinoseki 92 38.55 N 141.08 E
Ichino-tani ⊥ 96 34.39 N 135.07 E
Ichiu 96 33.57 N 134.04 E
Ichkeul, Lac ⊜ 36 37.10 N 9.40 E
Ichoa ≃ 248 15.44 S 65.15 W
Ichoca 248 17.12 S 67.17 W
Ich'on, C.M.I.K. 98 38.30 N 126.50 E
Ich'ŏn, Taehan 98 37.17 N 127.27 E
Ich Ovoo uul ∧ 90 44.40 N 95.08 E
Ichtamir 88 47.30 N 100.52 E
Ichtegem 50 51.06 N 3.00 E
Ichtershausen 54 50.52 N 10.58 E
Ich'un
→ Yichun 90 47.42 N 128.55 E
Ich Uul, Mong. 88 48.33 N 98.40 E
Ich Uul, Mong. 88 49.27 N 101.27 E
Icicle Creek ≃ 224 47.34 N 120.40 W
Ičinskaja Sopka, vulkan ∧[1] 74 55.42 N 157.35 E
Ička, gora ∧[2] 80 51.13 N 50.15 E
Ickenham ◆[8] 260 51.34 N 0.27 W
Ickern 263 51.36 N 7.21 E
Ickesburg 208 40.27 N 77.21 W
Icking 64 47.57 N 11.25 E
İçme 130 38.37 N 39.34 E
Ičn'a 78 50.52 N 32.24 E
Icó 250 6.24 S 38.51 W
Icoca 152 6.11 S 16.19 E
Iconha 255 20.48 S 40.48 W
Icy Bay c 180 60.00 N 141.15 W
Icy Cape > 180 70.20 N 161.52 W
Icy Strait ʊ 180 58.18 N 135.30 W
Ida 216 41.54 N 83.34 W
Ida, Mount ∧, Austl. 162 29.14 S 120.25 E
Ida, Mount ∧, Jam. 241q 17.58 N 77.43 W
Idabel 194 33.53 N 94.49 W
Idaga Hamus 144 14.12 N 39.48 E
Ida Grove 198 42.20 N 95.28 W
Idah 150 7.07 N 6.43 E
Idaho □[3], U.S. 178 45.00 N 115.00 W
Idaho □[3], U.S. 202 45.00 N 115.00 W
Idaho City 202 43.49 N 115.50 W
Idaho Falls 202 43.28 N 112.02 W
Idaho National Engineering Laboratory ◆[3] 202 43.40 N 112.45 W
Idaho Springs 200 39.44 N 105.00 W
Idalou 196 33.39 N 101.40 W
Idanha-a-Nova 34 39.55 N 7.14 W
Idāppādi 122 11.35 N 77.51 E
Idar 120 23.50 N 73.00 E
Idarkopf ∧ 56 49.51 N 7.16 E
Idar-Oberstein 56 49.42 N 7.19 E
Idarwald ◆[3] 56 49.49 N 7.12 E
Idaville, In., U.S. 216 40.45 N 86.38 W
Idaville, Or., U.S. 224 45.30 N 123.51 W
Iddo ◆[8] 273a 6.28 N 3.23 E
Ide 96 34.47 N 135.49 E
Idel' 24 64.08 N 34.14 E
Idelès 148 23.58 N 5.53 E
Idemba 152 2.38 S 11.38 E
Iden 54 52.46 N 11.55 E
Ider 88 48.13 N 97.23 E
Iderijn ≃ 88 49.16 N 100.41 E
Idermeg 88 47.40 N 111.05 E
Idfīnā 142 31.18 N 30.31 E
Idfū 140 24.58 N 32.52 E
Ídhi Óros ∧ 38 35.18 N 24.43 E
Ídhra 38 37.20 N 23.29 E
Ídhra (Hydra) I 38 37.20 N 23.32 E
Idi 114 4.57 N 97.46 E
Idice ≃ 64 44.35 N 11.49 E
Idi-cut 114 4.59 N 97.42 E
Ididole 144 5.53 N 43.36 E
Idifina Barrage ◆[6] 142 31.17 N 30.31 E
İdil 130 37.21 N 41.54 E
Idimu 273a 6.35 N 3.17 E
Idio 116 11.37 N 122.06 E
Idiofa 152 5.02 S 19.36 E
Iditarod ≃ 180 63.02 N 158.58 W
Idjwi, Île I 154 2.09 S 29.04 E
Idkerberget 40 60.23 N 15.14 E
Idkū 142 31.18 N 30.18 E
Idkū, Buḥayrat ⊜ 142 31.16 N 30.17 E
Idle ≃ 44 53.27 N 0.49 W
Idle Hill 260 51.15 N 0.08 E
Idlib 130 35.55 N 36.38 E
Idlib □[8] 130 35.50 N 36.40 E
Idmū 142 28.09 N 30.41 E
Idnah 132 31.34 N 34.59 E
Idodi 154 7.47 S 35.11 E
Idomogu 273a 6.43 N 3.30 E
Idracowra 162 25.00 S 133.47 E
Idre 26 61.52 N 12.43 E
Idria 226 36.25 N 120.40 W
Idrica 76 56.21 N 28.53 E
Idrigill Point > 46 57.20 N 6.35 W
Idrija 36 46.00 N 14.01 E
Idrijca ≃ 64 46.09 N 13.45 E
Idrinskoje 86 54.21 N 92.07 E
Idro 64 45.44 N 10.29 E
Idro, Lago d' ⊜ 64 45.47 N 10.30 E
Idroscalo ⊜ 266b 45.28 N 9.18 E
Idstedt 41 54.35 N 9.31 E
Idstein 56 50.13 N 8.16 E
Idutywa 158 32.02 S 28.16 E
Idyllwild 204 33.45 N 116.43 W
Idylside 216 41.31 N 88.07 W
Idylwood 284c 38.54 N 77.12 W
Idževan 84 40.53 N 45.07 E
Ie 174m 26.42 N 127.48 E
Iecava 76 56.36 N 24.12 E
Iecava ≃ 76 56.41 N 23.42 E
Ielsi 66 41.30 N 14.48 E
Ienne 66 41.53 N 13.10 E
Iepê 255 22.40 S 51.05 W
Ieper (Ypres) 50 50.51 N 2.53 E
Ierápetra 38 35.00 N 25.45 E
Ierisós 38 40.24 N 23.52 E
Ierzu 71 39.47 N 9.31 E
Ieshima 96 34.40 N 134.32 E
Ie-shima I 174m 26.43 N 127.47 E
Ieshima-shotō II 96 34.40 N 134.32 E
Iesolo 64 45.32 N 12.38 E
Ie-suidō ʊ 174m 26.42 N 127.51 E
If, Château d' ⊥ 62 43.17 N 5.19 E
Ifakara 154 8.08 S 36.41 E
Ifako 273a 6.39 N 3.20 E
Ifalik I[1] 108 7.15 N 144.27 E
Ifanadiana 157b 21.19 S 47.39 E
Ife 150 7.30 N 4.30 E
Iferouâne 150 19.04 N 8.24 E
Iferten
→ Yverdon 58 46.47 N 6.39 E
Iffezheim 56 48.49 N 8.08 E
Ifni □[9] 148 29.15 N 10.08 W
Ifôghas, Adrar des ⋏ 150 20.00 N 2.00 E
Ifon 150 6.58 N 5.45 E
Ifould Lake ⊜ 162 30.53 S 132.09 E
Ifrane 148 33.32 N 5.06 W
Ifrane □[4] 148 33.15 N 5.05 W
Ifta 56 51.04 N 10.11 E
Ifugao □[4] 116 16.45 N 121.15 E
Iga 94 34.49 N 136.13 E
Iga ≃ 94 34.45 N 136.01 E
Igal 30 46.31 N 17.55 E
Igalula, Tan. 154 5.14 S 33.00 E
Igalula, Tan. 154 5.38 S 32.38 E
Igan 112 2.49 N 111.43 E
Igan ≃ 112 2.51 N 111.39 E
Iganga 154 0.37 N 33.29 E
Iganmu ◆[8] 273a 6.29 N 3.22 E
Iganna 150 7.59 N 3.14 E
Igaporã 255 13.46 S 42.43 W
Igara 250 10.24 S 40.07 W
Igaraí 256 21.25 S 46.49 W
Igara Paraná ≃ 246 2.09 S 71.47 W
Igarapé-Açu 250 1.07 S 47.37 W
Igarapé Grande 250 4.41 S 44.58 W
Igarapé-Miri 250 1.59 S 48.58 W
Igaratá 256 23.12 S 46.07 W
Igarka 74 67.28 N 86.35 E
Igarra 150 7.18 N 6.07 E
Igarukiro 154 3.08 S 33.31 E
Igatpuri 122 19.42 N 73.33 E
Igaun 273a 6.42 N 3.23 E
Igawa 154 8.35 S 34.28 E
Igbaja 150 8.23 N 4.52 E
Igbobi 273a 6.32 N 3.22 E
Igboho 150 8.51 N 3.45 E
Igbologun 273a 6.25 N 3.20 E
Igbo-Ora 150 7.26 N 3.17 E
Igbor 150 7.27 N 8.34 E
Igdir, Īrān 84 39.20 N 47.30 E
Iğdır, Tür. 84 39.55 N 44.02 E
Iğdır, Tür. 130 41.14 N 33.07 E
Iğdır, Tür. 130 40.16 N 35.38 E
Igdy 128 39.54 N 56.54 E
Igea Marina 66 44.08 N 12.29 E
Igel 56 49.42 N 6.32 E
Igelfors 40 58.51 N 15.41 E
Igelsberg 58 48.32 N 8.26 E
Igel'vejem ≃ 180 65.40 N 172.50 W
Igersheim 56 49.29 N 9.49 E
Iggensbach 60 48.44 N 13.08 E
Iggesund 26 61.38 N 17.04 E
Igharghar, Oued V, Afr. 148 20.25 N 6.10 E
Igharghar, Oued V, Alg. 148 28.03 N 6.15 E
Ightham 260 51.17 N 0.17 E
Ightham Mote ⊥ 260 51.15 N 0.16 E
Igikpak, Mount ∧ 180 67.25 N 154.58 W
Igirma 88 56.59 N 103.37 E
Igiugig 180 59.20 N 155.55 W
Iglau
→ Jihlava 30 49.24 N 15.36 E
Iglesia 252 30.24 S 69.13 W
Iglesias 71 39.19 N 8.32 E
Iglesiente ◆[1] 71 39.18 N 8.40 E
Igli 148 30.25 N 2.12 W
Iglino 86 54.50 N 56.26 E
Igloolik 176 69.24 N 81.49 W
Iglovo 82 55.47 N 36.40 E
Igls 64 47.14 N 11.25 E
Ignacej 38 47.41 N 28.40 E
Ignacio, Ca., U.S. 226 38.05 N 122.32 W
Ignacio, Co., U.S. 200 37.06 N 107.37 W
Ignacio de la Llave 234 18.43 N 95.59 W
Ignacio Zaragoza, Méx. 232 29.35 N 107.30 W
Ignacio Zaragoza, Méx. 234 23.15 N 98.50 W
Ignacio Zaragoza, Méx. 234 23.55 N 103.42 W
Ignalina 76 55.21 N 26.10 E
Ignatjevcy 80 57.32 N 51.39 E
Ignatovka 80 53.57 N 47.38 E
Ignatovo 82 56.10 N 37.32 E
İğneada 130 41.52 N 27.58 E
İğneada Burnu > 130 41.54 N 28.03 E
Igney 58 48.17 N 6.24 E
Ignon ≃ 58 47.31 N 5.10 E
Igny 261 48.45 N 2.14 E
Igodovo 80 58.01 N 42.21 E
Igombe ≃ 154 4.38 S 31.40 E
Igoumenítsa 38 39.30 N 20.16 E
Igra 80 57.33 N 53.04 E
Igreja Nova 250 10.07 S 36.39 W
Iguaçu ≃, Bra. 256 22.45 S 43.14 W
Iguaçu ≃, S.A. 252 25.36 S 54.36 W
Iguaçu, Cataratas do (Iguassu Falls) ∟ 252 25.41 S 54.26 W
Iguaçu, Parque Nacional do ♦ 252 25.30 S 53.50 W
Iguaí 255 14.45 S 40.04 W
Iguala 234 18.21 N 99.32 W
Igualada 34 41.35 N 1.38 E
Iguana ≃ 246 7.54 N 65.46 W
Iguape 252 24.43 S 47.33 W
Iguará ≃ 250 3.28 S 43.55 W
Iguassu Falls
→ Iguaçu, Cataratas 99do ∟ 252 25.41 S 54.26 W
Iguatemi 255 23.40 S 54.34 W
Iguatemi ≃ 255 23.55 S 54.10 W
Iguatu 250 6.22 S 39.18 W
Iguazú, Parque Nacional ♦ 252 25.35 S 54.20 W
Iguéla 152 1.55 S 9.19 E
Iguéla, Lagune c 152 1.55 S 9.25 E
Iguetti, Sebkhet ≚ 148 25.05 N 9.50 W
Iguîdi, 'Erg ⊥[8] 148 26.35 N 5.40 W
Iguig 116 17.45 N 121.44 E
Igumale 150 6.49 N 7.59 E
Igumnovo 82 55.37 N 38.18 E
Igvak, Cape > 180 57.26 N 156.00 W
Igžej 88 53.59 N 103.10 E
Ihavandiffulu Atoll I[1] 122 7.00 N 72.55 E
Iheya-shima I 93b 27.04 N 127.58 E
Ihiala 150 5.51 N 6.51 E
Ihirène, Oued V 148 20.25 N 4.35 E
Ihle ≃ 54 52.17 N 11.52 E
Ihlienworth 52 53.44 N 8.55 E
Ihlow 52 53.25 N 7.27 E
Ihmert 56 51.20 N 7.44 E
Ihnāsiyat al-Madīnah 142 29.05 N 30.56 E
Ihorombe 157b 23.00 S 47.33 E
Ihosy 157b 22.24 S 46.08 E
Ihosy ≃ 157b 21.44 S 45.53 E
Ihotry, Lac ⊜ 157b 21.56 S 43.41 E
Ihringen 58 48.02 N 7.39 E
Ihringshausen 52 51.21 N 9.31 E
Ihrlerstein 60 48.56 N 11.52 E
İhsangazi 130 41.11 N 33.33 E
Ih Tal 89 43.13 N 122.15 E
Ihtiman 38 42.26 N 23.49 E
Ihu 164 7.55 S 145.25 E
Ihugh 150 7.02 N 9.00 E
Ihwah 142 29.03 N 31.00 E
Iida 94 35.31 N 137.50 E
Iidaan 144 6.06 N 48.59 E
Iijima 94 35.40 N 137.56 E
Iijoki ≃ 24 65.20 N 25.17 E
Iiktu, gora ∧ 86 49.51 N 87.40 E
Iinan 94 34.27 N 136.24 E
Iinashi ≃ 96 35.27 N 133.13 E
Iioka 94 35.42 N 140.43 E
Iisaku 76 59.06 N 27.19 E
Iisalmi 26 63.34 N 27.11 E
Iisvesi 26 62.40 N 27.02 E
Iitaka 94 34.26 N 136.21 E
Iittala 26 61.04 N 24.10 E
Iiyama 94 36.51 N 138.22 E
Iizuka 96 33.38 N 130.41 E
Ij ≃ 88 52.34 N 96.10 E
Ija ≃ 88 55.05 N 101.05 E
Ijâfene ◆[2] 134 20.30 N 8.00 W
Ijaiye 273a 6.40 N 3.18 E
Ijaji 144 8.59 N 37.13 E
Ijara 154 1.36 S 40.31 E
Ijebu-Igbo 150 6.56 N 4.01 E
Ijebu-Ode 150 6.50 N 3.56 E
Ijesa-Tedo 273a 6.30 N 3.19 E
Ijin 98 42.05 N 130.08 E
Ijira 94 35.31 N 136.44 E
IJmuiden 52 52.27 N 4.36 E
IJssel ≃ 52 52.35 N 5.50 E
IJsselmeer (Zuiderzee) ⊤[2] 52 52.45 N 5.25 E
IJsselmuiden 52 52.34 N 5.56 E
IJsselstein 52 52.02 N 5.03 E
Ijuí 252 28.23 S 53.55 W
Ijuí ≃ 252 27.58 S 55.20 W
Iju Junction 273a 6.40 N 3.19 E
Ijuw 174b 0.30 S 166.57 E
Iju Water Works ◆[3] 273a 6.40 N 3.20 E
IJzendijke 52 51.19 N 3.38 E
IJzer (Yser) ≃ 50 51.09 N 2.43 E
Ik ≃ 80 55.55 N 52.36 E
Ika 88 59.18 N 106.12 E
Ikaalinen 26 61.46 N 23.03 E
Ikaho 94 36.30 N 138.55 E
Ikalamavony 157b 21.09 S 46.35 E
Ikali 152 2.02 S 21.02 E
Ikalou 152 4.03 S 11.48 E
Ikamatua 172 42.16 S 171.41 E
Ikamba 273b 4.22 S 15.16 E
Ikang 150 4.50 N 8.32 E
Ikara 150 11.12 N 8.15 E
Ikare 150 7.32 N 5.45 E
Ikaría I 38 37.41 N 26.20 E
Ikari-dam ◆[6] 94 36.52 N 139.42 E
Ikari-ko ⊜ 94 36.56 N 139.41 E
Ikaruga 96 34.36 N 135.44 E
Ikast 41 56.08 N 9.10 E
Ikatan 180 54.45 N 163.19 W
Ikatskij chrebet ⋏ 88 54.00 N 111.00 E
Ikawa 94 35.13 N 138.15 E
Ikawa-dam ◆[6] 94 35.12 N 138.13 E
Ikawhenua Range ⋏ 172 38.20 S 176.56 E
Ikazaki 96 33.32 N 132.39 E
Ikeda, Nihon 92a 42.55 N 143.27 E
Ikeda, Nihon 94 35.53 N 136.21 E
Ikeda, Nihon 94 35.26 N 136.34 E
Ikeda, Nihon 94 36.25 N 137.53 E
Ikeda, Nihon 96 34.49 N 135.25 E
Ikeda, Nihon 96 34.01 N 133.48 E
Ikegawa 96 33.36 N 133.11 E
Ikej 88 54.12 N 100.04 E
Ikeja 150 6.36 N 3.21 E
Ikeja □[8] 273a 6.30 N 3.25 E
Ikela 152 1.11 S 23.16 E
Ikélemba 152 1.14 N 16.31 E
Ikelemba ≃ 152 0.07 N 18.17 E
Ikema-jima I 175d 24.56 N 125.16 E
Ikerre 150 7.31 N 5.14 E
Ike-shima I 174m 26.23 N 128.00 E
Ikeura 270 34.30 N 135.25 E
Iki I 92 33.47 N 129.43 E
Iki-Burul 80 45.49 N 44.39 E
Ikimba, Lake ⊜ 154 1.28 S 31.30 E
Īkinjī Maryūt 142 31.00 N 29.45 E
Ikire 150 7.23 N 4.12 E
Ikirun 150 7.55 N 4.41 E
İkizce 130 39.36 N 32.40 E
İkizdere 130 40.47 N 40.33 E
Iko 152 0.35 S 16.01 E
Ikole 150 7.49 N 5.30 E
Ikolik, Cape > 180 57.17 N 154.48 W
Ikom 150 5.58 N 8.42 E
Ikoma, Nihon 96 34.41 N 135.42 E
Ikoma, Tan. 154 2.04 S 34.37 E
Ikoma-sanchi ⋏ 270 34.40 N 135.40 E
Ikoma-tunnel ◆[5] 270 34.41 N 135.41 E
Ikoma-yama ∧ 270 34.40 N 135.41 E
Ikon-Chal' 84 44.18 N 41.55 E
Ikopa ≃ 157b 17.01 S 46.45 E
Ikorec ≃ 78 50.58 N 39.45 E
Ikorodu 150 6.37 N 3.31 E
Ikot Ekpene 150 5.12 N 7.40 E
Ikoy ≃ 152 0.53 S 10.36 E
Ikoyi ◆[8] 273a 6.27 N 3.26 E
Ikoyi Island I 273a 6.27 N 3.26 E
Ikoyi Prison ◆ 273a 6.25 N 3.25 E
Ikozi 154 2.32 S 27.37 E
Ikpikpuk ≃ 180 70.50 N 154.25 W
Ikra 126 23.42 N 87.07 E
Ikr'anoje 80 46.06 N 47.45 E
Ikrāsh 142 30.45 N 31.30 E
Ikša 82 56.10 N 37.31 E
Iksa ≃ 86 57.48 N 82.36 E
Ikti, Cape > 180 56.00 N 158.30 W
Ikuata 273a 6.25 N 3.22 E
Ikuchi-shima I 96 34.17 N 133.07 E
Ikuji-hana > 94 36.54 N 137.25 E
Ikuktlitlig Mountain ∧ 180 59.16 N 161.27 W
Ikungu 154 1.34 S 33.40 E
Ikuno 96 35.10 N 134.48 E
Ikuno ◆[8] 270 34.39 N 135.34 E
Ikurangi, Mount ∧[2] 174k 21.13 S 159.45 W
Ikusaka 94 36.25 N 137.56 E
Ikusu ≃ 273b 4.24 S 15.14 E
Ikuta 268 35.36 N 139.32 E
Ikva ≃, Magy. 61 47.42 N 16.58 E
Ikva ≃, Ukr. 78 50.33 N 25.24 E
Ikwah 142 30.41 N 31.28 E
Ila, Nig. 150 8.01 N 4.55 E
Ila, Zaïre 152 2.53 S 21.05 E
Ilabaya 248 17.25 S 70.31 W
Ilacaon Point > 116 11.00 N 123.12 E
Ilagala 154 5.12 S 29.50 E
Ilagan 116 17.10 N 121.54 E
Ilagan ≃ 116 17.09 N 121.54 E
Ilaiyānkudi 122 9.38 N 78.38 E
Ilaka, Madag. 157b 19.33 S 48.52 E
Ilaka, Madag. 157b 20.20 S 47.09 E
Īlām, Īrān 128 33.38 N 46.26 E
Ilām, Nepāl 124 26.55 N 87.56 E
Īlām □[4] 128 33.15 N 46.45 E
Ilam
→ Sri Lanka □[1] 122 7.00 N 81.00 E
Ilām Bāzār 126 23.38 N 87.32 E
Ilan 100 24.46 N 121.45 E
Ilan ≃ 100 24.43 N 121.49 E
Ilanskij 88 56.14 N 96.03 E
Ilanz 58 46.46 N 9.12 E
Ilara 273a 6.42 N 3.27 E
Ilaro 150 6.53 N 3.03 E
Ilasco 219 39.40 N 91.18 W
Ilave 248 16.06 S 69.41 W
Iława 30 53.37 N 19.33 E
Ilawe-Ekiti 150 7.37 N 5.06 E
Ilay 58 46.37 N 5.53 E
Ilbenge 74 62.49 N 124.24 E
Ilberstedt 54 51.48 N 11.40 E
Il Catalano I 71 39.53 N 8.17 E
Ilchester, Eng., U.K. 42 51.01 N 2.41 W
Ilchester, Md., U.S. 284b 39.15 N 76.45 W
Ildefonso, Islas II 254 55.44 S 69.26 W
Île-à-la-Crosse 184 55.27 N 107.53 W
Île-à-la-Crosse, Lac ⊜ 184 55.40 N 107.45 W
Ilebo (Port-Francqui) 152 4.19 S 20.35 E
Île-Cadieux 275a 45.25 N 74.01 W
Île-de-France □[9] 50 49.00 N 2.20 E
Île-de-Montréal □[6] 206 45.30 N 73.40 W
Île-Jésus □[6] 206 45.35 N 73.45 W
Ilek 80 51.30 N 53.22 E
Ilek ≃ 72 51.30 N 53.20 E
Ilen ≃ 48 51.33 N 9.19 W
Île-Perrot 206 45.23 N 73.57 W
Ileret 154 4.19 N 36.13 E
Îles, Grand lac des ⊜ 206 46.43 N 73.30 W
Îles, Lac des ⊜, P.Q., Can. 206 46.06 N 74.02 W
Îles, Lac des ⊜, Sk., Can. 184 54.26 N 109.25 W
Ilesha 150 7.38 N 4.45 E
Ilesha Ibarida 150 8.56 N 3.25 E
Ilet' ≃ 80 55.56 N 48.14 E
Ilevskij Pogost 24 60.41 N 43.46 E
Ileza 24 60.43 N 43.54 E
Ilfeld 54 51.34 N 10.47 E
Ilford, Austl. 170 32.58 S 149.51 E
Ilford, Mb., Can. 184 56.04 N 95.35 W
Ilford ◆[8] 260 51.33 N 0.05 E
Ilfov □[6] 38 44.30 N 26.15 E
Ilfracombe, Austl. 166 23.30 S 144.30 E
Ilfracombe, Eng., U.K. 42 51.13 N 4.08 W
Il Fuorn 58 46.40 N 10.12 E
Ilga ≃ 88 55.00 N 105.04 E
Ilgaz 130 40.56 N 33.38 E
Ilgaz Dağları ⋏ 130 41.00 N 33.35 E
Ilgın 130 38.17 N 31.55 E
Ilha ◆[8] 256 23.00 S 43.33 W
Ilhabela 256 23.47 S 45.21 W
Ilha das Flores 250 10.27 S 36.33 W
Ilha Grande, Baía da c 256 23.09 S 44.30 W
Ilhas, Cachoeira das ∟ 250 1.03 S 57.33 W
Ilha Solteira, Represa de ⊜[1] 255 20.20 S 51.20 W
Ilhavo 34 40.36 N 8.40 W
Ilhea Point > 156 23.25 S 14.27 E
Ilhéos
→ Ilhéus 255 14.49 S 39.02 W
Ilhéus 255 14.49 S 39.02 W
Ili ≃ 86 45.24 N 74.02 E
Ilia 38 45.56 N 22.39 E
Iliamna 180 59.45 N 154.54 W
Iliamna Lake ⊜ 180 59.30 N 155.00 W
Ilian, Mount ∧ 116 10.26 N 119.33 E
Iliatenco 234 16.58 N 98.40 W
İliç 130 39.28 N 38.34 E
Ilıca, Tür. 130 39.52 N 27.46 E
Ilıca, Tür. 130 39.57 N 41.07 E
Ilicínia 255 20.56 S 45.50 W
Iliff 198 40.45 N 103.03 W
Iliff, Lake ⊜ 276 41.02 N 74.43 W
Iligan 116 8.14 N 124.14 E
Iligan Bay c 116 8.25 N 124.05 E
Ilijan 116 13.38 N 121.04 E
Ilijsk 85 43.53 N 77.10 E
Ilim ≃ 88 57.38 N 102.34 E
Ilimsk 88 56.46 N 103.52 E
Ilin 116 12.15 N 121.02 E
Ilinge 158 31.59 S 27.02 E
Ilin Island I 116 12.14 N 121.05 E
Ilinka 82 54.04 N 38.12 E
Ilinza ∧ 246 0.40 S 78.42 W
Ilion 210 43.00 N 75.02 W
Ilio Point > 229a 21.13 N 157.15 W
Ilioúpolis 267c 37.56 N 23.45 E
Ilir 88 55.13 N 100.40 E
Ilirska Bistrica 36 45.34 N 14.15 E
Ilisós ≃ 267c 37.57 N 23.41 E
Ilizi 148 26.29 N 8.28 E
Ilja 76 54.25 N 27.18 E
Iljak 86 60.11 N 77.59 E
Iljič 85 40.50 N 68.27 E
Iljičovsk 78 46.18 N 30.39 E
Iljincy 78 49.07 N 29.12 E
Iljinka 80 48.32 N 41.05 E
Iljino 76 55.57 N 31.40 E
Iljinskij, Ross. 24 61.02 N 32.41 E
Iljinskij, Ross. 86 58.35 N 55.41 E
Iljinskij, Ross. 88 52.05 N 114.10 E
Iljinskij, Ross. 89 47.58 N 142.12 E
Iljinskij, Ross. 265b 55.37 N 38.06 E
Iljinskij Pogost 82 55.28 N 38.54 E
Iljinskoje, Ross. 76 56.58 N 37.11 E
Iljinskoje, Ross. 76 58.47 N 44.36 E
Iljinskoje, Ross. 76 53.14 N 35.26 E
Iljinskoje, Ross. 76 57.19 N 38.32 E
Iljinskoje, Ross. 80 56.29 N 52.49 E
Iljinskoje, Ross. 82 54.59 N 36.11 E
Iljinskoje, Ross. 82 56.34 N 35.57 E
Iljinskoje, Ross. 265b 55.46 N 37.15 E
Iljinskoje-Chovanskoje 80 56.58 N 39.46 E
Iljinsko-Podomskoje 24 61.08 N 47.56 E
Iljinsko-Zaborskoje 80 57.16 N 44.23 E
Iljiny gory ⋏[2] 76 56.34 N 34.12 E
Il'ka 88 51.43 N 108.32 E
Ilkal 122 15.58 N 76.08 E

Symbols in the index entries represent the broad categories identified in the key at the right. Symbols with superior numbers (⋏[1]) identify subcategories (see complete key on page *I · 1).*

Symbole im Register stellen die rechts im Schlüssel erklärten Kategorien dar. Symbole mit hochgestellten Ziffern (⋏[1]) bezeichnen Unterabteilungen einer Kategorie (vgl. vollständiger Schlüssel auf Seite *I · 1).*

Los símbolos incluídos en el texto del índice representan las grandes categorías identificadas con la clave a la derecha. Los símbolos con numeros en su parte superior (⋏[1]) identifican las subcategorías (véase la clave completa en la página *I · 1).*

Les symboles de l'index représentent les catégories indiquées dans la légende à droite. Les symboles suivis d'un indice (⋏[1]) représentent des sous-catégories (voir légende complète à la page *I · 1).*

Os símbolos incluídos no texto do índice representam as grandes categorias identificadas com a chave à direita. Os símbolos com números em sua parte superior (⋏[1]) identificam as subcategorias (veja-se a chave completa à página *I · 1).*

	ENGLISH	DEUTSCH			
∧	Mountain	Berg	Montaña	Montagne	Montanha
⋏	Mountains	Gebirge	Montañas	Montagnes	Montanhas
)(	Pass	Paß	Paso	Col	Passo
V	Valley, Canyon	Tal, Cañon	Valle, Cañón	Vallée, Canyon	Vale, Canhão
≚	Plain	Ebene	Llano	Plaine	Planície
>	Cape	Kap	Cabo	Cap	Cabo
I	Island	Insel	Isla	Île	Ilha
II	Islands	Inseln	Islas	Îles	Ilhas
⊥	Other Topographic Features	Andere Topographische Objekte	Otros Elementos Topográficos	Autres données topographiques	Outros acidentes topográficos

Name | Page | Lat.°′ | Long.°′ — Name | Seite | Breite°′ | Länge°′ E = Ost

ESPAÑOL FRANÇAIS PORTUGUÊS Ilke-Inve I · 77

| Nombre | Página | Lat.ᵒʳ | Long.ᵒʳ W=Oeste | Nom | Page | Lat.ᵒʳ | Long.ᵒʳ W=Ouest | Nome | Página | Lat.ᵒʳ | Long.ᵒʳ W=Oeste |

Nombre	Página	Lat.	Long.
Ilkeston	42	52.59 N	1.18 W
Il'kino	80	55.13 N	41.36 E
Ilkley	44	53.55 N	1.50 W
Ill ≃, Fr.	58	48.40 N	7.53 E
Ill ≃, Öst.	58	47.17 N	9.33 E
Illabot Creek ≃	224	48.29 N	121.30 W
Illampu, Nevado ∧	248	15.50 S	68.34 W
Illana Bay c	116	7.25 N	123.45 E
Illapel	252	31.38 S	71.10 W
Illarionovo	78	48.25 N	35.16 E
Illasi ≃	64	45.28 N	11.10 E
Illawarra, Lake c	170	34.32 S	150.50 E
Illbillee, Mount ∧	162	27.02 S	132.30 E
Ille-et-Vilaine □⁵	32	48.10 N	1.30 W
Illéla	150	14.28 N	5.15 E
Iller ≃	58	48.23 N	9.58 E
Illertissen	58	48.13 N	10.06 E
Illescas, Esp.	34	40.07 N	3.50 W
Illescas, Méx.	234	23.13 N	102.07 W
Illfurth	58	47.40 N	7.16 E
Illhaeusern	58	48.11 N	7.26 E
Illi, Ba ≃	146	10.44 N	15.21 E
Illiers	50	48.18 N	1.15 E
Illimani, Nevado ∧	248	16.50 S	67.54 W
Illimo	248	6.28 S	79.51 W
Illingen	58	48.57 N	8.55 E
Illingworth	262	53.45 N	1.54 W
Illinois □³, U.S.	178	40.00 N	89.00 W
Illinois □³, U.S.	194	40.00 N	89.00 W
Illinois ≃, U.S.	194	35.30 N	95.06 W
Illinois ≃, Co., U.S.	200	40.45 N	106.18 W
Illinois ≃, Il., U.S.	194	38.58 N	90.27 W
Illinois ≃, Or., U.S.	202	42.33 N	124.03 W
Illinois and Michigan Canal ≖	278	41.32 N	88.05 W
Illinois at Chicago, University of ⩊²	278	41.52 N	87.39 W
Illinois Beach State Park ♦	212	42.26 N	87.48 W
Illinois Institute of Technology ⩊²	278	41.50 N	87.38 W
Illinois Peak ∧	202	47.02 N	115.04 W
Illiopolis	219	39.51 N	89.14 W
Illkirch-Graffenstaden	58	48.32 N	7.43 E
Illminster	42	50.56 N	2.55 W
Illo	150	11.33 N	3.42 E
Illovo, S. Afr.	158	30.05 S	30.50 E
Illovo, S. Afr.	273d	26.08 S	28.03 E
Illzach	58	47.47 N	7.20 E
Ilm ≃, Dtsch.	54	51.07 N	11.40 E
Ilm ≃, Dtsch.	60	48.49 N	11.45 E
Ilmajoki	26	62.44 N	22.34 E
Il'men', ozero ◎	76	58.17 N	31.20 E
Ilmenau ≃	54	50.41 N	10.55 E
Ilmenau ≃	54	53.23 N	10.10 E
Il'menskij zapovednik ♦	86	55.16 N	60.17 E
Il'mino	80	53.47 N	43.40 E
Ilo	248	17.38 S	71.20 W
Ilobasco	236	13.51 N	83.51 W
Ilobu	150	7.51 N	4.30 E
Iloc Island I	116	11.18 N	119.41 E
Ilocos Norte □⁴	116	18.10 N	120.45 E
Ilocos Sur □⁴	116	17.05 N	120.35 E
Iloilo	116	10.42 N	122.34 E
Iloilo □⁴	116	11.00 N	122.35 E
Iloilo Strait ⋃	116	10.40 N	122.35 E
Ilomantsi	24	62.40 N	30.55 E
Ilondola Mission	154	10.42 S	31.47 E
Ilongero	154	4.40 S	34.52 E
Ilop	166	2.54 S	141.13 E
Ilopango, Lago de ◎	236	13.40 N	89.03 W
Ilora	150	7.45 N	3.50 E
Ilorin	150	8.30 N	4.32 E
Iller ≃	83	47.66 N	36.13 E
Ilovatka	80	50.31 N	45.55 E
Ilovka	78	50.43 N	38.38 E
Ilovl'a	80	49.18 N	43.59 E
Ilovl'a ≃	80	49.14 N	43.54 E
Ilowa	50	30.10 N	15.12 E
Il'Palone ∧	64	46.02 N	11.04 E
Il'pyrskij	74	59.56 N	164.10 E
Ilsan-ni	271b	37.41 N	126.46 E
Ilse ≃	54	52.06 N	10.35 E
Ilshofen	58	49.10 N	9.55 E
Il'skij	78	44.51 N	38.35 E
Ilskov	61	56.14 N	9.06 E
Il Telegrafo ∧	64	42.22 N	11.10 E
Ilten	52	52.21 N	9.55 E
Ilu	152	4.12 N	23.02 E
Ilubabor □⁴	144	7.50 N	35.00 E
Iluhār	126	22.48 N	90.06 E
Ilūkste	76	55.58 N	26.18 E
Ilverich	263	51.17 N	6.42 E
Ilwaco	224	46.19 N	124.03 W
Ilwaki	112	7.56 S	126.26 E
Ilwŏl-san ∧	98	36.50 N	129.06 E
Ilyasbey	130	40.13 N	29.52 E
Ilz ≃	61	47.05 N	15.55 E
Ilz ≃	60	48.35 N	13.29 E
Ilża	30	51.11 N	21.14 E
Ima	88	55.13 N	115.55 E
Ima	96	33.45 N	131.01 E
Imabari	96	34.03 N	133.00 E
Imadate	250	0.44 S	37.02 W
Imadomi	268	35.24 N	139.41 E
Imaichi	96	36.43 N	139.41 E
Imajō	96	35.46 N	136.12 E
Imajuku	268	35.58 N	139.21 E
Imajuku ⨀⁸	268	35.29 N	139.32 E
Imaki ∧	96	34.34 N	135.46 E
Imakoto ≃	157b	23.27 S	45.13 E
Imambara ∗¹	272b	22.54 N	88.25 E
Imanbaj ≃	88	43.13 N	60.25 E
Imandan-Makit, gora ∧	88	54.07 N	117.43 E
Imandra, ozero ◎	24	67.30 N	33.00 E
Imanombo	157b	24.26 S	45.49 E
Imantau	86	52.58 N	68.22 E
Imari	96	33.16 N	129.53 E
Imaruí	252	28.21 S	48.49 W
Imaruí, Lagoa do c	252	28.21 S	48.52 W
Imasa	140	18.01 N	36.12 E
Imatra	26	61.10 N	28.46 E
Imavere	76	58.44 N	25.48 E
Imazu	96	35.24 N	136.02 E
Imbābah ⨀⁸	142	30.04 N	31.13 E
Imbabura □⁴	246	0.22 N	78.25 W
Imba-numa ◎	96	35.45 N	140.12 E
Imbarié	256	22.39 S	43.13 W
Imbituba	252	28.14 S	48.40 W
Imbituva	252	25.13 S	50.36 W
Imboçu, Canal ⮝	287a	22.48 S	43.04 W
Imboden	194	36.12 N	91.10 W
Imbonga	152	0.43 S	19.46 E
Imbundi	152	5.44 S	15.16 E
Ime, Beinn ∧	46	56.14 N	4.49 W
Imeni 0206 Bakinskich Komissarov	84	39.19 N	49.12 E
Imeni Abaja	86	53.04 N	69.30 E
Imeni Babuškina	76	59.45 N	43.07 E
Imeni Capajeva	85	43.28 N	76.50 E
Imeni C'urupy	80	55.30 N	38.39 E
Imeni Dzěmbula, Kaz.	86	50.26 N	74.24 E
Imeni Džambula, Kaz.	86	44.52 N	71.22 E
Imeni Frunze	86	46.23 N	71.07 E
Imeni Il-Go Okt'abr'a	88	55.54 N	119.36 E
Imeni Kalinina, Kaz.	86	43.16 N	76.10 E
Imeni Kalinina, Kyrg.	85	41.28 N	76.22 E
Imeni Kalinina, Ross.	80	51.51 N	52.43 E
Imeni Kalinina, Uzb.	86	43.40 N	59.07 E
Imeni Karla Libknechta	78	51.37 N	35.27 E
Imeni Kirova, Kaz.	86	46.27 N	77.13 E
Imeni Kirova, Ross.	74	59.42 N	126.12 E
Imeni Leninskogo Komsomola	86	50.45 N	68.44 E
Imeni Marta	86	46.57 N	58.56 E

Nom	Page	Lat.	Long.
Imeni Michajla Ivanoviča Kalinina	80	57.59 N	45.07 E
Imeni Molodogvardejcev	86	54.03 N	70.44 E
Imeni Panfilova	85	43.23 N	77.07 E
Imeni Poliny Osipenko	92	52.25 N	136.28 E
Imeni Sardarova Karachana	85	38.26 N	68.46 E
Imeni Seredy	83	46.52 N	40.03 E
Imeni Ševčenko	86	45.58 N	61.04 E
Imeni Stepana Razina	80	54.54 N	44.18 E
Imeni Tel'mana	88	48.36 N	134.59 E
Imeni Timir'azeva	86	53.39 N	65.31 E
Imeni Vladimira Iljiča Lenina	80	53.36 N	46.58 E
Imeni Vorovskogo, Ross.	80	55.43 N	41.06 E
Imeni Vorovskogo, Ross.	82	55.43 N	38.20 E
Imeni XXI Partsjezda	86	50.43 N	67.50 E
Imeni Žel'abova	76	58.57 N	36.36 E
Imera ≃	70	37.59 N	13.49 E
Imerimandroso	157b	17.23 S	48.38 E
Imese	152	2.07 N	18.06 E
Imgenbroich	56	50.34 N	6.16 E
Imi	144	6.28 N	42.18 E
Imías	240p	20.04 N	74.38 W
Imilac	252	24.14 S	68.53 W
Imilili ⨀⁴	148	23.18 N	15.54 W
Imi-n'Tanout	148	31.10 N	8.50 W
Imiši	84	39.52 N	48.04 E
Imittós	267c	37.57 N	23.45 E
Imittós Óros ∧	267c	37.55 N	23.47 E
Imja-do I	98	35.05 N	126.05 E
Imjin-gang ≃	98	37.47 N	126.40 E
Imlay	204	40.39 N	118.08 W
Imlay City	190	43.01 N	83.04 W
Imlaystown	268	40.10 N	74.31 W
Imler	214	40.12 N	78.31 W
Immarna	162	30.30 S	132.09 E
Immendingen	58	47.56 N	8.44 E
Immenhausen	56	51.25 N	9.28 E
Immensen	52	52.23 N	10.04 E
Immenstaad	58	47.40 N	9.22 E
Immenstadt	58	47.33 N	10.13 E
Immigrath	263	51.06 N	6.57 E
Immingham	44	53.36 N	0.13 W
Immokalee	220	26.25 N	81.25 W
Imnaha ≃	202	45.49 N	116.46 W
Imo □³	150	5.30 N	7.25 E
Imo ≃	150	4.36 N	7.35 E
Imogiri	115a	7.55 S	110.23 E
Imokt'an	98	38.50 N	126.41 E
Imola	66	44.21 N	11.42 E
Imonda	164	3.20 S	141.10 E
Imore	273a	6.26 N	3.17 E
Imoro	273a	6.43 N	3.30 E
Im Ostholz ⨀⁸	263	51.26 N	7.12 E
Imotski	36	43.27 N	17.13 E
Impa ∧	98	35.59 N	126.49 E
Impasugong ≃	116	8.19 N	125.05 E
Impe	152	2.44 S	15.17 E
Impendle	158	29.37 S	29.55 E
Imperatore, Campo ≃	66	42.25 N	13.40 E
Imperatriz	250	5.32 S	47.29 W
Imperia	62	43.53 N	8.03 E
Imperia □⁴	62	43.58 N	7.47 E
Imperial, Sk., Can.	184	51.22 N	105.27 W
Imperial, Perú	248	13.04 S	76.21 W
Imperial, Ca., U.S.	204	32.50 N	115.34 W
Imperial, Mo., U.S.	219	38.22 N	90.24 W
Imperial, Ne., U.S.	198	40.31 N	101.38 W
Imperial, Pa., U.S.	214	40.26 N	80.14 W
Imperial, Tx., U.S.	196	31.16 N	102.41 W
Imperial ≃	254	38.48 S	73.24 W
Imperial Beach	228	32.35 N	117.06 W
Imperial Dam ⨀⁶	204	32.55 N	114.30 W
Imperial de Aragón, Canal ≖	34	42.02 N	1.33 W
Imperiale	68	40.07 N	16.35 E
Imperial Mills	200	54.55 N	111.44 W
Imperial Palace ∗	268	35.41 N	139.45 E
Imperial Valley ⩗	204	32.50 N	115.30 W
Impfingen	56	49.10 N	8.07 E
Impfondo	152	1.37 N	18.04 E
Imphāl	126	24.49 N	93.57 E
Impilachti	24	61.40 N	31.04 E
Impruneta	66	43.41 N	11.15 E
Imroz	130	40.11 N	25.55 E
Imsil	98	35.37 N	127.15 E
Imst	64	47.14 N	10.44 E
Imuris	132	30.47 N	110.52 W
Imuruan Bay c	116	10.40 N	119.16 E
Imuruk Basin c	180	65.06 N	165.30 W
Imuruk Lake ◎	180	65.36 N	163.10 W
Imute	273a	6.42 N	3.29 E
Imwŏn-ni	98	37.15 N	129.20 E
Ina, Nihon	96	37.19 N	139.32 E
Ina, Nihon	96	35.49 N	140.03 E
Ina, Nihon	96	35.50 N	137.57 E
Ina, Nihon	268	35.59 N	139.38 E
In'a, Ross.	74	59.24 N	144.48 E
Ina, Ross.	86	53.31 N	82.40 E
Ina, Ross.	86	50.48 N	86.37 E
Ina, II., U.S.	219	38.09 N	88.54 W
Ina ≃, Nihon	96	34.43 N	135.28 E
Ina ≃, Pol.	54	53.32 N	14.38 E
In'a ≃, Ross.	74	59.23 N	144.54 E
In'a ≃, Ross.	86	54.59 N	82.59 E
Inaba	270	34.36 N	135.27 E
Inabe	34	35.07 N	136.33 E
Ina-bonchi ⩊¹	96	35.30 N	137.50 E
Inabu	96	35.13 N	137.30 E
Inaccessible Island I	10	37.17 S	12.45 W
Inada	270	34.53 N	135.08 E
Inagawa	96	34.53 N	135.22 E
Inagawa ≃	96	34.39 N	135.25 E
Inage	268	35.38 N	140.05 E
Inagi	96	35.38 N	139.30 E
Inagi	268	35.38 N	139.30 E
In'akino	88	50.26 N	41.37 E
Inakona	175e	9.49 S	160.02 E
Inala	179	27.35 S	152.58 E
Inamangando ≃	152	11.03 S	12.23 E
Inambari ≃	248	12.41 S	69.44 W
In Amguel	148	23.40 N	5.10 E
Inami, Nihon	96	36.33 N	136.58 E
Inami, Nihon	96	34.45 N	134.54 E
Inami, Nihon	96	33.48 N	135.13 E
In Amnas	148	28.03 N	9.38 E
Inampulgan Island I	116	10.28 N	122.42 E
Inamuragasaki Point >	268	35.18 N	139.32 E
Inanda	158	29.43 S	30.52 E
Inanda ⨀⁸	273d	26.07 S	28.03 E
Inanghua Junction	172	41.51 S	171.57 E
Inanwatan	164	2.08 S	132.10 E
Iñapari	248	10.57 S	69.35 W
Inaporok	98	8.15 S	141.55 E
In'aptuk, gora ∧	88	56.31 N	112.10 E
Inari	24	68.54 N	27.01 E
Inarigda	74	63.14 N	107.27 E
Inarijärvi ◎	24	69.00 N	28.00 E
Inas, Gunong ∧	114	5.15 N	100.56 E
Inasa	96	34.50 N	137.40 E
Inatsuki	96	33.36 N	130.43 E
Inawini ≃	248	8.30 S	67.24 W
Inawashiro-ko ◎	92	37.29 N	140.06 E
In-n-Azaoua ⩗¹	148	20.49 N	7.30 E
Inazawa	96	35.15 N	136.47 E
Inba	96	35.46 N	140.12 E
Inba-numa ◎	96	35.46 N	140.12 E
In Belbel	148	27.54 N	1.10 E

Nome	Página	Lat.	Long.
Inca	34	39.43 N	2.54 E
Inca de Oro	252	26.45 S	69.54 W
Incaguasi	252	29.13 S	71.03 W
Incahuasi, Nevado de ∧	252	27.02 S	68.18 W
Ince	262	53.17 N	2.49 W
Ince Blundell	262	53.31 N	3.02 W
Ince Burun >	130	42.06 N	34.56 E
Ince-in-Makerfield	262	53.32 N	2.37 W
Incekurr Burnu >	130	36.13 N	33.58 E
Incesu	130	38.38 N	35.11 E
Inch	48	52.08 N	9.59 W
I-n-Chacuag ≃	150	16.23 N	0.10 E
Inchard, Loch c	46	58.27 N	5.04 W
Inchas Military Base ✈	142	30.20 N	31.27 E
Inchbare	46	56.47 N	2.38 W
Inchcape I²	46	56.26 N	2.23 W
Inchelium	182	48.17 N	118.11 W
Inchiri □⁴	150	19.50 N	15.00 W
Inchmarnock I	46	55.47 N	5.09 W
Inchnadamph	46	58.09 N	4.59 W
Inch'ŏn	98	37.28 N	126.38 E
Inch'ŏn □⁴	98	37.28 N	126.38 E
Inchture	46	56.26 N	3.10 W
Inchwang Lake ◎	281	42.27 N	83.41 W
incirliova	130	37.50 N	27.43 E
Incisa in Va d'Arno	66	43.40 N	11.27 E
Incline Village	226	39.16 N	119.56 W
Incomáti (Komati) ≃	156	25.46 S	32.43 E
Inconfidência	256	22.16 S	43.13 W
Incondentes	256	22.20 S	46.20 W
Indoun	180	66.18 N	170.17 W
Incudine	64	46.14 N	10.22 E
Incudine, Monte ∧	36	41.51 N	9.12 E
Incy	24	65.48 N	40.26 E
Indaal, Loch c	46	55.45 N	6.21 W
Indaiá ≃	255	18.27 S	45.22 W
Indaiatuba	256	23.05 S	47.14 W
Indalsälven ≃	26	62.31 N	17.27 E
Indanan	116	5.58 N	120.59 E
Indaparapec	234	19.47 N	100.58 W
Inda Silase	144	14.05 N	38.20 E
Indaw	110	23.40 N	94.46 E
Indawgyi Lake ◎	110	25.10 N	96.19 E
Indé	232	25.54 S	105.13 W
— India □¹	118	20.00 N	77.00 E
Inde ≃	56	50.54 N	6.21 E
Indemini	58	46.06 N	8.50 E
Independence, Ca., U.S.	204	36.48 N	118.11 W
Independence, Ia., U.S.	216	40.20 N	87.10 W
Independence, Ia., U.S.	190	42.28 N	91.53 W
Independence, Ks., U.S.	198	37.13 N	95.42 W
Independence, Ky., U.S.	218	38.56 N	84.32 W
Independence, La., U.S.	194	30.38 N	90.30 W
Independence, Mo., U.S.	194	39.05 N	94.24 W
Independence, Oh., U.S.	279a	41.23 N	81.38 W
Independence, Or., U.S.	202	44.51 N	123.11 W
Independence, Va., U.S.	214	40.15 N	80.31 W
Independence, Va., U.S.	222	30.19 N	96.21 W
Independence, Wi., U.S.	192	36.37 N	81.09 W
Independence ≃	190	44.21 N	91.25 W
Independence Creek ≃	188	43.45 N	75.20 W
Independence Hall ⊥	285	39.57 N	75.09 W
Independence Lake ◎	226	39.26 N	120.18 W
Independence Mountains ∧	204	41.15 N	115.55 W
Independência, Bol.	248	17.07 S	66.53 W
Independência, Bra.	250	5.23 S	40.19 W
Independência, Chile	286e	33.23 S	70.40 W
Independência, Perú	248	14.15 S	75.42 W
Independência, Isla I	248	14.15 S	76.12 W
Independencia ◎	152	13.53 S	13.39 E
Inderborskij	80	48.33 N	51.44 E
In der Bredde	263	51.20 N	7.23 E
Inderesi	137	37.50 N	35.40 E
Index	224	47.49 N	121.33 W
Index, Mount ∧	224	47.46 N	121.35 W
India (Bhārat) □¹	118	20.00 N	77.00 E
India Brook ≃	276	40.47 N	74.37 W
India Gate ⊥	272a	28.37 N	77.18 E
Indialantic	220	28.05 N	80.34 W
Indian ≃, On., Can.	212	48.15 N	76.14 W
Indian ≃, On., Can.	212	44.13 N	78.08 W
Indian ≃, La., U.S.	283	38.36 N	75.10 W
Indian ≃, Mi., U.S.	190	45.59 N	86.15 W
Indian ≃, N.Y., U.S.	190	43.50 N	74.39 W
Indiana	214	40.37 N	79.09 W
Indiana □³	178	40.00 N	86.15 W
Indiana □³, U.S.	194	40.00 N	86.15 W
Indiana Dunes National Lakeshore ♦	281	41.40 N	87.00 W
Indiana Dunes State Park ♦	216	41.40 N	87.02 W
Indian Agricultural Research Institute ⩊³	272a	28.38 N	77.10 E
Indiana Harbor	278	41.40 N	87.27 W
Indiana Harbor Canal ≖	278	41.40 N	87.27 W
Indianapolis	218	39.46 N	86.09 W
Indianapolis Motor Speedway ♦	281	39.43 N	86.16 W
Indian Bayou ≃	194	34.14 N	91.52 W
Indian Brook ≃	186	46.23 N	60.32 W
Indian Caverns ⊥ ⁵	214	40.38 N	78.05 W
Indian Church	232	17.45 N	88.40 W
Indian Creek ≃	182	42.14 N	87.59 W
Indian Creek ≃, Ca., U.S.	228	35.18 N	118.26 W
Indian Creek ≃, II., U.S.	219	39.56 N	90.32 W
Indian Creek ≃, In., U.S.	216	41.26 N	88.46 W
Indian Creek ≃, Md., U.S.	283	38.59 N	76.55 W
Indian Creek ≃, Mo., U.S.	194	36.33 N	94.29 W
Indian Creek ≃, Mt., U.S.	219	39.13 N	91.11 W
Indian Creek ≃, N.M., U.S.	200	36.11 N	108.23 W
Indian Creek ≃, N.Y., U.S.	276	43.06 N	73.06 W

Nome	Página	Lat.	Long.
Indian Creek ≃, Oh., U.S.	218	39.19 N	84.38 W
Indian Creek ≃, Oh., U.S.	279a	41.17 N	81.31 W
Indian Creek ≃, S.D., U.S.	198	44.39 N	103.19 W
Indian Creek ≃, Tn., U.S.	216	35.13 N	88.08 W
Indianford	216	42.49 N	88.35 W
Indian Grave Mountain ∧	192	32.59 N	84.21 W
Indian Harbor Beach	220	28.08 N	80.35 W
Indian Head, Sk., Can.	184	50.32 N	103.40 W
Indian Head, Md., U.S.	208	38.36 N	77.09 W
Indian Head ≃	283	42.04 N	70.52 W
Indian Head Park	281	41.47 N	87.54 W
Indian Head Pond ◎	283	42.03 N	70.51 W
Indian Heights	216	40.25 N	86.07 W
Indian Island I	224	48.04 N	122.43 W
Indian Kentuck Creek ≃	218	38.43 N	85.16 W
Indian Lake, Mi., U.S.	216	41.56 N	86.12 W
Indian Lake, N.Y., U.S.	188	43.46 N	74.16 W
Indian Lake ◎, On., Can.	190	47.08 N	82.08 W
Indian Lake ◎, Mi., U.S.	190	45.59 N	86.20 W
Indian Lake ◎, Mi., U.S.	216	42.09 N	85.29 W
Indian Lake ◎, N.J., U.S.	276	42.00 N	86.13 W
Indian Lake ◎, Oh., U.S.	216	40.29 N	83.53 W
Indian Lake Estates	220	27.47 N	81.19 W
Indian Lakes ≃	216	41.33 N	85.25 W
Indian Lake State Park ♦	216	40.23 N	83.52 W
Indian Mills Brook ≃	285	39.47 N	74.44 W
Indian Mills Lake ◎	285	39.48 N	74.44 W
Indian Neck	207	41.15 N	72.48 W
Indian Ocean ⛨¹	4	10.00 S	70.00 E
Indian Ocean ⛨¹	6	10.00 S	70.00 E
Indianola, a., U.S.	190	41.21 N	93.33 W
Indianola, Ms., U.S.	194	33.27 N	90.39 W
Indianola, Pa., U.S.	279b	40.34 N	79.51 W
Indianópolis ⨀⁸	255	19.02 S	47.55 W
Indianópolis ⨀⁸	287b	23.36 S	46.38 W
Indian Pea ≃, Ut., U.S.	200	38.16 N	113.53 W
Indian Pea ≃, Wy., U.S.	202	44.47 N	109.51 W
Indian Point ⩗	212	44.37 N	78.49 W
Indian Prairie Canal ≖	220	27.02 N	80.57 W
Indian Queen Estates	284c	38.46 N	77.02 W
Indian River	190	45.24 N	84.36 W
Indian River ≃	220	27.43 N	80.36 W
Indian River ≃	208	38.36 N	80.30 W
Indian River Bay c	208	38.36 N	75.05 W
Indian River Inlet ⋃	208	38.37 N	75.03 W
Indian Rock ∧	224	45.59 N	120.49 W
Indian Rock Dam ⨀⁶	208	39.57 N	76.45 W
Indian Rock Paintings ⊥	224	46.38 N	120.31 W
Indian Rocks Beach	220	27.52 N	82.51 W
Indian Springs, Nv., U.S.	204	36.34 N	115.40 W
Indian Springs, Va., U.S.	284c	38.49 N	77.10 W
Indian Stream ≃	206	45.03 N	71.26 W
Indiantown	220	27.01 N	80.29 W
Indian Town Point >	240c	17.06 N	61.40 W
Indian Valley, In., U.S.	216	40.40 N	86.15 W
Indian Village, In., U.S.	216	41.15 N	85.22 W
Indian Village, N.Y., U.S.	210	42.57 N	76.10 W
Indiaporã	255	19.57 S	50.17 W
Indiaroba	250	11.32 S	37.31 W
Indibir	144	8.05 N	37.58 E
Índico, Océano ⛨¹	— Indian Ocean	4	10.00 S	70.00 E
Índico, Océano ⛨¹	— Indian Ocean	6	10.00 S	70.00 E
Indien □¹ — India	118	20.00 N	77.00 E
Indien, Océan ⛨¹ — Indian Ocean	6	10.00 S	70.00 E
Indien, territoires britanniques de l'Ocean — British Indian Ocean Territory □²	12	7.00 S	72.00 E
Indiera Alta	240m	18.09 N	66.53 W
Indiga	24	67.41 N	49.00 E
Indigirka ≃	74	70.48 N	148.54 E
Indija	38	45.03 N	20.05 E
Indin	120	20.16 N	92.57 E
Indin ◎	200	64.36 N	115.12 W
Indio, Nic. ≃	236	10.57 N	83.44 W
Indio, Pan. ≃	238	9.12 N	80.11 W
Indio, Punta >	258	35.16 S	57.13 W
Indios, Cana de los ⮝	240p	21.56 N	83.16 W
Indira Gandhi Canal ≖	120	31.10 N	75.00 E
Indira Gandhi International Airport ✈	272a	28.35 N	77.07 E
Indischer Ozean ⛨¹ — Indian Ocean	6	10.00 S	70.00 E
Indispensable Reefs ⛝²	160	12.40 S	160.25 E
Indispensable Strait ⋃	175e	9.00 S	160.30 E
Indo — Indus ≃	108	24.20 N	67.47 E
Indom	108	16.00 N	107.00 E
Indom	24	64.36 N	55.22 E
Indonesia □¹	108	5.00 S	120.00 E
Indonesia, University of ⩊²	269e	6.12 S	106.51 E
Indonesia in Miniature — Indonesia □¹	108	5.00 S	120.00 E
Indonesia Culture, Museum of ⩗³	269e	6.09 N	106.49 E
— Indonesia □¹	108	5.00 S	120.00 E
Indonesien — Indonesia □¹	108	5.00 S	120.00 E
Indooroopilly	171a	27.30 S	152.58 E
Indore	120	22.43 N	75.50 E
— Yining	86	43.54 N	81.21 E
Indra	76	55.53 N	27.32 E
Indragiri ≃	112	0.23 S	103.11 E
Indramayu, Ujung >	115a	6.20 S	108.19 E
Indrapura	115	0.26 S	108.17 E
Indravati ≃	120	18.44 N	80.16 E
Indre □⁵	32	46.45 N	1.30 E
Indre ≃	32	47.16 N	0.19 E
Indre-et-Loire □⁵	50	47.15 N	0.45 E
Induno Olona	62	45.52 N	8.51 E
Indura	76	53.27 N	23.53 E
Industry, II., U.S.	194	40.20 N	90.36 W
Industry, Tx., U.S.	222	29.58 N	96.30 W
Indwe	158	31.28 S	27.23 E

Nome	Página	Lat.	Long.
Indwe	158	32.01 S	27.21 E
Ine	96	35.39 N	135.17 E
Inebolu	130	41.58 N	33.46 E
Inece	130	41.41 N	27.04 E
Inecik	130	40.56 N	27.16 E
In Ecker	148	24.09 N	5.03 E
Inegöl	130	40.05 N	29.31 E
Inerie, Gunung ∧	115b	8.52 S	120.56 E
Inés, Monte ∧	254	48.29 S	69.40 W
Ineu	38	46.26 N	21.49 E
Inez, Ky., U.S.	192	37.51 N	82.32 W
Inez, Tx., U.S.	222	28.54 N	96.47 W
Inez, Lake ◎	276	41.01 N	74.17 W
Infanta, Pil.	116	15.50 N	119.55 E
Infanta, Pil.	116	14.45 N	121.39 E
Infanta, Kaap >	158	34.29 S	20.51 E
Inferior, Laguna c	234	16.20 N	94.40 W
Infierno, Cachoeira do ⛝	—		
Infiernillo, Presa del ⛝¹	234	18.35 N	101.45 W
Infiesto	34	43.21 N	5.22 W
Infreschi, Ponta degli >	68	40.00 N	15.26 E
Ingá	250	7.17 S	35.36 W
Ingabu	110	17.49 N	95.16 E
Ingai	256	21.24 S	44.55 W
Ingai ≃	256	21.23 S	44.52 W
Ingal	150	16.47 N	6.56 E
Ingalls	218	39.57 N	85.48 W
Ingalls Creek ≃	224	47.28 N	120.39 W
Ingalls Park	216	41.32 N	88.03 W
Inganda	152	0.05 S	20.57 E
Inganno ≃	70	38.04 N	14.37 E
Ingarö I	40	59.16 N	18.28 E
Ingatestone	42	51.41 N	0.22 E
Ingatestone Hall ⊥	260	51.39 N	0.23 E
Ingelheim	56	49.18 N	9.39 E
Ingelheim	56	49.59 N	8.03 E
Ingelmunster	50	50.55 N	3.15 E
Ingelstad	26	56.45 N	14.55 E
Ingende	152	0.15 S	18.57 E
Ingeniería, Universidad Nacional de ⩊²	286d	12.02 S	77.02 W
Ingeniero Budge ⨀¹	264	34.43 S	58.28 W
Ingeniero Jacobacci	254	41.18 S	69.35 W
Ingeniero Juan Allan	258	34.53 S	58.11 W
Ingeniero Luiggi	252	35.25 S	64.29 W
Ingeniero Luis A. Huergo	252	39.05 S	67.14 W
Ingeniero Maschwitz	264	34.23 S	58.44 W
Ingeniero Romulo Otamendi	258	34.13 S	58.54 W
Ingeniero White	252	38.47 S	62.16 W
Ingeniero Williams	258	34.54 S	59.22 W
Ingenio La Esperanza	252	24.13 S	64.51 W
Ingenio Santa Ana	252	27.28 S	65.41 W
Ingeringbach ≃	61	47.12 N	14.49 E
Ingersheim	58	48.06 N	7.18 E
Ingersoll	212	43.02 N	80.53 W
Ingham	166	18.39 S	146.10 E
Ingham ≃	216	42.37 N	84.22 W
Ingička	85	39.52 N	67.20 E
Ingleborough ∧	44	54.11 N	2.23 W
Ingleburn	170	34.00 S	150.52 E
Inglesa, Costa — English Coast ⛨	9	73.45 S	73.00 W
Ingleside, Austl.	274a	33.41 S	151.13 E
Ingleside, On., Can.	206	45.00 N	75.00 W
Ingleside, II., U.S.	216	42.23 N	88.09 W
Ingleside, Tx., U.S.	196	27.52 N	97.12 W
Ingleside ⨀⁸	282	37.43 N	122.28 W
Inglewood, Austl.	166	28.25 S	151.05 E
Inglewood, Austl.	166	36.34 S	143.52 E
Inglewood, N.Z.	172	39.09 S	174.12 E
Inglewood, Ca., U.S.	228	33.57 N	118.21 W
Inglewood, Wa., U.S.	224	47.44 N	122.11 W
Inglewood Forest ⩗¹	44	54.45 N	2.50 W
Inglis, Mb., Can.	184	50.53 N	101.15 W
Inglis, Fl., U.S.	220	29.02 N	82.40 W
Inglis Lock ⨀⁵	220	29.02 N	82.47 W
Ingoda ≃	88	51.42 N	115.48 E
Ingogo	158	27.33 S	29.56 E
Ingoldmells	44	53.11 N	0.20 E
Ingoldstadt	60	48.46 N	11.27 E
Ingomar	279b	40.35 N	80.03 W
Ingonish	186	46.42 N	60.22 W
Ingornachoix Bay c	186	50.38 N	57.20 W
Ingraham, Lake ◎	220	25.15 N	81.08 W
Ingrāj Bāzār	124	25.00 N	88.09 E
Ingram, Pa., U.S.	279b	40.26 N	80.04 W
Ingram, Tx., U.S.	196	30.04 N	99.14 W
Ingram Bay c	208	37.48 N	76.17 W
Ingrave	260	51.36 N	0.20 E
Ingrid Christensen Coast ⛨	9	69.30 S	76.00 E
In Guezzam	150	19.32 S	5.42 E
Ingul ≃	78	47.20 N	31.59 E
Ingulec	288	47.43 N	33.14 E
Ingulo-Kamenka	78	48.17 N	32.30 E
Inguri ≃	84	42.24 N	41.33 E
Ingushetia — Čečnja-Ingušetija □³	84	43.15 N	45.40 E
Inguzet	88	58.50 N	83.52 E
Ingvallsbenning	40	60.15 N	15.53 E
Ingwavuma	158	27.09 S	31.58 E
Ingwe	154	23.00 S	26.00 E
Ingwiller	56	48.52 N	7.29 E
Inhaca, Ilha da I	158	26.03 S	32.57 E
Inhafenga	156	20.35 S	33.53 E
Inhambane	156	23.51 S	35.29 E
Inhambane, Baía de c	156	23.00 S	34.30 E
Inhaminga	156	18.24 S	35.00 E
Inhanduí ≃	255	21.37 S	52.59 W
Inhanduí-Mirim ≃	255	19.33 S	50.07 W
Inhangapi	250	1.26 S	47.55 W
Inharrime	156	24.29 S	35.01 E
Inhassoro	156	21.32 S	35.11 E
Inhaúma	255	19.29 S	44.22 W
Inhaúma ⨀⁸	287a	22.53 S	43.17 E
Inhisar	130	40.03 N	30.10 E
Inhoaiba ⨀⁸	287a	22.55 S	43.34 W
Inhomirim	256	22.35 S	43.13 W
Inhumas	287a	22.34 S	43.11 W
Ini	146	6.40 N	41.42 W
Iniesta	34	39.26 N	1.45 W
Inimutaba	255	18.40 S	44.23 W
Ining — Yining	86	43.54 N	81.21 E
Inírida ≃	246	3.55 N	67.52 W
Inisa	150	7.52 N	4.22 E
Inishbofin I, Ire.	48	53.37 N	10.13 W
Inishbofin I, Ire.	48	55.09 N	8.10 W
Inishcrone	48	54.13 N	9.06 W
Inisheer I	48	53.04 N	9.31 W
Inishkea North I	48	54.08 N	10.12 W
Inishkea South I	48	54.07 N	10.10 W
Inishmaan I	48	53.05 N	9.35 W
In'va ≃	88	58.59 N	54.40 E
Inishmurray I	48	54.26 N	8.40 W
Inishowen Head >	48	55.14 N	6.56 W
Inishshark I	48	53.37 N	10.18 W
Inishturk I	48	53.43 N	10.07 W
Inishvickillane I	48	52.02 N	10.35 W
Initao	116	8.30 N	124.18 E
Inje	98	38.05 N	128.09 E

Nome	Página	Lat.	Long.
Injibara	144	11.00 N	36.59 E
Injune	166	25.51 S	148.34 E
Inkeroinen	26	60.42 N	26.51 E
Inketete	152	2.37 S	21.53 E
Inkisi (Zadi) ≃	152	4.46 S	14.52 E
Inkom	202	42.47 N	112.15 W
Inkster, Mi., U.S.	216	42.17 N	83.18 W
Inkster, N.D., U.S.	198	48.09 N	97.38 W
Inland Kaikoura Range ∧	172	42.00 S	173.40 E
Inland Lake ◎, Mb., Can.	184	52.17 N	96.44 W
Inland Lake ◎, Ak., U.S.	180	66.27 N	159.47 W
Inland Sea — Seto-naikai ⛨²	96	34.20 N	133.30 E
Inle ≃	110	20.30 N	96.55 E
Inman, Ks., U.S.	198	38.13 N	97.46 W
Inman, S.C., U.S.	192	35.02 N	82.05 W
Inman Mills	192	35.02 N	82.06 W
Inman Valley	163b	35.30 S	138.28 E
Inn (En) ≃	32	48.35 N	13.28 E
Innamincka	166	27.45 S	140.44 E
Innbach ≃	61	48.18 N	14.07 E
Innellan	46	55.54 N	4.57 W
Inner Bay c	214	42.37 N	80.24 W
Innerbraz	64	47.09 N	9.55 E
Inner Channel ⋃	232	16.35 N	88.17 W
Innerferrera	58	46.31 N	9.28 E
Innerfragant	64	46.58 N	13.04 E
Inner Harbor c	276	40.52 N	73.28 W
Inner Hebrides I	46	56.30 N	6.00 W
Innerkip	212	43.13 N	80.42 W
Innerleithen	46	55.38 N	3.05 W
Inner Mongolia — Nei Monggol Zizhiqu □⁴	90	43.00 N	115.00 E
Inner Sister Island I	166	39.42 S	147.55 E
Innerschwand	61	47.55 N	13.25 E
Innerste ≃	52	52.15 N	9.52 E
Innerstalsperre ⛝⁶	52	51.55 N	10.17 E
Innerthal	58	47.06 N	8.56 E
Innerkirchen	58	46.42 N	8.14 E
Innervillgraten	64	46.48 N	12.23 E
Innichen	— San Candido	64	46.44 N	12.17 E
Inning	60	48.05 N	11.09 E
Innisfail, Austl.	166	17.32 S	146.02 E
Innisfail, Ab., Can.	182	52.02 N	113.57 W
Innisfl Creek ≃	212	44.08 N	79.49 W
Innisfree	182	53.22 N	111.32 W
Innisplair	171a	28.10 S	152.55 E
Innokent'evka	89	49.42 N	136.17 E
Innokent'evskij	89	48.37 N	140.10 E
Innoko ≃	180	62.14 N	159.45 W
Innolovo	262	59.47 N	29.59 E
Innoshima	96	34.17 N	133.11 E
Inno-shima I	96	34.17 N	133.11 E
Innsbruck	64	47.16 N	11.24 E
Innviertel ⮝¹	61	48.14 N	13.15 E
Ino ≃, Eng., U.K.	42	50.35 N	4.17 W
Ino, Va., U.S.	208	37.46 N	76.48 W
Inoã	256	22.55 S	42.57 W
Inobonto	112	0.52 N	123.57 E
Inocência	255	19.44 S	51.48 W
Inokashira Park ♦	268	35.42 N	139.34 E
Inola	196	36.09 N	95.30 W
Inongo	152	1.57 S	18.16 E
Inoni	152	3.04 S	15.39 E
Inōnū	130	39.48 N	30.09 E
Inoue	270	34.48 N	135.23 E
Inovroclaw	30	52.48 N	18.15 E
Inozemcevo	84	44.08 N	43.06 E
Inp'ung-dong	98	41.25 N	126.24 E
Inrath ⨀⁸	263	51.21 N	6.32 E
Isle of Man □²	44	54.15 N	4.30 W
Inta	160	8.49 N	9.40 E
Inshas ar-Raml	142	30.23 N	31.27 E
Ińsko	30	53.27 N	15.33 E
In Sokki, Oued ⩗	148	29.47 N	4.13 E
Inspiration	200	33.24 N	110.52 W
Insterburg — Čern'achovsk	76	54.38 N	21.49 E
Instow	184	49.30 N	108.16 W
Insurgente José María Morelos, Parque Nacional ♦	234	19.35 N	100.55 W
Insuil	150	19.32 S	5.42 E
Intaca	255	35.14 S	63.35 W
Inta Gulec	252	36.20 S	63.20 W
Intercession City	220	28.15 N	81.30 W
Intercourse	208	40.02 N	76.05 W
Interlachen	220	29.37 N	81.53 W
Interlaken, Schw.	58	46.41 N	7.51 E
Interlaken, N.J., U.S.	276	40.14 N	74.01 W
Interlaken, N.Y., U.S.	210	42.37 N	76.43 W
Interlândia	256	16.12 S	49.02 W
Internacional (Guarulhos), Aeroporto ✈	287b	23.29 S	46.28 W
International Amphitheatre ⊥	281	41.49 N	87.39 W
International Falls	190	48.36 N	93.24 W
International Peace Garden ♦	198	49.00 N	100.04 W
International Trade Fair ♦	267d	35.47 N	51.24 E
Interstate State Park ♦	190	45.35 N	92.40 W
Inthanon, Doi ∧	110	18.35 N	98.29 E
Intibucá □⁵	236	14.16 N	88.10 W
Intibucá	236	14.19 N	88.10 W
Intiyaco	252	28.39 S	60.05 W
Intracoastal Waterway ≃, La., U.S.	192	30.53 N	81.46 W
Intracoastal Waterway ≃, Tx., U.S.	196	26.04 N	97.12 W
Intragna	58	46.11 N	8.42 E
Intrånget	40	60.20 N	16.09 E
Introbio	62	45.59 N	9.27 E
Introdacqua	66	42.00 N	13.54 E
Intu	112	0.15 S	115.21 E
Inubō-saki >	96	35.42 N	140.52 E
Inukai	96	33.04 N	131.38 E
Inúquil	248	9.26 S	77.49 W
Inútil, Bahía c	254	53.30 S	70.00 W
Inuvik	176	68.25 N	133.30 W
Inuyama	96	35.23 N	136.57 E
Inverallochy	46	57.40 N	1.56 W
Inveraray	46	56.13 N	5.05 W
Inverbervie	46	56.51 N	2.17 W
Inverdruie	46	57.10 N	3.48 W
Inverell	166	29.47 S	151.07 E

Symbol	English	Deutsch	Español	Français	Português
≃	River	Fluß	Río	Rivière	Rio
≖	Canal	Kanal	Canal	Canal	Canal
⌇	Waterfall, Rapids	Wasserfall, Stromschnellen	Cascada, Rápidos	Cascade, Rápides	Chute d'eau, Rapides	Cascata, Rápidos
⋃	Strait	Meerestraße	Estrecho	Détroit	Estreito
c	Bay, Gulf	Bucht, Golf	Bahía, Golfo	Baie, Golfe	Baía, Golfo
◎	Lake, Lakes	See, Seen	Lago, Lagos	Lac, Lacs	Lago, Lagos
⌇	Swamp	Sumpf	Pantano	Marais	Pântano
⛝	Ice Features, Glacier	Eis- und Gletscherformen	Accidentes Glaciares	Formes glaciaires	Acidentes glaciares
⛨	Other Hydrographic Features	Andere Hydrographische Objekte	Otros Elementos Hidrográficos	Autres données hydrographiques	Outros acidentes hidrográficos

Symbol	English	Deutsch	Español	Français	Português
□	Political Unit	Politische Einheit	Unidad Política	Entité politique	Unidade política
⊥	Cultural Institution	Kulturelle Institution	Institución Cultural	Institution culturelle	Instituição cultural
⊥	Historical Site	Historische Stätte	Sitio Histórico	Site historique	Sítio histórico
♦	Recreational Site	Erholungs- und Ferienort	Sitio de Recreo	Centre de loisirs	Área de Lazer
✈	Airport	Flughafen	Aeropuerto	Aéroport	Aeroporto
⨀	Military Installation	Militäranlage	Instalación Militar	Installation militaire	Instalação militar
⌇	Miscellaneous	Verschiedenes	Misceláneo	Divers	Diversos

Symbol	English	Deutsch	Español	Français	Português
⩗	Submarine Features	Untermeerische Objekte	Accidentes Submarinos	Formes de relief sous-marin	Acidentes submarinos

Invergarry	46	57.02 N	4.47 W	Ipole	154	5.47 S	32.44 E	Iron Bridge, Eng.,				Işalniţa	38	44.24 N	23.44 E
Invergordon	46	57.42 N	4.10 W	Ipoly (Ipel') ≃	30	47.49 N	18.52 E	U.K.	42	52.38 N	2.29 W	Isla	234	18.01 N	95.30 W
Inverkeilor	46	56.38 N	2.32 W	Iporã, Bra.	255	16.28 S	51.07 W	Iron Bridge Dam ◆⁶	222	32.50 N	95.54 W	Isla	46	57.30 N	2.47 W
Inverkeithing	46	56.02 N	3.25 W	Iporã, Bra.	255	23.59 S	53.37 W	Iron City	194	35.01 N	87.34 W	Isla, Salar de la ≃	252	25.49 S	68.53 W
Inverkeithny	46	57.30 N	2.37 W	Ipota	175f	18.48 S	169.16 E	Iron Cove C	274a	33.52 S	151.10 E	Isla, Parc National			
Inverleigh	169	38.06 S	144.03 E	Ippari ≃	70	36.52 N	14.26 E	Iron Creek ≃	182	52.43 N	111.14 W	de l' ◆	157b	22.45 S	45.15 E
Inverloch	169	38.38 S	145.43 E	Ippinghausen	56	51.17 N	9.08 E	Irondale, Al., U.S.	194	33.32 N	86.42 W	Isana (Içana)	246	0.26 N	67.19 W
Invermay	184	51.48 N	103.09 W	Ipplepen	42	50.29 N	3.38 W	Irondale, Mo., U.S.	194	37.49 N	90.40 W	Işanagar	124	26.27 N	81.13 E
Invermere	182	50.30 N	116.02 W	Ippy	152	6.15 N	21.12 E	Irondale ≃	214	40.34 N	80.43 W	Isandō	273d	26.09 S	28.12 E
Invermoriston	46	57.13 N	4.37 W	Ipsala	130	40.55 N	26.23 E	Irondale ≃	212	44.49 N	78.37 W	Isanga	152	1.26 S	22.18 E
Inverness, N.S., Can.	186	46.14 N	61.18 W	Ipswich, Austl.	171a	27.36 S	152.46 E	Irondequoit	210	43.12 N	77.36 W	Isangano National			
Inverness, P.Q., Can.	206	46.15 N	71.31 W	Ipswich, Eng., U.K.	42	52.04 N	1.10 E	Irondequoit Bay C	210	43.12 N	77.32 W	Park ◆	154	11.10 S	30.40 E
Inverness, Scot., U.K.	46	57.27 N	4.15 W	Ipswich, Ma., U.S.	207	42.40 N	70.50 W	Iron Gate V	38	44.41 N	22.31 E	Isangel	175f	19.32 S	169.16 E
Inverness, Ca., U.S.	204	38.06 N	122.51 W	Ipswich, S.D., U.S.	198	45.26 N	99.01 W	Iron Gate Reservoir				Isangi	152	0.46 N	24.15 E
Inverness, Fl., U.S.	220	28.50 N	82.19 W	Ipswich ≃	207	42.42 N	70.48 W	⊜¹	38	44.30 N	22.00 E	Is'angulovo	26	52.12 N	56.36 E
Inverness, Il., U.S.	218	42.07 N	88.05 W	Ipswich Bay C	207	42.41 N	70.42 W	Ironia	276	40.49 N	74.37 W	Isanlu Makutu	150	8.17 N	5.46 E
Inverness, Ms., U.S.	194	33.21 N	90.35 W	Ipu	250	4.20 S	40.42 W	Iron Knob	166	32.44 S	137.08 E	Isan-ni	98	40.46 N	128.55 E
Inveruglas	46	56.15 N	4.43 W	Ipubi	250	7.39 S	40.07 W	Iron Mountain	190	45.49 N	88.03 W	Isanti	190	45.29 N	93.14 W
Inveruno	62	45.31 N	8.51 E	Ipueiras	250	4.33 S	40.43 W	Iron Mountain ∧, Az.,				Isar ≃	58	48.49 N	12.58 E
Inverurie	46	57.17 N	2.23 W	Ipuh	112	3.00 S	101.30 E	U.S.	200	33.27 N	111.10 W	Isara	150	6.59 N	3.41 E
Inverway	162	17.50 S	129.38 E	Ipuiúna	256	22.06 S	46.11 W	Iron Mountain ∧, Ca.,				Isarco (Eisack) ≃	64	46.27 N	11.18 E
Investigator Group II	162	33.45 S	134.30 E	Ipun, Isla I	252	44.37 S	74.46 W	U.S.	280	34.17 N	117.43 W	Isarco, Valle ∨	64	46.45 N	11.37 E
Investigator Shoal				Ipupiara	255	11.49 S	42.37 W	Iron Mountains ✗	192	36.30 N	81.50 W	Isaroag, Mount ∧	116	13.39 N	123.23 E
⊜²	108	8.09 N	114.44 E	Iput' ≃	76	52.26 N	31.02 E	Iron Range	164	12.42 S	143.18 E	Isasi	273a	6.40 N	3.23 E
Investigator Strait U	166	35.25 S	137.10 E	Iqaluit	176	63.44 N	68.28 W	Iron Range National				Isawa	94	35.39 N	138.38 E
Inwood, Mb., Can.	184	50.30 N	97.30 W	Iqe ≃	102	38.14 N	94.18 E	Park ◆	164	12.44 S	143.16 E	Isbergues	50	50.37 N	2.27 E
Inwood, On., Can.	214	42.49 N	81.59 W	Iqfahs	142	28.47 N	30.49 E	Iron River, Mi., U.S.	190	46.05 N	88.38 W	Isbister	46a	60.36 N	1.19 W
Inwood, Fl., U.S.	220	28.02 N	81.45 W	Iquique	248	20.13 S	70.10 W	Iron River, Wi., U.S.	190	46.34 N	91.24 W	Iscehisar	130	38.51 N	30.45 E
Inwood, In., U.S.	216	41.19 N	86.12 W	Iquitos	246	3.46 S	73.15 W	Iron Springs	208	39.46 N	77.25 W	Iščeino	76	52.57 N	38.50 E
Inwood, Ia., U.S.	198	43.18 N	96.25 W	Ira	196	32.35 N	101.00 W	Ironton, Mn., U.S.	190	46.29 N	93.58 W	Iščerskaja	44	43.43 N	45.08 E
Inwood, N.Y., U.S.	276	40.37 N	73.44 W	Iran, Pil.	116	10.04 N	117.42 E	Ironton, Mo., U.S.	194	37.35 N	90.37 W	Ischgl	58	47.01 N	10.17 E
Inwood Hill Park ◆	276	40.52 N	73.56 W	Iran, Tx., U.S.	196	30.54 N	101.53 W	Ironton, Oh., U.S.	188	38.32 N	82.40 W	Ischia	68	40.44 N	13.57 E
Inyanga	154	18.13 S	32.46 E	Ira Banda	152	5.57 N	22.04 E	Ironwood	190	46.27 N	90.10 W	Ischia, Isola d' I	68	40.44 N	13.54 E
Inyanga Mountains ✗	154	18.00 S	33.00 E	Irabu	175d	24.50 N	125.09 E	Ironworks Creek ≃	285	40.10 N	74.59 W	Ischia di Castro	66	42.33 N	11.45 E
Inyangani ∧	154	18.20 S	32.50 E	Irabu-jima I	175d	24.50 N	125.10 E	Iroquois, Il., U.S.	216	40.50 N	87.35 W	— Išim ≃	86	57.45 N	71.12 E
Inyan Kara Mountain				Iracajá, Cachoeira do				Iroquois, S.D., U.S.	198	44.22 N	97.51 W	— Išim ≃	86	57.45 N	71.12 E
∧	198	44.13 N	104.21 W	∧	248	10.29 S	64.05 W	Iroquois ⊜	216	40.47 N	87.44 W	— Ižma ≃	24	65.19 N	52.54 E
Inyantue	154	18.32 S	26.41 E	Iracema	250	5.48 S	38.18 W	Iroquois ≃	216	40.47 N	87.49 W	Ischnja	76	57.19 N	39.30 E
Inyati	154	19.39 S	28.54 E	Iracoubo	250	5.29 N	53.13 W	Iroquois Falls	190	48.46 N	80.41 W	Ischl ≃	58	47.54 N	13.37 E
Inyo, Mount ∧	204	36.44 N	117.59 W	Irago-misaki >	94	34.35 N	137.01 E	Iroquois Lock and				Ischnja	76	57.19 N	39.30 E
Inyokern	204	35.38 N	117.48 W	Irago-suidō U	94	34.35 N	137.00 E	Dam ◆⁵	212	44.45 N	75.23 W	Ischua Creek ≃	210	42.10 N	78.23 W
Inyo Mountains ✗	204	36.40 N	118.10 W	Irai	252	27.11 S	53.15 W	Irosin	116	12.42 N	124.02 E	Iscuandé	246	2.38 N	78.04 W
Inywa	110	23.56 N	96.17 E	Irajá ◆⁸	287a	22.51 S	43.19 W	Irottkó				Isdell ≃	162	16.27 S	124.51 E
Inza	80	53.51 N	46.21 E	Irajoť	24	64.27 N	55.08 E	(Geschriebenstein)	58	47.21 N	16.26 E	Isdes	50	47.40 N	2.15 E
Inza ≃	80	53.54 N	45.44 E	Irak				∧	61	47.21 N	16.26 E	Ise (Uji-yamada)	94	34.29 N	136.42 E
Inzago	62	45.32 N	9.29 E	— Iraq □¹	128	33.00 N	44.00 E	Irō-zaki >	94	34.36 N	138.51 E	Ise ≃	54	52.30 N	10.33 E
Inzai	94	35.50 N	140.09 E	Iráklia I	38	36.50 N	25.26 E	Irpen'	78	50.31 N	30.15 E	Isefjord C	41	55.52 N	11.49 E
Inzana Lake ⊜	182	54.58 N	124.40 W	Iráklion, Ellás	38	35.20 N	25.09 E	Irpen' ≃	78	50.31 N	30.15 E	Isehara	94	35.24 N	139.18 E
Inžavino	52	52.19 N	42.30 E	Iráklion, Ellás	287c	38.04 N	23.46 E	Irrawaddy				Išejevka	80	54.25 N	48.16 E
Inzell	86	54.14 N	57.34 E	Iran (Īrān) □¹, Asia	128	32.00 N	53.00 E	— Ayeyarwady ≃	110	20.32 N	96.55 E	Isel ≃	64	46.50 N	12.47 E
Inzer	86	54.30 N	56.28 E	Iran, Pegunungan ∧	112	2.05 N	114.55 E	Irrawaddy, Mouths of				Iselin, N.J., U.S.	210	40.34 N	74.19 W
Inzersdorf ◆⁸	264b	48.09 N	16.21 E	Iran National Arts				the ≃¹	110	15.45 N	94.50 E	Iselin, Pa., U.S.	214	40.33 N	79.23 W
Inzia ≃	152	3.45 S	17.57 E	Museum ◆	267d	35.41 N	51.27 E	Irrel	56	49.51 N	6.28 E	Iselle	58	46.12 N	8.12 E
Ioanna, gora ∧	180	64.50 N	178.08 E	Tränshahr	128	27.13 N	60.41 E	Irricana	182	51.19 N	113.37 W	Iseltwald	58	46.40 N	7.58 E
Ioánnina	38	39.40 N	20.50 E	Irapa	246	10.34 N	62.35 W	Irrigon	202	45.53 N	119.29 W	Isen	60	48.13 N	12.04 E
Ioco	224	49.18 N	122.52 W	Irapuato	234	20.41 N	101.21 W	Irša ≃	78	50.31 N	29.30 E	Isen ≃	60	48.13 N	12.04 E
Iokanga ≃	24	68.00 N	39.43 E	Iraq (Al-'Irāq) □¹,				Irshad ≃	78	48.20 N	23.03 E	Isenbüttel	52	52.26 N	10.34 E
Iola, Ks., U.S.	198	37.55 N	95.23 W	Asia	118	33.00 N	44.00 E	Irschenberg	54	47.50 N	11.55 E	Isenya	154	8.36 S	33.30 E
Iola, Pa., U.S.	210	45.08 N	76.32 W	Iraq (Al-'Irāq) □¹,				Irsee	58	47.54 N	10.34 E	Iseo	64	45.39 N	10.03 E
Iola, Tx., U.S.	222	30.46 N	96.05 W	Asia	128	33.00 N	44.00 E	Irsina	68	40.45 N	16.15 E	Iseo, Lago d' ⊜	64	45.43 N	10.04 E
Iola, Wi., U.S.	190	44.30 N	89.07 W	Iratapuru ≃	250	0.36 S	52.35 W	Irt ≃	44	54.22 N	3.26 W	Iseramagazi	154	4.40 S	32.09 E
Iolgo, chrebet ✗	86	51.36 N	86.25 E	Irati	252	25.27 S	50.39 W	Irthing ≃	44	54.55 N	7.02 E	Iseran, Col de l' ✗	62	45.10 N	7.02 E
Iolotan'	72	37.18 N	62.21 E	Iraú ≃	34	42.35 N	1.16 W	Irthingborough	42	52.20 N	0.37 W	Isère ≃	62	45.10 N	4.51 E
Ioma	164	8.20 S	147.50 E	Iraúçuba	250	3.45 S	39.47 W	Irtyš	86	54.55 N	74.22 E	Isère □⁵	62	45.10 N	5.50 E
Iôna, ang.	152	16.50 S	12.20 E	Irazú, Volcán ∧¹	236	9.58 N	83.53 W	Irtyš (Ertix) ≃	74	61.04 N	68.52 E	Iseri	273a	6.39 N	3.23 E
Iona, N.S., Can.	186	45.58 N	60.48 W	Irba	88	58.07 N	99.00 E	Irtysch				Iseri-Oke	273a	6.38 N	3.23 E
Iona, Id., U.S.	202	43.31 N	111.55 W	Irbejskoje	88	55.39 N	95.28 E	— Irtyš ≃	72	61.04 N	68.52 E	Iseri-Osun	273a	6.31 N	3.17 E
Iona I	46	56.19 N	6.25 W	Irbeni väin (Irbes				Irtysch				Iserlohn	56	51.22 N	7.41 E
Iôna, Parque				jūras šaurums) U	76	57.48 N	22.05 E	— Irtyš ≃	72	61.04 N	68.52 E	Isernhagen	52	52.26 N	9.51 E
Nacional do ◆	152	16.30 S	12.00 E	Irbes jūras šaurums				Irun	34	43.21 N	1.47 W	Isernia	68	41.36 N	14.14 E
Iona, Sound of U	46	56.19 N	6.24 W	(Irbeni väin) U	76	57.48 N	22.05 E	Irupana	248	16.28 S	67.28 W	Isernia □⁵	66	41.40 N	14.15 E
Iona College ◆²	276	40.56 N	73.47 W	Irbid	132	32.33 N	35.51 E	Iruma	94	35.50 N	139.24 E	Isesaki	94	36.19 N	139.12 E
Ione, Ca., U.S.	226	38.21 N	120.55 W	Irbid □⁴	132	32.30 N	35.45 E	Iruma Air Base ■	268	35.50 N	139.24 E	Ise-Shima-kokuritsu-			
Ione, Or., U.S.	202	45.30 N	119.50 W	Irbil	128	36.11 N	44.01 E	Iruma-kichi, Kaijō-				kōen ◆	92	34.23 N	136.48 E
Ione, Wa., U.S.	202	48.44 N	117.24 W	Irbil □⁴	128	36.10 N	44.00 E	jieitai- ■	94	35.53 N	139.24 E	Iset' ≃	86	56.36 N	66.24 E
Ionia, Mi., U.S.	216	42.59 N	85.04 W	Irbit	86	57.41 N	63.03 E	Irumu	154	1.27 N	29.52 E	Isetskoje	86	56.29 N	65.21 E
Ionia, N.Y., U.S.	210	42.56 N	77.30 W	Irby	262	53.21 N	0.38 W	Irún	34	43.21 N	1.47 W	Ise-wan C	94	34.43 N	136.43 E
Ionia ⊜⁶	216	42.56 N	85.04 W	Irching	61	47.33 N	14.01 E	Irupana	248	16.28 S	67.28 W	Iseyin	150	7.58 N	3.36 E
Ionian Islands				Irdyn' ≃	78	49.23 N	31.44 E	Irurzun	34	42.55 N	1.50 W	— Isesaki	92	36.19 N	139.12 E
— Iónioi Nísoi II	38	38.30 N	20.30 E	Ire, Mount ∧	175e	9.10 S	161.05 E	Irú Tepuy ∧	246	5.25 N	61.02 W	Isfahan			
Ionian Sea ▽²	22	39.00 N	19.00 E	Irebu	152	0.37 S	17.45 E	Irvine, Ab., Can.	184	49.57 N	110.16 W	— Eşfahān	128	32.40 N	51.38 E
Ionia State				Irecê	250	11.18 S	41.52 W	Irvine, Scot., U.K.	46	55.37 N	4.40 W	Isfana	85	39.50 N	69.31 E
Recreation Area ◆	216	42.58 N	85.36 W	Iregua ≃	34	42.27 N	2.24 W	Irvine, Ca., U.S.	192	33.40 N	117.49 W	Isfara	85	40.13 N	69.26 E
Ionico, Mare				Ireland (Éire) □¹,				Irvine, Ky., U.S.	192	37.42 N	83.58 W	Isfra	85	40.07 N	70.38 E
— Ionian Sea ▽²	22	39.00 N	19.00 E	Europe	22	53.00 N	8.00 W	Irvine, Pa., U.S.	214	41.50 N	79.17 W	Isfjorden C	24	78.10 N	13.50 E
Ionienne, Mer				Ireland (Éire) □¹,				Irvine ≃	46	55.37 N	4.41 W	'Isfiyā	132	32.43 N	35.04 E
— Ionian Sea ▽²	22	39.00 N	19.00 E	Europe	48	53.00 N	8.00 W	Irvine, Mount ∧	222	42.03 N	78.40 W	Ishenga Oswe	152	3.46 S	22.34 E
Iónioi Nísoi II	38	38.30 N	20.30 E	Ireland Brook ≃	276	40.25 N	74.29 W	Irvine Creek ≃	212	43.41 N	80.25 W	Isheri-Olofin	273a	6.35 N	3.17 E
Ionische Inseln				Iren' ≃	86	57.24 N	56.56 E	Irvine Park ◆	280	33.48 N	117.45 W	Isherton	246	2.19 N	59.22 W
— Iónioi Nísoi II	38	38.30 N	20.30 E	Irene, S. Afr.	155	25.52 S	28.13 E	Irvines Landing	182	49.38 N	124.03 W	Ishi	270	34.35 N	135.38 E
Ionisches Meer				Irene, Tx., U.S.	196	32.05 N	96.52 W	Irving, Il., U.S.	218	39.12 N	89.24 W	Ishibashi	94	36.26 N	139.52 E
— Ionian Sea ▽²	22	39.00 N	19.00 E	Irene, Mount ∧	172	45.10 S	167.22 E	Irving, N.Y., U.S.	214	39.07 N	79.07 W	Ishibe	94	35.00 N	136.04 E
Ionivejem ≃	180	66.12 N	174.00 W	Ireng (Maú) ≃	246	3.33 N	59.51 W	Irving, Tx., U.S.	210	32.49 N	96.56 W	Ishigaki	175d	24.20 N	124.09 E
Iony, ostrov I	74	56.26 N	143.25 E	Iresick Brook ≃	276	42.04 N	74.22 W	Irving Park ◆⁸	278	41.57 N	87.43 W	Ishigaki-shima I	175d	24.24 N	124.12 E
Ioppolo	68	38.35 N	15.53 E	Ireton	198	42.58 N	96.19 W	Irvington, Il., U.S.	218	38.26 N	89.10 W	Ishige	94	36.07 N	139.58 E
Ioppolo Giancaxio	70	37.23 N	13.33 E	Irfon ≃	42	52.10 N	3.27 W	Irvington, Ky., U.S.	194	37.53 N	86.17 W	Ishii	96	34.04 N	134.26 E
Iori ≃	84	41.03 N	46.17 E	Irgakly	84	44.22 N	44.45 E	Irvington, N.J., U.S.	210	40.44 N	74.13 W	Ishikari ≃	92a	43.15 N	141.23 E
Iorskoje ploskogorje				Irgiz	86	48.37 N	61.16 E	Irvington, N.Y., U.S.	210	41.02 N	73.52 W	Ishikari-heiya ≃	92a	43.33 N	143.02 E
∧¹	85	39.30 N	67.53 E	Irgiz ≃	86	48.13 N	62.08 E	Irvington, Oh., U.S.	218	39.51 N	84.15 W	Ishikari-sanchi ✗	92a	43.35 N	143.00 E
Iory	85	39.30 N	24.17 E	Iri	98	35.56 N	126.57 E	Irvington, Va., U.S.	216	37.39 N	76.25 W	Ishikari-wan C	92a	43.25 N	141.01 E
Íos	38	36.44 N	25.17 E	Irian Jaya □⁴	164	5.00 S	138.00 E	Irvona	214	40.46 N	78.33 W	Ishikawa, Nihon	94	37.09 N	140.27 E
Íos I	38	36.42 N	25.24 E	Iriba	146	15.07 N	22.15 E	Irvin	44	53.27 N	2.17 W	Ishikawa, Nihon	174m	26.25 N	127.50 E
Iooscoe, Lake ⊜	276	44.12 N	74.19 W	Iriba ≃	58	8.17 N	9.11 W	Irwell ≃	44	53.42 N	2.21 W	Ishikawa □⁵	94	36.45 N	136.46 E
Iosegun ≃	182	54.44 N	116.50 W	Iriga	116	13.25 N	123.25 E	Irwin, Austl.	168	29.12 S	115.04 E	Ishikari □⁵	270	34.41 N	135.39 E
Iosegun Lake ⊜	182	54.29 N	116.50 W	Irigny	62	45.42 N	4.49 E	Irwin, Id., U.S.	218	40.07 N	83.29 W	Ishi-hama I	96	33.51 N	130.24 E
Iō-shima I	93b	30.48 N	130.18 E	Irigui ∧¹	150	16.43 N	5.30 W	Irwin, Pa., U.S.	279b	40.19 N	79.42 W	Ishinomaki	92	38.26 N	141.18 E
Iota	194	30.19 N	92.29 W	Iriklinskij	86	51.39 N	58.38 E	Irwin ≃	162	29.15 S	114.56 E	Ishinomaki-wan C	92	38.24 N	141.24 E
Iovlevo	82	56.10 N	38.20 E	Iringa	154	7.46 S	35.42 E	Irwindale	280	34.07 N	117.59 W	Ishioka	94	36.11 N	140.16 E
Iowa □³	194	30.14 N	93.00 W	Iringa □⁴	154	9.00 S	35.00 E	Irwinton	192	32.48 N	83.10 W	Ishiyama	270	34.58 N	135.55 E
Iowa □³	178	42.15 N	93.15 W	Irinjālakuda	122	10.20 N	76.14 E	Is, Jabal ∧	140	21.49 N	35.39 E	Ishizuchi-san ∧	96	33.46 N	133.07 E
Iowa, South Fork ≃	190	42.18 N	93.04 W	Iriona	236	15.57 N	85.11 W	Iŝa	138	54.48 N	59.42 E	Ishkuman	122	29.12 N	31.11 E
Iowa City	190	41.39 N	91.31 W	Iriri ≃, Bra.	250	3.52 S	52.37 W	Iŝa ≃	86	58.48 N	59.43 E	Ishpeming	190	46.29 N	87.40 W
Iowa Falls	190	42.31 N	93.15 W	Iriri ≃, Bra.	287a	22.51 S	43.05 W	Isa, Ra's >	154	15.11 N	42.39 E	Ishuizu ≃	204	34.33 N	135.27 E
Iowa Park	196	33.57 N	98.40 W	Iriri Novo ≃	250	8.46 S	53.22 W	Isaac ≃	166	22.52 S	149.20 E	Ishurdi	124	24.09 N	89.05 E
Iō-zen ∧	94	36.31 N	136.48 E	Irische See				Isaac Lake ⊜, B.C.,				Isidro Casanova	288	34.42 S	58.35 W
Ipa ≃	76	52.13 N	29.08 E	— Irish Sea ▽²	28	53.30 N	5.20 W	Can.	182	53.10 N	120.50 W	Isigny	32	49.19 N	1.06 W
Ipala	44	4.30 S	32.53 E	Irish, Mount ∧	204	37.38 N	115.24 W	Isaac Lake ⊜, On.,				Isiki	94	36.32 N	140.29 E
Ipameri	254	48.09 N	19.45 E	Irish Sea ▽²	28	53.30 N	5.20 W	Can.	212	44.47 N	81.14 W	Isik Daği ∧	36	40.38 N	32.57 E
Ipanema ◆⁸	256	22.59 S	43.12 W	Irish Sea ▽²	28	53.30 N	5.20 W	Isaba	34	44.47 N	0.55 W	Isikli Burnu >	267b	41.14 N	29.15 E
Ipanema ≃	256	9.53 S	37.15 W	Irishtown	166	40.55 S	145.08 E	Isabel, Pil.	116	10.56 N	124.26 E	Isili	71	39.44 N	9.06 E
Ipanguaçu	250	5.30 S	36.52 W	Irituia	250	1.46 S	47.26 W	Isabel, S.D., U.S.	198	45.23 N	101.25 W	Isiolo	154	0.21 N	37.35 E
Ipat	24	66.13 N	56.33 E	Iriyamazu	94	36.19 N	139.39 E	Isabel □⁴	175f	7.55 S	159.10 E	Isiro	152	2.47 N	27.37 E
Ipatinga	255	19.30 S	42.32 W	Irkâs, Wādī V	142	28.50 N	32.00 E	Isabel I	175f	8.00 S	159.00 E	Isisford	164	24.16 S	144.26 E
Ipatovo	255	45.43 N	42.53 E	Irkeštam	85	39.41 N	73.55 E	Isabela, Pil.	116	10.12 N	122.59 E	Iskandar	85	41.36 N	69.43 E
Ipaumirim	250	6.43 N	38.48 E	Irki ≃	58	44.40 N	101.14 E	Isabela (Basilan), Pil.	116	6.42 N	121.58 E	Iskār ≃	38	43.44 N	24.27 E
Ipava	194	40.21 N	90.19 W	Irkineyevo ≃	88	58.30 N	96.49 E	Isabela, P.R.	240m	18.30 N	67.01 W	Iskār, jazovir ⊜¹	38	42.28 N	23.35 E
Ipeiros □⁹	38	39.40 N	20.50 E	Irkljiev	78	49.32 N	32.18 E	Isabela I	244m	17.00 N	62.00 W	İskārū	142	30.08 N	31.12 E
Ipel' (Ipoly) ≃	54	47.49 N	18.52 E	Irkljievskaja	44	45.51 N	39.39 E	Isabela, Cabo >	238	19.56 N	71.01 W	İşkāŝim	80	36.43 N	71.34 E
Iperu	150	6.52 N	3.38 E	Irkoutsk				Isabela, Canal U	246a	0.20 S	90.55 W	Ismaskaja step' ≃	86	55.00 N	70.00 E
Iphigenia Bay C	180	55.40 N	133.55 W	— Irkutsk	88	52.18 N	104.15 E	Isabela, Isla I, Ec.	246a	0.50 S	91.00 W	Isinga	88	51.23 N	112.00 E
Iphofen	58	49.42 N	10.15 E	Irkutsk	88	52.18 N	104.15 E	Isabela, Isla I, Méx.	234	21.51 N	105.55 W	Isinga	88	51.23 N	112.00 E
Ipiabas	256	22.23 S	43.53 W	Irkutsk Oblast' □⁴	88	56.00 N	106.00 E	Isabela, Cordillera ✗	236	13.45 N	85.15 W	Isiolo Game Reserve			
Ipiales	248	0.50 N	77.37 W	Irkut'skij	88	56.00 N	106.00 E	Isabela Indian				◆	154	0.32 N	37.34 E
Ipiaú	255	14.08 S	39.44 W	Irlam	44	53.28 N	2.25 W	Reservation ◆⁴	212	43.41 N	84.48 W	Isipingo	158	29.59 S	30.56 E
Ipiíba	256	22.52 S	42.57 W	Irlanda				Isabella Lake ⊜	204	35.40 N	118.26 W	Isipingo Beach	158	29.59 S	30.58 E
Ipil	116	7.47 N	122.35 E	— Ireland □¹	48	53.00 N	8.00 W	Isabella Lake ⊜	212	45.29 N	79.49 W	Isiro (Paulis)	154	2.47 N	27.37 E
Ipin				Irlande, Mer d'				Isabelle	190	46.59 N	92.41 W	Isis ≃	166	25.12 S	152.13 E
— Yibin	107	28.47 N	104.38 E	— Irish Sea ▽²	28	53.30 N	5.20 W	Isafjördur	24a	66.10 N	23.10 W	Isisford	164	24.16 S	144.26 E
Ipirá, Bra.	255	12.09 S	39.37 W	Irlanda, Mer d'				İşaghür	142	24.50 N	77.53 E	İskadar	85	41.36 N	69.43 E
Ipiranga, Bra.	252	25.01 S	50.35 W	— Irish Sea ▽²	48	53.00 N	5.20 W	Isagen	273a	6.32 N	3.20 E	Iskele	130	36.37 N	36.07 E
Ipiranga ◆⁸, Bra.	287b	23.21 S	46.35 W	Irma	182	52.55 N	111.14 W	Isahaya	92	32.50 N	130.03 E	Iskenderun	130	36.35 N	36.10 E
Ipiranga, Bra.	287b	23.21 S	45.10 W	Irmak	164	7.25 S	131.42 E	Isaka ≃	154	3.54 S	32.56 E	Iskenderun Körfezi			
Ipiranga, Canal ≃	255	22.46 S	43.37 W	Irmenach	56	49.58 N	7.08 E	Isaka, Tan.	152	3.54 S	32.56 E	(Gulf of			
Ipiranga, Museu do	287b	23.34 S	46.37 W	Irmjärvi ⊜	28	65.36 N	29.05 E	Isaka, Zaïre	152	2.35 S	18.48 E	Alexandretta) C	130	36.30 N	35.40 E
Ipita	248	19.02 S	63.31 W	Irmsum	88	55.47 N	37.37 E	Isaka-Buku	152	2.35 S	18.48 E	Iske-R'az'ap	52	55.37 N	49.17 E
Ipixuna	248	5.22 S	44.34 W	Iro, Lac ⊜	146	10.06 N	19.25 E	Isakly	80	54.08 N	51.34 E	Iskilip	130	40.45 N	34.29 E
Ipixuna ≃, Bra.	248	7.11 S	71.51 W	Iroise C	32	48.15 N	4.45 W	Isakova, Ross.	74	54.08 N	75.22 E	Iskininskij	80	47.13 N	52.41 E
Ipixuna ≃, Bra.	248	6.16 S	61.52 W	Iron Baron	166	33.00 S	137.09 E	Isakova, Ross.	88	56.38 N	87.24 E	Iskitim	74	54.38 N	83.18 E
Ipixuna, Igarapé ≃	250	4.32 S	62.30 W	Iron Belt	190	46.24 N	90.19 W	Isakova, Ross.	76	58.38 N	41.13 E	Iškovci	85	39.31 W	
Ipoh	114	4.35 N	101.05 E	Iron Bottom Sound U	175e	9.15 S	160.00 E	Isakova, Ross.	88	60.30 N	84.13 E	İskovci	85	37.15 N	68.49 E
Ipojuca ◆⁸	255	8.25 S	35.04 W	Iron Bridge, On.,				Isakovskaja	76	60.14 N	42.30 E	Iskra	86	52.48 N	66.00 E
Ipokera	152	8.03 S	35.41 E	Can.	46	46.17 N	83.14 W	Isakovo, Ross.	265b	55.59 N	37.23 E	İskut ≃	180	56.42 N	131.45 W

Itam-Jama I · 79

ESPAÑOL

Nombre	Página	Lat.°′	Long.°′ W = Oeste
Itamarati de Minas	256	21.25 S	42.49 W
Itamari	255	13.47 S	39.37 W
Itamataré	250	2.16 S	46.24 W
Itambacuri	255	18.01 S	41.42 W
Itambé	255	15.15 S	40.37 W
Itambi	256	22.44 S	42.58 W
Itami	96	34.46 N	135.25 E
Itami, Camp ■	270	34.47 N	135.24 E
Itamonte	256	22.17 S	44.53 W
Itampolo	157b	24.41 S	43.57 E
Itānagar	120	27.09 N	93.33 E
Itandéua, Lago ⊜	250	2.01 S	55.10 W
Itandrano	157b	21.47 S	45.17 E
Itanhaém	255	24.11 S	46.47 W
Itanhandu	256	22.18 S	44.57 W
Itanhauã ≐	248	4.45 S	63.48 W
Itanhém	255	17.09 S	40.20 W
Itanhomi	255	19.10 S	41.52 W
Itano	96	34.07 N	134.28 E
Itaobim	255	16.34 S	41.30 W
Itaocaia	287a	22.58 S	43.01 W
Itapaci	255	14.57 S	49.34 W
Itapagipe	255	19.54 S	49.22 W
Itapajé	250	3.41 S	39.34 W
Itapanhaú ≐	256	23.51 S	46.10 W
Itaparaná ≐	248	5.47 S	63.03 W
Itaparica, Ilha de I	255	13.00 S	38.42 W
Itaparica, Reprêsa de ⊜[1]	250	8.50 S	38.40 W
Itapaya	248	17.34 S	66.21 W
Itapé	255	14.54 S	39.26 W
Itapebi	255	15.56 S	39.32 W
Itapecerica	255	20.28 S	45.07 W
Itapecerica da Serra	256	23.43 S	46.50 W
Itapecerica da Serra □[7]	287b	23.44 S	46.52 W
Itapecuru-Mirim	250	3.24 S	44.20 W
Itapemirim	255	21.01 S	40.50 W
Itapera	250	2.32 S	43.47 W
Itaperina, Pointe ›	157b	24.59 S	47.06 E
Itaperuna	255	21.12 S	41.54 W
Itapetim	250	7.22 S	37.11 W
Itapetinga	255	15.15 S	40.15 W
Itapetininga	255	23.36 S	48.03 W
Itapetininga ≐	255	23.35 S	48.27 W
Itapeva, Bra.	255	23.58 S	48.52 W
Itapeva, Bra.	256	22.46 S	46.13 W
Itapevi	256	23.33 S	46.56 W
Itapevi □[7]	287b	23.31 S	46.55 W
Itapicuru	250	11.19 S	38.15 W
Itapicuru ≐, Bra.	250	2.52 S	44.12 W
Itapicuru ≐, Bra.	250	11.47 S	37.32 W
Itapipoca	250	3.30 S	39.35 W
Itapira	256	22.26 S	46.50 W
Itapiranga, Bra.	250	2.45 S	58.01 W
Itapiranga, Bra.	252	27.08 S	53.43 W
Itapirapuã	255	15.52 S	50.36 W
Itapitanga	255	14.26 S	39.34 W
Itapiúna	250	4.33 S	38.57 W
Itápolis	255	21.35 S	48.46 W
Itaporã	255	22.01 S	54.54 W
Itaporã de Goiás	250	8.02 S	48.39 W
Itaporanga, Bra.	250	7.18 S	38.10 W
Itaporanga, Bra.	255	23.42 S	49.29 W
Itaporanga d'Ajuda	250	10.59 S	37.18 W
Itapúa □[5]	252	26.50 S	55.50 W
Itapuranga	255	15.35 S	49.59 W
Itaquaí ≐	246	4.20 S	70.12 W
Itaquaquecetuba	256	23.29 S	46.21 W
Itaquaquecetuba □[7]	287b	23.28 S	46.20 W
Itaquara	255	13.27 S	39.57 W
Itaquari	255	20.20 S	40.22 W
Itaquaxiara	287b	23.47 S	46.51 W
Itaquaxiara, Ribeirão ≐	287b	23.44 S	46.47 W
Itaquera ◆[8]	256	23.32 S	46.27 W
Itaquera, Ribeirão ≐	287b	23.28 S	46.26 W
Itaqui	252	29.08 S	56.33 W
Itaquyry	252	24.56 S	55.13 W
Itarantim	255	15.39 S	40.03 W
Itararé	255	24.07 S	49.20 W
Itārsi	124	22.37 N	77.45 E
Itarumã	255	18.42 S	51.25 W
Itasca, Il., U.S.	278	41.58 N	88.00 W
Itasca, Tx., U.S.	222	32.09 N	97.08 W
Itasca, Lake ⊜	198	47.11 N	95.12 W
Itasca State Park ♠	198	47.18 N	95.18 W
Itata ≐	252	36.23 S	72.52 W
Itatí	252	27.16 S	58.15 W
Itatiaia	256	22.30 S	44.34 W
Itatiaia, Parque Nacional do ♠	256	22.28 S	44.37 W
Itatiba	256	23.00 S	46.51 W
Itatinga	255	23.07 S	48.36 W
Itatira	250	4.30 S	39.37 W
Itatka	86	56.49 N	85.37 E
Itatolo	273b	4.09 S	15.15 E
Itatskij	86	56.04 N	89.05 E
Itatupã	250	0.37 S	51.12 W
Itaú	250	5.50 S	37.59 W
Itaueira	250	7.36 S	43.02 W
Itaueira ≐	250	6.41 S	42.55 W
Itaúna	255	20.04 S	44.34 W
Itaúna, Morro do ʌ[2]	287a	22.46 S	43.02 W
Itāwa	124	25.32 N	76.22 E
Itazuke-kūkō ⊠	96	33.35 N	130.28 E
Itbayat Island I	108	20.46 N	121.50 E
Itéa	38	38.26 N	22.24 E
Itenes (Guaporé) ≐	248	11.54 S	65.01 W
Ith ʌ	52	52.05 N	9.35 E
Ithaca, Mi., U.S.	190	43.17 N	84.36 W
Ithaca, N.Y., U.S.	210	42.26 N	76.29 W
Itháki	38	38.23 N	20.42 E
Itháki I	38	38.24 N	20.42 E
Ithan Creek ≐	285	40.00 N	75.21 W
Ithnayn	142	30.41 N	32.21 E
Ithon ≐	42	52.12 N	3.27 W
Itigi	154	5.42 S	34.29 E
Itikawa → Ichikawa	94	35.44 N	139.55 E
Itimādpur	124	27.15 N	78.12 E
Itimbiri ≐	152	2.02 N	22.44 E
Itinga	255	16.36 S	41.47 W
Itinga ≐	255	16.35 S	41.45 W
Itinomiya → Ichinomiya	94	35.18 N	136.48 E
Itipo	152	0.50 S	18.35 E
Itiquira	255	17.12 S	54.07 W
Itiquira ≐	248	17.21 S	55.37 W
Itirapina	255	22.15 S	47.49 W
Itire	273a	6.31 N	3.21 E
Itiruçu	255	13.31 S	40.09 W
Itiúba	250	10.43 S	39.51 W
Itkillik ≐	180	70.08 N	150.57 W
Itlar'	82	56.51 N	39.17 E
Itlīdim	142	27.52 N	30.48 E
Itmīdah	142	30.46 N	31.20 E
Itmuryn, ozero ⊜	80	49.30 N	52.22 E
Itō	94	34.58 N	139.05 E
Itobi	256	21.44 S	46.58 W
Itobo	154	4.10 S	33.01 E
Itoculo	154	14.42 S	40.18 E
Itoigawa	94	37.02 N	137.51 E
Itoko	152	1.00 S	21.45 E
Itomamo, Lac ⊜	186	49.11 N	70.28 W
Itoman	174m	26.08 N	127.40 E
Iton ≐	50	49.09 N	1.12 E
Itonamas ≐	248	12.28 S	64.24 W
Itororó	255	15.07 S	40.06 W
Itri	66	41.17 N	13.32 E
Itsā	142	29.15 N	30.48 E
Itsukaichi, Nihon	94	35.44 N	139.13 E
Itsukaichi, Nihon	96	34.24 N	132.22 E
Itsuki	92	32.24 N	130.50 E
Itsuku-shima I	96	34.16 N	132.19 E
Itsuwa	92	32.30 N	130.10 E
Itta Bena	194	33.29 N	90.19 W
Ittel, Oued V	148	34.19 N	6.01 E
Itter ≐	263	51.09 N	6.52 E
Ittersum	52	52.28 N	6.07 E

FRANÇAIS

Nom	Page	Lat.°′	Long.°′ W = Ouest
Itteville	261	48.31 N	2.21 E
Ittiri	71	40.36 N	8.34 E
Itú	255	23.16 S	47.19 W
Itu ≐	252	29.25 S	55.51 W
Ituaçu	255	13.49 S	41.18 W
Ituango	246	7.04 N	75.45 W
Ituberá	255	13.44 S	39.09 W
Itucumã ≐	248	6.59 S	69.48 W
Itueta	255	19.23 S	41.11 W
Ituí	256	21.32 S	42.55 W
Ituí ≐	246	4.38 S	70.19 W
Ituim ≐	252	28.35 S	51.20 W
Ituiutaba	255	18.58 S	49.28 W
Itula	154	3.29 S	27.52 E
Itumbiara	255	18.25 S	49.13 W
Itumirim	256	21.19 S	44.53 W
Itum-Kale	84	42.43 N	45.35 E
Ituna	184	51.10 N	103.30 W
Itungi Port	154	9.35 S	33.56 E
Ituni	246	5.30 N	58.14 W
Itupararanga, Reprêsa de ⊜[1]	256	23.37 S	47.16 W
Itupeva	256	23.09 S	47.04 W
Itupeva, Rio da ≐	256	22.03 S	47.15 W
Itupiranga	250	5.09 S	49.20 W
Ituporanga	252	27.25 S	49.36 W
Iturama	255	19.44 S	50.11 W
Iturbe	252	26.01 S	56.30 W
Iturbide	232	19.40 N	89.37 W
Ituri ≐	154	1.40 N	27.01 E
Iturup, ostrov (Etorofu-tō) I	92a	44.35 N	147.10 E
Itutinga	256	21.18 S	44.40 W
Ituverava	255	20.20 S	47.47 W
Ituxi ≐	248	7.18 S	64.51 W
Ituzaingó, Arg.	252	27.36 S	56.41 W
Ituzaingó, Arg.	258	34.40 S	58.40 W
Ituzaingó, Ur.	258	34.25 S	56.26 W
Itwa	124	27.20 N	82.42 E
Ityāy al-Bārūd	142	30.53 N	30.40 E
Ityopiya → Ethiopia □[1]	144	9.00 N	39.00 E
Itz ≐	56	49.58 N	10.52 E
Itzehoe	52	53.55 N	9.31 E
Iubundha ≐	126	24.06 N	90.20 E
Iuka, Il., U.S.	219	38.37 N	88.47 W
Iuka, Ms., U.S.	194	34.48 N	88.11 W
Iul'tin	180	67.50 N	178.48 W
Iul'tin, gora ʌ	180	67.50 N	178.25 W
Iúna	255	20.21 S	41.32 W
Iupeba	256	23.41 S	46.22 W
Iva	192	34.18 N	82.39 W
Ivacevići	76	52.43 N	25.21 E
Ivačovo	76	60.32 N	36.22 E
Ivahona	157b	23.27 S	46.10 E
Ivaí ≐	255	23.18 S	53.42 W
Ivaiporã	252	24.15 S	51.45 W
Ivajlovgrad	38	41.32 N	26.08 E
Ivakoany, Massif de l' ⋀	157b	23.50 S	46.25 E
Ivalo	24	68.42 N	27.30 E
Ivalojoki ≐	24	68.43 N	27.36 E
Ivancevo	82	55.58 N	36.07 E
Ivančice	61	49.06 N	16.23 E
Ivancovo	82	56.39 N	35.50 E
Ivanec	36	46.13 N	16.08 E
Ivane-Puste	78	48.39 N	26.11 E
Ivangorod	76	59.24 N	28.10 E
Ivangrad	38	42.50 N	19.52 E
Ivanhoe, Austl.	166	32.54 S	144.18 E
Ivanhoe, Austl.	274b	37.46 S	145.03 E
Ivanhoe, Ca., U.S.	226	36.23 N	119.13 W
Ivanhoe, Il., U.S.	278	42.17 N	88.02 W
Ivanhoe, Mn., U.S.	198	44.27 N	96.14 W
Ivanhoe, Va., U.S.	192	36.50 N	80.58 W
Ivanhoe ≐	190	48.40 N	82.11 W
Ivanhoe Lake ⊜	190	48.05 N	82.38 W
Ivanica	78	50.47 N	32.36 E
Ivanić Grad	36	45.42 N	16.24 E
Ivaniči	78	50.39 N	24.20 E
Ivanišči, Ross.	76	56.36 N	35.13 E
Ivanišči, Ross.	80	55.46 N	40.26 E
Ivanjci	61	46.38 N	15.54 E
Ivanjica	38	43.35 N	20.14 E
Ivankov	78	50.56 N	29.54 E
Ivankovcy	89	49.06 N	134.28 E
Ivan'kovo	82	54.44 N	37.57 E
Ivan'kovskij	80	56.39 N	40.05 E
Ivan'kovskoje vodochranilišče ⊜[1]	82	56.37 N	36.32 E
Ivanof Bay	180	55.54 N	159.29 W
Ivano-Frankovo	78	49.55 N	23.43 E
Ivano-Frankovsk	78	48.55 N	24.43 E
Ivano-Frankovsk □[4]	78	48.45 N	24.30 E
Ivanopol'	78	49.52 N	28.12 E
Ivanopolje	83	48.28 N	37.46 E
Ivano-Šamševo	83	46.52 N	39.54 E
Ivanov	78	49.28 N	28.21 E
Ivanovka, Kyrg.	85	42.54 N	75.05 E
Ivanovka, Ross.	80	52.51 N	53.48 E
Ivanovka, Ross.	80	51.54 N	43.46 E
Ivanovka, Ross.	80	52.15 N	41.35 E
Ivanovka, Ross.	89	50.22 N	128.02 E
Ivanovka, Ross.	89	43.58 N	132.30 E
Ivanovka, Ukr.	78	46.43 N	34.33 E
Ivanovka, Ukr.	78	46.58 N	30.28 E
Ivanovka, Ukr.	83	48.14 N	38.58 E
Ivanovka, Ukr.	83	47.35 N	37.19 E
Ivanovo, Bela.	76	52.09 N	25.32 E
Ivanovo, Ross.	80	57.00 N	40.59 E
Ivanovo Oblast' □[4]	76	57.00 N	41.00 E
Ivanovo-Voznesensk → Ivanovo	80	57.00 N	40.59 E
Ivanovskaja, Ross.	24	60.48 N	55.52 E
Ivanovskaja, Ross.	78	45.17 N	38.29 E
Ivanovskoje, Ross.	76	59.17 N	28.49 E
Ivanovskoje, Ross.	78	51.37 N	34.57 E
Ivanovskoje, Ross.	82	55.05 N	37.50 E
Ivanovskoje, Ross.	82	54.55 N	36.50 E
Ivanovskoje, Ross.	82	55.52 N	36.55 E
Ivanovskoje, Ross.	82	56.23 N	37.07 E
Ivanovskoje, Ross.	265a	59.46 N	30.47 E
Ivan-Ozero	82	54.04 N	38.20 E
Ivan-Ozero, ozero ⊜	82	54.07 N	38.17 E
Ivanpah Lake ⊜	204	35.35 N	115.25 W
Ivantejevka, Ross.	80	52.16 N	49.07 E
Ivantejevka, Ross.	82	55.58 N	37.55 E
Ivantejevo	76	57.48 N	33.09 E
Ivato	157b	20.37 S	47.12 E
Ivatuba	255	23.37 S	52.13 W
Ivdel'	72	60.42 N	60.24 E
Ivel ≐	42	52.10 N	0.18 W
Ivenec	76	53.53 N	26.45 E
Iver	260	51.31 N	0.30 W
Iver Heath	260	51.32 N	0.31 W
Iverny	261	49.00 N	2.47 E
Ivigtut	176	61.12 N	48.10 W
Ivindo ≐	152	0.09 S	12.09 E
Ivinghoe	42	51.50 N	0.37 W
Ivinheima ≐	255	23.14 S	53.42 W
Ivje	76	53.56 N	25.46 E
Ivn'a	78	51.04 N	36.08 E
Ivnica	78	50.09 N	29.03 E
Ivohibe	157b	22.29 S	46.52 E
Ivolginsk	88	51.45 N	107.14 E
Ivón ≐	248	11.06 S	66.08 W
Ivondro	157b	24.47 S	46.52 E
Ivor	208	36.54 N	76.54 W
Ivorogbo	150	5.30 N	6.21 E
Ivory Coast ⊥[2]	150	5.10 N	5.00 W
Ivory Coast → Cote d'Ivoire □[1]	150	8.00 N	5.00 W
Ivoryton	207	41.20 N	72.26 W
Ivösjön ⊜	26	56.06 N	14.27 E
Ivot, Ross.	76	53.42 N	34.12 E
Ivot, Ukr.	78	51.58 N	33.28 E
Ivotka ≐	78	51.57 N	33.22 E
Ivrea	62	45.28 N	7.52 E
İvrindi	130	39.34 N	27.29 E
Ivry-la-Bataille	50	48.53 N	1.28 E

PORTUGUÊS

Nome	Página	Lat.°′	Long.°′ W = Oeste
Ivry [-sur-Seine]	50	48.49 N	2.23 E
Ivujivik	176	62.24 N	77.55 W
Ivybridge	42	50.23 N	3.56 W
Ivy Hatch	260	51.16 N	0.16 E
Ivyland	285	40.12 N	75.04 W
Iwade	96	34.15 N	135.19 E
Iwafune, Nihon	94	36.19 N	139.40 E
Iwafune, Nihon	270	34.44 N	135.54 E
Iwagi	96	34.15 N	133.09 E
Iwai	94	36.03 N	139.54 E
Iwai-shima I	96	33.47 N	131.58 E
Iwaizumi	92	39.50 N	141.48 E
Iwaki (Taira)	94	37.03 N	140.55 E
Iwaki ≐	92	41.01 N	140.22 E
Iwaki-san ʌ	92	40.39 N	140.18 E
Iwakuni	96	34.09 N	132.11 E
Iwakuni Marine Corps Air Station ■	96	34.08 N	132.14 E
Iwakura	94	35.17 N	136.52 E
Iwama	94	36.18 N	140.16 E
Iwami, Nihon	96	34.53 N	132.26 E
Iwami, Nihon	96	35.35 N	134.20 E
Iwami-kōgen ⋀[1]	96	35.00 N	132.30 E
Iwami-kokubun-ji ʊ[1]	96	34.56 N	132.08 E
Iwamizawa	92a	43.12 N	141.46 E
Iwamura	94	35.22 N	137.26 E
Iwanai	92a	42.58 N	140.30 E
Iwanowo → Ivanovo	80	57.00 N	40.59 E
Iwanuma	92	38.06 N	140.52 E
Iwaoka ◆[8]	270	34.44 N	134.58 E
Iwase, Nihon	94	36.21 N	140.06 E
Iwase, Nihon	268	35.17 N	139.52 E
Iwata	94	34.42 N	137.48 E
Iwataki	96	35.34 N	135.09 E
Iwate □[5]	92	39.37 N	141.22 E
Iwate-san ʌ	92	39.51 N	141.00 E
Iwatsuki	94	35.57 N	139.42 E
Iwaya → Awaji, Nihon	96	34.35 N	135.01 E
Iwaya, Nihon	270	34.35 N	135.02 E
Iwayama	270	34.52 N	135.52 E
Iwazono	270	34.45 N	135.19 E
Iwo	150	7.38 N	4.11 E
Iwo Jima → Iō-jima I	174f	24.47 N	141.20 E
Iwŏn	98	40.19 N	128.39 E
Iwuy	50	50.14 N	3.19 E
Ixcán ≐	236	16.07 N	91.05 W
Ixchiguán	236	15.12 N	91.53 W
Ixelles	56	50.50 N	4.22 E
Ixhuatlán	234	19.04 N	96.59 W
Ixiamas	248	13.45 S	68.09 W
Iximché ⊥	236	14.44 N	90.59 W
Ixmiquilpan	234	20.29 N	99.14 W
Ixonia	216	43.09 N	88.36 W
Ixopo	158	30.08 S	30.00 E
Ixtahuacán	236	15.25 N	91.46 W
Ixtapa	234	17.39 N	101.36 W
Ixtapa, Punta ›	234	17.39 N	101.40 W
Ixtapan de la Sal	234	18.50 N	99.41 W
Ixtepec	234	16.34 N	95.06 W
Ixtlahuacán del Río	234	20.52 N	103.15 W
Ixtlán	234	20.11 N	102.24 W
Ixtlán de Juárez	234	17.20 N	96.29 W
Ixtlán del Río	234	21.02 N	104.22 W
Ixworth	42	52.18 N	0.50 E
Iya ≐	96	33.58 N	133.47 E
'Iyādh	144	14.59 N	46.51 E
'Iyāl Bakhīt	140	13.25 N	28.41 E
Iyang, Taehan	98	34.53 N	127.01 E
Iyang → Yiyang, Zhg.	102	28.36 N	112.20 E
Iyang, Gili I	115a	6.59 S	114.10 E
Iyo	96	33.46 N	132.42 E
Iyo-mishima	96	33.58 N	133.33 E
Iyo-nada ⊤[2]	96	33.40 N	132.20 E
Iž ≐	80	55.58 N	52.38 E
Izabal	236	15.24 N	89.08 W
Izabal □[5]	236	15.30 N	89.00 W
Izabal, Lago de ⊜	236	15.30 N	89.10 W
'Izab al-Başārīţah	142	31.23 N	31.47 E
Īzad Khvāst	128	31.31 N	52.07 E
Izalco	236	13.45 N	89.40 W
'Izam, Jabal al- ʌ	132	30.51 N	35.46 E
Izamal	232	20.56 N	89.01 W
Izapa ⊥	232	14.55 N	92.10 W
Iz'aslav	78	50.07 N	26.51 E
'Izbat Abū Suqī	132	31.09 N	33.49 E
Izberbaš	84	42.33 N	47.52 E
Izbica, Pol.	30	50.54 N	23.09 E
Izbica, Pol.	30	54.42 N	17.26 E
Izd'oškovo	76	55.08 N	33.37 E
Izegem	50	50.55 N	3.12 E
Īzeh	128	31.50 N	49.50 E
Izena-shima I	174m	26.56 N	127.56 E
Izendy	86	45.48 N	59.28 E
Izernore	58	46.13 N	5.33 E
Iževsk	80	56.51 N	53.14 E
Iževskoje	80	54.34 N	40.53 E
Izkī	128	22.56 N	57.46 E
Ižma	24	65.02 N	53.55 E
Ižma ≐	24	65.19 N	52.54 E
Izmail	78	45.21 N	28.50 E
Izmajlovo	80	53.43 N	47.14 E
Izmajlovo ◆[8]	265b	55.48 N	37.46 E
Izmajlovo Park ♠	265b	55.46 N	37.47 E
Izmalkovo	76	52.41 N	37.58 E
İzmir	130	38.25 N	27.09 E
İzmir □[4]	130	38.30 N	27.15 E
İzmir Körfezi ⊂	130	38.30 N	26.50 E
İzmit (Kocaeli)	130	40.46 N	29.55 E
İzmit Körfezi ⊂	130	40.45 N	29.35 E
Ižmorskij	86	56.11 N	86.38 E
Iznajar, Embalse de ⊜[1]	34	37.15 N	4.30 W
Iznalloz	34	37.23 N	3.31 W
İznik	130	40.26 N	29.43 E
İznik Gölü ⊜	130	40.26 N	29.30 E
Iznoski	76	54.59 N	35.19 E
Izola	64	45.32 N	13.40 E
Izoplit	82	56.38 N	36.12 E
Izopo, Punta ›	236	15.48 N	87.23 W
Ižora ≐	265a	59.48 N	30.36 E
Izozog, Bañados del ≡	248	18.48 S	62.10 W
Izra'	132	32.51 N	36.15 E
Izsák	30	46.48 N	19.22 E
Iztacalco ◆[8]	286a	19.23 N	99.07 W
Iztaccíhuatl, Volcán ʌ[1]	234	19.11 N	98.39 W
Iztaccíhuatl y Popocatéptl, Parques Nacionales ♠	234	19.10 N	98.38 W
Iztapa	236	13.56 N	90.43 W
Iztapalapa ◆[8]	286a	19.21 N	99.06 W
Izucar de Matamoros	234	18.36 N	98.28 W
Izu-hantō ›[1]	94	34.45 N	139.00 E
Izuhara	92	34.12 N	129.17 E
Iz'um	83	49.12 N	37.19 E
Izumi, Nihon	92	38.20 N	140.53 E
Izumi, Nihon	92	32.05 N	130.22 E
Izumi, Nihon	94	35.54 N	136.40 E
Izumi, Nihon	96	34.55 N	134.55 E
Izumi, Nihon	96	34.29 N	135.26 E
Izumi ◆[8]	268	35.25 N	139.30 E
Izumi-ōtsu	96	34.30 N	135.24 E
Izumi-sano	96	34.25 N	135.19 E
Izumizaki	94	37.09 N	140.17 E
Izumo	96	35.22 N	132.46 E
Izumo ≐	94	34.38 N	136.33 E
Izumo-kokubun-ji ʊ[1]	96	35.26 N	133.06 E
Izumrud	86	57.05 N	61.23 E
Izu-nagaoka	94	35.02 N	138.56 E
Izushi	96	35.28 N	134.52 E
Izu-shotō II	6	32.00 N	140.00 E
Izu Trench ✦[1]	6	31.00 N	142.00 E
Izuwara	270	34.53 N	135.32 E
Izvarino	83	48.17 N	39.52 E

Izvestij CIK, ostrova II	74	75.55 N	82.30 E
Izvestkovyj	89	48.59 N	131.33 E
Izvorul Muntelui, Lacul ⊜[1]	38	47.00 N	26.00 E
Izynžul'	86	52.24 N	90.13 E

J

Ja'ār, Birkat al- ⊜	142	30.28 N	30.10 E
Jääsjärvi ⊜	26	61.36 N	26.07 E
Jaba, Ityo.	144	6.17 N	35.12 E
Jaba, Pap. N. Gui.	175e	6.32 S	155.12 E
Jabā, Sūrīy	132	33.10 N	35.56 E
Jabal, Bahr al- → Mountain Nile ≐	136	9.30 N	30.30 E
Jabal Abyad Plateau ⋀[1]	140	19.00 N	29.00 E
Jabal al-Awliyā'	140	15.14 N	32.30 E
Jabal al-Awliyā', Khazzān (White Nile Dam) ◆[6]	140	15.14 N	32.29 E
Jabalambre ʌ	34	40.06 N	1.03 W
Jabal an-Nūr	142	28.57 N	31.02 E
Jabal Aţ-Ţayr	142	28.14 N	30.45 E
Jabal Dūd	140	13.25 N	33.09 E
Jabal Lubnān □[4]	132	33.50 N	35.40 E
Jabalón ≐	34	38.53 N	4.05 W
Jabal os Sarāj	120	35.07 N	69.14 E
Jabalpur	124	23.10 N	79.57 E
Jabal Qerri	140	16.15 N	32.48 E
Jabal 'Uwaybid	142	30.09 N	32.12 E
Jabālyah	132	31.32 N	34.29 E
Jabal Zuqar, Jazīrat I	144	14.00 N	42.45 E
Jabbān, Arḑ al- ◆[1]	132	32.08 N	36.35 E
Jabbeke	50	51.11 N	3.05 E
Jabbi	123	32.24 N	72.06 E
Jabbū, Qā' ≚	132	29.35 N	36.13 E
Jabbūl, Sabkhat al- ⊜	130	36.03 N	37.39 E
Jabel	54	53.32 N	12.32 E
Jabi	114	2.32 N	102.48 E
Jabiru	164	12.40 S	132.53 E
Jabjabah, Wādī V	140	22.37 N	33.17 E
Jablah	130	35.21 N	35.55 E
Jablanac	36	44.42 N	14.54 E
Jablanica	36	43.39 N	17.45 E
Jablanica ≐	38	43.07 N	21.57 E
Jablaničko Jezero ⊜[1]	36	43.40 N	17.50 E
Jablines	261	48.55 N	2.46 E
Jabločnoje	78	50.18 N	35.14 E
Jabločnyj	89	47.10 N	142.04 E
Jablonec nad Nisou	30	50.44 N	15.10 E
Jablonica	30	48.37 N	17.25 E
Jabłonka	30	49.29 N	19.41 E
Jablonné v Podještědí	54	50.48 N	14.47 E
Jablonoj — Jablonovyj chrebet ⋀	88	53.30 N	115.00 E
Jablonov	78	48.24 N	24.57 E
Jablonovo	88	51.51 N	112.49 E
Jablonovyj chrebet ⋀	88	53.30 N	115.00 E
Jabłonowo	30	53.24 N	19.09 E
Jablonowy-Gebirge → Jablonovyj chrebet ⋀	88	53.30 N	115.00 E
Jablunkov	30	49.35 N	18.47 E
Jaboatão	250	8.07 S	35.01 W
Jaboncillos Creek ≐	196	27.23 N	97.45 W
Jabonga	116	9.20 N	125.32 E
Jaborandi	255	20.40 S	48.25 W
Jaboticabal	255	21.16 S	48.19 W
Jabrat Sa'īd ⊤[4]	140	16.06 N	31.50 E
Jabron ≐	62	44.33 N	4.45 E
Jabron, Torrent le ≐	62	44.09 N	5.57 E
Jabung	115a	5.29 S	105.40 E
Jabung, Tanjung ›	112	1.01 S	104.22 E
Jaca	34	42.34 N	0.33 W
Jacala	234	21.01 N	99.11 W
Jacaleapa	236	14.00 N	86.40 W
Jacaltenango	236	15.40 N	91.44 W
Jacana	274b	37.42 S	144.55 E
Jacaraci	255	14.51 S	42.26 W
Jacaré ≐, Bra.	248	5.49 S	63.35 W
Jacaré ≐, Bra.	250	10.10 S	41.58 W
Jacaré ≐, Bra.	255	13.50 S	40.42 W
Jacareí	256	23.19 S	45.58 W
Jacareí ≐	256	22.54 S	46.28 W
Jacarepaguá ◆[8]	256	22.56 S	43.20 W
Jacarepaguá, Lagoa de ⊂	256	22.59 S	43.24 W
Jacarezinho	255	23.09 S	49.59 W
Jaceel V	144	10.25 N	51.01 E
Jaceruba	256	22.35 S	43.34 W
Jáchal ≐	252	30.44 S	68.08 W
Jachenau	64	47.36 N	11.25 E
Jachniki	78	50.26 N	33.10 E
Jachroma	82	56.17 N	37.30 E
Jachroma ≐	82	56.31 N	37.07 E
Jáchymov	54	50.20 N	12.55 E
Jaciara	255	15.59 S	54.57 W
Jacinto	255	16.10 S	40.17 W
Jacinto Aráuz	252	38.04 S	63.26 W
Jacinto City	222	29.46 N	95.14 W
Jacinto Machado	252	29.00 S	49.46 W
Jaciparaná	248	9.15 S	64.23 W
Jaciparaná ≐	248	9.22 S	64.22 W
Jackass Creek ≐	226	37.22 N	119.23 W
Jack Creek ≐	202	42.59 N	121.32 W
Jackfish Lake ⊜	184	53.05 N	108.25 W
Jackhead Harbour	184	51.52 N	97.16 W
Jack Lake ⊜	212	44.42 N	78.03 W
Jack London State Historical Park ♠	226	38.21 N	122.32 W
Jackman	188	45.38 N	70.15 W
Jackman Creek ≐	224	48.30 N	121.43 W
Jack Mountain ʌ, Mt., U.S.	202	46.21 N	112.18 W
Jack Mountain ʌ, Wa., U.S.	224	48.47 N	120.57 W
Jackpot	204	41.59 N	114.40 W
Jacksboro, Tn., U.S.	192	36.19 N	84.11 W
Jacksboro, Tx., U.S.	196	33.13 N	98.09 W
Jacks Creek ≐	208	40.35 N	77.33 W
Jacks Fork ≐	194	37.12 N	91.17 W
Jacks Island I	279b	40.37 N	79.43 W
Jacks Mountain ʌ	210	40.45 N	77.30 W
Jackson, Al., U.S.	194	31.30 N	87.53 W
Jackson, Ca., U.S.	226	38.20 N	120.46 W
Jackson, Ga., U.S.	192	33.17 N	83.57 W
Jackson, Ky., U.S.	192	37.33 N	83.23 W
Jackson, La., U.S.	194	30.50 N	91.13 W
Jackson, Mi., U.S.	216	42.14 N	84.24 W
Jackson, Mn., U.S.	198	43.37 N	94.59 W
Jackson, Ms., U.S.	194	32.17 N	90.11 W
Jackson, Mo., U.S.	194	37.22 N	89.39 W
Jackson, N.J., U.S.	208	40.08 N	74.19 W
Jackson, N.C., U.S.	192	36.23 N	77.25 W
Jackson, Oh., U.S.	188	39.03 N	82.38 W
Jackson, Pa., U.S.	210	41.50 N	75.36 W
Jackson, S.C., U.S.	192	33.19 N	81.47 W
Jackson, Tn., U.S.	194	35.36 N	88.48 W
Jackson, Wy., U.S.	200	43.28 N	110.45 W
Jackson □[6], In., U.S.	218	38.53 N	86.03 W
Jackson □[6], Mi., U.S.	216	42.15 N	84.24 W
Jackson □[6], Tx., U.S.	222	29.00 N	96.35 W
Jackson ≐	188	37.47 N	79.46 W
Jackson, Cape ›	172	41.00 S	174.18 E
Jackson, Lake ⊜, Fl., U.S.	192	30.30 N	84.17 W
Jackson, Lake ⊜, Fl., U.S.	220	27.29 N	81.28 W
Jackson, Lake ⊜, Fl., U.S.	220	27.55 N	81.10 W
Jackson, Mount ʌ, Ant.	9	71.23 S	63.22 W

Jackson, Mount ʌ, Austl.	162	30.15 S	119.16 E
Jackson, Port ⊂	170	33.50 S	151.16 E
Jackson Bay ⊂	172	43.58 S	168.42 E
Jackson Brook ≐	276	40.53 N	74.34 W
Jackson Butte ʌ	226	38.20 N	120.43 W
Jackson Center, Oh., U.S.	216	40.27 N	84.02 W
Jackson Center, Pa., U.S.	214	41.16 N	80.09 W
Jackson Creek ≐, Can.	184	49.18 N	100.50 W
Jackson Creek ≐, Ca., U.S.	226	38.18 N	121.01 W
Jackson Creek ≐, Il., U.S.	216	41.26 N	88.10 W
Jackson Head ›	172	43.58 S	168.37 E
Jackson Heights ◆[8]	276	40.45 N	73.53 W
Jackson Lake ⊜	202	43.55 N	110.40 W
Jackson Lake ⊜[1]	192	33.22 N	83.52 W
Jackson Meadows Reservoir ⊜[1]	226	39.29 N	120.32 W
Jackson Mountain ʌ	188	44.46 N	70.32 W
Jackson Park ♠, On., Can.	281	42.17 N	83.01 W
Jackson Park ♠, Il., U.S.	278	41.47 N	87.35 W
Jackson's Arm	186	49.52 N	56.47 W
Jacksons Creek ≐	169	37.40 S	144.48 E
Jacksonville, Al., U.S.	194	33.48 N	85.45 W
Jacksonville, Ar., U.S.	194	34.51 N	92.06 W
Jacksonville, Fl., U.S.	192	30.19 N	81.39 W
Jacksonville, Il., U.S.	219	39.44 N	90.13 W
Jacksonville, N.J., U.S.	285	40.03 N	74.46 W
Jacksonville, N.Y., U.S.	210	42.31 N	76.37 W
Jacksonville, N.C., U.S.	192	34.45 N	77.25 W
Jacksonville, Or., U.S.	202	42.18 N	122.57 W
Jacksonville, Tx., U.S.	222	31.57 N	95.16 W
Jacksonville, Vt., U.S.	207	42.47 N	72.49 W
Jacksonville, Lake ⊜[1]	222	31.55 N	95.17 W
Jacksonville Beach	192	30.17 N	81.23 W
Jacksonville Naval Air Station ■	192	30.14 N	81.41 W
Jacks Reef	210	43.06 N	76.25 W
Jacks Run ≐	279b	40.13 N	79.35 W
Jacktown Acres	279b	40.19 N	79.45 W
Jacmel	238	18.14 N	72.32 W
Jaco	232	27.50 N	104.00 W
Jacob, Morne ʌ	240e	14.46 N	61.06 W
Jacobābād	120	28.17 N	68.26 E
Jacobina	250	11.11 S	40.31 W
Jacob Island I	212	44.28 N	78.28 W
Jacob Riis Park ♠	276	40.34 N	73.52 W
Jacobs Creek ≐	214	40.07 N	79.44 W
Jacobsdal	158	29.13 S	24.41 E
Jacobus	208	39.53 N	76.43 W
Jacona de Plancarte	234	19.57 N	102.16 W
Jacques, Lac à ⊜	180	66.10 N	127.25 W
Jacques-Cartier	275a	45.31 N	73.29 W
Jacques-Cartier ≐	206	46.40 N	71.45 W
Jacques-Cartier, Détroit de ⊔	186	50.00 N	63.30 W
Jacques-Cartier, Mont ʌ	186	48.59 N	65.57 W
Jacques-Cartier, Pont ◆[5]	275a	45.31 N	73.32 W
Jacquet River	186	47.55 N	66.00 W
Jacqueville	150	5.12 N	4.25 W
Jacquinot Bay ⊂	164	5.35 S	151.30 E
Jacu ≐, Bra.	250	6.13 S	35.09 W
Jacú ≐, Bra.	256	23.05 S	45.08 W
Jacu, Rio do ≐	287b	23.29 S	46.27 W
Jacuba ≐	255	18.25 S	52.28 W
Jacuecanga	256	23.01 S	44.13 W
Jacuí ≐	252	30.02 S	51.15 W
Jacuípe ≐	255	12.30 S	39.05 W
Jacumba	204	32.37 N	116.11 W
Jacundá	250	4.33 S	49.28 W
Jacundá ≐	250	1.57 S	50.26 W
Jacupiranga	252	24.42 S	48.00 W
Jacuriaí ≐	250	10.57 S	39.35 W
Jacutinga	256	22.17 S	46.37 W
Jada	146	8.46 N	12.09 E
Jada'ah, Jabal ʌ[2]	142	29.58 N	30.40 E
Jādabpur	126	22.29 N	88.23 E
Jaddi, Rās ›	128	25.14 N	63.31 E
Jade	52	53.20 N	8.14 E
Jade Buddha, Temple of the ʊ[1]	269b	31.14 N	121.26 E
Jadebusen ⊂	52	53.30 N	8.10 E
Jäder	40	59.25 N	16.41 E
Jäderfors	40	60.41 N	16.40 E
Jade Run ≐	285	39.56 N	74.45 W
Jadīdah	128	34.01 N	42.28 E
Jadito Wash V	200	35.22 N	110.50 W
J.A.D. Jensens Nunatakker ʌ	176	62.45 N	48.00 W
Jadotville → Likasi	154	10.59 S	26.44 E
Jadraque	34	40.55 N	2.55 W
Jadrin	80	55.56 N	46.12 E
Jadromino	82	55.57 N	36.36 E
Jādū	146	31.57 N	12.01 E
Jaduty	78	51.22 N	32.19 E
Jægerspris	41	55.51 N	11.59 E
Jaeger Summit ʌ	154	2.52 S	35.47 E
Jaén, Esp.	34	37.46 N	3.47 W
Jaén, Perú	248	5.42 S	78.47 W
Jaén □[4]	34	38.00 N	3.30 E
Jæren ◆[1]	26	58.45 N	5.45 E
Jāfarābād, India	120	20.52 N	71.22 E
Ja'farābād, Īrān	128	35.43 N	50.43 E
Jāfarpur	126	22.29 N	89.06 E
Jāfarpur ◆[8]	272a	28.40 N	77.01 E
Jaffa, Cape ›	166	36.58 S	139.40 E
Jaffa, Tel Aviv- → Tel Aviv-Yafo	132	32.04 N	34.46 E
Jaffna	122	9.40 N	80.00 E
Jaffna Lagoon ⊂	122	9.35 N	80.15 E
Jaffrey	207	42.48 N	72.01 W
Jafr, Qā' al- ⊥[7]	132	30.17 N	36.20 E
Jagādhri	124	30.10 N	77.18 E
Jägala ≐	76	59.29 N	25.09 E
Jagalūr	122	14.32 N	76.21 E
Jāgan	120	28.05 N	68.30 E
Jagannāthganj Ghāt	124	24.45 N	89.49 E
Jagannāthpūr	272b	22.43 N	88.19 E
Jagati	126	23.54 N	89.06 E
Jagatnagar	272b	22.47 N	88.13 E
Jagatpur ◆[8]	272a	28.44 N	77.14 E
Jagatsingpur	120	20.16 N	86.10 E
Jagdalpur	122	19.04 N	82.02 E
Jagdīspur	124	25.29 N	84.25 E
Jagel	41	54.27 N	9.32 E
Jagel'urta, gora ʌ[2]	24	67.33 N	38.02 E
Jagenbach	61	48.38 N	15.02 E
Jägerndorf → Krnov	30	50.05 N	17.41 E
Jagersfontein	158	29.44 S	25.29 E
Jaggayyapeta	122	16.54 N	80.06 E
Jagged Mountain ʌ	180	58.38 N	162.02 W
Jagīn ≐	128	25.35 N	58.18 E
Jagnob ≐	85	39.15 N	68.35 E
Jagny-sous-Bois	261	49.05 N	2.27 E
Jagodnoje, Ross.	74	62.33 N	149.40 E
Jagodnoje, Ross.	80	53.36 N	49.04 E
Jagodnyj	86	59.44 N	65.04 E
Jagorlyckij zaliv ⊂	78	46.24 N	31.50 E
Jagotin	78	50.17 N	31.46 E
Jagraon	123	30.47 N	75.29 E
Jagst ≐	56	49.14 N	9.11 E
Jagsthausen	56	49.19 N	9.28 E
Jagstzell	56	49.02 N	10.05 E
Jagtiāl	122	18.48 N	78.56 E

Jaguaquara	255	13.32 S	39.58 W
Jaguarão	252	32.34 S	53.23 W
Jaguarão (Yaguarón) ≐	252	32.39 S	53.12 W
Jaguarari	250	10.16 S	40.12 W
Jaguaretama	250	5.37 S	38.46 W
Jaguari	252	29.30 S	54.41 W
Jaguari ≐, Bra.	256	23.10 S	45.55 W
Jaguari ≐, Bra.	256	22.41 S	47.17 W
Jaguariaíva	252	24.15 S	49.42 W
Jaguaribara	250	5.40 S	38.37 W
Jaguaribe	250	5.53 S	38.37 W
Jaguaribe ≐	250	4.25 S	37.45 W
Jaguari-Mirim ≐	256	21.59 S	47.17 W
Jaguaripe	255	13.06 S	38.53 W
Jaguariúna	256	22.41 S	46.59 W
Jaguaruna	252	28.36 S	49.02 W
Jagüé	252	28.38 S	68.24 W
Jagüey Grande	240p	22.32 N	81.08 W
Jāguli	126	22.56 N	88.32 E
Jāgulia	272b	22.44 N	88.32 E
Jagungal, Mount ʌ	171b	36.09 S	148.23 E
Jagunovskij	86	55.17 N	85.59 E
Jahānābād, India	124	25.13 N	84.59 E
Jahānābād, Pāk.	123	32.11 N	72.29 E
Jahāngīra	123	33.58 N	72.13 E
Jahāngīrābād	124	28.25 N	78.06 E
Jahangirpur ◆[8]	272a	28.44 N	77.13 E
Jahānia	123	30.02 N	71.49 E
Jahannam, Qārat ʌ[2]	142	29.19 N	30.09 E
Jahdānīyah, Wādī al- V	132	30.12 N	36.22 E
Jahnsdorf	54	50.44 N	12.51 E
Jahrom	128	28.31 N	53.33 E
Jahú → Jaú	255	22.18 S	48.33 W
Jaicós	250	7.21 S	41.08 W
Jaidak	120	31.58 N	66.43 E
Jaihti ≐	126	24.08 N	86.48 E
Jaijon	123	31.21 N	76.09 E
Jailolo	108	1.05 N	127.30 E
Jaimanitas ≐	286b	23.05 N	82.29 W
Jainca	102	35.59 N	102.02 E
Jainti	124	26.42 N	89.36 E
Jaintiāpur	120	25.08 N	92.07 E
Jaipur	120	26.55 N	75.49 E
Jaipur Hāt	124	25.06 N	89.01 E
Jais	124	26.15 N	81.32 E
Jaisalmer	120	26.55 N	70.54 E
Jaito	123	30.28 N	74.53 E
Jaja	86	56.12 N	86.26 E
Jaja ≐	86	56.58 N	86.23 E
Jājapur	120	20.51 N	86.20 E
Jājarkot	124	28.42 N	82.12 E
Jājarm	128	36.58 N	56.27 E
Jajce	36	44.21 N	17.16 E
Jajichi	174m	26.47 N	128.13 E
Jajjha	123	28.45 N	70.34 E
Jajl'u	86	51.48 N	87.36 E
Jajpan	85	40.23 N	70.48 E
Jajsan	86	50.51 N	56.14 E
Jajva	86	59.20 N	57.15 E
Jajva ≐	86	59.13 N	56.40 E
Ják	61	47.08 N	16.35 E
Jakarta, Indon.	115a	6.10 S	106.48 E
Jakarta, Indon.	269e	6.10 S	106.48 E
Jakarta, Teluk ⊂	115a	6.05 S	106.48 E
Jakarta Kota Station ◆[5]	269e	6.08 S	106.49 E
Jakarta Raya □[4]	115a	6.10 S	106.45 E
Jakdūl ⊜	140	17.39 N	32.59 E
Jake Creek Mountain ʌ	204	41.13 N	116.54 W
Jakenan	115a	6.45 S	111.11 E
Jākhal	123	29.48 N	75.50 E
Jakhāu	120	23.13 N	68.43 E
Jakkonen	24	66.33 N	29.52 E
Jakobsberg	40	59.26 N	17.50 E
Jakobsdalsberget ʌ[2]	40	58.41 N	16.07 E
Jakobshavn (Ilulissat)	176	69.13 N	51.06 W
Jakobstad (Pietarsaari)	26	63.40 N	22.42 E
Jakovleviči	76	54.20 N	30.31 E
Jakovlevka	89	44.26 N	133.28 E
Jakovlevo, Ross.	78	50.51 N	36.27 E
Jakovlevo, Ross.	82	54.48 N	37.26 E
Jakša	24	61.48 N	56.49 E
Jakšanga	80	58.23 N	45.56 E
Jakšur-Bodja	80	57.11 N	53.09 E
Jakupica ⋀	38	41.43 N	21.26 E
Jakutija □[3]	74	67.00 N	125.00 E
Jakutsk	74	62.00 N	129.40 E
Jal	196	32.06 N	103.11 W
Jalacingo	234	19.48 N	97.18 W
Jalaid Qi	89	46.40 N	122.55 E
Jalājil	128	25.41 N	45.28 E
Jalālābād, Afg.	120	34.26 N	70.28 E
Jalālābād, India	123	30.37 N	74.15 E
Jalālābād, India	124	27.43 N	79.40 E
Jalālah al-Bahrīyah, Jabal ⋀[1]	142	29.20 N	32.00 E
Jalālat al-Qiblīyah, Jabal al- ⋀	142	28.42 N	32.22 E
Jalālpur, India	124	26.19 N	82.44 E
Jalālpur, Pāk.	123	32.38 N	74.12 E
Jalālpur Pīrwāla	123	29.30 N	71.13 E
Jalama	84	41.44 N	48.34 E
Jalan'	86	58.21 N	91.53 E
Jalán ≐	236	14.39 N	86.12 W
Jalan Besar Stadium ♠	271c	1.18 N	103.52 E
Jalandhar	123	31.19 N	75.34 E
Jalangi	126	24.08 N	88.42 E
Jalangi ≐	126	23.25 N	88.22 E
Jalan Kayu	271c	1.24 N	103.52 E
Jalapa, Guat.	236	14.38 N	89.59 W
Jalapa, Méx.	234	17.43 N	92.49 W
Jalapa, Nic.	236	13.55 N	86.08 W
Jalapa □[5]	236	14.35 N	89.55 W
Jalasjärvi	26	62.30 N	22.45 E
Jalaud ≐	116	10.45 N	122.40 E
Jālaun	124	26.09 N	79.21 E
Jal'čiki	80	55.09 N	48.01 E
Jalcocotán	234	21.28 N	105.07 W
Jalda	126	21.56 N	87.30 E
Jaleaca de Catalán	234	17.26 N	99.51 W
Jalesar	124	27.29 N	78.19 E
Jaleshwar	126	21.49 N	87.13 E
Jaleśwar	124	26.38 N	85.48 E
Jālgaon, India	122	21.01 N	75.34 E
Jālgaon, India	122	21.03 N	76.32 E
Jal'gelevo	265a	59.44 N	29.57 E
Jalhay	56	50.34 N	5.58 E
Jalingo	146	8.53 N	11.22 E
Jalirpār	126	23.13 N	89.58 E
Jalisco □[3]	234	20.20 N	103.40 W
Jallas ≐	34	42.54 N	9.08 W
Jālna	122	19.50 N	75.53 E
Jalón ≐	34	41.47 N	1.04 W
Jālor	120	25.21 N	72.37 E
Jalostotitlán	234	21.12 N	102.28 W
Jalpa	234	21.38 N	102.58 W
Jalpa de Méndez	234	18.08 N	93.05 W
Jalpāiguri	124	26.31 N	88.44 E
Jalpan de Serra	234	21.14 N	99.29 W
Jalpug ≐	78	45.41 N	28.35 E
Jalpug, ozero ⊜	78	45.25 N	28.37 E
Jalta (Yalta), Ukr.	78	44.30 N	34.10 E
Jalta, Ukr.	83	46.58 N	37.16 E
Jaltepec ≐	234	17.26 N	94.59 W
Jáltipan de Morelos	234	17.58 N	94.42 W
Jaltuškov	78	48.58 N	27.30 E
Jaluit I[1]	14	6.00 N	169.35 E
Jalūlā'	128	34.16 N	45.10 E
Jalutorovsk	86	56.40 N	66.18 E
Jam, Ross.	82	55.29 N	37.45 E
Jam, Uzb.	85	40.07 N	68.11 E
Jām ≐	128	35.10 N	61.06 E
Jama	83	48.52 N	38.06 E

≐ River	Fluß	Río	Rivière	Rio
≚ Canal	Kanal	Canal	Canal	Canal
⌊ Waterfall, Rapids	Wasserfall, Stromschnellen	Cascada, Rápidos	Chute d'eau, Rapides	Cascata, Rápidos
⊔ Strait	Meeresstraße	Estrecho	Détroit	Estreito
⊂ Bay, Gulf	Bucht, Golf	Bahía, Golfo	Baie, Golfe	Baía, Golfo
⊜ Lake, Lakes	See, Seen	Lago, Lagos	Lac, Lacs	Lago, Lagos
≡ Swamp	Sumpf	Pantano	Marais	Pântano
⊓ Ice Features, Glacier	Eis- und Gletscherformen	Accidentes Glaciales	Formes glaciaires	Acidentes glaciares
⊤ Other Hydrographic Features	Andere Hydrographische Objekte	Otros Elementos Hidrográficos	Autres données hydrographiques	Outros acidentes hidrográficos

✦ Submarine Features	Untermeerische Objekte	Accidentes Submarinos	Formes de relief sous-marin	Acidentes submarinos
□ Political Unit	Politische Einheit	Unidad Politica	Entité politique	Unidade política
ʊ Cultural Institution	Kulturelle Institution	Institución Cultural	Institution culturelle	Instituição cultural
⊥ Historical Site	Historische Stätte	Sitio Histórico	Site historique	Sitio histórico
♠ Recreational Site	Erholungs- und Ferienort	Sitio de Recreo	Centre de loisirs	Area de Lazer
⊠ Airport	Flughafen	Aeropuerto	Aéroport	Aeroporto
■ Military Installation	Militäranlage	Instalación Militar	Installation militaire	Instalação militar
◆ Miscellaneous	Verschiedenes	Misceláneo	Divers	Diversos

Jamaame (Margherita) 144 0.04 N 42.45 E
Jamaare ≃ 146 12.06 N 10.14 E
Jāmāibāti 272b 22.51 N 88.08 E
Jamaica 240p 20.12 N 75.09 W
Jamaica •[8] 276 40.42 N 73.47 W
Jamaica □[1], N.A. 230 18.15 N 77.30 W
Jamaica □[1], N.A. 241q 18.15 N 77.30 W
Jamaica Bay c 210 40.36 N 73.51 W
Jamaica Channel ⊔ 238 18.00 N 75.30 W
Jamaica Plain •[8] 283 42.19 N 71.06 W
Jamaica Pond ⊜ 283 42.19 N 71.07 W
Jamaika → Jamaica □[1] 241q 18.15 N 77.30 W
Jamaïque → Jamaica □[1] 241q 18.15 N 77.30 W
Jamal, poluostrov >[1] 74 70.00 N 70.00 E
Jam-Alin', chrebet ⋏ 89 53.00 N 134.36 E
Jamālīyah •[8] 273c 30.03 N 31.16 E
Jamalo-Neneckij □[3] 72 67.00 N 75.00 E
Jamālpur, Bngl. 124 24.55 N 89.56 E
Jamālpur, India 124 25.18 N 86.30 E
Jamālpurganj 126 23.04 N 87.59 E
Jamanchalinka 80 47.40 N 51.35 E
Jamanota ∧[2] 241s 12.29 N 69.57 W
Jamantau, gora ∧ 86 54.15 N 58.06 E
Jamanxim ≃ 250 4.43 S 56.18 W
Jamapará 256 21.55 S 42.43 W
Jamari ≃ 248 8.27 S 63.30 W
Jamarovka 88 50.38 N 110.16 E
Jamašurma 80 55.58 N 49.36 E
Jamay 234 20.18 N 102.43 W
Jamba 152 13.50 S 15.30 E
Jāmbād 126 22.42 N 86.35 E
Jambeiro 256 23.16 S 45.41 W
Jambeiro, Serra do ⋏[2] 256 23.13 S 45.38 W
Jambelí, Canal de ⊔ 246 3.00 S 80.00 W
Jamberoo 170 34.39 S 150.47 E
Jambes 56 50.28 N 4.52 E
Jambi 112 1.36 S 103.37 E
Jambi □[4] 112 1.30 S 103.00 E
Jambin 166 24.12 S 150.22 E
Jamboaye ≃ 114 5.16 N 97.29 E
Jambol 38 42.29 N 26.30 E
Jambongan, Pulau I 116 6.40 N 117.27 E
Jambuair, Tanjung > 114 5.16 N 97.30 E
Jambusar 120 22.03 N 72.48 E
James ≃, Austl. 166 20.36 S 137.41 E
James ≃, Ab., Can. 182 51.55 N 114.34 W
James ≃, U.S. 198 42.52 N 97.18 W
James ≃, Mo., U.S. 194 36.45 N 93.30 W
James ≃, Va., U.S. 192 36.57 N 76.26 W
James, Isla I 254 44.57 S 74.07 W
James, Lake ⊜ 216 41.42 N 85.02 W
James, Lake ⊜[1] 192 35.45 N 81.55 W
James Bay c 176 53.30 N 80.30 W
Jamesburg 208 40.21 N 74.26 W
James Bypass ≅ 226 36.41 N 120.16 W
James City, N.C., U.S. 192 35.05 N 77.02 W
James City, Pa., U.S. 214 41.37 N 78.50 W
James City □[6] 208 37.17 N 76.48 W
James Craik 252 32.09 S 63.28 W
James Creek 214 40.23 N 78.10 W
James Gardens ♦ 275b 43.40 N 79.31 W
James Island, B.C., Can. 224 48.37 N 123.22 W
James Island, S.C., U.S. 192 32.44 N 79.57 W
James Island I 208 38.31 N 76.20 W
Jameson Raid Memorial ⊥ 273d 26.11 S 27.49 E
James Point > 192 25.21 N 76.24 W
Jamesport 194 39.58 N 93.48 W
James Price Point > 162 17.30 S 122.08 E
James Ranges ⋏ 162 24.06 S 132.30 E
James River Bridge •[5] 208 37.00 N 76.30 W
James Ross, Cape > 176 74.40 N 114.25 W
James Ross Island I 9 64.15 S 57.45 W
James Ross Strait ⊔ 176 69.40 N 95.30 W
James Smith Indian Reserve •[4] 184 53.08 N 104.52 W
Jamestown, Austl. 166 33.12 S 138.36 E
Jamestown, Ire. 48 53.55 N 8.02 W
Jamestown, S. Afr. 158 31.06 S 26.45 E
Jamestown, Ca., U.S. 226 37.57 N 120.25 W
Jamestown, Ks., U.S. 198 39.35 N 97.51 W
Jamestown, Ky., U.S. 194 36.59 N 85.03 W
Jamestown, Mi., U.S. 216 42.50 N 85.51 W
Jamestown, N.Y., U.S. 214 42.05 N 79.14 W
Jamestown, N.C., U.S. 192 35.59 N 79.56 W
Jamestown, N.D., U.S. 198 46.54 N 98.42 W
Jamestown, Oh., U.S. 218 39.39 N 83.44 W
Jamestown, Pa., U.S. 214 41.29 N 80.26 W
Jamestown, R.I., U.S. 207 41.29 N 71.22 W
Jamestown, Tn., U.S. 194 36.25 N 84.55 W
Jamestown ⊥ 208 37.12 N 76.46 W
Jamestown Festival Park ♦ 208 37.14 N 76.48 W
Jamestown Island I 208 37.12 N 76.46 W
Jamestown Reservoir ⊜[1] 198 47.15 N 98.40 W
Jamesville, N.Y., U.S. 210 42.59 N 76.04 W
Jamesville, Va., U.S. 208 37.30 N 75.55 W
Jamet, Lac ⊜ 206 46.34 N 74.30 W
Jametz 56 49.26 N 5.23 E
Jamieson ≃ 169 37.18 S 146.08 E
Jaminauá ≃ 248 9.20 S 70.59 W
Jaminsk 76 52.46 N 28.16 E
Jaminskij 80 50.21 N 42.14 E
Jāmira ≃ 126 21.45 N 87.02 E
Jamira ≃[1] 126 21.35 N 88.28 E
Jamison 208 40.16 N 75.05 W
Jamison City 210 41.18 N 76.22 W
Jamison Town 274a 33.46 S 150.41 E
Jam-Ižora 265a 59.42 N 30.36 E
Jām Jodhpur 120 21.54 N 70.01 E
Jamkhandi 122 16.31 N 75.18 E
Jamki 86 59.33 N 66.47 E
Jamkino 82 55.55 N 38.24 E
Jamm 76 58.26 N 28.03 E
Jammalamadugu 122 14.50 N 78.24 E
Jammerbugten c 26 57.20 N 9.30 E
Jammerland Bugt c 41 55.35 N 11.05 E
Jammu 123 32.42 N 74.52 E
Jammu Airport ⊠ 123 32.42 N 74.51 E
Jammu and Kashmīr □[2] 120 34.00 N 76.00 E
Jamnagar 120 22.28 N 70.04 E
Jamoigne 56 49.42 N 5.25 E
Jamor ≃ 266c 38.42 N 9.15 W
Jampang-kulon 115a 7.16 S 106.37 E
Jampol', Ukr. 78 48.16 N 28.17 E
Jampol', Ukr. 78 49.58 N 26.14 E
Jampol', Ukr. 78 51.57 N 33.46 E
Jampol', Ukr. 83 48.56 N 37.58 E
Jāmpur, India 272b 22.56 N 88.12 E
Jāmpur, Pāk. 123 29.39 N 70.36 E
Jämsä 26 61.52 N 25.12 E
Jamsah 140 27.38 N 33.35 E
Jämsänkoski 26 61.55 N 25.11 E
Jamshedpur 126 22.48 N 86.11 E
Jamsk 74 59.35 N 154.10 E
Jamskaja Sloboda 82 55.29 N 36.01 E
Jāmtāra 126 23.57 N 86.48 E
Jämtland □[9] 26 63.30 N 14.00 E
Jämtlands Län □[6] 24 63.00 N 14.40 E
Jamuāni 126 21.57 N 86.14 E
Jamuga 82 56.24 N 36.40 E
Jamūi 124 24.55 N 86.13 E
Jamuna ≃, Bngl. 124 23.51 N 89.45 E
Jamuna ≃, India 272b 22.57 N 88.35 E
Jamundí 246 3.15 N 76.32 W

Jāmuria 126 23.44 N 87.02 E
Jāmurki 126 24.09 N 90.02 E
Jana ≃ 74 71.31 N 136.32 E
Janāi 272b 22.43 N 88.16 E
Janāj 142 31.00 N 30.46 E
Janajkino 80 50.43 N 51.06 E
Janakpur 124 26.39 N 85.55 E
Janakpur □[8] 124 27.15 N 86.00 E
Janas 266c 38.49 N 9.26 W
Janauacá, Lago ⊜ 246 3.28 S 60.17 W
Janaúba 255 15.48 S 43.19 W
Janaucu, Ilha I 250 0.30 N 50.10 W
Janaul 86 56.16 N 54.56 E
Jand 123 33.26 N 72.01 E
Janda, Laguna de la ⊜ 34 36.15 N 5.51 W
Jandaia 255 17.06 S 50.07 W
Jandaia do Sul 255 23.36 S 51.39 W
Jandaíra 250 11.34 S 37.47 W
Jandalī, Wādī al- V 142 30.05 N 31.52 E
Jandaq 128 34.02 N 54.26 E
Jandelsbrunn 60 48.44 N 13.42 E
Jandiāla 123 31.36 N 75.03 E
Jandiatuba ≃ 246 3.28 S 68.42 W
Jandira 256 23.31 S 46.54 W
Jandira □[7] 287b 23.32 S 46.54 W
Jandowae 166 26.47 S 151.06 E
Jandrakinot 180 64.54 N 172.32 W
Jándula ≃ 34 38.03 N 4.06 W
Jándula, Embalse de ⊜[1] 34 38.30 N 4.00 W
Janeiro, Rio de ≃ 250 11.51 S 45.09 W
Jane Peak ∧ 172 45.20 S 168.19 E
Janes Island I 208 38.00 N 75.52 W
Janes Island State Park ♦ 208 38.00 N 75.52 W
Janesville, Ca., U.S. 204 40.17 N 120.31 W
Janesville, Mn., U.S. 190 44.06 N 93.42 W
Janesville, Wi., U.S. 216 42.40 N 89.01 W
Jangal Bādhāl 126 23.07 N 89.21 E
Jangamo 156 24.06 S 35.21 E
Jangany 157b 23.14 S 45.27 E
Jangarej 24 68.46 N 61.25 E
Jangel'skij 86 53.08 N 58.59 E
Jangeru 112 2.20 S 116.29 E
Jangiabad 85 41.08 N 70.05 E
Jangi-Bazar 85 41.40 N 70.53 E
Jangijer 85 40.17 N 68.50 E
Jangijul' 85 41.07 N 69.03 E
Jangikišlak 85 40.25 N 67.10 E
Jangikurgan, Uzb. 85 40.34 N 71.09 E
Jangikurgan, Uzb. 85 41.12 N 71.44 E
Jangipāra 126 22.45 N 88.04 E
Jangīpur 124 24.28 N 88.04 E
Jangong 114 4.23 N 96.48 E
Jangoon 122 17.43 N 79.11 E
Jangulovo 80 56.26 N 50.25 E
Janikowo 30 52.45 N 18.07 E
Janīn 132 32.28 N 35.18 E
Janina → Ioánnina 38 39.40 N 20.50 E
Janino 265a 59.56 N 30.36 E
Janisjarvi, ozero ⊜ 24 61.59 N 30.57 E
Janiuay 116 10.58 N 122.30 E
Janja 38 44.40 N 19.15 E
Janjina, Hrv. 36 42.56 N 17.26 E
Janjina, Madag. 157b 20.30 S 45.50 E
Janka 126 21.52 N 87.56 E
Jankan, chrebet ⋏ 88 55.45 N 118.00 E
Jankāpur 126 21.54 N 87.23 E
Jan Kempdorp (Andalusia) 158 27.55 S 24.51 E
Jan Lake ⊜ 184 54.55 N 102.55 W
Janlohong 112 2.15 N 117.03 E
Jan Mayen I 12 71.00 N 8.20 W
Jan Mayen Ridge ✢[3] 10 69.00 N 8.00 W
Jannaale 144 1.48 N 44.42 E
Jannali 274a 34.01 S 151.04 E
Jannali Park ♦ 274a 34.01 S 151.03 E
Janos 232 30.54 N 108.10 W
Jánoshalma 30 46.18 N 19.20 E
Jánosháza 30 47.08 N 17.10 E
János-hegy ∧ 264c 47.31 N 18.58 E
Jánossomorja 61 47.47 N 17.08 E
Janoviči 76 55.17 N 30.42 E
Janowiec Wielkopolski 30 52.46 N 17.31 E
Janów Lubelski 30 50.43 N 22.24 E
Jānsath 124 29.20 N 77.51 E
Jansen 184 51.47 N 104.43 W
Jansenville 158 32.56 S 24.40 E
Janskij 74 68.28 N 134.48 E
Janskij zaliv c 74 71.50 N 136.00 E
Jantarnyj 76 54.52 N 19.57 E
Jantetelco 234 18.42 N 98.46 W
Jantikovo 80 55.32 N 47.48 E
Jantra ≃ 38 43.38 N 25.34 E
Januária 255 15.29 S 44.22 W
Januário Cicco 250 6.09 S 35.35 W
Jan Van Riebeeck Park ♦ 273d 26.10 S 27.59 E
Janvarcevo 80 51.26 N 52.15 E
Janville 50 48.12 N 1.53 E
Janville-sur-Juine 261 48.31 N 2.16 E
Janvry 261 48.39 N 2.09 E
Jany-Kurgan 85 43.55 N 67.15 E
Janzé 32 47.58 N 1.30 W
Janzūr 142 30.41 N 31.02 E
Jaora 120 23.38 N 75.08 E
Japan (Nihon) □[1], Asia 90 36.00 N 138.00 E
Japan (Nihon) □[1], Asia 92 36.00 N 138.00 E
Japan, Sea of ⊤[2] 90 40.00 N 135.00 E
Japan Basin ✢[1] 12 40.00 N 135.00 E
Japanisches Meer → Japan, Sea of ⊤[2] 90 40.00 N 135.00 E
Japan Trench ✢[1] 6 37.00 N 143.00 E
Japaratinga 250 9.05 S 35.15 W
Japaratuba 250 10.35 S 36.57 W
Japeri 256 22.39 S 43.40 W
Japi 250 6.27 S 35.56 W
Japim 248 7.37 S 72.54 W
Japla 124 24.33 N 84.01 E
Japoatã 250 10.20 S 36.48 W
Japon → Japan □[1] 92 36.00 N 138.00 E
Japón, Mar del → Japan, Sea of ⊤[2] 90 40.00 N 135.00 E
Japtiksal'a 74 69.21 N 72.32 E
Japuíba 256 22.35 S 42.42 W
Japurá 246 1.48 S 66.30 W
Japurá (Caquetá) ≃ 246 3.08 S 64.46 W
Jaqué 246 7.31 N 78.10 W
Jaqueri-mirim ≃ 287b 23.31 S 46.51 W
Jaquí 248 15.30 S 74.26 W
Jar 80 58.15 N 52.06 E
Jār, Jabal ∧ 128 24.34 N 38.18 E
Jarābulus 130 36.49 N 38.01 E
Jarad 144 18.59 N 41.24 E
Jaradū 142 29.18 N 30.42 E
Jaraguá 255 15.45 S 49.20 W
Jaraguá •[8] 287b 23.27 S 46.44 W
Jaraguá, Pico do ∧ 287b 23.26 S 46.46 W
Jaraguá do Sul 252 26.29 S 49.04 W
Jaraicejo 34 39.40 N 5.49 W
Jaraiz de la Vera 34 40.04 N 5.45 W
Jaral del Progreso 234 20.22 N 101.04 W
Jarales 200 34.36 N 106.45 W
Jarama ≃ 34 40.02 N 3.39 W
Jarama, Canal del ≅ 266a 40.18 N 3.32 W
Jaramānah 132 33.29 N 36.21 E
Jaramillo 254 47.11 S 67.09 W
Jaramor 80 56.07 N 48.44 E
Jaran' ≃ 80 57.35 N 48.14 E
Jarandilla 34 40.08 N 5.39 W
Jaraniyo 144 10.42 N 39.55 E
Jaransk 80 57.19 N 47.54 E
Jarānwāla 123 31.20 N 73.26 E

Jarash 132 32.17 N 35.54 E
Jaraucu ≃ 250 1.48 S 52.22 W
Jarawī, Wādī V 142 29.47 N 31.19 E
Jarbah, Jabal al- ∧ 142 30.16 N 32.03 E
Jarbah, Wāḥat ⊤[4] 140 29.21 N 25.20 E
Jarbidge ≃ 202 42.19 N 115.39 W
Järbo 40 60.43 N 16.36 E
Jarcevo 76 55.04 N 32.41 E
Jardas al-ʿAbīd 146 32.19 N 20.56 E
Jardim, Bra. 248 21.28 S 56.09 W
Jardim, Bra. 250 7.35 S 39.16 W
Jardim América •[8] 287b 23.34 S 46.41 W
Jardim de Piranhas 250 6.22 S 37.20 W
Jardim do Seridó 250 6.35 S 36.46 W
Jardim Paraiso 256 22.48 S 43.35 W
Jardim Paulista •[8] 287b 23.35 S 46.40 W
Jardín América 252 27.03 S 55.14 W
Jardine ≃ 164 10.55 S 142.13 E
Jardine River National Park ♦ 164 11.20 S 142.40 E
Jardines de la Reina, Archipiélago de los II 240p 20.50 N 78.55 W
Jardinópolis 255 21.02 S 47.46 W
Jardymly 84 38.55 N 48.15 E
Jaredi 150 12.46 N 5.05 E
Jaremča 78 48.27 N 24.33 E
Jaren'ga, Ross. 24 63.27 N 53.26 E
Jarenga, Ross. 24 62.43 N 49.30 E
Jarensk 24 62.11 N 49.02 E
Järfälla 40 59.24 N 17.50 E
Jargalang 89 43.06 N 122.54 E
Jargara 38 46.27 N 28.27 E
Jargeau 50 47.52 N 2.07 E
Jari ≃, Bra. 248 5.07 S 62.21 W
Jari ≃, Bra. 250 1.09 S 51.54 W
Jari, Lago ⊜ 246 5.00 S 62.19 W
Jāria Jhānjail 124 25.02 N 90.39 E
Jaridih 124 23.38 N 86.04 E
Jarinu 256 23.06 S 46.44 W
Jarīr, Wādī al- V 128 25.38 N 42.30 E
Jarkino 88 59.08 N 99.23 E
Jarkovo 86 57.24 N 67.05 E
Jarkul'-Mat'uškino 86 55.51 N 76.06 E
Järlåsa 40 59.53 N 17.12 E
Jarmen 54 53.55 N 13.20 E
Jarmolincy 78 49.12 N 26.50 E
Järna 40 59.06 N 17.34 E
Jarnac 32 45.41 N 0.10 W
Jarny 56 49.09 N 5.53 E
Jaro 116 11.11 N 124.47 E
Jarochta 88 58.58 N 98.58 E
Jarocin 30 51.59 N 17.31 E
Jaroměř 30 50.21 N 15.55 E
Jaroměřice 61 49.05 N 15.53 E
Jaropolec 82 56.08 N 35.49 E
Jaroslavec 78 51.33 N 33.40 E
Jaroslavl' 80 57.37 N 39.52 E
Jaroslavl' Oblast' □[4] 76 57.45 N 39.00 E
Jaroslavl' Station •[5] 265b 55.47 N 37.39 E
Jaroslavskaja 84 44.36 N 40.27 E
Jaroslavskij 89 44.10 N 132.13 E
Jarosław 30 50.02 N 22.42 E
Jarovaja 83 49.03 N 37.37 E
Järpen 26 63.21 N 13.29 E
Jarrahdale 168a 32.21 S 116.04 E
Jarratt 208 36.48 N 77.28 W
Jarreau 194 30.39 N 91.29 W
Jarrell 222 30.49 N 97.36 W
Jarrettsville 208 39.36 N 76.28 W
Jarrīs 142 27.55 N 30.46 E
Jarrow 44 54.59 N 1.29 W
Jarry, Parc ♦ 275a 45.32 N 73.38 W
Jar-Sale 74 66.50 N 70.50 E
Jarsomovy 86 60.15 N 73.38 E
Jartai Yanchi ⊜ 102 39.43 N 105.41 E
Jaru 248 10.26 S 62.27 W
Jaru ≃ 248 10.05 S 61.59 W
Jarud Qi 89 44.37 N 120.58 E
Jaruu 88 48.08 N 96.45 E
Järva-Jaani 76 59.02 N 25.53 E
Järvakandi 76 58.47 N 24.49 E
Järvelä 26 60.52 N 25.17 E
Järvenpää 26 60.28 N 25.06 E
Jarvie 182 54.27 N 113.59 W
Jarville-la-Malgrange 58 48.40 N 6.13 E
Jarvis 212 42.53 N 80.06 W
Jarvisburg 192 36.12 N 75.52 W
Jarvis Island I 14 0.23 S 160.02 W
Järvsö 26 61.43 N 16.10 E
Jarwa 124 27.39 N 82.31 E
Jasaan 116 8.39 N 124.45 E
Jasai 272c 18.56 N 73.01 E
Jašalta 80 46.20 N 42.17 E
Jasašnaja Tašla 80 53.55 N 48.16 E
Jaša Tomić 38 45.27 N 20.51 E
Jasdan 120 22.02 N 71.12 E
Jasel'da ≃ 76 52.07 N 26.28 E
Jasenevo •[8] 265b 55.36 N 37.33 E
Jasenki 78 51.32 N 38.12 E
Jasenovoje 82 54.10 N 36.47 E
Jasenovskij 83 48.10 N 39.10 E
Jasenskaja 78 46.22 N 38.16 E
Jashpurnagar 124 22.54 N 84.09 E
Jāshpur Pāts •[1] 124 22.55 N 84.00 E
Jasidih 124 24.31 N 86.39 E
Jasień 30 51.46 N 15.01 E
Jasienica 54 53.37 N 14.32 E
Jasikan 150 7.24 N 0.28 E
Jašil'kul', ozero ⊜ 120 37.45 N 72.55 E
Jasin 114 2.19 N 102.26 E
Jasin'a 78 48.16 N 24.20 E
Jasinga 115a 6.29 S 106.27 E
Jasinovataja 83 48.08 N 37.51 E
Jasinovka 83 48.08 N 37.57 E
Jāsk 128 25.38 N 57.46 E
Jaskhar 272c 18.54 N 72.59 E
Jaškino, Ross. 80 52.41 N 53.26 E
Jaškino, Ross. 86 55.54 N 85.26 E
Jaskino, Ross. 265b 55.40 N 37.16 E
Jaškul' 80 46.11 N 45.21 E
Jaškul' ≃ 80 46.15 N 45.05 E
Jasło 30 49.45 N 21.29 E
Jasmine Estates 220 28.17 N 82.42 W
Jasmund >[1] 54 54.32 N 13.35 E
Jasnaja Pol'ana ⊥ 82 54.05 N 37.32 E
Jasnogorka 83 48.47 N 37.33 E
Jasnogorsk 82 54.29 N 37.42 E
Jasnomorskij 89 46.45 N 141.54 E
Jasnyj, Ross. 86 51.04 N 59.58 E
Jasnyj, Ross. 89 53.17 N 127.59 E
Jason Islands II 254 51.05 S 61.00 W
Jason Peninsula >[1] 9 66.10 S 61.00 W
Jasonville 194 39.09 N 87.11 W
Jasper, Ab., Can. 182 52.53 N 118.05 W
Jasper, Al., U.S. 194 33.49 N 87.16 W
Jasper, Ar., U.S. 194 36.00 N 93.11 W
Jasper, Fl., U.S. 192 30.31 N 82.56 W
Jasper, Ga., U.S. 192 34.28 N 84.25 W
Jasper, In., U.S. 194 38.23 N 86.55 W
Jasper, Mi., U.S. 216 41.48 N 84.02 W
Jasper, Mn., U.S. 198 43.51 N 96.23 W
Jasper, Mo., U.S. 194 37.20 N 94.18 W
Jasper, N.Y., U.S. 210 42.07 N 77.30 W
Jasper, Tn., U.S. 194 35.04 N 85.37 W
Jasper, Tx., U.S. 194 30.55 N 93.59 W
Jasper □[6] 216 40.57 N 87.09 W
Jasper Lake ⊜ 182 53.07 N 118.00 W
Jasper National Park ♦ 182 52.53 N 118.03 W
Jaspur 124 29.17 N 78.49 E
Jasra 124 25.17 N 81.48 E
Jassans-Riottier 58 45.59 N 4.45 E
Jassar 123 32.06 N 74.57 E
Jassy → Iași 38 47.10 N 27.35 E
Jassy ≃ 85 40.46 N 73.05 E
Jastarnia 30 54.43 N 18.40 E
Jastrebarsko 36 45.40 N 15.39 E
Jastrebovka, Ross. 78 51.27 N 37.32 E
Jastrebovka, Ross. 82 54.36 N 36.24 E

Jastrowie 30 53.26 N 16.49 E
Jaswantnagar 124 26.53 N 78.55 E
Jászapáti 30 47.31 N 20.09 E
Jászberény 30 47.30 N 19.55 E
Jász-Nagykun-Szolnok □[6] 30 47.12 N 20.11 E
Jataí 255 17.53 S 51.43 W
Jatapu ≃ 246 2.13 S 58.17 W
Jatatė ≃ 232 16.15 N 91.17 W
Jati, Bra. 250 7.41 S 39.01 W
Jāti, Pāk. 120 24.21 N 68.16 E
Jatibarang 115a 6.28 S 108.17 E
Jatibonico 240p 21.56 N 79.10 W
Jatibonico del Sur ≃ 240p 21.33 N 79.09 W
Jatilawang 115a 7.32 S 109.06 E
Jatiluhur, Waduk ⊜[1] 115a 6.35 S 107.20 E
Jatinegara •[8] 269e 6.13 S 106.52 E
Jatiroto 115a 8.07 S 113.21 E
Jatisrono 115a 7.49 S 111.07 E
Jatiwangi 115a 6.44 S 108.15 E
Jatni 120 20.10 N 85.42 E
Jatniel 273d 26.07 S 28.19 E
Jatobá ≃ 255 12.23 S 54.07 W
Jatobá, Ribeirão ≃ 256 21.28 S 42.49 W
Jatoi Janūbi 123 29.31 N 70.51 E
Jātrāpur 126 22.44 N 89.45 E
Jatt (Tel Gat) 132 32.24 N 35.02 E
Jatznick 54 53.35 N 13.56 E
Jáu, Ang. 152 15.12 S 13.31 E
Jaú, Bra. 255 22.18 S 48.33 W
Jaú ≃ 246 1.54 S 61.26 W
Jaú, Parque Nacional do ♦ 246 2.30 S 63.00 W
Jauaperi ≃ 246 1.26 S 61.35 W
Jauerling ∧ 61 48.20 N 15.20 E
Jaugrām 126 23.06 N 88.05 E
Jauja 248 11.48 S 75.30 W
Jauli 272a 28.44 N 77.21 E
Jaumave 234 23.25 N 99.23 W
Jaunde → Yaoundé 152 3.52 N 11.31 E
Jaune, Mer → Yellow Sea ⊤[2] 90 36.00 N 123.00 E
Jaungulbene 76 57.04 N 26.36 E
Jaunjelgava 76 56.37 N 25.05 E
Jaunpass)(58 46.36 N 7.20 E
Jaunpiebalga 76 57.11 N 26.03 E
Jaunpils 76 56.44 N 23.01 E
Jaunpur 124 25.44 N 82.41 E
Jaupaci 255 16.18 S 50.54 W
Jauquara ≃ 248 15.06 S 57.06 W
Jáuregui 258 34.36 S 59.10 W
Jauru 250 11.06 S 57.30 W
Jauru ≃, Bra. 248 16.22 S 57.46 W
Jauru ≃, Bra. 255 18.40 S 54.36 W
Jausiers 62 44.25 N 6.44 E
Jauza ≃, Ross. 82 56.25 N 36.05 E
Jauza ≃, Ross. 265b 55.45 N 37.38 E
Java 198 45.30 N 99.53 W
Java → Jawa I 115a 7.30 S 110.00 E
Java Center 210 42.39 N 78.23 W
Javādi Hills ⋏[2] 122 12.35 N 78.50 E
Javan 85 38.19 N 69.02 E
Javari (Yavarí) ≃ 242 4.21 S 70.02 W
Javas 80 54.26 N 42.51 E
Java Sea → Jawa, Laut ⊤[2] 112 5.00 S 110.00 E
Java Trench ✢[1] 12 10.30 S 110.00 E
Java Village 210 42.40 N 78.26 W
Jävenitz 54 52.31 N 11.30 E
Javier, Isla I 254 47.06 S 74.24 W
Javkino 78 47.16 N 32.37 E
Javlenka 86 54.21 N 68.27 E
Javor ⋏ 38 44.05 N 18.55 E
Javořice ∧ 61 49.14 N 15.20 E
Javorie ∧ 30 48.27 N 19.18 E
Javorná 60 49.13 N 13.18 E
Javorník 30 50.23 N 17.00 E
Javorov 78 49.56 N 23.23 E
Javorová skála ∧ 30 49.31 N 14.30 E
Javr ≃ 24 68.09 N 30.06 E
Jävre 26 65.09 N 21.59 E
Jawa (Java) I 115a 7.30 S 110.00 E
Jawa, Laut (Java Sea) ⊤[2] 112 5.00 S 110.00 E
Jawa Barat □[4] 115a 7.00 S 107.00 E
Jawʿālīyāt, Jabal al- ∧ 132 31.26 N 36.26 E
Jawāla Mukhi 123 31.53 N 76.19 E
Jawa Tengah □[4] 115a 7.30 S 110.00 E
Jawa Timur □[4] 115a 8.00 S 113.00 E
Jawbar 132 33.31 N 36.19 E
Jawf, Wādī V 144 15.50 N 45.30 E
Jawi 112 0.48 S 109.16 E
Jawor 30 51.03 N 16.11 E
Jaworzno 30 50.13 N 19.15 E
Jay, Fl., U.S. 194 30.57 N 87.09 W
Jay, Ok., U.S. 196 36.25 N 94.47 W
Jay □[6] 216 40.26 N 84.59 W
Jaya, Puncak ∧ 164 4.05 S 137.11 E
Jayanca 248 6.24 S 79.50 W
Jayapura (Sukarnapura) 164 2.32 S 140.42 E
Jayb, Wādī al- (Haʿ Arava) V 132 30.58 N 35.24 E
Jay Cooke State Park ♦ 190 46.41 N 92.23 W
Jay Creek Aboriginal Reserve •[4] 162 23.45 S 133.35 E
Jaydebpur 124 24.00 N 90.26 E
Jaynagar 126 22.36 N 90.42 E
Jaynagar Majilpur 126 22.11 N 88.25 E
Jaynes 200 32.16 N 111.01 W
Jay Peak ∧ 188 44.55 N 72.32 W
Jaypur, India 122 18.51 N 82.35 E
Jaypur, India 126 23.03 N 87.27 E
Jayrūd 130 33.49 N 36.44 E
Jayton 196 33.15 N 100.34 W
Jayuya 240m 18.13 N 66.36 W
Jaywick 42 51.47 N 1.08 E
Jaz 80 54.54 N 45.13 E
Jaželbicy 76 58.02 N 32.58 E
Jazevec 24 65.43 N 46.30 E
Jazgulem ≃ 85 38.12 N 71.21 E
Jazīrat Muḥammad 273c 30.07 N 31.12 E
Jazjavan 85 40.39 N 71.44 E
Jažma 24 66.56 N 44.29 E
Jaz Mūrīān, Hāmūn-e ⊜ 128 27.20 N 58.55 E
Jazovaja 86 49.27 N 85.20 E
Jazykovo 80 54.18 N 47.24 E
Jazzīn 132 33.32 N 35.34 E
Jbāʿ 132 33.29 N 35.31 E
J.B. Thomas, Lake ⊜[1] 196 32.35 N 101.10 W
J. C. Murphey Lake ⊜ 216 40.58 N 87.30 W
Jdiouia 34 35.57 N 0.50 E
Jeanerette 194 29.54 N 91.39 W
Jeanesville 210 40.56 N 75.58 W
Jeannette 214 40.19 N 79.36 W
Jebba 150 9.08 N 4.50 E
Jebel 38 45.33 N 21.14 E
Jebeniana 148 35.02 N 10.55 E
Jeber-Bergfrieden 54 51.59 N 12.20 E
Jeberos 248 5.17 S 76.13 W
Jebri 120 27.18 N 65.44 E
Jebus 112 1.44 S 105.29 E
Jechegnadzor 84 39.46 N 45.21 E
Jéci, Serra ∧ 154 12.48 S 35.12 E
Jedane, Oued ti-n- V 148 24.55 N 6.30 E
Jedarma 88 58.44 N 102.36 E
Jedburgh 44 55.29 N 2.34 W
Jedburgh Abbey ⴷ[1] 44 55.27 N 2.34 W
Jeddah → Jiddah 144 21.30 N 39.12 E
Jeddore Lake ⊜[1] 186 48.03 N 55.55 W
Jedelevo 80 53.24 N 47.45 E
Jedepo 150 5.16 N 8.20 W
Jedincy 38 48.10 N 27.19 E

ENGLISH — Name, Page, Lat.°′, Long.°′

Jedisa 84 42.31 N 44.16 E
Jedlesee •[8] 264b 48.16 N 16.23 E
Jednevo 82 56.06 N 36.14 E
Jedogon 88 54.15 N 100.15 E
Jedrovo 76 57.55 N 33.38 E
Jędrzejów 30 50.39 N 20.18 E
Jedwabne 30 53.17 N 22.19 E
Jed Water ≃ 46 55.32 N 2.33 W
Jeetzel (Jeetze) ≃ 54 53.09 N 11.04 E
Jefawa 140 10.57 N 23.48 E
Jeffara (Al-Jifārah) ≚ 146 32.30 N 11.45 E
Jeffers 198 44.03 N 95.11 W
Jefferson, Ga., U.S. 192 34.07 N 83.34 W
Jefferson, In., U.S. 216 40.17 N 86.36 W
Jefferson, Ia., U.S. 198 42.00 N 94.22 W
Jefferson, Md., U.S. 208 39.21 N 77.31 W
Jefferson, Ma., U.S. 207 42.21 N 71.52 W
Jefferson, N.J., U.S. 285 39.45 N 75.13 W
Jefferson, N.Y., U.S. 210 42.14 N 73.54 W
Jefferson, N.Y., U.S. 210 42.29 N 74.37 W
Jefferson, N.C., U.S. 192 36.25 N 81.28 W
Jefferson, Oh., U.S. 214 41.44 N 80.46 W
Jefferson, Or., U.S. 202 44.43 N 123.00 W
Jefferson, Pa., U.S. 279b 40.18 N 80.03 W
Jefferson, S.C., U.S. 192 34.39 N 80.23 W
Jefferson, S.D., U.S. 198 42.36 N 96.33 W
Jefferson, Tx., U.S. 194 32.45 N 94.20 W
Jefferson, Wi., U.S. 216 43.00 N 88.48 W
Jefferson □[6], Il., U.S. 219 38.19 N 88.55 W
Jefferson □[6], In., U.S. 218 38.44 N 85.23 W
Jefferson □[6], Ky., U.S. 218 38.14 N 85.10 W
Jefferson □[6], Mo., U.S. 219 38.20 N 90.34 W
Jefferson □[6], N.Y., U.S. 212 43.59 N 75.55 W
Jefferson □[6], Oh., U.S. 214 40.22 N 80.37 W
Jefferson □[6], Pa., U.S. 214 41.09 N 79.05 W
Jefferson □[6], Wa., U.S. 224 47.50 N 122.36 W
Jefferson □[6], Wi., U.S. 216 43.02 N 88.46 W
Jefferson ≃ 202 45.56 N 111.30 W
Jefferson, Mount ∧, U.S. 202 44.34 N 111.30 W
Jefferson, Mount ∧, Nv., U.S. 204 38.46 N 116.55 W
Jefferson, Mount ∧, Or., U.S. 202 44.40 N 121.47 W
Jefferson City, Mo., U.S. 219 38.34 N 92.10 W
Jefferson City, Tn., U.S. 192 36.07 N 83.29 W
Jefferson Farms 285 39.40 N 75.34 W
Jefferson Manor 284c 38.47 N 77.04 W
Jefferson Park •[8] 278 41.59 N 87.46 W
Jefferson Proving Ground ▪ 218 38.50 N 85.25 W
Jeffersonton 188 38.38 N 77.55 W
Jeffersontown 218 38.11 N 85.33 W
Jefferson Village 284c 38.52 N 77.10 W
Jeffersonville, Ga., U.S. 192 32.41 N 83.20 W
Jeffersonville, In., U.S. 218 38.16 N 85.44 W
Jeffersonville, N.Y., U.S. 210 41.46 N 74.56 W
Jeffersonville, Oh., U.S. 218 39.39 N 83.33 W
Jeffrey City 200 42.29 N 107.49 W
Jeffreys Bay 158 34.02 S 24.54 E
Jeffries Creek ≃ 192 34.05 N 79.32 W
Jefimovka 80 52.13 N 52.03 E
Jefimovskij 76 59.30 N 35.02 E
Jefremov 76 53.09 N 38.07 E
Jefremova 82 56.13 N 38.59 E
Jefremovka 83 47.19 N 38.29 E
Jefremovo-Stepanovka 78 48.43 N 40.50 E
Jefremovskaja 82 55.25 N 38.59 E
Jega 150 12.15 N 4.23 E
Jegenstorf 58 47.03 N 7.30 E
Jegindybulak, Kaz. 86 49.45 N 76.23 E
Jegindybulak, Kaz. 86 48.42 N 81.48 E
Jegizkara, gora ∧ 86 46.24 N 64.09 E
Jegorjevka 89 50.42 N 127.42 E
Jegorjevsk 82 55.23 N 39.02 E
Jegorlyk ≃ 80 46.33 N 41.52 E
Jehol → Chengde 105 40.58 N 117.53 E
Jeja ≃ 78 46.41 N 38.36 E
Jejsk 78 46.42 N 38.16 E
Jejskij liman c 78 46.42 N 38.25 E
Jeju → Cheju 90 33.31 N 126.32 E
Jejur 272b 22.53 N 88.08 E
Jēkabpils 76 56.29 N 25.51 E
Jekaterinburg (Sverdlovsk) 86 56.51 N 60.36 E
Jekaterinburg Oblast' □[4] 86 58.00 N 62.00 E
Jekaterinino 76 55.49 N 33.58 E
Jekaterininskoje 86 56.53 N 74.34 E
Jekaterinoslav → Dnepropetrovsk 78 48.27 N 34.59 E
Jekaterinoslavka 89 50.23 N 129.08 E
Jekaterinovka, Kaz. 86 54.36 N 70.58 E
Jekaterinovka, Ross. 78 46.42 N 38.46 E
Jekaterinovka, Ross. 80 53.04 N 49.28 E
Jekaterinovka, Ross. 80 46.32 N 41.42 E
Jekaterinovka, Ross. 80 52.03 N 44.21 E
Jekaterinovka, Ross. 83 47.33 N 38.23 E
Jekaterinovka •[8] 265b 55.46 N 37.23 E
Jekaterinovskaja 78 46.20 N 39.58 E
Jekateriny, proliv ⊔, Ross. 74 44.30 N 146.45 E
Jekateriny, proliv ⊔, Ross. 92a 44.25 N 146.40 E
Jekimoviči 76 54.07 N 33.18 E
Jekpindykurylys 80 47.49 N 47.17 E
Jekyll Island I 192 31.04 N 81.25 W
Jekyll Island State Park ♦ 192 31.02 N 81.25 W
Jelabuga 80 55.47 N 52.04 E
Jelai ≃, Indon. 112 2.59 S 110.45 E
Jelai ≃, Malay. 114 4.04 N 102.20 E
Jelan', Ross. 80 52.13 N 44.11 E
Jelan', Ross. 80 50.57 N 43.44 E
Jelan', Ross. 83 48.41 N 39.47 E
Jelan', Ross. 86 57.39 N 63.42 E
Jelan' ≃, Ross. 78 51.07 N 41.25 E
Jelan' ≃, Ross. 80 50.57 N 43.44 E
Jelan' ≃, Ross. 80 51.07 N 41.26 E
Jelancy 88 52.49 N 106.25 E
Jelanec 78 47.42 N 31.51 E
Jelanka 86 55.37 N 75.18 E
Jelan'-Koleno 78 51.09 N 41.14 E
Jelan'-Kolenovskij 78 51.10 N 41.10 E
Jelat'ma 80 54.58 N 41.45 E
Jelaur, Ross. 80 54.34 N 50.21 E
Jelaur, Ross. 80 53.50 N 48.48 E
Jelchovka 80 53.51 N 50.18 E
Jel'covka 86 53.15 N 86.15 E
Jel'cy, Ross. 76 56.40 N 33.51 E
Jel'cy, Ross. 82 56.11 N 38.46 E
Jelec 76 52.37 N 38.30 E
Jeleckij 24 67.03 N 64.10 E
Jelenia Góra (Hirschberg) 30 50.55 N 15.46 E
Jelenia Góra □[4] 30 51.10 N 15.30 E
Jelenskij 76 53.29 N 35.23 E
Jelep La Pass)(124 27.23 N 88.51 E
Jelgava 76 56.39 N 23.42 E
Jelgavkrasti 76 57.28 N 24.26 E
Jelisejevka 78 47.02 N 36.24 E
Jelizarovo, Ross. 80 58.33 N 44.50 E
Jelizarovo, Ukr. 78 48.12 N 34.33 E
Jelizavetgradka 78 48.48 N 32.24 E

DEUTSCH — Name, Seite, Breite°′, Länge°′ E = Ost

Jelizavetinka 86 51.28 N 71.12 E
Jelizavetopol'skoje 86 52.51 N 60.36 E
Jelizavetovka 78 46.39 N 38.53 E
Jelizavety, mys > 89 54.26 N 142.42 E
Jelizovo 76 53.24 N 29.01 E
Jelli 154 5.22 N 31.48 E
Jellico 192 36.35 N 84.07 W
Jelling 41 55.45 N 9.26 E
Jelloway 214 40.33 N 82.18 W
Jelm Mountain ∧ 200 41.06 N 105.58 W
Jel'n'a 76 54.35 N 33.11 E
Jelnat' 80 57.20 N 42.49 E
Jel'niki 80 54.37 N 43.53 E
Jeloguj ≃ 74 63.13 N 87.45 E
Jel'onovka, Ukr. 83 48.39 N 38.01 E
Jel'onovka, Ukr. 83 47.50 N 37.40 E
Jelošnoje 86 55.27 N 66.44 E
Jelovo 80 57.03 N 54.54 E
Jels 41 55.21 N 9.12 E
Jelšanka, Ross. 80 51.49 N 46.23 E
Jelšanka, Ross. 80 52.35 N 47.59 E
Jelšanka Pervaja 80 52.53 N 52.02 E
Jelšava 30 48.39 N 20.14 E
Jel'sk 78 51.48 N 29.09 E
Jema ≃ 144 10.09 N 38.20 E
Jemaa 150 9.27 N 8.23 E
Jemaja, Pulau I 112 2.55 N 105.45 E
Jemaluang 114 2.17 N 103.52 E
Jemantajevo 80 53.34 N 53.50 E
Jemanželinsk 86 54.45 N 61.20 E
Jember 115a 8.10 S 113.42 E
Jemca 24 63.04 N 40.20 E
Jemca ≃ 24 63.15 N 41.20 E
Jemeljanovka 78 45.32 N 34.53 E
Jemeljanovo 86 56.11 N 92.40 E
Jemel'stan 24 61.13 N 52.29 E
Jemen → Yemen □[1] 144 15.00 N 47.00 E
Jemen, Volksrepublik → Yemen □[1] 144 15.00 N 47.00 E
Jemez ≃ 200 35.22 N 106.31 W
Jemez Canyon Reservoir ⊜[1] 200 35.28 N 106.39 W
Jemez Indian Reservation •[4] 200 35.35 N 106.45 W
Jemez Springs 200 35.46 N 106.41 W
Jemgum 52 53.16 N 7.23 E
Jemil'čino 78 50.52 N 27.48 E
Jeminary 86 47.32 N 85.38 E
Jemmal 148 35.38 N 10.46 E
Jemnice 61 49.01 N 15.35 E
Jempang, Kenohan ⊜ 112 0.26 S 116.12 E
Jena, Dtsch. 54 50.56 N 11.35 E
Jena, La., U.S. 194 31.40 N 92.08 W
Jenakijevo 83 48.14 N 38.13 E
Jenašimskij Polkan, gora ∧ 74 59.50 N 92.52 E
Jenaz 58 46.55 N 9.45 E
Jenbach 64 47.24 N 11.47 E
Jenbek 86 48.53 N 77.12 E
Jendarata 114 3.55 N 100.57 E
Jendongin 88 53.27 N 113.01 E
Jendouba (Souk el Arba) 148 36.30 N 8.47 E
Jendouba □[8] 148 36.30 N 8.45 E
Jeneponto 112 5.41 S 119.42 E
Jenera 216 40.54 N 83.44 W
Jeniang 114 5.49 N 100.38 E
Jenisej (Yenisey) ≃ 72 71.50 N 82.40 E
Jenisejsk 86 58.27 N 92.10 E
Jenisejskij kr'až ⋏ 74 59.00 N 93.00 E
Jenisejskij zaliv c 74 72.30 N 80.00 E
Jenison 216 42.54 N 85.47 W
Jenkins, Ky., U.S. 192 37.10 N 82.37 W
Jenkins, Tx., U.S. 222 32.59 N 94.44 W
Jenkins, Mount ∧ 162 25.36 S 129.41 E
Jenkinson Lake ⊜[1] 226 38.44 N 120.33 W
Jenkinsville 192 34.16 N 81.17 W
Jenkintown 208 40.05 N 75.07 W
Jenks 196 36.01 N 95.58 W
Jenli 100 23.15 N 120.08 E
Jenners 214 40.08 N 79.02 W
Jennersdorf 61 46.57 N 16.08 E
Jennerstown 214 40.10 N 79.04 W
Jennifer Branch ≃ 284b 39.25 N 76.30 W
Jennings, Fl., U.S. 192 30.36 N 83.05 W
Jennings, La., U.S. 194 30.13 N 92.39 W
Jennings, Mo., U.S. 219 38.43 N 90.15 W
Jennings □[6] 218 38.59 N 85.36 W
Jennings Creek ≃ 216 40.53 N 84.17 W
Jennings Lodge 224 45.23 N 122.36 W
Jenotajevka 80 47.15 N 47.03 E
Jenpeg Dam •[6] 184 54.33 N 98.02 W
Jensen 200 40.22 N 109.20 W
Jensen Beach 220 27.15 N 80.13 W
Jens Munk Island I 176 69.42 N 79.30 W
Jens Munks Ø I 176 64.40 N 40.30 W
Jenu 112 0.36 S 109.52 E
Jen'uka 88 57.58 N 121.42 E
Jeonju → Chŏnju 98 35.49 N 127.08 E
Jepač 24 66.58 N 61.22 E
Jepara 115a 6.35 S 110.39 E
Jeparit 166 36.09 S 141.59 E
Jepelacio 248 6.07 S 76.57 W
Jepichin 80 48.16 N 45.14 E
Jepifan' 76 53.49 N 38.33 E
Jeppener 258 35.17 S 58.12 W
Jeptha Knob ∧[2] 218 38.11 N 85.07 W
Jepua (Jeppo) 26 63.24 N 22.37 E
Jequeri 255 20.27 S 42.40 W
Jequetepeque ≃ 248 7.21 S 79.36 W
Jequié 255 13.51 S 40.05 W
Jequitaí 255 17.15 S 44.28 W
Jequitinhonha 255 16.26 S 41.00 W
Jequitinhonha ≃ 255 15.51 S 38.53 W
Jerachtur 80 54.43 N 41.09 E
Jerada 148 34.17 N 2.13 W
Jeradou 36 36.15 N 10.23 E
Jerangle 171b 35.52 S 149.22 E
Jeransang 114 3.52 N 102.22 E
Jerantut 114 3.56 N 102.22 E
Jerba, Île de I 148 33.48 N 10.54 E
Jerbar 140 5.39 N 31.05 E
Jerbent 128 39.19 N 58.36 E
Jerbogačon 74 61.16 N 108.00 E
Jercevo 24 60.48 N 40.05 E
Jerdenevo 82 54.55 N 36.27 E
Jerécuaro 234 20.09 N 100.31 W
Jeremejevka 83 46.58 N 39.33 E
Jeremejevo 82 55.57 N 37.01 E
Jérémie 238 18.39 N 74.07 W
Jeremino 82 56.27 N 37.58 E
Jeremoabo 250 10.04 S 38.21 W
Jeremy Hill ∧[2] 207 42.45 N 71.21 W
Jeremy Point > 207 41.53 N 70.04 W
Jerevan 84 40.11 N 44.30 E
Jerez ≃ 234 22.15 N 103.11 W
Jerez de García Salinas 234 22.39 N 103.00 W
Jerez de la Frontera 34 36.41 N 6.08 W
Jerez de los Caballeros 34 38.19 N 6.46 W
Jergač 86 57.28 N 56.39 E
Jergeni ⋏[2] 80 47.00 N 44.00 E
Jergeninskij 80 47.07 N 44.28 E
Jericho, Austl. 166 23.36 S 146.08 E
Jericho → Arīḥā, Isr. Occ 132 31.52 N 35.27 E
Jericho, N.J., U.S. 285 39.48 N 75.09 W
Jericho, N.Y., U.S. 210 40.47 N 73.32 W
Jericho Dam ⊜[1] 158 26.39 S 30.28 E
Jerichow 54 52.30 N 12.01 E
Jericó, Bra. 250 6.33 S 37.48 W
Jericó, Col. 246 5.47 N 75.47 W
Jericoacoara, Ponta de > 250 2.48 S 40.29 W
Jerid, Chott ≋ 148 33.42 N 8.26 E
Jerik ≃ 83 48.59 N 38.30 E
Jerilderie 166 35.22 S 145.44 E
Jerimoth Hill ∧[2] 207 41.52 N 71.47 W

Symbols in the index entries represent the broad categories identified in the key at the right. Symbols with superior numbers (⋏[1]) identify subcategories (see complete key on page *I · 1).*

Symbole im Register stellen die rechts im Schlüssel erklärten Kategorien dar. Symbole mit hochgestellten Ziffern (⋏[1]) bezeichnen Unterabteilungen einer Kategorie (vgl. vollständiger Schlüssel auf Seite *I · 1).*

Los símbolos incluídos en el texto del índice representan las grandes categorías identificadas con la clave a la derecha. Los símbolos con numeros en su parte superior (⋏[1]) identifican las subcategorías (véase la clave completa en la página *I · 1).*

Les symboles de l'index représentent les catégories indiquées dans la légende à droite. Les symboles suivis d'un indice (⋏[1]) représentent des sous-catégories (voir légende complète à la page *I · 1).*

Os símbolos incluídos no texto do índice representam as grandes categorias identificadas com a chave à direita. Os símbolos com números em sua parte superior (⋏[1]) identificam as subcategorias (veja-se a chave completa à página *I · 1).*

∧ Mountain	Berg	Montaña	Montagne	Montanha
⋏ Mountains	Gebirge	Montañas	Montagnes	Montanhas
)(Pass	Paß	Paso	Col	Passo
V Valley, Canyon	Tal, Cañon	Valle, Cañón	Vallée, Canyon	Vale, Canhão
≚ Plain	Ebene	Llano	Plaine	Planície
> Cape	Kap	Cabo	Cap	Cabo
I Island	Insel	Isla	Île	Ilha
II Islands	Inseln	Islas	Îles	Ilhas
⊥ Other Topographic Features	Andere Topographische Objekte	Otros Elementos Topográficos	Autres données topographiques	Outros acidentes topográficos

ESPAÑOL: Nombre | Página | Lat.°′ | Long.°′ W = Oeste
FRANÇAIS: Nom | Page | Lat.°′ | Long.°′ W = Ouest
PORTUGUÊS: Nome | Página | Lat.°′ | Long.°′ W = Oeste

Jerki 78 48.59 N 31.00 E
Jermak 86 52.02 N 76.55 E
Jermakovo 80 53.11 N 49.38 E
Jermakovskaja 80 48.03 N 41.17 E
Jermakovskoje 86 53.16 N 92.24 E
Jermekejevo 80 54.05 N 53.40 E
Jermentau 86 51.38 N 73.10 E
Jermentau ⋏ 86 51.10 N 73.10 E
Jermica 24 66.56 N 52.15 E
Jermilovka 86 57.40 N 72.55 E
Jermiš' 80 54.46 N 42.16 E
Jermolajevo, Ross. 86 52.46 N 55.47 E
Jermolajevo, Ross. 86 55.13 N 92.10 E
Jermolino, Ross. 82 55.12 N 36.36 E
Jermolino, Ross. 82 55.57 N 36.54 E
Jermolino, Ross. 82 56.48 N 37.49 E
Jermolino, Ross. 86 57.20 N 64.43 E
Jermyn 210 41.31 N 75.32 W
Jernhatten ∧[2] 41 56.15 N 10.48 E
Jernih 114 4.25 N 97.43 E
Jeroaquara 255 15.23 S 50.25 W
Jerofej Pavlovič 89 53.58 N 122.01 E
Jerome, Az., U.S. 200 34.44 N 112.06 W
Jerome, Id., U.S. 202 42.43 N 114.31 W
Jerome, Il., U.S. 219 39.46 N 89.41 W
Jerome, Mi., U.S. 216 42.01 N 84.28 W
Jerome, Pa., U.S. 214 40.12 N 78.59 W
Jeromesville 214 40.48 N 82.11 W
Jer'omino 86 58.35 N 79.25 E
Jerónimos, Mosteiro dos ♁[1] 266c 38.42 N 9.12 W
Jeröö 88 49.45 N 106.40 E
Jeröö ≃ 88 49.54 N 106.08 E
Jeropol 74 65.15 N 168.40 E
Jerpoint Abbey ⊥ 48 52.29 N 7.08 W
Jerry City 216 41.15 N 83.36 W
Jerry Slough ≃ 226 35.33 N 119.31 W
Jersey 214 40.03 N 82.46 W
Jersey □[5] 219 39.07 N 90.20 W
Jersey □[2], Europe 22 49.15 N 2.10 W
Jersey □[2], Europe 43b 49.15 N 2.10 W
Jersey City 210 40.43 N 74.04 W
Jersey City State College ♁[2] 276 40.43 N 74.05 W
Jersey Mountain ∧ 202 45.29 N 115.34 W
Jersey Shore 210 41.12 N 77.16 W
Jersey Village 222 29.52 N 95.35 W
Jerseyville 219 39.07 N 90.19 W
Jerši 76 54.24 N 34.12 E
Jeršiči 76 53.40 N 32.44 E
Jeršov 80 51.20 N 48.17 E
Jeršovka 86 54.07 N 64.59 E
Jeršovo 82 55.46 N 36.52 E
Jeršovskij 86 52.29 N 59.08 E
Jertarskij 86 56.47 N 64.18 E
Jerte ≃ 34 39.58 N 6.17 W
Jerteh 114 5.45 N 102.30 E
Jertoma 24 63.32 N 47.48 E
Jerumenha 250 7.05 S 43.30 W
Jerusalem → Yerushalayim 132 31.46 N 35.14 E
Jerusalem Airport ⊠ 132 31.52 N 35.12 E
Jerusalim (Talusan) 116 7.26 N 122.49 E
Jeruslan ≃ 80 50.15 N 45.42 E
Jervaulx Abbey ♁[1] 44 54.16 N 1.43 W
Jervis, Cape ⟩ 168b 35.38 S 138.06 E
Jervis Bay 170 35.08 S 150.42 E
Jervis Bay ⊂ 170 35.05 S 150.44 E
Jervis Inlet ⊂ 182 49.46 N 124.10 W
Jervois Range ⋏ 162 22.38 S 136.05 E
Jerxheim 54 52.05 N 10.54 E
Jerykly 80 55.11 N 51.26 E
Jerzens 58 47.10 N 10.45 E
Jesaulovka 83 48.03 N 39.02 E
Jesenankaty ≃ 80 50.32 N 51.47 E
Jesenice, Česká Rep. 54 50.04 N 13.29 E
Jesenice, Slvn. 61 46.27 N 14.04 E
Jesenice, údolní nádrž ⊜[1] 60 50.04 N 12.27 E
Jeseník 30 50.14 N 17.13 E
Jesenoviči 76 57.17 N 34.14 E
Jesensaj 80 49.54 N 51.28 E
Ješera 84 43.04 N 40.55 E
Jeserig bei Wiesenburg 54 52.05 N 12.27 E
Jesi 66 43.31 N 13.14 E
Jesil' 86 51.58 N 66.24 E
Jes'ki 76 57.56 N 36.23 E
Jesönbulag → Altaj 90 46.20 N 96.18 E
Jessej 74 68.29 N 102.10 E
Jesselton → Kota Kinabalu 112 5.59 N 116.04 E
Jessen 54 51.47 N 12.58 E
Jessentuki 84 44.03 N 42.51 E
Jesser Point ⟩ 158 27.32 S 32.40 E
Jessheim 26 60.09 N 11.11 E
Jessnitz 54 51.41 N 12.17 E
Jessore 124 23.10 N 89.13 E
Jessup, Md., U.S. 208 39.08 N 76.46 W
Jessup, Pa., U.S. 210 41.28 N 75.33 W
Jessup Park ♠ 280 34.15 N 118.24 W
Jestetten 58 47.39 N 8.34 E
Jestřebí 54 50.38 N 14.36 E
Jésuite, Lac du ⊜ 206 46.53 N 72.36 W
Jesup, Ga., U.S. 192 31.36 N 81.53 W
Jesup, Ia., U.S. 190 42.28 N 92.03 W
Jesup, Lake ⊜ 220 28.43 N 81.14 W
Jesús 252 27.03 S 55.47 W
Jésus, Île I 206 45.35 N 73.45 W
Jesús Carranza 234 17.26 N 95.02 W
Jesús de Otoro 236 14.26 N 87.59 W
Jesús María, Arg. 252 30.59 S 64.06 W
Jesús María, Méx. 232 25.06 N 107.28 W
Jesús María, Méx. 234 21.58 N 102.21 W
Jesús María, Perú 286d 12.04 S 77.04 W
Jesús María ≃ 234 21.51 N 104.42 W
Jesús María, Punta ⟩ 258 34.39 S 56.55 W
Jesús Menéndez 240p 21.10 N 76.29 W
Jet 196 36.39 N 98.10 W
Jeta, Ilha de I 150 11.53 N 16.15 W
Jetafe 116 10.09 N 124.09 E
Jetmore 198 38.05 N 99.53 W
Jet Propulsion Laboratory ♁[3] 280 34.12 N 118.11 W
Jetpur 120 21.44 N 70.37 E
Jetřichovice 54 50.49 N 14.25 E
Jett 218 38.11 N 84.49 W
Jette 50 50.52 N 4.20 E
Jettingen 58 48.23 N 10.26 E
Jeumont 50 50.18 N 4.06 E
Jeune Landing 182 50.27 N 127.30 W
Jeunieb 114 5.10 N 96.29 E
Jeuram 114 4.14 N 96.18 E
Jever 52 53.34 N 7.54 E
Jeverland ◆[1] 52 53.35 N 8.00 E
Jevgaščino 86 56.26 N 74.41 E
Jevgenjevka 85 43.31 N 77.40 E
Jevíčko 30 49.38 N 16.43 E
Jevišovice 61 48.59 N 16.00 E
Jevišovka ≃ 61 48.49 N 16.28 E
Jevlach 84 40.36 N 47.09 E
Jevlaš'ovo 80 53.07 N 46.51 E
Jevnaker 26 60.15 N 10.28 E
Jevpatorija 78 45.12 N 33.22 E
Jevra 86 59.56 N 64.27 E
Jevrej □[3] 89 48.30 N 132.00 E
Jevsug 83 49.13 N 39.18 E
Jevsug ≃ 83 48.47 N 39.19 E
Jewel Cave National Monument ♠ 198 43.42 N 103.50 W
Jewell, Ia., U.S. 190 42.18 N 93.38 W
Jewell, Ks., U.S. 198 39.40 N 98.09 W
Jewell, N.Y., U.S. 210 43.13 N 75.48 W
Jewell, Oh., U.S. 216 41.20 N 84.17 W
Jewell, Or., U.S. 224 45.56 N 123.30 W
Jewell Ridge 192 37.11 N 81.47 W
Jewell Village 218 39.10 N 85.51 W
Jewett, Il., U.S. 194 39.13 N 88.15 W
Jewett, Oh., U.S. 214 40.22 N 81.00 W
Jewett, Tx., U.S. 222 31.22 N 96.09 W
Jewett City 207 41.36 N 71.58 W
Jewett Creek ≃ 212 44.22 N 75.45 W
Jewett Lake ⊜ 184 56.09 N 104.40 W
Jewettville 284a 42.43 N 78.52 W
Jey ◆[8] 267d 35.41 N 51.21 E
Jeyretān 120 37.10 N 67.20 E
Jezerce ∧ 38 42.26 N 19.49 E
Jezerišče 76 55.50 N 29.59 E
Jezerní hora ∧ 60 49.10 N 13.11 E
Ježicha 80 58.06 N 47.40 E
Jeziorany 30 53.58 N 20.46 E
Ježovo 80 58.02 N 52.14 E
Jezreel, Valley of → Yizre'el, 'Émeq ⋁ 132 32.36 N 35.14 E
J. G. Strijdomdam ⊜[1] 158 27.25 S 32.05 E
Jhābua 120 22.46 N 74.36 E
Jhāhtipahāri 126 23.22 N 86.54 E
Jha Jha 124 24.46 N 86.22 E
Jhajjar 124 28.37 N 76.39 E
Jhal 120 28.17 N 67.27 E
Jhālakāti 124 22.39 N 90.12 E
Jhālārāpātan 124 24.33 N 76.10 E
Jhālāwār 124 24.36 N 76.09 E
Jhalida 124 23.22 N 85.58 E
Jhal Jhao 120 26.18 N 65.35 E
Jhālod 120 23.06 N 74.09 E
Jhang Sadar 123 31.16 N 72.19 E
Jhānsi 124 25.26 N 78.35 E
Jhānsi Post 123 33.52 N 71.24 E
Jhāpā 124 26.29 N 87.51 E
Jhārgrām 126 22.27 N 86.59 E
Jharia 126 23.45 N 86.24 E
Jhārpokhariā 126 22.10 N 86.38 E
Jhārsuguda 120 21.51 N 84.02 E
Jhawāriān 123 32.22 N 72.38 E
Jhelum 123 32.56 N 73.44 E
Jhelum ≃ 123 31.12 N 72.08 E
Jhenida 124 23.33 N 89.10 E
Jhenkāri 272b 22.46 N 88.18 E
Jhikergacha 126 23.07 N 89.07 E
Jhikra 126 22.37 N 87.55 E
Jhilimili 126 22.49 N 86.37 E
Jhil Kuranga ◆[8] 272a 28.40 N 77.17 E
Jhilla ≃[1] 126 21.58 N 88.56 E
Jhinkpāni 124 22.25 N 85.47 E
Jhok Rind 120 31.27 N 70.26 E
Jhumra 123 31.34 N 73.11 E
Jhunjhunūn 120 28.08 N 75.24 E
Jiaban, Zhg. 102 25.10 N 107.03 E
Jiaban, Zhg. 102 25.38 N 107.07 E
Jiabong 116 11.46 N 124.57 E
Jiacha 120 29.11 N 92.44 E
Jiading 106 31.23 N 121.15 E
Jiāganj 126 24.14 N 88.16 E
Jiagedan 89 51.35 N 120.55 E
Jiahashitai 89 46.25 N 122.17 E
Jiahe 102 25.43 N 112.05 E
Jiajiachang, Zhg. 107 29.44 N 105.06 E
Jiajiachang, Zhg. 107 30.26 N 104.21 E
Jiajiagou, Zhg. 104 41.44 N 120.58 E
Jiajiagou, Zhg. 104 42.20 N 121.46 E
Jiajiang 107 29.45 N 103.34 E
Jiajiayuan 106 32.18 N 120.55 E
Jiakou 100 30.10 N 119.03 E
Jiakou Wa ≡ 105 38.58 N 116.50 E
Jiali 120 30.47 N 93.24 E
Jialing ≃ 102 29.34 N 106.35 E
Jialou 100 32.54 N 113.26 E
Jialu 106 30.26 N 118.50 E
Jialu ≃ 100 33.38 N 114.36 E
Jiamingzhen 107 29.16 N 105.20 E
Jiamusi (Kiamusze) 89 46.50 N 130.21 E
Jiamuyingzi 104 41.56 N 121.43 E
Ji'an, Zhg. 98 41.06 N 126.08 E
Ji'an, Zhg. 100 27.07 N 114.58 E
Jian ≃, Zhg. 100 26.38 N 118.12 E
Jian ≃, Zhg. 104 40.59 N 121.51 E
Jian'an 89 43.04 N 125.03 E
Jianba 106 31.59 N 120.35 E
Jianbi 106 32.11 N 119.35 E
Jianchang, Zhg. 98 40.51 N 119.46 E
Jianchang, Zhg. 98 39.58 N 122.35 E
Jianchang, Zhg. 98 41.16 N 124.29 E
Ji'anchang, Zhg. 107 30.31 N 106.02 E
Jianchangying 98 40.06 N 118.49 E
Jianchapu 105 39.06 N 116.31 E
Jianchaxi, Zhg. 102 28.08 N 108.04 E
Jianchaxi, Zhg. 107 30.22 N 104.03 E
Jianchuan 102 26.34 N 99.53 E
Jiande 100 29.29 N 119.16 E
Jiang'an 107 28.44 N 105.05 E
Jiangba 100 33.08 N 118.45 E
Jiangbei (Lianglukou) 107 29.44 N 106.38 E
Jiangbeixu 100 26.20 N 115.26 E
Jiangbian 102 24.03 N 103.37 E
Jiangbianzhai 102 23.49 N 100.11 E
Jiangcheng, Zhg. 102 22.40 N 101.48 E
Jiangcheng, Zhg. 105 38.52 N 115.22 E
Jiangcun 100 28.17 N 117.49 E
Jiangdi 102 25.08 N 104.45 E
Jiangdihe 102 25.55 N 101.31 E
Jiangdu 100 32.26 N 119.34 E
Jiangduo 100 32.22 N 120.15 E
Jiange 102 32.06 N 105.29 E
Jianggezhuang 98 39.27 N 119.09 E
Jianghua (Shuikou) 102 24.58 N 111.38 E
Jianghuaqiao 106 32.05 N 120.00 E
Jiangji 100 32.19 N 115.44 E
Jiangjia, Zhg. 106 31.40 N 121.09 E
Jiangjia, Zhg. 106 31.58 N 121.28 E
Jiangjiadian 104 41.41 N 121.03 E
Jiangjiagou 104 41.44 N 121.44 E
Jiangjiaji 100 31.59 N 115.16 E
Jiangjiatun, Zhg. 104 41.42 N 122.02 E
Jiangjiatun, Zhg. 104 41.42 N 122.25 E
Jiangjin 107 29.17 N 106.15 E
Jiangjing 100 25.34 N 119.25 E
Jiangjunmiao 86 44.43 N 90.05 E
Jiangjunqiao 102 31.18 N 100.55 E
Jiangkou, Zhg. 100 29.43 N 121.25 E
Jiangkou, Zhg. 100 27.27 N 118.03 E
Jiangkou, Zhg. 100 25.29 N 119.12 E
Jiangkou, Zhg. 100 27.21 N 115.31 E
Jiangkou, Zhg. 100 27.44 N 114.49 E
Jiangkou, Zhg. 102 23.31 N 110.17 E
Jiangkou, Zhg. 102 27.37 N 108.48 E
Jiangkou, Zhg. 102 30.26 N 111.42 E
Jiangkou, Zhg. 102 33.39 N 107.12 E
Jiangkou, Zhg. 102 29.38 N 110.20 E
Jiangkou, Zhg. 107 30.14 N 103.55 E
Jiangkouji 100 32.50 N 116.16 E
Jiangkoutang 100 27.30 N 112.44 E
Jiangle 100 26.42 N 117.25 E
Jiangliadian 98 42.33 N 117.27 E
Jiangling 102 30.20 N 112.06 E
Jianglingxi 102 31.28 N 107.13 E
Jiangmen 100 22.35 N 113.05 E
Jiangmifeng 89 43.58 N 126.45 E
Jiangning 106 31.58 N 118.50 E
Jiangpu 100 32.04 N 118.37 E
Jiangqiao 89 46.48 N 123.45 E
Jiangqiaotou 106 30.37 N 120.38 E
Jiangshan 100 28.45 N 118.37 E
Jiangshan ≃ 100 28.57 N 118.50 E
Jiangshe 106 31.34 N 120.08 E
Jiangshui 98 37.13 N 113.59 E
Jiangsu (Kiangsu) □[4] 90 33.00 N 120.00 E
Jiangtian 100 25.52 N 119.34 E
Jiangtun, Zhg. 102 23.41 N 112.37 E
Jiangtun, Zhg. 104 41.37 N 122.22 E
Jiangwakou 105 39.31 N 117.42 E
Jiangwan, Zhg. 100 29.25 N 118.02 E
Jiangwan, Zhg. 106 31.18 N 121.29 E
Jiangwan Airport ⊠ 269b 31.20 N 121.30 E
Jiangxi 102 22.51 N 101.50 E
Jiangxi (Kiangsi) □[4] 100 28.00 N 116.00 E
Jiangxiacun 106 31.44 N 121.50 E
Jiangxiang 100 32.16 N 117.37 E
Jiangxikou 100 27.36 N 118.23 E
Jiangya 102 29.17 N 110.39 E
Jiangyi 100 29.12 N 115.46 E
Jiangyin 106 31.55 N 120.16 E
Jiangyou 102 31.47 N 104.45 E
Jiangyu, Zhg. 98 36.16 N 118.40 E
Jiangyu, Zhg. 100 27.50 N 112.46 E
Jiangyuanzhen 107 30.35 N 103.48 E
Jiangzaogang 106 32.01 N 121.03 E
Jiangzhasiji 120 30.28 N 88.55 E
Jiangzhong 120 29.10 N 93.32 E
Jianhe, Zhg. 102 26.27 N 108.33 E
Jianhe, Zhg. 105 39.14 N 118.03 E
Jianhu 100 33.28 N 119.50 E
Jianli 100 29.49 N 112.53 E
Jianling 100 32.45 N 113.12 E
Jianning 100 26.50 N 116.49 E
Jian'ou 100 27.03 N 118.19 E
Jianping (Yebaishou) 98 41.24 N 119.37 E
Jianqiao 106 30.20 N 120.12 E
Jianqigou 104 40.54 N 123.17 E
Jianshan, Zhg. 100 29.14 N 120.44 E
Jianshan, Zhg. 100 29.58 N 120.16 E
Jian Shan ∧ 104 41.49 N 121.44 E
Jianshi 102 30.36 N 109.38 E
Jianshui 102 23.38 N 102.49 E
Jiantiao 100 29.04 N 121.36 E
Jiantou 105 39.26 N 115.41 E
Jiantouji 98 34.35 N 117.34 E
Jianyang, Zhg. 100 27.22 N 118.04 E
Jianyang, Zhg. 100 33.27 N 119.40 E
Jianyang, Zhg. 107 30.24 N 104.32 E
Jiao ≃ 100 26.48 N 119.42 E
Jiaocheng 102 37.33 N 112.02 E
Jiaodao 105 39.39 N 116.06 E
Jiaodianzi 104 41.32 N 121.49 E
Jiaodonggou 104 40.50 N 123.58 E
Jiaohe, Zhg. 89 43.42 N 127.19 E
Jiaohe, Zhg. 98 38.01 N 116.17 E
Jiaojiapuzi 104 40.47 N 123.48 E
Jiaolai ≃, Zhg. 89 43.43 N 123.05 E
Jiaolai ≃, Zhg. 98 37.07 N 119.35 E
Jiaolai ≃, Zhg. 98 42.47 N 120.44 E
Jiaoling 100 24.41 N 116.10 E
Jiaomei 100 24.32 N 117.54 E
Jiaonan (Wanggezhuang) 98 35.51 N 119.59 E
Jiao Shan I 106 31.21 N 120.06 E
Jiaoshanhe 100 29.38 N 112.33 E
Jiaoxi 106 31.49 N 120.10 E
Jiaoxian 98 36.18 N 119.58 E
Jiaoyang 100 27.56 N 119.16 E
Jiaozhou Wan ⊂ 98 36.10 N 120.15 E
Jiaozhuang 100 33.14 N 114.02 E
Jiaozuo 102 35.15 N 113.13 E
Jiapu 106 31.06 N 119.56 E
Jiashan, Zhg. 100 32.47 N 118.00 E
Jiashan, Zhg. 106 30.51 N 120.54 E
Jiashi 85 39.28 N 76.45 E
Jiashun Hu ⊜ 120 34.35 N 86.05 E
Jiasi 107 29.06 N 106.24 E
Jiatan 107 30.12 N 106.29 E
Jiatanchang 107 29.09 N 106.16 E
Jiawang 98 34.27 N 117.27 E
Jiaxian, Zhg. 100 33.58 N 113.13 E
Jiaxian, Zhg. 102 38.01 N 110.31 E
Jiaxiang 98 35.25 N 116.21 E
Jiaxing 106 30.46 N 120.45 E
Jiayin 89 48.53 N 130.24 E
Jiayu 100 29.58 N 113.55 E
Jiayun Hu ⊜ 120 35.02 N 85.40 E
Jiaze 106 31.42 N 119.47 E
Jiazhai 98 34.33 N 115.48 E
Jiazhuang 105 39.19 N 117.22 E
Jiazi 100 22.55 N 116.04 E
Jiazier 85 38.40 N 76.33 E
Jibacoa ≃ 240p 20.15 N 77.12 W
Jibagalle 144 8.04 N 48.39 E
Jibalei 144 10.09 N 50.53 E
Jibannagar 126 23.25 N 88.50 E
Jíbaro ≃ 286b 23.03 N 82.23 W
Jibat ∧ 144 8.45 N 37.29 E
Jibiya 150 13.05 N 7.12 E
Jiboa ≃ 236 13.22 N 89.04 W
Jibóia, Ilha da I 256 23.03 S 44.22 W
Jibuti → Djibouti 144 11.36 N 43.09 E
Jicamarca, Quebrada ⋁ 286d 12.02 S 76.57 W
Jicarilla Apache Indian Reservation ◆[4] 200 36.40 N 107.00 W
Jicarón, Isla I 246 7.16 N 81.47 W
Jicatuyo ≃ 236 14.59 N 88.16 W
Jicheng 105 39.23 N 116.17 E
Jičín 30 50.26 N 15.21 E
Jicotea ≃ 286b 23.01 N 82.14 W
Jidād 140 11.05 N 24.44 E
Jiddah (Jeddah) 144 21.30 N 39.12 E
Jidingxilin 120 32.52 N 92.21 E
Jidy, Wādī al- ⋁ 142 30.13 N 32.46 E
Jiebu 100 28.15 N 115.02 E
Jiedong 100 26.02 N 113.00 E
Jiegou 100 33.21 N 117.55 E
Jiehe 98 35.16 N 117.04 E
Jieji 100 33.33 N 118.24 E
Jiejiang 106 31.58 N 120.43 E
Jiejinkou 89 47.57 N 132.50 E
Jielingkou 98 40.09 N 119.15 E
Jielongchang 107 29.13 N 106.32 E
Jiemian 100 25.56 N 118.02 E
Jiepai, Zhg. 100 26.41 N 112.46 E
Jiepai, Zhg. 100 29.34 N 115.06 E
Jiepai, Zhg. 106 30.55 N 119.32 E
Jiepai, Zhg. 107 29.28 N 104.43 E
Jiepaiji 100 32.15 N 117.50 E
Jiesheng 100 22.45 N 115.25 E
Jieshi, Zhg. 100 22.51 N 115.49 E
Jieshi, Zhg. 107 29.27 N 105.17 E
Jieshi Wan ⊂ 100 22.46 N 115.40 E
Jieshou, Zhg. 100 33.18 N 115.20 E
Jieshou, Zhg. 100 27.22 N 117.40 E
Jieshou, Zhg. 100 33.00 N 119.27 E
Jiexi 100 23.28 N 115.56 E
Jiexiu 102 37.05 N 111.51 E
Jieyang 100 23.35 N 116.21 E
Jiezhongdian 100 32.41 N 112.29 E
Jieznas 76 54.36 N 24.10 E
Jifjāfah, Bi'r ⊤[4] 140 30.27 N 33.11 E
Jiftūn, Jazā'ir II 140 27.13 N 33.56 E
Jiggalong 162 23.25 S 120.47 E
Jiggalong Creek ≃ 162 22.53 S 120.14 E
Jigongying 102 26.18 N 104.48 E
Jigongzhen 98 34.02 N 115.32 E
Jiguaní 240p 20.22 N 76.26 W
Jiguanshan, Zhg. 98 40.32 N 123.55 E
Jiguanshan, Zhg. 104 42.08 N 124.15 E
Jiguanshan, Zhg. 104 41.18 N 123.36 E
Jigüey, Bahía de ⊂ 240p 22.08 N 78.05 W
Jigzhi 102 33.28 N 101.29 E
Jihe 100 32.15 N 112.48 E
Jiheier 85 38.11 N 75.46 E
Jihlava 30 49.24 N 15.36 E
Jihlava ≃ 61 48.55 N 16.37 E
Jihočeský Kraj □[4] 30 49.05 N 14.30 E
Jihomoravský Kraj □[4] 30 49.10 N 16.40 E
Jiiqley 144 4.25 N 45.22 E
Jijel 148 36.48 N 5.46 E
Jijel □[5] 148 36.45 N 6.00 E
Jijia ≃ 38 46.54 N 28.05 E
Jijiadianzi 98 35.31 N 118.59 E
Jijiamiao 107 29.18 N 104.06 E
Jijiapuzi 104 41.16 N 124.12 E
Jijiashi 106 32.08 N 120.18 E
Jijiaying 105 40.20 N 115.24 E
Jijiga 144 9.22 N 42.47 E
Jikawo 144 8.22 N 33.46 E
Jikawo ≃ 144 8.22 N 33.47 E
Jike 102 31.00 N 99.41 E
Jilalin 89 51.19 N 119.55 E
Jilantai 102 39.47 N 105.45 E
Jilbānah, Bi'r al- ⊤[4] 142 30.55 N 32.29 E
Jilemutu 89 52.14 N 120.47 E
Jilib 144 0.29 N 42.46 E
Jilibulake 120 33.05 N 93.10 E
Jili Hu ⊜ 86 46.57 N 87.27 E
Jilin (Kirin) 89 43.51 N 126.33 E
Jilin (Kirin) □[4] 90 44.00 N 126.00 E
Jiliu ≃ 89 52.04 N 120.48 E
Jill, Kediet ej ∧ 148 22.38 N 12.33 W
Jill, Sebkhet ej ⊜ 148 22.47 N 12.53 W
Jiloca ≃ 34 41.21 N 1.39 W
Jilotepec de Abasolo 234 19.58 N 99.32 W
Jilotlán de los Dolores 234 19.14 N 102.59 W
Jílové 54 50.46 N 14.07 E
Jima 144 7.36 N 36.50 E
Jimbaran 115b 8.46 S 115.11 E
Jimbolia 38 45.47 N 20.43 E
Jimboomba 171a 27.50 S 153.02 E
Jimei 100 24.37 N 118.07 E
Jimena de la Frontera 34 36.26 N 5.27 W
Jiménez, Méx. 232 29.02 N 100.41 W
Jiménez, Méx. 232 27.08 N 104.55 W
Jimenez, Pil. 116 8.20 N 123.50 E
Jiménez, Arroyo ≃ 288 34.44 S 58.13 W
Jiménez, Laguna de ⊜ 258 35.26 S 59.01 W
Jiménez del Téul 234 23.10 N 104.05 W
Jimeta 146 9.16 N 12.27 E
Jimi ≃ 164 5.20 S 144.20 E
Jimingcun 105 39.19 N 116.09 E
Jiminghe 100 30.36 N 115.32 E
Jim Ned Creek ≃ 196 31.50 N 99.07 W
Jimo 98 36.23 N 120.27 E
Jimsar 86 44.00 N 89.04 E
Jim Thorpe 210 40.52 N 75.43 W
Jimuganayaji 85 38.36 N 75.39 E
Jin (Gam) ≃, Asia 110 21.55 N 105.12 E
Jin ≃, Zhg. 100 24.54 N 118.35 E
Jin ≃, Zhg. 100 28.24 N 115.49 E
Jin ≃, Zhg. 100 26.51 N 117.46 E
Jināh 140 25.20 N 30.31 E
Jinan (Tsinan), Zhg. 98 36.40 N 116.57 E
Jin'an, Zhg. 100 28.38 N 119.18 E
Jinbang 100 25.01 N 118.01 E
Jinbo ≃ 107 28.54 N 103.40 E
Jincang 89 43.20 N 130.30 E
Jince 60 49.47 N 13.59 E
Jinchanggouliang 98 41.56 N 120.19 E
Jincheng, Zhg. 102 35.30 N 112.50 E
Jincheng, Zhg. 104 41.12 N 121.25 E
Jinchengshai 102 26.43 N 111.00 E
Jincheng Shan ∧ 107 30.47 N 106.32 E
Jinchuan 102 31.25 N 102.08 E
Jinchuanqiao 102 27.18 N 101.48 E
Jincun 106 31.08 N 119.49 E
Jīnd 123 29.19 N 76.19 E
Jindabyne 171b 36.25 S 148.38 E
Jindabyne, Lake ⊜[1] 171b 36.22 S 148.37 E
Jindachang 107 29.43 N 104.49 E
Jindāī, Bi'r ⊤[4] 142 29.55 N 31.40 E
Jindřichovice 54 50.15 N 12.37 E
Jindřichův Hradec 30 49.09 N 15.00 E
Jinfeng 100 26.01 N 119.36 E
Jinfosi 102 39.29 N 99.00 E
Jing ≃, Zhg. 86 44.52 N 82.50 E
Jing ≃, Zhg. 102 34.28 N 109.00 E
Jing'an 100 28.52 N 115.20 E
Jin'gangpo 107 29.38 N 106.25 E
Jingangtou 100 27.54 N 113.40 E
Jingangtuo 107 29.10 N 106.07 E
Jing'anji 98 34.30 N 116.55 E
Jingbian 102 37.25 N 108.21 E
Jingbohu ⊜ 89 43.54 N 128.54 E
Jingcheng 100 24.36 N 117.30 E
Jingde 100 30.19 N 118.31 E
Jingdezhen (Kingtechen) 100 29.16 N 117.11 E
Jingdong 102 24.28 N 100.52 E
Jingellic 171b 35.56 S 147.42 E
Jingeryu 105 39.43 N 115.36 E
Jinggang 100 28.28 N 112.46 E
Jinggangshan (Ciping) 100 26.36 N 114.05 E
Jinggongqiao 100 29.45 N 117.11 E
Jinggu 102 23.32 N 100.41 E
Jingguanzhen 107 29.55 N 106.33 E
Jinghai, Zhg. 100 23.03 N 116.31 E
Jinghai, Zhg. 105 38.56 N 116.55 E
Jinghaiwei 98 36.52 N 122.13 E
Jinghe 86 44.39 N 82.50 E
Jinghong 102 22.01 N 100.49 E
Jinghuiling 105 40.22 N 117.27 E
Jingjiang, Zhg. 102 26.19 N 100.33 E
Jingjiang, Zhg. 106 32.01 N 120.15 E
Jingjiayu 104 41.40 N 123.51 E
Jingle 102 38.24 N 111.54 E
Jinglou 100 32.39 N 112.56 E
Jingmen 102 31.00 N 112.09 E
Jingning, Zhg. 100 27.59 N 119.38 E
Jingning, Zhg. 102 35.25 N 105.56 E
Jingou 104 41.38 N 120.35 E
Jingoutun 98 41.03 N 117.27 E
Jingshan 100 31.02 N 113.05 E
Jingtai 102 37.17 N 104.09 E
Jingu 100 25.13 N 118.07 E
Jingxi 102 23.08 N 106.29 E
Jingxian, Zhg. 98 37.42 N 116.16 E
Jingxian, Zhg. 100 30.42 N 118.24 E
Jingxian, Zhg. 102 26.40 N 109.25 E
Jingxin 100 24.14 N 115.56 E
Jingxing, Zhg. 89 47.04 N 123.01 E
Jingxing, Zhg. 98 38.02 N 114.08 E
Jingyan 107 29.40 N 104.04 E
Jingyu 98 42.22 N 126.50 E
Jingyuan, Zhg. 102 36.38 N 104.37 E
Jingyuan, Zhg. 102 35.30 N 106.48 E
Jingzhi 98 36.19 N 119.23 E
Jingzichang 107 29.00 N 104.41 E
Jinhae → Chinhae 98 35.09 N 128.40 E
Jinhu 100 33.00 N 119.02 E
Jinhua 100 29.07 N 119.39 E
Jinhua ≃ 100 29.06 N 119.39 E
Jinhui 106 30.59 N 121.29 E
Jining, Zhg. 98 35.25 N 116.36 E
Jining, Zhg. 102 40.57 N 113.02 E
Jinja 154 0.26 N 33.12 E
Jinjiadian 98 41.39 N 118.18 E
Jinjiang, Zhg. 100 24.50 N 118.35 E
Jinjiang, Zhg. 110 26.19 N 100.33 E
Jinjiawopeng 104 41.38 N 122.16 E
Jinjiawopu 104 42.32 N 122.10 E
Jinjiazhen 89 42.49 N 123.40 E
Jinjing, Zhg. 100 24.37 N 118.36 E
Jinjing, Zhg. 100 28.31 N 113.25 E
Jinjini 150 7.26 N 2.39 W
Jinju → Chinju 98 35.11 N 128.05 E
Jinkeng 100 27.15 N 117.14 E
Jinkichi-mori ∧ 96 33.41 N 134.07 E
Jinkou, Zhg. 98 36.35 N 120.46 E
Jinkou, Zhg. 100 30.22 N 114.10 E
Jinkou, Zhg. 100 29.18 N 115.15 E
Jinkuang 102 28.20 N 101.54 E
Jinlijing 107 29.48 N 104.45 E
Jinlingsi 104 41.42 N 120.49 E
Jinlingyu 105 40.06 N 117.32 E
Jinlingzhen 98 36.49 N 118.11 E
Jinlonggou 89 51.45 N 125.51 E
Jinmachi-chūtonchi, Rikujō-jieitai- ■ 92 38.25 N 140.27 E
Jinmu Jiao ⟩ 110 18.09 N 109.34 E
Jinnah Barrage ◆[6] 123 32.57 N 71.30 E
Jinning 102 24.41 N 102.35 E
Jinniu, Zhg. 100 31.24 N 117.12 E
Jinniu, Zhg. 100 29.59 N 114.38 E
Jinotega 236 13.06 N 86.00 W
Jinotega □[5] 236 14.00 N 85.25 W
Jinotepe 236 11.51 N 86.12 W
Jinping, Zhg. 102 26.38 N 109.03 E
Jinping, Zhg. 102 22.50 N 103.10 E
Jinpingchang 107 28.54 N 104.43 E
Jinpo 105 39.18 N 115.15 E
Jinqian ≃ 102 32.52 N 110.01 E
Jinqiao 100 31.46 N 116.50 E
Jinrui 100 27.57 N 114.12 E
Jinseki 96 34.48 N 133.11 E
Jinsen → Inch'ŏn 98 37.28 N 126.38 E
Jinsha, Zhg. 100 26.12 N 118.39 E
Jinsha, Zhg. 102 27.18 N 106.10 E
Jinsha, Zhg. 106 32.06 N 121.05 E
Jinsha (Yangtze) ≃ 102 28.50 N 104.36 E
Jinshan, Zhg. 89 51.51 N 126.30 E
Jinshan, Zhg. 106 30.54 N 121.09 E
Jinshanwei 106 30.44 N 121.19 E
Jinshanxiang 107 30.35 N 104.52 E
Jinshanzui 106 30.44 N 121.22 E
Jinshi 102 29.39 N 111.52 E
Jinshijing 107 29.23 N 104.08 E
Jinshuzhen 106 31.23 N 120.24 E
Jinsiniangqiao 106 30.43 N 121.15 E
Jinta 102 40.03 N 98.53 E
Jintan 106 31.45 N 119.34 E
Jintang, Zhg. 102 30.54 N 104.19 E
Jintang, Zhg. 102 30.19 N 102.19 E
Jintian 100 27.10 N 114.27 E
Jintotolo Channel ʮ 116 11.48 N 123.05 E
Jintotolo Island I 116 11.51 N 123.08 E
Jinxi, Zhg. 100 27.54 N 116.43 E
Jinxi, Zhg. 104 40.45 N 120.50 E
Jinxian, Zhg. 98 38.02 N 115.02 E
Jinxian, Zhg. 98 39.04 N 121.40 E
Jinxian, Zhg. 100 28.22 N 116.14 E
Jinxian (Dalinghe), Zhg. 104 41.11 N 121.22 E
Jinxiang, Zhg. 98 35.05 N 116.18 E
Jinxiang, Zhg. 100 27.26 N 120.35 E
Jin-ya ⊥ 94 36.06 N 137.15 E
Jinyun 100 28.40 N 120.03 E
Jinz, Qā' al- ≡ 132 30.45 N 36.04 E
Jinze 106 31.02 N 120.56 E
Jinzhai 100 31.44 N 115.54 E
Jinzhaizhen 100 31.32 N 115.46 E
Jinzhen 100 33.39 N 118.17 E
Jinzhong ≃ 105 39.08 N 117.42 E
Jinzhou (Chinchou) 104 41.07 N 121.08 E
Jinzisi 107 29.09 N 106.22 E
Jinzū ≃ 94 36.46 N 137.13 E
Jiō 270 34.58 N 135.28 E
Ji-Paraná 248 10.52 S 61.57 W
Jipijapa 246 1.20 S 80.35 W
Jipioca, Ilha I 250 1.53 N 50.12 W
Jiquí ≃ 240p 21.22 N 78.32 W
Jiquilisco 236 13.19 N 88.35 W
Jiquilisco, Bahía de ⊂ 236 13.10 N 88.28 W
Jiquilpan de Juárez 234 19.59 N 102.43 W
Jiquipilas 234 16.40 N 93.39 W
Jiquipilco 234 19.32 N 99.36 W
Jiquiriçá ≃ 255 13.12 S 38.57 W
Jirāfī, Wādī al- (Naḥal Paran) ⋁ 132 30.24 N 35.10 E
Jirbān 140 11.03 N 30.36 E
Jiřetín 54 50.50 N 14.35 E
Jiri ≃ 120 24.42 N 93.06 E
Jiříkov 54 50.59 N 14.35 E
Jirjā 140 26.20 N 31.53 E
Jirkov 54 50.30 N 13.27 E
Jīroft 128 28.40 N 57.46 E
Jīsh (Gush Ḥalav) 132 33.02 N 35.27 E
Jishou 102 28.17 N 109.29 E
Jishui, Zhg. 100 27.14 N 115.06 E
Jishui, Zhg. 100 33.46 N 115.24 E
Jisr ash-Shughūr 130 35.48 N 36.19 E
Jitan 100 24.56 N 115.43 E
Jitarning 162 32.48 S 117.59 E
Jitaúna 255 14.01 S 39.57 W
Jitianzhen 107 30.19 N 104.01 E
Jitotol 234 17.02 N 92.52 W
Jitra 114 6.16 N 100.25 E
Jituo 120 34.15 N 82.05 E
Jiu ≃ 38 43.47 N 23.48 E
Jiubao 100 25.57 N 115.48 E
Jiubingtai 104 41.39 N 124.07 E
Jiucheng, Zhg. 98 38.12 N 117.18 E
Jiucheng, Zhg. 105 39.23 N 116.44 E
Jiuchuchang 107 29.55 N 104.38 E
Jiudaoliang 102 31.35 N 110.12 E
Jiudhara 126 22.24 N 89.44 E
Jiudian 106 32.10 N 120.57 E
Jiudongle 102 38.49 N 101.05 E
Jiudu 106 30.31 N 119.53 E
Jiufanxian 98 35.51 N 115.41 E
Jiufeng, Zhg. 100 24.20 N 117.02 E
Jiufeng, Zhg. 100 25.33 N 119.08 E
Jiugang 105 39.03 N 116.12 E
Jiugongan 102 29.52 N 112.00 E
Jiugongkou 105 39.50 N 114.43 E
Jiugong Shan ∧ 100 29.26 N 114.42 E
Jiuguan, Zhg. 98 37.26 N 121.53 E
Jiuguan, Zhg. 106 30.51 N 120.16 E
Jiuguantao 98 36.40 N 115.25 E
Jiuhe 100 23.32 N 115.04 E
Jiuhongshui 102 37.14 N 103.57 E
Jiuhu 98 37.03 N 117.36 E
Jiuhuai'an 98 40.24 N 114.31 E
Jiuhuajie 100 30.25 N 117.51 E
Jiuhuaxian 100 23.30 N 113.16 E
Jiuhuinan 98 42.37 N 126.14 E
Jiujiang, Zhg. 100 29.44 N 115.59 E
Jiujiang, Zhg. 100 22.51 N 113.02 E
Jiujiang, Zhg. 100 29.36 N 115.52 E
Jiujiawopeng 104 40.59 N 121.22 E
Jiujiji 98 35.09 N 114.48 E
Jiujing 107 29.05 N 103.54 E
Jiukou 100 30.52 N 112.38 E
Jiuli 107 29.32 N 103.32 E
Jiulian Shan ⋏ 100 24.40 N 114.46 E
Jiuliguan 100 31.50 N 114.14 E
Jiuling Shan ⋏ 100 28.46 N 114.45 E
Jiulong → Kowloon, H.K. 271d 22.18 N 114.10 E
Jiulong, Zhg. 100 24.08 N 112.55 E
Jiulong, Zhg. 102 29.00 N 101.50 E
Jiulong ≃, Zhg. 100 25.59 N 117.18 E
Jiulong ≃, Zhg. 100 24.28 N 117.48 E
Jiulongchang 107 29.32 N 106.05 E
Jiulonggang 100 32.38 N 117.03 E
Jiulongpo 107 29.29 N 106.32 E
Jiulongzhen 106 31.54 N 121.34 E
Jiumen 98 40.42 N 120.27 E
Jiumianyang 100 30.16 N 113.13 E
Jiumiao 104 42.24 N 121.36 E
Jiumu 100 28.11 N 118.27 E
Jiuninghe 105 39.28 N 117.46 E
Jiuningyang 100 25.38 N 117.21 E
Jiupu, Zhg. 100 32.50 N 118.45 E
Jiupu, Zhg. 105 40.21 N 115.18 E
Jiuquan (Suzhou) 102 39.45 N 98.34 E
Jiurongcheng 98 37.21 N 122.32 E
Jiushangshui 100 33.32 N 114.32 E
Jiushan Liedao II 100 29.26 N 122.12 E
Jiushenqiu 100 33.11 N 115.08 E
Jiusiyang 100 33.41 N 118.39 E
Jiusongyu 105 40.27 N 116.58 E
Jiutai 89 44.08 N 125.50 E
Jiuwuqing 105 39.31 N 116.52 E
Jiuxian, Zhg. 98 37.53 N 117.06 E
Jiuxian, Zhg. 100 31.11 N 118.04 E
Jiuxian, Zhg. 100 33.15 N 115.35 E
Jiuxian, Zhg. 100 25.14 N 116.31 E
Jiuxian, Zhg. 100 33.32 N 113.17 E
Jiuxian, Zhg. 100 25.54 N 113.22 E
Jiuxian, Zhg. 107 30.27 N 103.51 E
Jiuxian, Zhg. 107 29.51 N 106.13 E
Jiuxian ≃ 100 25.07 N 116.24 E
Jiuxiangcheng 100 33.13 N 114.49 E
Jiuyingkou 105 39.42 N 114.44 E
Jiuyingzi 104 42.03 N 121.38 E
Jiuyuanqu 102 35.09 N 111.51 E
Jiuyuhang 106 30.17 N 119.56 E
Jiuyunjie 86 44.12 N 88.05 E
Jiuzhan 89 43.57 N 126.29 E
Jiuzhen 100 24.05 N 117.42 E
Jiuzhou 105 39.30 N 116.33 E
Jiuzhuangwo 105 40.11 N 115.36 E
Jiwangmiao 269b 31.14 N 121.17 E
Jiwangtun 104 41.02 N 122.58 E
Jīwani 128 25.03 N 61.45 E
Jiwen 89 50.32 N 123.15 E
Jixi, Zhg. 89 45.17 N 130.59 E
Jixi, Zhg. 100 30.06 N 118.35 E
Jixian, Zhg. 98 35.26 N 114.05 E
Jixian, Zhg. 98 37.36 N 115.31 E
Jixian, Zhg. 105 40.03 N 117.24 E
Jixiangsi 107 30.39 N 105.32 E
Jixiashi 100 28.22 N 118.44 E
Jixingji 100 32.55 N 116.46 E
Jiyang, Zhg. 98 36.59 N 117.11 E
Jiyang, Zhg. 100 27.10 N 118.07 E
Jiyang, Zhg. 105 39.38 N 115.59 E
Jiyi 102 35.50 N 110.23 E
Jiyuan 102 35.08 N 112.35 E
Jiyun ≃ 105 39.07 N 117.43 E
Jiz', Wādī al- ⋁ 144 16.19 N 52.00 E
Jīzah, Ahrāmāt al- (Pyramids of Giza) ⊥ 142 29.59 N 31.08 E
Jīzah, Tur'at al- ≅ 273c 29.50 N 31.16 E
Jīzān 144 16.54 N 42.29 E
Jizayy 142 30.28 N 30.51 E
Jize 98 36.54 N 114.52 E
Jizera ≃ 54 50.10 N 14.43 E
Jizl, Wādī al- ⋁ 128 25.38 N 38.21 E
Jizō-dake ∧ 94 36.36 N 139.28 E
Jizō-zaki ⟩ 96 35.34 N 133.20 E
Joaçaba 252 27.10 S 51.30 W
Joachimsthal → Jáchymov, Česká Rep. 54 50.20 N 12.55 E
Joachimsthal, Dtsch. 54 52.58 N 13.44 E
Joaíma 255 16.39 S 41.02 W
Joal Fadiout 150 14.10 N 16.51 W
Joana Coeli 250 1.58 S 49.23 W
Joana Peres 250 3.18 S 49.42 W
Joanes 250 0.51 S 48.31 W
Joanicó 258 34.36 S 56.15 W
Joanna 192 34.24 N 81.48 W
Joanópolis 256 22.56 S 46.17 W
João Câmara 250 5.32 S 35.48 W
João Mendes ≃ 287a 22.57 S 43.03 W
João Neiva 255 19.45 S 40.24 W
João Pessoa 250 7.07 S 34.52 W
João Pinheiro 255 17.45 S 46.10 W
Joaquim Egídio 256 22.53 S 46.59 W
Joaquim Távora 255 23.30 S 49.58 W
Joaquin 194 31.58 N 94.03 W
Joaquin Miller Park ♠ 282 37.49 N 122.11 W
Joaquín Suárez 258 34.44 S 56.02 W
Joaquín V. González 252 25.05 S 64.11 W
Job 62 45.37 N 3.45 E
Jobabo 240p 20.54 N 77.17 W
Jobat 120 22.25 N 74.34 E
Jobo Point ⟩ 116 8.42 N 126.15 E
Jobos 240m 17.58 N 66.10 W
Jobos, Bahía de ⊂ 240m 17.56 N 66.13 W
Job Peak ∧ 204 39.35 N 118.14 W
Jobstown 285 40.02 N 74.41 W
Jochberg 64 47.23 N 12.24 E
Jock ≃ 212 45.16 N 75.43 W
Jocketa 54 50.33 N 12.10 E
Jockgrim 56 49.06 N 8.17 E
Jocko ≃ 202 47.20 N 114.17 W
Jocolí 252 32.35 S 68.41 W
Jo Co Marsh ≡ 276 40.37 N 73.47 W
Jocón 236 15.17 N 86.58 W
Jocoro 236 13.37 N 88.01 W
Jocotán 236 14.49 N 89.23 W
Jocotepec 234 20.18 N 103.26 W
Jocotitlán 234 19.42 N 99.48 W
Jódar 34 37.50 N 3.21 W
Jodhpur 120 26.17 N 73.02 E
Jodiya 120 22.42 N 70.18 E
Jodoigne 56 50.43 N 4.52 E
Jodrell Bank Radio Telescope ♁[3] 262 53.14 N 2.18 W
Joe ≃ 220 25.17 N 81.05 W
Joe Batt's Arm 186 49.44 N 54.10 W
Joel 158 28.42 S 28.21 E
Joensuu 26 62.36 N 29.46 E
Joetsu 94 37.06 N 138.15 E
Jœuf 56 49.14 N 6.01 E
Jofane 156 21.17 S 34.16 E
Joffre, Mount ∧ 182 50.32 N 115.13 W
Jōganzi ≃ 94 36.46 N 137.18 E
Jōga-shima I 94 35.08 N 139.37 E
Jōgawara 268 35.42 N 139.22 E
Jōge 96 34.42 N 133.07 E
Jogeshvari ◆[8] 272c 19.08 N 72.51 E
Jogeshvari Cave ⊥[5] 272c 19.08 N 72.51 E
Jõgeva 76 58.45 N 26.24 E
Jog Falls ⌊ 122 14.13 N 74.45 E
Joggins 186 45.42 N 64.27 W
Joghatāy 128 36.36 N 57.01 E
Jogindarnagar 123 31.59 N 76.46 E
Jogjakarta → Yogyakarta 115a 7.48 S 110.22 E
Jogui ≃ 255 23.45 S 54.40 W
Jōhana 94 36.31 N 136.54 E
Johannesburg, S. Afr. 158 26.12 S 28.05 E
Johannesburg, S. Afr. 273d 26.12 S 28.05 E
Johannesburg, Ca., U.S. 228 35.22 N 117.38 W
Johannesburg □[5] 273d 26.13 S 28.02 E
Johannesburg (Jan Smuts) Airport ⊠ 273d 26.08 S 28.14 E
Johanngeorgenstadt 54 50.26 N 12.43 E
Johanniskreuz 56 49.20 N 7.49 E
Johannisthal ◆[8] 264a 52.26 N 13.30 E
Jōhen 92 32.57 N 132.35 E
Johi 120 26.41 N 67.37 E
Johilla ≃ 124 23.37 N 81.14 E
John ≃ 180 66.55 N 151.35 W
John Boyd Thacher State Park ♠ 210 42.38 N 74.01 W
John Carroll University ♁[2] 279a 41.29 N 81.32 W
John Day 202 44.24 N 118.57 W
John Day ≃ 202 45.44 N 120.39 W
John Day, Middle Fork ≃ 202 44.55 N 119.18 W
John Day, North Fork ≃ 202 44.45 N 119.38 W
John Day, South Fork ≃ 202 44.28 N 119.31 W
John Day Dam ◆[6] 224 45.43 N 120.41 W
John Day Fossil Beds National Monument ♠ 202 44.34 N 119.39 W
John F. Kennedy International Airport ⊠ 210 40.38 N 73.47 W
John F. Kennedy National Historic Site ⊥ 283 42.21 N 71.08 W
John F. Kennedy Space Center ♁[3] 220 28.40 N 80.40 W
John Forrest National Park ♠ 168a 31.53 S 116.06 E
John Hancock Center ♁ 278 41.55 N 87.37 W
John H. Kerr Reservoir ⊜[1] 192 36.35 N 78.35 W
John J. Duffy Preserve ♠ 278 41.39 N 87.55 W

Symbol	English	Deutsch	Español	Français	Português
≃	River	Fluß	Río	Rivière	Rio
≅	Canal	Kanal	Canal	Canal	Canal
⌊	Waterfall, Rapids	Wasserfall, Stromschnellen	Cascada, Rápidos	Chute d'eau, Rapides	Cascata, Rápidos
ʮ	Strait	Meeresstraße	Estrecho	Détroit	Estreito
⊂	Bay, Gulf	Bucht, Golf	Bahía, Golfo	Baie, Golfe	Baía, Golfo
⊜	Lake, Lakes	See, Seen	Lago, Lagos	Lac, Lacs	Lago, Lagos
≡	Swamp	Sumpf	Pantano	Marais	Pântano
⊓	Ice Features, Glacier	Eis- und Gletscherformen	Accidentes Glaciales	Formes glaciaires	Acidentes glaciares
⊤	Other Hydrographic Features	Andere Hydrographische Objekte	Otros Elementos Hidrográficos	Autres données hydrographiques	Outros acidentes hidrográficos

Symbol	English	Deutsch	Español	Français	Português
✦	Submarine Features	Untermeerische Objekte	Accidentes Submarinos	Formes de relief sous-marin	Acidentes submarinos
□	Political Unit	Politische Einheit	Unidad Politica	Entité politique	Unidade política
♁	Cultural Institution	Kulturelle Institution	Institución Cultural	Institution culturelle	Instituição cultural
⊥	Historical Site	Historische Stätte	Sitio Histórico	Site historique	Sítio histórico
♠	Recreational Site	Erholungs- und Ferienort	Sitio de Recreo	Centre de loisirs	Area de Lazer
⊠	Airport	Flughafen	Aeropuerto	Aéroport	Aeroporto
■	Military Installation	Militäranlage	Instalación Militar	Installation militaire	Instalação militar
◆	Miscellaneous	Verschiedenes	Misceláneo	Divers	Diversos

I · 82 John-Kabo

ENGLISH — Name | Page | Lat.°′ | Long.°′
DEUTSCH — Name | Seite | Breite°′ | Länge°′ E = Ost

John Martin Reservoir ⊜[1] 198 38.05 N 103.02 W
John McLaren Park ♠ 282 37.43 N 122.25 W
John Muir National Historic Site ⊥ 282 37.59 N 122.08 W
Johnny Run ≃ 216 41.17 N 88.21 W
John o' Groats 46 58.38 N 3.05 W
John Pennekamp Coral Reef State Park ♠ 220 25.11 N 80.15 W
John Redmond Reservoir ⊜[1] 198 38.18 N 95.55 W
Johns ≃ 224 46.54 N 124.01 W
Johns Creek ≃ 192 37.30 N 80.06 W
Johnshaven 46 56.47 N 2.20 W
Johns Hopkins University ⓥ[2] 284b 39.20 N 76.37 W
Johns Island I 192 32.40 N 80.05 W
Johnson, Ar., U.S. 194 36.07 N 94.09 W
Johnson, Ks., U.S. 198 37.34 N 101.45 W
Johnson, Ne., U.S. 198 40.24 N 95.59 W
Johnson, N.Y., U.S. 210 41.22 N 74.30 W
Johnson, Vt., U.S. 188 44.38 N 72.40 W
Johnson □[6], In., U.S. 218 39.29 N 86.03 W
Johnson □[6], Tx., U.S. 222 32.20 N 97.20 W
Johnson, Mount ∧ 226 36.37 N 121.19 W
Johnson Bay ⊂ 208 38.03 N 75.20 W
Johnsonburg, N.J., U.S. 210 40.58 N 74.53 W
Johnsonburg, N.Y., U.S. 210 42.44 N 78.18 W
Johnsonburg, Pa., U.S. 214 41.29 N 78.40 W
Johnson City, N.Y., U.S. 210 42.06 N 75.57 W
Johnson City, Tn., U.S. 192 36.18 N 82.21 W
Johnson City, Tx., U.S. 196 30.16 N 98.24 W
Johnson Creek, N.Y., U.S. 210 43.15 N 78.31 W
Johnson Creek, Wi., U.S. 216 43.04 N 88.46 W
Johnson Creek ≃, Id., U.S. 202 44.58 N 115.30 W
Johnson Creek ≃, Ky., U.S. 218 38.27 N 84.04 W
Johnson Creek ≃, N.Y., U.S. 210 43.22 N 78.16 W
Johnson Creek ≃, Tx., U.S. 222 32.02 N 94.59 W
Johnson Creek ≃, Wa., U.S. 224 46.35 N 121.42 W
Johnsondale 204 35.58 N 118.32 W
Johnson Drain ≊ 281 42.26 N 83.28 W
Johnson Draw V, Tx., U.S. 196 31.58 N 101.41 W
Johnson Draw V, Tx., U.S. 196 30.08 N 101.07 W
Johnson Hall State Historic Site ⊥ 210 43.01 N 74.23 W
Johnson Park ♠ 276 40.30 N 74.27 W
Johnson Point ≻ 241h 13.07 N 61.12 W
Johnsons Crossing 180 60.29 N 133.16 W
Johnsons Point ≻ 240c 17.02 N 61.53 W
Johnsons Pond ⊜ 283 42.44 N 71.03 W
Johnsons Station 222 32.42 N 97.08 W
Johnsonville, N.Z. 172 41.14 S 174.47 E
Johnsonville, N.Y., U.S. 210 42.55 N 73.31 W
Johnsonville, S.C., U.S. 192 33.49 N 79.26 W
Johnston, Wales, U.K. 42 51.46 N 5.00 W
Johnston, Ia., U.S. 190 41.40 N 93.41 W
Johnston, R.I., U.S. 207 41.46 N 71.21 W
Johnston, S.C., U.S. 192 33.49 N 81.48 W
Johnston, Lake ⊜ 162 32.25 S 120.30 E
Johnston Atoll I[1] 14 16.45 N 169.32 W
Johnston City 194 37.49 N 88.55 W
Johnstone 46 55.50 N 4.31 W
Johnstone Peak ∧ 280 34.10 N 117.48 W
Johnstone Strait ⋓ 182 50.25 N 126.00 W
Johnston Falls ∟ 154 10.35 S 28.40 E
Johnstown, Co., U.S. 200 40.20 N 104.54 W
Johnstown, N.Y., U.S. 210 43.00 N 74.22 W
Johnstown, Oh., U.S. 214 40.09 N 82.41 W
Johnstown, Pa., U.S. 214 40.19 N 78.55 W
Johnstown Center 216 42.42 N 88.50 W
Johnstown Flood National Memorial ⊥ 214 40.21 N 78.47 W
John Tyler Arboretum ♠ 285 39.56 N 75.26 W
Jōhoku 94 36.28 N 140.22 E
Johol 114 2.36 N 102.16 E
Johor □[3] 114 2.00 N 103.30 E
Johor ≃ 114 1.27 N 104.02 E
Johor, Selat ⋓ 271c 1.28 N 103.48 E
Johor Baharu 114 1.28 N 103.45 E
Jöhstadt 54 50.30 N 13.05 E
Joice Island I 282 38.08 N 122.02 W
Joigny 50 47.59 N 3.24 E
Joiner 194 35.30 N 90.08 W
Joinerville 222 32.11 N 94.55 W
Joinvile 252 26.18 S 48.50 W
Joinville 58 48.27 N 5.08 E
Joinville, Lac ⊜ 206 46.18 N 75.12 W
Joinville Island I 9 63.15 S 55.45 W
Joinville-le-Pont 261 48.49 N 2.28 E
Jōjima 96 33.15 N 130.26 E
Jojogan 115a 6.58 S 111.46 E
Jojutla 234 18.37 N 99.11 W
Joka 272b 22.27 N 88.18 E
Jokau 140 8.24 N 33.49 E
Jokioinen 26 60.49 N 23.28 E
Jokkmokk 24 66.37 N 19.50 E
Jökulsá á Brú ≃ 24a 65.41 N 14.13 W
Jökulsårgljúfur National Park ♠ 24a 66.00 N 16.20 W
Jolārpettai 122 12.34 N 78.35 E
Jolfā 128 38.57 N 45.38 E
Joliet, Il., U.S. 216 41.31 N 88.04 W
Joliet, Mt., U.S. 202 45.29 N 108.58 W
Joliet Correctional Center ⓥ 278 41.33 N 88.04 W
Joliett 208 40.37 N 76.27 W
Joliette 206 46.01 N 73.27 W
Joliette □[6] 206 46.25 N 74.00 W
Jolietville 218 40.03 N 86.15 W
Jollyville 222 30.27 N 97.47 W
Jolo 116 6.03 N 121.00 E
Jolo Group II 116 6.00 N 121.09 E
Jolo Island I 116 5.58 N 121.06 E
Jølstravatnet ⊜ 26 61.32 N 6.13 E
Jomalig Island I 116 14.42 N 122.22 E
Jomba 102 31.27 N 98.15 E
Jombang 115a 7.33 S 112.14 E
Jombo ≃ 152 10.36 S 17.32 E
Jona 58 47.14 N 8.52 E
Jonacatepec 234 18.41 N 98.48 W
Jonah 222 30.38 N 97.32 W
Jönåker 40 58.44 N 16.40 E
Jonathan Dickinson State Park ♠ 220 27.01 N 80.08 W
Jonava 76 55.05 N 24.17 E
Jones, Pil. 116 16.33 N 121.42 E
Jones, Mi., U.S. 216 41.54 N 85.48 W
Jones, Ok., U.S. 196 35.33 N 97.17 W
Jones ≃ 283 42.00 N 70.42 W
Jones and Laughlin Steel Corporation ⓥ[3], Pa., U.S. 279b 40.26 N 79.58 W
Jones and Laughlin Steel Corporation ⓥ[3], Pa., U.S. 279b 40.37 N 80.14 W
Jones Beach State Park ♠ 210 40.35 N 73.31 W
Jonesboro, Ar., U.S. 194 35.50 N 90.42 W
Jonesboro, Ga., U.S. 192 33.31 N 84.21 W
Jonesboro, Il., U.S. 194 37.27 N 89.16 W
Jonesboro, In., U.S. 216 40.28 N 85.37 W
Jonesboro, La., U.S. 194 32.14 N 92.42 W
Jonesboro, Tn., U.S. 192 36.17 N 82.28 W
Jonesburg 219 38.51 N 91.18 W
Jones Creek 222 28.58 N 95.27 W
Jones Creek ≃, On., Can. 212 44.30 N 75.49 W
Jones Creek ≃, Tx., U.S. 222 29.08 N 96.03 W
Jones Falls ≃ 284b 39.18 N 76.37 W
Jones Falls, North Branch ≃ 284b 39.25 N 76.42 W
Jones Inlet ⊂ 210 40.35 N 73.34 W
Jones Mill 194 34.27 N 92.50 W
Jones Mountains ⋏ 9 73.32 S 94.00 W
Jonesport 188 44.31 N 67.35 W
Jones Sound ⋓ 176 76.00 N 85.00 W
Jonestown 194 34.19 N 90.27 W
Jonesville, In., U.S. 218 39.04 N 85.53 W
Jonesville, La., U.S. 194 31.37 N 91.49 W
Jonesville, Mi., U.S. 216 41.59 N 84.40 W
Jonesville, N.Y., U.S. 210 42.55 N 73.49 W
Jonesville, N.C., U.S. 192 36.14 N 80.50 W
Jonesville, S.C., U.S. 192 34.50 N 81.40 W
Jonesville, Va., U.S. 192 36.41 N 83.06 W
Jong ≃ 150 7.32 N 12.23 W
Jonglei Canal ≊ 136 9.21 N 31.32 E
Jongunjärvi ⊜ 26 65.17 N 27.15 E
Jónico, Mar → Ionian Sea ⊤[2] 22 39.00 N 19.00 E
Joniškėlis 76 56.02 N 24.10 E
Joniškis 76 56.14 N 23.37 E
Jonkersberg 158 33.55 S 22.15 E
Jönköping 26 57.47 N 14.11 E
Jönköpings Län □[6] 26 57.30 N 14.30 E
Jonquière 186 48.24 N 71.15 W
Jonquières 62 44.07 N 4.54 E
Jonsdorf 54 50.51 N 14.43 E
Jonstorp 41 56.14 N 12.40 E
Jonuta 232 18.05 N 92.08 W
Jonvilliers 261 48.34 N 1.42 E
Jonzac 32 45.27 N 0.26 W
Joondalup, Lake ⊜ 168a 31.45 S 115.47 E
Joplin, Mo., U.S. 194 37.05 N 94.30 W
Joplin, Mt., U.S. 202 48.33 N 110.46 W
Joppa, Il., U.S. 194 37.12 N 88.50 W
Joppa, Md., U.S. 208 39.26 N 76.21 W
Jóquei Clube ♠ 287b 23.35 S 46.41 W
Joquicingo 234 19.03 N 99.33 W
Jora 124 26.20 N 77.49 E
Jordan, Pil. 116 10.40 N 122.35 E
Jordan, Mn., U.S. 190 44.40 N 93.37 W
Jordan, Mt., U.S. 202 47.19 N 106.54 W
Jordan, N.Y., U.S. 210 43.03 N 76.28 W
Jordan (Al-Urdun) □[1], Asia 118 31.00 N 36.00 E
Jordan (Al-Urdun) □[1], Asia 128 31.00 N 36.00 E
Jordan (Nahr al-Urdunn) (HaYarden) ≃, Asia 132 31.46 N 35.33 E
Jordan ≃, B.C., Can. 224 48.26 N 124.08 W
Jordan ≃, Ut,. U.S. 200 40.49 N 112.08 W
Jordan Creek ≃ 202 42.52 N 117.38 W
Jordânia 255 15.54 S 40.11 W
Jordania → Jordan □[1] 128 31.00 N 36.00 E
Jordanie → Jordan □[1] 128 31.00 N 36.00 E
Jordanien → Jordan □[1] 128 31.00 N 36.00 E
Jordan Lake ⊜ 216 42.46 N 85.09 W
Jordanów 30 49.40 N 19.50 E
Jordans 260 51.37 N 0.36 W
Jordan Valley 202 42.58 N 117.03 W
Jordanville 210 42.55 N 74.57 W
Jordão ≃ 252 25.46 S 52.07 W
Jordbro 40 59.09 N 18.07 E
Jördenstorf 54 53.52 N 12.37 E
Jordet 26 61.25 N 12.09 E
Jorge Chávez, Aeropuerto Internacional ⊠ 286d 12.02 S 77.07 W
Jorge Grego, Ilha I 256 23.13 S 44.09 W
Jorge Montt, Isla I 254 51.20 S 74.45 W
Jorge V, Costade → George V Coast ⩡[2] 9 68.30 S 147.30 E
Jorge VI, Estrecho de → George VI Sound ⋓ 9 71.00 S 68.00 W
Jorhāt 120 26.46 N 94.13 E
Jork 52 53.32 N 9.41 E
Jorm 120 36.52 N 70.51 E
Jörn 26 65.04 N 20.02 E
Jornado del Muerto ◆[2] 200 33.20 N 106.50 W
Joroinen 26 62.11 N 27.50 E
Jorong 112 3.58 S 114.56 E
Jørpeland 26 59.01 N 6.03 E
J'orzovka 80 48.56 N 44.38 E
Jos 150 9.55 N 8.53 E
Jose Abad Santos 116 5.38 N 125.27 E
José Batlle y Ordóñez 252 33.28 S 55.07 W
José Bonifácio 255 21.03 S 49.41 W
José Cardel 234 19.22 N 96.22 W
José C. Paz 258 34.30 S 58.45 W
José de Freitas 250 4.45 S 42.35 W
José de San Martín 254 44.02 S 70.29 W
José Enrique Rodó (Drabble) 258 33.41 S 57.34 W
José Francisco Vergara 252 22.28 S 69.38 W
Joselândia 248 16.32 S 56.12 W
José Martí, Aeropuerto Internacional ⊠ 286b 23.00 N 82.24 W
Jose Panganiban 116 14.17 N 122.41 E
José Pedro Varela 252 33.27 S 54.32 W
Joseph 202 45.21 N 117.13 W
Joseph, Lac ⊜ 176 52.45 N 65.15 W
Joseph, Lake ⊜ 212 45.10 N 79.44 W
Joseph Bonaparte Gulf ⊂ 164 14.15 S 128.30 E
Joseph City 200 34.57 N 110.20 W
Joseph Creek ≃ 202 46.03 N 117.01 W
Joseph Davis State Park ♠ 284a 43.13 N 79.03 W
Josephine, Pa., U.S. 214 40.29 N 79.11 W
Josephine, Tx., U.S. 222 33.04 N 96.19 W
Josephine, Lake ⊜ 220 27.24 N 81.26 W
Josephine Peak ∧ 280 34.17 N 118.09 W
Josephstaal 164 4.44 S 145.01 E
José Santos Arévalo 258 35.10 S 59.14 W
Joshīmath 120 30.34 N 79.34 E
Jōshin-Etsu-kōgen-kokuritsu-kōen ♠ 94 36.46 N 138.40 E
Joshua 222 32.28 N 97.23 W
Joshuas Creek ≃ 275b 43.29 N 79.37 W
Joshua Tree 204 34.08 N 116.18 W
Joshua Tree National Monument ♠ 204 33.55 N 116.00 W
Joshua Trees State Park ♠ 228 34.41 N 117.47 W
Joškar-Ola 80 56.38 N 47.52 E
Jos Plateau ⋏[1] 150 9.30 N 9.00 E
Jossa 56 50.14 N 9.35 E
Josselin 32 47.57 N 2.33 W
Jossigny 50 48.50 N 2.45 E
Jostedalsbreen ⊓ 26 61.40 N 7.00 E
Jost Van Dyke I 240m 18.28 N 64.45 W
Jōtō ◆[8] 270 34.42 N 135.34 E
Jotunheimen ⋏ 26 61.38 N 8.18 E
Jotunheimen Nasjonalpark ♠ 26 61.35 N 8.30 E
Jouarre 50 48.56 N 3.08 E
Jouars-Pontchartrain 261 48.47 N 1.54 E
Joubertina 158 33.50 S 23.51 E
Joué-lès-Tours 50 47.21 N 0.40 E
Jougne 58 46.46 N 6.24 E
Jouques 62 43.38 N 5.38 E
Jourdanton 196 28.55 N 98.32 W
Joure 52 52.57 N 5.47 E
Joutsa 26 61.44 N 26.07 E
Joutseno 26 61.06 N 28.30 E
Joutsijärvi 24 66.40 N 28.00 E
Joux, Lac de ⊜ 58 46.38 N 6.18 E
Joux, Vallée de V 58 46.35 N 6.15 E
Jouy 50 48.31 N 1.33 E
Jouy-en-Josas 261 48.46 N 2.10 E
Jouy-le-Moutier 261 49.01 N 2.03 E
Jouy-le-Potier 50 47.45 N 1.49 E
Jovellanos 240p 22.48 N 81.12 W
Jovellar 116 13.04 N 123.36 E
Jovet, Mont ∧ 62 45.30 N 6.39 E
Joveyn ≃ 128 36.48 N 56.28 E
Joviânia 255 17.49 S 49.30 W
Jowai 120 25.27 N 92.12 E
Jowhar 144 2.46 N 45.31 E
Jowlaenga, Mount ∧ 162 17.21 S 122.56 E
Jowzjān □[4] 120 36.30 N 66.00 E
Joy 190 41.12 N 90.55 W
Joy, Mount ∧ 180 63.46 N 132.55 W
Joyce 194 31.56 N 92.35 W
Joyeuse 62 44.29 N 4.14 E
Jōyō 96 34.51 N 135.47 E
Joyous Pavilion Park ♠ 271a 39.52 N 116.22 E
Joyuda 240m 18.07 N 67.11 W
Józefów 30 52.09 N 21.12 E
J. Percy Priest Lake ⊜[1] 194 36.05 N 86.30 W
Ju ≃, Zhg. 100 30.38 N 114.51 E
Ju ≃, Zhg. 105 39.45 N 117.35 E
Juaba 250 2.23 S 49.33 W
Juagdan 116 10.00 N 124.35 E
Juami ≃ 246 1.45 S 67.30 W
Juanacatlán 234 20.31 N 103.10 W
Juana Díaz 240m 18.03 N 66.31 W
Juan Aldama 232 24.19 N 103.21 W
Juan Anchorena ◆[8] 288 34.29 S 58.30 W
Juan Atucha 258 35.32 S 59.21 W
Juan B. Arruabarrena 252 30.20 S 58.19 W
Juan Bautista Alberdi 252 27.35 S 65.37 W
Juan Blanco, Arroyo ≃ 258 35.05 S 57.26 W
Juancheng 98 35.35 N 115.29 E
Juan de Fuca, Strait of ⋓ 224 48.18 N 124.00 W
Juan de Garay 254 38.52 S 64.34 W
Juan de Mena 252 24.55 S 56.44 W
Juan de Nova, Île I 138 17.03 S 42.45 E
Juan Díaz Covarrubias 234 18.07 N 95.09 W
Juan E. Barra 252 37.48 S 60.29 W
Juan Eugenio 232 25.10 N 103.20 W
Juan Fernández, Archipiélago II 244 33.00 S 80.00 W
Juan González Grande, Arroyo ≃ 258 34.00 S 58.14 W
Juan González Romero ◆[8] 286a 19.30 N 99.04 W
Juangriego 246 11.05 N 63.57 W
Juan Gualberto Gómez 240p 22.52 N 81.33 W
Juan Guerra 248 6.35 S 76.21 W
Juanita 224 47.42 N 122.13 W
Juan Jorba 252 33.37 S 65.16 W
Juan José Castelli 252 25.57 S 60.37 W
Juán José Perez 248 15.14 S 68.58 W
Juanjuí 248 7.11 S 76.45 W
Juankoski 26 63.04 N 28.21 E
Juan-les-Pins 62 43.34 N 7.06 E
Juan L. Lacaze 258 34.26 S 57.27 W
Juan N. Fernández 252 38.00 S 59.16 W
Juan Perez Sound ⋓ 182 52.30 N 131.18 W
Juan Ramírez, Isla I 234 21.50 N 97.40 W
Juan Rodríguez Clara 234 18.00 N 95.25 W
Juan Tronconi 258 35.30 S 59.15 W
Juan Viñas 236 9.54 N 83.45 W
Juárez, Méx. 232 27.37 N 100.44 W
Juárez → Ciudad Juárez, Méx. 232 31.44 N 106.29 W
Juárez, Méx. 232 30.19 N 108.05 W
Juárez, Méx. 234 17.39 N 93.10 W
Juárez, Cerro ∧ 234 20.37 N 99.17 W
Juárez, Sierra ⋏ 234 17.30 N 96.30 W
Juárez, Sierra de ⋏ 232 32.00 N 115.50 W
Juarzon 150 5.20 N 8.52 W
Juatinga, Ponta de ≻ 256 23.17 S 44.30 W
Juazeirinho 250 7.04 S 36.35 W
Juàzeiro 250 9.25 S 40.30 W
Juazeiro do Norte 250 7.12 S 39.20 W
Jūbā 154 4.51 N 31.37 E
Juba ≃ 248 14.59 S 57.44 W
Jubachstausee ⊜[1] 263 51.10 N 7.37 E
Jūbāl, Maḍīq ⋓ 140 27.40 N 33.55 E
Jubal, Strait of → Jūbāl, Maḍīq ⋓ 140 27.40 N 33.55 E
Jubayl (Byblos) 130 34.07 N 35.39 E
Jubaysho 144 5.48 N 37.22 E
Jubayt 140 18.57 N 36.50 E
Jubba (Genale) ≃ 144 0.15 S 42.38 E
Jubbada Dhexe □[4] 144 1.00 N 43.00 E
Jubbada Hoose □[4] 144 0.00 42.00 E
Jubbah 128 28.02 N 40.56 E
Jubb al-Jarrāḥ 130 34.49 N 37.19 E
Jubbātā al-Khashab 132 33.13 N 35.49 E
Jubb Jannīn 132 33.37 N 35.47 E
Jubbulpore → Jabalpur 124 23.10 N 79.57 E
Jubilee Downs 162 18.22 S 125.17 E
Jubilee Lake ⊜, Austl. 162 29.12 S 126.38 E
Jubilee Lake ⊜, Nf., Can. 186 48.04 N 55.11 W
Jubones ≃ 246 3.13 S 79.57 W
Jūbu-san ∧ 270 34.50 N 135.55 E
Juby, Cap ≻ 148 27.58 N 12.55 W
Júcar (Xúquer) ≃ 34 39.09 N 0.14 W
Juçara 255 15.53 S 50.51 W
Júcaro 240p 21.37 N 78.51 W
Jucás 250 6.32 S 39.32 W
Jüchen 56 51.06 N 6.30 E
Juchhöh 54 50.24 N 11.52 E
Juchipila 234 21.25 N 103.07 W
Juchipila ≃ 234 21.03 N 103.25 W
Juchitán de Zaragoza 234 16.26 N 95.01 W
Juchitepec 234 19.06 N 98.53 W
Juchitlán 234 20.05 N 104.07 W
Juchnov 76 54.45 N 35.14 E
Juchoviči 76 56.02 N 28.39 E
Jucuapa 236 13.31 N 88.24 W
Jucurucu ≃ 255 17.21 S 39.13 W
Jucurutu 250 6.02 S 37.01 W
Judaea □[9] 132 31.35 N 35.00 E
Judas, Punta ≻ 236 9.31 N 84.32 W
Judaydat al-Khās 132 33.24 N 36.33 E
Judaydat ʿArṭūz 132 33.26 N 36.10 E
Juddah → Jiddah 144 21.30 N 39.12 E
Jude Island I 186 47.15 N 54.49 W
Judenau 61 48.17 N 16.00 E
Judenburg 61 47.10 N 14.40 E
Judges Hill ∧[2] 283 42.12 N 70.49 W
Judian 102 27.20 N 99.36 E
Judinki, Ross. 82 54.37 N 37.17 E
Judinki, Ross. 82 55.27 N 35.48 E
Judino, Ross. 76 58.43 N 39.17 E
Judino, Ross. 80 55.51 N 48.55 E
Judino, Ross. 82 54.09 N 38.19 E
Judino, Ross. 265b 55.40 N 37.12 E
Judío, Rambla del ≃ 34 38.15 N 1.27 W
Judique 186 45.52 N 61.30 W
Judith ≃ 202 47.44 N 109.38 W
Judith, Point ≻ 207 41.22 N 71.29 W
Judith Gap 202 46.40 N 109.45 W
Judith Mountains ⋏ 202 47.12 N 109.15 W
Judith Peak ∧ 202 47.13 N 109.13 W
Judoma ≃ 74 59.08 N 135.06 E
Judson, S.C., U.S. 192 34.50 N 82.27 W
Judson, Tx., U.S. 222 32.35 N 94.45 W
Judsonia 194 35.16 N 91.38 W
Jue ≃ 100 31.42 N 113.20 E
Juehedian 105 39.26 N 117.06 E
Juelsminde 41 55.43 N 10.01 E
Juexi 100 29.27 N 121.57 E
Juexizhen 107 28.55 N 104.16 E
Jufari ≃ 246 1.13 S 62.00 W
Jufayr, Bi'r al- ⊤[4] 142 30.49 N 32.40 E
Jufrah, Wādī al- V 142 30.24 N 31.35 E
Jug 86 57.43 N 56.10 E
Jug ≃ 24 60.45 N 46.20 E
Jughna 140 12.24 N 25.06 E
Jugo-Kamskij 86 57.42 N 55.35 E
Jugon 32 48.25 N 2.20 W
Jugo-Osetija (South Ossetia) □[9] 84 42.20 N 44.00 E
Jugoslavija → Yugoslavia □[1] 22 44.00 N 21.00 E
Jugoslawien → Yugoslavia □[1] 22 44.00 N 21.00 E
Jugo-Zapad ◆[8] 265b 55.40 N 37.32 E
Juḥā 144 16.41 N 42.54 E
Jühnsdorf 264a 52.18 N 13.23 E
Jühnsdorfer Heide ◆[3] 264a 52.19 N 13.24 E
Juhu ◆[8] 272c 19.07 N 72.49 E
Juhua Dao I 98 40.29 N 120.47 E
Juhu Airport ⊠ 272c 19.06 N 72.50 E
Jui 272c 19.01 N 73.05 E
Juidongshan 100 23.46 N 117.31 E
Juigalpa 236 12.05 N 85.24 W
Juillac 32 45.19 N 1.19 E
Juilly 261 49.01 N 2.42 E
Juína ≃ 248 12.36 S 58.57 W
Juine ≃ 50 48.32 N 2.23 E
Juist 52 53.40 N 6.59 E
Juist I 52 53.40 N 7.00 E
Juisui 100 23.30 N 121.21 E
Juiz de Fora 256 21.45 S 43.20 W
Jūjō Base ■ 268 35.45 N 139.43 E
Jujurieux 58 46.02 N 5.25 E
Jujuy → San Salvador de Jujuy 252 24.11 S 65.18 W
Jujuy □[4] 252 23.00 S 66.00 W
Jukagirskoje ploskogorje ⋏[1] 74 66.00 N 155.00 E
Jukamenskoje 80 57.53 N 52.15 E
Jukonda ≃ 86 59.38 N 67.26 E
Juksa 86 56.55 N 85.10 E
Juksejevo 24 59.52 N 54.19 E
Jukskei ≃ 273d 26.06 S 28.06 E
Jukta 74 63.23 N 105.41 E
Jula ≃ 24 63.49 N 44.44 E
Julāna 124 29.08 N 76.25 E
Julayfah, Bi'r al- ⊤[4] 142 30.43 N 29.35 E
Julbach 60 48.40 N 13.52 E
Juldybajevo 86 52.20 N 57.52 E
Julebu 98 40.09 N 113.36 E
Julesburg 198 40.59 N 102.15 W
Juli 248 16.13 S 69.27 W
Juliaca 248 15.30 S 70.08 W
Julia Creek 166 20.39 S 141.45 E
Julia Creek ≃ 166 20.00 S 141.11 E
Julian 214 40.52 N 77.56 W
Juliana, Lake ⊜ 220 28.07 N 81.48 W
Julianakanaal ≊ 56 51.05 N 5.50 E
Julian Alps ⋏ 36 46.00 N 14.00 E
Juliana Top ∧ 250 3.41 N 56.32 W
Julianehåb (Qaqortoq) 176 60.43 N 46.01 W
Julia Pfeiffer Burns State Park ♠ 226 36.10 N 120.40 W
Jülich 56 50.55 N 6.21 E
Juliénas 58 46.14 N 4.43 E
Juliette, Lake ⊜[1] 192 33.05 N 83.50 W
Julijske Alpe → Julian Alps ⋏ 36 46.00 N 14.00 E
Julimes 232 28.25 N 105.27 W
Júlio de Castilhos 252 29.14 S 53.41 W
Julio Prestes, Estação ◆[5] 287b 23.32 S 46.38 W
Julita ⓥ 40 59.09 N 16.02 E
Juliuhe 104 42.03 N 122.55 E
Juliustown 285 40.00 N 74.40 W
Julu 98 37.13 N 115.01 E
Juma 24 65.07 N 33.16 E
Juma ≃ 98 39.34 N 115.42 E
Jumaguzino 86 52.54 N 56.23 E
Jumapolo 115a 7.42 S 111.00 E
Jumaševo 80 54.59 N 54.25 E
Jumay, Volcán ∧[1] 236 14.41 N 89.59 W
Jumbilla 248 5.54 S 77.45 W
Jumbo 154 17.28 S 30.55 E
Jumbo, Raas ≻ 144 1.39 S 41.36 E
Jumboo 144 0.15 S 42.38 E
Jumbo Peak ∧ 204 36.12 N 114.11 W
Jumeauville 261 48.55 N 1.47 E
Jumentos Cays II 238 22.42 N 75.55 W
Jumet 50 50.26 N 4.25 E
Jumièges 50 49.26 N 0.49 E
Jumilla 34 38.29 N 1.17 W
Jumlā 124 29.17 N 82.10 E
Jummayzat Banī ʿAmr 142 30.48 N 31.32 E
Jump ≃ 190 45.17 N 91.05 W
Jump, North Fork ≃ 190 45.25 N 90.40 W
Jump, South Fork ≃ 190 45.25 N 90.40 W
Jumt uul ∧ 102 44.29 N 97.10 E
Jūn 132 33.35 N 35.27 E
Jun ≃ 100 25.57 N 118.03 E
Jūnāgadh 120 21.31 N 70.28 E
Junan (Shizilu) 98 35.11 N 118.51 E
Junayfah 142 30.12 N 32.25 E
Junaynah, Ra's al- ∧ 140 29.01 N 33.58 E
Juncal, Isla I 258 33.58 S 58.24 W
Juncal do Norte ≋ 266c 38.52 N 8.59 W
Juncal do Sul ≋ 266c 38.51 N 8.58 W
Juncheng 98 38.57 N 114.41 E
Juncos 240m 18.14 N 65.55 W
Junction, Tx., U.S. 196 30.29 N 99.46 W
Junction, Ut,. U.S. 200 38.14 N 112.13 W
Junction City, Ar., U.S. 194 33.00 N 92.43 W
Junction City, Il., U.S. 219 38.34 N 89.07 W
Junction City, Ks., U.S. 198 39.01 N 96.49 W
Junction City, Ky., U.S. 194 37.35 N 84.47 W
Junction City, Or., U.S. 202 44.13 N 123.12 W
Junction City, Wa., U.S. 224 46.58 N 123.46 W
Jundah 166 24.50 S 143.04 E
Jundiaí 256 23.11 S 46.52 W
Jundiaí ≃, Bra. 256 23.32 S 46.15 W
Jundiaí ≃, Bra. 256 23.11 S 47.16 W
Jundiaí do Sul 255 23.27 S 50.17 W
Jundiaí-mirim ≃ 256 23.10 S 46.56 W
Jundiapeba 256 23.33 S 46.15 W
Jundu Shan ⋏ 105 40.30 N 116.05 E
Juneau, Ak., U.S. 180 58.20 N 134.27 W
Juneau, Wi., U.S. 190 43.24 N 88.42 W
Junee 166 34.52 S 147.35 E
June in Winter, Lake ⊜ 220 27.18 N 81.24 W
June Lake 226 37.46 N 119.04 W
June Park 220 28.04 N 80.41 W
Jungapeo de Juárez 234 19.27 N 100.29 W
Jungar Qi 102 39.49 N 111.10 E
Jungbluth Ditch ≊ 279a 41.27 N 82.07 W
Jungfernheide ◆[3] 264a 52.34 N 13.17 E
Jungfernheide, Volkspark ♠ 264a 52.33 N 13.16 E
Jungfern-Inseln → Virgin Islands □[2] 240m 18.20 N 64.50 W
Jungfern-See ⊜ 264a 52.25 N 13.05 E
Jungfrau ∧ 58 46.32 N 7.58 E
Jungfraujoch ◆ 58 46.33 N 7.58 E
Junggar Pendi (Dzungarian Basin) ⊻[1] 86 45.00 N 88.00 E
Jungle Habitat ♠ 276 41.08 N 74.21 W
Junglinster 56 49.43 N 6.15 E
Jungshāhi 120 24.51 N 67.46 E
Juniata 198 40.35 N 98.30 W
Juniata □[6] 208 40.34 N 77.24 W
Juniata ◆[8] 285 40.01 N 75.07 W
Juniata ≃ 188 40.24 N 77.01 W
Juniata, Frankstown Branch ≃ 214 40.34 N 78.03 W
Juniata, Raystown Branch ≃ 214 40.25 N 77.58 W
Juniata Gap 214 40.33 N 78.26 W
Juniata Terrace 208 40.35 N 77.34 W
Junín, Arg. 252 34.35 S 60.57 W
Junín, Ec. 246 0.56 S 80.13 W
Junín, Perú 248 11.10 S 76.00 W
Junín □[5] 248 11.30 S 75.00 W
Junín, Lago de ⊜ 248 11.02 S 76.06 W
Junín de los Andes 254 39.56 S 71.05 W
Junior 188 38.59 N 79.57 W
Juniper 186 46.33 N 67.13 W
Junipero Serra Peak ∧ 226 36.08 N 121.25 W
Juniville 50 49.24 N 4.23 E
Jūniyah 130 33.59 N 35.38 E
Junk Bay ⊂ 271d 22.17 N 114.15 E
Jun Kharchanai 123 36.52 N 75.01 E
Junk Island I 271d 22.17 N 114.16 E
Junkou 100 26.42 N 116.49 E
Junlian 102 28.08 N 104.35 E
Junliangcheng 105 39.04 N 117.27 E
Junling 100 28.17 N 116.28 E
Junnar 122 19.12 N 73.53 E
Juno Beach 220 26.52 N 80.04 W
Junokommunarskoje ◆[8] 83 48.13 N 38.18 E
Junqalī □[4] 140 7.30 N 32.20 E
Junqueiro 250 9.56 S 36.29 W
Junqueirópolis 255 21.32 S 51.26 W
Junsele 26 63.41 N 16.54 E
Juntas 236 10.16 N 85.00 W
Jun Ul Shan ⋏ 102 37.30 N 97.00 E
Junxian 102 32.31 N 111.30 E
Jūō 94 36.40 N 140.41 E
Juodkrantė 76 55.33 N 21.08 E
Juodupė 76 56.05 N 25.37 E
Juojärvi ⊜ 26 62.43 N 28.33 E
Juozapinės kalnas ∧[2] 76 54.32 N 25.37 E
Juparanã, Lagoa ⊜ 255 19.35 S 40.18 W
Jupilingo ≃ 236 14.48 N 89.14 W
Jupille 56 50.39 N 5.38 E
Jupiter 220 26.56 N 80.05 W
Jupiter ≃ 186 49.29 N 63.37 W
Jupiter Inlet ⊂ 220 26.57 N 80.04 W
Jupiter Island I 220 27.04 N 80.07 W
Juqueri ≃ 256 23.24 S 46.52 W
Juqueri, Reservatório do ⊜[1] 256 23.20 S 46.38 W
Juqueriquerê, Serra do ⋏ 256 23.43 S 45.37 W
Juquiá 252 24.19 S 47.38 W
Juquiá ≃ 256 23.56 S 47.09 W
Juquiá, Ponta do ≻ 252 24.25 S 47.00 W
Juquiá-guaçu ≃ 256 24.00 S 47.16 W
Juquitiba 256 23.57 S 47.03 W
Jur 74 59.52 N 137.39 E
Jur ≃ 140 8.39 N 29.18 E
Jura □[3] 58 47.20 N 7.15 E
Jura □[5] 58 46.50 N 5.50 E
Jura ⋏ 58 46.45 N 6.30 E
Jura I 46 56.00 N 5.50 W
Jūra ≃ 76 55.03 N 22.09 E
Jura, Sound of ⋓ 46 55.57 N 5.48 W
Juramento 255 16.50 S 43.35 W
Juratiški 76 54.02 N 25.54 E
Jurayrah, Jabal al- ∧ 128 24.06 N 39.16 E
Jurays wa ʿIzbatuhā 142 30.19 N 30.55 E
Jurbarkas 76 55.05 N 22.48 E
Jurcevo 76 60.02 N 32.36 E
Juréia 256 21.17 S 46.22 W
Jurenino 76 59.24 N 42.47 E
Jurevičì 78 51.57 N 29.32 E
Jurf ad-Darāwīsh 132 30.42 N 35.52 E
Jurga 86 55.42 N 84.51 E
Jurgamyš 86 55.21 N 64.28 E
Jurgenson Woods ♠ 278 41.34 N 87.36 W
Jurien 162 30.19 S 115.02 E
Juriesfontein 158 31.40 S 22.08 E
Juring 164 6.26 S 134.20 E
Jurino 80 56.18 N 46.18 E
Jurja 24 59.03 N 49.14 E
Jurjev → Tartu 76 58.23 N 26.43 E
Jurjevec 80 57.18 N 43.06 E
Jurjevka, Ukr. 78 48.44 N 36.02 E
Jurjevka, Ukr. 83 48.30 N 39.00 E
Jurjev-Pol'skij 80 56.30 N 39.41 E
Jurjevskoje 82 55.05 N 36.13 E
Jurla 86 59.17 N 54.19 E
Jurlovo, Ross. 82 55.54 N 37.16 E
Jurlovo, Ross. 82 55.19 N 35.52 E
Jūrmala 76 56.58 N 23.42 E
Jurong, Sing. 271c 1.19 N 103.43 E
Jurong, Zhg. 106 31.57 N 119.10 E
Jurong ≃ 271c 1.18 N 103.44 E
Jurong, Selat ⋓ 271c 1.18 N 103.42 E
Jurovo, Ross. 80 57.30 N 43.50 E
Jurovo, Ross. 82 55.30 N 38.22 E
Jurovo, Ukr. 78 51.22 N 27.50 E
Jurovskoje 86 59.29 N 69.02 E
Jursla 40 58.40 N 16.11 E
Jurty 88 56.03 N 97.37 E
Juruá 246 3.27 S 66.03 W
Juruá ≃ 242 2.37 S 65.44 W
Juruaia 256 21.15 S 46.35 W
Juruá-mirim ≃ 248 8.08 S 72.48 W
Juruena ≃ 248 7.20 S 58.03 W
Jurujuba, Enseada de ⊂ 287a 22.56 S 43.07 W
Jurumirim, Reprêsa ⊜[1] 255 23.20 S 49.15 W
Jurumkuvejem ≃ 180 66.14 N 173.35 E
Jurupari ≃ 248 7.45 S 70.10 W
Jurupari, Arquipélago II 250 0.07 N 50.30 W
Jurupari, Ilha de I 250 0.20 N 50.07 W
Juruti 250 2.09 S 56.04 W
Jur'uzan' 86 54.52 N 58.26 E
Jur'uzan' ≃ 86 55.42 N 57.00 E
Jurva 26 62.41 N 21.59 E
Jušala 86 57.04 N 64.17 E
Juscelândia 255 15.20 S 51.19 W
Jusepín 246 9.45 N 63.31 W
Jushiguan 102 24.47 N 97.38 E
Jūshiyama 94 35.06 N 136.46 E
Juskatla 182 53.37 N 132.18 W
Jus'ki 80 56.39 N 53.05 E
Juškovo 76 59.46 N 45.11 E
Juškozero 24 64.44 N 32.06 E
Jūsō ◆[8] 270 34.43 N 135.28 E
Jussey 58 47.49 N 5.54 E
Justa 80 47.07 N 46.18 E
Justice 278 41.44 N 87.50 W
Justin 222 33.05 N 97.18 W
Justineberg ∧[2] 40 58.43 N 15.04 E
Justiniano Posse 252 32.53 S 62.40 W
Justo Daract 252 33.52 S 65.11 W
Justus 214 40.42 N 81.35 W
Jušut ≃ 80 56.12 N 48.23 E
Jus'va 24 58.56 N 54.57 E
Jutaí 248 5.11 S 68.54 W
Jutaí ≃ 242 2.43 S 66.57 W
Jutaza 80 54.35 N 53.16 E
Jütchendorf 264a 52.16 N 13.10 E
Jüterbog 54 51.59 N 13.04 E
Juththah, Jabal al- ∧ 132 30.12 N 35.36 E
Juti 255 22.52 S 54.37 W
Jutiapa 236 14.17 N 89.54 W
Jutiapa □[5] 236 14.10 N 89.50 W
Juticalpa 236 14.42 N 86.15 W
Jutiquile 236 14.45 N 86.08 W
Jutland → Jylland ◆[1] 26 56.00 N 9.15 E
Jutogh 123 31.06 N 77.07 E
Jutrosin 30 51.40 N 17.10 E
Juupajoki 26 61.47 N 24.27 E
Juuru 76 59.04 N 24.59 E
Juva 26 61.54 N 27.51 E
Juventud, Isla de la (Isla de Pinos) I 240p 21.40 N 82.50 W
Juvisy-sur-Orge 50 48.41 N 2.23 E
Juvuln ⊜ 26 63.43 N 13.09 E
Juwana 115a 6.42 S 111.09 E
Juwangi 115a 7.10 S 110.45 E
Juxi 100 27.30 N 119.08 E
Juxian 98 35.37 N 118.54 E
Juxing 106 31.56 N 121.33 E
Juyanhai → Gaxun Nur ⊜ 102 42.22 N 100.34 E
Juye 98 35.23 N 116.06 E
Jūyom 128 28.34 N 53.56 E
Juyongguan 105 40.18 N 116.04 E
Juža 80 56.35 N 42.01 E
Juzennecourt 58 48.11 N 4.59 E
Juzi ≃ 98 40.18 N 123.35 E
Juziers 261 49.00 N 1.51 E
Južna Morava ≃ 38 43.41 N 21.24 E
Južno-Aleksandrovka 88 55.51 N 96.10 E
Južno-Aličurskij chrebet ⋏ 120 37.30 N 73.20 E
Južno-Golodnostepskij kanal ≊ 85 40.15 N 69.08 E
Južno-Jenisejskij 86 58.48 N 94.39 E
Južno-Mujskij chrebet ⋏ 88 55.40 N 114.00 E
Južno-Sachalinsk 89 46.58 N 142.42 E
Južno-Suchokumsk 84 44.37 N 45.34 E
Južno-Ural'sk 86 54.26 N 61.15 E
Južnyj, Kaz. 86 49.21 N 73.01 E
Južnyj, Ross. 80 56.08 N 44.09 E
Južnyj, Ross. 80 47.20 N 41.51 E
Južnyj, Ross. 86 53.14 N 83.42 E
Južnyj, Ross. 86 53.33 N 60.02 E
Južnyj, mys ≻ 74 57.45 N 156.45 E
Južnyj-Alamyšik 85 40.46 N 72.38 E
Južnyj Bug ≃ 78 46.59 N 31.58 E
Južnyj Prijut 84 43.12 N 41.55 E
Južnyj Ural ⋏ 86 54.00 N 58.30 E
Juzovka → Doneck 83 48.00 N 37.48 E
Jwālahari ◆[8] 272a 28.40 N 77.06 E
Jwayyā 132 33.14 N 35.19 E
Jyderup 41 55.40 N 11.26 E
Jylland (Jutland) ◆[1] 26 56.00 N 9.15 E
Jyllinge 41 55.45 N 12.07 E
Jyväskylä 26 62.14 N 25.44 E

K

K2 (Qogir Feng) ∧ 123 35.53 N 76.30 E
Ka ≃ 150 11.40 N 4.10 E
Kaaawa 229c 21.33 N 157.51 W
Kaabong 154 3.31 N 34.08 E
Kaachka 128 37.21 N 59.36 E
Kaala ∧ 229c 21.31 N 158.09 W
Kaalaea 229c 21.28 N 157.51 W
Kaala-Gomén 175f 20.40 S 164.25 E
Kaalspruit 158 29.15 S 26.10 E
Kaapahu Bay ⊂ 229a 20.39 N 156.05 W
Kaapmuiden 156 25.33 S 31.20 E
Kaappunt ≻ 158 34.21 S 18.30 E
Kaapstad → Cape Town 158 33.55 S 18.22 E
Kaarli 76 59.24 N 26.27 E
Kaarssen 54 53.12 N 11.02 E
Kaarst 56 51.14 N 6.37 E
Kaaterskill Creek ≃ 210 42.13 N 73.53 W
Kaatoan, Mount ∧ 116 8.07 N 124.55 E
Kaatsheuvel 52 51.40 N 5.02 E
Kaavi 26 62.59 N 28.30 E
Kaba 150 10.09 N 11.40 W
Kaba ≃ 86 47.53 N 86.12 E
Kaba, Goulbin V 150 13.42 N 6.19 E
Kabacan 116 7.08 N 124.49 E
Kabacan ≃ 116 7.08 N 124.50 E
Kabadak 126 22.13 N 89.19 E
Kabadak ≃[1] 126 22.13 N 89.18 E
Kabadüz 130 40.53 N 37.56 E
Kabaena, Pulau I 112 5.15 S 121.55 E
Kabaena, Selat ⋓ 112 5.00 S 122.00 E
Kabah ⊥ 232 20.07 N 89.29 W
Kabala 150 9.35 N 11.33 W
Kabale 154 1.15 S 29.59 E
Kabalebo ≃ 250 5.02 N 57.21 W
Kabalega Falls ∟ 154 2.17 N 31.41 E
Kabalega Falls National Park ♠ 154 2.15 N 31.50 E
Kabali, Indon. 112 1.42 S 121.54 E
Kabalı, Tür. 130 41.52 N 35.05 E
Kabalo 154 6.03 S 26.55 E
Kabambare 154 4.42 S 27.43 E
Kaban' 86 54.39 N 66.28 E
Kabangu Kuta 154 14.00 S 24.03 E
Kabanjahe 114 3.06 N 98.30 E
Kabanje 83 49.13 N 38.12 E
Kabankalan 116 9.59 N 122.49 E
Kabanovka 80 53.39 N 51.18 E
Kabanovo 86 55.20 N 70.52 E
Kabansk 88 52.03 N 106.39 E
Kabardinka 78 44.39 N 37.57 E
Kabardino-Balkarija □[3] 84 43.30 N 43.30 E
Kabasalan 116 7.48 N 122.45 E
Kabayan 116 16.37 N 120.51 E
Kabba 150 7.50 N 6.03 E
Kabbani ≃ 122 12.13 N 76.54 E
Kåbdalis 24 66.10 N 20.00 E
Kabd aṣ-Ṣārim ◆[1] 130 34.34 N 39.33 E
Kabd Warqah ◆[1] 130 34.20 N 39.37 E
Kabel ◆[8] 263 51.24 N 7.29 E
Kabenung Lake ⊜ 190 48.16 N 85.00 W
Kabetogama Lake ⊜ 190 48.28 N 92.59 W
Kabeya 154 5.40 S 27.58 E
Kab-hegy ∧ 30 47.03 N 17.39 E
Kabia ≃ 146 9.54 N 15.10 E
Kabid, Wādī V 132 30.08 N 36.31 E
Kabinakagami Lake ⊜ 190 48.54 N 84.25 W
Kabin Buri 110 13.59 N 101.43 E
Kabinda 152 6.08 S 24.29 E
Kabinu 112 4.00 N 116.05 E
Kabir 112 8.17 S 124.13 E
Kabira 175d 24.27 N 124.08 E
Kabīr Kili 123 33.11 N 71.19 E
Kabīr Kūh ⋏ 128 33.25 N 46.45 E
Kabīrwāla 123 30.24 N 71.52 E
Kabkābīyah 140 13.39 N 24.05 E
Kablow 264a 52.18 N 13.44 E
Kablower Ziegelei 264a 52.19 N 13.43 E
Kablukovo, Ross. 82 56.50 N 36.12 E
Kablukovo, Ross. 82 56.02 N 38.10 E
Kablumgu, Cape ≻ 164 6.20 S 150.00 E
Kabna 140 19.10 N 32.41 E
Kabo 152 7.39 N 18.37 E
Kabobo 154 5.07 S 29.03 E
Kaboe ≃ 158 28.55 S 19.17 E
Kābol 120 34.31 N 69.12 E
Kābol □[4] 120 34.30 N 69.15 E
Kābol ≃ 120 33.55 N 72.14 E
Kabompo 154 13.36 S 24.12 E
Kabompo ≃ 138 14.10 S 23.11 E
Kabondo-Dianda 154 8.53 S 25.40 E
Kabongo, Zaïre 154 7.19 S 25.35 E

Symbols in the index entries represent the broad categories identified in the key at the right. Symbols with superior numbers (⋏[1]) identify subcategories (see complete key on page *I · 1).*

Symbole im Register stellen die rechts im Schlüssel erklärten Kategorien dar. Symbole mit hochgestellten Ziffern (⋏[1]) bezeichnen Unterabteilungen einer Kategorie (vgl. vollständiger Schlüssel auf Seite *I · 1).*

Los símbolos incluídos en el texto del índice representan las grandes categorías identificadas con la clave a la derecha. Los símbolos con numeros en su parte superior (⋏[1]) identifican las subcategorías (véase la clave completa en la página *I · 1).*

Les symboles de l'index représentent les catégories indiquées dans la légende à droite. Les symboles suivis d'un indice (⋏[1]) représentent des sous-catégories (voir légende complète à la page *I · 1).*

Os símbolos incluídos no texto do índice representam as grandes categorias identificadas com a chave à direita. Os símbolos com números em sua parte superior (⋏[1]) identificam as subcategorias (veja-se a chave completa à página *I · 1).*

∧	Mountain	Berg	Montaña	Montagne	Montanha
⋏	Mountains	Gebirge	Montañas	Montagnes	Montanhas
)(	Pass	Paß	Paso	Col	Passo
V	Valley, Canyon	Tal, Cañon	Valle, Cañón	Vallée, Canyon	Vale, Canhão
⊻	Plain	Ebene	Llano	Plaine	Planície
≻	Cape	Kap	Cabo	Cap	Cabo
I	Island	Insel	Isla	Île	Ilha
II	Islands	Inseln	Islas	Îles	Ilhas
⩡	Other Topographic Features	Andere Topographische Objekte	Otros Elementos Topográficos	Autres données topographiques	Outros acidentes topográficos

ESPAÑOL Nombre	Página	Lat.°′	Long.°′ W = Oeste
Kabongo, Zaïre	154	8.43 S	28.11 E
Kabongo-Lunda, Chutes ∟	152	7.34 S	17.17 E
Kaboro	152	6.59 N	17.33 E
Kabot	150	10.48 N	14.57 W
Kabotshome	154	3.46 S	26.54 E
Kabou, Centraf.	152	5.20 N	21.43 E
Kabou, Togo	150	9.27 N	0.49 E
Kaboudia, Rass ›	148	35.14 N	11.10 E
Kaboul → Kābol	120	34.31 N	69.12 E
Kabr	140	10.54 N	26.50 E
Kabri	132	33.01 N	35.09 E
Kabūdarāhang	128	35.12 N	48.44 E
Kabūd Gonbad	128	37.00 N	59.45 E
Kābul → Kābol	120	34.30 N	69.11 E
Kabunda	154	12.25 S	29.22 E
Kabunga	154	1.42 S	28.08 E
Kabura ≃	94	36.17 N	139.04 E
Kaburuang, Pulau I	108	3.48 N	126.48 E
Kabūshīyah	140	16.53 N	33.42 E
Kabwanga	152	7.01 S	22.37 E
Kabwe (Broken Hill)	154	14.27 S	28.27 E
Kabwe-Katanda	152	7.59 S	24.29 E
Kabyčovka	83	49.28 N	39.45 E
Kabylie ◆[1]	34	36.30 N	4.30 E
Kača	78	44.47 N	33.32 E
Kačalinskaja	80	49.07 N	44.03 E
Kačanik	38	42.13 N	21.14 E
Kačanovo	76	57.28 N	27.46 E
Kacbachskij	86	52.58 N	59.40 E
Kačerginė	76	54.56 N	23.44 E
Kacha ≃[1]	126	22.23 N	89.54 E
Kachagalau ∧	154	2.19 N	35.03 E
Kach'ang-ni	98	38.24 N	126.11 E
Kachati	84	42.30 N	41.46 E
Kachchh, Gulf of ⊂	120	22.36 N	69.30 E
Kachemak Bay ⊂	180	59.35 N	151.30 W
Kachess Lake ⊜[1]	224	47.20 N	121.14 W
Kachhwa	124	25.13 N	82.43 E
Kachi	84	41.26 N	46.56 E
Kachia	150	9.53 N	7.58 E
Kachib	84	42.25 N	46.36 E
Kachin □[3]	102	26.00 N	97.30 E
Kach'i-ri	98	34.27 N	126.08 E
Kachisi	144	9.39 N	37.50 E
Kachovka	78	46.47 N	33.30 E
Kachovskoje vodochranilišče ⊜[1]	78	47.25 N	34.10 E
Kachowka-Stausee → Kachovskoje vodochranilišče ⊜[1]	78	47.25 N	34.10 E
K'achta	88	50.26 N	106.25 E
Kachua, Bngl.	126	22.39 N	89.53 E
Kachua, Bngl.	126	23.21 N	90.54 E
Kachul (Kagul)	38	45.54 N	28.11 E
Kačiry	86	53.05 N	76.07 E
Kačkanar	86	58.42 N	59.38 E
Kačkanar, gora ∧	86	58.47 N	59.23 E
Kaçkar Daği ∧	130	40.50 N	41.10 E
Kačkarovka	78	47.06 N	33.44 E
Kačug	88	53.58 N	105.52 E
Kada ≃	88	55.03 N	102.04 E
Kadada ≃	80	53.09 N	46.01 E
Kadaingti	110	17.37 N	97.32 E
Kadaiyanallūr	122	9.05 N	77.21 E
Kadamatt Island I	122	11.14 N	72.47 E
Kadaň	54	50.20 N	13.15 E
Kadanai (Kadaney) ≃	120	31.02 N	66.09 E
Kadaney (Kadanai) ≃	120	31.02 N	66.09 E
Kadan Kyun I	110	12.30 N	98.22 E
Kadapongan, Pulau I	112	4.43 S	115.44 E
Kadassa ≃	115b	9.24 S	120.02 E
Kaddam ⊜[1]	122	19.07 N	78.46 E
Kade	150	6.05 N	0.50 W
Kadéï ≃	152	3.31 N	16.05 E
Kadena	174m	26.22 N	127.45 E
Kadena Airfield ⊠	174m	26.22 N	127.45 E
Kadeshiki	80	58.08 N	49.11 E
Kadetrenden (Kadet Rinne) ʮ	41	54.30 N	12.15 E
Kadet Rinne (Kadetrenden) ʮ	41	54.30 N	12.15 E
Kadgo, Lake ⊜	162	26.42 S	127.18 E
Kadi	120	23.18 N	72.20 E
Kadiana	150	10.45 N	6.30 W
Kadıköy	130	40.46 N	26.46 E
Kadina	168b	33.58 S	137.43 E
Kading ≃	110	18.19 N	104.00 E
Kadınhanı	130	38.15 N	32.14 E
Kadiolo	150	10.33 N	5.46 W
Kadipaten	115a	6.46 S	108.10 E
Kādīpur	124	26.10 N	82.23 E
Kadiri	122	14.07 N	78.10 E
Kadirli	130	37.23 N	36.05 E
Kadışehri	130	40.00 N	35.49 E
Kadiyevka → Stachanov	83	48.34 N	38.40 E
Kadja, Ouadi (Wādī Kaja) V	146	12.02 N	22.28 E
Kadkan	128	35.35 N	58.50 E
Kadnikov	76	59.30 N	40.20 E
Kadnikovskij	76	60.19 N	40.15 E
Kado	150	7.39 N	9.44 E
Ka-do I	98	39.33 N	124.40 E
Kadodo	140	11.04 N	29.31 E
Kadogawa	92	32.28 N	131.39 E
Kadoka	198	43.50 N	101.30 W
Kadom	80	54.34 N	42.30 E
Kadoma, Nihon	270	34.44 N	135.35 E
Kadoma, Zimb.	154	18.21 S	29.55 E
Kadoškino	80	54.01 N	44.25 E
Kadov	60	49.24 N	13.47 E
Kaduj	76	59.12 N	37.09 E
Kadumbul ≃	115b	9.42 S	120.32 E
Kaduna	150	10.33 N	7.27 E
Kaduna □[3]	150	10.30 N	7.45 E
Kaduna ≃	150	8.45 N	5.45 E
Kāduqlī	140	11.01 N	29.43 E
Kadūr	122	13.34 N	76.01 E
Kadyj	80	57.47 N	43.11 E
Kadykčan	74	63.02 N	146.50 E
Kadyšovo	80	54.20 N	46.45 E
Kadžerom	24	64.41 N	55.54 E
Kadži-Saj	85	42.08 N	77.10 E
Kaech'ŏn	98	39.42 N	125.53 E
Kaédi	150	16.09 N	13.30 W
Kaedo-ri	98	34.35 N	127.39 E
Kaegudeck Lake ⊜	186	48.07 N	55.11 W
Kaélé	146	10.07 N	14.27 E
Kaena Point ›	229c	21.35 N	158.17 W
Kaeo	172	35.06 S	173.47 E
Kaesŏng	98	37.59 N	126.33 E
Kāf	128	31.24 N	37.24 E
Kafakumba	152	9.41 S	23.44 E
Kafan	84	39.13 N	46.24 E
Kafanchan	150	9.36 N	8.17 E
Kaffraria □[9]	158	31.30 S	28.30 E
Kaffrine	150	14.06 N	15.33 W
Kafia Kingi	140	9.16 N	24.25 E
Kafin	150	9.30 N	7.04 E
Kafinda	154	12.39 S	30.20 E
Kafin Madaki	150	10.41 N	9.46 E
Kafirévs, Ákra ›	38	38.09 N	24.36 E
Kafirnigan ≃	120	36.58 N	68.02 E
Kafo ≃	154	1.08 N	31.05 E
Kafr ad-Dawwār	142	31.08 N	30.07 E
Kafr ad-Difrāwī	142	31.03 N	30.40 E
Kafr al-'Ā'id	142	30.27 N	31.35 E
Kafr al-Baṭṭīkh	142	31.24 N	31.44 E
Kafr al-Jarā'idah	142	31.13 N	31.16 E
Kafr ash-Shaykh	142	31.07 N	30.56 E
Kafr ash-Shaykh □[4]	142	31.15 N	30.50 E
Kafrat Ṭā'il Mūsā	142	30.53 N	29.44 E
Kafr at-Tamīmī	142	30.37 N	31.21 E
Kafr az-Zayyāt	142	30.49 N	30.49 E
Kafr Diyamā	142	30.48 N	30.52 E
Kafr el-Zaiyat → Kafr az-Zayyāt	142	30.49 N	30.49 E

FRANÇAIS Nom	Page	Lat.°′	Long.°′ W = Ouest
Kafr Ḥakīm	273c	30.05 N	31.07 E
Kafr Ḥūnah	132	33.29 N	35.35 E
Kafr Kanna	132	32.45 N	35.20 E
Kafr Kilā al-Bāb	142	30.41 N	31.09 E
Kafr Nabrakh	132	33.42 N	35.38 E
Kafr Naffākh	132	33.04 N	35.44 E
Kafr Nāsij	132	33.09 N	36.03 E
Kafr Rabī'	142	30.42 N	30.50 E
Kafr Sa'd	142	31.19 N	31.39 E
Kafr Salīm	142	31.09 N	30.06 E
Kafr Ṣaqr	142	30.48 N	31.37 E
Kafr Shanawān	142	30.30 N	31.01 E
Kafr Shibīn	142	30.18 N	31.18 E
Kafr Shīmā	132	33.49 N	35.32 E
Kafr Shukr	142	30.33 N	31.16 E
Kafr Sūsah	132	33.29 N	36.16 E
Kafr Takhārīm	130	36.07 N	36.31 E
Kafr Ṭarkhān al-Gharbī	142	29.29 N	31.13 E
Kafr Yasif	132	32.57 N	35.10 E
Kafue	154	15.47 S	28.11 E
Kafue ≃	154	15.56 S	28.55 E
Kafue Flats ≡	154	15.40 S	27.25 E
Kafue Gorge V	154	15.54 S	28.34 E
Kafue National Park ♠	154	15.00 S	25.45 E
Kafulwe Mission	154	9.00 S	29.02 E
Kafumba	152	5.23 S	18.55 E
Kafwira	154	12.10 S	27.33 E
Kaga	94	36.18 N	136.18 E
Kaga Bandoro	152	6.59 N	19.11 E
Kagalaska Island I	180	51.47 N	176.23 W
Kagal'nickaja	83	46.53 N	40.09 E
Kagal'nik	83	47.05 N	39.19 E
Kagal'nik ≃	83	47.04 N	39.18 E
Kagami	96	33.37 N	133.26 E
Kagamigahara	94	35.24 N	136.54 E
Kagamil Island I	180	53.00 N	169.43 W
Kagamino	96	35.05 N	133.56 E
Kāgān, Pāk.	123	34.47 N	73.32 E
Kagan, Uzb.	128	39.43 N	64.33 E
Kagan Valley V	123	34.25 N	73.17 E
Kagarko	150	9.29 N	7.41 E
Kagarlyk	78	49.51 N	30.50 E
Kagawa	96	34.15 N	134.02 E
Kagawa □[5]	96	34.15 N	134.00 E
Kagawong, Lake ⊜	190	45.49 N	82.18 W
Kagaznagar	122	19.18 N	79.50 E
Kåge	26	64.50 N	20.59 E
Kagelike	120	37.20 N	87.02 E
Kagera (Akagera) ≃	154	0.57 S	31.47 E
Kågeröd	41	56.01 N	13.06 E
Kâgheț ◆[1]	148	24.00 N	7.30 W
Kâğıthane ◆[8]	267b	41.04 N	28.58 E
Kagitumba	154	1.04 S	30.27 E
Kağızman	84	40.09 N	43.08 E
Käglan ⋏[2]	40	59.23 N	15.31 E
Kagmar	140	14.24 N	30.25 E
Kagopal	146	8.17 N	16.27 E
Kagoshima	92	31.36 N	130.33 E
Kagoshima □[5]	93b	29.00 N	129.30 E
Kagoshima-wan ⊂	92	31.25 N	130.38 E
Kagran ◆[8]	264b	48.15 N	16.27 E
Kagulu	154	1.15 N	33.18 E
Kagyo-ri	98	34.25 N	126.48 E
Kahalīya, Jabal ∧	142	29.55 N	32.09 E
Kahaluu	229c	21.27 N	157.50 W
Kahama	154	3.50 S	32.36 E
Kahana Bay ⊂	229c	21.34 N	157.52 W
Kahayan ≃	112	3.20 S	114.04 E
Kahe	154	3.30 S	37.26 E
Kahemba	152	7.17 S	19.00 E
Kahia	154	6.21 S	28.24 E
Kahiu Point ›	229a	21.13 N	156.58 W
Kaḥk	142	29.25 N	30.38 E
Kahl ≃	56	50.04 N	9.00 E
Kahla	54	50.48 N	11.35 E
Kahl am Main	56	50.04 N	9.00 E
Kahlenberg ∧[2]	264b	48.16 N	16.21 E
Kahler Asten ∧	56	51.11 N	8.29 E
Kahlersberg ∧	64	47.32 N	13.02 E
Kāhna	123	31.22 N	74.22 E
Kahnūj	128	27.58 N	57.45 E
Kahoka	194	40.25 N	91.43 W
Kahoku, Nihon	96	33.39 N	133.47 E
Kahoku, Nihon	96	33.06 N	130.41 E
Kahoku-gata ⊜	94	36.40 N	136.41 E
Kahoolawe I	229a	20.33 N	156.37 W
Kahouanne, Îlet à I	241o	16.22 N	61.47 W
Kahoué, Mont ∧	150	7.06 N	7.15 W
Kahramanmaraş	130	37.36 N	36.55 E
Kahraman Maraş □[4]	130	38.00 N	37.05 E
Kahror Pakka	123	29.37 N	71.55 E
Kahshe Lake ⊜	212	44.52 N	79.16 W
Kâhta	130	37.46 N	38.36 E
Kahuku	229c	21.40 N	157.57 W
Kahuku Point ›	229c	21.43 N	157.59 W
Kahului	229a	20.54 N	156.28 W
Kahului Airport ⊠	229a	20.54 N	156.26 W
Kahului Bay ⊂	229a	20.54 N	156.28 W
Kahurangi Point ›	172	40.47 S	172.13 E
Kahūta	123	33.35 N	73.23 E
Kahuzi-Biega, Parc National de ♠	154	1.50 N	28.40 E
Kahyŏn-bong ∧	271b	37.38 N	126.39 E
Kahyŏn-ni	271b	37.32 N	126.44 E
Kai	164	2.15 S	136.32 E
Kai, Kepulauan II	164	5.35 S	132.45 E
Kai, Tanjung ›	112	2.52 S	118.45 E
Kaia, Wādī V	140	11.31 N	24.15 E
Kaiai, Jabal ∧	140	19.54 N	36.48 E
Kaiama	150	9.37 N	3.58 E
Kaiapit	164	6.15 S	146.15 E
Kaiapoi	172	43.23 S	172.40 E
Kaibab Indian Reservation ◆[4]	200	36.55 N	112.40 W
Kaibab Plateau ⋏[1]	200	36.30 N	112.15 W
Kaibara	96	35.08 N	135.05 E
Kai Beab	164	7.29 S	139.40 E
Kaibing	61	47.12 N	15.50 E
Kaibito Plateau ⋏[1]	200	36.40 N	111.20 W
Kaichengqiao	100	31.18 N	117.44 E
Kaida	94	35.56 N	137.36 E
Kaidori	268	35.37 N	139.27 E
Kaidu ≃	90	41.55 N	86.38 E
Kaiedin	140	9.45 N	32.11 E
Kaieteur Fall ∟	246	5.10 N	59.28 W
Kaieteur National Park ♠	246	5.10 N	59.45 W
Kaifeng	98	34.51 N	114.21 E
Kaifu	96	33.35 N	134.21 E
Kaifu ≃	96	33.35 N	134.22 E
Kaihe	98	35.42 N	116.20 E
Kaihu	172	35.46 S	173.42 E
Kaihua	100	29.09 N	118.23 E
Kai Iwi	172	39.51 S	174.56 E
Kaijian	102	23.42 N	111.48 E
Kaijiang	102	31.05 N	107.55 E
Kaijo → Kaesŏng	98	37.59 N	126.33 E
Kai Kecil I	164	5.45 S	132.40 E
Kaikohe	172	35.25 S	173.48 E
Kaikoura	172	42.25 S	173.41 E
Kaikoura Peninsula ›[1]	172	42.26 S	173.42 E
Kaikukang	89	53.07 N	124.46 E
Kailahun	150	8.17 N	10.34 W
Kailas → Kangrinboqê Feng ∧	120	31.04 N	81.18 E
Kailāshahar	120	24.20 N	92.01 E
Kaili	102	26.35 N	107.55 E
Kailu	89	43.36 N	121.14 E
Kailua	229c	21.24 N	157.44 W
Kailua Bay ⊂	229c	21.25 N	157.44 W
Kailua Kona	229d	19.22 N	155.59 W
Kaim ≃	164	6.40 S	141.45 E
Kaimai Range ⋏	172	37.45 S	175.55 E
Kaïmaktsalán ∧	38	40.58 N	21.48 E
Kaimana	164	3.39 S	133.45 E

PORTUGUÊS Nome	Página	Lat.°′	Long.°′ W = Oeste
Kaimanawa Mountains ⋏	172	39.15 S	175.54 E
Kaiman-Inseln → Cayman Islands □[2]	238	19.30 N	80.40 W
Kaimenshan	104	41.03 N	123.08 E
Kaimganj	124	27.34 N	79.21 E
Kaimon-dake ∧	92	31.11 N	130.32 E
Kain	50	50.38 N	3.22 E
Käina	76	58.50 N	22.45 E
Kainab ≃	158	28.31 S	19.35 E
Kainach ≃	61	46.54 N	15.31 E
Kainan, Nihon	96	33.36 N	134.22 E
Kainan, Nihon	96	34.09 N	135.12 E
Kainantu	164	6.15 S	145.55 E
Kainda	85	42.50 N	73.41 E
Kai-Ndunda	152	5.42 S	12.42 E
Kaingan ≃	115a	7.44 S	107.54 E
Kainji Lake ⊜[1]	150	10.30 N	4.35 E
Kaioba	112	5.20 S	122.37 E
Kaipara Harbour ⊂	172	36.25 S	174.13 E
Kaiparowits Plateau ⋏[1]	200	37.20 N	111.15 W
Kaiping, Zhg.	102	22.23 N	112.35 E
Kaiping, Zhg.	105	39.41 N	118.16 E
Kaipuri, Pulau I	164	1.51 S	137.01 E
Kairābani	126	24.08 N	87.02 E
Kairaku-en ♠	94	36.22 N	140.27 E
Kairāna	124	29.24 N	77.12 E
Kairatu	164	3.21 S	128.22 E
Kairiru Island I	164	3.20 S	143.35 E
Kairo → Al-Qāhirah	142	30.03 N	31.15 E
Kairouan	148	35.41 N	10.07 E
Kairouan □[8]	148	35.30 N	9.55 E
Kairuku	164	8.50 S	146.35 E
Kairy	78	46.57 N	33.43 E
Kaisarganj	124	27.15 N	81.33 E
Kaisariani	267c	37.58 N	23.47 E
Kaisariani Monastery ʊ[1]	267c	37.58 N	23.47 E
Kaisergebirge ⋏	64	47.36 N	12.20 E
Kaisermühlen ◆[8]	264b	48.14 N	16.26 E
Kaiser Pass ✕	226	37.17 N	119.06 W
Kaisersesch	56	50.14 N	7.08 E
Kaiserslautern	56	49.26 N	7.46 E
Kaiserstuhl ⋏[2]	58	48.06 N	7.40 E
Kaiserswerth ◆[8]	263	51.18 N	6.44 E
Kaiser-Wilhelm-Museum ʊ	263	51.20 N	6.34 E
Kaishantun	98	42.43 N	129.43 E
Kaisheim	56	48.46 N	10.48 E
Kaišiadorys	76	54.52 N	24.27 E
Kait, Tanjung ›	112	3.14 S	106.05 E
Kaita	96	34.20 N	132.32 E
Kaitaia	172	35.07 S	173.16 E
Kaitaichi-chūtonchi, Rikujō-jieitai- ■	96	34.21 N	132.32 E
Kai Tak Airport ⊠	271d	22.20 N	114.12 E
Kaitangata	172	46.18 S	169.51 E
Kaitersberg ⋏	60	49.11 N	12.57 E
Kaithal	124	29.48 N	76.23 E
Kaituma ≃	246	8.11 N	59.41 W
Kaiwaka	172	36.10 S	174.27 E
Kaiwatu	164	8.07 S	127.49 E
Kaiwi Channel ʮ	229b	21.15 N	157.30 W
Kaixian	102	31.13 N	108.25 E
Kaiyang	102	26.58 N	106.40 E
Kaiyuan, Zhg	102	23.44 N	103.11 E
Kaiyuan, Zhg	104	42.32 N	124.01 E
Kaiyuancheng	98	42.37 N	124.04 E
Kaiyuh Mountains ⋏	180	64.00 N	158.00 W
Kaizhou	104	41.22 N	121.19 E
Kaizu	94	35.13 N	136.38 E
Kaizuka	96	34.27 N	135.21 E
Kaja, Wādī (Ouadi Kadja) V	146	12.02 N	22.28 E
Kajaani	26	64.14 N	27.41 E
Kajabbi	166	20.02 S	140.02 E
Kajakī, Band-e ⊜[1]	128	32.22 N	65.16 E
Kajang, Indon.	112	5.20 S	120.21 E
Kajang, Malay.	114	2.59 N	101.47 E
Kajang, Gunong ∧	114	2.46 N	104.09 E
Kajasan	86	55.12 N	62.16 E
Kajasula	84	44.19 N	44.59 E
Kajen	115a	7.02 S	109.34 E
Kajgy	86	50.55 N	64.43 E
Kajiado	154	1.51 S	36.47 E
Kajikazawa	94	35.33 N	138.27 E
Kajiki	92	31.44 N	130.40 E
Kājlāgarh	126	22.02 N	87.47 E
Kajmanačicha	86	53.32 N	75.11 E
Kajmonovo	88	56.50 N	104.54 E
Kajmysovy	86	59.48 N	76.31 E
Kajnar	86	49.12 N	77.25 E
Kajo Kaji	154	3.53 N	31.40 E
Kajrakkum	85	40.16 N	69.49 E
Kajrakkumskoje vodochranilišče ⊜[1]	85	40.20 N	70.10 E
Kajrakty	86	48.31 N	73.14 E
Kajsackoje	80	49.44 N	46.51 E
Kājū ≃	128	25.34 N	61.13 E
Kājulia	126	23.01 N	89.57 E
Kajuru	150	10.21 N	7.40 E
Kaka, Centraf.	140	6.01 N	26.30 E
Kākā, Sūd.	140	10.36 N	32.11 E
Kaka, Lae o ›	229a	20.31 N	156.33 W
Kakabeka Falls ∟	190	48.24 N	89.37 W
Kakabia, Pulau I	112	6.54 S	122.13 E
Kakadu National Park ♠	164	13.00 S	132.45 E
Kakagi Lake ⊜	184	49.13 N	93.52 W
Kakamas	158	28.45 S	20.33 E
Kakamega	154	0.17 N	34.45 E
Kakamigahara	94	35.24 N	136.54 E
Kakana	110	9.07 N	92.49 E
Kakanui Mountains ⋏	172	45.09 S	170.26 E
Kaka Point	172	46.23 S	169.47 E
Kakaramea	172	39.43 S	174.27 E
Kakasa	164	9.20 S	148.45 E
Kakata	150	6.35 N	10.19 W
Kakatahi	172	39.41 S	175.20 E
Kākdwīp	126	21.53 N	88.11 E
Kake, Nihon	96	34.36 N	132.19 E
Kake, Ak., U.S.	180	56.58 N	133.56 W
Kakegawa	94	34.46 N	138.01 E
Kakehashi ≃	94	36.25 N	136.25 E
Kakelwe	154	4.49 S	29.00 E
Kakenge	152	4.51 S	21.55 E
Kakeya	96	35.11 N	132.49 E
Kakhonak	180	59.26 N	154.51 W
Kakhra	126	21.38 N	87.27 E
Kākī	128	28.19 N	51.34 E
Kākināda	122	16.56 N	82.13 E
Kakino	80	55.12 N	44.53 E
Kakinoki	96	34.26 N	131.52 E
Kakisa Lake ⊜	176	60.55 N	117.40 W
Kakizaki	92	37.15 N	138.25 E
Kako ≃, Guy.	246	5.46 N	60.35 W
Kako ≃, Nihon	96	34.44 N	134.49 E
Kakoaka	156	18.40 S	24.22 E
Kakogawa	96	34.46 N	134.51 E
Kakrāla	272a	28.33 N	77.25 E
Kāksa	126	23.28 N	87.28 E
Kaktovik	180	70.08 N	143.37 W
Kakuda	92	37.58 N	140.47 E
Kakui-shima I	96	34.43 N	134.19 E
Kakuma	154	3.43 N	34.52 E
Kakunodate	92	39.35 N	140.34 E
Kakus ≃	112	2.46 N	113.01 E
Kakwa ≃	182	54.36 N	118.28 W
Kala	146	12.05 N	14.27 E
Kala ≃	122	8.18 N	79.50 E
Kalaa Kebira	148	35.52 N	10.32 E
Kalaallit Nunaat → Greenland □[2]	16	70.00 N	40.00 W
Kalaa Sghira	36	35.49 N	10.33 E
Kālābāgh	123	32.58 N	71.34 E
Kalabahi	112	8.13 S	124.31 E
Kalabáka	38	39.42 N	21.43 E

Kalabakan	112	4.25 N	117.29 E
Kalabo	152	14.57 S	22.40 E
Kalabula	86	43.24 N	83.06 E
Kalač	78	50.25 N	41.01 E
Kalačinsk	86	55.03 N	74.34 E
Kalač-Kurtlak	80	49.00 N	42.26 E
Kalač-na-Donu	80	48.43 N	43.31 E
Kalačskaja vozvyšennost' ⋏[1]	80	50.30 N	41.30 E
Kaladan ≃	110	20.09 N	92.57 E
Kaladar	212	44.39 N	77.07 W
Kalae	229a	21.10 N	157.00 W
Ka Lae ›	229d	18.55 N	155.41 W
Kalaena ≃	112	2.40 S	120.53 E
Kalagan	89	50.30 N	119.55 E
Kalagwe	110	22.31 N	96.31 E
Kalahari Desert ◆[2]	156	24.00 S	21.30 E
Kalahari Gemsbok National Park ♠	156	25.30 S	20.30 E
Kalaheo	229b	21.55 N	159.31 W
Kālaia	126	22.23 N	90.36 E
Kalai-Chumb	85	38.28 N	70.46 E
Kalai-Mor	128	35.39 N	62.33 E
Kalais	80	52.38 N	42.38 E
Kalaiyā	124	27.02 N	85.00 E
Kalajka	88	58.28 N	111.46 E
Kalajoki	26	64.15 N	23.57 E
Kalajoki ≃	26	64.17 N	23.55 E
Kalakamate	156	20.39 S	27.21 E
Kalakan	88	55.08 N	116.45 E
Kalakan ≃	88	55.07 N	116.46 E
Kalakepen	114	2.45 N	97.50 E
Kalām	123	35.32 N	72.35 E
Kalama, Wa., U.S.	224	46.00 N	122.50 W
Kalama, Zaïre	154	2.55 S	28.33 E
Kalama ≃	224	46.02 N	122.52 W
Kalama, Pulau I	112	3.15 N	125.28 E
Kalámai	38	37.04 N	22.07 E
Kalamákion	267c	37.55 N	23.43 E
Kalamalka Lake ⊜	182	50.09 N	119.22 W
Kalamariá	0	40.35 N	22.58 E
Kalamazoo	216	42.17 N	85.35 W
Kalamazoo □[6]	216	42.14 N	85.32 W
Kalamazoo ≃	216	42.40 N	86.10 W
Kalamazoo, North Branch ≃	216	42.14 N	84.44 W
Kalamazoo, South Branch ≃	216	42.14 N	84.44 W
Kalamazoo Lake ⊂	216	42.39 N	86.13 W
Kalamb	122	19.03 N	73.57 E
Kalamba	152	0.26 S	18.17 E
Kalambau, Pulau I	112	4.55 S	115.39 E
Kalambo Falls ∟	154	8.36 S	31.14 E
Kalamboli	272c	19.01 N	73.06 E
Kalamitskij zaliv ⊂	78	45.05 N	33.23 E
Kalamo	216	42.32 N	85.01 W
Kalampising	112	3.44 N	116.42 E
Kalamunda	168a	31.57 S	116.03 E
Kalamunda National Park ♠	168a	31.59 S	116.04 E
Kalana	150	10.47 N	8.12 W
Kalančak	78	46.16 N	33.17 E
Kalandula	152	9.06 S	15.57 E
Kalange-Bushimaie ≃	152	7.55 S	23.11 E
Kalanguj	88	51.01 N	116.31 E
Kalankalan	150	10.07 N	8.54 W
Kalannie	162	30.21 S	117.04 E
Kalanshiyū ar-Ramlī al-Kabīr, Sarīr ⊥[8]	146	28.00 N	23.00 E
Kālānwāli	123	29.51 N	74.57 E
Kalao, Pulau I	112	7.18 S	120.58 E
Kalaong	116	6.04 N	124.28 E
Kalaotoa, Pulau I	112	7.22 S	121.47 E
Kalapana	229d	19.21 N	154.58 W
Kalāpāra	126	21.59 N	90.14 E
Kalar ≃	88	55.23 N	116.18 E
Kalār, Kūh-e ∧	128	31.50 N	50.53 E
Kalaraš	38	47.16 N	28.19 E
Kälarne	26	62.59 N	16.05 E
Kālāroa	126	22.52 N	89.02 E
Kalasarv	84	39.11 N	48.03 E
Kalasi	86	48.43 N	86.59 E
Kalasin, Indon.	112	0.12 N	114.16 E
Kalasin, Thai	110	16.29 N	103.30 E
Kalašnikovo	76	57.17 N	35.13 E
Kalāt	120	29.02 N	66.35 E
Kalatungan Mountain ∧	116	7.58 N	124.47 E
Kalaupapa	229a	21.11 N	156.59 W
Kalaupapa National Historical Park ♠	229a	21.12 N	156.58 W
Kalaupapa Peninsula ›[1]	229a	21.13 N	156.58 W
Kalauri	84	41.49 N	45.42 E
Kalaus ≃	80	45.43 N	44.07 E
Kalaus-Kr'akovka	83	48.46 N	38.52 E
Kalavárdha	38	36.20 N	27.57 E
Kalávrita	38	38.01 N	22.06 E
Kalaw	110	20.38 N	96.34 E
Kalawao □[6]	229a	21.12 N	156.58 W
Kal'azin	76	57.15 N	37.52 E
Kalb, Nahr al- ≃	132	33.57 N	35.35 E
Kalb, Ra's al- ›	144	14.02 N	48.41 E
Kalbā'	128	25.03 N	56.21 E
Kalbar	171a	27.56 S	152.37 E
Kalbarri	162	27.42 S	114.09 E
Kalbarri National Park ♠	162	27.45 S	114.25 E
Kalbe	54	52.40 N	11.25 E
Kalbinskij chrebet ⋏	86	49.10 N	83.00 E
Kalchās	120	29.21 N	69.42 E
Kal'čik ≃	83	47.07 N	37.36 E
Kaldırım ≃	267b	41.10 N	29.12 E
Kaldygajty ≃	80	49.20 N	52.38 E
Kale, Tür.	130	40.23 N	39.39 E
Kale, Tür.	130	37.26 N	28.51 E
Kale, Tür.	130	36.14 N	29.59 E
Kalecik, Tür.	130	37.17 N	39.02 E
Kalecik, Tür.	130	40.06 N	33.25 E
Kaleden	182	49.23 N	119.35 W
Kaledupa, Pulau I	112	5.32 S	123.47 E
Kalegauk Island I	110	15.32 N	97.40 E
Kalehe	154	2.06 S	28.55 E
Kaleindaung ≃	110	18.50 N	94.00 E
Kalema, Tan.	154	1.12 S	31.50 E
Kalema, Zaïre	152	4.08 S	24.15 E
Kalemie (Albertville)	154	5.56 S	29.12 E
Kalemyo	120	23.12 N	94.10 E
Kalene Hill	152	11.11 S	24.10 E
Kaleščatovka	83	49.35 N	39.55 E
Kaletwa	110	21.45 N	92.48 E
Kalety	30	50.34 N	18.54 E
Kalevala	24	65.13 N	31.08 E
Kalewa	110	23.12 N	94.17 E
Kale Water ≃	46	55.32 N	2.28 W
Kaleybar	128	38.47 N	47.02 E
Kálfafell	24a	63.58 N	17.40 W
Kalga	88	50.57 N	118.48 E
Kalgačicha	24	63.20 N	36.44 E
Kalgan, Aust.	162	34.53 S	118.01 E
Kalgan → Zhangjiakou, Zhg.	105	40.50 N	114.53 E
Kalgin Island I	180	60.28 N	151.55 W
Kalgoorlie-Boulder	162	30.45 S	121.28 E
Kalhe	272c	18.52 N	73.06 E
Kali	150	12.10 N	11.29 W
Kāli ≃[1]	126	23.40 N	89.12 E
Kālia	126	23.03 N	89.38 E
Kāliāganj	124	25.38 N	88.19 E
Kāliāghaj ≃	126	22.10 N	87.50 E
Kāliākair	126	24.05 N	90.14 E
Kaliakra, nos ›	38	43.21 N	28.27 E
Kalianda	115a	5.45 S	105.38 E
Kalianget	115a	7.03 S	113.56 E
Kalibek, ozero ⊜	86	53.52 N	70.40 E
Kālībhīt Hills ⋏[2]	124	22.10 N	77.30 E
Kalibo	116	11.43 N	122.22 E
Kalida	216	40.59 N	84.12 W

Kalifornien, Golf von → California, Golfo de ⊂	232	28.00 N	112.00 W
Kālī Gaṇḍakī ≃	124	27.42 N	84.25 E
Kāliganga ≃	126	23.43 N	90.15 E
Kālīganj, Bngl.	126	23.55 N	90.34 E
Kālīganj, Bngl.	126	23.25 N	89.08 E
Kālīganj, Bngl.	126	22.28 N	89.02 E
Kāliganj, India	126	23.44 N	88.14 E
Kalihiwai ≃	229b	22.13 N	159.26 W
Kalijati	115a	6.32 S	107.40 E
Kālikāpur, Bngl.	126	22.43 N	89.26 E
Kālikāpur, Bngl.	126	23.46 N	89.55 E
Kālikāpur, India	126	22.37 N	86.17 E
Kālikāpur, India	272b	22.29 N	88.32 E
Kalikino, Ross.	76	52.57 N	39.50 E
Kalikino, Ross.	80	52.55 N	54.05 E
Kalima, Zaïre	154	2.34 S	26.37 E
Kalima, Zhg.	104	41.32 N	122.40 E
Kalimantan → Borneo I	112	0.30 N	114.00 E
Kalimantan Barat □[4]	112	0.30 N	110.00 E
Kalimantan Selatan □[4]	112	2.30 S	115.30 E
Kalimantan Tengah □[4]	112	2.00 S	113.30 E
Kalimantan Timur □[4]	112	1.30 N	116.30 E
Kálimnos	38	36.57 N	26.59 E
Kálimnos I	38	37.00 N	27.00 E
Kālimpang	124	27.04 N	88.29 E
Kalina, Pointe de ›	273b	4.18 S	15.16 E
Kālīnadi ≃	122	14.50 N	74.08 E
Kālinagar	126	22.26 N	88.51 E
Kalinga-Apayao □[4]	116	17.50 N	121.10 E
Kalinga Bil ⊜	272b	22.33 N	88.33 E
Kalinin, Ross.	80	47.11 N	42.10 E
Kalinin → Tver', Ross.	82	56.52 N	35.55 E
Kalininabad	85	39.45 N	69.08 E
Kaliningrad (Königsberg), Ross.	76	54.43 N	20.30 E
Kaliningrad, Ross.	82	55.55 N	37.49 E
Kaliningrad Oblast' □[4]	76	54.45 N	21.15 E
Kalinino, Ross.	78	45.07 N	39.00 E
Kalinino, Ross.	80	46.21 N	48.53 E
Kalinino, Ross.	86	57.20 N	56.20 E
Kalinino, Ross.	89	49.24 N	129.20 E
Kalinino, Ukr.	83	47.27 N	37.28 E
Kalininsk, Kyrg.	85	42.29 N	72.06 E
Kalininsk, Ross.	80	51.30 N	44.28 E
Kalininskaja, Ross.	78	45.29 N	38.40 E
Kalininskaja, Ross.	80	47.52 N	42.15 E
Kalininskij	83	48.01 N	39.36 E
Kalininskoje, Kyrg.	85	42.50 N	73.49 E
Kalininskoje, Ukr.	78	47.07 N	32.59 E
Kalinkoviči	76	52.08 N	29.21 E
Kalinku	154	11.12 S	33.12 E
Kalinovik	38	43.31 N	18.26 E
Kalinovka, Kaz.	86	49.58 N	55.22 E
Kalinovka, Ross.	78	51.54 N	34.28 E
Kalinovka, Ukr.	78	50.14 N	30.14 E
Kalinovka, Ukr.	78	49.27 N	28.32 E
Kalinovo, Ross.	82	54.54 N	37.17 E
Kalinovo, Ukr.	83	48.34 N	38.31 E
Kālipur	272b	22.41 N	88.17 E
Kaliro	154	0.54 N	33.30 E
Kalis	144	8.23 N	49.05 E
Kalisat	115a	8.08 S	113.48 E
Kalisch → Kalisz	30	51.46 N	18.06 E
Kāli Sindh ≃	124	25.32 N	76.17 E
Kalispell	202	48.11 N	114.18 W
Kalistraticha	86	52.59 N	83.35 E
Kalisz	30	51.46 N	18.06 E
Kalisz □[4]	30	51.40 N	17.45 E
Kalisz Pomorski	30	53.19 N	15.54 E
Kalitva ≃	78	48.10 N	40.46 E
Kaliua	154	5.04 S	31.48 E
Kaliveli Tank ⊜[1]	122	12.05 N	79.50 E
Kaliwiro	115a	7.27 S	109.51 E
Kaliwungu	115a	6.57 S	110.14 E
Kalix	26	65.51 N	23.08 E
Kalixälven ≃	24	65.50 N	23.11 E
Kālka	123	30.50 N	76.56 E
Kālkāji ◆[8]	272a	28.33 N	77.16 E
Kalkaman	86	51.58 N	76.02 E
Kalkan	130	36.15 N	29.24 E
Kalkar	52	51.44 N	6.18 E
Kalkaska	190	44.44 N	85.10 W
Kalkfeld	156	20.53 S	16.11 E
Kalkfontein	156	22.08 S	20.53 E
Kalkfonteindam ⊜[1]	158	29.30 S	25.15 E
Kalkhorst	54	53.58 N	11.02 E
Kalkım	130	39.48 N	27.13 E
Kālkini	126	23.06 N	90.16 E
Kalkmond	158	28.40 S	20.26 E
Kalkrand	156	24.03 S	17.33 E
Kalksburg ◆[8]	264b	48.08 N	16.15 E
Kalk-See ⊜	264a	52.26 N	13.46 E
Kalkstasie	158	30.00 S	18.55 E
Kalkum ◆[8]	263	51.18 N	6.46 E
Kalkutta → Calcutta	126	22.32 N	88.22 E
Kalkwerf	158	28.39 S	21.43 E
Kall	56	50.32 N	6.32 E
Kallakkurichchi	122	11.44 N	78.58 E
Kallakoopah Creek ≃	166	27.29 S	138.15 E
Kållandsö I	26	58.40 N	13.09 E
Kallang ≃	271c	1.19 N	103.52 E
Kallar Kahār	123	32.47 N	72.42 E
Kallaste	76	58.39 N	27.09 E
Kallavesi ⊜	26	62.50 N	27.45 E
Kalletal	52	52.06 N	8.56 E
Källfallet	40	59.50 N	15.31 E
Kallhäll	40	59.27 N	17.48 E
Kalliecahoolie Lake ⊜	184	54.14 N	95.29 W
Kallinge	26	56.14 N	15.17 E
Kallista	274b	37.53 S	145.22 E
Kallithéa	267c	37.57 N	23.42 E
Kallmünz	60	49.09 N	11.58 E
Kallnach	58	47.01 N	7.14 E
Kallsjön ⊜	26	63.37 N	13.00 E
Kalmakkora	86	44.03 N	78.44 E
Kalmakkyrgan ≃	86	46.58 N	64.30 E
Kalmar	26	56.40 N	16.22 E
Kalmar Län □[6]	26	57.20 N	16.00 E
Kalmarsund ʮ	26	56.40 N	16.25 E
Kalmit ∧	56	49.19 N	8.05 E
Kal'mius ≃	83	47.05 N	37.34 E
Kalmthout	50	51.23 N	4.28 E
Kalmyckije Mysy	86	51.53 N	82.16 E
Kalmykia → Kalmykija □[3]	72	46.30 N	45.30 E
Kalmykija □[3]	72	46.30 N	45.30 E
Kalmykov	80	49.01 N	42.49 E
Kalmykovka, Ukr.	83	49.17 N	38.39 E
Kalmykovka, Ukr.	83	49.17 N	39.52 E
Kalmykovo	80	49.03 N	51.47 E
Kālna	126	23.13 N	88.22 E
Kalnciems	76	56.50 N	23.37 E
Kal'niboloto	78	48.44 N	31.00 E
Kalnibolotskaja	78	46.01 N	40.28 E
Kalničko Gorje ⋏	36	46.10 N	16.30 E
Kalo	164	10.00 S	147.45 E
Kálócfa	61	46.45 N	16.34 E
Kalocsa	30	46.32 N	18.59 E
Kalofer	38	42.37 N	24.59 E
Kalohi Channel ʮ	229a	21.00 N	156.56 W
Kaloko	154	6.47 S	25.48 E
Kalol, India	120	22.36 N	73.27 E
Kālol, India	120	23.15 N	72.29 E
Kalole	154	3.42 S	27.22 E
Kalolio	112	0.11 S	121.38 E
Kaloli Point ›	229d	19.38 N	154.57 W
Kalomo	154	17.02 S	26.30 E
Kalomo ≃	154	17.57 S	26.24 E
Kalona	190	41.28 N	91.42 W
Kalonda	152	4.48 S	17.33 E
Kalone Peak ∧	182	52.38 N	126.37 W

Kalonga	154	9.10 S	27.25 E
Kalorama	274b	37.49 S	145.22 E
Kaloran	115a	7.15 S	110.15 E
Kalø Vig ⊂	41	56.15 N	10.25 E
Kalpáki	38	39.53 N	20.38 E
Kalpeni Island I	122	10.05 N	73.38 E
Kālpi	124	26.07 N	79.44 E
Kāl Qal'eh	128	32.38 N	62.32 E
Kalri	123	31.39 N	72.33 E
Kalsdorf bei Graz	61	46.57 N	15.28 E
Kalskag	180	61.30 N	160.23 W
Kalsūbai ∧	122	19.36 N	73.43 E
Kaltag	180	64.20 N	158.44 W
Kaltan	86	53.30 N	87.17 E
Kaltbrunn	58	47.12 N	9.02 E
Kalte Herberge ∧	56	50.03 N	7.59 E
Kalteneber	56	51.19 N	10.08 E
Kaltenhouse	56	48.48 N	7.50 E
Kaltenkirchen	52	53.50 N	9.58 E
Kaltenleutgeben	264b	48.07 N	16.12 E
Kaltennordheim	56	50.38 N	10.10 E
Kaltensundheim	56	50.36 N	10.10 E
Kalter Gang ≃	264b	48.02 N	16.25 E
Kalthof	263	51.26 N	7.40 E
Kal'tino	265a	59.58 N	30.40 E
Kaltungo	146	9.50 N	11.19 E
Kaluga	82	54.31 N	36.16 E
Kaluga Oblast' □[4]	76	54.30 N	35.30 E
Kalugino, Kaz.	80	48.22 N	51.33 E
Kalugino, Ross.	82	54.59 N	37.11 E
Kalukalukuang, Pulau I	112	5.14 S	117.38 E
Kālu Khuhar	120	25.08 N	67.46 E
Kalulushi	154	12.50 S	28.03 E
Kalumba, Mount ∧	166	31.49 S	146.22 E
Kalumburu	164	14.18 S	126.39 E
Kalumburu Aboriginal Reserve ◆[4]	164	14.15 S	126.50 E
Kalundborg	41	55.41 N	11.06 E
Kalundborg Fjord ⊂	41	55.41 N	11.00 E
Kālundri	272c	18.59 N	73.08 E
Kalundu, Zaïre	154	3.26 S	29.08 E
Kalundu, Zam.	154	10.16 S	29.24 E
Kalungwishi ≃	154	9.01 S	28.57 E
Kalūr Kot	123	32.09 N	71.16 E
Kaluš	78	49.03 N	24.23 E
Kałuszyn	30	52.13 N	21.49 E
Kalutara	122	6.35 N	79.58 E
Kalvåg	26	61.46 N	4.53 E
Kalvarija	76	54.21 N	23.14 E
K'alvaz	84	38.39 N	48.18 E
Kalvehave	41	55.00 N	12.10 E
Kälviä	26	63.52 N	23.26 E
Kalwa	272c	19.12 N	72.59 E
Kalwang	61	47.26 N	14.46 E
Kalwaria Zebrzydowska	30	49.52 N	19.41 E
Kalyān	122	19.15 N	73.09 E
Kalyāndurg	122	14.33 N	77.06 E
Kam ≃	146	8.15 N	11.00 E
Kama, Mya.	110	19.02 N	95.06 E
Kama, Ross.	80	56.19 N	54.06 E
Kama, Ross.	86	60.08 N	62.10 E
Kama, Zaïre	154	3.32 S	27.07 E
Kama ≃, Ross.	72	55.45 N	52.00 E
Kama ≃, Ross.	86	55.35 N	76.54 E
Kamachumu	154	1.35 S	31.37 E
Kamado-zaki ›	96	33.04 N	132.02 E
Kamae	92	32.48 N	131.56 E
Kamagaya	94	35.45 N	140.01 E
Kamaiki Point ›	229a	20.46 N	156.50 W
Kamaishi	92	39.16 N	141.53 E
Kama-iwa I	174f	24.47 N	141.17 E
Kamajai	76	55.49 N	25.30 E
Kamakou ∧	229a	21.07 N	156.52 W
Kamakura	94	35.19 N	139.33 E
Kamakwie	150	9.30 N	12.14 W
Kamal	115a	7.10 S	112.42 E
Kamālia	123	30.44 N	72.39 E
Kamamaung	110	17.21 N	97.40 E
Kāman, India	124	27.39 N	77.16 E
Kaman, Tür.	130	39.22 N	33.44 E
Kaman ≃	110	14.48 N	106.51 E
Kamana	154	5.59 S	24.56 E
Kamanashi ≃	94	35.33 N	138.28 E
Kamango	154	0.39 N	29.53 E
Kamaniskeg Lake ⊜	212	45.25 N	77.42 W
Kamanjab	156	19.35 S	14.51 E
Kamapanda	152	12.00 S	24.10 E
Kamara Forest ♠	264c	47.26 N	19.00 E
Kamarān I	144	15.21 N	42.35 E
Kamaran, Hadjer ∧	146	12.41 N	21.46 E
Kamarang ≃	246	5.53 N	60.35 W
Kāmāreddi	122	18.19 N	78.21 E
Kāmārhāti	272b	22.40 N	88.22 E
Kamarik	130	39.37 N	39.18 E
Kāmārkhāli Ghāt	126	23.32 N	89.33 E
Kāmārkunda	272b	22.49 N	88.13 E
Kamas	200	40.38 N	111.16 W
Kamata ◆[8]	268	35.33 N	139.43 E
Kamatsi Lake ⊜	184	56.10 N	102.15 W
Kamay	196	33.51 N	98.48 W
Kamba	150	11.53 N	3.36 E
Kamba Kota	152	7.10 N	17.54 E
Kambalda	162	31.12 S	121.40 E
Kambam	122	9.44 N	77.18 E
Kambang	112	1.42 S	100.42 E
Kambanga	152	13.23 S	23.03 E
Kambar	120	27.36 N	68.00 E
Kambara	94	35.07 N	138.36 E
Kambara Island I	175g	18.57 S	178.57 W
Kambara-tunnel ◆[5]	94	35.02 N	138.31 E
Kambarka	80	56.17 N	54.12 E
Kambia	150	9.07 N	12.55 W
Kambja	76	58.14 N	26.42 E
Kambolé	150	8.45 N	1.36 E
Kambole Mission	154	8.46 S	30.46 E
Kambove	154	10.52 S	26.38 E
Kambu	115b	8.23 S	118.20 E
Kambuye	152	7.18 S	22.50 E
Kamčatka ≃	74	56.15 N	162.30 E
Kamčatka, poluostrov (Kamchatka) ›[1]	74	56.00 N	160.00 E
Kamčatskij poluostrov ›[1]	74	56.15 N	163.00 E
Kamčatskij zaliv ⊂	74	55.35 N	162.21 E
Kamchatka → Kamčatka, poluostrov ›[1]	74	56.00 N	160.00 E
Kâmchay Méa	110	11.35 N	105.40 E
Kamčija ≃	38	43.02 N	27.53 E
Kāmdebpur, India	272b	22.47 N	88.30 E
Kāmdebpur, India	272b	22.54 N	88.20 E
Kāmdeysh	123	35.24 N	71.20 E
Kameari ◆[8]	268	35.46 N	139.51 E
Kameda	92	37.52 N	139.07 E
Kameel	158	26.38 S	24.58 E
Kamegamori ∧	96	33.47 N	133.12 E
Kameido ◆[8]	268	35.42 N	139.50 E
Kamelik ≃	80	52.06 N	49.30 E
Kamen', Bela.	76	55.01 N	28.53 E
Kamen, Dtsch.	52	51.35 N	7.40 E
Kamen', gora ∧	74	69.06 N	94.48 E
Kamenda	154	6.28 S	24.33 E
Kamenec	76	52.24 N	23.49 E
Kamenec-Podol'skij	78	48.41 N	26.36 E
Kameng ≃	120	26.38 N	92.54 E
Kamenický Šenov	54	50.45 N	14.29 E
Kamenjak, Rt ›	36	44.46 N	13.55 E
Kamenka, Kaz.	80	51.07 N	50.19 E
Kamenka, Kaz.	85	42.55 N	72.50 E
Kamenka, Kaz.	86	52.22 N	69.04 E
Kamenka, Mol.	38	48.03 N	28.42 E
Kamenka, Ross.	24	65.54 N	44.05 E
Kamenka, Ross.	78	50.43 N	39.25 E
Kamenka, Ross.	80	56.11 N	45.35 E
Kamenka, Ross.	80	57.23 N	41.49 E
Kamenka, Ross.	80	53.13 N	44.03 E
Kamenka, Ross.	80	52.04 N	41.49 E
Kamenka, Ross.	82	54.43 N	38.19 E

≃ River	Fluß	Río	Rivière	Rio
≅ Canal	Kanal	Canal	Canal	Canal
∟ Waterfall, Rapids	Wasserfall, Stromschnellen	Cascada, Rápidos	Chute d'eau, Rapides	Cascata, Rápidos
ʮ Strait	Meeresstraße	Estrecho	Détroit	Estreito
⊂ Bay, Gulf	Bucht, Golf	Bahía, Golfo	Baie, Golfe	Baía, Golfo
⊜ Lake, Lakes	See, Seen	Lago, Lagos	Lac, Lacs	Lago, Lagos
≡ Swamp	Sumpf	Pantano	Marais	Pântano
⍓ Ice Features, Glacier	Eis- und Gletscherformen	Accidentes Glaciales	Formes glaciaires	Acidentes glaciares
⍑ Other Hydrographic Features	Andere Hydrographische Objekte	Otros Elementos Hidrográficos	Autres données hydrographiques	Outros acidentes hidrográficos

✧ Submarine Features	Untermeerische Objekte	Accidentes Submarinos	Formes de relief sous-marin	Acidentes submarinos
□ Political Unit	Politische Einheit	Unidad Politica	Entité politique	Unidade política
ʊ Cultural Institution	Kulturelle Institution	Institución Cultural	Institution culturelle	Institução cultural
⊥ Historical Site	Historische Stätte	Sitio Histórico	Site historique	Sítio histórico
♠ Recreational Site	Erholungs- und Ferienort	Sitio de Recreo	Centre de loisirs	Área de Lazer
⊠ Airport	Flughafen	Aeropuerto	Aéroport	Aeroporto
■ Military Installation	Militäranlage	Instalación Militar	Installation militaire	Instalação militar
◆ Miscellaneous	Verschiedenes	Misceláneo	Divers	Diversos

Name	Page	Lat.°′	Long.°′
Kamenka, Ross.	82	56.11 N	37.18 E
Kamenka, Ross.	82	55.13 N	36.59 E
Kamenka, Ross.	86	58.33 N	95.51 E
Kamenka, Ross.	89	44.28 N	136.01 E
Kamenka, Ross.	265a	59.59 N	30.53 E
Kamenka, Ukr.	78	49.02 N	32.06 E
Kamenka, Ukr.	83	49.38 N	39.22 E
Kamenka, Ukr.	83	49.07 N	37.18 E
Kamenka, Ukr.	83	47.25 N	37.42 E
Kamenka ◆[8]	265a	60.03 N	30.11 E
Kamenka ≐, Ross.	83	47.30 N	38.54 E
Kamenka ≐, Ross.	88	58.33 N	95.51 E
Kamenka ≐, Ross.	265a	60.01 N	30.12 E
Kamenka ≐, Ukr.	78	49.47 N	30.01 E
Kamenka ≐, Ukr.	78	47.39 N	34.02 E
Kamenka ≐, Ukr.	83	49.35 N	39.05 E
Kamenka-Bugskaja	78	50.07 N	24.20 E
Kamenka-Dneprovskaja	78	47.29 N	34.25 E
Kamen'-Kaširskij	78	51.38 N	24.58 E
Kamen'-na-Obi	86	53.47 N	81.20 E
Kamennogorsk	24	60.58 N	29.07 E
Kamennoje, Ukr.	78	51.31 N	27.38 E
Kamennoje, Ukr.	78	47.53 N	35.25 E
Kamennomostskij	84	44.18 N	40.12 E
Kamennye Mogily, zapovednik ♠	78	47.18 N	37.04 E
Kamennyj Brod, Ross.	83	47.26 N	39.51 E
Kamennyj Brod, Ukr.	78	50.25 N	27.49 E
Kamennyj Jar	80	48.27 N	45.34 E
Kamenolomni	83	47.40 N	40.13 E
Kamen'-Rybolov	89	44.46 N	132.02 E
Kamensk	88	51.58 N	106.36 E
Kamenskij	80	50.53 N	45.29 E
Kamenskoje, Ross.	74	62.30 N	166.12 E
Kamenskoje, Ross.	82	55.16 N	36.50 E
Kamenskoje, Ukr.	78	45.49 N	29.16 E
Kamensk-Šachtinskij	83	48.21 N	40.19 E
Kamensk-Ural'skij	86	56.28 N	61.54 E
Kamenz	54	51.16 N	14.06 E
Kameoka	96	35.00 N	135.35 E
Kamerik	52	52.06 N	4.54 E
Kamerun → Cameroon □[1]	134	6.00 N	12.00 E
Kamerunberg → Cameroon Mountain ∧	152	4.12 N	9.11 E
Kames	46	55.54 N	5.15 W
Kameškovo	80	56.21 N	41.00 E
Kāmet ∧	120	30.54 N	79.37 E
Kameur, Bahr ≐	146	9.26 N	20.50 E
Kameyama	94	34.51 N	136.27 E
Kami, Nihon	94	34.41 N	137.42 E
Kami, Nihon	96	35.05 N	134.53 E
Kamiah	202	46.13 N	116.01 W
Kamiak Butte ∧	202	46.52 N	117.10 W
Kamiakotani	270	34.56 N	135.23 E
Kamiasō	268	35.35 N	139.30 E
Kamień Krajeńskie	30	53.33 N	17.32 E
Kamienna ≐	30	51.06 N	21.47 E
Kamienna Góra	30	50.47 N	16.01 E
Kamień Pomorski	30	53.58 N	14.46 E
Kamieńsk	30	51.12 N	19.30 E
Kamieskroon	156	30.09 S	17.56 E
Kamifukuoka	94	35.52 N	139.32 E
Kamigōri	96	34.52 N	134.22 E
Kamigyō ◆[8]	270	35.02 N	135.45 E
Kamiichi	94	36.42 N	137.22 E
Kamiishihara	268	35.39 N	139.32 E
Kamiiso	92a	41.49 N	140.39 E
Kamiita	96	34.07 N	134.24 E
Kami-jima I	94	34.33 N	136.59 E
Kamikamagari-jima I	96	34.11 N	132.44 E
Kamikatsu	96	33.53 N	134.24 E
Kamikawa, Nihon	92a	43.51 N	142.46 E
Kamikawa, Nihon	94	36.13 N	139.07 E
Kamikitazawa ◆[8]	268	35.40 N	139.38 E
Kamikume	270	34.55 N	135.03 E
Kâmil	130	41.07 N	34.47 E
Kamilukuak Lake ⊜	176	62.22 N	101.40 W
Kamimaki	270	34.34 N	135.43 E
Kamimizo	268	35.33 N	139.22 E
Kamina	154	8.44 S	25.00 E
Kaminaka, Nihon	94	35.28 N	135.51 E
Kaminaka, Nihon	96	33.48 N	134.22 E
Kaminak Lake ⊜	176	62.10 N	95.00 W
Kaminaljuyú ⊥	236	14.38 N	90.33 W
Kaminoho	94	35.37 N	137.03 E
Kaminokawa	94	36.26 N	139.55 E
Kaminokuni	92a	41.48 N	140.06 E
Kaminoseki	96	33.49 N	132.07 E
Kaminoyama	92	38.09 N	140.17 E
Kaminskij	80	57.10 N	41.28 E
Kaminuriak Lake ⊜	176	63.00 N	95.40 W
Kamioka	94	36.16 N	137.18 E
Kamiotawa	270	34.54 N	135.31 E
Kamioyamada	268	35.35 N	139.24 E
Kámiros ⊥	38	36.19 N	27.57 E
Kamisato	94	36.15 N	139.09 E
Kamishak Bay c	180	59.15 N	153.45 W
Kamishii	94	36.04 N	136.24 E
Kamishinden	270	34.49 N	135.30 E
Kamisunagawa	92a	43.30 N	142.00 E
Kamitaira	94	36.24 N	136.54 E
Kamitakara	94	36.17 N	137.22 E
Kamitakino	270	34.57 N	134.59 E
Kamitomi	268	35.49 N	139.31 E
Kamitonda	96	33.43 N	135.27 E
Kamitsuruma	268	35.31 N	139.25 E
Kamitsushima	92	34.50 N	129.28 E
Kamituga	154	3.04 S	28.11 E
Kamiura	96	33.03 N	131.55 E
Kamiyahagi	94	35.18 N	137.29 E
Kamiyama	96	33.58 N	134.23 E
Kamiyamada	94	36.28 N	138.09 E
Kamiyama-jima I	174m	26.15 N	127.35 E
Kamiyugi	268	35.37 N	139.23 E
Kamīzgān	84	38.58 N	47.44 E
Kamkhat Muḥaywir ∧[2]	132	31.08 N	36.30 E
Kamku	120	27.30 N	96.30 E
Kamla (Kamlā) ≐	124	25.37 N	86.40 E
Kamlach ≐	58	48.30 N	10.22 E
Kamloops	182	50.40 N	120.20 W
Kamloops Indian Reserve ◆[4]	182	50.42 N	120.20 W
Kamloops Lake ⊜	182	50.43 N	120.33 W
Kammon-kaikyō ⩌	96	33.56 N	130.56 E
Kammon-kyō ◆[5]	96	33.56 N	130.55 E
Kammuri-yama ∧	96	34.28 N	132.05 E
Kamnik	36	46.13 N	14.37 E
Kamniokan	88	56.17 N	111.57 E
Kamo, Haya.	84	40.22 N	45.08 E
Kamo, N.Z.	172	35.41 S	174.19 E
Kamo, Nihon	92	37.39 N	139.03 E
Kamo, Nihon	94	34.50 N	138.46 E
Kamo, Nihon	96	34.45 N	135.52 E
Kamo, Nihon	96	35.10 N	134.04 E
Kamo, Nihon	96	35.20 N	132.55 E
Kamo, Nihon	270	34.55 N	135.13 E
Kamo ≐, Nihon	94	35.06 N	140.06 E
Kamo ≐, Nihon	96	33.56 N	133.09 E
Kamo ≐, Nihon	270	34.56 N	135.44 E
Kamoa Mountains ⩘	246	1.37 N	59.00 W
Kamoda-misaki ›	96	33.50 N	134.45 E
Kamogata	96	34.32 N	133.35 E
Kamogawa, Nihon	94	35.06 N	140.06 E
Kamogawa, Nihon	96	34.51 N	133.49 E
Kamohio Bay c	229a	20.31 N	156.36 W
Kamojima	96	34.04 N	134.21 E
Kāmoke	123	31.58 N	74.13 E
Kamoshida ◆[8]	268	35.34 N	139.30 E
Kamoto	96	33.00 N	130.45 E
Kamp	56	50.14 N	7.37 E
Kamp ≐	61	48.23 N	15.48 E
Kāmpa	272b	22.56 N	88.28 E
Kampala	154	0.19 N	32.25 E
Kampar	114	4.18 N	101.09 E
Kampar ≐	112	0.32 N	103.08 E
Kamparkalns ∧[2]	76	57.18 N	22.47 E
Kampar Kanan ≐	112	0.16 N	101.41 E
Kampen	52	52.33 N	5.54 E
Kampene	154	3.36 S	26.40 E
Kampfe, Lake ⊜	276	41.02 N	74.21 W
Kamphaeng, Khao ∧	110	14.37 N	99.18 E
Kamphaeng Phet	110	16.28 N	99.30 E
Kampil	124	27.37 N	79.17 E
Kampinoski Park Narodowy ♠	30	52.20 N	20.35 E
Kampire Dior ∧	123	36.38 N	74.23 E
Kamp-Lintfort	52	51.30 N	6.31 E
Kamp'o	98	35.48 N	129.29 E
Kampolombo, Lake ⊜	154	11.37 S	29.42 E
Kampong Ayer Puteh	114	4.16 N	103.12 E
Kampong Baharu	114	3.43 N	103.17 E
Kampong Benta	114	3.32 N	103.22 E
Kampong Buloh	114	5.32 N	102.45 E
Kâmpóng Cham	110	12.00 N	105.27 E
Kampong Chenor	114	3.29 N	102.36 E
Kâmpóng Chhnăng	110	12.15 N	104.40 E
Kampong Dong	114	3.54 N	101.54 E
Kampong Guchil	114	5.33 N	102.14 E
Kampong Jabor	114	3.57 N	103.20 E
Kampong Jerangau	114	4.51 N	103.12 E
Kampong Kandang	114	2.11 N	102.18 E
Kâmpóng Kântuŏt	110	11.26 N	104.49 E
Kampong Kenyam	114	4.31 N	102.28 E
Kampong Kuala Kemaman	114	4.14 N	103.27 E
Kampong Lamir	114	3.36 N	103.21 E
Kampong Lawa	114	5.40 N	101.42 E
Kampong Mengkarak	114	3.19 N	102.27 E
Kampong Merang	114	5.32 N	102.57 E
Kampong Nuri	114	5.02 N	102.23 E
Kampong Penarek	114	5.37 N	102.48 E
Kampong Raja	114	5.48 N	102.35 E
Kampong Renggong	114	4.33 N	102.35 E
Kâmpóng Saôm	110	10.38 N	103.30 E
Kâmpóng Saôm, Chhâk c	110	10.50 N	103.32 E
Kampong Sebuyau	112	1.31 N	110.56 E
Kampong Sekendi	114	3.43 N	100.56 E
Kampong Surau	114	5.49 N	100.54 E
Kampong Tanjong Batu	114	3.12 N	103.27 E
Kampong Tebing Runtoh	271c	1.26 N	103.40 E
Kâmpóng Thum	110	12.42 N	104.54 E
Kâmpóng Trâlach	110	11.54 N	104.47 E
Kampong Ulu	110	10.03 N	98.33 E
Kampong Ulu Chalok	114	5.26 N	102.50 E
Kâmpôt	110	10.37 N	104.11 E
Kampsville	194	39.18 N	90.37 W
Kampti	150	10.08 N	3.27 W
Kâmpŭchéa → Cambodia □[1]	110	13.00 N	105.00 E
Kampung ≐	164	5.44 S	138.24 E
Kampungbaru	112	1.12 S	102.57 E
Kampville	219	38.51 N	90.33 W
Kāmrānga	126	23.14 N	90.47 E
Kamrau, Teluk c	164	3.32 S	133.37 E
Kamsack	184	51.34 N	101.54 W
Kamsdorf	54	50.38 N	11.28 E
Kamskij	24	60.04 N	53.13 E
Kamskoje Ustje	80	55.13 N	49.16 E
Kamskoje vodochranilišče ⊜[1]	86	58.52 N	56.15 E
Kamslybas, ozero ⊜	86	46.12 N	61.48 E
Kamsu-ri	98	38.03 N	125.54 E
Kamsuuma	144	0.15 N	42.47 E
Kāmthi	120	21.14 N	79.12 E
Kam Tin	271d	22.27 N	114.03 E
Kamuchawie Lake ⊜	184	56.18 N	101.59 W
Kamudilo	154	7.42 S	27.18 E
Kamuela (Waimea)	229d	20.01 N	155.48 W
Kamui-misaki ›	92a	43.20 N	140.21 E
Kámuk, Cerro ∧	236	9.17 N	83.04 W
Kamuli	154	0.57 N	33.07 E
Kamundan ≐	164	2.17 S	132.39 E
Kamutambaie ≐	152	7.17 S	23.41 E
Kamwandu	152	6.04 S	22.42 E
Kamyšet	88	55.12 N	98.42 E
Kamyšev, Ross.	80	46.39 N	42.38 E
Kamyšev, Ross.	80	46.53 N	42.31 E
Kamyševacha, Ukr.	78	47.43 N	35.32 E
Kamyševacha, Ukr.	83	48.42 N	38.23 E
Kamyševatskaja	78	46.25 N	37.57 E
Kamyševskaja	80	47.37 N	41.49 E
Kamyšin	80	50.06 N	45.24 E
Kamyškurgon	85	40.34 N	70.24 E
Kamyšla	80	54.07 N	52.10 E
Kamyšlov	86	56.52 N	62.43 E
Kamyslybas	86	46.11 N	61.57 E
Kamyšnaja ≐	83	48.55 N	39.55 E
Kamyšnoje	86	51.58 N	61.47 E
Kamyšovyj	80	46.26 N	45.12 E
Kamyš-Samarskich Ozer, razlivy ≡	80	48.50 N	50.50 E
Kamyz'ak	80	46.07 N	48.05 E
Kamyz'ak ≐	80	46.00 N	48.06 E
Kan, Īrān	128	35.45 N	51.16 E
Kan, Sūd.	140	9.01 N	31.47 E
Kan ≐	86	56.31 N	93.47 E
Kana ≐	154	18.30 S	27.22 E
Kanaaupscow ≐	176	53.39 N	77.09 W
Kanab	200	37.02 N	112.31 W
Kanab Creek ≐	200	36.24 N	112.38 W
Kanab Plateau ⩘[1]	200	36.40 N	112.45 W
Kanada	96	33.41 N	130.47 E
Kanada → Canada □[1]	176	60.00 N	95.00 W
Kanadej	80	53.10 N	47.30 E
Kanae	94	35.30 N	137.49 E
Kanafis	140	9.48 N	25.40 E
Kanaga Island I	180	51.45 N	177.10 W
Kanaga Volcano ∧[1]	180	51.50 N	177.09 W
Kanagawa □[5]	94	35.30 N	139.30 E
Kanagawa ◆[8]	268	35.28 N	139.38 E
Kanagi	96	34.53 N	132.11 E
Kanai	268	35.35 N	139.28 E
Kānāipur	126	23.33 N	89.47 E
Kanairiktok ≐	176	55.05 N	60.20 W
Kanā'is, Ra's al- ›	140	31.15 N	27.51 E
Kanajevka, Ross.	80	53.07 N	45.35 E
Kanajevka, Ross.	80	52.12 N	49.40 E
Kanaka Creek ≐	226	39.25 N	120.57 W
Kanakapura	122	12.33 N	77.25 E
Kanakeswar	126	23.09 N	90.25 E
Kanākir	132	33.15 N	36.05 E
Kanal	64	46.05 N	13.38 E
Kanal-Inseln → Channel Islands II	28	49.20 N	2.20 W
Kanam	164	3.25 S	152.10 E
Kanamachi ◆[8]	268	35.46 N	139.53 E
Kanamori	268	35.32 N	139.28 E
Kanan	270	34.29 N	135.38 E
Kananaskis ≐	182	51.05 N	115.03 W
Kananga (Luluabourg)	152	5.54 S	22.25 E
Kananggar	115b	10.03 S	120.22 E
Kanangra-Boyd National Park ♠	170	34.00 S	150.06 E
Kananikol'skoje	86	52.47 N	57.29 E
Kanaoka	270	34.33 N	135.32 E
Kanapou Bay c	229a	20.33 N	156.33 W
Kanarase-yama ∧	96	33.26 N	131.15 E
Kanarraville	200	37.32 N	113.10 W
Kanaš	80	55.31 N	47.30 E
Kanasagō	94	36.33 N	140.28 E
Kanata	212	45.19 N	75.54 W
Kanaudi	124	23.36 N	81.23 E
Kanava, Ross.	24	61.07 N	54.58 E
Kanava, Ross.	80	47.13 N	45.24 E
Kanavka	80	50.19 N	48.33 E
Kanawha	190	42.56 N	93.47 W
Kanawha ≐	188	38.50 N	82.08 W
Kanaya, Nihon	94	34.49 N	138.08 E
Kanaya, Nihon	94	34.04 N	135.15 E
Kanaya, Nihon	268	35.10 N	139.50 E
Kanaya, Nihon	94	35.39 N	137.09 E
Kanazawa	94	36.34 N	136.39 E
Kanazawa ◆[8]	268	35.20 N	139.38 E
Kanazu	94	36.13 N	136.14 E
Kanbalu	110	23.12 N	95.31 E
Kanbauk	110	14.36 N	98.02 E
Kančalan ≐	180	65.08 N	176.25 E
Kanchanaburi	110	14.01 N	99.32 E
Kanchanadit	110	9.10 N	99.28 E
Kānchenjunga (Kañchanjanggā) ∧	124	27.42 N	88.08 E
Kānchipuram	122	12.50 N	79.43 E
Kanchow → Ganzhou	100	25.54 N	114.55 E
Kānchrāpāra	126	22.57 N	88.28 E
Kańczuga	30	49.59 N	22.24 E
Kanda	96	33.47 N	130.59 E
Kanda ◆[8]	268	35.42 N	139.46 E
Kandabulak	80	53.58 N	50.44 E
Kandāghāt	123	30.59 N	77.07 E
Kandahar	184	51.46 N	104.21 W
Kandāhu	120	27.33 N	69.24 E
Kanda-Kanda	152	6.56 S	23.36 E
Kandala	152	6.02 S	19.24 E
Kandalakša	24	67.09 N	32.21 E
Kandalakšskaja guba c	24	66.55 N	32.45 E
Kandalakšskij zapovednik ♠	24	68.50 N	37.30 E
Kandang	114	3.03 N	97.20 E
Kandangan	112	2.47 S	115.16 E
Kandanghaur	115a	6.21 S	108.06 E
Kandat	86	57.08 N	89.02 E
Kandava	76	57.05 N	22.49 E
Kandavu Island I	175g	19.03 S	178.13 E
Kandavu Passage ⩌	175g	18.45 S	178.00 E
Kandé	150	9.57 N	1.03 E
Kandel	56	49.05 N	8.11 E
Kandel ∧	58	48.04 N	8.01 E
Kander ≐	58	46.43 N	7.38 E
Kandern	58	47.43 N	7.40 E
Kandersteg	58	46.30 N	7.40 E
Kandhkot	120	28.14 N	69.11 E
Kāndhla	124	29.19 N	77.16 E
Kandi, Bénin	150	11.08 N	2.56 E
Kandi, India	126	23.57 N	88.02 E
Kandi, Tanjung ›	112	1.19 N	121.28 E
Kandia ≐	123	35.28 N	73.18 E
Kandiāro	120	27.04 N	68.13 E
Kandik ≐	180	65.24 N	142.34 W
Kandilli ◆[8]	267b	41.04 N	29.03 E
Kandıra	130	41.04 N	30.09 E
Kandivli ◆[8]	272c	19.12 N	72.51 E
Kandla	120	23.02 N	70.14 E
Kando ≐	96	35.22 N	132.40 E
Kandor, Ouadi V	146	17.13 N	20.52 E
Kandos	170	32.52 S	149.58 E
Kāndra	126	23.44 N	87.58 E
Kandrāch	120	25.29 N	65.29 E
Kandreho	157b	17.29 S	46.06 E
Kandrian	164	6.15 S	149.35 E
Kandry	80	54.34 N	54.07 E
Kandufuri I	122	7.05 N	72.48 E
Kandute I	122	6.20 N	72.57 E
Kandy	122	7.18 N	80.38 E
Kane, Il., U.S.	219	39.11 N	90.21 W
Kane, Pa., U.S.	214	41.39 N	78.48 W
Kane □[6]	216	41.53 N	88.18 W
Kaneda	268	35.28 N	139.22 E
Kaneilio Point ›	229c	21.27 N	158.12 W
Kanektok ≐	180	59.45 N	161.55 W
Kanem □[5]	146	15.00 N	16.00 E
Kanemi	116	6.55 N	123.58 E
Kaneohe	229c	21.25 N	157.48 W
Kaneohe Bay c	229c	21.28 N	157.49 W
Kaneohe Bay Marine Corps Air Station ■	229c	21.27 N	157.46 W
Kaneville	216	41.50 N	88.31 W
Kanevskaja	78	46.05 N	38.57 E
Kaneyama	94	35.28 N	137.06 E
Kanfanar	64	45.07 N	13.51 E
Kang	156	23.41 S	22.50 E
Kangaba	150	11.56 N	8.25 W
Kangal	130	39.15 N	37.24 E
Kangalassy	74	62.23 N	129.59 E
Kangān	128	27.50 N	52.03 E
Kānganheri ◆[8]	272a	28.33 N	76.59 E
Kanganpur	123	30.46 N	74.08 E
Kangar	114	6.26 N	100.12 E
Kangaré	150	11.35 N	8.10 W
Kangarilla	168b	35.09 S	138.40 E
Kangaroo ≐	170	34.46 S	150.18 E
Kangaroo Creek Reservoir ⊜[1]	168b	34.52 S	138.46 E
Kangaroo Flat	168b	34.33 S	138.40 E
Kangaroo Ground	274b	37.41 S	145.13 E
Kangaroo Island I	166	35.50 S	137.06 E
Kangaroo Valley	170	34.44 S	150.32 E
Kangasala	26	61.28 N	24.05 E
Kangasniemi	26	61.59 N	26.38 E
Kangāvar	128	34.30 N	47.58 E
Kangaz	38	46.07 N	28.33 E
Kangbao	98	41.53 N	114.40 E
Kangding	102	30.03 N	102.02 E
Kangdong	98	39.09 N	126.05 E
Kangdu	100	27.00 N	116.36 E
Kangean, Kepulauan II	112	6.55 S	115.30 E
Kangean, Pulau I	112	6.54 S	115.20 E
Kangen ≐	140	6.47 N	33.09 E
Kanggezhuang	105	40.26 N	116.44 E
Kanggup'o	98	41.07 N	127.31 E
Kanggye	98	40.58 N	126.34 E
Kanggyŏng	98	36.10 N	127.00 E
Kanghwa	98	37.45 N	126.30 E
Kanghwa-do I	98	37.40 N	126.27 E
Kanghwa-man c	98	37.20 N	126.35 E
Kangil	88	52.15 N	116.20 E
Kangiqsualujjuaq	176	58.41 N	65.57 W
Kangiqsujuaq	176	61.36 N	71.58 W
Kangirsuk	176	60.01 N	70.01 W
Kangjin	98	34.39 N	126.45 E
Kangjinjing	89	46.12 N	126.48 E
Kangkar Lenggor	114	2.16 N	103.44 E
Kangkar Teberau	114	1.32 N	103.45 E
Kangley	216	41.09 N	88.53 W
Kangly	85	40.07 N	67.54 E
Kangmaer	124	30.45 N	85.34 E
Kangmar	120	28.34 N	89.51 E
Kangnam ◆[8]	271b	37.30 N	127.01 E
Kangnam-sanmaek ⩘	98	40.30 N	125.30 E
Kangnichumike	120	33.10 N	80.59 E
Kangnŭng	98	37.45 N	128.54 E
Kango	152	0.09 N	10.08 E
Kangoku-iwa I	174f	24.48 N	141.17 E
Kangombe	152	14.03 S	23.40 E
Kangongo	152	17.57 S	21.02 E
Kangowa	152	9.55 S	22.48 E
Kangping	98	42.44 N	123.21 E
Kāngpokpi	120	25.08 N	93.58 E
Kangpu	102	27.43 N	99.00 E
Kāngra	123	32.06 N	76.16 E
Kangrinboqê Feng ∧	120	31.04 N	81.18 E
Kangshan	100	22.48 N	120.17 E
Kangsŏ	98	38.58 N	125.26 E
Kangsŏ-ri	98	38.06 N	126.58 E
Kangto ∧	120	27.52 N	92.30 E
Kangtuyingzi	104	41.47 N	121.31 E
Känguruh-Insel → Kangaroo Island I	166	35.50 S	137.06 E
Kangwŏn Do □[4], C.M.I.K.	98	38.45 N	127.35 E
Kangwŏn Do □[4], Taehan	98	37.45 N	128.15 E
Kangxianzhuang	105	39.06 N	116.27 E
Kangyidaung	110	16.56 N	94.54 E
Kangzhuang	105	40.23 N	115.53 E
Kanhar ≐	124	24.28 N	83.08 E
Kanheri Caves ◆[5]	272c	19.13 N	72.52 E
Kanholmsfjärden ⩌	40	59.20 N	18.47 E
Kanhsien → Ganzhou	100	25.54 N	114.55 E
Kani, C. Iv.	150	8.29 N	6.36 W
Kani, Mya.	110	22.26 N	94.50 E
Kani, Nihon	94	35.22 N	137.04 E
Kaniama	152	7.31 S	24.11 E
Kaniamba	154	7.27 S	26.57 E
Kanibadam	85	40.17 N	70.25 E
Kanie	94	35.08 N	136.48 E
Kaniepa	154	9.00 S	27.21 E
Kaniere	172	42.45 S	171.00 E
Kaniere, Lake ⊜	172	42.50 S	171.09 E
Kaniet Islands II	164	0.53 S	145.30 E
Kanifay	174q	9.32 N	138.06 E
Kanigiri	122	15.24 N	79.31 E
Kanihāula ◆[8]	272a	28.44 N	77.01 E
Kanin	54	52.17 N	12.50 E
Kanin, poluostrov ›[1]	24	68.00 N	45.00 E
Kanina	124	28.20 N	76.19 E
Kaningo	154	0.49 S	38.32 E
Kanin-Kamen' ∧	24	68.18 N	45.00 E
Kanin Nos	24	68.39 N	43.14 E
Kanin Nos, mys ›	24	68.39 N	43.16 E
Kaniva	166	36.23 S	141.15 E
Kanjiža	38	46.04 N	20.04 E
Kānjur ◆[8]	272c	19.08 N	72.56 E
Kanjut Sār ∧	123	36.14 N	75.22 E
Kankaanpää	26	61.48 N	22.25 E
Kankakee	216	41.07 N	87.51 W
Kankakee □[6]	216	41.07 N	87.52 W
Kankakee ≐	216	41.23 N	88.16 W
Kankakee River State Park ♠	216	41.12 N	87.59 W
Kankan	150	10.23 N	9.18 W
Kankar ◆[8]	272a	28.46 N	77.06 E
Kankéla	150	10.50 N	6.40 W
Kānker	122	20.17 N	81.29 E
Kankō → Hamhŭng	98	39.54 N	127.32 E
Kankossa	150	15.56 N	11.31 W
Kankunskij	74	57.37 N	126.08 E
Kanlıavşar	130	37.13 N	38.16 E
Kanlıca ◆[8]	267b	41.06 N	29.04 E
Kanmaw Kyun I	110	11.40 N	98.28 E
Kanmen	100	28.06 N	121.16 E
Kanmuri-jima I	96	35.41 N	135.25 E
Kanmuri-yama ∧	92	34.28 N	132.05 E
Kanna ≐	94	36.17 N	139.09 E
Kannabe	96	34.32 N	133.23 E
Kannabi-san ∧[2]	270	34.48 N	135.44 E
Kannack	110	14.07 N	108.37 E
Kannad	122	20.16 N	75.08 E
Kanna-kō c	174m	26.28 N	127.58 E
Kannami	94	35.05 N	138.57 E
Kannapolis	192	35.29 N	80.37 W
Kannauj	124	27.04 N	79.55 E
Kanniyākumari	122	8.05 N	77.34 E
Kannod	124	22.40 N	76.44 E
Kannonkoski	26	62.58 N	25.15 E
Kannon-zaki ›	268	35.15 N	139.45 E
Kannose ≐	96	34.54 N	132.49 E
Kannus	26	63.54 N	23.54 E
Kano, Nig.	150	12.00 N	8.30 E
Kano, Nihon	96	34.14 N	131.49 E
Kano □[3]	150	11.45 N	9.00 E
Kano ≐, Nig.	150	11.50 N	8.31 E
Kano ≐, Nihon	94	35.05 N	138.52 E
Kanona	210	42.22 N	77.22 W
Kanoneiland	158	28.39 S	21.05 E
Kanonerskij, ostrov I	265a	59.54 N	30.13 E
Kanonji	96	34.07 N	133.39 E
Kanopolis	198	38.42 N	98.09 W
Kanopolis Lake ⊜[1]	198	38.38 N	98.00 W
Kanorado	198	39.19 N	102.02 W
Kanosh	200	38.48 N	112.26 W
Kanouse Brook ≐	276	41.02 N	74.26 W
Kanouse Mountain ∧	276	41.04 N	74.25 W
Kan'ov	78	49.44 N	31.28 E
Kan'ovka	24	67.08 N	39.40 E
Kanovlei	156	19.10 S	19.23 E
Kan'ovskoje vodochranilišče ⊜[1]	78	50.00 N	31.20 E
Kanowit	112	2.06 N	112.09 E
Kanoya	92	31.23 N	130.51 E
Kanō-zan ∧[2]	268	35.15 N	139.57 E
Kanpetlet	110	21.12 N	94.02 E
Kanpoli	272c	19.04 N	73.09 E
Kānpur	124	26.28 N	80.21 E
Kanra	94	36.13 N	138.55 E
Kansa ≐	94	34.55 N	137.34 E
Kansaj	85	40.30 N	69.41 E
Kansanshi	154	12.05 S	26.26 E
Kānsāripāra	272b	22.56 N	88.14 E
Kansas, Il., U.S.	194	39.33 N	87.56 W
Kansas, Oh., U.S.	214	41.14 N	83.17 W
Kansas □[3], U.S.	178	38.45 N	98.15 W
Kansas □[3], U.S.	198	38.45 N	98.15 W
Kansas ≐	198	39.07 N	94.36 W
Kansas City, Ks., U.S.	198	39.06 N	94.37 W
Kansas City, Mo., U.S.	194	39.05 N	94.34 W
Kansau	110	23.50 N	93.35 E
Kansei Gakuin University ⚘[2]	270	34.46 N	135.21 E
Kansei University ⚘[2]	270	34.46 N	135.31 E
Kansenia	154	10.19 S	26.02 E
Kanshan	106	30.12 N	120.25 E
Kanshi	100	24.56 N	116.54 E
Kansk	86	56.13 N	95.41 E
Kansŏng	98	38.22 N	128.29 E
Kansu	85	39.45 N	75.02 E
Kansu → Gansu □[4]	102	37.00 N	103.00 E
Kansyat	164	2.15 S	138.51 E
Kant	85	42.55 N	74.55 E
Kantabrisches Gebirge → Cantábrica, Cordillera ⩘	34	43.00 N	5.00 W
Kantalvi	272c	18.54 N	73.03 E
Kantang	110	7.25 N	99.31 E
Kāntāphor	124	22.35 N	76.34 E
Kantchari	150	12.29 N	1.31 E
Kantché	150	13.33 N	8.28 E
Kantemirovka, Kaz.	85	42.51 N	70.20 E
Kantemirovka, Ross.	83	49.41 N	39.51 E
Kānth	124	29.04 N	78.38 E
Kantharalak	110	14.39 N	104.39 E
Kānthi Coastal Plain ≚	126	21.45 N	87.45 E
Kantishna ≐	180	64.45 N	149.58 W
Kantner	214	40.06 N	78.56 W
Kantō-heiya ≚	94	36.00 N	139.30 E
Kanton → Guangzhou	100	23.06 N	113.16 E
Kanton (Canton) I	174h	2.50 S	171.40 W
Kantorp	40	59.01 N	16.28 E
Kantō-sanchi ⩘, Nihon	92	35.50 N	138.50 E
Kantō-sanchi ⩘, Nihon	94	35.59 N	138.43 E
Kantuanji	100	32.59 N	116.19 E
Kantubek	86	45.07 N	59.16 E
Kantu-long	110	19.57 N	97.36 E
Kantunilkin	232	21.06 N	87.29 W
Kanturk	48	52.10 N	8.55 W
Kanuku Mountains ⩘	246	3.12 N	59.30 W
Kanuma	94	36.33 N	139.44 E
Kanus	156	27.54 S	18.40 E
Kanuti ≐	180	66.26 N	153.02 W
Kan'utino	76	55.33 N	33.14 E
Kanye	156	24.59 S	25.19 E
Kanygtokynmangkyn, laguna c	180	69.20 N	178.45 E
Kanyu	156	20.05 S	24.39 E
Kanyutkwin	110	18.19 N	96.34 E
Kanzaki ◆[8]	270	34.42 N	135.25 E
Kanzanavolok	24	62.23 N	36.58 E
Kanzenze	154	10.31 S	25.12 E
Kanzi	98	39.34 N	122.39 E

ENGLISH Name	Page	Lat.°′	Long.°′
Kaohiung → Kaohsiung	100	22.38 N	120.17 E
Kaohsiung	100	22.38 N	120.17 E
Kaohsiunghsien	100	22.38 N	120.21 E
Kaoje	150	11.14 N	4.07 E
Kaoka Bay c	175e	9.42 S	160.40 E
Kaokoland □[5]	156	18.15 S	13.00 E
Kaoko Otavi	156	18.14 S	13.40 E
Kaoko Veld ⩘[1]	156	20.00 S	14.00 E
Kaolack	150	14.09 N	16.04 W
Kaolack □[4]	150	14.00 N	15.30 W
Kaolin	285	39.48 N	75.43 W
Kaolun → Kowloon	271d	22.18 N	114.10 E
Kaoma	154	14.47 S	24.48 E
Kaongweshi ≐	152	7.53 S	22.20 E
Kaoping → Changzhi	102	36.11 N	113.08 E
Kaoshanji	105	40.11 N	117.17 E
Kaoshanpu	100	30.54 N	114.32 E
Kaouadja ≐	140	6.45 N	24.15 E
Kaouar ◆[1]	146	19.00 N	12.40 E
Kao Valley V	158	28.54 S	18.06 E
Kapaa	229b	22.04 N	159.19 W
Kapadvanj	120	23.01 N	73.04 E
Kapahiang	112	3.39 S	102.34 E
Kapal	86	45.08 N	79.03 E
Kapalong	116	7.35 N	125.42 E
Kapan	112	9.44 S	124.17 E
Kapanga, Zaïre	152	8.21 S	22.35 E
Kapanga, Zaïre	152	5.04 S	16.58 E
Kapangan	116	16.35 N	120.35 E
Kapaonik ⩘	38	43.20 N	20.50 E
Kāpāsia	126	24.07 N	90.32 E
Kapatagan	116	7.52 N	123.44 E
Kapatu	154	9.43 S	30.42 E
Kapčagaj	85	43.53 N	77.12 E
Kapčagajskoje vodochranilišče ⊜[1]	86	43.50 N	78.00 E
Kapchorwa	154	1.24 N	34.27 E
Kapedo	154	1.10 N	36.06 E
Kapelle	52	51.28 N	3.58 E
Kapellen, Bel.	50	51.19 N	4.26 E
Kapellen, Dtsch.	56	51.25 N	6.35 E
Kapellen, Dtsch.	263	51.08 N	6.38 E
Kapellen, Öst.	61	47.38 N	15.37 E
Kapelle-op-den-Bos	50	51.01 N	4.22 E
Kapellerfeld	264b	48.19 N	16.30 E
Kapelln	61	48.15 N	15.45 E
Kapellskär	40	59.43 N	19.04 E
Kapema	154	10.42 S	28.24 E
Kapenguria	154	1.04 N	35.07 E
Kapfenberg	61	47.26 N	15.18 E
Kapia	152	4.17 S	19.46 E
Kapıdağ Yarımadası ›[1]	130	40.28 N	27.50 E
Kapikik Lake ⊜	184	51.32 N	91.57 W
Kapikog Lake ⊜	212	45.09 N	79.53 W
Kapilmuni	126	22.42 N	89.20 E
Kapingamarangi I[1]	14	1.04 N	154.46 E
Kapiri Mposhi	154	13.58 S	28.41 E
Kāpīsā □[4]	120	34.45 N	69.30 E
Kapiskau ≐	176	52.47 N	81.55 W
Kapit	112	2.01 N	112.56 E
Kapitanovka	78	48.54 N	31.42 E
Kapiti Island I	172	40.52 S	174.54 E
Kapiura ≐	164	5.45 S	150.35 E
Kapka, Massif du ⩘	146	15.07 N	21.45 E
Kapkataš	85	40.23 N	74.20 E
Kapkatas, chrebet ⩘	85	41.50 N	76.10 E
Kapkinka	80	48.08 N	43.51 E
Kaplan	194	29.59 N	92.17 W
Kaplice	61	48.45 N	14.30 E
Kapoe	110	9.35 N	98.40 E
Kapoeta	154	4.47 N	33.35 E
Kapona	154	7.11 S	29.09 E
Kaponga	172	39.26 S	174.09 E
Kaporskoje	265a	59.45 N	29.58 E
Kapos ≐	30	46.44 N	18.30 E
Kaposvár	30	46.22 N	17.47 E
Kaposvar Creek ≐	184	50.31 N	101.55 W
Kapotn'a ◆[8]	265b	55.38 N	37.48 E
Kapowsin	224	46.59 N	122.13 W
Kapowsin, Lake ⊜	224	46.58 N	122.13 W
Kapp	26	60.42 N	10.52 E
Kappar	128	25.19 N	62.42 E
Kappel	56	50.00 N	7.21 E
Kappeln	41	54.40 N	9.56 E
Kappelshamn	26	57.51 N	18.47 E
Kapps	156	22.22 S	17.52 E
Kapralicha	86	56.11 N	67.15 E
Kaprijke	50	51.13 N	3.36 E
Kaprun	64	47.16 N	12.46 E
Kapsabet	154	0.12 N	35.06 E
Kapsan	98	41.04 N	128.19 E
Kapstadt → Cape Town	158	33.55 S	18.22 E
Kaptai	120	22.21 N	92.17 E
Kaptipada	126	21.31 N	86.32 E
Kaptol	36	45.26 N	17.44 E
Kapuas ≐, Indon.	112	0.25 S	109.40 E
Kapuas ≐, Indon.	112	3.01 S	114.20 E
Kapuas Hulu, Pegunungan ⩘	112	1.15 N	113.30 E
Kapulo	154	8.18 S	29.15 E
Kapunda	168b	34.21 S	138.54 E
Kapūrthala	123	31.23 N	75.23 E
Kapur Utara, Pegunungan ⩘	115a	6.52 S	111.30 E
Kapuskasing	176	49.25 N	82.26 W
Kapuskasing ≐	176	49.49 N	82.00 W
Kapuskasing Lake ⊜	190	48.30 N	82.55 W
Kapustin Jar	80	48.36 N	45.45 E
Kapustino	78	48.57 N	31.14 E
Kapuvár	30	47.36 N	17.02 E
Kap Verde → Cape Verde □[1]	150a	16.00 N	24.00 W
Kapyrevščina	76	55.15 N	32.53 E
Kapytdžuch, gora ∧	84	39.13 N	46.00 E
Kara	74	69.14 N	65.00 E
Kara ≐	150	10.01 N	0.25 E
Karaali	130	39.40 N	32.57 E
Karaaul	86	48.57 N	79.15 E
Karababa Dağı ∧	130	39.31 N	36.10 E
Karabachskij chrebet ⩘	84	39.42 N	46.36 E
Karabagl'ar	84	39.26 N	45.12 E
Kara-Balta	85	42.50 N	73.52 E
Karabanovo	82	56.19 N	38.42 E
Karabaš, Ross.	80	54.42 N	52.36 E
Karabaš, Ross.	86	55.29 N	60.14 E
Karabau	80	48.26 N	52.54 E
Karabekaul	128	38.30 N	64.08 E
Karabiğa	130	40.24 N	27.18 E
Karabil', vozvyšennost' ⩘[1]	128	36.25 N	64.00 E
Kara-Bogaz-Gol, zaliv c	72	41.00 N	53.15 E
Karabudachkent	84	42.41 N	47.34 E
Karabük	130	41.12 N	32.37 E
Karabula	88	58.08 N	97.23 E
Karabula ≐	88	58.22 N	97.02 E
Karabulak, Kaz.	85	42.32 N	69.46 E
Karabulak, Kaz.	86	44.54 N	78.30 E
Karabulak, Kaz.	86	47.34 N	84.41 E
Karabulak, Kyrg.	85	39.51 N	69.38 E
Karabulduk	130	40.50 N	38.34 E
Karaburun	130	38.37 N	26.31 E
Karabutak	86	49.59 N	60.10 E
Karacabey	130	40.13 N	28.21 E
Karacadağ, Tür.	130	37.43 N	39.37 E
Karacadağ, Tür.	130	41.57 N	27.40 E
Karaca Dağ ∧	130	37.40 N	39.50 E
Karačaj ≐	84	41.28 N	49.00 E
Karačajevo-Čerkesija □[3]	84	44.00 N	42.00 E
Karačajevsk	84	43.45 N	41.54 E
Karacaköy	130	41.24 N	28.22 E
Karačala	84	39.48 N	48.57 E
Karacaoğlan	130	41.31 N	27.07 E
Karacasu	130	37.43 N	28.37 E

DEUTSCH Name	Seite	Breite°′	Länge°′ E = Ost
Karacaviran	130	39.44 N	38.08 E
Karaçay	130	36.10 N	36.02 E
Karaçayır	130	39.55 N	37.01 E
Karačev	76	53.07 N	35.00 E
Karachay → Karačajevo-Čerkesija □[3]	84	44.00 N	42.00 E
Karāchi	120	24.52 N	67.03 E
Karachtaj	85	40.55 N	69.46 E
Karači	80	57.59 N	50.28 E
Karād	122	17.17 N	74.12 E
Kara Dağ ∧	130	40.22 N	39.05 E
Karadarja ≐	85	40.54 N	71.45 E
Karadeniz → Black Sea ▾[2]	22	43.00 N	35.00 E
Karadere	130	40.40 N	30.50 E
Karadirek	130	38.34 N	30.11 E
Karaftit	88	54.12 N	111.54 E
Karagaj, Kaz.	80	48.39 N	47.38 E
Karagaj, Ross.	80	58.16 N	54.56 E
Karagajly	86	49.20 N	75.48 E
Karaganda	86	49.50 N	73.10 E
Karaganda □[8]	86	50.00 N	74.00 E
Karagel	128	39.23 N	53.11 E
Karagičevskij	80	50.11 N	42.55 E
Karaginskij, ostrov I	74	58.50 N	164.00 E
Karaginskij zaliv c	74	58.50 N	164.00 E
Karagola Road	124	25.29 N	87.23 E
Karagöl Dağı ∧	130	40.32 N	38.10 E
Kara Gölü ⊜	130	36.42 N	29.50 E
Karagoš, gora ∧	86	51.44 N	89.24 E
Karagužicha	86	50.47 N	83.00 E
Karahallı	130	38.20 N	29.32 E
Karaia	124	25.54 N	78.01 E
Karaičev	80	48.37 N	42.13 E
Karaidel'	86	55.50 N	56.53 E
Karaidel'skij	86	55.49 N	57.05 E
Kāraikāl	122	10.55 N	79.50 E
Kāraikkudi	122	10.04 N	78.47 E
Karaisalı	130	37.16 N	35.03 E
Karaitivu I	122	8.23 N	79.47 E
Karaj	128	35.48 N	50.59 E
Karaj ≐	267d	35.35 N	51.11 E
Karajantak	85	40.03 N	67.54 E
Karak	114	3.24 N	102.02 E
Karakabak	86	50.33 N	75.09 E
Karakain	85	41.26 N	74.19 E
Kara-Kala	128	38.26 N	56.18 E
Karakalpak Respublika □[3]	86	43.00 N	59.00 E
Karakaralong, Pulau II	112	4.30 N	125.30 E
Karakastek	85	43.08 N	76.06 E
Karakavak	85	39.41 N	72.43 E
Karakax ≐	120	37.00 N	79.45 E
Karakaya Barajı ⊜[1]	130	38.25 N	38.45 E
Karakeçi	130	37.26 N	39.26 E
Karakeçili	130	39.36 N	33.23 E
Karakelong, Pulau I	108	4.15 N	126.48 E
Karakemer	85	42.55 N	75.20 E
Karakendža	85	39.14 N	71.31 E
Karakitang, Pulau I	112	3.11 N	125.32 E
Karakoin, ozero ⊜	86	46.10 N	68.45 E
Karakojsu ≐	84	42.33 N	46.58 E
Karakojun ≐	85	41.10 N	75.45 E
Karakol (Prževal'sk)	85	42.29 N	78.24 E
Karakolka	85	41.32 N	77.23 E
Karakoram Pass)(	120	35.30 N	77.50 E
Karakoram Range ⩘	120	35.30 N	77.00 E
Karakoro ≐	150	14.43 N	12.03 W
Karaksar	88	51.16 N	115.58 E
Karakudžur ≐	85	41.59 N	75.42 E
Karakul', Ross.	86	57.26 N	70.51 E
Karakul', Taj.	85	39.02 N	73.33 E
Karakul', Uzb.	128	39.32 N	63.50 E
Karakul', ozero ⊜	85	39.05 N	73.25 E
Karakulak	130	39.59 N	40.01 E
Kara-Kul'dža	85	40.37 N	73.35 E
Karakul'dža ≐	85	40.39 N	73.26 E
Karakulino	80	56.01 N	53.43 E
Karakul'skoje	86	54.04 N	62.26 E
Karakum	86	46.49 N	79.33 E
Karakumskij kanal ⩮	128	37.35 N	61.50 E
Karakumy ◆[2]	72	39.00 N	60.00 E
Karakuni	270	34.28 N	135.28 E
Karakurt	130	40.10 N	42.36 E
Karala ◆[8]	272a	28.44 N	77.02 E
Karalat	80	45.55 N	48.18 E
Karalon	88	57.02 N	115.52 E
Karalundi	162	26.07 S	118.41 E
Karam	88	55.09 N	107.37 E
Karama ≐	112	2.18 S	119.06 E
Karamağara	130	39.42 N	35.31 E
Karamai → Karamay	86	45.30 N	84.55 E
Karaman	130	37.11 N	33.14 E
Karaman □[4]	130	37.00 N	33.00 E
Karamanlı	130	37.22 N	29.49 E
Karamay	86	45.30 N	84.55 E
Karambu	112	3.51 S	116.04 E
Karamea	172	41.15 S	172.07 E
Karamea ≐	172	41.16 S	172.06 E
Karamea Bight c[3]	172	41.30 S	171.40 E
Karamıkbataklığı ≡	130	38.25 N	30.50 E
Karamnisa Nāla ⊜[1]	124	25.42 N	83.25 E
Karamoja □[5]	154	2.50 N	34.15 E
Karamola, gora ∧	86	47.58 N	66.35 E
Karamürsel	130	40.42 N	29.36 E
Karamurt	85	42.19 N	69.58 E
Karamyš ≐	80	51.20 N	45.00 E
Karamyševo, Ross.	76	57.45 N	28.45 E
Karamyševo, Ross.	82	54.46 N	36.07 E
Karamyševo, Ross.	88	57.34 N	100.55 E
Karamzino	76	56.00 N	34.33 E
Karang, Gunung ∧	115a	6.16 S	106.03 E
Karang, Tanjung ›	112	0.38 S	119.44 E
Karangagung	112	2.22 S	104.27 E
Karangampel	115a	6.28 S	108.27 E
Karangana	150	12.13 N	5.02 W
Karangasem	115b	8.27 S	115.37 E
Karangbinangun	115a	7.01 S	112.30 E
Karangbolang, Ujung ›	115a	7.46 S	109.02 E
Karangbolong	115a	7.45 S	109.28 E
Karanggede	115a	7.22 S	110.37 E
Karangkates, Waduk ⊜[1]	115a	8.11 S	112.34 E
Karangkobar	115a	7.16 S	109.44 E
Karangnunggal	115a	7.38 S	108.06 E
Karangpandan	115a	7.37 S	111.04 E
Karangsembung	115a	6.51 S	108.39 E
Kāranja	122	20.29 N	77.29 E
Karanjia	120	21.47 N	85.58 E
Karanpura	123	29.50 N	73.27 E
Karaoba, Kaz.	86	53.17 N	65.06 E
Karaoba, Kaz.	86	47.03 N	56.20 E
Karaoğlan	130	39.14 N	39.13 E
Karaoj	86	45.54 N	74.45 E
Karaozek, Kaz.	85	43.43 N	77.23 E
Karaozek, Kaz.	86	45.03 N	65.18 E
Karaozek, Uzb.	86	43.16 N	58.40 E
Karapınar, Tür.	130	37.43 N	33.33 E
Karapınar, Tür.	130	41.30 N	32.12 E
Karapyši	78	49.38 N	30.47 E
Karaš	80	56.54 N	39.24 E
Karas, Pulau I	164	3.27 S	132.40 E
Karasaj	85	41.34 N	77.49 E
Kara-Sal ≐	80	47.22 N	43.38 E
Karaşar	130	40.20 N	32.00 E
Karasay	120	36.47 N	83.48 E
Karasburg	156	28.00 S	18.43 E
Karasburg □[5]	156	28.00 S	18.45 E
Kara Sea → Karskoje more ▾[2]	72	76.00 N	80.00 E
Karašengel'	86	47.29 N	75.35 E
Karašjåkka ≐	24	69.26 N	25.49 E
Karasjok	24	69.27 N	25.30 E
Karaskan	85	41.03 N	71.49 E
Karasor, ozero ⊜, Kaz.	86	51.57 N	75.45 E

Symbols in the index entries represent the broad categories identified in the key at the right. Symbols with superior numbers (⩘[1]) identify subcategories (see complete key on page I · 1).

Symbole im Register stellen die rechts im Schlüssel erklärten Kategorien dar. Symbole mit hochgestellten Ziffern (⩘[1]) bezeichnen Unterabteilungen einer Kategorie (vgl. vollständiger Schlüssel auf Seite I · 1).

Los símbolos incluídos en el texto del índice representan las grandes categorías identificadas con la clave a la derecha. Los símbolos con numeros en su parte superior (⩘[1]) identifican las subcategorías (véase la clave completa en la página I · 1).

Les symboles de l'index représentent les catégories indiquées dans la légende à droite. Les symboles suivis d'un indice (⩘[1]) représentent des sous-catégories (voir légende complète à la page I · 1).

Os símbolos incluídos no texto do índice representam as grandes categorias identificadas com a chave à direita. Os símbolos com números em sua parte superior (⩘[1]) identificam as subcategorias (veja-se a chave completa à página I · 1).

∧ Mountain	Berg	Montaña	Montagne	Montanha
⩘ Mountains	Gebirge	Montañas	Montagnes	Montanhas
)(Pass	Paß	Paso	Col	Passo
V Valley, Canyon	Tal, Cañon	Valle, Cañón	Vallée, Canyon	Vale, Canhão
≚ Plain	Ebene	Llano	Plaine	Planície
› Cape	Kap	Cabo	Cap	Cabo
I Island	Insel	Isla	Île	Ilha
II Islands	Inseln	Islas	Îles	Ilhas
◆ Other Topographic Features	Andere Topographische Objekte	Otros Elementos Topográficos	Autres données topographiques	Outros acidentes topográficos

ESPAÑOL				FRANÇAIS				PORTUGUÊS			
Nombre	Página	Lat.ᵒʳ	Long.ᵒʳ W=Oeste	Nom	Page	Lat.ᵒʳ	Long.ᵒʳ W=Ouest	Nome	Página	Lat.ᵒʳ	Long.ᵒʳ W=Oeste

Karasor, ozero ⊚, Kaz. 86 49.54 N 75.32 E
Karasu, Azer. 84 40.11 N 48.41 E
Karasu, Kaz. 86 52.40 N 65.28 E
Karasu, Kaz. 86 51.20 N 62.21 E
Karasu, Kyrg. 85 43.03 N 73.57 E
Kara-Su, Kyrg. 85 40.44 N 72.53 E
Karasu, Nihon 94 34.39 N 136.32 E
Karasu, Tür. 130 41.06 N 30.41 E
Karasu ≃, Nihon 94 36.15 N 139.17 E
Karasu ≃, Tür. 130 39.07 N 38.44 E
Karasuk 86 53.44 N 78.02 E
Karasuk ≃ 86 53.35 N 77.30 E
Karasuyama 36 39.39 N 140.09 E
Karata 84 42.35 N 46.21 E
Karatal, Kaz. 86 45.07 N 77.54 E
Karatal, Kaz. 86 47.36 N 35.12 E
Karatal ≃ 86 46.26 N 77.10 E
Karataş, Tür. 130 38.34 N 28.17 E
Karataş, Tür. 130 36.36 N 35.21 E
Karataş Burun ᐳ 130 36.35 N 35.22 E
Karatau 85 43.10 N 70.28 E
Karatau, chrebet ⋏, Kaz. 72 43.50 N 68.30 E
Karatau, chrebet ⋏, Taj. 85 38.10 N 69.00 E
Karateginskij chrebet ⋏ 85 38.50 N 69.40 E
Karatia 126 24.14 N 89.58 E
Karatobe 80 49.41 N 53.31 E
Karatogaj 86 48.42 N 59.40 E
Karaton 86 46.25 N 53.30 E
Karatoya ≃ 124 24.13 N 89.36 E
Karatschi → Karāchi 120 24.52 N 67.03 E
Karatsu 92 33.26 N 129.58 E
Karaturuk 85 43.33 N 77.59 E
Karatuzskoje 86 53.36 N 92.53 E
Karau 164 3.45 S 144.20 E
Karaul 74 70.06 N 83.08 E
Karauli 124 26.30 N 77.01 E
Karaunk'ur ≃ 85 40.54 N 72.20 E
Karaurġan 130 40.15 N 42.17 E
Karauzak 86 42.59 N 60.02 E
Karauzek 85 41.30 N 45.12 E
Karavanroje, Ross. 85 45.59 N 47.08 E
Karavanroje, Ross. 80 57.47 N 47.41 E
Karave 272c 19.01 N 73.01 E
Karawa 152 3.20 N 20.18 E
Karawang 115a 6.19 S 107.17 E
Karawang, Tanjung ᐳ 115a 5.56 S 107.00 E
Karawanken ⋏ 36 46.30 N 14.30 E
Karayaka 130 40.45 N 36.37 E
Karayazı 130 39.41 N 42.08 E
Karaye 150 11.48 N 8.02 E
Karaylın 130 39.41 N 37.19 E
Karažal 86 48.02 N 70.49 E
Karballā' 128 32.00 N 42.15 E
Karbenning 40 60.02 N 15.04 E
Kårberg 40 58.58 N 14.57 E
Karbeyaz 130 36.02 N 36.12 E
Kårböle 26 61.59 N 15.19 E
Karby 40 56.18 N 18.13 E
Karcag 30 47.19 N 20.55 E
Karczew 30 52.06 N 21.15 E
Kardail ≃ 80 50.43 N 52.14 E
Kardašova Řečice 61 49.11 N 14.53 E
Kardeljevo 36 43.04 N 17.26 E
Karden 56 50.11 N 7.17 E
Kardhámaina 38 36.47 N 27.09 E
Kardhámila 38 38.32 N 26.05 E
Kardhitsa 38 39.22 N 21.55 E
Kárdla 76 59.00 N 22.45 E
Kardymovo 76 54.54 N 32.26 E
Kårdžali 38 41.39 N 25.22 E
Kardžin 84 43.16 N 44.16 E
Karea 272b 22.42 N 88.33 E
Kareeberge ⋏ 158 30.53 S 21.57 E
Kareedouw 158 33.57 S 24.18 E
Kareli 84 42.01 N 43.54 E
Karelia → Kareliia ⬡³ 24 64.00 N 32.30 E
Kareliia ⬡⁹ 24 63.00 N 32.00 E
Kareliia ⬡³ 24 64.00 N 32.30 E
Karel'skij Gorodok 76 58.04 N 36.30 E
Karema, Pap. N. Gui. 164 9.12 S 147.14 E
Karema, Tan. 154 6.49 S 30.26 E
Karen 110 12.51 N 92.55 E
Karenga ≃ 88 54.28 N 116.32 E
Karepino 24 61.02 N 57.02 E
Karera 272a 28.41 N 77.23 E
Karesuando 24 68.25 N 22.30 E
Kärevere 76 58.26 N 26.29 E
Kåreyz-e Elyās 82 80 55.12 N 50.54 E
Kargalinskaja 84 43.44 N 46.30 E
Karganaj 180 65.21 N 175.25 E
Kargapazan Dağları ⋏ 130 40.07 N 41.35 E
Kargasok 86 59.07 N 80.53 E
Kargat 86 55.10 N 80.17 E
Kargat ≃ 86 55.10 N 78.12 E
Kargil 130 41.08 N 34.30 E
Kargil 123 34.34 N 76.06 E
Karginskaja 84 60.21 N 41.38 E
Karginski ≃ 265a 59.50 N 30.01 E
Kargopol' 24 61.30 N 38.58 E
Karguéri 130 27.01 N 10.25 E
Karhal 124 27.01 N 78.57 E
Karhijärvi ⊚ 40 61.35 N 22.16 E
Karhula 26 60.31 N 26.57 E
Kari 84 11.14 N 10.34 E
Karia-ba-Mohammed 148 34.14 N 5.10 W
Kariai 38 40.16 N 24.15 E
Karianga 157b 22.22 S 47.26 E
Kariba 158 16.31 S 28.45 E
Kariba, Lake ⊜¹ 154 17.00 S 28.00 E
Karibib 156 21.58 S 15.51 E
Karibib ⬡⁵ 156 22.20 S 16.00 E
Karibisches Meer → Caribbean Sea ᐧ²⁻² 230 15.00 N 73.30 W
Kariega ≃ 158 33.42 S 26.41 E
Karigasniemi 24 69.24 N 25.50 E
Karikari, Cape ᐳ 162 34.47 S 173.24 E
Karimata, Kepulauan ⬡¹ 112 1.25 S 109.05 E
Karimata, Selat ⊔ 112 1.36 S 108.55 E
(Karimata Strait) ⊔ 112 2.05 S 108.40 E
Karīmganj 128 24.52 N 92.21 E
Karimnagar 122 18.26 N 79.09 E
Karimun, Pulau I 114 1.03 N 103.22 E
Karimunjawa, Kepulauan II 115a 5.50 S 110.25 E
Karimunjawa, Pulau I 115a 5.51 S 110.27 E
Karin, Som. 144 10.59 N 49.13 E
Karin, Som. 144 10.51 N 45.47 E
Karingal ᐧ³ 154 17.55 N 38.56 E
Karin Seamount ⋏³ 154 17.55 N 38.56 E
Karintorf 24 59.00 N 50.11 E
Karis (Karjaa) 26 60.05 N 23.40 E
Karise 54 55.18 N 12.13 E
Karisimbi, Volcan ⋏¹ 154 1.30 S 29.27 E
Káristos 38 38.00 N 24.24 E
Kariya 94 34.59 N 136.59 E
Kariye Museum ⬧¹ 267b 41.01 N 28.55 E
Karjat 128 34.49 N 60.47 E
Karjaa → Karis 26 60.05 N 23.40 E
Karjepolje 24 65.34 N 43.40 E
Kārkal 122 13.12 N 74.59 E

Karkalaj 80 57.00 N 52.24 E
Karkaralinsk 86 49.23 N 75.21 E
Karkar Dümän ⬟⬟⁸ 272a 28.39 N 77.18 E
Karkar Island I 164 4.40 S 146.00 E
Karkas, Küh-e ⋏ 128 33.29 N 51.50 E
Karkheh ≃ 128 31.46 N 47.55 E
Karkïndar 128 25.47 N 59.15 E
Karki 78 45.55 N 33.00 E
Karklia 26 60.32 N 24.11 E
Karklu 26 61.25 N 23.01 E
Karkom, Har ⋏ 132 30.17 N 34.44 E
Karkonoski Park Narodowy ⬥ 30 50.45 N 15.35 E
Kärla 76 58.20 N 22.15 E
Karlholmsbruk 40 60.31 N 17.35 E
Karlik Shan ⋏ 102 43.08 N 94.20 E
Karlino 30 54.03 N 15.51 E
Karlova 130 39.18 N 41.01 E
Karl-Marx-Stadt → Chemnitz 54 50.50 N 12.55 E
Karlobag 36 44.32 N 15.05 E
Karlo-Libknechtovsk 83 48.42 N 38.04 E
Karlo-Marksovo 83 48.16 N 38.09 E
Karloske ≃ 184 55.29 N 15.34 E
Karlova 78 49.27 N 35.08 E
Karlovo 38 42.38 N 24.48 E
Karlovy Vary (Carlsbad) 54 50.11 N 12.52 E
Karlsbad → Karlovy Vary 54 50.11 N 12.52 E
Karlsborg, Sve. 26 59.32 N 14.31 E
Karlsburg, Sve. 26 65.48 N 23.17 E
Karlsburg → Alba Iulia 38 46.04 N 23.35 E
Karlsby 40 58.38 N 15.08 E
Karlsfeld 60 48.13 N 11.28 E
Karlshafen 52 51.38 N 9.27 E
Karlshamn 26 56.10 N 14.51 E
Karlshorst, Trabrennbahn ⬥ 264a 52.29 N 13.32 E
Karlshuld 60 48.41 N 11.18 E
Karlskoga 40 59.20 N 14.31 E
Karlskrona 26 56.10 N 15.35 E
Karlslunde Strand 41 55.34 N 12.14 E
Karlsøarna II 26 57.17 N 17.58 E
Karlsruhe, Ross. 96 49.03 N 8.24 E
Karlsruhe ⬥⁵, Dtsch. 56 49.20 N 8.45 E
Karlsruhe ⬥⁸, Dtsch. 58 48.30 N 8.30 E
Karlstad, Sve. 40 59.22 N 13.30 E
Karlstad, Mn., U.S. 198 48.34 N 96.31 W
Karlstadt 58 49.57 N 9.45 E
Karlsøyt 85 48.35 N 14.45 E
Karluk, Ross. 88 53.27 N 105.58 E
Karluk, Ak., U.S. 180 57.34 N 154.28 W
Karl'uk, Uzb. 85 36.12 N 67.42 E
Karma, Ouadi ⩔ 146 15.38 N 20.01 E
Karmah 140 19.38 N 30.25 E
Karmäla 122 18.25 N 75.12 E
Karmanovka 80 45.24 N 50.22 E
Karmanovo 76 55.52 N 34.52 E
Karmansbo 40 59.42 N 15.44 E
Karmatän 126 24.05 N 86.42 E
Karmel, Har (Mount Carmel) ⋏ 132 32.44 N 35.02 E
Karmi'el 132 32.55 N 35.18 E
Karmiyya 132 31.36 N 34.23 E
Karmøy I 26 59.15 N 5.15 E
Karnack 194 32.40 N 94.10 W
Karnak → Al-Karnak, Miṣr 140 25.43 N 32.39 E
Karnak, Il., U.S. 194 37.17 N 88.58 W
Karnāl 124 29.41 N 76.59 E
Karnāla Fort ⬧ 272c 18.53 N 73.07 E
Karnāli ≃⁸ 124 29.30 N 82.30 E
Karnāli ≃ 124 28.15 N 81.05 E
Karnaphuli Reservoir ⊜¹ 120 22.42 N 92.12 E
Karnātaka ⬡³ 122 14.00 N 76.00 E
Karnauchovka 78 48.28 N 34.44 E
Karnes ⬡⁴ 122 29.00 N 97.47 W
Karnes City 196 28.53 N 97.54 W
Karni 150 10.40 N 2.37 W
Karniki 84 54.12 N 38.05 E
Karnische Alpen (Alpi Carniche) ⋏ 64 46.40 N 13.00 E
Karnobat 38 42.39 N 26.59 E
Kärnten ⬡³ 60 46.50 N 13.50 E
Kärnten ⬡³ 54 52.59 N 12.26 E
Karoi 154 16.50 S 29.40 E
Karoli 124 24.28 N 62.35 E
Karolinenhof ⬥⁸ 264a 52.23 N 13.38 E
Karomatan 116 7.46 N 123.44 E
Karompa Lompo, Pulau I 112 7.15 S 121.45 E
Karonga 154 24.07 N 86.44 E
Karonie 162 30.58 S 122.32 E
Karoonda 164 35.06 S 139.54 E
Karora 123 31.13 N 70.57 E
Karos 140 17.42 N 38.22 E
Káros I 38 36.53 N 25.39 E
Karoso, Tanjung ᐳ 115b 9.33 S 118.50 E
Karotho Post 154 5.11 N 35.50 E
Karow, Dtsch. 54 52.20 N 12.15 E
Karow, Dtsch. 54 53.31 N 12.15 E
Karow ⬥⁸ 264a 52.37 N 13.29 E
Karpathen → Carpathian Mountains ⋏ 22 48.00 N 24.00 E
Kárpathos, Ellás 38 35.30 N 27.14 E
Kárpathos I 38 35.31 N 27.12 E
Kárpathos I 38 35.40 N 27.10 E
Karpenísion 38 38.55 N 21.40 E
Karpinsk 86 59.46 N 60.01 E
Karpogory 83 64.00 N 44.27 E
Karpovka, Ukr. 83 49.10 N 37.43 E
Karpovo, Ross. 80 47.57 N 39.36 E
Karpovo, Ross. 76 60.00 N 36.40 E
Karpovo, Ross. 80 55.35 N 38.34 E
Karpovo-Ross. 80 55.42 N 45.20 E
Karpuninskij 86 58.43 N 61.50 E
Karpuzlu 130 37.33 N 27.50 E
Karratha 162 20.53 S 116.40 E
Karrats Fjord c² 176 71.20 N 54.00 W
Kärrbäcksminde 55 51.11 N 11.40 E
Karrebæk 54 47.13 N 10.47 E
Kärrgruvan 40 60.05 N 15.56 E
Karridale 162 34.13 S 115.05 E
Kärsämäki 26 63.58 N 25.46 E
Karši 30 53.54 N 17.56 E
Karskaja step'≃ 128 39.10 N 66.41 E
Karskije Vorota, proliv ⊔ 72 70.30 N 58.00 E
Karskoje more (Kara Sea) ᐧ² 72 76.00 N 80.00 E
Karsol 80 58.14 N 53.11 E
Karst → Kras ⩚¹ 64 45.48 N 14.00 E
Kärsta, Sve. 26 59.44 N 18.00 E
Kärsta, Sve. 40 59.40 N 16.49 E

Karstädt 54 53.09 N 11.44 E
Karstula 26 62.52 N 24.47 E
Karsun 80 54.11 N 46.59 E
Kartajol' 24 64.32 N 53.14 E
Kartala ⋏ 157a 11.45 S 43.22 E
Kartaly 86 53.03 N 60.40 E
Kartārpur 128 31.27 N 75.30 E
Karthaus 214 41.07 N 78.07 W
Kartijiski chrebet ⋏ 84 42.10 N 44.55 E
Kartosuro 115a 7.33 S 110.44 E
Karttula 26 62.53 N 26.58 E
Kartuzy 30 54.20 N 18.12 E
Kartzow 54 52.29 N 12.58 E
Käru 76 58.50 N 25.11 E
Karuah ≃ 170 32.39 S 151.58 E
Karufa 164 3.50 S 133.27 E
Karukh 94 36.21 N 138.38 E
Karukuwisa 156 18.56 S 19.40 E
Karumai 92 40.19 N 141.28 E
Karumba 166 17.29 S 140.50 E
Kārūn ≃ 128 30.26 N 48.10 E
Karungi 26 66.03 N 23.57 E
Karungu 154 0.51 S 34.09 E
Karunjie 164 16.18 S 127.12 E
Karup 41 56.18 N 9.10 E
Karup ≃ 41 56.18 N 9.10 E
Karūr 122 10.57 N 78.05 E
Karuscia, Punta ᐳ 66 36.41 N 11.59 E
Karvala 265a 64.41 N 30.09 E
Karviná 30 49.50 N 18.30 E
Kārwār 122 14.48 N 74.08 E
Karwendel ⋏ 64 47.27 N 11.20 E
Karwi 124 25.12 N 80.54 E
Karym 86 55.53 N 66.41 E
Karymskoje, Ross. 88 51.37 N 114.21 E
Karymskoje, Ross. 88 54.07 N 101.49 E
Karzi ≃ 86 58.35 N 60.50 E
Karzachi 84 41.15 N 43.16 E
Kaş, Süd. 140 12.30 N 24.17 E
Kaş, Tür. 130 36.12 N 29.38 E
Kasaan 180 55.32 N 132.24 W
Kasabi ≃ 152 14.48 S 23.42 E
Kasach ≃ 84 40.03 N 43.52 E
Kasadi ≃ 272c 19.01 N 73.03 E
Kasa-do I 98 34.28 N 126.03 E
Kasado-shima I 96 33.57 N 131.51 E
Kasagi 94 34.45 N 135.56 E
Kasagi-sanchi ⋏ 270 34.45 N 135.56 E
Kasagi-yama ⋏ 94 35.31 N 137.21 E
Kasahara 94 35.21 N 137.11 E
Kasai 268 35.54 N 139.25 E
Kasai 96 34.56 N 134.50 E
Kasai ≃, Incia 124 22.09 N 87.50 E
Kasai-Occidental ⬡⁴ 152 5.30 S 21.40 E
Kasai-Oriental c⁴ 152 4.00 S 23.30 E
Kasaji 152 10.22 S 23.27 E
Kasakake 94 36.23 N 139.17 E
Kasama, Nihon 94 36.23 N 140.16 E
Kasama, Zam. 154 10.13 S 31.12 E
Kasan → Kazan', Ross. 80 55.49 N 49.08 E
Kasan, Uzb. 128 39.02 N 65.35 E
Kasan-dong 98 41.18 N 126.55 E
Kasane 156 17.50 S 25.05 E
Kasanga 154 8.28 S 31.09 E
Kasangale 152 6.20 S 22.42 E
Kasangeshi ≃ 152 8.24 S 21.56 E
Kasangulu 152 4.36 S 15.10 E
Kasanka National Park ⬥ 154 12.35 S 30.12 E
Kasano-misaki ᐳ 94 36.21 N 136.18 E
Kasansaj 85 40.40 N 71.32 E
Kasansaj ≃ 85 40.57 N 71.30 E
Kasaoka 94 34.30 N 133.30 E
Kāsaragod 122 12.30 N 75.00 E
Kasāragod 154 12.30 N 75.00 E
Kasba 26 25.51 N 87.33 E
Kasbagoas 126 24.11 N 88.30 E
Kasba Kamarda 126 21.46 N 87.21 E
Kasba Lake ⊜ 176 60.18 N 102.07 W
Kasba Mirgoda 126 21.42 N 87.28 E
Kasba Nārāyangarh 126 22.10 N 87.23 E
Kasba-Tadla 148 32.34 N 6.18 W
Kaschau → Košice 30 48.43 N 21.15 E
Kāseberga 92 55.23 N 14.04 E
Kaseda 92 31.25 N 130.19 E
Kasempa 154 13.27 S 25.50 E
Kasenga 154 10.22 S 28.38 E
Kasenyi 154 1.24 N 30.26 E
Kasese, Ug. 154 0.10 N 30.05 E
Kasese, Zaïre 154 1.38 S 27.07 E
Kaset Sombun 110 16.17 N 101.57 E
Kasfareet Military Base ⬥ 142 30.15 N 32.24 E
Kāsganj 124 27.49 N 78.39 E
Kashabowie Lake ⊜ 198 48.42 N 90.25 W
Kashaf ≃ 128 35.58 N 61.07 E
Kashabwigamog Lake ⊜ 212 44.59 N 78.37 W
Kāshān 128 33.59 N 51.29 E
Kashasha 154 1.44 S 31.37 E
Kashegelok 180 60.50 N 157.50 W
Kashgar → Kashi 85 39.29 N 75.59 E
Kashi 85 39.29 N 75.59 E
Kashiba 94 34.33 N 135.42 E
Kashihara 96 34.31 N 135.46 E
Kashiji Plain ≃ 152 13.20 S 22.30 E
Kashikishi ≃ 152 9.46 S 29.05 E
Kashima, Nihon 92 35.04 N 130.06 E
Kashima, Nihon 94 35.58 N 140.38 E
Kashima, Nihon 92 35.58 N 136.55 E
Kashima, Nihon 96 35.30 N 133.01 E
Kashima, Nihon 96 35.30 N 133.01 E
Kashima-nada ᐧ² 96 36.15 N 140.45 E
Kashima-Yariga-take ⋏ 94 36.37 N 137.45 E
Kashimo 94 35.43 N 137.23 E
Kāshīnāthpur 126 23.58 N 89.37 E
Kashing → Jiaxing 106 30.46 N 120.45 E
Kāshīpur, India 124 29.13 N 78.57 E
Kāshīpur, India 126 23.26 N 86.40 E
Kashiwa 268 35.52 N 139.58 E
Kashiwara 94 34.35 N 135.38 E
Kashiwara ≃ 94 34.35 N 135.37 E
Kashiwazaki, Nihon 94 37.22 N 138.33 E
Kashiwazaki, Nihon 268 35.56 N 139.42 E
Kāshmīr → Jammu and Kāshmīr ⬡³ 123 34.00 N 76.00 E
Kashmir, Vale of ⩔ 123 34.00 N 75.00 E
Kashmünd Ghar ⋏ 128 34.42 N 70.31 E
Kashunuk ≃ 180 61.18 N 165.36 W
Kashwakamak Lake ⊜ 212 44.50 N 77.04 W
Kasia 124 26.45 N 83.55 E
Kasiguncu 115b 23.14 N 89.45 E
Kasiidji ≃ 152 7.57 S 23.12 E
Kasiguaj 94 35.48 N 136.11 E
Kasigluk 180 60.52 N 162.32 W
Kasilof 180 60.24 N 151.18 W

Kasilovo 78 50.38 N 35.37 E
Kasimbar 112 0.09 S 120.00 E
Kāsimov 80 54.56 N 41.24 E
Kāsimpur, Engl. 126 23.59 N 90.19 E
Kāsimpur, India 272b 22.46 N 88.31 E
Kāšin 76 57.21 N 37.37 E
Kāsināthpur 272b 22.35 N 88.31 E
Kasinge 154 6.20 S 26.59 E
Kasinka 156 18.13 S 24.22 E
Kāšipur 272b 22.25 N 88.10 E
Kāšira 82 54.51 N 38.10 E
Kāšira 82 54.52 N 38.13 E
Kasiruta, Pulau I 108 0.25 S 127.12 E
Kasiui, Pulau I 108 4.33 N 131.40 E
Kasiwa → Kashiwa 94 35.52 N 139.59 E
Kaskabulak 86 49.34 N 79.52 E
Kaškadarja ≃⁸ 128 39.00 N 66.00 E
Kaskaden-Kette → Cascade Range ⋏ 202 45.00 N 121.30 W
Kaskana 85 40.45 N 69.36 E
Kaskaskia ≃ 194 37.59 N 89.56 W
Kaskaskia, East Fork ≃ 219 38.43 N 89.09 W
Kaskaskia, North Fork ≃ 219 38.46 N 89.09 W
Kaskattama ≃ 176 57.03 N 90.07 W
Kaskelen 85 43.12 N 76.37 E
Kaskelen ≃ 85 43.53 N 77.08 E
Kaskinen → Kaskö 26 62.23 N 21.13 E
Kaskö (Kaskinen) 26 62.23 N 21.13 E
Kaślağač ≃ 83 47.45 N 37.16 E
Kaslātu ⋏ 124 23.58 N 84.54 E
Kasli 86 55.53 N 60.46 E
Kaslo 182 49.55 N 116.55 W
Kasn'a ≃ 76 55.24 N 34.20 E
Kasn'a ≃ 76 55.51 N 34.25 E
Kaso ≃ 115a 7.25 S 106.40 E
Kasongo 154 4.27 S 26.40 E
Kasongo-Lunda 152 6.28 S 16.49 E
Kásos I 38 35.22 N 26.56 E
Kasota 190 44.18 N 93.57 W
Kašperovka 85 49.26 N 29.41 E
Kaspi 84 41.57 N 44.25 E
Kaspijsk 84 42.52 N 47.38 E
Kaspijskij 82 48.22 N 47.24 E
Kaspijskoje more → Caspian Sea ᐧ² 72 42.00 N 50.30 E
Kaspiiskaja → Prikaspijskaja niznmennosti ≃ 80 48.00 N 52.00 E
Kaspisches Meer → Caspian Sea ᐧ² 72 42.00 N 50.30 E
Kaspl'a ≃ 76 55.00 N 31.38 E
Kaspl'a ≃ 76 55.24 N 30.43 E
Kaspl'a ≃ 76 55.24 N 31.08 E
Kasr, Ra's ᐳ 140 18.02 N 38.35 E
Kasrik 38 38.13 N 41.54 E
Kassa → Košice 30 48.43 N 21.15 E
Kassab 153 35.56 N 35.59 E
Kassai → Cassai (Kasai) ≃ 152 3.02 S 16.57 E
Kassalā 140 15.28 N 36.24 E
Kassalā ⬡⁴ 140 15.00 N 35.00 E
Kassándra ᐳ¹ 38 40.06 N 23.22 E
Kassándras, Kólpos ⊂ 38 40.06 N 23.30 E
Kassel 56 51.19 N 9.29 E
Kassel ⬡⁵ 56 51.10 N 9.20 E
Kasserine 148 35.11 N 8.48 E
Kasserine ≃⁸ 148 35.00 N 8.45 E
Kashabog Lake ⊜ 212 44.30 N 78.05 W
Kassikaitiy ≃ 246 1.49 N 58.32 W
Kassinger 140 18.45 N 31.54 E
Kassīr, Sabkhat al- ≃ 85 35.03 N 41.07 E
Kasslerfeld ⬥⁸ 263 51.26 N 6.45 E
Kasson 190 44.01 N 92.45 W
Kassou 150 11.35 N 2.03 W
Kassoum 150 11.35 N 2.03 W
Kastamonu 130 41.22 N 33.47 E
Kastamonu ⬡⁴ 130 41.40 N 33.45 E
Kastanéai 38 41.38 N 26.28 E
Kastelholm 26 60.14 N 20.04 E
Kastellaun 56 50.04 N 7.26 E
Kasterlee 56 51.15 N 4.57 E
Kastiyu, Puntan ᐳ 174n 14.57 N 145.40 E
Kastl, Dtsch. 60 49.22 N 11.42 E
Kastl, Dtsch. 60 48.12 N 12.24 E
Kastoría 38 40.30 N 21.15 E
Kastorías, Límni ⊜ 38 40.30 N 21.17 E
Kastornoje 78 51.50 N 38.06 E
Kastsina 154 12.07 N 7.32 E
Kastsina Ala ≃ 154 7.46 N 8.08 E
Kastsina Ala 152 7.10 N 9.17 E
Kastwa 84 54.59 N 28.03 E
Kasuga 92 33.32 N 130.27 E
Kasuga, Nihon 94 35.14 N 136.58 E
Kasugai 94 35.15 N 136.58 E
Kasugai, Nihon 94 35.14 N 136.58 E
Kasugai, Nihon 94 35.39 N 138.39 E
Kasuka-kōbūkichi, Nihon 94 35.39 N 138.39 E
Kasuga Shrine ⬧ 270 34.41 N 135.51 E
Kasugi 164 33.40 S 26.41 E
Kasukabe 268 35.58 N 139.45 E
Kasukawa 94 36.24 N 139.13 E
Kasulu 154 4.34 S 30.06 E
Kasumi 94 35.38 N 134.38 E
Kasumiga-ura ⊜ 94 36.00 N 140.25 E
Kasum-Ismailov 84 40.36 N 46.29 E
Kasungu 154 13.02 S 33.29 E
Kasungu National Park ⬥ 154 12.55 S 33.15 E
Kasūr 123 31.07 N 74.27 E
Kaszuby ᐧ⁸ 30 54.10 N 17.45 E
Kata ≃ 88 58.46 N 102.40 E
Kataeregi 150 9.22 N 6.17 E
Katagum ≃ 150 12.20 N 10.57 E
Katahdin, Mount ⋏ 188 45.55 N 68.55 W
Katako-Kombe 152 3.24 S 24.25 E
Katakura 270 34.29 N 135.31 E
Katalla 180 60.12 N 144.31 W
Katamatite 170 36.07 S 145.41 E
Katanga ⬡⁹ 154 8.00 S 26.00 E
Katanga ≃ 88 58.20 N 101.50 E
Katanga ≃ 88 58.36 N 103.01 E
Katangi, India 124 21.46 N 79.48 E
Katangi, India 124 23.27 N 79.47 E
Katangli 89 51.42 N 143.14 E
Katanning 162 33.42 S 117.33 E
Katano 270 34.46 N 135.40 E
Katano-hana ᐳ 94 24.49 N 141.20 E
Katārkān Ghāt 128 24.58 N 81.09 E
Katase 268 35.19 N 139.29 E
Katashina ≃ 94 36.43 N 139.20 E
Katav-Ivanovsk 86 54.43 N 58.12 E
Katchall Island I 110 7.57 N 93.22 E

Katchewanooka Lake ⊜ 212 44.27 N 78.16 W
Katchin-wan c 174m 26.19 N 127.53 E
Katchirga 154 14.03 N 0.06 E
Katchiungo 152 12.35 S 16.13 E
Katech 84 41.33 N 46.34 E
Katélé 150 10.33 N 7.12 E
Katena-wan c 174m 26.50 N 128.05 E
Katepwa Beach 184 50.42 N 103.38 W
Katerbow 54 52.59 N 12.39 E
Kateríni 38 40.16 N 22.30 E
Katerinopol' 78 48.56 N 30.59 E
Katerloch ⋏⁵ 61 47.16 N 15.32 E
Katernberg ⬥⁸, Dtsch. 263 51.16 N 7.06 E
Katernberg ⬥⁸, Dtsch. 263 51.29 N 7.04 E
Katesbridge 48 54.18 N 6.08 W
Kates Needle ⋏ 180 57.03 N 132.03 W
Katešovo 82 54.08 N 37.00 E
Katete, Malaŵi 154 12.17 S 33.39 E
Katete, Zam. 154 14.05 S 32.07 E
Katghora 124 22.30 N 82.33 E
Katha 110 24.11 N 96.21 E
Kathangor, Jabal ⋏ 140 14.28 N 33.59 E
Katharine ≃ 164 14.28 S 132.16 E
Katherine ≃ 164 14.39 S 131.42 E
Katherine Creek ≃ 166 23.48 S 143.42 E
Katherine Gorge National Park ⬥ 144 14.10 S 132.30 E
Kāthgodām 124 29.16 N 79.32 E
Kāthiāwār Peninsula ᐳ¹ 120 22.00 N 71.00 E
Kathi, Ra's ᐳ 144 14.55 S 42.53 E
Kathia 123 31.59 N 76.47 E
Kathleen 220 28.07 N 82.01 W
Kathleen Valley 162 27.23 S 120.38 E
Kathiow 54 53.14 N 14.29 E
Kāthmāndau 124 27.43 N 85.19 E
Kathmandu → Kāthmāndau 124 27.43 N 85.19 E
Kathor 120 21.18 N 72.56 E
Kathrabbā 132 31.08 N 35.37 E
Kathua 123 32.22 N 75.31 E
Kāthuli 126 23.52 N 88.40 E
Kati 150 12.44 N 8.04 W
Katīādi 126 24.15 N 90.48 E
Katibas ≃ 112 2.01 N 112.33 E
Katihār 124 25.32 N 87.35 E
Katikati 172 37.33 S 175.55 E
Katima Mulilo 152 17.27 S 24.14 E
Katimik Lake ⊜ 184 52.54 N 99.22 W
Katioa 150 8.08 N 5.06 W
Katiola 150 8.08 N 5.06 W
Katiti Aboriginal Land Reserve ⬥ 162 25.10 S 131.15 E
Kātlang 123 34.22 N 72.05 E
Katlenburg-Duhm 52 51.41 N 10.06 E
Katmai, Mount ⋏ 180 58.17 N 154.56 W
Katmai National Park ⬥ 180 58.30 N 155.00 W
Kātmāndu → Kāthmāndau 124 27.43 N 85.19 E
Katni → Murwāra, India 124 23.51 N 80.24 E
Katni, Ross. 87 57.59 N 47.46 E
Káto Akhaïa 38 38.09 N 21.32 E
Kātol 124 21.16 N 78.35 E
Katomp 60 6.11 S 26.20 E
Katonah 210 41.16 N 73.41 W
Katonga ≃ 154 0.34 N 31.50 E
Katon-Karagaj 86 49.11 N 85.37 E
Katoomba 170 33.42 S 150.18 E
Katopa 154 2.45 S 25.06 E
Katori-jingū ⬧¹ 94 35.52 N 140.33 E
Katovice 60 49.16 N 13.49 E
Katowice 30 50.15 N 19.00 E
Katowice ⬡⁴ 30 50.30 N 19.00 E
Katra 123 32.59 N 74.57 E
Kātrās 126 23.48 N 86.17 E
Katrîčev 80 49.23 N 45.33 E
Kātrîná, Jabal ⋏ 140 28.31 N 33.57 E
Katrine, Loch ⊜ 46 56.15 N 4.31 W
Katrineholm 40 59.00 N 16.12 E
Katsch, Golf von → Kachchh, Gulf of c 120 22.36 N 69.30 E
Katschbach ≃ 61 47.14 N 14.17 E
Katsepe 157b 15.45 S 46.15 E
Katshungu 154 2.07 S 27.23 E
Katsina 154 12.20 N 7.32 E
Katsina Ala ≃ 154 7.10 N 9.17 E
Katsina Ala 152 7.10 N 9.17 E
Katsuragi ⋏ 270 34.59 N 135.42 E
Katsura ≃ 270 34.59 N 135.42 E
Katsura → Nihon 94 34.53 N 135.08 E
Katsura, Nihon 94 34.53 N 135.08 E
Katsurao 94 37.30 N 140.46 E
Katsuren-hantō ᐳ¹ 174m 26.20 N 128.02 E
Katsushika-san ⋏ 94 36.41 N 138.45 E
Katsushika ᐳ¹ 268 35.43 N 139.51 E
Katsuura 94 35.08 N 140.18 E
Katsuyama, Nihon 94 36.03 N 136.30 E
Katsuyama, Nihon 96 35.05 N 133.41 E
Kattakurgan 72 39.55 N 66.15 E
Kattara-Senke → Qaṭṭārah, Munkhafad al- ⋏⁷ 140 30.00 N 27.30 E
Kattaviá 41 35.57 N 27.46 E
Katta-Taldyk 85 40.19 N 72.12 E
Kattegat ⊔ 26 57.00 N 11.00 E
Katterat 263 51.09 N 7.22 E
Katthammarsvik 26 57.26 N 18.50 E
Kattowitz → Katowice 30 50.16 N 19.00 E
Katttuppūttūr 124 11.29 N 78.13 E
Katul, Jabal ⋏ 140 14.16 N 29.23 E
Katuma ≃ 154 6.10 S 30.34 E
Katumba 154 6.10 S 30.34 E
Katun' ≃ 86 52.25 N 85.05 E
Katuni ≃ 86 55.50 N 87.16 E
Katuri ≃ 80 56.50 N 43.14 E
Katwijk aan de Rijn 56 52.12 N 4.25 E
Katwijk aan Zee 56 52.12 N 4.23 E
Katy 196 29.47 N 95.49 W
Katy Wrocławskie 54 51.02 N 16.44 E
Katzenbuckel ⋏ 58 49.29 N 9.02 E
Katzenelnbogen 56 50.17 N 7.59 E
Kau 108 1.11 N 127.54 E
Kaua 120 21.15 N 78.51 E
Kauai I 229b 22.00 N 159.30 W
Kauai Channel ⊔ 229b 21.45 N 158.50 W
Kaub 56 50.05 N 7.46 E
Kaufbeuren 60 47.53 N 10.37 E
Kaufering 60 48.06 N 10.52 E
Kaufman 196 32.35 N 96.18 W
Kaufman ⬡⁴ 196 32.38 N 96.18 W
Kaukakahi Channel ⊔ 229b 22.00 N 159.53 W
Kauhava 26 63.06 N 23.05 E
Kauiki Head ᐳ 229a 20.45 N 155.59 W
Kaukapakapa 172 36.37 S 174.30 E
Kaukasus → Bol'šoj Kavkaz ⋏ 84 42.30 N 45.00 E
Kaukauna 190 44.16 N 88.16 W
Kaukau Veld ⋏¹ 156 19.30 S 20.30 E
Kaukhéli 126 22.38 N 90.04 E
Kaukura I¹ 14 15.45 S 146.42 W
Kaula I 229a 21.45 N 160.30 W
Kaulakahi Channel ⊔ 229b 22.00 N 159.53 W
Kaulille 56 51.11 N 5.31 E
Kauliranta 24 66.27 N 23.41 E
Kaül-li 98 37.58 N 124.37 E
Kaulsdorf 54 50.37 N 11.26 E
Kaulsdorf ⬥⁸ 264a 52.31 N 13.33 E
Kaulsdorf-Süd ⬥⁸ 264a 52.29 N 13.34 E
Kaumakani 229b 21.55 S 159.37 W
Kaumalapau 229a 20.47 N 156.59 W
Kaunakakai 229a 21.05 N 157.01 W
Kaunas 76 54.54 N 23.54 E
Kaune ≃ 210 41.41 N 74.50 W
Kauner Tal ⩔ 64 47.01 N 10.44 E
Kaunghein 110 25.40 N 95.26 E
Kauniainen → Grankulla 26 60.13 N 24.45 E
Kaunun.ii ᐳ 229b 21.56 N 160.10 W
Kaup 26 61.11 N 7.14 E
Kaupanger 26 61.05 N 7.22 E
Kaura Namoda 150 12.35 N 6.35 E
Kauriyãla Ghāt 124 28.23 N 81.02 E
Kauru 150 10.33 N 8.12 E
Kausa 272c 19.10 N 73.02 E
Kaušany 78 46.38 N 29.25 E
Kaustinen 26 63.32 N 23.42 E
Kauswagar 116 8.11 N 124.05 E
Kautokeino 24 69.00 N 23.02 E
Kauttua 26 61.06 N 22.10 E
Kau-ye Kyun I 110 11.00 N 98.32 E
Kavaca 74 60.16 N 169.51 E
Kavacik 130 39.40 N 28.30 E
Kavadarci 38 41.26 N 22.00 E
Kavajë 38 41.11 N 19.33 E
Kavak, Tür. 130 38.24 N 39.26 E
Kavak, Tür. 130 41.05 N 36.03 E
Kavak, Tür. 130 39.18 N 37.30 E
Kavála 38 38.29 N 41.49 E
Kavaklidere 130 37.26 N 28.22 E
Kavála 38 40.56 N 24.25 E
Kavalerovo 89 44.15 N 135.04 E
Kävali 122 14.55 N 79.59 E
Kavango ≃⁵ 156 18.30 S 20.15 E
Kavaratti 110 10.34 N 72.39 E
Kavaratti Island I 122 10.33 N 72.38 E
Kavarna 38 43.25 N 28.20 E
Kavendou, Mont ⋏ 150 10.41 N 12.12 W
Kāveri ≃ 122 11.09 N 79.52 E
Kāveri Falls ⩇ 122 12.18 N 77.17 E
Kaverino, Ross. 80 54.04 N 41.47 E
Kaverino, Ross. 82 56.11 N 36.15 E
Kavieng 158 23.5 S 150.50 E
Kavirondo ⊔ 156 18.02 S 24.38 E
Kavir, Dasht-e ≃² 128 34.40 N 54.30 E
Kavkazskij zapovednik ⬥ 84 43.55 N 40.30 E
Kävlinge 41 55.48 N 13.06 E
Kävlingeán ≃ 41 55.47 N 13.06 E
Kavungo 152 11.31 S 23.03 E
Kaw, Guy. fr. 250 4.29 N 52.02 W
Kaw, Ok., U.S. 196 36.46 N 96.50 W
Kawa 110 17.05 N 96.28 E
Kawabe, Nihon 94 34.01 N 139.07 E
Kawabe, Nihon 94 33.55 N 135.31 E
Kawabe, Nihon 96 34.01 N 133.07 E
Kawachi, Nihon 94 36.37 N 139.56 E
Kawachi-nagano 94 34.27 N 135.34 E
Kawagama Lake ⊜ 212 45.18 N 78.45 W
Kawage 94 34.47 N 136.33 E
Kawagoe 94 35.55 N 139.29 E
Kawaguchi 94 35.48 N 139.43 E
Kawaguchi 94 35.30 N 138.46 E
Kawahara 94 35.23 N 134.12 E
Kawai, Nihor 94 34.18 N 137.07 E
Kawai, Nihor 94 36.37 N 137.07 E
Kawai, Nihon 92 39.33 N 141.35 E
Kawailoa Beach 229c 21.36 N 158.03 W
Kawakami, Nihon 96 34.55 N 133.32 E
Kawakami, Nihon 94 34.44 N 135.29 E
Kawakubo 94 34.59 N 139.04 E
Kawali 115a 7.11 S 108.22 E
Kawama Mission 154 10.04 S 28.37 E
Kawambwa 154 9.47 S 29.05 E
Kawanbwa 154 9.47 S 29.05 E
Kawanishi, Nihon 94 34.35 N 135.47 E
Kawanishi, Nihon 94 34.50 N 135.25 E
Kawara 92 33.37 N 130.50 E
Kawardha 124 22.01 N 81.15 E
Kawarau ≃ 172 44.57 S 169.10 E
Kawartha Lakes ⊜ 212 44.32 N 78.12 W
Kawasaki, Nihon 94 35.32 N 139.43 E
Kawasaki-kō ⊂ 268 35.29 N 139.45 E
Kawasaki Stadium ⬥ 94 35.31 N 139.42 E
Kawashima, Nihon 94 35.44 N 136.35 E
Kawashima, Nihon 94 35.04 N 134.11 E
Kawashiri-misaki ᐳ 96 34.26 N 130.52 E
Kawau Island I 172 36.25 S 174.51 E
Kawayan 116 11.41 N 124.21 E
Kawdut 110 15.13 N 98.08 E
Kawela 229a 21.05 N 157.02 E
Kawerau 172 38.05 S 176.42 E
Kawhia Harbour c 172 38.05 S 174.48 E
Kawia 144 2.45 S 150.45 E
Kawit 116b 14.27 N 120.54 E
Kawkareik 110 16.33 N 98.14 E
Kawludo 110 18.40 N 97.19 E

ENGLISH — Name / Page / Lat.°′ / Long.°′
DEUTSCH — Name / Seite / Breite°′ / Länge°′ E = Ost

Kawm al-Farā'in (Buto) ⊥ 142 31.11 N 30.45 E
Kawm ar-Rāhib 142 28.20 N 30.37 E
Kawm Birah 273c 30.05 N 31.08 E
Kawm Dafanah (Daphnæ) ⊥ 142 30.52 N 32.11 E
Kawm Ḥamādah 142 30.46 N 30.42 E
Kawm Ishfīn 273c 30.11 N 31.15 E
Kawm Ishū 142 31.07 N 30.00 E
Kawm Ju'ayf (Naucratis) ⊥ 142 30.54 N 30.36 E
Kawm Umbū 140 24.28 N 32.57 E
Kawnglanghpu 102 27.04 N 98.21 E
Kawnipi Lake ⊜ 190 48.24 N 91.14 W
Kawthaung 110 9.59 N 98.33 E
Kax ≃ 86 43.40 N 81.45 E
Kaxgar ≃ 85 39.40 N 78.00 E
Kaya, Burkina 150 13.05 N 1.05 W
Kaya, Nihon 96 35.30 N 135.06 E
Kayaapu 112 5.26 S 102.24 E
Kayadibi, Tür. 130 39.29 N 36.43 E
Kayadibi, Tür. 130 39.55 N 34.15 E
Kayah □[3] 110 19.15 N 97.30 E
Kayak Island I 180 59.52 N 144.30 W
Kāyalpattinam 122 8.34 N 78.07 E
Kāyamba 272b 22.41 N 88.32 E
Kayambi 154 9.27 S 31.58 E
Kayan 110 16.54 N 96.34 E
Kayan ≃ 112 2.55 N 117.35 E
Kayangel Islands II 108 8.04 N 134.43 E
Kayang-san ∧[2] 271b 37.33 N 126.43 E
Kāyankulam 122 9.11 N 76.30 E
Kayapa 116 16.22 N 120.53 E
Kayapınar 130 37.34 N 41.10 E
Kayaş 130 39.56 N 32.58 E
Kaya-san ∧ 98 35.49 N 128.07 E
Kaya-san Kukrip Kongwŏn ♦ 98 35.47 N 128.06 E
Kaycee 200 43.42 N 106.38 W
Kayeli 164 3.23 S 127.06 E
Kayembe-Mukulu 152 9.03 S 23.57 E
Kayen 115a 6.54 S 110.59 E
Kayenta 200 36.43 N 110.15 W
Kayes, Congo 152 4.25 S 11.41 E
Kayes, Mali 150 14.27 N 11.26 W
Kayes □[4] 150 14.00 N 11.00 W
Kay Gardens 285 39.45 N 75.25 W
Kayima 150 8.53 N 11.10 W
Kayin □[3] 110 17.30 N 97.45 E
Kayış Dağı ∧ 267b 40.59 N 29.10 E
Kaymakçı 130 38.10 N 28.08 E
Kaymaz, Tür. 130 39.31 N 31.11 E
Kaymaz, Tür. 130 40.55 N 30.18 E
Kayna 54 50.59 N 12.14 E
Kaynar 130 38.55 N 36.28 E
Kayō, Nihon 96 34.51 N 133.42 E
Kayō, Nihon 174m 26.33 N 128.07 E
Kayoa, Pulau I 164 0.05 S 127.25 E
Kayombo 154 9.36 S 25.37 E
Kaypak 130 37.08 N 36.27 E
Kay Point › 180 69.18 N 138.22 W
Kayser Gebergte ⋀ 250 3.03 N 56.35 W
Kayseri 130 38.43 N 35.30 E
Kayseri □[4] 130 38.30 N 35.55 E
Kaysersberg 58 48.08 N 7.15 E
Kaysville 200 41.02 N 111.56 W
Kayuadi, Pulau I 112 6.49 S 120.47 E
Kayuagung 112 3.24 S 104.50 E
Kayumas 115a 7.50 S 114.08 E
Kayuta Lake ⊜ 210 43.25 N 75.12 W
Kayuyu 154 3.39 S 26.21 E
Kazach 84 41.06 N 45.22 E
Kazachskij melkosopočnik ⋀[2] 86 49.00 N 72.00 E
Kazachstan → Kazakhstan □[1] 72 48.00 N 68.00 E
Kazačij 83 46.58 N 40.03 E
Kazačinskoje, Ross. 86 57.49 N 93.17 E
Kazačinskoje, Ross. 88 56.16 N 107.36 E
Kazačja Lopan' 78 50.21 N 36.11 E
Kazačje 74 70.44 N 136.13 E
Kazačji Lageri 78 46.42 N 32.59 E
Kazačka 80 51.28 N 43.56 E
Kazackij 86 49.20 N 58.31 E
Kazackoje 78 51.18 N 33.29 E
Kazakdarja 86 43.27 N 59.46 E
Kazakevičevo 89 48.17 N 134.46 E
Kazakhstan □[1], Asia 72 48.00 N 68.00 E
Kazakhstan □[1], Asia 86 47.00 N 76.00 E
Kazaki 76 52.38 N 38.16 E
Kazaklija 38 46.00 N 28.37 E
Kazakstan → Kazakhstan □[1] 72 48.00 N 68.00 E
Kazal'cevo 86 59.18 N 80.30 E
Kazalinsk 86 45.46 N 62.07 E
Kazan' 80 55.49 N 49.08 E
Kazan ≃ 176 64.02 N 95.30 W
Kazanbulak 84 40.38 N 46.41 E
Kazancı 130 36.30 N 32.53 E
Kazandžik 128 39.16 N 55.32 E
Kazanka, Kaz. 86 53.20 N 67.27 E
Kazanka, Ukr. 78 47.50 N 32.49 E
Kazanka ≃ 80 55.48 N 49.01 E
Kazanlâk 38 42.38 N 25.21 E
Kazan Lake ⊜ 184 55.33 N 108.21 W
Kazanlı 130 36.50 N 34.45 E
Kazanovka 76 53.46 N 38.34 E
Kazan-rettō (Volcano Islands) II 14 25.00 N 141.00 E
Kazanskaja 78 49.48 N 41.09 E
Kazanskoje, Ross. 82 54.59 N 37.39 E
Kazanskoje, Ross. 86 55.38 N 69.14 E
Kazan' Station ⊕[5] 265b 55.46 N 37.40 E
Kazantip, mys › 78 45.28 N 35.51 E
Kazarman 85 41.24 N 74.03 E
Kazatin 78 49.43 N 28.50 E
Kazatkul' 86 55.02 N 76.03 E
Kazbegi 84 42.39 N 44.39 E
Kazbek, gora ∧ 84 42.42 N 44.31 E
Kaz Dağı ∧ 130 39.42 N 26.50 E
Kazembe 154 12.11 S 32.37 E
Kāzerūn 128 29.37 N 51.38 E
Kazgorodok, Kaz. 86 49.56 N 71.36 E
Kazgorodok, Kaz. 86 52.53 N 70.42 E
Kažim 24 60.20 N 51.30 E
Kazi-Magomed 84 40.03 N 48.56 E
Kazimierza Wielka 30 50.16 N 20.30 E
Kazimierz Dolny 30 51.20 N 21.58 E
Kazincbarcika 30 48.16 N 20.37 E
Kazinka, Ross. 76 52.32 N 39.42 E
Kazinka, Ross. 78 50.14 N 37.50 E
Kāzipāra 272b 22.43 N 88.31 E
Kāzīr Char 126 22.46 N 90.33 E
Kaziza 152 10.42 S 23.52 E
Kazlų Rūda 76 54.46 N 23.30 E
Kaz'minskoje 84 44.35 N 41.41 E
Kaznačejevo 82 54.31 N 37.16 E
Kazo 94 36.07 N 139.36 E
Kaz'onnyj Torec ≃ 83 48.54 N 37.46 E
Kaztalovka 80 49.46 N 48.42 E
Kazuma Pan National Park ♦ 154 18.15 S 25.33 E
Kazumba 152 6.25 S 22.02 E
Kazungula 154 17.45 S 25.20 E
Kazuno 92 40.11 N 140.47 E
Kazvin → Qazvīn 128 36.16 N 50.00 E
Kazy 128 39.13 N 57.30 E
Kazym 74 63.40 N 67.14 E
Kazym ≃ 74 63.54 N 65.50 E
Kazyr ≃ 86 53.47 N 92.53 E
Kbal Dâmrei 110 14.07 N 105.21 E
Kbelnice 60 49.18 N 13.59 E
Kbely ⊕[8] 54 50.07 N 14.32 E
Kcynia 30 53.00 N 17.30 E
Kdyně 60 49.23 N 13.02 E
Kéa 38 37.38 N 24.21 E
Kéa I 38 37.34 N 24.22 E
Keaau 229d 19.37 N 155.02 W
Keady 48 54.15 N 6.42 W
Keahole Point › 229d 19.44 N 156.03 W
Keal, Loch na ⊂ 46 56.28 N 6.04 W
Kealaikahiki, Lae o › 229a 20.32 N 156.42 W
Kealaikahiki Channel ⋓ 229a 20.37 N 156.50 W
Kealakekua Bay ⊂ 229d 19.28 N 155.56 W
Kealia 229b 22.06 N 159.18 W
Keams Canyon 200 35.48 N 110.11 W
Keanae 229a 20.51 N 156.09 W
Keanapapa Point › 229a 20.54 N 157.04 W
Kean College of New Jersey ʋ[2] 276 40.41 N 74.14 W
Keansburg 208 40.25 N 74.12 W
Kearney, Mo., U.S. 194 39.22 N 94.21 W
Kearney, Ne., U.S. 198 40.41 N 99.04 W
Kearney, Pa., U.S. 214 40.08 N 78.12 W
Kearns 200 40.39 N 111.59 W
Kearny, Az., U.S. 200 33.03 N 110.54 W
Kearny, N.J., U.S. 210 40.46 N 74.08 W
Kearsley 262 53.32 N 2.23 W
Kearsley Creek ≃ 216 43.04 N 83.40 W
Keasbey 276 40.31 N 74.19 W
Keb' ≃ 76 57.44 N 28.28 E
Kebajoran ⊕[8] 269e 6.13 S 106.46 E
Keban 130 38.48 N 38.45 E
Keban Barajı ⊜[1] 130 38.50 N 39.20 E
Kebanyartimur 115a 7.09 S 112.52 E
Kébara 152 2.27 S 14.25 E
Kebbi 150 12.08 N 4.44 E
Kebeiti 120 36.47 N 79.29 E
Kébémer 150 15.22 N 16.27 W
Kébi, Mayo ≃ 146 9.18 N 13.33 E
Kebili 148 33.42 N 8.58 E
Kebîr, Oued el ≃ 34 36.50 N 6.07 E
Kebnekaise ∧ 24 67.53 N 18.33 E
Kebock Head › 46 58.01 N 6.20 W
Kebri Dehar 144 6.47 N 44.17 E
Kebumen 115a 7.40 S 109.39 E
Keb'uty 80 45.50 N 44.14 E
Keče 85 43.14 N 71.22 E
Kecel 30 46.32 N 19.16 E
Kech ≃ 128 26.00 N 62.44 E
Kechika ≃ 176 59.36 N 127.05 W
Keçiborlu 130 37.57 N 30.18 E
Kecksburg 214 40.11 N 79.28 W
Kecskemét 30 46.54 N 19.42 E
Kedabek 84 40.34 N 45.49 E
Kedah □[3] 114 6.00 N 100.40 E
Kėdainiai 76 55.17 N 24.00 E
Kédange-sur-Canner 56 49.19 N 6.20 E
Kedārnāth 124 30.44 N 79.04 E
Kedārpur 126 23.18 N 90.27 E
Kedges Straits ⋓ 208 38.03 N 76.02 W
Kedgwick 186 47.39 N 67.21 W
Kedgwick ≃ 186 47.40 N 67.29 W
Kédhron 38 39.13 N 22.03 E
Kedian 100 31.23 N 112.51 E
Kediri 115a 7.49 S 112.01 E
Kedjebi 150 8.12 N 0.25 E
Kedon 74 64.08 N 159.14 E
Kedong 89 48.02 N 126.15 E
Kédougou 150 12.33 N 12.11 W
Kedrasju 24 64.36 N 60.24 E
Kedrovka 86 55.32 N 86.03 E
Kedu 102 26.33 N 104.21 E
Kedungdung 115a 7.06 S 113.15 E
Kedungjati 115a 7.10 S 110.37 E
Kedungwuni 115a 6.58 S 109.39 E
Kedvavom 24 64.15 N 53.27 E
Kędzierzyn Kozle 30 50.20 N 18.12 E
Keecheus Lake ⊜ 224 47.22 N 121.22 W
Keefer 218 38.32 N 84.38 W
Keefers 182 50.02 N 121.33 W
Keego Harbor 216 42.36 N 83.20 W
Keelby 44 53.34 N 0.15 W
Keele 42 53.00 N 2.17 W
Keele ≃ 180 64.24 N 124.50 W
Keele Peak ∧ 180 63.26 N 130.19 W
Keeley Lake ⊜ 184 54.54 N 108.08 W
Keeling Islands → Cocos Islands □[2] 12 12.10 S 96.55 E
Keels 186 48.36 N 53.24 W
Keelung → Chilung 100 25.08 N 121.44 E
Keen, Mount ∧ 46 56.58 N 2.54 W
Keene, On., Can. 212 44.15 N 78.10 W
Keene, Ca., U.S. 228 35.13 N 118.33 W
Keene, Ky., U.S. 192 37.56 N 84.38 W
Keene, N.H., U.S. 188 42.56 N 72.16 W
Keene, Oh., U.S. 214 40.21 N 81.52 W
Keene, Tx., U.S. 222 32.23 N 97.19 W
Keenesburg 200 40.06 N 104.31 W
Keeney Knob ∧ 192 37.47 N 80.42 W
Keeneyville 278 41.59 N 88.07 W
Keep River National Park ♦ 164 15.48 S 129.03 E
Keerbergen 56 51.00 N 4.37 E
Keer-Weer, Cape › 164 13.58 S 141.30 E
Keeseg ∧ 64 46.58 N 12.14 E
Keeseville 188 44.30 N 73.28 W
Keesler Air Force Base ■ 194 30.26 N 88.55 W
Keetmanshoop 156 26.36 S 18.08 E
Keetmanshoop □[5] 156 26.30 S 19.00 E
Keewatin, On., Can. 184 49.46 N 94.34 W
Keewatin, Mn., U.S. 190 47.23 N 93.04 W
Kefa □[4] 144 6.50 N 36.00 E
Kefallinía I 38 38.15 N 20.35 E
Kéfalos 38 36.45 N 27.00 E
Kefamenanu 112 9.27 S 124.29 E
Kefar 'Azza 132 31.29 N 34.32 E
Kefar Blum 132 33.10 N 35.36 E
Kefar 'Eẕyon 132 31.39 N 35.08 E
Kefar Naḥum (Capernaum) ⊥ 132 32.53 N 35.34 E
Kefar Sava 132 32.10 N 34.54 E
Kefar Shammay 132 32.57 N 35.27 E
Kefar Szold 132 33.11 N 35.39 E
Kefar Vitkin 132 32.23 N 34.53 E
Kefar Warburg 132 31.43 N 34.44 E
Kefar Yona 132 32.19 N 34.55 E
Kefermarkt 61 48.26 N 14.32 E
Keffi 150 8.51 N 7.52 E
Keffin Hausa 150 12.15 N 9.58 E
Keflavík 24a 64.02 N 22.36 W
Keftya 144 13.54 N 37.07 E
Kega 24 65.10 N 36.54 E
Ke Ga, Mui ›, Viet 110 10.42 N 107.58 E
Ke Ga, Mui ›, Viet 110 12.53 N 109.28 E
Kegalla 122 7.15 N 80.21 E
Kégashka 186 50.12 N 61.17 W
Kégashka, Lac ⊜ 186 50.20 N 61.25 W
Kegejli 86 42.45 N 59.35 E
Kegičovka 78 49.17 N 35.46 E
Kegnæs ›[1] 41 54.52 N 9.59 E
Kegon-no-taki ∟ 94 36.44 N 139.31 E
Kegonsa, Lake ⊜ 216 42.58 N 89.15 W
Kegonzhake 120 33.00 N 87.53 E
Keg River 176 57.48 N 117.52 W
Kegums 76 56.46 N 24.45 E
Kegworth 42 52.50 N 1.16 W
Kehdingen, Land ⊕[1] 52 53.45 N 9.15 E
Kehiwin Indian Reserve ⊕[4] 182 54.07 N 110.48 W
Kehl 56 48.35 N 7.50 E
Kehlen 58 47.41 N 9.33 E
Kehoe 218 38.28 N 83.03 W
Kehra 76 59.20 N 25.20 E
Kehrigk 54 52.09 N 13.55 E
Ke-hsi Mānsām 110 21.56 N 97.50 E
Keig 46 57.15 N 2.39 W
Keighley 44 53.52 N 1.54 W
Keihoku 96 35.09 N 135.38 E
Keijō → Sŏul 98 37.33 N 126.58 E
Keila 76 59.18 N 24.25 E
Keilor 169 37.43 S 144.50 E
Keimoes 158 28.41 S 21.00 E
Kei Mouth 158 32.41 S 28.22 E
Keio University ʋ[2] 268 35.38 N 139.45 E
Kei Road 158 32.42 S 27.32 E
Keiser 194 35.40 N 90.05 W
Keiskammahoek 158 32.41 S 27.09 E
Keiskammapunt › 158 32.40 S 27.10 E
Keïta 150 14.46 N 5.46 E
Kéita, Bahr ≃ 146 9.14 N 18.21 E
Keitele 26 63.11 N 26.22 E
Keitele ⊜ 26 62.55 N 26.00 E
Keith, Austl. 166 36.06 S 140.21 E
Keith, Scot., U.K. 46 57.32 N 2.57 W
Keith Arm ⊂ 176 65.20 N 122.15 W
Keithley Creek 182 52.45 N 121.24 W
Keithsburg 190 41.05 N 90.56 W
Keiyasi 175g 17.54 S 177.45 E
Keizer 224 44.59 N 123.01 W
Kejaman 112 2.39 N 113.45 E
Kejimkujik National Park ♦ 186 44.21 N 65.18 W
Kejngypil'gyn, laguna ⊂ 180 63.30 N 178.50 E
Kejni, gora ∧ 180 64.30 N 174.54 W
Kejvy ⋀ 24 67.35 N 38.00 E
Kekaha 229b 21.58 N 159.42 W
Kekek ≃ 190 48.24 N 75.48 W
Kekerengu 172 42.00 S 174.01 E
Kékes ∧ 30 47.55 N 20.02 E
Kekeyaer 85 38.02 N 75.05 E
Kek Lok Si ʋ[1] 114 5.23 N 100.14 E
Kekpāra 126 22.27 N 86.35 E
Kekri 120 25.58 N 75.09 E
Kekurnoi, Cape › 180 57.44 N 155.15 W
Kelafo 144 5.40 N 44.20 E
Kelai ≃ 112 2.10 N 117.29 E
Kelan 102 38.43 N 111.32 E
Kelanang 114 2.48 N 101.26 E
Kelang 114 3.02 N 101.27 E
Kelang, Pulau I, Indon. 164 3.12 S 127.44 E
Kelang, Pulau I, Malay. 114 3.00 N 101.18 E
Kelani ≃ 122 6.58 N 79.52 E
Kelantan 114 0.51 N 101.40 E
Kelantan □[3] 114 5.20 N 102.00 E
Kelantan ≃ 114 6.11 N 102.15 E
Kelapa 112 1.52 S 105.42 E
Kelasuri 84 43.08 N 41.13 E
Kelat 218 38.32 N 84.19 W
Kelayres 210 40.54 N 76.00 W
Kelb, Ouadi V 146 15.19 N 18.51 E
Kel'badžar 84 40.07 N 46.02 E
Kelberg 56 50.17 N 6.55 E
Kelbia, Sebkhet ⊜ 36 35.51 N 10.16 E
Kelbra 54 51.26 N 11.02 E
Keld Ula ∧ 86 43.20 N 85.25 E
Kel'd'ušovo 80 55.01 N 44.59 E
Keleft 128 37.21 N 66.15 E
Kelegou 98 41.57 N 118.11 E
Kélékélé 273b 4.20 S 15.08 E
Kelem 144 4.48 N 35.58 E
Kelenföld ⊕[8] 264c 47.28 N 19.03 E
Kelenken, gora ∧ 180 66.07 N 170.52 W
Keles, Tür. 130 39.55 N 29.14 E
Keles, Uzb. 85 41.24 N 69.12 E
Keles ≃ 85 41.02 N 68.37 E
Keleti-főcsatorna ≡ 30 48.01 N 21.20 E
Keleti Pályaudvar ⊕[5] 264c 47.30 N 19.06 E
Kelheim 60 48.55 N 11.52 E
Kelibia 148 36.51 N 11.06 E
Kelkheim 56 50.08 N 8.26 E
Kelkit 130 40.08 N 39.27 E
Kelkit ≃ 130 40.46 N 36.32 E
Kell 219 38.30 N 88.54 W
Kellé 152 0.06 S 14.33 E
Kellen 52 51.48 N 6.10 E
Kellenhusen 54 54.11 N 11.03 E
Keller, Tx., U.S. 222 32.56 N 97.15 W
Keller, Va., U.S. 208 37.37 N 75.45 W
Keller, Wa., U.S. 182 48.04 N 118.41 W
Kellerberg 64 46.40 N 13.42 E
Kellerberrin 162 31.38 S 117.43 E
Kellerjoch ∧ 64 47.19 N 11.46 E
Keller Lake ⊜, N.T., Can. 176 64.00 N 121.30 W
Keller Lake ⊜, Sk., Can. 184 56.04 N 106.46 W
Kellerovka 86 53.50 N 69.17 E
Keller Peak ∧ 228 34.12 N 117.03 W
Kellett, Cape › 176 71.59 N 125.34 W
Kellettville 214 41.33 N 79.16 W
Kelleys Island 214 41.36 N 82.42 W
Kelleys Island I 214 41.36 N 82.42 W
Kelliher 184 51.15 N 103.44 W
Kellinghusen 52 53.57 N 9.43 E
Kellmünz 58 48.07 N 10.08 E
Kelloe 44 54.43 N 1.28 W
Kellogg, Id., U.S. 202 47.32 N 116.07 W
Kellogg, Ia., U.S. 190 41.43 N 92.54 W
Kellogg, Mn., U.S. 190 44.18 N 91.59 W
Kellogg Marsh 224 48.05 N 122.07 W
Kelloggsville 214 41.52 N 80.36 W
Kellojärvi ⊜ 26 64.16 N 29.03 E
Kelloselkä 24 66.56 N 28.50 E
Kells → Ceanannus Mór, Ire. 48 53.44 N 6.53 W
Kells, N. Ire., U.K. 44 54.48 N 6.13 E
Kells, N. Ire., U.K. 48 54.48 N 6.13 E
Kelly Air Force Base ■ 196 29.24 N 98.35 W
Kelly Lake ⊜ 180 65.30 N 126.10 W
Kelly Run ≃, Pa., U.S. 279b 40.15 N 79.55 W
Kelly Run ≃, Pa., U.S. 279b 40.13 N 79.45 W
Kellyville, Austl. 274a 33.43 S 150.57 E
Kellyville, Ok., U.S. 196 35.56 N 96.12 W
Kelmė 76 55.38 N 22.56 E
Kel'mency 78 48.27 N 26.50 E
Kelmet 144 16.04 N 38.55 E
Kelmscott 168a 32.07 S 116.01 E
Kelo 146 9.19 N 15.48 E
Kelolokan 112 1.08 N 117.54 E
Kelottijärvi 24 68.31 N 22.04 E
Kelowna 182 49.53 N 119.29 W
Kelsall 44 53.13 N 2.43 W
Kelsey Bay 182 50.24 N 125.57 W
Kelsey Head › 42 50.24 N 5.08 W
Kelsey Lake ⊜ 184 53.37 N 101.02 W
Kelseyville 204 38.58 N 122.50 W
Kelso, Scot., U.K. 46 55.36 N 2.25 W
Kelso, Wa., U.S. 224 46.08 N 122.54 W
Kelsterbach 56 50.04 N 8.32 E
Kel'temašat 85 42.30 N 70.17 E
Kelty 46 56.08 N 3.23 W
Keluang 114 2.02 N 103.19 E
Keluang, Tanjung › 112 3.02 S 110.39 E
Kelud, Gunung ∧ 115a 7.56 S 112.18 E
Keluo ≃ 89 49.22 N 125.15 E
Keluotun 89 49.16 N 125.44 E
Kelvedon 42 51.51 N 0.42 E
Kelvedon Hatch 260 51.40 N 0.16 E
Kelvington 184 52.10 N 103.30 W
Kelvin Seamount ✣[3] 16 38.50 N 64.00 W
Kelyexeed 144 8.46 N 49.12 E
Kelzenberg 263 51.07 N 6.30 E
Kem' 24 64.57 N 34.36 E
Kem' ≃, Ross. 24 64.57 N 34.41 E
Kem' ≃, Ross. 86 58.31 N 92.04 E
Kema 112 1.23 N 125.04 E
Kema ≃, Ross. 76 60.16 N 37.20 E
Kema ≃, Ross. 76 59.21 N 44.29 E
Ké Macina 150 13.58 N 5.22 W
Kémah, Congo 273b 4.11 S 15.13 E
Kemah, Tür. 130 39.36 N 39.02 E
Kemah, Tx., U.S. 222 29.32 N 95.01 W
Kemaliye 130 39.16 N 38.29 E
Kemalpaşa, Tür. 130 41.30 N 41.30 E
Kemalpaşa, Tür. 130 38.25 N 27.26 E
Kemano 182 53.34 N 127.56 W
Kemasik 114 4.25 N 103.27 E
Kemayan 114 3.08 N 102.22 E
Kemayoran Airport ⊠ 269e 6.09 S 106.51 E
Kembani 112 1.34 S 122.54 E
Kembé 152 4.36 N 21.54 E
Kemberg 54 51.46 N 12.38 E
Kemblesville 208 39.45 N 75.50 W
Kembolcha 144 11.02 N 39.43 E
Kembs 58 47.41 N 7.30 E
Kembul 164 5.55 S 150.40 E
Kemčug ≃ 86 57.14 N 90.31 E
Kemena ≃ 112 3.10 N 113.03 E
Kemeneshát ⋀[2] 61 46.58 N 16.40 E
Kemer, Tür. 130 36.38 N 29.21 E
Kemer, Tür. 130 36.36 N 30.34 E
Kemer, Tür. 130 37.21 N 30.04 E
Kemer ≃ 267b 41.04 N 29.07 E
Kemer Barajı ⊜[1] 130 37.34 N 28.31 E
Kemerburgaz ⊕[8] 267b 41.09 N 28.54 E
Kemerhisar 130 37.49 N 34.36 E
Kemerovo 86 55.20 N 86.05 E
Kemerovo Oblast' □[4] 86 55.00 N 87.00 E
Kemi 26 65.49 N 24.32 E
Kemie 26 62.14 N 30.20 E
Kemijärvi 24 66.40 N 27.25 E
Kemijärvi ⊜ 24 66.36 N 27.24 E
Kemijoki ≃ 24 65.47 N 24.30 E
Kemiö → Kimito 26 60.10 N 22.45 E
Keml'a 80 54.42 N 45.15 E
Kemmel 50 50.47 N 2.49 E
Kemmelberg ∧[2] 50 50.47 N 2.50 E
Kemmerer 200 41.47 N 110.32 W
Kemminghausen ⊕[8] 263 51.34 N 7.29 E
Kemmuna (Comino) I 36 36.00 N 14.20 E
Kemnader See ⊜ 263 51.25 N 7.15 E
Kemnath 60 49.52 N 11.54 E
Kemnay 46 57.14 N 2.27 W
Kemnitz 54 54.04 N 13.31 E
Kémo-Gribingui □[5] 152 6.00 N 19.00 E
Kemp 222 32.26 N 96.13 W
Kemp, Lake ⊜[1] 196 33.45 N 99.13 W
Kemparana 150 12.50 N 4.56 W
Kemp Coast ⊥[2] 9 67.10 S 58.00 E
Kempele 26 64.55 N 25.30 E
Kempen 56 51.22 N 6.25 E
Kempen ⊕[1] 56 51.10 N 5.20 E
Kempener Land ⊕[1] 263 51.19 N 6.29 E
Kempenfelt Bay ⊂ 212 44.23 N 79.36 W
Kempenich 56 50.25 N 7.07 E
Kemper → Quimper 32 48.00 N 4.06 W
Kempisch Kanaal ≡ 56 51.10 N 4.49 E
Kemp Mill 284c 39.02 N 77.01 W
Kempner 196 31.05 N 98.00 W
Kemp Peninsula ›[1] 9 73.08 S 60.15 W
Kemps Bay 238 24.02 N 77.33 W
Kemps Creek ≃ 274a 33.51 S 150.46 E
Kempsey, Austl. 166 31.05 S 152.50 E
Kempsey, Eng., U.K. 42 52.08 N 2.12 W
Kempston 42 52.07 N 0.30 W
Kempt, Lac ⊜ 176 47.25 N 74.22 W
Kempten (Allgäu) 58 47.43 N 10.19 E
Kempton, Il., U.S. 216 40.56 N 88.14 W
Kempton, In., U.S. 216 40.17 N 86.13 W
Kempton Park 158 26.06 S 28.14 E
Kempton Park □[5] 273d 26.06 S 28.14 E
Kempton Park Race Course ♦ 260 51.25 N 0.23 W
Kemptville 212 45.01 N 75.38 W
Kemptville Creek ≃ 212 45.03 N 75.39 W
Kemsing 260 51.18 N 0.14 E
Kemubu 114 5.18 N 102.01 E
Kemujan, Pulau I 115a 5.48 S 110.28 E
Kemul, Kong ∧ 112 1.52 N 116.11 E
Ken ≃ 124 25.46 N 80.31 E
Ken, Loch ⊜ 44 55.02 N 4.02 W
Ken, Water of ≃ 44 55.04 N 4.08 W
Kena ≃ 24 62.05 N 39.06 E
Kenai 180 60.33 N 151.15 W
Kenai Fjords National Park ♦ 180 59.45 N 150.00 W
Kenai Mountains ⋀ 180 60.00 N 150.00 W
Kenai Peninsula ›[1] 180 60.10 N 150.00 W
Kenamuke Swamp ≡ 140 6.15 N 33.48 E
Kenansville, Fl., U.S. 220 27.52 N 80.59 W
Kenansville, N.C., U.S. 192 34.57 N 77.57 W
Kenaral 85 42.32 N 72.08 E
Kenašči 80 50.32 N 53.20 E
Kenashiga-sen ∧ 96 35.14 N 133.31 E
Kenaston 184 51.30 N 106.18 W
Kenberma 283 42.17 N 70.52 W
Kenbridge 192 36.57 N 78.07 W
Kenda 126 23.12 N 86.32 E
Kendai 124 22.45 N 82.37 E
Kendal, Sk., Can. 184 50.15 N 103.37 W
Kendal, Indon. 115a 6.55 S 110.12 E
Kendal, S. Afr. 158 26.04 S 28.58 E
Kendal, Eng., U.K. 44 54.20 N 2.45 W
Kendall, Austl. 166 31.38 S 152.43 E
Kendall, Fl., U.S. 220 25.40 N 80.19 W
Kendall, Mi., U.S. 216 42.22 N 85.49 W
Kendall, N.Y., U.S. 210 43.20 N 78.02 W
Kendall, Wi., U.S. 190 43.47 N 90.22 W
Kendall □[6] 216 41.38 N 88.27 W
Kendall, Cape › 176 63.36 N 87.09 W
Kendall, Mount ∧ 172 41.22 S 172.24 E
Kendall Park 208 40.31 N 74.24 W
Kendallville 216 41.26 N 85.15 W
Kendari 112 3.57 S 122.35 E
Kendari, Teluk ⊂ 112 3.57 S 122.38 E
Kendawangan 112 2.32 S 110.12 E
Kende 150 11.30 N 4.12 E
Kendenup 162 34.29 S 117.39 E
Kendghāta 126 24.05 N 87.10 E
Kendikolu I 122 5.57 N 73.24 E
Kendiktas ⋀ 85 43.35 N 74.45 E
Kendleton 222 29.27 N 96.00 W
Kendrāparha 120 20.30 N 86.25 E
Kendrew 158 32.31 S 24.30 E
Kendrick, Fl., U.S. 192 29.22 N 82.12 W
Kendrick, Id., U.S. 202 46.36 N 116.38 W
Kendrick Creek ≃ 226 38.00 N 119.50 W
Kendua 272b 22.34 N 88.10 E
Kendu Bay 154 0.22 S 34.39 E
Kendujhargarh 120 21.38 N 85.35 E
Kendyrlik 86 47.30 N 85.12 E
Kenedy 196 28.49 N 97.50 W
Kenefick 222 30.07 N 94.51 W
Kenema 150 7.52 N 11.12 W
Kenes, Kaz. 85 43.41 N 67.49 E
Kenes, Kaz. 85 43.59 N 73.35 E
Kenesaw 198 40.37 N 98.39 W
Kenga 86 57.27 N 80.57 E
Kenga ≃ 86 58.05 N 80.37 E
Kenge 152 4.52 S 16.59 E
Kengeja 154 5.25 S 39.44 E
Kēng Hkam, Mya. 110 21.01 N 98.29 E
Keng Hkam, Mya. 110 21.27 N 97.03 E
Kengkou, Zhg. 100 29.48 N 117.22 E
Kengkou, Zhg. 100 28.27 N 120.26 E
Kengtian 100 25.54 N 119.26 E
Kēng Tung 110 21.17 N 99.36 E
Kengun-chūtonchi, Rikujō-jieitai- ■ 92 32.46 N 130.45 E
Kenhardt 158 29.19 S 21.12 E
Kenhorst 208 40.18 N 75.57 W
Kenia 152 2.43 S 17.04 E
Kenia → Kenya □[1] 154 1.00 N 38.00 E
Kenia → Kirinyaga ∧ 154 0.10 S 37.20 E
Kéniéba 150 12.50 N 11.14 W
Kenilworth, Eng., U.K. 42 52.21 N 1.34 W
Kenilworth, Il., U.S. 278 42.05 N 87.43 W
Kenilworth, N.J., U.S. 276 40.40 N 74.17 W
Kenilworth, Pa., U.S. 208 40.14 N 75.38 W
Kenilworth, Ut,. U.S. 200 39.41 N 110.48 W
Kenilworth Castle ⊥ 42 52.21 N 1.34 W
Keningau 112 5.20 N 116.10 E
Kenitra 148 34.16 N 6.40 W
Kenitra □[4] 148 34.30 N 6.00 W
Kenley ⊕[8] 260 51.19 N 0.06 W
Kenli (Xishuanghe) 98 37.40 N 118.35 E
Kenly 192 35.35 N 78.07 W
Kenmare, Ire. 48 51.53 N 9.35 W
Kenmare, N.D., U.S. 198 48.40 N 102.04 W
Kenmare River ≃ 48 51.45 N 10.00 W
Kenmawr 279b 40.28 N 80.06 W
Kenmore, Scot., U.K. 46 56.34 N 3.59 W
Kenmore, N.Y., U.S. 210 42.57 N 78.52 W
Kenmore, Wa., U.S. 224 47.45 N 122.14 W
Kennard, In., U.S. 218 39.54 N 85.31 W
Kennard, Pa., U.S. 214 41.28 N 80.20 W
Kennard, Tx., U.S. 222 31.22 N 95.11 W
Kennebec 198 43.54 N 99.51 W
Kennebec ≃ 188 44.00 N 69.50 W
Kennebecasis Bay ⊂ 186 45.25 N 66.00 W
Kennebec Lake ⊜ 212 44.43 N 77.00 W
Kennebunk 188 43.23 N 70.32 W
Kennedale 222 32.38 N 97.13 W
Kennedy, Al., U.S. 194 33.35 N 87.59 W
Kennedy, N.Y., U.S. 214 42.09 N 79.06 W
Kennedy, Zimb. 154 18.52 S 27.10 E
Kennedy, Cape → Canaveral, Cape › 220 28.27 N 80.32 W
Kennedy, Mount ∧, B.C., Can. 182 50.49 N 125.33 W
Kennedy, Mount ∧, Yk., Can. 180 60.30 N 139.00 W
Kennedy Entrance ⋓ 180 59.00 N 152.00 W
Kennedy Lake ⊜ 182 49.05 N 125.40 W
Kennedy Peak ∧ 110 23.19 N 93.45 E
Kennedy Range ⋀ 162 24.30 S 115.00 E
Kennedyville 208 39.18 N 75.59 W
Kennemerduinen, Nationale Park de ♦ 52 52.25 N 4.35 E
Kenner 194 29.59 N 90.14 W
Kennerdell 214 41.16 N 79.51 W
Kennet ≃ 42 51.28 N 0.57 W
Kennetcook 186 45.11 N 63.44 W
Kenneth City 220 27.49 N 82.44 W
Kennett 194 36.14 N 90.03 W
Kennett ≃ 42 52.26 N 0.28 E
Kennett Square 208 39.50 N 75.42 W
Kennewick 202 46.12 N 119.08 W
Kenney 219 40.06 N 89.05 W
Kenney Dam ⊕[6] 182 53.37 N 124.58 W
Kennington, Eng., U.K. 42 51.10 N 0.54 E
Kennington, Eng., U.K. 42 51.43 N 1.15 W
Kennisis Lake ⊜ 212 45.13 N 78.39 W
Kenn Reef ✣[2] 160 21.12 S 155.46 E
Kenny 222 30.03 N 96.20 W
Kennydale 224 47.31 N 122.12 W
Kennywood Park ♦ 279b 40.23 N 79.52 W
Kénogami 186 48.26 N 71.14 W
Kenogami ≃ 176 51.06 N 84.28 W
Kénogami, Lac ⊜ 186 48.20 N 71.23 W
Kenogamissi Lake ⊜ 190 48.15 N 81.31 W
Keno Hill 180 63.55 N 135.18 W
Kenora 184 49.47 N 94.29 W
Kenosha 216 42.35 N 87.49 W
Kenosha □[6] 216 42.35 N 88.03 W
Kenova 188 38.23 N 82.34 W
Kenoza Lake 210 41.44 N 74.57 W
Kenoza Lake ⊜ 283 42.47 N 71.03 W
Kenozero, ozero ⊜ 24 62.03 N 38.14 E
Ken Rock 216 42.15 N 89.03 W
Kensal 198 47.18 N 98.43 W
Kense 86 46.49 N 68.20 E
Kensett 194 35.13 N 91.40 W
Kensico Lake ⊜ 276 41.07 N 73.45 W
Kensico Reservoir ⊜[1] 210 41.05 N 73.46 W
Kensington, Austl. 274a 33.55 S 151.14 E
Kensington, P.E., Can. 186 46.26 N 63.38 W
Kensington, Ca., U.S. 226 37.54 N 122.16 W
Kensington, Ct., U.S. 207 41.38 N 72.46 W
Kensington, Ks., U.S. 198 39.46 N 99.01 W
Kensington, Md., U.S. 284c 39.01 N 77.04 W
Kensington, Oh., U.S. 214 40.44 N 80.57 W
Kensington ⊕[8], S. Afr. 273d 26.12 S 28.06 E
Kensington ⊕[8], N.Y., U.S. 276 40.39 N 73.58 W
Kensington ⊕[8], Pa., U.S. 285 39.58 N 75.08 W
Kensington and Chelsea ⊕[8] 260 51.29 N 0.11 W
Kensington Estates 284c 39.02 N 77.05 W
Kensington Metropolitan Park ♦ 281 42.32 N 83.39 W
Kensington Park 220 27.22 N 82.31 W
Kent, S.L. 150 8.10 N 13.10 W
Kent, Ct., U.S. 207 41.43 N 73.28 W
Kent, N.Y., U.S. 210 43.20 N 78.08 W
Kent, Oh., U.S. 214 41.09 N 81.21 W
Kent, Or., U.S. 224 45.11 N 120.41 W
Kent, Wa., U.S. 224 47.22 N 122.14 W
Kent □[6], On., Can. 214 42.25 N 82.10 W
Kent □[6], Eng., U.K. 42 51.15 N 0.40 E
Kent □[6], De., U.S. 208 39.10 N 75.32 W
Kent □[6], Md., U.S. 208 39.13 N 76.04 W
Kent □[6], Mi., U.S. 216 42.56 N 85.33 W
Kent □[6], R.I., U.S. 207 41.40 N 71.38 W
Kent ≃ 44 54.15 N 2.48 W
Kent, Vale of V 42 51.10 N 0.30 E
Kent Acres 208 39.07 N 75.31 W
Kentallen 46 56.39 N 5.15 W
Kentani 158 32.31 S 28.19 E
Kentau 85 43.36 N 68.36 E
Kent Bridge 214 42.31 N 82.04 W
Kent County Airport ⊠ 216 42.54 N 85.39 W
Kentfield 282 37.57 N 122.33 W
Kent Group II 166 39.27 S 147.20 E
Kenthurst 274a 33.40 S 151.00 E
Kent Island I 208 38.55 N 76.20 W
Kent Lake ⊜ 216 42.32 N 83.40 W
Kentland, In., U.S. 216 40.46 N 87.26 W
Kentland, Md., U.S. 284c 38.55 N 76.53 W
Kenton, Eng., U.K. 42 50.38 N 3.28 W
Kenton, De., U.S. 208 39.13 N 75.39 W
Kenton, Mi., U.S. 190 46.29 N 88.53 W
Kenton, Oh., U.S. 216 40.38 N 83.36 W
Kenton, Tn., U.S. 194 36.12 N 89.00 W
Kenton □[6] 218 38.56 N 84.33 W
Kent Park 283 42.06 N 70.41 W
Kent Park ♦ 273d 26.08 S 28.04 E
Kent Peninsula ›[1] 176 68.30 N 107.00 W
Kent Point › 208 38.50 N 76.22 W
Kentucky □[3] 178 37.30 N 85.15 W
Kentucky ≃ 218 38.41 N 85.11 W
Kentucky, Middle Fork ≃ 192 37.35 N 83.40 W
Kentucky, North Fork ≃ 192 37.34 N 83.42 W
Kentucky, South Fork ≃ 192 37.34 N 83.42 W
Kentucky Horse Park ♦ 218 38.08 N 84.31 W
Kentucky Lake ⊜[1] 194 36.25 N 88.05 W
Kent Village 284c 38.55 N 76.53 W
Kentville 186 45.05 N 64.30 W
Kentwood, La., U.S. 194 30.56 N 90.30 W
Kentwood, Mi., U.S. 216 42.52 N 85.38 W
Kent Woodlands 282 37.57 N 122.34 W
Kenvil 276 40.52 N 74.37 W
Kenwick 168a 32.02 S 115.58 E
Kenwood, Ca., U.S. 226 38.25 N 122.33 W
Kenwood, Md., U.S. 284b 39.21 N 76.31 W
Kenwood, Oh., U.S. 218 39.12 N 84.22 W
Kenwood ⊕[8] 278 41.49 N 87.36 W
Kenwood ⊥ 260 51.34 N 0.10 W
Kenya □[1] 154 1.00 N 38.00 E
Kenya, Mount → Kirinyaga ∧ 154 0.10 S 37.20 E
Kenyon, Eng., U.K. 262 53.27 N 2.34 W
Kenyon, Mn., U.S. 190 44.16 N 92.59 W
Kenyon, R.I., U.S. 207 41.26 N 71.37 W
Ken-zaki › 268 35.08 N 139.41 E
Kenzingen 58 48.11 N 7.46 E
Kenzou 152 4.10 N 15.02 E
Keokea 229a 20.42 N 156.21 W
Keokuk 190 40.23 N 91.23 W
Keoladeo National Park ♦ 124 27.10 N 77.20 E
Keonchi 124 22.38 N 81.47 E
Keo Neua, Col de)(110 18.23 N 105.09 E
Keon Park 274b 37.42 S 145.01 E
Keosauqua 190 40.43 N 91.57 W
Keota, Ia., U.S. 190 41.21 N 91.57 W
Keota, Ok., U.S. 196 35.15 N 94.55 W
Keowee, Lake ⊜[1] 192 34.45 N 82.55 W
Kepa (Mittagskogel) ∧ 61 46.31 N 13.57 E
Kepala Batas 114 5.31 N 100.26 E
Kepanjen 115a 8.07 S 112.34 E
Kepi 164 6.32 S 139.19 E
Kępice 30 54.15 N 16.52 E
Kepina 24 65.24 N 41.50 E
Keping Shan ⋀ 85 40.00 N 77.10 E
Kępno 30 51.17 N 17.59 E
Kepo 112 2.56 S 106.33 E
Keppel Bay ⊂ 166 23.21 S 150.55 E
Keppel Harbour ⊂ 271c 1.16 N 103.50 E
Kepsut 130 39.41 N 28.09 E
Keptown 219 39.05 N 88.40 W
Kequan 98 36.04 N 114.00 E
Kerala □[3] 122 10.00 N 76.30 E
Keram ≃ 164 4.07 S 144.07 E
Keramian, Pulau I 112 5.04 S 114.36 E
Kerandin 112 0.12 S 104.46 E
Kerang 166 35.44 S 143.55 E
Keranyo 144 5.04 N 38.18 E
Keratéa 38 37.48 N 23.59 E
Keratsínion 267c 37.58 N 23.37 E
Keraudren, Cape › 162 19.57 S 119.45 E
Kerava 26 60.24 N 25.07 E
Keravat 164 4.19 S 152.01 E
Kerbat ≃ 114 5.01 N 102.51 E
Kerbela → Karbalā' 128 32.36 N 44.02 E
Kerbi ≃ 89 52.28 N 136.25 E
Kerby 202 42.11 N 123.39 W
Kerč' 78 45.22 N 36.27 E
Kerčel' 86 59.18 N 64.46 E
Kerčemja 24 61.28 N 53.50 E
Kerčenskij poluostrov ›[1] 78 45.15 N 36.00 E
Kerčenskij proliv ⋓ 78 45.22 N 36.38 E
Kerčevskij 24 59.55 N 56.17 E
Kerch → Kerč' 78 45.22 N 36.27 E
Kerckhoff Lake ⊜[1] 226 37.09 N 119.31 W
Kéré 154 5.16 N 26.11 E
Kéré ≃ 140 5.19 N 25.40 E
Kerec, mys › 24 65.20 N 39.40 E
Kerej, ozero ⊜ 86 50.08 N 68.45 E
Kerema 164 8.00 S 145.45 E
Keremeos 182 49.12 N 119.50 W
Kerem Maharal 132 32.39 N 34.59 E
Kerempe Burnu › 130 42.01 N 33.21 E
Keren 144 15.46 N 38.28 E
Kerend 128 34.16 N 46.15 E
Kerens 222 32.07 N 96.13 W
Kerepes 264c 47.34 N 19.18 E
Keret' 24 66.16 N 33.34 E
Keret', ozero ⊜ 24 65.55 N 32.56 E
Kerewan 150 13.29 N 16.10 W
Kerga 24 62.39 N 46.00 E
Kergez 84 40.18 N 49.38 E
Kerguélen, Îles II 6 49.15 S 69.10 E
Kerguelen Plateau ✣[3] 6 55.00 S 75.00 E
Kerhonkson 210 41.46 N 74.17 W
Kerian ≃ 114 5.10 N 100.26 E
Kericho 154 0.22 S 35.17 E
Keri Kera 140 12.21 N 32.46 E
Kerikeri 172 35.13 S 173.58 E
Kerimäki 26 61.55 N 29.17 E
Kerinci, Gunung ∧ 112 1.42 S 101.16 E
Kerio ≃ 154 2.59 N 36.07 E
Keríon 38 37.40 N 20.48 E
Keritang 112 0.51 S 102.39 E
Keriya ≃ 120 38.30 N 82.10 E
Kerka ≃ 61 46.28 N 16.36 E
Kerkafalva 61 46.46 N 16.30 E
Kerkdriel 52 51.46 N 5.20 E
Kerkebet 144 16.18 N 37.24 E
Kerken 56 51.27 N 6.22 E
Kerkenna, Îles II 148 34.44 N 11.12 E
Kerkhove 50 50.48 N 3.30 E
Kerkhoven 198 45.11 N 95.19 W
Kerki, Ross. 24 63.43 N 54.05 E
Kerki, Turk. 128 37.50 N 65.12 E
Kérkira (Corfu) 38 39.36 N 19.56 E
Kérkira (Corfu) I 38 39.40 N 19.45 E
Kerkrade [-Holz] 56 50.52 N 6.04 E
Kerling 114 3.35 N 101.36 E
Kermadec Islands II 14 29.16 S 177.55 W
Kermadec Ridge ✣[3] 14 30.30 S 178.30 W
Kermadec Trench ✣[1] 14 30.00 S 177.00 W
Kermajärvi ⊜ 26 62.28 N 28.40 E
Kermān, Īrān 128 30.17 N 57.05 E
Kerman, Ca., U.S. 226 36.43 N 120.04 W
Kermān □[4] 128 29.00 N 57.30 E
Kermit 196 31.51 N 103.05 W
Kermit Roosevelt Seamount ✣[3] 16 39.35 N 146.00 W
Kermode, Mount ∧ 182 52.57 N 131.51 W
Kern □[6] 228 35.20 N 118.55 W
Kern ≃ 204 35.13 N 119.17 W
Kern, South Fork ≃ 204 35.40 N 118.27 W
Kern City 228 35.18 N 119.05 W
Kernersville 192 36.07 N 80.04 W
Kernforschungszentrum ʋ[3] 56 49.07 N 8.26 E
Kernhof 61 47.49 N 15.32 E
Kern Island Canal ≡ 228 35.22 N 119.01 W
Kern Lake Bed ⊜ 228 35.10 N 119.05 W
Kern River Channel ≃[1] 226 35.49 N 119.40 W
Kernville 204 35.45 N 118.25 W
Keroh 114 5.43 N 101.00 E
Keros 24 60.44 N 52.50 E
Kérou 150 10.50 N 2.06 E
Kérouané 150 9.16 N 9.01 W
Kerowagi 164 5.50 S 144.50 E
Kerpen 56 50.52 N 6.41 E
Kerpinen' 38 46.47 N 28.22 E
Kerr 214 41.03 N 78.25 W
Kerrera I 46 56.23 N 5.34 W
Kerridge 262 53.17 N 2.06 W
Kerridge Hill ∧[2] 262 53.17 N 2.06 W
Kerrobert 184 51.55 N 109.08 W
Kerrtown 214 41.38 N 80.10 W
Kerruish Park ♦ 279a 41.26 N 81.34 W
Kerrville 196 30.02 N 99.08 W
Kerry 42 52.30 N 3.16 W
Kerry □[6] 48 52.10 N 9.30 W
Kerry Head › 48 52.25 N 9.57 W
Kersa 144 9.28 N 41.53 E
Kersbrook 168b 34.47 S 138.51 E
Kersey 214 41.21 N 78.35 W
Kershaw 192 34.33 N 80.35 W
Kersinyane 150 15.24 N 10.10 W
Kersley 182 52.49 N 122.25 W
Kerspestausee ⊜[1] 263 51.08 N 7.30 E
Kerstenhausen 56 51.04 N 9.13 E
Kert, Oued ≃ 34 35.15 N 3.15 W
Kertamulia 112 0.23 S 109.09 E
Kerteh 114 4.31 N 103.27 E
Kerteminde 41 55.27 N 10.40 E
Kertosono 115a 7.35 S 112.06 E
Kerulen (Cherlen) (Herlen) ≃ 90 48.48 N 117.00 E
Kerva 80 55.37 N 39.35 E

Symbols in the index entries represent the broad categories identified in the key at the right. Symbols with superior numbers (⋀[1]) identify subcategories (see complete key on page *I* · *1*).

Symbole im Register stellen die rechts im Schlüssel erklärten Kategorien dar. Symbole mit hochgestellten Ziffern (⋀[1]) bezeichnen Unterabteilungen einer Kategorie (vgl. vollständiger Schlüssel auf Seite *I* · *1*).

Los símbolos incluídos en el texto del índice representan las grandes categorías identificadas con la clave a la derecha. Los símbolos con numeros en su parte superior (⋀[1]) identifican las subcategorías (véase la clave completa en la página *I* · *1*).

Les symboles de l'index représentent les catégories indiquées dans la légende à droite. Les symboles suivis d'un indice (⋀[1]) représentent des sous-catégories (voir légende complète à la page *I* · *1*).

Os símbolos incluídos no texto do índice representam as grandes categorias identificadas com a chave à direita. Os símbolos com números em sua parte superior (⋀[1]) identificam as subcategorias (veja-se a chave completa à página *I* · *1*).

∧	Mountain	Berg	Montaña	Montagne	Montanha
⋀	Mountains	Gebirge	Montañas	Montagnes	Montanhas
)(	Pass	Paß	Paso	Col	Passo
V	Valley, Canyon	Tal, Cañon	Valle, Cañón	Vallée, Canyon	Vale, Canhão
≃	Plain	Ebene	Llano	Plaine	Planície
›	Cape	Kap	Cabo	Cap	Cabo
I	Island	Insel	Isla	Île	Ilha
II	Islands	Inseln	Islas	Îles	Ilhas
⊥	Other Topographic Features	Andere Topographische Objekte	Otros Elementos Topográficos	Autres données topographiques	Outros acidentes topográficos

ESPAÑOL

Nombre	Página	Lat.°′	Long.°′ W = Oeste
Kerzaz	148	29.30 N	1.37 W
Kerzendorf	264a	52.16 N	13.17 E
Kerženec	80	56.28 N	44.26 E
Kerženec ≃	80	56.05 N	45.03 E
Kerzers	58	46.58 N	7.12 E
Kesabpur	126	22.55 N	89.13 E
Ke Sach	110	9.46 N	105.59 E
Kesagami Lake ⊜	176	50.23 N	80.15 W
Kesälahti	26	61.54 N	29.50 E
Keşan	130	40.51 N	26.37 E
Keşap	130	40.55 N	38.31 E
Kesbern	263	51.20 N	7.42 E
Kesch, Piz ∧	58	46.38 N	9.52 E
Kesem ≃	144	9.14 N	40.06 E
Kesennuma	92	38.54 N	141.35 E
Kesh	48	54.32 N	7.43 W
Keshan	89	48.02 N	125.51 E
Keshena	190	44.53 N	88.38 W
Keshendeh	120	36.05 N	66.51 E
Keshequa Creek ≃	210	42.43 N	77.50 W
Keshod	120	21.18 N	70.15 E
Keşiş Dağları ⋏	130	39.50 N	39.45 E
Keskastel	56	48.58 N	7.02 E
Keskin	130	39.41 N	33.37 E
Keski-Suomen lääni □[4]	26	62.30 N	25.30 E
Keskozero	24	61.24 N	33.12 E
Keskuvejem, gora ∧	180	66.12 N	177.40 W
Kes'ma	76	58.27 N	37.04 E
Kesova Gora	76	57.35 N	37.17 E
Kespur	126	22.35 N	87.29 E
Kesra	36	35.49 N	9.22 E
Kessebüren	263	51.31 N	7.43 E
Kessel	56	51.08 N	4.37 E
Kesselsdorf	54	51.02 N	13.35 E
Kessingland	42	52.25 N	1.42 E
Kesswil	58	47.36 N	9.20 E
Kestel Gölü ⊜	130	37.24 N	30.28 E
Kestell	158	28.19 S	28.38 E
Kesten'ga	24	65.55 N	31.47 E
Kestilä	26	64.21 N	26.17 E
Keston ◆[3]	260	51.22 N	0.02 E
Keswick, On., Can.	212	44.15 N	79.28 W
Keswick, Eng., U.K.	44	54.37 N	3.08 W
Keszthely	30	46.46 N	17.15 E
Ket' ≃	86	58.55 N	81.32 E
Keta	150	5.55 N	1.00 E
Keta ≃	94	34.56 N	137.50 E
Keta, ozero ⊜	74	68.44 N	90.00 E
Ketaka	96	35.30 N	134.03 E
Keta Lagoon c	150	5.54 N	0.56 E
Ketam, Pulau I	271c	1.24 N	103.57 E
Ketama	34	34.50 N	4.37 W
Ketang	100	22.58 N	115.28 E
Ketapang, Indon.	112	1.52 S	109.59 E
Ketapang, Indon.	115a	5.44 S	105.48 E
Ketapang, Indon.	115a	6.54 S	113.17 E
Ketaun	112	3.23 S	101.49 E
Ketčenery	80	47.18 N	44.31 E
Ketchikan	182	55.21 N	131.35 W
Ketchum	202	43.40 N	114.21 W
Kete Krachi	150	7.46 N	0.03 W
Ketelmeer ⊜	52	52.35 N	5.45 E
Keti Bandar	120	24.08 N	67.27 E
Ketingwan ∧	154	0.40 N	35.50 E
Ketoj, ostrov I	74	47.20 N	152.28 E
Kétou	150	7.22 N	2.36 E
Ketovo	86	55.21 N	65.18 E
Kętrzyn (Rastenburg)	30	54.06 N	21.23 E
Ketsch	56	49.22 N	8.31 E
Ketta	152	1.28 N	15.56 E
Kettering, Eng., U.K.	42	52.24 N	0.44 W
Kettering, Md., U.S.	284c	38.53 N	76.49 W
Kettering, Oh., U.S.	218	39.41 N	84.10 W
Kettinge	41	54.42 N	11.45 E
Kettle ≃, Mb., Can.	184	56.23 N	94.34 W
Kettle ≃, N.A.	182	48.42 N	118.07 W
Kettle ≃, Mn., U.S.	190	45.52 N	92.45 W
Kettle Creek ≃, On., Can.	212	42.40 N	81.13 W
Kettle Creek ≃, Pa., U.S.	210	41.18 N	77.51 W
Kettle Creek State Park ♦	214	41.23 N	77.56 W
Kettle Falls	202	48.36 N	118.03 W
Kettleman City	226	36.00 N	119.57 W
Kettleman Hills ⋏[2]	226	36.00 N	120.00 W
Kettle Rapids Dam ◆[6]	184	56.23 N	94.38 W
Kettlersville	216	40.22 N	84.16 W
Kettleshulme	262	53.19 N	2.01 W
Kettlewell	44	54.09 N	2.02 W
Kettwig	56	51.22 N	6.56 E
Kęty	30	49.53 N	19.13 E
Ketzin	54	52.28 N	12.50 E
Keudemane	114	5.15 N	96.55 E
Keudepasi	114	4.18 N	95.56 E
Keudeteunom	114	4.27 N	95.48 E
Keudeunga	114	5.01 N	95.22 E
Keuka Lake ⊜	210	42.27 N	77.10 W
Keuka Lake, West Branch c	210	42.33 N	77.09 W
Keuka Park	210	42.37 N	77.06 W
Keukenhof ♦	52	52.16 N	4.33 E
Keul'	88	58.25 N	102.49 E
Keula	54	51.20 N	10.31 E
Keum ≃	86	59.32 N	70.35 E
Keurboomsrivier	158	34.00 S	23.24 E
Keurusselkä ⊜	26	62.10 N	24.40 E
Keuruu	26	62.16 N	24.42 E
Kevdo-Mel'sitovo	80	53.09 N	43.54 E
Kevelaer	52	51.35 N	6.15 E
Kevin	202	48.44 N	111.57 W
Kevsala	80	45.48 N	42.41 E
Kew, Austl.	169	37.49 S	145.02 E
Kew, T./C. Is.	238	21.54 N	72.02 W
Kewanee	190	41.14 N	89.55 W
Kewanna	216	41.01 N	86.25 W
Kewaunee	190	44.27 N	87.30 W
Keweenaw Bay c	190	46.56 N	88.23 W
Keweenaw Peninsula ›[1]	190	47.12 N	88.25 W
Keweenaw Point ›	190	47.30 N	87.50 W
Kew Gardens ♦, On., Can.	275b	43.40 N	79.18 W
Kew Gardens ♦, Eng., U.K.	260	51.28 N	0.18 W
Key, Lough ⊜	48	54.00 N	8.15 W
Keyala	154	4.27 N	32.52 E
Keyangkeer Shan ∧	120	31.20 N	87.13 E
Keya Paha ≃	198	42.54 N	99.00 W
Key Biscayne	220	25.42 N	80.10 W
Keyes, Ca., U.S.	226	37.33 N	120.54 W
Keyes, Ok., U.S.	196	36.48 N	102.15 W
Keyesport	219	38.44 N	89.17 W
Keyhole Reservoir ⊜[1]	198	44.21 N	104.51 W
Keyhole State Park ♦	198	44.19 N	104.43 W
Keyihe	89	50.40 N	122.27 E
Keyingham	44	53.42 N	0.07 W
Key Largo	220	25.04 N	80.23 W
Key Largo I	220	25.16 N	80.19 W
Keymer	42	50.55 N	0.08 W
Keynes Hill ∧[2]	168b	34.37 S	139.06 E
Keyneton	168b	34.34 S	139.08 E
Keynsham	42	51.26 N	2.30 W
Keynshamburg	154	19.15 S	29.39 E
Keyport, N.J., U.S.	276	40.25 N	74.12 W
Keyport, Wa., U.S.	224	47.42 N	122.38 W
Keyport Harbor c	276	40.26 N	74.12 W
Keysborough	274b	38.00 S	145.10 E
Keysbrook	168a	32.26 S	115.59 E
Keyser	188	39.26 N	78.58 W
Keystone, In., U.S.	216	40.36 N	85.16 W
Keystone, Ia., U.S.	190	41.59 N	92.11 W
Keystone, S.D., U.S.	198	43.53 N	103.25 W
Keystone, W.V., U.S.	192	37.24 N	81.27 W
Keystone Lake ⊜[1], Ok., U.S.	196	36.15 N	96.25 W
Keystone Lake ⊜[1], Pa., U.S.	214	40.45 N	79.15 W

FRANÇAIS

Nom	Page	Lat.°′	Long.°′ W = Ouest
Keystone Peak ∧	200	31.53 N	111.13 W
Keystone State Park ♦	214	40.23 N	79.24 W
Keysville, Fl., U.S.	220	27.52 N	82.06 W
Keysville, Va., U.S.	192	37.02 N	78.29 W
Keytesville	194	39.26 N	92.56 W
Key West	220	24.33 N	81.46 W
Key West Island I	220	24.33 N	81.47 W
Key West Naval Air Station ■	220	24.34 N	81.41 W
Keyworth	42	52.52 N	1.05 W
Kez	80	57.53 N	53.43 E
Kezi	154	20.58 S	28.32 E
Kezilesu Zizhizhou □[8]	85	40.00 N	75.30 E
Kežma	88	58.59 N	101.09 E
Kežmarok	30	49.08 N	20.25 E
Kgalagadi □[5]	156	25.00 S	22.00 E
Kgatleng □[5]	156	24.28 S	26.05 E
Kgokgole ≃	158	26.44 S	22.28 E
Kgun Lake ⊜	180	61.32 N	163.45 W
Khaanziir, Ras ›	144	10.55 N	45.47 E
Khabab	132	33.00 N	36.16 E
Khabīr, Kūh-e ∧	128	28.48 N	56.26 E
Khābūr, Nahr al- (Habur) ≃	130	35.08 N	40.26 E
Khādar	272a	28.33 N	77.22 E
Khadari, Wādī al- V	140	10.29 N	26.15 E
Khadaungnge Taung ∧	110	18.57 N	94.37 E
Khadki (Kirkee)	122	18.34 N	73.52 E
Khadra	34	36.15 N	0.35 E
Khafūrī, Wādī V	142	29.37 N	32.04 E
Khagaria	124	25.30 N	86.29 E
Khagdon ≃[1]	126	22.09 N	90.05 E
Khāgrāmuri	272b	22.26 N	88.14 E
Khaïdhárion	267c	38.01 N	23.33 E
Khair	124	27.57 N	77.50 E
Khairābād	124	27.32 N	80.45 E
Khairāgarh	120	21.25 N	80.53 E
Khairbani	126	24.14 N	87.05 E
Khairna	272c	19.06 N	73.01 E
Khairpur, Pāk.	120	27.32 N	68.46 E
Khairpur, Pāk.	123	29.35 N	72.14 E
Khairwāra	120	23.59 N	73.35 E
Khajrāho	120	24.50 N	79.58 E
Khajuri	126	21.52 N	87.58 E
Khajuri ◆[8]	272a	28.43 N	77.16 E
Khakassia → Chakasija □[3]	86	53.00 N	90.00 E
Kha Khaeng ≃	110	14.55 N	99.07 E
Khakhea	156	24.51 S	23.20 E
Khalándrion	267c	38.01 N	23.48 E
Khalatse	123	34.20 N	76.49 E
Khālidī, Khirbat al- ⊥	132	29.39 N	35.14 E
Khalkhāl	128	37.37 N	48.32 E
Khalkhalah	132	33.04 N	36.32 E
Khálki I	38	36.17 N	27.35 E
Khalkidhikí □[9]	38	40.25 N	23.27 E
Khalkís	38	38.28 N	23.36 E
Khālsar	120	34.31 N	77.41 E
Khambhāliya	120	22.12 N	69.39 E
Khambhāt	120	22.18 N	72.37 E
Khambhāt, Gulf of c	122	21.00 N	72.30 E
Khāmgaon	122	20.41 N	76.34 E
Khamir	144	16.05 N	43.55 E
Khāmis, Ash-Shallāl al- (Fifth Cataract) ⌊	140	18.23 N	33.47 E
Khamīs Mushayṭ	144	18.18 N	42.44 E
Khamkeut	110	18.15 N	104.43 E
Khamma	70	36.47 N	12.02 E
Khammam	122	17.15 N	80.09 E
Khamsah	142	30.25 N	32.23 E
Khan ≃, Lao	110	19.54 N	102.09 E
Khan ≃, Namibia	156	22.37 S	14.56 E
Khāna	126	23.20 N	87.44 E
Khānābād	120	36.41 N	69.07 E
Khān Abū Shāmāt	132	33.40 N	36.54 E
Khānākul	126	22.43 N	87.51 E
Khān al-Baghdādī	128	33.51 N	42.33 E
Khānaqīn	128	34.21 N	45.22 E
Khān Arnabah	132	33.11 N	35.53 E
Khancoban	171b	36.12 S	148.05 E
Khandaghosh	126	23.13 N	87.41 E
Khandela	120	27.36 N	75.30 E
Khandwa	124	21.50 N	76.20 E
Khān-e Chahār Bāgh, Afg.	120	35.58 N	69.38 E
Khān-e Chahār Bāgh, Afg.	128	37.00 N	65.14 E
Khāneh Khvodī	128	36.02 N	55.59 E
Khānewāl	123	30.18 N	71.56 E
Khāngāh Dogrān	123	31.50 N	73.37 E
Khāngarh, Pāk.	120	28.22 N	71.43 E
Khāngarh, Pāk.	123	29.55 N	71.10 E
Khangkhai	110	19.28 N	103.15 E
Khaniá	38	35.31 N	24.02 E
Khaníon, Kólpos c	38	35.34 N	23.48 E
Khānkurda	126	22.00 N	87.25 E
Khanna	123	30.42 N	76.13 E
Khannā, Qā' ≡	132	32.04 N	36.26 E
Khānozai	120	30.37 N	67.19 E
Khānpur, India	272b	22.40 N	88.16 E
Khānpur, Pāk.	123	28.39 N	70.39 E
Khānpur ◆[8], India	272a	28.34 N	77.01 E
Khānpur ◆[8], India	272a	28.31 N	77.14 E
Khān Shaykhūn	130	35.26 N	36.38 E
Khanty-Mansiysk → Chanty-Mansijsk	74	61.00 N	69.06 E
Khān Yūnus	132	31.21 N	34.19 E
Khao Laem Reservoir ⊜[1]	110	14.50 N	98.30 E
Khao Saming	110	12.21 N	102.27 E
Khao Sok National Park ♦	110	8.55 N	98.35 E
Khao Yoi	110	13.14 N	99.50 E
Khapalu	123	35.10 N	76.20 E
Khaptad National Park ♦	124	29.28 N	81.10 E
Kharab, Ghoubet al c	144	11.30 N	42.35 E
Kharabā	132	32.34 N	36.27 E
Kharagdiha	124	24.25 N	86.10 E
Kharagpur, India	124	25.07 N	86.33 E
Kharagpur, India	126	22.20 N	87.20 E
Kharak	123	33.07 N	71.06 E
Khārān	120	28.35 N	65.25 E
Kharānoq	128	32.20 N	54.39 E
Kharar, India	123	30.45 N	76.39 E
Kharar, India	126	22.42 N	87.41 E
Khāravli ∧[2]	272c	18.54 N	72.55 E
Kharāyij, Sabkhat al- ⊜	130	35.40 N	37.20 E
Kharaz, Jabal ∧	144	12.44 N	44.09 E
Kharbatā	132	31.57 N	35.04 E
Kharbine → Harbin	89	45.45 N	126.41 E
Khardaha	126	22.44 N	88.22 E
Khārghar	272c	19.03 N	73.04 E
Kharg Island → Khārk, Jazīreh-ye I	128	29.15 N	50.20 E
Khargon	120	21.49 N	75.36 E
Khāriān Cantonment	123	32.49 N	73.52 E
Khariār Road	122	20.54 N	82.31 E
Khārijah, Al-Wāḥāt al- ⊤[4]	140	25.20 N	30.35 E
Kharīm, Jabal ∧	132	30.17 N	33.58 E
Kharīṭ, Wādī al- V	140	24.26 N	33.03 E
Khārk, Jazīreh-ye (Kharg Island) I	128	29.15 N	50.20 E
Kharkov → Char'kov	78	50.00 N	36.15 E
Kharmān, Kūh-e ∧	128	29.13 N	53.35 E
Kharri	272b	22.55 N	88.14 E
Kharsāwān	124	22.48 N	85.50 E
Kharsia	124	21.58 N	83.07 E
Khartoum → Al-Kharṭūm	140	15.36 N	32.32 E

PORTUGUÊS

Nome	Página	Lat.°′	Long.°′ W = Oeste
Khartoum North → Al-Kharṭūm Baḥrī	140	15.38 N	32.33 E
Khartum → Al-Kharṭūm	140	15.36 N	32.32 E
Kharumwa	154	3.12 S	32.39 E
Khāsbāti	272b	22.55 N	88.25 E
Khasebake	156	20.41 S	24.29 E
Khāsh, Afg.	128	31.31 N	62.52 E
Khāsh, Īrān	128	28.14 N	61.14 E
Khāsh ≃	128	31.11 N	62.05 E
Khāsh, Dasht-e ◆[2]	128	31.50 N	62.30 E
Khashab, Jabal al- ∧[2]	142	29.56 N	31.01 E
Khashm al-Qirbah	140	14.58 N	35.55 E
Khashm al-Qirbah, Khazzān ⊜[1]	140	14.40 N	35.55 E
Khashshab, Tur at al- ≍	273c	29.53 N	31.17 E
Khashum	140	12.27 N	28.02 E
Khāş Konar	120	34.39 N	70.54 E
Khaskovo → Haskovo	38	41.56 N	25.33 E
Khatauli	124	29.17 N	77.43 E
Khātegaon	124	22.36 N	76.55 E
Khātra	126	22.59 N	86.51 E
Khatt, Oued al V	148	26.45 N	13.03 W
Khaur	123	33.16 N	72.28 E
Khāvda	120	23.51 N	69.43 E
Khawrah	144	14.26 N	46.09 E
Khawsa	110	15.03 N	97.50 E
Khayāla ◆[8]	272a	28.40 N	77.06 E
Khaybar, Ḥarrat ⊥[9]	128	25.30 N	39.45 E
Khayerpur	272b	22.35 N	88.33 E
Khayl, Kathīb al- ⊥[8]	142	30.33 N	32.28 E
Khayra Bil ⊜	272b	22.52 N	88.29 E
Khayrasole	126	23.48 N	87.16 E
Khayung ≃	110	15.07 N	104.42 E
Kheardaha	272b	22.29 N	88.28 E
Khe Bo	110	19.08 N	104.41 E
Khed	122	17.43 N	73.23 E
Khefapur	272a	28.30 N	77.05 E
Khejurdaha	272b	22.59 N	88.10 E
Khemis	148	36.16 N	2.13 E
Khemis el Khechna	34	36.39 N	3.20 E
Khemisset	148	33.50 N	6.03 W
Khemisset □[4]	148	33.50 N	6.05 W
Khem Karan	123	31.09 N	74.34 E
Khemmarat	110	16.03 N	105.13 E
Khenchla	148	35.28 N	7.11 E
Khenifra	148	33.00 N	5.40 W
Khenifra □[4]	148	32.35 N	5.10 W
Khenjān	120	35.36 N	70.59 E
Khenyen	272b	22.59 N	88.19 E
Khera ◆[8]	272a	28.46 N	77.08 E
Kheri	124	27.54 N	80.48 E
Kheri Branch ≍	124	28.11 N	80.25 E
Kherli	124	27.12 N	77.02 E
Kherrata	148	36.31 N	5.26 E
Khersān ≃	128	31.33 N	50.22 E
Kherson → Cherson	78	46.38 N	32.35 E
Khetia	120	21.40 N	74.35 E
Khevāj	120	38.13 N	71.02 E
Khewāri	120	26.36 N	68.52 E
Khewra	123	32.39 N	73.01 E
Kheyr Khāneh	128	34.57 N	63.37 E
Khichīwāra Plateau ⋏[1]	124	24.25 N	77.30 E
Khichripur ◆[8]	272a	28.37 N	77.19 E
Khilchipur	124	24.02 N	76.34 E
Khilkāpur	272b	22.46 N	88.29 E
Khimki → Chimki	82	55.54 N	37.26 E
Khíos	38	38.22 N	26.08 E
Khíos (Chios) I	38	38.22 N	26.00 E
Khipro	120	25.50 N	69.22 E
Khirbat al-Ghazālah	132	32.44 N	36.12 E
Khirbat 'Awwād	132	32.19 N	36.43 E
Khirbat Qanāfār	132	33.38 N	35.43 E
Khirbat Umm as-Surab	132	32.26 N	36.19 E
Khirbitā	142	30.45 N	30.40 E
Khiri Mat	110	16.50 N	99.48 E
Khirpai	126	22.42 N	87.37 E
Khirr, Wādī al- V	128	31.51 N	44.29 E
Khisfīn	132	32.51 N	35.49 E
Khiuri Khala ∧	124	29.58 N	81.18 E
Khiva → Chiva	72	41.24 N	60.22 E
Khlong Khlung	110	16.12 N	99.43 E
Khlong Thom	110	7.56 N	99.09 E
Khlong Yai	110	11.46 N	102.54 E
Khlung	110	12.27 N	102.14 E
Khmel'nitskiy → Chmel'nickij	78	49.25 N	27.00 E
Khoai, Hon I	110	8.26 N	104.50 E
Khogali	140	6.08 N	27.47 E
Khojāng ∧	124	28.41 N	85.09 E
Khok Kloi	110	8.17 N	98.19 E
Khok Pho	110	6.43 N	101.06 E
Khoksa	126	23.48 N	89.17 E
Khok Samrong	110	15.04 N	100.44 E
Kholargós	267c	38.00 N	23.48 E
Kholm	120	36.42 N	67.41 E
Kholombidzo Falls ⌊	154	15.54 S	34.44 E
Khomām	128	37.22 N	49.40 E
Khomas Hochland ⋏[1]	156	22.30 S	16.30 E
Khomeyn	128	33.38 N	50.04 E
Khomeynīshahr	128	32.41 N	51.31 E
Khomodimo	156	22.46 S	23.52 E
Khondmāl Hills ⋏[2]	122	20.20 N	84.00 E
Khong → Mekong ≃	12	10.33 N	105.24 E
Khoni	272c	19.10 N	73.07 E
Khon Kaen	110	16.26 N	102.50 E
Khóra	38	37.04 N	21.43 E
Khorāsān □[4]	128	35.00 N	58.00 E
Khóra Sfakíon	38	35.12 N	24.09 E
Khordha	120	20.11 N	85.37 E
Khorel	272b	22.42 N	88.19 E
Khorramābād	128	33.30 N	48.20 E
Khorram Daraq	128	36.26 N	48.35 E
Khorramshahr	128	30.25 N	48.11 E
Khoru	272b	22.51 N	88.31 E
Khossanto	150	13.08 N	11.53 W
Khouribga	148	32.54 N	6.57 W
Khouribga □[4]	148	32.50 N	6.30 W
Khowai	120	24.06 N	91.38 E
Khowāng	120	27.16 N	94.53 E
Khowst	120	33.22 N	69.57 E
Khrisokhoús, Kólpos c	130	35.06 N	32.25 E
Khrisoúpolis	38	40.58 N	24.42 E
Khudiān	123	30.59 N	74.17 E
Khuff	128	24.57 N	44.42 E
Khugaung	110	26.07 N	98.18 E
Khūgīānī Sānī	120	31.31 N	66.12 E
Khuis	156	26.37 S	21.45 E
Khuīyāla	120	27.14 N	70.30 E
Khu Khan	110	14.42 N	104.12 E
Khulna	124	22.48 N	89.33 E
Khulna □[5]	126	22.45 N	89.30 E
Khŭm Bathéay	110	11.59 N	104.57 E
Khumbur Khūlē Ghar ∧	120	32.49 N	68.47 E
Khungdugang ⋏	124	27.31 N	89.02 E
Khūnjerāb Pass ✕	123	36.52 N	75.27 E
Khun Tan, Doi ∧	110	18.30 N	99.20 E
Khunti	124	23.05 N	85.17 E
Khūr	128	32.57 N	58.26 E
Khurai	124	24.03 N	78.19 E
Khuralji Khās ◆[8]	272a	28.39 N	77.17 E
Khuria Tank ⊜[1]	124	22.25 N	81.36 E
Khurigāchi	272b	22.49 N	88.20 E
Khurīyā Murīyā, Jazā'ir II	118	17.30 N	56.00 E
Khurja	124	28.15 N	77.51 E
Khurli	128	28.59 N	65.52 E
Khurramshahr → Khorramshahr	128	30.25 N	48.11 E
Khūsf	128	32.46 N	58.53 E
Khushāb	123	32.18 N	72.21 E
Khushālgarh	123	33.30 N	71.54 E
Khushk Khurd ◆[8]	272a	28.46 N	77.10 E
Khutubi ≃	86	44.45 N	86.25 E
Khuwayy	140	13.05 N	29.14 E
Khuzdār	120	27.48 N	66.37 E
Khūzestān □[4]	128	31.00 N	49.00 E
Khvāf	128	34.33 N	60.08 E
Khvājeh Moḥammad, Kūh-e ⋏	120	36.22 N	70.17 E
Khvājeh Ra'ūf	120	33.19 N	64.43 E
Khvor	128	33.47 N	55.03 E
Khvormūj	128	28.39 N	51.23 E
Khvoy	128	38.33 N	44.58 E
Khwae Noi ≃	110	14.01 N	99.32 E
Khyber Pass ✕	123	34.05 N	71.10 E
Kia	175e	7.33 S	158.26 E
Kialwe	154	9.22 S	27.08 E
Kiama, Austl.	170	34.41 S	150.51 E
Kiama, Zaïre	152	7.15 S	17.44 E
Kiamba	116	5.59 N	124.37 E
Kiambi	154	7.20 S	28.01 E
Kiamboni, Kap → Jumbo, Raas ›	144	1.39 S	41.36 E
Kiambu	154	1.10 S	36.50 E
Kiamesha Lake	210	41.41 N	74.40 W
Kiamichi ≃	194	33.57 N	95.14 W
Kiamika ≃	206	46.38 N	75.15 W
Kiamika, Barrage ◆[6]	206	46.37 N	75.08 W
Kiamika, Réservoir ⊜[1]	206	46.40 N	75.05 W
Kiamusze → Jiamusi	89	46.50 N	130.21 E
Kian → Ji'an	100	27.07 N	114.58 E
Kiana	180	66.59 N	160.25 W
Kiandra	171b	35.53 S	148.30 E
Kiangara	157b	17.58 S	47.02 E
Kiangarow, Mount ∧	166	26.49 S	151.33 E
Kiangsi → Jiangxi □[4]	100	28.00 N	116.00 E
Kiangsu → Jiangsu □[4]	90	33.00 N	120.00 E
Kiantajärvi ⊜	26	65.03 N	29.07 E
Kiaohsien → Jiaoxian	98	36.18 N	119.58 E
Kibæk	41	56.02 N	8.51 E
Kibaha	154	6.46 S	38.55 E
Kibali ≃	154	3.37 N	28.34 E
Kibali-Sturi Game Reserve ◆[4]	154	2.45 N	29.33 E
Kibamba	154	4.53 S	26.33 E
Kibanga Port	154	0.11 N	32.52 E
Kibangou	152	3.27 S	12.21 E
Kibanseke	273b	4.26 S	15.23 E
Kibar	120	32.20 N	78.01 E
Kibara	154	2.09 S	33.27 E
Kibāsī	128	30.34 N	47.50 E
Kibau Iyayi	154	8.52 S	34.32 E
Kibawe	116	7.34 N	125.00 E
Kibaya	154	5.18 S	36.34 E
Kibenga	152	7.55 S	17.35 E
Kibeni	164	7.25 S	143.48 E
Kiberashi	154	5.23 S	37.26 E
Kiberege	154	7.57 S	36.52 E
Kibi	150	6.10 N	0.33 W
Kibi-kōgen ⋏[1]	96	34.45 N	133.15 E
Kibila	154	8.14 S	26.23 E
Kibiti	154	7.44 S	38.57 E
Kibler Park	273d	26.18 S	28.00 E
Kiboga	154	1.02 N	30.58 E
Kiboko	154	2.15 S	37.42 E
Kibombo	154	3.54 S	25.55 E
Kibondo	154	3.35 S	30.42 E
Kibouendé, Congo	273b	4.19 S	15.11 E
Kibouendé, Congo	273b	4.17 S	15.09 E
Kibouendé I	273b	4.11 S	15.09 E
Kibouendé II	273b	4.12 S	15.09 E
Kibre Mengist	144	5.52 N	39.00 E
Kıbrıs → Cyprus □[1]	130	35.00 N	33.00 E
Kıbrısçık	130	40.25 N	31.51 E
Kibumbu	154	3.32 S	29.45 E
Kibungo	154	2.10 S	30.32 E
Kibuye, Bdi.	154	3.40 S	29.59 E
Kibuye, Rw.	154	2.03 S	29.21 E
Kibwesa	154	6.28 S	29.57 E
Kibwezi	154	2.25 S	37.58 E
Kibworth Harcourt	42	52.32 N	0.59 W
Kičevo	38	41.31 N	20.57 E
Kichčik	74	53.24 N	156.03 E
Kichijōji	268	35.42 N	139.35 E
Kickany	38	46.47 N	29.36 E
Kickapoo ≃	190	43.05 N	90.53 W
Kickapoo Creek ≃, Il., U.S.	194	40.08 N	89.27 W
Kickapoo Creek ≃, Il., U.S.	219	40.08 N	89.27 W
Kickapoo Creek ≃, Tx., U.S.	196	31.31 N	99.58 W
Kickapoo Creek ≃, Tx., U.S.	222	30.47 N	95.08 W
Kickapoo Creek ≃, Tx., U.S.	222	32.16 N	95.28 W
Kicking Horse Pass ✕	182	51.27 N	116.18 W
Kičkino	80	47.05 N	44.02 E
Kičma	80	57.12 N	48.55 E
Kicman'	78	48.27 N	25.44 E
Kičmengskij Gorodok	24	59.59 N	45.48 E
Kičuj ≃	80	55.13 N	51.16 E
Kidal	150	18.26 N	1.24 E
Kidapawan	116	7.01 N	125.03 E
Kidatu	154	7.42 S	36.57 E
Kidbrooke ◆[8]	260	51.28 N	0.02 E
Kidderminster	42	52.23 N	2.14 W
Kidderpore ◆[8]	272b	22.31 N	88.19 E
Kidderpore Docks ◆[5]	272b	22.33 N	88.19 E
Kidd's Beach	158	33.09 S	27.42 E
Kidepo National Park ♦	154	3.50 N	33.40 E
Kidete, Tan.	154	6.25 S	37.16 E
Kidete, Tan.	154	6.39 S	36.42 E
Kidira	150	14.28 N	12.13 W
Kidlington	42	51.50 N	1.17 W
Kidnappers, Cape ›	172	39.39 S	177.07 E
Kido	164	9.15 S	146.55 E
Kidričevo	61	46.24 N	15.47 E
Kidron	214	40.44 N	81.45 W
Kidsgrove	44	53.06 N	2.15 W
Kidston	166	18.53 S	144.10 E
Kidugallo	154	6.47 S	38.12 E
Kidul, Pegunungan ⋏	115a	8.13 S	111.30 E
Kidwelly	42	51.45 N	4.18 W
Kiefersfelden	64	47.37 N	12.11 E
Kiekebusch	264a	52.21 N	13.33 E
Kiel, Dtsch.	41	54.20 N	10.08 E
Kiel, Wi., U.S.	190	43.54 N	88.02 W
Kiel Canal → Nord-Ostsee-Kanal ≍	30	53.53 N	9.08 E
Kielce	30	50.52 N	20.37 E
Kielce □[4]	30	50.30 N	20.30 E
Kielder	44	55.14 N	2.35 W
Kielder Reservoir ⊜[1]	44	55.11 N	2.30 W
Kieler Bucht (Kiel Bay) c	41	54.35 N	10.35 E
Kieler Förde c	41	54.24 N	10.12 E
Kiembara	150	13.15 N	2.44 W
Kienberg	264a	52.40 N	12.54 E
Kienge	154	10.34 S	27.33 E
Kienitz	54	52.40 N	14.26 E
Kiens → Chienes	64	46.48 N	11.50 E
Kiental	58	46.35 N	7.43 E
Kierling	264b	48.19 N	16.17 E
Kierspe	56	51.08 N	7.35 E
Kierspe-Bahnhof	263	51.08 N	7.37 E
Kiester	190	43.32 N	93.42 W
Kieta	175e	6.13 S	155.38 E
Kietrz	30	50.05 N	18.01 E
Kietz	54	52.34 N	14.36 E
Kiev → Kijev	78	50.26 N	30.31 E
Kiev Station ◆[5]	265b	55.45 N	37.34 E
Kiew → Kijev	78	50.26 N	30.31 E
Kifaya	150	12.10 N	13.04 W
Kiffa	150	16.37 N	11.24 W
Kifisiá	38	38.04 N	23.48 E
Kifisós ≃, Ellás	38	38.26 N	23.15 E
Kifisós ≃, Ellás	267c	37.57 N	23.40 E
Kifrī	128	34.42 N	44.58 E
Kifrī, Jabal ∧	142	27.48 N	32.50 E
Kigač ≃	80	46.28 N	49.12 E
Kigali	154	1.57 S	30.04 E
Kiği	130	39.19 N	40.21 E
Kigille	140	8.40 N	34.02 E
Kigoma	154	4.52 S	29.38 E
Kigoma □[4]	154	4.30 S	30.30 E
Kigun, Cape ›	180	52.00 N	175.21 W
Kigwa	154	5.10 S	33.08 E
Kihei	229a	20.47 N	156.27 W
Kihikihi	172	38.02 S	175.21 E
Kihniö	26	62.12 N	23.11 E
Kihnu I	76	58.08 N	24.00 E
Kiholo Bay c	229d	19.52 N	155.56 W
Kihundo	154	9.25 S	38.59 E
Kihurio	154	4.28 S	38.04 E
Kii-hantō ›[1]	92	34.00 N	135.45 E
Kiik	86	47.31 N	72.55 E
Kiikkaškan	86	49.28 N	77.04 E
Kiiminginjoki ≃	26	65.12 N	25.18 E
Kii-nagashima	92	34.12 N	136.20 E
Kiirun → Chilung	100	25.08 N	121.44 E
Kii-sanchi ⋏	92	34.00 N	135.50 E
Kii-suidō ʊ	96	33.55 N	134.55 E
Kija ≃	86	56.52 N	86.39 E
Kijabe	154	0.56 S	36.34 E
Kijakty, ozero ⊜	86	50.00 N	69.15 E
Kijal	114	4.21 N	103.29 E
Kijaly	86	54.17 N	69.41 E
Kijasovo	80	56.21 N	53.07 E
Kijev (Kiev)	78	50.26 N	30.31 E
Kijev □[4]	78	50.15 N	30.30 E
Kijevka, Kaz.	86	50.16 N	71.34 E
Kijevka, Ross.	80	46.05 N	42.57 E
Kijevka, Ross.	80	50.46 N	48.28 E
Kijevskoje	78	45.03 N	37.52 E
Kijevskoje vodochranilišče ⊜[1]	78	51.00 N	30.25 E
Kijima-chosuichi ⊜	96	35.04 N	132.44 E
Kijimadaira	94	36.51 N	138.24 E
Kijima-dam ◆[6]	96	35.05 N	132.44 E
Kijma	86	51.35 N	67.34 E
Kijoka	174m	26.42 N	128.09 E
Kikagati	154	1.02 S	30.40 E
Kikai-shima I	93b	28.19 N	129.59 E
Kikale	154	7.50 S	39.12 E
Kikati ≃	152	14.48 S	12.28 E
Kikenka ≃	265a	59.52 N	30.04 E
Kikerino	76	59.28 N	29.35 E
Kikerk Lake ⊜	176	67.20 N	113.20 W
Kikimi	273b	4.26 S	15.25 E
Kikimorka	80	58.10 N	49.27 E
Kikinda	38	45.50 N	20.28 E
Kikládhes (Cyclades) II	38	37.30 N	25.00 E
Kiklah	146	32.05 N	12.41 E
Kiknur	80	57.19 N	47.14 E
Kikombo, Zaïre	152	5.59 S	18.09 E
Kikombo, Zaïre	152	5.40 S	18.48 E
Kikongo	152	4.16 S	17.11 E
Kikori	164	7.25 S	144.15 E
Kikori ≃	164	7.10 S	144.05 E
Kikorze	54	53.39 N	15.01 E
Kiku ≃	94	34.39 N	138.04 E
Kikuchi	96	32.59 N	130.49 E
Kikuchi ≃	96	32.56 N	130.35 E
Kikugawa, Nihon	94	34.45 N	138.05 E
Kikugawa, Nihon	96	34.07 N	131.02 E
Kikuka	96	33.02 N	130.46 E
Kikuma	96	34.03 N	132.53 E
Kikuna	268	35.10 N	139.40 E
Kikusui	96	32.58 N	130.36 E
Kikvidze, Ross.	80	50.53 N	42.46 E
Kikvidze, Ross.	80	50.44 N	43.03 E
Kikvorsberg ⋏	158	31.17 S	25.20 E
Kikwit	152	5.02 S	18.49 E
Kil	26	59.30 N	13.19 E
Kilaån ≃	40	58.44 N	17.01 E
Kilafors	26	61.14 N	16.34 E
Kila Kila	164	9.30 S	147.10 E
Kīlakkarai	122	9.14 N	78.47 E
Kilambé, Cerro ∧	236	13.34 N	85.42 W
Kilauea	229b	22.12 N	159.24 W
Kilauea Crater ⊥[6]	229d	19.25 N	155.17 W
Kilauea Point ›	229b	22.14 N	159.24 W
Kilb	61	48.06 N	15.24 E
Kilbaha	48	52.33 N	9.52 W
Kilbarchan	46	55.50 N	4.33 W
Kılbasan	130	37.20 N	33.12 E
Kilbeggan	48	53.22 N	7.29 W
Kilbirnie	46	55.46 N	4.41 W
Kilbourne, Il., U.S.	219	40.09 N	90.01 W
Kilbourne, Oh., U.S.	214	40.20 N	82.58 W
Kilbrannan Sound ʊ	46	55.40 N	5.25 W
Kilbride	46	57.05 N	7.27 W
Kilbuck Mountains ⋏	180	60.50 N	159.45 W
Kilbuck Run ≃	279b	40.31 N	80.08 W
Kilcar	48	54.38 N	8.35 W
Kilchberg	58	47.19 N	8.33 E
Kilchis ≃	224	45.30 N	123.52 W
Kilchoan	46	56.42 N	6.06 W
Kilchreest	48	53.10 N	8.38 W
Kilchrenan	46	56.21 N	5.11 W
Kilchu	98	40.58 N	129.20 E
Kilcock	48	53.24 N	6.40 W
Kilcolgan	48	53.13 N	8.52 W
Kilconnell	48	53.20 N	8.25 W
Kilcoole	48	53.06 N	6.04 W
Kilcormac	48	53.10 N	7.43 W
Kilcoy	171a	26.57 S	152.33 E
Kilcreggan	46	55.59 N	4.50 W
Kilcullen	48	53.08 N	6.45 W
Kildare (Saint-Ambroise-de-Kildare), P.Q., Can.	206	46.05 N	73.32 W
Kildare, Ire.	48	53.10 N	6.55 W
Kildare □[6]	48	53.15 N	6.45 W
Kildare, Cape ›	186	46.52 N	63.58 W
Kildeer	278	42.10 N	88.03 W
Kil'din, ostrov I	24	69.22 N	34.12 E
Kil'dinstroj	24	68.48 N	33.06 E
Kildonan, B.C., Can.	182	49.00 N	125.00 W
Kildonan, Scot., U.K.	46	58.10 N	3.51 W
Kildonan, Zimb.	154	17.21 S	30.37 E
Kildonan, Strath of V	46	58.09 N	3.51 W
Kildorrery	48	52.14 N	8.26 W
Kildrummy Castle ⊥	46	57.14 N	2.52 W
Kildurk	164	16.26 S	129.37 E
Kilemary	80	56.47 N	46.52 E
Kilembe, Ug.	154	0.12 N	30.00 E
Kilembe, Zaïre	152	5.42 S	19.55 E
Kilfenora	48	52.59 N	9.13 W
Kilfinnane	48	52.21 N	8.28 W
Kilgard	224	49.03 N	122.12 W
Kilgarvan	48	51.54 N	9.27 W
Kilgore, Oh., U.S.	214	40.28 N	81.00 W
Kilgore, Tx., U.S.	222	32.23 N	94.52 W
Kilham	44	54.04 N	0.23 W
Kili I	14	5.39 N	169.04 E
Kilian Island I	176	73.35 N	107.53 W
Kilibo	150	8.34 N	2.36 E
Kiliç	130	40.38 N	29.23 E
Kilifi	154	3.38 S	39.51 E
Kilija	78	45.27 N	29.16 E
Kilikollūr	122	8.54 N	76.39 E
Kilima	154	0.59 S	29.12 E
Kilimanjaro □[4]	154	3.45 S	37.45 E
Kilimanjaro ∧	154	3.04 S	37.22 E
Kilimanjaro Game Reserve ◆[4]	154	3.05 S	37.20 E
Kilimatinde	154	5.51 S	34.57 E
Kilimavony	157b	23.48 S	43.41 E
Kilimli	130	41.28 N	31.50 E
Kilindoni	154	7.55 S	39.39 E
Kilingi-Nõmme	76	58.09 N	24.58 E
Kilis	130	36.44 N	37.05 E
Kilkare Woods	282	37.38 N	121.55 W
Kilkee	48	52.41 N	9.38 W
Kilkeel	48	54.04 N	6.00 W
Kilkelly	48	53.53 N	8.51 W
Kilkenny (Cill Chainnigh)	48	52.39 N	7.15 W
Kilkenny □[6]	48	52.40 N	7.20 W
Kilkerrin	48	53.33 N	8.34 W
Kilkhampton	42	50.53 N	4.29 W
Kilkieran	48	53.19 N	9.43 W
Kilkieran Bay c	48	53.15 N	9.45 W
Kilkís	38	41.00 N	22.53 E
Killadoon	48	53.42 N	9.56 W
Killadysert	48	52.41 N	9.06 W
Killala	48	54.13 N	9.13 W
Killala Bay c	48	54.15 N	9.10 W
Killaloe	48	52.48 N	8.27 W
Killaloe Station	190	45.33 N	77.25 W
Killam	182	52.47 N	111.51 W
Killara	274a	33.46 S	151.09 E
Killarney, Austl.	166	28.20 S	152.18 E
Killarney, Mb., Can.	184	49.12 N	99.42 W
Killarney, On., Can.	190	45.58 N	81.31 W
Killarney, Ire.	48	52.03 N	9.30 W
Killarney, Lake ⊜	240b	25.03 N	77.27 W
Killarney, Lakes of ⊜	48	52.01 N	9.30 W
Killarney Heights	274a	33.46 S	151.13 E
Killarney Provincial Park ♦	190	46.05 N	81.30 W
Killashandra	48	54.00 N	7.32 W
Killavally	48	53.45 N	9.23 W
Killawog	210	42.24 N	76.01 W
Killbear Provincial Park ♦	212	45.21 N	80.12 W
Kill Buck, N.Y., U.S.	210	42.10 N	78.41 W
Killbuck, Oh., U.S.	214	40.29 N	81.59 W
Killbuck Creek ≃, Il., U.S.	216	42.10 N	89.06 W
Killbuck Creek ≃, In., U.S.	218	40.07 N	85.41 W
Killbuck Creek ≃, Oh., U.S.	214	40.20 N	81.57 W
Killdeer	198	47.22 N	102.45 W
Killean	46	55.39 N	5.40 W
Killearn	46	56.03 N	4.22 W
Killeen	222	31.07 N	97.43 W
Killen	194	34.51 N	87.32 W
Killenaule	48	52.34 N	7.40 W
Killeter	48	54.40 N	7.41 W
Kıllıdağ ∧	130	40.21 N	42.10 E
Killik ≃	180	69.00 N	153.58 W
Killilan	46	57.19 N	5.25 W
Killimor	48	53.10 N	8.17 W
Killin	46	56.28 N	4.19 W
Killington Peak ∧	188	43.36 N	72.49 W
Killingworth	207	41.21 N	72.33 W
Killíni	38	37.55 N	21.09 E
Killíni ∧	38	37.57 N	22.23 E
Killiniq Island I	176	60.24 N	64.40 W
Killinkoski	26	62.24 N	23.52 E
Killorglin	48	52.06 N	9.47 W
Killough	48	54.16 N	5.39 W
Killpecker Creek ≃	202	41.35 N	109.14 W
Killucan	48	53.31 N	7.07 W
Kill Van Kull ʊ	276	40.39 N	74.05 W
Killybegs	48	54.38 N	8.27 W
Killyleagh	48	54.24 N	5.39 W
Kilmacolm	46	55.54 N	4.38 W
Kilmacthomas	48	52.12 N	7.25 W
Kilmaine	48	53.34 N	9.09 W
Kilmallock	48	52.23 N	8.34 W
Kilmaluag	46	57.41 N	6.17 W
Kilmarnock, Scot., U.K.	46	55.36 N	4.30 W
Kilmarnock, Va., U.S.	208	37.42 N	76.22 W
Kilmartin	46	56.07 N	5.29 W
Kilmar Tor ∧[2]	42	50.33 N	4.28 W
Kilmaurs	46	55.39 N	4.32 W
Kilmelford	46	56.16 N	5.29 W
Kil'mez', Ross.	80	56.57 N	51.04 E
Kil'mez', Ross.	80	57.04 N	51.21 E
Kil'mez' ≃	80	56.58 N	50.28 E
Kilmichael	194	33.26 N	89.34 W
Kilmichael Point ›	48	52.44 N	6.10 W
Kilmore	169	37.18 S	144.57 E
Kilmore Creek ≃	216	40.20 N	86.38 W
Kilmory	46	57.03 N	6.22 W
Kilnaleck	48	53.52 N	7.19 W
Kilninver	46	56.20 N	5.31 W
Kilo	115b	8.21 S	118.24 E
Kilokri ◆[8]	272a	28.35 N	77.16 E
Kiloli	154	6.50 S	33.23 E
Kilombero ≃	154	8.31 S	37.22 E
Kilomines	154	1.48 N	30.14 E
Kilondo	154	9.46 S	34.21 E
Kilosa	154	6.50 S	36.59 E
Kilpisjärvi	24	69.03 N	20.48 E
Kilrea	48	54.58 N	6.35 W
Kilrenny	46	56.14 N	2.41 W
Kilrush	48	52.39 N	9.30 W
Kilsbergen ⋏[2]	40	59.20 N	14.47 E
Kilsmo	40	59.04 N	15.31 E
Kilsyth, Austl.	274b	37.48 S	145.19 E
Kilsyth, Scot., U.K.	46	55.59 N	4.04 W
Kiltealy	48	52.34 N	6.45 W
Kiltimagh	48	53.51 N	9.01 W
Kiltoom	48	53.28 N	8.01 W
Kilttān Island I	122	11.29 N	73.00 E
Kiltu-ri	98	34.35 N	127.20 E
Kilwa	154	9.18 S	28.25 E
Kilwa Island I	154	9.20 S	28.33 E
Kilwa Kivinje	154	8.45 S	39.24 E
Kilwa Masoko	154	8.56 S	39.31 E
Kilwinning	46	55.40 N	4.42 W
Kim	198	37.14 N	103.21 W
Kim ≃	152	5.28 N	11.07 E
Kima	154	1.26 S	26.43 E
Kimaam	164	7.58 S	138.53 E
Kimamba	154	6.47 S	37.08 E
Kimande	154	7.22 S	35.30 E
Kīmān Fāris (Crocodilopolis) (Arsinoe) ⊥	142	29.19 N	30.50 E
Kimba	166	33.09 S	136.25 E
Kimball, Mn., U.S.	190	45.19 N	94.18 W
Kimball, Ne., U.S.	198	41.14 N	103.39 W
Kimball, S.D., U.S.	198	43.44 N	98.57 W
Kimball, Mount ∧	180	63.14 N	144.39 W
Kimbanda	152	4.07 S	17.59 E
Kimbe	164	5.31 S	150.10 E
Kimbe Bay c	164	5.30 S	150.30 E
Kimberley, B.C., Can.	182	49.41 N	115.59 W
Kimberley, S. Afr.	158	28.43 S	24.46 E
Kimberley, Eng., U.K.	44	52.59 N	1.16 W
Kimberley Downs	162	17.24 S	124.22 E
Kimberley Plateau ⋏[1]	160	17.00 S	127.00 E
Kimberling City	194	36.38 N	93.28 W
Kimberly, Id., U.S.	202	42.32 N	114.21 W
Kimberly, Wi., U.S.	190	44.16 N	88.20 W
Kimberton	208	40.08 N	75.34 W
Kimbolton, N.Z.	172	40.03 S	175.47 E
Kimbolton, Eng., U.K.	42	52.18 N	0.24 W
Kimbolton, Oh., U.S.	214	40.09 N	81.34 W
Kimbongo	152	6.08 S	18.01 E
Kimbwala	273b	4.22 S	15.12 E
Kimch'aek (Sŏngjin)	98	40.41 N	129.12 E
Kimch'ŏn	98	36.07 N	128.05 E

≃	River	Fluß	Río	Rivière	Rio
≍	Canal	Kanal	Canal	Canal	Canal
⌊	Waterfall, Rapids	Wasserfall, Stromschnellen	Cascada, Rápidos	Chute d'eau, Rapides	Cascata, Rápidos
ʊ	Strait	Meeresstraße	Estrecho	Détroit	Estreito
c	Bay, Gulf	Bucht, Golf	Bahía, Golfo	Baie, Golfe	Baía, Golfo
⊜	Lake, Lakes	See, Seen	Lago, Lagos	Lac, Lacs	Lago, Lagos
≡	Swamp	Sumpf	Pantano	Marais	Pântano
⊓	Ice Features, Glacier	Eis- und Gletscherformen	Accidentes Glaciales	Formes glaciaires	Acidentes glaciares
⊤	Other Hydrographic Features	Andere Hydrographische Objekte	Otros Elementos Hidrográficos	Autres données hydrographiques	Outros acidentes hidrográficos

✢	Submarine Features	Untermeerische Objekte	Accidentes Submarinos	Formes de relief sous-marin	Acidentes submarinos
□	Political Unit	Politische Einheit	Unidad Política	Entité politique	Unidade política
▪	Cultural Institution	Kulturelle Institution	Institución Cultural	Institution culturelle	Instituição cultural
⊥	Historical Site	Historische Stätte	Sitio Histórico	Site historique	Sítio histórico
♦	Recreational Site	Erholungs- und Ferienort	Sitio de Recreo	Centre de loisirs	Área de Lazer
⊠	Airport	Flughafen	Aeropuerto	Aéroport	Aeroporto
■	Military Installation	Militäranlage	Instalación Militar	Installation militaire	Instalação militar
◆	Miscellaneous	Verschiedenes	Misceláneo	Divers	Diversos

ENGLISH — Name | Page | Lat. °′ | Long. °′
DEUTSCH — Name | Seite | Breite °′ | Länge °′ E = Ost

Kimerka ≃ 82 56.52 N 37.22 E
Kimhae 98 35.14 N 128.52 E
Kimhwa 98 38.26 N 127.36 E
Kími 38 38.37 N 24.06 E
Kimil'tej 88 54.08 N 101.59 E
Kimito (Kemiö) 26 60.10 N 22.45 E
Kimito I 26 60.07 N 22.40 E
Kimi-tōge ∧[2] 270 34.43 N 135.06 E
Kimi-tōge)(96 34.23 N 135.37 E
Kimitsu 94 35.20 N 139.54 E
Kimiwan Lake ⊜ 182 55.45 N 116.54 W
Kimje 98 35.48 N 126.52 E
Kim Kim ≃ 271c 1.26 N 103.58 E
Kimmell 216 41.23 N 85.32 W
Kim-me-ni-oli Wash V 200 36.07 N 108.11 W
Kímolos I 38 36.48 N 24.34 E
Kimongo 152 4.29 S 12.58 E
Kimovsk 76 53.58 N 38.32 E
Kimpangu 152 5.51 S 15.01 E
Kim Plan 279b 40.20 N 79.44 W
Kimp'o 271b 37.37 N 126.43 E
Kimp'o Airport ⊠ 271b 37.33 N 126.48 E
Kimpombo 273b 4.17 S 15.10 E
Kimpō-zan ∧ 94 35.53 N 138.38 E
Kimry 82 56.52 N 37.21 E
Kimsquit 182 52.49 N 126.58 W
Kimstad 40 58.32 N 15.58 E
Kimu ≃ 268 35.56 N 139.57 E
Kimuenza 273b 4.27 S 15.17 E
Kimvula 152 5.44 S 15.58 E
Kimwanga 154 7.08 S 28.42 E
Kin 174m 26.26 N 127.55 E
Kinabalian, Mount ∧ 116 8.14 N 125.25 E
Kinabalu, Gunong ∧ 112 6.05 N 116.33 E
Kinabalu National Park ♠ 112 6.05 N 116.33 E
Kinabatangan ≃ 112 5.42 N 118.23 E
Kınalı ✦[8] 267b 40.55 N 29.03 E
Kınalı Ada I 267b 40.55 N 29.03 E
Kinangaly ∧ 157b 19.12 S 45.40 E
Kinango 154 4.08 S 39.19 E
Kinapusan Island I 116 5.13 N 120.40 E
Kinara 164 2.16 S 132.44 E
Kinasa 94 36.42 N 138.01 E
Kinaūni 272a 28.39 N 77.23 E
Kinbasket Lake ⊜[1] 182 51.58 N 118.03 W
Kinbrace 46 58.15 N 3.56 W
Kinbuck 46 56.13 N 3.57 W
Kincaid, Sk., Can. 184 49.39 N 107.00 W
Kincaid, Il., U.S. 219 39.35 N 89.24 W
Kincardine, On., Can. 190 44.11 N 81.38 W
Kincardine, Scot., U.K. 46 56.04 N 3.44 W
Kinchafoonee Creek ≃ 192 31.38 N 84.10 W
Kinchang 110 26.32 N 98.02 E
Kinchara 272b 22.53 N 88.32 E
Kinchega National Park ♠ 166 32.30 S 142.20 E
Kincheloe Air Force Base ■ 190 46.15 N 84.28 W
Kincolith 182 55.00 N 129.57 W
Kincraig 46 57.08 N 3.55 W
Kinda, Zaïre 152 4.47 S 21.48 E
Kinda, Zaïre 154 9.18 S 25.04 E
Kindadal 112 1.35 S 123.11 E
Kindanba 152 3.44 S 14.31 E
Kindarun Mountain ∧ 170 32.49 S 150.41 E
Kindberg 61 47.31 N 15.27 E
Kinde 190 43.56 N 82.59 W
Kindeje 152 7.07 S 13.44 E
Kindel'a 80 51.36 N 52.58 E
Kindel'a ≃ 80 51.30 N 52.45 E
Kindelbrück 54 51.16 N 11.05 E
Kindele 152 8.39 S 24.11 E
Kinder 194 30.29 N 92.51 W
Kinderhook, Il., U.S. 219 39.42 N 91.09 W
Kinderhook, Mi., U.S. 216 41.48 N 85.00 W
Kinderhook, N.Y., U.S. 210 42.23 N 73.41 W
Kinderhook Creek ≃ 210 42.19 N 73.45 W
Kinder Reservoir ⊜[1] 262 53.23 N 1.55 W
Kinder Scout ∧ 44 53.23 N 1.52 W
Kindersley 184 51.27 N 109.10 W
Kindia 150 10.04 N 12.51 W
Kindikan 88 56.02 N 115.15 E
Kinding 60 49.00 N 11.23 E
Kindley Field ⊠ 240a 32.22 N 64.40 W
Kindred 198 46.38 N 97.01 W
Kindu 154 2.57 S 25.56 E
Kindykty, ozero ⊜ 86 51.15 N 62.14 E
Kinel' 80 53.14 N 50.39 E
Kinel'-Čerkasy 80 53.29 N 51.29 E
Kinel'skije jary ⋏[1] 80 53.42 N 52.00 E
Kineo, Mount ∧ 188 45.42 N 69.44 W
Kinesi 154 1.28 S 33.52 E
Kinešma 80 57.26 N 42.09 E
Kineton 42 52.10 N 1.30 W
Kinfauns 46 56.22 N 3.21 W
King 192 36.16 N 80.21 W
King □[6] 224 47.26 N 121.48 W
King ≃, Austl. 164 14.41 S 131.59 E
King ≃, Austl. 169 36.41 S 146.25 E
King, Lake ⊜ 162 25.38 S 120.06 E
King, Mont ∧ 212 45.29 N 75.52 W
King, Mount ∧ 166 25.10 S 147.31 E
Kingabwa ✦[8] 273b 4.19 S 15.20 E
King and Queen □[6] 208 37.42 N 76.50 W
King and Queen Court House 208 37.40 N 76.52 W
Kingaroy 166 26.33 S 151.50 E
Kingarth 46 55.46 N 5.03 W
King City, On., Can. 212 43.56 N 79.32 W
King City, Ca., U.S. 226 36.12 N 121.07 W
King City, Mo., U.S. 194 40.03 N 94.31 W
King Cove 180 55.04 N 162.19 W
Kingdom City 219 38.58 N 91.56 W
King Edward ≃ 164 14.14 S 126.35 E
Kingersheim 58 47.48 N 7.20 E
King Ferry 210 42.39 N 76.37 W
Kingfield 188 44.57 N 70.09 W
Kingfisher 196 35.51 N 97.55 W
King George 208 38.16 N 77.11 W
King George □[6] 208 38.15 N 77.10 W
King George, Mount ∧ 182 50.35 N 115.24 W
King George Bay ⊂ 254 51.33 S 60.37 W
King George Island I 9 62.00 S 58.15 W
King George Islands II 176 57.20 N 78.25 W
King George's Dock ✦[5] 272b 22.32 N 88.18 E
King George Sound ⊔ 162 35.03 S 117.57 E
King George's Reservoir ⊜[1] 260 51.39 N 0.01 W
King George VI Reservoir ⊜[1] 260 51.27 N 0.32 W
King Hill 202 43.00 N 115.12 W
Kinghorn 46 56.04 N 3.10 W
Kingie ≃ 46 57.04 N 5.08 W
Kingisepp 76 59.22 N 28.36 E
King Island I, Austl. 166 39.50 S 144.00 E
King Island I, B.C., Can. 182 52.12 N 127.42 W
King Island I, Ak., U.S. 180 64.58 N 168.05 W
Kinglake National Park ♠ 169 37.35 S 145.25 E
King Lear Peak ∧ 204 41.12 N 118.34 W
King Leopold Ranges ⋏ 160 17.30 S 125.45 E
Kingman, Az., U.S. 200 35.11 N 114.03 W
Kingman, Ks., U.S. 198 37.38 N 98.06 W
Kingman Reef +[2] 14 6.24 N 162.22 W
King Mountain ∧, B.C., Can. 180 58.17 N 128.54 W
King Mountain ∧, Ok., U.S. 196 34.52 N 99.17 W
King Mountain ∧, Or., U.S. 202 42.42 N 123.14 W
King Mountain ∧, Or., U.S. 202 43.49 N 118.52 W
King of Prussia 208 40.05 N 75.23 W
King of Prussia Plaza ✦[9] 285 40.05 N 75.25 W
Kingoma 152 5.11 S 13.34 E
Kingoma-Ngoma 152 5.50 S 16.49 E
Kingombe, Zaïre 154 3.56 S 26.35 E
Kingombe, Zaïre 154 7.24 S 26.11 E
Kingoonya 162 30.54 S 135.18 E
Kingoué 152 3.43 S 14.09 E
King Peak ∧ 204 40.10 N 124.08 W
King Peninsula >[1] 9 73.12 S 101.00 W
Kingri 120 30.27 N 69.49 E
Kings, Il., U.S. 216 42.00 N 89.06 W
Kings, Ms., U.S. 194 32.23 N 90.51 W
Kings □[6], Ca., U.S. 226 36.20 N 119.39 W
Kings □[6], N.Y., U.S. 210 40.42 N 74.00 W
Kings ≃, Ar., U.S. 194 36.29 N 93.35 W
Kings ≃, Ca., U.S. 226 36.03 N 119.49 W
Kings ≃, Nv., U.S. 204 41.31 N 118.08 W
Kings, Middle Fork ≃ 204 36.50 N 118.52 W
Kings, North Fork ≃, Ca., U.S. 204 36.52 N 119.08 W
Kings, North Fork ≃, Ca., U.S. 226 36.18 N 119.52 W
Kings, South Fork ≃ 226 36.18 N 119.52 W
King Salmon 180 58.41 N 156.39 W
King Salmon ≃ 180 58.15 N 157.30 W
Kingsbarns 46 56.18 N 2.39 W
Kings Beach 226 39.14 N 120.01 W
Kingsbridge 42 50.17 N 3.46 W
Kingsburg 226 36.30 N 119.33 W
Kingsbury, Eng., U.K. 42 52.35 N 1.40 W
Kingsbury, In., U.S. 216 41.31 N 86.42 W
Kingsbury ✦[8] 260 51.35 N 0.17 W
Kings Canyon National Park ♠ 204 36.48 N 118.30 W
Kingsclere 42 51.20 N 1.14 W
Kingscote 168b 35.40 S 137.38 E
Kingscourt 48 53.53 N 6.48 W
Kings Creek 218 40.10 N 83.44 W
Kings Creek ≃, Austl. 171a 27.57 S 151.42 E
Kings Creek ≃, Tx., U.S. 222 32.25 N 96.15 W
King's Cross Station ✦[5] 260 51.32 N 0.07 W
Kings Dominion ♠ 208 37.51 N 77.27 W
Kingsdown, Eng., U.K. 42 51.11 N 1.25 E
Kingsdown, Eng., U.K. 260 51.21 N 0.17 E
Kings Falls ∟ 212 43.55 N 75.38 W
Kingsford, Austl. 274a 33.56 S 151.14 E
Kingsford, Mi., U.S. 190 45.47 N 88.04 W
Kingsford Heights 216 41.29 N 86.42 W
Kingsford Smith Airport ⊠ 170 33.57 S 151.11 E
Kingsgate 182 49.00 N 116.11 W
Kingsgrove 274a 33.57 S 151.06 E
Kingshill 241n 17.44 N 64.48 W
Kingshouse 46 56.21 N 4.19 W
Kings Island ♠ 218 39.21 N 84.16 W
Kingskerswell 42 50.30 N 3.33 W
Kingsland, Eng., U.K. 42 52.15 N 2.47 W
Kingsland, Ar., U.S. 194 33.51 N 92.17 W
Kingsland, Ga., U.S. 192 30.47 N 81.41 W
Kingsland, Tx., U.S. 196 30.40 N 98.26 W
Kingsland, Va., U.S. 208 37.24 N 77.26 W
Kings Langley 42 51.43 N 0.28 W
Kingsley, S. Afr. 158 27.55 S 30.33 E
Kingsley, Eng., U.K. 42 53.01 N 1.59 W
Kingsley, Eng., U.K. 262 53.16 N 2.40 W
Kingsley, Ia., U.S. 198 42.35 N 95.58 W
Kingsley, Mi., U.S. 190 44.35 N 85.32 W
Kingsley, Pa., U.S. 210 41.46 N 75.45 W
Kingsley Dam ✦[6] 198 41.11 N 101.39 W
King's Lynn 42 52.45 N 0.24 E
Kings Manor 285 40.05 N 75.21 W
Kingsmere Lake ⊜ 184 54.06 N 106.27 W
Kings Mills 218 39.21 N 84.14 W
Kings Mountain 192 35.14 N 81.20 W
Kings Mountain National Military Park ♠ 192 35.07 N 81.33 W
King Solomon's Mines → Mikhrot Shelomo Hamelekh ⊥ 132 29.45 N 34.56 E
King Sound ⊔ 162 17.00 S 123.30 E
Kings Park, N.Y., U.S. 210 40.53 N 73.16 W
Kings Park, Va., U.S. 284c 38.48 N 77.14 W
Kings Park ♠ 168a 31.57 S 115.49 E
Kings Peak ∧ 200 40.46 N 110.22 W
Kings Plaza ✦[9] 276 40.37 N 73.55 W
King's Point, Nf., Can. 186 49.35 N 56.11 W
Kings Point, N.Y., U.S. 210 40.49 N 73.44 W
Kingsport 192 36.32 N 82.33 W
King's Sutton 42 52.01 N 1.16 W
Kingsteignton 42 50.33 N 3.35 W
King Sterndale 262 53.15 N 1.52 W
Kingsthorpe 171a 27.29 S 151.49 E
Kingston, Austl. 171a 27.40 S 153.07 E
Kingston, N.S., Can. 186 44.59 N 64.57 W
Kingston, On., Can. 212 44.14 N 76.30 W
Kingston, Jam. 241q 18.00 N 76.48 W
Kingston, N.Z. 172 45.20 S 168.42 E
Kingston, Norf. I. 174c 29.03 S 167.58 E
Kingston, Ga., U.S. 192 34.14 N 84.56 W
Kingston, Il., U.S. 216 42.06 N 88.46 W
Kingston, Ma., U.S. 207 41.59 N 70.43 W
Kingston, Mo., U.S. 194 39.38 N 94.02 W
Kingston, N.J., U.S. 276 40.22 N 74.36 W
Kingston, N.Y., U.S. 210 41.55 N 73.59 W
Kingston, Oh., U.S. 218 39.28 N 82.54 W
Kingston, Ok., U.S. 196 33.59 N 96.43 W
Kingston, Pa., U.S. 210 41.15 N 75.53 W
Kingston, R.I., U.S. 207 41.29 N 71.31 W
Kingston, Tn., U.S. 192 35.52 N 84.30 W
Kingston, Wa., U.S. 224 47.48 N 122.30 W
Kingston Bay ⊂ 283 42.00 N 70.42 W
Kingston Mills 212 44.17 N 76.27 W
Kingston Southeast 166 36.50 S 139.51 E
Kingston upon Hull 44 53.45 N 0.20 W
Kingston [upon Thames] 28 51.25 N 0.19 W
Kingston [upon Thames] ✦[8] 42 51.25 N 0.19 W
Kingstown → Dún Laoghaire, Ire. 48 53.17 N 6.08 W
Kingstown, St. Vin. 241h 13.09 N 61.14 W
Kingstree 192 33.40 N 79.49 W
Kingsville, Austl. 274b 37.49 S 144.52 E
Kingsville, On., Can. 214 42.02 N 82.45 W
Kingsville, Md., U.S. 284b 39.26 N 76.25 W
Kingsville, Oh., U.S. 214 41.53 N 80.41 W
Kingsville, Tx., U.S. 196 27.30 N 97.51 W
Kingsville Naval Air Station ■ 196 27.31 N 97.47 W
Kingswear 42 50.21 N 3.34 W
Kingswinford 42 52.29 N 2.10 W
Kingswood, Austl. 274a 33.46 S 150.43 E
Kingswood, S. Afr. 158 27.29 S 25.46 E
Kingswood, Eng., U.K. 42 51.27 N 2.22 W
Kingswood, Eng., U.K. 260 51.17 N 0.13 W
Kingswood Park 285 40.07 N 74.51 W
King's Worthy 42 51.06 N 1.18 W
Kingtechen → Jingdezhen 100 29.16 N 117.11 E
Kington 42 52.12 N 3.01 W
Kingunda 152 6.34 S 16.58 E
Kingungi 152 5.24 S 17.56 E
Kingussie 46 57.05 N 4.03 W
King William 208 37.41 N 77.00 W
King William □[6] 208 37.42 N 77.05 W
King William Island I 176 69.00 N 97.30 W
King William's Town 158 32.51 S 27.22 E
Kingwood, Tx., U.S. 222 29.54 N 95.18 W
Kingwood, W.V., U.S. 188 39.28 N 79.41 W
Kinh Duc 110 11.49 N 107.58 E
Kinhwa → Jinhua 100 29.07 N 119.39 E
Kınık 130 39.05 N 27.23 E
Kinira ≃ 158 31.12 S 29.17 E
Kinistino 184 52.57 N 105.00 W
Kinjar Khās 123 29.55 N 70.58 E
Kinkala 152 4.22 S 14.46 E
Kinker Creek ≃ 282 38.02 N 121.52 W
Kinkony, Lac ⊜ 157b 16.08 S 45.50 E
Kinkora 285 40.07 N 74.45 W
Kinleith 172 38.16 S 175.54 E
Kinloch 46 57.01 N 6.17 W
Kinlochbervie 46 58.28 N 5.03 W
Kinlocheil 46 56.51 N 5.20 W
Kinlochewe 46 57.36 N 5.20 W
Kinloch Hourn 46 57.06 N 5.22 W
Kinlochleven 46 56.42 N 4.58 W
Kinloch Rannoch 46 56.42 N 4.11 W
Kinloss 46 57.37 N 3.34 W
Kinmount 212 44.47 N 78.39 W
Kinmundy 219 38.46 N 88.50 W
Kinn 26 61.36 N 4.45 E
Kinna 26 57.30 N 12.41 E
Kinnaird 182 49.17 N 117.39 W
Kinnaird Head > 46 57.42 N 2.00 W
Kinnegad 48 53.26 N 7.05 W
Kinnekulle ∧[2] 26 58.35 N 13.23 E
Kinnelon 210 40.59 N 74.23 W
Kinnel Water ≃ 44 55.08 N 3.25 W
Kinneret 132 32.43 N 35.33 E
Kinneret, Yam (Sea of Galilee) ⊜ 132 32.48 N 35.35 E
Kinneret-Negev Conduit ≌[1] 132 32.52 N 35.32 E
Kinnerley 42 52.47 N 2.59 W
Kinniconick Creek ≃ 218 38.37 N 83.09 W
Kinnula 26 63.22 N 24.58 E
Kino ≃ 96 34.13 N 135.09 E
Kinoe 96 34.14 N 132.55 E
Kinogitan 116 9.00 N 124.48 E
Kinojévis ≃ 190 48.23 N 78.21 W
Kinomoto 94 35.30 N 136.13 E
Kinonge ≃ 206 45.39 N 74.55 W
Kinoni 154 0.39 S 30.27 E
Kinosaki 96 35.37 N 134.49 E
Kinpoku-san ∧ 92 38.05 N 138.22 E
Kinrola 166 23.46 S 148.45 E
Kinross, S. Afr. 158 26.22 S 29.03 E
Kinross, Scot., U.K. 46 56.13 N 3.27 W
Kin-saki > 174m 26.26 N 127.57 E
Kinsale, Ire. 48 51.42 N 8.32 W
Kinsale, Va., U.S. 208 38.01 N 76.34 W
Kinsale, Old Head of > 48 51.36 N 8.32 W
Kinsale Harbour ⊂ 48 51.41 N 8.30 W
Kinsarvik 26 60.23 N 6.43 E
Kinschasa → Kinshasa 152 4.18 S 15.18 E
Kinshasa (Léopoldville), Zaïre 152 4.18 S 15.18 E
Kinshasa (Léopoldville), Zaïre 273b 4.18 S 15.18 E
Kinshasa □[4] 152 4.18 S 15.18 E
Kinshasa (Ndjili) Airport ⊠, Zaïre 273b 4.23 S 15.27 E
Kinshasa (Ndolo) Airport ⊠, Zaïre 273b 4.20 S 15.19 E
Kinshasa-Est ✦[8] 273b 4.18 S 15.18 E
Kinshasa-Ouest ✦[8] 273b 4.20 S 15.15 E
Kinsley 198 37.55 N 99.24 W
Kinsman, Il., U.S. 216 41.11 N 88.34 W
Kinsman, Oh., U.S. 214 41.27 N 80.36 W
Kinston, Al., U.S. 194 31.12 N 86.10 W
Kinston, N.C., U.S. 192 35.15 N 77.34 W
Kintamani 115b 8.14 S 115.19 E
Kintamo, Rapides de ∟ 273b 4.19 S 15.15 E
Kintampo 150 8.03 N 1.43 W
Kintap 112 3.51 S 115.13 E
Kintari, Mont ∧[2] 273b 4.08 S 15.23 E
Kintélé 273b 4.09 S 15.21 E
Kintinian 150 11.36 N 9.23 W
Kintinku 154 5.53 S 35.14 E
Kintobongo-Bunge 154 8.54 S 26.23 E
Kintore 46 57.13 N 2.21 W
Kintore, Mount ∧ 162 26.34 S 130.30 E
Kintore Range ⋏ 162 23.25 S 129.20 E
Kintsana 273b 4.19 S 15.10 E
Kintus 86 60.09 N 71.25 E
Kintyre >[1] 46 55.32 N 5.35 W
Kintyre, Mull of > 46 55.17 N 5.55 W
Kinu ≃ 94 35.56 N 139.57 E
Kinuseo Falls ∟ 182 54.47 N 121.12 W
Kinuso 182 55.20 N 115.25 W
Kinvarra 48 53.08 N 8.55 W
Kinver 42 52.27 N 2.14 W
Kin-wan ⊂ 174m 26.25 N 127.54 E
Kinwood 222 29.56 N 95.23 W
Kinyangiri 154 4.27 S 34.37 E
Kinyeti ∧ 154 3.57 N 32.54 E
Kinzia 152 3.36 S 18.26 E
Kinzig ≃, Dtsch. 56 50.08 N 8.54 E
Kinzig ≃, Dtsch. 58 48.37 N 7.49 E
Kinzua 202 44.59 N 120.03 W
Kinzua Creek ≃ 214 41.47 N 78.50 W
Kinzua Dam ✦[6] 214 41.50 N 79.01 W
Kioga-See → Kyoga, Lake ⊜ 154 1.30 N 33.00 E
Kioshkokwi Lake ⊜ 190 46.05 N 78.52 W
Kioto → Kyōto 94 35.00 N 135.45 E
Kiowa, Co., U.S. 198 39.20 N 104.27 W
Kiowa, Ks., U.S. 198 37.01 N 98.29 W
Kiowa, Ok., U.S. 196 34.43 N 95.53 W
Kiowa Creek ≃, U.S. 196 36.46 N 99.55 W
Kiowa Creek ≃, Co., U.S. 198 40.20 N 104.05 W
Kipahigan Lake ⊜ 184 55.20 N 101.55 W
Kipandi 152 5.19 S 16.46 E
Kipanga 154 6.14 S 35.21 E
Kiparissía 38 37.14 N 21.40 E
Kiparissiakós Kólpos ⊂ 38 37.37 N 21.24 E
Kipatimu 154 8.29 S 38.56 E
Kipawa ≃ 190 47.03 N 79.23 W
Kipawa, Lac ⊜ 190 46.55 N 79.00 W
Kipawa, Réserve ♠ 190 47.15 N 78.15 W
Kipembawe 154 7.39 S 33.24 E
Kipengere Range ⋏ 154 9.10 S 34.15 E
Kiperčeny 38 47.32 N 28.50 E
Kipijevo 24 65.40 N 54.30 E
Kipili 154 7.26 S 30.36 E
Kipini 154 2.32 S 40.31 E
Kipling 184 50.10 N 102.38 W
Kipnuk 180 59.56 N 164.03 W
Kippax 44 53.46 N 1.22 W
Kippen 46 56.08 N 4.11 W
Kippenheim 58 48.17 N 7.49 E
Kippure ∧ 48 53.10 N 6.20 W
Kípros → Cyprus □[1] 130 35.00 N 33.00 E
Kipsdorf 54 50.47 N 13.32 E
Kipton 214 41.16 N 82.18 W
Kipushi 154 11.46 S 27.14 E
Kipushia, Zaïre 154 6.10 S 25.12 E
Kipushia, Zaïre 154 12.58 S 29.30 E
Kira, Nihon 94 34.49 N 137.05 E
Kir'a, Ross. 80 55.04 N 46.53 E
Kirakira 175e 10.27 S 161.55 E
Kirandul 122 18.40 N 81.16 E
Kirane 150 15.25 N 10.14 W
Kiranlık 130 39.07 N 41.41 E
Kiranomena 157b 18.17 S 46.03 E
Kīratpur 124 29.31 N 78.12 E
Kiraz 130 38.13 N 28.13 E
Kirazlı 130 40.02 N 26.41 E
Kırbaçbayırı ∧ 267b 40.56 N 29.10 E
Kırbaşı 130 40.01 N 31.50 E
Kirbla 76 58.44 N 23.57 E
Kirby Muxloe 42 52.38 N 1.13 W
Kirbys Creek ≃ 208 36.28 N 77.06 W
Kirbyville 194 30.39 N 93.53 W
Kırçal 130 41.39 N 35.16 E
Kırcasalih 130 41.23 N 26.48 E
Kirchardt 56 49.12 N 8.59 E
Kirchbach in Steiermark 61 46.54 N 15.44 E
Kirchberg, Dtsch. 54 50.37 N 12.32 E
Kirchberg, Dtsch. 56 49.12 N 9.58 E
Kirchberg, Dtsch. 56 49.56 N 7.24 E
Kirchberg, Dtsch. 60 48.54 N 13.11 E
Kirchberg, Schw. 58 47.05 N 7.35 E
Kirchberg, Schw. 58 47.25 N 9.03 E
Kirch-Berg ∧[2] 264a 52.27 N 13.02 E
Kirchberg am Wagram 61 48.26 N 15.53 E
Kirchberg an der Pielach 61 48.02 N 15.26 E
Kirchberg in Tirol 64 47.27 N 12.19 E
Kirchbichl 64 47.31 N 12.05 E
Kirchderne ✦[8] 263 51.33 N 7.30 E
Kirchdorf, Dtsch. 52 52.36 N 8.49 E
Kirchdorf, Dtsch. 54 54.00 N 11.26 E
Kirchdorf an der Krems 61 47.56 N 14.07 E
Kirchdorf im Wald 60 48.55 N 13.16 E
Kirchen 56 50.48 N 7.53 E
Kirchende 263 51.25 N 7.26 E
Kirchenlaibach 60 49.53 N 11.46 E
Kirchenlamitz 54 50.09 N 11.56 E
Kirchenthumbach 60 49.45 N 11.43 E
Kirchhain 56 50.49 N 8.55 E
Kirchham 60 48.21 N 13.16 E
Kirchheiligen 54 51.11 N 10.42 E
Kirchheimbolanden 56 49.40 N 8.00 E
Kirchheim in Schwaben 58 48.10 N 10.30 E
Kirchheim unter Teck 56 48.39 N 9.27 E
Kirchhellen 52 51.36 N 6.55 E
Kirchhellen Heide ✦[3] 263 51.36 N 6.53 E
Kirchhofen 264a 52.22 N 13.53 E
Kirchhörde ✦[8] 263 51.27 N 7.27 E
Kirchhundem 56 51.05 N 8.05 E
Kirchlengern 52 52.12 N 8.35 E
Kirchlinde ✦[8] 263 51.32 N 7.22 E
Kirchlinteln 52 52.56 N 9.19 E
Kirchmöser 54 52.22 N 12.25 E
Kirchroth 60 48.57 N 12.33 E
Kirchschlag in der Buckligen Welt 61 47.31 N 16.18 E
Kirchveischede 56 51.05 N 7.59 E
Kirchwalsede 52 53.01 N 9.23 E
Kirchwerder ✦[8] 52 53.25 N 10.11 E
Kirchzarten 58 47.58 N 7.56 E
Kircubbin 48 54.29 N 5.32 W
Kirda 85 41.06 N 69.00 E
Kirdāsah 142 30.02 N 31.07 E
Kireç 130 39.33 N 28.22 E
Kirej ≃ 88 54.12 N 100.40 E
Kirejevo 80 50.01 N 44.29 E
Kirejevsk 76 53.56 N 37.56 E
Kirejkovo 76 53.38 N 35.49 E
Kirenga ≃ 88 57.47 N 108.07 E
Kirensk 88 57.46 N 108.08 E
Kirghizia → Kyrgyzstan □[1] 72 41.30 N 75.00 E
Kirgili 85 40.24 N 71.43 E
Kirgizija → Kyrgyzstan □[1] 72 41.30 N 75.00 E
Kirgiziya → Kyrgyzstan □[1] 72 41.30 N 75.00 E
Kirgiz-Mijaki 86 53.38 N 54.47 E
Kirgizskij chrebet ⋏ 85 42.30 N 74.00 E
Kiri 152 1.27 S 19.00 E
Kiribati □[1] 14 5.00 S 170.00 W
Kiribati II 14 0.30 S 174.00 E
Kiries West 158 26.34 S 19.00 E
Kiriga-mine ∧ 94 36.06 N 138.12 E
Kırıkhan, Tür. 130 39.32 N 41.20 E
Kırıkhan, Tür. 130 36.32 N 36.19 E
Kirikiri Prisons ʊ 273a 6.27 N 3.19 E
Kırıkkale 130 39.50 N 33.31 E
Kırıkkale □[4] 130 40.00 N 33.45 E
Kirikovka 78 50.22 N 35.07 E
Kirillov 76 59.52 N 38.23 E
Kirillovka 265b 55.57 N 37.20 E
Kirillovo, Ross. 80 57.07 N 45.27 E
Kirillovo, Ross. 80 53.47 N 42.40 E
Kirillovskoje 76 60.28 N 29.17 E
Kirin → Jilin 89 43.51 N 126.33 E
Kirin → Jilin □[4] 90 44.00 N 126.00 E
Kirinyaga (Mount Kenya) ∧ 154 0.10 S 37.20 E
Kirishima-Yaku-kokuritsu-kōen ♠ 92 31.55 N 130.51 E
Kirishima-yama ∧ 92 31.56 N 130.52 E
Kiriši 76 59.27 N 32.02 E
Kiritimati (Christmas Island) I[1] 174o 1.52 N 157.20 W
Kiriwina Island I 164 8.35 S 151.05 E
Kiriwina Islands II 164 8.35 S 151.05 E
Kirizume-tōge ∧[2] 270 34.56 N 135.16 E
Kirjanovskaja Kontora 88 58.18 N 104.13 E
Kırka 130 39.17 N 30.33 E
Kirkabister 46a 60.07 N 1.08 W
Kırkağaç 130 39.06 N 27.40 E
Kirkbride 44 54.54 N 3.12 W
Kirkburton 44 53.37 N 1.42 W
Kirkby 44 53.29 N 2.54 W
Kirkby in Ashfield 44 53.06 N 1.15 W
Kirkby Lonsdale 44 54.13 N 2.36 W
Kirkby Malzeard 44 54.11 N 1.38 W
Kirkbymoorside 44 54.16 N 0.55 W
Kirkby Stephen 44 54.28 N 2.20 W
Kirkcaldy 46 56.07 N 3.10 W
Kirkcolm 44 54.58 N 5.05 W
Kirkconnel 44 55.23 N 4.00 W
Kirkcudbright 44 54.50 N 4.03 W
Kirkcudbright Bay ⊂ 44 54.48 N 4.04 W
Kirkdale ✦[8] 262 53.26 N 2.59 W
Kirkeby 41 56.09 N 9.27 E
Kirkee → Khadki 122 18.34 N 73.52 E
Kirkenær 26 60.28 N 12.03 E
Kirkenes 24 69.40 N 30.03 E
Kirke Stillinge 41 55.26 N 11.15 E
Kirkham 44 53.47 N 2.53 W
Kirkhill 46 57.28 N 4.26 W
Kirkintilloch 46 55.57 N 4.10 W
Kirkjubæjarklaustur 24a 63.47 N 18.04 W
Kirkkonummi → Kyrkslätt 26 60.07 N 24.26 E
Kirkland, P.Q., Can. 275a 45.27 N 73.52 W
Kirkland, Il., U.S. 216 42.05 N 88.51 W
Kirkland, Tx., U.S. 196 34.23 N 100.04 W
Kirkland, Wa., U.S. 224 47.40 N 122.12 W
Kirkland Creek ≃ 200 34.32 N 113.00 W
Kirkland Lake 190 48.09 N 80.02 W
Kırklar Dağı ∧ 130 40.32 N 40.35 E
Kırklareli 130 41.44 N 27.12 E
Kırklareli □[4] 130 41.40 N 27.30 E
Kirklees □[8] 262 53.36 N 1.52 W
Kirkleyditch 262 53.18 N 2.12 W
Kirklin 194 40.11 N 86.21 W
Kirkliston 46 55.58 N 3.25 W
Kirk Michael, I. of Man 44 54.17 N 4.35 W
Kirkmichael, Scot., U.K. 46 56.43 N 3.29 W
Kirkmuirhill 46 55.40 N 3.55 W
Kirkness Lake ⊜ 184 51.32 N 93.56 W
Kirkpatrick, Mount ∧ 9 84.20 S 166.19 E
Kirkpatrick Lake ⊜ 182 51.52 N 111.18 W
Kirk Sandall 44 53.33 N 1.04 W
Kirksville, Il., U.S. 219 39.34 N 88.40 W
Kirksville, Mo., U.S. 194 40.11 N 92.34 W
Kirkton 46 56.13 N 2.55 W
Kirkton of Culsalmond 46 57.23 N 2.34 W
Kirkton of Glenisla 46 56.44 N 3.17 W
Kirktown of Auchterless 46 57.27 N 2.28 W
Kirkūk 128 35.28 N 44.28 E
Kirkville 210 43.05 N 75.57 W
Kirkwall 46 58.59 N 2.58 W
Kirkwood, S. Afr. 158 33.24 S 25.26 E
Kirkwood, De., U.S. 208 39.34 N 75.41 W
Kirkwood, Il., U.S. 190 40.51 N 90.44 W
Kirkwood, Mo., U.S. 219 38.35 N 90.24 W
Kirkwood, N.J., U.S. 285 39.50 N 75.01 W
Kirkwood, N.Y., U.S. 210 42.02 N 75.48 W
Kirmir ≃ 130 40.07 N 31.43 E
Kirn 56 49.47 N 7.28 E
Kirnāhar 126 23.45 N 87.52 E
Kirotshe 154 1.37 S 29.02 E
Kirov, Ross. 76 54.05 N 34.20 E
Kirov, Ross. 80 58.38 N 49.42 E
Kirova, zaliv ⊂ 84 39.09 N 49.03 E
Kirovabad → Gjandža 84 40.40 N 46.22 E
Kirovakan 84 40.48 N 44.30 E
Kirovgrad 86 57.26 N 60.04 E
Kirovka 86 47.07 N 82.00 E
Kirovo, Bela. 78 51.29 N 29.24 E
Kirovo, Ross. 86 55.33 N 63.46 E
Kirovo, Ukr. 78 47.41 N 35.46 E
Kirovo, Ukr. 83 48.23 N 37.55 E
Kirovo, Ukr. 83 48.50 N 38.03 E
Kirovo, Uzb. 85 40.26 N 70.34 E
Kirov Oblast' □[4] 24 59.00 N 50.00 E
Kirovo-Čepeck 80 58.33 N 50.01 E
Kirovograd 78 48.30 N 32.18 E
Kirovograd □[4] 78 48.30 N 32.00 E
Kirovsk, Azer. 84 38.48 N 48.43 E
Kirovsk, Bela. 76 53.16 N 29.29 E
Kirovsk, Ross. 24 67.37 N 33.35 E
Kirovsk, Ross. 265a 59.52 N 31.00 E
Kirovsk, Turk. 128 37.42 N 60.23 E
Kirovsk, Ukr. 83 49.01 N 37.56 E
Kirovsk, Ukr. 83 48.38 N 38.39 E
Kirovskij, Azer. 84 40.26 N 49.51 E
Kirovskij, Kaz. 86 44.52 N 78.12 E
Kirovskij, Ross. 74 54.18 N 155.47 E
Kirovskij, Ross. 80 45.51 N 48.07 E
Kirovskij, Ross. 89 54.26 N 126.55 E
Kirovskij, Ross. 89 45.07 N 133.30 E
Kirovskije ostrova II 265a 59.58 N 30.15 E
Kirovskoje, Kyrg. 85 42.39 N 71.35 E
Kirovskoje, Ukr. 78 48.33 N 34.53 E
Kirovskoje, Ukr. 78 45.14 N 35.13 E
Kirovskoje, Ukr. 83 48.09 N 38.21 E
Kirov Stadium ♠ 265a 59.58 N 30.14 E
Kirov Theatre ʊ 265a 59.55 N 30.18 E
Kirpičnyj Zavod 265a 60.01 N 30.48 E
Kirpil'skaja 78 45.23 N 39.43 E
Kirriemuir 46 56.41 N 3.01 W
Kirs 86 59.21 N 52.14 E
Kirsanov 80 52.38 N 42.43 E
Kirsanovka 80 52.30 N 52.53 E
Kirschau 54 51.04 N 14.27 E
Kırşehir 130 39.09 N 34.10 E
Kırşehir □[4] 130 39.20 N 34.10 E
Kīrthar National Park ♠ 120 25.50 N 67.40 E
Kīrthar Range ⋏ 120 27.00 N 67.10 E
Kirtland, N.M., U.S. 200 36.44 N 108.21 W
Kirtland, Oh., U.S. 214 41.37 N 81.21 W
Kirtland Air Force Base ■ 200 35.02 N 106.37 W
Kirtland Hills 214 41.37 N 81.24 W
Kirtle Water ≃ 44 54.58 N 3.05 W
Kirton 42 52.56 N 0.04 W
Kirton in Lindsey 44 53.28 N 0.36 W
Kirtorf 56 50.46 N 9.06 E
Kiruna 24 67.51 N 20.16 E
Kirundu 154 0.44 S 25.32 E
Kirurumo 154 5.53 S 34.11 E
Kirvin 222 31.46 N 96.20 W
Kirwan Heights 279b 40.22 N 80.06 W
Kirwee 172 43.30 S 172.13 E
Kirwin 198 39.40 N 99.07 W
Kirwin Reservoir ⊜[1] 198 39.39 N 99.10 W
Kiryandongo 154 1.53 N 32.03 E
Kiryū 94 36.24 N 139.20 E
Kirza 86 54.14 N 81.40 E
Kiržač 82 56.09 N 38.52 E
Kiržač ≃ 82 55.52 N 39.04 E
Kisa, Nihon 96 34.43 N 132.59 E
Kisa, Sve. 26 57.59 N 15.37 E
Kisai 94 36.06 N 139.35 E
Kisaichi 270 34.46 N 135.42 E
Kisakata 92 39.13 N 139.54 E
Kisaki 154 7.28 S 37.36 E
Kis Alföld ≃ 61 47.35 N 17.00 E
Kišaly 76 54.23 N 43.12 E
Kisambo 152 6.25 S 18.14 E
Kisanga 154 2.29 N 26.35 E
Kisangani (Stanleyville) 154 0.30 S 25.12 E
Kisantu 152 5.07 S 15.05 E
Kisar, Pulau I 112 8.05 S 127.10 E
Kisaralik ≃ 180 60.51 N 161.16 W
Kisaran 114 2.59 N 99.37 E
Kisarawe 154 6.54 S 39.04 E
Kisarazu 94 35.23 N 139.55 E
Kisarazu-Kichi, Kōkū-jieitai ■ 94 35.24 N 139.55 E
Kisawa 96 33.49 N 134.18 E
K.I. Sawyer Air Force Base ■ 190 46.21 N 87.25 W
Kisbér 30 47.30 N 18.02 E
Kisbey 184 49.38 N 102.41 W
Kise ≃ 94 35.06 N 138.53 E
Kiselevsk → Kisel'ovsk 86 54.00 N 86.39 E
Kisel'ovka 80 47.18 N 44.07 E
Kisel'ovsk 86 54.00 N 86.39 E
Kisengwa 154 6.00 S 25.50 E
Kisen-yama ∧[2] 270 34.54 N 135.51 E
Kiser Lake ⊜ 218 40.11 N 83.58 W
Kīsh, Jazīreh-ye I 128 26.32 N 53.56 E
Kishanda 154 1.42 S 31.34 E
Kishanganga ≃ 123 34.22 N 73.30 E
Kishanganj 124 26.07 N 87.56 E
Kishangarh 120 27.52 N 70.34 E
Kishangarh ✦[8] 272a 28.31 N 77.08 E
Kishangarh Bās 120 26.34 N 74.52 E
Kishb, Ḥarrat al- ⊥[9] 144 23.00 N 41.25 E
Kishi, Nig. 150 9.05 N 3.52 E
Kishi, Zaïre 154 10.04 S 26.26 E
Kishida ≃ 96 35.38 N 134.27 E
Kishigawa 96 34.13 N 135.20 E
Kishikas ≃ 184 52.45 N 91.43 W
Kishimoto 96 35.23 N 133.25 E
Kishinev → Kišin'ov 38 47.00 N 28.50 E
Kishiwada 96 34.28 N 135.22 E
Kishorganj 124 24.26 N 90.46 E
Kishorn, Loch ⊂ 46 57.21 N 5.41 W
Kishtwār 123 33.19 N 75.46 E
Kishwaukee ≃ 216 42.11 N 89.08 W
Kishwaukee, South Branch ≃ 216 42.12 N 88.59 W
Kisia 152 4.35 S 18.22 E
Kisigo ≃ 154 7.03 S 35.50 E
Kisii 154 0.41 S 34.46 E
Kisiju 154 7.24 S 39.20 E
Kiši-Karoj, ozero ⊜ 86 54.03 N 71.20 E
Kisika-zaki > 93b 30.50 N 131.04 E
Kısıklı ✦[8] 267b 41.01 N 29.03 E
Kišin 78 51.08 N 27.41 E
Kišin'ov (Kishinev) 38 47.00 N 28.50 E
Kısır Dağı ∧ 84 40.58 N 43.04 E
Kısırkaya ✦[8] 267b 41.14 N 28.58 E
Kısırmandıra ✦[8] 267b 41.14 N 28.49 E
Kisiwada → Kishiwada 96 34.28 N 135.22 E
Kisiwani 154 4.08 S 37.57 E
Kisizi 154 1.00 S 29.56 E
Kiska Island I 181a 52.00 N 177.30 E
Kiskatinaw ≃ 182 56.06 N 120.08 W
Kiska Volcano ∧[1] 181a 52.07 N 177.36 E
Kis-Kevély ∧[2] 264c 47.38 N 18.59 E
Kiski Lake ⊜ 184 54.46 N 98.55 W
Kiskimere 279b 40.37 N 79.35 W
Kiskiminetas ≃ 214 40.41 N 79.40 W
Kiskittogisu Lake ⊜ 184 54.13 N 98.20 W
Kiskitto Lake ⊜ 184 54.16 N 98.34 W
Kiskörei-víztároló ⊜[1] 30 47.35 N 20.40 E
Kiskőrös 30 46.38 N 19.17 E
Kiskunfélegyháza 30 46.43 N 19.52 E
Kiskunhalas 30 46.26 N 19.30 E
Kiskunmajsa 30 46.30 N 19.45 E
Kiskunsági Nemzeti Park ♠ 30 46.40 N 19.25 E
Kisl'akovka 78 46.44 N 31.59 E
Kisl'akovskaja 78 46.27 N 39.40 E
Kislovka 83 49.38 N 37.53 E
Kislovo 80 49.54 N 45.25 E
Kislovodsk 84 43.55 N 42.44 E
Kismaayo 144 0.22 S 42.32 E
Kismet 276 40.38 N 73.12 W
Kisnema 76 60.20 N 37.39 E
Kiso, Nihon 94 35.56 N 137.47 E
Kiso, Nihon 268 35.34 N 139.26 E
Kiso ≃ 94 35.02 N 136.45 E
Kisofukushima 94 35.51 N 137.42 E
Kisogawa 94 35.20 N 136.47 E
Kisoripur 126 22.05 N 88.34 E
Kisoro 154 1.17 S 29.41 E
Kiso-sammyaku ⋏ 94 35.43 N 137.50 E
Kisozaki 94 35.04 N 136.44 E
Kispest ✦[8] 264c 47.27 N 19.08 E
Kispiox 182 55.21 N 127.41 W
Kispiox ≃ 182 55.16 N 127.41 W
Kispiox Mountain ∧ 182 55.25 N 127.57 W
Kissamos 38 35.30 N 23.38 E
Kissena Park ♠ 276 40.45 N 73.49 W
Kisseynew Lake ⊜ 184 54.58 N 101.35 W
Kissidougou 150 9.11 N 10.06 W
Kissimmee 220 28.17 N 81.24 W
Kissimmee ≃ 220 27.10 N 80.53 W
Kissimmee, Lake ⊜ 220 27.55 N 81.16 W
Kissing 60 48.18 N 10.59 E
Kississing 184 55.07 N 101.07 W
Kississing Lake ⊜ 184 55.10 N 101.20 W
Kisslegg 58 47.47 N 9.53 E
Kissū, Jabal ∧ 140 21.35 N 25.09 E
Kista 80 46.05 N 43.06 E
Kistanje 36 43.59 N 15.58 E
Kistarcsa 264c 47.33 N 19.16 E
Kistendej 80 52.08 N 43.39 E
Kistigan Lake ⊜ 184 54.38 N 92.37 W
Kistler 214 40.22 N 77.51 W
Kisújszállás 30 47.13 N 20.46 E
Kisuki 96 35.17 N 132.54 E
Kisumu 154 0.06 S 34.45 E
Kisvárda 30 48.13 N 22.05 E
Kiswere 154 9.26 S 39.33 E
Kita 150 13.03 N 9.29 W
Kita ✦[8], Nihon 268 35.45 N 139.44 E
Kita ✦[8], Nihon 270 34.45 N 135.08 E
Kita ✦[8], Nihon 270 34.42 N 135.30 E
Kita ✦[8], Nihon 270 35.03 N 135.45 E
Kitaaiki 94 36.04 N 138.34 E
Kita-Daitō-jima I 90 25.57 N 131.18 E
Kitafuji-enshūjō ■ 94 35.25 N 138.48 E
Kitagata 94 35.26 N 136.41 E
Kitagawa 96 33.27 N 134.03 E
Kitagi-shima I 96 34.23 N 133.32 E
Kitaibaraki 94 36.48 N 140.45 E
Kitain Temple ʊ[1] 268 35.54 N 139.30 E
Kita-Iō-jima I 14 25.26 N 141.17 E
Kitairiso 268 35.50 N 139.26 E
Kitajima 96 34.05 N 134.35 E
Kitakami 92 39.18 N 141.07 E
Kitakami ≃ 92 38.25 N 141.19 E
Kitakami-kōchi ⋏ 92 39.30 N 141.30 E
Kitakata 92 37.39 N 139.52 E
Kitakyuschu → Kitakyūshū 96 33.53 N 130.50 E
Kitakyūshū 96 33.53 N 130.50 E
Kitakyushu-kokutei-kōen ♠ 96 33.45 N 130.50 E
Kitale 154 1.01 N 35.00 E
Kitamachi ✦[8] 268 35.46 N 139.39 E
Kitamba ✦[8] 273b 4.19 S 15.14 E
Kitami 92a 43.48 N 143.54 E
Kitami-sanchi ⋏ 92a 44.22 N 142.43 E
Kitamoto 94 36.02 N 139.32 E
Kita-Nagato-kaigan-kokutei-kōen ♠ 96 34.24 N 131.16 E
Kitanakagusuku 174m 26.21 N 127.51 E
Kitanda, Zaïre 154 6.36 S 26.27 E
Kitanda, Zaïre 154 9.59 S 27.28 E
Kitangari 154 10.39 S 39.20 E
Kitangiri, Lake ⊜ 154 4.05 S 34.19 E
Kitangua 152 6.17 S 20.22 E
Kitano, Nihon 96 33.20 N 130.35 E
Kitano, Nihon 268 35.47 N 139.26 E
Kitanoshinden 268 35.48 N 139.26 E
Kitatachibana 94 36.29 N 139.03 E
Kitatajima 268 35.56 N 139.30 E
Kitatawara 270 34.44 N 135.42 E
Kitaura 94 36.04 N 140.32 E
Kita-ura ⊜ 94 36.00 N 140.34 E
Kitava Island I 164 8.40 S 151.20 E
Kitaya 154 10.39 S 40.10 E
Kit Carson, Ca., U.S. 226 38.41 N 120.07 W
Kit Carson, Co., U.S. 198 38.45 N 102.47 W
Kitchener, Austl. 162 31.02 S 124.11 E
Kitchener, On., Can. 212 43.27 N 80.29 W
Kitee 26 62.06 N 30.09 E
Kitega → Gitega 154 3.26 S 29.56 E
Kiteiyab 140 17.12 N 33.43 E
Kitenda 152 6.53 S 17.21 E
Kitenevo 82 56.21 N 36.13 E
Kitengo 152 7.26 S 24.08 E
Kitéssa 154 5.20 N 25.20 E
Kitgum 154 3.18 N 32.53 E
Kíthira 38 36.09 N 23.00 E
Kíthira I 38 36.20 N 22.58 E
Kíthnos 38 37.26 N 24.26 E
Kíthnos I 38 37.25 N 24.28 E
Kitimat 182 54.03 N 128.33 W
Kitimat ≃ 182 54.06 N 128.38 W
Kitimat Ranges ⋏ 182 53.30 N 128.50 W
Kitinen ≃ 24 67.08 N 27.29 E
Kitíou, Akrotírion > 130 34.48 N 33.36 E
Kitlope ≃ 182 53.10 N 127.45 W
Kitlope Lake ⊜ 182 53.07 N 127.47 W
Kitō, Nihon 94 34.42 N 138.03 E
Kitō, Nihon 96 33.46 N 134.12 E
Kitoj ≃ 88 52.39 N 103.56 E
Kitridge Point > 241g 13.09 N 59.25 W
Kitsap □[6] 224 47.41 N 122.44 W
Kitscoty 184 53.20 N 110.20 W
Kit's Coty House ʊ 260 51.19 N 0.30 E
Kitshua-Nseke 152 4.26 S 19.36 E
Kitsuki 92 33.25 N 131.37 E
Kitsuregawa 94 36.43 N 140.01 E
Kittanning 214 40.48 N 79.31 W
Kittatinny Mountain ∧ 210 41.10 N 74.55 W
Kittatinny Tunnel ✦[5] 214 40.09 N 77.41 W
Kittendorf 54 53.37 N 12.54 E
Kittery 188 43.05 N 70.44 W
Kitt Green 262 53.33 N 2.41 W
Kittilä 24 67.40 N 24.54 E
Kittitas 202 46.59 N 120.24 W
Kittitas □[6] 224 47.13 N 121.01 W
Kitt Peak National Observatory ʊ[3] 200 31.58 N 111.36 W

Symbols in the index entries represent the broad categories identified in the key at the right. Symbols with superior numbers (⋏[1]) identify subcategories (see complete key on page *I · 1).*

Symbole im Register stellen die rechts im Schlüssel erklärten Kategorien dar. Symbole mit hochgestellten Ziffern (⋏[1]) bezeichnen Unterabteilungen einer Kategorie (vgl. vollständiger Schlüssel auf Seite *I · 1).*

Los símbolos incluídos en el texto del índice representan las grandes categorías identificadas con la clave a la derecha. Los símbolos con numeros en su parte superior (⋏[1]) identifican las subcategorías (véase la clave completa en la página *I · 1).*

Les symboles de l'index représentent les catégories indiquées dans la légende à droite. Les symboles suivis d'un indice (⋏[1]) représentent des sous-catégories (voir légende complète à la page *I · 1).*

Os símbolos incluídos no texto do índice representam as grandes categorias identificadas com a chave à direita. Os símbolos com números em sua parte superior (⋏[1]) identificam as subcategorias (veja-se a chave completa à página *I · 1).*

Symbol	English	Deutsch	Español	Français	Português
∧	Mountain	Berg	Montaña	Montagne	Montanha
⋏	Mountains	Gebirge	Montañas	Montagnes	Montanhas
)(	Pass	Paß	Paso	Col	Passo
V	Valley, Canyon	Tal, Cañon	Valle, Cañón	Vallée, Canyon	Vale, Canhão
≃	Plain	Ebene	Llano	Plaine	Planície
>	Cape	Kap	Cabo	Cap	Cabo
I	Island	Insel	Isla	Île	Ilha
II	Islands	Inseln	Islas	Îles	Ilhas
⊥	Other Topographic Features	Andere Topographische Objekte	Otros Elementos Topográficos	Autres données topographiques	Outros acidentes topográficos

ESPAÑOL

Nombre | Página | Lat.°′ | Long.°′ W = Oeste

Kittsee 61 48.05 N 17.04 E
Kitu 154 7.38 S 27.42 E
Kitui 154 1.22 S 38.01 E
Kitumbeine ∧[1] 154 2.44 S 36.16 E
Kitunda 154 6.48 S 33.13 E
Kitutu 154 3.17 S 28.05 E
Kitwanga 182 55.06 N 128.03 W
Kitwangar Indian Reserve ⊸[4] 182 55.06 N 128.04 W
Kitwe 154 12.49 S 28.13 E
Kitwitwi 156 17.25 S 18.25 E
Kityang → Jieyang 100 23.35 N 116.21 E
Kitzbühel 64 47.27 N 12.23 E
Kitzbüheler Alpen ⩘ 64 47.20 N 12.20 E
Kitzingen 56 49.44 N 10.09 E
Kitzscher 54 51.09 N 12.33 E
Kiukiang → Jiujiang 100 29.44 N 115.59 E
Kiukiu, Pointe ≻ 174x 9.47 S 139.09 W
Kiul 124 25.09 N 86.06 E
Kiunga, Kenya 154 1.45 S 41.29 E
Kiunga, Pap. N. Gui. 164 6.10 S 141.15 E
Kiuruvesi 26 63.39 N 26.37 E
Kiuschu → Kyūshū I 92 33.00 N 131.00 E
Kivak 180 64.16 N 172.57 W
Kivalina 180 67.44 N 164.33 W
Kivercy 78 50.50 N 25.27 E
Kiveriči 76 57.22 N 36.36 E
Kivijärvi 26 63.04 N 25.03 E
Kivijärvi ⊜ 26 63.10 N 25.09 E
Kivik 26 55.41 N 14.15 E
Kiviõli 76 59.21 N 26.57 E
Kivu □[4] 154 2.30 S 27.00 E
Kivu, Lac ⊜ 154 2.00 S 29.10 E
Kiwaba N'zogi 152 8.57 S 16.32 E
Kiwai Island I 164 8.30 S 143.25 E
Kiwalik 180 66.02 N 161.50 W
Kiwanis Lake 214 41.28 N 81.09 W
Kiyama 96 33.25 N 130.32 E
Kīyāmakī Dāgh ∧ 84 38.47 N 45.51 E
Kiyan 174m 26.05 N 127.40 E
Kiyan-zaki ≻ 174m 26.05 N 127.39 E
Kıyıköy 130 41.38 N 28.05 E
Kiyiu Lake ⊜ 184 51.38 N 108.55 W
Kiyl ≏ 86 49.25 N 54.50 E
Kiyokawa 94 35.29 N 139.17 E
Kiyomi 94 36.07 N 137.11 E
Kiyosawa 94 35.03 N 138.15 E
Kiyose 94 35.47 N 139.32 E
Kiyosu 94 35.13 N 136.50 E
Kiyosumi-yama ∧ 94 35.09 N 140.09 E
Kiyotani 270 34.52 N 134.59 E
Kiyotsu ≏ 94 37.03 N 138.41 E
Kizel 86 59.03 N 57.40 E
Kizevatovo 80 53.13 N 45.18 E
Kızıl ≏ 130 41.44 N 35.58 E
Kızıl Adalar II 130 40.52 N 29.05 E
Kızılcabölük 130 37.37 N 29.01 E
Kızılcadağ 130 37.01 N 29.58 E
Kızılcahamam 130 40.28 N 32.39 E
Kızılçakçak 84 40.46 N 43.37 E
Kızıldağ Milli Parkı ♦ 130 37.58 N 31.28 E
Kızıldikme 130 39.05 N 37.01 E
Kızılhisar 130 37.33 N 29.18 E
Kızılırmak 130 40.21 N 33.59 E
Kızılören 130 37.52 N 32.07 E
Kizil'skoje 86 52.44 N 58.54 E
Kızılsu 130 37.28 N 42.13 E
Kiziltašskij liman ⊂ 78 45.07 N 37.05 E
Kızıltepe 130 37.12 N 40.36 E
Kızıltoprak ⊸[8] 267b 40.58 N 29.03 E
Kizil'urt 84 43.12 N 46.53 E
Kızılyaka 130 37.09 N 32.54 E
Kižimiz, gora ∧ 24 63.12 N 58.48 E
Kizimkazi 154 6.27 S 39.28 E
Kižinga 88 51.51 N 109.55 E
Kizir ≏ 86 53.51 N 93.06 E
Kızkalesi ⊥ 130 36.28 N 34.04 E
Kızkulesi ⊸[5] 267b 41.01 N 29.00 E
Kizl'ar 84 43.50 N 46.40 E
Kizl'arskij zaliv ⊂ 84 44.33 N 46.55 E
Kizner 80 56.17 N 51.31 E
Kiz'oma 24 61.08 N 44.50 E
Kizu 96 34.44 N 135.49 E
Kizu ≏ 94 34.53 N 135.42 E
Kizuki 268 35.34 N 139.40 E
Kizuri 270 34.39 N 135.34 E
Kizyl-Ajak 128 37.40 N 65.23 E
Kizyl-Arvat 128 38.58 N 56.15 E
Kizyl-Atrek 128 37.36 N 54.46 E
Kizyl-Su 128 39.48 N 53.01 E
Kjellerup 41 56.17 N 9.26 E
Kjøbenhavn → København 41 55.40 N 12.35 E
Kjustendil 38 42.17 N 22.41 E
Klaarstroom 158 33.20 S 22.32 E
Klaaswaal 52 51.46 N 4.26 E
Klabat, Gunung ∧ 112 1.28 N 125.02 E
Kladanj 38 44.13 N 18.41 E
Kladbišči 80 55.32 N 45.33 E
Kläden 54 52.38 N 11.39 E
Kladkovo 82 55.24 N 38.51 E
Kladno 54 50.08 N 14.05 E
Kladovo 38 44.37 N 22.37 E
Kladow ⊸[8] 54 52.27 N 13.09 E
Kladruby 60 49.43 N 12.59 E
Klaeng 110 12.47 N 101.39 E
Klagan 112 5.58 N 117.27 E
Klagenfurt 61 46.37 N 14.18 E
Klågerup 41 55.36 N 13.15 E
Klagshamn 41 55.32 N 12.55 E
Klagstorp 41 55.24 N 13.22 E
Klahoose Indian Reserve ⊸[4] 182 50.31 N 124.19 W
Klaipėda (Memel) 76 55.43 N 21.07 E
Klakah 115a 7.59 S 113.15 E
Klamath 204 41.31 N 124.02 W
Klamath ≏ 204 41.33 N 124.04 W
Klamath Falls 202 42.13 N 121.46 W
Klamath Marsh ≡ 202 42.54 N 121.44 W
Klamath Mountains ⩘ 204 41.40 N 123.20 W
K. Lamido 146 9.21 N 11.12 E
Klämmingen ⊜ 40 59.07 N 17.15 E
Klammpass)(64 47.17 N 13.05 E
Klamono 164 1.08 S 131.30 E
Klang → Kelang 114 3.02 N 101.27 E
Klangenan 115a 6.42 S 108.26 E
Klangpi 110 22.59 N 93.20 E
Klarälven (Trysilelva) ≏ 26 59.23 N 13.32 E
Kl'as'ma 265b 55.59 N 37.50 E
Klášterec 54 50.24 N 13.10 E
Kl'asticy 76 55.53 N 28.36 E
Klaten 115a 7.42 S 110.35 E
Klatovy 60 49.24 N 13.18 E
Klausdorf, Dtsch. 54 54.20 N 13.01 E
Klausdorf, Dtsch. 54 54.18 N 10.15 E
Klausenburg → Cluj-Napoca 38 46.47 N 23.36 E
Klausenpass)(58 46.52 N 8.51 E
Kl'avlino 80 54.17 N 52.01 E
Klawer 158 31.44 S 18.36 E
Klawock 182 55.33 N 133.06 W
Klazienaveen 52 52.44 N 7.00 E
Kl'az'ma 82 55.58 N 37.27 E
Kl'az'ma ≏ 80 56.10 N 42.58 E
Kl'az'minskoje vodochranilišče ⊜[1] 265b 55.59 N 37.35 E
Kleberg 222 32.40 N 96.37 W
Kleck 76 53.04 N 26.38 E
Klecko 30 52.38 N 17.26 E
Kleczew 30 52.23 N 18.10 E
Kledering ⊸[8] 264b 48.08 N 16.26 E
Kleef 263 51.11 N 6.56 E
Kleena Kleene 182 51.57 N 124.50 W
Kleinasien → Asia Minor □[9] 22 39.00 N 32.00 E

FRANÇAIS

Nom | Page | Lat.°′ | Long.°′ W = Ouest

Kleinbegin 158 28.50 S 21.36 E
Klein-Blesbokspruit ≏ 273d 26.16 S 28.29 E
Kleinbodungen 54 51.28 N 10.32 E
Klein Bonaire I 241s 12.10 N 68.18 W
Klein Bünzow 54 53.53 N 13.48 E
Kleinburg 275b 43.50 N 79.38 W
Klein Curaçao I 241s 12.00 N 68.40 W
Kleine Elster ≏ 54 51.32 N 13.23 E
Kleine Emme ≏ 58 47.04 N 8.17 E
Kleine Emscher ≏ 263 51.31 N 6.43 E
Kleine Erlauf ≏ 61 48.07 N 15.08 E
Kleineichen 263 51.08 N 7.21 E
Kleine Laber ≏ 60 48.55 N 12.31 E
Kleinenberg 52 51.35 N 8.58 E
Kleinenbroich 263 51.12 N 6.35 E
Kleinengstingen 58 48.23 N 9.18 E
Kleiner Jasmunder Bodden ⊂ 54 54.28 N 13.32 E
Kleiner Ravens-Berg ∧[2] 264a 52.22 N 13.04 E
Kleiner Wannsee ⊜ 264a 52.25 N 13.10 E
Kleiner Zern-See ⊜ 264a 52.26 N 12.55 E
Kleine Spree ≏ 54 51.31 N 14.24 E
Kleines Walsertal V 64 47.23 N 10.12 E
Kleinfeltersville 208 40.18 N 76.15 W
Kleinglödnitz 61 46.51 N 14.08 E
Kleinhammer 263 51.14 N 7.46 E
Klein-Jukskei ≏ 273d 26.08 S 27.56 E
Klein-Karas 156 27.32 S 18.06 E
Klein Karroo → Little Karroo ⩘[1] 158 33.45 S 21.30 E
Klein Kienitz 264a 52.18 N 13.29 E
Kleinlützel 58 47.26 N 7.25 E
Kleinmachnow 54 52.24 N 13.15 E
Klein Marzehns 54 52.01 N 12.37 E
Kleinmond 158 34.21 S 19.03 E
Klein-Olifants ≏ 158 25.41 S 29.19 E
Kleinschönebeck 264a 52.29 N 13.43 E
Klein-Soutpan 158 30.26 S 22.26 E
Klein-Vis ≏ 158 33.05 S 26.00 E
Klein Wanzleben 54 52.04 N 11.21 E
Klein Ziethen 264a 52.23 N 13.27 E
Klein Ziethener-Berge ∧[2] 264a 52.22 N 13.26 E
Klekovača ∧ 36 44.26 N 16.31 E
Klementjevka 86 50.16 N 80.56 E
Klementjevo 82 55.38 N 36.01 E
Klemme 190 43.00 N 93.36 W
Klemtu 182 52.36 N 128.31 W
Klenovka 80 57.45 N 54.19 E
Klenovo 82 55.19 N 37.21 E
Klerksdorp 158 26.58 S 26.39 E
Klerkskraal 158 26.15 S 27.10 E
Klesov 78 51.19 N 26.54 E
Klésso 150 10.57 N 3.59 W
Klet' ∧ 61 48.52 N 14.17 E
Kletn'a 76 53.23 N 33.12 E
Kletskij 80 49.19 N 43.04 E
Kletsko-Počtovskij 80 49.36 N 43.03 E
Klettgau ⊸[1] 58 47.40 N 8.25 E
Klettwitz 54 51.32 N 13.53 E
Klevan' 78 50.44 N 26.02 E
Kleve 52 51.48 N 6.09 E
Klevenka 80 52.07 N 49.33 E
Kley ⊸[8] 263 51.30 N 7.22 E
Klibreck, Ben ∧ 46 58.14 N 4.22 W
Kličev 76 53.29 N 29.21 E
Klička 88 50.26 N 118.00 E
Klickitat 224 45.49 N 121.09 W
Klickitat □[6] 224 45.50 N 121.07 W
Klickitat ≏ 224 45.42 N 121.17 W
Kliedbruch ⊸[1] 263 51.22 N 6.33 E
Klietz 54 52.40 N 12.04 E
Klimino 88 58.39 N 98.42 E
Klimoviči 76 53.37 N 31.58 E
Klimovo, Ross. 76 52.23 N 32.11 E
Klimovo, Ross. 82 55.22 N 38.52 E
Klimovsk 82 55.22 N 37.32 E
Klimovskoje 82 54.42 N 37.48 E
Klimov Zavod 76 54.50 N 34.55 E
Klimpfjäll 24 65.04 N 14.52 E
Klin, Ross. 82 56.20 N 36.44 E
Klin, Ross. 82 55.19 N 36.20 E
Klinaklini ≏ 182 51.05 N 125.36 W
Klin-Bel'din 82 54.45 N 39.13 E
Klincovka 80 51.41 N 49.11 E
Klincy 76 52.47 N 32.14 E
Kline Ditch ≊ 279a 41.28 N 82.04 W
Kling 116 5.58 N 124.42 E
Klingbach ≏ 56 49.10 N 8.20 E
Klingenberg 54 50.55 N 13.31 E
Klingenberg am Main 56 49.47 N 9.11 E
Klingenmünster 56 49.08 N 8.01 E
Klingenthal 54 50.21 N 12.28 E
Klinger Lake ⊜ 216 41.47 N 85.33 W
Klingerstown 208 40.40 N 76.41 W
Klinghardtberge ∧ 156 27.18 S 15.48 E
Klingnau 58 47.35 N 8.15 E
Klink 54 53.29 N 12.37 E
Klinkino 83 47.17 N 38.15 E
Klínovec ∧ 54 50.24 N 12.58 E
Klinsko-Dmitrovskaja gr'ada ∧ 82 56.15 N 37.30 E
Klintehamn 26 57.24 N 18.12 E
Klintsy → Klincy 76 52.47 N 32.14 E
Klip ≏, S. Afr. 158 27.03 S 29.03 E
Klip ≏, S. Afr. 273d 26.19 S 27.53 E
Klipbakken 158 28.50 S 21.21 E
Klipdale 158 34.19 S 19.57 E
Klipdam 158 27.35 S 19.56 E
Kliplev 41 54.56 N 9.25 E
Klippan 41 56.08 N 13.06 E
Klipplaat 158 33.02 S 24.21 E
Klippoortjie 273d 26.13 S 28.10 E
Klipriviersberg ⩘ 273d 26.17 S 28.02 E
Kliptown 273d 26.17 S 27.53 E
Klipwerf 158 31.09 S 19.52 E
Kliškovcy 78 48.26 N 26.15 E
Klisura 38 42.42 N 24.27 E
Klitmøller 26 57.02 N 8.31 E
Klitten 54 51.20 N 14.36 E
Klixbüll 41 54.48 N 8.53 E
Ključ 36 44.32 N 16.47 E
Klobbicke 264a 52.46 N 13.48 E
Klobouky 61 49.00 N 16.52 E
Kłobuck 30 50.55 N 18.57 E
Klobuticy 76 58.35 N 29.35 E
Kłodawa 30 52.16 N 18.55 E
Kłodzko 30 50.27 N 16.39 E
Kløfta 26 60.04 N 11.09 E
Kłomnice 30 50.56 N 19.21 E
Klondike 216 40.28 N 86.57 W
Klondike □[9] 180 63.30 N 139.00 W
Klondike ≏ 180 64.05 N 139.26 W
Klöntaler See ⊜ 58 47.02 N 8.58 E
Klooga 76 59.19 N 24.16 E
Kloosterveen 52 52.59 N 6.33 E
Kloosterzande 52 51.22 N 4.02 E
Kloster 54 54.35 N 13.06 E
Klosterfelde 54 52.48 N 13.28 E
Klosterhardt ⊸[8] 263 51.31 N 6.53 E
Klösterle 58 47.08 N 10.05 E
Klostermansfeld 54 51.35 N 11.29 E
Klosterneuburg 61 48.18 N 16.20 E
Kloster Oesede 52 52.12 N 8.07 E
Klosters 58 46.54 N 9.53 E
Klostertal V 58 47.08 N 9.59 E
Kloster Zinna 54 52.01 N 13.07 E
Kloten, Schw. 58 47.27 N 8.35 E
Kloten, Sve. 40 59.54 N 15.17 E
Klotz, Lac ⊜ 176 60.32 N 73.40 W
Klötze 54 52.38 N 11.10 E
Kloulklubed 175b 7.02 N 134.15 E
Klouto 150 6.57 N 0.34 E
Kluane ≏ 180 61.53 N 139.43 W
Kluane Lake ⊜ 180 61.15 N 138.40 W
Kluane National Park ♦ 180 60.45 N 139.30 W
Kluang 112 2.41 S 103.54 E

PORTUGUÊS

Nome | Página | Lat.°′ | Long.°′ W = Oeste

Kl'učevaja 24 65.16 N 41.32 E
Kl'učevskaja Sopka, vulkan ∧[1] 74 56.04 N 160.38 E
Kl'učevskij 88 53.33 N 119.26 E
Kluchorskij, pereval)(84 43.15 N 41.54 E
Kl'uči, Ross. 74 56.18 N 160.51 E
Kl'uči, Ross. 80 51.59 N 46.31 E
Kl'uči, Ross. 80 51.26 N 45.11 E
Kl'uči, Ross. 86 52.16 N 79.10 E
Kl'učovka, Kyrg. 85 42.34 N 71.48 E
Kl'učovka, Ross. 86 51.22 N 55.48 E
Kluczbork 30 50.59 N 18.13 E
Kluess 54 53.46 N 12.14 E
Kluet ≏ 114 3.04 N 97.20 E
Kl'ukvenka 86 58.34 N 85.55 E
Klukwan 180 59.24 N 135.54 W
Klundert 52 51.40 N 4.32 E
Klungkung 115b 8.32 S 115.24 E
Klüppelberg 56 51.06 N 7.28 E
Klüterthöhle ⊼[5] 52 51.18 N 7.21 E
Klutina Lake ⊜ 180 61.37 N 146.55 W
Klütz 54 53.58 N 11.10 E
Knaben gruver 26 58.39 N 7.04 E
Knaddah 130 35.45 N 36.12 E
Kn'aginino 80 55.49 N 45.03 E
Knaik ≏ 46 56.14 N 3.52 W
Knapdaar 158 30.43 S 26.09 E
Knapdale ⊸[1] 46 55.55 N 5.30 W
Knaphill 260 51.19 N 0.37 W
Knapp 190 44.57 N 92.04 W
Knapp Creek 210 42.00 N 78.30 W
Knappenberg 61 46.56 N 14.35 E
Knäred 26 56.32 N 13.19 E
Knaresborough 44 54.00 N 1.27 W
Knargram 126 24.01 N 87.59 E
Knauertown 285 40.10 N 75.44 W
Knauthain ⊸[8] 54 51.16 N 12.18 E
Kn'ažaja Bajgora 76 52.23 N 40.02 E
Kn'azevka 86 57.35 N 74.10 E
Kn'ažji Gory 76 56.05 N 35.14 E
Kn'ažovo 76 59.40 N 43.54 E
Knebel 41 56.13 N 10.30 E
Knebworth 42 51.52 N 0.12 W
Kneehills Creek ≏ 182 51.30 N 112.50 W
Knee Lake ⊜, Mb., Can. 184 55.03 N 94.40 W
Knee Lake ⊜, Sk., Can. 184 55.51 N 107.00 W
Knesebeck 54 52.41 N 10.42 E
Knesselare 50 51.08 N 3.25 E
Knetzgau 56 50.00 N 10.33 E
Knevicy 76 57.56 N 32.14 E
Kneža 38 43.30 N 24.05 E
Knić 38 43.55 N 20.43 E
Knickerbocker 196 31.16 N 100.38 W
Kniebis 58 48.28 N 8.17 E
Knife ≏ 198 47.20 N 101.23 W
Knife Lake ⊜ 184 53.47 N 91.20 W
Knife River Indian Villages National Historic Site ⊥ 198 47.21 N 101.23 W
Knight Inlet ⊂ 182 50.41 N 125.40 W
Knight Island I 180 60.20 N 147.45 W
Knighton 42 52.21 N 3.03 W
Knightsen 226 37.58 N 121.40 W
Knights Landing 226 38.47 N 121.43 W
Knightstown 218 39.47 N 85.31 W
Knightville Dam ⊸[6] 207 42.17 N 72.52 W
Knik Arm ⊂ 180 61.25 N 149.45 W
Knin 36 44.02 N 16.12 E
Knippa 196 29.18 N 99.38 W
Knislinge 26 56.11 N 14.05 E
Knittelfeld 61 47.14 N 14.50 E
Knittlingen 56 49.01 N 8.45 E
Knivsbjerg ∧[2] 41 55.08 N 9.27 E
Knivsta 40 59.43 N 17.48 E
Knjaževac 38 43.34 N 22.16 E
Knob, Cape ≻ 162 34.32 S 119.16 E
Knobby Head ≻ 162 29.40 S 114.58 E
Knob Noster 194 38.45 N 93.33 W
Knob Peak ∧ 116 12.28 N 121.21 E
Knoc 48 52.38 N 9.20 W
Knock 46 57.33 N 2.45 W
Knockholt 260 51.18 N 0.06 E
Knockholt Pound 260 51.19 N 0.08 E
Knocklayd ∧ 48 55.09 N 6.15 W
Knocklong 48 52.26 N 8.24 W
Knockmealdown Mountains ⩘ 48 52.10 N 8.00 W
Knokke 50 51.21 N 3.17 E
Knole ⊥ 260 51.16 N 0.12 E
Knolls Green 262 53.19 N 2.18 W
Knollwood, Ct., U.S. 207 41.16 N 72.23 W
Knollwood, Il., U.S. 278 42.17 N 87.53 W
Knollwood, Md., U.S. 284c 39.02 N 76.58 W
Knollwood Park 216 42.14 N 84.22 W
Knon ⊜ 40 60.12 N 13.40 E
Knossós ⊥ 38 35.20 N 25.10 E
Knottingley 44 53.43 N 1.14 W
Knott's Berry Farm ♦ 280 33.50 N 118.00 W
Knotts Island 208 36.31 N 75.56 W
Knotty Ash ⊸[8] 262 53.25 N 2.54 W
Knotty Green 260 51.37 N 0.39 W
Knowland State Arboretum and Park ♦ 282 37.45 N 122.09 W
Knowle 42 52.23 N 1.43 W
Knowlesville 210 43.14 N 78.19 W
Knowlton Lake ⊜ 212 44.28 N 76.41 W
Knowltonwood 285 39.53 N 75.24 W
Knowsley 262 53.27 N 2.51 W
Knowsley □[8] 262 53.27 N 2.50 W
Knowsley Hall ʋ 262 53.26 N 2.50 W
Knowsley Park ♦ 262 53.27 N 2.49 W
Knox, In., U.S. 216 41.17 N 86.37 W
Knox, N.Y., U.S. 210 42.40 N 74.07 W
Knox, Pa., U.S. 214 41.14 N 79.32 W
Knox □[6], Mo., U.S. 219 40.08 N 92.09 W
Knox □[6], Oh., U.S. 214 40.23 N 82.29 W
Knox, Cape ≻ 182 54.11 N 133.04 W
Knoxboro 210 42.58 N 75.36 W
Knox City, Mo., U.S. 219 40.08 N 92.00 W
Knox City, Tx., U.S. 196 33.25 N 99.49 W
Knox Coast ⊼[2] 9 66.30 S 105.00 E
Knox Dale 214 41.05 N 79.02 W
Knoxfield 274b 37.53 S 145.15 E
Knox Lake ⊜[1] 214 40.31 N 82.30 W
Knoxville, Ga., U.S. 192 32.43 N 83.59 W
Knoxville, Il., U.S. 190 40.54 N 90.17 W
Knoxville, Ia., U.S. 190 41.19 N 93.06 W
Knoxville, Pa., U.S. 210 41.57 N 77.26 W
Knoxville, Tn., U.S. 192 35.57 N 83.55 W
Knuckles ∧ 122 7.24 N 80.48 E
Knudshoved Odde ≻[1] 41 55.03 N 11.45 E
Knüll ∧ 56 50.53 N 9.24 E
Knutby 40 59.55 N 18.15 E
Knuthenborg 41 54.50 N 11.30 E
Knutsford 44 53.19 N 2.22 W
Knysna 158 34.02 S 23.02 E
Knyszyn 30 53.19 N 22.55 E
Koala Sanctuary ⊸[4] 274a 33.40 S 151.10 E
Koani 154 6.08 S 39.17 E
Kob' 88 55.25 N 101.24 E
Koba 112 2.29 S 106.24 E
Kob'aj 74 63.34 N 126.30 E
Kőbánya ⊸[8] 264c 47.29 N 19.10 E
Kobarid 36 46.15 N 13.35 E
Kobar Sink ⊼[7] 144 13.35 N 40.50 E
Kobayashi 92 31.59 N 130.59 E
Kōbe, Nihon 96 34.41 N 135.10 E
Kōbe, Nihon 270 34.41 N 135.10 E
Kōbe-kō ⊂ 270 34.40 N 135.12 E
Kobel'aki 78 49.09 N 34.12 E
København (Copenhagen) 41 55.40 N 12.35 E
København □[6] 41 55.45 N 12.25 E
Kōbe University ʋ[2] 270 34.43 N 135.14 E
Kobi 84 42.33 N 44.32 E
Koblenz, Dtsch. 56 50.21 N 7.35 E
Koblenz, Schw. 58 47.37 N 8.14 E
Koblenz □[5] 56 50.10 N 7.30 E
Kobo, Ityo. 144 12.11 N 39.33 E
Kobo, Zaïre 152 4.54 S 17.09 E
Ko-boke ♦ 96 33.50 N 133.46 E
Koboko 154 3.25 N 30.58 E
Koboldo 89 52.58 N 132.42 E
Kobona 76 60.01 N 31.36 E
Kobou ≏ 152 6.13 N 23.19 E
Kobowen Swamp ≡ 144 5.38 N 33.54 E
Koboža 76 58.49 N 35.01 E
Koboža ≏ 76 58.52 N 36.17 E
Kobra 24 60.03 N 50.44 E
Kobrin 76 52.13 N 24.21 E
Kobrinskoje 76 59.25 N 30.07 E
Kobroor, Pulau I 164 6.12 S 134.32 E
Kobuchizawa 94 35.52 N 138.19 E
Kobuga-hara ♦ 94 36.40 N 139.35 E
Kobuk 180 66.54 N 156.52 W
Kobuk ≏ 180 66.45 N 161.00 W
Kobuk Valley National Park ♦ 180 67.20 N 159.00 W
Kobuleti 84 41.50 N 41.47 E
Kobushiga-take ∧ 94 35.54 N 138.44 E
Kobylanka 54 53.19 N 14.50 E
Kobylin 30 51.43 N 17.13 E
Kobyl'nik 76 54.56 N 26.41 E
Kobyžča 78 50.49 N 31.30 E
Kocaali 130 41.03 N 30.52 E
Kocaaliler 130 37.19 N 30.44 E
Kocaavşar ≏ 130 40.08 N 27.57 E
Kocaeli → İzmit 130 40.46 N 29.55 E
Kocaeli □[4] 130 40.55 N 29.55 E
Koçali 130 37.55 N 38.15 E
Kočani 38 41.55 N 22.25 E
Koçarlı 130 37.45 N 27.42 E
Kocasinan ⊸[8] 267b 41.01 N 28.50 E
Koçbaşı Tepe ∧ 84 39.25 N 43.21 E
Kočečum ≏ 74 64.17 N 101.10 E
Kočelajevo 80 54.01 N 44.02 E
Kočemary 80 54.50 N 40.58 E
Kočen'ajevka 80 53.52 N 46.59 E
Kočen'ga, Ross. 76 60.09 N 43.33 E
Kočenga, Ross. 88 55.55 N 104.06 E
Kočenga ≏ 88 55.55 N 104.06 E
Kočerdyk 86 54.35 N 62.58 E
Kočerga 88 55.15 N 103.46 E
Kočerov 78 50.21 N 29.21 E
Kočetovka, Ross. 80 55.16 N 46.07 E
Kočetovka, Ross. 80 52.58 N 40.29 E
Kočevar 76 60.26 N 42.11 E
Kočevje 36 45.38 N 14.52 E
Kočevo 86 59.36 N 54.18 E
Koch'am-ni 98 41.06 N 129.23 E
Kŏch'ang, Taehan 98 35.26 N 126.42 E
Kŏch'ang, Taehan 98 35.41 N 127.55 E
Kochanoviči 76 55.52 N 28.08 E
Kochanovo 76 54.28 N 30.01 E
Koch Bihār 124 26.19 N 89.26 E
Kochel 64 47.39 N 11.22 E
Kochelsee ⊜ 64 47.38 N 11.20 E
Kochena 158 27.00 S 18.50 E
Kocher ≏ 56 49.14 N 9.12 E
Kōchi, Nihon 96 33.33 N 133.33 E
Kōchi, Nihon 96 34.28 N 132.53 E
Kōchi □[5] 96 33.40 N 133.30 E
Kōchi-dani ♦ 94 34.34 N 136.10 E
Kochinda 174m 26.08 N 127.43 E
Koch Island I 176 69.38 N 78.15 W
Kochiu → Gejiu 90 23.22 N 103.06 E
Kochma 80 56.56 N 41.06 E
Koch Peak ∧ 202 45.02 N 111.28 W
Kochugaon 124 26.34 N 90.04 E
Kock 30 51.39 N 22.27 E
Kočki, Ross. 86 52.24 N 80.40 E
Kočki, Ross. 86 54.20 N 80.29 E
Kočkor-Ata 85 41.04 N 72.29 E
Kočkorka 85 42.14 N 75.45 E
Kocksoord 273d 26.13 S 27.39 E
Kočkurovo 80 54.02 N 45.26 E
Kočmes 24 66.12 N 60.44 E
Kočon'ovo 86 55.02 N 82.12 E
Kočov 60 49.49 N 12.44 E
Kočubej 84 44.24 N 46.33 E
Kočubejevskoje 84 44.41 N 41.41 E
Kōda, Nihon 94 34.52 N 137.10 E
Kōda, Nihon 96 34.42 N 132.45 E
Kodačdikost 24 63.11 N 55.49 E
Kodaikānal 122 10.14 N 77.29 E
Kodaira 94 35.44 N 139.29 E
Kodama 94 36.11 N 139.08 E
Kodar, chrebet ⩘ 88 57.15 N 118.10 E
Kodāri 124 27.56 N 85.56 E
Kodarma 124 24.28 N 85.36 E
Kodera ⊸[8] 270 34.41 N 135.04 E
Kodersdorf 54 51.15 N 14.53 E
Kodi 152 3.34 S 22.12 E
Kodiak 180 57.48 N 152.23 W
Kodiak Island I 180 57.30 N 153.30 W
Kodiang 114 6.24 N 100.18 E
Kodinār 120 20.47 N 70.42 E
Kodino 24 63.43 N 39.41 E
Kodo ≏ 152 7.05 N 19.10 E
Kodo, Jabal ∧ 140 12.26 N 23.38 E
Kodok 140 9.53 N 32.07 E
Kodori ≏ 84 42.47 N 41.10 E
Kodorskij chrebet ⩘ 84 43.00 N 42.00 E
Kodra 78 50.36 N 29.34 E
Kodry ⩘[2] 38 47.10 N 28.25 E
Kodyma 78 48.07 N 29.07 E
Kodyma ≏ 78 48.01 N 30.48 E
Kodžori 84 41.40 N 44.41 E
Koegas 158 29.16 S 22.20 E
Koehn Lake ⊜ 228 35.20 N 117.53 W
Koekelare 50 51.05 N 2.58 E
Koekenaap 158 31.30 S 18.18 E
Koeltztown 219 38.19 N 92.03 W
Koenigsmacker 56 49.24 N 6.17 E
Koersel 56 51.04 N 5.16 E
Koes 156 25.59 S 19.08 E
Kofa Mountains ⩘ 200 33.20 N 114.00 W
Kofçaz 130 41.58 N 27.12 E
Kofeld 58 47.44 N 9.41 E
Köfering 60 48.56 N 12.12 E
Koffiefontein 158 29.30 S 25.00 E
Kofiau, Pulau I 164 1.11 S 129.50 E
Köflach 61 47.04 N 15.05 E
Koforidua 150 6.03 N 0.17 W
Kōfu, Nihon 94 35.39 N 138.35 E
Kōfu, Nihon 96 35.17 N 133.30 E
Koga, Nihon 94 36.11 N 139.43 E
Koga, Nihon 96 33.40 N 130.30 E
Koga, Tan. 154 6.14 S 32.25 E
Kogaluc ≏ 176 59.40 N 77.35 W
Kogaluc, Baie ⊂ 176 59.20 N 77.50 W
Kogaluk ≏ 176 56.12 N 61.44 W
Kogan 166 27.03 S 150.46 E
Kogane 268 35.50 N 139.56 E
Koganei 94 35.42 N 139.32 E
Kogarah 274a 33.58 S 151.08 E
Kogarah Bay ⊂ 274a 33.59 S 151.07 E
Køge, Dan. 41 55.27 N 12.11 E
Kōge, Nihon 96 35.24 N 134.15 E
Køge Bugt ⊂, Dan. 41 55.30 N 12.20 E
Køge Bugt ⊂, Kal. Nun. 176 65.00 N 40.30 W
Kogil'nik ≏ 78 45.51 N 29.38 E
Kogin Baba 146 7.55 N 11.30 E
Koglhof 61 47.19 N 15.40 E
Kogon ≏ 150 11.09 N 14.42 W
Kogoni 150 14.44 N 6.02 W
Kogŭm-do I 98 34.27 N 127.11 E
Kohak 128 25.44 N 62.33 E
Kohala Mountains ⩘ 229d 20.05 N 155.45 W
Kohama-shima I 175d 24.19 N 123.59 E
Kohāt 123 33.35 N 71.26 E
Kohāt ≏ 123 33.24 N 71.48 E
Kohatk Wash V 200 32.38 N 111.55 W
Kohila 76 59.10 N 24.45 E
Kohīma 120 25.40 N 94.07 E
Kohistān □[9] 123 35.03 N 72.52 W
Kohlberg ∧[2] 263 51.18 N 7.46 E
Kohler 190 43.44 N 87.46 W
Kohlstädt 52 51.50 N 8.52 E
Kohoku 94 35.26 N 136.15 E
Kōhoku ⊸[8] 268 35.31 N 139.38 E
Kohren-Sahlis 54 51.01 N 12.36 E
Kohsān 128 34.39 N 61.12 E
Kohtla-Järve 76 59.24 N 27.15 E
Kohu → Kōfu 94 35.39 N 138.35 E
Kohukohu 172 35.21 S 173.32 E
Kohŭng 98 34.37 N 127.16 E
Kohunlich ⊥ 232 18.27 N 89.01 W
Kohuratahi 172 39.06 S 174.46 E
Koide 94 37.13 N 138.57 E
Koidern 180 61.58 N 140.25 W
Koidu 150 8.38 N 10.59 W
Koigi 76 58.50 N 25.45 E
Koihoa 110 8.12 N 93.29 E
Koil-Aligarh → Alīgarh 124 27.53 N 78.05 E
Koimbani 157a 11.37 S 43.23 E
Koindu 150 8.26 N 10.19 W
Koin-ni 98 40.28 N 126.22 E
Koito ≏ 94 35.21 N 139.52 E
Kojandy 86 49.51 N 75.40 E
Kojda 24 66.23 N 42.31 E
Kŏje-do I 98 34.52 N 128.37 E
Kojetin 30 49.21 N 17.18 E
Kojgorodok 24 60.26 N 50.58 E
Ko-jima I 92a 41.22 N 139.48 E
Kojima-ko ⊜[1] 96 34.37 N 134.00 E
Kojŏ 98 38.57 N 127.51 E
Kojonup 162 33.50 S 117.09 E
Kojsary 85 42.33 N 78.10 E
Kojsug 83 47.07 N 39.41 E
Kojtas, Kaz. 86 51.32 N 76.15 E
Kojtaš, Uzb. 85 40.11 N 67.19 E
Kok (Hkok) ≏ 110 20.14 N 100.09 E
Kōka 94 34.54 N 136.13 E
Koka, Lake ⊜[1] 144 8.23 N 39.05 E
Kokai ≏ 94 35.52 N 140.08 E
K'okajgyr 85 40.43 N 75.37 E
Kokalaat 86 49.47 N 64.15 E
Kokand 85 40.33 N 70.57 E
Kokanee Glacier Provincial Park ♦ 182 49.47 N 117.10 W
Kokankišlak 85 40.56 N 72.30 E
Kökar I 26 59.56 N 20.55 E
Kokas 164 2.42 S 132.26 E
Kokašice 60 49.53 N 12.57 E
Kokava nad Rimavicou 30 48.34 N 19.50 E
Kokawa 96 34.16 N 135.24 E
K'okbel' 85 40.17 N 72.55 E
Kokčetav 86 53.17 N 69.25 E
Kokčetav □[8] 86 53.30 N 70.00 E
Kokčetavskaja vozvyšennost' ⩘[1] 86 52.50 N 69.00 E
Kokee State Park ♦ 229b 22.08 N 159.40 W
Kokemäenjoki ≏ 26 61.33 N 21.42 E
Kokemäki 26 61.15 N 22.21 E
Kokenau 164 4.43 S 136.26 E
Ko Kha 110 18.11 N 99.24 E
Kokhav HaYarden (Belvoir) ⊥ 132 32.36 N 35.31 E
Kókhi, Ákra ≻ 267c 37.53 N 23.27 E
Koki 150 15.30 N 15.59 W
Kokinu 268 35.59 N 139.59 E
Kokiu → Gejiu 102 23.22 N 103.06 E
Kok-Jangak 85 41.02 N 73.12 E
Kokka 140 20.00 N 30.35 E
Kokkilai Lagoon ⊂ 122 9.00 N 80.56 E
Kokkola (Karleby) 26 63.50 N 23.07 E
Kokku 98 40.22 N 128.44 E
Koknese 76 56.39 N 25.29 E
Koko 150 11.26 N 4.32 E
Kokoda 164 8.52 S 147.45 E
Koko Head ≻ 229c 21.16 N 157.42 W
Kokola 154 0.47 N 29.36 E
Kokole Point ≻ 229b 21.59 N 159.46 W
Kokolik ≏ 180 69.45 N 163.00 W
Kokolopozo 150 5.03 N 6.05 W
K'ok'omeren ≏ 85 41.43 N 73.54 E
Kokomo, Hi., U.S. 229a 20.52 N 156.18 W
Kokomo, In., U.S. 216 40.29 N 86.08 W
Kokomo, Ms., U.S. 194 31.11 N 90.00 W
Kokong 156 24.27 S 23.03 E
Kokonoe 96 33.10 N 131.10 E
Koko Nor → Qinghai Hu ⊜ 102 36.50 N 100.20 E
Kokopo 164 4.20 S 152.15 E
Kokorevka 76 52.35 N 34.16 E
Kokosing ≏ 214 40.22 N 82.12 W
Kokos-Inseln → Cocos (Keeling) Islands □[2] 14 12.10 S 96.55 E
Kokoškino 265b 55.38 N 37.11 E
Kokpāra Narsinghgarh 126 22.31 N 86.33 E
Kokpaš 86 51.12 N 87.45 E
Kokpekty 86 48.45 N 82.24 E
Kokrājhār 124 26.24 N 90.16 E
Kokrines 180 64.56 N 154.42 W
Kokrines Hills ⩘[2] 180 65.15 N 154.00 W
Koksa ≏ 86 50.16 N 85.36 E
Kokšaalatau, chrebet ⩘ 72 41.00 N 78.00 E
Koksan 98 38.46 N 126.40 E
Koksaraj 85 42.40 N 68.08 E
Kokšekol', ozero ⊜ 86 46.05 N 62.00 E
Koksijde 50 51.07 N 2.38 E
Koksilah 224 48.40 N 123.38 W
Koksilah ≏ 224 48.45 N 123.39 W
Koksoak ≏ 176 58.32 N 68.10 W
Koksŏng 98 35.17 N 127.17 E
Koksovyj 78 48.12 N 40.39 E
Kokstad 158 30.32 S 29.29 E
Koksu, Kaz. 85 41.27 N 68.01 E
Koksu, Kaz. 86 44.59 N 77.56 E
Koktal 86 44.09 N 79.48 E
Koktas, Kaz. 86 47.33 N 70.55 E
Koktas, Kaz. 86 45.59 N 73.32 E
Kok-Taš, Kyrg. 85 41.12 N 72.25 E
Kokterek 80 49.25 N 49.15 E
Koktubek 86 48.07 N 56.51 E
Kokubu, Nihon 92 31.44 N 130.46 E
Kokubu, Nihon 96 34.56 N 132.07 E
Kokubunji, Nihon 94 36.22 N 139.51 E
Kokubunji, Nihon 96 34.18 N 133.58 E
Kokubunji, Nihon 268 35.42 N 139.29 E
Kokubunji Temple ʋ[1] 268 35.44 N 139.55 E
Kokufu 96 35.28 N 134.16 E
Kokuj 88 52.13 N 117.33 E
Kokujbel' ≏ 85 38.21 N 72.46 E
Kokžar 86 49.01 N 60.10 E
Kol ≏ 128 26.59 N 55.47 E
Kola, Indon. 164 5.26 S 134.29 E
Kola, Ross. 24 68.53 N 33.01 E
Kola ≏ 24 68.53 N 33.02 E
Kolachel 122 8.10 N 77.15 E
Kolāchi ≏ 120 27.08 N 67.02 E
Kol'adovka 83 49.05 N 39.12 E
Kolageran 84 40.58 N 44.37 E
Kolahun 150 8.24 N 10.02 W
Kolaka 112 4.03 S 121.36 E
Kolambo 152 7.34 S 21.58 E
Kolambugan 116 8.07 N 123.55 E
Kolangār 120 34.02 N 69.01 E
Kola Peninsula → Kol'skij poluostrov ≻[1] 24 67.30 N 37.00 E
Kolār 122 13.08 N 78.08 E
Kolāras 124 25.14 N 77.36 E
Kolār Gold Fields 122 12.55 N 78.17 E
Kolari 24 67.20 N 23.48 E
Kolarovgrad → Šumen 38 43.16 N 26.55 E
Kolárovo 30 47.52 N 18.02 E
Kolašin 38 42.49 N 19.31 E
Kolāyat 120 27.50 N 72.57 E
Kolbači 89 54.22 N 123.02 E
Kolbäck 40 59.34 N 16.15 E
Kolbäcksån ≏ 40 59.32 N 16.16 E
Kol'baj, gora ∧[2] 86 43.43 N 53.57 E
Kolbano 112 10.02 S 124.31 E
Kolbasna 38 47.47 N 29.13 E
Kolbča 76 53.39 N 29.14 E
Kolberg → Kołobrzeg 30 54.12 N 15.33 E
Kolbermoor 64 47.51 N 12.04 E
Kolbio 144 1.10 S 41.15 E
Kolbnitz 64 46.52 N 13.19 E
Kolbotn 26 59.49 N 10.48 E
Kolbuszowa 30 50.15 N 21.47 E
Kolby Kås 41 55.48 N 10.33 E
Kolchida ≚ 84 42.15 N 42.00 E
Kolchozabad 120 37.27 N 68.31 E
Kol'covo 82 54.27 N 36.40 E
Kol'čuga 82 55.43 N 37.12 E
Kol'čugino 80 56.18 N 39.23 E
Kołczewo 54 53.58 N 14.38 E
Kolda 150 12.53 N 14.57 W
Kolda □[4] 150 12.50 N 14.50 W
Kolding 41 55.31 N 9.29 E
Kolding Fjord ⊂ 41 55.30 N 9.35 E
Kole, Zaïre 152 3.27 S 22.29 E
Kole, Zaïre 154 2.07 N 25.26 E
Kolea 34 36.38 N 2.46 E
Kolebīra 124 22.43 N 84.42 E
Kole Kalyan ⊸[8] 272c 19.06 N 72.51 E
Kolenfeld 52 52.24 N 9.27 E
Koleno 80 51.52 N 44.07 E
Kolenté 150 10.06 N 12.37 W
Kolenté (Great Scarcies) ≏ 150 8.55 N 13.08 W
Kolga 76 59.32 N 25.42 E
Kolgujev, ostrov I 24 69.05 N 49.15 E
Kolhāpur, India 122 16.06 N 78.16 E
Kolhāpur, India 122 16.42 N 74.13 E
Kolho 26 62.08 N 24.31 E
Koli 76 59.30 N 34.30 E
Koli ∧[2] 26 63.06 N 29.48 E
Koli, Jabal ∧ 140 14.05 N 25.31 E
Kolia 150 9.46 N 6.28 W
Koliba (Corubal) ≏ 150 11.57 N 15.06 W
Koliganek 180 59.48 N 157.25 W
Kolima ⊜ 26 63.16 N 25.50 E
Kolimbine ≏ 150 14.26 N 11.23 W
Kolín 30 50.01 N 15.13 E
Kolka 76 57.45 N 22.35 E
Kølkær 41 56.04 N 9.06 E
Kolkasrags ≻ 76 57.47 N 22.36 E
Kolki, Ukr. 78 51.37 N 26.37 E
Kolki, Ukr. 78 51.07 N 25.41 E
Kolkwitz 54 51.45 N 14.15 E
Kollbach ≏ 60 48.36 N 12.58 E
Kölleda 54 51.11 N 11.15 E
Kollegāl 122 12.09 N 77.07 E
Kolleru Lake ⊜ 122 16.39 N 81.13 E
Kollum 52 53.16 N 6.09 E
Kollund 41 54.51 N 9.27 E
Kolmanskop 156 26.40 S 15.12 E
Kolmården 40 58.40 N 16.23 E
Kolmården ⩘[2] 40 58.41 N 16.35 E
Kolmårdens Djurpark ♦ 40 58.40 N 16.29 E
Kolmogorovo 86 59.15 N 91.20 E
Köln (Cologne) 56 50.56 N 6.59 E
Köln □[5] 56 50.55 N 6.40 E
Köln-Bonn, Flughafen ⊠ 56 50.50 N 7.10 E
Kolno 30 53.25 N 21.56 E
Kolo, Niger 150 13.14 N 2.20 E
Koło, Pol. 30 52.12 N 18.38 E
Kolo, Tan. 154 4.44 S 35.50 E
Koloa 229b 21.54 N 159.28 W
Kolobovo 80 56.42 N 41.21 E
Kołobrzeg 30 54.12 N 15.33 E
Koloč' ≏ 82 55.34 N 35.52 E
Kolochau 54 51.44 N 13.16 E
Kolodn'a 76 54.48 N 32.09 E
Kologriv 76 58.51 N 44.17 E
Kologrivovka 80 51.44 N 45.20 E
Kolojar 80 52.34 N 46.58 E
Kolok (Golok) ≏ 114 6.15 N 102.05 E
Kolokani 150 13.35 N 8.02 W
Koloko 150 11.05 N 5.19 W
Kolokol'covka, Ross. 80 52.36 N 49.48 E
Kolokol'covka, Ross. 80 51.12 N 44.36 E
Kololo 144 7.29 N 41.58 E
Kolom'agi ⊸[8] 265a 60.00 N 30.17 E
Kolom'agi Airport ⊠ 265a 60.01 N 30.17 E
Kolomak 78 49.50 N 35.18 E
Kolombangara Island I 175e 8.00 S 157.05 E
Kolomea → Kolomyja 78 48.32 N 25.04 E
Kolomenka ≏ 82 55.06 N 38.46 E
Kolomenskaja Sloboda 82 54.22 N 38.15 E
Kolomenskoje ⊸[8] 265b 55.40 N 37.41 E
Kolomna 82 55.05 N 38.49 E
Kolomyja 78 48.32 N 25.04 E
Kolondiéba 150 11.05 N 6.54 W
Kolonga 174w 21.08 S 175.04 W
Kolonia 174r 6.58 N 158.13 E
Kolonie Stolp 264a 52.28 N 13.46 E
Kolono 112 4.18 S 122.41 E
Kolonodale 112 2.00 S 121.19 E
Kolora 272b 22.55 N 88.22 E
Kolosib 120 24.14 N 92.42 E
Kol'osnoje 78 46.02 N 29.56 E
Kolosovka 86 56.28 N 73.36 E
Kolovai 174w 21.06 S 175.20 W
Kolovertnoje 80 50.36 N 51.06 E
Kolowana Watobo, Teluk ⊂ 112 5.00 S 123.06 E
Kolozsvár → Cluj-Napoca 38 46.47 N 23.36 E
Kolp' ≏ 76 59.20 N 36.49 E
Kolpaševo 86 58.20 N 82.50 E
Kolpino 76 59.45 N 30.36 E
Kölpinsee ⊜ 54 53.30 N 12.34 E
Kolpny 76 52.15 N 37.02 E
Kölsa 54 51.28 N 12.13 E
Kol'skij poluostrov (Kola Peninsula) ≻[1] 24 67.30 N 37.00 E
Kolsnaren ⊜ 40 59.02 N 16.01 E
Kolsva 40 59.36 N 15.50 E
Kol'togan 85 43.51 N 67.25 E
Koltovskaja 80 52.47 N 44.16 E
Koltubanovskij 80 52.57 N 52.02 E
Koltuši 265a 59.56 N 30.40 E
Kol'ubakino 82 55.40 N 36.32 E
Kolubara ≏ 38 44.40 N 20.15 E
Kol'učinskaja guba ⊂ 180 66.40 N 174.30 W
Koluel Kayke 254 46.43 S 68.14 W
Kolumbien → Colombia □[1] 246 4.00 N 72.00 W
Kol'upanovo 82 54.26 N 36.14 E
Koluškino 78 48.39 N 40.56 E
Koluszki 30 51.44 N 19.49 E
Koluton 86 51.43 N 69.25 E
Koluton ≏ 86 51.42 N 69.10 E
Kolva ≏ 24 65.55 N 57.15 E
Kolvereid 24 64.51 N 11.32 E
Kølvrå 41 56.18 N 9.08 E
Kolwezi 154 10.43 S 25.28 E
Kolyberovo 82 55.16 N 38.44 E
Kolyčevo 82 55.30 N 37.52 E
Kolyma ≏ 74 69.30 N 161.00 E
Kolymskaja 74 68.44 N 158.44 E
Kolymskaja nizmennost' ≚ 74 68.30 N 154.00 E
Kolyšlej 80 52.42 N 44.32 E

	English	Deutsch	Español	Français	Português
≏	River	Fluß	Río	Rivière	Rio
≊	Canal	Kanal	Canal	Canal	Canal
ʟ	Waterfall, Rapids	Wasserfall, Stromschnellen	Cascada, Rápidos	Chute d'eau, Rapides	Cascata, Rápidos
)(	Strait	Meeresstraße	Estrecho	Détroit	Estreito
⊂	Bay, Gulf	Bucht, Golf	Bahía, Golfo	Baie, Golfe	Baía, Golfo
⊜	Lake, Lakes	See, Seen	Lago, Lagos	Lac, Lacs	Lago, Lagos
≡	Swamp	Sumpf	Pantano	Marais	Pântano
⍓	Ice Features, Glacier	Eis- und Gletscherformen	Accidentes Glaciales	Formes glaciaires	Acidentes glaciares
⍑	Other Hydrographic Features	Andere Hydrographische Objekte	Otros Elementos Hidrográficos	Autres données hydrographiques	Outros acidentes hidrográficos

	English	Deutsch	Español	Français	Português
✣	Submarine Features	Untermeerische Objekte	Accidentes Submarinos	Formes de relief sous-marin	Acidentes submarinos
□	Political Unit	Politische Einheit	Unidad Politica	Entité politique	Unidade política
ʋ	Cultural Institution	Kulturelle Institution	Institución Cultural	Institution culturelle	Instituição cultural
⊥	Historical Site	Historische Stätte	Sitio Histórico	Site historique	Sítio histórico
♦	Recreational Site	Erholungs- und Ferienort	Sitio de Recreo	Centre de loisirs	Area de Lazer
⊠	Airport	Flughafen	Aeropuerto	Aéroport	Aeroporto
■	Military Installation	Militäranlage	Instalación Militar	Installation militaire	Instalação militar
⊸	Miscellaneous	Verschiedenes	Misceláneo	Divers	Diversos

ENGLISH — Name, Page, Lat.°′, Long.°′ · DEUTSCH — Name, Seite, Breite°′, Länge°′ E = Ost

Name	Page	Lat.°′	Long.°′
Kolyšovo	82	54.54 N	36.57 E
Kolyvan', Ross.	86	55.18 N	82.45 E
Kolyvan', Ross.	86	51.18 N	82.34 E
Kom → Qom	128	34.39 N	50.54 E
Kom ∧	38	43.10 N	23.03 E
Kom ≃	152	2.18 N	11.40 E
Koma, Ityo.	144	8.27 N	36.52 E
Koma, Mya.	110	15.39 N	98.12 E
Koma, Ross.	86	55.02 N	91.19 E
Koma ≃	94	35.59 N	139.26 E
Komadougou Yobé (Komadugu Yobe) ≃	146	13.43 N	13.20 E
Komadugu Gana ≃	146	13.05 N	12.24 E
Komadugu Yobe (Komadougou Yobé) ≃	146	13.43 N	13.20 E
Komae	94	35.38 N	139.35 E
Komagane	94	35.43 N	137.55 E
Komaga-take ∧, Nihon	92a	42.04 N	140.41 E
Komaga-take ∧, Nihon	94	35.45 N	138.14 E
Komaga-take ∧, Nihon	94	35.47 N	137.48 E
Komagome -●-^{8}	268	35.44 N	139.45 E
Komaki	94	35.17 N	136.55 E
Komandorskije ostrova II	74	55.00 N	167.00 E
Komandorski Village	226	37.43 N	121.54 W
Komariči	76	52.27 N	34.47 E
Komarin	78	51.26 N	30.31 E
Komarniki	78	49.00 N	23.04 E
Komárno, Slvk.	30	47.45 N	18.09 E
Komarno, Ukr.	78	49.38 N	23.42 E
Komárom	30	47.44 N	18.08 E
Komárom-Esztergom □^{6}	30	47.40 N	18.15 E
Komarovka	78	51.14 N	32.07 E
Komarovo	76	58.39 N	33.26 E
Komarovy	86	60.26 N	75.50 E
Komati (Incomáti) ≃	156	25.46 S	32.43 E
Komatipoort	156	25.25 S	31.55 E
Komatsu, Nihon	94	36.24 N	136.27 E
Komatsu, Nihon	96	33.53 N	133.07 E
Komatsu-kūkō ⊠	94	36.24 N	136.26 E
Komatsushima	96	34.00 N	134.35 E
Kombissiri	150	12.04 N	1.20 W
Kombone	152	4.37 N	9.19 E
Komdhārā	272b	22.53 N	88.14 E
Kome Island I	154	0.06 S	32.45 E
Komen	64	45.49 N	13.44 E
Komenda	150	5.03 N	1.29 W
Komenoi	268	35.55 N	140.01 E
Komering ≃	112	2.59 S	104.50 E
Komeshia	154	8.01 S	27.07 E
Komfane	164	5.39 S	134.44 E
Komga	158	32.35 S	27.55 E
Komi □^{3}	72	64.00 N	54.00 E
Kominato → Amatsu-kominato	94	35.07 N	140.10 E
Kominternovskoje	78	46.49 N	30.56 E
Komin Yanga	150	11.42 N	0.08 E
Komi-Perm'ackij Avtonomnyj Okrug □^{8}	24	60.00 N	54.30 E
Komissarovka, Ross.	83	48.07 N	40.09 E
Komissarovka, Ukr.	83	48.23 N	38.32 E
Komissarovo	89	44.59 N	131.46 E
Komissarovskij	80	47.29 N	42.59 E
Komkans	158	31.16 S	18.09 E
Komló	30	46.12 N	18.16 E
Kommadagga	158	33.09 S	25.55 E
Kommandodrif	158	27.30 S	26.14 E
Kommandokraal	158	33.06 S	22.51 E
Kommetjie	158	34.08 S	18.21 E
Kommunal'naja	88	52.03 N	115.06 E
Kommunar, Ross.	80	58.10 N	43.33 E
Kommunar, Ross.	86	54.20 N	89.18 E
Kommunarka	265b	55.34 N	37.29 E
Kommunary	26	60.54 N	29.47 E
Kommunizma, pik ∧	85	38.57 N	72.01 E
Komo ≃	152	0.09 N	9.50 E
Komodo	115b	8.35 S	119.30 E
Komodo, Pulau I	115b	8.36 S	119.30 E
Komoé ≃	150	5.12 N	3.44 W
Komoé, Parc National de la ♦	150	9.00 N	3.30 W
Komoka	214	42.57 N	81.26 W
Komono, Congo	152	3.15 S	13.14 E
Komono, Nihon	94	35.00 N	136.31 E
Komoran, Pulau I	164	8.18 S	138.45 E
Komoren → Comoros □^{1}	157a	12.10 S	44.10 E
Komorin, Kap → Comorin, Cape ›	122	8.04 N	77.34 E
Komorn → Komárno	30	47.45 N	18.09 E
Komoro	94	36.19 N	138.26 E
Komotau → Chomutov	54	50.28 N	13.26 E
Komotiní	38	41.08 N	25.25 E
Kompanejevka	78	48.15 N	32.12 E
Kompasberg ∧	158	31.45 S	24.32 E
Kompiam	164	5.20 S	143.55 E
Kompot	112	0.24 N	124.10 E
Komrat	38	46.18 N	28.38 E
Komsomolabad	85	38.52 N	69.57 E
Komsomolec	86	53.45 N	62.02 E
Komsomolec, ostrov I	74	80.30 N	95.00 E
Komsomolec, zaliv ⊂	72	45.30 N	52.45 E
Komsomol'sk, Ross.	80	57.02 N	40.21 E
Komsomol'sk, Ross.	86	55.38 N	88.11 E
Komsomol'sk, Ross.	86	57.27 N	86.02 E
Komsomol'sk, Turk.	128	39.02 N	63.36 E
Komsomol'skij, Kaz.	86	51.40 N	66.39 E
Komsomol'skij, Kaz.	86	47.20 N	53.42 E
Komsomol'skij, Ross.	80	54.27 N	45.49 E
Komsomol'skij, Ross.	89	50.22 N	142.10 E
Komsomol'skij, Ukr.	83	47.40 N	37.26 E
Komsomol'sk-na-Amure	89	50.35 N	137.02 E
Komsomol'sk-na-Ust'urte	86	44.03 N	58.20 E
Komsomol'skoje, Ross.	80	55.16 N	47.33 E
Komsomol'skoje, Ross.	80	50.46 N	47.03 E
Komsomol'skoje, Ross.	88	52.29 N	111.06 E
Komsomol'skoje, Ukr.	78	49.35 N	36.30 E
Komsomol'skoje, Ukr.	78	49.43 N	28.40 E
Komsomol'skoje, Ukr.	83	47.40 N	38.05 E
Komsomol'skoj Pravdy, ostrova II	74	77.20 N	107.40 E
Kŏmun-do I	98	34.02 N	127.19 E
Kömürcüpınar -●-^{8}	267b	41.15 N	28.51 E
Komusan	98	42.08 N	129.41 E
Komyšn'a	78	50.12 N	33.41 E
Kona, India	272b	22.37 N	88.18 E
Kona, Mali	150	14.57 N	3.53 W
Kona Coast ⊥^{2}	229d	19.25 N	155.55 W
Konagkend	84	41.04 N	48.37 E
Konakovo	82	56.42 N	36.46 E
Konakpınar, Tür.	130	39.26 N	27.53 E
Konakpınar, Tür.	130	38.53 N	37.22 E
Konan → Hŭngnam, C.M.I.K.	98	39.50 N	127.38 E
Konan, C. Iv.	150	8.21 N	8.00 W
Kōnan, Nihon	94	35.20 N	136.53 E
Kōnan, Nihon	94	34.56 N	136.11 E
Kōnan -●-^{8}	268	35.22 N	139.35 E
Konar (Kunar) ≃	123	34.25 N	70.32 E
Konārak	120	19.54 N	86.07 E
Konār Dam -●-^{6}	124	23.58 N	85.45 E
Konarhā □^{4}	120	35.15 N	71.00 E
Konawa	196	34.57 N	96.45 W
Končanskoje-Suvorovskoje	76	58.39 N	34.04 E
Konceba	78	48.07 N	29.56 E
Konch	124	25.59 N	79.09 E
Konda	74	61.20 N	63.58 E
Konda ≃, Ross.	86	60.40 N	69.46 E
Konda ≃, Ross.	88	53.30 N	113.32 E
Kondagaon	122	19.36 N	81.40 E
Konde	154	4.57 S	39.45 E
Kondega	76	60.14 N	33.30 E
Kondiaronk, Lac ⊜	190	46.56 N	76.45 W
Kondinin	162	32.30 S	118.16 E
Kondinskoje	86	59.40 N	67.22 E
Kondli -●-^{8}	272a	28.37 N	77.19 E
Kondoa	154	4.54 S	35.47 E
Kondol'	80	52.49 N	45.03 E
Kondolole	154	1.20 N	25.58 E
Kondopoga	24	62.12 N	34.17 E
Kondorfa	61	46.54 N	16.24 E
Kondratjevo, Ross.	76	60.38 N	28.08 E
Kondratjevo, Ross.	88	57.21 N	98.11 E
Kondrovka	80	54.36 N	43.17 E
Kondrovo	82	54.48 N	35.56 E
Konduga	146	11.39 N	13.24 E
Kondukūr	122	15.13 N	79.55 E
Kondurča ≃	80	53.31 N	50.24 E
Kondūz	120	37.45 N	68.51 E
Kondūz □^{4}	120	36.45 N	68.30 E
Koné	175f	21.04 S	164.52 E
Koné, Passe de ʯ	175f	21.08 S	164.41 E
Konecbor	24	64.52 N	57.44 E
Konergino	180	65.54 N	178.50 W
Konfara	150	11.55 N	8.50 W
Kong, C. Iv.	150	9.09 N	4.37 W
Køng, Dan.	41	55.07 N	11.50 E
Kông ≃	110	13.32 N	105.58 E
Kŏng, Kaôh I	110	11.20 N	103.00 E
Kongakut ≃	180	69.48 N	141.50 W
Kongbo	152	4.44 N	21.23 E
Kongcheng	100	31.02 N	117.05 E
Kongeå ≃	41	55.23 N	8.40 E
Kongens Lyngby	41	55.46 N	12.31 E
Kongfang	100	27.58 N	116.53 E
Kongiganak	180	59.58 N	162.45 W
Konginkangas	26	62.46 N	25.48 E
Kongjiamatou	105	39.07 N	116.10 E
Kongjiatun	104	40.42 N	124.04 E
Kongjiawopeng	89	43.58 N	122.41 E
Kongjiazhuang	105	40.47 N	114.48 E
Kongju	98	36.27 N	127.07 E
Konglong	100	29.56 N	115.54 E
Konglongshan	105	40.33 N	117.17 E
Konglu	102	27.16 N	97.56 E
Kongmoon → Jiangmen	100	22.35 N	113.05 E
Kongo → Congo ≃	138	6.04 S	12.24 E
Kongo, Republik → Zaire □^{1}	138	4.00 S	25.00 E
Kongō-Ikoma-kokutei-kōen ♦	96	34.28 N	135.40 E
Kongolo, Zaïre	154	5.26 S	24.49 E
Kongolo, Zaïre	154	5.23 S	27.00 E
Kongor	140	7.10 N	31.21 E
Kongō-sanchi ⋌	270	34.27 N	135.41 E
Kongoussi	150	13.19 N	1.32 W
Kongō-zan ∧	96	34.25 N	135.41 E
Kongsberg	26	59.39 N	9.39 E
Kongsvinger	26	60.12 N	12.00 E
Kongsvoll	26	62.18 N	9.37 E
Kongtan	107	29.10 N	104.42 E
Kongur Shan ∧	85	38.37 N	75.20 E
Kongwa	154	6.12 S	36.25 E
Kongyangcun	106	31.23 N	118.54 E
Kongzhen	106	31.29 N	119.00 E
Koni	154	10.42 S	27.15 E
Koni ≃	150	13.05 N	5.37 W
Koniakari	150	14.34 N	10.54 W
Konice	30	49.35 N	16.53 E
Koniecpol	30	50.48 N	19.41 E
Königgrätz → Hradec Králové	30	50.12 N	15.50 E
Königheim	56	49.37 N	9.35 E
Königin Alexandra-Kette → Queen Alexandra Range ⋌	9	84.00 S	168.00 E
Königin Fabiola-Gebirge → Queen Fabiola Mountains ⋌	9	71.30 S	35.40 E
Königin Mary-Küste → Queen Mary Coast ⊥^{2}	9	67.00 S	96.00 E
Königin Maud-Land → Queen Maud Land -●-^{1}	9	72.30 S	12.00 E
König-Otto-Höhle ⊥^{5}	60	49.15 N	11.42 E
Königsbach	56	48.58 N	8.36 E
Königsberg, Dtsch.	56	50.05 N	10.34 E
Königsberg → Kaliningrad, Ross.	76	54.43 N	20.30 E
Königsborn	263	51.33 N	7.41 E
Königsbrück	54	51.16 N	13.54 E
Königsbrunn, Dtsch.	58	48.16 N	10.53 E
Königsbrunn, Öst.	264b	48.21 N	16.25 E
Königsdorf	64	47.49 N	11.28 E
Königsee	54	50.39 N	11.05 E
Königsfelden υ^{1}	58	47.29 N	8.14 E
Königsfeld im Schwarzwald	58	48.08 N	8.25 E
Königshain	54	51.11 N	14.52 E
Königshardt -●-^{8}	263	51.33 N	6.51 E
Königsheim	58	48.06 N	8.51 E
Königshofen im Grabfeld	54	50.18 N	10.29 E
Königslutter	54	52.15 N	10.49 E
Königsmoor -●-^{3}	52	53.15 N	9.40 E
Königssee	64	47.33 N	12.58 E
Königssee ⊜	64	47.36 N	12.59 E
Königsstuhl ⊥^{4}	54	54.34 N	13.40 E
Königstein, Dtsch.	54	50.55 N	14.04 E
Königstein, Dtsch.	56	50.11 N	8.29 E
Königstein, Dtsch.	60	49.37 N	11.38 E
Königstetten	264b	48.18 N	16.09 E
Königswalde	54	50.33 N	13.02 E
Königswartha	54	51.18 N	14.20 E
Königswiesen	61	48.24 N	14.50 E
Königswinter	56	50.40 N	7.11 E
Königs Wusterhausen	54	52.18 N	13.37 E
Konin	30	52.13 N	18.16 E
Konin □^{4}	30	52.20 N	18.20 E
Konispol	38	39.39 N	20.10 E
Kónitsa	38	40.02 N	20.45 E
Köniz	58	46.56 N	7.25 E
Konjic	38	43.39 N	17.57 E
Konka ≃	78	47.40 N	35.22 E
Könkämäälven ≃	24	68.29 N	22.17 E
Konkapot ≃	210	42.03 N	73.20 W
Konkiep ≃	156	28.03 S	17.21 E
Konkō	96	34.32 N	133.37 E
Kon'-Kolodez'	76	52.08 N	39.11 E
Konkouré ≃	150	9.58 N	13.42 W
Kon'kovo	83	47.20 N	38.10 E
Konkudera	88	57.33 N	112.30 E
Konkug University υ^{2}	271b	37.32 N	127.05 E
Konnagar	126	22.42 N	88.22 E
Könnern	54	51.40 N	11.46 E
Konnevesi ⊜	26	62.40 N	26.35 E
Konnur	122	16.12 N	74.45 E
Kōno	94	35.49 N	136.04 E
Konobejevo	82	55.24 N	38.40 E
Konohana -●-^{8}	270	34.41 N	135.26 E
Kōnoike	270	34.42 N	135.37 E
Konolfingen	58	46.53 N	7.38 E
Konongo	150	6.37 N	1.11 W
Konoša	24	60.58 N	40.15 E
Kōno-shima I	96	34.28 N	133.31 E
Kōnosu	94	36.03 N	139.31 E
Konotop	78	51.14 N	33.12 E
Konovalovka	80	53.06 N	51.34 E
Kon'ovo, Ross.	24	62.08 N	39.16 E
Kon'ovo, Ross.	86	56.18 N	70.43 E
Konqi ≃	90	40.40 N	90.10 E
Konradshöhe -●-^{8}	264a	52.35 N	13.14 E
Konradsreuth	54	50.16 N	11.50 E
Konsankoro	150	9.02 N	9.00 W
Konsen-daichi ⋌^{1}	92a	43.25 N	144.52 E
Końskie	30	51.12 N	20.26 E
Konstabel	158	33.16 S	20.17 E
Konstantinopel → İstanbul	130	41.01 N	28.58 E
Konstantinovka, Ross.	80	56.41 N	50.53 E
Konstantinovka, Ross.	265a	59.47 N	30.08 E
Konstantinovka, Ukr.	78	49.57 N	35.07 E
Konstantinovka, Ukr.	78	47.51 N	31.09 E
Konstantinovka, Ukr.	83	48.32 N	37.43 E
Konstantinovka, Ukr.	83	47.52 N	37.24 E
Konstantinovo	82	56.33 N	38.02 E
Konstantinovsk	80	47.35 N	41.06 E
Konstantinovskij	76	57.50 N	39.36 E
Konstantinovskije Porogi	76	60.34 N	37.04 E
Konstantynów Łódzki	30	51.45 N	19.20 E
Konstanz	58	47.40 N	9.10 E
Kontagora	150	10.24 N	5.28 E
Kontcha	152	7.58 N	12.14 E
Kontejevo	80	58.26 N	41.21 E
Kontha	110	19.30 N	96.03 E
Kontich	50	51.08 N	4.27 E
Kontiolahti	26	62.46 N	29.51 E
Kontiomäki	26	64.21 N	28.09 E
Kon Tum	110	14.21 N	108.00 E
Kontum, Plateau du ⋌^{1}	110	13.55 N	108.05 E
Kōnu	96	34.42 N	133.05 E
Kon'uchovo	86	55.08 N	70.38 E
Konus, gora ∧	180	67.34 N	178.10 E
Konya	130	37.52 N	32.31 E
Konya □^{4}	130	38.00 N	33.00 E
Konyr	80	50.25 N	53.25 E
Konyrat	80	49.36 N	47.01 E
Konyrolen	86	44.16 N	79.19 E
Konyševka	78	51.51 N	35.18 E
Konystanu	80	48.51 N	53.20 E
Konz	56	49.42 N	6.34 E
Konza	154	1.45 S	37.07 E
Konžakovskij Kamen', gora ∧	86	59.38 N	59.08 E
Konzell	60	49.04 N	12.43 E
Koocanusa, Lake ⊜^{1}	202	49.00 N	115.10 W
Koog [aan de Zaan]	52	52.27 N	4.49 E
Kookynie	162	29.20 S	121.29 E
Koolamarra	166	20.12 S	140.14 E
Koolatah	164	15.53 S	142.27 E
Koolau Range ⋌	229c	21.35 N	158.00 W
Kooloonong	166	34.53 S	143.09 E
Koolskamp	50	51.00 N	3.12 E
Koolyanobbing	162	30.50 S	119.35 E
Koolywurtie	168b	34.38 S	137.37 E
Koombana Bay ⊂	168a	33.18 S	115.36 E
Koonap ≃	158	33.03 S	26.39 E
Koondrook	166	35.39 S	144.08 E
Koonga	76	58.35 N	24.12 E
Koonibba	162	31.58 S	133.27 E
Koontz Lake	216	41.25 N	86.29 W
Koontz Lake ⊜	216	41.25 N	86.28 W
Koopan-Noord	158	26.53 S	20.41 E
Koopan-Suid	158	27.15 S	20.22 E
Koopmansfontein	158	28.14 S	24.01 E
Koorawatha	166	34.02 S	148.33 E
Koorda	162	30.50 S	117.29 E
Koosa	76	58.33 N	27.07 E
Koosfontein	158	27.22 S	25.27 E
Koosharem	200	38.30 N	111.52 W
Kooskia	202	46.08 N	115.58 W
Koossa	150	9.32 N	8.32 W
Kootenai (Kootenay) ≃	182	49.15 N	117.39 W
Kootenay (Kootenai) ≃	182	49.15 N	117.39 W
Kootenay Indian Reserve -●-^{4}	182	49.37 N	115.45 W
Kootenay Lake ⊜	182	49.35 N	116.50 W
Kootenay National Park ♦	182	51.00 N	116.00 W
Kootjieskolk	158	31.15 S	20.21 E
Kootwijk	52	52.12 N	5.45 E
Koo-wee-rup	169	38.12 S	145.30 E
Kopa	85	43.32 N	75.50 E
Kopa ≃	85	43.40 N	76.15 E
Kopāganj	124	26.01 N	83.34 E
Kopāi ≃	126	23.48 N	87.47 E
Kopajgorod	78	48.51 N	27.48 E
Kopanbulak	86	48.56 N	80.52 E
Kopang	115b	8.39 S	116.21 E
Kopanovka	80	47.27 N	46.48 E
Kopanskaja	78	46.17 N	38.29 E
Kopapan	80	50.20 N	50.26 E
Kopargaon	122	19.53 N	74.29 E
Koparkhairna	272c	19.06 N	72.59 E
Koparpāda	272c	19.02 N	73.04 E
Kópasker	24a	66.20 N	16.24 W
Kopatkeviči	76	52.19 N	28.49 E
Kópavogur	24a	64.06 N	21.50 W
Kopcevići	76	52.14 N	28.19 E
Kopé, Mont ∧^{2}	150	4.59 N	7.27 W
Kopejsk	86	55.07 N	61.37 E
Kopenhagen → København	41	55.40 N	12.35 E
Köpenick -●-^{8}	54	52.27 N	13.34 E
Köpenick, Schloss υ	264a	52.27 N	13.34 E
Koper	36	45.33 N	13.44 E
Köpernitz	54	53.04 N	12.56 E
Kopervik	26	59.17 N	5.18 E
Kopetdag, chrebet ⋌	128	37.50 N	58.00 E
Kopeysk → Kopejsk	86	55.07 N	61.37 E
Kop Geçidi)(	130	40.03 N	40.33 E
Kopice	54	53.44 N	14.32 E
Köping	40	59.31 N	16.00 E
Kopisty	54	50.34 N	13.35 E
Kopjevo	86	55.03 N	89.50 E
Koplik	38	42.13 N	19.26 E
Köpmanholmen	26	63.10 N	18.34 E
Kopnino	82	56.53 N	38.29 E
Kopondei, Tanjung ›	115b	8.04 S	122.52 E
Koporje	76	59.44 N	29.01 E
Koporskaja guba ⊂	76	59.52 N	28.55 E
Koppal	122	15.21 N	76.09 E
Koppang	26	61.34 N	11.04 E
Koppány ≃	30	46.35 N	18.26 E
Kopparberg	40	59.52 N	14.59 E
Kopparbergs Län □^{6}	26	61.00 N	14.30 E
Koppel	214	40.50 N	80.19 W
Kopperå	26	63.24 N	11.51 E
Kopperby	41	54.38 N	9.56 E
Kopperl	222	32.04 N	97.30 W
Koppi	89	48.32 N	140.07 E
Koppi ≃	89	48.33 N	140.08 E
Koppies	158	27.20 S	27.30 E
Koppom	26	59.43 N	12.09 E
Kopri	272c	19.11 N	72.58 E
Koprivnica	36	46.10 N	16.50 E
Köprü ≃	130	36.50 N	31.10 E
Köprülü Kanyon Milli Parkı ♦	130	37.20 N	31.18 E
Köprüören	130	39.30 N	29.47 E
Kopt'ovo	80	56.43 N	40.31 E
Kopyčincy	78	49.06 N	25.55 E
Kopyl'	76	53.09 N	27.05 E
Kopylovka	86	58.40 N	82.22 E
Kopylovo, Ross.	24	60.35 N	45.02 E
Kopylovo, Ross.	82	56.26 N	36.25 E
Kopys'	76	54.19 N	30.18 E
Kor ≃	128	29.36 N	53.18 E
Kōra	94	35.12 N	136.15 E
Koraa Shiir	144	3.18 N	46.16 E
Korab ⋌	38	41.47 N	20.34 E
Kor Aban	144	3.58 N	42.44 E
Korablino	80	53.55 N	40.01 E
Korahe	144	6.35 N	44.23 E
Kor'akovka	86	52.24 N	77.08 E
Kor'akskaja Sopka, vulkan ∧^{1}	74	53.20 N	158.43 E
Kor'akskoje nagorje ⋌	74	62.30 N	172.00 E
Kōrakuen ♦	96	34.38 N	133.53 E
Korakuen Stadium ♦	268	35.43 N	139.45 E
Korallenmeer → Coral Sea ⊤^{2}	14	20.00 S	158.00 E
Koralpe ⋌	61	46.50 N	14.58 E
Korannaberg ⋌	158	27.25 S	22.32 E
Korapun	164	5.25 S	152.00 E
Korāput	122	18.49 N	82.43 E
Korarou, Lac ⊜	150	15.15 N	3.16 W
Korat → Nakhon Ratchasima	110	14.58 N	102.07 E
Koratla	122	18.49 N	78.43 E
Kor'ažma	24	61.18 N	47.06 E
Korba, India	124	22.21 N	82.41 E
Korba, Tun.	36	36.35 N	10.52 E
Korbach	56	51.16 N	8.52 E
Korbeta	144	13.03 N	39.43 E
Korbol	146	10.01 N	17.43 E
Korbous	36	36.49 N	10.35 E
Korbu, Gunong ∧	114	4.43 N	101.17 E
Korçë	38	40.37 N	20.46 E
Korcovo	76	58.52 N	42.13 E
Korčula	36	42.58 N	17.08 E
Korčula, Otok I	36	42.57 N	16.50 E
Korčulanski Kanal ʯ	36	43.03 N	16.40 E
Kordestān □^{4}	128	35.30 N	47.00 E
Kord Kūy	128	36.48 N	54.07 E
Kordovo	86	54.06 N	93.17 E
Korea, North □^{1}, Asia	90	40.00 N	127.00 E
Korea, North □^{1}, Asia	98	40.00 N	127.00 E
Korea, South □^{1}, Asia	90	36.30 N	128.00 E
Korea, South □^{1}, Asia	98	36.30 N	128.00 E
Korea Bay ⊂	98	39.00 N	124.00 E
Korea Strait ʯ	90	34.00 N	129.00 E
Korea University υ^{2}	271b	37.36 N	127.02 E
Korec	78	50.37 N	27.09 E
Korekozevo	82	54.20 N	36.11 E
Korelakša	24	65.33 N	32.22 E
Koreliči	76	53.34 N	26.08 E
Korem	144	12.30 N	39.30 E
Koré Mayroua	150	13.18 N	3.55 E
Koren (Die Wurzen))(	64	46.31 N	13.45 E
Korenkovo	78	45.07 N	36.24 E
Koren'ovo, Ross.	78	51.25 N	34.55 E
Koren'ovo, Ross.	265b	55.40 N	38.00 E
Korenovsk	78	45.29 N	39.28 E
Korf	74	60.19 N	165.50 E
Korfovskij	89	48.13 N	135.03 E
Korga	158	30.12 S	20.28 E
Korgan	130	40.44 N	37.13 E
Korgašino	82	54.45 N	37.41 E
Kõrgessaare	76	58.59 N	22.28 E
Korgonskij chrebet ⋌	86	50.45 N	84.30 E
Korgus	140	19.13 N	33.29 E
Korhogo	150	9.27 N	5.38 W
Kōri	270	34.47 N	135.39 E
Koridhallós	267c	37.59 N	23.39 E
Korido	164	0.50 S	135.35 E
Koriella	169	37.10 S	145.39 E
Korienzé	150	15.24 N	3.47 W
Korim	164	0.54 S	136.02 E
Korima, Oued el ∨	148	33.51 N	0.23 W
Koringberg	158	33.01 S	18.40 E
Koringplaas	158	32.48 S	20.58 E
Korinth	41	55.08 N	10.21 E
Korinthiakós Kólpos (Gulf of Corinth) ⊂	38	38.19 N	22.04 E
Kórinthos (Corinth)	38	37.56 N	22.56 E
Korínthou, Dhiórix ≡	38	37.57 N	22.56 E
Kőris-hegy ∧	30	47.18 N	17.45 E
Koritsa → Korçë	38	40.37 N	20.46 E
Köritz	54	52.51 N	12.27 E
Kōriyama, Nihon	92	37.24 N	140.23 E
Kōriyama → Yamato-kōriyama, Nihon	96	34.38 N	135.47 E
Korizo, Passe de)(	146	22.28 N	15.27 E
Korkino, Ross.	86	54.54 N	61.23 E
Korkino, Ross.	88	54.23 N	105.14 E
Korkinskoje, ozero ⊜	265a	59.55 N	30.44 E
Korkuteli	130	37.04 N	30.13 E
Korla	90	41.44 N	86.09 E
Korl'aki	80	57.06 N	46.57 E
Korliki	74	61.31 N	82.22 E
Korma, Bela.	76	53.08 N	30.48 E
Korma, Bela.	76	52.21 N	31.31 E
Körmend	30	47.01 N	16.37 E
Kormilovka	86	55.00 N	74.06 E
Kormovoje	80	46.17 N	43.30 E
Kornat, Otok I	36	43.50 N	15.16 E
Körnebach ≃	263	51.35 N	7.38 E
Kornejevka, Kaz.	86	54.01 N	68.27 E
Kornejevka, Kaz.	86	50.12 N	74.19 E
Kornejevka, Ross.	80	51.45 N	48.46 E
Kornelimünster	56	50.43 N	6.11 E
Körner, Dtsch.	54	51.13 N	10.35 E
Korner, Mt., U.S.	182	48.59 N	112.15 W
Kornešty	38	47.22 N	27.59 E
Korneuburg	61	48.21 N	16.20 E
Kórnik	30	52.17 N	17.04 E
Kornilovo	86	53.32 N	81.05 E
Kornin	78	50.06 N	29.32 E
Kornouchovo	80	55.33 N	49.53 E
Korn'ovo	265a	60.03 N	30.45 E
Kornsjø	26	58.57 N	11.39 E
Kornwestheim	56	48.52 N	9.11 E
Koro, C. Iv.	150	8.34 N	7.28 W
Koro, Mali	150	14.04 N	3.05 W
Koro I	175g	17.19 S	179.23 E
Koroba	164	5.40 S	142.45 E
Koroča	78	50.48 N	37.11 E
Korodougou Markala	150	12.26 N	6.17 W
Köroğlu Tepesi ∧	130	40.31 N	31.53 E
Korogwe	154	5.09 S	38.29 E
Koroit	166	38.17 S	142.22 E
Korolenko, gora ∧	88	58.15 N	115.01 E
Korolevskij Belok, gora ∧	86	51.00 N	83.43 E
Korol'ovo	78	48.09 N	23.08 E
Korol'ovščina	76	55.49 N	31.45 E
Korom, Bahr ≃	146	10.35 N	19.45 E
Koromba ∧	175g	17.53 S	177.34 E
Koromiri I	174k	21.15 S	159.43 W
Koromo → Toyota	94	35.05 N	137.09 E
Koronadal	116	6.30 N	124.51 E
Koróni	38	36.48 N	21.56 E
Korónia, Límni ⊜	38	40.41 N	23.05 E
Koronowo	30	53.19 N	17.57 E
Korop	78	51.34 N	32.56 E
Koropélé	152	4.44 N	17.11 E
Koropíon	38	37.54 N	23.53 E
Koror	175b	7.20 N	134.29 E
Koror I	175b	7.20 N	134.30 E
Kororoit Creek ≃	274b	37.52 S	144.52 E
Körös ≃	30	46.43 N	20.12 E
Koro Sea ⊤^{2}	175g	18.00 S	179.50 E
Korosten'	78	50.57 N	28.39 E
Korostyšev	78	50.19 N	29.03 E
Korotkova	88	56.43 N	107.55 E
Korotojak	78	50.59 N	39.10 E
Koro Toro	146	16.05 N	18.30 E
Korotovo	76	58.57 N	37.28 E
Korotyš	76	52.22 N	37.27 E
Korovincy	78	50.48 N	33.45 E
Korovin Island I	180	55.25 N	160.15 W
Korovino, Ross.	78	51.25 N	36.45 E
Korovino, Ross.	80	53.49 N	53.03 E
Korovin Volcano ∧^{1}	180	52.22 N	174.10 W
Korovou	175g	17.57 S	178.21 E
Koroyanitu ∧	175g	17.40 S	177.35 E
Korožečna ≃	76	57.32 N	38.18 E
Korpilahti	26	62.01 N	25.33 E
Korpo (Korppoo)	26	60.10 N	21.34 E
Korså	40	60.38 N	16.08 E
Korsakov	89	46.38 N	142.46 E
Korsakovo	76	53.16 N	37.21 E
Korschenbroich	56	51.11 N	6.31 E
Korselbränna	26	64.27 N	15.35 E
Korševo	78	51.11 N	40.07 E
Korsika → Corse I	36	42.00 N	9.00 E
Korsnäs, Suomi	26	62.47 N	21.12 E
Korsnäs, Sve.	40	60.35 N	15.43 E
Korsør	41	55.20 N	11.09 E
Korsør Nor ⊂	41	55.20 N	11.11 E
Korsun'	83	48.12 N	38.05 E
Koršunovo	88	58.37 N	110.10 E
Korsun'-Ševčenkovskij	78	49.26 N	31.16 E
Korsze	30	54.10 N	21.09 E
Kortgene	52	51.34 N	3.48 E
Kortilisy	78	51.51 N	24.25 E
Kortkeros	24	61.49 N	51.28 E
Kortrijk (Courtrai)	50	50.50 N	3.16 E
Kortuz, gora ∧	86	54.33 N	91.56 E
Koruçam Burnu ›	130	35.24 N	32.56 E
Korucu	130	39.28 N	27.22 E
Kor'ukovka	78	51.46 N	32.14 E
Korumburra	169	38.26 S	145.49 E
Korwai	124	24.08 N	78.03 E
Kōryō	96	34.33 N	135.45 E
Koryŏng	98	35.44 N	128.15 E
Koryst'	78	50.35 N	27.01 E
Koryta	60	49.24 N	13.13 E
Korženevskoj, pik ∧	85	39.04 N	72.00 E
Koržeuc'	38	48.13 N	27.02 E
Korževka	80	54.12 N	46.22 E
Kos	38	36.53 N	27.18 E
Kos (Cos) I	38	36.50 N	27.10 E
Kosa, Ityo.	144	7.51 N	36.51 E
Kosa, Ross.	24	59.56 N	54.55 E
Kosa, Ross.	88	54.47 N	108.52 E
Kosa ≃, Ross.	24	60.11 N	55.10 E
Kosa ≃, Ross.	80	58.26 N	51.15 E
Kosa ⊥	150	15.50 N	7.00 W
Koš-Agač	86	50.00 N	88.40 E
Kosai	94	34.43 N	137.33 E
Kosaja, šivera ∟	88	58.24 N	97.48 E
Kosaja Gora	82	54.07 N	37.33 E
Kosaka	92	40.19 N	140.44 E
Kosan	98	38.52 N	127.24 E
Košankol'	80	49.56 N	48.11 E
Koščagyl	86	46.51 N	53.48 E
Kösching	60	48.49 N	11.30 E
Kościan	30	52.06 N	16.38 E
Kościerzyna	30	54.08 N	18.00 E
Kosciusko	194	33.03 N	89.35 W
Kosciusko □^{6}	216	41.14 N	85.51 W
Kosciusko, Mount ∧	171b	36.27 S	148.16 E
Kosciusko National Park ♦	166	36.10 S	148.15 E
Kös Dağı ∧	130	40.59 N	34.25 E
Kosdaulet, peski -●-^{2}	80	47.45 N	49.30 E
Kose, Eesti	76	59.11 N	25.10 E
Kose, Nihon	270	34.25 N	135.46 E
Köse, Tür.	130	40.13 N	39.39 E
Kösedağı ∧	130	39.54 N	42.39 E
Kösefakılı	130	39.36 N	34.09 E
Koševka	82	55.09 N	38.05 E
Košelicha	80	55.02 N	43.33 E
Koševovo	82	55.38 N	38.22 E
Koserow	54	54.03 N	13.59 E
Kosha	140	20.49 N	30.32 E
Koshien Stadium ♦	270	34.42 N	135.22 E
Koshigaya	94	35.54 N	139.48 E
Koshigoe	268	35.18 N	139.30 E
Koshikijima-rettō II	92	31.45 N	129.49 E
Koshino	94	36.02 N	136.01 E
Koshk-e Kohneh	128	34.52 N	62.31 E
Koshkonong	194	36.35 N	91.38 W
Koshkonong, Lake ⊜	216	42.52 N	88.58 W
Koshkonong Creek ≃	216	42.53 N	88.59 W
Koshlong Lake ⊜	212	44.58 N	78.29 W
Kōshoku	94	36.32 N	138.06 E
Koshu → Kwangju	98	35.09 N	126.54 E
Kosī □^{8}	124	27.15 N	87.15 E
Kosi ≃	124	25.26 N	87.22 E
Košice	30	48.43 N	21.15 E
Kosigi	122	15.51 N	77.16 E
Kosi Kalan	124	27.48 N	77.26 E
Kosikovo	76	59.52 N	43.23 E
Kosimeer ⊜	158	26.55 S	32.52 E
Kosino, Ross.	80	58.23 N	51.17 E
Kosino, Ross.	82	55.43 N	37.52 E
Kosju	24	65.38 N	59.03 E
Kosju ≃	24	66.18 N	59.53 E
Kosjuvom	24	66.17 N	59.50 E
Köşk	130	37.51 N	28.03 E
Koskaecodde Lake ⊜	186	48.00 N	55.20 W
Koškar	80	47.27 N	53.29 E
Koški, Ross.	80	54.12 N	50.28 E
Koski, Suomi	26	60.39 N	23.09 E
Koškino	80	56.20 N	50.49 E
Koskol'	86	49.31 N	67.05 E
Koskuduk	86	44.06 N	77.22 E
Koskullskulle	24	67.12 N	20.50 E
Koslan	24	63.28 N	48.52 E
Köslin → Koszalin	30	54.12 N	16.09 E
Kosmonosy	54	50.26 N	15.00 E
Kosmynino	80	57.35 N	40.46 E
Kosoba, gora ∧	86	48.15 N	79.40 E
Kosogor	80	57.07 N	47.34 E
Kosoj, porog ∟, Ross.	86	57.30 N	95.30 E
Kosoj, porog ∟, Ross.	88	57.44 N	96.20 E
Kosolapovo	80	56.57 N	49.37 E
Kosŏng, C.M.I.K.	98	38.40 N	128.19 E
Kosŏng, Taehan	98	34.58 N	128.18 E
Kosov	78	48.19 N	25.05 E
Kosovo-Metohija □^{4}	38	42.35 N	21.00 E
Kosovska Mitrovica	38	42.53 N	20.52 E
Kosový potok ≃	60	49.46 N	12.48 E
Kosrae I	14	5.19 N	162.59 E
Kösreli	130	37.11 N	35.59 E
Kossdorf	54	51.29 N	13.14 E
Kosse	222	31.18 N	96.38 W
Kössen	64	47.40 N	12.24 E
Kossindi	152	3.51 N	16.19 E
Kösslarn	60	48.22 N	13.07 E
Kossol Passage ʯ	175b	7.52 N	134.36 E
Kossol Reef -+-^{2}	175b	7.57 N	134.41 E
Kossou, Lac de ⊜^{1}	150	7.25 N	5.45 W
Kossovo	76	52.45 N	25.09 E
Kossuth	214	41.17 N	79.35 W
Kosta	26	56.51 N	15.23 E
Kostajnica	36	45.14 N	16.33 E
Košt'any	54	50.39 N	13.45 E
Koš-Tegirmen	85	42.47 N	73.53 E
Kostelec nad Labem	54	50.11 N	14.35 E
Kostenec	38	42.16 N	23.49 E
Koster	158	25.57 S	26.42 E
Kosterevo	80	55.56 N	39.37 E
Kosteröarna I	26	58.54 N	11.02 E
Kostešty	38	46.52 N	28.44 E
Kostešty-Stynka, vodochranilišče (Lacul Stînca-Costeşti) ⊜^{1}	38	47.55 N	27.10 E
Koštice	54	50.24 N	13.55 E
Kostino, Ross.	80	52.11 N	51.20 E
Kostino, Ross.	80	52.24 N	51.39 E
Kostino, Ross.	82	56.18 N	37.43 E
Kostino, Ross.	265b	55.55 N	37.51 E
Kostino-Otdelec	78	51.33 N	41.26 E
Kost'kovo	76	60.02 N	33.14 E
Košt'ob'o	85	41.06 N	74.15 E
Kostomukša	24	64.41 N	30.49 E
Kostonjärvi ⊜	26	65.47 N	28.27 E
Kostopol'	78	50.53 N	26.26 E
Kostriževka	78	48.38 N	25.41 E
Kostroma	76	57.46 N	40.55 E
Kostroma ≃	24	57.47 N	40.55 E
Kostroma Oblast' □^{4}	24	58.30 N	44.00 E
Kostrovo	82	55.53 N	36.42 E
Kostrzyn	30	52.37 N	14.39 E
Kost'ukoviči	76	53.20 N	32.03 E
Kost'ukovka	76	52.32 N	30.56 E
Kosugaya -●-^{8}	268	35.22 N	139.33 E
Kosuge	94	35.45 N	138.57 E
Kosugi	94	36.43 N	137.06 E
Kosum Phisai	110	16.13 N	103.01 E
Koszalin (Köslin)	30	54.12 N	16.09 E
Koszalin □^{4}	30	54.00 N	16.00 E
Kőszeg	30	47.23 N	16.33 E
Koszyce	30	50.11 N	20.35 E
Kota, India	120	25.11 N	75.50 E
Kota, India	124	22.18 N	82.02 E
Kota, Malay.	114	5.35 N	100.23 E
Kota, Malay.	114	2.31 N	102.10 E
Kotaagung	112	5.30 S	104.38 E
Kotabaharu, Indon.	112	0.48 S	111.33 E
Kota Baharu, Malay.	114	6.08 N	102.15 E
Kotabangun	112	0.16 S	116.35 E
Kotabaru, Indon.	112	3.14 S	116.13 E
Kotabaru, Indon.	112	1.08 S	101.43 E
Kotabaru → Jayapura, Indon.	164	2.32 S	140.42 E
Kota Belud	112	6.25 N	116.31 E
Kotabumi	112	4.50 S	104.54 E
Kotabunan	112	0.49 N	124.38 E
Kotadabok	112	0.30 S	104.33 E
Kot Addu	123	30.28 N	70.58 E
Kotagiri	122	11.26 N	76.53 E
Kot'ajevka	80	46.33 N	48.46 E
Kotake	96	33.41 N	130.43 E
Kota Kinabalu (Jesselton)	112	5.59 N	116.04 E
Kota Kota → Nkhotakota	154	12.57 S	34.17 E
Kotālpur	126	23.02 N	87.36 E
Kotamobagu	112	0.46 N	124.19 E
Kotanemel', gora ∧	86	47.43 N	77.18 E
Kotapinang	114	1.53 N	100.05 E
Kotari ⋌	36	44.05 N	15.30 E
Kotaringin	114	0.53 N	102.03 E
Kota Sarang Semut	114	5.59 N	100.24 E
Kotatengah	114	1.05 N	100.33 E
Kota Tinggi	114	1.44 N	103.54 E
Kotawaringin	112	2.29 S	111.25 E
Kotchāndpur	124	23.24 N	89.01 E
Kotcho Lake ⊜	176	59.05 N	121.10 W
Kot Chutta	123	29.53 N	70.39 E
Kotdwāra	124	29.45 N	78.32 E
Kotel	38	42.53 N	26.27 E
Kotel'nič	80	58.18 N	48.20 E
Kotel'niki	82	55.39 N	37.52 E
Kotel'nikovo	80	47.38 N	43.09 E
Kotel'nyj, ostrov I	74	75.45 N	138.44 E
Kotel'va	78	50.05 N	34.45 E
Kot Fateh	123	30.07 N	75.05 E
Köthen	54	51.45 N	11.58 E
Koti → Kōchi	96	33.33 N	133.33 E
Kotido	154	3.00 N	34.06 E
Kotikovo	89	49.08 N	144.13 E
Kotka	26	60.28 N	26.55 E
Kot Kapūra	123	30.35 N	74.54 E
Kotkino	24	67.02 N	51.03 E
Kotla	123	32.15 N	76.02 E
Kotl'akovo	82	56.17 N	35.49 E
Kotlas	24	61.16 N	46.35 E
Kotli	123	33.31 N	73.55 E
Kotlik	180	63.02 N	163.33 W
Kotlin, ostrov I	76	60.00 N	29.46 E
Kotly	76	59.36 N	28.45 E
Kot Mūmin	123	32.11 N	73.02 E
Kotō	94	35.08 N	136.14 E
Kōtō -●-^{8}	268	35.41 N	139.48 E
Kotō ≃, Nihon	96	34.21 N	134.02 E
Koto ≃, Nihon	96	33.58 N	131.13 E
Kotobiki-san ∧	96	35.03 N	132.47 E
Kotohira	96	34.11 N	133.49 E
Kotohira-gu υ^{1}	96	34.11 N	133.49 E
Kotohira-yama ∧	96	34.11 N	133.48 E
Kotonami	96	34.10 N	133.56 E
Koton-Karifi	150	8.08 N	6.48 E
Kotonkoro	150	11.02 N	5.58 E
Kotor	38	42.25 N	18.46 E
Kotoriba	36	46.21 N	16.49 E
Kotorovo	80	54.54 N	41.35 E
Kotor Varoš	36	44.37 N	17.23 E
Kotouba	150	8.41 N	3.12 W
Kotovka	78	49.08 N	34.57 E
Kotovo	80	50.18 N	44.50 E
Kotovsk, Ross.	80	52.36 N	41.32 E
Kotovsk, Ukr.	78	47.45 N	29.33 E
Kot Pūtli	124	27.43 N	76.12 E
Kotra, India	120	24.22 N	73.10 E
Kotra, India	272b	22.46 N	88.34 E
Kot Rādha Kishan	123	31.10 N	74.06 E
Kotri	120	25.22 N	68.18 E
Kotri Allāhrakhio	120	24.24 N	67.50 E
Kotrung → Uttarpara-Kotrung	272b	22.40 N	88.21 E
Kötschach [-Mauthen]	64	46.40 N	13.00 E
Kot Sultān	123	30.46 N	70.56 E
Kōtsu-zan ∧	96	34.01 N	134.12 E
Kottagūdem	122	17.33 N	80.38 E
Kottas Mountains ⋌	9	74.20 S	12.00 W
Kottayam	122	9.35 N	76.31 E
Kotte → Sri Jayawardenepura	122	6.54 N	79.54 E
Kottingbrunn	61	47.57 N	16.14 E
Kotto ≃	136	4.14 N	22.02 E
Kotton	144	9.35 N	50.28 E
Kottūru	122	14.49 N	76.13 E
Kotuj ≃	74	71.55 N	102.05 E
Kot'užen'	38	47.51 N	28.36 E
Kotwālīpāra	126	22.59 N	89.59 E
Kotzebue	180	66.53 N	162.39 W
Kotzebue Sound ʯ	180	66.20 N	163.00 W
Kötzting	60	49.11 N	12.52 E
Koualé	150	11.24 N	7.01 W
Kou'an	106	32.19 N	119.52 E
Kouandé	150	10.20 N	1.42 E
Kouango	152	4.58 N	19.59 E
Kouassi-Datékro	150	7.49 N	3.31 W
Koubansaki	273b	4.22 S	15.09 E
Koubia	150	11.35 N	11.54 W
Kouchibouguac National Park ♦	186	46.50 N	65.00 W
Koudougou	150	12.15 N	2.22 W
Kouéré	150	10.27 N	3.59 W
Kouffo ≃	150	6.35 N	1.59 E
Kouga	146	9.56 N	21.03 E
Kouga ≃	158	33.37 S	22.14 E
Kougaberge ⋌	158	33.40 S	23.50 E
Kougarok Mountain ∧	180	65.41 N	165.13 W
K'ouhu	100	23.35 N	120.11 E
Kouilou □^{5}	152	4.30 S	12.00 E
Kouilou ≃	152	4.28 S	11.41 E
Koukdjuak ≃	176	66.45 N	73.09 W
Kouki	152	7.10 N	17.18 E
Koúklia	130	34.42 N	32.34 E
Koukourou ≃	152	7.32 N	19.42 E
Koukourou-Bamingui, Réserve de Faune du -●-^{4}	152	7.20 N	20.00 E
Koula ≃	229b	21.54 N	159.36 W

Symbols in the index entries represent the broad categories identified in the key at the right. Symbols with superior numbers (⋌^{1}) identify subcategories (see complete key on page *I · 1).*

Symbole im Register stellen die rechts im Schlüssel erklärten Kategorien dar. Symbole mit hochgestellten Ziffern (⋌^{1}) bezeichnen Unterabteilungen einer Kategorie (vgl. vollständiger Schlüssel auf Seite *I · 1).*

Los símbolos incluídos en el texto del índice representan las grandes categorías identificadas con la clave a la derecha. Los símbolos con numeros en su parte superior (⋌^{1}) identifican las subcategorías (véase la clave completa en la página *I · 1).*

Les symboles de l'index représentent les catégories indiquées dans la légende à droite. Les symboles suivis d'un indice (⋌^{1}) représentent des sous-catégories (voir légende complète à la page *I · 1).*

Os símbolos incluídos no texto do índice representam as grandes categorias identificadas com a chave à direita. Os símbolos com números em sua parte superior (⋌^{1}) identificam as subcategorias (veja-se a chave completa à página *I · 1).*

Symbol	English	Deutsch	Español	Français	Português
∧	Mountain	Berg	Montaña	Montagne	Montanha
⋌	Mountains	Gebirge	Montañas	Montagnes	Montanhas
)(	Pass	Paß	Paso	Col	Passo
∨	Valley, Canyon	Tal, Cañon	Valle, Cañón	Vallée, Canyon	Vale, Canhão
≚	Plain	Ebene	Llano	Plaine	Planície
›	Cape	Kap	Cabo	Cap	Cabo
I	Island	Insel	Isla	Île	Ilha
II	Islands	Inseln	Islas	Îles	Ilhas
⊥	Other Topographic Features	Andere Topographische Objekte	Otros Elementos Topográficos	Autres données topographiques	Outros acidentes topográficos

ESPAÑOL — Nombre | Página | Lat.°′ | Long.°′ W = Oeste
FRANÇAIS — Nom | Page | Lat.°′ | Long.°′ W = Ouest
PORTUGUÊS — Nome | Fágina | Lat.°′ | Long.°′ W = Oeste

Koulamoutou	152	1.08 S	12.29 E
Koulikoro	150	12.53 N	7.33 W
Koulikoro □[4]	150	13.00 N	8.00 W
Koulouguidi	150	13.27 N	11.03 W
Koulountou ≃	150	13.15 N	13.37 W
Koumac	175f	20.33 S	164.17 E
Koumac, Grand Récif de ✢[2]	175f	20.32 S	164.04 E
Koumala	166	21.37 S	149.15 E
Koumaméyong	152	0.11 N	11.51 E
Koumankou	150	12.06 N	6.08 W
Koumbakara	150	12.42 N	14.29 W
Koumbal	146	9.26 N	22.39 E
Koumbala ≃	146	9.14 N	20.42 E
Koumbia, Burkina	150	11.14 N	3.42 W
Koumbia, Guinée	150	11.48 N	13.30 W
Koumbisaleh ⊥	150	15.46 N	7.59 W
Koumbouma	150	10.24 N	12.56 W
Koumi	94	36.05 N	138.29 E
Koumpentoum	150	13.59 N	14.34 W
Koumra	146	8.55 N	17.33 E
Koundara	150	12.29 N	13.18 W
Koundé	152	6.07 N	14.38 E
Koundian ⊥	150	13.10 N	10.41 W
Koundougou	150	11.44 N	4.31 W
Koun-Fao	150	7.29 N	3.15 W
Koungheul	150	13.59 N	14.48 W
Koungoulou	152	3.32 S	13.20 E
Kouniohou	150	7.40 N	0.48 E
Kounradskij	86	46.59 N	75.00 E
Kountze	194	30.22 N	94.18 W
Koupé, Mont ∧	152	4.47 N	9.43 E
Koupéla	150	12.11 N	0.21 W
Kouragué	150	12.18 N	10.02 W
Kourak	86	54.50 N	84.40 E
Kouriles, Détroit des → Pervyj Kuril'skij proliv ʉ	74	50.50 N	156.36 E
Kouri-shima I	174m	26.42 N	128.01 E
Kourou	250	5.09 N	52.39 W
Kouroukoto	150	12.35 N	10.05 W
Kourouma	150	11.37 N	4.48 W
Kourouninkoto	150	13.52 N	9.35 W
Kouroussa	150	10.39 N	9.53 W
Koury	150	12.11 N	4.48 W
Koussanar	150	13.52 N	14.05 W
Koussané, Mali	150	14.53 N	11.14 W
Koussane, Sén.	150	14.08 N	12.26 W
Kousser, Massif de ∧	148	32.02 N	5.59 W
Koussi, Emi ∧	146	19.50 N	18.30 E
Koussili	150	13.30 N	11.38 W
Koutia Ba	150	14.11 N	14.28 W
Koutiala	150	12.23 N	5.28 W
Kouto	150	9.53 N	6.25 W
Koutou	98	38.35 N	114.24 E
Koutoumo, Île I	175f	22.40 S	167.33 E
Kouts	216	41.19 N	87.01 W
Kouvola	26	60.52 N	26.42 E
Kouya ≃	150	10.09 N	9.45 W
Kouyou ≃	152	0.45 S	16.38 E
Kova	88	58.18 N	100.21 E
Kova ≃	88	58.18 N	100.18 E
Kovada Milli Parkı ♠	130	37.32 N	30.53 E
Kovaksa	80	55.31 N	43.30 E
Koval'ovka	78	47.16 N	31.43 E
Kovarskas	76	55.26 N	24.55 E
Kovarzino	76	60.09 N	38.33 E
Kovdor	24	67.34 N	30.22 E
Kovdozero, ozero ⊜	24	66.47 N	32.00 E
Kovel'	78	51.14 N	24.41 E
Kovernino	80	57.07 N	43.49 E
Kovilpatti	122	9.10 N	77.52 E
Kovin	38	44.45 N	20.59 E
Kovno → Kaunas	76	54.54 N	23.54 E
Kovpyta	78	51.23 N	30.50 E
Kovrina Vtoraja	80	47.01 N	41.44 E
Kovrov	80	56.22 N	41.18 E
Kovševata	78	49.29 N	30.38 E
Kovsug ≃	83	48.48 N	39.17 E
Kovūr	122	14.29 N	79.59 E
Kovvur	122	17.01 N	81.44 E
Kovylkin	80	48.16 N	41.28 E
Kovylkino	80	54.02 N	43.56 E
Kovža	24	61.09 N	38.58 E
Kovžinskij Zavod	76	60.24 N	37.04 E
Kowal	30	52.32 N	19.09 E
Kowalewo Pomorskie	30	53.10 N	18.53 E
Kowangge	115b	8.16 S	118.32 E
Kowanyama	164	15.28 S	141.44 E
Kowanyama Aboriginal Reserve ⊕[4]	164	15.15 S	141.45 E
Kowār	126	24.13 N	86.11 E
Koweït → Kuwait □[1]	128	29.30 N	47.45 E
Kowel → Kovel'	78	51.14 N	24.41 E
Kowghān ≃	128	34.15 N	62.57 E
Kowhitirangi	172	42.52 S	171.01 E
Kowie → Port Alfred	158	33.36 S	26.55 E
Kowkcheh ≃	120	37.10 N	69.23 E
Kowloon City	271d	22.19 N	114.11 E
Kowloon Peak ∧	271d	22.21 N	114.13 E
Kowmung ≃	170	33.52 S	150.16 E
Kowŏn	98	39.26 N	127.14 E
Kowt-e 'Ashrow	120	34.27 N	68.48 E
Koxtag	120	37.23 N	78.05 E
Kōya	96	34.12 N	135.35 E
Koyadaira	96	33.56 N	134.13 E
Kōyaguchi	96	34.18 N	135.33 E
Koyama ⊕[8]	268	35.37 N	139.43 E
Koyama-ike ⊜	96	35.30 N	134.09 E
Kōyama-misaki ›	96	34.40 N	131.36 E
Koyambattur → Coimbatore	122	11.00 N	76.58 E
Koyang-ni	98	37.42 N	126.56 E
Kōya-Ryūjin-kokutei-kōen ♠	96	34.10 N	135.35 E
Köyceğiz	130	36.57 N	28.41 E
Köyceğiz Gölü ⊜	130	36.55 N	28.40 E
Koyna Reservoir ⊜[1]	122	17.25 N	73.45 E
Koyra ≃[1]	126	22.27 N	89.16 E
Koyuk	180	64.56 N	161.08 W
Koyuk ≃	180	64.55 N	161.12 W
Koyukuk	180	64.53 N	157.43 W
Koyukuk ≃	180	64.56 N	157.30 W
Koyukuk, Middle Fork ≃	180	67.03 N	151.04 W
Koyukuk, North Fork ≃	180	67.03 N	151.04 W
Koyukuk, South Fork ≃	180	66.35 N	151.57 W
Koyulhisar	130	40.18 N	37.51 E
Koža	80	57.47 N	48.57 E
Kozakai	94	34.48 N	137.22 E
Kōzaki	94	35.54 N	140.24 E
Kō-zaki ›	92	34.05 N	129.13 E
Kozaklı	130	39.14 N	34.49 E
Kōzan, Nihon	96	34.35 N	133.03 E
Kozan, Tür.	130	37.27 N	35.49 E
Kozáni	38	40.18 N	21.47 E
Kožanka	78	49.58 N	29.46 E
Koz'any, Bela.	76	55.18 N	26.52 E
Kožany, Ross.	76	52.48 N	31.44 E
Kozara ⋏	36	45.00 N	16.50 E
Kozarac	36	44.58 N	16.51 E
Kozdinga	24	63.43 N	47.32 E
Kozelec	78	50.55 N	31.08 E
Kozel'ščina	78	49.13 N	33.51 E
Kozel'sk	82	54.02 N	35.48 E
Koževnikovo	86	56.16 N	84.00 E
Kozhikode → Calicut	122	11.15 N	75.46 E
Koziegłowy	30	50.36 N	19.09 E
Kozienice	30	51.35 N	21.33 E
Kožim	24	65.48 N	59.28 E
Kozin	78	50.14 N	30.39 E
Kozino	265b	55.54 N	37.11 E
Kozjak (Possruck) ⋏	61	46.37 N	15.28 E
Kozlov	78	49.33 N	25.20 E
Kozlov Bereg	76	58.57 N	27.44 E
Kozlovka, Ross.	78	51.39 N	41.16 E
Kozlovka, Ross.	78	50.52 N	40.27 E
Kozlovka, Ross.	80	55.52 N	48.14 E
Kozlovka, Ross.	80	52.33 N	45.41 E
Kozlovo, Ross.	76	57.34 N	35.29 E
Kozlovo, Ross.	82	56.31 N	36.16 E
Kozlovščina	76	53.19 N	25.18 E
Kozlu, Tür.	130	41.26 N	31.46 E
Kozlu, Tür.	130	40.37 N	36.30 E
Kozluk	130	38.11 N	41.29 E
Koźmin	30	51.50 N	17.28 E
Koz'mino	24	61.56 N	48.19 E
Koz'modemjansk	80	56.20 N	46.36 E
Koz'mogorodskoje	24	65.32 N	44.55 E
Kozova	78	49.26 N	25.09 E
Kožpos'olok	24	63.10 N	38.06 E
Kožuchovo	265b	55.43 N	37.54 E
Kożuchów	30	51.45 N	15.35 E
Kozuka	268	35.09 N	139.57 E
Kōzuki	96	34.59 N	134.20 E
Kozukue ⊕[8]	268	35.30 N	139.36 E
Kozul'ka	86	56.10 N	91.24 E
Kožurla	86	55.21 N	79.02 E
Kōzu-shima I	92	34.13 N	139.10 E
Kozuya	270	34.52 N	135.45 E
Kpandae	150	8.28 N	0.01 W
Kpandu	150	7.00 N	0.18 E
Kpong	150	6.09 N	0.04 E
Kpo Range ⋏	150	7.15 N	10.15 W
Kra, Isthmus of ⊥[3]	110	10.20 N	99.00 E
Kraai ≃	158	30.40 S	26.45 E
Kraaifontein	158	33.50 S	18.43 E
Kraal	158	26.34 S	28.26 E
Kraankuil	158	29.52 S	24.10 E
Krabbendijke	52	51.26 N	4.07 E
Krabi	110	8.04 N	98.55 E
Krâchéh	110	12.29 N	106.01 E
Krackow	54	53.20 N	14.16 E
Kraftsdorf	54	50.52 N	11.55 E
Kragan	115a	6.42 S	111.37 E
Kragenæs	41	54.55 N	11.22 E
Kragerø	26	58.52 N	9.25 E
Kraghave	41	54.48 N	11.53 E
Kragujevac	38	44.01 N	20.55 E
Krahenhöhe ⊕[8]	263	51.10 N	7.06 E
Kraiburg	60	48.10 N	12.26 E
Kraichgau ⊕[1]	56	49.10 N	8.50 E
Krainburg → Kranj	36	46.15 N	14.21 E
Krainka	82	54.07 N	36.21 E
Krai-Russkije	80	57.23 N	46.50 E
Krajčikovo	86	56.16 N	73.20 E
Krajenka	30	53.19 N	17.00 E
Krajeva	89	44.54 N	131.08 E
Krajneje	80	47.29 N	46.01 E
Krajnik Dolny	54	53.05 N	14.25 E
Krajnovka	84	43.57 N	47.24 E
Krakatau ∧[1]	115a	6.07 S	105.24 E
Krakatoa → Krakatau ∧[1]	115a	6.07 S	105.24 E
Krakau → Kraków	30	50.03 N	19.58 E
Krâkôr	110	12.32 N	104.12 E
Krakovec	78	49.57 N	23.07 E
Krakovo	80	53.36 N	50.51 E
Krakow, Dtsch.	54	53.39 N	12.16 E
Kraków, Pol.	30	50.03 N	19.58 E
Kraków □[4]	30	49.50 N	20.00 E
Krakower See ⊜	54	53.37 N	12.17 E
Kraksaan	115a	7.46 S	113.25 E
Kraksdorf	54	54.18 N	11.04 E
Kralendijk	241s	12.10 N	68.17 W
Kralice	61	49.11 N	16.12 E
Kraljevica	36	45.16 N	14.34 E
Kraljevo	38	43.43 N	20.41 E
Kralovice	60	49.59 N	13.29 E
Královské Vinohrady ⊕[8]	54	50.01 N	14.29 E
Kralupy nad Vltavou	54	50.11 N	14.18 E
Kralupy u Chomutova	54	50.25 N	13.20 E
Králův Dvůr	60	49.56 N	14.02 E
Kramatorsk	83	48.43 N	37.32 E
Kramer	216	40.20 N	87.17 W
Kramfors	26	62.56 N	17.47 E
Krammer ʉ	52	51.38 N	4.15 E
Krampen	61	47.40 N	15.32 E
Krampnitz	264a	52.28 N	13.04 E
Krampnitzsee ⊜	264a	52.27 N	13.03 E
Kramsach	64	47.27 N	11.52 E
Kranebitten, Flughafen ⊠	64	47.16 N	11.20 E
Kranenburg	52	51.47 N	6.03 E
Krångede	26	63.09 N	16.05 E
Kranichfeld	54	50.51 N	11.12 E
Kranídhion	38	37.22 N	23.10 E
Kranj	36	46.15 N	14.21 E
Kranji, Sing.	271c	1.26 N	103.46 E
Kranji, Sing.	271c	1.26 N	103.45 E
Kranji ≃	271c	1.26 N	103.45 E
Kranji Reservoir ⊜[1]	271c	1.26 N	103.45 E
Kranji War Memorial ⊥	271c	1.26 N	103.45 E
Kranjska Gora	64	46.29 N	13.47 E
Kransaja Pol'ana	84	43.41 N	40.13 E
Kranskop	158	29.00 S	30.47 E
Kranskop ∧	158	27.43 S	29.41 E
Kranzberg	156	21.55 S	15.43 E
Krapina	36	46.10 N	15.52 E
Krapivinskij	86	55.00 N	86.49 E
Krapivna	76	53.38 N	35.31 E
Krapkowice	30	50.29 N	17.56 E
Krapperup	41	56.16 N	12.31 E
Krapuh	114	3.39 N	98.10 E
Kras (Karst) ⋏[1]	64	45.48 N	14.00 E
Krasavino	24	60.58 N	46.26 E
Krasavka	80	51.11 N	43.24 E
Krasieo ≃	110	14.49 N	100.05 E
Krasilov	78	49.39 N	26.59 E
Krasino	72	70.45 N	54.27 E
Krasivaja Meča ≃	76	52.55 N	39.03 E
Krasivka	80	52.16 N	42.31 E
Krasivoje	86	51.54 N	66.46 E
Kraskino	89	42.44 N	130.48 E
Kraskovo	265b	55.39 N	37.59 E
Krāslava	76	55.54 N	27.10 E
Kraslice	54	50.18 N	12.31 E
Krasnaja ≃	83	49.01 N	38.15 E
Krasnaja Gora, Ross.	76	53.01 N	31.37 E
Krasnaja Gora, Ross.	76	60.16 N	35.42 E
Krasnaja Gorbatka	80	55.52 N	41.46 E
Krasnaja Gorka	80	56.12 N	43.04 E
Krasnaja Jaranga	180	65.40 N	172.50 W
Krasnaja Jaruga	78	50.48 N	35.39 E
Krasnaja Pachra	82	55.27 N	37.17 E
Krasnaja Pol'ana, Ross.	80	56.15 N	51.09 E
Krasnaja Pol'ana, Ross.	80	52.13 N	53.38 E
Krasnaja Pol'ana, Ross.	80	46.06 N	41.30 E
Krasnaja Pol'ana, Ukr.	78	47.33 N	37.05 E
Krasnaja Popovka	83	49.08 N	38.09 E
Krasnaja Sloboda, Azer.	84	41.24 N	48.31 E
Krasnaja Sloboda, Bela.	76	52.51 N	27.10 E
Krasnaja Talovka	83	48.51 N	39.51 E
Krasnaja Vol'a	76	52.23 N	27.04 E
Krasnaja Zar'a	76	52.47 N	37.41 E
Krásná Lípa	54	50.54 N	14.31 E
Krasn'anka	80	51.04 N	47.56 E
Krasneno	180	64.38 N	174.48 E
Kraśnik	30	50.56 N	22.13 E
Krasnoarmejsk, Kaz.	86	53.50 N	69.42 E
Krasnoarmejsk, Ross.	80	51.02 N	45.42 E
Krasnoarmejsk, Ross.	82	56.08 N	38.08 E
Krasnoarmejsk, Ukr.	83	48.17 N	37.11 E
Krasnoarmejskaja	78	45.23 N	38.12 E
Krasnoarmejskij, Ross.	74	69.35 N	172.00 E
Krasnoarmejskij, Ross.	80	47.01 N	42.12 E
Krasnoarmejskoje, Ross.	80	55.46 N	47.11 E
Krasnoarmejskoje, Ross.	80	52.44 N	50.02 E
Krasnoarmejskoje, Ukr.	83	47.14 N	37.56 E
Krasnoborsk, Ross.	24	61.34 N	45.53 E
Krasnoborsk, Ross.	80	53.46 N	48.04 E
Krasnobród	30	50.33 N	23.13 E
Krasnobrodskij	86	54.10 N	86.28 E
Krasnodar	78	45.02 N	39.00 E
Krasnodar Kraj □[8]	78	45.30 N	39.00 E
Krasnodarskij	83	48.15 N	39.51 E
Krasnodarskoje vodochranilišče ⊜[1]	78	45.06 N	39.31 E
Krasnodon	83	48.17 N	39.48 E
Krasnofarfornyj	76	59.08 N	31.51 E
Krasnoflotskoje	80	50.04 N	41.14 E
Krasnogorka	85	43.15 N	75.10 E
Krasnogorodskoje	76	56.50 N	28.17 E
Krasnogorovka	83	48.00 N	37.31 E
Krasnogorsk, Ross.	82	55.50 N	37.20 E
Krasnogorsk, Ross.	89	48.24 N	142.06 E
Krasnogorskij, Ross.	80	56.09 N	48.20 E
Krasnogorskij, Ross.	86	54.36 N	61.15 E
Krasnogorskij, Uzb.	85	41.09 N	69.39 E
Krasnogorskoje, Ross.	80	57.42 N	52.30 E
Krasnogorskoje, Ross.	86	52.18 N	86.12 E
Krasnogovardejskij	86	57.22 N	62.20 E
Krasnograd	78	49.22 N	35.27 E
Krasnogvardejsk	85	39.46 N	67.16 E
Krasnogvardejskij	82	54.04 N	37.46 E
Krasnogvardejskoje, Kaz.	86	51.24 N	69.18 E
Krasnogvardejskoje, Ross.	78	50.39 N	38.24 E
Krasnogvardejskoje, Ross.	80	45.51 N	41.31 E
Krasnogvardejskoje, Ukr.	78	45.29 N	34.17 E
Krasnoil'sk	78	48.01 N	25.34 E
Krasnojar	80	48.54 N	51.46 E
Krasnojarka, Ross.	86	55.20 N	73.04 E
Krasnojarka, Ross.	86	59.26 N	60.30 E
Krasnoj Armii, proliv ʉ	74	80.00 N	94.35 E
Krasnojarovo	89	51.27 N	128.28 E
Krasnojarsk	86	56.01 N	92.50 E
Krasnojarskij	86	51.58 N	59.55 E
Krasnojarsk Kraj □[8]	86	56.00 N	92.22 E
Krasnojarskoje vodochranilišče ⊜[1]	86	55.00 N	92.00 E
Krasnoje, Bela.	76	54.14 N	27.05 E
Krasnoje, Mol.	38	46.38 N	29.50 E
Krasnoje, Ross.	24	59.12 N	47.49 E
Krasnoje, Ross.	76	53.06 N	33.55 E
Krasnoje, Ross.	76	52.51 N	38.47 E
Krasnoje, Ross.	78	50.56 N	38.41 E
Krasnoje, Ross.	78	50.21 N	38.50 E
Krasnoje, Ross.	78	46.44 N	39.34 E
Krasnoje, Ross.	82	54.26 N	38.38 E
Krasnoje, Ross.	86	54.37 N	85.23 E
Krasnoje, Ukr.	83	48.23 N	39.31 E
Krasnoje, Ukr.	83	48.25 N	37.19 E
Krasnoje, ozero ⊜	74	64.30 N	174.24 E
Krasnoje Echo	80	55.48 N	40.42 E
Krasnoje Gorodišče	82	54.04 N	38.44 E
Krasnoje-na-Volge	80	57.31 N	41.14 E
Krasnoje Selo, Ross.	80	48.02 N	45.13 E
Krasnoje Selo, Ross.	80	48.46 N	42.20 E
Krasnoje Selo, Ross.	265a	59.44 N	30.05 E
Krasnoje Znam'a, Ross.	76	57.26 N	35.13 E
Krasnoje Znam'a, Turk.	128	36.58 N	62.30 E
Krasnokamsk	86	58.04 N	55.48 E
Krasnokutsk, Kaz.	86	53.01 N	75.59 E
Krasnokutsk, Ukr.	78	50.06 N	35.09 E
Krasnolesje	76	54.24 N	22.23 E
Krasnolesnyj	78	51.53 N	39.35 E
Krasnoluki	76	54.37 N	28.50 E
Krasnomajskij	76	57.37 N	34.22 E
Krasnookt'abr'skij, Kyrg.	85	42.50 N	74.18 E
Krasnookt'abr'skij, Ross.	80	56.40 N	47.45 E
Krasnookt'abr'skij, Ross.	80	48.53 N	44.45 E
Krasnooskol'skoje vodochranilišče ⊜[1]	83	49.17 N	37.37 E
Krasnoostrovskij	76	60.18 N	28.40 E
Krasnopavlovka	78	49.08 N	36.19 E
Krasnoperekopsk	78	45.57 N	33.47 E
Krasnopolje, Bela.	76	53.20 N	31.24 E
Krasnopolje, Ukr.	78	50.46 N	35.16 E
Krasnorečenskij	89	44.41 N	135.14 E
Krasnoščelje	24	67.21 N	37.02 E
Krasnoščokovo	86	51.40 N	82.45 E
Krasnosel'kup	74	65.41 N	82.28 E
Krasnosel'skoje	78	45.25 N	32.42 E
Krasnosielc	30	53.03 N	21.10 E
Krasnoslobodsk, Ross.	80	54.26 N	43.48 E
Krasnoslobodsk, Ross.	80	48.42 N	44.34 E
Krasnotorka	83	48.41 N	37.31 E
Krasnoturansk	86	54.16 N	91.29 E
Krasnoturjinsk	86	59.46 N	60.12 E
Krasnoufimsk	86	56.37 N	57.46 E
Krasnoural'sk	86	58.21 N	60.03 E
Krasnousol'skij	86	53.54 N	56.27 E
Krasnovidovo	80	55.21 N	49.04 E
Krasnovišersk	24	60.23 N	56.59 E
Krasnovka, Ross.	83	48.47 N	40.07 E
Krasnovka, Ukr.	83	47.24 N	37.26 E
Krasnovodsk	128	40.00 N	53.00 E
Krasnovodskij poluostrov ›[1]	128	40.30 N	53.15 E
Krasnovodskij zaliv ⊂	128	39.55 N	53.15 E
Krasnoyarsk → Krasnojarsk	86	56.01 N	92.50 E
Krasnozatonskij	24	61.41 N	50.58 E
Krasnozavodsk	82	56.27 N	38.13 E
Krasnoznamensk	76	54.57 N	22.30 E
Krasnoznamenskij	86	51.03 N	69.30 E
Krasnoz'orskoje	86	53.59 N	79.14 E
Krásný Dvůr	54	50.10 N	13.24 E
Krasnyj, Ross.	76	54.34 N	31.26 E
Krasnyj, Ross.	92a	46.15 N	141.15 E
Krasnyj Aul	86	51.03 N	81.02 E
Krasnyj Bazar	84	39.41 N	46.58 E
Krasnyj Bogatyr'	80	56.02 N	41.08 E
Krasnyj Bor, Ross.	80	55.17 N	43.59 E
Krasnyj Bor, Ross.	80	55.53 N	53.06 E
Krasnyj Bor, Ross.	265a	59.41 N	30.41 E
Krasnyj Cholm, Ross.	76	58.03 N	37.07 E
Krasnyj Cholm, Ross.	80	54.11 N	40.42 E
Krasnyj Cholm, Ross.	86	51.35 N	54.09 E
Krasnyj Chuduk	80	46.18 N	46.56 E
Krasnyj Čikoj	88	50.22 N	108.15 E
Krasnyje Baki	80	57.08 N	45.10 E
Krasnyje Barrikady	80	46.14 N	47.53 E
Krasnyje Četai	80	55.42 N	46.09 E
Krasnyje Gory	76	58.57 N	29.29 E
Krasnyje Okny	78	47.32 N	29.27 E
Krasnyje Partizany	78	50.57 N	31.47 E
Krasnyje Tkači	80	57.30 N	39.45 E
Krasnyj Gorodok	76	57.11 N	33.44 E
Krasnyj Gul'aj	80	54.01 N	48.22 E
Krasnyj Jar, Kaz.	86	53.20 N	69.14 E
Krasnyj Jar, Ross.	80	46.33 N	48.21 E
Krasnyj Jar, Ross.	80	53.30 N	50.22 E
Krasnyj Jar, Ross.	80	51.38 N	46.25 E
Krasnyj Jar, Ross.	80	50.37 N	45.47 E
Krasnyj Jar, Ross.	80	50.42 N	44.46 E
Krasnyj Jar, Ross.	86	55.54 N	86.57 E
Krasnyj Jar, Ross.	86	55.14 N	72.56 E
Krasnyj Jar, Ross.	86	57.07 N	84.33 E
Krasnyj Kl'ič	86	55.26 N	56.12 E
Krasnyj Kut, Ross.	80	50.57 N	46.58 E
Krasnyj Kut, Ukr.	83	48.12 N	38.48 E
Krasnyj Liman, Ross.	78	51.32 N	39.50 E
Krasnyj Liman, Ukr.	83	48.59 N	37.49 E
Krasnyj Log	78	51.23 N	39.46 E
Krasnyj Luč, Ross.	76	57.04 N	30.05 E
Krasnyj Luč, Ukr.	83	48.08 N	38.56 E
Krasnyj Majak	80	56.03 N	41.23 E
Krasnyj Manyč, Ross.	80	46.33 N	42.10 E
Krasnyj Manyč, Ross.	80	45.31 N	44.42 E
Krasnyj Manyč, Ross.	80	46.59 N	41.07 E
Krasnyj Meliorator	80	50.02 N	46.06 E
Krasnyj Okt'abr', Kaz.	86	46.50 N	75.59 E
Krasnyj Okt'abr', Ross.	80	51.33 N	45.42 E
Krasnyj Okt'abr', Ross.	80	56.06 N	41.23 E
Krasnyj Okt'abr', Ross.	82	56.07 N	38.53 E
Krasnyj Okt'abr', Ross.	82	55.37 N	36.30 E
Krasnyj Okt'abr', Ross.	86	55.37 N	64.48 E
Krasnyj Okt'abr', Ukr.	83	48.15 N	38.12 E
Krasnyj Okt'abr', Ukr.	83	48.56 N	39.23 E
Krasnyj Oskol	83	49.11 N	37.26 E
Krasnyj Partizan	80	46.20 N	43.10 E
Krasnyj Perekop	78	46.41 N	33.46 E
Krasnyj Profintern	80	57.45 N	40.27 E
Krasnyj Rog	76	52.57 N	33.45 E
Krasnyj Steklovar	80	56.13 N	48.47 E
Krasnyj Stroitel' ⊕[8]	265b	55.35 N	37.37 E
Krasnyj Sulin	83	47.54 N	40.03 E
Krasnyj Tekstil'ščik	80	51.23 N	45.50 E
Krasnyj Tkač	82	55.28 N	39.05 E
Krasnystaw	30	50.59 N	23.10 E
Krasnyy Luch → Krasnyj Luč	83	48.08 N	38.56 E
Krasucha	76	57.23 N	33.12 E
Kras'ukovskaja	83	47.31 N	40.06 E
Kraszna (Crasna) ≃	38	48.09 N	22.20 E
Kratovo	38	42.05 N	22.11 E
Krauchenwies	58	48.01 N	9.14 E
Kraul Mountains ⋏	9	73.10 S	14.10 W
Krauschwitz	54	51.31 N	14.41 E
Kräuterin ⋏	61	47.41 N	15.05 E
Krautheim	56	49.23 N	9.38 E
Kravaře, Česká Rep.	30	49.56 N	18.01 E
Kravaře, Česká Rep.	54	50.38 N	14.23 E
Kray ⊕[8]	263	51.28 N	7.05 E
Kražiai	76	55.36 N	22.40 E
Krbava ⊕[1]	36	44.40 N	15.35 E
Kreamer Island I	220	26.46 N	80.44 W
Kreba	54	51.20 N	14.40 E
Krebs	196	34.55 N	95.42 W
Krečetovo	24	60.56 N	38.30 E
Krečevicy	76	58.37 N	31.21 E
Krefeld	56	51.20 N	6.34 E
Kregme	41	55.57 N	12.04 E
Kreiensen	52	51.51 N	9.58 E
Kreischa	54	50.56 N	13.45 E
Kremastón, Tekhnití Límni ⊜[1]	38	38.55 N	21.30 E
Kremenčug	78	49.04 N	33.25 E
Kremenčugskoje vodochranilišče ⊜[1]	78	49.20 N	32.30 E
Kremenec	78	50.07 N	25.45 E
Kremennaja	83	49.03 N	38.14 E
Kremen'ovka	83	47.20 N	37.29 E
Kremenskoj	80	47.49 N	41.08 E
Kremenskoje	82	55.06 N	35.57 E
Kremlin ʋ	265b	55.45 N	37.37 E
Kremmen	54	52.45 N	13.01 E
Kremmling	200	40.03 N	106.23 W
Kremnica	30	48.43 N	18.54 E
Krempe	52	53.50 N	9.29 E
Krems ≃, Öst.	61	48.14 N	14.19 E
Krems ≃, Öst.	61	48.25 N	15.36 E
Krems an der Donau	61	48.25 N	15.36 E
Kremsbrücke	64	46.57 N	13.37 E
Kremsmünster	61	48.03 N	14.08 E
Krenitzin Islands II	180	54.08 N	166.00 W
Krensitz	54	51.29 N	12.27 E
Krepenskij	83	48.06 N	39.03 E
Krepkaja ≃	83	47.35 N	39.23 E
Krepoljin	38	44.16 N	21.37 E
Krešchonka	86	55.52 N	80.06 E
Kresgeville	210	40.54 N	75.30 W
Kress	196	34.22 N	101.45 W
Kressbronn	58	47.35 N	9.36 E
Kressey Lake ⊜	285	39.44 N	75.07 W
Kresta, zaliv ⊂	180	66.00 N	179.15 W
Krestcy, Ross.	76	58.15 N	32.31 E
Krestcy, Ross.	76	58.23 N	39.00 E
Krestjanskij	85	40.32 N	69.02 E
Krestjanskoje	80	45.34 N	42.56 E
Krest-Major	74	67.37 N	144.45 E
Krestovaja Guba	72	74.07 N	55.33 E
Krestovo-Gorodišče	80	54.10 N	48.36 E
Krestovyj, pereval)(	84	42.32 N	44.28 E
Kresty	82	55.16 N	37.06 E
Kreta → Kríti I	38	35.15 N	25.00 E
Kretek	115a	7.59 S	110.19 E
Kretinga	76	55.53 N	21.13 E
Kreuth	64	47.38 N	11.44 E
Kreuzau	56	50.45 N	6.29 E
Kreuzberg	263	51.09 N	7.27 E
Kreuzberg ⊕[8]	264a	52.30 N	13.23 E
Kreuzberg ∧	56	50.22 N	9.58 E
Kreuzeck-Gruppe ⋏	64	46.51 N	13.06 E
Kreuzen	64	46.40 N	13.35 E
Kreuzlingen	58	47.39 N	9.11 E
Kreuznach → Bad Kreuznach	56	49.52 N	7.51 E
Kreuztal	56	50.58 N	7.59 E
Krevo	76	54.19 N	26.17 E
Kreyenhagen	54	52.55 N	10.52 E
Krian	115a	7.24 S	112.35 E
Kría Vrísi	38	40.41 N	22.18 E
Kribi	152	2.57 N	9.55 E
Kričov	76	53.42 N	31.43 E
Kriebstein, Burg ⊥	54	51.02 N	13.00 E
Krieglach	61	47.33 N	15.34 E
Kriel	158	26.16 S	29.14 E
Kriens	58	47.02 N	8.17 E
Krigujgun, mys ›	180	65.30 N	171.05 W
Kriljon, mys ›	89	45.53 N	142.05 E
Krim → Krymskij poluostrov ›[1]	78	45.00 N	34.00 E
Křimice	60	49.46 N	13.15 E
Krim-Krim	146	8.58 N	15.48 E
Krimmler Wasserfälle ∟	64	47.12 N	12.10 E
Krimnicksee ⊜	264a	52.18 N	13.39 E
Krimpen aan de IJssel	52	51.54 N	4.35 E
Krimskij	80	47.39 N	40.44 E
Krinično-Lugskoje	83	47.45 N	39.12 E
Krinički	78	48.22 N	34.27 E
Kriničnaja	83	48.08 N	38.02 E
Kriničnoje	78	45.32 N	28.40 E
Krishna ≃	122	15.57 N	80.59 E
Krishna, Mouths of the ≃[1]	122	15.43 N	80.55 E
Krishnachaadrapur	126	21.50 N	86.49 E
Krishnagiri	122	12.32 N	78.14 E
Krishnamāti	272b	22.40 N	88.32 E
Krishnanagar, India	126	23.24 N	88.30 E
Krishnanagar, India	126	23.13 N	87.33 E
Krishnapur, Bngl.	126	23.30 N	89.56 E
Krishnapur, India	272b	22.36 N	88.26 E
Krishnarāja Sāgara ⊜[1]	122	12.30 N	76.26 E
Krishnarājpet	122	12.40 N	76.30 E
Krishnarāmpur	126	22.43 N	88.14 E
Kristdala	26	57.24 N	16.11 E
Kristiania → Oslo	26	59.55 N	10.45 E
Kristianopel	26	56.15 N	16.02 E
Kristiansand	26	58.10 N	8.00 E
Kristianstad	26	56.02 N	14.08 E
Kristianstads Län □[6]	26	56.15 N	14.00 E
Kristiansund	26	63.07 N	7.45 E
Kristiinankaupunki → Kristinestad	26	62.17 N	21.23 E
Kristineberg	26	65.04 N	18.35 E
Kristinehamn	40	59.20 N	14.07 E
Kristinestad (Kristiinankaupunki)	26	62.17 N	21.23 E
Kríti (Crete) I	38	35.29 N	24.42 E
Kritikón Pélagos (Sea of Crete) ⊤[2]	38	35.46 N	23.54 E
Kritzendorf	264b	48.20 N	16.18 E
Kriul'any	38	47.13 N	29.09 E
Kriuša	82	54.28 N	36.24 E
Kriv'ačka	80	58.40 N	45.27 E
Krivaja ≃	38	44.27 N	18.09 E
Krivaja, kosa ›[2]	83	47.02 N	38.06 E
Krivaja Ruda	78	49.31 N	32.59 E
Kriv'anskaja	83	47.24 N	40.10 E
Kriva Palanka	38	42.12 N	22.20 E
Krivcy	82	55.28 N	38.12 E
Kriviči	76	54.43 N	27.17 E
Krivinka	86	51.08 N	78.10 E
Krivodol	38	43.23 N	23.29 E
Krivoj Buzan	80	46.31 N	48.33 E
Krivoje Ozero	78	47.56 N	30.21 E
Krivoj Rog	78	47.55 N	33.21 E
Krivoj Torec ≃	83	48.39 N	37.32 E
Křivoklát	60	50.02 N	13.54 E
Krivonosovo	78	49.55 N	39.16 E
Krivorožje, Ross.	78	48.51 N	40.45 E
Krivorožje, Ukr.	78	48.31 N	38.40 E
Krivorožje, Ukr.	83	48.31 N	38.40 E
Krivošeino	86	57.20 N	83.57 E
Krivošin	76	52.52 N	26.08 E
Krivoy Rog → Krivoj Rog	78	47.55 N	33.21 E
Kriwoi-Rog → Krivoj Rog	78	47.55 N	33.21 E
Križevci	36	46.02 N	16.33 E
Krizskoje	83	49.28 N	39.38 E
Krk, Otok I	36	45.05 N	14.35 E
Krkonošský národní park ♠	30	50.45 N	15.35 E
Krn ∧	64	46.16 N	13.40 E
Krnov	30	50.05 N	17.41 E
Krobia	30	51.47 N	16.58 E
Krøderen ⊜	26	60.15 N	9.38 E
Krogager	41	55.42 N	8.51 E
Krögis	54	51.07 N	13.22 E
Krokek	40	58.40 N	16.24 E
Kroken	24	65.22 N	14.20 E
Krokodil ≃, S. Afr.	156	25.26 S	31.58 E
Krokodil ≃, S. Afr.	156	24.12 S	26.52 E
Krokom	26	63.19 N	14.30 E
Krokowa	30	54.48 N	18.11 E
Krolevec	78	51.33 N	33.23 E
Kröller-Müller, Rijksmuseum ʋ	52	52.05 N	5.50 E
Kröpa	54	50.41 N	11.32 E
Krom ≃	158	30.53 S	19.01 E
Krombi Pits	156	19.30 S	25.02 E
Kroměříž	30	49.18 N	17.24 E
Krommenie	52	52.29 N	4.45 E
Krompachy	30	48.56 N	20.52 E
Kromy	76	52.43 N	35.46 E
Kronach	54	50.14 N	11.20 E
Kronberg	56	50.10 N	8.30 E
Kronborg ⊥	41	56.02 N	12.38 E
Krone	263	51.27 N	7.20 E
Krong Ana ⊜[1]	110	12.30 N	108.00 E
Krŏng Kaôh Kŏng	110	11.37 N	102.59 E
Krŏng Kêb	110	10.29 N	104.19 E
Kronobergs Län □[6]	26	56.40 N	14.40 E
Kronoby (Kruunupyy)	26	63.43 N	23.02 E
Kronockaja Sopka, vulkan ∧[1]	74	54.44 N	160.31 E
Kronockij zaliv ⊂	74	54.12 N	160.36 E
Kronoki	74	54.33 N	161.10 E
Kronshagen	41	54.20 N	10.05 E
Kronstadt → Braşov, Rom.	38	45.39 N	25.37 E
Kronštadt, Ross.	76	59.59 N	29.45 E
Kronwa	110	15.25 N	98.26 E
Kroondal	158	25.45 S	27.19 E
Kroonstad	158	27.46 S	27.12 E
Kröpelin	54	54.04 N	11.48 E
Kropotkin, Ross.	72	45.26 N	40.34 E
Kropotkin, Ross.	88	58.30 N	115.17 E
Kropotkina, gora ∧	88	53.43 N	117.32 E
Kropp	41	54.24 N	9.31 E
Kroppefjäll ∧[2]	26	58.40 N	12.13 E
Kroppenstedt	54	51.56 N	11.18 E
Kropstädt	54	51.58 N	12.44 E
Kropufino	76	60.23 N	39.10 E
Krościenko	30	49.27 N	20.26 E
Kröslin	54	54.07 N	13.45 E
Krošn'a	78	50.18 N	28.39 E
Krośniewice	30	52.16 N	19.10 E
Krosno	30	49.42 N	21.46 E
Krosno □[4]	30	49.30 N	22.00 E
Krosno Odrzańskie	30	52.04 N	15.05 E
Krossen	54	50.58 N	11.59 E
Krostitz	54	51.28 N	12.27 E
Krotoszyn	30	51.42 N	17.26 E
Krotovka	80	53.18 N	51.12 E
Krotovo	86	56.57 N	69.20 E
Krotz Springs	194	30.32 N	91.45 W
Kröv	56	49.59 N	7.05 E
Kroya	115a	7.38 S	109.14 E
Krško	36	45.58 N	15.29 E
Krsy	60	49.54 N	13.03 E
Kr'učkov	80	48.01 N	45.40 E
Kr'učkovo	76	57.03 N	35.34 E
Kruckow	54	53.54 N	13.14 E
Krudenburg	263	51.39 N	6.45 E
Kruenggeukueh	114	5.15 N	97.02 E
Kruengluak	114	2.50 N	97.45 E
Kruft	56	50.23 N	7.20 E
Kruger National Park ♠	156	24.00 S	31.40 E
Krugersdorp	158	26.05 S	27.35 E
Krugersdorp □[5]	273d	26.05 S	27.35 E
Krugersdorp Race Course ♠	273d	26.08 S	27.45 E
Krugersdorp West	273d	26.06 S	27.45 E
Krugloje, Bela.	76	54.15 N	29.48 E
Krugloje, Ross.	83	47.01 N	39.15 E
Kruglooz'ornoje	86	55.13 N	79.01 E
Kruglooz'ornyj	80	51.06 N	51.17 E
Kruglyži	80	58.31 N	47.42 E
Krugzell	58	47.47 N	10.16 E
Krui	112	5.11 S	103.56 E
Kruidfontein	158	32.51 S	21.57 E
Kruiningen	52	51.27 N	4.02 E
Kruis, Kaap ›	156	21.49 S	13.57 E
Kruisfontein	158	34.00 S	24.43 E
Kruishoutem	50	50.54 N	3.31 E
Kruisland	52	51.34 N	4.24 E
Kruisrivier	158	33.26 S	21.55 E
Kruisvallei	158	33.53 S	23.10 E
Krujë	38	41.30 N	19.48 E
Krukira, Laguna de ⊂	236	13.56 N	83.30 W
Kr'ukov	80	47.24 N	42.28 E
Kr'ukovo, Ross.	74	66.30 N	159.31 E
Kr'ukovo, Ross.	82	55.59 N	37.10 E
Kr'ukovo, Ross.	82	55.28 N	36.32 E
Kr'ukovo, Ross.	83	47.40 N	39.13 E
Krukut, Kali ≃	269e	6.12 S	106.48 E
Krulevščina	76	55.02 N	27.45 E
Krumasye	164	1.40 S	133.09 E
Krumbach, Dtsch.	58	47.58 N	9.02 E
Krumbach, Dtsch.	58	48.14 N	10.22 E
Krumme Lanke ⊜	264a	52.27 N	13.14 E
Krummendammer Heide ⊕[3]	264a	52.28 N	13.39 E
Krummensee	264a	52.36 N	13.42 E
Krumme Steyrling ≃	61	47.54 N	14.14 E
Krummhörn	52	53.26 N	7.06 E
Krummhörn ⊕[1]	52	53.25 N	7.10 E
Krumovgrad	38	41.28 N	25.39 E
Krumroy	214	39.58 N	81.24 W
Krün	64	47.30 N	11.16 E
Krung Thep (Bangkok), Thai	110	13.45 N	100.31 E
Krung Thep (Bangkok), Thai	269a	13.45 N	100.31 E
Krung Thep Mahanakhon □[4]	269a	13.47 N	100.43 E
Krung Thon Bridge ⊕[5]	269a	13.47 N	100.30 E
Krupá	54	50.08 N	13.41 E
Krupec	78	51.38 N	34.21 E
Krüpel-See ⊜	264a	52.18 N	13.42 E
Krupka	54	50.43 N	13.46 E
Krupki	76	54.19 N	29.08 E
Kruså	41	54.50 N	9.25 E
Kruščica jezero ⊜[1]	36	44.39 N	15.19 E
Krusenstern, Cape ›	180	67.07 N	163.43 W
Kruševac	38	43.35 N	21.20 E
Kruševo	38	41.22 N	21.14 E
Krušinovka	76	53.14 N	29.50 E
Krušné hory (Erzgebirge) ⋏	54	50.30 N	13.15 E
Kruszwica	30	52.41 N	18.19 E
Krutaja, Ross.	24	63.02 N	54.38 E
Krutaja, Ross.	86	57.24 N	76.27 E
Krutaja Gorka	86	55.25 N	73.15 E
Krutcy	76	57.10 N	29.23 E
Krutec, Ross.	76	60.17 N	39.25 E
Krutec, Ross.	82	56.10 N	38.33 E
Kruticha, Ross.	86	53.58 N	81.14 E
Kruticha, Ross.	86	56.49 N	77.10 E
Krutinka	86	56.01 N	71.31 E
Krutoje	76	52.26 N	37.28 E
Krutoj Log	86	57.53 N	58.14 E
Krutoj Majdan	80	55.35 N	44.04 E
Krutyje Verchi	82	54.19 N	36.26 E
Kruunupyy → Kronoby	26	63.43 N	23.02 E
Kruzenšterna, proliv ʉ	74	48.30 N	153.50 E
Kruzof Island I	180	57.10 N	135.40 W
Krydor	184	52.47 N	107.03 W
Krylatskoje ⊕[8]	265b	55.45 N	37.26 E
Krylbo	40	60.08 N	16.13 E
Krylovskaja	78	46.07 N	39.19 E
Krym	83	47.19 N	39.31 E
Krym, Respublika □[3]	78	45.00 N	34.00 E
Krymsk	78	44.56 N	37.59 E
Krymskij	78	47.40 N	40.46 E
Krymskije gory ⋏	78	44.45 N	34.25 E
Krymskij poluostrov (Crimea) ›[1]	78	45.00 N	34.00 E
Krymskij zapovednik ⊕[4]	78	44.42 N	34.12 E
Krymskoje	83	48.45 N	38.48 E
Krynica	30	49.25 N	20.56 E
Krynka ≃	83	47.36 N	38.47 E
Kryžina, chrebet ⋏	88	54.00 N	95.00 E
Kryžopol'	78	48.23 N	28.52 E
Krzepice	30	50.58 N	18.44 E
Krzeszowice	30	50.09 N	19.39 E
Krzeszyce	54	52.36 N	15.01 E
Krzna ≃	30	52.08 N	23.31 E
Krzywiń	30	51.58 N	16.49 E
Krzyż	30	52.54 N	16.01 E
Ksar Chellala	148	35.13 N	2.18 E
Ksar el Barka	150	18.24 N	12.13 W
Ksar-el-Kebir	148	35.01 N	5.54 W
Ksar-el-Seghir	34	35.50 N	5.32 W
Ksar Hellal	36	35.39 N	10.54 E
Ksaverovka	78	50.03 N	30.12 E
Ksel, Djebel ∧	148	33.44 N	1.10 E
Kšen' ≃	76	52.23 N	37.44 E
Ksenjevka	88	53.34 N	118.44 E
Ksenofontova	24	60.58 N	56.12 E
Kšenskij	78	51.52 N	37.43 E
Książ Wielkopolski	30	52.05 N	17.14 E
Ksob, Oued ≃	36	35.49 N	7.53 E
Ksour, Monts des ⋏	148	32.45 N	0.30 W
Ksour Essaf	148	35.25 N	11.00 E
Kstovo	80	56.11 N	44.11 E
Kū', Wādī al- V	140	13.37 N	25.15 E
Kuah	114	6.19 N	99.51 E
Kuai ≃	100	33.09 N	117.32 E
Kuala, Indon.	112	2.55 N	105.48 E
Kuala, Indon.	114	3.32 N	98.24 E
Kualabee	114	4.24 N	96.03 E
Kuala Berang	114	5.04 N	103.01 E
Kualacenako	112	0.28 S	102.40 E
Kuala Kangsar	114	4.46 N	100.56 E
Kualakapuas	112	3.01 S	114.21 E
Kuala Kedah	114	6.06 N	100.18 E
Kuala Kelawang	114	2.56 N	102.05 E
Kuala Kerai	114	5.32 N	102.12 E
Kuala Kerau	114	3.43 N	102.22 E
Kualakeriau	112	0.50 N	113.20 E
Kuala Ketil	114	5.36 N	100.39 E
Kuala Kubu Baharu	114	3.34 N	101.39 E
Kuala Kurau	114	5.01 N	100.26 E
Kualakurun	112	1.07 S	113.53 E
Kualalangsa	114	4.32 N	98.01 E
Kuala Lipis	114	4.11 N	102.03 E
Kuala Lumpur	114	3.10 N	101.42 E
Kuala Lumpur □[3]	114	3.10 N	101.42 E
Kualamanjual	112	1.25 S	112.00 E
Kuala Nerang	114	6.15 N	100.36 E
Kualapesaguan	112	2.01 S	110.08 E
Kuala Pilah	114	2.44 N	102.15 E
Kualapuu	229a	21.09 N	157.02 W
Kuala Selangor	114	3.21 N	101.15 E
Kualasimpang	114	4.17 N	98.03 E
Kuala Terengganu	114	5.20 N	103.08 E
Kualu ≃	114	2.45 N	100.00 E
Kuamut	112	5.13 N	117.30 E
Kuamut ≃	112	5.13 N	117.32 E
Kuanbang	98	40.29 N	120.04 E
Kuancheng, Zhg.	98	40.37 N	118.31 E
Kuancheng, Zhg.	105	40.38 N	118.27 E
Kuandang	112	0.52 N	122.55 E
Kuandian	98	40.43 N	124.44 E
Kuando → Cuando ≃	152	18.27 S	23.32 E
Kuanhsi	100	24.48 N	121.10 E
Kuanmiao	100	22.58 N	120.19 E
Kuanshan	100	23.03 N	121.09 E
Kuan Shan ∧	100	23.14 N	120.54 E
Kuantan	114	3.48 N	103.20 E
Kuantan ≃	114	3.50 N	103.17 E
Kuanyin	100	25.02 N	121.04 E
Kuanyün → Guanyun	98	34.20 N	119.17 E
Kuanza → Cuanza ≃	152	9.19 S	13.08 E
Kuba	84	41.22 N	48.31 E
Kuba → Cuba □[1]	240p	21.30 N	80.00 W
Kuban' ≃	72	45.20 N	37.30 E
Kubatly	84	39.22 N	46.34 E
Kubbī	140	11.08 N	25.14 E
Kubbum	140	11.47 N	23.47 E
Kubena ≃	76	59.36 N	39.39 E
Kubenskoje	76	59.26 N	39.40 E

≃ River	Fluß	Río	Rivière	Rio
≋ Canal	Kanal	Canal	Canal	Canal
∟ Waterfall, Rapids	Wasserfall, Stromschnellen	Cascada, Rápidos	Chute d'eau, Rapides	Cascata, Rápidos
ʉ Strait	Meeresstraße	Estrecho	Détroit	Estreito
⊂ Bay, Gulf	Bucht, Golf	Bahía, Golfo	Baie, Golfe	Baía, Golfo
⊜ Lake, Lakes	See, Seen	Lago, Lagos	Lac, Lacs	Lago, Lagos
≡ Swamp	Sumpf	Pantano	Marais	Pântano
⍓ Ice Features, Glacier	Eis- und Gletscherformen	Accidentes Glaciales	Formes glaciaires	Acidentes glaciares
⊤ Other Hydrographic Features	Andere Hydrographische Objekte	Otros Elementos Hidrográficos	Autres données hydrographiques	Outros acidentes hidrográficos
✢ Submarine Features	Untermeerische Objekte	Accidentes Submarinos	Formes de relief sous-marin	Acidentes submarinos
□ Political Unit	Politische Einheit	Unidad Politica	Entité politique	Unidade política
ʋ Cultural Institution	Kulturelle Institution	Institución Cultural	Institution culturelle	Institução cultural
⊥ Historical Site	Historische Stätte	Sitio Histórico	Site historique	Sitio histórico
♠ Recreational Site	Erholungs- und Ferienort	Sitio de Recreo	Centre de loisirs	Area de Lazer
⊠ Airport	Flughafen	Aeropuerto	Aéroport	Aeroporto
■ Military Installation	Militäranlage	Instalación Militar	Installation militaire	Instalação militar
⊕ Miscellaneous	Verschiedenes	Misceláneo	Divers	Diversos

Name	Page	Lat.	Long.
Kubenskoje, ozero ⊜	76	59.40 N	39.25 E
Kubiki	94	37.11 N	138.20 E
Kubinka	82	55.35 N	36.43 E
Kubitzer Bodden c	54	54.24 N	13.12 E
Küblis	58	46.55 N	9.47 E
Kubn'a ≃	80	55.31 N	48.27 E
Kubokawa	96	33.12 N	133.08 E
Kubor, Mount ∧	164	6.05 S	144.45 E
Kubr' ≃	82	56.52 N	38.17 E
Kubrat	38	43.48 N	26.30 E
Kubu	115b	8.16 S	115.35 E
Kubuchaj	88	50.30 N	114.48 E
Kubu Gajah	114	5.10 N	100.41 E
Kubumesaai	112	1.31 N	115.06 E
Kubutambahan	115b	8.05 S	115.10 E
Kučema	24	65.37 N	42.28 E
Kučen'ajevo	80	54.44 N	46.24 E
Kučevo	38	44.27 N	21.44 E
Kuchaiburi	126	22.16 N	86.10 E
Kuchāman	120	27.09 N	74.52 E
Kuch'ang-ni	98	40.09 N	124.46 E
Kuchelebai	154	1.29 N	35.01 E
Kuchen Spitze ∧	58	47.03 N	10.14 E
Kuchinarai	110	16.32 N	104.04 E
Kuching	112	1.33 N	110.20 E
Kuchinoerabu-jima I	93b	30.28 N	130.12 E
Kuchino-shima I	93b	29.57 N	129.57 E
Kuchiwa	96	34.53 N	132.55 E
Kuchl	64	47.37 N	13.09 E
Kūchnay Darweyshān	128	30.59 N	64.11 E
Kuchterin Lug	89	52.25 N	128.05 E
Kuchtinka	82	54.29 N	38.10 E
Kučino	265b	55.45 N	37.58 E
Kučkak	85	40.15 N	70.20 E
Kučki	80	53.01 N	44.29 E
Kuçovë	38	40.48 N	19.54 E
Küçük Ağrı Dağı ∧	84	39.40 N	44.25 E
Küçükbahçe	130	38.33 N	26.24 E
Küçükbakkal ◆8	267b	40.58 N	29.06 E
Küçükçekmece ◆8	267b	40.59 N	28.46 E
Küçükçekmece Gölü ⊜	267b	41.00 N	28.46 E
Küçükköy ◆8	267b	41.04 N	28.54 E
Küçükkuyu	130	39.32 N	26.36 E
Kučukskoje, ozero ⊜	86	52.42 N	79.46 E
Kucur, Tanjung >	115a	8.39 S	114.34 E
Kučurgan ≃	78	46.43 N	29.53 E
Kūd	123	33.05 N	75.17 E
Kuda ≃	88	52.25 N	104.08 E
Kudaka-jima I	174m	26.09 N	127.54 E
Kudamatsu	96	34.00 N	131.52 E
Kudanggou	104	41.06 N	124.00 E
Kudap	114	1.17 N	102.26 E
Kudara, Ross.	88	52.13 N	106.39 E
Kudara, Taj.	85	38.25 N	72.41 E
Kudara ≃	85	38.19 N	72.28 E
Kudara-Somon	88	50.10 N	107.25 E
Kudat	112	6.53 N	116.50 E
Kudejevskij	86	54.52 N	56.46 E
Kudene	164	6.14 S	134.39 E
Kudever'	76	56.47 N	29.23 E
Kudinovo	82	55.45 N	38.12 E
Kudirkos Naumiestis	76	54.46 N	22.53 E
Kudongho	98	35.31 N	126.29 E
Kudoyama	96	34.17 N	135.34 E
Kudremukh ∧	122	13.08 N	75.16 E
Kudrovo	265a	59.54 N	30.31 E
Kudus	115a	6.48 S	110.50 E
Kudyat al-Islām	142	27.32 N	30.45 E
Kudymkar	86	59.01 N	54.37 E
Kuee Ruins ⊥	229d	19.21 N	155.23 W
Kueishan Tao I	100	24.51 N	121.57 E
Kueisui → Hohhot	102	40.51 N	111.40 E
Kueiyang → Guiyang	102	26.35 N	106.43 E
Kuekvun' ≃	180	69.14 N	179.25 E
Kuĕnlun → Kunlun Shan ⋏	120	36.30 N	88.00 E
Kuerbin	89	49.25 N	128.59 E
K'uerhlo → Korla	90	41.44 N	86.09 E
Kufayr az-Zayt	132	33.26 N	35.44 E
Kufayr Yābūs	132	33.42 N	36.01 E
Kufrinjah	132	32.18 N	35.42 E
Kufstein	64	47.35 N	12.10 E
Kufūr Bilshāy	142	30.51 N	30.48 E
Kufūr Najm	142	30.44 N	31.35 E
Kuga, Nihon	96	34.05 N	132.05 E
Kuga, Nihon	96	33.56 N	132.16 E
Kugaluk ≃	180	69.10 N	131.00 W
Kugaly	86	44.29 N	78.40 E
Kugarčino	80	55.33 N	50.29 E
Kugart ≃	85	40.52 N	72.53 E
Kugas	85	38.21 N	70.48 E
Kugej	83	46.53 N	39.19 E
Kugesi	80	56.02 N	47.18 E
Kugmallit Bay c	180	69.33 N	133.25 W
Kugojeja ≃	78	46.34 N	39.38 E
Kuguno	94	36.03 N	137.16 E
Kuḥaylī	140	19.25 N	32.50 E
Kühbach	60	48.29 N	11.11 E
Kūhdasht	128	33.32 N	47.36 E
Kūh Lab, Ra's-e >	128	25.17 N	60.28 E
Kuḥlīyah, Wādī V	142	30.05 N	31.58 E
Kühlungsborn	54	54.09 N	11.43 E
Kuhmo	26	64.08 N	29.31 E
Kuhmoinen	26	61.34 N	25.11 E
Kühnhausen	54	51.02 N	10.58 E
Kühnsdorf	61	46.37 N	14.37 E
Kūhpāyeh	128	32.43 N	52.26 E
Kühren	54	51.20 N	12.50 E
Kuhstedt	52	53.23 N	8.58 E
Kui	164	7.30 S	147.15 E
Kuibyschew → Samara	80	53.12 N	50.09 E
Kuidesu	98	41.46 N	119.29 E
Kuidou	100	25.10 N	118.11 E
Kuikkol', ozero ⊜	86	50.57 N	64.30 E
Kuikui, Lae o >	229a	20.36 N	156.35 W
Kuilāpāl	126	22.50 N	86.38 E
Kuinre	52	52.47 N	5.50 E
Kuiseb ≃	156	22.59 S	14.31 E
Kuishi-yama ∧, Nihon	96	33.51 N	133.35 E
Kuishi-yama ∧, Nihon	96	33.40 N	133.31 E
Kuitan	100	23.05 N	115.58 E
Kuiten Uul ∧	86	49.08 N	87.49 E
Kuito	152	12.22 S	16.56 E
Kuiu Island I	180	56.45 N	134.10 W
Kuivaniemi	26	65.35 N	25.11 E
Kuivastu	76	58.35 N	23.22 E
Kuja, Ross.	24	67.46 N	53.10 E
Kuja, Ross.	24	65.05 N	40.06 E
Kujal'nickij liman ⊜	78	46.40 N	30.42 E
Kujang	98	39.52 N	126.01 E
Kujani Game Reserve ◆4	150	7.10 N	0.50 W
Kujawy ◆1	30	52.45 N	18.30 E
Kujbyšev → Samara, Ross.	80	53.12 N	50.09 E
Kujbyšev, Ross.	86	55.27 N	78.19 E
Kujbyševka	78	47.37 N	31.42 E
Kujbyševo, Ross.	83	47.49 N	38.55 E
Kujbyševo, Ukr.	78	44.38 N	33.52 E
Kujbyševo, Ukr.	78	47.22 N	36.39 E
Kujbyševo, Uzb.	85	40.22 N	71.17 E
Kujbyševskij, Kaz.	86	53.15 N	66.51 E
Kujbyševskij, Uzb.	72	37.52 N	68.44 E
Kujbyševskij Zaton	80	55.09 N	49.12 E
Kujbyševskoje vodochranilišče ⊜1	80	54.30 N	48.30 E
Kujeda	86	56.26 N	55.35 E
Kujgan	86	45.25 N	74.10 E
Kujgenkol'	80	49.17 N	47.59 E
Kuji	92	40.11 N	141.46 E
Kuji ≃	94	36.29 N	140.37 E
Kujirai	268	35.56 N	139.27 E
Kujl'uk	85	41.15 N	69.20 E
Kujman'	76	52.52 N	39.16 E
Kujŏng-ni	98	37.53 N	125.54 E
Kujtun	88	54.21 N	101.29 E
Kujū	96	33.01 N	131.18 E
Kujūkuri	94	35.32 N	140.25 E
Kujūkuri-hama ≛2	94	35.35 N	140.30 E
Kujū-san ∧	96	33.05 N	131.15 E
Kuk ∧	64	46.16 N	13.45 E
Kuk ≃	180	70.36 N	160.00 W
Kukaklek Lake ⊜	180	59.09 N	155.20 W
Kukalaya ≃	236	13.39 N	83.37 W
Kukan	89	49.12 N	133.28 E
Kukarino	82	55.31 N	35.59 E
Kukawa	146	12.56 N	13.35 E
Kukerin	162	33.11 S	118.05 E
Kukës	38	42.05 N	20.24 E
Kuke Shan ⋏	85	40.00 N	75.00 E
Kuki	94	36.04 N	139.40 E
Kukipi	164	8.10 S	146.05 E
Kukkola	26	65.59 N	24.04 E
Kukmirn	61	47.04 N	16.13 E
Kukmor	80	56.13 N	50.54 E
Kukoboj	76	58.42 N	39.54 E
Kukol'	76	59.52 N	32.35 E
Kükong → Shaoguan	100	24.50 N	113.37 E
Kukpowruk ≃	180	69.35 N	163.00 W
Kukpuk ≃	180	68.23 N	166.20 W
Kukshi	120	22.12 N	74.45 E
Kukuj	76	59.21 N	32.33 E
Kuku-Nor → Qinghai Hu ⊜	102	36.50 N	100.20 E
Kukup	114	1.19 N	103.27 E
Kuku Point >	174a	19.18 N	166.34 E
Kukuri Mukuri Char I	126	21.56 N	90.39 E
Kukuštan	86	57.38 N	56.30 E
Kula, Blg.	38	43.53 N	22.31 E
Kula, Jugo.	38	45.36 N	19.32 E
Kula, Tür.	130	38.32 N	28.40 E
Kula, Hi., U.S.	229a	20.52 N	156.40 W
Kul'ab	120	37.55 N	69.46 E
Kul'ab □4	85	38.15 N	69.45 E
Kulāchi	123	31.56 N	70.27 E
Kulagi	76	52.56 N	32.24 E
Kula Gulf ʯ	175e	8.05 S	157.18 E
Kulai	114	1.40 N	103.36 E
Kulaj	86	57.42 N	75.15 E
Kula Kangri ∧	124	28.03 N	90.27 E
Kulākh	144	21.18 N	40.41 E
Kulakovo, Ross.	82	55.06 N	37.28 E
Kulakovo, Ross.	86	58.06 N	93.57 E
Kulakši	86	47.12 N	55.24 E
Kulal, Mount ∧	154	2.43 N	36.56 E
Kulanak	85	41.22 N	75.31 E
Kulandy	86	46.08 N	59.31 E
Kulanutpes ≃	86	50.21 N	69.08 E
Kular	74	70.41 N	134.22 E
Kulassein Island I	116	6.25 N	120.41 E
Kulaura	120	24.32 N	92.03 E
Kulautuva	76	54.58 N	23.38 E
Kulaykilī	140	11.21 N	25.36 E
Kul'či	89	53.33 N	139.36 E
Kuldīga	76	56.58 N	21.59 E
Kuldja → Yining	86	43.54 N	81.21 E
Kul'dur	89	49.13 N	131.38 E
Kule	156	23.05 S	20.05 E
Kulebaki	80	55.24 N	42.32 E
Kulejevo	86	59.40 N	80.59 E
Kulen Vakuf	36	44.34 N	16.06 E
Kulešovka	83	47.05 N	39.33 E
Kulevčinskij	86	53.12 N	61.26 E
Kulgām	123	33.39 N	75.01 E
Kulgera	162	25.50 S	133.18 E
Kulgunino	86	53.35 N	56.56 E
Kuligi	80	58.11 N	53.46 E
Kulikov	78	49.58 N	24.04 E
Kulikovka, Ross.	80	52.14 N	47.36 E
Kulikovka, Ukr.	78	51.23 N	31.37 E
Kulikovo	76	52.14 N	39.35 E
Kulikovskij	80	50.51 N	42.34 E
Kulim	114	5.22 N	100.34 E
Kulin	162	32.40 S	118.10 E
Kuliushucun	105	40.07 N	116.34 E
Kulju	26	61.23 N	23.46 E
Kulkyne Creek ≃	166	30.16 S	144.12 E
Kullaberg ⋏2	41	56.18 N	12.30 E
Kullamaa	76	58.53 N	24.05 E
Küllenhahn ◆8	263	51.14 N	7.08 E
Küllstedt	56	51.16 N	10.17 E
Kullu	123	31.58 N	77.06 E
Kulm	198	46.18 N	98.57 W
Kulmbach	54	50.06 N	11.27 E
Kulnura	170	33.14 S	151.13 E
Kuloj, Ross.	24	64.58 N	43.28 E
Kuloj, Ross.	24	61.02 N	42.29 E
Kuloj ≃, Ross.	24	66.03 N	43.22 E
Kuloj ≃, Ross.	76	60.25 N	42.30 E
Kuloli	85	39.22 N	68.03 E
Kulongshan	98	41.43 N	116.54 E
Kulongshanpuzi	104	41.16 N	123.59 E
Kulotino	76	58.27 N	33.21 E
Kulp	130	38.30 N	41.02 E
Kulpahar	124	25.19 N	79.39 E
Kulpara	168b	34.04 S	138.02 E
Kulpawn ≃	150	10.21 N	1.05 W
Kulpi	126	22.06 N	88.15 E
Kul'pino	82	56.18 N	37.09 E
Kulpmont	208	40.47 N	76.28 W
Kulpsville	285	40.15 N	75.20 W
Kul'sary	86	46.59 N	54.01 E
Kulsbjerge ⋏2	41	55.01 N	12.01 E
Külsheim	56	49.40 N	9.31 E
Kültepe ⊥	130	38.44 N	35.34 E
Kulti	126	23.44 N	86.51 E
Kultikri	126	22.10 N	87.09 E
Kultuk	88	51.44 N	103.42 E
Kulu	130	39.06 N	33.05 E
Kuluha, Jabal ∧	140	15.31 N	23.25 E
Kulumadau	164	9.03 S	152.43 E
Kulunda	86	52.35 N	78.57 E
Kulunda ≃	86	52.59 N	79.48 E
Kulundinskaja step' ≚	86	53.00 N	79.00 E
Kulundinskoje, ozero ⊜	86	53.00 N	79.36 E
Kuluqi	89	50.23 N	124.13 E
Kulwin	166	35.02 S	142.33 E
Kum ≃	130	38.38 N	27.32 E
Kuma	96	33.39 N	132.54 E
Kuma ≃, Nihon	92	32.30 N	130.34 E
Kuma ≃, Ross.	72	44.56 N	47.00 E
Kuma ≃, Ross.	86	59.32 N	66.45 E
Kumagaya	94	36.08 N	139.23 E
Kumai, Indon.	112	3.23 S	112.33 E
Kumai, Indon.	112	2.44 S	111.43 E
Kumai, Teluk c	112	3.00 S	111.43 E
Kumaishi	92a	42.08 N	139.59 E
Kumajri	84	40.48 N	43.50 E
Kumakanda	88	52.44 N	116.55 E
Kumalarang	116	7.44 N	123.08 E
Kumamba, Kepulauan II	164	1.36 S	138.45 E
Kumamoto	92	32.48 N	130.43 E
Kumamoto □5	96	32.58 N	130.55 E
Kumano, Nihon	92	33.54 N	136.05 E
Kumano, Nihon	96	34.20 N	132.34 E
Kumano ≃	92	33.44 N	136.01 E
Kumano-nada ⊤2	92	33.47 N	136.20 E
Kumanovo	38	42.08 N	21.43 E
Kumār ≃1, Bngl.	126	23.11 N	90.10 E
Kumār ≃1, Bngl.	126	23.31 N	89.28 E
Kumara, N.Z.	172	42.38 S	171.11 E
Kumara, Ross.	89	51.37 N	126.47 E
Kumārapālaiyam	122	11.28 N	77.43 E
Kumardhubi	126	23.48 N	86.43 E
Kumarganj	126	22.59 N	87.44 E
Kumārghāt	120	24.04 N	92.04 E
Kumārgrām	124	26.37 N	89.50 E
Kumāri ≃	126	22.57 N	86.48 E
Kumārkhāli	124	23.51 N	89.15 E
Kumarl	162	32.47 S	121.33 E
Kumasi	150	6.41 N	1.35 W
Kumatori	270	34.24 N	135.22 E
Kumawa, Pegunungan ⋏	164	3.50 S	132.50 E
Kumba	152	4.38 N	9.25 E
Kumbakonam	122	10.58 N	79.23 E
Kumba Pits	156	18.45 S	24.45 E
Kumbar	140	12.03 N	30.16 E
Kumbarilla	166	27.19 S	150.53 E
Kumbe	164	8.21 S	140.13 E
Kumbel'	85	42.30 N	73.11 E
Kŭmch'ŏn	98	38.10 N	126.29 E
Kum-Dag	128	39.16 N	54.35 E
Kumdah ⊤4	144	20.23 N	45.05 E
Kumdan ∧	123	35.09 N	77.35 E
Kumdanlı	130	38.19 N	30.59 E
Kume	96	35.03 N	133.54 E
Kume-jima I	93b	26.20 N	126.47 E
Kumenan	96	34.56 N	133.58 E
Kumeny	80	58.07 N	49.56 E
Kŭm-gang ≃	98	36.00 N	126.40 E
Kŭmgang-san ∧	98	38.35 N	128.10 E
Kŭmhwa	98	38.17 N	127.28 E
Kumi	154	1.29 N	33.56 E
Kumihama	96	35.36 N	134.55 E
Kuminovskoje	86	57.48 N	64.07 E
Kuminskij	86	58.40 N	66.04 E
Kumiyama	270	34.53 N	135.45 E
Kumizawa ◆8	268	35.23 N	139.31 E
Kumköy ◆8	267b	41.15 N	29.02 E
Kumla	40	59.08 N	15.08 E
Kumli	84	43.58 N	46.04 E
Kumlinge I	26	60.16 N	20.47 E
Kumluca, Tür.	130	36.22 N	30.18 E
Kumluca, Tür.	130	41.27 N	32.28 E
Kummelnäs	40	59.21 N	18.17 E
Kummerow	54	54.17 N	12.53 E
Kummerower See ⊜	54	53.49 N	12.52 E
Kümmersbruck	60	49.25 N	11.53 E
Kumo	146	10.03 N	11.13 E
Kŭmŏ-do I	98	34.31 N	127.45 E
Kumon Range ⋏	102	26.30 N	97.15 E
Kumora	88	55.53 N	111.13 E
Kumosō-yama ∧	96	33.54 N	134.18 E
Kumotori-yama ∧	94	35.51 N	138.57 E
Kumphawapi	110	17.07 N	103.01 E
Kumrābād	126	24.10 N	87.16 E
Kumru	130	40.53 N	37.17 E
Kŭmsan	98	36.07 N	127.30 E
Kŭmsan-ni	98	37.55 N	125.41 E
Kumsenga	154	3.47 S	30.25 E
Kumta	122	14.25 N	74.24 E
Kumu	154	3.04 N	25.09 E
Kumu ≃	114	1.24 N	100.43 E
Kumuch	84	42.11 N	47.07 E
Kumukahi, Cape >	229d	19.31 N	154.49 W
Kumukuli	120	37.33 N	88.50 E
Kumusi ≃	164	8.35 S	148.00 E
Kümüx	86	42.14 N	88.11 E
Kumzār	128	26.20 N	56.25 E
Kuna	202	43.29 N	116.25 W
Kunar (Konar) ≃	123	34.25 N	70.32 E
Kunašak	86	55.43 N	61.36 E
Kunashiri-tō → Kunašir, ostrov I	92a	44.10 N	146.00 E
Kunašir, ostrov (Kunashiri-tō) I	92a	44.10 N	146.00 E
Kun'batar	84	44.17 N	45.34 E
Kuncheng Hu ⊜	106	31.35 N	120.45 E
Kunchhā	124	28.08 N	84.20 E
Kunc'ovo ◆8	265b	55.44 N	37.26 E
Kunda, Eesti	76	59.29 N	26.32 E
Kunda, Zaïre	154	3.57 S	26.35 E
Kunda Hills ⋏2	122	11.10 N	76.30 E
Kundahit	126	23.58 N	87.10 E
Kundam	124	23.13 N	80.21 E
Kundāpura	122	13.38 N	74.42 E
Kundar ≃	120	31.56 N	69.19 E
Kundat	86	55.14 N	87.51 E
Kundelungu, Parc National de ♦	154	10.30 S	27.45 E
Kunderu ≃	122	14.38 N	78.42 E
Kundi	154	1.08 S	40.41 E
Kundiān	123	32.27 N	71.28 E
Kundiawa	164	6.00 S	145.00 E
Kundima	164	4.14 S	143.52 E
Kundl	64	47.28 N	11.59 E
Kundla	120	21.20 N	71.18 E
Kundr'učje ≃	83	47.52 N	40.15 E
Kundur, Pulau I	112	0.45 N	103.26 E
Kunene (Cunene) ≃	152	17.20 S	11.50 E
Kunersdorf, Forst ◆3	264a	52.17 N	12.59 E
Kunes	24	70.21 N	26.31 E
Künes ≃	86	43.55 N	80.55 E
Kunga ≃1	126	21.45 N	89.30 E
Kungälv	26	57.52 N	11.58 E
Kungana	146	7.50 N	10.42 E
Kungchuling → Huaide	89	43.32 N	124.50 E
Kungej-Alatau, chrebet ⋏	85	42.50 N	77.00 E
Kunggyü Yumco ⊜	124	30.35 N	82.09 E
Kunghit Island I	182	52.06 N	131.04 W
Kunghsi	100	24.37 N	121.16 E
Kung-pei-tien	269d	25.06 N	121.38 E
Kungrad	86	43.06 N	58.54 E
Kungsängen	40	59.29 N	17.45 E
Kungsängen flygplats ⊠	40	58.36 N	16.15 E
Kungsbacka	26	57.29 N	12.04 E
Kungsgården	40	60.36 N	16.37 E
Kungshamn	26	58.22 N	11.15 E
Kungsör	40	59.25 N	16.05 E
Kungu	152	2.47 N	19.12 E
Kungur	86	57.25 N	56.57 E
Kunhār ≃	123	34.17 N	73.29 E
Kunhegyes	30	47.22 N	20.38 E
Kunhing	110	21.18 N	98.26 E
Kuni	94	36.35 N	138.38 E
Kunia	229c	21.29 N	158.07 W
Kunigami	174m	26.45 N	128.10 E
Kunimi	96	33.41 N	131.36 E
Kuningan	115a	6.59 S	108.29 E
Kunisaki	96	33.33 N	131.45 E
Kunisaki-hantō >1	96	33.30 N	131.40 E
Kunitachi	268	35.41 N	139.26 E
Kuni Vyselki	82	54.18 N	38.41 E
Kunja	76	56.18 N	30.59 E
Kunja ≃, Ross.	76	57.09 N	31.10 E
Kunja ≃, Ross.	82	56.31 N	38.12 E
Kunjāh	123	32.32 N	73.59 E
Kunje	83	49.23 N	37.15 E
Kunkle	216	41.38 N	84.30 W
Kunkletown	210	40.51 N	75.27 W
Kunkuri	124	22.45 N	83.57 E
Kunlong	110	23.25 N	98.39 E
Kunlun Shan ⋏	120	36.30 N	88.00 E
Kunming	102	25.05 N	102.40 E
Kunming Hu ⊜	271a	39.59 N	116.15 E
Kunmunya Aboriginal Reserve ◆4	164	15.45 S	124.45 E
Kunnamkulam	122	10.39 N	76.05 E
Kunost'	76	60.01 N	37.38 E
Kunovice	30	49.03 N	17.29 E
Kunow	54	53.00 N	12.07 E
Kunowice	54	52.20 N	14.50 E
Kunrau	54	52.35 N	11.01 E
Kunsan	98	35.58 N	126.41 E
Kunshan	106	31.23 N	120.57 E
Kunszentmárton	30	46.51 N	20.18 E
Kuntair	150	13.32 N	16.13 W
Kuntaur	150	13.40 N	14.48 W
Kuntiki	86	58.29 N	76.24 E
Kunting	100	29.48 N	121.56 E
Kuntshankoie	152	3.20 S	23.34 E
Kuntuolun	102	45.13 N	115.21 E
Kununurra	164	15.47 S	128.44 E
Kunwi	98	36.15 N	128.34 E
Kunya	150	12.14 N	8.34 E
Kunyo	144	6.17 N	42.33 E
Kunžak	61	49.07 N	15.11 E
Künzell	56	50.33 N	9.42 E
Künzelsau	56	49.16 N	9.41 E
Künzing	60	48.40 N	13.05 E
Kunzulu	152	3.29 S	16.09 E
Kuocang Shan ⋏	100	28.36 N	120.30 E
Kuohsing	100	24.02 N	120.51 E
Kuokegan	120	37.30 N	89.55 E
Kuolajarvi	24	66.58 N	29.12 E
Kuop I1	175c	7.03 N	151.56 E
Kuopio	26	62.54 N	27.41 E
Kuopion lääni □4	26	63.00 N	27.30 E
Kuortane	26	62.48 N	23.30 E
Kupa ≃	36	45.28 N	16.24 E
Kup'abal	271b	37.37 N	126.54 E
Kupang	112	10.10 S	123.35 E
Kupang, Teluk c	112	10.04 S	123.40 E
Kup'ansk	83	49.42 N	37.38 E
Kupanskoje	82	56.51 N	38.43 E
Kup'ansk-Uzlovoj	83	49.39 N	37.39 E
Kuparuk ≃	180	70.25 N	148.55 W
Kupava	80	51.07 N	42.57 E
Kupavna	265b	55.45 N	38.08 E
Kuper Island I	224	48.58 N	123.39 W
Kupferberg	263	51.09 N	7.27 E
Kupferdreh ◆8	263	51.23 N	7.05 E
Kupfermühle	41	54.50 N	9.24 E
Kupferzell	56	49.14 N	9.41 E
Kupiano	164	10.05 S	148.11 E
Kupičev	78	51.00 N	24.44 E
Kupino	86	54.22 N	77.18 E
Kupiškis	76	55.50 N	24.58 E
Küplü, Tür.	130	41.07 N	26.21 E
Küplü, Tür.	130	40.06 N	30.00 E
Kupol, gora ∧	180	68.38 N	174.45 E
Kuppenheim	56	48.49 N	8.15 E
Kupper Airport ⊠	276	40.31 N	74.36 W
Kupreanof	180	56.49 N	132.57 W
Kupreanof Island I	180	56.50 N	133.30 W
Kupreanof Point >	180	55.34 N	159.35 W
Kupres	36	44.00 N	17.17 E
Küps	54	50.11 N	11.16 E
Kupuri	89	54.44 N	130.30 E
Kuqa	90	41.43 N	82.54 E
Kur ≃	89	48.44 N	134.14 E
Kur, Pulau I	164	5.20 S	132.00 E
Kura (Kuruçay) ≃, Asia	84	39.24 N	49.19 E
Kura ≃, Ross.	84	44.06 N	44.57 E
Kurabuchi	94	36.25 N	138.48 E
Kur'ačeje	83	48.10 N	39.37 E
Kur'ačevka, Ukr.	83	49.39 N	38.42 E
Kur'ačevka, Ukr.	83	49.22 N	39.36 E
Kurach	84	41.36 N	47.46 E
Kurach ≃	84	41.40 N	48.11 E
Kurachovka	83	48.02 N	37.23 E
Kurachovo	83	47.59 N	37.16 E
Kuragaty	85	43.06 N	72.59 E
Kuragaty ≃	85	43.57 N	73.34 E
Kuragino	86	53.53 N	92.40 E
Kurahashi	96	34.06 N	132.30 E
Kurahashi-jima I	96	34.08 N	132.31 E
Kuraj	86	56.42 N	95.29 E
Kurajlysaj	80	50.07 N	51.51 E
Kurakaki	270	34.59 N	135.28 E
Kurakino, Ross.	80	52.33 N	44.03 E
Kurakino, Ross.	82	54.30 N	35.48 E
Kurakovo	82	54.05 N	37.14 E
Kūrāli	123	30.50 N	76.35 E
Kuram	85	43.33 N	78.08 E
Kuramā', Ḥarrat ≛9	128	24.30 N	40.15 E
Kurama-yama ∧	96	35.07 N	135.46 E
Kuraminskij chrebet ⋏	85	40.45 N	70.10 E
Kuramo Waters c	273a	6.26 N	3.26 E
Kuranami	268	35.27 N	140.00 E
Kuraon	124	24.59 N	82.05 E
Kurar ◆8	272c	19.11 N	72.52 E
Kurašasaj	86	50.18 N	56.55 E
Kurashiki	96	34.35 N	133.46 E
Kurasiki → Kurashiki	96	34.35 N	133.46 E
Kurate	96	33.47 N	130.41 E
Kurauli	124	27.24 N	78.59 E
Kuraymah	140	18.33 N	31.51 E
Kurayoshi	96	35.26 N	133.49 E
Kurayyimah	132	32.16 N	35.36 E
Kurba	80	57.34 N	39.32 E
Kurba ≃	88	52.02 N	108.30 E
Kurbağa Gölü ⊜	130	38.21 N	35.17 E
Kurbağalı ≃	267b	40.59 N	29.02 E
Kurbatovo	86	55.34 N	91.10 E
Kurbulik	88	53.45 N	108.57 E
Kurčaloj	84	43.12 N	46.05 E
Kurchatov	78	51.39 N	35.36 E
Kur-Čilik ≃	85	43.50 N	78.06 E
Kurčum	86	48.37 N	83.40 E
Kurdaj	85	43.21 N	74.59 E
K'urdamir	84	40.21 N	48.08 E
Kurdgelauri	84	41.58 N	45.32 E
Kurdistan □9	128	37.00 N	45.00 E
Kurdufān al-Janūbīyah □4	140	11.00 N	30.00 E
Kurdufān ash-Shamālīyah □4	140	14.00 N	29.45 E
Kurd'umovka	83	48.28 N	37.59 E
Kurduvādi	122	18.05 N	75.26 E
Kure, Austl.	164	15.27 S	124.33 E
Kure, Nihon	96	34.14 N	132.34 E
Küre, Tür.	130	41.48 N	33.43 E
Kure Atoll I1	14	28.25 N	178.25 W
Küre Dağları ⋏	130	41.45 N	34.00 E
Kurejka ≃	74	66.30 N	87.12 E
Kurejskaja	88	58.56 N	111.20 E
Kuren'	78	51.09 N	32.44 E
Kurenalus	26	65.21 N	26.59 E
Kurenec	76	54.33 N	26.57 E
Kuresaare	76	58.15 N	22.28 E
Kurgal'džinskij	86	50.36 N	70.01 E
Kurgan	86	55.26 N	65.18 E
Kurgan Mečetnyj, gora ∧2	83	48.06 N	39.21 E
Kurgan Oblast' □4	86	55.30 N	64.30 E
Kurgan-T'ube	120	37.50 N	68.48 E
Kurgan T'ube □4	85	38.15 N	68.50 E
Kurgasyn	86	49.15 N	66.43 E
Kurgatej	88	54.23 N	99.27 E
Kurgolovo	76	59.46 N	28.06 E
Kuria I	14	0.14 N	173.25 E
Kuria Muria Islands → Khurīyā Murīyā, Jazā'ir II	118	17.30 N	56.00 E
Kuriasol	126	22.06 N	86.39 E
Kuridala	166	21.17 S	140.30 E
Kurīgrām	124	25.49 N	89.39 E
Kurihama	268	35.13 N	139.43 E
Kurihashi	94	36.08 N	139.42 E
Kurikka	26	62.37 N	22.25 E
Kurilen → Kuril'skije ostrova II	74	46.10 N	152.00 E
Kurilen-Strasse → Pervyj Kuril'skij proliv ʯ	74	50.50 N	156.36 E
Kuriles, Islas → Kuril'skije ostrova II	74	46.10 N	152.00 E
Kuril Islands → Kuril'skije ostrova II	74	46.10 N	152.00 E
Kurilovka	80	50.44 N	48.02 E
Kuril'sk	74	45.14 N	147.53 E
Kuril'skije ostrova (Kuril Islands) II	74	46.10 N	152.00 E
Kuril Strait → Pervyj Kuril'skij proliv ʯ	74	50.50 N	156.36 E
Kuril Trench ⊕1	6	47.00 N	155.00 E
Kuřim	30	49.18 N	16.32 E
Kurimoto	94	35.49 N	140.30 E
Ku-Ring-Gai Chase National Park ♦	170	33.38 S	151.15 E
Kurinjippadi	122	11.34 N	79.36 E
Kurinskaja kosa >2	84	39.03 N	49.13 E
Kurinwás ≃	236	12.49 N	83.41 W

ENGLISH

Name	Page	Lat.°′	Long.°′
Kuripapango	172	39.23 S	176.21 E
Kuriyama, Nihon	92a	43.03 N	141.47 E
Kuriyama, Nihon	94	36.52 N	139.37 E
Kurja, Ross.	24	61.42 N	57.09 E
Kurja, Ross.	86	51.36 N	82.19 E
Kurjanovskaja	76	60.19 N	41.33 E
Kurkijoki	26	61.18 N	29.54 E
Kurkino, Ross.	76	53.26 N	38.40 E
Kurkino, Ross.	265b	55.53 N	37.23 E
Kurkliai	76	55.25 N	25.03 E
Kurl ◆8	263	51.35 N	7.35 E
Kurla ◆8	272c	19.05 N	72.53 E
Kurlackoje	83	47.21 N	39.03 E
Kurleja	88	52.11 N	119.11 E
Kurlin	80	51.48 N	51.00 E
Kurlovskij	80	55.27 N	40.36 E
Kurmanajevka	80	52.31 N	52.06 E
Kurmani	126	22.47 N	89.53 E
Kurmankol'	80	49.09 N	48.27 E
Kurmenty	85	42.48 N	78.15 E
Kurmuk	140	10.33 N	34.17 E
Kurnell	274a	34.01 S	151.13 E
Kurnell Peninsula >1	274a	34.02 S	15.11 E
Kurnool	122	15.50 N	78.03 E
Kurobane	94	36.51 N	140.07 E
Kurobe	94	36.51 N	137.26 E
Kurobe ≃	94	36.55 N	137.25 E
Kurobe-dam ◆6	94	36.36 N	137.38 E
Kurodashō	96	35.01 N	135.00 E
Kurogi	96	33.12 N	130.40 E
Kurohone	94	36.30 N	139.17 E
Kuroishi	92	40.38 N	140.36 E
Kuroiso	94	36.58 N	140.03 E
Kuroo-tōge)(	96	35.11 N	134.12 E
Kuropatkino, Ross.	80	46.32 N	45.20 E
Kuropatkino, Uzb.	85	39.57 N	67.27 E
Kurort-Darasun	88	51.12 N	113.44 E
Kurose	96	34.19 N	132.40 E
Kurose ≃	96	34.13 N	132.36 E
Kuro-shima I, Nihon	93b	30.50 N	129.57 E
Kuro-shima I, Nihon	175d	24.19 N	124.05 E
Kurosu	268	35.51 N	139.23 E
Kurovo	82	55.49 N	36.00 E
Kurovskoje	82	55.34 N	38.55 E
Kurow	172	44.44 S	170.28 E
Kuroya	268	35.55 N	139.44 E
Kurrajong	170	33.33 S	150.40 E
Kurram	120	30.06 N	66.31 E
Kurram ≃	123	32.36 N	71.20 E
Kurri Kurri	170	32.49 S	151.29 E
Kuršab ≃	85	40.46 N	73.06 E
Kursavka	84	44.28 N	42.31 E
Kursela	124	25.27 N	87.15 E
Kuršėnai	76	56.00 N	22.56 E
Kurseong	120	26.53 N	88.17 E
Kursk	78	51.42 N	36.12 E
Kurskaja	84	44.03 N	44.27 E
Kurskaja kosa >2	76	55.18 N	21.00 E
Kurskij zaliv c	76	55.00 N	21.00 E
Kursk Oblast' □4	78	51.40 N	36.00 E
Kursk Station ◆5	265b	55.46 N	37.40 E
Kuršumlija	38	43.08 N	21.17 E
Kurşunlu, Tür.	130	40.51 N	33.16 E
Kurşunlu, Tür.	130	38.40 N	37.51 E
Kurtalan	130	37.57 N	41.42 E
Kurtamyš	86	54.55 N	64.27 E
Kurtatsch → Cortaccia	64	46.19 N	11.13 E
Kürten, Dtsch.	56	51.03 N	7.16 E
Kurten, Tx., U.S.	222	30.47 N	96.16 W
Kurthasanlı	130	38.20 N	32.11 E
Kurth Lake ⊜	222	31.26 N	94.42 W
Kūrtī	140	18.07 N	31.33 E
Kurtino	82	54.59 N	38.17 E
Kurtinskoje vodochranilišče ⊜1	85	43.50 N	76.20 E
Kurtistown	229d	19.36 N	155.03 W
Kurtoğlu Burnu >	130	36.35 N	28.50 E
Kurtušibinskij chrebet ⋏	88	52.10 N	93.30 E
Kurty ≃	85	44.05 N	76.20 E
Kurtz	218	38.58 N	86.12 W
Kuru, Sūd.	140	7.43 N	26.31 E
Kuru, Suomi	26	61.52 N	23.44 E
Kuru ≃	140	9.08 N	26.57 E
Kurucaşile	130	41.50 N	32.43 E
Kuruçay	130	39.39 N	38.29 E
Kuruçay (Kura) ≃	84	39.24 N	49.19 E
Kuruçeşme ◆8	267b	41.03 N	29.02 E
Kuruktag ⋏	90	41.30 N	90.00 E
Kurum	164	4.45 S	145.55 E
Kuruman	158	27.28 S	23.28 E
Kuruman ≃	158	26.56 S	20.39 E
Kurumanheuwels ⋏2	158	27.40 S	23.25 E
Kurumdy, gora ∧	85	39.28 N	73.32 E
Kurume	96	33.19 N	130.31 E
Kurumkan	88	54.18 N	110.18 E
Kurun ≃	144	5.30 N	34.17 E
Kurunegala	122	7.29 N	80.22 E
Kurungbaja, Tanjung >	115b	8.15 S	120.35 E
Kurung Tank ⊜1	124	22.19 N	82.14 E
Kurunzulaj	88	51.00 N	117.10 E
Kuruqi	89	48.58 N	123.50 E
Kurur, Jabal ∧	140	20.31 N	31.32 E
Kurusaj	85	40.35 N	69.24 E
Kurushima-kaikyo ʯ	96	34.07 N	133.00 E
Kuruson-zan ∧	96	34.12 N	130.58 E
Kurylys	86	48.38 N	60.47 E
Kuryongp'o	98	35.59 N	129.32 E
Kurzeme □9	76	56.50 N	22.30 E
Kusa	86	55.20 N	59.29 E
Kusabe	270	34.31 N	135.29 E
Kuşadası	130	37.51 N	27.15 E
Kuşadası Körfezi c	130	37.50 N	27.08 E
Kusak ≃	86	47.50 N	75.45 E
Kušalino	76	57.07 N	36.05 E
Kusan-ni, Taehan	98	37.43 N	128.49 E
Kusan-ni, Taehan	271b	37.29 N	126.45 E
Kusatsu, Nihon	94	36.37 N	138.36 E
Kusatsu, Nihon	94	35.00 N	135.57 E
Kusawa Lake ⊜	180	60.20 N	136.15 W
Kusaybah, Bi'r ⊤4	140	22.41 N	29.55 E
Kuščovskaja	78	46.33 N	39.37 E
Kuse	96	35.04 N	133.45 E
Kusel	56	49.32 N	7.24 E
Kušen'ki	78	48.53 N	34.07 E
Kusey	54	52.36 N	11.05 E
Kuş Gölü ⊜	130	40.10 N	27.57 E
Kuş Gölü Milli Parkı ♦	130	40.15 N	27.55 E
Kushaka	150	10.32 N	6.48 E
Kushālgarh	120	23.10 N	74.27 E
Kusheriki	150	10.33 N	6.28 E
Kushi	174m	26.33 N	128.06 E
Kushida ≃	94	34.36 N	136.34 E
Kushigata	94	35.36 N	138.28 E
Kushihiki	268	35.55 N	139.36 E
Kushikino	92	31.44 N	130.16 E
Kushima	92	31.29 N	131.14 E
Kushimoto	92	33.28 N	135.47 E
Kushira	270	34.28 N	135.43 E
Kushiro	92a	42.58 N	144.23 E
Kushog Lake ⊜	212	45.05 N	78.48 W
Kushtia	124	23.55 N	89.07 E
Kushui	102	42.11 N	94.25 E
Kusiro → Kushiro	92a	42.58 N	144.23 E
Kusiyāra ≃	120	24.36 N	91.44 E
Kuška	128	35.16 N	62.20 E
Kuška ≃	128	36.00 N	62.40 E
Kuskokwim ≃	180	60.17 N	162.27 W
Kuskokwim, North Fork ≃	180	63.06 N	154.37 W
Kuskokwim, South Fork ≃	180	63.06 N	154.37 W
Kuskokwim Bay c	180	59.45 N	162.25 W
Kuskokwim Mountains ⋏	180	62.30 N	156.00 W
Kuskovo ◆8	265b	55.44 N	37.49 E
Kuškušara	24	64.58 N	40.21 E
Kuśmā	124	28.14 N	83.41 E

DEUTSCH

Name	Seite	Breite°′	Länge°′ E = Ost
Kušmurun	86	52.27 N	64.36 E
Kušmurun, ozero ⊜	86	52.40 N	64.48 E
Küsnacht	58	47.19 N	8.35 E
Kušnarenkovo	86	55.06 N	55.22 E
Kušnica	78	48.27 N	23.14 E
Kusŏng	98	39.59 N	125.15 E
Kusria	272b	22.58 N	88.14 E
Kussharo-ko ⊜	92a	43.38 N	144.21 E
Küssnacht am Rigi	58	47.05 N	8.27 E
Kustanaj	86	53.10 N	63.35 E
Kustanaj □8	86	53.00 N	63.00 E
Kustar'ovka	80	54.16 N	42.16 E
Küsten-Gebirge → Coast Mountains ⋏	176	55.00 N	129.00 W
Küstenkanal ≊	52	52.57 N	7.18 E
Küsten-Ketten → Coast Ranges ⋏	178	41.00 N	123.30 W
Kusthalia	126	23.29 N	87.03 E
Kūstī	140	13.10 N	32.40 E
Kusu, Nihon	94	34.55 N	136.38 E
Kusu, Nihon	96	33.16 N	131.09 E
Kušugum	78	47.42 N	35.14 E
Kušum ≃	80	48.54 N	50.32 E
Kusumba	272b	22.27 N	88.24 E
Kusumbāni ∧	126	21.57 N	86.26 E
Kušumskij	80	51.38 N	48.21 E
Kusung	98	36.18 N	128.55 E
Kusunoki	96	34.03 N	131.15 E
K'us'ur	74	70.39 N	127.15 E
Kušva	86	58.18 N	59.45 E
Kut, Ko I	110	11.40 N	102.35 E
Kuta	150	9.52 N	6.43 E
Kuta ≃	88	56.46 N	105.40 E
Kutabaru	112	0.44 S	102.56 E
Kutabuloh	114	3.28 N	97.04 E
Kutacane	114	3.30 N	97.48 E
Kütahya	130	39.25 N	29.59 E
Kütahya □4	130	39.20 N	29.30 E
Kutais	78	44.32 N	39.18 E
Kutaisi	84	42.15 N	42.40 E
Kutāmat al-Ghābah	142	30.55 N	30.54 E
Kutanibong	114	3.53 N	96.22 E
Kutaradja → Banda Aceh	114	5.34 N	95.20 E
Kutarere	172	38.03 S	177.09 E
Kutasawang	114	5.08 N	96.54 E
Kutch, Rann of (Rann of Kachchh) ◆1	120	24.05 N	70.10 E
Kutchan	92a	42.54 N	140.45 E
Kutcharo-ko ⊜	92a	45.09 N	142.19 E
Kutejnikovo, Ross.	83	47.34 N	39.46 E
Kutejnikovo, Ukr.	83	47.49 N	38.18 E
Kutenholz	52	53.29 N	9.19 E
Kutima	88	57.10 N	108.16 E
Kutima ≃	88	57.08 N	108.14 E
Kutina	36	45.29 N	16.46 E
Kutiyāna	120	21.38 N	69.59 E
Kutkai	110	23.27 N	97.56 E
Kutluškino	80	55.14 N	50.24 E
Kutná Hora	30	49.57 N	15.16 E
Kutno	30	52.15 N	19.23 E
Kutoarjo	115a	7.43 S	109.54 E
Kutomara	88	51.06 N	118.49 E
Kutse Game Reserve ◆4	156	23.30 S	24.05 E
Kutsuki	94	35.21 N	135.55 E
Küttigen	58	47.25 N	8.03 E
Kuttura	24	68.24 N	26.28 E
Kuttusoja	24	67.46 N	28.50 E
Kuttuzi	265a	59.45 N	30.04 E
Kutu	152	2.44 S	18.09 E
Kutubdia Island I	120	21.50 N	91.52 E
Kutubu, Lake ⊜	164	6.23 S	143.18 E
Kutukovo	80	54.26 N	40.31 E
Kutulik	88	53.21 N	102.48 E
Kutulo, Lagh ≃	154	2.08 N	40.56 E
Kutuluk ≃	80	53.19 N	51.09 E
Kutum	140	14.12 N	24.40 E
Kutu-Moke	152	3.12 S	17.21 E
Kúty, Slvk.	30	48.40 N	17.03 E
Kuty, Ukr.	78	48.16 N	25.10 E
Kutztown	210	40.31 N	75.46 W
Kuujjuaq	176	58.06 N	68.25 W
Kuuli-Majak	128	40.14 N	52.42 E
Kuurne	50	50.51 N	3.17 E
Kuusamo	26	65.58 N	29.11 E
Kuusankoski	26	60.54 N	26.38 E
Kuva	85	40.32 N	72.05 E
Kuvak-Nikol'skoje	80	53.37 N	43.30 E
Kuvandyk	86	51.28 N	57.21 E
Kuvango	152	14.28 S	16.20 E
Kuvasaj	85	40.18 N	71.58 E
Kuvet ≃	180	69.14 N	175.00 E
Kuvšinovo	76	57.02 N	34.10 E
Kuwabara	270	34.53 N	135.15 E
Kuwait → Al-Kuwayt	128	29.20 N	47.59 E
Kuwait (Al-Kuwayt) □1, Asia	118	29.30 N	47.45 E
Kuwait (Al-Kuwayt) □1, Asia	128	29.30 N	47.45 E
Kuwait Bay → Kuwayt, Jūn al- c	128	29.30 N	48.00 E
Kuwana	94	35.04 N	136.42 E
Kuwayt, Jūn al- (Kuwait Bay) c	128	29.30 N	48.00 E
Kuyāli	126	22.31 N	86.11 E
Kuybyshev → Samara	80	53.12 N	50.09 E
Kuye ≃	102	38.30 N	110.44 E
Kūysanjaq	128	36.05 N	44.38 E
Kuyucak, Tür.	130	37.51 N	38.21 E
Kuyucak, Tür.	130	37.55 N	28.28 E
Kuyuwini ≃	246	2.16 N	58.16 W
Kuyuyukak, Cape >	180	56.54 N	156.50 W
Kuzaranda	24	62.22 N	35.37 E
Kuze	94	35.33 N	136.30 E
Kuze ◆8	270	34.57 N	135.43 E
Kuzedejevo	86	53.20 N	87.10 E
Kuzemin	78	50.09 N	34.39 E
Kuzemovka	83	49.31 N	37.59 E
Kužener	80	56.48 N	48.56 E
Kuženkino	76	57.44 N	33.59 E
Kuzitrin ≃	180	65.10 N	165.28 W
Kuzkejevo	80	55.46 N	52.48 E
Kuz'miniči	76	54.16 N	33.42 E
Kuz'minka ≃	265a	59.48 N	30.31 E
Kuz'minki ◆8	265b	55.42 N	37.48 E
Kuz'mino, Ross.	82	55.09 N	37.53 E
Kuz'mino, Ross.	82	56.36 N	37.55 E
Kuzmiščevo	82	54.46 N	37.12 E
Kuz'movka	74	62.19 N	92.02 E
Kuznečicha	80	54.43 N	49.38 E
Kuznečikovo	82	56.13 N	36.35 E
Kuzneck, Ross.	80	53.07 N	46.36 E
Kuzneck → Novokuzneck, Ross.	86	53.45 N	87.06 E
Kuzneckij Alatau ⋏	86	54.45 N	88.00 E
Kuznečnoje	26	61.09 N	29.52 E
Kuznecova	89	46.16 N	138.03 E
Kuznecovka	76	56.18 N	28.33 E
Kuznecovo, Ross.	82	55.30 N	38.21 E
Kuznecovo, Ross.	82	55.27 N	36.57 E
Kuznecovo, Ross.	86	59.15 N	63.28 E
Kuznecovo-Michajlovka	83	47.27 N	38.13 E
Kuznecovskij	80	47.25 N	40.57 E
Kuznecy	82	55.51 N	38.40 E
Kuznetsk → Kuzneck	80	53.07 N	46.36 E
Kuznetsovsk	78	51.22 N	25.53 E
Kuzomen', Ross.	24	64.17 N	42.53 E
Kuzomen', Ross.	24	66.17 N	36.54 E
Kuzovatovo	80	53.33 N	47.41 E
Kuzucubelen	130	36.51 N	34.27 E
Kuzuha	270	34.52 N	135.41 E
Kuzuryū ≃	94	36.13 N	136.08 E
Kuzuu	94	36.24 N	139.37 E

Symbols in the index entries represent the broad categories identified in the key at the right. Symbols with superior numbers (⋏1) identify subcategories (see complete key on page *I · 1*).

Symbole im Register stellen die rechts im Schlüssel erklärten Kategorien dar. Symbole mit hochgestellten Ziffern (⋏1) bezeichnen Unterabteilungen einer Kategorie (vgl. vollständiger Schlüssel auf Seite *I · 1*).

Los símbolos incluídos en el texto del índice representan las grandes categorías identificadas con la clave a la derecha. Los símbolos con numeros en su parte superior (⋏1) identifican las subcategorías (véase la clave completa en la página *I · 1*).

Les symboles de l'index représentent les catégories indiquées dans la légende à droite. Les symboles suivis d'un indice (⋏1) représentent des sous-catégories (voir légende complète à la page *I · 1*).

Os símbolos incluídos no texto do índice representam as grandes categorias identificadas com a chave à direita. Os símbolos com números em sua parte superior (⋏1) identificam as subcategorias (veja-se a chave completa à página *I · 1*).

English	Deutsch	Español	Français	Português
∧ Mountain	Berg	Montaña	Montagne	Montanha
⋏ Mountains	Gebirge	Montañas	Montagnes	Montanhas
)(Pass	Paß	Paso	Col	Passo
V Valley, Canyon	Tal, Cañon	Valle, Cañón	Vallée, Canyon	Vale, Canhão
≚ Plain	Ebene	Llano	Plaine	Planície
> Cape	Kap	Cabo	Cap	Cabo
I Island	Insel	Isla	Île	Ilha
II Islands	Inseln	Islas	Îles	Ilhas
≛ Other Topographic Features	Andere Topographische Objekte	Otros Elementos Topográficos	Autres données topographiques	Outros acidentes topográficos

Kuzy-Lago I · 93

ESPAÑOL

Nombre	Página	Lat.°′	Long.°′ W = Oeste
Kuzyaka	130	41.14 N	33.44 E
Kvænangen c [2]	24	70.05 N	21.13 E
Kværndrup	41	55.10 N	10.32 E
Kvaisi	84	42.31 N	43.40 E
Kvaløy I	24	69.40 N	18.30 E
Kvaløya I	24	70.37 N	23.52 E
Kvam	26	61.40 N	9.42 E
Kvanløse	41	55.39 N	11.41 E
Kvanndal	26	60.29 N	6.36 E
Kvareli	84	41.56 N	45.54 E
Kvarner c	36	44.45 N	14.15 E
Kvarnerić ʉ	36	44.45 N	14.35 E
Kvarnsveden	40	60.31 N	15.24 E
Kvarntorp	40	59.08 N	15.15 E
Kvarsa	80	56.58 N	53.57 E
Kvarsebo	40	58.39 N	16.39 E
Kvašenki	82	56.48 N	37.33 E
Kvenna ≃	26	60.01 N	7.56 E
Kverkfjöll ʌ	24a	64.43 N	16.38 W
Kvichak Bay c	180	58.48 N	157.30 W
Kvicksund	40	59.27 N	16.19 E
Kvidinge	41	56.08 N	13.04 E
Kvien ⊜	40	60.24 N	13.48 E
Kvikkjokk	24	66.55 N	17.50 E
Kvilda	60	49.01 N	13.35 E
Kvina ≃	26	58.17 N	6.56 E
Kvismare kanal ≋	40	59.12 N	15.11 E
Kvissleby	26	62.17 N	17.21 E
Kvistbro	40	59.09 N	14.49 E
Kvistgård	41	55.59 N	12.30 E
Kvitok	88	56.03 N	98.30 E
Kwa ≃	152	3.10 S	16.11 E
Kwachaga	154	5.38 S	38.08 E
Kwada	164	6.09 S	141.53 E
Kwahae-ri ◆ [8]	271b	37.33 N	126.50 E
Kwahu Plateau ⩘ [1]	150	6.30 N	0.30 W
Kwai → Khwae Noi ≃	110	14.00 N	99.33 E
Kwajalein I [1]	14	9.05 N	167.20 E
Kwajok	140	8.19 N	28.00 E
Kwakoegron	250	5.15 N	55.20 W
Kwale, Kenya	154	4.11 S	39.27 E
Kwale, Nig.	150	5.46 N	6.26 E
Kwambilo ≃	273b	4.26 S	15.20 E
Kwa-Mbonambi	158	28.36 S	32.05 E
Kwamisa ʌ	150	7.08 N	1.53 W
Kwamouth	152	3.10 S	16.12 E
Kwa Mtoro	154	5.14 S	35.26 E
Kwanak-san ʌ	271b	37.27 N	126.58 E
Kwando (Cuando) ≃	152	18.27 S	23.32 E
Kwangchow → Guangzhou	100	23.06 N	113.16 E
Kwangju	98	35.09 N	126.54 E
Kwangju □ [4]	98	35.09 N	126.55 E
Kwango (Cuango) ≃	152	3.14 S	17.23 E
Kwangsi Chuang Autonomous Region → Guangxi Zhuangzu Zizhiqu □ [4]	102	24.00 N	109.00 E
Kwangtung → Guangdong □ [4]	90	23.00 N	113.00 E
Kwangwazi	154	7.47 S	38.15 E
Kwangyang	98	34.59 N	127.34 E
Kwania, Lake ⊜	154	1.45 N	32.45 E
Kwanmo-bong ʌ	98	41.42 N	129.13 E
Kwansan-ni	271b	37.43 N	126.51 E
Kwanto Plain → Kantō-heiya ≚	94	36.00 N	139.30 E
Kwara □ [3]	150	8.45 N	5.00 E
Kware	150	13.12 N	5.14 E
Kwa-Thema	273d	26.18 S	28.23 E
Kwatisore	164	3.15 S	134.57 E
Kweichow → Guizhou □ [4]	102	27.00 N	107.00 E
Kweihwa → Hohhot	102	40.51 N	111.40 E
Kweijang → Guiyang	102	26.35 N	106.43 E
Kweilin → Guilin	102	25.17 N	110.17 E
Kweisui → Hohhot	102	40.51 N	111.40 E
Kweiyang → Guiyang	102	26.35 N	106.43 E
Kwekwe	154	18.55 S	29.49 E
Kweneng □ [5]	156	24.00 S	24.00 E
Kwenge (Caengo) ≃	152	4.50 S	18.42 E
Kwesimintim	150	4.54 N	1.47 W
Kwethluk	180	60.49 N	161.27 W
Kwethluk ≃	180	60.46 N	161.26 W
Kwidzyn	30	53.45 N	18.56 E
Kwigillingok	180	59.51 N	163.08 W
Kwiguk	180	62.45 N	164.28 W
Kwiha	144	13.31 N	39.32 E
Kwikila	164	9.48 S	147.41 E
Kwilu (Cuilo) ≃	152	3.22 S	17.22 E
Kwinana	168a	32.15 S	115.48 E
Kwitaro ≃	246	3.19 N	58.47 W
Kwobrup	162	33.37 S	117.46 E
Kwoka, Gunung ʌ	164	0.31 S	132.27 E
Kwolla	150	9.00 N	9.15 E
Kwun Tong	271d	22.19 N	114.12 E
Kyabé	146	9.27 N	18.57 E
Kyabra	166	26.18 S	143.10 E
Kyabra Creek ≃	166	25.36 S	142.55 E
Kyabram	166	36.19 S	145.03 E
Kyaikkami	110	16.04 N	97.34 E
Kyaiklat	110	16.26 N	95.44 E
Kyaikto	110	17.18 N	97.01 E
Kya-in	110	16.02 N	98.08 E
Kyaka	154	1.16 S	31.25 E
Kyalite	166	34.57 S	143.29 E
Kyancutta	166	33.08 S	135.34 E
Ky Anh	110	18.05 N	106.18 E
Kyat-aw	110	12.29 N	98.19 E
Kyaukhnyat	110	18.15 N	97.31 E
Kyaukkyi	110	18.19 N	96.46 E
Kyaukme	110	22.32 N	97.02 E
Kyaukpa	110	13.05 N	98.59 E
Kyaukpyu, Mya.	110	19.05 N	93.52 E
Kyaukpyu, Mya.	110	19.26 N	93.33 E
Kyaukse	110	21.36 N	96.08 E
Kyauktaw	110	20.51 N	92.59 E
Kyaunggon	110	17.06 N	95.11 E
Kybartai	76	54.39 N	22.45 E
Kybean	171b	36.22 S	149.25 E
Kybeyan Range ⩘	171b	36.10 S	149.30 E
Kyburz	226	38.47 N	120.18 W
Kydra	171b	36.27 S	149.23 E
Kyeamba	171b	35.26 S	147.37 E
Kyeamba Creek ≃	171b	35.06 S	147.29 E
Kyebang-san ʌ	98	37.43 N	128.29 E
Kyegegwa	154	0.29 N	31.03 E
Kyeikdon	110	16.00 N	98.24 E
Kyeintali	110	18.00 N	94.29 E
Kyenjojo	154	0.37 N	30.38 E
Kyeryong-san Kukrip Kongwŏn ♦	98	36.21 N	127.13 E
Kyes Peak ʌ	224	47.57 N	121.19 W
Kyffhäuser-Denkmal ⊥	54	51.23 N	11.06 E
Kyffhäuser Gebirge ⩘	54	51.23 N	11.05 E
Kyidaunggan	110	19.53 N	96.12 E
Kyindwe	110	20.58 N	93.51 E
Kyje ◆ [8]	54	50.04 N	14.32 E
Kyjov	30	49.01 N	17.08 E
Kykladen → Kikládhes II	38	37.30 N	25.00 E
Kykotsmovi Village	200	35.52 N	110.37 W
Kykva	80	57.22 N	53.50 E
Kylås ʌ	124	25.18 N	90.45 E
Kyle, Sask., Can.	184	50.50 N	108.02 W
Kyle, S.D., U.S.	198	43.25 N	102.10 W
Kyle, Tx., U.S.	196	29.59 N	97.52 W
Kyle □ [9]	46	55.29 N	4.24 W
Kyle, Lake ⊜ [1]	154	20.14 S	31.00 E
Kyleakin	46	57.16 N	5.44 W
Kyle of Lochalsh	46	57.17 N	5.43 W

FRANÇAIS

Nom	Page	Lat.°′	Long.°′ W = Ouest
Kylerhea	46	57.14 N	5.41 W
Kylertown	214	41.00 N	78.10 W
Kylestrome	46	58.16 N	5.02 W
Kyll ≃	56	49.48 N	6.42 E
Kyllburg	56	50.02 N	6.35 E
Kym ≃	42	52.14 N	0.17 W
Kymen lääni □ [4]	26	61.00 N	28.00 E
Kymijoki ≃	26	60.30 N	26.52 E
Kyn	86	57.52 N	58.38 E
Kyndby	41	55.48 N	11.56 E
Kyneton	169	37.15 S	144.27 E
Kynnefjäll ʌ [2]	26	58.42 N	11.41 E
Kynšperk nad Ohří	54	50.04 N	12.32 E
Kynuna	166	21.35 S	141.55 E
Kyodong-do I	98	37.45 N	126.16 E
Kyoga, Lake ⊜	154	1.30 N	33.00 E
Kyōga-misaki ›	96	35.46 N	135.13 E
Kyogle	166	28.37 S	153.00 E
Kyoha-ri	271b	37.46 N	126.46 E
Kyohyŏn-ni	271b	37.43 N	126.58 E
Kyom ≃	140	8.58 N	28.13 E
Kyŏmip'o → Songnim	98	38.44 N	125.38 E
Kyonan	94	35.07 N	139.50 E
Kyondo	110	16.35 N	98.03 E
Kyŏnggi Do □ [4]	98	37.30 N	127.15 E
Kyŏnggi-man c	98	37.25 N	126.00 E
Kyŏngju	98	35.51 N	129.14 E
Kyŏngju Kukrip Kongwŏn ♦	98	35.47 N	129.15 E
Kyŏngsan	98	35.48 N	128.43 E
Kyŏngsang Namdo □ [4]	98	35.15 N	128.30 E
Kyŏngsang Pukdo □ [4]	98	36.15 N	128.45 E
Kyŏngsŏng, C.M.I.K.	98	41.35 N	129.36 E
Kyŏngsŏng → Sŏul, Taehan	98	37.33 N	126.58 E
Kyŏngwŏn	98	42.48 N	130.09 E
Kyônkadun	110	16.04 N	95.38 E
Kyonmange	110	16.30 N	95.50 E
Kyonpyaw	110	17.18 N	95.12 E
Kyotera	154	0.33 S	31.19 E
Kyōto, Nihon	94	35.00 N	135.45 E
Kyōto, Nihon	270	35.00 N	135.45 E
Kyōto □ [5]	94	35.05 N	135.45 E
Kyōto-bonchi ⩘	270	35.03 N	135.45 E
Kyōto Race Track ♦	270	34.54 N	135.44 E
Kyōto University ʋ [2]	270	35.02 N	135.46 E
Kyōwa	94	36.19 N	140.03 E
Kyōyomi-dake ʌ	96	33.31 N	131.02 E
Kypšak, ozero ⊜	86	50.09 N	68.28 E
Kyra	88	49.36 N	111.58 E
Kyra ≃	88	49.24 N	112.19 E
Kyrčany	80	57.37 N	50.10 E
Kyren	88	51.41 N	102.08 E
Kyrenia → Girne	130	35.20 N	33.19 E
Kyrgyzstan □ [1], Asia	72	41.30 N	75.00 E
Kyrgyzstan □ [1], Asia	85	41.30 N	75.00 E
Kyritz	54	52.56 N	12.23 E
Kyrkheden	40	60.10 N	13.29 E
Kyrkkazyk	85	42.30 N	72.20 E
Kyrksæterøra	26	63.17 N	9.06 E
Kyrkslätt (Kirkkonummi)	26	60.07 N	24.26 E
Kyrö	26	60.42 N	22.45 E
Kyrönjoki ≃	26	63.14 N	21.45 E
Kyrösjärvi ⊜	26	61.45 N	23.10 E
Kyröskoski	26	61.40 N	23.11 E
Kyrta	24	64.04 N	57.42 E
Kyrykkuduk	80	49.51 N	51.54 E
Ky Son	110	19.24 N	104.08 E
Kyštovka	86	56.33 N	76.38 E
Kyštym	86	55.42 N	60.34 E
Kysykkamys	80	49.14 N	50.19 E
Kyte ≃	190	42.00 N	89.19 W
Kytlym	86	59.30 N	59.12 E
Kytmanovo	86	53.28 N	85.28 E
Kyūhōji	270	34.38 N	135.35 E
Kyunchaung	110	15.33 N	98.15 E
Kyundon	110	20.31 N	95.44 E
Kyungyi I	110	15.04 N	97.44 E
Kyunhla	110	23.21 N	95.18 E
Kyuquot	182	50.02 N	127.23 W
Kyuquot Sound ʉ	182	50.05 N	127.15 W
Kyūroku-jima I	92	40.32 N	139.29 E
Kyū-shizudani-gakkō ⊥	96	34.45 N	134.13 E
Kyūshū I	92	33.00 N	131.00 E
Kyushu-Palau Ridge ✦ [3]	14	20.00 N	136.00 E
Kyūshū-sanchi ⩘	92	32.35 N	131.17 E
Kywebwe	110	18.42 N	96.25 E
Kywong	166	34.59 S	146.44 E
Kyyjärvi	26	63.02 N	24.34 E
Kyyvesi ⊜	26	61.58 N	27.07 E
Kyzas	86	52.20 N	89.20 E
Kyzyl	88	51.42 N	94.27 E
Kyzylagadžskij zapovednik ◆ [4]	84	39.10 N	49.00 E
Kyzylagaš	86	45.54 N	81.37 E
Kyzylaryk	85	43.57 N	70.42 E
Kyzylbejit	85	41.30 N	72.24 E
Kyzyl-Chaja	86	50.03 N	89.54 E
Kyzyl-Chem (Šišchid) ≃	88	51.21 N	96.58 E
Kyzyl-Džar	85	41.17 N	72.02 E
Kyzylemgek	85	41.57 N	74.56 E
Kyzylespe	86	47.27 N	73.53 E
Kyzylkak, ozero ⊜	86	53.25 N	73.48 E
Kyzyl-Kija	85	40.16 N	72.08 E
Kyzyl-Kommuna	86	48.44 N	67.32 E
Kyzylkum ◆ [2]	72	42.00 N	64.00 E
Kyzylkup	128	40.38 N	53.58 E
Kyzyl-Mažalyk	86	51.10 N	90.32 E
Kyzylmazar	85	39.39 N	68.25 E
Kyzyloba	80	49.37 N	50.38 E
Kyzylsu ≃	85	39.17 N	71.23 E
Kyzyltas, gory ⩘	86	48.30 N	74.50 E
Kyzyltau	86	47.53 N	72.05 E
Kyzylt'ob'o	85	42.13 N	75.16 E
Kyzyltu, Kaz.	86	47.46 N	59.08 E
Kyzyltu, Kaz.	86	47.43 N	75.42 E
Kyzyltu, Kyrg.	85	42.11 N	76.40 E
Kyzyluj	86	48.07 N	65.28 E
Kyzylžar	86	48.17 N	69.39 E
Kzyl-Kuga	80	48.28 N	53.01 E
Kzyl-Orda	86	44.48 N	65.28 E
Kzyl-Orda □ [8]	86	45.00 N	64.00 E
Kzyltu	86	53.38 N	72.20 E

L

Nom	Page	Lat.°′	Long.°′ W = Ouest
La'a	102	29.44 N	101.26 E
Laa an der Thaya	61	48.43 N	16.23 E
Laaben	61	48.06 N	15.52 E
Laaber	60	49.04 N	11.53 E
Laaberberg	60	48.46 N	12.01 E
Laab im Walde	264b	48.09 N	16.11 E
Laacher See ⊜	56	50.25 N	7.16 E
Laaerberg ʌ [2]	264b	48.09 N	16.24 E
Laage	54	53.56 N	12.20 E
La Aguja, Cabo de ›	246	11.18 N	74.12 W
Laakajärvi ⊜	26	63.50 N	27.55 E
Laakirchen	64	47.58 N	13.49 E
La Albuera	34	38.43 N	6.49 W
La Alcarria ◆ [1]	34	40.45 N	2.45 W
La Aldea	234	20.54 N	101.29 W
La Aldehuela	266a	40.18 N	3.36 W
La Algaba	34	37.28 N	6.01 W
La Almarcha	34	39.41 N	2.22 W
La Almunia de Doña Godina	34	41.29 N	1.22 W
Laanecoorie Reservoir ⊜ [1]	169	36.52 S	143.53 E
La Antigua, Salina ≃	252	30.00 S	66.06 W
La Antorcha, Cerro ʌ	234	21.43 N	102.45 W

PORTUGUÊS

Nome	Página	Lat.°′	Long.°′ W = Oeste
Laar ◆ [8]	263	51.28 N	6.43 E
La Araucanía □ [4]	252	38.45 S	72.30 W
La Arena, Pan.	236	7.58 N	80.28 W
La Arena, Perú	248	5.20 S	80.44 W
Laas → Lasa	64	46.37 N	10.42 E
Laas Caanood	144	8.28 N	47.21 E
La Ascención	232	24.20 N	99.55 W
Laas Dawaco	144	10.28 N	49.05 E
Laas Dhaareed	144	10.10 N	45.59 E
Laase	54	53.04 N	11.18 E
Laas Qoray	144	11.10 N	48.13 E
La Asunción	246	11.02 N	63.53 W
La Atravesada, Loma ʌ [2]	232	29.57 N	112.12 W
Laatzen	52	52.19 N	9.47 E
Laau Point ›	229a	21.06 N	157.19 W
La Aurora	286e	33.36 S	70.38 W
La Azufrosa	196	28.14 N	100.50 W
Laba ≃	78	45.11 N	39.42 E
La Babia	232	28.34 N	102.04 W
Labadie	219	38.31 N	90.51 W
Labadieville	194	29.50 N	90.57 W
La Baie	186	48.19 N	70.53 W
La Balme-de-Sillingy	58	45.58 N	6.02 E
La Balme-les-Grottes	62	45.51 N	5.20 E
Laban	208	37.24 N	76.17 W
La Banda	252	27.44 S	64.15 W
La Bandera, Cerro ʌ	232	24.35 N	105.07 W
La Bañeza	34	42.18 N	5.54 W
La Barca	234	20.17 N	102.34 W
La Barceloneta ◆ [8]	266d	41.22 N	2.11 E
La Barge	200	42.15 N	110.11 W
La Barge Creek ≃	200	42.14 N	110.10 W
La Barra	236	12.54 N	83.32 W
La Barre-en-Ouche	50	48.57 N	0.40 E
La Barrita	236	14.05 N	91.03 W
La Barr Meadows	226	39.11 N	121.02 W
Labason	116	8.04 N	122.31 E
La Bassée	50	50.32 N	2.48 E
Labastide-Murat	32	44.39 N	1.34 E
La Bastide-Puylaurent	62	44.36 N	3.54 E
La Bâte	261	48.35 N	2.01 E
La Baule-Escoublac	32	47.17 N	2.24 W
La Bazoche-Gouet	50	48.08 N	0.59 E
L'Abbé	261	48.34 N	1.50 E
Labdah (Leptis Magna) ⊥	146	32.38 N	14.18 E
Labé	150	11.19 N	12.17 W
Labe (Elbe) ≃	30	53.50 N	9.00 E
Labégude	62	44.39 N	4.22 E
La Bégude-Blanche	62	43.55 N	6.08 E
La Bégude-de-Mazenc	62	44.32 N	4.56 E
Labelle, P.Q., Can.	206	46.16 N	74.44 W
La Belle, Fl., U.S.	220	26.45 N	81.26 W
La Belle, Mo., U.S.	219	40.07 N	91.54 W
Labelle □ [6]	206	46.20 N	75.00 W
Labelle, Lac ⊜, P.Q., Can.	206	46.13 N	74.52 W
La Belle, Lac ⊜, Wi., U.S.	216	43.08 N	88.31 W
Labengke, Pulau I	112	3.27 S	122.25 E
La Bérarde	62	44.56 N	6.18 E
Laberge, Lake ⊜	180	61.11 N	135.12 W
La Berra ʌ	58	46.41 N	7.11 E
Laberweinting	60	48.48 N	12.19 E
La Besace	56	49.34 N	4.58 E
Labette Creek ≃	198	37.03 N	95.05 W
Labi	112	4.25 N	114.22 E
La Biche ≃	182	55.01 N	112.44 W
Labico	66	41.47 N	12.53 E
Labin	36	45.05 N	14.07 E
Labinsk	84	44.38 N	40.44 E
Labis	114	2.23 N	103.02 E
La Bisbal	34	41.57 N	3.03 E
Łabiszyn	30	52.57 N	17.55 E
Lablābah, Wādī al- V	273c	30.02 N	31.19 E
La Blanca	286e	33.31 S	70.41 W
La Blanca Grande, Laguna ⊜	252	38.26 S	63.55 W
Labná ⊥	232	20.11 N	89.34 W
Labo	116	14.09 N	122.51 E
Labo ≃	116	14.11 N	122.56 E
Labo, Mount ʌ	116	14.01 N	122.48 E
Laboe	54	54.24 N	10.15 E
La Boissière	261	48.46 N	1.59 E
La Boissière-Ecole	261	48.41 N	1.39 E
La Bollène-Vésubie	62	43.59 N	7.20 E
La Bonneville-sur-Iton	50	49.00 N	1.02 E
Laboratory	214	40.09 N	80.13 W
Laborde, Arg.	252	33.09 S	62.51 W
La Borde, Fr.	261	48.32 N	2.50 E
Laborec ≃	30	48.36 N	22.00 E
Laborie	241f	13.45 N	61.00 W
Labouchere, Mount ʌ	162	25.12 S	118.18 E
Labouheyre	32	44.13 N	0.55 W
Laboulaye	252	34.07 S	63.24 W
La Bouverie	50	50.24 N	3.52 E
La Boyera, Ven.	286c	10.25 N	66.50 W
La Boyera, Ven.	286c	10.23 N	66.57 W
Lābpur	126	23.50 N	87.49 E
Labrador ◆ [1]	176	54.00 N	62.00 W
Labrador Basin ✦ [1]	16	53.00 N	48.00 W
Labrador City	176	52.57 N	66.55 W
Labrador Sea ▽ [2]	176	57.00 N	53.00 W
Lábrea, Bra.	248	7.16 S	64.47 W
La Brea, Trin.	241r	10.15 N	61.37 W
Labrède	32	44.41 N	0.31 W
La Bresse	58	48.00 N	6.53 E
La Brévine	58	46.59 N	6.36 E
Labrieville, Réserve ♦	186	49.20 N	69.40 W
La Brigue	62	44.04 N	7.37 E
La Brillanne	62	43.55 N	5.53 E
Labrit	32	44.07 N	0.33 W
La Broquerie	184	49.28 N	96.27 W
Labroye	50	50.17 N	1.59 E
Labry	56	49.10 N	5.52 E
Labuan, Pulau I	112	5.21 N	115.13 E
Labuha	164	0.37 S	127.29 E
Labuhan	115a	6.22 S	105.50 E
Labuhanbajo	115b	8.29 S	119.54 E
Labuhanbatu	114	2.12 N	100.12 E
Labuhanbilik	114	2.31 N	100.10 E
Labuhandeli	114	3.45 N	98.41 E
Labuhanhaji, Indon.	114	3.33 N	97.00 E
Labuhanhaji, Indon.	115b	8.42 S	116.34 E
Labuhanmarege	112	7.06 S	120.40 E
Labuhanmaringgai	115a	5.21 S	105.48 E
Labuhanruku	114	3.13 N	99.35 E
Labuk ≃	112	5.54 N	117.30 E
Labuk, Telukan c	116	6.07 N	117.46 E
Labu Kananga	115b	8.08 S	117.47 E
Labutta	110	16.09 N	94.46 E
Labytnangi	72	66.39 N	66.21 E
Lač, Ross.	24	63.18 N	54.28 E
Laç, Shq.	38	41.38 N	19.43 E
Lac □ [5]	146	13.30 N	14.15 E
Lača, ozero ⊜	24	61.20 N	38.48 E
La Cadena	196	25.53 N	104.12 W
L'Acadie	275a	45.19 N	73.21 W
L'Acadie ≃	206	45.29 N	73.16 W
La Cadière-d'Azur	62	43.12 N	5.46 E
Lacadivas, Islas → Lakshadweep II	122	10.00 N	73.00 E
Laca Jahuira ≃	248	19.21 S	67.54 W
La Cal ≃	248	17.27 S	58.15 W
Lac-à-la-Tortue	206	46.37 N	72.38 W
La Calera, Chile	252	32.47 S	71.12 W
La Calera, Perú	286d	12.10 S	76.51 W
Lacamas Creek ≃	224	46.20 N	122.55 W
Lacamas Lake ⊜	224	45.37 N	122.26 W
La Campana, Esp.	34	37.34 N	5.26 W
La Campana, Méx.	234	22.45 N	105.35 W
La Cañada	234	20.37 N	100.19 W
La Cañada, Cerro ʌ	234	21.24 N	99.13 W
La Cañada Flintridge	228	34.12 N	118.12 W

La Canada Verde Creek ≃	280	33.52 N	118.02 W
Lacanau	32	44.59 N	1.05 W
Lacanau, Lac de c	32	44.58 N	1.07 W
La Candelaria, Arg.	252	26.06 S	65.06 W
La Candelaria, Méx.	200	31.07 N	106.29 W
La Cañiza	34	42.13 N	8.16 W
La Canourgue	32	44.26 N	3.13 E
Lacantún ≃	232	16.36 N	90.39 W
La Capelle-en-Thiérache	50	49.58 N	3.55 E
La Capelle-lès-Boulogne	50	50.44 N	1.42 E
Lacapelle-Marival	32	44.44 N	1.54 E
La Carlota, Arg.	252	33.26 S	63.18 W
La Carlota, Pil.	116	10.25 N	122.55 E
Lacarne	214	41.31 N	83.03 W
La Carolina	34	38.15 N	3.37 W
La Casita	234	23.43 N	104.46 W
La Castellana	116	10.20 N	123.03 E
Lacaune	32	43.43 N	2.42 E
Lac-Bellemare	206	46.34 N	72.55 W
Lac-Brome	206	45.13 N	72.31 W
Laccadive, Minicoy, and Amīndīvi → Lakshadweep □ [3]	122	10.00 N	73.00 E
Laccadive Islands → Lakshadweep II	122	10.00 N	73.00 E
Lacchiarella	62	45.19 N	9.08 E
Lacco Ameno	68	40.45 N	13.54 E
Lac Courte Oreilles Indian Reservation ◆ [4]	190	45.55 N	91.19 W
Lac du Flambeau	190	45.59 N	89.51 W
Lac du Flambeau Indian Reservation ◆ [4]	190	45.59 N	89.53 W
Laceby	44	53.32 N	0.10 W
Lacedonia	68	41.03 N	15.25 E
La Ceiba, Hond.	236	15.47 N	86.50 W
La Ceiba, Ven.	246	9.28 N	71.04 W
La Celle-les-Bordes	261	48.38 N	1.57 E
La Celle-Saint-Cloud	261	48.51 N	2.08 E
La Celle-Saint-Cyr	50	47.58 N	3.18 E
La Center, Ky., U.S.	194	37.04 N	88.58 W
La Center, Wa., U.S.	224	45.52 N	122.40 W
Lacepede Bay c	166	36.47 S	139.45 E
Lacerdónia	156	18.01 S	35.30 E
Laces (Latsch)	64	46.37 N	10.52 E
Lac-Etchemin	186	46.24 N	70.30 W
Lacey	224	47.02 N	122.49 W
Lacey Creek ≃	278	41.50 N	88.03 W
Laceyville	210	41.39 N	76.10 W
Lac-Frontière	186	46.42 N	70.00 W
La Chaise-Dieu	62	45.19 N	3.42 E
La Chambre	62	45.22 N	6.18 E
La Chapelle-d'Angillon	50	47.22 N	2.26 E
La Chapelle-en-Vercors	62	44.58 N	5.25 E
La Chapelle-Gauthier	261	48.33 N	2.54 E
La Chapelle-la-Reine	50	48.19 N	2.35 E
La Chapelle-Saint-Luc	50	48.20 N	4.03 E
La Chapelle-Vendômoise	50	47.40 N	1.15 E
La Charité-sur-Loire	50	47.11 N	3.01 E
La Chartre-sur-le-Loir	50	47.44 N	0.35 E
La Châtaigneraie	32	46.39 N	0.44 W
La Châtre	32	46.35 N	1.59 E
Lachaussée, Étang de ⊜	56	49.02 N	5.48 E
La Chaux-de-Fonds	58	47.06 N	6.50 E
Lachay, Punta ›	248	11.18 S	77.39 W
Lach Dennis	262	53.15 N	2.26 W
Lachdenpochja	24	61.31 N	30.08 E
Lachen	58	47.12 N	8.51 E
Lachenaie	275a	45.42 N	73.34 W
Lachendorf	52	52.37 N	10.14 E
Lachhmangarh Sīkar	120	27.49 N	75.02 E
L'achi	80	55.20 N	41.56 E
Lachine	206	45.26 N	73.40 W
Lachine, Canal de ≋	275a	45.26 N	73.40 W
Lachine, Rapides de ᒪ	275a	45.25 N	73.36 W
La Chira, Punta ›	286d	12.13 S	77.03 W
La Chivera	286c	10.37 N	66.54 W
Lachkaltsap Indian Reserve ◆ [4]	182	55.03 N	129.34 W
Lachlan ≃	166	34.21 S	143.57 E
La Chorrera, Col.	246	0.44 S	73.01 W
La Chorrera, Pan.	236	8.53 N	79.47 W
L'achoviči, Bela.	76	53.02 N	26.16 E
L'achoviči, Bela.	76	52.23 N	27.55 E
L'achovskije ostrova II	74	73.30 N	141.00 E
La Choza	258	34.47 S	59.07 W
La Choza, Arroyo ≃	258	34.40 S	58.58 W
Lachta ◆ [8]	265a	60.00 N	30.09 E
Lachtinskij Razliv, ozero ⊜	265a	60.00 N	30.11 E
Lachute	206	45.38 N	74.20 W
Lachva	76	52.13 N	27.04 E
La Ciénaga	252	27.30 S	66.57 W
La Ciénega	234	16.54 N	96.46 W
Lâçin	130	40.47 N	34.54 E
La Cinta Creek ≃	196	35.24 N	104.06 W
La Ciotat	62	43.10 N	5.36 E
La Cisterna	286e	33.33 S	70.41 W
La Citadelle ⊥	238	19.35 N	72.14 W
La Ciudad	234	23.44 N	105.42 W
Lack	48	54.33 N	7.35 W
Lackawanna	210	42.49 N	78.49 W
Lackawanna □ [6]	210	41.24 N	75.40 W
Lackawanna ≃	210	41.21 N	75.47 W
Lackawanna, Lake ⊜	276	40.57 N	74.42 W
Lackawanna State Park ♦	210	41.33 N	75.44 W
Lackawaxen	210	41.29 N	74.59 W
Lackawaxen ≃	210	41.29 N	74.59 W
Lackey	208	37.14 N	76.33 W
Lackland Air Force Base ■	196	29.27 N	98.37 W
Läckö	26	58.41 N	13.13 E
Lackoje	76	58.05 N	38.08 E
Lac La Belle	216	43.09 N	88.32 W
Lac la Biche	182	54.46 N	111.58 W
Lac la Hache	182	51.49 N	121.28 W
Lac la Ronge Provincial Park ♦	184	55.15 N	104.55 W
La Clayette	32	46.18 N	4.19 E
Laclede, Id., U.S.	182	48.10 N	116.45 W
La Clede, Il., U.S.	219	38.53 N	88.43 W
Laclede, Mo., U.S.	194	39.47 N	93.09 W
La Clotilde	252	27.08 S	60.40 W
La Clusaz	58	45.54 N	6.25 E
La Cluse	58	46.10 N	5.34 E
La Cluse-et-Mijoux	58	46.53 N	6.23 E
Lacmalac	171b	35.19 S	148.19 E
Lac-Masson	206	46.02 N	74.04 W
Lac-Mégantic	188	45.36 N	70.53 W
Lacob ti-duyong, Mount ʌ	116	17.35 N	121.09 E
La Cocha	252	27.47 S	65.34 W
Lacolle	206	45.05 N	73.22 W
Lacolle ≃	206	45.04 N	73.20 W
La Colle-sur-Loup	62	43.41 N	7.06 E
La Colmena	286a	19.36 N	99.18 W
La Colorada	232	28.41 N	110.25 W
La Columna → Bolívar, Pico ʌ	246	8.30 N	71.02 W
Lacombe, Ab., Can.	182	52.28 N	113.44 W
Lacombe, La., U.S.	194	30.18 N	89.56 W
Lacon	190	41.01 N	89.24 W
Lacona, Ia., U.S.	190	41.11 N	93.22 W
Lacona, N.Y., U.S.	210	43.38 N	76.04 W
La Concepción, Pan.	236	8.31 N	82.37 W
La Concepción, Ven.	246	10.38 N	71.50 W

La Condamine-Châtelard	62	44.27 N	6.45 E
Laconi	71	39.51 N	9.03 E
Laconia	188	43.31 N	71.28 W
La Conner	224	48.23 N	122.29 W
La Consulta	252	33.44 S	69.07 W
Lacoochee	220	28.27 N	82.10 W
La Coruña	34	43.22 N	8.23 W
La Coruña □ [4]	34	43.00 N	8.35 W
Lacoste, Fr.	62	43.50 N	5.18 E
La Coste, Tx., U.S.	196	29.19 N	98.49 W
La Côte-Saint-André	62	45.23 N	5.15 E
La Courneuve	261	48.56 N	2.23 E
La Couronne	62	43.20 N	5.03 E
La Courtine	32	45.42 N	2.16 E
Lac qui Parle ≃	198	45.01 N	95.53 W
Lac qui Parle, West Branch ≃	198	44.55 N	96.02 W
La Crau	62	43.09 N	6.04 E
Lacre Punt ›	241s	12.02 N	68.15 W
La Crescent	190	43.49 N	91.18 W
La Crescenta	228	34.13 N	118.14 W
La Croft	214	40.39 N	80.35 W
Lacroix-Saint-Ouen	50	49.21 N	2.47 E
La Crosse, In., U.S.	216	41.19 N	86.53 W
La Crosse, Ks., U.S.	198	38.31 N	99.18 W
La Crosse, Va., U.S.	192	36.41 N	78.05 W
Lacrosse, Wa., U.S.	202	46.49 N	117.53 W
La Crosse, Wi., U.S.	190	43.48 N	91.14 W
La Crosse ≃	190	43.49 N	91.16 W
La Cruz, Arg.	252	29.10 S	56.38 W
La Cruz, Col.	246	1.35 N	76.58 W
La Cruz, C.R.	236	11.04 N	85.39 W
La Cruz, Méx.	196	28.33 N	100.48 W
La Cruz, Ur.	258	33.56 S	56.15 W
La Cruz, Cerro ʌ	234	17.55 N	101.31 W
La Cruz de Río Grande	236	13.06 N	84.10 W
Lac-Saguay	206	46.30 N	75.09 W
Lac Seul	184	50.20 N	92.16 W
Lac Seul Indian Reserve ◆ [4]	184	50.15 N	92.10 W
La Cuchilla	234	18.54 N	103.19 W
La Cuesta, C.R.	236	8.30 N	82.50 W
La Cuesta, Méx.	234	20.10 N	104.51 W
La Cuesta, P.R.	240m	18.25 N	66.49 W
La Cumbre, Arg.	252	30.58 S	64.30 W
La Cumbre, Ven.	286c	10.32 N	66.57 W
La Cumbre, Volcán ʌ [1]	246a	0.20 S	91.30 W
La Cure	58	46.28 N	6.05 E
Lacy Fork ≃	222	32.24 N	96.08 W
La Cygne	198	38.21 N	94.45 W
Lacy-Lakeview	222	31.37 N	97.06 W
Lada, Teluk c	115a	6.29 S	105.44 E
Ladainha	255	17.39 S	41.44 W
Ladākh □ [9]	120	35.10 N	76.10 E
Ladākh Range ⩘	120	34.00 N	78.00 E
Ladan	78	50.31 N	32.35 E
La Dang, Ko I	114	6.33 N	99.18 E
Ladang Jagor	114	4.42 N	101.35 E
Ladara	114	1.28 N	97.28 E
Ladário	248	19.01 S	57.35 W
Ladbergen	52	52.08 N	7.44 E
Ladby	41	55.26 N	10.38 E
Ladd	190	41.22 N	89.13 W
Låddenhøj ʌ [2]	41	56.13 N	9.48 E
Ladder Creek ≃	198	38.48 N	100.52 W
Laddingford	260	51.12 N	0.25 E
Laddonia	219	39.14 N	91.38 W
Ladeburg	264a	52.42 N	13.35 E
La Défense ʋ	261	48.53 N	2.15 E
La Dehesa	286e	33.22 S	70.33 W
La Dent d'Oche ʌ	58	46.21 N	6.44 E
Ladera Heights	280	33.59 N	118.22 W
La Désirade I	241o	16.19 N	61.03 W
Ládhi	38	41.27 N	26.17 E
Ladhurka	126	23.22 N	86.32 E
La Digue I	138	4.21 S	55.50 E
Lâdik	130	40.55 N	35.55 E
Ladinger Spitze ʌ	61	46.51 N	14.39 E
L'adiny	24	61.33 N	38.20 E
Ladismith	158	33.30 S	21.16 E
Ladispoli	66	41.56 N	12.05 E
Lādīz	128	28.56 N	61.19 E
Ladner	224	49.05 N	123.05 W
Lādnūn	120	27.39 N	74.23 E
Ladoga	194	39.54 N	86.48 W
Ladoga, Lake → Ladožskoje ozero ⊜	24	61.00 N	31.30 E
La Dolorita	286c	10.29 N	66.47 W
Ladon	50	48.00 N	2.32 E
Ladonia	196	33.25 N	95.56 W
La Dorada	246	5.27 N	74.40 W
La Dormida	252	33.21 S	67.55 W
Lado Sarāi ◆ [8]	272a	28.32 N	77.12 E
L'adova ≃	78	48.28 N	27.37 E
Ladovskaja Balka	80	45.38 N	41.25 E
Ladožskaja	78	45.19 N	39.54 E
Ladožskoje Ozero	76	60.08 N	31.04 E
Ladožskoje ozero (Lake Ladoga) ⊜	24	61.00 N	31.30 E
Lādpur ◆ [8]	272a	28.44 N	76.59 E
Ladrillero, Golfo c	254	49.20 S	75.37 W
Ladson	192	32.59 N	80.06 W
Ladue	219	38.38 N	90.23 W
Ladue ≃	180	63.09 N	140.25 W
Laduozong	102	31.27 N	97.19 E
Laduškin	76	54.36 N	20.11 E
Ladva	24	61.21 N	34.34 E
Ladva-Vetka	24	61.21 N	34.27 E
Lādwa	124	29.59 N	77.03 E
L'ady, Bela.	76	54.36 N	31.10 E
Lady, Fr.	261	48.35 N	2.54 E
L'ady, Ross.	76	58.38 N	28.47 E
Lady Ann Strait ʉ	176	75.40 N	79.50 W
Ladybank	46	56.16 N	3.08 W
Lady Barron	166	40.12 S	148.14 E
Ladybower Reservoir ⊜ [1]	44	53.20 N	1.45 W
Ladybrand	158	29.19 S	27.25 E
Lady Elliot Island I	166	24.07 S	152.42 E
Lady Evelyn Lake ⊜	190	47.20 N	80.10 W
Lady Frere	158	31.44 S	27.16 E
Lady Grey	158	30.45 S	27.13 E
Lady Lake	220	28.55 N	81.55 W
Ladysmith, Austl.	171b	35.12 S	147.31 E
Ladysmith, B.C., Can.	182	48.58 N	123.49 W
Ladysmith, S. Afr.	158	28.34 S	29.45 E
Ladysmith, Wi., U.S.	190	45.27 N	91.06 W
Ladyženka	86	51.00 N	68.42 E
Ladyžin	78	48.41 N	29.15 E
Ladžanurges	84	42.37 N	42.50 E
Lae	164	6.45 S	147.00 E
Lae I [1]	14	8.56 N	166.14 E
Laem, Khao ʌ	110	14.27 N	101.30 E
Laem Ngop	110	12.10 N	102.26 E
La Encantada	232	25.17 N	101.04 W
La Encarnacion	234	23.23 N	98.01 W
Laer	52	52.03 N	7.21 E
Laer ◆ [8]	263	51.28 N	7.16 E
Lærdalsøyri	26	61.06 N	7.29 E
La Escondida	196	26.17 N	99.46 W
La Esmeralda, Méx.	232	27.17 N	103.39 W
La Esmeralda, Para.	252	22.13 S	62.38 W
La Esmeralda, Ven.	246	3.10 N	65.33 W
Læsø I	26	57.16 N	11.01 E
La Esperanza, Cuba	240p	22.46 N	83.44 W
La Esperanza, Hond.	236	14.20 N	88.10 W
La Esperanza, Méx.	196	26.46 N	104.00 W
La Esperanza, Méx.	232	21.39 N	98.19 W
La Esperanza, Perú	248	8.05 S	79.04 W
La Esperanza, P.R.	240m	18.22 N	66.07 W
La Estación ◆ [8]	266a	40.30 N	3.48 W
La Estrada	34	42.41 N	8.29 W
La Estrella, Bol.	248	16.30 S	63.45 W
La Estrella, Ven.	286c	10.25 N	65.48 W
La Estrella, Cerro ʌ	286a	19.20 N	99.05 W

Lafa	89	43.50 N	127.19 E
La Falda	252	31.05 S	64.30 W
La Farge	190	43.34 N	90.38 W
LaFargeville	212	44.11 N	75.57 W
Lafayette, Fr.	62	45.35 N	5.04 E
Lafayette, Al., U.S.	194	32.53 N	85.24 W
Lafayette, Ca., U.S.	226	37.53 N	122.07 W
Lafayette, Co., U.S.	198	39.59 N	105.05 W
Lafayette, Ga., U.S.	192	34.42 N	85.16 W
Lafayette, In., U.S.	216	40.25 N	86.52 W
Lafayette, La., U.S.	194	30.13 N	92.01 W
Lafayette, Mn., U.S.	190	44.26 N	94.23 W
Lafayette, N.J., U.S.	210	41.05 N	74.41 W
La Fayette, N.Y., U.S.	210	42.54 N	76.06 W
Lafayette, Oh., U.S.	216	40.46 N	83.57 W
Lafayette, Or., U.S.	224	45.14 N	123.06 W
La Fayette, R.I., U.S.	207	41.34 N	71.28 W
Lafayette, Tn., U.S.	194	36.31 N	86.01 W
La Fayette, Tx., U.S.	222	32.54 N	94.51 W
Lafayette, Mount ʌ	188	44.10 N	71.38 W
Lafayette Hill	285	40.05 N	75.15 W
Lafayette Reservoir ⊜ [1]	282	37.53 N	122.08 W
Lafayette Water Tunnel ◆ [5]	282	37.54 N	122.12 W
La Fé	240p	21.45 N	82.45 W
La Fère	50	49.40 N	3.22 E
La Feria	196	26.09 N	97.49 W
Laferrere	288	34.45 S	58.35 W
La Ferrière-sur-Risle	50	48.59 N	0.48 E
La Ferté-Alais	50	48.29 N	2.21 E
La Ferté-Bernard	50	48.11 N	0.40 E
La Ferté-Frênel	50	48.50 N	0.30 E
La Ferté-Gaucher	50	48.47 N	3.18 E
La Ferté-Imbault	50	47.23 N	1.58 E
La Ferté-Macé	32	48.36 N	0.22 W
La Ferté-Milon	50	49.10 N	3.07 E
La Ferté-Saint-Aubin	50	47.43 N	1.56 E
La Ferté-sous-Jouarre	50	48.57 N	3.08 E
Laferté-sur-Amance	58	47.50 N	5.42 E
La Ferté-Vidame	50	48.37 N	0.55 E
La Ferté-Villeneuil	50	47.59 N	1.21 E
Lafferty	214	40.06 N	81.01 W
Laffrey	62	45.02 N	5.46 E
Lafia	150	8.30 N	8.30 E
Lafiagi	150	8.52 N	5.25 E
Laflamme ≃	190	48.56 N	77.18 W
Laflèche, P.Q., Can.	275a	45.30 N	73.28 W
Lafleche, Sk., Can.	184	49.43 N	106.35 W
La Flèche, Fr.	32	47.42 N	0.05 W
La Floresta	266d	41.27 N	2.04 E
La Florida, Chile	286e	33.33 S	70.34 W
La Florida, Esp.	266d	41.31 N	2.12 E
La Florida, Guat.	232	16.33 N	90.27 W
Lafnitz ≃	61	46.57 N	16.16 E
La Foa	175f	21.43 S	165.50 E
La Foce	62	44.08 N	9.47 E
La Follette	192	36.22 N	84.07 W
Lafon	154	5.02 N	32.27 E
Lafontaine, P.Q., Can.	206	45.48 N	74.01 W
La Fontaine, In., U.S.	216	40.40 N	85.43 W
Lafontaine, Parc ♦	275a	45.32 N	73.34 W
Lafourche, Bayou ≃	194	29.05 N	90.14 W
La Foux, Fr.	62	43.16 N	6.35 E
La Foux, Fr.	62	44.17 N	6.34 E
La Fragua	252	26.05 S	64.20 W
La Francia	252	31.24 S	62.38 W
La Fregeneda	34	40.59 N	6.52 W
La Frette-sur-Seine	261	48.58 N	2.11 E
La Fría	246	8.13 N	72.15 W
Lafrimbolle	58	48.36 N	7.01 E
La Fuente de San Esteban	34	40.48 N	6.15 W
Laga, Monti della ⩘	66	42.37 N	13.24 E
La Gacilly	28	47.46 N	2.09 W
Lagaip ≃	164	5.05 S	142.40 E
La Galite I	36	37.32 N	8.56 E
La Gallareta	252	29.34 S	60.23 W
La Gallega	34	41.54 N	3.16 W
Lagan	26	56.55 N	13.59 E
Lagan ≃, Sve.	26	56.33 N	12.56 E
Lagan ≃, N. Ire., U.K.	48	54.37 N	5.53 W
Lagangzong	120	28.05 N	91.04 E
Lagantu	102	42.20 N	108.22 E
La Garde	62	43.07 N	6.01 E
La Garde-Freinet	62	43.19 N	6.28 E
La Garenne-Colombes	261	48.55 N	2.15 E
Lagarina, Val V	64	45.45 N	11.00 E
Lagarto, Bra.	250	10.54 S	37.41 W
Lagarto, C.R.	236	10.07 N	84.56 W
Lagarto Creek ≃	196	28.08 N	97.56 W
Lagawe	116	16.49 N	121.06 E
Lagay	116	14.06 N	122.12 E
Lagayan	116	17.43 N	120.42 E
Lage, Dtsch.	52	51.59 N	8.48 E
Lage, Esp.	34	43.13 N	9.00 W
Lage, Zhg.	120	29.26 N	85.51 E
Lagedu	102	26.24 N	101.11 E
Lågen ≃, Nor.	26	59.03 N	10.05 E
Lågen ≃, Nor.	26	61.08 N	10.25 E
Lägerdorf	52	53.53 N	9.34 E
Lages	252	27.48 S	50.19 W
Lageuen	114	4.44 N	95.31 E
Lage Zwaluwe	52	51.43 N	4.41 E
Laggan	46	57.02 N	4.16 W
Laggan, Loch ⊜ [1]	46	56.57 N	4.28 W
Laggan Bay c	46	55.41 N	6.19 W
Lagginhorn ʌ	58	46.11 N	8.01 E
Laghmān □ [4]	120	35.00 N	70.15 E
Laghouat	148	33.50 N	2.59 E
Laghouat □ [5]	148	32.00 N	3.30 E
Laghy	48	54.37 N	8.05 W
Lagič	84	40.51 N	48.24 E
La Giettaz	62	45.52 N	6.30 E
La Giganta, Cerro ʌ	234	21.08 N	101.19 W
La Giustiniana ◆ [8]	267a	41.59 N	12.24 E
La Gleize	56	50.25 N	5.51 E
La Gloria	246	8.37 N	73.48 W
Lagnieu	58	45.54 N	5.21 E
Lagny	50	48.52 N	2.43 E
Lagny-le-Sac	261	49.05 N	2.45 E
Lago	68	39.10 N	16.09 E
Lago, Mount ʌ	224	48.51 N	120.32 W
Lagoa Branca	256	21.54 S	47.02 W
Lagoa da Prata	255	20.01 S	45.33 W
Lagoa Formosa	255	18.47 S	46.24 W
Lago Argentino → Calafate	254	50.20 S	72.18 W
Lagoa Santa	255	19.38 S	43.53 W
Lagoa Vermelha	252	28.13 S	51.32 W
Lago Blanco	254	45.55 S	71.15 W
Lago da Pedra	250	4.20 S	45.10 W
Lagodechi	84	41.49 N	46.18 E
Lagodechskij zapovednik ♦	84	41.53 N	46.22 E
Lagoinha	256	23.06 S	45.11 W
Lagolândia	255	15.37 S	49.02 W
Lagolovo	265a	59.42 N	30.00 E
Lagonegro	68	40.07 N	15.46 E
Lagonglong	116	8.48 N	124.47 E
Lagonoy	116	13.44 N	123.31 E
Lagonoy Gulf c	116	13.35 N	123.45 E
Lagopesole, Castel di ⊥	68	40.48 N	15.45 E
Lago Posadas	254	47.32 S	71.45 W
Lagorai, Catena del ⩘	64	46.18 N	11.35 E
Lago Ranco	254	40.20 S	72.38 W
La Gorgue	50	50.38 N	2.42 E
Lagos, Ang.	152	16.04 S	17.03 E
Lagos, Nig.	150	6.27 N	3.24 E
Lagos, Nig.	273a	6.27 N	3.24 E
Lagos, Port.	34	37.06 N	8.40 W
Lagos □ [5]	150	6.30 N	3.20 E
Lagos (Ikeja) Airport ⊠	273a	6.35 N	3.20 E

≃ River	Fluß	Río	Rivière	Rio
≋ Canal	Kanal	Canal	Canal	Canal
ᒪ Waterfall, Rapids	Wasserfall, Stromschnellen	Cascada, Rápidos	Chute d'eau, Rapides	Cascata, Rápidos
ʉ Strait	Meeresstraße	Estrecho	Détroit	Estreito
c Bay, Gulf	Bucht, Golf	Bahía, Golfo	Baie, Golfe	Baía, Golfo
⊜ Lake, Lakes	See, Seen	Lago, Lagos	Lac, Lacs	Lago, Lagos
≡ Swamp	Sumpf	Pantano	Marais	Pântano
⁂ Ice Features, Glacier	Eis- und Gletscherformen	Accidentes Glaciales	Formes glaciaires	Acidentes glaciares
▽ Other Hydrographic Features	Andere Hydrographische Objekte	Otros Elementos Hidrográficos	Autres données hydrographiques	Outros acidentes hidrográficos

✦ Submarine Features	Untermeerische Objekte	Accidentes Submarinos	Formes de relief sous-marin	Acidentes submarinos
□ Political Unit	Politische Einheit	Unidad Política	Entité politique	Unidade política
ʋ Cultural Institution	Kulturelle Institution	Institución Cultural	Institution culturelle	Instituição cultural
⊥ Historical Site	Historische Stätte	Sitio Histórico	Site historique	Sítio histórico
♦ Recreational Site	Erholungs- und Ferienort	Sitio de Recreo	Centre de loisirs	Area de Lazer
⊠ Airport	Flughafen	Aeropuerto	Aéroport	Aeroporto
■ Military Installation	Militäranlage	Instalación Militar	Installation militaire	Instalação militar
◆ Miscellaneous	Verschiedenes	Misceláneo	Divers	Diversos

Symbols in the index entries represent the broad categories identified in the key at the right. Symbols with superior numbers (⍦ⁿ) identify subcategories (see complete key on page I · 1).

Symbole im Register stellen die rechts im Schlüssel erklärten Kategorien dar. Symbole mit hochgestellten Ziffern (⍦ⁿ) bezeichnen Unterabteilungen einer Kategorie (vgl. vollständiger Schlüssel auf Seite I · 1).

Los símbolos incluídos en el texto del índice representan las grandes categorías identificadas con la clave a la derecha. Los símbolos con números en su parte superior (⍦ⁿ) identifican las subcategorías (véase la clave completa a la página I · 1).

Les symboles de l'index représentent les catégories identifiées dans la légende à droite. Les symboles suivis d'un indice (⍦ⁿ) représentent des sous-catégories (voir légende complète à la page I · 1).

Os símbolos incluídos no texto do índice representam as grandes categorias identificadas com a chave à direita. Os símbolos com números em cima (⍦ⁿ) identificam as subcategorias (veja-se a chave completa à página I · 1).

Symbol	English	Deutsch	Español	Français	Português
▲	Mountain	Berg	Montaña	Montagne	Montanha
⩙	Mountains	Gebirge	Montañas	Montagnes	Montanhas
⌅	Pass	Paß	Paso	Col	Passo
ꝟ	Valley, Canyon	Tal, Cañon	Valle, Cañón	Vallée, Canyon	Vale, Canhão
▷	Plain	Ebene	Llano	Plaine	Llano
⊁	Cape	Kap	Cabo	Cap	Cabo
I	Island	Insel	Isla	Île	Ilha
II	Islands	Inseln	Islas	Îles	Ilhas
⊡	Other Topographic Features	Andere Topographische Objekte	Otros Elementos Topográficos	Autres données topographiques	Outros acidentes topográficos

ESPAÑOL	FRANÇAIS	PORTUGUÊS
Nombre — Página — Lat.°' — Long.°' W = Oeste	Nom — Page — Lat.°' — Long.°' W = Ouest	Nome — Página — Lat.°' — Long.°' W = Oeste

ESPAÑOL

Lampasas ≃ 196 30.59 N 97.24 W
Lampezos de Naranjo 232 27.01 N 100.31 W
Lampedusa 70a 35.30 N 12.56 E
Lampedusa, Isola di ∎ 70a 35.31 N 12.35 E
Lampertheim 56 49.35 N 8.28 E
Lampeter, Wales, U.K. 42 52.07 N 4.05 W
Lampeter, Pa., U.S. 208 39.58 N 73.14 W
Lamphun 110 18.35 N 99.01 E
Lampinsaari 26 64.25 N 25.09 E
Lampione, Isolotto di ∎ 70a 35.34 N 12.19 E
Lampman 184 49.23 N 102.45 W
Lamprechtshausen 64 47.59 N 12.57 E
Lampung □⁴ 112 5.00 S 105.00 E
Lampung, Teluk ⊂ 115a 5.40 S 105.20 E
Lamskoje 76 52.57 N 38.02 E
Lamspringe 52 51.58 N 10.00 E
Lamstedt 52 53.38 N 9.05 E
Lämta 124 22.08 N 80.07 E
Lam Tong Hoi Hap ∿ 271d 22.15 N 114.15 E
Lamu, Kenya 154 2.16 S 40.54 E
Lāmu, Mya. 110 19.14 N 94.10 E
Lamud 248 6.09 S 77.55 W
La Muerte, Cerro ∧ 236 9.33 N 83.44 W
Lam Uk Wei 271d 22.26 N 114.22 E
La Mure 62 44.54 N 5.47 E
Lamure-sur-Azergues 58 46.04 N 4.30 E
La Mutua 234 22.23 N 99.18 W
Lan' ≃ Bela. 76 52.09 N 27.18 E
Lan ≃, Zhg. 100 41.14 N 123.32 E
Lan, Loi ∧ 110 19.40 N 97.55 E
Lana 64 46.37 N 11.09 E
Lanai ∎ 229a 20.50 N 156.55 W
Lanai City 229a 20.49 N 156.55 W
Lanaihale ∧ 229a 20.49 N 156.52 W
Lanaken 56 50.53 N 5.39 E
Lanalhue, Lago ⊜ 222 37.55 S 73.18 W
La Nana, Bayou ≃ 222 31.27 N 94.43 W
Lanao del Norte □⁴ 116 8.10 N 124.00 E
Lanao del Sur □⁴ 116 7.50 N 124.25 E
La Napoule 62 43.31 N 6.56 E
Lanarce 62 44.44 N 4.00 E
Lanark, On., Can. 212 45.01 N 76.22 W
Lanark, Scot., U.K. 46 55.41 N 3.46 W
Lanark, Il., U.S. 190 42.06 N 89.50 W
Lanark, Pa., U.S. 208 40.33 N 75.26 W
Lanark □⁶ 212 45.05 N 76.20 W
La Nartelle 62 43.19 N 6.39 E
Lanas 112 5.20 N 116.30 E
La Nava de Ricomalillo 34 39.39 N 4.59 W
Lanbi Kyun ∎ 110 10.50 N 98.15 E
Lanboyan Point ⊁ 116 8.18 N 122.56 E
Lancang 102 23.00 N 100 02 E
— Mekong ≃ 12 10.33 N 105.24 E
Lancashire □⁶ 44 53.45 N 2.40 W
Lancashire Plain ≃ 44 53.40 N 2.40 W
Lancaster, On., Can. 206 45.08 N 74.30 W
Lancaster, Eng., U.K. 44 54.03 N 2.48 W
Lancaster, Ca., U.S. 228 34.41 N 118.08 W
Lancaster, Ky., U.S. 192 37.37 N 84.34 W
Lancaster, Ma., U.S. 207 42.27 N 71.40 W
Lancaster, Mn., U.S. 198 48.51 N 96.48 W
Lancaster, Mo., U.S. 194 40.31 N 92.31 W
Lancaster, N.H., U.S. 188 44.29 N 71.34 W
Lancaster, N.Y., U.S. 210 42.54 N 78.40 W
Lancaster, Oh., U.S. 198 39.43 N 82.36 W
Lancaster, Pa., U.S. 208 40.02 N 76.18 W
Lancaster, S.C., U.S. 192 34.43 N 80.46 W
Lancaster, Tx., U.S. 222 32.38 N 96.47 W
Lancaster, Va., U.S. 208 37.46 N 76.28 W
Lancaster, Wi., U.S. 190 42.50 N 90.42 W
Lancaster □⁶, Pa., U.S. 208 40.02 N 76.19 W
Lancaster □⁶, Va., U.S. 208 37.45 N 76.30 W
Lancaster Canal ≃ 262 53.46 N 2.43 W
Lancaster Sound ∪ 176 74.13 N 84.00 W
Lancaster Village 84 42.06 N 42.01 E
Lančhuti 84 42.06 N 42.01 E
Lance Creek 200 43.01 N 104.38 W
Lance Creek ≃ 198 43.21 N 104.55 W
Lancefield 167 37.17 S 144.44 E
Lancelin 162 31.02 S 115.20 E
Lancelot, Mount ∧ 162 26.13 S 123.12 E
Lancey 62 45.14 N 5.53 E
Lanchang 114 3.30 N 102.11 E
Lanchester 44 54.49 N 1.44 W
Lanchow
— Lanzhou 102 36.03 N 103.41 E
Lanciano 66 42.14 N 14.23 E
Lancín, Fr. 62 45.43 N 5.24 E
Lančín, Ukr. 48 48.34 N 24.45 E
Lancing 42 50.50 N 0.19 W
Lanco 254 39.24 S 72.46 W
Lancones 246 4.35 S 80.30 W
Lancun 98 36.24 N 120.10 E
Lancut 30 50.05 N 22.13 E
Lancy 58 46.11 N 6.07 E
Lândana 152 5.13 S 12.08 E
Landang Gua 116 6.58 N 122.15 E
Landau 54 49.12 N 8.07 E
Landau an der Isar 54 48.40 N 12.43 E
Landay 128 30.31 N 63.47 E
Land Between the Lakes ⫶ 194 36.55 N 88.05 W
Landeck 58 47.08 N 10.34 E
Landen 56 50.45 N 5.05 E
Landenberg 208 39.47 N 75.45 W
Landenhausen 56 50.36 N 9.47 E
Lander 200 42.49 N 108.43 W
Lander ≃ 162 20.25 S 132.00 E
Landerneau 62 48.27 N 4.15 W
Landes □¹ 62 44.00 N 1.00 W
Landes ⫶¹ 62 44.15 N 1.00 W
Landesbergen 52 52.33 N 9.07 E
Landeskrone ∧² 54 50.58 N 14.46 E
Landess 216 40.37 N 85.34 W
Landete 34 39.54 N 1.22 W
Landham Brook ≃ 263 42.22 N 71.25 W
Landhausen 263 51.24 N 7.45 E
Landi 98 34.35 N 119.59 E
Landi Kotal 124 34.06 N 71.09 E
Landina 86 53.10 N 67.02 E
Landing 210 40.54 N 74.40 W
Landing Lake ⊜ 184 55.17 N 97.26 W
Landis, Sk., Can. 184 52.12 N 108.28 W
Landis, N.C., U.S. 192 35.32 N 80.36 W
Landisburg 208 40.20 N 77.18 W
Landivisiau 62 48.31 N 4.04 W
Landkey 42 51.04 N 4.00 W
Landö 52 54.27 N 11.08 E
Lando 192 34.46 N 81.00 W
Land O'Lakes, Fl., U.S. 192 28.13 N 82.28 W
Land O'Lakes, Wi., U.S. 220 28.11 N 82.34 W
Landor 162 25.09 S 116.54 E
Landos 62 44.51 N 3.52 E
Landösjön ⊜ 26 63.35 N 14.04 E
Landover Estates 284c 38.56 N 76.54 W
Landover Hills 284c 38.56 N 76.53 W
Landover Mall ☒⁹ 284c 38.55 N 76.51 W
Landquart 58 46.58 N 9.32 E
Landquart ≃ 58 46.58 N 9.32 E
Landrecies 50 50.08 N 3.42 E
Landres 58 49.19 N 5.48 E
Landreth Draw ∨ 196 31.14 N 102.29 W
Landri Sales 58 44.15 N 9.15 E
Landri Sales 255 7.16 S 43.55 W
Landro (Höhlenstein) 63 46.39 N 12.14 E
Landrum 192 35.10 N 82.11 W
Landry 62 46.31 N 6.46 E
Landsberg 54 51.31 N 12.10 E
Landsberg am Lech 58 48.05 N 10.55 E

FRANÇAIS

Landsberg an der Warthe
— Gorzów Wielkopolski 30 52.44 N 15.15 E
Landsborough 166 26.49 S 152.58 E
Landsborough Creek ≃ 166 22.30 S 144.33 E
Landsbro 26 57.22 N 14.54 E
Land's End ⊁, Eng., U.K. 42 50.03 N 5.44 W
Lands End ⊁, Ca., U.S. 228 37.35 N 118.36 W
Lands End ⊁, R.I., U.S. 207 41.27 N 71.19 W
Landshut 60 48.33 N 12.09 E
Landskrona 41 55.52 N 12.50 E
Landsman Creek ≃ 198 39.35 N 102.19 W
Landsmeer 52 52.26 N 4.52 E
Landštejn 61 49.00 N 15.13 E
Landstuhl 56 49.25 N 7.34 E
Landweg 263 51.29 N 7.37 E
Landwehrbach ≃ 263 51.26 N 6.26 E
Lane 219 40.07 N 88.51 W
Lane City 222 29.13 N 96.02 W
Lane Cove 274a 33.49 S 151.10 E
Lane Cove ≃ 274a 33.48 S 151.09 E
Lane Cove River Park ⫶ 274a 33.47 S 151.09 E
La Negra 252 23.45 S 70.19 W
Lane Mountain ∧ 228 35.05 N 116.58 W
Lanesborough 64 47.09 N 11.44 E
Lanesboro, Ma., U.S. 207 42.31 N 73.14 W
Lanesboro, Mn., U.S. 190 43.43 N 91.58 W
Lanesboro, Pa., U.S. 210 41.57 N 75.35 W
Lanester 32 47.46 N 3.21 W
Lanesville, In., U.S. 218 38.14 N 85.59 W
Lanesville, N.Y., U.S. 210 42.08 N 74.16 W
Lanesville, Va., U.S. 208 37.37 N 76.59 W
Lanett 194 32.52 N 85.11 W
Lanexa 208 37.24 N 76.55 W
Lanezi Lake ⊜ 182 53.03 N 125.09 W
Lang 184 49.56 N 104.23 W
La'nga Co ⊜ 124 30.42 N 81.16 E
Langadas 38 40.45 N 23.04 E
Langádhia 38 37.41 N 22.02 E
Langa-Langa 152 3.54 S 15.56 E
Langao, Lake ⊜ 144 7.35 N 38.48 E
Langao 102 32.13 N 109.02 E
Langar, Afg. 120 37.02 N 73.47 E
L'angar, Kyrg. 123 40.25 N 72.07 E
L'angar, Taj. 123 37.02 N 72.42 E
Langara 112 4.02 S 123.00 E
Langara Island ∎ 182 54.14 N 133.00 W
Langarūd 128 37.11 N 50.10 E
L'angasovo 80 58.32 N 49.30 E
Langat ≃ 114 2.54 N 101.22 E
Langau 61 48.49 N 15.55 E
Langavat, Loch ⊜ 46 58.04 N 6.48 W
Långban 40 59.51 N 14.15 E
Langbank 184 50.05 N 102.20 W
Lang Bay 182 49.47 N 124.21 W
Langberg 158 28.20 S 22.35 E
Langburkersdorf 54 51.02 N 14.14 E
Langdai 102 26.06 N 105.20 E
Langdon 198 48.45 N 98.22 W
Langdondale 214 40.08 N 78.15 W
Langdon Hills 260 51.34 N 0.25 E
Langeac 32 45.06 N 3.30 E
Langeais 50 47.20 N 0.24 E
Langebaan 158 33.05 S 18.02 E
Langeberg ∧⁴ 158 33.55 S 20.30 E
Lange Berge ∧² 58 52.00 N 10.55 E
Langebrück 54 51.07 N 13.50 E
Langeland ∎ 41 54.50 N 10.50 E
Langelandsbælt ∿ 41 54.50 N 10.55 E
Längelmävesi ⊜ 26 61.32 N 24.22 E
Langeloth 214 40.21 N 80.24 W
Langelsheim 52 51.56 N 10.19 E
Langenburg, Sk., Can. 184 50.50 N 101.43 W
Langenburg, Dtsch. 54 49.15 N 9.50 E
Langendorf 54 51.11 N 11.58 E
Langendreer ≃⁸ 263 51.28 N 7.19 E
Langeneichstädt 54 51.25 N 11.41 E
Langenfeld, Dtsch. 56 51.07 N 6.56 E
Langenfeld, Öst. 58 52.35 N 12.08 E
Langenhagen 52 52.27 N 9.44 E
Langenhessen 54 50.45 N 12.22 E
Langenhorn 54 54.41 N 8.53 E
Langenhorst 263 52.29 N 7.02 E
Langenlois 61 48.28 N 15.40 E
Langennaundorf 54 51.36 N 13.20 E
Langenneufnach 54 48.16 N 10.36 E
Langenselbold 56 50.10 N 9.02 E
Langensteinach 54 49.30 N 10.16 E
Langenthal 58 47.13 N 7.47 E
Langenwang 61 47.34 N 15.37 E
Langenwetzendorf 54 50.41 N 12.04 E
Langenzenn 54 49.18 N 10.48 E
Langenzersdorf 61 48.18 N 16.22 E
Langeoog 52 53.45 N 7.29 E
Langeoog ∎ 52 53.45 N 7.32 E
Langerfeld ≃⁸ 263 51.16 N 7.15 E
Langerwehe 56 50.49 N 6.21 E
Langeskov 41 55.22 N 10.36 E
Langesund 26 59.00 N 9.45 E
Langevåg 26 62.10 N 5.11 E
Langewiesen 54 50.40 N 10.58 E
Langfang 98 39.31 N 116.41 E
— Anci 105 39.31 N 116.41 E
Langfjorden ⊂² 26 62.43 N 7.37 E
Langford, B.C., Can. 182 48.27 N 123.30 W
Langford, Eng., U.K. 260 51.45 N 0.02 E
Langford, S.D., U.S. 198 45.36 N 97.49 W
Langfurth 54 49.12 N 10.20 E
Langgapayung 114 1.43 N 99.59 E
Langgöns 56 50.30 N 8.40 E
Langhalsen ☒² 54 58.56 N 4.61 E
Langham 44 52.42 N 106.57 W
Langhirano 64 44.37 N 10.16 E
Langhoim 44 55.09 N 3.00 W
Langi Shan ∧ 100 28.32 N 121.36 E
Langjökull ☒ 24a 64.42 N 20.12 W
Langji Shan 100 28.32 N 121.36 E
Lang Ka, Doi ∧ 110 20.17 N 99.24 E
Lang Kawi, Pulau ∎ 114 6.22 N 99.50 E
Langkesi, Kepulauan ∎∎ 112 5.18 S 124.20 E
Langklip 158 28.12 S 20.20 E
Langkrans 158 27.47 S 21.03 E

PORTUGUÊS

Langlade ∎ 186 46.50 N 56.20 W
Lang Larg ≃ 169 38.17 S 145.31 E
Langley, B.C., Can. 224 49.06 N 122.39 W
Langley, Eng., U.K. 260 51.30 N 0.33 W
Langley, Eng., U.K. 260 51.14 N 0.35 W
Langley, Eng., U.K. 262 53.15 N 2.05 W
Langley, Ok., U.S. 196 36.27 N 95.02 W
Langley, S.C., U.S. 192 33.31 N 81.50 W
Langley, Wa., U.S. 224 48.02 N 122.24 W
Langley Air Force Base ∎ 208 37.05 N 76.21 W
Langley Forest 284c 38.57 N 77.10 W
Langley Hill ∧² 282 37.20 N 122.14 W
Langley Park 284c 38.59 N 76.58 W
Langleyvile 219 39.34 N 89.21 W
Langlois 166 26.26 S 146.05 E
Langlois 202 42.55 N 124.26 W
Langmazong 120 30.52 N 89.58 E
Lang Mo 110 17.14 N 106.27 E
Långnäs 26 60.06 N 20.17 E
Langnau 58 46.57 N 7.47 E
Langogne 62 44.43 N 3.51 E
Langon 32 44.33 N 0.15 W
Langping 102 30.38 N 110.21 E
Langport 42 51.02 N 2.50 W
Langqiao 100 30.30 N 118.24 E
Languquaid 60 48.49 N 12.03 E
Langreo
— Sama [de Langreo] 34 43.18 N 5.41 W
Langres 58 47.52 N 5.20 E
Langres, Plateau de ∧¹ 58 47.41 N 5.00 E
Langruth 184 50.24 N 98.38 W
Langruzong 120 31.50 N 91.25 E
Langsa 114 4.28 N 97.58 E
Langsa, Teluk ⊂ 114 4.35 N 98.00 E
Langschede 263 51.29 N 7.43 E
Längsele 26 63.11 N 17.04 E
Langshan, Zhg. 102 41.12 N 107.22 E
Langshan, Zhg. 105 40.22 N 115.41 E
Långshyttan 40 60.27 N 16.01 E
Långsjön ⊜ 40 59.00 N 17.27 E
Langsnek ⫶ 158 27.28 S 29.55 E
Lang Son 110 21.50 N 106.44 E
Langstaff 275b 43.50 N 79.25 W
Langst-Kierst 263 51.18 N 6.43 E
Lang Suan 110 9.57 N 99.04 E
Långsvan ≃ 40 59.43 N 15.49 E
Langtang National Park ⫶ 124 28.10 N 85.30 E
Langtian 120 25.11 N 113.28 E
Langting 120 25.30 N 93.07 E
Langton 212 42.45 N 80.35 W
Langtoutun 89 46.51 N 121.54 E
Langtuozi 104 41.01 N 121.43 E
Langu 100 27.56 N 118.11 E
Langue ≃ 236 13.37 N 87.39 W
Languedoc □⁹ 62 43.30 N 3.30 E
Langui Layo, Laguna de ⊜ 248 14.29 S 71.13 W
L'Anguille ≃ 194 34.44 N 90.40 W
Languila 54 51.09 N 10.25 E
Langundu, Tanjung ⊁ 115b 8.49 S 118.58 E
Langwarden 52 53.36 N 8.19 E
Langwedel 52 52.59 N 9.12 E
Langweer 52 52.57 N 5.43 E
Langweid 56 48.29 N 10.51 E
Langweiler 56 49.40 N 7.31 E
Langwies 58 46.49 N 9.43 E
Langwo 104 41.13 N 121.44 E
Langwozhuang 105 39.05 N 115.37 E
Langxi 106 31.08 N 119.10 E
Langxi ≃ 100 31.10 N 118.59 E
Langzhong 102 31.35 N 105.59 E
Langzishan 104 41.02 N 123.23 E
Lanham 284c 38.58 N 76.51 W
Lanhill Island ∎ 116 6.44 N 122.22 E
Laniba, Mount ∧ 116 10.27 N 123.56 E
Lanigan ≃ 184 51.52 N 105.02 W
Lanigan Creek ≃ 184 51.23 N 105.13 W
Lanín, Parque Nacional ⫶ 254 39.36 S 71.24 W
Lanín, Volcán ∧¹ 254 39.38 S 71.30 W
Lanjiang 107 30.24 N 105.11 E
Lankao (Lanfeng) 98 34.50 N 114.49 E
Lanker See ⊜ 54 54.12 N 10.17 E
Lankeys Creek 171b 35.49 S 147.39 E
Länkipohja 26 61.44 N 24.48 E
Lankivci ≃ 48 51.01 N 5.44 E
Lank-Latum 263 51.18 N 6.41 E
Lankou 100 23.59 N 115.05 E
Lankoviri 146 9.00 N 11.25 E
Lankwitz ⫶⁸ 264a 52.26 N 13.21 E
Lanling 89 45.15 N 126.12 E
Lannabruk 40 59.06 N 15.19 E
Linnahólm 41 66.56 N 15.19 E
Lannaja 78 49.21 N 35.06 E
Lannemezan 32 43.08 N 0.23 E
Lannilis 32 48.34 N 4.31 W
Lannion 32 48.44 N 3.28 W
L'Annonciation 206 46.25 N 74.52 W
Lanoka Harbor 208 39.52 N 74.10 W
Lanoraie 206 45.58 N 73.13 W
La Noria 258 35.10 S 58.48 W
Lanovcy 78 49.52 N 26.05 E
Lanping 102 26.29 N 99.23 E
Lanqiao 104 40.56 N 122.25 E
Lanqikoucur 104 40.52 N 122.26 E
Lanqu 104 22.13 N 123.15 E
Lansan 236 15.34 N 89.58 W
Lans, Montagnes de ∧ 62 45.04 N 5.30 E
Lansberg 62 44.52 N 5.28 E
Lansdale 208 40.14 N 75.17 W
Lansdowne, Austl. 162 17.53 S 126.39 E
Lansdowne, Austl. 274a 33.54 S 150.59 E
Lansdowne 212 44.24 N 76.01 W
Lansdowne, India 124 29.50 N 78.41 E
Lansdowne, Md., U.S. 284b 39.14 N 76.39 W
Lansdowne, Pa., U.S. 285 39.56 N 75.16 W
L'Anse, Mi., U.S. 196 46.45 N 88.27 W
Lanse, Pa., U.S. 214 40.59 N 78.08 W
L'Anse-aux-Meadows National Historic Park ⫶ 186 51.36 N 55.32 W
L'anse Creuse Bay ⊂ 214 42.34 N 82.49 W
L'Anse Indian Reservation ⫶ 190 46.48 N 88.22 W
Lans-en-Vercors 62 45.08 N 5.35 E
Lansford, N.D., U.S. 198 48.37 N 101.22 W
Lansford, Pa., U.S. 210 40.49 N 75.52 W
Lanshan 100 25.23 N 112.11 E
Lanshantou 98 35.07 N 119.21 E
Lansing, Il., U.S. 216 41.33 N 87.32 W
Lansing, Ks., U.S. 190 39.14 N 94.54 W
Lansing, Mi., U.S. 216 42.44 N 84.33 W
Lansing, N.Y., U.S. 210 42.32 N 76.30 W
Lansing, Oh., U.S. 214 40.04 N 80.45 W
La Penne-sur-Huveaune 62 43.17 N 5.31 E
Lansing 204 42.32 N 91.13 W
Lanslebourg 62 45.17 N 6.52 E
Lansing Municipal Airport ∎ 278 41.32 N 87.32 W
Lanstrop ≃⁸ 263 51.34 N 7.34 E
Lanta, Ko ∎ 110 7.35 N 99.04 E
Lantan Island ∎ 100 22.17 N 113.59 E
Lanta Yai, Ko ∎ 110 7.30 N 99.05 E
Lantau ☒ 271b 22.16 N 113.55 E
Lantern ∧ 146 9.53 N 8.04 E
Lapham Hill ∧² 216 40.07 N 88.24 W
Lanti ≃ 102 34.03 N 109.12 E
Lantian 102 34.03 N 109.12 E
Lantianbā 107 28.52 N 105.26 E

Lantiancheng 271a 39.58 N 116.17 E
Lantsch 58 46.41 N 9.34 E
Lantschou
— Lanzhou 102 36.03 N 103.41 E
Lantzville 224 49.15 N 124.05 W
La Nurra ≃¹ 71 40.45 N 8.15 E
Lanús 258 34.43 S 58.24 W
La Pintada 236 8.36 N 80.27 W
Lanusei 71 39.53 N 9.32 E
Lanuvio 66 41.40 N 12.42 E
Lanuza 116 9.14 N 126.04 E
Lanuza Bay ⊂ 116 9.17 N 126.04 E
Lanxi, Zhg. 89 46.15 N 126.14 E
Lanxi, Zhg. 100 29.12 N 119.28 E
Lanxian 102 38.22 N 111.48 E
Lan Yü 100 22.03 N 121.32 E
Lanzada 64 46.19 N 9.51 E
Lanzarote ∎ 148 29.00 N 13.40 W
Lanzhou (Lanchow) 102 36.03 N 103.41 E
Lanzo Torinese 62 45.16 N 7.28 E
Lao
— Laos □¹ 110 18.00 N 105.00 E
Lao ≃, It. 68 39.47 N 15.48 E
Lao ≃, Thai 110 19.55 N 99.54 E
Lao ≃, Zhg. 100 29.11 N 116.00 E
Laoag 116 18.12 N 120.36 E
Laoag ≃ 116 18.12 N 120.31 E
Laoang 116 12.34 N 125.00 E
Laoang Island ∎ 116 12.35 N 125.01 E
Lao Bao 110 16.37 N 106.36 E
Laobian, Zhg. 104 40.42 N 122.21 E
Laobian, Zhg. 104 41.58 N 123.10 E
Lao Cai 110 22.30 N 103.57 E
Laochang, Zhg. 102 24.34 N 104.11 E
Laochang, Zhg. 107 29.30 N 106.36 E
Laocheng 104 42.37 N 124.04 E
Laodaidian 104 41.40 N 122.40 E
Laodao ≃ 104 42.05 N 122.22 E
Laodaodian 89 51.16 N 126.40 E
Laofengkou 86 46.11 N 83.36 E
Laofu 98 42.13 N 118.17 E
Laogang 106 31.01 N 121.49 E
Laoge 100 32.49 N 119.52 E
Laoguanpu 100 27.38 N 113.36 E
Laoha ≃ 89 42.30 N 120.39 E
Laohaotuo 104 41.25 N 122.46 E
Laoheba 107 28.51 N 103.49 E
Laoheshan 89 43.45 N 130.52 E
Laoheshanqtai 104 40.43 N 120.49 E
Laohokow
— Guangrua 102 32.25 N 111.36 E
Laohuk'ou 100 24.53 N 121.03 E
Lachumiao 271a 39.58 N 116.20 E
Lachutuozi 104 42.25 N 122.34 E
Laois □⁶ 48 53.00 N 7.24 W
Laojunjuan 105 39.56 N 97.51 E
Laojunmiao
— Yumen 86 39.50 N 97.44 E
Laoka 89 54.47 N 125.52 E
Laolao, Bahia ⊂ 174n 15.08 N 145.46 E
Lao Ling ∧ 89 43.30 N 130.11 E
Laolongtan 107 30.01 N 104.48 E
Laomocun 106 30.51 N 119.11 E
Laona, N.Y., U.S. 214 42.26 N 79.19 W
Laona, Wi., U.S. 190 45.33 N 88.40 W
La Orchila, Isla ∎ 246 11.48 N 66.09 W
La Orotava 148 28.23 N 16.31 W
La Oroya 248 11.32 S 75.54 W
Laos (Lao) □¹, Asia 110 18.00 N 105.00 E
Laos (Lao) □¹, Asia 110 18.00 N 105.00 E
Laoshan Wan ⊂ 98 36.24 N 120.45 E
Laosolu 114 3.11 N 98.02 E
Laotto 216 41.17 N 85.12 W
Laou, Oued ≃ 34 35.29 N 5.04 W
Laowushi 100 31.43 N 121.00 E
Laoxinkou 100 30.12 N 112.50 E
Laoyeezhuang 98 41.03 N 119.53 E
Laoyingpan 100 32.16 N 120.04 E
Laoyingshan 100 31.34 N 115.10 E
Laozhen 100 31.34 N 118.19 E
La Puente 282 34.01 N 117.56 W
La Puerta 252 28.10 S 65.48 W
Laozhuangzi 105 39.44 N 118.05 E
Lapa 262 25.45 S 49.42 W
Lapa ≃⁸, Bra. 287a 22.55 S 43.11 W
Lapa ≃⁸, Bra. 287b 23.32 S 46.32 W
Lapac Island ∎ 116 5.32 N 120.47 E
Lapai 146 9.06 N 6.45 E
Lapaich, Sgurr na ∧ 46 57.21 N 5.04 W
Lapalisse 62 46.15 N 3.38 E
La Palma, Cuba 240 22.45 N 83.33 W
La Palma, El Sal. 236 14.19 N 89.11 W
La Palma, Méx. 234 17.05 N 99.20 W
La Palma, Pan. 246 8.25 N 78.09 W
La Palma, Pan. 246 7.42 N 80.12 W
La Palma, Ca., U.S. 282 33.50 N 118.02 W
La Palma ∎ 148 28.40 N 17.52 W
La Palma de Cervelló 266d 41.25 N 1.58 E
La Palma del Condado 34 37.23 N 6.33 W
La Palmita 252 25.57 N 99.18 W
La Paloma 258 34.40 S 54.10 W
La Paloma ≃ 252 34.38 S 54.10 W
La Paloma 252 34.40 S 70.59 W
La Panza Range ∧ 228 35.18 N 120.20 W
La Paragua 246 6.50 N 63.20 W
Laparan Island ∎ 116 5.54 N 119.59 E
La Parota 234 17.08 N 99.47 W
La Pasión, Laguna ⊜ 234 18.40 N 91.40 W
La Pasión, Río de ≃ 236 16.31 N 90.10 W
La Patrie 206 45.24 N 71.15 W
La Paz, Arg. 252 30.45 S 59.39 W
La Paz, Arg. 252 33.28 S 67.33 W
La Paz, Bol. 248 16.30 S 68.09 W
La Paz, Col. 246 10.25 N 73.10 W
La Paz, Hond. 236 14.20 N 87.41 W
La Paz, Méx. 234 24.10 N 110.18 W
La Paz, Méx. 234 23.41 N 100.43 W
La Paz, Pil. 116 8.19 N 126.43 E
La Paz, Ur. 258 34.46 S 56.15 W
La Paz □⁵, Bol. 248 15.00 S 68.00 W
La Paz □⁵, Hond. 236 14.15 N 87.55 W
La Paz, Bahía ⊂ 234 24.09 N 110.25 W
La Paz, Río de ≃ 248 20.47 S 66.20 W
La Paz Centro 236 12.20 N 86.41 W
La Pedrera 246 1.18 S 69.43 W
Lapel 216 40.04 N 85.50 W
Lapeer 218 43.03 N 83.19 W
La Pelada 258 30.56 S 60.00 W
La Perla, Méx. 234 25.48 N 103.33 W
La Perla, Méx. 232 28.18 N 104.38 W
La Perla, Perú 286d 12.04 S 77.08 W
La Perouse 274a 33.59 S 151.15 E
La Perouse, Bahía ⊂ 174z 27.05 S 109.18 W
La Perouse Strait ∿ 92 45.45 N 142.00 E
Lapesse 58 46.32 N 5.51 E
La Petite-Pierre 58 48.51 N 7.19 E
Lapham Hill ∧² 216 40.07 N 88.24 W
La Piedad de Cabadas 234 20.21 N 102.00 W

La Pimienta 234 21.28 N 99.01 W
La Pine 202 43.40 N 121.30 W
Lapinin Island ∎ 116 10.06 N 124.34 E
Lapin lääni □⁴ 24 68.00 N 27.00 E
Lapinlahti 26 63.22 N 27.24 E
Lapinjärvi (Lappträsk) 26 60.38 N 26.13 E
Lapland □⁹ 24 68.00 N 25.00 E
Laplandskij zapovednik ☒⁴ 24 67.50 N 32.10 E
La Plata, Arg. 258 34.55 S 57.57 W
La Plata, Col. 246 2.23 N 75.53 W
La Plata, Mo., U.S. 194 40.01 N 92.29 W
La Plata ≃ 200 36.54 N 108.15 W
La Plata, Lago ⊜ 254 44.53 S 71.50 W
La Plata, Universidad Nacional de ⋔ 258 35.55 S 57.57 W
La Plata Peak ∧ 200 39.02 N 106.28 W
La Playa ≃⁸ 286b 23.06 N 82.27 W
La Playa Corrida de San Juan, Punta ⊁ 234 18.36 N 103.42 W
La Plonge Indian Reserve ≃⁴ 184 55.15 N 107.36 W
La Plume 210 41.34 N 75.45 W
La Pobla de Segur 34 42.14 N 0.59 E
La Pocatière 186 47.22 N 70.02 W
La Poile 186 47.41 N 58.24 W
La Poile Bay ⊂ 186 47.38 N 58.20 W
Laporinika 24 64.48 N 40.28 E
La Pomme 62 43.25 N 5.35 E
Laponie
— Lapland □⁹ 24 68.00 N 25.00 E
Laporte, Co., U.S. 200 40.38 N 105.08 W
La Porte, In., U.S. 216 41.36 N 86.43 W
La Porte, Pa., U.S. 210 41.25 N 76.30 W
La Porte, Tx., U.S. 222 29.39 N 95.01 W
La Porte ≃ 216 41.36 N 86.43 W
La Porte City 190 42.18 N 92.11 W
La Potherie, Lac ⊜ 176 58.50 N 72.24 W
Lapoutroie 58 48.09 N 7.10 E
La Poveda 266a 40.19 N 3.29 W
Lapo Grande 232 25.50 N 112.05 W
Lappago (Lappach) 64 46.55 N 11.48 E
Lappajärvi 26 63.12 N 23.38 E
Lappajärvi ⊜ 26 63.03 N 23.40 E
Lappeenranta 26 61.04 N 28.11 E
Lappfjärd (Lapväärtti) 26 62.15 N 21.32 E
Lappi 26 61.06 N 21.50 E
Lapland
— Lapland □⁹ 24 68.00 N 25.00 E
Lapträsk
— Lapinjärvi 26 60.38 N 26.13 E
La Prairie 206 45.25 N 73.30 W
Laprairie □⁶ 206 45.20 N 73.35 W
La Prele Creek ≃ 198 42.54 N 105.34 W
La Presa ≃ 234 24.50 N 110.34 W
Laprida, Arg. 252 37.33 S 60.49 W
Laprida, Arg. 252 28.23 S 64.33 W
La Pryor 222 28.57 N 99.51 W
Lapseki 80 40.20 N 26.41 E
Lapta 130 35.20 N 33.10 E
Laptev Sea
— Laptevych, more ⫶² 74 76.00 N 126.00 E
Laptevych, more (Laptev Sea) ⫶² 74 76.00 N 126.00 E
Lapua 26 62.57 N 23.00 E
Lapuanjoki ≃ 26 63.34 N 22.30 E
La Puebla de Cazalla 34 37.14 N 5.19 W
La Puebla de Montalbán 34 39.52 N 4.21 W
La Puente 282 34.01 N 117.56 W
La Puerta 252 28.10 S 65.48 W
Lapu-Lapu (Opon) 116 10.19 N 123.57 E
La Purísima, Chile 286e 33.34 S 70.39 W
La Purísima, Méx. 232 26.10 N 112.04 W
Lapuş ≃ 48 47.30 N 21.01 E
La Push 224 47.54 N 124.38 W
Lapuyan 116 7.36 N 123.12 E
Lapväärtti
— Lappfjärd 26 62.15 N 21.32 E
Lapy 30 52.59 N 22.53 E
Laqiya Arba'in ☒ 144 28.02 N 26.40 E
Lar ≃ 123 35.48 N 51.55 E
La Queue-en-Brie 261 48.47 N 2.35 E
La Queue-lès-Yvelines 261 48.49 N 1.46 E
La Quiaca 252 22.06 S 65.37 W
L'Aquila 66 42.22 N 13.22 E
L'Aquila □⁴ 71 42.10 N 13.45 E
Lar 128 27.41 N 54.17 E
La Rabida 34 37.12 N 6.55 W
La Rambla 34 37.36 N 4.44 W
Laramie 200 41.18 N 105.35 W
Laramie ≃ 198 42.13 N 104.33 W
Laramie Mountains ∧ 200 42.00 N 105.40 W
Laramie Peak ∧ 200 42.16 N 105.27 W
Laranda
— Karaman 130 37.11 N 33.14 E
Laranjal ≃ 255 1.02 S 55.16 W
Laranjeiras 255 10.48 S 37.10 W
Laranjeiras ≃⁸ 287a 22.57 S 43.11 W
Laranjeiras do Sul 262 25.25 S 52.25 W
Larantuka 112 8.21 S 122.59 E
Larat 112 7.12 S 131.53 E
Larat, Pulau ∎ 164 7.10 S 131.50 E
Laravale 171a 28.12 S 153.02 E
La Raya, Abra ∿ 248 14.28 S 70.59 W
L'Arbaa Naït Irathen 34 36.38 N 4.13 E
Larbert 46 56.01 N 3.50 W
L'Arbresle 62 45.50 N 4.37 E
Lárbro 40 57.47 N 18.47 E
Larbut, Jezīra'l ∎ 144 7.50 S 30.15 E
L'Archevêque, Col de (Colle della Maddalena) ∿ 62 44.25 N 6.53 E
Larchmont 284a 40.55 N 73.45 W
Larchmont Harbor ⊂ 275b 40.55 N 73.44 W
Larchwood 190 43.27 N 96.27 W
Larde 154 16.28 S 39.43 E
Lardier, Cap ⊁ 62 43.13 N 6.41 E
Lardizábal 235 19.20 N 98.23 W
Lardos 38 36.05 N 28.01 E
Lardy 261 48.31 N 2.15 E
Laredo, Esp. 34 43.25 N 3.26 W
Laredo, Tx., U.S. 222 27.30 N 99.30 W
Laredo Sound ∿ 182 52.30 N 128.53 W
La Redorte 62 43.14 N 2.39 E
La Reforma, Méx. 232 27.59 N 101.47 W
La Reforma, Méx. 234 25.04 N 108.03 W
La Reina 286e 33.27 S 70.32 W
Laren 52 52.16 N 5.14 E
Larena 116 9.14 N 123.35 E
La Réole 62 44.35 N 0.02 W
Lares, Perú 248 13.04 S 72.05 W
Lares, P.R. 240m 18.18 N 66.53 W
Larga 38 48.23 N 26.50 E
Larga, Laguna ⊜ 196 27.30 N 97.25 W
Large, Île du ∎ 275a 45.19 N 73.52 W
L'Argentière-la-Bessée 62 44.47 N 6.33 E
Lar Gerd 120 35.29 N 66.46 E
Largo 220 27.54 N 82.47 W
Largo, Cañón □⁴ 200 36.40 N 107.43 W
Largo, Cayo ∎ 240p 21.38 N 81.28 W
Largo Creek ≃ 200 34.29 N 108.51 W
Largoward 46 56.15 N 2.51 W
Largs 46 55.48 N 4.52 W
Largu ≃ 62 43.51 N 5.52 E
Lari ≃ 66 43.34 N 10.35 E
Lari, Perú 248 15.37 S 71.46 W
Lariang 112 1.26 S 119.17 E
Lariang ≃ 112 1.25 S 119.17 E
La Ricamarie 62 45.24 N 4.22 E
Larimer 214 40.21 N 79.44 W
Larimore 198 47.54 N 97.37 W
La Rioja 252 29.26 S 66.51 W
La Rioja □⁴, Arg. 252 29.30 S 67.30 W
La Rioja □⁴, Esp. 34 42.15 N 2.30 W
Larisa 38 39.38 N 22.25 E
Larisa Station ≃⁵ 267c 37.59 N 23.43 E
Larjak 74 61.16 N 80.15 E
Lark ≃ 42 52.30 N 0.20 E
Larjegan ≃ 86 60.30 N 77.44 E
Larkana 124 27.33 N 68.13 E
Larkhall 46 55.45 N 3.59 W
Lark Harbour 186 49.06 N 58.23 W
Larkhill 42 51.12 N 1.50 W
Larkspur 226 37.56 N 122.30 W
Larksville 210 41.14 N 75.55 W
Lárnakos, Kólpos ⊂ 130 34.55 N 33.38 E
Lárnax (Larnaca) 130 34.55 N 33.38 E
Larne 48 54.51 N 5.49 W
Larne □⁶ 198 38.10 N 99.05 W
Larne Lough ⊂ 48 54.47 N 5.45 W
La Robla 34 42.48 N 5.37 W
La Roca de la Sierra 34 39.07 N 6.41 W
La Roche 62 46.42 N 7.08 E
La Roche-Bernard 62 47.31 N 2.18 W
La Roche-de-Rame 62 44.45 N 6.35 E
La Roche-Derrien 32 48.45 N 3.16 W
La Roche-des-Arnauds 62 44.34 N 5.57 E
La Roche-en-Ardenne 50 50.11 N 5.35 E
La Roche-en-Brenil 64 47.22 N 4.10 E
La Rochefoucauld 62 45.45 N 0.23 E
La Roche-Guyon 50 49.05 N 1.38 E
La Rochelle 62 46.10 N 1.10 W
Larocha-Saint-Cydrine 50 47.58 N 3.31 E
La Roche-sur-Foron 62 46.04 N 6.19 E
La Roche-sur-Yon 62 46.40 N 1.26 W
La Rochette, Fr. 261 48.30 N 2.40 E
La Rochette, Fr. 62 45.47 N 6.15 E
La Roda 34 39.13 N 2.09 W
La Romaine 186 50.13 N 60.40 W
La Romana 240 18.26 N 68.58 W
La Ronge 184 55.06 N 105.17 W
Laroquebrou 62 44.58 N 2.11 E
La Roquetrussanne 62 43.26 N 5.59 E
Larose 194 29.34 N 90.22 W
La Rosita 236 13.53 N 84.24 W
La Route 261 48.48 N 2.47 E
Larrabee State Park ⫶ 224 48.41 N 122.29 W
Larreynaga 236 12.40 N 86.34 W
Larrey Point ⊁ 162 19.58 S 119.07 E
Larriman 164 15.35 S 133.12 E
Larringes 58 46.22 N 6.35 E
Larrison Creek ≃² 222 31.27 N 93.23 W
Larroque 258 33.02 S 59.01 W
Larrys Creek ≃ 210 41.13 N 77.13 W
Larrys River 188 45.13 N 61.23 W
Larsen Bay 180 57.33 N 153.59 W
Larsen Ice Shelf ∆ 195 68.30 S 62.30 W
Larshamn 40 58.03 N 16.45 E
Larvik 26 59.04 N 10.00 E
Laruns 32 42.59 N 0.26 W
Larue, Tx., U.S. 222 32.07 N 95.41 W
La Rumorosa 204 32.34 N 116.06 W
Larvik 26 59.04 N 10.00 E
Larvotto ≃¹ 62 43.45 N 7.27 E
Larwill 216 41.11 N 85.37 W
Larzac, Causse du ∧¹ 62 44.00 N 3.25 E
Las (Leas) 124 28.18 N 65.31 E
Lasa (Lhasa) 120 29.40 N 91.10 E
Las Adjuntas 286c 10.26 N 67.01 W
La Sal 200 38.18 N 109.14 W
La Salceda 266a 40.52 N 4.12 W
La Salceta, Laguna ⊜ 234 18.34 N 91.36 W
La Salle ≃, On., Can. 214 42.43 N 83.06 W
La Salle, Il., U.S. 190 41.19 N 89.06 W
La Salle, P.Q., Can. 275a 45.26 N 73.38 W
Lasalle ≃ 184 51.17 N 94.40 W
La Salle College ▾² 285 40.02 N 75.09 W
La Salle Gardens 277b 42.22 N 83.05 W
Las Almejas, Bahía ⊂ 232 24.29 N 111.44 W
Las Animas 198 38.04 N 103.13 W
Las Arenas 252 31.59 S 65.34 W
La Sarraz 58 46.39 N 6.31 E
La Sarre 206 48.48 N 79.12 W
Lasaule 218 43.04 N 86.36 W
Lascano 258 33.40 S 54.12 W
— San Cristóbal de las Casas 234 16.45 N 92.38 W
Las Catitas 252 33.18 S 68.02 W
Las Catonas, Arroyo ≃ 286d 34.36 S 58.46 W
Lascaux, Grotte de ☒ 62 45.04 N 1.08 E
Las Cejas 252 26.53 S 64.44 W
Las Cruces 196 32.18 N 106.46 W
La Seca 34 41.24 N 4.54 W
Las Breñas 252 27.05 S 61.05 W
Las Cabezas de San Juan 34 36.59 N 5.56 W
Lascelle 58 49.39 N 6.31 E
La Selva 34 41.53 N 3.00 E
La Seu d'Urgell 34 42.22 N 1.28 E
La Seyne-sur-Mer 62 43.06 N 5.53 E
Las Flores, Arg. 252 36.03 S 59.07 W
Las Heras 252 32.51 S 68.49 W
Lashio 110 22.56 N 97.45 E

Lantschou
— Lanzhou 102 36.03 N 103.41 E

≃ River	Fluß	Río	Rivière	Rio	⫶ Submarine Features	Untermeerische Objekte	Accidentes Submarinos	Formes de relief sous-marin	Acidentes submarinos
≊ Canal	Kanal	Canal	Canal	Canal	□ Political Unit	Politische Einheit	Unidad Política	Entité politique	Unidade política
⫶ Waterfall, Rapids	Wasserfall, Stromschnellen	Cascada, Rápidos	Cascade, Rapides	Chute d'eau, Rapides	Cascata, Rápidos	⋔ Cultural Institution	Kulturelle Institution	Institución Cultural	Institution culturelle	Instituição cultural
∿ Strait	Meeresstraße	Estrecho	Détroit	Estreito	☒ Historical Site	Historische Stätte	Sitio Histórico	Site historique	Sítio histórico
⊂ Bay, Gulf	Bucht, Golf	Bahía, Golfo	Baie, Golfe	Baía, Golfo	▾ Recreational Site	Erholungs- und Ferienort	Sitio de Recreo	Centre de loisirs	Area de Lazer
⊜ Lake, Lakes	See, Seen	Lago, Lagos	Lac, Lacs	Lago, Lagos	∎ Airport	Flughafen	Aeropuerto	Aéroport	Aeroporto
☐ Swamp	Sumpf	Pantano	Marais	Pântano	⫶ Military Installation	Militäranlage	Instalación Militar	Installation militaire	Instalação militar
∆ Ice Features, Glacier	Eis- und Gletscherformen	Accidentes Glaciales	Formes glaciaires	Acidentes glaciares	☒ Miscellaneous	Verschiedenes	Misceláneo	Divers	Diversos
⫶ Other Hydrographic Features	Andere Hydrographische Objekte	Otros Elementos Hidrográficos	Autres données hydrographiques	Outros acidentes hidrográficos					

Las Choapas 234 17.55 N 94.05 W
La Scie 186 49.57 N 55.36 W
Las Coloradas 254 39.33 S 70.35 W
Las Condes 286e 33.22 S 70.31 W
Lascone, Monte ∧[2] 267a 41.59 N 12.23 E
Las Cruces 200 32.18 N 106.46 W
Las Cuevas 232 29.38 N 101.19 W
Las Delicias 232 15.58 N 91.50 W
La Selle, Morne ∧ 238 18.22 N 71.59 W
La Selva Beach 226 36.55 N 121.51 W
Lasem 115a 6.42 S 111.26 E
La Serena 252 29.54 S 71.16 W
La Serena ◆[1] 34 38.45 N 5.30 W
La Seyne-sur-Mer 62 43.06 N 5.53 E
Las Flores, Arg. 252 36.03 S 59.07 W
Las Flores, Arg. 252 30.19 S 69.12 W
Las Flores, Méx. 234 18.22 N 93.10 W
Las Flores, P.R. 240m 18.03 N 66.22 W
Las Flores, Ven. 286c 10.34 N 66.56 W
Las Flores, Arroyo ≃ 252 35.36 S 59.01 W
Las Flores, Cerro ∧ 234 16.43 N 95.30 W
Las Flores Canyon V 280 34.03 N 118.38 W
Las Flores Chica, Laguna ⊜ 258 35.30 S 59.01 W
Las Flores Grande, Laguna ⊜ 258 35.34 S 59.02 W
Las Garcitas 252 26.35 S 59.48 W
Las Guacamayas 234 18.02 N 102.12 W
Las Guayabas 232 24.00 N 97.45 W
Lasham 42 51.11 N 1.03 W
Las Harquetas, Arroyo ≃ 288 34.29 S 58.38 W
Lashburn 184 53.08 N 109.36 W
Lāsh-e Joveyn 128 31.43 N 61.37 E
Las Heras, Arg. 252 32.51 S 68.49 W
Las Heras, Arg. 254 46.33 S 68.57 W
Lashio 110 22.56 N 97.45 E
Lashkar → Gwalior 124 26.13 N 78.10 E
Lashkar Gāh 128 31.35 N 64.21 E
Las Hormigas 232 25.30 N 98.44 W
Lasht 123 36.48 N 73.01 E
Lasia, Pulau I 114 2.10 N 96.39 E
La Sierra, Montaña ⋏ 236 14.04 N 87.54 W
Las Iglesias 196 27.35 N 101.21 W
Las Iglesias, Cerro ∧ 232 26.16 N 106.38 W
La Sila ⋏ 68 39.15 N 16.30 E
La Siligata 66 43.56 N 12.45 E
La Silla de Caracas ∧ 286c 10.33 N 66.51 W
Łasin 30 53.32 N 19.05 E
Lašino 80 58.16 N 49.59 E
Lāsjerd 128 35.24 N 53.04 E
Łask 30 51.36 N 19.07 E
Łaskarzew 30 51.48 N 21.35 E
L'askel'a 24 61.45 N 30.59 E
Laško 36 46.09 N 15.14 E
L'askoviči 78 52.07 N 28.09 E
Las Lajas, Arg. 252 38.31 S 70.22 W
Las Lajas, Pan. 236 8.15 N 81.52 W
Las Lajitas 252 24.41 S 64.15 W
Las Lomas 246 4.40 S 80.15 W
Las Lomitas 252 24.42 S 60.36 W
Lašma 80 54.56 N 41.09 E
Las Malvinas 252 34.50 S 68.15 W
Lašmanka 80 54.44 N 51.28 E
Las Mareas 240m 17.56 N 66.09 W
Las Margaritas 232 16.19 N 91.59 W
Las Margaritas, Laguna ⊜ 258 35.28 S 57.56 W
Las Marianas 258 35.04 S 59.31 W
Las Marías 240m 18.15 N 67.00 W
Las Marismas ≡ 34 37.00 N 6.15 W
Las Mayas 286c 10.26 N 66.56 W
Las Mercedes 246 9.07 N 66.24 W
Las Mesas de San Isidro 234 21.55 N 100.15 W
Las Minas 286c 10.27 N 66.52 W
Las Minas, Cerro ∧ 236 14.33 N 88.39 W
Las Minillas, Cerro ∧ 286e 33.31 S 70.29 W
Las Moras Creek ≃ 196 29.00 N 100.39 W
Las Mulas, Laguna ⊜ 258 35.32 S 57.54 W
Las Navas 116 12.21 N 125.02 E
Las Nieves 232 26.24 N 105.22 W
Las Nopaleras, Cerro ∧ 232 25.08 N 103.14 W
La Solana 34 38.56 N 3.14 W
La Soledad, Cerro ∧ 232 26.32 N 107.17 W
Lasolo 112 3.29 S 122.04 E
Lasolo ≃ 112 3.28 S 122.06 E
Las Ortegas, Arroyo ≃ 288 34.45 S 58.32 W
Las Ovejas 252 37.01 S 70.45 W
Las Palmas, Arg. 252 27.04 S 58.42 W
Las Palmas, Arg. 258 34.05 S 59.10 W
Las Palmas, Pan. 236 8.08 N 81.27 W
Las Palmas, P.R. 240m 17.59 N 66.02 W
Las Palmas □[4] 148 28.25 N 14.15 W
Las Palmas de Gran Canaria 148 28.06 N 15.24 W
Las Palomas 200 31.44 N 107.37 W
Las Perdices, Canal ⌶ 286e 33.31 S 70.33 W
La Spezia 62 44.07 N 9.50 E
La Spezia □[4] 62 44.15 N 9.42 E
Las Piedras, P.R. 240m 18.11 N 65.52 W
Las Piedras, Ur. 258 34.44 S 56.13 W
Las Piedras, Río de ≃ 248 12.30 S 69.14 W
Las Piñas, Pil. 269f 14.29 N 120.59 E
Las Piñas, P.R. 240m 18.15 N 65.55 W
Las Plumas 254 43.43 S 67.15 W
Lasqueti Island I 182 49.29 N 124.17 W
Las Raices Creek ≃ 196 28.09 N 99.02 W
Las Ratas, Cerro ∧ 234 18.37 N 103.37 W
Las Rejas 286e 33.28 S 70.44 W
Las Rosas, Arg. 252 32.28 S 61.34 W
Las Rosas, Chile 286e 33.35 S 70.37 W
Las Rosas, Méx. 232 16.24 N 92.23 W
Las Rozas de Madrid 266a 40.29 N 3.52 W
Las Sales, Canal ⌶ 286a 19.26 N 99.03 W
Lassan 54 53.57 N 13.50 E
Lassance 255 17.54 S 44.34 W
Lassater 222 32.49 N 94.30 W
Lassay 32 48.26 N 0.30 W
Lassee 61 48.13 N 16.49 E
Lassellsville 210 43.03 N 74.36 W
Lassen Peak ∧[1] 204 40.29 N 121.31 W
Lassen Volcanic National Park ♠ 204 40.30 N 121.19 W
Lassigny 50 49.35 N 2.51 E
Lassnitz ≃ 61 46.46 N 15.32 E
Lassnitzhöhe 61 47.05 N 15.35 E
Lasso ∧[2] 174n 15.02 N 145.38 E
L'Assomption 206 45.50 N 73.25 W
L'Assomption □[6] 206 45.48 N 73.35 W
L'Assomption ≃ 206 45.43 N 73.29 W
Lasswade 46 55.53 N 3.08 W
Lassy 261 49.06 N 2.27 E
Las Tablas 246 7.46 N 80.17 W
Lastarrio, Parque Nacional ♠ 254 44.50 S 72.05 W
Las Tinajas 252 27.27 S 62.55 W
Last Mountain ∧ 184 51.07 N 104.54 W
Last Mountain Lake ⊜ 184 51.05 N 105.10 W
Las Toscas 252 28.21 S 59.17 W
Lastoursville 152 0.49 S 12.42 E
Lastovo, Otok I 36 42.45 N 16.53 E
Lastovski Kanal ⊔ 36 42.50 N 16.59 E
Lastra a Signa 66 43.46 N 11.06 E
Las Trampas Creek ≃ 282 37.53 N 122.03 W
Las Trampas Peak ∧ 282 37.50 N 122.03 W
Las Trampas Regional Park ♠ 282 37.50 N 122.03 W
Las Trampas Ridge ∧ 282 37.49 N 122.02 W
Lästringe 40 58.54 N 17.18 E
Las Truchas 234 17.55 N 102.12 W
Lastrup 52 52.48 N 7.52 E
Las Tunas 240p 20.58 N 76.57 W
Las Tunas □[4] 240p 21.00 N 77.00 W
Las Tunas, Arroyo ≃ 288 34.27 S 58.41 W
Las Tunas, Punta › 240m 18.30 N 66.38 W
Las Tunas Beach ♠ 280 34.02 N 118.36 W
Las Tunas Grandes, Laguna ⊜ 252 35.58 S 62.25 W
La Suze 32 47.54 N 0.02 E
Las Varas, Méx. 232 29.29 N 108.01 W
Las Varas, Méx. 234 21.10 N 105.10 W
Las Varillas 252 31.52 S 62.43 W
Las Vegas, P.R. 240m 18.11 N 67.02 W
Las Vegas, Nv., U.S. 204 36.10 N 115.08 W
Las Vegas, N.M., U.S. 200 35.36 N 105.13 W
Las Vegas, Ven. 246 9.35 N 68.37 W
Las Vigas de Ramirez 234 19.38 N 97.05 W
La Tabatière 186 50.50 N 58.58 W
Latacunga 246 0.56 S 78.37 W
Latady Island I 9 70.45 S 74.35 W
La Tagua 246 0.03 S 74.40 W
Latakia → Al-Lādhiqīyah 130 35.31 N 35.47 E
Latakia □[9] 130 35.20 N 36.00 E
Latambar 123 33.07 N 70.52 E
Lata Mountain ∧ 174y 14.14 S 169.29 W
La Tapona 234 22.48 N 100.38 W
Låtefossen ∟ 26 59.57 N 6.37 E
Latehar 124 23.45 N 84.30 E
Lately Common 262 53.29 N 2.30 W
Latera 66 42.38 N 11.50 E
Laterina 66 43.31 N 11.43 E
Laterns 58 47.16 N 9.43 E
Laterrière 186 48.18 N 71.06 W
Laterza 68 40.37 N 16.48 E
La Teste-de-Buch 32 44.38 N 1.09 W
La Tetilla, Cerro ∧ 234 20.21 N 104.59 W
Latexo 222 31.24 N 95.29 W
Latgale □[9] 76 56.20 N 27.10 E
Latham, Austl. 162 29.45 S 116.26 E
Latham, Il., U.S. 219 39.58 N 89.10 W
Latham, N.Y., U.S. 210 42.44 N 73.45 W
Latham, Oh., U.S. 218 39.06 N 83.15 W
Lathan ≃ 50 47.27 N 0.08 E
Lathen 52 52.52 N 7.19 E
Latheron 46 58.17 N 3.23 W
Lāthi 120 21.43 N 71.23 E
Lathrop, Ca., U.S. 226 37.49 N 121.16 W
Lathrop, Mo., U.S. 194 39.32 N 94.19 W
Lathrup Village 281 42.29 N 83.14 W
La Thuile 62 45.43 N 6.57 E
La Tiama 286c 10.26 N 66.46 W
Latian, Mount ∧ 116 6.13 N 125.30 E
Latiano 68 40.33 N 17.43 E
Latimer, Eng., U.K. 260 51.41 N 0.33 W
Latimer, Ia., U.S. 190 42.45 N 93.22 W
Latina 66 41.28 N 12.52 E
Latina □[4] 66 41.27 N 13.06 E
Latiri 140 9.10 N 25.43 E
Latisana 64 45.47 N 13.00 E
Latjuga 24 64.16 N 48.46 E
Latnaja 78 51.43 N 38.55 E
La Toma 252 33.03 S 65.37 W
Laton 226 36.26 N 119.41 W
Latonovo 83 47.29 N 38.38 E
Latorica ≃ 30 48.28 N 21.50 E
Latornell ≃ 182 54.58 N 118.00 W
La Torrecilla ∧ 240m 18.12 N 66.20 W
La Tortuga, Isla I 246 10.56 N 65.20 W
Latouche Island I 180 60.00 N 147.55 W
Latouche Treville, Cape › 162 18.27 S 121.49 E
La Tour 62 43.57 N 7.11 E
La Tour-d'Aigues 62 43.44 N 5.33 E
La Tour-d'Auvergne 32 45.32 N 2.41 E
La Tour-de-Peilz 58 46.27 N 6.49 E
La Tour-du-Pin 62 45.34 N 5.27 E
La Tourette Park ♠ 276 40.35 N 74.08 W
Latowicz 30 52.02 N 21.48 E
Lat Phrao, Khlong ⌶ 269a 13.48 N 100.35 E
La Tremblade 32 45.46 N 1.08 W
La Trimouille 32 46.28 N 1.02 E
La Trinidad, Arg. 252 27.24 S 65.31 W
La Trinidad, Nic. 236 12.58 N 86.14 W
La Trinidad, Pil. 116 16.28 N 120.35 E
La Trinidad, Ven. 286c 10.27 N 66.52 W
La Trinidad de Orichuna 246 7.07 N 69.45 W
La Trinitaria 232 16.07 N 92.03 W
La Trinité 240e 14.44 N 60.58 W
Latrobe, Austl. 166 41.14 S 146.24 E
Latrobe, Pa., U.S. 214 40.19 N 79.22 W
La Trobe ≃ 169 38.10 S 146.32 E
Latrobe University ʊ[2] 274b 37.43 S 145.03 E
La Tronche 62 45.12 N 5.44 E
Latronico 68 40.05 N 16.01 E
Latsch → Laces 64 46.37 N 10.52 E
Latta 192 34.20 N 79.25 W
Lattarico 68 39.28 N 16.08 E
Lattasburg 214 40.53 N 82.06 W
Latterbach 58 46.40 N 7.35 E
Lattingtown 276 40.54 N 73.36 W
Latty 216 41.05 N 84.35 W
La Tuilerie 261 48.34 N 2.08 E
La Tuilière 62 44.11 N 5.32 E
Latuna 112 8.23 S 124.06 E
La Tuque 176 47.26 N 72.47 W
Lātūr 122 18.24 N 76.35 E
La Turbie 62 43.45 N 7.24 E
Latvia (Latvija) □[1], Europe 22 57.00 N 25.00 E
Latvia (Latvija) □[1], Europe 76 57.00 N 25.00 E
Lau, Nig. 146 9.13 N 11.17 E
Lau, Pap. N. Gui. 164 5.50 S 151.20 E
Laubach 56 50.33 N 8.59 E
Lau Basin ✢[1] 14 20.00 S 177.00 W
Laubusch 54 51.28 N 14.10 E
Laubuseschbach 56 50.24 N 8.20 E
Lauca ≃ 248 19.10 S 68.10 W
Lauca, Parque Nacional ♠ 248 18.20 S 69.15 W
Laucha 54 51.13 N 11.41 E
Lauchhammer 54 51.30 N 13.47 E
Lauchheim 56 48.52 N 10.14 E
Lauda-Königshofen 56 49.34 N 9.41 E
Lauder 46 55.43 N 2.45 W
Lauderdale 194 32.31 N 88.30 W
Lauderdale V 46 55.43 N 2.42 W
Lauderdale-by-the-Sea 220 26.12 N 80.07 W
Lauderdale Lakes 220 26.09 N 80.12 W
Lauderhill 220 26.08 N 80.12 W
Laudun 62 44.06 N 4.40 E
Lauenbrück 52 53.12 N 9.33 E
Lauenburg, Dtsch. 52 53.22 N 10.33 E
Lauenburg → Lębork, Pol. 30 54.33 N 17.44 E
Lauenförde 52 51.39 N 9.23 E
Lauenstein, Dtsch. 52 52.04 N 9.33 E
Lauenstein, Dtsch. 54 50.47 N 13.49 E
Lauenstein, Dtsch. 54 50.31 N 11.20 E
Lauer ≃ 56 50.18 N 10.10 E
Lauerzer See ⊜ 58 47.02 N 8.36 E
Lauf an der Pegnitz 60 49.30 N 11.17 E
Läufelfingen 58 47.24 N 7.51 E
Laufen, Dtsch. 64 47.57 N 12.56 E
Laufen, Schw. 58 47.25 N 7.30 E
Laufenburg (Baden), Dtsch. 58 47.35 N 8.04 E
Laufenburg (Baden), Schw. 58 47.33 N 8.04 E
Laufersfort, Schloss ⊥ 263 51.25 N 6.37 E
Lauffen am Neckar 56 49.05 N 9.10 E
Laugharne 42 51.47 N 4.28 W
Laughery Creek ≃ 218 39.02 N 84.53 W
Laughlen, Mount ∧ 162 23.23 S 134.23 E
Laughlin Air Force Base ■ 196 29.22 N 100.47 W
Laughlin Peak ∧ 196 36.38 N 104.12 W
Laughlintown 214 40.13 N 79.12 W
Lau Group II 175g 18.20 S 178.30 W
Lauingen 56 48.34 N 10.25 E
Lauis → Lugano 58 46.01 N 8.58 E
Laukaa 26 62.25 N 25.57 E
Laukuva 76 55.37 N 22.14 E
Laul'u 89 45.46 N 135.16 E
Laun 110 10.07 N 98.46 E
Launceston, Austl. 166 41.26 S 147.08 E
Launceston, Eng., U.K. 42 50.38 N 4.21 W
Laundi, Tanjung › 115b 9.28 S 120.12 E
Laune ≃ 48 52.07 N 9.48 W
Launglon 110 13.58 N 98.07 E
Laungowāl 123 30.13 N 75.41 E
La Unión, Chile 254 40.17 S 73.05 W
La Unión, Col. 246 1.36 N 77.09 W
La Unión, El Sal. 236 13.20 N 87.51 W
La Unión, Esp. 34 37.37 N 0.52 W
La Unión, Méx. 234 17.58 N 101.49 W
La Unión, Perú 248 9.46 S 76.48 W
La Unión, Perú 248 5.24 S 80.45 W
La Union, Pil. 116 6.42 N 126.05 E
La Union, N.M., U.S. 200 31.57 N 106.39 W
La Unión, Ven. 246 8.13 N 67.46 W
La Unión, Ven. 286c 10.25 N 66.48 W
La Union □[4] 116 16.35 N 120.25 E
Launois-sur-Vence 56 49.39 N 4.32 E
Launsdorf 61 46.46 N 14.27 E
Laupen 58 46.54 N 7.14 E
Laupendahl ◆[8] 263 51.21 N 6.56 E
Laupheim 58 48.14 N 9.52 E
Laur 116 15.35 N 121.11 E
Laura, Austl. 164 15.34 S 144.28 E
Laura, Oh., U.S. 218 39.59 N 84.24 W
La Urbana 246 7.08 N 66.56 W
Laureana di Borrello 68 38.30 N 16.05 E
Laurel, De., U.S. 208 38.33 N 75.34 W
Laurel, Fl., U.S. 220 27.07 N 82.27 W
Laurel, In., U.S. 218 39.30 N 85.11 W
Laurel, Md., U.S. 208 39.05 N 76.50 W
Laurel, Ms., U.S. 194 31.41 N 89.07 W
Laurel, Mt., U.S. 202 45.40 N 108.46 W
Laurel, Ne., U.S. 198 42.25 N 97.05 W
Laurel, Va., U.S. 208 37.38 N 77.30 W
Laurel, Wa., U.S. 224 45.57 N 121.23 W
Laurel ≃ 192 36.57 N 84.18 W
Laurel, Mount ∧[2] 285 39.56 N 74.53 W
Laurel Bay 192 32.33 N 80.44 W
Laureldale, N.J., U.S. 208 39.29 N 74.41 W
Laureldale, Pa., U.S. 208 40.23 N 75.55 W
Laureles 252 31.22 S 55.51 W
Laureles, Isla de los I 258 33.45 S 59.23 W
Laurel Gardens 279b 40.31 N 80.01 W
Laurel Hill, Austl. 171b 35.37 S 148.05 E
Laurel Hill, N.C., U.S. 192 34.48 N 79.32 W
Laurel Hill ∧ 214 40.15 N 79.05 W
Laurel Hollow 276 40.52 N 73.28 W
Laurel Reservoir ⊜[1] 276 41.10 N 73.33 W
Laurel Ridge State Park ♠ 188 39.58 N 79.23 W
Laurel River Lake ⊜[1] 192 36.55 N 84.15 W
Laurel Run 210 41.13 N 75.51 W
Laurel Run ≃ 208 40.20 N 77.20 W
Laurel Springs 285 39.49 N 75.00 W
Laurelton 210 40.52 N 77.11 W
Laurelville, Oh., U.S. 188 39.28 N 82.44 W
Laurelville, Pa., U.S. 214 40.09 N 79.29 W
Laurenburg 56 50.20 N 7.54 E
Laurence Harbor 276 40.27 N 74.14 W
Laurencekirk 46 56.50 N 2.29 W
Laurens, Ia., U.S. 198 42.50 N 94.51 W
Laurens, N.Y., U.S. 210 42.32 N 75.06 W
Laurens, S.C., U.S. 192 34.29 N 82.00 W
Laurentides 206 45.51 N 73.46 W
Laurentides, Les ⋏[1] 176 48.00 N 71.00 W
Laurentides, Parc Provincial des ♠ 186 47.40 N 71.30 W
Laurenzana 68 40.28 N 15.58 E
Lauria 68 40.02 N 15.50 E
Lau Ridge ✢[3] 14 21.00 S 178.30 W
Laurie Island I 9 60.45 S 44.35 W
Laurie Lake ⊜ 184 56.34 N 101.54 W
Laurier, Mb., Can. 184 50.54 N 99.33 W
Laurier, P.Q., Can. 206 46.32 N 71.38 W
Laurière 32 46.05 N 1.28 E
Laurierville 206 46.18 N 71.39 W
Laurinburg 192 34.46 N 79.27 W
Laurino 68 40.20 N 15.20 E
Laurito 68 40.10 N 15.24 E
Lauritsala 26 61.04 N 28.16 E
Lauritzen Bay c 9 69.05 S 156.50 E
Laurium 190 47.14 N 88.26 W
Lauriya Nandangarh 124 26.59 N 84.24 E
Lauro, Monte ∧ 70 37.07 N 14.49 E
Laurys Station 208 40.43 N 75.32 W
Lausanne 58 46.31 N 6.38 E
Lauscha 54 50.28 N 11.10 E
Laut 86 59.18 N 66.02 E
Laut, Pulau I, Indon. 112 3.40 S 116.10 E
Laut, Pulau I, Indon. 112 4.43 N 107.59 E
Laut, Selat ⊔ 112 3.25 S 116.03 E
Lauta 54 51.27 N 14.04 E
Lautaro 252 38.31 S 72.27 W
Lautaro, Volcán ∧[1] 254 49.00 S 73.32 W
Lautem 112 8.22 S 126.54 E
Lautenbach 58 47.57 N 7.09 E
Lautenthal 52 51.52 N 10.17 E
Lauter ≃, Dtsch. 56 49.39 N 7.35 E
Lauter ≃, Europe 56 48.58 N 8.11 E
Lauterach 58 47.29 N 9.44 E
Lauterbach, Dtsch. 56 50.38 N 9.24 E
Lauterbach, Dtsch. 58 48.14 N 8.20 E
Lauterbourg 56 48.59 N 8.11 E
Lauterbrunnen 58 46.36 N 7.55 E
Lauterecken 56 49.39 N 7.35 E
Lauterhofen 60 49.22 N 11.37 E
Lauter [Sachsen] 54 50.33 N 12.44 E
Laut Kecil, Kepulauan II 112 4.50 S 115.45 E
Lautoka 175g 17.37 S 177.27 E
Lauttakylä → Huittinen 26 61.11 N 22.42 E
Laut Tawar, Danau ⊜ 114 4.38 N 96.54 E
Lauwe 50 50.48 N 3.11 E
Lauwerszee c 52 53.20 N 6.12 E
Lauzerte 32 44.15 N 1.08 E
Lauzon 206 46.50 N 71.10 W
Lauzun 32 44.38 N 0.28 E
Lava (Łyna) ≃ 76 54.37 N 21.14 E
Lava, Nosy I 157b 14.33 S 47.36 E
Lava Beds National Monument ♠ 204 41.42 N 121.30 W
Lavaca □[6] 222 29.22 N 96.55 W
Lavaca ≃ 196 28.50 N 96.36 W
Lavaca Bay c 196 28.35 N 96.35 W
La Vacherie 62 44.53 N 5.11 E
Lavagh More ∧ 48 54.45 N 8.05 W
Lavagna 62 44.18 N 9.20 E
Lavagna ≃ 62 44.21 N 9.20 E
Lava Hot Springs 202 42.37 N 112.00 W
Lavaisse 252 33.49 S 65.25 W
Laval, P.Q., Can. 206 45.35 N 73.45 W
Laval, Fr. 32 48.04 N 0.46 W
Laval-des-Rapides ◆[8] 275a 45.33 N 73.42 W
La Valette → Valletta 36 35.54 N 14.31 E
La Valette-du-Var 62 43.08 N 5.59 E
La Vall d'Uixo 34 39.49 N 0.14 W
Lavalle, Arg. 252 29.01 S 59.11 W
Lavalle, Arg. 252 28.12 S 65.08 W
Lavalleja → Minas 252 34.23 S 55.14 W
Lavallette 208 39.58 N 74.04 W
La Valley 200 37.06 N 105.20 W
Laval-Ouest ◆[8] 275a 45.33 N 73.52 W
Lavaltrie 206 45.53 N 73.17 W
Lavamünd 61 46.39 N 14.56 E
Lāvān, Jazīreh-ye I 128 26.48 N 53.15 E
Lavan, Naḥal V 132 30.57 N 34.21 E
Lavanono 157b 25.24 S 44.55 E
Lavant ≃ 61 46.38 N 14.57 E
Lavapié, Punta › 252 37.09 S 73.35 W
Lávara 38 41.16 N 26.22 E
Lavaraty 157b 23.16 S 46.59 E
Lavardac 32 44.11 N 0.18 E
Lavarone 64 45.56 N 11.15 E
Lavassaare 76 58.31 N 24.22 E
Lava-Tudo ≃ 252 28.26 S 50.25 W
Laveaga Peak ∧ 226 36.53 N 121.11 W
La Vecilla de Curueño 34 42.51 N 5.24 W
La Vega 238 19.13 N 70.31 W
La Vega ◆[8] 286c 10.28 N 66.57 W
Lavela 24 63.38 N 45.31 E
La Vela, Cabo de › 246 12.15 N 72.11 W
La Vela de Coro 246 11.27 N 69.34 W
Lavelanet 32 42.56 N 1.51 E
Lavelle 208 40.46 N 76.22 W
Lavello 68 41.03 N 15.48 E
Laven 41 56.07 N 9.43 E
La Venada 196 25.50 N 97.30 W
Lavendon 42 52.11 N 0.40 W
Lavenham 42 52.06 N 0.47 E
Laveno 58 45.55 N 8.37 E
Lavenone 64 45.44 N 10.26 E
La Venta ≃ 234 16.59 N 93.46 W
La Venta ⊥ 234 18.08 N 94.03 W
Laventie 50 50.38 N 2.46 E
La Ventura 232 24.38 N 100.54 W
Laver ≃ 44 54.08 N 1.30 W
Lavéra 62 43.23 N 5.02 E
La Vera ◆[1] 34 40.20 N 5.30 W
La Verde, Arg. 252 27.08 S 59.23 W
La Verde, Arg. 258 34.44 S 59.16 W
Laverdière, Lac ⊜ 206 46.50 N 74.28 W
L'Averdy, Cape › 175e 5.33 S 155.04 E
La Vérendrye, Réserve ♠ 190 47.30 N 77.30 W
La Vergne 194 36.00 N 86.34 W
La Verna ʊ[1] 66 43.42 N 11.54 E
La Verne, Ca., U.S. 280 34.06 N 117.46 W
Laverne, Ok., U.S. 196 36.42 N 99.53 W
La Vernia 196 29.21 N 98.07 W
Laverock 285 40.05 N 75.11 W
La Verpillière 62 45.38 N 5.09 E
La Verrière 261 48.45 N 1.57 E
Lavers Hill 169 38.40 S 143.24 E
Laverton, Austl. 162 28.38 S 122.25 E
Laverton, Austl. 169 37.52 S 144.45 E
Laverton Royal Australian Air Force Base ■ 169 37.52 S 144.43 E
La Veta 200 37.30 N 105.00 W
Lavezares 116 12.32 N 124.20 E
Lavezzi, Îles II 71 41.20 N 9.15 E
Lavezzola 66 44.34 N 11.52 E
Lavia 26 61.36 N 22.36 E
Laviano 68 40.47 N 15.18 E
Lavic Lake ⊜ 204 34.40 N 116.21 W
La Victoria, Perú 286d 12.04 S 77.02 W
La Victoria, Ven. 246 10.14 N 67.20 W
Lavieille, Lake ⊜ 190 45.51 N 78.14 W
Lavik 26 61.06 N 5.30 E
La Vila Joiosa 34 38.30 N 0.14 W
La Villa 64 46.36 N 11.54 E
La Villa ≃ 236 7.59 N 80.23 W
La Ville-du-Bois 261 48.40 N 2.16 E
La Villeneuve-Saint-Martin 261 49.04 N 1.58 E
Lavillette 186 47.16 N 65.18 W
Lavin 58 46.46 N 10.06 E
La Viña, Arg. 252 25.27 S 65.35 W
Lavina, Mt., U.S. 202 46.17 N 108.56 W
Lavinio Lido di Enea 66 41.30 N 12.05 E
Laviolette, Lac ⊜ 206 46.51 N 73.58 W
La Virginia 246 4.54 N 75.53 W
Lavis 64 46.08 N 11.07 E
La Vista 198 41.11 N 96.01 W
Lavon 222 33.02 N 96.26 W
Lavonia 192 34.26 N 83.06 W
Lavon Lake ⊜[1] 222 33.05 N 96.28 W
Lavougba 152 5.46 N 23.21 E
La Voulte-sur-Rhône 62 44.48 N 4.47 E
Lavoûte-sur-Loire 62 45.07 N 3.54 E
Lavoutte, Anse c 241f 14.06 N 60.56 W
Lavradia 266c 38.40 N 9.03 W
Lavras 256 21.14 S 45.00 W
Lavras ≃ 287a 23.00 S 43.33 W
Lavras da Mangabeira 250 6.45 S 38.57 W
Lavras do Sul 252 30.49 S 53.55 W
Lavrentija 180 65.35 N 171.00 W
Lavrentija, zaliv c 180 65.40 N 171.15 W
Lavrinhas 256 22.35 S 44.54 W
Lávrion 38 37.44 N 24.04 E
Lavumisa 158 27.19 S 31.54 E
Lavushi Manda National Park ♠ 154 12.20 S 30.50 E
Lawa 116 6.12 N 125.41 E
Lawai 229b 21.55 N 159.30 W
Lawang 115a 7.49 S 112.42 E
La Wantzenau 58 48.40 N 7.50 E
La Ward 222 28.51 N 96.28 W
Lawas 112 4.51 N 115.24 E
Lawatu 112 2.53 S 120.18 E
Lawdar 144 13.53 N 45.52 E
Lawele 112 5.13 S 122.57 E
Lawers, Ben ∧ 46 56.34 N 4.13 W
Laweueng 114 5.31 N 95.52 E
Lawford Lake ⊜ 184 54.30 N 96.43 W
Lawgi 166 24.34 S 150.39 E
Lawin 114 5.18 N 101.04 E
Lawin, Pulau I 164 1.31 S 128.44 E
Lawit, Gunong ∧ 114 5.25 N 102.35 E
Lawksawk 110 21.15 N 96.52 E
Lawler 190 43.04 N 92.09 W
Lawlor, Mount ∧ 280 34.16 N 118.06 W
Lawn, Nf., Can. 186 46.57 N 55.32 W
Lawn, Pa., U.S. 208 40.13 N 76.32 W
Lawn, Tx., U.S. 196 32.08 N 99.49 W
Lawn Bay c 186 46.53 N 55.35 W
Lawndale, Ca., U.S. 228 33.53 N 118.21 W
Lawndale, Il., U.S. 219 40.13 N 89.17 W
Lawndale, N.C., U.S. 192 35.24 N 81.33 W
Lawndale ◆[8], Il., U.S. 278 41.51 N 87.43 W
Lawndale ◆[8], Pa., U.S. 285 40.03 N 75.05 W
Lawnes Creek ≃ 208 37.08 N 76.40 W
Lawn Hill 166 18.35 S 138.35 E
Lawn Hill Creek ≃ 166 18.03 S 139.09 E
Lawn Hill National Park ♠ 166 18.45 S 138.27 E
Lawnside 285 39.51 N 75.01 W
Lawowa 112 4.26 S 122.56 E
Lawqah 128 29.49 N 42.45 E
Lawra 150 10.39 N 2.52 W
Lawrence, N.Z. 172 45.55 S 169.41 E
Lawrence, In., U.S. 218 39.50 N 86.01 W
Lawrence, Ks., U.S. 198 38.58 N 95.14 W
Lawrence, Ma., U.S. 207 42.42 N 71.09 W
Lawrence, Mi., U.S. 216 42.13 N 86.03 W
Lawrence, Ne., U.S. 198 40.17 N 98.15 W
Lawrence, N.Y., U.S. 276 40.36 N 73.43 W
Lawrence, Pa., U.S. 279b 40.18 N 80.09 W
Lawrence, Tx., U.S. 222 32.45 N 96.21 W
Lawrence □[6], In., U.S. 218 38.52 N 86.29 W
Lawrence □[6], Pa., U.S. 214 41.00 N 80.20 W
Lawrence, Lake ⊜ 224 46.51 N 122.34 W
Lawrence Brook ≃ 276 40.29 N 74.24 W
Lawrenceburg, In., U.S. 218 39.05 N 84.51 W
Lawrenceburg, Ky., U.S. 218 38.02 N 84.54 W
Lawrenceburg, Tn., U.S. 194 35.14 N 87.20 W
Lawrence Fork ≃ 198 41.36 N 103.14 W

ENGLISH Name	Page	Lat.°′	Long.°′

Lawrence Institute of Technology ʊ[2] 281 42.28 N 83.15 W
Lawrence Marsh ≡ 276 40.36 N 73.42 W
Lawrence Municipal Airport ⊠ 283 42.43 N 71.07 W
Lawrence Park 214 42.09 N 80.01 W
Lawrencepur 123 33.50 N 72.30 E
Lawrenceville, Il., U.S. 194 38.43 N 87.40 W
Lawrenceville, N.J., U.S. 208 40.17 N 74.43 W
Lawrenceville, Pa., U.S. 210 42.00 N 77.08 W
Lawrenceville, Va., U.S. 192 36.45 N 77.50 W
Lawrenceville ◆[8] 279b 40.28 N 79.57 W
Lawson, Austl. 170 33.43 S 150.26 E
Lawson, Mo., U.S. 194 39.26 N 94.12 W
Lawson Heights 214 40.18 N 79.23 W
Lawsonia 208 37.58 N 75.50 W
Lawsons Creek ≃ 170 32.35 S 149.43 E
Lawtey 192 30.02 N 82.04 W
Lawton, Ky., U.S. 218 38.16 N 83.13 W
Lawton, Mi., U.S. 216 42.10 N 85.50 W
Lawton, N.D., U.S. 198 48.18 N 98.22 W
Lawton, Ok., U.S. 196 34.36 N 98.23 W
Lawton ◆[8] 286b 23.06 N 82.21 W
Lawu, Gunung ∧ 115a 7.38 S 111.11 E
Lawyer Creek ≃ 202 46.14 N 116.01 W
Lawyersville 210 42.42 N 74.30 W
Lawz, Jabal al- ∧ 128 28.40 N 35.18 E
Laxå 40 58.59 N 14.37 E
Laxay 46 58.09 N 6.35 W
Laxenburg 264b 48.04 N 16.21 E
Laxenburger Park ♠ 264b 48.04 N 16.22 E
Laxey 44 54.14 N 4.23 W
Laxford, Loch c 46 58.23 N 5.06 W
Lax Kw'alaams 182 54.33 N 130.25 W
Laxou 58 48.41 N 6.09 E
Layang Layang 114 1.49 N 103.29 E
Laye ≃ 62 43.54 N 5.48 E
La Yesca 234 21.19 N 104.02 W
Layhill 208 39.05 N 77.03 W
Laylā 144 22.17 N 46.45 E
Lay Lake ⊜[1] 194 33.10 N 86.35 W
Layou 241h 13.12 N 61.17 W
Layou ≃ 240d 15.23 N 61.26 W
La'youn □[4] 148 27.55 N 12.15 W
Lay-Saint-Christophe 56 48.45 N 6.12 E
Laysan Island I 14 25.50 N 171.50 W
Layton, N.J., U.S. 210 41.13 N 74.50 W
Layton, Ut,. U.S. 200 41.03 N 111.58 W
Laytons Lake ⊜ 285 39.42 N 75.26 W
Laytonville 204 39.41 N 123.28 W
Laytown 48 53.40 N 6.14 W
Laž 80 57.11 N 49.14 E
La Zarca 232 25.50 N 104.44 W
Lazarev 89 52.13 N 141.32 E
Lazarevo 80 56.49 N 50.15 E
Lazarevskoje 84 43.55 N 39.20 E
Lazarivo 157b 23.54 S 44.59 E
Lazaro Cárdenas, Méx. 196 25.23 N 103.10 W
Lázaro Cárdenas, Méx. 232 30.33 N 115.56 W
Lázaro Cárdenas, Méx. 234 17.57 N 102.12 W
Lázaro Cárdenas, Presa ⊜[1] 232 25.35 N 105.02 W
Lazdijai 76 54.14 N 23.31 E
Lazha 102 26.26 N 101.50 E
Lazhulong 120 35.08 N 81.33 E
Lazi 116 9.08 N 123.38 E
Lazio □[4] 66 42.00 N 12.30 E
Lazise 64 45.30 N 10.44 E
Lazo 89 43.25 N 133.55 E
Lazorki 78 50.06 N 32.39 E
La Zorra, Quebrada ≃ 286c 10.36 N 67.03 W
Lazovskij zapovednik ♠ 89 43.00 N 133.55 E
Lazzaro 68 37.58 N 15.40 E
Lazzate 266b 45.40 N 9.05 E
Lea ≃ 42 51.30 N 0.01 E
Léach 110 12.21 N 103.46 E
Leach ≃ 42 51.41 N 1.39 W
Leach Pond ⊜ 283 42.04 N 71.09 W
Leachville 194 35.56 N 90.15 W
Leacock 208 40.05 N 76.12 W
Lead 198 44.21 N 103.45 W
Leadbetter Point › 224 46.38 N 124.03 W
Leadburn 46 55.47 N 3.14 W
Leadenham 44 53.05 N 0.34 W
Leaden Roding 260 51.48 N 0.19 E
Leader 184 50.53 N 109.31 W
Leader Water ≃ 46 55.36 N 2.41 W
Leadgate 44 54.52 N 1.48 W
Lead Hill ∧[2] 194 37.06 N 92.38 W
Leadhills 44 55.25 N 3.47 W
Leadon ≃ 42 51.53 N 2.16 W
Leadore 202 44.40 N 113.21 W
Leadville 200 39.15 N 106.17 W
Leaf ≃, Mn., U.S. 198 46.29 N 94.53 W
Leaf ≃, Ms., U.S. 194 31.00 N 88.45 W
Leaf Lake ⊜ 184 53.02 N 102.07 W
Leaghur, Lake ⊜ 166 33.35 S 143.04 E
League, Slieve ∧ 48 54.39 N 8.44 W
League City 222 29.30 N 95.05 W
Leakesville 194 31.09 N 88.33 W
Leakey 196 29.43 N 99.45 W
Leakin Park ♠ 284b 39.18 N 76.42 W
Leak Run ≃ 279b 40.27 N 79.47 W
Leaksville 192 36.29 N 79.53 W
Lealman 220 27.49 N 82.40 W
Lealui 152 15.10 S 23.02 E
Leam ≃ 42 52.17 N 1.14 W
Leamington 214 42.03 N 82.36 W
Leamington Spa → Royal Leamington Spa 42 52.18 N 1.31 W
Le'an 100 27.24 N 115.48 E
Leán ≃ 236 15.47 N 87.20 W
Leander Point › 162 29.16 S 114.56 E
Leandro 250 5.59 S 44.55 W
Leandro N. Alem 252 27.36 S 55.19 W
Leane, Lough ⊜ 48 52.05 N 9.35 W
Leannan ≃ 48 55.02 N 7.38 W
Leano, Monte ∧ 66 41.20 N 13.13 E
Learmonth 162 22.15 S 114.05 E
Leary 192 31.29 N 84.30 W
Leaside □[8] 275b 43.42 N 79.22 W
Leask 184 53.00 N 106.45 W
Leatherhead 42 51.18 N 0.20 W
Leatherman Peak ∧ 202 44.05 N 113.44 W
Leatherwood Creek ≃ 218 38.49 N 86.30 W
Lea Town 262 53.46 N 2.48 W
Leavenworth, Ks., U.S. 198 39.18 N 94.55 W
Leavenworth, Wa., U.S. 224 47.35 N 120.39 W
Leavesden Aerodrome ⊠ 260 51.42 N 0.27 W
Leavittsburg 214 41.14 N 80.52 W
Leawood 194 37.03 N 94.31 W
Łeba 30 54.47 N 17.33 E
Łeba ≃ 30 54.47 N 17.33 E
Lebach 56 49.24 N 6.54 E
Lebak 116 6.32 N 124.03 E
Lebam 224 46.33 N 123.32 W
Lébamba 152 2.12 S 11.30 E
Lebango 152 0.22 N 14.49 E
Lebanon, Ct., U.S. 207 41.38 N 72.13 W
Lebanon, Il., U.S. 219 38.36 N 89.48 W
Lebanon, In., U.S. 218 40.02 N 86.28 W
Lebanon, Ks., U.S. 198 39.48 N 98.33 W
Lebanon, Ky., U.S. 194 37.34 N 85.15 W
Lebanon, Mo., U.S. 194 37.40 N 92.39 W
Lebanon, N.H., U.S. 188 43.38 N 72.15 W
Lebanon, N.J., U.S. 210 40.38 N 74.50 W
Lebanon, N.Y., U.S. 210 42.47 N 75.39 W

DEUTSCH Name	Seite	Breite°′	Länge°′ E = Ost

Lebanon, Oh., U.S. 218 39.26 N 84.12 W
Lebanon, Or., U.S. 202 44.32 N 122.54 W
Lebanon, Pa., U.S. 208 40.20 N 76.24 W
Lebanon, S.D., U.S. 198 45.04 N 99.46 W
Lebanon, Tn., U.S. 194 36.12 N 86.17 W
Lebanon, Va., U.S. 192 36.54 N 82.04 W
Lebanon □[6] 208 40.20 N 76.25 W
Lebanon (Lubnān) □[1], Asia 118 34.00 N 36.00 E
Lebanon (Lubnān) □[1], Asia 128 34.00 N 36.00 E
Lebanon Junction 194 37.50 N 85.43 W
Lebanon Mountains → Lubnān, Jabal ⋏ 132 34.00 N 36.00 E
Lebanon Springs 210 42.29 N 73.23 W
Le Bar-sur-le-Loup 62 43.42 N 6.59 E
Leb'ažje, Kaz. 86 51.28 N 77.46 E
Leb'ažje, Ross. 80 57.25 N 49.32 E
Leb'ažje, Ross. 86 55.16 N 66.29 E
Lebbeke 50 51.00 N 4.08 E
Le Béage 62 44.51 N 4.07 E
Le Beausset 62 43.12 N 5.48 E
Lebec 228 34.50 N 118.51 W
Lebed'an' 76 53.01 N 39.09 E
Lebedevka, Kaz. 86 50.09 N 54.07 E
Lebedevka, Ross. 80 51.06 N 47.09 E
Lebedevka, Ross. 86 56.48 N 66.57 E
Lebedi 78 51.17 N 37.38 E
Lebedin, Ukr. 78 48.59 N 31.31 E
Lebedin, Ukr. 78 50.36 N 34.30 E
Lebedino 80 55.14 N 49.50 E
Leben, Oued el V 148 34.37 N 10.01 E
Lebesby 24 70.34 N 26.59 E
Le Bessat 62 45.22 N 4.31 E
Le Bihan Falls ∟ 158 29.51 S 28.03 E
Le Biot 58 46.16 N 6.38 E
Lebir ≃ 114 5.33 N 102.12 E
Le Blanc 32 46.38 N 1.04 E
Le Blanc-Mesnil 261 48.56 N 2.28 E
Le Bleymard 62 44.29 N 3.44 E
Leblon ◆[8] 287a 22.59 S 43.13 W
Lebo, Ks., U.S. 198 38.25 N 95.51 W
Lebo, Zaïre 152 4.29 N 23.57 E
Le Bois-de-Cise 50 50.05 N 1.26 E
Le Bois-Dieu 261 48.39 N 1.43 E
Le Bois-d'Oingt 58 45.55 N 4.35 E
Lebombo Mountains ⋏[2] 156 25.15 S 32.00 E
Lebongtandai 112 3.01 S 101.54 E
Le Boréon 62 44.07 N 7.17 E
Lębork 30 54.33 N 17.44 E
Le Boulay 261 48.47 N 1.40 E
Le Bourg-d'Oisans 62 45.03 N 6.02 E
Le Bourget 261 48.56 N 2.26 E
Le Bourget-du-Lac 62 45.39 N 5.52 E
Le Brassus 58 46.35 N 6.13 E
Lebrija 34 36.55 N 6.04 W
Lebrija ≃ 246 8.08 N 73.47 W
Le Broc 62 43.49 N 7.10 E
Le Brugeron 62 45.43 N 3.43 E
Łebsko, Jezioro c 30 54.44 N 17.24 E
Lebu 252 37.37 S 73.39 W
Le Bugue 32 44.55 N 0.56 E
Le Buisson de Massoury ≡ 261 48.30 N 2.43 E
Lebus 54 52.25 N 14.32 E
Le Caire → Al-Qāhirah 142 30.03 N 31.15 E
Le Camp-du-Castellet 62 43.15 N 5.45 E
Le Cannet 62 43.34 N 7.01 E
Lecanto 220 28.51 N 82.29 W
Le Cap → Cap-Haïtien, Haï. 238 19.45 N 72.12 W
Le Cap → Cape Town, S. Afr. 158 33.55 S 18.22 E
Le Carbet 240e 14.43 N 61.11 W
Le Cateau 50 50.06 N 3.33 E
Le Catelet 50 50.00 N 3.15 E
Lecce 68 40.23 N 18.11 E
Lecce □[4] 68 40.13 N 18.10 E
Lecce, Tavoliere di ≚ 68 40.30 N 17.35 E
Lecce nei Marsi 66 41.56 N 13.41 E
Lečchumskij chrebet ⋏ 84 42.45 N 43.05 E
Lecco 62 45.51 N 9.23 E
Lecco, Lago di ⊜ 58 45.55 N 9.19 E
Le Center 190 44.23 N 93.43 W
Lech 58 47.12 N 10.09 E
Lech ≃ 30 48.44 N 10.56 E
Le Châble, Fr. 58 46.06 N 6.06 E
Le Châble, Schw. 58 46.05 N 7.12 E
L'Échalp 62 44.45 N 7.00 E
Le Chambon-Feugerolles 62 45.24 N 4.19 E
Le Chambon-sur-Lignon 62 45.03 N 4.18 E
Le Champ-Renault 261 49.06 N 2.31 E
Lechang 100 25.09 N 113.21 E
Le Chasseral ∧ 58 47.08 N 7.03 E
Le-Château-d'Oléron 32 45.53 N 1.11 W
Le Châtelard, Fr. 62 45.41 N 6.08 E
Le Châtelard, Schw. 58 46.04 N 6.58 E
Le Châtelet 32 46.39 N 2.17 E
Le Châtelet-en-Brie 50 48.30 N 2.48 E
Lechbruck 58 47.42 N 10.47 E
Leche, Laguna de la c 240p 22.13 N 78.38 W
Le Chêne-Rogneux 261 48.46 N 1.46 E
Le Chesnay 261 48.50 N 2.07 E
Le Chesne 56 49.31 N 4.46 E
Le Cheylard 62 44.54 N 4.25 E
Lechfeld ≚ 58 48.10 N 10.50 E
Lechiguanas, Islas de las II 252 33.26 S 59.42 W
Lechlade 42 51.43 N 1.41 W
Lechleiten 58 47.16 N 10.12 E
Lechta 24 60.49 N 48.28 E
Lechtaler Alpen ⋏ 64 47.15 N 10.30 E
Lechuga, Arroyo ≃ 286b 23.01 N 82.16 W
Lechuguilla, Cerro ∧ 234 22.19 N 104.15 W
Lecinone, Monte ∧ 267a 41.59 N 12.48 E
Leck 41 54.46 N 8.58 E
Le Claire 190 41.36 N 90.21 W
Lecompte 194 31.05 N 92.24 W
Leconfield 44 53.52 N 0.27 W
Léconi 152 1.35 S 14.14 E
Lecontes Mills 214 41.05 N 78.17 W
Le Cornate ∧ 66 43.10 N 10.57 E
Le Coudray-Montceaux 261 48.34 N 2.31 E
Le Coudray-Saint-Germer 50 49.25 N 1.50 E
Le Creusot 58 46.48 N 4.26 E
Le Croci di Acerno)(68 40.47 N 15.02 E
Le Croisic 32 47.18 N 2.31 W
Le Crotoy 50 50.13 N 1.37 E
Łęczna 30 51.19 N 22.52 E
Łęczyca 30 52.04 N 19.13 E
Leda ≃ 52 53.12 N 7.26 E
Ledaig 46 56.30 N 5.23 W
Led'anaja, gora ∧ 74 61.53 N 171.09 E
Ledang, Gunong ∧ 114 2.22 N 102.37 E
Ledava ≃ 61 46.29 N 16.35 E
Ledbetter 222 30.09 N 96.48 W
Ledbury 42 52.02 N 2.25 W
Lede 50 50.58 N 3.58 E
Ledenice 61 48.57 N 14.37 E
Lederach 285 40.16 N 75.24 W
Le Deschaux 58 46.57 N 5.30 E
Ledesma 34 41.05 N 6.00 W
Ledgewood 276 40.52 N 74.39 W
Ledi, Ben ∧ 46 56.15 N 4.19 W
Le Diamant 240e 14.29 N 61.02 W
Lediba 152 3.03 S 16.32 E
Lédignan 62 43.59 N 4.06 E
Ledkovo 24 67.14 N 50.30 E
Lednice 61 48.48 N 16.48 E
Ledo, India 120 27.18 N 95.44 E
Ledo, Indon. 112 1.02 N 109.36 E

Symbols in the index entries represent the broad categories identified in the key at the right. Symbols with superior numbers (⋏[1]) identify subcategories (see complete key on page *I · 1*).

Symbole im Register stellen die rechts im Schlüssel erklärten Kategorien dar. Symbole mit hochgestellten Ziffern (⋏[1]) bezeichnen Unterabteilungen einer Kategorie (vgl. vollständiger Schlüssel auf Seite *I · 1*).

Los símbolos incluídos en el texto del índice representan las grandes categorías identificadas con la clave a la derecha. Los símbolos con numeros en su parte superior (⋏[1]) identifican las subcategorías (véase la clave completa en la página *I · 1*).

Les symboles de l'index représentent les catégories indiquées dans la légende à droite. Les symboles suivis d'un indice (⋏[1]) représentent des sous-catégories (voir légende complète à la page *I · 1*).

Os símbolos incluídos no texto do índice representam as grandes categorias identificadas com a chave à direita. Os símbolos com números em sua parte superior (⋏[1]) identificam as subcategorias (veja-se a chave completa à página *I · 1*).

∧	Mountain	Berg	Montaña	Montagne	Montanha
⋏	Mountains	Gebirge	Montañas	Montagnes	Montanhas
)(	Pass	Paß	Paso	Col	Passo
V	Valley, Canyon	Tal, Cañon	Valle, Cañón	Vallée, Canyon	Vale, Canhão
≚	Plain	Ebene	Llano	Plaine	Planície
›	Cape	Kap	Cabo	Cap	Cabo
I	Island	Insel	Isla	Île	Ilha
II	Islands	Inseln	Islas	Îles	Ilhas
⊥	Other Topographic Features	Andere Topographische Objekte	Otros Elementos Topográficos	Autres données topographiques	Outros acidentes topográficos

ESPAÑOL

Nombre	Página	Lat.°′	Long.°′ W = Oeste
Lêdo, Cabo ›	152	9.41 S	13.12 E
Ledong	110	18.45 N	109.12 E
Le Donjon	32	46.21 N	3.48 E
Le Dorat	32	46.13 N	1.05 E
Le Doré, Lac ⊜	186	51.17 N	61.23 W
Ledra ≃	64	46.13 N	13.02 E
Ledsham	262	53.16 N	2.58 W
Ledu	102	36.32 N	102.25 E
Leduc	182	53.16 N	113.33 W
Ledung	114	2.45 N	99.59 E
Ledyard Bay c	180	69.30 N	164.30 W
Lędyczek	30	53.33 N	16.58 E
Lee, Il., U.S.	216	41.48 N	88.56 W
Lee, Ma., U.S.	207	42.18 N	73.14 W
Lee □[6], Fl., U.S.	220	26.34 N	81.55 W
Lee □[6], Il., U.S.	216	41.50 N	89.29 W
Lee □[6], Tx., U.S.	222	30.20 N	96.55 W
Lee ≃	48	51.54 N	8.22 W
Lee Boulevard Heights	284c	38.52 N	77.09 W
Lee Center	210	43.18 N	75.31 W
Leechburg	214	40.37 N	79.36 W
Leechburg Airport ⊠	279b	40.37 N	79.34 W
Leech Lake ⊜, Sk., Can.	184	51.04 N	102.30 W
Leech Lake ⊜, Mn., U.S.	190	47.09 N	94.23 W
Leech Lake Indian Reservation ⬥[4]	190	47.30 N	94.27 W
Leechtown	224	48.30 N	123.42 W
Leedey	196	35.52 N	99.20 W
Leedom Estates	285	39.41 N	75.35 W
Leeds, Eng., U.K.	44	53.50 N	1.35 W
Leeds, Al., U.S.	194	33.32 N	86.32 W
Leeds, N.Y., U.S.	210	42.15 N	73.54 W
Leeds, N.D., U.S.	198	48.17 N	99.26 W
Leeds and Bradford (Yeadon) Airport ⊠	44	53.52 N	1.38 W
Leeds and Grenville □[6]	212	44.45 N	75.50 W
Leeds and Liverpool Canal ≊	262	53.25 N	2.59 W
Leeds Point	208	39.29 N	74.25 W
Leedstown	42	50.10 N	5.22 W
Leegebruch	54	52.43 N	13.11 E
Leek, Ned.	52	53.09 N	6.24 E
Leek, Eng., U.K.	44	53.06 N	2.01 W
Leelanau, Lake ⊜	190	44.55 N	85.43 W
Leelanau Peninsula ›[1]	190	45.10 N	85.35 W
Leeming	44	54.17 N	1.32 W
Leenaun	48	53.36 N	9.45 W
Leende	52	51.21 N	5.33 E
Lee-on-the-Solent	42	50.47 N	1.12 W
Lee Park	210	41.14 N	75.55 W
Leeper	214	41.22 N	79.18 W
Leer	52	53.14 N	7.26 E
Leerdam	52	51.54 N	5.05 E
Leerhafe	52	53.32 N	7.47 E
Leersum	52	52.01 N	5.26 E
Lees	262	53.32 N	2.04 W
Leesburg, Fl., U.S.	220	28.48 N	81.52 W
Leesburg, Ga., U.S.	192	31.43 N	84.10 W
Leesburg, In., U.S.	216	41.19 N	85.51 W
Leesburg, N.J., U.S.	208	39.15 N	74.59 W
Leesburg, Oh., U.S.	218	39.20 N	83.33 W
Leesburg, Tx., U.S.	222	32.59 N	95.05 W
Leesburg, Va., U.S.	208	39.06 N	77.33 W
Lees Creek ≃	218	39.21 N	83.29 W
Leese	52	52.30 N	9.06 E
Leesport	208	40.27 N	75.58 W
Lees Summit	194	38.55 N	94.23 W
Leeste	52	52.59 N	8.49 E
Leeston	172	43.46 S	172.18 E
Leesville, Il., U.S.	216	41.01 N	87.33 W
Leesville, In., U.S.	218	38.51 N	86.18 W
Leesville, La., U.S.	194	31.08 N	93.15 W
Leesville, Oh., U.S.	214	40.27 N	81.13 W
Leesville, S.C., U.S.	192	33.54 N	81.30 W
Leesville, Tx., U.S.	222	29.24 N	97.45 W
Leesville Lake ⊜[1], Oh., U.S.	214	40.30 N	81.10 W
Leesville Lake ⊜[1], Va., U.S.	192	37.05 N	79.25 W
Leeton	166	34.33 S	146.24 E
Leetonia	214	40.52 N	80.45 W
Leetsdale	214	40.33 N	80.12 W
Leeudoringstad	158	27.15 S	26.10 E
Leeu-Gamka	158	32.47 S	21.59 E
Leeupan ≃	273d	26.14 S	28.19 E
Leeuwarden	52	53.12 N	5.46 E
Leeuwin, Cape ›	162	34.22 S	115.08 E
Lee Vining	226	37.57 N	119.07 W
Leeward Islands II	238	17.00 N	63.00 W
Le Faouët	28	48.02 N	3.29 W
Le Fayet	58	45.55 N	6.42 E
Lefèvre, Pointe ›	175f	20.54 S	167.01 E
Leffe	62	45.48 N	9.53 E
Lefferts, Lake ⊜	276	40.25 N	74.14 W
Léfini ≃	152	2.57 S	16.10 E
Léfini, Réserve de Chasse de la ⬥[4]	152	2.58 S	15.25 E
Lefke	130	35.07 N	32.51 E
Le Focette	64	43.55 N	10.13 E
Leforest	50	50.26 N	3.04 E
Lefors	196	35.26 N	100.48 W
Le François	240e	14.37 N	60.54 W
Le Freney-d'Oisans	62	45.02 N	6.07 E
Lefroy	212	44.16 N	79.34 W
Lefroy, Lake ⊜	162	31.15 S	121.40 E
Leftrook Lake ⊜	184	56.05 N	98.36 W
Lega Hida	144	7.56 N	41.04 E
Legal	182	53.57 N	113.35 W
Leganés	34	40.19 N	3.45 W
Le Gardeur	206	45.45 N	73.28 W
Legaspi	116	13.08 N	123.44 E
Legau	58	47.51 N	10.07 E
Legden	52	52.02 N	7.07 E
Legendre ≃	206	45.44 N	71.08 W
Legendre Island I	162	20.23 S	116.54 E
Leggett, Ca., U.S.	204	39.51 N	123.42 W
Leggett, Tx., U.S.	222	30.49 N	94.52 W
Leghorn → Livorno	66	43.33 N	10.19 E
Legion Mine	154	21.23 S	28.33 E
Legion of Honor, Palace of the ʊ	282	37.47 N	122.30 W
Legionowo	30	52.25 N	20.56 E
Legnago	64	45.11 N	11.18 E
Legnano	62	45.36 N	8.54 E
Legnica (Liegnitz)	30	51.13 N	16.09 E
Legnica □[4]	30	51.25 N	16.10 E
Le Gosier	241o	16.12 N	61.30 W
Le Grand	226	37.13 N	120.14 W
LeGrand, Cape ›	162	34.01 S	122.06 E
Le Grand-Lucé	50	47.52 N	0.28 E
Le Grand-Quevilly	50	49.25 N	1.02 E
Le Grand-Serre	62	45.16 N	5.06 E
Le Grand Wintersberg ∧[2]	56	48.59 N	7.37 E
Le Grau-du-Roi	62	43.32 N	4.08 E
Le Gua	62	45.01 N	5.37 E
Le Guelta	34	36.22 N	0.50 E
Leguga	154	3.23 N	25.02 E
Legume	166	28.25 S	152.19 E
Legundi, Pulau I	115a	5.50 S	105.16 E
Leh	123	34.10 N	77.35 E
Le Havre	50	49.30 N	0.08 E
Lehčevo	38	43.32 N	23.32 E
Le Hérie-la-Viéville	50	49.49 N	3.38 E
Lehesten	54	50.29 N	11.28 E
Lehi	200	40.23 N	111.50 W
Lehigh, Ia., U.S.	190	42.21 N	94.03 W
Lehigh, Ok., U.S.	196	34.28 N	96.12 W
Lehigh □[6]	208	40.36 N	75.29 W
Lehigh ≃	210	40.41 N	75.12 W
Lehigh Acres	220	26.37 N	81.37 W
Lehighton	210	40.50 N	75.42 W
Lehinch	48	52.56 N	9.21 W
Lehnin	54	52.19 N	12.44 E

FRANÇAIS

Nom	Page	Lat.°′	Long.°′ W = Ouest
Lehnitz	54	52.44 N	13.15 E
Lehnitz See ⊜	264a	52.45 N	13.16 E
Leho	140	7.07 N	33.52 E
Le Hohwald	58	48.24 N	7.20 E
Le Houlme	50	49.31 N	1.02 E
Lehr	198	45.59 N	99.32 W
Lehra Gāga	123	29.55 N	75.49 E
Lehrbach	56	50.47 N	9.04 E
Lehrberg	56	49.21 N	10.30 E
Lehre	54	52.19 N	10.40 E
Lehrte	52	52.22 N	9.59 E
Lehstedt	52	52.14 N	10.12 E
Lehtimäki	26	62.47 N	23.55 E
Lehtrār Bāla	123	33.42 N	73.26 E
Lehtse	76	59.15 N	25.50 E
Lehua I	229b	22.01 N	160.06 W
Lehututu	156	23.58 S	21.51 E
Lei ≃	100	26.54 N	112.39 E
Leiah	123	30.58 N	70.56 E
Leião	266c	38.44 N	9.18 W
Leibnitz	61	46.47 N	15.32 E
Leibo	102	28.19 N	103.21 E
Leicester, Eng., U.K.	42	52.38 N	1.05 W
Leicester, Ma., U.S.	207	42.14 N	71.54 W
Leicester, N.Y., U.S.	210	42.46 N	77.53 W
Leicestershire □[6]	42	52.40 N	1.10 W
Leichhardt	274a	33.53 S	151.07 E
Leichhardt ≃	166	17.35 S	139.48 E
Leichhardt Falls ∟	166	18.14 S	139.53 E
Leichhardt Range ⩘	166	20.40 S	147.25 E
Leichlingen	56	51.06 N	7.01 E
Leiden	52	52.09 N	4.30 E
Leiderdorp	52	52.09 N	4.32 E
Leidschendam	52	52.05 N	4.24 E
Leie (Lys) ≃	50	51.03 N	3.43 E
Leiferde	52	52.26 N	10.26 E
Leigh, N.Z.	172	36.17 S	174.49 E
Leigh, Eng., U.K.	44	53.30 N	2.33 W
Leigh, Eng., U.K.	260	51.12 N	0.13 E
Leigh ≃	169	38.06 S	144.03 E
Leigh Canal ≊	262	53.28 N	2.21 W
Leigh Creek	166	30.28 S	138.25 E
Leighlinbridge	48	52.44 N	6.59 W
Leigh-on-Sea	42	51.33 N	0.38 E
Leighton	194	34.42 N	87.31 W
Leighton Buzzard	42	51.55 N	0.40 W
Leikanger	26	61.10 N	6.52 E
Leiktho	110	19.13 N	96.35 E
Leimbach	54	51.36 N	11.28 E
Leimstruth	56	50.59 N	8.19 E
Lein ≃	56	48.54 N	10.01 E
Leinan	184	50.30 N	107.46 W
Leinburg	60	49.27 N	11.19 E
Leine ≃	52	52.43 N	9.36 E
Leinefelde, Dtsch.	52	51.23 N	10.20 E
Leinefelde, Dtsch.	54	51.23 N	10.20 E
Leinfelden-Echterdingen	56	48.41 N	9.08 E
Leinster	162	27.51 S	120.36 E
Leinster □[9]	48	53.05 N	7.00 W
Leinster, Mount ∧	48	52.37 N	6.44 W
Leintwardine	42	52.23 N	2.51 W
Leipalingis	76	54.05 N	23.51 E
Leipheim	58	48.27 N	10.13 E
Leipoldtville	158	32.14 S	18.30 E
Leipsic, De., U.S.	208	39.14 N	75.31 W
Leipsic, In., U.S.	218	38.40 N	86.22 W
Leipsic, Oh., U.S.	216	41.05 N	83.59 W
Leipsic ≃	208	39.15 N	75.24 W
Leipzig	54	51.19 N	12.20 E
Leiria	34	39.45 N	8.48 W
Leirvik	26	59.45 N	5.30 E
Leisach	64	46.48 N	12.45 E
Leishendian	107	28.58 N	106.40 E
Leisi	76	58.34 N	22.39 E
Leisler, Mount ∧	162	23.28 S	129.17 E
Leisnig	54	51.09 N	12.56 E
Leiston	42	52.12 N	1.34 E
Leisure City	220	25.29 N	80.25 W
Leitariegos, Puerto de ʯ	34	43.00 N	6.25 W
Leitchfield	194	37.28 N	86.17 W
Leiters Ford	216	41.07 N	86.23 W
Leith	46	55.59 N	3.10 W
Leith, Water of ≃	46	55.59 N	3.11 W
Leitha (Lajta) ≃	61	47.54 N	17.17 E
Leithagebirge ⩘	61	47.52 N	16.35 E
Leithe ⬥[8]	263	51.29 N	7.06 E
Leith Hill ∧[2]	42	51.11 N	0.23 W
Leitre	164	2.50 S	141.40 E
Leitrim	48	54.00 N	8.04 W
Leitrim □[6]	48	54.20 N	8.20 W
Leitzkau	54	52.03 N	11.57 E
Leixi	100	27.10 N	112.52 E
Leixlip	48	53.22 N	6.29 W
Leiyang	100	26.24 N	112.51 E
Lei Yue Mun ʯ	271d	22.16 N	114.14 E
Leizhou Bandao ›[1]	102	21.15 N	110.09 E
Leizhuang	98	39.47 N	118.34 E
Lejasciems	76	57.17 N	26.35 E
Lek ≃	52	51.55 N	4.34 E
Lékana	152	2.19 S	14.36 E
Le Kef → El Kef	148	36.11 N	8.43 E
Lékéti ≃	152	1.36 S	14.57 E
Lekhainá	38	37.56 N	21.17 E
Lekir	114	4.07 N	100.44 E
Lekitobi	112	1.58 S	124.33 E
Lekkeroog	158	30.43 S	20.00 E
Lekkerwater	156	23.38 S	17.14 E
Lekma ≃	80	58.18 N	52.04 E
Łęknice	54	51.35 N	14.45 E
Lékoni ≃	152	1.11 S	13.16 E
Lekotero	152	0.46 S	23.51 E
Lékoumou □[5]	152	3.00 S	13.30 E
Le Kreïder	148	34.06 N	0.02 E
Le Kremlin-Bicêtre	261	48.49 N	2.21 E
Leksand	26	60.44 N	14.59 E
Leksberg	40	59.41 N	13.49 E
Leksozero, ozero ⊜	24	63.46 N	30.58 E
Leksvik	26	63.40 N	10.37 E
Lela	152	5.03 S	12.29 E
Le Lac-d'Issarlès	62	44.49 N	4.04 E
Le Lamentin	240e	14.37 N	61.01 W
Leland, Il., U.S.	216	41.37 N	88.48 W
Leland, Mi., U.S.	190	45.01 N	85.45 W
Leland, Ms., U.S.	194	33.24 N	90.53 W
Leland Grove	219	39.47 N	89.41 W
Leland Lake ⊜	224	47.53 N	122.53 W
Lelång ⊜	26	59.08 N	12.10 E
Lelant	42	50.11 N	5.26 W
Le Laus	62	44.31 N	6.09 E
Le Lauzet-Ubaye	62	44.26 N	6.26 E
Le Lavandou	62	43.08 N	6.22 E
Lel'čicy	78	51.47 N	28.19 E
Leleiwi Point ›	229d	19.44 N	155.00 W
Leleque	254	42.23 S	71.03 W
Leles	115a	7.07 S	107.53 E
Lelewau	112	3.02 S	121.05 E
Lélex	58	46.18 N	5.57 E
Le Liège	50	47.13 N	1.06 E
Le Limbé	238	19.42 N	72.24 W
Leling	98	37.45 N	117.12 E
Lelingluang	164	7.09 S	131.43 E
Lelintah	164	2.03 S	130.16 E
Le Lion-d'Angers	32	47.38 N	0.43 W
Leli Shan ∧	120	33.26 N	81.42 E
Le Locle	58	47.03 N	6.45 E
Lelogama	112	9.44 S	123.57 E
Le Lorrain	240e	14.50 N	61.04 W
Le Luc	62	43.23 N	6.19 E
Le Lude	50	47.39 N	0.09 E
Lelydorp	250	5.42 N	55.16 W
Lelystad	52	52.31 N	5.27 E
Lema	150	12.57 N	4.14 E
Lemahabang	115a	6.17 S	107.27 E
Le Maire, Estrecho de ʯ	254	54.50 S	65.00 W
Léman, Lac → Geneva, Lake ⊜	58	46.25 N	6.30 E

PORTUGUÊS

Nome	Página	Lat.°′	Long.°′ W = Oeste
Lemankoa	175e	5.02 S	154.35 E
Le Mans	50	48.00 N	0.12 E
Le Marin	240e	14.28 N	60.53 W
Le Markstein	58	47.56 N	7.02 E
Le Mars	198	42.47 N	96.09 W
Lema Shilindi	144	4.55 N	42.02 E
Lemay	219	38.32 N	90.17 W
Lemay, Lac ⊜	186	50.35 N	68.25 W
Lembach	56	49.00 N	7.48 E
Lembach im Mühlkreis	60	48.29 N	13.53 E
Lemba-Gaba	273b	4.27 S	15.18 E
Lembak	112	0.52 N	117.32 E
Lembang	115a	6.49 S	107.36 E
Lembeck	52	51.45 N	7.00 E
Lembeek	50	50.43 N	4.13 E
Lembeh, Pulau I	112	1.26 N	125.13 E
Lembeni	154	3.47 S	37.37 E
Lemberg, Sk., Can.	184	50.44 N	103.13 W
Lemberg, Fr.	56	49.00 N	7.23 E
Lemberg → L'vov, Ukr.	78	49.50 N	24.00 E
Lemberg ∧	58	48.09 N	8.45 E
Lembruch	52	52.31 N	8.22 E
Lembu, Gunung ∧	114	4.12 N	97.24 E
Lemdiyya	148	36.12 N	2.50 E
Lemdiyya □[5]	148	35.50 N	3.00 E
Leme	255	22.12 S	47.24 W
Leme, Morro do ∧[2]	287a	22.58 S	43.10 W
Le Mée-sur-Seine	261	48.32 N	2.38 E
Lemei Rock ∧	224	46.01 N	121.46 W
Lemele	52	52.27 N	6.25 E
Le Mêle-sur-Sarthe	50	48.31 N	0.21 E
Lemene ≃	64	45.37 N	12.53 E
Lemeris, Cape ›	164	3.15 S	152.03 E
Le Merlerault	50	48.42 N	0.18 E
Lemery	116	13.53 N	120.55 E
Lemeškino	80	51.01 N	44.27 E
Le Mesle	261	48.43 N	1.41 E
Le Mesnil-Amelot	261	49.01 N	2.36 E
Le Mesnil-Aubry	261	49.03 N	2.24 E
Le Mesnil-le-Roi	261	48.56 N	2.08 E
Le Mesnil-Saint-Denis	261	48.45 N	1.58 E
Le Mesnil-sur-Oger	50	48.57 N	4.01 E
Lemesós (Limassol)	130	34.40 N	33.02 E
Lemešovka	78	52.04 N	31.38 E
Lemeta	180	64.52 N	147.44 W
Lemförde	52	52.28 N	8.22 E
Lemfu	152	5.18 S	15.13 E
Lemgo	52	52.02 N	8.54 E
Lemhi ≃	202	45.12 N	113.53 W
Lemhi Pass ʯ	202	44.58 N	113.27 W
Lemhi Range ⩘	202	44.30 N	113.25 W
Lemie	62	45.14 N	7.17 E
Lemierzyce	54	52.35 N	14.56 E
Lemieux Islands II	176	64.30 N	64.40 W
Lemin	102	21.11 N	109.42 E
Leming	196	29.04 N	98.29 W
Lemitar	200	34.09 N	106.54 W
Lemke	52	52.39 N	9.09 E
Lemland I	26	60.03 N	20.09 E
Lemmatsi	76	58.20 N	26.37 E
Lemmenjoen kansallispuisto ♠	24	68.40 N	26.00 E
Lemmer	52	52.50 N	5.42 E
Lemmon	198	45.56 N	102.09 W
Lemmon, Mount ∧	200	32.26 N	110.47 W
Lemnos → Límnos I	38	39.54 N	25.21 E
Lemoenshoek	158	33.51 S	20.51 E
Lemoine, Lac ⊜	190	48.00 N	78.00 W
Lemon, Lake ⊜	218	39.16 N	86.25 W
Le Monastier	62	44.56 N	4.00 E
Lemoncove	204	36.23 N	119.01 W
Lemon Creek ≃	276	40.31 N	74.12 W
Le Monêtier-les-Bains	62	44.59 N	6.31 E
Lemon Grove	228	32.44 N	117.01 W
Lemon Heights	280	33.46 N	117.48 W
Lemont, Il., U.S.	216	41.40 N	88.00 W
Lemont, Pa., U.S.	214	40.49 N	77.49 W
Le Montet	32	46.25 N	3.03 E
Le Mont-Saint-Michel ʊ[1]	32	48.38 N	1.32 W
Lemoore	226	36.18 N	119.46 W
Lemoore Naval Air Station ■	226	36.15 N	119.57 W
Lemoro	112	1.25 S	121.05 E
Le Moule	241o	16.20 N	61.21 W
Le Moutier	261	48.50 N	1.42 E
LeMoyne, P.Q., Can.	275a	45.31 N	73.29 W
Lemoyne, Oh., U.S.	214	41.30 N	83.28 W
Lemoyne, Pa., U.S.	208	40.15 N	76.54 W
Lempa ≃	236	13.14 N	88.49 W
Lempäälä	26	61.19 N	23.45 E
Lempe	112	1.40 S	120.14 E
Lempira □[5]	236	14.20 N	88.40 W
Lemro ≃	110	20.25 N	93.20 E
Lemsid	148	26.32 N	13.49 E
Lemukutan, Pulau I	112	0.45 N	108.43 E
Le Murge ⩘[1]	68	40.52 N	16.42 E
Lemutan	112	3.03 N	115.49 E
Le Muy	62	43.28 N	6.33 E
Lemva ≃	24	66.30 N	61.48 E
Lemvig	26	56.32 N	8.18 E
Lemyethna	110	17.36 N	95.09 E
Len ≃	260	51.16 N	0.31 E
Lena, Il., U.S.	190	42.22 N	89.49 W
Lena, Wi., U.S.	190	44.57 N	88.02 W
Lena ≃	74	72.25 N	126.40 E
Lenangguar	115b	8.44 S	117.24 E
Lenape	285	39.55 N	75.38 W
Lenart	36	46.35 N	15.50 E
Lenasia	273d	26.17 S	27.50 E
Lenawee □[6]	216	41.53 N	84.04 W
Lencloître	32	46.49 N	0.20 E
Lençóis	255	12.34 S	41.23 W
Lençois Maranhenses, Parque Nacional dos ♠	250	2.25 S	43.15 W
Lend	64	47.18 N	13.04 E
Lenda ≃	154	1.20 N	28.01 E
Lendava	61	46.34 N	16.27 E
Lendelede	50	50.53 N	3.14 E
Lendery	24	63.26 N	31.03 E
Lendinara	64	45.05 N	11.36 E
Lendorf	64	46.50 N	13.26 E
Lendringsen	56	51.24 N	7.49 E
Le Neubourg	50	49.09 N	0.55 E
Lenga	114	2.17 N	102.49 E
Lengduqiao	106	30.27 N	119.15 E
Lengede	52	52.12 N	10.18 E
Lengefeld	54	50.43 N	13.11 E
Lengelscheid	263	51.08 N	7.40 E
Lengenfeld, Dtsch.	54	50.34 N	12.22 E
Lengenfeld, Dtsch.	56	51.13 N	10.13 E
Lenger	85	42.12 N	69.54 E
Lengerich, Dtsch.	52	52.11 N	7.50 E
Lengerich, Dtsch.	52	52.33 N	7.32 E
Lenggor ≃	114	2.25 N	103.37 E
Lenggries	64	47.41 N	11.34 E
Lenghu	90	38.30 N	93.15 E
Lengjiagou	104	41.40 N	121.37 E
Lengkong	115a	7.32 S	112.04 E
Lenglingen ⊜	26	64.14 N	13.45 E
Lengnau	58	47.11 N	7.22 E
Lengoué	152	1.13 N	15.43 E
Lengoué ≃	152	0.49 N	15.47 E
Lengshuichang	107	29.27 N	106.26 E
Lengshuikeng	100	27.55 N	117.08 E
Lengshuitan	102	26.27 N	111.35 E
Lengua de Vaca, Punta ›	252	30.14 S	71.38 W
Lengulu	154	3.15 N	26.30 E
Lengwe National Park ♠	154	16.15 S	34.45 E
Lengzipu	104	41.42 N	122.47 E
Lenham	42	51.14 N	0.43 E
Lenhartsville	208	40.34 N	75.53 W
Lenhovda	26	57.00 N	15.17 E
Lenina, gora ∧[2]	265b	55.42 N	37.31 E
Lenina, ozero ⊜	78	48.33 N	35.12 E
Lenina, pik ∧	85	39.20 N	72.55 E
Leninabad → Chudžand	85	40.17 N	69.37 E
Leninakan → Kumajri	84	40.48 N	43.50 E
Lenin Central Stadium ♠	265b	55.43 N	37.33 E
Lenin-Džol	85	41.03 N	72.38 E
Leningori	84	42.07 N	44.29 E
Leningrad → Sankt-Peterburg	76	59.55 N	30.15 E
Leningrado → Sankt-Peterburg	76	59.55 N	30.15 E
Leningrad Oblast' □[4]	24	60.00 N	32.00 E
Leningradskaja	78	46.19 N	39.24 E
Leningradskaja ʊ[3]	9	69.30 S	159.23 E
Leningradskij	85	38.06 N	70.01 E
Leningradskoje	86	53.33 N	71.35 E
Lenino	78	45.18 N	35.47 E
Lenino ⬥[8]	265b	55.37 N	37.41 E
Leninogorsk, Kaz.	86	50.27 N	83.32 E
Leninogorsk, Ross.	80	54.36 N	52.30 E
Leninpol'	85	42.29 N	71.55 E
Leninsk, Kaz.	86	45.40 N	63.20 E
Leninsk, Ross.	80	46.08 N	43.46 E
Leninsk, Ross.	80	48.42 N	45.11 E
Leninsk, Ross.	86	54.55 N	59.54 E
Leninsk, Uzb.	85	40.38 N	72.15 E
Leninskaja Sloboda	80	56.05 N	44.28 E
Leninskij, Kaz.	86	52.13 N	76.47 E
Leninskij, Mol.	38	47.53 N	28.23 E
Leninskij, Ross.	80	46.31 N	44.28 E
Leninskij, Ross.	80	56.34 N	45.56 E
Leninskij, Ross.	82	54.18 N	37.28 E
Leninskij, Ukr.	83	48.05 N	39.31 E
Leninsk-Kuzneckij	86	54.38 N	86.10 E
Leninskoje, Kaz.	80	49.03 N	49.56 E
Leninskoje, Kaz.	85	41.45 N	69.23 E
Leninskoje, Kaz.	86	54.04 N	65.22 E
Leninskoje, Kaz.	86	50.44 N	57.53 E
Leninskoje, Kyrg.	85	40.42 N	73.11 E
Leninskoje, Ross.	80	58.19 N	47.06 E
Leninskoje, Ross.	89	47.56 N	132.38 E
Leninskoje, Ukr.	78	45.16 N	35.54 E
Leninskoje, Ukr.	78	51.27 N	33.18 E
Lenin-Stausee → Kujbyševskoje vodochranilišče ⊜[1]	80	54.30 N	48.30 E
Leninžol	80	49.20 N	47.05 E
Lenk	58	46.28 N	7.27 E
Lenkerville	208	40.32 N	76.58 W
Len'ki	86	52.57 N	80.26 E
Lenkoran'	84	38.45 N	48.50 E
Lenmalu	164	1.44 S	130.13 E
Lennard, Mount ∧[2]	168a	33.21 S	115.53 E
Lenne ≃	56	51.25 N	7.30 E
Lennegebirge ⩘	52	51.15 N	8.00 E
Lennep	56	51.12 N	7.16 E
Lennep ⬥[8]	52	51.12 N	7.16 E
Lennestadt	56	51.08 N	8.01 E
Lenni	285	39.54 N	75.27 W
Lennon	216	42.59 N	83.56 W
Lennonville	162	27.58 S	117.50 E
Lennox, Ca., U.S.	228	33.56 N	118.21 W
Lennox, S.D., U.S.	198	43.21 N	96.53 W
Lennox □[9]	46	56.02 N	4.15 W
Lennox, Isla I	254	55.18 S	66.50 W
Lennox and Addington □[6]	212	44.30 N	77.00 W
Lennoxtown	46	55.59 N	4.12 W
Lennoxville	206	45.22 N	71.51 W
Leno	64	45.22 N	10.13 E
Lenoir	192	35.54 N	81.32 W
Lenoir City	192	35.47 N	84.15 W
Le Noirmont	58	47.13 N	6.58 E
Lenola	66	41.24 N	13.28 E
Lenora	60	48.56 N	13.48 E
Lenore Lake ⊜	184	52.30 N	105.00 W
Le Nouvion-en-Thiérache	50	50.01 N	3.47 E
Lenox, Ga., U.S.	192	31.16 N	83.27 W
Lenox, Ia., U.S.	198	40.52 N	94.33 W
Lenox, Ma., U.S.	207	42.22 N	73.17 W
Lenox, Tn., U.S.	194	36.05 N	89.29 W
Lenox Dale	207	42.20 N	73.14 W
Lens	50	50.26 N	2.50 E
Lensahn	54	54.13 N	10.52 E
Lensk	74	61.00 N	114.50 E
Lenskoje	86	58.09 N	63.11 E
Lenswood	168b	34.55 S	138.49 E
Lentate sul Seveso	266b	45.41 N	9.07 E
Lentechi	84	42.48 N	42.44 E
Lenti	30	46.37 N	16.33 E
Lenting	60	48.48 N	11.28 E
Lentini	70	37.17 N	15.00 E
Lentner	219	39.43 N	92.09 W
Lentua ⊜	26	64.14 N	29.36 E
Lentvaris	76	54.39 N	25.03 E
Lenwood	228	34.53 N	117.07 W
Lenya	110	11.28 N	99.00 E
Lenya ≃	110	11.40 N	98.43 E
Lenz	273d	26.19 S	27.49 E
Lenzburg	58	47.23 N	8.11 E
Lenzen	54	53.05 N	11.28 E
Lenzerheide (Lai)	58	46.44 N	9.33 E
Lenzinghausen	52	52.07 N	8.28 E
Lenzkirch	58	47.52 N	8.12 E
Léo, Burkina	150	11.06 N	2.06 W
Leo, In., U.S.	216	41.13 N	85.00 W
Leoben	61	47.23 N	15.06 E
Leo Carrillo State Beach ♠	228	34.03 N	118.56 W
Léogâne	238	18.31 N	72.38 W
Leogang	64	47.26 N	12.45 E
Leola, Ar., U.S.	194	34.10 N	92.35 W
Leola, Pa., U.S.	208	40.05 N	76.11 W
Leola, S.D., U.S.	198	45.43 N	98.56 W
Leominster, Eng., U.K.	42	52.14 N	2.45 W
Leominster, Ma., U.S.	207	42.31 N	71.45 W
León, Esp.	34	42.36 N	5.34 W
Léon, Fr.	32	43.53 N	1.18 W
León, Nic.	236	12.26 N	86.53 W
Leon, Pil.	116	10.47 N	122.23 E
Leon, Ia., U.S.	190	40.44 N	93.44 W
Leon, Ks., U.S.	198	37.41 N	96.46 W
Leon, N.Y., U.S.	210	42.18 N	79.01 W
León □[4]	34	42.35 N	6.00 W
León □[5]	236	12.35 N	86.35 W
Leon □[6]	222	31.18 N	95.55 W
León □[9]	34	42.00 N	6.00 W
Leon ≃	196	30.59 N	97.24 W
Leon, Arroyo ≃	282	37.28 N	122.25 W
León, Montes de ⩘	34	42.30 N	6.18 W
Leona	222	31.09 N	95.58 W
Leona ≃	196	28.45 N	99.11 W
Leona, Punta ›	236	9.41 N	84.41 W
Leonard, Mi., U.S.	214	42.51 N	83.08 W
Leonard, Mo., U.S.	219	39.53 N	92.10 W
Leonard, N.D., U.S.	198	46.39 N	97.14 W
Leonard, Tx., U.S.	196	33.22 N	96.14 W
Leonardo	276	40.25 N	74.03 W
Leonardo da Vinci Aeroporto Intercontinentale ⊠	66	41.48 N	12.13 E
Leonardsburg	214	40.21 N	82.59 W
Leonardsville	210	42.48 N	75.15 W
Leonardtown	208	38.17 N	76.38 W
Leonardville, Namibia	156	23.29 S	18.49 E
Leonardville, Ks., U.S.	198	39.21 N	96.51 W
Leona Vicario	200	32.10 N	115.10 W
Leonberg	56	48.48 N	9.01 E
Leonbronn	56	49.03 N	8.53 E
Leondale	273d	26.18 S	28.12 E
Leondárion	267c	37.59 N	23.51 E
León [de los Aldamas]	234	21.07 N	101.40 W
Leonding	61	48.16 N	14.15 E
Leone	174u	14.20 S	170.47 W
Leone, Golfo del → Lion, Golfe du c	32	43.00 N	4.00 E
Leone, Monte ∧	58	46.15 N	8.06 E
Leones	252	32.39 S	62.18 W
Leonessa	66	42.34 N	12.58 E
Leonforte	70	37.38 N	14.23 E
Leongatha	169	38.29 S	145.57 E
León Guzmán	196	25.31 N	103.34 W
Leonia	276	40.51 N	73.59 W
Leonicha	76	59.37 N	38.51 E
Leonidas	216	42.01 N	85.21 W
Leonídhion	38	37.10 N	22.52 E
Leonidovo	89	49.17 N	142.50 E
Leon Junction	222	31.20 N	97.36 W
Leonora	162	28.53 S	121.20 E
Leonovo	82	55.26 N	38.42 E
Leontjevka	85	43.03 N	69.50 E
Leontjevo	76	58.58 N	36.37 E
Leonville	194	30.28 N	91.58 W
Leopard	285	40.01 N	75.27 W
Leopold	169	38.11 S	144.28 E
Leopold and Astrid Coast ⊥[2]	9	67.10 S	84.10 E
Leopoldau ⬥[8]	264b	48.16 N	16.27 E
Leopold Downs	162	17.52 S	125.25 E
Léopold II, Lac → Mai-Ndombe, Lac ⊜	152	2.00 S	18.20 E
Leopoldina	256	21.32 S	42.38 W
Leopoldkanaal ≊	50	51.14 N	3.46 E
Leopoldo de Bulhões	255	16.37 S	48.46 W
Leopoldo y Astrid, Costa → Leopold and Astrid Coast ⊥[2]	9	67.10 S	84.10 E
Leopoldsburg	56	51.07 N	5.15 E
Leopoldsdorf	264b	48.06 N	16.24 E
Leopoldshagen	54	53.46 N	13.53 E
Leopoldstadt ⬥[8]	264b	48.13 N	16.23 E
Léopoldville → Kinshasa	152	4.18 S	15.18 E
Leoti	198	38.28 N	101.21 W
Leoville	184	53.37 N	107.35 W
Leovo	38	46.29 N	28.15 E
Le Pailly	58	47.48 N	5.25 E
Le Palais	32	47.21 N	3.09 W
Lepanto, C.R.	236	9.57 N	85.02 W
Lepanto → Návpaktos, Ellás	38	38.23 N	21.50 E
Lepanto, Ar., U.S.	194	35.36 N	90.19 W
Lepar, Pulau I	112	2.57 S	106.50 E
Le Parcq	50	50.23 N	2.06 E
Le Pâté	261	48.32 N	2.18 E
Lepe	34	37.15 N	7.12 W
Le Péage-de-Roussillon	62	45.22 N	4.48 E
Le Pecq	261	48.54 N	2.07 E
Lepel'	76	54.53 N	28.42 E
Le Pellerin	32	47.12 N	1.45 W
Lepembusu, Keli ∧	115b	8.40 S	121.49 E
Le Perray-en-Yuelines	261	48.42 N	1.51 E
Le Perreux-sur-Marne	261	48.51 N	2.30 E
Lepeški	82	56.05 N	38.07 E
Le Petit-Clamart ʊ	261	48.47 N	2.14 E
Le Petit-Couronne	50	49.23 N	1.01 E
Le Petit-Quevilly	50	49.26 N	1.02 E
Lephepe	156	23.20 S	25.50 E
Lépi	152	12.52 S	15.26 E
Le Piastre	66	44.00 N	10.50 E
Lepihué	254	41.37 S	73.36 W
Le Pin	261	48.55 N	2.38 E
Le Pin-au-Haras	50	48.44 N	0.09 E
L'Épine, Fr.	56	48.58 N	4.28 E
L'Épine, Fr.	261	48.32 N	2.21 E
Leping	100	28.57 N	117.05 E
Lepini, Monti ⩘	66	41.35 N	13.00 E
Lépin-le-Lac	62	45.32 N	5.47 E
L'Épiphanie	206	45.51 N	73.30 W
Lepl'avo	78	49.48 N	31.32 E
Le Plessis-aux-Bois	261	49.00 N	2.46 E
Le Plessis-Belleville	50	49.06 N	2.46 E
Le Plessis-Bouchard	261	49.00 N	2.14 E
Le Plessis-Pâté	261	48.37 N	2.20 E
Le Plessis-Trévise	261	48.49 N	2.34 E
Lépo, Lagoa de ⊜	152	17.08 S	19.00 E
Le Poët	62	44.17 N	5.53 E
Le Pont	58	46.40 N	6.20 E
Le Pont-de-Beauvoisin	62	45.32 N	5.40 E
Le Pont-de-Montvert	62	44.22 N	3.45 E
Le Pontel	261	48.49 N	1.53 E
Lepontine, Alpi ⩘	58	46.25 N	8.40 E
Leporano	68	40.23 N	17.20 E
Le Port	157c	20.55 S	55.18 E
Le Portel	50	50.42 N	1.34 E
Le Port-Marly	261	48.53 N	2.06 E
Le Pouzin	62	44.45 N	4.45 E
Leppävirta	26	62.29 N	27.47 E
Lepperton	172	39.04 S	174.13 E
Leppin	54	52.53 N	11.34 E
Leppington	274a	33.58 S	150.49 E
Le Pradet	62	43.06 N	6.01 E
Lepreau, Point ›	186	45.04 N	66.27 W
Le Prêcheur	240e	14.48 N	61.14 W
Le Pré-Saint-Gervais	261	48.53 N	2.25 E
Le Prese	58	46.18 N	10.04 E
Lepsinsk	86	45.32 N	80.37 E
Lepsy, Kaz.	86	46.15 N	78.55 E
Lepsy, Kaz.	86	46.18 N	78.20 E
Le Puy	62	45.02 N	3.53 E
Le Quesnoy	50	50.15 N	3.38 E
Léraba ≃	150	9.42 N	4.35 W
Le Raincy	261	48.54 N	2.31 E
Le Rayol-Canadel-sur-Mer	62	43.10 N	6.28 E
Le Raysville	210	41.51 N	76.11 W
Lerberget	41	56.11 N	12.33 E
Lercara Friddi	70	37.45 N	13.36 E
Lerche ⬥[8]	263	51.37 N	7.43 E
Lerderderg ≃	169	37.42 S	144.30 E
Lerdo → Ciudad Lerdo	196	25.32 N	103.32 W
Léré, Fr.	50	47.28 N	2.52 E
Léré, Mali	150	15.43 N	4.55 W
Lere, Nig.	150	9.43 N	9.21 E
Léré, Tchad	146	9.39 N	14.13 E
Lereh	164	3.08 S	139.54 E
Lerek ∧	114	3.47 N	102.47 E
Le Reposoir	58	46.00 N	6.33 E
Leri ≃	42	52.32 N	4.02 W
Leribe	158	28.58 S	28.00 E
Lerici	64	44.04 N	9.55 E
Lérida, Col.	246	0.10 N	70.42 W
Lérida → Lleida, Esp.	34	41.37 N	0.37 E
Lerik	84	38.46 N	48.25 E
Lérins, Îles de II	62	43.31 N	7.03 E
Lerma	34	42.02 N	3.45 W
Lerma ≃	234	20.13 N	102.46 W
Lermontovka	89	47.10 N	134.20 E
Lermoos	64	47.24 N	10.53 E
Lerno, Monte ∧	71	40.37 N	9.10 E
Le Robert	240e	14.41 N	60.57 W
Léros I, Ellás	38	37.08 N	26.52 E
Léros I, Ellás	267c	37.59 N	23.32 E
Lérouville	56	48.47 N	5.33 E
Leroux Wash V	200	34.54 N	110.12 W
Le Roy, Il., U.S.	216	40.21 N	88.45 W
Leroy, In., U.S.	216	41.22 N	87.16 W
Le Roy, Ks., U.S.	198	38.05 N	95.38 W
Le Roy, Mn., U.S.	190	43.30 N	92.30 W
Le Roy, N.Y., U.S.	210	42.58 N	77.59 W
Le Roy, Pa., U.S.	210	41.41 N	76.43 W
Leroy, Tx., U.S.	222	31.44 N	97.01 W
Lerum	26	57.46 N	12.16 E
Le Russey	58	47.10 N	6.44 E
Lerwick	46a	60.09 N	1.09 W
Léry	206	45.21 N	73.48 W
Lesa	62	45.50 N	8.34 E
Les Abrets	62	45.32 N	5.35 E
Les Abymes	241o	16.16 N	61.31 W
Lesage, Lac ⊜	206	46.19 N	75.03 W
Le Saint-Esprit	240e	14.34 N	60.57 W
Les Aix-d'Angillon	50	47.12 N	2.34 E
Les Allues	62	45.26 N	6.33 E
Les Alluets-le-Roi	261	48.55 N	1.55 E
Les Andelys	50	49.15 N	1.25 E
Les Anses-d'Arlets	240e	14.29 N	61.05 W
Le Sappy-en-Chartreuse	62	45.16 N	5.47 E
Les Arcs	62	43.27 N	6.29 E
Lesatima, Oldoinyo ∧	154	0.19 S	36.37 E
Le Sauze	62	44.22 N	6.41 E
Les Baux-en-Provence	62	43.45 N	4.48 E
Les Bézards	50	47.48 N	2.44 E
Les Bordes	261	48.39 N	1.58 E
Les Borges Blanques	34	41.31 N	0.52 E
Lesbos → Lésvos I	38	39.10 N	26.20 E
Les Bouchoux	58	46.18 N	5.49 E
Les Bréviaires	261	48.42 N	1.49 E
Lesbury	44	55.24 N	1.36 W
L'Escarène	62	43.50 N	7.21 E
Les Cayes	238	18.12 N	73.45 W
Les Chaises	261	48.39 N	1.42 E
Les Chapieux	62	45.42 N	6.44 E
Leschenault, Cape ›	162	31.18 S	115.27 E
Leschenault Estuary c[1]	168a	33.15 S	115.42 E
Lesches	261	48.54 N	2.47 E
Leščinovka	78	49.16 N	34.14 E
Les Clayes-sous-Bois	261	48.49 N	1.59 E
Les Contamines-Montjoie	62	45.50 N	6.44 E
Les Diablerets	58	46.21 N	7.10 E
Les Diablerets ∧	58	46.19 N	7.12 E
Lesdiboderi	146	8.28 N	12.35 E
Les Echarmeaux	58	46.10 N	4.27 E
Les Échelles	62	45.26 N	5.45 E
Les Écureuils	206	46.39 N	71.43 W
Le Semnoz ∧	62	45.48 N	6.07 E
Leseru	154	0.35 N	35.10 E
Les Essarts	32	46.46 N	1.14 W
Les Essarts-le-Roi	261	48.43 N	1.54 E
Les Estables	62	44.54 N	4.10 E
Les Étangs	56	49.09 N	6.23 E
Les Fonts	266d	41.32 N	2.02 E
Les Fourgs	58	46.50 N	6.25 E
Les Galleries d'Anjou ⬥[9]	275a	45.35 N	73.34 W
Les Gâtines	261	48.48 N	1.58 E
Les Gets	58	46.09 N	6.40 E
Les Granges-le-Roi	261	48.30 N	2.01 E
Les Grésillons	261	48.56 N	2.01 E
Les Halles	62	45.43 N	4.26 E
Leshan	107	29.34 N	103.45 E
Les Haudères	58	46.05 N	7.31 E
Les Hautes-Rivières	56	49.53 N	4.50 E
Les Herbiers	32	46.52 N	1.01 W
Les Houches	62	45.53 N	6.48 E
Lesignano de'Bagni	64	44.39 N	10.18 E
Lésigny	261	48.45 N	2.37 E
Lesima, Monte ∧	62	44.41 N	9.15 E
Lesina	68	41.52 N	15.21 E
Lesina, Lago di c	68	41.53 N	15.26 E
Les Islettes	56	49.06 N	5.00 E
Lesjaskog	26	62.15 N	8.22 E
Lesjöfors	40	59.59 N	14.11 E
Lesken	84	43.16 N	43.48 E
Les'ki	78	49.19 N	32.13 E
Lesko	30	49.29 N	22.21 E
Leskovac	38	42.59 N	21.57 E
Leskov Island I	18	56.40 S	28.10 W
Les Laumes	58	47.32 N	4.27 E
Les Lecques	62	43.11 N	5.40 E
Leslie, S. Afr.	158	26.27 S	28.55 E
Leslie, Scot., U.K.	46	56.12 N	3.13 W
Leslie, Ar., U.S.	194	35.49 N	92.33 W
Leslie, Ga., U.S.	192	31.57 N	84.05 W
Leslie, Mi., U.S.	216	42.27 N	84.25 W
Leslie, W.V., U.S.	188	38.02 N	80.43 W
Les Lilas	261	48.53 N	2.25 E
Les Loges	261	48.34 N	2.03 E
Les Loges-en-Josas	261	48.46 N	2.09 E
Lesmahagow	46	55.39 N	3.55 W
Les Marécottes	58	46.07 N	7.00 E
Les Mées	62	44.02 N	5.59 E
Les Mesnuls	50	48.45 N	1.50 E
Lesmo	266b	45.39 N	9.18 E
Les Molières	261	48.40 N	2.04 E
Les Monges ∧	62	44.16 N	6.12 E
Lesmont	50	48.26 N	4.25 E
Les Mosses	58	46.24 N	7.07 E
Lesmurdie Falls National Park ♠	168a	32.01 S	116.04 E
Les Mureaux	261	49.00 N	1.55 E
Leśna	30	51.02 N	15.16 E
Lesna ≃	76	52.10 N	23.33 E
Lesnaja	76	52.59 N	25.46 E
Lesneven	32	48.34 N	4.19 W
Les Neyrolles	58	46.08 N	5.38 E
Lešnica	38	44.39 N	19.19 E
Lesnoj, Ross.	24	59.48 N	52.08 E
Lesnoj, Ross.	80	54.11 N	40.27 E
Lesnoj, Ross.	86	56.57 N	67.15 E
Lesnoj ⬥[8]	265a	60.00 N	30.19 E
Lesnoje	76	58.17 N	35.32 E
Lesnoje Konobejevo	80	54.02 N	41.55 E
Lesnoje Mat'unino	80	53.27 N	47.26 E
Lesnoj Gorodok	265b	55.39 N	37.13 E
Lesnoj park ♠	265a	59.59 N	30.21 E
Lesný ∧	60	50.02 N	12.37 E
Lesnyje Pol'any, Ross.	24	58.58 N	52.26 E
Lesnyje Pol'any, Ross.	265b	55.57 N	37.53 E
Lesogorsk, Ross.	80	55.06 N	43.56 E
Lesogorsk, Ross.	88	56.03 N	99.33 E
Lesogorsk, Ross.	89	49.27 N	142.08 E
Lesogorskij	24	61.02 N	28.53 E
Lesong, Gunong ∧	114	2.44 N	103.17 E
Lesopil'noje	89	46.44 N	134.20 E
Lesosibirsk	86	58.16 N	92.29 E
Lesotho □[1], Afr.	138	29.30 S	28.30 E
Lesotho □[1], Afr.	158	29.30 S	28.30 E
Lesovščina	78	50.47 N	28.35 E
Lesozavodsk	89	45.28 N	133.27 E
Lesozavodskij	24	66.44 N	32.49 E
Les Pavillons-sous-Bois	261	48.55 N	2.30 E
Les Pieux	32	49.31 N	1.48 W
Les Planches-en-Montagne	58	46.40 N	6.01 E
Les Ponts-de-Martel	58	46.54 N	6.41 E
Les Posets ∧	34	42.39 N	0.25 E
Les Praz-de-Chamonix	58	45.56 N	6.52 E
Lesquin	50	50.35 N	3.07 E
Les Riceys	50	47.59 N	4.22 E
Les Roches-l'Evêque	50	47.47 N	0.53 E
Les Rousses	58	46.29 N	6.04 E
Les Ruelles	261	48.40 N	1.37 E
Les Sables-d'Olonne	32	46.30 N	1.47 W
Lessach	64	47.11 N	13.49 E
Les Saintes II	241o	15.52 N	61.37 W
Les Salles-sur-Verdon	62	43.46 N	6.12 E
Lessay	32	49.13 N	1.32 W
Les Scaffarels	62	43.57 N	6.41 E
Lesse ≃	56	50.14 N	4.54 E
Lessebo	26	56.45 N	15.16 E
Lessen → Lessines	50	50.43 N	3.50 E
Lesser Antilles II	238	15.00 N	61.00 W

≃ River	Fluß	Río	Rivière	Rio
≊ Canal	Kanal	Canal	Canal	Canal
∟ Waterfall, Rapids	Wasserfall, Stromschnellen	Cascada, Rápidos	Chute d'eau, Rapides	Cascata, Rápidos
ʯ Strait	Meeresstraße	Estrecho	Détroit	Estreito
c Bay, Gulf	Bucht, Golf	Bahía, Golfo	Baie, Golfe	Baía, Golfo
⊜ Lake, Lakes	See, Seen	Lago, Lagos	Lac, Lacs	Lago, Lagos
≡ Swamp	Sumpf	Pantano	Marais	Pântano
⊓ Ice Features, Glacier	Eis- und Gletscherformen	Accidentes Glaciales	Formes glaciaires	Acidentes glaciares
∓ Other Hydrographic Features	Andere Hydrographische Objekte	Otros Elementos Hidrográficos	Autres données hydrographiques	Outros acidentes hidrográficos

✢ Submarine Features	Untermeerische Objekte	Accidentes Submarinos	Formes de relief sous-marin	Acidentes submarinos
□ Political Unit	Politische Einheit	Unidad Politica	Entité politique	Unidade política
ʊ Cultural Institution	Kulturelle Institution	Institución Cultural	Institution culturelle	Instituição cultural
⊥ Historical Site	Historische Stätte	Sitio Histórico	Site historique	Sitio histórico
♠ Recreational Site	Erholungs- und Ferienort	Sitio de Recreo	Centre de loisirs	Area de Lazer
⊠ Airport	Flughafen	Aeropuerto	Aéroport	Aeroporto
■ Military Installation	Militäranlage	Instalación Militar	Installation militaire	Instalação militar
⬥ Miscellaneous	Verschiedenes	Misceláneo	Divers	Diversos

Name	Page	Lat.°′	Long.°′
Lesser Khingan Range → Xiao Hinggan Ling ⋏	89	48.45 N	127.00 E
Lesser Slave ≃	182	55.10 N	114.03 W
Lesser Slave Lake ⊜	182	55.25 N	115.30 W
Lesser Sunda Islands → Tenggara, Nusa II	108	9.00 S	120.00 E
Lessines (Lessen)	50	50.43 N	3.50 E
Lessini, Monti ⋏	64	45.41 N	11.13 E
L'Estaque	62	43.22 N	5.20 E
Leste ≃	250	6.20 S	57.46 W
Lester, Pa., U.S.	285	39.52 N	75.17 W
Lester, Wa., U.S.	224	47.12 N	121.29 W
Lester B. Pearson International Airport ⊠	212	43.41 N	79.38 W
Les Tessiers	62	44.24 N	4.16 E
Les Thilliers-en-Vexin	50	49.14 N	1.36 E
Lestijärvi	26	63.32 N	24.39 E
Lestijoki ≃	26	64.04 N	23.38 E
Lestkov	60	49.54 N	12.52 E
Lestock	184	51.18 N	104.00 W
L'Estréchure	62	44.06 N	3.47 E
Les Trois-Îlets	240e	14.32 N	61.02 W
Les Trois Lacs ⊜	206	45.48 N	71.54 W
Le Sueur	190	44.30 N	93.52 W
Le Sueur ≃	190	44.07 N	94.03 W
Lesueur, Mount ∧ 2	162	30.10 S	115.11 E
Lešukonskoje	24	64.54 N	45.40 E
Les Ulis	261	48.41 N	2.11 E
Lesung, Tanjung ›	115a	6.28 S	105.40 E
Lesunovo	80	55.40 N	43.07 E
Les Vans	62	44.24 N	4.08 E
Les Verrières	58	46.54 N	6.30 E
Lésvos (Lesbos) I	38	39.10 N	26.20 E
Leszno	30	51.51 N	16.35 E
Leszno □ 4	30	51.45 N	16.45 E
Letälven ≃	40	59.05 N	14.20 E
L'Étang-la-Ville	261	48.52 N	2.05 E
Letcher	198	43.53 N	98.08 W
Letchmore Heath	260	51.40 N	0.20 W
Letchworth	42	51.58 N	0.14 W
Letchworth State Park ♦	210	42.42 N	77.56 W
Letea, Ostrovul I	38	45.20 N	29.20 E
Le Teil	62	44.33 N	4.41 E
Le Temple	261	49.00 N	1.58 E
Letenye	30	46.26 N	16.43 E
Le Tertre-Saint-Denis	261	48.56 N	1.36 E
Lethbridge, Austl.	274a	33.44 S	150.48 E
Lethbridge, Ab., Can.	182	49.42 N	112.50 W
Lethbridge, Nf., Can.	186	48.21 N	53.52 W
Le Theil-sur-Huisne	50	48.16 N	0.42 E
Lethem	246	3.23 N	59.48 W
Le Thillay	261	49.00 N	2.28 E
Le Thillot	58	47.53 N	6.46 E
Le Tholy	58	48.05 N	6.45 E
Le Thor	62	43.56 N	5.00 E
Le Thoronet	62	43.27 N	6.18 E
Leti, Kepulauan II	164	8.13 S	127.50 E
Leti, Pulau I	112	8.12 S	127.41 E
Letičev	78	49.23 N	27.37 E
Leticia	246	4.09 S	69.57 W
Leting	98	39.27 N	118.53 E
Letino	68	41.26 N	14.17 E
Letjiesbos	158	32.34 S	22.16 E
Letka	24	59.36 N	49.22 E
Letlhakane	156	21.27 S	25.30 E
Letlhakeng	156	24.08 S	25.02 E
Letmathe	56	51.22 N	7.37 E
Letn'aja Zolotica	24	64.57 N	36.50 E
Letnerečenskij	24	64.17 N	34.23 E
Le Touquet-Paris-Plage	50	50.31 N	1.35 E
Le Touvet	62	45.21 N	5.57 E
Letovo	265b	55.34 N	37.24 E
Letpadan	110	17.47 N	95.45 E
Le Trait	50	49.28 N	0.49 E
Le Trayas	62	43.28 N	6.55 E
Le Tremblay-sur-Mauldre	261	48.47 N	1.53 E
Le Tréport	50	50.04 N	1.22 E
Letschin	54	52.39 N	14.21 E
Letsôk-aw Kyun I	110	11.37 N	98.15 E
Letter	52	52.24 N	9.38 E
Letterfrack	48	53.33 N	10.00 W
Letterkenny	48	54.57 N	7.44 W
Lettermullan	48	53.13 N	9.42 W
Letterston	42	51.56 N	5.00 W
Lettonie → Latvia □ 1	72	57.00 N	25.00 E
Letts	218	39.14 N	85.35 W
Letung	112	2.58 N	105.42 E
Letzlingen	54	52.26 N	11.29 E
Leu	38	44.11 N	24.00 E
Léua	152	11.34 S	20.32 E
Leubnitz	54	50.43 N	12.21 E
Leubsdorf	54	50.48 N	13.08 E
Leuca	68	39.48 N	18.21 E
Leucadia	228	33.04 N	117.18 W
Leucate, Étang de C	32	42.51 N	3.00 E
Leuchars	46	56.23 N	2.53 W
Leuchtenberg	60	49.36 N	12.15 E
Leudeville	261	48.34 N	2.20 E
Leuenberger Forst ⊸ 3	264a	52.40 N	13.53 E
Leuglay	58	47.49 N	4.48 E
Leuk	58	46.19 N	7.38 E
Leukerbad	58	46.23 N	7.38 E
Leulumoega	175a	13.49 S	171.55 W
Leumeah	274a	34.03 S	150.50 E
Leuna	54	51.19 N	12.01 E
Leupoldsgrün	54	50.17 N	11.47 E
Leura	170	33.43 S	150.20 E
Leura, Mount ∧ 2	169	38.15 S	143.09 E
Leuser, Gunung ∧	114	3.45 N	97.11 E
Leušinskij Tuman, ozero ⊜	86	59.42 N	65.35 E
Leutenberg	54	50.34 N	11.28 E
Leutersdorf	54	50.57 N	14.40 E
Leutershausen	56	49.18 N	10.24 E
Leutesdorf	56	50.27 N	7.23 E
Leutkirch	58	47.49 N	10.01 E
Leuven (Louvain)	56	50.53 N	4.42 E
Leuville-sur-Orge	261	48.37 N	2.16 E
Leuwiliang	115a	6.34 S	106.37 E
Leuze, Bel.	50	50.36 N	3.36 E
Leuze, Bel.	56	50.34 N	4.54 E
Levack	190	46.38 N	81.23 W
Levádhia	38	38.25 N	22.54 E
Levaja Mama ≃	88	57.10 N	111.54 E
Le Val-d'Ajol	58	47.55 N	6.29 E
Le Val-d'Albian	261	48.45 N	2.11 E
Levallois-Perret	261	48.54 N	2.18 E
Le Val-Saint-Germain	261	48.34 N	2.04 E
Levan	200	39.33 N	111.51 W
Levanger	26	63.45 N	11.18 E
Levanna, Monte ∧	62	45.24 N	7.12 E
Levant, Île du I	62	43.03 N	6.28 E
Levante, Riviera di ± 2	62	44.15 N	9.30 E
Levanto	62	44.10 N	9.38 E
Levanzo	70	37.59 N	12.20 E
Levanzo, Isola di I	70	38.00 N	12.20 E
Levaši	84	42.27 N	47.20 E
Le Vauclin	240e	14.33 N	60.51 W
Levdym	86	60.29 N	66.19 E
Leveaux Mountain ∧ 2	190	47.37 N	90.47 W
Levél	61	47.54 N	17.12 E
Level, Isla I	254	44.29 S	74.23 W
Level Green	279b	40.24 N	79.43 W
Levelland	196	33.35 N	102.22 W
Levelock	180	59.07 N	156.52 W
Level Park	216	42.22 N	85.18 W
Leven, Eng., U.K.	44	53.53 N	0.19 W
Leven, Scot., U.K.	46	56.12 N	3.00 W
Leven ≃, Eng., U.K.	44	54.14 N	3.01 W
Leven ≃, Eng., U.K.	44	54.31 N	1.21 W
Leven, Loch ⊜, Scot., U.K.	46	56.41 N	5.07 W
Leven, Loch ⊜, Scot., U.K.	46	56.12 N	3.22 W
Leven Point ›	158	27.55 S	32.35 E
Levens	62	43.52 N	7.13 E
Levenshulme ⊸ 8	262	53.27 N	2.10 W
Levent	130	38.27 N	37.52 E
Leventina, Valle V	58	46.25 N	8.52 E
Leveque, Cape ›	162	16.24 S	122.56 E
Leverano	68	40.17 N	18.00 E
Leverburgh	46	57.45 N	7.00 W
Leveretts Chapel	222	32.19 N	94.55 W
Levering	190	45.38 N	84.47 W
Leverkusen	56	51.03 N	6.59 E
Levern	52	52.22 N	8.26 E
Lever Park ♦	262	53.37 N	2.34 W
Le Vésinet	261	48.54 N	2.08 E
Le Vésuve → Vesuvio ∧ 1	68	40.49 N	14.26 E
Leviathan Peak ∧	226	38.41 N	119.37 W
Levice	30	48.13 N	18.37 E
Levicha	86	57.36 N	59.55 E
Levick, Mount ∧	9	74.08 S	163.12 E
Levico	64	46.01 N	11.18 E
Levie	36	41.42 N	9.07 E
Levier	58	46.57 N	6.08 E
Le Vigan	32	43.59 N	3.35 E
Levin	172	40.37 S	175.17 E
Levino	76	60.29 N	37.30 E
Lévis	206	46.48 N	71.11 W
Lévis □ 6	206	46.40 N	71.15 W
Levisa Fork ≃	192	38.06 N	82.36 W
Lévis-Saint Nom	261	48.43 N	1.58 E
Levítha I	38	37.00 N	26.28 E
Levittown, P.R.	240m	18.27 N	66.14 W
Levittown → Willingboro, N.J., U.S.	208	40.03 N	74.53 W
Levittown, N.Y., U.S.	210	40.43 N	73.30 W
Levittown, Pa., U.S.	208	40.09 N	74.49 W
Levittown Discount World ⊸ 9	285	40.09 N	74.49 W
Lévka Óri ∧	38	35.18 N	24.01 E
Levkás	38	38.50 N	20.41 E
Levkás I	38	38.39 N	20.27 E
Levkímmi	38	39.25 N	20.04 E
Levoča	30	49.02 N	20.36 E
Levokumskoje	84	44.48 N	44.39 E
Levroux	32	46.59 N	1.37 E
Levski	38	43.22 N	25.08 E
Lev Tolstoj	76	53.13 N	39.27 E
Levuka	175g	17.41 S	178.50 E
Lėvuo ≃	76	56.04 N	24.23 E
Levyj Tuzlov ≃	83	47.35 N	39.23 E
Lewapaku	115b	9.43 S	119.55 E
Lewbeach	210	42.00 N	74.47 W
Lewe	110	19.38 N	96.07 E
Lewedorp	52	51.30 N	3.45 E
Lewellen	198	41.19 N	102.08 W
Lewer ≃	156	25.30 S	17.45 E
Lewes, Eng., U.K.	42	50.52 N	0.01 E
Lewes, De., U.S.	208	38.46 N	75.08 W
Lewin Brzeski	30	50.46 N	17.37 E
Lewis, Ia., U.S.	198	41.18 N	95.04 W
Lewis, Ks., U.S.	198	37.56 N	99.15 W
Lewis □ 6, Ky., U.S.	218	38.32 N	83.21 W
Lewis □ 6, Mo., U.S.	219	40.08 N	91.45 W
Lewis □ 6, N.Y., U.S.	212	43.47 N	75.29 W
Lewis □ 6, Wa., U.S.	224	46.35 N	122.22 W
Lewis ≃	224	45.51 N	122.48 W
Lewis, Butt of ›	46	58.31 N	6.16 W
Lewis, East Fork ≃	224	45.52 N	122.43 W
Lewis, Isle of I	46	58.10 N	6.40 W
Lewis, Mount ∧	204	40.24 N	116.51 W
Lewis and Clark ≃	224	46.10 N	123.52 W
Lewis and Clark Cavern State Park ♦	202	45.49 N	111.13 W
Lewis and Clark Lake ⊜ 1	198	42.50 N	97.45 W
Lewis and Clark Range ⋏	202	47.30 N	113.00 W
Lewisberry	208	40.08 N	76.52 W
Lewisburg, Ky., U.S.	194	36.59 N	86.56 W
Lewisburg, Oh., U.S.	218	39.50 N	84.32 W
Lewisburg, Pa., U.S.	210	40.57 N	76.53 W
Lewisburg, Tn., U.S.	194	35.26 N	86.47 W
Lewisburg, W.V., U.S.	188	37.48 N	80.26 W
Lewis Center	214	40.12 N	83.01 W
Lewis Creek ≃, Ca., U.S.	226	35.17 N	120.58 W
Lewis Creek ≃, In., U.S.	218	39.22 N	85.51 W
Lewis Creek Reservoir ⊜ 1	222	30.26 N	95.32 W
Lewisdale	284c	38.58 N	76.58 W
Lewisetta	208	38.01 N	76.28 W
Lewis Gut C	276	41.09 N	73.09 W
Lewisham	273d	26.07 S	27.49 E
Lewisham ⊸ 8	42	51.27 N	0.01 E
Lewisham Location	273d	26.10 S	27.47 E
Lewis-Lockport Airport ⊠	278	41.36 N	88.05 W
Lewis Pass)(	172	42.23 S	172.24 E
Lewisport	194	37.56 N	86.54 W
Lewisporte	186	49.15 N	55.03 W
Lewis Range ⋏, Austl.	162	20.20 S	128.40 E
Lewis Range ⋏, Mt., U.S.	202	48.35 N	113.40 W
Lewis Run	214	41.52 N	78.39 W
Lewis Run ≃	279b	40.17 N	79.55 W
Lewis Smith Lake ⊜ 1	194	34.05 N	87.07 W
Lewiston, Ca., U.S.	204	40.43 N	122.48 W
Lewiston, Id., U.S.	202	46.25 N	117.01 W
Lewiston, Me., U.S.	188	44.06 N	70.12 W
Lewiston, Mi., U.S.	190	44.53 N	84.18 W
Lewiston, Mn., U.S.	190	43.59 N	91.52 W
Lewiston, N.Y., U.S.	210	43.10 N	79.02 W
Lewiston, Ut,. U.S.	200	41.58 N	111.51 W
Lewiston Orchards	202	46.23 N	116.59 W
Lewistown, Il., U.S.	194	40.23 N	90.09 W
Lewistown, Md., U.S.	208	39.32 N	77.24 W
Lewistown, Mo., U.S.	219	40.05 N	91.48 W
Lewistown, Mt., U.S.	202	47.03 N	109.25 W
Lewistown, Oh., U.S.	216	40.25 N	83.53 W
Lewistown, Pa., U.S.	208	40.35 N	77.34 W
Lewisville, N.B., Can.	186	46.06 N	64.46 W
Lewisville, Ar., U.S.	194	33.21 N	93.34 W
Lewisville, In., U.S.	218	39.48 N	85.21 W
Lewisville, Pa., U.S.	208	39.43 N	75.53 W
Lewisville, Tx., U.S.	222	33.02 N	96.59 W
Lewisville Dam ⊸ 6	222	33.05 N	96.55 W
Lewisville Lake ⊜ 1	196	33.08 N	97.00 W
Lewoleba	112	8.23 S	123.24 E
Lewotobi-lakilaki, Ili ∧	115b	8.32 S	122.46 E
Lewvan	184	50.00 N	104.06 W
Lexa	194	34.35 N	90.44 W
Lexington, Ga., U.S.	192	33.52 N	83.06 W
Lexington, Il., U.S.	216	40.38 N	88.47 W
Lexington, In., U.S.	218	38.39 N	85.37 W
Lexington, Ky., U.S.	218	38.02 N	84.30 W
Lexington, Ma., U.S.	207	42.26 N	71.13 W
Lexington, Mi., U.S.	190	43.16 N	82.31 W
Lexington, Ms., U.S.	194	33.06 N	90.03 W
Lexington, Mo., U.S.	194	39.11 N	93.52 W
Lexington, Ne., U.S.	198	40.46 N	99.44 W
Lexington, N.Y., U.S.	210	42.15 N	74.22 W
Lexington, N.C., U.S.	192	35.49 N	80.15 W
Lexington, Oh., U.S.	214	40.40 N	82.34 W
Lexington, Ok., U.S.	196	35.00 N	97.20 W
Lexington, Or., U.S.	202	45.26 N	119.41 W
Lexington, S.C., U.S.	192	33.58 N	81.14 W
Lexington, Tn., U.S.	194	35.39 N	88.23 W
Lexington, Tx., U.S.	222	30.25 N	97.01 W
Lexington, Va., U.S.	192	37.47 N	79.26 W
Lexington Park	208	38.16 N	76.27 W
Lexington Reservoir ⊜ 1	226	37.12 N	121.59 W
Lexton	169	37.17 S	143.31 E
Leybourne	260	51.18 N	0.25 E
Leyburn	44	54.19 N	1.49 W
Leyden → Leiden	52	52.09 N	4.30 E
Leye	102	24.48 N	106.34 E
Leyland	44	53.42 N	2.42 W
Leyond ≃	184	51.40 N	96.32 W
Léyou ≃	152	1.07 S	13.08 E
Leyre ≃	32	44.39 N	1.01 W
Leysdown-on-Sea	42	51.24 N	0.55 E
Leysin	58	46.21 N	7.01 E
Leyte	116	11.23 N	124.29 E
Leyte □ 4	116	10.50 N	124.55 E
Leyte I	116	10.50 N	124.50 E
Leyte Gulf C	116	10.50 N	125.25 E
Leyton ⊸ 8	260	51.33 N	0.01 W
Leyu	106	31.55 N	120.43 E
Lèz ≋	62	43.31 N	3.55 E
Leža	76	58.56 N	40.45 E
Leža ≃	76	59.15 N	40.10 E
Leżajsk	30	50.16 N	22.24 E
Lezama	246	9.43 N	66.24 W
Lézarde ≃	240e	14.36 N	61.01 W
Lézat	58	46.30 N	5.56 E
Lèze ≃	62	43.40 N	5.28 E
Lezhë	38	41.47 N	19.39 E
Lezhi	107	30.17 N	105.02 E
Ležn'ovo	80	56.46 N	40.53 E
Lezzeno	58	45.56 N	9.11 E
L'gov	78	51.43 N	35.17 E
Lhasa	120	29.40 N	91.09 E
Lhasa ≃	120	29.21 N	90.45 E
L'Hautil	261	49.00 N	2.01 E
Lhazê	120	29.10 N	87.42 E
L'Hillil	34	35.41 N	0.19 E
Lhokkruet	114	4.52 N	95.24 E
Lhoknga	114	5.29 N	95.15 E
Lhokseumawe	114	5.10 N	97.08 E
Lhoksukon	114	5.03 N	97.19 E
L'Hôpital-sous-Rochefort	62	45.46 N	3.56 E
Lhorong	102	30.45 N	96.09 E
L'Hospitalet de Llobregat	34	41.22 N	2.08 E
Lhotse ∧	124	27.57 N	86.56 E
Lhozhag	120	28.24 N	90.49 E
Lhuis	62	45.45 N	5.32 E
Lhuntsi Dzong	120	27.39 N	91.09 E
Lhünzê	120	28.25 N	92.31 E
Li	110	17.48 N	98.57 E
Li ≃, Thai	110	18.26 N	98.42 E
Li ≃, Zhg.	100	33.11 N	115.07 E
Li ≃, Zhg.	102	29.24 N	112.01 E
Lian ≃, Zhg.	100	24.02 N	113.18 E
Lian ≃, Zhg.	100	25.46 N	115.38 E
Lian ≃, Zhg.	102	24.02 N	113.18 E
Lian ≃, Zhg.	102	27.48 N	112.52 E
Liancheng	100	25.44 N	116.46 E
Liancourt	50	49.20 N	2.28 E
Liane ≃	50	50.43 N	1.36 E
Liang	164	3.30 S	128.19 E
Lianga	116	8.38 N	126.06 E
Lianga Bay C	116	8.37 N	126.12 E
Liang'anchang	107	30.30 N	104.56 E
Liangbao	102	34.37 N	110.45 E
Liangbingbao	89	45.48 N	128.19 E
Liangbingtai	89	43.12 N	128.47 E
Liangbuaya	112	0.05 N	116.46 E
Liangchahe	107	29.03 N	106.18 E
Liangcheng	98	35.35 N	119.35 E
Liangcun	100	26.36 N	115.34 E
Liangdang	102	33.56 N	106.12 E
Liangdawa	105	40.39 N	117.37 E
Liangfengwu	107	30.11 N	105.22 E
Lianggezhuang	105	39.21 N	115.22 E
Lianghe, Zhg.	89	45.09 N	128.45 E
Lianghe, Zhg.	102	24.51 N	98.25 E
Liangheguan	102	32.52 N	109.19 E
Lianghekou, Zhg.	102	33.42 N	104.25 E
Lianghekou, Zhg.	102	29.14 N	108.40 E
Lianghekou, Zhg.	102	31.27 N	102.13 E
Lianghekou, Zhg.	107	28.55 N	106.03 E
Liangiu	98	35.12 N	117.47 E
Liangjia	107	29.29 N	105.33 E
Liangjiadian	98	39.10 N	121.54 E
Liangjiafang	98	41.04 N	117.18 E
Liangjianfang	105	40.45 N	117.20 E
Liangjiang	102	23.23 N	108.22 E
Liangjiangkou	98	42.38 N	128.05 E
Liangjiawazi	104	40.40 N	120.42 E
Liangjiazi	104	42.13 N	122.31 E
Liangkou	100	23.43 N	113.43 E
Lianglukou	107	29.18 N	106.15 E
Liangmen	98	35.34 N	114.54 E
Liangmentou	100	28.58 N	121.12 E
Liangmushi	106	30.46 N	119.35 E
Liangpa	102	24.10 N	106.13 E
Liangpeng	106	30.47 N	119.38 E
Liangping	102	30.41 N	107.49 E
Liang Shan ∧	102	23.45 N	99.45 E
Liangshui ≃	271a	39.49 N	116.40 E
Liangtian	100	25.37 N	113.00 E
Liangtinghe	100	30.20 N	116.12 E
Liangtoumen	100	29.31 N	120.45 E
Liangtun	98	40.14 N	122.34 E
Liangwangzhuang	105	39.01 N	116.58 E
Liangxiangzhen	105	39.44 N	116.08 E
Liangying	100	23.14 N	116.21 E
Liangyuan	100	32.00 N	117.34 E
Liangzhu	106	30.23 N	120.03 E
Liangzi Hu ⊜	100	30.16 N	114.34 E
Lianhe	98	42.36 N	125.37 E
Lian Hu ⊜	106	32.02 N	119.32 E
Lianhua	100	27.07 N	113.57 E
Lianhuachi	105	40.28 N	116.33 E
Lianhuapao	89	45.32 N	129.50 E
Lianhua Shan ⋏	100	23.40 N	116.00 E
Lianjiang, Zhg.	100	26.12 N	119.31 E
Lianjiang, Zhg.	102	21.38 N	110.15 E
Lianjiechang	107	29.41 N	104.30 E
Liannan (Sanjiang)	102	24.38 N	112.10 E
Lianozovo ⊸ 8	265b	55.54 N	37.35 E
Lianping	100	24.22 N	114.31 E
Lianpu	100	26.02 N	118.38 E
Lianshanguan	104	40.58 N	123.46 E
Lianshi	106	30.42 N	120.26 E
Lianshui	100	33.47 N	119.16 E
Liansiji	98	33.58 N	114.24 E
Liantang	106	31.37 N	120.38 E
Lianxian	102	24.48 N	112.25 E
Lianyin	89	53.28 N	123.51 E
Lianyuan (Lantian)	102	27.42 N	111.19 E
Lianyungang, Zhg.	98	34.44 N	119.30 E
Lianyungang (Xinpu), Zhg.	98	34.39 N	119.16 E
Lianyun Shan ∧	100	28.32 N	113.50 E
Lianzhou → Hepu	102	21.39 N	109.11 E
Liao ≃	90	40.50 N	121.48 E
Liaobinta	104	42.08 N	123.04 E
Liaocheng	98	36.30 N	115.59 E
Liaodong Bandao (Liaotung Peninsula) › 1	98	40.00 N	122.20 E
Liaodong Wan (Gulf of Liaotung) C	98	40.30 N	121.30 E
Liaohe Kou C 1	104	40.42 N	122.05 E
Liaojiangshi	100	26.05 N	113.17 E
Liaoning □ 4	90	41.00 N	123.00 E
Liaotung, Gulf of → Liaodong Wan C	98	40.30 N	121.30 E
Liaotung Peninsula → Liaodong Bandao › 1	98	40.00 N	122.20 E
Liaoyang	104	41.17 N	123.11 E
Liaoyangwopu	89	43.00 N	123.28 E
Liaoyuan	89	42.54 N	125.07 E
Liaozhong	104	41.31 N	122.44 E
Liapádhes	38	39.40 N	19.44 E
Liāquatpur	123	28.56 N	70.57 E
Liard ≃	176	61.52 N	121.18 W
Liāri	120	25.41 N	66.29 E
Liart	50	49.46 N	4.20 E
Liat, Pulau I	112	2.53 S	107.05 E
Liathach ∧	46	57.35 N	5.29 W
Lib I	14	8.19 N	167.25 E
Libagon	116	10.18 N	125.03 E
Liban → Lebanon □ 1	128	34.00 N	36.00 E
Libanga	152	0.19 N	18.41 E
Líbano	246	4.55 N	75.04 W
Libano → Lebanon □ 1	128	34.00 N	36.00 E
Libanon → Lebanon □ 1	128	34.00 N	36.00 E
Libau → Liepāja	76	56.31 N	21.01 E
Libby	202	48.23 N	115.33 W
Libby Dam ⊸ 6	202	48.24 N	115.20 W
Libčeves	54	50.26 N	13.50 E
Libčice nad Vltavou	54	50.10 N	14.20 E
Liběchov	54	50.20 N	14.28 E
Libenge	152	3.39 N	18.38 E
Liberal, Ks., U.S.	198	37.02 N	100.55 W
Liberal, Mo., U.S.	194	37.33 N	94.31 W
Liberdade	256	22.01 S	44.19 W
Liberdade ⊸ 8	287b	23.35 S	46.37 W
Liberdade ≃, Bra.	248	7.10 S	71.51 W
Liberdade ≃, Bra.	250	9.40 S	52.17 W
Liberec	30	50.46 N	15.03 E
Liberia	236	10.38 N	85.27 W
Liberia □ 1, Afr.	134	6.30 N	9.30 W
Liberia □ 1, Afr.	150	6.30 N	9.30 W
Liberta	240c	17.02 N	61.47 W
Libertad, Arg.	258	34.42 S	58.41 W
Libertad, Ur.	258	34.38 S	56.39 W
Libertad, Ven.	246	8.20 N	69.37 W
Libertad, Ven.	246	9.23 N	68.44 W
Libertador □ 5	286c	10.27 N	66.57 W
Libertador General Bernardo O'Higgins □ 4	252	34.30 S	71.00 W
Libertador General San Martín	252	23.48 S	64.48 W
Liberty, Il., U.S.	219	39.53 N	91.06 W
Liberty, In., U.S.	218	39.38 N	84.55 W
Liberty, Ky., U.S.	194	37.19 N	84.56 W
Liberty, Ms., U.S.	194	31.09 N	90.48 W
Liberty, Mo., U.S.	194	39.14 N	94.25 W
Liberty, Ne., U.S.	198	40.05 N	96.28 W
Liberty, N.Y., U.S.	210	41.48 N	74.44 W
Liberty, N.C., U.S.	192	35.51 N	79.34 W
Liberty, Pa., U.S.	210	41.34 N	77.06 W
Liberty, Pa., U.S.	279b	40.20 N	79.51 W
Liberty, S.C., U.S.	192	34.47 N	82.41 W
Liberty, Tx., U.S.	222	30.03 N	94.47 W
Liberty □ 6	222	30.12 N	94.50 W
Liberty Acres	280	34.04 N	118.12 W
Liberty Center, In., U.S.	216	40.41 N	85.16 W
Liberty Center, Oh., U.S.	216	41.26 N	84.00 W
Liberty City	222	32.27 N	94.57 W
Liberty Corner	276	40.39 N	74.34 W
Liberty Ditch ≋	226	36.31 N	120.02 W
Liberty Farms	226	38.19 N	121.42 W
Liberty Hill	196	30.40 N	97.55 W
Liberty Island I	276	40.41 N	74.03 W
Liberty Lake ⊜ 1	208	39.25 N	76.53 W
Liberty Manor	284b	39.21 N	76.47 W
Liberty Mills	216	41.02 N	85.44 W
Liberty Park	216	41.26 N	87.22 W
Libertytown	208	39.29 N	77.14 W
Liberty Tree Mall ⊸ 9	283	42.33 N	70.57 W
Liberty Tunnel ⊸ 5	279b	40.26 N	80.01 W
Libertyville	216	42.16 N	87.57 W
Líbeznice	54	50.10 N	14.30 E
Libia → Libya □ 1	146	27.00 N	17.00 E
Libibi	152	14.42 S	17.44 E
Libishan	106	30.45 N	119.20 E
Lībiyā → Libya □ 1	146	27.00 N	17.00 E
Lībīyah, Aṣ-Ṣaḥrā' al- (Libyan Desert) ⊸ 2	136	24.00 N	25.00 E
Liblín	60	49.55 N	13.32 E
Libni, Jabal ∧ 2	132	30.44 N	33.50 E
Libo	102	25.28 N	107.53 E
Libobo, Tanjung ›	164	0.54 S	128.28 E
Liboc ≃	54	50.10 N	13.31 E
Libochovice	54	50.22 N	14.03 E
Libode	158	31.33 S	29.02 E
Liboi	154	0.24 N	40.57 E
Liboko	152	2.43 N	21.28 E
Libomyšl	60	49.52 N	14.00 E
Libona	116	8.20 N	124.44 E
Liboumba ≃	152	0.38 N	12.54 E
Libourne	32	44.55 N	0.14 W
Libramont	56	49.55 N	5.23 E
Library	214	40.18 N	80.02 W
Librazhd	38	41.11 N	20.19 E
Libres	234	19.28 N	97.41 W
Libreville	152	0.23 N	9.27 E
Librizzi	70	38.06 N	14.57 E
Libro Point ›	116	11.26 N	119.29 E
Libu	102	23.41 N	111.30 E
Libucan Island I	116	11.54 N	124.39 E
Libuganon ≃	116	7.27 N	125.47 E
Libunga	154	1.49 N	26.35 E
Liburung	112	3.55 S	120.09 E
Libušín	54	50.09 N	14.04 E
Libya (Lībiyā) □ 1, Afr.	136	27.00 N	17.00 E
Libya (Lībiyā) □ 1, Afr.	146	27.00 N	17.00 E
Libyan Desert → Lībīyah, Aṣ-Ṣaḥrā' al- ⊸ 2	136	24.00 N	25.00 E
Libyan Plateau → Aḍ-Ḍiffah ⋏ 1	140	30.30 N	25.30 E
Libye → Libya □ 1	146	27.00 N	17.00 E
Libyen → Libya □ 1	146	27.00 N	17.00 E
Libysche Wüste → Lībīyah, Aṣ-Ṣaḥrā' al- ⊸ 2	136	24.00 N	25.00 E
Licancábur, Volcán ∧ 1	248	22.50 S	67.50 W
Licantén	252	34.59 S	72.00 W
Licata	70	37.06 N	13.56 E
Licciana Nardi	64	44.16 N	10.02 E
Lice	130	38.28 N	40.39 E
Lich	56	50.33 N	8.50 E
Lichačova, mys ›	89	42.44 N	132.51 E
Lichaja ≃	83	48.08 N	40.15 E
Lichang	107	28.53 N	104.26 E
Licheng	102	36.30 N	113.21 E
Lichères-Près-Aigremont	50	47.43 N	3.51 E
Lichfield	42	52.42 N	1.48 W
Lichinga	154	13.18 S	35.14 E
Lichitiseni	38	46.23 N	27.17 E
Lichoborka ≃	265b	55.50 N	37.38 E
Lichoslavl'	76	57.07 N	35.28 E
Lichovka	78	48.41 N	33.55 E
Lichovskoj	83	48.07 N	40.12 E
Lichtaart	56	51.14 N	4.54 E
Lichte	54	50.31 N	11.10 E
Lichtenau	56	48.43 N	8.01 E
Lichtenberg, Dtsch.	54	50.23 N	11.40 E
Lichtenberg, Fr.	56	48.55 N	7.29 E
Lichtenberg ⊸ 8	264a	52.31 N	13.29 E
Lichtenburg	158	26.08 S	26.08 E
Lichtendorf	263	51.28 N	7.37 E
Lichtenfels	56	50.09 N	11.04 E
Lichtenplatz ⊸ 8	263	51.15 N	7.12 E
Lichtenrade ⊸ 8	264a	52.23 N	13.25 E
Lichtensee	54	51.23 N	13.22 E
Lichtensteig	58	47.19 N	9.05 E
Lichtenstein	54	50.45 N	12.37 E
Lichtenstein, Schloss ✪	58	48.24 N	9.15 E
Lichtentanne	54	50.42 N	12.25 E
Lichtenvoorde	52	51.59 N	6.34 E
Lichterfelde ⊸ 8	264a	52.26 N	13.19 E
Lichtervelde	50	51.02 N	3.09 E
Lichuan, Zhg.	100	27.18 N	116.53 E
Lichuan, Zhg.	102	30.18 N	108.51 E
Lick Creek ≃, Il., U.S.	219	39.42 N	89.41 W
Lick Creek ≃, In., U.S.	218	38.33 N	86.31 W
Lick Creek ≃, Mo., U.S.	219	39.31 N	91.39 W
Lick Creek ≃, Oh., U.S.	216	41.21 N	84.25 W
Lick Creek ≃, Tn., U.S.	192	36.11 N	83.10 W
Lickershamn	26	57.50 N	18.31 E
Licking	194	37.29 N	91.51 W
Licking □ 6	214	40.10 N	82.30 W
Licking ≃, Ky., U.S.	188	39.06 N	84.30 W
Licking ≃, Oh., U.S.	214	40.03 N	82.20 W
Licking, North Fork ≃, Ky., U.S.	218	38.35 N	84.13 W
Licking, North Fork ≃, Oh., U.S.	214	40.03 N	82.23 W
Licking, South Fork ≃	218	38.41 N	84.20 W
Lickingville	214	41.23 N	79.22 W
Lick Observatory ✪ 3	226	37.22 N	121.37 W
Ličko Polje ≚	36	44.35 N	15.25 E
Lick Run ≃, Pa., U.S.	210	41.12 N	77.32 W
Lick Run ≃, Pa., U.S.	279b	40.17 N	79.57 W
Licodia Eubea	70	37.09 N	14.42 E
Licosa, Punta ›	68	40.15 N	14.54 E
Licun	98	38.32 N	117.08 E
Licungo ≃	154	17.40 S	37.15 E
Lid'	76	59.39 N	35.05 E
Lida	76	53.53 N	25.18 E
Lidan ≃	26	58.31 N	13.09 E
Lidao	98	37.15 N	122.32 E
Lidarentuncun	104	41.32 N	123.12 E
Lidcombe	274a	33.52 S	151.03 E
Liddel Water ≃	44	55.04 N	2.57 W
Liddesdale V	44	55.12 N	2.46 W
Liddon Gulf C	176	75.03 N	113.00 W
Liden	26	62.42 N	16.48 E
Lidesi	100	33.33 N	115.53 E
Lidgerwood	198	46.04 N	97.09 W
Lidgetton	158	29.25 S	30.05 E
Lidian	107	28.57 N	103.44 E
Lídice, Bra.	256	22.51 S	44.12 W
Lídice, Pan.	236	8.45 N	79.54 W
Lidice ⊥	54	50.03 N	14.08 E
Lidingö	40	59.22 N	18.08 E
Lidköping	26	58.30 N	13.10 E
Lido	64	45.25 N	12.22 E
Lido, Litorale di ± 2	64	45.23 N	12.21 E
Lido, Porto di C	64	45.26 N	12.25 E
Lido Beach	276	40.35 N	73.38 W
Lido di Camaiore	64	43.54 N	10.13 E
Lido di Castel Fusano ⊸ 8	66	41.43 N	12.20 E
Lido di Iesolo	64	45.30 N	12.39 E
Lido di Metaponto	68	40.22 N	16.50 E
Lido di Ostia ⊸ 8	66	41.44 N	12.14 E
Lido di Pomposa	66	44.45 N	12.14 E
Lido di Siponto	68	41.37 N	15.55 E
Lido Key I	220	27.19 N	82.35 W
Lidsjön ⊜	40	58.55 N	16.51 E
Lidu	107	30.35 N	106.04 E
Lidzbark	30	53.17 N	19.49 E
Lidzbark Warmiński	30	54.09 N	20.35 E
Liebenau, Dtsch.	52	52.36 N	9.05 E
Liebenau, Öst.	61	48.32 N	14.49 E
Liebenbergsvlei ≃	158	27.20 S	28.31 E
Liebenburg	52	52.01 N	10.26 E
Liebenwalde	54	52.52 N	13.23 E
Lieberhausen	56	51.03 N	7.40 E
Lieberose	54	51.59 N	14.17 E
Liebertwolkwitz	54	51.17 N	12.28 E
Liebig, Mount ∧	162	23.18 S	131.22 E
Liebstadt	54	50.52 N	13.51 E
Liechtenstein □ 1, Europe	22	47.09 N	9.35 E
Liechtenstein □ 1, Europe	58	47.09 N	9.35 E
Liechtensteinklamm V	64	47.18 N	13.12 E
Liedberg	263	51.10 N	6.32 E
Liedekerke	50	50.52 N	4.05 E
Liège (Luik)	56	50.38 N	5.34 E
Liège □ 4	56	50.30 N	5.30 E
Liège, Aéroport ⊠	56	50.39 N	5.30 E
Liegnitz → Legnica	30	51.13 N	16.09 E
Lieja → Liège	56	50.38 N	5.34 E
Lieksa	26	63.19 N	30.01 E
Lielais Liepu kalns ∧ 2	76	56.25 N	27.50 E
Lielupe ≃	76	57.01 N	23.56 E
Lielvārde	76	56.43 N	24.51 E
Liemienzhen	107	30.29 N	106.05 E
Lienart	154	3.04 N	25.31 E
Lienchou → Hepu	102	21.39 N	109.11 E
Lienen	52	52.09 N	7.58 E
Lienz	64	46.50 N	12.47 E
Liepāja	76	56.31 N	21.01 E
Liepājas ezers ⊜	76	56.27 N	21.03 E
Liepe	54	53.58 N	13.56 E
Liepna	76	57.25 N	27.25 E
Liepnitzsee ⊜	264a	52.45 N	13.30 E
Lièpvre	58	48.16 N	7.17 E
Lier (Lierre)	50	51.08 N	4.34 E
Lierenfeld ⊸ 8	263	51.13 N	6.51 E
Lierna	58	45.57 N	9.18 E
Liernais	50	47.12 N	4.17 E
Lierneux	56	50.18 N	5.48 E
Liershizhai	104	41.49 N	123.43 E
Liesborn	52	51.43 N	8.15 E
Lieser ≃, Dtsch.	56	49.55 N	7.01 E
Lieser ≃, Öst.	64	46.47 N	13.39 E
Lieshout	52	51.32 N	5.35 E
Liesing ⊸ 8	264b	48.08 N	16.17 E
Liesing ≃	264b	48.08 N	16.28 E
Liesingbach ≃	61	47.20 N	15.02 E
Liesjärven kansallispuisto ♦	26	60.40 N	23.54 E
Lieskau	54	51.37 N	13.48 E
Liesse	50	49.37 N	3.48 E
Liessies	50	50.07 N	4.05 E
Liestal	58	47.29 N	7.44 E
Liești	38	45.38 N	27.32 E
Lietuva → Lithuania □ 1	72	56.00 N	24.00 E
Lietzow	54	54.29 N	13.30 E
Lieurey	50	49.14 N	0.29 E
Lieusaint	261	48.38 N	2.33 E
Lieutel ≃	261	48.49 N	1.52 E
Lieutenant Robert J. Palenscar Memorial Airport ⊠	285	39.51 N	75.03 W
Liévin	50	50.25 N	2.46 E
Lièvre, Rivière du ≃	176	45.31 N	75.26 W
Lièvres, Île aux I	186	47.51 N	69.44 W
Liezen	61	47.35 N	14.15 E
Lifanga	152	0.19 N	21.57 E
Liffey ≃	48	53.21 N	6.16 W
Liffol-le-Grand	58	48.19 N	5.35 E
Lifford	48	54.50 N	7.29 W
Liffré	32	48.13 N	1.30 W
Lifjell ∧	26	59.30 N	8.52 E
Lifoku	152	0.04 S	21.18 E
Lifou I	175f	20.53 S	167.13 E
Lifoula	273b	4.06 S	15.25 E
Lifton	42	50.39 N	4.17 W
Liftwood	285	39.47 N	75.31 W
Lifune ≃	152	8.21 S	13.22 E
Ligačovo	265b	55.56 N	37.15 E
Ligang	100	30.04 N	121.52 E
Ligao, Pil.	116	13.14 N	123.32 E
Ligao, Pil.	116	6.17 N	124.09 E
Ligasa	152	0.42 N	23.45 E
Ligezhuang, Zhg.	105	39.49 N	115.56 E
Ligezhuang, Zhg.	105	39.42 N	118.12 E
Light ≃	168b	34.35 S	138.22 E
Lightfoot	208	37.20 N	76.45 W
Lighthouse Beach ± 2	273a	6.24 N	3.22 E
Lighthouse Point	220	26.16 N	80.05 W
Lighthouse Point ›, On., Can.	214	41.50 N	82.38 W
Lighthouse Point ›, Fl., U.S.	192	29.54 N	84.21 W
Lighthouse Point ›, Mi., U.S.	190	45.13 N	85.32 W
Lighthouse Reef ✢ 2	232	17.20 N	87.32 W
Lightning Creek ≃, Sk., Can.	184	49.12 N	101.43 W
Lightning Creek ≃, N.A.	224	48.50 N	121.03 W
Lightning Creek ≃, Wy., U.S.	198	43.11 N	104.44 W
Lightning Ridge	166	29.26 S	147.59 E
Lightstreet	210	41.02 N	76.25 W
Lightsville	216	40.18 N	84.42 W
Ligist	61	46.59 N	15.12 E
Lignano Pineta	64	45.40 N	13.07 E
Lignano Sabbiadoro	64	45.42 N	13.09 E
Lignières	32	46.45 N	2.11 E
Lignite	198	48.52 N	102.33 W
Lignon ≃	62	45.44 N	4.08 E
Lignumvitae Key I	220	24.55 N	80.42 W
Ligny-en-Barrois	58	48.41 N	5.20 E
Ligny-en-Cambrésis	50	50.06 N	3.22 E
Ligny-le-Châtel	50	47.54 N	3.45 E
Ligny-le-Ribault	50	47.41 N	1.47 E
Ligonha ≃	154	16.54 S	39.09 E
Ligonier, In., U.S.	216	41.27 N	85.35 W
Ligonier, Pa., U.S.	214	40.14 N	79.14 W
Ligovka	78	49.08 N	36.03 E
Ligovo	76	60.13 N	31.48 E
Ligovo ⊸ 8	265a	59.50 N	30.12 E
Ligovskij kanal ≋	265a	59.47 N	30.10 E
Liguantu	105	40.24 N	115.45 E
Ligueil	32	47.03 N	0.49 E
Ligui	232	25.43 N	111.16 W
Ligure, Mar → Ligurian Sea ⊤ 2	36	43.30 N	9.00 E
Liguria □ 4	36	44.30 N	8.50 E
Liguria, Mar de → Ligurian Sea ⊤ 2	36	43.30 N	9.00 E
Ligurian Sea ⊤ 2	36	43.30 N	9.00 E
Ligurisches Meer → Ligurian Sea ⊤ 2	36	43.30 N	9.00 E
Lihir Group II	164	3.05 S	152.40 E
Lihir Island I	164	3.05 S	152.35 E
Lihoi Seamount ✢ 3	14	18.56 N	155.16 W
Lihou Reef and Cays ✢ 2	166	17.25 S	151.40 E
Lihu	100	23.23 N	116.03 E
Lihue	229b	21.58 N	159.22 W
Lihue Airport ⊠	229b	21.59 N	159.21 W
Lihuel Calel, Parque Nacional ♦, Arg.	252	37.58 S	65.32 W
Lihuel Calel, Parque Nacional ♦, Arg.	254	37.58 S	65.32 W
Lihula	76	58.41 N	23.50 E
Liji, Zhg.	100	31.59 N	115.51 E
Liji, Zhg.	100	33.48 N	117.48 E
Lijia, Zhg.	98	37.49 N	118.01 E
Lijia, Zhg.	104	41.43 N	122.20 E
Lijiaba	107	29.37 N	105.33 E
Lijiadian	104	42.07 N	121.14 E
Lijiajie	107	29.49 N	105.30 E
Lijiakou	105	39.12 N	116.29 E
Lijiang	102	26.57 N	100.15 E
Lijiapuzi	104	40.59 N	123.38 E
Lijiaqiao, Zhg.	105	40.03 N	116.40 E
Lijiaqiao, Zhg.	105	39.47 N	117.47 E
Lijiaqiao, Zhg.	106	31.38 N	120.00 E
Lijiatun	104	41.19 N	121.23 E
Lijiatuo	107	29.28 N	106.33 E
Lijiawobao	104	41.00 N	122.26 E
Lijiaxiang	106	30.57 N	119.59 E
Lijiazao	105	39.17 N	118.19 E
Lijin, Zhg.	98	37.29 N	118.16 E
Lijin, Zhg.	104	41.40 N	121.20 E
Lik ≃	110	18.31 N	102.31 E
Likako	152	0.15 N	21.00 E
Likang	100	22.47 N	120.29 E
Likasi (Jadotville)	154	10.59 S	26.44 E
Likati	152	3.21 N	23.53 E
Likati ≃	152	2.53 N	24.03 E
Likely	182	52.37 N	121.34 W
Likėnai	76	56.12 N	24.37 E
Likete	152	0.43 S	21.25 E
Likhu ≃	124	27.15 N	86.12 E
Liki	112	1.36 S	101.11 E
Likimi	152	2.50 N	20.45 E
Likino	82	55.38 N	37.08 E
Likino-Dulevo	82	55.43 N	38.58 E
Liknes	26	58.19 N	6.59 E
Likoma Island I	154	12.05 S	34.45 E
Likou, Zhg.	100	29.53 N	117.28 E
Likou, Zhg.	100	33.51 N	113.20 E
Likou, Zhg.	106	31.24 N	120.37 E
Likouala □ 5	152	2.00 N	17.30 E
Likouala ≃	152	1.13 S	16.48 E
Likouala aux Herbes ≃	152	0.50 S	17.11 E
Likova ≃	265b	55.34 N	37.21 E
Likstammen ⊜	40	58.58 N	17.12 E
Liku	174v	19.02 S	169.47 W
Likupang	112	1.41 N	125.04 E
Likus ≃	236	14.14 N	83.35 W
Likuyu	154	10.20 S	36.14 E
Lilanchengzhen	105	39.12 N	116.43 E
Lilanga	152	0.34 S	23.55 E
Lilasi	124	29.22 N	84.30 E
Lilbert	222	31.44 N	94.54 W
Lilbourn	194	36.35 N	89.36 W
L'Île-Bouchard	32	47.07 N	0.25 E
Lilenga	152	0.54 N	22.06 E
L'Île-Rousse	36	42.38 N	8.56 E
Lili	106	31.00 N	120.42 E
Lilian Point ›	174d	0.53 S	169.35 E
Lilienfeld	61	48.03 N	15.36 E
Lilienthal	52	53.08 N	8.55 E
Liling	100	27.40 N	113.30 E
Lilio	116	14.08 N	121.26 E
Liljendal	40	60.08 N	14.04 E
Lilla Bharwana	123	32.34 N	72.45 E
Lilla Edet	26	58.08 N	12.08 E
Lillån	40	59.19 N	15.13 E
Lillby	26	63.28 N	23.00 E
Lille	50	50.38 N	3.04 E
Lillebælt ⊔	41	55.20 N	9.45 E
Lillebonne	50	49.31 N	0.33 E
Lillehammer	26	61.08 N	10.30 E
Lille-Lesquin, Aéroport ⊠	50	50.35 N	3.07 E
Lillerød	41	55.52 N	12.22 E
Lillers	50	50.34 N	2.29 E
Lillesand	26	58.15 N	8.24 E
Lilleshall	42	52.44 N	2.21 W
Lillestrøm	26	59.57 N	11.05 E
Lille Værløse	41	55.47 N	12.23 E
Lillhärdal	26	61.51 N	14.04 E
Lillian	222	32.30 N	97.11 W
Lillington	192	35.23 N	78.48 W
Lillinonah Lake ⊜ 1	207	41.28 N	73.21 W
Lilli Pilli	274a	34.04 S	151.07 E
Lillo	34	39.43 N	3.18 W
Lillooet	182	50.42 N	121.56 W
Lillooet ≃	182	49.45 N	122.08 W
Lillooet Lake ⊜	182	50.13 N	122.29 W
Lilly	214	40.25 N	78.37 W
Lilly Creek ≃	222	32.47 N	94.56 W
Liloan	116	10.09 N	125.07 E
Lilongwe	154	13.59 S	33.44 E

Symbols in the index entries represent the broad categories identified in the key at the right. Symbols with superior numbers (⋏ 1) identify subcategories (see complete key on page I · 1).

Symbole im Register stellen die rechts im Schlüssel erklärten Kategorien dar. Symbole mit hochgestellten Ziffern (⋏ 1) bezeichnen Unterabteilungen einer Kategorie (vgl. vollständiger Schlüssel auf Seite I · 1).

Los símbolos incluídos en el texto del índice representan las grandes categorías identificadas con la clave a la derecha. Los símbolos con numeros en su parte superior (⋏ 1) identifican las subcategorías (véase la clave completa en la página I · 1).

Les symboles de l'index représentent les catégories indiquées dans la légende à droite. Les symboles suivis d'un indice (⋏ 1) représentent des sous-catégories (voir légende complète à la page I · 1).

Os símbolos incluídos no texto do índice representam as grandes categorias identificadas com a chave à direita. Os símbolos com números em sua parte superior (⋏ 1) identificam as subcategorias (veja-se a chave completa à página I · 1).

	English	Deutsch	Español	Français	Português
∧	Mountain	Berg	Montaña	Montagne	Montanha
⋏	Mountains	Gebirge	Montañas	Montagnes	Montanhas
)(	Pass	Paß	Paso	Col	Passo
V	Valley, Canyon	Tal, Cañon	Valle, Cañón	Vallée, Canyon	Vale, Canhão
≚	Plain	Ebene	Llano	Plaine	Planície
›	Cape	Kap	Cabo	Cap	Cabo
I	Island	Insel	Isla	Île	Ilha
II	Islands	Inseln	Islas	Îles	Ilhas
±	Other Topographic Features	Andere Topographische Objekte	Otros Elementos Topográficos	Autres données topographiques	Outros acidentes topográficos

ESPAÑOL Nombre	Página	Lat.°	Long.° W=Oeste
FRANÇAIS Nom	Page	Lat.°	Long.° W=Ouest
PORTUGUÊS Nome	Página	Lat.°	Long.° W=Oeste

Name	Página	Lat.	Long.
Lilo Viejo	252	26.56 S	62.58 W
Liloy	116	8.08 N	122.40 E
Lilulh	272b	22.35 N	83.23 E
Lily	192	37.01 N	84.04 W
Lily Cache Creek ≃	278	41.41 N	87.07 W
Lilydale, Austl.	166	41.15 S	147.13 E
Lilydale, Austl.	169	37.45 S	145.21 E
Lily Dale, N.Y., U.S.	214	42.21 N	79.19 W
Lilyfield	274a	33.52 S	151.10 E
Lilyvale	273d	26.06 S	28.25 E
Lim ≃, Afr.	152	7.54 N	15.46 E
Lim ≃, Europe	34	43.45 N	19.13 E
Lima, Arg.	258	34.03 S	59.12 W
Lima, Pará.	252	23.54 S	56.20 W
Lima, Perú	248	12.03 S	77.03 W
Lima, Perú	286d	12.03 S	77.03 W
Lima, Sve.	26	60.56 N	13.26 E
Lima, Il., U.S.	219	40.11 N	91.23 W
Lima, Mt., U.S.	202	44.38 N	112.35 W
Lima, N.Y., U.S.	210	42.54 N	77.36 W
Lima, Oh., U.S.	216	40.44 N	84.06 W
Lima, Pa., U.S.	285	39.55 N	75.26 W
Lima ◻⁵	248	12.00 S	76.35 W
Lima (L'mia) ≃, Europe	34	41.41 N	8.50 W
Lima ≃ It.	44	44.00 N	10.35 E
Lima, Punta ﹥	240m	18.11 N	65.41 W
Lima Center	216	42.47 N	88.49 W
Limache	252	33.01 S	71.16 W
Lima Duarte	256	21.51 S	43.48 W
Liman, Ross.	80	45.47 N	47.14 E
Liman, Ukr.	78	49.36 N	36.27 E
Liman, Ukr.	78	45.41 N	29.45 E
Liman, Ukr.	83	49.21 N	38.57 E
Liman, Yis.	132	33.03 N	35.06 E
Liman ≃	115a	6.29 S	105.48 E
Limanowa	30	49.43 N	20.26 E
Limanskoje	78	46.38 N	30.30 E
Limão ➤⁸	287b	23.30 S	46.40 W
Limapuluh	114	3.10 N	99.26 E
Lima Reservoir ◙¹	202	44.38 N	112.17 W
Limari ≃	252	30.44 S	71.43 W
Limas	112	0.14 N	104.31 E
Limasawa Island I	116	9.56 N	125.05 E
Limassa	152	4.14 N	22.02 E
Limassol — Lemesós	130	34.40 N	33.02 E
Limavady	48	55.03 N	6.57 W
Limaville	214	40.59 N	81.09 W
Limay, Fr.	52	49.00 N	1.44 E
Limay, Pil.	116	14.34 N	120.36 E
Limay ≃	254	38.59 S	68.00 W
Limay Mahuida	252	37.12 S	66.42 W
Limbach-Oberfrohna	54	50.51 N	12.45 E
Limbdi	68	38.33 N	15.58 E
Limbang	112	4.45 N	115.00 E
Limbang ≃	112	4.50 N	115.01 E
Limbani	248	14.08 S	69.42 W
Limbara, Monte ʌ	71	40.51 N	9.10 E
Limbaži	76	57.31 N	24.42 E
Limbdi	28	22.34 N	71.48 E
Limbe	154	15.49 S	35.03 E
Limbiate	62	45.36 N	9.07 E
Limboto	112	0.37 N	122.57 E
Limbourg	56	50.37 N	5.56 E
Limbrick	262	53.38 N	2.36 W
Limbueta	152	13.20 S	18.42 E
Limbunya	164	17.14 S	129.50 E
Limburg ◻⁴, Bel.	56	51.00 N	5.30 E
Limburg ◻⁴, Ned.	52	51.15 N	6.00 E
Limburg an der Lahn	52	50.23 N	8.04 E
Limburgerhof	54	49.29 N	8.24 E
Lim Chu Kang	271c	1.26 N	103.43 E
Limecrest	218	39.54 N	83.48 W
Limefield	255	53.37 N	2.18 W
Limeira	255	22.34 S	47.24 W
Limekiln Canyon V	280	34.18 N	118.33 W
Lime Lake	210	42.26 N	78.29 W
Limen	100	27.07 N	119.19 E
Limena	64	45.29 N	11.50 E
Limentra ≃	64	44.14 N	11.03 E
Limerick, Sk., Can.	184	49.40 N	106.15 W
Limerick (Luimneach), Ire.			
Limerick ◻⁶	48	52.30 N	8.38 W
Limerick ⌾¹	285	40.14 N	75.32 W
Limerick ⌾⁶	48	52.30 N	8.45 W
Limerock	207	41.55 N	71.28 W
Limerick Lake ◙	212	44.54 N	77.37 W
Lime Springs	216	43.27 N	92.17 W
Limestone, Austl.	162	21.11 S	119.50 E
Limestone, Fl., U.S.	220	27.21 N	81.53 W
Limestone, Me., U.S.	186	46.54 N	67.49 W
Limestone, N.Y., U.S.	214	42.01 N	78.37 W
Limestone ≃⁶	214	41.08 N	79.20 W
Limestone ≃⁶	222	38.51 N	96.35 W
Limestone ≃	184	56.31 N	94.07 W
Limestone, Lake ◙²	222	31.25 N	96.20 W
Limestone Bay c	184	53.50 N	98.50 W
Limestone Canyon V	280	33.45 N	117.41 W
Limestone Creek ≃	210	43.06 N	75.58 W
Limestone Lake ◙, Mb., Can.	184	56.35 N	96.00 W
Limestone Lake ◙, Sk., Can.	184	53.50 N	103.18 W
Limestone Point ﹥¹	184	53.50 N	98.50 W
Limestone Point Lake ◙	184	55.07 N	100.32 W
Lime Street Station ⋆⁵	262	53.25 N	2.59 W
Lime Village	180	61.21 N	155.23 W
Limfjorden ☒	26	56.55 N	9.10 E
Limhamn ⋆	41	55.35 N	12.54 E
Limia (Lima) ≃	34	41.41 N	8.50 W
Limina	70	37.56 N	15.17 E
Liminka	26	64.49 N	25.24 E
Liminzhen	98	34.31 N	115.56 E
Limit Brook ≃	283	42.42 N	71.25 W
Limmared	26	57.32 N	13.21 E
Limmaren ◙	40	59.44 N	18.43 E
Limmen	52	52.34 N	4.41 E
Limmen Bight c³	164	14.45 S	135.42 E
Limmen Bight ≃	164	15.07 S	135.44 E
Límnos I	38	39.54 N	25.21 E
Limoeiro	250	7.52 S	35.27 W
Limoeiro do Norte	250	5.08 S	38.05 W
Limoges, On., Can.	212	45.20 N	75.15 W
Limoges, Fr.	52	45.50 N	1.16 E
Limoges-Fourches	261	48.38 N	2.40 E
Limogne	52	44.24 N	1.46 E
Limón, Hond.	236	15.52 N	85.33 W
Limon, Co., U.S.	198	39.15 N	103.41 W
Limón ≃	236	10.00 N	83.15 W
Limonar	240d	22.57 N	81.24 W
Limone Piemonte	62	44.12 N	7.34 E
Limone sul Garda	62	45.49 N	10.47 E
Limours	50	48.39 N	2.05 E
Limousin, Plateaux du ʌ¹	32	45.50 N	1.15 E
Limoux	32	43.04 N	2.14 E
Limpopo ≃	156	25.15 S	33.30 E
Limpsfield	64	51.15 N	0.01 E
Limski kanal c	62	45.10 N	13.38 E
Limru	102	25.02 N	110.51 E
Limuru	154	1.06 S	36.39 E
Linachamari	24	69.40 N	31.02 E
Lin'an	108	28.21 N	119.43 E
Linao Bay c	116	6.45 N	124.00 E
Linapacan Island I	116	11.27 N	119.43 E
Linapacan Strait ☒	116	11.37 N	119.56 E
Linares, Chile	252	35.51 S	71.36 W
Linares, Col.	246	1.23 N	77.31 W
Linares, Esp.	34	38.05 N	3.38 W
Linares, Méx.	232	24.52 N	99.34 W
Linariá	38	38.50 N	24.32 E
Linaro, Capo ﹥	68	42.02 N	11.50 E
Linas	261	48.38 N	2.16 E
Linas, Monte ʌ	71	39.27 N	8.37 E
Linas-Monthléry, Domaine Militaire de ⚔	261	48.37 N	2.13 E
Linate, Aeroporto di ⍝	62	45.27 N	9.16 E
Lincang	102	23.45 N	102.20 E
Lince	286d	12.06 S	77.03 W
Linch	200	43.36 N	106.11 W
Lincheng, Zhg.	98	37.27 N	114.29 E
Lincheng, Zhg.	106	30.55 N	119.47 E
Linch'ing — Linqing	98	36.53 N	115.41 E
Lincoln, Arg.	252	34.52 S	61.32 W
Lincoln, On., Can.	212	43.10 N	79.29 W
Lincoln, N.Z.	172	43.39 S	172.29 E
Lincoln, Eng., U.K.	44	53.14 N	0.33 W
Lincoln, Ar., U.S.	194	35.56 N	94.25 W
Lincoln, Ca., U.S.	226	38.53 N	121.17 W
Lincoln, De., U.S.	222	38.52 N	75.25 W
Lincoln, Il., U.S.	219	40.08 N	89.21 W
Lincoln, In., U.S.	216	40.37 N	86.12 W
Lincoln, Ks., U.S.	198	39.02 N	98.08 W
Lincoln, Me., U.S.	188	45.21 N	68.30 W
Lincoln, Ma., U.S.	207	42.25 N	71.18 W
Lincoln, Mi., U.S.	190	44.41 N	83.24 W
Lincoln, Mo., U.S.	198	38.23 N	93.20 W
Lincoln, Mt., U.S.	202	46.57 N	112.41 W
Lincoln, Ne., U.S.	198	40.48 N	96.40 W
Lincoln, N.H., U.S.	198	42.40 N	71.40 W
Lincoln, Pa., U.S.	208	40.12 N	76.12 W
Lincoln, Pa., U.S.	279b	40.19 N	79.51 W
Lincoln, R.I., U.S.	207	41.54 N	71.25 W
Lincoln, Tx., U.S.	222	30.17 N	96.52 W
Lincoln ◻⁶, Mo., U.S.	219	39.05 N	90.57 W
Lincoln ◻⁶, Or., U.S.	224	44.59 N	123.52 W
Lincoln, Mount ʌ	200	39.21 N	106.07 W
Lincoln Acres	228	32.40 N	117.04 W
Lincoln Boyhood National Memorial ⚹	194	38.10 N	86.58 W
Lincoln Cathedral ☩¹	44	53.14 N	0.33 W
Lincoln Center ≃, Ne., U.S.	198	40.54 N	97.06 W
Lincoln City	224	44.57 N	124.00 W
Lincoln Creek ≃, Ne., U.S.	198	40.54 N	97.06 W
Lincoln Creek ≃, Wa., U.S.	224	46.45 N	123.02 W
Lincolndale	210	41.19 N	73.43 W
Lincoln Estates	278	41.31 N	87.49 W
Lincoln Heights, Oh., U.S.	214	40.47 N	82.30 W
Lincoln Heights, Oh., U.S.	218	39.15 N	84.28 W
Lincoln Heights, Pa., U.S.	279b	40.19 N	79.37 W
Lincoln Home National Historic Site ⚹	219	39.47 N	89.38 W
Lincolnia Heights	284c	38.50 N	77.09 W
Lincoln Memorial ⚹	284c	38.53 N	77.03 W
Lincoln Park, Co., U.S.	200	38.25 N	105.13 W
Lincoln Park, Ga., U.S.	192	32.52 N	84.19 W
Lincoln Park, Mi., U.S.	215	42.15 N	83.10 W
Lincoln Park, N.J., U.S.	208	40.55 N	74.18 W
Lincoln Park, N.Y., U.S.	210	41.57 N	74.00 W
Lincoln Park ◂, Ca., U.S.	282	37.46 N	122.30 W
Lincoln Park Airport ⍝	276	40.57 N	74.19 W
Lincoln Place ➤⁸	279b	40.22 N	79.55 W
Lincoln Sea ⲧ²	16	33.00 N	56.00 W
Lincolnshire	216	42.11 N	87.54 W
Lincolnshire ◻⁶	262	53.10 N	0.22 W
Lincoln's New Salem State Park ✦	219	39.58 N	89.52 W
Lincoln Tomb State Memorial ⚹	219	39.50 N	89.39 W
Lincolnton, Ga., U.S.	192	33.47 N	82.28 W
Lincolnton, N.C., U.S.	192	35.28 N	81.15 W
Lincoln Tunnel ⋆⁵	276	40.46 N	74.01 W
Lincoln University	208	39.48 N	75.55 W
Lincoln Village, Ca., U.S.	226	38.00 N	121.19 W
Lincoln Village, Oh., U.S.	218	39.57 N	83.08 W
Lincolnville	214	41.47 N	79.51 W
Lincolnwood	216	42.00 N	87.44 W
Lincolnwood Hills	278	41.31 N	87.54 W
Linconia	285	40.08 N	74.59 W
Lincroft	208	40.19 N	74.07 W
Lind	202	46.58 N	118.36 W
Linda, Ross.	80	56.37 N	44.07 E
Linda, Ca., U.S.	226	39.07 N	121.32 W
Linda-a-Velha	34a	38.42 N	9.47 E
Lindale, Ga., U.S.	192	34.11 N	85.10 W
Lindale, Tx., U.S.	222	32.30 N	95.24 W
Lindau, Dtsch.	41	54.36 N	9.47 E
Lindau, Dtsch.	52	51.39 N	10.07 E
Lindau, Dtsch.	54	52.02 N	12.06 E
Lindau, Dtsch.	54	47.33 N	9.41 E
Lindau, Dtsch.	58	47.33 N	9.41 E
Lindbergh Field ⍝	228	32.44 N	117.11 W
Lind Coulee V	202	47.00 N	119.10 W
Linde	74	74.07 N	124.36 E
Lindelse	41	54.52 N	10.44 E
Linden, Guy.	246	6.00 N	58.18 W
Linden, Al., U.S.	194	32.18 N	87.47 W
Linden, In., U.S.	194	40.11 N	86.54 W
Linden, Mi., U.S.	216	42.48 N	83.46 W
Linden, N.J., U.S.	208	40.37 N	74.14 W
Linden, Tn., U.S.	194	35.37 N	87.50 W
Linden, Tx., U.S.	194	33.00 N	94.21 W
Linden Airport ⍝	276	40.37 N	74.15 W
Lindenberg, Dtsch.	54	52.36 N	13.31 E
Lindenberg, Dtsch.	54	53.33 N	13.31 E
Lindenberg im Allgäu	58	47.36 N	9.53 E
Linden-Dahlhausen			
Lindenfels	56	49.41 N	8.47 E
Lindenhorst	263	51.33 N	7.27 E
Lindenhurst, Il., U.S.	216	42.24 N	88.01 W
Lindenhurst, N.Y., U.S.	210	40.41 N	73.22 W
Lindenwold	208	39.49 N	74.59 W
Lindenwood, In., U.S.	218	39.43 N	89.02 W
Lindenwood, In., U.S.	218	39.41 N	86.09 W
Lindenhausen	263	51.26 N	7.09 E
Lindern	52	52.50 N	7.46 E
Linderödsåsen ʌ²	26	55.53 N	13.56 E
Lindesberg	40	59.35 N	15.15 E
Lindesnäs	26	58.00 N	7.02 E
Lindfield, Austl.	274a	33.47 S	151.10 E
Lindfield, Eng., U.K.	42	51.01 N	0.05 W
Lindholmen	40	59.04 N	18.31 E
Lindhos	38	36.06 N	28.04 E
Lindhos	38	36.06 N	28.05 E
Lindi	154	10.00 S	39.43 E
Lindi ◻⁴	154	9.15 S	38.45 E
Lindi ≃	154	0.33 N	25.05 E
Lindian	89	47.11 N	124.52 E
Lindis Pass ⤬	172	44.36 S	169.40 E
Lindkirchen	60	48.40 N	11.47 E
Lindlar	56	51.01 N	7.23 E
Lindley, S. Afr.	158	28.00 S	27.57 E
Lindley, N.Y., U.S.	210	42.02 N	77.08 W
Lindö	40	58.37 N	16.15 E
Lindóia	256	22.31 S	46.39 W
Lindome	26	57.34 N	12.05 E
Lindon	198	29.44 N	103.24 W
Lindong, Zhg.	100	26.03 N	118.49 E
Lindong, Zhg.	105	39.51 N	117.41 E
Lindow	54	52.58 N	13.00 E
Lind Point ﹥	240m	18.20 N	64.48 W
Lindsay, On., Can.	212	44.21 N	78.44 W
Lindsay, Ca., U.S.	204	36.12 N	119.05 W
Lindsay, Ne., U.S.	198	41.42 N	97.41 W
Lindsay, Ok., U.S.	198	34.50 N	97.36 W
Lindsborg	198	38.34 N	97.40 W
Lindsey	214	41.25 N	83.13 W
Lindved	41	55.47 N	9.35 E
Lindy Lake	276	41.05 N	74.22 W
Lineboro	208	39.43 N	76.50 W
Line Creek ≃	192	33.20 N	88.42 W
Line Islands II	14	0.05 N	157.00 W
Line Lexington	208	40.17 N	75.16 W
Line Mountain ʌ	210	40.45 N	76.37 W
Linesville	214	41.39 N	80.25 W
Lineville, Al., U.S.	194	33.18 N	85.45 W
Lineville, Ia., U.S.	190	40.34 N	93.31 W
Línevo	86	54.05 N	76.21 E
Linfen	102	36.05 N	111.32 E
Linfield	208	40.13 N	75.34 W
Linford	260	51.29 N	0.25 E
Ling ≃	46	57.19 N	5.27 W
Ling'an	106	30.36 N	120.30 E
Linganamakki Reservoir ◙¹	122	14.04 N	74.54 E
Lingao	102	19.54 N	109.40 E
Lingayen	116	16.01 N	120.14 E
Lingayen Gulf c	116	16.15 N	120.14 E
Lingbi	100	33.33 N	117.33 E
Lingbo	26	61.03 N	16.41 E
Lingchuan, Zhg.	102	25.26 N	110.15 E
Lingchuan, Zhg.	102	35.46 N	113.26 E
Lingda	106	31.12 N	119.18 E
Lingdale	44	54.32 N	0.57 W
Lingdianzhen	106	31.51 N	121.25 E
Lingdou	100	26.22 N	118.56 E
Lingen	52	52.31 N	7.19 E
Lingesestausee ◙¹	263	51.06 N	7.32 E
Lingfengwei	100	24.18 N	115.03 E
Lingfield	42	51.11 N	0.01 W
Lingga, Kepulauan II	112	0.05 S	104.35 E
Lingga, Pulau I	112	0.12 S	104.35 E
Lingham Lake ◙	212	44.46 N	77.25 W
Linghe	98	36.23 N	119.03 E
Linghu	106	30.44 N	120.10 E
Lingig	116	8.02 N	126.24 E
Lingjiachang	100	29.28 N	104.54 E
Lingjiaqiao	106	30.09 N	120.04 E
Lingjiar Dzong	124	28.45 N	90.36 E
Lingkou, Zhg.	100	29.16 N	120.38 E
Lingkou, Zhg.	106	31.57 N	119.38 E
Lingle	200	42.08 N	104.20 W
Linglestown	208	40.21 N	76.48 W
Lingling	106	26.13 N	111.37 E
Linglongta	102	23.20 N	107.53 E
Lingoleheim	58	48.34 N	7.41 E
Lingomo	152	0.38 N	21.57 E
Lingqiu	98	39.24 N	114.13 E
Lingshan, Zhg.	98	36.33 N	120.27 E
Lingshan, Zhg.	102	22.28 N	109.17 E
Lingshanwei	102	35.58 N	120.13 E
Lingshi	98	36.51 N	111.46 E
Lingshou	98	38.18 N	114.24 E
Lingshui	100	18.31 N	110.01 E
Lingtangqiao	100	32.43 N	119.14 E
Linguaglossa	70	37.50 N	15.08 E
Linguère	150	15.24 N	15.07 W
Lingwala	273b	4.22 S	15.17 E
Lingwood	42	52.36 N	1.30 E
Lingwu	102	38.06 N	106.21 E
Lingxian, Zhg.	98	37.21 N	116.34 E
Lingxian, Zhg.	106	26.30 N	113.46 E
Lingxiazhu	100	29.03 N	119.46 E
Lingyuan	105	41.15 N	119.16 E
Lingzhuangzi	105	39.04 N	117.09 E
Lingzinan	105	39.29 N	115.15 E
Linh, Ngoc ʌ	110	15.50 N	107.58 E
Linhai	100	28.51 N	121.07 E
Linhares	255	19.25 S	40.04 W
Linh Cam	110	18.31 N	105.34 E
Linhe	102	40.51 N	107.30 E
Linhezhuang	105	40.04 N	117.39 E
Linhigh	284b	39.21 N	76.31 W
Linhsia — Linxia	102	35.35 N	103.13 E
Linhuaiguan	100	32.55 N	117.40 E
Linhuanji	100	33.42 N	116.33 E
Lini — Linyi	98	35.04 N	118.22 E
Linjiang, Zhg.	98	41.44 N	126.55 E
Linjiang, Zhg.	100	27.50 N	118.26 E
Linjiang, Zhg.	105	39.41 N	118.21 E
Linjiangchang	100	29.14 N	105.58 E
Linjiangsi	100	28.41 N	117.54 E
Linjin	100	35.15 N	110.40 E
Linkang	106	31.37 N	120.04 E
Linkenheim	58	49.07 N	8.24 E
Linköping	26	58.25 N	15.37 E
Linkou	100	45.17 N	130.16 E
Linksfield	273d	26.10 S	28.06 E
Linksmakalnis	46	54.52 N	23.57 E
Linksness	46	58.56 N	3.19 W
Linkuva	46	56.05 N	23.59 E
Linkwood	208	38.32 N	75.52 W
Linli	102	29.26 N	111.39 E
Linlithgow	46	55.59 N	3.37 W
Linmeyer	273d	26.16 S	28.04 E
Linn, Ks., U.S.	198	39.40 N	97.05 W
Linn, Mo., U.S.	198	38.29 N	91.51 W
Linn ◻⁶	216	42.01 N	91.11 W
Linn, Cerro ʌ	248	21.53 S	66.52 W
Liñola	34	41.42 N	0.54 E
Linong	102	34.21 N	109.11 E
Linqing	98	36.51 N	115.42 E
Linqu	98	36.31 N	118.33 E
Linru	100	34.11 N	112.52 E
Linruzhen	100	34.17 N	112.35 E
Lins	255	21.40 S	49.45 W
Linshanhe	100	30.09 N	120.59 E
Linshengpu	105	41.34 N	123.20 E
Linshui	102	30.56 N	106.59 E
Linslade	42	51.55 N	0.41 W
Linstead	241q	18.08 N	77.02 W
Linta ≃	157b	25.02 S	44.05 E
Lintan	102	34.37 N	103.40 E
Lintao	102	35.27 N	103.46 E
Linté	152	5.24 N	11.42 E
Linth ≃	58	47.07 N	9.07 E
Linthal, Fr.	58	47.56 N	7.08 E
Linthal, Schw.	58	46.55 N	9.00 E
Linthicum Heights	284b	39.12 N	76.39 W
Linthkanal ☒	58	47.13 N	8.57 E
Linthwaite	262	53.37 N	1.51 W
Lintingkou	105	39.39 N	117.30 E
Linton, Austl.	169	37.41 S	143.34 E
Linton, N.Z.	172	40.26 S	175.33 E
Linton, Eng., U.K.	42	52.06 N	0.17 E
Linton, Eng., U.K.	260	51.13 N	0.31 E
Linton, In., U.S.	194	39.02 N	87.09 W
Linton, N.D., U.S.	198	46.16 N	100.13 W
Lintong	102	34.21 N	109.11 E
Linton Park ✦	260	51.13 N	0.31 E
Linum	264a	52.46 N	12.53 E
Linville, Austl.	171a	26.51 S	152.16 E
Linville, N.C., U.S.	192	36.03 N	81.52 W
Linwood, Austl.	168b	34.21 S	138.46 E
Linwood, In., U.S.	218	40.12 N	85.41 W
Linwood, Ma., U.S.	207	42.05 N	71.38 W
Linwood, N.J., U.S.	208	39.20 N	74.34 W
Linwood, Pa., U.S.	285	39.49 N	75.24 W
Linworth	214	40.06 N	83.04 W
Linwu, Zhg.	98	36.14 N	119.17 E
Linwu, Zhg.	106	25.16 N	112.20 E
Linxi, Zhg.	90	43.30 N	118.00 E
Linxi, Zhg.	98	36.52 N	115.32 E
Linxia	102	35.35 N	103.13 E
Linxian, Zhg.	78	36.04 N	113.50 E
Linxian, Zhg.	98	37.58 N	110.59 E
Linxiang	100	29.28 N	113.30 E
Linyanti	156	18.04 S	24.01 E
Linyanti ≃	156	17.58 S	24.16 E
Linyi, Zhg.	98	35.04 N	118.22 E
Linyi, Zhg.	98	37.13 N	116.51 E
Linyi, Zhg.	102	35.15 N	110.59 E
Linying	100	33.49 N	113.56 E
Linyü — Shanhaiguan	98	40.01 N	119.44 E
Linz, Dtsch.	56	50.34 N	7.17 E
Linz, Öst.	61	48.18 N	14.18 E
Linze, Zhg.	102	33.03 N	119.38 E
Linze, Zhg.	102	39.19 N	100.17 E
Linzhang	98	36.21 N	114.36 E
Linzhi	100	29.25 N	94.22 E
Linzikou	98	42.24 N	112.46 E
Linzolo	152	4.25 S	15.07 E
Lioko, Zaïre	152	0.02 N	22.04 E
Lioko, Zaïre	152	1.25 N	23.07 E
Lio Matoh	112	3.10 N	115.14 E
Liomer	50	49.51 N	1.49 E
Lion, Golfe du c	32	43.00 N	4.00 E
Lionel Town	241q	17.48 N	77.14 W
Lioni	68	40.52 N	15.11 E
Lion Rock ʌ²	271d	22.22 N	114.11 E
Lion Rock Tunnel ⋆⁵	271d	22.21 N	114.09 E
Lions Den	154	17.16 S	30.02 E
Lion's Head	212	44.59 N	81.15 W
Lionville	208	40.03 N	75.39 W
Lioppa	102	23.20 N	107.53 E
Liouesso	152	1.02 N	15.43 E
Liozno	76	55.02 N	30.48 E
Lipa	116	13.57 N	121.10 E
Lipany	30	49.10 N	20.58 E
Lipari	70	38.28 N	14.57 E
Lipari, Isola I	70	38.29 N	14.56 E
Lipatkain	112	0.01 S	101.13 E
Lipayan	116	12.13 N	123.23 E
Lipcy	78	50.13 N	36.25 E
Lipeck	76	52.37 N	39.35 E
Lipeck Oblast' ◻⁴	76	52.30 N	39.00 E
Lipeckoje Vtoroje	76	46.55 N	42.21 E
Lipen ≃	26	62.32 N	29.22 E
Lipetsk → Lipeck	76	52.37 N	39.35 E
Liphook	42	51.05 N	0.49 W
Lipiany	30	53.00 N	14.58 E
Lipicy	76	53.22 N	37.17 E
Lipin Bor	76	60.16 N	37.57 E
Lipis ≃	114	4.10 N	102.04 E
Lipiu	104	41.09 N	123.36 E
Lipka	30	53.24 N	17.10 E
Lipki	76	53.58 N	37.42 E
Lipnik nad Bečvou	30	49.31 N	17.35 E
Lipništi	76	54.00 N	25.37 E
Lipno	30	52.51 N	19.10 E
Lipno, údolní Nádrž ◙¹	61	48.14 N	14.04 E
Lipno nad Vltavou	61	48.38 N	14.14 E
Lpoa Point ﹥	229a	21.02 N	156.38 W
Lpova ≃	76	60.05 N	21.40 E
Lipovaja Dolina	78	50.35 N	34.48 E
Lipovcy	86	44.13 N	131.44 E
Lipovec	30	49.23 N	16.49 E
Lipovka, Ross.	76	50.52 N	40.02 E
Lipovka, Ross.	80	49.46 N	44.56 E
Lippborg	263	51.39 N	8.03 E
Lippe ≃	52	51.39 N	6.38 E
Lippetal	263	51.41 N	8.02 E
Lippoldsberg	52	51.37 N	9.33 E
Lippstadt	52	51.40 N	8.20 E
Lipscomb	196	36.14 N	100.16 W
Lipsko	30	51.09 N	21.39 E
Lipsói I, Ellás	38	37.20 N	26.45 E
Lipsói I, Ellás	38	37.17 N	26.46 E
Liptovská Teplička	30	48.57 N	20.00 E
Liptovský Mikuláš	30	49.06 N	19.37 E
Liptrap, Cape ﹥	166	38.54 S	145.55 E
Lipu	102	24.30 N	110.23 E
Lipu La ⤬	124	30.21 N	81.05 E
Lira	154	2.15 N	32.54 E
Lirang I	113	8.04 S	125.44 E
Lircay	248	12.59 S	74.43 W
Lire	52	47.14 N	0.58 W
Lirey	50	48.12 N	4.05 E
Liri ≃	68	41.25 N	13.52 E
Liro ≃	62	46.21 N	9.22 E
Lisakovsk	82	52.33 N	62.37 E
Lisala	152	2.09 N	21.31 E
Lisavy	86	56.33 N	38.23 E
Lisboa (Lisbon), Port.	34	38.43 N	9.08 W
Lisboa (Lisbon), Port.	266c	38.46 N	9.16 W
Lisboa ◻⁵	34	39.10 N	9.10 W
Lisbon — Lisboa	34	38.43 N	9.08 W
Lisbon, Md., U.S.	208	39.20 N	77.04 W
Lisbon, N.D., U.S.	198	46.26 N	97.40 W
Lisbon, Oh., U.S.	214	40.46 N	80.46 W
Lisbon Falls	207	43.59 N	70.03 W
Lisburn	48	54.31 N	6.03 W
Lisburne, Cape ﹥	180	68.53 N	166.13 W
Liscannor Bay c	48	52.55 N	9.25 W
Liscarney	48	53.43 N	9.35 W
Liscia ≃	71	41.11 N	9.19 E
Liscia, Lago di ◙	71	41.00 N	9.16 E
Lisdoonvarna	48	53.01 N	9.15 W
Lisec	78	48.52 N	24.36 E
Liseleje	41	56.01 N	11.59 E
Lishan, Zhg.	100	31.50 N	113.16 E
Lishan, Zhg.	104	41.10 N	123.00 E
Lishanzhuang	105	39.35 N	118.11 E
Lishanke	98	40.41 N	119.53 E
Lishe	100	29.48 N	121.26 E
Lishe	102	24.18 N	101.32 E
Lishi, Zhg.	102	37.32 N	111.09 E
Lishi, Zhg.	106	31.14 N	118.52 E
Lishi, Zhg.	107	29.10 N	105.42 E
Lishizhen, Zhg.	107	29.20 N	105.24 E
Lishizhen, Zhg.	107	29.04 N	106.15 E
Lishu	89	43.21 N	124.57 E
Lishui, Zhg.	100	28.27 N	119.54 E
Lishui, Zhg.	106	31.39 N	119.01 E
Lishuzhen	89	45.05 N	130.41 E
Lisianski Island I	14	26.02 N	174.00 W
Lisica ≃	86	58.34 N	85.11 E
Lisičansk	83	48.55 N	38.26 E
Lisičansk — Lisičansk	83	48.55 N	38.26 E
Lisica	82	56.47 N	36.21 E
Lisie, Il., U.S.	216	41.48 N	88.04 W
Lisle, N.Y., U.S.	210	42.21 N	76.00 W
L'Isle-Adam	50	49.07 N	2.14 E
L'Isle Jourdain	32	46.14 N	0.41 E
L'Isle-sur-la-Sorgue	62	43.55 N	5.03 E
L'Isle-sur-le-Doubs	58	47.27 N	6.35 E
L'Isle-sur-Serein	50	47.35 N	4.00 E
Lisman	232	40.01 N	88.16 W
Lismore, Austl.	166	28.48 S	153.17 E
Lismore, Austl.	169	37.58 S	143.20 E
Lismore, N.S., Can.	186	45.42 N	62.16 W
Lismore, Ire.	48	52.08 N	7.55 W
Lismore Castle ⊥	48	52.08 N	7.52 W
Lismore Island I	46	56.29 N	5.33 W
Lisnaskea	48	54.15 N	7.27 W
Liso ﹥¹	68	40.58 N	17.45 E
Lišov	61	49.01 N	14.37 E
Lišov'ka	78	50.59 N	39.30 E
Liss	42	51.03 N	0.55 W
Lissabon → Lisboa	34	38.43 N	9.08 W
Lisse	56	52.15 N	4.33 E
Lisses	261	48.36 N	2.26 E
Lissewege	56	51.18 N	3.11 E
Lissie	222	29.30 N	96.13 W
Lissingen	56	50.14 N	6.38 E
Lisso	62	45.37 N	9.14 E
Lissy	261	48.38 N	2.42 E
Lista ﹥¹	80	57.44 N	45.54 E
Lista ﹥¹	26	58.07 N	6.40 E
Lister ≃	263	51.05 N	7.45 E
Lištica	36	43.21 N	17.36 E
Listowel, On., Can.	212	43.44 N	80.57 W
Listowel, Ire.	48	52.27 N	9.29 W
Listv'anka	88	51.52 N	104.51 E
Listv'anskij	105	54.28 N	87.26 E
Liszki	30	50.05 N	16.44 E
Lita	86	59.02 N	63.19 E
Litang, Malay.	112	5.20 N	118.31 E
Litang, Zhg.	102	23.11 N	109.05 E
Litang, Zhg.	102	30.00 N	100.16 E
Litang ≃	102	28.04 N	101.30 E
Litani, Nahr al- ≃	132	33.20 N	35.14 E
Litava ≃	61	48.02 N	16.36 E
Litchfield, Ct., U.S.	207	41.44 N	73.11 W
Litchfield, Il., U.S.	219	39.10 N	89.39 W
Litchfield, Mi., U.S.	216	42.02 N	84.45 W
Litchfield, Mn., U.S.	198	45.07 N	94.31 W
Litchfield, Ne., U.S.	198	41.09 N	99.09 W
Litchfield ◻⁶	207	41.45 N	73.11 W
Litchfield Park	228	33.29 N	112.21 W
Litchville	198	46.39 N	98.11 W
Liteberry	219	39.51 N	90.12 W
Lith, Wådī al- V	144	20.40 N	40.35 E
Litherland	262	53.28 N	2.59 W
Lithgow	170	33.29 S	150.09 E
Lithia	220	27.51 N	82.10 W
Lithinon, Ákra ﹥	38	34.55 N	24.44 E
Lithonia	192	33.43 N	84.06 W
Lithuania (Lietuva) ◻¹	22	56.00 N	24.00 E
Lithuania (Lietuva) ◻¹, Europe	26	55.00 N	24.00 E
Litija	62	46.03 N	14.50 E
Litin	78	49.20 N	28.06 E
Lititz	208	40.09 N	76.18 W
Litke	89	54.16 N	131.20 E
Litochoron	38	40.06 N	22.29 E
Litoměřice	54	50.33 N	14.10 E
Litomyšl	30	49.52 N	16.19 E
Litoo	154	9.54 S	38.24 E
Litovel	30	49.42 N	17.05 E
Litovko	89	49.15 N	135.11 E
Litschau	61	48.57 N	15.03 E
Littau	58	47.03 N	8.16 E
Little ≃, On., Can.	281	48.30 N	80.01 W
Little ≃, U.S.	222	33.44 N	92.17 W
Little ≃, U.S.	222	31.41 N	91.17 W
Little ≃, U.S.	194	33.55 N	95.05 W
Little Abaco I	240c	26.53 N	77.43 W
Little Alföld ☲	30	47.30 N	17.00 E
Little Amwell	260	51.47 N	0.01 W
Little Andaman I	111	10.45 N	92.30 E
Little Arkansas ≃	198	37.48 N	97.26 W
Little Auglaize ≃	216	41.05 N	84.25 W
Little Averill Lake ◙	207	44.57 N	71.44 W
Little Baddow	260	51.44 N	0.35 E
Little Barrier Island I	172	36.12 S	175.05 E
Little Bay	186	47.41 N	58.24 W
Little Bay c	276	40.48 N	73.47 W
Little Bay Islands	186	49.39 N	55.47 W
Little Bear ≃	200	41.42 N	111.57 W
Little Bear Creek Reservoir ◙¹	194	34.50 N	87.57 W
Little Beaver Creek ≃, U.S.	198	46.17 N	103.56 W
Little Beaver Creek ≃, U.S.	198	39.49 N	101.03 W
Little Beaver Creek ≃, U.S.	214	40.38 N	80.31 W
Little Beaver Creek ≃, Wa., U.S.	224	48.54 N	121.06 W
Little Beaver Creek, Middle Fork ≃	214	40.43 N	80.37 W
Little Beaver Creek, North Fork ≃	214	40.43 N	80.33 W
Little Beaver Creek, West Fork ≃	214	40.43 N	80.37 W
Little Eel ≃	226	39.53 N	123.19 W
Little Belt Mountains ʌ	202	46.45 N	110.35 W
Little Berkhamsted	260	51.45 N	0.08 W
Little Bighorn ≃	200	45.44 N	107.34 W
Little Billabong	171b	35.35 S	147.32 E
Little Bitter Lake — Murrah aṣ-Ṣughrā, Al- ◙	142	30.13 N	32.33 E
Little Bitterroot ≃	202	47.30 N	114.19 W
Little Black ≃, U.S.	194	35.29 N	90.45 W
Little Black ≃, Ak., U.S.	180	66.26 N	143.49 W
Little Black Bear Indian Reserve ◂⁴	184	51.00 N	103.23 W
Little Blackfoot ≃	202	46.31 N	112.48 W
Little Blue ≃, U.S.	198	39.41 N	96.40 W
Little Blue ≃, In., U.S.	218	39.41 N	96.40 W
Littleborough	44	53.39 N	2.05 W
Little Bow ≃	182	49.53 N	112.29 W
Little Brazos ≃	222	30.38 N	96.31 W
Little Brokenstraw Creek ≃	214	41.50 N	79.23 W
Little Brosna ≃	48	53.10 N	8.05 W
Little Buffalo ≃	176	61.00 N	113.46 W
Little Bullhead	184	51.46 N	96.51 W
Little Burstead	260	51.36 N	0.24 E
Little Caiumet ≃	278	41.39 N	87.34 W
Little Catalina	186	48.33 N	53.10 W
Little Cayman I	238	19.41 N	80.03 W
Little Cedar ≃	190	43.40 N	92.31 W
Little Chalfont	260	51.40 N	0.34 W
Little Chartiers Creek ≃	279b	40.17 N	80.08 W
Little Choptank River ≃	208	38.32 N	76.13 W
Little Churchill ≃	184	57.15 N	95.21 W
Little Chute	216	44.16 N	88.19 W
Little Coco Island I	110	14.00 N	93.13 E
Little Colorado ≃	200	36.11 N	111.48 W
Little Compton	207	41.30 N	71.10 W
Little Cooley	214	41.44 N	79.53 W
Little Cottonwood ≃	198	44.15 N	94.20 W
Little Creek	285	38.07 N	6.40 W
Little Creek Naval Amphibious Base ◂	212	36.55 N	76.11 W
Little Creek Reservoir ◙¹	208	37.20 N	76.50 W
Little Cumbrae Island I	46	55.43 N	4.57 W
Little Current	184	45.58 N	81.56 W
Little Current ≃	176	50.57 N	84.36 W
Little Cypress Bayou ≃	194	32.41 N	94.15 W
Little Cypress Creek ≃	222	32.39 N	94.42 W
Little Darby Creek ≃	218	39.53 N	83.13 W
Little Dart ≃	260	50.54 N	3.51 W
Little Deep Creek ≃, In., U.S.	216	40.36 N	86.28 W
Little Deer Creek ≃, Pa., U.S.	279b	40.33 N	79.50 W
Little Deschutes ≃	202	43.51 N	121.27 W
Little Desert ◂²	166	36.35 S	141.20 E
Little Desert National Park ✦	166	36.25 S	141.25 E
Little Diomade Island I	180	65.45 N	168.57 W
Little Don ≃	275b	43.42 N	79.20 W
Little Dry Creek ≃, Ca., U.S.	226	39.22 N	121.52 W
Little Dry Creek ≃, Mt., U.S.	202	47.21 N	106.22 W
Little Ease Run ≃	285	39.40 N	75.04 W
Little Eau Pleine ≃	216	44.40 N	89.43 W
Little Egg Harbor c	208	39.35 N	74.18 W
Little Elkhart ≃	216	41.43 N	85.49 W
Littlefield	196	33.55 N	102.20 W
Little Etobicoke Creek ≃	275b	43.37 N	79.34 W
Little Exuma I	238	23.25 N	75.37 W
Little Fabius ≃	219	39.59 N	91.59 W
Little Falls, U.S.	210	43.02 N	74.51 W
Little Falls, Mn., U.S.	198	45.58 N	94.21 W
Little Falls, N.J., U.S.	276	40.53 N	74.13 W
Little Falls, Pa., U.S.	279b	40.51 N	79.40 W
Little Farms	218	40.55 N	80.13 W
Little Ferry	276	40.51 N	74.02 W
Little Flatrock ≃	218	39.26 N	85.33 W
Littlefork	198	48.24 N	93.33 W
Little Fork ≃	198	48.31 N	93.35 W
Littleham	260	50.47 N	3.15 W
Little Genesee	214	42.00 N	78.13 W
Little Goose ≃	202	44.25 N	106.48 W
Little Gunpowder Falls ≃	208	39.23 N	76.22 W
Littlehampton	42	50.48 N	0.33 W
Little Hawk Creek ≃	198	44.29 N	94.27 W
Little Hawk Lake ◙	212	45.11 N	78.42 W
Little Hope	214	40.05 N	79.49 W
Little Hulton	262	53.32 N	2.25 W
Little Humboldt ≃	204	41.00 N	117.43 W
Little Humboldt, North Fork ≃	226	41.24 N	117.10 W
Little Humboldt, South Fork ≃	226	41.04 N	117.00 W
Little Hurricane Creek ≃	192	31.23 N	82.19 W
Little Inagua I	238	21.30 N	73.00 W
Little Indian Creek ≃, Il., U.S.	216	41.31 N	88.46 W
Little Island Pond ◙	283	42.43 N	71.17 W
Little Jim ≃	216	41.34 N	87.06 W
Little Juniata ≃	208	40.35 N	78.03 W
Little Kanawha ≃	188	39.16 N	81.34 W
Little Kanawha, West Fork ≃	188	38.57 N	81.16 W
Little Karroo (Klein Karroo) ☲	158	33.45 S	21.30 E
Little Kentucky ≃	218	38.41 N	85.12 W
Little Koniuji Island I	180	55.01 N	159.26 W
Little Lake ◙, On., Can.	212	44.26 N	79.40 W

Symbol	English	Deutsch	Español	Français	Português
≃	River	Fluß	Río	Rivière	Rio
☒	Canal	Kanal	Canal	Canal	Canal
ᶫ	Waterfall, Rapids	Wasserfall, Stromschnellen	Cascada, Rápidos	Chute d'eau, Rapides	Cascata, Rápidos
☒	Strait	Meerestraße	Estrecho	Détroit	Estreito
c	Bay, Gulf	Bucht, Golf	Bahía, Golfo	Baie, Golfe	Baía, Golfo
◙	Lake, Lakes	See, Seen	Lago, Lagos	Lac, Lacs	Lago, Lagos
☲	Swamp	Sumpf	Pantano	Marais	Pântano
☒	Ice Features, Glacier	Eis- und Gletscherformen	Accidentes Glaciales	Formes glaciaires	Accidentes glaciares
⌁	Other Hydrographic Features	Andere Hydrographische Objekte	Otros Elementos Hidrográficos	Autres données hydrographiques	Outros acidentes hidrográficos
✛	Submarine Features	Untermeerische Objekte	Accidentes Submarinos	Formes de relief sous-marin	Acidentes submarinos
◻	Political Unit	Politische Einheit	Unidad Política	Entité politique	Unidade política
☩	Cultural Institution	Kulturelle Institution	Institución Cultural	Institution culturelle	Instituição cultural
⊥	Historical Site	Historische Stätte	Sitio Histórico	Site historique	Sítio histórico
✦	Recreational Site	Erholungs- und Ferienort	Sitio de Recreo	Centre de loisirs	Area de Lazer
⍝	Airport	Flughafen	Aeropuerto	Aéroport	Aeroporto
◂	Military Installation	Militäranlage	Instalación Militar	Installation militaire	Instalação militar
⚹	Miscellaneous	Verschiedenes	Misceláneo	Divers	Diversos

ENGLISH — Name · Page · Lat.°′ · Long.°′
DEUTSCH — Name · Seite · Breite°′ · Länge°′ E = Ost

Name	Page	Lat.°′	Long.°′
Little Lake ⊜, La., U.S.	194	29.30 N	90.10 W
Little Laramie ≃	200	41.28 N	105.44 W
Little Laver	260	51.46 N	0.14 E
Little Leigh	262	53.17 N	2.35 W
Little Lever	262	53.34 N	2.22 W
Little Limestone Lake ⊜	184	53.46 N	99.18 W
Little London	241q	18.15 N	78.13 W
Little Lost ≃	202	43.46 N	112.58 W
Little Lun ≃	116	6.02 N	125.17 E
Little Mahoning Creek ≃	214	40.49 N	79.00 W
Little Maitland ≃	212	43.52 N	81.18 W
Little Manatee ≃	220	27.42 N	82.28 W
Little Manatee, South Fork ≃	220	27.39 N	82.18 W
Little Manistee ≃	190	44.15 N	86.19 W
Little Manitou Lake ⊜	184	51.45 N	105.30 W
Little Marco Pass ⊂	220	26.01 N	81.46 W
Little Marsh	210	41.53 N	77.24 W
Little Meadows	210	41.59 N	76.08 W
Little Mecatina ≃	176	50.28 N	59.35 W
Little Medicine Bow ≃	200	41.58 N	106.18 W
Little Mexico	196	30.57 N	102.52 W
Little Miami ≃	218	39.05 N	84.26 W
Little Miami, East Fork ≃	218	39.09 N	84.18 W
Little Miami, North Fork ≃	218	39.48 N	83.47 W
Littlemill	46	57.32 N	3.49 W
Little Mississippi ≃	212	45.17 N	77.35 W
Little Missouri ≃, U.S.	198	47.30 N	102.25 W
Little Missouri ≃, Ar., U.S.	194	33.49 N	92.54 W
Little Mountain ∧	208	40.47 N	76.40 W
Little Muddy ≃, Il., U.S.	194	37.50 N	89.11 W
Little Muddy ≃, N.D., U.S.	198	48.12 N	103.36 W
Little Mulberry Creek ≃	194	32.26 N	86.51 W
Little Naches ≃	224	46.58 N	121.08 W
Little Nahant	283	42.25 N	70.56 W
Little Namaqualand □ 9	156	29.00 S	17.00 E
Little Neck	283	42.42 N	70.48 W
Little Neck ◆ 8	276	40.46 N	73.44 W
Little Neck Bay ⊂	276	40.47 N	73.46 W
Little Nemaha ≃	198	40.19 N	95.40 W
Little Neshaminy Creek ≃	285	40.15 N	75.02 W
Little Niangua ≃	194	38.04 N	92.54 W
Little Nicobar I	110	7.20 N	93.40 E
Little Ohoopee ≃	192	32.27 N	82.24 W
Little Osage ≃	194	38.02 N	94.14 W
Little Otter Creek ≃	212	42.44 N	80.51 W
Little Ouse ≃	42	52.30 N	0.22 E
Little Panoche Creek ≃	226	36.50 N	120.42 W
Little Patuxent ≃	284b	39.11 N	76.52 W
Little Paxton	42	52.15 N	0.15 W
Little Peconic Bay ⊂	207	40.59 N	72.24 W
Little Pee Dee ≃	192	33.42 N	79.11 W
Little Pic ≃	190	48.48 N	86.37 W
Little Pine and Lucky Man Indian Reserve ◆ 4	184	52.56 N	109.05 W
Little Pine Creek ≃, Pa., U.S.	210	41.18 N	77.22 W
Little Pine Creek ≃, Pa., U.S.	279b	40.31 N	79.57 W
Little Pine Island I	220	26.36 N	82.05 W
Little Pine Key I	220	24.44 N	81.19 W
Little Pine State Park ♠	210	41.22 N	77.20 W
Little Pipe Creek ≃	208	39.36 N	77.16 W
Little Platte ≃	194	39.24 N	94.41 W
Little Plum Creek ≃	279b	40.30 N	79.51 W
Little Popo Agie ≃	202	42.54 N	108.35 W
Little Porcupine Creek ≃, Mt., U.S.	202	46.18 N	106.34 W
Little Porcupine Creek ≃, Mt., U.S.	202	48.02 N	106.04 W
Littleport	42	52.28 N	0.19 E
Little Portage Creek ≃	216	42.00 N	85.27 W
Little Powder ≃	198	45.28 N	105.20 W
Little Pucketa Creek ≃	279b	40.33 N	79.45 W
Little Quill Lake ⊜	184	51.55 N	104.05 W
Little Rann of Kachchh ≚	120	23.25 N	71.15 E
Little Red ≃	194	35.11 N	91.27 W
Little Red, Middle Fork ≃	194	35.37 N	92.11 W
Little Red Deer ≃	182	52.04 N	114.09 W
Little Red River Indian Reserve ◆ 4	184	53.30 N	105.58 W
Little Redstone Lake ⊜	212	45.13 N	78.34 W
Little River, Austl.	169	37.58 S	144.30 E
Little River, N.Z.	172	43.46 S	172.47 E
Little River, Ks., U.S.	198	38.23 N	98.00 W
Little River, Tx., U.S.	222	30.59 N	97.22 W
Little Rock, Ar., U.S.	194	34.44 N	92.17 W
Littlerock, Ca., U.S.	228	34.31 N	117.59 W
Little Rock, Il., U.S.	216	41.43 N	88.34 W
Little Rock, Ia., U.S.	198	43.26 N	95.52 W
Littlerock, Wa., U.S.	224	46.54 N	123.01 W
Little Rock ≃	198	43.16 N	96.15 W
Little Rock Air Force Base ■	194	34.55 N	92.10 W
Little Rock Creek ≃	228	34.28 N	118.01 W
Little Rock Wash V	228	34.42 N	118.02 W
Little Rocky Mountains ⩘	202	47.50 N	108.10 W
Little Rouge Creek ≃	212	43.48 N	79.08 W
Little Ruaha ≃	154	7.17 S	35.28 E
Little Sable Point >	190	43.38 N	86.32 W
Little Sac ≃	194	37.39 N	93.46 W
Little Sachigo Lake ⊜	184	54.09 N	92.11 W
Little Saint Bernard Pass → Petit-Saint-Bernard, Col du)(	62	45.41 N	6.53 E
Little Salkehatchie ≃	192	32.37 N	80.53 W
Little Salmon ≃, Id., U.S.	202	45.25 N	116.19 W
Little Salmon ≃, N.Y., U.S.	212	43.32 N	76.16 W
Little Salmon, North Branch ≃	212	43.24 N	76.09 W
Little Salmon, South Branch ≃	212	43.24 N	76.09 W
Little Salmon Lake ⊜	180	62.12 N	134.45 W
Little Salt Lake ⊜	200	37.55 N	112.53 W
Little Sandy ≃	188	38.35 N	82.51 W
Little Sandy, East Fork ≃	188	38.30 N	82.50 W
Little Sandy Creek ≃	200	42.06 N	109.27 W
Little Sandy Desert ◆ 2	162	24.20 S	120.50 E
Little Saskatchewan ≃	184	49.52 N	100.07 W
Little Scarcies ≃	150	8.51 N	13.09 W
Little Scioto ≃, Oh., U.S.	214	40.31 N	83.12 W
Little Scioto ≃, Oh., U.S.	218	38.46 N	82.53 W
Little Sewickley Creek ≃, Pa., U.S.	279b	40.15 N	79.45 W
Little Sewickley Creek ≃, Pa., U.S.	279b	40.33 N	80.12 W
Little Silver	276	40.20 N	74.02 W
Little Sioux ≃	198	41.49 N	96.04 W
Little Sioux, West Fork ≃	198	42.04 N	96.00 W
Little Sitkin Island I	181a	51.55 N	178.30 E
Little Smoky ≃	182	55.42 N	117.38 W
Little Snake ≃	200	40.27 N	108.26 W
Little Sodus Bay ⊂	210	43.20 N	76.43 W
Little Southwest Miramichi ≃	186	46.57 N	65.50 W
Little Stanney	262	53.15 N	2.53 W
Little Stony Creek ≃	226	39.20 N	122.31 W
Little Stour ≃	42	51.19 N	1.15 E
Littlestown	208	39.44 N	77.05 W
Little Stukeley	42	52.21 N	0.13 W
Little Sugarloaf ∧ 2	274b	37.41 S	145.19 E
Little Sur ≃	226	36.20 N	121.54 W
Little Sutton	262	53.17 N	2.57 W
Little Swatara Creek ≃	208	40.24 N	76.29 W
Little Tallapoosa ≃	192	33.18 N	85.34 W
Little Tanaga Island I	180	51.48 N	176.10 W
Little Tennessee ≃	192	35.47 N	84.15 W
Little Thurrock	260	51.28 N	0.21 E
Little Timber Creek ≃	285	39.53 N	75.08 W
Little Tinicum Island I	285	39.51 N	75.17 W
Little Tobago I, Br. Vir. Is.	240m	18.26 N	64.51 W
Little Tobago I, Trin.	241r	11.18 N	60.30 W
Little Toby Creek ≃	214	41.22 N	78.49 W
Littleton, Eng., U.K.	260	51.24 N	0.28 W
Littleton, Co., U.S.	200	39.36 N	105.00 W
Littleton, Ma., U.S.	207	42.32 N	71.30 W
Littleton, N.H., U.S.	188	44.18 N	71.46 W
Littleton, N.C., U.S.	192	36.26 N	77.54 W
Littleton, W.V., U.S.	188	39.41 N	80.31 W
Little Traverse Bay ⊂	190	45.24 N	85.03 W
Little Truckee ≃	226	39.25 N	120.05 W
Little Turtle ≃	184	48.46 N	92.36 W
Little Turtle State Recreation Area ♠	216	40.50 N	85.26 W
Little Valley	210	42.15 N	78.48 W
Little Vermilion ≃	216	41.20 N	89.05 W
Little Vermilion Lake ⊜	184	51.16 N	93.50 W
Little Vienna Estates	284c	38.54 N	77.18 W
Little Wabash ≃	194	37.54 N	88.05 W
Little Walsingham	42	52.54 N	0.51 E
Little Waltham	260	51.47 N	0.29 E
Little Warley	260	51.35 N	0.19 E
Little Washita ≃	196	34.58 N	97.51 W
Little Wellington, Isla I	254	48.30 S	74.45 W
Little White ≃	198	43.44 N	100.40 W
Little White Mountain ∧	182	49.42 N	119.20 W
Little White Salmon ≃	224	45.43 N	121.38 W
Little Wichita ≃	196	33.54 N	97.59 W
Little Wichita, East Fork ≃	196	33.52 N	98.07 W
Little Wind ≃	202	42.57 N	108.29 W
Little Wind, North Fork ≃	202	43.01 N	108.53 W
Little Wind, South Fork ≃	202	43.01 N	108.53 W
Little Wolf ≃	190	44.23 N	88.48 W
Little Wood ≃	202	42.57 N	114.21 W
Little York, In., U.S.	218	38.42 N	85.54 W
Little York, N.Y., U.S.	210	42.42 N	76.10 W
Little Zab (Zāb-e Kūchek) (Az-Zāb aṣ-Ṣaghīr) ≃	128	35.12 N	43.25 E
Littoral □ 4	152	4.13 N	10.25 E
Litunga	152	13.17 S	16.43 E
Litvínov	54	50.37 N	13.36 E
Litvinovka	83	49.18 N	39.27 E
Litvinovo	76	59.34 N	38.01 E
Litvinskoje	86	50.42 N	72.42 E
Litzmannstadt → Łódź	30	51.46 N	19.30 E
Liu ≃, Zhg.	98	41.48 N	122.43 E
Liu ≃, Zhg.	98	42.45 N	126.04 E
Liu ≃, Zhg.	98	40.38 N	118.09 E
Liu ≃, Zhg.	102	23.52 N	109.45 E
Liu ≃, Zhg.	105	40.38 N	118.09 E
Liu ≃, Zhg.	106	31.31 N	121.18 E
Liuanzhuang	105	39.14 N	117.11 E
Liuba	102	33.32 N	107.07 E
Liubotong	100	31.26 N	116.00 E
Liucao	106	31.07 N	121.41 E
Liuchen	102	23.09 N	110.29 E
Liucheng, Zhg.	100	24.03 N	115.08 E
Liucheng, Zhg.	100	28.36 N	119.34 E
Liucheng, Zhg.	102	24.32 N	109.21 E
Liuchengba	102	27.27 N	102.53 E
Liuch'iu Hsü I	100	22.21 N	120.22 E
Liuchow → Liuzhou	102	24.19 N	109.24 E
Liucun	106	30.44 N	119.23 E
Liucura	252	38.39 S	71.05 W
Liudaogou	98	41.34 N	127.12 E
Liudaohe	105	40.39 N	116.12 E
Liudongqiao	106	31.03 N	119.32 E
Liudu	100	26.44 N	119.33 E
Liuduo	100	34.01 N	120.17 E
Liuduzhuang	105	39.27 N	117.50 E
Liuerbao	104	41.13 N	122.55 E
Liufang	100	27.56 N	116.22 E
Liufangling	100	30.27 N	114.27 E
Liufentzu	269d	24.57 N	121.35 E
Liugezhuang, Zhg.	98	38.33 N	116.30 E
Liugezhuang, Zhg.	105	40.03 N	118.16 E
Liugou	105	40.57 N	118.18 E
Liugu ≃	98	40.22 N	120.26 E
Liuguan	100	29.56 N	113.08 E
Liuguantun	104	41.20 N	121.21 E
Liuhang	106	31.21 N	121.22 E
Liuhe, Zhg.	98	42.15 N	125.43 E
Liuhe, Zhg.	100	33.20 N	112.48 E
Liuhe, Zhg.	100	30.46 N	113.12 E
Liuhe, Zhg.	100	32.22 N	118.49 E
Liuhe, Zhg.	100	30.20 N	115.36 E
Liuhe, Zhg.	105	39.31 N	118.17 E
Liuhe, Zhg.	106	31.30 N	121.15 E
Liuhegou	104	41.56 N	122.44 E
Liuheita	104	42.09 N	123.56 E
Liuhejie	102	24.26 N	101.35 E
Liuhekou	105	40.39 N	118.09 E
Liuheng Dao I	100	29.43 N	122.08 E
Liuhuang	100	23.58 N	116.28 E
Liuhudang	104	42.31 N	122.22 E
Liujia	102	24.54 N	107.49 E
Liujiachang	107	29.46 N	103.49 E
Liujiachuan	105	40.07 N	114.47 E
Liujiadai	106	31.57 N	120.23 E
Liujiadian	89	50.07 N	124.17 E
Liujiadu	106	32.15 N	120.33 E
Liujiafen	105	39.58 N	115.47 E
Liujiagangzi	104	41.28 N	122.33 E
Liujiagou	98	37.47 N	120.53 E
Liujiahe, Zhg.	100	32.06 N	113.21 E
Liujiahe, Zhg.	104	40.40 N	123.58 E
Liujiang	98	40.04 N	119.34 E
Liujiashan	105	40.14 N	114.49 E
Liujiatun, Zhg.	104	41.52 N	122.44 E
Liujiatun, Zhg.	104	41.51 N	122.05 E
Liujiatun, Zhg.	104	42.08 N	122.44 E
Liujiawopeng	104	42.16 N	123.01 E
Liujiazhai	269b	31.21 N	121.27 E
Liujiazhen	106	32.04 N	121.30 E
Liujiazi, Zhg.	98	41.00 N	120.13 E
Liujiazi, Zhg.	104	42.36 N	122.15 E
Liujiazi, Zhg.	104	41.48 N	123.47 E
Liujingcun	105	39.27 N	115.26 E
Liujisu	105	40.01 N	117.13 E
Liukeshu	86	44.59 N	90.12 E
Liuku	102	25.48 N	98.52 E
Liuli	154	11.05 S	34.38 E
Liulicun	271a	39.56 N	116.28 E
Liulidian	106	31.31 N	119.17 E
Liuligou	104	41.24 N	121.29 E
Liulihezhen	105	39.36 N	116.01 E
Liulin	100	31.34 N	113.14 E
Liuliwei	100	24.20 N	114.03 E
Liulongtai	104	41.32 N	120.56 E
Liumachang	107	29.51 N	104.54 E
Liumaogou	89	48.12 N	127.13 E
Liupangtun	104	41.36 N	123.28 E
Liupan Shan ⩘	102	35.40 N	106.40 E
Liuqianhutun	104	42.01 N	123.41 E
Liuqiao	106	32.11 N	120.51 E
Liuquan, Zhg.	98	34.27 N	117.20 E
Liuquan, Zhg.	105	39.22 N	116.18 E
Liurenba	100	29.57 N	114.49 E
Liushi, Zhg.	98	38.33 N	115.44 E
Liushi, Zhg.	100	28.03 N	120.51 E
Liushilipu	100	32.45 N	115.58 E
Liushi Shan ∧	120	36.15 N	82.05 E
Liushouying	98	39.48 N	119.19 E
Liushudian	98	35.54 N	119.30 E
Liushudixia	104	42.26 N	121.14 E
Liushui	89	44.17 N	124.15 E
Liushuigou	100	31.34 N	112.27 E
Liushuquan	105	39.21 N	118.06 E
Liusiqiao	100	29.47 N	116.21 E
Liusong	105	39.40 N	117.08 E
Liuta	98	35.52 N	115.18 E
Liutai	98	41.20 N	113.43 E
Liutaizi	104	41.46 N	122.39 E
Liutang	102	24.58 N	110.21 E
Liutiaozhaicun	104	41.29 N	123.12 E
Liutuan	98	36.56 N	119.22 E
Liutuhutun	104	40.44 N	120.32 E
Liuwanglou	98	34.48 N	116.28 E
Liuwa Plain ≚	152	14.30 S	22.40 E
Liuwa Plain National Park ♠	152	14.30 S	22.40 E
Liuwei	106	32.16 N	119.28 E
Liuwudian	100	24.36 N	118.13 E
Liuxi ≃	100	23.22 N	112.54 E
Liuxia	106	30.15 N	120.03 E
Liuyang	100	28.09 N	113.38 E
Liuyang ≃	100	28.13 N	112.58 E
Liuyuan	98	36.10 N	114.34 E
Liuyuankou	98	34.54 N	114.20 E
Liuzhai	102	25.15 N	107.20 E
Liuzhou	102	24.19 N	109.24 E
Liuzhuang	100	33.10 N	120.19 E
Livada	38	47.52 N	23.07 E
Livadija	89	42.50 N	132.39 E
Livanátai	38	38.42 N	23.03 E
Līvāni	76	56.22 N	26.11 E
Livanjsko Polje ≚	36	43.55 N	16.45 E
Livanovka	86	52.06 N	61.59 E
Livarot	50	49.01 N	0.09 E
Lively, On., Can.	190	46.26 N	81.09 W
Lively, Va., U.S.	208	37.47 N	76.31 W
Lively Island I	254	52.02 S	58.30 W
Livengood	180	65.32 N	148.33 W
Livenka, Ross.	78	50.26 N	38.18 E
Livenka, Ross.	78	50.44 N	40.14 E
Livenza ≃	64	45.35 N	12.51 E
Live Oak, Ca., U.S.	226	39.16 N	121.39 W
Live Oak, Fl., U.S.	192	30.17 N	82.59 W
Live Oak Creek ≃	196	30.39 N	101.42 W
Liverdun	56	48.45 N	6.03 E
Liverdy-en-Brie	261	48.42 N	2.47 E
Livergnano	66	44.19 N	11.21 E
Liveringa	162	18.03 S	124.10 E
Livermore, Ca., U.S.	226	37.40 N	121.46 W
Livermore, Ia., U.S.	190	42.52 N	94.11 W
Livermore, Ky., U.S.	194	37.29 N	87.07 W
Livermore, Mount ∧	196	30.38 N	104.10 W
Livermore Falls	188	44.28 N	70.11 W
Liverpool, Austl.	170	33.54 S	150.56 E
Liverpool, N.S., Can.	186	44.02 N	64.43 W
Liverpool, Eng., U.K.	44	53.25 N	2.55 W
Liverpool, Eng., U.K.	262	53.25 N	2.55 W
Liverpool, In., U.S.	216	41.34 N	87.18 W
Liverpool, N.Y., U.S.	210	43.06 N	76.13 W
Liverpool, Pa., U.S.	208	40.34 N	76.59 W
Liverpool, Tx., U.S.	222	29.18 N	95.17 W
Liverpool □ 8	262	53.25 N	2.55 W
Liverpool ≃	164	12.02 S	134.13 E
Liverpool (Speke) Airport ⊠	44	53.21 N	2.52 W
Liverpool, Cape >	176	73.38 N	78.06 W
Liverpool, University of ʋ 2	262	53.24 N	2.58 W
Liverpool Bay ⊂, N.T., Can.	180	69.45 N	130.00 W
Liverpool Bay ⊂, N.S., Can.	186	44.02 N	64.41 W
Liverpool Bay ⊂, Eng., U.K.	44	53.30 N	3.16 W
Liverpool Football Ground ♠	262	53.26 N	2.57 W
Liverpool Heights	210	43.07 N	76.13 W
Liverpool Range ⩘	166	31.40 S	150.30 E
Livet-et-Gavet	62	45.06 N	5.56 E
Livigno	64	46.32 N	10.04 E
Livilliers	261	49.06 N	2.06 E
Lívingston, Guat.	236	15.50 N	88.45 W
Livingston, Scot., U.K.	46	55.53 N	3.32 W
Livingston, Al., U.S.	194	32.35 N	88.11 W
Livingston, Ca., U.S.	226	37.23 N	120.43 W
Livingston, Il., U.S.	194	38.58 N	89.45 W
Livingston, Ky., U.S.	192	37.17 N	84.12 W
Livingston, La., U.S.	194	30.30 N	90.44 W
Livingston, Mt., U.S.	202	45.39 N	110.33 W
Livingston, N.J., U.S.	210	40.47 N	74.18 W
Livingston, N.Y., U.S.	210	42.09 N	73.47 W
Livingston, Tn., U.S.	194	36.23 N	85.19 W
Livingston, Tx., U.S.	222	30.42 N	94.55 W
Livingston, Wi., U.S.	190	42.54 N	90.25 W
Livingston □ 6, Il., U.S.	216	40.53 N	88.38 W
Livingston □ 6, Mi., U.S.	216	42.38 N	83.50 W
Livingston □ 6, N.Y., U.S.	210	42.48 N	77.49 W
Livingstone	154	17.50 S	25.53 E
Livingstone, Chutes de (Livingstone Falls) ⌊	152	4.50 S	14.30 E
Livingstone, Lake ⊜ 1	222	30.50 N	95.30 W
Livingstone Falls → Livingstone, Chutes de ⌊	152	4.50 S	14.30 E
Livingstone Lake ⊜	212	45.22 N	78.43 W
Livingstonia	154	10.36 S	34.07 E
Livingston Island I	9	62.35 S	60.30 W
Livingston Mall ◆ 9	276	40.47 N	74.21 W
Livingston Manor	210	41.54 N	74.49 W
Livno	36	43.50 N	17.01 E
Livny	76	52.25 N	37.37 E
Livojoki ≃	26	65.24 N	26.48 E
Livonia, In., U.S.	218	38.34 N	86.17 W
Livonia, La., U.S.	194	30.33 N	91.33 W
Livonia, Mi., U.S.	216	42.22 N	83.21 W
Livonia, N.Y., U.S.	210	42.49 N	77.40 W
Livonia Center	210	42.49 N	77.38 W
Livonia Mall ◆ 9	281	42.26 N	83.20 W
Livorno (Leghorn)	66	43.33 N	10.19 E
Livorno □ 4	66	43.14 N	10.35 E
Livorno Ferraris	62	45.17 N	8.05 E
Livourne → Livorno	66	43.33 N	10.19 E
Livramento → Santana do Livramento	252	30.53 S	55.31 W
Livramento do Brumado	255	13.39 S	41.50 W
Livron-sur-Drôme	62	44.46 N	4.51 E
Livry-Gargan	261	48.56 N	2.33 E
Livry-sur-Seine	261	48.31 N	2.41 E
Liwa	112	5.04 S	104.06 E
Liwale	154	9.46 S	37.56 E
Liwale Chini	154	9.41 S	38.01 E
Liwan	154	4.54 N	35.40 E
Liwonde	154	14.52 S	35.28 E
Liwonde National Park ♠	154	14.50 S	35.20 E
Liwung ≃	115a	6.08 S	106.49 E
Lixi, Zhg.	100	29.15 N	114.46 E
Lixi, Zhg.	100	27.39 N	116.19 E
Lixian, Zhg.	98	38.29 N	115.34 E
Lixian, Zhg.	102	34.11 N	105.02 E
Lixian, Zhg.	102	29.30 N	111.37 E
Lixian, Zhg.	105	39.33 N	116.26 E
Lixian → Black ≃	110	21.15 N	105.20 E
Lixin, Zhg.	100	33.06 N	116.08 E
Lixin, Zhg.	100	26.52 N	116.42 E
Lixing	100	33.28 N	115.28 E
Lixingzhuang	105	39.25 N	117.56 E
Lixoúrion	38	38.12 N	20.26 E
Lixus ⊥	34	35.16 N	6.13 W
Liyang, Zhg.	98	37.28 N	113.37 E
Liyang, Zhg.	106	31.26 N	119.29 E
Liyuanbao	100	25.16 N	112.55 E
Liyujiang	100	25.57 N	113.15 E
Lizard	42	49.58 N	5.12 W
Lizarda	250	9.36 S	46.41 W
Lizard Head Peak ∧	200	42.47 N	109.11 W
Lizard Island I	164	14.40 S	145.28 E
Lizard Point >	42	49.56 N	5.13 W
Lizard Point Indian Reserve ◆ 4	184	50.40 N	100.57 W
Lize	107	30.08 N	106.11 E
Lizhai	106	31.34 N	121.45 E
Lizhou	102	28.08 N	102.10 E
Lizhu	100	29.56 N	120.30 E
Lizhuang, Zhg.	100	34.24 N	116.30 E
Lizhuang, Zhg.	107	28.47 N	104.46 E
Lizhuangqiao	106	31.48 N	119.37 E
Lizino	83	49.33 N	38.51 E
Lizinovka	78	50.08 N	39.28 E
Liziwei	107	30.19 N	106.39 E
Lizy-sur-Ourcq	50	49.01 N	3.02 E
Lizzana	64	45.51 N	11.03 E
Lizzanello	68	40.18 N	18.13 E
Lizzano	68	40.23 N	17.27 E
Lizzano in Belvedere	64	44.10 N	10.53 E
Ljalovo	82	56.03 N	37.14 E
Ljan	26	59.51 N	10.48 E
Ljubelj (Loiblpass))(	61	46.26 N	14.16 E
Ljubija	36	44.56 N	16.37 E
Ljubimec	38	41.50 N	26.05 E
Ljubinje	38	42.57 N	18.05 E
Ljubljana	36	46.03 N	14.31 E
Ljubovija	38	44.11 N	19.22 E
Ljubuški	36	43.12 N	17.33 E
Ljugarn	26	57.19 N	18.42 E
Ljunga	40	58.31 N	16.21 E
Ljungan ≃	26	62.19 N	17.23 E
Ljungaverk	26	62.29 N	16.03 E
Ljungby	26	56.50 N	13.56 E
Ljungbyhed	41	56.04 N	13.12 E
Ljungbyholm	26	56.38 N	16.10 E
Ljungdalen	26	62.51 N	12.47 E
Ljungsbro	26	58.31 N	15.30 E
Ljungskile	26	58.14 N	11.55 E
Ljusdal	26	61.50 N	16.05 E
Ljusfallshammar	40	58.47 N	15.29 E
Ljusnan ≃	26	61.12 N	17.08 E
Ljusnaren ⊜	40	59.51 N	14.56 E
Ljusne	26	61.13 N	17.08 E
Ljusterö I	40	59.31 N	18.37 E
Ljutomer	36	46.31 N	16.12 E
Llagas Creek ≃	226	36.58 N	121.31 W
Llaima, Volcán ∧ 1	252	38.43 S	71.43 W
Llamara, Salar de ≚	248	21.13 S	69.40 W
Llanaber	42	52.45 N	4.05 W
Llanaelhaearn	42	52.59 N	4.24 W
Llanarth	42	52.12 N	4.18 W
Llanarthney	42	51.52 N	4.09 W
Llanbedrog	42	52.52 N	4.29 W
Llanberis, Pass of V	44	53.06 N	4.04 W
Llanbister	42	52.21 N	3.18 W
Llanboidy	42	51.54 N	4.36 W
Llanbryde	46	57.37 N	3.13 W
Llanbrynmair	42	52.37 N	3.57 W
Llançà	34	42.22 N	3.09 E
Llancanelo, Laguna ⊜	252	35.35 S	69.09 W
Llandaff	42	51.30 N	3.14 W
Llandaff Cathedral ʋ 1	42	51.29 N	3.15 W
Llanddewi Brefi	42	52.10 N	3.57 W
Llandeilo	42	51.52 N	3.59 W
Llandilo	274a	33.43 S	150.45 E
Llandinam	42	52.29 N	3.26 W
Llandissilio	42	51.53 N	4.44 W
Llandovery	42	51.59 N	3.48 W
Llandrindod Wells	42	52.15 N	3.23 W
Llandudno	44	53.19 N	3.49 W
Llandybie	42	51.50 N	4.00 W
Llandysul	42	52.02 N	4.19 W
Llanelli	42	51.42 N	4.10 W
Llanelltyd	42	52.45 N	3.54 W
Llanelly	169	36.44 S	143.51 E
Llanenddwyn	42	52.49 N	4.06 W
Llanerchymedd	44	53.20 N	4.22 W
Llanes	34	43.25 N	4.45 W
Llanfaethlu	44	53.21 N	4.32 W
Llanfair-Caereinion	42	52.39 N	3.20 W
Llanfairfechan	44	53.15 N	3.58 W
Llanfairpwllgwyngyll	44	53.13 N	4.12 W
Llanfrynach	42	51.56 N	3.21 W
Llanfyllin	42	52.46 N	3.17 W
Llanfynydd	42	51.56 N	4.06 W
Llanfyrnach	42	51.57 N	4.35 W
Llangadog	42	51.56 N	3.53 W
Llangefni	44	53.16 N	4.18 W
Llangennech	42	51.41 N	4.04 W
Llangollen	42	52.58 N	3.10 W
Llangollen Estates	208	39.39 N	75.37 W
Llangranog	42	52.09 N	4.29 W
Llangurig	42	52.25 N	3.36 W
Llangwyryfon	42	52.19 N	4.03 W
Llangynog	42	52.50 N	3.25 W
Llanharan	42	51.33 N	3.25 W
Llanidloes	42	52.27 N	3.32 W
Llanilar	42	52.21 N	4.01 W
Llanllyfni	44	53.03 N	4.17 W
Llano	196	30.45 N	98.40 W
Llano ≃	196	30.35 N	98.25 W
Llano Colorado	204	31.38 N	115.55 W
Llanon	42	52.17 N	4.10 W
Llanos ≚	246	5.00 N	70.00 W
Llanpumsaint	42	51.56 N	4.18 W
Llanquihue	254	41.15 S	73.01 W
Llanquihue, Lago ⊜	254	41.08 S	72.48 W
Llanrhaeadr-ym-Mochnant	42	52.51 N	3.17 W
Llanrhidian	42	51.37 N	4.11 W
Llanrhystud	42	52.18 N	4.09 W
Llanrwst	44	53.08 N	3.48 W
Llansantffraid-ym-Mechain	42	52.47 N	3.08 W
Llansawel	42	52.01 N	4.00 W
Llantrisant	42	51.33 N	3.23 W
Llantwit Major	42	51.25 N	3.30 W
Llanuwchllyn	42	52.52 N	3.41 W
Llanwenog	42	52.06 N	4.12 W
Llanwrda	42	51.58 N	3.53 W
Llanwrtyd Wells	42	52.07 N	3.38 W
Llanybydder	42	52.04 N	4.09 W
Llata	248	9.25 S	76.47 W
Llavallol ◆ 8	288	34.48 S	58.28 W
Llay	44	53.06 N	2.59 W
Lleida	34	41.37 N	0.37 E
Lleida □ 4	34	42.00 N	1.10 E
Llentrisca, Cap >	34	38.51 N	1.14 E
Llera de Canales	234	23.19 N	99.01 W
Llerena	34	38.14 N	6.01 W
Lleulleu, Lago ⊜	252	38.09 S	73.20 W
Lleyn Peninsula > 1	42	52.54 N	4.30 W
Llica	248	19.52 S	68.16 W
Llico	252	34.46 S	72.05 W
Lliria	34	39.38 N	0.36 W
Llivia	32	42.28 N	1.59 E
Llobregat ≃	34	41.19 N	2.09 E
Llobregat, Delta del ≚ 2	266d	41.17 N	2.08 E
Llorente	116	11.25 N	125.33 E
Llorente ≃	116	11.25 N	125.33 E
Llorona, Punta >	236	8.39 N	83.45 W
Lloyd	218	38.37 N	82.51 W
Lloyd Harbor	210	40.54 N	73.27 W
Lloyd Harbor ⊂	276	40.55 N	73.27 W
Lloydminster	184	53.17 N	110.00 W
Lloyd Neck > 1	276	40.56 N	73.28 W
Lloyd Point >	210	40.57 N	73.29 W
Lloyds ≃	186	48.33 N	57.13 W
Llucena	34	40.08 N	0.17 W
Llucmajor	34	39.29 N	2.54 E
Llullaillaco, Volcán ∧ 1	252	24.43 S	68.33 W
Llusco	248	14.21 S	72.07 W
Lluta ≃	248	18.24 S	70.19 W
Llyn Brianne Reservoir ⊜ 1	42	52.08 N	3.45 W
Llyswen	42	52.02 N	3.17 W
Llys-y-frân Reservoir ⊜ 1	42	51.53 N	4.51 W
Lnáře	60	49.28 N	13.47 E
Lo (Panlong) ≃	110	21.18 N	105.25 E
Loa	200	38.24 N	111.38 W
Loa ≃, Chile	244	21.26 S	70.04 W
Loa ≃, Congo	273b	4.20 S	15.11 E
Loami	194	39.40 N	89.51 W
Loanda → Luanda, Ang.	152	8.48 S	13.14 E
Loanda, Bra.	255	22.54 S	53.10 W
Loanda, Gabon	152	0.55 S	9.00 E
Loande ≃	152	8.41 S	17.56 E
Loange (Luangue) ≃	152	4.17 S	20.02 E
Loango Buele	152	5.10 S	12.59 E
Loanhead	46	55.53 N	3.09 W
Loanja ≃	154	17.22 S	24.48 E
Loano	62	44.08 N	8.15 E
Loantaka Brook ≃	276	40.43 N	74.28 W
Lo Aranguiz	286e	33.23 S	70.40 W
Loay	116	9.36 N	124.01 E
Lob' ≃	82	56.29 N	35.51 E
Lobamba	158	26.27 S	31.12 E
Loban	24	65.44 N	45.25 E
Loban' ≃	80	56.58 N	51.12 E
Lobanovo	76	53.04 N	38.14 E
Lobanovskije Vyselki	82	54.18 N	38.58 E
Lo Barnechea	286e	33.21 S	70.31 W
Lobaski	80	54.38 N	45.09 E
Lobatos	234	22.49 N	103.24 W
Lobatse	156	25.11 S	25.40 E
Löbau	54	51.05 N	14.40 E
Lobau ≚	264b	48.10 N	16.32 E
Lobaye □ 5	152	4.00 N	18.30 E
Lobaye ≃	152	3.41 N	18.35 E
Lobbes	50	50.21 N	4.15 E
Lobbs Run ≃	279b	40.15 N	79.55 W
Lobdell Lake ⊜	216	42.48 N	83.48 W
Löbejün	54	51.38 N	11.53 E
Lobelville	194	35.46 N	87.47 W
Lo Benitez	286e	33.34 S	70.42 W
Lobenstein	54	50.26 N	11.38 E
Lobería	252	38.09 S	58.47 W
Lo Bernales	286e	33.34 S	70.34 W
Löberöd	41	55.47 N	13.30 E
Lobethal	168b	34.54 S	138.52 E
Łobez	30	53.39 N	15.36 E
Lobito	152	12.20 S	13.34 E
Lobitos	246	4.26 S	81.17 W
Lobitos Creek ≃	282	37.22 N	122.24 W
Lobkoviči	76	53.50 N	31.45 E
Lobn'a	82	56.01 N	37.30 E
Löbnitz, Dtsch.	54	51.35 N	12.28 E
Löbnitz, Dtsch.	54	54.17 N	12.43 E
Lobo, Indon.	164	3.45 S	134.05 E
Lobo, Pil.	116	13.39 N	121.13 E
Lobo ≃	150	6.02 N	6.47 W
Loboko	152	0.45 S	16.38 E
Lobos	258	35.11 S	59.06 W
Lobos, Cay I	238	22.24 N	77.32 W
Lobos, Isla I	232	27.20 N	110.36 W
Lobos, Isla de I, Esp.	148	28.45 N	13.49 W
Lobos, Isla de I, Méx.	234	21.27 N	97.13 W
Lobos, Laguna de ⊜	258	35.17 S	59.07 W
Lobos, Point >	226	37.47 N	122.31 W
Lobos, Punta >	248	21.01 S	70.11 W
Lobos de Afuera, Islas II	248	6.57 S	80.42 W
Lobos de Tierra, Isla I	248	6.27 S	80.52 W
Lo Boza	286e	33.23 S	70.46 W
Lobskoje	24	62.45 N	35.16 E
Lobstädt	54	51.08 N	12.29 E
Löbtau ◆ 8	54	51.03 N	13.42 E
Loburg	54	52.07 N	12.05 E
Lobva	86	59.12 N	60.30 E
Łobżenica	30	53.16 N	17.15 E
Locana	62	45.25 N	7.27 E
Locana, Val di V	62	45.25 N	7.27 E
Locarno	58	46.10 N	8.48 E
Lo Castillo, Aeropuerto ⊠	286e	33.23 S	70.36 W
Locate Triulzi	62	45.21 N	9.13 E
Loccum	52	52.27 N	9.08 E
Loceri	71	39.51 N	9.35 E
Loch	169	38.22 S	145.43 E
Lochaber ◆ 1	46	56.57 N	5.06 W
Lochailort	46	56.53 N	5.40 W
Lochaline	46	56.32 N	5.47 W
Locharbriggs	44	55.06 N	3.35 W
Lochar Water ≃	44	54.59 N	3.27 W
Lochboisdale	46	57.09 N	7.19 W
Lochcarron	46	57.24 N	5.30 W
Lochdon	46	56.26 N	5.41 W
Lochearn	284b	39.21 N	76.43 W
Lochearnhead	46	56.23 N	4.17 W
Lochem	52	52.09 N	6.25 E
Loches	50	47.08 N	1.00 E
Lochgair	46	56.03 N	5.20 W
Loch Garman → Wexford	48	52.20 N	6.27 W
Lochgelly	46	56.08 N	3.19 W
Lochgilphead	46	56.03 N	5.26 W
Lochgoilhead	46	56.10 N	4.54 W
Lochiel	168b	33.56 S	138.10 E
Lochindorb ⊜	46	57.24 N	3.43 W
Lochino	265b	55.42 N	37.19 E
Lochinvar National Park ♠	154	15.55 S	27.15 E
Lochinver	46	58.09 N	5.15 W
Lochmaben	44	55.08 N	3.27 W
Lochmaddy	46	57.36 N	7.11 W
Lochnagar ∧	46	56.57 N	3.16 W
Lochovice	60	49.51 N	13.59 E
Lochranza	46	55.42 N	5.18 W
Loch Raven Dam ◆ 6	284b	39.26 N	76.33 W
Loch Raven Reservoir ⊜ 1	208	39.27 N	76.34 W
Lochristi	50	51.06 N	3.50 E
Lochsa ≃	202	46.08 N	115.36 W
Loch Sheldrake	210	41.46 N	74.39 W
Loch Sport	166	38.03 S	147.36 E
Lochvica	78	50.22 N	33.16 E
Lochwinnoch	46	55.48 N	4.39 W
Lochy, Loch ⊜	46	56.57 N	4.53 W
Lock	166	33.34 S	135.46 E
Lock and Dam No. 20 ◆ 6, U.S.	219	40.09 N	91.30 W
Lock and Dam No. 21 ◆ 6, U.S.	219	39.54 N	91.26 W
Lock and Dam No. 24 ◆ 6, U.S.	219	39.22 N	90.55 W
Lock and Dam No. 25 ◆ 6, U.S.	219	39.01 N	90.41 W
Lock and Dam No. 22 ◆ 6, U.S.	219	39.39 N	91.16 W
Locke, Ca., U.S.	226	38.15 N	121.31 W
Locke, In., U.S.	216	41.28 N	86.00 W
Locke, N.Y., U.S.	210	42.39 N	76.25 W
Lockeford	226	38.10 N	121.09 W
Lockenhaus	61	47.24 N	16.25 E
Lockeport	186	43.42 N	65.07 W
Lockerbie	44	55.07 N	3.22 W
Lockesburg	194	33.58 N	94.10 W
Lockhart, Austl.	166	35.14 S	146.43 E
Lockhart, Fl., U.S.	220	28.37 N	81.26 W
Lockhart, Tx., U.S.	222	29.53 N	97.40 W
Lockhart River Aboriginal Reserve ◆ 4	164	13.00 S	143.15 E
Lock Haven	210	41.08 N	77.26 W
Lockheed Aircraft Corporation ʋ 3, Ca., U.S.	280	34.12 N	118.22 W
Lockheed Aircraft Corporation ʋ 3, Ca., U.S.	282	37.25 N	122.02 W
Lockington	216	40.12 N	84.13 W
Lock Mountain ∧	214	40.25 N	78.18 W
Lockney	196	34.07 N	101.26 W
Löcknitz	54	53.27 N	14.12 E
Löcknitz ≃, Dtsch.	54	53.07 N	11.16 E
Löcknitz ≃, Dtsch.	264a	52.25 N	13.49 E
Lockport, Mb., Can.	184	50.05 N	96.56 W
Lockport, Il., U.S.	216	41.35 N	88.03 W
Lockport, La., U.S.	194	29.39 N	90.32 W
Lockport, N.Y., U.S.	210	43.10 N	78.41 W
Lockport Lock ◆ 5	278	41.35 N	88.04 W
Locks Heath	42	50.52 N	1.15 W
Locksley Park	210	42.45 N	78.52 W
Lockvattnet ⊜	40	59.03 N	17.05 E
Lockview	279b	40.10 N	79.55 W
Lockwood, Ca., U.S.	226	35.56 N	121.05 W
Lockwood, Mo., U.S.	194	37.23 N	93.57 W
Lockwood Corners	214	41.00 N	81.34 W
Lockyer Creek ≃	171a	27.25 S	152.36 E
Locminé	28	47.53 N	2.50 W
Loc Ninh	110	11.51 N	106.36 E
Loco, Bayou ≃	222	31.28 N	94.44 W
Locon	50	50.34 N	2.40 E
Locorotondo	68	40.45 N	17.20 E
Locri	68	38.14 N	16.16 E
Locri Epizefiri ⊥	68	38.12 N	16.13 E
Locroja	248	12.41 S	74.26 W
Locsin	116	13.09 N	123.43 E
Locumba	248	17.36 S	70.46 W
Locumba ≃	248	17.54 S	70.57 W
Locust	208	40.18 N	73.59 W
Locust Creek ≃	194	39.40 N	93.17 W
Locust Fork ≃	194	33.33 N	87.11 W
Locust Grove, N.Y., U.S.	276	40.48 N	73.30 W
Locust Grove, Ok., U.S.	196	36.12 N	95.10 W
Locust Lake State Park ♠	208	40.46 N	76.08 W
Locust Point >	276	40.49 N	73.48 W
Locust Valley	210	40.53 N	73.36 W
Lod (Lydda)	132	31.58 N	34.54 E
Lod, Nemel-Te'ufa (Ben Gurion Airport) ⊠	132	31.59 N	34.53 E
Loda	216	40.31 N	88.04 W
Lodal Creek ≃	285	40.14 N	75.27 W
Löddeköpinge	41	55.46 N	13.01 E
Loddon	42	52.32 N	1.29 E
Loddon ≃, Austl.	166	35.32 S	143.52 E
Loddon ≃, Eng., U.K.	42	51.30 N	0.53 W
Lodè	71	40.35 N	9.32 E
Lodejnoje Pole	76	60.44 N	33.30 E
Lodenau	54	51.24 N	14.57 E
Löderburg	54	51.52 N	11.32 E
Lodève	32	43.43 N	3.19 E
Lodge Creek ≃	202	48.35 N	109.10 W
Lodge Grass	202	45.18 N	107.21 W
Lodgepole, Ab., Can.	182	53.06 N	115.19 W
Lodgepole, Ne., U.S.	198	41.08 N	102.38 W
Lodgepole Creek ≃	198	40.57 N	102.22 W
Lodhāsuli	126	22.19 N	87.03 E
Lodhrān	123	29.32 N	71.38 E
Lodi, It.	62	45.19 N	9.30 E
Lodi, Ca., U.S.	226	38.07 N	121.16 W
Lodi, N.J., U.S.	210	40.52 N	74.05 W
Lodi, N.Y., U.S.	210	42.36 N	76.49 W
Lodi, Oh., U.S.	214	41.02 N	82.00 W
Lodi, Wi., U.S.	190	43.18 N	89.31 W
Lodi Park ♠	272a	28.36 N	77.13 E
Lodi Vecchio	62	45.18 N	9.24 E
Lodja	152	3.29 S	23.26 E
Lodosa	34	42.25 N	2.05 W
Lodoyo	115a	8.10 S	112.13 E
Lodrone	64	45.50 N	10.32 E
Lods	58	47.03 N	6.15 E
Lodsch → Łódź	30	51.46 N	19.30 E
Lodwar	154	3.07 N	35.36 E
Łódź	30	51.46 N	19.30 E
Łódź □ 4	30	51.50 N	19.25 E
Loe Āgra	123	34.35 N	71.43 E
Loei	110	17.29 N	101.35 E
Loei ≃	110	17.51 N	101.37 E
Loen	26	61.52 N	6.52 E
Loenen	52	52.07 N	6.01 E
Loengo	154	4.45 S	26.27 E
Loeriesfontein	158	30.56 S	19.26 E
Lo Espejo	286e	33.32 S	70.43 W
Lo Espejo, Canal ≊	286e	33.32 S	70.43 W
Lofa ≃	150	6.36 N	11.08 W
Lofer	64	47.35 N	12.41 E
Löffingen	58	47.53 N	8.20 E
Lofoten II	24	68.30 N	15.00 E
Lofoten Basin ◆ 1	10	70.00 N	4.00 E
Lofthouse	44	53.44 N	1.29 W
Lofthus	26	60.20 N	6.40 E
Loftus, Austl.	274a	34.03 S	151.03 E
Loftus, Eng., U.K.	44	54.33 N	0.53 W
Lofty, Mount ∧, Austl.	168b	34.59 S	138.42 E
Lofty, Mount ∧, Austl.	274b	37.43 S	145.17 E
Log	80	49.29 N	43.52 E
Loga, Dtsch.	52	53.14 N	7.29 E
Loga, Niger	150	13.37 N	3.14 E
Logačovka	80	52.23 N	52.21 E
Logan, Ia., U.S.	198	41.38 N	95.47 W
Logan, Ks., U.S.	198	39.39 N	99.34 W
Logan, N.M., U.S.	196	35.22 N	103.25 W
Logan, Oh., U.S.	188	39.32 N	82.24 W
Logan, Ut., U.S.	200	41.44 N	111.50 W
Logan, W.V., U.S.	188	37.50 N	81.59 W
Logan □ 6, Il., U.S.	219	40.09 N	89.22 W
Logan □ 6, Oh., U.S.	216	40.22 N	83.46 W
Logan ◆ 8	285	40.02 N	75.09 W
Logan ≃, Austl.	171a	27.43 S	153.18 E
Logan ≃, Ab., Can.	182	55.09 N	111.42 W
Logan ≃, Ut., U.S.	200	41.44 N	111.57 W
Logan, Mount ∧, Yk., Can.	180	60.34 N	140.24 W
Logan, Mount ∧, Wa., U.S.	224	48.32 N	120.57 W
Logan Creek ≃, Ca., U.S.	226	39.22 N	122.06 W
Logan Creek ≃, Mo., U.S.	194	37.11 N	90.49 W
Logan Creek ≃, Ne., U.S.	198	41.37 N	96.29 W
Logandale	204	36.35 N	114.29 W
Logan International Airport ⊠	283	42.22 N	71.00 W
Logan Lake ⊜	212	44.52 N	78.59 W
Logan Martin Lake ⊜ 1	194	33.40 N	86.15 W
Logan Mountains ⩘	180	61.45 N	128.38 W
Logan Pass)(	202	48.42 N	113.43 W
Logansport, In., U.S.	216	40.45 N	86.21 W
Logansport, La., U.S.	194	31.58 N	93.59 W
Logan Square ◆ 8	278	41.56 N	87.42 W
Loganton	210	41.02 N	77.18 W
Loganville, Ga., U.S.	192	33.50 N	83.54 W
Loganville, Pa., U.S.	208	39.52 N	76.42 W
Logärden ⊜	40	60.37 N	16.00 E
Lögdeälven ≃	26	63.33 N	19.25 E
Logduz	76	60.00 N	44.41 E
Loge ≃, Ang.	152	10.12 S	17.00 E
Loge ≃, Ang.	152	7.49 S	13.06 E
Logia	164	2.55 S	151.27 E

Symbols in the index entries represent the broad categories identified in the key at the right. Symbols with superior numbers (⩘ 1) identify subcategories (see complete key on page *I · 1).*

Symbole im Register stellen die rechts im Schlüssel erklärten Kategorien dar. Symbole mit hochgestellten Ziffern (⩘ 1) bezeichnen Unterabteilungen einer Kategorie (vgl. vollständiger Schlüssel auf Seite *I · 1).*

Los símbolos incluídos en el texto del índice representan las grandes categorías identificadas con la clave a la derecha. Los símbolos con numeros en su parte superior (⩘ 1) identifican las subcategorías (véase la clave completa en la página *I · 1).*

Les symboles de l'index représentent les catégories indiquées dans la légende à droite. Les symboles suivis d'un indice (⩘ 1) représentent des sous-catégories (voir légende complète à la page *I · 1).*

Os símbolos incluídos no texto do índice representam as grandes categorias identificadas com a chave à direita. Os símbolos com números em sua parte superior (⩘ 1) identificam as subcategorias (veja-se a chave completa à página *I · 1).*

∧	Mountain	Berg	Montaña	Montagne	Montanha
⩘	Mountains	Gebirge	Montañas	Montagnes	Montanhas
)(	Pass	Paß	Paso	Col	Passo
V	Valley, Canyon	Tal, Cañon	Valle, Cañón	Vallée, Canyon	Vale, Canhão
≚	Plain	Ebene	Llano	Plaine	Planície
>	Cape	Kap	Cabo	Cap	Cabo
I	Island	Insel	Isla	Île	Ilha
II	Islands	Inseln	Islas	Îles	Ilhas
♠	Other Topographic Features	Andere Topographische Objekte	Otros Elementos Topográficos	Autres données topographiques	Outros acidentes topográficos

ESPAÑOL	FRANÇAIS	PORTUGUÊS
Nombre · Página · Lat.°´ · Long.°´ W=Oeste	Nom · Page · Lat.°´ · Long.°´ W=Ouest	Nome · Página · Lat.°´ · Long.°´ W=Oeste

Símbolo	English	Deutsch	Español	Français	Português
≈	River	Fluß	Río	Rivière	Rio
≈	Canal	Kanal	Canal	Canal	Canal
⇃	Waterfall, Rapids	Wasserfall, Stromschnellen	Cascada, Rápidos	Chute d'eau, Rapides	Cascata, Rápidos
⊔	Strait	Meeresstraße	Estrecho	Détroit	Estreito
⊂	Bay, Gulf	Bucht, Golf	Bahía, Golfo	Baie, Golfe	Baía, Golfo
∅	Lake, Lakes	See, Seen	Lago, Lagos	Lac, Lacs	Lago, Lagos
≃	Swamp	Sumpf	Pantano	Marais	Pântano
⊠	Ice Features, Glacier	Eis- und Gletscherformen	Accidentes Glaciales	Formes glaciaires	Accidentes glaciares
⇁	Other Hydrographic Features	Andere Hydrographische Objekte	Otros Elementos Hidrográficos	Autres données hydrographiques	Outros acidentes hidrográficos
←	Submarine Features	Untermeerische Objekte	Accidentes Submarinos	Formes de relief sous-marin	Acidentes submarinos
□	Political Unit	Politische Einheit	Unidad Política	Entité politique	Unidade política
∙	Cultural Institution	Kulturelle Institution	Institución Cultural	Institution culturelle	Instituição cultural
∙	Historical Site	Historische Stätte	Sitio Histórico	Site historique	Sítio histórico
◆	Recreational Site	Erholungs- und Ferienort	Sitio de Recreo	Centre de loisirs	Area de Lazer
≈	Airport	Flughafen	Aeropuerto	Aéroport	Aeroporto
∙	Military Installation	Militäranlage	Instalación Militar	Installation militaire	Instalação militar
≋	Miscellaneous	Verschiedenes	Misceláneo	Divers	Diversos

Name	Page	Lat.°′	Long.°′
Los Angeles, Ca., U.S.	280	34.03 N	118.14 W
Los Angeles □[6]	228	34.20 N	118.10 W
Los Angeles ≃	228	33.46 N	118.12 W
Los Angeles Aqueduct ≊[1]	204	35.22 N	118.05 W
Los Angeles Coliseum and Sports Arena ♦	280	34.01 N	118.17 W
Los Angeles Convention Center ◈	280	34.03 N	118.17 W
Los Angeles County Fairgrounds ♦	280	34.05 N	117.46 W
Los Angeles County Museum of Art ◈	280	34.05 N	118.22 W
Los Angeles Harbor c	280	33.42 N	118.16 W
Los Angeles International Airport ⊠	228	33.56 N	118.24 W
Los Antiguos	254	46.33 S	71.37 W
Losantville	218	40.01 N	85.10 W
Losap I[1]	14	6.54 N	152.44 E
Los Arabos	240p	22.44 N	80.43 W
Losarang	115a	6.24 S	108.10 E
Los Aros	234	22.46 N	102.57 W
Los Banos	226	37.03 N	120.50 W
Los Banos Creek ≃	226	37.20 N	120.57 W
Los Banos Creek, North Fork ≃	226	36.57 N	121.07 W
Los Banos Creek, South Fork ≃	226	36.57 N	121.07 W
Los Banos Reservoir ⊜[1]	226	36.59 N	120.57 W
Los Berros	252	31.57 S	68.39 W
Los Blancos	252	23.36 S	62.36 W
Los Bolones, Cerro ∧, Méx.	232	16.50 N	92.38 W
Los Bolones, Cerro ∧, Méx.	234	16.39 N	92.34 W
Los Cardales	258	34.20 S	58.59 W
Los Cerrillos, Arg.	252	31.57 S	65.28 W
Los Cerrillos, Ur.	258	34.37 S	56.22 W
Los Cerrillos, Aeropuerto ⊠	286e	33.30 S	70.43 W
Los Cerritos Center ⇾[9]	280	33.52 N	118.05 W
Los Chacos	248	14.33 S	62.11 W
Löschenrod	56	50.30 N	9.41 E
Los Chiles	236	11.02 N	84.43 W
Los Conquistadores	252	30.36 S	58.28 W
Los Coronados, Islas II	204	32.25 N	117.15 W
Los Coyotes Indian Reservation ⇾[4]	204	33.20 N	116.35 W
Los Cuatro Álamos	286e	33.32 S	70.44 W
Los Dos Caminos	286c	10.31 N	66.50 W
Los Ebanos	196	26.14 N	98.34 W
Loseley House ⊥	260	51.13 N	0.36 W
Los Esclavos ≃	236	13.50 N	90.20 W
Losevo	78	50.40 N	40.02 E
Los Flamencos, Laguna ⊜	258	35.36 S	58.42 W
Los Frailes, Picacho ∧	234	23.53 N	106.03 W
Los Frentones	252	26.25 S	61.25 W
Los Fresnos	196	26.04 N	97.29 W
Los Garzas	196	26.23 N	99.46 W
Los Gatos	226	37.13 N	121.58 W
Los Gatos Creek ≃, Ca., U.S.	226	36.13 N	120.08 W
Los Gatos Creek ≃, Ca., U.S.	226	37.20 N	121.54 W
Los Glaciares, Parque Nacional ♦	254	49.52 S	73.05 W
Los Guerras	196	26.25 N	99.05 W
Loshan → Leshan	107	29.34 N	103.45 E
Losheim	56	49.30 N	6.44 E
Los Hermanos, Islas II	246	11.45 N	64.25 W
Los Herreras	196	25.55 N	99.24 W
Los Huacales, Cerro ∧	234	22.19 N	101.34 W
Losi	273a	6.40 N	3.31 E
Łosice	30	52.14 N	22.43 E
Los Idolos, Parque Arquelógico de ⊥	246	1.55 N	76.10 W
Lošinj, Otok I	36	44.36 N	14.24 E
Losinoborskaja	86	58.27 N	89.28 E
Losino-Petrovskij	82	55.52 N	38.12 E
Losinovka	78	50.51 N	31.54 E
Los Jazmines, Presa ⊜[1]	286a	19.25 N	99.16 W
Los Juríes	252	28.28 S	62.06 W
Loškar'ovka	78	47.57 N	34.12 E
Loskopdam ⊜[1]	156	25.23 S	29.20 E
Loskop Dam Game Reserve ⇾[4]	156	25.23 S	29.20 E
Los Lagos	254	39.51 S	72.50 W
Los Lagos □[4]	254	41.45 S	73.00 W
Los Llanos	240m	18.03 N	66.24 W
Los Llanos [de Aridane]	148	28.39 N	17.54 W
Los López	196	26.15 N	99.05 W
Los Lunas	200	34.48 N	106.43 W
Los Manglares de Tumbes, Santuario Nacional ♦	246	2.25 S	80.20 W
Los Maribios, Cordillera ⋀	236	12.35 N	86.50 W
Los Médanos, Istmo de ⊥[3]	241s	11.35 N	69.45 W
Los Menucos	254	40.50 S	68.08 W
Los Micos, Laguna de c	236	15.45 N	87.36 W
Los'mino	76	55.04 N	34.24 E
Los Mochis	232	25.45 N	108.57 W
Los Molinos	204	40.01 N	122.05 W
Los Muermos	254	41.24 S	73.29 W
Los Naranjos	286c	10.27 N	66.48 W
Los Navalmorales	34	39.43 N	4.38 W
Lošnica	76	54.17 N	28.46 E
Los Nietos	280	33.58 N	118.04 W
Løsning	41	55.48 N	9.42 E
Los Nogales	196	26.16 N	99.43 W
Losolava	175f	14.11 S	167.34 E
Los Olmos Creek ≃, Tx., U.S.	196	27.20 N	97.40 W
Los Olmos Creek ≃, Tx., U.S.	196	26.21 N	98.48 W
Los Osos	226	35.19 N	120.50 W
Los Oyameles	234	19.43 N	97.32 W
Los Padillas	200	34.58 N	106.41 W
Los Palacios, Arg.	252	29.22 S	68.11 W
Los Palacios, Cuba	240p	22.35 N	83.15 W
Los Palacios y Villafranca	34	37.10 N	5.56 W
Los Perros, Arroyo ≃	288	34.37 S	58.46 W
Los Pinos ⇾[8]	286b	23.04 N	82.23 W
Los Pinos ≃	200	36.56 N	107.36 W
Los Placeres del Oro	234	18.13 N	100.54 W
Los Polvorines	288	34.30 S	58.41 W
Los Quillayes	286e	33.34 S	70.37 W
Los Quirquinchos	252	33.22 S	61.43 W
Los Rábanos	240m	18.11 N	66.50 W
Los Ramones	196	25.42 N	99.37 W
Los Remedios ≃	286a	19.31 N	99.05 W
Los Reyes de Salgado	234	19.35 N	102.29 W
Los Reyes la Paz	286a	19.21 N	98.58 W
Los Ríos □[4]	246	1.30 S	79.25 W
Los Rodríguez	232	27.11 N	101.21 W
Los Roques, Islas II	246	11.50 N	66.45 W
Lossa ≃	54	51.18 N	11.10 E
Los Santos □[4]	236	7.55 N	80.25 W
Los Santos de Maimona	34	38.27 N	6.23 W
Los Sauces	252	37.58 S	72.50 W
Lossburg	58	48.25 N	8.27 E
Lössel	263	51.21 N	7.39 E
Losser	52	52.15 N	7.00 E
Los Serranos	228	33.59 N	117.42 W
Lossie ≃	46	57.43 N	3.16 W
Lossiemouth	46	57.43 N	3.18 W
Lössnitz	54	50.37 N	12.43 E
Lost ≃, U.S.	202	41.56 N	121.30 W
Lost ≃, In., U.S.	194	38.33 N	86.49 W
Lost ≃, Mn., U.S.	198	47.51 N	96.02 W
Lost ≃, W.V., U.S.	188	39.05 N	78.36 W
Lostant	216	41.09 N	89.04 W
Los Taques	246	11.50 N	70.16 W
Lost Bridge State Recreation Area ♦	216	40.45 N	85.37 W
Lost Creek ≃, Al., U.S.	194	33.38 N	87.14 W
Lost Creek ≃, Ar., U.S.	194	34.10 N	92.31 W
Lost Creek ≃, Oh., U.S.	218	39.58 N	84.09 W
Lost Creek ≃, Ut,. U.S.	200	41.04 N	111.32 W
Lost Creek ≃, Wy., U.S.	200	42.01 N	108.11 W
Lost Draw V	196	32.58 N	102.02 W
Los Telares	252	28.59 S	63.26 W
Los Teques	246	10.21 N	67.02 W
Los Testigos, Islas II	246	11.22 N	63.06 W
Lost Hills	226	35.36 N	119.41 W
Lostine ≃	202	45.33 N	117.29 W
Lost Lake ⊜, Or., U.S.	224	45.29 N	121.49 W
Lost Lake ⊜, Wa., U.S.	224	47.20 N	121.24 W
Lost Nation	190	41.57 N	90.49 W
Lostock ≃	262	53.40 N	2.48 W
Lostock Gralam	262	53.16 N	2.28 W
Los Trancos Creek ≃	282	37.25 N	122.12 W
Los Trancos Woods	282	37.21 N	122.12 W
Lost River Range ⋀	202	44.10 N	113.35 W
Lost Trail Pass)(	202	45.41 N	113.57 W
Lostwithiel	42	50.25 N	4.40 W
Losuia	164	8.32 S	151.04 E
Los Vidrios	232	31.59 N	113.28 W
Los Vilos	252	31.55 S	71.31 W
Los Yébenes	34	39.34 N	3.53 W
Lot □[5]	32	44.35 N	1.40 E
Lot ≃	32	44.18 N	0.20 E
Lota	252	37.05 S	73.10 W
Lotagipi Swamp (Lotikipi Plain) ≚	144	4.36 N	34.55 E
Lotak	112	0.11 S	115.54 E
Lotbinière □[6]	206	46.30 N	71.40 W
Lotela, Lake ⊜	220	27.34 N	81.29 W
Løten	26	60.49 N	11.19 E
Lot-et-Garonne □[5]	32	44.20 N	0.20 E
Lotfābād	128	37.32 N	59.20 E
Lothair, S. Afr.	158	26.26 S	30.27 E
Lothair, Ky., U.S.	192	37.14 N	83.10 W
Lothian □[4]	46	55.55 N	3.05 W
Lothringen → Lorraine □[9]	32	49.00 N	6.00 E
Lotikipi Plain (Lotagipi Swamp) ≚	144	4.36 N	34.55 E
Loto	152	2.49 S	22.29 E
Loto ≃	152	1.55 S	22.09 E
Lotofaga	175a	13.59 S	171.50 W
Lotoi ≃	152	1.35 S	18.30 E
Lotorp	40	58.44 N	15.50 E
Lotošino	76	56.14 N	35.38 E
Lotrului, Munții ⋀	38	45.30 N	23.52 E
Lotsane ≃	156	22.41 S	28.11 E
Lötschberg Tunnel ⇾[5]	58	46.25 N	7.45 E
Lötschental V	58	46.25 N	7.50 E
Lotseninsel I	41	54.40 N	10.01 E
Lott	222	31.12 N	97.02 W
Lotta ≃	24	68.36 N	31.06 E
Lotte	52	52.17 N	7.55 E
Lottivue	214	42.40 N	82.46 W
Löttringhausen ⇾[8]	263	51.27 N	7.27 E
Lottsburg	208	37.57 N	76.31 W
Lotts Creek ≃	192	32.09 N	81.47 W
Lottsford Branch ≃	284c	38.55 N	76.49 W
Lottstetten	58	47.38 N	8.34 E
Lotuke, Jabal ∧	154	4.07 N	33.48 E
Lotung	100	24.41 N	121.46 E
Lotzorai	71	39.58 N	9.39 E
Louang Namtha	110	20.57 N	101.25 E
Louangphrabang	110	19.52 N	102.08 E
L'Ouarsenis, Massif de ⋀	34	35.40 N	1.50 E
Loubaresse	62	44.36 N	4.03 E
Loube, Montagne de la ∧	62	43.22 N	5.59 E
Loubetsi	152	3.12 S	12.10 E
Louchi	24	66.04 N	33.00 E
Loučim	60	49.22 N	13.07 E
Loučná ∧	54	50.39 N	13.37 E
Loude	98	35.54 N	117.18 E
Loudéac	32	48.10 N	2.45 W
Louden Cove c	276	41.05 N	73.43 W
Loudes	62	45.05 N	3.45 E
Loudima Poste	152	4.07 S	13.04 E
Loudon	192	35.43 N	84.20 W
Loudonville, N.Y., U.S.	210	42.42 N	73.45 W
Loudonville, Oh., U.S.	214	40.38 N	82.14 W
Loudoun □[6]	208	39.05 N	77.30 W
Loudun	32	47.01 N	0.05 E
Loué	32	48.00 N	0.09 W
Loue ≃	58	47.01 N	5.27 E
Louga	150	15.37 N	16.13 W
Louga □[4]	150	15.25 N	15.30 W
Louge	252	36.57 S	61.40 W
Louge ≃	32	43.27 N	1.20 E
Lougguéré ≃	150	15.35 N	14.47 W
Loughborough	42	52.47 N	1.11 W
Loughborough Lake ⊜	212	44.23 N	76.30 W
Loughermore ∧[2]	48	54.59 N	7.05 W
Loughman	220	28.14 N	81.34 W
Loughor	42	51.40 N	4.04 W
Loughor ≃	42	51.40 N	4.04 W
Loughrea	48	53.12 N	8.34 W
Loughros More Bay c	48	54.47 N	8.35 W
Loughton	260	51.39 N	0.03 E
Louhans	58	46.38 N	5.13 E
Louin	194	32.04 N	89.15 W
Louisa, Ky., U.S.	192	38.06 N	82.36 W
Louisa, Va., U.S.	192	38.01 N	78.00 W
Louisa, Lake ⊜, On., Can.	212	45.28 N	78.30 W
Louisa, Lake ⊜, Fl., U.S.	220	28.29 N	81.44 W
Louisbourg	186	45.55 N	59.58 W
Louis Bull Indian Reserve ⇾[4]	182	52.53 N	113.31 W
Louisburg, Ks., U.S.	198	38.37 N	94.40 W
Louisburg, N.C., U.S.	192	36.05 N	78.18 W
Louisburgh	48	53.46 N	9.51 W
Louisdale	186	45.36 N	61.04 W
Louise, Ms., U.S.	194	32.58 N	90.35 W
Louise, Tx., U.S.	222	29.06 N	96.25 W
Louise, Lac ⊜, P.Q., Can.	206	45.43 N	71.25 W
Louise, Lac ⊜, P.Q., Can.	206	45.46 N	74.25 W
Louise, Lake ⊜	180	62.20 N	146.30 W
Louise Island I	182	52.58 N	131.50 W
Louiseville	206	46.15 N	72.57 W
Louis Gentil → Youssoufia	148	32.16 N	8.33 W
Louisiade Archipelago II	160	11.00 S	153.00 E
Louisiana	219	39.26 N	91.03 W
Louisiana □[3], U.S.	178	31.15 N	92.15 W
Louisiana □[3], U.S.	194	31.15 N	92.15 W
Louisiana ◈	41	55.58 N	12.33 E
Lou Island I	164	2.25 S	147.20 E
Louis Trichardt	156	23.01 S	29.43 E
Louisvale	158	28.33 S	21.12 E
Louisville, On., Can.	214	42.28 N	82.07 W
Louisville, Al., U.S.	194	31.47 N	85.33 W
Louisville, Ga., U.S.	192	33.00 N	82.24 W
Louisville, Il., U.S.	194	38.46 N	88.30 W
Louisville, Ky., U.S.	218	38.15 N	85.45 W
Louisville, Ms., U.S.	194	33.07 N	89.03 W
Louisville, Ne., U.S.	198	40.59 N	96.09 W
Louisville, Oh., U.S.	214	40.50 N	81.15 W
Louisville Ridge ✣[3]	14	31.00 S	172.30 W
Louisville Seamount ✣[3]	14	31.15 S	172.15 W
Louis-XIV, Pointe ›	176	54.37 N	79.45 W
Loujiaying	98	42.04 N	116.04 E
Loukanga	273b	4.20 S	15.09 E
Loukkos, Oued ≃	34	35.12 N	6.09 W
Loukoua ≃	273b	4.09 S	15.08 E
Loulé	34	37.08 N	8.02 W
Loum	152	4.43 N	9.44 E
Loumou	273b	4.08 S	15.09 E
Lount Lake ⊜	184	50.10 N	94.20 W
Louny	54	50.19 N	13.46 E
Loup ≃, Fr.	62	43.38 N	7.09 E
Loup ≃, Ne., U.S.	198	41.24 N	97.19 W
Loup, Gorge du V	56	49.47 N	6.23 E
Loup, Rivière du ≃	206	46.13 N	72.55 W
Loup City	198	41.16 N	98.57 W
Loups Marins, Lacs des ⊜	176	56.30 N	73.45 W
Lourches	50	50.19 N	3.21 E
Lourdes, Nf., Can.	186	48.39 N	59.00 W
Lourdes, Fr.	32	43.06 N	0.03 W
Lourel de Baixo	266c	38.49 N	9.22 W
Lourenço	250	2.30 N	51.40 W
Lourenço Marques → Maputo	156	25.58 S	32.35 E
Lourenço Velho	256	22.22 S	45.19 W
Lourenço Velho ≃, Bra.	256	23.26 S	45.35 W
Lourenço Velho ≃, Bra.	256	22.22 S	45.31 W
Loures	34	38.50 N	9.10 W
Loures ≃	266c	38.50 N	9.08 W
Lourinhã	34	39.14 N	9.19 W
Lourmarin	62	43.46 N	5.22 E
Lourosa	34	40.19 N	7.56 W
Loury	50	48.00 N	2.05 E
Lousã, Port.	34	40.07 N	8.15 W
Lousa, Port.	266c	38.53 N	9.12 W
Louse Creek ≃	198	46.22 N	100.57 W
Lou Shan ∧	89	45.15 N	128.58 E
Louta	150	13.30 N	3.10 W
Loutang	106	31.26 N	121.12 E
Loutézou, Île de I	273b	4.22 S	15.10 E
Louth, Austl.	166	30.32 S	145.07 E
Louth, Ire.	44	53.57 N	6.33 W
Louth, Ire.	48	53.57 N	6.33 W
Louth, Eng., U.K.	44	53.22 N	0.01 W
Louth □[6]	48	53.55 N	6.30 W
Louth Bay c	166	34.34 S	136.02 E
Louti, Mayo ≃	146	9.38 N	13.56 E
Loutit Bay c	169	38.33 S	144.00 E
Loutrá Aidhipsoú	38	38.51 N	23.02 E
Loutre ≃	219	38.42 N	91.25 W
Loutre, Bayou de ≃	194	32.41 N	92.08 W
Loutrópirgos	267c	38.02 N	23.28 E
Louvain → Leuven	56	50.53 N	4.42 E
Louveciennes	261	48.52 N	2.07 E
Louveigné	56	50.32 N	5.42 E
Louveira	256	23.04 S	46.58 W
Louviers, Fr.	50	49.13 N	1.10 E
Louviers, Co., U.S.	200	39.28 N	105.00 W
Louvre ◈	261	48.52 N	2.20 E
Louvres	50	49.02 N	2.30 E
Louvroil	50	50.16 N	3.58 E
Louwsburg	158	27.37 S	31.07 E
Lou Yaeger, Lake ⊜[1]	219	39.10 N	89.37 W
Lövånger	26	64.22 N	21.18 E
Lovászi	61	46.33 N	16.34 E
Lovat' ≃	76	58.14 N	31.28 E
Lovcy	82	55.00 N	39.15 E
Love	184	53.29 N	104.09 W
Loveč	38	43.08 N	24.43 E
Love Clough	262	53.44 N	2.17 W
Lovedale	279b	40.17 N	79.52 W
Lovejoy	219	38.39 N	90.10 W
Lovelady	222	31.08 N	95.27 W
Loveland, Co., U.S.	200	40.23 N	105.04 W
Loveland, Oh., U.S.	218	39.16 N	84.16 W
Lovell	202	44.50 N	108.23 W
Lovell Island I	283	42.20 N	70.56 W
Lovelock	204	40.10 N	118.28 W
Lovely	192	37.49 N	82.24 W
Love Point ›	208	39.02 N	76.18 W
Lovere	64	45.49 N	10.04 E
Lovering, Lac ⊜	206	45.10 N	72.09 W
Lovero	64	46.14 N	10.14 E
Loves Green	260	51.43 N	0.24 E
Loves Park	216	42.19 N	89.03 W
Loviisa → Lovisa	26	60.27 N	26.14 E
Lovilia	190	41.08 N	92.54 W
Loving, N.M., U.S.	196	32.17 N	104.05 W
Loving, Tx., U.S.	196	33.16 N	98.31 W
Lovingston	192	37.45 N	78.52 W
Lovington, Il., U.S.	219	39.42 N	88.37 W
Lovington, N.M., U.S.	196	32.56 N	103.20 W
Lovisa (Loviisa)	26	60.27 N	26.14 E
Lövő	61	47.30 N	16.47 E
Lovö I	40	59.20 N	17.50 E
Lovoi ≃	154	8.14 S	26.39 E
Lovosice	54	50.31 N	14.03 E
Lovozero, Ross.	24	68.00 N	35.00 E
Lovozero, Ross.	24	65.00 N	29.50 E
Lovozero, ozero ⊜	24	67.54 N	35.12 E
Lovrenc	61	46.32 N	15.23 E
Lövstabruk	40	60.24 N	17.53 E
Lövstabukten c	40	60.35 N	17.45 E
Lövstad slott ⊥	40	58.33 N	16.02 E
Lóvua, Ang.	152	11.36 S	23.53 E
Lóvua, Ang.	152	7.20 S	20.16 E
Lovua (Lóvua) ≃	152	6.07 S	20.35 E
Low	188	45.48 N	75.57 W
Low, Cape ›	176	63.07 N	85.18 W
Lowa	154	1.24 S	25.51 E
Lowa ≃	154	1.24 S	25.51 E
Lowāda	126	22.27 N	87.37 E
Lowat → Lovat' ≃	76	58.14 N	31.28 E
Lowber	279b	40.15 N	79.46 W
Lowden	190	41.51 N	90.55 W
Lowder Brook ≃	283	43.14 N	71.11 W
Lowell, Ar., U.S.	194	36.15 N	94.07 W
Lowell, In., U.S.	216	41.17 N	87.25 W
Lowell, Ma., U.S.	207	42.38 N	71.19 W
Lowell, Mi., U.S.	216	42.56 N	85.20 W
Lowell, Or., U.S.	202	43.55 N	122.46 W
Lowell, Lake ⊜[1]	202	43.33 N	116.40 W
Lowell, University of ◈[2]	283	42.39 N	71.20 W
Lowell-Dracut State Forest ♦	283	42.40 N	71.22 W
Lowelli	140	5.59 N	33.45 E
Lowellville	214	41.02 N	80.32 W
Löwen → Leuven	56	50.53 N	4.42 E
Löwen ≃	158	26.51 S	18.17 E
Löwenberg	54	52.54 N	13.08 E
Löwenbruch	264a	52.18 N	13.19 E
Löwenstein	56	49.06 N	9.22 E
Lowe Pond ⊜	283	42.41 N	70.59 W
Lower Aetna Lake ⊜	285	39.51 N	74.48 W
Lower Arrow Lake ⊜	182	49.40 N	118.08 W
Lower Bay c	208	40.33 N	74.02 W
Lower Bear River Reservoir ⊜[1]	226	38.33 N	120.14 W
Lower Bershire Valley	276	40.54 N	74.37 W
Lower Beverley Lake ⊜	212	44.36 N	76.09 W
Lower Broughton ⇾[8]	262	53.29 N	2.15 W
Lower Brule Indian Reservation ⇾[4]	198	44.05 N	99.44 W
Lower Buckhorn Lake ⊜	212	44.33 N	78.17 W
Lower Burrell	214	40.33 N	79.45 W
Lower California → Baja California ›[1]	232	28.00 N	113.30 W
Lower Chittering	168a	31.34 S	116.06 E
Lower Crystal Springs Reservoir ⊜[1]	226	37.32 N	122.22 W
Lower Darwen	262	53.43 N	2.28 W
Lower Egypt → Mișr Baḥrī □[9]	140	31.00 N	31.00 E
Lower Eltham Park ♦	274b	37.45 S	145.09 E
Lower Elwha Indian Reservation ⇾[4]	224	48.09 N	123.33 W
Lower Fort Garry National Historic Park ♦	184	50.07 N	96.55 W
Lower Ganga Canal ≊	124	26.27 N	80.17 E
Lower Gap c	212	44.10 N	76.35 W
Lower Halstow	260	51.22 N	0.40 E
Lower Hay Lake ⊜	212	45.25 N	78.13 W
Lower Higham	260	51.26 N	0.28 E
Lower Huron Metropolitan Park ♦	281	42.12 N	83.25 W
Lower Hutt	172	41.13 S	174.55 E
Lower Kalskag	180	61.31 N	160.22 W
Lower Keechi Creek ≃	222	31.08 N	95.46 W
Lower Klamath Lake ⊜	204	41.55 N	121.42 W
Lower Lake	226	38.55 N	122.36 W
Lower Lake ⊜	204	41.15 N	120.02 W
Lower Loteni	158	29.32 S	29.36 E
Lower Manitou Lake ⊜	184	49.15 N	93.00 W
Lower Matecumbe Key I	220	24.51 N	80.43 W
Lower Montville	276	40.54 N	74.22 W
Lower Mystic Lake ⊜	283	42.26 N	71.09 W
Lower Nazeing	260	51.44 N	0.01 E
Lower Otay Lake ⊜[1]	228	32.37 N	116.55 W
Lower Paia	229a	20.55 N	156.23 W
Lower Paudash Lake ⊜	212	44.58 N	78.01 W
Lower Peirce Reservoir ⊜[1]	271c	1.22 N	103.49 E
Lower Peover	262	53.16 N	2.23 W
Lower Place	262	53.36 N	2.09 W
Lower Plenty	274b	37.44 S	145.06 E
Lower Portland	170	33.27 S	150.53 E
Lower Post	176	59.55 N	128.30 W
Lower Red Lake ⊜	198	48.00 N	94.50 W
Lower River Rouge ≃	281	42.18 N	83.14 W
Lower Rouge Parkway ♦	281	42.18 N	83.20 W
Lower Saxony → Niedersachsen □[3]	30	52.40 N	9.00 E
Lower Stoke	260	51.27 N	0.38 E
Lower Trajan's Wall ⊥	38	45.40 N	28.30 E
Lower Ugashik Lake ⊜	180	57.30 N	156.56 W
Lower Van Norman Lake ⊜[1]	280	34.17 N	118.29 W
Lower West Pubnico	186	43.38 N	65.48 W
Lower Whitley	262	53.18 N	2.35 W
Lower Wood's Harbour	186	43.31 N	65.44 W
Lowery, Lake ⊜	220	28.07 N	81.41 W
Lower Zambezi International Game Park ⇾[4]	154	15.30 S	29.35 E
Lowestoft	42	52.29 N	1.45 E
Lowgar □[4]	120	33.50 N	69.00 E
Lowick	44	55.38 N	2.00 W
Łowicz	30	52.07 N	19.56 E
Lowman	210	42.02 N	76.44 W
Lowmoor	192	37.47 N	79.53 W
Lowood	171a	27.28 S	152.35 E
Lowrah (Pishīn Lora) ≃	120	29.09 N	64.55 E
Lowries Run ≃	279b	40.30 N	80.05 W
Low Rocky Point ›	166	43.00 S	145.30 E
Lowry Air Force Base ■	198	39.43 N	104.53 W
Lowry City	194	38.08 N	93.43 W
Lowther ≃	44	54.39 N	2.44 W
Lowther Hills ⋀[2]	44	55.19 N	3.38 W
Lowton	262	53.28 N	2.35 W
Lowton Common	262	53.29 N	2.33 W
Lowville, N.Y., U.S.	212	43.47 N	75.29 W
Lowville, Pa., U.S.	214	42.01 N	79.49 W
Loxahatchee	220	26.49 N	80.13 W
Loxley	194	30.37 N	87.45 W
Loxstedt	52	53.28 N	8.38 E
Loxten	52	52.03 N	8.08 E
Loxton, Austl.	166	34.27 S	140.35 E
Loxton, S. Afr.	158	31.30 S	22.22 E
Loyal	190	44.44 N	90.29 W
Loyal, Loch ⊜	46	58.23 N	4.22 W
Loyalhanna	214	40.19 N	79.21 W
Loyalhanna Creek ≃	214	40.28 N	79.27 W
Loyalhanna Lake ⊜[1]	214	40.25 N	79.28 W
Loyalsock Creek ≃	210	41.14 N	76.56 W
Loyalton	204	39.40 N	120.14 W
Loyalty Islands → Loyauté, Îles II	175f	21.00 S	167.00 E
Loyang, Sing.	271c	1.22 N	103.58 E
Loyang → Luoyang, Zhg.	102	34.41 N	112.28 E
Loyauté, Îles (Loyalty Islands) II	175f	21.00 S	167.00 E
Loyne, Loch ⊜	46	57.06 N	5.00 W
Loyola College ◈[2]	284b	39.21 N	76.37 W
Loyola Marymount University ◈[2]	280	33.58 N	118.25 W
Loyola University ◈[2]	278	42.00 N	87.39 W
Loyoro	154	3.21 N	34.16 E
Loysburg	214	40.10 N	78.23 W
Loysville	208	40.22 N	77.21 W
Lozano	258	34.51 S	59.03 W
Lozère □[5]	32	44.30 N	3.30 E
Lozère, Mont ⋀	62	44.25 N	3.46 E
Loznica	38	44.32 N	19.13 E
Ložnikovo, Ross.	86	56.54 N	73.56 E
Ložnikovo, Ross.	88	51.22 N	117.03 E
Lozno-Aleksandrovka	78	49.50 N	38.44 E
Loznoje	80	49.17 N	44.26 E
L'Ozone ⇾[8]	273b	4.21 S	15.14 E
Lozovaja, Kaz.	86	53.17 N	77.45 E
Lozovaja, Ukr.	78	48.54 N	36.20 E
Lozovaja, Ukr.	83	49.28 N	37.54 E
Lozovoje, Ukr.	78	49.18 N	27.18 E
Lozovoje, Ukr.	83	49.13 N	37.36 E
Lozovskij	83	48.33 N	38.54 E
Lozoyuela	34	40.55 N	3.37 W
Loz'va ≃	86	59.36 N	62.20 E
Lozzo di Cadore	64	46.29 N	12.27 E
Lu	62	45.00 N	8.29 E
Lu ≃	100	27.04 N	115.00 E
Lua ≃	152	2.46 N	18.26 E
Luabo	156	18.30 S	36.10 E
Luabu ≃	152	2.46 S	18.19 E
Luachimo ≃	152	6.33 S	20.59 E
Luaha-sibuha	110	0.31 S	98.28 E
Luala ≃	154	17.57 S	36.30 E
Lualaba ≃	154	0.26 N	25.20 E
Luali	152	5.06 S	12.29 E
Lualoje ≃	152	12.18 S	21.38 E
Luama ≃	154	4.46 S	26.53 E

ENGLISH

Name	Page	Lat.°′	Long.°′
Luambe National Park ♦	154	12.25 S	32.15 E
Luambimba ≃	152	15.00 S	22.48 E
Luampa	154	15.03 S	24.28 E
Luampa ≃	154	14.33 S	24.10 E
Lu'an	100	31.44 N	116.31 E
Luan ≃	98	39.20 N	119.10 E
Luana ≃	152	7.56 S	21.06 E
Luan Balu	114	2.38 N	96.13 E
Luancheng, Zhg.	98	37.53 N	114.39 E
Luancheng, Zhg.	102	22.45 N	108.51 E
Luanchuan	102	33.51 N	111.36 E
Luancundo ≃	152	16.25 S	21.27 E
Luanda	152	8.48 S	13.14 E
Luanda □[5]	152	9.00 S	13.15 E
Luando ≃	152	10.19 S	16.40 E
Luando, Réserva do ⇾[4]	152	11.10 S	17.30 E
Luang, Khao ∧	110	8.31 N	99.47 E
Luang, Thale c	110	7.30 N	100.15 E
Luang Chiang Dao, Doi ∧	110	19.23 N	98.54 E
Luanginga (Luanguinga) ≃	152	15.11 S	22.56 E
Luang Prabang → Louangphrabang	110	19.52 N	102.08 E
Luang Prabang Range ⋀	110	18.30 N	101.15 E
Luangue	152	7.19 S	19.38 E
Luangue (Loange) ≃	152	4.17 S	20.02 E
Luanguinga (Luanginga) ≃	152	15.11 S	22.56 E
Luangwa (Aruângua) ≃	154	15.36 S	30.25 E
Luanhaizi	120	34.27 N	93.12 E
Luanhe	105	40.57 N	117.44 E
Luannan (Bencheng)	98	39.32 N	118.39 E
Luanping (Anjiangying)	98	40.57 N	117.20 E
Luanshishan	104	42.10 N	123.41 E
Luanshya	154	13.08 S	28.24 E
Luán Toro	252	36.12 S	65.06 W
Luanxian	98	39.45 N	118.44 E
Luanza	154	8.42 S	28.42 E
Luapula □[4]	154	10.55 S	29.00 E
Luapula ≃	154	9.26 S	28.33 E
Luar, Danau ⊜	112	0.55 N	112.15 E
Luarca	34	43.32 N	6.32 W
Luashi	152	10.56 S	23.37 E
Luashi ≃	152	10.41 S	22.55 E
Luassinga ≃	152	15.47 S	18.50 E
Luati	152	14.35 S	21.13 E
Luatira	152	12.52 S	17.14 E
Luau	152	10.42 S	22.12 E
Lua-Vindu ≃	152	3.38 N	19.16 E
Luba	152	3.27 N	8.33 E
Lubaantun ⊥	232	16.17 N	88.58 W
Lubaczów	30	50.10 N	23.07 E
Lubalo	152	9.12 S	19.16 E
Lubalo ≃	152	7.22 S	19.20 E
Lubamiti	152	2.29 S	17.47 E
L'uban', Bela.	76	52.37 N	29.08 E
L'uban', Bela.	76	52.48 N	27.59 E
Lubań, Pol.	30	51.08 N	15.18 E
L'uban', Ross.	76	59.21 N	31.13 E
Lubāna	76	56.54 N	26.43 E
Lubang	116	13.52 N	120.07 E
Lubang Island I	116	13.46 N	120.11 E
Lubang Islands II	116	13.46 N	120.15 E
Lubango	152	14.55 S	13.30 E
Lubanowo	54	53.09 N	14.36 E
Lubāns ⊜	76	56.46 N	26.53 E
Lubansenshi ≃	154	11.21 S	30.35 E
Lub'any	80	56.02 N	51.24 E
Lubao	100	23.22 N	112.55 E
L'ubar	78	49.55 N	27.44 E
Lübars, Dtsch.	54	52.39 N	12.02 E
Lübars, Dtsch.	54	52.10 N	12.09 E
Lübars ⇾[8]	264a	52.37 N	13.22 E
Lubartów	30	51.28 N	22.38 E
L'ubašovka	78	47.51 N	30.15 E
Lubawa	30	53.30 N	19.45 E
Lubaynī, Baḥr al- ≊	273c	29.56 N	31.11 E
Lübbecke	52	52.18 N	8.36 E
Lübben	54	51.56 N	13.53 E
Lübbenau	54	51.52 N	13.57 E
Lubber Brook ≃	283	42.33 N	71.09 W
Lubbers Run ≃	276	40.56 N	74.43 W
Lübbesee ⊜	54	53.05 N	13.34 E
Lubbock	196	33.34 N	101.51 W
Lübbow	54	52.54 N	11.10 E
Lubbub Creek ≃	194	33.04 N	88.10 W
L'ubča	76	53.45 N	26.03 E
L'ubeč, Ukr.	78	51.42 N	30.39 E
Lubec, Me., U.S.	188	44.51 N	66.59 W
Lübeck	54	53.52 N	10.40 E
Lübecker Bucht c	54	54.00 N	10.55 E
Lubefu	152	4.43 S	24.25 E
Lubefu ≃	152	4.10 S	23.00 E
Lubelska, Wyżyna ⋀[2]	30	51.00 N	23.00 E
Lubembe (Luembe) ≃	152	6.37 S	21.05 E
Lüben → Lubin	30	51.24 N	16.13 E
Lubenec	54	50.06 N	13.20 E
L'ubercy	82	55.41 N	37.53 E
Lubéron, Montagne du ⋀	62	43.48 N	5.22 E
Lubersac	32	45.27 N	1.24 E
L'ubešov	78	51.46 N	25.31 E
Lübesse	54	53.29 N	11.28 E
Lubi ≃	152	4.58 S	23.26 E
Lubiana → Ljubljana	36	46.03 N	14.31 E
Lubic Island I	116	10.58 N	120.44 E
L'ubickoje	80	51.46 N	49.19 E
Lubień Kujawski	30	52.25 N	19.10 E
Lubilash ≃	152	6.02 S	23.45 E
Lubile	154	2.55 S	26.45 E
L'ubim	80	58.22 N	40.41 E
L'ubimovka, Kaz.	86	52.15 N	66.45 E
L'ubimovka, Ross.	78	51.31 N	35.37 E
L'ubimovka, Ukr.	78	46.47 N	33.34 E
L'ubimyj	83	47.53 N	39.28 E
Lubin, Pol.	30	51.24 N	16.13 E
Lubin, Pol.	54	53.50 N	14.25 E
L'ubino	86	57.30 N	88.47 E
L'ubinskij	86	55.09 N	72.42 E
Lubishi ≃	152	6.54 S	24.09 E
Lubja ≃	265a	59.58 N	30.30 E
Lublin	30	51.15 N	22.35 E
Lublin □[4]	30	51.30 N	22.30 E
Lubliniec	30	50.40 N	18.41 E
L'ublino ⇾[8]	265b	55.41 N	37.44 E
Lubmin	54	54.08 N	13.37 E
Lubnān → Lebanon □[1]	128	34.00 N	36.00 E
Lubnān, Jabal (Lebanon Mountains) ⋀	132	34.00 N	36.00 E
L'ubnica	76	57.58 N	32.42 E
Lubny	78	50.01 N	33.00 E
L'ubochna	76	53.31 N	34.23 E
Lubok China	114	2.27 N	102.04 E
Lubomierz	30	51.01 N	15.30 E
L'uboml'	78	51.14 N	24.01 E
Luboń	30	52.23 N	16.54 E
Lubondai	152	6.34 S	22.39 E
Lubondoi	154	8.02 S	26.31 E
L'ubostan'	78	51.19 N	35.44 E
L'ubotin	78	49.57 N	35.57 E
Lubraniec	30	52.33 N	18.50 E
Lubsko	30	51.46 N	14.59 E
Lubsza ≃	54	51.56 N	14.43 E
Lübtheen	54	53.18 N	11.04 E
Lubu, Indon.	112	0.46 S	122.30 E
Lubu, Zhg.	102	23.09 N	112.13 E
Lubuagan	116	17.21 N	121.10 E
L'ubučany	82	55.15 N	37.33 E
Lubudi, Zaïre	152	6.51 S	21.18 E

DEUTSCH

Name	Seite	Breite°′	Länge°′ E = Ost
Lubudi, Zaïre	154	9.57 S	25.58 E
Lubudi ≃, Zaïre	152	4.03 S	21.23 E
Lubudi ≃, Zaïre	154	9.13 S	25.38 E
Lubue	152	4.09 S	19.52 E
Lubue ≃	152	4.10 S	19.53 E
Lubukambacang	112	0.37 S	101.25 E
Lubukbatang	112	4.03 S	104.12 E
Lubukbertubung	112	0.02 N	102.08 E
Lubuklinggau	112	3.18 S	102.52 E
Lubukpakam	114	3.33 N	98.52 E
Lubukraya, Dolok ∧	114	1.29 N	99.13 E
Lubuksikaping	112	0.08 N	100.10 E
Lubumbaschi → Lubumbashi	154	11.40 S	27.28 E
Lubumbashi (Élisabethville)	154	11.40 S	27.28 E
Lubunda	154	5.10 S	26.40 E
Lubutu	154	0.44 S	26.35 E
Luby	54	50.12 N	12.25 E
L'ubytino	76	58.49 N	33.23 E
Lübz	54	53.27 N	12.01 E
Lučak	85	38.23 N	67.25 E
Lucala	152	9.16 S	15.15 E
Lucala ≃, Ang.	152	9.37 S	14.14 E
Lucala ≃, Ang.	152	6.38 S	12.34 E
Lucan, On., Can.	190	43.11 N	81.24 W
Lucan, Ire.	48	53.22 N	6.27 W
Lucanas	248	14.36 S	74.15 W
Lucania □[9]	68	40.30 N	16.00 E
Lucania, Mount ∧	180	61.01 N	140.28 W
Lucano	152	11.16 S	21.38 E
Lucaogou	102	42.26 N	96.55 E
Lucapa	152	8.36 S	20.54 E
Lucas, Ia., U.S.	190	41.01 N	93.27 W
Lucas, Ks., U.S.	198	39.03 N	98.32 W
Lucas, Oh., U.S.	214	40.45 N	82.30 W
Lucas, Tx., U.S.	222	33.05 N	96.35 W
Lucas □[6]	214	41.39 N	83.32 W
Lucas González	252	32.24 S	59.33 W
Lucas Heights	274a	34.02 S	150.58 E
Lucas Valley	282	38.03 N	122.35 W
Lucasville	218	38.52 N	82.59 W
Lucban	116	14.06 N	121.33 E
Lucca	66	43.50 N	10.29 E
Lucca □[4]	64	44.02 N	10.27 E
Lucca Sicula	70	37.35 N	13.18 E
Lucé	50	48.26 N	1.28 E
Luce, Water of ≃	44	54.52 N	4.48 W
Lucea	241q	18.27 N	78.10 W
Luce Bay c	44	54.47 N	4.50 W
Luce Bayou ≃	222	30.03 N	95.07 W
Lucedale	194	30.55 N	88.35 W
Lucena, Esp.	34	37.24 N	4.29 W
Lucena, Pil.	116	13.56 N	121.37 E
Lucenay-l'Évêque	32	47.05 N	4.15 E
Luc-en-Diois	62	44.37 N	5.27 E
Lučenec	30	48.20 N	19.40 E
Lucens	58	46.42 N	6.50 E
Luceque	152	14.41 S	15.04 E
Lucera	68	41.30 N	15.20 E
Lucéram	62	43.53 N	7.22 E
Lucerne → Luzern, Schw.	58	47.03 N	8.18 E
Lucerne, Ca., U.S.	204	39.05 N	122.47 W
Lucerne, In., U.S.	216	40.52 N	86.24 W
Lucerne, Lake → Vierwaldstätter See ⊜	58	47.00 N	8.28 E
Lucerne Lake ⊜	228	34.31 N	116.57 W
Lucernemines	214	40.33 N	79.09 W
Lucerne Valley	228	34.26 N	116.58 W
Lucero	200	30.49 N	106.30 W
Lucero, Lake ⊜	200	32.42 N	106.25 W
Lučesa ≃	76	55.10 N	30.11 E
Luch	80	57.01 N	42.15 E
Luch ≃	80	56.14 N	42.25 E
Luchang	102	26.23 N	102.18 E
Luchena ≃	34	37.44 N	1.50 W
Lucheng, Zhg.	102	24.21 N	106.00 E
Lücheng, Zhg.	106	31.55 N	119.44 E
Lucheng, Zhg.	106	31.47 N	120.02 E
Luché-Pringé	50	47.42 N	0.05 E
Lucheringo ≃	154	11.43 S	36.17 E
Luchibe ≃	152	12.07 S	21.13 E
Luchico (Lushiko) ≃	152	6.13 S	19.40 E
Luchou	269d	25.05 N	121.28 E
Luchovicy	82	54.59 N	39.03 E
Lüchow, Dtsch.	54	52.58 N	11.10 E
Luchow → Luzhou, Zhg.	107	28.54 N	105.27 E
Lüchtringen	52	51.47 N	9.25 E
Luchuan	102	22.19 N	110.11 E
Luci	100	29.52 N	119.47 E
Luciara	250	10.27 S	50.32 W
Lucie ≃	250	3.35 N	57.38 W
Lucikou	100	28.56 N	116.04 E
Lučin	76	53.01 N	30.01 E
Lucinda, Austl.	166	18.32 S	146.20 E
Lucinda, Pa., U.S.	214	41.19 N	79.22 W
Lucindale	166	36.59 S	140.22 E
Lucio Vázquez	234	22.47 N	99.46 W
Lucipara, Kepulauan II	164	5.30 S	127.33 E
Lucira	152	13.51 S	12.31 E
Lucito	66	41.44 N	14.41 E
Luci Yu I	100	25.07 N	119.22 E
Luck, Ukr.	78	50.44 N	25.20 E
Luck, Wi., U.S.	190	45.34 N	92.28 W
Luck, Mount ∧[2]	162	28.47 S	123.33 E
Lucka	54	51.06 N	12.20 E
Luckau	54	51.51 N	13.43 E
Luckeesarai	124	25.11 N	86.05 E
Luckenwalde	54	52.05 N	13.10 E
Luckey	214	41.27 N	83.29 W
Luckhoff	158	29.44 S	24.43 E
Luckiamute ≃	202	44.45 N	123.09 W
Luck Lake ⊜	184	51.05 N	107.07 W
Lucknow, On., Can.	190	43.57 N	81.31 W
Lucknow, India	124	26.51 N	80.55 E
Lucknow, Pa., U.S.	208	40.20 N	76.54 W
Lucknow Branch ≊	124	27.57 N	80.03 E
Lucky Lake	184	51.00 N	107.10 W
Lucky Peak Lake ⊜[1]	202	43.33 N	116.00 W
Luco dei Marsi	66	41.58 N	13.28 E
Lucomagno, Passo del)(	58	46.33 N	8.49 E
Luçon, Fr.	32	46.27 N	1.10 W
Lucon, Pa., U.S.	285	40.14 N	75.25 W
Luconha ≃	152	12.54 S	21.15 E
Lucun, Zhg.	98	36.12 N	118.01 E
Lucun, Zhg.	106	30.49 N	119.26 E
Lucunga ≃	152	6.57 S	12.48 E
Lucungu ≃	152	6.41 S	14.26 E
Lucusse	152	12.32 S	20.48 E
Lucy Creek	166	22.25 S	136.20 E
Lüda → Dalian	98	38.53 N	121.35 E
Luda Kamčija ≃	38	43.03 N	27.29 E
Ludao	89	43.51 N	129.19 E
Ludbreg	36	46.15 N	16.37 E
Luddan	123	29.54 N	72.34 E
Luddenden	262	53.44 N	1.56 W
Luddenham	274a	33.53 S	150.41 E
Luddesdown	260	51.22 N	0.24 E
Lüdenscheid	56	51.13 N	7.38 E
Lüder ≃	56	50.31 N	9.27 E
Lüderitz, Dtsch.	54	52.30 N	11.44 E
Lüderitz, Namibia	156	26.38 S	15.10 E
Lüderitz □[5]	156	26.30 S	15.45 E
Lüdersdorf	54	53.47 N	10.46 E
Ludgershall	42	51.16 N	1.37 W
Ludgo	40	58.55 N	17.08 E
Ludhiāna	123	30.54 N	75.51 E
Ludian	102	27.11 N	103.33 E
Luding	102	29.55 N	102.15 E
Lüdinghausen	52	51.46 N	7.26 E
Ludington	190	43.57 N	86.27 W
Ludingtonville	210	41.29 N	73.39 W
L'udinovo	76	53.52 N	34.27 E
L'udkovo	76	54.36 N	34.43 E
Ludlam Bay c	208	39.10 N	74.42 W

Symbols in the index entries represent the broad categories identified in the key at the right. Symbols with superior numbers (⋀[1]) identify subcategories (see complete key on page *I · 1)*.

Symbole im Register stellen die rechts im Schlüssel erklärten Kategorien dar. Symbole mit hochgestellten Ziffern (⋀[1]) bezeichnen Unterabteilungen einer Kategorie (vgl. vollständiger Schlüssel auf Seite *I · 1)*.

Los símbolos incluídos en el texto del índice representan las grandes categorías identificadas con la clave a la derecha. Los símbolos con numeros en su parte superior (⋀[1]) identifican las subcategorías (véase la clave completa en la página *I · 1)*.

Les symboles de l'index représentent les catégories indiquées dans la légende à droite. Les symboles suivis d'un indice (⋀[1]) représentent des sous-catégories (voir légende complète à la page *I · 1)*.

Os símbolos incluídos no texto do índice representam as grandes categorias identificadas com a chave à direita. Os símbolos com números em sua parte superior (⋀[1]) identificam as subcategorias (veja-se a chave completa à página *I · 1)*.

∧ Mountain	Berg	Montaña	Montagne	Montanha
⋀ Mountains	Gebirge	Montañas	Montagnes	Montanhas
)(Pass	Paß	Paso	Col	Passo
V Valley, Canyon	Tal, Cañon	Valle, Cañón	Vallée, Canyon	Vale, Canhão
≚ Plain	Ebene	Llano	Plaine	Planície
› Cape	Kap	Cabo	Cap	Cabo
I Island	Insel	Isla	Île	Ilha
II Islands	Inseln	Islas	Îles	Ilhas
⊥ Other Topographic Features	Andere Topographische Objekte	Otros Elementos Topográficos	Autres données topographiques	Outros acidentes topográficos

ESPAÑOL · FRANÇAIS · PORTUGUÊS

Nombre / Nom / Nome	Página / Page / Página	Lat.°′	Long.°′ W = Oeste / W = Ouest / W = Oeste
Ludlow, Eng., U.K.	42	52.22 N	2.43 W
Ludlow, Il., U.S.	216	40.23 N	83.08 W
Ludlow, Ky., U.S.	218	39.05 N	84.32 W
Ludlow, Ma., U.S.	207	42.09 N	72.28 W
Ludlow, Pa., U.S.	214	41.43 N	78.56 W
Ludlow, Vt., U.S.	188	43.23 N	72.42 W
Ludlow Falls	218	40.00 N	84.20 W
Ludlowville	210	42.33 N	76.32 W
Ludogorie ◆[1]	38	43.46 N	26.55 E
Ludonghe	102	25.53 N	103.33 E
Ludoni	76	58.12 N	29.21 E
Ludowici	192	31.42 N	81.44 W
Luduș	38	46.29 N	24.05 E
Ludvika	40	60.09 N	15.11 E
Ludwigkanal ≅	60	49.05 N	11.27 E
Ludwigsburg	56	48.53 N	9.11 E
Ludwigsfelde	54	52.17 N	13.16 E
Ludwigsfelder-Heide ◆[3]	264a	52.18 N	13.14 E
Ludwigshafen	56	49.29 N	8.26 E
Ludwigshafen am Bodensee	58	47.49 N	9.03 E
Ludwigslust	54	53.19 N	11.30 E
Ludwigsort → Laduškin	76	54.36 N	20.11 E
Ludwigsstadt	54	50.30 N	11.23 E
Ludwigstein, Burg ⊥	56	51.20 N	9.55 E
Ludza	76	56.33 N	27.43 E
Lue	170	32.39 S	149.51 E
Luebo	152	5.21 S	21.25 E
Lueders	196	32.48 N	99.37 W
Lueg, Pass)(	64	47.34 N	13.12 E
Lueki	154	3.22 S	25.51 E
Luele ≃	152	7.55 S	20.09 E
Luemba	154	3.42 S	28.40 E
Luembe (Lubembe) ≃, Afr.	152	6.37 S	21.05 E
Luembé ≃, Zaïre	154	6.43 S	24.11 E
Luena, Ang.	152	11.47 S	19.52 E
Luena, Zaïre	154	9.27 S	25.47 E
Luena ≃, Ang.	152	12.31 S	22.34 E
Luena ≃, Zam.	152	14.45 S	23.25 E
Luena Flats ≡	152	14.50 S	23.20 E
Luengué ≃	152	16.54 S	21.52 E
Luenha (Ruenya) ≃	154	16.24 S	33.48 E
Lueo ≃	152	9.06 S	23.51 E
Luepa	246	5.43 N	61.31 W
Lueta	152	7.19 S	22.06 E
Lueta ≃	152	7.04 S	21.40 E
Lueyang	102	33.20 N	106.10 E
Lüfangsicun	104	41.25 N	123.22 E
Lufeng, Zhg.	100	22.57 N	115.38 E
Lufeng, Zhg.	102	25.07 N	102.07 E
Lufico	152	6.24 S	13.23 E
Lufira ≃	154	8.16 S	26.27 E
Lufkin	222	31.20 N	94.43 W
Luftekopf ∧[2]	56	50.05 N	7.37 E
Lufubu ≃	154	8.36 S	30.47 E
Lufuidje ≃	152	12.52 S	22.47 E
Lufupa	154	10.37 S	24.56 E
Lufupa ≃	154	14.37 S	26.12 E
Luga	76	58.44 N	29.52 E
Luga ≃	76	59.40 N	28.18 E
Lugagnano Val d'Arda	62	44.49 N	9.50 E
Lugan' ≃	83	48.37 N	39.27 E
Lugančik ≃	83	48.35 N	39.32 E
Lugang, Zhg.	100	31.17 N	118.22 E
Lugang, Zhg.	100	27.23 N	115.36 E
Luganga	154	7.31 S	35.32 E
Lugano	58	46.01 N	8.58 E
Lugano, Lago di ⊜	58	46.00 N	9.00 E
Lugansk (Vorošilovgrad)	83	48.34 N	39.20 E
Lugansk □[4]	78	49.00 N	39.00 E
Luganskoje	83	48.26 N	38.15 E
Luganville	175f	15.32 S	167.10 E
Lugards Falls ⊾	154	3.03 S	38.42 E
Lugareño	240p	21.33 N	77.28 W
Lugarno	274a	33.59 S	151.03 E
Lugau	54	50.44 N	12.44 E
Lügde	52	51.57 N	9.15 E
Lugela	154	16.25 S	36.43 E
Lugenda	154	12.30 S	37.43 E
Lugenda ≃	154	11.25 S	38.33 E
Lugg ≃	42	52.02 N	2.38 W
Luggarus → Locarno	58	46.10 N	8.48 E
Luginino	76	57.43 N	35.17 E
Luginy	78	51.04 N	28.24 E
Lugnano in Teverina	66	42.34 N	12.20 E
Lugnaquillia Mountain ∧	48	52.58 N	6.27 W
Lugnås	40	58.39 N	13.42 E
Lugny	58	46.28 N	4.49 E
Lugo, Esp.	34	43.00 N	7.34 W
Lugo, It.	66	44.25 N	11.54 E
Lugo □[4]	34	43.00 N	7.25 W
Lugoj	38	45.41 N	21.54 E
Lugongshi	106	31.38 N	121.12 E
Lugos → Lugoj	38	45.41 N	21.54 E
Lugouqiao	105	39.51 N	116.13 E
Lugovaja Subbota	86	59.52 N	69.45 E
Lugovoj, Kaz.	85	42.56 N	72.45 E
Lugovoj, Ross.	86	59.44 N	65.55 E
Lugovoje	85	42.55 N	72.43 E
Lugovskij	88	58.02 N	112.54 E
Lugovskoje	80	50.38 N	46.28 E
Lugu	102	28.21 N	102.09 E
Lugulu ≃	154	2.17 S	26.32 E
Lugunga ∧	154	6.47 S	36.19 E
Luguru	154	2.55 S	33.58 E
Lugus Island I	116	5.41 N	120.50 E
Luhanka	26	61.47 N	25.42 E
Luhe	60	49.35 N	12.09 E
Luhe ≃	52	53.18 N	10.11 E
Lühedian	100	32.33 N	114.28 E
Lühmannsdorf	54	54.00 N	13.33 E
Luhombero ≃	154	8.24 S	37.12 E
Luhsien → Luzhou	107	28.54 N	105.27 E
Luhuo	102	31.26 N	100.48 E
Lui ≃, Ang.	152	8.41 S	17.56 E
Lui ≃, Zam.	152	16.21 S	23.18 E
Lui, Beinn ∧	46	56.24 N	4.49 W
Luia	152	8.26 S	21.45 E
Luia (Ruya) ≃, Afr.	154	16.34 S	33.12 E
Luia ≃, Ang.	152	8.24 S	21.42 E
Lúia ≃, Moç.	154	15.34 S	32.58 E
Luiana	152	17.23 S	23.03 E
Luiana ≃	152	17.27 S	23.14 E
Luichart, Loch ⊜	46	57.37 N	4.46 W
Luido	156	21.31 S	34.41 E
Luie ≃	152	4.33 S	17.41 E
Luik → Liège	56	50.38 N	5.34 E
Luilaka ≃	152	0.52 S	20.12 E
Luilu ≃	152	6.22 S	23.50 E
Luimbale	152	12.15 S	15.19 E
Luimneach → Limerick	48	52.40 N	8.38 W
Luing I	46	56.13 N	5.40 W
Luino	58	46.00 N	8.44 E
Luio ≃	152	13.15 S	21.39 E
Luipaardsvlei	273d	26.16 S	27.42 E
Luiro ≃	24	67.08 N	27.29 E
Luisant	50	48.25 N	1.29 E
Luís Correia	250	2.53 S	41.40 W
Luisen-Berg ∧[2]	264a	52.27 N	13.07 E
Luisenthal	54	50.47 N	10.43 E
Luís Gomes	250	6.25 S	38.23 W
Luis Guillón	288	34.48 S	58.27 W
Luishia	154	11.10 S	27.02 E
Luis Moya, Méx.	234	22.25 N	102.15 W
Luis Moya, Méx.	234	23.05 N	103.56 W
Luis Muñoz Marin, Aeropuerto Internacional ⊠	240m	18.27 N	66.00 W
Luis Peña, Cayo de I	240m	18.18 N	65.20 W
Luis Pereira, Arroyo ≃	258	34.33 S	57.02 W
Luita	152	8.04 S	19.25 E
Luitpold Coast ⊥[2]	9	78.30 S	32.00 W
Luiza	152	7.12 S	22.25 E
Luiza ≃	152	7.35 S	22.40 E
Luizavo ≃	152	11.42 S	23.12 E
Luizi	154	6.03 S	27.28 E
Luiziânia	255	21.41 S	50.17 W
Luján, Arg.	252	33.03 S	68.52 W
Luján, Arg.	252	32.22 S	65.57 W
Luján, Arg.	258	34.34 S	59.07 W
Luján ≃	288	34.26 S	58.32 W
Lujia, Zhg.	106	31.15 N	121.37 E
Lujia, Zhg.	106	31.19 N	121.03 E
Lujia, Zhg.	269b	31.22 N	121.18 E
Lujiabang	106	31.20 N	121.01 E
Lujiachang	107	30.14 N	105.34 E
Lujiagangzi	104	42.05 N	122.59 E
Lujiang	100	31.14 N	117.17 E
Lujiao	100	29.10 N	112.52 E
Lujiaoxi	107	28.55 N	105.48 E
Lujiaqiao, Zhg.	106	31.47 N	120.27 E
Lujiaqiao, Zhg.	107	28.50 N	106.21 E
Lujiatun, Zhg.	98	40.14 N	122.11 E
Lujiatun, Zhg.	104	41.58 N	122.38 E
Lujiatun, Zhg.	104	42.18 N	124.15 E
Lujiatun, Zhg.	104	41.10 N	121.56 E
Lujiazhou	100	28.16 N	114.35 E
L'uk	80	56.55 N	52.48 E
Lukachukai Wash V	200	36.39 N	109.36 W
Lukačok	89	53.03 N	132.16 E
Lukala	152	5.31 S	14.32 E
Lukang	100	24.03 N	120.25 E
Lukanga, Zaïre	152	1.00 S	18.08 E
Lukanga, Zaïre	152	1.41 S	18.09 E
Lukanga Swamp ≡	154	14.25 S	27.45 E
Luk'anovo	82	54.52 N	37.25 E
Lukašin	84	40.12 N	44.01 E
Lukaškin Jar	86	60.20 N	78.24 E
Luke, Mount ∧	162	27.13 S	116.48 E
Luke Air Force Base ■	200	33.32 N	112.22 W
Lukenie ≃	152	2.44 S	18.09 E
Lukens, Mount ∧	280	34.16 N	118.14 W
Lukeville	200	31.52 N	112.48 W
Luki	76	53.29 N	26.15 E
Lukino, Ross.	82	55.26 N	37.04 E
Lukino, Ross.	82	55.50 N	36.49 E
Lukka	140	14.33 N	23.42 E
Luknovo	80	56.12 N	42.03 E
Lukojanov	80	55.02 N	44.30 E
Lukolela, Zaïre	152	5.23 S	24.32 E
Lukolela, Zaïre	152	1.03 S	17.12 E
Lukong	107	29.31 N	105.39 E
Lukoshi ≃	152	10.05 S	22.59 E
Lukosi	154	18.30 S	26.30 E
Lukoškino	82	55.19 N	37.16 E
Lukou, Zhg.	100	27.14 N	114.04 E
Lukou, Zhg.	106	31.48 N	118.52 E
Lukoupu	100	29.30 N	113.26 E
Lukouyu	100	28.24 N	113.18 E
Lukov	78	51.13 N	24.19 E
Lukovit	38	43.12 N	24.10 E
Lukovskaja	80	50.35 N	41.52 E
Łuków	30	51.56 N	22.23 E
Lükqün	86	42.44 N	89.42 E
Lukuga ≃	154	5.40 S	26.55 E
Lukula	152	5.23 S	12.57 E
Lukula ≃, Afr.	152	5.08 S	12.28 E
Lukula ≃, Zaïre	152	4.13 S	17.58 E
Lukuledi ≃	154	10.05 S	39.42 E
Lukulu	152	14.25 S	23.12 E
Lukulu ≃	154	10.56 S	31.05 E
Lukumburu	154	9.45 S	35.09 E
Lukunga ≃	273b	4.25 S	15.14 E
Lukuni	152	5.52 S	17.11 E
Lukusashi ≃	154	14.38 S	30.00 E
Lukusuzi National Park ♠	154	12.50 S	32.35 E
Lula, It.	71	40.28 N	9.29 E
Lula, Ms., U.S.	194	34.27 N	90.28 W
Lula, Zaïre	152	5.22 S	16.02 E
Luleå	26	65.34 N	22.10 E
Luleälven ≃	24	65.35 N	22.03 E
Lüleburgaz	130	41.24 N	27.21 E
Lules	252	26.56 S	65.21 W
Luliang	102	25.05 N	103.36 E
Lüliang Shan ⋏	102	37.25 N	111.20 E
Luliāni	123	31.15 N	74.25 E
Luliao	269d	25.07 N	121.39 E
Luling	222	29.40 N	97.38 W
Lullingstone Castle ⊥	260	51.21 N	0.12 E
Lulo ≃	152	9.25 S	18.14 E
Lulong	98	39.54 N	118.50 E
Lulonga	152	0.37 N	18.23 E
Lulonga ≃	152	0.43 N	18.23 E
Lulu ≃	152	1.18 N	23.42 E
Lulua ≃	152	5.02 S	21.07 E
Luluabourg → Kananga	152	5.54 S	22.25 E
Lulu Island I, B.C., Can.	224	49.09 N	123.05 W
Lulu Island I, Ak., U.S.	182	55.28 N	133.30 W
Luluo	98	37.06 N	113.58 E
Lulworth, Mount ∧	162	26.53 S	117.42 E
Lumai	152	13.31 S	21.21 E
Lumajang	115a	8.08 S	113.13 E
Lumajangdong Co ⊜	120	34.00 N	81.45 E
Lumaku, Gunong ∧	112	4.52 N	115.38 E
Lumaling	120	29.53 N	92.37 E
Lumb	262	53.42 N	1.58 W
Lumbala ≃	152	12.38 S	22.34 E
Lumbala Kaquengue	152	12.39 S	22.34 E
Lumbala N'guimbo	152	14.08 S	21.25 E
Lumbangaraga	114	1.53 N	99.04 E
Lumbanlobu	114	2.31 N	99.08 E
Lumbe ≃	152	16.42 S	23.42 E
Lumber ≃	192	34.12 N	79.10 W
Lumber City	192	31.55 N	82.40 W
Lumberport	188	39.22 N	80.20 W
Lumberton, Ms., U.S.	194	31.00 N	89.27 W
Lumberton, N.J., U.S.	285	39.57 N	74.48 W
Lumberton, N.C., U.S.	192	34.37 N	79.00 W
Lumberton, Tx., U.S.	194	30.16 N	94.10 W
Lumbinī □[8]	124	27.45 N	83.30 E
Lumbis	112	4.18 N	116.15 E
Lumbo	154	15.00 S	40.44 E
Lumbovka	24	67.44 N	40.30 E
Lumbrales	34	40.56 N	6.43 W
Lumbrein	58	46.41 N	9.08 E
Lumbres	50	50.42 N	2.08 E
Lumbwa	154	0.12 S	35.28 E
Lumby	182	50.15 N	118.58 W
Lumding	120	25.45 N	93.10 E
Lumege ≃	152	11.55 S	20.58 E
Lumerau ≃	116	5.21 N	118.53 E
Lumi	164	3.29 S	142.02 E
Lumiei ≃	64	46.24 N	12.51 E
Luminárias	256	21.30 S	44.54 W
Luminosa	256	22.35 S	45.38 W
Lumintao ≃	116	12.43 N	120.55 E
Lummen	56	50.59 N	5.12 E
Lummi Bay ⊂	224	48.46 N	122.41 W
Lummi Indian Reservation ◆[4]	224	48.48 N	122.38 W
Lummi Island	224	48.42 N	122.40 W
Lummi Island I	224	48.42 N	122.40 W
Lumphanan	46	57.07 N	2.41 W
Lumphăt	110	13.30 N	106.59 E
Lumphini Park ♠	269a	13.44 N	100.33 E
Lumpkin	192	32.03 N	84.47 W
Lumpun ≃	80	57.01 N	51.22 E
Lumsån ≃	40	59.59 N	15.26 E
Lumsås	41	55.57 N	11.31 E
Lumsden, Nf., Can.	186	49.19 N	53.37 W
Lumsden, Sk., Can.	184	50.34 N	104.53 W
Lumsden, N.Z.	172	45.44 S	168.27 E
Lumsden, Scot., U.K.	46	57.15 N	2.52 W
Lumsheden	40	60.43 N	16.15 E
Lums Pond State Park ♠	208	39.34 N	75.43 W
Lumu, Indon.	112	2.11 S	119.09 E
Lumu, Zhg.	106	31.22 N	120.37 E
Lumuna	154	3.46 S	26.24 E
Lumuna ≃	152	16.59 S	21.25 E
Lumut, Indon.	114	1.33 N	98.56 E
Lumut, Malay.	114	4.14 N	100.38 E
Lumut, Tanjung ›	112	3.50 S	105.57 E
Lumwana	154	11.50 S	25.10 E
Lün, Mong.	88	47.24 N	102.52 E
Lün, Mong.	88	47.52 N	105.15 E
Luna, Pil.	116	16.51 N	120.23 E
Luna, Pil.	116	18.18 N	121.21 E
Luna ≃	246	4.32 S	60.41 W
Lunada Bay ⊂	280	33.46 N	118.25 W
Lunain ≃	50	48.20 N	2.47 E
Lunamatrona	71	39.39 N	8.54 E
Lunan	102	24.49 N	103.16 E
Lunan Bay ⊂	46	56.39 N	2.28 W
Lunano	66	43.44 N	12.26 E
Luna Pier	216	41.48 N	83.26 W
Lūnāvāda	120	23.08 N	73.37 E
Luncarty	46	56.27 N	3.28 W
Lund, B.C., Can.	182	49.58 N	124.44 W
Lund, Sve.	41	55.42 N	13.11 E
Lund, Nv., U.S.	204	38.51 N	115.00 W
Lunda ≃, Ang.	152	6.07 S	13.52 E
L'unda ≃, Ross	80	56.32 N	46.03 E
Lundåkrabukten ⊂	41	55.48 N	12.53 E
Lundale	188	37.48 N	81.44 W
Lunda Norte □[5]	152	8.45 S	19.45 E
Lundar	184	50.42 N	98.02 W
Lunda Sul □[5]	152	10.00 S	20.30 E
Lundazi	154	12.19 S	33.13 E
Lundby	41	55.07 N	11.53 E
Lunde	41	55.29 N	10.21 E
Lundeborg	41	55.08 N	10.47 E
Lunden	41	54.20 N	9.01 E
Lunderskov	41	55.29 N	9.18 E
Lundevatn ⊜	26	58.22 N	6.36 E
Lundi ≃	154	21.43 S	32.34 E
Lundsberg	40	59.30 N	14.10 E
Lundsfjärden ⊜	40	59.38 N	14.41 E
Lundy I	42	51.10 N	4.40 W
Lundys Lane	214	41.53 N	80.21 W
Lune ≃	44	54.02 N	2.50 W
Lüneburg	52	53.15 N	10.23 E
Lüneburg □[5]	52	53.15 N	10.00 E
Lüneburger Heide ◆[1]	52	53.10 N	10.20 E
Lunel	62	43.41 N	4.08 E
Lünen	52	51.36 N	7.32 E
Lunenburg, N.S., Can.	186	44.23 N	64.19 W
Lunenburg, Ma., U.S.	207	42.35 N	71.43 W
Lunenburg, Va., U.S.	192	36.57 N	78.15 W
Luneray	50	49.50 N	0.55 E
Lünern	263	51.33 N	7.46 E
Lunéville	56	48.36 N	6.30 E
Lunga I	46	56.13 N	5.42 W
Lunga ≃, Ang.	152	5.59 S	16.20 E
Lunga ≃, Zam.	154	14.34 S	26.25 E
Lungälven ≃	40	59.34 N	14.10 E
Lunga Reservoir ⊜[1]	208	38.32 N	77.28 W
Lungau ◆[1]	64	47.07 N	13.39 E
Lungavilla	62	45.02 N	9.04 E
Lungch'i → Zhangzhou	100	24.33 N	117.39 E
Lunge	152	12.12 S	16.05 E
Lunge'nake	120	31.45 N	85.55 E
Lungern	58	46.47 N	8.10 E
Lunggar	120	31.10 N	84.00 E
Lunghezza ◆[8]	267a	41.55 N	12.40 E
Lungi	150	8.38 N	13.13 W
Lunglei	120	22.53 N	92.44 E
Lungro	68	39.44 N	16.07 E
Lungsang	124	29.51 N	88.41 E
Lungt'an	100	24.52 N	121.12 E
Lungué-Bungo (Lungwebungu) ≃	152	14.19 S	23.14 E
Lunguya	154	3.23 S	32.24 E
Lungwebungu (Lungué-Bungo) ≃	152	14.19 S	23.14 E
Lūni	120	26.00 N	73.00 E
Lūni ≃	120	24.41 N	71.15 E
Luni ⊥	64	44.04 N	10.01 E
Lunia-Bubi	154	7.30 S	24.49 E
Lunigiana ◆[1]	64	44.15 N	9.50 E
Lunin	76	52.18 N	26.38 E
Luninec	76	52.15 N	26.48 E
Lunino, Ross.	80	53.35 N	45.14 E
Lunino, Ross.	82	54.09 N	38.29 E
Lunjiao	100	22.53 N	113.13 E
Lūnkaransar	120	28.29 N	73.44 E
Lunnaja, gora ∧	180	68.14 N	174.20 E
Lunndörrsfjällen ∧	26	63.00 N	13.00 E
Lunno	76	53.27 N	24.16 E
Lunongzha	106	31.59 N	120.55 E
Lunsar	150	8.41 N	12.32 W
Lunsemfwa ≃	154	14.54 S	30.12 E
Lunt	262	53.31 N	2.59 W
Lunteren	52	52.05 N	5.37 E
Lunyuk	115b	8.57 S	117.14 E
Lunz am See	61	47.51 N	15.03 E
Lunzenau	54	50.58 N	12.45 E
Lunzhen	98	36.47 N	116.34 E
Luo ≃, Zhg.	102	34.48 N	113.04 E
Luo ≃, Zhg.	102	34.42 N	110.15 E
Luoba, Zhg.	100	24.51 N	114.13 E
Luoba, Zhg.	107	29.08 N	106.11 E
Luobei (Fengxiang)	89	47.34 N	130.50 E
Luobo	102	28.22 N	101.38 E
Luobu	102	24.30 N	109.40 E
Luobumiao	102	40.19 N	107.30 E
Luochanghe	100	31.01 N	117.18 E
Luocheng, Zhg.	102	24.51 N	108.59 E
Luocheng, Zhg.	107	29.23 N	104.01 E
Luochuan	102	35.55 N	109.26 E
Luoci	102	25.19 N	102.18 E
Luodian	106	31.25 N	121.20 E
Luoding	102	22.47 N	111.31 E
Luoduzhen	107	30.22 N	106.35 E
Luofa	105	39.25 N	116.50 E
Luofang, Zhg.	100	28.40 N	115.04 E
Luofang, Zhg.	100	27.52 N	115.06 E
Luofu, Zaïre	154	0.10 S	29.14 E
Luofu, Zhg.	100	24.32 N	115.35 E
Luogang, Zhg.	100	23.11 N	113.30 E
Luogang, Zhg.	100	24.25 N	115.38 E
Luogosanto	71	41.03 N	9.13 E
Luoguhe	89	53.18 N	121.30 E
Luohan Shan ∧	100	25.51 N	119.13 E
Luohe	100	33.35 N	114.01 E
Luoheya	98	35.46 N	118.54 E
Luohua	100	26.35 N	118.43 E
Luoji	100	32.06 N	117.16 E
Luojiachang	107	30.49 N	106.32 E
Luojiang	102	31.21 N	104.28 E
Luojiatang	106	30.18 N	120.13 E
Luojiatun, Zhg.	98	40.11 N	118.34 E
Luojiatun, Zhg.	104	42.06 N	122.44 E
Luojiatun, Zhg.	104	40.55 N	122.04 E
Luojiawei	100	26.55 N	115.02 E
Luoke	100	24.07 N	114.28 E
Luokeng	100	24.32 N	113.23 E
Luokou, Zhg.	100	28.54 N	117.24 E
Luokou, Zhg.	100	25.46 N	115.39 E
Luolong	107	28.49 N	104.46 E
L'Uomo di Cagna ∧	71	41.33 N	9.04 E
Luonan	102	34.05 N	110.04 E
Luoning	102	34.25 N	111.42 E
Luoping	102	24.59 N	104.21 E
Luoqi	102	29.48 N	106.56 E
Luoqiao	100	26.28 N	119.01 E
Luoquanzhen	107	29.50 N	104.31 E
Luoshan, Zhg.	100	32.13 N	114.32 E
Luoshan, Zhg.	100	29.41 N	113.18 E
Luoshan, Zhg.	105	39.55 N	117.33 E
Luoshe, Zhg.	106	31.39 N	120.11 E
Luoshe, Zhg.	106	30.41 N	120.04 E
Luoshuihe	98	39.27 N	114.19 E
Luossa ≃	152	8.24 S	17.03 E
Luotian	100	30.48 N	115.22 E
Luotuodian	100	32.13 N	113.49 E
Luotuoqiao	100	29.56 N	121.32 E
Luotuo Shan ∧	104	42.14 N	121.42 E
Luowenba	102	31.48 N	107.48 E
Luowenyu	105	40.16 N	117.57 E
Luoxi	100	29.05 N	114.58 E
Luoxiao Shan ⋏	100	26.00 N	114.00 E
Luoyang (Loyang), Zhg.	102	34.41 N	112.28 E
Luoyang, Zhg.	106	31.39 N	120.05 E
Luoyuan	100	26.31 N	119.32 E
Luoyuan Wan ⊂	100	26.25 N	119.43 E
Luoyukou	102	38.23 N	110.43 E
Luozhexi	107	29.02 N	103.54 E
Luozi	152	4.57 S	14.08 E
Lupala	156	17.50 S	19.06 E
Lupani	154	18.54 S	27.44 E
Lupao	116	15.53 N	120.54 E
Lupar ≃	112	1.30 N	111.00 E
Łupawa	30	54.26 N	17.24 E
Lupberg	60	49.09 N	11.45 E
Lupembe	154	9.15 S	35.15 E
Lupeni	38	45.22 N	23.13 E
Lupire	152	14.36 S	19.29 E
Lupiro	154	8.23 S	36.40 E
Lupon	116	6.54 N	126.00 E
Luppa	54	51.20 N	12.57 E
Luputa	152	7.10 S	23.42 E
Luqiao, Zhg.	100	32.34 N	117.14 E
Luqiao, Zhg.	100	28.35 N	121.22 E
Luqu	102	34.41 N	102.22 E
Luque	34	37.33 N	4.16 W
Luquillo	240m	18.22 N	65.43 W
Luquillo, Sierra de ⋏	240m	18.17 N	65.47 W
Lūrah ≃	120	31.33 N	66.33 E
Luray	188	38.39 N	78.27 W
Lure	58	47.41 N	6.30 E
Lure, Montagne de ⋏	62	44.07 N	5.47 E
Lureco ≃	154	12.28 S	37.40 E
Luremo	152	8.31 S	17.50 E
Lurgan	48	54.28 N	6.20 W
Luribay	248	17.06 S	67.39 W
Lurigancho	286d	12.02 S	77.01 W
Lurín	248	12.17 S	76.52 W
Lúrio	154	13.35 S	40.30 E
Lúrio ≃	154	13.35 S	40.32 E
Lurisia	62	44.18 N	7.42 E
Lurnea	274a	33.56 S	150.54 E
Lurö I	26	58.48 N	13.14 E
Lürrip ◆[8]	263	51.12 N	6.28 E
Lusahunga	154	2.52 S	31.15 E
Lusaka, Zaïre	154	7.10 S	29.27 E
Lusaka, Zam.	154	15.25 S	28.17 E
Lusaka □[4]	154	15.25 S	29.00 E
Lusakert	84	40.23 N	44.36 E
Lusambo	152	4.58 S	23.27 E
Lusancay Islands and Reefs II	164	8.25 S	150.20 E
Lusanga	152	4.50 S	18.44 E
Lusangaye	154	4.54 S	26.00 E
Lusangi	154	4.37 S	27.08 E
Luscar	182	53.04 N	117.24 W
Luseke	152	2.51 S	23.08 E
Luseland	184	52.05 N	109.24 W
Lusen ∧	60	48.56 N	13.31 E
Lusenga Plain National Park ♠	154	9.30 S	29.10 E
Lusengo	152	1.46 N	19.29 E
Luserna San Giovanni	62	44.48 N	7.15 E
Lush, Mount ∧	164	17.02 S	127.30 E
Lushan, Zhg.	100	33.45 N	112.53 E
Lushan, Zhg.	102	30.15 N	102.58 E
Lu Shan ∧	100	29.31 N	115.58 E
Lu Shan ⋏	98	36.05 N	118.05 E
Lushanguanliju	100	29.33 N	115.58 E
Lushi	102	34.05 N	111.01 E
Lushiko (Luchico) ≃	152	6.13 S	19.40 E
Lüshikou	100	29.16 N	120.17 E
Lushnje	38	40.56 N	19.42 E
Lushoto	154	4.47 S	38.17 E
Lushui	102	26.00 N	98.51 E
Lüshun (Port Arthur)	98	38.48 N	121.16 E
Lüsi	106	32.03 N	121.36 E
Lusi ≃	115a	7.05 S	110.55 E
Lusiana	64	45.47 N	11.34 E
Lusignan	32	46.26 N	0.07 E
Lusignan, Lac ⊜	206	46.40 N	74.09 W
Lusigny-sur-Barse	50	48.15 N	4.16 E
Lusikisiki	158	31.25 S	29.30 E
L'usino	76	52.38 N	26.31 E
Lusk, Ire.	48	53.32 N	6.10 W
Lusk, Wy., U.S.	200	42.45 N	104.27 W
Lus-la-Croix-Haute	62	44.40 N	5.42 E
Lusongwa	152	12.58 S	24.16 E
Luspebryggan	24	67.01 N	19.51 E
Lussac-les-Châteaux	32	46.24 N	0.44 E
Lussan	62	44.09 N	4.22 E
Lușșān, Wādī V	132	30.30 N	34.18 E
Lustenau	58	47.26 N	9.39 E
Luster	26	61.26 N	7.24 E
Lustin	56	50.23 N	4.53 E
Lustrafjorden ⊂[2]	26	61.20 N	7.22 E
Lüstringen	52	52.16 N	8.08 E
Lusutfu (Maputo) (Great Usutu) ≃	158	26.11 S	32.42 E
Luswishi ≃	154	13.55 S	27.24 E
Lūt, Dasht-e ◆[2]	128	32.00 N	58.00 E
Lü-ta → Dalian	98	38.53 N	121.35 E
L'uta ≃	76	58.37 N	28.40 E
Lutago (Luttach)	64	46.57 N	11.55 E
Lutai	100	33.32 N	115.03 E
Lütan, Zhg.	98	34.07 N	114.27 E
Lütan, Zhg.	100	28.57 N	119.46 E
Lutang	100	25.39 N	112.46 E
Lutao	116	10.00 N	124.04 E
Lü Tao I	100	22.40 N	121.29 E
Lutcher	194	30.02 N	90.41 W
Lute	284c	39.04 N	77.03 W
Lutembo	152	13.26 S	21.16 E
Lutembo ≃	152	12.03 S	22.15 E
L'uten'ka	78	50.13 N	34.02 E
Lutesville	194	37.18 N	89.58 W
Lutéte ≃	152	9.21 S	15.14 E
Lutexu ≃	273b	4.24 S	15.12 E
Lütgendortmund ◆[8]	263	51.30 N	7.21 E
Luthe	52	52.26 N	9.28 E
Luther, Mi., U.S.	190	44.02 N	85.40 W
Luther, Ok., U.S.	196	35.39 N	97.11 W
Luther Lake ⊜	212	43.55 N	80.26 W
Luthersburg	214	41.03 N	78.43 W
Lutherville-Timonium	284b	39.25 N	76.37 W
Luthrie	46	56.21 N	3.05 W
Luti	175e	7.14 S	156.59 E
Lutian, Zhg.	100	26.33 N	114.38 E
Lütian, Zhg.	100	23.48 N	113.56 E
Lütjenburg	54	54.17 N	10.35 E
Lütjensee	52	53.39 N	10.22 E
Luton, Eng., U.K.	42	51.53 N	0.25 W
Luton, Eng., U.K.	260	51.22 N	0.32 E
Lutong	112	4.28 N	114.00 E
Lutosn'a ≃	82	56.26 N	36.52 E
Lutou	100	32.16 N	112.53 E
Lutry	58	46.30 N	6.41 E
Lutshi	154	4.09 S	26.30 E
Lutshima ≃	152	5.22 S	18.59 E
Lutsk → Luck	78	50.44 N	25.20 E
Luttach → Lutago	64	46.57 N	11.55 E
Lutter am Barenberge	52	51.59 N	10.16 E
Lutterbach	58	47.46 N	7.17 E
Lutterworth	42	52.28 N	1.10 W
Lüttich → Liège	56	50.38 N	5.34 E
Luttrell	192	36.11 N	83.44 W
Lüttringhausen ◆[8]	263	51.13 N	7.14 E
Lutuai ≃	152	12.33 S	20.16 E
Lutugino	83	48.24 N	39.13 E
Lutz	220	28.09 N	82.27 W
Lützel	56	50.58 N	8.10 E
Lutzelbourg	56	48.44 N	7.15 E
Lützelflüh	58	47.00 N	7.41 E
Lützen	54	51.15 N	12.08 E
Lutzerath	56	50.07 N	7.00 E
Lutz Hill	284b	39.20 N	76.32 W
Lützow	54	53.40 N	11.11 E
Lützow-Holm Bay ⊂	9	69.10 S	37.30 E
Lutzputs	158	28.03 S	20.40 E
Lützschena	54	51.23 N	12.16 E
Lutzville	158	31.33 S	18.22 E
Luud, Waadi V	144	10.17 N	50.14 E
Luuq	144	3.48 N	42.33 E
Luus	102	45.30 N	105.45 E
Luverne, Al., U.S.	194	31.42 N	86.15 W
Lu Verne, Ia., U.S.	190	42.54 N	94.04 W
Luverne, Mn., U.S.	198	43.39 N	96.12 W
Luvo	152	5.51 S	14.05 E
Luvo ≃	152	10.18 S	17.08 E
Luvua	154	8.48 S	25.19 E
Lúvua ≃, Ang.	152	11.57 S	22.30 E
Luvua ≃, Zaïre	154	6.46 S	26.58 E
Luvuvhu ≃	156	22.40 S	30.55 E
Luwegu ≃	154	8.31 S	37.23 E
Luwingu	154	10.15 S	29.55 E
Luwuk, Indon.	112	0.56 S	122.47 E
Luwuk → Banggai, Indon.	112	1.34 S	123.30 E
Luxana Bay ⊂	182	52.03 N	131.00 W
Luxapallila Creek ≃	194	33.28 N	88.26 W
Luxembourg	56	49.36 N	6.09 E
Luxembourg □[4]	56	50.00 N	5.30 E
Luxembourg □[1], Europe	22	49.45 N	6.05 E
Luxembourg □[1], Europe	56	49.45 N	6.05 E
Luxembourg, Aéroport de ⊠	56	49.37 N	6.10 E
Luxembourg, Jardin du ♠	261	48.51 N	2.19 E
Luxemburg	190	44.32 N	87.42 W
Luxemburg → Luxembourg □[1]	56	49.45 N	6.05 E
Luxemburgo → Luxembourg □[1]	56	49.45 N	6.05 E
Luxeuil-les-Bains	58	47.49 N	6.23 E
Luxi, Zhg.	102	24.32 N	103.41 E
Luxi (Mangshi), Zhg.	102	24.20 N	98.25 E
Lüxia	100	26.41 N	120.06 E
Luxian	107	28.55 N	105.29 E
Luxiang, Zhg.	106	31.32 N	120.45 E
Lüxiang, Zhg.	106	30.50 N	121.10 E
Luxi Dao I	100	27.59 N	121.11 E
Luxikou	100	29.54 N	113.42 E
Luxmanor	284c	39.02 N	77.07 W
Luxor → Al-Uqșur, Mișr	140	25.41 N	32.39 E
Luxor, Pa., U.S.	214	40.20 N	79.28 W
Luxora	194	35.45 N	89.55 W
Luxu	106	31.01 N	120.50 E
Lu Xun Museum ⊍	269b	31.16 N	121.28 E
Lüxuqiao	106	31.50 N	119.31 E
Luy ≃	32	43.39 N	1.08 W
Luyan	106	30.25 N	120.53 E
Lüyang	104	41.23 N	121.40 E
Luyanó ≃	286b	23.07 N	82.21 W
Luyeh	100	22.55 N	121.08 E
Luyi	100	33.53 N	115.28 E
Luynes	50	47.23 N	0.33 E
Luyu	106	31.34 N	121.41 E
Luyuan, Zhg.	106	31.51 N	120.38 E
Luyuan, Zhg.	271a	39.54 N	116.27 E
Luz, Bra.	255	19.48 S	45.40 W
Luz, Bra.	287a	22.48 S	43.05 W
Luz ◆[8]	266c	38.46 N	9.10 W
Luz, Estação da ◆[5]	287b	23.32 S	46.38 W
Luz, Isla I	254	45.30 S	73.59 W
Luz, Ponta da ›	287a	22.47 S	43.05 W
Luza, Ross.	24	62.42 N	37.06 E
Luza, Ross.	24	60.39 N	47.10 E
Luža, Ross.	76	59.58 N	31.56 E
Luža ≃	82	55.03 N	36.35 E
Luzarches	50	49.07 N	2.25 E
Luzern	58	47.03 N	8.18 E
Luzern □[3]	58	47.05 N	8.05 E
Luzerne	210	41.17 N	75.54 W
Luzerne □[6]	210	41.14 N	75.53 W
Luzhai, Zhg.	102	24.31 N	109.50 E
Luzhai, Zhg.	269b	31.20 N	121.22 E
Luzhi	106	31.16 N	120.52 E
Luzhou	107	28.54 N	105.27 E
Luziânia	255	16.15 S	47.56 W
Lužické hory ⋏	54	50.48 N	14.40 E
Luzilândia	250	3.28 S	42.22 W
Lužki, Bela.	76	55.21 N	27.52 E
Lužki, Ross.	82	54.51 N	37.36 E
Lužná	54	50.06 N	13.45 E
Lužnice ≃	30	49.14 N	14.23 E
Lužniki ◆[8]	265b	55.43 N	37.33 E
Luzon I	116	16.00 N	121.00 E
Luzon Strait ʮ	108	20.30 N	121.00 E
Lužskaja guba ⊂	76	59.45 N	28.20 E
Luzy	32	46.48 N	3.58 E
Luzzara	64	44.58 N	10.41 E
Luzzi	68	39.27 N	16.17 E
L'va ≃	78	52.00 N	27.36 E
L'va Tolstogo	82	54.37 N	36.03 E
L'vov	78	49.50 N	24.00 E
L'vov □[4]	78	49.30 N	24.00 E
L'vovskij	82	55.19 N	37.31 E
Lwów → L'vov	78	49.50 N	24.00 E
Lwówek	30	52.28 N	16.10 E
Lwówek Śląski	30	51.07 N	15.35 E
Lyall, Mount ∧	172	45.17 S	167.34 E
Lyallpur → Faisalabad	123	31.25 N	73.05 E
Lyantonde	154	0.24 S	31.09 E
Lybster	46	58.18 N	3.18 W
Lycaonia □[9]	130	37.50 N	33.15 E
Lychen	54	53.12 N	13.19 E
Lycia □[9]	130	36.20 N	30.00 E
Lyck → Ełk	30	53.50 N	22.22 E
Lyckeby	26	56.12 N	15.39 E
Lyčkovo, Ross.	76	57.55 N	32.24 E
Lyčkovo, Ukr.	78	49.06 N	35.12 E
Lycksele	26	64.36 N	18.40 E
Lycoming □[6]	210	41.14 N	77.00 W
Lycoming Creek ≃	210	41.13 N	77.02 W
Lydd	42	50.57 N	0.55 E
Lydda → Lod	132	31.58 N	34.54 E
Lydden ≃	42	50.56 N	2.22 W
Lydenburg	156	25.10 S	30.29 E
Lydenburgh County Park ♠	276	40.50 N	73.14 W
Lydford	42	50.39 N	4.06 W
Lydgate	262	53.44 N	2.07 W
Lydham	42	52.31 N	2.58 W
Lydia □[9]	130	38.40 N	27.30 E
Lydia Mills	192	34.28 N	81.55 W
Lydiate	262	53.32 N	2.57 W
Lydick	216	41.42 N	86.22 W
Lydney	42	51.44 N	2.32 W
Lye Green	260	51.43 N	0.35 W
Lyell, Mount ∧, Can.	182	51.57 N	117.06 W
Lyell, Mount ∧, Ca., U.S.	226	37.44 N	119.16 W
Lyell Brown, Mount ∧	162	23.21 S	130.24 E
Lyell Island I	182	52.40 N	131.30 W
Lyerly	192	34.24 N	85.24 W
Lyford	196	26.24 N	97.47 W
Lygnern ⊜	26	57.29 N	12.20 E
Lykens	208	40.34 N	76.42 W
Lykošino	76	58.07 N	33.43 E
Lyle, Mn., U.S.	190	43.30 N	92.56 W
Lyle, Wa., U.S.	224	45.41 N	121.17 W
Lyles	194	35.55 N	87.20 W
Lyman, Ne., U.S.	198	41.55 N	104.02 W
Lyman, S.C., U.S.	192	34.56 N	82.07 W
Lyman, Wa., U.S.	224	48.31 N	122.03 W
Lyman, Wy., U.S.	200	41.19 N	110.17 W
Lymbel'karamo	86	60.15 N	83.32 E
Lyme	207	41.18 N	72.19 W
Lyme Bay ⊂	42	50.38 N	3.00 W
Lyme Hall ⊥	262	53.20 N	2.03 W
Lyme Park ♠	262	53.21 N	2.04 W
Lyme Regis	42	50.44 N	2.57 W
Lyminge	42	51.08 N	1.05 E
Lymington	42	50.46 N	1.33 W
Lymkoj	86	59.31 N	70.22 E
Lymm	262	53.23 N	2.29 W
Lympne	42	51.05 N	1.02 E
Lympstone	42	50.39 N	3.25 W
Lyn	212	44.35 N	75.47 W
Łyna (Lava) ≃	76	54.37 N	21.14 E
Lynæs	41	55.57 N	11.52 E
Lynbrook	276	40.39 N	73.41 W
Lynch, Ky., U.S.	192	36.57 N	82.55 W
Lynch, Ne., U.S.	198	42.49 N	98.27 W
Lynch, Lac ⊜	190	46.25 N	77.05 W
Lynchburg, Oh., U.S.	218	39.14 N	83.47 W
Lynchburg, S.C., U.S.	192	34.03 N	80.04 W
Lynchburg, Tn., U.S.	194	35.16 N	86.22 W
Lynchburg, Va., U.S.	192	37.24 N	79.08 W
Lynches ≃	192	33.50 N	79.22 W
Lynchville	214	41.26 N	78.34 W
Lynd ≃	164	16.28 S	143.18 E
Lynde Creek ≃	212	43.51 N	78.57 W
Lynden, On., Can.	212	43.14 N	80.09 W
Lynden, Wa. U.S.	224	48.56 N	122.27 W
Lyndhurst, Austl.	166	19.12 S	144.23 E
Lyndhurst, Austl.	166	30.17 S	138.21 E
Lyndhurst, Austl.	274b	38.03 S	145.15 E
Lyndhurst, Eng., U.K.	42	50.52 N	1.34 W
Lyndhurst, N.J., U.S.	276	40.48 N	74.07 W
Lyndhurst, Oh., U.S.	214	41.31 N	81.29 W
Lyndoch	168b	34.37 S	138.53 E
Lyndon, Austl.	162	23.37 S	115.15 E
Lyndon, Ks., U.S.	198	38.38 N	95.41 W
Lyndon, Ky., U.S.	218	38.15 N	85.36 W
Lyndon ≃	162	23.29 S	114.06 E
Lyndon B. Johnson, Lake ⊜[1]	196	30.35 N	98.25 W
Lyndon B. Johnson Historical Park ♠	196	30.15 N	98.38 W
Lyndon B. Johnson Space Center ⊍[3]	222	29.34 N	95.05 W
Lyndonville, N.Y., U.S.	210	43.19 N	78.23 W
Lyndonville, Vt., U.S.	188	44.32 N	72.00 W
Lyndora	214	40.51 N	79.55 W
Lyne	260	51.23 N	0.33 W
Lyne ≃, Eng., U.K.	44	54.58 N	3.01 W
Lyne ≃, Eng., U.K.	44	55.12 N	1.31 W
Lyneham	42	51.31 N	1.58 W
Lynemouth	44	55.12 N	1.31 W
Lyne Water ≃	46	55.39 N	3.16 W
Lynga	80	57.17 N	53.04 E
Lyngdal	26	58.08 N	7.05 E
Lynge	41	55.51 N	12.17 E
Lyngen	24	69.34 N	20.10 E
Lyngen ⊂[2]	24	69.58 N	20.30 E
Lyngør	26	58.38 N	9.10 E
Lynher ≃	42	50.28 N	4.12 W
Lynmouth	42	51.15 N	3.50 W
Lynn, Al., U.S.	194	34.02 N	87.32 W
Lynn, In., U.S.	218	40.02 N	84.56 W
Lynn, Ma., U.S.	207	42.28 N	70.57 W
Lynn ≃	212	42.47 N	80.12 W
Lynn Canal ⊂	180	58.50 N	135.15 W
Lynndyl	200	39.31 N	112.22 W
Lynne Acres	284b	39.21 N	76.45 W
Lynnfield	207	42.32 N	71.02 W
Lynn Garden	192	36.34 N	82.34 W
Lynn Harbor ⊂	283	42.27 N	70.57 W
Lynn Haven	194	30.14 N	85.38 W
Lynn Lake	184	56.51 N	101.03 W
Lynnville	190	41.34 N	92.47 W
Lynnwood, Pa., U.S.	210	41.14 N	75.56 W
Lynnwood, Pa., U.S.	214	40.07 N	79.51 W
Lynnwood, Wa., U.S.	224	47.49 N	122.18 W
Lynn Woods ♠	283	42.29 N	70.59 W
Lynton	42	51.15 N	3.50 W
Lyntupy	76	55.03 N	26.19 E
Lynwood, Ca., U.S.	228	33.55 N	118.12 W
Lynwood, Il., U.S.	278	41.32 N	87.32 W
Lynx Lake ⊜	176	62.25 N	106.15 W
Lyø I	41	55.02 N	10.10 E
Lyon	62	45.45 N	4.51 E
Lyon □[6]	226	39.00 N	119.15 W
Lyon ≃	46	56.37 N	4.01 W
Lyon, Gare ◆[5]	261	48.51 N	2.23 E
Lyon, Glen V	46	56.35 N	4.20 W
Lyon, Loch ⊜	46	56.32 N	4.36 W
Lyon Inlet ⊂	176	66.32 N	83.53 W
Lyon Mountain	188	44.43 N	73.54 W
Lyon Mountain ∧	188	44.41 N	73.53 W
Lyonnais □[9]	62	45.45 N	4.30 E
Lyonnais, Monts du ⋏	62	45.40 N	4.30 E
Lyons, Co., U.S.	200	40.13 N	105.16 W
Lyons, Ga., U.S.	192	32.12 N	82.19 W
Lyons, Il., U.S.	216	41.48 N	87.49 W
Lyons, In., U.S.	194	38.59 N	87.04 W
Lyons, Ks., U.S.	198	38.20 N	98.12 W
Lyons, Mi., U.S.	216	42.58 N	84.56 W
Lyons, Ne., U.S.	198	41.56 N	96.28 W
Lyons, N.Y., U.S.	210	43.03 N	76.59 W
Lyons, Oh., U.S.	216	41.41 N	84.04 W
Lyons, Tx., U.S.	222	30.23 N	96.34 W
Lyons, Wi., U.S.	216	42.39 N	88.21 W
Lyons ≃	162	25.02 S	115.09 E
Lyon-Satolas, Aéroport de ⊠	62	45.43 N	5.04 E
Lyons Creek ≃	284a	43.03 N	79.04 W
Lyons Falls	212	43.37 N	75.22 W
Lyons-la-Forêt	50	49.24 N	1.28 E
Lyons Plains	207	41.13 N	73.21 W
Lyons Run ≃	279b	40.25 N	79.43 W
Lyon Station	208	40.28 N	75.45 W
Lyonsville	276	40.57 N	74.25 W
Lyracrumpane	48	52.20 N	9.30 W
Lyrestad	40	58.48 N	14.04 E
Lys (Leie) ≃, Europe	50	51.03 N	3.43 E
Lys ≃, It.	62	45.36 N	7.47 E
Lysá ∧	60	49.29 N	12.42 E
Lysaja Gora	78	48.11 N	31.06 E
Lysaker	26	59.54 N	10.36 E
Lys'anka	78	49.16 N	30.50 E
Lysá pod Makytou	30	49.12 N	18.13 E
Lysefjorden ⊂[2]	26	59.00 N	6.14 E
Lysekil	26	58.16 N	11.26 E
Łysica ∧	30	50.54 N	20.55 E
Lysjön ⊜	40	60.07 N	14.18 E
Lyskovo	80	56.04 N	45.02 E
Lysogorka	83	47.42 N	39.12 E
Lyss	58	47.04 N	7.18 E
Lysterfield	274b	37.56 S	145.18 E
Lysterfield ∧[2]	274b	37.56 S	145.16 E
Lysterfield Reservoir ⊜[1]	274b	37.58 S	145.18 E
Lyster Station	206	46.22 N	71.37 W
Lys'va	86	58.07 N	57.47 E
Lys'va ≃	80	58.15 N	54.47 E
Lysyje Gory	80	51.32 N	44.46 E
Lytham Saint Anne's	44	53.45 N	2.57 W
Lytkarino	82	55.35 N	37.54 E
Lytle	196	29.13 N	98.47 W
Lytle Creek ≃	228	34.09 N	117.23 W
Lyttelton, N.Z.	172	43.35 S	172.42 E

Symbol	English	Deutsch	Español	Français	Português
≃	River	Fluß	Río	Rivière	Rio
≅	Canal	Kanal	Canal	Canal	Canal
⊾	Waterfall, Rapids	Wasserfall, Stromschnellen	Cascada, Rápidos	Chute d'eau, Rapides	Cascata, Rápidos
ʮ	Strait	Meeresstraße	Estrecho	Détroit	Estreito
⊂	Bay, Gulf	Bucht, Golf	Bahía, Golfo	Baie, Golfe	Baía, Golfo
⊜	Lake, Lakes	See, Seen	Lago, Lagos	Lac, Lacs	Lago, Lagos
≡	Swamp	Sumpf	Pantano	Marais	Pântano
⊓	Ice Features, Glacier	Eis- und Gletscherformen	Accidentes Glaciales	Formes glaciaires	Acidentes glaciares
⊤	Other Hydrographic Features	Andere Hydrographische Objekte	Otros Elementos Hidrográficos	Autres données hydrographiques	Outros acidentes hidrográficos
✦	Submarine Features	Untermeerische Objekte	Accidentes Submarinos	Formes de relief sous-marin	Acidentes submarinos
□	Political Unit	Politische Einheit	Unidad Politica	Entité politique	Unidade política
⊍	Cultural Institution	Kulturelle Institution	Institución Cultural	Institution culturelle	Instituição cultural
⊥	Historical Site	Historische Stätte	Sitio Histórico	Site historique	Sitio histórico
♠	Recreational Site	Erholungs- und Ferienort	Sitio de Recreo	Centre de loisirs	Area de Lazer
⊠	Airport	Flughafen	Aeropuerto	Aéroport	Aeroporto
■	Military Installation	Militäranlage	Instalación Militar	Installation militaire	Instalação militar
◆	Miscellaneous	Verschiedenes	Misceláneo	Divers	Diversos

Symbols in the index entries represent the broad categories identified in the key at the right. Symbols with superior numbers (∧1) identify subcategories (see complete key on page I · 1).

Symbole im Register stellen die rechts im Schlüssel erklärten Kategorien dar. Symbole mit hochgestellten Ziffern (∧1) bezeichnen Unterteilungen einer Kategorie (vgl. vollständiger Schlüssel auf Seite I · 1).

Los símbolos incluidos en el texto del índice representan las grandes categorías identificadas con la clave a la derecha. Los símbolos con números en su parte superior (∧1) identifican las subcategorías (véase la clave completa en la página I · 1).

Os símbolos incluídos no texto do índice representam as grandes categorias identificadas na chave à direita. Os símbolos com números em sua parte superior (∧1) identificam as subcategorias (veja-se a chave completa na página I · 1).

Les symboles de l'index représentent les catégories indiquées dans la légende à droite. Les symboles suivis d'un indice (∧1) représentent des sous-catégories (voir légende complète à la page I · 1).

Symbol	English	Deutsch	Español	Português	Français	
∧	Mountain	Berg	Montaña	Montanha	Montagne	
⋋	Mountains	Gebirge	Montañas	Montanhas	Montagnes	
⋋	Pass	Paß	Paso	Passo	Col	
∨	Valley, Canyon	Tal, Cañon	Valle, Cañón	Vale, Canhão	Vallée, Canyon	
≃	Plain	Ebene	Llano	Planície	Plaine	
↦	Cape	Kap	Cabo	Cabo	Cap	
I	Island	Insel	Isla	Ilha	Île	
II	Islands	Inseln	Islas	Ilhas	Îles	
±	Other Topographic Features	Andere Topographische Objekte	Otros Elementos Topográficos	Outros acidentes topográficos	Autres données topographiques	

ESPAÑOL

Nombre	Página	Lat.°′	Long.°′ W = Oeste
Maḥallat Kayl	142	31.01 N	30.17 E
Maḥallat Marḥūm	142	30.48 N	30.57 E
Maḥallat Minūf	142	30.53 N	30.58 E
Maḥallat Zayyād	142	31.02 N	31.14 E
Maham	124	28.59 N	76.18 E
Mahamba	158	27.07 S	31.10 E
Mahānadi ≃	118	20.19 N	86.45 E
Mahānadpati	126	23.00 N	88.16 E
Mahānanda ≃	124	24.29 N	88.18 E
Mahanay Island I	116	10.12 N	124.14 E
Mahanoro	157b	19.54 S	48.48 E
Mahanoy City	208	40.48 N	76.08 W
Mahanoy Creek ≃	208	40.42 N	76.51 W
Mahantango Creek ≃	208	40.47 N	76.56 W
Mahantango Mountain ∧	208	40.40 N	76.45 W
Mahao	89	43.10 N	127.59 E
Mahape	272c	19.07 N	73.01 E
Mahārājganj, India	124	26.07 N	84.29 E
Mahārājganj, India	124	27.09 N	83.34 E
Mahārājpur, India	124	25.01 N	79.44 E
Mahārājpur, India	272a	28.39 N	77.20 E
Mahārāshtra □[3]	122	19.00 N	76.00 E
Maḥārīq, Wādī V	142	27.48 N	31.47 E
Mahārlū, Daryācheh-ye ⊜	128	29.25 N	52.50 E
Mahāsamund	120	21.06 N	82.06 E
Maha Sarakham	110	16.11 N	103.18 E
Maha Sawat, Khlong ≍	269a	13.47 N	100.28 E
Mahasoa	157b	22.12 S	46.06 E
Mahasolo	157b	19.07 S	46.22 E
Mahates	246	10.14 N	75.12 W
Mahatsinjo	157b	21.26 S	45.51 E
Maḥaṭṭat al-Ḥafīf	132	32.12 N	37.08 E
Mahaut	240d	15.21 N	61.25 W
Mahavavy ≃, Madag.	157b	15.57 S	45.54 E
Mahavavy ≃, Madag.	157b	13.00 S	48.55 E
Mahaweli ≃	122	8.27 N	81.13 E
Mahaxai	110	17.25 N	105.12 E
Maḥbas, Wādī al- V	140	15.50 N	29.45 E
Mahbūbābād	122	17.37 N	80.01 E
Mahbūbnagar	122	16.44 N	77.59 E
Mahd adh-Dhahab	128	23.30 N	40.52 E
Mahdāt, Bi'r al- ⍑[4]	142	30.44 N	32.32 E
Mahdia, Guy.	246	5.16 N	59.09 W
Mahdia, Tun.	148	35.30 N	11.04 E
Mahdia □[8]	148	35.18 N	10.45 E
Mahe	122	11.42 N	75.32 E
Mahébourg	157c	20.24 S	57.42 E
Mahé Island I	138	4.40 S	55.28 E
Mahendraganj	124	25.20 N	89.45 E
Mahendragarh	124	28.17 N	76.09 E
Mahendra Giri ∧	122	18.58 N	84.21 E
Mahendranagar	124	28.52 N	80.17 E
Mahenge, Tan.	154	7.38 S	36.16 E
Mahenge, Tan.	154	8.41 S	36.43 E
Maheno	172	45.10 S	170.50 E
Mahesāna	120	23.36 N	72.24 E
Mahesgādi	272b	22.39 N	88.33 E
Maheshmunda	126	24.13 N	86.24 E
Maheshtala	272b	22.30 N	88.15 E
Maheshwar	120	22.11 N	75.35 E
Mahespur	124	23.21 N	88.55 E
Mahgawān	124	26.29 N	78.37 E
Mahi ≃	120	22.16 N	72.58 E
Mahia Peninsula >[1]	172	39.10 S	177.53 E
Mahiāri	272b	22.35 N	88.14 E
Māhikpur	272b	22.32 N	88.14 E
Mahilāra	126	22.56 N	90.16 E
Māhīm ◆[8]	272c	19.03 N	72.49 E
Māhīm ≃	272c	19.03 N	72.51 E
Māhīm Bay c	272c	19.02 N	72.50 E
Mahina, Mali	150	13.46 N	10.51 W
Mahina, Poly. fr.	174s	17.31 S	149.30 W
Mahinerangi, Lake ⊜	172	45.51 S	169.57 E
Mahinog	116	9.09 N	124.47 E
Mahīshādal	126	22.11 N	87.59 E
Mahishdānga	272b	22.54 N	88.11 E
Mahlabatini	158	28.14 S	31.30 E
Mahlangasi	158	27.37 S	31.42 E
Mahlberg	58	48.17 N	7.48 E
Mahlow	54	52.22 N	13.24 E
Mahlsdorf	54	52.47 N	11.13 E
Mahlsdorf ◆[8]	264a	52.31 N	13.37 E
Mahlsdorf-Süd ◆[8]	264a	52.29 N	13.36 E
Mahmūdābād, India	124	27.18 N	81.07 E
Maḥmūdābād, Īrān	128	36.38 N	52.15 E
Maḥmūd-e Rāqī	120	35.01 N	69.20 E
Maḥmūdīyah, Tur'at al- ≍	142	31.11 N	29.53 E
Mahmudiye	130	39.30 N	31.00 E
Mahmūdpur, India	272a	28.46 N	77.22 E
Mahmudpur, India	272b	22.41 N	88.09 E
Mahmutbey ◆[8]	267b	41.03 N	28.49 E
Mahmutşevketpaşa	130	41.05 N	29.19 E
Mahmutşevketpaşa ◆[8]	267b	41.09 N	29.11 E
Mahnomen	198	47.18 N	95.58 W
Mahoba	124	25.17 N	79.52 E
Mahogany Mountain ∧	202	43.14 N	117.16 W
Mahomet	216	40.11 N	88.24 W
Mahone Bay	186	44.27 N	64.23 W
Mahone Bay c	186	44.30 N	64.15 W
Mahoning □[6]	214	41.06 N	80.39 W
Mahoning ≃	214	40.58 N	80.23 W
Mahoning, West Branch ≃	214	41.12 N	80.57 W
Mahoning Creek ≃	214	40.55 N	79.27 W
Mahoning Creek Lake ⊜[1]	214	40.50 N	79.10 W
Mahony Lake ⊜	180	65.30 N	125.20 W
Mahood Falls	182	51.50 N	120.39 W
Mahood Lake ⊜	182	51.55 N	120.24 W
Mahopac	210	41.22 N	73.44 W
Mahopac Falls	210	41.22 N	73.46 W
Mahora	34	39.13 N	1.44 W
Mahoras Brook ≃	276	40.25 N	74.08 W
Mahrāt, Jabal ⩘[1]	144	17.05 N	51.30 E
Mahrauli ◆[8]	272a	28.31 N	77.11 E
Mahrauni	124	24.35 N	78.43 E
Mähren → Morava □[9]	30	49.20 N	17.00 E
Mahres	148	34.32 N	10.30 E
Mähring	60	49.55 N	12.32 E
Mahuiling	100	29.24 N	115.48 E
Māhul ◆[8]	272c	19.01 N	72.53 E
Mahulia	126	22.39 N	86.24 E
Mahur Island I	164	2.50 S	152.40 E
Mahuta	154	10.52 S	39.27 E
Mahuva	120	21.05 N	71.48 E
Mahwa	124	27.03 N	76.56 E
Mahwah	276	41.06 N	74.09 W
Mahwah ≃	276	41.06 N	74.10 W
Mai, Île de I	275a	45.36 N	73.50 W
Maia, Am. Sam.	174y	14.13 S	169.28 W
Maia, Port.	34	41.14 N	8.37 W
Mai Aini	144	14.47 N	39.06 E
Maiala National Park ♠	171a	27.19 S	152.46 E
Maianga	152	14.12 S	21.45 E
Maiano	64	46.11 N	13.04 E
Maiauatá	250	1.51 S	49.02 W
Maicao	246	11.23 N	72.13 W
Maîche	58	47.15 N	6.48 E
Maichen	102	20.29 N	109.59 E
Maici ≃	248	6.30 S	61.43 W
Maicuru ≃	250	2.14 S	54.17 W
Maida	68	38.51 N	16.22 E
Maidan ♠	272b	22.33 N	88.21 E
Maiden	192	35.34 N	81.12 W
Maidenhead	42	51.32 N	0.44 W
Maiden Newton	42	50.46 N	2.35 W
Maidstone, Austl.	274b	37.47 S	144.52 E
Maidstone, On., Can.	214	42.13 N	82.53 W
Maidstone, Sk., Can.	184	53.06 N	109.18 W
Maidstone, Eng., U.K.	42	51.17 N	0.32 E
Maidstone □[8]	260	51.17 N	0.35 E

FRANÇAIS

Nom	Page	Lat.°′	Long.°′ W = Ouest
Maiduguri	146	11.51 N	13.10 E
Maie	154	2.46 N	30.34 E
Maiella, Montagna della ⩘	66	42.05 N	14.07 E
Maienfeld	58	47.00 N	9.32 E
Maierato	68	38.42 N	16.11 E
Maifeld ◆[1]	56	50.20 N	7.20 E
Maigatari	150	12.46 N	9.27 E
Maignelay	50	49.33 N	2.31 E
Maigo	116	8.10 N	123.57 E
Mai Gudo ∧	144	7.29 N	37.12 E
Maigue ≃	48	52.39 N	8.48 W
Maihar	124	24.16 N	80.45 E
Maihara	94	35.19 N	136.17 E
Maijoma	196	28.55 N	104.21 W
Maikala Plateau ⩘[1]	124	22.30 N	81.00 E
Maikala Range ⩘	122	22.30 N	81.30 E
Maikammer	56	49.18 N	8.08 E
Maiko ≃	154	0.14 N	25.33 E
Maiko, Parc National de la ♠	154	3.30 N	27.45 E
Maikoor, Pulau I	164	6.15 S	134.15 E
Mailand → Milano	62	45.28 N	9.12 E
Mailāni	124	28.17 N	80.21 E
Mailasqui	256	23.33 S	47.04 W
Maili	229c	21.25 N	158.10 W
Maillane	62	43.50 N	4.47 E
Mailley-et-Chazelot	58	47.32 N	6.03 E
Maillezais	32	46.22 N	0.44 W
Mailly-le-Camp	50	48.40 N	4.13 E
Mailly-le-Château	50	47.36 N	3.38 E
Mailly-Maillet	50	50.04 N	2.36 E
Mailsi	123	29.48 N	72.11 E
Maimbung	116	5.56 N	121.02 E
Mai Mefales	144	14.59 N	38.16 E
Mā'īn	132	31.41 N	35.44 E
Main ≃, Dtsch.	30	50.00 N	8.18 E
Main ≃, N. Ire., U.K.	48	54.43 N	6.18 W
Maināguri	124	26.34 N	88.49 E
Mainau	58	47.42 N	9.11 E
Mainburg	60	48.38 N	11.47 E
Main Camp	174o	2.01 N	157.25 W
Main Canal ≍, Ca., U.S.	226	37.25 N	121.05 W
Main Canal ≍, Ca., U.S.	226	37.23 N	120.26 W
Main Canal ≍, Wa., U.S.	224	47.07 N	120.44 W
Main Channel Ʉ	190	45.22 N	81.50 W
Maincourt-sur-Yvette	261	48.43 N	1.58 E
Main Creek ≃	276	40.34 N	74.11 W
Maincy	261	48.33 N	2.42 E
Mai-Ndombe, Lac ⊜	152	2.00 S	18.20 E
Main-Donau-Kanal ≍	60	49.02 N	11.36 E
Main Duck Island I	212	43.56 N	76.37 W
Maine	210	42.11 N	76.03 W
Maine □[9]	32	48.15 N	0.05 W
Maine □[3], U.S.	178	45.15 N	69.15 W
Maine □[3], U.S.	188	45.15 N	69.15 W
Maine ≃	48	52.09 N	9.45 W
Maine, Gulf of c	178	43.00 N	68.00 W
Maine-et-Loire □[5]	32	47.25 N	0.30 W
Mainesburg	210	41.47 N	77.07 W
Maïné-Soroa	146	13.12 N	12.02 E
Maineville	218	39.18 N	84.13 W
Mainguerin	261	48.32 N	1.51 E
Mainhardt	56	49.04 N	9.33 E
Mainit	116	9.32 N	125.32 E
Mainit, Lake ⊜	116	9.26 N	125.32 E
Mainland	285	40.15 N	75.22 W
Mainland I, Scot., U.K.	46	59.00 N	3.15 W
Mainland I, Scot., U.K.	46a	60.16 N	1.16 W
Mainleus	54	50.06 N	11.22 E
Mainoru	164	14.02 S	134.05 E
Mainpuri	124	27.14 N	79.01 E
Main Range National Park ♠	171a	28.01 S	152.22 E
Maintal	56	50.09 N	8.54 E
Maintenon	50	48.35 N	1.35 E
Maintirano	157b	18.03 S	44.01 E
Main Topsail ∧	186	49.08 N	56.33 W
Mainvilliers	50	48.27 N	1.28 E
Mainz	56	50.01 N	8.16 E
Maio I	150a	15.15 N	23.10 W
Maiolati Spontini	66	43.28 N	13.06 E
Maiori	68	40.39 N	14.38 E
Maiori, Nuraghe ⊥	71	40.56 N	9.06 E
Maipa	164	8.21 S	146.33 E
Maipo ≃	252	33.37 S	71.39 W
Maipo, Volcán ∧[1]	252	34.10 S	69.50 W
Maipú, Arg.	252	36.52 S	57.52 W
Maipú, Arg.	252	32.58 S	68.47 W
Maipú, Chile	252	33.31 S	70.46 W
Maiqihamiao	89	43.22 N	120.46 E
Maiquetía	246	10.36 N	66.57 W
Maira ≃	62	44.49 N	7.38 E
Maira, Valle V	62	44.30 N	7.08 E
Mairābāri	120	26.28 N	92.26 E
Mairi	250	11.43 S	40.08 W
Mairinque	256	23.33 S	47.10 W
Mairiporã	256	23.19 S	46.35 W
Mairiporã □[7]	287b	23.24 S	46.37 W
Mairipotaba	255	17.18 S	49.28 W
Maisach	60	48.13 N	11.16 E
Maisaka	94	34.41 N	137.37 E
Maishi	100	29.11 N	113.58 E
Maišiagala	76	54.52 N	25.04 E
Maiskhāl Island I	120	21.36 N	91.56 E
Maison de Pierre, Lac de la ⊜	206	46.53 N	74.42 W
Maisonneuve, Parc ♠	275a	45.33 N	73.34 W
Maisons-Alfort	261	48.48 N	2.26 E
Maisons-Laffitte	50	48.57 N	2.09 E
Maisons-Laffitte, Château de ⊥	261	48.57 N	2.09 E
Maisse	50	48.24 N	2.23 E
Maissin	56	49.58 N	5.11 E
Maitani	270	34.49 N	135.22 E
Maitengwe	156	20.06 S	27.13 E
Maitengwe ≃	156	19.59 S	26.26 E
Maithon Reservoir ⊜[1]	126	23.50 N	86.43 E
Maitland, Austl.	168b	34.22 S	137.40 E
Maitland, Austl.	170	32.44 S	151.33 E
Maitland, N.S., Can.	186	45.19 N	63.30 W
Maitland, On., Can.	212	44.38 N	75.37 W
Maitland, Fl., U.S.	220	28.37 N	81.21 W
Maitland ≃	190	43.45 N	81.43 W
Maitland, Lake ⊜	162	27.11 S	121.03 E
Maixie	100	27.38 N	115.29 E
Maíz ≃	236	11.17 N	83.52 W
Maíz, Islas del II	236	12.15 N	83.00 W
Maizefield	158	26.28 S	29.31 E
Maizhokunggar	120	29.50 N	91.45 E
Maizières-lès-Metz	56	49.13 N	6.09 E
Maizières-lès-Vic	58	48.43 N	6.46 E
Maizuru	96	35.28 N	135.24 E
Maja ≃, Ross.	74	60.24 N	134.30 E
Maja ≃, Ross.	89	54.31 N	134.41 E
Majābirah, Minqār al- ⊥[4]	142	30.16 N	29.49 E
Majačka ≃	83	48.44 N	37.33 E
Majačnyj	86	52.41 N	55.44 E
Majadahonda	266a	40.29 N	3.52 W
Majagua	240p	21.55 N	79.00 W
Majagual	246	8.33 N	74.38 W
Majaki, Ukr.	78	46.25 N	30.16 E
Majaki, Ukr.	83	48.57 N	37.37 E
Majalaya	115a	7.03 S	107.45 E
Majalengka	115a	6.50 S	108.13 E
Majana, Ensenada de c	240p	22.41 N	82.45 W
Majanji	154	0.15 N	33.59 E
Majari ≃	246	3.29 N	60.58 W
Majayjay	116	14.09 N	121.28 E
Majchura	85	39.02 N	68.35 E
Majdantal	85	43.41 N	68.02 E
Majd el Kurūm	132	32.55 N	35.15 E

PORTUGUÊS

Nome	Página	Lat.°′	Long.°′ W = Oeste
Majé	256	22.39 S	43.02 W
Majeigha	140	11.33 N	24.40 E
Majenang	115a	7.18 S	108.45 E
Majene	112	3.33 S	118.57 E
Majenica	216	40.46 N	85.27 W
Majevica ⩘	38	44.30 N	18.55 E
Maji	144	6.11 N	35.38 E
Majia	100	32.32 N	118.50 E
Majia ≃	98	38.09 N	117.53 E
Majiacun	106	30.08 N	119.58 E
Majiahe	102	35.20 N	104.46 E
Majian, Zhg.	100	29.19 N	119.36 E
Majian, Zhg.	100	29.43 N	120.00 E
Majiang, Zhg.	102	23.48 N	111.09 E
Majiang, Zhg.	110	26.28 N	107.28 E
Majiangzong	120	30.27 N	90.03 E
Majiaoba	102	32.14 N	104.35 E
Majiaping	102	36.31 N	103.20 E
Majiasi	105	39.03 N	117.05 E
Majiawopu	104	41.46 N	121.06 E
Majiayan	100	27.26 N	112.56 E
Majiazhai	104	42.22 N	124.04 E
Majiazhou	100	26.46 N	114.47 E
Majidun Creek ≃	273a	6.38 N	3.28 E
Majie, Zhg.	102	23.50 N	105.07 E
Majie, Zhg.	102	25.03 N	103.45 E
Majin	100	29.18 N	118.24 E
Majin ≃	100	29.00 N	118.21 E
Majinzhuangzi	104	41.55 N	123.53 E
Maji Shan I	106	31.26 N	120.06 E
Majītha	123	31.46 N	74.57 E
Majja	74	61.44 N	130.18 E
Majkain	86	51.27 N	75.52 E
Majkop	84	44.35 N	40.07 E
Majkor	86	59.01 N	55.54 E
Majlibaš	86	45.49 N	62.39 E
Majli-Saj	85	41.17 N	72.29 E
Majlispur	126	24.13 N	90.53 E
Majmak	85	42.40 N	71.15 E
Majna, Ross.	80	54.07 N	47.37 E
Majna, Ross.	86	53.00 N	91.28 E
Majnan	272b	22.59 N	88.09 E
Majnic, ozero ⊜	180	63.15 N	176.40 E
Majno-Gytkino	180	63.36 N	176.30 E
Majŏn-ni, C.M.I.K.	98	39.06 N	127.07 E
Majŏn-ni, Taehan	271b	37.36 N	126.41 E
Major, Puig ∧	34	39.48 N	2.48 E
Majorca → Mallorca I	34	39.30 N	3.00 E
Major Creek ≃	169	36.51 S	145.05 E
Major Isidoro	250	9.32 S	37.00 W
Majorque, Île → Mallorca I	34	39.30 N	3.00 E
Majrūr	140	14.01 N	30.27 E
Majrūr, Wādī V	140	15.44 N	26.26 E
Majsk	86	57.49 N	77.16 E
Majskij, Ross.	83	47.43 N	40.03 E
Majskij, Ross.	84	43.38 N	44.04 E
Majskij, Ross.	89	52.18 N	129.38 E
Majskij, Ross.	89	49.00 N	140.10 E
Majskoje, Kaz.	86	50.55 N	78.15 E
Majskoje, Ross.	82	56.08 N	37.55 E
Majtan	86	45.46 N	74.20 E
Majtobe	85	43.01 N	70.35 E
Māju	126	22.37 N	88.05 E
Majuba Hill ⊥	158	27.28 S	29.51 E
Majuqiao	105	39.46 N	116.32 E
Majuro I[1]	14	7.09 N	171.12 E
Majuzigou	104	41.49 N	121.38 E
Maka	150	13.40 N	14.17 W
Makabana	152	2.48 S	12.29 E
Makabe	94	36.16 N	140.06 E
Makadasa ≃	116	7.22 N	124.36 E
Makaha, Hi., U.S.	229c	21.28 N	158.13 W
Makaha, Zimb.	154	17.17 S	32.37 E
Makaha Point >	229b	22.08 N	159.44 W
Makah Indian Reservation ◆[4]	224	48.20 N	124.41 W
Makahuena Point >	229b	21.52 N	159.27 W
Makak	152	3.33 N	11.02 E
Makala	273b	4.25 S	15.17 E
Makalamabedi	156	20.19 S	23.51 E
Makale	112	3.06 S	119.51 E
Makallé	252	27.13 S	59.17 W
Makālu ∧	124	27.54 N	87.06 E
Makamba	154	4.08 S	29.49 E
Makanapur	272a	28.38 N	77.21 E
Makanči	86	46.48 N	82.00 E
Makanya	154	4.20 S	37.51 E
Makanza	152	1.36 N	19.07 E
Makaoo Indian Reserve ◆[4]	184	53.40 N	110.02 W
Makapu Point >	174v	18.59 S	169.56 W
Makapuu Head >	229c	21.19 N	157.39 W
Makarakomburu, Mount ∧	175e	9.43 S	160.02 E
Makarakskij	86	55.36 N	88.03 E
Makarapan Mountain ∧	246	4.00 N	58.51 W
Makarewa	172	46.20 S	168.21 E
Makari	146	12.35 N	14.28 E
Makar-Ib	24	63.39 N	49.24 E
Makaricha	24	66.15 N	58.20 E
Makarje	80	58.35 N	48.11 E
Makarjev	80	57.52 N	43.48 E
Makarjevo	80	56.06 N	45.06 E
Makarov, Ross.	89	48.38 N	142.48 E
Makarov, Ukr.	78	50.28 N	29.49 E
Makarovo, Ross.	80	52.18 N	43.20 E
Makarovo, Ross.	82	54.22 N	36.40 E
Makarovo, Ross.	88	57.29 N	107.52 E
Makarska	36	43.18 N	17.02 E
Makasar → Ujungpandang	112	5.07 S	119.24 E
Makasar, Selat (Makassar Strait) Ʉ	112	2.00 S	117.30 E
Makaševka	80	51.30 N	42.36 E
Makassar Strait → Makasar, Selat Ʉ	112	2.00 S	117.30 E
Makasuko	154	6.00 S	34.56 E
Makat	80	47.39 N	53.19 E
Makatea I	14	15.50 S	148.15 W
Makati	269f	14.34 N	121.02 E
Makaw, Mya.	110	26.27 N	96.42 E
Makaw, Zaïre	152	3.29 S	18.19 E
Makawao	229a	20.51 N	156.18 W
Makaweli	229b	21.55 N	159.38 W
Makay, Massif du ⩘	157b	21.15 S	45.15 E
Makaya	152	3.22 S	18.02 E
Makedonija → Macedonia □[1]	38	41.50 N	22.00 E
Makefu	174v	18.59 S	169.55 W
Makejevka, Ukr.	78	50.40 N	31.50 E
Makejevka, Ukr.	83	48.02 N	37.58 E
Makejevka, Ukr.	83	49.14 N	37.59 E
Makemie Park	208	37.55 N	75.34 W
Makemo I[1]	14	16.35 S	143.40 W
Makena	229a	20.39 N	156.27 W
Makeni	150	8.53 N	12.03 W
Makere	154	4.17 S	30.25 E
Maketu	172	37.46 S	176.27 E
Makeyevka → Makejevka	83	48.02 N	37.58 E
Makgadikgadi ≡	156	20.45 S	25.30 E
Makgadikgadi Pans Game Reserve ◆[4]	156	20.30 S	24.45 E
Makhachkala → Machačkala	84	42.58 N	47.30 E
Makhad	123	33.08 N	71.44 E
Makhaleng ≃	158	30.20 S	27.23 E
Mākhālpur	272b	22.56 N	88.10 E
Makham	110	12.40 N	102.12 E
Makhdūmnagar	124	26.28 N	82.46 E
Makhfar al-Quwayrah	132	29.48 N	35.19 E
Makhfar Ramn	132	29.42 N	35.25 E
Makhrūq, Wādī al- V	132	31.30 N	37.10 E
Makhyah, Wādī V	144	17.40 N	49.01 E
Maki, Indon.	164	3.11 S	134.14 E
Maki, Nihon	92	37.45 N	138.53 E
Maki, Nihon	94	37.05 N	138.23 E
Maki, Nihon	270	34.52 N	135.04 E
Makika, Lua ⊥[6]	229a	20.34 N	156.34 W
Makikih	172	44.38 S	171.09 E
Makilala	116	6.55 N	125.05 E
Makindu	154	2.17 S	37.49 E
Makino, Nihon	94	35.28 N	136.05 E
M'akino, Ross.	265b	55.48 N	37.22 E
Makinsk	86	52.37 N	70.26 E
Makio-dam ◆[6]	94	35.50 N	137.36 E
Makioka	94	35.45 N	138.43 E
Makira □[4]	175e	11.00 S	162.30 E
Makira Harbour c	175e	10.25 S	161.29 E
M'akiševo	76	56.34 N	28.53 E
M'akit	74	61.24 N	152.09 E
Makkah (Mecca)	144	21.27 N	39.49 E
Makkavejevo	88	51.44 N	113.58 E
Makkum	52	53.04 N	5.24 E
Makó, Magy.	30	46.13 N	20.29 E
Mako, Sén.	150	12.52 N	12.21 W
Makoaneng ∧	158	29.47 S	28.57 E
Makobe Lake ⊜	190	47.27 N	80.25 W
Makoka	154	2.34 S	25.29 E
Makok-ni	271b	37.43 N	126.38 E
Makokou	152	0.34 N	12.52 E
Makoli	154	17.27 S	26.05 E
Makongai Island I	175g	17.27 S	178.58 E
Makongo	154	3.25 N	26.22 E
Makongolosi	154	8.24 S	33.09 E
Makopse	84	43.59 N	39.13 E
Makorako ∧	172	39.09 S	176.02 E
Makoro	154	3.08 N	29.44 E
Makoshika State Park ♠	198	47.03 N	104.41 W
Makošino	78	51.27 N	32.18 E
Makotuku	172	40.07 S	176.14 E
Makoua	152	0.01 N	15.39 E
Makov	30	49.23 N	18.30 E
Makovskoje	86	58.12 N	90.52 E
Maków Mazowiecki	30	52.52 N	21.06 E
Maków Podhalański	30	49.44 N	19.41 E
Makrai	124	22.04 N	77.06 E
Makrampur	126	22.44 N	90.14 E
Makrāna	120	27.03 N	74.43 E
Makran Coast ⊥[2]	128	25.15 N	61.00 E
M'aksa	76	58.54 N	38.12 E
Maksaticha	76	57.48 N	35.53 E
Maksimicha	88	53.15 N	108.43 E
Maksimkin Jar	86	58.42 N	86.48 E
Maksimoviči	78	51.13 N	29.37 E
Maksimovka, Ross.	80	52.59 N	51.10 E
Maksimovka, Ross.	89	46.04 N	137.51 E
Maksimovka, Ukr.	83	47.38 N	37.34 E
Maksimovo	82	56.20 N	35.58 E
Maksudangarh	124	24.03 N	77.15 E
Maktar	148	35.51 N	9.12 E
Maktau	154	3.24 S	38.08 E
Mākū, Īrān	128	39.17 N	44.31 E
Maku, Zhg.	105	39.33 N	114.46 E
Makuhari	268	35.39 N	140.03 E
Makuliro	154	9.35 S	37.26 E
Makumbako	154	8.51 S	34.50 E
Makumbi	152	5.51 S	20.41 E
Makung (P'enghu)	100	23.34 N	119.34 E
Makunudu I	122	6.25 N	72.41 E
Makunudu Atoll I[1]	122	6.20 N	72.36 E
Makuragi-san ∧	96	35.32 N	133.08 E
Makurazaki	92	31.16 N	130.19 E
Makurdi	150	7.45 N	8.32 E
Makushin Volcano ∧[1]	180	53.53 N	166.50 W
Makušino	86	55.13 N	67.13 E
Makuyuni	154	3.33 S	36.06 E
Makwa Lake ⊜	184	54.04 N	109.15 W
Makwassie	158	27.26 S	26.00 E
Makwende-Bayo	154	7.08 S	28.06 E
Makwiro	154	17.58 S	30.28 E
Māl, India	124	26.52 N	88.44 E
Mal, Maur.	150	16.58 N	13.23 W
Mala, Perú	248	12.39 S	76.38 W
Malå, Sve.	26	65.11 N	18.44 E
Mala ≃	248	12.40 S	76.41 W
Mala, Punta >	246	7.28 N	80.00 W
Malabang	116	7.38 N	124.03 E
Malabar, Austl.	274a	33.58 S	151.15 E
Malabar, Fl., U.S.	220	28.00 N	80.33 W
Malabar Coast ⊥[2]	122	11.00 N	75.00 E
Malabar Farm State Park ♠	214	40.38 N	82.25 W
Malabar Hill ∧[2]	272c	18.57 N	72.48 E
Malabar Point >	272c	18.57 N	72.47 E
Malabo	152	3.45 N	8.47 E
Mal Abrigo	258	34.09 S	56.57 W
Malabrigo Point >	116	13.36 N	121.15 E
Malabuyoc	116	9.39 N	123.19 E
Malaca, Estrecho de → Malacca, Strait of Ʉ	110	2.30 N	101.20 E
Malacacheta	255	17.50 S	42.05 W
Malacañang Palace ʊ	269f	14.36 N	120.59 E
Malacatepec, Volcán ∧[1]	286a	19.10 N	99.16 W
Malacca, Strait of Ʉ	110	2.30 N	101.20 E
Malachovka	82	55.39 N	38.00 E
Malachovo, Ross.	82	54.45 N	37.27 E
Malachovo, Ross.	82	54.22 N	37.31 E
Malachovskij	80	49.08 N	41.43 E
Malacky	30	48.27 N	17.00 E
Mālād ◆[3]	272c	19.11 N	72.51 E
Malad ≃	200	41.35 N	112.07 W
Malad City	202	42.11 N	112.15 W
Malad Creek ≃	272c	19.08 N	72.48 E
Malafede ≃	267a	41.47 N	12.24 E
Málaga, Col.	246	6.42 N	72.44 W
Málaga, Esp.	34	36.43 N	4.25 W
Malaga, Ca., U.S.	226	36.42 N	119.46 W
Malaga, N.J., U.S.	208	39.34 N	75.02 W
Malaga, N.M., U.S.	196	32.13 N	104.04 W
Málaga □[4]	34	36.50 N	4.40 W
Malagarasi	154	5.06 S	30.50 E
Malagarasi ≃	154	5.12 S	29.47 E
Malagash	186	45.46 N	63.23 W
Malagasy Republic → Madagascar □[1]	157b	19.00 S	46.00 E
Malago ≃	116	10.55 N	123.02 E
Malagón	34	39.10 N	3.51 W
Malagón ≃	34	37.35 N	7.29 W
Malagrotta ◆[8]	66	41.53 N	12.20 E
Mal'agurt	80	57.39 N	52.32 E
Malahat	224	48.32 N	123.34 W
Malahide	48	53.27 N	6.09 W
Malaimbandy	157b	20.20 S	45.36 E
Malaisie → Malaysia □[1]	112	2.30 N	112.30 E
Malaita □[4]	175e	9.00 S	161.00 E
Malaita I	175e	9.00 S	161.00 E
Malaja Beloz'orka	78	47.14 N	34.56 E
Malaja → Bessergenovka	83	47.09 N	38.36 E
Malaja Borščovka	82	56.33 N	36.53 E
Malaja Bykovka	80	51.54 N	47.45 E
Malaja Čuja ≃	88	58.56 N	112.13 E
Malaja Devica	78	50.41 N	32.10 E
Malaja Doroginka	82	54.06 N	38.56 E
Malaja Dubna	82	55.52 N	38.58 E
Malaja Istra ≃	82	55.54 N	36.50 E
Malaja Ižmora	80	53.32 N	42.48 E
Malaja Janisol'	83	47.22 N	37.20 E
Malaja Jekaterinovka	80	51.26 N	44.17 E
Malaja Kinel' ≃	80	53.29 N	51.30 E
Malaja Kokšaga ≃	80	56.09 N	47.53 E
Malaja Konkudera ≃	88	57.26 N	112.37 E
Malaja Kuril'skaja Gr'ada (Habomai-Shotō) I	92a	43.30 N	146.10 E
Malaja Laba ≃	84	44.16 N	40.53 E
Malaja Neva ≃[1]	265a	59.57 N	30.15 E
Malaja Ochta ◆[8]	265a	59.56 N	30.24 E
Malaja Orlovka	80	47.18 N	41.24 E
Malaja Pera	24	64.11 N	54.47 E
Malaja Serdoba	80	52.28 N	44.56 E
Malaja Sestra ≃	82	56.17 N	35.57 E
Malaja Tokmačevka	78	47.32 N	35.54 E
Malaja Višera	76	58.51 N	32.14 E
Malaja Viska	78	48.39 N	31.38 E
Malaka → Melaka	114	2.12 N	102.15 E
Malaka, Sempitan Ʉ	114	5.44 N	95.30 E
Malakāl	140	9.31 N	31.39 E
Malākand	123	34.34 N	71.56 E
Mala Kapela ⩘	36	44.50 N	15.30 E
Malakka, Strasse von → Malacca, Strait of Ʉ	110	2.30 N	101.20 E
Malakoff, Fr.	261	48.49 N	2.19 E
Malakoff, Tx., U.S.	222	32.10 N	96.00 W
Malakpur ◆[8]	272a	28.42 N	77.12 E
Malakula □[6]	175f	16.20 S	167.20 E
Malakula I	175f	16.15 S	167.30 E
Malakwāl	123	32.34 N	73.13 E
Malala	164	5.15 S	147.10 E
Malalag	116	6.36 N	125.24 E
Malalbergo	64	44.43 N	11.32 E
Malamala	112	3.21 S	120.55 E
Mala Mala Game Reserve ◆[4]	156	24.52 S	31.30 E
Malamaui Island I	116	6.44 N	121.58 E
Malambo	246	10.52 N	74.47 W
Malambo, Arroyo ≃	258	33.43 S	58.46 W
Malambunga	116	9.02 N	117.38 E
Malamocco	64	45.22 N	12.20 E
Malampaya Sound Ʉ	116	10.51 N	119.20 E
Malān	110	25.37 N	96.21 E
Malān, Rās >	128	25.18 N	65.11 E
Malanao Island I	116	9.27 N	118.37 E
Malanas ≃	116	17.41 N	120.43 E
Mālancha	272b	22.55 N	88.26 E
Mālancha ≃[1]	126	21.40 N	89.20 E
Mālandighi	126	23.33 N	87.24 E
Malandji	152	5.56 S	22.18 E
Malang	115a	7.59 S	112.37 E
Malang, Gunung ∧	115a	7.02 S	107.01 E
Malangali	154	8.34 S	34.51 E
Malangas	116	7.37 N	123.01 E
Malanggwā	124	26.52 N	85.34 E
Malangka, Tanjung >	112	1.20 N	120.48 E
Malan Guan ⩘	105	40.16 N	117.39 E
Malanipa Island I	116	6.53 N	122.16 E
Malanje	152	9.32 S	16.20 E
Malanje □[5]	152	9.30 S	16.30 E
Malanut Bay c	116	9.16 N	117.59 E
Malanville	150	11.52 N	3.23 E
Malanyu	105	40.11 N	117.42 E
Malanzán	252	30.48 S	66.37 W
Mała Panew ≃	30	50.44 N	17.52 E
Malapantao, Mount ∧	116	9.54 N	122.37 E
Malapardis Brook ≃	276	40.49 N	74.25 W
Mälaren ⊜	40	59.30 N	17.12 E
Malargüe	252	35.28 S	69.35 W
Mälar-See → Mälaren ⊜	40	59.30 N	17.12 E
Malartic	190	48.08 N	78.08 W
Malartic, Lac ⊜	190	48.15 N	78.07 W
Malasia → Malaysia □[1]	112	2.30 N	112.30 E
Malasiqui	116	15.55 N	120.25 E
Malaspina	254	44.56 S	66.54 W
Malaspina Glacier ⊓	180	59.50 N	140.30 W
Malaspina Strait Ʉ	182	49.44 N	124.20 W
Malassis	261	48.38 N	2.03 E
Malāṭīyah	142	28.42 N	30.51 E
Malatya	130	38.21 N	38.19 E
Malatya □[4]	130	38.30 N	38.10 E
Malau	175f	15.10 S	166.48 E
Malaucène	62	44.10 N	5.08 E
Malaunay	50	49.32 N	1.02 E
Malaut	123	30.13 N	74.29 E
Malavalli	122	12.23 N	77.05 E
Malawali, Pulau I	116	7.03 N	117.18 E
Malawi □[1], Afr.	138	13.30 S	34.00 E
Malawi □[1], Afr.	154	13.30 S	34.00 E
Malawi, Lake → Nyasa, Lake ⊜	154	12.00 S	34.30 E
Malawiya	140	15.16 N	36.12 E
Malaya → Semenanjung Malaysia □[9]	114	4.00 N	102.00 E
Malayagiri ∧	120	21.23 N	85.16 E
Malayal	116	7.12 N	121.57 E
Malaybalay	116	8.09 N	125.05 E
Malāyer	128	34.17 N	48.50 E
Malay Peninsula >[1]	110	6.00 N	101.00 E
Malay Reef ✢[2]	166	17.59 S	149.18 E
Malaysia □[1], Asia	108	2.30 N	112.30 E
Malaysia □[1], Asia	112	2.30 N	112.30 E
Malazgirt	130	39.09 N	42.31 E
Malbaie ≃	186	47.39 N	70.09 W
Malbaie, La c	186	48.35 N	64.14 W
Malbon	166	21.04 S	140.18 E
Malbooma	162	30.41 S	134.11 E
Malborghetto Valbruna	64	46.30 N	13.26 E
Malbork	30	54.02 N	19.01 E
Malbrán	252	29.21 S	62.27 W
Malbuisson	58	46.48 N	6.18 E
Malbun	58	47.35 N	9.33 E
Malcesine	64	45.46 N	10.48 E
Mal'cevo	265b	55.56 N	37.57 E
Mal'čevskaja	78	49.04 N	40.21 E
Mal'čevsko-Polnenskaja	83	48.58 N	40.12 E
Malchanskij chrebet ⩘	88	50.45 N	109.30 E
Malchin	54	53.44 N	12.46 E
Malchiner See ⊜	54	53.43 N	12.38 E
Malching	60	48.19 N	13.12 E
Malchow	54	53.28 N	12.25 E
Malchow ◆[8]	264a	52.35 N	13.29 E
Malčin	88	49.44 N	93.18 E
Malcolm	162	28.56 S	121.30 E
Malcolm, Point >	162	33.48 S	123.45 E
Malcolm Island I	182	50.40 N	127.00 W
Malcom	190	41.42 N	92.33 W
Malcompeth → Mahābaleshwar	122	17.55 N	73.40 E
Malcontenta	64	45.25 N	12.13 E
Malczyce	30	51.14 N	16.29 E
Māldah	124	25.02 N	88.09 E
Maldegem	50	51.13 N	3.27 E
Malden, Ma., U.S.	207	42.25 N	71.04 W
Malden, Mo., U.S.	194	36.33 N	89.57 W
Malden I	14	4.03 S	154.59 W
Malden ≃	283	42.24 N	71.05 W
Malden Bridge	210	42.28 N	73.35 W
Malden on Hudson	210	42.06 N	73.56 W
Maldivas → Maldives □[1]	12	3.15 N	73.00 E
Maldive Islands → Maldives □[1]	12	3.15 N	73.00 E
Mal di Ventre, Isola di I	71	39.59 N	8.18 E
Maldives □[1]	12	3.15 N	73.00 E
Maldon, Austl.	169	37.00 S	144.04 E
Maldon, Eng., U.K.	42	51.45 N	0.40 E
Maldon □[8]	260	51.43 N	0.40 E
Maldonado	252	34.54 S	54.57 W
Maldonado, Punta >	234	16.20 N	98.35 W
Male, It.	64	46.21 N	10.55 E
Male', Mald.	12	4.10 N	73.30 E
Male, Mya.	110	23.02 N	95.58 E
Maléa, Ákra >	38	36.26 N	23.12 E
Malea, Dolok ∧	114	0.56 N	99.38 E
Malebo, Pool ⊜	152	4.17 S	15.20 E
Malediven → Maldives □[1]	12	3.15 N	73.00 E
Mālegaon	122	20.33 N	74.32 E
Malegno, It.	64	45.56 N	10.14 E
Malegno, It.	64	46.40 N	11.08 E
Malehra	124	24.34 N	79.19 E
Maleit, Lake ⊜	140	7.55 N	28.35 E
Malejevka	78	47.29 N	32.43 E
Malek, Kaz.	85	40.47 N	68.37 E
Malek, Sūd.	140	6.04 N	31.36 E
Malé Karpaty ⩘	30	48.30 N	17.20 E
Malek Dīn	120	32.25 N	68.04 E
Malek Kandī	128	37.09 N	46.06 E
Malek Sīāh, Kūh-e ∧	128	29.51 N	60.52 E
Malela, Zaïre	154	2.28 S	26.09 E
Malela, Zaïre	154	4.22 S	26.08 E
Malema	154	14.57 S	37.20 E
Malenga	24	63.50 N	36.25 E
Malengoya	154	3.32 N	25.25 E
Malente	54	54.10 N	10.33 E
Maleo	62	45.10 N	9.46 E
Māler Kotla	124	30.31 N	75.53 E
Malesco	58	46.08 N	8.30 E
Malesherbes	50	48.18 N	2.25 E
Malestroit	32	47.49 N	2.23 W
Maleta	88	50.50 N	108.25 E
Maletto	70	37.49 N	14.52 E
Malfa	70	38.35 N	14.50 E
Malgas	158	34.18 S	20.35 E
Malgersdorf	60	48.32 N	12.45 E
Malgobek	84	43.32 N	44.34 E
Malgomaj ⊜	26	64.47 N	16.12 E
Malha Wells	140	15.08 N	26.12 E
Malheur ≃	202	44.03 N	116.59 W
Malheur, North Fork ≃	202	43.45 N	118.04 W
Malheur, South Fork ≃	202	43.33 N	118.10 W
Malheureux, Cap >	157c	19.59 S	57.36 E
Malheur Lake ⊜	202	43.20 N	118.45 W
Mali, Guinée	150	12.05 N	12.18 W
Mali, Zaïre	154	2.48 S	26.08 E
Mali □[1], Afr.	134	17.00 N	4.00 W
Mali □[1], Afr.	150	17.00 N	4.00 W
Mali ≃	102	25.43 N	97.29 E
Maliangping	102	31.29 N	111.20 E
Malianjingzi	102	41.32 N	95.23 E
Malibamatšo ≃	158	29.20 S	29.28 E
Malibu	228	34.02 N	118.42 W
Malibu Lake ⊜[1]	228	34.07 N	118.45 W
Malien ≃	269d	25.11 N	121.41 E
Malienkang	269d	25.10 N	121.39 E
Maligay Bay c	116	7.30 N	123.14 E
Malighati	126	22.33 N	87.40 E
Maligne ≃	182	52.56 N	118.02 W
Maligne Lake ⊜	182	52.40 N	117.31 W
Malihābād	124	26.55 N	80.43 E
Māliḥah, Wādī V	142	29.21 N	32.35 E
Malik	112	0.34 S	123.14 E
Malik, Wādī al- V	140	18.02 N	30.58 E
Mali Kyun I	110	13.06 N	98.16 E
Malili	112	2.38 S	121.06 E
Målilla	26	57.23 N	15.48 E
Malimba, Monts ⩘	154	7.32 S	29.30 E
Malim Nawar	114	4.21 N	101.07 E
Malimono	116	9.34 N	125.25 E
Malin, Ire.	48	55.18 N	7.15 W
Malin, Ukr.	78	50.46 N	29.15 E
Malin, Or., U.S.	202	42.00 N	121.24 W
Malinalco ⊥	234	18.57 N	99.30 W
Malinaltepec	234	17.03 N	98.40 W
Malinau	112	3.35 N	116.38 E
Malin Beg	48	54.40 N	8.48 W
Malindang, Mount ∧	116	8.13 N	123.38 E
Malindi	154	3.13 S	40.07 E
Malindi Marine National Park ♠	154	3.15 S	40.10 E
Malines → Mechelen	50	51.02 N	4.28 E
Malinga	152	2.25 S	12.14 E
Malingping	115a	6.46 S	106.01 E
Malingsbosjön ⊜	40	59.55 N	15.27 E
Malin Head >	48	55.23 N	7.24 W
Malinki	82	54.05 N	38.59 E
Malinniki	82	56.17 N	38.24 E
Malino, Indon.	112	5.15 S	119.51 E
Malino, Ross.	82	55.06 N	38.11 E
Malino, Ross.	265b	55.58 N	37.13 E
Malino, Bukit ∧	112	0.45 N	120.47 E
Malinoa I	174w	21.02 S	175.08 W
Malinovka, Ross.	80	51.47 N	43.26 E
Malinovka, Ross.	86	53.24 N	87.17 E
Malinovka, Ukr.	78	49.47 N	36.43 E
Malinta	216	41.19 N	84.02 W
Malinyi	154	8.56 S	36.08 E
Malipara	272b	22.57 N	88.14 E
Mali Rajinac ∧	36	44.48 N	15.02 E
Malita	116	6.25 N	125.36 E
Malitbog	116	10.10 N	125.00 E
Maliuchang	107	29.05 N	104.07 E
Maliuping	107	29.55 N	106.23 E
Ma Liu Shui	271d	22.25 N	114.12 E
Malivo	82	55.07 N	39.02 E
Maliwun	110	10.14 N	98.37 E
Malizhen	102	23.10 N	104.35 E
Maljamar	196	32.51 N	103.46 W
Malka, Ross.	74	53.20 N	157.30 E
Malka, Ross.	84	43.47 N	43.21 E
Malka ≃	84	43.44 N	44.15 E
Malkāpur	120	20.53 N	76.12 E
Malkara	130	40.53 N	26.54 E
Malkerns	158	26.32 S	31.11 E
Malko Târnovo	38	41.59 N	27.32 E
Mallāḥ	132	32.30 N	36.51 E
Mallaig, Ab., Can.	182	54.13 N	111.22 W
Mallaig, Scot., U.K.	46	57.00 N	5.50 W
Mallala	168b	34.26 S	138.30 E
Mallaoua	150	13.02 N	9.36 E
Mallapunyah	164	16.59 S	135.49 E
Mallaranny	48	53.54 N	9.49 W
Mallard Reservoir ⊜[1]	282	38.01 N	122.03 W
Mallawī	142	27.44 N	30.50 E
Mallee Cliffs National Park ♠	166	34.15 S	142.40 E
Mallemort	62	43.44 N	5.11 E
Mallersdorf	60	48.47 N	12.16 E
Mallery Lake ⊜	176	63.55 N	98.25 W
Malles Venosta (Mals)	64	46.41 N	10.32 E
Mallet	252	25.55 S	50.50 W
Mallig	116	17.08 N	121.41 E
Malligasta	252	29.11 S	67.26 W
Mallina	162	20.53 S	118.02 E
Malling	41	56.02 N	10.10 E
Mallnitz	64	46.59 N	13.10 E
Mallorca I	34	39.30 N	3.00 E
Mallorytown	212	44.29 N	75.53 W
Mallow	48	52.08 N	8.39 W
Mallwood	216	42.51 N	89.02 W
Malm	26	64.04 N	11.13 E
Malmbäck	26	57.35 N	14.28 E
Malmberget	24	67.10 N	20.40 E
Malmédy	56	50.25 N	6.02 E
Malmesbury, S. Afr.	158	33.28 S	18.44 E
Malmesbury, Eng., U.K.	42	51.36 N	2.06 W
Malmesbury, Vale of V	42	51.22 N	2.10 W
Malmköping	40	59.08 N	16.44 E
Malmlången ⊜	40	59.27 N	14.42 E
Malmö	41	55.36 N	13.00 E
Malmöhus Län □[6]	26	55.45 N	13.30 E
Malmsbury	169	37.12 S	144.23 E
Malmsbury Reservoir ⊜[1]	169	37.13 S	144.22 E
Malmslätt	26	58.25 N	15.30 E
Malmstrom Air Force Base ■	202	47.30 N	111.10 W
Malmyž	80	56.31 N	50.41 E
Malna	116	8.08 N	124.27 E
Malnate	62	45.48 N	8.53 E
Malnoue	261	48.50 N	2.36 E
Malo	64	45.39 N	11.24 E
Malo I	175f	15.40 S	167.11 E
Malo, Arroyo ≃	258	33.43 S	58.52 W
Maloarchangel'sk	76	52.24 N	36.30 E
Maloarchangel'skoje	88	50.24 N	108.50 E
Maloba	154	6.18 S	27.39 E
Malodel'skaja	80	50.11 N	43.53 E

	English	Deutsch	Español	Français	Português
≃	River	Fluß	Río	Rivière	Rio
≍	Canal	Kanal	Canal	Canal	Canal
L	Waterfall, Rapids	Wasserfall, Stromschnellen	Cascada, Rápidos	Chute d'eau, Rapides	Cascata, Rápidos
Ʉ	Strait	Meeresstraße	Estrecho	Détroit	Estreito
c	Bay, Gulf	Bucht, Golf	Bahía, Golfo	Baie, Golfe	Baía, Golfo
⊜	Lake, Lakes	See, Seen	Lago, Lagos	Lac, Lacs	Lago, Lagos
≡	Swamp	Sumpf	Pantano	Marais	Pântano
⊓	Ice Features, Glacier	Eis- und Gletscherformen	Accidentes Glaciales	Formes glaciaires	Acidentes glaciares
⍑	Other Hydrographic Features	Andere Hydrographische Objekte	Otros Elementos Hidrográficos	Autres données hydrographiques	Outros acidentes hidrográficos
✢	Submarine Features	Untermeerische Objekte	Accidentes Submarinos	Formes de relief sous-marin	Acidentes submarinos
□	Political Unit	Politische Einheit	Unidad Politica	Entité politique	Unidade política
ʊ	Cultural Institution	Kulturelle Institution	Institución Cultural	Institution culturelle	Instituição cultural
⊥	Historical Site	Historische Stätte	Sitio Histórico	Site historique	Sitio histórico
♠	Recreational Site	Erholungs- und Ferienort	Sitio de Recreo	Centre de loisirs	Area de Lazer
⊠	Airport	Flughafen	Aeropuerto	Aéroport	Aeroporto
■	Military Installation	Militäranlage	Instalación Militar	Installation militaire	Instalação militar
◆	Miscellaneous	Verschiedenes	Misceláneo	Divers	Diversos

Symbols in the index entries represent the broad categories identified in the key at the right. Symbols with superior numbers (∧¹) identify subcategories (see complete key on page *I · 1*).

Symbole im Register stellen die rechts im Schlüssel erklärten Kategorien dar. Symbole mit hochgestellten Ziffern (∧¹) bezeichnen Unterteilungen einer Kategorie (vgl. vollständiger Schlüssel auf Seite *I · 1*).

Los símbolos incluídos en el texto del índice representan las grandes categorías identificadas con la clave a la derecha. Los símbolos con números en su clave superior (∧¹) identifican las subcategorías (véase la clave completa en la página *I · 1*).

Os símbolos incluídos no texto do índice representam as grandes categorias identificadas na chave à direita. Os símbolos com números em sua parte superior (∧¹) identificam as subcategorias (veja-se a chave completa à página *I · 1*).

Les symboles de l'index représentent les catégories indiquées dans la légende à droite. Les symboles suivis d'un indice (∧¹) représentent des sous-catégories (voir légende complète à la page *I · 1*).

	English	Deutsch	Español	Français	Português
∧	Mountain	Berg	Montaña	Montagne	Montanha
∧	Mountains	Gebirge	Montañas	Montagnes	Montanhas
✕	Pass	Paß	Paso	Col	Passo
∨	Valley, Canyon	Tal, Cañon	Valle, Cañón	Vallée, Canyon	Vale, Canhão
⌐	Plain	Ebene	Llano	Plaine	Planície
⊃	Cape	Kap	Cabo	Cap	Cabo
I	Island	Insel	Isla	Île	Ilha
II	Islands	Inseln	Islas	Îles	Ilhas
⌄	Other Topographic Features	Andere Topographische Objekte	Otros Elementos Topográficos	Autres données topographiques	Outros acidentes topográficos

ESPAÑOL

Nombre	Página	Lat.°′	Long.°′ W = Oeste
Mansfield Hollow Lake ◎[1]	207	41.45 N	72.11 W
Mansfield Hollow State Park ♠	207	41.46 N	72.10 W
Mansfield Municipal Airport ⊠	283	42.00 N	71.12 W
Mansfield Woodhouse	44	53.11 N	1.12 W
Man Shan I	106	31.14 N	120.17 E
Mansieville Location	273d	26.05 S	27.45 E
Mānsinhapur	272b	22.39 N	88.09 E
Mansión	236	10.06 N	85.22 W
Manskoje belogorje ⋏	88	54.35 N	94.00 E
Mansle	32	45.53 N	0.11 E
Manso ≃	248	14.42 S	56.16 W
Mansôa	150	12.10 N	14.36 W
Manson, Ia., U.S.	198	42.32 N	94.32 W
Manson, Wa., U.S.	182	47.53 N	120.09 W
Manson ≃	182	55.42 N	123.47 W
Manson Creek	182	55.41 N	124.29 W
Mansonville	206	45.03 N	72.23 W
Mansourah	34	36.04 N	4.28 E
Mansucum	246	9.02 N	77.49 W
Mansura → Al-Manṣūrah, Miṣr	142	31.03 N	31.23 E
Mansura, La., U.S.	194	31.03 N	92.02 W
Manṣūrīyah, Tur'at al- ≅	142	31.03 N	31.24 E
Mansurovo	82	55.52 N	36.36 E
Manta, Ec.	246	0.57 S	80.44 W
Manta, It.	62	44.37 N	7.29 E
Manta, Bahía de c	246	0.54 S	80.42 W
Mantabuan Island I	116	5.02 N	120.13 E
Mantagao ≃	184	51.50 N	97.48 W
Mantalingajan, Mount ∧	116	8.48 N	117.40 E
Mantalingajan Range ⋏	116	8.46 N	117.40 E
Mantanani Besar, Pulau I	112	6.45 N	116.17 E
Mantangule Island I	116	8.10 N	117.10 E
Mantantale	152	2.10 S	20.06 E
Mantare	154	2.43 S	33.13 E
Mantaro ≃	248	12.15 S	73.58 W
Manteca	226	37.47 N	121.12 W
Mantecal	246	7.33 N	69.09 W
Mantel	60	49.39 N	12.03 E
Mantena	255	18.47 S	40.59 W
Manteno	216	41.15 N	87.49 W
Manteo	192	35.54 N	75.40 W
Mantes-Chérence, Aérodrome de ⊠	261	49.05 N	1.41 E
Mantes-la-Jolie	50	48.59 N	1.43 E
Mantes-la-Ville	261	48.58 N	1.42 E
Manteswar	126	23.26 N	88.06 E
Manteuil-le-Haudouin	50	49.08 N	2.48 E
Manthelan	50	47.08 N	0.47 E
Manti	200	39.16 N	111.38 W
Manticao	116	8.24 N	124.17 E
Mantilla ⬥[8]	286b	23.04 N	82.20 W
Mantin	114	2.49 N	101.54 E
Mantiqueira, Serra da ⋏	256	22.00 S	44.45 W
Mantok	112	1.09 S	123.14 E
Manton	190	44.24 N	85.23 W
Mantorville	190	44.04 N	92.45 W
Mantos Blancos	252	23.25 S	70.05 W
Mantou	104	42.27 N	122.26 E
Mantova	64	45.09 N	10.48 E
Mantova □[4]	64	45.10 N	10.47 E
Māntri	126	21.39 N	86.49 E
Mänttä	26	62.02 N	24.38 E
Mantua, Cuba	240p	22.17 N	84.17 W
Mantua → Mantova, It.	64	45.09 N	10.48 E
Mantua, N.J., U.S.	208	39.47 N	75.10 W
Mantua, Oh., U.S.	214	41.17 N	81.13 W
Mantua, Va., U.S.	284c	38.51 N	77.15 W
Mantua ≃	240p	22.12 N	84.25 W
Mantua Creek ≃	285	39.51 N	75.14 W
Mantua Creek, Chestnut Branch ≃	285	39.47 N	75.10 W
Mantua Creek, Porch Branch ≃	285	39.46 N	75.07 W
Mantua Hills	284c	38.51 N	77.16 W
Mantua Terrace	285	39.48 N	75.10 W
Manturovo, Ross.	78	51.28 N	37.07 E
Manturovo, Ross.	80	58.20 N	44.46 E
Mäntyharju	26	61.25 N	26.53 E
Mäntyluoto	26	61.35 N	21.29 E
Manu	248	12.15 S	70.50 W
Manú ≃	248	12.16 S	70.51 W
Manu, Parque Nacional del ♠	248	12.15 S	71.40 W
Manuae I[1], Cook Is.	14	19.21 S	158.56 W
Manuae I[1], Poly. fr.	14	16.30 S	154.40 W
Manua Islands II	174y	14.13 S	169.35 W
Manuel	234	22.44 N	98.19 W
Manuel Alves ≃	250	11.19 S	48.28 W
Manuel Alves Grande ≃	250	7.27 S	47.35 W
Manuel Antonio, Parque Nacional ♠	236	9.25 N	84.10 W
Manuel Avila Camacho, Presa ◎[1]	234	18.55 N	98.10 W
Manuel Benavides	232	29.05 N	103.55 W
Manuel Derqui	252	27.50 S	58.48 W
Manuel Duarte	256	22.06 S	43.34 W
Manuel Ribeiro	256	22.54 S	42.47 W
Manuel Rodríguez, Isla I	254	52.35 S	73.50 W
Manuel Urbano	248	8.53 S	69.18 W
Manués-Açu ≃	250	3.22 S	57.44 W
Manuguru	122	17.59 N	80.43 E
Manuhangi I[1]	14	19.12 S	141.16 W
Manuherikia ≃	172	45.16 S	169.24 E
Manui, Pulau I	112	3.35 S	123.08 E
Manuilovskaja	76	60.29 N	40.40 E
Manu Island I	164	1.17 S	143.35 E
Manūjān	128	27.24 N	57.32 E
Manuk ≃	115a	6.14 S	108.13 E
Manuk, Pulau I	164	5.33 S	130.18 E
Manukan	116	8.31 N	123.06 E
Manukau	172	37.02 S	174.54 E
Manukau Harbour c	172	37.01 S	174.44 E
Manulla ≃	48	53.57 N	9.12 W
Manulu Lagoon c	174o	1.56 N	157.20 W
Manumuskin ≃	208	39.18 N	75.00 W
Manund, Tanjung ›	164	0.38 S	135.22 E
Manunui	172	38.53 S	175.20 E
Manuoha ∧	172	38.39 S	177.07 E
Manuripe (Mamuripi) ≃	248	11.06 S	67.36 W
Manuripi ≃	248	11.42 S	67.16 W
Manursing Island I	276	40.58 N	73.40 W
Manursing Island Park ♠	276	40.58 N	73.40 W
Manus □[5]	164	2.00 S	147.00 E
Mānushmuria	126	22.22 N	86.47 E
Manus Island I	164	2.05 S	147.00 E
Manutahi	172	39.40 S	174.24 E
Manutuke	172	38.41 S	177.55 E
Manvel, N.D., U.S.	198	48.04 N	97.10 W
Manvel, Tx., U.S.	222	29.28 N	95.22 W
Manville, N.J., U.S.	210	40.32 N	74.35 W
Manville, R.I., U.S.	207	41.58 N	71.28 W
Mānwat	122	19.18 N	76.30 E
Many	194	31.34 N	93.29 W
Manyal Shīḥah	273c	29.57 N	31.14 E
Manyana	156	23.23 S	21.44 E
Manyani	154	3.05 S	38.30 E
Manyara, Lake ◎	154	3.35 S	35.50 E
Manyberries	184	49.24 N	110.42 W
Manyč ≃	72	47.15 N	40.00 E
Manyč-Gudilo, ozero ◎	80	46.24 N	42.38 E
Manyeleti Game Reserve ⬥[4]	156	25.42 S	31.30 E

FRANÇAIS

Nom	Page	Lat.°′	Long.°′ W = Ouest
Many Island Lake ◎	184	50.08 N	110.03 W
Manyoni	154	5.45 S	34.50 E
Many Peaks	166	24.33 S	151.23 E
Manytsch → Manyč ≃	72	47.15 N	40.00 E
Manz'a	86	58.29 N	96.15 E
Mānzai	120	30.07 N	68.52 E
Manzanares	34	39.00 N	3.22 W
Manzanares ≃	34	40.19 N	3.32 W
Manzanares, Canal del ≅	266a	40.23 N	3.41 W
Manzanillo, Cuba	240p	20.21 N	77.07 W
Manzanillo, Méx.	234	19.03 N	104.20 W
Manzanillo, Bahía c	234	19.04 N	104.22 W
Manzanillo, Bahía de c	234	19.12 N	104.43 W
Manzanillo, Punta ›, Pan.	236	9.38 N	79.32 W
Manzanillo, Punta ›, Ven.	241s	11.32 N	69.17 W
Manzanillo Bay c	238	19.45 N	71.46 W
Manzanita, Or., U.S.	224	45.43 N	123.56 W
Manzanita, Wa., U.S.	224	47.42 N	122.33 W
Manzano, It.	64	45.59 N	13.23 E
Manzano, N.M., U.S.	200	34.38 N	106.20 W
Manzanola	198	38.06 N	103.51 W
Manzano Peak ∧	200	34.35 N	106.26 W
Manželija	78	49.19 N	33.38 E
Manzhouli	88	49.35 N	117.22 E
Manziana	66	42.08 N	12.08 E
Manzil	128	29.15 N	63.05 E
Manzilah, Birkat al- ◎	142	31.08 N	31.56 E
Manzilah, Buḥayrat al- ◎	142	31.15 N	32.00 E
Manzini	158	26.30 S	31.25 E
Manzone	258	34.29 S	58.52 W
Manzurka	88	53.30 N	106.04 E
Maó, Esp.	34	39.53 N	4.15 E
Mao, Rep. Dom.	238	19.34 N	71.05 W
Mao, Tchad	136	14.07 N	15.19 E
Maoba	102	30.02 N	108.59 E
Maocifan	100	31.40 N	112.53 E
Maocun	98	34.25 N	117.16 E
Maodianzi, Zhg.	107	29.45 N	104.55 E
Maodianzi, Zhg.	107	30.42 N	104.25 E
Mao'ertuo	107	29.19 N	106.24 E
Maojiagou	104	40.58 N	120.51 E
Maojiaji	100	31.32 N	114.16 E
Maojiakou	100	29.53 N	112.58 E
Maojiaping	105	40.34 N	114.43 E
Maojiapuzi	104	41.10 N	123.32 E
Maojiatun	104	41.05 N	121.58 E
Maojiazao	98	39.53 N	113.26 E
Maoke, Pegunungan ⋏	164	4.00 S	138.00 E
Maolin, Zhg.	89	43.58 N	123.24 E
Maolin, Zhg.	100	30.32 N	118.14 E
Maomao Shan ∧	102	37.12 N	103.10 E
Maoming	102	21.39 N	110.54 E
Maomu	102	40.18 N	99.28 E
Ma On Shan ∧	271d	22.25 N	114.15 E
Ma On Shan Tsuen	271d	22.24 N	114.14 E
Maoping	102	30.23 N	110.33 E
Maopora, Pulau I	112	7.35 S	127.35 E
Maoshan	105	40.17 N	117.26 E
Mao Shan ⋏	106	31.43 N	119.17 E
Maoshi	100	26.57 N	113.05 E
Maospati	115a	7.36 S	111.26 E
Maouri, Dallol V	150	12.05 N	3.32 E
Maowen	102	31.30 N	103.39 E
Maoxing	89	45.32 N	124.33 E
Mao Yü I	100	23.19 N	119.19 E
Maozhou	105	38.51 N	116.06 E
Mapaga	112	0.06 S	119.48 E
Mapam Yumco ◎	120	30.42 N	81.27 E
Mapan	112	2.21 S	111.10 E
Mapanda	152	9.32 S	24.16 E
Mapane	112	1.24 S	120.40 E
Mapanza	154	16.15 S	26.55 E
Mapaoni ≃	250	1.55 N	54.13 W
Mapari ≃, Bra.	246	1.49 S	66.48 W
Mapari ≃, Bra.	250	0.45 N	53.07 W
Mapastepec	234	15.26 N	92.54 W
Mapaville	219	38.14 N	90.29 W
Mapi	164	7.07 S	139.23 E
Mapi ≃	164	7.00 S	139.16 E
Mapia, Kepulauan II	108	0.50 N	134.20 E
Mapida	112	0.33 S	119.46 E
Mapimí	232	25.49 N	103.51 W
Mapimí, Bolsón de ⬥[2]	232	26.30 N	104.00 W
Mapimí, Bufa de ∧	196	25.47 N	103.48 W
Maping, Zhg.	100	24.16 N	117.54 E
Maping, Zhg.	100	31.36 N	113.32 E
Mapinga	154	6.36 S	39.04 E
Mapinhane	156	22.19 S	35.03 E
Mapire	246	7.45 N	64.42 W
Mapiri	248	15.15 S	68.10 W
Mapiri ≃	248	9.52 S	66.21 W
Mapixari, Ilha I	246	2.10 S	65.08 W
Maple ⬥[8]	275b	43.51 N	79.31 W
Maple ≃, U.S.	198	45.47 N	98.33 W
Maple ≃, Ia., U.S.	198	42.00 N	95.59 W
Maple ≃, Mi., U.S.	190	42.59 N	84.57 W
Maple ≃, Mn., U.S.	190	44.05 N	94.00 W
Maple ≃, N.D., U.S.	198	46.56 N	96.55 W
Maple Airfield ⊠	275b	43.51 N	79.32 W
Maple Bay	224	48.49 N	123.36 W
Maple Bluff	216	43.07 N	89.22 W
Maple Creek	184	49.55 N	109.27 W
Maple Creek ≃	198	41.33 N	96.27 W
Maplecrest	210	42.17 N	74.11 W
Maple Cross	260	51.37 N	0.30 W
Mapledale	214	41.23 N	79.51 W
Maple Falls	224	48.55 N	122.04 W
Maple Glen	285	40.11 N	75.11 W
Maple Grove, On., Can.	212	43.55 N	78.44 W
Maple Grove, P.Q., Can.	206	45.19 N	73.50 W
Maple Heights	214	41.24 N	81.33 W
Maple Lake	190	45.13 N	94.00 W
Maple Lake ◎	212	45.06 N	78.40 W
Maple Lane	216	41.45 N	86.14 W
Maple Leaf Gardens ♠	275b	43.40 N	79.23 W
Maple Meadow Brook ≃	283	42.33 N	71.09 W
Maple Mount	194	37.42 N	87.26 W
Maple Park	216	41.55 N	88.36 W
Maples	216	41.01 N	84.58 W
Maple Shade	285	39.57 N	74.59 W
Maple Springs	214	42.12 N	79.25 W
Maplesville	194	32.47 N	86.52 W
Mapleton, S. Afr.	158	26.20 S	28.14 E
Mapleton, Ia., U.S.	198	42.09 N	95.47 W
Mapleton, Mn., U.S.	190	43.55 N	93.57 W
Mapleton, Or., U.S.	202	44.01 N	123.51 W
Mapleton, Ut,. U.S.	200	40.07 N	111.34 W
Mapleton Depot	214	40.24 N	77.57 W
Maple Valley	224	47.25 N	122.03 W
Mapleville	207	41.56 N	71.38 W
Maplewood, Mo., U.S.	219	38.36 N	90.19 W
Maplewood, N.J., U.S.	276	40.43 N	74.14 W
Maplewood, Oh., U.S.	216	40.23 N	84.02 W
Maplewood, Wa., U.S.	224	47.30 N	122.07 W
Maplewood Terrace	279b	40.17 N	79.32 W
Mapocho ≃	286e	33.25 S	70.47 W
Mapocho, Estación ⬥[5]	286e	33.26 S	70.40 W
Mapoi	154	5.28 N	27.40 E
Mapoon Aboriginal Reserve ⬥[4]	164	11.40 S	142.25 E
Mappsville	208	37.51 N	75.34 W
Maprik	164	3.40 S	143.05 E
Mapuera ≃	250	1.05 S	57.02 W

PORTUGUÊS

Nome	Página	Lat.°′	Long.°′ W = Oeste
Mapujiang	105	40.24 N	114.56 E
Mapulanguene	156	24.29 S	32.06 E
Mapumulo	158	29.11 S	31.02 E
Maputa	158	26.59 S	32.46 E
Maputo	156	25.58 S	32.35 E
Maputo □[5]	156	26.00 S	32.25 E
Maputo (Great Usutu) (Lusutfu) ≃	158	26.11 S	32.42 E
Maputo, Baía de c	158	25.48 S	32.51 E
Maqên Gangri ∧	102	34.55 N	99.18 E
Maqiangou	105	39.30 N	115.02 E
Maqiao, Zhg.	100	29.48 N	114.22 E
Maqiao, Zhg.	106	30.28 N	120.42 E
Maqna	128	28.24 N	34.45 E
Maqteïr ⚲[4]	148	22.10 N	10.50 W
Maquan ≃	124	29.35 N	84.10 E
Maqueda	34	40.04 N	4.22 W
Maqueda Bay c	116	11.44 N	124.58 E
Maqueda Channel ɰ	116	13.42 N	124.01 E
Maquela do Zombo	152	6.03 S	15.07 E
Maquereau, Pointe au ›	186	48.12 N	64.47 W
Maquilaú ≃	246	1.23 N	63.24 W
Maquiling, Mount ∧	116	14.08 N	121.12 E
Maquinchao	254	41.15 S	68.44 W
Maquinchao ≃	254	41.13 S	69.25 W
Maquoketa	190	42.04 N	90.39 W
Maquoketa ≃	190	42.11 N	90.19 W
Maquoketa, North Fork ≃	190	42.05 N	90.40 W
Mar, Laguna c	286b	23.05 N	82.30 W
Mar, Serra do ≗[4]	252	26.00 S	48.00 W
Mara, India	120	28.11 N	94.06 E
Mara, Perú	248	14.06 S	72.07 W
Mara, Zhg.	120	28.11 N	94.08 E
Mara □[4]	154	1.45 S	34.30 E
Mara ≃, Afr.	154	1.31 S	33.56 E
Mara ≃, Ross.	88	58.06 N	104.06 E
Maraã, Bra.	246	1.50 S	65.22 W
Maraa, Poly. fr.	174s	17.46 S	149.34 W
Marabá	250	5.21 S	49.07 W
Marabahan	112	3.00 S	114.45 E
Marabut	116	11.07 N	125.13 E
Maracá, Ilha de I, Bra.	246	3.25 N	61.40 W
Maracá, Ilha de I, Bra.	250	2.05 N	50.25 W
Maracaçumé ≃	250	1.23 S	45.42 W
Maracaí	255	22.36 S	50.39 W
Maracaibo	246	10.40 N	71.37 W
Maracaibo, Lago de ◎	246	9.50 N	71.30 W
Maracaju	255	21.38 S	55.09 W
Maracaju, Serra de ⋏[2]	255	20.45 S	55.00 W
Maracalagonis	71	39.17 N	9.13 E
Maracanã	250	0.46 S	47.27 W
Maracanã ⬥[8]	287a	22.54 S	43.14 W
Maracanã ≃	248	8.22 S	59.41 W
Maracanã, Estádio do ♠	287a	22.55 S	43.14 W
Maracanaú	250	3.52 S	38.38 W
Maracás	255	13.26 S	40.27 W
Maracay	246	10.15 N	67.36 W
Maracossic Creek ≃	208	37.53 N	77.11 W
Marādah	146	29.14 N	19.13 E
Maradi	150	13.29 N	7.06 E
Maradi □[5]	150	14.00 N	7.00 E
Maradi, Goulbin ≃	150	13.38 N	6.20 E
Marāghah, Sabkhat al- ◎	130	35.39 N	37.39 E
Marāgheh	128	37.23 N	46.13 E
Maragiu, Capo ›	71	40.20 N	8.23 E
Maragogi	250	9.01 S	35.13 W
Maragogipe	255	12.46 S	38.55 W
Marahoué, Parc National de la ♠	150	7.00 N	6.00 W
Mārahra	124	27.44 N	78.35 E
Marahuaca, Cerro ∧	246	3.34 N	65.27 W
Maraial	250	8.47 S	35.50 W
Maraiche Lake ◎	184	54.28 N	102.01 W
Marainviller	58	48.35 N	6.36 E
Maraisburg → Roodepoort-Maraisburg	273d	26.11 S	27.56 E
Marais des Cygnes ≃	194	38.02 N	94.14 W
Marais Temps Clair ◎	219	38.54 N	90.24 W
Marajó, Baía de c	250	1.00 S	48.30 W
Marajó, Ilha de I	250	1.00 S	49.30 W
Marakabei	158	29.32 S	28.09 E
Ma'rakah	132	33.16 N	35.18 E
Mārākand	84	38.52 N	45.14 E
Marakwini	164	3.42 S	141.31 E
Maralal	154	1.06 N	36.42 E
Maralaleng	156	25.47 S	22.45 E
Maralal Game Sanctuary ⬥[4]	154	1.09 N	36.38 E
Maraldy	86	52.26 N	77.45 E
Marali	152	6.01 N	18.24 E
Maralik	84	40.35 N	43.52 E
Maralinga	162	30.10 S	131.35 E
Maralinga Lands ⬥[4]	162	29.15 S	130.50 E
Maram	120	25.25 N	94.06 E
Maramag	116	7.46 N	125.00 E
Maramasike I	175e	9.32 S	161.27 E
Marambaia ≃	256	21.44 S	46.25 W
Marambaia, Ilha da I	256	23.04 S	43.58 W
Marambaia, Pico da ∧	256	23.04 S	43.59 W
Marambaia, Restinga de ≗[2]	256	23.04 S	43.45 W
Marambio ʊ[3]	9	64.14 S	56.43 W
Marampa	150	8.41 N	12.28 W
Maramsilli Reservoir ◎[1]	122	20.32 N	81.41 E
Maramures □[6]	38	47.40 N	24.00 E
Maran	114	3.35 N	102.46 E
Mārān, Koh-i- ∧	120	29.26 N	66.48 E
Marana, Mali	150	14.38 N	11.55 W
Marana, Az., U.S.	200	32.26 N	111.13 W
Maranalgo	162	29.23 S	117.48 E
Maranboy	164	14.30 S	132.45 E
Maranchón	34	41.03 N	2.12 W
Marand	128	38.26 N	45.46 E
Maranello	64	44.32 N	10.52 E
Marang, Malay.	114	5.12 N	103.13 E
Marang, Mya.	110	10.27 N	98.47 E
Marangá ≃	287a	22.51 S	43.23 W
Marangani	248	14.22 S	71.10 W
Marangas	116	8.40 N	117.38 E
Marange-Zoncrange	56	49.07 N	6.32 E
Maranguape	250	3.53 S	38.40 W
Maranhão □[3]	250	5.00 S	45.00 W
Maranhão ≃	255	13.51 S	48.20 W
Marano	266b	45.38 N	8.38 E
Marano, Laguna di c	64	45.44 N	13.10 E
Maranoa ≃	166	27.50 S	148.37 E
Marano di Napoli	68	40.54 N	14.11 E
Marano Lagunare	64	45.46 N	13.10 E
Marañón ≃	242	4.30 S	73.27 W
Marano sul Panaro	64	44.27 N	10.58 E
Marano Vicentino	64	45.41 N	11.25 E
Marans	32	46.19 N	1.00 W
Maraoli ⬥[8]	272c	19.03 N	72.54 E
Marapanim	250	0.42 S	47.42 W
Marapendi, Lagoa de c	287a	23.01 S	43.24 W
Marapi ≃	250	0.37 N	55.58 W
Marapicu, Morro do ∧	287a	22.50 S	43.36 W
Mararoa ≃	172	45.34 S	167.36 E
Mararui	154	1.56 S	41.18 E
Maras, Perú	248	13.20 S	72.09 W
Maraş → Kahramanmaraş, Tür.	130	37.36 N	36.55 E
Marasany	80	57.27 N	54.25 E
Marasende, Pulau I	112	5.08 S	118.09 E
Mărăşeşti	38	45.52 N	27.14 E
Maratasã ≃	250	4.14 S	42.15 W
Maratea	68	39.59 N	15.45 E
Marathon, Austl.	166	20.49 S	143.34 E
Marathon, On., Can.	190	48.43 N	86.23 W
Marathón, Ellás	38	38.10 N	23.58 E
Marathon, Fl., U.S.	220	24.42 N	81.05 W
Marathon, N.Y., U.S.	210	42.26 N	76.01 W
Marathon, Tx., U.S.	196	30.12 N	103.15 W
Marathon, Wi., U.S.	190	44.55 N	89.50 W
Maratua, Pulau I	112	2.15 N	118.36 E
Marau, Bra.	252	28.27 S	52.12 W
Maraú, Bra.	255	14.06 S	39.00 W
Marauiá ≃	246	0.23 S	65.13 W
Marausa	70	37.56 N	12.30 E
Maravari	175e	7.51 S	156.42 E
Maravatío de Ocampo	234	19.54 N	100.27 W
Maravilha	252	26.47 S	53.09 W
Maravillas	232	27.22 N	104.29 W
Maravillas Creek ≃	196	29.34 N	102.47 W
Mara Vista	207	41.33 N	70.34 W
Marav Lake ◎	120	29.04 N	69.18 E
Maravovo	175e	9.17 S	159.38 E
Marāwah	146	32.29 N	21.25 E
Marawi, Pil.	116	8.01 N	124.18 E
Marawī, Sūd.	140	18.29 N	31.49 E
Marawwah I	128	24.18 N	53.18 E
Maraye-en-Othe	50	48.10 N	3.51 E
Marayes	252	31.29 S	67.20 W
Marayong	274a	33.45 S	150.54 E
Maraza	84	40.33 N	48.56 E
Marazion	42	50.08 N	5.28 W
Marbach, Dtsch.	54	51.02 N	13.13 E
Marbach, Dtsch.	56	50.37 N	9.43 E
Marbach, Schw.	58	46.52 N	7.55 E
Marbach am Neckar	56	48.56 N	9.14 E
Marbache	56	48.48 N	6.05 E
Marbais	50	50.33 N	4.31 E
Marbeck	52	51.49 N	6.52 E
Marbella	34	36.31 N	4.53 W
Marble, Mn., U.S.	190	47.19 N	93.17 W
Marble, N.C., U.S.	192	35.10 N	83.55 W
Marble, Pa., U.S.	214	41.20 N	79.26 W
Marble Arch ⊥	146	30.29 N	18.35 E
Marble Bar	162	21.11 S	119.44 E
Marble Canyon V	200	36.30 N	111.50 W
Marble Falls	196	30.34 N	98.16 W
Marble Hall	156	24.57 S	29.13 E
Marblehead, Il., U.S.	219	39.50 N	91.22 W
Marblehead, Ma., U.S.	207	42.30 N	70.51 W
Marblehead, Oh., U.S.	214	41.32 N	82.44 W
Marblehead Neck ›[1]	283	42.29 N	70.51 W
Marble Hill	194	37.18 N	89.58 W
Marble Lake ◎	216	41.54 N	84.54 W
Marblemount	224	48.31 N	121.26 W
Marble Rock	190	42.57 N	92.52 W
Marbleton	206	45.37 N	71.35 W
Marburg, Austl.	171a	27.34 S	152.35 E
Marburg, Dtsch.	56	50.49 N	8.46 E
Marburg, S. Afr.	158	30.44 S	30.26 E
Marburg, Lake ◎[1]	208	39.48 N	76.53 W
Marburg an der Drau → Maribor	36	46.33 N	15.39 E
Marbury	208	38.34 N	77.09 W
Marc ≃	50	50.43 N	3.50 E
Marca, Ponta da ›	152	16.31 S	11.42 E
Marcal ≃	30	47.41 N	17.32 E
Marcala	236	14.07 N	88.00 W
Marcali	30	46.35 N	17.25 E
Marcallo con Casone	266b	45.29 N	8.52 E
Marcaria	64	45.07 N	10.32 E
Marceau, Lac ◎	186	51.25 N	66.41 W
Marcedusa	68	39.02 N	16.50 E
Marcelin	184	52.55 N	106.47 W
Marceline	194	39.42 N	92.56 W
Marcelino Ramos	252	27.28 S	51.54 W
Marcella	276	40.59 N	74.28 W
Marcellina	66	42.01 N	12.48 E
Marcellus, Mi., U.S.	216	42.01 N	85.48 W
Marcellus, N.Y., U.S.	210	42.59 N	76.20 W
Marcellus Falls	210	43.00 N	76.20 W
Marcevo	83	47.15 N	38.53 E
March	42	52.33 N	0.06 E
March (Morava) ≃	30	48.10 N	16.59 E
Marcha	74	60.37 N	123.18 E
Marcha ≃	74	63.28 N	118.50 E
March Air Force Base ■	228	33.54 N	117.15 W
Marchais	261	48.31 N	2.03 E
Marchal	152	5.16 S	14.58 E
Marchamat	85	40.30 N	72.19 E
Marchand	214	40.51 N	79.02 W
Marchaux	58	47.19 N	6.08 E
Marche □[4]	66	43.30 N	13.15 E
Marche □[9]	32	46.05 N	2.10 E
Marche-en-Famenne	56	50.12 N	5.20 E
Marchegg	61	48.17 N	16.55 E
Marche-les-Dames	56	50.29 N	4.58 E
Marchémoret	261	49.03 N	2.46 E
Marchena	34	37.20 N	5.24 W
Marchena, Isla I	246a	0.21 N	90.29 W
Marchenoir	50	47.49 N	1.24 E
Marchesato ⬥[1]	68	39.07 N	16.58 E
Marchfeld ⬥[1]	264b	48.17 N	16.31 E
Marchienne-au-Pont	50	50.24 N	4.23 E
Marchinbar Island I	164	11.15 S	136.45 E
Marching	60	48.49 N	11.43 E
Mar Chiquita, Laguna c	252	37.37 S	57.24 W
Mar Chiquita, Laguna ◎	252	30.42 S	62.36 W
Marchtrenk	61	48.11 N	14.07 E
Marciana	66	42.47 N	10.10 E
Marciana Marina	66	42.48 N	10.12 E
Marcianise	68	41.02 N	14.17 E
Marciano della Chiana	66	43.18 N	11.47 E
Marčichina Buda	78	51.58 N	34.03 E
Marcigny	32	46.17 N	4.02 E
Marcillac-Vallon	32	44.29 N	2.28 E
Marcilloles	62	45.20 N	5.11 E
Marcilly	261	49.02 N	2.53 E
Marcilly-la-Campagne	50	48.50 N	1.13 E
Marcilly-le-Hayer	50	48.21 N	3.38 E
Marcilly-sur-Eure	50	48.49 N	1.21 E
Marck	50	50.57 N	1.57 E
Marckolsheim	58	48.10 N	7.33 E
Marco, Bra.	250	3.08 S	40.09 W
Marco, It.	64	45.51 N	11.01 E
Marco, Fl., U.S.	220	25.58 N	81.43 W
Marcoing	50	50.07 N	3.11 E
Marco Island I	220	25.55 N	81.45 W
Marcola	202	44.10 N	122.51 W
Marcolino, Igarapé ≃	250	11.03 S	58.35 W
Marcona	248	15.03 S	75.01 W
Marco Polo, Aeroporto ⊠	64	45.30 N	12.21 E
Marco Polo Bridge ⬥[5]	271a	39.52 N	116.12 E
Marcos Juárez	252	32.42 S	62.06 W
Marcos Paz	258	34.46 S	58.50 W
Marcos Paz □[5]	288	34.49 S	58.49 W
Marcotte, Lac ◎	206	46.47 N	73.12 W
Marcoussis	261	48.39 N	2.14 E
Marcq	261	48.52 N	1.49 E
Marcq-en-Barœul	50	50.40 N	3.05 E
Marčugi	82	55.21 N	38.33 E
Marcus	198	42.49 N	95.48 W
Marcus Baker, Mount ∧	180	61.26 N	147.45 W
Marcus Hook	208	39.49 N	75.25 W
Marcus Hook Creek ≃	285	39.49 N	75.25 W
Marcus Island → Minami-Tori-shima I	14	24.18 N	153.58 E
Marcy, Mount ∧	188	44.07 N	73.56 W
Marda	162	30.13 S	119.17 E
Mardakert	84	40.12 N	46.48 E
Mardalsfossen ᒪ	26	62.30 N	8.07 E
Mardān	123	34.12 N	72.02 E
Mardarovka	78	47.32 N	29.44 E
Mar de Cães, Vala de ≅	266c	38.51 N	8.59 W
Mar de Espanha	256	21.52 S	43.00 W
Mardela Springs	208	38.27 N	75.45 W
Mar del Plata	252	38.00 S	57.33 W
Marden	42	51.10 N	0.29 E
Mardie	162	21.11 S	115.57 E
Mardin	130	37.18 N	40.44 E
Mardin □[4]	128	37.25 N	41.00 E
Mar Dyke ≃	260	51.29 N	0.14 E
Maré I	175f	21.30 S	168.00 E
Mare a Brăilei, Insula I	38	45.00 N	28.00 E
Marea de Portillo	240p	19.55 N	77.11 W
Marecchia ≃	66	44.04 N	12.34 E
Marechal Cândido Rondon	252	24.34 S	54.04 W
Marechal Deodoro	250	9.43 S	35.54 W
Marechal Taumaturgo	248	8.57 S	72.48 W
Maree, Loch ◎	46	57.42 N	5.30 W
Mareeba	166	17.00 S	145.26 E
Mareetsane	158	26.09 S	25.25 E
Mareil-en-France	261	49.04 N	2.26 E
Mareil-le-Guyon	261	48.47 N	1.51 E
Mareil-Marly	261	48.53 N	2.05 E
Mare Island I	226	38.06 N	122.16 W
Mare Island Naval Shipyard ■	226	38.06 N	122.17 W
Mare Island Strait ɰ	282	38.06 N	122.17 W
Mareje, Gunung ∧	115b	8.46 S	116.08 E
Marek	112	4.48 S	120.21 E
Maremma ⬥[1]	66	42.30 N	11.30 E
Marene	62	44.39 N	7.44 E
Marengo, Il., U.S.	216	42.14 N	88.36 W
Marengo, In., U.S.	218	38.22 N	86.20 W
Marengo, Ia., U.S.	190	41.47 N	92.04 W
Marengo, Mi., U.S.	216	42.17 N	84.51 W
Marengo, Oh., U.S.	214	40.24 N	82.49 W
Marengo ⊥	62	44.49 N	8.40 E
Marengo Cave ≗[5]	218	38.23 N	86.21 W
Marenisco	190	46.22 N	89.41 W
Marennes	32	45.50 N	1.06 W
Marerano	157b	21.23 S	44.52 E
Maresias	256	23.48 S	45.33 W
Marettimo	70	37.58 N	12.04 E
Marettimo, Isola I	70	37.58 N	12.03 E
Mareuil-en-Brie	50	48.57 N	3.45 E
Mareuil-lès-Meaux	261	48.56 N	2.52 E
Mareuil-sur-Aÿ	50	49.03 N	4.02 E
Mareuil-sur-Belle	32	45.28 N	0.28 E
Marevo	76	57.19 N	32.05 E
Marey-sur-Tille	58	47.35 N	5.03 E
Marfa	196	30.18 N	104.01 W
Marfinka	83	47.36 N	38.32 E
Marfino	80	46.25 N	48.44 E
Mar Forest ⬥[3]	46	57.00 N	3.35 W
Margai Caka ◎	120	35.00 N	87.00 E
Margam, Īrān	84	39.09 N	44.57 E
Margam, Wales, U.K.	42	51.34 N	3.44 W
Marganec	78	47.38 N	34.40 E
Margao → Madgaon	122	15.18 N	73.57 E
Margaree	186	46.24 N	61.05 W
Margaree Harbour	186	46.26 N	61.07 W
Margaret ≃	162	18.10 S	125.37 E
Margaret, Mount ∧	224	46.18 N	122.08 W
Margaret Bay	182	51.20 N	127.29 W
Margaret Creek ≃	166	29.26 S	137.07 E
Margarethenhöhe ⬥[8]	263	51.26 N	6.58 E
Margaret River, Austl.	162	33.57 S	115.04 E
Margaret River, Austl.	162	18.38 S	126.52 E
Margaret Roding	260	51.47 N	0.19 E
Margaretting	260	51.41 N	0.25 E
Margarettsville	208	36.32 N	77.21 W
Margaretville	210	42.08 N	74.38 W
Margarita, Bahía → Marguerite Bay c	9	68.30 S	68.30 W
Margarita, Isla I	246	9.05 N	74.30 W
Margarita, Isla de I	246	11.00 N	64.00 W
Margarita Belén	252	27.16 S	58.58 W
Margarita Peak ∧	228	33.26 N	117.23 W
Margaritovka	83	46.55 N	38.52 E
Margate, S. Afr.	158	30.55 S	30.15 E
Margate, Eng., U.K.	42	51.24 N	1.24 E
Margate, Fl., U.S.	220	26.14 N	80.12 W
Margate City	208	39.19 N	74.30 W
Margecany	30	48.54 N	21.01 E
Margelan → Margilan	85	40.28 N	71.44 E
Margeride, Monts de la ⋏	32	44.50 N	3.30 E
Margès	62	45.09 N	5.03 E
Mārgherita, India	120	27.17 N	95.41 E
Margherita → Jamaame, Som.	144	0.04 N	42.45 E
Margherita di Savoia	68	41.23 N	16.09 E
Margherita Peak ∧	154	0.22 N	29.51 E
Marghī	120	34.58 N	66.31 E
Marghita	38	47.21 N	22.21 E
Margi ≃	70	37.16 N	14.58 E
Margilan	85	40.28 N	71.44 E
Margit Híd ⬥[5]	264c	47.31 N	19.02 E
Margit-sziget I	264c	47.32 N	19.03 E
Margny-lès-Compiègne	50	49.25 N	2.49 E
Margone	62	45.13 N	7.11 E
Margonin	30	52.59 N	17.05 E
Margos	248	10.04 S	76.26 W
Margosatubig	116	7.34 N	123.10 E
Margot Lake ◎	184	52.23 N	93.10 W
Mārgow, Dasht-e ⬥[2]	128	30.45 N	63.10 E
Margreid → Magrè	64	46.17 N	11.12 E
Marguerite, Pic → Margherita Peak ∧	154	0.22 N	29.51 E
Marguerite Bay c	9	68.30 S	68.30 W
Marguerittes	62	43.51 N	4.27 E
Margut	56	49.35 N	5.16 E
Margyang	124	29.57 N	90.09 E
Mari	164	9.10 S	141.40 E
Maria	116	9.12 N	123.39 E
Maria, Îles II	14	21.48 S	154.41 W
Mariabrunn ⬥[8]	264b	48.12 N	16.14 E
María Cleofas, Isla I	234	21.16 N	106.14 W
Maria da Fé	256	22.18 S	45.23 W
María Elena	252	22.21 S	69.40 W
Maria Enzersdorf	61	48.06 N	16.17 E
Maria Gail	64	46.36 N	13.52 E
Mariager	26	56.39 N	10.00 E
Mariāhu	124	25.37 N	82.37 E
María Ignacia (Vela)	252	37.24 S	59.30 W
Maria Island I, Austl.	164	14.52 S	135.40 E
Maria Island I, Austl.	166	42.39 S	148.04 E
Maria Island National Park ♠	166	42.39 S	148.06 E
Mariakani	154	3.52 S	39.28 E
Maria Laach ʊ[1]	56	50.24 N	7.14 E
María la Baja	246	9.59 N	75.17 W
Maria Lanzendorf	264b	48.06 N	16.25 E
Maria Luggau	64	46.42 N	12.45 E
María Madre, Isla I	234	21.35 N	106.33 W
María Magdalena, Isla I	234	21.25 N	106.24 W
Marian, Lake ◎	220	27.52 N	81.06 W
Mariana	255	20.23 S	43.25 W
Mariana Basin ✢[1]	14	17.30 N	145.00 E
Mariana Islands II	108	16.00 N	145.30 E
Mariana Ridge ✢[3]	14	17.00 N	146.00 E
Mariana Trench ✢[1]	14	15.00 N	147.30 E
Mariāni	120	26.40 N	94.20 E
Marian Lake ◎	176	63.00 N	116.10 W
Marianna, Ar., U.S.	194	34.46 N	90.45 W
Marianna, Fl., U.S.	192	30.46 N	85.13 W
Mariannelund	26	57.37 N	15.34 E
Mariannhill	158	29.52 S	30.50 E
Mariano Acosta	258	34.43 S	58.48 W
Mariano Comense	62	45.42 N	9.11 E
Mariano del Friuli	64	45.55 N	13.27 E
Mariano I. Loza	252	29.22 S	58.12 W
Mariano J. Haedo	288	34.38 S	58.36 W
Mariano Moreno, Arg.	252	38.44 S	70.01 W
Mariano Moreno → Moreno, Arg.	258	34.39 S	58.48 W
Marianopoli	70	37.36 N	13.55 E
Mariánské Lázně	60	49.59 N	12.43 E
Mariar	164	2.48 S	132.50 E
Mariarano	157b	15.29 S	46.42 E
Marias ≃	202	47.56 N	110.30 W
Marias, Dry Fork ≃	202	48.22 N	111.45 W
Marías, Islas II	234	21.25 N	106.28 W
Maria Saal	61	46.41 N	14.21 E
Marias Pass)(	202	48.19 N	113.21 W
Maria Stein	216	40.24 N	84.28 W
María Teresa	252	34.01 S	61.54 W
Maria-Theresiopel → Subotica	38	46.06 N	19.39 E
Mariato, Punta ›	246	7.13 N	80.53 W
Maria van Diemen, Cape ›	172	34.28 S	172.39 E
Mariaville	210	42.49 N	74.08 W
Mariazell	61	47.47 N	15.19 E
Ma'rib	144	15.30 N	45.20 E
Maribo	41	54.46 N	11.31 E
Maribojoc Bay c	116	9.42 N	123.50 E
Maribor	36	46.33 N	15.39 E
Maribyrnong	274b	37.46 S	144.54 E
Marica, Blg.	38	42.02 N	25.50 E
Maricá, Bra.	256	22.55 S	42.49 W
Marica, Ross.	78	51.45 N	35.16 E
Maricá □[7]	287a	22.57 S	42.59 W
Marica (Évros) (Meriç) ≃	38	40.52 N	26.12 E
Maricá, Lagoa de c	256	22.56 S	42.50 W
Maricaban Island I	116	13.39 N	120.53 E
Maricao	240m	18.11 N	66.59 W
Maricás, Ilhas II	256	23.01 S	42.55 W
Maricha Bil ◎	272b	22.55 N	88.31 E
Marico ≃	156	24.12 S	26.52 E
Maricopa, Az., U.S.	200	33.03 N	112.02 W
Maricopa, Ca., U.S.	204	35.03 N	119.24 W
Maricopa Indian Reservation ⬥[4]	200	33.02 N	112.05 W
Maricunga, Salar de ≃	252	26.55 S	69.05 W
Maridagao ≃	116	7.13 N	124.41 E
Marīdī	154	4.55 N	29.28 E
Marīdī ≃	140	6.05 N	29.24 E
Marié ≃	246	0.27 S	66.26 W
Marie Byrd Land ⬥[1]	9	80.00 S	120.00 W
Marie Curtis Park ♠	275b	43.35 N	79.33 W
Mariedamm	40	58.51 N	15.09 E
Mariefred	40	59.16 N	17.13 E
Marie-Galante I	241o	15.56 N	61.16 W
Mariehamn	26	60.06 N	19.57 E
Marieholm	41	55.52 N	13.09 E
Mariel	240p	22.59 N	82.45 W
Mari El → Marij El □[3]	80	56.30 N	48.00 E
Marie Lake ◎	184	54.37 N	110.18 W
Marie-Lefranc, Lac ◎	206	46.08 N	75.00 W
Mariembourg	50	50.06 N	4.31 E
Marienbad → Mariánské Lázně	60	49.59 N	12.43 E
Marienbaum	52	51.41 N	6.22 E
Marienberg, Dtsch.	54	50.39 N	13.10 E
Marienberg, Dtsch.	56	50.39 N	7.57 E
Marienberg, Pap. N. Gui.	164	3.55 S	144.15 E
Marien-Berg ∧[2]	264a	52.22 N	13.32 E
Marienborn	54	52.12 N	11.08 E
Marienburg → Malbork	30	54.02 N	19.01 E
Mariendorf ⬥[8]	264a	52.26 N	13.23 E
Marienfelde ⬥[8]	54	52.25 N	13.22 E
Marienhafe	52	53.31 N	7.16 E
Marienheide	56	51.05 N	7.32 E
Mariental, Dtsch.	54	52.16 N	10.59 E
Mariental, Namibia	156	24.36 S	17.59 E
Mariental □[5]	156	25.00 S	19.00 E
Marienville	214	41.28 N	79.07 W
Maries □[6]	219	38.15 N	91.56 W
Maries ≃	194	38.30 N	92.01 W
Mariestad	40	58.43 N	13.51 E
Marieta ≃	246	5.02 N	66.38 W
Marietta, Ga., U.S.	192	33.57 N	84.33 W
Marietta, In., U.S.	218	39.26 N	85.53 W
Marietta, Mn., U.S.	198	45.00 N	96.25 W
Marietta, Oh., U.S.	188	39.24 N	81.27 W
Marietta, Ok., U.S.	196	33.56 N	97.06 W
Marietta, Pa., U.S.	208	40.03 N	76.33 W
Marietta, Tx., U.S.	222	33.10 N	94.33 W
Marietta, Wa., U.S.	224	48.47 N	122.34 W
Marieville	206	45.26 N	73.10 W
Mariga ≃	150	9.40 N	5.55 E
Marignane	62	43.25 N	5.13 E
Marignier	58	46.06 N	6.31 E
Marigny-le-Châtel	50	48.24 N	3.44 E
Marigny-L'Église	50	47.22 N	3.56 E
Marigot, Dom.	240d	15.32 N	61.18 W
Marigot, Guad.	238	18.04 N	63.06 W
Marihatag	116	8.48 N	126.18 E
Mariinsk	86	56.13 N	87.45 E
Mariinskoje	89	51.43 N	140.13 E
Marijampole	76	54.33 N	23.21 E
Marijec	80	56.32 N	49.50 E
Marij El □[3]	80	56.30 N	48.00 E
Marikana	158	25.42 S	27.30 E
Marikina	269f	14.38 N	121.06 E
Marikina ≃	269f	14.33 N	121.04 E
Marília	255	22.13 S	49.56 W
Marilla	210	42.50 N	78.33 W
Mari-Malmyž	80	56.30 N	50.52 E
Marimari ≃	246	3.58 S	58.49 W
Marimba	152	8.28 S	17.08 E
Marín	34	42.23 N	8.42 W
Marin □[6]	226	38.03 N	122.33 W
Marina	226	36.41 N	121.48 W
Marina ⬥[8]	282	37.47 N	122.27 W
Marina del Rey	280	33.50 N	118.25 W
Marina del Rey c	280	33.58 N	118.27 W
Marina di Andora	62	43.57 N	8.08 E
Marina di Campo	66	42.44 N	10.14 E
Marina di Caronia	70	38.02 N	14.28 E
Marina di Carrara	64	44.02 N	10.02 E
Marina di Cecina	66	43.18 N	10.29 E
Marina di Gioiosa Ionica	68	38.18 N	16.20 E
Marina di Grosseto	66	42.43 N	10.59 E
Marina di Massa	64	44.00 N	10.06 E
Marina di Minturno	66	41.16 N	13.45 E
Marina di Orosei	71	40.22 N	9.43 E
Marina di Palma ⬥[8]	70	37.10 N	13.43 E
Marina di Pietrasanta	64	43.56 N	10.12 E
Marina di Pisa	66	43.40 N	10.16 E
Marina di Ragusa	70	36.47 N	14.33 E
Marina di Ravenna	66	44.29 N	12.17 E
Marina Fall ᒪ	246	5.22 N	59.29 W
Marin City	282	37.52 N	122.21 W
Marinduque □[4]	116	13.25 N	121.55 E
Marinduque Island I	116	13.24 N	121.58 E
Marine	219	38.47 N	89.46 W
Marine City	214	42.43 N	82.29 W
Marine-Ehrenmal ⊥	54	54.23 N	10.15 E
Marineland of the Pacific ʊ[3]	228	33.44 N	118.24 W
Marinella	70	37.35 N	12.50 E
Marine Museum ʊ	280	33.43 N	118.17 W
Marineo	70	37.57 N	13.25 E

≃	River	Fluß	Río	Rivière	Rio
≅	Canal	Kanal	Canal	Canal	Canal
ᒪ	Waterfall, Rapids	Wasserfall, Stromschnellen	Cascada, Rápidos	Chute d'eau, Rapides	Cascata, Rápidos
ɰ	Strait	Meeresstraße	Estrecho	Détroit	Estreito
c	Bay, Gulf	Bucht, Golf	Bahía, Golfo	Baie, Golfe	Baía, Golfo
◎	Lake, Lakes	See, Seen	Lago, Lagos	Lac, Lacs	Lago, Lagos
≡	Swamp	Sumpf	Pantano	Marais	Pântano
⛉	Ice Features, Glacier	Eis- und Gletscherformen	Accidentes Glaciales	Formes glaciaires	Acidentes glaciares
⚲	Other Hydrographic Features	Andere Hydrographische Objekte	Otros Elementos Hidrográficos	Autres données hydrographiques	Outros acidentes hidrográficos
✢	Submarine Features	Untermeerische Objekte	Accidentes Submarinos	Formes de relief sous-marin	Acidentes submarinos
□	Political Unit	Politische Einheit	Unidad Política	Entité politique	Unidade política
ʊ	Cultural Institution	Kulturelle Institution	Institución Cultural	Institution culturelle	Instituição cultural
⊥	Historical Site	Historische Stätte	Sitio Histórico	Site historique	Sitio histórico
♠	Recreational Site	Erholungs- und Ferienort	Sitio de Recreo	Centre de loisirs	Area de Lazer
⊠	Airport	Flughafen	Aeropuerto	Aéroport	Aeroporto
■	Military Installation	Militäranlage	Instalación Militar	Installation militaire	Instalação militar
⬥	Miscellaneous	Verschiedenes	Misceláneo	Divers	Diversos

Marine Park ♦ 283 42.20 N 71.01 W
Marine Parkway Bridge ➝[5] 276 40.34 N 73.53 W
Mariners Museum ⊕ 208 37.03 N 76.30 W
Marines 50 49.09 N 1.59 E
Marinette 190 45.06 N 87.37 W
Maringá 255 23.25 S 51.55 W
Maringa ≐ 152 1.14 N 19.48 E
Maringouin 194 30.29 N 91.31 W
Maringuè 154 17.55 S 34.24 E
Marinha Grande 34 39.45 N 8.56 W
Marinho ≐ 287a 23.00 S 43.27 W
Marin Mall ➝[9] 282 37.56 N 122.31 W
Marino, It. 66 41.46 N 12.39 E
Marino, Vanuatu 175f 15.00 S 168.09 E
Marinovka, Ross. 80 48.41 N 43.49 E
Marinovka, Ukr. 78 47.46 N 30.53 E
Marinovka, Ukr. 83 47.54 N 38.51 E
Marin Peninsula >[1] 282 37.51 N 122.31 W
Marinskij Posad 80 56.07 N 47.43 E
Marintu 112 0.34 N 110.00 E
Marinwood 226 38.02 N 122.32 W
Mario, Monte ∧[2] 267a 41.55 N 12.27 E
Marion, Austl. 168b 35.01 S 138.34 E
Marion, Al., U.S. 194 32.37 N 87.19 W
Marion, Ar., U.S. 194 35.12 N 90.11 W
Marion, Ct., U.S. 207 41.33 N 72.55 W
Marion, Il., U.S. 194 37.43 N 88.55 W
Marion, In., U.S. 216 40.33 N 85.39 W
Marion, Ia., U.S. 190 42.02 N 91.35 W
Marion, Ks., U.S. 198 38.20 N 97.01 W
Marion, Ky., U.S. 194 37.19 N 88.04 W
Marion, La., U.S. 194 32.54 N 92.14 W
Marion, Ma., U.S. 207 41.42 N 70.45 W
Marion, Mi., U.S. 190 44.06 N 85.08 W
Marion, Ms., U.S. 194 32.25 N 88.38 W
Marion, N.Y., U.S. 210 43.08 N 77.11 W
Marion, N.C., U.S. 192 35.41 N 82.00 W
Marion, N.D., U.S. 198 46.36 N 98.19 W
Marion, Oh., U.S. 214 40.35 N 83.07 W
Marion, S.C., U.S. 192 34.10 N 79.24 W
Marion, S.D., U.S. 198 43.25 N 97.15 W
Marion, Va., U.S. 192 36.50 N 81.30 W
Marion, Wi., U.S. 190 44.40 N 88.53 W
Marion □[6], Fl., U.S. 220 29.00 N 82.03 W
Marion □[6], Il., U.S. 219 38.38 N 88.57 W
Marion □[6], In., U.S. 218 39.46 N 86.09 W
Marion □[6], Mo., U.S. 219 39.50 N 91.37 W
Marion □[6], Oh., U.S. 214 40.35 N 83.08 W
Marion □[6], Or., U.S. 224 45.06 N 122.47 W
Marion □[6], Tx., U.S. 222 32.48 N 94.33 W
Marion, Lake ⊜ 220 28.05 N 81.32 W
Marion, Lake ⊜[1] 192 33.30 N 80.25 W
Marion Bay c 166 42.48 S 147.55 E
Marion Center 214 40.46 N 79.03 W
Marion Downs 166 23.22 S 139.39 E
Marion Heights 210 40.48 N 76.28 W
Marion Hill 214 40.44 N 80.18 W
Marion Junction 194 32.26 N 87.14 W
Marion Lake ⊜[1] 198 38.24 N 97.08 W
Marion Reef ✣[2] 166 19.10 S 152.17 E
Marion Station 208 38.02 N 75.46 W
Marionville 194 37.00 N 93.38 W
Mariópolis 252 26.20 S 52.33 W
Maripa 246 7.26 N 65.09 W
Maripá de Minas 256 21.48 S 42.58 W
Maripasoula 250 3.38 N 54.02 W
Maripipi Island I 116 11.47 N 124.19 E
Mariposa 226 37.29 N 119.57 W
Mariposa □[6] 226 37.29 N 119.58 W
Mariposa Creek ≐ 226 37.14 N 120.26 W
Mariposa Slough ≐ 226 37.12 N 120.46 W
Mariquita 246 5.12 N 74.54 W
Marisa 112 0.28 N 121.56 E
Marisa ≐ 112 0.28 N 121.56 E
Mariscal Estigarribia 252 22.02 S 60.38 W
Marisco, Ponta do > 287a 23.01 S 43.17 W
Mariškino 82 55.21 N 38.37 E
Marissa 219 38.15 N 89.45 W
Maritime Alps (Alpes Maritimes) (Alpi Marittime) ⩘ 62 44.15 N 7.10 E
Maritime Atlas → Atlas Tellien ⩘ 148 36.00 N 3.00 E
Maritimes, Alpes → Maritime Alps ⩘ 62 44.15 N 7.10 E
Marittime, Alpi → Maritime Alps ⩘ 62 44.15 N 7.10 E
Mari-Turek 80 56.47 N 49.36 E
Maritzburg → Pietermaritzburg 158 29.37 S 30.16 E
Mariupol' (Ždanov) 83 47.06 N 37.33 E
Mariusa, Caño ≐[1] 246 9.43 N 61.26 W
Mariusa, Isla I 241r 9.39 N 61.19 W
Marīvān 128 35.31 N 46.10 E
Mariveles 116 14.26 N 120.29 E
Märjamaa 76 58.54 N 24.26 E
Marjanovka, Ross. 86 54.58 N 72.38 E
Marjanovka, Ukr. 78 50.28 N 24.48 E
Marjanskaja 78 45.06 N 38.38 E
Marjevka 86 53.46 N 67.24 E
Marjina Gorka 76 53.31 N 28.09 E
Marjinka 83 47.56 N 37.31 E
Marjino, Ross. 82 54.28 N 37.12 E
Marjino, Ross. 89 48.31 N 130.38 E
Marjino, Ross. 265a 59.50 N 29.56 E
Marjino, Ross. 265a 59.54 N 31.00 E
Marjino, Ross. 265b 55.52 N 37.18 E
Marjinskaja 84 43.53 N 43.29 E
Marjinsko 76 58.49 N 28.32 E
Mār Jirjis, Jūn c 132 33.54 N 35.33 E
Marj 'Uyūn 132 33.22 N 35.35 E
Marka, Som. 144 1.43 N 44.53 E
Mārkā, Urd. 132 31.59 N 35.59 E
Markā I 144 18.13 N 41.19 E
Mark Acres 279b 40.21 N 79.42 W
Markakol', ozero ⊜ 86 48.45 N 85.48 E
Markala 150 13.41 N 6.05 W
Markam 102 29.40 N 98.30 E
Markansu 85 39.18 N 73.20 E
Mārkāpur 122 15.44 N 79.17 E
Markaryd 26 56.26 N 13.36 E
Markazī □[4] 128 34.30 N 50.30 E
Markdale 212 44.19 N 80.39 W
Markdorf 58 47.43 N 9.23 E
Marked Tree 194 35.31 N 90.25 W
Markelo 52 52.14 N 6.30 E
Markelovo 86 56.42 N 83.33 E
Marken I 52 52.28 N 5.03 E
Markendorf 54 51.59 N 13.10 E
Markermeer ⊜ 52 52.33 N 5.15 E
Markesan 190 43.42 N 88.59 W
Märket I 40 60.18 N 19.08 E
Market Bosworth 42 52.37 N 1.24 W
Market Deeping 42 52.41 N 0.19 W
Market Drayton 42 52.54 N 2.29 W
Market Harborough 42 52.29 N 0.55 W
Markethill 48 54.18 N 6.31 W
Market Lavington 42 51.18 N 1.59 W
Market Rasen 44 53.24 N 0.21 W
Market Weighton 44 53.52 N 0.40 W
Markfield 42 52.40 N 1.17 W
Markgröningen 56 48.54 N 9.05 E
Markham, On., Can. 212 43.52 N 79.16 W
Markham, Il., U.S. 278 41.35 N 87.41 W
Markham, Tx., U.S. 222 28.57 N 96.04 W
Markham ≐ 164 6.35 S 146.25 E
Markham, Mount ∧ 9 82.51 S 161.21 E
Markham Bay c 176 63.30 N 71.48 W
Markinch 46 56.12 N 3.08 W
Märkisch Buchholz 54 52.07 N 13.46 E
Markit 85 38.55 N 77.38 E
Markkleeberg 54 51.17 N 12.23 E
Markland Dam ➝[6] 218 38.47 N 84.58 W
Markle, In., U.S. 216 40.50 N 85.20 W
Markle, Pa., U.S. 279b 40.34 N 79.39 W
Markleeville 226 38.41 N 119.46 W
Markleville 218 39.58 N 85.36 W
Markley Canyon V 282 38.00 N 121.50 W
Marknesse 52 52.43 N 5.52 E
Markneukirchen 54 50.18 N 12.19 E
Markoldendorf 52 51.48 N 9.46 E
Markópoulon 267c 37.54 N 23.54 E
Markounda 152 7.37 N 16.59 E
Markovka 83 49.31 N 39.34 E
Markovo, Ross. 74 64.40 N 170.25 E
Markovo, Ross. 80 57.01 N 40.30 E
Markovo, Ross. 82 55.52 N 39.17 E
Markovo, Ross. 88 57.20 N 107.04 E
Markoy 150 14.39 N 0.02 E
Markranstädt 54 51.18 N 12.13 E
Marks, Ross. 80 51.42 N 46.46 E
Marks, Ms., U.S. 194 34.15 N 90.16 W
Marks Tey 42 51.52 N 0.47 E
Marksuhl 56 50.55 N 10.11 E
Marksville 194 31.07 N 92.03 W
Markt Bibart 56 49.39 N 10.26 E
Marktbreit 56 49.40 N 10.08 E
Markt Erlbach 56 49.29 N 10.38 E
Marktheidenfeld 56 49.50 N 9.36 E
Markt Indersdorf 60 48.22 N 11.23 E
Marktl 60 48.15 N 12.51 E
Marktleugast 54 50.10 N 11.38 E
Marktleuthen 54 50.08 N 12.00 E
Marktoberdorf 58 47.47 N 10.37 E
Marktredwitz 60 50.00 N 12.06 E
Markt Rettenbach 58 47.57 N 10.23 E
Marktschellenberg 64 47.42 N 13.02 E
Markt Schwaben 60 48.11 N 11.51 E
Mark Twain Cave ⊥[5] 219 39.42 N 91.21 W
Mark Twain Lake ⊜[1] 219 39.30 N 91.45 W
Mark Twain State Park ♦ 219 39.29 N 91.48 W
Markulešty 38 47.52 N 28.14 E
Markundi 140 11.33 N 23.49 E
Markvue Manor 279b 40.20 N 79.46 W
Mark West Creek ≐ 226 38.30 N 122.42 W
Marl 52 51.38 N 7.05 E
Marlasi 164 5.30 S 134.38 E
Marlboro, Ab., Can. 182 53.33 N 116.45 W
Marlboro, N.J., U.S. 208 40.18 N 74.14 W
Marlboro, N.Y., U.S. 210 41.36 N 73.58 W
Marlboro, Oh., U.S. 214 40.53 N 81.12 W
Marlboro, Pa., U.S. 285 39.54 N 75.42 W
Marlborough, Austl. 166 22.49 S 149.53 E
Marlborough, Guy. 246 7.29 N 58.38 W
Marlborough, Eng., U.K. 42 51.26 N 1.43 W
Marlborough, Ct., U.S. 207 41.37 N 72.27 W
Marlborough, Ma., U.S. 207 42.20 N 71.33 W
Marlborough Downs ⩘[1] 42 51.30 N 1.45 W
Marldon 42 50.28 N 3.36 W
Marle 50 49.44 N 3.46 E
Marlenheim 58 48.37 N 7.30 E
Marles-en-Brie 261 48.44 N 2.53 E
Marles-les-Mines 50 50.30 N 2.31 E
Marlette 190 43.19 N 83.04 W
Marlette Lake ⊜ 226 39.10 N 119.54 W
Marley, Il., U.S. 278 41.33 N 87.55 W
Marley, Md., U.S. 208 39.09 N 76.35 W
Marley Creek ≐ 278 41.31 N 87.57 W
Marley Neck >[1] 284b 39.12 N 76.33 W
Marlieux 58 46.04 N 5.04 E
Marlin 222 31.18 N 96.53 W
Marlinton 188 38.13 N 80.05 W
Marl-Loemühle, Flughafen ⊠ 263 51.39 N 7.10 E
Marlow, Dtsch. 54 54.09 N 12.34 E
Marlow, Eng., U.K. 42 51.35 N 0.48 W
Marlow, Ok., U.S. 196 34.38 N 97.57 W
Marlpit Hill 260 51.13 N 0.04 E
Marlton 208 39.53 N 74.55 W
Marlton Heights 285 39.40 N 75.21 W
Marly 50 50.20 N 3.32 E
Marly, Forêt de ♦ 261 48.52 N 2.03 E
Marly-la-Ville 261 49.05 N 2.30 E
Marly-le-Roi 50 48.52 N 2.05 E
Marma, Sve. 26 61.16 N 16.52 E
Marma, Sve. 40 60.30 N 17.25 E
Marmaduke 194 36.11 N 90.22 W
Marmagne 58 46.50 N 4.21 E
Marmande 32 44.30 N 0.10 E
Marmara, Sea of → Marmara Denizi ▽[2] 130 40.40 N 28.15 E
Marmara Adası I 130 40.38 N 27.37 E
Marmara Denizi (Sea of Marmara) ▽[2] 130 40.40 N 28.15 E
Marmara Ereğlisi 130 40.58 N 27.57 E
Marmara Gölü ⊜ 130 38.37 N 28.02 E
Marmaris 130 36.51 N 28.16 E
Marmarītā 130 34.47 N 36.15 E
Marmarth 198 46.17 N 103.55 W
Marmaton ≐ 194 38.00 N 94.19 W
Marmelopolis 256 22.27 S 45.10 W
Marmelos 248 6.08 S 61.50 W
Marmelos, Rio dos ≐ 248 6.06 S 61.46 W
Marmet 188 38.14 N 81.34 W
Marmion Lake ⊜[1] 190 48.54 N 91.30 W
Marmirolo 64 45.13 N 10.45 E
Marmolada ∧ 64 46.26 N 11.51 E
Marmora, On., Can. 212 44.29 N 77.41 W
Marmora, N.J., U.S. 208 39.16 N 74.38 W
Marmore 66 42.33 N 12.43 E
Marmore ≐ 62 45.44 N 7.37 E
Marmore, Cascàta delle ⌊ 66 42.33 N 12.43 E
Marmot Bay c 180 58.00 N 152.20 W
Marmot Island I 180 58.13 N 151.51 W
Marmoutier 58 48.41 N 7.23 E
Mar Muerto, Laguna c 234 16.10 N 94.10 W
Marnate 266b 45.38 N 8.54 E
Marnay 58 47.17 N 5.46 E
Marnaz 58 46.04 N 6.32 E
Marne, Dtsch. 52 53.57 N 9.00 E
Marne, Mi., U.S. 216 43.02 N 85.49 W
Marne □[5] 32 48.55 N 4.10 E
Marne ≐, Austl. 168b 34.40 S 139.18 E
Marne ≐, Fr. 32 48.49 N 2.24 E
Marne à la Saône, Canal de la ≋ 58 48.44 N 4.36 E
Marne au Rhin, Canal de la ≋ 56 48.35 N 7.47 E
Marneuli 84 41.28 N 44.50 E
Marnhull 42 50.58 N 2.18 W
Marnitz 54 53.19 N 11.56 E
Maroa, Il., U.S. 219 40.02 N 88.57 W
Maroa, Ven. 246 2.43 N 67.33 W
Maroala 157b 15.23 S 47.59 E
Maroantsetra 157b 15.26 S 49.44 E
Marobi Raghza 120 32.36 N 69.52 E
Maroc → Morocco □[1] 148 32.00 N 5.00 W
Maroelaboom 156 19.15 S 18.53 E
Marofandilia 157b 20.07 S 44.34 E
Maroglio ≐ 70 37.03 N 14.15 E
Marokko → Morocco □[1] 148 32.00 N 5.00 W
Marol ➝[8] 272c 19.07 N 72.53 E
Marolambo 157b 20.02 S 48.07 E
Maroldsweisach 56 50.12 N 10.39 E
Marolles-en-Brie 261 48.44 N 2.33 E
Marolles-en-Hurepoix 261 48.34 N 2.18 E
Marolles-les-Braults 50 48.15 N 0.19 E
Maromandia 157b 14.13 S 48.08 E
Maromme 50 49.28 N 1.02 E
Maromokotro ∧ 157b 14.01 S 48.59 E
Marondera 154 18.10 S 31.36 E
Marone 64 45.44 N 10.05 E
Marong 102 31.07 N 99.20 E
Maronghi Creek ≐ 171a 26.58 S 152.22 E
Maroni (Marowijne) ≐ 250 5.45 N 53.58 W
Maroon 171a 28.10 S 152.44 E
Maroon, Mount ∧ 171a 28.13 S 152.44 E
Maroondah Aqueduct ≋[1] 274b 37.42 S 145.01 E
Maros 112 5.00 S 119.34 E
Maros (Mureș) ≐ 38 46.15 N 20.13 E
Maroseranana 157b 18.32 S 48.51 E
Marostica 64 45.45 N 11.39 E
Marosvásárhely → Tîrgu Mureș 38 46.33 N 24.33 E
Marotandrano 157b 16.10 S 48.50 E
Marotiri, Îles II 14 27.55 S 143.26 W
Marotta 66 43.46 N 13.08 E
Maroua 146 10.36 N 14.20 E
Maroubra 274a 33.57 S 151.16 E
Marouini ≐ 250 3.18 N 54.04 W
Marovato, Madag. 157b 13.59 S 48.36 E
Marovato, Madag. 157b 15.48 S 48.05 E
Marovato, Madag. 157b 16.28 S 48.25 E
Marovoay 157b 16.06 S 46.39 E
Marovoay Nord 157b 16.57 S 44.34 E
Marowijne □[5] 250 5.40 N 54.20 W
Marowijne (Maroni) ≐ 250 5.45 N 53.58 W
Marpent 50 50.18 N 4.05 E
Marple 44 53.24 N 2.03 W
Marquam 224 45.04 N 122.41 W
Marquand 194 37.25 N 90.10 W
Marquard 158 28.54 S 27.28 E
Marquardt 54 52.27 N 12.57 E
Marquartstein 64 47.45 N 12.28 E
Marquesas Islands → Marquises, Îles II 6 9.00 S 139.30 W
Marquesas Keys II 220 24.34 N 82.08 W
Marquette, Ks., U.S. 198 38.33 N 97.50 W
Marquette, Mi., U.S. 190 46.32 N 87.23 W
Marquette Park ♦ 278 41.46 N 87.42 W
Márquez, Perú 286d 11.57 S 77.08 W
Marquez, Tx., U.S. 222 31.14 N 96.15 W
Marquion 50 50.13 N 3.05 E
Marquis 241k 12.06 N 61.37 W
Marquis, Cape > 241f 14.03 N 60.54 W
Marquise 50 50.49 N 1.42 E
Marquises, Îles (Marquesas Islands) II 6 9.00 S 139.30 W
Marrabel 168b 34.08 S 138.53 E
Marra Creek ≐ 166 30.05 S 147.05 E
Marradi 66 44.04 N 11.37 E
Marradong 168a 32.52 S 116.27 E
Marrah, Jabal ∧ 140 13.04 N 24.21 E
Marra Hills ⩘[2] 140 6.05 N 27.33 E
Marrakech 148 31.38 N 8.00 W
Marrakech □[4] 148 31.30 N 8.05 W
Marramarra National Park ♦ 170 33.32 S 151.04 E
Marrawah 166 40.56 S 144.41 E
Marree 166 29.39 S 138.04 E
Marrero 194 29.53 N 90.06 W
Marrickville 274a 33.55 S 151.09 E
Marromeu 156 18.20 S 35.56 E
Marrowstone Island I 224 48.04 N 122.41 W
Marrubiu 71 39.45 N 8.38 E
Marruecos → Morocco □[1] 148 32.00 N 5.00 W
Marrupa 154 13.08 S 37.30 E
Mars 214 40.41 N 80.00 W
Marsā al-Burayqah 146 30.25 N 19.34 E
Marsabit 154 2.20 N 37.59 E
Marsabit National Park ♦ 154 2.20 N 38.00 E
Marsac-en-Livradois 62 45.29 N 3.44 E
Marṣafā wa Kafr Aḥmad Ḥashīsh 142 30.25 N 31.15 E
Marsal 56 48.48 N 6.36 E
Marsala 70 37.48 N 12.26 E
Marsā Maṭrūḥ 140 31.21 N 27.14 E
Marsā Maṭrūḥ □[4] 142 29.00 N 30.00 E
Marsange ≐ 261 48.43 N 2.45 E
Marsangue ≐ 261 48.40 N 2.47 E
Marsannay-la-Côte 58 47.16 N 4.59 E
Marsanne 62 44.39 N 4.52 E
Marsassoum 150 12.50 N 16.00 W
Mars'aty 86 60.05 N 60.29 E
Marsberg 52 51.28 N 8.50 E
Marscheid ➝[8] 263 51.14 N 7.14 E
Marsciano 66 42.54 N 12.20 E
Marsden, Austl. 166 33.45 S 147.32 E
Marsden, Eng., U.K. 262 53.36 N 1.56 W
Marsden, Point > 168b 35.35 S 137.38 E
Marsden Park 274a 33.42 S 150.50 E
Marsdiep ⊔ 52 52.59 N 4.45 E
Marseille 62 43.18 N 5.24 E
Marseille-en-Beauvaisis 50 49.35 N 1.57 E
Marseille-Marignane, Aéroport de ⊠ 62 43.27 N 5.13 E
Marseilles, Il., U.S. 216 41.19 N 88.42 W
Marseilles, Oh., U.S. 214 40.42 N 83.23 W
Marsella → Marseille 62 43.18 N 5.24 E
Marsfield 274a 33.47 S 151.07 E
Marsfjället ∧ 24 65.05 N 15.28 E
Marshall, Liber. 150 6.10 N 10.23 W
Marshall, Ar., U.S. 194 35.54 N 92.37 W
Marshall, Il., U.S. 194 39.23 N 87.41 W
Marshall, Mi., U.S. 216 42.16 N 84.57 W
Marshall, Mn., U.S. 198 44.26 N 95.47 W
Marshall, Mo., U.S. 194 39.07 N 93.11 W
Marshall, N.C., U.S. 192 35.47 N 82.41 W
Marshall, Tx., U.S. 194 32.32 N 94.22 W
Marshall, Va., U.S. 188 38.51 N 77.51 W
Marshall, Wi., U.S. 216 43.10 N 89.04 W
Marshall □[6], Il., U.S. 216 41.02 N 89.24 W
Marshall □[6], In., U.S. 216 41.21 N 86.19 W
Marshall ≐ 162 22.59 S 136.59 E
Marshall Bennett Islands II 164 8.50 S 151.50 E
Marshallberg 192 34.43 N 76.30 W
Marshall Canyon Regional Park ♦ 280 34.09 N 117.43 W
Marshall Gold Discovery State Historical Park ♦ 226 38.48 N 120.53 W
Marshall Hall 208 38.41 N 77.06 W
Marshall Islands □[1] 14 11.00 N 168.00 E
Marshall Islands II 14 9.00 N 168.00 E
Marshalls Creek 210 41.03 N 75.08 W
Marshallton, De., U.S. 208 39.43 N 75.39 W
Marshallton, Pa., U.S. 210 40.47 N 76.33 W
Marshallton, Pa., U.S. 285 39.57 N 75.41 W
Marshalltown 190 42.02 N 92.54 W
Marshallville, Ga., U.S. 192 32.27 N 83.56 W
Marshallville, Oh., U.S. 214 40.54 N 81.44 W
Marshbank Metropolitan Park ♦ 281 42.36 N 83.23 W
Marsh Creek ≐, Ca., U.S. 282 37.53 N 121.49 W
Marsh Creek ≐, Mi., U.S. 281 42.06 N 83.13 W
Marsh Creek ≐, Pa., U.S. 214 41.03 N 77.36 W
Marsh Creek ≐, Pa., U.S. 285 40.03 N 75.43 W
Marsh Creek ≐, Wi., U.S. 216 42.13 N 89.04 W
Marsh Creek Lake ⊜[1] 208 40.04 N 75.44 W
Marshes Creek ≐ 276 40.36 N 74.13 W
Marshfield, Eng., U.K. 42 51.28 N 2.19 W
Marshfield, Ma., U.S. 207 42.05 N 70.42 W
Marshfield, Mo., U.S. 194 37.20 N 92.54 W
Marshfield, Wi., U.S. 190 44.40 N 90.10 W
Marshfield Airport ⊠ 283 42.06 N 70.40 W
Marshfield Center 283 42.07 N 70.43 W
Marshfield Hills 207 42.08 N 70.44 W
Marsh Harbour 238 26.33 N 77.03 W
Marsh Hill 210 41.29 N 76.58 W
Mars Hill, In., U.S. 218 39.43 N 86.09 W
Mars Hill, Me., U.S. 186 46.30 N 67.52 W
Mars Hill, N.C., U.S. 192 35.49 N 82.32 W
Marsh Island I 194 29.35 N 91.53 W
Marsh Lake ⊜ 180 60.25 N 134.18 W
Marsh Peak ∧ 200 40.43 N 109.50 W
Marshside 262 53.40 N 2.58 W
Marshville 192 34.59 N 80.22 W
Marshyhope Creek ≐ 208 38.32 N 75.45 W
Marsica ➝[1] 66 41.50 N 13.45 E
Marsico Nuovo 68 40.25 N 15.44 E
Marsico Vetere 68 40.23 N 15.49 E
Marsillargues 62 43.40 N 4.11 E
Marsimang, Tanjung > 164 3.27 S 130.49 E
Marsing 202 43.32 N 116.48 W
Marske-by-the-Sea 44 54.36 N 1.01 W
Mars-la-Tour 56 49.06 N 5.54 E
Marson 56 48.55 N 4.32 E
Marssum 52 53.12 N 5.42 E
Märsta 40 59.37 N 17.51 E
Marstal 41 54.51 N 10.31 E
Marsteller 214 40.39 N 78.48 W
Märstetten 58 47.36 N 9.04 E
Marston 262 53.16 N 2.30 W
Marston Moor ≍ 44 53.57 N 1.17 W
Marston Moor Battlesite ⊥ 44 53.57 N 1.17 W
Marstons Mills 207 41.39 N 70.25 W
Marstrand 26 57.53 N 11.35 E
Marsyāngdī ≐ 124 28.05 N 84.28 E
Mart 222 31.32 N 96.50 W
Marta 66 42.32 N 11.55 E
Marta ≐ 66 42.14 N 11.42 E
Martaban 110 16.32 N 97.37 E
Martaban, Gulf of c 110 16.30 N 97.00 E
Martano 68 40.12 N 18.18 E
Martap 152 6.54 N 13.03 E
Martapura, Indon. 112 3.25 S 114.51 E
Martapura, Indon. 112 4.19 S 104.22 E
Marte 146 12.22 N 13.51 E
Marteg ≐ 42 52.20 N 3.33 W
Martel, Fr. 32 44.56 N 1.37 E
Martel, Oh., U.S. 214 40.40 N 82.55 W
Martelange 56 49.50 N 5.44 E
Martell 226 38.22 N 120.48 W
Martello 64 46.34 N 10.47 E
Martello, Val V 64 46.31 N 10.45 E
Martemjanovskij 86 55.54 N 80.22 E
Marten ➝[8] 263 51.31 N 7.23 E
Marten Lake ⊜ 190 46.42 N 79.41 W
Marten Mountain ∧ 182 55.28 N 114.43 W
Marte R. Gomez, Presa ⊜[1] 196 26.10 N 99.00 W
Martfeld 52 52.52 N 9.04 E
Marthaguy Creek ≐ 166 30.16 S 147.35 E
Martha Lake 224 47.51 N 122.20 W
Marthall 262 53.17 N 2.18 W
Martham 42 52.42 N 1.38 E
Marthasville 219 38.37 N 91.03 W
Martha's Vineyard I 207 41.25 N 70.40 W
Martí, Cuba 240p 21.09 N 77.27 W
Martí, Cuba 240p 22.57 N 80.55 W
Martí, Pico ∧ 240p 20.01 N 76.35 W
Martignacco 64 46.05 N 13.08 E
Martignat 58 46.13 N 5.36 E
Martigny 58 46.06 N 7.04 E
Martigny-les-Bains 58 48.06 N 5.49 E
Martigues 62 43.24 N 5.03 E
Martil 34 35.37 N 5.17 W
Martim Francisco 256 22.31 S 46.57 W
Martin, Slvk. 30 49.05 N 18.55 E
Martin, Ky., U.S. 192 37.34 N 82.45 W
Martin, Mi., U.S. 216 42.32 N 85.38 W
Martin, N.D., U.S. 198 47.49 N 100.06 W
Martin, Oh., U.S. 214 41.33 N 83.20 W
Martin, S.D., U.S. 198 43.10 N 101.43 W
Martin, Tn., U.S. 194 36.20 N 88.51 W
Martin □[6] 220 27.07 N 80.31 W
Martín ≐ 34 41.18 N 0.19 W
Martín, Arroyo ≐ 288 34.51 S 58.04 W
Martin, Isle I 46 57.55 N 5.14 W
Martina 58 46.53 N 10.30 E
Martina Franca 68 40.42 N 17.21 E
Martinborough 172 41.13 S 175.28 E
Martín Chico, Punta > 258 34.10 S 58.13 W
Martindale 196 29.50 N 97.51 W
Martindale Creek ≐, Austl. 170 32.32 S 150.42 E
Martindale Creek ≐, In., U.S. 218 39.48 N 85.09 W
Martindale Pond ⊜ 284a 43.11 N 79.16 W
Martin-Église 50 49.54 N 1.09 E
Martinengo 62 45.34 N 9.46 E
Mărtinești 38 45.30 N 27.18 E
Martinez, Ca., U.S. 226 38.01 N 122.07 W
Martinez, Ga., U.S. 192 33.31 N 82.04 W
Martínez ➝[8] 258 34.29 S 58.30 W
Martínez de la Torre 234 20.04 N 97.03 W
Martín García, Isla I 258 34.13 S 58.15 W
Martinho Campos 255 19.20 S 45.13 W
Martinica → Martinique □[2] 240e 14.40 N 61.00 W
Martini Creek ≐ 282 37.33 N 122.31 W
Martinique □[2], N.A. 230 14.40 N 61.00 W
Martinique □[2], N.A. 240e 14.40 N 61.00 W
Martinique Passage ⊔ 238 15.10 N 61.15 W
Martin Lake ⊜[1], Al., U.S. 194 32.50 N 85.55 W
Martin Lake ⊜[1], Tx., U.S. 222 32.15 N 94.35 W
Martin Marietta Corporation ⊕[3] 284b 39.20 N 76.26 W
Martinniemi 26 65.13 N 25.18 E
Martinópole 250 3.15 S 40.41 W
Martin Peninsula >[1] 9 74.25 S 114.10 W
Martín Pérez ≐ 286b 23.07 N 82.20 W
Martin Point > 180 70.08 N 143.16 W
Martin Run ≐ 279a 41.27 N 82.12 W
Martins 250 6.05 S 37.55 W
Martinsberg 61 48.22 N 15.09 E
Martins Brook ≐ 283 42.34 N 71.06 W
Martinsburg, Mo., U.S. 219 39.06 N 91.38 W
Martinsburg, N.Y., U.S. 212 43.44 N 75.28 W
Martinsburg, Oh., U.S. 214 40.16 N 82.21 W
Martinsburg, Pa., U.S. 214 40.18 N 78.19 W
Martinsburg, W.V., U.S. 188 39.27 N 77.57 W
Martins Creek 208 40.47 N 75.11 W
Martins Creek ≐ 210 41.37 N 75.46 W
Martinscroft 262 53.24 N 2.31 W
Martins Ferry 214 40.05 N 80.43 W
Martins Mills 222 32.25 N 95.47 W
Martins Pond ⊜ 283 42.36 N 71.08 W
Martinstein 56 49.48 N 7.32 E
Martinsthal 56 50.03 N 8.07 E
Martinsville, Austl. 170 33.03 S 151.25 E
Martinsville, Il., U.S. 194 39.20 N 87.52 W
Martinsville, In., U.S. 218 39.25 N 86.25 W
Martinsville, N.J., U.S. 276 40.36 N 74.34 W
Martinsville, Oh., U.S. 218 39.19 N 83.48 W
Martinsville, Va., U.S. 192 36.41 N 79.52 W
Martinton 216 40.55 N 87.44 W
Martintown 206 45.09 N 74.42 W
Martin Van Buren National Historic Site ⊥ 210 42.22 N 73.43 W
Martin Vaz, Ilhas II 244 20.30 S 28.51 W
Martis 71 40.47 N 8.49 E
Martisovo 76 56.34 N 31.55 E
Martock 42 50.59 N 2.46 W
Martofte 41 55.33 N 10.40 E
Marton, N.Z. 172 40.05 S 175.23 E
Marton, Eng., U.K. 262 53.12 N 2.13 W
Martorell 266d 41.28 N 1.56 E
Martorelles de Baix 266d 41.32 N 2.14 E
Martos 34 37.43 N 3.58 W
Martovaja 78 49.57 N 36.57 E
Martre, Lac la ⊜ 176 63.15 N 117.55 W
Martti 24 67.28 N 28.28 E
Martūbah 146 32.35 N 22.46 E
Martuk 86 50.46 N 56.31 E
Martuni, Azer. 84 39.48 N 47.06 E
Martuni, Haya. 84 40.08 N 45.19 E
Martvili 84 42.25 N 42.22 E
Martville 210 43.17 N 76.38 W
Martynoviči 78 51.17 N 29.37 E
Martynovka 78 49.38 N 31.18 E
Martynovo 80 50.43 N 50.23 E
Martynovskij 80 50.29 N 42.18 E
Maru 150 12.22 N 6.22 E
Marua 164 9.30 S 149.20 E
Marudi 112 4.11 N 114.19 E
Marudu, Telukan c 112 6.45 N 116.55 E
Marugame 96 34.17 N 133.47 E
Maruggio 68 40.19 N 17.34 E
Maruia 172 42.11 S 172.13 E
Maruia ≐ 172 41.47 S 172.12 E
Maruim 250 10.45 S 37.05 W
Maruko 94 36.19 N 138.16 E
Marula 154 20.26 S 28.06 E
Marulan 170 34.43 S 150.00 E
Marulan South 170 34.46 S 150.02 E
Marum 52 53.08 N 6.16 E
Marum, Mont ∧ 175f 16.15 S 168.07 E
Marunga 152 17.27 S 20.02 E
Marungu 154 3.44 S 30.48 E
Marungu ⩘ 154 7.42 S 30.00 E
Maruoka 94 36.09 N 136.16 E
Mårup 41 55.57 N 10.35 E
Marusino 265b 55.42 N 37.59 E
Maruškino 82 55.36 N 37.12 E
Ma'rūt 120 31.34 N 67.03 E
Marutea I[1] 14 17.00 S 143.10 W
Maruyama 94 35.01 N 139.58 E
Maruyama ≐ 96 35.39 N 134.50 E
Marv Dasht 128 29.50 N 52.40 E
Marve ➝[8] 272c 19.12 N 72.49 E
Marvejols 32 44.33 N 3.18 E
Marvell 194 34.33 N 90.54 W
Marvel Loch 162 31.28 S 119.28 E
Marviken 40 58.34 N 16.51 E
Marvila ➝[8] 266c 38.44 N 9.06 W
Marville 56 49.27 N 5.27 E
Marvin Creek ≐ 214 41.48 N 78.26 W
Marvine, Mount ∧ 200 38.40 N 111.39 W
Mar Vista ➝[8] 280 34.00 N 118.27 W
Mārwār 120 25.44 N 73.36 E
Marwayne 184 53.32 N 110.20 W
Marwitz 264a 52.41 N 13.09 E
Marwitzer Heide ➝[3] 264a 52.40 N 13.06 E
Marwood 214 40.48 N 79.47 W
Marxhagen 54 53.37 N 12.36 E
Marxloh ➝[8] 263 51.31 N 6.46 E
Mary 128 37.36 N 61.50 E
Mary □[8] 128 37.30 N 62.30 E
Mary ≐, Austl. 164 12.53 S 131.38 E
Mary ≐, Austl. 166 25.26 S 152.55 E
Mary Anne Group II 162 21.13 S 115.32 E
Maryborough, Austl. 166 25.32 S 152.42 E
Maryborough, Austl. 169 37.03 S 143.45 E
Maryborough → Port Laoise, Ire. 48 53.02 N 7.17 W
Mary D 208 40.45 N 76.04 W
Marydale 158 29.23 S 22.05 E
Marydel 208 39.06 N 75.44 W
Maryfield 184 49.48 N 101.32 W
Maryhill 224 45.41 N 120.49 W
Mary Jane, Lake ⊜ 220 28.22 N 81.11 W
Mary Kathleen 166 20.49 S 139.58 E
Maryknoll 210 41.11 N 73.50 W
Mary Lake ⊜ 212 45.15 N 79.15 W
Maryland 210 42.32 N 74.53 W
Maryland □[3], U.S. 178 39.00 N 76.45 W
Maryland □[3], U.S. 188 39.00 N 76.45 W
Maryland, University of (Baltimore County Campus) ⊕[2], Md., U.S. 284b 39.15 N 76.43 W
Maryland, University of ⊕[2], Md., U.S. 284c 38.59 N 76.57 W
Maryland City 208 39.05 N 76.49 W
Maryland Gardens Park ♦ 275b 43.47 N 79.32 W
Maryland Heights 219 38.42 N 90.25 W
Maryland Historical Society ⊕ 284b 39.18 N 76.37 W
Maryland Line 208 39.42 N 76.39 W
Maryland Park 284c 38.53 N 76.54 W
Marylebone 262 53.34 N 2.38 W
Maryneal 196 32.14 N 100.27 W
Marypark 46 57.26 N 3.21 W
Maryport 44 54.43 N 3.30 W
Marys ≐, Il., U.S. 194 37.53 N 89.47 W
Marys ≐, Nv., U.S. 204 41.04 N 115.16 W
Marys Creek ≐ 202 42.18 N 115.48 W
Mary's Igloo 180 65.09 N 165.04 W
Marys Peak ∧ 202 44.30 N 123.33 W
Marystown 186 47.10 N 55.09 W
Marysvale 200 38.26 N 112.13 W
Marysville, Austl. 169 37.31 S 145.45 E
Marysville, B.C., Can. 182 49.38 N 115.57 W
Marysville, N.B., Can. 186 45.59 N 66.35 W
Marysville, Ca., U.S. 226 39.08 N 121.35 W
Marysville, Ks., U.S. 198 39.50 N 96.38 W
Marysville, Mi., U.S. 214 42.54 N 82.29 W
Marysville, Oh., U.S. 214 40.14 N 83.22 W
Marysville, Pa., U.S. 208 40.20 N 76.55 W
Marysville, Wa., U.S. 224 48.03 N 122.10 W
Maryūṭ, Buḥayrat ⊜ 142 31.08 N 29.56 E
Maryvale 171a 28.05 S 152.15 E
Maryvale ➝[8] 275b 43.46 N 79.18 W
Maryville, Mo., U.S. 194 40.20 N 94.52 W
Maryville, Tn., U.S. 192 35.45 N 83.58 W
Marywell 46 57.02 N 2.42 W
Marywood 216 41.48 N 88.18 W
Marzabotto 64 44.20 N 11.12 E
Marzagão 255 17.59 S 48.39 W
Marzahn ➝[8] 264a 52.33 N 13.33 E
Marzahna 54 52.00 N 12.46 E
Marzahne 54 52.31 N 12.31 E
Marzal, Aven de ⊥[5] 62 44.22 N 4.31 E
Marzo, Punta > 246 6.50 N 77.42 W
Marzolara 64 44.38 N 10.10 E
Marzūq 146 25.55 N 13.55 E
Marzūq, Ḥamādat ➝[2] 146 26.10 N 12.45 E
Marzūq, Ṣaḥrā' ➝[2] 146 24.30 N 13.00 E
Masa 152 3.45 S 15.29 E
Masachapa 236 11.47 N 86.31 W
Masada → Meẓada, Ḥorvot ⊥ 132 31.19 N 35.21 E
Mas'adah (Cæsarea Philippi) 132 33.14 N 35.45 E
Más Afuera, Isla → Alejandro Selkirk, Isla I 244 33.45 S 80.46 W
Masagua 236 14.12 N 90.51 W
Masaguisi 116 12.41 N 121.32 E
Masai 114 1.29 N 103.53 E
Masai Mara Game Reserve ➝[4] 154 1.15 S 35.15 E
Masai Steppe ⩘[1] 154 4.45 S 37.00 E
Masak 85 43.37 N 78.18 E
Masaka 154 0.20 S 31.44 E
Masaki, Nihon 96 33.47 N 132.42 E
Masaki, Nihon 268 35.13 N 140.02 E
Masalembu Besar, Pulau I 112 5.34 S 114.26 E
Masally 84 39.03 N 48.40 E
Masalok, Puntan > 174n 15.01 N 145.41 E
Masamba 112 2.32 S 120.20 E
Masan 98 35.11 N 128.32 E
Masangwe ∧ 154 5.28 S 30.05 E
Masānjor 126 24.07 N 87.19 E
Masapelid Island I 116 9.42 N 125.39 E
Masapun 112 7.47 S 126.38 E
Masaraḥ 142 27.29 N 30.50 E
Masaran 115a 7.28 S 110.55 E
Ma'ṣarat Samālūṭ 142 28.19 N 30.43 E
Masaryktown 220 28.26 N 82.27 W
Masasi 154 10.43 S 38.48 E
Masatepe 236 11.55 N 86.09 W
Más a Tierra, Isla → Róbinson Crusoe, Isla I 244 33.38 S 78.52 W
Masaya 236 11.58 N 86.06 W
Masaya □[5] 236 12.00 N 86.10 W
Masba 146 11.30 N 13.00 E
Masbate 116 12.22 N 123.36 E
Masbate □[4] 116 12.20 N 123.30 E
Masbate Island I 116 12.15 N 123.30 E
Masbate Pass ⊔ 116 12.30 N 123.35 E
Mascali 70 37.45 N 15.12 E
Mascarene Basin ✣[1] 12 15.00 S 56.00 E
Mascarene Islands II 157c 21.00 S 57.00 E
Mascarene Plateau ✣[3] 12 10.00 S 60.00 E
Mascasín 252 31.22 S 66.59 W
Maschen 52 53.24 N 10.02 E
Maschito 68 40.54 N 15.50 E
Mascot, Austl. 274a 33.56 S 151.12 E
Mascot, Tn., U.S. 192 36.03 N 83.44 W
Mascota 234 20.32 N 104.49 W
Mascota ≐ 234 20.38 N 104.59 W
Mascotte 220 28.35 N 81.53 W
Mascouche 206 45.45 N 73.36 W
Mascouche ≐ 206 45.41 N 73.40 W
Mascoutah 219 38.29 N 89.47 W
Mascuppic Lake ⊜ 283 42.41 N 71.23 W
Mase 102 27.16 N 104.08 E
Masefield 184 49.09 N 107.48 W
Masela, Pulau I 164 8.09 S 129.50 E
Masenberg ∧ 61 47.21 N 15.53 E
Maser 64 45.48 N 11.59 E
Maserada sul Piave 64 45.45 N 12.17 E
Maseru 158 29.28 S 27.30 E
Masevaux 58 47.47 N 7.00 E
Maševka 78 49.26 N 34.52 E
Maševo 78 52.06 N 32.48 E
Masha 100 27.26 N 117.50 E
Mashaba 154 20.02 S 30.29 E
Mashaba Mountains ⩘ 154 18.45 S 30.32 E
Mash'abbe' Sade 132 31.00 N 34.47 E
Mashābih I 128 25.37 N 36.29 E
Mashalah 142 30.44 N 31.08 E
Masham 44 54.13 N 1.40 W
Mashan, Zhg. 89 45.13 N 130.35 E
Mashan, Zhg. 100 27.33 N 113.46 E
Mashan, Zhg. 102 23.50 N 108.16 E
Mashar 140 9.14 N 26.52 E
Mashbury 260 51.47 N 0.24 E
Mashel ≐ 224 46.51 N 122.20 W
Mashenqiao 105 40.04 N 117.36 E
Masherbrum ∧ 123 35.43 N 76.18 E
Mashgharah 132 33.32 N 35.39 E
Mashhad, Īrān 128 36.18 N 59.36 E
Mash-had, Yis. 132 32.44 N 35.19 E
Mashi, Nig. 150 13.00 N 7.54 E
Mashi, Zhg. 100 29.05 N 114.22 E
Mashi, Zhg. 100 25.01 N 114.09 E
Mashike 92a 43.51 N 141.31 E
Mashiko 94 36.28 N 140.06 E
Mashita ≐ 94 35.40 N 137.10 E
Mashīz 128 29.56 N 56.37 E
Mashkai ≐ 128 26.02 N 65.19 E
Māshkel, Hāmūn-i- ⊜ 128 28.15 N 63.00 E
Māshkel, Rūd-i- (Māshkīd) ≐ 128 28.02 N 63.25 E
Mashki Chāh 128 29.01 N 62.27 E
Māshkīd (Rūd-i-Māshkel) ≐ 128 28.02 N 63.25 E
Mashonaland North □[4] 154 16.30 S 30.00 E
Mashonaland South □[4] 154 18.15 S 30.45 E
Mashpee 207 41.38 N 70.28 W
Mashra'ur-Raqq 140 8.25 N 29.16 E
Mashtūl as-Sūq 142 30.22 N 31.22 E
Mashū-ko ⊜ 92a 43.35 N 144.32 E
Masibi 152 11.08 S 22.42 E
Masihi 114 2.47 N 99.40 E
Masīlah, Wādī al- V 144 15.10 N 51.08 E
Masi-Manimba 152 4.46 S 17.55 E
Masin 164 6.15 S 139.19 E
Masina 272b 22.55 N 88.32 E
Masindi 154 1.41 N 31.43 E
Masini Port 154 1.42 N 32.05 E
Masinloc 116 15.32 N 119.57 E
Masīr 142 31.03 N 31.00 E
Maṣīrah I 118 20.25 N 58.50 E
Maṣīrah, Khalīj c 118 20.10 N 58.15 E
Masis 84 40.00 N 44.29 E
Masisea 248 8.36 S 74.19 W
Masisi 154 1.24 S 28.49 E
Masjed-e Soleymān 128 31.58 N 49.18 E
Masjid Tanah 114 2.21 N 102.07 E
Mask, Lough ⊜ 48 53.35 N 9.20 W
Maska 150 11.20 N 7.20 E
Maskan, Ras > 144 11.10 N 43.33 E
Maskanah 130 36.01 N 38.05 E
Maskin 128 23.35 N 56.39 E
Maškino 82 54.53 N 36.08 E
Maskinongé □[6] 206 46.35 N 73.30 W
Maskinongé ≐, P.Q., Can. 206 46.10 N 73.01 W
Maskinongé ≐, P.Q., Can. 206 45.49 N 74.40 W
Maskinongé, Lac ⊜ 206 46.19 N 73.23 W
Maškoviči 82 54.11 N 36.17 E
Masku 26 60.34 N 22.06 E
Maskūtān 128 26.51 N 59.49 E
Maskwa ≐ 184 50.33 N 96.08 W
Masl'anino 86 54.20 N 84.13 E
Masl'anskaja 86 55.56 N 70.08 E
Maslova 265a 59.47 N 30.48 E
Maslovka 78 51.33 N 39.14 E
Maslovo 86 60.07 N 60.30 E
Masnières 50 50.07 N 3.13 E
Maso 150 7.14 N 2.53 W
Masoala 157b 15.59 S 50.10 E
Masoala, Cap > 157b 15.59 S 50.13 E
Masoala, Presqu'île de >[1] 157b 15.40 S 50.12 E
Masoarivo 157b 19.03 S 44.19 E
Masomeloka 157b 20.17 S 48.37 E
Mason, Mi., U.S. 216 42.34 N 84.26 W
Mason, Oh., U.S. 218 39.21 N 84.18 W
Mason, Tn., U.S. 194 35.24 N 89.31 W
Mason, Tx., U.S. 196 30.44 N 99.13 W
Mason, W.V., U.S. 188 39.01 N 82.01 W
Mason □[6], Il., U.S. 219 40.18 N 90.04 W
Mason □[6], Ky., U.S. 218 38.35 N 83.48 W
Mason □[6], Wa., U.S. 224 47.20 N 123.09 W
Mason, Lake ⊜ 162 27.39 S 119.34 E
Mason Bay c 172 46.56 S 167.44 E
Mason City, Il., U.S. 219 40.12 N 89.41 W
Mason City, Ia., U.S. 190 43.09 N 93.12 W
Mason City, Ne., U.S. 198 41.13 N 99.18 W
Masone 62 44.30 N 8.42 E
Masonicus Brook ≐ 276 41.06 N 74.09 W
Mason Lake ⊜ 224 47.20 N 122.57 W
Masons Creek ≐ 285 39.59 N 74.51 W
Mason Valley V 226 39.07 N 119.10 W
Masonville, N.J., U.S. 285 39.59 N 74.52 W
Masonville, N.Y., U.S. 210 42.15 N 75.23 W
Maspeth ➝[8] 276 40.43 N 73.55 W
Masqaṭ (Muscat) 128 23.37 N 58.35 E
Maṣra' 142 27.14 N 31.02 E
Massa 64 44.01 N 10.09 E
Massa-Carrara □[4] 64 44.15 N 10.03 E
Massachusetts □[3], U.S. 178 42.15 N 71.50 W
Massachusetts □[3], U.S. 207 42.15 N 71.50 W
Massachusetts (Boston), University of ⊕[2] 283 42.19 N 71.03 W
Massachusetts Bay c 207 42.20 N 70.50 W

Symbols in the index entries represent the broad categories identified in the key at the right. Symbols with superior numbers (⩘[1]) identify subcategories (see complete key on page *I · 1).*

Symbole im Register stellen die rechts im Schlüssel erklärten Kategorien dar. Symbole mit hochgestellten Ziffern (⩘[1]) bezeichnen Unterabteilungen einer Kategorie (vgl. vollständiger Schlüssel auf Seite *I · 1).*

Los símbolos incluídos en el texto del índice representan las grandes categorías identificadas con la clave a la derecha. Los símbolos con numeros en su parte superior (⩘[1]) identifican las subcategorías (véase la clave completa en la página *I · 1).*

Les symboles de l'index représentent les catégories indiquées dans la légende à droite. Les symboles suivis d'un indice (⩘[1]) représentent des sous-catégories (voir légende complète à la page *I · 1).*

Os símbolos incluídos no texto do índice representam as grandes categorias identificadas com a chave à direita. Os símbolos com números em sua parte superior (⩘[1]) identificam as subcategorias (veja-se a chave completa à página *I · 1).*

ENGLISH	DEUTSCH	ESPAÑOL	FRANÇAIS	PORTUGUÊS
∧ Mountain	Berg	Montaña	Montagne	Montanha
⩘ Mountains	Gebirge	Montañas	Montagnes	Montanhas
)(Pass	Paß	Paso	Col	Passo
V Valley, Canyon	Tal, Cañon	Valle, Cañón	Vallée, Canyon	Vale, Canhão
≍ Plain	Ebene	Llano	Plaine	Planície
> Cape	Kap	Cabo	Cap	Cabo
I Island	Insel	Isla	Île	Ilha
II Islands	Inseln	Islas	Îles	Ilhas
⊥ Other Topographic Features	Andere Topographische Objekte	Otros Elementos Topográficos	Autres données topographiques	Outros acidentes topográficos

Nombre	Página	Lat.°′	Long.°′ W=Oeste
Massachusetts Correctional Institution ⊻	283	42.07 N	71.18 W
Massachusetts Institute of Technology ⊻²	283	42.21 N	71.06 W
Massaciuccoli, Lago di ⊘	66	43.50 N	10.20 E
Massacre Lake ⊘	204	41.39 N	119.35 W
Massa Fermana	66	43.09 N	13.28 E
Massa Fiscaglia	66	44.48 N	12.01 E
Massafra	88	40.35 N	17.07 E
Massaguet	148	12.28 N	15.26 E
Massakory	146	13.00 N	15.44 E
Massalassef	146	11.43 N	17.08 E
Massa Lombarda	66	44.27 N	11.49 E
Massa Lubrense	68	40.36 N	14.20 E
Massa Marittima	66	43.03 N	10.53 E
Massa Martana	66	42.46 N	12.31 E
Massandra	78	44.32 N	34.12 E
Massangano	152	9.37 S	14.15 E
Massangena	156	21.32 S	32.57 E
Massapê	250	3.31 S	40.19 W
Massapequa	210	40.40 N	73.28 W
Massapequa Park	276	40.40 N	73.27 W
Massapequa Reserve County Park ⊹	276	40.42 N	73.27 W
Massapoag Brook ≃	283	42.09 N	71.09 W
Massapoag Lake ⊘	283	42.06 N	71.11 W
Massara	156	18.20 S	34.09 E
Massarosa	66	43.52 N	10.20 E
Massasoit State Park ⊹	207	41.53 N	71.01 W
Massaua — Mitsiwa	144	15.38 N	39.28 E
Massawa — Mitsiwa	144	15.38 N	39.28 E
Massawippi ≃	206	45.22 N	71.51 W
Massawippi, Lake ⊘	206	45.14 N	72.00 W
Massay	50	47.09 N	2.00 E
Massé, Ruisseau ≃	275a	45.28 N	73.17 W
Massello	62	44.57 N	7.04 E
Massen	52	51.32 N	7.38 E
Massena, Ia., U.S.	198	41.15 N	94.46 W
Massena, N.Y., U.S.	206	44.55 N	74.53 W
Massenya	146	11.24 N	16.10 E
Masset	52	54.02 N	132.09 W
Masset Inlet ⊂	182	53.42 N	132.20 W
Masseube	32	42.46 N	0.35 E
Massey	190	46.12 N	82.05 W
Massiac	32	45.15 N	3.12 E
Massiaru	76	58.00 N	24.35 E
Massico, Monte ∧	68	41.10 N	13.55 E
Massieville	218	39.16 N	82.58 W
Massif Central — Central, Massif ∧	32	45.00 N	3.10 E
Massillon	214	40.48 N	81.32 W
Massima Camp	152	1.27 S	11.42 E
Massina	273b	4.22 S	15.22 E
Massina ⊻¹	150	14.30 N	5.00 W
Massinga	156	23.20 S	35.25 E
Massingir	156	23.51 S	32.04 E
Massive, Mount ∧	200	39.12 N	106.28 W
Masson, Lac ⊘	206	45.03 N	74.02 W
Masson Island I	9	66.08 S	96.34 E
Massy	261	48.44 N	2.17 E
Mastābah	144	20.49 N	39.20 E
Maštaga	84	40.32 N	50.00 E
Masterson	196	35.38 N	101.58 W
Masterton	172	41.05 S	175.42 E
Mas-Thibert	62	43.34 N	4.44 E
Mastic Point	192	25.03 N	77.57 W
Mastigouche ≃	206	46.20 N	73.24 W
Mastigouche Nord ≃	206	46.24 N	73.25 W
Mastůj	123	36.17 N	72.31 E
Mastūj ⊻	123	35.54 N	71.49 E
Masturug	128	29.48 N	66.51 E
Masturah	128	23.06 N	38.50 E
Masu	146	12.10 N	13.19 E
Masua	126	24.16 N	90.46 E
Masuda	96	34.40 N	131.51 E
Masuho	94	35.34 N	138.28 E
Masuika	152	7.37 S	22.32 E
Masuku	154	17.12 S	27.07 E
Māsüleh	128	37.10 N	48.59 E
Masulipatam — Machilīpatnam	122	16.10 N	81.08 E
Masura	126	23.16 N	90.24 E
Masurai, Gunung ∧	112	2.30 S	101.51 E
Masury	214	41.12 N	80.32 W
Masvingo	154	20.05 S	30.50 E
Maşyāf	130	35.03 N	36.21 E
Maszewo, Pol.	30	53.29 N	15.02 E
Maszewo, Pol.	54	52.06 N	14.55 E
Mat ≃	38	41.39 N	19.34 E
Mata, Indon.	115b	8.12 S	122.56 E
Mata, Zaïre	152	7.53 S	21.58 E
Mata Amarilla	254	49.36 S	71.13 W
Mataba, Mount ∧	269f	14.42 N	121.10 E
Matabeleland North □⁴			
Matabeleland South □⁴	154	21.00 S	29.15 E
Mātābhānga	126	26.20 N	89.13 E
Matabuena	34	41.10 N	3.40 W
Matachel ≃	34	38.50 N	6.17 W
Matachewan	190	47.56 N	80.39 W
Matacuni ≃	246	3.02 N	65.16 W
Matad	98	46.20 N	115.32 E
Mata de Plátano, Quebrada ≃	286c	18.15 N	66.46 W
Matadero Creek ≃	282	37.26 N	122.08 W
Mata de São João	255	12.31 S	38.17 W
Matadi	152	5.49 S	13.27 E
Matador	196	34.00 N	100.49 W
Matagalpa	236	12.55 N	85.55 W
Matagalpa □⁵	236	13.00 N	85.30 W
Matagami	186	49.45 N	77.38 W
Matag-ob	116	11.07 N	124.29 E
Matagorda	196	28.41 N	95.58 W
Matagorda □⁶	222	28.57 N	96.00 W
Matagorda Bay ⊂	196	28.35 N	96.20 W
Matagorda Island I	196	28.15 N	96.30 W
Matagorda Peninsula ⊃	196	28.32 N	96.07 W
Mata Grande	250	9.07 S	36.44 W
Matalhäe, Pointe ⊳	174s	17.49 S	149.17 W
Mataiea	174s	17.45 S	149.23 W
Mataiva I¹	14	14.53 S	148.40 W
Mataj	46	45.53 N	78.43 E
Matajing	107	19.33 N	104.00 E
Matak, Pulau I	112	3.18 N	106.16 E
Matakana, Austl.	168	33.00 S	145.54 E
Matakana, N.Z.	172	36.21 S	174.43 E
Matakana Island I	172	37.35 S	176.05 E
Matakitaki ≃	172	41.48 S	172.19 E
Matala	154	14.46 S	15.04 E
Matale	122	7.28 N	80.37 E
Matam	150	15.40 N	13.15 W
Matama	156	33.36 N	131.28 E
Matamata	172	37.49 S	175.47 E
Matameye	152	13.26 N	8.28 E
Matamoras	210	41.22 N	74.42 W
Matamoros, Méx.	232	25.53 N	97.30 W
Matamoros, Méx.	232	25.32 N	103.15 W
Matan	172	1.52 S	110.00 E
Matana	154	3.46 S	29.41 E
Matana, Danau ⊘	112	2.28 S	121.20 E
Matanem, Cape ⊳	164	2.28 S	149.57 E
Matandu ≃	154	9.26 S	39.33 E
Matane	186	48.51 N	67.32 W
Matang, Malay.	186	48.51 N	67.32 W
Matang, Zhg.	100	29.07 N	113.05 E
Matangi	173	17.49 S	178.57 E
Mataní	84	32.40 N	45.13 E
Matanuska ≃	180	61.30 N	149.15 W

Nom	Page	Lat.°′	Long.°′ W=Ouest
Matanza — San Justo	258	34.40 S	58.33 W
Matanza, Aeródromo ⊛	288	34.44 S	58.30 W
Matanza, Río de la ≃	258	34.42 S	58.28 W
Matanzas, Cuba	240p	23.03 N	81.35 W
Matanzas, Méx.	234	21.37 N	101.38 W
Matanzas ⊡⁴	240p	22.40 N	81.20 W
Matanzas, Bahía de ⊂	240p	23.04 N	81.30 W
Matapa	156	23.11 S	24.39 E
Matapalo, Cabo ⊳	236	8.23 N	83.19 W
Matape ≃	232	28.25 N	110.26 W
Matapédia	186	47.58 N	66.57 W
Matapédia, Lac ⊘	186	48.33 N	67.33 W
Matapi ≃	250	0.03 S	51.12 W
Mata Point ⊳	174v	19.07 S	169.51 W
Matapu	172	39.29 S	174.14 E
Mataquito ≃	252	34.59 S	72.12 W
Matará, Perú	248	7.16 S	78.16 W
Matara, S. Lan.	122	5.56 N	80.33 E
Mataram	115b	8.35 S	116.07 E
Matarani	248	17.00 S	72.06 W
Matarinao Bay ⊂	116	11.14 N	125.34 E
Mataró	34	41.32 N	2.27 E
Matarraña ≃	34	41.14 N	0.22 E
Matas ≃	266d	41.30 N	2.16 E
Matasiri, Pulau I	112	4.48 S	115.48 E
Mätäsvaara	26	63.26 N	29.36 E
Matata	172	37.53 S	176.45 E
Matatepai, Pointe ⊳	174x	9.43 S	139.02 W
Matatiele	158	30.24 S	28.43 E
Mätäfila Dam → ⁶	124	25.06 N	78.22 E
Matatindoo Point ⊳	116	9.43 N	122.23 E
Matatula, Cape ⊳	174u	14.15 S	170.34 W
Mataura	172	45.11 S	168.52 E
Mataurá ≃, Bra.	248	5.30 S	60.45 W
Mataura ≃, N.Z.	172	46.34 S	168.43 E
Matautu	175a	13.57 S	171.56 W
Matavai, Baie de ⊂	174s	17.30 S	149.30 W
Matavai	174s	21.13 S	159.44 W
Matateri	174z	27.10 S	109.27 E
Matateri Airstrip ⊛	174z	27.10 S	109.25 E
Matawai	172	38.21 S	177.32 E
Matawan	208	40.24 N	74.13 W
Matawin ≃	206	46.54 N	72.56 W
Matåy	142	28.25 N	30.46 E
Matbûl	142	31.05 N	31.02 E
Matča	85	39.27 N	69.39 E
Matchaponix Brook ≃	276	40.23 N	74.23 W
Matching	260	51.47 N	0.13 E
Matching Green	260	51.47 N	0.14 E
Matching Tye	260	51.47 N	0.12 E
Mateare	236	12.14 N	86.26 W
Mateba, Île de I	152	5.54 S	12.50 E
Matehuala	234	23.39 N	100.39 W
Mateke Hills ⊻²	154	21.48 S	31.00 E
Mateko	152	4.03 S	18.55 E
Matelica	66	43.15 N	13.00 E
Materno, Ilha I	154	12.13 S	40.58 E
Matera	68	40.40 N	16.37 E
Matera □⁴	68	40.30 N	16.25 E
Materborn	52	51.46 N	6.06 E
Matese, Lago del ⊘	68	41.25 N	14.25 E
Matese, Monti del ∧	68	41.27 N	14.22 E
Mátészalka	30	47.57 N	22.19 E
Matetsi	154	18.16 S	25.56 E
Mateur	148	37.03 N	9.40 E
Matewan	214	37.37 N	82.09 W
Matfield	207	42.02 N	70.59 W
Matfors	26	62.21 N	17.02 E
Matha	32	45.52 N	0.19 W
Mathaura	126	26.08 N	89.57 E
Mathematicians Seamounts → ³	16	15.00 N	111.00 W
Mather, Mb., Can.	184	49.06 N	99.07 W
Mather, Ca., U.S.	226	37.53 N	119.52 W
Mather Air Force Base ⊛	226	38.34 N	121.18 W
Mather Gorge V	284c	38.59 N	77.15 W
Matheson	190	48.32 N	80.28 W
Matheson Island	184	51.44 N	96.56 W
Matheu	258	34.22 S	58.50 W
Mathews	208	37.26 N	76.19 W
Mathews □⁶	208	37.25 N	76.20 W
Mathews, Lake ⊘	228	33.51 N	117.26 W
Mathis	62	45.15 N	7.32 E
Mathis	196	28.05 N	97.49 W
Mäthle	272b	22.35 N	88.14 E
Mathry	42	51.57 N	5.05 W
Mathura, India	124	27.30 N	77.41 E
Mathura, India	124	27.30 N	77.41 E
Mathura Bil ⊘	272b	22.56 N	88.12 E
Mathurai — Madurai	122	9.56 N	78.07 E
Mathurāpur, Bngl.	126	24.02 N	88.47 E
Mathurāpur, Bngl.	126	23.17 N	89.15 E
Mati	116	6.57 N	126.13 E
Matiacoali	150	12.23 N	1.02 E
Matiakoula	273b	4.26 S	14.35 E
Mätiāri	124	25.36 N	68.44 E
Matiāri	120	25.36 N	68.27 E
Matias Barbosa	256	21.53 S	43.20 W
Matías Romero	234	16.53 N	95.02 W
Mätibhānga	126	22.49 N	89.56 E
Maticora ≃	246	11.03 N	71.09 W
Matignon	32	48.36 N	2.18 W
Matiguás	236	12.50 N	85.28 W
Matinecock	276	40.52 N	73.38 W
Matinenda Lake ⊘	190	46.22 N	82.57 W
Matinha	250	3.06 S	45.02 W
Matinicock Point ⊳	276	40.54 N	73.38 W
Matinicus Island I	188	43.52 N	68.53 W
Matinho	68	40.02 N	18.08 E
Matipó	255	20.17 S	42.21 W
Matir Täris	148	35.29 N	11.00 E
Matiyure ≃	246	7.36 N	67.39 W
Matjiesfontein	158	33.14 S	20.35 E
Matkaset'kja	26	61.58 N	30.33 E
Matla ≃	126	21.40 N	88.09 E
Matlaa Bäzär	126	23.20 N	90.43 E
Matlacha	220	26.37 N	82.05 W
Matlacha Pass ⋃	220	26.37 N	82.04 W
Matlamanyane	156	19.33 S	25.57 E
Matlapa	234	21.15 N	98.50 W
M'atlevo	76	54.54 N	35.39 E
Matli	124	25.02 N	68.39 E
Matlock, Eng., U.K.	44	53.08 N	1.32 W
Matlock, Wa., U.S.	222	47.14 N	123.25 W
Matlock, Mount ∧	169	35.45 S	146.11 E
Matmata	148	33.33 N	9.58 E
Matnog	116	12.35 N	124.05 E
Mato ≃	246	8.01 S	24.55 E
Mato, Cerro ∧	246	7.15 N	65.07 W
Matoaca	208	37.13 N	77.28 W
Matobe	112	2.42 S	100.11 E
Matočkin Šar	82	73.16 N	56.27 E
Matočkin Šar, proliv ⋃	72	73.20 N	55.21 E
Mato Grosso □³	242	12.00 S	57.00 W
Mato Grosso, Planalto de ∧	242	15.30 S	56.00 W
Matola-Rio	156	25.58 S	32.26 E
Matombo	154	7.03 S	37.46 E
Mato Mole, Serra do ∧	256	20.40 S	46.12 W
Matonipi ≃	164	5.35 S	151.45 E
Matope	186	51.21 N	69.45 W
	154	15.20 S	34.59 E

Nome	Página	Lat.°′	Long.°′ W=Oeste
Matopo Hills ⊼²	154	20.36 S	28.28 E
Matopos	154	20.24 S	28.28 E
Matopos ≃	248	14.07 S	65.25 W
Matosinhos	34	41.11 N	8.42 W
Matoso, Ponta do ⊳	287a	22.50 S	43.11 W
Matou, T'aiwan	100	23.11 N	120.14 E
Matou, Zhg.	98	36.29 N	114.26 E
Matou, Zhg.	100	25.14 N	118.22 E
Matou, Zhg.	100	29.49 N	115.35 E
Matou, Zhg.	100	30.48 N	118.29 E
Matou, Zhg.	105	39.46 N	116.49 E
Matou, Zhg.	105	39.19 N	116.45 E
Matou, Zhg.	105	33.32 N	116.07 E
Matouji	98	35.02 N	115.07 E
Matour	58	46.18 N	4.29 E
Matoury	250	4.51 N	52.20 W
Matouxi	107	30.15 N	106.31 E
Matouying	98	39.18 N	118.47 E
Matouzhen, Zhg.	98	39.19 N	118.18 E
Matouzhen, Zhg.	100	33.32 N	118.56 E
Mato Verde	255	15.23 S	42.52 W
Matozinhos	255	19.35 S	44.07 W
Mátra ⊼	30	47.55 N	20.00 E
Matrah	128	23.38 N	58.34 E
Matraville	274a	33.54 S	151.18 E
Matrei am Brenner	64	47.08 N	11.27 E
Matrei in Osttirol	64	47.00 N	12.32 E
Matsap	158	28.38 S	22.47 E
Matsapha	158	26.29 S	31.23 E
Matsari	152	5.21 N	12.14 E
Matsena	152	13.05 N	10.05 E
Matsiatra ≃	157b	21.25 S	45.33 E
Matsieng	158	29.36 S	27.32 E
Matschnutsgårcarna	40	60.28 N	15.22 E
Matsqui	224	49.12 N	122.25 W
Matsu — Matsu Tao I	100	26.09 N	119.56 E
Matsubara	96	34.34 N	135.33 E
Matsubushi	268	35.55 N	139.49 E
Matsuda	95	35.21 N	139.09 E
Matsudo	94	37.08 N	138.37 E
Matsudo Race Track ⊹	268	35.47 N	139.54 E
Matsue	96	35.28 N	139.55 E
Matsugasaki	268	35.53 N	139.58 E
Matsuida	96	36.19 N	138.48 E
Matsukawa, Nihon	94	35.36 N	137.51 E
Matsukawa, Nihon	94	35.36 N	137.55 E
Matsumae	92	41.26 N	140.07 E
Matsumoto	94	36.14 N	137.58 E
Matsuno	96	33.13 N	132.42 E
Matsunoyama	94	37.05 N	138.37 E
Matsuo	95	35.38 N	140.28 E
Matsudji	268	35.00 N	140.01 E
Matsuo-san ∧	270	34.38 N	135.44 E
Matsusaka	94	34.34 N	136.32 E
Matsushima	92	38.22 N	141.04 E
Matsu Tao I	100	26.09 N	119.56 E
Matsutō	94	36.31 N	136.34 E
Matsuura	92	33.22 N	129.42 E
Matsuyama	96	33.50 N	132.45 E
Matsuzaki	94	34.45 N	138.47 E
Matta ≃	208	38.07 N	77.26 W
Mattagami ≃	176	50.43 N	81.29 W
Mattagami Heights	190	48.49 N	81.22 W
Mattagami Lake ⊘	190	47.54 N	81.35 W
Mattamuskeet, Lake ⊘			
	208	35.30 N	76.11 W
Mattapan	283	42.16 N	71.06 W
Mattapoisett	207	41.39 N	70.49 W
Mattaponi ≃	208	37.32 N	76.46 W
Mattaponi	208	37.31 N	76.47 W
Mattarana	62	44.15 N	9.37 E
Mattarello	64	46.00 N	11.07 E
Mattawa, On., Can.	190	46.19 N	78.42 W
Mattawa, Wa., U.S.	222	46.44 N	119.54 W
Mattawa ≃	190	46.19 N	78.43 W
Mattawamkeag	188	45.30 N	68.21 W
Mattawamkeag ≃	188	45.30 N	68.24 W
Mattawan	216	42.12 N	85.47 W
Mattawana	214	40.30 N	77.44 W
Mattawoman Creek ≃	208	38.34 N	77.12 W
Matterhorn (Cervino) ∧, Europe	58	45.59 N	7.43 E
Matterhorn ∧, Nv., U.S.	204	41.49 N	115.23 W
Mattersburg	64	47.44 N	16.25 E
Mattertal V	58	46.10 N	7.49 E
Matteson	216	41.30 N	87.42 W
Matteson Lake ⊘	216	41.56 N	85.12 W
Matthew Flinders Memorial ⊥	169	38.19 S	145.04 E
Matthews	216	40.23 N	85.29 W
Matthews Mountain ∧	194	37.39 N	90.21 W
Matthews Ridge	246	7.30 N	60.10 W
Matthew Town	238	20.57 N	73.40 W
Matthias Church ⊻	264c	47.30 N	19.02 E
Matthiessen State Park ⊹	216	41.17 N	89.01 W
Matti, Sabkhat ⊘	128	23.30 N	52.00 E
Mattie, Lake ⊘	220	28.08 N	81.46 W
Mattighofen	60	48.06 N	13.04 E
Mattinata	68	41.42 N	16.03 E
Mattishall	42	52.39 N	1.02 E
Mattituck	210	40.59 N	72.32 W
Mattmar	26	63.19 N	13.54 E
Mattoon, Il., U.S.	200	39.28 N	88.22 W
Mattoon, Wi., U.S.	190	45.30 N	90.14 W
Mattox Creek ≃	208	38.12 N	76.58 W
Mattox Draw V	198	38.03 N	101.11 W
Mattsee	64	47.58 N	13.06 E
Mattsee ⊘	64	47.59 N	13.07 E
Mattydale	210	43.05 N	76.08 W
Matu	112	2.41 N	111.32 E
Matua	156	24.27 S	32.55 E
Matucana	248	11.51 S	76.24 W
Matudo — Matsudo	95	35.47 N	139.54 E
Matue — Matsue	96	35.28 N	133.04 E
Matukituki ≃	172	44.32 S	169.09 E
Matumoto — Matsumoto	94	36.14 N	137.58 E
Matungo ≃	152	16.25 S	21.27 E
Matunuck	207	41.23 N	71.32 W
Matuog	116	6.37 N	121.33 E
Matura Bay ⊂	241r	10.38 N	61.01 W
Maturín	246	9.45 N	63.11 W
Matusadona National Park ⊹	154	16.35 S	28.30 E
Matusov	78	49.03 N	31.34 E
Matutina	255	19.13 S	45.58 W
Matutúm, Mount ∧	116	6.22 N	125.05 E
Matuzaka — Matsusaka	94	34.34 N	136.32 E
Matveev Kurgan	83	47.35 N	38.52 E
Matvejevka, Ross.	82	47.35 N	43.30 E
Matvejevo, Ross.	86	57.47 N	57.11 E
Matvejevo ≃ → ⁸	80	57.45 N	48.21 E
Matýšev	76	52.38 N	49.38 E
Mau (Ireng) ≃	246	20.36 S	59.51 W
Maú, Bra.	250	3.54 S	46.27 W
Maúa, Moç.	154	13.51 S	37.10 E
Maū □⁷	287b	20.47 S	156.20 W
Mau Aīmma	124	25.41 N	81.55 E
Mauban	116	14.12 N	121.45 E
Maubara	112	8.37 S	125.12 E
Maubeuge	50	50.17 N	3.58 E

Nom	Page	Lat.°′	Long.°′ W=Ouest
Mauchamps	261	48.32 N	2.12 E
Mauchline	46	55.31 N	4.24 W
Maud, Scot., U.K.	46	57.31 N	2.06 W
Maud, Mo., U.S.	219	39.37 N	92.15 W
Maud, Oh., U.S.	218	39.21 N	84.23 W
Maud, Ok., U.S.	196	35.08 N	96.46 W
Maud, Tx., U.S.	194	33.20 N	94.21 W
Maud, Point ⊳	162	23.06 S	113.45 E
Maudaha	124	25.41 N	80.07 E
Maude	168	34.28 S	144.18 E
Maudétour-en-Vexin	261	49.06 N	1.47 E
Mau-é-ele	156	24.21 S	34.07 E
Mauense	58	47.10 N	8.04 E
Mauer → ⁸	264b	48.09 N	16.16 E
Mauerbach	264b	48.15 N	16.10 E
Mauerbach ≃	264b	48.12 N	16.14 E
Mauerkirchen	60	48.11 N	13.08 E
Maués	248	3.24 S	57.42 W
Maués ≃	246	3.22 S	57.44 W
Mauganj	124	24.41 N	81.53 E
Mauga Silisili ∧	175a	13.35 S	172.27 W
Maughold	44	54.18 N	4.17 W
Maug Islands II	108	20.01 N	145.13 E
Mauguio	62	43.37 N	4.01 E
Mauguio, Étang de ⊂	62	43.35 N	4.02 E
Maui I → ⁶	162	23.06 S	106.30 E
Mauk	115a	6.04 S	106.30 E
Mauke I	14	20.09 S	157.23 W
Maulbach	56	50.43 N	9.04 E
Maulbronn	56	49.00 N	8.49 E
Maulde ≃	50	50.30 N	3.26 E
Mauldin	192	34.46 N	82.18 W
Maule □⁴	252	35.30 S	71.30 W
Maule ≃	252	35.19 S	72.25 W
Maule, Laguna del ⊘	252	36.04 S	70.30 W
Mauléon	32	46.56 N	0.45 W
Mauléon-Licharre	32	43.14 N	0.53 W
Maulette	261	48.48 N	1.37 E
Maulin	254	41.38 S	73.37 W
Mauivi Bāzār	120	24.29 N	91.47 E
Maumapaki ∧	172	36.58 S	175.35 E
Maumee	214	41.33 N	83.39 W
Maumee ≃	216	41.42 N	83.28 W
Maumee Bay ⊂	214	41.43 N	83.26 W
Maumelle, Lake ⊘	194	34.50 N	92.40 W
Maun	156	20.00 S	23.25 E
Maunabo	240m	18.01 N	65.54 W
Mauna Kea ∧¹	229d	19.50 N	155.28 W
Maunaloa	229a	21.08 N	157.13 W
Mauna Loa ∧¹	229a	19.29 N	155.36 W
Maunalua Bay ⊂	229c	21.17 N	157.44 W
Maurath Bhanjan	126	25.32 S	27.28 E
Maunesha ≃	216	43.13 N	88.57 W
Maungahaumi ∧	172	38.18 S	177.40 E
Maunga Roa ∧	174k	21.13 S	159.48 W
Maungatapere	172	35.45 S	174.12 E
Maungaturoto	172	36.06 S	174.22 E
Maungdaw	110	20.50 N	92.22 E
Maungmagan	110	14.09 N	98.06 E
Maupin	154	3.33 S	38.45 E
Maunoir, Lac ⊘	180	67.30 N	125.00 W
Maupihaa I¹	14	16.50 S	153.55 W
Maupin	222	45.10 N	121.04 W
Maur	123	30.05 N	75.15 E
Mau Rānīpur	124	25.15 N	79.08 E
Maurecourt	261	49.00 N	2.04 E
Maure-de-Bretagne	32	47.54 N	1.59 W
Mauregard	261	49.02 N	2.35 E
Maurepas	261	48.45 N	1.55 E
Maurepas, Lake ⊘	194	30.15 N	90.30 W
Maures ⊼	62	43.16 N	6.23 E
Mauretanien — Mauritania □¹	134	20.00 N	12.00 W
Mauri ≃	248	17.18 S	68.41 W
Mauria, Passo della ⋊	64	46.27 N	12.31 E
Mauriac	32	45.13 N	2.20 E
Maurice (Île)			
— Mauritius □¹	157c	20.17 S	57.33 E
Maurice ≃	208	39.13 N	75.02 W
Maurice K. Goddard State Park ⊹	214	41.23 N	81.10 W
Mauricetown	208	39.17 N	74.58 W
Mauricie	190	46.47 N	72.54 W
Mauricio — Mauritius □¹	157c	20.17 S	57.33 E
Mauritania □¹, Afr.	162	45.13 S	6.30 E
Maurinho, Canal ≃	286e	33.34 S	70.32 W
Mauritania (Mauritanie) □¹	134	20.00 N	12.00 W
Mauriti	250	7.23 S	38.46 W
Mauritius □¹, Afr.	157c	20.17 S	57.33 E
Mauritius □¹, Afr.	157c	20.17 S	57.33 E
Mauron	32	48.05 N	2.18 W
Maurs	32	44.43 N	2.11 E
Maury □⁶	192	35.37 N	87.05 W
Maury Channel ⋃	46	58.16 N	6.55 W
Maury Island I¹	224	47.20 N	122.24 W
Maussane	62	43.43 N	4.48 E
Māyir, Şürīy.	130	34.47 N	36.09 E
Māyir, Şürīy.	130	32.39 N	36.41 E
Maūtau, Pointe ⊳	174x	9.42 S	138.58 W
Mautern an der Donau	60	48.24 N	15.35 E
Mauterndorf	64	47.08 N	13.40 E
Mautern in Steiermark	64	47.24 N	14.50 E
Mauth	60	48.53 N	13.35 E
Mauthausen	64	48.15 N	14.30 E
Mauva-Loup	198	40.40 N	99.06 W
Mauvaise Terre Creek ≃	219	39.43 N	90.09 W
Mauvaise Terre Lake ⊘	219	39.42 N	90.12 W
Mauvezin	32	43.44 N	0.55 E
Meva	164	6.50 S	141.25 E
Mevaca	152	10.50 S	35.11 W
Meva ≃	156	22.43 S	35.08 E
MevNuota, Mount ∧	204	41.40 N	109.32 W
Meverick	200	35.50 N	109.12 W
Mevinga	156	15.50 S	20.21 E
Mavita	156	19.33 S	33.10 E
Mavone ≃	156	18.32 S	33.02 E
Mavrova	38	40.18 N	20.31 E
Mavuradonha Mountains ⊼	156	16.30 S	31.20 E
Mawa	154	2.45 N	26.42 E
Mawa Wan I	271d	22.21 N	114.03 E
Mawāna	124	29.06 N	77.55 E
Mawangkanli Shan ⊼	105	34.19 N	110.03 E
Mawangmu	107	24.47 N	116.46 E
Mawangsanka	112	5.33 S	122.18 E
Mawchi	110	18.49 N	97.09 E
Maw-Daung Pass ⋊	110	11.25 N	99.36 E
Mawdesley	262	53.38 N	2.46 W
Mawdesley Lake ⊘	184	54.40 N	100.29 W
Mawgan	42	50.06 N	5.12 W
Mawjib, Wādī al- V	130	31.28 N	35.34 E
Mawkmai	110	20.14 N	97.38 E
Mawlaik	110	23.38 N	94.24 E
Mawlamyaing — Moulmein	110	16.30 N	97.38 E
Mawnan	42	50.06 N	5.08 W
Māwr, Wādī V	144	15.43 N	43.11 E
Mawshij	144	13.43 N	43.17 E

Nombre	Página	Lat.°′	Long.°′ W=Oeste
Mawson ⊻³	9	67.40 S	63.43 E
Mawson Escarpment ⊼			
⊹¹ ⊼	9	73.05 S	68.10 E
Mawson Peninsula ⊳¹	9	68.35 S	154.11 E
Maw Taung ∧	110	11.39 N	99.35 E
Mawuba	102	29.50 N	108.11 E
Max	198	47.49 N	101.17 W
Maxaranguape	250	5.31 S	35.16 W
Maxatawny	208	40.33 N	75.41 W
Maxcanú	232	20.35 N	89.59 W
Maxéville	58	48.43 N	6.10 E
Maximo, Flughafen ⊛	64	47.48 N	13.02 E
Maxhütte Haidhof	60	49.12 N	12.05 E
Maxiang	100	24.41 N	118.15 E
Maximo	264b	48.03 N	81.11 W
Maximo Paz	258	34.56 S	58.37 W
Maxinkuckee, Lake ⊘	216	41.12 N	86.24 W
Maxixe	156	23.51 S	35.21 E
Maxon Creek ≃	196	29.53 N	102.24 W
Maxton	192	34.44 N	79.20 W
Maxville	206	45.17 N	74.51 W
Maxwell, Ca., U.S.	226	39.16 N	122.11 W
Maxwell, In., U.S.	218	39.51 N	85.46 W
Maxwell, Ia., U.S.	190	41.53 N	93.23 W
Maxwell, Ne., U.S.	198	41.04 N	100.31 W
Maxwell, N.M., U.S.	196	36.32 N	104.32 W
Maxwell, Tx., U.S.	222	29.53 N	97.48 W
Maxwell Air Force Base ⊛	194	32.23 N	86.21 W
Maxwell Bay ⊂	176	74.35 N	89.00 W
May	196	31.59 N	98.59 W
May, Austl.	162	17.07 S	123.50 E
May ≃, Ab., Can.	182	55.43 N	111.22 W
May, Cape ⊳¹	208	38.58 N	74.55 W
May, Isle of I	46	56.11 N	2.34 W
May, Mount ∧	182	54.02 N	119.58 W
Maya, Pulau I	112	1.10 S	109.35 E
May Aché	146	12.00 N	15.44 E
Mayaguana I	238	22.23 N	72.57 W
Mayaguana Passage ⋃	238	22.32 N	73.15 W
Mayagüez	240m	18.12 N	67.09 W
Mayagüez, Aeropuerto ⊛	240m	18.15 N	67.09 W
Mayagüez, Bahía de ⊂	240m	18.12 N	67.10 W
Mayahi	150	13.58 N	7.40 E
Mayajigua	240p	22.14 N	79.04 W
Mayaka	152	5.17 N	16.52 E
Mayala	273b	4.21 S	15.09 E
Mayales, Punta ⊳	236	11.52 N	85.26 W
Mayang	152	3.51 S	14.54 E
Mayang-do I	98	40.00 N	128.12 E
Mayantoc	116	15.37 N	120.23 E
Mayao	106	30.50 N	120.23 E
Mayapan ⊥	232	20.28 N	89.08 E
Māyāpur	272b	22.57 N	88.08 E
Mayari	240p	20.40 N	75.41 W
Mayarí Arriba	240p	20.30 N	75.32 W
Mayaro Bay ⊂	241r	10.15 N	60.58 W
Maya-san ∧	96	34.44 N	135.12 E
Maybee	216	42.00 N	83.30 W
Maybeury	192	37.22 N	81.22 W
Maybole	46	55.21 N	4.41 W
Maybrook	210	41.29 N	74.13 W
Maychew	144	13.02 N	39.34 E
Maydelle	222	31.48 N	95.18 W
Maydena	166	42.55 S	146.30 E
Maydh	144	11.00 N	47.06 E
Maydī	144	16.20 N	42.46 E
Maydolong	116	11.30 N	125.30 E
Mayen	142	29.22 N	31.10 E
Mayen	52	50.19 N	7.14 E
Mayence — Mainz	56	50.01 N	8.16 E
Mayenne	32	48.18 N	0.37 W
Mayenne □⁵	32	48.05 N	0.40 W
Mayenne ≃	47	47.30 N	0.33 W
Mayer	200	34.23 N	112.14 W
Mayerling	61	48.03 N	16.06 E
Mayersville	194	32.54 N	91.03 W
Mayerthorpe	182	53.57 N	115.08 W
Mayet	32	47.41 N	0.16 E
Mayfair → ⁸, S. Afr.	273d	26.12 S	28.01 E
Mayfair → ⁸, Pa., U.S.	285	40.02 N	75.03 W
Mayfield, N.Z.	172	43.49 S	171.25 E
Mayfield, Eng., U.K.	42	51.01 N	0.16 E
Mayfield, Eng., U.K.	44	53.01 N	1.45 W
Mayfield, Scot., U.K.	46	55.52 N	3.05 W
Mayfield, Ky., U.S.	200	36.44 N	88.38 W
Mayfield, N.Y., U.S.	210	43.06 N	74.16 W
Mayfield, Ut., U.S.	200	39.06 N	111.42 W
Mayfield Creek ≃	194	36.51 N	89.03 W
Mayfield Heights	214	41.31 N	81.27 W
Mayfield Lake ⊘	224	46.32 N	122.34 W
Mayford	260	51.20 N	0.33 W
May Inlet ⊂	176	75.00 N	105.45 W
Maykop — Majkop	80	44.35 N	40.07 E
Mayland	222	44.35 N	40.07 E
Maylodn	184	50.48 N	98.23 W
Maymaō, Wādī V	130	30.18 N	37.36 E
Maymyo	110	22.02 N	96.28 E
Maynal ≃	80	60.40 N	56.24 E
Maynard, Ia., U.S.	190	42.47 N	91.52 W
Maynard, Ma., U.S.	207	42.26 N	71.26 W
Maynard, Mn., U.S.	198	44.54 N	95.28 W
Maynard, Oh., U.S.	214	40.04 N	80.53 W
Maynardville	192	36.15 N	83.48 W
Mayne ≃	168	26.50 S	141.55 E
Mayenne	32	48.10 N	0.37 W
Mayo, Ire.	44	53.53 N	9.20 W
Mayo, Yk., Can.	180	63.35 N	135.54 W
Mayo □⁶	44	53.50 N	9.30 W
Mayo ≃, Arg.	254	45.40 S	70.15 W
Mayo ≃, Col.	244	1.26 N	77.17 W
Mayo ≃, Méx.	232	26.45 N	109.39 W
Mayo ≃, Perú	248	6.21 S	76.24 W
Mayodan	192	36.25 N	79.58 W
Mayo-Kébbi □⁵	148	9.05 N	15.30 E
Mayo Lake ⊘	180	63.40 N	135.10 W
Mayon Volcano ∧¹	116	13.15 N	123.41 E
Mayor Buratovich	252	39.15 S	62.37 W
Mayor Pablo Lagerenza	248	19.58 S	60.45 W
Mayotte □², Afr.	157a	12.50 S	45.10 E
Mayotte □², Afr.	138	12.50 S	45.10 E
Mayoyao	116	16.53 N	121.14 E
Mayra	110	18.35 N	97.17 E
Maypen	238	17.58 N	77.14 W
Mayport Naval Station ⊛	241q	30.24 N	81.24 W
Mayraira Point ⊳	116	18.39 N	120.51 E

Nombre	Página	Lat.°′	Long.°′ W=Oeste
Mayrán, Desierto de — ²	196	25.45 N	102.45 W
Mayres	62	44.40 N	4.07 E
Mayrhofen	64	47.10 N	11.52 E
Mays	218	39.45 N	85.26 W
Maysah, Tall al- ∧	132	31.08 N	35.40 E
Maysán □⁴	128	32.00 N	47.00 E
Maysfield	222	30.54 N	96.51 W
Mays Landing	208	39.27 N	74.43 W
Mays Lick	218	38.31 N	83.50 W
Maysville, Ky., U.S.	218	38.38 N	83.46 W
Maysville, Mo., U.S.	194	39.53 N	94.21 W
Maysville, N.C., U.S.	192	34.54 N	77.13 W
Maysville, Ok., U.S.	196	34.49 N	97.24 W
Maythalūr	132	32.21 N	35.16 E
Maytiguid Islanc I	116	11.03 N	119.36 E
Maytown	208	40.04 N	76.35 W
Mayu	100	27.48 N	120.26 E
Mayumba	152	3.25 S	10.39 E
Mayuram	122	11.06 N	79.40 E
Māyūran	122	11.06 N	79.40 E
Mayville, Mi., U.S.	216	43.20 N	83.21 W
Mayville, N.Y., U.S.	214	42.15 N	79.30 W
Mayville, N.D., U.S.	198	47.29 N	97.19 W
Mayville, Wi., U.S.	190	43.29 N	88.32 W
Maywood, Ca., U.S.	280	33.59 N	118.11 W
Maywood, Il., U.S.	216	41.52 N	87.51 W
Maywood, Mo., U.S.	219	39.57 N	91.36 W
Maywood, Ne., U.S.	198	40.39 N	100.37 W
Maywood, N.J., U.S.	276	40.54 N	74.03 W
Maywood, N.Y., U.S.	210	42.42 N	73.52 W
Maywood Race Track ⊹	278	41.44 N	87.50 W
Mayyit, Al-Bahr al- — Dead Sea □	132	31.30 N	35.30 E
Maza, Arg.	252	36.50 S	63.19 W
Maza, Ross.	80	57.14 N	44.13 E
Mazabuka	154	15.51 S	27.46 E
Mazagan — El-Jadida	148	33.16 N	8.30 W
Mazagão	250	0.07 S	51.17 W
Mazagão → ⁸	272e	18.57 N	72.50 E
Mazagão Velho	250	0.09 S	51.25 W
Ma'zah, Jaoal ∧	130	35.51 N	40.38 E
Mazamet	32	43.30 N	2.24 E
Mazamitla	234	19.55 N	103.02 W
Mazán	246	3.28 S	73.11 W
Mãzandarān □⁴	128	36.30 N	53.30 E
Mazanovo	89	51.40 N	128.52 E
Mazar, Jabal ∧	132	33.34 N	36.03 E
Mazar, Oued V	148	31.50 N	1.36 E
Mazār-i-Sharīf → ¹	100	36.42 N	67.06 E
Mazara del Vallo	70	37.39 N	12.35 E
Mazār-e Sharīf	128	36.42 N	67.06 E
Mazargues	62	43.15 N	5.24 E
Mazaro ≃	70	37.39 N	12.35 E
Mazarredo	254	47.05 S	66.42 W
Mazarrón	34	37.36 N	1.19 W
Mazarrón, Golfo de ⊂	34	37.30 N	1.18 W
Mazaruni ≃	246	6.25 N	58.38 W
Mazatenango	236	14.32 N	91.30 W
Mazatlán	234	23.13 N	106.25 W
Mazatlán Villa de Flores	234	18.02 N	96.54 W
Mazatzal Mountains ⊼	200	34.00 N	111.55 W
Mazatzal Peak ∧	200	34.00 N	111.28 W
Mazāy	152	3.20 N	15.40 E
Mazenod	184	49.50 N	106.32 W
Mazeppa, Pa., U.S.	214	40.59 N	76.59 W
Mazha	102	28.21 N	114.00 E
Māzhān, Īrān	128	32.35 N	59.01 E
Mazhan, Zhg.	106	30.45 N	118.45 E
Mazhang	107	21.16 N	110.19 E
Mazhangfang, Zhg.	104	40.44 N	120.53 E
Mazhangjie, Zhg.	102	30.23 N	122.26 E
Mazhuang, Zhg.	98	32.54 N	114.03 E
Mazhuang, Zhg.	105	39.11 N	116.15 E
Mazhūr, Khabb al-			
⊥	128	27.45 N	43.55 E
Mazidaği	130	37.30 N	40.30 E
Mazières → ⁸	288	37.14 N	48.02 E
Mazinan Lake ⊘	182	56.18 N	56.46 W
Mazinān	128	36.18 N	56.46 E
Maziwa	154	5.30 S	39.00 E
Mazoco	154	16.32 S	33.25 E
Mazomanie	190	43.10 N	89.47 W
Mazomin	258	22.53 S	43.49 W
Mazon	216	41.14 N	88.25 W
Mazon, East Fork ≃	278	41.10 N	88.15 W
Mazon, West Fork ≃	278	41.15 N	88.25 W
Mazong Shan ∧	98	41.40 N	97.20 E
Mazong Shan ⊼	98	41.45 N	97.00 E
Mazour, Zhg.	105	39.11 N	116.15 E
Mazra at-Bayt Jinn	132	33.19 N	35.55 E
Mazsalaca	76	57.52 N	25.03 E
Mazul'skij	82	56.16 N	90.28 E
Mazury → ¹	30	53.45 N	21.00 E
Mazzarino	70	37.19 N	14.13 E
Mazzarrà			
Sant'andrea	70	38.05 N	15.08 E
Mba	175g	17.33 S	177.41 E
Mbabane	158	26.18 S	31.06 E
Mbabo, Tchabal ∧	152	7.16 N	12.07 E
Mbaéré ≃	152	3.42 N	17.31 E
Mbai ≃	152	9.53 N	18.52 E
M'bahiakro	150	7.27 N	4.20 W
Mbaïki	152	3.53 N	18.00 E
Mbakaou, Barrage de ⊹	152	6.19 N	12.46 E
Mbala, Centraf.	152	7.48 N	20.51 E
Mbalam	152	2.13 N	13.49 E
Mbale	154	1.05 N	34.10 E
Mbali ≃	152	4.05 N	18.12 E
Mbalmayo	152	3.31 N	11.30 E
Mbam ≃	152	4.27 N	11.19 E
Mbamba Bay	154	11.17 S	34.46 E
Mbandaka	152	0.04 N	18.16 E
Mbandjok	152	4.27 N	11.54 E
Mban, Massif du ∧	152	7.08 N	13.52 E
Mbanga	152	4.30 N	9.34 E
Mbanika Island I	164	9.06 S	159.12 E
Mbanza Congo	152	6.16 S	14.15 E
M'banza-Ngungu	152	5.15 S	14.52 E
Mbarangandu ≃	154	9.57 S	37.24 E
Mbarara	154	0.36 S	30.39 E
Mbari ≃	152	4.34 N	22.43 E
Mbata	152	3.41 N	18.18 E
Mbé, Cam.	152	7.48 N	13.33 E
Mbé, Congo	152	3.28 S	16.12 E
Mbengga I	175g	18.24 S	178.08 E
Mbengga Passage ⋃	175g	18.23 S	178.15 E
M'béré ≃	152	7.45 N	15.36 E

≃ River / Fluß / Río / Rivière / Rio	⊹ Submarine Features / Untermeerische Objekte / Accidentes Submarinos / Formes de relief sous-marin / Acidentes submarinos
≋ Canal / Kanal / Canal / Canal / Canal	□ Political Unit / Politische Einheit / Unidad Política / Entité politique / Unidade política
ᴧ Waterfall, Rapids / Wasserfall, Stromschnellen / Cascada, Rápidos / Chute d'eau, Rapides / Cascata, Rápidos	⊻ Cultural Institution / Kulturelle Institution / Institution Cultural / Institution culturelle / Instituição Cultural
⋃ Strait / Meeresstraße / Estrecho / Détroit / Estreito	⊥ Historical Site / Historische Stätte / Sitio Histórico / Site historique / Sítio histórico
⊂ Bay, Gulf / Bucht, Golf / Bahía, Golfo / Baie, Golfe / Baía, Golfo	⊹ Recreational Site / Erholungs- und Ferienort / Sitio de Recreo / Centre de loisirs / Área de Lazer
⊘ Lake, Lakes / See, Seen / Lago, Lagos / Lac, Lacs / Lago, Lagos	⊛ Airport / Flughafen / Aeropuerto / Aéroport / Aeroporto
⸬ Swamp / Sumpf / Pantano / Marais / Pântano	⊠ Military Installation / Militäranlage / Instalación Militar / Installation militaire / Instalação militar
⊠ Ice Features, Glacier / Eis- und Gletscherformen / Accidentes Glaciales / Formes glaciaires / Acidentes glaciares	→ Miscellaneous / Verschiedenes / Misceláneo / Divers / Diversos
▾ Other Hydrographic Features / Andere Hydrographische Objekte / Otros Elementos Hidrográficos / Autres données hydrographiques / Outros acidentes hidrográficos	

ENGLISH: Name | Page | Lat.°′ | Long.°′
DEUTSCH: Name | Seite | Breite°′ | Länge°′ E = Ost

Mberengwa 154 20.30 S 29.53 E
Mbereshi Mission 154 9.45 S 28.46 E
Mberubu 150 6.10 N 7.38 E
Mbeya 154 8.54 S 33.27 E
Mbeya □[4] 154 8.00 S 33.30 E
Mbi ≃ 152 4.26 N 18.16 E
Mbia 140 6.15 N 29.19 E
M'bigou 152 1.53 S 11.56 E
Mbinda 152 2.00 S 12.55 E
Mbindawina 152 15.57 S 23.18 E
Mbinga 154 10.56 S 35.01 E
Mbini 152 1.35 N 9.37 E
Mbini ≃ 152 1.35 N 9.37 E
Mbirira 154 4.21 S 30.10 E
Mbirizi 154 0.23 S 31.27 E
Mbogo 154 7.26 S 33.26 E
Mboie 152 6.56 S 21.54 E
Mbola 175e 9.37 S 160.39 E
Mboli 152 4.08 N 23.09 E
Mbomou □[5] 152 5.00 N 23.30 E
Mbomou (Bomu) ≃ 136 4.08 N 22.26 E
Mbonge 152 4.33 N 9.05 E
Mboro, Sén. 150 15.09 N 16.54 W
Mboro, Sūd. 140 6.18 N 28.45 E
Mborokua I 175e 9.00 S 158.40 E
Mborong 115b 8.49 S 120.37 E
Mboté 152 3.56 S 12.43 E
Mbotou ≃ 152 6.49 N 24.14 E
Mbouda 152 5.38 N 10.15 E
Mboula 152 4.27 N 16.29 E
Mbour 150 14.24 N 16.58 W
Mbout 150 16.02 N 12.35 W
Mbrès 152 6.40 N 19.48 E
M'Bridge ≃ 152 7.14 S 12.52 E
Mbua 175g 16.48 S 178.37 E
Mbua Bay c 175g 16.49 S 178.35 E
Mbuji-Mayi (Bakwanga) 152 6.09 S 23.38 E
Mbulu 154 3.51 S 35.32 E
Mbulula 154 5.26 S 27.26 E
Mbuluzane ≃ 158 26.08 S 31.52 E
Mbuluzi ≃ 158 26.08 S 31.52 E
Mbuma 154 3.32 N 24.50 E
Mburucuyá 252 28.03 S 58.14 W
Mbutha 175g 16.39 S 179.50 E
Mbwemkuru ≃ 154 9.29 S 39.39 E
McAdam 186 45.36 N 67.20 W
McAdam National Park ♠ 164 7.15 S 145.40 E
McAdams Peak ∧[2] 219 38.58 N 90.32 W
McAdoo 210 40.54 N 75.59 W
McAdoo Heights 210 40.54 N 76.01 W
McAfee 210 41.10 N 74.32 W
McAlester 196 34.56 N 95.46 W
McAlisterville 208 40.38 N 77.16 W
McAllen 196 26.12 N 98.13 W
McAlpine 208 39.16 N 76.50 W
McAlpine Dam ◆[6] 218 38.16 N 85.47 W
McAlveys Fort 214 40.39 N 77.50 W
McArthur 188 39.14 N 82.28 W
McArthur ≃ 164 15.54 S 136.40 E
McArthur River 164 16.27 S 136.07 E
McAuley 184 50.16 N 101.23 W
McBain 190 44.11 N 85.12 W
McBee 192 34.28 N 80.15 W
McBeth 222 29.11 N 95.30 W
McBeth Fjord c[2] 176 69.38 N 68.30 W
McBride 182 53.18 N 120.10 W
McCall 202 44.54 N 116.05 W
McCall Creek 194 31.30 N 90.41 W
McCallum 186 47.38 N 56.15 W
McCallum Creek ≃ 169 37.03 S 143.49 E
McCamey 196 31.08 N 102.13 W
McCammon 202 42.39 N 112.11 W
McCandless, Pa., U.S. 214 40.35 N 80.01 W
McCandless, Pa., U.S. 279b 40.34 N 80.02 W
McCarteney Creek ≃ 202 47.13 N 120.05 W
McCarthy 180 61.26 N 142.55 W
McCauley Island I 182 53.40 N 130.15 W
McCaysville 192 34.59 N 84.22 W
McChord Air Force Base ■ 224 47.08 N 122.29 W
McClarens Run ≃ 279b 40.27 N 80.12 W
McClarty Lake ⊜ 184 54.28 N 100.20 W
McCleary 224 47.03 N 123.15 W
McClees Creek ≃ 276 40.22 N 74.03 W
McClellan Air Force Base ■ 226 38.39 N 121.23 W
McClellan Creek ≃ 196 35.22 N 100.34 W
McClellanville 192 33.05 N 79.27 W
McClintock, Mount ∧ 9 80.13 S 157.26 E
McCloud 204 41.15 N 122.08 W
McCloud ≃ 204 40.46 N 122.18 W
McClure, Il., U.S. 194 37.19 N 89.26 W
McClure, Oh., U.S. 216 41.22 N 83.56 W
McClure, Pa., U.S. 210 40.42 N 77.18 W
McClure, Lake ⊜[1] 226 37.37 N 120.16 W
McClusky 198 47.29 N 100.26 W
McColl 192 34.40 N 79.32 W
McComas 192 37.23 N 81.17 W
McComb, Ms., U.S. 194 31.14 N 90.27 W
McComb, Oh., U.S. 216 41.06 N 83.47 W
McConaughy, Lake ⊜[1] 198 41.15 N 101.50 W
McConnell Air Force Base ■ 198 37.38 N 97.15 W
McConnell Range ⋏ 180 64.00 N 123.50 W
McConnellsburg 188 39.55 N 77.59 W
McConnells Mill 279b 40.15 N 80.15 W
McConnells Mill State Park ♠ 214 40.57 N 80.11 W
McConnellstown 214 40.27 N 78.05 W
McConnellsville 210 43.16 N 75.42 W
McConnelsville 188 39.38 N 81.51 W
McCook, Il., U.S. 278 41.48 N 87.50 W
McCook, Ne., U.S. 198 40.12 N 100.37 W
McCordsville 218 39.53 N 85.55 W
McCormick 192 33.54 N 82.17 W
McCormick Place ʋ 278 41.51 N 87.37 W
McCoy 224 45.03 N 123.13 W
McCoy Creek ≃ 202 43.02 N 118.50 W
McCoy Lake ⊜ 184 52.35 N 92.19 W
McCraney Creek ≃ 219 39.39 N 91.12 W
McCreary 184 50.46 N 99.30 W
McCrory 194 35.15 N 91.12 W
McCulloch, Mount ∧ 162 25.10 S 129.52 E
McCullom Lake 216 42.22 N 88.18 W
McCullough 279b 40.22 N 79.38 W
McCullough Mountain ∧ 204 35.36 N 115.11 W
McCune 198 37.21 N 95.00 W
McCurtain 196 35.08 N 94.58 W
McCusker ≃ 184 55.32 N 108.40 W
McCutchenville 214 40.59 N 83.15 W
McDade 222 30.17 N 97.15 W
McDavid 194 30.51 N 87.19 W
McDermitt 204 41.59 N 117.43 W
McDermott 218 38.50 N 83.03 W
McDonald, Ks., U.S. 198 39.47 N 101.22 W
McDonald, Pa., U.S. 214 40.22 N 80.14 W
McDonald, Lac ⊜ 206 45.52 N 74.35 W
McDonald, Lake ⊜ 202 48.35 N 113.55 W
McDonald Park ♠ 282 37.18 N 122.17 W
McDonogh 284b 39.24 N 76.46 W
McDonough, Ga., U.S. 192 33.26 N 84.08 W
McDonough, N.Y., U.S. 210 42.30 N 75.46 W
McDouall Peak 162 29.51 S 134.55 E
McDougal, Mount ∧ 200 42.54 N 110.36 W
McDowell Peak ∧ 200 33.40 N 111.50 W
McElhattan 210 41.09 N 77.22 W
McElmo Creek ≃ 200 37.13 N 109.12 W
Mc Ennen Airport ⊠ 281 42.12 N 83.37 W
Mcensk 76 53.17 N 36.35 E
McEwen 194 36.06 N 87.37 W
McEwensville 210 41.05 N 76.49 W
McFadden 200 41.39 N 106.07 W
McFarland, Ca., U.S. 226 35.40 N 119.13 W
McFarland, Wi., U.S. 216 43.00 N 89.17 W
McGavock Lake ⊜ 184 56.32 N 101.25 W
McGehee 194 33.37 N 91.23 W
McGill 204 39.24 N 114.46 W
McGill, Université ʋ[2] 275a 45.30 N 73.35 W
McGillivray, Lac ⊜ 190 46.04 N 77.06 W
McGinnis Slough Wildlife Refuge ◆[4] 278 41.39 N 87.52 W
McGovern 214 40.14 N 80.13 W
McGrann 214 40.47 N 79.31 W
McGrath 180 62.58 N 155.38 W
McGraw 210 42.35 N 76.05 W
McGregor, On., Can. 214 42.09 N 82.58 W
McGregor, S. Afr. 158 33.57 S 19.50 E
McGregor, Ia., U.S. 190 43.01 N 91.10 W
McGregor, Tx., U.S. 222 31.26 N 97.24 W
McGregor ≃ 182 54.11 N 122.00 W
McGregor Creek ≃ 214 42.24 N 82.11 W
McGregor Lake ⊜ 182 50.31 N 112.53 W
McGregor Range ⋏ 166 26.40 S 142.45 E
McGuffey 216 40.41 N 83.47 W
McGuire, Mount ∧ 202 45.10 N 114.36 W
McGuire Air Force Base ■ 208 40.02 N 74.35 W
McGuire Reservoir ⊜ 224 45.19 N 123.26 W
M'Chedallah 34 36.21 N 4.16 E
McHenry, Il., U.S. 216 42.20 N 88.16 W
McHenry, Ms., U.S. 194 30.42 N 89.08 W
McHenry □[6] 216 42.19 N 88.27 W
Mcherrah ◆[1] 148 27.00 N 4.40 W
Mchinga 154 9.44 S 39.42 E
Mchinji 154 13.41 S 32.55 E
Mchungo 154 7.42 S 39.17 E
McInnes Lake ⊜ 184 52.12 N 93.45 W
McIntosh, Al., U.S. 194 31.15 N 88.01 W
McIntosh, Il., U.S. 216 42.03 N 88.23 W
McIntosh, Mn., U.S. 198 47.38 N 95.53 W
McIntosh, S.D., U.S. 198 45.55 N 101.20 W
McIntosh Lake ⊜ 184 55.45 N 105.08 W
McIntyre 214 40.34 N 79.17 W
McIntyre Bay c 182 54.05 N 131.55 W
McKay, Mount ∧ 162 22.26 S 120.01 E
McKay Creek ≃ 202 45.40 N 118.50 W
McKean 214 41.59 N 80.09 W
McKean □[6] 214 41.49 N 78.27 W
McKeand ≃ 176 65.26 N 68.10 W
McKee 192 37.25 N 83.59 W
McKee City 208 39.27 N 74.38 W
McKee Creek ≃ 219 39.46 N 90.36 W
McKeesport 214 40.20 N 79.51 W
McKees Rocks 214 40.27 N 80.03 W
McKenna 224 46.56 N 122.33 W
McKenzie, Al., U.S. 194 31.32 N 86.42 W
McKenzie, Tn., U.S. 194 36.07 N 88.31 W
McKenzie ≃ 202 44.07 N 123.06 W
McKenzie Bridge 202 44.10 N 122.09 W
McKenzie Creek ≃ 212 43.02 N 79.53 W
McKenzie Island 184 51.05 N 93.48 W
McKenzie Lake ⊜, On., Can. 212 45.22 N 78.02 W
McKenzie Lake ⊜, Sk., Can. 184 54.12 N 102.30 W
McKerrow, Lake ⊜ 172 44.26 S 168.03 E
McKillip Ditch ≊ 216 40.50 N 86.51 W
McKinlay 166 21.16 S 141.17 E
McKinlay ≃ 166 20.50 S 141.28 E
McKinley, Mount ∧ 180 63.04 N 151.00 W
McKinley Airport ⊠ 281 42.33 N 82.58 W
McKinley Park ♠ 279b 40.25 N 80.00 W
McKinleyville, Ca., U.S. 204 40.56 N 124.05 W
McKinleyville, W.V., U.S. 214 40.15 N 80.36 W
McKinney 222 33.11 N 96.36 W
McKittrick, Ca., U.S. 226 35.18 N 119.37 W
McKittrick, Mo., U.S. 219 38.44 N 91.27 W
McKittrick Summit ∧ 226 35.18 N 119.46 W
McKnight Lake ⊜ 184 56.03 N 101.08 W
McKnightstown 208 39.52 N 77.20 W
McKnight Village 279b 40.31 N 80.00 W
McKownville 210 42.41 N 73.50 W
McLain 194 31.06 N 88.49 W
McLaren Vale 168b 35.14 S 138.32 E
McLarty Hills ⋏[2] 162 19.29 S 123.33 E
McLaughlin 198 45.48 N 100.48 W
McLaughlin ≃ 184 53.46 N 97.38 W
McLaughlin Run ≃ 279b 40.22 N 80.07 W
McLaurin 194 31.10 N 89.13 W
McLean, Sk., Can. 184 50.30 N 104.04 W
McLean, Il., U.S. 194 40.18 N 89.10 W
McLean, N.Y., U.S. 210 42.33 N 76.17 W
McLean, Tx., U.S. 196 35.13 N 100.35 W
McLean, Va., U.S. 208 38.56 N 77.10 W
McLean □[6] 216 40.29 N 88.45 W
McLean Hamlet 284c 38.56 N 77.13 W
McLean Lake ⊜ 184 56.27 N 109.15 W
McLean Mountain ∧ 186 47.07 N 68.50 W
McLeansboro 194 38.05 N 88.32 W
McLennan 182 55.42 N 116.54 W
McLennan □[6] 222 31.35 N 97.13 W
McLeod ≃ 182 54.08 N 115.42 W
McLeod Bay c 176 62.53 N 110.00 W
McLeodganj 123 30.15 N 73.42 E
McLeod Lake 182 54.59 N 123.02 W
M'Clintock Channel ʮ 176 72.00 N 102.00 W
McLoughlin, Mount ∧ 202 42.27 N 122.19 W
McLoughlin Bay c 176 67.50 N 99.00 W
McLoughlin House National Historic Site ⊥ 224 45.20 N 122.33 W
McLouth 198 39.11 N 95.12 W
McLure 182 51.03 N 120.14 W
M'Clure Strait ʮ 176 74.30 N 116.00 W
McMahan 222 29.51 N 97.31 W
McMahon 184 50.05 N 107.32 W
McMasterville 206 45.33 N 73.15 W
McMichael Art Collection ʋ 275b 43.50 N 79.37 W
McMillan, Lake ⊜[1] 196 32.40 N 104.20 W
McMinnville, Or., U.S. 224 45.12 N 123.11 W
McMinnville, Tn., U.S. 194 35.41 N 85.46 W
McMurdo ʋ[3] 9 77.50 S 166.25 E
McMurdo Sound ʮ 9 77.30 S 165.00 E
McMurray 214 40.17 N 80.05 W
McNair 222 29.48 N 95.02 W
McNary 200 34.04 N 109.51 W
McNeil, Ar., U.S. 194 33.20 N 93.12 W
McNeil, Tx., U.S. 222 30.27 N 97.43 W
McNeil, Mount ∧ 182 54.35 N 130.14 W
McNeil Island I 224 47.13 N 122.41 W
McNeill 194 30.40 N 89.38 W
McNulty 224 45.50 N 122.50 W
McPhail ≃ 184 52.44 N 96.31 W
McPhee Bay c 212 44.35 N 79.19 W
McPhee Reservoir ⊜[1] 200 37.32 N 108.35 W
McPherson 198 38.22 N 97.39 W
McPherson Range ⋏ 166 28.20 S 153.00 E
McQueeney 196 29.35 N 98.02 W
McRae, Ar., U.S. 194 35.06 N 91.49 W
McRae, Ga., U.S. 192 32.04 N 82.54 W
McRae, Mount ∧ 162 22.17 S 117.35 E
McRae Point Provincial Park ♠ 212 44.34 N 79.19 W
McRoberts 192 37.12 N 82.40 W
McSherrystown 208 39.48 N 77.00 W
McVeigh 192 37.32 N 82.15 W
McVeytown 214 40.30 N 77.44 W
McVickers Brook ≃ 276 40.45 N 74.38 W
McVille 198 47.45 N 98.10 W
McWilliams 194 31.49 N 87.05 W
Mdandu 154 9.09 S 34.42 E
Mdantsana 158 32.56 S 27.42 E
M'Daourouch 36 36.05 N 7.49 E
Meacham 184 52.08 N 105.45 W
Mead 198 41.14 N 96.30 W
Mead, Lake ⊜[1] 200 36.05 N 114.25 W
Meade, Ks., U.S. 198 37.17 N 100.20 W
Meade, Mi., U.S. 214 42.43 N 82.52 W
Meade ≃ 180 70.50 N 156.25 W
Meaden Peak ∧ 200 40.46 N 107.03 W
Meade Peak ∧ 202 42.30 N 111.15 W
Meadie, Loch ⊜ 46 58.20 N 4.33 W
Meadow, Tx., U.S. 196 33.20 N 102.12 W
Meadow, Ut,. U.S. 200 38.53 N 112.24 W
Meadowbank Park ♠ 274a 33.49 S 151.06 E
Meadowbrook, Il., U.S. 219 38.54 N 90.01 W
Meadowbrook, In., U.S. 216 41.03 N 85.03 W
Meadow Brook ≃, Ma., U.S. 283 42.03 N 70.58 W
Meadow Brook ≃, Pa., U.S. 285 40.07 N 75.04 W
Meadow Creek ≃ 202 46.03 N 115.18 W
Meadow Flat 170 33.26 S 149.56 E
Meadow Island I 276 40.36 N 73.33 W
Meadow Lake 184 54.08 N 108.26 W
Meadow Lake ⊜, Sk., Can. 184 54.07 N 108.20 W
Meadow Lake ⊜, N.Y., U.S. 276 40.44 N 73.50 W
Meadow Lake Provincial Park ♠ 184 54.28 N 109.10 W
Meadow Lands 214 40.13 N 80.13 W
Meadowlands Race Track ♠ 276 40.49 N 74.05 W
Meadowlark Airport ⊠ 280 33.43 N 118.02 W
Meadowood, De., U.S. 285 39.43 N 75.47 W
Meadowood, Md., U.S. 284c 39.04 N 77.00 W
Meadows 168b 35.11 S 138.46 E
Meadows, Island of I 276 40.34 N 74.12 W
Meadows Field ⊠ 226 35.26 N 119.03 W
Meadowvale ◆[8] 275b 43.37 N 79.43 W
Meadow Valley Wash V 204 36.39 N 114.35 W
Meadowview 192 36.46 N 81.52 W
Meadow Vista 226 39.06 N 121.01 W
Meads Creek ≃ 210 42.10 N 77.07 W
Meadville, Ms., U.S. 194 31.28 N 90.53 W
Meadville, Mo., U.S. 194 39.47 N 93.18 W
Meadville, Pa., U.S. 214 41.38 N 80.09 W
Meaford 212 44.36 N 80.35 W
Meaghers Grant 186 44.55 N 63.15 W
Me-akan-dake ∧ 92a 43.23 N 144.01 E
Mealasta Isle I 46 58.05 N 7.08 W
Mealhada 34 40.22 N 8.27 W
Méan 56 50.22 N 5.20 E
Meana 128 36.55 N 60.30 E
Meana Sardo 71 39.57 N 9.04 E
Meandarra 166 27.20 S 149.53 E
Meander Creek Reservoir ⊜[1] 214 41.09 N 80.47 W
Meander River 176 59.02 N 117.42 W
Mearim ≃ 250 3.04 S 44.35 W
Measham 42 52.43 N 1.29 W
Meath □[6] 48 53.35 N 6.40 W
Meath □[9] 48 53.40 N 7.00 W
Meaux 50 48.57 N 2.52 E
Meaux-Esbly, Aérodrome de ⊠ 261 48.55 N 2.50 E
Mebane 192 36.05 N 79.16 W
Mebisere 273a 6.42 N 3.31 E
Mebtoûh, Oued el ≃ 34 35.16 N 0.32 W
Meča ≃ 82 54.50 N 39.10 E
Meca, La → Makkah 144 21.27 N 39.49 E
Mecanhelas 154 15.12 S 35.54 E
Mecatán 234 21.32 N 105.08 W
Mecatlán 234 20.13 N 97.41 W
Mecaya ≃ 246 0.29 N 75.11 W
Mecca → Makkah 144 21.27 N 39.49 E
Mečebilovo 78 49.04 N 36.41 E
Mečetinskaja 78 46.46 N 40.27 E
Mečetka 78 50.54 N 40.05 E
Mechanic Falls 188 44.06 N 70.23 W
Mechanicsburg, Il., U.S. 219 39.48 N 89.24 W
Mechanicsburg, In., U.S. 218 40.09 N 86.28 W
Mechanicsburg, Oh., U.S. 218 40.04 N 83.33 W
Mechanicsburg, Pa., U.S. 208 40.12 N 77.00 W
Mechanicstown, N.Y., U.S. 210 41.27 N 74.24 W
Mechanicstown, Oh., U.S. 214 40.37 N 80.57 W
Mechanicsville, Ia., U.S. 190 41.54 N 91.15 W
Mechanicsville, Md., U.S. 208 38.26 N 76.44 W
Mechanicsville, Va., U.S. 192 37.36 N 77.22 W
Mechanicville 210 42.54 N 73.41 W
Mechara 144 8.32 N 40.22 E
Mechelen (Malines) 50 51.02 N 4.28 E
Mechel'ta 84 42.48 N 46.30 E
Mechernich 56 50.35 N 6.38 E
Mechī □[8] 124 27.15 N 87.45 E
Mechī ≃ 124 26.14 N 87.58 E
Mechita 252 35.04 S 60.24 W
Mechlin → Mechelen 50 51.02 N 4.28 E
Mechonskoje 86 56.09 N 64.34 E
Mechra Safsaf 34 34.52 N 2.36 W
Mechren'ga 24 61.46 N 40.57 E
Mechrenga ≃ 24 63.15 N 41.20 E
Mechriyya 148 33.35 N 0.18 W
Mechroha 36 36.21 N 7.51 E
Mecidiye, Tür. 130 40.38 N 26.32 E
Mecidiye, Tür. 130 38.53 N 27.42 E
Mečigmen 180 65.28 N 172.05 W
Mečigmeskij zaliv c 180 65.25 N 172.00 W
Meçitözü 130 40.31 N 35.19 E
Meckelfeld 52 53.25 N 10.01 E
Meckenbeuren 58 47.42 N 9.34 E
Meckenheim 56 50.37 N 7.07 E
Meckering 162 31.38 S 117.01 E
Meckesheim 56 49.19 N 8.49 E
Meckinghoven 263 51.37 N 7.19 E
Mecklenburg, Dtsch. 54 53.47 N 11.28 E
Mecklenburg, N.Y., U.S. 210 42.27 N 76.43 W
Mecklenburg □[9] 54 53.30 N 13.00 E
Mecklenburger Bucht c 54 54.20 N 11.40 E
Mecklenburgische Seenplatte ◆[1] 54 53.30 N 12.00 E
Mecklenburg-Vorpommern □[3] 54 53.45 N 12.30 E
Meclov 60 49.31 N 12.52 E
Meco 210 43.03 N 74.23 W
Mecoacán 234 18.23 N 93.07 W
Mecoacán, Laguna c 234 18.22 N 93.09 W
Meconta 154 14.49 S 39.50 E
Mecox Bay c 207 40.54 N 72.20 W
Mecque, La → Makkah 144 21.27 N 39.49 E
Mecsek ⋏ 30 46.15 N 18.05 E
Mecubúri 154 14.39 S 38.54 E
Mecubúri ≃ 154 14.10 S 40.31 E
Mecúfi 154 13.17 S 40.30 E
Mecula 154 12.04 S 37.40 E
Meda, It. 62 45.40 N 9.09 E
Meda, Port. 34 40.58 N 7.16 W
Medak 122 18.02 N 78.16 E
Medākul 126 23.03 N 90.11 E
Médan, Fr. 261 48.57 N 2.00 E
Medan, Indon. 114 3.35 N 98.40 E
Medang 114 2.06 N 101.38 E
Medang, Pulau I 115b 8.09 S 117.23 E
Medang, Tanjung > 114 2.08 N 101.39 E
Médanos 252 38.50 S 62.41 W
Medanosa, Punta > 254 48.06 S 65.55 W
Medaryville 216 41.04 N 86.53 W
Mede 62 45.06 N 8.44 E
Medebach 56 51.12 N 8.42 E
Medeiros Neto 255 17.20 S 40.14 W
Medel, Val V 58 46.37 N 8.50 E
Medellín, Col. 246 6.15 N 75.35 W
Medellin, Pil. 116 11.08 N 123.58 E
Medelpad □[9] 26 62.40 N 16.15 E
Medemblik 52 52.46 N 5.06 E
Měděnec 54 50.25 N 13.05 E
Medenica 78 49.26 N 23.45 E
Médenine 148 33.21 N 10.30 E
Médenine □[8] 148 32.00 N 10.00 E
Mederdra 150 16.55 N 15.39 W
Medesano 64 44.45 N 10.08 E
Medevi 40 58.40 N 14.57 E
Medfield 207 42.11 N 71.18 W
Medford, Ma., U.S. 207 42.25 N 71.06 W
Medford, N.J., U.S. 208 39.54 N 74.49 W
Medford, N.Y., U.S. 210 40.49 N 73.00 W
Medford, Ok., U.S. 196 36.48 N 97.44 W
Medford, Or., U.S. 202 42.19 N 122.52 W
Medford, Wi., U.S. 190 45.08 N 90.20 W
Medford Farms 285 39.52 N 74.45 W
Medford Lakes 285 39.51 N 74.48 W
Medfra 180 63.06 N 154.44 W
Medgidia 38 44.15 N 28.16 E
Medgyes → Mediaș 38 46.10 N 24.21 E
Medi 154 5.04 N 30.44 E
Media 208 39.55 N 75.23 W
Mediapolis 190 41.00 N 91.09 W
Mediaș 38 46.10 N 24.21 E
Medical Lake 202 47.34 N 117.40 W
Medicina 66 44.28 N 11.38 E
Medicine Bow 200 41.53 N 106.12 W
Medicine Bow ≃ 200 42.00 N 106.40 W
Medicine Bow Mountains ⋏ 200 41.10 N 106.10 W
Medicine Bow Peak ∧ 200 41.21 N 106.19 W
Medicine Creek ≃, Mo., U.S. 194 39.43 N 93.24 W
Medicine Creek ≃, Ne., U.S. 198 40.17 N 100.10 W
Medicine Creek ≃, S.D., U.S. 198 44.06 N 99.42 W
Medicine Hat 184 50.03 N 110.40 W
Medicine Knoll Creek ≃ 198 44.19 N 100.05 W
Medicine Lake 198 48.30 N 104.30 W
Medicine Lake ⊜ 198 48.28 N 104.24 W
Medicine Lodge 198 37.16 N 98.34 W
Medicine Lodge ≃ 196 36.49 N 98.20 W
Medicine Rocks State Park ♠ 198 46.01 N 104.35 W
Medina → Al-Madīnah, Ar. Su. 128 24.28 N 39.36 E
Medina, Bra. 255 16.15 S 41.29 W
Medina, Pil. 116 8.55 N 125.01 E
Medina, N.Y., U.S. 210 43.13 N 78.23 W
Medina, N.D., U.S. 198 46.53 N 99.17 W
Medina, Oh., U.S. 214 41.08 N 81.51 W
Medina, Tx., U.S. 196 29.48 N 99.15 W
Medina, Wa., U.S. 224 47.37 N 122.13 W
Medina □[6] 214 41.08 N 81.52 W
Medina ≃ 196 29.12 N 98.20 W
Medinaceli 34 41.10 N 2.26 W
Medina del Campo 34 41.18 N 4.55 W
Medina de Ríoseco 34 41.53 N 5.02 W
Médina Gonasse 150 13.08 N 13.45 W
Medinah 278 41.59 N 88.01 W
Medina Lake ⊜[1] 196 29.35 N 98.58 W
Médina Sabak 150 13.36 N 15.35 W
Medina-Sidonia 34 36.27 N 5.55 W
Medinat al-Faiyum → Al-Fayyūm 142 29.19 N 30.50 E
Medininkai 76 54.32 N 25.40 E
Medinīpur 126 22.26 N 87.20 E
Medino 164 9.40 S 149.40 E
Medio, Arroyo del ≃ 258 33.49 S 57.43 W
Medio, Punta > 252 27.07 S 70.57 W
Medio Creek ≃ 196 28.19 N 97.19 W
Mediterranean Sea ⩧[2] 10 35.00 N 20.00 E
Mediterraneo, Mare → Mediterranean Sea ⩧[2] 10 35.00 N 20.00 E
Medjana 34 36.08 N 4.41 E
Medje 154 2.25 N 27.18 E
Medjerda, Monts de la ⋏ 36 36.35 N 8.15 E
Medkovec 38 43.37 N 23.10 E
Mednogorsk 86 51.24 N 57.37 E
Mednoje 76 56.56 N 35.29 E
Mednyj, ostrov I 74 54.45 N 167.35 E
Médoc ◆[1] 32 45.20 N 1.00 W
Mêdog 120 29.20 N 95.15 E
Medolla 64 44.51 N 11.04 E
Medora, Il., U.S. 219 39.11 N 90.09 W
Medora, In., U.S. 218 38.49 N 86.10 W
Medora, N.D., U.S. 198 46.54 N 103.31 W
Médouneu 152 0.57 N 10.47 E
Medow 54 53.50 N 13.32 E
Medstead, Sk., Can. 184 53.19 N 108.02 W
Medstead, Eng., U.K. 42 51.08 N 1.04 W
Medua 126 22.38 N 90.44 E
Meductic 186 46.00 N 67.29 W
Medulla 220 27.58 N 81.58 W
Međumurje ◆[1] 61 46.25 N 16.30 E
Meduna ≃ 64 45.49 N 12.34 E
Medveđa 38 42.50 N 21.35 E
Medvedevo, Ross. 76 60.02 N 43.01 E
Medvedevo, Ross. 80 56.37 N 47.47 E
Medvedevo, Ross. 86 60.37 N 77.21 E
Medvedevskoje 76 58.58 N 35.58 E
Medvedica ≃, Ross. 76 57.05 N 37.32 E
Medvedica ≃, Ross. 80 49.35 N 42.41 E
Medvedickij 80 50.47 N 44.43 E
Medvědí hora ∧ 60 48.59 N 13.25 E
Medvedkovo ◆[8] 265b 55.53 N 37.38 E
Medvedok 80 57.23 N 50.05 E
Medvedovskaja 78 45.27 N 39.01 E
Medvenka, Ross. 78 51.26 N 36.07 E
Medvenka, Ross. 82 54.15 N 37.42 E
Medvežij, ostrov I 89 54.41 N 136.18 E
Medvežinka 83 48.10 N 39.31 E
Medvežje, ozero ⊜ 86 55.07 N 68.00 E
Medvežjegorsk 24 62.55 N 34.23 E
Medvežji ostrova II 74 70.52 N 161.26 E
Medvežji ozera ⊜ 265b 55.52 N 38.00 E
Medvežji Oz'ora 265b 55.52 N 37.59 E
Medvežskaja 24 64.57 N 57.34 E
Medviagalis ∧[2] 76 55.38 N 22.45 E
Medvin 78 49.23 N 30.47 E
Medv'onka ≃ 265b 55.44 N 37.12 E
Medway, Ma., U.S. 207 42.08 N 71.23 W
Medway, Oh., U.S. 218 39.53 N 83.59 W
Medway □[8] 260 51.24 N 0.31 E
Medway ≃, N.S., Can. 186 44.08 N 64.36 W
Medway ≃, Eng., U.K. 42 51.27 N 0.44 E
Medyn' 82 54.58 N 35.52 E
Medynka ≃ 82 54.44 N 36.02 E
Medynskij Zavorot, mys > 24 68.58 N 59.17 E
Medžibož 78 49.26 N 27.25 E
Medzilaborce 30 49.16 N 21.55 E
Meeberrie 162 26.58 S 115.58 E
Meekatharra 162 26.36 S 118.29 E
Meeker, Co., U.S. 200 40.02 N 107.54 W
Meeker, Oh., U.S. 214 40.39 N 83.18 W
Meeks Bay 226 39.02 N 120.08 W
Meelpaeg Lake ⊜[1] 186 48.16 N 56.35 W
Meenaar 168a 31.38 S 116.53 E
Meentheena 162 21.17 S 120.28 E
Meer 56 51.27 N 4.44 E
Meeralpen → Maritime Alps ⋏ 62 44.15 N 7.10 E
Meerane 54 50.51 N 12.28 E
Meerbeck 263 51.28 N 6.39 E
Meerbeke 50 50.50 N 4.02 E
Meerbusch 56 51.15 N 6.41 E
Meerhout 56 51.08 N 5.05 E
Meerhusener Moor ◆[3] 52 53.35 N 7.30 E
Meerkerk 52 51.55 N 5.00 E
Meerle 52 51.28 N 4.48 E
Meersburg 58 47.41 N 9.16 E
Meerssen 56 50.53 N 5.45 E
Meerut 124 28.59 N 77.42 E
Meese ≃ 42 52.40 N 2.39 W
Meeteetse 202 44.09 N 108.52 W
Mega, Indon. 164 0.41 S 131.53 E
Mega, Ityo. 144 4.07 N 38.16 E
Mega, Pulau I 112 4.00 S 101.02 E
Megalo 144 6.55 N 41.48 E
Megálon Khoríon 38 36.27 N 27.21 E
Megalópolis 38 37.24 N 22.08 E
Meganom, mys > 78 44.48 N 35.05 E
Mégantic □[6] 206 46.10 N 71.30 W
Mégantic, Lac ⊜ 188 45.32 N 70.53 W
Mégantic, Mont ∧ 206 45.28 N 71.09 W
Mégara 38 38.01 N 23.21 E
Megargel 196 33.27 N 98.56 W
Mégaron, Kólpos c 267c 37.56 N 23.20 E
Megaruma ≃ 154 13.28 S 40.32 E
Megasini ∧ 126 21.38 N 86.21 E
Meget 88 52.24 N 104.03 E
Megève 62 45.52 N 6.37 E
Mégevette 58 46.12 N 6.30 E
Megezez ∧ 144 9.17 N 39.32 E
Megget Reservoir ⊜[1] 46 55.29 N 3.17 W
Meghālaya □[3] 120 25.30 N 91.15 E
Meghna ≃ 120 22.50 N 90.50 E
Megi-jima I 96 34.24 N 134.03 E
Mégiscane ≃ 190 48.29 N 77.08 W
Mégiscane, Lac ⊜ 190 48.35 N 75.55 W
Meglino, ozero ⊜ 76 58.25 N 35.07 E
Megra, Ross. 24 66.09 N 41.37 E
Megra, Ross. 76 60.10 N 37.13 E
Megri 84 38.56 N 46.16 E
Meguro ◆[8] 268 35.38 N 139.42 E
Meguro ≃ 268 35.37 N 139.45 E
Mehadia 38 44.55 N 22.22 E
Méhaigne ≃ 56 50.32 N 5.13 E
Mehaïguene, Oued V 148 32.15 N 2.59 E
Mehakit 112 2.51 S 115.57 E
Mehar 120 27.11 N 67.49 E
Meharry, Mount ∧ 162 22.59 S 118.35 E
Mehdia 148 35.26 N 1.40 E
Mehede 40 60.27 N 17.24 E
Mehedinți □[6] 38 44.30 N 22.50 E
Meheisa 140 19.37 N 32.57 E
Mehekar 122 20.09 N 76.34 E
Mehendiganj 126 22.49 N 90.32 E
Meherpur 124 23.46 N 88.38 E
Meherrin ≃ 192 36.26 N 76.57 W
Mehetia I 14 17.52 S 148.03 W
Mehidpur 120 23.49 N 75.40 E
Mehikoorma 76 58.14 N 27.28 E
Mehlteuer 54 50.32 N 12.02 E
Mehlville 219 38.30 N 90.19 W
Mehnagar 124 25.53 N 83.07 E
Mehndāwal 124 26.59 N 83.07 E
Mehoopany 210 41.34 N 76.04 W
Mehoopany Creek ≃ 210 41.34 N 76.03 W
Mehpālpur ◆[8] 272a 28.33 N 77.08 E
Mehrābād 128 36.53 N 47.55 E
Mehrābād ◆[8] 267d 35.40 N 51.20 E
Mehram Nagar ◆[8] 272a 28.34 N 77.07 E
Mehrān 128 33.07 N 46.10 E
Mehrān ≃ 128 26.52 N 55.24 E
Mehring 56 49.48 N 6.49 E
Mehrīz 128 31.35 N 54.28 E
Mehrow 264a 52.34 N 13.37 E
Mehrum 263 51.35 N 6.37 E
Mè-hsa-tè 110 19.33 N 97.38 E
Mehtarlām 120 34.39 N 70.10 E
Mehun-sur-Yèvre 50 47.09 N 2.13 E
Mei ≃, Zhg. 100 24.24 N 116.34 E
Mei ≃, Zhg. 100 26.00 N 115.23 E
Mei ≃, Zhg. 105 39.21 N 117.50 E
Meia Meia 154 5.49 S 35.48 E
Meia Ponte, Rio da ≃ 255 18.32 S 49.36 W
Meichang 105 39.22 N 117.10 E
Meichuan 100 30.10 N 115.36 E
Meicun, Zhg. 100 25.30 N 116.56 E
Meicun, Zhg. 106 30.22 N 119.01 E
Meicun, Zhg. 106 30.40 N 119.04 E
Meicun, Zhg. 106 31.33 N 120.24 E
Meide 263 51.11 N 6.55 E
Meiderich ◆[8] 263 51.28 N 6.46 E
Meidling ◆[8] 264b 48.11 N 16.20 E
Meierij ◆[1] 52 51.35 N 5.40 E
Meierkaisong 120 30.54 N 84.31 E
Meiersberg 263 51.17 N 6.57 E
Meig ≃ 46 57.34 N 4.41 W
Meiganga 152 6.31 N 14.11 E
Meigle 46 56.35 N 3.09 W
Meigs 192 31.04 N 84.05 W
Meigs Field ⊠ 278 41.51 N 87.36 W
Meihsien → Meixian 100 24.21 N 116.08 E
Meihua 100 26.02 N 119.40 E
Meihuajie 100 25.14 N 113.05 E
Meijel 52 51.21 N 5.53 E
Meijino-Mori-Minō-kokutei-kōen ♠ 94 34.51 N 135.29 E
Meiji Shrine ʋ[1] 268 35.41 N 139.42 E
Meikeng 100 23.59 N 114.05 E
Meikle Millyea ∧ 44 55.07 N 4.19 W
Meikle Says Law ∧ 46 55.55 N 2.40 W
Meiktila 110 20.52 N 95.52 E
Meila 54 51.09 N 13.13 E
Meilen 58 47.16 N 8.38 E
Meili 106 31.42 N 120.53 E
Meilie 100 26.18 N 117.38 E
Meilin, Zhg. 100 23.18 N 115.58 E
Meilin, Zhg. 106 30.35 N 119.04 E
Meillerie 58 46.24 N 6.43 E
Meilong 100 22.56 N 115.17 E
Meilunyingzi 104 42.18 N 122.10 E
Meina 62 45.47 N 8.32 E
Meine 52 52.23 N 10.32 E
Meiners Oaks 228 34.26 N 119.17 W
Meinerzhagen 56 51.06 N 7.38 E
Meiningen 54 50.34 N 10.25 E
Meinung 100 22.54 N 120.32 E
Meio, Ilha do I 287a 23.02 S 43.17 W
Meiringen 58 46.43 N 8.12 E
Meisburg 56 50.06 N 6.41 E
Meisenheim 56 49.42 N 7.40 E
Meishan, Zhg. 106 31.06 N 119.43 E
Meishan, Zhg. 107 30.02 N 103.49 E
Meissen 54 51.10 N 13.28 E
Meissendorf 52 52.43 N 9.50 E
Meiss Lake ⊜ 204 41.52 N 122.04 W
Meissner ∧ 56 51.12 N 9.50 E
Meitan 102 27.46 N 107.35 E
Meitian 100 25.21 N 112.47 E
Meitingen 56 48.32 N 10.50 E
Meiwa 94 34.33 N 136.39 E
Meixi 106 30.48 N 119.45 E
Meixian, Zhg. 100 24.21 N 116.08 E
Meixian, Zhg. 100 28.52 N 113.38 E
Meiyao 89 49.37 N 124.30 E
Meiyino 140 6.12 N 34.40 E
Meizhai 102 25.30 N 108.50 E
Meizhou 100 23.50 N 117.20 E
Meizhou Dao I 100 25.06 N 119.07 E
Meizhou Wan c 100 25.06 N 119.00 E
Meizhu 106 31.16 N 119.13 E
Meječkyn, ostrov I 180 65.26 N 178.00 W
Mejerda, Oued (Oued Medjerda) ≃ 36 37.07 N 10.13 E
Mejez el Bab 148 36.39 N 9.37 E
Mejia 126 23.34 N 87.06 E
Mejicanos 236 13.43 N 89.12 W
Mejillones 252 23.06 S 70.27 W
Mejillones, Península >[1] 252 23.17 S 70.34 W
Mejillones del Sur, Bahía de c 252 23.03 S 70.27 W
Mejnypil'gyno 74 62.32 N 177.02 E
Mejorada del Campo 266a 40.24 N 3.29 W
Meka 162 27.26 S 116.48 E
Mekada, Garaet el ≋ 36 36.48 N 8.00 E
Mékambo 152 1.01 N 13.56 E
Mekele 144 13.33 N 39.30 E
Mekerra, Oued ≃ 34 35.00 N 0.45 W
Mekhé 150 15.07 N 16.38 W
Mekhliganj 124 26.21 N 88.55 E
Mekhtar 120 30.28 N 69.22 E
Mékinac ≃ 206 46.51 N 72.46 W
Mekka → Makkah 144 21.27 N 39.49 E
Meknès 148 33.53 N 5.37 W
Meknès □[4] 148 33.50 N 5.30 W
Mekong ≃ 12 10.33 N 105.24 E
Mekongga, Gunung ∧ 112 3.38 S 121.15 E
Mekongga, Pegunungan ⋏ 112 3.35 S 121.15 E
Mékôngk → Mekong ≃ 12 10.33 N 105.24 E
Mekoryuk 180 60.23 N 166.12 W
Mékrou ≃ 150 12.24 N 2.49 E
Mel 64 46.04 N 12.05 E
Melado ≃ 252 35.43 S 71.05 W
Melah, Oued el V, Alg. 148 28.21 N 6.00 E
Melah, Oued el V, Tun. 148 34.03 N 8.06 E
Melah, Sebkhet el ⊜ 148 29.05 N 1.10 W
Melaka 114 2.12 N 102.15 E
Melaka □[3] 114 2.15 N 102.15 E
Melalap 112 5.14 N 116.00 E
Melandro ≃ 68 40.37 N 15.27 E
Melanesia II 14 13.00 S 164.00 E
Melanesian Basin ✦[1] 14 0.05 N 160.35 E
Melappālaiyam 122 8.42 N 77.43 E
Melara 64 45.03 N 11.11 E
Melaune 54 51.11 N 14.44 E
Melawi ≃ 112 0.05 N 111.29 E
Melayu ≃ 271c 1.27 N 103.42 E
Melbern 216 41.28 N 84.39 W
Melbost 46 58.15 N 6.22 W
Melbourn 42 52.05 N 0.01 E
Melbourne, Austl. 169 37.49 S 144.58 E
Melbourne, Austl. 274b 37.49 S 144.58 E
Melbourne, On., Can. 214 42.49 N 81.33 W
Melbourne, Eng., U.K. 42 52.49 N 1.25 W
Melbourne, Ar., U.S. 194 36.03 N 91.54 W
Melbourne, Fl., U.S. 220 28.04 N 80.36 W
Melbourne, Ia., U.S. 190 41.56 N 93.06 W
Melbourne, University of ʋ[2] 274b 37.48 S 144.58 E
Melbourne Beach 220 28.04 N 80.33 W
Melbourne Island I 176 68.30 N 104.45 W
Melbourne Regional Airport ⊠ 220 28.06 N 80.38 W
Mel'cany 80 54.28 N 44.43 E
Melcher 190 41.13 N 93.14 W
Melchor, Isla I 254 45.08 S 73.57 W
Melchor Múzquiz 232 27.53 N 101.31 W
Melchor Ocampo 196 26.03 N 99.33 W
Melchor Romero ◆[8] 258 34.56 S 58.03 W
Melchtal 58 46.50 N 8.17 E
Melcroft 214 40.03 N 79.24 W
Melderskin ∧ 26 60.01 N 6.05 E
Meldola 66 44.07 N 12.05 E
Meldorf 30 54.05 N 9.05 E
Meldrum Bay 190 45.56 N 83.07 W
Meldrum Creek 182 52.07 N 122.20 W
Mélé, Centraf. 146 9.46 N 21.33 E
Mele, India 272b 22.49 N 88.09 E
Mele, It. 62 44.27 N 8.45 E
Mélé, Baie c 175f 17.43 S 168.15 E
Mele, Capo > 62 43.57 N 8.10 E
Melechovo 80 56.17 N 41.17 E
Meleck 86 57.25 N 90.12 E
Meleden 144 10.25 N 49.51 E
Melegnano 62 45.21 N 9.19 E
Meleješt' 38 46.59 N 29.33 E
Melekeok 175b 7.29 N 134.38 E
Melekess → Dimitrovgrad 80 54.14 N 49.39 E
Melela ≃ 154 17.04 S 38.36 E
Melena del Sur 240p 22.47 N 82.09 W
Melendiz Dağı ∧ 130 38.07 N 34.25 E
Melendugno 68 40.16 N 18.20 E
Melenki 80 55.20 N 41.38 E
Meleškoviči 78 51.56 N 28.59 E
Meleuz 86 52.58 N 55.55 E
Mélèzes, Rivière aux ≃ 176 57.40 N 69.29 W
Melfa 208 37.39 N 75.45 W
Melfa ≃ 66 41.30 N 13.35 E
Melfi, It. 68 41.00 N 15.39 E
Melfi, Tchad 146 11.04 N 17.56 E
Melfort, Sk., Can. 184 52.52 N 104.36 W
Melfort, Zimb. 154 17.59 S 31.19 E
Melfort, Loch c 46 56.15 N 5.31 W
Melgaço, Bra. 250 1.47 S 50.44 W
Melgaço, Port. 34 42.07 N 8.16 W
Melgar 246 4.12 N 74.39 W
Melghir, Chott ⊜ 148 34.20 N 6.20 E
Mel'guny 80 52.09 N 40.52 E
Melhus 26 63.17 N 10.16 E
Meli ≃ 150 8.16 N 10.42 W
Meliane, Oued ≃ 36 36.46 N 10.18 E
Meliau 112 0.08 S 110.18 E
Meliau, Gunong ∧ 116 5.50 N 117.14 E
Melibocus ∧ 56 49.42 N 8.40 E
Melichovo, Ross. 78 50.42 N 36.48 E
Melichovo, Ross. 82 55.07 N 37.39 E
Melicuccà 68 38.18 N 15.53 E
Melide, Esp. 34 42.55 N 8.00 W
Melide, Schw. 58 45.57 N 8.57 E
Meligalás 38 37.13 N 21.59 E
Melilla 34 35.19 N 2.58 W
Melilli 70 37.11 N 15.07 E
Melimoyu, Cerro ∧ 254 44.05 S 72.52 W
Melincué 252 33.39 S 61.27 W
Melipilla 252 33.42 S 71.13 W
Mélisey 58 47.45 N 6.35 E
Melissa 68 39.18 N 17.01 E
Melissano 68 39.58 N 18.07 E
Melíssia 267c 38.03 N 23.50 E
Melita 184 49.16 N 101.00 W
Melito di Porto Salvo 68 37.55 N 15.47 E
Melitopol' 78 46.50 N 35.22 E
Melívoia 38 39.45 N 22.48 E
Melk 61 48.14 N 15.20 E
Melk ≃ 61 48.14 N 15.19 E
Melk ʋ[1] 61 48.14 N 15.20 E
Melka Teka 144 6.05 N 43.08 E
Melkbosstrand 158 33.43 S 18.27 E
Melksham 42 51.23 N 2.09 W
Mella ≃ 64 45.13 N 10.13 E
Mellansel 26 63.26 N 18.19 E
Mellau 58 47.21 N 9.53 E
Melle, Dtsch. 52 52.12 N 8.20 E
Melle, Fr. 32 46.13 N 0.09 W
Melleck 64 47.40 N 12.45 E
Mellègue, Oued ≃ 36 36.32 N 8.51 E
Mellen 190 46.19 N 90.39 W
Mellendorf 52 52.33 N 9.43 E
Mellenville 210 42.15 N 73.40 W
Mellerud 26 58.42 N 12.28 E
Mellette 198 45.09 N 98.29 W
Mellier ≃ 56 49.43 N 5.32 E
Melling 262 53.30 N 2.56 W
Mellingen 54 50.56 N 11.23 E
Mellish Reef I[1] 160 17.25 S 155.50 E
Mellish Rise ✦[3] 14 17.00 S 156.00 E
Mellit 140 14.08 N 25.33 E
Mellone, Monte ∧[2] 267a 41.50 N 12.43 E
Mellong Range ⋏ 170 33.06 S 150.43 E
Mellon Udrigle 46 57.55 N 5.39 W
Mellor 262 53.46 N 2.32 W

Symbols in the index entries represent the broad categories identified in the key at the right. Symbols with superior numbers (⋏[1]) identify subcategories (see complete key on page *I · 1).*

Symbole im Register stellen die rechts im Schlüssel erklärten Kategorien dar. Symbole mit hochgestellten Ziffern (⋏[1]) bezeichnen Unterabteilungen einer Kategorie (vgl. vollständiger Schlüssel auf Seite *I · 1).*

Los símbolos incluídos en el texto del índice representan las grandes categorías identificadas con la clave a la derecha. Los símbolos con numeros en su parte superior (⋏[1]) identifican las subcategorías (véase la clave completa en la página *I · 1).*

Les symboles de l'index représentent les catégories indiquées dans la légende à droite. Les symboles suivis d'un indice (⋏[1]) représentent des sous-catégories (voir légende complète à la page *I · 1).*

Os símbolos incluídos no texto do índice representam as grandes categorias identificadas com a chave à direita. Os símbolos com números em sua parte superior (⋏[1]) identificam as subcategorias (veja-se a chave completa à página *I · 1).*

	English	Deutsch	Español	Français	Português
∧	Mountain	Berg	Montaña	Montagne	Montanha
⋏	Mountains	Gebirge	Montañas	Montagnes	Montanhas
)(	Pass	Paß	Paso	Col	Passo
V	Valley, Canyon	Tal, Cañon	Valle, Cañón	Vallée, Canyon	Vale, Canhão
≚	Plain	Ebene	Llano	Plaine	Planície
>	Cape	Kap	Cabo	Cap	Cabo
I	Island	Insel	Isla	Île	Ilha
II	Islands	Inseln	Islas	Îles	Ilhas
⊥	Other Topographic Features	Andere Topographische Objekte	Otros Elementos Topográficos	Autres données topographiques	Outros acidentes topográficos

ESPAÑOL — Nombre | Página | Lat.°′ | Long.°′ W = Oeste
FRANÇAIS — Nom | Page | Lat.°′ | Long.°′ W = Ouest
PORTUGUÊS — Nome | Página | Lat.°′ | Long.°′ W = Oeste

Mellor Brook 262 53.47 N 2.33 W
Mellösa 40 59.06 N 16.33 E
Mellrichstadt 56 50.26 N 10.18 E
Mellum I 52 53.40 N 8.10 E
Melmerby 44 54.44 N 2.35 W
Melmore 214 41.02 N 83.07 W
Melmoth 158 28.38 S 31.24 E
Mel'nica-Podol'skaja 78 48.37 N 26.10 E
Mělník 54 50.20 N 14.29 E
Mel'nikovo, Ross. 26 61.05 N 29.22 E
Mel'nikovo, Ross. 86 56.34 N 84.05 E
Mel'nikovo, Taj. 85 40.19 N 70.19 E
Melo 252 32.22 S 54.11 W
Melo ≃ 248 21.27 S 57.52 W
Melo, Ilha de I 150 11.02 N 15.13 W
Melocheville 206 45.19 N 73.56 W
Meloco 154 13.25 S 39.08 E
Melolo 115b 9.53 S 120.40 E
Melolo ≃ 115b 9.52 S 120.41 E
Melong 152 5.07 N 9.57 E
Melos → Mílos I 38 36.41 N 24.15 E
Melovaja ≃ 83 49.23 N 40.16 E
Melovatka 83 49.21 N 38.11 E
Melovoje 83 49.22 N 40.06 E
Melovoj Syrt ∧ 80 52.15 N 52.35 E
Melozitna ≃ 180 64.46 N 155.29 W
Melrose, Austl. 162 27.56 S 121.19 E
Melrose, Austl. 166 32.42 S 146.58 E
Melrose, Scot., U.K. 46 55.36 N 2.44 W
Melrose, Ma., U.S. 207 42.27 N 71.04 W
Melrose, Mn., U.S. 198 45.40 N 94.48 W
Melrose, N.M., U.S. 196 34.25 N 103.37 W
Melrose, N.Y., U.S. 210 42.50 N 73.37 W
Melrose, Oh., U.S. 216 41.05 N 84.25 W
Melrose, Wi., U.S. 190 44.07 N 90.59 W
Melrose ◆[8] 276 40.49 N 73.55 W
Melrose Abbey ʋ[1] 46 55.37 N 2.45 W
Melrose Park, Fl., U.S. 220 26.06 N 80.12 W
Melrose Park, Il., U.S. 216 41.54 N 87.51 W
Melrose Park, N.Y., U.S. 212 42.54 N 76.32 W
Melrose Park, Pa., U.S. 285 40.04 N 75.08 W
Mels 58 47.03 N 9.25 E
Melstone 202 46.35 N 107.52 W
Melsungen 56 51.08 N 9.32 E
Meltaus 24 66.54 N 25.22 E
Meltham, Eng., U.K. 44 53.35 N 1.51 W
Meltham, Eng., U.K. 262 53.36 N 1.51 W
Melton, Austl. 168b 34.05 S 137.59 E
Melton, Austl. 169 37.41 S 144.35 E
Melton Constable 42 52.53 N 1.01 E
Melton Hill Lake ⊜[1] 192 36.00 N 84.15 W
Melton Mowbray 42 52.46 N 0.53 W
Melton Reservoir ⊜[1] 169 37.43 S 144.32 E
Melúa 246 3.55 N 72.50 W
Meluan 112 1.52 N 111.56 E
Meluco 154 12.36 S 39.38 E
Melúli ≃ 154 16.28 S 39.44 E
Melun, Fr. 50 48.32 N 2.40 E
Melun, Mya. 110 20.14 N 93.24 E
Melunga 152 17.16 S 16.24 E
Melūr 122 10.03 N 78.20 E
Melvaig 46 57.48 N 5.49 W
Melvern 198 38.30 N 95.38 W
Melvern Lake ⊜[1] 198 38.30 N 95.50 W
Melvich 46 58.33 N 3.55 W
Melville, Austl. 168a 32.03 S 115.49 E
Melville, Sk., Can. 184 50.55 N 102.48 W
Melville, La., U.S. 194 30.41 N 91.44 W
Melville, N.Y., U.S. 276 40.47 N 73.24 W
Melville ◆[8] 273d 26.11 S 28.00 E
Melville, Cape ≻, Austl. 164 14.11 S 144.30 E
Melville, Cape ≻, Pil. 116 7.49 N 117.01 E
Melville, Détroit de → Viscount Melville Sound ʯ 176 74.10 N 108.00 W
Melville, Lake ⊜ 176 53.45 N 59.30 W
Melville Bugt c 16 75.30 N 63.00 W
Melville Hall Airport ⊠ 240d 15.33 N 61.18 W
Melville Hills ↗[2] 180 69.15 N 124.00 W
Melville Island I, Austl. 164 11.40 S 131.00 E
Melville Island I, N.T., Can. 16 75.15 N 110.00 W
Melville Island Aboriginal Reserve ◆[4] 164 11.40 S 131.00 E
Melville Peninsula ≻[1] 176 68.00 N 84.00 W
Melville Sound ʯ, N.T., Can. 176 68.05 N 107.30 W
Melville Sound ʯ, On., Can. 212 44.57 N 81.05 W
Melvin, Il., U.S. 216 40.34 N 88.15 W
Melvin, Ky., U.S. 192 37.21 N 82.41 W
Melvin, Tx., U.S. 196 31.13 N 99.35 W
Melvin, Lough ⊜ 48 54.26 N 8.10 W
Melvindale 214 42.16 N 83.10 W
Melvin Lake ⊜ 184 57.08 N 100.15 W
Melyana 148 36.15 N 2.15 E
Mélykút 30 46.13 N 19.24 E
Melzo 62 45.30 N 9.25 E
Memala 112 1.44 S 112.36 E
Mêmar Co ⊜ 120 34.15 N 82.20 E
Memāri 126 23.12 N 88.07 E
Memba 154 14.11 S 40.30 E
Membalong 112 3.09 S 107.38 E
Memboro 115b 9.22 S 119.32 E
Membre 56 49.52 N 4.54 E
Même ≃ 50 48.11 N 0.39 E
Memel → Klaipėda, Liet. 76 55.43 N 21.07 E
Memel, S. Afr. 158 27.43 S 29.30 E
Memel → Nemunas ≃ 76 55.18 N 21.23 E
Mēmele ≃ 76 56.24 N 24.10 E
Memewin, Lac ⊜ 190 46.29 N 78.42 W
Memmert I 52 53.39 N 6.53 E
Memmingen 58 47.59 N 10.11 E
Memo ≃ 246 9.16 N 66.40 W
Memori, Tanjung ≻ 164 0.52 S 134.08 E
Memorial Bridge ◆[5] 269a 13.44 N 100.30 E
Memorial Stadium ♦ 284b 39.20 N 76.36 W
Mémót 110 11.49 N 106.11 E
Mempawah 112 0.22 N 108.58 E
Memphis, Fl., U.S. 220 27.32 N 82.33 W
Memphis, In., U.S. 218 38.29 N 85.45 W
Memphis, Mi., U.S. 214 42.54 N 82.46 W
Memphis, Mo., U.S. 194 40.27 N 92.10 W
Memphis, Tn., U.S. 194 35.08 N 90.02 W
Memphis, Tx., U.S. 196 34.43 N 100.32 W
Memphis → Mīt Ruhaynah ⊥ 142 29.51 N 31.15 E
Memphis Naval Air Station ■ 194 35.21 N 89.52 W
Memphremagog, Lake ⊜ 206 45.05 N 72.15 W
Memsie 46 57.39 N 2.02 W
Mena, Ityo. 144 6.25 N 39.51 E
Mena, Ukr. 78 51.31 N 32.13 E
Mena, Ar., U.S. 194 34.35 N 94.14 W
Menado → Manado 112 1.29 N 124.51 E
Menaggio 58 46.01 N 9.14 E
Menahga 198 46.45 N 95.06 W
Menai 274a 34.01 S 151.01 E
Menai Bridge 44 53.14 N 4.10 W
Menai Strait ʯ 44 53.12 N 4.12 W
Ménaka 150 15.55 N 2.24 E
Menaldum 52 53.12 N 5.39 E
Menan 202 43.43 N 111.59 W
Menands 210 42.41 N 73.43 W
Menangina 162 29.50 S 121.54 E
Menantico Creek ≃ 208 39.20 N 75.00 W
Menarandra ≃ 157b 25.17 S 44.30 E
Menard 196 30.55 N 99.47 W
Menard □[6] 219 40.01 N 89.51 W
Menard Creek ≃ 222 30.29 N 94.50 W
Menars 50 47.38 N 1.24 E
Menasha 190 44.12 N 88.26 W
Menate 112 0.14 S 113.02 E
Menawashei 140 12.40 N 24.59 E
Menchang 105 38.54 N 117.01 E
Menčikury 78 47.04 N 34.48 E
Mencué 254 40.25 S 69.38 W
Mend 89 43.40 N 123.08 E
Mendanau, Pulau I 112 2.51 S 107.26 E
Mendarik, Pulau I 112 1.18 N 107.02 E
Mendatai 102 38.51 N 94.39 E
Mendatica 62 44.05 N 7.49 E
Mendawai 112 2.59 S 113.16 E
Mendawai ≃ 112 3.17 S 113.21 E
Mendaya 115a 8.23 S 114.42 E
Mende 32 44.30 N 3.30 E
Mendebo ↗ 144 6.50 N 39.40 E
Mendel' ≃ 86 58.13 N 90.08 E
Mendelejevsk 80 55.54 N 52.20 E
Menden 56 51.26 N 7.47 E
Menden ◆[8] 263 51.24 N 6.54 E
Mendenhall, Ms., U.S. 194 31.57 N 89.52 W
Mendenhall, Pa., U.S. 285 39.51 N 75.38 W
Mendenhall, Cape ≻ 180 59.51 N 166.15 W
Mendes 256 22.32 S 43.44 W
Méndez 232 25.07 N 98.34 W
Mendez-Nuñez 116 14.08 N 120.54 E
Mendham 210 40.46 N 74.36 W
Mendi, Ityo. 144 9.50 N 35.06 E
Mendi, Pap. N. Gui. 164 6.10 S 143.40 E
Mendig 56 50.21 N 7.15 E
Mendip Hills ↗[2] 42 51.15 N 2.40 W
Mendlesham 42 52.16 N 1.05 E
Mendocino 204 39.18 N 123.47 W
Mendocino, Cape ≻ 204 40.25 N 124.25 W
Mendocino Fracture Zone ✣ 16 40.00 N 145.00 W
Mendola ≃ 70 37.44 N 13.32 E
Mendon, Il., U.S. 219 40.05 N 91.17 W
Mendon, Ma., U.S. 207 42.06 N 71.33 W
Mendon, Mi., U.S. 216 42.00 N 85.27 W
Mendon, N.Y., U.S. 210 43.00 N 77.34 W
Mendon, Oh., U.S. 216 40.40 N 84.31 W
Mendon, Pa., U.S. 279b 40.11 N 79.41 W
Mendota, Ca., U.S. 226 36.45 N 120.22 W
Mendota, Il., U.S. 216 41.32 N 89.07 W
Mendota, Lake ⊜ 216 43.05 N 89.25 W
Mendoza, Arg. 252 32.53 S 68.49 W
Mendoza, Perú 248 6.20 S 77.24 W
Mendoza, Ur. 258 34.17 S 56.13 W
Mendoza □[4] 252 34.30 S 68.30 W
Mendoza ≃ 252 32.21 S 68.18 W
Mendoza, Arroyo de ≃ 258 34.21 S 56.18 W
Mendrisio 58 45.52 N 8.59 E
Mend'ukino 82 54.47 N 38.51 E
Mendung 112 0.31 N 103.13 E
Ménéac 32 48.09 N 2.28 W
Mene de Mauroa 246 10.43 N 71.01 W
Mene Grande 246 9.49 N 70.56 W
Menemen 130 38.36 N 27.04 E
Menen 50 50.48 N 3.07 E
Meneng Point ≻ 174b 0.32 S 166.57 E
Menes 115a 6.23 S 105.55 E
Menfi 70 37.36 N 12.58 E
Mengalum, Pulau I 112 6.16 N 115.12 E
Mengban 102 23.08 N 100.19 E
Mengbang 102 21.28 N 101.19 E
Mengcheng 100 33.17 N 116.33 E
Mengchi ≃ 107 29.47 N 104.56 E
Mengcun 98 38.06 N 117.05 E
Mengdapu 104 41.35 N 123.12 E
Mengede ◆[8] 263 51.34 N 7.23 E
Mengeh Jek 120 37.02 N 66.07 E
Mengen, Dtsch. 58 48.03 N 9.20 E
Mengen, Tür. 130 40.56 N 32.04 E
Mengeringhausen 56 51.22 N 8.59 E
Mengersgereuth-Hämmern 54 50.24 N 11.07 E
Menges Mills 208 39.52 N 76.54 W
Menggala 112 4.28 S 105.17 E
Menggu 102 26.34 N 102.57 E
Menggubao 104 42.27 N 122.23 E
Menggudai 102 38.10 N 108.15 E
Menghai 102 22.00 N 100.26 E
Menghe 106 32.03 N 119.47 E
Menghun 102 21.44 N 100.23 E
Mengjiacun 106 31.33 N 118.46 E
Mengjiagang 89 46.22 N 130.40 E
Mengjiatai 104 42.06 N 123.21 E
Mengjiawan 102 38.35 N 109.25 E
Mengjiawopeng 104 41.22 N 121.51 E
Mengjiayuanjia 105 40.52 N 118.08 E
Mengjiazhai 269b 31.18 N 121.19 E
Mengka 102 25.10 N 98.01 E
Mengkibol 114 1.58 N 103.20 E
Mengkuang 114 3.11 N 102.24 E
Menglian 102 22.20 N 99.38 E
Menglinghausen ◆[8] 263 51.28 N 7.25 E
Mengluchang 107 29.19 N 103.35 E
Mengmucun 106 31.59 N 119.01 E
Mengong 152 2.56 N 11.25 E
Mengqigou 104 42.00 N 121.08 E
Mengshan 102 24.07 N 110.33 E
Meng Shan ↗, Zhg. 98 35.44 N 117.45 E
Meng Shan ↗, Zhg. 104 41.50 N 121.10 E
Mengtong 107 30.44 N 105.53 E
Mengulek, gora ∧ 86 50.58 N 89.30 E
Mengwang 102 22.26 N 100.34 E
Mengyin 98 35.45 N 117.57 E
Mengzhe 102 22.02 N 100.16 E
Mengzhi 102 24.10 N 99.46 E
Mengzi 102 23.22 N 103.20 E
Menihek Lakes ⊜ 176 54.00 N 66.35 W
Ménil-la-Tour 56 48.46 N 5.52 E
Menindee 166 32.24 S 142.26 E
Menindee Lake ⊜ 166 32.21 S 142.20 E
Meningie 166 35.42 S 139.20 E
Menjiaqiangzi 104 42.29 N 121.19 E
Menkoutang 106 31.01 N 119.27 E
Menlo 224 46.37 N 123.38 W
Menlo Park 226 37.27 N 122.10 W
Menlo Park Mall ◆[9] 276 40.32 N 74.20 W
Menlo Park Terrace 276 40.32 N 74.20 W
Mennecy 261 48.34 N 2.26 E
Mennetou-sur-Cher 50 47.16 N 1.53 E
Mennighüffen 52 52.13 N 8.43 E
Menno 198 43.14 N 97.34 W
Meno, Indon. 164 3.52 S 135.31 E
Meno, Ok., U.S. 196 36.23 N 98.10 W
Menominee 190 45.06 N 87.36 W
Menominee ≃ 190 45.05 N 87.36 W
Menominee Indian Reservation ◆[4] 190 45.00 N 88.45 W
Menomonee ≃ 216 43.02 N 87.54 W
Menomonee Falls 216 43.10 N 88.07 W
Menomonie 190 44.52 N 91.55 W
Menongue 152 14.36 S 17.48 E
Menor, Mar c 34 37.43 N 0.48 W
Menorca I 34 40.00 N 4.00 E
Mens 62 44.49 N 5.45 E
Menslage 52 52.41 N 7.49 E
Menston 44 53.53 N 1.44 W
Menstrup 41 55.13 N 11.36 E
Mentana 66 42.02 N 12.38 E
Mentasta Lake 180 62.55 N 143.45 W
Mentasta Mountains ↗ 180 62.40 N 143.07 W
Mentawai, Kepulauan II 108 2.00 S 99.30 E
Mentawai, Selat ʯ 108 1.45 S 100.00 E
Mentekab 114 3.29 N 102.21 E
Menteke, peski ◆[2] 80 47.20 N 50.40 E
Menteng ◆[8] 269e 6.12 S 106.50 E
Menteroda 54 51.18 N 10.33 E
Menthon-Saint-Bernard 62 45.51 N 6.12 E
Menton 62 43.47 N 7.30 E
Mentone, Austl. 274b 37.59 S 145.05 E
Mentone → Menton, Fr. 62 43.47 N 7.30 E
Mentone, Ca., U.S. 228 34.05 N 117.08 W
Mentone, In., U.S. 216 41.10 N 86.02 W
Mentone, Tx., U.S. 196 31.42 N 103.36 W
Mentor, Ky., U.S. 218 38.53 N 84.14 W
Mentor, Oh., U.S. 214 41.39 N 81.20 W
Mentor-on-the-Lake 214 41.42 N 81.21 W
Mentougou 105 39.56 N 116.03 E
Mentzdam ⊜[1] 158 33.10 S 25.09 E
Menucourt 261 49.02 N 1.59 E
Menuma 94 36.13 N 139.23 E
Men'uša 76 58.23 N 30.42 E
Menyamya 164 7.10 S 146.00 E
Menyapa, Gunung ∧ 112 1.05 N 116.05 E
Menyuan 102 37.27 N 101.48 E
Menza ≃ 88 50.14 N 108.38 E
Menzel Bourguiba 148 37.10 N 9.48 E
Menzel Bou Zelfa 36 36.41 N 10.36 E
Menzel Djemil 36 37.14 N 9.55 E
Menzelen 52 51.37 N 6.32 E
Menzelerheide 263 51.37 N 6.31 E
Menzelinsk 80 55.43 N 53.08 E
Menzel Temime 148 36.47 N 10.59 E
Menzenschwand 58 47.49 N 8.04 E
Menzies 162 29.41 S 121.02 E
Menzies, Mount ∧ 9 73.30 S 61.50 E
Menziken 58 47.14 N 8.12 E
Meobbaai c 156 24.25 S 14.34 E
Meola Āgri 272a 28.42 N 77.23 E
Meolo 64 45.37 N 12.27 E
Meon ≃ 42 50.48 N 1.15 W
Meopham 260 51.22 N 0.22 E
Meopham Station 260 51.23 N 0.21 E
Meoqui 232 28.17 N 105.29 W
Meota 184 53.02 N 108.27 W
Méouge ≃ 62 44.16 N 5.50 E
Méounes-lès-Montrieux 62 43.17 N 5.58 E
Mepal 42 52.24 N 0.07 E
Mepisckaro, gora ∧ 84 41.50 N 42.40 E
Meppel 52 52.42 N 6.11 E
Meppen 52 52.41 N 7.17 E
Meqerghane, Sebkha ≡ 148 26.19 N 1.20 E
Meqruur 174q 9.31 N 138.09 E
Mequinenza, Embalse de ⊜[1] 34 41.20 N 0.05 E
Mequon 216 43.13 N 87.59 W
Mer 50 47.42 N 1.30 E
Mera ≃ 58 46.11 N 9.25 E
Merah 112 0.50 N 116.48 E
Merai 164 4.50 S 152.20 E
Meråker 26 63.26 N 11.45 E
Merakurak 115a 6.53 S 111.59 E
Meramangye, Lake ⊜ 162 28.25 S 132.13 E
Merambéllou, Kólpos c 38 35.14 N 25.47 E
Meramec ≃ 194 38.23 N 90.21 W
Meramec Caverns ⊥[5] 219 38.15 N 91.06 W
Meramec State Park ♦ 219 38.14 N 91.05 W
Meran → Merano, It. 64 46.40 N 11.09 E
Meran, Nig. 273a 6.38 N 3.16 E
Meranggau 112 0.12 S 110.17 E
Merangin ≃ 112 2.09 S 102.47 E
Merano (Meran) 64 46.40 N 11.09 E
Merapi, Gunung ∧ 115a 8.03 S 114.15 E
Merapoh 114 4.41 N 101.59 E
Merasheen 186 47.25 N 54.21 W
Merasheen Island I 186 47.30 N 54.15 W
Merate 62 45.42 N 9.25 E
Meratus, Pegunungan ↗ 112 2.45 S 115.40 E
Merauke 164 8.28 S 140.20 E
Merauke ≃ 164 8.30 S 140.24 E
Merbabu, Gunung ∧ 115a 7.27 S 110.26 E
Merbau, Indon. 114 1.07 N 102.33 E
Merbau, Indon. 114 2.16 N 99.50 E
Merbein 166 34.11 S 142.04 E
Merca → Marka 144 1.43 N 44.53 E
Mercaderes 246 1.47 N 77.10 W
Mercantour, Parc National du ♦ 62 44.10 N 7.00 E
Mercāra 122 12.25 N 75.44 E
Mercatale 66 43.15 N 12.08 E
Mercato San Severino 68 40.47 N 14.46 E
Mercato Saraceno 66 43.57 N 12.12 E
Merced 226 37.18 N 120.28 W
Merced □[6] 226 37.15 N 120.40 W
Merced ≃ 226 37.21 N 120.58 W
Merced, Lake ⊜ 282 37.43 N 122.29 W
Merced, North Fork ≃ 226 37.37 N 120.03 W
Merced, South Fork ≃ 226 37.39 N 119.53 W
Merced Airport ⊠ 226 37.17 N 120.31 W
Mercedario, Cerro ∧ 252 31.59 S 70.07 W
Mercedes, Arg. 252 29.12 S 58.05 W
Mercedes, Arg. 252 33.40 S 65.28 W
Mercedes, Arg. 258 34.39 S 59.27 W
Mercedes, Pil. 116 14.07 N 123.01 E
Mercedes, Tx., U.S. 196 26.08 N 97.54 W
Mercedes, Ur. 252 33.16 S 58.01 W
Mercer, N.Z. 172 37.16 S 175.03 E
Mercer, Mo., U.S. 194 40.30 N 93.31 W
Mercer, Oh., U.S. 216 40.40 N 84.35 W
Mercer, Pa., U.S. 214 41.13 N 80.14 W
Mercer, Wi., U.S. 190 46.09 N 90.03 W
Mercer □[6], N.J., U.S. 208 40.13 N 74.45 W
Mercer □[6], Oh., U.S. 216 40.33 N 84.34 W
Mercer □[6], Pa., U.S. 214 41.14 N 80.15 W
Mercer Island 224 47.35 N 122.15 W
Mercersburg 188 39.49 N 77.54 W
Mercerville 208 40.14 N 74.41 W
Mercês, Bra. 256 21.12 S 43.21 W
Mercês, Port. 266c 38.47 N 9.19 W
Merchants Bay c 176 67.10 N 62.50 W
Merchants Millpond ⊜ 208 36.26 N 76.41 W
Merchantville 285 39.56 N 75.04 W
Merchong ≃ 114 3.03 N 103.27 E
Merchtem 50 50.58 N 4.14 E
Mercier (Saint-Philomène) 275a 45.19 N 73.45 W
Mercier, Pont ◆[5] 275a 45.25 N 73.39 W
Mercoal 182 53.10 N 117.05 W
Mercogliano 68 40.55 N 14.44 E
Mercury 204 36.40 N 115.59 W
Mercury Islands II 172 36.35 S 175.55 E
Mercy, Cape ≻ 176 64.53 N 63.32 W
Mercy Bay c 176 74.05 N 119.00 W
Mercy-le-Bas 56 49.23 N 5.45 E
Merdeka Bridge ◆[5] 271c 1.18 N 103.53 E
Méré, Fr. 261 48.47 N 1.49 E
Mere, Eng., U.K. 42 51.06 N 2.16 W
Mere, Eng., U.K. 262 53.20 N 2.25 W
Mere Brow 262 53.40 N 2.53 W
Mereckij 85 43.48 N 74.42 E
Mereclough 262 53.46 N 2.11 W
Meredale 273d 26.17 S 27.59 E
Meredith, Austl. 169 37.51 S 144.04 E
Meredith, N.H., U.S. 188 43.39 N 71.30 W
Meredith, Cape ≻ 254 52.15 S 60.39 W
Meredith, Lake ⊜[1] 196 35.36 N 101.42 W
Meredosia 219 39.50 N 90.34 W
Meredosia Lake ⊜ 219 39.52 N 90.33 W
Mereeg 144 3.46 N 47.18 E
Merefa 78 49.49 N 36.03 E
Méré Lava I 175f 14.25 S 168.03 E
Merelbeke 50 51.00 N 3.45 E
Merenkurkku (Norra Kvarken) ʯ 26 63.36 N 20.43 E
Mereny 38 46.58 N 29.04 E
Merevari ≃ 246 4.28 N 63.57 W
Méréville 50 48.19 N 2.05 E
Merewa 144 7.40 N 37.00 E
Merewether 170 32.57 S 151.46 E
Mereworth 260 51.15 N 0.23 E
Mergenevo 80 49.56 N 51.17 E
Mergozzo 58 45.58 N 8.26 E
Mergui (Myeik) 110 12.26 N 98.36 E
Mergui Archipelago II 110 12.00 N 98.00 E
Merḥavya 132 32.36 N 35.19 E
Meria 272b 22.59 N 88.20 E
Meribah 166 34.42 S 140.51 E
Méribel 62 45.25 N 6.34 E
Meriç 130 41.11 N 26.25 E
Meriç (Marica) (Évros) ≃ 38 40.52 N 26.12 E
Méricourt 50 50.24 N 2.52 E
Mérida, Esp. 34 38.55 N 6.20 W
Mérida, Méx. 200 32.39 N 114.58 W
Mérida, Méx. 232 20.58 N 89.37 W
Mérida, Pil. 116 10.55 N 124.32 E
Mérida, Ven. 246 8.36 N 71.08 W
Mérida □[3] 246 8.30 N 71.10 W
Mérida, Cordillera de ↗ 246 8.40 N 71.00 W
Meridale 210 42.22 N 74.57 W
Meriden, Eng., U.K. 42 52.26 N 1.37 W
Meriden, Ct., U.S. 207 41.32 N 72.48 W
Meriden, N.J., U.S. 276 40.57 N 74.28 W
Meridian, Ca., U.S. 226 39.09 N 121.55 W
Meridian, Ga., U.S. 192 31.27 N 81.22 W
Meridian, Id., U.S. 202 43.36 N 116.23 W
Meridian, Ms., U.S. 194 32.21 N 88.42 W
Meridian, N.Y., U.S. 210 43.09 N 76.32 W
Meridian, Pa., U.S. 214 40.51 N 79.58 W
Meridian, Tx., U.S. 222 31.55 N 97.39 W
Meridian Hills 218 39.53 N 86.09 W
Meridian Naval Air Station ■ 194 32.33 N 88.34 W
Meridianville 194 34.51 N 86.34 W
Mériel 261 49.05 N 2.12 E
Mérignac 32 44.50 N 0.42 W
Merigold 194 33.50 N 90.43 W
Merikarvia 26 61.51 N 21.30 E
Merille, Laga ≃ 154 1.25 N 38.26 E
Merimbula 166 36.53 S 149.54 E
Merín, Laguna (Lagoa Mirim) c 252 32.45 S 52.50 W
Merinda 166 20.01 S 148.10 E
Mering 60 48.16 N 10.59 E
Meringa 146 10.44 N 12.09 E
Merin Gubai 144 1.26 N 44.20 E
Meringur 166 34.24 S 141.16 E
Merino 198 40.28 N 103.21 W
Merinos 252 32.24 S 56.54 W
Merion Station 285 39.59 N 75.15 W
Merir I 108 4.19 N 132.19 E
Merishausen 58 47.45 N 8.37 E
Merit 222 33.13 N 96.17 W
Merivale Gardens 212 45.19 N 75.44 W
Meriwether Farms 285 39.58 N 75.34 W
Merizo 174p 13.16 N 144.40 E
Merke 85 42.52 N 73.11 E
Merkel 196 32.28 N 100.00 W
Merkem 50 50.57 N 2.51 E
Merkendorf 56 49.12 N 10.42 E
Merkinė 76 54.10 N 24.10 E
Merklin 60 49.34 N 13.07 E
Merklingen 58 48.30 N 9.44 E
Merkourovoúni ∧ 267c 37.54 N 23.48 E
Merksem 50 51.15 N 4.27 E
Merksplas 56 51.22 N 4.52 E
Merkuloviči 76 52.58 N 30.36 E
Merkys ≃ 76 54.10 N 24.11 E
Merlara 64 45.10 N 11.26 E
Merlejevo 82 55.05 N 37.13 E
Merlimau, Pulau I 271c 1.17 N 103.42 E
Merlimont-Plage 50 50.28 N 1.35 E
Merlin, On., Can. 214 42.14 N 82.14 W
Merlin, Or., U.S. 202 42.31 N 123.25 W
Merlin Seamount ✣[3] 14 9.05 S 150.44 W
Merlo, Arg. 252 32.21 S 65.02 W
Merlo, Arg. 258 34.40 S 58.45 W
Merlo □[5] 288 34.40 S 58.45 W
Merlo, Aeródromo ⊠ 288 34.41 S 58.45 W
Merlynston 274b 37.43 S 144.58 E
Mermaid Beach 171a 28.03 S 153.27 E
Mern 41 55.03 N 12.04 E
Merna 198 41.29 N 99.45 W
Mernye 30 46.30 N 17.50 E
Meroe ⊥ 140 16.56 N 33.43 E
Meron 132 32.59 N 35.26 E
Meron, Hare ∧ 132 32.58 N 35.25 E
Meros, Ponta dos ≻ 256 23.13 S 44.21 W
Merotai Besar 112 4.26 N 117.46 E
Merouana 34 35.38 N 5.55 E
Merouane, Chott ⊜ 148 34.00 N 6.02 E
Mer'oža 76 59.02 N 36.23 E
Merredin 162 31.29 S 118.16 E
Merrick 276 40.39 N 73.33 W
Merrick ∧ 44 55.08 N 4.29 W
Merrick Bay c 276 40.38 N 73.33 W
Merrickville 212 44.55 N 75.50 W
Merri Creek ≃ 169 37.48 S 145.01 E
Merriewold Lake 210 41.22 N 74.12 W
Merrifield 284c 38.52 N 77.13 W
Merrill, Ia., U.S. 198 42.43 N 96.14 W
Merrill, Mi., U.S. 190 43.24 N 84.19 W
Merrill, Or., U.S. 202 42.01 N 121.35 W
Merrill, Wi., U.S. 190 45.10 N 89.41 W
Merrillan 190 44.27 N 90.50 W
Merrill C. Meigs Field ⊠ 278 41.52 N 87.37 W
Merrill Lake ⊜ 212 44.55 N 77.24 W
Merrillville 216 41.28 N 87.19 W
Merrimac 207 42.49 N 71.00 W
Merrimack ≃ 188 42.49 N 70.49 W
Merrimack College ʋ[2] 283 42.40 N 71.08 W
Merrimac Terrace 283 42.49 N 71.00 W
Merriman, S. Afr. 158 31.13 S 23.38 E
Merriman, Ne., U.S. 198 42.55 N 101.42 W
Merrionette Park 278 41.41 N 87.42 W
Merriott 42 50.54 N 2.48 W
Merritt, B.C., Can. 182 50.07 N 120.47 W
Merritt, Wa., U.S. 224 47.47 N 120.51 W
Merritt, Lake ⊜[1] 282 37.48 N 122.16 W
Merritt Island 220 28.21 N 80.42 W
Merritt Island I 220 28.33 N 80.40 W
Merritt Reservoir ⊜[1] 198 42.35 N 100.55 W
Merriwa 166 32.08 S 150.21 E
Mer Rouge 194 32.46 N 91.47 W
Merrow 207 41.49 N 72.18 W
Merrygoen 166 31.50 S 149.14 E
Merrylands 274a 33.50 S 150.59 E
Merrymount Park ♦ 283 42.16 N 71.01 W
Merryville 194 30.45 N 93.32 W
Mersa Fatma 144 14.55 N 40.20 E
Mersa Matruh → Marsā Maṭrūḥ 140 31.21 N 27.14 E
Mersch 56 49.46 N 6.06 E
Merscheid ◆[8] 263 51.10 N 7.01 E
Merse V 46 55.39 N 2.15 W
Merse ≃ 66 43.05 N 11.22 E
Mersea Island I 42 51.47 N 0.55 E
Merseburg 54 51.21 N 11.59 E
Mersey ≃, Austl. 166 41.10 S 146.22 E
Mersey ≃, N.S., Can. 186 44.02 N 64.43 W
Mersey ≃, Eng., U.K. 44 53.25 N 3.00 W
Merseyside □[6] 44 53.25 N 2.50 W
Mersey Tunnel ◆[5] 262 53.24 N 3.00 W
Mersin → İçel 130 36.48 N 34.38 E
Mersing 114 2.26 N 103.50 E
Mers-les-Bains 50 50.04 N 1.23 E
Mērsrags 76 57.21 N 23.07 E
Merstham 260 51.16 N 0.09 W
Merta 120 26.39 N 74.02 E
Merta Road 120 26.43 N 73.55 E
Merthyr Tydfil 42 51.46 N 3.23 W
Merti 154 1.04 N 38.40 E
Mertingen 56 48.39 N 10.47 E
Mértola 34 37.38 N 7.40 W
Merton, Austl. 169 36.59 S 145.42 E
Merton, Wi., U.S. 216 43.08 N 88.18 W
Merton ◆[8] 42 51.25 N 0.12 W
Mertz Glacier Tongue ⊼ 9 67.40 S 144.45 E
Mertzon 196 31.16 N 100.49 W
Mertztown 208 40.30 N 75.40 W
Méru, Fr. 50 49.14 N 2.08 E
Meru, Kenya 154 0.03 N 37.39 E
Meru, Mount ∧ 154 3.14 S 36.45 E
Meru National Park ♦ 154 0.10 N 38.15 E
Meruoca 250 3.28 S 40.28 W
Merv → Mary 128 37.36 N 61.50 E
Mervans 58 46.48 N 5.11 E
Merville 50 50.38 N 2.38 E
Mervin 184 53.20 N 108.53 W
Merwede 158 31.38 S 23.48 E
Merweville 158 32.40 S 21.31 E
Merwin, Lake ⊜[1] 224 45.59 N 122.26 W
Merxleben 54 51.07 N 10.40 E
Mery 82 55.49 N 36.36 E
Méry-la-Bataille 50 49.33 N 2.38 E
Méry-sur-Oise 261 49.04 N 2.11 E
Méry-sur-Seine 50 48.30 N 3.53 E
Merzdorf 54 51.23 N 14.32 E
Merzhausen 58 47.58 N 7.49 E
Merzifon 130 40.53 N 35.29 E
Merzig 56 49.27 N 6.36 E
Mesa, Micron. 175c 7.21 N 151.51 E
Mesa, Moç. 154 13.00 S 39.33 E
Mesa, S. Afr. 158 26.29 S 26.59 E
Mesa, Az., U.S. 200 33.25 N 111.49 W
Mesa ≃ 34 41.15 N 1.48 W
Mesa, Cerro ∧ 254 48.46 S 71.29 W
Mesabi Range ↗[2] 190 47.30 N 92.50 W
Mesachie Lake 224 48.49 N 124.07 W
Mesa del Nayar 234 22.16 N 104.35 W
Mesa de Santa Rita 234 23.04 N 105.31 W
Mesagne 68 40.33 N 17.49 E
Mes'agutovo 86 55.35 N 58.20 E
Mesaména 152 3.44 N 12.50 E
Mesa Mountain ∧ 200 37.55 N 106.38 W
Mesarás, Kólpos c 38 34.58 N 24.36 E
Mesa Verde National Park ♦ 200 37.13 N 108.30 W
Mescalero 200 33.09 N 105.46 W
Mescalero Apache Indian Reservation ◆[4] 200 33.12 N 105.40 W
Meščerino, Ross. 76 53.37 N 37.23 E
Meščerino, Ross. 82 55.11 N 38.21 E
Meščerskij 265b 55.40 N 37.25 E
Meščerskoje 82 55.17 N 37.38 E
Meschede 56 51.20 N 8.17 E
Meschetskij chrebet ↗ 84 41.48 N 42.30 E
Mescit Tepe ∧ 130 40.22 N 41.11 E
Meščovsk 76 54.19 N 35.17 E
Meščura 24 63.20 N 50.52 E
Mese 58 46.17 N 9.21 E
Mèsè Atet 110 18.38 N 97.39 E
Mesen-Bucht → Mezenskaja guba c 24 66.40 N 43.45 E
Mesero 266b 45.30 N 8.51 E
Mesewa → Mitsiwa 144 15.38 N 39.28 E
Mesfinto 144 13.20 N 37.19 E
Mesgarābād 267d 35.37 N 51.31 E
Mesgouez, Lac ⊜ 176 51.24 N 75.05 W
Meshed → Mashhad 128 36.18 N 59.36 E
Meshgīn Shahr 128 38.24 N 47.40 E
Meshomasic Mountain ∧ 207 41.38 N 72.32 W
Meshoppen 210 41.34 N 76.03 W
Meshoppen Creek ≃ 210 41.37 N 76.03 W
Mesick 190 44.24 N 85.42 W
Mesier, Canal ʯ 254 48.20 S 74.33 W
Mesilinka ≃ 182 56.09 N 124.28 W
Mesilla 200 32.16 N 106.48 W
Mesillas, Méx. 234 23.14 N 106.03 W
Mesillas, Méx. 234 23.33 N 103.35 W
Mesima ≃ 68 38.30 N 15.55 E
Meskiana 148 35.39 N 7.41 E
Meskiana, Oued ≃ 36 35.49 N 7.53 E
Meskine 146 11.25 N 15.21 E
Meškuičiai 76 56.05 N 23.28 E
Meskum 114 1.34 N 102.01 E
Meslay-du-Maine 32 47.57 N 0.33 W
Meslay-le-Grenet 50 48.22 N 1.23 E
Mesnil-Val-Plage 50 50.03 N 1.20 E
Mesocco 58 46.23 N 9.14 E
Mesola 66 44.55 N 12.14 E
Mesolcina, Valle V 58 46.20 N 9.10 E
Mesolóngion 38 38.21 N 21.17 E
Mesomikenda Lake ⊜ 190 47.40 N 81.53 W
Mesopotamia 214 41.27 N 80.57 W
Mesopotamia □[9] 128 34.00 N 44.00 E
Mesoraca 68 39.05 N 16.48 E
Mesóyia □[9] 267c 37.56 N 23.53 E
Mespelbrunn ⊥ 56 49.54 N 9.19 E
Mesquita, Bra. 255 19.13 S 42.35 W
Mesquita, Bra. 256 22.48 S 43.26 W
Mesquite, Nv., U.S. 204 36.48 N 114.03 W
Mesquite, Tx., U.S. 222 32.46 N 96.35 W
Messach Mellet ↗[2] 146 24.30 N 11.35 E
Messalo ≃ 154 11.40 S 40.26 E
Messaoud, Oued V 148 27.28 N 0.21 W
Messdorf 54 52.43 N 11.33 E
Messina, It. 70 38.11 N 15.33 E
Messina, S. Afr. 156 22.23 S 30.00 E
Messina □[4] 70 38.03 N 14.52 E
Messina, Stretto di ʯ 70 38.15 N 15.35 E
Messinge ≃ 154 11.34 S 35.25 E
Messingham 44 53.32 N 0.39 W
Messíni 38 37.04 N 22.00 E
Messíni ⊥ 38 37.11 N 21.57 E
Messiniakós Kólpos c 38 36.58 N 22.00 E
Messix Peak ∧ 202 41.29 N 112.31 W
Messkirch 58 47.59 N 9.07 E
Messojacha ≃ 74 67.52 N 77.27 E
Messondo 152 3.43 N 10.28 E
Messtetten 58 48.11 N 8.58 E
Messy 261 48.58 N 2.42 E
Mestá 38 38.15 N 25.55 E
Mesta (Néstos) ≃ 38 40.41 N 24.44 E
Mestasa 148 35.07 N 4.25 W
Městečko 60 50.03 N 13.52 E
Mestghanem 148 35.51 N 0.07 E
Mestghanem □[5] 148 36.00 N 0.30 E
Mestia 84 43.03 N 42.43 E
Mestlin 54 53.35 N 11.56 E
Město Touškov 60 49.46 N 13.15 E
Mestre 64 45.29 N 12.15 E
Mestrino 64 45.26 N 11.45 E
Mesudiye 130 40.28 N 37.46 E
Mesuji ≃ 112 4.08 S 105.52 E
Mesum 52 52.13 N 7.29 E
Meszah Peak ∧ 180 58.28 N 131.26 W
Meta, It. 68 40.39 N 14.24 E
Meta, Mo., U.S. 219 38.18 N 92.09 W
Meta □[5] 246 3.30 N 73.00 W
Meta ≃ 246 6.12 N 67.28 W
Métabief 58 46.47 N 6.21 E
Metagācha 272b 22.38 N 88.31 E
Metahara 144 8.54 N 39.55 E
Meta Incognita Peninsula ≻[1] 176 62.45 N 68.30 W
Metairie 194 29.59 N 90.09 W
Metaline Falls 202 48.51 N 117.22 W
Metallifere, Colline ↗ 66 43.15 N 11.00 E
Metallostroj 265a 59.47 N 30.33 E
Metamora, Il., U.S. 190 40.47 N 89.21 W
Metamora, In., U.S. 218 39.26 N 85.08 W
Metamora, Mi., U.S. 216 42.56 N 83.17 W
Metamora, Oh., U.S. 216 41.42 N 83.54 W
Metán 252 25.29 S 64.57 W
Metangula 154 12.43 S 34.49 E
Metapán 236 14.20 N 89.27 W
Metaportum ⊥ 68 40.23 N 16.50 E
Metarica 154 14.20 S 36.48 E
Metates 234 23.46 N 106.02 W
Metaurilia 66 43.49 N 13.03 E
Metauro ≃ 66 43.50 N 13.03 E
Metcalfe 212 45.14 N 75.28 W
Metchosin 224 48.22 N 123.33 W
Metechi 84 41.55 N 44.21 E
Metedeconk, South Branch ≃ 208 40.04 N 74.09 W
Meteghan 186 44.11 N 66.10 W
Meteleen 52 52.08 N 7.12 E
Metema 144 12.57 N 36.12 E
Metéora ʋ[1] 38 39.46 N 21.36 E
Meteor Crater ⊥[6] 200 35.02 N 111.02 W
Meteor Seamount ✣[3] 8 48.00 S 8.30 E
Metepec, Méx. 234 19.15 N 99.36 W
Metepec, Méx. 234 18.56 N 98.28 W
Metharaw 110 16.12 N 98.08 E
Metheringham 44 53.08 N 0.24 W
Methil 46 56.10 N 3.01 W
Methler 263 51.35 N 7.37 E
Methlick 46 57.25 N 2.14 W
Methóni 38 36.50 N 21.43 E
Methow 182 48.07 N 120.00 W
Methow ≃ 202 48.03 N 119.53 W
Methuen 207 42.43 N 71.11 W
Methven, N.Z. 172 43.38 S 171.39 E
Methven, Scot., U.K. 46 56.25 N 3.34 W
Methwold 42 52.31 N 0.33 E
Metica ≃ 246 4.09 N 72.55 W
Metiskow 184 52.24 N 110.38 W
Metković 36 43.03 N 17.39 E
Metlakatla, B.C., Can. 182 54.20 N 130.27 W
Metlakatla, Ak., U.S. 182 55.08 N 131.35 W
Metlaoui 148 34.20 N 8.24 E
Metlatonoc 234 17.11 N 98.20 W
Metlika 36 45.39 N 15.19 E
Metlili, Oued V 148 31.54 N 4.53 E
Metlili ech Chaâmba 148 32.18 N 3.40 E
Metnitz 61 46.59 N 14.13 E
Meto, Bayou ≃ 194 34.05 N 91.26 W
Metolius ≃ 202 44.36 N 121.17 W
Metompkin Bay c 208 37.43 N 75.35 W
Metompkin Inlet c 208 37.41 N 75.35 W
Metro 115a 5.05 S 105.20 E
Metropolis 194 37.09 N 88.43 W
Metropolitan 190 46.00 N 87.53 W
Metropolitan Beach ♦ 281 42.35 N 82.48 W
Metropolitan Museum of Art ʋ 276 40.47 N 73.58 W
Metropolitan Oakland International Airport ⊠ 226 37.43 N 122.13 W
Metschow 54 53.49 N 12.58 E
Metsematluku 156 24.01 S 24.40 E
Metsera 154 2.35 S 26.07 E
Métsovon 38 39.46 N 21.11 E
Mettawa 278 42.14 N 87.56 W
Metten 60 48.52 N 12.55 E
Mettendorf 56 49.57 N 6.19 E
Metter 192 32.23 N 82.03 W
Mettet 56 50.19 N 4.40 E
Mettetal Airport ⊠ 281 42.21 N 83.27 W
Mettingen 52 52.18 N 7.46 E
Mettlach 56 49.30 N 6.36 E
Mettmach 60 48.10 N 13.21 E
Mettmann 56 51.15 N 6.58 E
Mettray 50 47.27 N 0.39 E
Mettuppālaiyam 122 11.18 N 76.57 E
Mettūr 122 11.48 N 77.48 E
Metu 144 8.20 N 35.36 E
Metuchen 210 40.32 N 74.21 W
Metuge 154 12.58 S 40.20 E
Metulla 132 33.16 N 35.35 E
Metundo, Ilha I 154 11.10 S 40.41 E
Metz 56 49.08 N 6.10 E
Metzervisse 56 49.19 N 6.17 E
Metzger 224 45.26 N 122.45 W
Metzingen 56 48.32 N 9.17 E
Metzkausen 263 51.16 N 6.57 E
Metztitlán 234 20.36 N 98.45 W
Metztitlán, Laguna ⊜ 234 20.40 N 98.50 W
Meu ≃ 32 48.02 N 1.47 W
Meudon 261 48.48 N 2.14 E
Meudon, Bois de ♦ 261 48.47 N 2.12 E
Meul ≃ 158 27.56 S 28.50 E
Meulaboh 114 4.09 N 96.08 E
Meulan 50 49.01 N 1.54 E
Meulebeke 50 50.57 N 3.17 E
Meung-sur-Loire 50 47.50 N 1.42 E
Meureubo ≃ 114 4.09 N 96.09 E
Meureudu 114 5.16 N 96.16 E
Meursault 58 46.59 N 4.46 E
Meurthe ≃ 32 48.47 N 6.09 E
Meurthe-et-Moselle □[5] 32 48.35 N 6.10 E
Meuse 58 47.59 N 5.33 E
Meuse □[5] 32 49.00 N 5.30 E
Meuse (Maas) ≃ 30 51.49 N 5.01 E
Meuselwitz 54 51.02 N 12.17 E
Meuvette ≃ 50 48.45 N 1.08 E
Meux Creek ≃ 212 44.07 N 81.02 W
Mevagissey 42 50.16 N 4.48 W
Mevang 152 0.07 N 11.05 E
Mewāt Plain ≡ 124 27.40 N 77.15 E
Mexborough 44 53.30 N 1.17 W
Mexia 222 31.40 N 96.28 W
Mexia Lake ⊜[1] 222 31.39 N 96.36 W
Mexiana, Ilha I 250 0.02 S 49.35 W
Mexicali 232 32.40 N 115.29 W
Mexican Hat 200 37.09 N 109.52 W
Mexico, In., U.S. 216 40.49 N 86.06 W
Mexico, Me., U.S. 188 44.33 N 70.32 W
Mexico, Mo., U.S. 219 39.10 N 91.52 W
Mexico, N.Y., U.S. 212 43.27 N 76.13 W
Mexico, Pa., U.S. 208 40.32 N 77.21 W
México □[3] 234 19.20 N 99.45 W
Mexico (Mexico) □[1], N.A. 230 23.00 N 102.00 W
Mexico (México) □[1], N.A. 232 23.00 N 102.00 W
México, Golfo de → Mexico, Gulf of c 230 25.00 N 90.00 W
Mexico, Gulf of c 230 25.00 N 90.00 W
Mexico Basin ✣[1] 16 25.00 N 92.00 W
Mexico Bay c 212 43.31 N 76.17 W
Mexico Beach 192 29.58 N 85.24 W
Mexico City → Ciudad de México 234 19.24 N 99.09 W
Mexiko → Ciudad de México 234 19.24 N 99.09 W
Mexiko → Mexico □[1] 232 23.00 N 102.00 W
Mexiko, Golf von → Mexico, Gulf of c 230 25.00 N 90.00 W
Meximieux 58 45.54 N 5.12 E
Mexique → Mexico □[1] 230 23.00 N 102.00 W
Mexique, Golfe du → Mexico, Gulf of c 230 25.00 N 90.00 W
Mexticacán 234 21.13 N 102.43 W
Mey, Castle of ⊥ 46 58.38 N 3.14 W
Meyanodas 164 7.38 S 131.38 E
Meycauayan 116 14.44 N 120.58 E
Meydan 130 38.21 N 41.47 E
Meydancık 130 41.25 N 42.14 E
Meydān-e Gel ≡ 128 29.04 N 54.50 E
Meydān Khvolah 120 33.36 N 69.51 E
Meyenburg 54 53.18 N 12.14 E

Symbol	English	Deutsch	Español	Français	Português
≃	River	Fluß	Río	Rivière	Rio
≍	Canal	Kanal	Canal	Canal	Canal
ᒪ	Waterfall, Rapids	Wasserfall, Stromschnellen	Cascada, Rápidos	Chute d'eau, Rapides	Cascata, Rápidos
ʯ	Strait	Meeresstraße	Estrecho	Détroit	Estreito
c	Bay, Gulf	Bucht, Golf	Bahía, Golfo	Baie, Golfe	Baía, Golfo
⊜	Lake, Lakes	See, Seen	Lago, Lagos	Lac, Lacs	Lago, Lagos
≡	Swamp	Sumpf	Pantano	Marais	Pântano
⊼	Ice Features, Glacier	Eis- und Gletscherformen	Accidentes Glaciales	Formes glaciaires	Acidentes glaciares
⫧	Other Hydrographic Features	Andere Hydrographische Objekte	Otros Elementos Hidrográficos	Autres données hydrographiques	Outros acidentes hidrográficos

Symbol	English	Deutsch	Español	Français	Português
✣	Submarine Features	Untermeerische Objekte	Accidentes Submarinos	Formes de relief sous-marin	Acidentes submarinos
□	Political Unit	Politische Einheit	Unidad Politica	Entité politique	Unidade política
ʋ	Cultural Institution	Kulturelle Institution	Institución Cultural	Institution culturelle	Instituição cultural
⊥	Historical Site	Historische Stätte	Sitio Histórico	Site historique	Sítio histórico
♦	Recreational Site	Erholungs- und Ferienort	Sitio de Recreo	Centre de loisirs	Area de Lazer
⊠	Airport	Flughafen	Aeropuerto	Aéroport	Aeroporto
■	Military Installation	Militäranlage	Instalación Militar	Installation militaire	Instalação militar
◆	Miscellaneous	Verschiedenes	Misceláneo	Divers	Diversos

I · 112 Meye-Mill

ENGLISH — Name | Page | Lat.°′ | Long.°′ — DEUTSCH — Name | Seite | Breite°′ | Länge°′ E = Ost

Meyers Chuck 182 55.44 N 132.15 W
Meyersdale 188 39.48 N 79.01 W
Meyers Lake 214 40.52 N 81.24 W
Meyersville 222 28.55 N 97.21 W
Meyerton 158 26.33 S 28.01 E
Meyísti I 130 36.08 N 29.34 E
Meymac 32 45.32 N 2.09 E
Meymaneh 120 35.55 N 64.47 E
Meymeh 128 33.27 N 51.10 E
Meymeh ≃ 128 32.05 N 47.16 E
Meynypilgino 180 62.32 N 177.02 E
Meyo Centre 152 2.33 N 11.02 E
Meyrargues 62 43.38 N 5.32 E
Meyrin 58 46.14 N 6.05 E
Meyronne 184 49.39 N 106.50 W
Meyrueis 32 44.10 N 3.26 E
Meyungs 175b 7.20 N 134.27 E
Meža ≃ 61 46.35 N 15.02 E
Mezada, Horvot (Masada) ⊥ 132 31.19 N 35.21 E
Mezapa 236 15.33 N 87.23 W
Mezcala 234 17.56 N 99.37 W
Mezcala ≃ 234 18.00 N 99.47 W
Mezcalapa 234 17.37 N 93.22 W
Mezcalapa ≃ 234 18.00 N 92.54 W
Mezdra 38 43.09 N 23.42 E
Meždurečensk 86 53.42 N 88.03 E
Meždurečenskij 86 59.36 N 65.53 E
Mèze 32 43.25 N 3.36 E
Mézel 62 43.59 N 6.12 E
Mezen' 24 65.50 N 44.13 E
Mezen' ≃ 24 66.11 N 43.59 E
Mézenc, Mont ∧ 62 44.55 N 4.11 E
Mezenskaja guba ⊂ 24 66.40 N 43.45 E
Meževaja 78 48.16 N 36.44 E
Mežgorje 78 48.32 N 23.30 E
Meziadin Lake ⊜ 182 56.04 N 129.18 W
Mežica 61 46.31 N 14.52 E
Mézières-en-Brenne 32 46.49 N 1.13 E
Mézières-sur-Seine 261 48.58 N 1.48 E
Mézilhac 62 44.48 N 4.21 E
Mézin 32 44.03 N 0.16 E
Mezinovskij 76 55.30 N 40.21 E
Mežirič 78 50.43 N 34.29 E
Mezőberény 30 46.50 N 21.02 E
Mezőcsát 30 47.49 N 20.55 E
Mezőkovácsháza 30 46.25 N 20.55 E
Mezőkövesd 30 47.50 N 20.34 E
Mezőtúr 30 47.00 N 20.38 E
Mežoz'ornyj 86 54.09 N 59.23 E
Mezquital 234 23.29 N 104.23 W
Mezquital ≃ 232 22.35 N 104.54 W
Mezquital del Oro 234 21.10 N 103.23 W
Mezquitic 234 22.23 N 103.41 W
Mezraa 130 41.12 N 35.08 E
Mézy 261 49.00 N 1.53 E
Mezzana 64 46.19 N 10.48 E
Mezzano 64 46.09 N 11.48 E
Mezzenile 62 45.17 N 7.23 E
Mezzocorona 64 46.13 N 11.07 E
Mezzoiuso 70 37.52 N 13.28 E
Mezzola, Lago di ⊜ 58 46.12 N 9.26 E
Mezzoldo 58 46.01 N 9.40 E
Mezzolombardo 64 46.13 N 11.05 E
Mezzomerico 266b 45.37 N 8.36 E
Mfangano Island I 154 0.28 S 34.01 E
Mfolozi ≃ 158 28.25 S 32.26 E
Mfou 152 3.43 N 11.38 E
Mfuwe 154 13.04 S 31.46 E
Mgači 89 51.05 N 142.17 E
Mgeni ≃ 158 29.48 S 31.02 E
Mgeta 154 8.19 S 36.08 E
Mglin 76 53.04 N 32.51 E
M'goun, Irhil ∧ 148 31.31 N 6.25 W
M'hai, B'nom ∧ 110 11.21 N 107.50 E
Mhasvād 122 17.38 N 74.47 E
Mhlatuze ≃ 158 28.47 S 32.06 E
Mhlume 158 26.02 S 31.50 E
Mholach, Beinn ∧ 2 46 58.14 N 6.31 W
Mhòr, Beinn ∧ 46 57.17 N 7.19 W
Mhòr, Loch ⊜ 46 57.14 N 4.26 W
Mhow 120 22.33 N 75.46 E
Mi ≃, Zhg. 98 37.12 N 119.10 E
Mi ≃, Zhg. 100 27.09 N 112.51 E
Mia, Oued V 148 30.47 N 4.54 E
Miacatlán 234 18.46 N 99.22 W
Mia-dong ⊶ 8 271b 37.37 N 127.01 E
Miagao 116 10.39 N 122.14 E
Miahuatlán de Porfirio Díaz 234 16.20 N 96.36 W
Miajadas 34 39.09 N 5.54 W
Miaméré 146 8.52 N 19.50 E
Miami, Mb., Can. 184 49.21 N 98.11 W
Miami, Az., U.S. 200 33.23 N 110.52 W
Miami, Fl., U.S. 220 25.46 N 80.11 W
Miami, In., U.S. 216 40.36 N 86.06 W
Miami, Ok., U.S. 196 36.52 N 94.52 W
Miami, Tx., U.S. 196 35.42 N 100.38 W
Miami □ 6, In., U.S. 216 40.45 N 86.04 W
Miami □ 6, Oh., U.S. 218 40.02 N 84.13 W
Miami ≃ 224 45.33 N 123.53 W
Miami Beach, On., Can. 212 44.13 N 79.29 W
Miami Beach, Fl., U.S. 220 25.47 N 80.07 W
Miami Canal ≋ 220 25.47 N 80.15 W
Miami Creek ≃ 226 37.21 N 119.44 W
Miami International Airport ⊠ 220 25.48 N 80.17 W
Miami Lakes 220 25.53 N 80.18 W
Miamisburg 218 39.38 N 84.17 W
Miamisburg Mound State Memorial ⊥ 218 39.38 N 84.17 W
Miami Shores 220 25.51 N 80.11 W
Miami Springs 220 25.49 N 80.17 W
Miami State Recreation Area ♠ 216 40.40 N 85.55 W
Miamiville 218 39.13 N 84.18 W
Miān Channūn 123 30.27 N 72.22 E
Mianchi 102 34.48 N 111.49 E
Mīāndoāb 128 36.58 N 46.06 E
Miandrivazo 157b 19.31 S 45.28 E
Mianduhe 89 49.05 N 121.06 E
Miane 64 45.57 N 12.06 E
Mīāneh 128 37.26 N 47.42 E
Miang, Phu ∧ 110 17.42 N 101.01 E
Miangas, Pulau I 108 5.35 N 126.35 E
Mianhu 100 23.28 N 116.09 E
Mianhuadi 104 41.15 N 120.49 E
Miāni 123 32.32 N 73.04 E
Miāni Hōr ⊂ 120 25.34 N 66.19 E
Mianning 102 28.39 N 102.09 E
Mianus ≃ 207 41.03 N 73.35 W
Mianus, East Branch ≃ 276 41.06 N 73.35 W
Mianus Reservoir ⊜ 1 276 41.08 N 73.37 W
Miānwāli 123 32.35 N 71.33 E
Mianxian 102 33.09 N 106.48 E
Mianyang, Zhg. 100 30.23 N 113.25 E
Mianyang, Zhg. 102 31.30 N 104.49 E
Mianzhu 102 31.20 N 104.09 E
Miao Dao I 98 37.56 N 120.45 E
Miaodao Qundao II 98 38.10 N 120.40 E
Miao'ergou 86 45.32 N 83.52 E
Miaofengshan 105 40.04 N 116.13 E
Miaogou 104 41.12 N 120.40 E
Miaojiagou 104 42.16 N 123.22 E
Miaojiatun 104 40.54 N 120.55 E
Miaokou 98 35.48 N 114.09 E
Miaoli 100 24.34 N 120.49 E
Miao Ling ⋏ 102 26.15 N 107.26 E
Miaopu 106 31.00 N 118.44 E
Miaoqian 100 30.33 N 117.44 E
Miaotou 106 30.58 N 120.33 E
Miaowan 100 33.07 N 114.41 E
Miaoyang 98 40.49 N 124.24 E
Miaozhen 106 31.43 N 121.21 E
Miaozigou 107 30.17 N 104.35 E
Miarayon 116 8.04 N 124.50 E
Miarinarivo, Madag. 157b 16.38 S 48.15 E
Miarinarivo, Madag. 157b 18.57 S 46.55 E
Miarinavaratra 157b 20.13 S 47.31 E
Miasa 94 36.34 N 137.53 E
Miass 86 54.59 N 60.06 E
Miass ≃ 86 56.06 N 64.30 E
Miasteczko Krajeńskie 30 53.06 N 17.01 E
Miastko 30 54.01 N 17.00 E
Miboro-dam ⊶ 6 94 36.08 N 136.55 E
Mibu 94 36.25 N 139.48 E
Mibu ≃ 94 35.49 N 137.57 E
Mica 156 24.10 S 30.48 E
Mica Mountain ∧ 200 32.13 N 110.33 W
Micang Shan ⋏ 102 32.45 N 107.20 E
Micanopy 192 29.30 N 82.16 W
Micaúne 156 18.18 S 36.35 E
Mičavičevnik 24 64.14 N 57.58 E
Miccosukee, Lake ⊜ 1 192 30.34 N 83.58 W
Miccosukee Indian Reservation ⊶ 4 220 26.10 N 80.50 W
Michael, Mount ∧ 164 6.25 S 145.20 E
Michael J. Kirwan Reservoir ⊜ 1 214 41.10 N 81.10 W
Michajlo-Koc'ubinskoje 78 51.27 N 31.04 E
Michajlov 82 54.14 N 39.02 E
Michajlovka, Kaz. 85 43.06 N 71.36 E
Michajlovka, Kaz. 85 42.50 N 75.42 E
Michajlovka, Kaz. 86 53.51 N 76.32 E
Michajlovka, Kyrg. 85 42.37 N 78.20 E
Michajlovka, Ross. 78 49.53 N 39.38 E
Michajlovka, Ross. 80 47.38 N 46.54 E
Michajlovka, Ross. 80 50.05 N 43.15 E
Michajlovka, Ross. 86 51.49 N 79.45 E
Michajlovka, Ross. 86 56.26 N 78.53 E
Michajlovka, Ross. 88 50.26 N 104.10 E
Michajlovka, Ross. 88 55.30 N 114.09 E
Michajlovka, Ross. 88 51.07 N 119.20 E
Michajlovka, Ross. 88 52.57 N 103.18 E
Michajlovka, Ross. 89 49.13 N 129.56 E
Michajlovka, Ross. 89 43.56 N 132.00 E
Michajlovka, Ross. 265a 60.04 N 30.14 E
Michajlovka, Ross. 265a 59.43 N 30.01 E
Michajlovka, Ukr. 78 49.19 N 36.28 E
Michajlovka, Ukr. 78 47.16 N 35.14 E
Michajlovka, Ukr. 83 48.30 N 38.54 E
Michajlovka, Ukr. 83 48.09 N 37.22 E
Michajlovka, Ukr. 83 48.44 N 37.16 E
Michajlovo 80 56.56 N 45.04 E
Michajlovo-Aleksandrovskij 83 49.13 N 40.15 E
Michajlovskaja 80 50.58 N 41.52 E
Michajlovskaja Celina, zapovednik ♠ 78 50.45 N 34.10 E
Michajlovskij, Kaz. 86 50.17 N 55.23 E
Michajlovskij, Ross. 76 60.05 N 43.29 E
Michajlovskij, Ross. 86 51.41 N 79.47 E
Michajlovskoje, Ross. 76 58.23 N 37.40 E
Michajlovskoje, Ross. 80 56.11 N 45.47 E
Michajlovskoje, Ross. 82 55.50 N 36.20 E
Michajlovskoje, Ross. 265b 55.35 N 37.35 E
Michalevo 82 55.27 N 38.26 E
Michali 82 55.17 N 39.05 E
Michalkovo 82 54.11 N 37.33 E
Michalovce 30 48.45 N 21.55 E
Michalovy Hory 60 49.55 N 12.47 E
Michanoviči 76 53.45 N 27.40 E
Michaud, Point › 186 45.34 N 60.40 W
Micheal Peak ∧ 182 53.35 N 126.26 W
Michejevo 88 57.10 N 104.53 E
Michel 182 49.43 N 114.49 W
Michelago 171b 35.43 S 149.10 E
Michelau 56 50.10 N 11.06 E
Micheldever 42 51.09 N 1.15 W
Micheldorf in Oberösterreich 61 47.52 N 14.08 E
Michelsneukirchen 60 49.08 N 12.33 E
Michelson, Mount ∧ 180 69.19 N 144.17 W
Michel'sonovskij 265b 55.42 N 37.54 E
Michelstadt 56 49.41 N 9.00 E
Michendorf 54 52.18 N 13.01 E
Miches 238 18.59 N 69.03 W
Micheta 84 41.52 N 44.44 E
Michiana 216 41.46 N 86.48 W
Michiana Regional Airport ⊠ 216 41.42 N 86.19 W
Michigamme ≃ 190 46.04 N 88.13 W
Michigan 198 48.01 N 98.07 W
Michigan □ 3, U.S. 178 44.00 N 85.00 W
Michigan □ 3, U.S. 190 44.00 N 85.00 W
Michigan ≃ 200 40.52 N 106.20 W
Michigan, Lake ⊜ 190 44.00 N 87.00 W
Michigan, University of ♥ 2 281 42.17 N 83.44 W
Michigan Center 216 42.13 N 84.19 W
Michigan City 216 41.42 N 86.53 W
Michigan International Speedway ♠ 216 42.03 N 84.15 W
Michigan Stadium ♠ 281 42.16 N 83.45 W
Michigan State Fair Grounds ♠ 281 42.27 N 83.07 W
Michigantown 216 40.19 N 86.23 W
Michika 146 10.38 N 13.24 E
Michillinda 280 34.07 N 118.05 W
Michinmahuida, Volcán ∧ 1 254 42.49 S 72.28 W
Michipicoten Bay ⊂ 190 47.55 N 84.56 W
Michipicoten Island I 190 47.45 N 85.45 W
Michnevo 82 55.07 N 37.58 E
Michninskaja 24 60.26 N 46.14 E
Michoacán 204 32.28 N 115.20 W
Michoacán □ 3 234 19.10 N 101.50 W
Michoacanejo 234 21.33 N 102.36 W
Michów 30 51.32 N 22.19 E
Michurinsk → Mičurinsk 80 52.54 N 40.30 E
Mickle Fell ∧ 44 54.37 N 2.18 W
Mickleham 260 51.16 N 0.19 W
Mickleover 42 52.54 N 1.32 W
Mickleton, Eng., U.K. 42 52.05 N 1.46 W
Mickleton, N.J., U.S. 285 39.47 N 75.14 W
Mickle Trafford 262 53.13 N 2.50 W
Mickleyville 218 39.45 N 86.16 W
Mico ≃ 236 12.11 N 84.16 W
Mico, Montañas del ⋏ 236 15.30 N 88.55 W
Miconge 152 4.26 S 12.51 E
Micoud 241f 13.50 N 60.54 W
Micronesia II 14 11.00 N 159.00 E
Micronesia, Federated States of □ 1 14 5.00 N 152.00 E
Mičurin 38 42.10 N 27.51 E
Mičurinsk 80 52.54 N 40.30 E
Midai, Pulau I 112 3.00 N 107.47 E
Midale 184 49.22 N 103.27 W
Midar 148 34.58 N 3.30 W
Mid-Atlantic Ridge ✣ 3 8 0.00 20.00 W
Midbar Yehuda → Wilderness of Judæa ⊶ 2 132 31.30 N 35.18 E
Middalya 162 23.55 S 114.45 E
Middelburg, Ned. 52 51.30 N 3.37 E
Middelburg, S. Afr. 158 25.47 S 29.28 E
Middelburg, S. Afr. 158 31.30 S 25.00 E
Middelfart 41 55.30 N 9.45 E
Middelharnis 52 51.45 N 4.11 E
Middelkerke 50 51.11 N 2.49 E
Middelkerke, Vliegveld ⊠ 50 51.12 N 2.52 E
Middelpos 158 31.55 S 20.13 E
Middelstum 52 53.20 N 6.38 E
Middelwater 156 23.17 S 30.16 E
Middelwit 156 24.58 S 27.00 E
Middenbeemster 52 52.33 N 4.55 E
Middenin 158 27.43 S 28.02 E
Middenmeer 52 52.47 N 5.00 E
Middle ≃, B.C., Can. 182 54.50 N 125.08 W
Middle ≃, Ca., U.S. 226 38.03 N 121.31 W
Middle ≃, Ia., U.S. 194 41.29 N 93.24 W
Middle ≃, Mn., U.S. 198 48.22 N 97.04 W
Middle ≃, Mo., U.S. 219 38.39 N 91.53 W
Middle Alkali Lake ⊜ 204 41.28 N 120.04 W
Middle America Trench ✣ 1 16 15.00 N 95.00 W
Middle Andaman I 110 12.30 N 92.50 E
Middle Barton 42 51.56 N 1.22 W
Middle Bass 214 41.41 N 82.50 W
Middle Bass Island I 214 41.41 N 82.49 W
Middle-Bay 186 51.28 N 57.30 W
Middle Bay ⊂ 276 40.37 N 73.36 W
Middleboro 207 41.53 N 70.54 W
Middle Bosque ≃ 222 31.31 N 97.16 W
Middlebourne 188 39.29 N 80.54 W
Middlebranch 214 40.54 N 81.20 W
Middle Breakwater ⊶ 5 280 33.43 N 118.13 W
Middlebro 184 49.01 N 95.21 W
Middle Brook 186 48.45 N 54.13 W
Middle Brook ≃, N.J., U.S. 276 40.39 N 74.41 W
Middle Brook ≃, N.J., U.S. 276 40.33 N 74.33 W
Middle Brook, East Branch ≃ 276 40.35 N 74.33 W
Middle Brook, West Branch ≃ 276 40.35 N 74.33 W
Middleburg, Md., U.S. 208 39.35 N 77.12 W
Middleburg, N.Y., U.S. 210 42.36 N 74.20 W
Middleburg, Oh., U.S. 216 40.17 N 83.34 W
Middleburg, Pa., U.S. 208 40.47 N 77.02 W
Middleburg Heights 214 41.22 N 81.48 W
Middlebury, Ct., U.S. 207 41.31 N 73.07 W
Middlebury, In., U.S. 216 41.40 N 85.42 W
Middlebury, Vt., U.S. 188 44.00 N 73.10 W
Middlebush 276 40.29 N 74.32 W
Middle Caicos I 238 21.47 N 71.43 W
Middle Cape › 220 25.09 N 81.09 W
Middle Castor ≃ 212 45.16 N 75.24 W
Middle Channel ≃ 1, N.T., Can. 180 69.21 N 135.33 W
Middle Channel ≃ 1, Mi., U.S. 281 42.33 N 82.42 W
Middle Concho ≃ 196 31.27 N 100.25 W
Middle Creek ≃, U.S. 208 39.41 N 76.18 W
Middle Creek ≃, Pa., U.S. 210 40.46 N 76.52 W
Middle Creek ≃, Pa., U.S. 210 41.28 N 75.11 W
Middle Fabius ≃ 194 39.58 N 91.35 W
Middle Falls 210 43.07 N 73.32 W
Middlefield, Ct., U.S. 207 41.31 N 72.42 W
Middlefield, N.Y., U.S. 210 42.41 N 74.50 W
Middlefield, Oh., U.S. 214 41.27 N 81.04 W
Middle Fork Reservoir ⊜ 1 218 39.51 N 84.51 W
Middle Ground I 272c 18.55 N 72.51 E
Middle Ground ✣ 2 174g 28.15 N 177.25 W
Middle Grove, Mo., U.S. 219 39.24 N 92.16 W
Middle Grove, N.Y., U.S. 210 43.05 N 73.55 W
Middle Haddam 207 41.33 N 72.33 W
Middleham 44 54.17 N 1.49 W
Middle Harbour ⊂ 274a 33.48 S 151.14 E
Middle Head › 274a 33.50 S 151.16 E
Middle Hope 210 41.34 N 74.01 W
Middle Island 210 40.53 N 72.56 W
Middle Island I 162 34.07 S 123.12 E
Middle Level Main Drain ≋ 42 52.43 N 0.22 E
Middle Loup ≃ 198 41.17 N 98.23 W
Middle Maitland ≃ 212 43.53 N 81.19 W
Middlemarch 172 45.31 S 170.07 E
Middlemount 166 22.49 S 148.40 E
Middle Musquodoboit 186 45.03 N 63.09 W
Middle Nodaway ≃ 194 40.54 N 95.00 W
Middle Pease ≃ 196 34.15 N 100.07 W
Middle Point 216 40.51 N 84.27 W
Middleport, N.Y., U.S. 210 43.12 N 78.28 W
Middleport, Oh., U.S. 188 39.00 N 82.02 W
Middleport, Pa., U.S. 208 40.44 N 76.05 W
Middle Raccoon ≃ 198 41.34 N 94.12 W
Middle Reservoir ⊜ 1 283 42.27 N 71.07 W
Middle River 208 39.20 N 76.26 W
Middle River ⊂ 208 39.19 N 76.25 W
Middle River Neck › 1 284b 39.22 N 76.23 W
Middle River Rouge ≃ 281 42.20 N 83.15 W
Middle Rouge Parkway ♠ 281 42.21 N 83.21 W
Middle Run ≃ 285 39.41 N 75.43 W
Middlesboro 192 36.36 N 83.43 W
Middlesbrough 44 54.35 N 1.14 W
Middlesex, Belize 232 17.02 N 88.31 W
Middlesex, N.J., U.S. 276 40.34 N 74.29 W
Middlesex, N.Y., U.S. 210 42.42 N 77.16 W
Middlesex, N.C., U.S. 192 35.47 N 78.12 W
Middlesex □ 6, On., Can. 212 43.00 N 81.08 W
Middlesex □ 6, Ct., U.S. 207 41.33 N 72.39 W
Middlesex □ 6, Ma., U.S. 207 42.30 N 71.25 W
Middlesex □ 6, N.J., U.S. 208 40.29 N 74.27 W
Middlesex □ 6, Va., U.S. 208 37.40 N 76.35 W
Middlesex Fells Reservation ♠ 283 42.27 N 71.07 W
Middlesex Reservoir ⊜ 1 276 40.37 N 74.19 W
Middle Stewiacke 186 45.13 N 63.08 W
Middle Swan 168a 31.52 S 116.00 E
Middle Thames ≃ 212 42.59 N 80.58 W
Middleton, Austl. 166 22.22 S 141.32 E
Middleton, N.S., Can. 186 44.57 N 65.04 W
Middleton, Eng., U.K. 42 52.43 N 0.28 E
Middleton, Eng., U.K. 44 53.33 N 2.13 W
Middleton, Ma., U.S. 207 42.35 N 71.01 W
Middleton, Mi., U.S. 190 43.11 N 84.42 W
Middleton, Tn., U.S. 194 35.03 N 88.53 W
Middleton, Wi., U.S. 216 43.05 N 89.30 W
Middleton-in-Teesdale 44 54.38 N 2.04 W
Middleton Island I 180 59.25 N 146.25 W
Middleton-on-the-Wolds 44 53.56 N 0.33 W
Middleton Pond ⊜ 283 42.36 N 71.02 W
Middleton Reef I 1 160 29.28 S 159.06 E
Middleton Saint George 44 54.30 N 1.28 W
Middletown, N. Ire., U.K. 48 54.18 N 6.50 W
Middletown, Ca., U.S. 226 38.45 N 122.36 W
Middletown, Ct., U.S. 207 41.33 N 72.39 W
Middletown, De., U.S. 208 39.26 N 75.43 W
Middletown, Il., U.S. 219 40.11 N 89.35 W
Middletown, In., U.S. 218 40.03 N 85.32 W
Middletown, Ky., U.S. 218 38.14 N 85.32 W
Middletown, Md., U.S. 208 39.26 N 77.32 W
Middletown, Mo., U.S. 219 39.07 N 91.24 W
Middletown, N.J., U.S. 208 40.23 N 74.07 W
Middletown, N.Y., U.S. 210 41.26 N 74.25 W
Middletown, Oh., U.S. 218 39.30 N 84.23 W
Middletown, Pa., U.S. 208 40.11 N 76.43 W
Middletown, R.I., U.S. 207 41.32 N 71.17 W
Middletown, Va., U.S. 188 39.01 N 78.16 W
Middletown Park 218 40.09 N 85.26 W
Middle Tuolumne ≃ 226 37.50 N 120.01 W
Middleville, Mi., U.S. 216 42.42 N 85.27 W
Middleville, N.Y., U.S. 210 43.08 N 74.58 W
Middleville, N.Y., U.S. 276 43.08 N 74.58 W
Middlewich 44 53.11 N 2.27 W
Middle Yegua Creek ≃ 222 30.19 N 96.47 W
Middle Yuba ≃ 226 39.22 N 121.12 W
Midelt 148 32.41 N 4.43 W
Midfield 222 28.56 N 96.13 W
Midge Hall 262 53.42 N 2.45 W
Midgic 186 45.59 N 64.18 W
Mid Glamorgan □ 6 42 51.40 N 3.30 W
Midgley 262 53.44 N 1.58 W
Midhurst, On., Can. 212 44.27 N 79.44 W
Midhurst, Eng., U.K. 42 50.59 N 0.45 W
Midi, Aiguille du ∧ 62 45.52 N 6.53 E
Midi, Canal du ≋ 32 43.26 N 1.58 E
Midi de Bigorre, Pic du ∧ 32 42.56 N 0.08 E
Mid Illovo 158 29.59 S 30.25 E
Mid-Indian Basin ✣ 1 12 10.00 S 80.00 E
Mid-Indian Ridge ✣ 3 6 12.00 S 66.00 E
Midland, Austl. 168a 31.53 S 116.00 E
Midland, On., Can. 212 44.45 N 79.53 W
Midland, Ca., U.S. 204 33.52 N 114.48 W
Midland, Mi., U.S. 190 43.36 N 84.14 W
Midland, N.C., U.S. 192 35.13 N 80.30 W
Midland, Oh., U.S. 218 39.18 N 83.54 W
Midland, Pa., U.S. 214 40.37 N 80.26 W
Midland, Pa., U.S. 214 40.37 N 80.26 W
Midland, S.D., U.S. 198 44.04 N 101.09 W
Midland, Tx., U.S. 196 31.59 N 102.04 W
Midland, Wa., U.S. 224 47.10 N 122.24 W
Midland Bay ⊂ 212 44.47 N 79.52 W
Midland Beach ⊶ 8 276 40.34 N 74.05 W
Midland City 219 40.09 N 89.08 W
Midland Park, Mi., U.S. 216 42.23 N 85.22 W
Midland Park, N.J., U.S. 276 40.59 N 74.08 W
Midland Park Lake ⊜ 212 44.44 N 79.53 W
Midlands □ 4 154 19.00 S 29.45 E
Midleton 48 51.55 N 8.10 W
Midlothian, Il., U.S. 216 41.37 N 87.43 W
Midlothian, Tx., U.S. 222 32.28 N 96.59 W
Midlothian Creek ≃ 278 41.39 N 87.40 W
Midlum 52 53.43 N 8.37 E
Midnapore 182 50.55 N 114.05 W
Midnapore Canal ≋ 126 22.25 N 87.53 E
Midnapore Plain ≚ 126 22.00 N 87.45 E
Mid-Ohio Sports Car Course ♠ 214 40.40 N 82.38 W
Midongy Nord 157b 20.45 S 46.13 E
Midongy Sud 157b 23.35 S 47.01 E
Midori 96 34.43 N 132.37 E
Midori ⊶ 8 268 35.32 N 139.34 E
Midori ≃ 92 32.42 N 130.37 E
Midou ≃ 32 43.54 N 0.30 W
Mid-Pacific Mountains ✣ 3 14 20.00 N 170.00 E
Midpines 226 37.32 N 119.55 W
Midreshet Ben Gurion 132 30.51 N 34.46 E
Midsayap 116 7.12 N 124.32 E
Midshipman Point › 282 38.07 N 122.27 W
Midsland 52 53.22 N 5.16 E
Midsomer Norton 42 51.18 N 2.28 W
Midu 102 25.22 N 100.31 E
Midvale, De., U.S. 285 39.39 N 75.37 W
Midvale, Id., U.S. 202 44.28 N 116.44 W
Midvale, Oh., U.S. 214 40.26 N 81.22 W
Midville 192 32.49 N 82.14 W
Midway, B.C., Can. 182 49.01 N 118.47 W
Midway, B.C., Can. 202 49.01 N 118.46 W
Midway, Al., U.S. 194 32.04 N 85.31 W
Midway, In., U.S. 216 41.37 N 85.55 W
Midway, Ky., U.S. 218 38.09 N 84.41 W
Midway, Pa., U.S. 279b 40.22 N 80.17 W
Midway, Tx., U.S. 222 31.02 N 95.45 W
Midway, Ut,. U.S. 200 40.30 N 111.28 W
Midway City 280 33.45 N 118.00 W
Midway Islands □ 2, Oc. 6 28.13 N 177.22 W
Midway Islands □ 2, Oc. 174g 28.13 N 177.22 W
Midway Mall ⊶ 9 279a 41.24 N 82.07 W
Midway Naval Station ■ 174g 28.13 N 177.26 W
Midway Park 192 34.43 N 77.21 W
Midwest 200 43.24 N 106.16 W
Midwest City 196 35.26 N 97.23 W
Midwolda 52 53.12 N 7.00 E
Midyan ⊶ 1 128 27.40 N 35.35 E
Midyat 130 37.25 N 41.23 E
Midyobe 152 1.21 N 10.18 E
Midžor (Midžur) ∧ 38 43.23 N 22.42 E
Mie 96 32.58 N 131.35 E
Mie □ 5 92 34.30 N 136.30 E
Miechów 30 50.23 N 20.01 E
Miedwie, Jezioro ⊜ 54 53.17 N 14.52 E
Międzybórz 30 51.24 N 17.40 E
Międzychód 30 52.36 N 15.55 E
Międzylesie 30 50.10 N 16.40 E
Międzyrzec Podlaski 30 52.00 N 22.47 E
Międzyrzecz 30 52.28 N 15.35 E
Międzyzdroje 30 53.55 N 14.28 E
Miehuapu 105 39.11 N 117.44 E
Miejska Górka 30 51.40 N 16.58 E
Miélan 32 43.26 N 0.19 E
Mielec 30 50.18 N 21.25 E
Mielno 30 54.16 N 16.01 E
Mien ⊜ 26 56.25 N 14.51 E
Mienga 152 17.17 S 19.48 E
Mienhua Yü I 100 25.29 N 122.06 E
Mient'ienhuo Shan ∧ 269d 25.11 N 121.30 E
Mier 232 26.26 N 99.09 W
Miercurea-Ciuc 38 46.22 N 25.48 E
Mieres 34 43.15 N 5.46 W
Mierlo 52 51.27 N 5.37 E
Mieroszów 30 50.41 N 16.10 E
Miersdorf 264a 52.20 N 13.37 E
Miersig 38 46.53 N 21.51 E
Mier y Noriega 234 23.25 N 100.07 W
Miesaituo 120 35.52 N 93.40 E
Miesbach 64 47.47 N 11.50 E
Miesenbach 61 47.22 N 15.46 E
Mieso 144 9.15 N 40.48 E
Mieste 54 52.28 N 11.11 E
Miesterhorst 54 52.27 N 11.09 E
Mieszkowice 30 52.46 N 14.30 E
Mifflin, Oh., U.S. 214 40.47 N 82.22 W
Mifflin, Pa., U.S. 208 40.34 N 77.24 W
Mifflin □ 6 210 40.40 N 77.33 W
Mifflinburg 210 40.55 N 77.02 W
Mifflintown 208 40.34 N 77.23 W
Mifflinville 210 41.01 N 76.18 W
Miftāḥ, Wādī V 142 30.15 N 31.46 E
Migdal 132 32.50 N 35.30 E
Migdal Ha'Emeq 132 32.41 N 35.15 E
Migdol 158 26.54 S 25.27 E
Migennes 50 47.58 N 3.31 E
Migliarino 66 44.46 N 11.56 E
Migliaro 64 44.48 N 11.58 E
Miglionico 68 40.34 N 16.30 E
Mignano Monte Lungo 68 41.23 N 13.58 E
Mignone ≃ 66 42.11 N 11.44 E
Mignovillard 58 46.48 N 6.08 E
Migori ≃ 154 0.59 S 34.15 E
Miguel Alemán, Presa ⊜ 1 234 18.13 N 96.32 W
Miguel Alves 250 4.10 S 42.54 W
Miguel Auza 232 24.18 N 103.25 W
Miguel Calmon 250 11.26 S 40.36 W
Miguel Couto 287a 22.43 S 43.27 W
Miguel de la Borda 236 9.09 N 80.19 W
Migueles, Arroyo de los ≃ 266a 40.20 N 3.32 W
Miguelete 258 34.01 S 57.39 W
Miguelete, Arroyo ≃ 258 34.14 S 57.54 W
Miguel Hidalgo, Presa ⊜ 1 232 26.30 N 108.35 W
Miguelópolis 255 20.12 S 48.03 W
Miguel Pereira 256 22.27 S 43.22 W
Miguel Riglos 252 36.51 S 63.42 W
Migulinskaja 80 49.42 N 41.16 E
Migvie 46 57.08 N 2.56 W
Migyaunglaung 110 14.40 N 98.09 E
Mihăești 38 45.07 N 25.00 E
Mihai Viteazu 38 44.39 N 28.41 E
Mihajlovgrad 38 43.25 N 23.13 E
Mihalgazi 130 40.02 N 30.34 E
Mihalıççık 130 39.52 N 31.30 E
Mihama, Nihon 94 34.46 N 136.54 E
Mihama, Nihon 94 35.36 N 135.56 E
Mihama, Nihon 96 33.54 N 135.08 E
Mihara, Nihon 96 34.24 N 133.05 E
Mihara, Nihon 96 34.17 N 134.46 E
Mihara, Nihon 96 34.32 N 135.34 E
Mihara-yama ∧ 94 34.43 N 139.23 E
Mihla 54 51.04 N 10.20 E
Miho 94 36.00 N 140.18 E
Mihonoseki 96 35.34 N 133.19 E
Miho-wan ⊂ 96 35.30 N 133.23 E
Mihuangzhuang 105 39.07 N 116.12 E
Mijaly 86 48.57 N 53.42 E
Mijares ≃ 34 39.55 N 0.01 W
Mijdaḥah 144 14.00 N 48.26 E
Mijdrecht 52 52.13 N 4.52 E
Mijiang 98 43.01 N 130.08 E
Mijoux 58 46.22 N 6.00 E
Mikabo-yama ∧ 94 36.09 N 138.55 E
Mikame 96 33.25 N 132.27 E
Mikamo, Nihon 96 35.09 N 133.37 E
Mikamo, Nihon 96 34.05 N 133.57 E
Mikasa 92a 43.14 N 141.53 E
Mikaševiči 76 52.13 N 27.28 E
Mikata 94 35.33 N 135.55 E
Mikata-ko ⊜ 94 35.34 N 135.53 E
Mikatou 273b 4.16 S 15.08 E
Mikawa, Nihon 94 36.29 N 136.29 E
Mikawa, Nihon 96 33.37 N 132.58 E
Mikawa-wan ⊂ 94 34.43 N 137.10 E
Mikawa-wan-kokutei-kōen ♠ 94 34.42 N 137.10 E
Mikazuki 96 34.58 N 134.27 E
Mikese 154 6.46 S 37.54 E
Mikhaylov, Cape › 9 66.51 S 118.33 E
Mikhrot Shelomo Hamelekh (Timna') (King Solomon's Mines) ⊥ 132 29.45 N 34.56 E
Miki, Nihon 96 34.48 N 134.59 E
Miki, Nihon 96 34.17 N 134.05 E
Mikínai ⊥ 38 37.44 N 22.45 E
Mikindani 154 10.17 S 40.07 E
Mikinduri 154 0.07 N 37.50 E
Mikkabi 94 34.48 N 137.33 E
Mikkaichi 270 34.26 N 135.35 E
Mikkeli 26 61.41 N 27.15 E
Mikkelin lääni □ 4 26 62.00 N 27.30 E
Mikkwa ≃ 176 58.25 N 114.45 W
Mikołajki 30 53.49 N 21.36 E
Mikołów 30 50.11 N 18.55 E
Mikomeseng 152 2.08 N 10.37 E
Mikomoto-jima I 94 34.34 N 138.56 E
Míkonos 38 37.26 N 25.20 E
Míkonos I 38 37.29 N 25.25 E
Mikope 152 5.03 S 20.48 E
Mikre 38 43.02 N 24.31 E
Mikrí Préspa, Límni ⊜ 38 40.46 N 21.04 E
Miksimil 126 22.52 N 89.23 E
Mikšino 76 57.15 N 35.43 E
Mikstat 30 51.32 N 17.59 E
Mikulášovice 54 50.58 N 14.20 E
Mikulincy 78 49.24 N 25.38 E
Mikulino 76 55.02 N 31.07 E
Mikulkin, mys › 24 67.48 N 46.40 E
Mikulov 61 48.49 N 16.39 E
Mikumi 154 7.24 S 36.59 E
Mikumi National Park ♠ 154 7.12 S 37.05 E
Mikun' 24 62.21 N 50.06 E
Mikuni 94 36.13 N 136.09 E
Mikuni-sammyaku ⋏ 94 36.50 N 138.40 E
Mikuni-tōge)(94 36.46 N 138.50 E
Mikuni-yama ∧ 94 35.59 N 138.43 E
Mikura-jima I 92 33.52 N 139.36 E
Mila 34 36.27 N 6.16 E
Milaca 190 45.45 N 93.39 W
Miladummadulu Atoll I 1 122 6.15 N 73.15 E
Milagre 256 21.18 S 47.00 W
Milagres 250 7.17 S 38.57 W
Milagro 246 2.07 S 79.36 W
Milagros 116 12.13 N 123.30 E
Milam □ 6 222 30.47 N 96.57 W
Milan → Milano, It. 62 45.28 N 9.12 E
Milan, Ga., U.S. 192 32.01 N 83.03 W
Milan, In., U.S. 218 39.07 N 85.07 W
Milan, Mi., U.S. 216 42.05 N 83.40 W
Milan, Mn., U.S. 198 45.06 N 95.54 W
Milan, Mo., U.S. 194 40.12 N 93.07 W
Milan, N.M., U.S. 200 35.10 N 107.53 W
Milan, Oh., U.S. 214 41.17 N 82.36 W
Milan, Pa., U.S. 210 41.54 N 76.32 W
Milan, Tn., U.S. 194 35.55 N 88.45 W
Milando 152 8.45 S 17.36 E
Milan Federal Correctional Institution ♥ 281 42.06 N 83.40 W
Milang 168b 35.25 S 138.58 E
Milano (Milan), It. 62 45.28 N 9.12 E
Milano (Milan), It. 266b 45.28 N 9.12 E
Milano, Tx., U.S. 222 30.43 N 96.52 W
Milano □ 4 62 45.30 N 9.30 E
Milanoa 157b 13.35 S 49.47 E
Milano Marittima 66 44.16 N 12.21 E
Milanville 210 41.40 N 75.04 W
Milâs 130 37.19 N 27.47 E
Milaševiči 78 51.39 N 27.56 E
Mil'atino, Ross. 76 54.29 N 34.18 E
Mil'atino, Ross. 82 55.41 N 35.48 E
Milazzo 70 38.13 N 15.14 E
Milazzo, Capo di › 70 38.16 N 15.14 E
Milazzo, Golfo di ⊂ 70 38.15 N 15.20 E
Milbank 198 45.13 N 96.38 W
Milbanke Sound ʊ 182 52.18 N 128.33 W
Milborne Port 42 50.58 N 2.27 W
Milbuk 116 6.10 N 124.16 E
Milburn 196 34.14 N 96.32 W
Milburn Creek ≃ 276 40.38 N 73.36 W
Milden 184 51.30 N 107.31 W
Mildenau 54 50.35 N 13.04 E
Mildenhall 42 52.21 N 0.30 E
Milders 64 47.06 N 11.16 E
Mildmay 212 44.03 N 81.07 W
Mildred, Il., U.S. 219 39.46 N 89.38 W
Mildred, Pa., U.S. 210 41.28 N 76.22 W
Mildura 166 34.12 S 142.09 E
Mile 102 24.26 N 103.26 E
Miléai 38 39.20 N 23.09 E
Milena 70 37.28 N 13.44 E
Milendella 168b 34.49 S 139.12 E
Milepa 154 11.43 S 36.20 E
Miles, Austl. 166 26.40 S 150.11 E
Miles, Tx., U.S. 196 31.35 N 100.10 W
Miles ≃ 283 42.40 N 70.51 W
Milesburg 214 40.56 N 77.47 W
Miles City 202 46.24 N 105.50 W
Miles Creek ⊂ 208 38.46 N 76.12 W
Miles Creek ≃ 226 37.12 N 120.21 W
Mile Seven Hundred Thirty Three 180 60.03 N 131.07 W
Milešovka ∧ 54 50.33 N 13.56 E
Milestone 184 50.00 N 104.30 W
Milesville 279b 40.12 N 79.52 W
Milet (Miletus) ⊥ 130 37.28 N 27.15 E
Mileto 68 38.36 N 16.04 E
Miletto, Monte ∧ 68 41.27 N 14.22 E
Miletus → Milet ⊥ 130 37.28 N 27.15 E
Mileura 162 26.23 S 117.20 E
Milevsko 30 49.27 N 14.22 E
Milford, Eng., U.K. 42 51.11 N 0.38 W
Milford, Ct., U.S. 207 41.13 N 73.04 W
Milford, De., U.S. 208 38.54 N 75.25 W
Milford, Il., U.S. 216 40.37 N 87.41 W
Milford, In., U.S. 216 41.24 N 85.50 W
Milford, Ia., U.S. 198 43.19 N 95.08 W
Milford, Ky., U.S. 218 38.34 N 84.09 W
Milford, Me., U.S. 188 44.56 N 68.38 W
Milford, Md., U.S. 284b 39.21 N 76.44 W
Milford, Ma., U.S. 207 42.08 N 71.31 W
Milford, Mi., U.S. 216 42.35 N 83.35 W
Milford, N.H., U.S. 207 42.50 N 71.38 W
Milford, N.J., U.S. 210 40.34 N 75.05 W
Milford, N.Y., U.S. 210 42.35 N 74.56 W
Milford, Oh., U.S. 218 39.10 N 84.17 W
Milford, Pa., U.S. 210 41.19 N 74.48 W
Milford, Tx., U.S. 222 32.07 N 96.57 W
Milford, Ut,. U.S. 200 38.23 N 113.00 W
Milford, Va., U.S. 208 38.01 N 77.22 W
Milford Brook ≃ 276 40.19 N 74.17 W
Milford Center 218 40.10 N 83.26 W
Milford Cross Roads 285 39.43 N 75.44 W
Milford Haven 42 51.40 N 5.02 W
Milford Haven ⊂ 42 51.42 N 5.03 W
Milford Lake ⊜ 1 198 39.15 N 97.00 W
Milford on Sea 42 50.44 N 1.36 W
Milford Ridge 284b 39.21 N 76.45 W
Milford Sound 172 44.40 S 167.54 E
Milford Sound ʊ 172 44.35 S 167.47 E
Milford Station 186 45.03 N 63.26 W
Milgis ≃ 154 1.48 N 38.06 E
Milgoo ∧ 162 28.51 S 118.07 E
Mil'guvejem ≃ 180 68.22 N 171.30 E
Milḥ, Baḥr al- ⊜ 128 32.40 N 43.35 E
Milḥat Ashqar ≡, 'Īrāq 128 35.18 N 41.55 E
Milḥat Ashqar ≡, 'Īrāq 130 35.18 N 41.55 E
Milhaud 62 43.47 N 4.18 E
Mili I 1 14 6.08 N 171.55 E
Milian ≃ 112 5.13 N 117.25 E
Milibangalala, Ponta › 158 26.26 S 32.56 E
Milicia ≃ 70 38.04 N 13.33 E
Milicz 30 51.32 N 17.17 E
Milieu, Rivière du ≃ 206 46.47 N 73.56 W
Milīj 142 30.36 N 31.03 E
Milim 164 5.10 S 152.00 E
Milín 60 49.39 N 14.02 E
Miling 162 30.30 S 116.21 E
Milis 71 40.03 N 8.38 E
Militello in Val di Catania 70 37.16 N 14.48 E
Militello Rosmarino 70 38.03 N 14.41 E
Milk ≃ 202 48.05 N 106.15 W
Milk Creek ≃, Co., U.S. 200 40.24 N 107.45 W
Milk Creek ≃, Or., U.S. 224 45.15 N 122.41 W
Milk Hill ∧ 2 42 51.23 N 1.51 W
Mil'kovo 74 54.43 N 158.37 E
Milk River 182 49.09 N 112.05 W
Milk River Ridge Reservoir ⊜ 1 182 49.22 N 112.35 W
Mill 52 51.41 N 5.47 E
Mill ≃, Ct., U.S. 276 41.08 N 73.16 W
Mill ≃, Ma., U.S. 207 42.18 N 72.37 W
Mill ≃, Ma., U.S. 283 42.38 N 70.41 W
Mill ≃, Ma., U.S. 283 42.12 N 70.57 W
Mill ≃, Ma., U.S. 283 42.08 N 71.21 W
Mill ≃, Ma., U.S. 283 42.44 N 70.52 W
Mill ≃, N.Y., U.S. 276 40.38 N 73.39 W
Millard 198 41.13 N 96.07 W
Millau 32 44.06 N 3.05 E
Mill Bay 224 48.39 N 123.34 W
Millboro 192 37.59 N 79.36 W
Millbourne 285 39.58 N 75.15 W
Millbrae 226 37.35 N 122.23 W
Millbrook, On., Can. 212 44.09 N 78.27 W
Millbrook, Eng., U.K. 42 50.20 N 4.13 W
Millbrook, Ma., U.S. 283 42.03 N 70.41 W
Millbrook, N.J., U.S. 276 40.52 N 74.33 W
Millbrook, N.Y., U.S. 210 41.47 N 73.41 W
Mill Brook ≃, Ma., U.S. 283 42.31 N 71.18 W
Mill Brook ≃, N.J., U.S. 276 40.53 N 74.32 W
Mill Brook ≃, N.J., U.S. 276 40.25 N 74.06 W
Mill Brook ≃, N.J., U.S. 276 40.29 N 74.23 W
Millburn 276 40.44 N 74.18 W
Millbury, Ma., U.S. 207 42.11 N 71.45 W
Millbury, Oh., U.S. 214 41.33 N 83.25 W
Mill City 202 44.45 N 122.29 W
Mill Creek, Pa., U.S. 214 40.26 N 77.56 W
Millcreek, Ut,. U.S. 200 40.27 N 111.54 W
Mill Creek, W.V., U.S. 188 38.43 N 79.58 W
Mill Creek ≃, Austl. 274a 33.59 S 151.01 E
Mill Creek ≃, Ca., U.S. 226 36.49 N 119.21 W
Mill Creek ≃, Ca., U.S. 228 34.05 N 117.06 W
Mill Creek ≃, De., U.S. 285 39.42 N 75.39 W
Mill Creek ≃, Il., U.S. 219 39.50 N 91.24 W
Mill Creek ≃, In., U.S. 194 39.30 N 86.57 W
Mill Creek ≃, In., U.S. 216 41.01 N 86.36 W
Mill Creek ≃, Ia., U.S. 198 42.47 N 95.31 W
Mill Creek ≃, Ks., U.S. 198 39.55 N 96.56 W
Mill Creek ≃, Ky., U.S. 218 38.28 N 84.20 W
Mill Creek ≃, N.J., U.S. 276 40.48 N 74.03 W
Mill Creek ≃, N.J., U.S. 285 40.02 N 74.55 W
Mill Creek ≃, N.Y., U.S. 212 43.57 N 76.08 W
Mill Creek ≃, Oh., U.S. 214 40.14 N 83.09 W
Mill Creek ≃, Oh., U.S. 214 41.06 N 80.40 W
Mill Creek ≃, Oh., U.S. 218 39.06 N 84.32 W
Mill Creek ≃, Oh., U.S. 279a 41.25 N 81.38 W
Mill Creek ≃, Or., U.S. 224 45.36 N 121.11 W
Mill Creek ≃, Pa., U.S. 208 40.00 N 76.18 W
Mill Creek ≃, Pa., U.S. 210 41.53 N 77.08 W
Mill Creek ≃, Pa., U.S. 214 41.09 N 79.03 W
Mill Creek ≃, Pa., U.S. 285 40.03 N 75.16 W
Mill Creek ≃, Pa., U.S. 285 40.08 N 74.52 W
Mill Creek ≃, Tx., U.S. 222 32.46 N 95.46 W
Mill Creek ≃, Tx., U.S. 222 29.50 N 96.07 W
Mill Creek ≃, Tx., U.S. 222 30.08 N 95.37 W
Mill Creek ≃, Va., U.S. 208 38.09 N 77.10 W
Mill Creek, North Fork ≃ 224 45.33 N 121.18 W
Mill Creek, South Fork ≃ 224 45.36 N 121.12 W
Millcreek Township 214 42.05 N 80.10 W
Milldale 207 41.33 N 72.53 W
Milledgeville, Ga., U.S. 192 33.04 N 83.13 W
Milledgeville, Il., U.S. 190 41.57 N 89.46 W

Symbols in the index entries represent the broad categories identified in the key at the right. Symbols with superior numbers (⋏¹) identify subcategories (see complete key on page I · 1).

Symbole im Register stellen die rechts im Schlüssel erklärten Kategorien dar. Symbole mit hochgestellten Ziffern (⋏¹) bezeichnen Unterabteilungen einer Kategorie (vgl. vollständiger Schlüssel auf Seite I · 1).

Los símbolos incluídos en el texto del índice representan las grandes categorías identificadas con la clave a la derecha. Los símbolos con numeros en su parte superior (⋏¹) identifican las subcategorías (véase la clave completa en la página I · 1).

Les symboles de l'index représentent les catégories indiquées dans la légende à droite. Les symboles suivis d'un indice (⋏¹) représentent des sous-catégories (voir légende complète à la page I · 1).

Os símbolos incluídos no texto do índice representam as grandes categorias identificadas com a chave à direita. Os símbolos com números em sua parte superior (⋏¹) identificam as subcategorias (veja-se a chave completa à página I · 1).

∧ Mountain	Berg	Montaña	Montagne	Montanha
⋏ Mountains	Gebirge	Montañas	Montagnes	Montanhas
)(Pass	Paß	Paso	Col	Passo
V Valley, Canyon	Tal, Cañon	Valle, Cañón	Vallée, Canyon	Vale, Canhão
≚ Plain	Ebene	Llano	Plaine	Planície
› Cape	Kap	Cabo	Cap	Cabo
I Island	Insel	Isla	Île	Ilha
II Islands	Inseln	Islas	Îles	Ilhas
⊥ Other Topographic Features	Andere Topographische Objekte	Otros Elementos Topográficos	Autres données topographiques	Outros acidentes topográficos

ESPAÑOL — Nombre, Página, Lat.°′, Long.°′ W = Oeste
FRANÇAIS — Nom, Page, Lat.°′, Long.°′ W = Ouest
PORTUGUÊS — Nome, Página, Lat.°′, Long.°′ W = Oeste

Milledgeville, Oh., U.S. 218 39.36 N 83.35 W
Mille Îles, Rivière des ≃ 206 45.42 N 73.32 W
Mille Lacs, Lac des ⊜ 190 48.50 N 90.30 W
Mille Lacs Kathio State Park ♠ 190 46.08 N 93.43 W
Mille Lacs Lake ⊜ 190 46.15 N 93.40 W
Millemont 261 48.49 N 1.45 E
Millen 192 32.48 N 81.56 W
Millendon 168a 31.48 S 116.02 E
Miller, Mo., U.S. 194 37.13 N 93.50 W
Miller, S.D., U.S. 198 44.31 N 98.59 W
Miller □ [6] 219 38.15 N 92.15 W
Miller, Mount ∧ 180 60.25 N 142.23 W
Miller City 216 41.06 N 84.08 W
Miller Creek ≃ 282 38.02 N 122.30 W
Miller House 180 65.32 N 145.11 W
Miller Mountain ∧ 204 38.03 N 118.12 W
Millerovo, Ross. 78 48.55 N 40.25 E
Millerovo, Ross. 83 47.49 N 39.15 E
Miller Peak ∧ 200 31.23 N 110.17 W
Miller Place 210 40.58 N 73.00 W
Millers ≃ 207 42.35 N 72.30 W
Millersburg, In., U.S. 216 41.31 N 85.41 W
Millersburg, In., U.S. 218 41.31 N 85.41 W
Millersburg, Ky., U.S. 218 38.18 N 84.08 W
Millersburg, Mi., U.S. 190 45.20 N 84.03 W
Millersburg, Oh., U.S. 214 40.33 N 81.55 W
Millersburg, Pa., U.S. 208 40.32 N 76.57 W
Millers Creek ≃ 196 33.27 N 99.14 W
Miller Seamount ✣ [3] 16 53.30 N 144.20 W
Millers Falls 207 42.34 N 72.29 W
Millers Ferry 194 32.05 N 87.22 W
Millers Flat 172 45.40 S 169.25 E
Millers Island 284b 39.14 N 76.24 W
Millers Pond ⊜ 276 40.51 N 73.12 W
Millersport 188 39.54 N 82.32 W
Millers Run ≃ 279b 40.22 N 80.07 W
Millerstown 210 40.32 N 77.09 W
Millersville, Il., U.S. 219 39.25 N 89.07 W
Millersville, Oh., U.S. 214 41.18 N 83.16 W
Millersville, Pa., U.S. 208 39.59 N 76.21 W
Millerton, N.Y., U.S. 210 41.57 N 73.30 W
Millerton, Pa., U.S. 210 41.59 N 76.56 W
Millerton Lake ⊜ [1] 226 37.01 N 119.41 W
Millerton Lake State Recreation Area ♠ 226 37.02 N 119.37 W
Millertown 186 48.49 N 56.33 W
Millertown Junction 186 49.01 N 56.21 W
Millesimo 62 44.22 N 8.12 E
Millet 182 53.06 N 113.28 W
Millett, Mi., U.S. 216 42.42 N 84.38 W
Millett, Tx., U.S. 196 28.35 N 99.12 W
Milleur Point › 44 55.01 N 5.06 W
Millevaches, Plateau de ⋏ [1] 32 45.30 N 2.10 E
Millford 48 55.07 N 7.43 W
Mill Green 260 51.41 N 0.22 E
Mill Grove 216 40.25 N 85.17 W
Mill Hall 210 41.06 N 77.29 W
Millheim 210 40.53 N 77.28 W
Mill Hill ◆ [8] 260 51.37 N 0.13 W
Mill Hill ∧ [2] 262 53.25 N 1.54 W
Millhousen 218 39.13 N 85.26 W
Millican 222 30.28 N 96.12 W
Millicent 166 37.36 S 140.22 E
Milligan, Fl., U.S. 194 30.45 N 86.38 W
Milligan, Ne., U.S. 198 40.30 N 97.23 W
Milligan Gulch V 200 33.37 N 107.02 W
Milligantown 279b 40.33 N 79.41 W
Milliken 275b 43.49 N 79.18 W
Millingen aan de Rijn 52 51.52 N 6.02 E
Millington, Il., U.S. 216 41.34 N 88.36 W
Millington, Md., U.S. 208 39.15 N 75.50 W
Millington, Mi., U.S. 190 43.16 N 83.31 W
Millington, N.J., U.S. 210 40.40 N 74.31 W
Millington, Tn., U.S. 194 35.20 N 89.53 W
Millinocket 188 45.39 N 68.42 W
Millionnyj 89 54.30 N 126.19 E
Millis 207 42.10 N 71.21 W
Mill Island I, Ant. 9 65.30 S 100.40 E
Mill Island I, N.T., Can. 176 64.00 N 78.00 W
Millisle 48 54.36 N 5.32 W
Mill Lake ⊜ 212 45.22 N 80.00 W
Millmerran 166 27.52 S 151.16 E
Millmont 210 40.53 N 77.08 W
Mill Neck 276 40.52 N 73.34 W
Mill Neck › [1] 276 40.53 N 73.33 W
Mill Neck Creek ⊂ 276 40.54 N 73.33 W
Millom 44 54.13 N 3.18 W
Mill Pond ⊜ 276 40.53 N 73.22 W
Millport, Scot., U.K. 46 55.46 N 4.55 W
Millport, Al., U.S. 194 33.33 N 88.04 W
Millport, N.Y., U.S. 210 42.16 N 76.50 W
Millport, Pa., U.S. 214 41.55 N 78.07 W
Millrift 210 41.25 N 74.45 W
Mill River 207 42.06 N 73.16 W
Mill Run Acres 284c 38.58 N 77.17 W
Millry 194 31.38 N 88.18 W
Mills, Pa., U.S. 214 41.57 N 77.41 W
Mills, Wy., U.S. 202 42.50 N 106.21 W
Mills, Lake ⊜ [1] 224 47.59 N 123.36 W
Millsboro 208 38.35 N 75.17 W
Mills Creek ≃, Austl. 166 22.23 S 143.05 E
Mills Creek ≃, Ca., U.S. 282 37.27 N 122.25 W
Mills Lake ⊜ 176 61.30 N 118.10 W
Mills Mansion State Historic Site ⊥ 210 41.52 N 73.57 W
Millstadt 219 38.27 N 90.05 W
Millstatt 64 46.48 N 13.35 E
Millstätter See ⊜ 64 46.47 N 13.35 E
Millstone 276 40.29 N 74.35 W
Millstone ≃ 276 40.33 N 74.34 W
Millstream, Austl. 162 21.35 S 117.04 E
Millstream, B.C., Can. 224 48.30 N 123.31 W
Millstream Chichester National Park ♠ 162 21.25 S 117.20 E
Millstreet 48 52.03 N 9.04 W
Milltown, Scot., U.K. 46 57.14 N 2.52 W
Milltown, In., U.S. 218 38.20 N 86.16 W
Milltown, Mt., U.S. 202 46.52 N 113.52 W
Milltown, N.J., U.S. 208 40.27 N 74.26 W
Milltown, Wi., U.S. 190 45.31 N 92.30 W
Milltown Malbay 48 52.50 N 9.23 W
Millvale 279b 40.28 N 79.58 W
Mill Valley 226 37.54 N 122.32 W
Mill Village 214 41.53 N 79.58 W
Millville, Ma., U.S. 207 42.01 N 71.34 W
Millville, N.J., U.S. 208 39.24 N 75.02 W
Millville, Oh., U.S. 218 39.24 N 84.40 W
Millville, Pa., U.S. 210 41.07 N 76.31 W
Millville Lake 283 42.48 N 71.13 W
Millville Lake ⊜ 283 42.48 N 71.13 W
Millwood, Md., U.S. 284c 38.53 N 76.53 W
Millwood, N.Y., U.S. 210 41.11 N 73.48 W
Millwood, Va., U.S. 188 39.04 N 78.02 W
Millwood Lake ⊜ [1] 194 33.45 N 94.00 W
Milly-la-Forêt 50 48.24 N 2.28 E
Milly-Lamartine 58 46.21 N 4.42 E
Milmay 208 39.26 N 74.51 W
Milmersdorf 54 53.06 N 13.38 E
Milmine 219 39.54 N 88.39 W
Milmont Park 285 39.53 N 75.20 W
Milne Bay □ [5] 164 10.00 S 152.30 E
Milne Bay ⊂ 164 10.22 S 150.30 E
Milner 224 49.20 N 122.42 W
Milnesville 210 40.59 N 75.59 W
Milngavie 46 55.57 N 4.20 W
Milnor 198 46.15 N 97.27 W
Milnrow 44 53.37 N 2.06 W
Milnthorpe 44 54.14 N 2.46 W
Milo, Ab., Can. 182 50.34 N 112.53 W
Milo, Ia., U.S. 190 41.17 N 93.26 W
Milo, Me., U.S. 188 45.15 N 68.59 W
Milo ≃ 150 11.04 N 9.14 W
Milon-la-Chapelle 261 48.44 N 2.03 E

Mílos 38 36.45 N 24.27 E
Mílos I 38 36.41 N 24.15 E
Miloslaviči 76 53.41 N 32.15 E
Miloslavskoje 76 53.34 N 39.24 E
Miłosław 30 52.13 N 17.29 E
Milow, Dtsch. 54 53.11 N 11.32 E
Milow, Dtsch. 54 52.31 N 12.18 E
Milpa Alta ◆ [8] 286a 19.11 N 99.01 W
Milparinka 166 29.44 S 141.53 E
Milpitas 226 37.25 N 121.54 W
Milpitas Wash V 204 33.18 N 114.44 W
Milroy, In., U.S. 218 39.29 N 85.28 W
Milroy, Pa., U.S. 208 40.42 N 77.35 W
Milseburg ∧ 56 50.32 N 9.53 E
Mil'skaja ravnina ≚ 84 40.00 N 48.00 E
Milspe 263 51.18 N 7.21 E
Miltach 60 49.09 N 12.46 E
Miltenberg 56 49.42 N 9.15 E
Miltitz 54 51.19 N 12.16 E
Milton, Austl. 170 35.19 S 150.26 E
Milton, On., Can. 212 43.31 N 79.53 W
Milton, N.Z. 172 46.07 S 169.58 E
Milton, Eng., U.K. 42 52.14 N 0.09 E
Milton, De., U.S. 208 38.46 N 75.18 W
Milton, Fl., U.S. 194 30.37 N 87.02 W
Milton, Il., U.S. 219 39.34 N 90.39 W
Milton, In., U.S. 218 38.58 N 85.01 W
Milton, In., U.S. 218 39.47 N 85.09 W
Milton, Ia., U.S. 190 40.40 N 92.09 W
Milton, Ky., U.S. 218 38.43 N 85.22 W
Milton, Ma., U.S. 207 42.15 N 71.05 W
Milton, N.J., U.S. 276 41.02 N 74.32 W
Milton, N.Y., U.S. 210 41.39 N 73.57 W
Milton, N.D., U.S. 198 48.37 N 98.02 W
Milton, Pa., U.S. 210 41.00 N 76.50 W
Milton, Vt., U.S. 188 44.38 N 73.06 W
Milton, Wa., U.S. 224 47.14 N 122.18 W
Milton, W.V., U.S. 188 38.26 N 82.07 W
Milton, Wi., U.S. 216 42.46 N 88.56 W
Milton, Lake ⊜ 214 41.06 N 80.58 W
Milton Abbot 42 50.35 N 4.15 W
Milton-Freewater 202 45.55 N 118.23 W
Milton Harbor ⊂ 276 40.57 N 73.42 W
Milton Keynes 42 52.02 N 0.42 W
Milton Point › 276 40.57 N 73.42 W
Miltonvale 198 39.20 N 97.26 W
Miltou 146 10.14 N 17.26 E
Miltzow 54 54.12 N 13.13 E
Milumba 154 7.06 S 31.04 E
Miluo 100 28.50 N 113.04 E
Miluo ≃ 100 28.50 N 113.06 E
Mil'utinskaja 80 48.38 N 41.40 E
Mil'utkej, gora ∧ 180 65.42 N 178.03 W
Milverton, On., Can. 212 43.34 N 80.55 W
Milverton, Eng., U.K. 42 51.02 N 3.16 W
Milwaukee 216 43.02 N 87.54 W
Milwaukee □ [6] 216 43.02 N 87.58 W
Milwaukee ≃ 190 43.02 N 87.54 W
Milwaukee Bay ⊂ 216 43.02 N 87.53 W
Milwaukie 224 45.26 N 122.38 W
Mim 150 6.54 N 2.34 W
Mima 96 33.17 N 132.36 E
Mimasaka 96 35.00 N 134.10 E
Mimbres ≃ 200 32.13 N 107.28 W
Mimbres Mountains ⋏ 200 32.45 N 107.45 W
Mimi ≃ 92 32.20 N 131.37 E
Mimico ◆ [8] 275b 43.37 N 79.30 W
Mimico Creek ≃ 275b 43.37 N 79.29 W
Mimizan 32 44.12 N 1.14 W
Mimmaya 92 41.12 N 140.26 E
Mimoň 54 50.40 N 14.44 E
Mimongo 152 1.11 S 11.36 E
Mimoso, Bra. 248 16.17 S 55.48 W
Mimoso, Bra. 255 15.10 S 48.05 W
Mimoso do Sul 255 21.04 S 41.22 W
Mims 220 28.39 N 80.50 W
Mimuro-yama ∧ 96 35.14 N 134.28 E
Min ≃, Zhg. 100 26.05 N 119.32 E
Min ≃, Zhg. 102 28.46 N 104.38 E
Mina, Méx. 196 26.01 N 100.32 W
Mina, Nv., U.S. 204 38.23 N 118.06 W
Mina ≃ 112 10.09 S 124.12 E
Mîna, Oued ≃ 34 35.47 N 0.30 E
Mīnā' al-Aḥmadī 128 29.04 N 48.08 E
Mīnāb 128 27.09 N 57.05 E
Mīnāb ≃ 128 27.01 N 56.53 E
Minabe 96 33.46 N 135.19 E
Minabegawa 96 33.47 N 135.20 E
Mina El Limón 236 12.45 N 86.44 W
Minago ≃ 184 54.34 N 98.08 W
Minahasa › [1] 112 1.00 N 124.35 E
Mināj ≃ [1] 126 22.31 N 89.22 E
Minakami 94 36.46 N 138.58 E
Minakuchi 94 34.58 N 136.10 E
Minam ≃ 202 45.37 N 117.43 W
Minamata 92 32.13 N 130.24 E
Minami 94 35.39 N 136.57 E
Minami ◆ [8], Nihon 268 35.24 N 139.36 E
Minami ◆ [8], Nihon 270 34.40 N 135.31 E
Minami ◆ [8], Nihon 270 34.58 N 135.45 E
Minami ≃ 94 35.30 N 135.49 E
Minamiaiki 94 36.02 N 138.33 E
Minami-Alps-kokuritsu-kōen ♠ 94 35.40 N 138.13 E
Minamiashigara 94 35.19 N 139.07 E
Minami-Bōsō-kokutei-kōen ♠ 94 35.10 N 140.05 E
Minamichita 94 34.44 N 136.52 E
Minami-Daitō-jima I 90 25.50 N 131.15 E
Minami-Iō-jima I 14 24.14 N 141.28 E
Minamiizu 94 34.39 N 138.50 E
Minamimaki 94 36.00 N 138.30 E
Minaminasu 94 36.39 N 140.06 E
Minamisenju ◆ [8] 268 35.44 N 139.48 E
Minamishinano 94 35.19 N 137.56 E
Minami-Tori-shima (Marcus Island) I 14 24.18 N 153.58 E
Minano 94 36.04 N 139.06 E
Mina Pirquitas 252 22.41 S 66.31 W
Minard, S. Afr. 158 31.17 S 27.35 E
Minard, Scot., U.K. 46 56.07 N 5.15 W
Minas, Cuba 240p 21.29 N 77.37 W
Minas, Indon. 114 0.50 N 101.29 E
Minas, Ur. 252 34.23 S 55.14 W
Minas, Sierra de las ⋏ 236 15.10 N 89.40 W
Minas Basin ⊂ 186 45.20 N 64.00 W
Minas Channel ц 186 45.15 N 64.45 W
Minas de Barroterán 232 27.40 N 101.20 W
Minas de Corrales 252 31.35 S 55.28 W
Minas de Matahambre 240p 22.35 N 83.57 W
Minas de Oro 236 14.46 N 87.20 W
Minas de Ríotinto 34 37.42 N 6.35 W
Minas Gerais □ [3] 255 18.00 S 44.00 W
Minas Novas 255 17.15 S 42.36 W
Mînăstirea 38 44.13 N 26.54 E
Minatare 198 41.48 N 103.30 W
Minatitlán 234 17.59 N 94.31 W
Minato 268 35.13 N 139.52 E
Minato ◆ [8], Nihon 268 35.39 N 139.45 E
Minato ◆ [8], Nihon 270 34.39 N 135.26 E
Minato ≃ 268 35.13 N 139.52 E
Minbāl 142 28.24 N 30.41 E
Minbu 110 20.11 N 94.52 E
Minbulak 85 41.30 N 75.53 E
Minbya 110 20.22 N 93.15 E
Minbyin 110 19.17 N 93.32 E
Minchinābād 123 30.10 N 73.34 E
Minchinhampton 42 51.42 N 2.10 W
Minchumina, Lake ⊜ 180 63.52 N 152.15 W
Mincio ≃ 64 45.04 N 10.59 E
Minco 196 35.18 N 97.56 W
Minčol ∧ 30 49.15 N 20.59 E
Mind'ak 86 54.02 N 58.48 E
Mindanao I 116 8.00 N 125.00 E
Mindanao ≃ 116 7.07 N 124.24 E
Mindego Creek ≃ 282 37.18 N 122.15 W
Mindego Hill ∧ [2] 282 37.18 N 122.13 W
Mindel ≃ 58 48.31 N 10.23 E

Mindelheim 58 48.03 N 10.29 E
Mindelo 150a 16.53 N 25.00 W
Mindemoya 190 45.44 N 82.10 W
Minden, On., Can. 212 44.55 N 78.43 W
Minden, Dtsch. 52 52.17 N 8.55 E
Minden, La., U.S. 194 32.36 N 93.17 W
Minden, Ne., U.S. 198 40.29 N 98.56 W
Minden, Nv., U.S. 226 38.57 N 119.45 W
Minden, W.V., U.S. 188 37.58 N 81.07 W
Minden City 190 43.40 N 82.46 W
Mindenmines 194 37.28 N 94.35 W
Minderoo 162 22.00 S 115.02 E
Mindif 146 10.24 N 14.26 E
Mindiptana 164 5.45 S 140.42 E
Mindon 110 19.21 N 94.44 E
Mindoro I 116 12.50 N 121.05 E
Mindoro Occidental □ [4] 116 13.00 N 121.00 E
Mindoro Oriental □ [4] 116 13.00 N 121.20 E
Mindoro Strait ц 116 12.20 N 120.40 E
Mindouli 152 4.17 S 14.21 E
Mindourou, Cam. 152 4.06 N 14.34 E
Mindourou, Cam. 152 3.25 N 13.32 E
Minduri 256 21.41 S 44.37 W
Mindživan 84 39.03 N 46.42 E
Mine, Ityo. 144 8.20 N 40.09 E
Mine, Nihon 96 33.17 N 130.26 E
Mine, Nihon 96 34.10 N 131.13 E
Minear Lake ⊜ 278 42.17 N 87.57 W
Minebank Run ≃ 284b 39.25 N 76.32 W
Mine Brook ≃, Ma., U.S. 283 42.08 N 71.26 W
Mine Brook ≃, Ma., U.S. 283 42.09 N 71.15 W
Mine Brook ≃, N.J., U.S. 276 40.41 N 74.38 W
Mine Centre 190 48.45 N 92.37 W
Minehead 42 51.13 N 3.29 W
Mine Hill 210 40.52 N 74.35 W
Mineiros 255 17.34 S 52.34 W
Mineo 70 37.16 N 14.42 E
Mineola, N.Y., U.S. 210 40.44 N 73.38 W
Mineola, Tx., U.S. 222 32.39 N 95.29 W
Miner ≃ 180 66.30 N 138.25 W
Mineral 224 46.43 N 122.10 W
Mineral City 214 40.36 N 81.21 W
Mineral Creek ≃ 224 46.45 N 122.08 W
Mineral de Cucharas 234 22.52 N 105.19 W
Mineral del Monte 234 20.08 N 98.40 W
Mineral de Pozos 234 21.14 N 100.29 W
Mineral'nyje Vody 84 44.12 N 43.08 E
Mineral Point, Pa., U.S. 214 40.23 N 78.50 W
Mineral Point, Wi., U.S. 190 42.51 N 90.10 W
Mineral Ridge 214 41.08 N 80.46 W
Mineral Springs, Ar., U.S. 194 33.52 N 93.54 W
Mineral Springs, Pa., U.S. 214 41.00 N 78.22 W
Mineral Wells 196 32.48 N 98.06 W
Minerbe 64 45.14 N 11.20 E
Minerbio 64 44.37 N 11.29 E
Minersville, Pa., U.S. 208 40.41 N 76.16 W
Minersville, Ut., U.S. 200 38.12 N 112.55 W
Mine Run ≃ 285 40.15 N 75.28 W
Minerva, Ky., U.S. 218 38.42 N 83.55 W
Minerva, Oh., U.S. 214 40.43 N 81.06 W
Minerva, Tx., U.S. 222 30.46 N 96.59 W
Minerva, Embalse ⊜ [1] 240p 22.25 N 79.48 W
Minerva Park 214 40.04 N 83.00 W
Minervino Murge 68 41.05 N 16.05 E
Minesing Swamp ≡ 212 44.23 N 79.51 W
Minetto 210 43.23 N 76.28 W
Mineville 188 44.05 N 73.31 W
Mineyama 96 35.37 N 135.04 E
Minfeng 120 37.05 N 82.40 E
Minga 154 11.08 S 27.57 E
Mingala 152 5.06 N 21.49 E
Mingan 186 50.18 N 64.02 W
Mingan ≃ 186 50.18 N 63.59 W
Mingan, Îles de II 186 50.12 N 63.35 W
Mingan Archipelago National Park ♠ 186 50.12 N 63.35 W
Mingan Mountains ⋏ 116 15.29 N 121.24 E
Mingāora 123 34.47 N 72.22 E
Mingardo ≃ 68 40.02 N 15.18 E
Mingary 166 32.08 S 140.44 E
Mingcheng 89 43.11 N 125.59 E
Mingečaur 84 40.45 N 47.03 E
Mingečaurskoje vodochranilišče ⊜ [1] 84 40.50 N 46.50 E
Mingela 166 19.53 S 146.38 E
Mingenew 162 29.11 S 115.26 E
Mingera Creek ≃ 166 20.38 S 138.10 E
Minggang 100 32.29 N 114.03 E
Minggao 100 34.20 N 112.15 E
Minghuang 106 31.41 N 119.56 E
Mingin 110 22.52 N 94.39 E
Mingjuesi 106 31.34 N 118.53 E
Minglanilla 34 39.32 N 1.36 W
Ming Ming 164 5.30 S 146.10 E
Mingo, Congo 152 1.55 S 14.59 E
Mingo, Oh., U.S. 216 40.13 N 83.38 W
Mingo Creek ≃, Pa., U.S. 279b 40.13 N 79.57 W
Mingo Creek ≃, Pa., U.S. 285 40.10 N 75.32 W
Mingo Junction 214 40.19 N 80.36 W
Mingorría 34 40.45 N 4.40 W
Mingoville 214 40.56 N 77.39 W
Mingoyo 154 10.06 S 39.38 E
Mingrel'skaja 78 45.01 N 38.20 E
Mingshantou 100 29.18 N 112.33 E
Mingshui, Zhg. 89 47.10 N 125.55 E
Mingshui, Zhg. 102 42.06 N 96.04 E
Mingulay I 46 56.49 N 7.38 W
Mingwan 106 31.04 N 120.17 E
Mingxi 100 26.24 N 117.13 E
Mingyuegou 89 43.07 N 128.54 E
Mingyuelu 85 39.34 N 75.26 E
Minhang 106 31.01 N 121.24 E
Minhla, Mya. 110 19.58 N 95.03 E
Minhla, Mya. 110 17.59 N 95.43 E
Minho □ [9] 34 41.40 N 8.30 W
Minho (Miño) ≃ 34 41.52 N 8.51 W
Minhou 100 26.12 N 119.06 E
Minianko 150 9.58 N 8.22 W
Minićevo 38 43.41 N 22.18 E
Minicoy Island I 122 8.17 N 73.02 E
Minier 194 40.26 N 89.18 W
Minigwal, Lake ⊜ 162 29.35 S 123.12 E
Minija ≃ 76 55.21 N 21.17 E
Minilya 162 23.51 S 113.58 E
Minilya ≃ 162 23.56 S 113.51 E
Minimarg 123 34.47 N 75.05 E
Minīn 132 33.39 N 36.18 E
Miniota 184 50.08 N 101.00 W
Minisinakwa Lake ⊜ 190 47.40 N 81.43 W
Ministikwan Lake ⊜ 184 54.01 N 109.39 W
Ministro Ramos Mexía 254 40.30 S 67.17 W
Ministro Rivadavia 288 34.51 S 58.22 W
Minitonas 184 52.07 N 101.00 W
Minj 164 5.54 S 144.39 E
Minjar 86 55.04 N 57.33 E
Minjary, Mount ∧ 171b 35.14 S 148.08 E
Minjiadianzi 104 41.35 N 121.41 E
Minjiaji 100 31.08 N 115.01 E
Minkamman 140 6.03 N 31.32 E
Min'kovo 76 59.42 N 43.28 E
Min-Kuš 85 41.41 N 74.28 E
Minlaton 168b 34.46 S 137.36 E
Minle, Zhg. 100 22.59 N 112.58 E
Minle, Zhg. 102 38.27 N 100.56 E
Minna 150 9.37 N 6.33 E
Minna Bluff › [1] 9 78.32 S 166.30 E
Minna-shima I, Nihon 174m 26.39 N 127.49 E
Minna-shima I, Nihon 175d 24.45 N 124.42 E

Minneapolis, Ks., U.S. 198 39.07 N 97.42 W
Minneapolis, Mn., U.S. 190 44.58 N 93.15 W
Minnechaduza Creek ≃ 198 42.54 N 100.29 W
Minnedosa 184 50.14 N 99.51 W
Minnehaha 224 45.39 N 122.37 W
Minnehaha, Lake ⊜ 220 28.31 N 81.46 W
Minneola, Fl., U.S. 220 28.35 N 81.45 W
Minneola, Ks., U.S. 198 37.26 N 100.00 W
Minneola, Lake ⊜ 220 28.34 N 81.46 W
Minneosa Creek ≃ 196 35.31 N 102.48 W
Minneota 198 44.34 N 95.59 W
Minnertsga 52 53.15 N 5.35 E
Minnesota □ [3] 178 46.00 N 94.15 W
Minnesota ≃ 178 44.54 N 93.10 W
Minnesota Lake 190 43.50 N 93.49 W
Minnewanka, Lake ⊜ 182 51.15 N 115.20 W
Minnewaukan 198 48.04 N 99.15 W
Minnie Creek 162 24.02 S 115.42 E
Minnigaff 44 54.58 N 4.30 W
Minnipa 162 32.51 S 135.09 E
Minnitaki Lake ⊜ 184 49.58 N 92.00 W
Minnoch, Water of ≃ 44 55.02 N 4.33 W
Mino, Nihon 94 35.32 N 136.55 E
Minō, Nihon 96 34.50 N 135.28 E
Miño (Minho) ≃, Europe 34 41.52 N 8.51 W
Minō ≃, Nihon 270 34.47 N 134.57 E
Minoa 210 43.04 N 76.00 W
Minobu 94 35.22 N 138.26 E
Minobu-san ∧ 94 35.24 N 138.25 E
Minobu-sanchi ⋏ 94 35.14 N 138.20 E
Minocqua 190 45.52 N 89.42 W
Minokamo 94 35.26 N 137.01 E
Mino-Mikawa-kōgen ⋏ [1] 94 35.11 N 137.23 E
Minong 190 46.05 N 91.49 W
Minonk 216 40.54 N 89.02 W
Minooka 216 41.27 N 88.16 W
Minorca → Menorca I 34 40.00 N 4.00 E
Minori 94 36.14 N 140.21 E
Minorsville 218 38.20 N 84.42 W
Minoshō 270 34.39 N 135.49 E
Minot, Ma., U.S. 283 42.14 N 70.45 W
Minot, N.D., U.S. 198 48.13 N 101.17 W
Minot Air Force Base ■ 198 48.26 N 101.21 W
Minowa 94 35.55 N 137.59 E
Minqiao 100 32.53 N 119.13 E
Minqin 102 38.42 N 103.11 E
Minqing 100 26.12 N 118.51 E
Minquadale 285 39.42 N 75.34 W
Minquan 98 34.41 N 115.11 E
Minquiers, Plateau des II 32 48.57 N 2.09 W
Minsen 52 53.42 N 7.58 E
Min Shan ⋏ 102 33.35 N 103.00 E
Minshāt adh-Dhahab 142 28.00 N 30.42 E
Minshat al-Amir Muhammad 'Ali 142 29.10 N 30.38 E
Minshāt al-Bakkārī 273c 30.01 N 31.08 E
Minshāt al-Ikhwah 142 30.56 N 31.21 E
Minshāt al-Mughālaqah 142 27.44 N 30.47 E
Minshāt Būlīn 142 31.11 N 30.10 E
Minshāt Sulṭān 142 30.32 N 30.55 E
Minsk 76 53.54 N 27.34 E
Minsk □ [8] 76 53.45 N 27.45 E
Minskaja vozvyšennost' ⋏ [1] 76 54.00 N 27.10 E
Mińsk Mazowiecki 30 52.11 N 21.34 E
Minster, Eng., U.K. 42 51.20 N 1.19 E
Minster, Eng., U.K. 42 51.26 N 0.49 E
Minster, Oh., U.S. 216 40.24 N 84.23 W
Minsterley 42 52.39 N 2.55 W
Minta 152 4.35 N 12.48 E
Mintaka Pass)(123 37.00 N 74.50 E
Mintard 263 51.22 N 6.54 E
Mintaro 168b 33.55 S 138.43 E
Mint Canyon 228 34.26 N 118.25 W
Mintlaw 46 57.31 N 2.00 W
Minto, Austl. 274a 34.01 S 150.51 E
Minto, Mb., Can. 184 49.25 N 100.01 W
Minto, N.B., Can. 186 46.05 N 66.05 W
Minto, Yk., Can. 180 62.34 N 136.51 W
Minto, Ak., U.S. 180 65.09 N 149.21 W
Minto, N.D., U.S. 198 48.17 N 97.22 W
Minto, Lac ⊜ 176 57.13 N 75.00 W
Minto, Mount ∧ 9 71.55 S 169.33 E
Minto Inlet ⊂ 176 71.20 N 117.00 W
Mintom II 152 2.42 N 13.17 E
Minton 184 49.10 N 104.35 W
Mintoum 152 0.27 N 12.16 E
Minturn 200 39.35 N 106.25 W
Minturnae ⊥ 68 41.14 N 13.45 E
Minturno 66 41.15 N 13.45 E
Minūf 142 30.28 N 30.56 E
Minulovo 265a 60.03 N 30.45 E
Minumadai-yōsui ≍ 268 35.50 N 139.42 E
Minur'uk 85 40.56 N 73.22 E
Minusinsk 86 53.43 N 91.42 E
Minutang 120 28.13 N 96.32 E
Minute Man National Historical Park ♠ 207 42.27 N 71.17 W
Minvoul 152 2.09 N 12.08 E
Minwakh 144 16.50 N 48.05 E
Minxian 102 34.26 N 104.02 E
Minya → Al-Minyā 142 28.06 N 30.45 E
Minyā al-Qamḥ 142 30.31 N 31.21 E
Minya Konka → Gongga Shan ∧ 102 29.35 N 101.51 E
Minyat an-Naṣr 142 31.07 N 31.39 E
Minyat as-Sīrij ◆ [8] 273c 30.05 N 31.15 E
Minyat Sandūb 142 31.00 N 31.23 E
Minžir 38 46.40 N 28.19 E
Minzow 54 53.23 N 12.30 E
Mio 190 44.39 N 84.07 W
Mioglia 62 44.29 N 8.25 E
Mionica 38 44.15 N 20.05 E
Miory 76 55.37 N 27.38 E
Mipi 120 28.57 N 95.48 E
Miquan 86 44.06 N 87.35 E
Miquelon I 186 47.03 N 56.20 W
Miquihuana 234 23.34 N 99.47 W
Miquon 285 40.04 N 75.16 W
Mir, Bela. 76 53.27 N 26.28 E
Mir, Cuba 240p 20.46 N 76.36 W
Mīr, Miṣr 142 27.27 N 30.44 E
Mir, Niger 146 14.05 N 11.59 E
Mira 34 40.26 N 8.44 W
Mira ≃, N.S., Can. 186 46.03 N 60.00 W
Mira ≃, Col. 246 1.36 N 79.01 W
Mira ≃, Port. 34 37.43 N 8.47 W
Mīrābād 128 30.25 N 61.50 E
Mira Bay ⊂ 186 46.02 N 59.56 W
Mirabeau 62 43.42 N 5.39 E
Mirabel 206 45.39 N 74.05 W
Mirabel, Aéroport International de ⊠ 206 45.41 N 74.02 W
Mirabella Eclano 68 41.02 N 14.59 E
Mirabella Imbaccari 70 37.19 N 14.27 E
Mirabello, Ippodromo ♠ 266b 45.36 N 9.17 E
Mirabello Monferrato 62 45.02 N 8.31 E
Miracema do Tocantins 250 9.33 S 48.24 W
Mirada Hills → La Mirada 228 33.54 N 118.01 W
Mirador 250 6.22 S 44.22 W
Mirador, Cerro ∧ 286d 11.57 S 77.02 W
Mirador, Paso de)(254 40.42 S 71.56 W
Miradouro 255 20.53 S 42.21 W
Miraflores, Arg. 252 28.36 S 65.55 W
Miraflores, Col. 246 5.12 N 73.12 W
Miraflores, Col. 246 1.25 N 72.13 W
Miraflores, Perú 286d 12.07 S 77.02 W

Miraflores, Esclusas de ◆ [5] 236 9.00 N 79.36 W
Miraflores, Palacio ʋ 286c 10.31 N 66.55 W
Mīrah, Wādī al- V 128 32.26 N 41.42 E
Miraí 256 21.12 S 42.37 W
Miraj 122 16.50 N 74.38 E
Miraki 85 39.02 N 67.10 E
Miraleste 228 33.46 N 118.19 W
Mira Loma 228 34.01 N 117.31 W
Miramar, Arg. 252 38.16 S 57.51 W
Miramar, Arg. 252 30.54 S 62.40 W
Miramar, C.R. 236 10.06 N 84.44 W
Miramar, Fr. 62 43.30 N 6.57 E
Miramar, Moç. 156 23.50 S 35.34 E
Miramar, Fl., U.S. 220 25.59 N 80.13 W
Miramar ◆ [8] 286b 23.07 N 82.25 W
Miramar, Laguna ⊜ 236 16.23 N 91.16 W
Miramare 66 44.02 N 12.38 E
Miramare, Aeroporto di ⊠ 66 44.02 N 12.35 E
Miramare, Castello di ⊥ 64 45.42 N 13.43 E
Miramar Naval Air Station ■ 228 32.52 N 117.07 W
Miramas 62 43.35 N 5.00 E
Mirambeau 32 45.23 N 0.34 W
Miramichi Bay ⊂ 186 47.08 N 65.08 W
Mira Monte 228 36.42 N 119.03 W
Mīram Shāh 120 33.01 N 70.04 E
Mīrān 123 31.24 N 70.43 E
Miranda, Austl. 274a 34.02 S 151.06 E
Miranda, Bra. 248 20.14 S 56.22 W
Miranda, Col. 246 3.15 N 76.14 W
Miranda, Ca., U.S. 204 40.14 N 123.49 W
Miranda □ [3] 246 10.15 N 66.25 W
Miranda ≃ 248 19.25 S 57.20 W
Miranda, Aerodromo ⊠ 286c 10.29 N 66.50 W
Miranda de Ebro 34 42.41 N 2.57 W
Miranda do Douro 34 41.30 N 6.16 W
Mirande 32 43.31 N 0.25 E
Mirandela 34 41.29 N 7.11 W
Mirando City 196 27.26 N 99.00 W
Mirandola 64 44.53 N 11.04 E
Mirano 64 45.30 N 12.07 E
Mirantão 256 22.15 S 44.30 W
Mirante do Paranapanema 255 22.17 S 51.54 W
Mirapuxi ≃ 255 13.06 S 51.10 W
Mirasaka 96 34.46 N 132.58 E
Mira Taglio 64 45.26 N 12.08 E
Miravalles, Volcán ∧ [1] 236 10.45 N 85.10 W
Miravete, Puerto de)(34 39.43 N 5.43 W
Mīr Bacheh Kowt 120 34.45 N 69.08 E
Mirbāṭ 118 17.00 N 54.45 E
Mirboo North 169 38.24 S 146.10 E
Mirebeau-sur-Bèze 58 47.24 N 5.19 E
Mirecourt 58 48.18 N 6.08 E
Miren 64 45.54 N 13.37 E
Mirfield 44 53.40 N 1.41 W
Mirgorod 78 49.58 N 33.36 E
Mirgorodka 80 50.58 N 53.33 E
Miri 112 4.23 N 113.59 E
Miriam Vale 166 24.20 S 151.34 E
Mirim, Lagoa (Laguna Merín) ⊂ 252 32.45 S 52.50 W
Mirimichi, Lake ⊜ 283 42.02 N 71.18 W
Mírina 38 39.52 N 25.04 E
Miriñay ≃ 252 30.10 S 57.39 W
Mirinzal 250 2.01 S 44.43 W
Miritiparaná ≃ 246 1.11 S 70.02 W
Miriyama 164 3.57 S 141.45 E
Mīrjāveh 128 29.01 N 61.28 E
Mirke ◆ [8] 263 51.16 N 7.09 E
Mirna ≃ 64 45.19 N 13.36 E
Mirnock ∧ 64 46.46 N 13.43 E
Mirnoje Ozero 86 57.44 N 78.45 E
Mirnyj, Ross. 74 62.33 N 113.53 E
Mirnyj, Ross. 80 53.30 N 50.18 E
Mirnyj, Ukr. 78 50.57 N 28.34 E
Mirnyy ʋ [3] 9 66.33 S 93.00 E
Mirond Lake ⊜ 184 55.06 N 102.47 W
Mironeasa 38 46.58 N 27.25 E
Mironovka 78 49.39 N 30.59 E
Mironovo 88 58.19 N 109.38 E
Mironovskij 83 48.29 N 38.17 E
Miropol' 78 50.07 N 27.41 E
Miropolje 78 51.02 N 35.16 E
Miroslav 61 48.57 N 16.18 E
Mirosławiec 30 53.21 N 16.05 E
Mirošov 60 49.41 N 13.40 E
Mirotice 60 49.26 N 14.02 E
Mirovice 60 49.31 N 14.02 E
Mirovoje 78 47.45 N 34.45 E
Mirovskoje 78 48.05 N 33.23 E
Mirow 54 53.16 N 12.49 E
Mīrpur, Bngl. 126 23.47 N 90.21 E
Mīrpur, Bngl. 126 23.56 N 88.59 E
Mīrpur, Pāk. 123 33.11 N 73.47 E
Mīrpur Batoro 120 24.44 N 68.16 E
Mīrpur Bībīwāri 120 28.32 N 67.44 E
Mīrpur Khās 120 25.32 N 69.00 E
Mīrpur Sakro 120 24.33 N 67.37 E
Mirria 150 13.43 N 9.07 E
Mirror 182 52.28 N 113.07 W
Mirror Lake ⊜, Ma., U.S. 283 42.05 N 71.20 W
Mirror Lake ⊜, N.J., U.S. 276 40.29 N 74.22 W
Mirtağ 130 38.23 N 41.56 E
Mirto 70 38.05 N 14.45 E
Mirtóön Pélagos ⊤ [2] 38 36.51 N 23.18 E
Miryang 98 35.31 N 128.44 E
Miry Run ≃ 285 40.15 N 74.49 W
Mirza-Aki 85 40.45 N 73.25 E
Mirzaani 84 41.23 N 46.09 E
Mirzāganj 126 22.21 N 90.14 E
Mīrzākalu 126 22.29 N 90.48 E
Mirzāpur, Bngl. 126 24.06 N 90.06 E
Mirzāpur, India 124 25.09 N 82.35 E
Mirzāpur, India 272b 22.50 N 88.24 E
Mis, It. 64 46.09 N 12.05 E
Mis, It. 64 46.12 N 11.57 E
Misa ≃ 66 43.43 N 13.14 E
Misāḥah, Bi'r ⊤ [4] 140 22.12 N 27.57 E
Misailovo 265b 55.34 N 37.49 E
Misaka 94 35.38 N 138.40 E
Misaka-tōge)(96 33.42 N 132.52 E
Misaki, Nihon 94 35.18 N 140.22 E
Misaki → Miura, Nihon 94 35.08 N 139.37 E
Misaki, Nihon 96 33.23 N 132.07 E
Misaki, Nihon 96 34.19 N 135.09 E
Misakubo 94 35.09 N 137.52 E
Misallah, Ra's › 142 29.50 N 32.36 E
Misamis Occidental □ [4] 116 8.20 N 123.42 E
Misamis Oriental □ [4] 116 8.45 N 125.00 E
Misano Adriatico 66 43.57 N 12.39 E
Misantla 234 19.56 N 96.50 W
Misasa 96 35.24 N 133.54 E
Misasagi → Fujiidera 96 34.34 N 135.36 E
Misato, Nihon 94 36.23 N 138.57 E
Misato, Nihon 94 34.43 N 136.24 E
Misato, Nihon 94 36.15 N 137.54 E
Misato, Nihon 96 34.09 N 135.22 E
Misato, Nihon 268 35.50 N 139.53 E
Misawa 92 40.41 N 141.24 E
Misbourne ≃ 260 51.34 N 0.29 W
Misburg 52 52.23 N 9.51 E
Miscou Centre 186 47.57 N 64.34 W
Miscou Island I 186 47.57 N 64.33 W
Miscou Point › 186 48.03 N 64.32 W
Miševka 88 52.51 N 103.09 E
Misema ≃ 190 47.54 N 79.53 W
Mi-sen ∧ 96 34.16 N 132.19 E
Misenheimer 192 35.29 N 80.17 W
Miseno 68 40.47 N 14.05 E

Misericórdia, Serra da ∧ 287a 22.51 S 43.17 W
Misery, Mount ∧ 169 37.24 S 143.36 E
Misgār 123 36.47 N 74.47 E
Mish'āb, Ra's al- › 128 28.12 N 48.39 E
Mishagua ≃ 248 11.13 S 72.59 W
Mishan 89 45.33 N 131.52 E
Mishawaka 216 41.39 N 86.09 W
Mishawum Lake ⊜ 283 42.30 N 71.08 W
Mishbiḥ, Jabal ∧ 140 22.38 N 34.44 E
Misheguk Mountain ∧ 180 68.15 N 161.03 W
Mishe-Mokwa, Lake ⊜ 285 39.52 N 74.48 W
Mishibishu Lake ⊜ 190 48.05 N 85.25 W
Mishicot 190 44.14 N 87.38 W
Mishima, Nihon 94 35.07 N 138.55 E
Mishima → Settsu, Nihon 96 34.46 N 135.33 E
Mi-shima I 96 34.46 N 131.09 E
Mishmar HaNegev 132 31.21 N 34.43 E
Mishmi Hills ⋏ [2] 120 29.00 N 96.00 E
Mishō 96 32.57 N 132.34 E
Mishqal, Jabal al- ∧ 132 31.53 N 36.08 E
Mišicha 88 51.38 N 105.35 E
Misikan 120 35.45 N 89.25 E
Misilmeri 70 38.02 N 13.27 E
Misima Island I 164 10.40 S 152.45 E
Misinto 266b 45.40 N 9.05 E
Misiones □ [4] 252 27.00 S 55.00 W
Misiones □ [5] 252 27.00 S 57.00 W
Misión San Francisco de Laishí 252 26.14 S 58.38 W
Misión San Vicente 232 31.20 N 116.15 W
Misirevo 82 56.16 N 36.45 E
Miskī 140 14.51 N 24.13 E
Miski, Enneri V 146 20.00 N 17.55 E
Miškino, Ross. 86 55.20 N 63.55 E
Miškino, Ross. 265a 59.42 N 30.45 E
Miskito Channel ц 236 14.20 N 83.08 W
Miskitos, Cayos II 236 14.23 N 82.46 W
Miskitos Reef ✣ [2] 236 14.28 N 82.42 W
Miskolc 30 48.06 N 20.47 E
Misli 130 38.10 N 34.52 E
Mislinja 61 46.28 N 15.14 E
Mislinja ≃ 61 46.35 N 15.02 E
Mislippi 146 10.00 N 15.37 E
Mislivna ∧ 61 48.40 N 14.44 E
Mismār 140 18.13 N 35.38 E
Mismār, Jabal ∧ 140 18.06 N 35.42 E
Mismi, Nevado ∧ 248 15.30 S 71.42 W
Mišn'ovo 76 53.58 N 36.21 E
Miscke 154 1.06 S 28.38 E
Miscol, Pulau I 164 1.52 S 130.10 E
Mispillion ≃ 208 38.57 N 75.20 W
Misquamaebin Lake ⊜ 184 53.30 N 91.05 W
Misquamicut 207 41.20 N 71.49 W
Miṣr → Egypt □ [1] 140 27.00 N 30.00 E
Miṣr al-Jadīdah (Heliopolis) ◆ [8] 273c 30.06 N 31.20 E
Miṣr al-Qadīmah (Old Cairo) ◆ [8] 273c 30.00 N 31.14 E
Misrātah 146 32.23 N 15.06 E
Miṣr Baḥrī □ [9] 140 31.00 N 31.00 E
Misrikh 124 27.27 N 80.31 E
Missanello 68 40.17 N 16.10 E
Missão Santa Cruz 152 16.14 S 21.57 E
Missão Velha 250 7.15 S 39.08 W
Misserghin 34 35.37 N 0.45 W
Missinaibi ≃ 176 50.44 N 81.29 W
Missinaibi Lake ⊜ 190 48.23 N 83.40 W
Missinaibi Lake Provincial Park ♠ 190 48.25 N 83.35 W
Mission, S.D., U.S. 198 43.18 N 100.39 W
Mission, Tx., U.S. 196 26.12 N 98.19 W
Mission ◆ [8] 282 37.45 N 122.25 W
Mission Bay ⊂ 228 32.47 N 117.15 W
Mission Beach 166 17.52 S 146.06 E
Mission City 224 49.08 N 122.18 W
Mission Creek ≃ 282 37.32 N 121.55 W
Mission Hills ◆ [8] 280 34.16 N 118.27 W
Mission Mountain ∧ [2] 194 36.02 N 94.35 W
Mission Peak ∧ 282 37.31 N 121.53 W
Mission Range ⋏ 202 47.30 N 113.55 W
Mission Texas State Historic Park ♠ 222 31.33 N 95.15 W
Mission Valley 222 28.54 N 97.12 W
Mission Viejo 228 33.36 N 117.40 W
Missisquoi □ [6] 206 45.10 N 72.55 W
Missisquoi ≃ 206 45.00 N 73.08 W
Missisquoi Bay ⊂ 206 45.05 N 73.10 W
Missisquoi-Nord ≃ 206 45.02 N 72.26 W
Mississagagon Lake ⊜ 212 44.52 N 77.05 W
Mississag ≃ 190 46.10 N 83.01 W
Mississag Provincial Park ♠ 190 46.35 N 82.45 W
Mississagua ≃ 212 44.34 N 78.20 W
Mississagua Lake ⊜ 212 44.42 N 78.19 W
Mississauga 212 43.35 N 79.39 W
Mississinewa ≃ 216 40.46 N 86.02 W
Mississinewa Lake ⊜ [1] 216 40.42 N 85.52 W
Mississippi □ [3], U.S. 178 32.50 N 89.30 W
Mississippi □ [3], U.S. 194 32.50 N 89.30 W
Mississippi ≃, On., Can. 212 45.26 N 76.16 W
Mississippi ≃, U.S. 178 29.00 N 89.15 W
Mississippi Bay ⊂ 162 34.00 S 122.17 E
Mississippi Delta ≚ [2] 194 29.10 N 89.15 W
Mississippi Lake ⊜ 212 45.05 N 76.12 W
Mississippi Sound ц 194 30.15 N 88.40 W
Mississippi State 194 33.26 N 88.47 W
Missolonghi → Mesolóngion 38 38.21 N 21.17 E
Missoula 202 46.52 N 113.59 W
Missouri □ [3], U.S. 178 38.30 N 93.30 W
Missouri □ [3], U.S. 194 38.30 N 93.30 W
Missouri ≃ 178 38.50 N 90.08 W
Missouri, Coteau du ⋏ [2] 198 46.00 N 99.30 W
Missouri Buttes ∧ 198 44.37 N 104.47 W
Missouri City 222 29.37 N 95.32 W
Missouri Creek ≃ 219 40.07 N 90.43 W
Missouri Valley 198 41.33 N 95.53 W
Mistake, Mount ∧ 171a 27.52 S 152.20 E
Mistake Creek 164 17.06 S 129.04 E
Mistake Creek ≃ 166 21.38 S 146.50 E
Mistake Mountains ⋏ 171a 27.52 S 152.22 E
Mistaken Point › 186 46.38 N 53.10 W
Mistanipisipou ≃ 186 51.32 N 61.50 W
Mistassibi ≃ 176 48.53 N 72.13 W
Mistassibi Nord-Est ≃ 186 49.50 N 71.56 W
Mistassini 176 50.25 N 73.52 W
Mistassini, Lac ⊜ 176 51.00 N 73.37 W
Mistatim 184 52.52 N 103.22 W
Mistawasis Indian Reserve ◆ [4] 184 53.06 N 106.48 W
Mistelbach, Dtsch. 60 49.55 N 11.31 E
Mistelbach, Öst. 61 48.34 N 16.35 E
Mistelgau 60 49.55 N 11.28 E
Misteln ⊜ 40 59.07 N 16.57 E
Misterbianco 70 37.31 N 15.00 E
Misterei 140 13.07 N 22.09 E
Misteriosa Bank ✣ [2] 238 18.50 N 83.50 W
Misterton, Eng., U.K. 42 50.52 N 2.47 W
Misterton, Eng., U.K. 44 53.27 N 0.51 W
Misti, Volcán ∧ [1] 248 16.18 S 71.24 W
Mistikokan ≃ 184 57.01 N 91.27 W
Mistley 42 51.56 N 1.05 E
Mistrás ⊥ 38 37.04 N 22.21 E
Mistretta 70 37.56 N 14.22 E
Misugi 94 34.33 N 136.16 E
Misumi, Nihon 92 32.37 N 130.27 E
Misumi, Nihon 96 34.46 N 131.58 E
Misumi, Nihon 96 34.22 N 131.15 E
Misumi ≃ 96 34.47 N 131.56 E
Misurina 64 46.35 N 12.15 E

Symbol	English	Deutsch	Español	Français	Português
≃	River	Fluß	Río	Rivière	Rio
≍	Canal	Kanal	Canal	Canal	Canal
∟	Waterfall, Rapids	Wasserfall, Stromschnellen	Cascada, Rápidos	Chute d'eau, Rapides	Cascata, Rápidos
ц	Strait	Meeresstraße	Estrecho	Détroit	Estreito
⊂	Bay, Gulf	Bucht, Golf	Bahía, Golfo	Baie, Golfe	Baía, Golfo
⊜	Lake, Lakes	See, Seen	Lago, Lagos	Lac, Lacs	Lago, Lagos
≡	Swamp	Sumpf	Pantano	Marais	Pântano
⍓	Ice Features, Glacier	Eis- und Gletscherformen	Accidentes Glaciales	Formes glaciaires	Acidentes glaciares
⊤	Other Hydrographic Features	Andere Hydrographische Objekte	Otros Elementos Hidrográficos	Autres données hydrographiques	Outros acidentes hidrográficos
✣	Submarine Features	Untermeerische Objekte	Accidentes Submarinos	Formes de relief sous-marin	Acidentes submarinos
□	Political Unit	Politische Einheit	Unidad Politica	Entité politique	Unidade política
ʋ	Cultural Institution	Kulturelle Institution	Institución Cultural	Institution culturelle	Institução cultural
⊥	Historical Site	Historische Stätte	Sitio Histórico	Site historique	Sitio histórico
♠	Recreational Site	Erholungs- und Ferienort	Sitio de Recreo	Centre de loisirs	Area de Lazer
⊠	Airport	Flughafen	Aeropuerto	Aéroport	Aeroporto
■	Military Installation	Militäranlage	Instalación Militar	Installation militaire	Instalação militar
◆	Miscellaneous	Verschiedenes	Misceláneo	Divers	Diversos

Name	Page	Lat.	Long.
Mišurin Rog	78	48.50 N	33.58 E
Mišutino, Ross.	76	59.31 N	36.01 E
Mišutino, Ross.	82	56.23 N	38.06 E
Mita, Punta ⸧	234	20.47 N	105.33 W
Mīt Abū Ghālib	142	31.17 N	31.40 E
Mita Hills Dam ⬩⁶	154	14.15 S	29.06 E
Mit'ajevo, Ross.	82	55.16 N	36.32 E
Mit'ajevo, Ross.	86	60.17 N	61.06 E
Mitaka	94	35.40 N	139.33 E
Mitake, Nihon	94	35.25 N	137.08 E
Mitake, Nihon	94	35.51 N	137.32 E
Mit'akinka ⱥ	83	48.35 N	39.50 E
Mit'akino	82	54.24 N	38.50 E
Mit'akinskaja	83	48.36 N	39.47 E
Mīt al-'Āmil	142	30.54 N	31.21 E
Mitatib	140	16.03 N	36.11 E
Mitau — Jelgava	76	56.39 N	23.42 E
Mīt Badr Halāwah	142	30.51 N	31.14 E
Mīt Bashnīh	142	30.31 N	31.24 E
Mitcham, Austl.	168b	34.59 S	138.36 E
Mitcham, Austl.	274b	37.49 S	145.12 E
Mitcham ⬩⁸	260	51.24 N	0.10 W
Mitcheldean	42	51.53 N	2.30 W
Mitchell, Austl.	166	26.29 S	147.58 E
Mitchell, On., Can.	212	43.27 N	81.12 W
Mitchell, Il., U.S.	219	38.46 N	90.06 W
Mitchell, In., U.S.	218	38.43 N	86.28 W
Mitchell, Ne., U.S.	198	41.56 N	103.48 W
Mitchell, Or., U.S.	202	44.34 N	120.09 W
Mitchell, S.D., U.S.	198	43.42 N	98.01 W
Mitchell ⱥ, Austl.	164	15.12 S	141.35 E
Mitchell ⱥ, Austl.	166	34.28 S	125.43 E
Mitchell ⱥ, Austl.	166	37.53 S	147.41 E
Mitchell, Lake ⬵	194	32.50 N	86.30 W
Mitchell, Mount ⱥ	192	35.46 N	82.16 W
Mitchell and Alice Rivers National Park ⬩	164	15.30 S	142.05 E
Mitchell Bay ⸦	214	42.28 N	82.26 W
Mitchell Corners	212	43.57 N	78.48 W
Mitchell Field ⬩	261	45.51 N	88.15 W
Mitchell Lake ⬵, B.C., Can.	182	52.53 N	120.36 W
Mitchell Lake ⬵, On., Can.	212	44.34 N	78.58 W
Mitchell Point ⸧	214	42.26 N	82.26 W
Mitchellville	190	41.40 N	93.21 W
Mitchelstown	42	52.16 N	8.16 W
Mīt Fāris	142	31.02 N	31.36 E
Mīt Ghamr	142	30.43 N	31.16 E
Mīt Halfah	273c	30.10 N	31.14 E
Mīt Hamal	142	30.26 N	31.32 E
Mithapur	120	22.25 N	69.00 E
Mitha Tiwāna	123	32.15 N	72.07 E
Mithi	102	24.44 N	69.48 E
Mithimna	38	39.22 N	26.10 E
Mitiaro I	14	19.49 S	157.43 W
Mitidja, Plaine de la ⬵	34	36.45 N	3.00 E
Mitilini	38	39.06 N	26.32 E
Mitino	265b	55.51 N	37.21 E
Mitis, Lac ⬵	186	48.17 N	67.45 W
Mitishto ⱥ	184	54.50 N	98.58 W
Mitiškovo	76	54.40 N	33.31 E
Mitiwanga	214	41.22 N	82.27 W
Mitkof Island I	180	56.45 N	132.50 W
Mitla ⱥ	156	15.55 N	96.17 W
Mitla, Laguna ⸦	234	17.03 N	100.25 W
Mitla, Mamarr (Mitla Pass) ⱶ	142	30.00 N	32.53 E
Mitla Pass — Mitla, Mamarr ⱶ	142	30.00 N	32.53 E
Mito, Nihon	94	34.49 N	137.19 E
Mito, Nihon	94	36.22 N	140.28 E
Mito, Nihon	94	34.40 N	131.59 E
Mitō, Nihon	94	34.13 N	131.21 E
Mitō, Nihon	268	35.10 N	137.16 E
Mitomi	94	35.47 N	138.44 E
Mitoya	96	35.17 N	132.52 E
Mitra, Monte ⱥ	152	1.23 N	9.57 E
Mitra do Bispo ⱥ	256	22.10 S	44.34 W
Mitre ⱥ	172	40.48 S	175.27 E
Mitre, Península ⸧¹	254	54.48 S	65.40 W
Mitre Peak ⱥ	142	44.38 S	167.50 E
Mitrofania Island I	180	55.51 N	158.49 W
Mitrofanovka	78	48.58 N	39.42 E
Mitrofanovo	24	63.13 N	56.00 E
Mīt Ruhaynah	273c	29.51 N	31.15 E
Mīt Ruhaynah (Memphis) ⱥ	142	29.51 N	31.15 E
Mitry-le-Neuf	261	48.40 N	1.39 E
Mitry-Mory	261	48.59 N	2.37 E
Mitsamiouli	157a	11.23 S	43.18 E
Mitsinjo	157b	16.01 S	45.52 E
Mitsio, Nosy I	157b	12.54 S	48.36 E
Mitsiwa (Massawa)	144	15.38 N	39.28 E
Mitsiwa Channel ⱶ	144	15.30 N	40.00 E
Mitsu, Nihon	96	34.44 N	134.33 E
Mitsu, Nihon	96	34.48 N	133.56 E
Mitsubori	268	35.56 N	139.56 E
Mitsue	94	34.29 N	136.10 E
Mitsugi	96	34.30 N	133.09 E
Mitsuike Park ⬩	268	35.31 N	139.39 E
Mitsukaidō	94	36.01 N	139.59 E
Mitsumarenge-dake ⱥ	94	36.23 N	137.35 E
Mitsushima	92	34.15 N	129.18 E
Mitsuzaku	268	35.25 N	140.00 E
Mitsuzawa Park Race Track ⬩	268	35.27 N	139.36 E
Mitta, Oued el ⱥ	34	36.16 N	6.44 E
Mittagong	170	34.27 S	150.27 E
Mittagskogel (Kepa) ⱥ	61	46.31 N	13.57 E
Mittainville	261	48.40 N	1.39 E
Mitta Mitta	171b	36.12 S	147.11 E
Mitte ⬩⁸	264a	36.13 N	13.24 E
Mittelberg, Dtsch.	58	48.10 N	10.25 E
Mittelberg, Öst.	58	47.20 N	10.10 E
Mittelfischach	58	49.02 N	9.52 E
Mittelfranken ⬩⁵	58	49.20 N	10.40 E
Mittellandkanal ⱶ	30	52.16 N	11.41 E
Mittelmeer — Mediterranean Sea ⱶ	10	35.00 N	20.00 E
Mittelsaida	54	50.48 N	13.18 E
Mittelstetten	58	48.15 N	11.05 E
Mittenwald	58	47.27 N	11.15 E
Mittenwalde, Dtsch.	54	53.11 N	13.39 E
Mittenwalde, Dtsch.	54	51.56 N	13.32 E
Mitterndorf	64	47.33 N	13.55 E
Mittersill	64	47.16 N	12.29 E
Mitterskirchen	60	48.21 N	12.44 E
Mitterteich	60	49.57 N	12.14 E
Mittewald an der Drau	64	46.46 N	12.36 E
Mittweida	54	50.59 N	12.59 E
Mitú	246	1.08 N	70.03 W
Mitumba, Monts ⱥ	154	6.00 S	29.00 E
Mituo	107	28.53 N	105.37 E
Mitwaba	154	8.38 S	27.20 E
Mitwitz	55	50.15 N	11.12 E
Mityana	154	0.24 N	32.03 E
Mīt Yazīd	142	30.30 N	31.20 E
Mitzic	152	0.47 N	11.34 E
Miura	94	35.08 N	139.37 E
Miura-chosuichi ⬵¹	268	35.13 N	139.37 E
Miura-dam ⬵⬩	268	35.13 N	139.37 E
Miura-hantō ⸧¹	94	35.12 N	139.38 E
Mius ⱥ	78	47.11 N	38.50 E
Mius ⱥ	82	51.26 N	47.56 E
Miusinsk	83	48.05 N	38.53 E
Miusskij liman ⸦¹	83	47.15 N	38.40 E
Miwa, Nihon	95	35.11 N	136.47 E
Miwa, Nihon	94	34.13 N	132.14 E
Miwa, Nihon	94	34.13 N	132.16 E
Miwa, Nihon	94	34.31 N	135.51 E
Miwa, Nihon	270	34.31 N	136.10 E
Mi-Wuk Village	204	38.06 N	120.11 W

Name	Page	Lat.	Long.
Mixcoac ⬩⁸	286a	19.23 N	99.12 W
Mixcoac, Presa de ⬵	286a	19.22 N	99.14 W
Mixco Viejo ⱥ	236	14.52 N	90.40 W
Mixian	100	34.31 N	113.22 E
Mixin	107	30.23 N	105.46 E
Mixquiahuala	234	20.14 N	99.13 W
Mixtán	234	17.55 N	95.51 W
Mixteco ⱥ	234	18.11 N	98.30 W
Mixtlán	234	20.26 N	104.25 W
Miya ⱥ, Nihon	94	36.05 N	137.15 E
Miya ⱥ, Nihon	94	34.32 N	136.44 E
Miya ⱥ, Nihon	94	36.28 N	137.15 E
Miyagawa, Nihon	94	36.19 N	137.09 E
Miyagawa, Nihon	94	34.22 N	136.21 E
Miyagi ⬩⁵	92	38.22 N	140.52 E
Miyagi-jima I	174m	26.21 N	127.57 E
Miyah, Wādī al- ⱥ	140	25.00 N	33.22 E
Miyahara	268	35.56 N	139.37 E
Miyajima	96	34.18 N	132.19 E
Miyake	270	34.35 N	135.47 E
Miyake-jima I	92	34.05 N	139.32 E
Miyako	92	39.38 N	141.57 E
Miyakojima ⬩⁸	270	34.43 N	135.33 E
Miyako-jima I	175d	24.47 N	125.20 E
Miyakonojō	92	31.44 N	131.04 E
Miyako-rettō II	175d	24.24 N	125.00 E
Miyama, Nihon	92	34.06 N	136.14 E
Miyama, Nihon	92	34.00 N	136.22 E
Miyama, Nihon	94	35.33 N	136.45 E
Miyama, Nihon	96	35.16 N	135.33 E
Miyama, Nihon	96	33.59 N	135.22 E
Miyāni	120	21.51 N	69.23 E
Miyanoura-dake ⱥ	93b	30.20 N	130.31 E
Miyara	175d	24.20 N	124.14 E
Miyata	96	33.44 N	130.40 E
Miyazaki, Nihon	92	31.54 N	131.26 E
Miyazaki, Nihon	94	35.56 N	136.05 E
Miyazakino-hana ⸧	96	35.04 N	134.05 E
Miyazu	96	35.32 N	135.11 E
Miyi	102	27.00 N	102.08 E
Miyoshi, Nihon	96	33.57 N	133.03 E
Miyoshi, Nihon	96	34.48 N	132.51 E
Miyoshi, Nihon	96	34.02 N	133.52 E
Miyoshi, Nihon	268	35.50 N	139.31 E
Miyota	96	36.18 N	138.30 E
Miyun Shuiku ⬵¹	105	40.30 N	116.58 E
Mizan Teferi	144	6.53 N	35.28 E
Mizdah	146	31.26 N	12.59 E
Mize	194	31.52 N	89.33 W
Mizen Head ⸧, Ire.	48	52.51 N	6.01 W
Mizen Head ⸧, Ire.	48	51.27 N	9.49 W
Miževiči	76	52.59 N	25.05 E
Mizhhir'ja	78	48.32 N	23.30 E
Mizil	38	45.00 N	26.26 E
Mizoč	78	50.24 N	26.09 E
Mizoguchi	96	35.21 N	133.26 E
Mizonokuchi	268	35.36 N	139.37 E
Mizonuma	268	35.48 N	139.36 E
Mizoram ⬩³	120	23.30 N	93.00 E
Mizpah	198	48.17 N	104.49 W
Mizpah Creek ⱥ	198	46.16 N	105.17 W
Mizpé Ramon	132	30.36 N	34.48 E
Mizque	248	17.56 S	65.19 W
Mizque ⱥ	248	18.39 S	64.20 W
Mizue ⬩⁸	268	35.41 N	139.54 E
Mizuho, Nihon	94	35.46 N	139.21 E
Mizuho, Nihon	96	35.10 N	135.22 E
Mizuho, Nihon	96	34.51 N	132.31 E
Mizukaidō — Mitsukaidō	94	36.01 N	139.59 E
Mizuko	268	35.50 N	139.34 E
Mizumaki	96	33.51 N	130.42 E
Mizunami	94	35.22 N	137.15 E
Mizunuko-jima I	96	33.02 N	132.11 E
Mizusawa	92	39.08 N	141.08 E
Mizushima-nada ⸦	96	34.25 N	133.40 E
Mizutori	270	34.47 N	135.45 E
Mizuwake-tōge ⱶ	96	33.15 N	131.17 E
Mjällom	26	62.59 N	18.26 E
Mjangad	86	48.15 N	91.57 E
Mjarvana	158	31.50 S	28.10 E
Mjöby	26	58.19 N	15.08 E
Mjøndalen	26	59.45 N	10.01 E
Mjörn ⬵	26	57.54 N	12.25 E
Mjøsa ⬵	26	60.40 N	11.00 E
Mkalama	154	4.07 S	34.38 E
Mkata	154	5.47 S	38.17 E
Mkhondvo ⱥ	158	26.39 S	31.25 E
Mkokotoni	154	5.52 S	39.15 E
Mkomazi ⱥ	158	30.12 S	30.50 E
Mkomazi Game Reserve ⬩⁴	154	4.10 S	38.10 E
Mkulwe	154	8.35 S	32.19 E
Mkumvura ⱥ	155	15.55 S	31.07 E
Mkurumbi	154	2.18 S	40.42 E
Mkushi	154	13.40 S	29.20 E
Mkushi River	154	14.40 S	29.07 E
Mkuze ⱥ	158	27.53 S	32.29 E
Mkuzi Game Reserve ⬩⁴	158	27.40 S	32.15 E
Mkwaja	154	5.48 S	38.51 E
Mkwaya	154	10.06 S	39.40 E
Mladá Boleslav	54	50.25 N	14.59 E
Mladenovac	38	44.26 N	20.42 E
Mladotice	60	49.58 N	13.18 E
Mlala Hills ⱥ²	154	6.41 S	31.45 E
M'Lang	116	6.55 N	124.53 E
Mlava ⱥ	38	44.45 N	21.13 E
Mława	30	53.06 N	20.23 E
Mlawula	158	26.11 S	32.01 E
Mlenvo	265b	50.45 N	37.28 E
Mnevniki ⬩⁸	265b	55.45 N	37.28 E
Mnichov	60	50.03 N	12.49 E
Mníšek pod Brdy	60	49.52 N	14.16 E
Mo	24	66.15 N	14.08 E
Mo ⱥ	150	8.45 N	11.26 W
Moa, Afr.	150	6.59 N	11.36 W
Moa, Bra.	248	7.39 S	72.41 W
Moa, Pulau I	164	8.10 S	127.56 E
Moab	200	38.34 N	109.32 W
Moabi	152	2.15 S	11.00 E
Moaco ⱥ	248	7.41 S	68.18 W
Moa Island I	164	10.12 S	142.16 E
Moala Island I	175g	18.36 S	179.53 E
Moalboal	116	9.56 N	123.23 E
Moama	168	36.07 S	144.47 E
Moana	172	42.35 S	171.00 E
Moanza	152	5.25 S	17.30 E
Moar Lake	184	52.00 N	95.09 W
Moatize	154	16.08 S	33.45 E
Moba, Nig.	273a	9.35 N	3.28 E
Moba, Zaïre	154	7.03 S	29.47 E
Mobara	94	35.26 N	140.18 E
Mobārakpur	126	22.69 N	76.10 E
Mobay-Mbongo	152	4.18 N	21.11 E
Mobberley	262	53.19 N	2.19 W
Mobeetie	196	35.31 N	100.26 W

Name	Page	Lat.	Long.
Mobenzélé	152	0.54 N	17.51 E
Moberly	194	39.25 N	92.26 W
Moberly ⱥ	182	56.12 N	120.55 W
Moberly Lake	182	55.49 N	121.45 W
Moberly Lake ⬵	182	55.49 N	121.45 W
Mobile, Al., U.S.	194	30.41 N	88.02 W
Mobile, Az., U.S.	200	33.03 N	112.16 W
Mobile ⱥ	194	30.29 N	88.01 W
Mobile Bay ⸦	194	30.25 N	88.00 W
Mobjack	208	37.23 N	76.21 W
Mobjack Bay ⸦	208	37.19 N	76.21 W
Mobridge	198	45.32 N	100.25 W
Moca, P.R.	240m	18.24 N	67.07 W
Moca, Rep. Dom.	238	19.24 N	70.31 W
Moča ⱥ	82	55.25 N	37.28 E
Mocajuba	250	2.35 S	49.30 W
Mocal ⱥ	236	14.00 N	88.33 W
Močalejevka	80	53.38 N	51.46 E
Močališče	80	56.21 N	48.23 E
Moçambique	154	15.03 S	40.45 E
Moçambique — Mozambique ⬩¹	138	18.15 S	35.00 E
Mocanaqua	210	41.08 N	76.08 W
Mocangué Grande, Ilha I	287a	22.52 S	43.08 W
Mocassins, Lac des ⬵	206	46.35 N	74.25 W
Mo Cay	110	10.08 N	106.20 E
Moccasin, Ca., U.S.	226	37.49 N	120.18 W
Moccasin, Il., U.S.	219	39.09 N	88.45 W
Moc Chau	110	20.51 N	104.37 E
Moccoidumis	144	1.36 N	44.26 E
Mocha, Isla I	252	38.22 S	73.56 W
Moche	248	8.10 S	79.03 W
Moche ⱥ	248	8.06 S	79.05 W
Mocheng	106	31.35 N	120.43 E
Mochgah	123	32.45 N	71.31 E
Mochigase	96	35.04 N	134.05 E
Mochitlan	234	17.30 N	99.18 W
Mochizuki	94	36.16 N	138.22 E
Mocho, Arroyo ⱥ	226	37.41 N	121.55 W
Mochov	54	50.08 N	14.50 E
Mochtín	60	49.22 N	13.21 E
Mochudi	156	24.28 S	26.05 E
Močily	82	54.20 N	38.41 E
Mocímboa da Praia	154	11.20 S	40.21 E
Mocímboa do Rovuma	154	11.20 S	39.18 E
Möckeln ⬵, Sve.	26	56.40 N	14.10 E
Möckeln ⬵, Sve.	40	59.18 N	14.30 E
Möckern	54	52.08 N	11.57 E
Mockfjärd	40	60.30 N	14.58 E
Mockhorn Island I	208	37.13 N	75.53 W
Möckmühl	58	49.19 N	9.22 E
Mockrehna	54	51.30 N	12.49 E
Mocksville	192	35.53 N	80.33 W
Moclips	226	47.14 N	124.12 W
Mõco, Serra do ⱥ	152	12.28 S	15.10 E
Mocoa	246	1.09 N	76.37 W
Mococa	256	21.28 S	47.01 W
Mocoduene	154	23.40 S	35.10 E
Mocoretá	252	30.38 S	57.58 W
Mocoretá ⱥ	252	25.29 N	107.55 W
Moctezuma, Méx.	234	29.48 N	109.42 W
Moctezuma, Méx.	232	22.45 N	101.05 W
Moctezuma, Méx.	234	29.09 N	109.40 W
Moctezuma ⱥ, Méx.	234	21.59 N	98.34 W
Mocuba	154	16.50 S	36.59 E
Mocúrica ⱥ	38	42.31 N	26.32 E
Modane	62	45.12 N	6.40 E
Modãsa	120	23.28 N	73.18 E
Modbury	42	50.21 N	3.53 W
Modder ⱥ	158	29.02 S	24.37 E
Modderbee	273d	26.10 S	28.24 E
Modderfontein	273d	26.06 S	28.09 E
Modderfontein ⬩	273d	26.11 S	28.26 E
Modderrivier	158	29.02 S	24.38 E
Model City	284a	43.11 N	78.59 W
Modena, It.	64	44.40 N	10.55 E
Modena, N.Y., U.S.	210	41.40 N	74.07 W
Moder ⱥ	54	48.43 N	8.00 E
Moderbrugg	61	48.49 N	8.06 E
Modern Art, Museum of ⬩	276	40.46 N	73.58 W
Modeste, Mount ⱥ	224	48.37 N	124.06 W
Modesto, Ca., U.S.	226	37.38 N	120.59 W
Modesto, Il., U.S.	219	39.29 N	89.59 W
Modesto City-County Airport ⬩	226	37.39 N	120.57 W
Modesto Main Canal ⱶ	226	37.39 N	120.27 W
Modesto Reservoir ⬵	226	37.26 N	121.58 W
Modica	70	36.52 N	14.46 E
Modigliana	66	44.09 N	11.47 E
Modinagar	124	28.51 N	77.37 E
Modione ⱥ	70	37.34 N	12.49 E
Modjamboli	152	2.28 N	22.06 E
Modjeska	280	33.43 N	117.37 W
Mödling	64	48.05 N	16.17 E
Modoc	218	40.02 N	85.07 W
Modowi	164	4.05 S	134.39 E
Modra, Slvk.	60	48.21 N	17.18 E
Modra, Tchad	146	20.43 N	17.42 E
Modra Špilja ⱥ⁵	72	43.01 N	16.01 E
Modriča	38	44.57 N	18.18 E
Módřice	60	49.07 N	16.37 E
Moe ⱥ	169	38.10 S	146.15 E
Moe ⱥ, Austl.	168	38.08 S	146.17 E
Moe ⱥ, P.Q., Can.	206	45.19 N	71.49 W
Moecherville	216	40.14 N	88.17 W
Moengo	255	5.37 N	54.24 W
Moenkopi	200	36.06 N	111.13 W
Moenkopi Wash ⱥ	200	35.54 N	111.26 W
Moeraki Point ⸧	172	45.22 S	170.52 E
Moerbeke, Bel.	50	51.10 N	3.56 E
Moerbeke, Bel.	50	50.59 N	3.54 E
Moerdijk	52	51.40 N	4.38 E
Moers	54	51.27 N	6.37 E
Moeskroen — Mouscron	50	50.44 N	3.13 E
Moesa ⱥ	58	46.13 N	9.03 E
Moffat	44	55.20 N	3.27 W
Moffat, Lac ⬵	206	46.13 N	74.49 W
Moffat Water ⱥ	44	55.18 N	3.25 W
Moffett Field Naval Air Station ⬩	226	37.24 N	122.03 W
Moffit	198	46.40 N	100.17 W
Mofoluku	273a	6.33 N	3.28 E
Moga	123	30.48 N	75.10 E
Mogadiscio — Muqdisho	144	2.04 N	45.22 E
Mogadishu — Muqdisho	144	2.04 N	45.22 E

Name	Page	Lat.	Long.
Mogadore	214	41.02 N	81.23 W
Mogadore Reservoir ⬵¹	214	41.04 N	81.21 W
Mogadouro	34	41.20 N	6.39 W
Mogalakwena ⱥ	156	23.00 S	28.40 E
Mogalo	152	3.10 N	19.04 E
Mogami ⱥ	92	38.55 N	139.48 E
Mogan Shan ⱥ	106	30.36 N	119.52 E
Mogapinyana	156	22.19 S	27.27 E
Mogaung	110	25.18 N	96.56 E
Mogdy	89	50.35 N	133.51 E
Mogees	285	40.06 N	75.19 W
Mogeltænder	41	54.56 N	8.49 E
Mogenstrup	41	55.11 N	11.53 E
Mogent ⱥ	266d	41.53 N	2.15 E
Moggio Udinese	64	46.25 N	13.12 E
Mogi, Serra do ⱥ	287b	23.47 S	46.20 W
Mogielnica	30	51.42 N	20.43 E
Mogila-Bel'mak, gora ⱥ²	78	47.20 N	36.35 E
Mogila-Mečetnaja, gora ⱥ²	83	48.16 N	38.53 E
Mogilev — Mogil'ov	76	53.54 N	30.21 E
Mogilno	30	52.40 N	17.58 E
Mogil'ov, Bela.	76	53.54 N	30.21 E
Mogil'ov, Ukr.	78	48.52 N	34.29 E
Mogil'ov ⬩⁸	76	53.45 N	30.30 E
Mogil'ov-Podol'skij	78	48.27 N	27.48 E
Mogincual	154	15.35 S	40.25 E
Mogla, Wādī ⱥ	140	19.18 N	34.29 E
Moglia	64	44.56 N	10.55 E
Mogliano Veneto	64	45.33 N	12.14 E
Mogoča	88	53.44 N	119.44 E
Mogoča ⱥ	86	58.00 N	36.26 E
Mogočin	86	57.43 N	83.34 E
Mogogh	140	8.26 N	31.19 E
Mogojto	88	54.25 N	110.27 E
Mogojtuj	88	51.17 N	114.55 E
Mogok	110	22.55 N	96.30 E
Mogollon Mountains ⱥ	200	33.25 N	108.40 W
Mogollon Rim ⱥ⁴	200	34.25 N	110.50 W
Mogor	200	34.25 N	67.47 E
Mogorella	71	39.52 N	8.51 E
Mogoro	71	39.41 N	8.47 E
Mogotes	246	6.30 N	72.58 W
Mogotón ⱥ	236	13.45 N	86.23 W
Mograt Island I	140	19.30 N	33.15 E
Mogroum	148	11.06 N	15.25 E
Moguer	34	37.16 N	6.50 W
Mogyoród	264c	47.36 N	19.20 E
Mogyoródi-patak ⱥ	264c	47.36 N	19.05 E
Mogzon	88	51.45 N	111.58 E
Mohács	38	45.59 N	18.42 E
Mohaka ⱥ	172	39.07 S	177.11 E
Mohaka ⱥ	172	39.07 S	177.12 E
Mohall	198	48.45 N	101.30 W
Mohammadābād	124	30.53 N	61.28 E
Mohammedia (Fedala)	148	33.44 N	7.24 W
Mohana	124	25.54 N	77.45 E
Mohangi	154	0.03 N	29.05 E
Mohanpur, Bngl.	124	23.24 N	90.36 E
Mohanpur, India	126	21.51 N	87.26 E
Mohanpur, India	272a	28.44 N	77.10 E
Mohave, Lake ⬵	204	35.25 N	114.38 W
Mohawk, Mi., U.S.	190	47.18 N	88.21 W
Mohawk, N.Y., U.S.	210	43.01 N	75.00 W
Mohawk ⱥ	210	42.47 N	73.42 W
Mohawk, East Branch ⱥ	212	43.22 N	75.28 W
Mohawk, Lake ⬵	276	41.02 N	74.41 W
Mohawk Dam ⱥ⁶	214	40.20 N	82.05 W
Mohawk Mountain ⱥ	207	41.49 N	73.17 W
Mohawk Point ⸧	212	42.51 N	79.29 W
Mohe	89	53.29 N	122.19 E
Moheda	26	57.00 N	14.34 E
Mohegan	207	41.28 N	72.06 W
Mohegan Lake	210	41.19 N	73.51 W
Mohelnice	30	49.46 N	16.55 E
Mohican, Black Fork ⱥ	214	40.22 N	82.09 W
Mohican, Clear Fork ⱥ	214	40.35 N	82.17 W
Mohican, Cape ⸧	180	60.12 N	167.28 W
Mohican, Jerome Fork ⱥ	214	40.45 N	82.23 W
Mohican, Lake Fork ⱥ	214	40.37 N	82.12 W
Mohican, Muddy Fork ⱥ	214	40.45 N	82.08 W
Mohican State Park ⬩	214	40.44 N	82.09 W
Mohicanville Dam ⱥ⁶	214	40.44 N	82.09 W
Mohill	48	53.56 N	7.52 W
Mohlakeng	273d	26.13 S	27.42 E
Möhlin	58	47.34 N	7.51 E
Möhne ⱥ	54	51.44 N	7.51 E
Möhnesee ⬵¹	54	51.29 N	8.08 E
Mohns Ridge ⱥ³	16	72.30 N	5.00 W
Mohnton	210	40.17 N	75.59 W
Mohnyin	110	24.47 N	96.22 E
Mohon	236	16.04 N	88.52 W
Mohokare (Caledon) ⱥ	158	30.31 S	26.05 E
Moholm	40	58.37 N	14.02 E
Mohon	36	49.47 N	4.44 E
Mohon Peak ⱥ	200	34.54 N	113.11 W
Mohoro	154	8.09 S	39.10 E
Moi	56	58.28 N	6.32 E
Moia	144	5.37 S	54.24 W
Moian	268	35.50 N	139.51 E
Moimenta da Beira	34	40.59 N	7.37 W
Moineşti	38	46.28 N	26.29 E
Moingona	216	42.02 N	94.01 W
Moinkum	84	44.30 N	72.53 E
Moio Alcantara	70	37.54 N	15.03 E
Moira ⱥ, Austl.	168	35.04 S	144.45 E
Moira ⱥ	212	44.50 N	74.17 W
Moira Lake ⬵	212	44.27 N	77.27 W
Moirang	126	24.30 N	93.45 E
Moirans	62	45.20 N	5.34 E
Moirans-en-Montagne	62	46.26 N	5.44 E
Mõisaküla	26	58.05 N	25.11 E
Moisburg	54	53.18 N	9.43 E
Moisdon	32	47.37 N	1.22 W
Moisés Ville	252	30.43 S	61.28 W
Moisevka	82	58.05 N	38.40 E
Moisie ⱥ	186	50.12 N	66.06 W
Moisie ⱥ	186	50.11 N	66.05 W
Moisselles	261	49.03 N	2.20 E
Moissac	62	44.06 N	1.05 E
Moisson	261	49.05 N	1.42 E
Moissy-Cramayel	261	48.37 N	2.36 E
Moitaco	246	8.01 N	64.21 W
Moivre ⱥ	36	48.54 N	4.36 E
Mojácar	34	37.08 N	1.51 W
Mojados	34	41.26 N	4.40 W
Mojanga, Brazo ⱥ	246	4.22 N	69.28 W
Mojang	102	23.08 N	103.33 E
Mojave	204	35.03 N	118.10 W
Mojave ⱥ	204	35.06 N	116.04 W
Mojave Desert ⬵²	204	35.00 N	117.00 W

Name	Page	Lat.	Long.
Mojave River Forks Reservoir ⬵¹	228	34.20 N	117.15 W
Moji	85	38.59 N	74.24 E
Mojiang	102	23.26 N	101.39 E
Mojiaçu ⱥ	255	20.53 S	48.10 W
Moji das Cruzes	256	23.31 S	46.11 W
Mojiguaçu	256	22.22 S	46.57 W
Mojimirim	256	22.26 N	46.57 W
Mojjero ⱥ	74	68.44 N	103.42 E
Mojnalyk	88	51.18 N	95.33 E
Mojo	144	8.36 N	39.07 E
Mojoagung	115a	7.34 S	112.21 E
Mojokerto	115a	7.28 S	112.26 E
Mojosari	115a	7.31 S	112.33 E
Mojstrana	64	46.27 N	13.56 E
Moju	250	1.53 S	48.46 W
Moju ⱥ	250	1.40 S	48.25 W
Mõka	94	36.26 N	140.01 E
Mokai	172	38.32 S	175.54 E
Mokāma	124	25.24 N	85.55 E
Mokāne	219	38.40 N	91.52 W
Mokapu Peninsula ⸧	229c	21.27 N	157.45 W
Mokaria	152	2.00 N	23.20 E
Mokarta, Castello di ⱥ	70	37.48 N	12.45 E
Mokau ⱥ	172	38.41 S	174.37 E
Mokau ⱥ	172	38.42 S	174.37 E
Moke	102	30.14 N	100.01 E
Mokelumne, Middle Fork ⱥ	226	38.13 N	121.28 W
Mokelumne, North Fork ⱥ	226	38.22 N	120.37 W
Mokelumne, South Fork ⱥ	226	38.23 N	120.35 W
Mokelumne Aqueduct ⱶ¹	226	37.54 N	122.07 W
Mokelumne Hill	226	38.18 N	120.42 W
Mokemane	216	41.31 N	87.53 W
Mokhotlong	158	29.22 S	29.02 E
Mokil I	1	6.40 N	159.47 E
Mokimbo	154	6.20 S	28.42 E
Mokmer	164	1.13 S	136.04 E
Möklinta	40	60.05 N	16.32 E
Mokochu, Khao ⱥ	110	15.56 N	99.06 E
Mokohinau Islands II	172	35.55 S	175.07 E
Mokokchũng	120	26.30 N	94.30 E
Mokolo, Cam.	146	10.45 N	13.48 E
Mokolo, Zaïre	152	1.57 N	18.05 E
Mokolo ⱥ	156	23.14 S	27.43 E
Mokombe	152	0.14 S	23.48 E
Mokoreta ⱥ	172	46.21 S	168.51 E
Mokpalin	110	17.26 N	96.53 E
Mokp'o	98	34.48 N	126.22 E
Mokra Jel'muta ⱥ	80	46.51 N	41.41 E
Mokra Ol'chovka ⱥ	80	50.28 N	44.59 E
Mokraja Sura ⱥ	78	48.39 N	35.09 E
Mokrany	78	51.49 N	24.14 E
Mokrisset	34	34.59 N	5.20 W
Mokro-Jelančik ⱥ	83	47.42 N	38.31 E
Mokrous	82	51.14 N	47.37 E
Mokrous	86	55.48 N	66.45 E
Mokrousovo	86	55.37 N	93.11 E
Mokryje Jaly ⱥ	78	48.05 N	36.44 E
Mokryj Jelančik ⱥ	80	46.53 N	42.45 E
Mokryj Kor	82	54.44 N	41.53 E
Mokša ⱥ	80	54.44 N	41.53 E
Moku	154	2.57 N	39.22 E
Mokuleia	229c	21.35 N	158.09 W
Mokumbusu	152	0.14 N	24.08 E
Mokwa	150	9.18 N	5.02 E
Mol	56	51.11 N	5.06 E
Mola di Bari	68	41.04 N	17.05 E
Molale	144	10.08 N	39.42 E
Molalla	224	45.08 N	122.34 W
Molalla ⱥ	224	45.18 N	122.43 W
Molalla, North Fork ⱥ	224	45.04 N	122.20 W
Molanda	152	2.08 N	20.48 E
Molango	234	20.53 N	98.46 W
Moláoi	72	36.48 N	22.52 E
Molara, Isola I	71	40.52 N	9.43 E
Molaretto	62	45.11 N	7.11 E
Molat, Otok I	66	44.15 N	14.49 E
Molatón ⱥ	34	38.47 N	1.15 W
Molčanovka	80	57.35 N	43.48 E
Molčanovo	86	57.35 N	83.48 E
Moldau — Vltava ⱥ	30	50.21 N	14.30 E
Moldavia	38	47.00 N	27.15 E
Moldavija — Moldova ⬩¹	38	47.00 N	29.00 E
Moldavija ⬩¹	24	52.15 N	25.05 E
Moldavskoje	38	44.11 N	28.59 E
Molde	26	62.44 N	7.11 E
Moldotau, chrebet ⱥ	84	41.50 N	73.40 E
Moldova ⱥ, Europe	30	46.20 N	29.00 E
Moldova ⱥ, Europe	38	47.56 N	26.42 E
Moldova Nouă	38	44.44 N	21.40 E
Moldoveanu, Vîrful ⱥ	38	45.36 N	24.44 E
Moldovei, Podişul ⱥ	38	47.10 N	27.00 E
Mole ⱥ, Eng., U.K.	42	51.24 N	0.20 W
Mole ⱥ, Eng., U.K.	260	51.16 N	0.18 W
Mole, Cap du ⸧	238	19.50 N	73.25 W
Moledet	132	32.31 N	35.22 E
Mole Game Reserve ⬩⁴	150	9.30 N	1.50 W
Molega Lake ⬵	207	44.22 N	64.53 W
Molegbe	152	4.14 N	20.53 E
Molenbeek-St-Jean	50	50.51 N	4.19 E
Molepolole	156	24.25 S	25.30 E
Moléson ⱥ	61	46.33 N	7.02 E
Molfetta	68	41.12 N	16.36 E
Molí	34	41.33 N	2.40 E
Molières-sur-Cèze	62	44.15 N	4.11 E
Molina de Aragón	34	40.50 N	1.53 W
Molina de Segura	34	38.03 N	1.12 W
Molina di Ledro	64	45.53 N	10.46 E
Moline, Il., U.S.	190	41.30 N	90.30 W
Moline, Ks., U.S.	216	37.22 N	96.18 W
Molinella	64	44.37 N	11.40 E
Molinges	62	46.24 N	5.46 E
Molini di Tures (Mühlen)	64	46.54 N	11.56 E
Molinière Point ⸧	241k	12.01 N	61.45 W
Molino de Rosas ⬩⁸	286a	19.22 N	99.12 W
Molinos	252	25.25 S	66.19 W
Molise ⬩¹	68	41.43 N	14.30 E
Moliterno	68	40.14 N	15.43 E
Molkau	54	51.19 N	12.28 E
Molkom	40	59.36 N	13.43 E
Mollahat	124	22.56 N	89.43 E
Mollakendi	128	38.38 N	39.23 E
Mollaoba	128	39.15 N	38.46 E
Mölle	41	56.17 N	12.29 E
Monaš	—	—	—

Name	Page	Lat.	Long.
Möllen	263	51.35 N	6.42 E
Möllenbeck, Dtsch.	54	53.17 N	11.44 E
Möllenbeck, Dtsch.	54	53.23 N	13.20 E
Mollendo	248	17.02 S	72.01 W
Mollepata	248	22.26 S	65.57 W
Mollepata	248	13.31 S	72.32 W
Moller, Port ⸦	180	55.51 N	160.25 W
Möllersdorf	264b	40.10 N	16.18 E
Mollet del Vallès	266d	41.33 N	2.13 E
Mollia	71	45.49 N	8.02 E
Molliens-Vidame	50	49.53 N	2.01 E
Mollina	34	37.08 N	4.40 W
Mollis	58	47.05 N	9.05 E
Mölln, Dtsch.	58	53.37 N	10.41 E
Mölln, Dtsch.	61	47.53 N	14.15 E
Mollösund	26	58.04 N	11.28 E
Mollusk	208	37.43 N	76.32 W
Molly Ann Brook ⱥ	276	40.55 N	74.11 W
Mölnbo	40	59.03 N	17.25 E
Möindal	26	57.39 N	12.09 E
Mölntorp	40	59.39 N	16.15 E
Molochio	68	38.18 N	16.02 E
Moločnaja ⱥ	78	46.30 N	35.20 E
Moločnoje	76	59.17 N	39.41 E
Moločnoje, ozero ⬵	78	46.30 N	35.20 E
Moločo ⱥ	154	17.03 S	38.52 E
Molodečno	76	54.19 N	26.49 E
Molodežnaja ⬩³	9	67.40 S	45.51 E
Molodi	82	55.17 N	37.31 E
Molodo	150	14.04 N	6.02 W
Molodogvardejsk	83	48.20 N	39.40 E
Molodoj Tud	76	56.26 N	33.36 E
Molodožnyj	89	50.23 N	136.48 E
Mologa ⱥ	76	58.50 N	37.11 E
Molokai I	229a	21.07 N	157.00 W
Molokai Fracture Zone ⬩	16	23.00 N	130.00 W
Moločka ⱥ	80	56.15 N	38.45 E
Molokovo, Ross.	76	58.10 N	36.45 E
Molokovo, Ross.	82	55.34 N	37.52 E
Moloma ⱥ	24	58.20 N	48.28 E
Molong	166	33.06 S	148.52 E
Molonglo ⱥ	171b	35.15 S	148.58 E
Molopo ⱥ	156	28.30 S	20.13 E
Molotovič	76	55.55 S	175.07 E
Molotov — Perm'	86	58.00 N	56.15 E
Molotovsk — Severodvinsk	24	64.34 N	39.50 E
Molou	146	13.42 N	21.44 E
Moloundou	152	2.03 N	15.10 E
Molowaie	152	5.47 S	23.20 E
Molsheim	54	48.32 N	7.29 E
Molson Lake ⬵	184	54.12 N	96.45 W
Molteno	158	31.22 S	26.22 E
Moltrasio	58	45.52 N	9.05 E
Molu, Pulau I	1	6.45 S	131.33 E
Moluccas — Maluku, Laut ⱶ²	108	0.00	125.00 E
Molucca Sea — Maluku, Laut ⱶ²	108	0.00	125.00 E
Moluccas, Islas — Maluku, Islas II	108	2.00 S	128.00 E
Moluccas — Maluku, Islas II	108	2.00 S	128.00 E
Molukken — Maluku, Islas II	108	2.00 S	128.00 E
Molundo	116	7.56 N	124.23 E
Moluques — Maluku, Islas II	108	2.00 S	128.00 E
Molveno, Lago di ⬵	64	46.08 N	10.57 E
Molvoticy	76	57.55 N	32.20 E
Molžaninovo	82	55.56 N	37.22 E
Moma, Moç.	154	16.44 S	39.14 E
Moma, Zaïre	152	1.36 S	23.57 E
Moma ⱥ	74	66.26 N	143.06 E
Momanga	74	66.28 N	143.06 E
Mombaça, Corrego ⱥ	287b	23.46 S	46.47 W
Mombachito, Cerro ⱥ	236	12.28 N	85.34 W
Mombango	152	1.45 N	24.26 E
Mombaruzzo	62	44.46 N	8.27 E
Mombasa	154	4.03 S	39.40 E
Mombetsu	92a	44.21 N	143.22 E
Mombuca ⱥ	256	22.26 N	51.35 E
Mombuey	34	42.01 N	6.20 W
Mombum	164	7.51 S	139.01 E
Mömbris	58	50.04 N	9.10 E
Momčilgrad	38	41.33 N	25.25 E
Momence	216	41.10 N	87.39 W
Momfafa, Tanjung ⸧	164	4.41 S	132.27 E
Mommark	41	54.55 N	10.02 E
Momignies	50	50.02 N	4.10 E
Momingou	116	7.29 N	121.12 E
Mommark	41	54.55 N	10.02 E
Momnabela	152	1.18 N	27.03 E
Momoiwa ⱥ	92	45.25 N	141.01 E
Momote	170	2.04 S	147.25 E
Momotombo, Volcán ⱥ	236	12.25 N	86.33 W
Momozaka	268	34.51 N	135.02 E
Mompog Pass ⱶ	116	13.31 N	122.11 E
Mompós	246	9.14 N	74.26 W
Mömpölö	58	66.00 N	146.00 E
Mon ⱥ	110	17.30 N	97.00 E
Mon ⬩¹	110	17.30 N	97.30 E
Mona, Canal de la ⱶ	238	18.05 N	67.45 W
Mona, Isla I	238	18.05 N	67.54 W
Mona, Punta ⸧	236	9.42 N	82.37 W
Monach, Sound of ⱶ	46	57.31 N	7.40 W
Monach Islands II	46	57.32 N	7.40 W
Monaci, Fiume dei ⱥ	71	40.48 N	14.48 E
Monaco []	62	43.43 N	7.23 E
Monaco ⬩¹, Europe	62	43.43 N	7.23 E
Monadhliath Mountains ⱥ	46	57.10 N	4.00 W
Monadnock Mountain ⱥ	207	42.52 N	72.07 W
Monagas ⬩³	246	9.20 N	63.00 W
Monaghan	48	54.15 N	6.58 W
Monaghan ⬩⁶	48	54.10 N	7.00 W
Monahans	196	31.35 N	102.54 W
Monahans Sandhills State Park ⬩	196	31.38 N	103.02 W
Monamolin	48	52.33 N	6.20 W
Monango	198	46.10 N	98.35 W
Monapo	154	14.57 S	40.19 E
Monarch	196	32.36 N	99.18 W
Monarch Mountain ⱥ	182	51.54 N	125.53 W
Monarch Pass ⱶ	196	38.30 N	106.20 W
Monarto South	171b	35.08 S	139.03 E
Monaš	60	48.02 N	16.18 E
Monashee Mountains ⱥ	182	51.00 N	118.43 W

Symbols in the index entries represent the broad categories identified in the key at the right. Symbols with superscript numbers (ⱥ¹) identify subcategories (see complete key on page *I · 1*).

Symbole im Register stellen die rechts im Schlüssel erklärten Kategorien dar. Symbole mit hochgestellten Ziffern (ⱥ¹) bezeichnen Unterteilungen einer Kategorie (vgl. vollständiger Schlüssel auf Seite *I · 1*).

Los símbolos incluidos en el texto del índice representan las grandes categorías identificadas con la clave a la derecha. Los símbolos con numeros en la parte superior (ⱥ¹) identifican las subcategorías (véase la clave completa en la página *I · 1*).

Les symboles de l'index représentent les catégories indiquées dans la légende à droite. Les symboles suivis d'un indice (ⱥ¹) représentent des sous-catégories (voir légende complète à la page *I · 1*).

Os símbolos incluídos no texto do índice representam as grandes categorias identificadas com a chave à direita. Os símbolos com números (ⱥ¹) identificam as subcategorias (veja-se a chave completa à página *I · 1*).

ⱥ Mountain	Berg	Montaña	Montaña	Montagne	Montanha
ⱥ Mountains	Gebirge	Montañas	Montañas	Montagnes	Montanhas
ⱶ Pass	Paß	Paso	Paso	Col	Passo
⥜ Valley, Canyon	Tal, Cañon	Valle, Cañón	Vallée, Canyon		Vale, Canhão
⬵ Plain	Ebene	Llano	Llanura	Plaine	Planície
⸦ Cape	Kap	Cabo	Cabo	Cap	Cabo
I Island	Insel	Isla	Isla	Île	Ilha
II Islands	Inseln	Islas	Islas	Îles	Ilhas
⬩ Other Topographic Features	Andere Topographische Objekte	Otros Elementos Topográficos	Autres données topographiques		Outros acidentes topográficos

ESPAÑOL Nombre	Página	Lat.	Long. W=Oeste
Monashee Mountains ✗	182	50.30 N	118.30 W
Monashee Provincial Park ♦	182	50.28 N	118.11 W
Monash University ●²	274b	37.55 S	145.08 E
Monasterace	68	38.27 N	16.33 E
Monasterevin	48	53.07 N	7.02 W
Monasterolo di Savigliano	62	44.40 N	7.37 E
Monastir, It.	71	39.23 N	9.02 E
Monastir — Bitola, Mak.	38	41.01 N	21.20 E
Monastir, Tun.	148	35.47 N	10.50 E
Monastir □⁸	148	35.15 N	10.45 E
Monastyrišče	78	49.00 N	29.49 E
Monastyriska	78	49.06 N	25.11 E
Monastyrščina	76	54.21 N	51.50 E
Monaélélé	152	4.16 N	11.12 E
Mona Vale	170	33.41 S	151.18 E
Monbulk	274b	37.52 S	145.25 E
Monbulk Creek ≈	274b	37.54 S	145.15 E
Moncada	116	15.44 N	120.34 E
Moncalieri	62	45.00 N	7.41 E
Moncalvo	62	45.03 N	8.16 E
Monção, Bra.	250	3.30 S	45.15 W
Monção, Port.	34	42.05 N	8.29 W
Monceau-sur-Sambre	50	50.25 N	4.22 E
Mončegorsk	24	67.54 N	52.58 E
Mönchdorf	56	48.21 N	14.48 E
Mönchengladbach	56	51.12 N	6.28 E
Mönchengladbach, Flughafen ⊠	263	51.14 N	6.29 E
Mönchhof	61	47.52 N	16.56 E
Monchique	34	37.19 N	8.33 W
Mönchweiler	58	48.06 N	8.24 E
Moncks Corner	192	33.11 N	80.00 W
Moncloa	232	26.54 N	101.25 W
Moncontour	32	48.21 N	2.39 W
Moncoutant	32	46.43 N	0.35 W
Moncton	186	46.06 N	64.47 W
Mondaí	252	27.05 S	53.25 W
Mondaino	66	43.51 N	12.41 E
Mondavio	66	43.40 N	12.58 E
Mondego ≈	34	40.09 N	8.52 W
Mondego, Cabo ➤	34	40.11 N	8.55 W
Mondello	70	38.13 N	13.20 E
Mondeodo	112	3.33 S	122.12 E
Mondeor	273d	26.17 S	28.00 E
Mondimbi	152	1.43 N	22.58 E
Mondo, Tan.	154	4.59 S	35.54 E
Mondo, Tchad	146	13.47 N	15.32 E
Mondolé, Monte ▲	62	44.13 N	7.46 E
Mondolfo	66	43.45 N	13.06 E
Mondombe	152	0.53 S	22.45 E
Mondoñedo	34	43.26 N	7.22 W
Mondorf-les-Bains	56	49.31 N	6.16 E
Mondoro	150	40.14 N	1.57 W
Mondoubleau	50	47.59 N	0.54 E
Mondovi	190	44.34 N	91.40 W
Mondragon, Fr.	62	44.14 N	4.43 E
Mondragon, Pil.	116	12.31 N	124.45 E
Mondragone	68	41.07 N	13.53 E
Mondrain Island I	162	34.08 S	122.15 E
Mondsee	44	47.52 N	13.21 E
Monds Island I	64	47.49 N	13.21 E
Mondy	88	51.40 N	100.59 E
Monee	216	41.25 N	87.45 W
Moneglia	62	44.14 N	9.30 E
Monemvasía	38	36.41 N	23.03 E
Monero	200	36.54 N	106.52 W
Moneron, ostrov I	89	46.17 N	141.15 E
Monesiglio	62	44.28 N	8.07 E
Monessen	214	40.08 N	79.53 W
Monesterio	34	38.05 N	6.16 W
Monestier-de-Clermont	62	44.54 N	5.38 E
Monetnyj	86	57.03 N	60.53 E
Monett	56	36.55 N	93.55 W
Monette	194	35.53 N	90.20 W
Money Creek ≈	216	40.40 N	88.58 W
Moneygall	48	52.53 N	7.57 W
Moneymore	48	54.42 N	6.40 W
Monfalcone	66	45.49 N	13.32 E
Monferrato □⁹	62	44.55 N	8.05 E
Monflanquin	32	44.32 N	0.46 E
Monforte	34	39.03 N	7.26 W
Monforte de Lemos	34	42.31 N	7.30 W
Monforte San Giorgio	70	38.09 N	15.23 E
Monfort Heights	218	39.12 N	84.37 W
Monga	152	4.12 N	22.49 E
Mongaguá	256	24.06 S	46.37 W
Mongai-Musenge	152	4.04 S	19.34 E
Mongala ≈	152	1.53 N	19.46 E
Mongalla	154	5.12 N	31.46 E
Mongalla Game Reserve ●⁴	154	5.12 N	31.33 E
Mongango	152	1.21 N	24.20 E
Mongarlowe ≈	170	35.15 S	149.52 E
Mongat	266d	41.28 N	2.17 E
Mongaup ≈	212	41.25 N	74.45 W
Mongaup Valley	210	41.40 N	74.47 W
Mongbwalu	154	1.57 N	30.02 E
Mongbyón-ni	271b	37.40 N	126.44 E
Mong Cai	110	21.32 N	107.58 E
Monge ≈	266c	38.46 N	9.26 E
Monger, Îles II	58	51.05 N	58.45 W
Mongeri	150	8.19 N	11.44 W
Mongers Lake @	162	29.15 S	117.05 E
Monggon Qulu	89	48.35 N	119.49 E
Monggǔmp'o	98	38.09 N	124.47 E
Mǒng Hai	110	20.46 N	99.49 E
Mǒng Hawm	110	23.51 N	98.20 E
Mǒnghidoru	66	44.13 N	11.19 E
Mǒng Hpayak	110	20.53 N	99.54 E
Mǒng Hsat	110	20.32 N	99.15 E
Mongi — Munger	124	25.23 N	88.28 E
Mongia	164	6.35 S	147.35 E
Mongiana	38	38.31 N	16.19 E
Mongibello — Etna, Monte ▲¹	70	37.46 N	15.00 E
Mongiuffri	70	37.55 N	15.17 E
Mǒng Küng	110	21.36 N	97.32 E
Mǒng Ma	110	21.37 N	99.54 E
Mǒng Mit	110	23.07 N	95.41 E
Mǒng Nai	110	20.31 N	97.52 E
Mǒng Nawng	110	21.39 N	93.08 E
Mongc, Tchad	146	12.11 N	13.42 E
Mongc, In., U.S.	216	41.41 N	85.17 W
Mongc □	150	9.34 N	12.11 W
Mongcj	88	53.57 N	113.50 E
Mongcl Altajn nuruu ✗	90	46.30 N	93.00 E
Mongcl Ard Uls — Mongolia □¹	90	46.00 N	105.00 E
Mongclei — Mongolia □¹	90	46.00 N	105.00 E
Mongcl els ●⁸	88	47.45 N	94.30 E
Mongolia (Mongol Ard Uls) □¹	90	46.00 N	105.00 E
Mongclie — Mongolia □¹	90	46.00 N	105.00 E
Mongumo	152	1.38 N	11.19 E
Mongǒn Mor't	88	48.11 N	103.29 E
Mongoro	146	12.01 N	22.28 E
Mongoumba	152	3.38 N	18.36 E
Mǒng Pai	110	19.44 N	97.05 E
Mǒng Pan	110	20.19 N	98.22 E
Mǒng Pawn	110	20.19 N	97.28 E
Mǒng Ping	110	21.22 N	99.02 E
Mongpong ≈	116	12.44 N	120.48 E
Mongrando	62	45.31 N	8.00 E
Mǒng Si	110	23.40 N	98.23 E
Mǒng Tung Hang ≈	271d	22.20 N	118.12 E
Mongu	152	15.15 S	23.09 E
Mongua	152	16.29 S	15.24 E
Monguelfo (Welsberg)	64	46.45 N	12.06 E
Mongumba	146	12.40 N	13.38 E

FRANÇAIS Nom	Page	Lat.	Lng. W=Ouest
Mǒng Yai	110	22.25 N	98.02 E
Mǒng Yawng	110	21.11 N	100.22 E
Monheim, Dtsch.	56	48.50 N	10.51 E
Monheim, Dtsch.	56	51.05 N	6.52 E
Moniaive	44	55.12 N	3.55 W
Mónichkirchen	61	47.31 N	16.02 E
Monico	190	45.34 N	89.09 W
Monida Pass ✗	202	44.33 N	112.18 W
Mon Idée	50	49.53 N	4.23 E
Monie	152	4.00 S	17.22 E
Monie Bay c	208	38.13 N	75.51 W
Monie Creek ≈	208	38.14 N	75.50 W
Monifieth	46	56.29 N	2.49 W
Monimail	46	56.18 N	3.08 W
Moninger	214	40.14 N	80.13 W
Monino	82	55.50 N	38.11 E
Moniquirá	246	5.52 N	73.36 W
Mǒniste	76	57.35 N	26.33 E
Monistrol-d'Allier	62	44.57 N	3.38 E
Monistrol-sur-Loire	62	45.17 N	4.10 E
Monitor Range ✗	204	38.45 N	116.30 W
Monitor Valley ✔	204	39.00 N	116.40 W
Monival	48	53.23 N	8.43 W
Monjolo	256	22.49 S	42.57 W
Monk, Pointe ➤	275a	45.29 N	73.57 W
Monkayo	116	7.50 N	126.03 E
Mönkebude	54	53.46 N	13.57 E
Monken Hadley ●⁸	260	51.40 N	0.11 W
Monkey Bay	154	14.05 S	34.55 E
Monkey River	238	16.22 N	88.29 W
Mǒnki	30	53.24 N	22.49 E
Monkira	166	24.49 S	140.34 E
Monkoto	152	1.38 S	20.39 E
Monks Heath	262	53.16 N	2.14 W
Monkton	212	43.35 N	81.05 W
Monmouth, Wales, U.K.	42	51.50 N	2.43 W
Monmouth, Il., U.S.	190	40.54 N	90.38 W
Monmouth, In., U.S.	216	40.52 N	84.57 W
Monmouth, Or., U.S.	202	44.50 N	123.13 W
Monmouth □⁶	208	40.16 N	74.17 W
Monmouth Beach	276	40.19 N	73.58 W
Monmouth Hills	276	40.24 N	74.00 W
Monmouth Junction	208	40.22 N	74.33 W
Monmouth Mountain ▲	182	51.00 N	123.47 W
Monnickendam	52	52.27 N	5.02 E
Monnow ≈	42	51.48 N	2.42 W
Mono ≈⁵	150	6.45 N	1.50 E
Mono ≈⁶	150	38.18 N	119.22 W
Mono, Ca., U.S.	204	6.17 N	1.57 E
Mono, Carbo ≈	246	4.25 N	67.47 W
Mono, Punta ➤	236	11.36 N	83.39 W
Monobe ≈	96	33.42 N	133.53 E
Monobe ≈	96	33.32 N	133.41 E
Monocacy ≈	208	39.13 N	77.27 W
Monocacy Station	208	40.16 N	75.46 W
Monogarovo	82	54.42 N	38.45 E
Mono Island I	175e	7.21 S	155.34 E
Mono Lake @	204	38.00 N	119.00 W
Monolith	228	35.07 N	118.22 W
Monomoy Island I	207	41.35 N	69.59 W
Monomoy Point ➤	207	41.33 N	70.02 W
Monon	216	40.52 N	86.52 W
Monona, Ia., U.S.	190	43.03 N	91.23 W
Monona, Wi., U.S.	216	43.03 N	89.20 W
Monona, Lake @	216	43.03 N	89.22 W
Monongahela ≈	214	40.12 N	79.55 W
Monongahela ≈	188	40.27 N	80.00 W
Monongahela Brook ≈	285	39.47 N	75.09 W
Monopoli	68	40.57 N	17.18 E
Monor	30	47.21 N	19.27 E
Mono Road Station	275b	43.51 N	79.51 W
Monòver	34	38.26 N	0.50 W
Monowai, Lake @	172	45.52 S	167.27 E
Monponsett	207	42.01 N	70.50 W
Monponsett Pond @	283	42.01 N	70.51 W
Monreal	34	42.42 N	1.30 W
Monreal del Campo	34	40.47 N	1.21 W
Monreale	70	38.05 N	13.17 E
Monreale, Castello di ✗	71	39.38 N	8.49 E
Monroe, Ct., U.S.	207	41.19 N	73.12 W
Monroe, Fl., U.S.	220	25.52 N	81.06 W
Monroe, Ga., U.S.	192	33.47 N	83.42 W
Monroe, In., U.S.	216	40.44 N	84.56 W
Monroe, Ia., U.S.	190	41.31 N	93.06 W
Monroe, La., U.S.	194	32.30 N	92.07 W
Monroe, Mi., U.S.	214	41.54 N	83.23 W
Monroe, N.C., U.S.	192	34.59 N	80.32 W
Monroe, N.Y., U.S.	210	41.19 N	74.11 W
Monroe, N.J., U.S.	276	41.06 N	74.38 W
Monroe, Or., U.S.	202	44.19 N	123.18 W
Monroe, Ut., U.S.	200	38.37 N	112.07 W
Monroe, Wa., U.S.	224	47.51 N	121.58 W
Monroe, Wi., U.S.	190	42.36 N	89.38 W
Monroe □⁶, Fl., U.S.	220	25.10 N	81.10 W
Monroe □⁶, Ga., U.S.	192	30.09 N	89.00 W
Monroe City, In., U.S.	194	38.36 N	87.21 W
Monroe City, Mo., U.S.	219	39.39 N	91.44 W
Monroe City, Tx., U.S.	222	29.47 N	94.35 W
Monroe Lake @¹	218	39.05 N	86.25 W
Monroe Manor	194	31.31 N	86.40 W
Monroeton	210	41.43 N	76.30 W
Monroeville, Al., U.S.	194	31.31 N	87.19 W
Monroeville, In., U.S.	216	40.58 N	84.52 W
Monroeville, N.J., U.S.			
Monroeville, Oh., U.S.	208	39.37 N	75.09 W
Monroeville, Pa., U.S.	214	40.26 N	79.47 W
Monroeville Mall ●⁸	279b	40.26 N	79.45 W
Monrovia □⁶, Liber.	150	6.18 N	10.47 W
Monrovia, Ca., U.S.	228	34.09 N	117.59 W
Monrovia, In., U.S.	216	39.34 N	86.29 W
Monrovia Mountain ▲	280	34.13 N	117.58 W
Monrovia Peak ▲	228	34.13 N	117.57 W
Mons (Bergen), Bel.	50	50.27 N	3.56 E
Mons, Fr.	62	43.41 N	6.13 E
Monschau	56	50.33 N	6.14 E
Monse	112	4.07 S	123.15 E
Monsefú	248	6.52 S	79.52 W
Monselice	64	45.14 N	11.45 E
Monsenhor Hipólito	250	6.59 S	41.07 W
Monsenhor Paulo	256	21.46 S	45.33 W
Monsenhor Tabosa	250	4.47 S	40.04 W
Monsey	210	41.06 N	74.04 W
Mǿns Klint ≈⁴	41	54.59 N	12.33 E
Monsols	58	46.13 N	4.31 E
Monson, Ma., U.S.	58	42.06 N	72.19 W
Monster	52	52.00 N	4.10 E
Mönsterås	26	57.02 N	16.26 E
Monsummano Terme	66	43.52 N	10.49 E
Montà	62	44.48 N	7.51 E
Montabaur	56	50.26 N	7.50 E
Montafon ▾	58	47.02 N	9.57 E
Montagano	68	41.39 N	14.40 E
Montagna	64	45.14 N	11.28 E

PORTUGUÊS Nome	Página	Lat.	Long. W=Oeste
Montagnareale	70	38.07 N	14.57 E
Montagne d'Ambre, Parque Nacional de la ✗	157b	12.40 S	49.05 E
Montagnola ✗	66	43.17 N	11.11 E
Montagrier	32	45.16 N	0.29 E
Montagu	158	33.45 S	20.08 E
Montague, P.E., Can.	186	46.10 N	62.39 W
Montague, Ca., U.S.	204	41.43 N	122.31 W
Montague, Mi., U.S.	190	43.25 N	86.21 W
Montague, Tx., U.S.	196	33.40 N	97.43 W
Montague, Isla I	232	31.45 N	114.48 W
Montague City	207	42.35 N	72.35 W
Montague Island I	180	60.00 N	147.30 W
Montague Peak ▲	180	60.15 N	147.01 W
Montague Island I	18	58.25 S	26.20 W
Montaigle, Château de ✗	56	50.18 N	4.49 E
Montaigu	32	46.59 N	1.19 W
Montaigut-en-Combraille	32	46.11 N	2.48 E
Montainville	261	48.53 N	1.52 E
Montaione	66	43.33 N	10.55 E
Montaj-Taš	85	42.06 N	68.58 E
Montalbá	222	33.53 N	95.38 W
Montalbén	34	40.50 N	0.48 W
Montalto di Castro	66	42.21 N	11.37 E
Montalto Ligure	62	43.56 N	7.51 E
Montalbano Ionico	70	38.02 N	15.01 E
Montalcino	66	40.17 N	16.34 E
Montalto Uffugo	68	39.25 N	16.10 E
Montalvo Manor	226	37.59 N	122.21 W
Montalvo ≈	228	34.15 N	119.12 W
Montana, Schw.	58	46.18 N	7.29 E
Montana, Ak., U.S.	180	62.05 N	150.04 W
Montana □³, U.S.	178	47.00 N	110.00 W
Montana □³, U.S.	202	47.00 N	110.00 W
Montana de Oro State Park ●	226	35.15 N	120.50 W
Montana Incian Reserve ●⁴	182	52.43 N	113.25 W
Montana'o ≈	62	45.14 N	7.51 E
Montánchez	34	39.13 N	6.09 W
Montandon	208	40.58 N	76.51 W
Montanha	255	10.08 S	40.21 W
Montánttila	68	40.10 N	15.22 E
Montara	226	37.33 N	122.31 W
Montara Beach ≈	282	37.33 N	122.31 W
Montara Mountain ✗	282	37.32 N	122.27 W
Montargil	34	39.05 N	8.10 W
Montargis	50	48.00 N	2.45 E
Montauban	32	44.01 N	1.21 E
Montauban, Lac @	206	46.52 N	72.10 W
Montauban-les-Mines	206	46.50 N	72.20 W
Montauk	207	41.02 N	71.57 W
Montauk Lake @	207	41.04 N	71.55 W
Montauk Point ➤	207	41.04 N	71.52 W
Montauroux	62	43.37 N	6.46 E
Mont Vista	226	37.19 N	122.03 W
Montazrrail	46	41.57 N	14.26 E
Montbard	50	47.37 N	4.20 E
Montbarrey	58	47.01 N	5.39 E
Montbazon	58	47.01 N	0.43 E
Montbéliard	58	47.31 N	6.48 E
Mont Belvieu	222	29.50 N	94.53 W
Montbenoît	58	46.59 N	6.28 E
Montbleux	34	41.22 N	1.10 E
Mont Blanc, Tunnel du ●⁵	58	45.50 N	6.53 E
Mont-Bonvillers	58	49.22 N	5.51 E
Montbovon	58	46.29 N	7.03 E
Montbrison	32	45.36 N	4.03 E
Montbron	32	45.40 N	0.30 E
Montbronn	58	48.59 N	7.19 E
Montcada i Reixas	266d	29.29 N	2.11 E
Montceau-les-Mines	58	46.40 N	4.22 E
Montcenis	58	46.47 N	4.23 E
Mont Cenis, Col du ✗	62	45.15 N	6.54 E
Montcevelles, Lac @	186	51.07 N	60.38 W
Montchanin, Fr.	58	46.45 N	4.27 E
Montchanin, De., U.S.	285	39.47 N	75.35 W
Montchauvet	261	48.54 N	1.38 E
Montclair, Ca., U.S.	228	34.04 N	117.41 W
Montclair, N.J., U.S.	276	40.49 N	74.12 W
Montclair State College ●²	276	40.51 N	74.11 W
Mont Clare	285	40.08 N	75.30 W
Montcorret	50	49.41 N	4.01 E
Montdale	50	41.34 N	75.37 W
Mont-de-Marsan	32	43.53 N	0.30 W
Montdidier	50	49.39 N	2.34 E
Mont-Dore	175f	22.16 S	166.34 E
Monte, Cima del ▲	66	42.16 N	10.23 E
Monte, Laguna del @, Arg.	252	37.00 S	62.28 W
Monte, Laguna del @, Arg.	252	37.00 S	62.28 W
Montea ▲	68	39.40 N	15.57 E
Monte Adone, Galleria di ●⁵	64	44.21 N	11.25 E
Monteagle	194	35.15 N	85.50 W
Monteagudo	248	19.49 S	63.59 W
Monte Alban ⊥	234	17.02 N	96.45 W
Monte Alegre, Bra.	250	2.01 S	54.04 W
Monte Alegre, Bra.	250	6.04 S	35.20 W
Monte Alegre de Goiás	255	13.14 S	47.10 W
Monte Alegre de Minas	255	18.52 S	48.52 W
Monte Alegre de Sergipe	250	10.02 S	37.33 W
Monte Alegre do Piauí	250	9.46 S	45.18 W
Monte Alegre do Sul	256	22.40 S	46.41 W
Monte Azul	255	15.09 S	42.53 W
Monte Azul Paulista	255	20.55 S	48.38 W
Montebelo, P.Q., Can.	186	45.39 N	74.56 W
Montebello, It.	62	45.00 N	9.06 E
Montebello, P.R.	240m	18.22 N	66.31 W
Montebello, Ca., U.S.	228	34.00 N	118.06 W
Montebello, Ga., U.S.	192	33.81 N	83.41 W
Montebello, Il., U.S.	216	40.41 N	89.31 W
Montebelluna	64	45.47 N	12.03 E
Montebello Vicentino	64	45.27 N	11.23 E
Monte Bello Islands II	162	20.25 S	115.32 E
Montebourg	50	49.29 N	1.23 W
Monte Buey	252	32.55 S	62.27 W
Monte Carmelo	255	18.43 S	47.29 W
Monte Caseros	252	30.15 S	57.39 W
Montecassino, Abbazia de ✗	68	41.29 N	13.48 E
Montecatini-Terme	64	43.53 N	10.46 E

(cont.) Nombre	Página	Lat.	Long.
Monte Cavallo	66	42.59 N	13.00 E
Montecchio	66	43.51 N	12.46 E
Montecchio Emilia	64	44.42 N	10.27 E
Montecchio Maggiore	64	45.30 N	11.24 E
Montecelio	66	42.01 N	12.44 E
Monte Ceneri, Passo ✗	58	46.08 N	8.55 E
Montechiaro d'Asti	62	45.01 N	8.07 E
Montechiarugolo	64	44.42 N	10.25 E
Monte Chingolo ●⁸	288	34.45 S	58.20 W
Monteciccardo	66	43.49 N	12.48 E
Montecilfone	68	41.54 N	14.50 E
Montecillos, Cordillera de ✗	236	14.25 N	87.51 W
Montecito	204	34.26 N	119.37 W
Monte Comán	252	34.36 S	67.54 W
Montecorice	68	40.14 N	15.00 E
Montecorvino Pugliano	68	40.41 N	14.57 E
Montecorvino Rovella	68	40.42 N	14.59 E
Montecristi, Ec.	246	1.03 S	80.40 W
Monte Cristi, Rep. Dom.	238	19.52 N	71.39 W
Monte Cristo	248	14.43 S	61.14 W
Montecristo, Isola di I	36	42.20 N	10.19 E
Montecucolo ●¹	64	44.19 N	10.50 E
Montedonne ≈	64	42.58 N	13.35 E
Monteforte d'Alpone	64	45.25 N	11.17 E
Monteforte Irpino	68	40.54 N	14.42 E
Montefrío	34	37.19 N	4.01 W
Montegallo	68	42.50 N	13.19 E
Montegiordano	68	40.02 N	16.32 E
Montegiorgio	66	43.08 N	13.32 E
Monte Giovi, Passo di (Jaufen Pass) ✗	64	46.50 N	11.19 E
Montego Bay	241q	18.28 N	77.55 W
Montegranaro	66	43.14 N	13.38 E
Monte Grande	252	30.06 S	70.31 W
Monte Grimano	66	43.52 N	12.29 E
Montegrotto Terme	64	45.19 N	11.46 E
Montegut	194	29.28 N	90.33 W
Monteiasi	68	40.30 N	17.23 E
Monteiro	250	7.53 S	37.04 W
Monteiro Lobato	256	22.58 S	45.50 W
Monteith, Mount ▲	182	55.45 N	122.30 W
Montejicar	34	37.34 N	3.30 W
Montejinni	166	16.40 S	131.45 E
Montelavar	266c	38.51 N	9.20 W
Monteleone di Puglia	68	41.10 N	15.15 E
Monteleone di Spoleto	66	42.39 N	12.58 E
Monteleone Rocca Doria	71	40.29 N	8.34 E
Monteleone Sabino	66	42.14 N	12.51 E
Montelepre	70	38.05 N	13.10 E
Montélibano	246	8.05 N	75.29 W
Montélimar	32	44.34 N	4.45 E
Montélindo ≈	252	23.56 S	57.12 W
Montella	68	40.51 N	15.01 E
Montellano	34	37.00 N	5.34 W
Montello, Nv., U.S.	204	41.15 N	114.11 W
Montello, Wi., U.S.	190	43.47 N	89.19 W
Monteluco ●¹	66	42.43 N	12.45 E
Montelupo Fiorentino	64	44.24 N	9.54 E
Montelupone	66	43.21 N	13.22 E
Montemaggiore Belsito	70	37.51 N	13.46 E
Montemagno	62	44.59 N	8.20 E
Monte Maíz	252	33.12 S	62.36 W
Montemarano	68	40.55 N	15.00 E
Montemarciano	66	43.38 N	13.19 E
Montemayor, Meseta de ✗	254	44.20 S	66.10 W
Montemesola	68	40.35 N	17.20 E
Montemiletto	68	41.01 N	14.54 E
Montemilone	68	41.02 N	15.58 E
Montemor ≈	266c	38.49 N	9.12 W
Montemor-o-Novo	34	38.39 N	8.13 W
Montemor-o-Velho	34	40.10 N	8.41 W
Montemorelos	232	25.12 N	99.49 W
Montemurro	68	40.18 N	16.00 E
Montendre	32	45.17 N	0.24 W
Montenegro	252	29.42 S	51.28 W
Montenegro — Crna Gora □³	38	42.30 N	19.18 E
Montenero di Bisaccia	68	41.57 N	14.47 E
Monteodorisio	68	42.05 N	14.39 E
Monte Oliveto Maggiore, Abbazia del ✗	66	43.12 N	11.32 E
Montepescali	66	42.54 N	11.05 E
Monte Porzio Catone	267a	41.49 N	12.43 E
Monteprandone	66	42.55 N	13.52 E
Montepuez	154	13.07 S	39.00 E
Montepuez ≈	154	12.32 S	40.27 E
Montepulciano	66	43.05 N	11.47 E
Monte Quemado	252	25.48 S	62.52 W
Monterado	112	0.45 N	109.08 E
Monte Real	34	39.51 N	8.50 W
Montereale	68	42.31 N	13.15 E
Montereale Valcellina	64	46.10 N	12.39 E
Montereau-Faut-Yonne	50	48.23 N	2.57 E
Montereau-sur-le-Jard	261	48.35 N	2.40 E
Monterey, Ca., U.S.	226	36.36 N	121.53 W
Monterey, Ky., U.S.	218	38.25 N	84.52 W
Monterey, Ma., U.S.	207	42.10 N	73.12 W
Monterey, Tn., U.S.	194	36.08 N	85.16 W
Monterey, Va., U.S.	188	38.24 N	79.34 W
Monterey Bay c	226	36.45 N	121.51 W
Monterey Park	228	34.03 N	118.07 W
Monterey Peninsula Airport ⊠	226	36.35 N	121.51 W
Monteriggioni	66	43.23 N	11.13 E
Monteroni d'Arbia	66	43.14 N	11.25 E
Monteroni di Lecce	68	40.19 N	18.05 E
Monteros	252	27.10 S	65.30 W
Monterosi	66	42.12 N	12.19 E
Monterosso al Mare	62	44.09 N	9.39 E
Monterosso Almo	70	37.05 N	14.46 E
Monterosso Calabro	68	38.43 N	16.17 E
Monterotondo	66	42.03 N	12.37 E
Monterotondo Maríttimo	66	43.09 N	10.51 E
Monterrey, Méx.	232	25.40 N	100.19 W
Monterrico, Hipódromo de ✗	286d	12.06 S	76.59 W

(cont.) Nombre	Página	Lat.	Long.
Monterubbiano	66	43.05 N	13.43 E
Montes Altos	250	5.50 S	47.04 W
Monte San Biagio	66	41.21 N	13.21 E
Monte San Giovanni Campano	66	41.38 N	13.31 E
Montesano	224	46.58 N	123.36 W
Montesano sulla Marcellana	68	40.16 N	15.42 E
Monte San Savino	66	43.20 N	11.43 E
Monte Santa Maria Tiberina	66	43.26 N	12.09 E
Monte Sant'Angelo	68	41.42 N	15.57 E
Monte Santo	250	10.26 S	39.20 W
Monte Santo de Minas	256	21.12 S	46.59 W
Monte Santu, Capo di ➤	71	40.05 N	9.44 E
Montesarchio	68	41.04 N	14.38 E
Montescaglioso	68	40.33 N	16.40 E
Montes Claros	255	16.43 S	43.52 W
Montescudaic	66	43.19 N	13.37 E
Montese	64	44.16 N	10.56 E
Monte Sereno	226	37.15 N	122.01 W
Monte Sião	256	22.26 S	46.34 W
Montesilvano Marina	66	42.31 N	14.09 E
Montespaccato ●⁸	267a	41.54 N	12.23 E
Montespertoli	66	43.38 N	11.04 E
Monte Vago	70	37.42 N	12.58 E
Montevago	70	37.42 N	12.58 E
Montevallo	194	33.06 N	86.51 W
Montevarchi	66	43.31 N	11.34 E
Monte Verde ≈	256	21.55 S	43.33 W
Monteverde Nuovo ●⁸	267a	41.51 N	12.27 E
Montedoro	70	37.27 N	13.49 E
Monte Escobedo	234	22.18 N	103.35 W
Monte Estoril	266c	38.42 N	9.24 W
Montefalcone	68	40.58 N	14.53 E
Montefalco	66	42.54 N	12.39 E
Montefalcone di Val Fortore	68	41.20 N	15.00 E
Montefano	66	43.25 N	13.26 E
Montefeltro ●¹	66	43.50 N	12.15 E
Montefiascone	66	42.32 N	12.02 E
Montefiorino	64	44.19 N	10.37 E
Montevergine, Santuario di ✗¹	68	40.55 N	14.45 E
Montevideo, Mn., U.S.	198	44.56 N	95.43 W
Montevideo, Ur.	258	34.53 S	56.11 W
Montevideo □⁵	258	34.50 S	56.12 W
Montevideo, Cerro de ▲²	258	33.54 S	56.15 W
Monte Vista	200	37.34 N	106.08 W
Montévrain	261	48.53 N	2.45 E
Montezemolo	62	44.22 N	8.08 E
Montezuma, In., U.S.	194	39.47 N	87.22 W
Montezuma, Ks., U.S.	196	37.35 N	100.26 W
Montezuma, N.Y., U.S.	210	43.00 N	76.42 W
Montezuma, Oh., U.S.	216	40.29 N	84.33 W
Montezuma Castle National Monument ✦	200	34.38 N	110.49 W
Montezuma Creek ≈	200	37.17 N	109.20 W
Montezuma Hills ✗²	282	38.07 N	121.51 W
Montezuma Slough ≈	282	38.04 N	121.52 W
Montfaucon, Fr.	62	49.17 N	5.08 E
Montfaucon, Fr.	62	45.10 N	4.18 E
Montfaucon, Schw.	58	47.17 N	7.03 E
Montfermeil	261	48.54 N	2.34 E
Montfleur	58	46.19 N	5.26 E
Montfort, Fr.	32	48.08 N	1.58 W
Montfort, Wi., U.S.	190	42.58 N	90.25 W
Montfort-l'Amaury	50	48.47 N	1.49 E
Montfort-le-Rotrou	50	48.03 N	0.25 E
Montfort-sur-Risle	50	49.18 N	0.40 E
Montfrin	62	43.55 N	4.36 E
Montgai	261	49.02 N	2.45 E
Montgenèvre	58	44.56 N	6.44 E
Montgenèvre, Col de ✗	58	44.56 N	6.44 E
Montgeron	261	48.42 N	2.27 E
Montgeroult	261	49.04 N	2.27 E
Montgesoye	58	47.05 N	6.12 E
Montgomery, Wales, U.K.	42	52.33 N	3.03 W
Montgomery, Al., U.S.	192	32.23 N	86.18 W
Montgomery, Il., U.S.	216	41.43 N	88.20 W
Montgomery, La., U.S.	194	31.40 N	92.53 W
Montgomery, Mi., U.S.	216	41.46 N	84.48 W
Montgomery, N.Y., U.S.	210	41.31 N	74.14 W
Montgomery, Oh., U.S.	218	39.13 N	84.21 W
Montgomery, Tx., U.S.	222	30.23 N	95.42 W
Montgomery, W.V., U.S.	188	38.11 N	81.19 W
Montgomery □⁶, Al.	192	32.15 N	86.19 W
Montgomery □⁶, Md.	208	39.09 N	77.12 W
Montgomery □⁶, Oh.	216	39.45 N	84.16 W
Montgomery □⁶, Tx.	222	30.18 N	95.30 W
Montgomery City	198	38.58 N	91.30 W
Montgomery Dam	214	40.24 N	80.24 W
Montgomery Knolls	284c	39.14 N	76.48 W
Montgomery Mall ●⁸	284c	39.01 N	77.09 W
Montgomery Square	285	39.14 N	75.19 W
Montgomeryville	285	40.15 N	75.15 W
Montgomeryville Airport ⊠	285	40.15 N	75.14 W
Montguyon	32	45.13 N	0.11 W
Monthermé	58	49.53 N	4.44 E
Monthey	58	46.15 N	6.57 E
Monthois	58	49.19 N	4.43 E
Monthyon	261	49.00 N	2.52 E
Monticelli d'Ongina	64	45.06 N	9.55 E
Monticello, Ar., U.S.	194	33.38 N	91.47 W
Monticello, Ga., U.S.	192	33.18 N	83.41 W
Monticello, Il., U.S.	216	40.01 N	88.34 W
Monticello, In., U.S.	216	40.45 N	86.46 W
Monticello, Ky., U.S.	188	36.49 N	84.51 W
Monticello, Me., U.S.	186	46.18 N	67.50 W
Monticello, Mn., U.S.	198	45.18 N	93.47 W
Monticello, Ms., U.S.	194	31.33 N	90.07 W
Monticello, N.Y., U.S.	210	41.39 N	74.41 W
Monticello, Ut., U.S.	200	37.52 N	109.20 W
Monticello Dam ●⁶	226	38.31 N	122.06 W
Monticello Woods	284c	41.31 N	73.10 W
Montichiari	64	45.25 N	10.23 E
Montiel, Campo de ≈	34	38.46 N	2.44 W
Monticn-en-Der	58	48.29 N	4.46 E

(cont.) Nombre	Página	Lat.	Long.
Monteri	66	43.08 N	11.01 E
Monteri, Poggio di ▲	66	43.08 N	11.00 E
Montiers-sur-Saulx	58	48.32 N	5.16 E
Montignac	32	45.04 N	1.10 E
Montigny	58	48.31 N	6.48 E
Montigny-Devant-Sassey	56	49.26 N	5.09 E
Montigny-le-Bretonneux	261	48.46 N	2.02 E
Montigny-le-Roi	58	48.00 N	5.30 E
Montigny-lès-Cormeilles	261	48.59 N	2.12 E
Montigny-lès-Metz	58	49.06 N	6.09 E
Montigny-sur-Aube	58	47.57 N	4.46 E
Montijo, Esp.	34	38.55 N	6.37 W
Montijo, Pan.	236	7.59 N	81.03 W
Montijo, Port.	34	38.42 N	8.58 W
Montijo, Aeroporto ⊠	266c	38.42 N	9.02 W
Montjo, Golfo de c	246	7.40 N	81.07 W
Montilla	34	37.35 N	4.38 W
Montividiu	255	17.24 S	51.14 W
Montivilliers	50	49.33 N	0.12 E
Montjay-la-Tour	261	48.55 N	2.40 E
Montoie, Lac ⊜, P.Q., Can.	206	46.17 N	75.08 W
Montoie, Lac ⊜, P.Q., Can.	206	46.15 N	72.06 W
Montova □	186		68.11 W
Montovet	182	45.43 N	7.40 E
Montoure, Estadio de ✗	266d	41.22 N	2.09 E
Montuich, Faro de ✗	266d	41.21 N	2.11 E
Montuich, Parque de ✗	266d	41.21 N	2.09 E
Mont-Laurier	176	46.33 N	75.30 W
Montebon	58	47.02 N	6.37 E
Monthéry	50	48.38 N	2.16 E
Monthéry, Tour de ♦	261	48.38 N	2.16 E
Montou	261	49.01 N	2.17 E
Montouet	261	48.01 N	1.43 E
Mont-Louis	32	42.31 N	2.07 E
Montoulis-sur-Loire	50	47.23 N	0.50 E
Montouon	62	45.51 N	5.03 E
Montmagny, P.Q., Can.	186	46.59 N	70.33 W
Montmagny, Fr.	261	48.58 N	2.21 E
Montmajour, Abbaye de ✗¹	62	43.43 N	4.40 E
Montmartre	261	48.53 N	2.21 E
Montméal	50	49.31 N	5.22 E
Montmélian	62	45.30 N	6.04 E
Montméal □	266d	41.33 N	2.15 E
Montmerle-sur-Saône	58	46.05 N	4.46 E
Montmirail, Fr.	50	48.52 N	3.32 E
Montmirail, Fr.	50	48.08 N	0.48 E
Montmirey-le-Château	58	47.13 N	5.32 E
Montmoreau-Saint-Cybard	32	45.24 N	0.08 E
Montmorenci	50	40.28 N	87.02 W
Montmorency, Austl.	274b	37.43 S	145.07 E
Montmorency — Beauport, P.Q., Can.	186	46.52 N	71.11 W
Montmorency, Fr.	261	49.00 N	2.20 E
Montmorency ≈	186	46.53 N	71.07 W
Montmorency, Forêt de ♦	261	49.02 N	2.16 E
Montmorillon	32	46.26 N	0.52 E
Montmort-Lucy	58	48.55 N	3.49 E
Montne	166	24.52 S	151.07 E
Montodine	64	45.17 N	9.42 E
Montoggio	62	44.31 N	9.03 E
Montoir-de-Bretagne	50	47.19 N	2.09 W
Montoire-sur-le-Loir	50	47.45 N	0.52 E
Montone ≈	62	44.29 N	12.20 E
Montone ≈	66	43.40 N	10.45 E
Mont Orford, Parc du ♦	206	45.22 N	72.05 W
Montorio al Vomano	66	42.35 N	13.38 E
Montorio nei Frentani	66	41.46 N	14.55 E
Montoro	34	38.01 N	4.23 W
Mont Orso, Galleria di ●⁵			
Montoursville	210	41.15 N	76.55 W
Montparnasse, Gare ●	261	48.51 N	2.19 E
Mont Peko, Parc National du ♦	150	7.00 N	7.15 W
Montpelier, Jam.	241q	18.22 N	77.56 W
Montpelier, Id., U.S.	202	42.19 N	111.17 W
Montpelier, In., U.S.	216	40.33 N	85.16 W
Montpelier, Md., U.S.	284c	39.06 N	76.51 W
Montpelier, Ms., U.S.	194	33.43 N	88.56 W
Montpelier, Oh., U.S.	216	41.35 N	84.36 W
Montpelier, Vt., U.S.	188	44.15 N	72.34 W
Montpellier	32	43.36 N	3.53 E
Montpellier-Fréjorgues, Aéroport de ⊠	62	43.33 N	4.00 E
Montpezat-de-Bauzon	62	44.43 N	4.12 E
Montpon-Ménestérol	32	45.00 N	0.10 E
Montpont-en-Bresse	58	46.33 N	5.09 E
Montréal, P.Q., Can.	206	45.31 N	73.34 W
Montréal, Fr.	32	47.32 N	0.42 E
Montreal, Wi., U.S.	190	46.35 N	90.14 W
Montreal City	219	38.58 N	91.30 W
Montreal Dam	190	47.14 N	84.39 W
Montréal ≈, Ont., Can.	214	47.08 N	79.27 W
Montreal ≈, Sk., Can.	184	55.06 N	105.19 W
Montreal, Base des Forces Canadiennes ●	275a	45.31 N	73.34 W
Montréal, Université de ●	206	45.30 N	73.37 W
Montréal-Est	206	45.38 N	73.31 W
Montreal International Airport ⊠	206	45.28 N	73.45 W
Montreal Lake @	184	54.20 N	105.40 W
Montreal Lake Indian Reserve ●⁴	184	54.00 N	105.46 W
Montréal-Nord	206	45.36 N	73.38 W
Montréal-Ouest	275a	45.27 N	73.39 W
Montreal Water Works Aqueduct ●	275a	45.26 N	73.35 W
Montréjeau	32	43.05 N	0.34 E
Montrésor	50	47.09 N	1.12 E
Montret	58	46.41 N	5.07 E
Montreuil-Bellay	32	47.08 N	0.09 W
Montrevault	50	47.17 N	1.04 W
Montrevel-en-Bresse	58	46.20 N	5.08 E
Montrichard	50	47.20 N	1.11 E
Montrichard	50	47.20 N	1.11 E
Montréjeau	32	43.05 N	0.34 E
Montreux	58	46.26 N	6.55 E
Montri	71	40.09 N	9.07 E
Montreuil-sur-Mer	50	50.28 N	1.46 E
Montrichard	50	47.20 N	1.11 E
Montrichard	50	47.20 N	1.11 E
Mont-Rolland	206	45.57 N	74.07 W
Montrond-les-Bains	62	45.38 N	4.14 E
Montrose, Scot., U.K.	46	56.43 N	2.29 W

Montrose, Ca., U.S. 228 34.12 N 118.13 W
Montrose, Co., U.S. 200 38.28 N 107.52 W
Montrose, Ia., U.S. 190 40.31 N 91.24 W
Montrose, Mi., U.S. 190 43.10 N 83.53 W
Montrose, N.Y., U.S. 210 41.15 N 73.56 W
Montrose, Oh., U.S. 214 41.08 N 81.37 W
Montrose, Pa., U.S. 210 41.50 N 75.52 W
Montrose, S.D., U.S. 198 43.41 N 97.11 W
Montrose Harbor c 278 41.58 N 87.38 W
Montrose Hill 279b 40.30 N 79.51 W
Montross 208 38.05 N 76.49 W
Montrouge 261 48.49 N 2.19 E
Mont-Royal 206 45.31 N 73.39 W
Mont Royal, Parc ♦ 275a 45.31 N 73.35 W
Mont Royal Tunnel ➔[5] 275a 45.31 N 73.38 W
Montry 261 48.53 N 2.50 E
Monts 50 47.17 N 0.37 E
Monts, Pointe des › 186 49.20 N 67.23 W
Mont-Saint-Aignan 50 49.28 N 1.05 E
Mont-Sainte-Anne, Parc du ♦ 186 47.08 N 70.55 W
Mont-Saint-Hilaire 206 45.34 N 73.11 W
Mont-Saint-Martin 56 49.32 N 5.47 E
Mont-Saint-Michel → Le Mont-Saint-Michel ♁[1] 32 48.38 N 1.32 W
Mont-Saint-Vincent 58 46.38 N 4.29 E
Montsauche 50 47.13 N 4.01 E
Montsec 56 48.53 N 5.43 E
Montserrat □[2], N.A. 230 16.45 N 62.12 W
Montserrat □[2], N.A. 238 16.45 N 62.12 W
Montserrat, Monasterio de ♁[1] 34 41.36 N 1.49 E
Montsoult 261 49.04 N 2.19 E
Montsûrs 28 48.08 N 0.33 W
Mont-sur-Vaudrey 58 46.58 N 5.36 E
Mont-Tremblant, Parc provincial du ♦ 206 46.42 N 74.20 W
Montuenga 34 41.03 N 4.37 W
Montvale, N.J., U.S. 276 41.02 N 74.01 W
Montvale, Va., U.S. 192 37.23 N 79.43 W
Montverde 220 28.36 N 81.41 W
Montville, Ct., U.S. 207 41.27 N 72.08 W
Montville, N.J., U.S. 276 40.54 N 74.23 W
Montville, Oh., U.S. 214 41.36 N 81.03 W
Montville Airpark ⊠ 276 40.56 N 74.20 W
Monument, S. Afr. 273d 26.06 S 27.43 E
Monument, Or., U.S. 202 44.49 N 119.25 W
Monument, Pa., U.S. 214 41.07 N 77.42 W
Monument Beach 207 41.43 N 70.36 W
Monument Draw V, U.S. 196 32.27 N 102.20 W
Monument Draw V, Tx., U.S. 196 30.51 N 102.33 W
Monument Hill State Historic Site ⊥ 222 29.53 N 96.54 W
Monumento 256 22.44 S 43.51 W
Monument Peak ʌ, Co., U.S. 200 39.43 N 107.55 W
Monument Peak ʌ, Id., U.S. 202 42.07 N 114.14 W
Monument Valley V 200 37.05 N 110.20 W
Monundilla, Mount ʌ 170 32.45 S 150.29 E
Monveda 152 2.57 N 21.27 E
Monymusk 46 57.13 N 2.31 W
Monyo 110 17.59 N 95.30 E
Monywa 110 22.05 N 95.08 E
Monza 62 45.35 N 9.16 E
Monze 154 16.16 S 27.28 E
Monzen 92 37.17 N 136.46 E
Monzie 46 56.24 N 3.48 W
Monzón, Esp. 34 41.55 N 0.12 E
Monzón, Perú 248 9.10 S 76.23 W
Moóca ➔[8] 287b 23.33 S 46.35 W
Moóca, Ribeirão da ≃ 287b 23.36 S 46.35 W
Moodie Island I 176 64.37 N 65.30 W
Moodus 207 41.30 N 72.27 W
Moodus Reservoir ⊜[1] 207 41.30 N 72.24 W
Moody 222 31.18 N 97.21 W
Moody Air Force Base ■ 192 30.59 N 83.11 W
Moody Wood Dale Airport ⊠ 278 41.59 N 87.58 W
Mooers 206 44.58 N 73.35 W
Mooi ≃, S. Afr. 158 28.45 S 30.34 E
Mooi ≃, S. Afr. 158 26.53 S 26.56 E
Mooirivier 158 29.13 S 29.50 E
Mook 52 51.45 N 5.54 E
Mookane 156 24.59 S 24.33 E
Mooketsi 156 23.35 S 30.05 E
Moolawatana 166 29.55 S 139.43 E
Moolman 158 27.10 S 30.53 E
Mooloogool 162 26.06 S 119.05 E
Moon 214 40.31 N 80.14 W
Moon ≃ 212 45.08 N 79.59 W
Moon, Mountains of the → Ruwenzori Range ʌʌ 154 0.23 N 29.54 E
Moonachie 276 40.50 N 74.02 W
Moonah Creek ≃ 166 22.03 S 138.33 E
Moon Crest 279b 40.32 N 80.11 W
Moondarra Reservoir ⊜[1] 169 38.04 S 146.22 E
Moonee Valley Racecourse ♦ 274b 37.46 S 144.56 E
Moonie 166 27.43 S 150.22 E
Moonie ≃ 166 29.19 S 148.43 E
Moon Island I, On., Can. 212 45.09 N 80.01 W
Moon Island I, Ma., U.S. 283 42.18 N 71.00 W
Moon Run 214 40.27 N 80.06 W
Moonta 168b 34.04 S 137.35 E
Moor, Kepulauan II 164 2.57 S 135.45 E
Moora 162 30.39 S 116.00 E
Moorabbin 169 37.56 S 145.02 E
Moorabbin Airport ⊠ 274b 37.59 S 145.09 E
Mooraberree 166 25.14 S 140.59 E
Moorabool ≃ 169 38.09 S 144.19 E
Moorarie 162 25.56 S 117.35 E
Moorburg 52 53.17 N 7.53 E
Moorcroft 198 44.15 N 104.56 W
Moordorf 52 53.28 N 7.23 E
Moordrecht 52 51.59 N 4.40 E
Moore, Austl. 171a 26.53 S 152.18 E
Moore, Eng., U.K. 262 53.21 N 2.38 W
Moore, Id., U.S. 202 43.44 N 113.21 W
Moore, Mt., U.S. 202 46.58 N 109.41 W
Moore, Ok., U.S. 196 35.20 N 97.29 W
Moore, Tx., U.S. 196 29.03 N 99.01 W
Moore ≃ 162 31.22 S 115.29 E
Moore, Lake ⊜ 162 29.50 S 117.35 E
Moorea I 174s 17.32 S 149.50 W
Moorebank 274a 33.56 S 150.56 E
Moore Creek ≃ 212 45.29 N 77.58 W
Moorefield, Ky., U.S. 218 38.16 N 83.55 W
Moorefield, Oh., U.S. 214 40.12 N 81.10 W
Moorefield, W.V., U.S. 188 39.03 N 78.58 W
Moore Haven 220 26.49 N 81.05 W
Moore Haven Lock ➔[5] 220 26.51 N 81.05 W
Moore Lake ⊜, On., Can. 212 45.26 N 78.01 W
Moore Lake ⊜, On., Can. 212 44.48 N 78.48 W
Moore Lake ⊜, Mi., U.S. 281 42.37 N 83.36 W
Mooreland, In., U.S. 218 39.59 N 85.15 W
Mooreland, Ok., U.S. 196 36.26 N 99.12 W
Moore Point › 275b 43.48 N 79.03 W
Moore Reservoir ⊜[1] 188 44.25 N 71.50 W
Mooresburg 210 40.59 N 76.43 W
Moores Creek National Battlefield ♦ 192 34.24 N 78.08 W
Moores Hill 218 39.06 N 85.05 W
Moore Station 222 32.11 N 95.35 W
Moorestown 208 39.58 N 74.56 W
Moorestown Mall ➔[9] 285 39.56 N 74.58 W
Mooresville, In., U.S. 218 39.36 N 86.22 W
Mooresville, N.C., U.S. 192 35.35 N 80.48 W
Mooreville 281 42.06 N 83.44 W
Moorfoot Hills ʌʌ[2] 46 55.45 N 3.02 W
Moorhead, Mn., U.S. 198 46.52 N 96.46 W
Moorhead, Ms., U.S. 194 33.27 N 90.30 W
Mooring 222 30.41 N 96.33 W
Mooringsport 194 32.41 N 93.57 W
Moormerland 52 53.20 N 7.27 E
Moornanyah Lake ⊜ 166 33.02 S 143.58 E
Moorooka 171a 27.32 S 153.02 E
Mooroolbark 274b 37.47 S 145.19 E
Moorpark 228 34.17 N 118.53 W
Moorreesburg 158 33.08 S 18.40 E
Moorrege 52 53.40 N 9.39 E
Moorriem 52 53.15 N 8.19 E
Moorsel 50 50.57 N 4.06 E
Moorside 262 53.34 N 2.04 W
Moorslede 50 50.53 N 3.04 E
Moos → Moso, It. 64 46.41 N 12.23 E
Moos → Moso in Passiria, It. 64 46.50 N 11.10 E
Moosach ➔[8] 60 48.11 N 11.31 E
Moosbrunn 264b 48.01 N 16.28 E
Moosburg 61 46.39 N 14.10 E
Moosburg an der Isar 60 48.29 N 11.57 E
Moose ≃, Me., U.S. 188 45.40 N 69.42 W
Moose ≃, N.Y., U.S. 212 43.37 N 75.22 W
Moose Creek 206 45.15 N 74.58 W
Moose Creek ≃ 206 45.23 N 75.04 W
Moosehead Lake ⊜ 188 45.40 N 69.40 W
Mooseheart 216 41.49 N 88.20 W
Moose Heights 182 53.05 N 122.30 W
Moose Hill ʌ[2] 283 42.07 N 71.13 W
Moose Island I 184 51.42 N 97.10 W
Moose Jaw 184 50.23 N 105.32 W
Moose Jaw ≃ 184 50.34 N 105.17 W
Moose Lake, Mb., Can. 184 53.43 N 100.20 W
Moose Lake, Mn., U.S. 190 46.27 N 92.45 W
Moose Lake ⊜, Ab., Can. 182 54.15 N 110.55 W
Moose Lake ⊜, Mb., Can. 184 53.55 N 99.45 W
Moose Lake ⊜, On., Can. 212 45.09 N 78.28 W
Mooselookmeguntic Lake ⊜ 188 44.53 N 70.48 W
Moose Mountain ʌ 184 49.45 N 102.37 W
Moose Mountain Creek ≃ 184 49.12 N 102.10 W
Moose Mountain Provincial Park ♦ 184 49.48 N 102.25 W
Moose Pass 180 60.29 N 149.22 W
Moosomin 184 50.07 N 101.40 W
Moosomin Indian Reserve ➔[4] 184 53.06 N 108.14 W
Moosonee 176 51.17 N 80.39 W
Moosup 207 41.42 N 71.52 W
Mooti 144 0.35 N 41.56 E
Moots Creek ≃ 216 40.32 N 86.47 W
Mootwingee National Park ♦ 166 31.07 S 142.23 E
Mopane 156 22.37 S 29.52 E
Mopeia Velha 156 17.59 S 35.44 E
Mopipi 156 21.07 S 24.55 E
Mopo 100 33.07 N 113.02 E
Moppo → Mokp'o 98 34.48 N 126.22 E
Mopti 150 14.30 N 4.12 W
Mopti □[4] 150 14.40 N 4.15 W
Moqokorei 144 4.04 N 46.08 E
Moquegua 248 17.12 S 70.56 W
Moquegua □[5] 248 16.50 S 70.55 W
Mór 30 47.23 N 18.12 E
Mor ≃ 126 24.01 N 88.03 E
Mòr, Glen V 46 57.10 N 4.40 W
Mor, Sgurr ʌ 46 57.42 N 5.03 W
Mora, Cam. 146 11.03 N 14.09 E
Mora, Esp. 34 39.41 N 3.46 W
Mora, India 272c 18.54 N 72.56 E
Mora, Port. 34 38.56 N 8.10 W
Mora, Sve. 26 61.00 N 14.33 E
Mora, Mn., U.S. 190 45.52 N 93.17 W
Mora, N.M., U.S. 200 35.58 N 105.19 W
Mora ≃ 196 35.44 N 104.23 W
Mora, Arroyo de la ≃ 196 34.05 N 104.18 W
Moraby 40 60.23 N 15.35 E
Morača, Manastir ♁[1] 38 42.44 N 19.20 E
Morada 226 38.01 N 121.15 W
Morādābād 124 28.50 N 78.47 E
Morada Nova 250 5.07 S 38.23 W
Morada Nova de Minas 255 18.37 S 45.22 W
Moradel, Montaña de ʌ 236 15.06 N 86.16 W
Mora de Rubielos 34 40.15 N 0.45 W
Moraduccio 66 44.10 N 11.29 E
Morafenobe 157b 17.49 S 44.55 E
Morąg 30 53.56 N 19.56 E
Moraga 226 37.50 N 122.08 W
Mórahalom 30 46.13 N 19.54 E
Moraine 218 39.42 N 84.13 W
Moraine Hills State Park ♦ 216 42.18 N 88.15 W
Moraine State Park ♦ 214 40.56 N 80.07 W
Morainvilliers 261 48.56 N 1.56 E
Morākhi ≃ 126 24.01 N 88.10 E
Morākhi Reservoir ⊜[1] 126 24.10 N 87.15 E
Mor'akovskij Zaton 86 56.45 N 84.41 E
Moral de Calatrava 34 38.50 N 3.35 W
Moraleda, Canal ⊔ 254 44.30 S 73.30 W
Morales, Guat. 236 15.29 N 88.49 W
Morales, Perú 248 6.28 S 76.28 W
Morales, Arroyo ≃ 258 34.48 S 58.36 W
Morales, Laguna c 234 23.35 N 97.47 W
Moramanga 157b 18.56 S 48.12 E
Moran, Ks., U.S. 198 37.54 N 95.10 W
Moran, Mi., U.S. 190 45.59 N 84.49 W
Moran, Tx., U.S. 196 32.33 N 99.10 W
Moran ≃ 164 15.16 S 125.33 E
Moranbah 166 22.00 S 148.02 E
Morangis 261 48.42 N 2.20 E
Morangup Hill ʌ[2] 168a 31.41 S 116.19 E
Morann 214 40.48 N 78.21 W
Morano Calabro 68 39.50 N 16.08 E
Morano sul Po 62 45.10 N 8.22 E
Moran State Park ♦ 224 48.41 N 122.52 W
Morant Bay 241q 17.53 N 76.25 W
Morant Cays II 238 17.24 N 75.59 W
Morant Point › 241q 17.55 N 76.10 W
Morar, Loch ⊜ 46 56.57 N 5.43 W
Mörarp 41 56.04 N 12.52 E
Morasverdes 34 40.36 N 6.16 W
Morat, Lac de (Murtensee) ⊜ 58 46.55 N 7.05 E
Moratalla 34 38.12 N 1.53 W
Morattico 208 37.47 N 76.37 W
Moratuwa 122 6.46 N 79.53 E
Morava □[9] 30 49.30 N 17.00 E
Morava (March) ≃ 30 48.10 N 16.59 E
Morāveh Tappeh 128 37.55 N 55.57 E
Moravia, C.R. 236 9.51 N 83.26 W
Moravia, Ia., U.S. 190 40.53 N 92.48 W
Moravia, N.Y., U.S. 210 42.42 N 76.25 W
Moravia → Morava □[9] 30 49.20 N 17.00 E
Moravian Indian Reserve ➔[4] 214 42.34 N 81.53 W
Moravská Dyje ≃ 61 48.51 N 15.30 E
Moravská Ostrava → Ostrava 30 49.50 N 18.17 E
Moravská Třebová 30 49.45 N 16.40 E
Moravské Budějovice 61 49.03 N 15.49 E
Moravský Krumlov 61 49.03 N 16.19 E
Morawa 162 29.13 S 116.00 E
Morawhanna 246 8.16 N 59.45 W
Moraya 248 21.45 S 65.32 W
Morayfield 171a 27.07 S 152.57 E
Moray Firth c[1] 46 57.50 N 3.30 W
Morazán, Guat. 236 14.56 N 90.09 W
Morazán, Hond. 236 15.17 N 87.34 W
Morbach 56 49.48 N 7.07 E
Morbegno 58 46.08 N 9.34 E
Morbi 120 22.49 N 70.50 E
Morbihan □[5] 32 47.55 N 2.50 W
Mörbisch am See 61 47.45 N 16.40 E
Morbras ≃ 261 48.47 N 2.29 E
Mörbylånga 26 56.31 N 16.23 E
Morcenx 32 44.02 N 0.55 W
Morciano di Romagna 66 43.55 N 12.38 E
Morcone 68 41.20 N 14.40 E
Morcote 58 45.56 N 8.55 E
Morcy 80 51.18 N 47.51 E
Morden 184 49.11 N 98.05 W
Morden ➔[8] 260 51.24 N 0.12 W
Mordialloc 169 38.00 S 145.05 E
Mordino 24 61.21 N 51.52 E
Mordoğan 130 38.30 N 26.37 E
Mordovija □[3] 80 54.30 N 44.00 E
Mordovo, Ross. 80 51.07 N 45.48 E
Mordovo, Ross. 80 52.05 N 40.46 E
Mordovo-Adel'akovo 80 53.47 N 51.36 E
Mordovskij Buguruslan 80 53.48 N 52.31 E
Mordovskij zapovednik ➔[4] 80 54.48 N 43.20 E
Mordves 82 54.34 N 38.13 E
Mordvinia → Mordovija □[3] 80 54.30 N 44.00 E
Mordy 30 52.13 N 22.31 E
More, Ben ʌ, Scot., U.K. 46 56.25 N 6.01 W
More, Ben ʌ, Scot., U.K. 46 56.21 N 4.35 W
More, Loch ⊜ 46 58.17 N 4.52 W
More Assynt, Ben ʌ 46 58.08 N 4.53 W
Moreau ≃, Mo., U.S. 219 38.33 N 92.06 W
Moreau ≃, S.D., U.S. 198 45.18 N 100.43 W
Moreau, North Fork ≃ 198 45.09 N 102.50 W
Moreau, South Fork ≃ 198 45.09 N 102.50 W
Moreau Peak ʌ 198 45.21 N 103.43 W
Moreauville 194 31.02 N 91.58 W
Morec 80 51.03 N 44.03 E
Morecambe 44 54.04 N 2.53 W
Morecambe Bay c 44 54.07 N 3.00 W
Moree, Austl. 166 29.28 S 149.51 E
Morée, Fr. 50 47.54 N 1.14 E
Morehead, Pap. N. Gui. 164 8.40 S 141.35 E
Morehead, Ky., U.S. 218 38.11 N 83.25 W
Morehead ≃ 164 9.00 S 141.25 E
Morehead City 192 34.43 N 76.43 W
Morehouse 194 36.50 N 89.41 W
Moreira César 256 22.55 S 45.22 W
Moreland, Austl. 274b 37.45 S 144.58 E
Moreland, Ga., U.S. 192 33.17 N 84.46 W
Moreland, Ky., U.S. 194 37.30 N 84.48 W
Moreland Hills 279a 41.27 N 81.29 W
Morelia 234 19.42 N 101.07 W
Morell 186 46.25 N 62.42 W
Morella, Austl. 166 22.59 S 143.52 E
Morella, Esp. 34 40.37 N 0.06 W
Morello ≃ 70 37.29 N 14.08 E
Morelos, Méx. 196 28.25 N 100.53 W
Morelos, Méx. 232 26.42 N 107.40 W
Morelos, Méx. 234 22.53 N 102.37 W
Morelos □[3] 234 18.45 N 99.00 W
Moremi Wildlife Reserve ➔[4] 156 19.10 S 23.15 E
Morena 124 26.30 N 78.09 E
Morena, Sierra ʌ 282 37.25 N 122.18 W
Morena, Sierra ʌʌ 34 38.00 N 5.00 W
Morenci, Az., U.S. 200 33.04 N 109.21 W
Morenci, Mi., U.S. 216 41.43 N 84.13 W
Moreni 38 45.00 N 25.39 E
Moreno, Arg. 258 34.39 S 58.48 W
Moreno, Ca., U.S. 228 33.55 N 117.09 W
Moreno □[5] 288 34.36 S 58.48 W
Moreno, Bahía c 252 23.35 S 70.30 W
Møre og Romsdal □[6] 26 62.40 N 7.50 E
Mores 71 40.33 N 8.50 E
Moresby Island I, B.C., Can. 182 52.50 N 131.55 W
Moresby Island I, B.C., Can. 224 48.40 N 123.20 W
Mores Island I 238 26.18 N 77.33 W
Moresnet 56 50.43 N 5.59 E
Morestel 62 45.40 N 5.28 E
Moreton, Austl. 164 12.28 S 142.38 E
Moreton, Eng., U.K. 44 53.24 N 3.07 W
Moreton, Eng., U.K. 260 51.44 N 0.14 E
Moreton, Cape › 171a 27.02 S 153.28 E
Moreton Bay c 171a 27.20 S 153.15 E
Moretonhampstead 42 50.40 N 3.45 W
Moreton-in-Marsh 42 51.59 N 1.42 W
Moreton Island I 171a 27.10 S 153.25 E
Moreton Island National Park ♦ 171a 27.09 S 153.25 E
Moret-sur-Loing 50 48.22 N 2.49 E
Moretta 62 44.46 N 7.32 E
Moreuil 50 49.46 N 2.29 E
Morey Park 210 42.33 N 73.43 W
Morey Peak ʌ 204 38.37 N 116.17 W
Morez 58 46.31 N 6.02 E
Morfa Nefyn 42 52.56 N 4.33 W
Mörfelden-Walldorf 56 49.58 N 8.34 E
Morga 80 54.26 N 46.29 E
Morgan, Austl. 166 34.02 S 139.40 E
Morgan, Ga., U.S. 192 31.32 N 84.35 W
Morgan, Ky., U.S. 218 38.36 N 84.23 W
Morgan, Mn., U.S. 198 44.25 N 94.55 W
Morgan, Pa., U.S. 279b 40.22 N 80.08 W
Morgan, Tx., U.S. 222 32.01 N 97.37 W
Morgan, Ut,. U.S. 200 41.02 N 111.40 W
Morgan □[6], Il., U.S. 219 39.44 N 90.14 W
Morgan □[6], In., U.S. 218 39.30 N 86.25 W
Morgan, Mount ʌ 171b 35.44 S 148.47 E
Morgan City, Al., U.S. 194 34.28 N 86.34 W
Morgan City, La., U.S. 194 29.41 N 91.12 W
Morgan Creek ≃ 196 32.19 N 100.55 W
Morganfield 194 37.41 N 87.55 W
Morgan Hill 226 37.07 N 121.39 W
Morganito 246 5.04 N 67.44 W
Morgan Park ➔[8] 278 41.42 N 87.40 W
Morgan's Bay 158 32.43 S 28.20 E
Morgan's Point 222 29.41 N 94.59 W
Morgans Point › 212 42.52 N 79.21 W
Morgan State College ♁[2] 284b 39.21 N 76.35 W
Morgantina ⊥ 70 37.25 N 14.29 E
Morganton 192 35.44 N 81.41 W
Morgantown, In., U.S. 218 39.22 N 86.15 W
Morgantown, Ky., U.S. 194 37.13 N 86.41 W
Morgantown, Md., U.S. 208 38.21 N 76.58 W
Morgantown, Ms., U.S. 194 31.18 N 89.54 W
Morgantown, Ms., U.S. 194 31.34 N 91.20 W
Morgantown, Oh., U.S. 218 39.08 N 83.13 W
Morgantown, Pa., U.S. 208 40.09 N 75.54 W
Morgantown, W.V., U.S. 188 39.37 N 79.57 W
Morganville 208 40.23 N 74.15 W
Morgan Whyalla Pipeline ≅[1] 168b 33.48 S 138.56 E
Morganza 194 30.44 N 91.35 W
Morgårdshammar 40 60.09 N 15.23 E
Morgauši 80 55.58 N 46.47 E
Morgenzon 158 26.45 S 29.36 E
Morges 58 46.31 N 6.30 E
Morgex 62 45.45 N 7.02 E
Morghāb (Murgab) ≃ 128 38.18 N 61.12 E
Morghar 126 23.40 N 89.37 E
Morghūm, Kūh-e ʌ 128 33.06 N 57.30 E
Morgongåva 40 59.56 N 16.57 E
Morgongiori 71 39.45 N 8.46 E
Morguilla, Punta › 252 37.46 S 73.40 W
Morhange 56 48.55 N 6.38 E
Mori, It. 64 45.51 N 10.59 E
Mori, Nihon 92a 42.06 N 140.35 E
Mori, Nihon 94 34.50 N 137.56 E
Mori, Nihon 270 34.32 N 135.00 E
Mori ≃ 164 10.00 S 148.30 E
Moriah 241r 11.15 N 60.43 W
Moriah, Mount ʌ 204 39.17 N 114.12 W
Morialta Conservation Park ♦ 168b 34.55 S 138.40 E
Moriarty 200 34.59 N 106.02 W
Moriarty, Mount ʌ 224 49.08 N 124.26 W
Morib 114 2.45 N 101.26 E
Moribaya 150 9.53 N 9.33 W
Morice ≃ 182 54.24 N 126.45 W
Morice Lake ⊜ 182 54.00 N 127.37 W
Morichal Largo ≃ 246 9.27 N 62.25 W
Moricsala rezervāts ♦ 76 57.17 N 22.11 E
Morie, Loch ⊜ 46 57.44 N 4.28 W
Morienval 50 49.18 N 2.56 E
Morigerati 68 40.08 N 15.33 E
Moriguchi 96 34.44 N 135.34 E
Morija 158 29.34 S 27.31 E
Moriki 150 12.52 N 6.30 E
Morin Dawa 89 48.28 N 124.27 E
Moringen 52 51.42 N 9.52 E
Morino, It. 66 41.53 N 13.25 E
Morino, Ross. 76 57.54 N 30.22 E
Morinville 182 53.48 N 113.39 W
Morioka 92 39.42 N 141.09 E
Morīri, Tso ⊜ 120 32.54 N 78.20 E
Morisset 170 33.06 S 151.29 E
Moriston ≃ 46 57.12 N 4.36 W
Moritzburg ⊥ 54 51.09 N 13.40 E
Morivione ➔[8] 266b 45.26 N 9.12 E
Moriya 94 35.56 N 140.00 E
Moriyama 94 35.04 N 135.59 E
Moriyama-chūtonchi, Rikujō-jieitai- ■ 94 35.12 N 136.57 E
Moriyoshi-zan ʌ 92 39.58 N 140.33 E
Morki 80 56.25 N 49.01 E
Morkill ≃ 182 53.42 N 120.30 W
Morkiny Gory 76 57.33 N 36.18 E
Mörkö I 40 58.59 N 17.40 E
Morkoka ≃ 74 65.10 N 115.52 E
Mørkøv 41 55.40 N 11.32 E
Morlaix 32 48.35 N 3.50 W
Morlanwelz 50 50.27 N 4.14 E
Morles 56 50.38 N 9.51 E
Morley, Eng., U.K. 44 53.46 N 1.36 W
Morley, Mi., U.S. 190 43.29 N 85.26 W
Morley, N.Y., U.S. 212 44.40 N 75.12 W
Morley Green 262 53.20 N 2.16 W
Mörlunda 26 57.19 N 15.51 E
Mormal' 76 52.45 N 29.53 E
Mormanno 68 39.53 N 16.00 E
Mormant 50 48.36 N 2.53 E
Mormoiron 62 44.04 N 5.11 E
Mormon Bar 226 37.28 N 119.57 W
Mormon Lake ⊜ 200 34.57 N 111.27 W
Mormon Peak ʌ 204 36.57 N 114.30 W
Mormon Reservoir ⊜[1] 202 43.16 N 114.49 W
Mormon Slough ≃ 226 37.57 N 121.18 W
Mormon Station Historical State Monument ♦ 226 39.00 N 119.50 W
Mormugao 122 15.24 N 73.48 E
Morna 272a 28.35 N 77.22 E
Mornant 62 45.37 N 4.40 E
Mornas 62 44.12 N 4.44 E
Morne-à-l'Eau 241o 16.21 N 61.31 W
Morne Trois Pitons National Park ♦ 240d 15.19 N 61.19 W
Morney 166 25.22 S 141.28 E
Morningdale 207 42.18 N 71.45 W
Morningside 284c 38.50 N 76.53 W
Morningside Park ♦ 275b 43.47 N 79.12 W
Morningstar ≃ 48 52.27 N 8.41 W
Morning Sun 190 41.05 N 91.15 W
Mornington 169 38.13 S 145.03 E
Mornington, Isla I 254 49.45 S 75.23 W
Mornington Island I 164 16.33 S 139.24 E
Mornington Island Aboriginal Land Trust ➔[4] 164 16.20 S 139.20 E
Mornington Peninsula ›[1] 169 38.20 S 145.05 E
Morno 150 8.41 N 1.31 W
Mornou, Hadjer ʌ 146 17.12 N 23.08 E
Moro, Indon. 114 0.46 N 103.43 E
Moro, Or., U.S. 224 45.29 N 120.43 W
Moro ≃ 150 7.25 N 11.03 W
Morobe 164 7.45 S 147.35 E
Morobe □[5] 164 7.00 S 146.30 E
Moroč' 76 52.34 N 27.36 E
Moroč' ≃ 76 52.35 N 27.35 E
Morocco 216 40.56 N 87.27 W
Morocco (Al-Magreb) □[1], Afr. 134 32.00 N 5.00 W
Morocco (Al-Magreb) □[1], Afr. 148 32.00 N 5.00 W
Morococala 248 18.10 S 66.44 W
Morococha 248 11.37 S 76.09 W
Moro Creek ≃ 194 33.18 N 92.22 W
Morogoro 154 6.49 S 37.40 E
Morogoro □[4] 154 8.00 S 37.15 E
Moro Gulf c 116 6.51 N 123.00 E
Moroka 273d 26.16 S 27.52 E
Morokweng 158 26.12 S 23.45 E
Moroleón 234 20.08 N 101.12 W
Morombe 157b 21.45 S 43.22 E
Morón, Arg. 258 34.39 S 58.37 W
Morón, Cuba 240p 22.06 N 78.38 W
Mörön, Mong. 88 48.15 N 100.23 E
Mörön, Mong. 88 47.24 N 110.16 E
Mörön, Mong. 88 49.38 N 100.10 E
Morón, Ven. 246 10.29 N 68.11 W
Morón □[5] 288 34.37 S 58.37 W
Mörön ≃ 88 47.14 N 110.37 E
Morón, Aeródromo ⊠ 288 34.41 S 58.38 W
Morón, Arroyo ≃ 288 34.33 S 58.37 W
Morona ≃ 246 4.45 S 77.04 W
Morona-Santiago □[4] 246 2.30 S 78.00 W
Morondava 157b 20.17 S 44.17 E
Morón de Almazán 34 41.25 N 2.25 W
Morón de la Frontera 34 37.08 N 5.27 W
Morones, Sierra ʌʌ 234 21.45 N 103.10 W
Morong 116 14.41 N 120.16 E
Morongo Indian Reservation ➔[4] 204 33.59 N 116.50 W
Moroni, Comores 157a 11.41 S 43.16 E
Moroni, Ut,. U.S. 200 39.31 N 111.35 W
Moron Us ≃, Zhg. 90 34.42 N 94.50 E
Moron Us ≃, Zhg. 120 34.42 N 94.50 E
Moros ≃ 34 41.03 N 4.15 W
Morošečnoje 74 56.24 N 156.12 E
Morotai I 108 2.20 N 128.25 E
Moroto 154 2.32 N 34.39 E
Moroto ʌ 154 2.32 N 34.46 E
Morouba 152 6.11 N 20.13 E
Morovis 240m 18.20 N 66.24 W
Morovsk 78 51.06 N 30.50 E
Morowali 112 1.52 S 121.30 E
Moroyama 94 35.56 N 139.19 E
Morozkovo 86 59.29 N 61.01 E
Morozovka, Ross. 78 50.09 N 39.38 E
Morozovka, Ukr. 83 49.28 N 39.54 E
Morozovsk 80 48.22 N 41.50 E
Morozovskaja 24 61.10 N 50.18 E
Morpeth, On., Can. 214 42.23 N 81.51 W
Morpeth, Eng., U.K. 44 55.10 N 1.41 W
Morphett Vale 168b 35.07 S 138.31 E
Morra, Monte ʌ 267a 42.02 N 12.50 E
Morral 214 40.41 N 83.12 W
Morral, Arroyo del ≃ 266d 41.29 N 2.03 E
Morrelganj 126 22.28 N 89.51 E
Morrice 216 42.50 N 84.11 W
Morrill 198 41.57 N 103.55 W
Morrilton 194 35.09 N 92.44 W
Morrin 182 51.40 N 112.47 W
Morrinhos, Bra. 250 3.14 S 40.07 W
Morrinhos, Bra. 255 17.44 S 49.07 W
Morrinsville 172 37.39 S 175.32 E
Morris, Mb., Can. 184 49.21 N 97.22 W
Morris, Ct., U.S. 207 41.41 N 73.11 W
Morris, Il., U.S. 216 41.21 N 88.25 W
Morris, In., U.S. 218 39.16 N 85.10 W
Morris, Mn., U.S. 198 45.35 N 95.54 W
Morris, N.Y., U.S. 210 42.32 N 75.14 W
Morris, Ok., U.S. 196 35.36 N 95.51 W
Morris, Pa., U.S. 210 41.36 N 77.18 W
Morris □[6], N.J., U.S. 210 40.48 N 74.29 W
Morris □[6], Tx., U.S. 222 33.05 N 94.45 W
Morris ≃ 184 49.21 N 97.22 W
Morris, Mount ʌ 162 26.09 S 131.04 E
Morrisburg 212 44.54 N 75.11 W
Morrisdale 214 40.56 N 78.13 W
Morris Dam ➔[6] 280 34.11 N 117.53 W
Morris Jesup, Kap › 16 83.38 N 33.52 W
Morris Lake ⊜ 276 41.03 N 74.37 W
Morrison, Arg. 252 32.36 S 62.50 W
Morrison, Il., U.S. 190 41.48 N 89.57 W
Morrison, Mo., U.S. 219 38.40 N 91.38 W
Morrison, Point › 168b 35.44 S 137.47 E
Morrison Creek ≃ 275b 43.28 N 79.39 W
Morrison Lake ⊜, On., Can. 212 44.52 N 79.28 W
Morrison Lake ⊜, Mi., U.S. 216 42.53 N 85.13 W
Morrisonville 219 39.25 N 89.27 W
Morris Park ♦ 285 39.59 N 75.15 W
Morris Plains 210 40.49 N 74.28 W
Morris Reservoir ⊜[1] 228 34.12 N 117.52 W
Morris Run 210 41.40 N 77.01 W
Morristown, Az., U.S. 200 33.51 N 112.37 W
Morristown, Il., U.S. 216 42.10 N 89.03 W
Morristown, In., U.S. 218 39.40 N 85.41 W
Morristown, Mn., U.S. 190 44.14 N 93.26 W
Morristown, N.J., U.S. 210 40.47 N 74.28 W
Morristown, N.Y., U.S. 212 44.35 N 75.38 W
Morristown, Oh., U.S. 214 40.04 N 81.05 W
Morristown, S.D., U.S. 198 45.56 N 101.43 W
Morristown, Tn., U.S. 192 36.12 N 83.17 W
Morristown Airport ⊠ 276 40.48 N 74.25 W
Morristown National Historical Park ♦ 210 40.46 N 74.32 W
Morrisville, N.Y., U.S. 210 42.53 N 75.38 W
Morrisville, Pa., U.S. 208 40.12 N 74.47 W
Morrisville, Vt., U.S. 188 44.33 N 72.35 W
Morrito 236 11.37 N 85.05 W
Morro 246 2.39 S 80.19 W
Morro, Castillo del (Morro Castle) ⊥ 286b 23.09 N 82.21 W
Morro, Punta › 232 19.39 N 90.42 W
Morro Agudo 287a 22.45 S 43.29 W
Morro Bay 226 35.21 N 120.50 W
Morro Bay c 226 35.20 N 120.51 W
Morro Bay State Park ♦ 226 35.20 N 120.52 W
Morro Creek ≃ 226 35.23 N 120.52 W
Morro do Chapéu 250 11.33 S 41.09 W
Morro d'Oro 66 42.39 N 13.54 E
Morro Mazatán 234 16.07 N 95.27 W
Morrone del Sannio 66 41.43 N 14.47 E
Morropón 248 5.15 S 80.00 W
Morros 250 2.52 S 44.03 W
Morrosquillo, Golfo de c 246 9.35 N 75.40 W
Morrow, La., U.S. 194 30.49 N 92.04 W
Morrow, Oh., U.S. 218 39.21 N 84.07 W
Morrow □[6] 214 40.33 N 82.50 W
Morrow Island I 282 38.07 N 122.05 W
Morrow Mountain State Park ♦ 192 35.23 N 80.05 W
Morrow Point Reservoir ⊜[1] 200 38.25 N 107.30 W
Mörrum 26 56.11 N 14.45 E
Morrumbala 154 17.22 S 35.36 E
Morrumbene 156 23.39 S 35.20 E
Mörrumsån ≃ 26 56.09 N 14.44 E
Mors I 26 56.50 N 8.45 E
Morsains 50 48.48 N 3.32 E
Morsang-sur-Orge 261 48.40 N 2.21 E
Moršansk 80 53.26 N 41.49 E
Morsbach 56 50.52 N 7.43 E
Mörsch 56 48.58 N 8.17 E
Morschwiller-le-Bas 58 47.45 N 7.16 E
Morščichino 265b 55.56 N 37.20 E
Morse, Sk., Can. 184 50.25 N 107.03 W
Morse, La., U.S. 194 30.07 N 92.29 W
Morse, Tx., U.S. 196 36.04 N 101.29 W
Morse Mill 219 38.17 N 90.40 W
Mörsenbroich ➔[8] 263 51.15 N 6.48 E
Morse Reservoir ⊜[1] 218 40.06 N 86.02 W
Morses Pond ⊜ 283 42.18 N 71.19 W
Morsi 120 21.21 N 78.00 E
Morskaja Masel'ga 24 63.06 N 34.54 E
Morskoj Bir'učok, ostrov I 84 44.42 N 47.02 E
Morson 184 49.03 N 94.18 W
Morsott 36 35.40 N 8.01 E
Morstein 285 40.01 N 75.35 W
Mort 272a 28.43 N 77.25 E
Morta 272a 28.44 N 77.27 E
Mortagne 32 48.31 N 0.33 E
Mortagne ≃ 58 48.33 N 6.27 E
Mortagne-au-Perche 50 48.31 N 0.33 E
Mortagne-sur-Sèvre 32 47.00 N 0.57 W
Mortain 32 48.39 N 0.56 W
Mortana 162 33.02 S 134.07 E
Mortara 62 45.15 N 8.44 E
Morteau 58 47.04 N 6.37 E
Mortefontaine 50 49.07 N 2.36 E
Mortegliano 64 45.57 N 13.10 E
Morte Point › 42 51.11 N 4.13 W
Morteratsch, Piz ʌ 58 46.22 N 9.51 E
Morteros 252 30.42 S 62.00 W
Mortes, Rio das ≃, Bra. 255 11.45 S 50.44 W
Mortes, Rio das ≃, Bra. 256 21.18 S 43.58 W
Mortesoro 140 10.12 N 34.09 E
Mort-Homme, Forêt du ➔[3] 56 49.15 N 5.15 E
Mortimer 42 51.22 N 1.04 W
Mortlach 184 50.28 N 106.03 W
Mortlake, Austl. 166 38.05 S 142.48 E
Mortlake, Austl. 274a 33.51 S 151.07 E
Mortlake ➔[8] 260 51.28 N 0.16 W
Mortlock ≃ 168a 31.42 S 116.55 E
Mortlock Islands II 14 5.27 N 153.40 E
Mortlock North ≃ 168a 31.38 S 116.42 E
Mortola Inferiore 62 43.47 N 7.33 E
Morton, Il., U.S. 190 40.36 N 89.27 W
Morton, Mn., U.S. 198 44.33 N 94.59 W
Morton, Ms., U.S. 194 32.21 N 89.39 W
Morton, N.Y., U.S. 210 43.20 N 78.00 W
Morton, Pa., U.S. 285 39.55 N 75.20 W
Morton, Tx., U.S. 196 33.43 N 102.45 W
Morton, Wa., U.S. 224 46.33 N 122.16 W
Morton, Mount ʌ[2] 274b 37.56 S 145.20 E
Morton Arboretum ♦ 278 41.49 N 88.04 W
Morton Craig Range ʌʌ 162 28.12 S 124.41 E
Morton Grove 216 42.02 N 87.46 W
Morton National Park ♦ 170 35.00 S 150.10 E
Mortons Gap 194 37.14 N 87.28 W
Mortorio, Isola I 71 41.05 N 9.36 E
Mortornès del Vallès 266d 41.33 N 2.16 E
Mortrée 50 48.38 N 0.05 E
Mörtschach 64 46.55 N 12.55 E
Mortsel 50 51.10 N 4.28 E
M'ortvyj Donec ≃ 83 47.15 N 39.14 E
Morty 80 55.49 N 51.44 E
Morua 175f 16.54 S 168.32 E
Morumbi ➔[8] 287b 23.36 S 46.42 E
Morumbi, Estádio do ♦ 287b 23.37 S 46.43 W
Morungaba 256 22.52 S 46.48 W
Morungole ʌ 154 3.49 N 34.02 E
Moruya 166 35.55 S 150.05 E
Morvan ʌʌ 32 47.05 N 4.00 E
Morvant 241r 10.39 N 61.28 W
Morven, Austl. 166 26.25 S 147.07 E
Morven, N.Z. 172 44.50 S 171.07 E
Morven, Ga., U.S. 192 30.56 N 83.29 W
Morven, N.C., U.S. 192 34.51 N 80.00 W
Morven ʌ, Scot., U.K. 46 58.14 N 3.42 W
Morven ʌ, Scot., U.K. 46 57.07 N 3.02 W
Morwell 169 38.14 S 146.24 E
Morwell ≃ 169 38.10 S 146.23 E
Morwenstow 42 50.54 N 4.33 W
Moryń 30 52.49 N 14.13 E
Morženga 76 59.37 N 40.12 E
Morzhovoi 180 54.55 N 163.18 W
Morzine 58 46.11 N 6.43 E
Moržovec, ostrov I 24 66.44 N 42.35 E
Moša ≃, Ross. 24 62.25 N 39.46 E
M'oša ≃, Ross. 80 55.25 N 49.22 E
Mosal'sk 76 54.29 N 34.59 E
Mosambik → Mozambique □[1] 138 18.15 S 35.00 E
Mošanicy 82 54.56 N 38.23 E
Mosås 40 59.12 N 15.08 E
Mosbach 56 49.21 N 9.08 E
Mosborough 44 53.19 N 1.22 W
Mosby 26 58.14 N 7.54 E
Mosby Woods 284c 38.52 N 77.18 W
Moscavide 266c 38.47 N 9.06 W
Mosciano Sant'Angelo 66 42.45 N 13.53 E
Moščnyj, ostrov I 76 60.01 N 27.50 E
Moscos Islands II 110 14.00 N 97.45 E
Moscou → Moskva 82 55.45 N 37.35 E
Moscow → Moskva, Ross. 82 55.45 N 37.35 E
Moscow, Id., U.S. 202 46.43 N 116.59 W
Moscow, In., U.S. 218 39.29 N 85.34 W
Moscow, Oh., U.S. 218 38.51 N 84.13 W
Moscow, Pa., U.S. 210 41.20 N 75.31 W
Moscow, Tx., U.S. 222 30.55 N 94.50 W
Moscow Air Terminal ⊠ 265b 55.48 N 37.32 E
Moscow Circus ♦ 265b 55.43 N 37.33 E
Moscow Mills 219 38.56 N 90.55 W
Moscow Station ➔[5] 265a 59.56 N 30.22 E
Moscow Victory Park ♦ 265a 59.52 N 30.20 E
Moscow Zoo ♦ 265b 55.46 N 37.34 E
Moscú → Moskva 82 55.45 N 37.35 E
Moscufo 66 42.25 N 14.03 E
Mosel 54 50.47 N 12.28 E
Mosel (Moselle) ≃ 32 50.22 N 7.36 E
Moselebe ≃ 156 25.03 S 23.13 E
Moselle, Ms., U.S. 194 31.30 N 89.16 W
Moselle, Mo., U.S. 219 38.23 N 90.54 W
Moselle □[5] 56 49.00 N 6.30 E
Moselle (Mosel) ≃ 32 50.22 N 7.36 E
Moselotte ≃ 58 48.01 N 6.38 E
Mošenskoje 76 58.31 N 34.35 E
Mosermandl ʌ 64 47.12 N 13.24 E
Mosers River 186 44.59 N 62.15 W
Moses Lake 202 47.07 N 119.16 W
Moses Lake ⊜[1] 202 47.10 N 119.20 W
Moses Point 180 64.42 N 162.03 W
Moses Power Plant ➔[6] 284a 43.09 N 79.02 W
Mosetse 156 20.37 S 26.32 E
Mosgiel 172 45.53 S 170.21 E
Moshannon 214 41.02 N 78.00 W
Moshannon Creek ≃ 214 41.04 N 78.06 W
Moshanpu 100 29.34 N 112.41 E
Moshaweng ≃ 158 26.35 S 22.50 E
Mosheim, Tn., U.S. 192 36.11 N 82.57 W
Mosheim, Tx., U.S. 222 31.38 N 97.36 W
Moshi 154 3.21 S 37.20 E
Moshi ≃ 150 9.18 N 4.38 E
Moshiyu 104 41.15 N 124.05 E
Mosier 224 45.41 N 121.23 W
Mosier Hill ʌ[2] 214 40.06 N 80.24 W
Mosina 30 52.16 N 16.51 E
Mosinee 190 44.47 N 89.42 W
Mosjøen 24 65.50 N 13.10 E
Moskal'onki 86 54.59 N 71.54 E
Moskal'vo 89 53.35 N 142.30 E
Moskau → Moskva 82 55.45 N 37.35 E
Moskenesøya I 24 67.59 N 13.00 E
Moskháton 267c 37.57 N 23.41 E
Moškino 80 57.45 N 45.20 E
Moskito-Golf → Mosquitos, Golfo de los c 236 9.00 N 81.15 W
Moškovo 86 55.18 N 83.37 E
Moskovskaja Slav'anka 265a 59.45 N 30.30 E
Moskovskaja vozvyšennost' ʌʌ[1] 76 56.15 N 37.30 E
Moskva (Moscow), Ross. 82 55.45 N 37.35 E
Moskva (Moscow), Ross. 265b 55.45 N 37.35 E
Moskva ≃ 76 55.05 N 38.50 E
Moskva, Gorod □[7] 265b 55.45 N 37.35 E
Moskva, pik ʌ 85 38.57 N 71.49 E
Moskva Oblast' □[4] 76 55.30 N 37.30 E
Moskvy, kanal imeni ≅ 82 56.43 N 37.08 E
Mosman 170 33.49 S 151.14 E
Mosman Park 168a 32.01 S 115.46 E
Mošny 78 49.32 N 31.44 E
Moso (Moos) 64 46.41 N 12.23 E
Moso in Passiria (Moos) 64 46.50 N 11.10 E
Mošok 80 55.48 N 41.17 E
Mosolovo 80 54.17 N 40.32 E
Mosomane 156 24.04 S 26.15 E
Mosoni-Duna ≃ 61 47.54 N 17.17 E
Mosonmagyaróvár 30 47.51 N 17.17 E
Mosonszolnok 61 47.51 N 17.11 E
Mosopa 156 24.50 S 25.31 E
Mospino 83 47.53 N 38.03 E
Mosqueiro 250 1.10 S 48.28 W
Mosquera 246 2.30 N 78.29 W
Mosquero 196 35.46 N 103.57 W
Mosquic, Lac ⊜ 206 46.39 N 74.28 W
Mosquito, Punta › 246 9.07 N 77.53 W
Mosquito, Riacho ≃ 252 22.02 S 57.57 W
Mosquito Brook ≃ 283 42.40 N 71.02 W
Mosquito Creek ≃, Ia., U.S. 198 41.11 N 95.50 W
Mosquito Creek ≃, Oh., U.S. 214 41.10 N 80.45 W
Mosquito Creek ≃, Pa., U.S. 214 41.07 N 78.07 W
Mosquito Creek Lake ⊜[1] 214 41.22 N 80.45 W

Symbols in the index entries represent the broad categories identified in the key at the right. Symbols with superior numbers (ʌʌ[1]) identify subcategories (see complete key on page I · 1).

Symbole im Register stellen die rechts im Schlüssel erklärten Kategorien dar. Symbole mit hochgestellten Ziffern (ʌʌ[1]) bezeichnen Unterabteilungen einer Kategorie (vgl. vollständiger Schlüssel auf Seite I · 1).

Los símbolos incluidos en el texto del índice representan las grandes categorías identificadas con la clave a la derecha. Los símbolos con números en su parte superior (ʌʌ[1]) identifican las subcategorías (véase la clave completa en la página I · 1).

Les symboles de l'index représentent les catégories indiquées dans la légende à droite. Les symboles suivis d'un indice (ʌʌ[1]) représentent des sous-catégories (voir légende complète à la page I · 1).

Os símbolos incluídos no texto do índice representam as grandes categorias identificadas com a chave à direita. Os símbolos com números em sua parte superior (ʌʌ[1]) identificam as subcategorias (veja-se a chave completa à página I · 1).

Symbol	English	Deutsch	Español	Français	Português
ʌ	Mountain	Berg	Montaña	Montagne	Montanha
ʌʌ	Mountains	Gebirge	Montañas	Montagnes	Montanhas
✕	Pass	Paß	Paso	Col	Passo
V	Valley, Canyon	Tal, Cañon	Valle, Cañón	Vallée, Canyon	Vale, Canhão
≍	Plain	Ebene	Llano	Plaine	Planície
›	Cape	Kap	Cabo	Cap	Cabo
I	Island	Insel	Isla	Île	Ilha
II	Islands	Inseln	Islas	Îles	Ilhas
⊥	Other Topographic Features	Andere Topographische Objekte	Otros Elementos Topográficos	Autres données topographiques	Outros acidentes topográficos

ESPAÑOL — Nombre | Página | Lat.°′ | Long.°′ W = Oeste
FRANÇAIS — Nom | Page | Lat.°′ | Long.°′ W = Ouest
PORTUGUÊS — Nome | Página | Lat.°′ | Long.°′ W = Oeste

Nombre / Nom / Nome	Página / Page	Lat.°′	Long.°′
Mosquito Creek State Park ♦	214	41.22 N	80.45 W
Mosquito Indian Reserve -◆- [4]	184	52.30 N	108.15 W
Mosquito Lagoon c	220	28.45 N	80.45 W
Mosquitos, Costa de □ [9]	236	13.00 N	83.45 W
Mosquitos, Golfo de los c	236	9.00 N	81.15 W
Moss	26	59.26 N	10.42 E
Mossaka	152	1.13 S	16.48 E
Mossâmedes	255	16.07 S	50.11 W
Mossbank, Sk., Can.	184	49.55 N	105.59 W
Moss Bank, Eng., U.K.	262	53.29 N	2.44 W
Mossbank, Scot., U.K.	46a	60.27 N	1.12 W
Moss Bank Park ♦	262	53.36 N	2.28 W
Moss Beach	282	37.32 N	122.31 W
Mossburn	172	45.40 S	168.15 E
Mosselbaai (Mossel Bay)	158	34.11 S	22.08 E
Mosselbaai c	158	34.06 S	22.20 E
Mossendjo	152	2.57 S	12.44 E
Mosses, Col des)(	58	46.24 N	7.06 E
Mossgiel	166	33.15 S	144.34 E
Moss Hill	222	30.15 N	94.45 W
Mossig ≐	58	48.33 N	7.30 E
Mössingen	58	48.24 N	9.03 E
Moss Landing	226	36.48 N	121.47 W
Mossleigh	182	50.43 N	113.20 W
Mossley	262	53.32 N	2.02 W
Mossley Hill -◆- [8]	262	53.23 N	2.55 W
Mossman	164	16.28 S	145.22 E
Mossmans Brook ≐	276	41.03 N	74.27 W
Moss Moor -◆- [3]	262	53.37 N	2.00 W
Moss Mountain ∧	194	34.50 N	92.40 W
Mossø ⊜	41	56.02 N	9.48 E
Mosson ≐	62	43.33 N	3.54 E
Mossoró	250	5.11 S	37.20 W
Mosso Santa Maria	62	45.38 N	8.08 E
Moss Point	194	30.24 N	88.32 W
Moss Point ›	279a	41.37 N	81.32 W
Moss Side	262	53.46 N	2.57 W
Mossuril	154	14.58 S	40.42 E
Moss Vale	170	34.33 S	150.22 E
Mossy ≐, Mb., Can.	184	51.39 N	99.55 W
Mossy ≐, Sk., Can.	184	54.05 N	103.00 W
Mossyrock	224	46.31 N	122.29 W
Mossyrock Dam -◆- [6]	224	46.32 N	122.25 W
Most	54	50.32 N	13.39 E
Mosta	80	56.32 N	42.10 E
Mostar	36	43.20 N	17.49 E
Mostardas, Bra.	252	31.06 S	50.57 W
Mostardas, Bra.	256	23.44 S	46.38 W
Møsting, Kap ›	176	64.00 N	41.00 W
Mostiska	78	49.48 N	23.09 E
Mostiştea ≐	38	44.15 N	27.10 E
Mostizzolo	64	46.24 N	11.01 E
Mostki	83	49.19 N	38.30 E
Most na Soči	64	46.09 N	13.44 E
Mostok	76	53.59 N	30.28 E
Móstoles	266a	40.19 N	3.51 W
Mostoos Hills ∧∧ [2]	184	55.00 N	109.15 W
Mostovaja	76	56.13 N	33.08 E
Mostovka	86	58.10 N	65.31 E
Mostovoje	78	47.24 N	30.59 E
Mostovskoj	84	44.25 N	40.48 E
Mostovskoje	86	55.46 N	66.22 E
Mostrim (Edgeworthstown)	48	53.42 N	7.36 W
Mostva ≐	78	52.00 N	27.33 E
Mosty	76	53.25 N	24.32 E
Mostyn, Malay.	112	4.40 N	118.11 E
Mostyn, Wales, U.K.	44	53.19 N	3.16 W
Mosul → Al-Mawṣil	128	36.20 N	43.08 E
Møsvatnet ⊜	26	59.52 N	8.05 E
Mota	144	11.02 N	37.52 E
Mota I	175f	13.49 S	167.42 E
Motaba ≐	152	2.03 N	18.03 E
Mota del Cuervo	34	39.30 N	2.52 W
Mota del Marqués	34	41.38 N	5.10 W
Motagua ≐	236	15.44 N	88.14 W
Motala	26	58.33 N	15.03 E
Motala ström ≐	40	58.38 N	16.10 E
Mota Lava I	175f	13.40 S	167.40 E
Motane I	174x	9.59 S	138.49 W
Motatán	246	9.24 N	70.36 W
Motaze	156	24.48 S	32.52 E
Motegi	94	36.32 N	140.11 E
Mote Park ♦	260	51.17 N	0.34 E
Moteve, Cap ›	174x	9.58 S	139.02 W
Moth	124	25.43 N	78.57 E
Mother Brook ≅	283	42.15 N	71.10 W
Motherwell	46	55.48 N	4.00 W
Motihāri	124	26.39 N	84.55 E
Motilla del Palancar	34	39.34 N	1.53 W
Motiong	116	11.47 N	125.00 E
Motiti Island I	172	37.38 S	176.26 E
Motjärnshyttan	40	59.56 N	13.58 E
Motloutse	156	21.28 S	27.24 E
Motloutse ≐	156	22.15 S	29.00 E
Moto-ara ≐	94	35.53 N	139.50 E
Motobu	174m	26.39 N	127.54 E
Motol'	76	52.19 N	25.36 E
Motola, Monte ∧	68	40.22 N	15.26 E
Motopu	174x	9.55 S	139.03 W
Motor Island I	284a	42.58 N	78.56 W
Motorki	80	56.53 N	51.29 E
Motorovo	86	56.31 N	71.10 E
Motosu	94	35.29 N	136.40 E
Motosu-ko ⊜	94	35.28 N	138.35 E
Motou	106	32.18 N	120.34 E
Motovilovo	80	55.36 N	43.51 E
Motovun	64	45.20 N	13.50 E
Motoyama	96	33.45 N	133.35 E
Moto-yama ∧ [2]	174f	24.48 N	141.20 E
Motozintla de Mendoza	232	15.22 N	92.14 W
Motril	34	36.45 N	3.31 W
Motrone	64	43.54 N	10.12 E
Motru	38	44.50 N	23.00 E
Mott	198	46.22 N	102.19 W
Motta	64	45.36 N	11.29 E
Motta Camastra	70	37.54 N	15.10 E
Motta d'Affermo	70	37.59 N	14.18 E
Motta di Livenza	64	45.47 N	12.36 E
Mottafollone	68	39.39 N	16.04 E
Motta Montecorvino	68	41.30 N	15.07 E
Motta San Giovanni	68	38.00 N	15.41 E
Motta Sant'Anastasia	70	37.31 N	14.58 E
Motta Visconti	62	45.17 N	8.59 E
Möttingen	56	48.48 N	10.35 E
Mottingham -◆- [8]	260	51.26 N	0.03 E
Mottisfont	42	51.02 N	1.32 W
Mottola	68	40.38 N	17.03 E
Mottram in Longdendale	262	53.27 N	2.01 W
Motts Creek ≐	276	40.38 N	73.45 W
Mottville, Mi., U.S.	216	41.48 N	85.45 W
Mottville, N.Y., U.S.	210	42.59 N	76.27 W
Motu ≐	172	37.51 S	177.35 E
Motueka	172	41.07 S	173.00 E
Motueka ≐	172	41.05 S	173.01 E
Motul [de Felipe Carrillo Puerto]	232	21.06 N	89.17 W
Motu One I [1]	14	15.48 S	154.33 W
Motupe	248	6.09 S	79.44 W
Motupena Point ›	175e	6.32 S	155.09 E
Motutapu I	174k	21.14 S	159.43 W
Motygino	86	58.11 N	94.40 E
Motyklejka	74	59.26 N	148.38 E
Motyžin	78	50.23 N	29.55 E
Motyzlej	80	54.54 N	42.54 E
Mou	175f	21.05 S	165.26 E
Mouanko	152	3.39 N	9.49 E
Mouans-Sartoux	62	43.37 N	6.58 E
Mouaskar	148	35.45 N	0.01 E
Mouaskar □ [5]	148	35.10 N	0.00
Mouchard	58	46.58 N	5.48 E
Mouchoir Bank ✣ [2]	238	20.57 N	70.42 W
Mouchoir Passage ⨉	238	21.10 N	71.00 W
Moúdhros	38	39.52 N	25.16 E
Mouding	102	25.24 N	101.35 E
Moudjéria	150	17.53 N	12.20 W
Moudon	58	46.40 N	6.48 E
Moudongouma ≐	152	1.36 N	17.24 E
Mouila	152	1.52 S	11.01 E
Mouit	150	16.35 N	13.05 W
Mouka	152	7.16 N	21.52 E
Moukden → Shenyang	104	41.48 N	123.27 E
Moulamein	166	35.05 S	144.02 E
Moulay-bou-Selham	34	34.53 N	6.15 W
Moulay-Idriss	148	34.02 N	5.27 W
Mouldsworth	262	53.14 N	2.44 W
Moule à Chique, Cap ›	241f	13.43 N	60.57 W
Moulhoulé	144	12.36 N	43.12 E
Moulin, Île du I	275a	45.41 N	73.32 W
Moulin-des-Ponts	58	46.20 N	5.19 E
Moulineaux	50	49.21 N	0.58 E
Moulinet	62	43.57 N	7.25 E
Moulins	32	46.34 N	3.20 E
Moulins-la-Marche	50	48.39 N	0.29 E
Moulmein → Mawlamyine	110	16.30 N	97.38 E
Moulmeingyun	110	16.23 N	95.16 E
Moulouya, Oued ≐	148	35.05 N	2.25 W
Moulton, Eng., U.K.	44	53.13 N	2.31 W
Moulton, Al., U.S.	194	34.28 N	87.17 W
Moulton, Ia., U.S.	190	40.41 N	92.40 W
Moulton, Tx., U.S.	222	29.34 N	97.09 W
Moultrie	192	31.10 N	83.47 W
Moultrie □ [6]	219	39.36 N	88.37 W
Moultrie, Lake ⊜ [1]	192	33.20 N	80.05 W
Mouly	175f	20.42 S	166.25 E
Mound	222	31.21 N	97.38 W
Mound Bayou	194	33.52 N	90.43 W
Mound City, Il., U.S.	194	37.05 N	89.09 W
Mound City, Ks., U.S.	198	38.08 N	94.48 W
Mound City, Mo., U.S.	194	40.07 N	95.13 W
Mound City, S.D., U.S.	198	45.43 N	100.04 W
Mound City Group National Monument ♦	218	39.23 N	83.00 W
Mound Lake ⊜	219	40.05 N	90.17 W
Moundou	146	8.34 N	16.05 E
Moundridge	198	38.12 N	97.31 W
Mounds, Il., U.S.	194	37.06 N	89.11 W
Mounds, Ok., U.S.	196	35.52 N	96.03 W
Mounds State Park ♦	218	40.07 N	85.37 W
Mounds State Recreation Area ♦	218	39.30 N	84.59 W
Moundsville	188	39.55 N	80.44 W
Moundville	194	32.59 N	87.37 W
Moungali -◆- [8]	273b	4.15 S	15.17 E
Moung Roessei	110	12.46 N	103.27 E
Mounianzé ≐	152	0.32 N	12.52 E
Mounier, Mont ∧	62	44.09 N	6.58 E
Mounlapamôk	110	14.20 N	105.52 E
Mount Aetna	208	40.25 N	76.18 W
Mountain	190	45.11 N	88.28 W
Mountain □ [4]	116	17.20 N	121.10 E
Mountain ≐	180	65.41 N	128.50 W
Mountainair	200	34.31 N	106.14 W
Mountainaire	200	35.05 N	111.39 W
Mountain Ash	42	51.42 N	3.24 W
Mountain Brook	194	33.30 N	86.45 W
Mountain Chute Dam -◆- [6]	212	45.11 N	76.54 W
Mountain City, Ga., U.S.	192	34.55 N	83.23 W
Mountain City, Nv., U.S.	204	41.50 N	115.57 W
Mountain City, Tn., U.S.	192	36.28 N	81.48 W
Mountain Creek	194	32.43 N	86.29 W
Mountain Creek ≐, Pa., U.S.	208	40.09 N	77.11 W
Mountain Creek ≐, Tx., U.S.	222	32.42 N	96.58 W
Mountain Creek Lake ⊜ [1]	222	32.43 N	96.58 W
Mountain Dale	210	41.41 N	74.31 W
Mountain Grove	194	37.07 N	92.15 W
Mountain Home, Ar., U.S.	194	36.20 N	92.23 W
Mountain Home, Id., U.S.	202	43.07 N	115.41 W
Mountainhome, Pa., U.S.	210	41.11 N	75.17 W
Mountain Home Air Force Base ■	202	43.03 N	115.52 W
Mountain Iron	190	47.31 N	92.37 W
Mountain Lake, Fl., U.S.	220	27.57 N	81.36 W
Mountain Lake, Mn., U.S.	198	43.56 N	94.55 W
Mountain Lake ⊜, On., Can.	212	44.42 N	81.03 W
Mountain Lake ⊜, On., Can.	212	44.59 N	78.43 W
Mountain Lake ⊜, N.J., U.S.	276	40.53 N	74.27 W
Mountain Lakes	210	40.53 N	74.26 W
Mountain Lodge	210	41.23 N	74.09 W
Mountain Nile (Baḥr al-Jabal) ≐	136	9.30 N	30.30 E
Mountain Park	182	52.55 N	117.14 W
Mountain Pine	194	34.34 N	93.10 W
Mountain Point	182	55.18 N	131.32 W
Mountain Ranch	226	38.14 N	120.33 W
Mountainside	208	40.40 N	74.21 W
Mountain Spring Lakes	276	41.02 N	74.23 W
Mountain Valley Lake ⊜	279b	40.18 N	79.35 W
Mountain View, Ar., U.S.	194	35.52 N	92.07 W
Mountain View, Ca., U.S.	226	37.23 N	122.04 W
Mountain View, Mo., U.S.	194	36.59 N	91.42 W
Mountain View, Ok., U.S.	196	35.05 N	98.44 W
Mountain View, Wy., U.S.	200	41.16 N	110.20 W
Mountain View, Wy., U.S.	200	42.51 N	106.23 W
Mountain View Acres	228	34.31 N	117.24 W
Mountain Village	180	62.05 N	163.44 W
Mountain Zebra National Park ♦	158	32.16 S	25.29 E
Mount Airy, Md., U.S.	208	39.22 N	77.09 W
Mount Airy, N.C., U.S.	192	36.29 N	80.36 W
Mount Airy -◆- [8]	285	40.04 N	75.12 W
Mount Albert	212	44.08 N	79.19 W
Mount Alford	171a	28.04 S	152.36 E
Mount Alida	158	29.09 S	30.18 E
Mount Angel	224	45.04 N	122.47 W
Mount Ann Park ♦	283	42.37 N	70.44 W
Mount Arlington	210	40.55 N	74.38 W
Mount Assiniboine Provincial Park ♦	182	50.54 N	115.40 W
Mount Auburn	219	39.46 N	89.16 W
Mount Augustus	162	24.19 S	116.54 E
Mount Ayliff	158	30.54 S	29.20 E
Mount Ayr, In., U.S.	216	40.57 N	87.18 W
Mount Ayr, Ia., U.S.	198	40.42 N	94.14 W
Mount Baldy	280	34.14 N	117.40 W
Mount Barker, Austl.	162	34.38 S	117.40 E
Mount Barker, Austl.	168b	35.04 S	138.52 E
Mount Bellew Bridge	48	53.28 N	8.29 W
Mount Berry	194	34.17 N	85.11 W
Mount Bethel	210	40.54 N	75.07 W
Mount Blanchard	216	40.53 N	83.33 W
Mount Bold Reservoir ⊜ [1]	168b	35.07 S	138.42 E
Mount Brydges	214	42.54 N	81.29 W
Mount Buffalo National Park ♦	166	36.45 S	146.45 E
Mount Buller	169	37.10 S	146.27 E
Mount Calm	222	31.45 N	96.53 W
Mount Carleton Provincial Park ♦	186	47.23 N	66.50 W
Mount Carmel, Nf., Can.	186	47.09 N	53.29 W
Mount Carmel, Il., U.S.	194	38.24 N	87.45 W
Mount Carmel, Ky., U.S.	218	38.29 N	83.38 W
Mount Carmel, Oh., U.S.	218	39.06 N	84.18 W
Mount Carmel, Pa., U.S.	208	40.47 N	76.24 W
Mount Carmel Heights	218	39.07 N	84.18 W
Mount Carroll	190	42.05 N	89.58 W
Mount Cavenagh	162	25.58 S	133.15 E
Mount Charles	275b	43.41 N	79.40 W
Mount Clare	188	39.13 N	80.21 W
Mount Clemens	214	42.35 N	82.52 W
Mount Colah	274a	33.41 S	151.07 E
Mount Compass	168b	35.22 S	138.37 E
Mount Cook	172	43.44 S	170.06 E
Mount Cook National Park ♦	172	43.35 S	170.15 E
Mount Coot-tha Park ♦	171a	27.28 S	152.56 E
Mount Cory	216	40.56 N	83.50 W
Mount Crawford	168b	34.40 S	138.57 E
Mount Crosby	171a	27.32 S	152.48 E
Mount Currie Indian Reserve -◆- [4]	182	50.19 N	122.42 W
Mount Dandenong	274b	37.50 S	145.22 E
Mount Dennis -◆- [8]	275b	43.42 N	79.30 W
Mount Desert Island I	188	44.20 N	68.20 W
Mount Diablo Creek ≐	282	38.02 N	122.02 W
Mount Diablo State Park ♦	226	37.51 N	121.55 W
Mount Dora	220	28.48 N	81.38 W
Mount Doreen	162	22.03 S	131.18 E
Mount Druitt	274a	33.46 S	150.49 E
Mount Eaton	214	40.42 N	81.42 W
Mount Eba	166	30.12 S	135.40 E
Mount Eden	226	37.38 N	122.06 W
Mount Edgecumbe	180	57.03 N	135.21 W
Mount Edwards	171a	28.01 S	152.31 E
Mount Elgon National Park ♦	154	1.07 N	34.44 E
Mount Elizabeth	164	16.15 S	126.12 E
Mount Emu Creek ≐	169	38.18 S	142.55 E
Mount Enterprise	222	31.55 N	94.41 W
Mount Ephraim	285	39.52 N	75.05 W
Mount Evelyn	274b	37.47 S	145.23 E
Mount Fern	276	40.52 N	74.34 W
Mount Field National Park ♦	166	42.40 S	146.35 E
Mount Fletcher	158	30.40 S	28.30 E
Mount Forest	212	43.59 N	80.44 W
Mount Freedom	210	40.49 N	74.34 W
Mount Frere	158	31.00 S	28.58 E
Mount Gambier	166	37.50 S	140.46 E
Mount Garnet	166	17.41 S	145.07 E
Mount Gay	188	37.51 N	82.00 W
Mount Gilead, N.C., U.S.	192	35.12 N	80.00 W
Mount Gilead, Oh., U.S.	214	40.32 N	82.49 W
Mount Gravatt	171a	27.33 S	153.06 E
Mount Greenwood -◆- [8]	278	41.42 N	87.43 W
Mount Gunson	162	31.27 S	137.11 E
Mount Hagen	164	5.50 S	144.15 E
Mount Hawke	42	50.17 N	5.12 W
Mount Hawthorn	168a	31.55 S	115.50 E
Mount Healthy	218	39.14 N	84.32 W
Mount Hebron	284b	39.18 N	76.50 W
Mount Helena	168a	31.53 S	116.13 E
Mount Hermon, Ca., U.S.	226	37.03 N	122.04 W
Mount Hermon, Ma., U.S.	207	42.40 N	72.29 W
Mount Holly, N.J., U.S.	208	39.59 N	74.47 W
Mount Holly, N.C., U.S.	192	35.17 N	81.00 W
Mount Holly Springs	208	40.07 N	77.11 W
Mount Hope, Austl.	166	34.07 S	135.23 E
Mount Hope, On., Can.	212	43.09 N	79.55 W
Mount Hope, Ks., U.S.	198	37.52 N	97.39 W
Mount Hope, N.J., U.S.	276	40.56 N	74.33 W
Mount Hope, Oh., U.S.	214	40.38 N	81.47 W
Mount Hope, W.V., U.S.	188	37.53 N	81.09 W
Mount Hope Lake ⊜	276	40.56 N	74.32 W
Mount Horeb	190	43.00 N	89.44 W
Mount Houston	222	29.54 N	95.18 W
Mount Howitt	166	26.31 S	142.16 E
Mount Hunter Rivulet ≐	274a	34.02 S	150.40 E
Mount Ida	194	34.33 N	93.38 W
Mount Isa	166	20.44 S	139.30 E
Mount Jackson, Pa., U.S.	214	40.58 N	80.26 W
Mount Jackson, Va., U.S.	188	38.44 N	78.38 W
Mount Jewett	214	41.43 N	78.38 W
Mount Juliet	194	36.12 N	86.31 W
Mount Kaputar National Park ♦	166	30.16 S	150.10 E
Mount Kenya National Park ♦	154	0.09 S	37.19 E
Mount Kisco	210	41.12 N	73.43 W
Mount Kokeby	168a	32.13 S	116.58 E
Mountlake Terrace	224	47.47 N	122.18 W
Mount Laurel	285	39.56 N	74.54 W
Mount Lebanon	214	40.21 N	80.02 W
Mount Liberty	214	40.21 N	82.38 W
Mount Lofty Ranges ∧∧	168b	34.45 S	139.00 E
Mount Magnet	162	28.04 S	117.49 E
Mount Manara	166	32.29 S	143.56 E
Mount Margaret, Austl.	162	28.47 S	122.11 E
Mount Margaret, Austl.	166	26.54 S	143.21 E
Mount Marion	210	42.02 N	73.59 W
Mount Martha	169	38.17 S	145.01 E
Mount Maunganui	172	37.37 S	176.11 E
Mount McKinley National Park → Denali National Park ♦	180	63.15 N	150.30 W
Mount Mee	171a	27.04 S	152.46 E
Mountmellick	48	53.07 N	7.20 W
Mount Misery Point ›	276	40.58 N	73.05 W
Mount Mistake National Park ♦	171a	27.53 S	152.20 E
Mount Molloy	164	16.41 S	145.20 E
Mount Monger	162	30.59 S	121.53 E
Mount Moorosi	158	30.16 S	27.53 E
Mount Morgan	166	23.39 S	150.23 E
Mount Morris, Il., U.S.	190	42.03 N	89.25 W
Mount Morris, Mi., U.S.	190	43.07 N	83.41 W
Mount Morris, N.Y., U.S.	210	42.43 N	77.52 W
Mount Morris Dam -◆- [6]	210	42.44 N	77.53 W
Mount Mulligan	166	16.51 S	144.52 E
Mount Nebo	279b	40.33 N	80.06 W
Mountnessing	260	51.39 N	0.21 E
Mount Olive, Il., U.S.	219	39.04 N	89.43 W
Mount Olive, Ms., U.S.	194	31.45 N	89.39 W
Mount Olive, N.C., U.S.	192	35.11 N	78.04 W
Mount Oliver	279b	40.28 N	79.59 W
Mount Olivet	218	38.31 N	84.02 W
Mount Orab	218	39.01 N	83.55 W
Mount Penn	208	40.20 N	75.54 W
Mount Perry	166	25.11 S	151.39 E
Mount Pleasant, Austl.	168b	34.47 S	139.02 E
Mount Pleasant, On., Can.	212	43.05 N	80.19 W
Mount Pleasant, In., U.S.	218	38.07 N	86.31 W
Mount Pleasant, Ia., U.S.	190	40.57 N	91.33 W
Mount Pleasant, Mi., U.S.	190	43.35 N	84.46 W
Mount Pleasant, N.C., U.S.	192	35.23 N	80.26 W
Mount Pleasant, Oh., U.S.	214	40.11 N	80.48 W
Mount Pleasant, Pa., U.S.	214	40.08 N	79.32 W
Mount Pleasant, S.C., U.S.	192	32.47 N	79.51 W
Mount Pleasant, Tn., U.S.	194	35.32 N	87.12 W
Mount Pleasant, Tx., U.S.	222	33.09 N	94.58 W
Mount Pleasant, Ut., U.S.	200	39.32 N	111.27 W
Mount Pleasant Mills	208	40.43 N	77.01 W
Mount Pleasant Park ♦	284b	39.22 N	76.35 W
Mount Pocono	210	41.07 N	75.21 W
Mount Pritchard	274a	33.54 S	150.54 E
Mount Prospect, S. Afr.	158	27.29 S	29.53 E
Mount Prospect, Il., U.S.	216	42.03 N	87.56 W
Mount Pulaski	219	40.00 N	89.16 W
Mount Rainier	284c	38.56 N	76.57 W
Mount Rainier National Park ♦	224	46.52 N	121.43 W
Mountrath	48	53.00 N	7.27 W
Mount Repose	218	39.10 N	84.14 W
Mount Revelstoke National Park ♦	182	51.06 N	118.00 W
Mount Riddock	162	23.03 S	134.40 E
Mount Robson Provincial Park ♦	182	52.58 N	118.50 W
Mount Rogers National Recreation Area ♦	192	36.42 N	81.30 W
Mount Roskill	172	36.55 S	174.45 E
Mount Royal	285	39.49 N	75.13 W
Mount Rushmore National Memorial ⊥	198	43.50 N	103.24 W
Mount Saint Helens National Volcanic Monument ♦	224	46.12 N	122.11 W
Mount Sandiman	162	24.24 S	115.23 E
Mount Sarah	162	26.57 S	135.22 E
Mount Savage	188	39.41 N	78.52 W
Mount's Bay c	42	50.03 N	5.25 W
Mount Selinda	154	20.25 S	32.43 E
Mount Selman	222	32.04 N	95.17 W
Mount Seymour Provincial Park ♦	182	49.23 N	122.57 W
Mount Shasta	204	41.18 N	122.18 W
Mount Sinai	276	40.57 N	73.02 W
Mount Sinai Harbor c	276	40.57 N	73.02 W
Mount Sinai Ridge ∧	218	39.04 N	84.58 W
Mount Somers	172	43.43 S	171.24 E
Mountsorrel	42	52.44 N	1.07 W
Mount Spokane State Park ♦	202	47.58 N	117.13 W
Mount Sterling, Il., U.S.	219	39.59 N	90.45 W
Mount Sterling, Ky., U.S.	192	38.03 N	83.56 W
Mount Sterling, Mo., U.S.	219	38.28 N	91.38 W
Mount Sterling, Oh., U.S.	218	39.43 N	83.15 W
Mount Stewart, P.E., Can.	186	46.22 N	62.52 W
Mount Stewart, S. Afr.	158	33.10 S	24.26 E
Mount Stromlo Observatory ☉ [3]	171b	35.20 S	149.00 E
Mount Summit	218	40.00 N	85.23 W
Mount Surprise	166	18.09 S	144.19 E
Mount Sylvia	171a	27.44 S	152.14 E
Mount Tamalpais State Park ♦	226	37.54 N	122.34 W
Mount Torrens	168b	34.52 S	138.57 E
Mount Tremper	210	42.03 N	74.17 W
Mount Uniacke	186	44.54 N	63.50 W
Mount Union	214	40.23 N	77.52 W
Mount Upton	210	42.25 N	75.23 W
Mount Vernon, Austl.	162	24.13 S	118.14 E
Mount Vernon, Al., U.S.	194	31.05 N	88.00 W
Mount Vernon, Ga., U.S.	192	32.10 N	82.35 W
Mount Vernon, Il., U.S.	219	38.19 N	88.54 W
Mount Vernon, In., U.S.	194	37.55 N	87.53 W
Mount Vernon, Ia., U.S.	190	41.55 N	91.25 W
Mount Vernon, Ky., U.S.	192	37.21 N	84.20 W
Mount Vernon, Md., U.S.	208	38.14 N	75.49 W
Mount Vernon, Mo., U.S.	194	37.06 N	93.49 W
Mount Vernon, N.Y., U.S.	210	42.45 N	78.53 W
Mount Vernon, N.Y., U.S.	210	40.54 N	73.50 W
Mount Vernon, Oh., U.S.	214	40.23 N	82.29 W
Mount Vernon, Or., U.S.	202	44.25 N	119.06 W
Mount Vernon, Pa., U.S.	279b	40.17 N	79.48 W
Mount Vernon, S.D., U.S.	198	43.42 N	98.15 W
Mount Vernon, Tx., U.S.	222	33.11 N	95.13 W
Mount Vernon, Wa., U.S.	224	48.25 N	122.19 W
Mount Vernon ⊥	208	38.47 N	77.06 W
Mount Victoria	170	33.35 S	150.15 E
Mount Victory	216	40.32 N	83.31 W
Mount View	207	41.38 N	71.24 W
Mountville	208	40.02 N	76.26 W
Mount Vision	210	42.35 N	75.04 W
Mount Washington	284b	39.23 N	76.41 W
Mount Washington -◆- [8]	284b	39.22 N	76.40 W
Mount Waverley	274b	37.53 S	145.08 E
Mount Wedge, Austl.	162	22.45 S	132.09 E
Mount Wedge, Austl.	162	33.29 S	135.10 E
Mount Wellington	172	36.54 S	174.51 E
Mount Wilhelm National Park ♦	164	5.45 S	145.05 E
Mount William National Park ♦	166	40.56 S	148.15 E
Mount Willoughby	162	27.58 S	134.08 E
Mount Wilson Observatory ☉ [3]	228	34.14 N	118.03 W
Mount Wolf	208	40.03 N	76.42 W
Mount Zion	219	39.46 N	88.53 W
Mounyaz	146	10.41 N	21.18 E
Moura, Austl.	166	24.35 S	149.58 E
Moura, Bra.	246	1.27 S	61.38 W
Moura, Port.	34	38.08 N	7.27 W
Moura, Tchad	146	13.47 N	21.13 E
Moura Brasil	256	22.07 S	43.09 W
Mouraya	146	11.27 N	20.59 E
Mourdi, Dépression du ⍊ [7]	146	18.10 N	23.00 E
Mourdiah	150	14.28 N	7.28 W
Mouriès	62	43.41 N	4.52 E
Mourindi	152	2.32 S	10.48 E
Mourmelon-le-Grand	50	49.08 N	4.22 E
Mourne ≐	48	54.49 N	7.28 W
Mourne Beg ≐	48	54.41 N	7.39 W
Mourne Mountains ∧∧	48	54.10 N	6.04 W
Mousa I	46a	60.00 N	1.11 W
Mouscron	50	50.44 N	3.13 E
Mousgougou	146	10.47 N	16.09 E
Moussa Ali ∧	144	12.28 N	42.24 E
Mousseaux-sur-Seine	261	49.03 N	1.39 E
Moussey	58	48.40 N	6.47 E
Moussoro	146	13.39 N	16.29 E
Moussy-le-Neuf	261	49.04 N	2.36 E
Moussy-le-Vieux	261	49.03 N	2.38 E
Moustiers-Sainte-Marie	62	43.51 N	6.13 E
Moustique, Morne ∧	241o	16.06 N	61.44 W
Mouthe	58	46.43 N	6.12 E
Mouthier-Haute-Pierre	58	47.02 N	6.16 E
Moutier	58	47.17 N	7.23 E
Moûtiers	62	45.29 N	6.32 E
Moutiers-au-Perche	50	48.29 N	0.51 E
Moutnice	61	49.02 N	16.46 E
Moutohora	172	38.17 S	177.32 E
Moutomoukadi	152	4.41 S	13.15 E
Moutong	112	0.28 N	121.13 E
Mouy	50	49.19 N	2.19 E
Mouydir ∧∧	148	24.45 N	4.05 E
Mouyondzi	152	3.58 S	13.57 E
Mouzákion	38	39.26 N	21.40 E
Mouzarak	146	13.11 N	15.58 E
Mouzon	56	49.36 N	5.05 E
Mouzon ≐	58	48.21 N	5.41 E
Moville, Ire.	48	55.11 N	7.03 W
Moville, Ia., U.S.	198	42.29 N	96.04 W
Mowang	100	30.31 N	113.34 E
Moweaqua	219	39.37 N	89.01 W
Mowein	140	7.36 N	28.11 E
Mowry Slough ≐	282	37.29 N	122.03 W
Mowrystown	218	39.02 N	83.44 W
Mowu	100	26.50 N	117.42 E
Moxhe	56	50.38 N	5.05 E
Moxi	107	30.18 N	105.41 E
Moxico □ [5]	152	13.00 S	20.30 E
Moxotó ≐	250	9.19 S	38.14 W
Moy	48	54.27 N	6.42 W
Moy ≐	48	54.12 N	9.08 W
Moy, Cnoc ∧ [2]	46	55.22 N	5.46 W
Moya, Comores	157a	12.18 S	44.27 E
Moya, Perú	248	12.24 S	75.10 W
Moyagee	162	27.45 S	117.54 E
Moyahua	234	21.16 N	103.10 W
Moyale, Ityo.	144	3.30 N	39.07 E
Moyale, Kenya	154	3.32 N	39.03 E
Moyamba	150	8.10 N	12.26 W
Moycullen	48	53.21 N	9.09 W
Moydans	62	44.24 N	5.30 E
Moÿ-de-l'Aisne	50	49.45 N	3.22 E
Moye Dao I	98	36.55 N	122.32 E
Moyen Atlas ∧∧	148	33.30 N	5.00 W
Moyen-Chari □ [5]	146	9.00 N	18.00 E
Moyenmoutier	58	48.23 N	6.55 E
Moyenne-Sido	146	8.13 N	18.43 E
Moyenneville	50	50.04 N	1.45 E
Moyen-Ogooué □ [4]	152	0.30 S	10.30 E
Moyenvic	56	48.47 N	6.33 E
Moyeuvre-Grande	56	49.15 N	6.02 E
Moyie	182	49.17 N	115.50 W
Moyie ≐	202	48.42 N	116.11 W
Moyie Springs	202	48.43 N	116.11 W
Moylan	285	39.54 N	75.23 W
Moyle ≐	48	52.24 N	7.39 W
Moyo	154	3.39 N	31.43 E
Moyo ≐	115b	8.26 S	117.28 E
Moyo, Pulau I	115b	8.15 S	117.34 E
Moyobamba	248	6.03 S	76.58 W
Moyock	208	36.31 N	76.10 W
Moyogalpa	236	11.32 N	85.42 W
Moyowosi ≐	154	4.50 S	31.24 E
Moyu	120	37.17 N	79.44 E
Moyuta, Volcán ∧ [1]	236	14.02 N	90.06 W
M'oža ≐, Europe	76	55.27 N	30.43 E
M'oža ≐, Ross.	80	58.23 N	44.54 E
Možajevka	83	48.44 N	39.45 E
Možajsk	82	55.30 N	36.01 E
Možajskij	265a	59.43 N	30.07 E
Možajskoje vodochranilišče ⊜ [1]	82	55.35 N	35.50 E
Mozambique → Moçambique	154	15.03 S	40.42 E
Mozambique (Moçambique) □ [1]	138	18.15 S	35.00 E
Mozambique Channel ⨉	138	19.00 S	41.00 E
Mozambique Plateau ✣ [3]	10	32.00 S	35.00 E
Mozarlândia	255	14.47 S	50.35 W
Možarovka	86	51.09 N	59.05 E
Možarov Majdan	80	55.37 N	45.53 E
Možary	80	53.53 N	41.02 E
Mozdok	84	43.44 N	44.38 E
Možga	80	56.23 N	52.17 E
Mozhabong Lake ⊜	190	46.57 N	82.05 W
Mozia ⊥	70	37.52 N	12.28 E
Mozichang	107	29.20 N	103.53 E
Mozolevo	76	59.19 N	33.51 E
Mozu	270	34.34 N	135.29 E
Mozuli	76	56.36 N	28.11 E
Mozyr'	78	52.03 N	29.14 E
Mozzanica	62	45.29 N	9.41 E
Mozzano	66	42.50 N	13.31 E
Mozzate	266b	45.41 N	8.57 E
Mpaka	158	26.26 S	31.47 E
Mpala	154	6.45 S	29.31 E
Mpama ≐	152	0.57 S	15.39 E
Mpanda	154	6.22 S	31.02 E
Mpé	152	2.54 S	14.43 E
Mpese	152	5.14 S	15.33 E
Mpessoba	150	12.40 N	5.43 W
Mphoengs	154	21.10 S	27.51 E
Mpigi	154	0.13 N	32.42 E
Mpika	154	11.54 S	31.26 E
Mpila -◆- [8]	273b	4.14 S	15.18 E
Mpoka	152	1.26 S	17.02 E
Mpoko ≐	152	4.19 N	18.33 E
Mporokoso	154	9.23 S	30.05 E
Mpouya	152	2.37 S	16.13 E
Mpraeso	150	6.35 N	0.44 W
Mpui	154	8.21 S	31.50 E
Mpulungu	154	8.46 S	31.07 E
Mpwapwa	154	6.21 S	36.29 E
Mqanduli	158	31.48 S	28.46 E
Mrągowo	30	53.52 N	21.19 E
Mrakovo	86	52.43 N	56.38 E
M'Ramani	157a	12.21 S	44.32 E
Mranggen	115a	7.01 S	110.31 E
Mras-Su ≐	86	53.45 N	87.49 E
Mrhila, Jebel ∧	36	35.25 N	9.14 E
Mrijo	154	5.10 S	36.15 E
Mrkonjić Grad	36	44.25 N	17.05 E
Mrkopalj	36	45.19 N	14.51 E
Mrocza	30	53.14 N	17.36 E
Msagali	154	6.21 S	36.18 E
M'Saken	148	35.44 N	10.35 E
Msata	154	6.20 S	38.23 E
Mšec	54	50.10 N	13.54 E
Mšeno	54	50.27 N	14.38 E
M'Sila	148	35.46 N	4.31 E
M'Sila □ [5]	148	35.00 N	4.20 E
M'Sila, Oued ≐	34	35.46 N	4.34 E
Mšinskaja	76	59.01 N	29.57 E
Msoro	154	13.36 S	31.55 E
Msta	76	57.55 N	34.29 E
Msta ≐	76	58.25 N	31.20 E
Mstera	80	56.23 N	41.56 E
Mstislavl	76	54.02 N	31.42 E
Mstiž	76	54.34 N	28.10 E
Mszana Dolna	30	49.42 N	20.05 E
Mszczonów	30	51.58 N	20.31 E
Mtakataka	154	14.12 S	34.32 E
Mtakuja	154	7.22 S	30.37 E
Mtama	154	10.18 S	39.22 E
Mtamvuna ≐	158	31.06 S	30.12 E
Mtarazi National Park ♦	154	18.36 S	32.50 E
Mtata ≐	158	31.58 S	29.10 E
Mtelo ∧	154	1.39 N	35.23 E
Mtilikwe ≐	154	21.09 S	31.30 E
Mtito Andei	154	2.41 S	38.10 E
Mtowabaga	154	2.30 S	35.53 E
Mtsensk → Mcensk	76	53.17 N	36.35 E
Mtubatuba	158	28.30 S	32.08 E
Mtunzini	158	28.57 S	31.46 E
Mtwara	154	10.16 S	40.11 E
Mtwara □ [4]	154	11.00 S	39.00 E
Mtyangimbori	154	10.16 S	35.31 E
Mu ≐, Mya.	110	21.56 N	95.38 E
Mu ≐, Nihon	92a	42.33 N	141.56 E
Mu, Cerro ∧	246	9.29 N	73.07 W
Mu'a	174w	21.11 S	175.07 W
Muacandala	152	10.02 S	19.40 E
Mualama	154	16.53 S	38.17 E
Mualang	112	0.42 N	111.18 E
Mu'allaqah, Lubnān	132	33.50 N	35.54 E
Mu 'Allaqah, Sūd.	140	13.28 N	23.57 E
Muan	98	34.58 N	126.26 E
Muaná	250	1.32 S	49.13 W
Muanda	152	5.56 S	12.21 E
Muangai	152	12.32 S	19.51 E
Muang Bèng	110	20.22 N	101.44 E
Muang Hay	110	21.03 N	101.49 E
Muang Hinboun	110	17.35 N	104.36 E
Muang Hôngsa	110	19.43 N	101.20 E
Muang Houn	110	20.09 N	101.27 E
Muang Hounxianghoung	110	21.37 N	102.18 E
Muang Huang	110	18.45 N	103.42 E
Muang Khammouan	110	17.24 N	104.48 E
Muang Khao	110	19.47 N	103.29 E
Muang Khi	110	18.27 N	101.46 E
Muang Không	110	14.07 N	105.51 E
Muang Khôngxédôn	110	15.34 N	105.49 E
Muang La	110	20.52 N	102.07 E
Muang Liap	110	18.29 N	101.40 E
Muang Long	110	20.57 N	100.48 E
Muang Meung	110	20.43 N	100.28 E
Muang Ngoy, Lao	102	20.43 N	102.41 E
Muang Ngoy, Lao	110	20.43 N	102.41 E
Muang Nong	110	16.22 N	106.30 E
Muang Ou Nua	110	22.18 N	101.48 E
Muang Ou Tai	110	22.07 N	101.48 E
Muang Pakbèng	110	19.54 N	101.08 E
Muang Pak-Lay	110	18.12 N	101.25 E
Muang Paktha	110	20.06 N	100.36 E
Muang Pakxan	110	18.22 N	103.39 E
Muang Peun	110	20.13 N	103.52 E
Muang Phalan	110	16.39 N	105.34 E
Muang Phiang	110	19.06 N	101.32 E
Muang Phônthong	110	15.05 N	105.39 E
Muang Phoun	110	19.07 N	102.43 E
Muang Sam Sip	110	15.31 N	104.44 E
Muang Sing	110	21.11 N	101.09 E
Muang Soum	110	18.45 N	102.36 E
Muang Souvannakhili	110	15.23 N	105.49 E
Muang Souy	110	19.33 N	102.52 E
Muang Sung	110	20.19 N	102.27 E
Muang Thadua	110	19.26 N	101.50 E
Muang Thatèng	110	15.26 N	106.23 E
Muang Thathôm	110	19.00 N	103.36 E
Muang Va	110	21.53 N	102.19 E
Muang Vangviang	110	18.56 N	102.27 E
Muang Vapi	110	15.40 N	105.55 E
Muang Xaignabouri	110	19.15 N	101.45 E
Muang Xamtong	110	19.51 N	103.51 E
Muang Xay	110	20.42 N	101.59 E
Muang Xépôn	110	16.41 N	106.14 E
Muang Xon	110	20.27 N	103.19 E
Muang Yo	110	21.31 N	101.51 E
Muang You	110	19.49 N	102.50 E
Muanza	156	18.59 S	34.48 E
Muar (Bandar Maharani)	114	2.02 N	102.34 E
Muar ≐	114	2.03 N	102.35 E
Muara	112	5.02 N	115.02 E
Muaraaman	112	3.07 S	102.12 E
Muaraancalung	112	0.27 N	116.41 E
Muarabeliti	112	3.15 S	103.02 E
Muaraberangin	112	0.58 S	115.19 E
Muarabinuangeun	115a	6.50 S	105.53 E
Muarabulian	112	1.43 S	103.15 E
Muaraburgo	112	1.28 S	102.07 E
Muaradua	112	4.32 S	104.05 E
Muaraenim	112	3.39 S	103.48 E
Muaragusung	112	1.35 N	117.17 E
Muarajuloi	112	0.12 S	114.03 E
Muarakaman	112	0.09 S	116.43 E
Muarakelingi	112	3.05 S	103.14 E
Muarakumpe	112	1.24 S	104.00 E
Muaralabuh	112	1.29 S	101.03 E
Muaralakitan	112	2.51 S	103.19 E
Muaralasan	112	1.48 N	117.12 E
Muaralembu	112	0.24 S	101.21 E
Muaramawai	112	0.37 N	116.49 E
Muarapangean	112	2.38 N	116.41 E
Muarapartai	112	0.45 S	101.43 E
Muarapayang	112	1.32 S	115.48 E
Muararupit	112	2.44 S	102.54 E
Muarasabak	112	1.08 S	103.51 E
Muarasiberut	108	1.36 S	99.11 E
Muarasipongi	112	0.37 N	99.51 E
Muaratais	114	1.17 N	99.21 E
Muaratebo	112	1.30 S	102.26 E
Muarateladang	112	2.50 S	103.58 E
Muaratembesi	112	1.42 S	103.07 E
Muaratewe	112	0.57 S	114.53 E
Muaratuhup	112	0.37 S	114.50 E
Muaratunan	112	1.24 S	116.39 E
Muarawahau	112	1.02 N	116.52 E
Muāri, Rās ›	120	24.49 N	66.40 E
Muasdale	46	55.36 N	5.41 W
Muá Ximica	152	9.50 S	18.41 E
Mubārakpur	124	26.05 N	83.18 E
Mubārakpur Dabās -◆- [8]	272a	28.43 N	77.03 E
Mubayyac ⫧ [4]	142	30.55 N	32.48 E
Mubende	154	0.35 N	31.23 E
Mubi	146	10.18 N	13.20 E
Mubur, Pulau I	112	3.20 N	106.12 E
Mucaitá ≐	250	6.59 S	42.40 W
Mucajaí ≐	246	2.25 N	60.52 W
Mucambo	250	3.54 S	40.44 W
Mucári	152	9.30 S	16.54 E
Muccan	162	20.38 S	120.04 E
Muccia	66	43.05 N	13.02 E
Much	56	50.54 N	7.25 E
Mucha	269d	24.59 N	121.34 E
Muchangpu	100	31.55 N	116.35 E
Muchanovo	82	56.31 N	38.20 E
Muchavec ≐	76	52.05 N	23.39 E
Much Dewchurch	42	51.59 N	2.46 W
Muchea	168a	31.35 S	115.59 E
Mücheln	54	51.18 N	11.48 E
Muchen	89	48.10 N	136.13 E

Symbol	English	Deutsch	Español	Français	Português
≐	River	Fluß	Río	Rivière	Rio
≅	Canal	Kanal	Canal	Canal	Canal
⌞	Waterfall, Rapids	Wasserfall, Stromschnellen	Cascada, Rápidos	Chute d'eau, Rapides	Cascata, Rápidos
⨉	Strait	Meeresstraße	Estrecho	Détroit	Estreito
c	Bay, Gulf	Bucht, Golf	Bahía, Golfo	Baie, Golfe	Baía, Golfo
⊜	Lake, Lakes	See, Seen	Lago, Lagos	Lac, Lacs	Lago, Lagos
⩦	Swamp	Sumpf	Pantano	Marais	Pântano
☖	Ice Features, Glacier	Eis- und Gletscherformen	Accidentes Glaciales	Formes glaciaires	Acidentes glaciares
⫧	Other Hydrographic Features	Andere Hydrographische Objekte	Otros Elementos Hidrográficos	Autres données hydrographiques	Outros acidentes hidrográficos
✣	Submarine Features	Untermeerische Objekte	Accidentes Submarinos	Formes de relief sous-marin	Acidentes submarinos
□	Political Unit	Politische Einheit	Unidad Política	Entité politique	Unidade política
☉	Cultural Institution	Kulturelle Institution	Institución Cultural	Institution culturelle	Instituição cultural
⊥	Historical Site	Historische Stätte	Sitio Histórico	Site historique	Sítio histórico
♦	Recreational Site	Erholungs- und Ferienort	Sitio de Recreo	Centre de loisirs	Área de Lazer
✈	Airport	Flughafen	Aeropuerto	Aéroport	Aeroporto
■	Military Installation	Militäranlage	Instalación Militar	Installation militaire	Instalação militar
-◆-	Miscellaneous	Verschiedenes	Misceláneo	Divers	Diversos

Muchengzhen 107 29.47 N 103.29 E
Much Hoole 262 53.42 N 2.48 W
Muchinga
 Escarpment ±⁴ 154 14.45 S 29.30 E
Muchinga Mountains ▲ 154 12.20 S 31.00 E
Muchino, Ross. 80 58.11 N 51.02 E
Muchino, Ross. 89 52.16 N 127.14 E
Muchor-Konduj 88 52.25 N 113.16 E
Muchrani 84 41.56 N 44.35 E
Muchtadir 84 41.41 N 48.46 E
Muchtolovo 80 55.27 N 43.13 E
Muchtuan 107 28.55 N 103.58 E
Much Wenlock 42 52.36 N 2.34 W
Mucifal 266c 38.48 N 9.26 W
Muck 46 56.50 N 6.15 W
Mücka 54 51.18 N 14.40 E
Muckadilla 166 26.35 S 148.23 E
Muckalee Creek ≃ 192 31.38 N 84.09 W
Muckamore 48 54.41 N 6.10 W
Muckapskij 80 51.52 N 44.28 E
Muckas 24 64.02 N 48.27 E
Mücke 56 50.38 N 9.03 E
Muckendorf an der
 Donau 264b 48.20 N 16.09 E
Mucking 260 51.30 N 0.26 E
Muckle Roe I 46a 60.22 N 1.27 W
Muckleshoot Indian
 Reservation ▲ 224 47.16 N 122.09 W
Muckno Lough ≃ 48 54.07 N 6.42 W
Mucojo 154 12.04 S 40.28 E
Mucoma 152 15.18 S 13.39 E
Muconda 152 10.34 S 21.17 E
Mucope, Ang. 152 16.24 S 14.53 E
Mucope, Ang. 152 8.42 S 21.43 E
Mucrone, Monte ▲ 62 45.36 N 7.56 E
Mucubela 154 16.55 S 37.52 E
Mucuchíes 246 8.45 N 70.55 W
M'uc'ucl'u 84 40.28 N 47.55 E
Mucugé 255 13.00 S 41.23 W
Mucuim ≃ 248 6.33 S 64.18 W
Muculo 152 16.47 S 14.61 E
Mucurn 252 29.10 S 51.53 W
Mucumbura 154 16.09 S 31.31 E
Mucun 100 26.44 N 114.00 E
Mucupia 156 18.01 S 36.48 E
Mucupina, Monte ▲ 236 15.08 N 86.38 W
Mucur 130 39.04 N 34.23 E
Mucuri ≃ 255 18.05 S 39.34 W
Mucusso 152 18.01 S 21.25 E
Mud ≃, Ky., U.S. 194 37.13 N 86.54 W
Mud ≃, W.V., U.S. 188 38.20 N 82.17 W
Muda 114 5.33 N 100.22 E
Mudan ≃ 89 46.22 N 129.33 E
Mudanjiang 89 44.35 N 129.36 E
Mudanya 130 40.22 N 28.52 E
Mudau 56 49.32 N 9.11 E
Mudayslsät, Jabal ▲ 132 31.39 N 36.14 E
Mud Creek ≃, N.A. 206 45.01 N 72.24 W
Mud Creek ≃, U.S. 198 43.17 N 96.15 W
Mud Creek ≃, Il., U.S. 219 38.21 N 89.48 W
Mud Creek ≃, In., U.S. 216 41.06 N 86.21 W
Mud Creek ≃, Ne., U.S. 216 40.26 N 85.55 W
Mud Creek ≃, N.Y., U.S. 210 42.17 N 77.13 W
Mud Creek ≃, N.Y., U.S. 210 42.59 N 77.23 W
Mud Creek ≃, N.Y., U.S. 210 43.05 N 78.43 W
Mud Creek ≃, Ok., U.S. 196 33.55 N 97.28 W
Mud Creek ≃, S.D., U.S. 198 45.11 N 98.24 W
Mud Creek ≃, Tx., U.S. 222 31.48 N 94.58 W
Muddus Nationalpark ▲ 24 67.00 N 20.16 E
Muddy ≃, Nv., U.S. 204 36.27 N 114.22 W
Muddy ≃, Wa., U.S. 224 46.04 N 122.04 W
Muddy Boggy Creek ≃ 196 34.03 N 95.47 W
Muddy Branch ≃ 284c 39.03 N 77.18 W
Muddy Brook ≃ 276 41.07 N 73.20 W
Muddy Creek ≃, U.S. 274 41.03 N 74.02 W
Muddy Creek ≃, Mo., U.S. 194 38.53 N 93.03 W
Muddy Creek ≃, Mt., U.S. 202 47.56 N 111.46 W
Muddy Creek ≃, Oh., U.S. 214 41.27 N 83.03 W
Muddy Creek ≃, Pa., U.S. 208 39.47 N 76.18 W
Muddy Creek ≃, Ut,. U.S. 200 38.24 N 110.42 W
Muddy Creek ≃, Wy., U.S. 198 42.35 N 104.57 W
Muddy Creek ≃, Wy., U.S. 202 41.59 N 106.08 W
Muddy Creek ≃, Wy., U.S. 202 41.32 N 110.13 W
Muddy Creek ≃, Wy., U.S. 200 41.01 N 107.42 W
Muddy Creek ≃, Wy., U.S. 202 43.17 N 108.14 W
Muddy Fork ≃ 224 46.22 N 121.34 W
Muddy Gut c 284b 39.17 N 76.26 W
Muddy Peak ▲ 204 36.18 N 114.42 W
Müden, Dtsch. 52 52.52 N 10.22 E
Müden, Dtsch. 52 52.31 N 10.22 E
Mudgee 166 32.36 S 149.35 E
Mudgeeraba 171a 28.04 S 153.22 E
Mudhol 122 16.21 N 75.17 E
Mud Island I 171a 27.20 S 153.15 E
Mud Island II 169 38.17 S 144.45 E
Mudjatik ≃ 184 56.02 N 107.36 W
Mudjuga 24 63.46 N 39.15 E
Mud Lake ≃, Id., U.S. 202 43.53 N 112.24 W
Mud Lake ≃, N.Y., U.S. 204 37.52 N 117.04 W
Mud Lake ≃, N.Y., U.S. 210 42.34 N 75.07 W
Mud Lake Reservoir ≃ 198 45.50 N 98.10 W
Mudon 110 16.15 N 97.44 E
Mudongzhen 102 29.35 N 106.51 E
Mudu 106 31.15 N 120.30 E
Mudug □⁴ 144 6.15 N 48.00 E
Mudurnu 130 40.28 N 31.13 E
Mudurnu ≃ 130 40.49 N 30.33 E
M'ud'ur'um ≃ 85 40.55 N 76.36 E
Mueda 154 11.39 S 39.33 E
Muelle de los Bueyes 236 12.04 N 84.32 W
Mueller, Mount ▲ 154 19.54 S 127.51 E
Muenster 196 33.39 N 97.23 W
Mu'er 162 34.29 N 106.37 E
Muerte, Valle de la
 — Death Valley ⌵ 204 36.30 N 117.00 W
Muerto ▲ 252 23.02 S 62.29 W
Muerto, Mar
 — Dead Sea ≃ 132 31.30 S 35.30 E
Mufulira 154 12.33 S 28.14 E
Mufu Shan ▲ 100 31.30 N 114.00 E
Mufu Shan ▲ 100 29.02 N 113.54 E
Mufu Shan ▲ 100 29.44 N 115.14 E
Muganskaja ravnina ≃ 84 39.45 N 48.30 E
Mugazine 158 26.07 S 32.30 E
Mugegawa 94 35.31 N 136.51 E
Mugello ⌵ 66 43.55 N 11.30 E
Mügeln 154 51.24 N 13.02 E
Muger ≃ 144 9.54 N 37.57 E
Müggelberge ▲² 264a 52.25 N 13.39 E
Müggelheim ▲⁸ 264a 52.25 N 13.40 E

Muggia 64 45.36 N 13.46 E
Muggio 266b 45.36 N 9.14 E
Mughal Saräi 124 25.18 N 83.07 E
Mugi, Nihon 94 35.34 N 137.01 E
Mugi, Nihon 96 33.40 N 134.25 E
Mu Gia, Deo ⌂ 110 17.40 N 105.47 E
Muginga 152 8.20 S 17.37 E
Mugla 130 37.12 N 28.22 E
Mugla □⁴ 130 37.10 N 28.30 E
Mugodžarskaja ▲ 86 48.36 N 58.27 E
Mugodžary, gory ▲² 86 49.00 N 58.40 E
Mugo-ri 98 38.58 N 126.31 E
Mugrejevskij 80 56.36 N 42.21 E
Mugur-Aksy 86 50.21 N 90.30 E
Mugur Karnälï ≃ 124 29.38 N 81.52 E
Muhala 154 5.40 S 28.43 E
Muhamdi 124 27.57 N 80.13 E
Muhammad, Ra's ➤ 140 27.44 N 34.15 E
Muhammadäbäd 124 26.02 N 83.23 E
Muhammadpur 126 23.24 N 89.36 E
Muhammad Qawl 140 20.54 N 37.05 E
Muhayshir, Birkat ≃ 142 30.43 N 31.56 E
Muheza 154 5.10 S 38.47 E
Muhît, Maṣrif al- ≃ 273c 30.07 N 31.06 E
Mühlacker 56 48.57 N 8.50 E
Mühlau 54 50.54 N 12.45 E
Mühlbach am
 Hochkönig 64 47.22 N 13.08 E
Mühlbach-sur-
 Munster 58 48.02 N 7.05 E
Mühlberg 54 51.26 N 13.13 E
Mühldorf ≃ 61 48.22 N 15.21 E
Mühldorf am Inn 60 48.15 N 12.32 E
Mühlen
 — Molini di Tures 64 ...
Mühlenbeck 54 52.40 N 13.22 E
Mühlenbecker See ≃ 264a 52.41 N 13.24 E
Mühlenberg 210 41.14 N 76.09 W
Mühlen-Berg ▲² 248 52.23 N 13.15 E
Mühlen Eichsen 54 53.45 N 11.15 E
Mühlenfliess ≃ 264a 52.26 N 13.41 E
Mühlenrähmede 263 51.16 N 7.40 E
Mühlhausen ≃ 263 51.12 N 10.27 E
Mühlhausen, Dtsch. 263 51.33 N 7.44 E
Mühlhausen im Täle 56 16.30 S 37.30 E
Mühlheim an der
 Donau 58 48.01 N 8.52 E
Mühlig-Hofmann
 Mountains ▲ 9 72.00 S 5.20 E
Mühlleiten 264b 48.10 N 16.34 E
Mühltroff 54 50.32 N 11.55 E
Mühlviertel ≃¹ 30 48.25 N 14.10 E
Muhola 26 63.20 N 25.05 E
Muhos 154 1.01 S 34.07 E
Muhradah 30 35.15 N 36.35 E
Mühringen 58 48.25 N 8.46 E
Muhu 76 58.38 N 23.15 E
Muhu I 76 58.36 N 23.15 E
Mülhausen
 — Mulhouse 58 47.45 N 7.20 E
Mülheim 58 49.54 N 7.01 E
Mülheim an der Ruhr 56 51.24 N 6.54 E
Mülheimer
 Ruhrtalbrücke ▲⁵ 263 51.23 N 6.54 E
Mülheim-Karlich 56 50.21 N 7.28 E
Mulhouse 58 47.45 N 7.20 E
Muli 102 27.50 N 101.15 E
Muling, Zhg. 89 44.56 N 130.31 E
Muling, Zhg. 89 44.34 N 130.13 E
Muling ≃ 89 45.53 N 133.30 E
Mulin, Capo ➤ 70 37.34 N 15.10 E
Mulino 224 45.13 N 122.34 W
Mulinu'u, Cape ➤ 175a 13.26 S 172.43 W
Mulita 116 7.18 N 124.52 E
Muli 48 52.40 N 8.33 W
Mülki 122 13.06 N 74.48 E
Mull, Island of I 46 56.27 N 6.00 W
Mull, Sound of ⌂ 46 56.32 N 5.50 W
Mullagh 58 53.49 N 6.57 W
Mullagharirk
 Mountains ▲ 48 52.20 N 9.10 W
Mullaghcleevaun ▲ 48 53.06 N 6.24 W
Mullaghmore ▲ 48 54.52 N 6.51 W
Mullaloo Point ➤ 168a 31.48 S 115.44 E
Mullan 202 47.28 N 115.48 W
Müllen 198 42.02 N 101.02 W
Müllenbach 56 50.19 N 6.55 E
Mullengudgery 166 31.41 S 147.26 E
Mullens 188 37.34 N 81.22 W
Muller, Pegunungan ▲ 112 0.40 N 113.50 E
Muller Creek ≃ 162 22.29 S 134.30 E
Muller Range ≃ 164 5.35 S 142.15 E
Mullerup 41 55.30 N 11.13 E
Mullet Key I 220 27.37 N 82.44 W
Mullet Peninsula ➤¹ 48 54.12 N 10.00 W
Mullet Lake ≃ 190 45.30 N 84.30 W
Mullewa 162 28.33 S 115.31 E
Mullica ≃ 274 39.33 N 74.27 W
Mull Head ➤, Scot., U.K. 46 59.23 N 2.54 W
Mull Head ➤, Scot., U.K. 46 58.58 N 2.43 W
Müllheim 40 59.09 N 14.41 E
Mullhyttan 40 59.09 N 14.41 E
Mullica, Alquatka Branch ≃ 285 39.47 N 74.48 W
Mullica, Sleeper Branch ≃ 285 39.39 N 74.40 W
Mullica Hill 208 39.44 N 75.13 W
Mulligan ≃ 166 25.00 S 138.30 E
Mullin 196 31.33 N 98.40 W
Mullinahone 48 52.30 N 7.30 W
Mullinavat 48 52.21 N 7.10 W
Mullingar 48 53.32 N 7.20 W
Mullins 200 34.12 N 79.15 W
Mullinville 196 37.35 N 99.25 W
Mullion 42 50.01 N 5.15 W
Mullon Creek ≃ 171b 30.55 S 149.38 E
Mullovka 80 54.13 N 49.25 E
Mullröse 54 52.14 N 14.25 E
Mullsjö 26 57.55 N 13.53 E
Mullumbimby 166 28.33 S 153.30 E
Mullum Mullum Creek ≃ 274b 37.44 S 145.10 E
Mulobezi 154 16.48 S 25.09 E
Mulonda Funda 154 11.06 S 25.28 E
Mulondo 152 15.39 S 15.14 E
Mulshi Lake ≃ 122 18.30 N 73.30 E
Multai 120 21.46 N 78.15 E
Multan 120 30.11 N 71.29 E
Multia 26 62.24 N 24.47 E
Multiă 120 49.09 N 14.37 E
Mulungushi Dam ▲⁶ 154 14.40 S 28.50 E
Mulvane 198 37.28 N 97.14 W
Mulyah Mountain ▲ 166 30.37 S 144.31 E
Mumbles Head ➤ 42 51.34 N 3.59 W
Mumbondo 152 10.05 S 14.15 E
Mumbwa 154 14.59 S 27.04 E
Mumcular 130 37.05 N 27.40 E
Mumford, N.Y., U.S. 210 43.00 N 77.52 W
Mumford, Tx., U.S. 222 30.44 N 96.34 W

Mulaly 86 45.27 N 78.19 E
Mulan 89 45.57 N 128.03 E
Muland ▲⁸ 272c 19.10 N 72.57 E
Mulanda 152 14.41 S 21.48 E
Mulanje, Malaŵi 154 16.03 S 35.31 E
Mulanje, Moç. 154 16.03 S 35.45 E
Mulargia, Lago ⌀¹ 71 39.37 N 9.14 E
Mulas, Punta ➤ 240m 18.09 N 65.27 W
Mulas, Punta de ➤ 240p 21.01 N 75.35 W
Mulatos 232 28.39 N 108.51 W
Mulayit Taung ▲ 110 16.11 N 98.32 E
Mulazzo 64 44.19 N 9.53 E
Mulbägal 122 13.10 N 78.24 E
Mulben 46 57.31 N 3.06 W
Mulberry, Ar., U.S. 194 35.30 N 94.03 W
Mulberry, Fl., U.S. 220 27.53 N 81.58 W
Mulberry, In., U.S. 216 40.20 N 86.39 W
Mulberry, Oh., U.S. 218 39.11 N 84.14 W
Mulberry ≃ 194 35.28 N 94.03 W
Mulberry Creek ≃, Tx., U.S. 196 34.37 N 100.55 W
Mulberry Creek ≃, U.S. 194 32.27 N 86.52 W
Mulberry Fork ≃ 194 33.33 N 87.11 W
Mulberry Grove 219 38.55 N 89.16 W
Mulberry Mountain ▲ 194 35.42 N 92.56 W
Mulchatna ≃ 180 59.39 N 157.08 W
Mulchén 252 37.43 S 72.14 W
Mulde, Dtsch. 54 50.48 N 13.25 E
Mul'da, Ross. 24 67.28 N 63.34 E
Mulde ≃ 54 51.52 N 12.15 E
Muldenstein 54 51.40 N 12.19 E
Muldersdrif se Loop ≃ 273d 26.06 S 27.51 E
Muldersvlei 158 30.41 S 22.13 E
Muldoon 222 29.49 N 97.04 W
Muldraugh 194 37.56 N 85.59 W
Mule, Lac la ⌀ 186 51.33 N 65.35 W
Muleba 154 1.49 S 31.40 E
Mule Creek ≃ 198 37.05 N 99.00 W
Mulegé 232 26.53 N 112.01 W
Mulegns 58 46.33 N 9.37 E
Mulei 86 43.49 N 90.11 E
Mules (Mauls) 64 46.51 N 11.31 E
Mules, Pulau I 115b 8.54 S 120.17 E
Muleshoe 196 34.13 N 102.43 W
Mulevala 154 16.30 S 37.30 E
Mulga Downs 162 22.08 S 118.26 E
Mulgathing 162 30.15 S 134.00 E
Mulgathing Rocks ▲ 162 30.14 S 133.58 E
Mulghar 126 22.46 N 89.45 E
Mulgoa 170 33.50 S 150.40 E
Mulgoa Creek ≃ 274a 33.50 S 150.39 E
Mulgowie 171a 27.43 S 152.22 E
Mulgrave, Austl. 170 37.56 S 145.12 E
Mulgrave, N.S., Can. 186 45.37 N 61.23 W
Mulgrave Hills ▲² 180 67.42 N 163.24 W
Mulgul 162 24.49 S 118.26 E
Mulhacén ▲ 34 37.03 N 3.19 W
Mulhall 196 36.03 N 97.24 W

Mumias 154 0.20 N 34.29 E
Mümling ≃ 56 49.50 N 9.09 E
Mumoni ▲ 154 0.31 S 38.01 E
Mumra 80 45.47 N 47.41 E
Mumu 140 12.06 N 23.42 E
Mumungwe 154 16.23 S 26.24 E
Mun ≃ 110 15.19 N 105.30 E
Mun, Jabal ▲ 140 14.08 N 22.42 E
Munä, Ar. Su. 144 21.25 N 39.52 E
Muna, Méx. 232 20.29 N 89.43 W
Muna ≃ 74 67.52 N 123.06 E
Muna, Pulau I 112 5.00 S 122.30 E
Muna, Selat ⌂ 112 5.15 S 122.10 E
Munä al-Amïr 142 29.54 N 31.15 E
Munäbäo 120 25.45 N 70.17 E
Munajly 86 46.47 N 54.31 E
Munakata 96 33.50 N 130.35 E
Munam-ni 98 38.41 N 126.54 E
Munbong-ni 271b 37.43 N 126.49 E
Muncar 115a 8.26 S 114.20 E
München 60 48.08 N 11.34 E
Münchberg 56 50.11 N 11.47 E
München (Munich) 60 48.08 N 11.34 E
Münchenbernsdorf 54 50.49 N 11.56 E
Münchenbuchsee 58 47.01 N 7.27 E
München-Erding, Flughafen ≋ 60 48.22 N 11.48 E
München-Gladbach
 — Mönchengladbach 56 51.12 N 6.28 E
München-Riem, Flughafen ≋ 60 48.08 N 11.41 E
Münchenstein 56 47.31 N 7.37 E
Münchhausen 56 50.57 N 8.43 E
Munchique, Cerro ▲ 246 2.32 N 76.57 W
Munch'ŏn 98 39.16 N 127.15 E
Muncie 216 40.11 N 85.23 W
Muncy 210 41.12 N 76.47 W
Muncy Creek ≃ 210 41.13 N 76.48 W
Muncy Valley 210 41.21 N 76.35 W
Mundare 182 53.36 N 112.20 W
Munday 196 33.26 N 99.37 W
Mundelein 216 42.15 N 88.00 W
Mündelheim ▲⁸ 263 51.21 N 6.41 E
Münden 56 51.25 N 9.39 E
Munderfing 60 48.05 N 13.11 E
Munderkingen 56 48.14 N 9.38 E
Munderoo ▲ 171b 35.48 S 147.47 E
Mundesley 42 52.53 N 1.26 E
Mundiwindi 162 23.52 S 120.09 E
Mundka ▲⁸ 272a 28.41 N 77.02 E
Mundo ≃ 34 38.19 N 1.40 W
Mundon Hill 260 51.41 N 0.42 E
Mundo Novo 255 11.52 S 40.28 W
Mundra 120 22.51 N 69.44 E
Mundrabilla 162 31.52 S 127.51 E
Mundubbera 166 25.36 S 151.18 E
Mundybaš 86 53.14 N 87.19 E
Mundytau, gora ▲ 86 58.00 N 68.27 E
Munene 152 20.38 S 30.03 E
Munenga 152 10.02 S 14.41 E
Munera 34 39.02 N 2.28 W
Munford 196 35.26 N 89.48 W
Munfordville 194 37.16 N 85.53 W
Mungallala 166 26.27 S 147.33 E
Mungallala Creek ≃ 166 28.05 S 147.15 E
Mungana 166 17.07 S 144.24 E
Mungaoli 124 24.25 N 78.06 E
Mungári 154 17.12 S 33.31 E
Mungar Junction 166 25.36 S 152.36 E
Mungbere 154 2.38 N 28.30 E
Mungeli 124 22.04 N 81.41 E
Munger 124 25.23 N 86.28 E
Mungeranie 162 28.00 S 138.36 E
Mungindi 166 28.58 S 148.59 E
Munglinup 162 33.43 S 120.51 E
Mungo National Park ▲ 166 33.44 S 143.02 E
Mungo Badshähpur 124 25.40 N 82.11 E
Mungun-Tajga, gora ▲ 86 50.16 N 90.05 E
Mun'gyŏng 98 36.44 N 128.07 E
Munhall 214 40.23 N 79.54 W
Munhamade 152 16.37 S 36.58 E
Munhango 152 12.12 S 18.42 E
Munhango ≃ 152 11.20 S 19.50 E
Munhoz 256 22.37 S 46.22 W
Munhye-ri 98 38.10 N 127.19 E
Munich
 — München 60 48.08 N 11.34 E
Muniesa 34 41.02 N 0.48 W
Munising 190 46.24 N 86.38 W
Munith 250 42.23 N 84.15 W
Muñiz 258 34.33 S 58.42 W
Muniz Freire 255 20.28 S 41.25 W
Munkács
 — Mukačevo 78 48.27 N 22.45 E
Munkebo 41 55.28 N 10.34 E
Munkebjerg ▲² 41 55.41 N 9.37 E
Munkedal 40 58.28 N 11.40 E
Munkerud 58 59.50 N 13.31 E
Munkfors 26 59.50 N 13.32 E
Munksund 26 65.17 N 21.29 E
Munktorp 40 59.32 N 16.08 E
Munku-Sardyk, gora ▲ 88 51.45 N 100.32 E
Munlochy 46 57.32 N 4.15 W
Münnerstadt 56 50.15 N 10.11 E
Munnsville 210 42.58 N 75.35 W
Muñoz 116 15.43 N 120.54 E
Munozero 24 67.05 N 34.12 E
Munpal-i 271b 37.45 N 126.43 E
Munro Falls 208 41.08 N 81.26 W
Munro Lake ≃ 154 18.58 S 95.16 W
Munsan 98 37.51 N 126.48 E
Munsarpur 124 26.15 N 85.28 E
Munsey Park 279a 40.48 N 73.41 W
Munshiganj 124 23.33 N 90.32 E
Münsing 60 47.54 N 11.22 E
Münsingen, Dtsch. 56 48.25 N 9.34 E
Münsingen, Schw. 58 46.52 N 7.34 E
Munson, Ab., Can. 182 51.34 N 112.45 W
Munson, Pa., U.S. 210 41.02 N 78.24 W
Munson Knob ▲ 210 40.51 N 81.54 W
Munsons Corners 210 42.34 N 76.11 W
Münster, Fr. 58 48.03 N 7.08 E
Münster, Schw. 58 46.29 N 8.16 E
Munster, In., U.S. 216 41.33 N 87.30 W
Münsterkirche ▲¹ 263 51.23 N 7.09 E
Münsterland ≃¹ 56 51.55 N 7.35 E
Münsterlingen 58 47.38 N 9.14 E
Münstermaifeld 56 50.15 N 7.22 E
Munte 112 0.30 N 119.55 E

Muntele Mare, Vîrful ▲ 38 46.29 N 23.14 E
Muntenia ≃¹ 38 44.30 N 26.00 E
Muntendam 52 53.07 N 6.53 E
Muntok 112 2.04 S 105.11 E
Mununga 154 0.36 N 29.15 E
Munuscong Lake ≃ 190 46.10 N 84.08 W
Munyamadzi ≃ 154 14.30 S 30.30 E
Munzur ≃ 130 39.40 N 39.10 E
Munzur Dağlari ▲ 130 39.30 N 39.10 E
Munzur Vadisi Milli Parki ▲ 130 39.25 N 39.30 E
Muolea Point ➤ 229a 20.41 N 156.01 W
Muong Het 110 20.49 N 104.01 E
Muong Hinh 110 19.49 N 105.03 E
Muong Khoua 110 21.05 N 102.31 E
Muong Saiapoun 110 18.24 N 101.31 E
Muong Te 110 22.28 N 102.37 E
Muonio 24 67.57 N 23.42 E
Muotathal 58 46.59 N 8.46 E
Mupa 152 16.10 S 15.44 E
Mupa, Parque Nacional da ▲ 152 16.00 S 15.35 E
Muping 98 37.24 N 121.36 E
Mupini 156 17.50 S 19.40 E
Mup'ungjang 98 35.58 N 127.49 E
Muqaddam, Wädï V 140 18.04 N 31.30 E
Muqatta' 140 14.40 N 35.51 E
Muqaybirah, Bi'r al- ▲⁴ 142 30.53 N 32.50 E
Muqayshit I 128 24.10 N 53.45 E
Muqdisho (Mogadishu) 144 2.04 N 45.22 E
Muqi 98 41.46 N 124.39 E
Muqsam, Jabal ▲ 140 13.38 N 27.42 E
Muquequete 152 14.50 S 14.16 E
Muqui 255 20.57 S 41.20 W
Mur (Mura) ≃ 30 46.18 N 16.53 E
Mura ≃, Ross. 88 52.26 N 98.34 E
Muradiye, Tür. 84 38.59 N 43.46 E
Muradiye, Tür. 130 38.39 N 27.21 E
Murädnagar 124 28.47 N 77.30 E
Murafa ≃ 78 48.13 N 28.14 E
Murăgācha 126 23.32 N 88.24 E
Muraglione, Passo del ⌂ 64 44.06 N 11.39 E
Murat Reservoir ⌀¹ 271c 1.24 N 103.41 E
Murajä 250 0.47 S 47.57 W
Murakami 92 38.14 N 139.29 E
Murallón, Cerro ▲ 254 49.48 S 73.25 W
Murambi 144 1.46 S 30.23 E
Muramvya 144 3.33 S 133.49 E
Murang'a 154 0.43 S 37.09 E
Murano, Isola di I 268 45.27 N 12.21 E
Muranskij porog ▲ 88 58.02 N 112.16 E
Muraoka 96 35.28 N 134.35 E
Muraši 24 59.24 N 48.55 E
Muraški 265b 59.59 N 37.45 E
Murat ≃ 84 38.39 N 39.50 E
Murat Daği ▲ 130 38.55 N 29.43 E
Murath 130 41.10 N 27.30 E
Muratovo 85 44.48 N 38.45 E
Muratpur 272b 22.59 N 88.27 E
Murau 61 47.07 N 14.10 E
Muravera 71 39.25 N 9.34 E
Muravjovka 89 49.50 N 127.44 E
Muravjovo 90 56.14 N 34.14 E
Murayama 92 38.28 N 140.22 E
Murayama-chosuichi ⌀¹ 268 ...
Muraysah, Ra's al- ➤ 146 31.55 N 25.22 E
Murča 34 41.13 N 7.27 W
Murcanyo 144 11.41 N 50.27 E
Mürchen Khvort 128 33.06 N 51.30 E
Murchin 54 53.54 N 13.44 E
Murchison, Austl. 166 35.19 S 145.14 E
Murchison, N.Z. 172 41.48 S 172.20 E
Murchison, Tx., U.S. 222 32.17 N 95.45 W
Murchison, Mount ▲, Austl. 162 26.46 S 116.25 E
Murchison, Mount ▲, N.Z. 172 43.01 S 171.22 E
Murchison Falls
 — Kabalega Falls ▲ 154 2.17 N 31.41 E
Murchison Range ▲ 162 20.11 S 134.26 E
Murcia 34 37.59 N 1.07 W
Murcia, Pil. 116 10.36 N 123.02 E
Murcia ▲⁴, Esp. 34 38.00 N 1.30 W
Murcia ≃, Esp. 34 37.55 N 1.30 W
Murciélago, Islas II 236 10.51 N 85.57 W
Murciélagos Bay c 116 8.09 N 123.33 E
Mur-de-Barrez 32 44.51 N 2.39 E
Murdeudale, Lake ≃ 169 38.01 S 143.53 E
Murder Creek ≃, Al., U.S. 194 31.04 N 87.06 W
Murder Creek ≃, N.Y., U.S. 210 43.03 N 78.31 W
Murderkill ≃ 208 39.03 N 75.24 W
Murdo 198 43.53 N 100.42 W
Murdock 220 27.00 N 82.08 W
 — Morat, Lac de ⌀ 58 46.56 N 7.05 E
Murdochville 186 48.58 N 65.30 W
Murè, Otok I 36 43.48 N 15.37 E
Murefte 130 40.45 N 27.25 E
Mureck 61 46.42 N 15.46 E
Mures (Maros) ≃ 38 46.15 N 20.13 E
Muret 32 43.28 N 1.21 E
Murfreesboro, Ar., U.S. 194 34.03 N 93.41 W
Murfreesboro, N.C., U.S. 200 36.26 N 77.05 W
Murfreesboro, Tn., U.S. 194 35.50 N 86.23 W

Mürïtäniyä
 — Mauritania □¹ 134 20.00 N 12.00 W
Müritz ≃ 54 53.25 N 12.43 E
Muriwai 172 38.46 S 177.55 E
Murkong Selek 120 27.49 N 95.16 E
Murⁱganj 124 25.54 N 86.59 E
Murlo 66 43.09 N 11.23 E
Murmansk 24 68.58 N 33.05 E
Murmansk Oblast' □⁴ 24 68.00 N 35.00 E
Murmansk Rise ▲³ 12 75.00 N 37.00 E
Murmerwoude 52 53.16 N 6.00 E
Murmino 80 54.36 N 40.03 E
Murnau 64 47.40 N 11.12 E
Muro 140 12.57 N 22.52 E
Murö 94 34.34 N 136.02 E
Murö-Akame-Aoyama-kokutei-köen ▲ 94 34.30 N 136.10 E
Muro Lucano 68 40.45 N 15.29 E
Murom 80 55.34 N 42.02 E
Muromcevo 86 56.23 N 75.14 E
Muros 34 42.18 N 140.59 E
Muros y Noya, Ría de c¹ 34 42.45 N 9.00 W
Muroto 34 33.41 N 134.09 E
Muroto-Anan-kaigan-kokutei-köen ▲ 96 33.33 N 134.10 E
Muroto-zaki ➤ 96 33.15 N 134.11 E
Murovanyje Kurilovcy 78 48.43 N 27.31 E
Murowana Goślina 30 52.35 N 17.01 E
Murphy, Id., U.S. 202 43.13 N 116.33 W
Murphy, Mo., U.S. 219 38.29 N 90.29 W
Murphy, N.C., U.S. 192 35.05 N 84.02 W
Murphy Lake ≃ 182 52.03 N 121.14 W
Murphys 204 38.08 N 120.28 W
Murphysboro 194 37.45 N 89.20 W
Murphy Slough ≃ 226 36.28 N 120.00 W
Murr ≃ 56 48.57 N 9.16 E
Murr, Wädï V 142 38.27 N 32.18 E
Murrah, Qärat al- ≃² 142 30.00 N 32.41 E
Murrah al-Kubrä, Al-Buhayrah al- (Great Bitter Lake) ≃ 142 30.20 N 32.23 E
Murrah as-Sughrä, Al-Buhayrah al- (Little Bitter Lake) ≃ 142 30.13 N 32.33 E
Murra Murra 166 28.16 S 146.48 E
Murrät, Äbär V⁴ 141 21.03 N 32.55 E
Murray ≃, Ia., U.S. 190 43.10 N 93.56 W
Murray ≃, Ky., U.S. 194 36.36 N 88.18 W
Murray, Ut., U.S. 200 40.40 N 111.53 W
Murray ≃, Austl. 166a 35.22 S 139.22 E
Murray ≃, B.C., Can. 168a 32.35 S 115.46 E
Murray, Lake ≃ 164 7.00 S 141.30 E
Murray, Mount ▲ 192 34.30 N 81.23 W
Murray ≃, Yk., Can. 180 60.54 N 128.49 W
Murray Bay
 — La Malbaie 186 47.39 N 70.10 W
Murray Bridge 168b 35.07 S 139.17 E
Murray Canal ≋ 212 44.04 N 77.35 W
Murray City 208 39.30 N 82.09 W
Murray Fracture Zone ≃ 16 34.00 N 135.00 W
Murray Harbour 186 46.00 N 62.31 W
Murray Head ➤ 186 46.00 N 62.28 W
Murray Maxwell Bay c 176 70.00 N 80.00 W
Murray Mouth ≋ 168b 35.34 S 138.54 E
Murray River 186 46.01 N 62.37 W
Murraysburg 158 31.58 S 23.47 E
Murrayville, B.C., Can. 224 49.10 N 122.36 W
Murrayville, Il., U.S. 194 39.35 N 90.15 W
Murrayville, N.C. ≃¹ 192 34.18 N 77.52 W
Mürren 58 46.34 N 7.54 E
Murrhardt 56 48.59 N 9.35 E
Murri ≃ 246 6.33 N 76.52 W
Murrieta 228 33.33 N 117.12 W
Murro di Porca, Capo ➤ 70 37.00 N 15.20 E
Murrumbidgee ≃ 166 34.43 S 143.12 E
Murrumburrah 166 34.33 S 148.21 E
Murrundi 154 15.27 S 38.47 E
Murrurundi 166 31.46 S 150.50 E
Murry Hill 279b 40.17 N 80.09 W
Murrysville 208 40.26 N 79.41 W
Mursala, Pulau I 114 1.38 N 98.38 E
Mürshidäbäd 126 24.11 N 88.16 E
Mürsitpinar 130 36.54 N 38.19 E
Murska Sobota 36 46.40 N 16.10 E
Mursko Središče 61 46.31 N 16.27 E
Murtee 166 31.35 S 143.32 E
Murten 266c 46.56 N 7.07 E
Murtensee ≃
 — Morat, Lac de ⌀ 58 46.56 N 7.05 E
Murtle Lake ≃ 182 52.09 N 119.38 W
Murtoa 166 36.37 S 142.28 E
Murton 44 54.49 N 1.24 W
Muru ≃ 250 8.39 S 73.38 W
Muru ≃ 140 6.36 N 29.15 E
Murud 248 18.19 N 72.58 E
Murud, Gunong ▲ 112 3.52 N 115.30 E
Murukta 74 67.46 N 102.01 E
Mururoa 2 21.52 S 138.55 W
Murupara 172 38.28 S 176.42 E
Mururutia 246 3.26 S 59.12 W
Murvaul, Lake ≃¹ 222 30.10 N 94.30 W
Murvaul Creek ≃ 222 32.05 N 94.12 W
Murwāra 124 23.51 N 80.24 E
Murwillumbah 166 28.19 S 153.24 E
Mürz ≃ 61 47.24 N 15.17 E
Mürzsteg 61 47.40 N 15.29 E
Mürzzuschlag 61 47.36 N 15.41 E
Muş 130 38.44 N 41.30 E
Muş □⁴ 130 38.44 N 41.30 E
Muša ≃, Europe 76 56.20 N 24.10 E
Muša ≃, Pap. N. Gui. 164 9.25 S 148.50 E
Müsá (Mount Sinai) ▲ 140 28.32 N 33.59 E
Müsá, 'Uyün (Springs of Moses) V 140 29.52 N 32.39 E
Musá Khel Bāzār 120 30.52 N 69.49 E
Musala ▲ 38 42.11 N 23.34 E
Musan 98 42.14 N 129.13 E
Musandam Peninsula ➤¹ 128 26.18 N 56.24 E
Musay'id 128 24.57 N 51.36 E
Musaymir 142 13.27 N 44.37 E

Symbols in the index entries represent the broad categories identified in the key at the right. Symbols with superior numbers (≠¹) identify subcategories (see complete key on page I · 1).

Symbole im Register stellen die rechts im Schlüssel erklärten Kategorien dar. Symbole mit hochgestellten Ziffern (≠¹) bezeichnen Unterteilungen einer Kategorie (vgl. vollständiger Schlüssel auf Seite I · 1).

Los símbolos incluidos en el texto del índice representan las grandes categorías identificadas con la clave a la derecha. Los símbolos con números en su parte superior (≠¹) identifican las subcategorías (véase la clave completa en la página I · 1).

Les symboles de l'index représentent les catégories indiquées dans la légende à droite. Les symboles suivis d'un indice (≠¹) représentent des sous-catégories (voir légende complète à la page I · 1).

Os símbolos incluídos no texto do índice representam as grandes categorias identificadas com a clave à direita. Os símbolos com números em sua parte superior (≠¹) identificam as subcategorias (veja-se a chave completa à página I · 1).

▲	Mountain	Berg	Montaña	Montagne	Montanha
▲	Mountains	Gebirge	Montañas	Montagnes	Montanhas
⌂	Pass	Paß	Paso	Col	Passo
⌵	Valley, Canyon	Tal, Cañon	Valle, Cañón	Vallée, Canyon	Vale, Canhão
≖	Plain	Ebene	Llano	Plaine	Planície
≖	Cape	Kap	Cabo	Cap	Cabo
I	Island	Insel	Isla	Île	Ilha
II	Islands	Inseln	Islas	Îles	Ilhas
±	Other Topographic Features	Andere Topographische Objekte	Otros Elementos Topográficos	Autres données topographiques	Outros acidentes topográficos

Nombre — Página — Lat.ᵒ' — Long.ᵒ' W = Oeste / Nom — Page / Nome — Página

Nombre / Nom / Nome	Página	Lat.	Long.
Mūsāzai	120	30.23 N	66.32 E
Muscat — Masqat	128	23.37 N	58.35 E
Muscat and Oman — Oman ◻¹	118	22.00 N	58.00 E
Muscatatuck ≈	218	38.46 N	86.10 W
Muscatatuck, Grassy Fork ≈	218	38.45 N	85.07 W
Muscatatuck, Vernon Fork ≈	218	38.46 N	85.54 W
Muscatine	190	41.25 N	91.03 W
Müsch	56	50.23 N	6.49 E
Mus-Chaja, gora ▲	74	62.35 N	140.50 E
Muschu Island I	164	3.25 S	143.35 E
Muschwitz	54	51.11 N	12.07 E
Muscle Shoals	194	34.44 N	87.40 W
Musclow, Mount ▲	182	53.17 N	127.09 W
Musclow Lake ⊜	184	51.25 N	94.56 W
Muscoda	190	43.11 N	90.26 W
Musconetcong ≈	210	40.36 N	75.11 W
Musconetcong, Lake ⊜	276	40.54 N	74.42 W
Muscongus Bay c	188	43.55 N	69.20 W
Muscote Bay c	212	44.06 N	77.18 W
Muscowpetung Indian Reserve ◄◄	184	50.45 N	104.15 W
Muscoy	228	34.09 N	117.20 W
Muse	214	40.17 N	80.12 W
Musengezi ≈	154	15.43 S	31.14 E
Musgrave, Austl.	164	14.47 S	143.30 E
Musgrave, B.C., Can.	224	48.45 N	123.32 W
Musgrave, Mount ▲	172	43.48 S	170.43 E
Musgrave Ranges ≈	162	26.10 S	131.50 E
Musgravetown	186	48.24 N	53.53 W
Mūshā	142	27.08 N	31.18 E
Mushābani	126	22.31 N	86.27 E
Mushāsh, Jabal al- ▲²	142	28.54 N	31.11 E
Mushenge	152	4.32 S	21.21 E
Mushie	152	3.01 S	16.54 E
Mushima	154	14.13 S	25.05 E
Mushin	164	6.30 N	3.22 E
Mūsi ≈, India	122	16.41 N	79.40 E
Musi ≈, Indon.	112	2.20 S	104.56 E
Musicians Seamounts ◄³	6	31.00 N	162.00 W
Muskauer Heide ◄³	54	51.25 N	14.40 E
Muskeg ≈	182	54.01 N	119.03 W
Muskeget Channel ⊔	207	41.25 N	70.20 W
Muskeget Island I	207	41.20 N	70.18 W
Muskeg Lake Indian Reserve ◄◄	184	52.58 N	106.57 W
Muskego	216	42.54 N	88.08 W
Muskego Lake ⊜	216	42.53 N	88.07 W
Muskeçon ◻	216	43.14 N	86.14 W
Muskeçon ≈	216	43.14 N	86.08 W
Muskeçon ≈	190	43.14 N	86.20 W
Muskeçon County Airport ≈	216	43.10 N	86.14 W
Muskeçon Heights	216	43.12 N	86.14 W
Muskeçon Lake ⊜	216	43.14 N	86.17 W
Muskeçon State Park ≈	216	43.14 N	86.20 W
Mušketova, gora ▲	88	53.35 N	113.32 E
Muskingum ◻⁶	214	40.06 N	81.51 W
Muskingum ≈	188	32.27 N	81.54 W
Muskingum Brook ≈	285	39.48 N	74.44 W
Muskira	124	25.40 N	79.48 E
Muskö I	49	59.00 N	18.06 E
Muskocay Indian Reserve ◄◄	184	53.06 N	105.30 W
Muskogee	196	35.44 N	95.22 W
Muskoka ◻⁶	212	45.00 N	79.03 W
Muskoka, Lake ⊜	212	45.00 N	79.25 W
Muskoka, North Branch ≈	212	45.02 N	79.19 W
Muskoka, South Branch ≈	212	45.02 N	79.19 W
Muskosh Channel ⊔	212	44.55 N	79.53 W
Muskowekwan Indian Reserve ◄◄	184	51.19 N	104.06 W
Muskrat Creek ≈	285	43.09 N	108.11 W
Muskrat Dam Lake ⊜	184	53.25 N	91.40 W
Muskrat Lake ⊜	190	43.40 N	76.55 W
Muskwa ≈	176	58.45 N	122.35 W
Muskwa Lake ⊜	182	56.09 N	114.38 W
Muslimbāgh	120	30.49 N	67.45 E
Musl'umovo	80	55.18 N	53.12 E
Musmus	132	32.32 N	35.09 E
Musococo ◄⁸	266b	46.30 N	9.08 E
Musofu Mission	154	13.31 S	29.02 E
Musoma	154	1.30 S	33.48 E
Musone ≈, It.	64	45.50 N	11.55 E
Musone ≈, It.	66	43.28 N	13.38 E
Musoshi	154	11.54 S	27.46 E
Musquaϸousse, Lac ⊜	186	50.22 N	61.05 W
Musquaϸsink Brook ≈	276	40.59 N	74.01 W
Musquaro, Lac ⊜	186	50.38 N	61.05 W
Musquash ≈	212	44.57 N	79.52 W
Musquash Brook ≈	283	42.13 N	71.26 W
Musquashcut Pond ⊜	283	42.12 N	70.46 W
Musquodoboit Harbour	186	44.47 N	63.09 W
Mussau Island I	164	1.30 S	149.40 E
Musselburgh	46	55.57 N	3.04 W
Musselkanaal	52	52.56 N	7.00 E
Mussel'nell ≈	202	47.21 N	107.58 W
Mussende	154	10.32 S	16.05 E
Mussidan	32	45.02 N	0.22 E
Mussomeli	76	37.35 N	13.45 E
Mussoorie	124	30.27 N	78.05 E
Mussuco	154	17.08 S	19.35 E
Mussum	154	51.48 N	6.34 E
Mussuma	152	14.14 S	21.59 E
Mussy-sur-Seine	58	47.58 N	4.30 E
Mustafakemalpaşa	138	40.02 N	28.24 E
Mustafa Kemal Paşa ≈	130	40.07 N	28.33 E
Mustahil	144	5.12 N	44.17 E
Mustair	58	46.37 N	10.27 E
Mustang	78	57.59 N	26.58 E
Mustang	124	29.11 N	83.58 E
Mustang Draw V	196	32.12 N	101.36 W
Mustang Island I	196	27.45 N	97.10 W
Mustja ≈	142	30.37 N	31.09 E
Musters, Lago ⊜	254	45.27 S	69.13 W
Mustjala	78	58.30 N	22.14 E
Mustla	198	45.45 N	98.58 W
Mustla	78	58.14 N	25.52 E
Musturud	273c	30.08 N	31.17 E
Mustvee	78	58.51 N	26.56 E
Musu-dan ▸	98	40.50 N	129.43 E
Musun	84	39.42 N	43.49 E
Muswellbrook	160	32.15 S	150.55 E
Musyma	30	49.21 N	20.54 E
Müt, Misr	140	25.29 N	28.59 E
Müt, Tür	130	36.39 N	33.26 E
Muta	61	46.37 N	15.10 E
Mutá, Pcnta do ▸	255	13.52 S	38.56 W
Mu'tah	132	31.06 N	35.42 E
Mutamba	174v	16.56 S	169.50 W
Mutambara	154	19.36 S	32.33 E
Mutanchiang — Mudanjiang	94	44.35 N	129.36 E
Mutanda, Moç.	156	21.02 S	33.31 E
Mutanda, Zaïre	152	5.17 S	16.34 E
Mutanda Mission	154	12.24 S	26.16 E
Mutarara — Mudanjiang	94	44.35 N	129.36 E
Mutarammil, Jabal al- ▲	132	31.04 N	36.06 E
Mutare	154	18.58 S	32.40 E
Mutbin	132	33.09 N	36.15 E
Mutějovice	54	50.09 N	13.41 E
Mutha	154	1.48 S	38.26 E

Nom	Page	Lat.	Long.
Muthill	46	56.19 N	3.50 W
Mutiko	154	1.39 S	28.12 E
Muting	164	7.23 S	140.20 E
Mutis, Gunung ▲	112	9.34 S	124.14 E
Mutlu (Rezovska) ≈	38	41.59 N	28.01 E
Mutoko	154	17.24 S	32.13 E
Mutombo-Mukulu	152	7.58 S	24.00 E
Mutoraj	74	61.20 N	100.30 E
Mutoto	152	5.42 S	22.42 E
Mutouchengzi	98	41.20 N	119.59 E
Mutouhao	107	28.49 N	105.04 E
Mutsamudu	157a	12.09 S	44.25 E
Mutsu	92	41.17 N	141.10 E
Mutsui	268	35.08 N	139.38 E
Mutsumi	96	34.26 N	131.34 E
Mutsuura ◄⁸	268	35.19 N	139.37 E
Mutsu-wan c	92	41.05 N	140.55 E
Muttaburra	166	22.36 S	144.33 E
Mutte Kopf ▲	58	47.16 N	10.39 E
Muttenz	58	47.32 N	7.39 E
Mutters	64	47.14 N	11.23 E
Mutterstadt	56	49.26 N	8.21 E
Muttonbird Islands II	172	47.15 S	167.24 E
Muttonbird — Mathura	276	40.49 N	73.33 W
Muttra — Mathura	124	27.30 N	77.41 E
Mutual, Oh., U.S.	218	40.05 N	83.38 W
Mutual, Pa., U.S.	279b	40.14 N	79.30 W
Mutūbis	142	31.18 N	30.31 E
Mutuca, Ribeirão da ≈	256	21.36 S	45.39 W
Mutuca, Lago ⊜	250	1.21 N	50.24 W
Mutupie	153	13.15 S	39.31 W
Mutum	255	19.49 S	41.26 W
Mutum Biyu	146	8.38 N	10.46 E
Mutumbo	152	13.14 S	17.17 E
Mutunópolis	255	13.40 S	49.15 W
Muturi ≈	164	2.06 S	133.43 E
Muturi ≈	164	2.13 S	133.40 E
Mututi, Ilha do I	250	0.45 S	51.00 W
Mutzig	58	48.32 N	7.28 E
Mutzschen	54	51.16 N	12.53 E
Mu Us Shamo ◄²	102	38.45 N	109.10 E
Müvattupula	122	9.58 N	76.35 E
Muvukoni	154	0.24 S	38.14 E
Muwala ≈	104	41.03 N	121.12 E
Muxaluando	152	8.07 S	14.17 E
Muxihe	101	31.03 N	115.21 E
Muxima	152	9.31 S	13.56 E
Muyaga	152	3.14 S	30.33 E
Muyang	100	27.06 N	119.34 E
Muyang ≈	100	27.00 N	119.41 E
Muymano ≈	154	2.51 S	30.20 E
Muymano ≈	248	11.57 S	69.03 W
Muy Muy	236	12.46 N	85.38 W
Muyua Island I	164	9.05 S	152.50 E
Muyuka	152	4.17 N	9.25 E
Muyumba	154	7.15 S	26.59 E
Mužaž⁸	84	22.54 N	36.21 E
Muzaffarābād	123	34.22 N	73.28 E
Muzaffargarh	123	30.04 N	71.12 E
Muzaffarnagar	124	29.28 N	77.41 E
Muzaffarpur	124	26.07 N	85.24 E
Muzambinho	256	21.22 S	46.32 W
Muzambinho ≈	256	21.15 S	46.26 W
Muzarabani ≈	256	21.17 S	46.16 W
Muzat ≈	90	41.15 N	83.27 E
Muzayrib	132	32.42 N	36.01 E
Muzbek, gora ▲	85	40.23 N	69.39 E
Muzbel'⁴·¹	86	50.15 N	70.50 E
Muzeze	152	15.03 S	17.43 E
Muzhan	100	34.43 N	117.56 E
Muži	74	65.22 N	64.40 E
Mužiksu	86	43.03 N	44.59 E
Mužiľac	32	47.33 N	2.29 W
Muzkol, chrebet ▲	85	38.25 N	73.30 E
Muzoka	154	16.41 S	27.19 E
Muzon, Cape ▸	182	54.41 N	132.44 W
Muztag ▲, Zhg.	120	36.03 N	80.07 E
Muztag ▲, Zhg.	90	38.17 N	75.06 E
Muztagata ▲	85	38.17 N	75.11 E
Muz Tau ▲	86	43.50 N	85.40 E
Muzūrah	142	28.53 N	30.48 E
Muzzana del Turgnano	64	45.49 N	13.08 E
Mvam	152	0.13 S	9.39 E
Mveia	154	14.46 S	35.16 E
Mvengué	152	3.17 N	11.01 E
Mvolo	140	6.03 N	29.56 E
Mvomero	154	6.20 S	37.25 E
Mvoti ≈	158	29.24 S	31.22 E
Mvoung ≈	152	0.04 N	12.18 E
Mvuha	152	4.15 S	12.29 E
Mvuma	154	7.12 S	37.51 E
Mvuma	154	19.19 S	30.35 E
Mwadi-Kalumba	152	7.53 S	18.46 E
Mwadui	154	3.33 S	33.36 E
Mwali (Mohéli) I	157a	12.15 S	43.45 E
Mwami	156	16.40 S	29.46 E
Mwanagumune	152	6.51 S	24.13 E
Mwanza, Malaŵi	154	15.37 S	34.31 E
Mwanza, Tan.	154	2.31 S	32.54 E
Mwanza, Zaïre	154	7.54 S	26.45 E
Mwanza, Zam.	152	17.02 S	24.27 E
Mwanza Gulf c	154	2.45 S	32.45 E
Mwaya, Tan.	154	9.33 S	33.57 E
Mwaya, Tan.	154	8.55 S	36.56 E
Mwe-kerea ≈	48	53.38 N	9.50 W
Mwehu	154	5.44 S	26.40 E
Mweka	152	4.51 S	21.34 E
Mwemena	154	10.19 S	27.28 E
Mwenda	152	7.53 S	18.51 E
Mwenda	154	7.12 S	18.51 E
Mwene-Ditu	152	7.03 S	23.27 E
Mwenezi	154	21.22 S	30.45 E
Mwenga	154	3.02 S	28.26 E
Mwepo	154	11.56 S	26.11 E
Mwerasandu	154	0.59 S	30.23 E
Mweru, Lake ⊜	154	4.20 S	39.08 E
Mweru, Lake ⊜	154	9.00 S	28.45 E
Mweru Wantipa, Lake ⊜	154	8.45 S	29.40 E
Mweru Wantipa National Park ♦	154	8.45 S	29.40 E
Mwetshi	152	4.42 S	22.39 E
Mwilambwe	154	7.18 S	25.00 E
Mwimbi	154	8.39 S	31.40 E
Mwingi	154	0.56 S	38.04 E
Mwinilunga	152	11.44 S	24.26 E
Mwitikira	154	6.31 S	35.39 E
Mwombezhi ≈	154	12.52 S	25.00 E
Myajing	120	26.15 N	70.23 E
Myakka ≈	220	26.56 N	82.11 W
Myakka City	220	27.20 N	82.09 W
Myakka River State Park ♦	220	27.15 N	82.17 W
Myanaung	110	18.17 N	95.19 E
Myanmar (Burma) ◻¹	110	22.00 N	98.00 E
Myaungmya	110	16.36 N	94.56 E
Myawadi	110	16.41 N	98.31 E
Mÿbster	46	58.27 N	3.23 W
Myckelgensjö	26	63.34 N	17.37 E
Myebon	110	20.03 N	93.22 E
Myeik — Mergui	110	12.26 N	98.36 E
Myers, N.Y., U.S.	210	42.32 N	76.32 W
Myerstown	208	40.22 N	76.19 W

Nome	Página	Lat.	Long.
Myingyan	110	21.28 N	95.23 E
Myinmoletkat Taung ▲	110	13.28 N	98.48 E
Myitkyinä	110	25.23 N	97.24 E
Myitnge ≈	110	21.52 N	95.59 E
Myitta	110	14.10 N	98.31 E
Myittha	110	21.25 N	96.08 E
Myittha ≈	110	23.12 N	94.17 E
Myjava	30	48.45 N	17.34 E
Myjeldino	24	61.46 N	54.48 E
Myjlybulak	86	48.57 N	75.13 E
Myla	24	65.25 N	50.48 E
Mylau	54	50.37 N	12.16 E
Myl'džino	88	59.03 N	78.29 E
Myllendonk, Schloss 🏛	263	51.13 N	6.29 E
Myllykoski	26	60.47 N	26.48 E
Myllymäki	26	62.32 N	24.17 E
Mylor	168b	35.03 S	138.45 E
Mymensingh	124	24.45 N	90.24 E
Mynämäki	26	60.40 N	22.00 E
Mynaral	85	45.25 N	73.41 E
Mynbulak, gcra ▲	85	41.43 N	69.49 E
Mynfontein	158	30.55 S	23.57 E
Mynydd Bach ▲²	42	52.15 N	4.05 W
Mynydd Eppynt ▲	42	52.05 N	3.30 W
Mynydd Hiraethog ▲	44	53.05 N	3.33 W
Mynydd Pencarreg ▲	42	52.04 N	4.04 W
Mynydd Presali ▲	42	51.58 N	4.42 W
Myōgata	96	35.17 N	137.02 E
Myōgi	94	36.17 N	138.49 E
Myōgi-Arafune-Saku-kōgen-kokutei-kōen ♦	94	36.12 N	138.10 E
Myōgi-san ▲	94	36.17 N	138.44 E
Myo-gyi	110	21.27 N	96.22 E
Myohyang	110	20.36 N	93.10 E
Myohyang-san ▲	98	40.02 N	126.17 E
Myohyang-sanmaek ▲	98	40.30 N	127.00 E
Myojin-dake ▲	270	34.57 N	135.36 E
Myōjin-san ▲	96	34.30 N	133.04 E
Myōken-san ▲	96	35.24 N	134.39 E
Myōken-zan ▲	270	34.56 N	135.28 E
Myōken-zan ▲²	270	34.30 N	134.57 E
Myōkō	94	36.56 N	138.13 E
Myōkō-kōgen	94	36.52 N	138.12 E
Myōkō-san ▲	94	36.52 N	138.07 E
Myōnmong-ni ◄⁸	271b	37.35 N	127.05 E
Myponga	168b	35.24 S	138.28 E
Myponga Reservoir ⊜¹	168b	35.24 S	138.26 E
Myra	130	36.15 N	29.54 E
Mýrdalsjökull ⊘	24a	63.40 N	19.05 W
Myrnam	182	53.40 N	111.14 W
Myroodah	162	18.08 S	124.16 E
Myrskylä (Mörskom)	26	60.40 N	25.51 E
Myrtle Beach	192	33.41 N	78.53 W
Myrtle Beach Air Force Base ▪	192	33.41 N	78.56 W
Myrtle Beach State Park ♦	192	33.37 N	78.58 W
Myrtle Creek	202	43.01 N	123.17 W
Myrtle Grove	194	30.25 N	87.18 W
Myrtle Point	202	43.04 N	124.08 W
Myrtle Springs	222	32.37 N	95.56 W
Myrtletowne	204	40.47 N	124.04 W
Myrtleville	170	34.29 S	149.49 E
Mÿšega	82	54.31 N	37.02 E
Mysen	26	59.33 N	11.20 E
Mysia ◄⁹	130	39.15 N	28.00 E
Mysingen ⊔	40	59.00 N	18.15 E
Myski	86	53.42 N	87.48 E
Mýškino	76	57.47 N	38.27 E
Mýšla ≈	54	52.40 N	14.29 E
Myślenice	30	49.51 N	19.56 E
Myślibórz	30	52.55 N	14.52 E
Mysłowice	30	50.15 N	19.07 E
Mysore	122	12.18 N	76.39 E
Mys Smīdta	66	68.56 N	179.26 W
Mystic, Ct., U.S.	207	41.21 N	71.58 W
Mystic, Ia., U.S.	190	40.46 N	92.56 W
Mystic ≈	283	42.23 N	71.03 W
Mystic Seaport ♦	207	41.22 N	71.58 W
Mys Vchodno;	74	73.53 N	86.43 E
Mysy	24	60.34 N	53.57 E
Myš Želanija	72	76.55 N	68.00 E
Myszków	30	50.36 N	19.20 E
Myszyniec	30	53.24 N	21.21 E
Myt	82	56.48 N	42.21 E
My Tho	110	10.21 N	106.21 E
Mytholm	262	53.44 N	2.01 W
Mytholmroyd	262	53.44 N	1.59 W
Mytilene — Mitilíni	38	39.06 N	26.32 E
Mytišči	82	55.55 N	37.46 E
Mytishchi — Mytišči	82	55.55 N	37.46 E
Mýto	60	49.47 N	13.44 E
Myton	200	40.12 N	110.04 W
Myvatn ⊜	24a	65.36 N	16.58 W
Mýzovo	78	51.22 N	24.31 E
M'zab, Oued ≈	148	32.19 N	5.24 E
Mže ≈	60	49.46 N	13.24 E
Mzenga	154	6.56 S	38.43 E
Mziha	154	5.54 S	37.47 E
Mzimba	154	11.52 S	33.34 E
Mzimkulu ≈	158	30.44 S	30.28 E
Mzimvubu ≈	158	31.38 S	29.32 E
Mzintlava ≈	158	31.12 S	29.18 E
Mzuzu	154	11.27 S	33.55 E
Mzymta ≈	84	43.27 N	39.56 E

N

Nom	Page	Lat.	Long.
Na ≈	174r	6.52 N	158.22 E
Na (Tengtiao) ≈	112	22.05 N	103.09 E
Naab ≈	54	49.01 N	12.02 E
Naach, Jbel ▲	34	34.53 N	3.22 W
Naaldwijk	52	51.59 N	4.12 E
Naalehu	229d	19.03 N	155.35 W
Na'ām ≈	140	9.42 N	28.27 E
Na'āma, Sebkhet en ⊜	148	33.20 N	0.16 E
Naaman Creek ≈	285	39.48 N	75.27 W
Naantali	26	60.27 N	22.02 E
Naarden	52	52.17 N	5.10 E
Naarn ≈	61	48.11 N	14.49 E
Naas (An Nás)	48	53.13 N	6.39 W
Nababiep	158	29.36 S	17.46 E
Nabadwip	272b	23.25 N	88.22 E
Nabaganga ≈	272b	22.59 N	89.34 E
Nabagram	272b	24.30 N	88.06 E
Nabari	96	34.37 N	136.05 E
Nabari ≈	270	34.45 N	136.01 E
Nabas	116	11.50 N	122.05 E
Nabasta	116	23.15 N	88.01 E
Nabawa	162	28.31 S	114.47 E
Nabb	218	38.36 N	85.38 W
Nabberu, Lake ⊜	162	25.50 S	120.30 E
Nabburg	54	49.28 N	12.11 E
Nabeina	174t	1.26 N	173.05 E

Legend

Símbolo / Symbol	FLUSS (German)	RÍO	RIVIÈRE	RIO	English	Untermeerische Objekte	Accidentes Submarinos	Formes de relief sous-marin	Acidentes submarinos
≈ River	Fluß	Río	Rivière	Rio	☩ Submarine Features	Untermeerische Objekte	Accidentes Submarinos	Formes de relief sous-marin	Acidentes submarinos
≋ Cana	Kanal	Canal	Canal	Canal	◻ Political Unit	Politische Einheit	Unidad Política	Entité politique	Unidade política
⅃ Waterfall, Rapids	Wasserfall, Stromschnellen	Cascada, Rápidos	Chute d'eau, Rapides	Cascata, Rápidos	⅃ Cultural Institution	Kulturelle Institution	Institución Cultural	Institution culturelle	Instituição Cultural
⊔ Strait	Meeresstraße	Estrecho	Détroit	Estreito	🏛 Historical Site	Historische Stätte	Sitio Histórico	Site historique	Sitio histórico
c Bay, Gulf	Bucht, Golf	Bahía, Golfo	Baie, Golfe	Baía, Golfo	♦ Recreational Site	Erholungs- und Ferienort	Sitio de Recreo	Centre de loisirs	Area de Lazer
⊜ Lake, Lakes	See, Seen	Lago, Lagos	Lac, Lacs	Lago, Lagos	≈ Airport	Flughafen	Aeropuerto	Aéroport	Aeroporto
≈ Swamp	Sumpf	Pantano	Marais	Pântano	▪ Military Installation	Militäranlage	Instalación Militar	Installation militaire	Instalação militar
⊘ Ice Features, Glacier	Eis- und Gletscherformen	Accidentes Glaciales	Formes glaciaires	Acidentes glaciares	◄ Miscellaneous	Verschiedenes	Misceláneo	Divers	Diversos
▾ Other Hydrographic Features	Andere Hydrographische Objekte	Otros Elementos Hidrográficos	Autres données hydrographiques	Outros acidentes hidrográficos					

Nallihan 130 40.11 N 31.21 E
Na Logu 64 46.23 N 13.45 E
Nalolo 152 15.35 S 23.07 E
Nalón ≃ 34 43.32 N 6.04 W
Nalong 102 23.35 N 106.05 E
Nalusa 152 14.55 S 22.13 E
Nalüt 146 31.52 N 10.59 E
Nalžovské Hory 60 49.20 N 13.33 E
Nam ≃ 110 21.33 N 98.38 E
Namaacha 156 25.58 S 32.01 E
Namachire 152 11.26 S 22.43 E
Namacunde 152 17.18 S 15.50 E
Namacurra 154 17.29 S 37.01 E
Namadgi National Park ♦ 171b 35.45 S 148.57 E
Namak, Daryācheh-ye ⌷ 128 34.30 N 51.50 E
Namak, Kavīr-e ⬟² 128 34.45 N 57.45 E
Namakan Lake ⌷ 190 48.27 N 92.35 W
Nãmakkal 122 11.14 N 78.10 E
Namakzãr, Kowl-e ⌷ 128 34.00 N 64.30 E
Namakula 174v 18.57 S 169.54 W
Namaland ≃ 156 25.50 S 18.00 E
Namamugi ⬟⁸ 268 35.29 N 139.41 E
Namanga 154 2.33 S 36.46 E
Namangan 85 41.00 N 71.40 E
Namangan □⁴ 85 41.00 N 71.15 E
Namanyere 154 7.31 S 31.03 E
Namarodu, Cape ➤ 164 3.38 S 152.30 E
Namarrói 154 15.58 S 36.55 E
Namasagali 154 1.01 N 32.57 E
Namatanai 164 3.40 S 152.25 E
Nambe Indian Reservation ⬟⁴ 200 35.52 N 105.57 W
Namber 164 1.04 S 134.49 E
Nambi 162 28.54 S 121.41 E
Nambour 166 26.38 S 152.58 E
Nambouwalu 175g 16.59 S 178.42 E
Nambuangongo 152 8.01 S 14.12 E
Nambucca Heads 166 30.39 S 153.00 E
Nam Can 110 8.46 N 104.59 E
Namcha Barwa → Namjagbarwa Feng ⌃ 102 29.38 N 95.04 E
Namch'ang 98 35.26 N 129.16 E
Nam Co ⌷ 120 30.42 N 90.30 E
Namdae-ch'ŏn 98 40.26 N 128.57 E
Namdanak 85 41.11 N 69.42 E
Nam Dinh 110 20.25 N 106.10 E
Namdöll I 40 59.12 N 18.41 E
Nãmdöfjärden ⌷ 40 59.12 N 18.34 E
Nam Du, Quan Dao II 110 9.42 N 104.22 E
Namegawa 94 36.04 N 139.22 E
Nameh 112 2.34 N 116.21 E
Nameigos Lake ⌷ 190 48.46 N 84.43 W
Namekagon ≃ 190 46.05 N 92.06 W
Namen → Namur 56 50.28 N 4.52 E
Namerikawa 94 36.46 N 137.20 E
Námĕšť 61 49.12 N 16.10 E
Nametil 154 15.43 S 39.21 E
Namew Lake ⌷ 184 54.13 N 101.56 W
Nam-gang ≃ 98 39.03 N 125.52 E
Namhae 94 34.50 N 127.54 E
Namhae-do I 98 34.48 N 127.57 E
Namhan-gang ≃ 98 37.31 N 127.18 E
Namhkam 110 23.50 N 97.41 E
Namho-ri 98 38.07 N 125.10 E
Namhsan 102 22.58 N 97.10 E
Namiai 94 35.22 N 137.41 E
Namib Desert ⬟² 156 23.00 S 15.00 E
Namibe 152 15.10 S 12.09 E
Namibe □⁵ 152 15.00 S 12.30 E
Namibia □¹, Afr. 138 22.00 S 17.00 E
Namibia □¹, Afr. 138 22.00 S 17.00 E
Namibie → Namibia □¹ 156 22.00 S 17.00 E
Namib-Naukluft Park ♦ 156 23.30 S 15.30 E
Namie 92 37.29 N 141.00 E
Namies 156 29.18 S 19.13 E
Namĭn 128 38.25 N 48.30 E
Naminga 88 56.33 N 118.41 E
Namjagbarwa Feng ⌃ 102 29.38 N 95.04 E
Nãmja La ⨽ 124 27.42 N 82.34 E
Nampi-ri 98 35.23 N 128.29 E
Nămkhãna 126 21.46 N 88.14 E
Nam Kwo Chau I 271d 22.15 N 114.21 E
Namlan 110 22.19 N 97.24 E
Nãmling ≃ 124 29.28 N 82.50 E
Namlea 164 3.18 S 127.06 E
Namling 120 29.41 N 89.04 E
Namses 58 47.21 N 10.40 E
Nam Ngum Reservoir ⌷¹ 110 18.30 N 102.40 E
Namno 110 30.06 N 98.38 E
Namoi ≃ 112 1.24 S 119.57 E
Namo 166 30.00 S 148.07 E
Namoluk I¹ 14 5.55 S 153.08 E
Namonuiti I¹ 14 8.46 N 150.02 E
Namorik I¹ 14 5.36 N 168.07 E
Namoruputh 154 4.34 N 35.57 E
Namouni 150 11.52 N 1.42 E
Namous, Oued en ∨ 148 31.00 N 0.15 W
Namoya 154 4.01 S 27.34 E
Nampa, Ab., Can. 182 56.02 N 117.08 W
Nampa, Id., U.S. 202 43.32 N 116.33 W
Nampala 150 15.17 N 5.33 W
Nam Pat 110 17.43 N 100.41 E
Nampawng 110 22.45 N 97.52 E
Nam Phan □⁹ 110 11.00 N 107.00 E
Nam Phong 110 16.42 N 102.52 E
Nampicuan 105 15.44 N 120.38 E
Nampô 98 38.45 N 125.23 E
Nampont-Saint-Martin 50 50.21 N 1.45 E
Namp'ot'ae-san ⌃ 98 41.44 N 128.24 E
Nampuecha 154 13.59 S 40.18 E
Nampula 154 15.07 S 39.15 E
Nampula □⁵ 154 15.00 S 39.00 E
Namsang 110 20.53 N 97.43 E
Namsan Park ♦ 271b 37.34 N 126.59 E
Namsanyŏng-ni 98 38.59 N 127.26 E
Namsen ≃ 34 64.27 N 11.28 E
Namsi 98 39.34 N 124.36 E
Namsos 24 64.29 N 11.30 E
Nam Tok 110 14.14 N 99.04 E
Namtu 110 23.05 N 97.25 E
Namu 182 51.49 N 127.52 W
Namu I¹ 14 8.00 N 168.10 E
Namukila-I-Lau I 175g 18.51 S 178.38 W
Namúli, Serra ⌃ 154 15.15 S 37.08 E
Namur, Bel. 56 50.28 N 4.52 E
Namur, P.Q., Can. 206 45.54 N 74.56 W
Namur □⁴ 56 50.20 N 4.50 E
Namuruputh 154 4.34 N 35.57 E
Namutoni 156 18.48 N 16.55 E
Namwala 154 15.45 S 26.26 E
Namwera 154 14.22 S 35.30 E
Namwŏn 98 35.25 N 127.23 E
Namyang, C.M.I.K. 98 42.57 N 129.53 E
Namyang, Taehan 98 37.14 N 126.44 E
Namyit Island I 108 10.11 N 114.22 E
Namysłów 30 51.05 N 17.42 E
Nan ≃, Thai. 110 15.42 N 100.07 E
Nan ≃, Zhg. 102 32.33 N 107.30 E
Nana ≃ 152 5.00 N 15.50 E
Nana Barya ≃ 152 5.00 N 15.50 E
Nana Barya, Réserve de Faune de ⬟➤ 146 7.30 N 17.30 E
Nanacamilpa 214 19.29 N 98.33 W
Nanaimo 224 49.10 N 123.56 W
Nanaimo ≃ 224 49.10 N 123.56 W
Nanaimo Lakes ⌷ 224 49.07 N 124.11 W
Nãnakhet ⬟⁸ 272a 18.31 S 23.07 E
Nana Kru 150 4.50 N 8.44 W
Nanakuli 229c 21.23 N 158.09 W
Nanakusa Sãhib 152 41.43 N 122.41 E
Nana-Mambéré □⁵ 152 5.30 N 15.30 E
Nan'an 100 24.58 N 118.23 E

Nan'anba 107 28.46 N 104.38 E
Nanango 166 26.40 S 152.00 E
Nanantun 110 24.45 N 95.41 E
Nanao, Nihon 94 37.03 N 136.58 E
Nanao, T'aiwan 100 24.28 N 121.48 E
Nan'ao, Zhg. 100 23.27 N 117.02 E
Nan'ao Dao I 100 23.26 N 117.03 E
Nanao-wan ⌷ 94 37.06 N 137.00 E
Nanas Channel ⨽ 271c 1.25 N 103.58 E
Nanatsu-jima II 94 37.36 N 136.53 E
Nanatsuka 94 36.44 N 136.41 E
Nanay ≃ 246 3.42 S 73.16 W
Nanba 102 32.20 N 104.58 E
Nanbaita 102 25.00 N 112.00 E
Nanbaixia 98 35.45 N 117.23 E
Nanbaozhen 106 31.32 N 121.37 E
Nanbu, Nihon 94 35.17 N 138.27 E
Nanbu, Zhg. 102 31.23 N 106.02 E
Nancaicun 105 39.28 N 117.01 E
Nancefield 273d 26.17 S 27.53 E
Nancha 89 47.08 N 129.19 E
Nanchang, Zhg. 100 28.41 N 115.53 E
Nanchang (Liantang), Zhg. 100 28.34 N 115.56 E
Nancheng, Zhg. 105 25.39 N 118.26 E
Nancheng, Zhg. 100 27.35 N 116.40 E
Nancheng → Hanzhong, Zhg. 102 33.08 N 107.02 E
Nancheng → Nanjing 106 32.03 N 118.47 E
Nanchital 234 18.04 N 94.24 W
Nanchong 107 30.48 N 106.04 E
Nanchuan 102 29.08 N 107.07 E
Nanchuang 100 24.36 N 120.59 E
Nanch'ung → Nanchong 107 30.48 N 106.04 E
Nancowry Island I 110 7.59 N 93.32 E
Nancroix 62 45.32 N 6.46 E
Nancun, Zhg. 96 36.32 N 120.06 E
Nancun, Zhg. 98 39.46 N 114.07 E
Nancy 58 48.41 N 6.12 E
Nanda Devi ⌃ 124 30.23 N 79.59 E
Nãndãha 272b 22.50 N 88.17 E
Nandaime 236 11.46 N 86.03 W
Nanda Kot ⌃ 124 30.17 N 80.05 E
Nandan 96 34.15 N 134.43 E
Nandarivatu 175g 17.34 S 177.58 E
Nandatad 100 29.01 N 112.43 E
Nãnded 122 19.09 N 77.20 E
Nãndgaon, India 122 20.19 N 74.39 E
Nãndgaon, India 272c 18.58 N 73.08 E
Nandi ≃ 175g 17.48 S 177.25 E
Nandi Bay c 175g 17.44 S 177.25 E
Nandi Drug ⌃ 122 13.25 N 77.42 E
Nandigrãm 126 22.01 N 87.58 E
Nandikotkūr 122 15.52 N 78.16 E
Nanding ≃, Asia 102 23.25 N 98.41 E
Nanding ≃, Asia 102 23.25 N 98.41 E
Nandisladt 60 48.32 N 11.48 E
Nandom 150 10.51 N 2.45 W
N'andoma 24 61.40 N 40.12 E
Nandu 106 31.27 N 119.19 E
Nandu ≃ 110 20.04 N 110.22 E
Nanduluohe 105 40.11 N 117.13 E
Nandurbãr 122 21.22 N 74.15 E
Nanduri 175g 16.27 S 179.09 E
Nanfen 96 41.06 N 123.44 E
Nanfeng, Zhg. 100 27.15 N 116.32 E
Nanfeng, Zhg. 100 29.16 N 116.32 E
Nangabadau 112 1.00 N 111.54 E
Nanga Eboko 152 4.41 N 12.22 E
Nangahale 115b 8.34 S 122.32 E
Nangahu 112 0.23 N 112.26 E
Nangala ≃ 112 31.24 N 76.14 E
Nangalaangki 112 1.15 S 111.40 E
Nangalao Island I 116 12.17 N 120.11 E
Nangal Dewat ⬟⁸ 272a 28.33 N 77.06 E
Nangamau 112 0.06 S 111.55 E
Nangan, Teluk c 115b 9.37 S 120.20 E
Nangapinoh 112 0.22 S 111.23 E
Nang Gang c 100 23.30 N 117.00 E
Nangang ⬟ 105 34.00 S 138.14 E
Nangatbat 112 0.57 N 113.13 E
Nangaocun 105 39.25 N 115.58 E
Nangata Parbat ⌃ 123 35.15 N 74.36 E
Nangatayap 112 1.32 S 110.34 E
Nangbéto ⌷ 150 39.31 N 116.23 E
Nangatayap 112 1.32 S 110.34 E
Nanggala Hill ⌃ 175e 8.16 S 157.43 E
Nanggulan 115a 7.46 S 110.12 E
Nangi 272b 22.31 N 88.13 E
Nangio 101 30.31 N 98.55 E
Nangka ≃ 269f 14.41 N 121.06 E
Nangka 150 43.33 N 3.00 E
Nanglu ≃ 126 24.20 N 90.04 E
Nangloi ⬟⁸, India 272a 28.41 N 77.05 E
Nangloi ⬟⁸, India 272a 28.41 N 77.02 E
Nangloi Jat ⬟⁸ 272a 28.41 N 77.04 E
Nangnim-sanmaek ⌃ 98 40.00 N 127.00 E
Nangô, Nihon 92 31.22 N 131.23 E
Nangô, Nihon 94 37.13 N 139.33 E
Nangola 150 12.40 N 6.36 W
Nangoma 89 37.24 N 115.22 E
Nangong 99 43.17 N 128.37 E
Nangô-yama-tunnel ⬟ 94 35.12 N 139.10 E
Nangqên 102 32.22 N 96.21 E
Nang Rong 110 14.38 N 102.48 E
Nangweshi 152 16.26 S 23.17 E
Nanhai 100 23.03 N 113.09 E
Nanhai → Foshan 100 23.03 N 113.09 E
Nanhai → South China Sea ⌷² 108 10.00 N 113.00 E
Nanhedian 100 33.23 N 112.25 E
Nanhezhao 105 39.05 N 115.56 E
Nanhsi 102 23.11 N 120.29 E
Nanhsi 102 39.57 N 94.13 E
Nanhualou 94 42.30 N 123.53 E
Nanhuang 98 36.58 N 121.47 E
Nanhui 100 31.03 N 121.45 E
Nanjangūd 122 12.06 N 76.42 E
Nanji ⌷ 100 27.58 N 121.04 E
Nanjiang, Zhg. 100 32.24 N 120.52 E
Nanjiang, Zhg. 102 32.33 N 107.30 E
Nanjie 100 29.11 N 105.00 E
Nanjing, Zhg. 100 24.32 N 117.22 E
Nanjing, Zhg. 100 24.24 N 117.22 E
Nanjing (Nanking), Zhg. 100 32.03 N 118.47 E
Nankang 100 25.40 N 114.47 E
Nankang 100 30.02 N 114.25 E
Nanking → Nanjing 106 32.03 N 118.47 E
Nanki-Shirahama 92 33.41 N 135.21 E
Nanku 100 24.24 N 103.04 E
Nankang ≃ 269d 25.03 N 121.36 E

Nankin 214 40.55 N 82.17 W
Nanking → Nanjing 106 32.03 N 118.47 E
Nanko-kŏen ♦ 94 37.05 N 140.14 E
Nankoku 96 33.39 N 133.44 E
Nankou 106 26.38 N 117.24 E
Nankouzhen 105 40.14 N 116.07 E
Nanku 106 31.06 N 120.37 E
Nankye 110 14.20 N 98.11 E
Nanle 98 36.04 N 115.10 E
Nanling, Zhg. 100 30.56 N 118.20 E
Nanling, Zhg. 105 23.21 N 115.25 E
Nanling, Zhg. 104 41.37 N 120.56 E
Nan Ling ⌃ 90 25.00 N 112.00 E
Nanliuqiao 100 29.35 N 114.19 E
Nan Liu ≃ 100 21.38 N 109.00 E
Nanliucun 105 40.10 N 116.04 E
Nanlongba 100 28.02 N 107.31 E
Nanlou Shan ⌃ 89 43.27 N 126.42 E
Nanma 100 24.17 N 101.03 E
Nanmatang 100 32.18 N 120.38 E
Nanmoku 94 36.11 N 116.22 E
Nanmu, Zhg. 94 36.10 N 138.44 E
Nanmerch 262 53.13 N 3.15 W
Nanmu, Zhg. 105 39.11 N 116.22 E
Nannine 226 26.53 S 118.20 E
Nanning 102 22.48 N 108.20 E
Nanniwan 102 36.29 N 109.40 E
Nannô 94 35.13 N 136.36 E
Nannup 226 33.59 S 115.45 E
Nanny ≃ 48 53.40 N 6.14 W
Na Noi 110 18.19 N 100.43 E
Nãnole ⬟⁸ 272c 19.01 N 72.55 E
Nanoose Bay 224 49.16 N 124.12 W
Nanoose Harbour c 224 49.20 N 124.10 W
Nanoshi 272c 18.56 N 73.05 E
Nanowin ≃ 112 53.13 N 97.13 W
Nanpan ≃, Zhg. 102 24.34 N 103.04 E
Nanpan ≃, Zhg. 102 25.07 N 106.00 E
Nãnpãra 124 27.52 N 81.30 E
Nanpengchang 107 29.21 N 106.38 E
Nanpi 98 38.02 N 116.42 E
Nanpiao 104 41.12 N 120.39 E
Nanping, Zhg. 106 32.43 N 129.05 E
Nanping, Zhg. 100 26.38 N 118.10 E
Nanping, Zhg. 102 21.50 N 107.28 E
Nanping, Zhg. 102 33.07 N 104.20 E
Nanpingji 100 33.30 N 116.51 E
Nanpu 100 39.16 N 118.12 E
Nanqingtuo 105 39.37 N 117.53 E
Nanqui 104 40.44 N 122.08 E
Nanquan 98 36.24 N 120.17 E
Nanri Dao I 100 25.13 N 119.30 E
Nansa ≃ 34 43.22 N 4.29 W
Nansei 92 34.22 N 136.41 E
Nansei-shotō (Ryukyu Islands) II 90 26.30 N 128.00 E
Nansemond ⌷⁶ 208 36.43 N 76.40 W
Nansen, Lago ⌷ 254 47.57 S 72.21 W
Nan Sha I 106 31.36 N 121.22 E
Nanshahe 96 35.03 N 117.12 E
Nanshan, Zhg. 100 26.38 N 118.20 E
Nanshan, Zhg. 105 39.21 N 115.34 E
Nanshan → Qilian Shan ⌃ 102 39.06 N 98.40 E
Nanshanchengzi 96 25.34 N 116.32 E
Nanshan Island I 108 10.45 N 115.49 E
Nanshankou 102 43.09 N 93.41 E
Nanshanlingcun 105 39.09 N 117.26 E
Nanshuang Dao I 100 26.35 N 120.08 E
Nansio 154 2.08 S 33.03 E
Nansol 154 2.08 S 33.03 E
Nanstal 154 11.05 S 39.36 E
Nans-les-Pins 63 43.22 N 5.47 E
Nansunzhai 269b 31.21 N 121.27 E
Nant 63 44.01 N 3.18 E
Nant 50 47.32 N 1.41 E
Nantai 100 40.55 N 122.47 E
Nantais, Lac ⌷ 176 60.59 N 74.00 W
Nantai-san ⌃ 94 36.43 N 140.26 E
Nantai-zan ⌃ 94 36.46 N 139.29 E
Nantang 106 28.08 N 115.12 E
Nantangdun 106 31.15 N 120.56 E
Nantangmei 105 38.51 N 114.56 E
Nantasket Beach 283 42.16 N 70.52 W
Nantawara ⬟ 105 34.00 S 138.14 E
Nant Bran ≃ 262 51.57 N 3.28 W
Nanterre 58 48.53 N 2.12 E
Nantes 32 47.13 N 1.33 W
Nanteuil-le-Haudouin 50 49.08 N 2.48 E
Nanteuil-lès-Meaux 261 48.56 N 2.54 E
Nantian, Zhg. 100 27.57 N 119.56 E
Nantian, Zhg. 106 28.00 N 121.56 E
Nantianmen 104 30.36 N 123.04 E
Nanticoke, On., Can. 212 42.54 N 80.11 E
Nanticoke, Md., U.S. 208 38.16 N 75.54 W
Nanticoke, Pa., U.S. 208 41.12 N 76.00 W
Nanticoke Creek ≃, On., Can. 212 42.48 N 80.04 W
Nanticoke Creek ≃, N.Y., U.S. 210 42.16 N 76.05 W
Nantmeal Village 285 40.08 N 75.40 W
Nanton 182 50.21 N 113.46 W
Nantong, Zhg. 100 32.02 N 120.53 E
Nantou, T'aiwan 100 23.55 N 120.41 E
Nantou, Zhg. 100 22.33 N 113.55 E
Nantouillet 261 49.00 N 2.42 E
Nantschang → Nanchang 100 28.41 N 115.53 E
Nantua 63 46.09 N 5.37 E
Nantucke 32 47.13 N 1.33 W
Nantucket I 207 41.17 N 70.06 W
Nantucket ≃, Ma., U.S. 207 41.17 N 70.06 W
Nantucket Island I 207 41.16 N 70.03 W
Nantucket Sound ⨽ 207 41.30 N 70.15 W
Nantuego 154 11.21 S 38.24 E
Nantulo 154 12.17 S 39.03 E
Nantun → Nantong 106 32.02 N 120.53 E
Nanwich 94 53.04 N 2.32 W
Nanty Glo 214 40.28 N 78.49 W
Nant-y-moch Reservoir ⌷¹ 42 52.27 N 3.50 W
Nanu 146 8.50 S 142.40 E
Nanuet 210 41.05 N 74.00 W
Nanuku Passage ⨽ 175g 16.45 S 179.15 W
Nanumanga I 4 6.18 S 176.20 E
Nanumea I¹ 14 5.39 S 176.08 E
Nanuque 255 17.50 S 40.21 W
Nanusa, Kepulauan II 118 4.42 N 127.06 E
Nanushuk ≃ 180 69.19 N 151.00 W
Nan'utou 269 39.01 N 117.40 E
Nanutuo ⬟⁸ 175g 18.09 S 178.25 E
Nanwan ⬟⁸ 269d 25.09 N 121.38 E
Nan Wan c 100 22.01 N 120.46 E
Nanwenquan 107 29.26 N 106.35 E
Nanxi, Zhg. 100 31.31 N 115.38 E
Nanxi, Zhg. 107 28.50 N 104.59 E
Nanxian 100 29.21 N 112.24 E
Nanxing 100 25.10 N 114.07 E
Nanxin Hu ⌷ 105 39.11 N 115.48 E
Nanxun 100 30.53 N 120.25 E
Nanyandang Shan ⌃ 100 27.26 N 120.04 E
Nanyang, Zhg. 100 33.00 N 112.32 E
Nanyang, Zhg. 106 28.25 N 119.49 E
Nanyanggangzi 100 31.53 N 121.43 E
Nanyanggangzi 89 43.13 N 125.27 E
Nanyang Hu ⌷ 96 35.12 N 116.41 E

Nanyang Shan ⌃ 106 31.20 N 120.28 E
Nanyang Technological Institute ⬟² 271c 1.21 N 103.41 E
Nanyi Hu ⌷ 106 31.07 N 118.57 E
Nan-yô 92 38.03 N 140.10 E
Nanyu 105 25.59 N 119.14 E
Nanyu 105 39.04 N 116.22 E
Nanyuan Airport ⬟ 271a 39.47 N 116.23 E
Nanyue 100 27.13 N 112.43 E
Nanyuki 154 0.01 N 37.04 E
Nanyunlin 105 40.09 N 115.23 E
Nanzamu 98 41.56 N 124.23 E
Nanzha 106 31.51 N 120.15 E
Nanzhai 106 31.34 N 120.02 E
Nanzhang, Zhg. 100 31.50 N 111.41 E
Nanzhang, Zhg. 105 39.03 N 115.46 E
Nanzhao 100 33.30 N 112.27 E
Nanzhaoji 100 32.38 N 115.58 E
Nanzhen 106 26.59 N 119.57 E
Nanzhenjie 106 31.48 N 119.17 E
Nanzhila 154 16.05 S 26.07 E
Nanzhuang, Zhg. 105 40.43 N 114.58 E
Nanzhuang, Zhg. 106 22.28 N 88.27 E
Nao 152 4.35 N 15.09 E
NaoãBãd 272b 22.09 N 88.22 E
NaoãPãra 126 22.45 N 89.39 E
Naococoane, Lac ⌷ 176 52.52 N 70.40 W
Naoetsu 94 37.11 N 138.15 E
Naogaon 124 24.47 N 88.56 E
Naori 98 33.04 N 131.23 E
Naokot 120 24.51 N 69.27 E
Naoli ≃ 89 47.20 N 134.10 E
Naolinco 234 19.39 N 96.51 W
Não-me-Toque 252 28.28 S 52.49 W
Naong, Bukit ⌃ 112 2.40 N 112.45 E
NãopãRa 100 39.04 N 88.54 E
Naopukuria 272b 22.55 N 88.16 E
Naoshima 96 34.26 N 133.59 E
Naours 50 50.02 N 2.17 E
Nãousa 38 40.37 N 22.05 E
Naozhou Dao I 102 20.57 N 110.34 E
Napa 226 32.18 N 122.17 W
Napa ≃ 226 38.08 N 122.17 W
Napa ≃ 226 38.07 N 122.18 W
Napacao Point ➤ 116 9.43 N 124.31 E
Napajedla 30 49.10 N 17.31 E
Napakiak 180 60.42 N 161.57 W
Napaku 100 2.32 N 115.58 E
Na Pali Coast State Park ♦ 229b 22.09 N 159.41 W
Napakovo 74 70.03 N 73.47 E
Napamute 180 61.33 N 158.42 W
Napanee 212 44.15 N 76.57 W
Napanee ≃ 212 44.12 N 77.02 W
Napanoch 210 41.44 N 74.22 W
Napareuli 84 59.53 N 81.58 E
Napas 86 59.53 N 81.58 E
Napaskiak 180 60.42 N 161.45 W
Napassoq 178 63.08 N 52.27 W
Napavine 224 46.34 N 122.54 W
Napayauan Island I 116 12.22 N 123.14 E
Napê 118 18.18 N 105.06 E
Napenay 252 26.54 S 60.37 W
Naperville 186 51.21 N 58.08 W
Napetpi ≃ 185 51.21 N 58.08 W
Napido 164 0.41 S 135.23 E
Napiéolédougou 150 9.18 N 5.43 W
Napier, N.Z. 172 39.29 S 176.55 E
Napier, S. Afr. 158 34.29 S 19.53 E
Napier, Mount ⌃ 162 17.32 S 129.10 E
Napier Mountains ⌃ 6 66.30 S 53.40 E
Napierville 206 45.10 N 73.35 W
Napierville ⬟⁶ 206 45.11 N 73.27 W
Napinka 184 49.19 N 100.50 W
Naplate 216 41.20 N 88.54 W
Naples → Napoli, It. 68 40.51 N 14.17 E
Naples, Fl., U.S. 226 26.08 N 81.47 W
Naples, Id., U.S. 202 48.34 N 116.23 W
Naples, Il., U.S. 219 39.45 N 90.36 W
Naples, Tx., U.S. 210 42.36 N 77.24 W
Naples Park 220 26.16 N 81.48 W
Napo 102 23.16 N 105.54 E
Napo ≃, Chn. 246 3.20 S 72.40 W
Napo ≃, S.A. 246 3.20 S 72.40 W
Napola 70 37.59 N 12.38 E
Napoleon, In., U.S. 218 39.12 N 85.19 W
Napoleon, Ky., U.S. 218 38.46 N 84.47 W
Napoleon, Mi., U.S. 215 42.19 N 84.25 W
Napoleon, N.D., U.S. 198 46.30 N 99.46 W
Napoleon, Oh., U.S. 214 41.23 N 84.07 W
Napoleonville 194 29.56 N 91.01 W
Nápoles → Napoli 68 40.51 N 14.17 E
Napoli (Naples) 68 40.51 N 14.17 E
Napoli, Golfo di c 68 40.42 N 14.10 E
Napoli ⬟⁹ 68 40.51 N 14.17 E
Nápoli ⬟⁹ 68 40.51 N 14.17 E
Napoli ≃ 68 40.51 N 14.17 E
Napomerry 166 27.36 S 141.07 E
Napomos 216 41.26 N 86.00 W
Nappan 212 45.46 N 64.14 W
Nappanee 218 41.27 N 85.59 W
Nappan River 212 45.46 N 64.14 W
Napton on the Hill 42 52.15 N 1.24 W
Napu 115b 2.45 S 119.56 E
Napudalutai Shan ⌃ 89 51.06 N 122.13 E
Naputo ≃ 102 35.36 N 104.35 E
Naqadeh 140 36.54 N 45.23 E
Nãqb, Ra's an- ⌷ 132 30.00 N 35.40 E
Nãqb, Ra's an- ⌷ 132 30.00 N 35.40 E
Nar ≃ 42 52.45 N 0.24 E
Nara, Mali 150 15.10 N 7.17 W
Nara, Nihon 96 34.41 N 135.50 E
Nara ≃ 96 34.41 N 135.50 E
Nara □⁵, Pãk. 120 24.07 N 69.07 E
Nara ≃, Ross. 247 37.09 N 107.32 E
Nara-bonchi ⌷ 270 34.38 N 135.50 E
Naracoorte 166 36.58 S 140.44 E
Naradhan 162 33.37 S 146.19 E
Narã̃l 124 36.20 N 137.55 E
Naraina ⬟⁸ 272a 28.34 N 77.09 E
Naraini 124 25.11 N 80.29 E
Narainpur 124 20.01 N 81.26 E
Narakal 122 10.03 N 76.16 E
Naramata 182 49.36 N 119.35 W
Naran 122 16.27 N 81.40 W
Naran Bulag 88 48.34 N 98.17 E
Nãrang 124 34.11 N 70.41 E
Narangba 176 27.12 S 152.58 E
Naranjal 246 2.32 S 79.37 W
Naranjal, Ec. 246 2.42 S 79.37 W
Naranjito, Hond. 236 14.57 N 88.41 W
Naranjito, P.R. 240m 18.18 N 66.15 W
Naranjos 234 21.21 N 97.41 W
Narao 92 32.51 N 129.04 E
Nara Park ♦ 270 34.41 N 135.52 E
Nara Visa 200 35.36 N 103.06 W
Nãrã̃yanganj 124 23.37 N 90.30 E
Nãrã̃yani ≃ 124 27.15 N 84.02 E
Nãrã̃yanpet 122 16.44 N 77.30 E
Narã̃yanpur 272a 22.29 N 88.34 E
Narazeni 272b 24.57 N 88.54 E
Narberth, Wales, U.K. 42 51.48 N 4.45 W
Narberth, Pa., U.S. 285 40.00 N 75.15 W

Narbonne 32 43.11 N 3.00 E
Narcao 71 39.10 N 8.40 E
Narcea ≃ 34 43.28 N 6.06 W
Narcisco, On., Can. 275b 43.50 N 79.40 W
Narcosli Creek 182 52.49 N 122.28 W
Nardò 68 40.11 N 18.02 E
Nare ≃ 246 6.12 N 74.35 W
Narellan 170 34.02 S 150.44 E
Naremeen 162 32.04 S 118.24 E
Narenbulake 89 49.52 N 120.23 E
Narendranagar 124 30.10 N 78.18 E
Nares Strait ⨽ 16 80.30 N 68.00 W
Naretha 162 31.00 S 124.50 E
Narew 30 52.26 N 22.42 E
Narew ≃ 30 52.26 N 20.42 E
Nargund 122 15.43 N 75.23 E
Narhan 272c 19.08 N 73.07 E
Nãri 120 28.35 N 67.50 E
Naria 124 23.18 N 90.25 E
Nariai 270 35.33 N 135.14 E
Nariel 171b 36.26 S 147.50 E
Narijn ⬟ 88 52.20 N 93.24 E
Narijnteel 102 45.57 N 101.29 E
Nãsir, Buhayrat (Lake Nasser) ⌷¹ 126 23.17 N 89.21 E
Nariman 85 40.34 N 72.48 E
Narimanabad 84 38.53 N 48.52 E
Narimba, Her Majesty's Air Station (Royal Australian Navy Airfield) ⬟ 274a 33.43 S 150.53 E
Narin ⬟ 120 36.54 N 92.51 E
Narince 130 37.52 N 38.46 E
Narinda, Baie de c 157b 14.55 S 47.32 E
Nariño □⁵ 246 1.30 N 78.00 W
Narita 94 35.47 N 140.19 E
Nariwa 96 34.47 N 133.33 E
Nãrjeh 140 35.44 N 49.08 E
Narjan-Mar 24 67.39 N 53.00 E
Nãrkanda 123 31.16 N 77.27 E
Narkatiãganj 124 27.06 N 84.28 E
Närke □⁹ 40 59.06 N 15.03 E
Närkes Marieberg 40 59.12 N 15.10 E
Narli 130 37.27 N 37.09 E
Narma 80 54.46 N 42.01 E
Narmada ≃ 124 21.38 N 72.36 E
Narmada Valley ∨ 124 22.30 N 77.00 E
Narmak ⬟⁸ 267d 35.43 N 51.29 E
Narman 130 40.21 N 41.52 E
Narmušað ⬟⁸ 80 54.41 N 67.10 E
Nar-Nar-Goon 169 38.05 S 145.34 E
Nãrnaul 124 28.03 N 76.07 E
Narni 66 42.31 N 12.31 E
Naro 70 37.18 N 13.47 E
Naro ≃ 70 37.18 N 13.37 E
Naroč ≃ 76 54.26 N 26.39 E
Naroč, ozero ⌷ 76 54.52 N 26.45 E
Narodiči 78 51.13 N 29.03 E
Narodnaja, gora ⌃ 24 65.04 N 60.09 E
Naro-Fominsk 82 55.23 N 36.43 E
Naro Island I 116 11.53 N 123.40 E
Narok 154 1.05 S 35.52 E
Narol 30 50.22 N 23.21 E
Narón 34 43.32 N 8.10 W
Narooma 166 36.14 S 150.08 E
Naro-Osakovo 82 55.33 N 36.43 E
Naroväat 80 53.52 N 43.41 E
Narpes (Närpiö) 26 62.28 N 21.20 E
Närpiö → Närpes 26 62.28 N 21.20 E
Narrabeen 170 33.43 S 151.18 E
Narrabeen Lagoon c 274a 33.43 S 151.18 E
Narrabri 166 30.19 S 149.47 E
Narragansett 207 41.26 N 71.27 W
Narragansett Bay c 207 41.40 N 71.20 W
Narran ≃ 166 29.45 S 147.20 E
Narra Narra ⌃ 171b 35.50 S 147.27 E
Narrandera 166 34.45 S 146.33 E
Narraway ≃ 182 54.48 N 119.56 W
Narre Warren 274b 38.02 S 145.19 E
Narre Warren North 274b 38.01 S 145.19 E
Narromine 166 32.14 S 148.15 E
Narrows, Md., U.S. 208 39.37 N 78.57 W
Narrows, Va., U.S. 208 37.19 N 80.48 W
Narrowsburg 210 41.36 N 75.03 W
Narsingdi 124 23.55 N 90.43 E
Narsimhapur 124 22.57 N 79.12 E
Narsinghgarh 124 23.42 N 77.06 E
Narsīpatnam 122 17.40 N 82.37 E
Narskije Prudy, ozero ⌷ 82 55.32 N 36.36 E
Nartkala 76 43.33 N 43.48 E
Nartuby ≃ 63 43.28 N 6.06 E
Naru 92 32.49 N 128.56 E
Narubis, Namibia 156 27.10 S 19.05 E
Narubis, Namibia 158 26.55 S 19.05 E
Naruja 196 40.33 N 44.33 E
Naruko 94 38.45 N 140.43 E
Narusawa 268 35.29 N 138.39 E
Naruto, Nihon 95 35.36 N 140.25 E
Naruto, Nihon 96 34.10 N 134.37 E
Naruto-kaikyô ⨽ 96 34.14 N 134.39 E
Narva, Eesti 75 59.23 N 28.12 E
Narva ≃, Ross. 76 59.28 N 28.02 E
Narva ≃ 65 59.27 N 28.02 E
Narva-Jõesuu 76 59.27 N 28.02 E
Narva laht (Narvskij zaliv) c 76 59.30 N 27.40 E
Narvik 24 68.26 N 17.25 E
Narvskij zaliv (Narva laht) c 76 59.30 N 27.40 E
Narvskoje vodochranilišče ⌷¹ 76 59.18 N 28.14 E
Nãrwãna 124 29.37 N 76.07 E
Narym 84 58.54 N 81.30 E
Naryn 85 41.26 N 75.59 E
Naryn ≃, Kyrg. 85 41.30 N 76.04 E
Naryn ≃, Ross. 84 50.54 N 87.10 E
Narynkol 86 42.43 N 80.12 E
Naryntau, gory ⌃ 85 41.29 N 74.30 E
Nãrõ-zaki ➤ 92 32.35 N 128.33 E
Narzole 66 44.37 N 7.52 E
Nãs, Sve. 40 60.27 N 16.20 E
Nãs, Sve. 40 60.21 N 15.00 E
Nasadkino 82 56.29 N 37.21 E
Näsåker 24 63.23 N 16.54 E
Na San, Thai. 110 19.04 N 103.42 E
Na San, Viet 110 21.13 N 104.02 E
Nasarawa 150 8.32 N 7.43 E
Nãsãud 34 47.17 N 24.24 E
Nasavrky 60 49.51 N 15.48 E
NASA Wallops Station ⬟³ 208 37.52 N 75.28 W
Naseby → Naze 93b 28.23 N 129.30 E
Naseby, Eng., U.K. 42 52.25 N 0.59 W
Naselle 224 46.21 N 123.48 W
Nash 216 36.39 N 97.57 W
Nashawena Island I 207 41.26 N 70.56 W
Nãshik 122 19.59 N 73.48 E
Nashoba Brook ≃ 283 42.31 N 71.24 W
Nashport 214 40.04 N 82.00 W
Nashton, Lake ⌷ 194 35.50 N 118.10 W
Nashua ≃ 207 42.46 N 71.27 W
Nashuixi 102 30.09 N 108.40 E
Nãshulutasjön ⌷ 40 59.14 N 16.21 E
Nashville, On., Can. 275b 43.50 N 79.40 W
Nashville, Ar., U.S. 194 33.56 N 93.50 W
Nashville, Ga., U.S. 192 31.12 N 83.15 W
Nashville, Il., U.S. 218 38.21 N 89.22 W
Nashville, In., U.S. 218 39.12 N 86.15 W
Nashville, Mi., U.S. 215 42.36 N 85.05 W
Nashville, N.C., U.S. 192 35.58 N 77.57 W
Nashville, Oh., U.S. 214 40.36 N 82.07 W
Nashville, Tn., U.S. 194 36.09 N 86.47 W
Nashwaak ≃ 186 45.57 N 66.37 W
Nashwaaksis 186 45.59 N 66.39 W
Nashwah 142 30.30 N 31.29 E
Nashwauk 190 47.22 N 93.10 W
Nasia 150 10.09 N 0.48 E
Nasib 132 32.33 N 36.11 E
Nasice 38 45.29 N 18.06 E
Nasielsk 30 52.36 N 20.48 E
Nãsijärvi ⌷ 26 61.37 N 23.42 E
Nãsir 140 8.36 N 33.04 E
Nãsir, Buhayrat (Lake Nasser) ⌷¹ 142 22.40 N 32.00 E
Nãsirãbãd, India 120 26.18 N 74.44 E
NãsirãBãd, Pãk. 120 28.23 N 68.24 E
Naskaftym 90 52.57 N 45.38 E
Naskaupi ≃ 176 53.45 N 60.50 W
Näsnaren ⌷ 40 58.51 N 16.18 E
Naso 70 38.07 N 14.47 E
Nasondoye 154 10.22 S 25.06 E
Naso Point ➤ 116 10.25 N 117.57 E
Nasoreleu ≃ 175g 16.38 S 178.42 E
Nasosnyj 84 40.37 N 49.34 E
Nasr 142 30.36 N 30.23 E
Nasrãbãd 128 34.08 N 51.26 E
Nasrãni, Jabal an- 132 34.06 N 37.24 E
Nasridinbek 85 40.41 N 71.55 E
Nass ≃ 182 55.00 N 129.50 W
Nassau, Ba. 240b 25.05 N 77.21 W
Nassau, Dtsch. 54 50.46 N 13.32 E
Nassau, Dtsch. 56 50.19 N 7.47 E
Nassau, N.Y., U.S. 210 42.30 N 73.36 W
Nassau ≃ 210 40.45 N 73.36 W
Nassau, Bahía c 254 55.25 S 67.40 W
Nassau Bay 222 29.32 N 95.05 W
Nassau Coliseum ♦ 276 40.43 N 73.36 W
Nassau International Airport ⬟ 240b 25.02 N 77.28 W
Nassau Island I 14 11.33 S 165.25 W
Nassau Shores 276 40.39 N 73.26 W
Nassawango Creek ≃ 208 38.10 N 75.25 W
Nassenfels 60 48.48 N 11.16 E
Nassenheide 54 52.49 N 13.12 E
Nasser, Lake → Nãsir, Buhayrat 140 22.40 N 32.00 E
Nassereith 58 47.19 N 10.50 E
Nassian 150 8.27 N 3.29 W
Nãssjö 26 57.39 N 14.41 E
Nastapoca ≃ 176 56.55 N 76.33 W
Nastapoka Islands II 176 57.00 N 76.50 W
Nasträsk 82 54.28 N 38.16 E
Nastätten 56 50.12 N 7.51 E
Nastauli 272a 28.43 N 77.22 E
Nastf, Bi'r ▼⁴ 132 32.44 N 23.34 E
Nasu 94 37.01 N 140.07 E
Nasu-dake ⌃, Nihon 94 37.07 N 139.58 E
Nasu-dake ⌃, Nihon 94 37.07 N 139.58 E
Nasukoin Mountain ⌃ 202 48.48 N 114.35 W
Nasva 76 56.35 N 30.10 E
Nat ≃ 190 48.48 N 82.07 W
Nata ≃ 156 20.12 S 26.12 E
Nata, Pan. 236 8.20 N 80.31 W
Nata ≃ 156 20.14 S 26.10 E
Natagaima 250 3.37 N 75.06 W
Nãtãgarh 272b 22.42 N 88.25 E
Natal, Bra. 250 5.47 S 35.13 W
Natal, B.C., Can. 182 49.44 N 114.50 W
Natal, Indon. 110 0.33 N 99.07 E
Natal □⁴ 158 29.00 S 30.00 E
Natal Basin ⬟¹ 10 30.00 S 40.00 E
Natalia 222 29.11 N 98.51 W
Natalevka 78 47.10 N 36.35 E
Nataljin Jar 80 41.17 N 63.55 W
Natalkuz Lake ⌷ 182 52.56 N 125.20 W
Natalspruit ≃ 273d 26.17 S 28.05 E
Natanes Plateau ▼⁷ 200 33.35 N 110.15 W
Natashi, Wãdī ∨ 132 28.25 N 34.55 E
Natashquan 176 50.11 N 61.49 W
Natashquan ≃ 176 50.06 N 61.49 W
Natashquan, Pointe de ➤ 186 50.06 N 61.44 W
Natashquan Est ≃ 186 50.11 N 61.44 W
Natchez 194 31.33 N 91.24 W
Natchez Trace Parkway ♦ 194 32.00 N 91.00 W
Natchitoches 194 31.45 N 93.05 W
Natco Lake ⌷ 276 40.26 N 74.02 W
Natércia 256 22.07 S 45.30 W
Naters 62 46.20 N 7.59 E
Naterei 256 46.20 N 7.59 E
Nathalia 162 36.03 S 145.13 E
Nathdwãra 124 24.56 N 73.49 E
Nathenje 154 14.00 S 33.37 E
Nathkaw 102 24.04 N 96.11 E
Nathula ⨽ 175g 15.43 S 177.25 E
Natick 207 42.17 N 71.21 W
National Laboratories ⬟ 283 42.17 N 71.21 W
Natimuk 166 36.45 S 141.57 E
Nation ≃ 182 55.30 N 123.32 W
National Agricultural Research Center ⬟ 284c 39.02 N 76.52 W
National Airport ⬟ 281 42.19 N 83.25 W
National Arboretum ⬟ 284c 38.54 N 76.58 W
National Assembly ♦ 269a 13.46 N 100.31 E
National Baseball Hall of Fame and Museum ♦ 210 42.42 N 74.57 W
National City 226 32.40 N 117.05 W
National Gallery ♦ 260 51.31 N 0.08 W
National Institute of Health ♦ 284c 39.00 N 77.06 W
National Maritime Museum ♦ 260 51.29 N 0.00
National Park 285 51.29 N 75.10 W
National Taiwan Normal University ♦ 269d 25.02 N 121.31 E
National Taiwan University ♦ 269d 25.01 N 121.32 E
National Zoological Park ♦ 284c 38.56 N 77.03 W
Natipi, Lac ⌷ 186 51.27 N 71.23 W
Natisone ≃ 64 45.57 N 13.22 E
Nativitas 214 19.14 N 98.20 W
Nativity, Church of the ♦ 132 31.43 N 35.12 E
Natõrp 40 55.18 N 97.32 W

	English	Deutsch			
⌃ Mountain	Berg	Montaña	Montagne	Montanha
⌃ Mountains	Gebirge	Montañas	Montagnes	Montanhas
⨽ Pass	Paß	Paso	Col	Passo
∨ Valley, Canyon	Tal, Cañon	Valle, Cañón	Vallée, Canyon	Vale, Canhão
≃ Plain	Ebene	Llano	Plaine	Planície
➤ Cape	Kap	Cabo	Cap	Cabo
I Island	Insel	Isla	Île	Ilha
II Islands	Inseln	Islas	Îles	Ilhas
⬟ Other Topographic Features	Andere Topographische Objekte	Otros Elementos Topográficos	Autres données topographiques	Outros acidentes topográficos

Nattai ≃ 170 34.05 S 150.25 E
Nattai River 170 34.04 S 150.27 E
Nattam 122 10.14 N 78.14 E
Nattarö I 40 58.52 N 18.07 E
Nattaset ▲ 24 68.12 N 27.20 E
Nattaung ▲ 110 18.48 N 97.02 E
Natters 64 47.14 N 11.22 E
Nattwerder 264a 52.26 N 12.56 E
Natuchajevskaja 78 44.54 N 37.34 E
Nātudaha 126 23.39 N 88.41 E
Natukanaoka Pan ≃ 156 18.40 S 15.45 E
Natuna Besar I 112 4.00 N 108.15 E
Natuna Besar, Kepulauan II 112 4.40 N 108.00 E
Natuna Selatan, Kepulauan II 112 2.45 N 109.00 E
Natural Bridge 212 44.04 N 75.29 W
Natural Bridge ♦ 192 37.38 N 79.33 W
Natural Bridges National Monument ♦ 200 37.30 N 110.08 W
Natural Bridge State Resort Park ♦ 192 37.47 N 33.42 W
Naturaliste, Cape > 162 33.32 S 115.01 E
Naturaliste Channel ⴑ 162 25.25 S 113.00 E
Naturita 200 38.13 N 108.34 W
Naturita Creek ≃ 200 38.13 N 108.32 W
Naturno (Naturns) 64 46.39 N 11.00 E
Natzungen 52 51.36 N 9.14 E
Nau 85 40.09 N 69.22 E
Nau, Cap de la > 34 38.44 N 0.14 E
Naucalpan de Juárez 286a 19.28 N 99.14 W
Naucelle 32 44.12 N 2.20 E
Naučnyj 78 44.44 N 34.01 E
Naude 272c 19.03 N 73.06 E
Nauders 58 46.53 N 10.30 E
Nauen 54 52.36 N 12.52 E
Nauener Luch ⊠ 264a 52.37 N 12.55 E
Nauener Stadtforst ♦ 264a 52.38 N 12.58 E
Naugachhia 124 25.24 N 87.06 E
Naugatuck 207 41.30 N 73.05 W
Naugatuck ≃ 207 41.19 N 73.05 W
Naughton 190 46.24 N 81.12 W
Naugol'noje 82 56.22 N 38.11 E
Naui 140 18.28 N 30.43 E
Naujamiestis 76 55.41 N 24.04 E
Naujan 116 13.20 N 121.18 E
Naujan, Lake ◎ 116 13.10 N 121.21 E
Naujoji Akmenė 76 56.19 N 22.55 E
Naukan 180 66.01 N 169.43 W
Naulavaara ▲[2] 26 63.53 N 29.13 E
Naulila 152 17.12 S 14.42 E
Naumburg, Dtsch. 54 51.09 N 11.48 E
Naumburg, Dtsch. 56 51.15 N 9.10 E
Naumovščina 76 58.23 N 23.20 E
Naunak 86 59.00 N 83.13 E
Naundorf 54 50.56 N 13.25 E
Naungion 110 16.48 N 97.45 E
Naungpale 110 19.33 N 97.08 E
Naunhof 54 51.16 N 12.35 E
Naupada ✈[8] 272c 19.04 N 72.50 E
Nā'ūr 132 31.53 N 35.50 E
Naurauhaun Brook ≃ 276 41.03 N 73.59 W
Nauroth 56 50.42 N 7.52 E
Nauroz Kalāt 128 28.47 N 65.38 E
Naurskaja 84 43.38 N 45.19 E
Nauru □[1], Oc. 14 0.32 S 166.55 E
Nauru □[1], Oc. 174b 0.32 S 166.55 E
Naurzumskij zapovednik ♦ 86 51.30 N 64.20 E
Naushahro Firoz 120 26.50 N 68.07 E
Naushon Island I 207 41.29 N 70.45 W
Nauški 88 50.28 N 106.07 E
Nausori 175g 18.02 S 178.32 E
Naussac, Barrage de ⚓[6] 62 44.46 N 3.49 E
Naustdal 26 61.31 N 5.43 E
Nauta 246 4.32 S 73.33 W
Nautanwa 124 27.26 N 83.25 E
Nautilus Park 207 41.22 N 72.05 W
Nautla 234 20.13 N 96.47 W
Nauvoo 190 40.33 N 91.23 W
Nava, It. 62 44.06 N 7.22 E
Nava, Méx. 232 28.25 N 100.46 W
Nava, Arroyo de la ≃ 266a 40.31 N 3.46 W
Nava, Colle di ⟩(62 44.05 N 7.53 E
Nava del Rey 34 41.20 N 5.05 W
Navadwip 126 23.25 N 88.22 E
Navahermosa 34 39.38 N 4.28 W
Navajo 200 35.55 N 109.01 W
Navajo ≃ 200 37.01 N 107.10 W
Navajo Creek ≃ 200 36.59 N 111.24 W
Navajo Hopi Joint Use Area ✈[4] 200 36.15 N 110.30 W
Navajo Indian Reservation ✈[4] 200 36.25 N 110.00 W
Navajo Mountain ▲ 200 37.02 N 110.52 W
Navajo National Monument ♦ 200 36.40 N 110.33 W
Navajo Reservoir ◎[1] 200 36.55 N 107.30 W
Naval 116 11.34 N 124.23 E
Navalmoral de la Mata 34 39.54 N 5.32 W
Naval Ordnance Test Station ■ 228 35.32 N 117.05 W
Navalvillar de Pela 34 39.06 N 5.28 W
Navan 48 53.39 N 6.41 W
Navāpur 122 21.09 N 73.48 E
Navarin, mys > 180 62.16 N 179.10 E
Navarino — Pílos 38 36.55 N 21.43 E
Navarino, Isla I 254 55.05 S 67.40 W
Navarra □[4] 34 42.40 N 1.30 W
Navarre, Austl. 169 36.54 S 143.07 E
Navarre, Oh., U.S. 214 40.43 N 81.31 W
Navarro 258 35.01 S 59.16 W
Navarro □[6] 222 32.05 N 96.30 W
Navarro ≃ 204 39.11 N 123.45 W
Navarro, Cañada ≃ 258 35.00 S 59.18 W
Navarro, Laguna ◎ 258 35.01 S 59.18 W
Navarro Mills Lake ◎[1] 222 31.56 N 96.45 W
Navašino 80 55.32 N 42.12 E
Navasota 222 30.23 N 96.05 W
Navasota ≃ 222 30.20 N 96.09 W
Navassa 192 34.15 N 78.00 W
Navassa Island I 238 18.24 N 75.01 W
Nave 64 45.35 N 10.17 E
Navekvarn 40 58.38 N 16.49 E
Navenne 58 47.36 N 6.10 E
Naver ≃ 46 58.32 N 4.15 W
Naver, Loch ◎ 46 58.17 N 4.23 W
Navesink 276 40.24 N 74.02 W
Navesink River ⊂ 276 40.23 N 73.58 W
Navesnoje 76 52.17 N 37.57 E
Nāves-Parmelan 58 45.56 N 6.11 E
Navesti ≃ 76 58.30 N 24.54 E
Navestock 260 51.39 N 0.13 E
Navestock Side 260 51.39 N 0.16 E
Navia, Arg. 252 34.47 S 66.35 W
Navia, Esp. 34 43.32 N 6.43 W
Navia ≃ 34 43.33 N 6.44 W
Navidad 252 33.57 S 71.50 W
Navidad ≃ 196 28.41 N 96.35 W
Navidad, Bahía de ⊂ 234 19.17 N 104.50 W
Navidad Bank ✈[3] 238 20.00 N 68.50 W
Navío, Riacho do ≃ 250 8.39 S 38.36 W
Navirai 255 23.08 S 54.13 W
Navis 64 47.07 N 11.32 E
Naviti I 175g 17.07 S 177.15 E
Navl'a 76 52.51 N 34.30 E
Navl'a ≃ 76 52.42 N 34.01 E
Navodari 38 44.19 N 28.36 E
Navoi 72 40.15 N 65.15 E
Navojoa 232 27.06 N 109.26 W
Navolato 232 24.47 N 107.42 W
Navoloki 80 57.28 N 41.59 E
Navotas 269f 14.39 N 120.57 E
Návpaktos 38 38.23 N 21.50 E

Návplion 38 37.34 N 22.48 E
Navrongo 150 10.54 N 1.06 W
Navsāri 120 20.51 N 72.55 E
Navua 175g 18.14 S 178.10 E
Navy Island I 284a 43.04 N 79.01 W
Navy Pier ✈[5] 278 41.53 N 87.36 W
Navy Yard City 224 47.32 N 122.41 W
Nawa, Nihon 96 35.30 N 133.30 E
Nawa — Naha, Nihon 174m 26.13 N 127.40 E
Nawā, Sūrīy. 132 32.53 N 36.03 E
Nawābganj, Bngl. 124 24.36 N 88.17 E
Nawābganj, Bngl. 126 23.40 N 90.10 E
Nawābganj, India 124 28.33 N 79.38 E
Nawābganj, India 124 26.52 N 82.08 E
Nawābganj, India 124 26.56 N 81.13 E
Nawābshāh 120 26.15 N 68.25 E
Nawāda 124 24.53 N 85.32 E
Nāwah 120 32.19 N 67.53 E
Nawa Kot 120 28.20 N 71.22 E
Nawalapitiya 122 7.03 N 80.32 E
Nawalgarh 120 27.51 N 75.16 E
Nawān Kot 123 31.06 N 71.32 E
Nawanshahr 123 31.07 N 76.08 E
Nawāpāra, Bngl. 126 23.02 N 89.23 E
Nawāpāra, India 122 20.58 N 81.51 E
Nawāpāra, India 126 23.29 N 88.15 E
Nawasā al-Ghayṭ 132 30.58 N 31.19 E
Nawāshahr 123 34.10 N 73.16 E
Nawāṣīf, Harrat ⊥[9] 144 21.20 N 42.10 E
Nawāy 142 27.47 N 30.46 E
Nawiliwili Bay ⊂ 229b 21.57 N 159.21 W
Nawinda Kuta 152 16.25 S 24.28 E
Nawon-ni 98 36.25 N 126.40 E
Naxera 208 37.20 N 76.27 W
Naxi 107 28.47 N 105.22 E
Náxos 38 37.06 N 25.23 E
Náxos I 38 37.02 N 25.35 E
Naxos ⊥ 70 37.49 N 15.17 E
Nayābās 272a 28.35 N 77.19 E
Nayāgaon 126 23.32 N 90.46 E
Nayāgarh 120 20.08 N 85.06 E
Nayāgrām 126 22.02 N 87.11 E
Nayak 120 34.44 N 66.57 E
Nayāpāra 126 21.35 N 87.01 E
Nayarit 204 32.20 N 115.19 W
Nayarit □[3] 234 22.00 N 105.00 W
Nayau Island I 175g 17.58 S 179.03 W
Nāy Band, Īrān 128 32.20 N 57.34 E
Nāy Band, Īrān 128 27.23 N 52.38 E
Nāy Band, Kūh-e ▲ 128 32.26 N 57.22 E
Nayland 42 51.59 N 0.52 E
Naylor 194 36.34 N 90.36 W
Nayong 102 26.50 N 105.13 E
Nayoro 92a 44.21 N 142.28 E
Nazāll Tāhā 142 28.11 N 30.42 E
Nazaré, Bra. 250 6.23 S 47.40 W
Nazaré, Bra. 255 13.02 S 39.00 W
Nazaré, Port. 34 39.36 N 9.04 W
Nazaré da Mata 250 7.44 S 35.14 W
Nazaré do Piauí 250 6.59 S 42.40 W
Nazareno 256 21.13 S 44.37 W
Nazaré Paulista 256 23.11 S 46.24 W
Nazareth, Bel. 50 50.58 N 3.36 E
Nazareth, Pa., U.S. 208 40.44 N 75.18 W
Nazareth, Vanuatu 175f 15.29 S 168.10 E
Nazareth — Nazerat, Yis. 132 32.42 N 35.18 E
Nazareth Bank ✈[4] 12 14.30 S 60.45 E
Nazário 255 16.36 S 49.54 W
Nazarjevo, Ross. 82 55.22 N 36.24 E
Nazarjevo, Ross. 265b 55.59 N 37.16 E
Nazarovo 86 56.01 N 90.26 E
Nazarovskij 78 49.33 N 40.56 E
Nazas 232 25.14 N 104.08 W
Nazas ≃ 232 25.35 N 105.00 W
Nazca 248 14.50 S 74.57 W
Nazca Ridge ✈[3] 18 22.00 S 82.00 W
Naze 93b 28.23 N 129.30 E
Nazeing 260 51.44 N 0.03 E
N'azepetrovsk 86 56.03 N 59.36 E
Nazerat (Nazareth) 132 32.42 N 35.18 E
Nazerat 'Illit 132 32.42 N 35.19 E
Nazija 76 59.50 N 31.35 E
Nazik Gölü ◎ 130 38.50 N 42.16 E
Nazilli 130 37.55 N 28.21 E
Nazimicha 265b 55.59 N 38.06 E
Nazimiye 130 39.11 N 39.50 E
Nazimovo 86 59.30 N 90.58 E
Nazina 86 60.07 N 78.52 E
Nazino 120 26.55 N 94.44 E
Nāzir Hāt 120 22.38 N 91.47 E
Nāzirpur 126 22.43 N 89.58 E
Nazko ≃ 182 53.07 N 123.34 W
Nazlat al-'Amūdayn 142 28.14 N 30.42 E
Nazlat al-Baḥḥāriyah 142 27.40 N 30.44 E
Nazlat as-Sammān 273c 29.59 N 31.08 E
Nazlat Khalīfah 273c 30.01 N 31.10 E
Nazlat Quftan Bāshā 142 28.57 N 30.49 E
Nazlat Thābit 142 28.25 N 30.47 E
Nazran' 84 43.13 N 44.46 E
Nazret 144 8.33 N 39.16 E
Nazyvajevsk 86 55.34 N 71.21 E
N. B. C. Studios ✈[3] 280 34.09 N 118.20 W
Nchelenge 154 9.21 S 28.44 E
Ncue 152 2.01 N 10.28 E
Ndabala 154 13.28 S 29.50 E
Ndala 154 4.46 S 33.16 E
N'dalatando 152 9.18 S 14.54 E
Ndali 150 9.51 N 2.43 E
Ndanda 152 5.12 N 22.21 E
Ndande 150 15.16 N 16.30 W
Ndarassa 152 6.49 N 22.15 E
Ndélé 146 8.24 N 20.39 E
Ndélélé 152 4.02 N 14.56 E
Ndemba 152 0.11 N 14.19 E
Ndendé 152 2.23 S 11.23 E
Ndikiniméki 152 4.46 N 10.50 E
Ndindi 152 3.46 S 11.09 E
N'Djamena 146 12.07 N 15.03 E
Ndji ≃ 152 6.47 N 22.14 E
Ndjili ✈[8] 273b 4.20 S 15.22 E
Ndjili ≃ 273b 4.20 S 15.23 E
Ndjili, Grande Île de la I 273b 4.19 S 15.24 E
Ndjim ≃ 152 4.38 N 11.24 E
Ndjo 152 1.15 S 14.30 E
Ndjolé 152 0.11 S 10.45 E
Ndogo, Lagune ⊂ 152 2.35 S 10.00 E
Ndola 154 12.58 S 28.38 E
Ndolo ✈[8] 273b 4.19 S 15.19 E
Ndoma 115b 8.46 S 121.45 E
Ndongo 152 2.19 S 13.38 E
Ndouba 152 0.11 S 14.09 E
Ndougou 152 1.39 S 9.40 E
Ndu 152 4.41 N 22.49 E
Nduguti 154 4.18 S 34.42 E
Nduindui 175f 15.24 S 167.46 E
Ndumbwe 154 10.14 S 39.58 E
Ndumu Game Reserve ✈[4] 158 26.53 S 32.15 E
Nduye 154 1.50 N 29.01 E
Ne 268 35.47 N 140.03 E
Nea ≃ 26 63.13 N 11.02 E
Neabul Creek ≃ 166 27.45 S 147.20 E
Néa Erithraía 267c 38.05 N 23.49 E
Néa Filadhélfia 267c 38.02 N 23.44 E
Neagari 94 36.27 N 136.27 E
Neagh, Lough ◎ 48 54.38 N 6.24 W
Neah Bay 224 48.22 N 124.37 W
Néa Ionía 267c 38.02 N 23.45 E
Neajlov ≃ 38 44.11 N 26.12 E
Néa Khalkidhón 267c 38.02 N 23.43 E
Neale, Lake ◎ 162 24.22 S 130.00 E
Neales ≃ 162 23.08 S 136.47 E
Neales Flat 168b 34.15 S 139.10 E
Néa Liósia 267c 38.02 N 23.42 E
Neamṭ □[6] 38 47.00 N 26.30 E

Neandertal, Naturschutzgebiet ♦ 263 51.15 N 7.00 E
Néa Páfos (Paphos) 130 34.45 N 32.25 E
Neapel — Napoli 68 40.51 N 14.17 E
Néa Pendéli 267c 38.04 N 23.52 E
Néa Péramos 267c 38.00 N 23.26 E
Neápolis, Ellás 38 36.30 N 23.04 E
Neápolis, Ellás 38 35.15 N 25.37 E
Neapolis, Oh., U.S. 216 41.29 N 83.52 W
Near Islands II 181a 52.40 N 173.30 E
Near North Side ✈[8] 278 41.54 N 87.38 W
Néa Smírni 267c 37.57 N 23.43 E
Neasons Hill 214 41.37 N 80.08 W
Neatahwanta, Lake ◎ 210 43.18 N 76.27 W
Neath 42 51.40 N 3.48 W
Neath ≃ 42 51.37 N 3.50 W
Neauphle-le-Château 50 48.49 N 1.54 E
Neauphle-le-Vieux 261 48.49 N 1.52 E
Neavitt 208 38.43 N 76.16 W
Neba 94 35.15 N 137.35 E
Nebaj 236 15.24 N 91.08 W
Nebbou 150 11.18 N 1.53 W
Nebelhorn ▲ 58 47.25 N 10.20 E
Nebesnaja, gora ▲ 86 43.19 N 80.44 E
Nebeur 36 36.17 N 8.47 E
Nebine Creek ≃ 166 29.07 S 146.56 E
Nebit-Dag 128 39.30 N 54.22 E
Neblina, Pico da ▲ 246 0.48 N 66.02 W
Nebo 194 39.27 N 90.47 W
Nebo, Mount ▲, Ut, U.S. 200 39.49 N 111.46 W
Nebo, Mount — Nabā, Jabal an- ▲, Urd. 132 31.46 N 35.45 E
Nebolči 76 59.08 N 33.18 E
Nebra 54 51.17 N 11.34 E
Nebraska 218 39.04 N 85.28 W
Nebraska □[3], U.S. 178 41.30 N 100.00 W
Nebraska □[3], U.S. 198 41.30 N 100.00 W
Nebraska City 198 40.40 N 95.51 W
Nebrodi ▲ 70 37.54 N 14.35 E
Nebyloje 80 56.22 N 39.59 E
Nečajannoje 78 46.57 N 31.33 E
Nečajevka 80 53.17 N 44.27 E
Nečajevo 82 54.42 N 37.23 E
Necaxa ≃ 234 20.16 N 97.27 W
Necedah 190 44.01 N 90.04 W
Nechajevskij 80 50.25 N 41.44 E
Nechako ≃ 182 53.56 N 122.42 W
Nechako Plateau ⊀[1] 182 54.00 N 124.30 W
Nechako Range ⊀ 182 53.20 N 124.30 W
Nechako Reservoir ◎[1] 182 53.25 N 125.10 W
Neche 198 48.59 N 97.33 W
Neches 222 31.52 N 95.30 W
Neches ≃ 194 29.55 N 93.52 W
Nechí 246 8.07 N 74.46 W
Nechí ≃ 246 8.08 N 74.46 W
Nechisar National Park ♦ 144 6.00 N 37.50 E
Nechmeya 36 36.36 N 7.31 E
Nechranická Přehradová Nádrž ◎[1] 54 50.20 N 13.20 E
Nechvorošča 78 49.09 N 34.44 E
Neckar ≃ 30 49.31 N 8.26 E
Neckarbischofsheim 56 49.17 N 8.57 E
Neckarelz 56 49.20 N 9.06 E
Neckargemünd 56 49.23 N 8.47 E
Neckarsteinach 56 49.25 N 8.53 E
Neckarsulm 56 49.12 N 9.13 E
Neckartailfingen 56 48.36 N 9.16 E
Neckartenzlingen 56 48.35 N 9.14 E
Neck Creek ≃ 276 40.36 N 74.12 W
Necker 284b 39.23 N 76.29 W
Necker Island I, Br. Vir. Is. 240m 18.33 N 64.21 W
Necker Island I, Hi., U.S. 14 23.35 N 164.42 W
Necker Ridge ✈[3] 14 22.00 N 167.15 W
Necochea 252 38.33 S 58.45 W
Necrópolis ✈ 266a 40.25 N 3.38 W
Nedalssjön ◎ 26 62.56 N 12.11 E
Nedančiči 78 51.30 N 30.37 E
Ned Brown Preserve ♦ 278 42.02 N 88.01 W
Nedel'noje 82 54.50 N 36.39 E
Nederland 194 29.58 N 93.59 W
Nederland — Netherlands □[1] 30 52.15 N 5.30 E
Nederlandse Antillen — Netherlands Antilles □[2] 241s 12.15 N 69.00 W
Neder-Rijn ≃[1] 52 51.58 N 5.20 E
Nederweert 52 51.17 N 5.45 E
Nederzwalm-Hermelgem 50 50.53 N 3.41 E
Nedlands 168a 31.59 S 115.49 E
Nedlitz 54 52.04 N 12.14 E
Nedlitz ✈[8] 264a 52.26 N 13.03 E
Nědong 120 29.14 N 91.46 E
Nedre Soppero 24 68.01 N 21.44 E
Nedre Vättern ◎ 40 58.49 N 15.44 E
Nedrigajlov 78 50.50 N 33.53 E
Nédroma 148 35.01 N 1.45 W
Nedrow 210 42.58 N 76.08 W
Nedstrand 26 59.21 N 5.51 E
Neebish Island I 190 46.16 N 84.09 W
Neede 52 52.08 N 6.36 E
Needham, In., U.S. 218 39.32 N 85.58 W
Needham, Ma., U.S. 207 42.17 N 71.14 W
Needham Market 42 52.09 N 1.03 E
Needhams Point > 241g 13.05 N 59.36 W
Needle Mountain ▲ 202 44.05 N 109.37 W
Needles 204 34.50 N 114.36 W
Needling Hill ▲[2] 168a 21.53 S 116.56 E
Needville 222 29.23 N 95.50 W
Neelyton 214 40.10 N 77.50 W
Ñeembucú □[5] 252 27.00 S 58.00 W
Neenah 190 44.11 N 88.27 W
Neepawa 184 50.13 N 99.29 W
Neerabup National Park ♦ 168a 31.41 S 115.43 E
Neerim South 169 38.01 S 145.58 E
Neermoor 52 53.18 N 7.26 E
Neeroeteren 56 51.05 N 5.42 E
Neerpelt 56 51.13 N 5.25 E
Neersen 263 51.15 N 6.29 E
Nee Soon 271c 1.24 N 103.49 E
Neetze 52 53.20 N 10.36 E
Neetze ≃ 54 53.20 N 10.36 E
Nefedjevo, Ross. 82 54.39 N 37.56 E
Nefedjevo, Ross. 265b 55.54 N 37.10 E
Neffs 208 40.42 N 75.37 W
Neffsville 208 40.06 N 76.18 W
Nef'odovo 86 58.48 N 72.34 E
Neftçala 84 39.23 N 49.16 E
Neftegorsk 84 44.22 N 39.42 E
Neftekumsk 84 44.45 N 44.58 E
Nefyn 42 52.57 N 4.31 W
Nefza 36 36.58 N 9.05 E
Negage 152 7.45 S 15.16 E
Negala 150 12.52 N 8.27 W
Negapatam — Nāgappattinam 122 10.46 N 79.50 E
Negara, Indon. 115a 8.22 S 114.37 E
Negara, Indon. 112 3.00 S 114.45 E
Negara ≃ 112 3.00 S 114.45 E
Negast 54 54.15 N 13.01 E
Negaunee 190 46.29 N 87.36 W
Negba 132 31.40 N 34.41 E
Negele 144 5.20 N 39.36 E
Negenborn 52 51.53 N 9.34 E
Negeribatin 112 4.35 S 104.32 E
Negeri Sembilan □[3] 114 2.45 N 102.10 E

Negev Desert — HaNegev ✈[1] 132 30.30 N 34.55 E
Negishi 268 35.51 N 139.23 E
Negley 214 40.47 N 80.32 W
Negola 152 14.10 S 14.30 E
Negomano 154 11.27 S 38.31 E
Negombo 122 7.13 N 79.50 E
Negoreloje 76 53.36 N 27.04 E
Negotin 38 44.14 N 22.32 E
Negra, Laguna ◎ 252 34.03 S 53.40 W
Negra, Punta >, 256 22.58 S 42.42 W
Negra, Punta >, Belize 232 16.17 N 88.34 W
Negra, Punta >, Perú 248 6.06 S 81.09 W
Negrais 266c 38.53 N 9.17 W
Negras, Lomas ▲[2] 286d 11.55 S 77.06 W
Negreira 34 42.54 N 8.44 W
Nègres, Pointe des > 240e 14.36 N 61.06 W
Negrești 38 46.50 N 27.27 E
Negrești-Oaș 38 47.52 N 23.25 E
Negritos 246 4.38 S 81.19 W
Negro ≃, Arg. 254 41.02 S 62.47 W
Negro ≃, Bol. 248 9.49 S 65.42 W
Negro ≃, Bol. 248 14.11 S 63.07 W
Negro ≃, Bra. 248 5.15 S 70.53 W
Negro ≃, Bra. 248 19.13 S 57.17 W
Negro ≃, Bra. 250 9.15 S 47.34 W
Negro ≃, Bra. 252 26.01 S 50.30 W
Negro ≃, Col. 246 5.44 N 74.39 W
Negro ≃, N.A. 236 13.02 N 87.17 W
Negro ≃, Para. 252 24.23 S 57.11 W
Negro ≃, S.A. 246 3.08 S 59.55 W
Negro ≃, S.A. 252 33.24 S 58.22 W
Negro, Baia del ⊂ 144 7.55 N 49.55 E
Negro, Cerro ▲, Arg. 254 44.09 S 69.30 W
Negro, Cerro ▲, Arg. 254 46.55 S 70.12 W
Negro, Cerro ▲, Méx. 234 17.19 N 97.25 W
Negro, Mar — Black Sea ✈[2] 22 43.00 N 35.00 E
Negros I 116 10.00 N 123.00 E
Negros Occidental □[4] 116 10.20 N 123.00 E
Negros Oriental □[4] 116 9.40 N 123.00 E
Negru-Vodă 38 43.50 N 28.12 E
Neguac 186 47.15 N 65.05 W
Nehalem 224 45.43 N 123.53 W
Nehalem ≃ 224 45.40 N 123.56 W
Nehawka 198 40.49 N 95.59 W
Nehbandān 128 31.32 N 60.02 E
Neheim-Hüsten 56 51.27 N 7.57 E
Nehonsey Brook ≃ 285 39.49 N 75.18 W
Néhoué, Baie de ⊂ 175f 20.21 S 164.09 E
Nehru Planetarium ♦ 272c 18.59 N 72.49 E
Neiba 238 18.28 N 71.25 W
Neichiang — Neijiang 107 29.35 N 105.03 E
Neidpath 184 50.13 N 107.15 W
Neiges, Crêt de la ▲ 58 46.16 N 5.56 E
Neiges, Piton des ▲ 157c 21.05 S 55.29 E
Neihart 202 46.56 N 110.44 W
Neihe ≃ 100 22.54 N 115.38 E
Neihu 269d 25.05 N 121.34 E
Neihuang 98 35.59 N 114.55 E
Neijiang 107 29.35 N 105.03 E
Neikiang — Neijiang 107 29.35 N 105.03 E
Neilburg 184 52.50 N 109.38 W
Neillsville 190 44.33 N 90.35 W
Neilston 46 55.47 N 4.27 W
Neimen 263 51.29 N 7.48 E
Nei Monggol Zizhiqu (Inner Mongolia) □[4] 90 43.00 N 115.00 E
Nein 132 32.38 N 35.21 E
Neindorf 54 52.20 N 10.50 E
Neinstedt 54 51.45 N 11.05 E
Neiqiu 98 37.17 N 114.31 E
Neira 246 5.10 N 75.32 W
Neirone 62 44.27 N 9.11 E
Neishuihan 269d 25.09 N 121.43 E
Neisse (Nysa Łużycka) (Nisa) ≃ 30 52.04 N 14.46 E
Neiva 246 2.56 N 75.18 W
Neiwufuquan 105 40.11 N 117.39 E
Neixiang 102 33.05 N 111.50 E
Neixpa ≃ 234 18.05 N 102.46 W
Neizeng Shan ▲ 100 24.02 N 117.32 E
Neja, Ross. 80 58.24 N 46.31 E
Neja, Ross. 80 58.18 N 43.54 E
Neja ≃ 80 57.48 N 43.42 E
Nejapa de Madero 234 16.37 N 95.59 W
Nejd — Najd ⊀[9] 118 25.00 N 44.30 E
Nejdek 54 50.17 N 12.42 E
Nejo 144 9.30 N 35.30 E
Nejva ≃ 86 57.54 N 62.18 E
Nejvo-Šajtanskij 86 57.44 N 61.15 E
Nekalagba 154 2.50 N 28.01 E
Nekemte 144 9.02 N 36.31 E
Nekhab ⊥ 140 25.07 N 32.48 E
Nekoosa 190 44.18 N 89.54 W
Nekor, Oued ≃ 34 35.14 N 3.45 W
Neko-zaki > 96 35.40 N 134.46 E
Nekrasino 82 56.18 N 36.33 E
Nekrasovka 265b 55.41 N 37.56 E
Nekrasovo, Ross. 80 51.10 N 45.18 E
Nekrasovo, Ross. 82 56.14 N 40.31 E
Nekrasovskoje 80 57.41 N 40.22 E
Nekselø I 41 55.47 N 11.18 E
Neksø 41 55.04 N 15.09 E
Nela Park ♦ 279a 41.33 N 81.33 W
Nel'aty 88 56.29 N 115.41 E
Nelichu ▲ 140 6.08 N 34.25 E
Nelidovo 76 56.13 N 32.46 E
Neligh 198 42.07 N 98.01 W
Nel'kan 74 57.40 N 136.13 E
Nell 214 40.20 N 82.04 W
Nellie 122 11.46 N 79.41 E
Nellikuppam 122 11.46 N 79.41 E
Nellingen 56 48.33 N 9.47 E
Nellis Air Force Base ■ 204 36.14 N 115.02 W
Nelliston 210 42.56 N 74.37 W
Nellis Weapons Range ■ 204 37.15 N 116.20 W
Nellore 122 14.26 N 79.58 E
Nel'ma 89 47.39 N 139.05 E
Nelson, B.C., Can. 182 49.29 N 117.17 W
Nelson, N.Z. 172 41.17 S 173.17 E
Nelson, Eng., U.K. 44 53.51 N 2.13 W
Nelson, Ne., U.S. 198 40.12 N 98.04 W
Nelson, Pa., U.S. 210 41.59 N 77.14 W
Nelson ≃ 184 57.04 N 92.30 W
Nelson, Cape >, Austl. 166 38.26 S 141.33 E
Nelson, Cape >, Pap. N. Gui. 164 9.00 S 149.15 E
Nelson, Estrecho ⴑ 254 51.37 S 75.00 W
Nelson Creek ≃ 222 30.56 N 95.31 W
Nelson House 184 55.47 N 98.51 W
Nelson Island I 180 60.35 N 164.45 W
Nelson-Kennedy Ledges State Park ♦ 214 41.18 N 81.04 W
Nelson Lakes National Park ♦ 172 41.50 S 172.40 E
Nelson Reservoir ◎[1] 202 48.30 N 107.34 W
Nelson's Dockyard ⊥ 240c 17.00 N 61.46 W
Nelsonville, N.Y., U.S. 210 41.25 N 73.57 W
Nelsonville, Oh., U.S. 188 39.27 N 82.14 W
Nelspoort 158 32.07 S 23.00 E
Nelspoortjie 158 29.58 S 22.25 E
Nelspruit 156 25.30 S 30.58 E
Nêma, Maur. 150 16.37 N 7.15 W
Nema, Ross. 80 57.31 N 50.31 E
Nêma, Dahr ⊥[4] 150 16.40 N 7.13 W
Nemadji ≃ 190 46.41 N 92.02 W
Nemah 224 46.31 N 123.51 W
Nemaha 198 40.20 N 95.40 W
Neman 76 55.02 N 22.02 E

Neman (Nemunas) ≃ 76 55.18 N 21.23 E
Nematābād ✈[8] 267d 35.38 N 51.21 E
Nembe 150 4.35 N 6.26 E
Nembrala 112 10.53 S 122.50 E
Nembro 62 45.45 N 9.45 E
Nemčinovka 265b 55.43 N 37.23 E
Nemda ≃, Ross. 80 57.35 N 48.56 E
Nemda ≃, Ross. 80 57.21 N 43.08 E
Nemegosenda ≃ 190 48.01 N 82.53 W
Nemegt uul ⊀ 102 43.40 N 101.10 E
Nemeiben Lake ◎ 184 55.20 N 105.20 W
Nemenčinė 76 54.51 N 25.29 E
Nementcha, Monts de ⊀ 148 34.52 N 7.05 E
Nemeriči 76 53.51 N 33.59 E
Nemi 66 41.43 N 12.43 E
Nemi, Lago di ◎ 267a 41.43 N 12.42 E
Nemira Mare, Vîrful ▲ 38 46.15 N 26.19 E
Nemirov, Ukr. 78 50.07 N 23.25 E
Nemirov, Ukr. 78 48.58 N 28.50 E
Nemirovo 82 55.54 N 36.12 E
Nemo 222 32.16 N 97.39 W
Nemoli 68 40.04 N 15.48 E
Nemor ≃ 89 48.23 N 124.32 E
Nemours 50 48.16 N 2.42 E
Nemovniči 80 54.51 N 39.02 E
Nemrut Gölü ◎ 130 38.37 N 42.12 E
Nemuna, Bjeshkët e ⊀ 38 42.27 N 19.47 E
Nemunas (Neman) ≃ 76 55.18 N 21.23 E
Nemuro 92a 43.20 N 145.35 E
Nemuro-hantō >[1] 92a 43.21 N 145.42 E
Nemuro Strait ⴑ 92a 44.00 N 145.20 E
Nemzeti Museum ♦ 264c 47.29 N 19.05 E
Nen ≃ 89 45.25 N 124.40 E
Nena Creek ≃ 224 45.07 N 121.07 W
Nenagh 48 52.52 N 8.12 W
Nenagh ≃ 48 52.56 N 8.17 W
Nenana 180 64.34 N 149.07 W
Nenana ≃ 180 64.30 N 149.00 W
Nenaševo 82 54.34 N 37.28 E
Nenasi 114 3.08 N 103.27 E
Nendaz 58 46.11 N 7.18 E
Nendeln 58 47.12 N 9.32 E
Nendo I 14 10.45 S 165.54 E
Nene ≃ 42 52.48 N 0.13 E
Neneckij □[3] 72 67.30 N 54.00 E
Nenetsia — Neneckij □[3] 72 67.30 N 54.00 E
Nenggiri ≃ 114 4.53 N 101.48 E
Nengjia 104 41.38 N 120.46 E
Nengo ≃ 152 14.27 S 22.09 E
Nengonengo I[1] 14 18.47 S 141.48 W
Nenneper Fleuth ≃ 263 51.32 N 6.26 E
Neno 154 15.24 S 34.39 E
Nentón ≃ 236 15.48 N 91.52 W
Nenzing 58 47.11 N 9.42 E
Neo 94 35.38 N 136.37 E
Neo ≃ 94 35.24 N 136.34 E
Neodesha 198 37.25 N 95.40 W
Neoga 194 39.19 N 88.27 W
Neola, Ia., U.S. 198 41.26 N 95.36 W
Neola, Ut., U.S. 200 40.26 N 110.01 W
Neoneli 71 40.04 N 8.57 E
Néon Fáliron 267c 37.57 N 23.40 E
Néon Karlovásion 38 37.48 N 26.44 E
Néon Psikhikón 267c 38.00 N 23.47 E
Neopit 190 44.58 N 88.49 W
Neópolis 250 10.18 S 36.35 W
Neosho 123 33.09 N 74.14 E
Neosho 194 36.52 N 94.22 W
Neosho ≃ 194 35.48 N 95.18 W
Neotsu 224 45.00 N 123.58 W
Nepa ≃ 88 59.16 N 108.16 E
Nepal (Nepāl) □[1], Asia 118 28.00 N 84.00 E
Nepal (Nepāl) □[1], Asia 124 28.00 N 84.00 E
Nepālgañj 124 28.03 N 81.37 E
Nepa Nagar 120 21.28 N 76.23 E
Nepaug Reservoir ◎[1] 207 41.48 N 72.57 W
Nepean 212 45.18 N 75.47 W
Nepean ≃ 170 33.27 S 150.53 E
Nepean, Point > 169 38.18 S 144.39 E
Nepean Bay ⊂ 168b 35.42 S 137.44 E
Nepean Island I 174c 29.04 S 167.58 E
Nepean Reservoir ◎[1] 170 34.22 S 150.35 E
Nepecino 82 55.12 N 38.37 E
Nepeña 248 9.13 S 78.23 W
Nepewassi Lake ◎ 190 46.23 N 80.40 W
Nephi 200 39.42 N 111.50 W
Nephin ▲ 48 54.01 N 9.22 W
Nephin Beg Range ⊀ 48 54.00 N 9.35 W
Nepi 66 42.14 N 12.21 E
Nepisiguit ≃ 186 47.37 N 65.38 W
Nepisiguit Bay ⊂ 186 47.46 N 65.32 W
Népliget ♦ 264c 47.29 N 19.07 E
Nepoko ≃ 154 1.40 N 27.01 E
Nepomuceno 256 21.14 S 45.15 W
Nepomuk 60 49.29 N 13.36 E
Neponset ≃ 283 42.17 N 71.02 W
Neponset Reservoir ◎[1] 283 42.05 N 71.15 W
Neponset River Reservation ♦ 283 42.13 N 71.08 W
Neppermin 54 53.56 N 14.02 E
Nepr'adva ≃ 76 53.40 N 38.39 E
Nép-sziget I 264c 47.34 N 19.05 E
Neptune, N.J., U.S. 208 40.12 N 74.02 W
Neptune, Oh., U.S. 216 40.36 N 84.30 W
Neptune Beach 192 30.18 N 81.23 W
Neptune City 208 40.12 N 74.02 W
Neqarot, Naḥal ∨ 132 30.40 N 35.15 E
Nera ≃, Europe 38 44.49 N 21.22 E
Nera ≃, It. 66 42.26 N 12.24 E
Nérac 32 44.08 N 0.20 E
Nerákion 267c 38.01 N 23.27 E
Nerang 171a 28.00 S 153.20 E
Nerang ≃ 171a 28.03 S 153.17 E
Neratovice 54 50.14 N 14.31 E
Nerča ≃ 88 51.56 N 116.40 E
Nerchau 54 51.16 N 12.47 E
Nerčinsk 88 51.58 N 116.35 E
Nerčinskij Zavod 88 51.19 N 119.36 E
Nerdvik 26 63.47 N 8.17 E
Nere 150 9.29 N 2.18 E
Nerechta 80 57.28 N 40.34 E
Nerenstetten 56 48.31 N 10.06 E
Neresheim 56 48.45 N 10.15 E
Nereta 76 56.13 N 25.18 E
Nereto 66 42.49 N 13.49 E
Neretva ≃ 36 43.01 N 17.27 E
Nerevoznoje 80 56.53 N 53.54 E
Nerima ✈[8] 268 35.44 N 139.39 E
Neris (Vilija) ≃ 76 54.54 N 23.53 E
Nerja 34 36.44 N 3.52 W
Nerka, Lake ◎ 180 59.30 N 158.45 W
Nerl', Ross. 76 57.03 N 37.59 E
Nerl', Ross. 80 56.40 N 40.24 E
Nerl' ≃, Ross. 76 57.07 N 37.59 E
Nerl' ≃, Ross. 80 56.11 N 40.34 E
Nero, ozero ◎ 80 57.07 N 39.27 E
Neroj 88 54.28 N 97.49 E
Neronde 62 45.50 N 4.14 E
Nérondes 32 47.00 N 2.49 E
Nerópolis 255 16.25 S 49.14 W
Nerriga 170 35.07 S 150.05 E
Nerrigundah 162 18.24 S 124.29 E
Nerrima 162 18.24 S 124.29 E
Nerrimunga Creek ≃ 170 34.57 S 150.04 E
Nersingen 58 48.25 N 10.07 E
Nerskogen 26 62.48 N 9.38 E
Nerul 272c 19.02 N 73.01 E
Nerusa ≃ 76 52.33 N 33.47 E
Nerva 34 37.42 N 6.32 W
Nervi 62 44.23 N 9.02 E
Nervia ≃ 62 43.47 N 7.38 E
Nerviano 266b 45.33 N 8.58 E
Nerville-la-Forêt 261 49.05 N 2.17 E
Nes, Ned. 52 53.04 N 5.51 E

Nes, Ned. 52 53.26 N 5.45 E
Nes, Nor. 26 60.34 N 9.59 E
Nes', Ross. 24 66.37 N 44.36 E
Nes, Har ▲ 132 30.22 N 34.37 E
Nesbyen 26 60.34 N 9.09 E
Nesčerdo, ozero ◎ 76 55.54 N 29.04 E
Nesčeratovo 83 49.24 N 38.48 E
Nesco 208 39.38 N 74.41 W
Nescochague Creek ≃ 285 39.39 N 74.41 W
Nescochague Creek, Great Swamp Branch ≃ 285 39.41 N 74.43 W
Nesconset 276 40.51 N 73.09 W
Nescopeck 210 41.03 N 76.13 W
Nescopeck Creek ≃ 210 41.03 N 76.14 W
Nescopeck Mountain ▲ 210 41.03 N 76.05 W
Nesebăr 38 42.39 N 27.44 E
Neshaminy Creek ≃ 208 40.04 N 74.55 W
Neshaminy Hills 285 40.10 N 74.57 W
Neshaminy Mall ✈[9] 285 40.08 N 74.57 W
Neshaminy State Park ♦ 285 40.05 N 74.55 W
Neshaminy Woods 285 40.10 N 74.57 W
Neshannock Creek ≃ 214 40.59 N 80.21 W
Nesher 132 32.46 N 35.03 E
Nesjøen ◎[1] 26 63.02 N 12.01 E
Neškan 180 67.03 N 173.01 W
Neskaupstaður 24a 65.10 N 13.43 W
Neskowin 224 45.06 N 123.58 W
Neskypil'gyn, laguna ⊂ 180 66.57 N 172.45 W
Nesle 50 49.46 N 2.55 E
Nesna 24 66.12 N 13.02 E
Nespelem 182 48.10 N 118.58 W
Nesque ≃ 62 43.59 N 4.59 E
Nesquehoning 210 40.51 N 75.48 W
Ness 262 53.17 N 3.03 W
Ness, Loch ◎ 46 57.15 N 4.30 W
Ness City 198 38.27 N 99.54 W
Nesse ≃ 54 50.59 N 10.32 E
Nesselrode, Mount ▲ 180 58.58 N 134.18 W
Nesselwang 58 47.37 N 10.30 E
Nesselwängle 58 47.29 N 10.37 E
Nessiau 58 47.13 N 9.13 E
Nessmersiel 52 53.40 N 7.21 E
Nesso 62 45.55 N 9.08 E
Neštěmice 54 50.40 N 14.07 E
Nesterkovo 76 59.10 N 30.33 E
Nesterov, Ross. 76 54.38 N 22.34 E
Nesterov, Ukr. 78 50.04 N 23.58 E
Nesterovka 80 52.26 N 53.42 E
Nesterovo, Ross. 80 54.31 N 41.49 E
Nesterovo, Ross. 82 56.45 N 36.30 E
Nesterovo, Ross. 88 52.22 N 107.53 E
Nestiary 80 56.34 N 45.21 E
Nestoita 78 47.47 N 29.21 E
Neston 44 53.18 N 3.04 W
Nestore ≃ 66 43.21 N 12.15 E
Néstos (Mesta) ≃ 38 40.41 N 24.44 E
Nesttun 26 60.19 N 5.20 E
Nestucca ≃ 224 45.12 N 123.57 W
Nesvetaj 83 47.27 N 39.40 E
Nesviž 76 53.13 N 26.40 E
Nes Ziyyona 132 31.55 N 34.48 E
Netanya 132 32.20 N 34.51 E
Netarhāt 124 23.29 N 84.16 E
Netarts 224 45.26 N 123.56 W
Netarts Bay ⊂ 224 45.24 N 123.56 W
Netcong 210 40.53 N 74.42 W
Nethan ≃ 46 55.42 N 3.52 W
Nether Alderley 262 53.17 N 2.14 W
Netherdale 166 21.08 S 148.32 E
Netherlands (Nederland) □[1], Europe 22 52.15 N 5.30 E
Netherlands (Nederland) □[1], Europe 30 52.15 N 5.30 E
Netherlands Antilles (Nederlandse Antillen) □[2], N.A. 230 12.15 N 68.45 W
Netherlands Antilles (Nederlandse Antillen) □[2], N.A. 241s 12.15 N 68.45 W
Netherton 262 53.30 N 2.58 W
Nethy Bridge 46 57.16 N 3.38 W
Netia 154 14.48 S 39.59 E
Netley Marsh 42 50.53 N 1.32 W
Neto ≃ 68 39.13 N 17.08 E
Netolice 61 49.03 N 14.12 E
Netphen 56 50.55 N 8.06 E
Netra 56 51.06 N 10.05 E
Netrakona 124 24.53 N 90.43 E
Netstal 58 47.03 N 9.03 E
Nettancourt 56 48.52 N 4.57 E
Nette 52 52.02 N 10.05 E
Nette ✈[8] 263 51.33 N 7.25 E
Nettelstedt 52 52.18 N 8.41 E
Nettetal 56 51.18 N 6.16 E
Nettilling Fiord ⊂[2] 176 66.02 N 68.12 W
Nettilling Lake ◎ 176 66.30 N 70.40 W
Nett Lake ◎ 190 48.10 N 93.10 W
Nett Lake Indian Reservation ✈[4] 190 48.06 N 93.10 W
Nettlebed 42 51.35 N 1.00 W
Nettle Creek ≃ 218 40.03 N 83.48 W
Nettleden 260 51.47 N 0.32 W
Nettleham 44 53.16 N 0.29 W
Nettlestead 260 51.15 N 0.25 E
Nettlestead Green 260 51.14 N 0.25 E
Nettleton 194 34.05 N 88.37 W
Nettuno 66 41.27 N 12.39 E
Nettuno, Grotta di ⊥[5] 71 40.34 N 8.09 E
Netzschkau 54 50.36 N 12.14 E
Neualbenreuth 60 49.59 N 12.27 E
Neu-Anspach 56 50.17 N 8.29 E
Neuastenberg 56 51.11 N 8.29 E
Neubeckum 52 51.48 N 8.01 E
Neubrandenburg 54 53.33 N 13.15 E
Neubraunschweig — New Brunswick □[4] 186 46.30 N 66.15 W
Neubritannien — New Britain I 164 6.00 S 150.00 E
Neu Büddenstedt 54 52.11 N 11.02 E
Neubukow 54 54.02 N 11.40 E
Neuburg am Inn 60 48.30 N 13.27 E
Neuburg an der Donau 60 48.44 N 11.12 E
Neuchâtel 58 46.59 N 6.56 E
Neuchâtel □[3] 58 47.00 N 6.55 E
Neuchâtel, Lac de ◎ 58 46.52 N 6.50 E
Neu-Delhi — New Delhi 124 28.36 N 77.12 E
Neudenau 56 49.17 N 9.16 E
Neudietendorf 54 50.55 N 10.55 E
Neudorf, Sk., Can. 184 50.44 N 102.59 W
Neudorf, Dtsch. 54 50.29 N 12.58 E
Neudorf ✈[8] 263 51.25 N 6.47 E
Neudörfl 61 47.48 N 16.17 E
Neue Hebriden — Vanuatu □[1] 175f 16.00 S 167.00 E
Neuemühle 264a 52.18 N 13.39 E
Neuenburg, Dtsch. 52 53.23 N 7.57 E
Neuenburg, Dtsch. 58 48.50 N 8.35 E
Neuenburg, Dtsch. 58 47.48 N 7.34 E
Neuenburg — Neuchâtel, Schw. 58 46.59 N 6.56 E
Neuendettelsau 56 49.17 N 10.47 E
Neuendorf 54 54.31 N 13.05 E
Neuendorfer See ◎ 54 52.07 N 13.55 E
Neuenegg 58 46.54 N 7.18 E
Neuenhagen bei Berlin 54 52.32 N 13.41 E
Neuenhaus 52 52.30 N 6.59 E
Neuenhof ✈[8] 263 51.13 N 6.25 E
Neuenhoven 263 51.08 N 6.31 E

≃ River | Fluß | Río | Rivière | Rio
≍ Canal | Kanal | Canal | Canal | Canal
ᒪ Waterfall, Rapids | Wasserfall, Stromschnellen | Cascada, Rápidos | Chute d'eau, Rapides | Cascata, Rápidos
ⴑ Strait | Meeresstraße | Estrecho | Détroit | Estreito
⊂ Bay, Gulf | Bucht, Golf | Bahía, Golfo | Baie, Golfe | Baía, Golfo
◎ Lake, Lakes | See, Seen | Lago, Lagos | Lac, Lacs | Lago, Lagos
⊠ Swamp | Sumpf | Pantano | Marais | Pântano
⊡ Ice Features, Glacier | Eis- und Gletscherformen | Accidentes Glaciales | Formes glaciaires | Acidentes glaciares
✈ Other Hydrographic Features | Andere Hydrographische Objekte | Otros Elementos Hidrográficos | Autres données hydrographiques | Outros acidentes hidrográficos

✈ Submarine Features | Untermeerische Objekte | Accidentes Submarinos | Formes de relief sous-marin | Acidentes submarinos
□ Political Unit | Politische Einheit | Unidad Política | Entité politique | Unidade política
♦ Cultural Institution | Kulturelle Institution | Institución Cultural | Institution culturelle | Instituição cultural
⊥ Historical Site | Historische Stätte | Sitio Histórico | Site historique | Sítio histórico
♦ Recreational Site | Erholungs- und Ferienort | Sitio de Recreo | Centre de loisirs | Área de Lazer
⊠ Airport | Flughafen | Aeropuerto | Aéroport | Aeroporto
■ Military Installation | Militäranlage | Instalación Militar | Installation militaire | Instalação militar
✈ Miscellaneous | Verschiedenes | Misceláneo | Divers | Diversos

Symbols in the index entries represent the broad categories identified in the key at the right. Symbols with superior numbers (⨯¹) identify subcategories (see complete key on page I · 1).

Symbole im Register stellen die rechts im Schlüssel erklärten Kategorien dar. Symbole mit hochgestellten Ziffern (⨯¹) bezeichnen Unterabteilungen einer Kategorie (vgl. vollständiger Schlüssel auf Seite I · 1).

Los símbolos incluidos en el texto del índice representan las grandes categorías identificadas con la clave a la derecha. Los símbolos con numeros en su parte superior (⨯¹) identifican las subcategorías (véase la clave completa en la página I · 1).

Os símbolos incluídos no texto do índice representam as grandes categorias identificadas com a chave à direita. Os símbolos com números em sua parte superior (⨯¹) representam as subcategorias (veja-se a chave completa à página I · 1).

Les symboles de l'index représentent les catégories indiquées dans la légende à droite. Les symboles suivis d'un indice (⨯¹) représentent les sous-catégories (voir légende complète à la page I · 1).

Symbol	English	Deutsch	Español	Français	Português
⋀	Mountain	Berg	Montaña	Montagne	Montanha
⨯	Mountains	Gebirge	Montañas	Montagnes	Montanhas
)(	Pass		Paso	Col	Passo
⋁	Valley, Canyon	Tal, Cañon	Valle, Cañón	Vallée, Canyon	Vale, Canhão
≍	Plain	Ebene	Llano	Plaine	Planicie
≃	Cape	Kap	Cabo	Cap	Cabo
I	Island	Insel	Isla	Île	Ilha
II	Islands	Inseln	Islas	Îles	Ilhas
⊥	Other Topographic Features	Andere Topographische Objekte	Otros Elementos Topográficos	Autres données topographiques	Outros acidentes topográficos

ESPAÑOL — Nombre | Página | Lat.°′ | Long.°′ W = Oeste
FRANÇAIS — Nom | Page | Lat.°′ | Long.°′ W = Ouest
PORTUGUÊS — Nome | Página | Lat.°′ | Long.°′ W = Oeste

New Terrell City Lake ⊜[1] 222 32.44 N 96.14 W
New Territories □[8] 271d 22.24 N 114.10 E
New Thunderchild Indian Reserve ◆[4] 184 53.30 N 108.50 W
Newtok 180 60.56 N 164.38 W
Newton, Eng., U.K. 44 53.57 N 2.27 W
Newton, Eng., U.K. 262 53.16 N 2.43 W
Newton, Ga., U.S. 192 31.18 N 84.20 W
Newton, Il., U.S. 194 38.59 N 88.09 W
Newton, Ia., U.S. 190 41.41 N 93.02 W
Newton, Ks., U.S. 198 38.02 N 97.20 W
Newton, Ma., U.S. 207 42.20 N 71.12 W
Newton, Ms., U.S. 194 32.19 N 89.09 W
Newton, N.J., U.S. 210 41.03 N 74.45 W
Newton, N.C., U.S. 192 35.40 N 81.13 W
Newton, Tx., U.S. 194 30.50 N 93.45 W
Newton □[6] 216 40.46 N 87.27 W
Newton Abbot 42 50.32 N 3.36 W
Newton Arlosh 44 54.53 N 3.15 W
Newton Aycliffe 44 54.36 N 1.32 W
Newton Brook ◆[8] 275b 43.48 N 79.24 W
Newton Center 283 42.20 N 71.12 W
Newton Falls, N.Y., U.S. 188 44.12 N 74.59 W
Newton Falls, Oh., U.S. 214 41.11 N 80.58 W
Newton Ferrers 42 50.18 N 4.02 W
Newton Flotman 42 52.32 N 1.16 E
Newton Hamilton 214 40.24 N 77.51 W
Newton Highlands 283 42.19 N 71.13 W
Newton-le-Willows 44 53.28 N 2.37 W
Newton Longville 42 51.58 N 0.46 W
Newton Lower Falls 283 42.19 N 71.23 W
Newtonmore 46 57.04 N 4.08 W
Newton Stewart 44 54.57 N 4.29 W
Newtonsville 218 39.11 N 84.05 W
Newton Upper Falls 283 42.19 N 71.13 W
Newtonville, On., Can. 212 43.56 N 78.30 W
Newtonville, Ma., U.S. 283 42.21 N 71.13 W
Newtonville, N.J., U.S. 208 39.33 N 74.51 W
New Toronto ◆[8] 275b 43.36 N 79.30 W
Newtown, Austl. 169 38.09 S 144.20 E
Newtown, Nf., Can. 186 49.12 N 53.31 W
Newtown, Eng., U.K. 262 53.21 N 2.00 W
Newtown, Wales, U.K. 42 52.32 N 3.19 W
Newtown, Ct., U.S. 207 41.24 N 73.18 W
Newtown, In., U.S. 216 40.12 N 87.08 W
Newtown, Ky., U.S. 218 38.13 N 84.57 W
New Town, N.D., U.S. 198 47.58 N 102.29 W
Newtown, Pa., U.S. 208 40.14 N 74.56 W
Newtown ◆[8] 274a 33.54 S 151.11 E
Newtownabbey 48 54.42 N 5.54 W
Newtownards 48 54.36 N 5.41 W
Newtownbutler 48 54.12 N 7.23 W
Newtown Creek ≐, N.Y., U.S. 276 40.44 N 73.58 W
Newtown Creek ≐, Pa., U.S. 285 40.13 N 74.56 W
Newtown Crommelin 48 54.59 N 6.13 W
Newtown Forbes 48 53.46 N 7.50 W
Newtownhamilton 48 54.12 N 6.35 W
Newtown Mount Kennedy 48 53.05 N 6.07 W
Newtown Saint Boswells 46 55.34 N 2.40 W
Newtown Square 208 39.59 N 75.24 W
Newtownstewart 48 54.43 N 7.24 W
New Tredegar 42 51.43 N 3.14 W
New Tripoli 208 40.41 N 75.45 W
New Troy 216 41.53 N 86.33 W
New Truxton 219 38.58 N 91.15 W
New Ulm, Mn., U.S. 190 44.18 N 94.27 W
New Ulm, Tx., U.S. 222 29.53 N 96.29 W
New Utrecht ◆[8] 276 40.36 N 73.59 W
New Vernon 276 40.45 N 74.30 W
New Vienna 218 39.19 N 83.41 W
Newville, In., U.S. 216 41.21 N 84.51 W
Newville, Pa., U.S. 208 40.10 N 77.23 W
New Vineyard 188 44.48 N 70.07 W
New Waltham 44 53.32 N 0.04 W
New Washington, Pil. 116 11.39 N 122.26 E
New Washington, In., U.S. 218 38.33 N 85.32 W
New Washington, Oh., U.S. 214 40.57 N 82.51 W
New Waterford, N.S., Can. 186 46.15 N 60.05 W
New Waterford, Oh., U.S. 214 40.50 N 80.36 W
New Waverly, In., U.S. 216 40.46 N 86.12 W
New Waverly, Tx., U.S. 222 30.32 N 95.29 W
New Westminster 224 49.12 N 122.55 W
New Whiteland 218 39.33 N 86.05 W
New Wilmington 214 41.07 N 80.19 W
New Windsor → Windsor, Eng., U.K. 42 51.29 N 0.38 W
New Windsor, Md., U.S. 208 39.32 N 77.06 W
New Windsor, N.Y., U.S. 210 41.30 N 74.01 W
New Woodbine Racetrack ♠ 275b 43.43 N 79.36 W
New Woodstock 210 42.50 N 75.51 W
New World Island I 186 49.35 N 54.40 W
New Year Creek ≐ 222 30.08 N 96.12 W
New York, N.Y., U.S. 210 40.43 N 74.01 W
New York, N.Y., U.S. 276 40.43 N 74.01 W
New York □[6] 276 40.47 N 73.58 W
New York □[3], U.S. 178 43.00 N 75.00 W
New York □[3], U.S. 188 43.00 N 75.00 W
New York, City College of ⊌[2] 276 40.49 N 73.57 W
New York, Polytechnic Institute of ⊌[2] 276 40.42 N 73.59 W
New York, State University of (Stony Brook) ⊌[2], N.Y., U.S. 276 40.55 N 73.08 W
New York, State University of (Buffalo) ⊌[2], N.Y., U.S. 284a 42.57 N 78.49 W
New York, State University of, College at Buffalo ⊌[2] 284a 42.56 N 78.53 W
New York at Buffalo, State University of ⊌[2] 284a 42.56 N 78.49 W
New York Mills, Mn., U.S. 198 46.31 N 95.22 W
New York Mills, N.Y., U.S. 210 43.06 N 75.18 W
New York State Barge Canal ≋ 210 43.05 N 78.43 W
New York Stock Exchange ⊌ 276 40.42 N 74.01 W
New Zealand □[1] 172 41.00 S 174.00 E
Nexapa ≐ 234 18.07 N 98.46 W
Nexon 32 45.41 N 1.11 E
Ney 216 41.23 N 84.32 W
Neyagawa 96 34.46 N 135.38 E
Neye 263 51.07 N 7.22 E
Neyestausee ⊜[1] 263 51.08 N 7.24 E
Ney Lake ⊜ 184 54.38 N 92.25 W
Neyland 42 51.43 N 4.57 W
Neylandville 222 33.12 N 96.00 W
Neyrīz 128 29.12 N 54.19 E
Neyshābūr 128 36.12 N 58.50 E
Neyyāttinkara 122 8.24 N 77.05 E
Nezahualcóyotl 234 19.27 N 99.03 W
Nezahualcóyotl, Presa ⊜[1] 234 17.10 N 93.40 W
Nezamajevskaja 78 46.09 N 40.16 E
Nezameno-toko ♠ 94 35.46 N 137.42 E
Nežárka ≐ 61 49.11 N 14.41 E
Nezavertajlovka 38 46.37 N 29.56 E
Nežin 78 51.03 N 31.54 E
Nezlobnaja 84 44.08 N 43.23 E
Neznanka ≐ 265b 55.34 N 37.21 E
Neznanovo 80 54.02 N 40.06 E
Nezperce 202 46.14 N 116.14 W
Nez Perce Indian Reservation ◆[4] 202 46.20 N 116.30 W
Nez Perce National Historical Park ♠ 202 45.50 N 116.15 W
Nezpique, Bayou ≐ 194 30.12 N 92.35 W
Nezvěstice 60 49.39 N 13.32 E
Ngabang 112 0.23 N 109.57 E
Ngabé 152 3.12 S 16.11 E
Ngabordamlu, Tanjung › 164 6.56 S 134.11 E
Ngadda ≐ 146 12.40 N 13.50 E
Ngadirojo 115a 8.13 S 111.19 E
Ngadza 152 5.10 N 20.12 E
Ngahere 172 42.24 S 171.27 E
Ngala 146 12.20 N 14.10 E
Ngale 152 2.56 N 21.20 E
Ngali 152 2.27 S 19.20 E
Ngaliema, Baie de ⊂ 273b 4.19 S 15.16 E
Ngalipaeng 112 3.24 N 125.37 E
Ngaloa Harbour ⊂ 175g 19.06 S 178.11 E
Ngamaba 273b 4.14 S 15.16 E
Ngamba ◆[8] 273b 4.15 S 15.18 E
Ngambé 152 4.14 N 10.37 E
Ngamdu 146 11.48 N 12.18 E
Ngami, Lake ⊜ 156 20.37 S 22.40 E
Ngamiland □[5] 156 19.09 S 22.47 E
Ngamo 154 19.08 S 27.32 E
Ngamouéri 273b 4.14 S 15.14 E
Ngamring 124 29.14 N 87.10 E
Nganda ∧ 154 10.25 S 33.50 E
Ngangala 154 4.42 N 31.55 E
Ngangla Ringco ⊜ 120 31.40 N 83.00 E
Nganglong Kangri ∧ 120 32.45 N 81.12 E
Nganglong Kangri ⋀ 120 32.00 N 83.00 E
Ngangzê Co ⊜ 120 31.05 N 86.55 E
Nganjuk 115a 7.36 S 111.55 E
Ngao 110 18.46 N 99.59 E
Ngaoui, Mont ∧ 152 6.40 N 14.57 E
Ngaoundéré 152 7.19 N 13.35 E
Ngapali 110 18.26 N 94.19 E
Ngapara 172 44.57 S 170.45 E
Ngape 110 20.04 N 94.38 E
Ngaputaw 110 16.32 N 94.42 E
Ngara 154 2.28 S 30.39 E
Ngaramasch 175b 6.54 N 134.08 E
Ngarimbi 154 8.28 S 38.36 E
Ngaruawahia 172 37.40 S 175.09 E
Ngaruroro ≐ 172 39.34 S 176.56 E
Ngasamo 154 2.33 S 33.53 E
Ngat ≐ 110 19.09 N 99.01 E
Ngatangiia 174k 21.14 S 159.43 W
Ngatangiia Harbour ⊂ 174k 21.14 S 159.45 W
Ngatea 172 37.17 S 175.30 E
Ngathainggyaung 110 17.24 N 95.05 E
Ngatik I[1] 14 5.51 N 157.16 E
Ngau I 175g 18.02 S 179.18 E
Ngauruhoe, Mount ∧ 172 39.09 S 175.38 E
Ngau Tau Kok → Kwun Tong 271d 22.19 N 114.12 E
Ngawen 115a 7.00 S 111.18 E
Ngawi 115a 7.24 S 111.26 E
Ngay Nua 110 21.50 N 101.54 E
Ngebel 115a 7.46 S 111.37 E
Ngele 152 0.29 S 20.25 E
Ngemelis Islands II 175b 7.07 N 134.15 E
Ngerengere 154 6.45 S 38.07 E
Ngerkeel 175b 7.25 N 134.30 E
Ngermechau 175b 7.35 N 134.39 E
Ngeruktabel I 175b 7.15 N 134.24 E
Ngetbong 175b 7.37 N 134.35 E
Ngetera 146 12.31 N 12.38 E
Nggamea Island I 175g 16.46 S 179.46 W
Nggatokae Island I 175e 8.46 S 158.11 E
Nggela Pile I 175e 9.05 S 160.15 E
Nggela Sule I 175e 9.05 S 160.15 E
Nggelelevu I 175g 16.05 S 179.09 W
Nggwavuma ≐ 158 26.58 S 32.17 E
Nghia Dan 110 19.18 N 105.26 E
Nghia Hanh 110 15.03 N 108.47 E
Nghia Lo 110 21.36 N 104.31 E
Ngiap ≐ 110 18.24 N 103.36 E
Ngidinga 152 5.37 S 15.17 E
Ngimbang 115a 7.17 S 112.12 E
Ng'iro ∧ 154 2.08 N 36.51 E
Ngiro, Ewaso ≐, Kenya 154 2.04 S 36.07 E
Ng'iro, Ewaso ≐, Kenya 154 0.28 N 39.55 E
Ngo 152 2.29 S 15.45 E
Ngoangoa ≐ 140 5.48 N 25.09 E
Ngoboli 154 4.57 N 32.37 E
Ngoko ≐, Afr. 152 1.40 N 16.03 E
Ngoko ≐, Congo 152 0.25 S 15.29 E
Ngol-Kedju Hill ∧[2] 152 6.20 N 9.45 E
Ngolo 146 9.56 N 22.16 E
Ngom ≐ 102 31.11 N 97.15 E
Ngomahuru 154 20.26 S 30.43 E
Ngomba 154 8.23 S 32.53 E
Ngomba ∧ 154 5.43 S 35.52 E
Ngombe, Zaïre 152 6.35 S 20.42 E
Ngombe, Zaïre 273b 4.24 S 15.11 E
Ngome 158 27.46 S 31.28 E
Ngomedzap 152 3.15 N 11.12 E
Ngomeni, Ras › 154 2.59 S 40.14 E
Ngong 154 1.22 S 36.39 E
Ngongotaha 172 38.05 S 176.12 E
Ngono ≐ 154 1.08 S 31.35 E
Ngonye Falls ⌞ 152 16.40 S 23.35 E
Ngop 140 6.16 N 30.12 E
Ngora 154 1.27 N 33.46 E
Ngorengore 154 1.02 S 35.30 E
Ngoring Hu ⊜ 102 34.50 N 97.35 E
Ngoro 115a 7.41 S 112.16 E
Ngorongoro Crater ⊼[6] 154 3.10 S 35.35 E
Ngote 154 2.14 N 30.48 E
Ngoto 152 4.00 N 17.21 E
Ngotwane ≐ 156 23.35 S 26.58 E
Ngoulémakong 152 3.07 N 11.25 E
Ngouma 150 15.38 N 3.22 W
Ngounié □[4] 152 1.30 S 11.00 E
Ngounié ≐ 152 0.37 S 10.18 E
Ngouri 146 13.38 N 15.22 E
Ngouroundou 152 6.27 N 22.37 E
Ngourti 146 15.19 N 13.12 E
Ngoywa 154 5.56 S 32.48 E
Ngozi 154 2.54 S 29.50 E
Ngqeleni 158 31.40 S 29.02 E
Ngudiabaka ≐ 273b 4.25 S 15.11 E
Nguélémendouka 152 4.23 N 12.55 E
Ngugha ≐ 156 19.21 S 23.15 E
Nguigmi 146 14.15 N 13.07 E
Nguila 152 4.43 N 11.41 E
Nguiu 164 11.45 S 130.38 E
Ngulu I[1] 108 8.27 N 137.29 E
Ngum ≐ 110 18.09 N 103.06 E
Nguna, Île I 175f 17.26 S 168.21 E
Ngunga 154 3.41 S 33.34 E
Ngunju, Tanjung › 115b 10.19 S 120.28 E
Ngunut 115a 8.06 S 112.01 E
Ngurore 146 9.18 N 12.14 E
Nguru 146 12.52 N 10.27 E
Ngwempisi ≐ 158 26.42 S 31.26 E
Ngweni 158 27.56 S 32.15 E
Ngwenya ∧ 158 26.11 S 31.02 E
Ngwerere 154 15.18 S 28.20 E
Ngweze ≐ 154 17.40 S 25.07 E
Nha Be 269c 10.42 N 106.44 E
Nhabe ≐, Bots. 156 20.22 S 22.58 E
Nha Be ≐, Viet 269c 10.39 N 106.44 E
Nhacoongo 156 24.18 S 35.14 E
Nhamacolomo 156 18.05 S 34.26 E
Nhamundá 250 2.14 S 56.43 W
Nhamundá ≐ 246 2.12 S 56.41 W
Nha Nam 110 21.27 N 106.06 E
Nhandeara 255 20.40 S 50.02 W
Nhareia 152 11.25 S 17.03 E
Nha Trang 110 12.15 N 109.11 E
Nhia ≐ 152 10.15 S 14.12 E
Nhill 166 36.20 S 141.39 E
Nhlangano 158 27.06 S 31.12 E
Nhlazatshe 158 28.10 S 31.14 E
Nhoma ≐ 156 18.52 S 20.53 E
Nhon Trach 269c 10.43 N 106.51 E
Nhulunbuy 164 12.11 S 136.47 E
Nhundo 152 14.25 S 21.23 E
Nhunguaçu 256 22.21 S 42.53 W
Niabembe 154 2.14 S 27.44 E
Niafounké 150 15.56 N 4.00 W
Niagara 190 45.46 N 87.59 W
Niagara □[5], On., Can. 212 43.05 N 79.20 W
Niagara □[6], N.Y., U.S. 210 43.10 N 78.42 W
Niagara ≐ 212 43.15 N 79.04 W
Niagara County Historical Center ⊌ 284a 43.10 N 78.43 W
Niagara Falls, On., Can. 212 43.06 N 79.04 W
Niagara Falls, On., Can. 284a 43.06 N 79.04 W
Niagara Falls, N.Y., U.S. 210 43.05 N 79.03 W
Niagara Falls, N.Y., U.S. 284a 43.05 N 79.03 W
Niagara Falls ⌞ 212 43.05 N 79.04 W
Niagara Falls Airport ⊠ 284a 43.02 N 79.08 W
Niagara Falls International Airport ⊠ 284a 43.06 N 78.56 W
Niagara-on-the-Lake 212 43.15 N 79.04 W
Niagara University ⊌[2] 284a 43.08 N 79.02 W
Niagassola 150 12.19 N 9.07 W
Niah 112 3.52 N 113.44 E
Niakaramandougou 150 8.40 N 5.17 W
Niamey 150 13.31 N 2.07 E
Niamey □[5] 150 14.00 N 2.00 E
Niamtougou 150 9.46 N 1.06 E
Nianbadu 100 28.17 N 118.28 E
Niandan ≐ 150 10.30 N 10.26 W
Niandan Koro 150 11.05 N 9.15 W
Nianforando 150 9.32 N 10.31 W
Niangara 154 3.42 N 27.52 E
Niangay, Lac ⊜ 150 15.50 N 3.00 W
Niangmake 102 30.14 N 99.40 E
Niangniangong 104 41.00 N 121.13 E
Niangniangmiao 98 42.34 N 118.05 E
Niangniangwa 105 40.33 N 117.30 E
Niangoloko 150 10.17 N 4.55 W
Niangua ≐ 194 37.58 N 92.48 W
Niangzizhuang 105 40.02 N 118.05 E
Nia-Nia 154 1.24 N 27.36 E
Nianpan 104 41.48 N 124.02 E
Niantic, Ct., U.S. 207 41.19 N 72.11 W
Niantic, Il., U.S. 219 39.51 N 89.10 W
Nianyugou 104 42.00 N 123.59 E
Nianyushan 100 29.11 N 117.04 E
Nianzhuang 98 34.19 N 117.47 E
Nianzigang 100 31.03 N 114.18 E
Nianzishan 89 47.32 N 122.52 E
Niapu 154 2.25 N 26.28 E
Niari □[5] 152 3.15 S 12.30 E
Niari ≐ 152 3.56 S 12.12 E
Niaro 140 10.38 N 31.31 E
Nias, Pulau I 114 1.05 N 97.35 E
Niassa □[5] 154 13.30 S 36.00 E
Niatupo 246 9.33 N 78.54 W
Nibbiano 62 44.54 N 9.19 E
Nibe 26 56.59 N 9.38 E
Nibong Tebal 114 5.10 N 100.29 E
Nibra 272b 22.36 N 88.16 E
Nīca 76 56.19 N 21.04 E
Nica ≐ 86 57.29 N 64.33 E
Nicaea → İznik 130 40.26 N 29.43 E
Nicaragua □[1], N.A. 230 13.00 N 85.00 W
Nicaragua □[1], N.A. 236 13.00 N 85.00 W
Nicaragua, Lago de ⊜ 236 11.30 N 85.30 W
Nicaro 240p 20.42 N 75.33 W
Nicastro 68 38.59 N 16.20 E
Ničatka, ozero ⊜ 88 57.45 N 117.30 E
Nice 62 43.42 N 7.15 E
Nice-Côte d'Azur, Aéroport de ⊠ 62 43.40 N 7.14 E
Niceville 194 30.31 N 86.28 W
Nichelino 62 44.59 N 7.38 E
Nicheng 106 30.55 N 121.49 E
Nichihara 96 34.33 N 131.50 E
Nichinan, Nihon 92 31.36 N 131.23 E
Nichinan, Nihon 96 35.09 N 133.16 E
Nicholas □[6] 218 38.20 N 84.02 W
Nicholas Channel ʊ 238 23.25 N 80.05 W
Nicholasville 192 37.52 N 84.34 W
Nicholls 192 31.31 N 82.38 W
Nicholl's Town 238 25.08 N 78.00 W
Nichols, Ca., U.S. 282 38.02 N 121.59 W
Nichols, Fl., U.S. 220 27.54 N 82.02 W
Nichols, N.Y., U.S. 210 42.01 N 76.22 W
Nichols Brook ≐ 283 42.37 N 70.59 W
Nicholson, Austl. 162 18.02 S 128.54 E
Nicholson, Ky., U.S. 218 38.54 N 84.33 W
Nicholson, Ms., U.S. 194 30.28 N 89.41 W
Nicholson, Pa., U.S. 210 41.37 N 75.46 W
Nicholson ≐, Austl. 162 17.34 S 128.38 E
Nicholson ≐, Austl. 166 17.31 S 139.36 E
Nicholson Island I 212 43.56 N 77.31 W
Nicholson Range ⋀ 162 27.15 S 116.45 E
Nicholson River Aboriginal Reserve ◆[4] 162 18.00 S 137.30 E
Nichols Run ≐ 284b 39.03 N 77.18 W
Nickerie □[5] 250 5.40 N 56.50 W
Nickerie ≐ 250 5.59 N 57.00 W
Nickerson 198 38.08 N 98.05 W
Nickol Bay ⊂ 162 20.39 S 116.52 E
Nicktown 214 40.37 N 78.48 W
Nicobar Islands II 110 8.00 N 93.30 E
Nicola 182 50.10 N 120.40 W
Nicola ≐ 182 50.25 N 121.18 W
Nicolae Bălcescu 38 47.34 N 26.52 E
Nicolai Mountain ∧ 224 46.05 N 123.28 W
Nicola Lake ⊜ 182 50.10 N 120.25 W
Nicola Mameet Indian Reserve ◆[4] 182 50.11 N 120.49 W
Nicolaus 226 38.54 N 121.35 W
Nicolet 206 46.13 N 72.37 W
Nicolet □[6] 206 46.15 N 72.20 W
Nicolet ≐ 206 46.14 N 72.39 W
Nicolet, Lac ⊜ 206 45.50 N 71.33 W
Nicolet, Lake ⊜ 190 46.20 N 84.15 W
Nicolet Centre ≐ 206 45.46 N 71.50 W
Nicolet Sud-Ouest ≐ 206 46.13 N 72.36 W
Nicoll Bay ⊂ 276 40.43 N 73.07 W
Nicollet 190 44.16 N 94.11 W
Nicoll Point › 276 40.42 N 73.09 W
Nicolosi 70 37.37 N 15.01 E
Nicosia, It. 70 37.45 N 14.24 E
Nicosia (Levkosía), Kípros 130 35.10 N 33.22 E
Nicosia (Lefkoşa), Kıbrıs 130 35.10 N 33.22 E
Nicotera 68 38.34 N 15.57 E
Nicoya 236 10.09 N 85.27 W
Nicoya, Golfo de ⊂ 236 9.47 N 84.48 W
Nicoya, Península de ›[1] 236 10.00 N 85.25 W
Nictheroy → Niterói 256 22.53 S 43.07 W
Nida 76 55.18 N 21.01 E
Nida ≐ 30 50.18 N 20.52 E
Nidadavole 122 16.55 N 81.40 E
Nidau 58 47.07 N 7.14 E
Nidd ≐ 44 54.01 N 1.12 W
Nidda 56 50.24 N 9.00 E
Nidda ≐ 56 50.06 N 8.34 E
Nidder ≐ 56 50.12 N 8.47 E
Nidderau 56 50.14 N 8.52 E
Nide 102 31.51 N 96.19 E
Nideggen 56 50.47 N 6.29 E
Nidelva ≐ 26 58.24 N 8.48 E
Nidwalden □[3] 58 46.55 N 8.28 E
Nidž 84 40.56 N 47.41 E
Nidzica 30 53.22 N 20.26 E
Niebüll 41 54.48 N 8.50 E
Nied ≐ 56 49.23 N 6.40 E
Nied Allemande ≐ 56 49.10 N 6.26 E
Nieddu, Monte ∧ 71 40.45 N 9.34 E
Niederanven 56 49.39 N 6.16 E
Niederau 54 51.10 N 13.32 E
Niederaula 56 50.48 N 9.36 E
Niederbayern □[5] 60 48.45 N 12.45 E
Niederbipp 58 47.16 N 7.39 E
Niederbobritzsch 54 50.54 N 13.26 E
Niederbonsfeld 263 51.23 N 7.08 E
Niederbronn-Les-Bains 56 48.57 N 7.38 E
Niederdonk 263 51.14 N 6.41 E
Niederelfringhausen 263 51.21 N 7.10 E
Niedere Tauern ⋀ 30 47.18 N 14.00 E
Niederfinow 54 52.50 N 13.55 E
Niederfrohna 54 50.53 N 12.43 E
Niederhaverbeck 52 53.09 N 9.54 E
Niederheimbach 56 50.02 N 7.48 E
Niederhone 56 51.13 N 10.06 E
Niederkassel 56 50.49 N 7.02 E
Nieder-Kassel ◆[8] 263 51.14 N 6.45 E
Niederkrüchten 56 51.12 N 6.13 E
Niederlande → Netherlands □[1] 30 52.15 N 5.30 E
Niederländische Antillen → Netherlands Antilles □[2] 241s 12.15 N 69.00 W
Niederlausitz □[9] 54 51.40 N 14.15 E
Niederlehme 54 52.19 N 13.39 E
Niedermarsberg 56 51.28 N 8.50 E
Niedermarschacht 52 53.25 N 10.21 E
Nieder-Mörlen 56 50.23 N 8.43 E
Niederndodeleben 54 52.08 N 11.30 E
Nieder-Neuendorf 264a 52.37 N 13.12 E
Niedernhall 56 49.17 N 9.36 E
Niedernwöhren 52 52.21 N 9.08 E
Niederoderwitz 54 50.57 N 14.44 E
Nieder-Ohmen 56 50.38 N 9.02 E
Nieder-Olm 56 49.55 N 8.11 E
Niederorschel 54 51.22 N 10.25 E
Niederösterreich □[3] 61 48.20 N 15.50 E
Niedersachsen □[3] 30 52.40 N 9.00 E
Niedersachswerfen 54 51.33 N 10.46 E
Niederschöneweide ◆[8] 264a 52.27 N 13.31 E
Niederschönhausen ◆[8] 54 52.35 N 13.23 E
Niedersonthofen 58 47.38 N 10.13 E
Niederstetten 56 49.24 N 9.55 E
Niederstotzingen 56 48.32 N 10.14 E
Niedersulz 61 48.29 N 16.40 E
Niederurnen 58 47.07 N 9.03 E
Niederwald 58 46.26 N 8.12 E
Niederwalgern 56 50.44 N 8.41 E
Niederweningen 58 47.30 N 8.23 E
Niederwiesa 54 50.51 N 13.01 E
Niederwürschnitz 54 50.43 N 12.45 E
Nied Française ≐ 56 49.10 N 6.26 E
Niedu 100 25.28 N 114.08 E
Niefang 152 1.50 N 10.14 E
Nieheim 52 51.48 N 9.06 E
Niekerkshoop 158 29.19 S 22.51 E
Niel 50 51.07 N 4.20 E
Niellé 150 10.12 N 5.38 W
Niellim 146 9.42 N 17.49 E
Niem 152 6.12 N 15.14 E
Niemba 154 5.57 S 28.26 E
Niemegk 54 52.04 N 12.41 E
Niemeyer ◆[8] 287a 23.00 S 43.15 W
Niemodlin 30 50.39 N 17.37 E
Niéna 150 11.26 N 6.21 W
Nienberge 52 52.00 N 7.34 E
Nienborg-Wigbold 52 52.08 N 7.06 E
Nienburg, Dtsch. 52 52.38 N 9.13 E
Nienburg, Dtsch. 54 51.50 N 11.46 E
Niendorf 54 53.59 N 10.50 E
Nienhagen, Dtsch. 52 52.33 N 10.05 E
Nienhagen, Dtsch. 54 51.57 N 11.09 E
Niénokoué, Mont ∧[2] 150 5.26 N 7.10 W
Niepkuhlen ≐ 263 51.29 N 6.31 E
Niepołomice 30 50.03 N 20.13 E
Nieppe 50 50.42 N 2.50 E
Nier ≐ 48 52.17 N 7.48 W
Niéré 146 14.30 N 21.09 E
Niéré, Hadjer ∧ 146 14.21 N 21.40 E
Nieri Ko ≐ 150 13.21 N 13.23 W
Niers ≐ 52 51.43 N 5.57 E
Nierst 263 51.19 N 6.43 E
Nierstein 56 49.52 N 8.20 E
Niesen ∧ 58 46.39 N 7.39 E
Niesky 54 51.17 N 14.49 E
Nieszawa 30 52.50 N 18.55 E
Nieto, Cañada de ≐ 258 34.00 S 58.15 W
Nieu Bethesda 158 31.51 S 24.34 E
Nieuw-Amsterdam, Ned. 52 52.44 N 6.51 E
Nieuw Amsterdam, Sur. 250 5.53 N 55.05 W
Nieuw-Buinen 52 52.57 N 6.55 E
Nieuwefontein 158 28.01 S 19.06 E
Nieuwegein 52 52.03 N 5.05 E
Nieuwe-Niedorp 52 52.45 N 4.54 E
Nieuwe-Pekela 52 53.04 N 6.58 E
Nieuweschans 52 53.11 N 7.12 E
Nieuwkoop 52 52.08 N 4.47 E
Nieuw Nickerie 250 5.57 N 56.59 W
Nieuwolda 52 53.14 N 6.59 E
Nieuwoudtville 158 31.23 S 19.07 E
Nieuwpoort, Bel. 50 51.08 N 2.45 E
Nieuwpoort, Ned. Ant. 241s 12.03 N 68.49 W
Nieuwpoort-Bad 50 51.09 N 2.42 E
Nieuw-Schoonebeek 52 52.38 N 6.59 E
Nieuw-Vennep 52 52.16 N 4.38 E
Nieuw-Weerdinge 52 52.52 N 6.59 E
Nieva ≐ 246 4.35 S 77.53 W
Nievenheim 56 51.07 N 6.46 E
Nievería 286d 11.59 S 76.55 W
Nièvre □[5] 32 47.05 N 3.30 E
Nièvre ≐ 50 47.10 N 3.13 E
Niga 150 13.38 N 5.27 W
Nigan 126 23.30 N 87.59 E
Niğde 130 37.59 N 34.42 E
Niğde □[4] 130 38.15 N 34.15 E
Nigei Island I 182 50.55 N 127.50 W
Nigel 158 26.30 S 28.28 E
Niger □[3] 150 10.00 N 6.00 E
Niger □[1] 134 16.00 N 8.00 E
Niger ≐ 150 5.33 N 6.33 E
Niger Delta ≡[2] 150 4.50 N 6.00 E
Nigeria □[1] 134 10.00 N 8.00 E
Nigerian Museum ⊌ 273a 6.20 N 3.24 E
Nigg 46 57.43 N 4.00 W
Nighāsan 124 28.14 N 80.52 E
Nightcaps 172 45.58 S 168.02 E
Nighthawk 182 48.58 N 119.38 W
Night Hawk Lake ⊜ 190 48.28 N 81.00 W
Nightingale Island I 10 37.24 S 12.28 W
Nightmute 180 60.29 N 164.43 W
Nigríta 38 40.55 N 23.30 E
Nihe 104 41.27 N 121.13 E
Nihing (Nahang) ≐ 128 26.00 N 62.44 E
Nihoa I 14 23.06 N 161.58 W
Nihommatsu 92 37.35 N 140.26 E
Nihon → Japan □[1] 92 36.00 N 138.00 E
Nihonbashi ◆[8] 268 35.41 N 139.47 E
Nihon-kai → Japan, Sea of ⊤[2] 90 40.00 N 135.00 E
Nihon University ⊌[2] 268 35.42 N 139.45 E
Nihtaur 124 29.20 N 78.23 E
Nihuil, Embalse del ⊜[1] 252 35.05 S 68.45 W
Niida ≐ 96 33.11 N 132.58 E
Niigata 92 37.55 N 139.03 E
Niigata □[5] 94 37.08 N 138.30 E
Niihama 96 33.58 N 133.16 E
Niihari 94 36.07 N 140.09 E
Niiharu 94 36.41 N 138.55 E
Niihau I 229b 21.55 N 160.10 W
Nii-jima I 92 34.22 N 139.16 E
Niimi 96 34.59 N 133.28 E
Niinisalo 26 61.50 N 22.29 E
Niitsu 92 37.48 N 139.07 E
Niiza 94 35.48 N 139.34 E
Níjar 34 36.58 N 2.12 W
Nijiaqiao 269b 31.14 N 121.21 E
Nijil 132 30.31 N 35.33 E
Nijkerk 52 52.13 N 5.30 E
Nijlen 56 51.10 N 4.39 E
Nijmegen 52 51.50 N 5.50 E
Nijo Castle ⊥ 270 35.01 N 135.45 E
Nijvel → Nivelles 50 50.36 N 4.20 E
Nijverdal 52 52.22 N 6.27 E
Níkaia 267c 37.58 N 23.39 E
Nikel' 24 69.24 N 30.12 E
Nikel'tau 86 50.23 N 58.13 E
Nikiforovo 265b 55.50 N 38.05 E
Nikiniki 112 9.49 S 124.28 E
Nikip Lake ⊜ 184 52.53 N 91.53 W
Nikitovka, Ross. 78 50.23 N 38.25 E
Nikitovka, Ukr. 83 48.21 N 38.02 E
Nikitsch 61 47.32 N 16.40 E
Nikitskoje, Ross. 82 55.18 N 38.28 E
Nikitskoje, Ross. 82 55.13 N 35.46 E
Nikki 150 9.56 N 3.12 E
Nikkō 94 36.45 N 139.37 E
Nikkō-kokuritsu-kōen ♠ 94 36.49 N 139.33 E
Niklā al-'Inab 142 30.55 N 30.46 E
Niklasdorf 61 47.24 N 15.10 E
Nikobaren → Nicobar Islands II 110 8.00 N 93.30 E
Nikolai 180 62.58 N 154.09 W
Nikolajev, Ukr. 78 46.58 N 32.00 E
Nikolajev, Ukr. 78 49.32 N 23.58 E
Nikolajev □[4] 78 47.15 N 31.45 E
Nikolajevka, Kaz. 86 49.10 N 81.59 E
Nikolajevka, Ross. 80 52.28 N 49.14 E
Nikolajevka, Ross. 80 52.11 N 48.04 E
Nikolajevka, Ross. 80 53.08 N 47.12 E
Nikolajevka, Ross. 80 46.21 N 47.44 E
Nikolajevka, Ross. 83 47.18 N 38.50 E
Nikolajevka, Ross. 86 56.29 N 95.06 E
Nikolajevka, Ross. 86 54.57 N 75.44 E
Nikolajevka, Ross. 88 55.46 N 98.10 E
Nikolajevka, Ross. 89 48.34 N 134.47 E
Nikolajevka, Ukr. 78 47.38 N 33.12 E
Nikolajevka, Ukr. 78 47.06 N 34.14 E
Nikolajevka, Ukr. 78 44.58 N 33.37 E
Nikolajevka, Ukr. 78 46.23 N 29.24 E
Nikolajevka, Ukr. 78 47.33 N 30.25 E
Nikolajevka, Ukr. 78 51.04 N 34.02 E
Nikolajevka, Ukr. 83 48.46 N 38.20 E
Nikolajevka, Ukr. 83 48.51 N 37.46 E
Nikolajevka, Ukr. 83 47.39 N 37.41 E
Nikolajevo 76 58.16 N 29.29 E
Nikolajevo-Kozlovskij 83 47.13 N 38.21 E
Nikolajevsk 80 50.01 N 45.28 E
Nikolajevskaja 80 47.37 N 41.29 E
Nikolajevsk-Na-Amure 89 53.08 N 140.44 E
Nikolajevskoje, Ross. 78 45.08 N 39.36 E
Nikolajevskoje, Ross. 88 51.04 N 111.48 E
Nikolajevskoje, Ross. 88 52.21 N 117.00 E
Nikolassee ◆[8] 264a 52.26 N 13.12 E
Nikolayev → Nikolajev 78 46.58 N 32.00 E
Nikolo-Berezovec 76 58.38 N 42.17 E
Nikolo-Berjozovka 80 56.06 N 54.17 E
Nikolo-Chovanskoje 265b 55.36 N 37.27 E
Nikologory 80 56.09 N 41.59 E
Nikolo-Kropotki 82 56.44 N 37.55 E
Nikolo-L'vovsk 89 43.54 N 131.23 E
Nikolo-Makarovo 80 57.38 N 43.34 E
Nikolsdorf 64 46.47 N 12.55 E
Nikol'sk, Ross. 24 59.30 N 45.27 E
Nikol'sk, Ross. 80 53.45 N 46.05 E
Nikolski 180 52.56 N 168.52 W
Nikol'skij, Ross. 24 60.55 N 34.00 E
Nikol'skij, Ross. 86 56.18 N 68.58 E
Nikol'skij Toržok 76 59.53 N 38.46 E
Nikol'skoje, Ross. 74 55.12 N 166.00 E
Nikol'skoje, Ross. 76 52.39 N 36.04 E
Nikol'skoje, Ross. 76 55.26 N 35.04 E
Nikol'skoje, Ross. 76 59.23 N 44.36 E
Nikol'skoje, Ross. 76 59.30 N 42.32 E
Nikol'skoje, Ross. 78 50.35 N 41.10 E
Nikol'skoje, Ross. 80 47.46 N 46.24 E
Nikol'skoje, Ross. 80 52.37 N 43.49 E
Nikol'skoje, Ross. 82 54.51 N 35.53 E
Nikol'skoje, Ross. 82 54.27 N 36.24 E
Nikol'skoje, Ross. 82 54.30 N 36.50 E
Nikol'skoje, Ross. 82 54.03 N 37.10 E
Nikol'skoje, Ross. 82 54.18 N 35.53 E
Nikol'skoje, Ross. 82 55.37 N 36.41 E
Nikol'skoje, Ross. 82 55.15 N 36.04 E
Nikol'skoje, Ross. 82 56.09 N 36.43 E
Nikol'skoje, Ross. 82 55.53 N 36.26 E
Nikol'skoje, Ross. 86 57.12 N 84.21 E
Nikol'skoje, Ross. 86 52.02 N 55.43 E
Nikol'skoje, Ross. 265a 59.41 N 30.47 E
Nikol'skoje, Ross. 265b 55.46 N 37.54 E
Nikol'skoje, Ukr. 83 47.46 N 37.18 E
Nikol'skoje-na-Čeremšane 80 54.03 N 49.14 E
Nikol'skoje-na-Dnepre 78 48.12 N 35.12 E
Nikol'skoje-Ur'upino 265b 55.48 N 37.13 E
Nikonga ≐ 154 4.40 S 31.28 E
Nikonorovka 83 49.07 N 39.59 E
Nikonova Gora 76 60.22 N 36.07 E
Nikonovskoje 82 55.17 N 38.10 E
Nikopol, Blg. 38 43.42 N 24.54 E
Nikopol', Ukr. 78 47.35 N 34.25 E
Niksar 130 40.36 N 36.58 E
Nīkshahr 128 26.13 N 60.12 E
Nikšić 38 42.46 N 18.56 E
Nikulino, Ross. 76 55.16 N 33.46 E
Nikulino, Ross. 80 58.05 N 44.14 E
Nikulino, Ross. 82 56.48 N 35.50 E
Nikulino ◆[8] 265b 55.40 N 37.28 E
Nikulkino 82 56.07 N 38.38 E
Nikul'skoje 82 55.10 N 38.41 E
Nikumaroro I[1] 14 4.40 S 174.32 W
Nikunau I 14 1.23 S 176.26 E
Nil → Nile ≐ 140 30.10 N 31.06 E
Nīl, Nahr an- → Nile ≐ 140 30.10 N 31.06 E
Nila, Pulau I 164 6.44 S 129.31 E
Nilakka ⊜ 26 63.07 N 26.33 E
Niland 204 33.14 N 115.31 W
Nil Blanc → White Nile ≐ 140 15.38 N 32.31 E
Nile □[5] 154 3.00 N 31.30 E
Nile (Nahr an-Nīl) ≐ 140 30.10 N 31.05 E
Niles, Il., U.S. 216 42.01 N 87.43 W
Niles, Mi., U.S. 216 41.49 N 86.15 W
Niles, Oh., U.S. 214 41.10 N 80.45 W
Niles Canyon V 282 37.36 N 121.56 W
Niles Pond ⊜ 283 42.35 N 70.40 W
Nilgani 272b 22.46 N 88.26 E
Nilgaut, Lac ⊜ 190 46.36 N 77.15 W
Nīlgiri 126 21.28 N 86.46 E
Nilka 86 43.47 N 82.20 E
Nilkitkwa ≐ 182 55.27 N 126.43 W
Nillahcootie, Lake ⊜[1] 169 36.54 S 146.00 E
Nilo → Nile ≐ 140 30.10 N 31.06 E
Nilo Azul → Blue Nile ≐ 140 15.38 N 32.31 E
Nilo Blanco → White Nile ≐ 140 15.38 N 32.31 E
Nilópolis 256 22.49 S 43.25 W
Nilópolis □[7] 287a 22.49 S 43.26 W
Nilphāmāri 124 25.56 N 88.51 E
Nilsiä 26 63.12 N 28.05 E
Niltepec 234 16.34 N 94.37 W
Nilüfer ≐ 130 40.18 N 28.27 E
Nīlwāl ◆[8] 272a 28.40 N 76.59 E
Nilwood 219 39.24 N 89.49 W
Nima 96 35.09 N 132.24 E
Nīmach 120 24.28 N 74.52 E
Niman ≐ 89 51.24 N 132.45 E
Nimančik 89 52.09 N 133.47 E
Nimba, Mount ∧ 150 7.37 N 8.25 W
Nimbāhera 120 24.37 N 74.41 E
Nimba Range ⋀ 150 7.30 N 8.30 W
Nimboran, Pegunungan ⋀ 164 2.45 S 140.20 E
Nimelen ≐ 89 52.27 N 136.32 E
Nîmes 62 43.50 N 4.21 E
Nimis 64 46.12 N 13.16 E
Nimishillen Creek ≐ 214 40.38 N 81.22 W
Nimisila 214 40.56 N 81.34 W
Nimisila Reservoir ⊜[1] 214 40.57 N 81.31 W
Nīm Ka Thāna 120 27.44 N 75.48 E
Nimmitabel 166 36.31 S 149.16 E
Nimmonsburg 210 42.09 N 75.55 W
Nimpkish Lake ⊜ 182 50.25 N 126.59 W
Nimrod Lake ⊜[1] 194 34.55 N 93.20 W
Nīmrūz □[4] 128 30.30 N 62.00 E
Nims ≐ 56 49.51 N 6.28 E
Nimta 272b 22.40 N 88.25 E
Nimule 154 3.36 N 32.03 E
Nimule National Park ♠ 154 3.50 N 31.35 E
Nimy 50 50.28 N 3.57 E
Niña Bonita, Presa ⊜[1] 286b 23.02 N 82.29 W
Nīnah, Wādī V 146 30.02 N 15.22 E
Nīnawā □[4] 128 36.10 N 42.35 E
Nīnawá (Nineveh) ⊥ 128 36.25 N 43.10 E
Nin Bay ⊂ 116 12.13 N 123.15 E
Ninda 152 14.47 S 21.24 E
Nindigully 166 28.21 S 148.49 E
Nindirí 236 12.00 N 86.08 W
Nine Ashes 260 51.42 N 0.18 E
Nine Degree Channel ʊ 122 9.00 N 73.00 E
Ninemile Creek ≐, N.Y., U.S. 210 43.24 N 76.38 W
Ninemile Creek ≐, N.Y., U.S. 210 43.11 N 75.20 W
Ninemile Creek ≐, N.Y., U.S. 210 43.06 N 76.14 W
Nine Mile Creek ≐, Ut., U.S. 200 39.50 N 109.53 W
Ninemile Island I 279b 40.29 N 79.52 W
Nine Mile Lake ⊜ 212 44.57 N 79.34 W
Nine Mile Point › 212 44.09 N 76.34 W
Ninepin Group II 271d 22.16 N 114.21 E
Nineteen Hundred Five Memorial Cemetery ◆ 265a 59.51 N 30.27 E
Ninette 184 49.24 N 99.38 W
Ninetyeast Ridge ✦[3] 6 4.00 S 90.00 E
Ninety Mile Beach ⊼[2], Austl. 166 38.13 S 147.23 E
Ninety Mile Beach ⊼[2], N.Z. 172 34.48 S 173.00 E
Ninety Six 192 34.10 N 82.01 W
Nineveh, In., U.S. 218 39.22 N 86.05 W
Nineveh, N.Y., U.S. 210 42.12 N 75.36 W
Nineveh → Nīnawá ⊥ 128 36.25 N 43.10 E
Ninfa ⊥ 66 41.36 N 12.58 E
Ninfas, Punta › 254 42.56 S 64.20 W
Ninfield 42 50.53 N 0.25 E
Ninga 184 49.13 N 99.51 W
Ningaloo 162 22.42 S 113.40 E
Ning'an 89 44.22 N 129.25 E
Ningari 150 14.40 N 3.16 W
Ningbo 100 29.52 N 121.31 E
Ningcheng (Tianyi) 98 41.33 N 119.20 E
Ningde 100 26.43 N 119.33 E
Ningdu 100 26.31 N 115.58 E
Ningerum 164 5.41 S 141.08 E
Ninggang 100 26.50 N 114.02 E
Ningguo 106 30.38 N 118.58 E
Ninghai 100 29.17 N 121.25 E
Ninghe (Lutai) 105 39.20 N 117.48 E
Ninghepu 105 40.43 N 116.07 E
Ninghua 100 26.15 N 116.38 E
Ningi 150 11.04 N 9.32 E
Ningjin, Zhg. 98 37.37 N 114.55 E
Ningjin, Zhg. 98 37.39 N 116.48 E
Ningjing Shan ⋀ 102 29.45 N 98.45 E
Ningling 98 34.27 N 115.21 E
Ningming 102 22.07 N 107.05 E
Ningnan 102 27.11 N 102.36 E
Ningpo → Ningbo 100 29.52 N 121.31 E
Ningqiang 102 32.44 N 106.19 E
Ningshan 102 33.04 N 108.39 E
Ningsia → Yinchuan 102 38.30 N 106.18 E
Ningsia Hui Autonomous Region → Ningxia Huizu Zizhiqu □[4] 102 37.00 N 106.00 E
Ningwu 102 39.01 N 112.21 E
Ningxi 100 28.35 N 121.00 E
Ningxia Huizu Zizhiqu (Ningsia Hui) □[4] 102 37.00 N 106.00 E
Ningxian 102 35.31 N 108.01 E
Ningxiang 100 28.15 N 112.33 E
Ningyang 98 35.47 N 116.47 E
Ningyō-tōge)(96 35.19 N 133.56 E
Ningyuan 102 25.37 N 111.46 E
Ningyuanbao 102 38.38 N 102.30 E
Ningyuanpu 105 40.44 N 114.54 E
Ninh Binh 110 20.15 N 105.59 E
Ninh Hoa 110 12.29 N 109.08 E
Ninhue 252 36.24 S 72.24 W
Ninigo Group II 164 1.15 S 144.15 E
Ninilchik 180 60.03 N 151.41 W
Ninnescah ≐ 198 37.20 N 97.10 W
Ninnescah, North Fork ≐ 198 37.34 N 97.42 W
Ninnescah, South Fork ≐ 198 37.34 N 97.42 W
Ninnis Glacier Tongue ⊓ 9 68.12 S 147.12 E
Ninocminda 84 41.18 N 43.35 E
Ninohe 92 40.16 N 141.18 E
Ninomiya, Nihon 94 35.18 N 139.16 E
Ninomiya, Nihon 94 36.22 N 139.58 E
Ninove 50 50.50 N 4.01 E
Niny 84 44.29 N 43.57 E
Nio 96 34.12 N 133.39 E
Nioaque 248 21.08 S 55.48 W
Nioaque ≐ 248 20.46 S 56.04 W
Niobe 214 42.01 N 79.27 W
Niobrara 198 42.45 N 98.01 W
Niobrara ≐ 198 42.45 N 98.00 W

	English	Deutsch	Español	Français	Português
≐	River	Fluß	Río	Rivière	Rio
≋	Canal	Kanal	Canal	Canal	Canal
⌞	Waterfall, Rapids	Wasserfall, Stromschnellen	Cascada, Rápidos	Chute d'eau, Rapides	Cascata, Rápidos
ʊ	Strait	Meeresstraße	Estrecho	Détroit	Estreito
⊂	Bay, Gulf	Bucht, Golf	Bahía, Golfo	Baie, Golfe	Baía, Golfo
⊜	Lake, Lakes	See, Seen	Lago, Lagos	Lac, Lacs	Lago, Lagos
≡	Swamp	Sumpf	Pantano	Marais	Pântano
⊓	Ice Features, Glacier	Eis- und Gletscherformen	Accidentes Glaciales	Formes glaciaires	Acidentes glaciares
⊤	Other Hydrographic Features	Andere Hydrographische Objekte	Otros Elementos Hidrográficos	Autres données hydrographiques	Outros acidentes hidrográficos
✦	Submarine Features	Untermeerische Objekte	Accidentes Submarinos	Formes de relief sous-marin	Acidentes submarinos
□	Political Unit	Politische Einheit	Unidad Política	Entité politique	Unidade política
⊌	Cultural Institution	Kulturelle Institution	Institución Cultural	Institution culturelle	Instituição cultural
⊥	Historical Site	Historische Stätte	Sitio Histórico	Site historique	Sítio histórico
♠	Recreational Site	Erholungs- und Ferienort	Sitio de Recreo	Centre de loisirs	Area de Lazer
⊠	Airport	Flughafen	Aeropuerto	Aéroport	Aeroporto
■	Military Installation	Militäranlage	Instalación Militar	Installation militaire	Instalação militar
◆	Miscellaneous	Verschiedenes	Misceláneo	Divers	Diversos

Column 1

Name	Page	Lat.	Long.
Nioka	154	2.10 N	30.39 E
Nioki	152	2.43 S	17.41 E
Niokolo Koba	150	13.04 N	12.43 W
Niokolo Koba, Parc National du ♦	150	13.00 N	13.00 W
Niono	150	14.15 N	6.00 W
Nionsamoridougou	150	8.43 N	8.50 W
Nioro du Rip	150	13.45 N	15.48 W
Nioro du Sahel	150	15.15 N	9.35 W
Niort	32	46.19 N	0.27 W
Niota	192	35.30 N	84.32 W
Nioût ▽⁴	150	16.03 N	6.32 W
Nipan	166	24.47 S	150.01 E
Nipāni	122	16.24 N	74.23 E
Nipawin	184	53.22 N	104.00 W
Nipawin Provincial Park ♦	184	54.00 N	104.40 W
Nipe, Bahía de c	240p	20.47 N	75.42 W
Nipekamew ±	184	54.59 N	104.52 W
Nipekamew Lake ⊜	184	54.24 N	104.58 W
Nipepe	154	14.01 S	37.55 E
Nipigon	190	49.01 N	88.16 W
Nipigon, Lake ⊜	176	49.50 N	88.30 W
Nipigon Bay c	190	48.53 N	87.50 W
Nipin ±	184	55.45 N	109.02 W
Nipisi Lake ⊜	182	55.47 N	114.57 W
Nipissing ◦⁶	212	45.30 N	78.50 W
Nipissing, Lake ⊜	190	46.17 N	80.00 W
Nipisso, Lac ⊜	186	51.02 N	66.10 W
Nipisso, Lac ⊜	186	50.52 N	65.50 W
Nipomo	204	35.02 N	120.28 W
Nippenicket, Lake ⊜	283	41.58 N	71.03 W
Nippers Harbour	186	49.48 N	55.52 W
Nippersink Creek ±	216	42.23 N	88.22 W
Niqu	100	33.25 N	115.38 E
Niquelândia	255	14.27 S	48.27 W
Niquero	240p	20.03 N	77.35 W
Niquivil	252	30.25 S	68.42 W
Nīr	128	38.02 N	47.59 E
Nīr, Jabal an- ʌ²	128	24.10 N	43.20 E
Nīra ±	122	17.59 N	75.07 E
Niʾar ±	132	31.31 N	34.35 E
Nirasaki	94	35.42 N	138.27 E
Nirayama	94	35.03 N	138.57 E
Nirgua	246	10.09 N	68.34 W
Nirim	132	31.20 N	34.24 E
Nirmal	122	19.06 N	78.21 E
Nirmāli	124	26.19 N	86.35 E
Nirsa	126	23.47 N	86.43 E
Niš	38	43.19 N	21.54 E
Nisa	38	39.31 N	7.39 W
Nisa (Neisse) (Nysa Łużycka) ±	30	52.04 N	14.46 E
Nisāb, Ar. Su.	128	24.25 N	44.43 E
Nisāb, Yaman	144	14.31 N	46.30 E
Nišava ±	38	43.22 N	21.46 E
Nisbet	210	41.13 N	77.07 W
Niscemi	70	37.09 N	14.23 E
Nischintpur	124	22.26 N	88.22 E
Nisf Thārī Bashbīsh	142	31.07 N	31.11 E
Nish → Niš	38	43.19 N	21.54 E
Nishan	120	33.05 N	85.30 E
Nishi ⬦⁸, Nihon	265	35.27 N	139.38 E
Nishi ⬦⁸, Nihon	270	34.41 N	135.30 E
Nishiarai ⬦⁸	268	35.47 N	139.47 E
Nishiazai	94	35.31 N	136.10 E
Nishibetsuin	270	34.58 N	135.31 E
Nishi-Chūgoku-sanchi-kokutei-kōen ♦	96	34.40 N	132.10 E
Nishigō	94	37.09 N	140.10 E
Nishiyayama	96	33.53 N	133.49 E
Nishizu	94	34.58 N	138.47 E
Nishi-jima I	94	34.39 N	134.29 E
Nishikata	94	36.28 N	139.45 E
Nishikatsura	94	35.31 N	138.51 E
Nishiki	96	34.16 N	131.57 E
Nishikiori	270	34.29 N	132.15 E
Nishikiyō ⬦⁸	270	34.59 N	135.40 E
Nishimori ⬦⁸	270	34.45 N	135.01 E
Nishinari ⬦⁸	270	34.38 N	135.28 E
Nishinasuno	94	36.53 N	139.59 E
Nishinomiya	96	34.43 N	135.20 E
Nishinoomote	93b	30.44 N	131.00 E
Nishio	96	34.52 N	137.03 E
Nishishita ⬦⁸	270	34.43 N	135.00 E
Nishitosa	96	33.09 N	132.47 E
Nishiwaki	96	34.59 N	134.58 E
Nishiyodogawa ⬦⁸	270	34.42 N	135.27 E
Nishinomiya → Nishinomiya	96	34.43 N	135.20 E
Nisiros I	38	36.35 N	27.10 E
Niska Lake ⊜	184	55.35 N	108.38 W
Niskayuna	210	42.46 N	73.50 W
Nisling ±	180	62.27 N	139.30 W
Nismes	56	50.05 N	4.33 E
Nispen	52	51.29 N	4.28 E
Nisporeny	38	47.06 N	28.11 E
Nisqually ±	224	47.06 N	122.42 W
Nisqually Indian Reservation ⬦⁴	224	47.02 N	122.42 W
Nisqually Reach c	224	47.07 N	122.45 W
Nissan ±	26	56.40 N	12.51 E
Nissequogue ⊜	276	40.54 N	73.12 W
Nissequogue ±	276	40.54 N	73.13 W
Nissequogue, Northeast Branch ±	276	40.50 N	73.13 W
Nissequogue River State Park ♦	276	40.51 N	73.13 W
Nisser	26	59.10 N	8.30 E
Nisshin	94	35.08 N	137.02 E
Nissoria	70	37.39 N	14.27 E
Nissum Bredning c	26	56.38 N	8.22 E
Nissum Fjord c²	26	56.21 N	8.14 E
Nisswa	190	46.31 N	94.17 W
Nistelrode	52	51.43 N	5.33 E
Nister ±	56	50.47 N	7.43 E
Nisutlin ±	180	60.10 N	132.30 W
Nita, Indon.	115b	8.40 S	122.11 E
Nita, Nihon	96	35.12 N	133.01 E
Nitabas	272c	19.06 N	78.08 E
Nītaure	76	57.10 N	25.10 E
Niterói	256	22.53 S	43.07 W
Niterói ◦⁷	287a	22.55 S	43.04 W
Nith ±, On., Can.	212	43.12 N	80.22 W
Nith ±, Scot., U.K.	44	55.00 N	3.35 W
Nithārī ⬦⁸	272a	28.42 N	77.03 E
Nithi River	182	54.01 N	125.01 W
Nithsdale V	44	55.14 N	3.46 W
Nitibe	112	9.19 S	124.12 E
Nitinat	224	48.49 N	124.37 W
Nitinat Lake ⊜	182	48.45 N	124.45 W
Niton	42	50.35 N	1.16 W
Nitra ±	30	48.19 N	18.05 E
Nitra ±	30	48.14 N	18.04 E
Nitro	188	38.24 N	81.50 W
Nitry	40	47.40 N	3.53 E
Nitta	94	36.17 N	139.18 E
Nittälven ±	40	59.51 N	14.50 E
Nittany Mountain ʌ	210	41.00 N	77.25 W
Nittedal	26	60.04 N	10.53 E
Nittenau	60	49.12 N	12.16 E
Nittendorf	60	49.02 N	11.58 E
Niu Aunfo Point ➤	174w	21.04 S	175.09 W
Niubautun	100	39.46 N	116.41 E
Niubu	100	31.07 N	117.39 E
Nioutuncun	104	41.28 N	120.28 E
Niue ◦², Oc.	14	19.02 S	169.52 W
Niue ◦², Oc.	174v	19.02 S	169.52 W
Niu'erhe	89	51.30 N	121.49 E
Niufentai	89	41.30 N	120.02 E
Niufozhen	107	29.23 N	105.02 E
Niuhang	100	28.44 N	115.51 E
Niuhuaxi	107	29.23 N	105.02 E
Niujie	102	27.47 N	104.16 E

Column 2

Name	Page	Lat.	Long.
Niujingjie	110	25.46 N	100.33 E
Niuke	120	30.41 N	82.01 E
Niulakita I	14	10.45 S	179.30 E
Niulan ±	102	27.28 N	103.10 E
Niulanshan	105	40.13 N	116.39 E
Niumaowu	98	40.58 N	124.59 E
Niupeng	106	31.32 N	121.50 E
Niupichang	107	30.35 N	103.40 E
Niushitun	98	35.18 N	114.24 E
Niut, Gunung ʌ	112	1.00 N	109.55 E
Niutan	107	29.05 N	105.21 E
Niutao I	14	6.06 S	177.17 E
Niutou I	100	32.58 N	113.35 E
Niutian	107	27.17 N	115.44 E
Niutoushan	89	45.09 N	126.45 E
Niutou Shan I	100	29.07 N	121.56 E
Niutuo	105	39.15 N	116.20 E
Niutuoshan	106	31.04 N	119.37 E
Niuxichang	107	28.47 N	104.31 E
Niuxintai	100	41.21 N	123.53 E
Niuyanzi	104	41.56 N	121.21 E
Niuyuanzi	105	40.20 N	117.47 E
Niuzhuang, Zhg.	98	37.21 N	118.29 E
Niuzhuang, Zhg.	104	40.58 N	122.32 E
Nivå	41	55.56 N	12.31 E
Nivala	26	63.55 N	24.58 E
Nivelle ±, Austl.	166	26.02 S	146.25 E
Nive ±, Fr.	32	43.30 N	1.29 W
Nivelles (Nijvel)	50	50.36 N	4.20 E
Nivernais ◦⁹	32	47.00 N	3.30 E
Nivernais, Canal du ꙍ	32	47.40 N	3.40 E
Niverville, Mb., Can.	184	49.37 N	97.01 W
Niverville, N.Y., U.S.	210	42.26 N	73.40 W
Nivillers	50	49.28 N	2.10 E
Nivnoje	76	53.11 N	32.35 E
Niwa ±	94	67.16 N	32.23 E
Niwāno	128	26.22 N	62.43 E
Nixa	194	37.02 N	93.17 W
Nixi	102	27.58 N	99.27 E
Nixis	107	30.08 N	106.19 E
Nixizhen	107	29.02 N	104.16 E
Nixon, Nv., U.S.	204	39.49 N	119.21 W
Nixon, Pa., U.S.	214	40.45 N	79.56 W
Nixon, Tx., U.S.	222	29.16 N	97.45 W
Niyodo	96	33.32 N	133.08 E
Niyodo ±	96	33.27 N	133.29 E
Niyor	114	2.05 N	103.17 E
Niyu Shan I	100	27.51 N	121.03 E
Niza	24	66.20 N	43.16 E
Nizāmābād	122	18.40 N	78.07 E
Nizamghāt	120	28.16 N	95.42 E
Nizam Sāgar ⊜¹	122	18.10 N	77.55 E
Nizāo ±	240p	18.11 N	70.12 W
Nizina ±	50	47.40 N	20.28 E
Nizip	128	37.01 N	37.47 E
Nízke Tatry ʌ	30	48.54 N	19.40 E
Nízke Tatry, národní park ♦	30	47.48 N	19.35 E
Nizna Čvorovaja	80	56.34 N	49.07 E
Nižnaja Duvanka	83	49.35 N	38.10 E
Nižnaja-Gerasimovka	83	48.46 N	39.44 E
Nižnaja Grajvoronka	78	51.47 N	37.45 E
Nižnʹaja Irga	86	56.51 N	57.26 E
Nižnʹaja Ivanovka ⬦⁸	88	57.55 N	107.44 E
Nižnʹaja Karelina	88	58.25 N	102.46 E
Nižnʹaja Keulʹskaja, Šivera ∪	88	58.07 N	38.11 E
Nižnʹaja Krynka	83	52.16 N	40.06 E
Nižnʹaja Matrenka	80	56.25 N	55.46 E
Nižnʹaja Ol'chovaja	88	48.44 N	39.35 E
Nižnʹaja Omka	86	55.26 N	74.55 E
Nižnʹaja Omra	24	62.46 N	55.46 E
Nižnʹaja Ošma	80	55.44 N	51.18 E
Nižnʹaja Peša	24	66.43 N	47.38 E
Nižnʹaja Pojma	88	56.11 N	97.13 E
Nižnʹaja Pokrovka	80	51.40 N	50.07 E
Nižnʹaja Šachtama	88	51.24 N	117.40 E
Nižnʹaja Salda	86	58.05 N	60.43 E
Nižnʹaja Syzranʹ	80	53.04 N	48.34 E
Nižnʹaja Tavda	86	57.40 N	66.12 E
Nižnʹaja Tunguska ±	74	65.48 N	88.04 E
Nižnʹaja Voʹdža	86	58.37 N	59.49 E
Nižnʹaja Voʹdža	86	58.19 N	79.20 E
Nižnʹaja Zaimka	88	56.09 N	98.14 E
Niženagarsk	88	55.47 N	109.33 E
Nižnebakanskij	78	44.52 N	37.52 E
Niže-Baranikovka	83	49.05 N	39.51 E
Niženčujskij	85	43.12 N	74.27 E
Niženčujskij	80	56.14 N	49.32 E
Niže-Gnilovskoj ⬦⁸	83	47.11 N	39.36 E
Nižengnutov	88	48.02 N	42.22 E
Niže-Iljimsk	88	45.27 N	34.44 E
Nižneie	83	48.46 N	38.37 E
Niže Al'kejevo	80	54.46 N	50.03 E
Niže Gir'unino	88	51.12 N	116.58 E
Niže Kučukovo	80	56.13 N	52.57 E
Niže Kujto, ozero	24	64.58 N	31.38 E
Niže M'ačkovo	82	55.35 N	37.59 E
Niže Platino	83	44.38 N	40.33 E
Nižnejepravaje ±	88	48.17 N	39.57 E
Niže Romanovo	86	59.47 N	69.35 E
Niže Sančelejevo	80	53.40 N	49.34 E
Nižnekamsk	80	55.32 N	51.58 E
Nižnekamskoje vodochranilišče ⊜¹	24	55.50 N	53.00 E
Nižnekundr'učen-Skaja	80	47.45 N	40.57 E
Nizin	86	64.01 N	56.16 E
Niže-Nagol'naja	83	49.00 N	39.59 E
Niže'ornoje	80	51.37 N	53.56 E
Niže-Podpol'nyj	83	47.12 N	40.01 E
Nižetambovskoje	89	50.54 N	138.13 E
Niže-T'oploje	83	48.48 N	39.23 E
Nižetisckij	80	54.54 N	30.17 E
Niže'udinsk	88	54.54 N	99.03 E
Niže'vartovsk	74	60.56 N	76.31 E
Niže'nij Baskunčak	80	48.13 N	46.50 E
Nižnij Čir	83	48.20 N	43.16 E
Nižnij Čulym	86	54.54 N	78.56 E
Nižnij Černi	80	47.41 N	43.26 E
Niže Čeršely	80	54.54 N	52.08 E
Niže Ostrovcy	76	55.35 N	38.01 E
Niže Sergi	86	56.40 N	59.18 E
Nižnij Serogozy	78	46.20 N	34.24 E
Niže Timers'any	80	54.34 N	47.45 E
Niže V'azovyje	80	55.43 N	48.32 E
Nižnij Ingaš	88	56.11 N	96.33 E
Nižnij Kisljaj	78	50.50 N	40.11 E
Niže Kuranach	74	58.50 N	125.30 E
Nor, Isla I	246	54.29 S	72.00 W
Nižnij Lomov	80	53.32 N	43.41 E
Nižnij Mamon	78	50.00 N	40.26 E
Nižnij Novgorod (Gorky)	80	56.20 N	44.00 E

Column 3

Name	Page	Lat.	Long.
Nizy-le-Comte	50	49.34 N	4.03 E
Nizza Monferrato	62	44.46 N	8.21 E
Nizzana	132	30.53 N	34.27 E
Nizzana, Nahal V	132	30.57 N	34.23 E
Nizzanim	132	31.43 N	34.38 E
Njassa-See → Nyasa, Lake ⊜	154	12.00 S	34.30 E
Njazidja (Grande Comore) I	157a	11.35 S	43.20 E
Njinjo	154	8.48 S	38.54 E
Njoko ±	152	17.10 S	24.05 E
Njombe ±	152	9.20 S	34.46 E
Njupeskär ∪	26	61.38 N	12.41 E
Njurunda	26	62.16 N	17.22 E
Nkambe	152	6.38 N	10.40 E
Nkandla	158	28.37 S	31.05 E
Nkawkaw	150	6.33 N	0.47 W
Nkayi	154	19.00 S	28.54 E
Nkhata Bay	154	11.33 S	34.18 E
Nkhotakota	154	12.57 S	34.17 E
Nkolabona	152	1.14 N	11.43 E
Nkomi, Lagune c	152	1.35 S	9.17 E
Nkongsamba	152	4.57 N	9.56 E
Nkonko	154	6.20 S	34.58 E
Nkoso	152	2.42 S	22.39 E
Nkoto	152	1.56 S	19.41 E
Nkunga	152	4.41 S	18.34 E
Nkurenkuru	152	17.38 S	18.35 E
Nkwalini	158	28.45 S	31.33 E
Nmai ±	102	25.42 N	97.30 E
Nnewi	150	6.00 N	6.59 E
Noādbād	272b	22.34 N	88.31 E
Noailles	50	49.22 N	2.12 E
Noākhāli	124	22.49 N	91.06 E
Noak Hill ⬦⁸	260	51.37 N	0.14 E
Noale	54	45.32 N	12.04 E
Noāmundi	124	22.09 N	85.32 E
Noank	207	41.19 N	71.59 W
Noarlunga	168b	35.11 S	138.30 E
Noasca	62	45.27 N	7.19 E
Noatak ±	180	67.34 N	162.59 W
Noatak	180	67.00 N	162.30 W
Nobby	171	27.51 S	151.54 E
Nobel	212	45.25 N	80.06 W
Nobeoka	92	32.35 N	131.40 E
Nobidome	268	35.48 N	139.35 E
Nobidome-yōsui ꙍ¹	268	35.44 N	139.27 E
Nōbi-heiya ≃	94	35.15 N	136.45 E
Noble	150	11.33 N	1.12 W
Noble, Il., U.S.	194	38.41 N	88.13 W
Noble, Ok., U.S.	196	35.08 N	97.23 W
Noble ±	216	41.24 N	85.25 W
Noble Park	274b	37.58 S	145.10 E
Noblestown	279b	40.24 N	80.12 W
Noblesville	218	40.02 N	86.00 W
Nobleton, On., Can.	212	43.54 N	79.40 W
Nobleton, Fl., U.S.	228	28.38 N	82.15 W
Noboribetsu	92a	42.27 N	141.11 E
Noborito	268	35.37 N	139.34 E
Nobsa	246	14.44 S	56.20 W
Nocatee	220	27.09 N	81.52 W
Noccundra	166	27.50 S	142.36 E
Nocé	64	48.22 N	0.42 E
Noce ±	54	46.09 N	11.04 E
Nocera Inferiore	68	40.44 N	14.38 E
Nocera Superiore	68	40.44 N	14.40 E
Nocera Tirinese	68	39.02 N	16.09 E
Nocera Umbra	66	43.05 N	12.47 E
Noceto	62	44.48 N	10.11 E
Nochistlán	234	21.22 N	102.51 W
Nochten	58	51.26 N	14.36 E
Nociglia	68	40.02 N	18.20 E
Nockamixon Lake ⊜¹	208	40.28 N	75.14 W
Nockamixon State Park ♦	208	40.27 N	75.16 W
Nockatunga	166	27.43 S	142.43 E
Nocona	196	33.47 N	97.43 W
Nocopétaro	234	18.48 N	101.04 W
Nocrich	38	45.56 N	24.25 E
Noda	94	35.56 N	139.52 E
Nodagawa	96	35.31 N	135.06 E
Nodaway ±	194	39.54 N	94.58 W
Nodera	272	45.20 N	141.41 E
Nods	58	47.06 N	6.20 E
Noé, Ouadi V	146	15.39 N	21.19 E
Noel	194	36.32 N	94.29 W
Noenieput	158	27.29 S	20.06 E
Noepoli	68	40.05 N	16.20 E
Noer	41	54.27 N	10.00 E

Column 4

Name	Page	Lat.	Long.
Nokami	96	34.15 N	135.20 E
Nokaneng	156	19.40 S	22.16 E
Nōke	270	34.26 N	135.29 E
Nokha Mandi	120	27.35 N	73.29 E
Nokia	26	61.28 N	23.30 E
Nokilalaki, Bulu ʌ	112	1.13 S	120.08 E
Nok Kundi	128	28.46 N	62.46 E
Nokogiri-yama ʌ²	268	35.09 N	139.51 E
Nokomis, Sk., Can.	184	51.30 N	105.00 W
Nokomis, Fl., U.S.	220	27.07 N	82.26 W
Nokomis, Il., U.S.	219	39.18 N	89.17 W
Nokomis Lake ⊜	184	56.58 N	103.02 W
Nokou	146	14.35 N	14.47 E
Nokpan-ni ⬦⁸	271b	37.36 N	126.56 E
Nokrek ʌ	124	25.27 N	90.20 E
Noku	175f	14.53 S	166.35 E
Nola, Centraf.	152	3.32 N	16.04 E
Nola, It.	68	40.55 N	14.33 E
Nolan ±	222	32.07 N	97.26 W
Nolan Creek ±	222	31.02 N	97.26 W
Nolands Fork ±	218	39.41 N	85.07 W
Nolands ±	222	31.05 N	97.36 W
Nolay	58	46.57 N	4.38 E
Nole	62	45.15 N	7.35 E
Noli, Capo di ➤	62	44.12 N	8.26 E
Nolichucky ±	192	36.07 N	83.14 W
Nolin ±	188	37.13 N	86.15 W
Nolin Lake ⊜¹	194	37.20 N	86.10 W
Nolinsk	80	57.33 N	49.57 E
Nomad	164	6.18 S	142.14 E
Nomahegan Brook ±	276	40.41 N	74.18 W
Nomans Land I	207	41.15 N	70.49 W
Nombre de Dios, Méx.	234	23.51 N	104.14 W
Nombre de Dios, Pan.	236	9.35 N	79.28 W
Nombre de Dios, Cordillera ʌ	236	15.35 N	86.55 W
Nome	180	64.30 N	165.24 W
Noměny	58	48.54 N	6.14 E
Nomexy	58	48.18 N	6.23 E
Nomgon, Mong.	102	42.50 N	105.07 E
Nomgon, Mong.	102	45.26 N	105.08 E
Nomgon uul ʌ	102	42.50 N	104.20 E
Nomingue, Petit lac ⊜	206	46.21 N	75.00 W
Nomini Bay c	208	38.09 N	76.43 W
Nomininge	206	46.24 N	75.02 W
Nomininge, Lac ⊜	206	46.26 N	74.59 W
Nomonas II	175c	7.24 N	151.53 E
Nomozaki	92	32.35 N	129.45 E
Nomtsas	156	24.22 S	16.47 E
Nomura	96	33.22 N	132.38 E
Nona, Lake ⊜	220	28.24 N	81.15 W
Nonacho Lake ⊜	176	61.42 N	109.40 W
Nonancourt	50	48.46 N	1.12 E
Nonant-le-Pin	50	48.42 N	0.13 E
Nonard	224	44.41 N	110.12 W
Nonburg	24	65.34 N	50.32 E
Nonceveux	56	50.28 N	5.44 E
Nondalton	180	60.00 N	154.49 W
Nondwa	154	6.26 S	35.20 E
None	158	28.11 S	30.49 E
Nonette ±	50	44.56 N	7.32 E
None-yama ʌ	96	33.29 N	134.10 E
Nong'an	98	44.25 N	125.10 E
Nong Bua Lamphu	110	17.11 N	102.25 E
Nong Han	110	17.21 N	103.07 E
Nong Hèt	110	19.29 N	103.59 E
Nong Khai	110	17.52 N	102.44 E
Nongoma	158	27.58 S	31.35 E
Nongoh	120	25.54 N	91.53 E
Nongston	120	25.31 N	91.16 E
Nonnenhorn	58	47.34 N	9.36 E
Nonning	166	32.30 S	136.30 E
Nonnweiler	58	49.36 N	6.58 E
Nonoai	248	27.21 S	52.47 W
Nonoava	232	27.27 N	106.44 W
Nono Island I	116	9.51 N	125.37 E
Nono de Julho, Túnel ⬦⁵	287b	23.35 S	46.39 W
Nonogasta	252	29.18 S	67.30 W
Nonoichi	94	36.32 N	136.37 E
Nonsuri I¹	94	40.45 N	124.21 E
Non Sung	110	15.11 N	102.16 E
Nonthaburi	110	13.50 N	100.29 E
Nonthaburi ◦⁵	269a	13.52 N	100.27 E
Nontron	32	45.32 N	0.40 E
Nonvianuk Lake ⊜	180	59.00 N	155.15 W
Nonza	64	42.48 N	9.21 E
Noonan	198	48.53 N	103.00 W
Noon Hill ʌ²	283	42.07 N	71.19 W
Noonkanbah	162	18.30 S	124.50 E
Noonkanbah ±	162	18.12 S	124.52 E
Noord-Beveland I	52	51.35 N	3.45 E
Noord-Brabant ◦⁴	52	51.30 N	5.00 E
Noord-Holland ◦⁴	52	52.40 N	4.50 E
Noordhollands Kanaal ꙍ	52	52.41 N	4.50 E
Noordhorn	52	53.13 N	6.20 E
Noordoewer	156	28.45 S	17.37 E
Noordoost Polder ⬦⁴ ¹	52	52.43 N	5.45 E
Noordpunt ➤	241s	12.23 N	69.10 W
Noord-Scharwoude	52	52.43 N	4.47 E
Noordwijk aan Zee	52	52.14 N	4.26 E
Noordwijk-Binnen	52	52.15 N	4.27 E
Noordwijkerhout	52	52.16 N	4.29 E
Noormarkku	26	61.35 N	21.52 E
Noorvik	180	66.50 N	161.02 W
Noosa	162	26.24 S	153.04 E
Noosa de Ángeles	234	22.27 N	105.01 E
Nootka Island I	182	49.32 N	126.40 W
Nootka Sound ﬗ	184	56.50 N	133.33 E
Nopaltepec	234	19.47 N	99.59 W
No Point, Point ➤	208	38.07 N	76.18 W
Nóqui	152	5.51 S	13.25 E
Nora ±	28	59.10 N	15.00 E
Nora, It.	68	38.59 N	9.01 E
Nora, In., U.S.	218	39.55 N	86.08 W
Nora, Sve.	28	59.31 N	15.02 E
Nora ±	71	55.40 N	121.03 E
Norah Head ➤	170	33.17 S	151.35 E
Norala	116	6.32 N	124.40 E
Noranda	190	48.15 N	79.02 W
Norashen	130	39.14 N	44.35 E
Norberg	28	60.04 N	15.56 E
Norcia	66	42.48 N	13.06 E
Norco	204	33.56 N	117.33 W
Norcross	226	33.56 N	84.12 W
Nord ◦⁴	32	50.16 N	3.00 E
Nord ±	146	20.30 N	18.15 E
Nord, Cap ➤ → Nordkapp V	24	71.11 N	25.48 E
Nord, Gare du ⬦⁸	261	48.53 N	2.21 E
Nord, Grand lac du ⊜	186	50.54 N	67.06 W

Column 5 (ENGLISH · DEUTSCH)

Name	Page	Lat.	Long.	Name	Seite	Breite	Länge
Nord, Petit lac du ⊜	186	50.50 N	67.10 W	Norman Island I	240m	18.20 N	64.37 W
Nord, Rivière du ≃	206	45.31 N	74.20 W	Normannische Inseln → Channel Islands II	28	49.20 N	2.20 W
Nordamerika → North America				Norman Park	192	31.16 N	83.41 W
Nordanholen	40	60.04 N	14.57 E	Normans Kill ±	210	42.36 N	73.44 W
Nordausques	50	50.49 N	2.05 E	Normanton, Austl.	166	17.40 S	141.05 E
Nordaustlandet I	12	79.48 N	22.24 E	Normanton, Eng., U.K.	44	53.41 N	1.27 W
Nordbögge	263	51.37 N	7.44 E	Normanville	168b	35.27 S	138.19 E
Nordborg	41	55.03 N	9.45 E	Norman Wells	180	65.17 N	126.51 W
Nordby	41	55.58 N	10.34 E	Nor Marsh ≃	260	51.24 N	0.38 E
Nord Dakota → North Dakota				Nornalup	162	35.00 S	116.49 E
Norddeich	52	53.37 N	7.09 E	Norogachi	232	27.15 N	107.07 W
Nordegg	182	52.28 N	116.04 W	Noroton ≃	276	41.03 N	73.31 W
Nordegg ±	182	52.53 N	115.18 W	Noroton Point ➤	276	41.03 N	73.26 W
Norden, Dtsch.	52	53.36 N	7.12 E	Norovlin	88	48.40 N	112.00 E
Norden, Ca., U.S.	262	53.38 N	2.13 W	Noroy-le-Bourg	58	47.37 N	6.18 E
Nordenberg	226	39.20 N	120.22 W	Norphlet	194	33.18 N	92.39 W
Nordenham	52	48.36 N	10.50 E	Norquay	184	51.53 N	102.05 W
Nordendorf	58	53.29 N	8.28 E	Norquinco	254	41.51 S	70.54 W
Nordenšel'da, archipelag II	74	76.45 N	96.00 E	Norra Barken ⊜	40	60.07 N	15.31 E
Nordenskiold ≃	180	62.05 N	136.18 W	Norrahammar	40	57.42 N	14.06 E
Norderney	52	53.42 N	7.08 E	Norra Hörken ⊜	40	60.04 N	14.53 E
Norderney I	52	53.42 N	7.10 E	Norra Kvarken (Merenkurkku) ﬗ	26	63.36 N	20.43 E
Norderstapel	41	54.24 N	9.14 E	Norra Kvills Nationalpark ♦	26	57.34 N	15.37 E
Norderstedt	52	53.43 N	10.00 E				
Nordfjord c²	26	61.54 N	5.12 E	Norrälgen ⊜	40	59.50 N	14.34 E
Nordfjordeid	26	61.54 N	6.00 E	Norrbottens Län ◦⁶	24	66.45 N	23.00 E
Nordfold	24	67.46 N	15.12 E	Norrbottens Län ◦⁶	24	66.45 N	23.00 E
Nordfriesische Inseln → North Frisian Islands II	24	54.50 N	8.12 E	Norrby	26	65.27 N	19.54 E
Nordfriesland ⬦⁸	41	54.40 N	9.10 E	Norrent-Fontes	50	50.35 N	2.24 E
Nordgermersleben	54	52.13 N	11.20 E	Nørre Snede	41	55.58 N	9.25 E
Nordhalben	54	50.22 N	11.30 E	Nørresundby	26	57.04 N	9.55 E
Nordhausen	54	51.30 N	10.47 E	Nørre Vejrup	41	55.31 N	8.47 E
Nordheim	222	28.55 N	97.36 W	Nørrfjärden	26	65.25 N	21.27 E
Nordheim von der Rhön	56	50.20 N	10.11 E	Norridge	216	41.57 N	87.49 W
Nordhorn ʌ²	263	51.09 N	10.11 E	Norridgewock	188	44.42 N	69.47 W
Nordhorn	52	52.27 N	7.05 E	Norris	192	36.11 N	84.04 W
Nordic Park	278	41.57 N	88.02 W	Norris, Lake ⊜	220	28.57 N	81.32 W
Nordingrå	26	62.56 N	18.16 E	Norris Arm	186	49.05 N	55.15 W
Nordirland → Northern Ireland	48	54.40 N	6.45 W	Norris Bridge ⬦⁵	208	37.37 N	76.26 W
Nordiyya	132	32.19 N	34.54 E	Norris City	194	37.58 N	88.19 W
Nordkanal ≃	263	51.10 N	6.42 E	Norris Dam State Park ♦	192	36.14 N	84.07 W
Nordkapp ➤	24	71.11 N	25.48 E	Norrish Creek ≃	224	49.10 N	122.08 W
Nordkinnhalvøya ʌ¹	24	70.55 N	27.45 E	Norris Lake ⊜	192	36.20 N	83.55 W
Nordkirchen	52	51.44 N	7.31 E	Norris Point	186	49.31 N	57.53 W
Nordkjosbotn	24	69.13 N	19.30 E	Norristown	208	40.03 N	122.41 W
Nord-Korea → Korea, North ◦¹	98	40.00 N	127.00 E	Norrköping	28	58.36 N	16.11 E
Nordländer	224	48.03 N	122.41 W	Norrnäs	26	62.53 N	21.11 E
Nordland ◦⁶	24	67.00 N	14.40 E	Norrsjön ⊜	40	58.36 N	16.16 E
Nördliche Dwina → Severnaja Dvina	24	64.32 N	40.30 E	Norrsundet	28	60.56 N	17.08 E
Nördliches Eismeer → Arctic Ocean				Norrtälje	40	59.46 N	18.42 E
Nördlingen	56	85.00 N	170.00 E	Norrtäljeviken c	40	59.47 N	18.53 E
Nördmaling	26	63.34 N	19.30 E	Norseman	162	32.12 S	121.46 E
Nordmark	40	59.50 N	14.06 E	Norsewood	172	40.04 S	176.13 E
Nordmarka ⬦¹	26	60.00 N	10.25 E	Norsjö ⊜	26	59.18 N	9.20 E
Nordostrundingen ➤	186	81.36 N	12.09 W	Norsjö	26	64.55 N	19.29 E
Nord-Ostsee-Kanal ≃	30	53.53 N	9.08 E	Norsk	89	52.20 N	129.55 E
Nord-Ouest ◦²	152	6.30 N	10.30 E	Norsminde	41	56.01 N	10.16 E
Nordpfälzer Bergland ±	56	49.40 N	7.40 E	Norsup	175f	16.05 S	167.23 E
Nordradde ≃	52	52.43 N	7.17 E	Norte, Cabo ➤, Bra.	256	1.40 N	49.55 W
Nordreisa	24	69.46 N	21.03 E	Norte, Cabo ➤, Chile	174z	27.03 S	109.24 W
Nordre Strømfjord c²	176	67.50 N	52.00 W	Nor. → Nordkapp ➤	24	71.11 N	25.48 E
Nordrhein-Westfalen ◦³	52	51.30 N	7.30 E	Norte ±	288	34.37 S	58.15 W
Nordsee → North Sea ▽²	22	55.20 N	3.00 E	Norte, Canal ﬗ	250	0.30 N	50.30 W
Nordstemmen	52	52.09 N	9.46 E	Norte, Cayo I	240m	18.20 N	65.15 W
Nordstrand I	41	54.30 N	8.53 E	Norte, Estación del → North Sea ▽²	266a	40.25 N	3.43 W
Nordstrandischmoor I	41	54.33 N	8.48 E	Norte, Mar del → North Sea ▽²	22	55.20 N	3.00 E
Nord-Trøndelag ◦⁶	24	64.25 N	12.00 E	Norte, Punta ➤	254	42.04 S	63.45 W
Nordvik	74	74.02 N	111.32 E	Norte, Serra do ʌ¹	248	11.20 S	59.00 W
Nordwalde	52	52.05 N	7.28 E	Nortelândia	248	14.25 S	56.48 W
Nordwest-Kap → North West Cape ➤	162	21.45 S	114.10 E	Norte de Santander ◦⁵	238	9.15 N	73.00 W
Nore ≃	26	60.10 N	9.01 E	Norte de Santander ◦⁵	246	8.00 N	73.00 W
Nore ±	48	52.25 N	6.58 W	Nörten-Hardenberg	52	51.38 N	9.56 E
Noremberg → Nürnberg	60	49.27 N	11.04 E	Norton, S.C., U.S.	192	33.36 N	81.06 W
Norf	263	51.11 N	6.44 E	Norton, s.Afr.	158	17.53 S	30.42 E
Norfolk, Ct., U.S.	207	41.59 N	73.12 W	Northam, Austl.	168a	31.39 S	116.40 E
Norfolk, Ne., U.S.	198	42.01 N	97.25 W	Northam, Eng., U.K.	42	51.02 N	4.13 W
Norfolk, Va., U.S.	208	36.50 N	76.17 W	North America ⬦¹	16	45.00 N	100.00 W
Norfolk ◦⁶ Ma., U.S.	207	42.10 N	71.15 W	North Adams, Ma., U.S.	207	42.42 N	73.06 W
Norfolk Broads ⬦¹	42	52.43 N	1.30 E	North Adams, Mi., U.S.	216	41.58 N	84.32 W
Norfolk-Insel → Norfolk Island I	174c	29.02 S	167.57 E	Northallerton	44	54.20 N	1.26 W
Norfolk International Airport ꙍ	208	36.54 N	76.12 W	Northam, Austl.	168a	31.39 S	116.40 E
Norfolk Island ◦², Oc.	14	29.02 S	167.57 E	Northam, S. Afr.	156	25.03 S	27.17 E
Norfolk Island ◦², Oc.	174c	29.02 S	167.57 E	North America ±	16	25.03 S	27.17 E
Norfolk Naval Aerodrome ꙍ	174c	29.03 S	167.57 E	North American Basin ⬦¹	8	30.00 N	60.00 W
Norfolk Naval Shipyard ꙍ				North Amherst	207	42.24 N	72.31 W
Norfolk Naval Station ꙍ	208	36.57 N	76.18 W	North Amityville	208	40.41 N	73.25 W
Norfolk Ridge ⬦³	8	29.00 S	168.00 E	North Andaman I	122	28.21 S	114.37 E
Nordfork Lake ⊜	194	36.25 N	92.11 W	North Andover	207	42.42 N	71.08 W
Norg	52	53.04 N	6.28 E	North Andover ◦⁶, Ma., U.S.	42	52.14 N	0.54 W
Norge	208	37.22 N	76.46 W	North Andover			
Norham	44	55.43 N	2.10 W	Northampton, Ma.	284c	38.52 N	76.49 W
Norheimsund	26	60.22 N	6.08 E	Northampton ◦⁶	232	27.15 N	107.07 W
Noria de Ángeles	234	22.27 N	101.56 W	Northampton, N.Y., U.S.	42	52.19 N	72.38 W
Norikura-dake ʌ	94	36.07 N	137.33 E	Northampton, Pa., U.S.	208	40.41 N	75.29 W
Nors'k	74	52.20 N	129.55 E	North Attleboro	207	41.59 N	71.18 W
Norci Creek ≃	284b	39.18 N	121.35 W	North Atlanta	284	33.54 N	84.18 W
Norchia ≃	66	42.15 N	11.57 E	North Attleboro	207	41.59 N	71.20 W
Norcia del Fisco				North Atlanta	207	42.42 N	73.06 W
Norseland	261	48.51 N	2.37 E				
Norslund	261	48.51 N	2.29 E	North Auburn	283	42.00 N	71.17 W
Norchia	162	33.56 N	117.33 W	North Augusta	192	33.30 N	81.57 W
Norcross	232	33.56 N	84.12 W	North Aulatsivik Island I	176	59.50 N	64.00 W
Nord, Canal du ≃	50	50.16 N	3.05 E	North Aurora	216	41.48 N	88.19 W
Nord, Cap ➤ → Nordkapp V	24	71.11 N	25.48 E	North Australian Basin ⬦¹	14	14.30 S	116.30 E
Nordamerika → North America				Northaw	260	51.42 N	0.10 W
Norf	162	25.04 S	122.32 E	North Babylon	276	40.42 N	73.19 W

Symbols in the index entries represent the broad categories identified in the key at the right. Symbols with superior numbers (ʌ¹) identify subcategories (see complete key on page I · 1).

Symbole im Register stellen die rechts im Schlüssel erklärten Kategorien dar. Symbole mit hochgestellten Ziffern (ʌ¹) bezeichnen Unterteilungen einer Kategorie (vgl. vollständiger Schlüssel auf Seite I · 1).

Los símbolos incluidos en el texto del índice representan las grandes categorías identificadas con la clave a la derecha. Los símbolos con números en su parte superior (ʌ¹) identifican las subcategorías (véase la clave completa en la página I · 1).

Les symboles de l'index représentent les catégories indiquées dans la légende à droite. Les symboles suivis d'un indice (ʌ¹) représentent les sous-catégories (voir légende complète à la page I · 1).

Os símbolos incluídos no texto do índice representam as grandes categorias identificadas com a chave à direita. Os símbolos com números em sua parte superior (ʌ¹) identificam as subcategorias (veja-se a chave completa à página I · 1).

ʌ	Mountain	Berg	Montaña	Montagne	Montanha
ʌ	Mountains	Gebirge	Montañas	Montagnes	Montanhas
x	Pass	Paß	Paso	Col	Col
V	Valley, Canyon	Tal, Cañon	Valle, Cañón	Vallée, Canyon	Vale, Canhão
≃	Plain	Ebene	Llano	Plaine	Planície
➤	Cape	Kap	Cabo	Cap	Cabo
I	Island	Insel	Isla	Île	Ilha
II	Islands	Inseln	Islas	Îles	Ilhas
±	Other Topographic Features	Andere Topographische Objekte	Otros Elementos Topográficos	Autres données topographiques	Outros acidentes topográficos

ESPAÑOL: Nombre · Página · Lat.°′ · Long.°′ W = Oeste
FRANÇAIS: Nom · Page · Lat.°′ · Long.°′ W = Ouest
PORTUGUÊS: Nome · Página · Lat.°′ · Long.°′ W = Oeste

Nombre / Nom / Nome	Página / Page	Lat.°′	Long.°′
North Balabac Strait ꭒ	116	8.10 N	117.04 E
North Baltimore	216	41.10 N	83.40 W
North Balwyn	274b	37.48 S	145.05 E
North Bannister	168a	32.35 S	116.26 E
North Bārākpur	126	22.46 N	88.22 E
North Bass Island I	214	41.43 N	82.49 W
North Battleford	184	52.47 N	108.17 W
North Bay, On., Can.	190	46.19 N	79.28 W
North Bay, N.Y., U.S.	210	43.14 N	75.45 W
North Bay, Wi., U.S.	216	42.46 N	87.47 W
North Bay c, On., Can.	212	44.53 N	79.48 W
North Bay c, Wa., U.S.	224	46.59 N	124.04 W
North Bay Shore	276	40.45 N	73.16 W
North Bay Village	220	25.51 N	80.08 W
North Beach	168a	31.52 S	115.45 E
North Beach ◆[8]	282	37.48 N	122.25 W
North Beach Peninsula ≻[1]	224	46.30 N	124.02 W
North Belle Vernon	214	40.08 N	79.52 W
North Bellmore	276	40.41 N	73.32 W
North Bend, B.C., Can.	182	49.53 N	121.27 W
North Bend, Ne., U.S.	198	41.27 N	96.46 W
North Bend, Oh., U.S.	218	39.09 N	84.44 W
North Bend, Or., U.S.	202	43.24 N	124.13 W
North Bend, Pa., U.S.	214	41.21 N	77.42 W
North Bend, Wa., U.S.	224	47.29 N	121.47 W
North Benfleet	260	51.35 N	0.32 E
North Bengal Plains ≚	124	26.20 N	88.30 E
North Bennington	210	42.55 N	73.14 W
North Bergen	276	40.47 N	74.02 W
North Berwick, Scot., U.K.	46	56.04 N	2.44 W
North Berwick, Me., U.S.	188	43.18 N	70.44 W
North Bethlehem	210	42.40 N	73.50 W
North Bihar Plains ≚	124	26.20 N	86.00 E
North Billerica	207	42.35 N	71.17 W
North Bloomfield	214	41.27 N	80.52 W
North Boggy Creek ≃	196	34.23 N	96.04 W
North Bonneville	224	45.38 N	121.58 W
Northborough	207	42.19 N	71.38 W
North Bosque ≃	196	31.40 N	97.24 W
North Boston	210	42.41 N	78.47 W
North Bourke	166	30.03 S	145.57 E
North Box Hill	274b	37.48 S	145.07 E
North Braddock	279b	40.23 N	79.50 W
North Branch, Mi., U.S.	190	43.13 N	83.11 W
North Branch, Mn., U.S.	190	45.30 N	92.58 W
North Branch, N.J., U.S.	210	40.36 N	74.41 W
North Branch Canal ≍	224	47.12 N	120.40 W
North Branford	207	41.19 N	72.46 W
North Breakers ✢[2]	174g	28.14 N	177.25 W
Northbridge, Austl.	274a	33.49 S	151.13 E
Northbridge, Ma., U.S.	207	42.09 N	71.39 W
North Bristol	214	41.24 N	80.52 W
Northbrook, On., Can.	212	44.44 N	77.10 W
Northbrook, Il., U.S.	216	42.07 N	87.49 W
Northbrook, Pa., U.S.	285	39.55 N	75.41 W
North Brookfield, Ma., U.S.	207	42.16 N	72.05 W
North Brookfield, N.Y., U.S.	210	42.51 N	75.24 W
North Brunswick	208	40.28 N	74.28 W
North Buganda □[5]	154	1.00 N	32.15 E
North Caicos I	238	21.56 N	71.59 W
North Caldwell	276	40.51 N	74.16 W
North Canadian ≃	196	35.17 N	95.31 W
North Canton, Ct., U.S.	207	41.53 N	72.53 W
North Canton, Ga., U.S.	192	34.14 N	84.29 W
North Canton, Oh., U.S.	214	40.52 N	81.24 W
North Cape	216	42.47 N	88.05 W
North Cape ≻, P.E., Can.	186	47.05 N	64.00 W
North Cape ≻, N.Z.	172	34.25 S	173.02 E
North Cape → Nordkapp ≻, Nor.	24	71.11 N	25.48 E
North Cape ≻, Pap. N. Gui.	164	2.32 S	150.49 E
North Cape ≻, Mi., U.S.	216	41.44 N	83.25 W
North Cape May	208	38.58 N	74.57 W
North Captiva Island I	220	26.35 N	82.13 W
North Caribou Lake ⊜	176	52.50 N	90.40 W
North Carolina □[3], U.S.	178	35.30 N	80.00 W
North Carolina □[3], U.S.	192	35.30 N	80.00 W
North Carver	207	41.55 N	70.48 W
North Cascades National Park ♦	224	48.30 N	121.00 W
North Castor ≃	212	45.16 N	75.24 W
North Catasauqua	208	40.40 N	75.29 W
North Chagrin Reservation ♦	279a	41.34 N	81.26 W
North Channel ꭒ, On., Can.	190	46.02 N	82.50 W
North Channel ꭒ, On., Can.	212	44.10 N	76.45 W
North Channel ꭒ, U.K.	44	55.10 N	5.40 W
North Channel ꭒ, N.Y., U.S.	276	40.36 N	73.53 W
North Channel ≃[1]	281	42.38 N	82.40 W
North Charleroi	214	40.09 N	79.54 W
North Charleston	192	32.51 N	79.58 W
North Chatham	210	42.29 N	73.38 W
North Chelmsford	207	42.38 N	71.23 W
North Chicago	216	42.19 N	87.50 W
North Chili	210	43.06 N	77.45 W
Northchurch	260	51.46 N	0.36 W
North City	224	47.45 N	122.18 W
North Cleveland	222	30.21 N	95.06 W
Northcliff ◆[8]	273d	26.09 S	27.58 E
Northcliffe	162	34.36 S	116.07 E
North Clymer	214	42.04 N	79.34 W
North Cohasset	283	42.15 N	70.50 W
North Cohocton	210	42.34 N	77.28 W
North College Hill	218	39.13 N	84.33 W
North Collins	210	42.35 N	78.56 W
North Commerce Lake ⊜	281	42.35 N	83.30 W
North Concho ≃	196	31.27 N	100.25 W
North Conway	188	44.03 N	71.07 W
North Cotabato □[4]	116	7.15 N	124.50 E
Northcote	274b	37.46 S	145.00 E
North Cray ◆[8]	260	51.26 N	0.08 E
North Creek	188	43.41 N	73.59 W
North Creek ≃	278	41.33 N	87.37 W
Northcrest	222	31.38 N	97.06 W
North Crossett	194	33.09 N	91.56 W
North Crosswicks	285	40.10 N	74.39 W
North Croton Creek ≃	196	33.24 N	100.00 W
North Dakota □[3], U.S.	178	47.30 N	100.15 W
North Dakota □[3], U.S.	198	47.30 N	100.15 W
North Dandalup	168a	32.31 S	115.58 E
North Dandalup ≃	168a	32.36 S	115.53 E
North Dartmouth	207	41.38 N	70.58 W
North Dighton	207	41.51 N	71.07 W
North Dorset Downs ⋏[1]	42	50.47 N	2.30 W
North Downs ⋏[1]	42	51.20 N	0.10 E
North Dum Dum	126	22.38 N	88.23 E
North Eagle Butte	198	45.02 N	101.15 W
North East, Md., U.S.	208	39.36 N	75.56 W
North East, Pa., U.S.	214	42.12 N	79.50 W
North-East □[5]	156	21.00 S	27.30 E
Northeast Cape	180	63.18 N	168.42 W
Northeast Cape ≻	180	63.17 N	168.45 W
Northeast Cape Fear ≃	192	34.11 N	77.57 W
Northeast Creek ≃	284b	39.18 N	76.29 W
North Eastern □[4]	154	1.00 N	40.15 E
Northeastern University ᵿ[2]	283	42.20 N	71.05 W
North Eastham	207	41.51 N	69.59 W
Northeast Henrietta	210	43.04 N	77.36 W
Northeast Islands II	175c	7.36 N	151.57 E
North Easton	207	42.04 N	71.06 W
Northeast Pass ꭒ	175c	7.30 N	151.59 E
North East Point ≻, Ba.	238	21.20 N	73.01 W
North East Point ≻, Ba.	238	22.43 N	73.50 W
North East Point ≻, Kiribati	174o	1.57 N	157.16 W
Northeast Point ≻, St. Vin.	241h	13.03 N	61.13 W
Northeast Providence Channel ꭒ	238	25.40 N	77.09 W
North Edwards	228	35.01 N	117.44 W
North Egremont	207	42.11 N	73.26 W
Northeim	52	51.42 N	10.00 E
North Elkhorn Creek ≃	218	38.13 N	84.48 W
North Elm Creek ≃	222	30.53 N	97.00 W
North English	190	41.30 N	92.04 W
Northern □[4], Ghana	150	9.30 N	1.00 W
Northern □[4], Malaŵi	154	11.00 S	34.00 E
Northern □[4], S.L.	150	9.15 N	11.45 W
Northern □[4], Zam.	154	11.00 S	31.00 E
Northern □[5], Pap. N. Gui.	164	9.00 S	148.30 E
Northern □[5], Ug.	154	2.50 N	32.45 E
Northern Arm	186	49.10 N	55.23 W
Northern Cheyenne Indian Reservation ◆[4]	202	45.31 N	106.45 W
Northern Circārs ⋏[2]	122	18.00 N	83.15 E
Northern Cook Islands II	14	10.00 S	161.00 W
Northern Division □[5]	175g	16.30 S	179.30 E
Northern Dvina → Severnaja Dvina ≃	24	64.32 N	40.30 E
Northern Indian Lake ⊜	176	57.20 N	97.20 W
Northern Ireland □[8]	48	54.40 N	6.45 W
Northern Light Lake ⊜	190	48.15 N	90.38 W
Northern Mariana Islands □[2]	14	16.00 N	149.00 E
Northern Samar □[4]	116	12.30 N	124.30 E
Northern Territory □[8]	160	20.00 S	134.00 E
North Esk ≃, Scot., U.K.	46	55.54 N	3.04 W
North Esk ≃, Scot., U.K.	46	56.44 N	2.28 W
North Essendon	274b	37.45 S	144.54 E
North Evans	210	42.42 N	78.56 W
Northey Island I	260	51.44 N	0.43 E
North Fabius ≃	194	39.54 N	91.30 W
North Fairfield	214	41.06 N	82.36 W
North Fair Oaks	282	37.28 N	122.12 W
North Falmouth	207	41.38 N	70.37 W
North Ferriby	44	53.43 N	0.30 W
Northfield, B.C., Can.	224	49.11 N	123.59 W
Northfield, Ct., U.S.	207	41.41 N	73.06 W
Northfield, Il., U.S.	278	42.05 N	87.46 W
Northfield, Ma., U.S.	207	42.41 N	72.27 W
Northfield, Mn., U.S.	190	44.27 N	93.09 W
Northfield, N.J., U.S.	208	39.22 N	74.33 W
Northfield, Oh., U.S.	214	41.20 N	81.32 W
Northfield, Vt., U.S.	188	44.09 N	72.39 W
Northfield Airport ⊠	279a	41.17 N	81.31 W
Northfield Center	279a	41.19 N	81.32 W
Northfield Park Race Track ♦	279a	41.21 N	81.31 W
Northfield Village	279a	41.21 N	81.31 W
Northfield Woods	278	42.05 N	87.52 W
North Fiji Basin ✢[1]	14	16.00 S	174.00 E
North Fillmore	228	34.24 N	118.56 W
North Fitzroy	274b	37.47 S	144.59 E
Northfleet	42	51.27 N	0.21 E
North Flinders Range ⋏	166	31.00 S	139.00 E
North Fond du Lac	190	43.48 N	88.29 W
Northford	207	41.23 N	72.47 W
North Foreland ≻	42	51.23 N	1.27 E
North Fork	226	37.13 N	119.30 W
North Fork ≃	194	36.13 N	92.17 W
North Fork Lake ⊜[1]	226	38.56 N	121.00 W
North Fork Reservoir ⊜[1]	224	45.13 N	122.15 W
North Fork Village	218	39.21 N	83.02 W
North Fort Myers	220	26.40 N	81.52 W
North Freedom	190	43.27 N	89.52 W
North Frisian Islands II	24	54.50 N	8.12 E
Northgate	216	43.01 N	85.36 W
Northgate ◆[9]	282	38.00 N	122.33 W
North Georgetown	214	40.51 N	80.59 W
North Glanford	212	43.11 N	79.54 W
North Glen Ellyn	278	41.54 N	88.04 W
Northglenn	200	39.53 N	104.59 W
North Gower	212	45.08 N	75.43 W
North Grafton	207	42.14 N	71.42 W
North Granby	207	41.59 N	72.49 W
North Grand Island Bridge ◆[5]	284a	43.04 N	78.59 W
North Great River	276	40.44 N	73.10 W
North Greece	212	43.15 N	77.44 W
North Grosvenordale	207	41.59 N	71.53 W
North Grove	216	40.37 N	85.58 W
North Gulfport	194	30.24 N	89.06 W
North Hadley	207	42.23 N	72.36 W
North Haledon	276	40.57 N	74.11 W
North Hampton	218	39.59 N	83.56 W
North Hanover	283	42.08 N	70.52 W
North Harbor c	269f	14.36 N	120.57 E
North Harbour c	274a	33.49 S	151.17 E
North Haven	207	41.23 N	72.51 W
North Head ≻, Austl.	274a	33.49 S	151.18 E
North Head ≻, N.Z.	172	36.25 S	174.03 E
North Henderson	192	36.21 N	78.22 W
North Henik Lake ⊜	176	61.45 N	97.40 W
North Hero	188	44.49 N	73.17 W
North Highlands	226	38.41 N	121.22 W
North Hill	42	50.34 N	4.25 W
North Hills, De., U.S.	285	39.46 N	75.30 W
North Hills, Il., U.S.	278	42.18 N	88.01 W
North Hills, N.Y., U.S.	276	40.47 N	73.41 W
North Hinksey	42	51.45 N	1.16 W
North Hogan Creek ≃	218	39.03 N	84.54 W
North Hollywood ◆[8]	280	34.10 N	118.23 W
North Holmwood	260	51.13 N	0.20 W
North Honcut Creek ≃	226	39.19 N	121.36 W
North Hoosick	210	42.56 N	73.21 W
North Hornell	210	42.21 N	77.40 W
North Horr	154	3.19 N	37.04 E
North Houston	222	29.54 N	95.31 W
Northiam	42	50.59 N	0.36 E
North Industry	214	40.44 N	81.22 W
North Irwin	279b	40.20 N	79.43 W
North Island I, India	122	10.08 N	72.20 E
North Island I, Kenya	154	4.04 N	36.03 E
North Island I, N.Z.	172	39.00 S	176.00 E
North Island Naval Air Station ■	228	32.42 N	117.12 W
North Islet I	116	8.56 N	120.02 E
North Jackson	214	41.06 N	80.52 W
North Java	210	42.41 N	78.20 W
North Judson	216	41.12 N	86.46 W
North Kenai	180	60.44 N	151.19 W
North Kingstown	207	41.38 N	71.25 W
North Kingsville	214	41.54 N	80.42 W
North Knife Lake ⊜	176	58.05 N	97.05 W
North Knob ∧	210	41.43 N	75.33 W
North Korea → Korea, North □[1]	98	40.00 N	127.00 E
North La Junta	198	37.59 N	103.31 W
North Lake	216	43.09 N	88.22 W
North Lake ⊜, N.Y., U.S.	276	41.09 N	73.41 W
North Lake ⊜, Tx., U.S.	222	32.57 N	96.58 W
North Lakhimpur	120	27.14 N	94.07 E
Northland ◆[9]	281	42.27 N	83.13 W
North Landing ≃	208	36.31 N	76.01 W
North Laramie ≃	198	42.08 N	104.56 W
North Las Vegas	204	36.11 N	115.07 W
North La Veta Pass)(	200	37.37 N	105.11 W
North Lawrence	214	40.51 N	81.38 W
Northleach	42	51.51 N	1.50 W
North Lewisburg	216	40.13 N	83.33 W
North Liberty	216	41.32 N	86.25 W
North Lima	214	40.56 N	80.39 W
North Lindenhurst	276	40.42 N	73.22 W
North Line Island I	276	40.38 N	73.29 W
Northline Terrace	222	29.55 N	95.25 W
North Little Rock	194	34.46 N	92.16 W
North Llano ≃	196	30.30 N	99.46 W
North Logan	202	41.46 N	111.48 W
North Loma Linda	228	34.02 N	117.05 W
North Loon Mountain ∧	202	45.07 N	115.52 W
North Loup	198	41.29 N	98.46 W
North Loup ≃	198	41.17 N	98.23 W
North Luangwa National Park ♦	154	11.50 S	32.15 E
North Luconia Shoals ✢[2]	108	5.40 N	112.35 E
North Macmillan ≃	180	63.03 N	133.18 W
North Madison	214	41.48 N	81.03 W
North Magnetic Pole ◆	16	77.19 N	101.49 W
North Malosmadulu Atoll I[1]	122	5.35 N	72.55 E
North Mamm Peak ∧	200	39.23 N	107.52 W
North Manchester	216	41.00 N	85.46 W
North Manitou Island I	190	45.06 N	86.01 W
North Mankato	190	44.10 N	94.02 W
North Manly	274a	33.46 S	151.16 E
North Maroota	170	33.29 S	150.56 E
North Marshfield	283	42.08 N	70.46 W
North Marysville	224	48.07 N	122.09 W
North Massapequa	276	40.42 N	73.27 W
Northmead, Austl.	274a	33.47 S	151.00 E
Northmead, S. Afr.	273d	26.10 S	28.20 E
North Merrick	276	40.41 N	73.33 W
North Miami	220	25.53 N	80.11 W
North Miami Beach	220	25.55 N	80.09 W
North Middleboro	207	41.56 N	70.58 W
North Milk ≃	202	49.08 N	112.23 W
North Mokelumne ≃	226	38.08 N	121.35 W
North Moose Lake ⊜	184	54.08 N	100.13 W
North Moreau Creek ≃	194	38.30 N	92.18 W
North Muskegon	216	43.15 N	86.16 W
North Myrtle Beach	192	33.49 N	78.40 W
North Nahanni ≃	180	62.05 N	124.30 W
North Naples	220	26.13 N	81.47 W
North Narrabeen	274a	33.42 S	151.18 E
North Nemah ≃	224	46.30 N	123.53 W
North New Hyde Park	276	40.44 N	73.41 W
North New River Canal ≍	220	26.05 N	80.12 W
North Newton	198	38.04 N	97.21 W
North Niles	216	41.52 N	86.15 W
North Norwich	210	42.37 N	75.31 W
North Oaks	222	30.22 N	97.41 W
North Ockendon ◆[8]	260	51.32 N	0.18 E
North Ogden	200	41.18 N	111.57 W
North Olmsted	214	41.24 N	81.55 W
Northolt Aerodrome ⊠	260	51.33 N	0.23 W
Northome	190	47.52 N	94.16 W
Northop	262	53.12 N	3.08 W
North Ore Creek ≃	281	42.43 N	83.47 W
North Orwell	210	41.55 N	76.19 W
North Ossetia → Severnaja Osetija □[3]	84	43.00 N	44.15 E
Northowram	262	53.44 N	1.50 W
North Oxford	207	42.09 N	71.52 W
North Palisade ∧	204	37.06 N	118.31 W
North Palm Beach	220	26.49 N	80.04 W
North Para ≃	168b	34.36 S	138.45 E
North Park ◆[8]	278	41.59 N	87.43 W
North Park ♦	279b	40.36 N	80.00 W
North Park Lake ⊜	279b	40.36 N	80.00 W
North Parramatta	274a	33.48 S	151.00 E
North Pass ꭒ	175c	7.41 N	151.48 E
North Patchogue	276	40.47 N	73.00 W
North Peak ∧, Ak., U.S.	180	62.34 N	162.23 W
North Peak ∧, Ca., U.S.	282	37.33 N	122.28 W
North Pease ≃	196	34.15 N	100.07 W
North Pelham, N.H., U.S.	283	42.46 N	71.21 W
North Pelham, N.Y., U.S.	276	40.55 N	73.48 W
North Pembroke	207	42.05 N	70.47 W
North Pender Island I	224	48.49 N	123.17 W
North Perry	214	41.47 N	81.07 W
North Petherton	42	51.06 N	3.01 W
North Philadelphia ◆[8]	285	39.58 N	75.09 W
North Philadelphia Airport ⊠	285	40.05 N	75.01 W
North Pine ≃	171a	27.17 S	153.01 E
North Pine Grove	214	41.24 N	79.13 W
North Piney Creek ≃	200	42.31 N	110.05 W
North Pitcher	210	42.37 N	75.49 W
North Plainfield	210	40.37 N	74.25 W
North Plains	224	45.35 N	122.59 W
North Plains ≚	200	34.40 N	108.15 W
North Platte	198	41.07 N	100.45 W
North Platte ≃	178	41.07 N	100.42 W
North Pleasureville	218	38.22 N	85.07 W
North Plympton	283	41.59 N	70.48 W
North Point, H.K.	271d	22.17 N	114.12 E
Northpoint, Pa., U.S.	214	40.54 N	79.08 W
North Point ≻, Barb.	241g	13.20 N	59.36 W
North Point ≻, Md., U.S.	284b	39.12 N	76.27 W
North Point ≻, Mi., U.S.	190	45.02 N	83.16 W
North Pole	180	64.45 N	147.21 W
North Pole ◆	16	90.00 N	0.00
Northport, Al., U.S.	194	33.13 N	87.34 W
North Port, Fl., U.S.	220	27.03 N	82.15 W
Northport, Mi., U.S.	190	45.07 N	85.37 W
Northport, N.Y., U.S.	210	40.53 N	73.20 W
Northport, Wa., U.S.	202	48.54 N	117.46 W
North Portal	184	49.00 N	102.33 W
Northport Bay c	276	40.55 N	73.23 W
Northport Harbor c	276	40.53 N	73.22 W
North Powder	202	45.01 N	117.55 W
North Pownal	207	42.47 N	73.15 W
North Prairie	216	42.56 N	88.24 W
North Providence	207	41.50 N	71.25 W
North Puyallup	224	47.12 N	122.17 W
North Queensferry	46	56.01 N	3.25 W
North Quincy	219	39.58 N	91.24 W
North Raccoon ≃	198	41.50 N	94.08 W
North Raisin ≃	206	45.09 N	74.43 W
North Ram ≃	182	52.16 N	115.38 W
North Randall	279a	41.27 N	81.32 W
North Reading	207	42.34 N	71.04 W
North Reservoir ⊜[1]	283	42.28 N	71.07 W
North Rhine-Westphalia → Nordrhein-Westfalen □[3]	30	51.30 N	7.30 E
North Richland Hills	222	32.50 N	97.13 W
North Richmond	282	37.57 N	122.22 W
Northridge, Oh., U.S.	218	39.59 N	83.46 W
Northridge, Oh., U.S.	218	39.48 N	84.11 W
Northridge ◆[8]	280	34.14 N	118.33 W
Northridge Fashion Center ◆[9]	280	34.13 N	118.33 W
North Ridge Village	218	39.57 N	86.09 W
North Ridgeville	214	41.23 N	82.01 W
North Rim	200	36.12 N	112.03 W
North River c	208	37.25 N	76.25 W
North Riverside	278	41.50 N	87.49 W
North Riverside Park Mall ◆[9]	278	41.51 N	87.49 W
North Robinson	214	40.48 N	82.51 W
North Rocks	274a	33.46 S	151.02 E
North Ronaldsay I	46	59.22 N	2.26 W
North Ronaldsay Firth ꭒ	46	59.20 N	2.25 W
North Rose	210	43.11 N	76.53 W
North Royalton	214	41.18 N	81.43 W
North Rustico	186	46.27 N	63.19 W
North Ryde	274a	33.48 S	151.07 E
North Salem	214	40.09 N	81.33 W
North Salt Lake	200	40.50 N	111.54 W
North San Juan	226	39.22 N	121.06 W
North Santiam ≃	202	44.41 N	123.00 W
North Saskatchewan ≃	176	53.15 N	105.05 W
North Saugeen ≃	212	44.19 N	81.17 W
North Scituate, Ma., U.S.	207	42.13 N	70.47 W
North Scituate, R.I., U.S.	207	41.49 N	71.35 W
North Sea ⊤[2]	22	56.00 N	3.00 E
North Seaton Colliery	44	55.11 N	1.32 W
North Sentinel Island I	110	11.33 N	92.15 E
North Shafter	226	35.31 N	119.18 W
North Shields	44	55.01 N	1.27 W
Norths Highland ⋏[1]	9	66.40 S	126.00 E
North Shoal Lake ⊜	184	50.29 N	97.40 W
North Shore	216	42.16 N	88.23 W
Northshore ◆[9]	283	42.32 N	70.57 W
North Shore Channel ≍	278	42.05 N	87.41 W
North Shores	216	41.50 N	83.25 W
North Shoshone Peak ∧	204	39.09 N	117.29 W
North Siberian Lowland → Severo-Sibirskaja nizmennost' ≚	74	73.00 N	100.00 E
Northside	174h	2.47 S	171.43 W
North Singa	126	23.16 N	89.30 E
North Sioux City	198	42.31 N	96.28 W
North Skunk ≃	190	41.15 N	92.02 W
North Somercotes	44	53.28 N	0.08 E
North Sound ꭒ, Antig.	240c	17.07 N	61.45 W
North Sound ꭒ, Ire.	48	53.11 N	9.43 W
North Sound ꭒ, Scot., U.K.	46	59.18 N	2.46 W
North Spicer Island I	176	68.30 N	78.55 W
North Spirit Lake ⊜	184	52.30 N	92.53 W
North Spot I	236	16.15 N	88.11 W
North Springfield, Pa., U.S.	214	41.59 N	80.26 W
North Springfield, Va., U.S.	284c	38.48 N	77.12 W
North Stamford Reservoir ⊜[1]	276	41.08 N	73.32 W
North Star, De., U.S.	285	39.46 N	75.43 W
North Star, Oh., U.S.	216	40.19 N	84.34 W
North Sterling Reservoir ⊜[1]	198	40.47 N	103.17 W
North Stradbroke Island I	171a	27.35 S	153.28 E
North Sudbury	283	42.24 N	71.24 W
North Sulphur ≃	196	33.23 N	95.18 W
North Sunday Creek ≃	202	46.27 N	105.54 W
North Sunderland	44	55.34 N	1.39 W
North Swansea	207	41.46 N	71.15 W
North Sydenham ≃	214	42.35 N	82.23 W
North Sydney, Austl.	274a	33.50 S	151.13 E
North Sydney, N.S., Can.	186	46.13 N	60.15 W
North Syracuse	210	43.08 N	76.07 W
North Tamborine	171a	27.56 S	153.11 E
North Taranaki Bight c[3]	172	38.42 S	174.15 E
North Tarrytown	276	41.05 N	73.51 W
North Tawton	42	50.48 N	3.53 W
North Tea Lake ⊜	190	45.56 N	79.03 W
North Terre Haute	194	39.31 N	87.21 W
North Tewksbury	283	42.38 N	71.14 W
North Thames ≃	212	42.59 N	81.16 W
North Thompson ≃	182	50.41 N	120.21 W
North Thoresby	44	53.28 N	0.03 W
North Tidworth	42	51.16 N	1.40 W
North Toe ≃	192	36.00 N	82.16 W
North Tolsta	46	58.20 N	6.13 W
North Tonawanda	210	43.02 N	78.51 W
North Towanda	210	41.47 N	76.28 W
North Troy	206	44.59 N	72.24 W
North Truro	207	42.02 N	70.05 W
North Tule Draw V	196	34.30 N	101.36 W
North Tunica	194	34.42 N	90.23 W
North Turlock	226	37.31 N	120.51 W
North Turramurra	274a	33.43 S	151.09 E
North Twin Lake ⊜	186	49.16 N	55.56 W
North Tyne ≃	44	54.59 N	2.08 W
North Ubian Island I	116	6.09 N	120.27 E
North Uist I	46	57.36 N	7.18 W
Northumberland	210	40.53 N	76.47 W
Northumberland □[6], On., Can.	212	44.10 N	78.00 W
Northumberland □[6], Eng., U.K.	44	55.15 N	2.05 W
Northumberland □[6], Pa., U.S.	210	40.49 N	76.39 W
Northumberland □[6], Va., U.S.	208	37.50 N	76.25 W
Northumberland Isles II	166	21.40 S	150.00 E
Northumberland National Park ♦	44	55.15 N	2.20 W
Northumberland Strait ꭒ	186	46.00 N	63.30 W
North Umpqua ≃	202	43.16 N	123.27 W
North Uxbridge	207	42.05 N	71.38 W
Northvale	276	41.00 N	73.56 W
North Valley Hills ⋏[2]	285	40.02 N	75.40 W
North Valley Stream	276	40.41 N	73.42 W
North Vancouver	224	49.19 N	123.04 W
North Vandergrift	279b	40.36 N	79.34 W
North Vernon	218	39.00 N	85.37 W
North Versailles	279b	40.22 N	79.48 W
North Vietnam → Vietnam □[1]	108	16.00 N	108.00 E
Northville, Mi., U.S.	216	42.25 N	83.29 W
Northville, N.Y., U.S.	210	43.13 N	74.10 W
Northville Downs ♦	281	42.26 N	83.29 W
Northvue	214	40.54 N	79.56 W
North Wabasca Lake ⊜	182	56.00 N	113.55 W
North Wales	208	40.12 N	75.16 W
Northwall	46	59.16 N	2.17 W
North Walsham	42	52.50 N	1.24 E
North Wantagh	276	40.41 N	73.30 W
North Warren	214	41.52 N	79.09 W
North Washington, Pa., U.S.	214	41.03 N	79.49 W
North Washington, Pa., U.S.	279b	40.32 N	79.36 W
North Watuppa Pond ⊜	207	41.42 N	71.06 W
Northway	180	62.58 N	141.56 W
North Weald Bassett	42	51.43 N	0.10 E
North Webster	216	41.19 N	85.41 W
North Weissport	210	40.50 N	75.41 W
Northwest ≃	208	36.31 N	76.05 W
North West Cape ≻, Austl.	162	21.45 S	114.10 E
Northwest Cape ≻, Ak., U.S.	180	63.43 N	171.45 W
Northwest Cape ≻, Fl., U.S.	220	25.13 N	81.11 W
North Westchester	207	41.34 N	72.24 W
North Western	210	43.20 N	75.22 W
North-Western □[4]	154	13.00 S	25.00 E
Northwestern University ᵿ[2], Il., U.S.	278	42.04 N	87.40 W
Northwestern University (Chicago Campus) ᵿ[2], Il., U.S.	278	41.54 N	87.37 W
Northwest Frontier □[4]	120	34.30 N	72.00 E
Northwest Gander ≃	186	48.50 N	55.00 W
Northwest Harbor c	284b	39.16 N	76.35 W
Northwest Head ≻	116	10.08 N	118.45 E
Northwest Miramichi ≃	186	46.58 N	65.35 W
Northwest Pacific Basin ✢[1]	6	40.00 N	155.00 E
North West Point ≻	174o	2.02 N	157.29 W
Northwest Providence Channel ꭒ	238	26.10 N	78.20 W
North West River	176	53.32 N	60.08 W
Northwest Territories □[4]	176	70.00 N	100.00 W
North Weymouth	283	42.15 N	70.57 W
Northwich	44	53.16 N	2.32 W
North Wichita ≃	196	33.43 N	99.29 W
North Wilbraham	207	42.09 N	72.25 W
North Wildwood	208	39.00 N	74.47 W
North Wilkesboro	192	36.09 N	81.08 W
North Willow Creek ≃	202	46.51 N	107.54 W
North Wilmington	283	42.34 N	71.09 W
North Windham, Ct., U.S.	207	41.44 N	72.09 W
North Windham, Me., U.S.	188	43.50 N	70.26 W
Northwold	42	52.33 N	0.35 E
Northwood, Eng., U.K.	42	50.44 N	1.19 W
Northwood, Ia., U.S.	190	43.26 N	93.13 W
Northwood, Mi., U.S.	216	42.19 N	85.38 W
Northwood, N.D., U.S.	198	47.44 N	97.33 W
Northwood, Oh., U.S.	214	41.36 N	83.28 W
Northwood ◆[8]	260	51.37 N	0.25 W
North Woodslee	281	42.13 N	82.43 W
Northwood Village	284c	39.02 N	77.01 W
North Yamhill ≃	224	45.13 N	123.08 W
North Yelta	168b	34.03 S	137.37 E
North York	212	43.46 N	79.25 W
North York Moors ⋏[2]	44	54.24 N	0.53 W
North York Moors National Park ♦	44	54.23 N	0.50 W
North Yorkshire □[6]	44	54.15 N	1.30 W
North Yuba ≃	226	39.22 N	121.08 W
North Zulch	222	30.55 N	96.07 W
Norton, N.B., Can.	186	45.38 N	65.42 W
Norton, Eng., U.K.	44	54.09 N	0.47 W
Norton, Eng., U.K.	262	53.20 N	2.40 W
Norton, Ks., U.S.	198	39.50 N	99.53 W
Norton, Ma., U.S.	207	41.58 N	71.11 W
Norton, Oh., U.S.	214	41.01 N	81.39 W
Norton, Vt., U.S.	206	45.00 N	71.47 W
Norton, Va., U.S.	192	36.56 N	82.37 W
Norton, Zimb.	154	17.53 S	30.42 E
Norton Air Force Base ■	228	34.06 N	117.14 W
Norton Basin c	276	40.36 N	73.47 W
Norton Bay c	180	64.45 N	161.15 W
Norton Creek ≃	281	42.34 N	83.34 W
Norton Fitzwarren	42	51.02 N	3.09 W
Norton Grove	207	42.00 N	71.12 W
Norton Heath	260	51.43 N	0.19 E
Norton Hill	210	42.25 N	74.04 W
Norton Pond ⊜	206	44.56 N	71.51 W
Norton Reservoir ⊜[1]	283	41.59 N	71.12 W
Norton Shores	216	43.10 N	86.15 W
Norton Sound ꭒ	180	63.50 N	164.00 W
Nortonville, On., Can.	275b	43.43 N	79.44 W
Nortonville, Ks., U.S.	198	39.25 N	95.20 W
Nortorf, Dtsch.	30	54.10 N	9.50 E
Nortorf, Dtsch.	52	53.55 N	9.16 E
Nort-sur-Erdre	32	47.26 N	1.30 W
Noruega → Norway □[1]	24	62.00 N	10.00 E
Noruega, Mar de → Norwegian Sea ⊤[2]	10	70.00 N	2.00 E
Norumbega Reservoir ⊜[1]	283	42.20 N	71.18 W
Nørup	41	55.43 N	9.19 E
Norval	212	43.39 N	79.51 W
Norvalspont	158	30.38 S	25.27 E
Norvège → Norway □[1]	24	62.00 N	10.00 E
Norvegia, Cape ≻	9	71.25 S	12.18 W
Norvell	216	42.10 N	84.11 W
Norvelt	214	40.12 N	79.32 W
Norvin Green State Forest ♦	276	41.03 N	74.20 W
Norwalk, Ca., U.S.	228	33.54 N	118.04 W
Norwalk, Ct., U.S.	207	41.07 N	73.24 W
Norwalk, Ia., U.S.	190	41.28 N	93.40 W
Norwalk, Oh., U.S.	214	41.14 N	82.36 W
Norwalk ≃	207	41.06 N	73.25 W
Norwalk Harbor c	276	41.06 N	73.24 W
Norwalk Islands II	276	41.03 N	73.23 W
Norway, In., U.S.	216	40.47 N	86.46 W
Norway, Ia., U.S.	190	41.54 N	91.55 W
Norway, Me., U.S.	188	44.12 N	70.32 W
Norway, Mi., U.S.	190	45.47 N	87.54 W
Norway (Norge) □[1], Europe	22	62.00 N	10.00 E
Norway (Norge) □[1], Europe	24	62.00 N	10.00 E
Norway Bay c	176	71.08 N	104.35 W
Norway House	184	53.59 N	97.50 W
Norway Lake ⊜	212	45.20 N	76.43 W
Norwegen → Norway □[1]	24	62.00 N	10.00 E
Norwegian Basin ✢[1]	10	68.00 N	2.00 W
Norwegian Sea ⊤[2]	10	70.00 N	2.00 E
Norwegian Trench ✢[1]	10	59.00 N	4.30 E
Norwell	283	42.09 N	70.47 W
Norwich, On., Can.	212	42.59 N	80.36 W
Norwich, Eng., U.K.	42	52.38 N	1.18 E
Norwich, Ct., U.S.	207	41.32 N	72.05 W
Norwich, Ks., U.S.	198	37.27 N	97.50 W
Norwich, N.Y., U.S.	210	42.31 N	75.31 W
Norwich Airport ⊠	42	52.41 N	1.15 E
Norwin Heights	279b	40.20 N	79.44 W
Norwood, On., Can.	212	44.23 N	77.59 W
Norwood, Co., U.S.	200	38.07 N	108.17 W
Norwood, Ma., U.S.	207	42.11 N	71.12 W
Norwood, Mn., U.S.	190	44.46 N	93.55 W
Norwood, N.J., U.S.	276	40.59 N	73.57 W
Norwood, N.Y., U.S.	188	44.45 N	74.59 W
Norwood, N.C., U.S.	192	35.13 N	80.07 W
Norwood, Oh., U.S.	218	39.10 N	84.27 W
Norwood, Pa., U.S.	285	39.53 N	75.17 W
Norwood ◆[8]	273d	26.10 S	28.04 E
Norwood Memorial Airport ⊠	283	42.11 N	71.10 W
Norwood Park ◆[8]	278	41.59 N	87.48 W
Norwood Pond ⊜	283	42.35 N	70.52 W
Norwoodville	190	41.39 N	93.33 W
Noryang	98	34.56 N	127.52 E
Nosaka	94	35.39 N	140.34 E
Nosappu-misaki ≻	92a	43.23 N	145.49 E
Nosate	266b	45.33 N	8.43 E
Nosbonsing, Lake ⊜	190	46.12 N	79.13 W
Nose	96	34.58 N	135.24 E
Nose ◆[8]	270	34.49 N	135.09 E
Nose Creek ≃	182	54.52 N	119.38 W
Noshiro	92	40.12 N	140.02 E
Noska ≃	86	58.53 N	68.40 E
Nosop (Nossob) ≃	156	26.55 S	20.37 E
Nosova	86	59.30 N	63.13 E
Nosovaja, Ross.	24	68.15 N	54.35 E
Nosovaja, Ross.	80	57.15 N	45.35 E
Nosovka	78	50.55 N	31.35 E
Nosovo, Ross.	76	57.07 N	27.50 E
Nosovo, Ross.	83	47.16 N	38.40 E
Nosovščina	24	62.56 N	37.03 E
Noṣratābād	128	29.54 N	59.59 E
Noss, Isle of I	46a	60.09 N	1.01 W
Nossa Senhora da Aparecida	256	22.02 S	42.48 W
Nossa Senhora das Dores	250	10.29 S	37.13 W
Nossa Senhora do Amparo	256	22.22 S	44.05 W
Nossa Senhora do Livramento	248	15.48 S	56.22 W
Nossa Senhora do Ó ◆[8]	287b	23.30 S	46.41 W
Nossebro	26	58.11 N	12.43 E
Nossen	54	51.03 N	13.17 E
Nossentiner Heide ◆[3]	54	53.35 N	12.25 E
Noss Head ≻	46	58.28 N	3.04 W
Nossob	156	22.18 S	17.10 E
Nossob (Nosop) ≃	156	26.55 S	20.37 E
Nossombougou	150	13.06 N	7.56 W
Nošul'	24	60.09 N	49.28 E
Nosy Varika	157b	20.35 S	48.32 E
Notasulga	194	32.33 N	85.40 W
Notch Cliff	284b	39.27 N	76.31 W
Notch Hill	182	50.52 N	119.26 W
Notch Peak ∧	200	39.08 N	113.24 W
Noteć ≃	30	52.44 N	15.26 E
Notigi Lake ⊜	184	55.57 N	99.18 W
Notikewin ≃	176	57.15 N	117.05 W
Noto, It.	70	36.53 N	15.04 E
Noto, Nihon	92	37.18 N	137.09 E
Noto, Golfo di c	70	36.50 N	15.12 E
Noto, Val di ◆[1]	70	37.05 N	14.35 E
Noto Antica ⊥	70	36.56 N	15.02 E
Notodden	26	59.34 N	9.17 E
Notogawa	94	35.10 N	136.10 E
Noto-hantō ≻[1]	92	37.20 N	137.00 E
Noto-hantō-kokutei-kōen ♦	94	37.10 N	136.50 E
Noto-jima	94	37.08 N	137.00 E
Noto-jima I	94	37.07 N	137.00 E
Nōtori-dake ∧	94	35.37 N	138.15 E
Notoro-ko ⊜	92a	44.05 N	144.10 E
Notozero, ozero ⊜	24	66.28 N	32.05 E
Notre-Dame	186	46.19 N	64.43 W
Notre-Dame ᵿ[1]	261	48.51 N	2.21 E
Notre-Dame, Bois ♦	261	48.45 N	2.35 E
Notre-Dame, Monts ⋏	186	48.10 N	68.00 W
Notre-Dame, Ruisseau ≃	275a	45.41 N	73.26 W
Notre Dame Bay c	186	49.45 N	55.15 W
Notre-Dame-de-Bellecombe	62	45.48 N	6.31 E
Notre-Dame-de-Lorette ᵿ[1]	50	50.25 N	2.42 E
Notre-Dame-de-Lourdes	184	49.32 N	98.33 W
Notre-Dame-de-Pierreville	206	46.06 N	72.53 W
Notre-Dame-des-Victoires ◆[8]	275a	45.35 N	73.34 W
Notre-Dame-du-Haut ᵿ[1]	58	47.43 N	6.37 E
Notre-Dame-du-Laus	188	46.05 N	75.37 W
Notre-Dame-du-Nord	190	47.36 N	79.30 W
Notrees	196	31.55 N	102.45 W
Notreure ≃	50	47.41 N	2.36 E
Notsu	96	33.02 N	131.42 E
Notsuharu	96	33.09 N	131.32 E
Nottawa	216	41.55 N	85.27 W
Nottawa Creek ≃	216	42.01 N	85.24 W
Nottawasaga ≃	212	44.32 N	80.01 W
Nottawasaga Bay c	212	44.35 N	80.15 W
Nottaway ≃	176	51.22 N	79.55 W
Nottingham, Eng., U.K.	42	52.58 N	1.10 W
Nottingham, Pa., U.S.	208	39.45 N	76.01 W
Nottingham, Pa., U.S.	285	40.07 N	74.58 W
Nottingham Island I	176	63.20 N	77.55 W
Nottingham Park	278	41.46 N	87.48 W
Nottingham Road	158	29.22 S	30.00 E
Nottinghamshire □[6]	44	53.00 N	1.00 W
Notting Hill	274b	37.54 S	145.08 E
Nottleben	54	50.58 N	10.50 E
Nottoway	192	37.08 N	78.05 W
Nottoway ≃	192	36.33 N	76.55 W
Nottuln	52	51.55 N	7.22 E
Notukeu Creek ≃	184	49.55 N	106.30 W
Nouâdhibou	148	20.54 N	17.04 W
Nouâdhibou, Râs ≻	148	20.46 N	17.03 W
Nouakchott	150	18.06 N	15.57 W
Nouâmghâr	150	19.22 N	16.31 W
Nouan-le-Fuzelier	50	47.32 N	2.02 E
Nouans-les-Fontaines	50	47.08 N	1.18 E
Nouméa	175f	22.16 S	166.27 E
Noun ≃	152	4.55 N	11.06 E
Nouna	150	12.44 N	3.52 W
Nounsley	260	51.46 N	0.36 E
Noupoort	158	31.10 S	24.57 E
Nous	158	28.44 S	19.52 E
Nouveau Brunswick → New Brunswick □[4]	186	46.30 N	66.15 W
Nouveau Mexique → New Mexico □[3]	178	34.30 N	106.00 W
Nouveau-Québec, Cratère du ⊥[6]	176	61.17 N	73.40 W
Nouvelle	186	48.08 N	66.19 W
Nouvelle ≃	186	48.07 N	66.18 W
Nouvelle-Calédonie → New Caledonia □[2]	175f	21.30 S	165.30 E
Nouvelle-Calédonie (New Caledonia) I	175f	21.30 S	165.30 E
Nouvelle Écosse → Nova Scotia □[4]	186	45.00 N	63.00 W
Nouvelle-France, Cap de ≻	176	62.27 N	73.42 W
Nouvelle Galles du Sud → New South Wales □[3]	166	33.00 S	146.00 E
Nouvelle-Orléans → New Orleans	194	29.58 N	90.07 W
Nouvelles-Hébrides → Vanuatu □[1]	175f	16.00 S	167.00 E
Nouvelle Zélande → New Zealand □[1]	172	41.00 S	174.00 E
Nouvelle Zemble → Novaja Zemlja II	72	74.00 N	57.00 E

Symbol	English	Deutsch	Español	Français	Português
≃	River	Fluß	Río	Rivière	Rio
≍	Canal	Kanal	Canal	Canal	Canal
⌞	Waterfall, Rapids	Wasserfall, Stromschnellen	Cascada, Rápidos	Chute d'eau, Rapides	Cascata, Rápidos
ꭒ	Strait	Meeresstraße	Estrecho	Détroit	Estreito
c	Bay, Gulf	Bucht, Golf	Bahía, Golfo	Baie, Golfe	Baía, Golfo
⊜	Lake, Lakes	See, Seen	Lago, Lagos	Lac, Lacs	Lago, Lagos
≚	Swamp	Sumpf	Pantano	Marais	Pântano
⊓	Ice Features, Glacier	Eis- und Gletscherformen	Accidentes Glaciales	Formes glaciaires	Acidentes glaciares
⊤	Other Hydrographic Features	Andere Hydrographische Objekte	Otros Elementos Hidrográficos	Autres données hydrographiques	Outros acidentes hidrográficos
✢	Submarine Features	Untermeerische Objekte	Accidentes Submarinos	Formes de relief sous-marin	Acidentes submarinos
□	Political Unit	Politische Einheit	Unidad Política	Entité politique	Unidade política
ᵿ	Cultural Institution	Kulturelle Institution	Institución Cultural	Institution culturelle	Instituição cultural
⊥	Historical Site	Historische Stätte	Sitio Histórico	Site historique	Sitio histórico
♦	Recreational Site	Erholungs- und Ferienort	Sitio de Recreo	Centre de loisirs	Area de Lazer
⊠	Airport	Flughafen	Aeropuerto	Aéroport	Aeroporto
■	Military Installation	Militäranlage	Instalación Militar	Installation militaire	Instalação militar
◆	Miscellaneous	Verschiedenes	Misceláneo	Divers	Diversos

I · 126 Nouv-Nyan

ENGLISH: Name Page Lat.°′ Long.°′
DEUTSCH: Name Seite Breite°′ Länge°′ E = Ost

Nouvion-en-Ponthieu 50 50.12 N 1.47 E
Nouvion-sur-Meuse 56 49.42 N 4.48 E
Nouzonville 56 49.49 N 4.45 E
Nova, Magy. 61 46.41 N 16.41 E
Nova, Oh., U.S. 214 41.02 N 82.18 W
Nova América 255 15.01 S 49.56 W
Nova Andradina 255 22.10 S 53.15 W
Novabad, Taj. 85 38.37 N 68.45 E
Novabad, Taj. 85 39.01 N 70.09 E
Nová Baňa 30 48.26 N 18.39 E
Nová Bystřice 61 49.01 N 15.06 E
Nova Cachoeirinha ◆[8] 287b 23.28 S 46.40 W
Nova Caipemba 152 7.26 S 14.38 E
Novacella ʊ[1] 64 46.44 N 11.39 E
Nova Era 255 19.45 S 43.03 W
Nova Esperança 255 23.08 S 52.13 W
Novafeltria 66 43.53 N 12.17 E
Nova Friburgo 256 22.16 S 42.32 W
Nova Goa → Panaji 122 15.29 N 73.50 E
Nova Gorica 64 45.57 N 13.39 E
Nova Gradiška 36 45.16 N 17.23 E
Nova Granada 255 20.29 S 49.19 W
Nova Iguaçu 256 22.45 S 43.27 W
Nova Iguaçu □[7] 287a 22.45 S 43.29 W
Novaja, Ross. 82 55.13 N 38.54 E
Novaja, Ross. 265b 55.48 N 38.03 E
Novaja ◆[8] 265a 60.02 N 30.28 E
Novaja Astrachan' 83 49.07 N 38.36 E
Novaja Belaja 78 49.46 N 39.11 E
Novaja Belokorovići 78 51.07 N 28.02 E
Novaja Binaradka 80 53.48 N 49.56 E
Novaja Borovaja 78 50.42 N 28.39 E
Novaja Čigla 78 51.13 N 40.28 E
Novaja Derevn'a, Ross. 82 54.01 N 38.53 E
Novaja Derevn'a, Ross. 88 57.15 N 103.08 E
Novaja Ivanovka 78 45.55 N 29.05 E
Novaja Janisol' 83 47.17 N 37.16 E
Novaja Kachovka 78 46.45 N 33.23 E
Novaja Kalitva 78 50.06 N 40.01 E
Novaja Kazanka 80 48.57 N 49.36 E
Novaja Kazmaska 80 56.49 N 53.31 E
Novaja Kriuša 78 50.16 N 41.16 E
Novaja Ladoga 76 60.05 N 32.16 E
Novaja L'al'a 86 59.03 N 60.36 E
Novaja Majačka 78 46.36 N 33.14 E
Novaja Maluksa 76 59.39 N 31.21 E
Novaja Malykla 80 54.13 N 49.57 E
Novaja Mojgora 82 54.27 N 38.32 E
Novaja Odessa 78 47.19 N 31.47 E
Novaja Porubežka 80 51.45 N 49.40 E
Novaja Praga 78 48.33 N 32.54 E
Novaja Ropša 265a 59.45 N 29.53 E
Novaja Sibir', ostrov I 74 75.00 N 149.00 E
Novaja Sloboda 78 51.23 N 34.08 E
Novaja Slobodka 82 54.56 N 36.47 E
Novaja Šul'ba 86 50.33 N 81.20 E
Novaja Uda 88 54.07 N 103.33 E
Novaja Ušica 78 48.49 N 27.16 E
Novaja Usman' 78 51.37 N 39.24 E
Novaja Vodolaga 78 49.43 N 35.52 E
Novaja Zburjevka 78 46.28 N 32.24 E
Novaja Zeml'a II 72 74.00 N 57.00 E
Nováky 30 48.43 N 18.34 E
Nova Lamego 150 12.19 N 14.11 W
Novale (Rauth) 64 46.24 N 11.30 E
Novalesa 62 45.11 N 7.01 E
Novaliches Reservoir ⊜[1] 269f 14.43 N 121.05 E
Nova Lima 255 19.59 S 43.51 W
Nova Lisboa → Huambo 152 12.44 S 15.47 E
Nova Lusitânia 156 19.54 S 34.35 E
Nova Mambone 156 20.59 S 35.01 E
Nova Milanese 266b 45.35 N 9.12 E
Nova Nabúri 154 16.46 S 38.57 E
Nova Odessa 256 23.09 S 46.51 W
Nova Olinda 250 7.06 S 39.40 W
Nova Olinda do Norte 246 3.45 S 59.03 W
Nová Paka 30 50.29 N 15.31 E
Nova Ponente (Deutschnofen) 64 46.25 N 11.25 E
Nova Ponte 255 19.08 S 47.41 W
Nova Prata 252 28.47 S 51.36 W
Novar 212 45.27 N 79.15 W
Novara 62 45.28 N 8.38 E
Novara □[4] 62 45.40 N 8.30 E
Novara di Sicilia 70 38.01 N 15.08 E
Nová Role 54 50.15 N 12.47 E
Nova Roma 255 13.51 S 46.57 W
Nova Russas 250 4.42 S 40.34 W
Nova Scotia □[4], Can. 176 45.00 N 63.00 W
Nova Scotia □[4], Can. 186 45.00 N 63.00 W
Nova Siri 68 40.09 N 16.32 E
Nova Sofala 156 20.09 S 34.42 E
Nova Soure 250 11.14 S 38.29 W
Novate Mezzola 58 46.15 N 9.27 E
Novate Milanese 266b 45.32 N 9.08 E
Nova Timboteua 250 1.12 S 47.24 W
Novato 226 38.06 N 122.34 W
Novato Creek ≃ 282 38.06 N 122.29 W
Nova Vandúzi 156 18.57 S 33.16 E
Nova Varoš 38 43.28 N 19.48 E
Nova Venécia 255 18.43 S 40.24 W
Nova Viçosa 255 17.53 S 39.22 W
Nova Vida 248 10.11 S 62.47 W
Nova Vida, Cachoeira ∟ 248 9.25 S 63.36 W
Nova Zagora 38 42.29 N 26.01 E
Nove 64 45.43 N 11.40 E
Nové Hrady 61 48.47 N 14.37 E
Novelda 34 38.23 N 0.46 W
Novellara 64 44.51 N 10.44 E
Novelty 219 40.00 N 92.12 W
Nové Město 30 50.21 N 16.09 E
Nové Město nad Váhom 30 48.46 N 17.49 E
Nové Město na Moravě 30 49.34 N 16.04 E
Nové Mlýny, údolní nádrž ⊜[1] 61 48.54 N 16.34 E
Noventa di Piave 64 45.39 N 12.31 E
Noventa Padovana 64 45.24 N 11.58 E
Noventa Vicentina 64 45.17 N 11.32 E
Noves 62 43.52 N 4.54 E
Nové Sedlo 54 50.10 N 12.42 E
Nové Strašecí 54 50.07 N 13.53 E
Nové Údolí 60 48.48 N 13.48 E
Nové Zámky 30 47.59 N 18.11 E
Novgorod 76 58.31 N 31.17 E
Novgorodka 78 48.21 N 32.39 E
Novgorod Oblast' □[4] 76 58.15 N 33.00 E
Novgorod-Severskij 78 51.59 N 33.16 E
Novgorodskoje 83 48.20 N 37.50 E
Novi 216 42.28 N 83.28 W
Novi Bečej 38 45.36 N 20.08 E
Novi Beograd 38 44.49 N 20.27 E
Novice 196 31.59 N 99.37 W
Novičicha 86 52.13 N 81.24 E
Novi di Modena 64 44.54 N 10.54 E
Novigrad, Hrv. 36 45.19 N 13.34 E
Novigrad, Hrv. 36 44.11 N 15.33 E
Novikovo, Ross. 86 58.15 N 80.39 E
Novikovo, Ross. 89 46.23 N 143.20 E
Novi Ligure 62 44.46 N 8.47 E
Noville 56 50.40 N 5.23 E
Novi Lyon Drain ≍ 281 42.30 N 83.38 W
Novinger 194 40.13 N 92.42 W
Novinka 76 59.49 N 33.20 E
Novion-Porcien 50 49.36 N 4.25 E
Novi Pazar, Blg. 38 43.21 N 27.12 E
Novi Pazar, Jugo. 38 43.08 N 20.31 E
Novi Sad 38 45.15 N 19.50 E
Novi Vinodolski 36 45.08 N 14.48 E
Novka 76 55.27 N 30.24 E
Novki 80 56.22 N 41.06 E
Novl'anka 80 55.48 N 41.44 E
Novlenskoje 76 59.37 N 39.20 E
Novo ≃, Bra. 248 4.55 S 70.33 W
Novo ≃, Bra. 250 4.30 S 53.50 W
Novo ≃, Bra. 250 6.22 S 55.42 W
Novo ≃, Bra. 256 21.23 S 42.44 W
Novo, Lago ⊜ 250 1.30 N 50.40 W
Novoachtyrka 83 48.55 N 38.49 E
Nôvo Acôrdo 255 13.10 S 46.48 W
Novoajdar 83 48.57 N 39.00 E
Novoaleksandrovka, Kaz. 86 51.47 N 68.49 E
Novoaleksandrovka, Ross. 80 51.56 N 52.26 E
Novoaleksandrovka, Ukr. 83 48.17 N 39.37 E
Novoaleksandrovka, Ukr. 83 49.08 N 39.17 E
Novoaleksandrovo 265b 55.59 N 37.33 E
Novoaleksandrovsk 80 45.29 N 41.16 E
Novoaleksejevka, Kaz. 86 52.56 N 64.41 E
Novoaleksejevka, Kaz. 86 52.47 N 74.54 E
Novoaleksejevka, Kaz. 86 50.08 N 55.39 E
Novoaleksejevka, Ukr. 78 46.06 N 32.30 E
Novoaleksejevka, Ukr. 78 46.13 N 34.39 E
Novoaltajsk 86 53.24 N 83.58 E
Novoamvrosijevskoje 83 47.49 N 38.29 E
Novoanninskij 80 50.32 N 42.41 E
Novoarchangel'sk 78 48.39 N 30.48 E
Novoarchangel'skoje 265b 55.55 N 37.33 E
Novo Aripuanã 246 5.08 S 60.22 W
Novoasbest 86 57.44 N 60.45 E
Novoazovsk 83 47.08 N 38.05 E
Novobachmutovka 83 48.15 N 37.48 E
Novobatajsk 83 46.54 N 39.47 E
Novobelaja 78 49.49 N 39.18 E
Novobessergenovka 83 47.11 N 38.51 E
Novobogatinskoje 80 47.22 N 51.11 E
Novobogdanovka 78 47.06 N 35.29 E
Novobogordskoje 80 53.11 N 53.56 E
Novoborovaja 83 49.15 N 38.33 E
Novo Brasil 255 16.11 S 50.38 W
Novobratcevskij 82 55.51 N 37.23 E
Novoburejskij 89 49.49 N 129.54 E
Novočeboksarsk 80 56.08 N 47.30 E
Novo Čeremšansk 80 54.21 N 50.10 E
Novočerkassk 83 47.25 N 40.06 E
Novočernorečenskij 86 56.16 N 91.06 E
Novocharitonovo 82 55.35 N 38.30 E
Novocherkassk → Novočerkassk 83 47.25 N 40.06 E
Novochop'orsk 80 51.07 N 41.37 E
Novochop'orskij 80 51.06 N 41.33 E
Novochovrino ◆[8] 265b 55.52 N 37.30 E
Novociml'anskaja 80 47.59 N 42.17 E
Novo Cruzeiro 255 17.29 S 41.53 W
Novodanilovka 78 46.38 N 35.00 E
Novoderev'ankovskaja 78 46.19 N 38.45 E
Novoderkul 83 49.08 N 39.38 E
Novodevičje 80 53.37 N 48.52 E
Novodolinka 86 51.12 N 72.33 E
Novodolinskij 86 49.44 N 72.45 E
Novodoroninskoje 88 51.08 N 112.08 E
Novodružesk 83 48.58 N 38.21 E
Novodubovoje 76 52.19 N 39.13 E
Novodugino 76 55.38 N 34.18 E
Novodvinsk 24 64.26 N 40.47 E
Novodžerelijevskaja 78 45.46 N 38.41 E
Novoekonomičeskoje 83 48.18 N 37.15 E
Novofetinino 82 56.14 N 39.17 E
Novogaritovo 80 52.47 N 40.07 E
Novogirejevo ◆[8] 265b 55.45 N 37.49 E
Novogorbovo 82 55.43 N 36.29 E
Novogornyj 86 55.37 N 60.47 E
Novograd-Volynskij 78 50.36 N 27.36 E
Novogrigorjevka 78 46.24 N 34.59 E
Novogrigorjevskaja 80 49.26 N 43.37 E
Novogrodovka 83 48.13 N 37.20 E
Novogroznenskij 84 43.15 N 46.15 E
Novogrudok 76 53.36 N 25.50 E
Novogupalovka 78 48.02 N 35.26 E
Novo Hamburgo 252 29.41 S 51.08 W
Novo Horizonte 255 21.28 S 49.13 W
Novoignatjevka 83 47.38 N 37.41 E
Novoiljinsk 88 51.42 N 108.41 E
Novoiljinskij 86 57.54 N 55.30 E
Novoivanovka, Kaz. 85 43.08 N 71.26 E
Novoivanovka, Ukr. 78 49.44 N 33.28 E
Novoivanovka, Ukr. 83 47.41 N 38.23 E
Novoivanovskoje 265b 55.43 N 37.22 E
Novoizborsk 76 57.50 N 27.59 E
Novojampol' 89 52.55 N 127.38 E
Novojamskoje 76 52.14 N 34.28 E
Novoje, Ross. 82 55.38 N 38.55 E
Novoje, Ross. 86 58.53 N 68.40 E
Novoje Alechnovo 82 56.02 N 36.49 E
Novojegorjevskoje 86 51.46 N 80.53 E
Novojekaterinovka 83 47.43 N 38.07 E
Novoje Koval'ovo 265a 59.59 N 30.34 E
Novoje Leušino 80 56.48 N 40.32 E
Novojel'n'a 76 53.28 N 25.35 E
Novojenisejsk 86 58.16 N 92.24 E
Novoje Pavšino 82 54.15 N 37.07 E
Novoje Zarečje 76 57.43 N 34.22 E
Novokačalinsk 89 45.06 N 132.01 E
Novokadinsk 88 54.46 N 101.24 E
Novokamala 88 55.58 N 94.58 E
Novokarasuk 86 56.16 N 71.46 E
Novokaširovo 80 54.58 N 52.32 E
Novokaširsk 82 54.51 N 38.15 E
Novokazalinsk 86 45.50 N 62.10 E
Novokijevskij 80 50.27 N 43.08 E
Novokorsunskaja 78 45.38 N 39.09 E
Novokrasn'anka 83 49.08 N 38.18 E
Novokrasnoje 78 48.01 N 31.21 E
Novokručininskij 88 51.46 N 113.48 E
Novokubanka 86 51.40 N 70.44 E
Novokujbyševsk 80 53.07 N 49.58 E
Novokurovka 89 48.51 N 134.20 E
Novokuzneck 86 53.45 N 87.06 E
Novokuznetsk → Novokuzneck 86 53.45 N 87.06 E
Novolakskoje 84 43.07 N 46.29 E
Novolazarevskaja ʊ[3] 9 70.45 S 11.50 E
Novoleuškovskaja 78 45.59 N 39.58 E
Novoli 68 40.23 N 18.03 E
Novolimarevka 83 49.17 N 39.36 E
Novolukoml' 76 54.40 N 29.08 E
Novol'vovsk 76 53.55 N 38.47 E
Novomalorossijskaja 78 45.38 N 39.53 E
Novomansurkino 80 53.52 N 51.52 E
Novomargaritovka 83 46.54 N 38.50 E
Novomariinka 88 55.27 N 96.01 E
Novomarkovka 86 51.44 N 72.17 E
Novomel'nikov 84 43.56 N 45.09 E
Novomelovatka 78 50.27 N 40.46 E
Novomelovoje 78 51.23 N 38.13 E
Novo Mesto 36 45.48 N 15.10 E
Novomichajlovka, Ross. 86 55.13 N 81.57 E
Novomichajlovka, Ukr. 78 47.19 N 36.04 E
Novomichajlovka, Ukr. 83 47.51 N 37.29 E
Novomichajlovskij 78 44.15 N 38.51 E
Novomichajlovskoje 82 55.25 N 37.10 E
Novominskaja 78 46.19 N 38.57 E
Novomirgorod 78 48.47 N 31.39 E
Novomoskovsk, Ross. 82 54.05 N 38.13 E
Novomoskovsk, Ukr. 78 48.37 N 35.12 E
Novomyšastovskaja 78 45.12 N 38.35 E
Novonagajevo 80 55.56 N 54.15 E
Novonikolajevka, Kaz. 85 42.26 N 70.28 E
Novonikolajevka, Ross. 83 46.59 N 39.36 E
Novonikolajevka, Ukr. 78 46.13 N 32.45 E
Novonikolajevka, Ukr. 78 47.59 N 35.55 E
Novonikolajevskij 80 50.58 N 42.22 E
Novonikolayevsk → Novosibirsk 86 55.02 N 82.55 E
Novonikol'skoje, Ross. 76 59.25 N 33.13 E
Novonikol'skoje, Ross. 80 49.09 N 45.00 E
Novonikol'skoje, Ross. 86 59.46 N 79.12 E
Novonikol'skoje, Ross. 265b 55.50 N 37.15 E
Novonikol'skoje, Ukr. 83 49.21 N 39.51 E
Novoomel'kovo 83 49.08 N 39.05 E
Novo Oriente 250 5.32 S 40.42 W
Novoorsk 86 51.23 N 58.58 E
Novopavlovka 88 51.13 N 109.14 E
Novopavlovskaja 84 43.58 N 43.38 E
Novopavlovskoje 88 50.56 N 111.35 E
Novopetrovo 86 57.11 N 69.10 E
Novopetrovskoje 82 55.59 N 36.28 E
Novopiscovo 76 57.19 N 41.54 E
Novopodrezkovo 82 55.57 N 37.21 E
Novopokrovka, Kaz. 86 53.43 N 67.45 E
Novopokrovka, Kaz. 86 50.41 N 80.28 E
Novopokrovka, Kyrg. 85 42.52 N 74.45 E
Novopokrovka, Ross. 89 45.52 N 134.28 E
Novopokrovka, Ukr. 78 48.03 N 34.37 E
Novopokrovskoje 80 51.35 N 43.36 E
Novopolevodino 80 51.46 N 47.29 E
Novopolock 76 55.31 N 28.38 E
Novopskov 83 49.33 N 39.05 E
Novorajčichinsk 89 49.47 N 129.38 E
Novor'ažsk 80 53.44 N 40.07 E
Novorepnoje 80 51.06 N 48.24 E
Novorossijka 85 42.44 N 76.07 E
Novorossijsk 78 44.45 N 37.45 E
Novorossijskoje 86 50.13 N 58.00 E
Novorossiysk → Novorossijsk 78 44.45 N 37.45 E
Novorossoš' 83 49.32 N 39.15 E
Novorudnyj 86 51.30 N 58.10 E
Novorybinka 86 51.51 N 71.14 E
Novorybnoje 74 72.50 N 105.50 E
Novoržev 76 57.02 N 29.20 E
Novošachtinsk 83 47.47 N 39.56 E
Novosaratovka 265a 59.50 N 30.32 E
Novoščerbinovskaja 78 46.28 N 38.38 E
Novosel'e 86 54.10 N 76.53 E
Novoselenginsk 88 51.06 N 106.37 E
Novoselica 78 48.14 N 26.17 E
Novoselickoje 84 44.45 N 43.26 E
Novoseliščе 78 49.48 N 25.03 E
Novoselje 265a 59.48 N 30.05 E
Novoselki, Ross. 82 55.08 N 37.33 E
Novoselki, Ross. 82 54.49 N 38.55 E
Novosel'nyj 86 50.00 N 54.38 E
Novoselovka Pervaja 83 48.12 N 37.31 E
Novoselovo 82 56.04 N 39.04 E
Novosel'skoje 78 45.20 N 28.33 E
Novosemejkino 80 53.23 N 50.22 E
Novosergijevka, Ross. 80 52.06 N 53.39 E
Novosergijevka, Ross. 265a 59.54 N 30.34 E
Novoseslavino 80 53.21 N 40.26 E
Novošešminsk 80 55.04 N 51.15 E
Novoshakhtinsk → Novošachtinsk 83 47.47 N 39.56 E
Novosibirsk 86 55.02 N 82.55 E
Novosibirskije ostrova II 74 75.00 N 142.00 E
Novosibirsk Oblast' □[4] 86 55.00 N 80.00 E
Novosibirskoje vodochranilišče ⊜[1] 86 54.35 N 82.35 E
Novosil' 76 52.58 N 37.03 E
Novosil'skoje 78 51.56 N 38.31 E
Novosokol'niki 76 56.21 N 30.10 E
Novos'olki, Bela. 76 52.24 N 28.33 E
Novos'olki, Bela. 76 52.02 N 24.21 E
Novos'olki, Ross. 76 56.01 N 33.37 E
Novos'olki, Ross. 80 55.48 N 42.41 E
Novos'olki, Ross. 80 54.50 N 39.46 E
Novos'olki, Ross. 265a 59.42 N 30.17 E
Novos'olovka 83 49.04 N 37.42 E
Novos'olovo, Ross. 86 55.04 N 91.07 E
Novos'olovo, Ross. 88 56.04 N 107.42 E
Novos'olovskoje 78 45.26 N 33.34 E
Novospasovka 83 47.42 N 39.04 E
Novospasskoje 80 53.08 N 47.45 E
Novostrel'covka 83 49.20 N 39.55 E
Novostrojevo 76 54.27 N 21.50 E
Novosvetlovka 83 48.30 N 39.30 E
Novosysojevka 89 44.14 N 133.22 E
Novotavolžanka 78 50.22 N 36.50 E
Novotitarovskaja 78 45.14 N 39.00 E
Novotroick, Ross. 86 56.11 N 78.41 E
Novotroick, Ross. 86 51.12 N 58.20 E
Novotroickoje, Kaz. 85 43.42 N 73.46 E
Novotroickoje, Ross. 80 58.28 N 47.06 E
Novotroickoje, Ukr. 78 46.22 N 34.20 E
Novotroickoje, Ukr. 83 47.43 N 37.35 E
Novo-Troitsk → Novotroick 86 51.12 N 58.20 E
Novotulka, Ross. 80 52.38 N 48.45 E
Novotulka, Ross. 80 50.50 N 47.34 E
Novotul'skij 82 54.10 N 37.43 E
Novoukolovo 78 51.02 N 38.25 E
Novoukrainka 78 48.19 N 31.32 E
Novouljanovsk 80 54.08 N 48.24 E
Novoural'sk 86 51.15 N 57.16 E
Novouzensk 80 50.28 N 48.08 E
Novovaršavka 86 54.11 N 74.42 E
Novovasiljevka, Ukr. 78 46.51 N 36.46 E
Novovasiljevka, Ukr. 78 46.48 N 35.44 E
Novov'atsk 80 58.29 N 49.44 E
Novov'azniki 80 56.12 N 42.10 E
Novovolynsk 78 50.50 N 24.05 E
Novovoroncovka 78 47.29 N 33.54 E
Novovoronežskij 78 51.16 N 39.11 E
Novovoskresenovka 85 42.50 N 73.32 E
Novovoskresenskoje 78 47.21 N 33.37 E
Novozacharkino 80 52.11 N 48.29 E
Novozagorje 82 55.39 N 38.38 E
Novozavidovskij 82 56.33 N 36.26 E
Novožilovskaja 24 64.50 N 51.20 E
Novozizevka 80 50.48 N 49.08 E
Novozybkov 76 52.32 N 31.56 E
Novska 36 45.21 N 16.59 E
Nový Bohumín 30 49.56 N 18.20 E
Nový Bor 54 50.45 N 14.33 E
Novyj 86 55.39 N 86.39 E
Novyj Afon 84 43.06 N 40.48 E
Novyj Bor 24 66.43 N 52.16 E
Novyj Bug 78 47.41 N 32.30 E
Novyj Bujan 80 53.41 N 50.04 E
Novyj Bykov 78 50.36 N 31.39 E
Novyj Donbass ◆[8] 83 48.05 N 38.46 E
Novyj Dvor 76 52.50 N 24.21 E
Novyje Ajbesi 80 54.49 N 47.02 E
Novyje Aneny 38 46.52 N 29.14 E
Novyje Basy 78 50.53 N 34.51 E
Novyje Burasy 80 52.08 N 46.06 E
Novyje Denisoviči 76 54.12 N 29.13 E
Novyje Gorki 80 56.42 N 41.06 E
Novyje Maty 80 55.15 N 54.04 E
Novyje Salty 80 54.06 N 53.26 E
Novyje Senžary 78 49.21 N 34.19 E
Novyje Z'atcy 80 57.27 N 52.36 E
Nový Jičín 30 49.36 N 18.00 E
Novyj Jaryčev 78 49.55 N 24.18 E
Novyj Jegorlyk 80 46.24 N 41.54 E
Novyj Karačaj 84 43.49 N 41.56 E
Novyj Karamass 80 56.11 N 48.58 E
Novyj Kiner 80 56.24 N 49.44 E
Novyj Multan 80 57.09 N 52.19 E
Novyj Nekouz 78 57.54 N 38.04 E
Novyj Oskol 78 50.46 N 37.53 E
Novyj Pogost 76 55.30 N 27.29 E
Novyj Port 74 67.40 N 72.52 E
Novyj Put' 85 43.29 N 73.52 E
Novyj Ropsk 76 52.18 N 32.19 E
Novyj Stan 82 56.18 N 37.00 E
Novyj Svet 83 47.48 N 38.00 E
Novyj Tap 86 57.04 N 67.49 E
Novyj Terek ≃ 84 43.37 N 47.25 E
Novyj Tevriz 86 59.04 N 78.08 E
Novyj Uzen 72 43.18 N 52.48 E
Novyj Vas'ugan 86 58.34 N 76.29 E
Novy Torjal 80 57.00 N 48.44 E
Nowa Dęba 30 50.26 N 21.46 E
Nowaja Semlja → Novaja Zeml'a II 72 74.00 N 57.00 E
Nowa Ruda 30 50.35 N 16.31 E
Nowa Sól (Neusalz) 30 51.48 N 15.44 E
Nowata 196 36.42 N 95.38 W
Nowater Creek ≃ 202 43.57 N 108.00 W
Nowbarān 128 35.08 N 48.42 E
Nowe 30 53.40 N 18.43 E
Nowe Miasto Lubawskie 30 53.27 N 19.35 E
Nowe Miasto nad Pilicą 30 51.38 N 20.35 E
Nowendoc 166 31.32 S 151.43 E
Nowe Warpno 30 53.44 N 14.16 E
Nowfel low Shātow 128 34.23 N 50.32 E
Nowgong 124 25.04 N 79.27 E
Nowingi 166 34.36 S 142.14 E
Nowitna ≃ 180 65.55 N 154.17 W
Nowogard 30 53.40 N 15.08 E
Nowogród 30 53.15 N 21.53 E
Nowogrodziec 30 51.12 N 15.25 E
Nowokusnezk → Novokuzneck 86 53.45 N 87.06 E
Nowood ≃ 202 44.17 N 107.58 W
Nowosibirsk → Novosibirsk 86 55.02 N 82.55 E
Nowra 170 34.53 S 150.36 E
Nowrangapur 122 19.14 N 82.33 E
Nowshāk ∧ 123 36.26 N 71.50 E
Nowshera 123 34.01 N 71.59 E
Nowy Dwór Gdański 30 54.13 N 19.06 E
Nowy Dwór Mazowiecki 30 52.26 N 20.43 E
Nowy Sącz 30 49.38 N 20.42 E
Nowy Sącz □[4] 30 49.30 N 20.15 E
Nowy Staw 30 54.09 N 19.00 E
Nowy Targ 30 49.29 N 20.02 E
Nowy Tomyśl 30 52.20 N 16.07 E
Now Zād 120 32.24 N 64.28 E
Noxapater 194 32.59 N 89.03 W
Noxe ≃ 50 48.33 N 3.35 E
Noxen 210 41.25 N 76.03 W
Noxon 202 48.00 N 115.47 W
Noxon Reservoir ⊜[1] 202 47.54 N 115.40 W
Noxubee ≃ 194 32.50 N 88.10 W
Noy ≃ 110 17.05 N 105.02 E
Noya 34 42.47 N 8.53 W
Noya ≃ 152 0.58 N 9.48 E
Noyant 50 47.31 N 0.08 E
Noye ≃ 50 49.51 N 2.20 E
Noyelles-sur Mer 50 50.11 N 1.43 E
Noyers 50 47.42 N 4.00 E
Noyers, Ruisseau des ≃ 275a 45.21 N 73.22 W
Noyers-sur-Jabron 62 44.10 N 5.50 E
Noyes Island I 182 55.30 N 133.40 W
Noyon 50 49.35 N 3.00 E
Nožaj-Jurt 84 43.05 N 46.24 E
Nozawa-onsen 94 36.55 N 138.27 E
Nozay, Fr. 32 47.34 N 1.38 W
Nozay, Fr. 261 48.40 N 2.14 E
Nozeroy 58 46.47 N 6.02 E
Nozori-dam ◆[6] 94 36.43 N 138.39 E
Nozori-ko ⊜ 94 36.42 N 138.39 E
Nozuta 268 35.35 N 139.27 E
Nqamakwe 158 32.12 S 27.56 E
Nqutu 158 28.13 S 30.32 E
N'Riquinha 152 15.45 S 21.42 E
N'Rougas 158 29.07 S 21.09 E
Nsa, Oued en V 148 32.28 N 5.24 E
Nsaba 150 5.39 N 0.45 W
Nsah 152 2.22 S 15.19 E
Nsang 152 2.02 N 10.56 E
Nsanje 154 16.55 S 35.12 E
Nsawam 150 5.50 N 0.20 W
Nsefu Game Reserve ◆[4] 154 13.07 S 32.10 E
Nsele ≃ 152 4.14 S 15.33 E
Nseleni 158 28.33 S 31.39 E
Nsok 152 1.08 N 11.16 E
Nsoko 158 27.02 S 31.57 E
Nsontin 152 3.09 S 18.00 E
Nsouélé 273b 4.12 S 15.11 E
Nsukka 150 6.52 N 7.24 E
Nsuta 150 5.17 N 1.58 W
Ntakat 150 16.49 N 11.43 W
Ntambanana 158 28.36 S 31.45 E
Ntandembele 152 2.11 S 17.08 E
Ntcheu 154 14.49 S 34.38 E
Ntem ≃ 152 2.15 N 9.45 E
Ntoum 152 0.23 N 9.47 E
Ntsama 152 0.32 S 14.38 E
N'Tsaoueni 157a 11.27 S 43.18 E
Ntui 152 4.27 N 11.38 E
Ntumba 154 8.20 S 32.05 E
Ntusi 154 0.03 N 31.13 E
Ntwetwe Pan ≍ 156 20.30 S 25.20 E
Nuala 154 13.27 S 28.16 E
Nuanchitang 104 41.02 N 120.41 E
Nuanetsi ≃ 156 22.40 S 31.50 E
Nuangola 210 41.09 N 75.58 W
Nuanli 102 23.26 N 100.51 E
Nuannuan 269d 25.06 N 121.44 E
Nuanshui 100 28.53 N 117.51 E
Nuanzhouying 100 25.22 N 117.22 E
Nuasjärvi ⊜ 26 64.10 N 28.05 E
Nuatabu 174t 1.33 N 172.59 E
Nuatja 150 6.57 N 1.10 E
Nu'aymah 132 32.38 N 36.10 E
Nūbah 142 30.29 N 31.33 E
Nūbah, Jibāl an- ⋀ 140 11.00 N 30.45 E
Nūbārīyah, Tur'at an- ≍ 142 30.43 N 30.46 E
Nubian Desert ◆[2] 140 20.30 N 33.00 E
Ñuble ≃ 252 36.39 S 72.27 W
Nubra ≃ 123 34.39 N 77.36 E
Nucet 38 46.28 N 22.35 E
Nucetto 62 44.20 N 8.04 E
Nucha → Šeki 84 41.12 N 47.12 E
Nuchatlitz Inlet ⊂ 182 49.45 N 126.55 W
N'uchča 24 63.27 N 46.28 E
Nuch'ŏn-ni 98 38.14 N 126.16 E
Nucla 200 38.16 N 108.32 W
Núcleo Colonial São Bento 287a 22.44 S 43.18 W
N'učpas 24 60.51 N 51.18 E
Nucuray ≃ 246 5.02 S 75.34 W
Nuda, Monte la ∧ 64 44.17 N 10.15 E
Nudaybah 142 30.59 N 30.22 E
Nudol' ≃ 82 56.07 N 36.42 E
Nudol'-Šarino 82 56.06 N 36.31 E
Nudow 264a 52.20 N 13.10 E
Nueces ≃ 196 27.50 N 97.30 W
Nueces Plains ≍ 196 28.30 N 99.15 W
Nueltin Lake ⊜ 176 60.20 N 99.50 W
Nuenen 52 51.29 N 5.33 E
Nü'er ≃ 98 40.57 N 121.19 E
Nü'erhe 104 41.04 N 121.00 E
Nuestra Señora de Talavera 252 25.26 S 63.48 W
Nueva, Isla I 254 55.13 S 66.30 W
Nueva Antioquia 246 6.05 N 69.26 W
Nueva Asunción □[5] 248 21.00 S 61.00 W
Nueva Atzacoalco ◆[8] 286a 19.29 N 99.05 W
Nueva Brunswick → New Brunswick □[4] 186 46.30 N 66.15 W
Nueva Caledonia → New Caledonia □[2] 175f 21.30 S 165.30 E
Nueva Chicago ◆[8] 288 34.40 S 58.30 W
Nueva Ciudad Guerrero 232 26.35 N 99.15 W
Nueva Concepción 236 14.08 N 89.18 W
Nueva Cuadrilla 234 18.04 N 101.33 W
Nueva Ecija □[4] 116 15.35 N 121.00 E
Nueva Escocia → Nova Scotia □[4] 186 45.00 N 63.00 W
Nueva Esparta □[3] 246 11.00 N 64.00 W
Nueva Francia 252 28.11 S 64.12 W
Nueva Galia 252 35.07 S 65.15 W
Nueva Germania 252 23.54 S 56.45 W
Nueva Gerona 240p 21.53 N 82.48 W
Nueva Guinea, Isla → New Guinea I 164 5.00 S 140.00 E
Nueva Hébridas → Vanuatu □[1] 175f 16.00 S 167.00 E
Nueva Helvecia 258 34.19 S 57.13 W
Nueva Imperial 252 38.44 S 72.57 W
Nueva Italia de Ruiz 234 19.01 N 102.06 W
Nueva Loja 246 0.06 N 76.52 W
Nueva Lubecka 254 44.32 S 70.24 W
Nueva Ocotepeque 236 14.24 N 89.13 W
Nueva Palmira 258 33.53 S 58.25 W
Nueva Paz 240p 22.46 N 81.45 W
Nueva Pompeya ◆[8] 288 34.39 S 58.25 W
Nueva Rosita 232 27.57 N 101.13 W
Nueva San Salvador 236 13.41 N 89.17 W
Nueva Segovia □[5] 236 13.40 N 86.10 W
Nueva Siberia, Islas → Novosibirskije ostrova II 74 75.00 N 142.00 E
Nueva Venecia 236 14.03 N 91.33 W
Nueva Vizcaya □[4] 116 16.25 N 121.10 E
Nueva Zelandia → New Zealand □[1] 172 41.00 S 174.00 E
Nueva Zembla, Isla de → Novaja Zeml'a II 72 74.00 N 57.00 E
Nueve, Canal Numero ≖ 252 36.11 S 57.18 W
Nueve de Julio 252 35.27 S 60.52 W
Nuevitas 240p 21.33 N 77.16 W
Nuevitas, Bahía de ⊂ 240p 21.30 N 77.12 W
Nuevo 228 33.48 N 117.09 W
Nuevo, Bajo ✢[4] 238 15.55 N 78.30 W
Nuevo, Cayo I 232 21.51 N 92.05 W
Nuevo, Golfo ⊂ 254 42.42 S 64.36 W
Nuevo Berlín 252 32.59 S 58.03 W
Nuevo Camarón 196 27.05 N 99.55 W
Nuevo Casas Grandes 232 30.25 N 107.55 W
Nuevo Chagres 236 9.14 N 80.05 W
Nuevo Delicias 232 26.15 N 102.50 W
Nuevo Laredo 232 27.30 N 99.31 W
Nuevo Léon 204 32.20 N 115.12 W
Nuevo León □[3] 232 25.40 N 100.00 W
Nuevo Morelos 234 17.31 N 95.02 W
Nuevo Necaxa 234 20.13 N 98.00 W
Nuevo Poblado el Oro 196 26.50 N 101.19 W
Nuevo Primero de Mayo 196 26.01 N 98.02 W
Nuevo Progreso 232 18.38 N 92.18 W
Nuevo Rocafuerte 246 0.56 S 75.24 W
Nuevo Saucillo 196 27.20 N 104.54 W
Nufcor 273d 26.17 S 27.44 E
Nugaal □[4] 144 8.30 N 49.00 E
Nugaaleed, Dooxo V 144 8.35 N 48.35 E
Nugget Point › 172 46.27 S 169.49 E
Nûgssuaq ›[1] 176 70.25 N 52.30 W
Nugu ⊜[1] 122 11.58 N 76.28 E
Nuguria Islands II 14 3.20 S 154.45 E
Nūh 124 28.07 N 77.01 E
Nūh, Rās › 128 25.05 N 62.24 E
Nuhaka 172 39.03 S 177.45 E
Nuhaydāt as-Sūd, Jabal an- ∧ 142 28.01 N 32.21 E
Nuhūd, Jabal an- ∧ 140 14.50 N 29.53 E
Nui I[1] 14 7.15 S 177.10 E
Nuia 76 58.04 N 25.33 E
Nuits-Saint-Georges 58 47.08 N 4.57 E
Nuits-sur-Armançon 50 47.44 N 4.12 E
N'uja 74 60.32 N 116.14 E
N'uja ≃ 74 60.32 N 116.20 E
Nujiang 102 29.58 N 97.25 E
N'uk, ozero ⊜ 24 64.27 N 31.45 E
Nuka Island I 180 59.21 N 150.42 W
Nukan 175c 7.23 N 151.53 E
Nukata 94 34.55 N 137.17 E
Nukatl', chrebet ⋀ 84 42.15 N 46.35 E
Nukey Bluff ≜[4] 166 32.33 S 135.40 E
Nukhayb 128 32.02 N 42.15 E
Nukhaylah ⊤[4] 140 19.03 N 26.19 E
Nukhaylah, Wādī an- V 132 31.27 N 35.49 E
Nukiki 175e 6.46 S 156.28 E
N'uksenica 24 60.25 N 44.13 E
Nuku'alofa 174w 21.08 S 175.12 W
Nukufetau I[1] 14 8.00 S 178.22 E
Nukuhu 164 5.35 S 149.25 E
Nukulaelae I[1] 14 9.23 S 179.52 E
Nukumanu Islands II 14 4.30 S 159.30 E
Nukunonu I 14 9.12 S 171.54 W
Nukunuku 174w 21.08 S 175.18 W
Nukuoro I[1] 14 3.51 N 154.58 E
Nukus 72 42.50 N 59.29 E
Nul 175f 16.49 S 168.24 E
Nulato 180 64.43 N 158.06 W
Nullagine 162 21.53 S 120.06 E
Nullagine ≃ 162 20.43 S 120.33 E
Nullarbor 162 31.26 S 130.55 E
Nullarbor National Park ♠ 162 31.30 S 130.30 E
Nullarbor Plain ≍ 162 31.00 S 129.00 E
Nulltown 218 39.35 N 85.10 W
Nul'vand 85 38.16 N 70.32 E
Nulvi 71 40.47 N 8.45 E
Num, Mios I 164 1.30 S 135.13 E
Numabin Bay ⊂ 184 56.30 N 103.08 W
Numakuma 96 34.23 N 133.20 E
Numan 146 9.28 N 12.02 E
Numana 66 43.31 N 13.37 E
Numancia 116 9.52 N 125.58 E
Numancia ⊥ 34 41.48 N 2.25 W
Numansdorp 52 51.44 N 4.26 E
Numara I 122 6.26 N 73.03 E
Numata, Nihon 92a 43.48 N 141.57 E
Numata, Nihon 94 36.38 N 139.03 E
Numata, Nihon 96 34.27 N 132.24 E
Numatinna ≃ 140 7.14 N 27.37 E
Numazu 94 35.06 N 138.52 E
Numbargulme, Mount ∧ 164 14.56 S 145.03 E
Number 5 Mine 214 41.08 N 80.11 W
Numedal V 26 60.06 N 9.06 E
Numeralla 171b 36.11 S 149.20 E
Numeralla ≃ 171b 36.06 S 149.11 E
Numfoor, Pulau I 164 1.03 S 134.54 E
Numidia 210 40.53 N 76.24 W
Numila 229b 21.54 N 159.33 W
Nu Mine 214 40.48 N 79.18 W
Numto 74 63.40 N 71.20 E
Numurkah 166 36.06 S 145.26 E
Nun ≃[1] 150 4.20 N 6.00 E
Nun'amo 180 65.37 N 170.40 W
Nunapitchuk 180 60.54 N 162.29 W
Nunawading 169 37.49 S 145.10 E
Nünchritz 54 51.18 N 13.23 E
Nunda 210 42.34 N 77.56 W
Nundah 171a 27.24 S 153.04 E
Nundu 154 3.49 S 29.05 E
Nuneaton 42 52.32 N 1.28 W
Núñes, Isla I 254 53.31 S 73.48 W
Núñez ◆[8] 288 34.33 S 58.27 W
Nunez ≃ 150 10.36 N 14.40 W
Nungarin 162 31.11 S 118.06 E
Nungesser Lake ⊜ 184 51.28 N 93.35 W
Nungwe 154 2.46 S 32.01 E
Nunica 216 43.04 N 86.04 W
Nunivak Island I 180 60.00 N 166.30 W
Nunjiang 89 49.10 N 125.11 E
Nunjikompita 162 32.16 S 134.19 E
Nunkini 232 20.20 N 90.11 W
Nunkun ∧ 123 33.59 N 76.01 E
Nunligran 180 64.48 N 175.24 W
Nunnelly 194 35.51 N 87.28 W
Ñuñoa 286e 33.28 S 70.36 W
Nunshan 89 48.59 N 125.14 E
Nunspeet 52 52.23 N 5.46 E
Nuomin ≃ 89 48.06 N 124.26 E
Nuomin Dashan ∧ 89 50.15 N 122.46 E
Nuon ≃ 150 6.30 N 8.36 W
Nuoro 71 40.19 N 9.20 E
Nuoro □[4] 71 40.10 N 9.20 E
Nuqruş, Jabal ∧ 140 24.49 N 34.36 E
Nuquí 246 5.42 N 77.17 W
Nura 86 48.53 N 62.20 E
Nura ≃ 86 50.30 N 69.59 E
Nurallao 71 39.47 N 9.05 E
Nuraminis 71 39.26 N 9.01 E
Nuratau, chrebet ⋀ 85 40.20 N 67.15 E
Nuraxi, Nuraghe su ⊥ 71 39.42 N 9.00 E
N'urba 74 63.17 N 118.20 E
Nürburg 56 50.21 N 6.57 E
Nürburgring ♠ 56 50.21 N 6.58 E
Nur Dağları ⋀ 130 36.45 N 36.20 E
Nure ≃ 62 45.03 N 9.49 E
Nurek 85 38.23 N 69.19 E
Nurekskoje vodochranilišče ⊜[1] 85 38.30 N 69.30 E
Nuremberg → Nürnberg, Dtsch. 60 49.27 N 11.04 E
Nuremberg, Pa., U.S. 210 40.56 N 76.10 W
Nürenbei 107 30.11 N 106.04 E
Nūrestān □[9] 123 35.30 N 70.45 E
Nurettin 130 39.14 N 42.25 E
Nurhak 130 37.58 N 37.25 E
Nuria, Monte ∧ 66 42.21 N 13.05 E
Nuriootpa 168b 34.29 S 139.00 E
Nurlat 80 54.26 N 50.46 E
Nurlaty 80 55.37 N 48.18 E
Nūrmahal 123 31.06 N 75.36 E
Nurmes 26 63.33 N 29.07 E
Nurmijärvi 26 60.28 N 24.48 E
Nūrnagar 126 22.20 N 89.03 E
Nürnberg 60 49.27 N 11.04 E
Nürnberg, Flughafen ⊠ 60 49.30 N 11.06 E
Nūrpur, India 123 31.10 N 76.29 E
Nūrpur, India 123 32.18 N 75.54 E
Nurpur, India 126 22.13 N 88.05 E
Nūrpur, Pāk. 123 31.53 N 71.54 E
Nurrari Lakes ⊜ 162 29.01 S 130.05 E
Nurri 71 39.43 N 9.14 E
Nurri, Mount ∧[2] 166 31.42 S 146.02 E
Nursery 222 28.56 N 97.06 W
Nürtingen 56 48.38 N 9.20 E
Nus 62 45.45 N 7.28 E
Nūsah 144 14.00 N 46.43 E
Nusa Tenggara Barat □[4] 115b 8.50 S 117.30 E
Nusa Tenggara Timur □[4] 112 9.30 S 122.00 E
Nusaybin 130 37.03 N 41.13 E
Nuşayrīyah, Jabal an- ⋀ 130 35.30 N 36.12 E
Nusco 68 40.53 N 15.05 E
Nushagak ≃ 180 59.00 N 158.30 W
Nushagak Bay ⊂ 180 58.40 N 158.40 W
Nushagak Peninsula ›[1] 180 58.30 N 159.00 W
Nu Shan ⋀ 102 27.00 N 99.00 E
Nüshan Hu ⊜ 100 32.57 N 118.03 E
Nu-shima I 96 34.10 N 134.50 E
Nushki 120 29.33 N 66.01 E
Nusplingen 58 48.08 N 8.53 E
Nušpoly 82 56.39 N 37.44 E
Nussdorf ◆[8] 264b 48.15 N 16.22 E
Nussdorf am Attersee 64 47.53 N 13.31 E
Nuta ≃ 96 34.23 N 133.04 E
Nutauge, laguna ⊂ 180 67.55 N 176.45 W
Nutepel'men, Ross. 180 67.26 N 174.56 W
Nutepelmen, Ross. 180 65.31 N 178.30 W
Nutfield 260 51.14 N 0.07 W
Nuth 56 50.55 N 5.54 E
Nuthe ≃, Dtsch. 54 51.58 N 11.53 E
Nuthe ≃, Dtsch. 54 52.23 N 13.04 E
Nut Lake Indian Reserve ◆[4] 184 52.20 N 103.30 W
Nutley 210 40.49 N 74.09 W
Nutrioso 200 33.57 N 109.12 W
Nut Swamp Brook ≃ 276 40.21 N 74.06 W
Nuttby Mountain ∧[2] 186 45.33 N 63.13 W
Nutter Fort 188 39.15 N 80.19 W
Nutting Lake 207 42.32 N 71.16 W
Nutting Lake ⊜ 283 42.32 N 71.16 W
Nutwood 219 39.05 N 90.39 W
Nutwood Downs 164 15.49 S 134.10 E
Nutzotin Mountains ⋀ 180 62.10 N 141.40 W
Nu'ūmīyah, Wādī an- V 142 29.31 N 31.17 E
Nuupere, Pointe › 174s 17.36 S 149.47 W
Nu'uuli 174u 14.18 S 170.42 W
N'uvčim 24 61.22 N 50.42 E
Nuwākoṭ 124 28.08 N 83.53 E
Nuwaybi' al-Muzayyinah 140 28.58 N 34.39 E
Nuwerus 158 31.08 S 18.24 E
Nuweveldberge ⋀ 158 32.13 S 22.10 E
Nuxis 71 39.09 N 8.44 E
Nuyakuk Lake ⊜ 180 60.00 N 158.40 W
Nuyts, Point › 162 35.04 S 116.37 E
Nuyts Archipelago II 162 32.35 S 133.17 E
Nūzvīd 122 16.47 N 80.51 E
N'Vinda 152 13.04 S 18.57 E
Nwa 152 6.30 N 11.00 E
Nxainxai 156 19.50 S 21.13 E
Nxai Pan National Park ♠ 156 19.45 S 24.50 E
Nxaunxau 156 18.19 S 21.04 E
Nyaake 150 4.52 N 7.37 W
Nyabéssan 152 2.24 N 10.24 E
Nyabing 162 33.32 S 118.09 E
Nyac 180 61.01 N 159.57 W
Nyack 210 41.05 N 73.55 W
Nyack Beach State Park ♠ 276 41.07 N 73.55 W
Nyadiri ≃ 154 16.44 S 32.33 E
Nyahanga 154 2.23 S 33.33 E
Nyahua 154 5.24 S 33.19 E
Nyahururu Falls 154 0.02 N 36.22 E
Nyah West 166 35.11 S 143.22 E
Nyainqêntanglha Feng ∧ 124 30.22 N 90.35 E
Nyainqêntanglha Shan ⋀ 120 30.00 N 90.00 E
Nyainrong 120 32.09 N 92.11 E
Nyakabindi 154 2.38 S 33.59 E
Nyakakiri 154 2.15 S 31.28 E
Nyakanazi 154 3.00 S 31.15 E
Nyakrom 150 5.37 N 0.48 W
Nyakulenga 152 13.03 S 23.29 E
Nyala 140 12.03 N 24.53 E
Nyalam 120 28.11 N 85.58 E
Nyalas 114 2.26 N 102.28 E
Nyamandhlovu 154 19.50 S 28.16 E
Nyamina 150 13.19 N 6.59 W
Nyamlell 140 9.07 N 26.58 E
Nyamougo 154 1.29 S 34.33 E
Nyamtumbo 154 10.29 S 36.02 E
Nyamwage 154 8.08 S 39.00 E
Nyandekwa 154 3.55 S 32.30 E
Nyanding, Khawr V 140 8.40 N 32.41 E
Nyang ≃ 124 29.25 N 94.22 E
Nyanga □[4] 152 3.00 S 11.00 E
Nyanga ≃ 152 2.58 S 10.15 E

Symbols in the index entries represent the broad categories identified in the key at the right. Symbols with superior numbers (⋀[1]) identify subcategories (see complete key on page I · 1).

Symbole im Register stellen die rechts im Schlüssel erklärten Kategorien dar. Symbole mit hochgestellten Ziffern (⋀[1]) bezeichnen Unterabteilungen einer Kategorie (vgl. vollständiger Schlüssel auf Seite I · 1).

Los símbolos incluídos en el texto del índice representan las grandes categorías identificadas con la clave a la derecha. Los símbolos con numeros en su parte superior (⋀[1]) identifican las subcategorías (véase la clave completa en la página I · 1).

Les symboles de l'index représentent les catégories indiquées dans la légende à droite. Les symboles suivis d'un indice (⋀[1]) représentent des sous-catégories (voir légende complète à la page I · 1).

Os símbolos incluídos no texto do índice representam as grandes categorias identificadas com a chave à direita. Os símbolos com números em sua parte superior (⋀[1]) identificam as subcategorias (veja-se a chave completa à página I · 1).

∧ Mountain	Berg	Montaña	Montagne	Montanha
⋀ Mountains	Gebirge	Montañas	Montagnes	Montanhas
✕ Pass	Paß	Paso	Col	Passo
V Valley, Canyon	Tal, Cañon	Valle, Cañón	Vallée, Canyon	Vale, Canhão
≍ Plain	Ebene	Llano	Plaine	Planície
› Cape	Kap	Cabo	Cap	Cabo
I Island	Insel	Isla	Île	Ilha
II Islands	Inseln	Islas	Îles	Ilhas
◆ Other Topographic Features	Andere Topographische Objekte	Otros Elementos Topográficos	Autres données topographiques	Outros acidentes topográficos

ESPAÑOL Nombre	Página	Lat.°′	Long.°′ W = Oeste
Nyanga, Lake @	162	29.57 S	126.10 E
Nyangana	156	18.00 S	20.41 E
Nyangui ∧	154	17.53 S	32.44 E
Nyanji Mission	154	14.23 S	31.48 E
Nyanza □⁴	154	0.30 S	34.30 E
Nyanza-Lac	154	4.21 S	29.36 E
Nyasa, Lake (Lake Malawi) @	154	12.00 S	34.30 E
Nyaunglebin	110	17.57 N	96.44 E
Nyavikungu	154	11.26 S	25.54 E
Nyazura	154	18.43 S	32.10 E
Nyazvidzi ≃	154	20.00 S	32.17 E
Nybergsund	26	61.15 N	12.19 E
Nyborg	41	55.19 N	10.48 E
Nybro	26	56.45 N	15.54 E
Nyda	74	66.36 N	72.54 E
Nyêmo	124	29.25 N	90.08 E
Nyengo Swamp ☰	152	14.51 S	22.07 E
Nyeri	154	0.25 S	36.57 E
Nyerol	140	8.41 N	32.02 E
Nyfer ≃	42	52.02 N	4.50 W
Nygčigen, mys ⊳	180	65.05 N	172.06 W
Nyhammar	40	60.17 N	14.58 E
Nyhyttan	40	59.40 N	14.48 E
Nyíel	140	6.06 N	31.13 E
Nyika National Park ♦	154	10.48 S	33.48 E
Nyika Flateau ∧¹	154	10.40 S	33.50 E
Nyimba	154	14.35 S	30.52 E
Nyingchi	120	29.32 N	94.25 E
Nyíradony	30	47.41 N	21.55 E
Nyírbátor	30	47.50 N	22.08 E
Nyíregyháza	30	47.59 N	21.43 E
Nykøbing, Dan.	26	56.48 N	8.52 E
Nykøbing, Dan.	41	55.55 N	11.41 E
Nykøbing, Dan.	41	54.46 N	11.53 E
Nyköping	40	58.45 N	17.00 E
Nykroppa	40	59.38 N	14.18 E
Nykvarn	40	59.11 N	17.26 E
Nyland	26	63.00 N	17.46 E
Nyland Acres	228	34.14 N	119.09 W
Nylga, Ross.	80	56.46 N	52.22 E
Nylga, Ross.	89	51.38 N	127.35 E
Nylstroom	156	24.42 S	28.20 E
Nymagee	166	32.04 S	146.20 E
Nymboida ≃	166	29.39 S	152.30 E
Nymbure	30	50.11 N	15.03 E
Nymphenburg ♦⁸	60	48.09 N	11.30 E
Nynäshamn	40	58.54 N	17 57 E
Nyngan	166	31.34 S	147 11 E
Nyoma	120	33.11 N	78.38 E
Nyon	58	46.23 N	6.14 E
Nyong ≃	152	3.17 N	9.54 E
Nyons	62	44.22 N	5.08 E
Nyons I	41	55.03 N	12.13 E
Nyou	150	12.46 N	1.56 W
Nyťany	90	49.43 N	13.12 E
Nyrov	24	60.42 N	56.40 E
Nyrsko	60	49.18 N	13.09 E
Nyš	89	51.31 N	142.46 E
Nysa, Pol.	30	50.29 N	17.20 E
Nysa, Ross.	80	56.23 N	51.51 E
Nysa Kłodzka ≃	30	52.04 N	17.50 E
Nysa Łużycka (Neisse) (Nisa) ≃	30	52.04 N	14.46 E
Nyslott → Savonlinna	26	61.52 N	28.53 E
Nyssa	41	55.08 N	12.32 E
Nyssa	202	43.52 N	116.39 W
Nysted	41	54.40 N	11.45 E
Nytva	86	57.56 N	55.20 E
Nyūdō-zaki ⊁	92	40.00 N	139.42 E
Nyugati Pályaudvar ♦⁸	264c	47.31 N	19.04 E
Nyúkawa	94	36.10 N	137.19 E
Nyumba ya Mungu Dam ♦⁶	154	3.51 S	37.28 E
Nyungwe	154	10.16 S	34.07 E
Nyunzu	154	5.57 S	28.01 E
Nyuri	120	27.42 N	92.13 E
Nyūzen	94	36.56 N	137.30 E
Nyvång	41	56.08 N	12.54 E
Nyvrovo	89	54.19 N	142.36 E
Nzaba	273b	4.06 S	15.16 E
Nzébéla	150	8.05 N	9.06 W
Nzega	154	4.13 S	33.11 E
Nzéla	152	1.25 S	12.39 E
Nzérékoré	150	7.45 N	8.49 W
N'zeto	152	7.14 S	12.52 E
Nzheledam @¹	156	22.44 S	30.06 E
Nzi ≃	150	5.57 N	4.50 W
Nzirna	154	3.03 S	32.48 E
Nziro	152	3.17 N	24.06 E
Nzo ≃	150	6.16 N	7.03 W
Nzoia ≃	154	0.03 N	33.57 E
Nzubuka	154	4.45 S	32.50 E
Nzwani (Anjouan) I	157a	12.15 S	44.25 E

O

Nombre	Página	Lat.	Long.
Oa, Mull of ⊁	46	55.35 N	6.20 W
Oacoma	198	43.47 N	99.23 W
Oadby	36	52.36 N	1.04 W
Oad Street	260	51.20 N	0.41 E
Oahe, Lake @¹	198	45.30 N	100.25 W
Oahe Dam ♦⁶	198	44.21 N	100.23 W
Oahu I	229c	21.30 N	158.00 W
Oak I	184	49.51 N	100.23 W
O-Aran-dake ∧	92	43.27 N	144.10 E
Oakbank, Austl.	162	33.03 S	140.35 E
Oakbank, Austl.	168b	34.59 S	138.51 E
Oak Bay	224	48.27 N	123.18 W
Oak Beach	276	40.38 N	73.17 W
Oak Bluffs	207	41.27 N	70.33 W
Oakboro	192	35.13 N	80.19 W
Oak Brook	74	41.49 N	87.55 W
Oakbrook Center ♦⁹	74	41.52 N	87.57 W
Oakbrook Terrace	74	41.52 N	87.58 W
Oakburn	184	50.50 N	100.32 W
Oak City, N.C., U.S.	192	35.57 N	77.18 W
Oak City, Ut., U.S.	200	39.22 N	112.20 W
Oak Creek, Co., U.S.	200	40.16 N	106.57 W
Oak Creek, Wi., U.S.	218	42.53 N	87.54 W
Oak Creek ≃, Az., U.S.	200	34.41 N	111.56 W
Oak Creek ≃, Co., U.S.	200	40.25 N	106.50 W
Oak Creek ≃, Ks., U.S.	198	39.29 N	98.28 W
Oak Creek ≃, N.D., U.S.	198	45.38 N	100.24 W
Oak Creek ≃, Tx., U.S.	196	31.48 N	100.13 W
Oakdale, Ct., U.S.	226	37.46 N	120.50 W
Oakdale, Ct., U.S.	207	41.27 N	72.09 W
Oakdale, Il., U.S.	194	38.16 N	89.30 W
Oakdale, La., U.S.	194	30.49 N	92.39 W
Oakdale, Ma., U.S.	207	42.21 N	71.47 W
Oakdale, N.J., U.S.	285	39.59 N	74.49 W
Oakdale, N.Y., U.S.	210	40.44 N	73.08 W
Oakdale Woods	278	41.56 N	87.58 W
Oakengates	42	52.42 N	2.28 W
Oakes	198	46.08 N	98.05 W
Oakesdale	202	47.07 N	117.14 W
Oakey	171a	27.26 S	151.43 E
Oakeys Brook ≃	276	40.21 N	74.27 W
Oakfield, Me., U.S.	188	46.05 N	68.09 W
Oakfield, N.Y., U.S.	210	43.03 N	78.16 W
Oakfield, Wi., U.S.	190	43.41 N	88.32 W
Oakford, In., U.S.	219	40.06 N	89.54 W
Oakford, Pa., U.S.	208	40.09 N	74.58 W
Oak Forest	216	41.36 N	87.44 W
Oakgrove, Eng., U.K.	262	53.13 N	2.07 W

FRANÇAIS Nom	Page	Lat.°′	Long.°′ W = Ouest
Oak Grove, La., U.S.	194	32.51 N	91.23 W
Oak Grove, Or., U.S.	224	45.25 N	122.38 W
Oak Hall	208	37.56 N	75.33 W
Oakham	42	52.40 N	0.43 W
Oak Harbor, Oh., U.S.	214	41.30 N	83.09 W
Oak Harbor, Wa., U.S.	224	48.17 N	122.38 W
Oak Hill, De., U.S.	285	39.44 N	75.36 W
Oak Hill, Fl., U.S.	220	28.51 N	80.51 W
Oak Hill, Mi., U.S.	224	44.13 N	86.18 W
Oak Hill, N.J., U.S.	210	42.25 N	74.09 W
Oak Hill, Oh., U.S.	188	38.54 N	82.34 W
Oak Hill, W.V., U.S.	188	37.58 N	81.08 W
Oakhurst, Ca., U.S.	226	37.19 N	119.40 W
Oakhurst, N.J., U.S.	208	40.16 N	74.01 W
Oakhurst, Tx., U.S.	222	30.44 N	95.19 W
Oak Island I, N.S., Can.	186	44.31 N	64.13 W
Oak Island I, N.Y., U.S.	276	40.39 N	73.17 W
Oak Knolls	204	34.51 N	120.27 W
Oak Lake @, Mb., Can.	184	49.47 N	100.33 W
Oak Lake @, On., Can.	184	50.26 N	93.50 W
Oak Lake @, On., Can.	212	44.36 N	77.55 W
Oakland, On., Can.	214	42.09 N	82.36 W
Oakland, Ca., U.S.	226	37.48 N	122.16 W
Oakland, Fl., U.S.	220	28.33 N	81.38 W
Oakland, Il., U.S.	194	39.39 N	88.01 W
Oakland, Ia., U.S.	198	41.18 N	95.23 W
Oakland, Me., U.S.	188	44.32 N	69.43 W
Oakland, Md., U.S.	188	39.24 N	79.24 W
Oakland, Md., U.S.	284c	38.51 N	76.55 W
Oakland, Ne., U.S.	198	41.50 N	96.28 W
Oakland, N.J., U.S.	210	41.00 N	74.15 W
Oakland, Or., U.S.	202	43.25 N	123.17 W
Oakland, Pa., U.S.	210	41.57 N	75.36 W
Oakland, Pa., U.S.	214	40.59 N	80.22 W
Oakland, Tx., U.S.	222	29.36 N	96.50 W
Oakland ♦, U.S.	216	42.40 N	83.23 W
Oakland ♦⁸	279b	40.26 N	79.58 W
Oakland-Alameda County Coliseum ♦	282	37.45 N	122.12 W
Oakland Army Base ♦	282	37.49 N	122.19 W
Oakland Beach	214	41.37 N	80.18 W
Oakland City	194	38.20 N	87.2C W
Oakland Gardens ♦⁸	284c	40.45 N	73.45 W
Oakland Mall ♦⁹	281	42.32 N	83.07 W
Oakland Park	283	42.26 N	80.07 W
Oakland-Pontiac Airport ♦	281	42.40 N	83.24 W
Oaklands	168b	30.05 S	137.41 E
Oaklands ♦⁸	273d	26.09 S	28.04 E
Oakland Southwest Airport ♦	281	42.30 N	83.37 W
Oakland University ♦	281	42.41 N	83.13 W
Oak Lane Manor	285	39.47 N	75.32 W
Oak Lawn, Il., U.S.	216	41.43 N	87.45 W
Oak Lawn, Ks., U.S.	198	37.36 N	97.17 W
Oaklawn, Md., U.S.	284c	38.47 N	76.55 W
Oakleigh	169	37.54 S	145.06 E
Oakleigh South	274b	37.56 S	145.05 E
Oakley, Eng., U.K.	42	51.15 N	1.11 W
Oakley, Scot., U.K.	46	56.04 N	3.33 W
Oakley, Ca., U.S.	226	37.58 N	121.43 W
Oakley, Id., U.S.	202	42.14 N	113.52 W
Oakley, Il., U.S.	219	39.53 N	88.48 W
Oakley, Ks., U.S.	198	39.08 N	100.51 W
Oakley Park	216	42.34 N	83.30 W
Oaklyn	285	39.54 N	75.05 W
Oakman	194	33.42 N	87.23 W
Oakmont	214	40.31 N	79.50 W
Oak Mountain State Park ♦	193	33.22 N	86.41 W
Oakmulgee Creek ≃	194	32.28 N	87.09 W
Oak Neck ⊁¹	276	40.54 N	73.34 W
Oak Neck Point ⊁	276	40.55 N	73.34 W
Oakohay Creek ≃	194	31.44 N	89.25 W
Oak Orchard Creek ≃	210	43.22 N	78.12 W
Oak Orchard Swamp ☰	210	43.07 N	78.18 W
Oakover ≃	162	20.43 S	120.33 E
Oak Park, Austl.	274b	37.43 S	144.55 E
Oak Park, Ca., U.S.	228	34.11 N	118.45 W
Oak Park, Il., U.S.	216	41.53 N	87.47 W
Oak Park, Mi., U.S.	216	42.28 N	83.10 W
Oak Park, Pa., U.S.	285	40.15 N	75.18 W
Oak Point	184	50.30 N	98.00 W
Oakridge, Ca., U.S.	228	38.03 N	121.21 W
Oakridge, N.J., U.S.	210	41.03 N	74.29 W
Oakridge, Or., U.S.	202	43.44 N	122.27 W
Oak Ridge, Pa., U.S.	210	41.00 N	79.18 W
Oak Ridge, Tn., U.S.	192	36.00 N	84.16 W
Oak Ridge Lake	276	41.00 N	74.32 W
Oak Ridge National Laboratory ♦	192	36.00 N	84.15 W
Oak Ridge Reservoir @	276	41.03 N	74.30 W
Oaks	285	40.08 N	81.28 W
Oaks Corners	210	42.56 N	77.01 W
Oak Shades	276	40.26 N	74.13 W
Oakton	284c	38.52 N	77.18 W
Oakura	172	39.07 S	173.57 E
Oak Valley, N.J., U.S.	285	39.48 N	75.09 W
Oak Valley, Va., U.S.	284c	36.51 N	77.15 W
Oak View, Ca., U.S.	228	34.24 N	119.18 W
Oak View, Md., U.S.	285	39.01 N	76.59 W
Oakview, N.J., U.S.	285	39.51 N	75.09 W
Oakview Beach	212	44.29 N	80.03 W
Oakville, Mb., Can.	184	49.56 N	97.58 W
Oakville, On., Can.	212	43.27 N	79.41 W
Oakville, Ct., U.S.	208	41.35 N	73.05 W
Oakville, In., U.S.	218	40.05 N	85.23 W
Oakville, Wa., U.S.	224	46.50 N	123.13 W
Oakwood, On., Can.	212	44.29 N	78.50 W
Oakwood, N.J., U.S.	285	39.52 N	74.50 W
Oakwood, Oh., U.S.	214	41.06 N	83.31 W
Oakwood, Oh., U.S.	218	39.44 N	84.10 W
Oakwood, Tx., U.S.	222	31.35 N	95.50 W
Oakwood Beach	208	39.23 N	75.23 W
Oakwood Park ♦	279a	41.26 N	82.06 W
Oamishirasato	268	35.31 N	140.18 E
Ōana	268	35.31 N	140.04 E
Oancea	38	45.55 N	28.06 E
Ōarai	92	36.18 N	140.34 E
Oaro	172	42.31 S	173.30 E
Oasis, Ca., U.S.	204	33.28 N	116.06 W
Oasis, Nv., U.S.	226	41.01 N	114.30 W
Oates Coast ⊁²	9	70.00 S	160.00 E
Oatka Creek ≃	210	43.01 N	77.44 W
Oatlands	166	42.18 S	147.21 E
Oatley	274a	33.59 S	151.05 E
Oatley Park ♦	274a	33.59 S	151.05 E
Oaxaca □³	234	16.30 N	96.30 W
Oaxaca [de Juárez]	234	17.03 N	96.43 W
Ob' ≃	72	66.45 N	69.30 E
Oba ≃	190	43.55 N	84.17 W
Obaba	152	2.00 S	16.10 E
Obabika Lake @	190	47.05 N	80.10 W
Ōbama, Nihon	92	33.45 N	130.13 E
Ōbama, Nihon	92	35.29 N	135.45 E
Obama-wan C	92	35.30 N	135.42 E
Oban, Nig.	152	5.17 N	8.35 E
Oban, Scot., U.K.	46	56.25 N	5.29 W

PORTUGUÊS Nome	Página	Lat.°′	Long.°′ W = Oeste
Obanazawa	92	38.36 N	140.24 E
Obando	269l	14.43 N	120.56 E
Oban Hills ∧²	150	5.35 N	8.35 E
Obara	94	35.15 N	137.18 E
Obata	94	34.30 N	136.40 E
Ob' Bay C	9	70.35 S	163.22 E
Obbo	144	3.36 N	38.54 E
Obbola	26	63.42 N	20.19 E
Občuga	76	54.30 N	29.22 E
Obdach	61	47.04 N	14.41 E
Obed	182	53.33 N	117.12 W
Obed ≃	192	36.04 N	84.39 W
Obeliai	76	55.56 N	25.48 E
Obelisk ∧	172	45.20 S	169.12 E
Oberá	252	27.29 S	55.08 W
Oberägeri	58	47.08 N	8.37 E
Oberalppass ⋋	58	46.39 N	8.40 E
Oberalpstock ∧	58	46.44 N	8.46 E
Oberammergau	64	47.35 N	11.04 E
Oberau	64	47.33 N	11.08 E
Oberaudorf	64	47.39 N	12.10 E
Oberbauer	263	51.17 N	7.26 E
Oberbayern □⁵	64	48.15 N	11.45 E
Oberbieber	56	50.28 N	7.29 E
Oberbonsfeld	263	51.22 N	7.08 E
Oberbrügge	263	51.11 N	7.34 E
Obercunnersdorf	54	51.02 N	14.40 E
Oberdiessbach	58	46.51 N	7.38 E
Oberdolling	48	48.50 N	11.35 E
Oberdorla	54	51.10 N	10.25 E
Oberdrauburg	64	46.45 N	12.58 E
Obereifinghausen	263	51.20 N	7.11 E
Ober Engadin ∨	58	46.37 N	9.58 E
Oberengstringen	58	47.25 N	8.28 E
Oberer See → Superior, Lake @	190	48.00 N	88.00 W
Oberfranken □⁵	60	49.50 N	11.20 E
Obergeis	56	50.54 N	9.38 E
Ober-Grafendorf	61	48.09 N	15.33 E
Obergum	52	53.20 N	6.31 E
Obergünzburg	58	47.51 N	10.25 E
Obergurgl	64	46.52 N	11.01 E
Obergurig	54	51.07 N	14.24 E
Oberhaan	263	51.13 N	7.02 E
Oberhaching	64	48.02 N	11.36 E
Oberharmersbach	58	48.22 N	8.07 E
Oberhasisch	58	48.33 N	7.20 E
Oberhausen	56	51.28 N	6.50 E
Oberhof	54	50.41 N	10.44 E
Oberhofen	58	46.44 N	7.40 E
Oberinntal ∨	64	47.13 N	10.45 E
Oberjettingen	64	48.34 N	8.46 E
Oberjoch	58	47.31 N	10.23 E
Ober-Kassel ♦⁸	263	51.14 N	6.46 E
Oberkirch	58	48.31 N	8.05 E
Oberkirchtach	264b	48.17 N	16.12 E
Oberkirchen	56	51.09 N	8.22 E
Oberkochen	58	48.47 N	10.06 E
Oberkotzau	56	50.16 N	11.56 E
Oberlaa ♦⁸	264b	48.08 N	16.23 E
Oberlaapark ♦	264b	48.08 N	16.25 E
Oberlausitz ∨	54	51.15 N	14.30 E
Oberlin, Ks., U.S.	198	39.49 N	100.31 W
Oberlin, La., U.S.	194	30.37 N	92.45 W
Oberlin, Oh., U.S.	214	41.17 N	82.13 W
Oberlin, Pa., U.S.	208	40.14 N	76.49 W
Oberloisdorf	61	47.26 N	16.30 E
Obermarchtal	58	48.14 N	9.34 E
Obermeiser	56	51.26 N	9.19 E
Obermiening	64	47.18 N	10.59 E
Obermodern	58	48.51 N	7.32 E
Obermoschel	56	49.44 N	7.46 E
Obermühl	61	48.27 N	13.56 E
Obermünstertal	58	47.52 N	7.49 E
Obernai	58	48.28 N	7.29 E
Obernbeck	52	52.12 N	8.41 E
Obernberg am Inn	60	48.19 N	13.20 E
Obernburg am Main	60	49.50 N	9.08 E
Oberndorf	56	53.44 N	9.08 E
Oberndorf am Neckar	58	48.18 N	8.34 E
Oberndorf bei Salzburg	64	47.57 N	12.56 E
Oberndorf in Tirol	64	47.30 N	12.23 E
Oberne	171b	35.24 S	147.50 E
Oberne Hill ∧²	171b	35.26 S	147.53 E
Obernhausen	56	50.29 N	9.56 E
Obernkirchen	56	52.16 N	9.07 E
Obernzell	60	48.34 N	13.38 E
Oberon	166	33.43 S	149.52 E
Oberösterreich □³	60	48.15 N	14.00 E
Oberpfalz □⁵	60	49.30 N	12.10 E
Oberpleis	56	50.43 N	7.16 E
Oberpullendorf	61	47.30 N	16.31 E
Ober-Ramstadt	56	49.49 N	8.45 E
Oberried	58	47.54 N	7.58 E
Oberriet	58	47.19 N	9.33 E
Oberrimsingen	48	48.00 N	7.40 E
Oberröblingen	54	51.26 N	11.18 E
Ober Sankt Veit ♦⁸	264b	48.11 N	16.16 E
Oberscheidental	56	49.32 N	9.09 E
Oberschleißheim	56	49.42 N	10.26 E
Oberschönau	56	50.44 N	8.20 E
Oberschleissheim	56	48.15 N	11.34 E
Oberschöneweide ♦⁸	264a	52.28 N	13.31 E
Obersiecke	56	48.58 N	7.59 E
Oberspier	54	52.13 N	10.38 E
Oberstadtfeld	56	50.10 N	6.46 E
Oberstarten	64	47.24 N	10.10 E
Oberstdorf	64	47.24 N	10.16 E
Obersteinbach	58	49.02 N	7.41 E
Oberstenfeld	58	49.00 N	9.12 E
Obersuhl	56	50.56 N	10.02 E
Obersulm	56	49.08 N	9.27 E
Obertauern	64	47.15 N	13.32 E
Oberthulba	56	50.14 N	9.59 E
Obertilliach	64	46.42 N	12.37 E
Obertraubling	60	48.58 N	12.10 E
Obertrum	64	47.56 N	13.05 E
Ober-türmer See @	56	47.56 N	12.50 E
Obertürken	60	48.58 N	12.50 E
Oberursel	56	50.12 N	8.34 E
Oberuzwil	58	47.26 N	9.08 E
Obervellach	60	46.56 N	13.12 E
Oberviechtach	60	49.28 N	12.25 E
Obervolta → Burkina Faso □¹	150	13.00 N	1.30 W
Oberwald	58	46.32 N	8.21 E
Oberwart	61	47.17 N	16.13 E
Oberweissbach	54	50.35 N	11.08 E
Oberwengern	263	51.23 N	7.22 E
Oberwesel	56	50.06 N	7.44 E
Oberweisenthal	54	50.25 N	12.59 E
Oberwil	58	47.30 N	7.33 E
Oberwölfach	58	48.18 N	8.13 E
Oberwölz Stadt	61	47.13 N	14.17 E
Oberzeiring	61	47.16 N	14.29 E
Obetz	218	39.52 N	82.57 W
Obey, East Fork ≃	192	36.27 N	85.07 W
Obey, West Fork ≃	192	36.27 N	85.19 W
Obfelden	58	47.16 N	8.26 E
Obi	150	8.22 N	8.46 E
Obi, Pulauan II	164	1.30 S	127.45 E
Obi, Pulau I	164	1.30 S	127.45 E
Obi, Selat ≃	164	0.52 S	127.33 E
Obiaruku	150	5.51 N	6.09 E
Obichody	269l	14.38 N	121.20 E
Obi-Garm	85	38.43 N	69.42 E
Obihiro	92a	42.55 N	143.12 E
Obikanda	91	37.07 N	68.05 E
Obilatu, Pulau I	164	1.25 S	127.20 E
Obil'noje	78	47.32 N	44.25 E

Nome	Página	Lat.	Long.
Obing	60	48.00 N	12.24 E
Obion	194	36.15 N	89.11 W
Obion ≃	194	35.55 N	89.39 W
Obion, Middle Fork ≃	194	36.13 N	88.56 W
Obion, Rutherford Fork ≃	194	36.17 N	89.01 W
Obion, South Fork ≃	194	36.17 N	89.03 W
Obion Creek ≃	194	36.35 N	89.11 W
Obiou, Grande Tête de l' ∧	62	44.40 N	5.50 E
Obira	92a	44.00 N	141.35 E
Obitočnaja kosa ⊁²	78	46.33 N	36.13 E
Obitočnyj zaliv C	78	46.35 N	36.00 E
Obitsu ≃	94	35.24 N	139.54 E
Objačevo	24	60.20 N	49.34 E
Oblatlaja, gora ∧	89	43.45 N	134.10 E
Öblarn	61	47.27 N	13.59 E
Oblastnaja	80	56.59 N	52.37 E
Oblivskaja	80	48.32 N	42.30 E
Oblong	194	39.00 N	87.54 W
Obluč'e	89	49.03 N	131.04 E
Obninsk	82	55.05 N	36.37 E
Obnora ≃	82	58.30 N	40.58 E
Obnova	38	43.26 N	24.59 E
Obo	154	5.24 N	26.30 E
Obobogorao	158	27.18 S	20.04 E
Obock	144	11.59 N	43.16 E
Obojan'	78	51.13 N	36.16 E
O-boke ≃	96	33.55 N	133.46 E
Obokote	154	0.52 S	26.19 E
Obol'	76	55.22 N	29.17 E
Obol' ≃	76	55.24 N	29.02 E
Oboldino	265b	55.53 N	37.56 E
Obolon'	78	49.36 N	32.52 E
Oborniki	30	52.39 N	16.51 E
Obot	144	4.30 N	37.20 E
Obouya	152	0.56 S	15.43 E
Oboz'orskij	24	63.28 N	40.18 E
Obrazcovo-Travino	80	45.58 N	48.02 E
Obree, Mount ∧	164	9.30 S	148.05 E
Obrenovac	38	44.39 N	20.12 E
O'Brien	202	42.04 N	123.42 W
O'Brien Coulee ∨	202	48.38 N	110.22 W
Obrighoven-Lackhausen	52	51.40 N	6.38 E
Obrovac	36	44.12 N	15.41 E
Obrovo	76	52.30 N	25.34 E
Obručeva, gora ∧	88	53.36 N	113.52 E
Obručevka	85	42.30 N	69.05 E
Obruk	130	38.10 N	33.12 E
Obryta	54	53.13 N	14.59 E
Obryvistoje	89	48.44 N	136.48 E
Obša ≃	76	55.55 N	32.32 E
Obšarovka	80	53.07 N	48.52 E
Obščij Syrt ∧	80	52.00 N	51.30 E
Observation Peak ∧	204	40.46 N	120.10 W
Observatoire, Caye de l' I	160	21.25 S	158.50 E
Observatory Inlet C	182	55.10 N	129.54 W
Obskaja guba C	72	69.00 N	73.00 E
Obsteig	64	47.18 N	10.56 E
Obtovo	78	51.37 N	33.13 E
Ob' Trench ♣¹	14	33.00 S	98.00 E
Ōbu	94	35.00 N	136.58 E
Obu ♦⁸	270	34.44 N	135.09 E
Obuasi	150	6.14 N	1.39 W
Obubra	150	6.06 N	8.21 E
Obuchova	78	50.08 N	30.37 E
Obuchovo	76	56.06 N	32.22 E
Obuchoviči	76	51.00 N	29.46 E
Obuchova, Ross.	86	46.13 N	81.05 E
Obuchovo, Ross.	82	55.50 N	38.16 E
Obuchovo, Ross.	82	56.09 N	36.55 E
Obudai	264c	47.33 N	19.02 E
Obudai-sziget I	264c	47.33 N	19.04 E
Obudu	150	6.40 N	9.09 E
Obuse	94	36.42 N	138.19 E
Obushkong Lake @	190	47.42 N	80.48 W
Obuškovo	82	55.47 N	37.02 E
Obu-tōge ⋋	270	34.44 N	135.10 E
Obva ≃	86	58.32 N	55.18 E
Obvärak	86	58.30 N	54.51 E
Obwalden □³	58	46.50 N	8.14 E
Obžerica	80	57.11 N	42.58 E
Očakov	78	46.37 N	31.33 E
Očakovo ♦⁸	265b	55.41 N	37.27 E
Ocala	192	29.11 N	82.08 W
Ocalí	248	6.09 S	78.18 W
Ocamo ≃	246	3.36 N	65.14 W
Ocampo, Méx.	232	28.11 N	108.23 W
Ocampo, Méx.	232	27.20 N	102.21 W
Ocampo, Méx.	234	22.50 N	99.20 W
Ocampo, Méx.	234	21.39 N	101.30 W
Ocaña, Col.	248	8.15 N	73.20 W
Ocaña, Esp.	34	39.56 N	3.31 W
Ocate Creek ≃	196	36.17 N	104.30 W
Occaquan ≃	284c	38.40 N	77.14 W
Occaquan Bay C	284c	38.37 N	77.13 W
Occaquan Reservoir @¹	208	38.43 N	77.22 W
Očchamuri	62	41.52 N	41.50 E
Occhieppo Inferiore	62	45.33 N	8.01 E
Occhiobello	64	44.55 N	11.35 E
Occhito, Lago di @¹	66	41.35 N	14.54 E
Occidental, Cordillera ∧, Col.	246	5.00 N	76.00 W
Occidental, Cordillera ∧, Perú	248	10.00 S	77.00 W
Occidental College ∨²	280	34.08 N	118.13 W
Occidental de Zapata, Ciénaga @	240p	22.25 N	81.20 W
Occoquan Bay C	284c	38.37 N	77.13 W
Oceana Naval Air Station ♦	208	36.49 N	76.02 W
Ocean Bay Park	207	40.39 N	73.08 W
Ocean Beach	207	40.38 N	73.09 W
Ocean Bluff	207	42.05 N	70.39 W
Ocean Breeze Park	220	27.53 N	80.30 W
Ocean Cape ⊁	180	59.30 N	139.45 W
Ocean City, N.J., U.S.	208	39.16 N	74.34 W
Ocean City, Wa., U.S.	224	47.04 N	124.09 W
Ocean Falls	182	52.21 N	127.41 W
Ocean Gate	208	39.55 N	74.08 W
Ocean Grove, Austl.	169	38.16 S	144.32 E
Ocean Grove, Ma., U.S.	207	41.43 N	71.12 W
Ocean Heights	207	40.19 N	70.33 W
Ocean Island → Banaba I	174d	0.52 S	169.35 E
Ocean Island → Kure Atoll I	128	28.25 N	178.20 W
Oceano	204	35.06 N	120.37 W
Ocean Park, B.C., Can.	224	49.02 N	122.53 W
Ocean Park, Wa., U.S.	224	46.29 N	124.02 W
Ocean Pines	208	38.23 N	75.09 W
Ocean Port	208	40.19 N	74.00 W
Ocean Shores	224	47.00 N	124.10 W
Oceanside, Ca., U.S.	228	33.11 N	117.22 W
Ocean Springs	194	30.24 N	88.49 W
Ocean View, De., U.S.	208	38.32 N	75.05 W

Nome	Página	Lat.	Long.
Ochagavía, Canal ≃	286e	33.30 S	70.49 W
Ochanomizu Women's University ∨²	268	35.43 N	139.44 E
Ochansk	86	57.43 N	55.23 E
Ochapowace Indian Reserve ♦⁴	184	50.30 N	102.24 W
Ocheyedan	198	43.08 N	95.32 W
Ocheyedan ≃	198	43.24 N	95.32 W
Ochi, Nihon	95	33.32 N	133.15 E
Ochi, Nihon	95	35.04 N	132.36 E
Ochi, Nihon	95	34.16 N	134.18 E
Ochiai	95	35.01 N	133.45 E
Ochiai ♦⁸	268	35.43 N	139.42 E
O'Chiese Indian Reserve ♦⁴	182	52.50 N	115.28 W
Ochil Hills ∧²	46	56.14 N	3.40 W
Ochiltree	44	55.28 N	4.23 W
Ochise ≃	94	35.03 N	137.46 E
Ochlocknee	192	30.58 N	84.03 W
Ochlockonee ≃	192	29.58 N	84.21 W
Ochoco Creek ≃	202	44.19 N	120.53 W
Ochoco Mountains ∧²	202	44.10 N	120.35 W
Ochoco Reservoir @¹	202	44.25 N	120.54 W
Ocho Rios	241q	18.25 N	77.07 W
Ochota	74	59.20 N	143.04 E
Ochotsk	74	59.23 N	143.18 E
Ochotskisches Meer → Okhotsk, Sea of ⊤²	74	53.00 N	150.00 E
Ochre River	184	51.03 N	99.47 W
Ochsenfurt	56	49.40 N	10.03 E
Ochsenhausen	58	48.04 N	9.56 E
Ochsenwerder ♦⁸	52	53.28 N	10.06 E
Ochta ≃	265a	59.57 N	30.24 E
Ochtrup	56	52.13 N	7.11 E
Ochvat	76	56.46 N	32.27 E
Oci ≃	152	15.14 S	15.16 E
Ocilla	192	31.35 N	83.15 W
Öck	42	51.39 N	1.17 W
Ockelbo	26	60.53 N	16.43 E
Ockenden	26	57.43 N	11.39 E
Ockerö	26	57.43 N	11.39 E
Ockham	260	51.18 N	0.27 W
Ockholm	41	54.40 N	8.49 E
Ockies	158	31.31 S	21.41 E
Ocklawaha, Lake @¹	192	29.30 N	81.50 W
Ocmulgee ≃	192	31.58 N	82.32 W
Ocmulgee National Monument ♦	192	32.43 N	83.38 W
Ocna Mureş	38	46.23 N	23.51 E
Ocoa, Bahía de C	238	18.22 N	70.39 W
Ocoee	220	28.34 N	81.32 W
Ocoee ≃	192	35.12 N	84.40 W
Ocoee (Toccoa) ≃	192	35.12 N	84.40 W
Ocoña	248	16.26 S	73.07 W
Ocoña ≃	248	16.28 S	73.07 W
Oconee	219	39.17 N	89.07 W
Oconee ≃	192	31.58 N	82.32 W
Oconee, Lake @¹	192	33.30 N	83.15 W
Ocongate	248	13.38 S	71.23 W
O'Connell	170	33.22 S	149.44 E
Oconomowoc	216	43.06 N	88.29 W
Oconomowoc ≃	216	43.07 N	88.37 W
Oconomowoc Lake @	216	43.06 N	88.27 W
Oconto	190	44.53 N	87.51 W
Oconto, North Branch ≃	190	45.00 N	88.23 W
Oconto Falls	190	44.52 N	88.08 W
Ocós	236	14.31 N	92.11 W
Ocosingo	232	16.54 N	92.05 W
Ocotal	234	13.38 N	86.29 W
Ocotepec	234	17.13 N	93.09 W
Ocotepeque □⁵	234	14.30 N	89.00 W
Ocotlán	234	20.21 N	102.46 W
Ocotlán de Morelos	234	16.48 N	96.40 W
Ocoyoacac	234	19.16 N	99.26 W
Ocozocoautla [de Espinosa]	234	16.46 N	93.22 W
Ocracoke	192	35.06 N	75.58 W
Ocracoke Island I	192	35.09 N	75.53 W
Ocre, Monte ∧	66	42.15 N	13.26 E
Ocros	248	10.24 S	77.24 W
Octoraro Creek ≃	208	39.39 N	76.09 W
Octoraro Creek, East Branch ≃	208	39.49 N	76.02 W
Octoraro Lake @¹	208	39.48 N	76.02 W
Ocú	234	7.57 N	80.47 W
Ocuilán de Arteaga	234	18.58 N	99.25 W
Ocumare del Tuy	244	10.07 N	66.47 W
Ocuri	248	18.50 S	65.50 W
Ocussi	112	9.12 S	124.21 E
Oda, Ghana	150	5.55 N	0.59 W
Ōda, Nihon	96	35.11 N	132.30 E
Ōda, Nihon	96	34.39 N	132.48 E
Oda, Jabal ∧	144	20.21 N	36.39 E
Odadahraun ∧	26a	65.00 N	17.00 W
Odaejin	98	41.34 N	129.40 E
Ōdaesan ∧	94	37.46 N	128.37 E
Ōdai	94	34.24 N	136.20 E
Ōdaigahara-zan ∧	92	34.11 N	136.06 E
Ōdaka	92	37.34 N	141.00 E
Odanakumadona	156	20.53 S	24.45 E
Odawara	92	35.15 N	139.10 E
Ōdate	92	40.16 N	140.34 E
Odda	26	60.04 N	6.33 E
Odden	41	55.58 N	11.22 E
Oddebolt	198	42.11 N	95.15 W

Nome	Página	Lat.	Long.
Odessa, Mo., U.S.	194	38.59 N	93.57 W
Odessa, N.Y., U.S.	210	42.20 N	76.47 W
Odessa, Tx., U.S.	196	31.50 N	102.22 W
Odessa, Wa., U.S.	202	47.20 N	118.41 W
Odessa ≃⁴	78	47.30 N	30.00 E
Odessa Lake @	212	44.14 N	72.58 W
Odiel ≃	34	37.10 N	6.54 W
Odienné	150	9.30 N	7.34 W
Odiham	42	51.15 N	0.57 W
Odin	219	38.37 N	89.03 W
Odin, Mount ∧	182	50.33 N	118.08 W
Odincovo, Ross.	82	55.41 N	37.17 E
Odincovo, Ross.	82	55.04 N	38.00 E
Odiongan	116	12.24 N	121.59 E
Odiongan Bay C	116	12.25 N	121.58 E
Odivelas	34	38.47 N	9.11 W
Odobeşti	38	45.45 N	27.04 E
Odojev	76	53.56 N	36.41 E
Odolanów	30	51.35 N	17.39 E
Odomari-chosuichi @⁹	96	33.43 N	132.18 E
Odon	194	38.50 N	86.59 W
Odónçk	110	11.48 N	104.45 E
O'Donnell	196	32.57 N	101.49 W
O'Donnell ≃	162	12.35 S	126.36 E
Odoorn	52	52.51 N	6.51 E
Odorheiu Secuiesc	38	46.18 N	25.18 E
Odra (Oder) ≃	30	53.32 N	14.38 E
Odra Port	54	53.32 N	14.14 E
Odrinhas	266c	38.53 N	9.22 W
Odrzywół	30	51.30 N	20.33 E
Ødsted	41	55.39 N	9.25 E
Odum	192	31.39 N	82.01 W
Odžaci	38	45.30 N	19.16 E
Odzala, Parc National de ♦	152	1.00 S	15.00 E
Odzi	154	18.58 S	32.23 E
Odzi ≃	154	19.45 S	32.23 E
Odziba	152	3.35 S	15.31 E
Oe	96	35.31 N	135.09 E
Oebisfelde	54	52.25 N	10.59 E
Oederan	54	50.51 N	13.09 E
Oederen	54	50.52 N	13.09 E
Oeding	52	51.56 N	6.49 E
Oedheim	56	49.17 N	9.15 E
Oegstgeest	52	52.10 N	4.29 E
Oeiras, Bra.	250	7.01 S	42.08 W
Oeiras, Port.	266c	38.41 N	9.21 W
Oeiras do Pará	250	1.58 S	49.51 W
Oelde	52	51.49 N	8.08 E
Oelenari ≃	250	3.13 N	54.09 W
Oella	284b	39.16 N	76.47 W
Oels → Oleśnica	30	51.13 N	17.23 E
Oelsig	54	51.41 N	13.22 E
Oelsnitz, Dtsch.	54	50.24 N	12.10 E
Oelsnitz, Dtsch.	54	50.43 N	12.41 E
Oelwein	190	42.41 N	91.54 W
Oenpelli	164	12.20 S	133.04 E
Oensingen	58	47.17 N	7.44 E
Oepping	60	48.36 N	13.56 E
Oeraro-do I	98	34.27 N	127.30 E
Oer-Erkenschwick	52	51.39 N	7.15 E
Oerlinghausen	52	51.57 N	8.39 E
Oermten	263	51.29 N	6.27 E
Oesede	52	52.12 N	8.04 E
Oeslau	54	50.17 N	11.01 E
Oespel ♦⁸	263	51.30 N	7.23 E
Oeste, Canal del ≃	266a	40.23 N	3.42 W
Oeste, Parque del ♦	266a	40.26 N	3.43 W
Oesterstrand ♦⁸	52	51.29 N	4.15 E
Oestrich	263	51.21 N	7.38 E
Oeting	58	49.10 N	6.50 E
Oetz	64	47.12 N	10.54 E
Oeuf ≃	50	48.11 N	2.21 E
Oeventrop	56	51.24 N	8.08 E
Oeversee	41	54.42 N	9.26 E
Oe-yama ∧	96	35.24 N	135.07 E
Oeyreluy	62	43.42 N	1.03 W

Legend (map feature glossary):

Symbol	English	Deutsch	Español	Français	Português
≃	River	Fluß	Rio	Rivière	Rio
≃ Canal	Canal	Kanal	Canal	Canal	Canal
⌣	Waterfall, Rapids	Wasserfall, Stromschnellen	Cascada, Rápidos	Chute d'eau, Rapides	Cascata, Rápidos
⋉	Strait	Meerenge	Estrecho	Détroit	Estreito
C	Bay, Gulf	Bucht, Golf	Bahía, Golfo	Baie, Golfe	Baía, Golfo
@	Lake, Lakes	See, Seen	Lago, Lagos	Lac, Lacs	Lago, Lagos
☰	Swamp	Sumpf	Pantano	Marais	Pântano
⧓	Ice Features, Glacier	Eis- und Gletscherformen	Accidentes Glaciales	Formes glaciaires	Acidentes glaciares
⊤	Other Hydrographic Features	Andere Hydrographische Objekte	Otros Elementos Hidrográficos	Autres données hydrographiques	Outros acidentes hidrográficos
⊁	Submarine Features	Untermeerische Objekte	Accidentes Submarinos	Formes de relief sous-marin	Acidentes submarinos
□	Political Unit	Politische Einheit	Unidad Politica	Entité politique	Unidade política
∨²	Cultural Institution	Kulturelle Institution	Institución Cultural	Institution culturelle	Instituição cultural
♦⁹	Historical Site	Historische Stätte	Sitio Histórico	Site historique	Sitio histórico
♦	Recreational Site	Erholungs- und Ferienort	Sitio de Recreo	Centre de loisirs	Área de Lazer
♦	Airport	Flughafen	Aeropuerto	Aéroport	Aeroporto
♦	Military Installation	Militäranlage	Instalación Militar	Installation militaire	Instalação militar
♦	Miscellaneous	Verschiedenes	Misceláneo	Divers	Diversos

Name	Page	Lat.	Long.
Ogeechee ≃	192	31.51 N	81.06 W
Oge-jima I	96	34.12 N	134.38 E
Ogema	184	49.35 N	104.55 W
Oggersheim	56	49.29 N	8.22 E
Oghi Fort	123	34.31 N	73.01 E
Ogibalovo	76	60.34 N	39.40 E
Ogidaki Mountain ∧²	190	46.58 N	83.58 W
Ogies	158	26.02 S	29.04 E
Ogi-jima I	96	34.26 N	134.04 E
Ogijo	273a	6.42 N	3.31 E
Ogilvie, Austl.	162	28.09 S	114.38 E
Ogilvie, Mn., U.S.	190	45.49 N	93.25 W
Ogilvie ≃	180	65.52 N	137.16 W
Ogilvie Mountains ∧	180	65.00 N	139.30 W
Ogilville	218	39.08 N	86.01 W
Ogimi	174m	26.42 N	128.07 E
Ogino-sen ∧	96	35.26 N	134.26 E
Ogle □⁶	216	42.01 N	89.20 W
Oglesby, Il., U.S.	190	41.17 N	89.03 W
Oglesby, Tx., U.S.	222	31.25 N	97.31 W
Oglethorpe	192	32.17 N	84.03 W
Ogliastra ∧¹	71	39.56 N	9.37 E
Ogliastro Cilento	68	40.21 N	15.03 E
Oglio ≃	64	45.02 N	10.39 E
Ogmore	166	22.37 S	149.40 E
Ogmore ≃	42	51.38 N	3.31 W
Ogmore Vale	42	51.38 N	3.31 W
Ogni	54	54.54 N	83.31 E
Ognica	54	53.07 N	14.27 E
Ognon ≃	58	47.20 N	5.29 E
Ogn'ov Jar	86	58.23 N	82.26 E
Ogn'ovka	86	49.36 N	83.25 E
Ogo	94	36.25 N	139.50 E
Ogo ⊶⁸	270	34.49 N	135.06 E
Ogo ≃	270	34.47 N	135.04 E
Ogoamas, Bulu ∧	112	0.40 N	120.12 E
Ogóchi-dam ⊶⁶	94	35.47 N	139.04 E
Ogodža	89	52.44 N	132.31 E
Ogoja	150	6.40 N	8.48 E
Ogoki □⁵	176	51.38 N	85.57 W
'Ogol, Khaṭṭ el V	150	20.01 N	15.29 W
Ogooué ≃	152	0.49 S	9.00 E
Ogooué-Ivindo □⁴	152	1.00 N	13.00 E
Ogooué-Lolo □⁴	152	1.00 S	12.30 E
Ogooué-Maritime □⁴	152	2.00 S	9.30 E
Ogōri, Nihon	96	33.22 N	130.32 E
Ogōri, Nihon	96	34.06 N	131.24 E
Ogorodnoje	78	45.53 N	28.50 E
Ogose	94	35.58 N	139.18 E
Ogosta ≃	38	43.45 N	23.51 E
Ogoyo	273a	6.26 N	3.29 E
Ogr	140	12.02 N	27.06 E
Ogre	76	56.51 N	24.36 E
Ogre ≃	76	56.48 N	24.36 E
Ogrodzieniec	30	50.27 N	19.31 E
Ogrosen	54	51.42 N	14.02 E
Oguchi	94	36.12 N	136.55 E
Ogu-dong	98	38.57 N	126.56 E
Ogudu	273a	6.34 N	3.24 E
Ogulin	36	45.16 N	15.14 E
Ogun □³	150	6.45 N	3.25 E
Ogun ≃	150	6.36 N	3.27 E
Ogun Forest Reserve ✦	273a	6.37 N	3.26 E
Oguni, Nihon	92	38.04 N	139.45 E
Ogunlogun	273a	6.41 N	3.28 E
Ogunquit	188	43.14 N	70.35 W
Ogura-san ∧	96	34.20 N	138.37 E
Ogurčinskij, ostrov I	128	38.55 N	53.02 E
Oguta	150	5.44 N	6.44 E
Oğuz, Tür.	130	37.49 N	41.22 E
Ōguzeli	130	36.59 N	37.30 E
Ogwashi-Uku	150	6.10 N	6.31 E
Ohakune	172	39.25 S	175.24 E
Ohanapecosh	224	46.38 N	121.37 W
Ohanet	148	28.45 N	8.55 E
Ohār	124	27.21 N	84.37 E
Ōhara, Nihon	94	35.15 N	140.23 E
Ōhara, Nihon	96	35.07 N	134.20 E
Ōharano ⊶⁸	270	34.58 N	135.40 E
Ōhara-tunnel ⊶⁵	94	35.12 N	137.50 E
Ōhata	92	41.24 N	141.10 E
Ōhatake	268	35.57 N	139.46 E
Ohau, Lake ⊜	172	44.15 S	169.51 E
Ohaupo	172	37.55 S	175.19 E
Ohey	56	50.26 N	5.08 E
O'Higgins, Cabo ⋗	174z	27.05 S	109.15 W
O'Higgins, Cerro ∧	254	48.48 S	73.11 W
O'Higgins, Lago ⊜ (Lago San Martín)	254	49.00 S	72.40 W
Ohingaiti	172	39.52 S	175.43 E
Ohio	190	41.34 N	89.28 W
Ohio □⁶, In., U.S.	218	38.57 N	84.51 W
Ohio □⁶, W.V., U.S.	214	40.09 N	80.35 W
Ohio □³, U.S.	178	40.15 N	82.45 W
Ohio □³, U.S.	178	40.15 N	82.45 W
Ohio ≃	178	36.59 N	89.08 W
Ohio Brush Creek ≃	218	38.41 N	83.27 W
Ohio Brush Creek, Baker Fork ≃	218	39.02 N	83.26 W
Ohio Brush Creek, Little West Fork ≃	218	38.58 N	83.34 W
Ohio Brush Creek, West Fork ≃	218	38.56 N	83.28 W
Ohio Canal ≌	279a	41.26 N	81.40 W
Ohio Caverns ∧⁵	218	40.14 N	83.41 W
Ohio City	216	40.46 N	84.36 W
Ohio Peak ∧	208	38.49 N	107.07 W
Ohiopyle State Park ✦	214	39.50 N	79.31 W
Ohioville, N.Y., U.S.	210	41.45 N	74.03 W
Ohioville, Pa., U.S.	214	40.40 N	80.29 W
Ōhira	94	36.20 N	139.42 E
Ōhira-yama ∧	96	34.20 N	133.57 E
Ōhito	94	35.01 N	138.56 E
Ohlau → Oława	30	50.57 N	17.17 E
Ohligs ⊶⁸	263	51.09 N	7.00 E
Ohlman	219	39.21 N	89.13 W
Ohlsdorf	54	47.57 N	13.47 E
Ohm ≃	56	50.51 N	8.48 E
Ōho	94	36.08 N	140.06 E
Ohoitom	164	5.56 S	132.41 E
'Ohonua	174w	21.20 S	174.57 W
Ohoopee ≃	192	31.54 N	82.07 W
Ohori	268	35.30 N	140.02 E
Ōhori	94	51.10 N	114.02 E
Ohra Stausee ⊜¹	52	50.50 N	10.42 E
Ohrdruf	54	50.50 N	10.44 E
Ohre ≃, Dtsch.	54	52.18 N	11.47 E
Ohře (Eger) ≃, Europe	54	50.32 N	14.08 E
Ohrid	38	41.07 N	20.47 E
Ohrid, Lake ⊜	38	41.02 N	20.43 E
Ohrigstad	156	24.49 S	30.33 E
Öhringen	52	49.12 N	9.30 E
Ohrnberg	56	49.15 N	9.27 E
Ohuira, Bahía ⊂	232	25.38 N	108.58 W
Ohura	172	38.50 S	174.59 E
Ōi, Nihon	94	35.51 N	139.10 E
Ōi, Nihon	268	35.51 N	139.30 E
Ōi ⊶⁸	268	35.35 N	139.45 E
Ōi ≃, Nihon	94	34.46 N	138.13 E
Ōi ≃, Nihon	96	35.01 N	135.18 E
Ōiapoque (Oyapock) ≃	254	4.08 N	51.40 W
Ōies, Ȋle aux I	186	47.07 N	70.34 W
Oignies	50	50.28 N	2.59 E
Oil Center	196	32.29 N	103.15 W
Oil City, La., U.S.	196	32.44 N	93.58 W
Oil City, Pa., U.S.	214	41.26 N	79.42 W
Oil Creek ≃	214	41.26 N	79.42 W
Oil Creek State Park ✦	214	41.33 N	79.40 W
Oildale	226	35.25 N	119.01 W

Name	Page	Lat.	Long.
Oilmont	182	48.44 N	111.50 W
Oil Springs	214	42.47 N	82.07 W
Oilton, Ok., U.S.	196	36.05 N	96.35 W
Oilton, Tx., U.S.	196	27.33 N	98.59 W
Oil Trough	194	35.37 N	91.27 W
Oinville-sur-Montcient	261	49.02 N	1.51 E
Oir, Beinn an ∧	46	55.54 N	6.00 W
Oirschot	52	51.30 N	5.18 E
Oise □⁵	50	49.30 N	2.30 E
Oise ≃	50	49.00 N	2.04 E
Oise à l'Aisne, Canal de l' ≌	50	49.36 N	3.11 E
Oisemont	50	49.57 N	1.46 E
Ōiso, Nihon	94	35.18 N	139.19 E
Ōiso, Nihon	270	34.33 N	135.01 E
Oissel	50	49.20 N	1.06 E
Oissery	261	49.04 N	2.49 E
Oisterwijk	52	51.35 N	5.12 E
Oistins	241g	13.04 N	59.32 W
Ōita	96	33.14 N	131.36 E
Ōita □⁵	96	33.15 N	131.30 E
Ōita ≃	96	33.15 N	131.37 E
Oiticica	250	5.03 S	41.05 W
Oituz, Pasul ⋋	38	46.03 N	26.23 E
Ōiwa	270	34.53 N	135.33 E
Oiyung	124	29.39 N	89.46 E
Ōizumi, Nihon	94	36.15 N	139.25 E
Ōizumi, Nihon	94	35.52 N	138.23 E
Ōizuruga-dake ∧	94	36.18 N	136.47 E
Oja ≃	40	58.45 N	17.52 E
Ōja ≃	86	53.26 N	91.55 E
Ōjaren ⊜	40	60.43 N	16.50 E
Ōjat' ≃	76	60.31 N	33.00 E
Ojcowski Park Narodowy ✦	30	50.15 N	19.50 E
Öje	26	60.49 N	13.51 E
Ōjgon nuur ⊜	88	49.10 N	96.36 E
Ōjigor	86	49.10 N	89.17 E
Ōjima	94	36.15 N	139.20 E
Ojinaga	232	29.34 N	104.25 W
Ojiya	92	37.18 N	138.48 E
Ojm'akon	74	63.28 N	142.49 E
Ojocaliente	234	22.34 N	102.15 W
Ojo de la Casa	200	31.23 N	106.32 W
Ojo del Carrizo	232	29.58 N	105.16 W
Ojo de Liebre, Laguna ⊂	232	27.45 N	114.15 W
Ojok	88	52.35 N	104.27 E
Ojo del Salado, Nevado ∧	252	27.06 S	68.32 W
Ojos Negros	232	31.54 N	116.15 W
Ojota	273a	6.35 N	3.23 E
Ōjtal, Kaz.	85	40.24 N	74.06 E
Ōjtal, Kyrg.	85	40.24 N	74.06 E
Oju	150	6.53 N	8.26 E
Ojuelos de Jalisco	234	21.52 N	101.35 W
Oka ≃, Ross.	80	56.20 N	43.59 E
Oka ≃, Ross.	88	55.15 N	102.10 E
Okaba	164	8.06 S	139.42 E
Okabe, Nihon	94	36.12 N	139.15 E
Okabe, Nihon	94	34.55 N	138.17 E
Okagaki	96	33.50 N	130.38 E
Okahandja	156	21.59 S	16.58 E
Okahandja ≃	156	21.30 S	17.00 E
Okahukura	172	38.47 S	175.13 E
Okahumpka	220	28.45 N	81.54 W
Okaihau	172	35.19 S	173.47 E
Okalataka	152	0.20 S	14.59 E
Okaloacoochee Slough ≌	220	26.16 N	81.17 W
Okamoto	270	34.55 N	135.58 E
Okamoto ⊶⁸	270	34.44 N	135.16 E
Okanagan (Okanogan) ≃	182	48.06 N	119.43 W
Okanagan Centre	182	50.03 N	119.27 W
Okanagan Falls	182	49.21 N	119.34 W
Okanagan Indian Reserve ⊶⁴	182	50.21 N	119.17 W
Okanagan Lake ⊜	182	50.00 N	119.28 W
Okanagan Landing	182	50.14 N	119.22 W
Okanagan Mountain Provincial Park ✦	182	49.45 N	119.40 W
Okanagan Range (Okanogan Range) ∧	182	49.00 N	120.00 W
Okanogan	182	48.22 N	119.34 W
Okanogan □⁶	202	48.21 N	119.41 W
Okanogan ≃	224	48.39 N	120.41 W
Okanogan (Okanagan) ≃	182	48.06 N	119.43 W
Okanogan Range → Okanagan Range ∧	182	49.00 N	120.00 W
Okapilco Creek ≃	192	30.45 N	83.30 W
Okaputa	156	20.09 S	16.56 E
Okāra	123	30.49 N	73.27 E
Okarche	196	35.44 N	97.58 W
Okarito	172	43.14 S	170.11 E
Okasaki	230	34.46 N	135.52 E
Okatibbee Reservoir ⊜¹	194	32.30 N	88.47 W
Okato	172	39.12 S	173.53 E
Okauchee	216	43.06 N	88.26 W
Okauchee Lake ⊜	216	43.07 N	88.26 W
Okaukuejo	156	19.10 S	15.54 E
Okavango (Cubango) ≃	138	18.50 S	22.25 E
Okavango Delta ≃²	156	18.45 S	22.45 E
Ōkawa, Nihon	94	33.12 N	130.23 E
Ōkawa, Nihon	96	33.05 N	138.15 E
Okawville	219	38.26 N	89.33 W
Okaya	94	36.03 N	138.03 E
Okayama	96	34.39 N	133.55 E
Okayama □⁵	96	35.00 N	134.00 E
Okazaki	94	34.57 N	137.10 E
Okch'ŏn	98	36.20 N	127.34 E
Oke-Aro	273a	6.41 N	3.19 E
Okeechobee	220	27.14 N	80.49 W
Okeechobee, Lake ⊜	220	26.55 N	80.45 W
Ōkeechobee Waterway ≌	220	26.51 N	80.46 W
Okeene	196	36.06 N	98.19 W
Okefenokee Swamp ≌	192	30.42 N	82.20 W
Okegawa	94	36.00 N	139.35 E
Okehampton	42	50.44 N	4.00 W
Okeigbo	150	7.09 N	4.43 E
Okemah	196	35.26 N	96.18 W
Okement ≃	42	50.50 N	4.01 W
Okemos	216	42.43 N	84.25 W
Oke-Odo	150	7.33 N	6.15 E
Oke Ogbe	273a	6.24 N	3.23 E
Okere ≃	154	2.07 N	33.55 E
Okhaldungā	124	27.19 N	86.30 E
Okhotsk, Sea of (Ochotskoje more) ⊽²	84	53.00 N	150.00 E
Okhotsk Basin ⊹	12	54.00 N	148.00 E
Okiep	156	29.39 S	17.53 E
Okinawa □⁵	174m	26.20 N	127.50 E
Okinawa-jima I	96	26.30 N	128.00 E
Okinawa-shotō II	93b	26.40 N	128.00 E
Okino-Daitō-jima I	90	24.28 N	131.11 E
Okino-Erabu-shima I	93b	27.22 N	128.35 E
Okino I'uchi	96	30.36 N	107.06 E
Okino-shima I, Nihon	96	35.12 N	136.44 E
Okino-Tori-shima (Parece Vela) I	90	20.25 N	136.00 E
Oki-shotō II	96	36.15 N	133.15 E

Name	Page	Lat.	Long.
Okitipupa	150	6.29 N	4.46 E
Okitsu-zaki ⋗	96	33.09 N	133.14 E
Okkang-ni	98	40.18 N	124.42 E
Okkerbil ≃	265a	59.56 N	30.26 E
Okladnevo	76	58.36 N	33.39 E
Oklahoma, Pa., U.S.	214	41.07 N	78.44 W
Oklahoma, Pa., U.S.	279b	40.35 N	79.35 W
Oklahoma □³, U.S.	178	35.30 N	98.00 W
Oklahoma □³, U.S.	196	35.30 N	98.00 W
Oklahoma City	196	35.30 N	97.30 W
Oklawaha	220	29.02 N	81.55 W
Oklawaha ≃, Fl., U.S.	276	40.47 N	73.28 W
Oklawaha ≃, Fl., U.S.	192	29.28 N	81.41 W
Oklee	198	47.50 N	95.51 W
Okmulgee	196	35.37 N	95.57 W
Oknica	38	48.24 N	27.29 E
Okno	78	48.34 N	25.58 E
Oko, Wādī V	140	21.15 N	35.56 E
Okobojo Creek ≃	198	44.38 N	100.28 W
Okok ≃	154	2.06 N	33.53 E
Okola	152	2.57 S	23.27 E
Okollo	152	4.01 N	31.23 E
Okollo	154	2.40 N	31.08 E
Okolona, Ar., U.S.	152	3.46 S	23.55 E
Okolona, Ar., U.S.	194	33.59 N	93.20 W
Okolona, Ms., U.S.	194	38.08 N	85.41 W
Okombahe	194	34.00 N	88.45 W
Okondja	156	21.23 S	15.22 E
Okonek	152	0.41 S	13.47 E
Okonešnikovo	30	53.33 N	16.50 E
Okotoks	86	54.50 N	75.05 E
Okpara ≃	182	50.44 N	113.59 W
Okrika	150	7.40 N	2.35 E
Oksbøl	150	4.44 N	7.04 E
Oksbøl	26	55.38 N	8.17 E
Oksskolten ∧	24	65.59 N	14.15 E
Oktemberjan → Armavir	130	40.09 N	44.03 E
Oktjab'rsk → Kandyagash	82	49.28 N	57.25 E
Oktjab'rskij, Kaz.	85	43.41 N	77.12 E
Oktjab'rsk, Kaz.	85	45.45 N	61.34 E
Oktjab'rsk, Ross.	76	57.50 N	37.26 E
Oktjab'rsk, Kaz.	80	53.11 N	48.40 E
Oktjab'rsk, Bela.	76	52.38 N	28.53 E
Oktjab'rskij, Kaz.	82	52.35 N	62.40 E
Oktjab'rskij, Ross.	24	61.04 N	43.08 E
Oktjab'rskij, Ross.	54	59.29 N	48.50 E
Oktjab'rskij, Ross.	85	40.12 N	69.15 E
Oku ≃, Taj.	120	38.09 N	73.57 E
Oktjab'rskij, Kaz.	85	43.41 N	77.12 E
Oktjab'rskij, Ross.	210	41.22 N	75.44 W
Oktjab'r'skoje, Ross.	76	50.46 N	43.59 E
Oktjab'rskij, Ross.	76	55.34 N	53.26 E
Oktjab'rskij, Ross.	76	58.19 N	44.19 E
Oktjab'r'skij, Taj.	85	38.33 N	68.22 E
Oktjab'r'skoje, Ross.	82	52.07 N	65.40 E
Oktjab'rskoje, Ross.	76	62.28 N	66.03 E
Oktjab'r'skoje, Ross.	76	52.18 N	39.44 E
Oktjab'r'skoje, Ross.	85	45.37 N	42.49 E
Oktjab'rskoje, Ross.	80	52.54 N	46.30 E
Oktjab'rskoje, Ross.	82	54.26 N	55.30 E
Oktjab'r'skoje, Ross.	86	54.14 N	71.20 E
Oktjab'r'skij, Ukr.	78	48.38 N	33.04 E
Oktjab'r'skoje, Ukr.	78	45.18 N	34.09 E
Oktjab'r'skij	82	52.38 N	37.22 E
Oktjab'r'skij Provincial Park ✦	182	49.45 N	119.40 W
Okt'abr'skij Revol'ucii, ostrov I	74	79.30 N	97.00 E
Ok Tedi	164	5.44 S	141.09 E
Oktemberjan → Armavir	130	40.09 N	44.03 E
Oktong-ni	98	38.27 N	127.07 E
Oktwin	110	18.49 N	96.26 E
Oktyabr'skiy → Oktjab'rskij	80	54.28 N	53.28 E
Oku, Nihon	96	34.39 N	134.05 E
Ōkubo, Nihon	268	35.21 N	138.17 E
Ōkubo, Nihon	270	34.41 N	135.57 E
Ōkubo ⊶⁸	268	35.24 N	139.35 E
Okuchi, Nihon	96	32.04 N	130.37 E
Ōkuchi, Nihon	94	36.17 N	136.39 E
Okuku ≃	172	43.16 S	172.28 E
Okuma	268	36.23 N	140.58 E
Okundi	150	6.22 N	8.44 E
Ōkun'ov Nos	24	66.15 N	52.28 E
Ōkura-yama ∧	94	35.08 N	133.22 E
Okusawa ⊶⁸	268	35.36 N	139.40 E
Okushiri-tō I	92a	42.10 N	139.27 E
Ōkusu-yama ∧²	268	35.15 N	139.38 E
Okuta	150	9.14 N	3.15 E
Okutadami Dam ⊶⁶	94	37.09 N	139.15 E
Okutama	94	35.47 N	139.02 E
Ōkutama-ko ⊜¹	268	35.47 N	139.02 E
Okuwa	94	35.41 N	137.40 E
Okwa (Chapman's) ≃	156	22.30 S	23.00 E
Okwoga	150	7.01 N	7.50 E
Olá, Pan.	230	8.26 N	80.39 W
Ola, Ross.	74	59.35 N	151.17 E
Olá ≃	230	8.20 N	80.39 W
Ólafsfjörður	26a	66.04 N	18.38 W
Olambwe Valley Game Reserve ✦	154	0.37 S	34.15 E
Olancha	226	36.16 N	118.00 W
Olancha Peak ∧	204	36.16 N	118.07 W
Olanchito	236	15.30 N	86.35 W
Olanchó □⁵	236	14.45 N	86.00 W
Öland I	26	56.45 N	16.38 E
Olanda ∧	40	60.20 N	16.14 E
Olango Island I	116	10.16 N	124.03 E
Olar	192	33.56 N	79.55 W
Olarevo	76	59.22 N	40.04 E
Olari	78	47.16 N	27.50 E
Ólari ⊶⁸	265b	60.14 N	25.04 E
Olary	166	32.17 S	140.19 E
Olascoaga	252	35.12 S	60.36 W
Olasore	273a	6.40 N	3.17 E
Olathe, Co., U.S.	208	38.36 N	108.04 W
Olathe, Ks., U.S.	198	38.52 N	94.49 W
Olavarría	252	36.54 S	60.17 W
Olavinlinna ⋗	26	61.52 N	28.36 E
Olavinlinna ⊽	30	50.57 N	17.17 E
Olawa	30	50.57 N	17.17 E
Oława ≃	30	51.09 N	17.22 E
Olbernhau	54	50.39 N	13.20 E
Olbersdorf	54	50.54 N	14.46 E
Olbersleben	54	51.09 N	11.20 E
Ólbia, Golfo di ⊂	71	40.55 N	9.31 E
Olby, Lyng ⊶⁸	41	55.29 N	12.09 E
Olca, Volcán ∧¹	248	20.57 S	68.30 W
Ōlchi	80	53.53 N	41.28 E
Ol'chon, ostrov I	88	53.10 N	107.24 E
Ol'chovskij	76	50.29 N	44.33 E
Ol'chovatka ≃, Ross.	78	48.47 N	40.15 E
Ol'chovatka, Ross.	78	50.17 N	39.17 E
Ol'chovatka, Ukr.	78	48.15 N	38.07 E
Ol'chovka, Ross.	86	49.00 N	81.30 E
Ol'chovka, Ross.	80	49.52 N	44.34 E

Name	Page	Lat.	Long.
Ol'chovka, Ross.	86	56.22 N	63.46 E
Ol'chovoje	83	48.40 N	39.34 E
Olcott	210	43.20 N	78.42 W
Old □⁶, Ca., U.S.	226	38.04 N	121.35 W
Old □⁶, Tx., U.S.	222	30.25 N	96.19 W
Old Bahama Channel ⊻	238	22.30 N	78.50 W
Old Bedford ≃	42	52.35 N	0.20 E
Old Bennington	210	42.52 N	73.12 W
Old Bethpage	276	40.45 N	73.27 W
Old Bethpage Village ✦	276	40.47 N	73.28 W
Old Brazoria	222	29.04 N	95.34 W
Old Bridge	276	40.24 N	74.21 W
Old Brookville	276	40.49 N	73.36 W
Oldbury	42	52.30 N	2.00 W
Old Cairo → Misr al-Qadīmah	273c	30.00 N	31.14 E
Oldcastle	48	53.46 N	7.10 W
Old Cork	166	22.56 S	141.52 E
Old Creek Estates	284c	38.50 N	77.16 W
Old Crow	180	67.35 N	139.50 W
Old Crow ≃	180	67.35 N	139.50 W
Oldeani	154	3.21 S	35.33 E
Oldebroek	52	52.26 N	5.54 E
Oldenburg ⊥	279b	40.36 N	80.14 W
Olden, Nor.	26	61.50 N	6.49 E
Olden, Tx., U.S.	196	32.25 N	98.45 W
Oldenbrok	52	53.17 N	8.23 E
Oldenburg, Dtsch.	52	53.08 N	8.13 E
Oldenburg, In., U.S.	218	39.20 N	85.12 W
Oldenburg in Holstein	52	54.17 N	10.52 E
Oldendorf	52	53.00 N	8.00 E
Oldenstadt	52	52.58 N	10.35 E
Oldenswort	41	54.22 N	8.56 E
Oldenzaal	52	52.19 N	6.56 E
Oldersum	52	53.20 N	7.22 E
Old Faithful Geyser ⊽⁴	202	44.30 N	110.45 W
Old Farm	284c	39.03 N	77.09 W
Old Field ≃	276	40.57 N	73.08 W
Old Field Point ⋗	276	40.58 N	73.07 W
Old Forge, N.Y., U.S.	188	43.42 N	74.58 W
Old Forge, Pa., U.S.	210	41.22 N	75.44 W
Old Forge Village	276	40.49 N	74.29 W
Old Fort	214	41.15 N	83.09 W
Old Fort Erie ⊥	284a	42.53 N	78.56 W
Old Fort Henry ⊥	182	44.14 N	76.28 W
Old Fort Mountain ∧	182	55.06 N	126.30 W
Old Fort Niagara ⊥	284a	43.16 N	79.03 W
Old Fort Parker State Historic Site ⊥	222	31.34 N	96.34 W
Old Fort Point ⋗	240b	25.03 N	77.29 W
Old Greenwich	276	41.02 N	73.34 W
Oldham, Eng., U.K.	44	53.33 N	2.07 W
Oldham, S.D., U.S.	198	44.13 N	97.18 W
Oldham □⁶	284	38.23 N	85.27 W
Oldham □⁶	218	38.23 N	85.27 W
Oldham Pines	283	42.05 N	70.50 W
Oldham Pond ⊜	283	42.03 N	70.51 W
Oldham Village	207	42.04 N	70.49 W
Old Harbor	180	57.12 N	153.19 W
Old Harbour	241q	17.56 N	77.07 W
Old Hickory Lake ⊜¹	194	36.18 N	86.30 W
Old Howe ≃	44	53.57 N	0.21 W
Old Lyme	207	41.18 N	72.19 W
Old Malden ⊶⁸	268	51.23 N	0.15 W
Oldman ≃	182	49.56 N	111.42 W
Old Man House ⊥	284	47.43 N	122.34 W
Old Man Range ∧	172	45.20 S	169.15 E
Old Manor	276	40.04 N	74.11 W
Oldmans Creek ≃	208	39.47 N	75.27 W
Oldmeldrum	46	57.20 N	2.20 W
Old Mkushi	154	14.22 S	29.22 E
Old Monroe	219	38.55 N	90.44 W
Old Mystic	207	41.23 N	71.57 W
Old Nene ≃	42	52.40 N	0.10 E
Old North Bridge ⊥	283	42.28 N	71.21 W
Old North Church ⊥	283	42.22 N	71.03 W
Old Ocean	222	29.05 N	95.45 W
Ol Doinyo Sapuk National Park ✦	154	1.09 S	37.12 E
Ol'doj ≃	89	53.33 N	123.21 E
Old Orchard ⊶⁸	278	42.04 N	87.45 W
Old Orchard Beach	188	43.31 N	70.22 W
Old Perlican	186	48.05 N	53.01 W
Old Place Creek ≃	276	40.36 N	74.10 W
Old Point Comfort ⋗	208	37.00 N	76.19 W
Old Rhodes Key I	220	25.22 N	80.14 W
Old Road Bay ⊂	240e	16.59 N	61.50 W
Old Road Bluff ⋗	240e	16.59 N	61.50 W
Old Round Rock	222	30.31 N	97.42 W
Olds	182	51.47 N	114.06 W
Old Saybrook	188	41.17 N	72.22 W
Oldsmar	220	28.02 N	82.39 W
Old Speck Mountain ∧	188	44.34 N	70.57 W
Old Sturbridge Village ✦	207	42.07 N	72.07 W
Old Swamp ≃	283	42.11 N	70.57 W
Old Swedes Church ⊥	208	39.44 N	75.32 W
Old Tampa Bay ⊂	220	27.56 N	82.35 W
Old Tappan	276	41.00 N	73.59 W
Old Tate	156	21.22 S	27.46 E
Old Town	188	44.56 N	68.38 W
Old Trafford Cricket Ground ∧	262	53.28 N	2.17 W
Old Trap	192	36.15 N	76.02 W
Olduvai Gorge V	154	2.58 S	35.22 E
Old Westbury	276	40.48 N	73.36 W
Old Westbury Gardens ✦	276	40.46 N	73.36 W
Old Wick	210	40.40 N	74.44 W
Old Windsor	261	51.28 N	0.35 W
Old Wives Lake ⊜	184	50.06 N	106.00 W
Old Woman Creek ≃	198	43.19 N	104.21 W
Oldziyt, Mong.	88	45.50 N	102.18 E
Old Zoinsville	208	39.19 N	75.31 W
Olean	214	42.04 N	78.25 W
Olean Creek ≃	210	42.04 N	78.25 W
O'Leary	186	46.42 N	64.13 W
Oleggio	64	45.36 N	8.38 E
Olekma ≃	74	60.22 N	120.42 E

Name	Page	Lat.	Long.
Ol'ga, Ross.	89	43.45 N	135.18 E
Olga, Wa., U.S.	224	48.37 N	122.50 W
Olga, Mount ∧, Austl.	162	25.19 S	130.46 E
Olga, Mount ∧, Vt., U.S.	207	42.51 N	72.48 W
Olgiata	267a	42.02 N	12.22 E
Olgiate Comasco	62	45.48 N	8.58 E
Olgiate Olona	62	45.38 N	8.53 E
Ōlgij, Mong.	86	48.56 N	89.57 E
Ōlgij, Mong.	86	48.59 N	92.01 E
Olginate	62	45.48 N	9.24 E
Ol'ginka, Ross.	78	44.14 N	38.53 E
Ol'ginka, Ukr.	78	47.42 N	37.31 E
Ol'ginskaja, Ross.	78	45.57 N	38.34 E
Ol'ginskaja, Ross.	83	47.11 N	39.56 E
Olgopol'	78	48.12 N	29.29 E
Ol'gopol'	78	48.12 N	29.29 E
Ølgod	26	55.49 N	8.37 E
Ol'govo	82	56.16 N	37.21 E
Olho	34	37.02 N	7.50 W
Olho d'Água das Cunhãs	250	4.43 S	44.34 W
Olho d'Água das Flores	250	9.33 S	37.17 W
Oli ≃	150	9.45 N	4.38 E
Olib, Otok I	36	44.22 N	14.48 E
Oliden	258	35.11 S	57.57 W
Oliena	71	40.16 N	9.24 E
Olifants (Rio dos Elefantes) ≃, Afr.	156	24.10 S	32.40 E
Olifants ≃, Namibia	156	25.30 S	19.30 E
Olifants ≃, S. Afr.	156	33.41 S	21.42 E
Olifants ≃, S. Afr.	158	31.42 S	18.12 E
Olifants ≃, S. Afr.	158	29.39 S	21.10 E
Olifantshoek	158	27.57 S	22.42 E
Olifantsrivierberge ∧	158	32.40 S	19.00 E
Oliki	265a	60.46 N	29.55 E
Olimarao I¹	108	7.41 N	145.52 E
Olímbía ⊥	38	37.38 N	21.41 E
Ólimbos ≃	38	35.44 N	27.11 E
Ólimbos ∧	130	34.56 N	32.52 E
Ólimbos, Óros (Mount Olympus) ∧	38	40.05 N	22.21 E
Oluvo	273a	6.34 N	3.18 E
Olivenstedt	54	52.09 N	11.34 E
Olvera	34	36.56 N	5.16 W
Olychovatka	78	50.13 N	37.31 E
Olyka	78	50.42 N	25.51 E
Olym ≃	78	52.42 N	38.10 E
— Ólimbos, Óros ∧	38	40.05 N	22.21 E
Olympe, Mont ∧	58	42.50 N	9.30 E
— Ólimbos, Óros ∧	38	40.05 N	22.21 E
Olympia	224	47.02 N	122.53 W
Olympía	38	37.38 N	21.41 E
Olympia Fields	216	41.32 N	87.42 W
Olympia Heights	220	25.43 N	80.21 W
Olympic, Park ∧	273d	25.15 S	80.01 W
Olympic-Stadion ∧	264	52.31 N	13.14 E
Olympic Mountains ∧	224	47.50 N	123.45 W
Olympic National Park ✦	224	47.48 N	123.30 W
Olympic Valley	226	39.13 N	120.14 W
Olympic View	224	47.43 N	122.45 W
Olympic, Stade ✦	267c	37.58 N	23.44 E
Olympique, Stade ✦	275a	45.33 N	73.33 W
— Ólimbos, Óros ∧	38	40.05 N	22.21 E
Olympos, Ellás ∧	38	40.05 N	22.21 E
Olympus, Mount ∧, Wa., U.S.	224	47.48 N	123.43 W
Olympus, Mount ∧²	192	38.03 N	87.36 W
Olzai	71	40.11 N	9.16 E
Olzony	88	52.57 N	105.15 E
Om ≃, Pap. N. Gui.	164	5.09 S	142.22 E
Om ≃, Ross.	54	54.59 N	73.22 E
Ōma	92	41.32 N	140.55 E
Ōma ≃	92	40.37 N	140.52 E
Ōmachi, Nihon	94	36.30 N	137.52 E
Ōmachi, Nihon	96	33.13 N	130.11 E
Ōmaezaki	94	34.36 N	138.13 E
Ōmae-zaki ⋗	94	34.36 N	138.14 E
Ōmagari	92	39.27 N	140.29 E
Omagh, On., Can.	275b	43.30 N	79.49 W
Omagh, N. Ire., U.K.	48	54.36 N	7.18 W
Ōmagi	268	35.52 N	139.43 E
Ōmaha, Ne., U.S.	198	41.15 N	95.56 W
Omaha, Tx., U.S.	222	33.11 N	94.45 W
Omaha Indian Reservation ⊶⁴	198	42.08 N	96.22 W
Omak	202	48.24 N	119.31 W
Omak Lake ⊜	182	48.16 N	119.23 W
Omalo	84	42.43 N	45.38 E
Ōmama	94	36.26 N	139.17 E
Oman □¹	118	22.00 N	58.00 E
Oman, Gulf of ⊂	118	24.30 N	58.30 E
Omapere, Lake ⊜	172	35.21 S	173.47 E
Omarama	172	44.29 S	169.58 E
Omaruru	156	21.00 S	16.00 E
Omaruru ≃	156	22.07 S	14.15 E
Omarama ≃	156	21.25 N	76.17 W
Omate	248	12.31 S	76.17 W
Ōmata	52	52.00 N	8.06 E
Ōmba	54	43.19 N	21.12 E
Ōmba ≃	108	15.24 S	167.57 E
Ōme	94	35.47 N	139.15 E
Omega, Oh., U.S.	218	39.09 N	82.51 W
Omega, Ga., U.S.	192	31.20 N	83.35 W
Omegna	64	45.53 N	8.24 E
Omemee	182	44.18 N	78.33 W
Ōmerbükü	130	37.26 N	34.52 E
Ōmerköy	40	39.58 N	28.08 E
Omerli Barajı ⊜¹	266	41.04 N	29.18 E
Ometepe, Isla de I	236	11.30 N	85.35 W
Ometepec	234	16.41 N	98.25 W
Ometepec ≃	234	16.30 N	98.35 W
Ōmi ≃	94	36.55 N	137.48 E
Omineca ≃	180	56.05 N	124.05 W
Omineca Mountains ∧	180	56.00 N	125.00 W
Omini-ni ⊶⁶	271b	37.27 N	127.01 E
Ōmi-shima I, Nihon	174z	34.15 N	133.01 E
Ōmi-shima I, Nihon	96	34.15 N	132.30 E
Ōmitama	94	36.18 N	140.30 E
Ōmiya, Nihon	94	35.54 N	139.38 E
Ōmiya, Nihon	94	35.34 N	139.38 E
Ōmiya, Nihon	96	35.35 N	135.06 E
— Mutsu			

	English	Berg	Montaña	Montagne	Montanha
∧	Mountain		Montañas	Montagnes	Montanhas
∧	Mountains	Gebirge			
⋋	Pass	Paß	Paso	Col	Passo
V	Valley, Canyon	Tal, Cañon	Valle, Cañón	Vallée, Canyon	Vale, Canhão
≃	Plain	Ebene	Llano	Plaine	Planície
⋗	Cape	Kap	Cabo	Cap	Cabo
I	Island	Insel	Isla	Île	Ilha
II	Islands	Inseln	Islas	Îles	Ilhas
⊥	Other Topographic Features	Andere Topographische Objekte	Otros Elementos Topográficos	Autres données topographiques	Outros acidentes topográficos

ESPAÑOL — Nombre | Página | Lat.°' | Long.°' W = Oeste
FRANÇAIS — Nom | Page | Lat.°' | Long.°' W = Ouest
PORTUGUÊS — Nome | Página | Lat.°' | Long.°' W = Oeste

Ōmiya-daichi ⋀[1] 268 35.56 N 139.38 E
Ōmiya Park Race Track ♦ 268 35.55 N 139.38 E
Øm Kloster ⊥ 41 56.03 N 9.45 E
Ommaney, Cape > 180 56.10 N 134.39 W
Ommanney Bay c 176 73.07 N 100.11 W
Omme ≃ 41 55.53 N 8.40 E
Ommen 52 52.32 N 6.25 E
Ömnödelger 88 47.52 N 109.55 E
Ömnögov' 86 49.06 N 91.43 E
Ömnögov' □[4] 102 43.00 N 104.00 E
Omø I 41 55.09 N 11.10 E
Omo ≃ 144 43.10 N 35.59 E
Omoa, Bahía de c 236 15.45 N 88.10 W
Omodeo, Lago ⊜ 71 40.08 N 8.55 E
Omogo 96 33.41 N 133.02 E
Omoi ≃ 94 36.09 N 139.41 E
Omoko 150 5.20 N 6.39 E
Omole 273a 6.38 N 3.22 E
Omoloj ≃ 74 71.10 N 132.08 E
Omolon ≃ 74 68.42 N 158.36 E
Omo National Park ♦ 144 6.00 N 35.45 E
Omono ≃ 92 39.46 N 140.03 E
Omont 56 49.36 N 4.44 E
Omo Ranch 226 38.35 N 120.35 W
Ōmori ●[8] 268 35.34 N 139.44 E
Omotegō 94 37.03 N 140.18 E
Omoy 152 1.21 S 13.09 E
Omrel'kaj ≃ 180 68.34 N 170.30 E
Omro 190 44.02 N 88.44 W
Omsino 80 58.36 N 50.28 E
Omsk 86 55.00 N 73.24 E
Omsk Oblast' □[4] 86 56.00 N 73.00 E
Omsukčan 74 62.32 N 155.48 E
O-mu, Mya. 110 22.58 N 99.18 E
Ōmu, Nihon 92a 44.34 N 142.58 E
Omu-Aran 150 8.09 N 5.07 E
Ōmuda → Ōmuta 96 33.02 N 130.27 E
Omul, Vîrful ∧ 38 45.26 N 25.26 E
Omulew ≃ 30 53.05 N 21.32 E
Ōmura 92 32.54 N 129.57 E
Ōmura-wan c 92 32.57 N 129.52 E
Ōmuro 268 35.54 N 139.58 E
Omurtag 38 43.06 N 26.25 E
Ōmuta 96 33.02 N 130.27 E
Omutinskij 86 56.31 N 67.41 E
Omutninsk 86 58.40 N 52.12 E
Ŏmyŏnbo 98 41.16 N 127.36 E
On 110 21.40 N 106.35 E
Ona, Nor. 26 62.52 N 6.34 E
Ona, Fl., U.S. 220 27.28 N 81.55 W
Ona ≃, Ross. 86 52.34 N 89.50 E
Ona → Bir'usa ≃, Ross. 88 57.43 N 95.24 E
Onabas 232 29.27 N 109.32 W
Onadikondo 152 3.52 S 24.10 E
Onaga 198 39.29 N 96.10 W
Onagawa 92 38.26 N 141.27 E
Onahama 94 36.57 N 140.54 E
Onalaska, Tx., U.S. 222 30.48 N 95.07 W
Onalaska, Wa., U.S. 224 46.34 N 122.43 W
Onamia 190 46.04 N 93.40 W
Onancock 208 37.42 N 75.44 W
Onangué, Lac ⊜ 152 0.57 S 10.04 E
Onaping ≃ 190 46.37 N 81.18 W
Onaping Lake ⊜ 190 47.00 N 81.30 W
Onarga 216 40.42 N 88.00 W
Ōnari 268 35.55 N 139.37 E
Onatchiway, Lac ⊜ 186 49.00 N 71.03 W
Onawa 198 42.01 N 96.05 W
Onaway 190 45.21 N 84.13 W
Oncativo 252 31.55 S 63.40 W
Once, Canal Numero ≍ 252 36.09 S 58.36 W
Onchāi 272b 22.57 N 88.19 E
Onchan 44 54.11 N 4.27 W
Onch'ŏn-dong 98 40.51 N 129.07 E
Oncócua 152 16.34 S 13.28 E
Onda, Esp. 34 39.58 N 0.15 W
Onda, India 126 23.08 N 87.12 E
Ondangwa 156 17.55 S 16.00 E
Ondas, Rio de ≃ 255 12.08 S 45.00 W
Ondava ≃ 30 48.27 N 21.48 E
Onderdijk 52 52.45 N 5.07 E
Onderstedorings 158 30.13 S 20.37 E
Ondjiva 152 17.03 S 15.47 E
Ondo, Nig. 150 7.04 N 4.47 E
Ondo, Nihon 96 34.11 N 132.32 E
Ondo □[3] 150 7.00 N 5.15 E
Ondo-ōhashi ●[5] 96 34.12 N 132.33 E
Öndörchaan 88 47.19 N 110.39 E
Öndörchangaj 88 49.20 N 94.50 E
Öndör-Önc 102 45.51 N 103.11 E
Öndöršireet 88 47.27 N 104.50 E
Öndör-Ulaan 88 48.03 N 100.30 E
Ondozero, ozero ⊜ 24 63.48 N 33.20 E
O'Neals 226 37.08 N 119.42 W
One Arrow Indian Reserve ●[4] 184 52.48 N 106.03 W
Oneco, Ct., U.S. 207 41.41 N 71.48 W
Oneco, Fl., U.S. 220 27.26 N 82.32 W
Onega 24 63.55 N 38.05 E
Onega ≃ 24 63.58 N 37.55 E
Onega, Lake → Onežskoje ozero ⊜ 24 61.30 N 35.45 E
Oneglia 62 43.53 N 8.02 E
One Hundred and Two ≃ 194 39.44 N 94.43 W
One Hundred and Two, West Fork ≃ 194 40.26 N 94.49 W
One Hundred Fifty Mile House 182 52.06 N 121.55 W
One Hundred Mile House 182 51.39 N 121.18 W
Oneida, Il., U.S. 190 41.04 N 90.13 W
Oneida, Ky., U.S. 192 37.16 N 83.38 W
Oneida, N.Y., U.S. 210 43.05 N 75.39 W
Oneida, Oh., U.S. 218 39.28 N 84.23 W
Oneida, Pa., U.S. 210 40.54 N 76.08 W
Oneida, Tn., U.S. 192 36.29 N 84.30 W
Oneida □[6] 210 43.10 N 75.20 W
Oneida ≃ 210 43.12 N 76.17 W
Oneida Castle 210 43.05 N 75.40 W
Oneida County Airport ⊠ 210 43.09 N 75.23 W
Oneida Creek ≃ 210 43.10 N 75.44 W
Oneida Indian Reservation ●[4] 190 44.30 N 88.10 W
Oneida Indian Reserve ●[4] 214 42.49 N 81.24 W
Oneida Lake ⊜ 210 43.13 N 76.00 W
O'Neil Forebay ⊜[1] 226 37.05 N 121.03 W
O'Neill 198 42.27 N 98.38 W
Onekama 190 44.21 N 86.12 W
Onekotan, ostrov I 74 49.25 N 154.45 E
Onema 152 4.33 S 24.31 E
Onemen, zaliv c 180 64.45 N 176.35 E
Oneonta, Al., U.S. 194 33.56 N 86.28 W
Oneonta, N.Y., U.S. 210 42.27 N 75.03 W
Oneroa I 174k 21.15 S 159.43 W
One Tree Hill 168b 34.43 S 138.46 E
One Tree Hill ∧[2] 274b 37.52 S 145.19 E
One Tree Hill Lookout ♦ 169 36.48 S 144.18 E
Onevai I 174w 21.05 S 175.07 W
Onex 58 46.10 N 6.06 E
Onežskaja guba c 24 64.20 N 36.30 E
Onežskij poluostrov >[1] 24 64.35 N 38.00 E
Onežskoje ozero (Lake Onega) ⊜ 24 61.30 N 35.45 E
Onga ≃ 96 33.54 N 130.39 E
Ongaonga 172 39.55 S 176.25 E
Ongarue 172 38.43 S 175.17 E
Ong Con, Cu Lao I 269c 10.45 N 106.50 E
Ongea Levu I 175g 19.08 S 178.24 W
Ongeluks ≃ 158 32.24 S 19.46 E
Ongers ≃ 158 31.04 S 23.13 E
Ongerup 162 33.58 S 118.29 E
Ongijn ≃ 102 44.30 N 103.40 E
Ongjin 98 37.57 N 125.21 E
Ongoka 154 1.23 S 26.02 E
Ongole 122 15.31 N 80.04 E
Ongon 102 45.21 N 113.09 E
Ongudaj 86 50.45 N 86.09 E
Oni 84 42.34 N 43.27 E
Onich 46 56.42 N 5.13 W
Onida 198 44.42 N 100.03 W
Onifai 71 40.24 N 9.39 E
Oniferi 71 40.16 N 9.10 E
Onigajō-yama ∧ 96 33.07 N 132.41 E
Onilahy ≃ 157b 23.34 S 43.45 E
Onin, Jazirah >[1] 164 2.50 S 132.05 E
Onion Creek ≃ 222 30.12 N 97.35 W
Onion Peak ∧ 224 45.49 N 123.53 W
Onishi 94 36.09 N 139.04 E
Onistagane, Lac ⊜ 186 50.42 N 71.19 W
Onitsha 150 6.09 N 6.47 E
Onji 270 34.37 N 135.38 E
Onjuku 94 35.11 N 140.22 E
Onkaparinga ≃ 168b 35.10 S 138.28 E
Onkivesi ⊜ 26 63.18 N 27.18 E
Onko 152 4.07 S 19.59 E
Onley 208 37.41 N 75.42 W
Onna 174m 26.30 N 127.51 E
Onnaing 50 50.23 N 3.36 E
Onno 58 45.55 N 9.17 E
Onny ≃ 42 52.23 N 2.45 W
Ōno, Nihon 94 35.59 N 136.29 E
Ōno, Nihon 94 35.28 N 136.38 E
Ōno, Nihon 96 34.18 N 132.17 E
Ono, Nihon 96 34.51 N 134.56 E
Ōno, Nihon 96 33.02 N 131.30 E
Ono, Nihon 270 34.57 N 135.14 E
Ono, Pa., U.S. 208 40.24 N 76.32 W
Ono I 175g 18.55 S 178.29 E
Ōno ≃ 96 33.15 N 131.43 E
Onochoj 88 51.58 N 108.01 E
Onoda 96 33.59 N 131.11 E
Ōno-dam ●[6] 96 35.15 N 135.27 E
Onogami 94 36.33 N 138.56 E
Ōnohara 96 34.05 N 133.40 E
Ono-I-Lau I 14 20.39 S 178.42 W
Ōnojō 96 33.32 N 130.28 E
Onolimbu 114 1.03 N 97.53 E
Ōnomi 96 33.21 N 133.09 E
Onomichi 96 34.25 N 133.12 E
Onon 88 49.08 N 112.38 E
Onon ≃ 88 51.42 N 115.50 E
Onondaga, Mi., U.S. 216 42.26 N 84.33 W
Onondaga, N.Y., U.S. 210 43.00 N 76.11 W
Onondaga □[6] 210 43.03 N 76.09 W
Onondaga Creek ≃ 210 43.04 N 76.11 W
Onondaga Indian Reservation ●[4] 210 42.55 N 76.09 W
Onor 89 50.11 N 142.40 E
Onota Lake ⊜ 207 42.28 N 73.17 W
Onoto 246 9.36 N 65.12 W
Onotoa I[1] 14 1.52 S 175.34 E
Onoway 182 53.42 N 114.12 W
Ons, Isla de I 34 42.23 N 8.56 W
Onsbjerg 41 55.51 N 10.35 E
Onseepkans 158 28.46 S 19.14 E
Onsen 96 35.33 N 134.29 E
Onset 207 41.44 N 70.39 W
Onslow 162 21.39 S 115.06 E
Onslow Bay c 192 34.20 N 77.20 W
Onslow Village 260 51.14 N 0.36 W
Onsted 216 42.00 N 84.11 W
Onstmettingen 58 48.17 N 9.00 E
Onstwedde 52 53.02 N 7.02 E
On-take ∧ 92 31.35 N 130.39 E
Ontake-san ∧ 94 35.53 N 137.29 E
Ontario, Ca., U.S. 228 34.03 N 117.39 W
Ontario, In., U.S. 216 41.43 N 85.23 W
Ontario, N.Y., U.S. 210 43.13 N 77.17 W
Ontario, Oh., U.S. 214 40.45 N 82.35 W
Ontario, Or., U.S. 202 44.01 N 116.57 W
Ontario □[6] 210 42.54 N 77.17 W
Ontario □[4] 176 51.00 N 85.00 W
Ontario, Lake ⊜ 212 43.45 N 78.00 W
Ontario Agricultural Museum ʊ 212 43.30 N 79.56 W
Ontario Center 210 43.14 N 77.19 W
Ontario International Airport ⊠ 228 34.04 N 117.36 W
Ontario Place ♦ 275b 43.38 N 79.25 W
Ontario Science Centre ʊ 275b 43.43 N 79.21 W
Ontelaunee, Lake ⊜ 208 40.27 N 75.55 W
Ontinyent (Onteniente) 34 38.49 N 0.37 W
Ontojärvi ⊜ 26 64.08 N 29.09 E
Ontonagon 190 46.52 N 89.18 W
Ontonagon ≃ 190 46.52 N 89.20 W
Ontonagon, East Branch ≃ 190 46.42 N 89.11 W
Ontonagon, Middle Branch ≃ 190 46.42 N 89.10 W
Ontonagon, West Branch ≃ 190 46.42 N 89.11 W
Ontong Java I[1] 175e 5.20 S 159.30 E
Onufrijevka 78 48.54 N 33.26 E
Onufrijevo 82 55.51 N 36.31 E
Ōnuma 268 35.32 N 139.25 E
Onverwacht 250 5.36 N 55.12 W
Onward 216 40.42 N 86.12 W
Ŏnyang, Taehan 98 36.47 N 127.00 E
Ŏnyang, Taehan 98 35.34 N 129.07 E
Onzain 50 47.30 N 1.11 E
Onzo ≃ 152 8.12 S 13.16 E
Oobagooma 162 16.46 S 123.59 E
Oodnadatta 162 27.33 S 135.28 E
Ood Weyne 144 9.25 N 45.04 E
Ōoka 94 36.30 N 137.59 E
Ooldea 162 30.27 S 131.50 E
Oolitic 218 38.54 N 86.31 W
Oologah 196 36.26 N 95.42 W
Oologah Lake ⊜[1] 196 36.33 N 95.36 W
Ooma 174d 0.53 S 169.36 E
Oombergen 50 50.54 N 3.50 E
Oona River 182 53.57 N 130.18 W
Ooratippra 162 22.00 S 136.00 E
Ooratippra Creek ≃ 162 21.55 S 136.05 E
Oorlogskloof ≃ 158 31.52 S 19.01 E
Oos 56 48.47 N 8.11 E
Oos-Londen → East London 158 33.00 S 27.55 E
Oostakker 50 51.06 N 3.46 E
Oostburg, Ned. 52 51.20 N 3.30 E
Oostburg, Wi., U.S. 190 43.37 N 87.47 W
Oost-Cappel 50 50.55 N 2.36 E
Oostduinkerke 50 51.07 N 2.41 E
Oostelijk Flevoland ●[1] 52 52.30 N 5.40 E
Oostende (Ostende) 50 51.13 N 2.55 E
Oosterbeek 52 52.00 N 5.50 E
Oosterend 52 53.05 N 4.52 E
Oosterhout 52 51.38 N 4.51 E
Oosterschelde c 52 51.33 N 4.00 E
Oosterscheldedam ●[6] 52 51.38 N 3.42 E
Oosterwolde 52 52.59 N 6.17 E
Oosterzele 50 50.57 N 3.48 E
Oosthuizen 52 52.35 N 5.00 E
Oostkamp 50 51.09 N 3.14 E
Oostmahorn 52 53.24 N 6.09 E
Oostmalle 56 51.18 N 4.44 E
Oostpunt > 241s 12.02 N 68.45 W
Oostrozebeke 50 50.55 N 3.20 E
Oost-Souburg 52 51.27 N 3.35 E
Oost-Vlaanderen □[4] 50 51.00 N 3.45 E
Oostvleteren 50 50.56 N 2.44 E
Oost-Vlieland 52 53.17 N 5.04 E
Oostvoorne 52 51.55 N 4.06 E
Ootmarsum 52 52.25 N 6.54 E
Ootsa Lake 182 53.47 N 126.03 W
Ootsa Lake ⊜ 182 53.49 N 126.18 W
Ootsi 156 25.02 S 25.45 E
Ootua, Mont ∧ 174x 9.47 S 138.58 W
Opaka 38 43.27 N 26.10 E
Opala 152 0.37 S 24.21 E
Opalaca, Cordillera ⋀ 236 14.30 N 88.20 W
Opal Cliffs 226 36.57 N 121.57 W
Opale, Côte d' ⊥[2] 50 50.40 N 1.35 E
Opalenica 30 52.19 N 16.23 E
Opalicha 265b 55.49 N 37.15 E
Opa-Locka 220 25.54 N 80.15 W
Opari 154 3.56 N 32.03 E
Oparino 24 59.52 N 48.17 E
Opasatica, Lac ⊜ 190 48.05 N 79.18 W
Opasatika Lake ⊜ 190 49.04 N 83.08 W
Opasquia 184 53.16 N 93.35 W
Opasquia Lake ⊜ 184 53.18 N 93.34 W
Opatija 36 45.21 N 14.19 E
Opatów 30 50.49 N 21.26 E
Opava 30 49.56 N 17.54 E
Opava ≃ 30 49.50 N 18.13 E
Opečenskij Posad 76 58.16 N 34.07 E
Opeepeesway Lake ⊜ 190 47.38 N 82.14 W
Opeilu 273a 6.42 N 3.18 E
Opelika 194 32.38 N 85.22 W
Opelousas 194 30.32 N 92.04 W
Open Bay c 164 4.50 S 151.20 E
Open Door 258 34.30 S 59.05 W
Opeongo ≃ 190 45.30 N 77.57 W
Opeongo Lake ⊜ 190 45.42 N 78.23 W
Opequon Creek ≃ 188 39.35 N 77.52 W
Opfikon 58 47.26 N 8.35 E
Ophain-Bois-Seigneur-Isaac 50 50.40 N 4.21 E
Ophasselt 50 50.49 N 3.53 E
Opheim 202 48.51 N 106.24 W
Opherdicke 263 51.29 N 7.38 E
Opheusden 52 51.56 N 5.38 E
Ophir, Ak., U.S. 180 63.10 N 156.31 W
Ophir, Or., U.S. 202 42.33 N 124.22 W
Ophirton ●[8] 273d 26.14 S 28.01 E
Ophthalmia Range ⋀ 162 23.17 S 119.30 E
Opi 66 41.47 N 13.50 E
Opienge 154 0.12 N 27.30 E
Opihikao 229d 19.25 N 154.53 W
Opinaca ≃ 176 52.15 N 78.02 W
Opinan 46 57.43 N 5.47 W
Opinicon Lake ⊜ 212 44.33 N 76.20 W
Opiscotéo, Lac ⊜ 176 53.10 N 68.10 W
Opladen 56 51.04 N 7.00 E
Opmeer 52 52.43 N 4.56 E
Opobo 150 4.34 N 7.27 E
Opobo Town 150 4.30 N 7.30 E
Opočka 76 56.43 N 28.38 E
Opoczno 30 51.23 N 20.17 E
Opol 116 8.31 N 124.34 E
Opole (Oppeln) 30 50.41 N 17.55 E
Opole □[4] 30 50.30 N 17.45 E
Opole Lubelskie 30 51.09 N 21.58 E
Opon → Lapu-Lapu 116 10.19 N 123.57 E
Oponono, Lake ⊜ 156 18.08 S 15.45 E
Opopeo 234 19.24 N 101.36 W
Oporto → Porto 34 41.11 N 8.36 W
Opošn'a 78 49.58 N 34.37 E
Opotiki 172 38.00 S 177.17 E
Opp 194 31.16 N 86.15 W
Oppach 54 51.03 N 14.30 E
Oppdal 26 62.36 N 9.40 E
Oppelhain 54 51.33 N 13.35 E
Oppeln → Opole 30 50.41 N 17.55 E
Oppenau 58 48.28 N 8.10 E
Oppenberg 61 47.29 N 14.16 E
Oppenheim, Dtsch. 56 49.51 N 8.21 E
Oppenheim, N.Y., U.S. 210 43.04 N 74.42 W
Oppenheim Park ♦ 284a 43.06 N 78.54 W
Oppenhuizen 52 53.00 N 5.42 E
Oppido Lucano 68 40.47 N 16.00 E
Oppido Mamertina 68 38.16 N 16.00 E
Oppio 66 44.03 N 10.50 E
Oppland □[6] 26 61.10 N 9.40 E
Opportunity, Mt., U.S. 202 46.07 N 112.49 W
Opportunity, Wa., U.S. 202 47.39 N 117.14 W
Oppum ●[8] 263 51.19 N 6.37 E
Opsa 76 55.32 N 26.47 E
Opsaheden 40 60.28 N 13.59 E
Optic Lake 184 54.46 N 101.13 W
Optima Lake ⊜[1] 196 36.40 N 101.10 W
Opua 172 35.19 S 174.07 E
Opunake 172 39.27 S 173.51 E
Opunohu, Baie d' c 174s 17.30 S 149.51 W
Opuwo 152 18.03 S 13.45 E
Opwijk 50 50.58 N 4.11 E
Oquawka 190 40.55 N 90.56 W
Oquendo, Perú 286d 11.58 S 77.08 W
Oquendo, Pil. 116 12.08 N 124.32 E
O'Quinn 222 29.50 N 96.58 W
Or' ≃ 86 51.12 N 58.30 E
Or, Côte d' ∧ 58 47.10 N 4.50 E
Or, Étang d' ⊜ 261 48.38 N 1.51 E
Ora (Auer), It 64 46.21 N 11.18 E
Ora, Lībiyā 146 28.33 N 19.24 E
Ōra, Nihon 174m 26.33 N 128.02 E
Ora Banda 162 30.22 S 121.04 E
Oracle 200 32.36 N 110.46 W
Oradea 38 47.03 N 21.57 E
Oradell 276 40.57 N 74.02 W
Oradell Reservoir ⊜[1] 276 40.58 N 74.01 W
Öræfajökull ⍓ 24a 64.03 N 16.38 W
Orahovica 38 45.31 N 17.53 E
Orai 124 25.59 N 79.28 E
Oraibi Wash V 200 35.26 N 110.49 W
Oraison 62 43.55 N 5.55 E
Oran → Wahran, Alg. 148 35.43 N 0.43 W
Oran, Mo., U.S. 194 37.05 N 89.39 W
Oran, Sebkha d' ⊜ 34 35.32 N 0.48 W
Orange, Austl. 166 33.17 S 149.06 E
Orange, Fr. 62 44.08 N 4.48 E
Orange, Ca., U.S. 228 33.47 N 117.51 W
Orange, Ct., U.S. 207 41.16 N 73.01 W
Orange, Ma., U.S. 207 42.35 N 72.18 W
Orange, N.J., U.S. 276 40.46 N 74.13 W
Orange, Oh., U.S. 279a 41.26 N 81.29 W
Orange, Tx., U.S. 194 30.05 N 93.44 W
Orange, Va., U.S. 188 38.14 N 78.06 W
Orange □[6], Ca., U.S. 228 33.43 N 117.54 W
Orange □[6], Fl., U.S. 220 28.32 N 81.16 W
Orange □[6], In., U.S. 218 38.33 N 86.28 W
Orange □[6], N.Y., U.S. 210 41.24 N 74.20 W
Orange (Oranje) ≃ 156 28.41 S 16.28 E
Orange, Cabo > 250 4.24 N 51.33 W
Orange Bowl ♦ 220 25.46 N 80.14 W
Orangeburg, Ky., U.S. 218 38.35 N 83.39 W
Orangeburg, N.Y., U.S. 210 41.03 N 73.57 W
Orangeburg, S.C., U.S. 192 33.29 N 80.51 W
Orange City, Fl., U.S. 220 28.57 N 81.17 W
Orange City, Ia., U.S. 198 43.00 N 96.03 W
Orange County Airport ⊠ 228 33.40 N 117.51 W
Orange Cove 226 36.37 N 119.19 W
Orange Free State (Oranje-Vrystaat) □[4] 158 28.30 S 27.00 E
Orange Grove 196 27.57 N 97.56 W
Orange Grove ●[8] 273d 26.10 S 28.05 E
Orange Lake, Fl., U.S. 192 29.25 N 82.13 W
Orange Lake, N.Y., U.S. 210 41.33 N 74.06 W
Orange Lake ⊜ 192 29.29 N 82.10 W
Orangemouth → Oranjemund 156 28.38 S 16.24 E
Orange Park 192 30.09 N 81.42 W
Orange Park Acres 280 33.48 N 117.47 W
Orange Reservoir ⊜[1] 276 40.46 N 74.17 W
Orangevale 226 38.40 N 121.13 W
Orangeville, On., Can. 212 43.55 N 80.06 W
Orangeville, Oh., U.S. 214 41.20 N 80.31 W
Orangeville, Pa., U.S. 210 41.05 N 76.25 W
Orangeville, Ut., U.S. 200 39.13 N 111.03 W
Orange Walk 232 18.06 N 88.33 W
Orango Grande I 150 11.10 N 16.08 W
Orani, It. 71 40.15 N 9.11 E
Orani, Pil. 116 14.49 N 120.32 E
Oranienbaum 54 51.48 N 12.24 E
Oranienburg 54 52.45 N 13.14 E
Oranje 52 52.55 N 6.28 E
Oranje → Orange ≃ 156 28.41 S 16.28 E
Oranjefontein 156 23.25 S 27.41 E
Oranje Gebergte ⋀ 250 3.00 N 55.05 W
Oranjemund 156 28.38 S 16.24 E
Oranjerivier 158 29.40 S 24.12 E
Oranjestad 241s 12.33 N 70.06 W
Oranjeville 158 27.00 S 28.15 E
Oranki 80 55.53 N 43.44 E
Oranmore 48 53.16 N 8.54 W
Ŏran-ni 98 34.22 N 126.29 E
Oranžerei 80 45.50 N 47.36 E
Or 'Aqiva 132 32.30 N 34.55 E
Orarak 140 6.15 N 32.23 E
Orari ≃ 172 44.15 S 171.25 E
Oras 116 12.09 N 125.26 E
Oras ≃ 116 12.08 N 125.26 E
Oras Bay c 116 12.07 N 125.28 E
Orăștie 38 45.50 N 23.12 E
Orașul Stalin → Brașov 38 45.39 N 25.37 E
Oratório, Ribeirão do ≃ 287b 23.37 S 46.32 W
Oratov 78 49.12 N 29.32 E
Oravais (Oravainen) 26 63.18 N 22.23 E
Oravița 38 45.02 N 21.41 E
Orawia 172 46.03 S 167.49 E
Orb ≃ 32 43.15 N 3.18 E
Orba ≃ 62 44.53 N 8.37 E
Orba Co ⊜ 120 34.32 N 81.03 E
Orbassano 62 45.01 N 7.32 E
Orbe 58 46.43 N 6.32 E
Orbe ≃ 58 46.47 N 6.39 E
Orbec-en-Auge 50 49.01 N 0.25 E
Orbetello 66 42.27 N 11.13 E
Orbetello, Laguna di c 66 42.27 N 11.14 E
Orbey 58 48.08 N 7.10 E
Orbieu ≃ 32 43.14 N 2.54 E
Orbigny 50 47.12 N 1.14 E
Órbigo ≃ 34 41.58 N 5.40 W
Orbiquet ≃ 50 49.09 N 0.14 E
Orbisonia 214 40.15 N 77.54 W
Orbost 166 37.42 S 148.27 E
Örbyhus 40 60.14 N 17.42 E
Orcadas ʊ[3] 9 60.45 S 44.43 W
Orcadas, Islas → Orkney Islands II 46 59.00 N 3.00 W
Orcadas del Sur, Islas → South Orkney Islands II 9 60.35 S 45.30 W
Orcades du Sud, Îles → South Orkney Islands II 9 60.35 S 45.30 W
Orcas 224 48.36 N 122.57 W
Orcas Island I 224 48.39 N 122.55 W
Orcemont 261 48.35 N 1.49 E
Orcera 34 38.19 N 2.39 W
Orchamps 58 47.09 N 5.40 E
Orchard, Ne., U.S. 198 42.20 N 98.14 W
Orchard, Tx., U.S. 222 29.36 N 95.58 W
Orchard City 200 38.49 N 107.58 W
Orchard Hills, Austl. 274a 33.47 S 150.43 E
Orchard Hills, Pa., U.S. 279b 40.35 N 79.32 W
Orchard Homes 202 46.51 N 114.02 W
Orchard Island 216 40.28 N 83.53 W
Orchard Lake ⊜ 281 42.35 N 83.22 W
Orchard Lake Village 281 42.35 N 83.21 W
Orchard Mesa 200 39.02 N 108.33 W
Orchard Park 210 42.46 N 78.44 W
Orchard Park Airport ⊠ 284a 42.48 N 78.45 W
Orchard Peak ∧ 226 35.44 N 120.08 W
Orchards 224 45.40 N 122.33 W
Orchard Valley 200 41.05 N 104.48 W
Orchard View 285 40.04 N 74.53 W
Orchej (Orgejev) 38 47.23 N 28.48 E
Orchha 124 25.21 N 78.39 E
Orchies 50 50.28 N 3.14 E
Orchon 88 49.09 N 105.21 E
Orchon ≃ 88 50.21 N 106.05 E
Orchon Tuul 88 48.58 N 104.59 E
Orcia ≃ 66 42.58 N 11.21 E
Orcières 62 44.41 N 6.20 E
Orčik ≃ 78 49.10 N 35.04 E
Orco ≃ 62 45.10 N 7.52 E
Ord 198 41.36 N 98.55 W
Ord ≃ 160 15.30 S 128.21 E
Ord, Mount ∧ 162 17.20 S 125.34 E
Orda 86 57.12 N 56.54 E
Ordenes 34 43.04 N 8.24 W
Orderville 200 37.16 N 112.38 W
Ordesa, Parque Nacional de ♦ 34 42.39 N 0.02 E
Ord Mountain ∧ 204 34.40 N 116.49 W
Ord Mountains ⋀ 228 34.42 N 117.10 W
Ordoqui 252 35.54 S 61.10 W
Ord River 162 17.23 S 128.51 E
Ordu 130 41.00 N 37.53 E
Ordu □[4] 130 40.45 N 37.30 E
Ordubad 84 38.56 N 46.02 E
Ordway 198 38.13 N 103.45 W
Ordynskoje 86 54.22 N 81.56 E
Ordzhonikidze → Vladikavkaz, Ross. 84 43.03 N 44.40 E
Ordžhonikidze → Vladikavkaz, Ross. 84 43.03 N 44.40 E
Ordzhonikidze → Jenakijevo, Ukr. 83 48.14 N 38.13 E
Ordžonikidze, Azer. 84 40.53 N 47.23 E
Ordžonikidze, Kaz. 86 52.28 N 61.46 E
Ordžonikidze, Ukr. 78 47.40 N 34.04 E
Ordžonikidze, Ukr. 78 44.57 N 35.22 E
Ordžonikidzeabad 85 38.34 N 69.01 E
Ordžonikidzevskaja 84 43.18 N 45.03 E
Ordžonikidzevskij, Ross. 84 43.51 N 41.54 E
Ordžonikidzevskij, Ross. 86 54.46 N 88.59 E
Ore 150 6.44 N 4.52 E
Ore ≃ 46 56.10 N 3.15 W
Öreälven ≃ 26 63.32 N 19.44 E
Oreana 219 39.56 N 88.51 W
Örebro 40 59.17 N 15.13 E
Örebro Län □[6] 40 59.30 N 15.00 E
Orechov 78 47.34 N 35.47 E
Orechovka, Ross. 80 52.56 N 48.14 E
Orechovka, Ukr. 83 48.17 N 39.13 E
Orechovo 80 58.28 N 41.58 E
Orechovo-Zujevo 82 55.49 N 38.59 E
Orechovsk 76 54.41 N 30.30 E
Orechov'skij ●[8] 83 48.01 N 38.42 E
Ore City 222 32.48 N 94.43 W
Oredež 76 58.49 N 30.20 E
Oredež ≃ 76 58.49 N 30.00 E
Orefield 208 40.38 N 75.35 W
Oregon, Il., U.S. 190 42.00 N 89.19 W
Oregon, Mo., U.S. 194 39.59 N 95.08 W
Oregon, Oh., U.S. 214 41.38 N 83.29 W
Oregon, Wi., U.S. 216 42.55 N 89.23 W
Oregon □[3], U.S. 178 44.00 N 121.00 W
Oregon □[3], U.S. 202 44.00 N 121.00 W
Oregon Caves National Monument ♦ 202 42.06 N 123.24 W
Oregon City 224 45.21 N 122.36 W
Oregon Creek ≃ 226 39.23 N 121.05 W
Oregon Dunes National Recreation Area ♦ 202 43.45 N 124.12 W
Oregon House 226 39.21 N 121.17 W
Öregrund 40 60.20 N 18.26 E
Öregrundsgrepen c 40 60.27 N 18.18 E
Orehoved 41 54.57 N 11.52 E
Orekhovo-Zuyevo → Orechovo-Zujevo 82 55.49 N 38.59 E
Orel 76 52.59 N 36.05 E
Orel', ozero ⊜ 89 53.30 N 139.42 E
Oreland 285 40.07 N 75.10 W
Orellana 248 6.54 S 75.04 W
Orellana, Embalse de ⊜[1] 34 39.00 N 5.25 W
Orel Oblast' □[4] 76 53.00 N 36.20 E
Orem 200 40.17 N 111.41 W
Ören 130 37.02 N 27.57 E
Orenburg 86 51.54 N 55.06 E
Orenburg Oblast' □[4] 86 52.30 N 54.00 E
Örencik 130 39.16 N 29.33 E
Oreng, Indon. 114 4.03 N 97.28 E
Oreng, Indon. 114 4.33 N 96.49 E
Orense, Arg. 252 38.40 S 59.47 W
Orense, Esp. 34 42.20 N 7.51 W
Orense □[4] 34 42.15 N 7.30 W
Örenşehir 130 39.00 N 36.39 E
Orepuki 172 46.17 S 167.44 E
Oreški 82 55.43 N 36.21 E
Oressa ≃ 76 52.33 N 28.45 E
Orestes 216 40.16 N 85.43 W
Orestes Pereyra 232 26.31 N 105.40 W
Orestiás 38 41.30 N 26.31 E
Orestimba Creek ≃ 226 37.25 N 121.00 W
Øresund → The Sound ⊔ 41 55.50 N 12.40 E
Oreti ≃ 172 46.28 S 168.17 E
Oreto ≃ 70 38.06 N 13.24 E
Orewa 172 36.34 S 174.42 E
Oreye 56 50.44 N 5.22 E
Orfanoú, Kólpos c 38 40.40 N 23.50 E
Orford, Eng., U.K. 42 52.06 N 1.31 E
Orford, Eng., U.K. 262 53.25 N 2.35 W
Orford, Mont ∧ 206 45.19 N 72.15 W
Orford Ness > 42 52.05 N 1.34 E
Orfordville 190 42.37 N 89.15 W
Organ Needle ∧ 200 32.21 N 106.33 W
Organ Pipe Cactus National Monument ♦ 200 32.00 N 112.55 W
Órgãos, Serra dos ⋀ 256 22.22 S 42.45 W
Orgaz 34 39.39 N 3.54 W
Orge ≃ 50 48.42 N 2.24 E
Orgelet 58 46.31 N 5.37 E
Orgères-en-Beauce 50 48.09 N 1.42 E
Orgerus 261 48.50 N 1.42 E
Orgeval 50 48.55 N 1.59 E
Orgeval ≃ 261 49.00 N 1.54 E
Orgiano 64 45.21 N 11.28 E
Orgnac, Aven d' ⊥[5] 62 44.19 N 4.27 E
Orgnac-l'Aven 62 44.19 N 4.27 E
Orgof 144 3.03 N 41.44 E
Orgon 62 43.47 N 5.02 E
Orgosolo 71 40.12 N 9.21 E
Orgtrud 80 56.12 N 40.37 E
Orgūn 120 32.51 N 69.07 E
Orhaneli 130 39.54 N 29.00 E
Orhangazi 130 40.30 N 29.18 E
Orhanlar 130 39.54 N 27.37 E
Oria, It. 68 40.30 N 17.38 E
Oria, Zaïre 154 3.17 N 30.41 E
Orica 236 14.41 N 86.56 W
Oriçanga, Rio do ≃ 256 22.18 S 47.03 W
Orichuna ≃ 246 7.25 N 68.58 W
Oriči 80 58.24 N 49.05 E
Orick 204 41.17 N 124.03 W
Oricola 66 42.02 N 13.02 E
Orient, Ia., U.S. 198 41.12 N 94.24 W
Orient, N.Y., U.S. 207 41.08 N 72.18 W
Orient, Oh., U.S. 218 39.48 N 83.09 W
Orient, Wa., U.S. 182 48.53 N 118.13 W
Oriental, Méx. 234 19.22 N 97.37 W
Oriental, N.C., U.S. 192 35.01 N 76.41 W
Oriental, Cordillera ⋀, Col. 246 6.00 N 73.00 W
Oriental, Cordillera ⋀, Perú 248 11.00 S 74.00 W
Oriental, Pico ∧ 286c 10.32 N 66.50 W
Oriental de Zapata, Ciénaga ≡ 240p 22.15 N 80.50 W
Oriental Park 214 42.09 N 79.22 W
Oriente 252 38.44 S 60.37 W
Orientos 166 28.05 S 141.14 E
Origgio 266b 45.36 N 9.01 E
Origny-en-Thiérache 50 49.54 N 4.01 E
Origny-Sainte-Benoite 50 49.50 N 3.30 E
Orillia 212 44.37 N 79.25 W
Orimattila 26 60.48 N 25.45 E
Orinda 226 37.52 N 122.10 W
Orinduik 246 4.42 N 60.01 W
Orini 172 37.34 S 175.18 E
Orinin 78 48.46 N 26.24 E
Orinoco ≃ 246 8.37 N 62.15 W
Orinoco, Delta del ⊤[2] 246 9.15 N 61.30 W
Oriola (Orihuela) 34 38.05 N 0.57 W
Oriole, Md., U.S. 208 38.10 N 75.48 W
Oriole, Pa., U.S. 210 41.08 N 77.13 W
Oriole Park ♦ 284b 39.18 N 76.37 W
Oriolo 68 40.03 N 16.27 E
Oriomo 164 8.50 S 143.15 E
Orion, Pil. 116 14.37 N 120.34 E
Orion, Il., U.S. 190 41.21 N 90.22 W
Oripää 26 60.51 N 22.41 E
Oriskany 210 43.09 N 75.19 W
Oriskany Battlefield State Historic Site ⊥ 210 43.11 N 75.23 W
Oriskany Creek ≃ 210 43.10 N 75.20 W
Oriskany Falls 210 42.56 N 75.27 W
Orissa □[3] 118 20.00 N 84.00 E
Orissaare 76 58.34 N 23.05 E
Orissa Coast Canal ≍ 126 21.51 N 87.41 E
Oristano 71 39.54 N 8.36 E
Oristano □[4] 71 39.55 N 8.40 E
Oristano, Golfo di c 71 39.50 N 8.29 E
Őriszentpéter 61 46.51 N 16.25 E
Orituco ≃ 246 8.45 N 67.27 W
Orivesi 26 61.41 N 24.21 E
Orivesi ⊜ 26 62.16 N 29.24 E
Oriximiná 250 1.45 S 55.52 W
Orizaba 234 18.51 N 97.06 W
Orizaba, Pico de (Volcán Citlaltépetl) ∧[1] 234 19.01 N 97.16 W
Orizona 255 17.03 S 48.18 W
Orjahovo 38 43.45 N 23.57 E
Ørje 26 59.29 N 11.39 E
Orjen ∧ 38 42.30 N 18.38 E
Orjiva 34 36.54 N 3.25 W
Ork, Ness of > 46 59.05 N 2.48 W
Orkanger 26 63.19 N 9.52 E
Örkelljunga 41 56.17 N 13.17 E
Orken 263 51.06 N 6.34 E
Orkla ≃ 26 63.18 N 9.50 E
Orkney, Sk., Can. 184 49.08 N 107.55 W
Orkney, S. Afr. 158 27.00 S 26.39 E
Orkney □[4] 46 59.00 N 3.00 W
Orkney Islands II 46 59.00 N 3.00 W
Orl'a 76 53.30 N 24.59 E
Orla ≃ 54 50.46 N 11.31 E
Orlamünde 54 50.47 N 11.31 E
Orland, Ca., U.S. 204 39.44 N 122.11 W
Orland, In., U.S. 216 41.43 N 85.10 W
Orlândia 255 20.43 S 47.53 W
Orland Lake ⊜ 278 41.38 N 87.52 W
Orlando, S. Afr. 273d 26.14 S 27.55 E
Orlando, Fl., U.S. 220 28.32 N 81.22 W
Orlando, Capo d' > 70 38.10 N 14.45 E
Orlando Dam ⊜[1] 273d 26.16 S 27.56 E
Orlando International Airport ⊠ 220 28.26 N 81.19 W
Orlando Naval Training Center ■ 220 28.34 N 81.20 W
Orlando West Extension 273d 26.15 S 27.54 E
Orland Park 216 41.37 N 87.51 W
Orland Square ●[9] 278 41.36 N 87.51 W
Orléanais □[9] 50 47.50 N 2.00 E
Orléans, On., Can. 212 45.28 N 75.31 W
Orléans, Fr. 50 47.55 N 1.54 E
Orleans, Ca., U.S. 204 41.18 N 123.32 W
Orleans, In., U.S. 218 38.39 N 86.27 W
Orleans, Ma., U.S. 207 41.47 N 69.59 W
Orleans, Ne., U.S. 198 40.07 N 99.27 W
Orleans, Vt., U.S. 188 44.48 N 72.12 W
Orleans □[6], N.Y., U.S. 210 43.15 N 78.12 W
Orleans □[6], Vt., U.S. 206 44.57 N 72.12 W
Orléans, Canal d' ≍ 50 47.54 N 1.55 E
Orléans, Île d' I 186 46.55 N 70.58 W
Orléansville → Ech Cheliff 148 36.10 N 1.20 E
Orlik, Kaz. 80 48.17 N 51.32 E
Orlik, Ross. 88 52.30 N 99.55 E
Orlinaja, gora ∧ 180 62.35 N 178.30 E
Orlinga 88 56.03 N 105.53 E
Orlinga ≃ 88 56.03 N 105.53 E
Orlov 80 58.33 N 48.50 E
Orlová 30 49.50 N 18.24 E
Orlov Gaj 80 50.57 N 48.12 E
Orlovista 220 28.32 N 81.28 W
Orlovka, Ross. 78 51.02 N 40.32 E
Orlovka, Ross. 86 59.03 N 85.59 E
Orlovka, Ukr. 78 51.54 N 32.47 E
Orlovka, Ukr. 78 45.40 N 33.21 E
Orlovka, Ukr. 83 48.10 N 37.39 E
Orlovka ≃ 86 58.40 N 86.08 E
Orlovo, Ross. 78 51.45 N 39.35 E
Orlovo, Ross. 265b 55.38 N 37.23 E
Orlovskij 80 46.52 N 42.03 E
Orlu 150 5.47 N 7.02 E
Orly 261 48.45 N 2.24 E
Ormanlı 130 41.10 N 31.39 E
Ormāra 128 25.12 N 64.38 E
Ormāra, Rās > 128 25.09 N 64.35 E
Orme, Rivière à l' ≃ 275a 45.27 N 73.56 W
Ormea 62 44.09 N 7.54 E
Ormesby 44 54.33 N 1.11 W
Ormesby Saint Margaret 42 52.40 N 1.42 E
Ormiston 184 49.45 N 105.22 W
Ormoc 116 11.00 N 124.37 E
Ormoc Bay c 116 10.58 N 124.35 E
Ormond 274b 37.54 S 145.03 E
Ormond Beach 192 29.17 N 81.03 W
Ormož 36 46.25 N 16.09 E
Ormsby 214 41.48 N 78.33 W
Ormsby □[6] 226 39.11 N 119.46 W
Ormsjön ⊜ 26 64.23 N 16.03 E
Ormskirk 44 53.35 N 2.54 W
Ormstown 206 45.08 N 74.00 W
Ormtjernkampen Nasjonalpark ♦ 26 61.12 N 9.48 E
Ornain ≃ 56 48.46 N 4.47 E
Ornans 58 47.06 N 6.09 E
Ornäs 40 60.31 N 15.32 E
Ornavasso 58 45.58 N 8.24 E
Orne □[5] 32 48.40 N 0.05 E
Orne ≃, Fr. 32 49.19 N 0.14 W
Orne ≃, Fr. 50 48.08 N 0.11 E
Orne ≃, Fr. 56 49.17 N 6.11 E
Ornes 26 61.18 N 7.22 E
Orneta 30 54.08 N 20.08 E
Ornö I 40 59.04 N 18.24 E
Örnsköldsvik 26 63.18 N 18.43 E
Oro 98 40.02 N 127.26 E
Orø I 41 55.46 N 11.49 E
Orobie, Alpi ⋀ 64 46.00 N 10.00 E
Oročanskij Golec, gora ∧ 88 53.29 N 114.18 E
Oročen 74 58.28 N 125.26 E
Orocovis 240m 18.14 N 66.23 W
Orocué 246 4.48 N 71.20 W
Orocuina 236 13.26 N 87.06 W
Orodara 150 10.59 N 4.55 W
Orofino 202 46.28 N 116.15 W
Orogen Zizhiqi 89 50.34 N 123.40 E
Örög nuur ⊜, Mong. 86 50.10 N 91.00 E
Orog nuur ⊜, Mong. 102 45.03 N 100.42 E
Oro Grande 228 34.35 N 117.20 W
Orohena, Mont ∧ 174s 17.37 S 149.28 W
Orok, Olcoinyo ∧ 154 2.29 S 36.46 E
Oroku 174m 26.12 N 127.39 E
Or'ol 86 59.21 N 56.35 E
Or'ol' ≃ 78 48.30 N 34.54 E
Oroluk I[1] 14 7.32 N 155.18 E
Oromocto 186 45.51 N 66.29 W
Oromocto Lake ⊜ 186 45.36 N 67.00 W
Oron, Nig. 150 4.48 N 8.14 E
Oron, Ross. 88 57.11 N 116.28 E
Oron ≃ 62 45.18 N 4.47 E
Oron, ozero ⊜ 88 57.06 N 116.30 E
Orona I[1] 14 4.29 S 172.10 W
Oron-la-Ville 58 46.34 N 6.50 E
Orono, On., Can. 212 43.59 N 78.37 W
Orono, Me., U.S. 188 44.52 N 68.40 W
Oronoque ≃ 246 2.45 N 57.25 W
Oronsay I 46 56.01 N 6.16 W
Orontes → Asi ≃ 130 36.02 N 35.58 E
Oropa, Santuario di ʊ[1] 62 45.38 N 7.58 E
Oropeo 234 18.50 N 101.48 W
Oroquieta 116 8.29 N 123.48 E
Orós 250 6.15 S 38.55 W
Orós, Açude ⊜[1] 250 6.15 S 39.05 W
Orosei 71 40.23 N 9.42 E
Orosei, Golfo di c 71 40.15 N 9.44 E
Orosháza 30 46.34 N 20.40 E
Orosi 226 36.33 N 119.17 W
Orosí, Volcán ∧[1] 236 10.59 N 85.29 W
Oroszlány 30 47.30 N 18.19 E
Orotelli 71 40.18 N 9.07 E
Orote Peninsula >[1] 174p 13.26 N 144.38 E
Oroville, Ca., U.S. 226 39.30 N 121.33 W
Oroville, Wa., U.S. 202 48.56 N 119.26 W
Oroville, Lake ⊜[1] 204 39.32 N 121.25 W
Orowoc Creek ≃ 276 40.43 N 73.13 W
Orpheus Island I 166 18.37 S 146.30 E
Orphin 261 48.35 N 1.47 E
Orpierre 62 44.19 N 5.41 E
Orpington ●[8] 260 51.23 N 0.06 E
Orrefors 26 56.50 N 15.45 E
Orrell 44 53.32 N 2.42 W
Orrick 194 39.12 N 94.07 W
Orrin 198 48.05 N 100.09 W
Orrin, Glen V 46 57.30 N 4.46 W
Orrin Reservoir ⊜[1] 46 57.30 N 4.45 W
Òrrius 266d 41.33 N 2.21 E
Orr Lake ⊜, Mb., Can. 184 56.07 N 97.11 W
Orr Lake ⊜, On., Can. 212 44.37 N 79.47 W
Orroroo 166 32.44 S 138.37 E
Orrs Island 188 43.45 N 69.58 W
Orrtanna 208 39.51 N 77.22 W
Orrville, Al., U.S. 194 32.18 N 87.14 W
Orrville, Oh., U.S. 214 40.50 N 81.45 W

Symbol	English	Deutsch	Español	Français	Português
≃	River	Fluß	Río	Rivière	Rio
≍	Canal	Kanal	Canal	Canal	Canal
ʟ	Waterfall, Rapids	Wasserfall, Stromschnellen	Cascada, Rápidos	Chute d'eau, Rapides	Cascata, Rápidos
⊔	Strait	Meeresstraße	Estrecho	Détroit	Estreito
c	Bay, Gulf	Bucht, Golf	Bahía, Golfo	Baie, Golfe	Baía, Golfo
⊜	Lake, Lakes	See, Seen	Lago, Lagos	Lac, Lacs	Lago, Lagos
≡	Swamp	Sumpf	Pantano	Marais	Pântano
⍓	Ice Features, Glacier	Eis- und Gletscherformen	Accidentes Glaciales	Formes glaciaires	Acidentes glaciares
⊤	Other Hydrographic Features	Andere Hydrographische Objekte	Otros Elementos Hidrográficos	Autres données hydrographiques	Outros acidentes hidrográficos
✦	Submarine Features	Untermeerische Objekte	Accidentes Submarinos	Formes de relief sous-marin	Acidentes submarinos
□	Political Unit	Politische Einheit	Unidad Politica	Entité politique	Unidade política
ʊ	Cultural Institution	Kulturelle Institution	Institución Cultural	Institution culturelle	Institução cultural
⊥	Historical Site	Historische Stätte	Sitio Histórico	Site historique	Sitio histórico
♦	Recreational Site	Erholungs- und Ferienort	Sitio de Recreo	Centre de loisirs	Area de Lazer
⊠	Airport	Flughafen	Aeropuerto	Aéroport	Aeroporto
■	Military Installation	Militäranlage	Instalación Militar	Installation militaire	Instalação militar
●	Miscellaneous	Verschiedenes	Misceláneo	Divers	Diversos

Column 1

Orrville, Pa., U.S. 279b 40.33 N 79.47 W
Orša, Bela. 76 54.30 N 30.24 E
Orsa, Sve. 26 61.07 N 14.37 E
Orša ≈ 82 56.48 N 36.11 E
Orsago 64 45.56 N 12.25 E
Orsan 62 44.08 N 4.40 E
Oršanka 80 56.55 N 47.53 E
Orsara di Puglia 68 41.17 N 15.16 E
Orsasjön ⊜ 26 61.07 N 14.34 E
Orsay 50 48.42 N 2.11 E
Orsett 260 51.31 N 0.22 E
Orsières 58 46.00 N 7.09 E
Orsjön ⊜ 26 61.35 N 16.20 E
Orsk 86 51.12 N 58.34 E
Örskär I 40 60.31 N 18.23 E
Orslev 41 55.02 N 11.59 E
Orsogna 66 42.13 N 14.17 E
Orsomarso 68 39.48 N 15.55 E
Orson 210 43.49 N 75.27 W
Orsova 38 44.42 N 22.24 E
Ørsta 26 62.12 N 6.09 E
Ørsted 41 55.20 N 10.04 E
Ørsundaån ≈ 40 59.44 N 17.21 E
Örsundsbro 40 59.44 N 17.18 E
Orta 130 40.38 N 33.06 E
Orta, Lago d' 62 45.49 N 8.24 E
Ortaca 130 36.49 N 28.47 E
Ortakent 130 37.02 N 27.21 E
Ortaklar 130 37.53 N 27.30 E
Ortaköy, Tür. 130 40.17 N 35.16 E
Ortaköy, Tür. 130 38.44 N 34.03 E
Ortaköy, Tür. 130 38.00 N 34.23 E
Ortaköy ≈ 130 40.27 N 38.02 E
Ortaköy → 8 267b 41.03 N 29.01 E
Orta Nova 68 41.19 N 15.42 E
Orta San Giulio 62 45.48 N 8.25 E
Orte 66 42.27 N 12.23 E
Ortega 246 3.56 N 75.13 W
Ortegal, Cabo › 34 43.45 N 7.53 W
Orteguaza ≈ 246 0.43 N 75.16 W
Ortelsburg
— Szczytno 30 53.34 N 21.00 E
Ortenberg, Dtsch. 56 50.21 N 9.02 E
Ortenberg, Dtsch. 58 48.27 N 7.58 E
Ortenburg 60 48.33 N 13.14 E
Orth 54 54.27 N 11.03 E
Orthez 32 43.29 N 0.46 W
Ortigalita Creek ≈ 226 36.57 N 120.52 W
Ortigalita Peak ▲ 226 36.48 N 120.55 W
Ortigara, Monte ▲ 64 46.00 N 11.29 E
Ortigueira 34 43.41 N 7.51 W
Ortigueira, Ría de c ¹ 34 43.42 N 7.51 W
Orting 224 47.05 N 122.12 W
Ortisei (Sankt Ulrich) 64 46.34 N 11.40 E
Ortiz, Méx. 232 28.17 N 110.43 W
Ortiz, Ven. 246 9.37 N 67.17 W
Ortles (Otler) ▲ 64 46.31 N 10.33 E
Ortles ▲ 64 46.30 N 10.40 E
Ortofta 41 55.47 N 13.14 E
Ortolo ≈ 71 41.30 N 8.55 E
Ortona 66 42.21 N 14.24 E
Ortona Lock ⊷ ⁵ 220 26.24 N 81.18 W
Orton Park ♦ 275b 43.46 N 79.12 W
Ortonura 85 41.29 N 76.12 E
Ortonville, Mi., U.S. 216 42.51 N 83.26 W
Ortonville, Mn., U.S. 198 45.18 N 96.26 W
Ortonville State
Recreation Area ♦ 216 42.52 N 83.26 W
Ortoroberk 85 41.56 N 71.21 E
Orto-Tokoj 85 42.21 N 76.01 E
Ortovero 62 44.03 N 8.07 E
Ortrand 54 51.22 N 13.45 E
Örträsk 26 64.08 N 18.59 E
Ortueri 71 40.02 N 8.59 E
Ortúzar, Canal ≋ 286e 33.33 S 70.47 W
Örtze ≈ 52 52.40 N 9.57 E
Oruanui 172 38.35 S 176.02 E
Oruba 273a 6.35 N 3.25 E
Orudjevo 82 56.26 N 37.32 E
Orümíyeh (Reẕā'īyeh) 128 37.33 N 45.04 E
Orümíyeh,
Daryācheh-ye
(Lake Urmia) ⊜ 128 37.40 N 45.30 E
Orune 71 40.24 N 9.22 E
Oruro 248 17.59 S 67.09 W
Oruro □ ⁵ 248 18.40 S 67.40 W
Or'us-Mljele ≈ 88 58.35 N 121.30 E
Orust I 26 58.10 N 11.38 E
Orüzgān (Qala-i-
Hazār Qadam) 120 32.56 N 66.38 E
Orüzgān □ ¹ 120 33.15 N 66.00 E
Orval, Abbaye d' �? ¹ 56 49.38 N 5.22 E
Orvanne ≈ 50 48.22 N 2.50 E
Orvieto 66 42.43 N 12.07 E
Orvilla 208 40.16 N 75.17 W
Orvilliers 261 48.49 N 1.39 E
Orvin ⍗ 54 48.28 N 3.23 E
Oriviston 214 41.06 N 77.45 W
Orvwyn, gora ▲ 180 65.14 N 175.20 W
Orwell, On., Can. 214 42.46 N 81.02 W
Orwell, N.Y., U.S. 212 43.35 N 76.00 W
Orwell, Oh., U.S. 214 41.32 N 80.52 W
Orwell ≈ 42 51.57 N 1.17 E
Orwigsburg 208 40.39 N 76.06 W
Orwin 208 40.35 N 76.31 W
Oroxon ≈ 82 59.40 N 117.41 E
Or Yehuda 132 32.01 N 34.51 E
Oryu-dong → ⁸ 271b 29.29 N 126.51 E
Orževo 80 37.49 N 26.07 E
Orževka 78 49.48 N 42.55 E
Orzinuovi 62 45.24 N 9.55 E
Orzyc ≈ 30 52.46 N 21.14 E
Orzysz 30 53.49 N 21.56 E
Oš, Kyrg. 85 40.33 N 72.48 E
Os, Nor. 26 62.30 N 11.12 E
Oš ≈ 4 40.00 N 72.30 E
Osa, Nig. 96 35.56 N 133.34 E
Osa, Ross. 82 57.17 N 55.26 E
Osa, Ross. 86 57.30 N 103.53 E
Oša ≈ 86 57.13 N 73.41 E
Osa, Península de › ¹ 236 8.34 N 83.31 W
Osage, Ia., U.S. 190 43.17 N 92.48 W
Osage, Mo., U.S. 219 38.25 N 92.02 W
Osage, N.J., U.S. 285 39.43 N 74.57 W
Osage, Wy., U.S. 188 43.58 N 104.25 W
Osage □ ⁵ 187 36.37 N 91.50 W
Osage ≈ 194 38.35 N 91.57 W
Osage Beach 194 38.09 N 92.37 W
Osage City 198 38.38 N 95.49 W
Ōsaka, Nihon 96 35.17 N 137.16 E
Ōsaka, Nihon 94 34.40 N 135.30 E
Ōsaka □ ³ 94 34.40 N 135.34 E
Ōsaka › ² 96 34.40 N 135.32 E
Ōsaka Castle ⊥ 270 34.41 N 135.32 E
Ōsaka-heiya ≃ 94 34.43 N 135.30 E
Ōsaka International
Airport ⊠ 270 34.48 N 135.26 E
Ōsaka-kō ⊂ 270 34.38 N 135.26 E
Ōsakarovka 86 50.32 N 72.39 E
Ōsaka-wan c 94 34.34 N 135.18 E
Ōsaka University › ² 270 34.49 N 135.31 E
Ōsakigahana ▸ 96 35.11 N 132.25 E
Ōsaki-Kami-jima I 96 34.15 N 132.56 E
Ōsaki-Shimo-jima I 96 34.10 N 132.50 E
Osäm ≈ 38 43.42 N 24.51 E
Osan 98 37.11 N 127.04 E
Osanovo 82 54.51 N 38.30 E
Osasco 256 23.32 S 46.46 W
Osasco □ ⁷ 287b 23.32 S 46.46 W
Osawano 94 36.34 N 137.12 E
Osawatomie 198 38.29 N 94.57 W
Ōsa-yama ▲ 96 34.03 N 134.18 E
Osbaldeston 262 53.47 N 2.32 W
Osborne, Pa., U.S. 279b 39.26 N 98.41 W

Column 2

Osborne, Pa., U.S. 279b 40.32 N 80.10 W
Osbourn Seamount
⍗ ³ 14 26.00 S 174.50 W
Osburger Hochwald
⍗ ⁴ 56 49.40 N 6.50 E
Osburn 202 47.30 N 115.59 W
Osby 26 56.22 N 13.59 E
Osbyholm 41 55.51 N 13.36 E
Oscar Peak ▲ 182 54.51 N 129.07 W
Oscarville 180 60.43 N 161.46 W
Oscawana Lake 210 41.23 N 73.52 W
Osceola, Ar., U.S. 194 35.42 N 89.58 W
Osceola, In., U.S. 216 41.39 N 86.04 W
Osceola, Ia., U.S. 190 41.02 N 93.45 W
Osceola, Ne., U.S. 198 41.10 N 97.32 W
Osceola, Ne., U.S. 210 41.59 N 77.21 W
Osceola, Tx., U.S. 222 32.08 N 97.14 W
Osceola, Wi., U.S. 190 45.19 N 92.42 W
Osceola ≈ ⁵ 220 28.00 N 81.15 W
Osceola Mills 214 40.51 N 78.16 W
Oščepkovo 86 57.35 N 70.42 E
Oschatz 54 51.17 N 13.07 E
Oschersleben 54 52.01 N 11.13 E
Oschiri 71 40.43 N 9.06 E
Oscoda 192 44.26 N 83.20 W
Ošečna ≈ 263 51.26 N 7.49 E
Ošečerka 76 57.33 N 34.48 E
Osečina 38 44.23 N 19.36 E
Osejevskaja 82 55.53 N 38.10 E
Ošejkino 82 56.15 N 35.54 E
Osek 54 50.37 N 13.40 E
Osen — Saaremaa I 58.25 N 22.30 E
Osen 24 64.17 N 10.30 E
Oševo 88 55.32 N 138.10 E
Oseretrovo 88 56.47 N 105.47 E
Ose-zaki ▸ 94 35.02 N 138.47 E
Osgood, In., U.S. 218 39.07 N 85.17 W
Osgood, Oh., U.S. 216 40.20 N 84.30 W
Osgoode 212 45.08 N 75.36 W
Osh
— Oš 85 40.33 N 72.48 E
Oshamambe 92a 42.30 N 140.22 E
O'Shanassy ≈ 166 18.59 S 138.46 E
O'Shaughnessy Dam
⍉ 226 37.57 N 119.47 W
O'Shaughnessy
Reservoir ⊜ ¹ 214 40.12 N 83.09 W
Oshawa 212 43.54 N 78.51 W
Oshawa Creek ≈ 212 43.52 N 78.49 W
Oshibe → ⁸ 270 34.45 N 135.04 E
Oshigambo 156 17.47 S 16.05 E
Oshika, Nihon 92 38.16 N 141.32 E
Oshika-hantō › ¹ 92 38.20 N 141.30 E
Oshikango 156 17.25 S 15.56 E
Oshima ≈ 92 33.03 N 129.33 E
Ōshima, Nihon 94 37.07 N 138.30 E
Ōshima, Nihon 94 34.45 N 139.22 E
Ō-shima I, Nihon 92a 41.30 N 139.22 E
Ō-shima I, Nihon 94 34.43 N 139.23 E
Ō-shima I, Nihon 96 36.15 N 136.07 E
Ō-shima I, Nihon 96 33.54 N 130.26 E
Ō-shima I, Nihon 96 34.30 N 131.25 E
Ō-shima I, Nihon 96 34.09 N 133.04 E
Ō-shima I, Nihon 96 33.38 N 134.30 E
Oshima-hantō › ¹ 92a 42.00 N 140.30 E
Oshimizu 94 36.46 N 136.46 E
Oshino 94 35.28 N 138.51 E
Oshivre → ⁸ 272c 19.09 N 72.51 E
Oshkosh, Ne., U.S. 188 41.24 N 102.20 W
Oshkosh, Wi., U.S. 190 44.01 N 88.32 W
Oshnov'lyeh 128 37.02 N 45.06 E
Oshodi 273a 6.34 N 3.21 E
Oshoek 158 26.13 S 30.59 E
Oshogbo 150 7.47 N 4.34 E
Oshtemo 216 42.15 N 85.41 W
Oshtorān Küh ▲ 128 33.20 N 49.16 E
Oshtorīnān 128 34.01 N 48.38 E
Oshwe 152 3.24 S 19.30 E
Osica de Jos 38 44.45 N 24.18 E
Osichi'ón-ni 94 41.25 N 128.16 E
Osiek 30 50.31 N 21.28 E
Osiglia 62 44.17 N 8.12 E
Osijek 38 45.33 N 18.41 E
Osilinka ≈ 182 56.05 N 124.29 W
Osilo 71 40.43 N 8.40 E
Osimo 66 43.29 N 13.29 E
Osini 71 39.50 N 9.29 E
Osinki 80 52.51 N 49.30 E
Osinniki, Ross. 86 58.03 N 47.02 E
Osinniki, Ross. 86 53.37 N 87.21 E
Osinovka, Ross. 76 56.19 N 109.27 E
Osinovka, Ross. 88 56.19 N 101.56 E
Osinovka, Ukr. 82 55.44 N 39.05 E
Osinovskij chrebet ≈ 180 67.10 N 175.00 E
Osínov Dolny 82 52.48 N 14.10 E
Osintorf 76 54.42 N 30.39 E
Osio Sotto 62 45.36 N 9.35 E
Osipaonica 38 44.33 N 21.04 E
Osipenko
— Berd'ansk, Ukr. 78 46.45 N 36.49 E
Osipenko, Ukr. 76 46.54 N 36.49 E
Osipovo 76 53.18 N 26.38 E
Osipovo Selo 156 20.59 S 17.19 E
Osiván 156 26.43 N 72.55 E
Oskaloosa, Ia., U.S. 190 41.17 N 92.38 W
Oskaloosa, Ks., U.S. 198 39.12 N 95.18 W
Oskar-Fredriksborg 26 59.19 N 18.21 E
Oskarshamn 26 57.16 N 16.26 E
Oskarström 26 56.48 N 12.58 E
Os'kino 78 51.14 N 39.02 E
Oskol ≈ 78 49.06 N 37.15 E
Oskolkovo 24 67.58 N 53.42 E
Oskü 128 30.55 N 133.34 E
Oskuja ≈ 76 59.17 N 32.05 E
Osl'anka, gora ▲ 86 59.14 N 31.54 E
Oslava ≈ 61 49.05 N 16.22 E
Ōsling → ¹ 56 49.55 N 6.00 E
Oslo 26 59.55 N 10.45 E
Oslob 116 9.31 N 123.26 E
Osløfjorden c² 26 59.20 N 10.35 E
Os'ma ≈, Ross. 76 54.55 N 33.24 E
Os'ma ≈, Ross. 82 57.52 N 47.45 E
Osmānābād 122 18.10 N 76.02 E
Osmancık 130 40.59 N 34.49 E
Osmaneli 130 40.22 N 30.01 E
Osmaniye 130 37.05 N 36.14 E
Ōsm'anskaja
vozvyšennosť ≈ ¹ 76 54.20 N 26.00 E
Ōšm'any 76 54.25 N 25.56 E
Osmington 116 10.11 N 125.31 E
Osmino 42 58.39 N 2.22 W
Os'mino 76 58.59 N 17.54 E
Osmond 198 42.21 N 97.35 W
Osmore 148 58.39 N 7.04 W
Osnabrück 54 52.16 N 8.03 E
Osno 30 52.28 N 14.50 E
Oso ≈ 246 4.48 N 71.40 W
Oso 154 3.08 N 121.56 W
Oso, Rango del Loo
— Great Bear 176 66.00 N 120.00 W

Column 3

Osorno, Chile 254 40.34 S 73.09 W
Osorno, Esp. 34 42.24 N 4.22 W
Osorno, Volcán ▲ ¹ 254 41.06 S 72.30 W
Osorun 273a 6.33 N 3.29 E
Os'otri ≈ 82 54.58 N 38.46 E
Osoyoos 182 49.02 N 119.28 W
Osoyoos Indian
Reserve ⊷ ⁴ 182 49.08 N 119.30 W
Osoyoos Lake ⊜ 182 49.00 N 119.26 W
Osøyra 26 60.11 N 5.28 E
Ospedaletti 62 43.48 N 7.43 E
Ospedaletto, It. 64 46.03 N 11.33 E
Ospedaletto, It. 64 46.17 N 13.07 E
Ospino 246 9.18 N 69.27 W
Ospitale di Cadore 64 46.20 N 12.19 E
Osprey 220 27.11 N 82.29 W
Osprey Reef ⍗ ² 166 13.55 S 146.38 E
Osqwagan Lake ⊜ 184 55.35 N 98.03 W
Ossa ≈ 52 51.46 N 5.31 E
Ossa, Mount ▲ 166 41.54 S 146.01 E
Ossabaw Island I 192 31.47 N 81.06 W
Osse ≈, Fr. 32 44.07 N 0.17 E
Osse ≈, Nig. 150 6.10 N 5.20 E
Ossenberg 263 51.34 N 6.35 E
Ossendrecht 52 51.24 N 4.19 E
Osseo, Mi., U.S. 216 41.53 N 84.33 W
Osseo, Wi., U.S. 190 44.34 N 91.13 W
Ossi 71 40.40 N 8.35 E
Ossiacher See ⊜ 64 46.40 N 13.55 E
Ossian, In., U.S. 216 40.52 N 85.09 W
Ossian, Ia., U.S. 190 43.08 N 91.45 W
Ossiaco, Loch ⊜ 46 56.46 N 4.38 W
Ossining 210 41.09 N 73.51 W
Ossjøen ⊜ 26 61.13 N 11.53 E
Ossora 86 59.20 N 163.13 E
Ossum-Bösinghoven 263 51.18 N 6.39 E
Ōšta 24 60.49 N 35.32 E
Ostaboningue, Lac ⊜ 190 47.09 N 78.53 W
Ōstanå, Sve. 26 59.33 N 18.35 E
Ōstanå, Sve. 40 60.38 N 16.48 E
Ostanbyn 40 60.39 N 16.48 E
Ostankino → ⁸ 265b 55.49 N 37.37 E
Ōstansjö 78 59.03 N 14.59 E
Ostašjo 78 49.33 N 33.46 E
Ostaškov 76 57.09 N 33.06 E
Ostašovo 82 55.52 N 35.52 E
Ostbevern 52 52.02 N 7.50 E
Ōstbirk 41 55.58 N 9.45 E
Ostbüren 263 51.31 N 7.46 E
Ōstby 26 61.15 N 12.32 E
Ostchinesisches
Meer
— East China Sea
⍗ ² 90 30.00 N 126.00 E
Oste ≈ 52 53.51 N 8.59 E
Osted 41 55.34 N 11.58 E
Osteen 220 28.50 N 81.09 W
Ostellato 64 44.45 N 11.56 E
Ostende
— Oostende 50 51.13 N 2.55 E
Ostenfelde 52 51.52 N 8.04 E
Oster 60 48.43 N 13.29 E
Osterath 54 51.16 N 6.37 E
Osterbönen 263 51.37 N 7.48 E
Osterburg, Dtsch. 54 52.47 N 11.44 E
Osterburg, Pa., U.S. 214 40.16 N 78.31 W
Osterburken 60 49.26 N 9.26 E
Østerbybruk 40 60.12 N 17.54 E
Ōsterbymo 40 57.50 N 15.16 E
Östercappeln 52 52.20 N 8.13 E
Ōsterdalälven ≈ 26 60.33 N 15.08 E
Østerfärnebo 40 60.18 N 16.48 E
Osterfeld 54 51.05 N 11.56 E
Osterfeld → ⁸ 263 51.30 N 6.53 E
Østergötland □ ⁹ 26 58.24 N 15.34 E
Östergötlands Län □ ⁶ 26 58.25 N 15.45 E
Osterhaninge 26 59.08 N 18.12 E
Osterhofen 60 48.42 N 13.01 E
Øster Hørst 41 59.40 N 9.03 E
Osterholz-
Scharmbeck 52 53.14 N 8.47 E
Osterley Park ♦ 260 51.30 N 0.21 W
Ōsterlövsta 40 60.26 N 17.47 E
Ostermundigen 58 46.58 N 7.29 E
Osternienburg 54 51.48 N 12.01 E
Osterode, Dtsch. 52 51.44 N 10.11 E
Osterode
— Ostróda, Pol. 30 53.43 N 19.59 E
Østerøya I 26 60.33 N 5.35 E
Ōsterreich
— Austria □ ¹ 30 47.20 N 13.20 E
Österreichisches
Freilichtmuseum ♦ 61 47.10 N 15.19 E
Osterrönfeld 41 54.17 N 9.41 E
Ōstersjön
— Baltic Sea ⍗ ² 24 57.00 N 19.00 E
Ōsterskär 40 59.28 N 18.18 E
Ōstersund 40 63.11 N 14.39 E
Ōstervåla 40 60.11 N 17.11 E
Osterwick 263 52.03 N 7.05 E
Ostfeld → ⁸ 263 51.05 N 7.45 E
Østfold □ ⁶ 26 59.20 N 11.30 E
Ostfriesische Inseln II 52 53.44 N 7.25 E
Ostfriesland □ ⁹ 52 53.30 N 7.30 E
Ost-Ghats
— Eastern Ghâts ≈ 122 14.00 N 78.50 E
Ōsthammar 40 60.16 N 18.22 E
Ostheim vor der
Rhön 56 50.26 N 10.14 E
Osthofen 56 49.42 N 8.19 E
Ostia, Bonifica di → 267a 41.43 N 12.17 E
Ostia Antica ≈ 1 66 41.45 N 12.18 E
Ostiano 64 45.13 N 10.15 E
Ostiglia 64 45.04 N 11.08 E
Ostki 78 51.16 N 27.22 E
Ōstliche Sierra Madre
— Madre Oriental,
Sierra ≈ 232 22.00 N 99.30 W
Ōstmark 26 60.17 N 12.48 E
Ostnäs 24 63.48 N 20.50 E
Ostnor 26 60.55 N 13.57 E
Ostorozyck ≈ 263 51.00 N 6.53 E
Ostra 66 43.37 N 13.09 E
Ōstraby 41 55.46 N 13.41 E
Ostrach 60 48.04 N 9.24 E
Ōstra Grevie 41 55.30 N 13.08 E
Ōstra Husby 40 58.35 N 16.33 E
Ōstra Laxsjön ⊜ 40 59.34 N 14.42 E
Ōstra Ljungby 40 56.11 N 13.04 E
Ōstra Ringsjön ⊜ 41 55.52 N 13.32 E
Ostrau
— Ostrava, Česká
Rep. 30 49.50 N 18.17 E
Ostrava 78 50.20 N 26.31 E
Ostrog 78 50.20 N 26.31 E
Ostrogožsk 78 50.52 N 39.03 E
Ostrokonp 76 59.52 N 40.22 E
Ostroleka 30 53.06 N 21.34 E
Ostroróg 30 52.30 N 16.27 E
Ostróv 30 53.00 N 21.30 E
Ostrožickij Gorodok 102 54.04 N 27.42 E

Column 4

Ostrov, Bela. 76 52.53 N 25.59 E
Ostrov, Česká Rep. 54 50.17 N 12.57 E
Ostrov, Rom. 38 44.06 N 27.22 E
Ostrov, Ross. 76 57.20 N 28.22 E
Ostrov, Ross. 76 60.34 N 37.55 E
Ostrov, Ross. 265b 55.35 N 37.51 E
Ostrov I 38 47.55 N 17.35 E
Ostrov'anskij 80 46.45 N 42.13 E
Ostrovec 76 54.37 N 25.57 E
Ostrovki 265a 59.48 N 30.50 E
Ostrovnoje 58 43.48 N 29.53 E
Ostrovskaja 80 50.26 N 44.27 E
Ostrovskoje 80 57.48 N 42.15 E
Ostrov-Zalit 58 58.01 N 28.04 E
Ostrowiec
Świętokrzyski 30 50.57 N 21.23 E
Ostrów Lubelski 30 51.30 N 22.52 E
Ostrów Mazowiecka 30 52.49 N 21.54 E
Ostrów Wielkopolski 30 51.39 N 17.49 E
Ostryna 76 53.44 N 24.32 E
Ostrzeszów 30 51.25 N 17.57 E
Ostsee
— Baltic Sea ⍗ ² 24 57.00 N 19.00 E
Ostseebad
Ahrenshoop 54 54.23 N 12.25 E
Ostseebad
Boltenhagen 54 54.00 N 11.12 E
Ostseebad Dierhagen 54 54.18 N 12.22 E
Ostseebad Graal-
Müritz 54 54.15 N 12.12 E
Ostseebad
Nienhagen 54 54.09 N 11.58 E
Ostseebad Rerik 54 54.06 N 11.37 E
Ostseebad Wustrow 54 54.21 N 12.23 E
Ost-Stürmeren 263 51.26 N 7.44 E
Osttirol □ ⁹ 64 46.55 N 12.30 E
Ostúa ≈ 236 14.17 N 89.33 W
Ostuacán 234 17.25 N 93.18 W
Ostula 234 18.30 N 103.28 W
Osum ≈ 68 40.44 N 1.35 E
Osund 88 48.33 N 7.43 E
Oswald 98 35.31 N 127.18 E
Osu 98 35.31 N 127.18 E
Osuga 76 56.02 N 34.18 E
Osuga ≈ 76 57.16 N 34.49 E
Ōsuka 94 34.41 N 137.59 E
O'Sullivan, Lac ⊜ 190 47.37 N 76.05 W
Ōsumi-hantō › ¹ 92 31.20 N 130.55 E
Ōsumi-kaikyō ≈ 92 31.20 N 131.00 E
Ōsumi-shotō II 93b 30.30 N 130.00 E
Osuna 34 37.14 N 5.07 W
Osupugo ▲ 154 1.40 N 35.49 E
Osvaldo Cruz 255 21.47 S 50.50 W
Osveja 76 56.01 N 28.06 E
Osvejskoje, ozero ⊜ 76 56.00 N 28.06 E
Oswaldtwistle 44 53.43 N 2.26 W
Oswaldtwistle Moor
⍗ ³ 262 53.43 N 2.23 W
Oswego, In., U.S. 216 41.20 N 85.50 W
Oswego, Ks., U.S. 198 37.10 N 95.06 W
Oswego, N.Y., U.S. 212 43.27 N 76.30 W
Oswego □ ⁷ 212 43.22 N 76.15 W
Oswego,
U.S. 208 39.40 N 74.32 W
Oswego ≈, N.J.,
U.S. 212 44.06 N 81.07 W
Oswego ≈, N.Y.,
U.S. 212 43.28 N 76.31 W
Oswestry 42 52.52 N 3.04 W
Oświęcim 30 50.03 N 19.12 E
Osyka 194 31.00 N 90.28 W
Ōta, Nihon 94 35.58 N 136.04 E
Ōta, Nihon 96 36.18 N 139.22 E
Ōta, Nihon 96 33.31 N 131.33 E
Ōta ≈, Nihon 96 34.21 N 132.26 E
Ōta → ⁸, Nihon 96 34.40 N 137.54 E
Ōtago □ ⁶ 172 45.00 N 170.00 E
Otago Peninsula › ¹ 172 45.52 S 170.40 E
Ōtaishi 172 36.57 S 174.51 E
Ōtake 94 34.12 N 132.13 E
Otaki, N.Z. 172 40.45 S 175.09 E
Ōtaki, Nihon 96 35.17 N 140.15 E
Ōtaki, Nihon 94 35.48 N 137.33 E
Ōtaki ≈ 94 35.49 N 137.40 E
Ōtaki-gawa ≈ 94 34.07 N 134.08 E
Ōta-Koizumi-hikojō ♦ 96 36.16 N 139.24 E
Otanmäki 24 64.08 N 27.06 E
Otar 82 43.33 N 75.13 E
Otaru 92a 43.13 N 141.00 E
Otatitlán 234 18.12 N 96.02 W
Otautau 172 46.09 S 168.00 E
Otava ≈ 61 49.26 N 14.12 E
Otavalo 246 0.14 N 78.16 W
Otavi 156 19.39 S 17.20 E
Otavi-Bergland ≈ 156 19.20 S 17.30 E
Ōtawa-yama ▲ 270 34.28 N 135.33 E
Ōtawara 96 36.52 N 140.02 E
Ōtchinjau 152 16.30 S 13.57 E
Oteapan 234 18.00 N 94.39 W
Otego 210 42.23 N 75.11 W
Otego Creek ≈ 210 42.25 N 75.07 W
Otélé 152 3.35 N 11.15 E
Otematata 172 44.37 S 170.16 E
Otepää 76 58.03 N 26.30 E
Oteppä ≈ 232 26.53 N 108.22 W
Oter ≈ 146 27.25 N 9.00 E
Otero, Co., U.S. 198 37.55 N 103.45 W
Otero, Ks., U.S. 198 38.32 N 99.40 W
Otero, Ms., U.S. 195 33.20 N 89.35 W
Otisco 218 39.40 N 86.54 W
Otisco Lake ⊜ 210 42.53 N 76.18 W
Otis, Co., U.S. 198 40.08 N 102.57 W
Otis, In., U.S. 216 41.36 N 86.54 W
Otis, Ks., U.S. 198 38.32 N 99.03 W
Otis, Ma., U.S. 208 42.11 N 73.05 W
Otisco 218 39.40 N 86.54 W
Otisville 212 43.18 N 85.40 W
Otjiseva 156 22.38 S 17.01 E
Otjimbingue 156 22.19 S 16.10 E
Otjiwarongo 156 20.25 S 16.39 E
Otjozondjou ≈ 156 20.18 S 20.50 E
Otley 44 53.54 N 1.41 W
Otm'ok, pereval ≈ 85 41.52 N 34.37 E
Otnuchovo 76 57.24 N 36.54 E
Otnes 26 61.45 N 11.14 E
Otobe 92a 41.59 N 140.07 E
Otočac 30 44.52 N 15.15 E
Otog Qi 90 39.05 N 108.00 E

Column 5

Ōtomi 175d 24.19 N 123.54 E
Oton 116 10.42 N 122.29 E
Otonabee ≈ 212 44.08 N 78.14 W
Otoque, Isla I 236 8.36 N 79.36 W
Ōtori-kita 270 34.33 N 135.27 E
Ōtorma 80 53.32 N 42.32 E
Otoro ≈ 236 15.00 N 88.16 W
Otorohanga 172 38.11 S 175.12 E
Otoskwin ≈ 176 52.13 N 88.06 W
Otowa 94 34.51 N 137.18 E
Otowa-yama ▲ 270 34.58 N 135.51 E
Otowa-yama-tunnel
⍗ 94 34.58 N 135.51 E
Ōtoyo 96 33.46 N 133.40 E
Otra ≈ 26 58.09 N 8.00 E
Otradnaja 84 44.23 N 41.31 E
Otradnoje 265a 59.47 N 30.49 E
Otradnyj 80 53.22 N 51.21 E
Otranto 68 40.09 N 18.30 E
Otranto, Capo d' › 68 40.06 N 18.31 E
Otranto, Strait of ⋃ 68 40.00 N 19.00 E
Otricoli 66 42.25 N 12.29 E
Otrokovice 30 49.13 N 17.31 E
Ōtscher ▲ 61 47.52 N 15.12 E
Otsego 216 42.27 N 85.41 W
Otsego ⊜ ² 210 42.42 N 74.56 W
Otsego Lake ⊜ 210 42.45 N 74.52 W
Otselic ≈ 210 42.20 N 75.58 W
Ōtsu, Nihon 96 35.00 N 135.52 E
Ōtsu, Nihon 268 35.16 N 139.42 E
Ōtsu ≈ 270 34.30 N 135.24 E
Ōtsuchi 92 39.21 N 141.54 E
Ōtsuki 94 35.36 N 138.57 E
Ōtsu-shima I 94 34.00 N 131.42 E
Otta, Nig. 150 6.42 N 3.10 E
Otta, Nor. 26 61.46 N 9.32 E
Ottakring → ⁸ 264b 48.12 N 16.19 E
Ottana 71 40.14 N 9.02 E
Otta Pass ⋃ 175c 72.09 N 151.53 E
Ottaric Pond ⊜ 283 42.46 N 71.25 W
Ottati 68 40.38 N 15.19 E
Ottavia → ⁸ 267a 41.58 N 12.24 E
Ottaviano 68 40.51 N 14.28 E
Ottawa, On., Can. 212 45.25 N 75.42 W
Ottawa, Il., U.S. 216 41.20 N 88.50 W
Ottawa, Ks., U.S. 198 38.36 N 95.16 W
Ottawa, Oh., U.S. 216 41.01 N 84.02 W
Ottawa ≈ 6, Mi., U.S. 216 42.57 N 84.50 W
Ottawa ≈ 6, Oh., U.S. 214 41.31 N 82.56 W
Ottawa ≈, Can. 176 45.20 N 73.58 W
Ottawa ≈, Can. 214 41.44 N 83.28 W
Ottawa-Carleton □ 6 212 45.15 N 75.45 W
Ottawa Hills 214 41.39 N 83.38 W
Ottawa International
Airport ⊠ 212 45.19 N 75.40 W
Ottawa Islands II 176 59.30 N 80.10 W
Ottbergen 52 51.42 N 9.18 E
Ottenby 26 56.14 N 16.25 E
Ottendorf-Okrilla 54 51.18 N 13.50 E
Ottenhöfen 58 48.34 N 8.09 E
Ottenschlag 61 48.25 N 15.13 E
Ottensheim 61 48.20 N 14.11 E
Ottenstein Stausee
⊜ ¹ 61 48.37 N 15.17 E
Otter ≈ 42 50.46 N 3.17 E
Otterbach ≈ 263 50.49 N 8.21 E
Otterbäcken 40 58.57 N 14.02 E
Otterbein 216 40.29 N 87.06 W
Otterburne 44 55.14 N 2.10 W
Otterburne 184 49.30 N 97.03 W
Otterburn Park 206 45.33 N 73.13 W
Otter Creek ≈, On.,
Can. 212 44.06 N 81.07 W
Otter Creek ≈, Il.,
U.S. 219 39.18 N 90.01 W
Otter Creek ≈, In.,
U.S. 218 38.58 N 85.37 W
Otter Creek ≈, Mo.,
U.S. 190 41.20 N 93.30 W
Otter Creek ≈, Mt.,
U.S. 219 39.31 N 91.51 W
Otter Creek ≈, N.Y.,
U.S. 202 45.36 N 106.17 W
Otter Creek ≈, N.Y.,
U.S. 212 43.43 N 75.23 W
Otter Creek ≈, Ut.,
U.S. 188 38.10 N 112.02 W
Otter Creek ≈, Vt.,
U.S. 212 44.13 N 73.17 W
Otter Creek
Reservoir ⊜ ¹ 200 38.10 N 111.59 W
Otterhöfen 56 48.33 N 8.12 E
Otter Lake, Mi., U.S. 216 43.13 N 83.28 W
Otter Lake ≈, Mn., U.S. 212 44.47 N 76.07 W
Otter Lake ≈, Sk.,
Can. 184 55.35 N 104.39 W
Otter Lake ⊜ — Uganda □ ¹ 154 1.00 N 32.00 E
Ottertail 190 46.26 N 95.54 W
Otter Tail □ ⁷ 190 46.25 N 95.45 W
Otter Tail ≈ 198 46.19 N 96.04 W
Otter Tail Lake ⊜ 198 46.24 N 95.35 W
Otter Tail Lake ⊜ 190 46.24 N 95.35 W
Otterup 41 55.31 N 10.24 E
Otterville, On., Can. 212 42.55 N 80.36 W
Otterville, Il., U.S. 194 39.03 N 84.46 W
Otterville, Mo., U.S. 194 38.41 N 92.54 W
Ottery ≈ 42 50.39 N 4.19 W
Ottery Saint Mary 42 50.45 N 3.17 W
Ottignies 52 50.40 N 4.34 E
Ottine 222 29.36 N 97.36 W
Ottley ≈ 246 6.13 N 58.30 W
Ottmarsbocholt 263 51.46 N 7.35 E
Ottnang 61 48.06 N 13.40 E
Ottnarov ≈ 52 46.49 N 119.10 W
Otto, In., U.S. 218 38.34 N 85.25 W
Otto, N.Y., U.S. 210 42.24 N 78.49 W
Otto, Tx., U.S. 222 31.27 N 96.49 W
Ottobeuren 60 47.56 N 10.18 E
Otto-Klein-
Klosterkirche ⍉ ¹ 54 47.20 N 11.25 E
Ottobrunn 60 48.04 N 11.40 E
Ottonia 152 7.15 S 146.30 E
Ottoshoop 158 25.45 S 25.55 E
Ottosdal 158 26.48 S 25.59 E
Ottoschwanden 263 51.14 N 7.59 E
Ottoville 216 40.56 N 84.20 W
Ottuk, Kyrg. 85 41.36 N 75.18 E
Ottumwa, Ia., U.S. 190 41.01 N 92.24 W
Ottweiler 56 49.24 N 7.10 E
Otuca 248 14.42 S 73.27 W
Otukpa 150 7.14 N 7.43 E
Otway, Bahía c 254 53.20 S 71.15 W
Otway, Cape › 166 38.52 S 143.31 E
Otway, Seno c 254 53.00 S 72.35 W
Ōtwock 30 52.07 N 21.16 E
Otztal → ⁸ 94 40.44 N 24.51 E
Ōtztal → ⁸ 94 40.44 N 24.51 E
Ötztaler Ache ≈ 64 47.14 N 10.50 E

Column 6

Ötztaler Alpen (Alpi
Venoste) ≈ 64 46.45 N 10.55 E
Ou ≈, Lao 110 20.04 N 102.13 E
Ou ≈, Zhg. 100 28.01 N 120.44 E
Ōu ≈, Zhg. 100 28.01 N 120.44 E
Oua ≈ 152 0.43 N 12.55 E
Ouachita ≈ 194 31.38 N 91.49 W
Ouachita, Lake ⊜ ¹ 194 34.40 N 93.25 W
Ouachita Mountains
≈ 194 34.40 N 94.25 W
Ouaco 175f 20.50 S 164.29 E
Ouadâne 152 20.56 N 11.37 W
Ouadda 152 8.04 N 22.24 E
Ouaddaï □ ⁵ 146 13.00 N 21.00 E
Ouadey, Ouadi el ≈ 146 13.34 N 18.03 E
Ouagadougou 150 12.22 N 1.31 W
Ouahigouya 150 13.35 N 2.25 W
Ouahran
— Wahran 148 35.43 N 0.43 W
Ouaka □ ³ 152 6.00 N 21.00 E
Ouaka ≈ 152 4.59 N 19.56 E
Oualâta 152 17.18 N 7.02 W
Oualâta, Dahr ≈ ⁴ 152 17.48 N 7.24 W
Oualé ≈ 150 10.52 N 0.51 E
Oualidia 152 32.44 N 9.08 W
Ouallam 150 14.19 N 2.05 E
Ouanary 250 3.01 N 51.38 W
Ouanda Djallé 146 8.54 N 22.48 E
Ouandago 146 7.10 N 18.42 E
Ouandja ≈ 146 9.35 N 21.43 E
Ouandja-Vakaga,
Réserve de la ♦ ⁴ 146 9.00 N 21.30 E
Ouango 152 4.19 N 22.33 E
Ouangolodougou 150 9.58 N 5.09 W
Ouanino ▲ 50 8.11 N 7.51 W
Ouanne ≈ 50 47.57 N 2.47 E
Ouan Taredert 148 27.33 N 9.32 E
Ouaquaga 210 42.08 N 75.39 W
Ouara ≈ 154 5.05 N 24.26 E
Ouarâne ≈ ¹ 134 21.00 N 10.30 W
Ouararda, Passe de ⋃ 146 21.01 N 13.03 W
Ouareau ≈ 206 45.56 N 73.25 W
Ouareau, Lac ⊜ ¹ 206 46.17 N 74.09 W
Ouargaye 150 11.32 N 0.01 E
Ouarkoye 150 12.05 N 3.40 W
Ouarkziz, Jbel ≈ 148 28.50 N 9.00 W
Ouarsenis, Djebel ▲ 34 36.53 N 1.38 E
Ouarville 50 48.21 N 1.46 E
Ouarzazate 148 30.57 N 6.50 W
Ouarzazate ≈ ⁴ 148 30.55 N 6.45 W
Ouassoulou ≈ 150 11.35 N 8.11 W
Ouatcha 152 13.22 N 9.18 E
Oubangui (Ubangi) ≈ 152 0.30 S 17.42 E
Ouche ≈ 58 47.06 N 5.16 E
Oucques 50 47.49 N 1.18 E
Ōuda 94 34.28 N 135.56 E
Oudaze Lake ⊜ 212 45.27 N 79.11 W
Oud-Beijerland 52 51.49 N 4.25 E
Ouddorp 52 51.48 N 3.56 E
Oude IJssel (Issel) ≈ 52 51.54 N 6.09 E
Oudenaarde 50 50.51 N 3.36 E
Oudenbosch 52 51.35 N 4.31 E
Oudenburg 50 51.11 N 3.00 E
Oude-Pekela 52 53.06 N 6.58 E
Oude Rijn ≈ 52 52.05 N 4.20 E
Oudeschild 52 53.03 N 4.52 E
Oude-Tonge 52 51.40 N 4.13 E
Oudewater 52 52.02 N 4.52 E
Oud-Gastel 52 51.35 N 4.27 E
Oudtja → ⁸
— Oujda 148 34.41 N 1.45 W
Oud-Loosdrecht 52 52.13 N 5.04 E
Oudtshoorn 158 33.35 S 22.14 E
Oudyoumoudi 150 14.04 N 0.28 W
Oued Athmenia 148 36.15 N 6.17 E
Oued Cheham 148 36.23 N 7.46 E
Oued edh Dheheb,
Khlij ≈ 148 23.45 N 15.47 W
Oued Fodda 148 36.11 N 1.32 E
Oued Meliz 148 36.27 N 8.34 E
Oued Rhiou 148 35.58 N 0.55 E
Oued Tielat 148 35.33 N 0.30 W
Oued Zarga 148 36.40 N 9.25 E
Oued-Zem 148 32.55 N 6.33 W
Ouellé 150 7.18 N 4.01 W
Ouémé □ ⁶ 150 7.00 N 2.35 E
Ouémé ≈ 150 6.29 N 2.32 E
Ouen, Île I 175f 22.26 S 166.49 E
Ouenza 148 35.57 N 8.05 E
Ouenza, Djebel ▲ 148 35.57 N 8.05 E
Ouessa 150 11.03 N 2.47 W
Ouessant, Île d'
(Ushant) I 32 48.28 N 5.05 W
Ouest □ ⁵ 152 1.37 N 16.04 E
Ouest → ¹ 150 10.45 N
Ouest, Pointe de l' › 206 49.52 N 64.31 W
Ouest, Rivière de l' ≈ 206 45.39 N 74.21 W
Ouezzane 148 34.52 N 5.35 W
Ouffet 52 50.26 N 5.28 E
Ouganda
— Uganda □ ¹ 154 1.00 N 32.00 E
Ougarou 150 12.05 N 0.56 E
Ougher, Lough ⊜ 48 54.00 N 7.20 W
Oughtbridge 262 53.26 N 1.35 W
Oughterard 48 53.26 N 9.17 W
Ouham □ ⁵ 152 8.30 N 17.30 E
Ouham ≈ 146 9.19 N 18.07 E
Ouham-Pendé □ ⁵ 152 6.30 N 16.30 E
Ouidah 150 6.22 N 2.08 E
Ouimet 190 48.47 N 88.40 W
Ouimet Canyon ⍗ 190 48.47 N 88.40 W
Ouistreham 50 49.17 N 0.15 W
Oujda 148 34.41 N 1.45 W
Oulad Naïl, Monts
≈ 148 34.05 N 2.10 E
Oulangan
kansallispuisto ♦ 24 66.12 N 29.30 E
Oulchy-le-Château 50 49.12 N 3.28 E
Oule ≈ 32 44.25 N 5.21 E
Oulebsir 148 36.00 N 4.53 E
Oulesbocholt 210 42.20 N 75.18 W
Oulle 146 22.20 N 11.04 E
Oullins 58 45.43 N 4.48 E
Oulou, Bahr ≈ 146 9.48 N 21.32 E
Oulton Broad 42 52.28 N 1.43 E
Oulu 24 65.01 N 25.28 E
Oulujärvi ⊜ 24 64.20 N 27.15 E
Oulujoki ≈ 24 65.01 N 25.25 E
Oulun lääni □ ⁴ 24 65.00 N 27.00 E
Oum-Chalouba 146 15.48 N 20.46 E
Oum El Bouaghi 148 35.53 N 7.07 E
Oum er Rbia, Oued
≈ 148 33.19 N 8.20 W
Oum Hadjer 146 13.18 N 19.41 E
Oumiao 150 7.09 N 1.13 W
Oun 102 31.55 N 112.09 E
Ounane, Djebel ▲ 148 24.03 N 11.45 W
Ouanâne, Bîr ⍗ ⁴ 148 21.28 N 3.56 W
Ounasjoki ≈ 24 66.30 N 25.45 W
Ounara 148 31.33 N 9.28 W
Ou=njo 148 35.30 N 8.09 E
Ounianga Kébir 146 19.04 N 20.29 E
Ouolosséougou 150 11.46 N 7.46 W
Our ≈ 56 49.53 N 6.18 E
Oura 175d 26.32 N 128.04 E

Bottom Legend

ESPAÑOL

Nombre	Página	Lat.°′	Long.°′ W = Oeste
Ouray	200	38.01 N	107.40 W
Ouray, Mount ∧	200	38.25 N	106.14 W
Ource ≃	58	48.06 N	4.23 E
Ourcq ≃	50	49.01 N	3.01 E
Ourcq, Canal de l' ≍	50	48.51 N	2.22 E
Ourém	250	1.33 S	47.06 W
Ouri	146	21.34 N	19.13 E
Ouri, Tarso ∧	146	21.25 N	18.56 E
Ouricuri	250	7.53 S	40.05 W
Ourimbah	170	33.22 S	151.23 E
Ourinhos	255	22.59 S	49.52 W
Ourique	34	37.39 N	8.13 W
Ournie	171b	35.56 S	147.51 E
Ouro, Paraná do ≃	248	8.29 S	70.30 W
Ouro, Ponta do ›	158	26.51 S	32.54 E
Ouro Branco	250	6.42 S	36.57 W
Ouro Fino	256	22.17 S	46.22 W
Ouro Preto	255	20.23 S	43.30 W
Ouro Preto ≃	248	11.02 S	65.13 W
Ouroula, Vallée d' V	150	14.42 N	7.00 E
Ours, Grand Lac de l' → Great Bear Lake ⊜	176	66.00 N	120.00 W
Oursi	150	14.41 N	0.27 W
Ourthe ≃	56	50.38 N	5.35 E
Ourthe Occidentale ≃	56	50.08 N	5.41 E
Ourthe Orientale ≃	56	50.08 N	5.41 E
Ourville-en-Caux	50	49.44 N	0.36 E
Ōu-sammyaku ⋏	92	38.45 N	140.50 E
Ouse ≃, On., Can.	212	44.17 N	78.03 W
Ouse ≃, Eng., U.K.	42	50.47 N	0.03 E
Ouse ≃, Eng., U.K.	44	53.42 N	0.41 W
Oust ≃	32	47.39 N	2.06 W
Outaouais, Rivière des → Ottawa ≃	176	45.20 N	73.58 W
Outardes, Baie aux c	186	49.02 N	68.30 W
Outardes, Rivière aux ≃	176	49.04 N	68.28 W
Outardes Est, Rivière aux ≃	206	45.06 N	74.04 W
Outardes Quatre, Réservoir ⊜[1]	186	49.50 N	68.58 W
Outardes Trois, Barrage ◆[6]	186	49.34 N	68.48 W
Outarville	50	48.13 N	2.01 E
Outcalt	276	40.23 N	74.24 W
Outeniekwaberge ⋏	158	33.53 S	22.35 E
Outerbridge Crossing ◆[5]	276	40.31 N	74.15 W
Outer Harbour	168b	34.47 S	138.30 E
Outer Hebrides II	46	57.45 N	7.00 W
Outer Island I	190	47.03 N	90.30 W
Outer Santa Barbara Passage ʊ	228	33.10 N	118.30 W
Outer Sister Island I	166	39.39 S	148.00 E
Outjo	156	20.08 S	16.08 E
Outjo □[5]	156	19.30 S	15.30 E
Outlane	262	53.39 N	1.53 W
Outlet Bay c	208	37.22 N	75.49 W
Outlook, Sk., Can.	184	51.30 N	107.03 W
Outlook, Mt., U.S.	198	48.53 N	104.46 W
Outokumpu	26	62.44 N	29.01 E
Outpost Mountain ∧	180	69.08 N	151.12 W
Outreau	50	50.42 N	1.35 E
Outremont	206	45.31 N	73.38 W
Outside Canal ≍	226	37.13 N	121.02 W
Out Skerries II	46a	60.25 N	0.42 W
Outwell	42	52.37 N	0.14 E
Ouvéa I	175f	20.30 S	166.35 E
Ouvéa, Lagon d' c	175f	20.33 S	166.27 E
Ouvèze ≃	62	43.59 N	4.51 E
Ouvidor	255	18.14 S	47.50 W
Ouye, Forêt de l' ♠	261	48.32 N	2.00 E
Ouyen	166	35.04 S	142.20 E
Ouzinkie	180	57.55 N	152.30 W
Ouzouer-le-Marché	50	47.55 N	1.32 E
Ouzouer-sur-Loire	50	47.46 N	2.29 E
Ouzzal, Oued i-n- V	148	21.35 N	2.00 E
Ovabag	130	37.43 N	39.59 E
Ovacık, Tür.	130	39.22 N	39.13 E
Ovacık, Tür.	130	41.05 N	32.55 E
Ovada	62	44.38 N	8.38 E
Ovakent	130	38.06 N	28.02 E
Oval	210	41.09 N	77.11 W
Ovalau I	175g	17.40 S	178.48 E
Ovalle	252	30.36 S	71.12 W
Ovamboland □[9]	156	17.45 S	16.30 E
Ovana, Cerro ∧	246	4.38 N	66.57 W
Ovar	34	40.52 N	8.38 W
Ovaro	64	46.29 N	12.52 E
Ovčinino	82	56.02 N	39.03 E
Ovcyno	265a	59.48 N	30.37 E
Övedskloster	41	55.41 N	13.38 E
Ovejas	246	9.32 N	75.14 W
Ovelgönne	52	53.20 N	8.25 E
Ovenden	262	53.44 N	1.53 W
Oveng	152	2.25 N	12.16 E
Overath	56	50.55 N	7.14 E
Overberge	263	51.37 N	7.41 E
Overbrook	198	38.46 N	95.33 W
Overbrook ◆[8], Pa., U.S.	279b	40.24 N	79.59 W
Overbrook ◆[8], Pa., U.S.	285	39.58 N	75.16 W
Overdinkel	52	52.14 N	7.01 E
Overflakkee I	52	51.45 N	4.10 E
Overflowing ≃	184	53.10 N	101.05 W
Overhalla	24	64.30 N	11.57 E
Overijse	56	50.46 N	4.32 E
Overijssel □[4]	52	52.25 N	6.30 E
Over Jerstal	41	55.12 N	9.18 E
Överkalix	24	66.21 N	22.56 E
Overland	219	38.42 N	90.21 W
Overland Park	198	38.58 N	94.40 W
Overlea	208	39.22 N	76.31 W
Overloon	52	51.35 N	5.57 E
Övermark (Ylimarkku)	26	62.38 N	21.30 E
Overpeck Creek ≃	276	40.51 N	74.02 W
Overpelt	56	51.13 N	5.25 E
Overseal	42	52.44 N	1.34 W
Overstrand	42	52.56 N	1.20 E
Overton, Eng., U.K.	42	51.15 N	1.15 W
Overton, Ne., U.S.	198	40.44 N	99.32 W
Overton, Nv., U.S.	204	36.32 N	114.26 W
Overton, Tx., U.S.	222	32.16 N	94.58 W
Overton Arm c	204	36.20 N	114.25 W
Övertorneå	24	66.23 N	23.40 E
Överum	26	57.59 N	16.19 E
Over Wallop	42	51.09 N	1.35 W
Ovett	194	31.29 N	89.01 W
Ovid, Mi., U.S.	216	43.00 N	84.22 W
Ovid, N.Y., U.S.	210	42.40 N	76.49 W
Ovidiopol'	78	46.17 N	30.27 E
Oviedo, Esp.	34	43.22 N	5.50 W
Oviedo, Fl., U.S.	220	28.40 N	81.13 W
Oviglio	62	44.52 N	8.29 E
Oviken	26	62.59 N	14.24 E
Oviksfjällen ⋏	26	63.02 N	13.51 E
Ovilla	222	32.32 N	96.53 W
Ovindoli	66	42.08 N	13.31 E
Ovinišče	76	58.22 N	37.02 E
Ovino	76	59.41 N	33.11 E
Ovīši	76	57.34 N	21.45 E
Övörchangaj □[4]	102	46.00 N	102.30 E
Øvre Anarjokka Nasjonalpark ♠	24	69.00 N	25.00 E
Øvre Årdal	26	61.19 N	7.48 E
Øvre Dividal Nasjonalpark ♠	24	68.39 N	19.45 E
Øvre Pasvik Nasjonalpark ♠	24	69.06 N	28.55 E
Øvre Rendal	26	61.53 N	11.05 E
Övre Vättern ⊜	40	59.52 N	15.40 E
Ovruč	78	51.21 N	28.49 E
Ovs'anikovo	76	60.09 N	45.16 E
Ovs'anka, Ross.	86	55.57 N	92.33 E
Ovs'anka, Ross.	89	53.35 N	126.57 E
Ovs'annikovo	82	56.54 N	37.33 E

FRANÇAIS

Nom	Page	Lat.°′	Long.°′ W = Ouest
Ovstug	76	53.24 N	33.52 E
Ōwada	268	35.49 N	139.33 E
Owaka	172	46.27 S	169.40 E
Owambo □[5]	156	18.00 S	16.00 E
Owambo ≃	156	18.45 S	17.03 E
Owando	152	0.29 S	15.55 E
Owaneco	219	39.29 N	89.12 W
Owariashi	94	35.12 N	137.02 E
Owasco	210	42.51 N	76.28 W
Owasco Inlet ≃	210	42.45 N	76.28 W
Owasco Lake ⊜	210	42.52 N	76.32 W
Owasco Outlet ≃	210	43.04 N	76.39 W
Owase	92	34.04 N	136.12 E
Owasso	196	36.16 N	95.51 W
Owatonna	190	44.05 N	93.13 W
Owbeh	128	34.22 N	63.10 E
Owe	272c	19.04 N	73.04 E
Owego	210	42.06 N	76.15 W
Owego Creek, East Branch ≃	210	42.10 N	76.15 W
Owego Creek, West Branch ≃	210	42.10 N	76.15 W
Owel, Lough ⊜	48	53.34 N	7.25 W
Owen, Austl.	168b	34.16 S	138.33 E
Owen, Dtsch.	56	48.35 N	9.27 E
Owen, In., U.S.	218	38.27 N	85.34 W
Owen, Wi., U.S.	190	44.57 N	90.33 W
Owen □[6]	218	38.33 N	84.49 W
Owen, Mount ∧	172	41.33 S	172.32 E
Owenboy ≃	48	51.48 N	8.18 W
Owendo	152	0.17 N	9.30 E
Owenea ≃	48	54.47 N	8.26 W
Owen Falls Dam ◆[6]	154	0.27 N	33.11 E
Owen Fracture Zone ✢	12	12.00 N	58.00 E
Owenkillew ≃	48	54.44 N	7.18 W
Owenmore ≃	48	54.07 N	9.50 W
Owen River	172	41.39 S	172.27 E
Owens ≃	204	36.31 N	117.57 W
Owensboro	194	37.46 N	87.06 W
Owens Creek ≃, Ca., U.S.	226	37.13 N	120.42 W
Owens Creek ≃, Md., U.S.	208	39.33 N	77.20 W
Owens Lake ⊜	204	36.25 N	117.56 W
Owen Sound	212	44.34 N	80.56 W
Owen Sound c	212	44.40 N	80.55 W
Owen Stanley Range ⋏	164	9.20 S	147.55 E
Owensville, In., U.S.	194	38.16 N	87.41 W
Owensville, Mo., U.S.	219	38.20 N	91.30 W
Owensville, Oh., U.S.	218	39.07 N	84.08 W
Owenton, Ky., U.S.	218	38.32 N	84.50 W
Owenton, Va., U.S.	208	37.53 N	77.06 W
Owentown	222	32.26 N	95.12 W
Owerri	150	5.29 N	7.02 E
Owhango	172	39.00 S	175.23 E
Owikeno Lake ⊜	182	51.41 N	127.00 W
Owings	208	38.43 N	76.36 W
Owings Mills	284b	39.25 N	76.46 W
Owingsville	188	38.08 N	83.45 W
Owl ≃, Ab., Can.	182	54.54 N	111.57 W
Owl ≃, Mb., Can.	176	57.51 N	92.44 W
Owl Creek ≃, U.S.	198	44.41 N	103.29 W
Owl Creek ≃, Mt., U.S.	202	45.18 N	107.21 W
Owl Creek ≃, Wy., U.S.	202	43.41 N	108.11 W
Owl Creek, South Fork ≃	202	43.43 N	108.32 W
Owl Creek Mountains ⋏	202	43.30 N	108.35 W
Owo	150	7.15 N	5.37 E
Oworonsoki	273a	6.33 N	3.24 E
Owosso	216	42.59 N	84.10 W
Owuru ≃	273a	6.39 N	3.27 E
Owyhee	204	41.56 N	116.05 W
Owyhee ≃	202	43.46 N	117.02 W
Owyhee, Lake ⊜[1]	202	43.28 N	117.20 W
Owyhee, South Fork ≃	202	42.26 N	116.53 W
Oxapampa	248	10.34 S	75.24 W
Öxarfjörður c	24a	66.15 N	16.45 W
Oxbow, Sk., Can.	184	49.14 N	102.11 W
Oxbow, Mi., U.S.	281	42.38 N	83.28 W
Oxbow, N.Y., U.S.	212	44.17 N	75.37 W
Oxbow Lake ⊜	281	42.38 N	83.28 W
Ox Creek ≃	198	48.37 N	100.17 W
Oxelösund	40	58.40 N	17.06 E
Oxford, N.S., Can.	186	45.44 N	63.52 W
Oxford, N.Z.	172	43.18 S	172.11 E
Oxford, Eng., U.K.	42	51.46 N	1.15 W
Oxford, Al., U.S.	194	33.36 N	85.50 W
Oxford, Ct., U.S.	207	41.26 N	73.07 W
Oxford, Fl., U.S.	220	28.55 N	82.02 W
Oxford, In., U.S.	216	40.31 N	87.14 W
Oxford, Ia., U.S.	190	41.43 N	91.47 W
Oxford, Ks., U.S.	198	37.16 N	97.10 W
Oxford, Ky., U.S.	218	38.16 N	84.30 W
Oxford, Me., U.S.	188	44.07 N	70.29 W
Oxford, Md., U.S.	208	38.41 N	76.10 W
Oxford, Ma., U.S.	207	42.07 N	71.51 W
Oxford, Mi., U.S.	216	42.49 N	83.15 W
Oxford, Ms., U.S.	194	34.21 N	89.31 W
Oxford, Ne., U.S.	198	40.15 N	99.38 W
Oxford, N.J., U.S.	210	40.48 N	74.59 W
Oxford, N.Y., U.S.	210	42.26 N	75.35 W
Oxford, N.C., U.S.	192	36.18 N	78.35 W
Oxford, Oh., U.S.	218	39.30 N	84.44 W
Oxford, Pa., U.S.	208	39.47 N	75.58 W
Oxford, Wi., U.S.	190	43.46 N	89.34 W
Oxford □[6]	212	43.08 N	80.50 W
Oxford Falls	274a	33.44 S	151.15 E
Oxford House	184	54.56 N	95.16 W
Oxford House Indian Reserve ◆[4]	184	54.54 N	95.15 W
Oxford Junction	190	41.59 N	90.57 W
Oxford Lake ⊜	184	54.51 N	95.37 W
Oxford Peak ∧	202	42.16 N	112.06 W
Oxfordshire □[6]	42	51.50 N	1.15 W
Oxford Valley Mall ◆[9]	285	40.11 N	74.53 W
Oxhey	260	51.39 N	0.23 W
Oxie	41	55.33 N	13.04 E
Oxkutzcab	232	20.18 N	89.25 W
Oxley	166	34.12 S	144.06 E
Oxley Creek ≃	171a	27.32 S	153.00 E
Oxnard	228	34.11 N	119.10 W
Oxnard Beach	228	34.09 N	119.13 W
Oxon Hill	284c	38.48 N	76.59 W
Oxon Run ≃	284b	38.49 N	77.00 W
Ox Pasture Brook ≃	283	42.45 N	70.54 W
Oxshott	260	51.20 N	0.21 W
Oxted	42	51.16 N	0.01 W
Oxtongue ≃	212	45.19 N	79.01 W
Oxtongue Lake ⊜	212	45.22 N	78.55 W
Oxus → Amu Darya ≃	72	43.40 N	59.01 E
Oy	58	47.38 N	10.28 E
Oya, Malay.	112	2.52 N	111.53 E
Ōya, Nihon	96	35.20 N	134.40 E
Oya ≃	112	2.52 N	111.52 E
Oyabe	94	36.40 N	136.52 E
Oyabe ≃	94	36.48 N	137.04 E
Ōya-ji ʋ[1]	94	36.38 N	139.48 E
Ōyake-yama ∧[2]	270	34.48 N	135.51 E
Oyalı	130	37.14 N	41.45 E
Oyama, B.C., Can.	182	50.07 N	119.22 W
Oyama, Nihon	94	35.21 N	139.00 E
Oyama, Nihon	94	36.18 N	139.48 E
Ōyama, Nihon	94	36.36 N	137.18 E
Oyama, Nihon	268	35.36 N	139.22 E
Ōyamada	94	34.46 N	136.13 E
Ōyamazaki	270	34.54 N	135.42 E
Oyameyo, Volcán ∧[1]	286a	19.10 N	99.11 W
Oyan	152	0.02 N	10.17 E
Ōyano	92	32.35 N	130.26 E
Oyapock (Oiapoque) ≃	250	4.08 N	51.40 W
Oyashirazu ♠	94	36.59 N	137.40 E

PORTUGUÊS

Nome	Página	Lat.°′	Long.°′ W = Oeste
Oybin	54	50.50 N	14.44 E
Oye-et-Pallet	58	46.51 N	6.20 E
Oyem	152	1.37 N	11.35 E
Oyen	184	51.22 N	110.28 W
Øyeren ⊜	26	59.48 N	11.14 E
Oykel ≃	46	57.56 N	4.25 W
Oykel Bridge	46	57.58 N	4.43 W
Oymyakon → Ojm'akon	74	63.28 N	142.49 E
Oyo, Congo	152	0.01 N	15.54 E
Oyo, Nig.	150	7.51 N	3.56 E
Oyo □[3]	150	8.00 N	3.50 E
Oyo ≃	115a	7.57 S	110.22 E
Ōyodo	96	34.23 N	135.48 E
Ōyodo ◆[8]	270	34.43 N	135.30 E
Ōyodo ≃	92	31.53 N	131.28 E
Oyón	248	10.39 S	76.47 W
Oyonnax	58	46.15 N	5.40 E
Ōyorogi-san ∧	96	35.05 N	132.51 E
Oyotún	248	6.51 S	79.19 W
Oyster	208	37.17 N	75.55 W
Oyster Bay	210	40.51 N	73.31 W
Oyster Bay c	276	40.55 N	73.30 W
Oyster Bay Cove	276	40.52 N	73.31 W
Oyster Bay Harbor c	276	40.53 N	73.32 W
Oyster Creek	222	29.00 N	95.20 W
Oyster Creek ≃	222	28.59 N	95.18 W
Oyster Point ∧	282	37.50 N	121.52 W
Oyster Point ›	168b	34.55 S	137.48 E
Oyster Rock I[2]	272c	18.54 N	72.50 E
Oysterville	224	46.33 N	124.02 W
Øystese	26	60.23 N	6.13 E
Oyten	52	53.04 N	9.01 E
Ozaki	268	35.59 N	139.51 E
Ozamiz	116	8.08 N	123.50 E
Ozanne ≃	50	48.11 N	1.22 E
Ozariči	76	52.28 N	29.16 E
Ozark, Al., U.S.	194	31.27 N	85.38 W
Ozark, Ar., U.S.	194	35.29 N	93.49 W
Ozark, Mo., U.S.	194	37.01 N	93.12 W
Ozark National Scenic Riverways ♠	194	37.10 N	91.10 W
Ozark Plateau ⋏[1]	194	37.00 N	93.00 W
Ozark Reservoir ⊜[1]	194	35.35 N	94.00 W
Ozarks, Lake of the ⊜[1]	194	38.10 N	92.50 W
Ozaukee □[6]	216	44.14 N	88.00 W
Ózd	30	48.14 N	20.18 E
Ozd'atiči	76	54.06 N	28.50 E
Oze ≃	96	34.12 N	132.14 E
Ozeblin ∧	36	44.35 N	15.53 E
Ozek	86	46.35 N	60.41 E
Ozereckoje	82	56.04 N	37.23 E
Oželelje	82	54.48 N	38.17 E
Oželelki	82	55.51 N	38.52 E
Ozerišče	76	54.48 N	33.13 E
Ozerki, Ross	80	51.13 N	53.56 E
Ozerki, Ross	80	51.32 N	45.16 E
Ozerki, Ross	80	52.01 N	45.29 E
Ozerki, Ross	86	53.38 N	83.44 E
Ozerki, Ross	265a	59.54 N	30.44 E
Ozerna ≃	82	55.44 N	36.08 E
Ozerninskoje vodochranilišče ⊜[1]	82	55.45 N	36.15 E
Ozernoje	78	50.11 N	28.42 E
Ozernovskij	74	51.30 N	156.31 E
Ozernyj	180	66.24 N	179.06 W
Ozero	80	56.58 N	44.43 E
Ozery	82	54.51 N	38.34 E
Ozette Lake ⊜	224	48.06 N	124.38 W
Ozgoryš	85	41.15 N	74.45 E
Ozieri	71	40.35 N	9.00 E
Ozimek	30	50.41 N	18.13 E
Ozinki	80	51.12 N	49.45 E
Ožogino, ozero ⊜	74	69.16 N	146.36 E
Ozoir-la-Ferrière	261	48.46 N	2.40 E
Ozona, Fl., U.S.	220	28.04 N	82.46 W
Ozona, Tx., U.S.	196	30.42 N	101.12 W
Ozone Park ◆[8]	276	40.40 N	73.51 W
Ozorków	30	51.58 N	19.19 E
Oz'ornaja, Kaz.	86	53.25 N	63.15 E
Oz'ornaja, Ross.	86	51.08 N	60.50 E
Oz'ornoje, Ross.	80	51.41 N	44.55 E
Oz'ornoje, Ross.	80	51.46 N	51.28 E
Oz'ornoje, Ross.	86	56.48 N	71.15 E
Oz'ornyj	80	57.10 N	40.59 E
Oz'orsk, Ross.	76	54.25 N	22.01 E
Oz'orsk, Ukr.	78	51.43 N	26.24 E
Oz'orskij	89	46.36 N	143.08 E
Oz'ory	76	53.43 N	24.11 E
Ozouer-le-Voulgis	261	48.40 N	2.47 E
Özpınar	130	37.57 N	42.16 E
Ōzu, Nihon	92	32.52 N	130.52 E
Ōzu, Nihon	96	33.30 N	132.33 E
Ozubulu	150	5.57 N	6.51 E
Ozuluama	234	21.40 N	97.51 W
Ozumba	234	19.03 N	98.48 W
Ozurgeti	84	41.56 N	42.00 E

P

Pâ	150	11.33 N	3.15 W
Paagoumène	175f	20.29 S	164.11 E
Paal	56	51.02 N	5.11 E
Paama □[8]	175f	16.28 S	168.18 E
Paama I	175f	16.28 S	168.14 E
Paar ≃	60	48.45 N	11.33 E
Paardekraal Monument ⊥	273d	26.06 S	27.47 E
Paaren	264a	52.39 N	12.59 E
Paarl	158	33.45 S	18.56 E
Paasbach ≃	263	51.25 N	7.11 E
Paauilo	229d	20.02 N	155.22 W
Pabarabuk	164	6.05 S	144.05 E
Pabbay I, Scot., U.K.	46	56.51 N	7.35 W
Pabbay I, Scot., U.K.	46	57.46 N	7.15 W
Pabbi	123	34.01 N	71.47 E
Pabbiring, Kepulauan II	112	4.55 S	119.25 E
Pabean	112	6.50 S	115.19 E
Pabellón, Punta ›	254	43.14 S	74.23 W
Pabellón de Arteaga	234	22.10 N	102.21 W
Pabellones, Ensenada c	232	24.27 N	107.36 W
Pabianice	30	51.40 N	19.22 E
Pabillonis	71	39.35 N	8.43 E
Pablo	202	47.36 N	114.07 W
Pābna	124	24.00 N	89.15 E
Pabo	154	3.00 N	32.09 E
Pabradė	76	54.59 N	25.44 E
Paca	115b	8.29 S	120.11 E
Pacaás Novas, Parque Nacional ♠	248	11.10 S	63.30 W
Pacaás Novos ≃	248	10.51 S	65.20 W
Pacaás Novos, Serra dos ⋏	248	10.45 S	64.15 W
Pacaembu	255	21.34 S	51.17 W
Pacaembú, Estádio do ♠	287b	23.33 S	46.39 W
Pacajá ≃	250	1.56 S	50.50 W
Pacajus	250	4.10 S	38.28 W
Pacaltsdorp	158	34.00 S	22.28 E
Pacaraima, Sierra de → Pakaraima Mountains ⋏	246	5.30 N	60.40 W
Pacarán	248	12.52 S	76.03 W
Pacaraos	248	11.11 S	76.44 W
Pacasmayo	248	7.24 S	79.34 W
Pacatuba	250	3.58 S	38.37 W
Pace, Fl., U.S	194	30.35 N	87.09 W
Pace, Ms., U.S.	194	33.47 N	90.51 W
Paceco	70	37.59 N	12.33 E
Pačelma, Ross.	80	53.15 N	43.21 E
Pačelma, Ross.	80	53.20 N	43.20 E
Pacet	115a	6.45 S	107.03 E
Pachača	74	60.34 N	169.03 E
Pachacamac ⊥	248	12.14 S	76.52 W

Pachamba	126	24.12 N	86.16 E
Pachaug Pond ⊜	207	41.34 N	71.54 W
Pacheco	226	37.59 N	122.04 W
Pacheco, Isla I	254	52.17 S	74.45 W
Pacheco Creek ≃	226	36.58 N	121.28 W
Pacheco Pass)(	226	37.03 N	121.13 W
Pāchh Elāsin	126	24.08 N	89.54 E
Pachino	70	36.43 N	15.05 E
Pachitea ≃	248	8.46 S	74.32 W
Pachiza	248	7.16 S	76.46 W
Pachkoli ◆[8]	272c	19.08 N	72.54 E
Pachmarhi	124	22.28 N	78.26 E
Pacho	246	5.08 N	74.10 W
Pachomovo	82	54.38 N	37.33 E
Pachor	124	23.42 N	76.44 E
Pāchora	122	20.40 N	75.21 E
Pachotnyj Ugol	80	52.58 N	41.56 E
Pachra ≃	82	55.32 N	37.59 E
Pachtaabad	85	38.28 N	68.10 E
Pachuca [de Soto]	234	20.07 N	98.44 W
Paciência ◆[8]	256	22.55 S	43.38 W
Pacific, B.C., Can.	182	54.46 N	128.17 W
Pacific, Mo., U.S.	219	38.28 N	90.44 W
Pacific, Wa., U.S.	224	47.15 N	122.14 W
Pacific □[6]	224	46.30 N	123.39 W
Pacifica	226	37.37 N	122.29 W
Pacific-Antarctic Ridge ✢[3]	6	62.00 S	157.00 W
Pacific Beach	224	47.12 N	124.12 W
Pacific City	224	45.12 N	123.57 W
Pacific Creek ≃	200	42.08 N	109.24 W
Pacific Gardens	226	37.58 N	121.20 W
Pacific Grove	226	36.38 N	121.56 W
Pacific Islands, Trust Territory of the → Palau □[2]	14	5.00 N	137.00 E
Pacific Missile Test Center ■	228	34.07 N	119.07 W
Pacífico, Océano → Pacific Ocean ⫪[1]	6	10.00 S	150.00 W
Pacific Ocean ⫪[1]	4	10.00 S	150.00 W
Pacific Ocean ⫪[1]	6	10.00 S	150.00 W
Pacifico Mountain ∧	228	34.23 N	118.02 W
Pacific Palisades ◆[8]	280	34.03 N	118.32 W
Pacific Ranges ⋏	182	50.45 N	125.30 W
Pacific Rim National Park ♠	182	48.45 N	125.40 W
Pacifique, Océan → Pacific Ocean ⫪[1]	6	10.00 S	150.00 W
Pacijan Island I	116	10.39 N	124.20 E
Pacinan, Tanjung ›	115a	7.36 S	114.02 E
Paciran	115a	6.52 S	112.20 E
Pacitan	115a	8.12 S	111.07 E
Pack	61	46.58 N	14.59 E
Packanack Lake ⊜	276	40.56 N	74.15 W
Packard Mountain ∧[2]	207	42.28 N	72.21 W
Páckevei-Duna ≃[1]	264c	47.19 N	19.02 E
Pack Monadnock Mountain ∧	207	42.52 N	71.52 W
Packsattel)(	61	46.58 N	14.58 E
Packwood	224	46.36 N	121.40 W
Packwood Lake ⊜	224	46.35 N	121.34 W
Pacllón	248	10.18 S	77.07 W
Pacock Brook ≃	276	41.05 N	74.31 W
Paço de Arcos	266c	38.42 N	9.17 W
Paço do Lumiar	250	2.31 S	44.07 W
Pacohuaras ≃	248	10.04 S	65.46 W
Pacoima ◆[8]	280	34.16 N	118.26 W
Pacolet ≃	192	34.50 N	81.27 W
Pacolet Mills	192	34.55 N	81.44 W
Pacora	246	9.05 N	79.17 W
Pacov	30	49.28 N	15.00 E
Pacquet	186	49.59 N	55.53 W
Pacuare ≃	236	10.14 N	83.17 W
Pacuí ≃	255	16.46 S	45.01 W
Pacuneiro ≃	255	13.02 S	53.25 W
Pacy-sur-Eure	50	49.01 N	1.23 E
Paczkow	30	50.27 N	17.00 E
Padada	116	6.42 N	125.22 E
Padada ≃	116	6.42 N	125.23 E
Padaido, Kepulauan II	164	1.15 S	136.30 E
Padam	123	33.28 N	76.53 E
Padamarang, Pulau I	112	4.07 S	121.24 E
Padamo ≃	246	2.54 N	65.17 W
Padampur	120	20.59 N	83.04 E
Padang, Indon.	112	1.39 S	108.55 E
Padang, Indon.	112	2.59 N	105.40 E
Padang, Indon.	112	6.11 S	120.26 E
Padang, Indon.	112	0.57 S	100.21 E
Padang, Pulau I	114	1.10 N	102.20 E
Padang Besar	114	6.40 N	100.19 E
Padangbetuah	112	3.39 S	102.13 E
Padang Endau	114	2.40 N	103.37 E
Padangpanjang	112	0.27 S	100.25 E
Padangsidempuan	114	1.22 N	99.16 E
Padangtiji	114	5.22 N	95.50 E
Padangtikar, Pulau I	112	0.50 S	109.30 E
Padang Tungku	114	4.14 N	101.59 E
Padany	24	63.17 N	33.22 E
Padas	115a	7.25 S	111.32 E
Padas ≃	112	5.14 N	115.34 E
Padasjoki	26	61.21 N	25.17 E
Padauari ≃	246	0.15 S	64.05 W
Padborg	41	54.49 N	9.22 E
Padcaya	248	21.52 S	64.48 W
Paddington ◆[8]	260	51.31 N	0.10 W
Paddington Station ◆[5]	260	51.31 N	0.11 W
Paddle ≃	182	54.05 N	114.15 W
Paddle Prairie	176	57.57 N	117.29 W
Paddock Lake	216	42.34 N	88.06 W
Paddock Wood	42	51.11 N	0.23 E
Padea	38	44.01 N	23.52 E
Padea-besar I	112	3.30 S	123.05 E
Padeghar	272c	18.58 N	73.03 E
Paden City	188	39.36 N	80.56 W
Paderborn	52	51.43 N	8.45 E
Paderno Dugnano	266b	45.34 N	9.10 E
Paderno Ponchielli	64	45.14 N	9.55 E
Padghe	272c	19.03 N	73.07 E
Padibe	154	3.28 N	32.50 E
Padiham	44	53.49 N	2.19 W
Padilla	248	19.19 S	64.20 W
Padilla Bay c	224	48.35 N	122.32 W
Padjelanta Nationalpark ♠	24	67.28 N	16.41 E
Padle	272c	19.09 N	73.03 E
Padloping Island I	176	67.07 N	62.35 W
Padma → Ganges ≃	124	23.22 N	90.32 E
Padola	64	46.36 N	12.28 E
Padoue → Padova	64	45.25 N	11.53 E
Padova	64	45.25 N	11.53 E
Padova □[4]	64	45.21 N	11.49 E
Padovka	80	52.28 N	49.31 E
Pādra	120	22.14 N	73.05 E
Padrão, Ponta do ›	152	6.03 S	12.18 E
Padrauna	124	26.55 N	83.59 E
Padre Bernardo	255	15.21 S	48.30 W
Padre Brito	256	21.18 S	43.59 W
Padre Burgos	116	10.02 N	125.01 E
Padre Island I	196	27.00 N	97.15 W
Padre Island National Seashore ♠	196	27.00 N	97.25 W
Padre Miguel ◆[8]	287a	22.53 S	43.26 W
Padre Paraíso	255	17.06 S	41.31 W
Padria	71	40.24 N	8.38 E
Padrón	34	42.44 N	8.40 W
Padrone, Cape ›	158	33.46 S	26.30 E
Padrt'	60	49.40 N	13.46 E
Padstow, Austl.	274a	33.57 S	151.02 E
Padstow, Eng., U.K.	42	50.33 N	4.56 W
Padua → Padova	64	45.25 N	11.53 E
Paducah, Ky., U.S.	194	37.05 N	88.36 W
Paducah, Tx., U.S.	196	34.00 N	100.18 W
Padula	68	40.20 N	15.39 E

Paduli	68	41.10 N	14.53 E
Padunskaja	86	55.02 N	85.02 E
Paea	174s	17.41 S	149.35 W
Paedun	98	35.03 N	128.21 E
Paekakariki	172	40.59 S	174.57 E
Paektu-san ∧	98	42.00 N	128.03 E
Paengaroa	172	37.49 S	176.25 E
Paengnyŏng-do I	98	37.57 N	124.40 E
Paerdegat Basin c	276	40.37 N	73.54 W
Paeroa	172	37.23 S	175.40 E
Paesana	62	44.41 N	7.16 E
Paese	64	45.40 N	12.10 E
Paestum ⊥	68	40.25 N	15.00 E
Paete	116	14.23 N	121.29 E
Páez ≃	246	2.28 N	75.34 W
Pafúri	156	22.27 S	31.21 E
Pag	36	44.27 N	15.04 E
Pag, Otok I	36	44.30 N	15.00 E
Paga	150	10.58 N	1.06 W
Pagadenbaru	115a	6.28 S	107.48 E
Pagadian	116	7.49 N	123.25 E
Pagadian Bay c	116	7.48 N	123.31 E
Pagai Selatan, Pulau I	112	3.00 S	100.20 E
Pagai Utara, Pulau I	112	2.42 S	100.07 E
Pagalungan	116	7.04 N	124.41 E
Pagan	110	21.10 N	94.51 E
Pagan I	108	18.07 N	145.46 E
Pagancillo	252	29.34 S	68.03 W
Paganella ∧	64	46.08 N	11.02 E
Pagani	68	40.45 N	14.37 E
Paganica	66	42.21 N	13.28 E
Paganico	66	42.56 N	11.16 E
Pagaralam	112	4.01 S	103.16 E
Pagasitikós Kólpos c	38	39.15 N	22.51 E
Pagatan	112	3.36 S	115.56 E
Pagato ≃	184	55.49 N	102.05 W
Pagato Lake ⊜	184	56.08 N	102.30 W
Pagbilao	116	13.58 N	121.41 E
Pagbilao Grande Island I	116	13.55 N	121.46 E
Pagdanan Bay c	116	10.31 N	119.15 E
Page, Az., U.S.	200	36.54 N	111.28 W
Page, N.D., U.S.	198	47.09 N	97.34 W
Page Field ⊠	220	26.35 N	81.52 W
Pagėgiai	76	55.09 N	21.54 E
Pageland	192	34.46 N	80.23 W
Page Manor	218	39.45 N	84.06 W
Pager ≃	154	3.09 N	32.30 E
Pagerdewa	112	3.46 S	105.18 E
Paget, Mount ∧	244	54.26 S	36.33 W
Paghmān	120	34.36 N	68.57 E
Paglia ≃	66	42.42 N	12.11 E
Pagliara	70	37.59 N	15.22 E
Paglieta	66	42.10 N	14.30 E
Pagliete, Bonifica delle ◆[1]	267a	41.53 N	12.12 E
Pagny-sur-Moselle	56	48.59 N	6.01 E
Pago Bay c	174p	13.25 N	144.48 E
Pagoda Peak ∧	200	40.10 N	107.20 W
Pagoda Point ›	110	15.57 N	94.15 E
Pagon, Bukit ∧	112	4.18 N	115.19 E
Pago Pago	174u	14.16 S	170.42 W
Pago Pago Harbor c	174u	14.17 S	170.40 W
Pago Pago International Airport ⊠	174u	14.20 S	170.43 W
Pagosa Springs	200	37.16 N	107.00 W
Pagote	272c	18.54 N	72.59 E
Pagouda	150	9.45 N	1.19 E
Pagri	124	27.44 N	89.09 E
Pagsangahan	116	13.13 N	122.33 E
Pagsanjan	116	14.15 N	121.25 E
Paguate	200	35.08 N	107.22 W
Pagudpud	116	18.34 N	120.47 E
Pagueras, Torrente de ≃	266d	41.28 N	1.58 E
Paguyaman ≃	112	0.31 N	122.38 E
Pagwi	164	4.03 S	143.02 E
Pah	84	39.08 N	39.40 E
Pahādi ◆[8]	272c	19.10 N	72.51 E
Pahala	229d	19.12 N	155.28 W
Pahalgam	123	34.02 N	75.20 E
Pahang □[3]	114	3.30 N	102.45 E
Pahang ≃	114	3.32 N	103.28 E
Páhara, Laguna c	236	14.18 N	83.15 W
Pahāsu	124	28.11 N	78.03 E
Pahau Point ›	229b	21.49 N	160.15 W
Pahi	114	5.28 N	102.13 E
Pahia Point ›	172	46.19 S	167.41 E
Pahiatua	172	40.27 S	175.50 E
Pahlād Garhi	272a	28.40 N	77.21 E
Pahlavī → Bandar-e Anzalī	128	37.28 N	49.27 E
Pahoa	229d	19.29 N	154.57 W
Pahokee	220	26.49 N	80.39 W
Pahrump	204	36.12 N	115.58 W
Pahsimeroi ≃	202	44.41 N	114.03 W
Pahuatlán de Valle	234	20.17 N	98.09 W
Pahvant Range ⋏	200	38.45 N	112.15 W
Pai	110	19.19 N	98.27 E
Pai ≃	110	19.09 N	97.33 E
Pai, Ilha do I	287a	22.59 S	43.05 W
Paia	229a	20.54 N	156.22 W
Paianía	267c	37.57 N	23.51 E
Paicines	226	36.44 N	121.17 W
Paico	248	14.02 S	73.39 W
Paide	76	58.54 N	25.33 E
Paidorzu, Monte ∧	71	40.30 N	9.05 E
Paifangchang	107	30.31 N	106.38 E
Paige	222	30.13 N	97.07 W
Paignton	42	50.26 N	3.34 W
Paiguano	252	30.01 S	70.32 W
Paihia	172	35.17 S	174.05 E
Paiho	100	23.21 N	120.25 E
Paiján	248	7.44 S	79.19 W
Päijänne ⊜	26	61.35 N	25.30 E
Pāikgācha	126	22.35 N	89.20 E
Paikü Co ⊜	124	28.48 N	85.36 E
Pail	123	32.38 N	72.27 E
Paila ≃	248	16.02 S	64.12 W
Paila, Sierra la ⋏	196	25.50 N	101.30 W
Pailin	110	12.51 N	102.36 E
Pailitas	246	8.58 N	73.38 W
Paillaco	254	40.04 S	72.53 W
Pailolo Channel ʊ	229a	21.05 N	156.42 W
Pailoutou	106	30.56 N	121.16 E
Pailoutun	104	40.44 N	122.49 E
Paimboeuf	32	47.17 N	2.02 W
Paimio	26	60.27 N	22.42 E
Paimpol	32	48.46 N	3.03 W
Painan	112	1.21 S	100.34 E
Paincourt	214	42.23 N	82.17 W
Painesdale	190	47.02 N	88.40 W
Painesville	214	41.43 N	81.14 W
Painscastle	42	52.07 N	3.12 W
Painshawfield	44	54.56 N	1.54 W
Painswick	42	51.48 N	2.11 W
Paint ≃	190	45.58 N	88.15 W
Paint Creek ≃, Mi., U.S.	281	42.06 N	83.36 W
Paint Creek ≃, Oh., U.S.	218	39.13 N	82.56 W
Paint Creek ≃, Pa., U.S.	214	41.10 N	79.28 W
Paint Creek ≃, Tx., U.S.	196	30.13 N	99.54 W
Paint Creek, East Fork ≃	218	39.32 N	83.25 W
Paint Creek, North Fork ≃	218	39.13 N	83.02 W
Paint Creek Lake ⊜[1]	218	39.15 N	83.22 W
Painted Desert ◆[2]	200	36.00 N	111.20 W
Painted Post	210	42.09 N	77.05 W
Painted Rock Reservoir ⊜[1]	200	33.00 N	112.50 W
Painten	60	49.00 N	11.49 E
Painter	208	37.35 N	75.47 W
Painter Creek ≃	218	40.05 N	84.21 W
Paintertown	279b	40.21 N	79.42 W

Paint Lake ⊜	184	55.28 N	97.57 W
Paint Rock	196	31.30 N	99.55 W
Paint Rock ≃	194	34.28 N	86.28 W
Paintsville	192	37.48 N	82.48 W
Paiolinho	256	21.52 S	45.54 W
Pai Pobre, Morro do ∧	287b	23.40 S	46.55 W
Paisco	64	46.04 N	10.17 E
Paisha	100	23.40 N	119.35 E
Paisley, Austl.	274b	37.51 S	144.51 E
Paisley, On., Can.	212	44.18 N	81.16 W
Paisley, Scot., U.K.	46	55.50 N	4.26 W
Paisley, Fl., U.S.	220	28.59 N	81.32 W
Paisley, Or., U.S.	202	42.41 N	120.32 W
Païta, N. Cal.	175f	22.08 S	166.22 E
Paita, Perú	248	5.06 S	81.07 W
Paita, Bahía de c	248	5.04 S	81.05 W
Paitan	100	23.31 N	113.46 E
Paitan ≃	116	6.30 N	117.30 E
Paitan, Teluk c	116	6.45 N	117.20 E
Paiton	115a	7.43 S	113.30 E
Paiva	256	21.18 S	43.25 W
Paiva ≃	34	41.04 N	8.16 W
Paizhou	100	30.13 N	113.56 E
Paj	24	61.13 N	34.24 E
Pajala	24	67.11 N	23.22 E
Pajan	246	1.34 S	80.25 W
Pajapan	234	18.15 N	94.42 W
Pajares, Puerto de)(	34	43.00 N	5.46 W
Pajaro	226	36.54 N	121.39 W
Pajaro ≃	226	36.51 N	121.48 W
Pajaros Point ›	240m	18.31 N	64.18 W
Paj-Choj ⋏[2]	72	69.00 N	63.00 E
Pajdugina ≃	86	58.50 N	81.47 E
Pajęczno	30	51.09 N	19.00 E
Pajeú ≃	250	8.55 S	38.42 W
Pajiangkou	100	23.46 N	113.14 E
Pajjer, gora ∧	24	66.42 N	64.25 E
Pajtug	85	40.53 N	72.15 E
Pak ≃	110	21.05 N	102.31 E
Páka, Magy.	61	46.36 N	16.39 E
Paka, Malay.	114	4.39 N	103.26 E
Paka ≃	114	4.40 N	103.27 E
Pākāla	122	13.28 N	79.07 E
Pakaraima Mountains ⋏	246	5.30 N	60.40 W
Pākaur	124	24.38 N	87.51 E
Pak Ban	110	21.14 N	102.28 E
Pakch'ŏn	98	39.45 N	125.35 E
Pak Chong	110	14.42 N	101.25 E
Pakeng	140	6.55 N	30.40 E
Pakenham, Austl.	169	38.04 S	145.29 E
Pakenham, On., Can.	212	45.20 N	76.17 W
Pākhāl ⊜[1]	122	17.57 N	79.59 E
Pákhi	267c	37.59 N	23.22 E
Pákhi I	267c	37.58 N	23.22 E
Pákhna	130	34.46 N	32.48 E
Pakhoi → Beihai	102	21.29 N	109.05 E
Pakin I[1]	14	7.04 N	157.48 E
Pakipaki	172	39.41 S	176.48 E
Pakistan (Pākistān) □[1], Asia	118	30.00 N	70.00 E
Pakistan (Pākistān) □[1], Asia	120	30.00 N	70.00 E
Pakistan, East → Bangladesh □[1]	120	24.00 N	90.00 E
Pak Kong	271d	22.23 N	114.15 E
Pak Kret	269a	13.55 N	100.30 E
Pak Kwo Chau I	271d	22.16 N	114.20 E
Paklenica Nacionalni Park ♠	36	44.21 N	15.23 E
Pakokku	110	21.20 N	95.05 E
Pakość	30	52.49 N	18.05 E
Pakouabo	150	7.10 N	5.48 W
Pakowki Lake ⊜	184	49.22 N	110.57 W
Pākpattan	123	30.21 N	73.24 E
Pak Phanang	110	8.21 N	100.12 E
Pak Phayun	110	7.21 N	100.19 E
Pak Phraek	110	8.13 N	100.12 E
Pakrac	36	45.26 N	17.12 E
Pākrāganj	126	24.00 N	90.41 E
Pakruojis	76	55.58 N	23.52 E
Paks	30	46.39 N	18.53 E
Pak Sane → Muang Pakxan	110	18.22 N	103.39 E
Pāksey	126	24.05 N	89.03 E
Pak Thong Chai	110	14.43 N	102.01 E
Paktīā □[4]	120	33.30 N	69.30 E
Paktīkā □[4]	120	32.30 N	68.45 E
Pākundia	126	24.20 N	90.42 E
P'akupur ≃	74	65.00 N	77.48 E
Pakwach	154	2.28 N	31.30 E
Pakwash Lake ⊜	184	50.45 N	93.30 W
Pakxé	110	15.07 N	105.47 E
Pala, Mya.	110	12.51 N	98.40 E
Pala, Tchad	146	9.22 N	14.54 E
Pala, Ca., U.S.	228	33.22 N	117.05 W
Palaau State Park ♠	229a	21.11 N	157.00 W
Palabek	154	3.26 N	32.34 E
Palacca Point ›	238	21.15 N	73.26 W
Palacios	196	28.42 N	96.13 W
Palacios ≃	248	16.36 S	64.18 W
Paladru	62	45.28 N	5.33 E
Palagano	64	44.20 N	10.39 E
Palagianello	68	40.37 N	16.58 E
Palagiano	68	40.35 N	17.02 E
Palagonia	70	37.19 N	14.45 E
Palagruža, Otoci II	36	42.24 N	16.15 E
Palai	122	9.44 N	76.41 E
Palai, Punta ∧	71	40.20 N	8.55 E
Palaia	66	43.36 N	10.46 E
Palaiá Epídhavros	38	37.38 N	23.09 E
Palaiá Psará	38	38.46 N	25.36 E
Palaikhóri	130	34.55 N	33.05 E
Pala Indian Reservation ◆[4]	228	33.21 N	117.04 W
Palaiokhóra	38	35.14 N	23.41 E
Palaión Fáliron	267c	37.55 N	23.41 E
Palaiseau	50	48.43 N	2.15 E
Pālakodu	122	16.32 N	81.44 E
Pālam ◆[8]	272a	28.35 N	77.05 E
Palam Airport ⊠	123	28.35 N	77.07 E
Palamás	38	39.28 N	22.05 E
Palamós	34	41.51 N	3.08 E
Pālampur	123	32.07 N	76.32 E
Palamuse	76	58.41 N	26.35 E
Palamut	130	38.59 N	27.41 E
Palana	74	59.07 N	159.58 E
Palanan, Mount ∧	116	17.03 N	122.15 E
Palanan Bay c	116	17.09 N	122.27 E
Palanan Point ›	116	17.09 N	122.30 E
Palanas	116	12.09 N	123.55 E
Palandöken Dağları ⋏	130	39.47 N	41.15 E
Pālang	126	23.13 N	90.21 E
Pālang ≃	126	23.15 N	90.21 E
Palanga	76	55.55 N	21.03 E
Palanganene	152	6.26 S	18.50 E
Palangkaraya	112	2.16 S	113.56 E
Palani	122	10.28 N	77.32 E
Pālanpur	120	24.10 N	72.26 E
Palanquinos	34	42.27 N	5.31 W
Palanzano	64	44.26 N	10.11 E
Palaoa Point ›	229a	20.44 N	156.58 W
Palapag	116	12.33 N	125.07 E
Palapye	156	22.37 S	27.06 E
Pālār ≃	122	12.28 N	80.10 E
Palasan Island I	116	14.52 N	122.03 E
Palas de Rei	34	42.52 N	7.52 W
Palāshdānga	126	23.24 N	87.22 E
Palāspol	126	22.43 N	89.05 E
Palasthali	126	23.51 N	87.03 E
Palata	66	41.53 N	14.47 E
Palatcy	86	49.09 N	83.43 E
Palatine	216	42.06 N	88.02 W
Palatine Bridge	210	42.55 N	74.35 W
Palatka, Ross.	74	60.06 N	150.54 E
Palatka, Fl., U.S.	192	29.38 N	81.38 W
Palau, It.	71	41.11 N	9.23 E
Palau, Méx.	196	27.54 N	101.26 W

≃ River	Fluß	Río	Rivière	Rio
≍ Canal	Kanal	Canal	Canal	Canal
ʟ Waterfall, Rapids	Wasserfall, Stromschnellen	Cascada, Rápidos	Chute d'eau, Rapides	Cascata, Rápidos
ʊ Strait	Meeresstraße	Estrecho	Détroit	Estreito
c Bay, Gulf	Bucht, Golf	Bahía, Golfo	Baie, Golfe	Baía, Golfo
⊜ Lake, Lakes	See, Seen	Lago, Lagos	Lac, Lacs	Lago, Lagos
≡ Swamp	Sumpf	Pantano	Marais	Pântano
⍓ Ice Features, Glacier	Eis- und Gletscherformen	Accidentes Glaciales	Formes glaciaires	Acidentes glaciares
⫪ Other Hydrographic Features	Andere Hydrographische Objekte	Otros Elementos Hidrográficos	Autres données hydrographiques	Outros acidentes hidrográficos

✢ Submarine Features	Untermeerische Objekte	Accidentes Submarinos	Formes de relief sous-marin	Acidentes submarinos
□ Political Unit	Politische Einheit	Unidad Politica	Entité politique	Unidade política
ʋ Cultural Institution	Kulturelle Institution	Institución Cultural	Institution culturelle	Instituição cultural
⊥ Historical Site	Historische Stätte	Sitio Histórico	Site historique	Sitio histórico
♠ Recreational Site	Erholungs- und Ferienort	Sitio de Recreo	Centre de loisirs	Area de Lazer
⊠ Airport	Flughafen	Aeropuerto	Aéroport	Aeroporto
■ Military Installation	Militäranlage	Instalación Militar	Installation militaire	Instalação militar
◆ Miscellaneous	Verschiedenes	Misceláneo	Divers	Diversos

ENGLISH / DEUTSCH

Name	Page	Lat.°′	Long.°′
Palau (Belau) □[2], Oc.	14	5.00 N	137.00 E
Palau (Belau) □[2], Oc.	175b	7.30 N	134.30 E
Palauig	116	15.26 N	119.54 E
Palaui Island I	116	18.33 N	122.08 E
Palau Islands II	175b	7.30 N	134.30 E
Palauk	110	13.16 N	98.38 E
Pal'avaam ≃	180	68.50 N	170.45 E
Pal'avaamskij chrebet ⋏	180	68.20 N	177.00 E
Palavas-les-Flots	62	43.32 N	3.56 E
Palaw	110	12.58 N	98.39 E
Palawai Basin ⩧[1]	229a	20.47 N	156.55 W
Palawan □[4]	116	10.00 N	118.50 E
Palawan I	116	9.30 N	118.30 E
Palawan Passage ⊔	116	10.00 N	118.00 E
Palayan	116	15.33 N	121.06 E
Pālayankottai	122	8.43 N	77.44 E
Palazzo Adriano	70	37.41 N	13.23 E
Palazzolo Acreide	70	37.04 N	14.54 E
Palazzolo dello Stella	64	45.48 N	13.05 E
Palazzolo sull'Oglio	62	45.36 N	9.53 E
Palazzolo Vercellese	62	45.11 N	8.14 E
Palazzo San Gervasio	68	40.56 N	16.00 E
Palazzuolo sul Senio	66	44.07 N	11.33 E
P'albong-san ʌ	98	40.16 N	127.57 E
Palca, Bol.	248	16.34 S	67.59 W
Palca, Perú	248	11.21 S	75.31 W
Palcamayo	248	11.18 S	75.46 W
Pal'co	76	53.17 N	34.56 E
Paldi	224	48.48 N	123.51 W
Paldiski	76	59.20 N	24.06 E
Pāldor ʌ	124	28.16 N	85.11 E
Palech	80	56.48 N	41.51 E
Palel	120	24.27 N	94.02 E
Paleleh	112	1.04 N	121.57 E
Palembang	112	2.55 S	104.45 E
Palena	66	41.59 N	14.08 E
Palena ≃	254	43.50 S	72.59 W
Palena, Lago (Lago General Vintter) ⊜	254	43.55 S	71.40 W
Palencia	34	42.01 N	4.32 W
Palencia □[4]	34	42.25 N	4.35 W
Palen Lake ⊜	204	33.46 N	115.12 W
Palenque	232	17.31 N	91.58 W
Palenque ⊥	232	17.30 N	92.00 W
Palenque, Punta ›	238	18.14 N	70.09 W
Palenville	210	42.10 N	74.01 W
Paleparto, Monte ʌ	68	39.28 N	16.34 E
Palermo, Col.	246	2.54 N	75.26 W
Palermo, It.	70	38.07 N	13.21 E
Palermo, Ca., U.S.	226	39.26 N	121.33 W
Palermo, Ur.	252	33.48 S	55.59 W
Palermo □[4]	70	37.49 N	13.35 E
Palermo ✦[8]	288	34.35 S	58.25 W
Palermo, Golfo di ⊂	70	38.08 N	13.26 E
Palese, Aeroporto di ⊠	68	41.10 N	16.47 E
Palestina, Bra.	255	20.23 S	49.25 W
Palestina, Méx.	196	29.10 N	100.55 W
Palestine, Ar., U.S.	194	34.58 N	90.54 W
Palestine, Il., U.S.	194	39.00 N	87.36 W
Palestine, Oh., U.S.	218	40.03 N	84.45 W
Palestine, Tx., U.S.	222	31.45 N	95.37 W
Palestine □[9]	132	32.00 N	35.15 E
Palestine, Lake ⊜[1]	222	32.06 N	95.27 W
Palestrina	66	41.50 N	12.53 E
Paletwa	110	21.18 N	92.51 E
Palézieux	58	46.33 N	6.50 E
Palfau	61	47.42 N	14.48 E
Pālghāt	122	10.47 N	76.39 E
Palgrave, Mount ʌ	162	23.22 S	115.58 E
Palgrave Point ›	156	20.45 S	13.20 E
Palhais	266c	38.37 N	9.03 W
Palhano	250	4.44 S	37.57 W
Palhano ≃	250	4.33 S	37.42 W
Pāli, India	120	25.46 N	73.20 E
Pali, India	124	25.51 N	76.33 E
Paliano	66	41.48 N	13.03 E
Palidoro ✦[8]	66	41.56 N	12.11 E
Palikea ʌ	229c	21.26 N	158.06 W
Palima	112	4.20 S	120.22 E
Palimanan	115a	6.42 S	108.26 E
Palimbang	116	6.12 N	124.12 E
Palimé	150	6.54 N	0.38 E
Palín	236	14.24 N	90.42 W
Palinges	32	46.33 N	4.13 E
Palinuro	68	40.02 N	15.17 E
Palinuro, Capo ›	68	40.02 N	15.16 E
Palisade, Co., U.S.	200	39.06 N	108.21 W
Palisade, Ne., U.S.	198	40.20 N	101.06 W
Palisades, Id., U.S.	202	43.21 N	111.13 W
Palisades, N.Y., U.S.	276	41.01 N	73.55 W
Palisades Amusement Park ♦	276	40.50 N	73.59 W
Palisades Interstate Park ♦	210	40.56 N	73.55 W
Palisades Park, Mi., U.S.	216	42.18 N	86.19 W
Palisades Park, N.J., U.S.	276	40.50 N	73.59 W
Palisades Reservoir ⊜[1]	202	43.15 N	111.05 W
Paliseul	56	49.54 N	5.08 E
Pālitāna	120	21.31 N	71.50 E
Palivere	76	58.59 N	23.52 E
Palizada	232	18.15 N	92.05 W
Palizzi	68	37.58 N	15.59 E
Paljakka ʌ[2]	26	64.41 N	28.08 E
Pälkäne	26	61.20 N	24.16 E
Palk Bay ⊂	122	9.30 N	79.15 E
Palkino, Ross.	76	57.32 N	28.01 E
Palkino, Ross.	80	58.15 N	42.56 E
Pālkonda	122	18.36 N	83.45 E
Pālkonda Range ⋏	122	14.05 N	79.05 E
Palk Strait ⊔	122	10.00 N	79.45 E
Palla Bianca (Weisskugel) ʌ	64	46.48 N	10.44 E
Pallagorio	68	39.18 N	16.54 E
Pallamana	168b	35.02 S	139.12 E
Pallasca	248	8.15 S	78.01 W
Pallas Grean	48	52.33 N	8.22 W
Pallaskenry	48	52.39 N	8.52 W
Pallas-Ounastunturin kansallispuisto ♦	24	68.06 N	24.00 E
Pallasovka	80	50.03 N	46.53 E
Pallastunturi ʌ	24	68.06 N	24.00 E
Pallejà	266d	41.25 N	2.00 E
Pallës, Bishti i ›	38	41.24 N	19.24 E
Palling	182	54.21 N	125.55 W
Pallíni	267c	38.00 N	23.53 E
Pallinup ≃	162	34.29 S	118.54 E
Pallisa	154	1.10 N	33.42 E
Palliser, Cape ›	172	41.37 S	175.17 E
Palliser Bay ⊂	172	41.25 S	175.05 E
Pallu	123	28.56 N	74.13 E
Palluau	32	46.48 N	1.37 W
Palma, Bra.	255	21.22 S	42.19 W
Palma, Moç.	154	10.46 S	40.29 E
P'al'ma, Ross.	24	62.26 N	35.53 E
Palma ≃	255	12.33 S	47.52 W
Palma, Badia de ⊂	34	39.27 N	2.35 E
Palmácia	250	4.08 S	38.50 W
Palma del Río	34	37.42 N	5.17 W
Palma [de Mallorca]	34	39.34 N	2.39 E
Palma di Montechiaro	70	37.11 N	13.46 E
Palmaḥim	132	31.56 N	34.42 E
Palmanova	64	45.54 N	13.19 E
Palma Pegada	234	22.42 N	101.48 W
Palmar ≃	246	10.10 N	71.50 W
Palmar, Lago Artificial del ⊜[1]	252	33.05 S	57.10 W
Palmar Camp	232	16.26 N	88.53 W
Palmar de Cariaco	286c	10.34 N	66.55 W
Palmar de los Sepúlveda	232	25.43 N	107.55 W
Palmar de Varela	246	10.45 N	74.45 W
Palmarejo	240m	18.03 N	67.05 W
Palmares, Bra.	250	8.41 S	35.36 W
Palmares, C.R.	236	10.03 N	84.26 W
Palmares, C.R.	236	9.21 N	83.40 W
Palmares do Sul	252	30.16 S	50.31 W
Palmaria, Isola I	62	44.02 N	9.51 E
Palmarito	246	7.37 N	70.10 W
Palmarola, Isola I	66	40.56 N	12.51 E
Palmar Sur	236	8.58 N	83.29 W
Palmas, Bra.	250	10.08 S	48.18 W
Palmas, Bra.	252	26.30 S	52.00 W
Palmas, Méx.	234	22.49 N	103.57 W
Palmas, Golfo di ⊂	71	39.02 N	8.31 E
Palmas, Ilha das I, Bra.	287a	23.04 S	43.31 W
Palmas, Ilha das I, Bra.	287a	23.02 S	43.12 W
Palmas Bellas	236	9.14 N	80.05 W
Palmas de Monte Alto	255	14.16 S	43.10 W
Palma Sola	220	27.31 N	82.38 W
Palma Soriano	240p	20.13 N	76.00 W
Palm Bay	220	28.02 N	80.35 W
Palm Beach, Austl.	170	33.36 S	151.19 E
Palm Beach, Austl.	171a	28.08 S	153.28 E
Palm Beach, Fl., U.S.	220	26.42 N	80.02 W
Palm Beach □[6]	220	26.38 N	80.27 W
Palm Beach Gardens	220	26.49 N	80.06 W
Palm Beach International Airport ⊠	220	26.41 N	80.05 W
Palm City	220	27.09 N	80.16 W
Palmdale, Ca., U.S.	228	34.34 N	118.06 W
Palmdale, Fl., U.S.	220	26.56 N	81.18 W
Palmdale, Pa., U.S.	208	40.18 N	76.37 W
Palmdale, Lake ⊜[1]	228	34.33 N	118.07 W
Palm Desert	204	33.43 N	116.23 W
Palmeira, Bra.	252	25.25 S	50.00 W
Palmeira, C.V.	150a	16.46 N	22.59 W
Palmeira das Missões	252	27.55 S	53.17 W
Palmeira d'Oeste	255	20.23 S	50.47 W
Palmeira dos Índios	250	9.25 S	36.37 W
Palmeirais	250	5.58 S	43.04 W
Palmeiral	256	21.38 S	46.31 W
Palmeiras	255	12.31 S	41.34 W
Palmeiras ≃, Bra.	250	12.22 S	47.08 W
Palmeiras ≃, Bra.	255	15.25 S	51.10 W
Palmeirina	250	8.56 S	36.17 W
Palmeirinhas, Ponta das ›	152	9.05 S	13.00 E
Palmela ≃	256	21.38 S	45.23 W
Palmelo	255	17.20 S	48.27 W
Palmer, Austl.	168b	34.51 S	139.10 E
Palmer, P.R.	240m	18.22 N	65.46 W
Palmer, Ak., U.S.	180	61.36 N	149.07 W
Palmer, Il., U.S.	219	39.27 N	89.24 W
Palmer, Ma., U.S.	207	42.09 N	72.19 W
Palmer, Ms., U.S.	194	31.16 N	89.15 W
Palmer, Ne., U.S.	198	41.13 N	98.15 W
Palmer, Tn., U.S.	194	35.21 N	85.34 W
Palmer, Tx., U.S.	222	32.26 N	96.40 W
Palmer ≃, Austl.	162	24.46 S	133.25 E
Palmer ≃, Austl.	164	15.34 S	142.26 E
Palmer ≃, P.Q., Can.	206	46.19 N	71.27 W
Palmer ᵾ[3]	9	64.46 S	64.03 W
Palmerah ✦[8]	269e	6.12 S	106.47 E
Palmer Heights	208	40.42 N	75.16 W
Palmer Lake	200	38.52 N	104.48 W
Palmer Land ✦[1]	9	71.30 S	65.00 W
Palmer Mill Brook ≃	283	41.58 N	70.52 W
Palmer Park	284c	38.55 N	76.52 W
Palmer Park ♦	281	42.26 N	83.07 W
Palmerston, On., Can.	212	43.50 N	80.51 W
Palmerston, N.Z.	172	45.29 S	170.43 E
Palmerston I[1]	14	18.04 S	163.10 W
Palmerston, Cape ›	166	21.32 S	149.29 E
Palmerston Lake ⊜	212	45.01 N	76.50 W
Palmerston North	172	40.21 S	175.37 E
Palmerton	210	40.48 N	75.36 W
Palmerville	164	15.59 S	144.05 E
Palmetto, Fl., U.S.	220	27.31 N	82.34 W
Palmetto, Ga., U.S.	192	33.31 N	84.40 W
Palmetto, La., U.S.	194	30.43 N	91.54 W
Palmford	158	27.11 S	29.42 E
Palm Harbor	220	28.04 N	82.45 W
Palmi	68	38.21 N	15.51 E
Palminópolis	255	16.47 S	50.08 W
Palmira, Arg.	252	33.03 S	68.34 W
Palmira, Col.	246	3.32 N	76.16 W
Palmira, Cuba	240p	22.14 N	80.23 W
Palmira, Ec.	246	2.05 S	78.43 W
Palmira, Méx.	196	28.58 N	100.47 W
Palmitas	252	33.31 S	57.49 W
Palmitos	252	27.05 S	53.08 W
Palmnicken → Jantarnyj	76	54.52 N	19.57 E
Palmoli	66	41.56 N	14.32 E
Palm River	220	27.56 N	82.23 W
Palms ✦[8]	280	34.02 N	118.25 W
Palm Shores	220	28.11 N	80.35 W
Palm Springs, Ca., U.S.	204	33.49 N	116.32 W
Palm Springs, Fl., U.S.	220	26.39 N	80.06 W
Palmyra → Tudmur, Sūrīy.	130	34.33 N	38.17 E
Palmyra, Il., U.S.	219	39.26 N	89.59 W
Palmyra, In., U.S.	218	38.24 N	86.06 W
Palmyra, Mi., U.S.	216	41.52 N	83.56 W
Palmyra, Mo., U.S.	219	39.47 N	91.31 W
Palmyra, N.J., U.S.	208	40.00 N	75.01 W
Palmyra, N.Y., U.S.	210	43.03 N	77.14 W
Palmyra, Oh., U.S.	214	41.07 N	81.02 W
Palmyra, Pa., U.S.	208	40.18 N	76.35 W
Palmyra, Va., U.S.	192	37.51 N	78.15 W
Palmyra, Wi., U.S.	216	42.52 N	88.35 W
Palmyra ⊥	130	34.33 N	38.17 E
Palmyra Atoll I[1]	14	5.52 N	162.06 W
Palo, It.	66	41.56 N	12.06 E
Palo, Pil.	116	11.10 N	124.59 E
Palo Alto, Méx.	196	26.32 N	99.45 W
Palo Alto, Ca., U.S.	226	37.26 N	122.08 W
Palo Alto, Pa., U.S.	208	40.41 N	76.11 W
Palo Alto Airport ⊠	282	37.28 N	122.07 W
Palo Blanco, Méx.	196	26.45 N	101.32 W
Palo Blanco, P.R.	240m	18.26 N	66.39 W
Palo Blanco Creek ≃	196	27.10 N	97.52 W
Paločka	86	58.25 N	84.32 E
Palo del Colle	68	41.03 N	16.42 E
Palo Duro Canyon State Park ♦	196	34.55 N	101.42 W
Palo Duro Creek ≃, U.S.	196	36.39 N	100.58 W
Palo Duro Creek ≃, Tx., U.S.	196	35.00 N	101.54 W
Paloe, Pulau I	115b	8.20 S	121.43 E
Paloemeu ≃	250	3.21 N	55.26 W
Palo Flechado Pass)(	200	36.25 N	105.20 W
Paloh, Indon.	112	1.43 N	109.18 E
Paloh, Malay.	112	2.25 N	111.15 E
Paloh, Malay.	114	2.11 N	103.12 E
Paloich, Sūd.	140	6.45 N	30.08 E
Paloich, Sūd.	140	10.28 N	32.32 E
Palojoensuu	24	68.17 N	23.05 E
Paloma Creek ≃	226	36.15 N	121.26 W
Palomares Creek ≃	282	37.42 N	122.02 W
Palomar Mountain ʌ	204	33.22 N	116.50 W
Palomar Mountain State Park ♦	228	33.19 N	116.53 W
Palomar Park	282	37.29 N	122.16 W
Palomas	196	28.43 N	103.45 W
Palomas Viejo	232	31.44 N	107.37 W
Palombara Sabina	66	42.04 N	12.46 E
Palominos, Isla I	240m	18.21 N	65.34 W
Palomonte	68	40.40 N	15.17 E
Palompon	116	11.03 N	124.23 E
Palo Negro	246	10.11 N	67.33 W
Palo Pinto	196	32.46 N	98.18 W
Palo Pinto Reservoir ⊜[1]	196	32.38 N	98.18 W
Palopo	112	3.00 S	120.12 E
Palora ≃	246	1.51 S	77.49 W
Palos, Cuba	240p	22.48 N	81.44 W
Palos → Palos de la Frontera, Esp.	34	37.14 N	6.53 W
Palos, Cabo de ›	34	37.38 N	0.41 W
Palo Santo	252	25.34 S	59.21 W
Palos de la Frontera	34	37.14 N	6.53 W
Palos Gardens	278	41.40 N	87.48 W
Palos Heights	216	41.40 N	87.47 W
Palos Hills	278	41.41 N	87.49 W
Palos Hills ♦	278	41.42 N	87.53 W
Palos Park	278	41.40 N	87.49 W
Palos Verdes Estates	228	33.48 N	118.23 W
Palos Verdes Hills ⋏[2]	280	33.46 N	118.21 W
Palos Verdes Point ›	228	33.47 N	118.26 W
Palotai-sziget I	264c	47.35 N	19.05 E
Paloúkia	267c	37.58 N	23.31 E
Palouse	202	46.54 N	117.04 W
Palouse ≃	202	46.35 N	118.13 W
Palouse, South Fork ≃	202	46.53 N	117.22 W
Palo Verde	204	33.25 N	114.43 W
Palo Verde, Parque Nacional ♦	236	10.15 N	85.10 W
P'alovskoje vodochranilišče ⊜[1]	82	56.03 N	37.40 E
Palpa	248	14.32 S	75.11 W
Palpalá	252	24.15 S	65.12 W
Pålsboda	40	59.04 N	15.20 E
Pālsit	126	23.12 N	88.03 E
Paltamo	26	64.25 N	27.50 E
Paltenbach ≃	61	47.34 N	14.20 E
Palu, Indon.	112	0.53 S	119.53 E
Palu, Tür.	130	38.42 N	39.57 E
Palu ≃	112	0.52 S	119.51 E
Palu, Teluk ⊂	112	0.40 S	119.45 E
Paluan	116	13.25 N	120.28 E
Paluan Bay ⊂	116	13.23 N	120.25 E
Palù del Fersina	64	46.08 N	11.21 E
Paludi	68	39.32 N	16.41 E
Paluga	24	65.16 N	45.11 E
Paluke	150	5.02 N	8.06 W
Paluška ʌ	61	48.45 N	14.24 E
Paluxy ≃	196	32.15 N	97.43 W
Paluzza	64	46.32 N	13.01 E
Palvantaš	85	40.34 N	72.12 E
Palvār, Kūh-e ʌ	128	30.04 N	57.28 E
Palvart	128	38.11 N	64.34 E
Palwal	124	28.09 N	77.20 E
Pal-Waukee Airport ⊠	278	42.07 N	87.54 W
Pam	175f	20.16 S	164.19 E
Pama	150	11.15 N	0.42 E
Pama ≃	152	4.23 N	18.27 E
Pamaluan	112	1.04 S	116.39 E
Pamanukan	115a	6.16 S	107.49 E
Pamarayan	115a	6.16 S	106.17 E
Pam'ati 0103 Borcov	86	56.13 N	92.20 E
Pam'atnaja	86	56.01 N	65.42 E
Pam'at' Parižskoj Kommuny	80	56.06 N	44.31 E
Pāmban Channel ⊔	122	9.17 N	79.10 E
Pāmban Island I	122	9.15 N	79.20 E
Pambeguwa	150	10.40 N	8.19 E
Pambuhan	116	13.59 N	123.05 E
Pambuhan ≃	116	12.34 N	124.55 E
Pambujan	116	12.34 N	124.56 E
Pamekasan	115a	7.10 S	113.28 E
Pamenang	112	2.07 S	102.31 E
Pameungpeuk	115a	7.38 S	107.43 E
Pamiers	32	43.07 N	1.36 E
Pamir ⋏	118	38.00 N	73.00 E
Pamlico ≃	192	35.20 N	76.30 W
Pamlico Sound ⊔	192	35.20 N	75.55 W
Pamotan	115a	6.46 S	111.29 E
Pampa	196	35.32 N	100.57 W
Pampã ≃	255	17.43 S	40.36 W
Pampa ✦[1]	252	35.00 S	63.00 W
Pampa Almirón	252	26.42 S	59.08 W
Pampacolca	248	15.43 S	72.33 W
Pampa del Castillo	254	45.48 S	68.05 W
Pampa del Chañar	252	30.11 S	68.43 W
Pampa del Indio	252	26.02 S	59.55 W
Pampa del Infierno	252	26.31 S	61.10 W
Pampa de los Guanacos	252	26.14 S	61.51 W
Pampa Grande	248	18.05 S	64.06 W
Pampana ≃	150	8.24 N	12.00 W
Pampanga □[4]	116	15.05 N	120.40 E
Pampanga ≃	116	14.47 N	120.39 E
Pampanua	112	4.14 S	120.08 E
Pamparato	62	44.17 N	7.55 E
Pampas	248	12.24 S	74.54 W
Pampas ≃	248	13.23 S	73.15 W
Pampas del Heath, Santuario Nacional ♦	248	12.40 S	68.15 W
Pampeluna → Pamplona	34	42.49 N	1.38 W
Pamphylia □[9]	130	37.00 N	31.00 E
Pamplico	192	33.59 N	79.34 W
Pamplona, Col.	246	7.23 N	72.39 W
Pamplona, Esp.	34	42.49 N	1.38 W
Pampoenpoort	158	31.03 S	22.40 E
Pampow	54	53.32 N	14.15 E
Pāmpur	123	34.01 N	74.56 E
Pamukkale (Hierapolis) ⊥	130	37.58 N	29.19 E
Pamukova	130	40.31 N	30.09 E
Pamunkey ≃	208	37.32 N	76.48 W
Pana	219	39.23 N	89.04 W
Panabá	232	21.17 N	88.16 W
Panabo	116	7.19 N	125.42 E
Panaca	204	37.47 N	114.23 W
Panacan	116	9.16 N	118.25 E
Panacea	192	30.02 N	84.23 W
Panache, Lake ⊜	190	46.15 N	81.20 W
Panadura	122	6.43 N	79.54 E
Panaeati Island I	164	10.40 S	152.20 E
Panāgar	124	23.18 N	79.59 E
Panagjurište	38	42.30 N	24.11 E
Panagtaran Point ›	116	9.41 N	118.45 E
Panahan	112	1.44 S	111.49 E
Panaitan, Pulau I	115a	6.36 S	105.12 E
Panaitan, Selat ⊔	115a	6.40 S	105.16 E
Panaji (Panjim)	122	15.29 N	73.50 E
Pānākua	272b	22.23 N	88.21 E
Panamá, Bra.	255	18.11 S	49.21 W
Panamá, Pan.	236	8.58 N	79.32 W
Panama, Il., U.S.	219	39.02 N	89.32 W
Panama, N.Y., U.S.	214	42.04 N	79.29 W
Panama, Ok., U.S.	194	35.10 N	94.40 W
Panamá □[4]	236	8.48 N	79.55 W
Panama (Panamá) □[1], N.A.	230	9.00 N	80.00 W
Panama (Panamá) □[1], N.A.	246	9.00 N	80.00 W
Panamá, Bahía de ⊂	246	8.50 N	79.20 W
Panamá, Canal de ≍	236	9.20 N	79.55 W
Panamá, Golfo de ⊂	246	8.00 N	79.30 W
Panamá, Istmo de ⩧[3]	246	9.00 N	80.00 W
Panama Basin ✧[1]	18	5.00 N	83.30 W
Panama City	194	30.09 N	85.39 W
Panamá Vieja ⊥	236	9.00 N	79.29 W
Panambi	252	28.18 S	53.30 W
Panamint Range ⋏	204	36.30 N	117.20 W
Panamint Valley V	204	36.15 N	117.20 W
Pan'an	100	29.06 N	120.27 E
Panao, Perú	248	9.49 S	76.00 W
Pan'ao, Zhg.	107	30.09 N	103.37 E
Panaon Island I	116	10.03 N	125.13 E
Panarea, Isola I	70	38.38 N	15.04 E
Panaro ≃	64	44.55 N	11.25 E
Panarukan	115a	7.42 S	113.56 E
Panasoffkee, Lake ⊜	220	28.47 N	82.08 W
Panatinane Island I	164	11.15 S	153.10 E
Panay I	116	11.15 N	122.30 E
Panay ≃	116	11.35 N	122.43 E
Panay Gulf ⊂	116	10.15 N	122.15 E
Panayía	38	39.59 N	25.24 E
Panay Island I	116	13.58 N	124.20 E
Pancalieri	62	44.50 N	7.35 E
Pancas	266c	38.48 N	8.55 W
Pančevo, Jugo.	38	44.52 N	20.39 E
Pančevo, Ukr.	78	48.44 N	31.51 E
Panchagarh	124	26.20 N	88.34 E
Pānchāl	126	23.15 N	87.18 E
Pānchet Hill ʌ[2]	126	23.37 N	86.47 E
Pānchet Reservoir ⊜[1]	126	23.40 N	86.45 E
Pānchghara	272b	22.44 N	88.16 E
Panchgram	126	24.12 N	88.01 E
Panch'iao	269d	25.01 N	121.27 E
Panchla	126	22.32 N	88.09 E
Panchor	114	2.10 N	102.43 E
Pancho Simón ≃	286b	23.03 N	82.21 W
Pānchur	272b	22.32 N	88.16 E
Pānchuria	272b	22.33 N	88.29 E
Panciu	38	45.55 N	27.05 E
Panda	156	24.02 S	34.45 E
Pandakan	115a	7.39 S	112.41 E
Pandamatenga	156	18.35 S	25.42 E
Pandan, Malay.	112	3.09 N	113.22 E
Pandan, Pil.	116	11.43 N	122.06 E
Pandan, Pil.	116	14.03 N	124.10 E
Pandan, Selat ⊔	271c	1.15 N	103.44 E
Pandanan Island I	116	8.17 N	117.13 E
Pandan Bay ⊂	116	11.43 N	122.04 E
Pandan Reservoir ⊜[1]	271c	1.19 N	103.44 E
Pandaria	124	22.14 N	81.25 E
Pandarochan Bay ⊂	116	12.12 N	121.10 E
Pandasan	112	6.28 N	116.32 E
Pan de Azúcar	252	34.48 S	55.14 W
Pan de Azucar, Cerro ʌ	286e	33.19 S	70.42 W
Pan de Azucar Island I	116	11.17 N	123.10 E
Pandegelang	115a	6.18 S	106.06 E
Pandėlys	76	56.01 N	25.13 E
Pāndharkawada	122	20.01 N	78.32 E
Pandharpur	122	17.40 N	75.20 E
Pāndhurna	122	21.36 N	78.31 E
Pandian	98	36.38 N	116.27 E
Pandino	62	45.24 N	9.33 E
Pando	252	34.43 S	55.57 W
Pando □[5]	248	11.20 S	67.40 W
Pando, Cerro ʌ	236	8.55 N	82.43 W
Pandora	216	40.56 N	83.57 W
Pandu	152	5.01 N	19.16 E
Pandua, India	124	25.08 N	88.10 E
Pāndua, India	126	23.05 N	88.17 E
P'andž (Panj) ≃	120	37.06 N	68.20 E
Panebianco ≃	70	37.24 N	15.04 E
Panelas	250	8.40 S	36.01 W
Paneveggio	64	46.18 N	11.44 E
Panevėžys	76	55.44 N	24.21 E
Panfang	100	27.54 N	115.57 E
Panfilov	86	44.10 N	80.01 E
Panfilovo	80	50.26 N	42.55 E
Pāng ≃	110	20.58 N	98.30 E
Panga	154	1.51 N	26.25 E
Pangala	152	3.19 S	14.34 E
Pangalanes, Canal des ≍	157b	22.40 S	47.50 E
Pangandaran	115a	7.41 S	108.39 E
Pangani	154	5.26 S	38.58 E
Pangani ≃	154	5.26 S	38.58 E
Panganiran	116	13.02 N	123.26 E
Pangantocan	116	7.50 N	124.49 E
Panganuran	116	7.24 N	122.03 E
Pangasinan □[4]	116	16.00 N	120.20 E
Pangbourne	42	51.29 N	1.05 W
Pangburn	194	35.25 N	91.50 W
Pange	56	49.05 N	6.22 E
Pangfou → Bengbu	100	32.58 N	117.24 E
Pangga, Tanjung ›	115b	8.55 S	116.02 E
Panggezhuang, Zhg.	105	39.38 N	116.19 E
Panggezhuang, Zhg.	105	39.16 N	115.49 E
Panghkam	110	23.53 N	97.37 E
Pangi	154	3.11 S	26.38 E
Pangian	112	1.06 S	119.24 E
Pangjiabu	105	40.36 N	115.27 E
Pangkah	115a	6.58 S	109.10 E
Pangkajene	112	4.50 S	119.32 E
Pangkalanbrandan	114	4.01 N	98.17 E
Pangkalanbuun	112	2.41 S	111.37 E
Pangkalansusu	114	4.06 N	98.14 E
Pangkalaseang, Tanjung ›	112	0.42 S	123.26 E
Pangkalpinang	112	2.08 S	106.08 E
Pangkatan	114	2.09 N	100.00 E
Pangke	114	1.01 N	103.10 E
Pangkor, Pulau I	114	4.13 N	100.33 E
Panglao	116	9.35 N	123.45 E
Panglao Island I	116	9.35 N	123.48 E
Pangman	184	49.39 N	104.38 W
Pangnirtung	176	66.08 N	65.44 W
Pango Aluquém	152	8.43 S	14.27 E
Pangŏjin	98	35.29 N	129.26 E
Pangong Tso ⊜	120	33.45 N	78.43 E
Pangp'u → Bengbu	100	32.58 N	117.24 E
Pāngsa	126	23.47 N	89.25 E
Pangtara	110	20.57 N	96.40 E
Pangubatan	116	6.57 N	125.47 E
Panguil Bay ⊂	116	8.01 N	123.43 E
Panguipulli	254	39.38 S	72.20 W
Panguipulli, Lago ⊜	254	39.43 S	72.13 W
Panguiranan	116	12.04 N	123.19 E
Panguitch	200	37.49 N	112.26 W
Panguruan	114	2.37 N	98.42 E
Pangutaran	116	6.18 N	120.35 E
Pangutaran Group II	116	6.15 N	120.30 E
Pangutaran Island I	116	6.18 N	120.34 E
Pangutaran Passage ⊔	116	6.13 N	120.30 E
Pangzidian	107	30.38 N	105.04 E
Panhandle	196	35.20 N	101.22 W
Paniai, Danau ⊜	164	3.50 S	136.15 E
Pania-Mutombo	152	5.11 S	23.51 E
Paniau ʌ	229b	21.57 N	160.05 W
Panié, Mont ʌ	175f	20.36 S	164.46 E
Pānihāti	126	22.42 N	88.22 E
Panika	80	50.59 N	50.11 E
Panindícuaro	234	19.59 N	101.46 W
Panino, Ross.	76	56.25 N	34.34 E
Panino, Ross.	78	51.38 N	40.08 E
Panino-Nesterovo	82	55.23 N	38.11 E
Panīpāt	124	29.23 N	76.58 E
Paniqui	116	15.40 N	120.35 E
Panissières	62	45.47 N	4.20 E
Panitan	116	11.28 N	122.46 E
Panitian	116	9.05 N	118.05 E
Panj (P'andž) ≃	120	37.06 N	68.20 E
Panjāb	120	34.22 N	67.01 E
Panjang	115a	5.28 S	105.18 E
Panjang, Pulau I	112	2.44 N	108.55 E
Panjang, Selat ⊔	114	0.40 N	102.30 E
Panje	272c	18.54 N	72.57 E
Panjgūr	128	26.58 N	64.06 E
Panji	114	2.34 N	97.50 E
Panjiapie	100	32.54 N	120.42 E
Panjiatun	104	41.04 N	121.38 E
Panjim → Panaji	122	15.29 N	73.50 E
Pānjkora ≃	123	34.39 N	71.44 E
Panjnad ≃	123	28.57 N	70.30 E
Panjpāi	120	29.55 N	66.30 E
Panjshār ≃	120	34.38 N	69.42 E
Pankakoski	26	63.19 N	30.09 E
Panke ≃	264a	52.32 N	13.22 E
Panker	54	54.20 N	10.34 E
Pānkhāli	126	22.37 N	89.31 E
Pankof, Cape ›	180	54.40 N	163.04 W
Pankow ✦[8]	54	52.34 N	13.25 E
Pankratovo	76	59.10 N	43.30 E
Pankshin	150	9.20 N	9.24 E
Panlong, Zhg.	100	25.52 N	114.52 E
Panlong, Zhg.	106	31.58 N	121.35 E
Panlong, Zhg.	106	31.11 N	121.16 E
Panlong (Lo) ≃	110	21.18 N	105.25 E
Panlongzhen	107	29.31 N	105.17 E
P'anmunjŏm	98	37.57 N	126.40 E
Panna	124	24.43 N	80.12 E
Pannawonica	162	21.44 S	116.22 E
Panni	68	41.13 N	15.16 E
Panningen	52	51.20 N	5.59 E
Pannonhalma ᵾ[1]	30	47.28 N	17.50 E
Panoche Creek ≃	226	36.44 N	120.31 W
Panola	194	31.58 N	86.23 W
Panola □[6]	222	32.07 N	94.30 W
Páno Lévkara	130	34.52 N	33.18 E
Panopah	112	1.56 S	111.11 E
Páno Panayiá	130	34.55 N	32.38 E
Páno Plátres	130	34.53 N	32.52 E
Panora	198	41.41 N	94.21 W
Panorama	255	21.21 S	51.51 W
Pánormos	38	37.38 N	25.02 E
Panovo, Ross.	24	59.48 N	46.27 E
Panovo, Ross.	88	58.58 N	101.58 E
P'anp'yŏng-ni	98	40.28 N	125.49 E
Panruti	122	11.46 N	79.33 E
Pansfelde	54	51.39 N	11.16 E
Panshan	104	41.12 N	122.04 E
Panshanger Aerodrome ⊠	260	51.48 N	0.08 W
Pansik, Rápido ∟	236	14.30 N	85.15 W
Pansionat	265b	55.59 N	37.41 E
Pānskura	126	22.25 N	87.42 E
Pantabangan	116	15.50 N	121.09 E
Pantajevka	78	48.41 N	32.53 E
Pantalica, Necropoli di ⊥	70	37.08 N	15.01 E
Pantanal Matogrossense, Parque Nacional do ♦	248	17.35 S	57.40 W
Pantanaw	110	16.59 N	95.28 E
Pântano	256	22.23 S	46.01 W
Pântano, Ribeirão do ≃	256	22.15 S	45.59 W
Pantar, Pulau I	112	8.25 S	124.07 E
Pantelejmonovka	83	48.12 N	37.59 E
Pantelleria	70	36.50 N	11.57 E
Pantelleria, Isola di I	70	36.47 N	12.00 E
Panteón Nacional ⊥	286c	10.31 N	66.55 W
Pantepec ≃	234	20.56 N	97.44 W
Pantha	110	23.49 N	94.33 E
Pantheon ⊥	267a	41.55 N	12.29 E
Panther Creek ≃, Id., U.S.	202	45.19 N	114.24 W
Panther Creek ≃, Ky., U.S.	194	37.45 N	87.19 W
Panther Creek, South Fork ≃	194	37.42 N	87.05 W
Panther Lake	210	43.19 N	75.54 W
Pantin	50	48.54 N	2.24 E
Pantitlán ✦[8]	286a	19.25 N	99.05 W
Panto, Tanjung ›	115a	6.51 S	105.54 E
Panton, Mount ʌ[2]	162	17.21 S	129.13 E
Pantonlabu	114	5.08 N	97.28 E
Pantry Brook ≃	283	42.24 N	71.22 W
Panu	152	3.48 S	19.07 E
Pánuco	234	22.03 N	98.10 W
Pánuco ≃	234	22.16 N	97.47 W
Panuke Lake ⊜	186	44.48 N	64.07 W
Panukulan	116	14.56 N	121.49 E
Pānuria	126	23.49 N	86.58 E
Pan'utino	78	48.56 N	36.17 E
Panvel	122	18.59 N	73.06 E
Panvel ≃	272c	19.01 N	73.04 W
Panvel Creek ≃	272c	18.59 N	73.00 E
Panwāri	124	25.27 N	79.29 E
Panxi	106	30.35 N	119.20 E
Panxian	102	25.50 N	104.36 E
Panxidu	98	35.39 N	115.52 E
Panyabungan	114	0.51 N	99.33 E
Panyam	150	9.25 N	9.13 E
Panyang	140	10.04 N	29.58 E
Panyčevo	86	57.05 N	81.49 E
Panyu	100	22.57 N	113.20 E
Panzerstausee ⊜[1]	263	51.11 N	7.16 E
Panzhuang	105	39.20 N	117.28 E
Panzi	152	7.13 S	17.58 E
Panzós	236	15.24 N	89.40 W
Pao ≃, Thai	110	16.13 N	103.43 E
Pao ≃, Ven.	246	8.06 N	64.17 W
Pao ≃, Ven.	246	8.33 N	68.01 W
Paochi → Baoji	102	34.23 N	107.09 E
Pão de Açúcar	250	9.45 S	37.26 W
Pão de Açúcar (Sugar Loaf) ʌ	287a	22.57 S	43.09 W
Paoki → Baoji	102	34.23 N	107.09 E
Paola, It.	68	39.22 N	16.03 E
Paola, Ks., U.S.	198	38.34 N	94.52 W
Paoli, In., U.S.	218	38.33 N	86.28 W
Paoli, Pa., U.S.	208	40.02 N	75.28 W
Paoli, Wi., U.S.	216	42.56 N	89.32 W
Paonia	200	38.52 N	107.35 W
Pāonta Sāhib	124	30.27 N	77.37 E
Paopao	174s	17.31 S	149.49 W
Paoshenmiao	98	41.12 N	118.17 E
Paotai Yingzi	98	41.48 N	115.12 E
Paoting → Baoding	105	38.52 N	115.29 E
Paotow → Baotou	102	40.40 N	109.59 E
Paoua	152	7.15 N	16.26 E
Paoying → Baoying	100	33.16 N	119.20 E
P'aozero, ozero ⊜	24	66.05 N	30.58 E
Paozi	104	42.13 N	122.19 E
Pap	85	40.53 N	71.07 E
Pápa	30	47.19 N	17.28 E
Papa, Sound of ⊔	46a	60.18 N	1.41 W
Papagaio	250	6.01 S	45.21 W
Papagaio ≃, Bra.	246	1.53 S	62.35 W
Papagaio ≃, Bra.	248	12.56 S	58.18 W
Papagayo ≃	234	16.46 N	99.43 W
Papagayo, Golfo de ⊂	236	10.42 N	85.50 W
Papago Indian Reservation ✦[4]	200	32.20 N	112.00 W
Papaikou	229d	19.47 N	155.05 W
Papakating Creek ≃	276	41.11 N	74.38 W
Papakura	172	37.04 S	174.57 E
Papalia	112	5.58 S	124.01 E
Papaloapan ≃	234	18.42 N	95.38 W
Papanoa	234	17.21 N	101.02 W
Papantla [de Olarte]	234	20.27 N	97.19 W
Papar, Indon.	115a	7.41 S	112.04 E
Papar, Malay.	112	5.44 N	115.56 E
Papara, Poly. fr.	174s	17.44 S	149.21 W
Papara, Sol.Is.	175e	7.02 S	156.48 E
Paparoa	172	36.06 S	174.14 E
Paparoa National Park ♦	172	42.05 S	171.25 E
Paparoa Range ⋏	172	42.00 S	171.35 E
Papasidero	68	39.52 N	15.54 E
Papa Stour I	46a	60.20 N	1.42 W
Papatoetoe	172	36.58 S	174.52 E
Papawai Point ›	229a	20.47 N	156.33 W
Papa Westray I	46	59.21 N	2.54 W
Papeari	174s	17.45 S	149.21 W
Papeete	174s	17.32 S	149.34 W
Papelón	286c	10.27 N	66.47 W
Papenburg	52	53.05 N	7.23 E
Papendrecht	52	51.50 N	4.40 E
Papenoo	174s	17.30 S	149.25 W
Papenoo ≃	174s	17.30 S	149.25 W
Papetoai	174s	17.29 S	149.52 W
Papey I	24a	64.37 N	14.11 W
Paphlagonia □[9]	130	41.10 N	32.45 E
Paphos → Néa Páfos	130	34.45 N	32.25 E
Papilė	76	56.09 N	22.48 E
Papillion	198	41.09 N	96.02 W
Papineau	216	40.58 N	87.43 W
Papineau □[6]	206	45.50 N	75.00 W
Papineau, Lac ⊜	206	45.48 N	74.46 W
Papineau Creek ≃	212	45.13 N	77.43 W
Papineau-Labelle, Réserve ♦	188	45.55 N	75.20 W
Papineau Lake ⊜	212	45.20 N	77.50 W
Papineauville	206	45.37 N	75.01 W
Paposo	252	25.01 S	70.28 W
Papouasie Nouvelle-Guinée → Papua New Guinea □[1]	164	6.00 S	150.00 E
Papozze	64	44.59 N	12.02 E
Pappenheim, Dtsch.	54	50.47 N	10.27 E
Pappenheim, Dtsch.	56	48.56 N	10.58 E
Paps of Jura ⋏	46	55.55 N	6.00 W
Papua, Gulf of ⊂	164	8.30 S	145.00 E
Papua Neuguinea → Papua New Guinea □[1]	164	6.00 S	150.00 E
Papua New Guinea □[1]	164	6.00 S	147.00 E
Papuasia Nueva Guinea → Papua New Guinea □[1]	164	6.00 S	150.00 E
Papucaia	256	22.37 S	42.44 W
Papudo	252	32.31 S	71.27 W
Papulovo	24	60.34 N	48.00 E
Papun	110	18.04 N	97.27 E
Papunáua ≃	246	2.09 N	70.32 W
Papunya	162	23.16 S	131.54 E
Papurí ≃	246	0.36 N	69.11 W
Paquequer ≃	256	22.12 S	42.54 W
Paquequer, Serra do ⋏	256	22.12 S	42.40 W
Paquera	236	9.50 N	84.56 W
Paquetá, Ilha de I	287a	22.46 S	43.06 W
Par	42	50.21 N	4.43 W
Pará → Belém	250	1.27 S	48.29 W
Pará □[3]	250	4.00 S	53.00 W
Para □[5]	250	5.30 N	55.15 W
Pará ≃, Bra.	250	1.30 S	48.55 W
Pará ≃, Bra.	255	19.13 S	45.07 W
Para ≃, Ross.	80	54.23 N	40.52 E
Pará, Ilha do I	250	0.18 S	51.15 W
Para, Pulau I	112	3.05 N	125.30 E
Parabel'	86	58.43 N	81.31 E
Parabel' ≃	86	58.44 N	81.35 E
Parabiago	62	45.33 N	8.57 E
Parabita	68	40.03 N	18.08 E
Paraburdoo	162	23.14 S	117.48 E
Paracale	116	14.17 N	122.48 E
Paracambi	256	22.37 S	43.43 W
Paracari ≃	250	4.36 S	57.47 W
Paracas, Bahía de ⊂	248	13.50 S	76.17 W
Paracas, Península de ›[1]	248	13.48 S	76.24 W
Paracatu	255	17.13 S	46.52 W
Paracatu ≃, Bra.	255	16.30 S	45.04 W
Paracatu ≃, Bra.	255	16.35 S	45.06 W
Paracel Islands → Xisha Qundao II	108	16.30 N	112.15 E
Parachilna	166	31.08 S	138.23 E
Pārachinār	120	33.54 N	70.06 E
Paracho de Verduzco	234	19.39 N	102.04 W
Parachute	200	39.27 N	108.03 W
Paraćin	38	43.52 N	21.24 E
Parácuaro	234	20.09 N	100.46 W
Paracuellos de Jarama	266a	40.30 N	3.32 W
Paracuru	250	3.24 S	39.04 W
Parád	30	47.55 N	20.02 E
Parada, Punta ›	248	15.22 S	75.12 W
Paradas	34	37.18 N	5.30 W
Paradino	76	53.59 N	31.51 E
Paradise, Guy.	246	6.45 N	58.00 W
Paradise, Ca., U.S.	204	39.44 N	121.38 W
Paradise, Mt., U.S.	202	47.23 N	114.48 W
Paradise, Nv., U.S.	204	36.09 N	115.10 W
Paradise, Pa., U.S.	208	40.01 N	76.08 W
Paradise, Tx., U.S.	222	33.09 N	97.41 W
Paradise Hill, Sk., Can.	184	53.32 N	109.28 W
Paradise Hill, Ak., U.S.	180	62.25 N	160.03 W
Paradise Island I	240b	25.05 N	77.19 W
Paradise Mountain ʌ	171a	27.45 S	152.02 E
Paradise Valley, Az., U.S.	200	33.31 N	111.56 W
Paradise Valley, Nv., U.S.	204	41.29 N	117.32 W
Parado	115b	8.45 S	118.36 E
Parado ≃	250	10.17 S	55.39 W
Pāradwīp	120	20.16 N	86.37 E
Parafield	168b	34.47 S	138.38 E
Parafijevka	78	50.53 N	32.38 E
Paragačaj	84	39.07 N	45.56 E
Paragon	218	39.23 N	86.33 W
Paragonah	200	37.53 N	112.46 W
Paragould	194	36.03 N	90.30 W
Paraguá ≃, Bol.	248	13.34 S	61.53 W
Paragua ≃, Ven.	246	6.55 N	62.55 W
Paraguaçu	256	21.33 S	45.44 W
Paraguaçu ≃	255	12.45 S	38.54 W
Paraguaçu Paulista	255	22.25 S	50.34 W
Paraguaipoa	246	11.21 N	71.57 W
Paraguaná, Península de ›[1]	246	11.55 N	70.00 W
Paraguarí	252	25.38 S	57.09 W
Paraguarí □[5]	252	26.00 S	57.10 W
Paraguay □[1], S.A.	244	23.00 S	58.00 W
Paraguay □[1], S.A.	252	23.00 S	58.00 W
Paraguay (Paraguai) ≃	18	27.18 S	58.38 W
Parahyba → João Pessoa	250	7.07 S	34.52 W
Parai, Represa do ⊜[1]	256	23.20 S	45.35 W
Paraíba □[3]	250	7.15 S	36.30 W
Paraíba do Sul	256	22.09 S	43.17 W
Paraíba do Sul ≃	255	21.37 S	41.03 W
Paraibano	250	6.30 S	44.01 W
Paraibuna	256	23.23 S	45.39 W
Paraibuna ≃, Bra.	256	22.06 S	43.08 W
Paraibuna ≃, Bra.	256	23.22 S	45.40 W
Paraibuna, Represa do ⊜[1]	256	23.25 S	45.30 W
Paraíso, Bra.	255	19.03 S	52.59 W
Paraíso, Bra.	256	22.19 S	45.42 W
Paraíso, C.R.	236	9.50 N	83.51 W
Paraíso, Méx.	234	18.24 N	93.14 W
Paraiso, Pan.	236	9.02 N	79.38 W
Paraíso do Norte	255	23.13 S	52.38 W
Paraíso Garcia	256	21.32 S	43.53 W
Paraíso Novillero	234	18.16 N	95.59 W
Paraisópolis	256	22.33 S	45.47 W
Paraitinga ≃, Bra.	256	23.34 S	46.02 W
Paraitinga ≃, Bra.	256	23.22 S	45.40 W
Parakan	115a	7.17 S	110.06 E
Parakou	150	9.21 N	2.37 E
Paralía Aspropírgos	267c	38.02 N	23.35 E
Paralímni	130	35.02 N	33.59 E
Parama Island I	164	9.00 S	143.25 E
Paramakkudi	122	9.33 N	78.36 E
Paramaribo	250	5.50 N	55.10 W
Parambu	250	6.13 S	40.43 W
Paramillo, Parque Nacional ♦	246	7.15 N	76.15 W
Paramirim	255	13.26 S	42.15 W
Paramirim ≃	250	11.34 S	43.18 W
Paramithiá	38	39.28 N	20.30 E
Paramonga	248	10.40 S	77.50 W
Paramoti	250	4.06 S	39.15 W
Paramount	228	33.53 N	118.09 W
Paramus	210	40.56 N	74.04 W
Paramušir, ostrov I	74	50.25 N	155.50 E
Paramus Park ✦[9]	276	40.57 N	74.04 W
Paran, Naḥal (Wādī al-Jirāfī) V	132	30.24 N	35.10 E
Paraná, Arg.	252	31.44 S	60.32 W
Paranã, Bra.	255	12.33 S	47.52 W
Paraná □[3]	252	24.00 S	51.00 W
Paranã ≃, Bra.	255	12.30 S	48.14 W

DEUTSCH: Name · Seite · Breite°′ · Länge°′ E = Ost

Symbols in the index entries represent the broad categories identified in the key at the right. Symbols with superior numbers (⋏[1]) identify subcategories (see complete key on page I · 1).

Symbole im Register stellen die rechts im Schlüssel erklärten Kategorien dar. Symbole mit hochgestellten Ziffern (⋏[1]) bezeichnen Unterabteilungen einer Kategorie (vgl. vollständiger Schlüssel auf Seite I · 1).

Los símbolos incluídos en el texto del índice representan las grandes categorías identificadas con la clave a la derecha. Los símbolos con numeros en su parte superior (⋏[1]) identifican las subcategorías (véase la clave completa en la página I · 1).

Les symboles de l'index représentent les catégories indiquées dans la légende à droite. Les symboles suivis d'un indice (⋏[1]) représentent des sous-catégories (voir légende complète à la page I · 1).

Os símbolos incluídos no texto do índice representam as grandes categorias identificadas com a chave à direita. Os símbolos com números em sua parte superior (⋏[1]) identificam as subcategorias (veja-se a chave completa à página I · 1).

ʌ Mountain	Berg	Montaña	Montagne	Montanha
⋏ Mountains	Gebirge	Montañas	Montagnes	Montanhas
)(Pass	Paß	Paso	Col	Passo
V Valley, Canyon	Tal, Cañon	Valle, Cañón	Vallée, Canyon	Vale, Canhão
⩧ Plain	Ebene	Llano	Plaine	Planície
› Cape	Kap	Cabo	Cap	Cabo
I Island	Insel	Isla	Île	Ilha
II Islands	Inseln	Islas	Îles	Ilhas
⊥ Other Topographic Features	Andere Topographische Objekte	Otros Elementos Topográficos	Autres données topographiques	Outros acidentes topográficos

Para-Pawa I · 133

ESPAÑOL

Nombre	Página	Lat.°'	Long.°' W = Oeste
Paraná ≏, S.A.	18	33.43 S	59.15 W
Paraná, Pico ∧	252	25.16 S	48.48 W
Paranabi	256	23.54 S	45.14 W
Paraná Bravo ≏ [1]	258	33.53 S	58.27 W
Paranacito ≏	258	33.44 S	58.33 W
Paraná de las Palmas ≏ [1]	258	34.18 S	58.33 W
Paranaguá	252	25.31 S	48.30 W
Paranaguá, Baía de ⊂	252	25.29 S	48.33 W
Paraná Guazú ≏ [1]	258	34.00 S	58.25 W
Paranaíba	255	19.40 S	51.11 W
Paranaíba ≏	255	20.07 S	51.05 W
Paranaidji	250	6.33 S	47.27 W
Paranaíta ≏	250	9.28 S	56.43 W
Paranam	250	5.37 N	55.06 W
Paraná Miní ≏ [1]	258	34.13 S	58.25 W
Paranapanema ≏	255	22.40 S	53.09 W
Paranapiacaba	256	23.47 S	46.19 W
Paranapiacaba, Serra do ⋌	252	24.20 S	49.00 W
Parañaque	269f	14.30 N	120.59 E
Paranavaí	255	23.04 S	52.28 W
Parang, Pil.	116	7.23 N	124.16 E
Parang, Pil.	116	5.55 N	120.54 E
Parang, Pulau I	115a	5.45 S	110.14 E
Paran'ga	80	56.43 N	49.24 E
Paranhos	255	23.55 S	55.25 W
Paranjang	98	37.08 N	126.55 E
Paranoá, Lago do ⊜	255	15.48 S	47.50 W
Párao de Masa, Puerto de)(	34	42.38 N	3.46 W
Paraopeba	255	19.18 S	44.25 W
Parapara	246	9.44 N	67.18 W
Paraparaumu	172	40.55 S	175.01 E
Paraparaumu Beach	172	40.54 S	174.59 E
Parapaye	58	45.55 N	7.32 E
Parapetí ≏	248	18.58 S	62.21 W
Parara	112	2.37 S	120.07 E
Parás, Méx.	196	26.30 N	99.31 W
Paras, Perú	248	13.30 S	74.35 W
Parasan	116	8.05 N	123.33 E
Parāsī	124	27.32 N	83.40 E
Parāsia	124	22.12 N	78.46 E
Parasida	126	23.46 N	87.20 E
Parasnāth	124	23.59 N	86.02 E
Paratei	256	23.14 S	46.00 W
Parateí ≏	256	23.12 S	46.00 W
Parati	256	23.13 S	44.43 W
Paratico	64	45.39 N	9.57 E
Parati-Mirim	256	23.14 S	44.38 W
Paratinga	255	12.42 S	43.10 W
Paratoo	166	32.42 S	139.22 E
Parauapebas ≏	250	5.35 S	49.41 W
Parauari ≏	250	4.36 S	57.47 W
Paraúna	255	17.02 S	50.26 W
Paravani, ozero ⊜	84	41.26 N	43.48 E
Para Wirra Recreation Park ♠	168b	34.43 S	138.50 E
Paray-le-Monial	32	46.27 N	4.07 E
Parbakalan	114	2.38 N	98.27 E
Pārbati ≏	124	25.51 N	76.36 E
Pārbatipur	124	25.39 N	88.55 E
Parbhani	122	19.16 N	76.47 E
Parbig	86	57.14 N	81.24 E
Parbig ≏	86	57.37 N	82.18 E
Parbold	262	53.36 N	2.46 W
Parburuan	114	1.52 N	99.55 E
Parchen	54	52.21 N	12.05 E
Parchim	54	53.25 N	11.51 E
Parchment	216	42.19 N	85.34 W
Parchomenko	83	48.34 N	39.43 E
Parchomovka	78	50.08 N	35.01 E
Parcines (Partschins)	64	46.41 N	11.04 E
Parczew	30	51.39 N	22.54 E
Pardee Reservoir ⊜ [1]	226	38.16 N	120.51 W
Pardeeville	190	43.32 N	89.18 W
Pardes Hanna-Karkur	132	32.28 N	34.58 E
Pārdi	122	20.31 N	72.57 E
Parding	120	32.52 N	88.39 E
Pardo ≏, Bra.	250	5.21 S	52.53 W
Pardo ≏, Bra.	252	29.59 S	52.23 W
Pardo ≏, Bra.	255	15.48 S	44.48 W
Pardo ≏, Bra.	255	20.10 S	48.38 W
Pardo ≏, Bra.	255	22.55 S	49.58 W
Pardo ≏, Bra.	255	15.39 S	38.57 W
Pardo ≏, Bra.	255	21.46 S	52.09 W
Pardo ≏, Bra.	256	23.32 S	45.30 W
Pardo ≏, Bra.	256	21.25 S	42.39 W
Pardomuan	114	2.06 N	98.20 E
Pardubice	30	50.02 N	15.47 E
Pare	115a	7.46 S	112.11 E
Parece Vela → Okino-Tori-shima I	90	20.25 N	136.00 E
Parecis	248	14.09 S	56.56 W
Parecis ≏	248	12.56 S	56.43 W
Parecis, Chapada dos ⋌	248	13.00 S	60.00 W
Parede	266c	38.41 N	9.21 W
Paredes de Nava	34	42.09 N	4.41 W
Paredón	232	25.56 N	100.58 W
Parelhas	250	6.41 S	36.39 W
Parelheiros ⊸ [8]	256	23.51 S	46.44 W
Pareloup, Lac de ⊜	32	44.15 N	2.45 E
Paremata	172	41.07 S	174.52 E
Parempei I	174r	7.01 N	158.15 E
Paren'	74	62.28 N	163.05 E
Paren' ≏	74	62.25 N	163.10 E
Parengarenga Harbour ⊂	172	34.31 S	172.57 E
Parent	176	47.55 N	74.37 W
Parent, Lac ⊜	190	48.38 N	77.03 W
Parentis-en-Born	32	44.21 N	1.05 W
Pareora	172	44.30 S	171.12 E
Parepare	112	4.01 S	119.38 E
Parera	252	35.08 S	64.32 W
Parets del Vallès	266d	41.34 N	2.14 E
Parey	54	52.22 N	11.59 E
Parfenjevo, Ross.	24	61.21 N	42.43 E
Parfenjevo, Ross.	80	58.29 N	43.25 E
Parfentevo	82	55.06 N	38.49 E
Parfino	76	57.58 N	31.41 E
Parforce-Heide ⊸ [3]	264a	52.22 N	13.10 E
Párga	38	39.17 N	20.23 E
Pārgaon	272c	18.59 N	73.05 E
Pargarutan	114	1.28 N	99.20 E
Pargas (Parainen)	26	60.18 N	22.18 E
Pargey Creek ≏	285	39.49 N	75.18 W
Pargny-sur-Saulx	56	48.46 N	4.50 E
Pargolovo ⊸ [8]	265a	60.04 N	30.18 E
Parham	240c	17.05 N	61.46 W
Parhebangan	114	2.15 N	98.45 E
Pari ⊸ [8]	287b	23.32 S	46.37 W
Paria ≏	200	36.52 N	111.36 W
Paria, Gulf of ⊂	246	10.20 N	62.00 W
Paria, Península de ≻ [1]	241r	10.40 N	62.10 W
Pariaguán	246	8.51 N	64.43 W
Pariaman	112	0.38 S	100.08 E
Pariamanu ≏	248	12.26 S	69.16 W
Pariči	76	52.48 N	29.25 E
Paricutín ∧ [1]	234	19.28 N	102.15 W
Parida, Isla I	236	8.07 N	82.20 W
Pariette Draw ⋁	200	40.02 N	109.45 W
Parigi, Indon.	112	0.48 S	120.10 E
Parigi, Indon.	115a	6.12 S	106.22 E
Parigné-L'Évêque	50	47.56 N	0.22 E
Parika	246	6.52 N	58.25 W
Parikkala	26	61.33 N	29.30 E
Parima ≏	246	3.34 N	63.47 W
Parima, Sierra ⋌	246	2.30 N	64.00 W
Pariñas, Punta ≻	246	4.40 S	81.20 W
Parîngu Mare, Vîrful ∧	38	45.22 N	23.33 E
Parintins	250	2.36 S	56.44 W
Paripiranga	250	10.41 S	37.52 W
Pariquera-Açu	252	24.43 S	47.53 W
Paris, On., Can.	212	43.12 N	80.23 W
Paris, Fr.	50	48.52 N	2.20 E
Paris, Fr.	261	48.52 N	2.20 E

FRANÇAIS

Nom	Page	Lat.°'	Long.°' W = Ouest
Paris, Ar., U.S.	194	35.17 N	93.43 W
Paris, Id., U.S.	202	42.13 N	111.24 W
Paris, Il., U.S.	194	39.36 N	87.41 W
Paris, Ky., U.S.	218	38.12 N	84.15 W
Paris, Me., U.S.	188	44.15 N	70.30 W
Paris, Mo., U.S.	219	39.28 N	92.00 W
Paris, Oh., U.S.	214	40.48 N	81.10 W
Paris, Pa., U.S.	214	40.24 N	80.31 W
Paris, Tn., U.S.	194	36.18 N	88.19 W
Paris, Tx., U.S.	196	33.39 N	95.33 W
Paris □ [5]	261	48.52 N	2.20 E
Paris, Port de ⊂	261	48.57 N	2.17 E
Parish	210	43.24 N	76.07 W
Parisien de Pantin, Cimetière ⊸	261	48.54 N	2.23 E
Parisienne, Ile I	190	46.41 N	84.44 W
Paris-le-Bourget, Aéroport de ⊠	50	48.52 N	2.25 E
Parismina	236	10.12 N	83.38 W
Parismina ≏	236	10.19 N	83.21 W
Paris-Orly, Aéroport de ⊠	50	48.43 N	2.22 E
Paris-Plage, Aéroport ⊠	50	50.31 N	1.38 E
Parit	112	3.10 S	104.38 E
Parita, Bahía de ⊂	236	8.08 N	80.24 W
Parit Bunga	114	2.04 N	102.33 E
Parit Buntar	114	5.07 N	100.30 E
Pariti	112	10.01 S	123.43 E
Parit Jawa	114	1.57 N	102.39 E
Parižskaja Kommuna ⊸ [8]	83	48.26 N	38.49 E
Park ≏	198	48.28 N	97.09 W
Park, North Branch ≏	198	48.26 N	97.27 W
Park, South Branch ≏	198	48.26 N	97.27 W
Parka	154	4.31 N	27.20 E
Parkano	26	62.01 N	23.01 E
Parkany	38	46.49 N	29.31 E
Parkchester	285	40.00 N	75.35 W
Park City, Il., U.S.	216	42.21 N	87.53 W
Park City, Ks., U.S.	198	37.48 N	97.19 W
Park City, Mt., U.S.	202	45.37 N	108.55 W
Park City, Ut,. U.S.	200	40.38 N	111.29 W
Park Creek ≏	285	40.13 N	75.08 W
Parkdale, P.E., Can.	186	46.15 N	63.07 W
Parkdale, Mo., U.S.	219	38.29 N	90.32 W
Parkdale, Or., U.S.	224	45.31 N	121.35 W
Parkdene	273d	26.14 S	28.16 E
Parkent	85	41.18 N	69.40 E
Parker, Az., U.S.	200	34.09 N	114.17 W
Parker, Co., U.S.	198	39.31 N	104.45 W
Parker, Fl., U.S.	194	30.07 N	85.36 W
Parker, Pa., U.S.	214	41.05 N	79.41 W
Parker, S.D., U.S.	198	43.23 N	97.08 W
Parker □ [6]	222	32.48 N	97.42 W
Parker ≏	207	42.45 N	70.49 W
Parker, Cape ≻	176	75.04 N	79.40 W
Parker, Lake ⊜	220	28.04 N	81.56 W
Parker City	218	40.11 N	85.12 W
Parker Dam	204	34.17 N	114.08 W
Parker Dam ⊸ [6]	200	34.18 N	114.10 W
Parker Ford	285	40.12 N	75.35 W
Parker Peak ∧	198	43.24 N	103.41 W
Parker Range	162	31.38 S	119.35 E
Parker River National Wildlife Refuge ⊸ [4]	283	42.45 N	70.48 W
Parkersburg, Il., U.S.	194	38.36 N	88.03 W
Parkersburg, Ia., U.S.	190	42.34 N	92.47 W
Parkersburg, W.V., U.S.	188	39.16 N	81.33 W
Parkers Creek ≏	285	40.00 N	74.53 W
Parkers Prairie	198	46.09 N	95.19 W
Parkerville	168a	31.53 S	116.09 E
Parker Volcano ∧ [1]	116	6.07 N	124.54 E
Parkes	166	33.08 S	148.11 E
Parkesburg	208	39.57 N	75.55 W
Park Falls	190	45.56 N	90.26 W
Park Forest	216	41.28 N	87.38 W
Parkgate, Eng., U.K.	262	53.18 N	3.05 W
Parkgate, Eng., U.K.	262	53.16 N	2.20 W
Park Hall	208	38.13 N	76.25 W
Parkhill, On., Can.	190	43.09 N	81.41 W
Parkhill, Pa., U.S.	214	40.22 N	78.52 W
Parkhill Gardens	273d	26.14 S	28.11 E
Parkin	194	35.15 N	90.34 W
Park Lake	216	42.48 N	84.27 W
Parkland, Pa., U.S.	285	40.09 N	74.56 W
Parkland, Wa., U.S.	224	47.09 N	122.25 W
Parklawn	284c	38.50 N	77.09 W
Park Layne	218	39.53 N	84.03 W
Parklea	274a	33.44 S	150.57 E
Parkman	214	41.22 N	81.03 W
Park Meadows	279b	40.18 N	79.44 W
Park Orchards	274b	37.46 S	145.13 E
Park Plateau ⋌ [1]	198	37.15 N	104.45 W
Park Range ⋌	200	40.40 N	106.40 W
Park Rapids	198	46.55 N	95.03 W
Park Ridge, Il., U.S.	216	42.00 N	87.50 W
Park Ridge, N.J., U.S.	276	41.02 N	74.02 W
Park Ridge Farms	285	40.10 N	74.42 W
Park River	198	48.23 N	97.44 W
Parkrose	224	45.33 N	122.33 W
Park Rynie	158	30.25 S	30.35 E
Parks	180	57.38 N	154.00 W
Parks Creek ≏	212	44.17 N	77.21 W
Park Shore Resort	216	41.55 N	85.59 W
Parkside, Md., U.S.	284c	39.02 N	77.06 W
Parkside, Pa., U.S.	285	39.52 N	75.23 W
Parksley	208	37.46 N	75.39 W
Park Station ⊸ [5]	273d	26.12 S	28.03 E
Parkstein	60	49.44 N	12.04 E
Parkstetten	60	48.55 N	12.36 E
Parkston	198	43.23 N	97.59 W
Parksville, B.C., Can.	182	49.19 N	124.19 W
Parksville, N.Y., U.S.	210	41.51 N	74.45 W
Parktown ⊸ [8]	273d	26.11 S	28.03 E
Parktown North ⊸ [8]	273d	26.09 S	28.02 E
Parkview	279b	40.30 N	79.56 W
Parkville, Md., U.S.	208	39.22 N	76.32 W
Parkville, Mo., U.S.	194	39.11 N	94.40 W
Parkwater	202	47.40 N	117.19 W
Parkway, Ca., U.S.	226	38.29 N	121.27 W
Parkway, Mo., U.S.	219	38.20 N	90.57 W
Parkwood	284c	39.01 N	77.05 W
Parla	34	40.14 N	3.46 W
Parlākimidi	122	18.47 N	84.06 E
Parle, Lac qui ⊜	198	45.07 N	96.00 W
Parli	122	18.51 N	76.32 E
Parliament, Houses of ⍦	260	51.30 N	0.07 W
Parlier	226	36.36 N	119.31 W
Parma, It.	64	44.48 N	10.20 E
Parma, Id., U.S.	202	43.47 N	116.56 W
Parma, Mi., U.S.	216	42.15 N	84.35 W
Parma, Mo., U.S.	194	36.36 N	89.48 W
Parma, Oh., U.S.	214	41.24 N	81.43 W
Parma □ [4]	64	44.40 N	10.10 E
Parma ≏	64	44.56 N	10.26 E
Parma Heights	214	41.23 N	81.45 W
Parmain	261	49.07 N	2.12 E
Parmatown Mall ⊸ [9]	279a	41.23 N	81.44 W
Parnaguá	250	10.13 S	44.38 W
Parnahyba → Parnaíba	250	2.54 S	41.47 W
Parnaíba	250	2.54 S	41.47 W
Parnaíba ≏	250	3.00 S	41.50 W
Parnaíbinha ≏	250	9.17 S	45.55 W
Parnamirim	250	8.05 S	39.34 W
Parnarama	250	5.41 S	43.06 W
Parnassós ∧	38	38.32 N	22.35 E
Parnassus	172	42.43 S	173.18 E
Parndorf	61	47.59 N	16.51 E
Parnell	216	40.14 N	88.42 W
Párnis ∧	38	38.11 N	23.42 E
Párnis Óros ⋌	267c	38.07 N	23.44 E
Parnon ⋌	38	37.05 N	22.40 E
Pärnu	76	58.24 N	24.32 E

PORTUGUÊS

Nome	Página	Lat.°'	Long.°' W = Oeste
Pärnu ≏	76	58.23 N	24.29 E
Pärnu-Jaagupi	76	58.37 N	24.30 E
Pärnu laht ⊂	76	58.15 N	24.25 E
Paro	124	27.26 N	89.25 E
Pārola	120	20.53 N	75.07 E
Paromaj	89	52.50 N	143.02 E
Paroo	162	26.16 S	119.46 E
Paroo ≏	166	31.28 S	143.32 E
Parorā	272b	22.48 N	88.09 E
Páros	38	37.04 N	25.08 E
Páros I	38	37.08 N	25.12 E
Parow	158	33.53 S	18.37 E
Parowan	200	37.50 N	112.49 W
Parpaillon ⋌	62	44.30 N	6.40 E
Parpan	58	46.46 N	9.33 E
Parr	216	41.02 N	87.13 W
Parral, Chile	252	36.09 S	71.50 W
Parral → Hidalgo del Parral, Méx.	232	26.56 N	105.40 W
Parral, Oh., U.S.	214	40.33 N	81.30 W
Parral ≏	232	27.39 N	105.07 W
Parramatta	170	33.49 S	151.00 E
Parramatta ≏	274a	33.51 S	151.14 E
Parramatta Park ♠	274a	33.49 S	151.00 E
Parramore Island I	208	37.32 N	75.38 W
Parras de la Fuente	232	25.25 N	102.11 W
Parrett ≏	42	51.13 N	3.01 W
Parrish, Al., U.S.	194	33.43 N	87.17 W
Parrish, Fl., U.S.	220	27.35 N	82.25 W
Parris Island Marine Corps Recruit Depot ■	192	32.21 N	80.41 W
Parrita	236	9.30 N	84.19 W
Parrita ≏	236	9.29 N	84.19 W
Parrsboro	186	45.24 N	64.20 W
Parry, Cape ≻	176	70.08 N	124.24 W
Parry, Mount ∧	182	52.53 N	128.45 W
Parry Bay ⊂	176	68.07 N	82.00 W
Parry Channel ⊔	16	74.20 N	98.00 W
Parry Island I	212	45.18 N	80.10 W
Parry Island Indian Reserve ⊸ [4]	212	45.18 N	80.10 W
Parry Peninsula ≻ [1]	180	69.45 N	124.30 W
Parry Sound	212	45.21 N	80.02 W
Parry Sound □ [6]	212	45.25 N	79.55 W
Parry Sound ⊔	212	45.21 N	80.06 W
Parryville	208	40.49 N	75.40 W
Parsberg	60	49.09 N	11.43 E
Parsdorf	60	48.09 N	11.47 E
Parseier Spitze ∧	58	47.10 N	10.28 E
Parsęta ≏	30	54.12 N	15.33 E
Parshād	120	24.11 N	73.42 E
Parshall	198	47.57 N	102.08 W
Parshallville	281	42.41 N	83.46 W
Paršino	88	59.10 N	111.48 E
Parsippany	210	40.51 N	74.25 W
Parsippany, Lake ⊜	276	40.51 N	74.26 W
Parsnāth ∧	124	23.53 N	86.08 E
Parsnip ≏	182	55.10 N	123.00 W
Parsoburan	114	2.19 N	99.20 E
Parsonage Island I	276	40.37 N	73.37 W
Parsons, Ks., U.S.	198	37.20 N	95.15 W
Parsons, Tn., U.S.	194	35.38 N	88.07 W
Parsons, W.V., U.S.	188	39.05 N	79.40 W
Parsons, Mount ∧ [2]	164	13.33 S	135.09 E
Parson's Pond	186	50.02 N	57.43 W
Parsons Pond ⊜	186	50.00 N	57.35 W
Parsons Range ⋌	164	13.30 S	135.15 E
Parsteiner See ⊜	54	52.55 N	13.59 E
Pärsti	76	58.25 N	25.32 E
Partābpur	124	23.29 N	83.13 E
Partanna	70	37.43 N	12.53 E
Partāppur	126	21.48 N	86.44 E
Partenen	58	46.58 N	10.03 E
Parthala	272a	28.36 N	77.24 E
Parthe ≏	54	51.22 N	12.21 E
Parthenay	32	46.39 N	0.15 W
Partington	262	53.25 N	2.26 W
Partinico	70	38.03 N	13.07 E
Partizansk	89	43.08 N	133.09 E
Partizánske	30	48.39 N	18.23 E
Partizanskoje	86	55.30 N	94.24 E
Parton	44	54.34 N	3.35 W
Partridge, Point ≻	224	48.13 N	122.46 W
Partridge Creek ≏	212	44.44 N	77.13 W
Partridge Crop Lake ⊜	184	55.38 N	97.27 W
Partridge Point ≻	186	50.09 N	56.10 W
Partry	48	53.41 N	9.19 W
Partschins → Parcines	64	46.41 N	11.04 E
Paru ≏, Bra.	250	1.33 S	52.38 W
Parú ≏, Ven.	246	4.20 N	66.27 W
Parubcan	116	13.43 N	123.45 E
Paru de Este ≏	250	1.10 N	54.40 W
Paru de Oeste ≏	250	1.30 S	56.00 W
Parung	115a	6.25 S	106.42 E
Pårup, Dan.	41	55.24 N	10.20 E
Pårup, Dan.	41	56.08 N	9.21 E
Parūr	122	10.09 N	76.14 E
Paruro	248	13.46 S	71.51 W
Parutino	78	46.43 N	31.53 E
Parvān □ [4]	120	35.15 N	69.30 E
Pārvatīpuram	122	18.47 N	83.26 E
Parvin State Park ♠	208	39.30 N	75.09 W
Pârvomaj	38	42.06 N	25.13 E
Paryang	120	30.11 N	83.09 E
Påryd	26	56.34 N	15.55 E
Parys	158	27.04 S	27.16 E
Paša ≏	76	60.29 N	32.55 E
Paşabahçe ⊸ [8]	267b	41.06 N	29.05 E
Pasacao	116	13.31 N	123.03 E
Pasaco	236	13.59 N	90.12 W
Pasadena, Nf., Can.	186	49.01 N	57.36 W
Pasadena, Ca., U.S.	228	34.08 N	118.08 W
Pasadena, Md., U.S.	208	39.06 N	76.34 W
Pasadena, Tx., U.S.	222	29.41 N	95.12 W
Pasado, Cabo ≻	246	0.22 S	80.30 W
Pasaje	246	3.20 S	79.49 W
Pasaje ≏	252	25.35 S	63.57 W
Pasaje Talavera ≏ [1]	258	33.53 S	58.55 W
Pa Sak ≏	110	14.21 N	100.35 E
Paşaköy	130	35.09 N	33.36 E
Pasaleng Bay ⊂	116	18.36 N	120.56 E
Paşalimanı Adası I	130	40.28 N	27.37 E
Pasān	124	22.51 N	82.12 E
Pasanauri	84	42.21 N	44.41 E
Pasangkayu	112	1.10 S	119.20 E
Pasarbantal	112	2.45 S	101.20 E
Pasarseluma	112	4.09 S	102.32 E
Pasar Senen Station ⊸ [5]	269e	6.10 S	106.50 E
Pasarsorkam	114	1.53 N	98.34 E
Pasarwajo	112	5.29 S	122.50 E
Pasatiempo	226	37.02 N	122.02 W
Pasaunda	272a	28.42 N	77.21 E
Pasawng	110	18.52 N	97.18 E
Pasay	269f	14.33 N	121.00 E
Pasayten ≏	224	49.08 N	120.35 W
Pasayten, Middle Fork ≏	224	48.53 N	120.37 W
Pasayten, West Fork ≏	224	48.53 N	120.37 W
Pascack Brook ≏	276	40.59 N	73.59 W
Pascagama, Lac ⊜	190	48.34 N	75.36 W
Pascagoula	194	30.21 N	88.33 W
Pascagoula ≏	194	30.21 N	88.34 W
Pascalis, Lac ⊜	190	48.16 N	77.24 W
Paşcani	38	47.15 N	26.44 E
Pasching	61	48.15 N	14.12 E
Pasco	202	46.13 N	119.05 W
Pasco □ [5]	248	10.30 S	75.15 W
Pasco □ [6]	220	28.20 N	82.27 W
Pascoag	207	41.57 N	71.42 W
Pascoe Vale	274b	37.44 S	144.56 E
Pascua ≏	254	48.13 S	73.22 W
Pascua, Isla de (Easter Island) (Rapa Nui) I	174z	27.07 S	109.22 W

Pas-de-Calais □ [5]	50	50.30 N	2.20 E
Pas-en-Artois	50	50.09 N	2.30 E
Pasewalk	54	53.30 N	14.00 E
Pashmāl	123	35.26 N	72.36 E
Pasian di Prato	64	46.03 N	13.11 E
Pasiano di Pordenone	64	45.51 N	12.37 E
Pasig	116	14.33 N	121.05 E
Pasig ≏	269f	14.36 N	120.58 E
Pāsighāt	120	28.04 N	95.20 E
Pašija	86	58.26 N	58.16 E
P'asina ≏	74	73.50 N	87.10 E
Pasinler (Hasankale)	130	39.59 N	41.41 E
Pašino	86	55.11 N	83.00 E
P'asino, ozero ⊜	74	69.45 N	87.45 E
P'asinskij zaliv ⊂	74	74.00 N	86.00 E
Pasirganting	112	2.02 S	100.53 E
Pasir Gudang	271c	1.27 N	103.53 E
Pasirian	115a	8.13 S	113.06 E
Pasir Mas	114	6.02 N	102.08 E
Pasir Panjang	271c	1.17 N	103.47 E
Pasirpengarayan	114	0.51 N	100.16 E
Pasir Puteh, Malay.	114	5.50 N	102.24 E
Pasir Puteh, Malay.	271c	1.26 N	103.56 E
Påskallavik	26	57.10 N	16.27 E
Paskeville	168b	34.02 S	137.54 E
Paškovo, Ross.	80	53.39 N	42.25 E
Paškovo, Ross.	89	48.54 N	130.42 E
Paškovskij	78	45.02 N	39.06 E
Pasłęk	30	54.05 N	19.39 E
Pasłęka ≏	30	54.26 N	19.45 E
Pasley, Cape ≻	162	33.57 S	123.31 E
Pasley Bay ⊂	176	70.40 N	96.27 W
Pašman, Otok I	36	43.58 N	15.21 E
Pasmore ≏	166	31.07 S	139.48 E
Pašn'a	24	63.21 N	56.28 E
Pasni	128	25.16 N	63.28 E
Paso de Indios	254	43.52 S	69.06 W
Paso del Cerro	252	31.29 S	55.50 W
Paso del Macho	234	18.58 N	96.43 W
Paso de los Libres	252	29.43 S	57.05 W
Paso de los Toros	252	32.49 S	56.31 W
Paso del Rey	288	34.39 S	58.46 W
Paso del Toro	234	19.02 N	96.07 W
Paso de Ovejas	234	19.17 N	96.26 W
Paso de Patria	252	27.13 S	58.35 W
Paso de San Antonio	196	29.05 N	103.55 W
Paso Hondo	232	15.49 N	92.02 W
Paso Limay	254	40.33 S	70.26 W
Pasorapa	248	18.16 S	64.37 W
Paso Robles	226	35.37 N	120.41 W
Paso Seco	240m	17.59 N	66.23 W
Paso Severino, Embalse ⊜ [1]	258	34.15 S	56.18 W
Pašozero	76	60.02 N	34.37 E
Pasqua Indian Reserve ⊸ [4]	184	50.45 N	104.02 W
Pasque Island I	207	41.27 N	70.50 W
Pasquel, Punta ≻	232	25.30 N	111.01 W
Pasquia Hills ⋌ [2]	184	53.13 N	102.37 W
Pasquotank □ [6]	208	36.26 N	76.26 W
Pasquotank ≏	192	36.10 N	76.03 W
Pasrūr	123	32.16 N	74.40 E
Passadumkeag	188	45.11 N	68.37 W
Passadumkeag Mountain ∧ [2]	188	45.10 N	68.20 W
Passage East	48	52.13 N	6.59 W
Passagem Franca	250	6.10 S	43.47 W
Passage Point ≻	176	73.29 N	115.17 W
Passage West	48	51.52 N	8.20 W
Passaic	210	40.51 N	74.07 W
Passaic □ [6]	210	40.55 N	74.10 W
Passaic ≏	276	40.43 N	74.07 W
Passaic Falls ʟ	276	40.55 N	74.11 W
Passamaquoddy Bay ⊂	186	45.06 N	66.59 W
Passa Quatro	256	22.23 S	44.58 W
Passa Três	256	22.42 S	44.00 W
Passau	60	48.35 N	13.28 E
Passa Vinte	256	22.13 S	44.15 W
Pass Creek ≏	198	43.45 N	101.28 W
Passero, Capo ≻	70	36.40 N	15.09 E
Passignano sul Trasimeno	66	43.11 N	12.08 E
Passirio (Passer) ≏	64	46.41 N	11.10 E
Pass Island	186	47.29 N	56.11 W
Pašskij Perevoz	76	60.24 N	32.59 E
Passo Corese	66	42.09 N	12.39 E
Passo Fundo	252	28.15 S	52.24 W
Passopisciaro	70	37.52 N	15.02 E
Passo Real, Represa do ⊜ [1]	252	28.55 S	53.10 W
Passos	255	20.43 S	46.37 W
Passow	54	53.08 N	14.06 E
Passy	58	45.55 N	6.41 E
Passy ⊸ [8]	261	48.52 N	2.17 E
Pastaza □ [4]	246	1.45 S	76.50 W
Pastaza ≏	246	4.50 S	76.25 W
Pastecho ≏	182	56.07 N	114.15 W
Pasteur, Lac ⊜	186	50.13 N	66.58 W
Pastillo	240m	17.59 N	66.29 W
Pasto	246	1.13 N	77.17 W
Pastol Bay ⊂	180	63.07 N	163.15 W
Pastora Peak ∧	200	36.47 N	109.10 W
Pastoria Creek ≏	228	35.01 N	118.51 W
Pastos Bons	250	6.36 S	44.05 W
Pastrana	34	40.25 N	2.55 W
Pastrengo	64	45.29 N	10.48 E
Pašukovo	82	55.55 N	38.16 E
Pasuquin	116	18.20 N	120.37 E
Pasuruan	115a	7.38 S	112.54 E
Pasvalys	76	56.04 N	24.24 E
Pásztó	30	47.55 N	19.42 E
Pata	116	5.51 N	121.10 E
Patacamaya	248	17.14 S	67.55 W
Pātāchārkuchi	120	26.31 N	91.16 E
Patagonia	200	31.32 N	110.45 W
Patagonia ⊸ [1]	254	44.00 S	68.00 W
Pataha Creek ≏	202	46.31 N	117.59 W
Pata Island I	116	5.49 N	121.10 E
Pātan, India	120	23.50 N	72.07 E
Pātan, India	124	23.18 N	79.42 E
Patapsco	208	39.32 N	76.53 W
Patapsco ≏	208	39.09 N	76.27 W
Patapsco, Cooks Branch ≏	284b	39.27 N	76.53 W
Patapsco, Davis Branch ≏	284b	39.19 N	76.51 W
Patapsco, North Branch ≏	208	39.21 N	76.53 W
Patapsco, Rockburn Branch ≏	284b	39.14 N	76.43 W
Patapsco, Soapstone Branch ≏	284b	39.13 N	76.43 W
Patapsco, South Branch ≏	208	39.21 N	76.53 W
Patapsco River Neck ≻ [1]	284b	39.14 N	76.27 W
Patapsco Valley State Park ♠	208	39.20 N	76.55 W
Patargān, Daqq-e ≡	128	33.30 N	60.40 E
Pataudi	124	28.19 N	76.47 E
Pataula Creek ≏	192	31.46 N	85.02 W
Patay	50	48.03 N	1.42 E
Pataz	248	7.44 S	77.37 W
Patchewollock	166	35.23 S	142.11 E
Patchogue	210	40.45 N	73.00 W
Patchogue Bay ⊂	276	40.44 N	73.01 W
Patchway	42	51.32 N	2.34 W
Pat Cleburne, Lake ⊜ [1]	222	32.25 N	97.30 W
Pate	154	2.08 S	41.00 E
Patea	172	39.45 S	174.28 E
Patea ≏	172	39.46 S	174.29 E
Patearoa	172	45.16 S	170.03 E
Pategi	150	8.44 N	5.44 E
Pate Island I	154	2.07 S	41.03 E
Pateley Bridge	44	54.05 N	1.45 W
Patel Nagar ⊸ [8]	272a	28.39 N	77.10 E
Patensie	158	33.46 S	24.49 E

Patéras Óros ⋌	267c	38.07 N	23.25 E
Patergassen	64	46.49 N	13.52 E
Paterna	34	39.30 N	0.26 W
Paternal ⊸ [8]	288	34.36 S	58.28 W
Paternion	64	46.43 N	13.38 E
Paternò	70	37.34 N	14.54 E
Pateros, Pil.	269f	14.33 N	121.04 E
Pateros, Wa., U.S.	202	48.03 N	119.54 W
Patersdorf	60	49.01 N	12.59 E
Paterson, Austl.	170	32.36 S	151.37 E
Paterson, S. Afr.	158	33.26 S	25.58 E
Paterson, N.J., U.S.	210	40.55 N	74.10 W
Paterson ≏	170	32.43 S	151.39 E
Paterson, Cape ≻	169	38.40 S	145.36 E
Paterson Inlet ⊂	172	46.55 S	168.03 E
Paterswolde	52	53.08 N	6.35 E
Pātghāti	126	22.53 N	89.55 E
Pathalgaon	124	22.34 N	83.28 E
Pathānkot	123	32.17 N	75.39 E
Pathānkot Airport ⊠	123	32.15 N	75.37 E
Pātharghāra	272b	22.34 N	88.35 E
Patharia	124	23.54 N	79.12 E
Pathein (Bassein)	110	16.47 N	94.44 E
Pathfinder Reservoir ⊜ [1]	200	42.30 N	106.50 W
Pathfinder Seamount ✢ [3]	16	50.55 N	143.15 W
Pathiong	140	6.46 N	30.54 E
Pathiu	110	10.42 N	99.19 E
Path of Condie	46	56.15 N	3.30 W
Pāthrāil	126	24.12 N	89.56 E
Pathro ≏	126	24.12 N	86.48 E
Pathum Thani	110	14.01 N	100.32 E
Pati, Indon.	112	0.33 S	111.19 E
Pati, Indon.	115a	6.45 S	111.01 E
Patía	246	2.04 N	77.04 W
Patía ≏	246	2.13 N	78.40 W
Patiāla	123	30.19 N	76.24 E
Patiāla ∧	123	32.32 N	72.11 E
P'atichatki	78	48.24 N	33.42 E
Pati do Alferes	256	22.25 S	43.25 W
P'atigorsk	84	44.03 N	43.04 E
Pātihāl	272b	22.39 N	88.08 E
Patikul	116	6.04 N	121.06 E
Patillas	240m	18.00 N	66.01 W
P'atimar	80	49.31 N	50.32 E
Patinti, Selat ⊔	164	0.30 S	127.45 E
Patipāda	272c	19.04 N	73.05 E
Pati Point ≻	174p	13.36 N	144.57 E
Pātiram	124	25.19 N	88.45 E
Patire, Convento del ⍦ [1]	68	39.34 N	16.35 E
Pătîrlagele	38	45.19 N	26.22 E
Pativilca	248	10.42 S	77.47 W
Pativilca ≏	248	10.44 S	77.48 W
Pātkai Range ⋌	120	27.00 N	96.00 E
Pat Mayse Reservoir ⊜ [1]	196	33.40 N	95.35 W
Pátmos I	38	37.20 N	26.33 E
Patna, India	124	25.36 N	85.07 E
Patna, India	126	21.56 N	87.52 E
Pātna, India	272b	22.59 N	88.18 E
Patna, Scot., U.K.	44	55.21 N	4.30 W
Patnāgarh	122	20.43 N	83.09 E
Patnanongan Island I	116	14.48 N	122.11 E
P'atnica, Ross.	82	54.46 N	38.09 E
P'atnica, Ross.	82	56.05 N	36.48 E
P'atnickoje, Ross.	78	50.25 N	37.51 E
P'atnickoje, Ross.	82	54.20 N	35.53 E
Pātnoli	272c	18.57 N	73.05 E
Patnoñgon	116	10.55 N	122.00 E
Patnos	84	39.14 N	42.52 E
Pato Branco	252	26.13 S	52.40 W
Patoka	219	38.45 N	89.05 W
Patoka ≏	194	38.25 N	87.44 W
Patoka Lake ⊜ [1]	194	38.20 N	86.40 W
Patokino	82	56.27 N	39.06 E
Patomskoje nagorje ⋌ [1]	88	59.00 N	115.00 E
Paton, Île I	275a	45.31 N	73.45 W
Patonga	154	2.46 N	33.18 E
Patos	250	7.01 S	37.16 W
Patos, Lagoa dos ⊂	252	31.06 S	51.15 W
Patos, Río de los ≏	252	31.18 S	69.25 W
Patos, Rio dos ≏	248	13.33 S	56.29 W
Patos de Minas	255	18.35 S	46.32 W
Patos Island I	224	48.47 N	122.56 W
P'atovskij	82	54.41 N	36.04 E
Patquía	252	30.03 S	66.53 W
Pátrai	38	38.15 N	21.44 E
Patraïkós Kólpos ⊂	38	38.14 N	21.15 E
Patras → Pátrai	38	38.15 N	21.44 E
Pātrasāer	124	23.13 N	87.31 E
Patricio Lynch, Isla I	254	48.37 S	75.26 W
Patrick Air Force Base ■	220	28.15 N	80.36 W
Patrick Henry International Airport ⊠	208	37.08 N	76.30 W
Patrick Point ≻	214	42.35 N	81.28 W
Patrington	44	53.41 N	0.02 W
Patriot	218	38.50 N	84.49 W
Patrocínio	255	18.57 S	46.59 W
Patrocínio Paulista	255	20.38 S	47.17 W
Patsaliga Creek ≏	194	31.22 N	86.31 W
Patscherkofel ∧	64	47.13 N	11.28 E
Pattada	71	40.35 N	9.06 E
Pattani	110	6.52 N	101.16 E
Pattani ≏	110	6.53 N	101.16 E
Patten	188	45.59 N	68.26 W
Pattenburg	210	40.38 N	75.01 W
Pattensen	52	52.15 N	9.46 E
Pattenville	283	42.35 N	71.14 W
Patterdale	44	54.32 N	2.56 W
Patterson, Ca., U.S.	226	37.28 N	121.07 W
Patterson, Ga., U.S.	192	31.23 N	82.08 W
Patterson, Il., U.S.	219	39.29 N	90.29 W
Patterson, La., U.S.	194	29.41 N	91.18 W
Patterson, N.Y., U.S.	210	41.30 N	73.36 W
Patterson, Oh., U.S.	216	40.47 N	83.32 W
Patterson ≏	274b	38.05 S	145.07 E
Patterson, Mount ∧	180	64.04 N	134.39 W
Patterson Creek ≏	188	39.34 N	78.44 W
Patterson Gardens	216	41.56 N	83.25 W
Patterson Heights	214	40.45 N	80.19 W
Patterson Island I	190	48.39 N	87.00 W
Patterson Park ♠	284b	39.17 N	76.35 W
Pattersonville	210	42.53 N	74.05 W
Patti, India	123	31.17 N	74.51 E
Patti, India	124	25.55 N	82.12 E
Patti, It.	70	38.08 N	14.58 E
Patti, Golfo di ⊂	36	38.12 N	15.05 E
Pattison, Ms., U.S.	194	31.53 N	90.53 W
Pattison, Tx., U.S.	222	29.49 N	95.60 W
Pattoki	123	31.01 N	73.51 E
Patton	214	40.37 N	78.39 W
Patton, Cape ≻	169	38.42 S	143.50 E
Patton Park ♠	281	42.19 N	83.10 W
Pattonsburg	194	40.02 N	94.08 W
Patton Seamounts ✢ [3]	16	54.20 N	149.30 W
Pattscheid ⊸ [8]	263	51.05 N	7.03 E
Pattukkottai	122	10.26 N	79.19 E
Pattullo, Mount ∧	180	56.14 N	129.39 W
Patu	250	6.06 S	37.38 W
Pātua	126	22.06 N	90.23 E
Patuākhāli	124	22.21 N	90.21 E
Patuca ≏	236	15.50 N	84.17 W
Patuca, Punta ≻	236	15.51 N	84.18 W
Patuha, Gunung ∧	115a	7.10 S	107.23 E
Pātul	272b	22.45 N	88.10 E
Patul, Cerro ∧	246	2.40 S	79.03 W
Pātuli	126	23.33 N	88.15 E
Patulul	236	14.25 N	91.10 W
Patumahoe	172	37.11 S	174.50 E
Pātūr	122	20.27 N	76.56 E
Patusi	164	2.10 S	147.10 E
Patutu ∧	172	39.15 S	175.51 E
Patuxent ≏	208	38.18 N	76.25 W

Patuxent, Western Branch ≏	208	38.47 N	76.43 W
Patuxent River Naval Air Test Center ■	208	38.17 N	76.25 W
Patuxent Wildlife Research Center ⍦ [3]	284c	39.03 N	76.48 W
Patvinsuon kansallispuisto ♠	24	63.10 N	30.55 E
Patwāri	272a	28.35 N	77.27 E
Pátzcuaro	234	19.31 N	101.36 W
Pátzcuaro, Lago de ⊜	234	19.35 N	101.35 W
Patzicía	236	14.38 N	90.56 W
Patzig	54	54.28 N	13.24 E
Patzún	236	14.41 N	91.01 W
Pau	32	43.18 N	0.22 W
Pau, Gave de ≏	32	43.33 N	1.12 W
Pau Brasil	255	15.27 S	39.39 W
Paucarbamba	248	12.25 S	74.36 W
Paucarpata	248	16.26 S	71.30 W
Paucartambo	248	13.18 S	71.40 W
Paudash Lake ⊜	212	44.58 N	78.04 W
Pau dos Ferros	250	6.07 S	38.10 W
Pauh	112	2.08 S	102.48 E
Pauhunri ∧	124	27.58 N	88.50 E
Pauini	248	7.40 S	66.58 W
Pauini ≏, Bra.	246	1.42 S	62.50 W
Pauini ≏, Bra.	248	7.47 S	67.05 W
Pauk	110	21.27 N	94.27 E
Pauksa Taung ∧	110	19.55 N	94.18 E
Paul	202	42.36 N	113.46 W
Paul, Lac à ⊜	186	49.52 N	70.46 W
Paula Lima	256	21.35 S	43.29 W
Paularo	64	46.32 N	13.07 E
Paulaya ≏	236	15.51 N	85.06 W
Paulding, Ms., U.S.	194	32.01 N	89.02 W
Paulding, Oh., U.S.	216	41.08 N	84.34 W
Paulding □ [6]	216	41.08 N	84.35 W
Paulhan	32	43.32 N	3.27 E
Paulicéia	255	21.17 S	51.51 W
Paulilatino	71	40.05 N	8.46 E
Paulina Peak ∧	202	43.41 N	121.15 W
Pauline, Mount ∧	182	53.33 N	119.54 W
Paulinenaue	54	52.40 N	12.43 E
Paulínia	256	22.45 S	47.10 W
Paulino Neves	250	2.43 S	42.33 W
Paulins Kill	210	41.03 N	74.49 W
Paulins Kill ≏	210	40.55 N	75.05 W
Paulinzella ⊥	54	50.42 N	11.06 E
Paulis → Isiro	154	2.47 N	27.37 E
Paulistana	250	8.09 S	41.09 W
Paulistas	255	18.25 S	42.52 W
Paullina	198	42.58 N	95.41 W
Paull Lake ⊜	184	56.08 N	104.50 W
Paullo	62	45.25 N	9.24 E
Paulo Afonso	250	9.21 S	38.14 W
Paulo Afonso, Cachoeira de ʟ	250	9.24 S	38.13 W
Paulo de Faria	255	20.02 S	49.24 W
Pauloff Harbor (Pavlof Harbor)	180	54.27 N	162.42 W
Paulpietersburg	158	27.30 S	30.51 E
Paul Roux	158	28.18 S	27.59 E
Paul-Sauvé, Parc ♠	275a	45.28 N	74.02 W
Paulsboro	208	39.49 N	75.14 W
Pauls Cross Roads	208	37.52 N	76.53 W
Paul Seamount ✢ [3]	14	23.26 N	172.36 W
Paulstown → Whitehall	48	52.41 N	7.01 W
Pauls Valley	196	34.44 N	97.13 W
Paulton, Eng., U.K.	42	51.18 N	2.30 W
Paulton, Pa., U.S.	279b	40.34 N	79.34 W
Pauma Indian Reservation ⊸ [4]	228	33.22 N	116.58 W
Pāunān	272b	22.57 N	88.17 E
Paung	110	16.37 N	97.28 E
Paungbyin	110	24.16 N	94.49 E
Paungde	110	18.29 N	95.30 E
Paunggyi	110	17.19 N	96.11 E
Paup	164	3.15 S	142.35 E
Paupack	210	41.24 N	75.14 W
Pauri	124	30.09 N	78.47 E
Pausa, Dtsch.	54	50.35 N	12.00 E
Pausa, Perú	248	15.16 S	73.20 W
Pausin	264a	52.38 N	13.03 E
Paute	246	2.47 S	78.50 W
Paute ≏	246	2.46 S	78.16 W
Pauto ≏	246	5.09 N	70.55 W
Pautou → Baotou	102	40.40 N	109.59 E
Pauwalu Point ≻	229a	20.52 N	156.08 W
Pauwela	229a	20.56 N	156.19 W
Pauwela Point ≻	229a	20.57 N	156.19 W
Pavai ⊸ [8]	272c	19.07 N	72.55 E
Pavai Lake ⊜	272c	19.07 N	72.55 E
Pavda	86	59.15 N	59.30 E
Pāveh	128	35.03 N	46.22 E
Pavel'cevo	82	56.15 N	36.26 E
Pavelec	76	53.50 N	39.16 E
Pavelec Station ⊸ [5]	265b	55.44 N	37.38 E
Pavia	62	45.10 N	9.10 E
Pavia □ [4]	62	45.07 N	9.08 E
Pavia, Naviglio di ≊	266b	45.27 N	9.11 E
Pavia di Udine	64	45.59 N	13.17 E
Pavilion, B.C., Can.	182	50.52 N	121.50 W
Pavilion, N.Y., U.S.	210	42.52 N	78.01 W
Pavilion Key I	220	25.42 N	81.22 W
Pavillion	200	43.14 N	108.41 W
Pavilly	50	49.34 N	0.58 E
Pāvilosta	76	56.53 N	21.14 E
Pavino	24	59.07 N	46.07 E
Pavione, Monte ∧	64	46.07 N	11.50 E
Pavlice	61	48.59 N	15.53 E
Pavlikeni	38	43.14 N	25.18 E
Pavliščevo, Ross.	82	55.11 N	35.59 E
Pavliščevo, Ross.	82	55.34 N	35.59 E
Pavlodar	86	52.18 N	76.57 E
Pavlodar □ [8]	86	52.00 N	76.00 E
Pavlof Bay ⊂	180	55.30 N	161.32 W
Pavlof Volcano ∧ [1]	180	55.24 N	161.52 W
Pavlograd	78	48.32 N	35.53 E
Pavlogradka	86	54.12 N	73.33 E
Pavlopol'	83	47.16 N	37.47 E
Pavlovka, Ross.	80	52.41 N	47.09 E
Pavlovka, Ross.	86	55.25 N	56.33 E
Pavlovka, Ross.	86	51.55 N	54.47 E
Pavlovka, Ukr.	78	47.45 N	37.14 E
Pavlovka, Ukr.	83	48.08 N	39.33 E
Pavlovka, Ukr.	83	49.36 N	38.42 E
Pavlovo, Ross.	76	60.05 N	45.17 E
Pavlovo, Ross.	80	55.58 N	43.04 E
Pavlovo, Ross.	265a	59.56 N	30.40 E
Pavlovo, Ross.	265a	59.49 N	30.54 E
Pavlovsk, Ross	76	59.41 N	30.27 E
Pavlovsk, Ross.	78	50.27 N	40.08 E
Pavlovsk, Ross.	86	53.20 N	82.59 E
Pavlovskaja	78	46.08 N	39.48 E
Pavlovskaja Sloboda	82	55.49 N	37.05 E
Pavlovskij, Kaz.	86	52.32 N	63.06 E
Pavlovskij, Ross.	80	57.50 N	54.51 E
Pavlovskij Posad	82	55.47 N	38.40 E
Pavlyš	78	48.55 N	33.21 E
Pavne	272c	19.05 N	73.01 E
Pavo	192	31.02 N	84.04 W
Pavón, Arg.	258	34.23 S	59.03 W
Pavón, Col.	246	3.37 N	72.15 W
Pavón, Arroyo ≏	258	34.30 S	57.05 W
Pavona	267a	41.43 N	12.37 E
Pavonia	214	40.49 N	82.26 W
Pavšino	265b	55.49 N	37.21 E
Pavšozero	76	60.38 N	35.34 E
Pavullo nel Frignano	64	44.20 N	10.50 E
Pavuna, Arroio ≏	287a	22.58 S	43.23 W
Pavuvu Island I	175e	9.03 S	159.06 E
Pavy	76	58.03 N	29.30 E
Pawai, Pulau I	271c	1.12 N	103.43 E
Pawan ≏	112	1.51 S	109.57 E
Pawāyān	124	28.04 N	80.06 E

Symbol	English	Deutsch	Español	Français	Português
≏	River	Fluß	Río	Rivière	Rio
≊	Canal	Kanal	Canal	Canal	Canal
ʟ	Waterfall, Rapids	Wasserfall, Stromschnellen	Cascada, Rápidos	Chute d'eau, Rapides	Cascata, Rápidos
⊔	Strait	Meeresstraße	Estrecho	Détroit	Estreito
⊂	Bay, Gulf	Bucht, Golf	Bahía, Golfo	Baie, Golfe	Baía, Golfo
⊜	Lake, Lakes	See, Seen	Lago, Lagos	Lac, Lacs	Lago, Lagos
≡	Swamp	Sumpf	Pantano	Marais	Pântano
⩍	Ice Features, Glacier	Eis- und Gletscherformen	Accidentes Glaciales	Formes glaciaires	Acidentes glaciares
⍑	Other Hydrographic Features	Andere Hydrographische Objekte	Otros Elementos Hidrográficos	Autres données hydrographiques	Outros acidentes hidrográficos

Symbol	English	Deutsch	Español	Français	Português
✢	Submarine Features	Untermeerische Objekte	Accidentes Submarinos	Formes de relief sous-marin	Acidentes submarinos
□	Political Unit	Politische Einheit	Unidad Politica	Entité politique	Unidade política
⍦	Cultural Institution	Kulturelle Institution	Institución Cultural	Institution culturelle	Institução cultural
⊥	Historical Site	Historische Stätte	Sitio Histórico	Site historique	Sitio histórico
♠	Recreational Site	Erholungs- und Ferienort	Sitio de Recreo	Centre de loisirs	Area de Lazer
⊠	Airport	Flughafen	Aeropuerto	Aéroport	Aeroporto
■	Military Installation	Militäranlage	Instalación Militar	Installation militaire	Instalação militar
⊸	Miscellaneous	Verschiedenes	Misceláneo	Divers	Diversos

Symbols in the index entries represent the broad categories identified in the key at the right. Categories with superior numbers (∧¹) identify subcategories (see complete key on page I · 1).

Symbole im Register stellen die rechts im Schlüssel erklärten Kategorien dar. Symbole mit hochgestellten Ziffern (∧¹) bezeichnen Unterteilungen einer Kategorie (vgl. vollständiger Schlüssel auf Seite I · 1).

Los símbolos incluídos en el texto del índice representan las grandes categorías identificadas con la clave a la derecha. Los símbolos con números en su superior (∧¹) identifican las subcategorías (véase la clave completa en la página I · 1).

Les symboles de l'index représentent les grandes catégories identifiées dans la légende à droite. Les symboles suivis d'un indice (∧¹) représentent des sous-catégories (voir légende complète à la page I · 1).

Os símbolos incluídos no texto do índice representam as grandes categorias identificadas à direita. Os símbolos com números em sua parte superior (∧¹) identificam as subcategorias (veja-se a chave completa à página I · 1).

Symbol	English	Deutsch	Español	Français	Português
∧	Mountain	Berg	Montaña	Montagne	Montanha
∧	Mountains	Gebirge	Montañas	Montagnes	Montanhas
⋏	Pass	Paß	Paso	Col	Passo
V	Valley, Canyon	Tal, Cañon	Valle, Cañón	Vallée, Canyon	Vale, Canhão
⟩	Plain	Ebene	Llano	Plaine	Planície
⟩	Cape	Kap	Cabo	Cap	Cabo
I	Island	Insel	Isla	Île	Ilha
II	Islands	Inseln	Islas	Îles	Ilhas
⊥	Other Topographic Features	Andere Topographische Objekte	Otros Elementos Topográficos	Autres données topographiques	Outros acidentes topográficos

| ESPAÑOL | | | | FRANÇAIS | | | | PORTUGUÊS | | | | | Penu-Phil I · 135 |

Nombre — Página — Lat.°′ — Long.°′ W=Oeste · Nom — Page — Lat.°′ — Long.°′ W=Ouest · Nome — Página — Lat.°′ — Long.°′ W=Oeste

Column 1 (ESPAÑOL)

Nombre	Página	Lat.	Long.
Penunjok, Tanjong ►	114	4.22 N	103.29 E
Pènwègon	110	18.13 N	96.34 E
Penweil	196	31.44 N	102.35 W
Peny	78	51.04 N	55.54 E
Penyagolosa ▲	34	40.13 N	0.21 W
Penyal d'Ifac ♦	34	38.38 N	0.05 E
Penyengat	114	0.54 N	102.20 E
Pen-y-Ghent ▲	44	54.09 N	2.14 W
Penygroes, Wales, U.K.	42	51.49 N	4.02 W
Penygroes, Wales, U.K.	44	53.04 N	4.17 W
Penyu, Kepulauan II	164	5.22 S	127.46 E
Penyu, Teluk C	115a	7.45 S	109.15 E
Penza	80	53.13 N	45.00 E
Penzance	42	50.07 N	5.33 W
Penza Oblast' □⁴	80	53.00 N	45.00 E
Penzberg	64	47.45 N	11.23 E
Penžina ≈	264b	48.12 N	165.18 E
Penzing ↝ᴮ	64	48.12 N	16.18 E
Penzino	80	52.07 N	50.27 E
Penžinskaja guba C	74	61.00 N	162.00 E
Penžinskij chrebet ↙	74	62.30 N	167.00 E
Penzlin	54	53.30 N	13.05 E
Péone	62	44.07 N	6.54 E
Peoples Creek ≈	202	48.24 N	108.19 W
Peoples Ditch ≈	226	36.15 N	119.41 W
Peoria, Az., U.S.	200	33.34 N	112.14 W
Peoria, Il., U.S.	190	40.41 N	89.35 W
Peoria, Oh., U.S.	216	40.19 N	83.27 W
Peoria Heights	190	40.44 N	89.34 W
Peotillos	234	22.30 N	100.37 W
Peotone	216	41.19 N	87.47 W
Peover Eye ≈	262	53.15 N	2.31 W
Peover Heath	262	53.15 N	2.19 W
Pepa	154	7.42 S	29.47 E
Pepacton Reservoir @¹	210	42.06 N	74.54 W
Pepaw ≈	184	52.40 N	102.23 W
Pepel	150	8.35 N	13.03 W
Peper	140	7.04 N	33.00 E
Pepin, Lake @	190	44.26 N	92.08 W
Pepinster	56	50.34 N	5.49 E
Pepperell	207	42.40 N	71.35 W
Pepper Park State Recreation Area ♦	220	27.30 N	80.18 W
Pepper Pike	279a	41.28 N	81.27 W
Peqi'in Hadasha	38	32.59 N	35.20 E
Peqin	38	41.03 N	19.45 E
Pequannock	210	40.57 N	74.17 W
Pequannock ≈	276	40.58 N	74.17 W
Pequanticut Brook ≈	283	42.01 N	71.08 W
Pequea Creek ≈	208	39.53 N	76.22 W
Pequeno ≈	287a	22.55 S	43.25 W
Pequeri	256	21.50 S	43.06 W
Pequest ≈	210	40.50 N	75.05 W
Pequez	250	39.53 N	76.22 W
Pequizeiro	250	8.32 S	48.58 W
Pequop Mountains ↙	204	40.45 N	114.40 W
Pequot Lakes	190	46.36 N	94.18 W
Perabumulih	112	3.27 S	104.15 E
Perak C	114	5.00 N	101.00 E
Perak ≈	114	3.58 N	100.53 E
Perak, Kuala C	114	4.00 N	100.47 E
Peralba, Monte ▲	64	46.37 N	12.43 E
Perales de Alfambra	34	40.38 N	1.00 W
Perales del Rio	266a	40.19 N	3.38 W
Peralillo	252	34.29 S	71.29 W
Peralta	200	34.50 N	106.41 W
Pérama	267c	37.58 N	23.34 E
Perambalur	122	11.14 N	78.53 E
Perímeri (Bottenviken) C	26	65.00 N	23.00 E
Peranãmbattu	122	12.56 N	78.43 E
Perani, Ákra ►	267c	37.54 N	23.31 E
Peraroic di Cadore	64	46.24 N	12.21 E
Peräseinäjoki	26	62.34 N	23.04 E
Percé	186	48.31 N	64.13 W
Percée, Pointe ▲	58	45.57 N	6.33 E
Perch ≈	240m	18.19 N	76.05 W
Perchau	61	47.06 N	14.27 E
Perchauer Sattel Ж	61	47.07 N	14.27 E
Perche, Collines du ↙²	50	48.25 N	0.40 E
Perche Creek ≈	194	38.49 N	92.24 W
Perch Lake @	212	48.07 N	76.17 W
Perchtoldsdorf	61	48.07 N	16.17 E
Perchuškovo	265b	55.41 N	37.10 E
Percival Lakes @	162	21.25 S	125.00 E
Percy Creek ≈	194	38.49 N	92.24 W
Percy Isles II	166	21.39 S	150.16 E
Percy Lake @	212	45.13 N	78.49 W
Percy Reach @	212	44.15 N	77.45 W
Perdagangan-tomuon	114	3.09 N	99.20 E
Perdasdefogu	71	39.41 N	9.26 E
Perdeberg	158	28.59 S	25.05 E
Perdekop	158	27.13 S	29.38 E
Perdices, Arroyo de las ≈	288	34.41 S	58.22 W
Perdida ≈	250	9.13 S	47.59 W
Perdido	194	31.00 N	87.37 W
Perdido ≈, Bra.	248	22.10 S	57.33 W
Perdido, U.S.	194	30.29 N	87.26 W
Perdido, Arroyo ≈	254	42.55 S	67.00 W
Perdido, Arroyo del ≈²	258	33.37 S	57.23 W
Perdido, Cuchilla del ↙²	258	33.43 S	57.17 W
Perdido, Monte ▲	34	42.40 N	0.05 E
Perdido Bay C	194	30.21 N	87.27 W
Perdifumo	68	40.16 N	15.01 E
Perdix	208	40.22 N	76.57 W
Perdizes	255	19.21 S	47.17 W
Perdreauville	261	48.58 N	1.38 E
Perdu, Lac @	186	50.44 N	70.14 W
Perdue	184	52.04 N	107.32 W
Perebrocy	78	51.43 N	27.00 E
Perečin	78	48.44 N	22.26 E
Peredel	80	55.12 N	35.41 E
Peredel'cy	80	55.36 N	37.21 E
Peredelkino	265b	55.39 N	37.21 E
Peregino	78	57.27 N	31.21 E
Pereginskoje	78	48.49 N	24.12 E
Peregonovka	78	48.32 N	30.31 E
Pereira	244	4.49 N	75.43 W
Pereira Barreto	255	20.38 S	51.07 W
Pereiro	250	6.03 S	38.28 W
Perejaslav-Chmel'nickij	78	48.58 N	31.20 E
Perejaslavka	89	47.58 N	135.06 E
Perejaslavskaja	83	45.51 N	39.02 E
Perejezdnoje	83	48.47 N	38.04 E
Perejezd'na	83	49.43 N	48.12 E
Perekopovka	80	51.13 N	48.14 E
Perekopca'naja	78	50.37 N	30.25 E
Perekopskaja	80	49.21 N	43.10 E
Père-Lachaise, Cimetière du ⌀	261	48.51 N	2.25 E
Perelazovskij	80	49.09 N	42.33 E
Perelazy	80	53.08 N	31.28 E
Pereleŝinskij	80	51.44 N	40.27 E
Pereľub	80	51.52 N	50.22 E
Pere Marquette ≈	190	43.57 N	86.27 W
Pere Marquette, Big South Branch ≈	190	43.56 N	86.10 W
Pere Marquette State Park ♦	219	39.00 N	90.30 W
Perem'otnoje	80	51.11 N	50.49 E
Peremyšl'	80	54.23 N	36.09 E
Peremyšl'any	78	49.41 N	24.33 E
Perenjori	162	29.26 S	116.17 E
Pereputje	92a	46.17 N	141.54 E
Pererov	78	52.04 N	23.00 E
Perešč̌epino	78	49.01 N	35.22 E
Perešč̌epnoje	80	50.32 N	45.03 E
Pereslavl'-Zalesskij	82	56.44 N	38.51 E
Peresypkino Pervoje	80	52.59 N	42.55 E

Column 2 (FRANÇAIS)

Nom	Page	Lat.	Long.
Peretrusovo	82	56.51 N	36.53 E
Pereval'sk	83	48.26 N	38.47 E
Perevoz, Ross.	80	55.56 N	44.32 E
Perevoz, Ross.	88	59.00 N	116.57 E
Perevoz, Ross.	265a	59.43 N	30.47 E
Pereyra, Arroyo ≈	288	34.47 S	58.08 W
Pereyra, Punta ►	258	34.14 S	58.04 W
Pérez	252	33.00 S	60.46 W
Perfugas	71	40.50 N	8.53 E
Perg	61	48.15 N	14.37 E
Pergamino	252	33.53 S	60.35 W
Pergamum ⌓	130	39.10 N	27.13 E
Pergau ≈	114	5.23 N	102.02 E
Pergine Valdarno	66	43.28 N	11.41 E
Pergine Valsugana	64	46.04 N	11.14 E
Pergola	66	43.34 N	12.50 E
Pergusa, Lago di @	70	37.31 N	14.18 E
Perham	198	46.35 N	95.34 W
Perho	26	63.13 N	24.25 E
Peri	64	45.39 N	10.54 E
Peri	130	38.50 N	39.35 E
Peribán de Ramos	234	19.32 N	102.28 W
Péribonca	176	48.45 N	72.05 W
Péribonca, Lac @	186	50.04 N	71.15 W
Perico, Arg.	252	24.23 S	65.06 W
Perico, Cuba	240p	22.46 N	81.01 W
Pericos	232	25.03 N	107.42 W
Pericumã ≈	250	2.17 S	44.42 W
Peridot	200	33.18 N	110.27 W
Périers	32	49.11 N	1.25 W
Perigiraja	112	0.16 S	103.30 E
Périgord ↙	32	45.20 N	1.00 E
Perigoso, Canal ⋃	250	0.05 N	49.40 W
Périgueux	32	45.11 N	0.43 E
Perijá, Serranía De ↙	246	10.00 N	73.00 W
Perim [—Barīm I]	144	12.39 N	43.25 E
Peri-Mirim	250	2.38 S	44.54 W
Perinaldo	62	43.52 N	7.40 E
Peringat	114	6.02 N	102.17 E
Periprava	38	45.24 N	29.32 E
Perisher Valley ♦	171b	36.23 S	145.24 E
Péristérion	267c	38.01 N	23.42 E
Perito	68	40.18 N	15.09 E
Perito Moreno	254	46.36 S	70.56 W
Peritoró	250	4.20 S	44.18 W
Perivale ↝ᴮ	260	51.32 N	0.19 W
Periyakulam	122	10.07 N	77.33 E
Periyar ≈	122	10.11 N	76.13 E
Perkasie	208	40.22 N	75.17 W
Perkins	196	38.58 N	97.02 W
Perkins Observatory	212	44.42 N	79.57 W
Perkins ↝³	214	40.14 N	83.02 W
Perkinston	194	30.46 N	89.08 W
Perkinsville, In., U.S.	218	40.09 N	85.52 W
Perkinsville, N.Y., U.S.	210	42.32 N	77.38 W
Perkiomen Creek ≈	208	40.07 N	75.28 W
Perkiomen Creek, East Branch ≈	208	40.15 N	75.27 W
Perkiomen Junction	285	40.06 N	75.28 W
Perkiomen Valley ⌓	285	40.17 N	75.25 W
Perl	56	49.28 N	6.23 E
Perlas, Archipiélago de las II	246	8.25 N	79.00 W
Perlas, Laguna de ⓒ	236	12.30 N	83.40 W
Perlas, Punta de ►	236	12.23 N	83.30 W
Perleberg	54	53.04 N	11.51 E
Perlez	69	45.12 N	20.23 E
Perlis □³	114	6.30 N	100.15 E
Perl'ovka	78	51.51 N	38.51 E
Perm'	80	58.00 N	56.15 E
Permanente Creek ≈	282	37.25 N	122.05 W
Permas	24	59.20 N	45.34 E
Përmet	80	40.14 N	20.21 E
Permian	80	54.06 N	45.48 E
Perm' Oblast' □⁴	86	58.00 N	58.00 E
Pernambuco [—Recife]	250	8.03 S	34.54 W
Pernambuco ↝³	250	8.00 S	37.00 W
Pernate	266b	45.27 N	8.41 E
Pernatty Lagoon @	166	31.31 S	137.14 E
Pernegg an der Mur	50	47.27 N	15.21 E
Pernem	122	15.44 N	73.48 E
Pernes-les-Fontaines	58	44.00 N	5.03 E
Pernik	38	42.36 N	23.02 E
Pernink	54	50.20 N	12.45 E
Perniö	26	60.12 N	23.08 E
Pernovo	82	61.40 N	41.54 E
Peroba, Ribeirão do ≈	287b	23.27 S	46.22 W
Pérols, Étang de C	58	43.33 N	3.56 E
Peron, Cape ►	168a	32.17 S	115.41 E
Péronne	32	49.56 N	2.56 E
Peron Peninsula ↦¹	166c	25.51 S	113.30 E
Perú Pinheiro	250	2.58 S	40.23 W
Perosa Argentina	62	44.58 N	7.10 E
Perote	234	19.34 N	97.14 W
Peroto	248	14.50 S	64.31 W
Pérou [—Peru ↙¹]	242	10.00 S	76.00 W
Pérouges	58	45.54 N	5.10 E
Peroulaz	62	46.51 N	7.35 E
Perow	182	54.31 N	126.26 W
Perpendicular, Point ►	170	35.06 S	150.48 E
Perpignan	32	42.41 N	2.53 E
Perranporth	42	50.20 N	5.09 W
Perrault Falls	184	50.19 N	93.11 W
Perray ≈	261	48.31 N	1.42 E
Perre	261	49.29 N	0.22 E
Perriers-sur-Andelle	50	49.24 N	1.22 E
Perrignier	58	46.18 N	6.27 E
Perrin	196	33.02 N	98.04 W
Perrineville	208	40.13 N	74.26 W
Perris	228	33.46 N	117.13 W
Perris, Lake @¹	228	33.51 N	117.11 W
Perro, Laguna del @	200	34.40 N	105.57 W
Perro, Punta del ►	34	36.48 N	6.22 W
Perros, Bahía de C	240p	22.25 N	78.30 W
Perros-Guirec	32	48.49 N	3.26 W
Perry, Fl., U.S.	194	30.07 N	83.34 W
Perry, Ga., U.S.	192	32.27 N	83.43 W
Perry, Ia., U.S.	190	41.50 N	94.06 W
Perry, Il., U.S.	190	39.47 N	90.45 W
Perry, Ks., U.S.	190	39.04 N	95.23 W
Perry, Me., U.S.	186	44.58 N	67.04 W
Perry, Mi., U.S.	216	42.49 N	84.13 W
Perry, N.Y., U.S.	210	42.43 N	78.00 W
Perry, Oh., U.S.	214	41.45 N	81.08 W
Perry, Ok., U.S.	196	36.17 N	97.17 W
Perry, Tx., U.S.	222	31.05 N	96.55 W
Perry, Ut., U.S.	204	41.27 N	112.02 W
Perrydale	224	45.01 N	123.11 W
Perry Hall	208	39.24 N	76.27 W
Perry Heights	214	40.47 N	81.28 W
Perry-Jōriku-kinenhi ⌓	94	35.14 N	139.43 E
Perryman	208	39.27 N	76.11 W
Perryopolis	279b	40.05 N	79.45 W
Perry Point	208	39.33 N	76.04 W
Perrysburg, Oh., U.S.	214	41.33 N	83.37 W
Perry's Landing	208	40.04 N	80.08 W
Perry's Victory and International Peace Memorial ⌓	214	41.39 N	82.50 W

Column 3 (PORTUGUÊS)

Nome	Página	Lat.	Long.
Perrysville	214	40.39 N	82.18 W
Perryton	196	36.24 N	100.48 W
Perryville Ak., U.S.	180	55.54 N	159.10 W
Perryville, Ar., U.S.	194	35.00 N	92.48 W
Perryville, Ky., U.S.	192	37.39 N	84.57 W
Perryville, Md., U.S.	208	39.33 N	76.04 W
Perryville, Mo., U.S.	194	37.43 N	89.51 W
Perryville, N.Y., U.S.	210	43.01 N	75.48 W
Peršaj	76	54.02 N	26.41 E
Persani	50	49.09 N	21.16 E
Persani, Munţii ↙	38	45.40 N	25.15 E
Persberg	40	59.45 N	14.15 E
Perschling ≈	61	48.20 N	15.58 E
Perşembe	130	41.04 N	37.46 E
Persepolis [—Takht-e Jamshīd ⌓]	128	29.57 N	52.52 E
Perseverance, Mount ▲	171a	27.25 S	152.10 E
Pershagen	40	59.10 N	17.39 E
Pershing	198	39.49 N	84.53 W
Pershore	42	52.07 N	2.05 W
Persia	198	41.34 N	95.34 W
Peshin Ján	128	34.05 N	61.28 E
Peshkopi	38	41.41 N	20.26 E
Peshtigo	190	45.03 N	87.44 W
Peshtigo ≈	190	44.58 N	87.40 W
Pesio ≈	62	44.28 N	7.53 E
Pesjane	82	56.01 N	38.48 E
Peski, Bela.	76	53.21 N	24.38 E
Peski, Ross.	82	55.13 N	38.46 E
Peski, Ross.	82	56.08 N	37.04 E
Peski, Ross.	82	55.13 N	38.46 E
Peski, Ukr.	78	50.23 N	33.27 E
Peski, Ukr.	83	49.26 N	38.59 E
Peski-Rad'kovskije	83	49.17 N	37.36 E
Peskovatskoje	83	54.03 N	36.16 E
Peskovka, Ross.	86	59.04 N	52.20 E
Peskovka, Jkr.	78	50.42 N	29.38 E
Peskovo	83	47.02 N	39.24 E
Peškovo Grecovo	82	54.26 N	37.36 E
Peškovskoje	86	53.45 N	62.23 E
Pesmes	58	47.17 N	5.34 E
Pesnica	61	46.36 N	15.41 E
Pesnica	61	46.36 N	16.05 E
Pešnoj, poluostrov ↦²	80	46.52 N	51.27 E
Pesočenski	82	54.10 N	36.06 E
Pesočnja ≈	80	49.57 N	36.06 E
Pesočn'a	80	54.07 N	40.50 E
Pesočnoje, Bela.	76	53.20 N	27.06 E
Pesočnoje, Ross.	82	58.01 N	39.10 E
Pesočnyj	76	60.07 N	30.08 E
Peso da Régua	34	41.10 N	7.47 W
Pespire	236	13.35 N	87.22 W
Pesqueira	250	8.22 S	36.42 W
Pesquería	196	25.47 N	100.03 W
Pesquería ≈	196	25.54 N	99.11 W
Pessac	32	44.48 N	0.38 W
Pessin	54	52.38 N	12.40 E
Pessinetto	62	45.18 N	7.22 E
Pest □⁶	61	47.25 N	19.20 E
Pest ≈	264c	47.30 N	19.04 E
Pest'aki	82	56.43 N	42.40 E
Peštera	38	42.02 N	24.18 E
Pesterzsébet ↝⁸	264c	47.26 N	19.07 E
Pesthidegkút ↝⁸	264c	47.34 N	18.58 E
Pestime ≈	264c	47.24 N	19.12 E
Pestôrinc ↝⁸	264c	47.06 N	19.12 E
Pestovo, Ross.	76	58.36 N	35.48 E
Pestovo, Ross.	86	57.12 N	46.44 E
Pestovskoje vodochranilišče @¹	82	56.06 N	37.40 E
Pestravka	80	52.24 N	49.58 E
Pestrecy	80	55.46 N	49.39 E
Pestrikovo	82	54.32 N	38.04 E
Pestyhely ↝	264c	47.32 N	19.07 E
Petacalco, Bahía C	234	17.57 N	102.05 W
Petah Tiqwa	132	32.05 N	34.53 E
Petäjävesi	26	62.15 N	25.12 E
Petal	194	31.20 N	89.15 W
Petalciingo	232	17.17 N	92.27 W
Petaling Jaya	114	3.06 N	101.39 E
Petalón, Kórpos C	38	37.59 N	24.02 E
Petaluma	226	38.13 N	122.38 W
Petaluma ≈	226	38.06 N	122.30 W
Pétange	56	49.34 N	5.52 E
Petare	246	10.29 N	66.49 W
Petatlán	234	17.31 N	101.16 W
Petauke	154	14.15 S	31.20 E
Petawawa	190	45.54 N	77.17 W
Petawawa ≈	190	45.55 N	77.15 W
Petegem	56	50.58 N	3.32 E
Petén □⁵	236	16.55 N	89.50 W
Petén Itzá, Lago @	236	16.59 N	89.50 W
Petenwell Lake @¹	190	44.10 N	89.57 W
Peter and Paul Fortress ⌓	265a	59.57 N	30.19 E
Peterborough, Austl.	166	32.58 S	138.50 E
Peterborough, On., Can.	212	44.18 N	78.19 W
Peterborough, Eng., U.K.	42	52.35 N	0.15 W
Peterborough, N.H., U.S.	210	42.52 N	71.57 W
Peterculter	46	57.05 N	2.16 W
Peterhead	46	57.30 N	1.47 W
Peter Hill ▲	46	56.58 N	2.42 W
Peter I Island I	9	68.50 S	90.35 W
Peter Island I	240m	18.22 N	64.35 W
Peter Lake @, N.T., Can.	184	63.08 N	92.48 W
Peter Lake @, Sk., Can.	184	57.15 N	103.53 W
Peterlee	44	54.46 N	1.19 W
Peter Lougheed Provincial Park ♦	182	50.45 N	115.15 W
Peterman	194	31.35 N	87.15 W
Petermann Reserve ♦	162	26.00 S	129.46 E
Peter Pond Lake @	184	55.55 N	108.44 W
Peter Pond Lake Indian Reserve ↝⁴	184	55.55 N	109.00 W
Peters Brook ≈	210	42.58 N	73.00 W
Petersburg, Ak., U.S.	180	56.49 N	132.57 W
Petersburg, Il., U.S.	194	40.01 N	89.51 W
Petersburg, In., U.S.	194	38.29 N	87.16 W
Petersburg, Mi., U.S.	216	41.53 N	83.42 W
Petersburg, N.D., U.S.	198	48.01 N	98.00 W
Petersburg, Tn., U.S.	194	35.19 N	86.38 W
Petersburg, Va., U.S.	192	37.13 N	77.24 W
Petersburg, W.V., U.S.	208	39.00 N	79.07 W
Petersburg National Battlefield ⌓	208	37.14 N	77.22 W
Peters Canyon Reservoir @¹	283	33.47 N	117.45 W
Peters Creek ≈, Ca., U.S.	282	37.15 N	122.13 W
Peters Creek, Piney Fork ≈	279b	40.18 N	79.28 W
Petersdorf	54	54.26 N	11.04 E
Petersfield, Eng., U.K.	42	51.00 N	0.56 W

Column 4

Nome	Página	Lat.	Long.
Pescantina	64	45.29 N	10.51 E
Pesčanyj	83	47.02 N	37.28 E
Pesčanyje, ostrova II	83	46.52 N	38.17 E
Pescara	66	42.28 N	14.13 E
Pescara □⁴	66	42.20 N	13.57 E
Pescara ≈	66	42.28 N	14.13 E
Pescasseroli	66	41.48 N	13.47 E
Pesch	263	51.11 N	6.32 E
Pesch, Schloss ⌓	263	51.18 N	6.39 E
Peschici	66	41.57 N	16.01 E
Peschiera del Garda	64	45.26 N	10.42 E
Peschio, Monte ▲	267a	41.43 N	13.23 E
Pescia	66	43.54 N	10.41 E
Pescina	66	42.00 N	13.39 E
Pescocostanzo	66	41.53 N	14.04 E
Pescolanciano	66	41.41 N	14.20 E
Pescopagano	68	40.50 N	15.24 E
Pescorocchiano	66	42.12 N	13.09 E
Pesco Sannita	68	41.14 N	14.49 E
Pesé	236	7.54 N	80.37 W
Pesek, Pulau I	271c	1.17 N	103.41 E
Peseux	58	46.59 N	6.53 E
Peshastin	224	47.34 N	120.36 W
Peshastin Creek ≈	224	47.33 N	120.35 W
Peshāwar	123	34.01 N	71.33 E
Peshāwar Ján	128	34.05 N	61.28 E
Peškovo	82	54.26 N	36.33 E
Peškovskoje	58	47.17 N	5.34 E
Pesmes	61	46.36 N	15.41 E
Pesnica	61	46.36 N	16.05 E
Pešnoj, poluostrov ↦²	80	46.52 N	51.27 E
Pesočenski	82	54.10 N	36.06 E
Pesočnja ≈	80	49.57 N	36.06 E
Pesočn'a	80	54.07 N	40.50 E
Pesočnoje, Bela.	76	53.20 N	27.06 E
Pesočnoje, Ross.	82	58.01 N	39.10 E
Pesočnyj	76	60.07 N	30.08 E
Peso da Régua	34	41.10 N	7.47 W
Pespire	236	13.35 N	87.22 W
Pesqueira	250	8.22 S	36.42 W
Pesquería	196	25.47 N	100.03 W
Pesquería ≈	196	25.54 N	99.11 W
Pessac	32	44.48 N	0.38 W
Pessin	54	52.38 N	12.40 E
Pessinetto	62	45.18 N	7.22 E
Pest □⁶	61	47.25 N	19.20 E
Pest ≈	264c	47.30 N	19.04 E
Pest'aki	82	56.43 N	42.40 E
Peštera	38	42.02 N	24.18 E
Pesterzsébet ↝⁸	264c	47.26 N	19.07 E
Pesthidegkút ↝⁸	264c	47.34 N	18.58 E
Pestime ≈	264c	47.24 N	19.12 E
Pestôrinc ↝⁸	264c	47.06 N	19.12 E
Pestovo, Ross.	76	58.36 N	35.48 E
Pestovo, Ross.	86	57.12 N	46.44 E
Pestovskoje vodochranilišče @¹	82	56.06 N	37.40 E
Pestravka	80	52.24 N	49.58 E
Pestrecy	80	55.46 N	49.39 E
Pestrikovo	82	54.32 N	38.04 E
Pestyhely ↝	264c	47.32 N	19.07 E
Petacalco, Bahía C	234	17.57 N	102.05 W
Petah Tiqwa	132	32.05 N	34.53 E
Petäjävesi	26	62.15 N	25.12 E
Petal	194	31.20 N	89.15 W
Petalciingo	232	17.17 N	92.27 W
Petaling Jaya	114	3.06 N	101.39 E
Petalón, Kórpos C	38	37.59 N	24.02 E
Petaluma	226	38.13 N	122.38 W
Petaluma ≈	226	38.06 N	122.30 W
Pétange	56	49.34 N	5.52 E
Petare	246	10.29 N	66.49 W
Petatlán	234	17.31 N	101.16 W
Petauke	154	14.15 S	31.20 E
Petawawa	190	45.54 N	77.17 W
Petawawa ≈	190	45.55 N	77.15 W
Petegem	56	50.58 N	3.32 E
Petén □⁵	236	16.55 N	89.50 W
Petén Itzá, Lago @	236	16.59 N	89.50 W
Petenwell Lake @¹	190	44.10 N	89.57 W
Peterdorf	54	54.26 N	11.04 E
Petersdorf	54	54.26 N	11.04 E
Petersfield, Mb., Can.	184	50.18 N	96.59 W
Petershagen, Dtsch.	52	52.23 N	8.58 E

Column 5

Nome	Página	Lat.	Long.
Petershagen, Dtsch.	52	52.23 N	8.58 E
Petershagen, Dtsch.	54	52.24 N	14.20 E
Petershagen bei Berlin	54	52.31 N	13.46 E
Petersham, Austl.	274a	33.54 S	151.09 E
Petersham, Ma., U.S.	207	42.29 N	72.11 W
Peters Hill ▲²	168b	34.11 S	138.50 E
Peterson	198	42.55 N	95.20 W
Peterson Air Force Base ▲	198	38.49 N	104.42 W
Peters Pond @	283	42.43 N	71.16 W
Peterswald Hill ▲²	162	26.43 S	123.39 E
Peter the Great Bay [—Petra Velikogo, zaliv C]	89	42.40 N	132.00 E
Peter the Great Monument ⌓	265a	59.56 N	30.18 E
Pétervására	30	48.01 N	20.06 E
Petilia Policastro	68	39.07 N	16.47 E
Pétionville	238	18.31 N	72.17 W
Petit	273d	26.06 S	28.22 E
Petit Bois Island I	194	30.12 N	88.26 W
Petit-Bourg	241o	16.12 N	61.36 W
Petit-Canal	241o	16.23 N	61.29 W
Petitcodiac	186	45.56 N	65.10 W
Petitcodiac ≈	186	45.50 N	64.33 W
Petit Cul-de-Sac Marin C	241o	16.12 N	61.33 W
Petite Nation, Rivière de la ≈	205	45.35 N	75.06 W
Petite Rivière du Chêne ≈	206	46.34 N	72.02 W
Petite Rivière Noire, Piton de la ▲	157c	20.24 S	57.24 E
Petite Rivière Rouge ≈		45.45 N	75.00 W
Petites-Anses	241o	15.51 N	61.39 W
Petite Sauldre ≈	50	47.26 N	2.05 E
Petite Terre, Îles de la ≈	241o	16.10 N	61.07 W
Petit Forte	186	44.54 N	54.40 W
Petit-Fort-Philippe	50	51.00 N	2.07 E
Petit-Goâve	238	16.26 N	72.52 W
Petit Jean ≈	194	35.06 N	92.57 W
Petit Jean State Park ♦	194	35.06 N	92.57 W
Petit Loango	152	2.16 S	9.35 E
Petit Loango, Parc National du ♦	152	2.15 S	9.36 E
Petit Mécatina, Île du ♦ I	186	50.33 N	59.20 W
Petit Morin ≈	50	48.56 N	3.07 E
Petit-ot ≈	176	60.14 N	123.29 W
Petit Piton ▲	241f	13.50 N	61.04 W
Petit Rhône ≈	62	43.27 N	4.24 E
Petit-Saint-Bernard, Col du Ж	62	45.41 N	6.53 E
Petitsikapau Lake @	176	54.45 N	66.25 W
Petkeljärven kansallispuisto ♦		62.35 N	31.12 E
Petkus	54	51.59 N	13.21 E
Petläd	120	22.28 N	72.48 E
Petlalcingo	234	18.05 N	97.54 W
Peto	232	20.08 N	88.55 W
Petoh	114	2.53 N	103.15 E
Petone ≈	172	41.13 S	174.52 E
Petorca	252	32.15 S	70.56 W
Petoskey	190	45.22 N	84.57 W
Petowninkip Lake @	190	52.56 N	92.00 W
Petra [—Batrā ⌓]	132	30.20 N	35.26 E
Petralia Soprana	70	37.47 N	14.06 E
Petralia Sottana	70	37.48 N	14.05 E
Petras, Mount ▲	9	75.52 S	128.38 W
Petra Velikogo, zaliv C [(Peter the Great Bay) C]	89	42.40 N	132.00 E
Petre, Point ►	212	43.50 N	77.09 W
Petreccoco	24	61.18 N	57.07 E
Petrella, Monte ▲	66	41.18 N	13.40 E
Petrella Tifernina	66	41.41 N	14.42 E
Petrič	38	41.24 N	23.13 E
Petrie	171a	27.16 S	152.59 E
Petrified Forest National Park ♦	200	34.55 N	109.49 W
Petrikov	76	52.08 N	28.30 E
Petrikovka	80	48.43 N	34.37 E
Petrila	38	45.27 N	23.25 E
Petrinja	38	45.26 N	16.18 E
Petriščevo, Ross.	82	54.37 N	36.57 E
Petriščevo, Ross.	82	55.50 N	36.18 E
Petriškės	76	54.37 N	25.27 E
Petrodvorec	76	59.53 N	29.54 E
Petroglyphs Provincial Park ♦	212	44.33 N	77.53 W
Petrograd [—Sankt-Peterburg ↝⁹]	76	59.55 N	30.15 E
Petrogrado-Doneckoje ↝⁹	83	48.42 N	38.41 E
Petrohué	254	41.08 S	72.37 W
Petrolândia	250	9.05 S	38.18 W
Petrólea	246	8.29 N	72.35 W
Petrolia, On., Can.	214	42.53 N	82.09 W
Petrolia, Tx., U.S.	196	34.01 N	98.14 W
Petrolina	250	9.24 S	40.30 W
Petrolina de Goiás	255	16.06 S	49.20 W
Petroná	66	39.03 N	16.45 E
Petronila Creek ≈	196	27.37 N	97.32 W
Petropavlovka, Ross.	86	50.35 N	105.19 E
Petropavlovka, Ross.	88	50.38 N	105.19 E
Petropavlovsk, Kaz.	86	54.54 N	69.06 E
Petropavlovsk-Kamčatskij	74	53.01 N	158.39 E
Petropavlovskaja	83	53.01 N	38.52 E (?)
Petropavlovskoje, Ross.	88	58.13 N	108.59 E
Petro-Slav'anka	265a	59.48 N	30.31 E
Petrovce, Monte ▲	66	43.26 N	13.15 E (?)
Petrópolis	255	22.31 S	43.10 W
Petros	192	36.05 N	84.26 W
Petrovsk	80	52.19 N	45.22 E
Petrovskij, Ross.	82	57.37 N	37.57 E
Petrovskij, Ross.	82	58.13 N	34.11 E
Petrovskoje, Ross.	82	56.04 N	41.59 E
Petrovskoje, Ross.	82	55.25 N	37.51 E
Petrovsk-Zabajkal'skij	88	51.17 N	108.50 E

Column 6

Nome	Página	Lat.	Long.
Petrov Val	80	50.09 N	45.12 E
Petrozavodsk	24	61.47 N	34.20 E
Petrozsény [—Petroşani]	38	45.25 N	23.22 E
Petrun'	24	66.28 N	60.43 E
Petrusburg	158	29.08 S	25.27 E
Petrušino	265a	59.48 N	30.50 E
Petrus Steyn	158	27.38 S	28.08 E
Petrusville	158	30.05 S	24.41 E
Petschora ≈ [—Pečora ≈]	24	68.13 N	54.15 E
Petten	52	52.45 N	4.39 E
Pettenbach	61	47.57 N	14.01 E
Petterill ≈	44	54.54 N	2.55 W
Petticoat Creek ≈	275b	43.48 N	79.06 W
Pettigoe	48	54.33 N	7.50 W
Pettinascura, Monte ▲	68	39.22 N	16.37 E
Pettineo	70	37.58 N	14.17 E
Pettisville	216	41.31 N	84.13 W
Pettnau	64	47.18 N	11.08 E
Pettneu am Arlberg	64	47.09 N	10.20 E
Pettus	196	28.37 N	97.48 W
Petty Harbour	186	47.28 N	52.43 W
Petty Island I	285	39.58 N	75.07 W
Petua	272b	22.25 N	88.27 E
Petuchovo	86	55.06 N	67.58 E
Petuški	80	55.55 N	39.28 E
Petworth	42	50.59 N	0.38 W
Petzow	264a	52.21 N	12.56 E
Peudada	114	5.12 N	96.35 E
Peuerbach	61	48.20 N	13.46 E
Peureulak	114	4.55 N	96.20 E
Peureulak ≈	114	4.54 N	97.53 E
Peureulak, Ujung ►	114	4.54 N	97.54 E
Peusangan ≈	114	5.16 N	96.51 E
Peusangan, Ujung ►	114	5.16 N	96.50 E
Pevek	74	69.42 N	170.17 E
Pevely	219	38.17 N	90.24 W
Pevensey	42	50.49 N	0.20 E
Pevensey Levels ≈	42	50.50 N	0.20 E
Peveragno	62	44.20 N	7.37 E
Pewamo	216	43.00 N	84.50 W
Pewaukee	216	43.04 N	88.15 W
Pewaukee Lake @	216	43.04 N	88.19 W
Pewee Valley	218	38.18 N	85.29 W
Pews Creek ≈	276	40.27 N	74.06 W
Pewsey	42	51.21 N	1.46 W
Pewsey, Vale of ⱴ	42	51.20 N	1.48 W
Péyia	130	34.53 N	32.23 E
Peyrolles-en-Provence	62	43.39 N	5.35 E
Peyruis	62	44.02 N	5.56 E
Peza ≈	24	65.36 N	45.23 E
Pezas	86	59.34 N	87.46 E
Pezawa Taung ▲	110	19.33 N	94.31 E
Pézenas	32	43.27 N	3.25 E
Pežeanga	76	59.10 N	44.16 E
Pezinok	30	48.18 N	17.17 E
Pezu	123	32.19 N	70.44 E
Pezzana	62	45.16 N	8.29 E
Pfäfers	58	46.59 N	9.30 E
Pfaffenhausen	58	48.07 N	10.27 E
Pfaffenhofen an der Ilm	60	48.31 N	11.30 E
Pfaffenhofen	56	47.51 N	7.37 E
Pfaffenhofen ▲²	264b	48.04 N	16.13 E
Pfäffikersee @	58	47.21 N	8.48 E
Pfäffikon	58	47.13 N	8.47 E
Pfaffnau	58	47.11 N	7.54 E
Pfaffstätten	264b	48.01 N	16.16 E
Pfalzdorf	263	51.42 N	6.11 E
Pfalzel	56	49.47 N	6.41 E
Pfänder ▲	58	47.30 N	9.47 E
Pfarrkirchen	60	48.25 N	12.56 E
Pfarrweisach	60	50.10 N	10.46 E
Pfastatt	58	47.47 N	7.18 E
Pfatter	60	48.58 N	12.23 E
Pfaueninsel, Schloss ⌓	264a	52.26 N	13.07 E
Pfeddersheim	56	49.38 N	8.16 E
Pfeffenhausen	60	48.31 N	11.30 E
Pfeiffer-Big Sur State Park ♦	226	36.15 N	121.47 W
Pferdenberg ≈		51.31 N	7.32 E
Pflugerville	222	30.26 N	97.37 W
Pforzen	60	47.55 N	10.37 E
Pforzheim	60	48.54 N	8.42 E
Pfreimd	60	49.29 N	12.11 E
Pfrimm ≈	56	49.39 N	8.22 E
Pfronten	60	47.35 N	10.33 E
Pfuhl	60	48.24 N	10.02 E
Pfullendorf	60	47.55 N	9.15 E
Pfullingen	60	48.28 N	9.14 E
Pfunds	60	46.58 N	10.33 E
Pfungstadt	56	49.48 N	8.36 E
Phae-an	110	16.53 N	97.38 E
Phachi ≈	110	15.11 N	100.32 E
Phalaborwa	158	23.56 S	31.13 E
Phalempin	261	50.31 N	3.01 E
Phalia	123	32.26 N	73.34 E
Phalodi	120	27.08 N	72.22 E
Phaltan	118	18.00 N	74.26 E
Phan	110	19.30 N	99.43 E
Phanat Nikhom	110	13.27 N	101.11 E
Phangan, Ko I	110	9.45 N	100.04 E
Phang Hoei, Khao ↙	110	15.15 N	101.23 E
Phangnga	110	8.27 N	98.32 E
Phaniang ≈	110	16.49 N	102.24 E
Phanom-Dongrak, Thiu Khao ↙	110	14.25 N	103.30 E
Phanom Thuan	110	13.58 N	99.52 E
Phan Rang	110	11.34 N	108.59 E
Phan Thiet	110	10.56 N	108.06 E
Phan Thong	110	13.27 N	100.59 E
Phariāri	126	27.12 N	68.59 E
Pharr	196	26.11 N	98.11 W
Phasi Charoen, Khlong ⱴ	269a	13.43 N	100.28 E
Phatthalung	110	7.37 N	100.05 E

ENGLISH | DEUTSCH

Name	Page	Lat.°′	Long.°′
Philadelphia, N.Y., U.S.	212	44.09 N	75.42 W
Philadelphia, Pa., U.S.	208	39.57 N	75.09 W
Philadelphia, Pa., U.S.	285	39.57 N	75.09 W
Philadelphia, Tn., U.S.	192	35.40 N	84.24 W
Philadelphia □6	285	39.57 N	75.07 W
Philadelphia International Airport ⊠	208	39.53 N	75.14 W
Philadelphia Museum of Art ⊍	285	39.58 N	75.11 W
Philadelphia Naval Shipyard ■	285	39.53 N	75.11 W
Philadelphia Park Race Track ♦	285	40.07 N	74.57 W
Philae ⊥	140	24.01 N	32.53 E
Phil Campbell	194	34.21 N	87.42 W
Philip	198	44.02 N	101.39 W
Philipp	194	33.45 N	90.12 W
Philippeville → Skikda, Alg.	148	36.50 N	6.58 E
Philippeville, Bel.	50	50.12 N	4.32 E
Philippi	188	39.09 N	80.02 W
Philippi, Lake ⊜	166	24.22 S	139.00 E
Philippine Basin ✦1	14	17.00 N	132.00 E
Philippine International Convention Center ♦	269f	14.32 N	120.59 E
Philippinen → Philippines □1	116	13.00 N	122.00 E
Philippines (Pilipinas) □1, Asia	108	13.00 N	122.00 E
Philippines (Pilipinas) □1, Asia	116	13.00 N	122.00 E
Philippines, University of the ⊍2	269f	14.39 N	121.04 E
Philippine Sea ⊤2	14	20.00 N	135.00 E
Philippine Trench ✦1	14	9.00 N	127.00 E
Philippolis	158	30.19 S	25.13 E
Philippopolis → Plovdiv	38	42.09 N	24.45 E
Philippsreut	60	48.52 N	13.41 E
Philippsthal	264a	52.20 N	13.09 E
Philipsburg, P.Q., Can.	206	45.02 N	73.05 W
Philipsburg, Ned. Ant.	238	17.59 N	63.10 W
Philipsburg, Mt., U.S.	202	46.19 N	113.17 W
Philipsburg, Pa., U.S.	214	40.53 N	78.13 W
Philipsburg Manor ⊥	276	41.05 N	73.52 W
Philipse Manor Hall State Historic Site ⊥	276	40.56 N	73.54 W
Philip Smith Mountains ⟁	180	68.30 N	148.00 W
Philipstown	158	30.26 S	24.29 E
Phillaur	123	31.01 N	75.47 E
Phillip Island I	169	38.29 S	145.14 E
Phillips, Me., U.S.	188	44.49 N	70.20 W
Phillips, Tx., U.S.	196	35.41 N	101.21 W
Phillips, Wi., U.S.	190	45.41 N	90.24 W
Phillipsburg, Ga., U.S.	192	31.34 N	83.31 W
Phillipsburg, Ks., U.S.	198	39.45 N	99.19 W
Phillipsburg, N.J., U.S.	210	40.41 N	75.11 W
Philmont	210	42.14 N	73.39 W
Philo, Il., U.S.	194	40.01 N	88.09 W
Philo, Oh., U.S.	188	39.51 N	81.54 W
Philomath	202	44.32 N	123.21 W
Philpots Island I	176	74.48 N	80.00 W
Phimai	110	15.13 N	102.30 E
Phinga	272b	22.41 N	88.25 E
Phitsanulok	110	16.50 N	100.15 E
Phnom Penh → Phnum Pénh	110	11.33 N	104.55 E
Phnum Pénh	110	11.33 N	104.55 E
Phnum Tbêng Méanchey	110	13.49 N	104.58 E
Pho ≏	124	27.41 N	89.53 E
Phoenicia	210	42.05 N	74.18 W
Phoenix, Az., U.S.	200	33.26 N	112.04 W
Phoenix, Il., U.S.	278	41.36 N	87.38 W
Phoenix, Md., U.S.	208	39.30 N	76.36 W
Phoenix, N.Y., U.S.	210	43.13 N	76.18 W
Phoenix Islands II	14	4.00 S	172.00 W
Phoenix Lake ⊜1	282	37.57 N	122.35 W
Phoenix Park ♦	281	42.24 N	83.27 W
Phoenixville	208	40.07 N	75.30 W
Phon	110	15.49 N	102.36 E
Phong ≏	110	16.23 N	102.56 E
Phôngsali	110	21.41 N	102.06 E
Phong Tho	110	22.32 N	103.21 E
Phon Phisai	110	18.01 N	103.05 E
Phosphate Hill	166	21.52 S	139.51 E
Phrae	110	18.09 N	100.08 E
Phra Khanong ◆8	269a	13.42 N	100.35 E
Phra Nakhon → Krung Thep	110	13.45 N	100.31 E
Phra Nakhon Si Ayutthaya	110	14.21 N	100.33 E
Phran Kratai	110	16.40 N	99.36 E
Phrao	110	19.22 N	99.13 E
Phra Pradaeng	269a	13.40 N	100.32 E
Phra Rop, Khao ∧	110	13.11 N	99.31 E
Phrom Phiram	110	17.02 N	100.12 E
Phrygia □9	130	39.00 N	30.00 E
Phsar Réam	110	10.30 N	103.37 E
Phu Cat	110	14.01 N	109.03 E
Phu Huu, Viet	110	18.58 N	105.31 E
Phu Huu, Viet	269c	10.43 N	106.47 E
Phuket	110	7.53 N	98.24 E
Phuket, Ko I	110	8.00 N	98.22 E
Phularwān	123	32.22 N	73.00 E
Phulbari	126	21.52 N	88.08 E
Phulbāria	126	23.22 N	89.50 E
Phuljhuri	126	22.12 N	90.04 E
Phulkusma	126	22.43 N	86.52 E
Phu Loc	110	16.16 N	107.53 E
Phūlpur	124	25.33 N	82.06 E
Phulra	123	34.20 N	73.03 E
Phultala	126	22.59 N	89.28 E
Phu Ly	110	20.32 N	105.56 E
Phum Duang ≏	110	9.10 N	99.20 E
Phumi Bâ Khâm	110	13.51 N	107.22 E
Phumi Banam	110	11.19 N	105.18 E
Phumi Béng	110	13.05 N	104.18 E
Phumi Châmbák	110	11.14 N	104.49 E
Phumi Chângho Andêng	110	12.39 N	104.35 E
Phumi Chhuk	110	10.50 N	104.28 E
Phumi Chruŏy Slêng	110	13.14 N	105.57 E
Phumi Dák Dâm	110	12.20 N	107.21 E
Phumi Kâmpóng Srâlau	110	14.05 N	105.46 E
Phumi Kâmpóng Trâbêk	110	13.06 N	105.14 E
Phumi Kântuŏt Sâmraông	110	14.12 N	104.37 E
Phumi Kaôh Kért	110	13.47 N	104.32 E
Phumi Kaôh Kông	110	11.26 N	103.11 E
Phumi Khpôb	110	11.02 N	105.12 E
Phumi Krêk	110	11.46 N	105.56 E
Phumi Lvéa Kraôm	110	13.21 N	102.54 E
Phumi Moŭng	110	13.45 N	103.35 E
Phumi Narŭng	110	13.53 N	105.34 E
Phumi Phnum Srâlau	110	11.03 N	103.42 E
Phumi Prêk Kák	110	12.15 N	105.32 E
Phumi Prêk Sândêk	110	11.51 N	105.22 E
Phumi Prey Toch	110	12.54 N	103.23 E
Phumi Puŏk Chás	110	13.26 N	103.44 E
Phumi Rôluŏs Chás	110	13.20 N	103.59 E
Phumi Sâmraông	110	14.11 N	103.31 E
Phumi Spœ Tbong	110	12.20 N	105.19 E
Phumi Srê Kôkir	110	13.08 N	106.04 E
Phumi Srê Rônéam	110	12.16 N	106.25 E
Phumi Thalabârivât	110	13.33 N	105.57 E
Phumi Thmâ Pôk	110	13.57 N	103.04 E
Phumi Tnaôt	110	12.56 N	104.34 E
Phumi Tœk Choŭ	110	13.36 N	103.24 E
Phu My	110	14.10 N	109.03 E
Phung Hiep	110	9.49 N	105.50 E
Phuntsholing	124	26.53 N	89.23 E
Phuoc Binh	110	11.50 N	106.58 E
Phuoc Khanh	269c	10.40 N	106.48 E
Phuoc Long	110	9.26 N	105.28 E
Phuoc Long Xa	269c	10.49 N	106.46 E
Phuoc Luong	269c	10.45 N	106.48 E
Phu Quoc	110	10.13 N	103.58 E
Phu Quoc, Dao I	110	10.12 N	104.00 E
Phurphura	272b	22.44 N	88.08 E
Phu Tho	110	21.24 N	105.13 E
Phu Tho Hoa	269c	10.46 N	106.38 E
Phu Tho Race Track ♦	269c	10.46 N	106.40 E
Phutthaisong	110	15.32 N	103.01 E
Phu Vang	110	16.31 N	107.37 E
Phu Yen	110	21.16 N	104.39 E
Pi ≏	100	32.26 N	116.34 E
Pia	154	4.00 N	26.17 E
Piaanu Pass ʯ	175c	7.20 N	151.26 E
Piabas	250	1.12 S	46.54 W
Piabetá	256	22.37 S	43.10 W
Piabonha ≏	256	22.07 S	43.08 W
Piaçabuçu	250	10.24 S	36.25 W
Piacatuba	256	21.29 S	42.47 W
Piacenza	62	45.01 N	9.40 E
Piacenza □4	62	44.53 N	9.35 E
Piacouadie, Lac ⊜	186	51.16 N	70.54 W
Piadena	64	45.08 N	10.22 E
Piaggine	68	40.21 N	15.23 E
Piako ≏	172	37.12 S	175.30 E
Pialba	166	25.17 S	152.51 E
Piāli ≏	272b	22.23 N	88.35 E
Piana	36	42.14 N	8.38 E
Piana, Isola I	71	40.58 N	8.13 E
Piana Crixia	62	44.29 N	8.18 E
Piana degli Albanesi	70	38.00 N	13.17 E
Piana degli Albanesi, Lago di ⊜	70	37.58 N	13.18 E
Piana Mwanga	154	7.40 S	28.10 E
Piancastagnaio	66	42.51 N	11.41 E
Piancó	250	7.12 S	37.57 W
Pian Creek ≏	166	30.02 S	148.12 E
Pian di Sco	66	43.38 N	11.33 E
Pianella	66	42.24 N	14.02 E
Pianello Val Tidone	62	44.57 N	9.24 E
Pianezza	62	45.06 N	7.33 E
Pianguan	102	39.24 N	111.30 E
Pianjiaojie	102	26.01 N	100.32 E
Piankatank ≏	208	37.32 N	76.18 W
Pianling	104	41.24 N	123.58 E
Piano	64	45.46 N	11.08 E
Piano d'Arta	64	46.29 N	13.01 E
Piano del Voglio	66	44.10 N	11.13 E
Pianoro	64	44.22 N	11.20 E
Pianosa, Isola I, It.	36	42.35 N	10.04 E
Pianosa, Isola I, It.	66	42.13 N	15.45 E
Pianosinatico	66	44.07 N	10.44 E
Pianottoli-Caldarello	71	41.29 N	9.03 E
Pians	58	47.08 N	10.30 E
Piapot	184	49.59 N	109.07 W
Piapot Indian Reserve ◆4	184	50.45 N	104.26 W
Piasa	219	39.07 N	90.07 W
Piasa Creek ≏	219	38.56 N	90.17 W
Piaseczno	30	52.05 N	21.01 E
Piashti, Lac ⊜	186	50.29 N	62.52 W
Piaski	30	51.08 N	22.51 E
Piat	116	17.48 N	121.29 E
Piatã	255	13.09 S	41.48 W
Piatra-Neamț	38	46.56 N	26.22 E
Piatra Olt	38	44.24 N	24.16 E
Piatt □6	219	40.00 N	88.35 W
Piau	256	21.31 S	43.19 W
Piauí □3	250	7.00 S	43.00 W
Piauí ≏, Bra.	250	6.38 S	42.42 W
Piauí ≏, Bra.	255	16.41 S	41.53 W
Piauí, Morro do ∧	255	14.59 S	47.31 W
Piaus ≏	255	12.27 S	49.32 W
Piave ≏	64	45.32 N	12.44 E
Piawaning	162	30.51 S	116.22 E
Piaxtla ≏	232	23.42 N	106.49 W
Piazza Armerina	70	37.23 N	14.22 E
Piazzi, Isla I	254	51.45 S	74.05 W
Piazzola sul Brenta	64	45.32 N	11.47 E
Piberegg	61	47.05 N	15.05 E
Pibor ≏	140	8.26 N	33.13 E
Pibor Post	140	6.48 N	33.08 E
Pibroch	182	54.16 N	113.52 W
Pic ≏	190	48.36 N	86.18 W
Pica	248	20.30 S	69.21 W
Picacho	200	32.42 N	111.29 W
Picacho, Cerro del ∧	286a	19.35 N	99.08 W
Pičajevo	80	53.15 N	42.12 E
Picanoc ≏	190	46.05 N	76.03 W
Picardie □9	50	49.45 N	2.50 E
Picatinny Arsenal ■	276	40.57 N	74.33 W
Picatinny Lake ⊜	276	40.57 N	74.33 W
Picayune	194	30.31 N	89.40 W
Piccadilly	186	48.34 N	58.55 W
Piccadilly Station ◆5	262	53.28 N	2.14 W
Piccione	66	43.11 N	12.31 E
Piccolo, Mar ⊤2	68	40.29 N	17.16 E
Piccotts End	260	51.46 N	0.28 W
Pic de Tio ∧	150	8.52 N	8.54 W
Piceance Creek ≏	200	40.05 N	108.14 W
Picentini, Monti ⟁	68	40.45 N	15.00 E
Picerno	68	40.38 N	15.38 E
Pičeury	80	54.19 N	45.50 E
Pīch ≏	123	34.52 N	71.09 E
Pichana ≏	246	3.31 S	71.43 W
Pichanal	252	23.19 S	64.13 W
Picheng	106	32.07 N	119.42 E
Picher	196	36.59 N	94.49 W
Pichhor	124	25.58 N	78.24 E
Pichilemu	252	34.23 S	72.00 W
Pichileufú, Arroyo ≏	254	40.35 S	70.39 W
Pichimá	246	4.24 N	77.21 W
Pichi-Mahuída	252	38.50 S	64.57 W
Pichincha □4	246	0.10 S	78.40 W
Pichis ≏	248	9.59 S	74.59 W
Pichl bei Wels	60	48.11 N	13.54 E
Pichor	124	25.11 N	78.11 E
Pichtovka	86	56.00 N	82.42 E
Pichucalco	234	17.31 N	93.09 W
Picinguaba	256	23.22 S	44.50 W
Picinisco	66	41.39 N	13.52 E
Pic Island I	190	48.43 N	86.38 W
Pickardville	182	54.03 N	113.53 W
Pickaway □6	218	39.36 N	82.57 W
Pickens, Ms., U.S.	194	32.53 N	89.58 W
Pickens, S.C., U.S.	192	34.53 N	82.42 W
Pickens, W.V., U.S.	188	38.39 N	80.12 W
Pickensville	194	33.14 N	88.16 W
Pickerel Lake ⊜	190	45.55 N	80.50 W
Pickerel Lake ⊜	184	52.36 N	99.30 W
Pickering, On., Can.	212	43.52 N	79.02 W
Pickering, Eng., U.K.	44	54.14 N	0.46 W
Pickering, Vale of V	44	54.12 N	0.45 W
Pickering Beach	212	43.50 N	78.59 W
Pickering Brook	168a	32.03 S	116.08 E
Pickering Creek ≏	285	40.08 N	75.31 W
Pickering Creek Reservoir ⊜1	285	40.07 N	75.30 W
Pickett, Lake ⊜	220	28.36 N	81.07 W
Pickford	190	46.09 N	84.21 W
Pičkir'ajevo	80	53.44 N	49.26 E
Pickle Crow	176	51.30 N	90.04 W
Pickmere	262	53.17 N	2.28 W
Pick Mere ⊜	262	53.17 N	2.29 W
Pickstown	198	43.04 N	98.31 W
Pickton	222	33.02 N	95.24 W
Pickwick Lake ⊜1	194	34.55 N	88.10 W
Pickwick Landing Dam ◆6	194	35.00 N	88.21 W
Picnic Point ≻	274b	37.57 S	145.04 E
Pico	66	41.27 N	13.34 E
Pico ∧	150a	14.56 N	24.21 W
Pico I	148a	38.28 N	28.20 W
Pico, Ponta do ∧	148a	38.28 N	28.25 W
Pico da Neblina, Parque Nacional ♦	246	0.30 N	66.00 W
Pico de Orizaba, Parque Nacional ♦	234	19.05 N	97.16 W
Pico Rivera	228	33.58 N	118.05 W
Picos	250	7.05 S	41.28 W
Picota	248	6.55 S	76.20 W
Pico Truncado	254	46.48 S	67.58 W
Picquigny	50	49.57 N	2.09 E
Picton, Austl.	170	34.11 S	150.36 E
Picton, On., Can.	212	44.00 N	77.08 W
Picton, N.Z.	172	41.18 S	174.01 E
Picton, Eng., U.K.	262	53.14 N	2.51 W
Picton, Isla I	254	55.02 S	66.57 W
Picton Bay C	212	44.03 N	77.08 W
Picton Junction	168a	33.21 S	115.41 E
Pictou	186	45.41 N	62.43 W
Pictou Island I	186	45.50 N	62.34 W
Picture Butte	182	49.53 N	112.47 W
Pictured Rocks National Lakeshore ♦	190	46.35 N	86.20 W
Picture Rocks	210	41.17 N	76.43 W
Picúa, Punta ≻	240m	18.25 N	65.46 W
Picuí	250	6.31 S	36.21 W
Picunda	84	43.12 N	40.21 E
Picún Leufú	254	39.31 S	69.15 W
Picún Leufú, Arroyo ≏	254	39.31 S	69.08 W
Picuris Indian Reservation ◆4	200	36.12 N	105.42 W
Pidálion, Akrotírion ≻	130	34.56 N	34.05 E
Pidarak	128	25.51 N	63.14 E
Piddle ≏	42	50.42 N	2.04 W
Piddletrenthide	42	50.48 N	2.25 W
Pide Adası I	267b	40.53 N	29.04 E
Pidie, Ujung ≻	114	5.30 N	95.53 E
Piding	64	47.46 N	12.55 E
Pidurutalagala ∧	122	7.00 N	80.46 E
Piedade	287a	22.41 S	43.05 W
Piedade ◆8	287a	22.53 S	43.19 W
Piedade do Baruel	287b	23.37 S	46.18 W
Piedade do Rio Grande	256	21.28 S	44.12 W
Piedecuesta	246	6.59 N	73.03 W
Piedicavallo	62	45.42 N	7.57 E
Piedicroce	36	42.23 N	9.23 E
Piediluco	66	42.32 N	12.45 E
Piedimonte Etneo	70	37.48 N	15.12 E
Piedimonte Matese	68	41.21 N	14.22 E
Piedimonte San Germano	66	41.30 N	13.45 E
Piedimulera	58	46.01 N	8.16 E
Piè di Ripa	66	43.15 N	13.29 E
Piedmont, Al., U.S.	194	33.55 N	85.36 W
Piedmont, Ca., U.S.	226	37.49 N	122.13 W
Piedmont, Mo., U.S.	194	37.09 N	90.41 W
Piedmont, Oh., U.S.	214	40.11 N	81.12 W
Piedmont, S.C., U.S.	192	34.54 N	82.21 W
Piedmont Lake ⊜1	214	40.08 N	81.11 W
Piedra, C.R.	236	9.29 N	83.40 W
Piedra, Ca., U.S.	226	36.48 N	119.22 W
Piedra ≏	200	37.01 N	107.24 W
Piedra, Cerro ∧	252	37.41 S	73.07 W
Piedra Azul, Quebrada ≏	286c	10.36 N	66.57 W
Piedrabuena	34	39.02 N	4.10 W
Piedra del Águila	254	40.03 S	70.05 W
Piedra del Águila, Embalse ⊜1	254	40.30 S	70.20 W
Piedrafita, Puerto de)(	34	42.40 N	7.01 W
Piedrahita	34	40.28 N	5.19 W
Piedra Roja	236	8.38 N	81.48 W
Piedras, Arroyo de las ≏	288	34.43 S	58.19 W
Piedras, Punta ≻, Arg.	258	35.25 S	57.08 W
Piedras, Punta ≻, Ven.	246	10.40 N	61.40 W
Piedras Blancas	252	31.11 S	59.56 W
Piedras Blancas, Point ≻	226	35.40 N	121.17 W
Piedras Coloradas	252	32.23 S	57.36 W
Piedras Negras, Guat.	232	17.11 N	91.15 W
Piedras Negras, Méx.	232	28.42 N	100.31 W
Piedras Negras ⊥	232	17.12 N	91.15 W
Piedra Sola	252	32.04 S	56.21 W
Piegaro	66	42.58 N	12.05 E
Pie Island I	190	48.15 N	89.05 W
Pieksämäki	26	62.18 N	27.08 E
Piéla	150	12.42 N	0.08 W
Pielach ≏	61	48.15 N	15.22 E
Pielavesi	26	63.14 N	26.45 E
Pielavesi ⊜	26	63.18 N	26.35 E
Pielinen ⊜	26	63.15 N	29.40 E
Pieljekaise Nationalpark ♦	24	66.18 N	16.58 E
Piemonte □4	36	45.00 N	8.00 E
Pienaarsrivier	156	25.15 S	28.18 E
Piendamó	246	2.38 N	76.30 W
Pieniężno	30	54.15 N	20.08 E
Pieniński Park Narodowy ♦	30	49.25 N	20.25 E
Pieni-Salpausselkä ∧	26	61.08 N	27.20 E
Piennes	56	49.19 N	5.47 E
Pieńsk	30	51.15 N	15.03 E
Pienza	66	43.04 N	11.41 E
Pierce, Co., U.S.	200	40.38 N	104.45 W
Pierce, Fl., U.S.	220	27.50 N	81.58 W
Pierce, Id., U.S.	202	46.29 N	115.47 W
Pierce, Ne., U.S.	198	42.11 N	97.31 W
Pierce, Tx., U.S.	222	29.14 N	96.12 W
Pierce □6	224	47.04 N	122.07 W
Pierce, Lake ⊜	220	27.58 N	81.31 W
Pierce City	194	36.56 N	94.00 W
Pierce Lake ⊜, Can.	184	54.10 N	92.56 W
Pierce Lake ⊜, Sk., Can.	184	54.30 N	109.42 W
Pierceton	216	41.12 N	85.42 W
Piermont	210	41.03 N	73.55 W
Pierowall	46	59.20 N	2.59 W
Pierpont, Oh., U.S.	214	41.45 N	80.34 W
Pierpont, S.D., U.S.	198	45.29 N	97.49 W
Pierre	198	44.22 N	100.21 W
Pierre, Bayou ≏, La., U.S.	194	31.51 N	93.06 W
Pierre, Bayou ≏, Ms., U.S.	194	31.55 N	91.11 W
Pierre-Buffière	32	45.42 N	1.21 E
Pierreclos	58	46.20 N	4.41 E
Pierre-de-Bresse	58	46.53 N	5.13 E
Pierrefeu-du-Var	62	43.13 N	6.08 E
Pierrefitte-sur-Aire	56	48.54 N	5.20 E
Pierrefitte-sur-Sauldre	58	47.30 N	2.09 E
Pierrefitte-sur-Seine	261	48.58 N	2.22 E
Pierrefonds, P.Q., Can.	206	45.29 N	73.52 W
Pierrefonds, Fr.	50	49.21 N	2.59 E
Pierrefontaine-les-Varans	58	47.13 N	6.33 E
Pierrelatte	62	44.23 N	4.42 E
Pierrelaye	261	49.01 N	2.09 E
Pierre Part	194	29.57 N	91.12 W
Pierre Pertuis, Col de)(	58	47.12 N	7.11 E
Pierrepont Manor	212	43.44 N	76.04 W
Pierre-sur-Haute ∧	62	45.39 N	3.49 E
Pierreville, P.Q., Can.	206	46.04 N	72.49 W
Pierreville, Trin.	241r	10.18 N	61.01 W
Pierron	219	38.53 N	89.36 W
Pierron, Lac ⊜	206	46.53 N	74.02 W
Pierry	50	49.01 N	3.56 E
Pierson	192	29.14 N	81.27 W
Piersonville	285	40.10 N	74.42 W
Pierz	190	45.58 N	94.06 W
Piesendorf	64	47.17 N	12.43 E
Piešťany	30	48.36 N	17.50 E
Piesting ≏	61	48.02 N	16.30 E
Pietarsaari → Jakobstad	26	63.40 N	22.42 E
Pieterburen	52	53.24 N	6.27 E
Pieterlen	58	47.11 N	7.20 E
Pietermaritzburg	158	29.37 S	30.16 E
Pietersburg	156	23.54 S	29.25 E
Pietrabbondante	66	41.45 N	14.23 E
Pietracamela	66	42.31 N	13.33 E
Pietracatella	66	41.35 N	14.52 E
Pietra del Pertusillo, Lago di ⊜	68	40.17 N	15.58 E
Pietragalla	68	40.45 N	15.53 E
Pietra Ligure	62	44.09 N	8.17 E
Pietralunga	66	43.26 N	12.26 E
Pietramala	66	44.10 N	11.20 E
Pietramelara	68	41.16 N	14.11 E
Pietramontecorvino	68	41.32 N	15.07 E
Pietrapaola	68	39.29 N	16.49 E
Pietrapertosa	68	40.31 N	16.04 E
Pietraperzia	70	37.25 N	14.08 E
Pietrasanta	64	43.57 N	10.14 E
Pietrelcina	68	41.12 N	14.51 E
Piet Retief	158	27.01 S	30.50 E
Pietrosu, Vîrful ∧, Rom.	38	47.08 N	25.11 E
Pietrosu, Vîrful ∧, Rom.	38	47.36 N	24.38 E
Pieve	64	45.46 N	10.45 E
Pieve d'Alpago	64	46.10 N	12.21 E
Pieve del Cairo	62	45.03 N	8.48 E
Pieve di Cadore	64	46.26 N	12.22 E
Pieve di Cento	64	44.43 N	11.18 E
Pieve di Soligo	64	45.53 N	12.10 E
Pieve di Teco	62	44.03 N	7.56 E
Pieve Fosciana	64	44.08 N	10.25 E
Pievepelago	64	44.12 N	10.37 E
Pieve Porto Morone	62	45.07 N	9.26 E
Pieve Santo Stefano	66	43.40 N	12.02 E
Piffard	210	42.50 N	77.51 W
Pigari	80	51.24 N	49.42 E
Pigeon, Mi., U.S.	190	43.49 N	83.16 W
Pigeon, Pa., U.S.	214	41.32 N	79.03 W
Pigeon ≏, Mb., Can.	184	52.15 N	97.00 W
Pigeon ≏, On., Can.	212	44.22 N	78.31 W
Pigeon ≏, N.A.	190	48.00 N	89.34 W
Pigeon ≏, U.S.	192	36.00 N	83.11 W
Pigeon ≏, U.S.	216	41.46 N	85.47 W
Pigeon ≏, Mi., U.S.	190	43.56 N	83.17 W
Pigeon ≏, Mi., U.S.	190	45.27 N	84.33 W
Pigeon ≏, Mi., U.S.	216	42.54 N	86.11 W
Pigeon Bay C	214	42.01 N	82.40 W
Pigeon Cove	207	42.40 N	70.38 W
Pigeon Creek ≏, Al., U.S.	194	31.20 N	86.42 W
Pigeon Creek ≏, In., U.S.	194	37.59 N	87.35 W
Pigeon Creek ≏, In., U.S.	216	41.41 N	85.17 W
Pigeon Creek ≏, Pa., U.S.	279b	40.12 N	79.55 W
Pigeon Creek ≏, Pa., U.S.	285	40.12 N	75.35 W
Pigeon Forge	192	35.47 N	83.33 W
Pigeon Lake ⊜, Ab., Can.	182	53.00 N	114.00 W
Pigeon Lake ⊜, On., Can.	212	44.30 N	78.30 W
Pigeon Run ≏	285	40.06 N	75.35 W
Pigeon Swamp ≋	276	40.23 N	74.29 W
Pigezhuang	105	39.39 N	116.15 E
Pigg ≏	192	37.00 N	79.29 W
Piggott	194	36.22 N	90.11 W
Piggs Peak	158	25.38 S	31.15 E
Pigkawagan	116	7.12 N	124.32 E
Piglio	66	41.49 N	13.08 E
Pigna	62	43.56 N	7.40 E
Pignans	62	43.18 N	6.13 E
Pignataro Maggiore	68	41.11 N	14.10 E
Pignola	68	40.34 N	15.47 E
Pigs, Bay of → Cochinos, Bahía de C	240p	22.07 N	81.10 W
Pigüé	252	37.37 S	62.25 W
Pigŭm-do I	98	34.45 N	125.55 E
Pihama	172	39.30 S	173.56 E
Piha Passage ʯ	174w	21.07 S	175.05 W
Pihāri	124	27.38 N	80.12 E
Pihlajavesi ⊜	26	61.45 N	28.50 E
Pihlava	26	61.33 N	21.36 E
Pihtipudas	26	63.23 N	25.34 E
Pihuamo	234	19.15 N	103.23 W
P'ihyŏn	98	40.01 N	124.37 E
Piikkiö	26	60.26 N	22.31 E
Piippola	26	64.10 N	25.58 E
Pijijiapan	234	15.42 N	93.14 W
Pijnacker	52	52.02 N	4.27 E
Pijol, Pico ∧	236	15.06 N	87.35 W
Pikal'ovo	76	59.31 N	34.06 E
Pikangikum	184	51.49 N	94.00 W
Pikangikum Lake ⊜	184	51.48 N	94.00 W
Pike	210	42.33 N	78.09 W
Pike □6, Il., U.S.	219	39.36 N	90.48 W
Pike □6, Mo., U.S.	219	39.21 N	91.10 W
Pike □6, Oh., U.S.	218	39.05 N	83.06 W
Pike □6, Pa., U.S.	210	41.19 N	74.48 W
Pike ≏, N.A.	206	45.04 N	73.06 W
Pike ≏, Wi., U.S.	190	45.26 N	87.52 W
Pike, North Branch ≏	190	45.30 N	88.01 W
Pike, South Branch ≏	190	45.30 N	88.01 W
Pike Creek ≏, On., Can.	281	42.19 N	82.51 W
Pike Creek ≏, De., U.S.	285	39.42 N	75.42 W
Pike Lake ⊜	212	44.46 N	76.21 W
Pikelot I	14	8.05 N	147.38 E
Pike Lowe ∧2	262	53.42 N	2.34 W
Pike Run ≏	276	40.25 N	74.38 W
Pikes Peak	218	39.08 N	86.09 W
Pikes Peak ∧	200	38.51 N	105.03 W
Pikes Rocks ∧2	214	41.56 N	79.24 W
Pikesville	208	39.22 N	76.43 W
Piketberg	158	32.54 S	18.46 E
Piketon	218	39.04 N	83.00 W
Pikeville, Ky., U.S.	192	37.28 N	82.31 W
Pikeville, Tn., U.S.	194	35.36 N	85.11 W
Pikkola	265a	59.42 N	30.08 E
Pikou	98	39.24 N	122.20 E
Pikounda	152	0.33 N	16.42 E
Pikwitonei	184	55.35 N	97.09 W
Pila, Arg.	252	36.01 S	58.08 W
Pila, It.	62	45.04 N	7.18 E
Piła (Schneidemühl), Pol.	30	53.10 N	16.44 E
Piła □4	30	53.15 N	16.30 E
Pilanesberg ∧	158	25.14 S	27.04 E
Pilanesberg Game Reserve ◆4	156	25.15 S	27.05 E
Pilão Arcado	250	9.56 S	42.29 W
Pilar, Arg.	252	31.41 S	63.54 W
Pilar, Arg.	252	31.27 S	61.15 W
Pilar, Arg.	258	34.27 S	58.54 W
Pilar, Bra.	250	9.36 S	35.56 W
Pilar, Bra.	287a	22.42 S	43.19 W
Pilar, Para.	252	26.52 S	58.23 W
Pilar, Pil.	116	11.29 N	123.00 E
Pilar, Pil.	116	9.52 N	126.06 E
Pilar □5	288	34.28 S	58.52 W
Pilar Bay C	116	11.34 N	123.00 E
Pilarcitos Creek ≏	282	37.28 N	122.27 W
Pilarcitos Lake ⊜	282	37.33 N	122.25 W
Pilar de Goiás	255	14.47 S	49.35 W
Pilar do Sul	256	23.49 S	47.42 W
Pilares	196	30.24 N	104.52 W
Pilas Group II	116	6.45 N	121.35 E
Pilas Island I	116	6.38 N	121.37 E
Pilatus ∧	58	46.59 N	8.15 E
Pilawa	30	51.58 N	21.32 E
Pilaya ≏	248	20.55 S	64.04 W
Pilcher Park ♦	278	41.32 N	88.01 W
Pilchuck ≏	224	47.55 N	122.02 W
Pilchuck Creek ≏	224	48.12 N	122.13 W
Pilcomayo ≏	18	25.21 S	57.42 W
Pilcomayo, Brazo Norte ≏	252	24.56 S	58.16 W
Pilcomayo, Brazo Sur ≏	252	24.56 S	58.16 W
Pil'dozero	24	65.43 N	33.28 E
Piles Creek ≏	276	40.37 N	74.12 W
Pilga	162	21.29 S	119.25 E
Pilger	198	42.00 N	97.03 W
Pilgrim Gardens	285	39.57 N	75.19 W
Pilgrim Memorial Monument ⊥	207	42.04 N	70.12 W
Pilgrims Hatch	260	51.38 N	0.17 E
Pilgrim's Rest	156	24.55 S	30.44 E
Pil'gyn	180	69.18 N	179.08 E
Pili	116	13.33 N	123.16 E
Pīlībhīt	124	28.38 N	79.48 E
Pilica ≏	30	51.52 N	21.17 E
Pilipinas → Philippines □1	116	13.00 N	122.00 E
Pilis ⟁	264c	47.37 N	18.59 E
Pilisborosjenő	264c	47.36 N	19.00 E
Pilkhua	124	28.43 N	77.39 E
Pillaro	246	1.10 S	78.32 W
Pillar Point ≻	282	37.30 N	122.30 W
Pillar Point ≻1	212	43.59 N	76.09 W
Pillau → Baltijsk	76	54.39 N	19.55 E
Pilley's Island	186	49.31 N	55.44 W
Pilliga	166	30.21 S	148.54 E
Pillings Pond ⊜	283	42.32 N	71.02 W
Pillnitz ◆8	54	51.00 N	13.52 E
Pillon, Col du)(	58	46.22 N	7.13 E
Pillow	208	40.38 N	76.48 W
Pillsbury Sound ʯ	240m	18.20 N	64.49 W
Pil'na	80	55.33 N	45.55 E
Pílos	38	36.55 N	21.43 E
Pilot ∧	166	36.45 S	148.13 E
Pilot Butte	184	50.28 N	104.25 W
Pilot Grove	194	38.52 N	92.54 W
Pilot Hill	226	38.50 N	121.02 W
Pilot Knob	194	37.37 N	90.38 W
Pilot Knob ∧, Ar., U.S.	194	35.42 N	93.57 W
Pilot Knob ∧, Id., U.S.	202	45.54 N	115.42 W
Pilot Mound	184	49.16 N	98.55 W
Pilot Mountain	192	36.23 N	80.28 W
Pilot Peak ∧, Nv., U.S.	204	38.21 N	117.58 W
Pilot Peak ∧, Nv., U.S.	204	41.02 N	114.06 W
Pilot Peak ∧, Wy., U.S.	202	44.58 N	109.53 W
Pilot Point, Ak., U.S.	180	57.34 N	157.35 W
Pilot Point, Tx., U.S.	196	33.23 N	96.57 W
Pilot Rock	202	45.29 N	118.49 W
Pilot Rock ∧	200	35.09 N	109.53 W
Pilot Station	180	61.56 N	162.54 W
Pilottown	194	29.10 N	89.15 W
Pilpah Range ⟁	166	20.23 S	138.34 E
Pilsen → Plzeň	60	49.45 N	13.23 E
Pilsensee ⊜	60	48.01 N	11.11 E
Pilsum	52	53.29 N	7.04 E
Piltene	76	57.13 N	21.40 E
Pilu ≏	110	19.33 N	97.24 E
Piluchang	107	29.13 N	105.37 E
Pil'ugino	80	53.25 N	52.26 E
Pilusi	106	32.05 N	120.05 E
Pilzno	30	49.59 N	21.17 E
Pim ≏	74	61.18 N	71.57 E
Pima	200	32.53 N	109.49 W
Pimah	110	15.36 N	107.25 E
Pimba	166	31.15 S	136.47 E
Pimelles	50	47.50 N	4.10 E
Pimenta Bueno ≏	248	11.39 S	61.11 W
Pimenteira, Vereda ≏	250	9.58 S	42.46 W
Pimenteiras	250	6.14 S	41.25 W
Pimentel, Bra.	250	3.43 S	45.30 W
Pimentel, Perú	248	6.50 S	79.57 W
Pimlico Race Course ♦	284b	39.21 N	76.40 W
Pimmit Hills	284c	38.54 N	77.12 W
Pimmit Run ≏	284c	38.55 N	77.07 W
Pimu-Lendo	152	1.46 N	20.54 E
Pimville ◆8	273d	26.16 S	27.54 E
Pina	34	41.29 N	0.32 W
Pina ≏	76	52.10 N	26.14 E
Pinacanauan ≏	116	17.37 N	121.44 E
Pináculo, Cerro ∧	254	50.45 S	72.16 W
Pinalón, Cerro ∧	236	15.05 N	89.55 W
Pinamalayan	116	13.02 N	121.29 E
Pinang → George Town	114	5.25 N	100.20 E
Pinang □3	114	5.20 N	100.20 E
Pinang, Pulau I	114	5.23 N	100.15 E
Pinangah	112	5.12 N	116.50 E
Pınarbaşı, Tür.	130	41.36 N	33.07 E
Pınarbaşı, Tür.	130	38.44 N	36.24 E
Pinar del Río	240p	22.25 N	83.42 W
Pinar del Río □4	240p	22.30 N	83.45 W
Pinardville	188	42.59 N	71.30 W
Pinarhisar	130	41.37 N	27.30 E
Pinarlar	130	38.53 N	39.29 E
Pinas, Arg.	252	31.09 S	65.29 W
Piñas, Ec.	246	3.42 S	79.42 W
Piñas, Cerro ∧	236	15.25 N	85.47 W
Pinatubo, Mount ∧	116	15.08 N	120.21 E
Pinazo, Arroyo ≏	288	34.24 S	58.48 W
Pinchbeck	42	52.48 N	0.09 W
Pincher Creek	182	49.29 N	113.57 W
Pinchi Lake ⊜	182	54.35 N	124.20 W
Pinckney	216	42.27 N	83.56 W
Pinckney State Recreation Area ♦	216	42.25 N	84.04 W
Pinckneyville	194	38.04 N	89.22 W
Pinconning	190	43.51 N	83.57 W
Pincourt	206	45.23 N	74.00 W
Pinčuga	86	58.23 N	96.59 E
Pińczów	30	50.32 N	20.35 E
Pindaíba, Ribeirão ≏	255	14.18 S	51.44 W
Pindale	110	21.11 N	95.51 E
Pindamonhangaba	256	22.55 S	45.28 W
Pindar	162	28.29 S	115.48 E
Pindaré ≏	250	3.17 S	44.47 W
Pindaré-Mirim	250	3.37 S	45.21 W
Pind Dādan Khān	123	32.35 N	73.03 E
Pinde → Píndhos Óros ⟁	38	39.49 N	21.14 E
Pinder Point ≻	192	26.28 N	78.39 W
Píndhos Óros (Pindus Mountains) ⟁	38	39.49 N	21.14 E
Pindi Bhattiān	123	31.54 N	73.16 E
Pindiga	146	9.59 N	10.54 E
Pindi Gheb	123	33.14 N	72.16 E
Pindo → Píndhos Óros ⟁	38	39.49 N	21.14 E
Pindobaçu	250	10.44 S	40.21 W
Pindorama de Goiás	255	10.55 S	47.40 W
Pinduši	24	62.56 N	34.35 E
Pindus Mountains → Píndhos Óros ⟁	38	39.49 N	21.14 E
Pindwāra	120	24.48 N	73.04 E
Pine ≏, B.C., Can.	182	56.08 N	120.41 W
Pine ≏, Mb., Can.	184	52.00 N	100.09 W
Pine ≏, On., Can.	212	44.20 N	79.52 W
Pine ≏, Mi., U.S.	190	44.15 N	85.55 W
Pine ≏, Mi., U.S.	190	46.03 N	84.40 W
Pine ≏, Mi., U.S.	190	44.26 N	83.21 W
Pine ≏, Mi., U.S.	190	43.15 N	83.45 W
Pine ≏, Wi., U.S.	190	44.08 N	88.54 W
Pine ≏, Wi., U.S.	190	45.50 N	88.08 W
Pine ≏, Wi., U.S.	190	43.12 N	90.18 W
Pine Apple	194	31.52 N	86.59 W
Pine Banks Park ♦	283	42.26 N	71.04 W

Name	Seite	Breite°′	Länge°′ E = Ost
Pine Barrens ◆1	208	39.48 N	74.35 W
Pine Beach	206	45.32 N	73.57 W
Pine Bluff	194	34.13 N	92.00 W
Pine Bluffs	198	41.10 N	104.04 W
Pine Brook	276	40.52 N	74.20 W
Pine Brook ≏, U.S.	276	41.04 N	74.05 W
Pine Brook ≏, Ma., U.S.	283	42.00 N	70.47 W
Pine Brook ≏, N.J., U.S.	276	40.19 N	74.20 W
Pine Bush	210	41.36 N	74.17 W
Pine Castle	220	28.28 N	81.22 W
Pine City, Mn., U.S.	190	45.49 N	92.58 W
Pine City, N.Y., U.S.	210	42.02 N	76.52 W
Pinecliff Lake ⊜	276	41.08 N	74.23 W
Pinecraft	220	27.19 N	82.30 W
Pine Creek	164	13.49 S	131.49 E
Pine Creek ≏, Ab., Can.	182	54.56 N	112.31 W
Pine Creek ≏, Ca., U.S.	204	40.40 N	120.46 W
Pine Creek ≏, Ca., U.S.	282	37.58 N	122.02 W
Pine Creek ≏, Nv., U.S.	204	40.36 N	116.10 W
Pine Creek ≏, Pa., U.S.	210	41.10 N	77.16 W
Pine Creek ≏, Pa., U.S.	279b	40.30 N	79.57 W
Pine Creek ≏, Pa., U.S.	285	40.05 N	75.37 W
Pine Creek, West Branch ≏	210	41.43 N	77.38 W
Pine Creek Indian Reserve ◆4	184	52.03 N	100.14 W
Pine Creek Lake ⊜1	196	34.05 N	95.05 W
Pine Creek Point ≻	276	41.07 N	73.16 W
Pine Crest, Fl., U.S.	220	28.01 N	82.32 W
Pinecrest, Va., U.S.	208	38.50 N	77.09 W
Pinecrest Lake ⊜	226	38.12 N	119.58 W
Pine Crest Point ≻	284a	42.52 N	79.11 W
Pinedale, Ca., U.S.	226	36.50 N	119.48 W
Pinedale, Wy., U.S.	200	42.52 N	109.51 W
Pine Falls	184	50.35 N	96.15 W
Pine Flat Lake ⊜1	226	36.52 N	119.18 W
Pinega	24	64.42 N	43.19 E
Pinega ≏	24	64.08 N	41.54 E
Pine Glen	212	45.19 N	75.43 W
Pine Grove, On., Can.	275b	43.48 N	79.35 W
Pine Grove, Ca., U.S.	226	38.25 N	120.39 W
Pine Grove, Fl., U.S.	220	28.16 N	81.11 W
Pine Grove, N.J., U.S.	285	39.53 N	74.52 W
Pine Grove, Pa., U.S.	208	40.32 N	76.23 W
Pine Grove, W.V., U.S.	188	39.33 N	80.40 W
Pine Grove Mills	214	40.44 N	77.53 W
Pine Hill, Austl.	166	23.39 S	146.58 E
Pine Hill, Al., U.S.	194	31.58 N	87.35 W
Pine Hill, N.J., U.S.	208	39.47 N	74.59 W
Pine Hill, N.Y., U.S.	210	42.08 N	74.29 W
Pinehill, Tx., U.S.	222	32.06 N	94.36 W
Pine Hills	220	28.33 N	81.27 W
Pinehouse Lake	184	55.31 N	106.36 W
Pinehouse Lake ⊜	184	55.32 N	106.35 W
Pinehurst, Ga., U.S.	192	32.11 N	83.45 W
Pinehurst, Id., U.S.	202	45.15 N	116.20 W
Pinehurst, Ma., U.S.	207	42.31 N	71.13 W
Pinehurst, N.Y., U.S.	284a	42.44 N	78.57 W
Pinehurst, N.C., U.S.	192	35.11 N	79.28 W
Pinehurst, Tx., U.S.	222	30.10 N	95.41 W
Pinehurst Lake ⊜	182	54.39 N	111.25 W
Pine Island, Mn., U.S.	190	44.12 N	92.38 W
Pine Island, N.Y., U.S.	210	41.17 N	74.27 W
Pine Island I	220	26.35 N	82.06 W
Pine Island Bay C	9	74.50 S	102.05 W
Pine Island Bayou ≏	194	30.10 N	94.07 W
Pine Island Creek ≏	283	42.47 N	70.48 W
Pine Island Dam ◆6	214	40.08 N	80.43 W
Pine Island Sound ʯ	220	26.33 N	82.10 W
Pine Lake, In., U.S.	216	41.38 N	86.45 W
Pine Lake, Ma., U.S.	283	42.23 N	71.27 W
Pine Lake ⊜, On., Can.	212	44.57 N	79.27 W
Pine Lake ⊜, Mi., U.S.	281	42.35 N	83.20 W
Pine Lake ⊜, N.Y., U.S.	210	43.12 N	74.31 W
Pineland	194	31.14 N	93.58 W
Pine Lawn	219	38.41 N	90.16 W
Pinellas □6	220	27.53 N	82.43 W
Pinellas, Point ≻	220	27.42 N	82.38 W
Pinellas Park	220	27.50 N	82.41 W
Pine Marsh ≋	276	40.37 N	73.34 W
Pine Meadow Lake ⊜	276	41.11 N	74.07 W
Pine Mountain ∧, U.S.	192	36.55 N	83.20 W
Pine Mountain ∧, Ca., U.S.	226	35.41 N	121.05 W
Pine Mountain ∧, Ca., U.S.	280	34.13 N	117.54 W
Pine Mountain ∧, Ct., U.S.	207	41.58 N	72.56 W
Pine Mountain ∧, Ga., U.S.	192	32.51 N	84.47 W
Pine Mountain ∧, Or., U.S.	202	43.47 N	120.54 W
Pine Mountain ∧, Wy., U.S.	200	41.02 N	109.01 W
Pine Nut Mountains ⟁	226	39.00 N	119.25 W
Pine Orchard Meadows	284b	39.17 N	76.52 W
Pine Pass)(	182	55.22 N	122.40 W
Pine Plains	210	41.59 N	73.40 W
Pine Point, Austl.	168b	34.34 S	137.52 E
Pine Point, N.T., Can.	176	61.01 N	114.15 W
Pine Point Park ♦	275b	43.43 N	79.33 W
Pine Portage Dam ◆6	176	49.18 N	88.19 W
Pine Prairie	194	30.47 N	92.25 W
Piner	218	38.50 N	84.32 W
Pine Rest	283	42.23 N	71.26 W
Pine Ridge, Pa., U.S.	285	39.55 N	75.22 W
Pine Ridge, S.D., U.S.	198	43.01 N	102.33 W
Pine Ridge, Va., U.S.	208	38.52 N	77.14 W
Pine Ridge ∧	198	42.40 N	103.00 W
Pine Ridge Estates	276	41.02 N	73.41 W
Pine Ridge Indian Reservation ◆4	198	43.25 N	102.21 W
Pine River, Mb., Can.	184	51.47 N	100.32 W
Pine River, Mn., U.S.	190	46.43 N	94.24 W
Piñero	258	34.32 S	60.48 W
Pinerolo	62	44.53 N	7.21 E
Piñeros, Isla I	240m	18.15 N	65.35 W
Pinerovka	80	51.34 N	43.04 E
Pine Run ≏	279b	40.30 N	79.35 W
Pines ≏	283	42.27 N	70.58 W
Pines, Isle of → Juventud, Isla de la I	240p	21.40 N	82.50 W
Pines, Lake o' the ⊜1	222	32.46 N	94.35 W
Pines, Point of ≻	283	42.26 N	70.58 W
Pine Shores	220	27.17 N	82.32 W
Pines Lake ⊜	276	41.00 N	74.16 W
Pine Swamp Knob ∧	188	39.33 N	79.57 W
Pineto	66	42.36 N	14.04 E
Pinetop	200	34.07 N	109.56 W
Pinetops	192	35.47 N	77.38 W
Pinetown	158	29.52 S	30.46 E
Pine Tree Hill ∧	114	3.43 N	101.42 E
Pine Valley, Md., U.S.	284b	39.26 N	76.39 W
Pine Valley, N.Y., U.S.	210	42.14 N	76.51 W
Pine Valley V	200	38.25 N	113.40 W
Pine Village	216	40.27 N	87.15 W
Pineville, Ky., U.S.	192	36.45 N	83.41 W
Pineville, La., U.S.	194	31.19 N	92.26 W

Symbols in the index entries represent the broad categories identified in the key at the right. Symbols with superior numbers (⟁1) identify subcategories (see complete key on page *I · 1*).

Symbole im Register stellen die rechts im Schlüssel erklärten Kategorien dar. Symbole mit hochgestellten Ziffern (⟁1) bezeichnen Unterabteilungen einer Kategorie (vgl. vollständiger Schlüssel auf Seite *I · 1*).

Los símbolos incluídos en el texto del índice representan las grandes categorías identificadas con la clave a la derecha. Los símbolos con numeros en su parte superior (⟁1) identifican las subcategorías (véase la clave completa en la página *I · 1*).

Les symboles de l'index représentent les catégories indiquées dans la légende à droite. Les symboles suivis d'un indice (⟁1) représentent des sous-catégories (voir légende complète à la page *I · 1*).

Os símbolos incluídos no texto do índice representam as grandes categorias identificadas com a chave à direita. Os símbolos com números em sua parte superior (⟁1) identificam as subcategorias (veja-se a chave completa à página *I · 1*).

∧ Mountain	Berg	Montaña	Montagne	Montanha
⟁ Mountains	Gebirge	Montañas	Montagnes	Montanhas
)(Pass	Paß	Paso	Col	Passo
V Valley, Canyon	Tal, Cañon	Valle, Cañón	Vallée, Canyon	Vale, Canhão
≃ Plain	Ebene	Llano	Plaine	Planície
≻ Cape	Kap	Cabo	Cap	Cabo
I Island	Insel	Isla	Île	Ilha
II Islands	Inseln	Islas	Îles	Ilhas
⊥ Other Topographic Features	Andere Topographische Objekte	Otros Elementos Topográficos	Autres données topographiques	Outros acidentes topográficos

ESPAÑOL / FRANÇAIS / PORTUGUÊS

Nombre / Nom / Nome	Página / Page / Página	Lat.°′	Long.°′ W = Oeste / W = Ouest
Pineville, Mo., U.S.	194	36.35 N	94.23 W
Pineville, N.C., U.S.	192	35.04 N	80.53 W
Pineville, Pa., U.S.	208	40.18 N	75.00 W
Pineville, W.V., U.S.	192	37.34 N	81.32 W
Pinewood, Fl., U.S.	220	25.53 N	80.14 W
Pinewood, S.C., U.S.	192	33.44 N	80.27 W
Piney	50	48.22 N	4.20 E
Piney ≃	194	35.49 N	87.33 W
Piney Branch ≃	284c	38.56 N	77.18 W
Piney Creek ≃, Tx., U.S.	222	31.03 N	94.34 W
Piney Creek ≃, Wy., U.S.	202	44.34 N	106.32 W
Piney Fork	214	40.15 N	80.50 W
Piney Point	222	29.46 N	95.31 W
Piney Point ›	208	38.08 N	76.32 W
Piney Run ≃	284c	38.58 N	77.17 W
Piney Woods	194	32.03 N	89.59 W
Pinfold	262	53.36 N	2.55 W
Ping ≃, Thai	110	15.42 N	100.09 E
Ping ≃, Zhg.	100	25.59 N	115.07 E
Pinga	154	1.01 S	28.42 E
Ping'an, Zhg.	89	45.20 N	123.42 E
Ping'an, Zhg.	104	41.11 N	123.26 E
Ping'an, Zhg.	107	30.36 N	104.42 E
Ping'anbu	98	41.45 N	116.13 E
Ping'ancheng	105	40.03 N	117.48 E
Ping'andi	104	42.34 N	121.52 E
Pingaring	162	32.45 S	118.37 E
Pingba, Zhg.	100	31.19 N	113.18 E
Pingba, Zhg.	102	26.22 N	106.09 E
Pingchang	102	31.35 N	107.03 E
Pingchao	106	32.07 N	120.45 E
Pingding	98	37.48 N	113.37 E
Pingdingpu	104	42.22 N	123.55 E
Pingdingshan, Zhg.	98	41.26 N	124.45 E
Pingdingshan, Zhg.	100	33.45 N	113.17 E
Pingding Shan ∧	89	46.38 N	128.27 E
Pingdu	98	36.47 N	119.54 E
Pingelap I[1]	14	6.13 N	160.42 E
Pingelly	162	32.32 S	117.05 E
Pingfang, Zhg.	100	30.07 N	113.48 E
Pingfang, Zhg.	104	41.17 N	120.40 E
Pingfang, Zhg.	104	41.28 N	120.48 E
Pingfang, Zhg.	104	42.14 N	120.38 E
Pingfang, Zhg.	104	42.27 N	120.38 E
Pingfang, Zhg.	271a	39.56 N	116.33 E
Pingfangdu	104	41.45 N	121.12 E
Pingfangzi	104	41.31 N	121.21 E
Pinggau	61	47.27 N	16.04 E
Pinggu	105	40.09 N	117.07 E
Pingguo	102	23.19 N	107.39 E
Pinghai, Zhg.	100	25.14 N	119.15 E
Pinghai, Zhg.	100	22.39 N	114.53 E
Pinghe, Zhg.	100	24.25 N	117.22 E
Pinghe, Zhg.	102	22.51 N	102.30 E
Pinghe ≃	100	24.25 N	116.36 E
P'inghsiang → Pingxiang	102	22.09 N	106.43 E
Pinghu, Zhg.	100	26.46 N	118.48 E
Pinghu, Zhg.	100	30.56 N	115.22 E
Pinghu, Zhg.	100	22.42 N	114.08 E
Pinghu, Zhg.	106	30.42 N	121.01 E
Pingjiang	100	28.44 N	113.34 E
Pingjing	105	39.20 N	116.06 E
Pinglan	100	22.22 N	113.27 E
Pingle, Zhg.	102	24.37 N	110.40 E
Pingle, Zhg.	102	24.31 N	106.59 E
Pingli	102	32.19 N	109.21 E
Pingliang	102	35.32 N	106.41 E
Pinglidian	98	37.17 N	119.59 E
Pingling	100	23.39 N	114.23 E
Pinglucheng	102	39.50 N	112.19 E
Pingluo	102	38.57 N	106.35 E
Pingluopu	104	41.56 N	123.20 E
Pingnan, Zhg.	100	26.56 N	119.02 E
Pingnan, Zhg.	102	23.30 N	110.30 E
Pingqiao	100	33.24 N	119.13 E
Pingquan	98	40.59 N	118.34 E
Pingrup	162	33.32 S	118.31 E
Ping Shan, H.K.	271d	22.27 N	114.00 E
Pingshan, Zhg.	100	25.36 N	117.52 E
Pingshan, Zhg.	100	23.26 N	113.15 E
Pingshan, Zhg.	100	22.43 N	114.22 E
Pingshan, Zhg.	102	38.15 N	114.10 E
Pingshang	98	35.11 N	119.07 E
Pingshi, Zhg.	100	32.32 N	113.03 E
Pingshi, Zhg.	100	25.20 N	113.02 E
Pingshui	100	29.53 N	120.38 E
Pingtaizi	105	40.44 N	116.25 E
Pingtan, Zhg.	100	25.31 N	119.47 E
Pingtan, Zhg.	100	23.04 N	114.38 E
Pingtan, Zhg.	107	29.50 N	105.56 E
Pingtan, Zhg.	107	29.38 N	105.16 E
Pingtan Dao I	100	25.33 N	119.48 E
Pingtang	102	25.50 N	107.19 E
Pingtian	100	25.19 N	113.31 E
P'ingtung	100	22.40 N	120.29 E
Pingües, Cayos II	240p	20.47 N	78.15 W
Pingwang	106	30.59 N	120.38 E
Pingwu	102	32.29 N	104.37 E
Pingxiang, Zhg.	100	27.38 N	113.50 E
Pingxiang, Zhg.	102	22.09 N	106.43 E
Pingyang, Zhg.	89	48.13 N	124.23 E
Pingyang, Zhg.	100	27.41 N	120.33 E
Pingyao, Zhg.	102	37.16 N	112.09 E
Pingyao, Zhg.	106	30.24 N	119.58 E
Pingyi	98	35.34 N	117.37 E
Pingyin	98	36.19 N	116.22 E
Pingyu	100	32.57 N	114.41 E
Pingyuan, Zhg.	98	37.11 N	116.25 E
Pingyuan, Zhg.	100	24.36 N	115.54 E
Pingzhai	102	24.07 N	104.22 E
Pingzhuang	98	42.03 N	119.22 E
Pinhal	256	22.12 S	46.45 W
Pinhal, Ribeirão do ≃	256	22.42 S	46.42 W
Pinhal Novo	34	38.38 N	8.55 W
Pinhalzinho	256	22.46 S	46.36 W
Pinhão	250	10.34 S	37.44 W
Pinheiral	256	22.31 S	43.59 W
Pinheirinhos	256	22.26 S	44.59 W
Pinheiro	250	2.31 S	45.05 W
Pinheiro de Loures	266c	38.50 N	9.12 W
Pinheiro Machado	252	31.34 S	53.23 W
Pinheiros, Bra.	255	18.21 S	40.14 W
Pinheiros, Bra.	256	22.32 S	44.54 W
Pinheiros ≃	287b	23.32 S	46.44 W
Pinhel	34	40.46 N	7.04 W
Pinhoe	42	50.44 N	3.27 W
Pinhuã ≃	248	6.21 S	65.00 W
Pini, Pulau I	110	0.08 N	98.40 E
Pinillos	246	8.55 N	74.28 W
Piniós ≃	38	39.54 N	22.45 E
Pinitos, Sierra de ⋀	200	31.08 N	110.50 W
Pinjar, Lake ⊜	168a	31.38 S	115.49 E
Pinjarra	168a	32.37 S	115.53 E
Pinjor Garden ♦	123	30.47 N	76.47 E
Pinka ≃	61	47.00 N	16.35 E
Pinkafeld	61	47.22 N	16.07 E
Pinkiang → Harbin	89	45.45 N	126.41 E
Pinlaung	110	20.08 N	96.47 E
Pinlebu	110	24.05 N	95.21 E
Pinn ≃	260	51.31 N	0.29 W
Pinnacle ∧, N.Z.	172	41.49 S	173.17 E
Pinnacle ∧, N.Y., U.S.	188	43.13 N	74.23 W
Pinnacle ∧, Va., U.S.	188	39.08 N	78.26 W
Pinnacle Buttes ∧	202	43.44 N	109.57 W
Pinnacle Island I	180	60.12 N	172.46 W
Pinnacle Peak ∧	224	46.45 N	121.43 W
Pinnacles National Monument ♦	226	36.28 N	121.19 W
Pinnaroo	166	35.16 S	140.55 E
Pinneberg	52	53.40 N	9.47 E
Pinner ◆[8]	260	51.36 N	0.23 W
Pino, Sierra del ⋀	196	28.15 N	103.03 W
Pin Oak Creek ≃	222	31.57 N	96.28 W
Pinocchio	66	43.35 N	13.30 E
Pinochle Peak ∧	224	45.43 N	123.36 W
Pinole	226	38.00 N	122.17 W
Pinole Creek ≃	282	38.01 N	122.18 W
Pinole Point ›	282	38.01 N	122.22 W
Pinole Ridge ∧	282	37.59 N	122.15 W
Pinos	234	22.18 N	101.34 W
Pinos, Mount ∧	228	34.50 N	119.09 W
Pinos, Point ›	226	36.38 N	121.56 W
Pinos-Puente	34	37.15 N	3.45 W
Pinotepa de Don Luis	234	16.25 N	97.55 W
Pinrang	112	3.48 S	119.38 E
Pins, Île de → Juventud, Isla de la I	240p	21.40 N	82.50 W
Pins, Île des I	175f	22.37 S	167.30 E
Pins, Pointe aux ›	214	42.15 N	81.51 W
Pins, Rivière des ≃	206	46.01 N	72.03 W
Pinsk	76	52.07 N	26.04 E
Pinson	194	33.41 N	86.41 W
Pinsot	62	45.21 N	6.06 E
Pinta, Isla I	246a	0.35 N	90.44 W
Pintada Arroyo V	196	34.53 N	104.39 W
Pintado	258	33.50 S	56.18 W
Pintado ≃	255	13.33 S	50.16 W
Pintado, Arroyo de ≃	258	34.08 S	56.14 W
Pintado, Cuchilla del ⋀[2]	258	34.12 S	56.25 W
Pintados	248	20.37 S	69.38 W
Pintados, Salar de ≚	248	20.30 S	69.42 W
Pintasan	112	5.26 N	117.43 E
Pinteus	266c	38.52 N	9.09 W
Pintlala Creek ≃	194	32.21 N	86.30 W
Pinto Butte ∧	184	49.22 N	107.25 W
Pinto Creek ≃, Ab., Can.	182	53.51 N	117.35 W
Pinto Creek ≃, Sk., Can.	184	49.40 N	106.42 W
Pintos, Arroyo de ≃	258	33.55 S	56.51 W
Pintos Negreiros	256	22.18 S	45.13 W
Pintoyacu ≃, Ec.	246	2.07 S	76.03 W
Pintoyacu ≃, Perú	246	3.35 S	73.55 W
Pinturas ≃	254	46.35 S	70.18 W
Pintuyan	116	9.57 N	125.15 E
Pin'ug	24	60.15 N	47.48 E
Pinukpuk	116	17.35 N	121.22 E
Pinwherry	44	55.09 N	4.50 W
Pinxton	44	53.06 N	1.19 W
Pinzano al Tagliamento	64	46.11 N	12.57 E
Pinzgau V	64	47.15 N	12.40 E
Pinzón, Isla I	246a	0.36 S	90.40 W
Piobbico	66	43.35 N	12.31 E
Pioche	204	37.55 N	114.27 W
Pio IX	250	6.50 S	40.37 W
Piolenc	62	44.11 N	4.46 E
Piombino	66	42.55 N	10.32 E
Piombino, Canale di ʮ	66	42.53 N	10.30 E
Pioneer, Austl.	162	31.48 S	121.43 E
Pioneer, Ca., U.S.	226	38.25 N	120.33 W
Pioneer, Oh., U.S.	216	41.40 N	84.33 W
Pioneer Mine	182	50.46 N	122.46 W
Pioneer Mountains ⋀	202	45.40 N	113.00 W
Pioneer Park ♦	273d	26.14 S	28.04 E
Pioner, ostrov I	74	79.50 N	92.30 E
Pionerskij	76	54.57 N	20.20 E
Pionierbivak	164	2.16 S	138.02 E
Pionki	30	51.30 N	21.27 E
Pio Pico State Historical Monument ♦	280	33.59 N	118.04 W
Piopio	172	38.28 S	175.01 E
Pioppo	70	38.03 N	13.14 E
Piora, Mount ∧	164	6.45 S	146.00 E
Pioraco	66	43.11 N	12.59 E
Piorini ≃	246	3.23 S	63.30 W
Piorini, Lago ⊜	246	3.34 S	63.15 W
Piotrków Trybunalski	30	51.25 N	19.42 E
Piotrków Trybunalski □[4]	30	51.30 N	19.45 E
Piotta	58	46.31 N	8.40 E
Pio V. Corpus (Limbujan)	116	11.53 N	124.03 E
Piove di Sacco	64	45.18 N	12.02 E
Piovene-Rocchette	64	45.45 N	11.25 E
Pio XII	250	3.53 S	45.17 W
Pipa	107	29.07 N	105.05 E
Pipalkoti	124	30.26 N	79.27 E
Pipanaco, Salar de ≚	252	28.07 S	66.25 W
Pīpār	120	26.23 N	73.32 E
Piparia	124	22.45 N	78.21 E
Pīpār Road	120	26.27 N	73.27 E
Pipas	152	14.56 S	12.12 E
Pipe Creek ≃, In., U.S.	194	40.08 N	85.52 W
Pipe Creek ≃, In., U.S.	216	40.45 N	86.13 W
Pipe Creek ≃, In., U.S.	218	39.26 N	85.06 W
Piper City	216	40.45 N	88.11 W
Pipe Spring National Monument ♦	200	36.43 N	112.33 W
Pipestem Creek ≃	198	46.54 N	98.43 W
Pipestem State Park ♦	192	37.32 N	81.00 W
Pipestone	198	44.00 N	96.19 W
Pipestone ≃	176	52.53 N	89.23 W
Pipestone Creek ≃, Can.	184	49.42 N	100.45 W
Pipestone Creek ≃, Mi., U.S.	216	42.04 N	86.24 W
Pipestone National Monument ♦	198	44.00 N	96.18 W
Pipi ≃	146	7.27 N	22.48 E
Pipinas	258	35.32 S	57.20 W
Piping Brook ≃	276	41.08 N	73.37 W
Pipiriki	172	39.29 S	175.03 E
Piplān	123	32.17 N	71.21 E
Piplūn	126	23.21 N	88.07 E
Pipmuacan, Réservoir ⊜[1]	186	49.35 N	70.30 W
Pipri	124	23.58 N	82.40 E
Pipriac	28	47.49 N	1.57 W
Piqiang	85	40.20 N	77.38 E
Piqiao	106	31.34 N	119.27 E
Piqua	218	40.08 N	84.14 W
Piquet Carneiro	250	5.48 S	39.25 W
Piquete	256	22.36 S	45.11 W
Piquete, Ribeirão ≃	256	22.36 S	45.01 W
Piquiri ≃, Bra.	248	17.39 S	55.09 W
Piquiri ≃, Bra.	248	17.18 S	56.44 W
Piquiri ≃, Bra.	252	24.03 S	54.14 W
Pira	150	8.30 N	1.44 E
Piracaia	256	23.03 S	46.21 W
Piracanjuba	255	17.18 S	49.01 W
Piracanjuba ≃	255	18.14 S	48.48 W
Piracão ≃	287a	23.02 S	43.36 W
Piracicaba	255	22.43 S	47.38 W
Piracicaba ≃	255	22.36 S	48.19 W
Piraçununga	255	21.59 S	47.25 W
Piracuruca	250	3.56 S	41.42 W
Pirae	174s	17.32 S	149.33 W
Piraeus → Piraiévs	38	37.57 N	23.38 E
Pirahmet	130	38.11 N	39.51 E
Piraí	256	22.38 S	43.54 W
Piraí ≃	256	22.28 S	43.50 W
Piraí do Sul	252	24.31 S	49.56 W
Piraiévs (Piraeus)	38	37.57 N	23.38 E
Piraino	70	38.10 N	14.52 E
Piraju	255	23.12 S	49.23 W
Pirajuba	255	19.54 S	48.42 W
Pirajucara, Ribeirão ≃	287b	23.34 S	46.43 W
Pirajuí	255	21.59 S	49.29 W
Pirakata	126	22.34 N	87.11 E
Piramida, gora ∧	88	54.15 N	95.45 E
Piramidal'nyj, pik ∧	85	39.34 N	69.57 E
Pirámide de Cuicuilco ⊥	286a	19.18 N	99.11 W
Pirámide de Santa Cecilia ⊥	286a	19.33 N	99.09 W
Pirámide de Tenayuca ⊥	286a	19.32 N	99.11 W
Piram Island I	120	21.36 N	72.41 E
Piran	36	45.32 N	13.34 E
Piraña, Arroyo ≃	288	34.24 S	58.30 W
Pirané	252	25.43 S	59.06 W
Piranga	255	20.41 S	43.18 W
Pirangaí	256	22.34 S	44.37 W
Piranguçu	256	22.31 S	45.30 W
Piranguinho	256	22.24 S	45.32 W
Piranhas	255	16.31 S	51.51 W
Piranhas ≃, Bra.	250	5.15 S	36.45 W
Piranhas ≃, Bra.	250	8.40 S	49.28 W
Piranhas ≃, Bra.	250	5.56 S	48.15 W
Piranji ≃	250	4.23 S	37.48 W
Pīrān Shahr	128	36.41 N	45.08 E
Pirapemas	250	3.43 S	44.14 W
Pirapetinga ≃	256	21.37 S	42.32 W
Pirapetinga, Ribeirão ≃	256	21.49 S	43.36 W
Pirapó ≃	255	22.30 S	52.01 W
Pirapora	255	17.21 S	44.56 W
Pirapora do Bom Jesus	256	23.24 S	47.00 W
Pirapora do Bom Jesus □[7]	287b	23.24 S	46.56 W
Piraputanga	255	20.26 S	55.32 W
Piraquara	252	25.26 S	49.04 W
Piraquê ≃	287a	23.01 S	43.37 W
Pirarajá	252	33.44 S	54.45 W
Pirata, Monte ∧[2]	240m	18.06 N	65.33 W
Pirate Creek ≃	282	37.33 N	121.52 W
Pir'atin	78	50.15 N	32.30 E
Piratinga ≃	255	15.41 S	46.07 W
Piratini	252	31.27 S	53.06 W
Piratini ≃	252	28.06 S	55.27 W
Piratininga	287a	22.57 S	43.04 W
Piratininga, Lagoa c	256	22.57 S	43.05 W
Piratuba	252	27.27 S	51.48 W
Piratuba, Lago c	250	1.37 N	50.10 W
Piratucu ≃	250	1.59 S	56.58 W
Piraúba	256	21.17 S	43.02 W
Piraube, Lac ⊜	186	50.33 N	71.42 W
Piray ≃	248	16.32 S	63.45 W
Piraziz	130	40.58 N	38.08 E
Pirbright	260	51.18 N	0.39 W
Pirdop	38	42.42 N	24.11 E
Pirenópolis	255	15.51 S	48.57 W
Pires, Ribeirão ≃	287b	23.43 S	46.25 W
Pires do Rio	255	17.18 S	48.17 W
Pírgos	38	37.41 N	21.28 E
Piriá	250	1.40 S	50.02 W
Piriápolis	252	34.54 S	55.17 W
Piribebuy	252	25.29 S	57.03 W
Pirin ⋀	38	41.40 N	23.30 E
Pirinçci ◆[8]	267b	41.10 N	28.50 E
Pirineos → Pyrenees ⋀	34	42.40 N	1.00 E
Piripiri	250	4.16 S	41.47 W
Piritiba	250	11.44 S	40.34 W
Píritu, Ven.	246	11.22 N	69.08 W
Píritu, Ven.	246	9.23 N	69.12 W
Pirituba ◆[8]	287b	23.29 S	46.43 W
Pirk	54	50.25 N	12.04 E
Pīr Mahal	123	30.46 N	72.26 E
Pirmasens	56	49.12 N	7.36 E
Pirna	54	50.58 N	13.56 E
Piroči	82	55.04 N	38.57 E
Pirogovka	78	51.54 N	33.18 E
Pirogovskij	265b	55.59 N	37.44 E
Pirogovskoje vodochranilišče ⊜[1]	82	55.58 N	37.40 E
Pirojpur	126	22.34 N	89.59 E
Pirón ≃	34	41.23 N	4.31 W
Pirongia	172	38.00 S	175.12 E
Pirot	38	43.09 N	22.35 E
Pirovano	252	36.30 S	61.34 W
Pirovskoje	86	57.37 N	92.16 E
Pīr Panjāl Range ⋀	123	33.37 N	74.32 E
Pirpirituba	250	6.46 S	35.30 W
Pirreşit Tepe ∧	84	38.56 N	43.55 E
Pirsagat	84	39.54 N	49.24 E
Pirsagat ≃	84	39.53 N	49.19 E
Pirtleville	200	31.22 N	109.34 W
Piru, Indon.	164	3.04 S	128.12 E
Piru, Ca., U.S.	228	34.25 N	118.48 W
Piru, Lake ⊜[1]	228	34.30 N	118.45 W
Piru, Teluk c	164	3.10 S	128.08 E
Piru Creek ≃	228	34.23 N	118.47 W
Pisa	66	43.43 N	10.23 E
Pisa □[4]	66	43.25 N	10.43 E
Pisa ∧[2]	26	63.13 N	28.18 E
Pisa ≃	30	53.15 N	21.52 E
Pisa, Certosa di ʋ[1]	66	43.45 N	10.31 E
Pisa, Mount ∧	172	44.52 S	169.11 E
Pisagua	248	19.36 S	70.13 W
Pisam-bong ∧	98	40.41 N	126.34 E
Pisang, Pulau I	164	1.23 S	128.55 E
Pisarevka	78	49.53 N	40.12 E
Pisarve	272c	19.06 N	73.05 E
Pisau, Tanjong ›	116	6.04 N	118.03 E
Piščalje	80	58.14 N	48.42 E
Piscasaw Creek ≃	216	42.16 N	88.49 W
Piscataway	210	40.29 N	74.23 W
Piscataway Creek ≃, Md., U.S.	208	38.42 N	77.02 W
Piscataway Creek ≃, Va., U.S.	208	37.54 N	76.50 W
Pişchia	38	45.55 N	21.20 E
Pisciotta	68	40.06 N	15.14 E
Pisco	248	13.42 S	76.13 W
Pisco ≃	248	13.42 S	76.15 W
Pişcolt	38	47.35 N	22.18 E
Piscovo	80	57.11 N	40.32 E
Piseco Lake ⊜	210	43.23 N	74.36 W
Písek	30	49.19 N	14.10 E
Pisgah, Md., U.S.	208	38.32 N	77.08 W
Pisgah, Oh., U.S.	218	39.19 N	84.22 W
Pisgah Forest	192	35.15 N	82.42 W
Pishan	120	37.37 N	78.18 E
Pishīn	120	30.35 N	67.00 E
Pishīn Lora (Lowrah) ≃	120	29.09 N	64.55 E
Pisidia □[9]	130	37.30 N	31.00 E
Pisinemo	200	32.02 N	112.18 W
Pising	112	5.05 S	121.54 E
Pis'mennoje	78	48.13 N	35.48 E
Pismo Beach	226	35.08 N	120.38 W
Pišnur	80	57.47 N	47.58 E
Piso, Lake ⊜	150	6.48 N	11.17 W
Pisogne	64	45.48 N	10.06 E
Pisqui ≃	248	7.45 S	75.01 W
Pissila	150	13.10 N	0.49 W
Pissos	32	44.19 N	0.47 W
Pistakee Highlands	216	42.25 N	88.11 W
Pistakee Lake ⊜	216	42.23 N	88.12 W
Pisticci	68	40.23 N	16.34 E
Pistoia	66	43.55 N	10.54 E
Pistoia □[4]	64	43.58 N	10.50 E
Pistolet Bay c	186	51.32 N	55.50 W
Pistuk Peak ∧	180	59.43 N	159.42 W
Pisuerga ≃	34	41.33 N	4.52 W
Pisz	30	53.38 N	21.49 E
Pit ≃	204	40.45 N	122.22 W
Pit, North Fork ≃	204	41.28 N	120.33 W
Pit, South Fork ≃	204	41.28 N	120.33 W
Pita	150	11.05 N	12.24 W
Pital	246	2.16 N	75.49 W
Pitalito	246	1.51 N	76.02 W
Pitampura Kālan ◆[8]	272a	28.42 N	77.08 E
Pitanga	252	24.46 S	51.44 W
Pitangueiras	255	21.02 S	48.13 W
Pitangueiras, Ribeirão das ≃	256	21.27 S	44.27 W
Pitangui	255	19.40 S	44.54 W
Pitcairn	279b	40.24 N	79.46 W
Pitcairn □[2], Oc.	6	25.04 S	130.05 W
Pitcairn □[2], Oc.	174s	25.04 S	130.05 W
Pitcher	207	42.35 N	75.52 W
Pitch Place	260	51.16 N	0.36 W
Piteå	26	65.20 N	21.30 E
Piteälven ≃	24	65.14 N	21.32 E
Piteglio	66	44.01 N	10.46 E
Pitelino	80	54.34 N	41.49 E
Piterka	80	50.42 N	47.27 E
Piteşti	38	44.52 N	24.52 E
Pithapuram	122	17.07 N	82.16 E
Pithara	162	30.24 S	116.40 E
Pithiviers	50	48.10 N	2.15 E
Pithorāgarh	124	29.35 N	80.13 E
Piti, Lagoa ⊜	158	26.34 S	32.53 E
Pitigliano	66	42.38 N	11.40 E
Pitim	80	53.12 N	42.21 E
Pitinga ≃	246	1.32 S	59.49 W
Pitiquito	232	30.42 N	112.02 W
Pitjantjatjara Lands ◆[4]	162	27.00 S	130.30 E
Pitk'aranta	24	61.34 N	31.27 E
Pitkas Point	180	62.02 N	163.17 W
Pitlochry	46	56.43 N	3.45 W
Pitman	208	39.43 N	75.07 W
Pitman Airport ⊠	285	39.45 N	75.08 W
Pitmedden	46	57.20 N	2.11 W
Pitner Ditch ≍	216	41.14 N	86.53 W
Pitogo	116	10.08 N	124.33 E
Pitomača	36	45.57 N	17.14 E
Pitou, Zhg.	100	25.01 N	114.35 E
Pitou, Zhg.	100	23.34 N	116.05 E
Pitou, Zhg.	100	24.26 N	114.22 E
Pitrufquén	254	38.59 S	72.39 W
Pitsea	260	51.34 N	0.31 E
Pitseng	158	28.58 S	28.16 E
Pitsford Reservoir ⊜[1]	42	52.20 N	0.52 W
Pitt ≃	224	49.12 N	122.47 W
Pitt, Mount ∧	174c	29.01 S	167.56 E
Pittem	50	51.00 N	3.16 E
Pitten ≃	61	47.44 N	16.14 E
Pittenweem	46	56.12 N	2.44 W
Pitti Island I	122	10.50 N	72.38 E
Pitt Island I	182	53.35 N	129.45 W
Pitt Lake ⊜	182	49.25 N	122.32 W
Pittsboro, In., U.S.	218	39.51 N	86.28 W
Pittsboro, Ms., U.S.	194	33.56 N	89.20 W
Pittsboro, N.C., U.S.	192	35.43 N	79.10 W
Pittsburg, Ca., U.S.	226	38.01 N	121.53 W
Pittsburg, In., U.S.	216	40.37 N	86.42 W
Pittsburg, Ks., U.S.	198	37.24 N	94.42 W
Pittsburg, N.H., U.S.	206	45.03 N	71.23 W
Pittsburg, Tx., U.S.	222	32.59 N	94.57 W
Pittsburgh, Pa., U.S.	214	40.26 N	79.59 W
Pittsburgh, Pa., U.S.	279b	40.26 N	79.59 W
Pittsburgh, University of ʋ[2]	279b	40.27 N	79.58 W
Pittsburgh-Monroeville Airport ⊠	279b	40.27 N	79.46 W
Pittsfield, Il., U.S.	219	39.36 N	90.48 W
Pittsfield, Me., U.S.	188	44.46 N	69.23 W
Pittsfield, Ma., U.S.	207	42.27 N	73.14 W
Pittsfield, N.H., U.S.	188	43.18 N	71.19 W
Pittsfield, Pa., U.S.	214	41.50 N	79.23 W
Pittsford, Mi., U.S.	216	41.52 N	84.28 W
Pittsford, N.Y., U.S.	210	43.05 N	77.31 W
Pitt Stadium ♦	279b	40.27 N	79.58 W
Pittston	210	41.19 N	75.47 W
Pittsview	194	32.11 N	85.09 W
Pittsville	208	38.23 N	75.24 W
Pittsworth	166	27.43 S	151.38 E
Pitt Water c	170	33.37 S	151.18 E
Pituil	252	28.34 S	67.27 W
Pitumarca	248	13.59 S	71.25 W
Pituri Creek ≃	166	22.58 S	138.50 E
Pitzbach ≃	64	47.13 N	10.46 E
Pitztal V	64	47.07 N	10.47 E
Pium	250	10.27 S	49.11 W
Pium ≃	250	10.12 S	49.57 W
Piura	248	5.12 S	80.38 W
Piura □[5]	248	5.10 S	80.00 W
Piura ≃	248	5.32 S	80.53 W
Piute Peak ∧	204	35.27 N	118.24 W
Piute Reservoir ⊜[1]	200	38.17 N	112.12 W
Piva ≃	38	43.21 N	18.51 E
Pivan'	89	50.29 N	137.06 E
Piverone	62	45.27 N	8.00 E
Pivijay	246	10.28 N	74.37 W
Piwniczna	30	49.27 N	20.42 E
Pixian	102	30.49 N	103.49 E
Pixley	226	35.58 N	119.17 W
Pižanka	80	57.28 N	48.33 E
Pižma	80	57.52 N	47.06 E
Pižma ≃	80	57.37 N	48.58 E
Pizzighettone	62	45.11 N	9.47 E
Pizzillo, Monte ∧	70	37.48 N	15.01 E
Pizzo	68	38.44 N	16.10 E
Pizzoferrato	66	41.55 N	14.14 E
Pizzoli	66	42.26 N	13.18 E
Pizzone	66	41.40 N	14.02 E
Pjalka	24	66.43 N	40.59 E
Pjana ≃	80	55.40 N	45.57 E
Pjöngjang → P'yŏngyang	98	39.01 N	125.45 E
P. K. le Rouxdam ⊜[1]	158	30.12 S	24.54 E
Placanica	68	38.25 N	16.27 E
Place Bonaventure ◆[9]	275a	45.30 N	73.34 W
Placentia, Nf., Can.	186	47.14 N	53.58 W
Placentia, Ca., U.S.	228	33.52 N	117.52 W
Placentia Bay c	186	47.15 N	54.30 W
Placer, Pil.	116	11.52 N	123.55 E
Placer, Pil.	116	9.39 N	125.36 E
Placer □[6]	226	38.54 N	121.04 W
Placeres del Oro ≃	234	18.27 N	100.57 W
Placeres de Picacho	234	23.11 N	105.42 W
Placerville	226	38.43 N	120.47 W
Placetas	240p	22.19 N	79.40 W
Place Versailles ◆[9]	275a	45.35 N	73.32 W
Plachino	76	54.28 N	39.20 E
Plachtejevka	78	46.07 N	29.43 E
Placid, Lake ⊜	220	27.14 N	81.22 W
Placida	220	26.49 N	82.15 W
Plácido de Castro	248	10.20 S	67.11 W
Plácido Rosas	252	32.45 S	53.44 W
Placita de Morelos	234	18.31 N	103.42 W
Plačkovica ⋀	38	41.45 N	22.35 E
Plaffeien	58	46.44 N	7.17 E
Plages, Lac des ⊜	206	45.59 N	74.54 W
Plage-Sainte-Cécile	50	50.34 N	1.35 E
Plailly	261	49.06 N	2.35 E
Plai Mat ≃	110	15.22 N	102.45 E
Plain	224	47.46 N	120.39 W
Plain City, Oh., U.S.	214	40.06 N	83.16 W
Plain City, Ut., U.S.	200	41.17 N	112.05 W
Plain Dealing	194	32.54 N	93.41 W
Plaines, Île aux I	275a	45.21 N	73.50 W
Plainfield, Ct., U.S.	207	41.40 N	71.54 W
Plainfield, Il., U.S.	216	41.37 N	88.12 W
Plainfield, In., U.S.	218	39.42 N	86.23 W
Plainfield, Ma., U.S.	207	42.30 N	72.55 W
Plainfield, N.J., U.S.	210	40.37 N	74.26 W
Plainfield, Oh., U.S.	214	40.13 N	81.43 W
Plainfield, Pa., U.S.	208	40.12 N	77.17 W
Plainfield, Wi., U.S.	190	44.12 N	89.29 W
Plainfield Heights	216	43.01 N	85.37 W
Plains, Ga., U.S.	192	32.02 N	84.23 W
Plains, Ks., U.S.	198	37.15 N	100.35 W
Plains, Mt., U.S.	202	47.27 N	114.52 W
Plains, Tx., U.S.	196	33.11 N	102.50 W
Plainsboro	208	40.20 N	74.36 W
Plainview, Ca., U.S.	226	36.08 N	119.08 W
Plainview, Il., U.S.	219	39.10 N	89.59 W
Plainview, Mn., U.S.	190	44.09 N	92.10 W
Plainview, Ne., U.S.	198	42.20 N	97.47 W
Plainview, N.Y., U.S.	210	40.46 N	73.28 W
Plainview, Tx., U.S.	196	34.11 N	101.42 W
Plainville, Ct., U.S.	207	41.40 N	72.51 W
Plainville, Il., U.S.	219	39.47 N	91.11 W
Plainville, In., U.S.	194	38.48 N	87.09 W
Plainville, Ks., U.S.	198	39.14 N	99.17 W
Plainville, Ma., U.S.	207	42.00 N	71.20 W
Plainville, N.Y., U.S.	210	43.10 N	76.27 W
Plainwell	216	42.26 N	85.38 W
Plaisance, Baie de c	186	47.18 N	61.53 W
Plaisir	261	48.49 N	1.57 E
Plaistow	207	42.50 N	71.05 W
Plaksino	76	56.11 N	30.42 E
Plamondon	182	54.51 N	112.19 W
Plampang	115b	8.48 S	117.48 E
Planá	60	49.52 N	12.44 E
Plana, Illa I	34	38.10 N	0.28 W
Planada	226	37.18 N	120.19 W
Planalto, Bra.	252	27.20 S	53.03 W
Planalto, Bra.	255	14.39 S	40.29 W
Planches	50	48.42 N	0.22 E
Plandome	276	40.48 N	73.42 W
Plandome Heights	276	40.48 N	73.42 W
Plandome Manor	276	40.49 N	73.42 W
Plan-d'Orgon	62	43.48 N	5.00 E
Plane ≃	54	52.23 N	12.30 E
Planegg	60	48.06 N	11.25 E
Planerskoje	78	44.57 N	35.14 E
Planeta Rica	246	8.25 N	75.36 W
Plangeross	64	46.59 N	10.52 E
Plankenfels	60	49.53 N	11.20 E
Plankinton	198	43.42 N	98.29 W
Plano, Il., U.S.	216	41.39 N	88.32 W
Plano, Tx., U.S.	222	33.01 N	96.41 W
Plansee ⊜	64	47.28 N	10.48 E
Plantagenet	206	45.32 N	75.00 W
Plantation, Fl., U.S.	220	26.07 N	80.14 W
Plantation, Fl., U.S.	220	24.59 N	80.33 W
Plantation, Ky., U.S.	218	38.17 N	85.36 W
Plantation Key I	220	24.58 N	80.33 W
Plant City	220	28.01 N	82.06 W
Plantersville, Al., U.S.	194	32.39 N	86.55 W
Plantersville, Ms., U.S.	194	34.12 N	88.39 W
Plantersville, Tx., U.S.	222	30.20 N	95.52 W
Planting Fields Arboretum State Park ♦	276	40.52 N	73.33 W
Plantsite	200	33.03 N	109.19 W
Plantsville	207	41.35 N	72.53 W
Plaquemine	194	30.17 N	91.14 W
Plaridel, Pil.	116	10.32 N	124.46 E
Plaridel, Pil.	116	8.37 N	123.43 E
Plasencia	34	40.02 N	6.05 W
Plaški	36	45.05 N	15.22 E
Plassenburg ⊥	60	50.06 N	11.28 E
Plassey	126	23.47 N	88.15 E
Plast	86	54.22 N	60.50 E
Plaster Rock	186	46.54 N	67.24 W
Plastovo	82	54.17 N	37.03 E
Plastun	89	44.45 N	136.19 E
Plastunovskaja	78	45.18 N	39.16 E
Plasy	60	49.56 N	13.24 E
Plata, Isla de la I	246	1.16 S	81.06 W
Plata, Río de la c[1]	258	35.00 S	57.00 W
Plata, Río de la ≃	240m	18.29 N	66.15 W
Platani ≃	70	37.24 N	13.16 E
Platania	68	39.00 N	16.19 E
Plátanos	288	34.47 S	58.11 W
Plátanos, Arroyo ≃	288	34.45 S	58.08 W
Plate, Île I	275a	45.22 N	73.48 W
Platea	214	41.57 N	80.20 W
Plateau □[3]	150	8.45 N	8.30 E
Plateau Creek ≃	200	39.11 N	108.18 W
Plateaux □[5]	152	2.15 S	15.30 E
Platì	68	38.13 N	16.03 E
Platinum	180	59.01 N	161.49 W
Platnirovskaja	78	45.23 N	39.23 E
Plato	246	9.47 N	74.47 W
Platono-Petrovka	83	46.59 N	39.28 E
Platonovka	80	52.43 N	41.57 E
Platón Sánchez	234	21.17 N	98.22 W
Platovo	83	48.05 N	39.53 E
Platrand	158	27.08 S	29.29 E
Platt	260	51.17 N	0.20 E
Platta	58	46.40 N	8.51 E
Platte	198	43.23 N	98.50 W
Platte ≃, U.S.	194	39.16 N	94.50 W
Platte ≃, Mn., U.S.	190	45.47 N	94.17 W
Platte ≃, Ne., U.S.	198	41.04 N	95.53 W
Platte ≃, Wi., U.S.	190	42.37 N	90.40 W
Platte Center	198	41.32 N	97.29 W
Platte City	194	39.22 N	94.46 W
Platte Creek ≃	198	43.19 N	99.00 W
Platte Island I	138	5.52 S	55.23 E
Plattekill	210	41.37 N	74.05 W
Platteville, Co., U.S.	200	40.12 N	104.49 W
Platteville, Wi., U.S.	190	42.44 N	90.28 W
Platt Hall ⊥	262	53.27 N	2.13 W
Plattling	60	48.47 N	12.53 E
Plattsburg	194	39.33 N	94.26 W
Plattsburgh	188	44.41 N	73.27 W
Plattsburgh Air Force Base ▪	188	44.40 N	73.28 W
Plattsmouth	198	41.00 N	95.52 W
Plattsville	212	43.18 N	80.37 W
Platveld	156	19.58 S	17.07 E
Plau	54	53.27 N	12.16 E
Plaue, Dtsch.	54	52.24 N	12.25 E
Plaue, Dtsch.	54	50.47 N	10.54 E
Plauen	54	50.30 N	12.08 E
Plauer See ⊜	54	53.30 N	12.20 E
Plav	38	42.36 N	19.56 E
Plave	64	46.02 N	13.36 E
Plaviņas	76	56.37 N	25.43 E
Plavsk	76	53.43 N	37.18 E
Plaxtol	260	51.15 N	0.18 E
Playa Azul	234	17.59 N	102.24 W
Playa Baracoa	286b	23.03 N	82.34 W
Playa Bonita	236	9.39 N	84.27 W
Playa de Fajardo	240m	18.20 N	65.38 W
Playa de Guayanés	240m	18.04 N	65.49 W
Playa de Guayanilla	240m	18.01 N	66.46 W
Playa del Carmen	232	20.36 N	87.06 W
Playa del Rey ◆[8]	280	33.58 N	118.26 W
Playa de Naguabo	240m	18.12 N	65.43 W
Playa de Ponce	240m	17.59 N	66.37 W
Playa Noriega, Laguna ⊜	232	29.10 N	111.50 W
Playas Lake ⊜	200	31.50 N	108.34 W
Playa Vicente	234	17.50 N	95.49 W
Play Cu	110	13.59 N	108.00 E
Playford ≃	162	19.03 S	135.35 E
Playgreen Lake ⊜	184	54.00 N	98.10 W
Playland ♦	276	40.58 N	73.41 W
Plaza	198	48.01 N	101.57 W
Plaza at Mid Island ◆[9]	276	40.46 N	73.32 W
Plaza de Caisán	236	8.46 N	82.45 W
Plaza de Mayo ♦	288	34.36 S	58.23 W
Plaza de Toros ♦	266a	40.26 N	3.39 W
Plaza de Toros Las Arenas ♦	266d	41.23 N	2.09 W
Plaza de Toros Monumental ♦	266d	41.24 N	2.11 E
Plaza Huincul	252	38.55 S	69.09 W
Plaza Park	285	40.04 N	74.53 W
Plazas de Soberanía en el Norte de África → Spanish North Africa □[2]	34	35.53 N	5.19 W
Pleasant	275b	43.41 N	79.49 W
Pleasant, Lake ⊜[1]	200	33.53 N	112.16 W
Pleasant, Mount ∧	192	37.44 N	79.10 W
Pleasant, Mount ∧[2]	186	45.26 N	66.49 W
Pleasant Bay	186	46.49 N	60.48 W
Pleasantdale, Sk., Can.	184	52.35 N	104.30 W
Pleasantdale, N.Y., U.S.	210	42.47 N	73.40 W
Pleasant Gap	214	40.52 N	77.44 W
Pleasant Garden	192	35.57 N	79.45 W
Pleasant Grove, Ca., U.S.	226	38.49 N	121.29 W
Pleasant Grove, Ut., U.S.	200	40.21 N	111.44 W
Pleasant Grove Creek ≃	226	38.48 N	121.32 W
Pleasant Hill, Ca., U.S.	226	37.56 N	122.03 W
Pleasant Hill, Il., U.S.	219	39.26 N	90.52 W
Pleasant Hill, La., U.S.	194	31.49 N	93.31 W
Pleasant Hill, Mo., U.S.	194	38.47 N	94.16 W
Pleasant Hill, N.C., U.S.	208	36.32 N	77.32 W
Pleasant Hill, Oh., U.S.	218	40.03 N	84.20 W
Pleasant Hill Lake ⊜[1]	214	40.38 N	82.21 W
Pleasant Hills	214	40.20 N	79.57 W
Pleasant Lake, In., U.S.	216	41.34 N	85.00 W
Pleasant Lake, Mi., U.S.	216	42.23 N	84.22 W
Pleasant Lake ⊜	216	42.13 N	83.56 W
Pleasant Mills	216	40.47 N	84.51 W
Pleasant Mount	210	41.44 N	75.26 W
Pleasanton, Ca., U.S.	226	37.39 N	121.52 W
Pleasanton, Ks., U.S.	198	38.10 N	94.42 W
Pleasanton, Tx., U.S.	196	28.58 N	98.28 W
Pleasanton Ridge ∧	282	37.40 N	121.55 W
Pleasant Plains, Il., U.S.	219	39.52 N	89.55 W
Pleasant Plains, N.J., U.S.	208	40.00 N	74.13 W
Pleasant Point	172	44.16 S	171.08 E
Pleasant Prairie	216	42.33 N	87.57 W
Pleasant Ridge	281	42.31 N	83.10 W
Pleasant Unity	214	40.15 N	79.28 W
Pleasant Valley, N.Y., U.S.	210	41.44 N	73.49 W
Pleasant Valley, Oh., U.S.	218	39.22 N	83.03 W
Pleasant Valley, Pa., U.S.	279b	40.31 N	75.18 W
Pleasantville, Ia., U.S.	190	41.23 N	93.16 W
Pleasantville, Md., U.S.	284b	39.11 N	76.38 W
Pleasantville, N.J., U.S.	208	39.23 N	74.31 W
Pleasantville, N.Y., U.S.	210	41.07 N	73.47 W
Pleasantville, Pa., U.S.	214	41.35 N	79.34 W
Pleasington	262	53.44 N	2.34 W
Pleasure Beach	207	41.18 N	72.08 W
Pleasure Ridge Park	218	38.09 N	85.51 W
Pleasureville	218	38.33 N	85.04 W
Pléaux	32	45.08 N	2.14 E
Plechanovo	82	54.14 N	37.33 E
Plechanovskoje	76	52.39 N	39.50 E
Plechovo	78	51.07 N	35.18 E
Plechý (Plöckenstein) ∧	60	48.46 N	13.51 E
Pledger	222	29.11 N	95.55 W
Pleebo	150	4.35 N	7.40 W
Pleiku → Play Cu	110	13.59 N	108.00 E
Pleinfeld	56	49.06 N	10.59 E
Pleissa	54	50.50 N	12.46 E
Pleisse ≃	54	51.20 N	12.22 E
Pléneuf	32	48.36 N	2.33 W
Plenty	184	51.47 N	108.36 W
Plenty ≃, Austl.	162	23.25 S	136.31 E
Plenty ≃, Austl.	274b	37.45 S	145.07 E
Plenty, Bay of c	172	37.40 S	177.00 E
Plentywood	198	48.46 N	104.33 W
Plered	115a	6.38 S	107.23 E
Pleščejevo, ozero ⊜	82	56.46 N	38.47 E
Pleščenicy	76	54.25 N	27.50 E
Pleseck	24	62.43 N	40.20 E
Plešivka	82	54.23 N	37.09 E
Plesna ≃	54	50.07 N	12.28 E
Pless, Dtsch.	58	48.05 N	10.08 E
Pless → Pszczyna, Pol.	30	49.59 N	18.57 E
Plessa	54	51.28 N	13.37 E
Plessisville	206	46.14 N	71.47 W
Pleszew	30	51.54 N	17.48 E
Pletenevka	82	54.31 N	36.06 E
Pleternica	38	45.17 N	17.48 E
Plétipi, Lac ⊜	176	51.44 N	70.06 W
Plet'onyj Tašlyk	78	48.29 N	31.40 E
Plettenberg	56	51.13 N	7.52 E
Plettenbergbaai	158	34.04 S	23.22 E
Pleurs	50	48.41 N	3.52 E
Pleven	38	43.25 N	24.37 E
Plevna, Mo., U.S.	219	39.58 N	92.05 W
Plevna, Mt., U.S.	198	46.25 N	104.31 W
Pleyben	32	48.14 N	3.58 W
Pleystein	60	49.39 N	12.25 E
Pliening	60	48.12 N	11.48 E
Pliezhausen	56	48.33 N	9.12 E
Plimmerton	172	41.05 S	174.52 E
Plimoth Plantation ⊥	207	41.57 N	70.38 W
Plintovka	265a	60.01 N	30.46 E
Pliski	78	51.07 N	32.24 E
Pliskov	78	49.23 N	29.18 E
Pliszka ≃	54	52.14 N	14.42 E
Plitvička Jezera Nacionalni Park ♦	36	44.53 N	15.38 E
Plješevica ⋀	36	44.40 N	15.45 E
Pljevlja	38	43.21 N	19.21 E
Ploaghe	71	40.40 N	8.45 E
Plochingen	56	48.42 N	9.25 E
Płock	30	52.33 N	19.43 E
Płock □[4]	30	52.25 N	19.45 E
Plöckenpass)(	64	46.36 N	12.58 E
Plöckenstein (Plechý) ∧	60	48.46 N	13.51 E
Plockton	46	57.20 N	5.39 W
Pločno ∧	36	43.36 N	17.34 E
Plodorodnoje	80	46.44 N	41.06 E
Ploegsteert	50	50.43 N	2.53 E
Ploërmel	32	47.56 N	2.24 W
Ploeşti → Ploieşti	38	44.56 N	26.02 E
Plogastel-Saint-Germain	28	47.59 N	4.16 W
Ploieşti	38	44.56 N	26.02 E
Plomárion	38	38.59 N	26.22 E
Plomb du Cantal ∧	32	45.03 N	2.46 E
Plombières-les-Bains	58	47.58 N	6.29 E
Plombières-lès-Dijon	58	47.20 N	4.58 E
Plomer	258	34.48 S	59.02 W
Plomer, Point ›	166	31.19 S	152.58 E
Plön	54	54.09 N	10.25 E
Plonge, Lac la ⊜	184	55.08 N	107.25 W
Płońsk	30	52.38 N	20.23 E
Pl'os	80	57.27 N	41.31 E
Plose, Cima delle ∧	64	46.42 N	11.44 E
Ploskij	78	46.17 N	40.15 E
Ploskoje	76	52.45 N	38.21 E
Ploskoš'	76	56.46 N	31.16 E
Pl'oso	76	59.47 N	35.43 E
Plotbišče	80	56.50 N	50.35 E
Plotina	83	48.33 N	40.05 E
Plotnica	76	52.03 N	26.39 E
Plottier	252	38.58 S	68.14 W
Płoty	30	53.49 N	15.16 E
Plötz	54	51.38 N	11.56 E
Plouay	32	47.55 N	3.20 W
Ploučnice ≃	54	50.47 N	14.13 E
Ploudalmézeau	32	48.32 N	4.39 W
Plouguenast	32	48.17 N	2.43 W
Plouha	32	48.41 N	2.56 W
Plovdiv	38	42.09 N	24.45 E
Plover ≃	190	44.29 N	89.35 W
Plover Islands II	180	71.15 N	155.30 W
Pluckemin	276	40.39 N	74.39 W
Plum, Pa., U.S.	214	40.31 N	79.45 W
Plum, Pa., U.S.	214	41.35 N	79.51 W
Plum, Tx., U.S.	222	29.56 N	96.58 W
Pluma Hidalgo	234	15.55 N	96.25 W
Plumas	184	50.25 N	99.02 W

≃	River	Fluß	Río	Rivière	Rio
≍	Canal	Kanal	Canal	Canal	Canal
L	Waterfall, Rapids	Wasserfall, Stromschnellen	Cascada, Rápidos	Chute d'eau, Rapides	Cascata, Rápidos
ʮ	Strait	Meeresstraße	Estrecho	Détroit	Estreito
c	Bay, Gulf	Bucht, Golf	Bahía, Golfo	Baie, Golfe	Baía, Golfo
⊜	Lake, Lakes	See, Seen	Lago, Lagos	Lac, Lacs	Lago, Lagos
⊟	Swamp	Sumpf	Pantano	Marais	Pântano
⊠	Ice Features, Glacier	Eis- und Gletscherformen	Accidentes Glaciales	Formes glaciaires	Acidentes glaciares
⊤	Other Hydrographic Features	Andere Hydrographische Objekte	Otros Elementos Hidrográficos	Autres données hydrographiques	Outros acidentes hidrográficos

✢	Submarine Features	Untermeerische Objekte	Accidentes Submarinos	Formes de relief sous-marin	Acidentes submarinos
□	Political Unit	Politische Einheit	Unidad Política	Entité politique	Unidade política
ʋ	Cultural Institution	Kulturelle Institution	Institución Cultural	Institution culturelle	Instituição cultural
⊥	Historical Site	Historische Stätte	Sitio Histórico	Site historique	Sítio histórico
♦	Recreational Site	Erholungs- und Ferienort	Sitio de Recreo	Centre de loisirs	Área de Lazer
⊠	Airport	Flughafen	Aeropuerto	Aéroport	Aeroporto
▪	Military Installation	Militäranlage	Instalación Militar	Installation militaire	Instalação militar
◆	Miscellaneous	Verschiedenes	Misceláneo	Divers	Diversos

I · *138* **Plum-Pont**

ENGLISH — Name, Page, Lat.°′, Long.°′ / DEUTSCH — Name, Seite, Breite°′, Länge°′ E = Ost

Name	Page	Lat.°′	Long.°′
Plumbridge	48	54.46 N	7.15 W
Plum Brook ≐	281	42.34 N	82.58 W
Plum Creek ≐, Il., U.S.	278	41.33 N	87.29 W
Plum Creek ≐, Ne., U.S.	198	41.52 N	96.44 W
Plum Creek ≐, Oh., U.S.	279a	41.18 N	82.09 W
Plum Creek ≐, Pa., U.S.	279b	40.31 N	79.51 W
Plum Creek ≐, S.D., U.S.	198	44.13 N	100.43 W
Plum Creek ≐, Tx., U.S.	196	29.38 N	97.36 W
Plum Creek, Clear Fork ≐	222	29.45 N	97.37 W
Plumerville	194	35.09 N	92.38 W
Plum Grove	222	30.15 N	95.05 W
Plum Grove Estates	278	42.04 N	88.02 W
Plum Island	283	42.49 N	70.59 W
Plum Island I, Ma., U.S.	207	42.45 N	70.48 W
Plum Island I, N.Y., U.S.	207	41.11 N	72.12 W
Plum Island Airport ⊠	283	42.48 N	70.50 W
Plum Island Sound ʉ	283	42.45 N	70.48 W
Plum Island State Park ♦	283	42.42 N	70.47 W
Plumley	262	53.17 N	2.25 W
Plummer	202	47.20 N	116.53 W
Plummers Landing	218	38.19 N	83.33 W
Plumper Sound ʉ	224	48.47 N	123.13 W
Plum Point ›	276	40.50 N	40.43 W
Plumpton	274a	33.45 S	150.50 E
Plumridge Lakes ⊜	162	29.30 S	125.25 E
Plum Run ≐	279b	40.15 N	80.13 W
Plumsteadville	208	40.23 N	75.09 W
Plumtree	154	20.30 S	27.50 E
Plumville	214	40.48 N	79.11 W
Plumwood	218	40.01 N	83.23 W
Plungė	76	55.55 N	21.51 E
Pl'uskovo	76	52.46 N	33.49 E
Pl'ussa	76	58.26 N	29.21 E
Pl'ussa ≐	76	59.19 N	28.11 E
Plutarco Elías Calles, Presa ⊜[1]	232	29.10 N	109.40 W
Pluvigner	32	47.46 N	3.01 E
Plym ≐	42	50.22 N	4.07 W
Plymouth, Monts.	238	16.42 N	62.13 W
Plymouth, Trin.	241r	11.13 N	60.47 W
Plymouth, Eng., U.K.	42	50.23 N	4.10 W
Plymouth, Ca., U.S.	226	38.29 N	120.51 W
Plymouth, Ct., U.S.	207	41.40 N	73.03 W
Plymouth, Il., U.S.	194	40.17 N	90.55 W
Plymouth, In., U.S.	216	41.20 N	86.18 W
Plymouth, Ma., U.S.	207	41.57 N	70.40 W
Plymouth, Mi., U.S.	216	42.22 N	83.28 W
Plymouth, Ne., U.S.	198	40.18 N	96.59 W
Plymouth, N.H., U.S.	188	43.45 N	71.41 W
Plymouth, N.Y., U.S.	210	42.37 N	75.36 W
Plymouth, N.C., U.S.	192	35.52 N	76.44 W
Plymouth, Oh., U.S.	214	41.00 N	82.40 W
Plymouth, Pa., U.S.	210	41.14 N	75.56 W
Plymouth, Wi., U.S.	190	43.44 N	87.58 W
Plymouth □[6]	207	41.58 N	70.41 W
Plymouth ≐	283	42.12 N	70.54 W
Plymouth Airport ⊠	42	50.25 N	4.06 W
Plymouth Bay c	207	41.57 N	70.37 W
Plymouth Harbor c	283	41.58 N	70.39 W
Plymouth Meeting	285	40.06 N	75.16 W
Plymouth Meeting Mall ◆[9]	285	40.07 N	75.17 W
Plymouth Rock ⊥	207	41.57 N	70.39 W
Plymouth Valley	285	40.07 N	75.23 W
Plympton, Eng., U.K.	42	50.23 N	4.03 W
Plympton, Ma., U.S.	207	41.57 N	70.48 W
Plymptonville	214	41.03 N	78.28 W
Plymstock	42	50.22 N	4.04 W
Plynlimon ʌ	42	52.28 N	3.47 W
Plzeň	60	49.45 N	13.23 E
Pniewy	30	52.31 N	16.15 E
Pô	150	11.10 N	1.09 W
Po ≐, It.	36	44.57 N	12.04 E
Po ≐, Zhg.	100	28.57 N	116.39 E
Po, Foci del (Mouths of the Po) ≐[1]	64	44.52 N	12.30 E
Pô, Parc National de ♦	150	11.30 N	1.15 W
Poá	256	23.32 S	46.20 W
Poá ≐	287b	23.37 S	46.45 W
Poana ≐	250	0.56 N	57.03 W
Poarta Orientală, Pasul)(	38	45.06 N	22.18 E
Poás, Volcán ʌ[1]	236	10.11 N	84.13 W
Pobé, Bénin	150	6.58 N	2.41 E
Pobé, Burkina	150	13.53 N	1.45 W
Pobeda, gora ʌ	74	65.12 N	146.12 E
Pobeda Ice Island I	9	64.30 S	97.00 E
Pobedino	74	49.51 N	142.49 E
Pobedy, pik ʌ	72	42.02 N	80.05 E
Pobershau	54	50.38 N	13.13 E
Poběžovice	60	49.31 N	12.48 E
Poblado Cerro Gordo	240m	18.29 N	66.20 W
Poblado Jacaguas	240m	18.03 N	66.32 W
Poblado Medianía Alta	240m	18.26 N	65.50 W
Poblado Sábalos	240m	18.11 N	67.09 W
Poblado Santana	240m	18.27 N	66.40 W
Poblet	258	35.04 S	57.57 W
Pocahontas, Ar., U.S.	194	36.15 N	90.58 W
Pocahontas, Il., U.S.	219	38.49 N	89.32 W
Pocahontas, Ia., U.S.	198	42.44 N	94.40 W
Pocahontas State Park ♦	208	37.23 N	77.34 W
Počajev	78	50.01 N	25.31 E
Pocantico Hills	276	41.06 N	73.50 W
Pocantico Lake ⊜	276	41.07 N	73.50 W
Poção	250	8.11 S	36.42 W
Pocasset	207	41.41 N	70.37 W
Pocatalico ≐	188	38.29 N	81.49 W
Pocatello	202	42.52 N	112.26 W
Počep	76	52.56 N	33.27 E
Počepy	76	53.17 N	31.20 E
Pocé-sur-Cisse	50	47.26 N	0.59 E
Pöchlarn	61	48.12 N	15.13 E
Pochvistnevo	80	53.38 N	52.08 E
Pocinhos, Bra.	250	7.04 S	36.03 W
Pocinhos, Bra.	256	21.56 S	46.25 W
Počinki	80	54.42 N	44.51 E
Počinnaja Sopka	76	58.25 N	34.22 E
Počinok	76	54.25 N	32.27 E
Pocitos, Salar ≚	252	24.30 S	67.03 W
Pockau	54	50.42 N	13.14 E
Pocking	60	48.24 N	13.19 E
Pocklington	44	53.56 N	0.46 W
Pocoata	248	18.41 S	66.11 W
Poço da Cruz, Açude ⊜[1]	250	8.30 S	37.35 W
Poço do Bispo ◆[8]	266c	38.44 N	9.06 W
Poções	255	14.31 S	40.21 W
Poço Fundo	256	21.48 S	45.58 W
Poço Fundo, Cachoeira do ⌞	256	22.10 S	44.13 W
Pocol	64	46.31 N	12.07 E
Pocola	194	35.13 N	94.28 W
Pocomoke ≐	208	37.58 N	75.39 W
Pocomoke City	208	38.04 N	75.34 W
Pocomoke Sound ʉ	208	37.52 N	75.49 W
Pocona	248	17.39 S	65.24 W
Poconé	248	16.15 S	56.37 W
Pocono International Raceway ♦	210	41.03 N	75.31 W
Pocono Lake	210	41.06 N	75.31 W
Pocono Manor	210	41.06 N	75.22 W
Pocono Mountains ᴧ[2]	210	41.10 N	75.20 W
Pocono Pines	210	41.05 N	75.29 W
Pocono Summit	210	41.07 N	75.25 W
Pocopson	285	39.54 N	75.37 W
Pocopson Creek ≐	285	39.54 N	75.37 W
Poço Redondo	250	9.49 S	37.41 W
Poços de Caldas	256	21.48 S	46.34 W
Poço Verde	250	10.42 S	38.11 W
Pocrane	255	19.37 S	41.37 W
Pocrí	236	8.16 N	80.33 W
Podbel'skaja	80	53.37 N	51.50 E
Podberezje, Ross.	76	56.57 N	30.38 E
Podberezje, Ross.	82	56.46 N	37.10 E
Podbořany	54	50.11 N	13.25 E
Podborki	82	54.11 N	35.56 E
Podborovje	76	59.30 N	35.02 E
Podbuž	78	49.22 N	23.15 E
Podbužje	76	53.30 N	34.56 E
Podčerje	24	63.57 N	57.34 E
Podchožeje	82	54.19 N	38.34 E
Podčinnyj	80	50.52 N	45.13 E
Poddębice	30	51.53 N	18.58 E
Poddemjur	24	64.05 N	53.26 E
Poddolgoje	76	53.12 N	38.04 E
Poddorje	76	57.28 N	31.07 E
Poděbrady	30	50.08 N	15.07 E
Po della Donzella ≐	64	44.48 N	12.25 E
Po delle Tolle ≐	64	44.50 N	12.28 E
Podensac	32	44.39 N	0.22 W
Podenzano	62	44.57 N	9.41 E
Podersdorf am See	61	47.51 N	16.50 E
Podgajcy	78	49.16 N	25.08 E
Podgorenskij	78	50.24 N	39.39 E
Podgorica	38	42.26 N	19.14 E
Podgornaja	78	50.28 N	41.10 E
Podgornoje, Kaz.	85	42.55 N	72.25 E
Podgornoje, Ross.	78	51.43 N	39.07 E
Podgornoje, Ross.	78	50.27 N	39.37 E
Podgornoje, Ross.	80	46.33 N	43.07 E
Podgornoje, Ross.	86	57.47 N	82.36 E
Podgorodnaja	78	48.07 N	30.51 E
Podgorodnoje	78	48.34 N	35.08 E
Podhůří	60	49.28 N	13.40 E
Podi	112	1.08 S	121.16 E
Po di Goro ≐	64	44.48 N	12.27 E
Po di Volano ≐	64	44.49 N	12.15 E
Podjom-Michajlovka	80	52.49 N	50.32 E
Podjuchy ◆[8]	54	53.20 N	14.36 E
Podkamen'	78	49.57 N	25.19 E
Podkamennaja Tunguska	74	61.36 N	90.09 E
Podkamennaja Tunguska ≐	74	61.36 N	90.18 E
Podkoren	64	46.30 N	13.45 E
Podkumok ≐	84	44.14 N	43.36 E
Podlasie ◆[1]	30	52.30 N	23.00 E
Podlesnoje, Ross.	80	51.50 N	47.03 E
Podlesnoje, Ukr.	78	48.47 N	32.15 E
Podlopatki	88	50.55 N	107.05 E
Podmošje	82	56.23 N	37.24 E
Podol'sk	82	55.26 N	37.33 E
Podol'skaja vozvyšennost' ᴧ[1]	78	49.00 N	27.00 E
Podor, Maur.	150	16.40 N	15.00 W
Podor, Sén.	150	16.40 N	14.57 W
Podora	24	62.22 N	54.19 E
Podosinovec	24	60.17 N	47.04 E
Podoz'orskij	80	57.14 N	40.20 E
Podporožje	24	60.53 N	34.07 E
Podravina ◆[1]	36	45.40 N	17.40 E
Podravska Slatina	38	45.42 N	17.42 E
Podrezčicha	24	59.22 N	51.28 E
Podstepnyj	80	51.08 N	51.28 E
Podsvilje	76	55.09 N	27.58 E
Podt'osovo	88	58.36 N	92.06 E
Pod'uga	24	61.06 N	40.53 E
Podujevo	38	42.55 N	21.11 E
Poduškino	265b	55.43 N	37.17 E
Podu Turcului	38	46.12 N	27.23 E
Podvoločisk	78	49.33 N	26.09 E
Podymachino	88	56.59 N	106.11 E
Podyvotje	78	52.03 N	34.08 E
Poe	216	40.56 N	85.05 W
Poechos, Embalse ⊜[1]	246	4.40 S	80.30 W
Poel I	54	54.00 N	11.26 E
Poeldijk	52	52.01 N	4.12 E
Poelela, Lagoa ⊜	156	24.38 S	35.00 E
Poelkapelle	50	50.55 N	2.57 E
Poestenkill	210	42.41 N	73.34 W
Poesten Kill ≐	210	42.43 N	73.42 W
Poetto	71	39.12 N	9.10 E
Pofadder	158	29.10 S	19.22 E
Pogamasing Lake ⊜	190	46.57 N	81.50 W
Pogan, Zhg.	100	28.18 N	116.46 E
Pogan, Zhg.	100	27.40 N	116.46 E
Pogăniş ≐	38	45.41 N	21.22 E
Pogar	76	52.33 N	33.16 E
Poge, Cape ›	207	41.25 N	70.27 W
Poggendorf	54	54.03 N	13.07 E
Poggiardo	68	40.03 N	18.23 E
Poggibonsi	66	43.28 N	11.09 E
Poggio	64	44.30 N	10.00 E
Poggio Berni	66	44.02 N	12.24 E
Poggio Bustone	66	42.30 N	12.53 E
Poggio Imperiale	68	41.49 N	15.22 E
Poggiomarino	68	40.48 N	14.32 E
Poggio Mirteto	66	42.16 N	12.41 E
Poggio Moiano	66	42.12 N	12.53 E
Poggioreale	70	37.47 N	13.01 E
Poggio Renatico	64	44.46 N	11.29 E
Poggiorsini	68	40.55 N	16.15 E
Poggio Rusco	64	44.59 N	11.07 E
Poggio Sannita	66	41.47 N	14.25 E
Pöggstall	61	48.19 N	15.12 E
Pogibi	89	52.12 N	141.42 E
Pogil-to I	98	34.09 N	126.33 E
Pogliano	266b	45.32 N	8.59 E
Pogny	56	48.52 N	4.29 E
Pogoanele	38	44.54 N	27.00 E
Pogodajev	80	51.37 N	51.04 E
Pogonianí	38	40.00 N	20.25 E
Pogoreloje Gorodišče	76	56.08 N	34.56 E
Pogoso	152	6.46 S	17.12 E
Pogost, Bela.	76	52.51 N	27.39 E
Pogost, Bela.	76	53.51 N	29.09 E
Pogost, Ross.	80	57.39 N	42.33 E
Pogost, Ross.	82	56.52 N	39.04 E
Pogožeje	78	51.36 N	37.16 E
Pogradec	38	40.54 N	20.39 E
Po Grande ≐	64	44.57 N	12.26 E
Pograničnoje	80	50.32 N	48.38 E
Pograničnyj, Ross.	80	46.57 N	45.46 E
Pograničnyj, Ross.	89	44.25 N	131.24 E
Pogrebišče	78	49.29 N	29.16 E
Pogromni Volcano ʌ[1]	180	54.33 N	164.45 W
Pogromnoje	80	52.35 N	52.32 E
Pogruznaja	80	54.14 N	50.29 E
Poh	112	0.46 S	122.49 E
P'ohang	98	36.03 N	129.20 E
Pohatcong Creek ≐	210	40.37 N	75.11 W
Pohénégamook	186	47.31 N	69.16 W
Pohick Creek ≐	284c	38.46 N	77.14 W
Pohick Creek, Rabbit Branch ≐	284c	38.48 N	77.17 W
Pohick Creek, Sideburn Branch ≐	284c	38.48 N	77.17 W
Pohjanmaa ◆[1]	26	64.00 N	25.00 E
Pohjois-Karjalan lääni □[4]	24	63.00 N	30.00 E
Pöhl, Talsperre ◆[6]	54	50.33 N	12.12 E
Pöhla	54	50.31 N	12.49 E
Pöhlde	52	51.37 N	10.18 E
Pohl-Göns	56	50.28 N	8.39 E
Pohlheim	56	50.34 N	8.45 E
Pohnpei I	174r	6.55 N	158.15 E
Pohořelice	61	48.59 N	16.32 E
Pohorje ᴧ	61	46.30 N	15.20 E
Pohri	124	25.32 N	77.21 E
Pohsien → Boxian	100	33.53 N	115.45 E
Pohue Bay c	229d	19.00 N	155.48 W
Poiana Mare	38	43.55 N	23.04 E
Poiana Ruscă, Munții ᴧ	38	45.41 N	22.30 E
Pöide	76	58.31 N	23.03 E
Poigny-la-Forêt	261	48.41 N	1.45 E
Poim	80	53.01 N	43.11 E
Poinsett, Cape ›	9	65.42 S	113.18 E
Poinsett, Lake ⊜, Fl., U.S.	220	28.20 N	80.50 W
Poinsett, Lake ⊜, S.D., U.S.	198	44.34 N	97.05 W
Point	222	32.56 N	95.52 W
Point Arena	204	38.54 N	123.41 W
Point Au Fer Island I	194	29.15 N	91.15 W
Point Baker	180	56.21 N	133.37 W
Pointblank	222	30.45 N	95.13 W
Point Chautauqua	214	42.14 N	79.28 W
Point Comfort	196	28.41 N	96.33 W
Point Cook	274b	37.56 S	144.45 E
Point Cook Royal Australian Air Force Station ■	169	37.56 S	144.45 E
Point du Jour, Ruisseau du ≐	206	45.50 N	73.25 W
Pointe-à-la-Frégate	186	49.12 N	64.55 W
Pointe-à-la-Garde	186	48.05 N	66.32 W
Pointe a la Hache	194	29.34 N	89.47 W
Pointe-à-Maurier	186	50.20 N	59.48 W
Pointe-à-Pitre	241o	16.14 N	61.32 W
Pointe-à-Pitre-le Raizet, Aéroport de ⊠	241o	16.17 N	61.32 W
Pointe-au-Chêne	206	45.38 N	74.45 W
Pointe Aux Peaux Farms	216	41.57 N	83.16 W
Pointe-aux-Trembles	206	45.39 N	73.30 W
Pointe-Calumet	275a	45.30 N	73.58 W
Pointe-Claire	206	45.26 N	73.50 W
Pointe-des-Cascades	275a	45.20 N	73.58 W
Pointe-des-Galets → Le Port	157c	20.55 S	55.18 E
Pointe-du-Moulin	275a	45.22 N	73.52 W
Point Edward	214	43.00 N	82.24 W
Pointe-Noire, Congo	152	4.48 S	11.51 E
Pointe-Noire, Guad.	241o	16.14 N	61.47 W
Point Enterprise	222	31.40 N	96.26 W
Pointers	208	39.35 N	75.26 W
Point Fortin	241r	10.11 N	61.41 W
Point Hope	180	68.21 N	166.41 W
Point Imperial ʌ	200	36.16 N	111.58 W
Point Independence	207	41.44 N	70.39 W
Point Lake ⊜	176	65.15 N	113.04 W
Point Leamington	186	49.20 N	55.24 W
Point Lookout, Md., U.S.	208	38.02 N	76.19 W
Point Lookout, N.Y., U.S.	276	40.35 N	73.35 W
Point Marion	188	39.44 N	79.53 W
Point McLeay	168b	35.32 S	139.06 E
Point Nepean National Park ♦	169	38.25 S	144.45 E
Point of Rocks	208	39.16 N	77.32 W
Point O'Woods	276	40.39 N	73.08 W
Point Pass	168b	34.05 S	139.03 E
Point Pelee National Park ♦	214	41.57 N	82.30 W
Point Peninsula ›[1]	212	44.01 N	76.15 W
Point Pleasant, Md., U.S.	284b	39.11 N	76.35 W
Point Pleasant, N.J., U.S.	208	40.04 N	74.04 W
Point Pleasant, Oh., U.S.	218	38.54 N	84.14 W
Point Pleasant, Pa., U.S.	208	40.25 N	75.04 W
Point Pleasant, W.V., U.S.	188	38.50 N	82.08 W
Point Pleasant Beach	208	40.05 N	74.02 W
Point Reyes National Seashore ♦	204	38.00 N	122.58 W
Point Roberts	224	48.59 N	123.04 W
Point Salines International Airport ⊠	241k	12.01 N	61.47 W
Point Samson	162	20.36 S	117.12 E
Point Sapin	186	46.58 N	64.50 W
Point View Reservoir ⊜[1]	276	40.58 N	74.15 W
Point Whiteshed	180	60.28 N	145.57 W
Poirino	62	44.55 N	7.51 E
Poisevo	80	55.32 N	53.30 E
Poison Creek ≐	202	43.15 N	108.09 W
Poison Spider Creek ≐	200	42.46 N	106.31 W
Poisson Blanc, Réservoir du ⊜[1]	188	46.00 N	75.45 W
Poissonnier Point ›	162	19.57 S	119.11 E
Poissons	58	48.25 N	5.13 E
Poissy	50	48.56 N	2.03 E
Poitiers	32	46.35 N	0.20 E
Poitou □[9]	32	46.20 N	0.30 W
Poix	50	49.47 N	1.59 E
Poix-Terron	56	49.39 N	4.39 E
Pojarkovo	89	49.38 N	128.38 E
Pojma ≐	88	56.54 N	97.48 E
Pojo	248	17.45 S	64.49 W
Pojoaque Valley	200	35.59 N	106.00 W
Pojuca	255	12.21 S	38.20 W
Pojuca ≐	255	12.34 S	38.03 W
Pokagon State Park ♦	216	41.43 N	85.01 W
Pokaran	120	26.55 N	71.55 E
Pokataroo	166	29.35 S	148.42 E
Pokatejeva	88	56.59 N	97.25 E
Pokatilovka, Kaz.	80	51.06 N	51.53 E
Pokatilovka, Kaz.	86	45.23 N	80.10 E
Poke Run ≐	279b	40.30 N	79.33 W
Pokharā	124	28.14 N	83.59 E
Pokharia	126	23.55 N	86.37 E
Poko, Sūd.	140	5.38 N	31.50 E
Poko, Zaïre	154	3.09 N	26.53 E
Pokoinu	174k	21.12 S	159.49 W
Pokojnoje	84	44.48 N	44.16 E
Pokok Sena	114	6.10 N	100.32 E
Pokol'ubiči	76	52.30 N	31.02 E
Pokrov	82	55.55 N	39.10 E
Pokrovka, Kaz.	86	54.17 N	68.15 E
Pokrovka, Kaz.	86	49.28 N	81.28 E
Pokrovka, Kyrg.	85	42.20 N	78.01 E
Pokrovka, Kyrg.	85	42.45 N	71.36 E
Pokrovka, Ross.	80	48.22 N	46.04 E
Pokrovka, Ross.	80	53.47 N	53.19 E
Pokrovka, Ross.	89	43.57 N	131.39 E
Pokrovo-Kirejevo	83	47.38 N	38.16 E
Pokrovsk	74	61.29 N	129.06 E
Pokrovskaja Arčada	80	52.56 N	44.13 E
Pokrovskij	78	46.32 N	31.38 E
Pokrovskoje, Ross.	76	52.38 N	36.51 E
Pokrovskoje, Ross.	80	54.04 N	43.37 E
Pokrovskoje, Ross.	80	53.54 N	40.26 E
Pokrovskoje, Ross.	82	56.25 N	37.03 E
Pokrovskoje, Ross.	82	55.53 N	36.19 E
Pokrovskoje, Ross.	83	47.25 N	38.54 E
Pokrovskoje, Ross.	86	57.14 N	66.48 E
Pokrovskoje, Ross.	265a	59.44 N	30.46 E
Pokrovskoje, Ukr.	78	49.44 N	38.13 E
Pokrovskoje, Ukr.	78	47.59 N	36.14 E
Pokrovskoje, Ukr.	83	48.37 N	38.09 E
Pokrovskoje ◆[8]	265b	55.37 N	37.37 E
Pokrovsko-Strešnevo ◆[8]	265b	55.49 N	37.29 E
Pokrovsk-Ural'skij	86	60.10 N	59.49 E
Pokur	74	61.02 N	75.26 E
Pola → Pula, Hrv.	64	44.52 N	13.50 E
Pola, Pil.	116	13.09 N	121.26 E
Pola, Ross.	76	57.56 N	31.50 E
Pola ≐	76	58.04 N	31.37 E
Pola Bay c	116	13.10 N	121.28 E
Polacca	200	35.50 N	110.22 W
Polacca Wash V	200	35.22 N	110.50 W
Pola de Laviana	34	43.15 N	5.34 W
Pola de Lena	34	43.10 N	5.49 W
Pola de Siero	34	43.23 N	5.40 W
Polān	128	25.35 N	61.12 E
Polanco	252	33.54 S	55.09 W
Poland, Kiribati	174o	1.59 N	157.32 W
Poland, N.Y., U.S.	210	43.13 N	75.03 W
Poland, Oh., U.S.	214	41.01 N	80.37 W
Poland (Polska) □[1], Europe	22	52.00 N	19.00 E
Poland (Polska) □[1], Europe	30	52.00 N	19.00 E
Polangui	116	13.17 N	123.29 E
Polanów	30	54.08 N	16.39 E
Polapare ≐	115b	9.43 S	119.06 E
Pol'arnik	180	67.03 N	178.53 W
Pol'arnyj, Ross.	24	69.12 N	33.22 E
Pol'arnyj, Ross.	74	69.10 N	178.48 E
Pol'arnyj Ural ᴧ	24	66.55 N	64.30 E
Polatlı	130	39.36 N	32.09 E
Polba	272b	22.57 N	88.18 E
Polbain	46	58.02 N	5.23 W
Polbeth	46	55.52 N	3.33 W
Polch	56	50.18 N	7.18 E
Polcirkeln	24	66.34 N	21.05 E
Polcura	252	37.17 S	71.43 W
Połczyn Zdrój	30	53.46 N	16.06 E
Polden Hills ᴧ[2]	42	51.08 N	2.50 W
Poldnevica	80	58.37 N	46.38 E
Pol'dorak	85	39.25 N	69.56 E
Poleang	112	4.42 S	121.46 E
Polebridge	182	48.45 N	114.17 W
Polecat Creek ≐	196	36.00 N	95.57 W
Poledník ʌ	60	49.04 N	13.24 E
Polee, Pulau I	164	2.12 S	130.15 E
Polegate	42	50.49 N	0.15 E
Pol-e Khomrī	120	35.56 N	68.43 E
Pole Moor	262	53.39 N	1.54 W
Polen → Poland □[1]	30	52.00 N	19.00 E
Polenezköy ◆[8]	267b	41.07 N	29.12 E
Pol-e Safīd	128	36.06 N	53.01 E
Polesden Lacey ⊥	260	51.15 N	0.22 W
Polesella	64	44.58 N	11.45 E
Polesine ◆[1]	64	45.00 N	11.45 E
Polesine Parmense	64	45.01 N	10.04 E
Polesje	76	53.05 N	31.17 E
Polesje ◆[1]	72	52.00 N	27.00 E
Polessk [Labiau]	76	54.52 N	21.05 E
Polesskoje	78	51.14 N	29.22 E
Polesworth	42	52.37 N	1.36 W
Polevaja	78	51.37 N	36.30 E
Polevskoj	86	56.26 N	60.11 E
Polewali	112	3.25 S	119.20 E
Pol-e Žahāb	128	34.28 N	45.52 E
Polgár	30	47.52 N	21.08 E
Polgooth	42	50.19 N	4.48 W
Pŏlgyo	98	34.52 N	127.21 E
Poli, Cam.	146	8.29 N	13.15 E
Poli, Zhg.	98	35.43 N	119.47 E
Poli, Zhg.	98	35.57 N	118.17 E
Polia	68	38.45 N	16.19 E
Políaigos I	38	36.46 N	24.38 E
Policastro, Golfo di c	68	40.00 N	15.30 E
Policastro Bussentino	68	40.09 N	15.32 E
Police	30	53.35 N	14.33 E
Polička	30	49.43 N	16.16 E
Policoro	68	40.13 N	16.41 E
Polignac	62	45.04 N	3.52 E
Polignano a Mare	68	41.00 N	17.13 E
Poligny	58	46.50 N	5.43 E
Polihale State Park ♦	229b	22.05 N	159.45 W
Políkastron	38	41.00 N	22.34 E
Polikhnítos	38	39.05 N	26.11 E
Polillo	116	14.43 N	121.56 E
Polillo Island I	116	14.50 N	121.57 E
Polillo Islands II	116	14.50 N	122.05 E
Polillo Strait ʉ	116	14.44 N	121.51 E
Polinesia Francesa → French Polynesia □[2]	14	15.00 S	140.00 W
Polinik ʌ	64	46.54 N	13.09 E
Polinyà de Vallès	266d	41.33 N	2.10 E
Pólis	130	35.02 N	32.25 E
Polist' ≐	76	58.06 N	31.31 E
Polistena	68	38.25 N	16.05 E
Politécnico Nacional, Instituto ʋ[2]	286a	19.30 N	99.08 W
Politotdel'skoje	83	47.33 N	39.05 E
Pölitz → Police	30	53.35 N	14.33 E
Polivanovo	80	53.36 N	47.23 E
Políyiros	38	40.23 N	23.27 E
Polizzi Generosa	70	37.49 N	14.00 E
Polizzo, Monte ʌ	70	37.52 N	12.47 E
Polk, Ne., U.S.	198	41.04 N	97.47 W
Polk, Oh., U.S.	214	40.57 N	82.13 W
Polk, Pa., U.S.	214	41.22 N	79.55 W
Polk □[6], Fl., U.S.	220	28.01 N	81.37 W
Polk □[6], Or., U.S.	224	45.00 N	123.23 W
Polk □[6], Tx., U.S.	222	30.45 N	94.48 W
Polk City	220	28.10 N	81.49 W
Pol'kino	74	71.10 N	99.13 E
Polkton	192	35.00 N	80.12 W
Polla	68	40.30 N	15.30 E
Pollāchi	122	10.40 N	77.01 E
Pollanten	60	49.09 N	11.28 E
Pöllau	61	47.18 N	15.51 E
Pöllauberg	61	47.19 N	15.52 E
Polleben	54	51.34 N	11.36 E
Pollenfeld	60	48.57 N	11.12 E
Pollenza	66	43.16 N	13.21 E
Pollica	68	40.11 N	15.03 E
Pollina	70	37.59 N	14.09 E
Polling	64	47.48 N	11.09 E
Pollino, Monte ʌ	68	39.55 N	16.11 E
Polloc Harbor c	116	7.23 N	124.12 E
Pollock, La., U.S.	194	31.31 N	92.24 W
Pollock, S.D., U.S.	198	45.54 N	100.17 W
Pollock Pines	226	38.46 N	120.34 W
Pollock Run ≐	279b	40.14 N	79.47 W
Pollok	222	31.27 N	94.52 W
Pollutri	66	42.08 N	14.35 E
Pollux ʌ	172	44.14 S	168.53 E
Polmak	24	70.04 N	28.00 E
Polmont	46	55.59 N	3.42 W
Polná	30	49.29 N	15.43 E
Polnaja ≐	83	48.54 N	39.50 E
Pol'noje-Jaltunovo	80	53.59 N	41.52 E
Polnovo-Seliger	76	57.32 N	32.55 E
Polo, Il., U.S.	190	41.59 N	89.34 W
Polo, Mo., U.S.	194	39.33 N	94.02 W
Polochic ≐	236	15.28 N	89.22 W
Polock, Bela.	76	55.31 N	28.46 E
Polock, Ross.	86	52.46 N	59.42 E
Pologi	78	47.29 N	36.15 E
Pologne → Poland □[1]	30	52.00 N	19.00 E
Pologoje Zajmišče	80	48.29 N	45.57 E
Pologrudovo	86	57.07 N	74.13 E
Polom, Ross.	24	59.13 N	50.50 E
Polom, Ross.	80	57.47 N	53.29 E
Polo Magnético del Sur → South Magnetic Pole ◆	9	65.18 S	139.30 E
Pölömäki ʌ[2]	26	63.21 N	27.03 E
Polomet' ≐	76	57.41 N	32.12 E
Polomolo	116	6.14 N	125.03 E
Polonia → Poland □[1]	30	52.00 N	19.00 E
Polonia, Arroyo ≐	258	34.10 S	57.15 W
Polonio, Cabo ›	252	34.24 S	53.46 W
Polonnaruwa	122	7.56 N	81.00 E
Polonnaruwa ⊥	122	7.56 N	81.00 E
Polonnoje	78	50.07 N	27.30 E
Pološkovo	82	54.08 N	35.53 E
Polo Sur → South Pole ◆	9	90.00 S	0.00
Polotn'anyj	82	54.45 N	36.00 E
Polotsk → Polock	76	55.31 N	28.46 E
Polovinkino	83	49.14 N	38.55 E
Polovinnoje, Ross.	86	54.43 N	63.50 E
Polovinnoje, Ross.	86	53.46 N	79.15 E
Polovo	76	57.03 N	32.27 E
Polperro	42	50.19 N	4.31 W
Polruan	42	50.19 N	4.36 W
Pöls	61	47.13 N	14.35 E
Pölsbach ≐	61	47.11 N	14.45 E
Polska → Poland □[1]	30	52.00 N	19.00 E
Polski Trâmbeš	38	43.22 N	25.38 E
Polson	202	47.41 N	114.09 W
Polster ʌ	61	47.32 N	14.58 E
Polsum	52	51.37 N	7.03 E
Poltava	78	49.35 N	34.34 E
Poltava □[4]	78	49.45 N	34.00 E
Poltavka	86	54.22 N	71.45 E
Poltevy Pen'ki	80	54.35 N	42.06 E
Poltimore	188	45.47 N	75.43 W
Põltsamaa	76	58.38 N	25.58 E
Põltsamaa ≐	76	58.27 N	26.09 E
Poludino	86	54.51 N	69.55 E
Poluj ≐	74	66.31 N	66.33 E
Polunočnoje	72	60.52 N	60.25 E
Polur	122	12.30 N	79.08 E
Polur'adinki	82	54.51 N	38.41 E
Poluškino	265b	55.41 N	38.05 E
Pol'ustrovo ◆[8]	265a	59.58 N	30.25 E
Põlva	76	58.03 N	27.03 E
Polvaredas	258	35.35 S	59.30 W
Polverigi	66	43.31 N	13.23 E
Polvijärvi	26	62.51 N	29.22 E
Polvilho	287b	23.23 S	46.50 W
Polvoranca	266a	40.19 N	3.48 W
Polynesia II	14	4.00 S	156.00 W
Polynesian Cultural Center ʋ	229c	21.39 N	157.55 W
Polynésie française → French Polynesia □[2]	14	15.00 S	140.00 W
Polynnoje	80	46.51 N	46.56 E
Polysajevo	86	54.35 N	86.14 E
Pölzig	54	50.57 N	12.11 E
Poma, Lago ⊜[1]	70	37.55 N	13.06 E
Pomabamba	248	8.50 S	77.28 W
Pomacanchi	248	14.02 S	71.34 W
Pomahaka ≐	172	46.09 S	169.34 E
Pomarance	66	43.18 N	10.52 E
Pomarico	68	40.31 N	16.33 E
Pomarkku	26	61.42 N	22.00 E
Pomata	248	16.16 S	69.18 W
Pomáz	264c	47.39 N	19.02 E
Pomba ≐	256	21.24 S	42.32 W
Pombais, Ribeira de ≐	266c	38.48 N	9.07 W
Pombal, Bra.	250	6.46 S	37.47 W
Pombal, Port.	34	39.55 N	8.38 W
Pombia	266b	45.39 N	8.38 E
Pomellen	54	53.20 N	14.23 E
Pomene	156	22.53 S	35.33 E
Pomerania □[9]	30	54.00 N	16.00 E
Pomeranian Bay c	54	54.00 N	14.15 E
Pomerene	200	31.59 N	110.17 W
Pomerode	252	26.45 S	49.11 W
Pomeroon ≐	246	7.37 N	58.45 W
Pomeroon-Supenaam □[4]	246	7.20 N	58.50 W
Pomeroy, S. Afr.	158	28.33 S	30.26 E
Pomeroy, N. Ire., U.K.	48	54.36 N	6.55 W
Pomeroy, Ia., U.S.	198	42.33 N	94.41 W
Pomeroy, Oh., U.S.	188	39.01 N	82.02 W
Pomeroy, Pa., U.S.	208	39.58 N	75.53 W
Pomeroy, Wa., U.S.	202	46.28 N	117.36 W
Pomezia	66	41.40 N	12.30 E
Pomfret, S. Afr.	156	25.50 S	23.32 E
Pomfret, Ct., U.S.	207	41.53 N	71.57 W
Pomfret, Md., U.S.	208	38.34 N	77.01 W
Pomi	38	47.42 N	23.19 E
Pomigliano	68	40.54 N	14.23 E
Pominovo	82	55.26 N	39.11 E
Pomio	164	5.30 S	151.30 E
Pommard	58	47.01 N	4.47 E
Pomme de Terre ≐, Mn., U.S.	198	45.10 N	96.05 W
Pomme de Terre ≐, Mo., U.S.	194	38.11 N	93.24 W
Pomme de Terre Lake ⊜[1]	194	37.51 N	93.19 W
Pommera	50	50.10 N	2.26 E
Pommern → Pomerania □[9]	30	54.00 N	16.00 E
Pommersche Bucht → Pomeranian Bay c	54	54.00 N	14.15 E
Pommersfelden	56	49.46 N	10.49 E
Pomona, Namibia	156	27.09 S	15.18 E
Pomona, Ca., U.S.	228	34.03 N	117.45 W
Pomona, Ks., U.S.	198	38.36 N	95.27 W
Pomona, N.J., U.S.	208	39.28 N	74.34 W
Pomona, N.Y., U.S.	276	41.10 N	74.02 W
Pomona College ʋ[2]	280	34.06 N	117.44 W
Pomona Estates	273d	26.06 S	28.15 E
Pomona Lake ⊜[1]	198	38.40 N	95.35 W
Pomona Park	192	29.30 N	81.35 W
Pomongo	152	5.00 S	19.08 E
Pomor'any	78	49.38 N	24.56 E
Pomorie	38	42.33 N	27.39 E
Pomorskij proliv ʉ	24	68.30 N	50.00 E
Pomorze → Pomerania □[9]	30	54.00 N	16.00 E
Pomošnaja	78	48.14 N	31.26 E
Pomozdino	24	62.12 N	54.06 E
Pompano Beach	220	26.14 N	80.07 W
Pompano Beach Highlands	220	26.16 N	80.06 W
Pompei	68	40.45 N	14.30 E
Pompei ⊥	68	40.45 N	14.30 E
Pompéia	255	22.08 S	50.10 W
Pompejevka	89	48.23 N	130.46 E
Pompeston Creek ≐	285	40.01 N	75.01 W
Pompéu	255	19.12 S	44.59 W
Pompey, Fr.	56	48.46 N	6.07 E
Pompey, N.Y., U.S.	210	42.54 N	76.01 W
Pomponio Creek ≐	282	37.18 N	122.25 W
Pomponio State Beach ♦	282	37.17 N	122.24 W
Pomponne	261	48.53 N	2.41 E
Pompon-yama ʌ	270	34.56 N	135.37 E
Pomposa	66	44.49 N	12.11 E
Pomposa, Abbazia di ʋ[1]	64	44.49 N	12.11 E
Pompton ≐	276	40.54 N	74.16 W
Pompton Lakes	210	41.00 N	74.17 W
Pompton Lakes ⊜	276	41.00 N	74.17 W
Pomquet	186	45.38 N	61.51 W
Pomssen	54	51.14 N	12.37 E
Ponape → Pohnpei I	174r	6.55 N	158.15 E
Ponask Lake ⊜	184	54.00 N	92.41 W
Ponass Lakes ⊜	184	52.18 N	103.58 W
Ponazyrevo	80	58.21 N	46.19 E
Ponca	198	42.33 N	96.42 W
Ponca City	196	36.42 N	97.05 W
Ponca Creek ≐	198	42.48 N	98.05 W
Ponce	240m	18.01 N	66.37 W
Ponce, Aeropuerto ⊠	240m	18.01 N	66.34 W
Ponce de Leon	194	30.43 N	85.56 W
Ponce de Leon Bay c	220	25.21 N	81.07 W
Ponce de Leon Inlet c	192	29.04 N	80.55 W
Poncé-sur-le-Loir	50	47.46 N	0.40 E
Poncha Pass)(	200	38.25 N	106.05 W
Ponchatoula	194	30.26 N	90.26 W
Poncin	58	46.05 N	5.24 E
Poncitlán	234	20.22 N	102.55 W
Pond ≐	194	37.32 N	87.21 W
Pond Brook ≐, N.J., U.S.	276	41.02 N	74.15 W
Pond Brook ≐, Oh., U.S.	279a	41.17 N	81.24 W
Pondcreek	196	36.40 N	97.48 W
Pond Creek ≐, U.S.	196	36.40 N	97.33 W
Pond Creek ≐, Tx., U.S.	222	31.02 N	96.46 W
Pond Eddy	210	41.27 N	74.49 W
Ponder	222	33.11 N	97.17 W
Pondera Coulee V	202	48.16 N	111.03 W
Ponders End ◆[8]	260	51.39 N	0.03 W
Pondicherry	122	11.56 N	79.53 E
Pondicherry □[8]	122	11.56 N	79.50 E
Pond Inlet	176	72.41 N	78.00 W
Pond Inlet c	176	72.46 N	77.00 W
Pondok Tanjong	114	5.00 N	100.44 E
Pondoland □[9]	158	31.10 S	29.30 E
Pondosa	204	41.12 N	121.41 W
Pond Run ≐	285	40.13 N	74.44 W
Poneas Island I	116	9.55 N	125.57 E
Ponente, Capo ›	70a	35.31 N	12.31 E
Ponente, Riviera di ⌓[2]	62	44.10 N	8.20 E
Ponérihouen	175f	21.05 S	165.24 E
Poneto	216	40.39 N	85.13 W
Ponežukaj	78	44.53 N	39.22 E
Ponferrada	34	42.33 N	6.35 W
Pong	110	19.10 N	100.17 E
Pongani	164	9.05 S	148.35 E
Pongara, Pointe ›	152	0.21 N	9.21 E
Pongaroa	172	40.33 S	176.11 E
Pongau V	64	47.21 N	13.14 E
Pong Dam ◆[6]	123	31.59 N	75.57 E
Ponghyŏn	98	37.49 N	125.36 E
Pongo ≐	140	8.42 N	27.40 E
Pongolo ≐	158	26.57 S	32.17 E
Pon'goma	24	65.21 N	34.25 E
Pong Tamale	150	9.41 N	0.49 W
Ponhook Lake ⊜	186	44.19 N	64.53 W
Poni ≐	208	38.07 N	77.26 W
Poniatowa	30	51.11 N	22.05 E
Poniec	30	51.47 N	16.50 E
Ponil Creek ≐	196	36.29 N	104.48 W
Poninka	78	50.12 N	27.32 E
Ponino	80	58.16 N	52.49 E
Ponitz, Dtsch.	54	50.51 N	12.25 E
Pönitz, Dtsch.	54	54.03 N	10.40 E
Ponizovje	76	55.17 N	31.04 E
Ponkapoag Pond ⊜	283	42.12 N	71.06 W
Pônley	110	12.26 N	104.27 E
Ponnaiyār ≐	122	11.46 N	79.47 E
Ponnāni	122	10.46 N	75.54 E
Ponnūru Nidubrolu	122	16.04 N	80.34 E
Pono	164	6.22 S	134.36 E
Ponoj	24	67.05 N	41.07 E
Ponoj ≐	24	66.59 N	41.17 E
Ponoka	182	52.42 N	113.35 W
Ponomar'ovka, Ross.	80	53.19 N	54.08 E
Ponomar'ovka, Ross.	86	56.08 N	82.23 E
Ponornica	78	51.43 N	32.49 E
Ponorogo	115a	7.52 S	111.27 E
Ponpāj	272b	22.56 N	88.15 E
Pons	32	45.35 N	0.33 W
Ponsacco	66	43.37 N	10.38 E
Ponson Island I	116	10.46 N	124.32 E
Ponsul ≐	34	39.40 N	7.31 W
Pont	62	45.34 N	7.07 E
Pont-à-Celles	50	50.30 N	4.21 E
Ponta Delgada	148a	37.44 N	25.40 W
Ponta Delgada □[5]	148a	37.40 N	25.30 W
Ponta de Pedras	250	1.23 S	48.52 W
Ponta Grossa	252	25.05 S	50.09 W
Pontalete	256	21.27 S	45.40 W
Pontalina	255	17.31 S	49.27 W
Pontallier-sur-Saône	58	47.18 N	5.25 E
Pont-à-Marcq	50	50.31 N	3.07 E
Pont-à-Mousson	56	48.54 N	6.04 E
Ponta Negra	256	22.57 S	35.10 W
Pontão	34	39.55 N	8.22 W
Ponta Porã	255	22.32 S	55.43 W
Pontardawe	42	51.44 N	3.51 W
Pontardulais	42	51.43 N	4.03 W
Pontarlier	58	46.54 N	6.22 E
Pontas de Pedra	250	7.38 S	34.48 W
Pontassieve	66	43.46 N	11.26 E
Pontaubert	50	47.29 N	3.52 E
Pont-Audemer	50	49.21 N	0.31 E
Pontault-Combault	261	48.47 N	2.36 E
Pontaumur	32	45.52 N	2.40 E
Pont-Aven	32	47.51 N	3.45 W
Pontbriand	206	46.09 N	71.15 W
Pont Canavese	62	45.25 N	7.36 E
Pontcarré	261	48.48 N	2.42 E
Pontcharra	62	45.26 N	6.01 E
Pontchartrain	261	48.48 N	1.54 E
Pontchartrain, Lake ⊜	194	30.10 N	90.10 W
Pontchâteau	32	47.26 N	2.05 W
Pont-Croix	32	48.02 N	4.29 W
Pont-d'Ain	58	46.03 N	5.20 E
Pont d'Arc ♦	62	44.23 N	4.26 E
Pont-de-Bonne	56	50.27 N	5.17 E
Pont-de-Chéruy	62	45.45 N	5.11 E
Pont-de-l'Arche	50	49.18 N	1.10 E
Pont-de-Pany	58	47.18 N	4.49 E
Pont-de-Poitte	58	46.35 N	5.41 E
Pont-de-Roide	58	47.23 N	6.46 E
Pont-de-Ruan	50	47.15 N	0.35 E
Pont-de-Salars	32	44.17 N	2.44 E
Pont-de-Vaux	58	46.26 N	4.56 E
Pont-de-Veyle	58	46.16 N	4.53 E
Ponte a Elsa	66	43.41 N	10.54 E
Ponte Alta do Bom Jesus	255	12.06 S	46.29 W
Ponte Alta do Norte	250	10.45 S	47.34 W
Ponte a Moriano	66	43.54 N	10.31 E
Ponteareas	34	42.11 N	8.30 W
Pontebba	64	46.30 N	13.18 E
Ponte Branca	255	16.27 S	52.40 W
Ponte Caffaro	64	45.50 N	10.32 E
Pontecagnano	68	40.39 N	14.52 E
Ponte Caldelas	34	42.23 N	8.30 W
Pontecchio Marconi	64	44.25 N	11.15 E
Pontecchio Polesine	64	45.01 N	11.49 E
Pontecorvo	66	41.27 N	13.40 E
Pontecurone	62	44.57 N	8.56 E
Ponte da Barca	34	41.48 N	8.25 W
Ponte d'Arbia	66	43.10 N	11.28 E
Ponte delle Arche	64	46.02 N	10.52 E
Ponte dell'Olio	62	44.52 N	9.39 E
Pontedera	66	43.40 N	10.38 E
Ponte de Sor	34	39.15 N	8.01 W
Pontedeume	34	43.24 N	8.10 W
Ponte di Barbarano	64	45.23 N	11.34 E
Ponte di Legno	64	46.16 N	10.31 E
Ponte di Nava	62	44.08 N	7.53 E
Ponte di Piave	64	45.43 N	12.28 E
Ponte do Lima	34	41.46 N	8.35 W
Ponte do Púngoè	156	19.30 S	34.32 E
Pontefract	44	53.42 N	1.18 W
Ponte Galeria ◆[8]	267a	41.49 N	12.21 E
Ponte Gardena (Waidbruck)	64	46.36 N	11.32 E
Ponte Ghiereto	66	43.59 N	11.15 E
Pontegrande	58	45.59 N	8.09 E
Ponte in Valtellina	64	46.12 N	9.59 E
Ponteix	184	49.45 N	107.29 W
Pontelagoscuro	64	44.53 N	11.36 E
Ponteland	44	55.03 N	1.44 W
Pontelandolfo	68	41.17 N	14.41 E
Pontelongo	64	45.15 N	12.02 E
Ponte nell'Alpi	64	46.11 N	12.16 E
Ponte Nova	255	20.24 S	42.54 W
Pont-en-Royans	62	45.04 N	5.21 E
Ponte Nuovo	66	43.01 N	12.28 E
Pontenure	62	44.59 N	9.47 E
Pontepetri	66	44.02 N	10.53 E
Pontericcioli	66	43.26 N	12.38 E
Ponte Rocchetta	64	46.14 N	11.04 E
Ponterwyd	42	52.25 N	3.50 W
Ponte San Giovanni	66	43.05 N	12.26 E
Ponte San Pietro	62	45.42 N	9.35 E
Pontesbury	42	52.39 N	2.54 W
Ponte Selva	64	45.52 N	9.54 E
Ponte Serrada	252	26.52 S	51.58 W
Pontestura	62	45.08 N	8.20 E
Ponte Tresa	58	45.58 N	8.52 E

Symbols in the index entries represent the broad categories identified in the key at the right. Symbols with superior numbers (ᴧ[1]) identify subcategories (see complete key on page *I · 1)*.

Symbole im Register stellen die rechts im Schlüssel erklärten Kategorien dar. Symbole mit hochgestellten Ziffern (ᴧ[1]) bezeichnen Unterabteilungen einer Kategorie (vgl. vollständiger Schlüssel auf Seite *I · 1)*.

Los símbolos incluídos en el texto del índice representan las grandes categorías identificadas con la clave a la derecha. Los símbolos con numeros en su parte superior (ᴧ[1]) identifican las subcategorías (véase la clave completa en la página *I · 1)*.

Les symboles de l'index représentent les catégories indiquées dans la légende à droite. Les symboles suivis d'un indice (ᴧ[1]) représentent des sous-catégories (voir légende complète à la page *I · 1)*.

Os símbolos incluídos no texto do índice representam as grandes categorias identificadas com a chave à direita. Os símbolos com números em sua parte superior (ᴧ[1]) identificam as subcategorias (veja-se a chave completa à página *I · 1)*.

ʌ Mountain	Berg	Montaña	Montagne	Montanha
ᴧ Mountains	Gebirge	Montañas	Montagnes	Montanhas
)(Pass	Paß	Paso	Col	Passo
V Valley, Canyon	Tal, Cañon	Valle, Cañón	Vallée, Canyon	Vale, Canhão
≚ Plain	Ebene	Llano	Plaine	Planície
› Cape	Kap	Cabo	Cap	Cabo
I Island	Insel	Isla	Île	Ilha
II Islands	Inseln	Islas	Îles	Ilhas
⌓ Other Topographic Features	Andere Topographische Objekte	Otros Elementos Topográficos	Autres données topographiques	Outros acidentes topográficos

ESPAÑOL

Nombre	Página	Lat.°′	Long.°′ W = Oeste
Pontevedra, Arg.	258	34.45 S	58.42 W
Pontevedra, Esp.	34	42.26 N	8.38 W
Pontevedra, Pil.	116	10.22 N	122.52 E
Pontevedra □ [4]	34	42.30 N	8.40 W
Pontevedra, Ría de c [1]	34	42.22 N	8.45 W
Ponte Vedra Beach	192	30.14 N	81.23 W
Pont-Évêque	62	45.32 N	4.55 E
Pontevico	64	45.16 N	10.05 E
Pontfaverger-Moronvilliers	50	49.18 N	4.19 E
Pontgibaud	32	45.50 N	2.52 E
Ponthévrard	261	48.33 N	1.55 E
Ponthierry	261	48.32 N	2.33 E
Ponthierville → Ubundu	154	0.21 S	25.29 E
Pontiac, Il., U.S.	216	40.52 N	88.37 W
Pontiac, Mi., U.S.	216	42.38 N	83.17 W
Pontiac □ [6]	212	46.30 N	77.00 W
Pontiac Lake	281	42.40 N	83.28 W
Pontiac Lake ⊜	281	42.40 N	83.28 W
Pontiac Lake State Recreation Area ♠	216	42.41 N	83.28 W
Pontiac Mall ◆ [9]	281	42.39 N	83.20 W
Pontiac State Recreation Area ♠	281	42.41 N	83.28 W
Pontianak	112	0.02 S	109.20 E
Pontian Kechil	114	1.29 N	103.23 E
Pontida	62	45.43 N	9.30 E
Pontigny	50	47.55 N	3.43 E
Pontinha ◆ [8]	266c	38.46 N	9.11 W
Pontinia	66	41.24 N	13.02 E
Pontivy	32	48.04 N	2.59 W
Pont-l'Abbé	32	47.52 N	4.13 W
Pont-lès-Moulins	58	47.19 N	6.22 E
Pont-l'Évêque	50	49.18 N	0.11 E
Pontlevoy	50	47.23 N	1.15 E
Pontoise	50	49.03 N	2.06 E
Pontoise-Cormeilles-en-Vexin, Aérodrome ⊠	261	49.06 N	2.02 E
Ponton Creek ≐	162	31.10 S	124.25 E
Pontonnyj	265a	59.47 N	30.38 E
Pontoon Beach	219	38.43 N	90.04 W
Pontorson	32	48.33 N	1.31 W
Pontotoc, Ms., U.S.	194	34.14 N	88.59 W
Pontotoc, Tx., U.S.	196	30.54 N	98.59 W
Pontremoli	62	44.22 N	9.53 E
Pont-Remy	50	50.03 N	1.55 E
Pontresina	58	46.28 N	9.53 E
Pontrhydfendigaid	42	52.17 N	3.51 W
Pont-Rouge	206	46.45 N	71.42 W
Pont-Royal	62	43.43 N	5.11 E
Ponts	34	41.55 N	1.12 E
Pont-Sainte-Marie	50	48.19 N	4.06 E
Pont-Sainte-Maxence	50	49.18 N	2.36 E
Pont-Saint-Esprit	62	44.15 N	4.39 E
Pont-Saint-Martin	62	45.36 N	7.48 E
Pont-Scorff	28	47.50 N	3.24 W
Ponts Quentin, Ruisseau des ≐	261	48.44 N	1.48 E
Pont-sur-Yonne	50	48.17 N	3.12 E
Pontuda, Ilha I	287a	23.02 S	43.18 W
Pontus □ [9]	130	40.15 N	38.00 E
Pontvallain	50	47.45 N	0.12 E
Pont-Viau ◆ [8]	275a	45.34 N	73.41 W
Pontyberem	42	51.17 N	4.09 W
Pontycymer	42	51.37 N	3.34 W
Pontypool	42	51.43 N	3.02 W
Pontypridd	42	51.37 N	3.22 W
Pony	202	45.39 N	111.53 W
Ponyri	76	52.19 N	36.20 E
Ponza	66	40.54 N	12.58 E
Ponza, Isola di I	66	40.55 N	12.57 E
Ponziane, Isole II	66	40.55 N	12.57 E
Ponzone	62	44.35 N	8.27 E
Poochera	162	32.43 S	134.51 E
Pool □ [5]	152	3.30 S	15.00 E
Poole	42	50.43 N	1.59 W
Poole, Mount ∧	166	29.37 S	141.46 E
Poole Bay c	42	50.42 N	1.52 W
Pooler	192	32.06 N	81.14 W
Poole's Cavern ⊥ [5]	262	53.14 N	1.56 W
Pooles Island I	208	39.17 N	76.16 W
Poolesville	208	39.08 N	77.25 W
Poolewe	46	57.45 N	5.37 W
Pooley Island I	182	52.44 N	128.16 W
Pool's Cove	186	47.41 N	55.26 W
Poolville	222	32.58 N	97.52 W
Poona → Pune	122	18.32 N	73.52 E
Pooncarie	166	33.23 S	142.34 E
Poondinna, Mount ∧	162	27.20 S	129.59 E
Poopo	248	18.23 S	66.59 W
Poopó, Lago ⊜	248	18.45 S	67.07 W
Pooraka	168b	34.50 S	138.37 E
Poor Knights Islands II	172	35.30 S	174.45 E
Poor Man Indian Reserve ◆ [4]	184	51.30 N	104.23 W
Poor Meadow Brook ≐	283	42.01 N	70.55 W
Poortjie	158	30.13 S	22.44 E
Poowong	169	38.21 S	145.46 E
Popa, Isla I	236	9.11 N	82.07 W
Popasnaja	83	48.37 N	38.20 E
Popasnoje	78	48.48 N	35.31 E
Popayán	246	2.27 N	76.36 W
Pope	194	34.12 N	89.56 W
Pope Creek ≐	226	38.37 N	122.17 W
Popel'n'a	78	49.57 N	29.27 E
Popel'nastoje	78	48.39 N	33.43 E
Poperečnoje	88	52.23 N	110.42 E
Poperinge	50	50.51 N	2.43 E
Popești	38	47.14 N	22.25 E
Popești-Leordeni	38	44.23 N	26.10 E
Pope Valley	226	38.37 N	122.26 W
Popham Bay c	176	64.10 N	65.10 W
Popigaj	74	71.55 N	110.47 E
Popigaj ≐	74	72.54 N	106.36 E
Popiltah Lake ⊜	166	33.10 S	141.43 E
Popinci	38	42.25 N	24.17 E
Popki	80	50.11 N	44.30 E
Popkum	224	49.12 N	121.44 W
Poplar, Ca., U.S.	226	36.03 N	119.08 W
Poplar, Mt., U.S.	198	48.06 N	105.11 W
Poplar, Wi., U.S.	190	46.35 N	91.47 W
Poplar ◆ [8]	260	51.31 N	0.01 W
Poplar ≐, Can.	184	53.00 N	97.24 W
Poplar ≐, N.A.	198	48.05 N	105.11 W
Poplar ≐, Mn., U.S.	198	47.51 N	96.04 W
Poplar, West Fork ≐	198	48.31 N	105.22 W
Poplar Bluff	194	36.45 N	90.23 W
Poplar Grove	216	42.22 N	88.49 W
Poplar Heights	284c	38.53 N	77.12 W
Poplar Hill	184	52.05 N	94.18 W
Poplar Mountain ∧	194	36.43 N	85.03 W
Poplar Point	184	50.04 N	97.57 W
Poplar Ridge	210	42.44 N	76.37 W
Poplar Springs	208	39.21 N	77.06 W
Poplarville	194	30.50 N	89.32 W
Poplevinskij	76	53.41 N	39.33 E
Popocatépetl, Volcán ∧ [1]	234	19.02 N	98.38 W
Popof Island I	180	55.17 N	160.25 W
Popoh	115a	8.15 S	111.48 E
Popokabaka	152	5.42 S	16.35 E
Popoli	66	42.10 N	13.50 E
Popondetta	164	8.46 S	148.14 E
Popova	89	42.58 N	131.42 E
Popovka, Ross.	76	60.08 N	39.21 E
Popovka, Ross.	80	49.14 N	41.12 E
Popovkino	82	56.07 N	36.01 E
Popovo	38	43.21 N	26.13 E
Poppberg ∧	60	49.25 N	11.35 E
Poppel	56	51.27 N	5.02 E
Poppenbüttel ◆ [8]	52	53.39 N	10.04 E
Poppenhausen	56	50.06 N	10.08 E
Poppi	66	43.43 N	11.46 E
Popple ≐	190	45.50 N	83.21 W

FRANÇAIS

Nom	Page	Lat.°′	Long.°′ W = Ouest
Poprad	30	49.03 N	20.18 E
Poprad ≐	30	49.38 N	20.42 E
Popricani	38	47.18 N	27.31 E
Pŏpsŏng	98	35.22 N	126.27 E
Pŏptong	98	38.59 N	127.05 E
Poptún	236	16.21 N	89.26 W
Populonia	66	42.59 N	10.29 E
Poputnaja	84	44.31 N	41.27 E
Poquessing Creek ≐	285	40.03 N	74.58 W
Poquetanuck	207	41.29 N	72.02 W
Poquonock	207	41.54 N	72.40 W
Poquonock Bridge	207	41.20 N	72.01 W
Poquoson	208	37.07 N	76.21 W
Poquoson ≐	208	37.10 N	76.24 W
Poquott	276	40.57 N	73.05 W
Porādaha	126	23.51 N	89.01 E
Porādiha	126	21.33 N	86.26 E
Porāli Nai ≐	120	25.58 N	66.26 E
Poranga	250	4.44 S	40.55 W
Porangahau	172	40.18 S	176.37 E
Porangatu	255	13.26 S	49.10 W
Porbandar	120	21.38 N	69.36 E
Porce ≐	246	7.28 N	74.53 W
Porchaman	128	33.08 N	63.51 E
Porcher Island I	182	53.57 N	130.30 W
Porcheville	261	48.58 N	1.47 E
Porchov	76	57.46 N	29.34 E
Porcia	64	45.57 N	12.36 E
Porciúncula	255	20.58 S	42.02 W
Porco	248	19.50 S	65.59 W
Porcos, Rio dos ≐	255	12.42 S	45.07 W
Porcuna	34	37.52 N	4.11 W
Porcupine ≐	180	66.35 N	145.15 W
Porcupine Brook ≐	283	42.46 N	71.13 W
Porcupine Creek ≐	202	48.07 N	106.20 W
Porcupine Creek, Middle Fork ≐	202	48.31 N	106.30 W
Porcupine Creek, West Fork ≐	202	48.31 N	106.30 W
Porcupine Dome ∧	180	65.31 N	145.31 W
Porcupine Hills ⋏ [2]	184	52.30 N	101.45 W
Porcupine Mountains State Park ♠	190	46.47 N	89.50 W
Pordenone	64	45.57 N	12.39 E
Pordenone □ [4]	64	46.00 N	12.45 E
Pordim	38	43.23 N	24.51 E
Poreč	36	45.13 N	13.37 E
Porecatu	255	22.43 S	51.24 W
Porečje, Bela.	76	53.55 N	24.07 E
Porečje, Ross.	76	55.43 N	35.33 E
Porečje, Ross.	76	56.06 N	30.29 E
Porečje-Rybnoje	80	57.06 N	39.23 E
Poreckoje	80	55.12 N	46.20 E
Porez	80	57.40 N	51.10 E
Pori	26	61.29 N	21.47 E
Poricy Brook ≐	276	40.21 N	74.05 W
Poringland	42	52.33 N	1.21 E
Porirua	172	41.08 S	174.51 E
Porjaguba	24	66.47 N	33.45 E
Porkkala	26	59.59 N	24.26 E
Porlamar	246	10.57 N	63.51 W
Porlezza	58	46.03 N	9.07 E
Porlock	42	51.14 N	3.36 W
Porma ≐	34	42.29 N	5.28 W
Pornassio	62	44.04 N	7.52 E
Pörnbach	60	48.37 N	11.28 E
Pornic	32	47.07 N	2.06 W
Poro ∧	154	1.14 N	36.37 E
Porog, Ross.	24	63.50 N	38.29 E
Porog, Ross.	76	59.16 N	33.24 E
Porogi	265a	59.46 N	30.47 E
Poro Island I	116	10.40 N	124.27 E
Porokylä	26	63.33 N	29.06 E
Poroma	248	18.29 S	65.30 W
Poronaj ≐	89	49.14 N	143.06 E
Poronajsk	89	49.14 N	143.04 E
Porong	115a	7.32 S	112.41 E
Porong ≐	115a	7.32 S	112.51 E
Poropotank ≐	208	37.27 N	76.42 W
Poroškovo	78	48.41 N	22.45 E
Porosozero	24	62.43 N	32.42 E
Poroto Mountains ⋏	154	9.00 S	33.45 E
Porozovo	76	52.56 N	24.22 E
Porožskij	88	56.04 N	101.46 E
Porpoise Bay c	9	66.30 S	128.30 E
Porpoise Channel ʊ	276	40.55 N	73.09 W
Porquerolles	62	43.00 N	6.12 E
Porquerolles, Île de I	62	43.00 N	6.13 E
Porrentruy	58	47.25 N	7.05 E
Porretta Terme	64	44.09 N	10.59 E
Porsangen c [2]	24	70.58 N	27.00 E
Porsangerhalvøya ≻ [1]	24	70.50 N	25.00 E
Porsea	114	2.27 N	99.09 E
Porsgrunn	26	59.09 N	9.40 E
Porsuk ≐	130	39.42 N	31.59 E
Port → Le Port	157c	20.55 S	55.18 E
Portachuelo	248	17.21 S	63.24 W
Portacloy	48	54.19 N	9.48 W
Port Adelaide	168b	34.51 S	138.30 E
Portadown	48	54.26 N	6.27 W
Portaferry	48	54.23 N	5.33 W
Portage, In., U.S.	216	41.34 N	87.10 W
Portage, Mi., U.S.	216	42.12 N	85.34 W
Portage, Oh., U.S.	216	41.20 N	83.39 W
Portage, Pa., U.S.	214	40.23 N	78.40 W
Portage, Ut,. U.S.	200	41.58 N	112.14 W
Portage, Wi., U.S.	190	43.32 N	89.27 W
Portage □ [6]	214	41.09 N	81.15 W
Portage ≐, Mi., U.S.	216	41.57 N	85.38 W
Portage ≐, Oh., U.S.	214	41.31 N	83.05 W
Portage, East Branch ≐	216	41.17 N	83.31 W
Portage, Middle Branch ≐	216	41.22 N	83.28 W
Portage, North Branch ≐	216	41.25 N	83.27 W
Portage, South Branch ≐	216	41.22 N	83.30 W
Portage Bay c	184	51.33 N	98.50 W
Portage Des Sioux	219	38.55 N	90.20 W
Portage Lake ⊜, Mi., U.S.	190	47.04 N	88.30 W
Portage Lake ⊜, Mi., U.S.	216	42.25 N	83.54 W
Portage Lake ⊜, Mi., U.S.	216	42.03 N	85.31 W
Portage Lakes	214	40.59 N	81.32 W
Portage Lakes ⊜	214	40.59 N	81.32 W
Portage Lakes State Park ♠	214	40.57 N	81.32 W
Portage-la-Prairie	184	49.59 N	98.18 W
Portage Park ◆ [8]	278	41.57 N	87.46 W
Portageville, Mo., U.S.	194	36.25 N	89.41 W
Portageville, N.Y., U.S.	210	42.34 N	78.02 W
Portal, Ga., U.S.	192	32.32 N	81.55 W
Portal, N.D., U.S.	198	48.59 N	102.32 W
Port Alberni	224	49.14 N	124.48 W
Portal del Infierno ʟ	236	14.22 N	85.38 W
Portalegre, Bra.	250	6.02 S	38.00 W
Portalegre, Port.	34	39.17 N	7.26 W
Portales	196	34.11 N	103.20 W
Port Alexander	180	56.15 N	134.39 W
Port Alfred (Kowie)	158	33.36 S	26.55 E
Port Alice	182	50.23 N	127.27 W
Port Allegany	214	41.48 N	78.16 W
Port Allen	194	30.27 N	91.12 W
Port Alma, Austl.	166	23.35 S	150.51 E
Port Alma, On., Can.	214	42.11 N	82.15 W
Port Alsworth	180	60.12 N	154.20 W
Port Angeles	224	48.07 N	123.25 W
Port Angeles Harbor c	224	48.07 N	123.24 W
Port Anson	186	49.32 N	55.50 W
Port Antonio	241q	18.11 N	76.28 W
Port Aransas	196	27.50 N	97.04 W
Portarlington, Austl.	169	38.07 S	144.39 E
Portarlington, Ire.	48	53.10 N	7.11 W

PORTUGUÊS

Nome	Página	Lat.°′	Long.°′ W = Oeste
Port Arthur, Austl.	166	43.09 S	147.51 E
Port Arthur → Thunder Bay, On., Can.	190	48.23 N	89.15 W
Port Arthur, Tx., U.S.	194	29.53 N	93.55 W
Port Arthur → Lüshun, Zhg.	98	38.48 N	121.16 E
Port Ashton	180	60.04 N	148.01 W
Port Askaig	46	55.51 N	6.07 W
Port Augusta	166	32.30 S	137.46 E
Port au Port	186	48.33 N	58.44 W
Port au Port Bay c	186	48.40 N	58.45 W
Port au Port Peninsula ≻ [1]	186	48.35 N	59.00 W
Port-au-Prince	238	18.32 N	72.20 W
Port-au-Prince, Baie de c	238	18.40 N	72.30 W
Port Austin	190	44.02 N	82.59 W
Port-aux-Basques → Channel-Port-aux-Basques	186	47.34 N	59.09 W
Portavogie	48	54.27 N	5.27 W
Porta Westfalica	52	52.14 N	8.55 E
Porta Westfalica ♠	52	52.14 N	8.55 E
Port Bannatyne	46	55.52 N	5.05 W
Port Barre	194	30.33 N	91.57 W
Port Bell	154	0.17 N	32.39 E
Port-Bergé	157b	15.33 S	47.40 E
Port Blair	110	11.40 N	92.45 E
Port Blakely	224	47.37 N	122.28 W
Port Blandford	186	48.21 N	54.10 W
Port Bolivar	222	29.23 N	94.46 W
Port Borden	186	46.15 N	63.42 W
Port-Bouët	150	5.15 N	3.58 W
Port Broughton	166	33.36 S	137.56 E
Port Burwell	212	42.39 N	80.49 W
Port Byron, Il., U.S.	190	41.36 N	90.20 W
Port Byron, N.Y., U.S.	210	43.02 N	76.37 W
Port Campbell	169	38.37 S	143.00 E
Port Campbell National Park ♠	169	38.38 S	142.55 E
Port Canning	126	22.18 N	88.40 E
Port Carbon	208	40.42 N	76.10 W
Port Carling	212	45.07 N	79.35 W
Port-Cartier	186	50.01 N	66.52 W
Port-Cartier Sept-Îles, Réserve ♠	186	50.35 N	67.10 W
Port Chalmers	172	45.49 S	170.37 E
Port Charlotte	220	26.58 N	82.05 W
Port Chester	210	41.00 N	73.39 W
Port Chester Harbor c	276	40.59 N	73.40 W
Port Chicago	226	38.03 N	122.01 W
Port Clements	182	53.42 N	132.11 W
Port Clinton, Austl.	168b	34.14 S	138.01 E
Port Clinton, Oh., U.S.	214	41.30 N	82.56 W
Port Clinton, Pa., U.S.	208	40.35 N	76.02 W
Port Clyde	188	43.55 N	69.15 W
Port Colborne	212	42.53 N	79.14 W
Port Colden	210	40.45 N	74.57 W
Port Columbus International Airport ⊠	218	40.00 N	82.53 W
Port Coquitlam	224	49.16 N	122.46 W
Port Costa	226	38.03 N	122.11 W
Port Crane	210	42.10 N	75.50 W
Port Credit	212	43.33 N	79.35 W
Port-Cros	62	43.00 N	6.23 E
Port-Cros, Île de I	62	43.00 N	6.24 E
Port-Cros, Parc National de ♠	62	43.01 N	6.24 E
Port-Daniel, Réserve ♠	186	48.18 N	64.55 W
Port-de-Bouc	62	43.24 N	4.59 E
Port-de-Paix	238	19.57 N	72.50 W
Port Deposit	208	39.36 N	76.06 W
Port Dickinson	210	42.08 N	75.53 W
Port Dickson	114	2.31 N	101.48 E
Porte Crayon, Mount ∧	188	38.56 N	79.27 W
Port Edward, B.C., Can.	182	54.14 N	130.18 W
Port Edward, S. Afr.	158	31.02 S	30.13 E
Port Edward → Weihai, Zhg.	98	37.28 N	122.07 E
Port Edwards	190	44.21 N	89.51 W
Portegolpe	236	10.20 N	85.46 W
Porteiras	250	7.31 S	39.07 W
Porteirinha	255	15.44 S	43.02 W
Portel, Bra.	250	1.57 S	50.49 W
Portel, Port.	34	38.18 N	7.42 W
Portela, Aeroporto da ⊠	266c	38.46 N	9.08 W
Port Elgin, N.B., Can.	186	46.03 N	64.05 W
Port Elgin, On., Can.	190	44.26 N	81.24 W
Port Elizabeth, St. Vin.	241h	13.03 N	61.13 W
Port Elizabeth, S. Afr.	158	33.58 S	25.40 E
Port Elizabeth, N.J., U.S.	208	39.18 N	74.58 W
Port Ellen	46	55.39 N	6.12 W
Port Elliot	168b	35.32 S	138.41 E
Port-en-Bessin	32	49.21 N	0.45 W
Porter, In., U.S.	216	41.36 N	87.04 W
Porter, Ok., U.S.	196	35.52 N	95.31 W
Porter, Tx., U.S.	222	30.06 N	95.14 W
Porter, Wa., U.S.	224	46.56 N	123.18 W
Porter □ [6]	216	41.28 N	87.04 W
Port'Ercole	66	42.23 N	11.12 E
Porter Corners	210	43.09 N	73.53 W
Porter Creek ≐	279a	41.41 N	81.56 W
Port Erin	44	54.06 N	4.44 W
Porter Lake ⊜	184	56.21 N	107.20 W
Porter Point ≻	241h	13.23 N	61.11 W
Porter Springs	222	31.16 N	95.36 W
Porters Retreat	170	34.00 S	149.48 E
Porters Run ≐	279b	40.27 N	79.33 W
Portersville	214	40.56 N	80.09 W
Porterville, S. Afr.	158	33.00 S	19.00 E
Porterville, Ca., U.S.	204	36.03 N	119.00 W
Porterville, Ms., U.S.	194	32.41 N	88.28 W
Portes-lès-Valence	62	44.52 N	4.53 E
Port Essington	182	54.09 N	129.57 W
Portete, Bahía c	246	12.13 N	71.55 W
Port-Étienne → Nouâdhibou	148	20.54 N	17.04 W
Port Ewen	210	41.54 N	73.58 W
Port-Eynon	42	51.33 N	4.13 W
Port-Eynon Point ≻	42	51.32 N	4.12 W
Portezuelo	234	20.25 N	102.31 W
Port Fairy	166	38.23 S	142.14 E
Port Fitzroy	172	36.10 S	175.21 E
Port Gamble	224	47.51 N	122.34 W
Port Gamble Indian Reservation ◆ [4]	224	47.53 N	122.34 W
Port Gentil	152	0.43 S	8.47 E
Port Germein	166	33.01 S	138.00 E
Port Gibson, Ms., U.S.	194	31.57 N	90.59 W
Port Gibson, N.Y., U.S.	210	43.02 N	77.09 W
Port Glasgow	46	55.57 N	4.41 W
Portglenone	48	54.52 N	6.29 W
Port Graham	180	59.21 N	151.50 W
Port Greville	186	45.24 N	64.33 W
Porth	42	51.38 N	3.25 W
Port Hacking	274a	34.04 S	151.08 E
Port Hacking Point ≻	170	34.05 S	151.10 E
Port Hammond	224	49.13 N	122.39 W
Port Harcourt	150	4.43 N	7.05 E
Port Hardy	182	50.43 N	127.29 W
Port Hawkesbury	186	45.37 N	61.21 W
Porthcawl	42	51.29 N	3.43 W
Port Hedland	162	20.19 S	118.34 E
Port Heiden	180	56.55 N	158.41 W
Port Henry	188	44.02 N	73.27 W
Port Hill	186	46.35 N	63.53 W
Porthleven	42	50.05 N	5.19 W
Porthmadog	42	52.55 N	4.08 W
Porth Neigwl c	42	52.48 N	4.34 W
Port Hood	186	46.01 N	61.32 W
Port Hope, On., Can.	212	43.57 N	78.18 W
Port Hope, Mi., U.S.	190	43.56 N	82.42 W
Port Howe	238	24.15 N	75.21 W
Port Hueneme	228	34.08 N	119.11 W
Port Hughes	168b	34.04 S	137.32 E
Port Huron	214	42.58 N	82.25 W
Portici	68	40.49 N	14.20 E
Portico di Romagna	66	44.01 N	11.47 E
Portigliola	68	38.14 N	16.13 E
Port-Il'ič	84	38.53 N	48.48 E
Portimão	34	37.08 N	8.32 W
Portinho, Rio do ≐	287a	23.03 S	43.35 W
Port Isaac	42	50.35 N	4.49 W
Port Isabel	196	26.04 N	97.12 W
Portishead	42	51.30 N	2.46 W
Port Jefferson, N.Y., U.S.	210	40.56 N	73.03 W
Port Jefferson, Oh., U.S.	216	40.19 N	84.05 W
Port Jefferson Harbor c	276	40.58 N	73.05 W
Port Jefferson Station	210	40.55 N	73.02 W
Port Jervis	210	41.22 N	74.41 W
Port Julia	168b	34.40 S	137.52 E
Port-Katon	83	46.52 N	38.46 E
Port Kembla	170	34.29 S	150.54 E
Port Kennedy	285	40.06 N	75.25 W
Port Kenny	162	33.10 S	134.42 E
Portknockie	46	57.41 N	2.51 W
Port Láirge → Waterford	48	52.15 N	7.06 W
Port Lambton	214	42.39 N	82.30 W
Portland, Austl.	166	38.21 S	141.36 E
Portland, Austl.	170	33.22 S	150.00 E
Portland, N.Z.	172	35.48 S	174.19 E
Portland, Ar., U.S.	194	33.14 N	91.30 W
Portland, Ct., U.S.	207	41.34 N	72.38 W
Portland, In., U.S.	216	40.26 N	84.58 W
Portland, Me., U.S.	188	43.39 N	70.15 W
Portland, Mi., U.S.	216	42.52 N	84.54 W
Portland, Mo., U.S.	219	38.42 N	91.43 W
Portland, N.Y., U.S.	214	42.22 N	79.28 W
Portland, N.D., U.S.	198	47.29 N	97.22 W
Portland, Or., U.S.	224	45.31 N	122.40 W
Portland, Pa., U.S.	210	40.55 N	75.06 W
Portland, Tn., U.S.	194	36.34 N	86.30 W
Portland, Tx., U.S.	196	27.52 N	97.19 W
Portland, Wi., U.S.	216	43.12 N	88.58 W
Portland, Bill of ≻	42	50.31 N	2.27 W
Portland, Cape ≻	166	40.45 S	147.57 E
Portland, Isle of I	42	50.33 N	2.27 W
Portland Bay c	166	38.19 S	141.47 E
Portland Bight c [3]	241q	17.53 N	77.08 W
Portland Canal c	182	55.10 N	130.08 W
Portland Creek Pond ⊜	186	50.12 N	57.34 W
Portland Inlet c	182	54.50 N	130.15 W
Portland International Airport ⊠	224	45.35 N	122.36 W
Portland Island I	172	39.17 S	177.52 E
Portland Mills	214	41.23 N	78.50 W
Portland Point ≻	241q	17.42 N	77.11 W
Portlandville	210	42.32 N	74.58 W
Port Laoise (Maryborough)	48	53.02 N	7.17 W
Port Lavaca	196	28.36 N	96.37 W
Portlaw	48	52.17 N	7.19 W
Port-Lesney	58	47.00 N	5.49 E
Portlethen	46	57.03 N	2.06 W
Port Leyden	212	43.35 N	75.21 W
Port Lincoln	166	34.44 S	135.52 E
Port Lions	180	57.52 N	152.53 W
Portlock Reefs ✢ [2]	164	9.30 S	144.45 E
Port Logan	44	54.43 N	4.56 W
Port Loko	150	8.46 N	12.47 W
Port-Louis Fr.	32	47.43 N	3.21 W
Port-Louis Guad.	241o	16.25 N	61.32 W
Port Louis Maus.	157c	20.10 S	57.30 E
Port Ludlow	224	47.55 N	122.40 W
Port-Lyautey → Kenitra	148	34.16 N	6.40 W
Port MacDonnell	166	38.03 S	140.42 E
Port Macquarie	166	31.26 S	152.55 E
Port Madison Indian Reservation ◆ [4]	224	47.45 N	122.35 W
Portmahomack	46	57.49 N	3.50 W
Port Maitland, N.S., Can.	186	43.59 N	66.09 W
Port Maitland, On., Can.	214	42.52 N	79.34 W
Port Maria	241q	18.22 N	76.54 W
Portmarnock	48	53.25 N	6.08 W
Port Matilda	214	40.48 N	78.03 W
Port Mayaca	220	27.08 N	80.12 W
Port McNeill	182	50.35 N	127.06 W
Port McNicoll	212	44.45 N	79.49 W
Port Melbourne	274b	37.51 S	144.56 E
Port Mellon	182	49.32 N	123.29 W
Port-Menier	186	49.48 N	64.20 W
Port Moller	180	55.59 N	160.34 W
Port Monmouth	276	40.25 N	74.05 W
Port Moody	224	49.17 N	122.51 W
Port Morant	241q	17.54 N	76.19 W
Portmore	241q	17.58 N	76.53 W
Port Moresby	164	9.30 S	147.10 E
Port Moresby □ [5]	164	9.30 S	147.10 E
Port Morien	186	46.08 N	59.52 W
Port Morris	276	40.54 N	74.41 W
Port Mouton	186	43.56 N	64.51 W
Port Murray	210	40.47 N	74.54 W
Portnaguran	46	58.17 N	6.13 W
Portnahaven	46	55.41 N	6.31 W
Port Neches	194	29.59 N	93.57 W
Port Neill	166	34.07 S	136.20 E
Port Nelson	184	57.03 N	92.36 W
Portneuf	206	46.42 N	71.53 W
Portneuf □ [6]	206	46.45 N	72.00 W
Portneuf ≐, P.Q., Can.	186	48.38 N	69.05 W
Portneuf ≐, P.Q., Can.	206	46.42 N	71.53 W
Portneuf ≐, Id., U.S.	202	42.58 N	112.35 W
Portneuf, Lac ⊜	186	49.08 N	70.18 W
Portneuf-Station	206	46.43 N	71.54 W
Portneuf-sur-Mer	186	48.37 N	69.06 W
Port Neville	182	50.29 N	126.05 W
Port Noarlunga	168b	35.09 S	138.28 E
Port Nolloth	156	29.17 S	16.51 E
Port Norris	208	39.14 N	75.02 W
Porto, Bra.	250	3.54 S	42.42 W
Porto, Port.	34	41.11 N	8.36 W
Porto, Bonifica di ◆ [1]	267a	41.48 N	12.16 E
Porto Acre	248	9.34 S	67.31 W
Porto Alegre, Bra.	252	30.04 S	51.11 W
Porto Alegre, S. Tom./P.	152	0.02 N	6.32 E
Porto Amboim	152	10.44 S	13.44 E
Porto Azzurro	66	42.46 N	10.24 E
Portobello	46	55.58 N	3.07 W
Porto Belo, Bra.	252	27.10 S	48.33 W
Portobelo, Pan.	236	9.33 N	79.39 W
Porto Calvo	250	9.04 S	35.24 W
Porto Ceresio	58	45.54 N	8.55 E
Port O'Connor	196	28.27 N	96.24 W
Porto das Caixas	256	22.42 S	42.53 W
Porto d'Ascoli	66	42.55 N	13.53 E
Porto das Flôres	256	22.05 S	43.34 W
Porto das Gabarras	250	3.07 S	44.34 W
Pôrto de Mós	34	39.36 N	8.39 W
Porto de Moz	250	1.45 S	52.14 W
Porto de Pedras	250	9.10 S	35.17 W
Porto di Potenza Picena	66	43.21 N	13.42 E
Porto di Traiano, Necropoli del ⊥	267a	41.46 N	12.16 E
Porto dos Gaúchos	250	11.29 S	57.22 W
Porto Empedocle	70	37.17 N	13.32 E
Porto Esperança	248	19.37 S	57.27 W
Porto Esperidião	248	15.51 S	58.28 W
Porto Farina	36	37.10 N	10.12 E
Porto Feliz	255	23.13 S	47.32 W
Portoferraio	66	42.49 N	10.19 E
Porto Ferreira	255	21.51 S	47.28 W
Portofino	62	44.18 N	9.12 E
Port of Ness	46	58.29 N	6.13 W
Porto Franco	250	6.20 S	47.24 W
Port of Spain	241r	10.39 N	61.31 W
Porto Garibaldi	66	44.41 N	12.14 E
Porto Grande	250	0.42 N	51.24 W
Portogruaro	64	45.47 N	12.50 E
Porto Inglês	150a	15.08 N	23.13 W
Portola	204	39.48 N	120.28 W
Portola State Park ♠	226	37.15 N	122.13 W
Portola Valley	226	37.23 N	122.13 W
Porto Lucena	252	27.51 S	55.01 W
Pörtom (Pirttikylä)	26	62.42 N	21.37 E
Portomaggiore	64	44.42 N	11.48 E
Porto Maurizio	62	43.52 N	8.01 E
Porto Mendes	252	24.30 S	54.20 W
Porto Murtinho	248	21.42 S	57.52 W
Porto Nacional	250	10.42 S	48.25 W
Porto-Novo, Bénin	150	6.29 N	2.37 E
Porto Novo, Bra.	256	23.40 S	45.28 W
Porto Novo, India	122	11.29 N	79.46 E
Porto Novo Creek c	273a	6.26 N	3.20 E
Portopalo, It.	70	36.41 N	15.08 E
Porto Palo, It.	70	37.34 N	12.54 E
Port Orange	192	29.06 N	80.59 W
Port Orchard	224	47.32 N	122.38 W
Porto Real	256	22.25 S	44.20 W
Porto Real do Colégio	250	10.11 S	36.49 W
Porto Recanati	66	43.26 N	13.40 E
Port Orford	202	42.44 N	124.29 W
Porto Rico	152	6.08 S	12.30 E
Porto Rico → Puerto Rico □ [2]	240m	18.15 N	66.30 W
Portorož	64	45.31 N	13.36 E
Porto Salvo	266c	38.43 N	9.18 W
Porto San Giorgio	66	43.11 N	13.48 E
Porto Santana	250	0.03 S	51.11 W
Porto Sant'Elpidio	66	43.15 N	13.45 E
Porto Santo I	148	33.04 N	16.20 W
Porto Santo Stefano	66	42.26 N	11.07 E
Porto São José	255	22.43 S	53.10 W
Portoscuso	71	39.12 N	8.23 E
Porto Seguro, Bra.	255	16.26 S	39.05 W
Porto-Séguro, Togo	150	6.12 N	1.29 E
Porto Torres	71	40.50 N	8.24 E
Porto União	252	26.15 S	51.05 W
Porto Válter	248	8.15 S	72.45 W
Porto Valtravaglia	58	45.58 N	8.41 E
Porto-Vecchio	36	41.35 N	9.16 E
Porto Velho	248	8.46 S	63.54 W
Porto Velho do Cunha	256	21.50 S	42.32 W
Portovenere	62	44.03 N	9.51 E
Portoviejo	246	1.03 S	80.27 W
Portpatrick, Scot., U.K.	44	54.51 N	5.07 W
Port Patrick, Vanuatu	175f	20.08 S	169.47 E
Port Penn	208	39.31 N	75.34 W
Port Perry	212	44.06 N	78.57 W
Port Phillip Bay c	169	38.07 S	144.48 E
Port Pirie	166	33.11 S	138.01 E
Port Providence	285	40.08 N	75.30 W
Portraine	48	53.30 N	6.07 W
Port Reading	276	40.33 N	74.15 W
Portree	46	57.24 N	6.12 W
Port Renfrew	224	48.33 N	124.25 W
Port Republic	208	39.31 N	74.29 W
Port Rexton	186	48.23 N	53.20 W
Port Richey	220	28.16 N	82.43 W
Port Richmond	208	37.33 N	76.49 W
Port Robinson	284a	43.02 N	79.13 W
Port Rowan	214	42.37 N	80.28 W
Port Royal, Jam.	241q	17.56 N	76.51 W
Port Royal, Ky., U.S.	218	38.33 N	85.04 W
Port Royal, Pa., U.S.	208	40.32 N	77.23 W
Port Royal, S.C., U.S.	192	32.22 N	80.41 W
Port Royal, Va., U.S.	208	38.10 N	77.11 W
Port-Royal-des-Champs, Abbaye de ʋ [1]	261	48.45 N	2.01 E
Port Royal National Historic Park ♠	186	44.44 N	65.40 W
Portrush	48	55.12 N	6.40 W
Port Said → Būr Sa'īd	142	31.16 N	32.18 E
Port-Sainte-Marie	32	44.15 N	0.24 E
Port Saint Joe	192	29.49 N	85.18 W
Port Saint Johns	158	31.38 S	29.33 E
Port-Saint-Louis	62	43.23 N	4.48 E
Port Saint Lucie	220	27.20 N	80.20 W
Port Saint Mary	44	54.05 N	4.43 W
Port-Saint-Servan	186	51.19 N	58.02 W
Port Salerno	220	27.08 N	80.12 W
Portsalon	48	55.13 N	7.37 W
Port Sanilac	190	43.25 N	82.32 W
Port Saunders	186	50.39 N	57.18 W
Pörtschach	61	46.37 N	14.08 E
Portsea	169	38.19 S	144.43 E
Port Seton	46	55.58 N	2.57 W
Port Shepstone	158	30.46 S	30.22 E
Portslade	42	50.50 N	0.11 W
Portsmouth, Dom.	240d	15.35 N	61.28 W
Portsmouth, Eng., U.K.	42	50.48 N	1.05 W
Portsmouth, N.H., U.S.	188	43.04 N	70.45 W
Portsmouth, Oh., U.S.	218	38.43 N	82.59 W
Portsmouth, R.I., U.S.	207	41.36 N	71.15 W
Portsmouth, Va., U.S.	208	36.50 N	76.17 W
Portsmouth Naval Shipyard ■	188	43.05 N	70.45 W
Portsoy	46	57.41 N	2.41 W
Port Stanley, On., Can.	214	42.40 N	81.13 W
Port Stanley → Stanley, Falk. Is.	254	51.42 S	57.51 W
Portstewart	48	55.11 N	6.43 W
Port Sudan → Būr Sūdān	140	19.37 N	37.14 E
Port Sulphur	194	29.28 N	89.41 W
Port Sunlight	262	53.21 N	2.59 W
Port-sur-Saône	58	47.41 N	6.03 E
Port Talbot	42	51.36 N	3.47 W
Port Taufiq → Būr Tawfīq	128	29.57 N	32.34 E
Porttipahdan tekojärvi ⊜ [1]	24	68.08 N	26.40 E
Port Tobacco River c	208	38.27 N	77.02 W
Port Townsend	224	48.07 N	122.45 W
Port Trevorton	208	40.42 N	76.52 W
Portugal □ [1], Europe	22	39.30 N	8.00 W
Portugal □ [1], Europe	34	39.30 N	8.00 W
Portugal, Cachoeira ʟ	248	9.55 S	64.16 W
Portugal Cove South	186	46.42 N	53.15 W
Portugalete	34	43.19 N	3.01 W
Portuguesa □ [3]	246	9.10 N	69.15 W
Portuguesa ≐	246	7.57 N	67.32 W
Portuguese Guinea → Guinea-Bissau □ [1]	150	12.00 N	15.00 W
Portumna	48	53.06 N	8.13 W
Port Union, Nf., Can.	186	48.30 N	53.05 W
Port Union, On., Can.	275b	43.47 N	79.08 W
Port-Vendres	32	42.31 N	3.07 E
Port Victoria → Victoria	138	4.38 S	55.27 E
Port Vila	175f	17.44 S	168.19 E
Portville	210	42.02 N	78.20 W
Port Vincent	168b	34.47 S	137.51 E
Port-Vladimir	24	69.25 N	33.06 E
Port Vue	279b	40.20 N	79.52 W
Port Waikato	172	37.23 S	174.44 E
Port Wakefield, Austl.	168b	34.11 S	138.09 E
Port Wakefield, Ak., U.S.	180	58.03 N	153.03 W
Port Washington, B.C., Can.	224	48.49 N	123.19 W
Port Washington, N.Y., U.S.	210	40.49 N	73.41 W
Port Washington, Oh., U.S.	214	40.27 N	81.37 W
Port Washington, Wi., U.S.	190	43.23 N	87.52 W
Port Weld	114	4.50 N	100.38 E
Port Welshpool	169	38.42 S	146.28 E
Port Wentworth	192	32.08 N	81.09 W
Port William, Scot., U.K.	44	54.46 N	4.35 W
Port William, Oh., U.S.	218	39.33 N	83.47 W
Port Wing	190	46.46 N	91.23 W
Porum	196	35.21 N	95.15 W
Porus	241q	18.02 N	77.25 W
Porvenir, Chile	254	53.18 S	70.22 W
Porvenir, Méx.	232	31.15 N	105.51 W
Porvoo (Borgå)	26	60.24 N	25.40 E
Porvoonjoki ≐	26	60.23 N	25.40 E
Porz	56	50.53 N	7.03 E
Porzdni	80	57.00 N	42.33 E
Porzuna	34	39.09 N	4.09 W
Posada	71	40.38 N	9.43 E
Posada ≐	71	40.39 N	9.45 E
Posadas, Arg.	252	27.23 S	55.53 W
Posadas, Esp.	34	37.48 N	5.06 W
Posavina V	36	45.10 N	17.20 E
Pošcharv	85	38.24 N	71.10 E
Poschiavino ≐	58	46.12 N	10.10 E
Poschiavo	58	46.18 N	10.04 E
Pošechon'e	76	58.30 N	39.07 E
Posen → Poznań, Pol.	30	52.25 N	16.55 E
Posen, Il., U.S.	278	41.37 N	87.40 W
Posen, Mi., U.S.	190	45.15 N	83.41 W
Poseritz	54	54.18 N	13.16 E
Posesión, Bahía c	254	52.17 S	69.14 W
Posevnaja	86	54.18 N	83.20 E
Poshan → Boshan	98	36.29 N	117.50 E
Poshiwu	106	30.22 N	119.36 E
Posieux	58	46.46 N	7.06 E
Posina	64	45.47 N	11.15 E
Pösing	60	49.14 N	12.33 E
Posio	26	66.06 N	28.09 E
Positano	68	40.38 N	14.29 E
Posjet	89	42.39 N	130.50 E
Poso	112	1.23 S	120.44 E
Poso, Danau ⊜	112	1.52 S	120.35 E
Poso, Teluk c	112	1.15 S	120.55 E
Poso Creek ≐	226	35.41 N	119.22 W
Posof	130	41.31 N	42.42 E
Pos'olki	80	53.08 N	46.29 E
Pos'olok	265a	59.43 N	30.12 E
Posŏng	98	34.47 N	127.04 E
Posooy, Mount ∧	116	17.21 N	120.48 E
Pospelicha	86	51.57 N	81.46 E
Possagno	64	45.51 N	11.51 E
Posse, Bra.	255	14.05 S	46.22 W
Posse, Bra.	256	22.16 S	43.06 W
Possel	152	5.01 N	19.15 E
Possendorf	54	50.57 N	13.42 E
Posses	256	21.43 S	46.08 W
Possession Islands II	9	71.27 S	171.08 E
Possession Sound ʊ	224	48.00 N	122.20 W
Possidhonia ⊥	38	37.40 N	24.00 E
Pössneck	54	50.42 N	11.37 E
Possruck (Kozjak) ⋏	61	46.37 N	15.28 E
Possum Kingdom Lake ⊜ [1]	196	32.55 N	98.28 W
Post	196	33.11 N	101.22 W
Posta	66	42.31 N	13.06 E
Postal (Burgstall)	64	46.36 N	11.11 E
Postau	60	48.39 N	12.20 E
Postavy	76	55.07 N	26.50 E
Postbauer	60	49.19 N	11.21 E
Post Creek ≐	210	42.09 N	77.02 W
Poste-de-la-Baleine	176	55.17 N	77.45 W
Postelle	192	35.02 N	84.22 W
Poste Ramartina	157b	19.38 S	45.58 E
Posterholt	52	51.07 N	6.03 E
Post Falls	202	47.43 N	116.57 W
Postiglione	68	40.33 N	15.13 E
Postmasburg	158	28.18 S	23.05 E
Postojna	36	45.47 N	14.13 E
Postojnska jama ⊥ [7]	36	45.47 N	14.12 E
Postoloprty	54	50.20 N	13.40 E
P'ostraja Dresva	74	61.34 N	156.41 E
Postrevalle	248	18.29 S	63.51 W
Postsee ⊜	54	54.13 N	10.13 E
Poststadion ♠	264a	52.32 N	13.21 E
Postville	190	43.05 N	91.34 W
Pota	115b	8.20 S	120.46 E
Potaizi	104	41.34 N	121.08 E
Potake Pond ⊜	276	41.08 N	74.13 W
Pótam	232	27.36 N	110.23 W
Potanino	76	60.16 N	32.47 E
Potaro ≐	246	5.22 N	58.54 W
Potaro Landing	246	5.23 N	59.08 W
Potaro-Siparuni □ [4]	246	5.00 N	59.30 W
Potato Creek ≐, Ga., U.S.	192	32.47 N	84.21 W
Potato Creek ≐, Pa., U.S.	214	41.53 N	78.23 W
Potawatomie Woods ♠	278	42.08 N	87.53 W
Potchefstroom	158	26.46 S	27.01 E
Poté	255	17.49 S	41.49 W
Poteau	194	35.03 N	94.37 W
Poteau ≐	194	35.23 N	94.26 W
Poteet	196	29.02 N	98.34 W
Potengi ≐	250	5.47 S	35.16 W
Pötenitz	54	53.57 N	10.58 E
Pötenitzer Wiek c	54	53.55 N	10.55 E
Potenji	250	7.06 S	40.00 W
Potenza	68	40.38 N	15.49 E
Potenza □ [4]	68	40.30 N	15.50 E
Potenza ≐	66	43.25 N	13.40 E
Potenza Picena	66	43.22 N	13.37 E
Poteriteri, Lake ⊜	172	46.06 S	167.08 E
Potes	34	43.09 N	4.37 W
Potfontein	158	30.12 S	24.08 E
Potgietersrus	156	24.15 S	28.55 E
Poth	196	29.04 N	98.05 W
Potholes Reservoir ⊜ [1]	202	47.01 N	119.19 W
Poti	84	42.09 N	41.40 E
Poti ≐	250	5.02 S	42.50 W
Potic Creek ≐	210	42.16 N	73.55 W
Potijevka	78	50.37 N	28.58 E
Potiraguá	255	15.36 S	39.53 W
Potirendaba	255	21.08 S	49.08 W
Potiskum	146	11.43 N	11.05 E
Potlatch	202	46.55 N	116.53 W
Potlatch ≐	202	46.28 N	116.46 W
Po Toi Island I	271d	22.10 N	114.15 E
Po Toi Island Group II	271d	22.11 N	114.16 E
Potol Point ≻	116	11.56 N	121.57 E
Potomac, Il., U.S.	216	40.18 N	87.48 W
Potomac, Md., U.S.	284c	39.01 N	77.12 W
Potomac ≐	188	38.00 N	76.18 W
Potomac, South Branch ≐	188	39.31 N	78.35 W

Symbol	English	Deutsch	Español	Français	Português
≐	River	Fluß	Río	Rivière	Rio
≚	Canal	Kanal	Canal	Canal	Canal
ʟ	Waterfall, Rapids	Wasserfall, Stromschnellen	Cascada, Rápidos	Chute d'eau, Rapides	Cascata, Rápidos
ʊ	Strait	Meeresstraße	Estrecho	Détroit	Estreito
c	Bay, Gulf	Bucht, Golf	Bahía, Golfo	Baie, Golfe	Baía, Golfo
⊜	Lake, Lakes	See, Seen	Lago, Lagos	Lac, Lacs	Lago, Lagos
⩸	Swamp	Sumpf	Pantano	Marais	Pântano
⍓	Ice Features, Glacier	Eis- und Gletscherformen	Accidentes Glaciales	Formes glaciaires	Acidentes glaciares
⫪	Other Hydrographic Features	Andere Hydrographische Objekte	Otros Elementos Hidrográficos	Autres données hydrographiques	Outros acidentes hidrográficos
✢	Submarine Features	Untermeerische Objekte	Accidentes Submarinos	Formes de relief sous-marin	Acidentes submarinos
□	Political Unit	Politische Einheit	Unidad Politica	Entité politique	Unidade política
ʋ	Cultural Institution	Kulturelle Institution	Institución Cultural	Institution culturelle	Instituição cultural
⊥	Historical Site	Historische Stätte	Sitio Histórico	Site historique	Sitio histórico
♠	Recreational Site	Erholungs- und Ferienort	Sitio de Recreo	Centre de loisirs	Area de Lazer
⊠	Airport	Flughafen	Aeropuerto	Aéroport	Aeroporto
■	Military Installation	Militäranlage	Instalación Militar	Installation militaire	Instalação militar
◆	Miscellaneous	Verschiedenes	Misceláneo	Divers	Diversos

I · *140* **Poto-Prit**

ENGLISH — Name | Page | Lat.°′ | Long.°′
DEUTSCH — Name | Seite | Breite°′ | Länge°′ E = Ost

Potomac, South Branch, North Fork ≃ **188** 38.59 N 79.11 W
Potomac, South Branch, South Fork ≃ **188** 39.04 N 78.59 W
Potomac Creek ≃ **208** 38.21 N 77.18 W
Potomac Creek, Long Branch ≃ **208** 38.23 N 77.29 W
Potomac Heights **208** 38.36 N 77.08 W
Poto-Poto ✦[8] **273b** 4.15 S 15.18 E
Potosí, Bol. **248** 19.35 S 65.45 W
Potosi, Mo., U.S. **194** 37.56 N 90.47 W
Potosí □[5] **248** 20.40 S 67.00 W
Pototan **116** 10.55 N 122.40 E
Potrerillos, Chile **252** 26.26 S 69.29 W
Potrerillos, Hond. **236** 15.11 N 87.58 W
Potrerillos Arriba **236** 8.41 N 82.30 W
Potrero **236** 10.28 N 85.47 W
Potrero ✦[8] **282** 37.48 N 122.24 W
Potrero de Gallegos **234** 22.38 N 103.41 W
Potrero del Llano **196** 29.12 N 104.28 W
Potrero Grande **236** 9.00 N 83.11 W
Potrite **248** 61.32 S 16.10 W
Potro, Cerro del ∧ **252** 28.24 S 69.39 W
Potsdam, Dtsch. **54** 52.24 N 13.04 E
Potsdam, N.Y., U.S. **188** 44.40 N 74.58 W
Potsdam, Oh., U.S. **218** 39.58 N 84.25 W
Potsdam, Staatsforst ♦ **264a** 52.26 N 13.04 E
Potshausen **52** 53.11 N 7.37 E
Pott, Île I **175f** 19.35 S 163.36 E
Pottawatomie Creek ≃ **198** 38.29 N 94.55 W
Pottawatomi Indian Reservation ✦[4] **198** 39.20 N 95.50 W
Pottendorf **61** 47.55 N 16.23 E
Potten End **260** 51.46 N 0.31 W
Pottenhofen **61** 48.46 N 16.33 E
Pottenstein **60** 49.46 N 11.25 E
Potter **198** 41.13 N 103.18 W
Potter □[6] **214** 41.47 N 78.01 W
Potter Hollow **210** 42.25 N 74.13 W
Potter Lake **216** 42.50 N 88.21 W
Potter Point › **274a** 34.03 S 151.13 E
Potters Bar **42** 51.42 N 0.11 W
Potters Mills **208** 40.48 N 77.32 W
Potter Street **260** 51.46 N 0.08 E
Pottersville **276** 40.42 N 74.43 W
Potterville **216** 42.38 N 84.45 W
Pöttmes **60** 48.35 N 11.06 E
Potton **42** 52.08 N 0.14 W
Potts Camp **194** 34.38 N 89.18 W
Potts Creek ≃ **192** 37.45 N 80.00 W
Potts Grove **210** 41.00 N 76.48 W
Potts Hill Reservoirs ⊜[1] **274a** 33.54 S 151.02 E
Pott Shrigley **262** 53.19 N 2.05 W
Pottstown **208** 40.14 N 75.39 W
Pottstown Landing **285** 40.14 N 75.40 W
Pottstown Limerick Airport ⊠ **285** 40.14 N 75.34 W
Pottstown Municipal Airport ⊠ **285** 40.16 N 75.40 W
Pottsville **208** 40.41 N 76.11 W
Potwin **198** 37.56 N 97.01 W
Pötzleinsdorf ✦[8] **264b** 48.15 N 16.19 E
Pötzleinsdorfer Park ♦ **264b** 48.14 N 16.18 E
P'otzu **100** 23.28 N 120.14 E
Pouancé **32** 47.44 N 1.11 W
Pouce-Coupe **182** 55.43 N 120.08 W
Pouce Coupé ≃ **182** 56.08 N 119.52 W
Pouch **54** 51.37 N 12.24 E
Pouch Cove **186** 47.46 N 52.46 W
Pouembout **175f** 21.08 S 164.53 E
Poughkeepsie **210** 41.42 N 73.55 W
Poughquag **210** 41.37 N 73.41 W
Pouilly-en-Auxois **58** 47.16 N 4.33 E
Pouilly-sur-Loire **50** 47.17 N 2.57 E
Pouilly-sur-Meuse **56** 49.32 N 5.07 E
Poulain, Étang ⊜ **261** 48.43 N 1.44 E
Poulan **192** 31.30 N 83.47 W
Poulaphouca Reservoir ⊜[1] **48** 53.08 N 6.31 W
Poulin-de-Courval, Lac ⊜ **186** 48.52 N 70.27 W
Poulsbo **224** 47.44 N 122.38 W
Poulter, Lac ⊜ **190** 47.07 N 76.45 W
Poultney **188** 43.31 N 73.14 W
Poulton-le-Fylde **44** 53.51 N 2.59 W
Poum **175f** 20.14 S 164.02 E
Poŭn **98** 36.29 N 127.43 E
Pound **192** 37.07 N 82.36 W
Poundmaker Indian Reserve ✦[4] **184** 52.51 N 109.00 W
Poundstock **42** 50.46 N 4.33 W
Pouoanuu, Mont ∧ **174x** 9.49 S 139.07 W
Pourri, Mont ∧ **62** 45.32 N 6.52 E
Pouru-Saint-Rémy **56** 49.41 N 5.05 E
Pourville-sur-Mer **50** 49.55 N 1.02 E
Pouso Alegre **256** 22.13 S 45.56 W
Pouso Alto **256** 22.11 S 44.58 W
Pouso Redondo **252** 27.15 S 49.57 W
Pouso Sêco **256** 22.41 S 44.10 W
Pouss **146** 10.51 N 15.03 E
Poutasi **175a** 14.01 S 171.41 W
Poŭthĭsăt **110** 12.32 N 103.55 E
Poŭthĭsăt ≃ **110** 12.41 N 104.09 E
Pouxeux **58** 48.06 N 6.34 E
Pouzauges **32** 46.47 N 0.50 W
Považská Bystrica **30** 49.08 N 18.27 E
Povenec **24** 62.51 N 34.45 E
Poverello, Monte ∧ **70** 38.05 N 15.22 E
Poverennyj **80** 46.45 N 43.12 E
Poverty Bay ⊂ **172** 38.42 S 177.58 E
Povetkino **82** 54.20 N 38.23 E
Poviglio **64** 44.51 N 10.32 E
Povljen ⋏ **38** 43.55 N 19.30 E
Póvoa, Mouchão da I **266c** 38.51 N 9.03 W
Povoação **148a** 37.45 N 25.15 W
Póvoa de Santa Iria **266c** 38.52 N 9.04 W
Póvoa de Santo Adrião **266c** 38.48 N 9.10 W
Póvoa de Varzim **34** 41.23 N 8.46 W
Povorino **80** 51.12 N 42.14 E
Povorotnyj, mys › **89** 42.42 N 133.04 E
Povorsk **78** 51.16 N 25.07 E
Povrly **54** 50.40 N 14.10 E
Povungnituk **176** 60.02 N 77.10 W
Povungnituk, Rivière de ≃ **176** 60.03 N 77.15 W
Powassan **190** 46.05 N 79.22 W
Poway **228** 32.57 N 117.02 W
Powder ≃, U.S. **178** 46.44 N 105.26 W
Powder ≃, Or., U.S. **202** 44.45 N 117.03 W
Powder, Dry Fork ≃ **200** 43.47 N 106.15 W
Powder, Middle Fork ≃ **200** 43.42 N 106.33 W
Powder, North Fork ≃ **202** 43.42 N 106.33 W
Powder, Red Fork ≃ **202** 43.39 N 106.47 W
Powder, South Fork ≃ **202** 43.40 N 106.30 W
Powder Horn Lake ⊜ **278** 41.38 N 87.32 W
Powderly, Ky., U.S. **194** 37.09 N 87.10 W
Powderly, Tx., U.S. **196** 33.49 N 95.31 W
Powdermaker Ditch ≊ **279a** 41.30 N 82.02 W
Powder Mill Village **284c** 39.03 N 76.57 W
Powder River Pass)(**202** 44.09 N 107.04 W
Powell, Oh., U.S. **214** 40.09 N 83.05 W
Powell, Pa., U.S. **210** 41.42 N 76.31 W
Powell, Tx., U.S. **222** 32.07 N 96.20 W
Powell, Wy., U.S. **202** 44.45 N 108.45 W
Powell ≃ **192** 36.29 N 83.42 W
Powell, Lake ⊜[1] **200** 37.25 N 110.45 W
Powell, Mount ∧ **200** 39.46 N 106.20 W
Powell Creek ≃, Austl. **166** 25.02 S 143.40 E
Powell Creek ≃, Oh., U.S. **216** 41.17 N 84.21 W
Powellhurst **224** 45.30 N 122.32 W
Powell Lake ⊜ **182** 50.11 N 124.24 W
Powell River **182** 49.52 N 124.33 W
Powells Valley **208** 40.26 N 76.56 W
Powellton **188** 38.05 N 81.19 W
Powellville **208** 38.19 N 75.22 W
Powers, Mi., U.S. **190** 45.41 N 87.31 W
Powers, Or., U.S. **202** 42.53 N 124.04 W
Powers Lake, N.D., U.S. **198** 48.33 N 102.38 W
Powers Lake, Wi., U.S. **216** 42.33 N 88.17 W
Powers Lookout ♦ **169** 36.50 S 146.22 E
Powhatan, La., U.S. **194** 31.52 N 93.12 W
Powhatan, Va., U.S. **192** 37.32 N 77.55 W
Powhatan Mill **284b** 39.20 N 76.43 W
Powhatan Point **188** 39.51 N 80.48 W
Powis, Vale of V **42** 52.38 N 3.08 W
Powissett Brook ≃ **283** 42.16 N 71.14 W
Powlett ≃ **169** 38.35 S 145.32 E
Pownal **210** 42.45 N 73.14 W
Powys □[6] **42** 52.17 N 3.20 W
Poxoréo **255** 15.50 S 54.23 W
Poya **175f** 21.19 S 165.07 E
Poyang Hu ⊜ **100** 29.00 N 116.25 E
Poyan Reservoir ⊜[1] **271c** 1.23 N 103.40 E
Poyen **194** 34.19 N 92.38 W
Poygan, Lake ⊜ **190** 44.09 N 88.50 W
Poyle **260** 51.28 N 0.31 W
Poynette **190** 43.23 N 89.24 W
Poynor **222** 32.04 N 95.36 W
Poynton **44** 53.21 N 2.07 W
Poyntz Pass **48** 54.18 N 6.23 W
Poyraz ✦[8] **267b** 41.12 N 29.07 E
Poyraz Burnu › **267b** 41.12 N 29.08 E
Poysdorf **61** 48.40 N 16.38 E
Pozantı **130** 37.25 N 34.52 E
Požarevac **38** 44.37 N 21.11 E
Poza Rica **234** 20.33 N 97.27 W
Požarskoje **89** 46.16 N 134.04 E
Pozdejevka **89** 50.36 N 128.56 E
Požega **38** 43.50 N 20.02 E
Poznań **30** 52.25 N 16.55 E
Poznań □[4] **30** 52.20 N 16.55 E
Pozo Alcón **34** 37.42 N 2.56 W
Pozo Almonte **248** 20.16 S 69.48 W
Pozoblanco **34** 38.22 N 4.51 W
Pozo-Cañada **34** 38.48 N 1.45 W
Pozo Colorado **252** 23.28 S 58.51 W
Pozo del Molle **252** 32.02 S 62.55 W
Pozo del Tigre **252** 24.54 S 60.19 W
Pozo Hondo **252** 27.10 S 64.30 W
Pozos, Punta › **254** 47.57 S 65.47 W
Pozsony → Bratislava **30** 48.09 N 17.07 E
Pozuelo de Alarcón, Esp. **34** 40.26 N 3.49 W
Pozuelo de Alarcón, Esp. **266a** 40.26 N 3.49 W
Pozuelos **246** 10.11 N 64.39 W
Pozuelos, Laguna ⊜ **252** 22.22 S 66.01 W
Pozuzo **248** 10.04 S 75.32 W
Pozuzo ≃ **248** 9.52 S 75.12 W
Požva **86** 59.05 N 56.05 E
Pozzallo **70** 36.43 N 14.51 E
Pozzillo, Lago di ⊜ **70** 37.40 N 14.35 E
Pozzolo Formigaro **62** 44.48 N 8.47 E
Pozzomaggiore **71** 40.24 N 8.39 E
Pozzuoli **68** 40.49 N 14.07 E
Pozzuolo del Friuli **64** 45.59 N 13.12 E
Pra ≃, Ghana **150** 5.01 N 1.37 W
Pra ≃, Ross. **80** 54.45 N 41.01 E
Prabuty **30** 53.46 N 19.10 E
Praça Cruzeiro **256** 22.43 S 42.38 W
Praça Sêca ✦[8] **287a** 22.54 S 43.21 W
Prachatice **30** 49.01 N 14.00 E
Prachin Buri **110** 14.03 N 101.22 E
Prachuap Khiri Khan **110** 11.49 N 99.48 E
Prackenbach **60** 49.06 N 12.50 E
Pracuí ≃ **250** 2.26 S 51.19 W
Pracupi ≃ **250** 2.06 S 51.30 W
Pradelles **62** 44.46 N 3.53 E
Pradera **246** 3.25 N 76.15 W
Prades **32** 42.37 N 2.26 E
Pradleves **62** 44.25 N 7.17 E
Prado **255** 17.21 S 39.13 W
Prado, Museo del ʊ **266a** 40.25 N 3.41 W
Prado Dam ✦[6] **280** 33.54 N 117.39 W
Prado Flood Control Basin ≚[1] **280** 33.54 N 117.38 W
Prados **255** 21.03 S 44.05 W
Pr'adovka **78** 48.55 N 34.41 E
Prads **62** 44.13 N 6.27 E
Præstø **41** 55.07 N 12.03 E
Prag → Praha **54** 50.05 N 14.26 E
Praga → Praha **54** 50.05 N 14.26 E
Pragelato **62** 45.01 N 6.57 E
Pragersko **61** 46.23 N 15.40 E
Praglia, Monastero di ʊ[1] **64** 45.23 N 11.45 E
Prägraten **64** 47.01 N 12.23 E
Prague → Praha, Česká Rep. **54** 50.05 N 14.26 E
Prague, Ne., U.S. **198** 41.18 N 96.48 W
Prague, Ok., U.S. **196** 35.29 N 96.41 W
Praha (Prague) **54** 50.05 N 14.26 E
Praha ∧ **60** 49.40 N 13.49 E
Prahova □[6] **38** 45.00 N 26.00 E
Prahova ≃ **38** 44.43 N 26.27 E
Prahran **274b** 37.51 S 144.59 E
Praia **150a** 14.55 N 23.31 W
Praia a Mare **68** 39.54 N 15.47 E
Praia da Cruz Quebrada **266c** 38.42 N 9.14 W
Praia da Enseada **256** 23.29 S 45.05 W
Praia das Maçãs **266c** 38.50 N 9.28 W
Praia da Vitória **148a** 38.44 N 27.04 W
Praia de Araçatiba **256** 23.15 S 44.21 W
Praia Funda, Ponta da › **287a** 23.05 S 43.33 W
Praia Grande, Bra. **252** 29.12 S 49.57 W
Praia Grande, Bra. **256** 24.01 S 46.25 W
Praiano **68** 40.37 N 14.32 E
Praikalogu **115b** 9.45 S 119.25 E
Prainha **250** 1.48 S 53.29 W
Prainha Nova **248** 7.16 S 60.23 W
Prairie **166** 20.52 S 144.36 E
Prairie ≃, Mi., U.S. **216** 41.55 N 85.38 W
Prairie ≃, Mn., U.S. **190** 47.18 N 93.29 W
Prairie ≃, Wi., U.S. **190** 45.10 N 89.42 W
Prairie City, Il., U.S. **190** 40.37 N 90.28 W
Prairie City, Ia., U.S. **190** 41.35 N 93.14 W
Prairie City, Or., U.S. **202** 44.27 N 118.42 W
Prairie Creek ≃, Fl., U.S. **220** 26.59 N 81.56 W
Prairie Creek ≃, Il., U.S. **216** 41.21 N 88.12 W
Prairie Creek ≃, Il., U.S. **216** 40.55 N 87.49 W
Prairie Creek ≃, Il., U.S. **278** 41.36 N 87.40 W
Prairie Creek ≃, Mi., U.S. **216** 42.59 N 85.01 W
Prairie Creek ≃, Ne., U.S. **198** 41.22 N 97.32 W
Prairie Creek Reservoir ⊜[1] **218** 40.08 N 85.17 W
Prairie Dog Creek ≃ **198** 40.00 N 99.23 W
Prairie du Chien **190** 43.03 N 91.08 W
Prairie du Sac **190** 43.17 N 89.43 W
Prairie Elk Creek ≃ **198** 48.00 N 105.51 W
Prairie Grove **194** 35.58 N 94.19 W
Prairie Hill **222** 31.39 N 96.47 W
Prairie Lea **222** 29.44 N 97.45 W
Prairie River **184** 52.52 N 103.00 W
Prairies, Coteau des ⋏[2] **198** 44.30 N 96.45 W
Prairies, Lake of the ⊜[1] **184** 51.05 N 101.25 W
Prairies, Rivière des ≃ **275a** 45.42 N 73.29 W
Prairie View, Il., U.S. **278** 42.12 N 87.57 W
Prairie View, Tx., U.S. **222** 30.05 N 95.59 W
Prairie Village **198** 38.59 N 94.38 W
Prajekan **115a** 7.47 S 113.59 E
Prakhon Chai **110** 14.37 N 103.05 E
Pralboino **64** 45.16 N 10.13 E
Prali **62** 44.54 N 7.03 E
Pralls Island I **276** 40.37 N 74.12 W
Pralognan-la-Vanoise **62** 45.23 N 6.43 E
Pram **60** 48.14 N 13.37 E
Pram ≃ **60** 48.28 N 13.26 E
Pramaggiore, Monte ∧ **64** 46.22 N 12.33 E
Prambachkirchen **60** 48.19 N 13.55 E
Prambanan **115a** 7.45 S 110.30 E
Pr'amicyno **78** 51.39 N 35.56 E
Pramort **54** 54.26 N 12.55 E
Prampram **150** 5.42 N 0.07 E
Pran Buri **110** 12.23 N 99.55 E
Pran Buri ≃ **110** 12.24 N 100.00 E
Prang **150** 7.59 N 0.53 W
Prangli I **76** 59.38 N 25.02 E
Prānhita ≃ **122** 18.49 N 79.55 E
Pranzo **64** 45.55 N 10.48 E
Prapa, Khlong ≊ **269a** 13.46 N 100.32 E
Prapat **114** 2.40 N 98.56 E
Praraye **58** 45.55 N 7.32 E
Prärien → Great Plains ≚ **16** 42.00 N 100.00 W
Praskoveja **84** 44.43 N 44.12 E
Praskovejevka **83** 48.40 N 38.00 E
Praslin, Lac ⊜ **186** 50.03 N 69.48 W
Praslin Island I **138** 4.19 S 55.44 E
Prasonísi, Ákra › **38** 35.52 N 27.46 E
Praszka **30** 51.04 N 18.26 E
Prat, Isla I **254** 48.15 S 75.00 W
Prata, Bra. **250** 7.41 S 37.06 W
Prata, Bra. **255** 19.18 S 48.55 W
Prata, Bra. **287a** 22.45 S 43.25 W
Prata, Rio da ≃, Bra. **255** 17.28 S 46.35 W
Prata, Rio da ≃, Bra. **255** 18.49 S 49.54 W
Prata, Rio da ≃, Bra. **287a** 22.56 S 43.34 W
Pratāpgarh, India **120** 24.02 N 74.47 E
Pratāpgarh, India **124** 25.54 N 81.58 E
Pratāpnagar **126** 22.23 N 89.13 E
Pratápolis **255** 20.45 S 46.52 W
Pratas Island → Tungsha Tao I **90** 20.42 N 116.43 E
Pratau **54** 51.50 N 12.38 E
Pratella **68** 41.24 N 14.11 E
Prater ♦ **264b** 48.12 N 16.25 E
Prathet Thai → Thailand □[1] **110** 15.00 N 100.00 E
Pratinha **255** 19.46 S 46.24 W
Prato **66** 43.53 N 11.06 E
Prato allo Stelvio **64** 46.37 N 10.35 E
Pratola Peligna **66** 42.06 N 13.52 E
Pratola Serra **68** 40.59 N 14.51 E
Pratolino **66** 43.52 N 11.18 E
Pratomagno ⋏ **66** 43.39 N 11.39 E
Pratt **198** 37.38 N 98.44 W
Pratteln **58** 47.31 N 7.42 E
Prättigau V **58** 46.55 N 9.45 E
Pratt's Bottom ✦[8] **260** 51.20 N 0.07 E
Prattsburg **210** 42.31 N 77.17 W
Prattsville **210** 42.18 N 74.26 W
Prattville **194** 32.27 N 86.27 W
Pratudão ≃ **255** 13.56 S 44.55 W
Prauthoy **58** 47.40 N 5.17 E
Pravaja Mama ≃ **88** 57.10 N 111.54 E
Pravda **89** 47.00 N 142.01 E
Pravdinsk, Ross. **76** 54.27 N 21.01 E
Pravdinsk, Ross. **80** 56.32 N 43.34 E
Pravdinskij **82** 56.04 N 37.51 E
Pravia **34** 43.29 N 6.07 W
Prawet Buri Rom, Khlong ≊ **269a** 13.42 N 100.35 E
Prawle Point › **42** 50.13 N 3.42 W
Praya **115b** 8.42 S 116.17 E
Pr'aža **24** 61.42 N 33.35 E
Praz-sur-Arly **62** 45.50 N 6.34 E
Prazzo **62** 44.29 N 7.03 E
Preakness Brook ≃ **276** 40.54 N 74.15 W
Preakness Mountain ∧ **276** 40.58 N 74.13 W
Preakness Valley Park ♦ **276** 40.55 N 74.14 W
Preble, In., U.S. **216** 40.50 N 85.01 W
Preble, N.Y., U.S. **210** 42.44 N 76.09 W
Preble □[6] **218** 39.45 N 84.38 W
Preci **66** 42.53 N 13.02 E
Prečistoje, Ross. **76** 55.41 N 34.56 E
Prečistoje, Ross. **76** 55.31 N 32.22 E
Prečistoje, Ross. **80** 58.27 N 40.19 E
Précy-sous-Thil **50** 47.23 N 4.19 E
Précy-sur-Marne **261** 48.56 N 2.47 E
Précy-sur-Oise **50** 49.12 N 2.22 E
Preda **58** 46.36 N 9.46 E
Predappio **66** 44.06 N 11.58 E
Predazzo **64** 46.19 N 11.36 E
Predeal **38** 45.30 N 25.35 E
Prédecelle ≃ **261** 48.35 N 2.07 E
Předenice **60** 49.37 N 13.24 E
Predeşti **38** 44.21 N 23.36 E
Predgornoje **86** 47.10 N 81.02 E
Predigtstuhl ∧ **61** 48.48 N 15.22 E
Předín **61** 49.12 N 15.40 E
Predivinsk **86** 57.04 N 93.27 E
Predlitz [-Turrach] **64** 47.04 N 13.55 E
Predmostnoje **78** 45.57 N 34.37 E
Predoi (Prettau) **64** 47.02 N 12.06 E
Predore **64** 45.40 N 10.01 E
Preeceville **184** 51.58 N 102.40 W
Pré-en-Pail **32** 48.27 N 0.12 W
Preesall **44** 53.55 N 2.58 W
Preetz **54** 54.14 N 10.16 E
Pregarten **61** 48.21 N 14.32 E
Pregel → Pregol'a ≃ **76** 54.41 N 20.22 E
Pregnana **266b** 45.31 N 9.00 E
Pregol'a ≃ **76** 54.41 N 20.22 E
Pregonero **246** 8.01 N 71.46 W
Pregos **256** 21.46 S 42.54 W
Pregradnaja **84** 43.58 N 41.12 E
Pregradnoje **80** 45.49 N 41.45 E
Preguiças ≃ **250** 2.34 S 42.44 W
Preila **76** 55.22 N 21.04 E
Preiļi **76** 56.18 N 26.43 E
Preissac, Lac ⊜ **190** 48.20 N 78.20 W
Prekestolen ♦ **26** 59.00 N 6.01 E
Preko **36** 44.05 N 15.11 E
Prekomurje ✦[1] **61** 46.40 N 16.10 E
Prĕk Poŭthĭ **110** 11.51 N 105.07 E
Prelate **184** 50.51 N 109.23 W
Přelouč **30** 50.02 N 15.34 E
Premana **58** 46.03 N 9.25 E
Prembun **115a** 7.43 S 109.48 E
Prémery **50** 47.10 N 3.20 E
Premià de Dalt **266d** 41.31 N 2.21 E
Premià de Mar **266d** 41.29 N 2.21 E
Premnitz **54** 52.32 N 12.19 E
Prémont, P.Q., Can. **206** 46.22 N 73.03 W
Premont, Tx., U.S. **196** 27.21 N 98.07 W
Prémontré **50** 49.33 N 3.24 E
Premuda, Otok I **36** 44.20 N 14.37 E
Prenestini, Monti ⋏ **66** 41.50 N 12.55 E
Prenjas **38** 41.04 N 20.32 E
Prentice **190** 45.32 N 90.17 W
Prentiss **194** 31.35 N 89.52 W
Prenton **262** 53.22 N 3.03 W
Prenzlau **54** 53.19 N 13.52 E
Prenzlauer Berg ✦[8] **264a** 52.32 N 13.26 E
Preobraženije **89** 42.57 N 133.55 E
Preobražennoje **83** 49.32 N 38.10 E
Preobraženovka **89** 48.04 N 131.55 E
Preparis Island I **110** 14.52 N 93.41 E
Preparis North Channel ʊ **110** 15.27 N 94.05 E
Preparis South Channel ʊ **110** 14.40 N 94.00 E
Přerov **30** 49.27 N 17.27 E
Prerow **54** 54.26 N 12.35 E
Pré-Saint-Didier **62** 45.46 N 6.59 E
Presanella, Cima ∧ **64** 46.13 N 10.40 E
Prescot **44** 53.26 N 2.48 W
Prescott, On., Can. **212** 44.43 N 75.31 W
Prescott, Az., U.S. **200** 34.32 N 112.28 W
Prescott, Ar., U.S. **194** 33.48 N 93.22 W
Prescott, Or., U.S. **224** 46.02 N 122.53 W
Prescott, Wi., U.S. **190** 44.44 N 92.48 W
Prescott and Russell □[6] **206** 45.25 N 75.00 W
Prescott Island I **176** 73.01 N 96.50 W
Preševo **38** 42.18 N 21.39 E
Presho **198** 43.54 N 100.03 W
Presicce **68** 39.54 N 18.16 E
Presidencia de la Plaza **252** 27.01 S 59.51 W
Presidencia Roca **252** 26.08 S 59.36 W
Presidencia Roque Sáenz Peña **252** 26.47 S 60.27 W
Presidente Costa e Silva, Ponte ✦[5] **287a** 22.53 S 43.10 W
Presidente Derqui **258** 34.29 S 58.51 W
Presidente Dutra **250** 5.15 S 44.30 W
Presidente Epitácio **255** 21.46 S 52.06 W
Presidente Getúlio **252** 27.03 S 49.37 W
Presidente Hayes □[5] **252** 24.00 S 59.00 W
Presidente Nicolás Avellaneda, Parque ♦ **288** 34.39 S 58.29 W
Presidente Olegário **255** 18.25 S 46.25 W
Presidente Prudente **255** 22.07 S 51.22 W
Presidente Ríos, Lago ⊜ **254** 46.28 S 74.25 W
Presidente Roosevelt, Estação ✦[5] **287b** 23.33 S 46.36 W
Presidente Venceslau **255** 21.52 S 51.50 W
Presidential Heights **279b** 40.34 N 80.03 W
President Roxas **116** 11.26 N 122.56 E
Presidio **196** 29.33 N 104.22 W
Presidio ≃ **234** 23.06 N 106.17 W
Presidio of San Francisco ■ **226** 37.48 N 122.28 W
Presles **56** 50.23 N 4.35 E
Presles-en-Brie **261** 48.43 N 2.45 E
Presnogor'kovka **86** 54.30 N 65.45 E
Presnovka **86** 54.40 N 67.09 E
Presolana, Passo della)(**64** 45.55 N 10.06 E
Prešov **30** 49.00 N 21.15 E
Prespa, Lake ⊜ **38** 40.55 N 21.00 E
Prespansko Jezero → Prespa, Lake ⊜ **38** 40.55 N 21.00 E
Presque Isle **186** 46.40 N 68.00 W
Presque Isle ›[1] **214** 42.09 N 80.06 W
Presque Isle ≃ **190** 46.43 N 89.59 W
Presque Isle State Park ♦ **214** 42.09 N 80.06 W
Presqu'ile Bay ⊂ **212** 44.01 N 77.43 W
Presqu'ile Peninsula ›[1] **212** 44.00 N 77.41 W
Presqu'ile Provincial Park ♦ **212** 44.00 N 77.42 W
Pressana **64** 45.17 N 11.24 E
Pressath **60** 49.46 N 11.56 E
Pressbaum **61** 48.11 N 16.05 E
Pressburg → Bratislava **30** 48.09 N 17.07 E
Pressel **54** 51.34 N 12.41 E
Prestatyn **44** 53.20 N 3.24 W
Prestbury **262** 53.17 N 2.09 W
Prestea **150** 5.27 N 2.08 W
Presteigne **42** 52.17 N 3.00 W
Přeštice **60** 49.34 N 13.20 E
Presto **279b** 40.23 N 80.07 W
Preston, Austl. **169** 37.45 S 145.01 E
Preston, Eng., U.K. **42** 50.39 N 2.25 W
Preston, Eng., U.K. **44** 53.46 N 2.42 W
Preston, Eng., U.K. **44** 53.46 N 0.12 W
Preston, Ga., U.S. **192** 32.03 N 84.32 W
Preston, Id., U.S. **202** 42.05 N 111.52 W
Preston, Ia., U.S. **190** 42.03 N 90.24 W
Preston, Ks., U.S. **198** 37.45 N 98.33 W
Preston, Md., U.S. **208** 38.42 N 75.54 W
Preston, Mn., U.S. **190** 43.40 N 92.04 W
Preston, Wa., U.S. **224** 47.31 N 121.55 W
Preston □[8] **262** 53.48 N 2.42 W
Preston ≃, Austl. **168a** 33.20 S 115.40 E
Preston ≃, P.Q., Can. **206** 46.05 N 75.04 W
Preston, Cape › **162** 20.51 S 116.12 E
Preston, Lac ⊜ **206** 46.05 N 75.04 W
Preston, Lake ⊜, Austl. **168a** 32.59 S 115.42 E
Preston, Lake ⊜, Fl., U.S. **220** 28.18 N 81.08 W
Preston Airport ⊠ **276** 40.22 N 74.15 W
Preston Brook **262** 53.19 N 2.39 W
Preston Brook Canal Tunnel ✦[5] **262** 53.19 N 2.38 W
Preston Heights **216** 41.28 N 88.08 W
Preston Hollow **210** 42.27 N 74.13 W
Preston North End Football Ground ♦ **262** 53.47 N 2.42 W
Prestonpans **46** 55.57 N 3.00 W
Preston Peak ∧ **204** 41.50 N 123.37 W
Prestonsburg **192** 37.39 N 82.46 W
Prestrud Inlet ⊂ **9** 78.18 S 156.00 W
Preststranda **26** 59.06 N 9.04 E
Prestville **182** 55.44 N 118.37 W
Prestwich **44** 53.32 N 2.17 W
Prestwick **46** 55.29 N 4.37 W
Prestwick Airport ⊠ **46** 55.30 N 4.36 W
Preto ≃, Bra. **246** 1.41 S 63.48 W
Preto ≃, Bra. **248** 8.03 S 62.54 W
Preto ≃, Bra. **250** 11.21 S 43.52 W
Preto ≃, Bra. **250** 3.32 S 43.46 W
Preto ≃, Bra. **255** 13.37 S 48.06 W
Preto ≃, Bra. **255** 17.00 S 46.12 W
Preto ≃, Bra. **255** 18.44 S 50.23 W
Preto ≃, Bra. **255** 20.08 S 49.38 W
Preto ≃, Bra. **256** 22.14 S 43.07 W
Preto ≃, Bra. **256** 22.01 S 43.20 W
Preto do Igapó-açu ≃ **246** 4.26 S 59.48 W
Pretoria **158** 25.45 S 28.10 E
Pretoriusvlei **158** 28.30 S 22.59 E
Prettau → Predoi **64** 47.02 N 12.06 E
Prettin **54** 51.39 N 12.55 E
Prettyboy Reservoir ⊜[1] **208** 39.38 N 76.45 W
Pretty Prairie **198** 37.46 N 98.01 W
Pretzfeld **60** 49.45 N 11.11 E
Pretzier **54** 52.49 N 11.15 E
Pretzsch **54** 51.42 N 12.48 E
Preussisch Eylau → Bagrationovsk **76** 54.23 N 20.39 E
Preussisch-Oldendorf **52** 52.18 N 8.30 E
Preussisch-Ströhen **52** 52.29 N 8.40 E
Prevalje **61** 46.32 N 14.55 E
Préveza **38** 38.57 N 20.44 E
Prévost **206** 45.52 N 74.05 W
Prevost Island I **224** 48.50 N 123.22 W
Prey Lvéa **110** 11.10 N 104.57 E
Prey Nób **110** 10.38 N 103.47 E
Prey Vêng **110** 11.29 N 105.19 E
Prezza, Monte ∧ **66** 42.02 N 13.49 E
Priaral'skije Karakumy ✦[2] **86** 47.00 N 63.30 E
Priargunsk **88** 50.27 N 119.00 E
Priay **58** 46.00 N 5.17 E
Priazovskaja vozvyšennost' ⋏[1] **83** 47.30 N 37.30 E
Priazovskoje **78** 46.43 N 35.38 E
Pribilof Islands II **180** 57.00 N 170.00 W
Priboj **38** 43.35 N 19.31 E
Příbram **30** 49.42 N 14.01 E
Pribylovo **76** 60.26 N 28.40 E
Priccio, Cozzo ∧ **70** 37.01 N 14.46 E
Price, Austl. **168b** 34.17 S 138.00 E
Price, Tx., U.S. **222** 32.08 N 94.57 W
Price, Ut,. U.S. **200** 39.35 N 110.48 W
Price ≃ **200** 39.10 N 110.06 W
Price, Cape › **110** 13.34 N 93.03 E
Price Bend ⊂ **276** 40.55 N 73.24 W
Price Island I **182** 52.23 N 128.36 W
Prichard **194** 30.44 N 88.04 W
Prickly Point › **241k** 11.59 N 61.45 W
Pričornomorskaja nizmennost' ≚ **78** 47.00 N 33.00 E
Priddy **196** 31.40 N 98.31 W
Pridneprovskaja nizmennost' ≚ **78** 50.00 N 32.00 E
Pridneprovskaja vozvyšennost' ⋏[1] **78** 49.00 N 32.00 E
Priego **34** 40.27 N 2.18 W
Priego de Córdoba **34** 37.26 N 4.11 W
Priekule, Lat. **76** 56.26 N 21.35 E
Priekule, Liet. **76** 55.33 N 21.19 E
Prienai **76** 54.38 N 23.57 E
Prien am Chiemsee **64** 47.51 N 12.20 E
Prieros **54** 52.13 N 13.46 E
Prieska **158** 29.40 S 22.42 E
Priest ≃ **202** 48.11 N 116.53 W
Priestewitz **54** 51.15 N 13.30 E
Priest Island I **46** 57.58 N 5.30 W
Priest Lake ⊜ **202** 48.34 N 116.52 W
Priestley, Mount ∧ **182** 55.13 N 128.53 W
Priest Rapids Lake ⊜[1] **202** 46.45 N 119.55 W
Priest River **202** 48.10 N 116.54 W
Prieta, Loma ∧ **226** 37.07 N 121.51 W
Prieta, Peña ∧ **34** 43.01 N 4.44 W
Prieto ≃ **240m** 18.15 N 66.54 W
Prieto Diaz **116** 13.02 N 124.12 E
Prievidza **30** 48.47 N 18.37 E
Prignitz ✦[1] **54** 53.05 N 12.15 E
Priiskovyj, Ross. **86** 54.39 N 88.42 E
Priiskovyj, Ross. **88** 51.57 N 116.39 E
Prijedor **36** 44.59 N 16.43 E
Prijepolje **38** 43.23 N 19.39 E
Prijutnoje **80** 46.06 N 43.31 E
Prijutovo **80** 53.54 N 53.56 E
Prikaspijskaja nizmennost' ≚ **80** 48.00 N 52.00 E
Prikolotnoje **78** 50.09 N 37.21 E
Prikro **150** 7.39 N 3.59 W
Prilep **38** 41.20 N 21.33 E
Prilepy **82** 54.03 N 37.42 E
Prilly **58** 46.32 N 6.36 E
Priluki, Ross. **76** 59.16 N 39.53 E
Priluki, Ross. **82** 54.51 N 37.53 E
Priluki, Ukr. **78** 50.36 N 32.24 E
Prima Porta ✦[8] **267a** 42.00 N 12.29 E
Primavera **250** 0.56 S 47.06 W
Přimda **60** 49.41 N 12.41 E
Primeira Cruz **250** 2.30 S 43.26 W
Primeiro de Maio **255** 22.48 S 51.01 W
Primera **196** 26.14 N 97.43 W
Primero ≃ **252** 31.00 S 63.12 W
Primero de Mayo **196** 27.12 N 101.15 W
Primghar **198** 43.05 N 95.37 W
Primolano **64** 45.58 N 11.42 E
Primorje [Warnicken] **76** 54.57 N 20.02 E
Primorka **83** 47.16 N 39.03 E
Primorsk, Azer. **84** 40.13 N 49.33 E
Primorsk, Ross. **76** 54.44 N 20.01 E
Primorsk, Ross. **76** 60.22 N 28.36 E
Primorsk, Ross. **80** 49.16 N 45.03 E
Primorsk, Ukr. **78** 46.44 N 36.20 E
Primorskij, Ross. **89** 43.07 N 131.38 E
Primorskij, Ukr. **78** 45.07 N 35.29 E
Primorskij chrebet ⋏ **88** 52.30 N 106.00 E
Primorskij Kraj □[8] **89** 45.25 N 135.25 E
Primorsko-Achtarsk **78** 46.03 N 38.11 E
Primorskoje **83** 47.11 N 37.42 E
Primos **285** 39.55 N 75.18 W
Primrose, S. Afr. **273d** 26.12 S 28.10 E
Primrose, Pa., U.S. **210** 40.42 N 76.17 W
Primrose, Pa., U.S. **279b** 40.21 N 80.16 W
Primrose Brook ≃ **276** 40.43 N 74.31 W
Primrose Lake ⊜ **184** 54.55 N 109.45 W
Prims ≃ **56** 49.20 N 6.44 E
Primstal **56** 49.32 N 6.58 E
Prince, Lake ⊜[1] **208** 36.48 N 76.38 W
Prince Albert, On., Can. **212** 44.05 N 78.58 W
Prince Albert, Sk., Can. **184** 53.12 N 105.46 W
Prince Albert, S. Afr. **158** 33.13 S 22.02 E
Prince Albert Mountains ⋏ **9** 76.00 S 161.30 E
Prince Albert National Park ♦ **184** 54.00 N 106.25 W
Prince Albert Road **158** 33.01 S 21.40 E
Prince Albert Sound ʊ **176** 70.25 N 115.00 W
Prince Alexander Mountains ⋏ **164** 3.30 S 142.50 E
Prince Alfred Hamlet **158** 33.18 S 19.20 E
Prince Charles Island I **176** 67.50 N 76.00 W
Prince Charles Mountains ⋏ **9** 72.00 S 67.00 E
Prince-de-Galles, Île du → Prince of Wales Island I, Austl. **164** 10.40 S 142.10 E
Prince-de-Galles, Île du → Prince of Wales Island I, N.T., Can. **176** 72.40 N 99.00 W
Prince Edward □[6] **212** 44.00 N 77.15 W
Prince Edward Bay ⊂ **212** 43.57 N 76.57 W
Prince Edward Island □[4], Can. **176** 46.20 N 63.20 W
Prince Edward Island □[4], Can. **186** 46.20 N 63.20 W
Prince Edward Island National Park ♦ **186** 46.31 N 63.26 W
Prince Edward Islands II **6** 46.35 S 37.56 E
Prince Edward Park ♦ **274a** 34.02 S 151.03 E
Prince Edward Point › **212** 43.56 N 76.52 W
Prince Frederick **208** 38.32 N 76.35 W
Prince Gallitzin State Park ♦ **214** 40.40 N 78.32 W
Prince George, B.C., Can. **182** 53.55 N 122.45 W
Prince George, Va., U.S. **208** 37.13 N 77.17 W
Prince George □[6] **208** 37.13 N 77.10 W
Prince Georges □[6] **208** 38.49 N 76.45 W
Prince Georges Plaza ✦[9] **284c** 38.58 N 76.57 W
Prince Leopold Island I **176** 74.02 N 89.55 W
Prince of Wales, Cape › **180** 65.40 N 168.05 W
Prince of Wales Island I, Austl. **164** 10.40 S 142.10 E
Prince of Wales Island I, N.T., Can. **176** 72.40 N 99.00 W
Prince of Wales Island I, Ak., U.S. **180** 55.47 N 132.50 W
Prince of Wales Strait ʊ **176** 73.00 N 117.00 W
Prince Olav Coast ±[2] **9** 68.30 S 42.30 E
Prince Patrick Island I **16** 76.45 N 119.30 W
Prince Regent ≃ **164** 15.28 S 125.05 E
Prince Regent Inlet ⊂ **176** 73.00 N 90.30 W
Prince Regent Nature Reserve ♦ **164** 15.30 S 125.30 E
Prince Rupert **182** 54.19 N 130.19 W
Prince Rupert Bay ⊂ **240d** 15.34 N 61.29 W
Prince Rupert Bluff Point › **240d** 15.35 N 61.29 W
Princesa, Puerto ⊂ **116** 9.45 N 118.43 E
Princesa Astrid, Costa → Princess Astrid Coast ±[2] **9** 70.45 S 12.30 E
Princesa Carlota, Bahía → Princess Charlotte Bay ⊂ **164** 14.25 S 144.00 E
Princesa Isabel **250** 7.44 S 38.00 W
Princesa Marta, Costa → Princess Martha Coast ±[2] **9** 72.00 S 7.30 W
Princesa Ragnhild, Costa → Princess Ragnhild Coast ±[2] **9** 70.15 S 27.30 E
Princes Bay ⊂ **276** 40.31 N 74.12 W
Princes Risborough **42** 51.44 N 0.51 W
Princess Anne **208** 38.12 N 75.41 W
Princess Astrid Coast ±[2] **9** 70.45 S 12.30 E
Princess Charlotte Bay ⊂ **164** 14.25 S 144.00 E
Princess Martha Coast ±[2] **9** 72.00 S 7.30 W
Princess Ragnhild Coast ±[2] **9** 70.15 S 27.30 E
Princess Ranges ⋏ **162** 26.08 S 121.55 E
Princess Royal Channel ʊ **182** 53.10 N 128.37 W
Princess Royal Island I **182** 52.57 N 128.49 W
Princes Town **241r** 10.16 N 61.23 W
Princeton, B.C., Can. **182** 49.27 N 120.31 W
Princeton, Nf., Can. **186** 48.25 N 53.36 W
Princeton, On., Can. **212** 43.10 N 80.32 W
Princeton, Ca., U.S. **226** 39.24 N 122.00 W
Princeton, Fl., U.S. **220** 25.32 N 80.24 W
Princeton, Il., U.S. **190** 41.22 N 89.27 W
Princeton, In., U.S. **194** 38.21 N 87.34 W
Princeton, Ky., U.S. **194** 37.06 N 87.52 W
Princeton, Me., U.S. **188** 45.13 N 67.34 W
Princeton, Mi., U.S. **190** 46.17 N 87.28 W
Princeton, Mn., U.S. **190** 45.34 N 93.34 W
Princeton, Mo., U.S. **194** 40.24 N 93.34 W
Princeton, N.J., U.S. **208** 40.20 N 74.39 W
Princeton, N.C., U.S. **192** 35.27 N 78.09 W
Princeton, Tx., U.S. **222** 33.11 N 96.30 W
Princeton, W.V., U.S. **192** 37.21 N 81.06 W
Princeton, Wi., U.S. **190** 43.51 N 89.07 W
Princeton Airfield ⊠ **276** 40.24 N 74.39 W
Princeton Battlefield Park ⊥ **276** 40.20 N 74.41 W
Princeton Junction **208** 40.19 N 74.37 W
Princeton Township **276** 40.22 N 74.40 W
Princeton University ʊ[2] **276** 40.21 N 74.39 W
Princetown **42** 50.33 N 4.00 W
Princeville, P.Q., Can. **206** 46.10 N 71.53 W
Princeville, Il., U.S. **190** 40.56 N 89.45 W
Princeville, N.C., U.S. **192** 35.53 N 77.31 W
Prince William □[6] **208** 38.42 N 77.27 W
Prince William Forest Park ♦ **208** 38.36 N 77.23 W
Prince William Sound ʊ **180** 60.40 N 147.00 W
Príncipe I **152** 1.37 N 7.25 E
Príncipe Alberto, Montes → Prince Albert Mountains ⋏ **9** 76.00 S 161.30 E
Príncipe Carlos, Montes → Prince Charles Mountains ⋏ **9** 72.00 S 67.00 E
Principe Channel ʊ **182** 53.28 N 130.00 W
Príncipe da Beira **248** 12.25 S 64.25 W
Príncipe de Gales, Isla → Prince of Wales Island I, Austl. **164** 10.40 S 142.10 E
Príncipe de Gales, Isla → Prince of Wales Island I, N.T., Can. **176** 72.40 N 99.00 W
Príncipe Eduardo, Isla → Prince Edward Island □[4] **186** 46.20 N 63.20 W
Príncipe Olav, Costa → Prince Olav Coast ±[2] **9** 68.30 S 42.30 E
Príncipe Patricio, Isla → Prince Patrick Island I **16** 76.45 N 119.30 W
Prineville **202** 44.18 N 120.51 W
Prineville Reservoir ⊜[1] **202** 44.08 N 120.42 W
Prineville Southeast **202** 44.17 N 120.53 W
Pringgabaja **115b** 8.34 S 116.37 E
Pringsewu **112** 5.24 S 104.55 E
Pringy **261** 48.31 N 2.34 E
Prinsenbeek **52** 51.36 N 4.42 E
Prinses Margrietkanaal ≊ **52** 53.10 N 5.55 E
Prinshof **158** 32.06 S 20.53 E
Prinzapolka **236** 13.24 N 83.34 W
Prinzapolka ≃ **236** 13.24 N 83.34 W
Prinzessin Astrid-Küste → Princess Astrid Coast ±[2] **9** 70.45 S 12.30 E
Prinzessin Charlotte Bucht → Princess Charlotte Bay ⊂ **164** 14.25 S 144.00 E
Prinzessin Martha-Küste → Princess Martha Coast ±[2] **9** 72.00 S 7.30 W
Prinzessin Ragnhild-Küste → Princess Ragnhild Coast ±[2] **9** 70.15 S 27.30 E
Priobskoje plato ⋏[1] **86** 52.40 N 83.00 E
Priioksko-Terrasnyj zapovednik ✦[4] **82** 54.51 N 37.36 E
Priolo Gargallo **70** 37.09 N 15.11 E
Prior, Cabo › **34** 43.34 N 8.19 W
Priort **264a** 52.31 N 12.58 E
Priozernyj **80** 47.23 N 45.14 E
Prioz'ornyj **86** 47.50 N 84.13 E
Prioz'orsk **24** 61.02 N 30.04 E
Prip'at' ≃ **78** 51.21 N 30.09 E
Pripet → Prip'at' ≃ **78** 51.21 N 30.09 E
Pripet Marshes → Polesje ✦[1] **72** 52.00 N 27.00 E
Pripol'arnyj Ural ⋏ **24** 65.00 N 60.00 E
Priputni **78** 50.57 N 32.14 E
Prirečje **88** 55.07 N 101.03 E
Prirečnyj **80** 51.03 N 52.26 E
Přísečnice **54** 50.27 N 13.06 E
Priselje **76** 55.09 N 32.49 E
Prišib, Azer. **84** 39.08 N 48.36 E
Prišib, Ukr. **78** 47.16 N 35.21 E
Prislon **82** 56.48 N 37.16 E
Pristan'-Prževal'sk **85** 42.34 N 78.18 E
Pristen', Ross. **78** 51.15 N 36.41 E
Pristen', Ukr. **83** 49.36 N 37.38 E
Priština **38** 42.39 N 21.10 E
Pritchett **198** 37.22 N 102.51 W
Přítluky **61** 48.51 N 16.46 E
Pritzerbe **54** 52.30 N 12.27 E
Pritzier **54** 53.22 N 11.04 E
Pritzwalk **54** 53.09 N 12.10 E

Symbols in the index entries represent the broad categories identified in the key at the right. Symbols with superior numbers (⋏[1]) identify subcategories (see complete key on page *I · 1).*

Symbole im Register stellen die rechts im Schlüssel erklärten Kategorien dar. Symbole mit hochgestellten Ziffern (⋏[1]) bezeichnen Unterabteilungen einer Kategorie (vgl. vollständiger Schlüssel auf Seite *I · 1).*

Los símbolos incluídos en el texto del índice representan las grandes categorías identificadas con la clave a la derecha. Los símbolos con numeros en su parte superior (⋏[1]) identifican las subcategorías (véase la clave completa en la página *I · 1).*

Les symboles de l'index représentent les catégories indiquées dans la légende à droite. Les symboles suivis d'un indice (⋏[1]) représentent des sous-catégories (voir légende complète à la page *I · 1).*

Os símbolos incluídos no texto do índice representam as grandes categorias identificadas com a chave à direita. Os símbolos com números em sua parte superior (⋏[1]) identificam as subcategorias (veja-se a chave completa à página *I · 1).*

∧ Mountain	Berg	Montaña	Montagne	Montanha
⋏ Mountains	Gebirge	Montañas	Montagnes	Montanhas
)(Pass	Paß	Paso	Col	Passo
V Valley, Canyon	Tal, Cañon	Valle, Cañón	Vallée, Canyon	Vale, Canhão
≚ Plain	Ebene	Llano	Plaine	Planície
› Cape	Kap	Cabo	Cap	Cabo
I Island	Insel	Isla	Île	Ilha
II Islands	Inseln	Islas	Îles	Ilhas
± Other Topographic Features	Andere Topographische Objekte	Otros Elementos Topográficos	Autres données topographiques	Outros acidentes topográficos

ESPAÑOL	FRANÇAIS	PORTUGUÊS
Nombre — Página — Lat. — Long. W=Oeste E	Nom — Page — Lat. — Long. W=Ouest E	Nome — Página — Lat. — Long. W=Oeste E

Column 1 (ESPAÑOL)

Nombre	Página	Lat.	Long.
Priural'nyj	80	51.29 N	53.06 E
Privas	62	44.44 N	4.36 E
Priverno	66	41.28 N	13.11 E
Privetnoje	78	44.50 N	34.41 E
Privodino	24	61.05 N	46.28 E
Privokzal'nyj, Ross.	82	55.59 N	35.56 E
Privokzal'nyj, Ross.	86	58.53 N	60.43 E
Privolje, Ukr.	83	49.01 N	38.18 E
Privolje, Ukr.	83	48.52 N	37.16 E
Privol'naja	78	46.09 N	38.42 E
Privol'n'anskij →⁸	83	48.41 N	38.28 E
Privol'noje, Ross.	80	57.57 N	46.06 E
Privol'noje, Ukr.	78	47.29 N	32.17 E
Privolžje	80	52.52 N	48.37 E
Privolžsk	80	57.23 N	41.17 E
Privolžskaja vozvyšennost' ⚹¹	80	52.00 N	46.00 E
Privolžskij, Ross.	80	46.24 N	48.00 E
Privolžskij, Ross.	80	51.24 N	46.02 E
Privolžskoje	80	51.06 N	45.57 E
Prizren	38	42.12 N	20.44 E
Prizzi	70	37.43 N	13.26 E
Prizzi, Lago di ⍝	70	37.44 N	13.25 E
Prnjavor	34	44.52 N	17.40 E
Probolinggo	115a	7.45 S	113.13 E
Proboštov	54	50.39 N	13.50 E
Probstzella	54	50.32 N	11.22 E
Probus	42	50.17 N	4.57 W
Procchio	68	42.47 N	10.15 E
Prochladnoje	86	48.30 N	82.41 E
Prochladnyj	84	43.46 N	44.00 E
Prochorkino	86	59.34 N	79.26 E
Prochorovka	82	54.07 N	38.11 E
Prochowice	54	51.17 N	16.22 E
Procida	68	40.46 N	14.02 E
Procida, Isola di I	68	40.45 N	14.01 E
Proctor	182	49.37 N	116.57 W
Proctor, Mn., U.S.	190	46.44 N	92.13 W
Proctor, Vt., U.S.	188	43.39 N	73.02 W
Proctor Brook ⚹	283	42.32 N	70.54 W
Proctor Lake ⍝	228	35.07 N	118.21 W
Proctor Lake ⍝¹	196	32.02 N	98.32 W
Proddatūr	122	14.44 N	78.33 E
Proença-a-Nova	34	39.45 N	7.55 W
Profen	54	51.07 N	12.13 E
Pro Football Hall of Fame I	214	40.49 N	81.25 W
Prognoj	83	48.45 N	39.51 E
Progreso, Méx.	196	27.28 N	100.59 W
Progreso, Méx.	232	21.17 N	89.40 W
Progreso, Méx.	234	20.15 N	99.12 W
Progreso, Méx.	234	23.48 N	103.18 W
Progreso, Ur.	258	34.40 S	56.13 W
Progress, Ross.	89	49.42 N	129.39 E
Progress, Or., U.S.	224	45.28 N	122.47 W
Progress, Pa., U.S.	208	40.08 N	76.34 W
Project City	204	40.41 N	122.21 W
Prokopjeva	88	58.03 N	100.39 E
Prokopjevsk	86	53.53 N	86.45 E
— Prokopjevsk	86	53.53 N	86.45 E
Prokuplje	38	43.14 N	21.36 E
Prokuševo	76	59.55 N	34.56 E
Proletarsk, Taj.	86	56.19 N	69.46 E
Proletarsk ⚹	76	58.26 N	31.44 E
Proletarsk, Taj.	85	40.10 N	69.30 E
Proletarsk, Ukr.	78	48.56 N	38.23 E
Proletarsk →⁸	83	48.56 N	38.23 E
Proletarskij, Ross.	78	50.47 N	35.47 E
Proletarskij, Ross.	82	55.01 N	37.23 E
Proletarskij →⁸	83	48.08 N	39.18 E
Prolivsovo	76	52.54 N	34.09 E
Prome (Pyè)	110	18.49 N	95.13 E
Promised Land State Park ⚹	210	41.18 N	75.11 W
Promissão	255	21.32 S	49.52 W
Promontogno	58	46.21 N	9.34 E
Prompton	210	41.35 N	75.19 W
Prompton Lake ⍝¹	210	41.36 N	75.20 W
Prompton Lake State Park ⚹	210	41.37 N	75.22 W
Promyšlennaja	86	54.55 N	85.40 E
Promyšlennovskij	86	55.29 N	86.12 E
Promyšlennyj	24	67.35 N	63.55 E
Promyslovka	80	45.44 N	47.10 E
Pron'a ⚹, Bela.	76	53.25 N	31.05 E
Pron'a ⚹, Ross.	82	54.21 N	40.24 E
Pron'a Gorodišče	82	54.15 N	38.43 E
Pronin	80	49.12 N	42.11 E
Pronsfeld	56	50.10 N	6.20 E
Pronsk	56	54.07 N	39.37 E
Prony, Baie du c	175f	22.22 S	166.53 E
Prophet ⚹	178	58.45 N	122.45 W
Prophetstown	190	41.40 N	89.56 W
Propriá	250	10.13 S	36.51 W
Propriano	36	41.40 N	8.55 E
Prorer Wiek c	54	54.31 N	13.38 E
Prorva	86	46.03 N	53.15 E
Proryvnoje	86	54.23 N	64.26 E
Pros'araja	78	48.07 N	36.23 E
Pros'anov	78	49.22 N	35.47 E
Prösen	54	51.25 N	13.30 E
Proserpine	166	20.24 S	148.34 E
Prosigk	54	51.42 N	12.03 E
Proskurov — Chmel'nickij	78	49.25 N	27.00 E
Prosna ⚹	30	52.10 N	17.39 E
Prosnica	80	58.25 N	50.15 E
Prosotsáni	38	41.10 N	23.59 E
Prospect, Austl.	168b	34.54 S	138.35 E
Prospect, Austl.	274a	33.48 S	150.56 E
Prospect, Ct., U.S.	207	41.30 N	72.58 W
Prospect, N.Y., U.S.	210	43.18 N	75.09 W
Prospect, Oh., U.S.	214	40.27 N	83.11 W
Prospect, Or., U.S.	204	42.45 N	122.29 W
Prospect Bay c	208	38.56 N	76.14 W
Prospect Creek ⚹	274a	33.55 S	150.59 E
Prospect Heights	168b	42.06 N	87.54 W
Prospect Hill	168b	35.13 S	138.44 E
Prospect Hill ⚹², Ma., U.S.	207	41.21 N	70.45 W
Prospect Hill Park ⚹	283	42.23 N	71.15 W
Prospect Park, N.J., U.S.	209	40.55 N	74.10 W
Prospect Park, Pa., U.S.	276	39.53 N	75.18 W
Prospect Park ⚹	214	41.31 N	78.13 W
Prospect Park Lake ⍝	276	40.40 N	73.58 W
Prospect Plains	276	40.39 N	73.57 W
Prospect Point	276	40.19 N	74.28 W
Prospect Point ⚹	276	40.58 N	74.38 W
Prospect Reservoir ⍝	274a	33.49 S	150.54 E
Prospectville	285	40.13 N	75.11 W
Prosperi Airport ⚹	227	41.33 N	87.47 W
Prosperidad	116	8.34 N	125.52 E
Prosser	202	46.12 N	119.46 W
Proštějov	30	49.29 N	17.07 E
Prostki	30	53.43 N	22.26 E
Proston	166	26.10 S	151.36 E
Proszowice	30	50.12 N	20.18 E
Protasovo, Ross.	82	53.58 N	42.16 E
Protasovo, Ross.	82	54.11 N	37.10 E
Protasovo, Ross.	86	56.08 N	37.36 E
Protasy	76	52.47 N	29.05 E
Protea	273d	26.17 S	27.51 E
Protection	198	37.12 N	99.29 W
Protection Island I	202	48.07 N	122.55 W
Protivín	54	49.16 N	14.13 E
Protoka ⚹	78	45.43 N	37.16 E

Column 2 (FRANÇAIS)

Nom	Page	Lat.	Long.
Protva ⚹	82	55.01 N	36.41 E
Protva ⚹	82	54.51 N	37.16 E
Protville	36	36.54 N	10.01 E
Prötzel	54	52.38 N	13.59 E
Proud Lake State Recreation Area ⚹	281	42.34 N	83.33 W
Prouxville	206	46.40 N	72.30 W
Provadija	38	43.11 N	27.26 E
Provencal	194	31.39 N	93.12 W
Provence ⚹⁹	44	44.00 N	6.00 E
Provence, Alpes de ⚹	62	43.40 N	6.00 E
Provenchères-sur-Fave	58	48.19 N	7.05 E
Providence, Ky., U.S.	194	37.23 N	87.45 W
Providence, R.I., U.S.	207	41.49 N	71.24 W
Providence, Ut., U.S.	200	41.42 N	111.48 W
Providence ◻⁶	207	41.52 N	71.36 W
Providence ◻⁶	207	41.43 N	71.21 W
Providence Forge	208	37.26 N	77.02 W
Providence Island I	138	9.14 S	51.02 E
Providência, Bra.	256	21.40 S	42.35 W
Providencia, Chile	286e	33.26 S	70.37 W
Providencia, Méx.	196	27.06 N	103.32 W
Providencia, Isla de I	236	13.21 N	81.22 W
Providenciales I	238	21.47 N	72.17 W
Providenija	180	64.23 N	173.18 W
Providenija, buchta c	180	64.30 N	173.20 W
Provincetown	207	42.03 N	70.10 W
Provins	50	48.33 N	3.18 E
Provo	200	40.14 N	111.39 W
Provo ⚹	200	40.14 N	111.39 W
Provost	184	52.21 N	110.16 W
Provost, Lac ⍝	206	46.22 N	74.00 W
Prozor	36	43.49 N	17.37 E
Pru ⚹	150	7.58 N	0.53 W
Prud'anka	78	50.14 N	36.09 E
Prudence Island I	207	41.37 N	71.19 W
Prudentópolis	252	25.12 S	50.57 W
Prudentov	80	49.39 N	46.19 E
Prudhoe	44	54.58 N	1.51 W
Prudhoe Bay c	180	70.20 N	148.20 W
Prudhoe Island I	166	21.19 S	149.40 E
Prudišči	82	54.24 N	38.26 E
Prudnik	30	50.19 N	17.34 E
Prudy	76	53.47 N	26.32 E
Pruggern	64	47.25 N	13.52 E
Prüm	56	50.12 N	6.25 E
Prüm ⚹	56	49.49 N	6.28 E
Pruna, Punta sa ⚹	71	40.11 N	9.26 E
Prunay-le-Temple	50	48.52 N	1.40 E
Prunay-sous-Ablis	261	48.32 N	1.48 E
Prunedale	226	36.47 N	121.40 W
Prunëřov	54	50.25 N	13.16 E
Prunières	62	44.33 N	6.20 E
Prunn, Schloss I	60	48.57 N	11.44 E
Pruszków	30	52.11 N	20.48 E
Prut ⚹	78	45.30 N	28.12 E
Pruth — Prut ⚹	78	45.30 N	28.12 E
Prutting	64	47.53 N	12.11 E
Prutz	58	47.05 N	10.40 E
Pružany	76	52.33 N	24.28 E
Prydz Bay c	9	69.00 S	76.00 E
Pryor	196	36.19 N	95.19 W
Pryor Mountain ⚹²	202	45.54 N	108.57 W
Pryor Mountain ⚹²	222	31.43 N	95.12 W
Prysor ⚹	42	52.56 N	4.00 W
Przasnysz	30	53.01 N	20.55 E
Przedbórz	30	51.06 N	19.53 E
Przemków	30	51.32 N	15.48 E
Przemocze	54	53.27 N	14.55 E
Przemyśl	30	49.47 N	22.47 E
Przemyśl ⚹²	30	50.00 N	22.40 E
Przeworsk	30	50.05 N	22.29 E
Przewóz	54	51.29 N	14.59 E
Przybiernów	54	53.46 N	14.46 E
Przysucha	30	51.22 N	20.38 E
Pšaga⚹	85	39.58 N	68.08 E
Psakhná	85	38.35 N	23.38 E
Psará I	38	38.35 N	25.37 E
Psárion	30	37.20 N	21.51 E
Psebaj	84	44.07 N	40.47 E
Pšecha ⚹	78	44.47 N	39.48 E
Psekups ⚹	78	45.00 N	39.09 E
Pselec	78	51.17 N	36.32 E
Psikhikón	267c	38.01 N	23.46 E
Pšiš ⚹	78	45.01 N	39.18 E
Pšiš, gora ⚹	84	43.24 N	41.12 E
Psittalia I	267c	37.56 N	23.35 E
Pskem	85	41.56 N	70.22 E
Pskem ⚹	85	41.38 N	70.01 E
Pskent	85	40.54 N	69.20 E
Pskov	76	57.50 N	28.20 E
Pskov Oblast' ◻⁴	76	58.00 N	29.00 E
Pskovskoje ozero ⍝	76	58.00 N	28.00 E
Pskowsee — Pskovskoje ozero ⍝	76	58.00 N	28.00 E
Ps'ol ⚹	78	49.02 N	33.33 E
Pšov	76	50.10 N	13.29 E
Pszczyna	30	49.59 N	18.57 E
Ptarmigan, Cape ⚹	176	71.04 N	118.07 W
Ptič ⚹	76	52.09 N	28.52 E
Ptolemaís	38	40.31 N	21.41 E
Ptolemaís	146	32.43 N	20.57 E
Ptuj	36	46.25 N	15.52 E
Pu ⚹, Zhg.	104	41.21 N	122.47 E
Pu ⚹, Zhg.	107	30.25 N	103.49 E
Puah, Pulau I	112	0.30 S	122.34 E
Puakonikai	174d	0.52 S	169.36 E
Puamau, Baie ⍝	174x	9.46 S	138.52 W
Puán, Arg.	252	37.33 S	62.45 W
Puan, Taehan	98	35.45 N	126.44 E
Pubei	104	22.16 N	109.33 E
Pubnico	186	43.42 N	65.47 W
Pucallpa	248	8.23 S	74.32 W
Pucará	248	16.43 S	64.11 W
Pucarani	248	16.23 S	68.30 W
Puccia, Serra di ⚹	70	37.44 N	13.56 E
Puces	214	41.18 N	82.47 W
Pučevejam ⚹	180	68.48 N	170.90 E
Pučež	80	56.59 N	43.11 E
Puchberg am Schneeberg	61	47.47 N	15.54 E
Pucheng, Zhg.	100	27.55 N	118.31 E
Pucheng, Zhg.	100	35.00 N	109.34 E
Pucheta	252	29.54 S	57.94 W
Puchheim	60	48.09 N	11.20 E
Púchov	30	49.08 N	18.20 E
Puchovičí	76	53.32 N	28.15 E
Pucioasa	38	45.04 N	25.26 E
Pucio Point ⚹	116	14.16 N	121.51 E
Pučišča	36	43.21 N	16.44 E
Puck	30	54.43 N	18.24 E
Puckapunyal	169	37.01 N	145.03 E
Pucketa Creek ⚹	279b	40.39 N	79.45 W
Pudahuel	286e	33.26 S	70.46 W
Pudding ⚹	224	45.04 N	122.44 W
Puddingstone Reservoir ⍝¹	280	34.05 N	117.48 W
Puddletown	42	50.45 N	2.21 W
Púdeh Tal I	128	31.03 N	62.15 E
Pudem	80	58.18 N	52.10 E
Pudi	102	29.08 N	99.05 E
Pudimoe	158	27.26 S	24.44 E
Pudino	86	57.07 N	75.54 E
Pudong	86	57.18 N	75.35 E
Pudops Dam ⚹⁶	186	48.09 N	56.50 W
Pudož	80	61.48 N	36.32 E
Pudsey	44	53.48 N	1.40 W
Pudu ⚹	102	26.16 N	102.45 E
Puduari ⚹	246	2.08 S	61.15 W
Puduc ⚹⁶	102	25.39 N	100.46 E
Pudukkottai	122	10.23 N	78.49 E
Puebla ⚹	234	18.50 N	98.00 W

Column 3 (PORTUGUÊS)

Nome	Página	Lat.	Long.
Puebla de Alcocer	34	38.59 N	5.15 W
Puebla de Don Fadrique	34	37.58 N	2.26 W
Puebla de Don Rodrigo	34	39.05 N	4.37 W
Puebla de Sanabria	34	42.03 N	6.38 W
Puebla de Trives	34	42.20 N	7.15 W
Puebla [de Zaragoza]	234	19.03 N	98.12 W
Pueblito de Ponce	240m	18.26 N	66.58 W
Pueblo	198	38.15 N	104.36 W
Pueblo Libertador	252	30.13 S	59.23 W
Pueblo Libre	286d	12.05 S	77.04 W
Pueblo Mountain ⚹	202	42.06 N	118.39 W
Pueblo Nuevo, Col.	246	8.31 N	75.15 W
Pueblo Nuevo, Méx.	234	20.31 N	101.22 W
Pueblo Nuevo, Nic	236	13.23 N	86.29 W
Pueblo Nuevo, P.R.	240m	18.28 N	66.51 W
Pueblo Nuevo, Ur.	258	34.26 S	56.29 W
Pueblo Nuevo, Ven.	246	11.58 N	69.55 W
Pueblo Nuevo →⁸	266a	40.26 N	3.39 W
Pueblo Nuevo Tiquisate	236	14.17 N	91.22 W
Pueblo of Acoma	200	35.03 N	107.35 W
Pueblo Reservoir ⍝¹	198	38.15 N	104.45 W
Pueblovíejc, Ec.	246	1.34 S	79.30 W
Pueblo Viejo, Méx.	234	23.13 N	100.05 W
Pueblo Viejo, Méx.	234	16.14 N	94.39 W
Pueblo Yacui	232	27.19 N	110.01 W
Pelches	252	38.09 S	65.55 W
Puente Alto	252	33.37 S	70.35 W
Puente de Arganda	266a	40.19 N	3.31 W
Puente de Ixtla	234	18.37 N	99.20 W
Puente-Genil	34	37.23 N	4.47 W
Puente-Hills ⚹²	280	34.00 N	117.55 W
Puente-Hills Mall →⁹	280	33.59 N	117.56 W
Puente la Reina	34	42.40 N	1.49 W
Puente Negro	196	23.51 N	101.01 W
Puente Nuevo, Embalse de ⍝¹	34	38.00 N	5.00 W
Puente Piedra	286d	11.57 S	77.05 W
Pueo Point ⚹	229b	21.54 N	160.04 W
Pu'er	102	23.07 N	101.00 E
Puerca, Punta ⚹	240m	18.14 N	65.36 W
Puerco ⚹	200	34.53 N	110.07 W
Puerco, Rio ⚹	200	34.22 N	106.50 W
Pu'erdu	102	28.08 N	104.24 E
Puerto Acosta	248	15.32 S	69.15 W
Puerto Adela	252	24.33 S	54.22 W
Puerto Aisén	252	45.24 S	72.42 W
Puerto Alegre	248	13.53 S	61.36 W
Puerto Ángel	234	15.40 N	96.29 W
Puerto Arista	234	15.56 N	93.48 W
Puerto Armuelles	236	8.17 N	82.52 W
Puerto Asís	246	0.30 N	76.31 W
Puerto Ayacucho	246	5.40 N	67.35 W
Puerto Ayora, Ec.	246a	0.45 S	90.19 W
Puerto Ayora, Ec.	246a	0.45 S	90.19 W
Puerto Bahía Negra	248	20.15 S	58.12 W
Puerto Baquerizo Moreno	246a	0.54 S	89.36 W
Puerto Barrios	236	15.43 N	88.36 W
Puerto Bermejo	252	26.56 S	58.30 W
Puerto Bermúdez	248	10.20 S	74.54 W
Puerto Berrío	246	6.29 N	74.24 W
Puerto Bolívar, Col.	246	12.15 N	71.58 W
Puerto Bolívar, Ec.	246	3.16 S	79.59 W
Puerto Boyacá	246	5.59 N	74.24 W
Puerto Busch	248	20.02 S	57.55 W
Puerto Cabello	246	10.28 N	68.01 W
Puerto Cabezas	236	14.02 N	83.23 W
Puerto Carreño	246	6.12 N	67.22 W
Puerto Casado	252	22.20 S	57.55 W
Puerto Castilla	236	16.01 N	86.01 W
Puerto Chicama	248	7.42 S	79.27 W
Puerto Colombia	246	10.59 N	74.58 W
Puerto Constanza	258	33.50 S	59.03 W
Puerto Cortés	236	15.48 N	87.56 W
Puerto Cumarebo	246	11.29 N	69.21 W
Puerto de Eten	248	6.54 S	79.52 W
Puerto de Delicia	236	26.12 S	54.35 W
Puerto de Lomas	248	15.34 S	74.50 W
Puerto Deseado	254	47.45 S	65.54 W
Puerto El Triunfo	236	13.17 N	88.33 W
Puerto Escondido	234	15.50 N	97.10 W
Puerto España — Port of Spain	241r	10.39 N	61.31 W
Puerto Esperanza	252	26.01 S	54.39 W
Puerto Felipe, Bahía — Port Phillip Bay c	169	38.07 S	144.48 E
Puerto Fonciere	252	22.29 S	57.48 W
Puerto Francisco de Orellana	246	0.28 S	76.58 W
Puerto Gonzalo Moreno	248	11.06 S	66.10 W
Puerto Guaraní	248	21.18 S	57.55 W
Puerto Heath	248	12.30 S	68.40 W
Puerto Ingeniero Ibáñez	254	46.18 S	71.56 W
Puerto Inírida	246	3.53 N	67.52 W
Puerto Jiménez	236	8.33 N	83.19 W
Puerto Juárez	232	21.11 N	86.49 W
Puerto la Cruz	246	10.13 N	64.38 W
Puerto la Plata, Zona Nacional ⚹	288	34.52 S	57.52 W
Puerto Leda	248	20.41 S	58.02 W
Puerto Leguízamo	246	0.12 S	74.46 W
Puerto Lempira	236	15.15 N	83.47 W
Puerto Libertad, Arg.	252	25.55 S	54.36 W
Puerto Libertad, Méx.	232	29.55 N	112.43 W
Puerto Limón, Col.	246	3.23 N	73.30 W
Puerto Limón, C.R.	236	10.00 N	83.02 W
Puertollano	34	38.43 N	4.07 W
Puerto Lobos	254	42.00 S	65.06 W
Puerto Madero	234	14.44 N	92.25 W
Puerto Madryn	254	42.46 S	65.03 W
Puerto Maldonado	248	12.36 S	69.11 W
Puerto Manatí	238	21.22 N	76.50 W
Puerto Marañón	240p	27.01 N	112.15 W
Puerto Mihanovich	248	20.17 S	58.11 W
Puerto Montt	254	41.28 S	72.57 W
Puerto Morazán	236	12.51 N	87.11 W
Puerto Morelos	232	20.51 N	86.52 W
Puerto Narño	246	3.46 S	70.21 W
Puerto Natales	254	51.44 S	72.31 W
Puerto Nuevo, Punta ⚹	240m	18.30 N	66.24 W
Puerto Octay	254	40.58 S	72.54 W
Puerto Ordaz — Ciudad Guayana	246	8.22 N	62.40 W
Puerto Padre	238	21.12 N	76.36 W
Puerto Páez	246	6.13 N	67.28 W
Puerto Peñasco	232	31.20 N	113.33 W
Puerto Pilón	236	9.23 N	79.40 W
Puerto Pinasco	248	22.43 S	57.50 W
Puerto Pirámide	254	42.35 S	64.17 W
Puerto Pirav	252	26.28 S	54.42 W
Puerto Píritu	246	10.04 N	65.03 W
Puerto Portillo	248	9.46 S	72.45 W
Puerto Princesa, Pil.	116	9.44 N	118.44 E
Puerto Princesa, Pil.	116	10.06 N	125.29 E
Puerto Real, Arg.	252	26.28 S	54.42 W
Puerto Real, P.R.	240m	18.05 N	67.11 W
Puerto Rico, Arg.	252	26.48 S	54.58 W
Puerto Rico, Bol.	248	11.06 S	67.33 W
Puerto Rico, Col.	246	1.54 N	75.10 W
Puerto Rico ◻², N.A.	240m	18.15 N	66.30 W
Puerto Rico Trench ⚹	16	20.00 N	66.00 W

Column 4

	Página	Lat.	Long.
Puerto Saavedra	252	38.47 S	73.24 W
Puerto Salgar	246	5.28 N	74.39 W
Puerto Sandino	236	12.12 N	86.46 W
Puerto San José	236	13.55 N	90.49 W
Puerto San Julián	254	49.18 S	67.43 W
Puerto Santa Cruz	254	50.01 S	68.31 W
Puerto Sastre	252	20.04 S	57.59 W
Puerto Siles	248	12.48 S	65.05 W
Puerto Suarez	248	18.57 S	57.51 W
Puerto Supe	248	10.49 S	77.45 W
Puerto Tejada	246	3.14 N	76.24 W
Puerto Tolosa	246	0.59 S	76.09 W
Puerto Umbría	246	0.52 N	76.33 W
Puerto Vallarta	234	20.37 N	105.15 W
Puerto Varas	254	41.19 S	72.59 W
Puerto Victoria, Arg.	252	26.20 S	54.39 W
Puerto Victoria, Perú	248	9.54 S	74.58 W
Puerto Viejo, C.R.	236	9.39 N	82.45 W
Puerto Viejo, C.R.	236	10.26 N	83.59 W
Puerto Villamil	246a	0.56 S	91.01 W
Puerto Villarroel	248	16.50 S	64.47 W
Puerto Visser	254	45.24 S	67.08 W
Puerto Wilches	246	7.21 N	73.54 W
Puerto Williams	254	54.56 S	67.37 W
Puerto Yapabobó	252	23.42 S	57.12 W
Pueyrredón, Lago (Lago Cochrane) ⍝	254	47.20 S	72.00 W
Puffendorf	56	50.56 N	6.13 E
Puffing Billy Railroad Station →⁵	274b	37.55 S	145.21 E
Pugačov	80	52.01 N	48.50 E
Pugač'ovo	80	56.35 N	53.02 E
Puge, Tan.	154	4.45 S	33.07 E
Puge, Zhg.	102	27.28 N	102.31 E
Puget, Cape ⚹	180	59.52 N	148.26 W
Puget Island I	224	46.10 N	123.23 W
Puget Sound ⚹	224	47.50 N	122.30 W
Puget Sound Naval Shipyard ⚹	224	47.33 N	122.38 W
Puget-sur-Argens	62	43.27 N	6.41 E
Puget-Théniers	62	43.57 N	6.54 E
Puget-Villa	62	43.17 N	6.08 E
Pugh Mountain ⚹	224	46.38 N	121.22 W
Pughtown	285	40.10 N	75.40 W
Puglia ◻⁴	68	41.15 N	16.15 E
Pugog-ni	271b	37.43 N	126.58 E
Pugô-ri	98	42.01 N	129.59 E
Pugwash	186	45.51 N	63.40 W
Puhe	104	41.57 N	123.36 E
Puhi	229b	21.58 N	159.23 W
Puhoi	176	36.30 S	174.39 E
Puhos	26	62.05 N	29.54 E
Puhosjärvi ⍝	26	65.19 N	27.55 E
Puica	248	15.04 S	72.42 W
Puiešti	38	46.25 N	27.33 E
Puigcerdá	34	42.26 N	1.56 E
Puigmal ⚹	34	42.23 N	2.07 E
Puimoisson	62	43.52 N	6.08 E
Puinahua, Canal de ⚹	248	5.20 S	74.13 W
Puinán	272b	22.56 N	88.13 E
Puir	89	53.10 N	141.25 E
Puisaye, Collines de la ⚹²	50	47.42 N	3.15 E
Puiseaux	50	48.00 N	2.28 E
Puiseux-en-France	261	49.04 N	2.29 E
Puiseux-Pontoise	261	49.03 N	2.01 E
Puisieux	50	50.07 N	2.42 E
Puits ⚹	50	47.31 N	4.15 E
Pujada Bay c	116	6.51 N	126.14 E
Pujehun	150	7.21 N	11.42 W
Puji, Zhg.	100	29.58 N	113.25 E
Puji, Zhg.	100	29.58 N	113.32 E
Pujiang, Zhg.	100	29.28 N	119.53 E
Pujiang, Zhg.	107	30.12 N	103.30 E
Pujili	246	0.57 S	78.41 W
Pujon	115a	7.50 S	112.28 E
Pujut	114	1.20 S	104.20 E
Pujut, Tanjung ⚹	115a	5.52 S	106.02 E
Pukaki, Lake ⍝	172	44.07 S	170.10 E
Pukalani	229a	20.50 S	156.20 W
Pukaskwa ⚹	190	48.00 N	85.53 W
Pukaskwa National Park ⚹	190	48.20 N	85.50 W
Pukch'ang	98	39.36 N	126.17 E
Pukchin	98	40.13 N	125.46 E
Pukch'ŏn	98	36.13 N	126.45 E
Pukë	38	42.03 N	19.54 E
Pukeashun Mountain ⚹	182	51.12 N	119.14 W
Pukekohe	172	37.12 S	174.55 E
Puketeraki Range ⚹	172	42.58 S	172.12 E
Puketoi Range ⚹	172	40.30 S	176.05 E
Pukeuri Junction	172	45.02 S	171.02 E
Pukhan-gang ⚹	98	37.31 N	127.18 E
Pükhan-san ⚹	271b	37.41 N	127.00 E
Pukhrāyān	124	26.14 N	79.51 E
Puksoozero	86	62.38 N	40.36 E
Puksubaek-san ⚹	98	40.42 N	127.44 E
Puktae-ch'ŏn ⚹	98	40.38 N	127.14 E
Pula, Hrv.	36	44.52 N	13.50 E
Pula, It.	71	39.01 N	9.00 E
Pulacayo	248	20.25 S	66.41 W
Pulandian Wan c	98	39.18 N	121.35 E
Pulanduta Point ⚹	116	11.54 N	123.01 E
Pulangi ⚹	116	8.10 N	124.50 E
Pulap I¹	14	7.39 N	149.24 E
Pular, Cerro ⚹	252	24.11 S	68.04 W
Pulaski, Ia., U.S.	216	40.39 N	90.59 W
Pulaski, Mi., U.S.	216	42.07 N	84.40 W
Pulaski, N.Y., U.S.	210	43.34 N	76.08 W
Pulaski, Oh., U.S.	214	41.30 N	84.26 W
Pulaski, Tn., U.S.	194	35.11 N	87.01 W
Pulaski, Va., U.S.	216	37.03 N	80.46 W
Pulaski, Wi., U.S.	216	44.40 N	88.14 W
Pulaski ◻⁶	216	37.05 N	80.45 W
Pulaski ◻⁶	216	43.34 N	89.16 W
Pulaukida	174	2.44 S	102.34 E
Pulaumerak, Indon.	115a	5.56 S	106.00 E
Pulauraja	114	2.49 N	99.37 E
Pulawy	30	51.25 N	21.58 E
Pul'chakim	85	38.50 N	67.21 E
Pulehu Gulch ⚹	229a	20.48 N	156.23 W
Pulfero	68	46.13 N	13.29 E
Pulgaon	124	20.44 N	78.19 E
Pulham Market	42	52.26 N	1.14 E
Pulheim	56	51.00 N	6.47 E
Puli	100	23.58 N	120.57 E
Pulicat	122	13.25 N	80.19 E
Pulicat Lake c	122	13.40 N	80.10 E
Pulivendla	122	14.25 N	78.15 E
Puliyangudi	122	9.10 N	77.24 E
Pulkau	61	48.43 N	15.51 E
Pülken	56	51.00 N	6.47 E
Pulkkila	26	64.16 N	25.52 E
Pullman, Mi., U.S.	216	42.29 N	86.05 W
Pullman, Wa., U.S.	202	46.44 N	117.10 W
Pullo	248	15.14 S	73.50 W
Pulo'm ⚹	154	3.30 S	21.35 E

Column 5

	Página	Lat.	Long.
Pulog, Mount ⚹	116	16.36 N	120.54 E
Pulogadung →⁸	269e	6.11 S	106.54 E
Pulon'ga	24	66.17 N	40.02 E
Púlpito do Sul	152	15.46 S	12.00 E
Pulsano	68	40.23 N	17.22 E
Pulsen	54	51.23 N	13.26 E
Pulsnitz	54	51.11 N	14.01 E
Pulsnitz ⚹	54	51.27 N	13.33 E
Pulteney	210	42.31 N	77.10 W
Pultneyville	210	43.17 N	77.11 W
Puttusk	30	52.43 N	21.05 E
Pulū, Zhg.	107	29.50 N	106.11 E
Pulu, Zhg.	120	36.11 N	81.30 E
Pulupandan	116	10.31 N	122.48 E
Puluur	130	40.10 N	39.53 E
Pulusuk I¹	14	6.42 N	149.19 E
Pulversheim	58	47.51 N	7.18 E
Puma Yumco ⍝	120	28.35 N	90.20 E
Pumbi	152	3.26 N	22.11 E
Pumei	102	23.28 N	105.15 E
Pumphrey	284b	39.13 N	76.38 W
Pumpkin Buttes ⚹	200	43.44 N	105.54 W
Pumpkin Center, U.S.	228	35.18 N	119.05 W
Pumpkin Creek ⚹, Mt., U.S.	198	46.15 N	105.45 W
Pumpkin Creek ⚹, Ne., U.S.	198	41.38 N	103.01 W
Pumsi	82	57.12 N	51.39 E
Puna, Isla I	246	2.50 S	80.08 W
Punaauia	174s	17.38 S	149.36 W
Punaauia, Pointe de ⚹	174s	17.38 S	149.36 W
Punakha	124	27.37 N	89.52 E
Punaluu	229c	21.35 N	157.53 W
Punan, Indon.	112	1.20 N	115.34 E
Punan, Indon.	112	3.24 N	116.16 E
Punan, Zhg.	100	24.39 N	117.41 E
Punata	248	17.32 S	65.50 W
Pünch	123	33.46 N	74.06 E
Pünch ⚹	123	33.12 N	73.40 E
Puncha	126	23.10 N	86.39 E
Punchaw	182	53.28 N	123.13 W
Punchbowl	274a	33.56 S	151.03 E
Pundaguitan	116	6.22 N	126.10 E
Punda Maria	156	22.40 S	31.05 E
Pünderich	56	50.02 N	7.08 E
Pündri	124	29.45 N	76.33 E
Pune (Poona)	122	18.32 N	73.52 E
P'ungam-ni	98	37.43 N	128.11 E
Pungarancho ⚹	234	18.47 N	100.41 W
Pungešti	271c	1.25 N	103.55 E
Punggol →⁸	271c	1.25 N	103.54 E
Pungi	114	4.17 N	96.13 E
Pungo ⚹	192	35.23 N	76.33 W
Pungo Andongo	152	9.40 S	15.35 E
Punia	154	1.28 S	26.27 E
Punín	98	40.47 N	128.10 E
P'ungsan, C.M.I.K.	98	38.28 N	125.01 E
P'ungsong-ni	98	36.36 N	127.11 E
Punilla, Sierra de la ⚹	252	28.55 S	69.00 W
Puning	100	23.18 N	116.12 E
Punitaqui	252	30.50 S	71.16 W
Punjab ◻³	123	31.00 N	75.30 E
Punjab ◻³	123	31.00 N	72.30 E
Punkaharju ⚹	26	61.47 N	29.20 E
Punkalaidun	26	61.07 N	23.06 E
Punnichy	184	51.23 N	104.18 W
Puno	248	15.50 S	70.02 W
Puno ◻⁵	248	15.00 S	70.00 W
Punta, Castillo de la ⚹	286b	23.09 N	82.21 W
Punta, Cerro de ⚹	240m	18.10 N	66.36 W
Punta Alegre	240p	22.23 N	78.49 W
Punta Alta	252	38.53 S	62.05 W
Punta Arenas	254	53.09 S	70.55 W
Punta Banda, Cabo ⚹	232	31.45 N	116.45 W
Punta Cardón	246	11.38 N	70.14 W
Punta Colnett	232	31.05 N	116.05 W
Punta de agua Creek (Tramperos Creek) ⚹	196	35.32 N	102.27 W
Punta de Bombón	248	17.11 S	71.48 W
Punta de Díaz	252	28.00 S	70.37 W
Punta del Cobre	252	27.30 S	70.16 W
Punta del Este	252	34.58 S	54.57 W
Punta Delgada	254	42.46 S	63.38 W
Punta de los Llanos	252	30.09 S	66.33 W
Punta de Piedras	246	10.54 N	64.06 W
Punta de Piedras	116	7.23 N	123.25 E
Punta Gorda, Belize	236	16.07 N	88.48 W
Punta Gorda, Nic.	236	11.31 N	83.47 W
Punta Gorda, Fl., U.S.	192	26.55 N	82.02 W
Punta Gorda, Bahía de ⚹	236	11.15 N	83.45 W
Punta Negra, Salar de ⚹	252	24.35 S	69.00 W
Punta Prieta	232	28.58 N	114.17 W
Punta Raisi, Aeroporto di ⚹	70	38.11 N	13.06 E
Punta Santiago	240m	18.10 N	65.45 W
Punta Santiago	236	9.58 N	84.50 W
Puntarenas ⚹	236	10.00 N	84.45 W
Puntas del Sauce	258	33.51 S	57.01 W
Punto Fijo	246	11.42 N	70.13 W
Puntzi Lake ⍝	182	52.12 N	124.02 W
Punung	115a	8.08 S	111.01 E
Puolanka	26	64.52 N	27.40 E
Puokio	26	64.49 N	27.26 E
Puolo Point ⚹	229b	21.54 N	159.36 W
Pupuya, Volcán ⚹¹	236	11.50 N	85.55 W
Puqi, Zhg.	100	29.43 N	113.52 E
Puqi, Zhg.	102	26.13 N	104.27 E
Puqian	103	20.01 N	110.36 E
Puquio	248	14.42 S	74.08 W
Puquios	252	23.36 S	70.18 W

Column 6

	Página	Lat.	Long.
Purificación ≃, Méx.	234	19.18 N	104.54 W
Purkari neem ⚹	76	59.40 N	25.43 E
Pursima	196	29.09 N	100.46 W
Pursima, Sierra de la ⚹	196	26.30 N	101.44 W
Pursima Creek ⚹	282	37.24 N	122.26 W
Pursima de Bustos	234	21.02 N	101.52 W
Purxersdorf	61	48.12 N	16.11 E
Pureign	260	51.41 N	0.40 E
Purey	222	33.05 N	95.16 W
Purey →⁸	260	51.20 N	0.07 W
Purfleet	210	42.17 N	74.00 W
Purmerend	52	52.31 N	4.57 E
Pūrna ⚹, India	122	19.07 N	77.02 E
Pūrna ⚹, India	122	21.05 N	76.00 E
Pūrnia	124	25.47 N	87.31 E
Purenga	76	60.09 N	40.54 E
Puruanque	254	40.55 S	73.10 W
Purorumba Hill ⚹	175b	35.10 S	149.23 E
Purros	156	18.38 S	12.59 E
Purumbete, Lake ⍝	169	38.17 S	143.14 E
Pursat			
— Poŭthisät	110	12.32 N	103.55 E
Purton	42	51.36 N	1.52 W
Puruándiro	234	20.05 N	101.30 W
Puruarén	234	20.00 N	101.32 W
Purui ⚹	246	1.40 S	68.08 W
Purukcahu	112	0.35 S	114.35 E
Puruliya	126	23.20 N	86.22 E
Pur, ni ⚹	246	6.00 N	59.12 W
Pur, s (Purús) ≃	242	3.42 S	61.28 W
Pur, vesi ⚹	26	61.50 N	29.27 E
Purvis	194	31.08 N	89.24 W
Purwakarta	115a	6.34 S	107.26 E
Purwantoro	115a	7.51 S	111.15 E
Purwareja	115a	7.28 S	109.25 E
Purwodadi, Indon.	115a	7.49 S	110.00 E
Purwodadi, Indon.	115a	7.05 S	110.54 E
Purwokerto	115a	7.25 S	109.14 E
Purworejo	115a	7.43 S	110.01 E
Puse	112	1.36 N	111.17 E
Pusen	122	19.54 N	77.35 E
Pusen	98	35.06 N	129.03 E
Pūse Road	124	25.59 N	85.41 E
Puset Gayo, Pegunungan ⚹	114	4.15 N	97.05 E
Pusho	82	54.50 N	37.36 E
Pusco Point ⚹	116	13.31 N	122.38 E
Pushang	98	36.08 N	119.42 E
Pushkar	120	26.30 N	74.33 E
Pushkin — Puškin	76	59.43 N	30.25 E
Pushkin Airport ≃	265a	59.41 N	30.21 E
Pushkin Drama Theatre ⚹	265a	59.56 N	30.21 E
Pushthrough	186	47.39 N	56.10 W
Puškin-cka	78	48.40 N	34.16 E
Pusong-ni	98	40.19 N	127.19 E
Puspóklédány	30	47.19 N	21.07 E
Pussay	50	48.21 N	2.00 E
Püssi	76	59.24 N	27.07 E
Pustertal V	64	46.45 N	12.20 E
Pustin'	76	56.45 N	35.32 E
Pustomy:y	78	49.42 N	23.56 E
Pustoš	76	60.07 N	42.45 E
Pustošb-ka	76	56.20 N	29.22 E
Pustozersk	24	67.33 N	52.27 E
Puszczykowo	30	52.17 N	16.52 E
Putaendc	252	32.38 S	70.44 W
Putah Creek ⚹	226	38.33 N	121.42 W
Putai	100	23.23 N	120.09 E
Putang, Tanjung ⚹	269e	6.13 S	106.54 E
Putanjqiao	98	34.34 N	118.59 E
Putao	110	27.21 N	97.24 E
Putaruru	172	38.03 S	175.47 E
Put'atino	80	54.28 N	41.07 E
Putaux	265	48.53 N	2.14 E
Putian, Pulau I	113	1.25 N	103.00 E
Putian	100	25.28 N	119.01 E
Putian Zhg.	100	25.26 N	119.01 E
Putignano	68	40.51 N	17.07 E
Putina	248	14.55 S	69.52 W
Putivli	78	51.20 N	33.53 E
Putjana, Volcán ⚹¹	236	11.50 N	85.55 W
Putla de Guerrero	234	17.02 N	97.56 W
Putlitz	54	53.15 N	12.02 E
Putnam, Ct., U.S.	207	41.55 N	71.54 W
Putnam, Tx., U.S.	196	32.22 N	99.12 W
Putnam ◻⁶, Oh., U.S.	216	41.03 N	73.41 W
Putnam ◻⁶, N.Y., U.S.	210	41.25 N	73.42 W
Putnam Valley	210	41.20 N	73.50 W
Putney, Ga., U.S.	192	31.29 N	84.07 W
Putney, Vt., U.S.	188	42.59 N	72.31 W
Putney →	260	51.28 N	0.13 W
Putney Island ⚹	260	51.28 N	0.13 W
Putorana Plain ⚹	88	69.00 N	95.00 E
Putorino	172	39.07 S	177.00 E
Putrajaya	113	2.56 N	101.42 E
Putsonderwater	158	29.14 S	21.53 E
Puttalam	122	8.02 N	79.49 E
Puttalam Lagoon c	122	8.15 N	79.45 E
Puttelange	58	49.03 N	6.56 E
Putten	52	52.15 N	5.36 E
Putten I	52	51.52 N	4.15 E
Puttgarden	54	54.30 N	11.13 E
Puttlingen	56	49.17 N	6.53 E
Putumayo (çá) ≃	242	3.07 S	67.58 W
Putuoshan	100	30.00 N	122.24 E
Putussibau	112	0.50 N	112.56 E
Puʻuanunu	229b	20.01 N	155.48 W
Puʻu Kaalaea ⚹	229c	21.30 N	157.54 W
Puʻu Keʻekeʻe ⚹	229b	20.01 N	155.48 W
Puʻu Keahiakahoe ⚹	229c	21.23 N	157.49 W

ENGLISH				DEUTSCH		
Name	Page	Lat.°ʳ	Long.°ʳ	Name	Seite	Breite°ʳ Länge°ʳ E = Ost

Column 1

Name	Page	Lat.	Long.
Puukohola Heiau National Historic Site ▲	229d	20.00 N	155.46 W
Puukolii	229a	20.56 N	156.40 W
Puu Kukui ▲	229a	20.52 N	156.35 W
Puula ⌀	26	61.50 N	26.42 E
Puumala	26	61.32 N	28.11 E
Puunene	229a	20.51 N	156.27 W
Pu'upu'a	175a	13.34 S	172.09 W
Puurmani	76	58.34 N	26.17 E
Puurs	50	51.05 N	4.17 E
Puuwai	229b	21.54 N	160.12 W
Puxi	100	25.10 N	119.08 E
Puxian	102	36.30 N	111.02 E
Puxico	194	36.56 N	90.09 W
Puxingchang	107	30.41 N	105.06 E
Puyallup	224	47.11 N	122.17 W
Puyallup ≃	224	47.15 N	122.24 W
Puyang	98	35.42 N	114.59 E
Puyang ⌀	100	30.05 N	120.11 E
Puyang (Tumbes) ≃	246	3.30 S	80.27 W
Puy-de-Dôme ⌀⁵	32	45.45 S	3.05 E
Puyehue	254	40.40 S	72.37 W
Puyehue, Volcán ▲¹	254	40.35 S	72.08 W
Puylaurens	32	43.34 N	2.01 E
Puy-l'Évêque	32	44.30 N	1.08 E
Puyloubier	32	43.31 N	5.41 E
Puymorens, Col de ✕	32	42.30 N	1.50 E
Puyo, Ec.	246	1.28 S	77.59 W
Puyö, Taehan	98	36.18 N	126.54 E
Puysegur Point ⟩	172	46.09 S	166.36 E
Puyuguapi, Canal ᴍ	254	44.45 S	72.48 W
Puyun-dong	98	41.55 N	129.30 E
Pūzak, Hāmūn-e ⌀	128	31.30 N	61.45 E
Puzhen	100	32.09 N	118.41 E
Puzzle Creek ≃	162	17.58 S	135.41 E
Puzzle Lake ⌀, On., Can.	212	44.36 N	76.58 W
Puzzle Lake ⌀, Fl., U.S.	220	28.41 N	81.02 W
Pwalagu	150	10.35 N	0.50 W
Pwani ⌀⁴	154	7.00 S	39.00 E
Pweto	154	8.28 S	28.54 E
Pwinbyu	110	20.22 N	94.40 E
Pwllheli	42	52.53 N	4.25 W
Pyalo	110	19.09 N	95.11 E
Pyalong	169	37.07 S	144.54 E
Pyamalaw ≃¹	110	15.49 N	94.42 E
Pyapon	110	16.17 N	95.41 E
Pyatigorsk — P'atigorsk	84	44.03 N	43.04 E
Pyawbwe	110	20.35 N	96.04 E
Pyaye	110	19.15 N	95.06 E
Pyčas	80	56.29 N	52.28 E
Pye Islands ᴵᴵ	180	59.22 N	150.25 W
Pygmalion Point ⟩	116	6.45 N	93.49 E
Pyhäjärvi ⌀, Europe	26	61.53 N	30.00 E
Pyhäjärvi ⌀, Suomi	26	60.00 N	22.18 E
Pyhäjärvi ⌀, Suomi	26	62.46 N	25.30 E
Pyhäjärvi ⌀, Suomi	26	63.35 N	25.57 E
Pyhäjärvi ⌀, Suomi	26	61.28 N	23.35 E
Pyhäjoki	26	64.28 N	24.14 E
Pyhäjoki ≃	26	64.28 N	24.13 E
Pyhärnaa ᴵ	26	60.57 N	21.20 E
Pyhän-Häkin kansallispuisto ♦	26	62.52 N	25.30 E
Pyhäsalmi	26	63.41 N	25.59 E
Pyhäselkä ⌀	26	62.26 N	29.58 E
Pyhäselkä ⌀	26	62.26 N	29.58 E
Pyhätunturi ▲	24	67.01 N	27.09 E
Pyhätunturin kansallispuisto ♦	24	67.01 N	27.10 E
Pyhra	61	48.10 N	15.41 E
Pyhtää (Pyttis)	26	60.29 N	26.32 E
Pyinbongyi	110	17.34 N	96.34 E
Pyingaing	110	23.09 N	94.51 E
Pyinkayaing	110	15.58 N	94.24 E
Pyinmana	110	19.44 N	96.13 E
Pyle	42	51.32 N	3.42 W
Pylos — Pilos	38	36.55 N	21.43 E
Pymatuning Creek ≃	214	41.18 N	80.27 W
Pymatuning Reservoir ⌀¹	214	41.37 N	80.30 W
Pymatuning State Park ♦, Oh., U.S.	214	41.38 N	80.33 W
Pymatuning State Park ♦, Pa., U.S.	214	41.30 N	80.27 W
Pymble	274a	33.45 S	151.09 E
Pyngodl'gyn, laguna ⌀	180	67.24 N	175.10 W
Pyŏktong	98	40.35 N	125.20 E
Pyŏlch'ang-ni	98	39.17 N	126.26 E
Pyŏngnam Namdo ⌀⁴	98	39.20 N	126.00 E
Pyŏngan Pukdo ⌀⁴	98	40.10 N	125.20 E
Pyŏngch'ŏng-ni	98	37.23 N	128.22 E
Pyŏngdong-ni	98	39.08 N	126.19 E
Pyŏnggang	98	38.46 N	129.28 E
Pyŏnghae	98	38.19 N	126.23 E
Pyŏngsan	98	37.00 N	127.05 E
Pyŏngt'aek	98	39.01 N	125.45 E
Pyŏngyang	98	39.05 N	125.50 E
Pyŏngyang ⌀⁴	98	40.48 N	126.32 E
Pyote	196	31.32 N	103.08 W
Pyramid Head ⟩	228	32.49 N	118.21 W
Pyramid Lake ⌀	204	40.00 N	119.35 W
Pyramid Lake ⌀	228	34.39 N	118.47 W
Pyramid Lake Indian Reservation ♦	204	40.20 N	119.35 W
Pyramid Peak ▲, Ca., U.S.	226	38.50 N	120.19 W
Pyramid Peak ▲, Wa., U.S.	224	47.07 N	121.24 W
Pyramid Peak ▲, Wy., U.S.	200	43.27 N	110.28 W
Pyramid Point ⟩	174h	2.52 S	171.37 W
Pyramids of Giza — Jizah, Ahrāmāt al-	142	29.59 N	31.08 E
Pyrenäen — Pyrenees ✕	34	42.40 N	1.00 E
Pyrenees ✕	34	42.40 N	1.00 E
Pyrénées-Atlantiques ⌀⁵	32	43.15 N	0.50 W
Pyrénées Occident., Parc National des ♦	32	42.48 N	0.08 W
Pyrénées-Orientales ⌀⁵	32	42.30 N	2.20 E
Pyre Peak ▲	180	52.20 N	172.31 W
Pyrford	260	51.19 N	0.30 W
Pyrgi ᴵ	66	42.01 N	11.58 E
Pyrgos — Pirgos	38	37.41 N	21.28 E
Pyrkanajan, gora ▲	180	69.14 N	175.50 E
Pyrkino	80	53.49 N	45.07 E
Pyrmont	216	40.28 N	86.41 W
Pyrzyce	30	53.10 N	14.55 E
Pyšma	56	56.56 N	63.13 E
Pyšma ≃	56	56.56 N	63.43 E
Pyšma ≃	56	57.04 N	27.56 E
Pytalovo	76	57.04 N	27.56 E
Pythonga, Lac ⌀	190	46.23 N	76.25 W
Pyu	110	18.29 N	96.26 E
Pyuntaza	110	17.52 N	96.44 E
Pyūthān	124	28.06 N	82.54 E
Pyvésa ≃	76	56.04 N	24.27 E
Pyzdry	30	52.11 N	17.41 E

Q

Name	Page	Lat.	Long.
Qabātīyah	132	32.25 N	35.17 E
Qabbāsîn	130	36.25 N	37.34 E
Qabb Ilyās	132	33.48 N	35.49 E
Qabr Hūd	144	16.00 N	49.37 E
Qacentina (Constantine)	148	36.22 N	6.37 E
Qacentina ✕	148	36.22 N	6.40 E

Column 2

Name	Page	Lat.	Long.
Qaddīs Antūn, Dayr al- (Monastery of Saint Anthony) ✝¹	142	28.55 N	32.21 E
Qaddīs Būlus, Dayr al- (Monastery of Saint Paul) ✝¹	142	28.52 N	32.33 E
Qāderābād	128	30.17 N	53.16 E
Qādīān	123	31.49 N	75.23 E
Qā'emshahr	128	36.28 N	52.53 E
Qagan	88	49.14 N	118.08 E
Qagan Nur ⌀, Zhg.	98	41.23 N	113.55 E
Qagan Nur ⌀, Zhg.	102	43.37 N	114.40 E
Qahā	142	30.17 N	31.12 E
Qahar Youyi Zhongqi	102	41.09 N	112.38 E
Qahbūna	142	30.48 N	31.54 E
Qaidam ⌀	102	36.39 N	96.20 E
Qaidam Pendi ⌀¹	120	37.00 N	95.00 E
Qakar	120	36.32 N	80.43 E
Qala' an-Nahl	140	13.38 N	34.57 E
Qalabshū	142	31.26 N	31.19 E
Qalandīyah	132	31.50 N	35.14 E
Qalandūl	142	27.49 N	30.50 E
Qalāt	120	32.07 N	66.54 E
Qal'at ash-Shaqīf (Beaufort Castle) ᴵ	132	33.19 N	35.32 E
Qal'at Bīshah	144	20.01 N	42.36 E
Qal'at Sālih	128	31.31 N	47.16 E
Qal'at Sukkar	128	31.51 N	46.05 E
Qal'eh Shahr	120	35.33 N	65.34 E
Qal'eh-ye Deh-e Bārez	128	27.26 N	57.12 E
Qal'eh-ye Now, Afg.	120	35.27 N	67.08 E
Qal'eh-ye Now, Afg.	120	34.59 N	63.08 E
Qal'eh-ye Panjeh	123	37.00 N	72.36 E
Qal'eh-ye Sarkārī	120	35.54 N	67.17 E
Qallābāt, Sūd.	140	12.43 N	23.26 E
Qallābāt, Sūd.	142	12.58 N	36.09 E
Qalīn	142	31.03 N	30.51 E
Qalqilīya	132	32.11 N	34.58 E
Qalyūb	142	30.11 N	31.12 E
Qamar, Ghubbat al- ᴄ	118	16.00 N	52.30 E
Qamata	158	32.00 S	27.21 E
Qamdo	102	31.11 N	97.15 E
Qamīnis	146	31.39 N	20.03 E
Qamr-ud-dīn Kārez	120	31.39 N	68.25 E
Qamsar	128	33.45 N	51.26 E
Qanā, Ar. Su.	128	27.47 N	41.25 E
Qānā, Lubnān	132	33.13 N	35.18 E
Qanāyah	132	33.01 N	36.11 E
Qandahār ⌀⁴	120	31.32 N	65.30 E
Qandahār ⌀⁴	120	31.00 N	65.45 E
Qandala	144	11.28 N	49.52 E
Qantaran. Jabal ▲²	142	30.09 N	30.15 E
Qantur	140	9.45 N	25.52 E
Qārah, Ar. Su.	128	29.52 N	40.15 E
Qārah, Sūrīy.	130	34.09 N	36.44 E
Qarah Bāgh	128	34.56 N	61.46 E
Qarak	85	38.23 N	76.58 E
Qardwol	120	37.14 N	68.46 E
Qardho	144	9.34 N	49.05 E
Qareh ≃	128	34.52 N	51.25 E
Qareh Sū ≃	128	39.27 N	47.23 E
Qareh Żīā' od Dīn	84	38.54 N	45.02 E
Qarqan ≃	90	39.25 N	88.22 E
Qarqīn	120	37.25 N	66.03 E
Qartabā	130	34.06 N	35.51 E
Qārūn, Birkat (Lake Moeris) ⌀	142	29.30 N	30.40 E
Qaryat al-Qaddāhīyah	146	31.22 N	15.14 E
Qaryat al-Zuwaytīnah	146	30.58 N	20.07 E
Qaşa-e Qand	128	26.13 N	60.45 E
Qāsh, Nahr al- (Gash) ≃	140	16.48 N	35.51 E
Qashqeh, Kūh-e ▲	128	28.23 N	55.18 E
Qāsim	132	32.59 N	36.05 E
Qāsimwāla	123	30.09 N	73.50 E
Qasr ad-Dayr, Jabal ▲	132	30.48 N	35.34 E
Qasr al-Azraq ᴵ	132	31.53 N	36.49 E
Qasr al-Dubārā (Garden City) ✦⁸	273c	30.02 N	31.14 E
Qasr al-Jibāll	142	29.20 N	30.38 E
Qasr al-Kharānah ᴵ	132	31.44 N	36.28 E
Qasr al-Mushāsh ᴵ	132	31.49 N	36.19 E
Qasr al-Mushattā ᴵ	132	31.44 N	36.01 E
Qasr al Qarābūllī	146	32.45 N	13.43 E
Qasr 'Amrah ᴵ	132	31.48 N	36.35 E
Qasr at-Tūbah ᴵ	132	31.20 N	36.34 E
Qasr Baghdād	128	30.44 N	40.53 E
Qasr Bū-Hādī	146	31.03 N	16.40 E
Qasr Dab'ah ᴵ	132	31.36 N	36.03 E
Qasr-e Fīrūzeh	267d	35.40 N	51.32 E
Qasr el-Boukhari	148	35.51 N	2.52 E
Qasr Shīrīn	128	34.31 N	45.35 E
Qasr Qārūn	142	29.25 N	30.25 E
Qa'tabah	144	13.51 N	44.42 E
Qatanā	132	33.26 N	36.05 E
Qatar (Qatar) ▫¹, Asia	118	25.00 N	51.10 E
Qatar (Qatar) ▫¹, Asia	128	25.00 N	51.10 E
Qaţia, Bi'r ☴⁴	132	30.58 N	32.45 E
Qatmah	130	36.36 N	36.57 E
Qaṭrānī, Jabal ▲²	142	29.41 N	30.35 E
Qaţţānīyah, Ghurd al- ☴⁸	142	29.50 N	30.17 E
Qattara Depression — Qaţţārah, Munkhafad al- ▲⁷	140	30.00 N	27.30 E
Qaţţārah, Munkhafad al- (Cattara Depression) ▲⁷	142	29.18 N	31.10 E
Qaţţīnah, Buhayrat ⌀	130	34.39 N	36.34 E
Qawz Rajab	140	16.04 N	35.34 E
Qāy	142	29.39 N	30.57 E
Qaytah	132	33.04 N	36.08 E
Qāzigund	123	33.38 N	75.09 E
Qazvīn	128	36.16 N	50.00 E
Qeh	102	42.18 N	100.59 E
Qena — Qinā	140	26.10 N	32.43 E
Qegertaq ᴵ	176	71.55 N	55.30 W
Qesari, Horbat (Caesarea) ᴵ	132	32.30 N	34.53 E
Qeshm	128	26.58 N	56.16 E
Qeshm, Jazīreh-ye ᴵ	128	26.45 N	55.45 E
Qetura	132	29.58 N	35.03 E
Qeydār	128	36.07 N	48.35 E
Qeys, Jazīreh-ye ᴵ	128	26.32 N	53.58 E
Qezel Owzan ≃	128	36.45 N	49.57 E
Qezel Qeshlāq	84	39.08 N	45.21 E
Qi ≃, Zhg.	100	35.30 N	114.17 E
Qi ≃, Zhg.	100	35.30 N	115.20 E
Qi ≃, Zhg.	102	34.55 N	105.26 E
Qian'an, Zhg.	89	29.15 N	106.24 E
Qian'an, Zhg.	107	45.00 N	124.01 E
Qiancaijiatun	104	41.34 N	121.28 E
Qiandiwu	105	39.16 N	116.58 E
Qiandongnan ⌀⁴	106	26.35 N	108.18 E
Qiandaohu	100	29.34 N	119.00 E
Qianfang	100	28.32 N	116.13 E
Qian Gorlos	89	45.05 N	124.47 E
Qiangzilu	105	40.26 N	117.13 E
Qianhonghepu	104	41.23 N	123.07 E
Qianhuang	100	31.36 N	119.58 E
Qianjiadian	89	43.42 N	120.35 E
Qianjiang, Zhg.	106	29.32 N	108.46 E
Qianjiang, Zhg.	107	30.23 N	109.00 E
Qianjian'gangzi	104	41.34 N	122.26 E
Qianjiawan	104	41.37 N	122.26 E

Column 3

Name	Page	Lat.	Long.
Qianjiaqiao	106	30.53 N	121.31 E
Qianjiaying	105	39.35 N	118.21 E
Qianjiazhuang	106	32.16 N	120.17 E
Qianjing	106	31.33 N	121.15 E
Qianjinmiao	105	25.09 N	118.20 E
Qiankeng	106	30.43 N	119.47 E
Qiankoutou	105	39.42 N	117.01 E
Qianlijiazhuang	105	39.25 N	118.17 E
Qianluanshanzi	104	42.17 N	122.26 E
Qianmajiagushanzi	104	42.23 N	123.33 E
Qianmitun	104	41.49 N	123.15 E
Qianning	102	30.30 N	101.31 E
Qianpai	102	22.22 N	111.11 E
Qianqi	107	27.20 N	120.20 E
Qianqianjianglugou	104	41.59 N	120.58 E
Qiansandaoliangzi	104	42.06 N	120.44 E
Qianshahezi	104	41.46 N	123.01 E
Qianshan, Zhg.	106	30.36 N	116.33 E
Qianshan, Zhg.	100	31.06 N	120.24 E
Qian Shan ▲	104	40.52 N	123.25 E
Qianshuangshanzi	104	41.22 N	121.13 E
Qiansuo	100	28.44 N	121.27 E
Qiantang ≃	106	30.23 N	120.33 E
Qiantangzhen	107	30.12 N	106.18 E
Qianwei, Zhg.	102	42.31 N	120.06 E
Qianwei, Zhg.	107	29.12 N	103.57 E
Qianxi	106	27.02 N	106.01 E
Qianxi, Zhg.	105	40.09 N	118.19 E
Qianxiatazi	104	42.23 N	123.53 E
Qianyamen	104	42.04 N	121.26 E
Qianyaopu	104	42.09 N	122.37 E
Qi anzhen	106	32.11 N	121.03 E
Qianyou ≃	106	31.42 N	120.13 E
Qiaodun	100	27.29 N	120.18 E
Qiaoershan ↗	102	31.48 N	99.10 E
Qiaogou	102	32.26 N	115.45 E
Qiaohengjin	102	29.30 N	99.50 E
Qiaojia	102	26.57 N	102.52 E
Qiaokou	269b	31.15 N	121.19 E
Qiaokou	100	25.55 N	113.10 E
Qiaolima	120	34.35 N	81.00 E
Qiaomai	110	31.57 N	118.32 E
Qiaomu	98	39.34 N	114.27 E
Qiaopurikebazha	85	38.48 N	76.19 E
Qiaoqi	102	31.49 N	120.18 E
Qiaoshe	102	30.21 N	120.18 E
Qiaosi	106	30.21 N	120.18 E
Qiaotou, Zhg.	100	33.05 N	112.46 E
Qiaotou, Zhg.	106	28.17 N	99.22 E
Qiaotou, Zhg.	104	41.13 N	123.44 E
Qiaotou, Zhg.	106	32.11 N	119.14 E
Qiaotou, Zhg.	107	29.18 N	104.39 E
Qiaotoucun	106	31.39 N	119.08 E
Qiaotun	100	31.45 N	117.04 E
Qiaotoupu	106	30.33 N	118.50 E
Qiaotouyi	100	28.24 N	112.58 E
Qiaotouzhen	100	30.49 N	119.13 E
Qiaowan	102	40.36 N	96.55 E
Qiaowei	102	22.51 N	109.50 E
Qiaoxia	100	31.09 N	119.35 E
Qiaoxiajie	100	28.10 N	120.34 E
Qiaozhuang	100	31.39 N	121.24 E
Qibao	106	31.09 N	121.20 E
Qibyā	132	31.59 N	35.01 E
Qichun	100	30.17 N	115.26 E
Qiddīsah Kātrīnā, Dayr al- (Monastery of Saint Catherine) ✝¹	140	28.29 N	34.01 E
Qidong, Zhg.	102	26.44 N	112.04 E
Qidong, Zhg.	100	31.49 N	121.40 E
Qidu	107	30.16 N	117.46 E
Qiemo	120	38.08 N	85.32 E
Qiesanglinzi	104	41.42 N	123.30 E
Qieshikou	271a	39.59 N	116.24 E
Qifeng	107	29.25 N	106.30 E
Qifosi	100	29.27 N	105.58 E
Qift (Coptos)	140	26.00 N	32.49 E
Qigong	102	28.38 N	100.38 E
Qigongtai	104	41.50 N	123.08 E
Qihe (Yancheng)	100	36.48 N	116.44 E
Qiji	98	37.16 N	115.21 E
Qijiadian	89	43.38 N	125.36 E
Qijiang	107	29.02 N	106.39 E
Qijiapuzi	104	40.54 N	122.31 E
Qijiawan	100	30.53 N	114.13 E
Qijiawopeng	104	41.02 N	121.26 E
Qijiazi	104	41.54 N	122.58 E
Qika	89	50.35 N	119.16 E
Qila Abdullāh	120	30.43 N	66.38 E
Qila Dīdār Singh	123	32.08 N	74.01 E
Qilagugani Shan ▲	124	28.46 N	87.38 E
Qila Lādgasht	128	27.54 N	62.57 E
Qila Saifullāh	120	30.43 N	68.21 E
Qila Sobha Singh	123	32.14 N	74.46 E
Qili	130	38.05 N	100.12 E
Qilian Shan ▲	102	39.06 N	98.40 E
Qilian Shan ▲	102	39.19 N	117.33 E
Qili Hai ⌀	105	39.19 N	117.33 E
Qilihe, Zhg.	106	41.21 N	121.16 E
Qilihe, Zhg.	104	41.30 N	121.15 E
Qilinezi	104	41.06 N	123.08 E
Qilinguicun	106	32.04 N	118.55 E
Qilinzhen	106	31.56 N	121.21 E
Qiliping	100	31.27 N	114.39 E
Qiliqiao	106	31.35 N	120.48 E
Qilizhen, Zhg.	100	31.46 N	120.28 E
Qilizhen, Zhg.	100	32.19 N	120.05 E
Qilt,' Ayn al- ≃⁴	132	31.50 N	35.23 E
Qimafang	98	40.08 N	114.31 E
Qiman al-'Arūs	142	29.18 N	31.10 E
Qimen, Zhg.	100	29.52 N	117.42 E
Qimen, Zhg.	106	25.18 N	113.15 E
Qimoudi	105	39.35 N	115.32 E
Qimu Jiao ⟩	98	37.46 N	120.67 E
Qin, Zhg.	89	23.48 N	117.24 E
Qin, Zhg.	106	26.16 N	115.57 E
Qinā	102	35.01 N	113.25 E
Qinā, Wādī V, Mişr	140	26.12 N	32.44 E
Qinā, Wādī V, Mişr	142	26.12 N	32.44 E
Qincaigou	104	40.38 N	120.37 E
Qing'an, Zhg.	89	46.52 N	127.30 E
Qing'an, Zhg.	89	48.23 N	125.04 E
Qingbaikou	105	40.01 N	115.58 E
Qingcaoge	100	31.26 N	116.46 E
Qingchengzi	104	40.44 N	123.36 E
Qingdu, Zhg.	100	30.35 N	120.09 E
Qingduizi	104	39.41 N	121.53 E
Qingfeng	98	35.54 N	115.07 E
Qinggang	89	46.43 N	126.07 E
Qinggil — Qinghe	90	46.40 N	90.23 E
Qinggil ≃	90	46.37 N	90.38 E
Qinggou	100	37.12 N	117.40 E
Qinggouzi	104	41.49 N	121.36 E
Qing Hai ⌀	102	36.50 N	100.20 E
Qinghai ⌀⁴	102	36.00 N	96.00 E
Qinghai Hu ⌀	102	36.50 N	100.20 E
Qinghe (Tsinghai) ⌀⁴	102	35.16 N	96.00 E

Column 4

Name	Page	Lat.	Long.
Qingjian	102	37.10 N	110.00 E
Qingjiang, Zhg.	100	28.05 N	115.29 E
Qingjiang, Zhg.	100	33.35 N	119.02 E
Qingjiang, Zhg.	100	29.17 N	105.34 E
Qingjujie	107	30.42 N	106.07 E
Qinglian	107	24.27 N	112.45 E
Qingliuzhen	107	29.56 N	105.19 E
Qinglong, Zhg.	98	40.24 N	118.54 E
Qinglong, Zhg.	105	25.28 N	114.28 E
Qinglong ≃, Zhg.	105	39.51 N	118.51 E
Qinglong ≃, Zhg.	98	39.51 N	118.51 E
Qinglongchang, Zhg.	107	28.50 N	106.31 E
Qinglongchang, Zhg.	102	29.51 N	105.40 E
Qinglonggang	100	31.51 N	121.15 E
Qinglongguan	100	30.25 N	104.48 E
Qinglongji	100	34.05 N	116.37 E
Qinglongwan ≃	106	39.19 N	117.32 E
Qingmuguan	107	29.41 N	106.18 E
Qingningsi	100	31.16 N	121.33 E
Qingping, Zhg.	98	36.47 N	116.06 E
Qingpu	106	31.09 N	121.06 E
Qingquan	107	30.14 N	106.12 E
Qingquan	102	26.57 N	106.00 E
Qingshan ≃, Zhg.	105	40.09 N	118.19 E
Qingshan, Zhg.	100	30.38 N	114.23 E
Qingshan, Zhg.	106	30.15 N	119.52 E
Qingshan, Zhg.	106	30.36 N	119.41 E
Qingshanpu	100	30.43 N	120.03 E
Qingshanpu	100	29.27 N	114.01 E
Qingshen	107	29.50 N	103.50 E
Qingshi, Zhg.	102	32.42 N	106.21 E
Qingshi, Zhg.	100	29.23 N	99.09 E
Qingshi ≃, Zhg.	102	30.10 N	104.03 E
Qingshi ≃, Zhg.	102	37.30 N	105.30 E
Qingshuihe	86	44.12 N	80.45 E
Qingshuijian	98	39.59 N	115.58 E
Qingshuilang Shan ↗	102	26.15 N	99.35 E
Qingshuixi	102	29.09 N	103.55 E
Qingtan	100	31.48 N	112.48 E
Qingtang, Zhg.	106	26.25 N	115.48 E
Qingtang, Zhg.	106	24.14 N	113.51 E
Qingtian	100	28.10 N	120.17 E
Qingtong	107	29.28 N	103.27 E
Qingtongxia	102	37.53 N	105.54 E
Qingtuosi	98	35.29 N	118.20 E
Qingtuozi, Zhg.	104	41.05 N	121.28 E
Qingtuozi, Zhg.	105	39.08 N	117.45 E
Qingxi, Zhg.	106	23.39 N	113.50 E
Qingxi, Zhg.	107	30.40 N	106.14 E
Qingxian	98	38.34 N	116.46 E
Qingxizhen	107	30.49 N	103.55 E
Qingyang, Zhg.	89	45.20 N	128.47 E
Qingyang, Zhg.	100	30.38 N	117.48 E
Qingyang, Zhg.	102	36.06 N	107.47 E
Qingyangzhen	107	31.46 N	120.15 E
Qingyi ≃¹	107	29.34 N	103.42 E
Qingyuan, Zhg.	100	42.13 N	124.56 E
Qingyuan, Zhg.	100	27.38 N	119.04 E
Qingyuan	100	23.42 N	113.02 E
Qingyun (Xiejiaji)	105	38.52 N	115.29 E
Qingyundian	105	39.38 N	116.29 E
Qing Zang Gaoyuan ▲¹	12	33.00 N	92.00 E
Qingzhen, Zhg.	102	26.29 N	106.22 E
Qingzhen, Zhg.	106	29.41 N	107.24 E
Qingzhou	100	23.39 N	116.57 E
Qinhuai ≃	106	32.01 N	118.50 E
Qinhuangdao	98	39.56 N	119.36 E
Qinija	89	46.47 N	127.00 E
Qinlan	100	22.37 N	119.08 E
Qin Ling (Tsinlingshan) ↗	102	34.00 N	108.00 E
Qinnan	100	33.16 N	119.55 E
Qinshui	98	35.41 N	112.11 E
Qintong	100	32.39 N	120.08 E
Qinxian	102	36.45 N	112.41 E
Qinyang	102	35.06 N	112.57 E
Qinyuan	102	36.30 N	112.15 E
Qinzhou	102	21.59 N	108.36 E
Qionghai (Jiaji)	110	19.20 N	110.30 E
Qionglai	107	30.25 N	103.27 E
Qionglaishan ▲	102	31.21 N	102.50 E
Qionglong Shan ▲	106	31.15 N	120.25 E
Qiongzhong, Zhg.	110	19.04 N	109.48 E
Qiongzhou Haixia ᴍ	102	20.10 N	110.15 E
Qipandi	105	39.46 N	115.12 E
Qipanshan	98	38.05 N	100.12 E
Qiqian	89	52.12 N	120.49 E
Qiqihar (Tsitsihar)	88	47.19 N	123.55 E
Qira	120	37.00 N	80.47 E
Qir'awn, Buhayrat al- ⌀¹	132	33.34 N	35.42 E
Qiryat	132	32.49 N	35.06 E
Qiryat 'Anavim	132	31.48 N	35.07 E
Qiryat Ata	132	32.04 N	35.06 E
Qiryat Bialik	132	32.50 N	35.05 E
Qiryat Gat	132	31.36 N	34.46 E
Qiryat Hayyim	132	32.50 N	35.04 E
Qiryat Mal'akhi	132	31.44 N	34.44 E
Qiryat Motzkin	132	32.50 N	35.05 E
Qiryat Ono	132	32.03 N	34.51 E
Qiryat Shemona	132	33.13 N	35.34 E
Qiryat Tiv'on	132	32.43 N	35.08 E
Qiryat Yam	132	32.51 N	35.04 E
Qirzah, Wādī V	146	30.56 N	14.31 E
Qiseqi Shan ▲	89	43.37 N	122.32 E
Qishan	102	34.26 N	107.38 E
Qishon ≃	132	32.49 N	35.02 E
Qishrān ᴵ	144	20.14 N	40.05 E
Qishudang	129	29.13 N	104.39 E
Qishuyan	106	31.44 N	120.04 E
Qisrāyā	130	34.53 N	36.26 E
Qitai	89	44.01 N	89.28 E
Qitaihe	89	45.48 N	130.53 E
Qitamu	89	44.22 N	126.20 E
Qitangzhen	107	29.51 N	106.16 E
Qitou	100	31.02 N	114.44 E
Qiubei	102	24.07 N	104.12 E
Qiujin	100	28.58 N	115.40 E
Qiujiatun	104	41.20 N	121.00 E
Qiujin	100	29.10 N	115.42 E
Qiuxi	107	29.58 N	104.40 E
Qiuxizhen	107	29.56 N	104.40 E
Qiuxigang	100	30.33 N	119.42 E
Qixia	98	37.17 N	120.48 E
Qixian (Zhaoge), Zhg.	98	35.38 N	114.11 E
Qixian, Zhg.	98	34.33 N	114.47 E
Qixian, Zhg.	98	37.23 N	111.07 E
Qi Xia Si ✝¹	106	32.12 N	118.58 E
Qixingtai	104	41.21 N	120.33 E
Qiyang	102	26.36 N	111.51 E
Qiyi	102	36.38 N	105.28 E
Qizhou	102	23.52 N	111.31 E
Qizil Jilga	120	35.19 N	78.52 E
Qizil Langar	120	36.41 N	74.58 E
Qogir Feng (K2) ▲	123	35.53 N	76.30 E
Qolnak ≃⁸	267d	35.44 N	51.26 E
Qom	128	34.39 N	50.54 E
Qom ≃	128	34.55 N	51.02 E

Column 5 (ENGLISH/DEUTSCH)

Name	Page	Lat.	Long.
Qomolangma Feng — Everest, Mount	124	27.59 N	86.56 E
Qomsheh	128	32.01 N	51.52 E
Qondūz ≃	120	37.00 N	68.16 E
Qorveh	128	35.10 N	47.48 E
Qotbābād	128	28.42 N	53.34 E
Qoţūr	128	38.28 N	44.25 E
Qu ≃, Zhg.	100	29.12 N	119.27 E
Qu ≃, Zhg.	102	30.10 N	106.24 E
Quabbin Reservoir ⌀¹	207	42.22 N	72.18 W
Quaddick Reservoir ⌀¹	207	41.57 N	71.49 W
Quadra Island ᴵ	182	50.08 N	125.16 W
Quadraro ⌀⁸	267a	41.51 N	12.33 E
Quadros, Lagoa dos ⌀	252	29.42 S	50.05 W
Quaidābād	123	32.20 N	71.52 E
Quail Lake ⌀¹	228	34.47 N	118.45 W
Quail Valley	228	33.43 N	117.15 W
Quairading	162	32.01 S	117.25 E
Quakake	214	40.51 N	76.02 W
Quakenbrück	52	52.40 N	7.57 E
Quaker Hill, Ct., U.S.	207	41.22 N	72.06 W
Quaker Hill N.Y., U.S.	210	41.35 N	73.33 W
Quakers Hill	170	33.43 S	150.53 E
Quakers Knob ▲²	214	40.21 N	80.24 W
Quaker Street	210	42.44 N	74.11 W
Quakertown, N.J., U.S.	210	40.33 N	74.56 W
Quakertown, Pa., U.S.	208	40.26 N	75.20 W
Qualicum Beach	182	49.21 N	124.27 W
Quambatook	166	35.51 S	143.31 E
Quanah	196	34.17 N	99.44 W
Quanbao Shan ▲	102	34.09 N	111.29 E
Quangang	100	28.10 N	115.34 E
Quang Trach	110	17.45 N	106.27 E
Quanjiang	100	27.43 N	113.59 E
Quanjiao	100	32.06 N	118.16 E
Quan Long — Ca Mau	110	9.11 N	105.08 E
Quanman	104	42.02 N	122.13 E
Quannan	100	24.44 N	114.31 E
Quannapowitt, Lake ⌀	283	42.31 N	71.05 W
Quanshang	106	26.25 N	116.55 E
Quanshengpu	104	41.59 N	123.22 E
Quanshui	104	41.18 N	124.11 E
Quanshuitou	105	40.24 N	116.39 E
Quantico, Md., U.S.	208	38.22 N	75.44 W
Quantico, Va., U.S.	208	38.31 N	77.17 W
Quantico Marine Corps Air Station ■	208	38.31 N	77.19 W
Quantock Hills ✕²	42	51.07 N	3.10 W
Quantou	89	52.52 N	124.07 E
Quanxishi	100	26.51 N	112.45 E
Quanyanhezi	104	40.52 N	123.26 E
Quanzhou (Chuanzhou)	100	24.54 N	118.35 E
Quanzhou Gang ᴄ	100	24.52 N	118.37 E
Quaohaning	184	50.33 N	103.52 W
Qu'Appelle	184	50.25 N	101.20 W
Qu'Appelle Dam ✦	184	51.00 N	106.25 W
Quarai	252	30.23 S	56.27 W
Quarai ≃	252	30.12 S	57.36 W
Quaregnon	50	50.26 N	3.51 E
Quarles, Pegunungan ▲	112	2.55 S	119.30 E
Quarrata	66	43.50 N	10.58 E
Quarré-les-Tombes	50	47.22 N	3.59 E
Quarry	226	38.01 N	120.30 W
Quarry Heights	255	32.18 N	96.30 W
Quarryville, Ca., U.S.	207	41.51 N	72.25 W
Quarryville, Pa., U.S.	208	39.53 N	76.09 W
Quartu Sant'Elena	71	39.14 N	9.11 E
Quartz Hill	228	34.39 N	118.13 W
Quartz Lake ⌀	176	70.55 N	80.33 W
Quartz Mountain ▲	202	43.10 N	122.40 W
Quartzsite	200	33.39 N	114.13 W
Quatre, Isle à ᴵ	241h	12.57 N	61.15 W
Quatsino Sound ᴍ	182	50.25 N	127.55 W
Qubei	124	28.18 N	86.53 E
Qūchān	128	37.06 N	58.30 E
Quchijie	128	28.03 N	111.53 E
Qudaym	130	35.03 N	38.25 E
Qudsia Gardens ♦	272a	28.40 N	77.13 E
Quê ⌀	152	14.45 S	14.45 E
Queanbeyan	171b	35.21 S	149.14 E
Queanbeyan ≃	171b	35.20 S	149.14 E
Québec	206	46.49 N	71.14 W
Québec Airport ■	176	52.00 N	72.00 W
Quebec House	260	51.14 N	0.04 E
Quebeck	215	35.49 N	85.34 W
Quebra-Anzol ≃	255	19.09 S	48.14 W
Quebra-Cangalha, Serra da ▲	254	22.55 S	45.10 W
Quebrada Seca	252	31.57 S	57.53 W
Quebradillas	240m	18.29 N	66.56 W
Quebrangulo	248	18.29 N	36.28 E
Quecholac	234	18.57 N	97.39 W
Quechultenango	234	17.25 N	99.13 W
Quedal, Cabo ⟩	254	40.06 S	73.59 W
Quedas	156	19.30 S	33.29 E
Quedlinburg	54	51.48 N	11.09 E
Queen	214	40.16 N	78.31 W
Queen Alexandra Range ▲	9	84.00 S	168.00 E
Queen Alia International Airport ■	132	31.44 N	35.59 E
Queen Anne	208	38.55 N	75.57 W
Queen Anne Creek ≃	285	40.08 N	74.53 W
Queen Anne's ⌀⁶	208	39.03 N	76.04 W
Queen Bess, Mount ▲	182	51.16 N	124.34 W
Queen Charlotte	182	53.16 N	132.05 W
Queen Charlotte Bay ᴄ	254	51.50 S	60.40 W
Queen Charlotte Islands ᴵᴵ	182	53.00 N	132.00 W
Queen Charlotte Mountains ▲	182	53.00 N	132.00 W
Queen Charlotte Sound ᴍ	182	51.00 N	129.30 W
Queen Charlotte Strait ᴍ	182	50.50 N	127.25 W
Queen City, Mo., U.S.	194	40.24 N	92.34 W
Queen City, Tx., U.S.	194	33.08 N	94.09 W
Queen Elizabeth II Reservoir ⌀¹	260	51.23 N	0.24 W
Queen Elizabeth Islands ᴵᴵ	16	78.00 N	95.00 W
Queen Fabiola Mountains ▲	9	71.30 S	35.40 E
Queen Mary ⌀	280	33.45 N	118.12 W
Queen Mary Coast ✕	9	67.00 S	96.00 E
Queen Mary Reservoir ⌀¹	260	51.25 N	0.28 W
Queen Maud Gulf ᴄ	176	68.25 N	102.30 W
Queen Maud Land ✕	9	72.30 S	12.00 E
Queen Maud Mountains ▲	9	86.00 S	160.00 W
Queens ⌀⁶	210	40.44 N	73.52 W
Queensburg	216	39.25 N	85.19 W
Queens Channel ᴍ, Austl.	164	14.46 S	129.24 E

Column 6 (DEUTSCH)

Name	Seite	Breite	Länge
Queens Channel ᴍ, N.T., Can.	176	76.11 N	96.00 W
Queenscliff	169	38.16 S	144.40 E
Queensferry, Scot., U.K.	46	55.59 N	3.25 W
Queensferry, Wales, U.K.	44	53.12 N	3.01 W
Queensland ⌀³	160	22.00 S	145.00 E
Queensland Plateau ▲³	14	17.00 S	150.00 E
Queens Park ♦, Austl.	274a	33.54 S	151.16 E
Queens Park ♦, On., Can.	275b	43.40 N	79.24 W
Queens Park ♦, Eng., U.K.	262	53.35 N	2.27 W
Queen's Park ♦, Eng., U.K.	262	53.44 N	2.28 W
Queensport	186	45.21 N	61.16 W
Queens Sound ᴍ	182	51.55 N	128.11 W
Queenston	284a	43.10 N	79.03 W
Queenston Chippawa Power Canal ≃	284a	43.08 N	79.03 W
Queenstown, Austl.	160	42.05 S	145.33 E
Queenstown, Guy.	246	7.12 N	58.29 W
Queenstown — Cobh, Ire.	48	51.51 N	8.17 W
Queenstown, N.Z.	172	45.02 S	168.40 E
Queenstown, S. Afr.	158	31.52 S	26.52 E
Queenstown, Md., U.S.			
Queensville	212	44.08 N	79.28 W
Queen Victoria Park ♦	284a	43.05 N	79.05 W
Que'ar'ao ᴵ	100	28.48 N	121.51 E
Queerhe	104	40.57 N	121.35 E
Queets	224	47.32 N	124.19 W
Queets ≃	224	47.33 N	124.21 W
Queguay Grande ≃	252	32.09 S	58.09 W
Queich ≃	56	49.14 N	8.23 E
Queimada, Ilha ᴵ	250	0.10 S	50.50 W
Queimada Nova	250	8.35 S	41.25 W
Queimadas	250	10.58 S	39.38 W
Queimados	256	22.42 S	43.34 W
Queiros, Cap ⟩	175f	14.55 S	167.01 E
Quela	152	9.16 S	17.02 E
Quelimane	156	17.53 S	36.51 E
Quelichen	106	30.54 N	121.26 E
Quelle	52	52.00 N	8.29 E
Quellendorf	54	51.45 N	12.07 E
Quellón	254	43.07 S	73.37 W
Quelo	152	6.27 S	12.48 E
Quelpart Island — Cheju-do ᴵ	90	33.20 N	126.30 E
Queluz — Conselheiro Lafaiete, Bra.	255	20.40 S	43.48 W
Queluz, Bra.	256	22.32 S	44.46 W
Queluz, Port.	266c	38.45 N	9.15 W
Quemado, N.M., U.S.	200	34.20 N	108.29 W
Quemado, Tx., U.S.	196	28.56 N	100.38 W
Quemado de Güines	240p	22.18 N	74.08 W
Quemado de Güines	240p	22.13 N	80.15 W
Quemchi	254	42.09 S	73.29 W
Quemoy — Chinmen Tao ᴵ	100	24.27 N	118.23 E
Quemú Quemú	252	36.03 S	63.33 W
Quend	50	50.19 N	1.38 E
Quend Plage	50	50.19 N	1.33 E
Queñi, Nevado de ▲	246	14.55 S	71.49 W
Quenouilles, Lac aux ⌀			
Quepem	206	46.10 N	74.23 W
Quepem	208	40.17 N	76.26 W
Quepos	236	9.27 N	84.09 W
Quepos, Punta ⟩	236	9.23 N	84.10 W
Queqúen	252	38.32 S	58.42 W
Querary ≃	246	1.04 N	69.51 W
Quercianella	66	43.27 N	10.22 E
Quercy ⌀⁹	32	44.30 N	1.25 E
Querecotillo	248	4.53 S	80.40 W
Querenhorst	54	52.10 N	10.57 E
Querétaro	234	20.36 N	100.23 W
Querétaro ⌀³	234	21.00 N	99.55 W
Querfurt	54	51.23 N	11.36 E
Quero	64	45.55 N	11.56 E
Queroabi	232	30.03 N	111.01 W
Quesada, C.R.	236	10.19 N	84.26 W
Quesada, Esp.	58	37.51 N	3.04 W
Queset Brook ≃	283	42.02 N	71.04 W
Quesnel	100	32.48 N	114.01 E
Quesnel	182	52.59 N	122.30 W
Quesnel Lake ⌀	182	53.00 N	121.05 W
Quesney	62	50.33 N	3.40 E
Que Son	110	15.43 N	108.13 E
Questa	200	36.42 N	105.35 W
Questembert	32	47.40 N	2.27 W
Quetico Lake ⌀	190	48.34 N	91.52 W
Quetico Provincial Park ♦			
Quetta	190	48.30 N	91.30 W
Quettehou	32	30.12 N	67.00 E
Quetta ▲	32	49.36 N	1.18 W
Quetzala ≃	236	16.35 N	98.30 W
Quetzalcoalco ≃	234	18.09 N	94.25 W
Quetzaltenango	236	14.50 N	91.31 W
Quetzaltenango ⌀⁵	236	14.45 N	91.40 W
Quevedo	246	1.02 S	79.29 W
Quezaltepeque, El Sal.	236	13.50 N	89.17 W
Quezaltepeque, Guat.	236	14.38 N	89.27 W
Quezon, Pil.	116	15.34 N	120.49 E
Quezon, Pil.	116	14.01 N	122.11 E
Quezon ⌀³	116	13.58 N	122.02 E
Quezon City	116	14.38 N	121.03 E
Quezon Memorial ᴵ	269c	14.39 N	121.03 E
Qufu	98	35.36 N	117.02 E
Qugou, Zhg.	102	35.36 N	113.59 E
Qugou, Zhg.	105	39.17 N	116.15 E
Quiaca	152	10.46 S	14.59 E
Quibala	152	10.48 S	14.59 E
Quibaxi	152	8.29 S	14.36 E
Quibdó	246	5.42 N	76.40 W
Quiberon	32	47.29 N	3.07 W
Quiberville	32	49.54 N	0.55 E
Quibor	242	9.56 N	69.37 W
Quibray Bay ᴄ	274a	34.01 S	151.11 E
Quibú ≃	268b	23.05 N	82.27 W
Quiçama, Parque Nacional de ♦	152	9.45 S	13.30 E
Qui Chau	110	19.33 N	105.06 E
Quichen	254	41.55 N	73.57 E
Quickborn	52	53.44 N	9.53 E
Quickborn	152	8.31 S	15.19 E
Quicksand	152	8.21 N	15.49 E
Quidal Point ⟩	116	6.49 N	122.01 E
Quidnessett	207	41.37 N	71.27 W
Quidnick	207	41.41 N	71.32 W
Quiebra ≃	116	16.37 N	95.59 W
Quien Sabe Creek ≃	226	36.51 N	121.21 W
Quiévrain	50	50.24 N	3.41 E
Quiévy	50	50.13 N	3.23 E
Quiindy	252	25.58 S	57.14 W
Quila	234	24.23 N	107.13 W
Quilates, Cap ⟩	34	35.20 N	3.45 W
Quilengues	152	14.09 S	14.04 E
Quileute Indian Reservation ♦	224	47.55 N	124.38 W
Quilcura	268c	33.22 S	70.45 W
Quilimari	252	32.07 S	71.30 W
Quilino	252	30.12 S	64.29 W
Quilitamba	248	16.49 S	12.43 W
Quilocán	246	17.26 S	66.17 W
Quillabamba	246	12.50 S	72.43 W
Quillacollo	248	17.26 S	66.17 W
Quillagua	248	21.39 S	69.33 W
Quillan	32	42.52 N	2.11 E
Quilleuf-sur-Seine	98	49.29 N	0.31 E

▲ Mountain	Berg	Montaña	Montagne	Montanha
▲ Mountains	Gebirge	Montañas	Montagnes	Montanhas
✕ Pass	Paß	Paso	Col	Passo
V Valley, Canyon	Tal, Cañon	Valle, Cañón	Vallée, Canyon	Vale, Canhão
≃ Plain	Ebene	Llano	Plaine	Planície
⟩ Cape	Kap	Cabo	Cap	Cabo
ᴵ Island	Insel	Isla	Île	Ilha
ᴵᴵ Islands	Inseln	Islas	Îles	Ilhas
☴ Other Topographic Features	Andere Topographische Objekte	Otros Elementos Topográficos	Autres données topographiques	Outros acidentes topográficos

ESPAÑOL — Nombre | Página | Lat.°′ | Long.°′ W = Oeste

FRANÇAIS — Nom | Page | Lat.°′ | Long.°′ W = Ouest

PORTUGUÊS — Nome | Página | Lat.°′ | Long.°′ W = Oeste

Nombre / Nom / Nome	Página / Page	Lat.°′	Long.°′
Quill Lake	184	52.05 N	104.15 W
Quillota	252	32.53 S	71.16 W
Quilmes	258	34.44 S	58.16 W
Quilmes □[5]	288	34.44 S	58.16 W
Quilmes, Aeródromo ⊠	288	34.42 S	58.15 W
Quilombo ≏	256	23.52 S	46.21 W
Quilon	122	8.53 N	76.36 E
Quilotosa Wash V	200	32.56 N	112.46 W
Quilpie	166	26.37 S	144.15 E
Quilpué	252	33.03 S	71.27 W
Quilty	48	52.47 N	9.26 W
Quimarí, Alto de ∧	246	8.07 N	76.23 W
Quimbango	152	11.01 S	17.26 E
Quimbaya	246	4.38 N	75.47 W
Quimbele	152	6.28 S	16.13 E
Quimbo	152	13.59 S	16.05 E
Quimbonge	152	8.36 S	18.30 E
Quimbumbe	152	7.50 S	14.03 E
Quimby	198	42.37 N	95.38 W
Quime	248	17.02 S	67.15 W
Quimichis	234	22.21 N	105.32 W
Quimilí	252	27.38 S	62.25 W
Quimper	32	48.00 N	4.06 W
Quimperlé	32	47.52 N	3.33 W
Quinalasag Island I	116	13.56 N	123.38 E
Quinault	224	47.28 N	123.50 W
Quinault ≏	224	47.23 N	124.18 W
Quinault, North Fork ≏	224	47.32 N	123.40 W
Quinault Indian Reservation ◆[4]	224	47.24 N	124.10 W
Quinault Lake ⊜	224	47.28 N	123.52 W
Quinby Inlet ⊂	208	37.28 N	75.40 W
Quincampoix	50	49.32 N	1.11 E
Quince Mil	248	13.16 S	70.38 W
Quinches	248	12.13 S	76.05 W
Quincy, Ca., U.S.	204	39.56 N	120.56 W
Quincy, Fl., U.S.	192	30.35 N	84.35 W
Quincy, Il., U.S.	219	39.56 N	91.24 W
Quincy, Ky., U.S.	218	38.37 N	83.07 W
Quincy, Ma., U.S.	207	42.15 N	71.00 W
Quincy, Mi., U.S.	216	41.56 N	84.53 W
Quincy, Oh., U.S.	216	40.17 N	83.58 W
Quincy, Or., U.S.	224	46.08 N	123.09 W
Quincy, Pa., U.S.	208	39.48 N	77.35 W
Quincy, Wa., U.S.	202	47.14 N	119.51 W
Quincy Bay ⊂	283	42.17 N	70.58 W
Quincy-sous-Sénart	261	48.40 N	2.33 E
Quincy-Voisins	261	48.54 N	2.53 E
Quindanning	168a	33.03 S	116.34 E
Quindío □[5]	246	4.30 N	75.40 W
Quinebaug	207	42.01 N	71.57 W
Quinebaug ≏	207	41.33 N	72.03 W
Quines	252	32.13 S	65.48 W
Quinga	154	15.49 S	40.15 E
Quingey	58	47.06 N	5.53 E
Quingyi ≏	100	31.12 N	118.29 E
Quinhagak	180	59.45 N	161.43 W
Qui Nhon	110	13.46 N	109.14 E
Quiniluban Islands II	116	11.27 N	120.48 E
Quinjenje	152	12.49 S	14.55 E
Quinlan	222	32.55 N	96.08 W
Quinn ≏	204	40.52 N	119.03 W
Quiñones, Arroyo de los ≏	266a	40.33 N	3.34 W
Quinson	62	43.42 N	6.02 E
Quinta da Boa Vista ♠	287a	22.54 S	43.15 W
Quintanar de la Orden	34	39.34 N	3.03 W
Quintana Roo □[3]	232	19.40 N	88.30 W
Quinta Normal	286e	33.27 S	70.42 W
Quinta Normal de Agricultura ⊌[2]	286e	33.27 S	70.42 W
Quinte, Bay of ⊂	212	44.07 N	77.15 W
Quinter	198	39.04 N	100.13 W
Quintero	252	32.47 S	71.32 W
Quintette Mountain ∧	182	54.52 N	120.53 W
Quintin	32	48.24 N	2.55 W
Quintino Sella, Canale ≊	266b	45.29 N	8.38 E
Quinto	34	41.25 N	0.29 W
Quinto ≏	252	34.14 S	64.10 W
Quinto Creek ≏	226	37.11 N	121.02 W
Quinto de Noviembre, Presa ◆[6]	236	13.59 N	88.44 W
Quinton, Sk., Can.	184	51.23 N	104.24 W
Quinton, N.J., U.S.	208	39.32 N	75.24 W
Quinton, Ok., U.S.	196	35.07 N	95.22 W
Quinto Romano ◆[8]	266b	45.29 N	9.05 E
Quinzano d'Oglio	64	45.19 N	10.00 E
Quinzáu	152	6.51 S	12.46 E
Quinze, Lac des ⊜	190	47.35 N	79.05 W
Quionga	154	10.37 S	40.30 E
Quipapá	250	8.50 S	36.02 W
Quipar ≏	34	38.14 N	1.36 W
Quipeio	152	12.26 S	15.30 E
Quipemba	152	7.12 S	15.06 E
Quipit ≏	116	8.04 N	122.29 E
Quipungo	152	14.51 S	14.30 E
Quiquive ≏	248	14.39 S	67.38 W
Quirauk Mountain ∧	208	39.42 N	77.31 W
Quiriguá ⊥	236	15.17 N	89.04 W
Quirihue	252	36.17 S	72.32 W
Quirima	152	10.48 S	18.09 E
Quirimba, Ilha I	154	12.20 S	40.36 E
Quirimbo	152	10.36 S	14.12 E
Quirindi	166	31.31 S	150.41 E
Quirino □[4]	116	16.25 N	121.35 E
Quirinópolis	255	18.32 S	50.30 W
Quiriquire	246	9.59 N	63.13 W
Quiriri ≏	152	15.13 S	18.47 E
Quiririm	256	23.02 S	45.38 W
Quirke Lake ⊜	190	46.28 N	82.33 W
Quiroga, Esp.	34	42.29 N	7.16 W
Quiroga, Méx.	234	19.40 N	101.32 W
Quirós	252	28.47 S	65.07 W
Quirpon Island I	186	51.35 N	55.25 W
Quirra, Salto di ◆[1]	71	39.35 N	9.33 E
Quissac	62	43.55 N	4.00 E
Quissanga	154	12.25 S	40.29 E
Quissico	156	24.42 S	34.44 E
Quissongo	152	10.01 S	15.07 E
Quistello	64	45.00 N	10.59 E
Quitapa	152	10.23 S	18.14 E
Quitaque	196	34.22 N	101.04 W
Quitasueño ✣[4]	236	14.20 N	81.15 W
Quiterajo	154	11.48 S	40.25 E
Quitilipi	252	26.52 S	60.13 W
Quitman, Ga., U.S.	192	30.47 N	83.33 W
Quitman, Ms., U.S.	194	32.02 N	88.43 W
Quitman, Tx., U.S.	222	32.47 N	95.27 W
Quitman, Lake ⊜[1]	222	32.52 N	95.27 W
Quito	246	0.13 S	78.30 W
Quitzdorf, Speicherbecken ⊜[1]	54	51.17 N	14.45 E
Quivilla	248	9.32 S	76.41 W
Quixadá	250	4.58 S	39.01 W
Quixeramobim	250	5.12 S	39.17 W
Quixeré	250	5.05 S	37.59 W
Quixico	152	7.59 S	14.25 E
Quixinge	152	9.52 S	14.23 E
Quixito ≏	246	4.29 S	70.18 W
Quizenga	152	9.21 S	15.28 E
Qujiadian	89	43.13 N	123.53 E
Qujiang, Zhg.	100	28.15 N	115.45 E
Qujiang, Zhg.	100	24.48 N	113.17 E
Qujiang, Zhg.	100	24.41 N	113.35 E
Qujing	102	25.32 N	103.41 E
Qujiu	102	22.28 N	107.40 E
Qukou	105	39.46 N	117.07 E
Qulay'ah, Ra's al- ≻	128	28.53 N	48.18 E
Qulin	194	36.35 N	90.14 W
Qulubbā	142	27.45 N	30.50 E
Qulūd, Jabal ∧[2]	140	11.41 N	29.31 E
Qulūṣanā	142	28.21 N	30.44 E
Qulzum, Baḥr al- ⊂	142	29.55 N	32.31 E
Qumar ≏, Zhg.	90	34.42 N	94.50 E
Qumar ≏, Zhg.	120	34.39 N	95.00 E
Qumarlêb	102	34.35 N	95.27 E
Qumbu	158	31.10 S	28.48 E
Qumrān, Khirbat ⊥	132	31.44 N	35.27 E
Qunayfidhah, Nafūd ⊼[8]	128	24.45 N	45.30 E
Qunbush Al-Ḥamrā'	142	29.00 N	30.59 E
Qungtag	120	29.59 N	87.33 E
Qunshen'guan	105	39.49 N	117.59 E
Quobba, Point ≻	162	24.23 S	113.24 E
Quoich ≏	176	64.00 N	93.30 W
Quoich, Loch ⊜	46	57.04 N	5.17 W
Quoile ≏	48	54.21 N	5.42 W
Quoin Point ≻	158	34.46 S	19.37 E
Quonochontaug	207	41.21 N	71.43 W
Quorn	166	32.21 S	138.03 E
Quorndon	42	52.45 N	1.09 W
Quoxo ≏	156	22.16 S	24.02 E
Qurayyah, Wādī V	132	30.26 N	34.01 E
Qurayyāt	128	23.17 N	58.55 E
Qurdūd	140	10.17 N	29.56 E
Qurrāṣah	140	14.38 N	32.12 E
Qurūn Ḥarḥash ∧[2]	142	28.09 N	31.42 E
Qūṣ	140	25.55 N	32.45 E
Quṣayr ad-Daffah ⊥	146	30.20 N	23.57 E
Qūshchī	128	37.59 N	45.03 E
Qushui	107	30.41 N	106.02 E
Qutang	100	32.30 N	120.21 E
Qutbapur ◆[8]	272a	28.35 N	77.01 E
Qutb Minar ⊌[1]	272a	28.32 N	77.11 E
Qutdligssat	176	70.04 N	53.01 W
Quthing	158	30.30 S	27.36 E
Quṭūr	142	30.59 N	30.57 E
Quwaysinā	142	30.34 N	31.09 E
Quxi, Zhg.	100	28.00 N	120.31 E
Quxi, Zhg.	100	23.36 N	116.26 E
Quxia	106	32.06 N	120.09 E
Quxian, Zhg.	100	28.58 N	118.52 E
Quxian, Zhg.	102	30.51 N	106.59 E
Quxingji	98	34.52 N	114.39 E
Quxiong	102	31.09 N	96.00 E
Qüxü	120	29.22 N	90.43 E
Quyang	98	38.34 N	114.42 E
Qūyjāq-e-Bālā	84	39.16 N	47.07 E
Quyon	188	45.31 N	76.14 W
Quyquyó	252	26.14 S	57.01 W
Quzaymah, Jabal ∧	132	30.34 N	36.21 E
Quzhou	98	36.46 N	114.57 E
Quzong	102	30.08 N	96.00 E

R

Nom / Nome	Page / Página	Lat.°′	Long.°′
Råå	41	56.00 N	12.44 E
Raab → Győr, Magy.	30	47.42 N	17.38 E
Raab, Öst.	60	48.21 N	13.39 E
Raab (Rába) ≏	30	47.42 N	17.38 E
Raabs an der Thaya	61	48.51 N	15.30 E
Raadt ◆[8]	263	51.24 N	6.56 E
Raahe	26	64.41 N	24.29 E
Rääkkylä	26	62.19 N	29.37 E
Raalte	52	52.24 N	6.16 E
Raamsdonksveer	52	51.42 N	4.56 E
Ra'ananna	132	32.11 N	34.53 E
Raas, Pulau I	115a	7.09 S	114.32 E
Raasay I	46	57.23 N	6.04 W
Raasay, Sound of ⊔	46	57.27 N	6.06 W
Raasdorf	264b	48.15 N	16.34 E
Raasiku	76	59.22 N	25.11 E
Rab	36	44.46 N	14.46 E
Rab, Otok I	36	44.47 N	14.45 E
Raba	115b	8.27 S	118.46 E
Rába (Raab) ≏, Europe	30	47.42 N	17.38 E
Raba ≏, Pol.	30	50.09 N	20.30 E
Rabaable	144	8.17 N	48.18 E
Rabaçal ≏	34	41.30 N	7.12 W
Rábade	34	43.07 N	7.37 W
Rábahidvég	61	47.04 N	16.45 E
Rabai	154	3.58 S	39.37 E
Rabak	140	13.09 N	32.44 E
Rabal	164	6.22 S	134.52 E
Rabaraba	164	10.00 S	149.50 E
Rabat, Magreb	148	34.02 N	6.51 W
Rabat, Malta	36	35.52 N	14.25 E
Rabat (Victoria), Malta	36	36.02 N	14.14 E
Rabat □[4]	148	33.57 N	6.50 W
Rabaul	164	4.12 S	152.12 E
Rabbit ≏	216	42.38 N	86.06 W
Rabbit, Lac ⊜	190	47.30 N	78.22 W
Rabbit Creek ≏, S.D., U.S.	198	45.13 N	102.10 W
Rabbit Creek ≏, Tx., U.S.	222	32.26 N	94.47 W
Rabbit Ears Pass)(	200	40.23 N	106.37 W
Rabbit Lake ⊜, On., Can.	190	47.00 N	79.37 W
Rabbit Lake ⊜, Ca., U.S.	228	34.27 N	117.01 W
Rabbs Creek ≏	222	29.59 N	96.55 W
Rábca ≏	61	47.43 N	17.17 E
R'abcevo	76	54.39 N	32.19 E
Rabeira, Ponta da ≻	287a	22.49 S	43.10 W
Rabenau	54	50.57 N	13.38 E
Rabette, Ruisseau la ≏	261	48.35 N	2.00 E
Rābi', Ash-Shallāl ar- (Fourth Cataract) ∟	140	18.47 N	32.03 E
Rābigh	128	22.48 N	39.01 E
Rabinal	236	15.06 N	90.27 W
Rabiusa ≏	58	46.48 N	9.20 E
Rabka	30	49.36 N	19.56 E
Rabkavi Banhatti	122	16.28 N	75.06 E
Rabnābād Channel ⊔	126	21.50 N	90.19 E
Rabnābād Islands II	126	21.58 N	90.24 E
Rabočeostrovsk	24	64.59 N	34.48 E
Rabočij	86	59.07 N	79.00 E
Rabong, Gunong ∧	114	4.48 N	102.07 E
Rabotki	80	56.03 N	44.38 E
R'abovskij	80	50.01 N	41.53 E
Rabun Bald ∧	192	34.58 N	83.18 W
Rabwāh	123	31.44 N	72.50 E
Raby	262	53.19 N	3.02 W
Rabyānah ⊤[4]	146	24.15 N	22.00 E
Rabyānah, Ṣaḥrā' ◆[2]	146	24.30 N	21.00 E
Racale	68	39.57 N	18.06 E
Racalmuto	70	37.24 N	13.44 E
Răcari	38	44.38 N	25.45 E
Raccoon ≏	194	41.35 N	93.37 W
Raccoon Creek ≏, N.J., U.S.	208	39.48 N	75.23 W
Raccoon Creek ≏, Oh., U.S.	188	38.43 N	82.11 W
Raccoon Creek ≏, Oh., U.S.	214	40.02 N	82.24 W
Raccoon Creek ≏, Pa., U.S.	214	40.38 N	80.22 W
Raccoon Creek ≏, Pa., U.S.	285	39.48 N	75.23 W
Raccoon Creek ≏, Va., U.S.	208	36.48 N	77.10 W
Raccoon Creek, South Branch ≏	285	39.44 N	75.15 W
Raccoon Creek State Park ♠	214	40.30 N	80.27 W
Raccoon Island I	285	39.49 N	75.22 W
Raccuia	70	38.03 N	14.54 E
Race, Cape ≻	186	46.40 N	53.10 W
Raceland	194	29.43 N	90.35 W
Race Point ≻	207	42.04 N	70.14 W
Racette, Lac ⊜	206	46.34 N	74.03 W
Racette, Ruisseau ≏	206	46.36 N	74.04 W
Raceview	273d	26.17 S	28.08 E
Rach'a	76	60.05 N	30.49 E
Rach Gia	110	10.01 N	105.05 E
Rach Gia, Vinh ⊂	110	10.00 N	105.00 E
Rachmanovka, Ross.	80	51.57 N	49.29 E
Rachmanovka, Ukr.	78	47.48 N	33.13 E
Rachmanovo	82	55.44 N	38.37 E
Rachny Lesovyje	78	48.47 N	28.29 E
Rachov	78	48.03 N	24.12 E
Raciąż	30	52.47 N	20.06 E
Racibórz (Ratibor)	30	50.06 N	18.13 E
Racine, Pa., U.S.	214	40.49 N	80.20 W
Racine, Wi., U.S.	216	42.43 N	87.46 W
Racine □[6]	216	42.45 N	88.05 W
Racines	64	46.52 N	11.18 E
Račinskij chrebet ⋏	84	42.30 N	43.30 E
Rackerby	226	39.26 N	121.20 W
Ráckeve	30	47.10 N	18.56 E
Rackwick	46	58.52 N	3.23 W
R'ad	76	57.56 N	35.04 E
Råda	40	60.00 N	13.36 E
Radama, Nosy II	157b	14.00 S	47.47 E
Radama, Presqu'île ≻[1]	157b	14.16 S	47.53 E
Rådasjön ⊜	40	59.58 N	13.38 E
Radaur	124	30.02 N	77.09 E
Rădăuți	38	47.51 N	25.55 E
Radbuza ≏	60	49.46 N	13.24 E
Radčenskoje	78	49.48 N	40.32 E
Radcliff	194	37.50 N	85.56 W
Radcliffe	44	53.34 N	2.20 W
Radcliffe on Trent	42	52.57 N	1.03 W
Radda in Chianti	66	43.29 N	11.22 E
Raddusa	70	37.28 N	14.32 E
Råde	26	59.21 N	10.51 E
Radebaugh	279b	40.19 N	79.35 W
Radeberg	54	51.07 N	13.55 E
Radebeul	54	51.06 N	13.40 E
Radeburg	54	51.13 N	13.43 E
Radeče	36	46.04 N	15.11 E
Radechov	78	50.18 N	24.37 E
Radegast	54	51.39 N	12.05 E
Radenci	61	46.38 N	16.03 E
Radenthein	64	46.48 N	13.43 E
Radevormwald	56	51.12 N	7.21 E
Radford	192	37.07 N	80.34 W
Rādhānagar, India	126	23.09 N	87.19 E
Rādhānagar, India	272b	22.27 N	88.28 E
Rādhanpur	120	23.50 N	71.36 E
Radici, Foce delle)(	64	44.12 N	10.31 E
Radicofani	66	42.54 N	11.46 E
Radicondoli	66	43.16 N	11.02 E
Rădinești	38	44.48 N	23.46 E
Radiščevo	80	52.51 N	47.53 E
Radisson	184	52.27 N	107.23 W
Radiumbad Brambach	54	50.13 N	12.19 E
Radium Hot Springs	182	50.38 N	116.03 W
Rad'kovka	78	51.06 N	36.58 E
Radlett	42	51.42 N	0.20 W
Radlett Aerodrome ⊠	260	51.43 N	0.19 W
Radley Run ≏	285	39.54 N	75.37 W
Radlje ob Dravi	61	46.37 N	15.13 E
Rådmansö ≻[1]	40	59.45 N	18.55 E
Radnevo	38	42.18 N	25.56 E
Radnice	60	49.51 N	13.37 E
Radnor, Oh., U.S.	214	40.23 N	83.09 W
Radnor, Pa., U.S.	285	40.02 N	75.21 W
Radnor Forest ∧	42	52.18 N	3.10 W
Radnor Mere ⊜	262	53.17 N	2.14 W
Radofinnikovo	76	59.09 N	30.55 E
Radogošča	76	59.47 N	34.51 E
Radoj'a	38	47.44 N	28.09 E
Radolfzell	58	47.44 N	8.58 E
Radom, Pol.	30	51.25 N	21.10 E
Radom, Il., U.S.	219	38.17 N	89.12 W
Radom □[4]	30	51.25 N	21.15 E
Radomicko	54	52.10 N	14.58 E
Radomir	38	42.33 N	22.58 E
Radomka	78	51.56 N	32.32 E
Radomka ≏	30	51.43 N	21.26 E
Radomsko	30	51.05 N	19.25 E
Radomyšl'	78	50.30 N	29.14 E
Radomyśl Wielki	30	50.12 N	21.16 E
Radošice	60	49.33 N	13.39 E
Radoškoviči	76	54.09 N	27.14 E
Radotín	30	50.00 N	14.22 E
Radovicy	80	55.06 N	39.32 E
Radoviš	38	41.38 N	22.28 E
Radovljica	36	46.21 N	14.11 E
Radstadt	64	47.23 N	13.27 E
Radstädter Tauern)(	64	47.15 N	13.34 E
Radstock	42	51.18 N	2.28 W
Radstock, Cape ≻	162	33.12 S	134.20 E
Raduha ∧	61	46.25 N	14.45 E
Radul'	78	51.49 N	30.42 E
Radun'	76	54.03 N	25.00 E
Radušnoje	78	47.49 N	33.29 E
Radutino	76	52.39 N	33.57 E
Radvaniči	76	52.02 N	24.02 E
Radviliškis	76	55.50 N	23.31 E
Radville	184	49.27 N	104.17 W
Radway	182	54.04 N	112.57 W
Radykovskoje	80	45.56 N	41.57 E
Radymno	30	49.57 N	22.48 E
Radyr	42	51.31 N	3.15 W
Radziejów	30	52.38 N	18.32 E
Radzyń Chełmiński	30	53.24 N	18.56 E
Radzyń Podlaski	30	51.48 N	22.38 E
Rae	176	62.50 N	116.03 W
Rae ≏	176	67.55 N	115.30 W
Rāe Bareli	124	26.13 N	81.14 E
Raeford	192	34.58 N	79.13 W
Rae Isthmus ⊼[3]	176	66.55 N	86.10 W
Rāenda	126	22.18 N	89.51 E
Raeren	56	50.41 N	6.07 E
Raesfeld	52	51.46 N	6.50 E
Raeside, Lake ⊜	162	29.30 S	122.00 E
Rae Strait ⊔	176	68.45 N	95.00 W
Raetihi	172	39.26 S	175.17 E
Rafaela	252	31.16 S	61.29 W
Rafael Calzada	258	34.48 S	58.22 W
Rafael Castillo	288	34.43 S	58.37 W
Rafael Perazza	258	34.32 S	56.47 W
Rafaḥ	132	31.18 N	34.15 E
Rafaï	152	4.58 N	23.56 E
Rafalovka	78	51.22 N	25.52 E
Raffadali	70	37.24 N	13.32 E
Raffelberg, Rennbahn ♠	263	51.26 N	6.50 E
Raffili Mission	140	6.53 N	27.58 E
Rafḥā'	128	29.42 N	43.30 E
Rafinesque, Mount ∧[2]	210	42.47 N	73.37 W
Rafsanjān	128	30.24 N	56.01 E
Raft ≏	202	42.37 N	113.15 W
Raft River Mountains ⋏	200	41.55 N	113.25 W
Rafz	58	47.37 N	8.32 E
Raga	140	8.28 N	25.41 E
Ragada	64	46.10 N	10.38 E
Ragang, Mount ∧	116	7.43 N	124.32 E
Ragay	116	13.49 N	122.47 E
Ragay Gulf ⊂	116	13.30 N	122.45 E
Rågeleje	41	56.06 N	12.10 E
Rägelin	54	53.01 N	12.38 E
Ragewitz	54	51.14 N	12.51 E
Ragged, Mount ∧	162	33.27 S	123.25 E
Ragged Island I	238	22.12 N	75.44 W
Ragged Island Range II	238	22.40 N	75.54 W
Ragged Lake ⊜	212	45.28 N	78.38 W
Ragged Top Mountain ∧	200	41.27 N	105.20 W
Raghabpur	272b	22.25 N	88.21 E
Rāghogarh	124	24.27 N	77.12 E
Raghumāthbār	126	22.22 N	87.47 E
Raghunāthpur, Bngl.	126	23.12 N	89.31 E
Raghunāthpur, India	126	23.33 N	86.40 E
Raglan, Austl.	170	33.26 S	149.36 E
Raglan, N.Z.	172	37.48 S	174.53 E
Raglan, Wales, U.K.	42	51.47 N	2.51 W
Ragland	194	33.44 N	86.09 W
Ragnitz	61	46.50 N	15.35 E
Rago Nasjonalpark ♠	24	67.26 N	16.00 E
Ragow	264a	52.17 N	13.33 E
Ragozino	86	59.15 N	77.52 E
Rågsveden	40	60.29 N	14.05 E
Raguda, Ghubbet ⊂	144	10.45 N	46.34 E
Raguhn	54	51.42 N	12.17 E
Raguli	80	45.38 N	43.42 E
Ragusa → Dubrovnik, Hrv.	38	42.38 N	18.07 E
Ragusa, It.	70	36.55 N	14.44 E
Ragusa □[4]	70	36.55 N	14.36 E
Raguva	76	55.34 N	24.36 E
Raha	112	4.51 S	122.43 E
Rahad, Nahr ar- (Rahad) ≏	140	14.28 N	33.31 E
Rahad al-Bardī	140	11.18 N	23.53 E
Rahad Game Reserve ◆[4]	140	13.06 N	35.05 E
Rahaṭ, Ḥarrat ⊼[9]	144	22.20 N	40.05 E
Rahatgaon	124	22.15 N	77.14 E
Rāhatgarh	124	23.47 N	78.22 E
Raḥbah	130	34.30 N	36.09 E
Rahden	52	52.26 N	8.36 E
Rahimatpur	122	17.36 N	74.12 E
Rahīm Ki Bāzār	120	24.19 N	69.09 E
Rahīmyār Khān	120	28.25 N	70.18 E
Rahlstedt ◆[8]	52	53.36 N	10.09 E
Rahm	263	51.26 N	6.26 E
Rahm ◆[8], Dtsch.	263	51.32 N	7.23 E
Rahm ◆[8], Dtsch.	263	51.21 N	6.47 E
Rahmede ≏	263	51.17 N	7.41 E
Rahmer See ⊜	264a	52.45 N	13.25 E
Rahns	285	40.12 N	75.27 W
Rahnsdorf ◆[8]	264a	52.26 N	13.42 E
Rāhon	123	31.03 N	76.07 E
Rahotu	172	39.20 S	173.48 E
Rahouia	34	35.32 N	1.01 E
Rāhwāli	123	32.15 N	74.10 E
Rahway	210	40.36 N	74.16 W
Rahway ≏	276	40.35 N	74.12 W
Rahway, East Branch ≏	276	40.42 N	74.18 W
Rahway, Robinsons Branch ≏	276	40.37 N	74.17 W
Rahway, South Branch ≏	276	40.36 N	74.17 W
Rahway, West Branch ≏	276	40.42 N	74.18 W
Rahway River Parkway ♠	276	40.41 N	74.19 W
Raiano	66	42.06 N	13.49 E
Raiatea I	14	16.50 S	151.25 W
Rāichūr	122	16.12 N	77.22 E
Raidak ≏	124	26.22 N	89.45 E
Rāidighi	126	22.00 N	88.26 E
Raiding	61	47.34 N	16.32 E
Raiford	192	30.03 N	82.14 W
Raiganj	124	25.37 N	88.07 E
Raigarh	122	21.54 N	83.24 E
Raijua, Pulau I	112	10.37 S	121.36 E
Rāikot	123	30.39 N	75.36 E
Railroad	208	39.46 N	76.42 W
Railroad Canyon Reservoir ⊜[1]	228	33.42 N	117.16 W
Railroad Creek ≏	224	48.12 N	120.36 W
Rail Road Flat	226	38.20 N	120.30 W
Railroad Valley V	204	38.25 N	115.40 W
Railton	166	41.21 S	146.25 E
Raimangal ≏	126	21.47 N	89.08 E
Rain, Dtsch.	56	48.41 N	10.55 E
Rain → Riva di Tures, It.	64	46.57 N	12.04 E
Rainbach im Innkreis	60	48.27 N	13.32 E
Rainbow	228	33.24 N	117.10 W
Rainbow Bridge ◆[5]	284a	43.05 N	79.04 W
Rainbow Bridge National Monument ♠	200	37.06 N	110.57 W
Rainbow Falls ∟	182	52.23 N	119.59 W
Rainbow Lakes	276	40.52 N	74.28 W
Rainbow Park ♠	278	41.46 N	87.33 W
Rainbow Shores	212	43.37 N	76.12 W
Rainelle	188	37.58 N	80.46 W
Rainford	44	53.30 N	2.48 W
Rainham	42	51.23 N	0.36 E
Rainham ◆[8]	260	51.31 N	0.12 E
Rainhill	262	53.26 N	2.46 W
Rainhill Stoops	262	53.24 N	2.45 W
Rainier, Or., U.S.	224	46.05 N	122.56 W
Rainier, Wa., U.S.	224	46.53 N	122.41 W
Rainier, Mount ∧	224	46.52 N	121.46 W
Rainow	262	53.17 N	2.04 W
Rains □[6]	222	32.50 N	95.47 W
Rainsboro	218	39.13 N	83.25 W
Rainsford Island I	283	42.18 N	70.57 W
Rainworth	44	53.07 N	1.08 W
Rainy ≏, N.A.	184	48.50 N	94.41 W
Rainy ≏, Mi., U.S.	190	45.27 N	84.13 W
Rainy Lake ⊜, On., Can.	212	45.32 N	79.30 W
Rainy Lake ⊜, N.A.	184	48.42 N	93.10 W
Rainy Pass)(	224	48.32 N	120.39 W
Rainy River	190	48.43 N	94.34 W
Rāipur, Bngl.	126	23.03 N	90.46 E
Raipur, India	122	21.14 N	81.38 E
Raipur, India	124	30.19 N	78.06 E
Raipur, India	126	22.48 N	86.57 E
Raipur, India	272a	28.32 N	77.20 E
Raipur, India	272b	22.24 N	88.09 E
Rāipura	126	23.59 N	90.53 E
Raipur Uplands ⋏[1]	122	21.00 N	82.20 E
Rairākhol	120	21.04 N	84.21 E
Ra'īs	128	23.34 N	38.36 E
Raisdorf	54	54.17 N	10.16 E
Raisen	124	23.20 N	77.48 E
Ráisi, Punta ≻	70	38.11 N	13.06 E
Raisin	226	36.36 N	119.54 W
Raisin ≏, On., Can.	206	45.08 N	74.29 W
Raisin ≏, Mi., U.S.	216	41.53 N	83.20 W
Rāisinghnagar	123	29.32 N	73.27 E
Raismes	50	50.23 N	3.29 E
Raita	126	24.07 N	88.57 E
Raitenbuch	60	49.01 N	11.08 E
Raití	236	14.35 N	85.02 W
Raivavae I	14	23.52 S	147.40 W
Rāiwind	123	31.15 N	74.13 E
Raizeux	261	48.37 N	1.41 E
Raja, Gili I	115a	7.14 S	113.47 E
Raja, Ujung ≻	114	3.45 N	96.33 E
Rājābāri	126	23.23 N	90.28 E
Rajabasa	112	5.25 S	104.24 E
Rājābhāt Khāwa	124	26.37 N	89.32 E
Rājābhita	126	23.52 N	86.20 E
Rājahmundry	122	16.59 N	81.47 E
Rajāj	140	10.55 N	24.43 E
Rāja Jang	123	31.13 N	74.16 E
Raja-Jooseppi	24	68.28 N	28.21 E
Rājākhera	124	26.55 N	78.11 E
Rājaldesar	120	28.02 N	74.28 E
Raj-Aleksandrovka	83	48.48 N	37.51 E
Rājāluka	126	22.09 N	86.38 E
Rajamäki	26	60.32 N	24.45 E
Rājampet	122	14.11 N	79.10 E
Rajang ≏	112	2.04 N	111.12 E
Rājanpur	120	29.06 N	70.19 E
Rājapālaiyam	122	9.27 N	77.34 E
Rājāpur, Bngl.	126	22.34 N	90.09 E
Rājāpur, India	122	16.40 N	73.31 E
Rājāpur, India	124	25.23 N	81.09 E
Rājāpur, India	272b	22.39 N	88.11 E
Rājapur Canal ≊	272b	22.30 N	88.07 E
Rājasthān □[3]	120	27.00 N	74.00 E
Rājauri	123	33.23 N	74.18 E
Rājbāri, Bngl.	124	23.46 N	89.39 E
Rājbāri, India	126	22.25 N	88.48 E
Raj Bhavan ⊌	272b	22.34 N	88.21 E
Rājbirāj	124	26.32 N	86.44 E
Rajčichinsk	89	49.46 N	129.25 E
Rājendrapur	126	24.06 N	90.27 E
Rajevskij	86	54.04 N	54.56 E
Rāj Gangpur	124	22.11 N	84.36 E
Rājganj ≏[1]	126	22.21 N	90.16 E
Rājgarh, India	123	28.38 N	75.23 E
Rājgarh, India	124	23.56 N	76.58 E
Rājgarh, India	124	27.14 N	76.38 E
Rajghat ⊌[1]	272a	28.39 N	77.15 E
Rājgīr	124	25.02 N	85.25 E
Rajgorod	80	48.26 N	44.55 E
Rajgorodka, Ukr.	83	49.22 N	37.57 E
Rajgorodka, Ukr.	83	48.50 N	39.04 E
Rajgorodok, Kaz.	80	48.48 N	52.53 E
Rajgorodok, Ukr.	83	48.54 N	37.43 E
Rajgród	30	53.44 N	22.42 E
Rājhāt	272b	22.56 N	88.21 E
Rajhrad	61	49.05 N	16.37 E
Rājibpur	272b	22.49 N	88.34 E
Rajik	112	2.36 S	105.56 E
Rajka	30	48.00 N	17.12 E
Rājkot	120	22.18 N	70.47 E
Rajkuzi	265a	59.47 N	29.57 E
Rājmahāl	124	25.03 N	87.50 E
Rājmahāl Hills ⋏[2]	124	24.40 N	87.25 E
Rājnagar	126	23.57 N	87.19 E
Rāj Nāndgaon	120	21.06 N	81.02 E
Rajokri ◆[8]	272a	28.31 N	77.07 E
Rājpipla	120	21.47 N	73.34 E
Rājpur, India	120	21.56 N	75.08 E
Rājpur, India	126	22.25 N	88.25 E
Rājpur, India	272a	28.44 N	77.22 E
Rājpur ◆[8]	272a	28.41 N	77.12 E
Rājpura	124	30.29 N	76.36 E
Rājshāhi	124	24.22 N	88.36 E
Rājshāhi □[5]	124	25.15 N	89.15 E
Rajskoje	83	48.34 N	37.25 E
Rājula	122	21.03 N	71.26 E
Raka	124	29.26 N	85.50 E
Raka ≏	124	29.24 N	87.58 E
Rakaia	172	43.45 S	172.01 E
Rakaia ≏	172	43.56 S	172.13 E
Rakamaz	30	48.08 N	21.30 E
Rakaposhi ∧	123	36.10 N	74.30 E
Rakata, Pulau I	115a	6.10 S	105.26 E
Rakha La)(	124	27.53 N	87.34 E
Rakhawt, Wādī V	144	17.40 N	51.40 E
Rakhine □[8]	110	19.00 N	94.15 E
Rakhneh	128	31.39 N	59.13 E
Rakhni	120	30.03 N	69.55 E
Rakhshān ≏	128	27.10 N	63.25 E
Rākīn	132	31.14 N	35.42 E
Rakitnoje, Ross.	78	50.51 N	35.50 E
Rakitnoje, Ross.	89	45.36 N	134.17 E
Rakitnoje, Ukr.	78	49.42 N	30.27 E
Rakitnoje, Ukr.	78	51.17 N	27.14 E
Rakke	76	58.59 N	26.15 E
Rakkestad	26	59.26 N	11.21 E
Rakoniewice	30	52.10 N	16.16 E
Rakops	156	21.00 S	24.32 E
Rákoscsaba ◆[8]	264c	47.29 N	19.17 E
Rákoshegy ◆[8]	264c	47.28 N	19.14 E
Rákoskeresztúr ◆[8]	264c	47.29 N	19.15 E
Rákoskert ◆[8]	264c	47.28 N	19.19 E
Rákosliget ◆[8]	264c	47.30 N	19.16 E
Rákospalota ◆[8]	264c	47.34 N	19.08 E
Rákos-patak ≏	264c	47.33 N	19.04 E
Rákosszentmihály ◆[8]	264c	47.32 N	19.11 E
Rakovnická plošina ⋏[1]	54	50.08 N	13.47 E
Rakovník	54	50.05 N	13.43 E
Rakovski	38	42.18 N	24.58 E
Rakša	80	53.33 N	41.37 E
Raksakiny	86	60.37 N	73.52 E
Rakuša	80	47.03 N	52.47 E
Råkvåg	26	63.46 N	10.05 E
Rakvere	76	59.22 N	26.20 E
Rakwa	164	2.42 S	134.30 E
Raleigh, Nf., Can.	186	51.34 N	55.44 W
Raleigh, Ms., U.S.	194	32.02 N	89.31 W
Raleigh, N.C., U.S.	192	35.46 N	78.38 W
Raleigh Hills	224	45.29 N	122.45 W
Raleighvallen Voltz Berg, Natuurreservaat ♠, Sur.	246	4.45 N	56.05 W
Raleighvallen Voltz Berg, Natuurreservaat ♠, Sur.	250	4.50 N	55.10 W
Ralik Chain II	14	8.00 N	167.00 E
Ralls	196	33.40 N	101.23 W
Ralls □[6]	219	39.34 N	91.30 W
Ralsko ∧	54	50.42 N	14.47 E
Ralston, Ne., U.S.	198	41.12 N	96.02 W
Ralston, Pa., U.S.	210	41.31 N	76.57 W
Ram ≏	182	52.23 N	115.25 W
Rama, Nic.	236	12.09 N	84.15 W
Rama, Yis.	132	32.56 N	35.22 E
Rama ≏	236	12.08 N	84.13 W
Ramacca	70	37.23 N	14.42 E
Rāmachandrapuram	122	16.51 N	82.01 E
Ramādah	144	13.38 N	43.56 E
Ramah	200	35.07 N	108.29 W
Ramah Indian Reservation ◆[4]	200	34.50 N	108.25 W
Rama Indian Reserve ◆[4]	212	44.41 N	79.15 W
Ramales de la Victoria	34	43.15 N	3.27 W
Rām Allāh	132	31.54 N	35.12 E
Rāman	123	29.58 N	74.58 E
Rāmanagaram	122	12.43 N	77.18 E
Rāmanāthapuram	122	9.23 N	78.50 E
Ramānāthpur	272b	22.41 N	88.14 E
Ramanbāti	272b	22.47 N	88.08 E
Rāmānuj Ganj	124	23.48 N	83.42 E
Ramapo	276	41.08 N	74.10 W
Ramapo ≏	276	40.58 N	74.17 W
Ramapo Lake ⊜	276	41.02 N	74.16 W
Ramapo Mountains ⋏	276	41.08 N	74.12 W
Ramas, Cape ≻	122	15.07 N	73.55 E
Ramasaig	46	57.24 N	6.44 W
Ramasucha	76	52.46 N	33.33 E
Ramat Gan	132	32.05 N	34.49 E
Ramat HaSharon	132	32.09 N	34.50 E
Ramat HaShofét	132	32.37 N	35.06 E
Ramathlabama	156	25.40 S	25.35 E
Ramatuelle	62	43.13 N	6.37 E
Rama VI Bridge ◆[5]	269a	13.48 N	100.31 E
Rāmban	123	33.15 N	75.15 E
Rambervillers	58	48.21 N	6.38 E
Rambi I	175g	16.30 S	179.59 E
Rambipuji	115a	8.13 S	113.36 E
Rambleton Acres	208	39.39 N	75.38 W
Ramblewood	285	39.55 N	74.56 W
Rambouillet	50	48.39 N	1.50 E
Rambouillet, Château de ⊥	261	48.39 N	1.49 E
Rambouillet, Forêt de ♠	261	48.40 N	1.50 E
Rambutyo Island I	164	2.20 S	147.50 E
Rām Dās	123	31.58 N	74.54 E
Rāmdia	126	23.42 N	89.32 E
Rāmdurg	122	15.57 N	75.18 E
Ramea	186	47.31 N	57.23 W
Ramea Islands II	186	47.31 N	57.21 W
Rāmechhāp	124	27.20 N	86.05 E
Rame Head ≻, Transkei	158	31.48 S	29.22 E
Rame Head ≻, Eng., U.K.	42	50.19 N	4.13 W
Rämen ⊜	40	60.18 N	15.10 E
Ramenje, Ross.	76	60.17 N	43.46 E
Ramenje, Ross.	82	56.34 N	37.13 E
Ramenka ◆[8]	265b	55.41 N	37.30 E
Ramenskoje	82	55.34 N	38.14 E
Ramer	194	32.03 N	86.13 W
Ramerupt	50	48.31 N	4.18 E
Rameški	76	57.21 N	36.03 E
Rāmeswaram	122	9.17 N	79.18 E
Ramey	214	40.48 N	78.24 W
Rāmganj	126	23.06 N	90.51 E
Rāmgarh, Bngl.	120	22.59 N	91.44 E
Rāmgarh, India	120	27.22 N	70.30 E
Rāmgarh, India	120	27.15 N	75.11 E
Rāmgarh, India	124	23.38 N	85.31 E
Rāmgarh, India	124	24.34 N	87.15 E
Rāmgarh, India	126	22.42 N	87.04 E
Rāmgarh Hills ⋏[2]	124	22.50 N	83.10 E
Ram Head ≻	240m	18.18 N	64.42 W
Rāmhormoz	128	31.16 N	49.36 E
Ramingining	164	12.19 S	135.03 E
Ramingstein	64	47.04 N	13.50 E
Ramírez, Méx.	196	27.20 N	100.58 W
Ramírez, Méx.	196	25.57 N	97.46 W
Ramiriquí	246	5.24 N	73.20 W
Ramis ≏	144	7.59 N	41.34 E
Rāmjībanpur	126	22.50 N	87.37 E
Rāmkānāli	126	23.35 N	86.45 E
Raml, Qārat ar- ∧[2]	142	30.02 N	30.39 E
Ramla	132	31.55 N	34.52 E
Ramlu ∧	144	13.24 N	41.51 E
Ramm, Jabal ∧	132	29.35 N	35.24 E
Rämmen	40	60.07 N	14.08 E
Rāmnagar, India	123	32.49 N	75.19 E
Rāmnagar, India	124	25.17 N	83.02 E
Rāmnagar, India	124	29.24 N	79.07 E
Rāmnagar, India	126	21.41 N	87.33 E
Rāmnagar, India	272b	22.23 N	88.19 E
Ramnäs	40	59.46 N	16.12 E
Ramo	144	6.42 N	41.23 E
Ramon'	78	51.54 N	39.20 E
Ramon, Har ∧	132	30.30 N	34.38 E
Ramon, Makhtésh ⊼[7]	132	30.36 N	34.49 E
Ramon, Naḥal V	132	30.36 N	34.55 E
Ramona, Ca., U.S.	228	33.02 N	116.52 W
Ramona, Ok., U.S.	196	36.31 N	95.55 W
Ramona, S.D., U.S.	198	44.07 N	97.12 W
Ramor, Lough ⊜	48	53.49 N	7.05 W
Ramos	234	22.50 N	101.55 W
Ramos ◆[8]	287a	22.51 S	43.15 W
Ramos ≏[1]	150	5.08 N	5.22 E
Ramosch	58	46.50 N	10.22 E
Ramos Island I	116	8.06 N	117.02 E
Ramos Mejía	258	34.38 S	58.34 W
Ramot	132	32.46 N	35.40 E
Ramotswa	156	24.56 S	25.50 E
Rāmpāl	126	22.34 N	89.39 E
Rampart	180	65.30 N	150.11 W
Ramparts ≏	180	66.11 N	129.03 W
Rampillon	50	48.33 N	3.04 E
Rampside	44	54.05 N	3.10 W
Rāmpur, India	120	31.27 N	77.38 E
Rāmpur, India	123	29.49 N	77.27 E
Rāmpur, India	124	28.49 N	79.02 E
Rāmpura	120	24.28 N	75.26 E
Rāmpura Phūl	123	30.17 N	75.14 E
Rampur Boalia → Rājshāhi	124	24.22 N	88.36 E
Rāmpur Hāt	126	24.10 N	87.47 E
Ramrath	263	51.06 N	6.41 E
Ramree Island I	110	19.06 N	93.48 E
Rāmsāgar	126	23.05 N	87.17 E
Ramsau	64	47.36 N	12.54 E
Ramsay Range ⋏	162	18.31 S	127.03 E
Ramsbeck	56	51.18 N	8.24 E
Ramsberg	40	59.46 N	15.17 E
Ramsbottom	44	53.40 N	2.19 W
Ramsden Bellhouse	260	51.37 N	0.29 E
Ramsden Heath	260	51.38 N	0.28 E
Ramsdorf	52	51.54 N	6.55 E
Ramsele	26	63.33 N	16.29 E
Ramsenthal	60	50.01 N	11.35 E
Ramseur	192	35.44 N	79.39 W
Ramsey, I. of Man	44	54.20 N	4.21 W
Ramsey, Eng., U.K.	42	51.56 N	1.14 E
Ramsey, Eng., U.K.	42	52.27 N	0.07 W
Ramsey, Il., U.S.	219	39.08 N	89.06 W
Ramsey, N.J., U.S.	210	41.03 N	74.08 W
Ramsey Bay ⊂	44	54.20 N	4.20 W
Ramsey Brook ≏	276	41.02 N	74.08 W
Ramsey Creek ≏	219	39.03 N	89.04 W
Ramsey Island I	42	51.52 N	5.10 W
Ramsey Lake ⊜	190	47.15 N	82.16 W
Ramsey Lake State Park ♠	219	39.10 N	89.08 W
Ramsgate, Austl.	274a	33.59 S	151.08 E
Ramsgate, S. Afr.	158	30.55 S	30.20 E
Ramsgate, Eng., U.K.	42	51.20 N	1.25 E
Rāmshai	124	26.44 N	88.51 E
Rāmshīr	128	30.54 N	49.24 E
Ramshorn Peak ∧	202	45.09 N	111.06 W
Rämshyttan	40	60.18 N	15.13 E
Ramsjö	26	62.11 N	15.39 E
Ramsloh	52	53.06 N	7.40 E
Ramstein	56	49.27 N	7.33 E
Rāmtek	120	21.24 N	79.20 E
Rāmu, Bngl.	120	21.25 N	92.07 E
Ramu, Kenya	154	3.56 N	41.13 E
Ramu ≏	164	4.02 S	144.41 E
Ramuševo	76	57.50 N	31.37 E
Ramvik	26	62.49 N	17.51 E
Ramville, Îlet I	240e	14.42 N	60.53 W
Ramygala	76	55.31 N	24.18 E
Ramzaj	80	53.18 N	44.44 E
Rānāghāt	126	23.11 N	88.35 E
Rana Kao, Volcán ∧[1]	174z	27.11 S	109.27 W
Ranalt	64	47.02 N	11.13 E
Rāna Pratāp Sāgar ⊜[1]	120	24.50 N	75.35 E
Rånäs	40	59.48 N	18.17 E
Ranau	112	5.58 N	116.41 E
Ranau, Danau ⊜	112	4.50 S	103.55 E
Ranbīrsinghpura	123	32.38 N	74.44 E
Ranburne	194	33.31 N	85.20 W
Rancabali	115a	7.08 S	107.21 E
Rancagua	252	34.10 S	70.45 W
Rancah	115a	7.12 S	108.30 E
Rance ≏	32	48.31 N	1.59 W
Rancevo, Ross.	76	56.56 N	34.03 E
Rancevo, Ross.	76	56.40 N	33.02 E
Rancharia	255	22.15 S	50.55 W
Rancheria	180	60.05 N	130.40 W
Ranchería ≏	246	11.34 N	72.54 W
Rancheria Rock ∧	202	44.53 N	120.08 W
Ranches of Taos	200	36.22 N	105.37 W
Ranchester	202	44.54 N	107.09 W
Rānchi	124	23.21 N	85.20 E
Ranchillos	252	26.57 S	65.03 W
Rānchi Plateau ⋏[1]	124	23.20 N	84.50 E
Ranch Lake ⊜	184	52.30 N	104.46 W
Rancho Colorado, Presa de ⊜[1]	286a	19.29 N	99.17 W
Rancho Cordova	226	38.35 N	121.18 W
Rancho Del Mar	226	38.10 N	122.15 W
Rancho Nuevo, Méx.	196	26.22 N	99.54 W
Rancho Nuevo, Méx.	234	23.12 N	97.48 W
Rancho Palos Verdes	228	33.45 N	118.24 W
Rancho Rinconado	226	37.18 N	122.01 W
Rancho Santa Fe	228	33.01 N	117.12 W
Rancho Veloz	240p	22.53 N	80.23 W
Ranchuelo	240p	22.23 N	80.09 W
Ranco, Lago ⊜	254	40.14 S	72.24 W
Rancocas	208	40.00 N	74.52 W
Rancocas Creek ≏	285	40.02 N	74.59 W
Rancocas Creek, North Branch ≏	208	40.00 N	74.52 W
Rancocas Creek, South Branch ≏	208	40.00 N	74.52 W
Rancocas Creek, Southwest Branch ≏	285	39.57 N	74.48 W
Rancocas Heights	285	39.59 N	74.51 W
Rancocas State Park ♠	285	40.00 N	74.50 W
Rancocas Woods	285	39.59 N	74.51 W
Rancul	252	35.03 S	64.42 W
Rand	166	35.36 S	146.35 E

≏	River	Fluß	Río	Rivière	Rio
≊	Canal	Kanal	Canal	Canal	Canal
∟	Waterfall, Rapids	Wasserfall, Stromschnellen	Cascada, Rápidos	Chute d'eau, Rapides	Cascata, Rápidos
⊔	Strait	Meeresstraße	Estrecho	Détroit	Estreito
⊂	Bay, Gulf	Bucht, Golf	Bahía, Golfo	Baie, Golfe	Baía, Golfo
⊜	Lake, Lakes	See, Seen	Lago, Lagos	Lac, Lacs	Lago, Lagos
≡	Swamp	Sumpf	Pantano	Marais	Pântano
⊓	Ice Features, Glacier	Eis- und Gletscherformen	Accidentes Glaciales	Formes glaciaires	Acidentes glaciares
⊤	Other Hydrographic Features	Andere Hydrographische Objekte	Otros Elementos Hidrográficos	Autres données hydrographiques	Outros acidentes hidrográficos
✣	Submarine Features	Untermeerische Objekte	Accidentes Submarinos	Formes de relief sous-marin	Acidentes submarinos
□	Political Unit	Politische Einheit	Unidad Politica	Entité politique	Unidade política
⊌	Cultural Institution	Kulturelle Institution	Institución Cultural	Institution culturelle	Instituição cultural
⊥	Historical Site	Historische Stätte	Sitio Histórico	Site historique	Sitio histórico
♠	Recreational Site	Erholungs- und Ferienort	Sitio de Recreo	Centre de loisirs	Area de Lazer
⊠	Airport	Flughafen	Aeropuerto	Aéroport	Aeroporto
■	Military Installation	Militäranlage	Instalación Militar	Installation militaire	Instalação militar
◆	Miscellaneous	Verschiedenes	Misceláneo	Divers	Diversos

Name	Page	Lat.°′	Long.°′
Rand (Germiston) Airport ⊠	273d	26.15 S	28.09 E
Randa	58	46.07 N	7.47 E
Randall Lake ⊜	216	41.57 N	85.02 W
Randall Park Mall ◆[9]	279a	41.26 N	81.32 W
Randalls Island I	276	40.48 N	73.55 W
Randallstown	284b	39.22 N	76.48 W
Randalstown	48	54.45 N	6.19 W
Randan	32	46.01 N	3.21 E
Rāndaveswar	126	23.43 N	87.17 E
Randazzo	70	37.53 N	14.57 E
Randbøl	41	55.42 N	9.16 E
Randburg	273d	26.06 S	27.59 E
Randers	26	56.28 N	10.03 E
Randfontein	158	26.11 S	27.42 E
Randfontein □[5]	273d	26.13 S	27.40 E
Randgate	273d	26.11 S	27.41 E
Randhurst ◆[9]	278	42.05 N	87.56 W
Randle	224	46.32 N	121.57 W
Randleman	192	35.49 N	79.48 W
Randlett	196	34.10 N	98.27 W
Randolph, Az., U.S.	200	32.55 N	111.30 W
Randolph, Me., U.S.	188	44.13 N	69.46 W
Randolph, Ma., U.S.	207	42.09 N	71.02 W
Randolph, Ne., U.S.	198	42.22 N	97.21 W
Randolph, N.Y., U.S.	210	42.09 N	78.58 W
Randolph, Oh., U.S.	214	41.01 N	81.14 W
Randolph, Ut,. U.S.	200	41.39 N	111.10 W
Randolph, Vt., U.S.	188	43.55 N	72.39 W
Randolph, Wi., U.S.	190	43.32 N	89.00 W
Randolph □[6], In., U.S.	218	40.10 N	85.00 W
Randolph □[6], Mo., U.S.	219	39.22 N	92.20 W
Randolph Air Force Base ■	196	29.32 N	98.16 W
Randolph Hills	284c	39.03 N	77.05 W
Randolph Village	284c	38.53 N	76.52 W
Random Island I	186	48.08 N	53.45 W
Random Lake	190	43.33 N	87.57 W
Randow ≃	54	53.41 N	14.04 E
Randowaya	164	1.52 S	136.31 E
Randowbruch ≡	54	53.15 N	14.10 E
Randsburg	228	35.22 N	117.39 W
Randse Afrikaanse Universiteit Ʊ[2]	273d	26.11 S	27.50 E
Randsfjorden ⊜	26	60.25 N	10.24 E
Rand Stadium ♠	273d	26.14 S	28.03 E
Randublatung	115a	7.12 S	111.23 E
Randudongkal	115a	7.06 S	109.19 E
Randwick	170	33.55 S	151.15 E
Randwick Racecourse ♠	274a	33.54 S	151.14 E
Råneå	26	65.52 N	22.18 E
Ranelagh	258	34.48 S	58.12 W
Rāner	123	28.53 N	73.17 E
Ranérou	150	15.18 N	13.58 W
Rāneswar	126	24.02 N	87.25 E
Raneue	114	5.03 N	95.20 E
Ranford	168a	32.48 S	116.31 E
Ranfurly, N.Z.	172	45.08 S	170.06 E
Ranfurly, Scot., U.K.	46	55.52 N	4.33 W
Rangae	114	6.17 N	101.44 E
Rāngāmāti	120	22.38 N	92.12 E
Rangantemiang	112	0.35 S	113.19 E
Rangas, Tanjung ›	112	2.38 S	118.49 E
Rangasa, Tanjung ›	112	3.33 S	118.56 E
Rangaunu Bay ⊂	172	34.50 S	173.15 E
Range Creek ≃	200	39.18 N	110.04 W
Range Indian Reserve ◆[4]	182	49.09 N	119.50 W
Rangeley	188	44.57 N	70.38 W
Rangely	200	40.05 N	108.48 W
Ranger	196	32.28 N	98.40 W
Ranger Lake ⊜	190	46.54 N	83.35 W
Rangersdorf	64	46.51 N	12.58 E
Ranghe	100	33.43 N	112.51 E
Rangia	120	26.28 N	91.38 E
Rangiora	172	43.18 S	172.36 E
Rangitaiki ≃	172	37.54 S	176.53 E
Rangitata ≃	172	44.12 S	171.30 E
Rangitikei ≃	172	40.18 S	175.14 E
Rangitukia	172	37.46 S	178.27 E
Rangkasbitung	115a	6.21 S	106.15 E
Rangkul'	85	38.29 N	74.22 E
Rangoon → Yangon	110	16.47 N	96.10 E
Rangoon ≃	110	16.29 N	96.21 E
Rangpo	124	27.11 N	88.32 E
Rangpur, Bngl.	124	25.45 N	89.15 E
Rangpur, Pāk.	123	30.31 N	71.34 E
Rangpuri ⊥	272a	28.33 N	77.08 E
Rangsang, Pulau I	114	1.00 N	102.55 E
Rangsdorf	54	52.17 N	13.25 E
Rangsdorfer See ⊜	264a	52.17 N	13.24 E
Ranguana Cay I	236	16.20 N	88.09 W
Ranguana Entrance ⊔	236	16.19 N	88.09 W
Rangun → Yangon	110	16.47 N	96.10 E
Ranholas	266c	38.47 N	9.22 W
Rānībāndh	126	22.52 N	86.47 E
Rānībennur	122	14.37 N	75.37 E
Rānīganj	126	23.37 N	87.08 E
Rānikhet	124	29.39 N	79.25 E
Ranino	80	52.58 N	40.15 E
Ranis	54	50.39 N	11.34 E
Rānīwāra	120	24.45 N	72.13 E
Rāniyah	128	36.15 N	44.53 E
Rankamhaeng National Park ♠	110	17.10 N	99.58 E
Ranken ≃	166	20.31 S	137.36 E
Ranken Store	166	19.35 S	136.55 E
Rankin, Il., U.S.	216	40.27 N	87.53 W
Rankin, Mi., U.S.	216	42.55 N	83.46 W
Rankin, Pa., U.S.	279b	40.24 N	79.52 W
Rankin, Tx., U.S.	196	31.13 N	101.56 W
Rankin Inlet	176	62.45 N	92.10 W
Rankins Springs	166	33.50 S	146.16 E
Rankūs	132	33.45 N	36.23 E
Rankweil	58	47.17 N	9.39 E
Ranlo	192	35.17 N	81.07 W
Ranneje	80	51.29 N	52.37 E
Rannersdorf	264b	48.08 N	16.28 E
Rannoch, Loch ⊜	46	56.41 N	4.20 W
Rannoch Moor ◆[3]	46	56.38 N	4.40 W
Rann of Kutch → Kutch, Rann of ◆[1]	120	24.05 N	70.10 E
Ranobe ≃	157b	17.10 S	44.08 E
Ranohira	157b	22.29 S	45.24 E
Ranomafana, Madag.	157b	18.57 S	48.50 E
Ranomafana, Madag.	157b	24.36 S	46.58 E
Ranomena	157b	23.25 S	47.17 E
Ranong	110	9.58 N	98.38 E
Ranongga Island I	175e	8.05 S	156.34 E
Ranopiso	157b	25.03 S	46.40 E
Ranot	110	7.46 N	100.19 E
Ranotsara Nord	157b	22.48 S	46.36 E
Rānsai	272c	18.53 N	73.05 E
Ransäter	40	59.46 N	13.26 E
Ransiki	164	1.30 S	134.10 E
Ransom, Il., U.S.	216	41.09 N	88.39 W
Ransom, Ks., U.S.	198	38.38 N	99.56 W
Ransom, Pa., U.S.	210	41.24 N	75.50 W
Ransom Creek ≃	284a	43.04 N	78.45 W
Ransomville	210	43.14 N	78.54 W
Ranson	188	39.17 N	77.51 W
Ransta	40	59.48 N	16.38 E
Ranstadt	56	50.21 N	8.59 E
Rantabe	157b	15.42 S	49.39 E
Rantasalmi	26	62.04 N	28.18 E
Rantau, Indon.	112	2.56 S	115.09 E
Rantau, Malay.	114	2.35 N	101.58 E
Rantaukampar	114	1.24 N	100.59 E
Rantaupanjang, Indon.	112	1.51 S	102.19 E
Rantaupanjang, Indon.	112	1.16 S	101.49 E
Rantaupanjang, Indon.	114	0.58 N	99.13 E
Rantauprapat	114	2.06 N	99.50 E
Rantekombola, Bulu ∧	112	3.21 S	120.01 E
Ranten	61	47.09 N	14.05 E
Rantepao	112	2.59 S	119.54 E
Rantigny	50	49.20 N	2.26 E
Rantoul	216	40.09 N	88.20 W
Rantsila	26	64.31 N	25.39 E
Rantzau	54	54.15 N	10.30 E
Ranua	26	65.55 N	26.32 E
Rānvād	272c	18.53 N	72.55 E
Ranwanalenaus	156	19.35 S	22.47 E
Råö	26	57.24 N	11.56 E
Rao'er	100	28.48 N	117.40 E
Raohe	89	46.47 N	134.00 E
Raon-L'Étape	58	48.24 N	6.51 E
Raon-sur-Plaine	58	48.31 N	7.06 E
Raoping	100	23.43 N	117.01 E
Raoui, 'Erg er ◆[2]	148	29.17 N	2.20 W
Raoul	192	34.27 N	83.36 W
Raoul Island I	14	29.16 S	177.54 W
Raoyang	98	38.16 N	115.44 E
Raoyang ≃	104	41.50 N	122.35 E
Raoyanghe	104	41.46 N	122.26 E
Rapa I	14	27.36 S	144.20 W
Rapa, Ponta do ›	252	27.22 S	48.26 W
Rapallo	62	44.21 N	9.14 E
Rapang	112	3.50 S	119.48 E
Rāpar	120	23.34 N	70.38 E
Raparo, Monte ∧	68	40.12 N	15.59 E
Rapatovo	80	55.04 N	54.37 E
Rāpch ≃	128	25.28 N	59.21 E
Rapel ≃	252	33.55 S	71.51 W
Rapel, Embalse ⊜[1]	252	34.12 S	71.30 W
Rapelli	252	26.24 S	64.29 W
Raphoe	48	54.52 N	7.36 W
Rapid ≃, Mi., U.S.	190	45.55 N	86.58 W
Rapid ≃, Mn., U.S.	198	48.42 N	94.26 W
Rapid ≃, Wa., U.S.	224	47.48 N	121.18 W
Rapidan ≃	188	38.22 N	77.37 W
Rapid Bay	168b	35.32 S	138.12 E
Rapid City, Mb., Can.	184	50.08 N	100.02 W
Rapid City, Mi., U.S.	190	44.50 N	85.16 W
Rapid City, S.D., U.S.	198	44.04 N	103.13 W
Rapid Creek ≃	198	43.54 N	102.37 W
Rapide Taureau, Barrage du ◆[6]	206	46.52 N	73.39 W
Rapid River	190	45.55 N	86.58 W
Räpina	76	58.06 N	27.27 E
Rapkan	85	40.22 N	70.40 E
Rapla	76	59.01 N	24.47 E
Rapness	46	59.14 N	2.51 W
Rapolano Terme	66	43.17 N	11.36 E
Rapolla	68	40.58 N	15.41 E
Rapone	68	40.51 N	15.30 E
Raposo ∧[2]	266c	38.40 N	9.11 W
Rappahannock ≃	208	37.34 N	76.18 W
Rappbodestausee ⊜[1]	54	51.44 N	10.53 E
Rappenlochschlucht ∟	58	47.23 N	9.47 E
Rappottenstein	61	48.31 N	15.05 E
Rāptī □[8]	124	28.15 N	82.30 E
Rāpti (Raptī) ≃, Asia	124	26.18 N	83.41 E
Rāptī ≃, Nepāl	124	27.33 N	84.07 E
Rapulo ≃	248	13.43 S	65.32 W
Rapu-Rapu	116	13.11 N	124.08 E
Rapu Rapu Island I	116	13.12 N	124.09 E
Raqabah, Khashm ar- ∧[2]	142	28.18 N	31.43 E
Raquette ≃	206	45.00 N	74.42 W
Raraka I[1]	14	16.10 S	144.54 W
Rara National Park ♠	124	29.35 N	82.05 E
Rārh Plains ≚	126	23.13 N	87.20 E
Rāribahāl	126	24.05 N	87.21 E
Raritan	210	40.34 N	74.38 W
Raritan ≃	208	40.29 N	74.17 W
Raritan, North Branch ≃	210	40.33 N	74.41 W
Raritan, South Branch ≃	210	40.33 N	74.41 W
Raritan Bay ⊂	208	40.28 N	74.12 W
Raroïa I	14	16.01 S	142.27 W
Raron	58	46.19 N	7.48 E
Rarotonga I	174k	21.14 S	159.46 W
Rarotonga International Airport ⊠	174k	21.12 S	159.49 W
Rarz	85	39.23 N	68.44 E
Rasa, Ilha I	287a	23.04 S	43.09 W
Rasa, Punta ›, Arg.	252	36.17 S	56.47 W
Rasa, Punta ›, Arg.	254	40.51 S	62.19 W
Rašaant	88	49.07 N	101.25 E
Rasa de Guaratiba, Ilha I	256	23.05 S	43.34 W
Rasa Island I	116	9.14 N	118.27 E
Ra's al-'Ayn	130	36.51 N	40.04 E
Ra's al-Barr	142	31.31 N	31.50 E
Ra's al-Khalīj	142	31.15 N	31.39 E
Ra's al-Khaymah	128	25.47 N	55.57 E
Ra's al-Unūf	146	30.31 N	18.34 E
Ra's al-Ushsh ◆[8]	142	31.08 N	32.18 E
Ra's an-Naqb, Miṣr	132	29.36 N	34.51 E
Ra's an-Naqb, Urd.	132	30.00 N	35.29 E
Rasawi	164	2.04 S	134.01 E
Ra's Ba'labakk	130	34.15 N	36.25 E
Rasbo	40	59.57 N	17.53 E
Raschau	54	50.32 N	12.50 E
Ras Dashen Terara ∧	144	13.16 N	38.24 E
Rasdorf	56	50.43 N	9.53 E
Raseborg	26	59.59 N	23.39 E
Raseiniai	76	55.24 N	23.07 E
Râs el Aïoun	36	35.30 N	8.18 E
Ras el Ma, Alg.	148	34.31 N	0.46 W
Râs el Mâ, Mali	150	16.37 N	4.28 W
Ras el Oued	34	35.57 N	5.03 E
Rasen-Antholz → Anterselva di Sopra	64	46.52 N	12.08 E
Raševka	78	50.14 N	33.54 E
Rashād	140	11.51 N	31.04 E
Rāshayyā	132	33.30 N	35.51 E
Rashīd (Rosetta)	142	31.24 N	30.25 E
Rashīd, Far' (Rosetta Branch) ≃	142	31.30 N	30.21 E
Rashīd, Maṣabb (Rosetta Mouth) ≃[1]	142	31.30 N	30.20 E
Rashīd Qal'eh	120	31.31 N	67.31 E
Rashin → Najin	98	42.15 N	130.18 E
Rasht	128	37.16 N	49.36 E
Rashtrapati Bhawan Ʊ	272a	28.37 N	77.12 E
Rasina ≃	38	43.37 N	21.22 E
Rāsipuram	122	11.28 N	78.10 E
Rasi Salai	110	15.20 N	104.09 E
Rāsk	128	26.13 N	61.25 E
Raška	38	43.17 N	20.37 E
Rask Mølle	41	55.52 N	9.37 E
Rās Koh ∧	128	28.50 N	65.12 E
Raškov	38	47.57 N	28.50 E
Raskunda	126	22.48 N	87.26 E
Rasm al-Arwām, Sabkhat ⊜	130	35.53 N	37.40 E
R'asna	76	54.01 N	31.12 E
R'asnopol'	78	47.04 N	31.12 E
Raso, Cabo ›	266c	38.43 N	9.29 W
Raso, Ilhéu I	150a	16.37 N	24.36 W
Rasocolmo, Capo ›	70	38.18 N	15.31 E
Rason Lake ⊜	162	28.46 S	124.20 E
Raspberry Peak ∧	194	34.23 N	94.01 W
Raspopinskaja	80	49.24 N	42.52 E
Rasra	124	25.51 N	83.51 E
Rass Jebel	36	37.13 N	10.09 E
Rasskazovka	265b	55.38 N	37.20 E
Rasskazovo	80	52.40 N	41.53 E
Rasšua, ostrov I	74	47.45 N	153.01 E
Rassudovo	82	55.29 N	36.54 E
Rassvet, Ross.	84	43.58 N	46.44 E
Rassvet, Ross.	84	43.58 N	46.44 E
Rassvet, Ross.	86	57.02 N	91.34 E
Rassvet, Ross.	88	57.02 N	91.34 E
Rassypnaja	80	51.35 N	53.37 E
Rassypnoje	83	48.08 N	38.34 E
Rast	38	43.53 N	23.17 E
Rastälven ≃	40	59.37 N	14.56 E
Ra's Tannūrah	128	26.42 N	50.06 E
Rastatt	56	48.51 N	8.12 E
Rastavica ≃	78	49.44 N	30.01 E
Rastede	52	53.15 N	8.11 E
Rastegai'sa ∧	24	70.00 N	26.18 E
Rastenberg	54	51.10 N	11.25 E
Rastenburg → Kętrzyn	30	54.06 N	21.23 E
Rastorf	54	54.16 N	10.19 E
Rastorgujevo	82	55.33 N	37.41 E
Rastovcy	82	56.39 N	37.35 E
Rastunovo	82	55.16 N	37.50 E
Rasu, Monte ∧	71	40.25 N	9.00 E
Rasūl	123	32.42 N	73.34 E
Rasūlnagar	123	32.20 N	73.47 E
Rasulpur	272a	28.37 N	77.22 E
Rasulpur ◆[8]	272a	28.42 N	77.01 E
Rasun di sopra	64	46.48 N	12.03 E
Rasun di sotto	64	46.47 N	12.02 E
Rasura	58	46.06 N	9.33 E
Råsvalen ⊜	40	59.40 N	15.10 E
Răsvani	38	44.25 N	26.53 E
Rat ≃, Mb., Can.	184	49.35 N	97.08 W
Rat ≃, Mb., Can.	184	55.41 N	99.04 W
Ratahan	112	1.04 N	124.48 E
Ratak Chain II	14	9.00 N	171.00 E
Ratangarh	120	28.05 N	74.36 E
Ratanpur, India	126	23.07 N	87.04 E
Ratanpur, India	272b	22.50 N	88.14 E
Rätansbyn	26	62.29 N	14.32 E
Rat Burana	269a	13.41 N	100.30 E
Ratčino, Ross.	80	53.02 N	39.55 E
Ratčino, Ross.	82	55.16 N	38.39 E
Ratcliff	222	31.24 N	95.08 W
Rateče	64	46.30 N	13.43 E
Ratekau	54	53.57 N	10.44 E
Rāth	124	25.35 N	79.34 E
Rath ◆[8]	263	51.17 N	6.49 E
Rathangan	48	53.12 N	6.59 W
Rathbone	210	42.08 N	77.19 W
Rathbun Lake ⊜	212	44.47 N	78.12 W
Rathbun Lake ⊜[1]	190	40.54 N	93.05 W
Rathcoole	48	53.16 N	6.28 W
Rathcormack	48	52.05 N	8.17 W
Rathdowney, Austl.	171a	28.12 S	152.52 E
Rathdowney, Ire.	48	52.50 N	7.34 W
Rathdrum, Ire.	48	52.56 N	6.13 W
Rathdrum, Id., U.S.	202	47.48 N	116.53 W
Rathebur	54	53.44 N	13.46 E
Ratheim	52	51.04 N	6.10 E
Rathen	46	57.38 N	2.02 W
Rathenow	54	52.36 N	12.20 E
Rathfriland	48	54.14 N	6.10 W
Rathkeale	48	52.32 N	8.56 W
Rathlin Island I	48	55.18 N	6.13 W
Rathlin Sound ⊔	48	55.15 N	6.15 W
Ráth Luirc (Charleville)	48	52.21 N	8.41 W
Rathmecke	263	51.15 N	7.38 E
Rathmelton	48	55.02 N	7.38 W
Rathmore	48	52.03 N	9.13 W
Rathmullan	48	55.06 N	7.33 W
Rathnew	48	53.00 N	6.05 W
Ratho	46	55.55 N	3.22 W
Rathowen	48	53.40 N	7.31 W
Rathstock	54	52.31 N	14.32 E
Rathwell	184	49.40 N	98.32 W
Ratibor → Racibórz	30	50.06 N	18.13 E
Raticosa, Passo della)(	66	44.10 N	11.20 E
Rätikon ⋏	58	47.03 N	9.40 E
Ratingen	56	51.18 N	6.51 E
Ratisbon → Regensburg	60	49.01 N	12.06 E
Rätische Alpen → Rhaetian Alps ⋏	58	46.30 N	10.00 E
Rat Island I	181a	51.55 N	178.20 E
Rat Islands II	181a	51.40 N	178.30 E
Rat'kovo	82	56.01 N	38.38 E
Rat Lake ⊜	184	56.10 N	99.40 W
Ratlām	120	23.19 N	75.04 E
Ratmanova, ostrov I	180	65.46 N	169.02 W
Ratnāgiri	122	16.59 N	73.18 E
Ratnapura	122	6.41 N	80.24 E
Ratno	78	51.40 N	24.31 E
Ratodero	120	27.48 N	68.18 E
Ratomka	76	53.56 N	27.21 E
Raton	196	36.54 N	104.26 W
Raton Pass)(	196	36.59 N	104.29 W
Ratqah, Wādī ar- V	130	34.25 N	40.55 E
Ratt ≃	224	47.27 N	124.21 W
Rattanaburi	110	15.19 N	103.51 E
Rattaphum	110	7.08 N	100.16 E
Ratten	61	47.29 N	15.43 E
Rattlesnake	202	46.56 N	113.59 W
Rattlesnake Creek ≃, Ks., U.S.	198	38.13 N	98.22 W
Rattlesnake Creek ≃, Oh., U.S.	218	39.16 N	83.23 W
Rattlesnake Creek ≃, Or., U.S.	202	42.44 N	117.47 W
Rattlesnake Creek ≃, Wa., U.S.	224	46.45 N	120.55 W
Rattlesnake Creek ≃, Wa., U.S.	224	45.48 N	121.29 W
Rattlesnake Mountain ∧	207	41.42 N	72.50 W
Rattlesnake Peak ∧	280	34.16 N	117.47 W
Rattling Brook	186	49.38 N	56.10 W
Rattling Run ≃	279b	40.33 N	79.32 W
Rattray	46	56.35 N	3.19 W
Rattray Head ›	46	57.37 N	1.49 W
Rattu	123	35.08 N	74.48 E
Rättvik	26	60.53 N	15.06 E
Ratz, Mount ∧	180	57.23 N	132.19 W
Ratzeburg	54	53.42 N	10.46 E
Ratzeburger See ⊜	54	53.45 N	10.47 E
Rätzlingen	54	52.23 N	11.08 E
Rau	112	0.34 N	100.01 E
Raub, Malay.	114	3.48 N	101.52 E
Raub, In., U.S.	216	40.44 N	87.29 W
Raubsville	208	40.38 N	75.12 W
Rauch	252	36.46 S	59.06 W
Raucheck ∧	64	47.30 N	13.14 E
Rauchenwarth	264b	48.05 N	16.32 E
Rauchtown	210	41.07 N	77.14 W
Raucourt-et-Flaba	56	49.36 N	4.57 E
Rauen	54	52.20 N	14.01 E
Rauenstein	54	50.24 N	11.03 E
Raufarhöfn	24a	66.30 N	15.57 W
Raufoss	26	60.43 N	10.37 E
Rauhe Ebrach ≃	56	49.50 N	10.56 E
Raukumara Range ⋏	172	37.47 S	178.02 E
Raul Soares	255	20.05 S	42.22 W
Rauma	26	61.08 N	21.30 E
Rauma ≃	26	62.33 N	7.43 E
Raumünzach	56	48.38 N	8.21 E
Rauna	76	57.20 N	25.43 E
Raunds	42	52.21 N	0.33 W
Raung, Gunung ∧	115a	8.08 S	114.03 E
Raunheim	56	50.01 N	8.28 E
Raupal'an	180	65.28 N	171.59 W
Raurimu	172	39.07 S	175.24 E
Rauris	64	47.13 N	13.00 E
Raurkela	124	22.13 N	84.53 E
Rauschenberg	56	50.53 N	8.55 E
Rausu	92a	44.01 N	145.12 E
Rautalampi	26	62.38 N	26.50 E
Rāutara	272b	22.51 N	88.28 E
Rautavaara	26	63.29 N	28.18 E
Ravahere I[1]	14	18.14 S	142.09 W
Ravalgaon	122	20.38 N	74.25 E
Ravanica, Manastir Ʊ[1]	38	43.58 N	21.26 E
Ravānsar	128	34.43 N	46.40 E
Ravanusa	70	37.16 N	13.58 E
Rāvar	128	31.15 N	56.53 E
Ravarano	64	44.35 N	10.04 E
Ravarino	64	44.44 N	11.06 E
Rava-Russkaja	78	50.14 N	23.37 E
Ravascletto	64	46.32 N	12.57 E
Ravat	85	39.54 N	70.12 E
Ravello	68	40.39 N	14.37 E
Ravelo	248	18.48 S	65.32 W
Raven	192	37.05 N	81.51 W
Ravena	210	42.28 N	73.49 W
Ravenglass	44	54.21 N	3.24 W
Raven Lake ⊜	212	45.13 N	78.51 W
Ravenna, It.	66	44.25 N	12.12 E
Ravenna, Ky., U.S.	192	37.41 N	83.57 W
Ravenna, Mi., U.S.	216	43.11 N	85.56 W
Ravenna, Ne., U.S.	198	41.01 N	98.54 W
Ravenna, Oh., U.S.	214	41.09 N	81.14 W
Ravenna □[4]	66	44.25 N	11.59 E
Ravensbourne	171a	27.22 S	152.10 E
Ravensbourne National Park ♠	171a	27.21 S	152.15 E
Ravensburg	58	47.47 N	9.37 E
Ravenscrag	184	49.30 N	109.05 W
Ravensdale	224	47.21 N	121.58 W
Ravenshoe	166	17.37 S	145.29 E
Ravensthorpe	162	33.35 S	120.02 E
Ravenswood, S. Afr.	273d	26.11 S	28.15 E
Ravenswood, Mi., U.S.	216	42.45 N	84.36 W
Ravenswood, W.V., U.S.	188	38.56 N	81.45 W
Ravenswood Park ♠	283	42.36 N	70.42 W
Ravenswood Point ›	282	37.30 N	122.08 W
Ravensworth	284c	38.48 N	77.13 W
Rāver	120	21.15 N	76.02 E
Ravernet ≃	48	54.30 N	6.04 W
Rāvi ≃	123	30.35 N	71.49 E
Ravières	50	47.45 N	4.17 E
Ravine	208	40.34 N	76.24 W
Ravine Lake ⊜[1]	276	40.43 N	74.38 W
Ravinia Park ♠	278	42.09 N	87.46 W
Ravna Gora	36	45.23 N	14.57 E
Ravne	61	46.33 N	14.58 E
Ravnina	128	37.57 N	62.40 E
Ravsted	41	55.01 N	9.08 E
Rāwah	128	34.28 N	41.55 E
Rawaki I[1]	14	3.43 S	170.43 W
Rāwala Kot	123	33.52 N	73.46 E
Rāwalpindi	123	33.36 N	73.04 E
Rawa Mazowiecka	30	51.46 N	20.16 E
Rāwāndūz	128	36.37 N	44.31 E
Rawang	114	3.19 N	101.35 E
Rawas ≃	112	2.42 S	103.24 E
Rāwatsar	123	29.17 N	74.23 E
Rawāwiṣ, Wādī V	146	30.26 N	15.24 E
Rawḍah ⊜	130	35.15 N	41.05 E
Rawḍah, Wādī ar- V	130	34.22 N	37.21 E
Rawd al-Faraj ◆[8]	273c	30.05 N	31.14 E
Rawḍaw, Jazīrat ar- I	273c	30.01 N	31.13 E
Rawdon	206	46.03 N	73.43 W
Rawene	172	35.24 S	173.30 E
Rawḥah	144	19.28 N	41.48 E
Rawhide Creek ≃	198	42.06 N	104.20 W
Rawhide Lake ⊜	190	46.39 N	82.37 W
Rawhide Mountain ∧	204	38.17 N	116.25 W
Rawi	112	2.07 S	113.56 E
Rawi, Ko I	114	6.33 N	99.14 E
Rawicz	30	51.37 N	16.52 E
Rawlinna	162	31.01 S	125.20 E
Rawlins	200	41.47 N	107.14 W
Rawlinson, Mount ∧	162	25.58 S	127.28 E
Rawlinson Range ⋏	162	24.51 S	128.00 E
Rawmarsh	44	53.27 N	1.21 W
Rawreth	260	51.37 N	0.35 E
Rawson, Arg.	252	34.36 S	60.04 W
Rawson, Arg.	254	43.18 S	65.06 W
Rawson, Oh., U.S.	216	40.57 N	83.47 W
Rawsonville	158	33.41 S	19.20 E
Rawtenstall	44	53.42 N	2.18 W
Rawu	102	29.30 N	96.45 E
Rax ⋏	61	47.42 N	15.43 E
Raxāul	124	26.59 N	84.51 E
Ray, Il., U.S.	219	40.12 N	90.29 W
Ray, In., U.S.	216	41.45 N	84.53 W
Ray, N.D., U.S.	198	48.20 N	103.09 W
Ray ≃	42	51.48 N	1.15 W
Ray, Cape ›	186	47.40 N	59.18 W
Raya	112	1.05 N	118.32 E
Raya, Bukit ∧	112	0.40 S	112.41 E
Raya, Gunong ∧	114	6.22 N	99.49 E
Raya, Pulau I	114	4.52 N	95.22 E
Rāyachoti	122	14.03 N	78.45 E
Rāyadurg	122	14.42 N	76.52 E
Rāyagarha	122	19.10 N	83.25 E
Rayburn	222	30.25 N	94.56 W
Rayen, Dtsch.	263	51.28 N	6.32 E
Rāyen, Īrān	128	29.34 N	57.26 E
Ray Hubbard, Lake ⊜[1]	222	32.53 N	96.35 W
Rāyikhah I	128	26.12 N	36.21 E
Rayland	214	40.11 N	80.41 W
Rayleigh	42	51.36 N	0.36 E
Raymond, Ab., Can.	182	49.27 N	112.39 W
Raymond, Ca., U.S.	226	37.13 N	119.54 W
Raymond, Il., U.S.	219	39.19 N	89.34 W
Raymond, Mn., U.S.	198	45.00 N	95.14 W
Raymond, Ms., U.S.	194	32.15 N	90.25 W
Raymond, Oh., U.S.	216	40.20 N	83.28 W
Raymond, Wa., U.S.	224	46.41 N	123.43 W
Raymond Terrace	170	32.46 S	151.44 E
Raymondville	196	26.29 N	97.47 W
Raymore	184	51.25 N	104.31 W
Ray Mountains ⋏	180	65.45 N	151.30 W
Rāyna	126	23.05 N	87.54 E
Rayne	194	30.14 N	92.16 W
Raynham	207	41.56 N	71.04 W
Raynham Greyhound Park ♠	283	41.59 N	71.04 W
Rayón, Méx.	232	29.43 N	110.35 W
Rayón, Méx.	234	17.12 N	93.00 W
Rayón, Méx.	234	21.51 N	99.40 W
Rayones	232	25.01 N	100.05 W
Rayong	110	12.40 N	101.17 E
Rāypur	272b	22.25 N	88.31 E
Rayrah ⊤[4]	140	15.21 N	34.41 E
Rayse Creek ≃	219	38.13 N	89.00 W
Raystown Lake ⊜[1]	214	40.20 N	78.05 W
Rayton	158	25.45 S	28.32 E
Raytown	194	39.00 N	94.27 W
Rayville	194	32.28 N	91.45 W
Raywood	222	30.02 N	94.40 W
Raz, Pointe du ›	32	48.02 N	4.44 W
Raza, Punta ›	234	21.02 N	105.20 W
Razan, Īrān	128	35.23 N	49.02 E
R'azan', Ross.	80	54.38 N	39.44 E
R'azancevo	82	56.42 N	39.12 E
Ražanj	38	43.40 N	21.33 E
R'azan' Oblast' □[4]	76	54.30 N	40.30 E
R'azanovo	82	55.29 N	37.31 E
Razbegaj	265a	59.47 N	29.56 E
Războeni	38	47.05 N	26.32 E
Razdan	84	40.30 N	44.46 E
Razdan ≃	84	39.58 N	44.27 E
Razdel'naja	78	46.51 N	30.05 E
Razdolinsk	86	58.25 N	94.38 E
Razdolje	88	52.27 N	103.13 E
Razdol'noje, Ross.	89	43.30 N	131.52 E
Razdol'noje, Ukr.	78	45.47 N	33.29 E
Razdol'noje, Ukr.	83	47.37 N	38.01 E
Razdol'nyj	80	46.38 N	42.57 E
Razdorskaja	78	47.33 N	40.38 E
Razdory, Ross.	265b	55.45 N	37.18 E
Razdory, Ukr.	78	48.21 N	35.42 E
R'aženoje	83	47.31 N	38.52 E
Raževo	86	56.09 N	68.25 E
Razgrad	38	43.32 N	26.31 E
Razim, Lacul ⊜	38	44.54 N	28.57 E
Razlog	38	41.53 N	23.28 E
Razmachnino	88	51.47 N	115.28 E
Razmitelevo	265a	59.54 N	30.41 E
Rāznas ezers ⊜	76	56.20 N	27.27 E
Raznočinovka	80	46.37 N	47.57 E
Raznomojka	86	52.29 N	55.52 E
Razorback Mountain ∧	182	51.35 N	124.42 W
R'ažsk	80	53.43 N	40.04 E
Razvil'noje	80	46.14 N	41.18 E
Razzoli, Isola I	71	41.18 N	9.21 E
Ré, Île de I	32	46.12 N	1.25 W
Rea ≃	42	52.18 N	2.32 W
Read	262	53.49 N	2.21 W
Reading, Eng., U.K.	42	51.28 N	0.59 W
Reading, Il., U.S.	216	41.05 N	88.51 W
Reading, Ks., U.S.	198	38.31 N	95.57 W
Reading, Ma., U.S.	207	42.31 N	71.05 W
Reading, Mi., U.S.	216	41.50 N	84.44 W
Reading, Oh., U.S.	218	39.13 N	84.26 W
Reading, Pa., U.S.	208	40.20 N	75.55 W
Reading Center	210	42.26 N	76.56 W
Reading Station ◆[5]	285	39.57 N	75.10 W
Readington	210	40.34 N	74.44 W
Readlyn	190	42.42 N	92.13 W
Readsboro	207	42.46 N	72.56 W
Readstown	190	43.26 N	90.45 W
Reagan	222	31.13 N	96.47 W
Real	116	14.40 N	121.36 E
Real ≃	250	11.27 S	37.22 W
Real, Cordillera ⋏	248	19.00 S	66.30 W
Real, Estero ≃	236	12.55 N	87.23 W
Real del Padre	252	34.50 S	67.46 W
Real de San Carlos	258	34.26 S	57.53 W
Realengo ◆[8]	256	22.53 S	43.25 W
Real Felipe, Museo Histórico del ⊥	286d	12.04 S	77.09 W
Realicó	252	35.02 S	64.15 W
Realitos	196	27.27 N	98.32 W
Realmonte	70	37.18 N	13.28 E
Reamstown	208	40.12 N	76.07 W
Reana del Roiale	64	46.12 N	13.13 E
Reardan	202	47.40 N	117.52 W
Reata	232	26.08 N	101.05 W
Reatini, Monti ⋏	66	42.28 N	13.00 E
Réau	261	48.37 N	2.38 E
Reay	46	58.33 N	3.47 W
Reay Forest ◆[3]	46	58.19 N	4.47 W
Rebecca, Lake ⊜	162	29.53 S	122.10 E
Rebecq-Rognon	50	50.40 N	4.08 E
Rebeida, Wādī V	140	20.45 N	34.06 E
Rebel Hill	285	40.04 N	75.20 W
Rebersburg	210	40.57 N	77.27 W
Rebi	164	6.23 S	134.06 E
Rebiana Sand Sea → Rabyānah, Ṣaḥrā' ◆[2]	146	24.20 N	20.37 E
Rebild Bakker ♠	26	56.50 N	9.51 E
Reboly	24	63.50 N	30.47 E
Rebouças	252	25.36 S	50.42 W
Reboucas, Túnel ◆[5]	287a	22.56 S	43.14 W
Rebricha	86	53.05 N	82.20 E
Rebun-tō I	92a	45.23 N	141.02 E
Recalde	252	36.39 S	61.05 W
Recanati	66	43.24 N	13.32 E
Rečane	76	56.25 N	31.39 E
Recco	62	44.22 N	9.09 E
Recey-sur-Ource	58	47.47 N	4.52 E
Rēchah Lām	120	34.58 N	70.51 E
Rechberghausen	56	48.44 N	9.38 E
Recherche, Archipelago of the II	162	34.05 S	122.45 E
Recherche, Cape ›	175e	10.11 S	161.19 E
Réchicourt-le-Château	58	48.40 N	6.51 E
Rechlin	54	53.21 N	12.43 E
Rechna Doāb ⋏[1]	123	31.35 N	73.30 E
Rechnitz	61	47.18 N	16.27 E
Rečica, Bela.	76	52.22 N	30.25 E
Rečica, Bela.	78	51.52 N	26.48 E
Recife	250	8.03 S	34.54 W
Recife, Kaap ›	158	34.02 S	25.44 E
Recinto	252	36.48 S	71.44 W
Recke	52	52.22 N	7.43 E
Rečki	78	51.07 N	34.30 E
Recklinghausen	52	51.36 N	7.13 E
Recknitz ≃	54	54.14 N	12.28 E
Recoaro Terme	64	45.42 N	11.13 E
Recogne	56	49.55 N	5.22 E
Recoleta	286e	33.23 S	70.38 W
Recologne	58	47.16 N	5.50 E
Reconquista	252	29.09 S	59.39 W
Reconquista, Río de la ≃	288	34.25 S	58.35 W
Recovery Glacier ⊓	9	81.10 S	28.00 W
Recreio	255	21.32 S	42.28 W
Recreo	252	29.16 S	65.04 W
Rector	194	36.15 N	90.17 W
Rectorville	218	38.34 N	83.39 W
Recuay	248	9.43 S	77.28 W
Recz	30	53.16 N	15.33 E
Red (Hong) (Yuan) ≃, Asia	110	20.17 N	106.34 E
Red ≃, N.A.	178	50.24 N	96.48 W
Red ≃, U.S.	178	31.00 N	91.40 W
Red ≃, U.S.	194	36.32 N	87.22 W
Red ≃, Ky., U.S.	192	37.51 N	84.05 W
Red ≃, N.M., U.S.	200	36.39 N	105.42 W
Red ≃, Wi., U.S.	190	44.49 N	88.38 W
Red, Elm Fork ≃	196	34.53 N	99.19 W
Red, North Fork ≃	196	34.24 N	99.14 W
Red, Prairie Dog Town Fork ≃	196	34.35 N	99.58 W
Red, Salt Fork ≃	196	34.27 N	99.22 W
Red, South Fork ≃	194	36.41 N	86.56 W
Red, West Fork ≃	194	36.32 N	87.21 W
Reda	30	54.37 N	18.21 E
Redang, Pulau I	114	5.47 N	103.00 E
Redange	56	49.46 N	5.54 E
Redang Panjang	114	5.07 N	100.47 E
Red Bank, N.J., U.S.	208	40.20 N	74.03 W
Red Bank, Tn., U.S.	194	35.07 N	85.17 W
Red Bank Battle Monument ⊥	285	39.52 N	75.11 W
Redbank Creek ≃	214	40.58 N	79.33 W
Red Banks	194	34.49 N	89.33 W
Red Bay, Nf., Can.	186	51.44 N	56.25 W
Red Bay, Al., U.S.	194	34.26 N	88.08 W
Redbay, Fl., U.S.	194	30.35 N	85.56 W
Red Bay ⊂	48	55.04 N	6.02 W
Redberry Lake ⊜	184	52.40 N	107.10 W
Redbird	214	41.48 N	81.06 W
Red Bluff	204	40.10 N	122.14 W
Red Bluff Reservoir ⊜[1]	196	31.57 N	103.56 W
Red Boiling Springs	194	36.31 N	85.50 W
Redbourn	42	51.48 N	0.24 W
Redbridge ◆[8]	42	51.34 N	0.05 E
Red Bud	219	38.12 N	89.59 W
Red Canyon V	198	43.18 N	103.49 W
Redcar	44	54.37 N	1.04 W
Red Cedar ≃, Mi., U.S.	216	42.43 N	84.33 W
Red Cedar ≃, Wi., U.S.	190	44.42 N	91.53 W
Red Cedar Lake ⊜	190	46.45 N	79.54 W
Red Clay Creek ≃	285	39.43 N	75.39 W
Red Clay Creek, East Branch ≃	285	39.49 N	75.42 W
Red Clay Creek, West Branch ≃	285	39.49 N	75.42 W
Redcliff, Ab., Can.	184	50.05 N	110.47 W
Red Cliff, Co., U.S.	200	39.31 N	106.22 W
Redcliff, Zimb.	154	19.02 S	29.50 E
Redcliffe	171a	27.14 S	153.07 E
Redcliffe, Mount ∧	162	28.25 S	121.32 E
Red Cliff Indian Reservation ◆[4]	190	46.50 N	90.47 W
Red Cliffs	166	34.19 S	142.11 E
Red Cloud	198	40.05 N	98.31 W
Red Creek	210	43.14 N	76.43 W
Red Creek ≃	194	30.41 N	88.40 W
Red Cross Lake ⊜	184	55.05 N	92.55 W
Red Deer	182	52.16 N	113.48 W
Red Deer ≃, Can.	176	50.56 N	109.54 W
Red Deer ≃, Can.	184	52.53 N	101.01 W
Red Deer Creek ≃	196	35.56 N	100.24 W
Red Deer Lake ⊜, Ab., Can.	182	52.43 N	113.02 W
Red Deer Lake ⊜, Mb., Can.	184	52.56 N	101.20 W
Reddersburg	158	29.38 S	26.07 E
Red Devil	180	61.46 N	157.18 W
Red Dial	44	54.48 N	3.10 W
Reddick	216	41.06 N	88.15 W
Redding, Ca., U.S.	204	40.35 N	122.23 W
Redding, Ct., U.S.	207	41.18 N	73.23 W
Redding Ridge	207	41.18 N	73.21 W
Reddish	262	53.26 N	2.09 W
Redditch	42	52.19 N	1.56 W
Rede ≃	44	55.08 N	2.13 W
Redefin	54	53.21 N	11.11 E
Redelinghuys	158	32.30 S	18.33 E
Redenção	250	4.13 S	38.43 W
Redenção da Serra	256	23.16 S	45.33 W
Redesdale V	44	55.17 N	2.16 W
Redes Mere ⊜	262	53.15 N	2.14 W
Redeye ≃	198	46.26 N	94.49 W
Redfield, Ia., U.S.	198	41.35 N	94.11 W
Redfield, N.Y., U.S.	212	43.32 N	75.49 W
Redfield, S.D., U.S.	198	44.52 N	98.31 W
Redfish Lake ⊜	202	44.07 N	114.56 W
Redford	196	29.47 N	104.10 W
Redford ◆[8]	281	42.25 N	83.16 W
Redford Township	216	42.25 N	83.16 W
Red Fox Forest	284c	38.49 N	77.15 W
Redhead	241r	10.47 N	60.57 W
Red Hill, Austl.	162	21.59 S	116.03 E
Redhill, Eng., U.K.	42	51.14 N	0.11 W
Red Hill, Ca., U.S.	280	33.45 N	117.48 W
Red Hill, Pa., U.S.	208	40.22 N	75.29 W
Red Hill ∧	172	41.38 S	173.04 E
Redhill Aerodrome ⊠	260	51.12 N	0.07 W
Red Hill Branch ≃	284b	39.14 N	76.51 W
Red Hook	210	41.59 N	73.52 W
Redhouse Creek ≃	284b	39.18 N	76.31 W
Rédics	61	46.36 N	16.30 E
Red Indian Lake ⊜	186	48.40 N	56.50 W
Redinger Lake ⊜[1]	226	37.09 N	119.26 W
Redington Beach	220	27.49 N	82.49 W
Redington Shores	220	27.50 N	82.50 W
Red Island I	186	47.23 N	54.11 W
Redja ≃	76	58.05 N	31.33 E
Redkey	216	40.21 N	85.09 W
Redkino	82	56.38 N	36.17 E
Red Lake, On., Can.	184	51.03 N	93.49 W
Redlake, Mn., U.S.	198	47.53 N	95.01 W
Red Lake ⊜, On., Can.	184	51.01 N	94.05 W
Red Lake ⊜, Az., U.S.	200	35.40 N	114.04 W
Red Lake ⊜, S.D., U.S.	198	43.44 N	99.13 W
Red Lake ⊜[1]	222	31.40 N	95.58 W
Red Lake ≃	198	47.55 N	97.01 W
Red Lake Falls	198	47.52 N	96.16 W
Red Lake Indian Reservation ◆[4]	198	48.05 N	95.05 W
Red Lake Road	184	49.58 N	93.22 W
Redland, Scot., U.K.	46	59.05 N	3.05 W
Redland, Tx., U.S.	222	31.25 N	94.43 W
Redland Bay	171a	27.37 S	153.18 E
Redlands, S. Afr.	158	29.52 S	22.57 E
Redlands, Ca., U.S.	228	34.01 N	117.12 W
Redlands, Co., U.S.	200	39.04 N	108.38 W
Red Level	194	31.24 N	86.36 W
Red Lick	194	31.47 N	90.58 W
Redlin	54	53.22 N	12.01 E
Red Lion, Pa., U.S.	208	39.54 N	76.36 W
Red Lion, Pa., U.S.	285	39.53 N	75.41 W
Red Lion Airport ⊠	285	39.54 N	74.45 W
Red Lodge	202	45.11 N	109.14 W
Red Mill	206	46.25 N	72.28 W
Redmond, Or., U.S.	202	44.16 N	121.10 W
Redmond, Ut,. U.S.	200	39.00 N	111.51 W
Redmond, Wa., U.S.	224	47.40 N	122.07 W
Red Mountain	228	35.21 N	117.36 W
Red Mountain ∧, Ca., U.S.	204	41.35 N	123.06 W
Red Mountain ∧, Ca., U.S.	228	35.21 N	117.36 W
Red Mountain ∧, Mt., U.S.	202	47.07 N	112.44 W
Red Mountain Pass)(	200	37.54 N	107.43 W
Rednitz ≃	56	49.28 N	10.59 E
Red Oak, Ia., U.S.	198	41.00 N	95.13 W
Red Oak, Ok., U.S.	196	34.57 N	95.04 W
Red Oak, Tx., U.S.	222	32.31 N	96.48 W
Red Oak Creek ≃	222	32.28 N	96.30 W
Red Oaks Mill	210	41.40 N	73.53 W
Redon	32	47.39 N	2.05 W
Redonda I	238	16.55 N	62.19 W
Redonda, Ilha I	256	23.04 S	43.12 W
Redonda, Isla I	241r	9.52 N	61.35 W
Redonda Islands II	182	50.13 N	124.48 W
Redondela	34	42.17 N	8.36 W
Redondo, Port.	34	38.39 N	7.33 W
Redondo, Wa., U.S.	224	47.20 N	122.19 W
Redondo, Mount ∧	116	10.21 N	125.38 E
Redondo Beach	228	33.50 N	118.23 W
Redondo Beach State Park ♠	280	33.50 N	118.24 W
Redoubt, Mount ∧	224	48.57 N	121.18 W
Redoubt Volcano ∧[1]	180	60.29 N	152.45 W
Red Pass	182	52.59 N	118.59 W
Red Pheasant Indian Reserve ◆[4]	184	52.30 N	108.07 W
Red Pine Lake ⊜	212	45.12 N	78.42 W
Red Point ›	170	34.29 S	150.55 E
Red Rock, B.C., Can.	182	53.39 N	122.41 W
Red Rock, On., Can.	190	48.58 N	88.15 W
Red Rock, Tx., U.S.	222	29.58 N	97.27 W
Red Rock I	282	37.56 N	122.26 W
Red Rock ≃	202	44.59 N	112.52 W
Red Rock, Lake ⊜[1]	190	41.30 N	93.02 W
Red Rock Canyon State Park ♠	228	35.23 N	118.00 W
Red Rock Creek ≃	196	36.36 N	97.03 W
Red Rocks Point ›	162	32.13 S	127.32 E
Red Root Creek ≃	276	40.30 N	74.19 W
Red Run ≃, Md., U.S.	284b	39.24 N	76.47 W
Red Run ≃, Mi., U.S.	281	42.34 N	82.58 W
Redruth	42	50.13 N	5.14 W
Red Sea ⊤[2]	136	20.00 N	38.00 E
Red Springs	192	34.48 N	79.11 W
Redstone	182	52.08 N	123.42 W
Redstone ≃, N.T., Can.	180	64.17 N	124.33 W
Redstone ≃, On., Can.	190	48.27 N	81.03 W
Redstone Arsenal ■	194	34.38 N	86.38 W
Redstone Creek ≃	198	44.04 N	98.05 W
Redstone Lake ⊜	212	45.11 N	78.32 W
Red Sucker ≃	184	55.19 N	92.31 W
Red Sucker Lake ⊜	184	54.09 N	93.40 W
Reduction	279b	40.11 N	79.46 W
Redut	80	47.22 N	51.53 E
Redvers	184	49.33 N	101.39 W
Redwater	182	53.57 N	113.06 W
Redwater ≃	198	48.03 N	105.13 W
Red Wharf Bay ⊂	44	53.18 N	4.10 W
Redwillow ≃	182	55.04 N	119.21 W
Red Willow Creek ≃	198	40.13 N	100.29 W
Red Wing	190	44.33 N	92.32 W
Redwood	212	44.18 N	75.48 W
Redwood ≃	198	44.34 N	95.05 W
Redwood City	226	37.29 N	122.14 W
Redwood Creek ≃, Ca., U.S.	204	41.18 N	124.05 W
Redwood Creek ≃, Ca., U.S.	226	38.18 N	122.18 W

Symbols in the index entries represent the broad categories identified in the key at the right. Symbols with superior numbers (⋏[1]) identify subcategories (see complete key on page *I · 1).*

Symbole im Register stellen die rechts im Schlüssel erklärten Kategorien dar. Symbole mit hochgestellten Ziffern (⋏[1]) bezeichnen Unterabteilungen einer Kategorie (vgl. vollständiger Schlüssel auf Seite *I · 1).*

Los símbolos incluídos en el texto del índice representan las grandes categorías identificadas con la clave a la derecha. Los símbolos con numeros en su parte superior (⋏[1]) identifican las subcategorías (véase la clave completa en la página *I · 1).*

Les symboles de l'index représentent les catégories indiquées dans la légende à droite. Les symboles suivis d'un indice (⋏[1]) représentent des sous-catégories (voir légende complète à la page *I · 1).*

Os símbolos incluídos no texto do índice representam as grandes categorias identificadas com a chave à direita. Os símbolos com números em sua parte superior (⋏[1]) identificam as subcategorias (veja-se a chave completa à página *I · 1).*

Symbol	English	Deutsch	Español	Français	Português
∧	Mountain	Berg	Montaña	Montagne	Montanha
⋏	Mountains	Gebirge	Montañas	Montagnes	Montanhas
)(	Pass	Paß	Paso	Col	Passo
V	Valley, Canyon	Tal, Cañon	Valle, Cañón	Vallée, Canyon	Vale, Canhão
≚	Plain	Ebene	Llano	Plaine	Planície
›	Cape	Kap	Cabo	Cap	Cabo
I	Island	Insel	Isla	Île	Ilha
II	Islands	Inseln	Islas	Îles	Ilhas
⊥	Other Topographic Features	Andere Topographische Objekte	Otros Elementos Topográficos	Autres données topographiques	Outros acidentes topográficos

ESPAÑOL — Nombre / Página / Lat.°′ / Long.°′ W = Oeste
FRANÇAIS — Nom / Page / Lat.°′ / Long.°′ W = Ouest
PORTUGUÊS — Nome / Página / Lat.°′ / Long.°′ W = Oeste

Nombre	Página	Lat.°′	Long.°′ W = Oeste
Redwood Creek ≃, Ca., U.S.	282	37.31 N	122.12 W
Redwood Creek ≃, Ca., U.S.	282	37.52 N	122.35 W
Redwood Estates	226	37.10 N	121.59 W
Redwood Falls	198	44.32 N	95.07 W
Redwood National Park ♦	204	41.30 N	124.05 W
Redwood Point >	282	37.32 N	122.12 W
Redwood Regional Park ♦	282	37.38 N	122.10 W
Redwood Terrace	282	37.19 N	122.18 W
Redwood Valley	204	39.15 N	123.12 W
Ree, Lough ⊜	48	53.35 N	8.00 W
Reed City	190	43.52 N	85.30 W
Reeder	198	46.06 N	102.56 W
Reeders	210	41.01 N	75.20 W
Reed Lake ⊜, Mb., Can.	184	54.37 N	100.30 W
Reed Lake ⊜, Sk., Can.	184	50.24 N	107.05 W
Reedley	226	36.35 N	119.26 W
Reedsburg, Oh., U.S.	214	40.49 N	82.07 W
Reedsburg, Wi., U.S.	190	43.31 N	90.00 W
Reeds Peak ∧	200	33.09 N	107.51 W
Reedsport	202	43.42 N	124.05 W
Reedsville, Pa., U.S.	208	40.39 N	77.35 W
Reedsville, Wi., U.S.	190	44.09 N	87.57 W
Reedurban	214	40.47 N	81.26 W
Reedville	208	37.50 N	76.16 W
Reedy Creek ≃	220	28.04 N	81.21 W
Reedy Creek Swamp ≡	220	28.17 N	81.31 W
Reedy Lake ⊜	220	27.44 N	81.22 W
Reefton	172	42.07 S	171.52 E
Reelfoot Lake ⊜	194	36.25 N	89.22 W
Reepham	42	52.46 N	1.07 E
Reersø >[1]	41	55.31 N	11.06 E
Rees	52	51.45 N	6.23 E
Reese	190	43.27 N	83.41 W
Reese ≃	204	40.39 N	116.54 W
Reese Air Force Base ▪	196	33.36 N	102.02 W
Reeseville	190	43.18 N	88.50 W
Reesville	218	39.29 N	83.41 W
Reetz	54	53.11 N	11.52 E
Refaa, Djebel ∧	34	35.34 N	5.52 E
Refahiye	130	39.54 N	38.46 E
Reform	194	33.22 N	88.00 W
Reforma de Pineda	234	16.24 N	94.28 W
Refton	208	39.57 N	76.14 W
Refuge Cove	182	50.07 N	124.50 W
Refugio	196	28.18 N	97.16 W
Refugio, Isla I	254	43.58 S	73.12 W
Refugio Creek ≃	282	38.01 N	122.17 W
Rega ≃	30	54.10 N	15.18 E
Regaïa	34	35.38 N	5.46 W
Regalbuto	70	37.39 N	14.38 E
Regau	64	47.59 N	13.41 E
Regen	60	48.59 N	13.07 E
Regen ≃	60	49.01 N	12.06 E
Regência	255	19.36 S	39.49 W
Regency Estates	284c	39.03 N	77.10 W
Regeneração	250	6.15 S	42.41 W
Regensburg	60	49.01 N	12.06 E
Regensdorf	58	47.26 N	8.28 E
Regenstauf	60	49.08 N	12.08 E
Regent, Austl.	274b	37.44 S	145.00 E
Regent, N.D., U.S.	198	46.25 N	102.33 W
Regent Park	284c	39.03 N	77.10 W
Regents Park	274a	33.53 S	151.02 E
Regents Park ✦[8]	273d	26.15 S	28.04 E
Regent's Park ♦	260	51.32 N	0.09 W
Regentville	274a	33.47 S	150.40 E
Reggâne	148	26.42 N	0.10 E
Regge ≃	52	52.31 N	6.22 E
Reggello	66	43.41 N	11.32 E
Reggio di Calabria	68	38.07 N	15.39 E
Reggio di Calabria □[4]	68	38.10 N	16.00 E
Reggiolo	64	44.55 N	10.48 E
Reggio nell'Emilia	64	44.43 N	10.36 E
Reggio nell'Emilia □[4]	64	44.37 N	10.37 E
Regharen ⊜	40	58.54 N	15.46 E
Reghin	38	46.47 N	24.42 E
Regina, Sk., Can.	184	50.25 N	104.39 W
Régina, Guy. fr.	250	4.19 N	52.08 W
Regina, S. Afr.	158	27.02 S	26.30 E
Regina Beach	184	50.47 N	105.00 W
Regina Elena, Canale ≅	266b	45.41 N	8.39 E
Región Metropolitana □[4]	252	33.30 S	70.30 W
Regis-Breitingen	54	51.05 N	12.26 E
Registro	252	24.30 S	47.50 W
Registro do Araguaia	255	15.44 S	51.50 W
Regiwar	120	25.57 N	65.44 E
Regla ✦[8]	286b	23.08 N	82.20 W
Regnéville	32	49.01 N	1.33 W
Regnitz ≃	56	49.54 N	10.49 E
Rego Park ✦[8]	276	40.44 N	73.52 W
Regozero	24	65.28 N	31.10 E
Regresso, Cachoeira do ∟	250	0.58 S	54.51 W
Regstrup	41	55.40 N	11.37 E
Reguengos de Monsaraz	34	38.25 N	7.32 W
Rehau	54	50.15 N	12.02 E
Rehbach ≃	56	49.27 N	8.27 E
Rehberg	54	52.43 N	12.10 E
Rehberge ∧[2]	264a	52.35 N	13.11 E
Rehberge, Volkspark ♦	264a	52.33 N	13.20 E
Rehburg	52	52.28 N	9.13 E
Rehden	52	52.37 N	8.29 E
Rehe	56	50.38 N	8.07 E
Rehefeld-Zaunhaus	54	50.43 N	13.42 E
Rehfelde	54	52.30 N	13.54 E
Rehli	124	23.38 N	79.05 E
Rehme	52	52.12 N	8.49 E
Rehna	54	53.47 N	11.03 E
Rehoboth, Namibia	156	17.53 S	15.04 E
Rehoboth, Namibia	156	23.18 S	17.03 E
Rehoboth □[5]	156	23.30 S	17.00 E
Rehoboth Bay ⊂	208	38.40 N	75.06 W
Rehoboth Beach	208	38.43 N	75.04 W
Rehoboth Seamount ✚[3]	16	37.30 N	59.50 W
Réhon	56	49.30 N	5.45 E
Reḥovot	132	31.54 N	34.49 E
Rehti	124	22.44 N	77.26 E
Reiche Ebrach ≃	56	49.49 N	10.58 E
Reiche Liesing ≃	264b	48.08 N	16.16 E
Reichelsheim	56	49.43 N	8.50 E
Reichenau, Dtsch.	58	47.41 N	9.03 E
Reichenau, Schw.	58	46.49 N	9.24 E
Reichenau an der Rax	61	47.42 N	15.50 E
Reichenbach, Dtsch.	54	51.08 N	14.48 E
Reichenbach, Dtsch.	54	50.37 N	12.18 E
Reichenbach → Dzierżoniów, Pol.	30	50.44 N	16.39 E
Reichenbach, Schw.	58	46.38 N	7.42 E
Reichenberg → Liberec	30	50.46 N	15.03 E
Reichenhofen	58	47.50 N	9.58 E
Reichensachsen	56	51.09 N	9.59 E
Reichen Spitze ∧	64	47.09 N	12.07 E
Reichertshausen	60	48.28 N	11.31 E
Reichertsheim	60	48.12 N	12.17 E
Reichertshofen	60	48.40 N	11.28 E
Reichraming	61	47.53 N	14.27 E
Reichsbrücke ✦[5]	264b	48.14 N	16.25 E
Reichshoffen	56	48.56 N	7.40 E
Reid	162	30.49 S	128.26 E
Reid, Mount ∧, Austl.	162	17.58 S	130.38 E
Reid, Mount ∧, Ak., U.S.	182	55.42 N	131.15 W
Reid Lake ⊜[1]	184	50.02 N	108.05 W
Reidsville, Ga., U.S.	192	32.05 N	82.07 W
Reidsville, N.C., U.S.	192	36.21 N	79.39 W
Reiffton	208	40.19 N	75.53 W
Reigate	42	51.14 N	0.13 W
Reigate and Banstead □[8]	260	51.17 N	0.12 W
Reignac-sur-Indre	50	47.13 N	0.55 E
Reignier	58	46.08 N	6.16 E
Reigoldswil	58	47.24 N	7.41 E
Reihoku	92	32.31 N	130.02 E
Reillanne	62	43.53 N	5.40 E
Reims	50	49.15 N	4.02 E
Reims, Montagne de ⋏[2]	50	49.08 N	4.00 E
Reina Alejandra → Queen Alexandra Range ⋏	9	84.00 S	168.00 E
Reina Carlota, Estrecho de la → Queen Charlotte Sound ∪	182	51.30 N	129.30 W
Reinach, Schw.	58	47.30 N	7.35 E
Reinach, Schw.	58	47.15 N	8.11 E
Reina Fabiola → Queen Fabiola Mountains ⋏	9	71.30 S	35.40 E
Reina Maria, Costa de la → Queen Mary Coast ±[2]	9	67.00 S	96.00 E
Reina Maud, Tierras de la → Queen Maud Land ✦[1]	9	72.30 S	12.00 E
Reinbeck	190	42.19 N	92.35 W
Reinbek	52	53.31 N	10.14 E
Reinberg	54	54.12 N	13.15 E
Reindeer ≃	184	55.36 N	103.11 W
Reindeer Island I	184	52.25 N	98.00 W
Reindeer Lake ⊜	176	57.15 N	102.40 W
Reindeer Station	180	68.42 N	134.06 W
Reine Charlotte, Détroit de la → Queen Charlotte Sound ∪	182	51.30 N	129.30 W
Reinerton	208	40.36 N	76.34 W
Reinfeld	52	53.49 N	10.28 E
Reinga, Cape >	172	34.25 S	172.41 E
Reinhardswald ⋏	52	51.30 N	9.30 E
Reinhardtsdorf	54	50.53 N	14.11 E
Reinheim	56	49.49 N	8.50 E
Reinickendorf ✦[8]	264a	52.35 N	13.21 E
Reinosa	34	43.00 N	4.08 W
Reino Unido → United Kingdom □[1]	28	54.00 N	2.00 W
Reinsdorf, Dtsch.	54	50.42 N	12.33 E
Reinsdorf, Dtsch.	54	51.54 N	12.37 E
Reinshagen ✦[8]	263	51.10 N	7.09 E
Reinstorf	54	53.50 N	11.38 E
Reis	130	38.16 N	31.35 E
Reisach	64	46.39 N	13.09 E
Reisaelva ≃	24	69.48 N	21.00 E
Reischach	60	48.17 N	12.44 E
Reisdorf	56	49.53 N	6.15 E
Reisdorf, Camp ▪	273b	4.21 S	15.15 E
Reisholz ✦[8]	263	51.11 N	6.52 E
Reisjärvi	26	63.37 N	24.54 E
Reiss	46	58.28 N	3.10 W
Reisterstown	208	39.28 N	76.49 W
Reisterstown Road Plaza ✦[9]	284b	39.02 N	76.42 W
Reitano	70	37.58 N	14.20 E
Reitdiep ≅	52	53.20 N	6.18 E
Reith bei Seefeld	64	47.18 N	11.12 E
Reit im Winkl	64	47.40 N	12.28 E
Reitz	158	27.53 S	28.31 E
Reitzenhain	54	50.33 N	13.13 E
Reivilo	158	27.36 S	24.08 E
Rejinagar	126	23.53 N	88.15 E
Rejmyra	40	58.50 N	15.55 E
Rejowiec Fabryczny	30	51.08 N	23.13 E
Rejštejn	60	49.09 N	13.31 E
Rekarne	40	59.26 N	16.20 E
Rekarne □[9]	40	59.17 N	16.25 E
Reken	52	51.50 N	7.02 E
Rekjoāti	272b	22.37 N	88.28 E
Reliance, N.T., Can.	176	62.42 N	109.08 W
Reliance, Wy., U.S.	200	41.40 N	109.11 W
Relief Reservoir ⊜[1]	226	38.16 N	119.44 W
Religione, Punta >	70	36.42 N	14.46 E
Reliz Creek ≃	226	36.19 N	121.18 W
Rellingen	52	53.39 N	9.49 E
Rellinghausen ✦[8]	263	51.25 N	7.04 E
Reloncaví, Seno ⊂	254	41.40 S	72.35 W
Remada	148	32.19 N	10.24 E
Remagen	56	50.34 N	7.13 E
Rémalard	50	48.26 N	0.47 E
Remanso	250	9.37 S	42.07 W
Remarde ≃	261	48.35 N	2.15 E
Remarkable, Mount ∧	162	32.48 S	138.10 E
Rembang	115a	6.42 S	111.20 E
Rembau	114	2.35 N	102.06 E
Rembia	114	2.20 N	102.13 E
Remchi	34	35.04 N	1.26 W
Remecó	252	37.38 S	63.39 W
Remedios, Col.	246	7.02 N	74.41 W
Remedios, Cuba	240p	22.30 N	79.33 W
Remedios, Pan.	236	8.14 N	81.51 W
Remedios, Punta >	236	13.31 N	89.49 W
Remedios, Santuario de los ʋ[1]	286a	19.28 N	99.15 W
Remedios de Escalada ✦[8]	258	34.43 S	58.23 W
Remels	52	53.18 N	7.44 E
Remennicy	82	56.43 N	36.36 E
Remer	190	47.03 N	93.54 W
Remeshk	128	26.50 N	58.49 E
Remhoogte	158	29.33 S	23.01 E
Remich	56	49.33 N	6.22 E
Remich Airport ⊠	279b	40.36 N	79.49 W
Rémigny, Lac ⊜	190	47.51 N	79.12 W
Rémilly	56	49.01 N	6.24 E
Reminderville	214	41.20 N	81.23 W
Remington, In., U.S.	216	40.45 N	87.09 W
Remington, Va., U.S.	188	38.32 N	77.48 W
Rémire	250	4.53 N	52.17 W
Remiremont	58	48.01 N	6.35 E
Remo □[8]	273a	6.42 N	3.29 E
Remolá, Estany del ⊂	266d	41.17 N	2.04 E
Remollon	62	44.28 N	6.10 E
Remontnoje	80	46.33 N	43.39 E
Remoray	58	46.46 N	6.14 E
Remoulins	62	43.56 N	4.34 E
Removka ✦[8]	83	47.59 N	38.43 E
Rempang, Pulau I	114	0.51 N	104.10 E
Remptendorf	54	50.31 N	11.39 E
Rems ≃	56	48.52 N	9.16 E
Remscheid	56	51.11 N	7.11 E
Remscheider-Stausee ⊜[1]	263	51.10 N	7.14 E
Remsen, Ia., U.S.	198	42.48 N	95.58 W
Remsen, N.Y., U.S.	210	43.19 N	75.11 W
Remsfeld	56	51.00 N	9.29 E
Remuna	126	21.33 N	86.54 E
Remus	190	43.36 N	85.09 W
Rémuzat	62	44.24 N	5.21 E
Rena	26	61.08 N	11.22 E
Renaix → Ronse	50	50.45 N	3.36 E
Renāla Khurd	123	30.53 N	73.36 E
Rena Point >	116	16.10 N	119.45 E
Renard Islands II	164	10.50 S	153.05 E
Renata	182	49.26 N	118.06 W
Renaud Island I	9	65.40 S	66.00 W
Renca	286e	33.24 S	70.44 W
Renca, Cerro ∧	286e	33.23 S	70.43 W
Rencēni	76	57.44 N	25.26 E
Renchen	56	48.35 N	8.01 E
Rencontre East	186	47.38 N	55.12 W
Rencun	98	36.19 N	113.50 E
Renda, Ityo.	144	14.30 N	39.53 E
Renda, Lat	76	57.09 N	22.22 E
Rende	68	39.19 N	16.11 E
Rendena, Valle V	64	46.08 N	10.42 E
Rend Lake ⊜[1]	194	38.05 N	88.58 W
Rendova Island I	175e	8.32 S	157.20 E
Rendsburg	41	54.18 N	9.40 E
Renens	58	46.32 N	6.35 E
Renesse	52	51.44 N	3.46 E
Renews	186	46.56 N	52.56 W
Renfrew, On., Can.	212	45.28 N	76.41 W
Renfrew, Scot., U.K.	46	55.53 N	4.24 W
Renfrew, Pa., U.S.	214	40.46 N	79.58 W
Renfrew □[6]	212	45.25 N	77.05 W
Rengam	114	1.53 N	103.24 E
Ren'gang	106	32.01 N	120.50 E
Rengasdengklok	115a	6.09 S	107.17 E
Rengat	112	0.24 S	102.33 E
Rengel	115a	7.04 S	112.00 E
Rengen ⊜	26	64.05 N	14.03 E
Rengezhuang	105	39.45 N	118.10 E
Rengit	114	1.41 N	103.09 E
Rengkang	112	1.07 N	112.10 E
Rengo	252	34.25 S	70.52 W
Rengsdorf	56	50.30 N	7.29 E
Reng Tlāng ∧	120	21.59 N	92.36 E
Renhe, Zhg.	100	33.32 N	114.02 E
Renhe, Zhg.	100	27.41 N	115.15 E
Renhechang	107	30.30 N	105.56 E
Renheji	100	31.56 N	115.07 E
Renhua	100	25.06 N	113.44 E
Renhuai	102	27.48 N	106.18 E
Reni	78	45.27 N	28.17 E
Renick	188	37.59 N	80.21 W
Renish Point >	46	57.44 N	6.59 W
Renjiawopeng	104	41.27 N	122.18 E
Renjiaxu	106	30.49 N	121.00 E
Renju	100	24.51 N	115.54 E
Renko	26	60.54 N	24.17 E
Renkum	52	51.58 N	5.45 E
Renliuchang	107	29.13 N	106.39 E
Renlong	107	30.32 N	105.47 E
Renmark	166	34.11 S	140.45 E
Renmei	100	25.50 N	117.56 E
Renmin	89	46.37 N	125.32 E
Renna, Monte ∧	70	36.52 N	14.41 E
Rennau	54	52.17 N	10.55 E
Renne, Lac du → Reindeer Lake ⊜	176	57.15 N	102.40 W
Renne, Rivière le ≃	206	45.41 N	72.39 W
Rennell I	160	11.40 S	160.10 E
Rennell, Islas II	254	52.00 S	74.00 W
Rennell Sound ∪	182	53.25 N	132.40 W
Renner	222	32.59 N	96.47 W
Rennerdale	279b	40.24 N	80.08 W
Rennerod	56	50.36 N	8.04 E
Renner Springs	162	18.20 S	133.48 E
Rennertshofen	60	48.45 N	11.02 E
Rennes	32	48.05 N	1.41 W
Rennick Bay ⊂	9	70.18 S	161.45 E
Rennick Glacier ⊓	9	70.30 S	161.45 E
Rennie	184	49.51 N	95.33 W
Rennie's Mill	271d	22.18 N	114.15 E
Renningen	56	48.46 N	8.56 E
Renntier-See → Reindeer Lake ⊜	176	57.15 N	102.40 W
Rennweg	64	47.01 N	13.37 E
Reno, Nv., U.S.	226	39.31 N	119.48 W
Reno, Pa., U.S.	214	41.25 N	79.45 W
Reno, Tx., U.S.	222	32.56 N	97.05 W
Reno ≃	64	44.37 N	12.16 E
Reno Beach	214	41.40 N	83.15 W
Reno Hill ∧	200	42.35 N	106.03 W
Reno International Airport ⊠	226	39.30 N	119.46 W
Renoster ≃	158	31.37 S	20.37 E
Renous	186	46.49 N	65.48 W
Renous ≃	186	46.50 N	65.50 W
Renovo	214	41.19 N	77.45 W
Renqiao	100	33.27 N	117.16 E
Renqiu	98	38.43 N	116.05 E
Rens	41	54.54 N	9.06 E
Renshan	100	22.50 N	114.48 E
Renshou, Zhg.	100	27.08 N	117.51 E
Renshou, Zhg.	107	30.00 N	104.08 E
Rensjön	24	68.05 N	19.49 E
Rensselaer, In., U.S.	216	40.56 N	87.09 W
Rensselaer, Mo., U.S.	219	39.40 N	91.33 W
Rensselaer, N.Y., U.S.	210	42.38 N	73.44 W
Rensselaer □[6]	210	42.43 N	73.40 W
Rensselaer Falls	212	44.35 N	75.19 W
Rensselaerville	210	42.30 N	74.08 W
Rentería	34	43.19 N	1.54 W
Rentfort ✦[8]	263	51.35 N	6.57 E
Renton	224	47.28 N	122.12 W
Rentuo	107	29.14 N	106.23 E
Rentweinsdorf	56	50.04 N	10.47 E
Renun ≃	114	3.05 N	97.55 E
Renville	198	44.47 N	95.12 W
Renwez	56	49.50 N	4.36 E
Renwick, N.Z.	172	41.30 S	173.50 E
Renwick, Ia., U.S.	190	42.49 N	93.58 W
Renyichang	107	29.29 N	105.28 E
Renziehausen Park ♦	279b	40.21 N	79.50 W
Réo, Burkina	150	12.19 N	2.28 W
Reo, Indon.	115b	8.19 S	120.30 E
Reola ✦[8]	272a	28.34 N	76.59 E
Repartimento ≃	250	6.06 S	50.40 W
Repaupo	285	39.48 N	75.18 W
Repbäcken	40	60.31 N	15.20 E
Répce ≃	30	47.41 N	17.03 E
Repentigny	206	45.44 N	73.28 W
Repetek	128	38.34 N	63.11 E
Repino	76	60.10 N	29.52 E
Repjovka, Ross.	78	51.05 N	38.39 E
Repjovka, Ross.	80	53.09 N	48.06 E
Repki	78	51.48 N	31.05 E
Repolka	76	59.16 N	29.34 E
Repolovo	86	60.40 N	69.50 E
Reporoa	172	38.26 S	176.21 E
Reposaari	26	61.37 N	21.27 E
Repton	194	31.24 N	87.14 W
Republic, Ks., U.S.	198	39.55 N	97.49 W
Republic, Mi., U.S.	190	46.24 N	87.58 W
Republic, Mo., U.S.	194	37.07 N	93.28 W
Republic, Oh., U.S.	214	41.07 N	83.00 W
Republic, Wa., U.S.	202	48.38 N	118.44 W
República Centroafricana → Central African Republic □[1]	136	7.00 N	21.00 E
Republic Airport ⊠	276	40.44 N	73.25 W
Republican ≃	198	39.03 N	96.48 W
Republican, North Fork ≃	198	40.01 N	101.59 W
Republican, South Fork ≃	198	40.03 N	101.31 W
Republic Observatory ʋ[3]	273d	26.11 S	28.05 E
Republic Steel Corporation ʋ[3]	279a	41.28 N	81.40 W
République centrafricaine → Central African Republic □[1]	136	7.00 N	21.00 E
Repueblo de Oriente	196	25.51 N	99.39 W
Repulse Bay	176	66.32 N	86.15 W
Repulse Bay ⊂	166	20.36 S	148.43 E
Repvåg	24	70.45 N	25.41 E
Requena, Esp.	34	39.29 N	1.06 W
Requena, Perú	248	4.58 S	73.50 W
Réquista	32	44.02 N	2.32 E
Rère ≃	50	47.22 N	1.50 E
Reriutaba	250	4.10 S	40.35 W
Reşadiye	130	40.24 N	37.21 E
Reşadiye ✦[8]	267b	41.05 N	29.15 E
Reşadiye Yarımadası >[1]	130	36.40 N	27.45 E
Resang, Tanjong >	114	2.35 N	103.51 E
Resarö	40	59.26 N	18.20 E
Rescalda	266b	45.38 N	8.56 E
Rescaldina	266b	45.37 N	8.57 E
Reschenpass (Passo di Resia))(	64	46.50 N	10.30 E
Rescue	208	36.59 N	76.33 W
Research	274b	37.42 S	145.11 E
Reseda ✦[8]	280	34.12 N	118.31 W
Resen	38	41.05 N	21.00 E
Resende	256	22.28 S	44.27 W
Reserva	252	24.38 S	50.52 W
Reserva, Parque de la ♦	286d	12.04 S	77.02 W
Reserve, La., U.S.	194	30.03 N	90.33 W
Reserve, N.M., U.S.	200	33.42 N	108.45 W
Reserve Township	279b	40.29 N	79.59 W
Reservoir	274b	37.43 S	145.00 E
Reservoir Pond ⊜	283	42.10 N	71.07 W
Rešetilovka	78	49.34 N	34.04 E
Rešetnikovo	82	56.27 N	36.34 E
Reshui	98	42.09 N	119.18 E
Reshuitang	102	24.10 N	103.09 E
Resia, Lago di ⊜	64	46.47 N	10.32 E
Resia, Passo di (Reschenpass))(	64	46.50 N	10.30 E
Resipol, Beinn ∧	46	56.43 N	5.39 W
Resistencia	252	27.27 S	58.59 W
Reşiţa	38	45.17 N	21.53 E
Resiutta	64	46.23 N	13.13 E
Resko	30	53.47 N	15.25 E
Rešma	80	57.24 N	42.34 E
Rešn'ovka	78	49.47 N	27.25 E
Resolute	176	74.41 N	94.54 W
Resolution Island I, N.T., Can.	176	61.30 N	65.00 W
Resolution Island I, N.Z.	172	45.40 S	166.40 E
Resolven	42	51.42 N	3.42 W
Resort, Loch ⊂	46	58.03 N	7.06 W
Resoty	76	57.09 N	28.30 E
Resplandes	250	6.17 S	45.13 W
Resplendor	255	19.20 S	41.15 W
Ressa ≃	76	54.45 N	35.10 E
Ressaca, Ribeirão da ≃	287b	23.38 S	46.51 W
Resse ✦[3]	263	51.34 N	7.07 E
Resseta ≃	76	53.49 N	35.15 E
Ressons-sur-Matz	50	49.33 N	2.45 E
Resta ≃	76	53.36 N	30.56 E
Resthaven	216	41.16 N	88.09 W
Restigouche (Ristigouche) ≃	186	48.04 N	66.20 W
Restín, Punta >	246	4.17 S	81.15 W
Restinga	34	35.42 N	5.23 W
Restinga Seca	252	29.49 S	53.23 W
Reston, Mb., Can.	184	49.35 N	101.02 W
Reston, Scot., U.K.	46	55.51 N	2.11 W
Reston, Va., U.S.	208	38.58 N	77.20 W
Restoule Lake ⊜	190	46.03 N	79.47 W
Restrepo, Col.	246	4.15 N	73.33 W
Restrepo, Col.	246	3.48 N	76.31 W
Resuttano	70	37.41 N	14.02 E
Retalhuleu	236	14.32 N	91.41 W
Retalhuleu □[5]	236	14.20 N	91.50 W
Retamosa	252	33.35 S	54.44 W
Retem, Oued er V	148	33.30 N	5.45 E
Řetenice	54	50.38 N	13.46 E
Retezat, Parcul Național ♦	38	45.20 N	22.50 E
Retezatului, Munții ⋏	38	45.25 N	23.00 E
Rethel	50	49.31 N	4.22 E
Rethem	52	52.45 N	9.23 E
Réthimnon	38	35.22 N	24.29 E
Retiche, Alpi → Rhaetian Alps ⋏	58	46.30 N	10.00 E
Retie	56	51.16 N	5.04 E
Retiers	28	47.55 N	1.23 W
Retiro, Estacion ✦[5]	288	34.36 S	58.22 W
Retiro, Parque del ♦	266a	40.25 N	3.41 W
Retournac	62	45.12 N	4.02 E
Retreat	222	32.03 N	96.29 W
Retreat ≃	170	34.07 S	149.38 E
Retsof	210	42.50 N	77.53 W
Rettenberg	58	47.35 N	10.17 E
Rettendon	260	51.39 N	0.33 E
Rettendon Place	260	51.38 N	0.34 E
Rettichovka	89	44.10 N	132.47 E
Rettin	54	54.06 N	10.53 E
Return Creek ≃	226	37.56 N	119.28 W
Retz	61	48.45 N	15.57 E
Retzow	54	52.37 N	12.41 E
Reuden	54	52.04 N	12.18 E
Reungeut	114	4.34 N	96.22 E
Reunion (Réunion) □[2], Afr.	138	21.06 S	55.36 E
Reunion (Réunion) □[2], Afr.	157c	21.06 S	55.36 E
Reus	34	41.09 N	1.07 E
Reuschenberg	263	51.10 N	6.42 E
Reusel	52	51.21 N	5.22 E
Reuss ≃	58	47.28 N	8.14 E
Reut ≃	38	47.15 N	29.09 E
Reuterstadt Stavenhagen	54	53.42 N	12.53 E
Reutlingen	58	48.29 N	9.11 E
Reutov	82	55.46 N	37.52 E
Reutte	58	47.29 N	10.43 E
Reuver	52	51.17 N	6.05 E
Revadim	132	31.46 N	34.48 E
Rev'akino	82	54.22 N	37.40 E
Reval → Tallinn	76	59.25 N	24.45 E
Revda, Ross.	24	67.58 N	34.32 E
Revda, Ross.	86	56.48 N	59.57 E
Réveillon, Ruisseau le ≃	261	48.42 N	2.30 E
Revel	62	45.11 N	5.52 E
Revelganj	124	25.47 N	84.40 E
Revelstoke	182	50.59 N	118.12 W
Reventazón	248	6.10 S	80.58 W
Reventazón ≃	236	10.17 N	83.24 W
Revere, It.	64	45.03 N	11.08 E
Revere, Ma., U.S.	207	42.24 N	71.00 W
Revere, Pa., U.S.	208	40.31 N	75.10 W
Revere Beach ±[2]	283	42.25 N	70.59 W
Revermont ⋏[2]	58	46.27 N	5.25 E
Revesby	274a	33.57 S	151.01 E
Revest-du-Bion	62	44.05 N	5.33 E
Révia	154	13.23 S	36.31 E
Reviga	38	44.42 N	27.06 E
Revigny-sur-Ornain	56	48.50 N	4.59 E
Revilla del Campo	34	42.13 N	3.32 W
Revillagigedo, Islas II	232	19.00 N	111.30 W
Revillagigedo Channel ∪	182	55.10 N	131.13 W
Revillagigedo Island I	182	55.35 N	131.23 W
Revillo	198	45.01 N	96.34 W
Revin	56	49.56 N	4.38 E
Revloc	214	40.29 N	78.45 W
Řevničov	54	50.08 N	13.45 E
Revò	64	46.23 N	11.03 E
Revol'ucii, pik ∧	85	38.31 N	72.21 E
Revolución Mexicana	234	16.03 N	93.04 W
Revolution, Museum of the ʋ	265b	55.46 N	37.36 E
Revsundssjön ⊜	26	62.49 N	15.17 E
Revúboè ≃	154	16.13 S	33.37 E
Revuè ≃	156	19.49 S	34.00 E
Rew	214	41.54 N	78.32 W
Rewa	124	24.32 N	81.18 E
Rewa ≃	246	3.53 N	58.45 W
Rewāri	124	28.11 N	76.37 E
Rewataya, Taka ✚[2]	112	6.05 S	118.55 E
Rex, Mount ∧	9	74.57 S	76.00 W
Rexburg	202	43.49 N	111.47 W
Rexdale ✦[8]	275b	43.43 N	79.35 W
Rexford, Ks., U.S.	198	39.28 N	100.44 W
Rexford, Mt., U.S.	202	48.52 N	115.13 W
Rexhame	283	42.06 N	70.40 W
Rexton	186	46.39 N	64.52 W
Rexville	210	42.05 N	77.40 W
Rey, Arroyo del ≃	288	34.46 S	58.27 W
Rey, Embalse del ⊜[1]	266a	40.18 N	3.32 W
Rey, Estrecho del → King Sound ∪	162	17.00 S	123.30 E
Rey, Isla del I	246	8.22 N	78.55 W
Rey, Laguna del ⊜	196	27.01 N	103.26 W
Rey Bouba	146	8.40 N	14.11 E
Reyes	248	14.19 S	67.23 W
Reyes, Point >	204	38.00 N	123.01 W
Reyes Peak ∧	228	34.38 N	119.17 W
Reyhanlı	130	36.18 N	36.32 E
Rey Jorge, Estrecho → King George Sound ∪	162	35.03 S	117.57 E
Rey Jorge, Isla → King George Island I	9	62.00 S	58.15 W
Reykjanes >[1]	24a	63.49 N	22.43 W
Reykjanes Ridge ✚[3]	10	62.00 N	27.00 W
Reykjavík	24a	64.09 N	21.51 W
Reynella	168b	35.06 S	138.32 E
Reyno	194	36.21 N	90.45 W
Reynolds, Ga., U.S.	192	32.33 N	84.05 W
Reynolds, In., U.S.	216	40.44 N	86.52 W
Reynolds, N.D., U.S.	198	47.57 N	97.45 W
Reynolds Channel ∪	276	40.36 N	73.40 W
Reynolds Creek ≃, Austl.	171a	27.56 S	152.36 E
Reynolds Creek ≃, On., Can.	212	43.00 N	80.58 W
Reynoldsville	214	41.05 N	78.53 W
Reynosa	232	26.07 N	98.18 W
Reyssouze ≃	58	46.27 N	4.54 E
Rež	86	57.23 N	61.24 E
Rež ≃	86	57.54 N	62.18 E
Reza, gora (Kūh-e Rīzeh) ∧	128	37.47 N	58.05 E
Rezé	32	47.12 N	1.34 W
Rēzekne	76	56.30 N	27.19 E
Rēzekne ≃	76	56.46 N	26.58 E
Rezeny	38	46.46 N	28.54 E
Rezina	38	47.44 N	28.58 E
Rezino	86	55.51 N	75.18 E
Rezovo	38	41.59 N	28.02 E
Rezovska (Mutlu) ≃	38	41.59 N	28.01 E
Rezvānshahr	128	37.33 N	49.09 E
Rezzato	64	45.31 N	10.19 E
Rezzoaglio	62	44.32 N	9.23 E
Rezzonico	58	46.04 N	9.16 E
Rhade	52	53.19 N	9.07 E
Rhadeswood Reservoir ⊜[1]	262	53.29 N	1.56 W
Rhaetian Alps (Rätische Alpen) (Alpi Retiche) ⋏	58	46.30 N	10.00 E
Rhallamane, Sebkha de ⊻	148	23.41 N	9.50 W
Rhame	198	46.13 N	103.39 W
Rharbi, Île I	148	34.39 N	11.03 E
Rharbi, Zahrez ⊜	148	34.50 N	2.50 E
Rhauderfehn	52	53.08 N	7.35 E
Rhaunen	56	49.52 N	7.20 E
Rhayader	42	52.18 N	3.30 W
Rhea Creek ≃	202	45.30 N	119.46 W
Rheda-Wiedenbrück	52	51.50 N	8.18 E
Rhede, Dtsch.	52	53.03 N	7.16 E
Rhede, Dtsch.	52	51.51 N	7.16 E
Rheden	52	52.01 N	6.02 E
Rheems	208	40.08 N	76.34 W
Rheem Valley	226	37.52 N	122.07 W
Rheidol ≃	42	52.25 N	4.05 W
Rheims → Reims	50	49.15 N	4.02 E
Rhein	184	51.22 N	102.10 W
Rhein → Rhine ≃	30	51.52 N	6.02 E
Rheinau	56	48.41 N	7.56 E
Rheinbach	56	50 37 N	6.57 E
Rheinberg	52	51 33 N	6.35 E
Rheinböllen	56	50 00 N	7.40 E
Rheinbrohl	56	50 30 N	7.19 E
Rheinbrücke ✦[5]	263	51 12 N	6.44 E
Rheindürkheim	56	49 42 N	8.21 E
Rheine	52	52 17 N	7.26 E
Rheineck	58	47 28 N	9.35 E
Rheinen	263	51 27 N	7.38 E
Rheinfall ∟	58	47 41 N	8.38 E
Rheinfelden, Dtsch.	58	47.33 N	7.47 E
Rheinfelden, Schw.	58	47.33 N	7.48 E
Rheinhausen	56	51.24 N	6.44 E
Rhein-Herne-Kanal ≅	263	51.27 N	6.47 E
Rheinhessen-Pfalz □[5]	56	49.30 N	8.00 E
Rheinkamp	52	51.30 N	6.37 E
Rheinland-Pfalz □[3]	56	50.00 N	7.00 E
Rheinsberg	54	53.06 N	12.53 E
Rheinstadion ♦	263	51.16 N	6.44 E
Rheinstein, Burg ⊥	56	50.00 N	7.50 E
Rheinwald V	58	46.32 N	9.17 E
Rheinwaldhorn ∧	58	46.30 N	9.02 E
Rheirs, Oued V	148	30.39 N	4.26 W
Rhêmes-Notre-Dame	62	45.34 N	7.07 E
Rhenen	52	51.57 N	5.34 E
Rhens	56	50.17 N	7.37 E
Rheurdt	56	51.27 N	6.28 E
Rheydt	56	51.10 N	6.25 E
Rheydt, Schloss ⊥	263	51.11 N	6.29 E
Rhin ≃, Dtsch.	54	52.59 N	12.55 E
Rhin → Rhine ≃, Europe	30	51.52 N	6.02 E
Rhinau	58	48.19 N	7.42 E
Rhine	192	31.59 N	83.12 W
Rhine (Rhein) (Rhin) ≃	30	51.52 N	6.02 E
Rhinebeck	210	41.55 N	73.54 W
Rhinecliff	210	41.55 N	73.57 W
Rhineland	219	38.43 N	91.31 W
Rhinelander	190	45.38 N	89.24 W
Rhin Kanal ≅	54	52.47 N	12.24 E
Rhinluch ≡	54	52.50 N	12.50 E
Rhinns of Kells ⋏	44	55.07 N	4.22 W
Rhinns Point >	46	55.40 N	6.30 W
Rhino Camp	154	2.58 N	31.24 E
Rhinow	54	52.45 N	12.20 E
Rhiou, Oued ≃	34	36.00 N	0.55 E
Rhir, Cap >	148	30.38 N	9.55 W
Rhis, Oued ≃	34	35.14 N	3.57 W
Rhiw ≃	42	52.36 N	3.11 W
Rho	62	45.32 N	9.02 E
Rhode Island □[3], U.S.	178	41.40 N	71.30 W
Rhode Island □[3], U.S.	207	41.40 N	71.30 W
Rhode Island I	207	41.33 N	71.15 W
Rhode Island Sound ∪	207	41.25 N	71.15 W
Rhoden	52	51.28 N	9.00 E
Rhodes, Austl.	274a	33.50 S	151.05 E
Rhodes → Ródhos, Ellás	38	36.26 N	28.13 E
Rhodes, S. Afr.	158	30.47 S	27.59 E
Rhodes, Eng., U.K.	262	53.33 N	2.14 W
Rhodes → Ródhos I	38	36.10 N	28.00 E
Rhodesia → Zimbabwe □[1]	154	20.00 S	30.00 E
Rhodes Inyanga National Park ♦	154	18.12 S	32.45 E
Rhodes Matopos National Park ♦	154	20.33 S	28.20 E
Rhodes Park ♦	273d	26.12 S	28.06 E
Rhodes Peak ∧	202	46.41 N	114.47 W
Rhodes' Tomb ⊥	154	20.30 S	28.30 E
Rhododendron	224	45.20 N	121.55 W
Rhododendron State Park ♦	207	42.47 N	72.12 W
Rhodon	261	48.43 N	2.04 E
Rhodon, Ruisseau le ≃	261	48.42 N	2.04 E
Rhodope Mountains (Rodopi) (Orosirá Rodhópis) ⋏	38	41.30 N	24.30 E
Rhodt	56	49.16 N	8.07 E
Rhome	222	33.03 N	97.28 W
Rhondda	42	51.40 N	3.27 W
Rhône □[5]	32	45.55 N	4.40 E
Rhône ≃	32	43.20 N	4.50 E
Rhône à Sète, Canal du ≅	62	43.25 N	3.42 E
Rhône au Rhin, Canal du ≅	58	47.06 N	5.19 E
Rhoose	42	51.24 N	3.20 W
Rhosesmor	262	53.12 N	3.10 W
Rhosllanerchrugog	44	53.00 N	3.03 W
Rhosneigr	44	53.14 N	4.31 W
Rhos-on-Sea	44	53.19 N	3.45 W
Rhossili	42	51.34 N	4.17 W
Rhourde-el-Baguel	148	31.24 N	6.57 E
Rhuddlan	44	53.18 N	3.27 W
Rhue ≃	32	45.23 N	2.29 E
Rhum I	46	57.00 N	6.20 W
Rhum, Sound of ∪	46	56.56 N	6.14 W
Rhyl	44	53.19 N	3.29 W
Rhymney	42	51.46 N	3.18 W
Rhymney ≃	42	51.28 N	3.10 W
Rhynie	46	57.19 N	2.50 W
Riaba	152	3.23 N	8.46 E
Riace	68	38.25 N	16.29 E
Riachão	250	7.22 S	46.37 W
Riachão do Dantas	250	11.04 S	37.44 W
Riachão do Jacuípe	250	11.48 S	39.21 W
Riacho de Santana	255	13.37 S	42.57 W
Riacho Grande	256	23.48 S	46.35 W
Riachos, Islas de los II	254	40.10 S	62.08 W
Riachuelo, Bra.	250	10.44 S	37.11 W
Riachuelo, Chile	254	40.49 S	73.21 W
Riachuelo, Ur.	258	34.28 S	57.43 W
Riachuelo ≃	288	34.38 S	58.22 W
Riachuelo, Arroyo ≃	258	34.27 S	57.44 W
Rialma	255	15.18 S	49.34 W
Rialto, Bra.	256	22.35 S	44.16 W
Rialto, Ca., U.S.	228	34.06 N	117.22 W
Riamkanan, Waduk ⊜[1]	112	3.30 S	115.05 E
Rianápolis	255	15.29 S	49.28 W
Riāng	120	27.32 N	92.56 E
Riangnom	140	9.55 N	30.01 E
Riaño	34	42.58 N	5.01 W
Rians	62	43.37 N	5.45 E
Riánsares ≃	34	39.32 N	3.18 W
Riāsi	123	33.05 N	74.50 E
Riau □[4]	112	1.00 N	102.00 E
Riau, Kepulauan II	112	1.00 N	104.30 E
Riaz	58	46.38 N	7.04 E
Riaza	34	41.17 N	3.28 W
Riaza ≃	34	41.42 N	3.55 W
Ribadavia	34	42.17 N	8.08 W
Ribadeo	34	43.32 N	7.02 W
Ribadesella	34	43.28 N	5.04 W
Ribas de Jarama	266a	40.23 N	3.31 W
Ribas do Rio Pardo	255	20.27 S	53.46 W
Ribauè	154	14.57 S	38.17 E
Ribble ≃	44	53.44 N	2.50 W
Ribbleton	262	53.46 N	2.40 W
Ribble Valley □[8]	262	53.48 N	2.31 W
Ribbon Fall ∟	226	37.44 N	119.39 W
Ribchester	262	53.49 N	2.32 W
Ribe	41	55.21 N	8.46 E
Ribe □[6]	41	55.35 N	8.50 E
Ribe ≃	41	55.21 N	8.40 E
Ribeauvillé	58	48.12 N	7.19 E
Ribécourt	50	49.31 N	2.55 E
Ribeira	252	24.40 S	49.01 W
Ribeira do Iguape ≃	252	24.40 S	47.24 W
Ribeira do Pombal	250	10.50 S	38.32 W
Ribeira Grande, C.V.	150a	17.11 N	25.04 W
Ribeira Grande, Port.	148a	37.49 N	25.31 W
Ribeirão	250	8.31 S	35.23 W
Ribeirão das Lajes, Reprêsa do ⊜[1]	256	22.45 S	43.55 W
Ribeirão de São Joaquim	256	22.17 S	44.11 W
Ribeirão do Pinhal	255	23.24 S	50.18 W
Ribeirão Pires	256	23.43 S	46.25 W
Ribeirão Preto	255	21.10 S	47.48 W
Ribeirão Vermelho	255	21.11 S	45.03 W
Ribeirãozinho	255	16.27 S	52.35 W
Ribeiro Gonçalves	250	7.32 S	45.14 W
Ribeiro Junqueira	256	21.28 S	42.31 W
Ribeiros	256	21.59 S	45.35 W
Ribemont	50	49.48 N	3.28 E
Ribera	70	37.30 N	13.16 E
Riberalta	248	10.59 S	66.06 W
Riberão Pires □[7]	287b	23.43 S	46.21 W
Ribiers	62	44.14 N	5.52 E
Rib Lake	190	45.19 N	90.12 W
Ribnica, Slvn.	36	45.44 N	14.44 E
Ribnica, Slvn.	61	46.32 N	15.16 E
Ribnitz-Damgarten	54	54.15 N	12.28 E
Ribstone Creek ≃	184	52.51 N	110.05 W
Ricadi	68	38.37 N	15.52 E
Ricarda, Estany de la ⊂	266d	41.18 N	2.07 E
Ricardo Flores Magón	232	29.58 N	106.58 W
Ricaurte	246	1.13 N	77.59 W
Riccall	44	53.50 N	1.04 W
Riccarton	172	43.32 S	172.36 E
Riccia	66	41.29 N	14.50 E
Riccione	66	43.59 N	12.39 E
Rice	222	32.15 N	96.30 W
Rice Creek ≃	216	42.16 N	84.57 W
Rice Lake	190	45.30 N	91.44 W
Rice Lake ⊜, On., Can.	190	47.42 N	82.08 W
Rice Lake ⊜, On., Can.	212	44.08 N	78.13 W
Rice Lake Indian Reserve ✦[4]	212	44.10 N	78.12 W
Riceville, Ia., U.S.	190	43.22 N	92.33 W
Riceville, Pa., U.S.	214	41.47 N	79.48 W
Riceville, Tn., U.S.	192	35.23 N	84.41 W
Rich, Cape >	212	44.43 N	80.38 W
Richan	184	49.59 N	92.49 W
Richard B. Russell Lake ⊜[1]	192	34.05 N	82.39 W
Richard Collinson Inlet ⊂	176	72.45 N	113.45 W
Richards	222	30.32 N	95.51 W
Richard's Bay	158	28.47 S	32.06 E
Richard's Bay ⊂	158	28.50 S	32.02 E
Richards-Gebaur Air Force Base ▪	194	38.51 N	94.33 W
Richard's Harbour	186	47.37 N	56.24 W
Richards Island I	180	69.20 N	134.30 W
Richardson	222	32.56 N	96.43 W
Richardson ≃	176	58.30 N	111.30 W
Richardson, Mount ∧	162	28.49 S	119.59 E
Richardson Bay ⊂	282	37.52 N	122.29 W
Richardson Mountains ⋏, Can.	180	67.15 N	136.30 W
Richardson Mountains ⋏, N.Z.	172	44.45 S	168.31 E
Richardson Park	285	39.44 N	75.35 W
Richardsville	214	41.14 N	79.01 W
Richard-Toll	150	16.28 N	15.41 W
Richardton	198	46.53 N	102.18 W
Rîchât, Guelb er ∧[2]	148	21.07 N	11.24 W
Richboro	208	40.13 N	75.01 W
Richburg	210	42.05 N	78.09 W
Riche, Pointe >	186	50.42 N	57.25 W
Richebourg	261	48.49 N	1.38 E
Richelieu, P.Q., Can.	206	45.27 N	73.15 W
Richelieu, Fr.	32	47.01 N	0.19 E
Richelieu □[6]	206	45.55 N	73.00 W

Symbol	English	Deutsch	Español	Français	Português
≃	River	Fluß	Río	Rivière	Rio
≅	Canal	Kanal	Canal	Canal	Canal
∟	Waterfall, Rapids	Wasserfall, Stromschnellen	Cascada, Rápidos	Chute d'eau, Rapides	Cascata, Rápidos
∪	Strait	Meeresstraße	Estrecho	Détroit	Estreito
⊂	Bay, Gulf	Bucht, Golf	Bahía, Golfo	Baie, Golfe	Baía, Golfo
⊜	Lake, Lakes	See, Seen	Lago, Lagos	Lac, Lacs	Lago, Lagos
≡	Swamp	Sumpf	Pantano	Marais	Pântano
⊓	Ice Features, Glacier	Eis- und Gletscherformen	Accidentes Glaciales	Formes glaciaires	Acidentes glaciares
⊻	Other Hydrographic Features	Andere Hydrographische Objekte	Otros Elementos Hidrográficos	Autres données hydrographiques	Outros acidentes hidrográficos
✚	Submarine Features	Untermeerische Objekte	Accidentes Submarinos	Formes de relief sous-marin	Acidentes submarinos
□	Political Unit	Politische Einheit	Unidad Política	Entité politique	Unidade política
ʋ	Cultural Institution	Kulturelle Institution	Institución Cultural	Institution culturelle	Instituição cultural
⊥	Historical Site	Historische Stätte	Sitio Histórico	Site historique	Sítio histórico
♦	Recreational Site	Erholungs- und Freizeitort	Sitio de Recreo	Centre de loisirs	Área de Lazer
⊠	Airport	Flughafen	Aeropuerto	Aéroport	Aeroporto
▪	Military Installation	Militäranlage	Instalación Militar	Installation militaire	Instalação militar
✦	Miscellaneous	Verschiedenes	Misceláneo	Divers	Diversos

Richelieu ≃ 206 46.03 N 73.07 W
Richer 184 49.39 N 96.28 W
Richey 198 47.38 N 105.04 W
Richfield, Id., U.S. 202 43.02 N 114.09 W
Richfield, Mn., U.S. 190 44.53 N 93.16 W
Richfield, Oh., U.S. 214 41.14 N 81.39 W
Richfield, Pa., U.S. 208 40.41 N 77.07 W
Richfield, Ut,. U.S. 200 38.46 N 112.05 W
Richfield Springs 210 42.51 N 74.59 W
Richford, N.Y., U.S. 210 42.21 N 76.12 W
Richford, Vt., U.S. 206 44.59 N 72.40 W
Rich Fountain 219 38.24 N 91.53 W
Richgrove 226 35.48 N 119.07 W
Richhill, N. Ire., U.K. 48 54.23 N 6.33 W
Rich Hill, Mo., U.S. 194 38.05 N 94.12 W
Richibucto 186 46.41 N 64.52 W
Richisau 58 47.02 N 8.54 E
Richland, Ga., U.S. 192 32.05 N 84.40 W
Richland, Mi., U.S. 216 42.22 N 85.27 W
Richland, Mo., U.S. 194 37.51 N 92.24 W
Richland, N.J., U.S. 208 39.29 N 74.52 W
Richland, N.Y., U.S. 212 43.34 N 76.03 W
Richland, Pa., U.S. 208 40.21 N 76.16 W
Richland, Tx., U.S. 222 31.56 N 96.26 W
Richland, Tx., U.S. 222 32.57 N 95.49 W
Richland, Wa., U.S. 202 46.17 N 119.17 W
Richland □[6] 214 40.46 N 82.31 W
Richland Center 190 43.20 N 90.23 W
Richland Creek ≃, Il., U.S. 219 38.14 N 89.54 W
Richland Creek ≃, Tn., U.S. 194 35.02 N 86.55 W
Richland Creek ≃, Tx., U.S. 222 31.58 N 96.03 W
Richlands, N.C., U.S. 192 34.53 N 77.32 W
Richlands, Va., U.S. 192 37.05 N 81.47 W
Richland Springs 196 31.16 N 98.57 W
Richmond, Austl. 166 20.44 S 143.08 E
Richmond, Austl. 170 33.36 S 150.46 E
Richmond, Austl. 274b 37.49 S 145.00 E
Richmond, B.C., Can. 224 49.09 N 123.06 W
Richmond, On., Can. 212 45.11 N 75.50 W
Richmond, P.Q., Can. 206 45.40 N 72.09 W
Richmond, N.Z. 172 41.20 S 173.11 E
Richmond, S. Afr. 158 31.23 S 23.56 E
Richmond, S. Afr. 158 29.54 S 30.08 E
Richmond, Eng., U.K. 44 54.24 N 1.44 W
Richmond, Ca., U.S. 226 37.56 N 122.20 W
Richmond, Il., U.S. 216 42.28 N 88.18 W
Richmond, In., U.S. 218 39.49 N 84.53 W
Richmond, Ks., U.S. 198 38.24 N 95.15 W
Richmond, Ky., U.S. 192 37.44 N 84.17 W
Richmond, Me., U.S. 188 44.05 N 69.47 W
Richmond, Ma., U.S. 207 42.22 N 73.22 W
Richmond, Mi., U.S. 214 42.48 N 82.45 W
Richmond, Mn., U.S. 190 45.27 N 94.31 W
Richmond, Mo., U.S. 194 39.16 N 93.58 W
Richmond, Oh., U.S. 214 40.26 N 80.46 W
Richmond, Tx., U.S. 222 29.34 N 95.45 W
Richmond, Ut,. U.S. 200 41.55 N 111.48 W
Richmond, Vt., U.S. 188 44.24 N 72.59 W
Richmond, Va., U.S. 208 37.33 N 77.27 W
Richmond □[6], P.Q., Can. 206 45.40 N 72.00 W
Richmond □[6], N.Y., U.S. 210 40.38 N 74.05 W
Richmond □[6], Va., U.S. 208 37.32 N 77.28 W
Richmond ⊸[8], Eng., U.K. 42 51.28 N 0.18 W
Richmond ⊸[8], Ca., U.S. 282 37.46 N 122.29 W
Richmond ⊸[8], Pa., U.S. 285 39.59 N 75.06 W
Richmond, Mount ∧ 172 41.29 S 173.24 E
Richmond, Point > 282 37.55 N 122.23 W
Richmond Beach 224 47.46 N 122.23 W
Richmond Creek ≃ 276 40.34 N 74.11 W
Richmond Heights, Fl., U.S. 220 25.37 N 80.22 W
Richmond Heights, Mo., U.S. 219 38.37 N 90.19 W
Richmond Heights, Oh., U.S. 214 41.33 N 81.30 W
Richmond Highlands 224 47.45 N 122.20 W
Richmond Hill, On., Can. 212 43.52 N 79.27 W
Richmond Hill, Ga., U.S. 192 31.56 N 81.18 W
Richmond Hill ⊸[8] 276 40.42 N 73.49 W
Richmond International Airport ⊠ 208 37.30 N 77.19 W
Richmond Mall ⊸[9] 279a 41.32 N 81.30 W
Richmond National Battlefield Park ♦ 208 37.25 N 77.23 W
Richmond Park ♦ 260 51.26 N 0.16 W
Richmond Peak ∧ 241h 13.17 N 61.13 W
Richmond Range ⋀ 172 41.27 S 173.30 E
Richmond Royal Australian Air Force Base ■ 170 33.37 S 150.48 E
Richmond-San Rafael Bridge ⊸[5] 282 37.56 N 122.27 W
Richmondtown Restoration ⊥ 276 40.34 N 74.09 W
Richmond Valley ⊸[8] 276 40.31 N 74.13 W
Richmondville 210 42.38 N 74.33 W
Richrath 263 51.08 N 6.56 E
Rich Square 192 36.16 N 77.17 W
Rich Stadium ♦ 284a 42.57 N 78.47 W
Richtenberg 54 54.12 N 12.53 E
Richterswil 58 47.13 N 8.42 E
Richton 194 31.20 N 88.56 W
Richton Park 216 41.29 N 87.42 W
Richvale, On., Can. 212 43.51 N 79.26 W
Richvale, Ca., U.S. 226 39.30 N 121.45 W
Richview 219 38.23 N 89.11 W
Richville, N.Y., U.S. 212 44.25 N 75.23 E
Richville, Oh., U.S. 214 40.45 N 81.27 W
Richwood, N.J., U.S. 285 39.43 N 75.10 W
Richwood, Oh., U.S. 214 40.25 N 83.17 W
Richwood, W.V., U.S. 188 38.13 N 80.32 W
Richwood Village 222 29.04 N 95.25 W
Ricinskij zapovednik ♦ 84 43.25 N 40.30 E
Rickenbacker Air Force Base ■ 218 39.48 N 82.56 W
Rickenpass)(58 47.14 N 9.02 E
Ricken Tunnel ⊸[5] 58 47.12 N 9.05 E
Ricketts Glen State Park ♦ 210 41.20 N 76.18 W
Ricketts Point > 274b 38.00 S 145.02 E
Rickleån ≃ 26 64.05 N 20.56 E
Rickling 54 54.01 N 10.13 E
Rickmansworth 42 51.39 N 0.29 W
Rico 200 37.41 N 108.01 W
Ricoa ≃ 241s 11.30 N 69.12 W
Ricobayo, Embalse de ⊜[1] 34 41.30 N 5.55 W
Ricupe 152 14.37 S 21.25 E
Ridā' 144 14.38 N 44.54 E
Ridanna (Ridnaun) 64 46.55 N 11.15 E
Riddarhyttan 40 59.48 N 15.33 E
Ridderkerk 52 51.52 N 4.36 E
Riddes 58 46.10 N 7.13 E
Riddle 202 42.57 N 123.21 W
Riddle Mountain ∧ 202 43.07 N 118.30 W
Riddlesburg 214 40.10 N 78.15 W
Riddlewood 285 39.54 N 75.26 W
Riddon, Loch ⊂ 46 55.58 N 5.12 W
Rideau ≃ 212 45.27 N 75.42 W
Ridge, Eng., U.K. 260 51.41 N 0.15 W
Ridge, N.Y., U.S. 207 40.54 N 72.53 W
Ridge, Tx., U.S. 222 31.09 N 96.19 W
Ridge Acres 276 40.41 N 74.32 W
Ridgecrest, Ca., U.S. 204 35.37 N 117.40 W
Ridgecrest, Wa., U.S. 224 47.45 N 122.21 W
Ridgedale 184 53.04 N 104.09 W
Ridge Farm 194 39.53 N 87.39 W
Ridgefield, Ct., U.S. 207 41.16 N 73.29 W
Ridgefield, Il., U.S. 216 42.16 N 88.22 W
Ridgefield, N.J., U.S. 210 40.50 N 74.00 W
Ridgefield, Wa., U.S. 224 45.48 N 122.44 W
Ridgefield Park 276 40.51 N 74.01 W
Ridgeland, Ms., U.S. 194 32.25 N 90.07 W
Ridgeland, S.C., U.S. 192 32.28 N 80.58 W
Ridgely, Md., U.S. 208 38.56 N 75.53 W
Ridgely, Tn., U.S. 194 36.15 N 89.29 W
Ridge Manor 220 28.31 N 82.10 W
Ridgemont 210 43.13 N 77.43 W
Ridgetown 214 42.26 N 81.54 W
Ridgeville, Mb., Can. 184 49.04 N 97.01 W
Ridgeville, In., U.S. 216 40.17 N 85.01 W
Ridgeville, S.C., U.S. 192 33.05 N 80.18 W
Ridgeville Corners 216 41.26 N 84.15 W
Ridgeway, On., Can. 284a 42.53 N 79.03 W
Ridgeway, Mi., U.S. 216 41.59 N 83.51 W
Ridgeway, Mo., U.S. 194 40.22 N 93.56 W
Ridgeway, N.J., U.S. 208 40.01 N 74.17 W
Ridgeway, Oh., U.S. 216 40.30 N 83.34 W
Ridgeway, Tx., U.S. 222 33.11 N 95.46 W
Ridgeway, Wi., U.S. 190 43.00 N 89.59 W
Ridgeway Ditch ≍ 279a 41.25 N 82.05 W
Ridgewood 210 40.58 N 74.07 W
Ridgewood ⊸[8] 276 40.42 N 73.53 W
Ridgewood Farm 285 39.57 N 75.34 W
Ridgewood Reservoir ⊜[1] 276 40.41 N 73.53 W
Ridgway, Co., U.S. 200 38.09 N 107.46 W
Ridgway, Il., U.S. 194 37.47 N 88.15 W
Ridgway, Pa., U.S. 214 41.25 N 78.43 W
Riding Mountain ∧ 184 50.37 N 99.37 W
Riding Mountain National Park ♦ 184 50.55 N 100.25 W
Ridīwajār 124 27.57 N 83.26 E
Ridley Creek ≃ 285 39.51 N 75.21 W
Ridley Creek State Park ♦ 285 39.57 N 75.27 W
Ridley Park 285 39.52 N 75.19 W
Ridnaun → Ridanna 64 46.55 N 11.15 E
Riebeek-Kasteel 158 33.23 S 18.53 E
Riebeek-Oos 158 33.10 S 26.10 E
Riebeek-Wes 158 33.21 S 18.52 E
Riecawr, Loch ⊜ 44 55.13 N 4.27 W
Riedau 60 48.18 N 13.38 E
Riedelbach 56 50.18 N 8.23 E
Rieden 60 49.19 N 11.57 E
Riedenburg 60 48.58 N 11.41 E
Rieder 54 51.44 N 11.10 E
Riederalp 58 46.23 N 8.01 E
Riedern 56 49.40 N 9.23 E
Ried im Innkreis 60 48.13 N 13.30 E
Ried im Oberinntal 58 47.03 N 10.39 E
Riedisheim 58 47.45 N 7.22 E
Riedlingen 58 48.09 N 9.28 E
Riedstadt 56 49.50 N 8.30 E
Riegel 58 48.09 N 7.45 E
Riegelsville, N.J., U.S. 210 40.49 N 74.52 W
Riegelsville, Pa., U.S. 208 40.36 N 75.12 W
Riegelwood 192 34.20 N 78.15 W
Riegersburg 61 47.00 N 15.56 E
Riegersburg, Schloss ⊥ 61 47.01 N 15.56 E
Riegersdorf 64 46.33 N 13.47 E
Riehen 58 47.35 N 7.39 E
Rieka → Rijeka 36 45.20 N 14.27 E
Rielasingen 58 47.44 N 8.50 E
Riemke ⊸[8] 263 51.30 N 7.13 E
Riemst 56 50.48 N 5.36 E
Rieneck 56 50.05 N 9.38 E
Rienza (Rienz) ≃ 64 46.43 N 11.39 E
Rienzi 194 34.45 N 88.31 W
Riesa 54 51.18 N 13.17 E
Riesco, Isla I 254 53.00 S 72.30 W
Rieseby 41 54.32 N 9.48 E
Riesel 222 31.28 N 96.56 W
Riesenbeck 52 52.16 N 7.37 E
Riese Pio X 64 45.44 N 11.55 E
Riesi 70 37.17 N 14.05 E
Riestedt 54 51.29 N 11.21 E
Riet ≃, S. Afr. 158 29.00 S 23.54 E
Riet ≃, S. Afr. 158 31.20 S 20.17 E
Rietavas 76 55.44 N 21.56 E
Rietberg 52 51.47 N 8.25 E
Rietbron 158 32.54 S 23.10 E
Rietfontein 156 21.58 S 20.58 E
Riethuiskraal 158 34.20 S 21.22 E
Rieti 66 42.24 N 12.51 E
Rieti □[4] 66 42.18 N 12.52 E
Rietschen 54 51.23 N 14.47 E
Rietspruit ≃, S. Afr. 273d 26.06 S 27.39 E
Rietspruit ≃, S. Afr. 273d 26.19 S 28.18 E
Rietvlei 158 30.29 S 29.51 E
Rietzer See ⊜ 54 52.22 N 12.39 E
Rievaulx Abbey ✿[1] 44 54.16 N 1.07 W
Riez 62 43.49 N 6.06 E
Riezlern 58 47.21 N 10.11 E
Rif ⋀ 148 35.00 N 4.00 W
Riffe Lake ⊜[1] 224 46.30 N 122.20 W
Rifflart 273b 4.25 S 15.21 E
Rifiano (Riffian) 64 46.42 N 11.11 E
Rifle 200 39.32 N 107.46 W
Rifle ≃ 190 44.00 N 83.49 W
Rifstangi > 24a 66.35 N 16.10 W
Rifton 210 41.50 N 74.03 W
Rift Valley □[4] 154 0.30 N 36.00 E
Rift Valley V 10 3.00 S 29.00 E
Rift Valley Lakes National Park ♦ 144 7.30 N 38.30 E
Rīga, Lat. 76 56.57 N 24.06 E
Riga, Ross. 88 56.36 N 106.17 E
Riga, Mi., U.S. 216 41.49 N 83.50 W
Riga, Gulf of (Rīgas jūras līcis) (Riia laht) ⊂ 76 57.30 N 23.35 E
Riga, Mount ∧ 162 21.59 S 116.25 E
Rigacikun 150 10.40 N 7.28 E
Rigaih 114 4.40 N 95.34 E
Rīgān 128 28.37 N 58.58 E
Rīgas jūras līcis → Riga, Gulf of ⊂ 76 57.30 N 23.35 E
Rīga Station ⊸[5] 265b 55.48 N 37.38 E
Rigaud 206 45.29 N 74.18 W
Rigaud ≃ 206 45.29 N 74.18 W
Rigby 202 43.40 N 111.54 W
Rīgestān ⊸[1] 128 31.00 N 65.00 E
Riggins 202 45.25 N 116.18 W
Riggisberg 58 46.48 N 7.29 E
Riggston 219 39.42 N 90.25 W
Rigi ∧ 58 47.05 N 8.30 E
Rignano Flaminio 66 42.12 N 12.29 E
Rignano Garganico 68 41.40 N 15.35 E
Rignano sull'Arno 66 43.43 N 11.27 E
Rigney 58 47.23 N 6.11 E
Rigney Bluff 210 43.19 N 77.38 W
Rigny-Ussé 50 47.15 N 0.18 E
Rigo 164 9.47 S 147.34 E
Rigolet 176 54.20 N 58.35 W
Rig-Rig 146 14.16 N 14.21 E
Rigside 46 55.36 N 3.47 W
Riguldi 76 59.08 N 23.33 E
Rīh, Jazīrat ar- I 140 18.10 N 38.27 E
Riḥāb 132 32.19 N 36.06 E
Rihand ≃ 124 24.33 N 82.59 E
Rihand Dam ⊸[6] 124 24.05 N 82.45 E
Riihimäki 26 60.45 N 24.46 E
Riiser-Larsen Peninsula >[1] 9 68.55 S 34.00 E
Rijau 150 11.07 N 5.14 E
Riječki Zaljev ⊂ 36 45.15 N 14.25 E
Rijeka 36 45.20 N 14.27 E
Rijen 52 51.35 N 4.55 E
Rijkevorsel 56 51.21 N 4.46 E
Rijksdorp 52 52.09 N 4.25 E
Rijn → Rhine ≃ 30 51.52 N 6.02 E
Rijnsburg 52 52.12 N 4.27 E
Rijssel → Lille 50 50.38 N 3.04 E
Rijssen 52 52.18 N 6.30 E
Rijswijk 52 52.04 N 4.20 E
Rikers Island I 276 40.47 N 73.53 W
Rikers Island Channel ⊔ 276 40.47 N 73.52 W
Rikkavesi ⊜ 26 62.50 N 28.44 E
Riksgränsen 24 68.24 N 18.12 E
Rikuchū-kaigan-kokuritsu-kōen ♦ 92 39.25 N 141.57 E
Rikuzen-takata 92 39.01 N 141.38 E
Rila ⋀ 38 42.08 N 23.33 E
Riley 198 39.17 N 96.49 W
Riley, Mount ∧ 200 31.55 N 107.07 W
Riley, Point > 168b 33.53 S 137.36 E
Riley Creek ≃ 216 41.02 N 84.00 W
Riley Lake ⊜ 212 44.50 N 79.11 W
Rileys Range ⋀ 170 34.21 S 150.10 E
Rilievo 70 37.55 N 12.33 E
Rillieux 62 45.49 N 4.54 E
Rillington 44 54.09 N 0.42 W
Rillito 200 32.24 N 111.09 W
Rillton 214 40.17 N 79.44 W
Rilly-la-Montagne 50 49.10 N 4.03 E
Rilski manastir ✿[1] 38 42.08 N 23.20 E
Rima ≃ 150 13.04 N 5.10 E
Rímac 286d 12.03 S 77.03 W
Rímac ≃ 248 12.02 S 77.09 W
Rimachi, Laguna ⊜ 246 4.25 S 76.43 W
Rimāh, Jabal ar- ∧ 132 32.19 N 36.52 E
Rima San Giuseppe 62 45.52 N 8.00 E
Rimatara I 14 22.38 S 152.51 W
Rimavská Sobota 30 48.23 N 20.02 E
Rimbey 182 52.38 N 114.14 W
Rimbo 40 59.45 N 18.22 E
Rimé, Ouadi V 146 14.02 N 18.03 E
Rimersburg 214 41.02 N 79.30 W
Rimforsa 26 58.08 N 15.40 E
Rimi 150 12.58 N 7.43 E
Rimini 66 44.04 N 12.34 E
Rîmna ≃ 38 45.39 N 27.19 E
Rîmnicu Sărat 38 45.23 N 27.03 E
Rîmnicu Vîlcea 38 45.06 N 24.22 E
Rimo Glacier ⊓ 123 35.25 N 77.30 E
Rimogne 56 49.50 N 4.33 E
Rimouski 186 48.26 N 68.33 W
Rimouski ≃ 186 48.27 N 68.32 W
Rimouski, Réserve ♦ 186 48.03 N 68.15 W
Rimpar 56 49.51 N 9.57 E
Rimrock Lake ⊜[1] 224 46.38 N 121.12 W
Rimsko-Korsakovka 80 51.34 N 48.31 E
Rín → Rhine ≃ 30 51.52 N 6.02 E
Rinbung 124 29.21 N 89.57 E
Rinca 115b 8.37 S 119.48 E
Rinca, Pulau I 115b 8.41 S 119.42 E
Rinchnach 60 48.57 N 13.12 E
Rinčin Lchumbe 88 51.07 N 99.40 E
Rincón, C.R. 236 8.42 N 83.29 W
Rincón, P.R. 240m 18.20 N 67.15 W
Rincon, Ga., U.S. 192 32.17 N 81.14 W
Rincon, N.M., U.S. 200 32.40 N 107.03 W
Rincón, Bahía de ⊂ 240m 17.58 N 66.20 W
Rinconada 252 22.26 S 66.10 W
Rinconada, Hipódromo de la ♦ 286c 10.26 N 66.56 W
Rincón de la Vieja, Parque Nacional ♦ 236 10.48 N 85.18 W
Rincón del Bonete, Lago Artificial de ⊜[1] 252 32.45 S 56.00 W
Rincón del Ocote, Cerro ∧ 236 13.36 N 87.10 W
Rincón de Romos 234 22.14 N 102.18 W
Rincon Indian Reservation ⊸[4] 228 33.15 N 116.57 W
Rincon Valley 226 38.28 N 122.39 W
Rindal 26 63.03 N 9.13 E
Rindown Castle ⊥ 48 53.32 N 7.59 W
Rīngas 120 27.21 N 75.34 E
Ringdove 175f 16.38 S 168.09 E
Ringe 41 55.14 N 10.29 E
Ringebu 26 61.31 N 10.10 E
Ringenwalde 54 53.03 N 13.42 E
Ringertown 279b 40.25 N 79.36 W
Ringford 44 54.54 N 4.03 W
Ringgau ⊸[1] 56 51.04 N 10.04 E
Ringgit, Gunung ∧ 115a 7.43 S 113.50 E
Ringgold, Ga., U.S. 192 34.54 N 85.06 W
Ringgold, La., U.S. 194 32.19 N 93.16 W
Ringgold, Pa., U.S. 214 41.00 N 79.10 W
Ringgold Isles II 175g 16.15 S 179.25 W
Ringim 150 12.08 N 9.10 E
Ringkøbing 26 56.05 N 8.15 E
Ringkøbing □[6] 41 56.10 N 8.50 E
Ringkøbing Fjord ⊂[2] 26 56.00 N 8.15 E
Ringlet 114 4.25 N 101.23 E
Ringling 196 34.10 N 97.35 W
Ringling Museums ✿ 220 27.23 N 82.34 W
Ringmer 42 50.53 N 0.04 E
Ringoes 208 40.26 N 74.52 W
Rings Island 283 42.49 N 70.52 W
Ringsted, Dan. 41 55.27 N 11.49 E
Ringsted, Ia., U.S. 198 43.17 N 94.30 W
Ringtown 210 40.51 N 76.14 W
Ringvassøy I 24 69.55 N 19.15 E
Ringville 48 52.02 N 7.34 W
Ringwood, Austl. 169 37.49 S 145.14 E
Ringwood, Eng., U.K. 42 50.51 N 1.47 W
Ringwood, N.J., U.S. 210 41.06 N 74.14 W
Ringwood Manor ⊥ 276 41.08 N 74.15 W
Ringwood North 274b 37.48 S 145.14 E
Ringwood State Park ♦ 210 41.08 N 74.16 W
Riñihue 254 39.49 S 72.27 W
Riñihue, Lago ⊜ 254 39.50 S 72.18 W
Rinjani, Gunung ∧ 115b 8.24 S 116.28 E
Rinkenæs 41 54.54 N 9.34 E
Rinkerode 52 51.50 N 7.41 E
Rinnes, Ben ∧ 46 57.23 N 3.15 W
Rinnthal 56 49.13 N 7.55 E
Rinsumageest 52 53.18 N 5.57 E
Rinteln 52 52.11 N 9.04 E
Rinxent 50 50.48 N 1.44 E
Rio, Fl., U.S. 220 27.13 N 80.14 W
Rio, Wi., U.S. 190 43.26 N 89.14 W
Rio Azul 252 25.43 S 50.47 W
Riobamba 246 1.40 S 78.38 W
Río Blanco, Chile 252 32.55 S 70.19 W
Río Blanco (Tenango de Rio Blanco), Méx. 234 18.50 N 97.09 W
Rio Bonito 256 22.43 S 42.37 W
Rio Bonito ⊸[8] 287b 23.43 S 46.41 W
Rio Branco, Bra. 248 9.58 S 67.48 W
Río Branco, Ur. 252 32.34 S 53.25 W
Río Bravo, Méx. 196 28.17 N 100.55 W
Río Bravo, Méx. 232 25.59 N 98.06 W
Rio Brilhante 255 21.48 S 54.33 W
Río Bueno 254 40.19 S 72.58 W
Río Caribe 246 10.42 N 63.07 W
Rio Casca 255 20.13 S 42.39 W
Río Cauto 240p 20.33 N 76.55 W
Río Ceballos 252 31.10 S 64.20 W
Río Chico, Arg. 254 41.43 S 70.30 W
Río Chico, Ven. 246 10.18 N 65.59 W
Rio Claro, Bra. 255 22.24 S 47.33 W
Rio Claro, Bra. 256 22.43 S 44.09 W
Rio Claro, Trin. 241r 10.18 N 61.11 W
Rio Claro, Represa do ⊜[1] 256 23.39 S 45.54 W
Río Colorado 252 39.01 S 64.05 W
Rio Comprido ⊸[8] 287a 22.55 S 43.12 W
Río Cuarto 252 33.08 S 64.21 W
Rio das Flores 256 22.10 S 43.35 W
Rio das Pedras 156 23.12 S 35.23 E
Rio de Contas 255 13.36 S 41.48 W
Rio de Janeiro, Bra. 256 22.54 S 43.14 W
Rio de Janeiro, Bra. 287a 22.54 S 43.14 W
Rio de Janeiro □[3] 255 22.00 S 42.30 W
Rio de Janeiro □[7] 287a 22.55 S 43.30 W
Río de Jesús 236 7.59 N 81.10 W
Rio Dell 204 40.29 N 124.06 W
Rio de Mouro 266c 38.46 N 9.20 W
Río de Oro 246 8.17 N 73.23 W
Rio do Prado 255 16.35 S 40.34 W
Rio do Sul 252 27.13 S 49.39 W
Rio Douro 287a 22.39 S 43.32 W
Rio Espera 255 20.51 S 43.29 W
Río Gallegos 254 51.38 S 69.13 W
Río Grande, Arg. 254 53.47 S 67.42 W
Rio Grande, Bra. 252 32.02 S 52.05 W
Río Grande, Méx. 234 15.59 N 97.27 W
Río Grande, Méx. 234 23.50 N 103.02 W
Río Grande, Nic. 236 12.53 N 86.32 W
Río Grande, P.R. 240m 18.23 N 65.50 W
Rio Grande, N.J., U.S. 208 39.00 N 74.52 W
Río Grande, Ven. 286c 10.35 N 66.57 W
Rio Grande → Grande, Rio ≃ 178 25.57 N 97.09 W
Rio Grande, Ponte do ⊸[5] 287b 23.46 S 46.31 W
Rio Grande City 196 26.22 N 98.49 W
Rio Grande Da Serra, Bra. 256 23.44 S 46.24 W
Rio Grande da Serra, Bra. 287b 23.44 S 46.24 W
Rio Grande da Serra □[7] 287b 23.45 S 46.23 W
Rio Grande do Norte □[3] 250 5.45 S 36.00 W
Rio Grande do Sul → Rio Grande 252 32.02 S 52.05 W
Rio Grande do Sul □[3] 252 30.00 S 54.00 W
Riograndina 256 22.11 S 42.30 W
Ríohacha 246 11.33 N 72.55 W
Río Hato 236 8.23 N 80.10 W
Río Hondo, Méx. 286a 19.25 N 99.16 W
Rio Hondo, Tx., U.S. 196 26.14 N 97.34 W
Rioja 248 6.05 S 77.09 W
Rio Jaguari, Reservatório do ⊜[1] 256 22.55 S 46.25 W
Río Jueyes 240m 18.01 N 66.20 W
Riola 64 44.16 N 11.04 E
Río Lagartos 232 21.36 N 88.10 W
Riolândia 255 19.59 S 49.40 W
Rio Largo 250 9.29 S 35.51 W
Riola Sardo 71 39.59 N 8.32 E
Rio Linda 226 38.41 N 121.26 W
Riolo Terme 66 44.16 N 11.43 E
Río Luján 258 34.17 S 58.54 W
Riom 32 45.54 N 3.07 E
Riomaggiore 62 44.06 N 9.44 E
Rio Marina 66 42.49 N 10.25 E
Río Mayo 254 45.41 S 70.16 W
Rio Mulatos 248 19.42 S 66.47 W
Río Muni □[4] 152 1.30 N 10.30 E
Riondel 182 49.46 N 116.52 W
Rio Negro, Bra. 252 26.06 S 49.48 W
Rio Negro, Bra. 255 19.27 S 54.58 W
Río Negro, Chile 254 40.47 S 73.14 W
Ríonegro, Col. 246 6.09 N 75.22 W
Ríonegro, Col. 246 7.16 N 73.09 W
Río Negro □[4] 254 40.00 S 67.00 W
Rio Negro, Pantanal do ≣ 248 19.00 S 56.00 W
Rionero in Vulture 68 40.56 N 15.41 E
Rionero Sannitico 66 41.42 N 14.08 E
Rioni ≃ 84 42.08 N 41.39 E
Rio Novo 256 21.29 S 43.08 W
Rio Novo do Sul 255 20.52 S 40.56 W
Riópar 34 38.30 N 2.27 W
Rio Pardo 252 29.59 S 52.22 W
Rio Pardo de Minas 255 15.37 S 42.33 W
Río Pico 254 44.13 S 71.21 W
Río Piedras, Arg. 252 25.18 S 64.54 W
Río Piedras, P.R. 240m 18.24 N 66.03 W
Río Pilcomayo, Parque Nacional ♦ 252 25.10 S 58.00 W
Rio Piracicaba 255 19.55 S 43.11 W
Rio Pomba 256 21.17 S 43.11 W
Rio Prêto, Bra. 256 22.06 S 43.50 W
Rio Prêto → São José do Rio Prêto, Bra. 256 22.10 S 42.57 W
Rio Rancho 200 35.14 N 106.38 W
Rio Real 250 11.28 S 37.56 W
Rio Saliceto 64 44.49 N 10.49 E
Río San Juan □[5] 236 11.10 N 84.30 W
Río Segundo 252 31.40 S 63.55 W
Ríosucio, Col. 246 5.25 N 75.42 W
Ríosucio, Col. 246 7.27 N 77.07 W
Río Tercero 252 32.11 S 64.06 W
Rio Tinto 250 6.48 S 35.05 W
Riotord 62 45.14 N 4.24 E
Rio Tuba 116 8.30 N 117.25 E
Riou, Île de I 62 43.11 N 5.24 E
Rioveggio 64 44.17 N 11.14 E
Rio Verde, Bra. 255 17.43 S 50.56 W
Ríoverde, Méx. 234 21.56 N 99.59 W
Rio Verde de Mato Grosso 255 18.56 S 54.52 W
Rio Vermelho 255 18.18 S 43.00 W
Rio Vista, Ca., U.S. 226 38.09 N 121.41 W
Rio Vista, Tx., U.S. 222 32.14 N 97.23 W
Rioz 58 47.25 N 6.04 E
Riozinho ≃, Bra. 246 2.55 S 67.07 W
Riozinho ≃, Bra. 250 10.22 S 49.50 W
Riozinho ≃, Bra. 250 8.25 S 45.43 W
Riozinho ≃, Bra. 250 7.06 S 51.40 W
Říp ∧ 54 50.24 N 14.18 E
Ripacandida 68 40.55 N 15.43 E
Ripalti, Punta dei > 66 42.42 N 10.25 E
Ripatransone 66 43.00 N 13.46 E
Ripley, Eng., U.K. 44 53.03 N 1.24 W
Ripley, Eng., U.K. 260 51.18 N 0.29 W
Ripley, Il., U.S. 219 40.01 N 90.38 W
Ripley, In., U.S. 216 41.06 N 86.39 W
Ripley, Ms., U.S. 194 34.43 N 88.57 W
Ripley, N.Y., U.S. 214 42.16 N 79.42 W
Ripley, Oh., U.S. 218 38.44 N 83.50 W
Ripley, Tn., U.S. 194 35.44 N 89.31 W
Ripley, W.V., U.S. 188 38.49 N 81.42 W
Ripley □[6] 218 39.04 N 85.15 W
Ripoll 34 42.12 N 2.12 E
Ripoll ≃ 266d 41.29 N 2.12 E
Ripollet 266d 41.30 N 2.10 E
Ripon, P.Q., Can. 206 45.47 N 75.06 W
Ripon, Eng., U.K. 44 54.08 N 1.31 W
Ripon, Ca., U.S. 226 37.44 N 121.07 W
Ripon, Wi., U.S. 190 43.50 N 88.50 W
Riposto 70 37.44 N 15.12 E
Rippling Ridge 284b 39.11 N 76.37 W
Ripponden 44 53.41 N 1.57 W
Rippowam ≃ 276 41.03 N 73.33 W
Riquewihr 58 48.10 N 7.18 E
Ririba, Laga ≃ 154 3.34 N 37.15 E
Ririe 202 43.37 N 111.46 W
Risālpur Cantonment 123 34.04 N 72.00 E
Risaralda □[5] 246 5.00 N 76.00 W
Risasi 154 0.25 S 25.44 E
Risbäck 26 64.42 N 15.32 E
Risca 42 51.37 N 3.07 W
Rischenau 52 51.53 N 9.17 E
Riscle 32 43.40 N 0.05 W
Risco, Ilha do I 246 3.07 S 58.19 W
Rishā', Wādī ar- V 128 25.33 N 44.05 E
Rīshahr 128 28.55 N 50.50 E
Rishīkesh 124 30.07 N 78.19 E
Rishiri-Rebun-Sarobetsu-kokuritsu-kōen ♦ 92a 45.10 N 141.35 E
Rishiri-suidō ⊔ 92a 45.10 N 141.25 E
Rishiri-tō I 92a 45.11 N 141.15 E
Rishiri-zan ∧ 92a 45.11 N 141.15 E
Rishmayyā 132 33.44 N 35.36 E
Rishon LeẔiyyon 132 31.58 N 34.48 E
Rishpon 132 32.12 N 34.49 E
Rishra 272b 22.43 N 88.21 E
Rishrāsh, Wādī V 142 29.29 N 31.16 E
Rishton 262 53.46 N 2.25 W
Rishworth 262 53.40 N 1.57 W
Rishworth Moor ⊸[3] 262 53.39 N 2.01 W
Risinge 40 58.42 N 15.51 E
Rising Star 196 32.05 N 98.57 W
Rising Sun, In., U.S. 218 38.56 N 84.51 W
Rising Sun, Md., U.S. 208 39.41 N 76.03 W
Risingsun, Oh., U.S. 214 41.16 N 83.25 W
Risle ≃ 50 49.26 N 0.23 E
Risnjak ∧ 36 45.26 N 14.37 E
Rîşnov 38 45.36 N 25.28 E
Risø 41 55.42 N 12.06 E
Rison, Ar., U.S. 194 33.57 N 92.11 W
Rison, Md., U.S. 208 38.32 N 77.10 W
Risør 26 58.43 N 9.14 E
Ris-Orangis 50 48.39 N 2.25 E
Riss ≃ 58 48.17 N 9.49 E
Rissani 148 31.23 N 4.09 W
Risskov ⊸[8] 41 56.11 N 10.14 E
Risstissen 58 48.16 N 9.49 E
Risti 76 58.59 N 24.03 E
Ristigouche (Restigouche) ≃ 186 48.04 N 66.20 W
Ristiina 26 61.30 N 27.16 E
Ristijärvi 26 64.30 N 28.13 E
Ristinge 41 54.50 N 10.38 E
Ristna 76 58.56 N 22.05 E
Risum-Lindholm 41 54.45 N 8.53 E
Rita Blanca Creek ≃ 196 35.40 N 102.29 W
Ritchie, S. Afr. 158 29.02 S 24.38 E
Ritchie, Md., U.S. 284c 38.52 N 76.52 W
Ritchie Branch ≃ 284c 38.53 N 76.52 W
Rithāla ⊸[8] 272a 28.43 N 77.06 E
Ritidian Point > 174p 13.39 N 144.51 E
Ritscher Upland ⋀[1] 9 73.20 S 9.30 W
Ritsumeikan University ✿[2] 270 35.01 N 135.46 E
Ritsurin-kōen ♦ 96 34.21 N 134.02 E
Ritta Island I 220 26.44 N 80.48 W
Ritter, Mount ∧ 226 37.42 N 119.12 W
Ritterhude 52 53.11 N 8.45 E
Rittersgrün 54 50.29 N 12.47 E
Rittman 214 40.58 N 81.46 W
Rittō 94 35.01 N 136.00 E
Ritzleben 54 52.50 N 11.21 E
Ritzville 202 47.07 N 118.22 W
Riu 120 28.19 N 95.03 E
Riva 208 38.57 N 76.35 W
Rivadavia, Arg. 252 35.28 S 62.57 W
Rivadavia, Arg. 252 33.11 S 68.28 W
Rivadavia, Arg. 252 24.11 S 62.53 W
Rivadavia, Arg. 252 31.33 S 68.37 W
Rivadavia, Chile 252 29.58 S 70.34 W
Riva del Garda 64 45.53 N 10.50 E
Riva del Sole 66 42.46 N 10.52 E
Riva di Tures (Rain) 64 46.57 N 12.04 E
Rivanazzano 62 44.56 N 9.01 E
Rivanna ≃ 192 37.45 N 78.10 W
Rivare 216 40.49 N 84.50 W
Rivarolo Canavese 62 45.19 N 7.43 E
Rivarolo Mantovano 64 45.04 N 10.26 E
Rivas 236 11.26 N 85.50 W
Rivas □[5] 236 11.25 N 85.50 W
Rivasdale 273d 26.17 S 27.56 E
Rīvash 128 35.26 N 58.26 E
Rivas-Vaciamadrid 266a 40.20 N 3.31 W
Riva Trigoso 62 44.16 N 9.26 E
Rive, Île de la I 273b 4.21 S 15.26 E
Rive d'Arcano 64 46.08 N 13.02 E
Rive-de-Gier 62 45.32 N 4.37 E
Rivello 68 40.04 N 15.45 E
Rivera, Arg. 252 37.12 S 63.14 W
Rivera, Col. 246 2.47 N 75.15 W
Rivera, Ur. 252 30.54 S 55.31 W
Riverbank 226 37.44 N 120.56 W
River Cess 150 5.28 N 9.32 W
Riverdale, Ca., U.S. 226 36.25 N 119.51 W
Riverdale, Il., U.S. 278 41.38 N 87.37 W
Riverdale, Md., U.S. 284c 38.57 N 76.55 W
Riverdale, N.J., U.S. 276 40.59 N 74.18 W
Riverdale, N.D., U.S. 198 47.29 N 101.22 W
Riverdale, Or., U.S. 224 45.27 N 122.41 W
Riverdale ⊸[8] 276 40.54 N 73.54 W
Riverdale Heights 284c 38.58 N 76.55 W
Riverdale Park ♦ 275b 43.40 N 79.21 W
River Drive Park 212 44.08 N 79.31 W
River Edge, N.J., U.S. 276 40.55 N 74.02 W
River Edge, Oh., U.S. 279a 41.25 N 81.51 W
River Falls, Al., U.S. 194 31.21 N 86.32 W
River Falls, Wi., U.S. 190 44.51 N 92.37 W
River Forest 278 41.53 N 87.48 W
Rivergaro 62 44.55 N 9.36 E
River Grove 278 41.55 N 87.50 W
Riverhaven 216 41.05 N 85.02 W
Riverhead, Eng., U.K. 260 51.17 N 0.10 E
Riverhead, N.Y., U.S. 207 40.55 N 72.39 W
River Hébert 186 45.42 N 64.23 W
River Hill 279b 40.12 N 79.54 W
River Hills 216 43.10 N 87.55 W
Riverhurst 184 50.53 N 106.52 W
Riverina ⊸[1] 166 35.30 S 145.30 E
River John 186 45.45 N 63.03 W
River Jordan 224 48.25 N 124.03 W
Riverlea 214 40.05 N 83.02 W
River Lea Navigation ≍ 260 51.32 N 0.02 W
River Meadow Brook ≃ 283 42.38 N 71.17 W
Rivermont 192 35.13 N 77.38 W
Rivero, Isla I 254 45.37 S 74.20 W
River Oaks 284c 38.57 N 77.11 W
River of Ponds 186 50.32 N 57.24 W
River Pines, Ca., U.S. 226 38.33 N 120.45 W
River Pines, Ma., U.S. 207 42.33 N 71.17 W
River Plaza 208 40.21 N 74.05 W
River Ridge Estates 284c 38.47 N 77.00 W
River Road 202 44.03 N 123.05 W
River Rouge 216 42.16 N 83.08 W
River Rouge Park ♦ 281 42.22 N 83.15 W
Rivers 184 50.02 N 100.12 W
Rivers □[3] 150 4.30 N 6.30 E
Rivers, Lake of the ⊜ 184 49.45 N 105.45 W
Riversdale, N.Z. 172 45.54 S 168.45 E
Riversdale, S. Afr. 158 34.07 S 21.15 E
Riverside, Ca., U.S. 228 33.57 N 117.23 W
Riverside, Ct., U.S. 276 41.02 N 73.35 W
Riverside, Il., U.S. 278 41.50 N 87.49 W
Riverside, Ia., U.S. 190 41.28 N 91.34 W
Riverside, Mi., U.S. 216 42.11 N 86.23 W
Riverside, Mi., U.S. 216 42.17 N 84.29 W
Riverside, N.J., U.S. 208 40.01 N 74.57 W
Riverside, N.Y., U.S. 210 42.55 N 73.40 W
Riverside, N.Y., U.S. 210 42.08 N 77.01 W
Riverside, Pa., U.S. 210 40.57 N 76.38 W
Riverside, Tx., U.S. 222 30.57 N 95.24 W
Riverside, Wa., U.S. 182 48.30 N 119.30 W
Riverside □[6] 228 33.45 N 117.10 W
Riverside ⊸[8] 281 42.20 N 82.57 W
Riverside International Raceway ♦ 228 33.57 N 117.17 W
Riverside Manors 284a 43.11 N 79.03 W
Riverside Park ♦, Mi., U.S. 281 42.22 N 83.26 W
Riverside Park ♦, N.Y., U.S. 284a 42.57 N 78.54 W
Rivers Inlet 182 51.41 N 127.15 W
Rivers Inlet ⊂ 182 51.39 N 127.30 W
Riversleigh 166 19.02 S 138.44 E
Riverstone 170 33.40 S 150.52 E
Riverton, Austl. 168b 34.09 S 138.45 E
Riverton, Mb., Can. 184 50.59 N 96.59 W
Riverton, N.Z. 172 46.21 S 168.01 E
Riverton, Il., U.S. 219 39.51 N 89.33 W
Riverton, Ne., U.S. 198 40.05 N 98.45 W
Riverton, N.J., U.S. 208 40.00 N 75.00 W
Riverton, Ut,. U.S. 200 40.31 N 111.56 W
Riverton, Va., U.S. 188 38.56 N 78.11 W
Riverton, Wy., U.S. 200 43.01 N 108.22 W
Riverton Heights 224 47.28 N 122.18 W
River Vale 276 40.59 N 74.00 W
Riverview, S. Afr. 158 28.27 S 32.10 E
River View, Al., U.S. 194 32.47 N 85.08 W
Riverview, Fl., U.S. 220 27.51 N 82.19 W
Riverview, Ks., U.S. 198 37.47 N 97.22 W
Riverview, Mi., U.S. 216 42.10 N 83.10 W
Riverview Park ♦ 279b 40.29 N 80.01 W
Riverwood, Austl. 274a 33.57 S 151.03 E
Riverwood, In., U.S. 218 40.06 N 85.58 W
Riverwoods 278 42.10 N 87.54 W
Rives, Fr. 62 45.21 N 5.30 E
Rives, Tn., U.S. 194 36.21 N 89.02 W
Rivesaltes 32 42.46 N 2.52 E
Rives Junction 216 42.23 N 84.27 W
Rive Sud, Canal de la ≍ 275a 45.25 N 73.41 W
Rivesville 188 39.31 N 80.07 W
Riviera, Az., U.S. 204 35.04 N 114.35 W
Riviera, Tx., U.S. 196 27.18 N 97.49 W
Riviera V 58 46.15 N 8.58 E
Riviera Beach, Fl., U.S. 220 26.46 N 80.03 W
Riviera Beach, Md., U.S. 208 39.10 N 76.30 W
Rivière-à-Claude 186 49.13 N 65.54 W
Rivière-au-Tonnerre 186 50.16 N 64.47 W
Rivière-Bleue 186 47.26 N 69.03 W
Rivière-Bois-Clair 206 46.34 N 71.50 W
Rivière-de-la-Chaloupe 186 49.08 N 62.32 W
Rivière-des-Prairies ⊸[8] 275a 45.39 N 73.33 W
Rivière-du-Loup 186 47.50 N 69.32 W
Rivière du Rempart 157c 20.06 S 57.41 E
Rivière-Matane 186 48.39 N 67.20 W
Rivière-Mékinac 206 46.47 N 72.48 W
Rivière-Pentecôte 186 49.47 N 67.10 W
Rivière-Pilote 240e 14.29 N 60.54 W
Rivière-Salée 240e 14.32 N 60.59 W
Rivière-Verte 186 47.19 N 68.09 W
Riviersonderend 158 34.09 S 19.55 E
Rivignano 64 45.52 N 13.03 E
Rivington 262 53.37 N 2.34 W
Rivington Reservoirs ⊜[1] 262 53.37 N 2.34 W
Rivisondoli 66 41.52 N 14.04 E
Rivoli 62 45.04 N 7.31 E
Rivoli Bay ⊂ 166 37.32 S 140.04 E
Rivolta d'Adda 62 45.28 N 9.31 E
Rivoltella 64 45.27 N 10.33 E
Riwaka 172 41.05 S 173.00 E
Rixford 214 41.55 N 78.30 W
Rixheim 58 47.46 N 7.24 E
Riyadh → Ar-Riyāḍ 128 24.38 N 46.43 E
Rīyāq 132 33.51 N 36.00 E
Rizal, Pil. 116 15.43 N 121.06 E
Rizal → Pasay, Pil. 269f 14.33 N 121.00 E
Rizal □[4] 116 14.35 N 121.10 E
Rizal Memorial Stadium ♦ 269f 14.34 N 120.59 E
Rize 130 41.02 N 40.31 E
Rize □[4] 130 40.55 N 40.55 E
Rīzeh, Kūh-e (gora Reza) ∧ 128 37.47 N 58.05 E
Rizhao 98 35.27 N 119.29 E
Rizziconi 68 38.25 N 15.57 E
Rizzuto, Capo > 68 38.54 N 17.06 E
Rjukan 26 59.52 N 8.34 E
Rkîz, Lac ⊜ 150 16.50 N 15.19 W
Rô 175f 21.22 S 167.50 E
Roa, Esp. 34 41.42 N 3.55 W
Roa, Nor. 26 60.17 N 10.37 E
Roa, Zaïre 154 3.49 N 24.56 E
Roachdale 194 39.50 N 86.48 W
Roade 42 52.09 N 0.53 W
Roadford Reservoir ⊜[1] 42 50.43 N 4.13 W
Roadhead 44 55.04 N 2.46 W
Roadknight, Point > 169 38.26 S 144.11 E
Roadside 158 27.31 S 28.52 E
Road Town 240m 18.27 N 64.37 W
Roag, East Loch ⊂ 46 58.14 N 6.48 W
Roag, West Loch ⊂ 46 58.13 N 6.53 W
Roaming Rock, Lake ⊜[1] 214 41.38 N 80.49 W
Roaming Shores 214 41.39 N 80.49 W
Roana 64 45.52 N 11.28 E
Roan Cliffs ±[4] 200 39.20 N 109.40 W
Roan Creek ≃ 200 39.20 N 108.13 W
Roan Fell ∧ 44 55.13 N 2.52 W
Roan Mountain 192 36.11 N 82.04 W
Roann 216 40.54 N 85.55 W
Roanne 32 46.02 N 4.04 E
Roanoke, Al., U.S. 194 33.09 N 85.22 W
Roanoke, Il., U.S. 190 40.47 N 89.11 W
Roanoke, In., U.S. 216 40.57 N 85.22 W
Roanoke, Tx., U.S. 222 33.01 N 97.14 W
Roanoke, Va., U.S. 192 37.16 N 79.56 W
Roanoke (Staunton) ≃ 192 35.56 N 76.43 W
Roanoke Island I 192 35.53 N 75.39 W
Roanoke Rapids 192 36.27 N 77.39 W
Roanoke Rapids Dam ⊸[6] 192 36.24 N 77.40 W
Roan Plateau ⋀[1] 200 39.30 N 109.40 W
Roans Prairie 222 30.35 N 95.57 W
Roaring ≃ 224 45.13 N 122.12 W
Roaring Branch 210 41.34 N 76.57 W
Roaring Brook ≃ 212 43.44 N 75.24 W
Roaring Fork ≃ 200 39.33 N 107.20 W
Roaring River Slough ≃ 282 38.05 N 121.55 W
Roaring Run ≃ 279b 40.33 N 79.32 W
Roaring Spring 214 40.20 N 78.23 W
Roaring Springs 196 33.54 N 100.52 W
Roaringwater Bay ⊂ 48 51.31 N 9.26 W
Roatán 236 16.18 N 86.35 W
Roatán, Isla de I 236 16.23 N 86.30 W
Robâa Oued Yahia 36 36.05 N 9.35 E
Robāṭ Karīm 128 35.28 N 51.05 E
Robbeneiland I 158 33.49 S 18.22 E
Robbers Cave State Park ♦ 196 35.01 N 95.27 W
Robbins, Ca., U.S. 226 38.53 N 121.42 W
Robbins, Il., U.S. 216 41.38 N 87.42 W
Robbins, N.C., U.S. 192 35.26 N 79.35 W
Robbins, Tn., U.S. 192 36.21 N 84.35 W
Robbins Airport ⊠ 283 42.34 N 70.58 W
Robbins Ditch ≍ 216 41.21 N 86.43 W
Robbins Island I 166 40.41 S 144.57 E
Robbins Pond ⊜ 283 42.00 N 70.55 W
Robbins Rest 276 40.39 N 73.10 W
Robbinsville, N.J., U.S. 208 40.13 N 74.37 W
Robbinsville, N.C., U.S. 192 35.19 N 83.48 W
Robbio 62 45.17 N 8.35 E
Robe, Austl. 166 37.11 S 139.45 E
Robe, Ityo. 144 7.52 N 39.38 E
Robe ≃, Austl. 162 21.19 S 115.40 E
Robe ≃, Ire. 48 53.37 N 9.16 W
Robe, Mount ∧[2] 166 31.40 S 141.20 E
Robecchetto con Induno 266b 45.32 N 8.46 E
Robecco d'Oglio 64 45.15 N 10.04 E
Robecco sul Naviglio 266b 45.26 N 8.53 E
Röbel 54 53.23 N 12.35 E
Robeline 194 31.41 N 93.18 W
Röberget ∧[2] 40 59.45 N 14.54 E
Robersonville 192 35.49 N 77.15 W
Robert, Havre du ⊂ 240e 14.40 N 60.55 W
Roberta 192 32.43 N 84.00 W
Roberta Mills 192 35.22 N 80.38 W
Robert E. Lee Memorial Park ♦ 284b 39.23 N 76.39 W
Robert E. Lee's Birthplace ⊥ 208 38.10 N 76.49 W
Robert-Espagne 56 48.45 N 5.02 E

Symbols in the index entries represent the broad categories identified in the key at the right. Symbols with superior numbers (⋀[1]) identify subcategories (see complete key on page *I · 1).*

Symbole im Register stellen die rechts im Schlüssel erklärten Kategorien dar. Symbole mit hochgestellten Ziffern (⋀[1]) bezeichnen Unterabteilungen einer Kategorie (vgl. vollständiger Schlüssel auf Seite *I · 1).*

Los símbolos incluídos en el texto del índice representan las grandes categorías identificadas con la clave a la derecha. Los símbolos con numeros en su parte superior (⋀[1]) identifican las subcategorías (véase la clave completa en la página *I · 1).*

Les symboles de l'index représentent les catégories indiquées dans la légende à droite. Les symboles suivis d'un indice (⋀[1]) représentent des sous-catégories (voir légende complète à la page *I · 1).*

Os símbolos incluídos no texto do índice representam as grandes categorias identificadas com a chave à direita. Os símbolos com números em sua parte superior (⋀[1]) identificam as subcategorias (veja-se a chave completa à página *I · 1).*

	English	Deutsch	Español	Français	Português
∧	Mountain	Berg	Montaña	Montagne	Montanha
⋀	Mountains	Gebirge	Montañas	Montagnes	Montanhas
)(	Pass	Paß	Paso	Col	Passo
V	Valley, Canyon	Tal, Cañon	Valle, Cañón	Vallée, Canyon	Vale, Canhão
≏	Plain	Ebene	Llano	Plaine	Planície
>	Cape	Kap	Cabo	Cap	Cabo
I	Island	Insel	Isla	Île	Ilha
II	Islands	Inseln	Islas	Îles	Ilhas
±	Other Topographic Features	Andere Topographische Objekte	Otros Elementos Topográficos	Autres données topographiques	Outros acidentes topográficos

| ESPAÑOL | | | FRANÇAIS | | | PORTUGUÊS | | | | | | | | | Robe-Rong I · 147 |

ESPAÑOL — Nombre · Página · Lat.°′ · Long.°′ W=Oeste
FRANÇAIS — Nom · Page · Lat.°′ · Long.°′ W=Ouest
PORTUGUÊS — Nome · Página · Lat.°′ · Long.°′ W=Oeste

≃ River / Fluß / Río / Rivière / Rio
≖ Canal / Kanal / Canal / Canal / Canal
⌣ Waterfall, Rapids / Wasserfall, Stromschnellen / Cascada, Rápidos / Chute d'eau, Rapides / Cascata, Rápidos
✕ Strait / Meeresstraße / Estrecho / Détroit / Estreito
c Bay, Gulf / Bucht, Golf / Bahía, Golfo / Baie, Golfe / Baía, Golfo
⊘ Lake, Lakes / See, Seen / Lago, Lagos / Lac, Lacs / Lago, Lagos
≖ Swamp / Sumpf / Pantano / Marais / Pântano
⊠ Ice Features, Glacier / Eis- und Gletscherformen / Accidentes Glaciares / Formes glaciaires / Acidentes glaciares
⊺ Other Hydrographic Features / Andere Hydrographische Objekte / Otros Accidentes Hidrográficos / Autres accidents hydrographiques / Outros acidentes hidrográficos

⊹ Submarine Features / Untermeerische Objekte / Accidentes Submarinos / Formes de relief sous-marin / Acidentes submarinos
⚬¹ Political Unit / Politische Einheit / Unidad Política / Entité politique / Unidade política
⊮ Cultural Institution / Kulturelle Institution / Institución Cultural / Institution culturelle / Instituição cultural
⊥ Historical Site / Historische Stätte / Sitio Histórico / Site historique / Sítio histórico
♦ Recreational Site / Erholungs- und Ferienort / Sitio de Recreo / Centre de loisirs / Área de Lazer
⌭ Airport / Flughafen / Aeropuerto / Aéroport / Aeroporto
■ Military Installation / Militäranlage / Instalación Militar / Installation militaire / Instalação militar
⊷ Miscellaneous / Verschiedenes / Misceláneo / Divers / Diversos

Rongjiang 102 25.52 N 108.37 E
Rongkop 115a 8.10 S 110.45 E
Rongola 158 27.22 S 31.37 E
Rongotea 172 40.18 S 175.25 E
Röngu 76 58.09 N 26.15 E
Rongui, Ilha I 154 10.50 S 40.40 E
Rongwanshi 100 28.10 N 112.57 E
Rongxian, Zhg. 102 22.50 N 110.38 E
Rongxian, Zhg. 107 29.28 N 104.25 E
Ronkiti Harbor c 174r 6.48 N 158.10 E
Ronkonkoma 276 40.48 N 73.06 W
Ronkonkoma, Lake ⊜ 276 40.50 N 73.07 W
Ronne 26 55.06 N 14.42 E
Rönne ≃ 41 56.16 N 12.50 E
Ronneburg 54 50.51 N 12.10 E
Ronneby 26 56.12 N 15.18 E
Ronne Entrance c 9 72.30 S 74.00 W
Ronne Ice Shelf ⊓ 9 78.30 S 61.00 W
Ronnenberg 52 52.20 N 9.40 E
Rönneshytta 40 58.56 N 15.02 E
Rönninge 40 59.12 N 17.44 E
Ronroni 175e 9.37 S 159.58 E
Rönsahl 263 51.07 N 7.30 E
Ronsdorf ◆[8] 263 51.14 N 7.12 E
Ronse (Renaix-Gleiche) 50 50.45 N 3.36 E
Röntgenmuseum v 263 51.12 N 7.16 E
Ronuro ≃ 255 11.56 S 53.33 W
Roodepoort □[5] 273d 26.10 S 27.52 E
Roodepoort-Maraisburg 158 26.11 S 27.54 E
Roodeschool 52 53.25 N 6.45 E
Roodhouse 219 39.29 N 90.22 W
Roof Butte ∧ 200 36.28 N 109.05 W
Rooiberge ∧ 158 28.27 S 28.26 E
Rooiboklaagte ≃ 156 20.50 S 21.00 E
Rooidam 158 28.07 S 21.15 E
Rooilyf 158 28.49 S 21.57 E
Rooiwal 158 27.18 S 27.32 E
Rooks Creek ≃ 216 40.57 N 88.44 W
Rookwood Cemetery ◆ 274a 33.53 S 151.04 E
Roon, Pulau I 164 2.23 S 134.33 E
Rooniu, Mont ∧ 174s 17.49 S 149.12 W
Roordahuizum 52 53.06 N 5.46 E
Roorkee 124 29.52 N 77.53 E
Roosboom 158 28.36 S 29.44 E
Roosendaal 52 51.32 N 4.28 E
Roosevelt, Az., U.S. 200 33.40 N 111.08 W
Roosevelt, Mn., U.S. 198 48.48 N 95.05 W
Roosevelt, N.J., U.S. 208 40.13 N 74.28 W
Roosevelt, N.Y., U.S. 276 40.40 N 73.35 W
Roosevelt, Ok., U.S. 196 34.50 N 99.01 W
Roosevelt, Ut., U.S. 200 40.17 N 109.59 W
Roosevelt ≃ 248 7.35 S 60.20 W
Roosevelt Beach 210 43.19 N 78.52 W
Roosevelt Campobello International Park ♦ 186 44.52 N 66.58 W
Roosevelt Field ◆[9] 276 40.45 N 73.37 W
Roosevelt Island I 9 79.30 S 162.00 W
Roosevelt Park 216 43.11 N 86.15 W
Roosevelt Park ♦ 276 40.33 N 74.21 W
Roosevelt Roads Naval Station ■ 240m 18.15 N 65.38 W
Roosevelt Terrace 226 38.08 N 122.16 W
Root 58 47.07 N 8.23 E
Root ≃, N.T., Can. 180 62.50 N 123.40 W
Root ≃, Mn., U.S. 190 43.46 N 91.15 W
Root ≃, Wi., U.S. 216 42.44 N 87.47 W
Root, North Branch ≃ 190 43.49 N 92.10 W
Root, South Branch ≃ 190 43.44 N 91.58 W
Root Lake ⊜ 184 54.04 N 101.24 W
Rootstown 214 41.05 N 81.14 W
Rooty Hill 170 33.46 S 150.50 E
Ropang 115b 8.52 S 117.29 E
Ropaži 76 57.08 N 24.30 E
Ropča 24 63.02 N 52.16 E
Ropczyce 30 50.03 N 21.37 E
Roper 192 35.52 N 76.36 W
Roper ≃ 164 14.43 S 135.27 E
Roper Bar 164 14.44 S 134.44 E
Roper Valley 164 14.56 S 134.00 E
Ropes Creek ≃ 274a 33.43 S 150.47 E
Ropesville 196 33.26 N 102.09 W
Roppe 58 47.40 N 6.55 E
Ropša 265a 59.44 N 29.52 E
Roque 250 3.01 S 45.23 W
Roquebillière 62 44.01 N 7.18 E
Roquebrune-Cap-Martin 62 43.46 N 7.28 E
Roquebrune-sur-Argens 62 43.26 N 6.38 E
Roquefavour, Aqueduc de ≡[1] 62 43.31 N 5.19 E
Roquefort 32 44.02 N 0.19 W
Roquemaure 62 44.03 N 4.47 E
Roque Pérez 258 35.25 S 59.20 W
Roquesteron 62 43.52 N 7.00 E
Roquevaire 62 43.21 N 5.36 E
Rora Head › 46 58.52 N 3.25 W
Roraima □[3] 246 1.00 N 61.00 W
Roraima, Mount ∧ 246 5.12 N 60.44 W
Rörbäcksnäs 26 61.08 N 12.49 E
Roreto Chisone 62 44.59 N 7.06 E
Rorke Lake ⊜ 180 66.55 N 128.25 W
Rorke Lake ⊜ 184 54.33 N 92.30 W
Rorke's Drift ⊥ 158 28.20 S 30.32 E
Rorketon 184 51.26 N 99.32 W
Røros 26 62.35 N 11.20 E
Rorschach 58 47.29 N 9.30 E
Rørvig 41 55.57 N 11.46 E
Rørvik 24 64.51 N 11.14 E
Ros' ≃ 78 49.39 N 31.35 E
Rosà, It. 64 45.43 N 11.45 E
Rosa, Zam. 154 9.38 S 31.21 E
Rosa, Cap › 36 36.58 N 8.14 E
Rosa, Lake ⊜ 238 21.00 N 73.30 W
Rosa, Monte ∧ 58 45.55 N 7.53 E
Rosairinho 266c 38.40 N 9.01 W
Rosal' 80 55.40 N 39.51 E
Rosales, Méx. 232 28.12 N 105.33 W
Rosales, Pil. 116 15.54 N 120.38 E
Rosalia 202 47.14 N 117.22 W
Rosalie, Lake ⊜ 220 27.58 N 81.28 W
Rosalind Bank ◆[4] 238 16.30 N 80.30 W
Rosamond, Ca., U.S. 228 34.51 N 118.09 W
Rosamond, Il., U.S. 219 39.23 N 89.10 W
Rosamond Lake ⊜ 228 34.50 N 118.04 W
Rosamorada 234 22.08 N 105.12 W
Rosana 255 22.33 S 53.00 W
Rosander, Mount ∧ 224 48.46 N 124.42 W
Rosanky 222 29.56 N 97.18 W
Rosanna 274b 37.45 S 145.04 E
Rosans 62 44.23 N 5.28 E
Rosario, Arg. 252 32.57 S 60.40 W
Rosário, Bra. 250 2.57 S 44.14 W
Rosario, Méx. 232 27.37 N 109.16 W
Rosario, Méx. 234 23.00 N 105.52 W
Rosario, Para. 252 24.27 S 57.03 W
Rosario, Pil. 116 13.51 N 121.12 E
Rosario, Pil. 116 16.14 N 120.29 E
Rosario, Ur. 258 34.19 S 57.21 W
Rosario, Ven. 246 10.19 N 72.19 W
Rosario ≃, Arg. 252 24.50 S 65.43 W
Rosario ≃, Ur. 258 34.26 S 57.21 W
Rosario, Bahía c 232 29.52 N 115.45 W
Rosario, Cayo el I 240p 21.38 N 81.53 W
Rosario, Islas del II 246 10.10 N 75.46 W
Rosario Bank ◆[2] 238 18.30 N 84.05 W
Rosario de Arriba 232 30.01 N 115.40 W
Rosario de la Frontera 252 25.48 S 64.58 W
Rosario de Lerma 252 24.59 S 65.35 W
Rosario del Tala 252 32.18 S 59.09 W
Rosário do Sul 252 30.15 S 54.55 W
Rosário Oeste 248 14.50 S 56.25 W
Rosario Strait ꝟ 224 48.30 N 122.45 W
Rosarito, Méx. 204 32.20 N 117.02 W
Rosarito, Méx. 232 26.27 N 111.38 W
Rosarito, Embalse de ⊜[1] 34 40.05 N 5.15 W
Rosarno 68 38.29 N 15.59 E
Rosas 196 26.09 N 103.27 W
Rosazza 62 45.41 N 7.58 E
Rošča 82 54.47 N 36.51 E
Roščino 76 60.15 N 29.37 E
Rosciolo 66 42.07 N 13.20 E
Roscoe, Il., U.S. 216 42.25 N 89.01 W
Roscoe, N.Y., U.S. 210 41.55 N 74.54 W
Roscoe, Pa., U.S. 214 40.04 N 79.51 W
Roscoe, S.D., U.S. 198 45.26 N 99.20 W
Roscoe, Tx., U.S. 196 32.26 N 100.32 W
Roscoe ≃ 180 69.40 N 120.57 W
Roscoe Village ⊥ 214 40.18 N 81.54 W
Roscoff 32 48.44 N 3.59 E
Roscommon, Ire. 48 53.38 N 8.11 W
Roscommon, Mi., U.S. 190 44.29 N 84.35 W
Roscommon □[6] 48 53.45 N 8.15 W
Roscrea 48 52.57 N 7.47 W
Rosdorf 52 51.30 N 9.53 E
Rose, It. 68 39.24 N 16.17 E
Rose, N.Y., U.S. 210 43.09 N 76.53 W
Rose, Monte ∧ 70 37.39 N 13.25 E
Rose, Mount ∧ 226 39.21 N 119.55 W
Rose, Pointe de la › 240e 14.40 N 60.53 W
Roseau, Dom. 240d 15.18 N 61.24 W
Roseau, Mn., U.S. 198 48.50 N 95.45 W
Roseau ≃, Dom. 240d 15.18 N 61.24 W
Roseau ≃, N.A. 198 49.08 N 97.15 W
Roseau ≃, St. Luc. 241f 13.58 N 61.02 W
Rosebank ◆[8] 273d 26.09 S 28.02 E
Rosebank Station 275b 43.47 N 79.07 W
Roseberry Lakes ⊜ 184 52.40 N 92.30 W
Roseberth 166 25.47 S 139.37 E
Rosebery 166 41.46 S 145.32 E
Rosebery ◆[8] 274a 33.55 S 151.12 E
Rose-Blanche 186 47.37 N 58.41 W
Roseboom 210 42.45 N 74.47 W
Roseboro 192 34.57 N 78.30 W
Rose Bowl ♦ 280 34.10 N 118.09 W
Rosebud, Austl. 169 38.21 S 144.54 E
Rosebud, Mo., U.S. 219 38.23 N 91.24 W
Rosebud, Mt., U.S. 202 46.16 N 106.26 W
Rose Bud, Pa., U.S. 214 40.45 N 78.33 W
Rosebud, S.D., U.S. 198 43.13 N 100.51 W
Rosebud, Tx., U.S. 222 31.04 N 96.58 W
Rosebud ≃ 182 51.25 N 112.37 W
Rosebud Creek ≃ 202 46.16 N 106.28 W
Rosebud Indian Reservation ◆[4] 198 43.25 N 100.28 W
Roseburg 202 43.13 N 123.20 W
Rosebush 190 43.41 N 84.46 W
Rose City 190 44.25 N 84.07 W
Rose Creek ≃, U.S. 198 40.04 N 97.07 W
Rose Creek ≃, Ca., U.S. 226 38.07 N 120.24 W
Rosecroft Raceway ♦ 284c 38.48 N 76.58 W
Rosedale, Austl. 166 24.38 S 151.55 E
Rosedale, Ab., Can. 182 51.25 N 112.38 W
Rosedale, B.C., Can. 224 49.11 N 121.48 W
Rosedale, In., U.S. 194 39.37 N 87.17 W
Rosedale, La., U.S. 194 30.27 N 91.27 W
Rosedale, Md., U.S. 284b 39.19 N 76.30 W
Rosedale, Ms., U.S. 194 33.51 N 91.01 W
Rosedale ◆[8], On., Can. 275b 43.41 N 79.22 W
Rosedale ◆[8], N.Y., U.S. 276 40.39 N 73.45 W
Rosedale Estates 284c 38.47 N 76.58 W
Rosedale Hills 218 39.42 N 86.07 W
Rosedene 158 32.01 S 22.07 E
Rosehall 246 6.16 N 57.21 W
Rosehearty 46 57.42 N 2.07 W
Rose-Hill, Maus. 157c 20.14 S 57.27 E
Rose Hill, N.C., U.S. 192 34.49 N 78.01 W
Rose Hill, Va., U.S. 192 36.40 N 83.22 W
Rose Hill, Wa., U.S. 224 47.42 N 122.10 W
Rosehill Cemetery ◆ 278 41.59 N 87.41 W
Rosehill Racecourse ♦ 274a 33.49 S 151.02 E
Rose Hills Memorial Park ◆ 280 34.01 N 118.02 W
Roseira 256 22.54 S 45.18 W
Rose Island I, Am. Sam. 14 14.32 S 168.08 W
Rose Island I, Ba. 192 25.06 N 77.14 W
Rose Lake 182 54.24 N 126.02 W
Roseland, Ca., U.S. 226 38.30 N 122.55 W
Roseland, In., U.S. 216 41.42 N 86.15 W
Roseland, La., U.S. 194 30.45 N 90.30 W
Roseland, N.J., U.S. 276 40.49 N 74.17 W
Roseland, Oh., U.S. 214 40.47 N 82.32 W
Roseland ◆[8] 278 41.42 N 87.38 W
Roselawn 216 41.09 N 87.19 W
Roselle, Il., U.S. 216 41.59 N 88.04 W
Roselle, N.J., U.S. 276 40.39 N 74.15 W
Roselle Field ⊠ 278 41.59 N 88.06 W
Rosellen 263 51.08 N 6.43 E
Roselle Park 276 40.39 N 74.15 W
Rosellerheide 263 51.07 N 6.44 E
Rose Lodge 224 45.01 N 123.52 W
Rosemary 182 50.46 N 112.05 W
Rosemary Brook ≃ 283 42.19 N 71.15 W
Rosemead 280 34.04 N 118.04 W
Rosemère 206 45.38 N 73.48 W
Rosemont, Ca., U.S. 226 38.34 N 121.20 W
Rosemont, Il., U.S. 278 41.59 N 87.52 W
Rosemont, Ky., U.S. 218 38.01 N 84.32 W
Rosemont, Oh., U.S. 214 41.03 N 80.53 W
Rosemont, Pa., U.S. 285 40.01 N 75.19 W
Rosemont Horizon ♦ 278 42.00 N 87.53 W
Rosenberg 222 29.33 N 95.48 W
Rosendaël 50 51.02 N 2.24 E
Rosendal, Nor. 26 59.59 N 6.01 E
Rosendal, S. Afr. 158 28.30 S 27.55 E
Rosendale 210 41.51 N 74.05 W
Roseneath 273d 26.17 S 28.11 E
Rosenfeld 58 48.17 N 8.43 E
Rosengarten 52 53.23 N 9.54 E
Rosenhayn 208 39.28 N 75.07 W
Rosenheim 64 47.51 N 12.07 E
Rosenhügel ◆[8] 263 51.10 N 7.12 E
Rosenthal, Dtsch. 54 50.51 N 14.04 E
Rosenthal, Dtsch. 56 50.58 N 8.52 E
Rosenthal ◆[8] 264a 52.36 N 13.23 E
Rose Peak ∧ 200 33.26 N 109.22 W
Rosepine 194 30.55 N 93.17 W
Rose Point › 182 54.13 N 131.35 W
Rosersberg 40 59.35 N 17.53 E
Rosersberg ⊥ 40 59.34 N 17.50 E
Roses, Golf de c 34 42.10 N 3.15 E
Roseto 210 40.52 N 75.12 W
Roseto Capo Spulico 68 39.59 N 16.36 E
Roseto degli Abruzzi 66 42.41 N 14.01 E
Roseto Valfortore 68 41.22 N 15.06 E
Rosetown 184 51.33 N 108.00 W
Rose Tree 285 39.56 N 75.23 W
Rose Tree Park ♦ 285 39.56 N 75.24 W
Rosetta → Rashīd 142 31.24 N 30.25 E
Rosetta Branch → Rashīd, Far' ≃ 142 31.30 N 30.21 E
Rosetta Mouth → Rashīd, Maṣabb ≃[1] 142 31.30 N 30.20 E
Rosettenville ◆[8] 273d 26.15 S 28.03 E
Rosevale 171a 27.51 S 152.29 E
Rose Valley, Sk., Can. 184 52.18 N 103.50 W
Rose Valley, Pa., U.S. 285 39.53 N 75.23 W
Rose Valley, Pa., U.S. 285 40.10 N 75.13 W
Rose Valley, Wa., U.S. 224 46.06 N 122.50 W
Roseville, Austl. 274a 33.47 S 151.11 E
Roseville, Ca., U.S. 226 38.45 N 121.17 W
Roseville, Il., U.S. 190 40.43 N 90.39 W
Roseville, Mi., U.S. 214 42.29 N 82.56 W
Roseville, Mn., U.S. 190 45.00 N 93.09 W
Roseville, Oh., U.S. 188 39.48 N 82.04 W
Roseville, Pa., U.S. 210 41.51 N 76.57 W
Roseville Park 285 39.42 N 75.43 W
Rosewood, Austl. 171a 27.39 S 152.35 E
Rosewood, Austl. 171b 35.41 S 147.52 E
Rosewood, Oh., U.S. 216 40.13 N 83.58 W
Rosewood Heights 219 38.53 N 90.05 W
Roseworthy 168b 34.32 S 138.44 E
Roshage › 26 57.07 N 8.38 E
Roshanara Gardens ♦ 272a 28.40 N 77.12 E
Rosharon 222 29.21 N 95.28 W
Rosheim 58 48.30 N 7.28 E
Rosherville Dam ⊜[1] 273d 26.14 S 28.07 E
Rosh Ha'Ayin 132 32.06 N 34.57 E
Rosholt, S.D., U.S. 198 45.52 N 96.43 W
Rosholt, Wi., U.S. 190 44.37 N 89.18 W
Rosh Pinna 132 32.58 N 35.32 E
Rosica ≃ 38 43.15 N 25.42 E
Rosice 30 49.11 N 16.23 E
Rosiclare 194 37.25 N 88.20 W
Rosières-aux-Salines 58 48.36 N 6.20 E
Rosières-en-Santerre 50 49.49 N 2.43 E
Rosiers, Rivière des ≃ 206 45.59 N 72.07 W
Rosignano Marittimo 66 43.24 N 10.28 E
Rosignano Solvay 66 43.23 N 10.26 E
Rosignol 246 6.17 N 57.32 W
Roșiori de Vede 38 44.07 N 25.00 E
Rositz 54 51.01 N 12.22 E
Roskilde 41 55.39 N 12.05 E
Roskilde □[6] 41 55.30 N 12.05 E
Roskilde Fjord c 41 55.56 N 12.00 E
Roskow 54 52.28 N 12.42 E
Roslagen □[9] 40 59.30 N 18.40 E
Roslags-Bro 40 59.50 N 18.44 E
Rosl'akovo 24 69.03 N 33.09 E
Rosl'atino 76 59.46 N 44.15 E
Roslavl' 76 53.57 N 32.52 E
Roslev 26 56.42 N 8.59 E
Roslindale ◆[8] 283 42.18 N 71.07 W
Roslyn, N.Y., U.S. 276 40.48 N 73.39 W
Roslyn, Pa., U.S. 208 40.07 N 75.08 W
Roslyn, Pa., U.S. 285 39.57 N 75.36 W
Roslyn, Wa., U.S. 224 47.13 N 120.59 W
Roslyn Estates 276 40.47 N 73.40 W
Roslyn Harbor 276 40.49 N 73.38 W
Roslyn Heights 276 40.47 N 73.38 W
Rosmalen 52 51.43 N 5.22 E
Rosman 192 35.08 N 82.49 W
Rosmead 158 31.29 S 25.08 E
Ros Mhic Thriúin → New Ross 48 52.24 N 6.56 W
Røsnæs ›[1] 41 55.44 N 10.59 E
Rosne, Ruisseau le ≃ 261 48.58 N 2.25 E
Rosneath 46 56.01 N 4.49 W
Rosny-sous-Bois 261 48.53 N 2.29 E
Rosny-sur-Seine 50 49.00 N 1.38 E
Rosolina 64 45.05 N 12.15 E
Rosolini 70 36.49 N 14.57 E
Rošore 85 38.20 N 72.19 E
Rosporden 32 47.58 N 3.50 W
Rösrath 56 50.54 N 7.11 E
Ross, Austl. 166 42.02 S 147.29 E
Ross', Bela. 76 53.17 N 24.24 E
Ross, N.Z. 172 42.54 S 170.49 E
Ross, Ca., U.S. 226 37.55 N 122.32 W
Ross, In., U.S. 278 41.32 N 87.23 W
Ross, Oh., U.S. 218 39.19 N 84.39 W
Ross □[6] 218 39.20 N 83.06 W
Ross ≃ 180 61.59 N 132.26 W
Ross, Cape › 116 10.56 N 119.13 E
Ross, Mount ∧ 172 41.28 S 175.21 E
Ross, Point › 174c 29.04 S 167.56 E
Ross, Pointe › 275a 45.21 N 73.48 W
Rossa 58 46.22 N 9.08 E
Rossach 56 50.09 N 10.56 E
Rossano 68 39.35 N 16.39 E
Rossasna 76 54.39 N 30.53 E
Rossau 54 52.47 N 11.38 E
Rossbach 54 51.15 N 11.53 E
Ross Behy 48 52.02 N 9.58 W
Ross-Béthio 150 16.16 N 16.08 W
Rossburg 216 40.17 N 84.38 W
Rossburn 184 50.40 N 100.52 W
Ross Carbery 48 51.35 N 9.01 W
Rosscott Manor 285 39.39 N 75.44 W
Ross Dam ◆[6] 224 48.44 N 121.04 W
Rossdorf 56 49.51 N 8.45 E
Rosseau 212 45.16 N 79.39 W
Rosseau, Lake ⊜ 212 45.10 N 79.35 W
Rossel, Cap › 175f 20.23 S 166.36 E
Rossell y Rius 252 33.11 S 55.42 W
Rossen ⊜ 40 60.19 N 16.26 E
Rossendale □[8] 262 53.43 N 2.14 W
Rosser 222 32.28 N 96.27 W
Rosses Bay c 48 55.02 N 8.27 W
Rosses Point 48 54.18 N 8.33 W
Rossford 214 41.37 N 83.33 W
Ross Fork Creek ≃ 202 47.05 N 109.43 W
Rosshaupten 58 47.39 N 10.43 E
Rosshyttan 40 60.04 N 16.21 E
Ross Ice Shelf ⊓ 9 81.30 S 175.00 W
Rossiglione 62 44.34 N 8.40 E
Rossignol, Lake ⊜ 186 44.10 N 65.10 W
Rossija → Russia □[1] 72 60.00 N 80.00 E
Rössing 156 22.31 S 14.52 E
Rossio, Estação do ◆[5] 266c 38.43 N 9.09 W
Ross Island I, Ant. 9 77.30 S 168.00 E
Ross Island I, Mb., Can. 184 54.14 N 97.45 W
Rossiter 214 40.53 N 78.55 W
Rossitten → Rybačij 76 55.09 N 20.51 E
Rossiya → Russia □[1] 72 60.00 N 80.00 E
Rossla 54 51.28 N 11.04 E
Ross Lake ⊜[1] 224 48.53 N 121.04 W
Ross Lake National Recreation Area ♦ 224 48.45 N 121.00 W
Rossland 182 49.05 N 117.48 W
Rosslare 48 52.17 N 6.23 W
Rosslare Harbour 48 52.15 N 6.22 W
Rosslau 54 51.53 N 12.14 E
Rosslea 48 54.14 N 7.11 W
Rosslyn Farms 279b 40.26 N 80.05 W
Rossmoor 280 33.47 N 118.05 W
Rossmore 274a 33.57 S 150.46 E
Rossmoyne 208 40.13 N 76.57 W
Rosso 150 16.30 N 15.49 W
Rossön 26 63.55 N 16.21 E
Ross-on-Wye 42 51.55 N 2.35 W
Rossony 76 55.53 N 28.49 E
Rossoš', Ross. 78 51.08 N 38.29 E
Rossoš', Ross. 78 50.12 N 39.34 E
Rossouw 158 31.09 S 27.18 E
Ross R. Barnett Reservoir ⊜[1] 194 32.30 N 90.00 W
Ross River 180 61.59 N 132.27 W
Ross-Schelfeis → Ross Ice Shelf ⊓ 9 81.30 S 175.00 W
Ross Sea ⊤[2] 9 76.00 S 175.00 W
Rosstal 56 49.25 N 10.52 E
Rosston 218 40.03 N 86.17 W
Ross Township 279b 40.32 N 80.01 W
Rossu, Capu › 36 42.14 N 8.33 E
Røssvatnet ⊜ 24 65.45 N 14.00 E
Rossville, Ga., U.S. 192 34.58 N 85.17 W
Rossville, Il., U.S. 216 40.22 N 87.40 W
Rossville, In., U.S. 216 40.25 N 86.35 W
Rossville, Ks., U.S. 198 39.08 N 95.57 W
Rossville, Md., U.S. 284b 39.20 N 76.29 W
Rosswein 54 51.03 N 13.10 E
Røst II 24 67.28 N 11.59 E
Rostāq 120 37.07 N 69.49 E
Röstånga 41 56.00 N 13.17 E
Rosthern 184 52.40 N 106.17 W
Rostherne 262 53.21 N 2.23 W
Rostherne Mere ⊜ 262 53.21 N 2.23 W
Roštkala 120 37.16 N 71.49 E
Rostock 54 54.05 N 12.07 E
Rostov 80 57.11 N 39.25 E
Rostov-na-Donu 83 47.14 N 39.42 E
Rostov Oblast' □[4] 78 48.00 N 40.00 E
Rostrataville 158 26.49 S 25.39 E
Rostraver Airport ⊠ 279b 40.13 N 79.50 W
Rostrevor 48 54.06 N 6.12 W
Rosvinskoje 24 66.32 N 52.26 E
Roswell, Ga., U.S. 192 34.01 N 84.21 W
Roswell, N.M., U.S. 196 33.23 N 104.31 W
Roswell, Oh., U.S. 214 40.28 N 81.21 W
Rosyth 46 56.03 N 3.26 W
Rot ≃ 58 48.19 N 9.54 E
Rota 34 36.37 N 6.21 W
Rota I 108 14.10 N 145.12 E
Rot am See 56 49.15 N 10.01 E
Rotan 196 32.51 N 100.27 W
Rotanda 156 19.33 S 32.50 E
Rotary Island I 285 40.14 N 74.49 W
Rotbach ≃ 263 51.34 N 6.41 E
Rotberg 264a 52.21 N 13.31 E
Rote-Erde, Stadion ♦ 263 51.30 N 7.27 E
Rotenburg 52 53.06 N 9.24 E
Rotenburg an der Fulda 56 51.00 N 9.45 E
Roter Main ≃ 60 50.04 N 11.24 E
Rotes Meer → Red Sea ⊤[2] 136 20.00 N 38.00 E
Roth, Dtsch. 56 50.46 N 7.42 E
Roth, Dtsch. 60 49.15 N 11.06 E
Roth ≃ 58 48.27 N 10.10 E
Rötha 54 51.12 N 12.25 E
Rothaargebirge ⋏ 56 51.05 N 8.15 E
Rothbury 44 55.19 N 1.55 W
Rothbury Forest ◆[3] 44 55.18 N 1.54 W
Rothemühl 54 53.36 N 13.49 E
Röthenbach, Dtsch. 58 47.37 N 9.59 E
Röthenbach, Schw. 58 46.51 N 7.45 E
Röthenbach an der Pegnitz 60 49.29 N 11.15 E
Rothenburg 54 51.20 N 14.58 E
Rothenburg ob der Tauber 56 49.23 N 10.10 E
Rothenkirchen 54 50.33 N 12.30 E
Rothenschirmbach 54 51.27 N 11.33 E
Rothenstein ∧[2] 263 51.07 N 7.41 E
Rother ≃, Eng., U.K. 42 50.57 N 0.32 W
Rother ≃, Eng., U.K. 42 50.54 N 0.42 E
Rothera v[3] 9 67.34 S 68.08 W
Rotherham, N.Z. 172 42.42 S 172.57 E
Rotherham, Eng., U.K. 44 53.26 N 1.20 W
Rothes 46 57.31 N 3.13 W
Rothesay, N.B., Can. 186 45.23 N 66.00 W
Rothesay, Scot., U.K. 46 55.51 N 5.03 W
Rothneusiedl ◆[8] 264b 48.08 N 16.23 E
Rothrist 58 47.19 N 7.53 E
Rothsay, Austl. 162 29.17 S 116.53 E
Rothsay, Mn., U.S. 198 46.28 N 96.16 W
Rothschild 190 44.53 N 89.37 W
Rothsville 208 40.09 N 76.15 W
Rothwell, N.B., Can. 186 46.04 N 66.04 W
Rothwell, Eng., U.K. 42 52.25 N 0.48 W
Rothwell, Eng., U.K. 44 53.46 N 1.29 W
Roti, Pulau I 112 10.45 S 123.10 E
Roti, Selat ꝟ 112 10.25 S 123.25 E
Roto 166 33.03 S 145.28 E
Rotoiti, Lake ⊜, N.Z. 172 41.50 S 172.50 E
Rotoiti, Lake ⊜, N.Z. 172 38.02 S 176.25 E
Rotomanu 172 42.39 S 171.32 E
Rotonda 68 39.57 N 16.02 E
Rotondella 68 40.10 N 16.32 E
Rotondo, Monte ∧ 36 42.13 N 9.03 E
Rotoroa, Lake ⊜ 172 41.52 S 172.38 E
Rotorua 172 38.09 S 176.15 E
Rotorua, Lake ⊜ 172 38.05 S 176.16 E
Rotowaro 172 37.36 S 175.05 E
Rott 64 47.54 N 10.59 E
Rott ≃ 60 48.27 N 13.26 E
Rottach-Egern 64 47.41 N 11.46 E
Rott am Inn 64 47.59 N 12.07 E
Röttenbach 60 49.09 N 11.02 E
Rottenbach-Tremersdorf 56 50.21 N 10.56 E
Rottenbuch 64 47.44 N 10.58 E
Rottenburg am Neckar 58 48.28 N 8.56 E
Rottenburg an der Laaber 60 48.42 N 12.02 E
Rottenmann 61 47.31 N 14.22 E
Rotterdam, Ned. 52 51.55 N 4.28 E
Rotterdam, N.Y., U.S. 210 42.48 N 73.59 W
Rotterdam, Luchthaven ⊠ 52 51.58 N 4.30 E
Rotterdam Junction 210 42.52 N 74.03 W
Rotthalmünster 60 48.21 N 13.12 E
Rotthausen ◆[8] 263 51.30 N 7.05 E
Rottingdean 42 50.48 N 0.04 W
Röttingen 56 49.31 N 9.58 E
Rottleberode 54 51.31 N 10.57 E
Rottnest Island I 168a 32.00 S 115.30 E
Rottofreno 62 45.03 N 9.34 E
Rottum 263 51.36 N 7.42 E
Rottumeroog I 52 53.33 N 6.35 E
Rottumerplaat I 52 53.32 N 6.30 E
Rottweil 58 48.10 N 8.37 E
Rotuma I 14 12.30 S 177.05 E
Rotwand ∧ 64 47.39 N 11.56 E
Rötz 60 49.21 N 12.32 E
Roubaix 50 50.42 N 3.10 E
Roubideau Creek ≃ 200 38.44 N 108.10 W
Roubidoux Creek ≃ 194 37.51 N 92.13 W
Roubion ≃ 62 44.31 N 4.42 E
Rouceux 58 48.22 N 5.41 E
Roudnice [nad Labem] 54 50.22 N 14.16 E
Rouen 50 49.26 N 1.05 E
Rougé 32 47.47 N 1.27 W
Rouge ≃, On., Can. 212 43.48 N 79.07 W
Rouge ≃, P.Q., Can. 206 45.39 N 74.42 W
Rouge ≃, P.Q., Can. 206 45.33 N 74.20 W
Rouge → Red ≃, U.S. 178 31.00 N 91.40 W
Rouge, Bell Branch ≃ 281 42.23 N 83.16 W
Rouge, Lac ⊜ 206 46.56 N 74.38 W
Rouge, Mer → Red Sea ⊤[2] 136 20.00 N 38.00 E
Rouge, River ≃ 281 42.17 N 83.06 W
Rougeau, Forêt de ♦ 261 48.35 N 2.30 E
Rougemont, Fr. 58 47.29 N 6.21 E
Rougemont, Schw. 58 46.29 N 7.12 E
Rougemont-le-Château 58 47.44 N 6.58 E
Rough ≃ 194 37.29 N 87.08 W
Rough And Ready 226 39.14 N 121.08 W
Rough River Lake ⊜[1] 194 37.40 N 86.25 W
Rouiba 34 36.44 N 3.17 E
Rouillac 32 45.47 N 0.04 W
Rouillon 261 48.33 N 2.00 E
Roulans 58 47.19 N 6.14 E
Rouleau 184 50.11 N 104.55 W
Roulers → Roeselare 50 50.57 N 3.08 E
Roulette 214 41.46 N 78.09 W
Roumanie → Romania □[1] 38 46.00 N 25.30 E
Round Harbour 186 49.51 N 55.40 W
Roundhead 216 40.34 N 83.50 W
Round Hill Head › 166 24.10 S 151.53 E
Round Hill Regional Park ♦ 279b 40.15 N 79.51 W
Round Knowe ∧[2] 48 55.08 N 6.55 W
Round Lake, Il., U.S. 278 42.21 N 88.05 W

ENGLISH — Name | Page | Lat.°′ | Long.°′

Round Lake, Mn., U.S. 198 43.32 N 95.28 W
Round Lake, N.Y., U.S. 210 42.56 N 73.47 W
Round Lake ⊜, Nf., Can. 186 51.08 N 56.33 W
Round Lake ⊜, On., Can. 190 45.38 N 77.32 W
Round Lake ⊜, On., Can. 212 44.30 N 77.52 W
Round Lake ⊜, On., Can. 212 45.28 N 79.24 W
Round Lake ⊜, Sk., Can. 184 50.33 N 102.23 W
Round Lake ⊜, Il., U.S. 278 42.22 N 88.05 W
Round Lake ⊜, Mi., U.S. 216 41.58 N 84.17 W
Round Lake Beach 216 42.22 N 88.05 W
Round Lake Park 216 42.21 N 88.04 W
Round Mound ∧[2] 198 38.55 N 99.39 W
Round Mountain 204 38.42 N 117.04 W
Round Mountain ∧, Austl. 166 30.27 S 152.14 E
Round Mountain ∧, Austl. 171b 36.15 S 148.34 E
Round Pond ⊜, Nf., Can. 186 48.10 N 56.00 W
Round Pond ⊜, Ma., U.S. 283 42.36 N 70.49 W
Round Rock 222 30.30 N 97.40 W
Roundstone 48 53.23 N 9.53 W
Round Top 210 42.16 N 74.02 W
Round Top ∧[2] 208 40.30 N 76.42 W
Round Top Regional Park ♦ 282 37.51 N 122.12 W
Roundup 202 46.26 N 108.32 W
Round Valley Indian Reservation ◆[4] 204 39.50 N 123.20 W
Round Valley Reservoir ⊜[1] 210 40.36 N 74.50 W
Roundwood 48 53.04 N 6.13 W
Roura 250 4.44 N 52.20 W
Rourkela → Raurkela 124 22.13 N 84.53 E
Rousay I 46 59.10 N 3.02 W
Rouse Hill 274a 33.41 S 150.56 E
Rouses Point 206 45.00 N 73.22 W
Rouseville 214 41.28 N 79.41 W
Rousies 50 50.16 N 4.00 E
Rousseau, Lake ⊜[1] 220 29.02 N 82.32 W
Rousset, Col de)(62 44.50 N 5.24 E
Roussigny 261 48.39 N 2.06 E
Roussillon, Fr. 62 45.22 N 4.49 E
Roussillon, Fr. 62 43.54 N 5.17 E
Roussillon □[9] 32 42.30 N 2.30 E
Roussy-le-Village 56 49.27 N 6.10 E
Routhierville 186 48.11 N 67.09 W
Routot 50 49.23 N 0.44 E
Rouveen 52 52.36 N 6.11 E
Rouvignies 50 50.20 N 3.26 E
Rouville □[6] 206 45.23 N 73.04 W
Rouvray 50 47.25 N 4.06 E
Rouvray, Lac ⊜ 186 49.18 N 70.49 W
Rouxville 158 30.29 S 26.46 E
Rouyn 190 48.15 N 79.01 W
Rouzerville 208 39.44 N 77.32 W
Rovaniemi 24 66.34 N 25.48 E
Rovasenda 62 45.32 N 8.19 E
Rovato 64 45.34 N 10.00 E
Rovbickskaja 76 52.40 N 24.05 E
Rove, Tunnel du ◆[5] 62 43.22 N 5.17 E
Rovegno 62 44.35 N 9.17 E
Rovellasca 62 45.40 N 9.03 E
Rovello Porro 62 45.39 N 9.02 E
Roven'ki, Ross. 78 49.56 N 38.54 E
Roven'ki, Ukr. 83 48.05 N 39.21 E
Rovenskaja Sloboda 76 52.13 N 30.19 E
Roverbella 64 45.16 N 10.46 E
Rovere 66 42.10 N 13.31 E
Roverè della Luna 64 46.15 N 11.10 E
Roveredo 58 46.14 N 9.08 E
Rovereto 64 45.53 N 11.02 E
Roverè Veronese 64 45.36 N 11.03 E
Rövershagen 54 54.10 N 12.15 E
Roversi 252 27.35 S 61.57 W
Roverud 26 60.15 N 12.03 E
Roviano 66 42.01 N 13.00 E
Rovigo 64 45.04 N 11.47 E
Rovigo □[4] 64 45.02 N 11.50 E
Rovinj 36 45.05 N 13.38 E
Rovira 246 4.14 N 75.14 W
Rovno 78 50.37 N 26.15 E
Rovno □[4] 78 51.00 N 26.30 E
Rovnoje, Kyrg. 85 42.53 N 73.32 E
Rovnoje, Ross. 80 50.47 N 46.05 E
Rovnoje, Ukr. 78 48.15 N 31.45 E
Rovubu (Ruvubu) ≃ 154 2.23 S 30.47 E
Rovuma (Ruvuma) ≃ 154 10.29 S 40.28 E
Rów 54 52.58 N 14.45 E
Rowan □[6] 218 38.17 N 83.26 W
Rowan Lake ⊜ 184 49.18 N 93.32 W
Rowanty Creek ≃ 208 36.58 N 77.21 W
Rowena, Austl. 166 29.49 S 148.54 E
Rowena, Tx., U.S. 196 31.39 N 100.03 W
Rowe Park ♦ 273a 6.30 N 3.23 E
Rowhill 273d 26.14 S 28.26 E
Rowland, N.C., U.S. 192 34.32 N 79.17 W
Rowland, Pa., U.S. 210 41.28 N 75.03 W
Rowland Flat 168b 34.35 S 138.56 E
Rowland Heights 280 33.58 N 117.54 W
Rowlands Gill 44 54.54 N 1.45 W
Rowlesburg 188 39.20 N 79.40 W
Rowlett 222 32.54 N 96.33 W
Rowlett, Isla I 254 44.48 S 74.25 W
Rowlett Creek ≃ 222 32.49 N 96.31 W
Rowley 207 42.43 N 70.52 W
Rowley ≃, N.T., Can. 176 70.16 N 77.45 W
Rowley ≃, Ma., U.S. 283 42.43 N 70.49 W
Rowley Island I 176 69.08 N 78.50 W
Rowley Shoals ◆[2] 162 17.30 S 119.00 E
Rowntree Mill Park ♦ 275b 43.45 N 79.35 W
Rowsburg 214 40.52 N 82.10 W
Rowville 274b 37.56 S 145.14 E
Roxa, Ilha I 150 11.15 N 15.40 W
Roxana 219 38.50 N 90.04 W
Roxas, Pil. 108 11.35 N 122.45 E
Roxas, Pil. 116 17.08 N 121.36 E
Roxas, Pil. 116 12.35 N 121.31 E
Roxas, Pil. 116 10.20 N 119.21 E
Roxas (Capiz), Pil. 116 11.35 N 122.45 E
Roxboro, P.Q., Can. 275a 45.31 N 73.48 W
Roxboro, N.C., U.S. 192 36.23 N 78.58 W
Roxborough 241r 11.15 N 60.35 W
Roxborough ◆[8] 285 40.02 N 75.13 W
Roxburgh, N.Z. 172 45.32 S 169.19 E
Roxburgh, Scot., U.K. 46 55.34 N 2.30 W
Roxbury, Ct., U.S. 207 41.33 N 73.18 W
Roxbury, N.Y., U.S. 210 42.17 N 74.33 W
Roxbury, Pa., U.S. 214 40.07 N 77.40 W
Roxbury, Va., U.S. 208 37.28 N 77.09 W
Roxbury ◆[8], Ma., U.S. 283 42.20 N 71.06 W
Roxbury ◆[8], N.Y., U.S. 276 40.34 N 73.54 W
Roxby Downs 162 30.43 S 136.46 E
Roxel 52 51.57 N 7.32 E
Roxen ⊜ 26 58.30 N 15.41 E
Roxie 194 31.30 N 91.04 W
Roxo, Cap › 150 12.20 N 16.43 W
Roxton 196 33.33 N 95.44 W
Roxton Pond (Sainte-Pudentienne) 206 45.29 N 72.40 W
Roxwell 260 51.45 N 0.23 E
Roy, N.M., U.S. 196 35.56 N 104.11 W
Roy, Ut,. U.S. 200 41.09 N 112.01 W
Roy, Wa., U.S. 224 47.00 N 122.32 W
Roya (Roia) ≃ 62 43.48 N 7.35 E
Royal 198 43.03 N 95.17 W
Royal Albert Hall v 260 51.30 N 0.11 W

DEUTSCH — Name | Seite | Breite°′ | Länge°′ E = Ost

Royal Australian Naval College v[2] 170 35.07 S 150.42 E
Royal Bangkok Sports Club ♦ 269a 13.44 N 100.33 E
Royal Botanic Gardens ♦, Austl. 274a 33.52 S 151.13 E
Royal Botanic Gardens ♦, Austl. 274b 37.50 S 144.59 E
Royal Canal ≋ 48 53.21 N 6.15 W
Royal Center 216 40.51 N 86.29 W
Royal Chitwan National Park ♦ 124 27.30 N 84.30 E
Royal City 202 46.54 N 119.38 W
Royale, Isle I 190 48.00 N 89.00 W
Royal Gorge V 200 38.17 N 105.45 W
Royal Island I 192 25.31 N 76.51 W
Royalla 171b 35.31 S 149.09 E
Royal Leamington Spa 42 52.18 N 1.31 W
Royal Natal National Park ♦ 158 28.45 S 28.57 E
Royal National Park ♦ 170 34.10 S 151.05 E
Royal Naval College ■ 260 51.29 N 0.01 W
Royal Oak, B.C., Can. 224 48.30 N 123.23 W
Royal Oak, Md., U.S. 208 38.44 N 76.10 W
Royal Oak, Mi., U.S. 216 42.29 N 83.08 W
Royal Oak Township 281 42.27 N 83.10 W
Royal Ontario Museum v 275b 43.40 N 79.24 W
Royal Palms State Beach ♦ 280 33.44 N 118.19 W
Royal Park ♦ 274b 37.47 S 144.57 E
Royal Roads c 224 48.26 N 123.26 W
Royalton, In., U.S. 218 39.56 N 86.21 W
Royalton, Mn., U.S. 190 45.49 N 94.17 W
Royalton, Pa., U.S. 208 40.11 N 76.44 W
Royal Tunbridge Wells 42 51.08 N 0.16 E
Royal Turf Club ♦ 269a 13.46 N 100.32 E
Royan 32 45.37 N 1.01 W
Royaume-Uni → United Kingdom □[1] 28 54.00 N 2.00 W
Roybon 62 45.15 N 5.15 E
Royce Brook ≃ 276 40.32 N 70.35 W
Roydon, Eng., U.K. 42 51.46 N 0.03 E
Roydon, Eng., U.K. 42 52.50 N 0.32 E
Roye 50 49.42 N 2.48 E
Royersford 208 40.11 N 75.32 W
Royerton 216 40.15 N 85.21 W
Roy Hill 162 22.38 S 119.57 E
Royse City 222 32.58 N 96.19 W
Royston, Eng., U.K. 42 52.03 N 0.01 W
Royston, Eng., U.K. 44 53.37 N 1.27 W
Royston, Ga., U.S. 192 34.17 N 83.06 W
Royton 44 53.34 N 2.08 W
Rožaj 38 42.50 N 20.10 E
Różan 30 52.53 N 21.25 E
Rozay-en-Brie 50 48.41 N 2.58 E
Roždestvenka, Kaz. 86 50.52 N 71.22 E
Roždestvenka, Ross. 86 55.21 N 77.29 E
Roždestvenka, Ross. 86 55.42 N 70.00 E
Roždestveno, Ross. 76 57.44 N 37.57 E
Roždestveno, Ross. 80 53.15 N 50.04 E
Roždestveno, Ross. 82 56.51 N 36.33 E
Roždestveno, Ross. 82 55.57 N 36.23 E
Roždestvenskaja Chava 78 51.38 N 39.40 E
Roždestvenskoje, Ross. 80 58.09 N 45.35 E
Roždestvenskoje, Ross. 80 52.47 N 42.10 E
Roždestvenskoje, Ross. 80 51.14 N 42.10 E
Roždestvo 76 57.36 N 33.48 E
Rozel 43b 49.14 N 2.03 W
Rozelle 274a 33.52 S 151.10 E
Roželov 60 49.33 N 13.48 E
Rozewie, Przylądek › 30 54.51 N 18.21 E
Rozhnof, Cape › 180 55.58 N 160.58 W
Rožišče 78 50.54 N 25.15 E
Rožki 80 56.41 N 50.31 E
Rožkov 80 51.39 N 52.19 E
Rožmberk ⊜ 61 49.04 N 14.47 E
Rožmberk nad Vltavou 61 48.39 N 14.22 E
Rožmitál pod Třemšínem 60 49.36 N 13.52 E
Rožn'atov 78 48.56 N 24.09 E
Rožňava 30 48.40 N 20.32 E
Roznov 38 46.50 N 26.31 E
Rožnov pod Radhoštěm 30 49.28 N 18.10 E
Rożnów 30 49.46 N 20.42 E
Rozovka 78 47.23 N 37.04 E
Rozoy-sur-Serre 50 49.43 N 4.08 E
Roztocze ⋏[2] 30 50.30 N 23.20 E
Roztoky 54 50.09 N 14.22 E
Rozzano 62 45.20 N 9.06 E
Rrëshen 38 41.47 N 19.54 E
Rrogozhinë 38 41.05 N 19.40 E
Rtiščevo 80 52.16 N 43.47 E
Ru ≃ 100 32.43 N 115.01 E
Ru, Tanjong › 114 2.50 N 101.17 E
Ruabon 42 52.59 N 3.02 W
Ruacaná 152 17.25 S 14.12 E
Ruacana Falls ᒪ 152 17.22 S 14.12 E
Ruaha National Park ♦ 154 7.30 S 34.40 E
Ruahine Range ⋏ 172 40.00 S 176.06 E
Ruahmi, Ra's › 142 28.44 N 32.50 E
Ruanda 154 10.33 S 34.57 E
Ruanda → Rwanda □[1] 154 2.00 S 30.00 E
Ruango 164 5.35 S 150.10 E
Ruapehu, Mount ∧ 172 39.17 S 175.34 E
Ruapuke Island I 172 46.47 S 168.30 E
Ruatahuna 172 38.33 S 176.57 E
Ruatapu 172 42.48 S 170.53 E
Ruathair, Loch an ⊜ 46 58.18 N 3.56 W
Ruatoria 172 37.53 S 178.20 E
Ruawai 172 36.08 S 174.02 E
Rub' al Khali → Ar-Rub' al-Khālī ◆[2] 118 20.00 N 51.00 E
Rubanovka 78 47.00 N 34.10 E
Rubbestadneset 26 59.49 N 5.17 E
Rubcovsk 86 51.33 N 81.10 E
Rubcy 83 49.12 N 37.33 E
Rubeho Mountains ⋏ 154 6.55 S 36.30 E
Rubel' 78 51.58 N 27.04 E
Rübeland 54 51.45 N 10.50 E
Rubelles 261 48.34 N 2.41 E
Rubery ◆[8] 42 52.24 N 2.00 W
Rubeshibe 92a 43.47 N 143.38 E
Rubežka 80 51.26 N 51.59 E
Rubežnoje 83 49.01 N 38.23 E
Rubí, Esp. 266d 41.29 N 2.02 E
Rubi, Zaïre 154 2.49 N 25.14 E
Rubí ≃, Esp. 266d 41.26 N 2.00 E
Rubi ≃, Zaïre 152 2.48 N 23.54 E
Rubiana 62 45.08 N 7.23 E
Rubiataba 255 15.08 S 49.48 W
Rubicon ≃ 226 39.00 N 120.44 W
Rubicone ≃ 66 44.08 N 12.28 E
Rubidoux 228 33.59 N 117.24 W
Rubiera 64 44.39 N 10.45 E
Rubim 255 16.23 S 40.32 W
Rubino 150 6.04 N 4.18 W
Rubio 246 7.43 N 72.22 W
Rubio Woods ♦ 278 41.38 N 87.46 W
Rubl'ovka 78 49.15 N 33.19 E
Rubl'ovo 82 55.47 N 37.21 E
Ruboani 140 8.06 N 30.45 E
Rubona 154 0.33 N 30.10 E
Rubondo Island I 154 2.20 S 31.52 E
Rubondo Island National Park ♦ 154 2.20 S 31.52 E

Symbols in the index entries represent the broad categories identified in the key at the right. Symbols with superior numbers (⋏[1]) identify subcategories (see complete key on page I · 1).

Symbole im Register stellen die rechts im Schlüssel erklärten Kategorien dar. Symbole mit hochgestellten Ziffern (⋏[1]) bezeichnen Unterabteilungen einer Kategorie (vgl. vollständiger Schlüssel auf Seite I · 1).

Los símbolos incluídos en el texto del índice representan las grandes categorías identificadas con la clave a la derecha. Los símbolos con números en su parte superior (⋏[1]) identifican las subcategorías (véase la clave completa en la página I · 1).

Les symboles de l'index représentent les catégories indiquées dans la légende à droite. Les symboles suivis d'un indice (⋏[1]) représentent des sous-catégories (voir légende complète à la page I · 1).

Os símbolos incluídos no texto do índice representam as grandes categorias identificadas com a chave à direita. Os símbolos com números em sua parte superior (⋏[1]) identificam as subcategorias (veja-se a chave completa à página I · 1).

∧ Mountain	Berg	Montaña	Montagne	Montanha
⋏ Mountains	Gebirge	Montañas	Montagnes	Montanhas
)(Pass	Paß	Paso	Col	Passo
V Valley, Canyon	Tal, Cañon	Valle, Cañón	Vallée, Canyon	Vale, Canhão
⩦ Plain	Ebene	Llano	Plaine	Planície
› Cape	Kap	Cabo	Cap	Cabo
I Island	Insel	Isla	Île	Ilha
II Islands	Inseln	Islas	Îles	Ilhas
⊥ Other Topographic Features	Andere Topographische Objekte	Otros Elementos Topográficos	Autres données topographiques	Outros acidentes topográficos

ESPAÑOL — Nombre | Página | Lat.°′ | Long.°′ W = Oeste
FRANÇAIS — Nom | Page | Lat.°′ | Long.°′ W = Ouest
PORTUGUÊS — Nome | Página | Lat.°′ | Long.°′ W = Oeste

Nombre	Página	Lat.°′	Long.°′ W = Oeste
Rubtsovsk → Rubcovsk	86	51.33 N	81.10 E
Ruby, Ak., U.S.	180	64.44 N	155.30 W
Ruby, N.Y., U.S.	210	42.01 N	74.01 W
Ruby ≃	202	45.34 N	112.21 W
Ruby Creek ≃	224	48.43 N	120.59 W
Ruby Dome ∧	204	40.37 N	115.28 W
Ruby Lake ⊞	204	40.10 N	115.30 W
Ruby Mountains ⩘	204	40.25 N	115.35 W
Ruby Valley V	204	40.30 N	115.15 W
Rucava	76	56.09 N	21.10 E
Ruchan'	76	53.33 N	32.48 E
Ruche	261	49.02 N	2.27 E
Rucheng	100	25.34 N	113.41 E
Ruciane-Nida	30	53.39 N	21.35 E
Ručji ✦[8]	265a	60.01 N	30.24 E
Ručjuvom	24	66.42 N	61.08 E
Rucphen	52	51.32 N	4.34 E
Ruda	64	45.50 N	13.24 E
Rudall	166	33.41 S	136.16 E
Rudall ≃	162	22.16 S	122.47 E
Rudall River National Park ♦	162	22.25 S	122.40 E
Ruda Śląska	30	50.18 N	18.51 E
Rudauli	124	26.45 N	81.45 E
Ruḍaymat al-Liwā'	132	33.01 N	36.35 E
Rūdbār, Afg.	128	30.09 N	62.36 E
Rūdbār, Īrān	128	36.48 N	49.24 E
Rudbøl	41	54.54 N	8.45 E
Ruddervoorde	50	51.06 N	3.12 E
Ruddiman Terrace	216	43.12 N	86.17 W
Rudelsburg ⊥	54	51.07 N	11.43 E
Ruden I	54	54.12 N	13.46 E
Rudensk	76	53.36 N	27.52 E
Rüdersdorf, Dtsch.	54	52.29 N	13.47 E
Rudersdorf, Öst.	61	47.03 N	16.07 E
Rüdersdorf, Forst ✦[3]	264a	52.26 N	13.50 E
Rüdesheim am Rhein	56	49.59 N	7.56 E
Rudeville	276	41.09 N	74.33 W
Rudewa	154	10.06 S	34.39 E
Rudge Ramos	287b	23.41 S	46.34 W
Rūdiškės	76	54.31 N	24.50 E
Rudki	78	49.39 N	23.29 E
Rudkino	78	51.27 N	39.01 E
Rudkøbing	41	54.56 N	10.43 E
Rudn'a, Ross.	76	54.57 N	31.06 E
Rudn'a, Ross.	80	50.48 N	44.33 E
Rudnaja Pristan'	89	44.22 N	135.48 E
Rudnevka ≃	265b	55.43 N	37.56 E
Rudnevo	82	54.44 N	38.09 E
Rudnica	78	48.15 N	28.55 E
Rudničnyj, Kaz.	86	44.40 N	78.55 E
Rudničnyj, Ross.	24	59.38 N	52.27 E
Rudničnyj, Ross.	86	56.08 N	86.12 E
Rudničnyj, Ross.	86	59.42 N	60.18 E
Rudnik	30	50.28 N	22.15 E
Rüdnitz	54	52.43 N	13.37 E
Rudnyj, Kaz.	86	52.57 N	63.07 E
Rudnyj, Ross.	89	44.21 N	134.58 E
Rudo	38	43.37 N	19.22 E
Rudolf, Lake (Lake Turkana) ⊜	144	3.30 N	36.00 E
Rudolfov	61	48.59 N	14.34 E
Rudolph	216	41.17 N	83.40 W
Rudolstadt	54	50.43 N	11.20 E
Rudong, Zhg.	102	21.39 N	111.23 E
Rudong, Zhg.	106	32.19 N	121.12 E
Rudovka, Ross.	80	53.07 N	42.23 E
Rudovka, Ukr.	83	49.24 N	38.27 E
Rudow ✦[8]	54	52.25 N	13.30 E
Rudrón ≃	34	42.47 N	3.45 W
Rūdsar	128	37.08 N	50.18 E
Ruds Vedby	41	55.33 N	11.23 E
Rudyard, Mi., U.S.	190	46.13 N	84.36 W
Rudyard, Mt., U.S.	202	48.33 N	110.33 W
Rudyerd Bay c	182	55.35 N	130.44 W
Rue, Fr.	50	50.16 N	1.40 E
Rue, Schw.	58	46.37 N	6.50 E
Ruecas ≃	34	39.00 N	5.55 W
Rueil-Malmaison	261	48.53 N	2.11 E
Ruen ∧	38	42.10 N	22.31 E
Ruenya (Luenha) ≃	154	16.24 S	33.48 E
Rufā'ah	140	14.46 N	33.22 E
Ruffano	68	39.59 N	18.15 E
Ruffec	32	46.01 N	0.12 E
Ruffieu	58	46.00 N	5.40 E
Ruffieux	62	45.51 N	5.50 E
Ruffin	192	33.00 N	80.48 W
Ruffle Bar I	276	40.36 N	46.51 W
Rufford	262	53.38 N	2.49 W
Rufford Old Hall ⊥	262	53.38 N	2.49 W
Ruffs Dale	279b	40.10 N	79.37 W
Rufidschi → Rufiji ≃	154	8.00 S	39.20 E
Rufiji ≃	154	8.00 S	39.20 E
Rufina	66	43.49 N	11.29 E
Rufino	252	34.16 S	62.42 W
Rufisque	150	14.43 N	17.17 W
Rufunsa	154	15.05 S	29.40 E
Rufus	224	45.41 N	120.44 W
Rufus, Mount ∧	168b	34.20 S	139.07 E
Rugāji	76	57.00 N	27.08 E
Rugao	100	32.25 N	120.36 E
Rugby, Eng., U.K.	42	52.23 N	1.15 W
Rugby, N.D., U.S.	198	48.22 N	99.59 W
Rugeley	42	52.46 N	1.55 W
Rügen I	54	54.25 N	13.24 E
Rüggeberg	263	51.16 N	7.22 E
Rugged Mountain ∧	182	50.02 N	126.41 W
Ruggles Beach	214	41.22 N	82.29 W
Rugles	50	48.49 N	0.42 E
Rugufu ≃	154	5.10 S	30.14 E
Ruguj	76	59.28 N	32.50 E
Ruḫama	132	31.30 N	34.42 E
Ruhea	124	26.10 N	88.25 E
Ruhengeri	154	1.30 S	29.38 E
Ruhla	54	50.53 N	10.22 E
Ruhland	54	51.27 N	13.52 E
Ruhlsdorf	264a	52.23 N	13.16 E
Ruhmannsfelden	60	48.59 N	12.59 E
Ruhner Berge ∧[2]	54	53.17 N	11.55 E
Ruhnu saar I	76	57.48 N	23.15 E
Ruhpolding	64	47.45 N	12.38 E
Ruhr ≃	52	51.27 N	6.44 E
Ruhrort ✦[8]	263	51.26 N	6.45 E
Ruhr-Universität ᵿ[2]	263	51.27 N	7.16 E
Ruhstorf an der Rott	60	48.26 N	13.20 E
Ruhudji ≃	154	8.52 S	36.01 E
Ruhuhu ≃	154	10.31 S	34.34 E
Ruhunu National Park ♦	122	6.30 N	81.30 E
Rui'an	100	27.49 N	120.38 E
Ruichang	100	29.41 N	115.40 E
Ruicheng	102	34.45 N	110.45 E
Ruidoso	200	33.19 N	105.40 W
Ruidoso, Rio ≃	200	33.23 N	105.16 W
Ruidoso Downs	200	33.19 N	105.36 W
Ruifeng Sha I	106	31.25 N	121.36 E
Ruihong	100	28.45 N	116.23 E
Ruijin	100	25.50 N	116.00 E
Ruinen	52	52.46 N	6.22 E
Ruiselede	50	51.03 N	3.24 E
Ruislip ✦[8]	260	51.34 N	0.25 W
Ruivo, Pico ∧	148	32.45 N	16.56 W
Ruiz	234	21.57 N	105.09 W
Ruiz, Nevado del ∧[1]	246	4.54 N	75.18 W
Ruiz de Montoya	252	26.59 S	55.03 W
Rūjiena	76	57.54 N	25.21 E
Rujm ar-Rashīd, Jabal ∧	132	31.53 N	36.18 E
Rujm aṣ-Ṣakhrī	132	31.02 N	35.43 E
Rukan-shō ✢[2]	174m	26.06 N	127.32 E
Ruki ≃	152	0.05 N	18.17 E
Rukni	126	23.33 N	86.33 E
Rukungiri	154	0.48 S	29.55 E
Rukwa □[4]	154	7.00 S	31.30 E
Rukwa, Lake ⊜	154	8.00 S	32.25 E
Rule	196	33.11 N	99.53 W
Rule Creek ≃	198	38.02 N	103.02 W
Ruleville	194	33.43 N	90.33 W
Rulle	52	52.20 N	8.04 E
Rully	58	46.52 N	4.45 E
Rulo	198	40.03 N	95.25 W
Rülzheim	56	49.09 N	8.16 E
Rum	61	47.08 N	16.51 E
Rum ≃	190	45.11 N	93.23 W
Ruma	38	45.00 N	19.49 E
Rumaat	164	5.49 S	132.48 E
Rumāh	128	25.34 N	47.09 E
Rumahtinggih	164	6.23 S	140.17 E
Rum'ancevo, Ross.	82	55.38 N	37.26 E
Rum'ancevo, Ross.	82	55.58 N	36.32 E
Rum'ancevo ✦[8]	83	48.21 N	38.06 E
Rumänien → Romania □[1]	38	46.00 N	25.30 E
Rumaysh	132	33.05 N	35.22 E
Rumbek	140	6.48 N	29.41 E
Rumbeke	50	50.56 N	3.10 E
Rumberpon, Pulau I	164	1.50 S	134.15 E
Rumbling Bridge	46	56.10 N	3.35 W
Rumburk	54	50.57 N	14.32 E
Rum Cay I	238	23.40 N	74.53 W
Rumelange	56	49.28 N	6.02 E
Rumelifeneri ✦[8]	267b	41.14 N	29.06 E
Rumelihisarı ✦[8]	267b	41.05 N	29.03 E
Rumelihisarı ⊥	267b	41.05 N	29.02 E
Rumelikavağı ✦[8]	267b	41.11 N	29.04 E
Rumford	188	44.33 N	70.33 W
Rumford ≃	283	41.58 N	71.11 W
Rumia	30	54.35 N	18.25 E
Rumigny	50	49.48 N	4.16 E
Rumilly	62	45.52 N	5.57 E
R'uminskoje	82	56.31 N	38.47 E
Rum Jungle	164	13.01 S	131.00 E
R'umki	265a	59.47 N	30.02 E
Rümlang	58	47.27 N	8.32 E
Rummah, Wādī ar- V	128	26.12 N	44.04 E
Rummānah	142	31.01 N	32.40 E
Rummānah, Bi'r ar- ⊤[4]	142	31.00 N	32.40 E
Rummel	214	40.13 N	78.48 W
Rummelsburg ✦[8]	264a	52.30 N	13.29 E
Rummenohl ✦[8]	263	51.17 N	7.32 E
Rumney	42	51.31 N	3.07 W
Rumoi	92a	43.56 N	141.39 E
Rumont	56	48.50 N	5.17 E
Rumphi	154	11.01 S	33.52 E
Rump Mountain ∧	188	45.12 N	71.04 W
Rumson	208	40.22 N	73.59 W
Rumst	50	51.05 N	4.25 E
Rumula	164	16.35 S	145.20 E
Rumung I	174q	9.37 N	138.10 E
Rumuruti	154	0.16 N	36.32 E
Runan	100	33.01 N	114.22 E
Runanga	172	42.24 S	171.16 E
Runaway, Cape ≻	172	37.32 S	177.59 E
Runazi	154	2.47 S	31.28 E
Runcorn ✦[8]	44	53.20 N	2.44 W
Rundeng	114	2.39 N	97.52 E
Rundēni	76	56.16 N	27.50 E
Rundu	156	17.52 S	19.43 E
Rundvik	26	63.32 N	19.26 E
Runere	154	3.06 S	33.16 E
Rŭng, Kaôh I	110	10.44 N	103.14 E
Rungāni	120	26.38 N	65.43 E
Runge	222	28.52 N	97.42 W
Rungis	261	48.45 N	2.21 E
Rungis-Halles, Marché de ᵿ	261	48.46 N	2.21 E
Rungsted	41	55.53 N	12.33 E
Rungus Point ≻	116	13.43 N	123.58 E
Rungwa, Tan.	154	7.21 S	31.40 E
Rungwa, Tan.	154	6.57 S	33.31 E
Rungwa ≃	154	7.36 S	31.50 E
Rungwa Game Reserve ✦[4]	154	7.00 S	34.10 E
Rungwe	154	9.10 S	33.36 E
Runhällen	40	60.02 N	16.49 E
Runheji	100	32.30 N	116.05 E
Runkel	56	50.24 N	8.10 E
Runmarö I	40	59.17 N	18.46 E
Runn ⊜	40	60.33 N	15.40 E
Runnemede	285	39.51 N	75.04 W
Running Springs	228	34.12 N	117.07 W
Running Water Draw V	196	33.58 N	101.30 W
Runnymede □[8]	260	51.24 N	0.32 W
Runnymede ⊥	42	51.26 N	0.34 W
Rünthe	263	51.39 N	7.39 E
Runwell	260	51.37 N	0.32 E
Ruo ≃, Afr.	154	16.33 S	35.09 E
Ruo ≃, Zhg.	102	41.00 N	100.10 E
Ruo'ergai	102	33.16 N	102.55 E
Ruoheng	100	28.24 N	121.31 E
Ruokolahti	26	61.17 N	28.50 E
Ruoms	62	44.27 N	4.21 E
Ruoqiang	90	38.30 N	88.05 E
Ruoti	68	40.43 N	15.41 E
Ruovesi	26	61.59 N	24.05 E
Ruoxi	100	29.18 N	115.20 E
Rupanco	254	40.46 S	72.42 W
Rupanco, Lago ⊜	254	40.49 S	72.28 W
Rupari	168b	35.37 S	139.09 E
Rupat, Pulau I	114	1.50 N	101.35 E
Rupat, Selat ꓴ	114	1.50 N	101.25 E
Rupdia	126	23.08 N	89.18 E
Rupea	38	46.02 N	25.13 E
Rupert, Id., U.S.	202	42.37 N	113.40 W
Rupert, Vt., U.S.	210	43.15 N	73.13 W
Rupert, W.V., U.S.	188	37.57 N	80.41 W
Rupert, Rivière de ≃	176	51.29 N	78.45 W
Rupert Creek ≃	166	20.53 S	142.23 E
Rupganj	126	23.48 N	90.31 E
Rūpnagar	123	30.59 N	76.31 E
Rūpnārāyan ≃	126	22.13 N	88.03 E
Ruponda	154	10.15 S	38.42 E
Ruppertenrod	56	50.37 N	9.05 E
Ruppiner See ⊜	54	52.48 N	12.50 E
Rupprechtseck ∧	61	47.14 N	14.00 E
Rupt de Mad ≃	56	49.01 N	6.02 E
Rupt-sur-Moselle	58	47.56 N	6.40 E
Rupununi ≃	246	4.03 N	58.34 W
Ruqqād, Wādī ar- V	132	32.44 N	35.46 E
Rur (Roer) ≃	56	51.12 N	5.59 E
Rural Hall	192	36.14 N	80.17 W
Rural Retreat	192	36.53 N	81.16 W
Rural Ridge	279b	40.35 N	79.50 W
Rural Valley	214	40.48 N	79.18 W
Rurberg	56	50.37 N	6.22 E
Ruri-kei ♦	96	35.03 N	135.26 E
Rurrenabaque	248	14.28 S	67.34 W
Rurstausee ⊜[1]	56	50.36 N	6.22 E
Rurutu I	14	22.26 S	151.20 W
Rusambo	154	16.35 S	32.12 E
Rušan	120	37.58 N	71.30 E
Rusanov	78	50.29 N	31.09 E
Rusanovka	78	50.32 N	33.44 E
Rusape	154	18.32 S	32.07 E
Rusavkina-Popovščina	265b	55.42 N	38.04 E
Ruṣayriṣ, Khazzān ar- ⊜[1]	140	11.40 N	34.20 E
Ruschuk → Ruse	38	43.50 N	25.57 E
Ruscom ≃	214	42.18 N	82.38 W
Ruscom Station	214	42.13 N	82.39 W
Ruse, Blg.	38	43.50 N	25.57 E
Ruše, Slvn.	61	46.32 N	15.31 E
Rusera	124	25.45 N	86.02 E
Rush, Ire.	48	53.32 N	6.06 W
Rush, N.Y., U.S.	210	42.59 N	77.39 W
Rush, Pa., U.S.	210	41.47 N	76.03 W
Rush □[6]	218	39.37 N	85.27 W
Rush ≃, N.D., U.S.	198	47.00 N	96.54 W
Rush ≃, Wi., U.S.	190	44.34 N	92.19 W
Rushan (Xiacun)	98	36.54 N	121.29 E
Rush Center	198	38.27 N	99.18 W
Rush City	190	45.41 N	92.57 W
Rush Creek ≃, Co., U.S.	198	38.22 N	102.32 W
Rush Creek ≃, Ne., U.S.	198	41.27 N	102.32 W
Rush Creek ≃, N.Y., U.S.	284a	42.00 N	78.52 W
Rush Creek ≃, Oh., U.S.	188	39.38 N	82.33 W
Rush Creek ≃, Oh., U.S.	214	40.34 N	83.20 W
Rush Creek ≃, Ok., U.S.	196	34.42 N	97.10 W
Rushden	42	52.17 N	0.36 W
Rushford, Mn., U.S.	190	43.48 N	91.45 W
Rushford, N.Y., U.S.	210	42.23 N	78.15 W
Rush Hill	219	39.13 N	91.43 W
Rush Lake ⊜, On., Can.	190	47.48 N	82.12 W
Rush Lake ⊜, Wi., U.S.	190	43.56 N	88.49 W
Rushland	285	40.15 N	75.02 W
Rushmore	198	43.37 N	95.48 W
Rusholme ✦[8]	262	53.27 N	2.12 W
Rush Springs	196	34.46 N	97.57 W
Rushsylvania	216	40.27 N	83.40 W
Rushville, Il., U.S.	219	40.07 N	90.33 W
Rushville, In., U.S.	218	39.36 N	85.26 W
Rushville, Ne., U.S.	198	42.43 N	102.27 W
Rushville, N.Y., U.S.	210	42.45 N	77.13 W
Rusinga Island I	154	0.24 S	34.10 E
Rusizi (Ruzizi) ≃	154	3.16 S	29.14 E
Rusk	222	31.47 N	95.09 W
Rusk □[6]	222	32.10 N	94.50 W
Rusken ⊜	26	57.17 N	14.20 E
Ruskin, B.C., Can.	224	49.12 N	122.28 W
Ruskin, Fl., U.S.	220	27.43 N	82.26 W
Ruskington	44	53.02 N	0.23 W
Rusnė	76	55.18 N	21.22 E
Rušons ⊜	76	56.11 N	27.02 E
Rusovce	61	48.04 N	17.10 E
Russa	272b	22.29 N	88.21 E
Russas	250	4.56 S	37.58 W
Russbach ≃	61	48.10 N	16.58 E
Russee	41	54.18 N	10.04 E
Russell, Mb., Can.	184	50.47 N	101.15 W
Russell, On., Can.	212	45.15 N	75.22 W
Russell, N.Z.	172	35.16 S	174.07 E
Russell, Ia., U.S.	190	40.58 N	93.11 W
Russell, Ks., U.S.	198	38.53 N	98.51 W
Russell, Ky., U.S.	188	38.31 N	82.41 W
Russell, Ma., U.S.	207	42.11 N	72.51 W
Russell, Mn., U.S.	198	44.19 N	95.57 W
Russell, Pa., U.S.	214	41.56 N	79.08 W
Russell, Cape ≻	176	75.15 N	117.35 W
Russell, Mount ∧	180	62.48 N	151.52 W
Russell Cave National Monument ♦	194	34.54 N	85.48 W
Russell Creek ≃	194	37.14 N	85.30 W
Russell Gardens	276	40.47 N	73.43 W
Russell Island I	176	73.55 N	98.25 W
Russell Islands II	175e	9.04 S	159.12 E
Russellkonda	120	19.56 N	84.35 E
Russell Lake ⊜	184	56.15 N	101.30 W
Russell Range ⩘	162	33.24 S	123.28 E
Russells Point	216	40.28 N	83.54 W
Russell Springs	194	37.03 N	85.05 W
Russellton	214	40.37 N	79.50 W
Russellville, Al., U.S.	194	34.30 N	87.43 W
Russellville, Ar., U.S.	194	35.16 N	93.08 W
Russellville, Ky., U.S.	194	36.50 N	86.53 W
Russellville, Mo., U.S.	194	38.30 N	92.26 W
Russellville, Oh., U.S.	218	38.51 N	83.47 W
Russellville, Or., U.S.	224	45.31 N	122.33 W
Rüsselsheim	56	50.00 N	8.25 E
Russi	66	44.22 N	12.02 E
Russia	216	40.14 N	84.24 W
Russia □[1], Europe	72	60.00 N	80.00 E
Russia □[1], Europe	74	60.00 N	100.00 E
Russian ≃	204	38.27 N	123.08 W
Russian Mission	180	61.47 N	161.19 W
Russiaville	216	40.25 N	86.16 W
Russka	76	58.59 N	28.30 E
Russkaja Bujlovka	78	50.22 N	40.03 E
Russkaja Gavan'	74	76.10 N	62.35 E
Russkaja Pol'ana	86	53.47 N	73.53 E
Russkaja Talovka	80	49.59 N	49.05 E
Russkaja Žuravka	80	50.21 N	40.33 E
Russkij	89	43.03 N	131.50 E
Russkij, ostrov I	74	77.00 N	96.00 E
Russkij Aktaš	80	55.02 N	52.07 E
Russkij Brod	76	52.36 N	37.22 E
Russkij Kameškir	80	52.52 N	46.06 E
Russkij Turek	80	57.03 N	50.13 E
Russkij Vožoj	80	56.57 N	53.22 E
Russkij Zavorot, mys ≻	24	68.58 N	54.34 E
Russkoje	83	47.45 N	38.56 E
Russkoje-Dobrino	80	54.22 N	52.28 E
Russko-Vysockoje	265a	59.42 N	29.56 E
Rust, Dtsch.	58	48.16 N	7.43 E
Rust, Öst.	61	47.48 N	16.41 E
Rustajskij	80	56.31 N	44.49 E
Rustam	123	34.21 N	72.17 E
Rustavi	84	41.33 N	45.02 E
Rustburg	192	37.16 N	79.06 W
Rustenburg	158	25.37 S	27.08 E
Rustfontein	158	30.28 S	29.17 E
Rustic Canyon V	280	34.04 N	118.31 W
Rustig	158	27.22 S	27.09 E
Rustington	42	50.48 N	0.31 W
Ruston, La., U.S.	194	32.31 N	92.38 W
Ruston, Wa., U.S.	224	47.17 N	122.30 W
Rusville	273d	26.10 S	28.18 E
Rutana	154	3.55 S	30.00 E
Rutčenkovo	83	47.57 N	37.44 E
Rute	34	37.19 N	4.22 W
Rütenbrock	52	52.50 N	7.10 E
Ruteng	115b	8.36 S	120.27 E
Rutenga	154	21.08 S	30.45 E
Rutersville	222	29.57 N	96.48 W
Rutgers University ᵿ[2], N.J., U.S.	276	40.30 N	74.27 W
Rutgers University (Newark) ᵿ[2], N.J., U.S.	276	40.44 N	74.10 W
Rutgers University (Camden) ᵿ[2], N.J., U.S.	285	39.56 N	75.07 W
Ruth, Ms., U.S.	194	31.22 N	90.18 W
Ruth, Nv., U.S.	204	39.16 N	114.59 W
Rüthen	52	51.29 N	8.25 E
Rutherford, Ca., U.S.	226	38.28 N	122.25 W
Rutherford, N.J., U.S.	210	40.49 N	74.06 W
Rutherford, Tn., U.S.	194	36.07 N	88.59 W
Rutherfordton	192	35.22 N	81.57 W
Rutherglen, Scot., U.K.	46	55.50 N	4.12 W
Ruther Glen, Va., U.S.	208	37.56 N	77.27 W
Ruthin	44	53.07 N	3.18 W
Ruthton	198	44.10 N	96.06 W
Ruthven, On., Can.	214	42.03 N	82.40 W
Ruthven, Ia., U.S.	198	43.07 N	94.53 W
Rüti	58	47.16 N	8.51 E
Rutigliano	68	41.01 N	17.00 E
Rutino	68	40.18 N	15.04 E
Rutka ≃	80	56.22 N	46.38 E
Rutland, B.C., Can.	182	49.53 N	119.24 W
Rutland, Fl., U.S.	220	28.51 N	82.13 W
Rutland, Il., U.S.	216	40.59 N	89.03 W
Rutland, Ma., U.S.	207	42.22 N	71.56 W
Rutland, N.D., U.S.	198	46.03 N	97.30 W
Rutland, Vt., U.S.	188	43.36 N	72.58 W
Rutland □[6]	210	43.21 N	73.15 W
Rutland Island I	110	11.25 N	92.40 E
Rutland State Park ♦	207	42.23 N	72.01 W
Rutland Water ⊜[1]	42	52.39 N	0.38 W
Rutledge, Ga., U.S.	192	33.37 N	83.36 W
Rutledge, Pa., U.S.	285	39.54 N	75.20 W
Rutledge, Tn., U.S.	192	36.16 N	83.30 W
Rutog	120	33.27 N	79.42 E
Rutshuru	154	1.11 S	29.27 E
Rüttenscheid ✦[8]	263	51.26 N	7.00 E
Rutter	190	46.06 N	80.40 W
Rutul	84	41.33 N	47.25 E
Ruukki	26	64.40 N	25.06 E
Ruurlo	52	52.05 N	6.26 E
Ruvo del Monte	68	40.51 N	15.32 E
Ruvo di Puglia	68	41.07 N	16.29 E
Ruvu	154	6.48 S	38.39 E
Ruvu ≃	154	6.23 S	38.52 E
Ruvubu (Rovubu) ≃	154	2.23 S	30.47 E
Ruvuma □[4]	154	11.00 S	36.00 E
Ruvuma (Rovuma) ≃	154	10.29 S	40.28 E
Ruwayān, Wādī ar- ≛[7]	142	29.07 N	30.10 E
Ruwaybah ⊤[4]	140	15.39 N	28.45 E
Ruwayfī, Jabal ar- ∧	132	31.12 N	36.00 E
Ruwenzori National Park ♦	154	0.15 S	30.00 E
Ruwenzori Range ⩘	154	0.23 N	29.54 E
Ruwer	56	49.47 N	6.43 E
Ruwer ≃	56	49.47 N	6.42 E
Ruya (Luia) ≃	154	16.34 S	33.12 E
Ruyang	100	34.10 N	112.26 E
Ruy Barbosa	255	12.18 S	40.27 W
Ruyigi	154	3.29 S	30.15 E
Ruyton-Eleven-Towns	42	52.48 N	2.54 W
Ruza	82	55.42 N	36.12 E
Ruza ≃	82	55.38 N	36.17 E
Ruzajevka, Kaz.	86	52.49 N	66.57 E
Ruzajevka, Ross.	80	54.04 N	44.57 E
Ružany	76	52.52 N	24.53 E
Ružičnaja	78	49.24 N	26.58 E
Ružin	78	49.43 N	29.14 E
Ruzizi (Rusizi) ≃	154	3.16 S	29.14 E
Ružomberok	30	49.06 N	19.18 E
Ruzskoje vodochranilišče ⊜[1]	82	55.47 N	36.00 E
Ruzyně ✈	54	50.06 N	14.17 E
Ruzzah, Jabal ∧[2]	142	30.01 N	30.26 E
Rwamagana	154	1.57 S	30.34 E
Rwanda □[1], Afr.	138	2.00 S	30.00 E
Rwanda □[1], Afr.	154	2.00 S	30.00 E
Rwashamaire	154	0.49 S	30.08 E
Ry	41	56.05 N	9.46 E
Ryal Fold	262	53.41 N	2.30 W
Ryan	196	34.01 N	97.57 W
Ryan ≃	182	50.25 N	122.43 W
Ryan, Loch c	44	54.58 N	5.02 W
Ryan Peak ∧	202	43.54 N	114.25 W
Ryans Creek ≃	169	36.43 S	146.12 E
Ryarsh	260	51.19 N	0.24 E
Ryazan' → R'azan'	80	54.38 N	39.44 E
Rybačij	76	55.09 N	20.51 E
Rybačij, poluostrov ≻[1]	24	69.42 N	32.36 E
Rybačje	86	46.27 N	81.32 E
Rybackaja ✦[8]	265a	60.00 N	30.30 E
Rybackoje ✦[8]	265a	59.50 N	30.30 E
Rybakovka	78	46.37 N	31.20 E
Rybinsk	76	58.03 N	38.52 E
Rybinsker Stausee → Rybinskoje vodochranilišče ⊜[1]	76	58.30 N	38.25 E
Rybinskije Budy	78	51.13 N	35.57 E
Rybinskoje	86	55.47 N	94.47 E
Rybinskoje vodochranilišče ⊜[1]	76	58.30 N	38.25 E
Rybkino	80	54.15 N	43.46 E
Rybnaja Sloboda	80	55.28 N	50.09 E
Rybnica	38	47.45 N	29.01 E
Rybnik	30	50.06 N	18.32 E
Rybnoje, Ross.	76	54.44 N	39.30 E
Rybnoje, Ross.	86	58.08 N	94.30 E
Rybnovsk	89	53.12 N	141.50 E
Ryburn ≃	262	53.43 N	1.54 W
Rybuška	80	51.17 N	45.26 E
Rychwał	30	52.05 N	18.09 E
Ryčkovo	86	58.09 N	61.43 E
Rycroft	182	55.45 N	118.43 W
Ryd	26	56.28 N	14.41 E
Rydaholm	26	56.59 N	14.16 E
Rydal, Austl.	170	33.29 S	150.02 E
Rydal, Pa., U.S.	285	40.06 N	75.06 W
Rydalmere	274a	33.49 S	151.02 E
Rydbo	40	59.28 N	18.11 E
Ryde, Austl.	170	33.49 S	151.06 E
Ryde, Eng., U.K.	42	50.44 N	1.10 W
Ryder	198	47.55 N	101.40 W
Ryder's Hill ∧[2]	42	50.31 N	3.53 W
Ryderwood	224	46.22 N	123.02 W
Rydsgård	41	55.28 N	13.35 E
Rydzyna	30	51.48 N	16.40 E
Rye, Austl.	169	38.23 S	144.49 E
Rye, Eng., U.K.	42	50.57 N	0.44 E
Rye, N.Y., U.S.	210	40.58 N	73.41 W
Rye, Tx., U.S.	222	30.27 N	94.46 W
Rye ≃	44	54.10 N	0.45 W
Ryegate	202	46.17 N	109.15 W
Rye Hills-Rye Brook	276	41.00 N	73.41 W
Rye Lake ⊜	276	41.04 N	73.43 W
Ryeosu → Yŏsu	98	34.46 N	127.44 E
Rye Patch Reservoir ⊜[1]	204	40.38 N	118.18 W
Ryer Island I	282	38.05 N	122.01 W
Ryes	32	49.19 N	0.37 W
Ryfoss	26	61.09 N	8.49 E
Ryfylke ✦[1]	26	59.30 N	5.30 E
Rygge	26	59.23 N	10.43 E
Rygnestad	26	59.16 N	7.29 E
Ryhope	44	54.52 N	1.21 W
Rykaartspos	158	26.32 S	26.39 E
Ryker Lake ⊜	276	41.03 N	74.33 W
Rykerts	182	49.00 N	116.35 W
Ryki	30	51.39 N	21.56 E
Rykonec	76	59.33 N	36.34 E
Ryley	182	53.17 N	112.26 W
Ryloviči	76	52.31 N	32.04 E
Ryl'sk	78	51.36 N	34.43 E
Rylstone	170	32.48 S	149.58 E
Rymanów	30	49.34 N	21.53 E
Rýmařov	30	49.56 N	17.16 E
Ryn	30	53.56 N	21.33 E
Rynfield	273d	26.09 S	28.20 E
Rynok	80	45.39 N	47.34 E
Ryn-Peski ✦[2]	80	48.24 N	49.00 E
Ryō	270	34.44 N	135.55 E
Ryōhaku-sanchi ⩘	94	36.09 N	136.45 E
Ryojun → Lüshun	98	38.48 N	121.16 E
Ryōkami	94	36.00 N	138.58 E
Ryōke	268	35.58 N	139.33 E
Ryōnan	96	33.15 N	133.55 E
Ryōtsu	92	38.05 N	138.26 E
Rypin	30	53.05 N	19.25 E
Ryškany	38	47.58 N	27.32 E
Ryslinge	41	55.15 N	10.33 E
Rysy ∧	30	49.12 N	20.04 E
Ryton	44	54.59 N	1.46 W
Ryton ≃	44	53.25 N	1.00 W
Ryton-on-Dunsmore	42	52.22 N	1.26 W
Ryūga-do ≛[5]	96	33.39 N	133.45 E
Ryūgasaki	94	35.54 N	140.11 E
Ryūjin	96	33.53 N	135.29 E
Ryukyu Islands → Nansei-shotō II	90	26.30 N	128.00 E
Ryukyu Trench ✢[1]	12	24.45 N	128.00 E
Ryūmon-dake ∧	270	34.26 N	135.53 E
Ryūō, Nihon	94	35.04 N	136.07 E
Ryūō, Nihon	94	35.39 N	138.30 E
Ryūsen	270	34.28 N	135.37 E
Ryūyō	94	34.40 N	137.48 E
Ržaksa	80	52.09 N	42.02 E
Ržanica	76	53.26 N	33.55 E
Ržava	78	51.14 N	36.43 E
Rzepin	30	52.22 N	14.50 E
Rzeszów	30	50.03 N	22.00 E
Rzeszów □[4]	30	50.00 N	22.00 E
Ržev	76	56.16 N	34.20 E
Ržiščov	78	49.58 N	31.03 E
Ržovka ✦[8]	265a	59.58 N	30.30 E
S			
Sa	110	18.34 N	100.45 E
Sa ≃	105	40.22 N	117.58 E
Saa	152	4.22 N	11.27 E
Sa'ad	132	31.28 N	34.32 E
Sa'ādatābād	128	30.06 N	53.08 E
Sääksjärvi ⊜	26	61.24 N	22.24 E
Saal	54	54.19 N	12.29 E
Saalach ≃	64	47.51 N	13.00 E
Saal an der Donau	60	48.54 N	11.56 E
Saal an der Saale	56	50.19 N	10.21 E
Saalbach	64	47.23 N	12.38 E
Saalburg	54	50.30 N	11.43 E
Saaldorf	54	50.27 N	11.41 E
Saale ≃	54	51.57 N	11.55 E
Saaler Bodden c	54	54.20 N	12.28 E
Saales	58	48.21 N	7.07 E
Saaletalsperre ✦[6]	54	50.30 N	11.43 E
Saalfeld	54	50.39 N	11.22 E
Saalfelden	64	47.25 N	12.51 E
Šaamar	88	50.08 N	106.10 E
Saâne ≃, Fr.	50	49.54 N	0.56 E
Saane ≃, Schw.	58	46.59 N	7.16 E
Saanen	58	46.29 N	7.16 E
Saanenmöser	58	46.31 N	7.18 E
Saanich Inlet c	224	48.38 N	123.30 W
Saar → Saarland □[3]	56	49.20 N	7.00 E
Saar (Sarre) ≃	56	49.42 N	6.34 E
Saarbrücken	56	49.14 N	6.59 E
Saarburg	56	49.36 N	6.33 E
Sääre	76	57.56 N	22.02 E
Saarelouis → Saarlouis	56	49.21 N	6.45 E
Saaremaa I	76	58.25 N	22.30 E
Saarijärvi	26	62.43 N	25.16 E
Saaristomeren kansallispuisto ♦	26	59.50 N	21.50 E
Saarland □[3]	56	49.20 N	7.00 E
Saarlautern → Saarlouis	56	49.21 N	6.45 E
Saarlouis	56	49.21 N	6.45 E
Saarmund	264a	52.19 N	13.07 E
Saarn ✦[8]	263	51.24 N	6.53 E
Saarnberg ✦[8]	263	51.25 N	6.53 E
Saas Almagell	58	46.07 N	7.58 E
Saas Fee	58	46.07 N	7.55 E
Saas Grund	58	46.08 N	7.56 E
Saastal V	58	46.10 N	7.56 E
Saatly	84	39.56 N	48.23 E
Saavedra	252	37.45 S	62.22 W
Saba I	238	17.38 N	63.10 W
Saba ≃, Nihon	96	34.02 N	131.30 E
Saba ≃, Ross.	76	59.08 N	29.00 E
Sabā', Wādī al- V	128	28.35 N	36.35 E
Saba Bank ✢[2]	238	17.30 N	63.30 W
Šabac	38	44.45 N	19.42 E
Sabadell	34	41.33 N	2.06 E
Sabae	94	35.57 N	136.11 E
Sab'ah	142	30.15 N	32.33 E
Sabah □[3]	112	5.20 N	117.10 E
Sabajevo	80	53.59 N	45.43 E
Sabak, Cape ≻	181a	52.20 N	173.45 E
Sabak Bernam	114	3.46 N	100.59 E
Sabal	112	0.59 S	123.14 E
Sabalān ∧	128	38.15 N	47.48 E
Sabalana, Kepulauan II	112	6.45 S	118.50 E
Sabalgarh	124	26.15 N	77.24 E
Sabaluka Game Reserve ✦[4]	140	16.18 N	32.40 E
Sabana	240m	18.20 N	65.44 W
Sabana, Archipiélago de II	240p	23.00 N	80.00 W
Sabana de La Mar	238	19.04 N	69.23 W
Sabana de Mendoza	246	9.26 N	70.46 W
Sabanagrande, Hond.	236	13.50 N	87.15 W
Sabana Grande, P.R.	240m	18.05 N	66.58 W
Sabanalamar, Ensenada c	240p	21.36 N	78.44 W
Sabanalarga	246	10.38 N	74.55 W
Sabana Llana	240m	18.02 N	66.15 W
Sabancuy	232	18.58 N	91.11 W
Sabaneta, Rep. Dom.	238	19.30 N	71.21 W
Sabaneta, Ven.	246	8.46 N	69.56 W
Sabaneta, Puntan ≻	174n	15.17 N	145.49 E
Sābang, India	126	22.11 N	87.36 E
Sabang (Dampelas), Indon.	112	0.11 N	119.51 E
Sabang, Indon.	114	5.55 N	95.19 E
Sabanillas	232	25.08 N	101.44 W
Šabanovo	82	55.38 N	38.43 E
Şabanözü	130	40.29 N	33.18 E
Sabará	255	19.54 S	43.48 W
Sabarei	154	4.20 N	36.55 E
Sābari ≃	122	17.34 N	81.15 E
Sābarmati ≃	120	22.18 N	72.22 E
Sabasṭīyah (Samaria)	132	32.17 N	35.12 E
Sab'atayn, Ramlat as- ≛[8]	144	15.30 N	46.10 E
Sabathu	123	30.59 N	76.59 E
Sabatini, Monti ⩘	66	42.10 N	12.15 E
Sabato ≃	66	41.08 N	14.45 E
Sabaudia	66	41.18 N	13.01 E
Sabaudia, Lago di c	66	41.16 N	13.02 E
Sabaúna	256	23.29 S	46.05 W
Saba Wanak	144	10.33 N	44.08 E
Sabaya	248	19.01 S	68.23 W
Ṣabāyā, Jabal I	144	18.35 N	41.03 E
Sabažo	84	42.14 N	41.48 E
Sabbioneta	64	45.00 N	10.29 E
Şabe	272c	19.11 N	73.02 E
Šabel'kovka	83	48.45 N	37.29 E
Šabel'sk	83	46.51 N	38.29 E
Ṣāberī, Hāmūn-e ⊜	128	31.30 N	61.20 E
Sabetha	198	39.54 N	95.48 W
Sabhā, Lībiyā	146	27.03 N	14.26 E
Ṣabḥā, Urd.	132	32.20 N	36.30 E
Sābhār	126	23.51 N	90.15 E
Sabi (Save) ≃, Afr.	156	21.00 S	35.02 E
Sabi ≃, Nihon	94	36.48 N	140.04 E
Sabicy	76	58.50 N	29.18 E
Sabidana, Jabal ∧	140	18.04 N	36.50 E
Sabie	156	25.10 S	30.48 E
Sábiè ≃	156	25.19 S	32.18 E
Sabile	76	57.03 N	22.35 E
Sabillasville	208	39.42 N	77.27 W
Sabina	218	39.29 N	83.38 W
Sabina □[9]	66	42.15 N	12.42 E
Sabinal	196	29.19 N	99.27 W
Sabinal ≃	196	29.06 N	99.27 W
Sabinal, Cayo I	240p	21.40 N	77.18 W
Sabiñánigo	34	42.31 N	0.22 W
Sabinas	232	27.51 N	101.07 W
Sabinas ≃, Méx.	232	27.37 N	100.42 W
Sabinas ≃, Méx.	232	26.51 N	99.34 W
Sabinas ≃, Méx.	234	22.59 N	98.58 W
Sabinas Hidalgo	232	26.30 N	100.10 W
Sabine ≃	178	30.00 N	93.45 W
Sabine, Mount ∧	169	38.38 S	143.44 E
Sabine, South Fork ≃	222	32.52 N	96.10 W
Sabine Bay c	176	75.35 N	109.30 W
Sabine Lake ⊜	194	29.50 N	93.50 W
Sabine Pass c	194	29.44 N	93.52 W
Sabine Peninsula ≻[1]	176	76.20 N	109.30 W
Sabini, Monti ⩘	66	42.13 N	12.50 E
Sabinópolis	255	18.40 S	43.06 W
Sabinov	30	49.06 N	21.06 E
Sabinsville	210	41.52 N	77.31 W
Sabir, Jabal ∧	144	13.30 N	44.03 E
Sabirabad	84	40.01 N	48.29 E
Šabla	38	43.32 N	28.32 E
Sabl'a, gora ∧	24	64.48 N	58.50 E
Sablayan	116	12.50 N	120.46 E
Sable, Anse au c	275a	45.21 N	73.56 W
Sable, Cape ≻	186	43.25 N	65.35 W
Sable, Cape ≻[1]	220	25.12 N	81.05 W
Sable, Île de I	160	19.15 S	159.56 E
Sable, Rivière du ≃	176	55.30 N	68.21 W
Sable Island I	186	43.55 N	59.50 W
Sables, Lac aux ⊜	206	46.53 N	72.22 W
Sables, River aux ≃	190	46.13 N	82.04 W
Sablé-sur-Sarthe	32	47.50 N	0.20 W
Sablinskoje	84	44.31 N	43.14 E
Sablūkah, Ash-Shallāl as- (Sixth Cataract) ↳	140	16.20 N	32.42 E
Šablykino	76	52.51 N	35.12 E
Sabo, Centraf.	152	7.50 N	17.49 E
Šabo, Ukr.	78	46.08 N	30.23 E
Saboeiro	250	6.32 S	39.54 W
Sabogal ≃	236	10.55 N	84.43 W
Sāboli ✦[8]	272a	28.43 N	77.18 E
Sabonkaf	150	14.38 N	8.45 E
Sabor ≃	34	41.10 N	7.07 W
Sabou	150	12.04 N	2.14 W
Sabourin, Lac ⊜	190	47.58 N	77.41 W
Sabra, Tanjung ≻	164	2.17 S	132.19 E
Ṣabrātah	146	32.47 N	12.29 E
Sabres	32	44.09 N	0.44 W
Sabrevois	206	45.12 N	73.14 W
Sabrina Coast ≛[2]	9	67.00 S	119.30 E
Sabuda, Pulau I	164	2.38 S	131.36 E
Sabugal	34	40.21 N	7.05 W
Sabugo	266c	38.49 N	9.18 W
Sabuka	273b	4.27 S	15.10 E
Sabula	190	42.04 N	90.10 W
Sabunči	84	40.26 N	49.56 E
Sabuncu	130	39.33 N	30.12 E
Saburovo	265b	55.53 N	37.16 E
Saburovo ✦[8]	265b	55.38 N	37.42 E
Ṣabyā	144	17.09 N	42.37 E
Sabyin	110	19.06 N	94.11 E
Sabyndy	86	50.53 N	70.33 E
Sabzevār	128	36.13 N	57.42 E
Sac ≃	194	38.01 N	93.43 W
Sacaba	248	17.23 S	66.02 W
Sacaca	248	18.05 S	66.26 W
Sacacomie, Lac ⊜	206	46.31 N	73.14 W
Sacagawea ≃	202	47.27 N	107.58 W
Sacajawea Peak ∧	202	45.15 N	117.17 W
Sacanche	248	7.05 S	76.44 W
Sacandaga ≃	210	43.19 N	73.50 W
Sacandaga, West Branch ≃	210	43.22 N	74.17 W
Sacandica	152	5.58 S	15.56 E
Sacaola	152	12.57 S	22.25 E
Sacariúra ≃	248	12.52 S	57.22 W
Sacaton	200	33.04 N	111.44 W
Sacavém	266c	38.47 N	9.06 W
Sačchere	84	42.21 N	43.23 E
Sac City	198	42.25 N	94.59 W
Sacco ≃	66	41.31 N	13.32 E
Sacedón	34	40.29 N	2.43 W
Săcele	38	45.37 N	25.42 E
Saç Geçidi ✕	130	39.54 N	42.22 E
Šacha ≃	82	56.45 N	39.10 E
Sachalin, ostrov (Sakhalin) I	89	51.00 N	143.00 E
Sachalin Oblast' □[4]	89	51.00 N	143.00 E
Sachalinskij zaliv c	89	53.45 N	141.30 E
Šachand	85	40.54 N	71.28 E
Sachayoj	252	26.41 S	61.50 W
Šachbuz	84	39.25 N	45.34 E
Šachdagskij chrebet ⩘	84	40.24 N	45.35 E
Saché	50	47.14 N	0.33 E
Šache ≃	84	43.47 N	39.27 E
Sachicapa	152	10.21 S	19.59 E
Sachigo ≃	176	55.06 N	88.58 W
Sachigo Lake ⊜	184	53.49 N	92.08 W
Sachimbo	152	9.14 S	20.16 E
Šachnovščina	78	49.08 N	35.53 E
Šachovskaja	76	56.02 N	35.29 E
Sachrang	64	47.41 N	12.15 E
Šachrichan	85	40.44 N	72.03 E
Šachrinau	85	38.34 N	68.20 E
Šachrisabz	72	39.03 N	66.50 E
Šachristan	85	39.47 N	68.49 E
Šachristan, pereval ✕	85	39.33 N	68.33 E
Šachrovka	80	58.34 N	52.12 E
Sachse	222	32.59 N	96.36 W
Sachseln	58	46.52 N	8.15 E
Sachsen □[3]	30	51.00 N	13.00 E
Sachsen □[9]	30	52.45 N	9.30 E
Sachsen-Anhalt □[3]	54	52.00 N	11.30 E
Sachsenbrunn	54	50.27 N	10.56 E
Sachsenburg	64	46.50 N	13.21 E
Sachsenhagen	52	52.24 N	9.16 E
Sachsenhausen, Dtsch.	54	52.47 N	13.14 E
Sachsenhausen, Dtsch.	56	51.15 N	9.00 E
Sachs Harbour	176	72.00 N	125.00 W
Sächsische Schweiz ✦[1]	54	50.55 N	14.10 E
Šachterskij	180	64.42 N	177.40 E
Šachtinsk	86	49.40 N	72.37 E
Šachtnoje	83	47.57 N	38.17 E
Šacht'orsk, Ross.	89	49.11 N	142.07 E
Šacht'orsk, Ukr.	83	48.03 N	38.28 E
Šacht'orskij ✦[8]	83	48.09 N	39.08 E
Šachty	83	47.42 N	40.13 E
Šachunja	80	57.40 N	46.37 E
Sachy	56	49.40 N	5.08 E
Sacile	64	45.57 N	12.30 E
Šack, Bela.	76	53.25 N	27.41 E
Šack, Ross.	80	54.01 N	41.43 E
Šack, Ukr.	78	51.31 N	23.57 E
Sackets Harbor	212	43.56 N	76.07 W
Sackville	186	45.54 N	64.22 W
Saclay	261	48.44 N	2.10 E
Saclay, Étang de ⊜	261	48.45 N	2.10 E
Saco, Me., U.S.	188	43.30 N	70.26 W
Saco, Mt., U.S.	202	48.27 N	107.20 W
Saco ≃	188	43.27 N	70.22 W
Saco Bay c	188	43.30 N	70.15 W
Sacol Island I	116	6.58 N	122.13 E
Sacotes	266c	38.48 N	9.20 W
Sacra, Isola I	267a	41.45 N	12.15 E
Sacra Família do Tinguá	256	22.29 S	43.36 W
Sacramento, Bra.	255	19.53 S	47.27 W
Sacramento, Ca., U.S.	226	38.34 N	121.29 W
Sacramento □[6]	226	38.35 N	121.30 W
Sacramento ≃, Ca., U.S.	204	38.03 N	121.56 W
Sacramento ≃, N.M., U.S.	200	32.16 N	105.31 W
Sacramento, Pampa del ≛	248	8.00 S	75.50 W
Sacramento Metropolitan Airport ✈	226	38.42 N	121.37 W
Sacramento Mountains ⩘	200	32.45 N	105.30 W
Sacramento River Deep Water Ship Channel ≡	226	38.15 N	121.40 W
Sacramento South	226	38.32 N	121.26 W
Sacramento Valley V	204	39.15 N	122.00 W
Sacramento Wash V	200	34.43 N	114.28 W
Sacre ≃	248	12.56 S	58.18 W
Sacré-Cœur ᵿ[1]	261	48.53 N	2.21 E
Sacred Heart	198	44.47 N	95.21 W
Sacriston	44	54.49 N	1.37 W
Sacro, Monte ∧	68	40.13 N	15.20 E
Sacro Monte ᵿ[1]	62	45.49 N	8.15 E

Symbol	English	Deutsch	Español	Français	Português
≃	River	Fluß	Río	Rivière	Rio
≡	Canal	Kanal	Canal	Canal	Canal
↳	Waterfall, Rapids	Wasserfall, Stromschnellen	Cascada, Rápidos	Chute d'eau, Rapides	Cascata, Rápidos
ꓴ	Strait	Meeresstraße	Estrecho	Détroit	Estreito
c	Bay, Gulf	Bucht, Golf	Bahía, Golfo	Baie, Golfe	Baía, Golfo
⊜	Lake, Lakes	See, Seen	Lago, Lagos	Lac, Lacs	Lago, Lagos
⊞	Swamp	Sumpf	Pantano	Marais	Pântano
⊼	Ice Features, Glacier	Eis- und Gletscherformen	Accidentes Glaciales	Formes glaciaires	Acidentes glaciares
⊤	Other Hydrographic Features	Andere Hydrographische Objekte	Otros Elementos Hidrográficos	Autres données hydrographiques	Outros acidentes hidrográficos
✢	Submarine Features	Untermeerische Objekte	Accidentes Submarinos	Formes de relief sous-marin	Acidentes submarinos
□	Political Unit	Politische Einheit	Unidad Política	Entité politique	Unidade política
ᵿ	Cultural Institution	Kulturelle Institution	Institución Cultural	Institution culturelle	Instituição cultural
⊥	Historical Site	Historische Stätte	Sitio Histórico	Site historique	Sitio histórico
♦	Recreational Site	Erholungs- und Ferienort	Sitio de Recreo	Centre de loisirs	Area de Lazer
✈	Airport	Flughafen	Aeropuerto	Aéroport	Aeroporto
■	Military Installation	Militäranlage	Instalación Militar	Installation militaire	Instalação militar
✦	Miscellaneous	Verschiedenes	Misceláneo	Divers	Diversos

ENGLISH: Name | Page | Lat.°′ | Long.°′ — DEUTSCH: Name | Seite | Breite°′ | Länge°′ E = Ost

Name	Page	Lat.°′	Long.°′
Sacrow ◆[8]	264a	52.26 N	13.06 E
Sacrower-Paretzer Kanal ≋	264a	52.28 N	12.55 E
Sacrower See ⊜	264a	52.27 N	13.06 E
Săcueni	38	47.21 N	22.06 E
Sacul	222	31.50 N	94.56 W
Sacupana	246	8.35 N	61.39 W
Sada, Esp.	34	43.21 N	8.15 W
Sada, Nihon	96	35.15 N	132.43 E
Sádaba	34	42.17 N	1.16 W
Sadābād, India	124	27.27 N	78.03 E
Sa'dābād, Īrān	128	29.23 N	51.07 E
Sa'dābād, Īrān	128	34.51 N	50.36 E
Ṣadad	130	34.18 N	36.56 E
Ṣa'dah	144	16.52 N	43.37 E
Sadaik Taung ∧	110	15.09 N	98.12 E
Sadali	71	39.49 N	9.16 E
Sada-misaki >	96	33.20 N	132.01 E
Sada-misaki-hantō >[1]	96	33.26 N	132.13 E
Sadamitsu	96	34.02 N	134.04 E
Sadane ≃	115a	6.01 S	106.37 E
Sadang ≃	112	3.43 S	119.27 E
Sadanga	116	17.09 N	121.02 E
Sadani	154	6.03 S	38.47 E
Sadao	110	6.38 N	100.26 E
Sadarpur, Bngl.	126	23.28 N	90.02 E
Sādarpur, India	272a	28.33 N	77.21 E
Sadčikovka	86	53.01 N	63.27 E
Sadda	120	33.42 N	70.20 E
Saddle ≃	276	40.52 N	74.07 W
Saddleback, Mount ∧	168a	32.58 S	116.28 E
Saddle Brook	276	40.54 N	74.06 W
Saddlebunch Keys II	220	24.37 N	81.37 W
Saddle Lake Indian Reserve ◆[4]	182	54.00 N	111.40 W
Saddle Mountain ∧, Co., U.S.	200	38.50 N	105.28 W
Saddle Mountain ∧, Or., U.S.	224	45.58 N	123.41 W
Saddle Mountains ⩘	202	46.50 N	119.55 W
Saddle Mountain State Park ♠	224	45.58 N	123.41 W
Saddle Peak ∧	110	13.09 N	93.01 E
Saddle River	276	40.54 N	74.05 W
Saddle Rock	276	40.48 N	73.45 W
Saddleworth, Austl.	168b	34.05 S	138.47 E
Saddleworth, Eng., U.K.	262	53.33 N	1.59 W
Saddleworth Moor ◆[3]	262	53.33 N	1.57 W
Sa Dec	110	10.18 N	105.46 E
Sadelkow	54	53.36 N	13.26 E
Sādhaura	124	30.23 N	77.13 E
Sādhuhāti	126	23.34 N	89.01 E
Sadieville	218	38.23 N	84.32 W
Sadiola	150	13.53 N	11.42 W
Sādiqābād	120	28.18 N	70.08 E
Sadiya	120	27.50 N	95.40 E
Sa'dīyah, Wādī V	144	20.35 N	39.38 E
Sa'dīyāt, Ra's as- >	132	33.41 N	35.25 E
Sadler Lake ⊜	184	55.17 N	103.45 W
Sado I	92	38.00 N	138.25 E
Sado ≃	34	38.29 N	8.55 W
Sado-kaikyō)(	92	37.50 N	138.40 E
Sadon	84	42.51 N	44.00 E
Sadovoje, Ross.	80	46.56 N	44.23 E
Sadovoje, Ross.	80	47.46 N	44.30 E
Sadovoje Pervoje	78	51.33 N	40.29 E
Sadowara	92	32.02 N	131.26 E
Ṣādri	120	25.11 N	73.26 E
Šadrina	89	51.33 N	130.22 E
Šadrino	86	55.52 N	91.06 E
Šadrinsk	86	56.05 N	63.38 E
Sadsburyville	208	39.59 N	75.53 W
Sādulpur	123	28.38 N	75.24 E
Sădvaluspen	24	66.24 N	16.51 E
Sæby, Dan.	26	57.20 N	10.32 E
Sæby, Dan.	41	55.33 N	11.19 E
Saegertown	214	41.43 N	80.09 W
Sae Islands II	164	0.45 S	145.15 E
Saeki, Nihon	96	34.22 N	132.11 E
Saeki, Nihon	96	34.51 N	134.06 E
Saeki → Saiki, Nihon	96	32.57 N	131.54 E
Saengil-to I	98	34.19 N	126.59 E
Saerbeck	52	52.10 N	7.38 E
Saerluojia Hu ⊜	120	33.55 N	86.55 E
Særslev, Dan.	41	55.31 N	10.11 E
Særslev, Dan.	41	55.43 N	11.23 E
Saeul	56	49.44 N	5.59 E
Ṣafā, Tulūl aṣ- ∧[1]	132	33.02 N	37.12 E
Safad → Ẓefat	132	32.58 N	35.30 E
Safājah, Jazīrat I	140	26.45 N	33.59 E
Safakulevo	86	54.59 N	62.33 E
Ṣafānīyah	142	28.49 N	30.48 E
Safdar Jang Airport ⊠	272a	28.37 N	77.13 E
Safdar Jang's Tomb ⊥	272a	28.36 N	77.13 E
Safed Koh Range ⩘	123	33.58 N	70.25 E
Safe Harbor Dam ◆[6]	208	39.59 N	76.28 W
Safenbach ≃	61	47.06 N	16.05 E
Safety Bay	168a	32.18 S	115.43 E
Safety Harbor	220	27.59 N	82.41 W
Säffle	26	59.08 N	12.56 E
Safford	200	32.50 N	109.42 W
Saffron Walden	42	52.01 N	0.15 E
Safi	148	32.20 N	9.17 W
Safi □[4]	148	32.05 N	9.00 W
Safia	164	9.35 S	148.40 E
Ṣafīābād	128	36.45 N	57.58 E
Safīd ≃	120	36.44 N	65.38 E
Safīd Kūh, Selseleh-ye ⩘	128	34.30 N	63.30 E
Safidon	124	29.25 N	76.40 E
Safiental V	58	46.40 N	9.18 E
Safioune, Sebkhet ≡	148	32.16 N	5.27 E
Safipur	126	23.01 N	90.22 E
Ṣāfītā	130	34.49 N	36.07 E
Safonovo, Ross.	24	65.42 N	47.39 E
Safonovo, Ross.	76	55.06 N	33.15 E
Safonovo, Ross.	82	55.33 N	38.17 E
Safrakköyü ◆[8]	267b	41.00 N	28.47 E
Safranbolu	130	41.15 N	32.45 E
Ṣaft al-'Inab	142	30.49 N	30.41 E
Ṣaft al-Khammār	142	28.02 N	30.42 E
Ṣaft al-Laban	273c	30.02 N	31.10 E
Ṣaft al-Mulūk	142	30.49 N	30.41 E
Ṣaft Rāshīn	142	28.58 N	30.55 E
Ṣaft Turāb	142	30.54 N	31.07 E
Ṣafwān	128	30.07 N	47.43 E
Saga, Kaz.	86	50.23 N	64.15 E
Saga, Kaz.	86	49.25 N	55.17 E
Saga, Nihon	92	33.15 N	130.18 E
Saga, Nihon	96	33.05 N	133.06 E
Saga, Zhg.	120	29.30 N	85.22 E
Saga □[5]	96	33.21 N	130.28 E
Sagaba	152	11.17 S	23.07 E
Sagae	92	38.22 N	140.17 E
Sagaing	110	21.52 N	95.59 E
Sagaing □[8]	110	24.00 N	95.00 E
Sagak, Cape >	180	52.48 N	169.08 W
Sagalaherang	115a	6.40 S	107.39 E
Sagalakasa	80	46.54 N	50.43 E
Sagamāthā □[8]	124	27.15 N	86.45 E
Sagami ≃	94	35.19 N	139.22 E
Sagamihara	94	35.34 N	139.23 E
Sagamihara-daichi ⩘[1]	268	35.27 N	139.27 E
Sagamiko	94	35.37 N	139.12 E
Sagami-ko ⊜	94	35.35 N	139.16 E
Sagami-nada c	94	35.00 N	139.30 E
Sagami-wan c	94	35.15 N	139.25 E
Sagamore, Ma., U.S.	207	41.46 N	70.31 W
Sagamore, Pa., U.S.	214	40.46 N	79.13 W
Sagamore Beach	207	41.47 N	70.31 W
Sagamore Hill National Historic Site ⊥	276	40.53 N	73.30 W
Sagamore Hills	279a	41.02 N	81.26 W
Sagan → Żagań	30	51.37 N	15.19 E
Šagan ≃, Kaz.	86	50.37 N	79.15 E
Sagån ≃, Sve.	40	59.35 N	16.54 E
Saganaga Lake ⊜	190	48.14 N	90.52 W
Saganashkee Slough ≃	278	41.41 N	87.53 W
Saganash Lake ⊜	190	49.04 N	82.35 W
Saganoseki	96	33.15 N	131.53 E
Ṣaganthit Kyun I	110	11.56 N	98.29 E
Šagany, ozero ⊜	78	45.43 N	29.53 E
Sagaon	272c	19.12 N	73.06 E
Sāgar, India	122	14.10 N	75.02 E
Sāgar, India	124	23.50 N	78.43 E
Sagara	94	34.41 N	138.12 E
Sagaranten	115a	7.13 S	106.52 E
Sagard	54	54.31 N	13.33 E
Sāgardīghi	126	24.17 N	88.06 E
Sagaredžo	84	41.44 N	45.20 E
Sāgar Island I	126	21.43 N	88.06 E
Sagarmatha → Everest, Mount ∧	124	27.59 N	86.56 E
Sagarmatha National Park ♠	124	27.50 N	86.45 E
Sāgar Plateau ⩘[1]	124	23.30 N	78.30 E
Sagavanirktok ≃	180	70.20 N	148.00 W
Sagay	116	10.57 N	123.25 E
Sage, Mount ∧	240m	18.25 N	64.39 W
Sage Creek ≃, N.A.	202	48.58 N	110.06 W
Sage Creek ≃, U.S.	202	44.50 N	108.26 W
Sage Creek ≃, Mt., U.S.	202	47.16 N	109.43 W
Sage Creek ≃, Mt., U.S.	202	48.20 N	110.03 W
Sagemace Bay c	184	51.49 N	100.03 W
Sagerton	196	33.05 N	99.58 W
Saggaubach ≃	61	46.43 N	15.24 E
Sag Harbor	207	40.59 N	72.17 W
Ṣaghbīn	132	33.37 N	35.42 E
Ṣaghīr, Al-Baḥr aṣ- ≋	142	31.09 N	31.56 E
Sagil	86	50.20 N	91.40 E
Saginaw, Mi., U.S.	190	43.25 N	83.56 W
Saginaw, Tx., U.S.	222	32.52 N	97.22 W
Saginaw ≃	190	43.39 N	83.51 W
Saginaw Bay c	190	43.50 N	83.40 W
Sagiz, Kaz.	80	47.31 N	53.16 E
Sagiz, Kaz.	86	48.12 N	54.56 E
Sagiz ≃	86	47.32 N	53.20 E
Sağkaya	130	37.11 N	35.41 E
Sagleipie	150	7.00 N	8.52 W
Saglek Bay c	176	58.35 N	63.00 W
Šaglyteniz, ozero ⊜	86	54.08 N	69.52 E
Šagonar	86	51.32 N	92.48 E
Sagra ∧	34	37.57 N	2.34 W
Sagrado	64	45.52 N	13.29 E
Sagres	34	37.00 N	8.56 W
Sag Sag	164	5.35 S	148.20 E
Sagsaj	86	48.54 N	89.37 E
Sagsajn ≃	102	44.50 N	96.26 E
Sagu, Indon.	112	8.15 S	123.13 E
Ṣagu, Rom.	38	46.03 N	21.17 E
Saguache	200	38.05 N	106.05 W
Saguache Creek ≃	200	37.52 N	105.51 W
Sagua de Tánamo	240p	20.35 N	75.14 W
Sagua la Chica ≃	240p	22.45 N	79.39 W
Sagua la Grande	240p	22.49 N	80.05 W
Saguaro National Monument ♠	200	32.12 N	110.38 W
Saguenay ≃	176	48.08 N	69.44 W
Saguna	272b	22.59 N	88.29 E
Sagunay Lake	216	41.43 N	86.34 W
Sagunovka	78	49.17 N	32.23 E
Sagunt	34	39.41 N	0.16 W
Saguny	78	50.36 N	39.43 E
Sagutjevo	76	52.28 N	33.28 E
Sāgwāra	120	23.41 N	74.01 E
Sagy	261	49.03 N	1.57 E
Sa'gya	120	28.55 N	88.05 E
Sagyndyk, mys >	84	44.02 N	50.52 E
Sah	150	15.38 N	4.03 W
Saḥāb	132	31.53 N	36.00 E
Sahaba	140	18.55 N	30.28 E
Sahagún, Col.	246	8.57 N	75.27 W
Sahagún, Esp.	34	42.22 N	5.02 W
Saḥam	132	32.42 N	35.47 E
Saḥam al-Jawlān	132	32.46 N	35.56 E
Sahana Ambodipont	157b	14.37 S	50.11 E
Sahand, Kūh-e ∧	128	37.44 N	46.27 E
Sahara ◆[2]	10	26.00 N	13.00 E
Sahāranpur	124	29.58 N	77.33 E
Sahara Occidental → Western Sahara □[2]	148	24.30 N	13.00 W
Sahara Occidentale → Western Sahara □[2]	148	24.30 N	13.00 W
Saharsa	124	25.53 N	86.36 E
Sahasinaka	157b	21.49 S	47.49 E
Sahasrail	126	23.19 N	89.43 E
Sahaswān	124	28.05 N	78.45 E
Sahel — Sudan ◆[1]	134	10.00 N	20.00 E
Sahel, Canal du ≋	150	13.44 N	6.05 W
Sahel, Oued ≃	34	36.26 N	4.33 E
Sāhibabad	272a	28.40 N	77.22 E
Sahibābad ◆[8]	272a	28.45 N	77.05 E
Sāhibganj	124	25.15 N	87.39 E
Sāhibi ≃	124	28.29 N	76.44 E
Şahin	130	41.01 N	26.50 E
Sāhīwāl, Pāk.	123	30.40 N	73.06 E
Sāhīwāl, Pāk.	123	31.58 N	72.20 E
Sahlenburg	52	53.52 N	8.38 E
Ṣaḥneh	128	34.29 N	47.41 E
Ṣaḥrā', Bi'r ⊤[4]	140	22.52 N	28.37 E
Ṣahrajat al-Kubrā wa Kafr Jirjis Yūsuf	142	30.38 N	31.17 E
Sahtlam	224	48.48 N	123.54 W
Sahuaripa	232	29.03 N	109.14 W
Sahuarita	200	31.57 N	110.58 W
Sahuayo de José María Morelos	234	20.04 N	102.43 W
Sahul Shelf ✧[4]	14	12.30 S	125.00 E
Sa Huynh	110	14.40 N	109.04 E
Ṣahwat al-Qamḥ	132	32.36 N	36.23 E
Šahy	30	48.05 N	18.57 E
Saï	150	13.50 N	5.00 W
Sai ≃, India	124	25.39 N	82.47 E
Sai ≃, Nihon	94	36.36 N	136.35 E
Sai ≃, Nihon	94	36.37 N	138.14 E
Saibai Island I	164	9.24 S	142.40 E
Sai Buri	110	6.42 N	101.37 E
Sai Buri ≃	110	6.43 N	101.39 E
Saïda	148	34.50 N	0.09 E
Saïda □[5]	148	33.00 N	0.30 W
Saidābād, Bngl.	126	24.18 N	89.43 E
Sa'īdābād, Īrān	267d	35.40 N	51.11 E
Saidaiji	96	34.39 N	134.02 E
Saïdia	148	35.04 N	2.15 W
Sa'īdīyeh	128	36.26 N	48.48 E
Saido	268	35.52 N	139.41 E
Saidor	164	5.35 S	146.30 E
Saidpur, Bngl.	124	25.47 N	88.54 E
Saidpur, India	124	25.33 N	83.11 E
Saidu	123	34.45 N	72.21 E
Saigawa	96	33.39 N	130.57 E
Saignelégier	58	47.15 N	7.00 E
Saignon	62	43.52 N	5.26 E
Saigō	92	36.12 N	133.20 E
Saigon → Thanh Pho Ho Chi Minh	269c	10.45 N	106.40 E
Sai Gon ≃	269c	10.45 N	106.45 E
Saihaku	96	35.20 N	133.20 E
Saihan Toroi	102	41.41 N	100.26 E
Saijō, Nihon	96	33.55 N	133.11 E
Saijō, Nihon	96	34.56 N	133.07 E
Saijō	96	34.48 N	132.51 E
Saikai-kokuritsu-kōen ♠	92	33.12 N	129.22 E
Sai Keng	271d	22.26 N	114.16 E
Saiki	96	32.57 N	131.54 E
Saiki-wan c	96	33.00 N	131.58 E
Sai Kung	271d	22.23 N	114.15 E
Saileati	85	38.57 N	74.45 E
Sailkupa	126	23.41 N	89.15 E
Saillans	62	44.42 N	5.11 E
Sailly	261	49.02 N	1.48 E
Sailmouille, Ruisseau ≃	261	48.37 N	2.17 E
Sailolof	164	1.15 S	130.46 E
Sailor Creek ≃	202	42.56 N	115.29 W
Ṣail-sous-Couzan	62	45.44 N	3.57 E
Šaim	86	60.21 N	64.14 E
Saima	98	41.00 N	124.14 E
Saimaa ⊜	26	61.15 N	28.15 E
Saimaa Canal ≋	26	61.05 N	28.18 E
Saimbeyli	130	38.00 N	36.06 E
Saín Alto	234	23.35 N	103.15 W
Saindak	128	29.17 N	61.34 E
Ṣā'īn Dezh	128	36.40 N	46.33 E
Sainghin-en-Weppes	50	50.33 N	2.54 E
Sainjang	98	39.15 N	125.51 E
Sainō-ha'iji ⊥	96	35.29 N	133.39 E
Sains-du-Nord	50	50.06 N	4.00 E
Sains-en-Gohelle	50	50.27 N	2.41 E
Sains-Richaumont	50	49.49 N	3.42 E
Saint Abb's Head >	46	55.54 N	2.09 W
Sainte-Adèle	206	45.57 N	74.07 W
Sainte-Adresse	50	49.30 N	0.05 E
Saint-Adrien	206	45.49 N	71.43 W
Saint-Affrique	32	43.57 N	2.53 E
Saint-Agapit	206	46.34 N	71.27 W
Saint Agatha	212	43.26 N	80.36 W
Sainte-Agathe, Mb., Can.	184	49.34 N	97.10 W
Sainte-Agathe, Fr.	62	45.49 N	3.37 E
Sainte-Agathe [-de-Lotbinière]	206	46.23 N	71.24 W
Sainte-Agathe-des-Monts	206	46.03 N	74.17 W
Sainte-Agnès, Fr.	62	43.48 N	7.28 E
Saint Agnes, Eng., U.K.	42	50.18 N	5.13 W
Saint Agnes I	42a	49.54 N	6.20 W
Saint-Agrève	62	45.01 N	4.24 E
Saint-Aignan	50	47.16 N	1.23 E
Saint-Aimé (Massueville)	206	45.55 N	72.56 W
Saint Albans, Austl.	169	37.44 S	144.48 E
Saint Albans, Austl.	170	33.17 S	150.59 E
Saint Alban's, Nf., Can.	186	47.52 N	55.51 W
Saint Albans, Eng., U.K.	42	51.46 N	0.21 W
Saint Albans, Mo., U.S.	219	38.35 N	90.46 W
Saint Albans, Vt., U.S.	188	44.48 N	73.05 W
Saint Albans, W.V., U.S.	188	38.23 N	81.50 W
Saint Albans □[8]	260	51.45 N	0.20 W
Saint Albans ◆[8]	276	40.42 N	73.46 W
Saint Albans, Cape >	168b	35.49 S	138.07 E
Saint Albans Cathedral ✝[1]	260	51.45 N	0.20 W
Saint Albert, Ab., Can.	182	53.38 N	113.38 W
Saint-Albert, P.Q., Can.	206	46.00 N	72.05 W
Saint Aldhelm's Head >	42	50.34 N	2.04 W
Saint-Alexandre-de-Kamouraska	186	47.41 N	69.38 W
Saint-Alexis-des-Monts	206	46.28 N	73.08 W
Saint-Amable	275a	45.39 N	73.18 W
Saint-Amand	56	48.49 N	4.36 E
Saint-Amand-en-Puisaye	50	47.31 N	3.04 E
Saint-Amand-les-Eaux	50	50.26 N	3.26 E
Saint-Amand-Longpré	50	47.41 N	1.01 E
Saint-Amand-Montrond	32	46.44 N	2.30 E
Saint-Amant-Roche-Savine	62	45.34 N	3.38 E
Saint-Amarin	58	47.53 N	7.01 E
Saint-Ambroix	62	44.15 N	4.11 E
Sainte-Amélie	184	50.59 N	99.21 W
Saint-Amour	58	46.26 N	5.21 E
Saint-André	157c	20.57 S	55.39 E
Saint-André, Cap >	157b	16.11 S	44.27 E
Saint-André, Ruisseau ≃	275a	45.22 N	73.29 W
Saint-André-Avellin	206	45.43 N	75.03 W
Saint-André-de-l'Eure	50	48.54 N	1.17 E
Saint-André-de-Valborgne	62	44.09 N	3.41 E
St.-André-Est	206	45.34 N	74.20 W
Saint-André-les-Alpes	62	43.58 N	6.30 E
Saint-André-les-Vergers	50	48.17 N	4.03 E
Saint Andrew	241g	13.15 N	59.33 W
Saint Andrew, Mount ∧	241h	13.11 N	61.13 W
Saint Andrew Lakes ⊜	212	44.36 N	76.40 W
Saint Andrews, N.B., Can.	186	45.05 N	67.03 W
Saint Andrews, Scot., U.K.	46	56.20 N	2.48 W
Saint Andrews, S.C., U.S.	192	32.46 N	79.59 W
Saint Andrews Bay c	46	56.22 N	2.50 W
Saint Andrew's Cathedral ✝[1]	271c	1.18 N	103.51 E
Saint Andrews Channel)(	186	46.03 N	60.38 W
Saint Ann	219	38.43 N	90.22 W
Sainte-Anne, Guad.	241o	16.14 N	61.23 W
Saint Anne, Guernsey	43b	49.42 N	2.12 W
Sainte-Anne, Mart.	240e	14.26 N	60.53 W
Saint Anne, Il., U.S.	216	41.01 N	87.42 W
Sainte-Anne ≃	206	46.33 N	72.12 W
Saint Anne, Cathedral of ✝[1]	273b	4.18 S	15.19 E
Sainte Anne, Lac ⊜, Ab., Can.	182	53.43 N	114.27 W
Sainte-Anne, Lac ⊜, P.Q., Can.	186	50.05 N	67.50 W
Sainte-Anne-de-Beaupré	186	47.02 N	70.56 W
Sainte-Anne-de-Bellevue	275a	45.24 N	73.57 W
Sainte-Anne-de-la-Pérade	206	46.35 N	72.12 W
Sainte-Anne-de-Madawaska	186	47.15 N	68.02 W
Sainte-Anne-des-Chênes	184	49.40 N	96.40 W
Sainte-Anne-des-Monts	186	49.08 N	66.30 W
Sainte-Anne-des-Plaines	186	45.46 N	73.48 W
Saint Anne of the Congo ✝[1]	273b	4.16 S	15.17 E
Saint Anne's	44	53.45 N	3.02 W
Saint Anns Bay	241q	18.26 N	77.08 W
Saint Anns Bay c	186	46.20 N	60.30 W
Saint Ann's Head >	42	51.41 N	5.10 W
Saint-Anselme	186	46.37 N	70.58 W
Saint Ansgar	190	43.22 N	92.55 W
Saint-Anthème	62	45.31 N	3.55 E
Saint Anthony, N.B., Can.	186	46.22 N	64.45 W
Saint Anthony, Nf., Can.	186	51.22 N	55.35 W
Saint Anthony, Id., U.S.	202	43.57 N	111.40 W
Saint-Antoine, P.Q., Can.	206	45.46 N	73.59 W
Saint-Antoine, Fr.	62	45.10 N	5.13 E
Saint-Antonin	32	44.09 N	1.45 E
Saint-Apollinaire (Francoeur)	206	46.37 N	71.31 W
Saint Arnaud, Austl.	166	36.37 S	143.15 E
Saint Arnaud, N.Z.	172	41.48 S	172.50 E
Saint-Arnoult, Forêt de ♠	261	48.35 N	1.55 E
Saint-Arnoult-en-Yvelines	50	48.34 N	1.56 E
Saint Arvans	42	51.40 N	2.41 W
Saint Asaph	44	53.16 N	3.26 W
Saint-Astier	32	45.09 N	0.32 E
Saint Athan	42	51.24 N	3.25 W
Saint-Auban	62	43.51 N	6.44 E
Saint-Aubert, Mont ∧[2]	50	50.39 N	3.24 E
Saint Aubert Island I	219	38.40 N	91.52 W
Saint-Aubin, Fr.	50	49.53 N	0.53 E
Saint-Aubin, Fr.	58	47.02 N	5.20 E
Saint Aubin, Jersey	43b	49.11 N	2.10 W
Saint-Aubin, Schw.	58	46.54 N	6.47 E
Saint-Aubin-lès-Elbeuf	50	49.18 N	1.01 E
Saint-Aubin-sur-Aire	58	48.42 N	5.27 E
Saint-Augustin	157b	23.33 S	43.46 E
Saint-Augustin ≃	176	51.14 N	58.41 W
Saint-Augustin-Deux-Montagnes	275a	45.38 N	73.59 W
Saint Augustine	192	29.53 N	81.18 W
Saint-Augustin Nord-Ouest ≃	186	51.16 N	58.42 W
Saint-Augustin-Saguenay	186	51.14 N	58.39 W
Saint-Aulaye	32	45.12 N	0.08 E
Saint Austell	42	50.20 N	4.48 W
Saint-Avertin	50	47.22 N	0.44 E
Saint-Avold	56	49.06 N	6.42 E
Saint-Ay	50	47.51 N	1.45 E
Saint-Aygulf	62	43.23 N	6.44 E
Saint Barbe	186	51.12 N	56.46 W
Saint Barnabas Chapel ✝[1]	174c	29.02 S	167.55 E
Saint-Barthélemy I	238	17.54 N	62.50 W
Saint-Basile	186	47.21 N	68.14 W
Saint-Basile-de-Portneuf	206	46.45 N	71.49 W
Saint-Basile-le-Grand	206	45.32 N	73.17 W
Saint Bathans, Mount ∧	172	44.44 S	169.46 E
Sainte-Baume, Chaîne de la ⩘	62	43.20 N	5.45 E
Saint-Béat	32	42.55 N	0.42 E
Saint Bees	44	54.30 N	3.37 W
Saint Bees Head >	44	54.32 N	3.38 W
Saint Benedict	214	40.38 N	78.44 W
Saint-Benoît, Fr.	261	48.40 N	1.55 E
Saint-Benoît, Réu.	157c	21.02 S	55.43 E
Saint-Benoît-du-Sault	32	46.27 N	1.23 E
Saint-Benoît-en-Woëvre	56	48.59 N	5.47 E
Saint Bernard	218	39.10 N	84.29 W
Saint-Bernard, Île I	275a	45.23 N	73.45 W
Saint-Bernard-de-Dorchester	206	46.30 N	71.08 W
Saint-Béron	62	45.30 N	5.43 E
Saint-Blaise, P.Q., Can.	206	45.13 N	73.17 W
Saint-Blaise, Schw.	58	47.01 N	6.59 E
Saint-Blaise-la-Roche	58	48.24 N	7.10 E
Saint Blaize, Cape >	158	34.11 S	22.10 E
Saint Blazey	42	50.22 N	4.43 W
Saint-Blin	58	48.16 N	5.25 E
Saint-Bonaventure, P.Q., Can.	206	45.58 N	72.41 W
Saint Bonaventure, N.Y., U.S.	210	42.05 N	78.28 W
Saint-Boniface-de-Shawinigan	206	46.30 N	72.49 W
Saint-Bonnet	62	44.41 N	6.05 E
Saint-Bonnet-de-Joux	58	46.29 N	4.27 E
Saint-Bonnet-le-Château	62	45.25 N	4.04 E
Saint-Bonnet-le-Froid	62	45.09 N	4.27 E
Saint Boswells	46	55.34 N	2.39 W
Saint Brendan's	186	48.52 N	53.40 W
Saint-Brice-sous-Forêt	261	49.00 N	2.21 E
Saint Bride, Mount ∧	182	51.30 N	115.57 W
Saint Bride's	186	46.55 N	54.10 W
Saint Brides Bay c	42	51.48 N	5.15 W
Saint Bride's Major	42	51.28 N	3.38 W
Saint-Brieuc	32	48.31 N	2.47 W
Saint-Brieux	184	52.38 N	104.52 W
Saint-Broing-les-Moines	58	47.41 N	4.50 E
Saint-Bruno	206	45.32 N	73.21 W
Saint-Bruno, Mont ∧[2]	275a	45.33 N	73.19 W
Saint-Calais	50	47.55 N	0.45 E
Saint-Calixte-de-Kilkenny	206	45.57 N	73.51 W
Saint-Cannat	62	43.37 N	5.18 E
Saint-Casimir	206	46.40 N	72.08 W
Saint-Cassien, Lac de ⊜[1]	62	43.35 N	6.48 E
Saint Catharines	212	43.10 N	79.15 W
Saint Catharines Airport ⊠	284a	43.11 N	79.10 W
Saint Catherine	220	28.37 N	82.08 W
Saint Catherine, Monastery of → Qiddīsah Kātrīnā, Dayr al- ✝[1]	140	28.29 N	34.01 E
Saint Catherine, Mount ∧	241k	12.10 N	61.40 W
Sainte-Catherine-de-Fierbois	50	47.09 N	0.39 E
Saint Catherines Island I	192	31.38 N	81.10 W
Saint Catherine's Point >	42	50.34 N	1.15 W
Saint-Célestin (Annaville)	206	46.13 N	72.26 W
Saint-Céré	32	44.52 N	1.53 E
Saint-Cergue	58	46.27 N	6.09 E
Saint-Césaire	206	45.25 N	73.00 W
Saint-Cézaire-sur-Siagne	62	43.39 N	6.48 E
Saint-Chamas	62	43.33 N	5.02 E
Saint-Chamond	62	45.28 N	4.30 E
Saint-Chaptes	62	43.58 N	4.17 E
Saint Charles, Ar., U.S.	194	34.22 N	91.08 W
Saint Charles, Id., U.S.	202	42.06 N	111.23 W
Saint Charles, Il., U.S.	216	41.54 N	88.18 W
Saint Charles, Md., U.S.	208	38.36 N	76.56 W
Saint Charles, Mi., U.S.	190	43.17 N	84.08 W
Saint Charles, Mn., U.S.	190	43.58 N	92.03 W
Saint Charles, Mo., U.S.	219	38.47 N	90.28 W
Saint Charles □[6]	219	38.47 N	90.43 W
Saint-Charles, Lac ⊜	206	46.55 N	71.23 W
Saint-Charles-de-Drummond	206	45.54 N	72.28 W
Saint Charles Mesa	198	38.15 N	104.32 W
Saint-Charles-sur-Richelieu	206	45.41 N	73.11 W
Saint-Chef	62	45.38 N	5.22 E
Saint-Chély-d'Apcher	32	44.48 N	3.17 E
Saint-Chéron	261	48.33 N	2.07 E
Saint-Christophe-en-Bazelle	50	47.11 N	1.43 E
Saint-Christophe-Nevis → Saint Kitts and Nevis □[1]	238	17.20 N	62.45 W
Saint Christopher (Saint Kitts) I	238	17.20 N	62.45 W
Saint Christopher-Nevis → Saint Kitts and Nevis □[1]	238	17.20 N	62.45 W
Saint-Chrysostome	206	45.06 N	73.46 W
Saint-Ciers-sur-Gironde	32	45.18 N	0.37 W
Saint Clair, Mi., U.S.	214	42.48 N	82.29 W
Saint Clair, Mo., U.S.	219	38.20 N	90.58 W
Saint Clair, Pa., U.S.	208	40.43 N	76.11 W
Saint Clair, Pa., U.S.	279b	40.16 N	79.33 W
Saint Clair □[6], Il., U.S.	219	38.31 N	90.00 W
Saint Clair □[6], Mi., U.S.	214	42.50 N	82.42 W
Saint Clair ≃	214	42.37 N	82.31 W
Saint Clair, Lake ⊜	214	42.25 N	82.41 W
Saint Clair Beach	281	42.19 N	82.51 W
Saint Clair Flats	214	42.32 N	82.37 W
Saint Clair Flats ≚	281	42.35 N	82.36 W
Saint Clair Flats Canal ≋	214	42.20 N	82.58 W
Saint Clair Flats State Wildlife Area ◆[4]	281	42.36 N	82.40 W
Saint Clair Haven	214	42.34 N	82.47 W
Saint Clair Shores	214	42.29 N	82.53 W
Saint-Clair-sur-Epte	50	49.12 N	1.41 E
Saint Clairsville, Oh., U.S.	214	40.04 N	80.54 W
Saint Clairsville, Pa., U.S.	214	40.09 N	78.31 W
Saint Clair Tunnel ◆[5]	214	42.57 N	82.25 W
Saint-Claud	32	45.53 N	0.23 E
Saint-Claude, Mb., Can.	184	49.40 N	98.22 W
Saint-Claude, Fr.	58	46.23 N	5.52 E
Saint-Claude, Guad.	241o	16.02 N	61.42 W
Saint-Claude, Ruisseau ≃	275a	45.25 N	73.28 W
Saint Clears	42	51.50 N	4.30 W
Saint-Clément	58	48.32 N	6.36 E
Saint Clements	212	43.31 N	80.39 W
Saint Clements Bay c	208	38.17 N	76.42 W
Sainte-Clothilde	206	45.59 N	72.14 W
Sainte-Clotilde-de-Châteauguay	206	45.10 N	73.41 W
Saint-Cloud, Fr.	50	48.50 N	2.11 E
Saint Cloud, Fl., U.S.	220	28.14 N	81.16 W
Saint Cloud, Mn., U.S.	190	45.33 N	94.09 W
Saint-Cloud, Parc de ♠	261	48.50 N	2.13 E
Saint-Colomban-des-Villards	62	45.18 N	6.14 E
Sainte-Colombe	58	47.52 N	4.32 E
Saint Columb Major	42	50.26 N	4.56 W
Saint Combs	46	57.39 N	1.54 W
Saint-Constant	206	45.22 N	73.37 W
Saint-Cosme-en-Vairais	50	48.16 N	0.28 E
Sainte-Croix, P.Q., Can.	206	46.38 N	71.44 W
Sainte-Croix, Schw.	58	46.49 N	6.31 E
Saint Croix I	241n	17.45 N	64.45 W
Saint Croix ≃, N.A.	186	45.10 N	67.10 W
Saint Croix ≃, U.S.	190	44.45 N	92.49 W
Sainte-Croix, Barrage de ◆[6]	62	43.45 N	6.08 E
Sainte-Croix-aux-Mines	58	48.16 N	7.13 E
Saint Croix Falls	190	45.24 N	92.38 W
Saint Croix Island I	158	33.48 S	25.45 E
Saint Croix Island National Monument ♠	188	45.08 N	67.08 W
Saint Croix National Scenic Riverway ♠	190	46.00 N	92.25 W
Saint Croix State Park ♠	190	46.00 N	92.40 W
Sainte-Croix-Vallée-Francaise	62	44.11 N	3.44 E
Saint-Cuthbert	206	46.09 N	73.14 W
Saint-Cyprien	32	44.52 N	1.02 E
Saint-Cyrille-de-Wendover	206	45.56 N	72.26 W
Saint-Cyr-l'École	50	48.48 N	2.04 E
Saint-Cyr-l'École, Aérodrome de ⊠	261	48.49 N	2.04 E
Saint Cyr Range ⩘	180	61.10 N	131.10 W
Sainte-Cyr-sous-Dourdan	261	48.34 N	2.02 E
Saint-Cyr-sur-Loire	50	47.24 N	0.40 E
Saint-Cyr-sur-Mer	62	43.11 N	5.43 E
Saint-Dalmas-de-Tende	62	44.03 N	7.35 E
Saint-Damien-de-Brandon	206	46.20 N	73.29 W
Saint David, Az., U.S.	200	31.54 N	110.12 W
Saint David, Il., U.S.	190	40.29 N	90.02 W
Saint David's, Nf., Can.	186	48.12 N	58.52 W
Saint Davids, On., Can.	284a	43.10 N	79.06 W
Saint David's, Wales, U.K.	42	51.54 N	5.16 W
Saint Davids, Pa., U.S.	285	40.02 N	75.22 W
Saint David's Cathedral ✝[1]	42	51.54 N	5.16 W
Saint David's Head >	42	51.55 N	5.19 W
Saint David's Island I	240a	32.22 N	64.39 W
Saint Day	42	50.14 N	5.11 W
Saint-Denis, Fr.	50	48.56 N	2.22 E
Saint-Denis, Réu.	157c	20.52 S	55.28 E
Saint-Denis, Basilique ✝[1]	261	48.56 N	2.22 E
Saint-Denis-de-l'Hôtel	50	47.52 N	2.07 E
Saint-Denis-en-Bugey	58	45.57 N	5.20 E
Saint-Denis-Rivière-Richelieu	206	45.47 N	73.09 W
Saint Dennis	42	50.23 N	4.53 W
Saint-Didier-en-Velay	62	45.18 N	4.17 E
Saint-Didier-les-Bains	62	44.00 N	5.07 E
Saint-Dié	58	48.17 N	6.57 E
Saint-Disdier	62	44.44 N	5.54 E
Saint-Dizier	58	48.38 N	4.57 E
Saint Dogmaels	42	52.05 N	4.40 W
Saint-Donat-de-Montcalm	206	46.19 N	74.13 W
Saint-Donat-sur-l'Herbasse	62	45.07 N	5.00 E
Sainte-Dorothée ◆[8]	275a	45.32 N	73.49 W
Saint-Dyé-sur-Loire	50	47.39 N	1.29 E
Saint-Édouard-de-Maskinongé	206	46.20 N	73.09 W
Saint Edward	198	41.34 N	97.52 W
Saint-Égrève	62	45.14 N	5.41 E
Saint Eleanor's	186	46.25 N	63.49 W
Saint Elias, Cape >	180	59.52 N	144.30 W
Saint Elias, Mount ∧	180	60.18 N	140.55 W
Saint Elias Mountains ⩘	180	60.30 N	139.30 W
Saint-Élie	250	4.50 N	53.17 W
Saint Elmo	219	39.01 N	88.50 W
Saint-Éloi	186	48.02 N	69.14 W
Saint-Émile-de-Montcalm	206	46.06 N	74.00 W
Saint-Émile-de-Québec	206	46.52 N	71.20 W
Saint-Émile-de-Suffolk	206	45.56 N	74.55 W
Sainte-Enimie	32	44.22 N	3.26 E
Saint-Épain	50	47.08 N	0.32 E
Saint-Esprit	206	45.52 N	73.27 W
Saint-Étienne	62	45.26 N	4.24 E
Saint-Étienne-de-Lugdarès	62	44.39 N	3.57 E
Saint-Étienne-de-Saint-Geoirs	62	45.20 N	5.21 E
Saint-Étienne-des-Grès	206	46.26 N	72.46 W
Saint-Étienne-de-Tinée	62	44.15 N	6.55 E
Saint-Étienne-du-Rouvray	50	49.23 N	1.06 E
Saint-Étienne-en-Dévoluy	62	44.42 N	5.56 E
Saint-Étienne-le-Laus	62	44.30 N	6.10 E
Saint-Étienne-les-Orgues	62	44.03 N	5.47 E
Saint-Étienne-lès-Remiremont	58	48.02 N	6.37 E
Saint-Eugène	206	45.30 N	74.28 W
Saint-Eustache	206	45.34 N	73.54 W
Saint-Evroult-Notre-Dame-du-Bois	50	48.48 N	0.28 E
Saint-Fabien	186	48.18 N	68.52 W
Saint Faith's	158	30.30 S	30.12 E
Saint-Fargeau	50	47.38 N	3.04 E
Saint-Fargeau-Ponthierry	261	48.33 N	2.32 E
Saint-Félicien, P.Q., Can.	176	48.39 N	72.26 W
Saint-Félicien, Fr.	62	45.05 N	4.38 E
Sainte-Félicité	186	48.54 N	67.20 W
Saint-Félix	62	45.48 N	5.58 E
Saint-Félix-de-Kingsey	206	45.48 N	72.12 W
Saint-Félix-de-Valois	206	46.10 N	73.26 W
Saint-Ferdinand (Bernierville)	206	46.06 N	71.34 W
Saintfield	48	54.28 N	5.50 W
Saint Fillans	46	56.23 N	4.07 W
Saint-Firmin	62	44.47 N	6.02 E
Saint-Firmin-sur-Loire	50	47.37 N	2.44 E
Saint-Flavien	206	46.31 N	71.36 W
Saint-Florent	36	42.41 N	9.18 E
Saint-Florentin	50	48.00 N	3.44 E
Saint-Florent-sur-Cher	32	46.59 N	2.15 E
Saint-Floris, Parc National ♠	146	9.40 N	21.35 E
Saint-Flour	32	45.02 N	3.05 E
Saint-Fons	62	45.42 N	4.52 E
Saint-Fortunat	206	45.58 N	71.36 W
Sainte-Foy	206	46.47 N	71.17 W
Sainte-Foy-la-Grande	32	44.50 N	0.13 E
Sainte-Foy-l'Argentière	62	45.42 N	4.28 E
Sainte-Foy-lès-Lyon	62	45.44 N	4.48 E
Sainte-Foy-Tarentaise	62	45.35 N	6.53 E
Saint Francis, Ks., U.S.	198	39.46 N	101.47 W
Saint Francis, S.D., U.S.	198	43.08 N	100.54 W
Saint Francis, Wi., U.S.	216	42.58 N	87.52 W
Saint Francis ≃, N.A.	186	47.10 N	68.57 W
Saint Francis ≃, U.S.	194	34.38 N	90.35 W
Saint Francis, Cape >, Nf., Can.	186	47.50 N	52.47 W
Saint Francis, Cape >, S. Afr.	158	34.14 S	24.49 E
Saint Francis, Lake ⊜	206	45.08 N	74.25 W
Saint Francis Bay c	158	34.35 S	25.10 E
Saint Francisville	194	30.46 N	91.22 W
Saint-François	241o	16.15 N	61.17 W
Saint-François ≃	206	46.07 N	72.55 W
Saint-François, Lac ⊜	206	45.55 N	71.10 W
Saint-François de Boundji	152	1.03 S	15.22 E
Saint-François-de-Laval ◆[8]	275a	45.40 N	73.34 W
Saint-François-du-Lac	206	46.04 N	72.50 W
Saint Francois Mountains ⩘[2]	194	37.30 N	90.35 W
Saint-François-sur-Bugeon	62	45.24 N	6.21 E
Saint-Front	62	44.59 N	4.08 E
Saint-Gabriel	206	46.17 N	73.23 W
Saint-Gabriel-de-Gaspé	186	48.31 N	64.32 W
Saint-Gabriel-de-Rimouski	186	48.25 N	68.10 W
Saint-Gall → Sankt Gallen	58	47.25 N	9.23 E
Saint-Galmier	62	45.35 N	4.19 E
Sainte-Gauburge-Sainte-Colombe	50	48.42 N	0.26 E
Saint-Gaudens	32	43.07 N	0.44 E
Saint-Gaudens National Historic Site ⊥	188	43.29 N	72.19 W
Saint-Gaultier	32	46.38 N	1.25 E
Saint-Gély-du-Fesc	62	43.42 N	3.48 E
Saint-Genest-Lerpt	62	45.27 N	4.20 E
Saint-Genest-Malifaux	62	45.20 N	4.25 E
Sainte-Geneviève, P.Q., Can.	275a	45.29 N	73.52 W
Sainte Genevieve, Mo., U.S.	194	37.59 N	90.03 W
Sainte-Geneviève-de-Batiscan	206	46.32 N	72.20 W
Sainte-Geneviève-des-Bois	50	48.38 N	2.20 E
Saint-Gengoux-le-National	58	46.37 N	4.39 E
Saint-Genis-de-Saintonge	32	45.29 N	0.34 W
Saint-Genis-Laval	62	45.41 N	4.48 E
Saint-Genis-Pouilly	58	46.15 N	6.01 E
Saint-Genix-sur-Guiers	62	45.36 N	5.38 E
Saint-Geoire-en-Valdaine	62	45.27 N	5.38 E
Saint George, Austl.	166	28.02 S	148.35 E
Saint George, Ber.	240a	32.22 N	64.40 W
Saint George, N.B., Can.	186	45.08 N	66.49 W
Saint George, On., Can.	212	43.15 N	80.15 W
Saint George, Pa., U.S.	214	41.15 N	79.47 W
Saint George, S.C., U.S.	192	33.11 N	80.34 W
Saint George, Ut., U.S.	200	37.06 N	113.34 W
Saint George ◆[8]	276	40.39 N	74.05 W
Saint George, Cape >, Nf., Can.	186	48.27 N	59.15 W
Saint George, Cape >, Pap. N. Gui.	164	4.52 S	152.52 E
Saint George, Cape >, Fl., U.S.	192	29.35 N	85.04 W
Saint George, Point >	204	41.47 N	124.15 W
Saint George Island, Ak., U.S.	180	56.36 N	169.32 W
Saint George Island, Md., U.S.	208	38.07 N	76.29 W
Saint George Island I, Ak., U.S.	180	56.35 N	169.35 W
Saint George Island I, Fl., U.S.	192	29.39 N	84.55 W
Saint George's, Nf., Can.	186	48.26 N	58.29 W
Saint-Georges, P.Q., Can.	186	46.07 N	70.40 W
Saint-Georges, P.Q., Can.	206	46.37 N	72.40 W
Saint-Georges, Fr.	58	48.40 N	6.56 E
Saint George's, Gren.	241k	12.03 N	61.45 W
Saint-Georges, Guy. fr.	250	3.54 N	51.48 W
Saint Georges, De., U.S.	208	39.33 N	75.39 W

Symbols in the index entries represent the broad categories identified in the key at the right. Symbols with superior numbers (⩘[1]) identify subcategories (see complete key on page I · 1).

Symbole im Register stellen die rechts im Schlüssel erklärten Kategorien dar. Symbole mit hochgestellten Ziffern (⩘[1]) bezeichnen Unterabteilungen einer Kategorie (vgl. vollständiger Schlüssel auf Seite I · 1).

Los símbolos incluidos en el texto del índice representan las grandes categorías identificadas con la clave a la derecha. Los símbolos con numeros en su parte superior (⩘[1]) identifican las subcategorías (véase la clave completa en la página I · 1).

Les symboles de l'index représentent les catégories indiquées dans la légende à droite. Les symboles suivis d'un indice (⩘[1]) représentent des sous-catégories (voir légende complète à la page I · 1).

Os símbolos incluídos no texto do índice representam as grandes categorias identificadas com a chave à direita. Os símbolos com números em sua parte superior (⩘[1]) identificam as subcategorias (veja-se a chave completa à página I · 1).

English	Deutsch	Español	Français	Português
∧ Mountain	Berg	Montaña	Montagne	Montanha
⩘ Mountains	Gebirge	Montañas	Montagnes	Montanhas
)(Pass	Paß	Paso	Col	Passo
V Valley, Canyon	Tal, Cañon	Valle, Cañon	Vallée, Canyon	Vale, Canhão
≚ Plain	Ebene	Llano	Plaine	Planície
> Cape	Kap	Cabo	Cap	Cabo
I Island	Insel	Isla	Île	Ilha
II Islands	Inseln	Islas	Îles	Ilhas
⊥ Other Topographic Features	Andere Topographische Objekte	Otros Elementos Topográficos	Autres données topographiques	Outros acidentes topográficos

ESPAÑOL — Nombre | Página | Lat.°′ | Long.°′ W = Oeste
FRANÇAIS — Nom | Page | Lat.°′ | Long.°′ W = Ouest
PORTUGUÊS — Nome | Página | Lat.°′ | Long.°′ W = Oeste

Nombre / Nom / Nome	Página / Page	Lat.°′	Long.°′
Saint Georges Basin ᑕ	170	35.07 S	150.36 E
Saint George's Bay ᑕ, Nf., Can.	186	48.20 N	59.00 W
Saint Georges Bay ᑕ, N.S., Can.	186	45.50 N	61.45 W
Saint George's Channel Ʉ, Europe	28	52.00 N	6.00 W
Saint George's Channel Ʉ, Pap. N. Gui.	164	4.30 S	152.30 E
Saint-Georges-de-Reneins	58	46.04 N	4.43 E
Saint-Georges-de-Windsor	206	45.42 N	71.50 W
Saint-Georges-en-Couzan	62	45.42 N	3.56 E
Saint Georges Head ›	170	35.12 S	150.42 E
Saint George's Island I	240a	32.22 N	64.40 W
Saint George Sound Ʉ	192	29.47 N	84.42 W
Saint-Gérard, Bel.	56	50.21 N	4.45 E
Saint-Gérard, P.Q., Can.	206	45.46 N	71.25 W
Saint-Germain ≃	206	45.55 N	72.30 W
Saint-Germain, Forêt de ♠	261	48.55 N	2.05 E
Saint-Germain-de-Calberte	62	44.13 N	3.48 E
Saint-Germain-de-Grantham	206	45.50 N	72.34 W
Saint-Germain-de-Joux	58	46.11 N	5.44 E
Saint-Germain-des-Champs	50	47.25 N	3.55 E
Saint-Germain-du-Bois	58	46.45 N	5.15 E
Saint-Germain-du-Plain	58	46.42 N	4.58 E
Saint-Germain-en-Laye	50	48.54 N	2.05 E
Saint-Germain-en-Laye, Château de ⊥	261	48.54 N	2.06 E
Saint-Germain-Laval	62	45.50 N	4.01 E
Saint-Germain-Laxis	261	48.35 N	2.43 E
Saint-Germain-Lembron	32	45.28 N	3.14 E
Saint-Germain-lès-Arlay	58	46.46 N	5.34 E
Saint-Germain-lès-Corbeil	261	48.37 N	2.29 E
Saint-Germain-l'Herm	32	45.28 N	3.33 E
Saint-Germain-sur-Morin	261	48.53 N	2.51 E
Saint Germans	42	50.24 N	4.18 W
Saint-Germer-de-Fly	50	49.27 N	1.47 E
Saint-Gervais-d'Auvergne	32	46.02 N	2.49 E
Saint-Gervais-les-Bains	62	45.54 N	6.43 E
Saint-Gervasy	62	43.53 N	4.29 E
Saint-Géry	32	44.29 N	1.35 E
Saint-Gilles, Bel.	50	50.49 N	4.20 E
Saint-Gilles, P.Q., Can.	206	46.31 N	71.22 W
Saint-Gilles, Fr.	62	43.41 N	4.26 E
Saint-Gilles-Croix-de-Vie	32	46.42 N	1.57 W
Saint-Gingolph	58	46.24 N	6.52 E
Saint-Girons	32	42.59 N	1.09 E
Saint-Gobain	50	49.36 N	3.23 E
Saint Gotthard Pass → San Gottardo, Passo del)(	58	46.33 N	8.34 E
Saint Govan's Head ›	42	51.36 N	4.55 W
Saint-Gratien	261	48.58 N	2.17 E
Saint-Grégoire (Larochelle)	206	46.16 N	72.30 W
Saint Gregory, Mount ∧	186	49.19 N	58.13 W
Saint-Guénolé	32	47.49 N	4.20 W
Saint-Guillaume-d'Upton	206	45.53 N	72.46 W
Saint-Héand	62	45.31 N	4.22 E
Saint Helena	226	38.30 N	122.28 W
Saint Helena □[2]	10	15.57 S	5.42 W
Saint Helena, Mount ∧	226	38.40 N	122.38 W
Saint Helena Sound Ʉ	192	32.27 N	80.25 W
Sainte-Hélène, Île I	275a	45.31 N	73.32 W
Sainte-Hélène-de-Bagot	206	45.44 N	72.44 W
Saint Helens, Austl.	166	41.20 S	148.15 E
Saint Helens, Eng., U.K.	42	50.42 N	1.06 W
Saint Helens, Eng., U.K.	44	53.28 N	2.44 W
Saint Helens, Or., U.S.	224	45.51 N	122.48 W
Saint Helens □[8]	262	53.28 N	2.45 W
Saint Helens, Mount ∧[1]	224	46.12 N	122.11 W
Saint Helens Canal ≊	262	53.27 N	2.42 W
Saint Helier	43b	49.11 N	2.06 W
Saint Henry	216	40.25 N	84.38 W
Sainte-Hermine	32	46.33 N	1.04 W
Saint-Hilaire-du-Harcouët	32	48.35 N	1.06 W
Saint-Hilarion	261	48.37 N	1.44 E
Saint-Hippolyte, Fr.	58	47.19 N	6.49 E
Saint-Hippolyte, Fr.	62	43.38 N	4.45 E
Saint-Hippolyte-de-Kilkenny	206	45.56 N	74.01 W
Saint-Hippolyte-du-Fort	62	43.58 N	3.51 E
Saint-Honorat, Mont ∧	62	44.05 N	6.46 E
Saint-Hubert, Bel.	56	50.01 N	5.23 E
Saint-Hubert, P.Q., Can.	206	45.30 N	73.25 W
Saint-Hubert, Étang de ⊜	261	48.43 N	1.51 E
Saint-Hubert-le-Roi	261	48.43 N	1.52 E
Saint-Hugues	206	45.48 N	72.52 W
Saint-Hyacinthe	206	45.37 N	72.57 W
Saint-Hyacinthe □[6]	206	45.40 N	73.05 W
Saint-Ignace, N.B., Can.	186	46.42 N	65.05 W
Saint Ignace, Mi., U.S.	190	45.52 N	84.43 W
Saint Ignace Island I	190	48.48 N	87.55 W
Saint Ignatius, Guy.	246	3.20 N	59.47 W
Saint Ignatius, Mt., U.S.	202	47.19 N	114.05 W
Saint-Imier	58	47.09 N	7.00 E
Saint-Imier, Vallon de V	58	47.10 N	7.00 E
Saint-Isidore	186	47.33 N	65.03 W
Saint-Isidore-d'Auckland	206	45.16 N	71.31 W
Saint-Isidore-de-Laprairie	275a	45.18 N	73.41 W
Saint Ives, Austl.	274a	33.44 S	151.10 E
Saint Ives, Eng., U.K.	32	50.12 N	5.29 W
Saint Ives, Eng., U.K.	42	52.20 N	0.05 W
Saint Ives Bay ᑕ	42	50.14 N	5.28 W
Saint Jacob	219	38.43 N	89.46 W
Saint Jacobs	212	43.32 N	80.33 W
Saint-Jacques	206	45.57 N	73.34 W
Saint-Jacques ≃	275a	45.26 N	73.29 W
Saint James, Il., U.S.	219	38.57 N	88.51 W
Saint James, Mi., U.S.	190	45.45 N	85.30 W
Saint James, Mn., U.S.	198	43.58 N	94.37 W
Saint James, Mo., U.S.	194	37.59 N	91.36 W
Saint James, N.Y., U.S.	210	40.52 N	73.09 W
Saint James, Cape ›	182	51.56 N	131.01 W
Saint James City	220	26.29 N	82.04 W
Saint James Islands II	240m	18.19 N	64.50 W
Saint-Janvier	275a	45.43 N	73.56 W
Saint-Jean □[6]	206	45.15 N	73.20 W
Saint-Jean ≃, P.Q., Can.	186	48.46 N	64.26 W
Saint-Jean ≃, P.Q., Can.	186	50.17 N	64.20 W
Saint-Jean, Île I	275a	45.41 N	73.39 W
Saint-Jean, Lac ⊜	176	48.35 N	72.05 W
Saint-Jean, Rapides de ∟	275a	45.19 N	73.15 W
Saint-Jean Airport ⊠	275a	45.18 N	73.17 W
Saint-Jean-aux-Bois	50	49.21 N	2.55 E
Saint-Jean-Baptiste	184	49.16 N	97.21 W
Saint-Jean-Baptiste-de-Rouville	206	45.31 N	73.07 W
Saint-Jean-Cap-Ferrat	62	43.41 N	7.20 E
Saint-Jean-d'Angély	32	45.57 N	0.31 W
Saint-Jean-d'Assé	50	48.09 N	0.07 E
Saint-Jean-de-Bournay	62	45.29 N	5.08 E
Saint-Jean-de-Braye	50	47.54 N	1.58 E
Saint-Jean-de-la-Roulle	50	47.55 N	1.52 E
Saint-Jean-de-Losne	58	47.06 N	5.15 E
Saint-Jean-de-Luz	32	43.23 N	1.40 W
Saint-Jean-de-Maurienne	62	45.17 N	6.21 E
Saint-Jean-de-Monts	32	46.48 N	2.03 W
Saint-Jean-des-Piles	206	46.41 N	72.45 W
Saint-Jean-du-Gard	62	44.06 N	3.53 E
Saint-Jean-en-Royans	62	45.01 N	5.18 E
Saint-Jean-Pied-de-Port	32	43.10 N	1.14 W
Saint-Jean-Port-Joli	186	47.13 N	70.16 W
Saint-Jean-Soleymieux	62	45.30 N	4.02 E
Saint-Jean-sur-Richelieu	206	45.19 N	73.16 W
Saint-Jeoire	58	46.09 N	6.28 E
Saint-Jérôme	206	45.47 N	74.00 W
Saint Jo	196	33.41 N	97.31 W
Saint Joachim	214	42.16 N	82.38 W
Saint Joe	216	41.18 N	84.54 W
Saint Joe ≃	202	47.21 N	116.42 W
Saint John, N.B., Can.	186	45.16 N	66.03 W
Saint John, Jersey	43b	49.15 N	2.08 W
Saint John, In., U.S.	216	41.27 N	87.28 W
Saint John, Ks., U.S.	198	38.00 N	98.45 W
Saint John, N.D., U.S.	198	48.56 N	99.42 W
Saint John, Wa., U.S.	202	47.05 N	117.34 W
Saint John I	240m	18.20 N	64.45 W
Saint John ≃, Liber.	150	6.40 N	9.10 W
Saint John ≃, N.A.	186	45.15 N	66.04 W
Saint John, Cape ›	186	50.00 N	55.32 W
Saint John, Lake ⊜, Nf., Can.	186	48.23 N	54.41 W
Saint John, Lake ⊜, On., Can.	212	44.41 N	79.20 W
Saint John Bay ᑕ	186	50.54 N	57.08 W
Saint John Island I	186	50.49 N	57.14 W
Saint John's, Antig.	240c	17.06 N	61.51 W
Saint John's, Nf., Can.	186	47.34 N	52.43 W
Saint Johns → Saint-Jean-sur-Richelieu, P.Q., Can.	206	45.19 N	73.16 W
Saint John's, I. of Man	44	54.13 N	4.38 W
Saint Johns, Az., U.S.	200	34.30 N	109.21 W
Saint Johns, Mi., U.S.	216	43.00 N	84.33 W
Saint Johns, Mo., U.S.	219	38.42 N	90.20 W
Saint Johns, Oh., U.S.	216	40.33 N	84.05 W
Saint Johns ≃, Ca., U.S.	226	36.25 N	119.25 W
Saint Johns ≃, Fl., U.S.	192	30.24 N	81.24 W
Saint Johnsburg	210	43.05 N	78.53 W
Saint Johnsbury	188	44.25 N	72.00 W
Saint Johns Creek ≃	219	38.34 N	91.01 W
Saint John's Jerusalem ⊥	260	51.25 N	0.14 E
Saint Johns Marsh ≡	220	27.45 N	80.40 W
Saint John's Point ›	48	54.13 N	5.40 W
Saint John's University ⊌[2]	276	40.43 N	73.48 W
Saint Johnsville	210	42.59 N	74.41 W
Saint Joseph, N.B., Can.	186	45.59 N	64.34 W
Saint Joseph, Dom.	240d	15.26 N	61.26 W
Saint-Joseph, Mart.	240e	14.40 N	61.03 W
Saint-Joseph, N. Cal.	175f	20.27 S	166.36 E
Saint-Joseph, Réu.	157c	21.22 S	55.36 E
Saint Joseph, Il., U.S.	194	40.06 N	88.02 W
Saint Joseph, La., U.S.	194	31.55 N	91.14 W
Saint Joseph, Mi., U.S.	216	42.05 N	86.29 W
Saint Joseph, Mn., U.S.	190	45.33 N	94.19 W
Saint Joseph, Mo., U.S.	194	39.46 N	94.50 W
Saint Joseph, Tn., U.S.	194	35.02 N	87.30 W
Saint Joseph □[6], In., U.S.	216	41.41 N	86.15 W
Saint Joseph □[6], Mi., U.S.	216	41.55 N	85.31 W
Saint Joseph ≃, U.S.	216	42.07 N	86.29 W
Saint Joseph ≃, U.S.	216	41.05 N	85.08 W
Saint Joseph, East Branch ≃	216	41.39 N	84.34 W
Saint-Joseph, Île I	275a	45.41 N	73.42 W
Saint-Joseph, Lac ⊜	206	46.54 N	71.38 W
Saint Joseph, Lake ⊜	176	51.05 N	90.35 W
Saint Joseph, West Branch ≃	216	41.39 N	84.34 W
Saint Joseph Bay ᑕ	192	29.47 N	85.21 W
Saint Joseph Channel Ʉ	190	46.19 N	84.04 W
Saint-Joseph-d'Alma → Alma	186	48.33 N	71.39 W
Saint-Joseph-de-Beauce	186	46.18 N	70.53 W
Saint-Joseph-de-Mékinac	206	46.55 N	72.42 W
Saint-Joseph-de-Sorel	206	46.02 N	73.07 W
Saint-Joseph-du-Lac	275a	45.32 N	74.00 W
Saint Joseph Island I	190	46.13 N	83.57 W
Saint Joseph's University ⊌[2]	285	40.00 N	75.14 W
Saint-Jouin-Bruneval	50	49.39 N	0.10 E
Saint-Jovite	206	46.07 N	74.36 W
Sainte-Julie	206	45.35 N	73.19 W
Saint-Julien	58	46.23 N	5.27 E
Saint-Julien-Chapteuil	62	45.02 N	4.04 E
Saint-Julien-du-Sault	50	48.02 N	3.18 E
Saint-Julien-du-Verdon	62	43.55 N	6.32 E
Saint-Julien-en-Beauchêne	62	44.37 N	5.42 E
Saint-Julien-en-Born	32	44.04 N	1.14 W
Saint-Julien-en-Genevois	58	46.08 N	6.05 E
Saint-Julien-en-Jarez	62	45.28 N	4.31 E
Saint-Julien-les-Villas	50	48.16 N	4.06 E
Saint-Julien-Molin-Molette	62	45.19 N	4.37 E
Sainte-Julienne	206	45.58 N	73.43 W
Saint-Junien	32	45.53 N	0.54 E
Saint Just, P.R.	240m	18.23 N	66.00 W
Saint Just, Eng., U.K.	42	50.07 N	5.42 W
Saint-Just-en-Chaussée	50	49.30 N	2.26 E
Saint-Just-en-Chevalet	32	45.55 N	3.50 E
Saint-Justin	206	46.15 N	73.05 W
Saint-Just-Malmont	62	45.20 N	4.19 E
Saint-Just-sur-Loire	62	45.29 N	4.16 E
Saint Keverne	42	50.03 N	5.06 W
Saint Kilda, Austl.	168b	34.44 S	138.32 E
Saint Kilda, Austl.	169	37.52 S	144.59 E
Saint Kilda, N.Z.	172	45.54 S	170.30 E
Saint Kilda I	28	57.49 N	8.36 W
Saint Kitts	168b	34.21 S	139.04 E
Saint Kitts → Saint Christopher I	238	17.20 N	62.45 W
Saint Kitts and Nevis □[1], N.A.	230	17.20 N	62.45 W
Saint Kitts and Nevis □[1], N.A.	238	17.20 N	62.45 W
Saint-Lambert, P.Q., Can.	206	45.30 N	73.30 W
Saint-Lambert, Fr.	261	48.44 N	2.01 E
Saint Landry	194	30.50 N	92.15 W
Saint-Laurent, Mb., Can.	184	50.24 N	97.56 W
Saint-Laurent, P.Q., Can.	206	45.30 N	73.40 W
Saint-Laurent, Fr.	58	48.09 N	6.27 E
Saint-Laurent → Saint Lawrence ≃	176	49.30 N	67.00 W
Saint-Laurent-Blangy	50	50.18 N	2.48 E
Saint-Laurent-de-Chamousset	62	45.44 N	4.28 E
Saint-Laurent-du-Maroni	250	5.30 N	54.02 W
Saint-Laurent-du-Maroni □[8]	250	4.00 N	53.30 W
Saint-Laurent-du-Pont	62	45.23 N	5.44 E
Saint-Laurent-du-Var	62	43.40 N	7.11 E
Saint-Laurent-en-Caux	50	49.45 N	0.53 E
Saint-Laurent-en-Grandvaux	58	46.35 N	5.57 E
Saint-Laurent-et-Benon	32	45.09 N	0.49 W
Saint-Laurent-les-Bains	62	44.37 N	3.58 E
Saint-Laurent-sur-Saône	58	46.18 N	4.50 E
Saint Lawrence, Austl.	166	22.21 S	149.31 E
Saint Lawrence, Nf., Can.	186	46.55 N	55.24 W
Saint Lawrence □[6]	212	44.30 N	75.27 W
Saint Lawrence ≃	176	49.30 N	67.00 W
Saint Lawrence Cape ›	186	47.03 N	60.37 W
Saint Lawrence, Gulf of ᑕ	186	48.00 N	62.00 W
Saint Lawrence, Lake ⊜	206	44.56 N	75.04 W
Saint Lawrence Island I	180	63.30 N	170.30 W
Saint Lawrence Islands National Park ♠	212	44.18 N	76.08 W
Saint-Lawrence Seaway ≊	275a	45.43 N	73.25 W
Saint-Lazare	184	50.26 N	101.16 W
Saint-Lazare, Gare ◆[5]	261	48.53 N	2.20 E
Saint-Léandre	186	48.44 N	67.36 W
Saint-Léger-en-Yvelines	50	48.43 N	1.46 E
Saint-Léger-sur-Dheune	58	46.51 N	4.38 E
Saint Leo	220	28.20 N	82.15 W
Saint Leon	218	39.17 N	84.57 W
Saint-Léonard, N.B., Can.	186	47.10 N	67.56 W
Saint-Léonard, P.Q., Can.	206	45.35 N	73.35 W
Saint Leonard, Md., U.S.	208	38.28 N	76.30 W
Saint-Léonard-d'Aston	206	46.06 N	72.22 W
Saint Leonards, Eng., U.K.	42	50.51 N	0.34 E
Saint Leonards, Eng., U.K.	42	50.49 N	1.51 W
Saint-Leu-d'Esserent	50	49.13 N	2.25 E
Saint-Leu-la-Forêt	50	49.01 N	2.15 E
Saint-Liboire	206	45.39 N	72.46 W
Saint-Lô	32	49.07 N	1.05 W
Saint-Louis, Sk., Can.	184	52.56 N	105.49 W
Saint-Louis, Fr.	58	47.35 N	7.34 E
Saint-Louis, Guad.	241o	15.57 N	61.19 W
Saint-Louis, Réu.	157c	21.16 S	55.25 E
Saint-Louis, Sén.	150	16.02 N	16.30 W
Saint Louis, Mi., U.S.	190	43.24 N	84.36 W
Saint Louis, Mo., U.S.	219	38.37 N	90.11 W
Saint Louis, Tx., U.S.	222	32.18 N	95.20 W
Saint-Louis □[4]	150	16.00 N	14.30 W
Saint Louis □[6]	219	38.39 N	90.25 W
Saint-Louis ≃, P.Q., Can.	275a	45.19 N	73.53 W
Saint Louis ≃, U.S.	190	46.45 N	92.06 W
Saint-Louis, Lac ⊜	206	45.24 N	73.48 W
Saint-Louis, Pointe ›	275a	45.19 N	73.53 W
Saint Louis Crossing	218	39.19 N	85.51 W
Saint-Louis-de-Champlain	206	46.25 N	72.36 W
Saint-Louis-de-Kent	186	46.44 N	64.58 W
Saint Louis Park	190	44.56 N	93.20 W
Saint Louisville	214	40.10 N	82.25 W
Saint-Loup-sur-Aujon	58	47.53 N	5.05 E
Saint-Loup-sur-Semouse	58	47.53 N	6.16 E
Saint-Luc, P.Q., Can.	206	45.22 N	73.18 W
Saint-Luc, Schw.	58	46.13 N	7.36 E
Sainte-Luce	240e	14.28 N	60.56 W
Saint Lucia □[1], N.A.	230	13.53 N	60.58 W
Saint Lucia □[1], N.A.	241f	13.53 N	60.58 W
Saint Lucia, Cape ›	158	28.25 S	32.25 E
Saint Lucia, Lake ⊜	158	28.05 S	32.26 E
Saint Lucia Channel Ʉ	238	14.09 N	60.57 W
Saint Lucia Estuary	158	28.22 S	32.25 E
Saint Lucia Game Reserve ◆[4]	158	28.10 S	32.28 E
Sainte-Lucie, Fr.	36	41.42 N	9.22 E
Saint Lucie, Fl., U.S.	220	27.29 N	80.20 W
Saint Lucie □[6]	220	27.23 N	80.26 W
Saint Lucie Canal ≊	220	27.10 N	80.15 W
Saint Lucie Inlet ᑕ	220	27.10 N	80.10 W
Saint Lucie Lock ◆[5]	220	27.07 N	80.17 W
Saint-Lucien	261	48.39 N	1.38 E
Saint-Lupicin	58	46.24 N	5.47 E
Sainte-Magnance	50	47.27 N	4.04 E
Saint Magnus Bay ᑕ	46a	60.24 N	1.34 W
Saint Magnus Cathedral ⊌[1]	46	58.58 N	2.57 W
Saint-Malo, P.Q., Can.	206	45.12 N	71.30 W
Saint-Malo, Fr.	32	48.39 N	2.01 W
Saint-Malo, Golfe de ᑕ	32	48.45 N	2.00 W
Saint-Mamert-du-Gard	62	43.53 N	4.12 E
Saint-Mammès	50	48.23 N	2.49 E
Saint-Mandé	261	48.50 N	2.25 E
Saint-Mandrier-sur-Mer	62	43.04 N	5.56 E
Saint-Marc	238	19.07 N	72.42 W
Saint-Marc, Canal de Ʉ	238	18.50 N	72.45 W
Saint-Marc-des-Carrières	206	46.41 N	72.03 W
Saint-Marcel	58	46.47 N	4.54 E
Saint-Marcellin	62	45.09 N	5.19 E
Saint-Marcelline-de-Kildare	206	46.07 N	73.36 W
Saint-Marc-sur-Richelieu	275a	45.41 N	73.12 W
Saint-Mard	261	49.02 N	2.42 E
Saint Margaret Bay ᑕ	186	51.01 N	56.58 W
Saint Margaret's at Cliffe	42	51.09 N	1.24 E
Saint Margarets Bay ᑕ	186	44.35 N	64.00 W
Saint Margaret's Hope	46	58.49 N	2.57 W
Sainte-Marguerite ≃	176	50.09 N	66.36 W
Sainte-Marguerite, Baie ᑕ	186	50.06 N	66.36 W
Sainte-Marguerite-sur-Mer	50	49.55 N	0.57 E
Sainte-Marie	240e	14.47 N	61.00 W
Sainte-Marie, Cap ›	157b	25.36 S	45.08 E
Sainte-Marie-aux-Mines (Markirch)	58	48.15 N	7.11 E
Saint Maries	202	47.18 N	116.33 W
Saint Maries ≃	202	47.19 N	116.33 W
Saint-Marin → San Marino □[1]	66	43.56 N	12.25 E
Saint Marks, S. Afr.	158	32.01 S	27.22 E
Saint Marks, Fl., U.S.	192	30.09 N	84.12 W
Saint Marks ≃	192	30.08 N	84.12 W
Sainte-Marthe-de-Gaspé	186	49.12 N	66.10 W
Sainte-Marthe-sur-le-Lac	275a	45.32 N	73.56 W
Saint-Martin (Sint Maarten) I	238	18.04 N	63.04 W
Saint-Martin, Cap ›	240e	14.52 N	61.13 W
Saint Martin, Lake ⊜	184	51.37 N	98.29 W
Saint-Martin-Boulogne	50	50.43 N	1.38 E
Saint-Martin-d'Ardèche	62	44.18 N	4.35 E
Saint-Martin-d'Auxigny	50	47.12 N	2.25 E
Saint-Martin-de-Belleville	62	45.23 N	6.30 E
Saint-Martin-de-Bossenay	50	48.26 N	3.41 E
Saint-Martin-de-Bréthencourt	261	48.31 N	1.56 E
Saint-Martin-de-Crau	62	43.38 N	4.49 E
Saint-Martin-de-Londres	62	43.47 N	3.44 E
Saint-Martin-de-Nigelles	261	48.37 N	1.37 E
Saint-Martin-d'Entraunes	62	44.08 N	6.46 E
Saint-Martin-des-Champs	261	48.53 N	1.43 E
Saint-Martin-de-Valamas	62	44.56 N	4.22 E
Saint-Martin-d'Hères	62	45.10 N	5.46 E
Saint-Martin-du-Puy	50	47.20 N	3.52 E
Saint-Martin-du-Tertre	261	49.06 N	2.21 E
Saint-Martin-du-Var	62	43.49 N	7.12 E
Sainte-Martine	206	45.15 N	73.48 W
Saint-Martin-en-Bresse	58	46.49 N	5.04 E
Saint-Martin-la-Garenne	261	49.02 N	1.41 E
Saint-Martin-la-Plaine	62	45.32 N	4.36 E
Saint Martins, N.B., Can.	186	45.21 N	65.32 W
Saint Martin's, Eng., U.K.	42	52.55 N	2.59 W
Saint Martin's I	42a	49.58 N	6.20 W
Saint Martins Keys II	220	28.47 N	82.44 W
Saint-Martin-Vésubie	62	44.04 N	7.15 E
Saint Martinville	194	30.07 N	91.49 W
Saint Mary	194	37.52 N	89.58 W
Saint Mary ≃, B.C., Can.	182	49.37 N	115.38 W
Saint Mary ≃, N.A.	182	49.37 N	112.52 W
Saint Mary, Cape ›	150	13.28 N	16.40 W
Saint Mary, Mount ∧	164	8.10 S	147.00 E
Saint Mary Bourne	42	51.16 N	1.24 W
Saint Mary Cray ◆[8]	260	51.23 N	0.07 E
Saint Mary Lake ⊜	202	48.40 N	113.30 W
Saint Marylebone ◆[8]	260	51.31 N	0.10 W
Saint Mary of the Lake Seminary ⊌[2]	278	42.17 N	88.00 W
Saint Mary Peak ∧	166	31.30 S	138.33 E
Saint Mary Reservoir ⊜[1]	182	49.19 N	113.12 W
Saint Marys, Austl.	166	41.35 S	148.10 E
Saint Marys, Austl.	170	33.47 S	150.47 E
Saint Mary's, Nf., Can.	186	46.55 N	53.34 W
Saint Mary's, On., Can.	212	43.16 N	81.08 W
Saint Marys, Ak., U.S.	180	62.04 N	163.10 W
Saint Marys, Ga., U.S.	192	30.43 N	81.32 W
Saint Marys, Ks., U.S.	198	39.11 N	96.04 W
Saint Marys, Oh., U.S.	216	40.32 N	84.23 W
Saint Marys, Pa., U.S.	214	41.25 N	78.33 W
Saint Marys, W.V., U.S.	188	39.23 N	81.12 W
Saint Marys □[6]	208	38.17 N	76.38 W
Saint Mary's I	42a	49.55 N	6.18 W
Saint Marys ≃, N.S., Can.	186	45.02 N	61.54 W
Saint Marys ≃, N.A.	190	45.58 N	83.54 W
Saint Marys ≃, U.S.	192	30.43 N	81.27 W
Saint Marys ≃, U.S.	216	41.05 N	85.08 W
Saint Marys ≃, Md., U.S.	208	38.06 N	76.26 W
Saint Mary's, Cape ›, Nf., Can.	186	46.49 N	54.12 W
Saint Marys, Cape ›, N.S., Can.	186	44.05 N	66.13 W
Saint Marys, North Prong ≃	192	30.22 N	82.06 W
Saint Marys, South Prong ≃	192	30.22 N	82.06 W
Saint Mary's Bay	42	51.00 N	0.58 E
Saint Mary's Bay ᑕ, Nf., Can.	186	46.50 N	53.47 W
Saint Marys Bay ᑕ, N.S., Can.	186	44.25 N	66.10 W
Saint Marys City	208	38.11 N	76.26 W
Saint Mary's Hoo	260	51.28 N	0.36 E
Saint Marys Lake ⊜	278	42.17 N	87.59 W
Saint Mary's Marshes ≡	260	51.28 N	0.35 E
Saint-Mathieu	32	45.42 N	0.46 E
Saint-Mathieu, Pointe de ›	32	48.20 N	4.46 W
Saint-Mathieu-de-Laprairie	275a	45.19 N	73.31 W
Saint Matthew Island I	180	60.30 N	172.45 W
Saint Matthews, Ky., U.S.	218	38.15 N	85.39 W
Saint Matthews, S.C., U.S.	192	33.39 N	80.46 W
Saint Matthias Group II	164	1.30 S	149.40 E
Saint-Maur-des-Fossés	50	48.48 N	2.30 E
Sainte-Maure-de-Touraine	32	47.07 N	0.37 E
Saint-Maurice, Fr.	261	48.49 N	2.25 E
Saint-Maurice, Schw.	58	46.13 N	7.00 E
Saint-Maurice □[6]	206	46.35 N	73.00 W
Saint-Maurice ≃	176	46.21 N	72.31 W
Saint-Maurice, Parc de ♠	206	46.52 N	73.10 W
Saint-Maurice-en-Montagne	58	46.34 N	5.50 E
Saint-Maurice-Montcouronne	261	48.35 N	2.07 E
Saint Mawes	42	50.09 N	5.01 W
Saint Mawgan	42	50.28 N	4.58 W
Saint-Max	58	48.42 N	6.13 E
Sainte-Maxime	62	43.18 N	6.38 E
Saint-Maximin-la-Sainte-Baume	62	43.27 N	5.52 E
Saint-Méen-le-Grand	32	48.11 N	2.12 W
Saint Meinrad	194	38.10 N	86.48 W
Sainte-Menehould	56	49.05 N	4.54 E
Saint-Menges	56	49.44 N	4.56 E
Sainte-Mère-Église	32	49.25 N	1.19 W
Saint Merryn	42	50.31 N	4.58 W
Saint-Méry	261	48.35 N	2.50 E
Sainte-Mesme	261	48.32 N	1.58 E
Saint-Mesmes	261	48.59 N	2.42 E
Saint Michael, Ak., U.S.	180	63.29 N	162.02 W
Saint Michael, Pa., U.S.	214	40.20 N	78.46 W
Saint Michaels	208	38.47 N	76.13 W
Saint-Michel, Fr.	50	49.55 N	4.08 E
Saint-Michel, Fr.	62	45.13 N	6.28 E
Saint-Michel ◆[8]	275a	45.35 N	73.35 W
Saint-Michel-de-Napierville	206	45.14 N	73.34 W
Saint-Michel-des-Saints	206	46.41 N	73.55 W
Saint-Michel-sur-Meurthe	58	48.19 N	6.54 E
Saint-Michel-sur-Orge	261	48.38 N	2.18 E
Saint-Mihiel	56	48.54 N	5.33 E
Saint Monance	46	56.12 N	2.46 W
Sainte-Monique-des-Deux-Montagnes	275a	45.40 N	74.00 W
Sainte-Montaine	50	47.29 N	2.19 E
Saint-Moritz → Sankt Moritz	58	46.30 N	9.50 E
Saint-Narcisse	206	46.34 N	72.28 W
Saint-Nazaire	32	47.17 N	2.12 W
Saint-Nazaire-en-Royans	62	45.04 N	5.15 E
Saint-Nazaire-le-Désert	62	44.34 N	5.17 E
Saint Nazianz	190	44.00 N	87.55 W
Saint Neots	42	52.14 N	0.17 W
Saint-Nicéphore	206	45.50 N	72.25 W
Saint-Nicolas → Sint-Niklaas, Bel.	50	51.10 N	4.08 E
Saint-Nicolas, Bel.	56	50.38 N	5.32 E
Saint-Nicolas, P.Q., Can.	206	46.42 N	71.24 W
Saint-Nicolas-aux-Bois	50	49.36 N	3.25 E
Saint-Nicolas-d'Aliermont	50	49.53 N	1.13 E
Saint-Nizier-du-Moucherotte	62	45.10 N	5.38 E
Saint-Nom-la-Bretèche	261	48.51 N	2.01 E
Saint Nora Lake ⊜	212	45.08 N	78.49 W
Saint-Norbert-d'Arthabaska	206	46.07 N	71.50 W
Sainte-Odile ⊌[1]	58	48.26 N	7.24 E
Saint-Omer	50	50.45 N	2.15 E
Saintonge □[9]	32	45.30 N	0.30 W
Saint-Ouen, Fr.	50	50.02 N	2.03 E
Saint-Ouen, Fr.	261	48.54 N	2.20 E
Saint-Ouen-l'Aumône	50	49.03 N	2.06 E
Saint-Pacôme	186	47.24 N	69.57 W
Saint-Pamphile	186	46.58 N	69.47 W
Saint Pancras ◆[8]	260	51.32 N	0.07 W
Saint Paris	218	40.07 N	83.57 W
Saint-Pascal	186	47.32 N	69.49 W
Saint-Paterne	50	48.24 N	0.07 E
Saint-Pathus	261	49.04 N	2.48 E
Saint-Patrice, Lac ⊜	190	46.22 N	77.20 W
Saint Paul, Ab., Can.	182	53.59 N	111.17 W
Saint-Paul, Fr.	62	43.42 N	7.07 E
Saint-Paul, Fr.	62	44.31 N	6.45 E
Saint-Paul, Réu.	157c	21.00 S	55.16 E
Saint Paul, In., U.S.	218	39.25 N	85.28 W
Saint Paul, Ks., U.S.	198	37.31 N	95.10 W
Saint Paul, Mn., U.S.	190	44.57 N	93.05 W
Saint Paul, Ne., U.S.	198	41.13 N	98.27 W
Saint Paul, Or., U.S.	224	45.12 N	122.58 W
Saint Paul, Va., U.S.	192	36.54 N	82.18 W
Saint-Paul ≃, Can.	176	51.26 N	57.40 W
Saint Paul ≃, Liber.	150	6.23 N	10.48 W
Saint Paul, Cape ›	150	5.49 N	0.57 E
Saint-Paul, Île I	6	38.43 S	77.29 E
Saint-Paul, Lac ⊜	206	46.18 N	72.29 W
Saint Paul Bay ᑕ	116	10.14 N	118.54 E
Saint-Paul-de-Chester (Chesterville)	206	45.57 N	71.49 W
Saint-Paul-en-Jarez	62	45.29 N	4.35 E
Saint-Paul-et-Valmalle	62	43.38 N	3.40 E
Saint-Paulien	62	45.08 N	3.49 E
Saint-Paulin	206	46.25 N	73.01 W
Saint Paul Island	180	57.07 N	170.17 W
Saint Paul Island I, N.S., Can.	186	47.15 N	60.10 W
Saint Paul Island I, Ak., U.S.	180	57.10 N	170.15 W
Saint Pauls	192	34.48 N	78.58 W
Saint Paul's Cathedral ⊌[1]	260	51.31 N	0.06 W
Saint Paul's Cray ◆[8]	260	51.24 N	0.07 E
Saint Pauls Inlet ᑕ	186	49.50 N	57.45 W
Saint Paul's Point ›	174e	25.04 S	130.05 W
Saint-Paul-Trois-Châteaux	62	44.21 N	4.46 E
Saint-Péravy-la-Colombe	50	48.00 N	1.42 E
Saint-Péray	62	44.57 N	4.50 E
Saint-Père	50	47.28 N	3.46 E
Saint Peter, Il., U.S.	219	38.52 N	88.51 W
Saint Peter, Mn., U.S.	190	44.19 N	93.57 W
Saint Peter, Lake ⊜	212	45.18 N	78.02 W
Saint Peter Island I	162	32.17 S	133.35 E
Saint Peter Port	43b	49.27 N	2.32 W
Saint Peters, N.S., Can.	186	45.40 N	60.52 W
Saint Peters, Mo., U.S.	219	38.48 N	90.37 W
Saint Peters, Pa., U.S.	285	40.11 N	75.44 W
Saint Peters Bay	186	46.25 N	62.35 W
Saint Petersburg → Sankt-Peterburg, Ross.	76	59.55 N	30.15 E
Saint Petersburg, Fl., U.S.	220	27.46 N	82.40 W
Saint Petersburg, Pa., U.S.	214	41.10 N	79.37 W
Saint Petersburg Beach	220	27.43 N	82.44 W
Saint Peter's College ⊌[2]	276	40.44 N	74.05 W
Saint-Philippe-d'Argenteuil	206	45.37 N	74.25 W
Saint-Philippe-de-Laprairie	275a	45.21 N	73.28 W
Saint-Pie	206	45.30 N	72.54 W
Saint-Pierre, P.Q., Can.	275a	45.27 N	73.39 W
Saint-Pierre, Fr.	62	45.40 N	3.45 E
Saint-Pierre, It.	62	45.42 N	7.14 E
Saint-Pierre, Mart.	240e	14.45 N	61.11 W
Saint-Pierre, Réu.	157c	21.19 S	55.29 E
Saint-Pierre, St. P./M.	186	46.47 N	56.11 W
Saint-Pierre I	186	46.47 N	56.11 W
Saint-Pierre ≃	275a	45.23 N	73.34 W
Saint-Pierre, Lac ⊜, P.Q., Can.	186	50.08 N	68.26 W
Saint-Pierre, Lac ⊜, P.Q., Can.	206	46.12 N	72.52 W
Saint Pierre and Miquelon (Saint-Pierre-et-Miquelon) □[2], N.A.	176	46.55 N	56.20 W
Saint Pierre and Miquelon (Saint-Pierre-et-Miquelon) □[2], N.A.	186	46.55 N	56.20 W
Saint-Pierre-d'Albigny	62	45.34 N	6.09 E
Saint-Pierre-de-Bœuf	62	45.22 N	4.45 E
Saint-Pierre-de-Broughton	206	46.15 N	71.12 W
Saint-Pierre-de-Chartreuse	62	45.20 N	5.49 E
Saint-Pierre-des-Corps	50	47.23 N	0.44 E
Saint-Pierre-de-Vacquière	62	43.52 N	4.13 E
Saint-Pierre-du-Vauvray	50	49.14 N	1.13 E
Saint-Pierre-Église	32	49.40 N	1.24 W
Saint-Pierre-en-Port	50	49.48 N	0.29 E
Saint-Pierre-et-Miquelon → Saint Pierre and Miquelon □[2]	186	46.55 N	56.20 W
Saint Pierre Island I	138	9.19 S	50.43 E
Saint Pierre-Jolys	184	49.26 N	96.59 W
Saint Pierre-le-Moûtier	32	46.48 N	3.07 E
Saint-Pierre-lès-Elbeuf	50	49.16 N	1.03 E
Saint-Pierre-sur-Dives	28	49.01 N	0.02 W
Saint-Pierreville	62	44.49 N	4.29 E
Saint-Point, Lac de ⊜	58	46.49 N	6.19 E
Saint-Pol-de-Léon	32	48.41 N	3.59 W
Saint-Pol-sur-Mer	50	51.02 N	2.21 E
Saint-Pol-sur-Ternoise	50	50.23 N	2.20 E
Saint-Polycarpe	206	45.18 N	74.18 W
Saint-Pons	32	43.29 N	2.46 E
Saint-Pourçain-sur-Sioule	32	46.19 N	3.17 E
Saint-Prex	58	46.29 N	6.28 E
Saint-Priest	62	45.42 N	4.57 E
Saint-Priest-en-Jarez	62	45.28 N	4.22 E
Saint-Prix	261	49.01 N	2.16 E
Saint-Prosper-de-Dorchester	188	46.13 N	70.29 W
Saint-Quentin, N.B., Can.	186	47.30 N	67.23 W
Saint-Quentin, Fr.	50	49.51 N	3.17 E
Saint-Quentin, Canal de ≊	50	49.36 N	3.11 E
Saint-Quentin, Étang de ⊜	261	48.47 N	2.01 E
Saint-Rambert-d'Albon	62	45.17 N	4.49 E
Saint-Rambert-en-Bugey	58	45.57 N	5.26 E
Saint-Rambert-sur-Loire	62	45.30 N	4.15 E
Saint-Raphaël	62	43.25 N	6.46 E
Saint-Raymond	206	46.54 N	71.50 W
Saint-Récempter-de-Lévis	206	46.42 N	71.17 W
Saint Regis	202	47.17 N	115.06 W
Saint-Régis ≃, P.Q., Can.	275a	45.24 N	73.34 W
Saint Regis ≃, N.A.	188	45.00 N	74.39 W
Saint Regis ≃, Mt. U.S.	202	47.18 N	115.05 W
Saint Regis, West Branch ≃	188	44.47 N	74.46 W
Saint Regis Falls	188	44.40 N	74.32 W
Saint Regis Indian Reservation ◆[4]	206	44.58 N	74.39 W
Saint-Rémi	206	45.16 N	73.37 W
Saint-Rémi-d'Amherst	206	46.01 N	74.46 W
Saint-Rémy (lès-Chevreuse), Fr.	50	48.42 N	2.05 E
Saint-Rémy, Fr.	58	46.46 N	4.50 E
Saint Remy, N.Y., U.S.	210	41.54 N	74.01 W
Saint-Rémy-de-Provence	62	43.47 N	4.50 E
Saint-Rémy-en-Bouzemont	58	48.38 N	4.39 E
Saint-Rémy-l'Honoré	261	48.45 N	1.53 E
Saint-Rémy-sur-Avre	50	48.46 N	1.15 E
Saint-Renan	32	48.26 N	4.37 W
Saint-Révérien	50	47.13 N	3.30 E
Saint-Rhémy	62	45.50 N	7.11 E
Saint-Riquier	50	50.08 N	1.57 E
Saint Robert	194	37.50 N	92.09 W
Saint-Roch-de-l'Achigan	206	45.51 N	73.36 W
Saint-Romain-de-Colbosc	50	49.32 N	0.22 E
Saint-Romain-le-Puy	62	45.33 N	4.07 E
Saint-Romans	62	45.07 N	5.19 E
Saint-Romuald	206	46.45 N	71.14 W
Sainte-Rosalie	206	45.38 N	72.54 W
Sainte-Rose	241o	16.20 N	61.42 W
Sainte-Rose ◆[8]	275a	45.36 N	73.47 W
Sainte-Rose-du-Lac	184	51.03 N	99.32 W
Saintry-sur-Seine	261	48.36 N	2.30 E
Saintes, Bel.	50	50.42 N	4.10 E
Saintes, Fr.	32	45.45 N	0.38 W
Saint-Saëns	50	49.40 N	1.17 E
Saint Sampson	43b	49.29 N	2.31 W
Saint-Satur	50	47.20 N	2.51 E
Saint-Saturnin-d'Apt	62	43.56 N	5.23 E
Saint-Sauveur, Fr.	50	47.37 N	3.12 E
Saint-Sauveur, Fr.	58	47.48 N	6.23 E
Saint-Sauveur-des-Monts	206	45.52 N	74.10 W
Saint-Sauveur-sur-Tinée	62	44.05 N	7.06 E
Saint-Savin	32	46.34 N	0.52 E
Saint-Savinien	32	45.53 N	0.41 W
Saint Saviour	43b	49.11 N	2.06 W
Saint Sebastian Bay ᑕ	158	34.25 S	21.00 E
Saint-Sébastien	206	45.07 N	73.09 W
Saint-Sébastien, Cap ›	157b	12.26 S	48.44 E
Saint-Seine-l'Abbaye	58	47.26 N	4.47 E
Saint Séverin	56	50.32 N	5.25 E
Saint Shotts	186	46.38 N	53.35 W
Sainte-Sigolène	62	45.14 N	4.15 E
Saint-Siméon	186	47.50 N	69.53 W
Saint-Simon	50	49.45 N	3.10 E
Saint Simons Island	192	31.09 N	81.22 W
Saint Simons Island I	192	31.14 N	81.21 W
Saint-Sixte ≃	206	45.39 N	75.08 W
Saintes-Maries, Golfe des ᑕ	62	43.25 N	4.31 E
Saintes-Maries-de-la-Mer	62	43.27 N	4.26 E
Sainte-Sophie-de-Mégantic	206	46.09 N	71.42 W
Saint-Soupplets	261	49.02 N	2.48 E
Saint Stanislas Bay ᑕ	174o	1.53 N	157.30 W
Saint-Stanislas-de-Kosta	206	45.11 N	74.08 W

≃ River	Fluß	Río	Rivière	Rio
≊ Canal	Kanal	Canal	Canal	Canal
∟ Waterfall, Rapids	Wasserfall, Stromschnellen	Cascada, Rápidos	Chute d'eau, Rapides	Cascata, Rápidos
Ʉ Strait	Meeresstraße	Estrecho	Détroit	Estreito
ᑕ Bay, Gulf	Bucht, Golf	Bahía, Golfo	Baie, Golfe	Baía, Golfo
⊜ Lake, Lakes	See, Seen	Lago, Lagos	Lac, Lacs	Lago, Lagos
≡ Swamp	Sumpf	Pantano	Marais	Pântano
⍓ Ice Features, Glacier	Eis- und Gletscherformen	Accidentes Glaciales	Formes glaciaires	Acidentes glaciares
⍑ Other Hydrographic Features	Andere Hydrographische Objekte	Otros Elementos Hidrográficos	Autres données hydrographiques	Outros acidentes hidrográficos

✣ Submarine Features	Untermeerische Objekte	Accidentes Submarinos	Formes de relief sous-marin	Acidentes submarinos
□ Political Unit	Politische Einheit	Unidad Politica	Entité politique	Unidade política
⊌ Cultural Institution	Kulturelle Institution	Institución Cultural	Institution culturelle	Institução cultural
⊥ Historical Site	Historische Stätte	Sitio Histórico	Site historique	Sitio histórico
♠ Recreational Site	Erholungs- und Ferienort	Sitio de Recreo	Centre de loisirs	Area de Lazer
⊠ Airport	Flughafen	Aeropuerto	Aéroport	Aeroporto
■ Military Installation	Militäranlage	Instalación Militar	Installation militaire	Instalação militar
◆ Miscellaneous	Verschiedenes	Misceláneo	Divers	Diversos

ENGLISH / DEUTSCH

Name / Name	Page / Seite	Lat.°′ / Breite°′	Long.°′ / Länge°′ E = Ost
Saint Stephen, N.B., Can.	186	45.12 N	67.17 W
Saint Stephen, S.C., U.S.	192	33.24 N	79.55 W
Saint-Sulpice-de-Favières	261	48.33 N	2.11 E
Saint-Sulpice-les-Feuilles	32	46.19 N	1.22 E
Sainte-Suzanne	58	47.30 N	6.46 E
Saint-Sylvestre	206	46.22 N	71.14 W
Saint-Symphorien, Fr.	32	44.26 N	0.30 W
Saint-Symphorien, Fr.	261	48.31 N	1.46 E
Saint-Symphorien-d'Ozon	62	45.38 N	4.52 E
Saint-Symphorien-sur-Coise	62	45.38 N	4.27 E
Sainte-Thècle	206	46.49 N	72.31 W
Saint-Théodore-d'Acton	206	45.41 N	72.35 W
Sainte-Thérèse	206	45.38 N	73.51 W
Sainte-Thérèse, Île I, P.Q., Can.	275a	45.41 N	73.28 W
Sainte-Thérèse, Île I, P.Q., Can.	275a	45.22 N	73.15 W
Saint-Thibault-des-Vignes	261	48.52 N	2.41 E
Saint Thomas, On., Can.	212	42.47 N	81.12 W
Saint Thomas, Mo., U.S.	219	38.22 N	92.13 W
Saint Thomas, N.D., U.S.	198	48.37 N	97.26 W
Saint Thomas → Charlotte Amalie, Vir. Is., U.S.	240m	18.21 N	64.56 W
Saint Thomas I	240m	18.21 N	64.55 W
Saint-Timothée	206	45.18 N	74.02 W
Saint-Tite	206	46.44 N	72.34 W
Saint-Tite-des-Caps	186	47.08 N	70.47 W
Saint-Trivier-de-Courtes	58	46.28 N	5.05 E
Saint-Trivier-sur-Moignans	58	46.04 N	4.54 E
Saint-Tropez	62	43.16 N	6.38 E
Saint Tudy	42	50.33 N	4.43 W
Sainte-Tulle	62	43.47 N	5.46 E
Saint-Ubald	206	46.45 N	72.16 W
Saint-Urbain-de-Charlevoix	186	47.33 N	70.32 W
Saint-Ursanne	58	47.22 N	7.10 E
Saint-Uze	62	45.11 N	4.52 E
Saint-Valérien	50	48.11 N	3.06 E
Saint-Valéry-en-Caux	50	49.52 N	0.44 E
Saint-Valéry-sur-Somme	50	50.11 N	1.38 E
Saint-Vallier, Fr.	58	46.38 N	4.22 E
Saint-Vallier, Fr.	62	45.10 N	4.49 E
Saint-Vallier-de-Thiey	62	43.42 N	6.51 E
Saint-Varent	32	46.53 N	0.14 W
Saint-Venant	50	50.37 N	2.33 E
Saint-Véran	62	44.42 N	6.52 E
Sainte-Victoire, Montagne ∧	62	43.32 N	5.39 E
Saint-Victoret	62	43.25 N	5.14 E
Saint-Vincent, It.	62	45.45 N	7.39 E
Saint Vincent, Mn., U.S.	198	48.58 N	97.13 W
Saint Vincent I	241h	13.15 N	61.12 W
Saint-Vincent, Baie de ⊂	175f	22.00 S	166.05 E
Saint-Vincent, Cap ›	157b	21.57 S	43.16 E
Saint Vincent, Cape ›, Austl.	166	43.18 S	145.50 E
Saint Vincent, Cape → São Vicente, Cabo de ›, Port.	34	37.01 N	9.00 W
Saint Vincent, Gulf ⊂	168b	35.00 S	138.05 E
Saint Vincent and the Grenadines □[1], N.A.	230	13.15 N	61.12 W
Saint Vincent and the Grenadines □[1], N.A.	241h	13.15 N	61.12 W
Saint-Vincent-de-Paul ◆[8]	275a	45.37 N	73.39 W
Saint-Vincent-de-Tyrosse	32	43.40 N	1.18 W
Saint Vincent Passage ⊔	238	13.30 N	61.00 W
Saint Vincent's	186	46.48 N	53.38 W
Saint-Vit	58	47.11 N	5.49 E
Saint-Vith	56	50.17 N	6.08 E
Saint-Vivien-de-Médoc	32	45.26 N	1.02 W
Saint-Vrain	261	48.33 N	2.20 E
Saint Walburg	184	53.39 N	109.12 W
Saint-Wandrille-Rançon	50	49.32 N	0.46 E
Saint-Wenceslas ≃	206	46.18 N	72.23 W
Saint Williams	212	42.40 N	80.25 W
Saint-Witz	261	49.05 N	2.34 E
Saint-Yrieix-la-Perche	32	45.31 N	1.12 E
Saint-Yvon	186	49.10 N	64.48 W
Saint-Zacharie	62	43.23 N	5.43 E
Saint-Zénon	206	46.33 N	73.49 W
Sāinthiya	126	23.57 N	87.40 E
Saipan I	174n	15.12 N	145.45 E
Saipan Channel ⊔	174n	15.05 N	145.41 E
Saipan International Airport ⊠	174n	15.07 N	145.43 E
Saiqi	100	27.00 N	119.43 E
Saishu-to → Cheju-do I	90	33.20 N	126.30 E
Saita	96	34.08 N	133.49 E
Saita ≃	96	34.08 N	133.38 E
Saitama □[5]	94	36.00 N	139.30 E
Saitama University ⊛[2]	268	35.52 N	139.36 E
Saito	92	32.06 N	131.24 E
Saiwai ◆[8]	268	35.33 N	139.41 E
Saiwa Swamp National Park ♠	154	1.06 N	35.12 E
Saiyidān ◆[8]	272a	28.40 N	77.05 E
Sai Yok	110	14.07 N	99.08 E
Sajak	86	47.02 N	77.22 E
Sajam	164	0.53 S	132.41 E
Sajama	248	18.07 S	69.00 W
Sajama, Nevado ∧	248	18.06 S	68.54 W
Sajan → Sayan Mountains ⋀	88	52.45 N	96.00 E
Sajanogorsk	86	53.08 N	91.29 E
Sajano-Šušenskoje vodochranilišče ⊜[1]	86	52.20 N	92.25 E
Sajantuj	88	51.44 N	107.30 E
Sajasan	84	43.03 N	46.17 E
Sajat	128	38.47 N	63.53 E
Sajchan	88	48.40 N	102.39 E
Sajchandulaan	102	44.40 N	109.01 E
Sajchan-Ovoo	102	45.27 N	103.54 E
Sajchin	80	48.50 N	46.47 E
Sajen	115a	7.40 S	112.31 E
Šajgino	80	57.46 N	46.51 E
Ṣajīd I	144	16.52 N	41.50 E
Šajmak'	120	37.27 N	74.44 E
Sajnšand	102	44.52 N	110.09 E
Sajó (Slaná) ≃	30	47.56 N	21.08 E
Sajószentpéter	30	48.13 N	20.44 E
Sajram	85	42.18 N	69.45 E
Sajukino	80	52.47 N	41.59 E
Sājūr (Bağırsak) ≃	130	36.40 N	38.05 E
Sak ≃	158	30.02 S	20.40 E
Saka, Kenya	154	0.09 S	39.20 E
Saka, Nihon	96	34.20 N	132.31 E
Sakado	94	35.57 N	139.24 E
Sakae, Nihon	94	35.50 N	140.15 E
Sakae, Nihon	94	36.58 N	138.35 E
Sa Kaeo	110	13.49 N	102.04 E
Sakahogi	94	35.26 N	136.59 E
Sakai, Nihon	94	36.10 N	136.14 E
Sakai, Nihon	94	36.16 N	139.15 E
Sakai, Nihon	94	36.06 N	139.48 E
Sakai, Nihon	96	34.35 N	135.28 E
Sakai, Nihon	268	35.25 N	139.22 E
Sakai ≃	94	35.18 N	139.29 E
Sakaide	96	34.19 N	133.52 E
Sakaigawa	94	35.35 N	138.37 E
Sakaiminato	96	35.33 N	133.15 E
Sakākah	128	29.59 N	40.06 E
Sakakawea, Lake ⊜[1]	198	47.50 N	102.20 W
Sakaki	94	36.28 N	138.11 E
Sakakita	94	36.25 N	138.01 E
Sakala, Pulau I	112	6.54 S	116.15 E
Sakami ≃	176	53.40 N	76.40 W
Sakami, Lac ⊜	176	53.15 N	76.45 W
Sakania	154	12.45 S	28.34 E
Sakar	128	38.56 N	63.45 E
Sakar ⋀	38	41.59 N	26.16 E
Sakaraha	157b	22.55 S	44.32 E
Sakar-Čaga	128	37.38 N	61.40 E
Sakar Island I	164	5.25 S	148.05 E
Sakartvelo → Georgia □[1]	22	42.00 N	44.00 E
Sakarya □[4]	130	40.45 N	30.35 E
Sakarya ≃	130	41.07 N	30.39 E
Sakashita	94	35.34 N	137.32 E
Sakassou	150	7.27 N	5.18 W
Sakata	92	38.55 N	139.50 E
Sakauchi	94	35.36 N	136.25 E
Sakawa	96	33.30 N	133.17 E
Sakawa ≃	94	35.15 N	139.11 E
Sakchu	98	40.23 N	125.01 E
Sakesar	123	32.33 N	71.56 E
Sakété	150	6.43 N	2.40 E
Sakhā	142	31.05 N	30.57 E
Sakhalin → Sachalin, ostrov I	89	51.00 N	143.00 E
Sākhar	120	32.57 N	65.32 E
Sakhi Sarwar	120	29.59 N	70.18 E
Sakhnin	132	32.52 N	35.17 E
Ṣakhrīyāt, Jabal aṣ- ∧	132	31.01 N	36.21 E
Sakht Sar	128	36.53 N	50.41 E
Saki	78	45.09 N	33.35 E
Ṣāki ◆[8]	272c	19.06 N	72.53 E
Šakiai	76	54.57 N	23.03 E
Sākib	132	32.17 N	35.49 E
Sakiet Sidi Youssef	36	36.13 N	8.22 E
Sakijang Bendera, Pulau I	271c	1.13 N	103.51 E
Sakijang Pelepah, Pulau I	271c	1.13 N	103.52 E
Sakishima-shotō II	175d	24.46 N	124.00 E
Sakito	92	33.02 N	129.32 E
Sakkara → Ṣaqqārah	142	29.51 N	31.13 E
Sakmara ≃	86	51.46 N	55.01 E
Sako	270	34.53 N	135.47 E
Sakon Nakhon	110	17.10 N	104.09 E
Sakonnet	207	41.28 N	71.12 W
Sakonnet Point ›	207	41.27 N	71.12 W
Sakoyra	150	14.17 N	1.24 E
Sakra, Pulau I	271c	1.16 N	103.42 E
Sakrand	120	26.08 N	68.16 E
Sakrivier	158	30.54 S	20.28 E
Saks	194	33.42 N	85.52 W
Saksagan' ≃	78	47.53 N	33.18 E
Saksauldala ◆[2]	86	44.30 N	73.00 E
Sakskøbing	41	54.48 N	11.39 E
Sakti	124	22.02 N	82.58 E
Saku, Nihon	94	36.09 N	138.30 E
Saku, Nihon	94	36.13 N	138.29 E
Sakubva	154	19.00 S	32.10 E
Sakugi	96	34.52 N	132.43 E
Sakuma	94	35.05 N	137.48 E
Sakuma-dam ◆[6]	94	35.05 N	137.47 E
Sakuma-ko ⊜[1]	94	35.08 N	137.47 E
Sakura	94	35.43 N	140.14 E
Sakura ≃	94	36.05 N	140.14 E
Sakurae	96	34.57 N	132.20 E
Sakurai	96	34.30 N	135.51 E
Sakura-tōge)(	270	34.36 N	135.53 E
Saku-shima I	94	34.43 N	137.03 E
Sakutō	96	35.01 N	134.14 E
Sakwaso Lake ⊜	184	53.01 N	91.55 W
Säkylä	26	61.02 N	22.20 E
Sakyō ◆[8]	270	35.02 N	135.48 E
Sal I	150a	16.45 N	22.55 W
Sal ≃	80	47.31 N	40.45 E
Sal, Cay I	238	23.42 N	80.24 W
Sal, Ponta do ›	266c	38.41 N	9.22 W
Sal, Punta ›	236	15.53 N	87.37 W
Šal'a, Ross.	86	57.15 N	58.43 E
Šal'a, Slvk.	30	48.09 N	17.52 E
Sala, Sve.	40	59.55 N	16.36 E
Sala, Ouadi V	146	17.00 N	20.53 E
Sala Baganza	64	44.43 N	10.14 E
Salabangka, Kepulauan II	112	3.02 S	122.25 E
Salaberry, Île de I	206	45.17 N	74.07 W
Salaberry-de-Valleyfield	206	45.15 N	74.08 W
Salaca ≃	76	57.45 N	24.21 E
Salacgrīva	76	57.45 N	24.21 E
Sala Consilina	68	40.24 N	15.36 E
Salada, Laguna ⊜, Arg.	258	35.17 S	59.24 W
Salada, Laguna ⊜, Méx.	232	32.20 N	115.40 W
Saladas	252	28.15 S	58.38 W
Saladillo	252	35.38 S	59.46 W
Saladillo ≃, Arg.	252	33.25 S	63.02 W
Saladillo ≃, Arg.	252	29.05 S	63.25 W
Saladillo, Arroyo ≃	258	35.33 S	59.04 W
Saladillo de Rodríguez, Arroyo ≃	258	35.29 S	59.01 W
Saladillo Dulce, Arroyo ≃	252	31.25 S	60.33 W
Salado, Arg.	252	28.18 S	67.15 W
Salado, Tx., U.S.	222	30.57 N	97.32 W
Salado ≃, Arg.	252	38.49 S	64.57 W
Salado ≃, Arg.	252	31.42 S	60.44 W
Salado ≃, Arg.	252	35.44 S	57.21 W
Salado ≃, Arg.	252	29.13 S	66.34 W
Salado ≃, Cuba	240p	20.36 N	76.56 W
Salado ≃, Méx.	232	26.52 N	99.19 W
Salado ≃, Méx.	234	18.44 N	103.36 W
Salado ≃, Méx.	234	17.55 N	96.58 W
Salado, Arroyo ≃, Arg.	254	41.37 S	65.02 W
Salado, Arroyo ≃, Arg.	254	40.35 S	66.33 W
Salado, Rio ≃	200	34.16 N	106.52 W
Salado Creek ≃, Tx., U.S.	196	29.14 N	98.25 W
Salado Creek ≃, Tx., U.S.	222	30.59 N	97.25 W
Salaga	150	8.33 N	0.31 W
Salagle	144	1.50 N	42.17 E
Sālah	132	32.38 N	36.46 E
Ṣalāh ad-Dīn □[4]	128	34.15 N	43.55 E
Salahin	144	2.57 N	46.26 E
Sala'ilua	175a	13.41 S	172.34 W
Salair	86	54.13 N	85.47 E
Salairskij kr'až ∧	86	54.15 N	85.30 E
Sălaj □[6]	38	47.15 N	23.00 E
Salak	114	2.34 N	98.20 E
Salak, Gunung ∧	115a	6.42 S	106.44 E
Šalakas	76	55.35 N	26.08 E
Šalakuša	24	62.15 N	40.17 E
Salal	146	14.51 N	17.13 E
Salala, Chile	252	30.41 S	71.32 W
Salala, Liber.	150	6.40 N	10.05 W
Salālah, Sūd.	140	21.19 N	36.13 E
Ṣalālah, 'Umān	118	17.00 N	54.06 E
Salamá, Guat.	236	15.06 N	90.16 W
Salamá, Hond.	236	14.50 N	86.36 W
Salamajärven kansallispuisto ♠	26	63.20 N	24.40 E
Salaman	115a	7.35 S	110.08 E
Salamanca, Chile	252	31.47 S	70.58 W
Salamanca, Esp.	34	40.58 N	5.39 W
Salamanca, Méx.	234	20.34 N	101.12 W
Salamanca, Perú	248	15.31 S	72.50 W
Salamanca, Perú	286d	12.05 S	77.00 W
Salamanca, N.Y., U.S.	210	42.09 N	78.42 W
Salamanca □[4]	34	40.45 N	6.00 W
Salamanga	158	26.28 S	32.39 E
Salamat □[5]	146	11.00 N	20.30 E
Salamat, Bahr ≃	146	9.27 N	18.06 E
Salāmbek	120	28.18 N	65.09 E
Salamina	246	5.25 N	75.29 W
Salamínos, Órmos ⊂	267c	37.56 N	23.27 E
Salamís	38	37.58 N	23.29 E
Salamís I	38	37.54 N	23.26 E
Salamis ⊥	130	35.10 N	33.54 E
Salamīyah	130	35.01 N	37.03 E
Salām Khān	120	31.47 N	66.45 E
Salamonia	216	40.23 N	84.52 W
Salamonie ≃	216	40.50 N	85.43 W
Salamonie Lake ⊜[1]	216	40.46 N	85.37 W
Salāmūn	142	31.04 N	31.28 E
Salandra	68	40.31 N	16.19 E
Sālang, Tūnel-e ◆[5]	120	35.19 N	69.02 E
Salani	175a	14.00 S	171.33 W
Salantai	76	56.04 N	21.32 E
Salaparuta	70	37.47 N	13.00 E
Salaquí	246	7.18 N	77.33 W
Salaquí ≃	246	7.27 N	77.07 W
Salāqūs	142	28.44 N	30.50 E
Salar	85	41.21 N	69.22 E
Salara	64	44.59 N	11.25 E
Salard	38	47.13 N	22.03 E
Salarjovo	265b	55.37 N	37.26 E
Salas	248	6.16 S	79.37 W
Salas de los Infantes	34	42.01 N	3.17 W
Salat ≃	32	43.10 N	0.58 E
Salatiga	115a	7.19 S	110.30 E
Salauš	80	55.59 N	52.53 E
Salavat	86	53.21 N	55.55 E
Salavaux	58	46.55 N	7.02 E
Salaverry	248	8.14 S	78.58 W
Salavina	252	28.48 S	63.25 W
Salawati I	164	1.07 S	130.52 E
Salawe	154	3.19 S	32.52 E
Salay	116	8.52 N	124.47 E
Salāya	120	22.19 N	69.35 E
Sala y Gómez, Isla I	18	26.28 S	105.28 W
Sala y Gomez Ridge ✦[3]	18	25.00 S	98.00 W
Salazgor'	80	54.07 N	43.09 E
Salba	88	53.14 N	92.36 E
Salbani	126	22.38 N	87.20 E
Salbohed	40	59.55 N	16.19 E
Salbosjön ⊜	40	59.50 N	14.54 E
Salbris	50	47.26 N	2.03 E
Šalbuzdag, gora ∧	84	41.19 N	47.48 E
Salcajá	236	14.53 N	91.27 W
Salccantay, Nevado ∧	248	13.20 S	72.33 W
Salcedo, Pil.	116	11.09 N	125.40 E
Salcedo, Rep. Dom.	238	19.23 N	70.25 W
Salcha ≃	180	64.29 N	147.00 W
Salching	60	48.49 N	12.34 E
Salcia	38	43.57 N	24.56 E
Šalčininkai	76	54.18 N	25.23 E
Salcombe	42	50.13 N	3.47 W
Salda ≃	86	58.48 N	61.20 E
Šaldaj	86	51.56 N	78.48 E
Saldaña	34	42.31 N	4.44 W
Saldaña ≃	246	4.01 N	74.52 W
Saldanha	158	33.00 S	17.56 E
Saldanhabaai ⊂	158	33.04 S	18.00 E
Šaldež	80	56.52 N	44.46 E
Saldungaray	252	38.12 S	61.47 W
Saldus	76	56.40 N	22.30 E
Sale, Austl.	166	38.06 S	147.04 E
Sale, It.	62	44.59 N	8.48 E
Salé, Magreb	148	34.04 N	6.50 W
Sale, Eng., U.K.	44	53.26 N	2.19 W
Salebabu, Pulau I	108	3.55 N	126.40 E
Salechard	74	66.33 N	66.40 E
Sale Creek	194	35.22 N	85.06 W
Salée, Rivière ⊔	241o	16.17 N	61.33 W
Saleh, Teluk ⊂	115b	8.34 S	117.57 E
Salelologa	175a	13.44 S	172.10 W
Salem, On., Can.	212	43.42 N	80.27 W
Salem, Dtsch.	58	47.46 N	9.16 E
Salem, India	122	11.39 N	78.10 E
Salem, S. Afr.	158	33.28 S	26.29 E
Salem, Sve.	40	59.13 N	17.44 E
Salem, Ar., U.S.	194	36.22 N	91.49 W
Salem, Il., U.S.	219	38.37 N	88.56 W
Salem, In., U.S.	218	38.03 N	86.15 W
Salem, Ia., U.S.	190	40.51 N	91.37 W
Salem, Ky., U.S.	194	37.15 N	88.14 W
Salem, Ma., U.S.	207	42.31 N	70.53 W
Salem, Mi., U.S.	281	42.24 N	83.34 W
Salem, Mo., U.S.	194	37.38 N	91.32 W
Salem, N.H., U.S.	207	42.47 N	71.12 W
Salem, N.J., U.S.	208	39.34 N	75.28 W
Salem, N.Y., U.S.	210	43.10 N	73.19 W
Salem, Oh., U.S.	214	40.54 N	80.51 W
Salem, Or., U.S.	224	44.56 N	123.02 W
Salem, S.D., U.S.	198	43.43 N	97.23 W
Salem, Ut,. U.S.	200	40.03 N	111.40 W
Salem, Va., U.S.	192	37.17 N	80.03 W
Salem, W.V., U.S.	188	39.16 N	80.33 W
Salem, Wi., U.S.	216	42.33 N	88.06 W
Salem □[6]	208	39.34 N	75.20 W
Salem ≃	208	39.34 N	75.31 W
Salem Airfield ⊠	281	42.25 N	83.34 W
Sale Marasino	64	45.43 N	10.06 E
Salem Canal ≊	285	39.41 N	75.31 W
Salem Depot	283	42.47 N	71.12 W
Salem Harbor ⊂	283	42.31 N	70.53 W
Salem Heights	214	40.54 N	80.53 W
Salemi	70	37.49 N	12.48 E
Salem Maritime National Historic Site ⊥	207	42.31 N	70.53 W
Salem State College ⊛[2]	283	42.30 N	70.54 W
Salem Upland ⋀[1]	194	37.25 N	91.30 W
Sälen, Sve.	26	61.10 N	13.16 E
Salen, Scot., U.K.	46	56.43 N	5.47 W
Salen, Scot., U.K.	46	56.31 N	5.57 W
Salentina, Penisola ›[1]	68	40.25 N	18.00 E
Salentine, Murge ◆[1]	68	40.02 N	18.13 E
Salento	68	40.15 N	15.11 E
Salernes	62	43.33 N	6.14 E
Salerno	68	40.41 N	14.47 E
Salerno □[4]	68	40.27 N	15.16 E
Salerno, Golfo di ⊂	68	40.32 N	14.42 E
Salers	32	45.08 N	2.30 E
Salesbury	262	53.47 N	2.30 W
Salesópolis	256	23.32 S	45.51 W
Salève, Mont ∧	58	46.07 N	6.10 E
Salford	44	53.28 N	2.18 W
Salford □[8]	262	53.28 N	2.23 W
Salfords	260	51.12 N	0.10 W
Šalgačova	24	62.19 N	39.35 E
Salgado	250	11.02 S	37.28 W
Salgan	80	55.14 N	45.30 E
Salgar	246	5.58 N	75.59 W
Šalgija	86	47.35 N	70.36 E
Salgir ≃	78	45.38 N	35.01 E
Salgótarján	30	48.07 N	19.48 E
Salgueiro	250	8.04 S	39.06 W
Salher ∧	122	20.43 N	73.56 E
Sali, Alg.	148	26.58 N	0.01 W
Sali, Hrv.	36	43.56 N	15.10 E
Šali, Ross.	80	55.41 N	49.40 E
Šali, Ross.	84	43.08 N	45.54 E
Salí ≃	252	27.33 S	64.57 W
Salice Salentino	68	40.23 N	17.58 E
Salice Terme	62	44.55 N	9.01 E
Salici, Monte ∧	70	37.44 N	14.38 E
Salida, Ca., U.S.	226	37.42 N	121.05 W
Salida, Co., U.S.	200	38.32 N	105.59 W
Salies-de-Béarn	32	43.29 N	0.55 W
Ṣalīf	144	15.18 N	42.40 E
Salignac-Eyvignes	32	44.59 N	1.19 E
Salihli	130	38.29 N	28.09 E
Ṣālikha	126	23.18 N	89.22 E
Šalikovo	82	55.30 N	36.13 E
Salim	140	12.52 N	28.40 E
Salima	154	13.47 S	34.26 E
Salīmah, Wāḥat ▼[4]	140	21.22 N	29.19 E
Salimani	157a	11.47 S	43.17 E
Salimbatu	112	2.57 N	117.21 E
Salimgarh Fort ⊥	272a	28.40 N	77.14 E
Salimi	152	9.24 S	23.35 E
Salin	110	20.35 N	94.39 E
Salina, Ks., U.S.	198	38.50 N	97.36 W
Salina, Ok., U.S.	196	36.17 N	95.09 W
Salina, Pa., U.S.	214	40.31 N	79.30 W
Salina, Ut,. U.S.	200	38.57 N	111.51 W
Salina, Canale di ⊔	70	38.32 N	14.54 E
Salina, Isola I	70	38.34 N	14.50 E
Salina Cruz	234	16.10 N	95.12 W
Salina Point ›	238	22.13 N	74.18 W
Salinas, Bra.	255	16.10 S	42.17 W
Salinas, Ec.	246	2.13 S	80.58 W
Salinas, P.R.	240m	17.59 N	66.18 W
Salinas, Ca., U.S.	226	36.40 N	121.39 W
Salinas ≃, Bra.	255	16.37 S	42.18 W
Salinas (Chixoy) ≃, N.A.	232	16.28 N	90.33 W
Salinas ≃, Ca., U.S.	226	36.45 N	121.48 W
Salinas, Pampa de las ≚	252	31.58 S	66.42 W
Salinas, Ponta das ›	152	12.50 S	12.56 E
Salinas, Sierra de ⋀	226	36.18 N	121.20 W
Salinas de Garci Mendoza	248	19.38 S	67.43 W
Salinas de Hidalgo	234	22.38 N	101.43 W
Salinas del Rey	196	27.38 N	102.24 W
Salinas Municipal Airport ⊠	226	36.40 N	121.40 W
Salinas National Monument ♠	200	34.05 N	106.14 W
Salinas Valley V	226	36.15 N	121.15 W
Salinas Victoria	196	25.53 N	100.19 W
Salin-de-Giraud	62	43.25 N	4.44 E
Salindres	62	44.10 N	4.10 E
Saline, La., U.S.	194	32.09 N	92.58 W
Saline, Mi., U.S.	216	42.10 N	83.46 W
Saline ≃, Ar., U.S.	194	33.44 N	93.58 W
Saline ≃, Ar., U.S.	194	33.10 N	92.08 W
Saline ≃, Il., U.S.	194	37.35 N	88.08 W
Saline ≃, Ks., U.S.	198	38.51 N	97.30 W
Saline ≃, Mi., U.S.	216	41.59 N	83.37 W
Saline, North Fork ≃	194	37.44 N	88.19 W
Saline Bayou ≃	194	31.45 N	92.58 W
Saline di Volterra	66	43.22 N	10.49 E
Saline Lake ⊜[1]	194	31.55 N	92.55 W
Salines, Point ›	241k	12.00 N	61.48 W
Salines, Pointe des ›	240e	14.24 N	60.53 W
Salineville	214	40.37 N	80.51 W
Salingyi	110	21.58 N	95.03 E
Salinópolis	250	0.37 S	47.20 W
Šalinskoje	86	55.43 N	93.46 E
Salins-les-Bains	58	46.57 N	5.53 E
Salins-les-Thermes	62	45.28 N	6.32 E
Salipolo	112	3.45 S	119.29 E
Salisbury, Austl.	168b	34.46 S	138.38 E
Salisbury, Dom.	240d	15.26 N	61.27 W
Salisbury, Eng., U.K.	42	51.05 N	1.48 W
Salisbury, Ct., U.S.	207	41.59 N	73.25 W
Salisbury, Md., U.S.	208	38.21 N	75.35 W
Salisbury, Ma., U.S.	207	42.50 N	70.51 W
Salisbury, Mo., U.S.	194	39.25 N	92.48 W
Salisbury, N.C., U.S.	192	35.40 N	80.28 W
Salisbury, Pa., U.S.	188	39.45 N	79.04 W
Salisbury → Harare, Zimb.	154	17.50 S	31.03 E
Salisbury Cathedral ⊛[1]	42	51.05 N	1.48 W
Salisbury Center	210	43.09 N	74.47 W
Salisbury Hall ⊥	260	51.43 N	0.16 W
Salisbury Island I, Austl.	162	34.21 S	123.32 E
Salisbury Island I, N.T., Can.	176	63.30 N	77.00 W
Salisbury Mills	210	41.26 N	74.08 W
Salisbury Plain ≚	42	51.12 N	1.55 W
Salisbury Plain ≃	283	42.02 N	70.58 W
Salish Mountains ⋀	202	48.15 N	114.45 W
Salito ≃	70	37.29 N	13.46 E
Salitpa	194	31.37 N	88.01 W
Salitre ≃	250	9.29 S	40.39 W
Salix	214	40.18 N	78.46 W
Saljany	84	39.34 N	48.58 E
Šalkar, Kaz.	80	48.03 N	48.56 E
Šalkar, Kaz.	80	50.32 N	51.51 E
Šalkar, ozero ⊜	80	50.33 N	51.40 E
Šalkar-Jega-Kara, ozero ⊜	86	50.45 N	60.54 E
Salkehatchie ≃	192	32.37 N	80.53 W
Ṣalkhad	132	32.29 N	36.43 E
Salkhia	272b	22.35 N	88.21 E
Salkum	224	46.31 N	122.37 W
Salla	24	66.50 N	28.40 E
Salladasburg	210	41.17 N	77.14 W
Sallagriffon	62	43.53 N	6.54 E
Sallanches	58	45.56 N	6.38 E
Salland ◆[1]	52	52.20 N	6.20 E
Salles-Curan	32	44.11 N	2.47 E
Salles-sous-Bois	62	44.27 N	4.56 E
Sallgast	54	51.35 N	13.51 E
Salling ◆[1]	26	56.40 N	9.00 E
Salliqueló	252	36.45 S	62.56 W
Sallisaw	196	35.27 N	94.47 W
Sallisaw Creek ≃	194	35.23 N	94.52 W
Salluit	176	62.14 N	75.38 W
Sallūm	140	19.23 N	37.06 E
Sallūm, Khalīj as- ⊂	146	31.41 N	25.21 E
Salm ≃, Bel.	56	50.22 N	5.52 E
Salm ≃, Dtsch.	56	49.51 N	6.51 E
Salmās	128	38.11 N	44.47 E
Salmchâteau	56	50.16 N	5.54 E
Salme	76	58.10 N	22.15 E
Salmi	24	61.22 N	31.53 E
Salmo	182	49.12 N	117.17 W
Salmon	202	45.10 N	113.53 W
Salmon ≃, B.C., Can.	182	54.05 N	122.34 W
Salmon ≃, N.B., Can.	186	46.06 N	65.56 W
Salmon ≃, On., Can.	212	44.11 N	77.15 W
Salmon ≃, N.A.	188	45.02 N	74.31 W
Salmon ≃, Ct., U.S.	207	41.29 N	72.29 W
Salmon ≃, Id., U.S.	202	45.51 N	116.46 W
Salmon ≃, N.Y., U.S.	212	43.35 N	76.12 W
Salmon ≃, Or., U.S.	224	45.22 N	122.02 W
Salmon ≃, Or., U.S.	224	45.03 N	124.00 W
Salmon, East Fork ≃	202	44.16 N	114.19 W
Salmon, Middle Fork ≃	202	45.18 N	114.36 W
Salmon, North Branch ≃	212	43.32 N	75.48 W
Salmon, South Fork ≃	202	45.23 N	115.31 W
Salmon Arm	182	50.42 N	119.16 W
Salmon-Bay	186	51.26 N	57.36 W
Salmon Creek ≃, N.Y., U.S.	210	43.16 N	77.02 W
Salmon Creek ≃, N.Y., U.S.	210	43.19 N	77.43 W
Salmon Creek ≃, Wa., U.S.	224	46.26 N	122.52 W
Salmon Creek ≃, Wa., U.S.	224	45.44 N	122.45 W
Salmon Falls Creek ≃	202	42.43 N	114.51 W
Salmon Falls Creek Reservoir ⊜[1]	202	42.08 N	114.45 W
Salmon Gums	162	32.59 S	121.38 E
Salmon Lake ⊜	212	44.49 N	78.28 W
Salmon Mountain ∧	188	45.14 N	71.08 W
Salmon Mountains ⋀	204	41.00 N	123.00 W
Salmon Peak ∧	196	29.28 N	100.10 W
Salmon Point ›	212	43.52 N	77.14 W
Salmon River Mountains ⋀	202	44.45 N	115.30 W
Salmon River Reservoir ⊜[1]	212	43.32 N	75.52 W
Salmon Valley	182	54.05 N	122.41 W
Salmyš ≃	86	52.01 N	55.21 E
Sal'nica	78	49.44 N	28.02 E
Salo, Centraf.	152	3.12 N	16.07 E
Salò, It.	64	45.36 N	10.31 E
Salo, Suomi	26	60.23 N	23.08 E
Salobel'ak	80	57.07 N	48.05 E
Salobra ≃	248	20.12 S	56.29 W
Salomatino	80	50.01 N	44.50 E
Salome	200	33.46 N	113.36 W
Salomon, Cap ›	240e	14.30 N	61.06 W
Salomon, Îles → Solomon Islands □[1]	175e	8.00 S	159.00 E
Salomón, Islas → Solomon Islands □[1]	175e	8.00 S	159.00 E
Salomone, Monte ∧	267a	41.47 N	12.44 E
Salomon-Inseln → Solomon Islands □[1]	175e	8.00 S	159.00 E
Salon ≃	58	47.32 N	5.41 E
Salona	210	41.05 N	77.28 W
Salon-de-Provence	62	43.38 N	5.06 E
Salonga ≃	152	0.10 S	19.50 E
Salonga, Parc National de la ♠	152	1.45 S	21.20 E
Salonika → Thessaloníki	38	40.38 N	22.56 E
Salonta	38	46.48 N	21.40 E
Salor ≃, Esp.	34	39.42 N	6.28 W
Salor ≃, Esp.	34	39.39 N	7.03 W
Salorno (Salurn)	64	46.14 N	11.13 E
Saloslovo	265b	55.42 N	37.09 E
Saloum ≃	150	13.50 N	16.45 W
Šalovka ≃	265b	55.47 N	38.12 E
Salpausselkä ∧	26	61.00 N	26.30 E
Şalpazarı	130	40.59 N	39.10 E
Şalqīn	130	36.08 N	36.27 E
Sal Rei	150a	16.11 N	22.55 W
Salsacate	252	31.19 S	65.05 W
Salsette Island I	272c	19.10 N	72.53 E
Salsilgo, Qawz ⊥[8]	140	10.49 N	22.54 E
Salsipuedes, Canal ⊔	232	28.37 N	113.00 W
Salsipuedes, Punta ›, C.R.	236	8.28 N	83.37 W
Salsipuedes, Punta ›, Méx.	232	32.05 N	116.53 W
Šal'sk	80	46.28 N	41.33 E
Šal'skij	24	61.48 N	35.58 E
Sal'sko-Manyčskaja gr'ada ∧	80	46.40 N	42.30 E
Salso ≃	70	37.06 N	13.57 E
Salsomaggiore Terme	64	44.49 N	9.59 E
Salt ≃, U.S.	202	43.08 N	111.02 W
Salt ≃, Az., U.S.	200	33.23 N	112.18 W
Salt ≃, Ky., U.S.	194	38.00 N	85.57 W
Salt ≃, Mi., U.S.	281	42.39 N	82.47 W
Salt ≃, Mo., U.S.	219	39.28 N	91.04 W
Salt, Elk Fork ≃	219	39.28 N	91.53 W
Salt, Middle Fork ≃	219	39.28 N	91.49 W
Salt, North Fork ≃	219	39.30 N	91.47 W
Salt, South Fork ≃	219	39.28 N	91.49 W
Salta	252	24.47 S	65.25 W
Salta □[4]	252	25.00 S	64.30 W
Saltaim, ozero ⊜	86	56.10 N	71.45 E
Saltair	224	48.57 N	123.46 W
Saltaire	276	40.39 N	73.12 W
Saltanovka	76	52.47 N	34.17 E
Saltara	66	43.45 N	12.54 E
Salt Ash, Austl.	170	32.47 S	151.55 E
Saltash, Eng., U.K.	42	50.24 N	4.12 W
Saltbæk Vig ⊂	41	55.43 N	11.12 E
Salt Basin ⊜	196	31.50 N	105.00 W
Saltburn-by-the-Sea	44	54.35 N	0.58 W
Salt Cay I	240b	25.06 N	77.18 W
Saltcoats, Sk., Can.	184	51.03 N	102.12 W
Saltcoats, Scot., U.K.	46	55.38 N	4.47 W
Salt Creek ≃, On., Can.	275b	43.48 N	79.42 W
Salt Creek ≃, Ca., U.S.	204	36.15 N	116.49 W
Salt Creek ≃, Il., U.S.	194	40.08 N	89.50 W
Salt Creek ≃, Il., U.S.	278	41.49 N	87.50 W
Salt Creek ≃, In., U.S.	216	41.37 N	87.09 W
Salt Creek ≃, In., U.S.	218	38.50 N	86.32 W
Salt Creek ≃, In., U.S.	218	39.27 N	85.09 W
Salt Creek ≃, Ks., U.S.	198	39.06 N	97.44 W
Salt Creek ≃, N.M., U.S.	196	33.35 N	104.23 W
Salt Creek ≃, Ok., U.S.	196	36.32 N	96.43 W
Salt Creek ≃, Or., U.S.	202	43.43 N	122.26 W
Salt Creek ≃, Or., U.S.	224	45.09 N	123.13 W
Salt Creek ≃, Wy., U.S.	202	43.41 N	106.20 W
Salt Creek, Middle Fork ≃	218	39.04 N	86.15 W
Salt Creek, North Fork ≃, Il., U.S.	216	40.13 N	88.50 W
Salt Creek, North Fork ≃, In., U.S.	218	39.08 N	86.21 W
Salt Creek, West Branch ≃	278	42.02 N	88.01 W
Salt Creek South Fork ≃	218	39.02 N	86.16 W
Salt Draw V	196	31.19 N	103.28 W
Saltee Islands II	48	52.07 N	6.36 W
Salten	41	56.05 N	9.35 E
Saltfleet	44	53.25 N	0.11 E
Saltford	42	51.24 N	2.27 W
Salt Fork Lake ⊜[1]	214	41.07 N	81.30 W
Salt Fork State Park ♠	214	40.06 N	81.29 W
Saltholm I	41	55.38 N	12.46 E
Saltillo, Méx.	232	25.25 N	101.00 W
Saltillo, Ms., U.S.	194	34.22 N	88.40 W
Saltillo, Pa., U.S.	214	40.13 N	78.01 W
Saltillo, Tn., U.S.	194	35.22 N	88.12 W
Saltillo, Tx., U.S.	222	33.11 N	95.20 W
Salt Island I	240m	18.23 N	64.31 W
Salt Lake	158	29.16 S	24.00 E
Salt Lake ⊜	196	34.05 N	103.05 W
Salt Lake City	200	40.45 N	111.53 W
Salto, Arg.	252	34.17 S	60.15 W
Salto, Ur.	252	31.23 S	57.58 W
Salto ≃	66	42.23 N	12.54 E
Salto, Lago del ⊜	66	42.15 N	13.02 E
Salto da Divisa	255	16.00 S	39.57 W
Salto de las Rosas	252	34.43 S	68.14 W
Salto del Fraile ›	286d	12.11 S	77.03 W
Salto del Guairá	252	24.03 S	54.17 W
Salto Grande	255	22.54 S	49.59 W
Salto Grande, Embalse ⊜[1]	252	31.00 S	57.55 W
Salton City	204	33.19 N	115.59 W
Salton Sea ⊜	204	33.19 N	115.50 W
Salton Sea State Recreation Area ♠	204	33.29 N	115.53 W
Saltonstall, Lake ⊜	283	42.47 N	71.04 W
Sāltora	126	23.32 N	86.56 E
Saltoro Range ⋀	123	35.17 N	77.03 E
Salto Santiago, Represa de ⊜[1]	252	25.40 S	52.30 W
Salt Pan Creek ≃	274a	33.59 S	151.02 E
Saltpeter Creek ⊂	284b	39.20 N	76.22 W
Salt Point	210	41.44 N	73.42 W
Saltpond	150	5.12 N	1.04 W
Salt Range ⋀	123	32.40 N	72.35 E
Salt River Indian Reservation ◆[4]	200	33.31 N	111.48 W
Saltsburg	214	40.29 N	79.27 W
Saltsjöbaden	40	59.17 N	18.18 E
Salt Slough ≃	226	37.18 N	120.54 W
Saltspring Island I	224	48.47 N	123.30 W
Salt Springs Reservoir ⊜[1]	226	38.30 N	120.11 W
Saltville	192	36.52 N	81.45 W
Salt Wells Creek ≃	200	41.39 N	108.59 W
Saltykovka, Ross.	80	52.07 N	44.05 E
Saltykovka, Ross.	265b	55.46 N	37.55 E
Saluda, S.C., U.S.	192	34.00 N	81.46 W
Saluda, Va., U.S.	208	37.36 N	76.35 W
Saluda ≃	192	34.00 N	81.04 W
Saludecio	66	43.52 N	12.40 E
Saluën → Salween ≃	12	16.31 N	97.37 E
Salue Timpaus, Selat ⊔	112	1.55 S	124.00 E
Salug	116	8.07 N	122.47 E
Saluggia	62	45.14 N	8.00 E
Sālūmbar	120	24.08 N	74.03 E
Salunga	208	40.06 N	76.26 W
Saluping Island I	116	6.20 N	122.02 E
Salūq 'Atīq	130	36.36 N	39.07 E
Sālūr	122	18.32 N	83.13 E
Salurn → Salorno	64	46.14 N	11.13 E
Salussola	62	45.27 N	8.07 E
Salutaris	256	22.10 S	43.17 W
Saluzzo	62	44.39 N	7.29 E
Salvación, Bahía ⊂	254	50.55 S	75.05 W
Salvado, Mount ∧	162	25.15 S	121.01 E
Salvador, Bra.	255	12.59 S	38.31 W
Salvador, Pil.	116	7.54 N	123.50 E
Salvador, Ca., U.S.	226	38.20 N	122.18 W
Salvador, El → El Salvador □[1]	236	13.50 N	88.55 W
Salvador, Lake ⊜	194	29.45 N	90.15 W
Salvador Island I	116	15.31 N	119.55 E
Salvador María	258	35.18 S	59.10 W
Salvador Mazza	252	22.04 S	63.43 W
Salvage	186	48.41 N	53.38 W
Salvail ≃	206	45.49 N	72.58 W
Salvaterra	250	0.46 S	48.31 W
Salvaterra de Magos	34	39.01 N	8.48 W
Salvatierra	234	20.13 N	100.53 W
Salve	68	39.51 N	18.17 E
Salviac	32	44.41 N	1.16 E
Salwā, Dawḥat ⊂	128	25.30 N	50.40 E
Salwā Baḥrī	140	24.44 N	32.56 E
Salween ≃	12	16.31 N	97.37 E
Salyān	124	28.22 N	82.10 E
Salyer	204	40.53 N	123.35 W
Salyersville	192	37.45 N	83.04 W
Šalygino	78	51.34 N	34.07 E
Salza ≃, Dtsch.	54	51.32 N	11.50 E
Salza ≃, Öst.	61	47.40 N	14.43 E
Salzach ≃	30	48.12 N	12.56 E
Salza Irpina	68	40.55 N	14.53 E
Salzbergen	52	52.19 N	7.20 E
Salzböde ≃	56	50.40 N	8.42 E
Salzbrunn	156	24.23 S	18.00 E
Salzburg	64	47.48 N	13.02 E
Salzburg □[3]	64	47.25 N	13.15 E
Salzgitter	52	52.10 N	10.25 E
Salzgitter-Bad ◆[8]	52	52.04 N	10.23 E
Salzgitter-Barum ◆[8]	52	52.07 N	10.25 E
Salzgitter-Immendorf ◆[8]	52	52.09 N	10.26 E
Salzgitter-Lebenstedt ◆[8]	52	52.09 N	10.20 E
Salzgitter-Thiede ◆[8]	52	52.11 N	10.29 E
Salzgitter-Watenstedt ◆[8]	54	52.06 N	10.22 E
Salzhaff ⊂	54	54.06 N	11.36 E
Salzhausen	52	53.13 N	10.09 E
Salzhemmendorf	52	52.04 N	9.35 E
Salzkammergut ◆[1]	64	47.45 N	13.30 E
Salzkotten	52	51.40 N	8.36 E
Salzmünde	54	51.31 N	11.49 E
Salzwedel	54	52.51 N	11.09 E
Sam, Gabon	152	0.58 N	11.16 E
Sām, India	120	26.50 N	70.31 E
Samā	132	32.28 N	36.14 E
Sama ≃	248	18.10 S	70.40 W
Sam A. Baker State Park ♠	194	37.16 N	90.34 W
Samacá	246	5.29 N	73.29 W
Samacimbo	152	13.33 S	16.59 E
Sama [de Langreo]	34	43.18 N	5.41 W
Samādūn	142	30.20 N	30.57 E
Samagaltaj	88	50.36 N	95.03 E
Samah	146	28.12 N	19.09 E
Samāika ◆[8]	272a	28.32 N	77.05 E
Samaipata	248	18.09 S	63.52 W
Samal (Peñaplata)	116	7.05 N	125.42 E
Samalá ≃	236	14.11 N	91.47 W
Samalanga	114	5.13 N	96.22 E
Samalayuca	200	31.21 N	106.28 W
Šamaldy-Saj	85	41.12 N	72.11 E
Samales Group II	116	6.00 N	121.45 E
Samalga Pass ⊔	180	52.48 N	169.25 W
Samal Island I	116	7.03 N	125.44 E
Sāmalkot	122	17.03 N	82.11 E
Samālūt	142	28.18 N	30.42 E
Samambaia ≃	255	22.45 S	53.21 W
Samāna, India	124	30.09 N	76.12 E
Samaná, Rep. Dom.	238	19.13 N	69.19 W
Samaná, Bahía de ⊂	238	19.10 N	69.25 W
Samaná, Cabo ›	238	19.18 N	69.09 W
Samana Cay I	238	23.06 N	73.42 W
Samandağı	130	36.07 N	35.56 E
Samandıra	130	40.59 N	29.13 E
Samandıra ≃	267b	40.59 N	29.15 E
Samangān	120	36.16 N	68.01 E
Samangān □[4]	120	36.15 N	67.40 E
Samangwa	152	4.24 S	24.10 E
Samani	92a	42.07 N	142.56 E
Samaniego	246	1.20 N	77.35 W
Samanlı Dağları ⋀	130	40.36 N	29.30 E
Samannūd	142	30.58 N	31.15 E
Samar	132	29.49 N	35.01 E
Samar □[4]	116	11.50 N	125.00 E
Samar I	116	12.00 N	125.00 E
Samara	80	53.12 N	50.09 E
Samara ≃, Ross.	80	53.10 N	50.04 E
Samara ≃, Ukr.	78	48.27 N	35.07 E
Samarai	164	10.37 S	150.40 E
Samara Oblast' □[4]	80	53.30 N	50.30 E
Samarate	62	45.38 N	8.47 E
Samarga	89	47.17 N	138.48 E
Samarga ≃	89	47.15 N	138.46 E
Samaria, Id., U.S.	202	42.07 N	112.20 W
Samaria, Mi., U.S.	216	41.48 N	83.35 W
Samaria (As-Sāmirah) □[9]	132	32.15 N	35.10 E
Samaria, Mount ∧	169	36.52 S	146.03 E
Samaria Gorge → Farángi Samariás V	38	35.18 N	24.00 E
Samariapo	246	5.15 N	67.48 W
Samarinda	112	0.30 S	117.09 E
Samarka	89	44.44 N	134.13 E
Samarkand	85	39.40 N	66.48 E
Samarkand □[4]	85	39.40 N	67.15 E
Sāmarrā'	128	34.12 N	43.52 E
Samar Sea ▼[2]	116	12.15 N	124.15 E
Samarskoje, Kaz.	86	49.00 N	83.23 E
Samarskoje, Ross.	83	46.56 N	39.41 E
Şamarskoje, Ross.	86	52.02 N	58.10 E
Šamary	86	57.21 N	58.14 E
Samasata	123	29.21 N	71.33 E
Samassi	71	39.29 N	8.54 E
Samastīpur	124	25.51 N	85.47 E
Samatya ◆[8]	267b	41.00 N	28.56 E

Symbols in the index entries represent the broad categories identified in the key at the right. Symbols with superior numbers (⋀[1]) identify subcategories (see complete key on page I · 1).

Symbole im Register stellen die rechts im Schlüssel erklärten Kategorien dar. Symbole mit hochgestellten Ziffern (⋀[1]) bezeichnen Unterabteilungen einer Kategorie (vgl. vollständiger Schlüssel auf Seite I · 1).

Los símbolos incluídos en el texto del índice representan las grandes categorías identificadas con la clave a la derecha. Los símbolos con numeros en su parte superior (⋀[1]) identifican las subcategorías (véase la clave completa en la página I · 1).

Les symboles de l'index représentent les catégories indiquées dans la légende à droite. Les symboles suivis d'un indice (⋀[1]) représentent des sous-catégories (voir légende complète à la page I · 1).

Os símbolos incluídos no texto do índice representam as grandes categorias identificadas com a chave à direita. Os símbolos com números em sua parte superior (⋀[1]) identificam as subcategorias (veja-se a chave completa à página I · 1).

∧ Mountain	Berg	Montaña	Montagne	Montanha
⋀ Mountains	Gebirge	Montañas	Montagnes	Montanhas
)(Pass	Paß	Paso	Col	Passo
V Valley, Canyon	Tal, Cañon	Valle, Cañón	Vallée, Canyon	Vale, Canhão
≚ Plain	Ebene	Llano	Plaine	Planície
› Cape	Kap	Cabo	Cap	Cabo
I Island	Insel	Isla	Île	Ilha
II Islands	Inseln	Islas	Îles	Ilhas
⊥ Other Topographic Features	Andere Topographische Objekte	Otros Elementos Topográficos	Autres données topographiques	Outros acidentes topográficos

ESPAÑOL Nombre	Página	Lat.°	Long.° W=Oeste
FRANÇAIS Nom	Page	Lat.	Long. W=Ouest
PORTUGUÊS Nome	Página	Lat.	Long. W=Oeste

Column 1

Name	Pg	Lat	Long
Semaúna	248	7.50 S	60.02 W
Semawãri	120	28.34 N	66.46 E
Semba, Centraf.	152	6.49 N	21.12 E
Samba, India	123	32.34 N	75.07 E
Samba, Zaïre	152	0.14 N	21.19 E
Samba, Zaïre	154	4.58 S	26.22 E
Samba Caju	152	8.46 S	15.24 E
Sambaetiba	256	22.41 S	42.48 W
Sambalba	250	7.08 S	45.21 W
Sambalpur	122	21.27 N	83.58 E
Sambar, Tanjung ▸	112	2.59 S	110.19 E
Sambas	112	1.20 N	109.15 E
Sambava	157b	14.15 S	50.10 E
Sambawizi	154	18.21 S	26.16 E
Sambayat	130	37.41 N	38.03 E
Sambaza	120	31.49 N	89.20 E
Sambek, Ross.	83	47.20 N	39.01 E
Sambek, Ross.	83	47.45 N	39.48 E
Sambek ≃	83	47.16 N	39.01 E
Sambesi — Zambezi ≃	138	18.55 S	36.04 E
Sambhal	124	28.35 N	78.33 E
Sâmbhar	120	26.55 N	75.12 E
Sâmbhar Lake ⊘	120	26.56 N	75.05 E
Sambia — Zambia ◻¹	154	14.30 C	27.30 E
Sambiase	68	38.58 N	16.17 E
Sambit, Pulau ▮	112	1.46 N	119.03 E
Sarrbito ≃	250	5.40 S	42.10 W
Sarrbo	152	12.57 S	16.05 E
Samboan	116	9.32 N	123.18 E
Sambola	112	1.02 S	117.02 E
Sambolabbo	152	7.05 N	11.59 E
Sâmbor, Kâm.	110	12.46 N	105.58 E
Sambor, Ukr.	78	49.32 N	23.11 E
Samoorombón ≃	252	35.43 S	57.20 W
Samoorombón, Bahía ⊂	258	30.5 N	57.12 W
Samborondón	246	1.57 S	79.44 W
Sambre ≃	32	50.28 N	4.52 E
Sambre à l'Oise, Canal de la ≅	50	49.39 N	3.20 E
Sambreville	56	50.26 N	4.37 E
Sambriãl	123	32.28 N	74.21 E
Sambú ≃	246	8.05 N	78.18 W
Sambuca di Sicilia	70	37.39 N	13.07 E
Sambuca Pistoiese	66	44.06 N	11.00 E
Sambughetti, Monte ∧	70	37.50 N	14.22 E
Sambungo	152	8.39 S	20.43 E
Sambusu	156	17.50 S	19.20 E
Samch'ôk	98	37.27 N	129.10 E
Sam Chom, Khao ∧	110	8.07 N	99.26 E
Samch'ônp'o	98	34.57 S	128.03 E
Samdžir, gora ∧	88	52.32 N	93.53 E
Same	154	4.04 S	37.44 E
Same ≃	94	36.54 N	140.49 E
Samedan	58	46.33 N	9.52 E
Samegawa	94	37.02 N	140.31 E
Sãmen	128	34.12 N	48.42 E
Samere, Oued ∇	148	26.49 N	7.08 E
Samer	50	50.38 N	1.45 E
Sameru Dando ∧	124	27.02 N	93.20 E
Samet	80	57.49 N	40.44 E
Samford	171a	27.23 S	152.53 E
Samfya	154	11.21 S	29.32 E
Samgóng	98	35.25 N	128.05 E
Samho	98	39.56 N	127.53 E
Saminka ≃	265b	55.45 N	37.17 E
Samiria ≃	246	4.42 S	74.13 W
Samish	224	48.33 N	122.33 W
Samish ≃	224	48.38 N	122.29 W
Samish Bay c	224	48.36 N	122.28 W
Samish Lake ⊘	224	48.39 N	122.24 W
Samj	132	32.27 N	36.30 E
Samka	110	20.09 N	96.57 E
Sâmkir	84	40.50 N	46.02 E
Samlesbury	262	53.46 N	2.38 W
Samlesbury Aerodrome c	262	53.47 N	2 34 W
Samlesbury Bottoms	262	53.45 N	2 34 W
Samlesbury Higher Hall ∆	262	53.46 N	2.34 W
Samli	130	39.48 N	27.51 E
Sammamish, Lake ⊘	224	47.36 N	122.06 W
Sammichele di Bari	68	40.53 N	16.57 E
Samnangjin	98	35.23 N	128.50 E
Samnaun	58	46.57 N	10.22 E
Samnaungruppe ∧	58	46.57 N	10.25 E
Sam Ngao	110	17.15 N	99.01 E
Samnû	146	27.17 N	14.53 E
Samnye	98	35.55 N	127.05 E
Samo	164	3.58 S	152.51 E
Samoa ◻¹ — Western Samoa ◻¹	175a	13.55 S	172.00 W
Samoa — American Samoa ◻²	175a	14.20 S	170.00 W
Samoa americane — American Samoa ◻²	175a	14.20 S	170.00 W
Samoa Basin ▾¹	14	16.00 S	166.00 W
Samoa i Sisifo — Western Samoa ◻¹	175a	13.55 S	172.00 W
Samoa Islands ▮	175a	14.00 S	171.00 W
Samo Alto	252	30.25 S	70.58 W
Samoa Occidental — Western Samoa ◻¹	175a	13.55 S	172.00 W
Samoa Occidentales — Western Samoa ◻¹	175a	13.55 S	172.00 W
Samobor	36	45.48 N	15.43 E
Samoded	24	63.38 N	40.29 E
Samodens	58	46.06 N	6.44 E
Samofalovka	80	48.57 N	44.13 E
Samoggia ≃	64	44.41 N	11.15 E
Samojlovka	80	51.12 N	43.43 E
Samokov	38	42.20 N	23.33 E
Samolaco	58	46.15 N	9.21 E
Samora ≃	266c	38.50 N	8.57 W
Samorín	64	48.01 N	17.27 E
Samos ▮	38	37.48 N	26.44 E
Samosdelka	80	46.02 N	47.53 E
Samoset	220	27.28 N	82.32 W
Samosir, Pulau ▮	114	2.35 N	98.50 E
Samotevici	76	53.13 N	31.50 E
Samothrace — Samothráki ▮	38	40.30 N	25.32 E
Samothráki	38	40.28 N	25.31 E
Samothráki (Samothrace) ▮	38	40.30 N	25.32 E
Samouco	266c	38.43 N	9.00 W
Samovo	76	54.12 N	31.22 E
Samovol'no-Ivanovka	80	52.30 N	50.53 E
S'amozero	24	61.54 N	33.13 E
Sampacho	252	33.23 S	64.43 W
Sampaga	112	2.19 S	119.07 E
Sampaio Correia	256	22.52 S	42.36 W
Sampalan	115b	8.41 S	115.34 E
Sampanahan	112	2.34 S	116.11 E
Sampang	115a	7.12 S	113.14 E
Sampawams Creek ≃	276	40.41 N	73.19 W
Sam Pervyj	86	54.38 N	56.06 E
Sampéyre	62	44.34 N	7.11 E
Sampford Peverell	42	50.56 N	3.22 W
Sampieri	70	36.43 N	14.44 E
Sampit	112	2.32 S	112.57 E
Sampit ≃	112	3.42 S	112.54 E
Sampit, Teluk c	112	3.05 S	113.03 E
Sampolawa	112	5.36 S	122.43 E
Sampson	279b	40.10 N	79.53 W
Sampson State Park ♦	210	42.44 N	76.55 W
Sampués	246	9.11 N	75.23 W
Sampwe	80	12.51 N	41.37 E

Column 2

Name	Pg	Lat	Long
Sampwe	154	9.20 S	27.26 E
Šamrajevka	78	49.46 N	29.49 E
Samrãla	123	30.51 N	76.11 E
Sam Rayburn Reservoir ⊘¹	194	31.27 N	94.37 W
Samre	144	13.07 N	39.10 E
Samreboi	150	5.36 N	2.34 W
Samro, ozero ⊘	76	58.57 N	28.49 E
Samrong, Khlong ≃	269a	13.39 N	100.34 E
Sams ≃	224	47.38 N	124.01 W
Samsang	120	30.31 N	82.37 E
Samsø ▮	41	55.52 N	10.37 E
Samsø Bælt ∪	41	55.48 N	10.47 E
Samson, Al., U.S.	194	31.06 N	86.02 W
Sam Son, Viet	110	19.44 N	105.54 E
Samson Indian Reserve ✦⁴	182	52.48 N	113.10 W
Samsonovka	85	44.47 N	132.09 E
Samsonvale, Lake ⊘¹	171a	27.15 S	152.55 E
Samsonville	210	41.53 N	74.18 W
Sams Point ∧	210	41.40 N	74.22 W
Samsu	98	41.19 N	127.59 E
Samsun	130	41.17 N	36.20 E
Samsun ◻¹	130	41.15 N	36.00 E
Samsun Körfezi c	130	41.18 N	36.21 E
Samtens	54	54.21 N	13.17 E
Samthar	124	25.51 N	78.55 E
Samtown	194	31.16 N	92.26 W
Samtredia	84	42.10 N	42.20 E
Samu	112	2.01 S	115.57 E
Samūdragarh	126	23.21 N	88.20 E
Samuel, Mount ∧	162	19.41 S	134.09 E
Samuel P. Taylor State Park ♦	226	38.01 N	122.44 W
Samugheo	71	39.57 N	8.56 E
Samui, Ko ▮	110	9.30 N	100.00 E
Samukawa	94	35.22 N	139.23 E
Samundri	123	31.04 N	72.58 E
Samur ≃	84	41.53 N	48.32 E
Samur-Apšeronskij kanal ≅	84	41.38 N	48.25 E
Samurskij chrebet ∡	84	41.35 N	47.35 E
Samusu'	86	56.46 N	84.44 E
Samusele	152	10.06 S	24.05 E
Samut Prakan	110	13.36 N	100.36 E
Samut Prakan ◻⁴	269a	13.35 N	100.35 E
Samut Sakhon	110	13.32 N	100.17 E
Samut Songkhram	110	13.24 N	100.00 E
Samuyi Shankou ⋊	124	29.55 N	84.46 E
S'amža	76	60.01 N	41.02 E
San (Xan) ≃, Asia	110	13.32 N	105.58 E
San ≃, Europe	30	50.44 N	21.50 E
San ≃, Zhg.	100	33.02 N	119.21 E
Saña, Perú	248	6.55 S	79.35 W
San 'ã', Yaman	144	15.23 N	44.12 E
San ≃, Ross.	82	54.41 N	35.55 E
Sanaag ◻⁴	144	10.30 N	47.45 E
Sanaba	150	12.25 N	3.49 W
Sanaba ≃	150	15.06 N	10.55 W
Sanabū	142	27.30 N	30.47 E
Sanada	94	36.27 N	138.20 E
Sanaga ≃	9	70.30 S	2.30 W
Sanafir ▮	142	30.47 N	31.21 E
Sanâfîr ▮	128	27.55 N	34.40 E
Sanaga ≃	152	3.35 N	9.38 E
Sanage-yama ∧	94	35.12 N	137.10 E
Sanagōchi	96	33.59 N	134.28 E
San Agustín, Arg.	252	38.01 S	58.21 W
San Agustín, Arg.	252	31.59 S	64.23 W
San Agustín, Bol.	248	21.05 S	67.45 W
San Agustín, Col.	246	1.53 N	76.16 W
San Agustín, Méx.	236	21.31 N	106.15 W
San Agustín, Pil.	116	16.30 N	121.45 E
San Agustín, Cape ▸	116	6.16 N	126.11 E
San Agustín, Plains of ⊂	200	33.50 N	108.00 W
San Agustín Atenango	234	17.38 N	97.59 W
San Agustín de Valle Fértil	252	30.38 S	67.27 W
San Agustín Loxicha	234	16.01 N	96.38 W
San Agustín Tlaxiaca	234	20.07 N	98.53 W
Sanak Islands ▮	180	54.25 N	162.35 W
San Alberto	196	27.30 N	102.30 W
San Alejo	236	13.26 N	87.58 W
Sãn al-Hajar, Birkat ⊘	142	31.03 N	31.54 E
Sãn al-Hajar al-Qiblîyah	142	30.58 N	31.52 E
Sanalona, Presa ⊘¹	232	24.53 N	107.00 W
San Ambrosio, Isla ▮	244	26.21 S	79.52 W
Sanam Chai, Khlong ≃	269b	13.38 N	100.27 E
Sanana	112	2.04 S	125.58 E
Sanana, Pulau ▮	112	2.12 S	125.55 E
Sãnandaj	128	35.19 N	47.00 E
Sanandita	248	21.40 S	63.35 W
San Andreas	226	38.11 N	120.40 W
San Andreas Fault ∇	282	37.25 N	122.15 W
San Andrés, Col.	246	6.49 N	72.52 W
San Andrés, Col.	246	5.23 N	81.42 W
San Andrés, Méx.	232	27.14 N	114.14 W
San Andrés, Pan.	236	8.36 N	82.44 W
San Andrés, Laguna c	234	22.40 N	97.52 W
San Andrés Calpan	234	19.06 N	98.27 W
San Andrés Cohamiata	232	22.12 N	104.03 W
San Andrés de Giles	258	34.27 S	59.27 W
San Andrés Mountains ∧	200	33.25 N	106.45 W
San Andres Point ▸	116	13.34 N	121.52 E
San Andrés Sajcabajá	236	15.13 N	90.55 W
San Andrés Timilpan	234	19.52 N	99.45 W
San Andrés Tototepec ❋⁸	286a	19.15 N	99.10 W
San Andrés Tuxtla	234	18.27 N	95.13 W
San Andrés y Providencia ◻⁸	238	12.30 N	81.45 W
Sananduva	252	27.57 S	51.48 W
San Angel — Álvaro Obregón	286a	19.21 N	99.12 W
San Angelo	196	31.27 N	100.26 W
San Anselmo	226	37.58 N	122.33 W
San Antero	246	9.23 N	75.46 W
San Antonio, Arg.	252	28.57 S	65.20 W
San Antonio, Chile	252	33.35 S	71.38 W
San Antonio, Col.	246	3.55 N	75.28 W
San Antonio, C.R.	236	10.12 N	85.26 W
San Antonio, N. Mar. Is.	174n	15.08 N	145.43 E
San Antonio, Perú	248	6.22 S	76.21 W
San Antonio, Pil.	116	12.35 N	124.17 E
San Antonio, Pil.	116	14.57 N	120.05 E
San Antonio, P.R.	240m	18.30 N	67.07 W
San Antonio, Fl., U.S.	220	28.20 N	82.16 W
San Antonio, N.M., U.S.	200	35.06 N	106.22 W
San Antonio, Tx., U.S.	196	29.25 N	98.29 W
San Antonio, Ur.	252	34.27 S	56.05 W
San Antonio ≃, Méx.	196	29.13 N	103.47 W
San Antonio ≃, Méx.	232	31.00 N	116.15 W

Column 3

Name	Pg	Lat	Long
San Antonio ≃, Tx., U.S.	196	28.30 N	96.50 W
San Antonio ≃¹	288	34.24 S	58.31 W
San Antonio, Cabo ▸	252	36.40 S	56.42 W
San Antonio, Cabo de ▸	240p	21.52 N	84.57 W
San Antonio, Lake ⊘¹	226	35.55 N	121.00 W
San Antonio, Mount ∧	228	34.17 N	117.39 W
San Antonio, Punta ▸, Méx.	232	29.46 N	115.42 W
San Antonio, Punta ▸, Méx.	232	26.31 N	111.28 W
San Antonio, Rio ≃	200	37.11 N	105.55 W
San Antonio Bay c, Pil.	116	8.38 N	117.35 E
San Antonio Bay c, Tx., U.S.	196	28.20 N	96.45 W
San Antonio Canyon ∇	280	34.12 N	117.40 W
San Antonio Creek ≃	226	38.09 N	122.33 W
San Antonio Dam ❋⁶	280	34.09 N	117.41 W
San Antonio de Areco	258	34.15 S	59.28 W
San Antonio de Galipán	286c	10.33 N	66.53 W
San Antonio de los Baños	240p	22.53 N	82.30 W
San Antonio de los Cobres	252	24.11 S	66.21 W
San Antonio del Táchira	246	7.50 N	72.27 W
San Antonio de Padua, Arg.	258	34.40 S	58.42 W
San Antonio de Padua, Méx.	234	22.35 N	104.30 W
San Antonio de Padua, Mission ∇¹	226	36.01 N	121.15 W
San Antonio de Tamanaco	246	9.41 N	66.03 W
San Antonio El Bravo	232	30.10 N	104.42 W
San Antonio Eloxochitlán	234	18.11 N	96.52 W
San Antonio Heights	228	34.10 N	117.40 W
San Antonio Mountain ∧	200	36.52 N	106.02 W
San Antonio Nogalar	234	23.04 N	98.22 W
San Antonio Oeste	254	40.44 S	64.56 W
San Antonio Reservoir ⊘¹	226	37.35 N	121.50 W
San Antonio Someyucan	286a	19.27 N	99.16 W
San Antonio Suchitepéquez	236	14.32 N	91.25 W
San Antonio Tecómitl ❋⁸	286a	19.13 N	98.59 W
San Antonio Ticino	266b	45.35 N	8.46 E
San Ardo	226	36.01 N	120.54 W
Sanaroa Island ▮	164	9.35 S	151.01 E
Sanary-sur-Mer	62	43.07 N	5.48 E
Sanatoga	285	40.15 N	75.36 W
Sanatoga Creek ≃	285	40.14 N	75.36 W
Sanatorium	194	31.53 N	89.46 W
San Augustine	194	31.31 N	94.06 W
San Augustin Pass ⋊	200	32.26 N	106.34 W
Sanaūr	124	30.18 N	76.27 E
Sanāw	144	17.50 N	51.00 E
Sanāwad	123	22.11 N	76.04 E
Sanāwān	123	30.19 N	70.59 E
Sanbao, Zhg.	102	43.00 N	93.19 E
Sanbao, Zhg.	105	40.20 N	116.02 E
Sanbe-yama ∧	96	35.08 N	132.37 E
San Bartolomeo in Galdo	68	41.24 N	15.01 E
San Basilio	71	39.32 N	9.11 E
San Benedetto, Alpe di ∧	66	43.53 N	11.43 E
San Benedetto del Alpe	66	43.59 N	11.41 E
San Benedetto in Alpe	66	43.59 N	11.41 E
San Benedetto, Isla ▮	232	19.18 N	110.49 W
San Benigno Canavese	62	45.13 N	7.46 E
San Benito, Bol.	248	17.31 S	65.55 W
San Benito, Guat.	232	16.55 N	89.54 W
San Benito, Perú	248	7.26 S	78.56 W
San Benito, Tx., U.S.	196	26.08 N	97.37 W
San Benito ≃	226	36.51 N	121.24 W
San Benito ◻⁶	226	36.53 N	121.34 W
San Benito Mountain ∧	226	36.22 N	120.38 W
San Bernard ≃	222	28.52 N	95.27 W
San Bernardino, Schw.	58	46.28 N	9.12 E
San Bernardino, Ca., U.S.	228	34.07 N	117.18 W
San Bernardino ◻⁶	228	34.07 N	117.17 W
San Bernardino Passo del ⋊	58	46.30 N	9.11 E
San Bernardino Mountains ∧	204	34.10 N	116.45 W
San Bernardino National Forest ♦	228	34.12 N	117.38 W
San Bernardino Strait ∪	116	12.32 N	124.10 E
San Bernardo, Arg.	252	27.17 S	60.42 W
San Bernardo, Chile	252	33.36 S	70.43 W
San Bernardo, Méx.	232	25.59 N	105.33 W
San Bernardo, Isla ▮	236	11.32 N	105.06 W
San Bernardo, Islas de ▮	246	9.45 N	75.50 W
San Bernardo del Viento	246	9.21 N	75.57 W
San Biagio di Callalta	64	45.41 N	12.22 E
San Biagio Platani	70	37.31 N	13.32 E
San Biagio Saracinisco	70	41.37 N	13.55 E
San Blas, Méx.	234	26.05 N	108.46 W
San Blas, Méx.	234	21.31 N	105.16 W
San Blas, Cape ▸	192	29.40 N	85.22 W
San Blas, Golfo de c	246	9.30 N	79.00 W
San Blas, Serranía De ∧	246	9.18 N	79.00 W
San Blas de los Sauces	252	28.24 S	67.05 W
San Bonifacio	64	45.24 N	11.16 E
San Borja	248	14.49 S	66.51 W
Sanborn, Ia., U.S.	198	43.11 N	95.39 W
Sanborn, Mn., U.S.	198	44.12 N	95.07 W
San Bovio	266b	45.28 N	9.17 E
San Bruno	282	37.37 N	122.24 W
San Bruno, Pt. ▸	282	37.39 N	122.22 W
San Bruno Mountain ∧	282	37.42 N	122.25 W
Sanbu	94	35.39 N	140.23 E
San Buenaventura, Bol.	248	14.28 S	67.35 W
San Buenaventura, Méx.	236	27.05 N	101.32 W
San Buenaventura — Ventura, Ca., U.S.	228	34.17 N	119.18 W
San Buono	68	41.59 N	14.34 E
San Calogero	68	38.34 N	16.01 E
San Calogero, Monte ∧	70	37.57 N	13.44 E
San Candido (Innichen)	64	46.44 N	12.17 E
Sancang	100	32.45 N	120.43 E
San Carlos, Arg.	252	25.56 S	65.56 W
San Carlos, Arg.	252	33.46 S	69.00 W

Column 4

Name	Pg	Lat	Long
San Carlos, Chile	252	36.25 S	71.58 W
San Carlos, Chile	286e	33.36 S	70.35 W
San Carlos, Méx.	232	29.01 N	100.51 W
San Carlos, Méx.	232	24.35 N	98.56 W
San Carlos, Nic.	236	11.07 N	84.47 W
San Carlos, Pan.	236	8.29 N	79.57 W
San Carlos, Para.	252	22.16 S	57.18 W
San Carlos, Pil.	116	10.30 N	123.25 E
San Carlos, Pil.	116	15.55 N	120.20 E
San Carlos, Az., U.S.	200	33.20 N	110.27 W
San Carlos, Ca., U.S.	282	37.29 N	122.15 W
San Carlos, Ur.	252	34.48 S	54.55 W
San Carlos, Ven.	246	9.40 N	68.36 W
San Carlos, C.R.	236	10.47 N	84.12 W
San Carlos Borromeo, Mission ∇¹	226	36.34 N	121.55 W
San Carlos Centro	252	31.44 S	61.06 W
San Carlos de Bariloche	254	41.09 S	71.18 W
San Carlos de Bolívar	252	36.15 S	61.06 W
San Carlos de Chena	286e	33.35 S	70.44 W
San Carlos de Guaroa	246	3.44 N	73.14 W
San Carlos del Zulia	246	9.01 N	71.55 W
San Carlos de Río Negro	246	1.55 N	67.04 W
San Carlos Indian Reservation ✦⁴	200	33.23 N	110.09 W
San Carlos Reservoir ⊘¹	200	33.13 N	110.24 W
San Carlos Viejo, Canal ≅	286e	33.25 S	70.38 W
San Carpoforo Creek ≃	226	35.47 N	121.19 W
San Casciano dei Bagni	66	42.52 N	11.53 E
San Casciano in Val di Pesa	66	43.39 N	11.11 E
San Catado, It.	68	40.23 N	18.17 E
San Catadò, It.	70	37.29 N	13.59 E
San Cayetano	252	38.20 S	59.37 W
Sancergues	50	47.09 N	2.55 E
Sancerre	50	47.20 N	2.51 E
Sancerrois, Collines du ∡²	50	47.25 N	2.45 E
San Cesario di Lecce	68	40.18 N	18.10 E
San Cesario sul Panaro	64	44.34 N	11.02 E
Sancey-le-Grand	58	47.18 N	6.35 E
Sancha, Zhg.	105	40.27 N	116.26 E
Sancha, Zhg.	105	31.52 N	119.06 E
Sancha ≃	102	26.55 N	106.06 E
Sanchahe	89	44.59 N	126.04 E
Sanchakou	105	39.47 N	117.19 E
Sanchazi	104	41.07 N	124.15 E
Sanchazi	104	42.03 N	123.59 E
Sanchenglong	89	44.02 N	120.58 E
Sánchez	238	19.14 N	69.36 W
Sánchez Magallanes	234	18.14 N	93.52 W
Sanchih	100	25.16 N	121.30 E
San Chirico Raparo	68	40.11 N	16.05 E
Sanch'ong	98	35.26 N	127.54 E
Sanchung	269d	25.04 N	121.30 E
Sanch'ungch'iao	269d	25.12 N	121.35 E
San Cipirello	70	37.58 N	13.10 E
San Ciro de Acosta	234	21.38 N	99.49 W
San Clemente, Esp.	34	39.24 N	2.26 W
San Clemente, Ca., U.S.	228	33.25 N	117.36 W
San Clemente, Cerro ∧	254	46.36 S	73.20 W
San Clemente a Casauria ∇¹	66	42.14 N	13.55 E
San Clemente Island ▮	228	32.54 N	118.29 W
Sancoins	32	46.50 N	2.55 E
San Colombano al Lambro	62	45.11 N	9.29 E
San Cono	70	37.17 N	14.22 E
Sanco Point ▸	116	8.15 N	126.27 E
San Cosme	252	27.22 S	58.31 W
San Cosmo Albanese	68	39.35 N	16.25 E
San Costantino Albanese	68	40.06 N	16.18 E
San Cristóbal, Cuba	240p	22.43 N	83.03 W
San Cristóbal, Rep. Dom.	238	18.25 N	70.06 W
San Cristóbal, Ven.	246	7.46 N	72.14 W
San Cristóbal, Bahía c	232	27.23 N	114.38 W
San Cristóbal, Cerro ∧, Chile	286e	33.25 S	70.39 W
San Cristóbal, Cerro ∧, Perú	286d	12.02 S	77.01 W
San Cristóbal, Isla ▮	246a	0.50 S	89.26 W
San Cristóbal, Nevis — Saint Kitts and Nevis ◻¹	238	17.20 N	62.45 W
San Cristóbal, Volcán ∧	236	12.42 N	87.01 W
San Cristóbal de la Barranca	234	21.03 N	103.26 W
San Cristóbal de la Laguna	148	28.29 N	16.19 W
San Cristóbal de las Casas	234	16.45 N	92.38 W
San Cristóbal Totonicapán	236	14.55 N	91.26 W
San Cristobal Trench ❋¹	14	11.15 S	162.45 E
San Cristóbal Verapaz	236	15.23 N	90.24 W
San Cristoforo	62	44.43 N	8.49 E
San Croce, Monte ∧	200	32.47 N	113.44 W
Sancti Spiritus	240p	21.56 N	79.27 W
Sancti Spiritus ◻⁶	240p	22.00 N	79.30 W
San Cugat, Riera de ≃	266d	41.29 N	2.11 E
Sancy, Puy de ∧	50	45.32 N	2.49 E
San Damián	248	12.05 S	76.24 W
San Damiano d'Asti	62	44.50 N	8.04 E
San Damiano Macra	62	44.29 N	7.16 E
Sandan, Chãn ⋊⁴	128	28.59 N	63.27 E
San Daniele del Friuli	64	46.09 N	13.00 E
Sandan-kyō ✦	96	34.38 N	132.13 E

Column 5

Name	Pg	Lat	Long
Sandanski	38	41.34 N	23.17 E
Sandaogang	89	46.08 N	130.05 E
Sandaogou, Zhg.	104	41.39 N	121.45 E
Sandaogou, Zhg.	105	39.33 N	115.27 E
Sandaohe	86	44.21 N	85.37 E
Sandaoliangzi	104	41.20 N	122.07 E
Sandaolingzi	104	40.58 N	124.08 E
Sandaozhen	89	47.25 N	126.25 E
Sandaré	150	14.42 N	10.18 W
Sandared	26	57.43 N	12.47 E
Sandarne	26	61.16 N	17.10 E
Sand Arroyo ∇	196	37.29 N	101.29 W
Sandata	80	46.16 N	41.46 E
Sanday ▮	46	59.15 N	2.35 W
Sanday Sound ∪	46	59.1 N	2.31 W
Sandbach	54	53.09 N	2.22 W
Sandbank	46	55.59 N	4.58 W
Sandbanks Provincial ≃	212	43.55 N	77.17 W
Sandbochum ∇⁸	263	51.40 N	7.41 E
Sand City	226	36.37 N	121.51 W
Sand Coulee	202	47.23 N	111.10 W
Sand Coulee Creek ≃¹	226	37.27 N	111.18 W
Sand Creek ≃, In., U.S.	218	39.03 N	85.51 W
Sand Creek ≃, Ks., U.S.	198	37.26 N	98.12 W
Sand Creek ≃, Mn., U.S.	190	45.56 N	92.39 W
Sand Creek ≃, Mt., U.S.	202	47.18 N	106.45 W
Sand Creek ≃, S.D., U.S.	198	44.02 N	98.05 W
Sand Creek ≃, Wy., U.S.	200	43.27 N	105.26 W
Sand Creek ≃, Wy., U.S.	200	41.02 N	107.52 W
Sand Cut	202	44.16 N	107.55 W
Sande, Dtsch.	52	51.45 N	8.39 E
Sande, Dtsch.	52	53.30 N	8.01 E
Sandefjord	26	59.08 N	10.14 E
San Demetrio ne'Vestini	66	42.17 N	13.34 E
Sandersdorf, Dtsch.	52	51.37 N	12.15 E
Sandersleben	54	51.40 N	11.34 E
Sanderson	196	30.08 N	102.23 W
Sanderstead ∇⁸	262	51.19 N	0.04 W
Sanderville, Ga., U.S.	192	32.58 N	82.48 W
Sandesneben	54	53.41 N	10.30 E
Sandfly Lake ⊘	184	55.45 N	106.05 W
Sand Fork	188	38.54 N	80.45 W
Sandgate, Austl.	171a	27.20 S	153.05 E
Sandgate, Eng., U.K.	42	51.04 N	1.09 E
Sandhamn ≃	26	55.23 N	14.12 E
Sandham	40	59.17 N	18.55 E
Sandhead	54	54.48 N	4.58 W
Sandheuvel	158	31.46 S	20.48 E
Sandhill, On., Can.	275b	43.50 N	79.49 W
Sand Hill, Ma., U.S.	207	42.13 N	70.44 W
Sand Hill ∧²	210	42.31 N	77.37 W
Sand Hill ∧²	286e	33.44 S	70.40 W
Sand Hills ∧	198	42.00 N	101.00 W
Sandhorst	52	53.29 N	7.29 E
Sandhurst	42	51.19 N	0.48 W
Sãndi	124	27.18 N	79.57 E
Sandia	248	14.17 S	69.26 W
Sandia Crest ∧	200	35.13 N	106.27 W
Sandia Indian Reservation ✦⁴	200	35.15 N	106.30 W
Sandian	100	30.56 N	114.48 E
San Diego, Ca., U.S.	228	32.42 N	117.09 W
San Diego ◻⁶	228	33.00 N	117.05 W
San Diego ≃, Cuba	240p	22.04 N	83.20 W
San Diego ≃, Ca., U.S.	282	32.46 N	117.13 W
San Diego, Cabo ▸	254	54.38 S	65.07 W
San Diego Aqueduct ≃¹	228	32.55 N	116.55 W
San Diego Bay c	228	32.37 N	117.07 W
San Diego Creek ≃	196	27.47 N	98.03 W
San Diego de Alcala, Mission ∇¹	228	32.48 N	117.06 W
San Diego de la Unión	234	21.28 N	100.52 W
San Diego Naval Training Center ◻⁸	228	32.44 N	117.13 W
San Dieguito ≃	228	32.58 N	117.16 W
Sandies Creek ≃	222	29.06 N	97.20 W
Sandila	124	27.05 N	80.31 E
Sandlands	168b	34.13 S	19.46 E
Sandlands Village	240b	20.07 N	77.18 W
San Dimas	228	34.06 N	117.48 W
San Dimas Canyon ∇	280	34.10 N	117.46 W
San Dimas Reservoir ⊘¹	280	34.09 N	117.43 W
San Dionisio, Nic.	236	12.45 N	85.51 W
San Dionisio, Pil.	116	11.16 N	123.06 E
Sand Island ▮, Mid. Is.	174g	28.12 N	177.23 W
Sand Island ▮, Hi., U.S.	229c	21.18 N	157.53 W
Sand Islet ▮	174g	28.16 N	177.23 W
Sandley	262	52.15 N	2.36 W
Sand Key ▮	220	24.27 N	81.53 W
Sandkrug	54	52.53 N	13.52 E
Sandl	61	48.29 N	14.38 E
Sand Lake ⊘, On., Can.	212	44.56 N	77.02 W
Sand Lake ⊘, On., Can.	184	53.02 N	93.00 W
San Domino, Isola ▮	68	42.07 N	15.29 E
Sandoná	246	1.17 N	77.28 W
San Donaci	68	40.27 N	17.55 E
San Donà di Piave	64	45.38 N	12.34 E
San Donato di Lecce	68	40.16 N	18.08 E
San Donato Milanese	62	45.25 N	9.16 E
San Donato Val di Comino	66	41.43 N	13.49 E
Sandongo	152	15.30 S	21.28 E
San Dorligo della Valle	64	45.36 N	13.51 E
Sandoval	218	38.37 N	89.07 W
Sandovo	76	58.28 N	36.25 E
Sandoway	110	18.28 N	94.22 E
Sandown	42	50.39 N	1.09 W

Column 6

Name	Pg	Lat	Long
Sandown Park Race Course ♦, Eng., U.K.	260	51.22 N	0.22 W
Sand Point, Ak., U.S.	180	55.20 N	160.30 W
Sandpoint, Id., U.S.	202	48.16 N	116.33 W
Sancrancourt	261	49.02 N	1.39 E
Sancray I	46	56.53 N	7.30 W
Sandridge, Eng., U.K.	260	51.47 N	0.18 W
Sand Ridge, N.Y., ≃	210	43.15 N	76.14 W
Sandringham, Austl.	166	24.05 S	139.04 E
Sandringham, Austl.	169	37.57 S	145.00 E
Sandringham ∇⁸	273d	26.09 S	28.07 E
Sandringham House ≃	42	52.50 N	0.30 E
Sand River Valley	158	28.28 S	29.33 E
Sandrovka	38	48.57 N	35.46 E
Sands Key ▮	220	25.30 N	80.11 W
Sandslân	26	63.01 N	17.47 E
Sandö	182	53.14 N	131.50 W
Sands Point ▸	276	40.51 N	73.43 W
Sands Point ▸	276	40.52 N	73.44 W
Sand Springs, Ok., U.S.	196	36.09 N	96.06 W
Sand Springs, Tx., U.S.	196	32.15 N	101.22 W
Sandspruit	158	27.18 S	29.48 E
Sandspruit ≃	273d	26.07 S	28.12 E
Sandstedt	52	53.31 N	8.31 E
Sandston	208	37.31 N	77.18 W
Sandstone, Austl.	162	27.59 S	119.17 E
Sandstone, Mn., U.S.	190	46.07 N	92.52 W
Sandstone Creek ≃	216	42.23 N	84.33 W
Sandu, Zhg.	100	29.46 N	120.12 E
Sandu, Zhg.	100	26.02 N	113.16 E
Sandu, Zhg.	100	29.12 N	114.40 E
Sandu, Zhg.	102	25.59 N	107.52 E
Sandu, Zhg.	100	41.10 N	121.27 E
Sandu Ao c	100	26.35 N	119.50 E
Sandumba	152	13.45 S	17.29 E
Sandun, Zhg.	100	31.52 N	121.50 E
Sandun, Zhg.	104	40.56 N	120.48 E
Sanduo	100	32.49 N	119.42 E
Sandusky, In., U.S.	218	39.25 N	85.29 W
Sandusky, Mi., U.S.	190	43.25 N	82.49 W
Sandusky, N.Y., U.S.	210	42.30 N	78.23 W
Sandusky, Oh., U.S.	214	41.26 N	82.42 W
Sandusky ≃	214	41.21 N	83.07 W
Sandusky ∇⁶	214	41.27 N	83.00 W
Sandusky Bay c	214	41.27 N	82.52 W
Sandusku uul ∧	102	43.27 N	104.04 E
Sandvig	26	55.17 N	14.47 E
Sandvika	26	59.54 N	10.31 E
Sandviken	40	60.37 N	16.46 E
Sandweier	54	48.49 N	6.13 E
Sandwell, Eng., U.K.	42	51.17 N	1.20 E
Sandwich, Il., U.S.	216	41.38 N	88.37 W
Sandwich, Ma., U.S.	207	41.46 N	70.29 W
Sandwich Bay c, Nf., Can.	176	53.35 N	57.15 W
Sandwich Bay c, Namibia	156	23.22 S	14.30 E
Sandwich del Sur, Islas — South Sandwich Islands ▮	18	57.45 S	26.30 W
Sandwick, B.C., Can.	182	49.42 N	124.59 W
Sandwick, Scot., U.K.	46a	60.00 N	1.15 W
Sand Wick c	46a	60.42 N	0.52 W
Sandy, B.C., Can.	182	54.24 N	125.59 W
Sandwip Channel ∪	124	22.30 N	91.26 E
Sandwip Island ▮	124	22.30 N	91.25 E
Sandy, Eng., U.K.	42	52.08 N	0.18 W
Sandy, Or., U.S.	224	45.23 N	122.15 W
Sandy, Pa., U.S.	214	41.07 N	78.47 W
Sandy, Ut., U.S.	200	40.35 N	111.53 W
Sandy ≃, Me., U.S.	188	44.45 N	69.52 W
Sandy ≃, Or., U.S.	224	45.34 N	122.24 W
Sandy Bay c, Nic.	236	14.28 N	83.16 W
Sandy Bay c, Ma., U.S.	207	42.40 N	70.37 W
Sandy Bay Indian Reserve ✦⁴	184	50.33 N	98.40 W
Sandy Bay Mountain ∧	188	45.47 N	70.25 W
Sandy Beach	210	43.04 N	78.55 W
Sandy Branch ≃	284c	39.03 N	77.16 W
Sandy Cape ▸, Austl.	166	41.25 S	144.45 E
Sandy Cape ▸, Austl.	166	24.42 S	153.17 E
Sandy Creek	212	43.38 N	76.05 W
Sandy Creek ≃, Austl.	166	32.10 S	144.39 E
Sandy Creek ≃, Oh., U.S.	196	36.50 N	98.10 W
Sandy Creek, North	210	43.17 N	75.58 W
Sandy Creek, West	210	43.18 N	76.00 W
Sandy Desert ≈	128	28.40 N	62.30 E
Sandy Hoek, Ct., U.S.	212	41.25 N	73.16 W
Sandy Hook, Ky., U.S.	192	38.05 N	83.07 W
Sandy Hook ▸	194	30.20 N	89.48 W
Sandy Hook ∇⁴	276	40.28 N	74.00 W
Sandy Hook Bay c	276	40.26 N	74.01 W
Sandy Key ▮	220	25.13 N	80.57 W
Sandy Lake ⊘, Nf., Can.	186	49.16 N	57.00 W
Sandy Lake ⊘, On., Can.	184	53.02 N	93.00 W
Sandy Lick Creek ≃	214	41.09 N	79.00 W
Sandy Point ▸, Trin.	241r	11.09 N	60.50 W
Sandy Point ▸, R.I., U.S.	207	41.14 N	71.35 W
Sandy Ridge	208	36.26 N	80.05 W
Sandy Springs	192	33.55 N	84.22 W
Sandyville, Oh., U.S.	214	40.38 N	81.23 W
Sandžak ∧⁹	38	43.10 N	19.30 E
San Eladio	258	34.46 S	59.11 W
San Emidio	226	35.06 N	119.11 W
San Emigdio Creek ≃	228	35.02 N	119.11 W
San Emilio	196	17.14 N	120.37 E
Sanen	115a	8.23 S	113.37 E
San Enrique	258	35.47 S	60.22 W
San Estanislao	252	24.39 S	56.26 W
San Esteban	252	15.17 N	85.52 W

Legend (footer)

	ESPAÑOL	FLUSS	RÍO	RIVIÈRE	RIO
≃	River	Fluß	Río	Rivière	Rio
≅	Canal	Kanal	Canal	Canal	Canal
⌣	Waterfall, Rapids	Wasserfall, Stromschnellen	Cascada, Rápidos	Chute d'eau, Rapides	Cascada, Rápidos
⋊	Strait	Meeresstraße	Estrecho	Détroit	Estreito
c	Bay, Gulf	Bucht, Golf	Bahía, Golfo	Baie, Golfe	Baía, Golfo
⊘	Lake, Lakes	See, Seen	Lago, Lagos	Lac, Lacs	Lago, Lagos
≈	Swamp	Sumpf	Pantano	Marais	Pântano
⊠	Ice Features, Glacier	Eis- und Gletscherformen	Accidentes Glaciales	Formes glaciaires	Acidentes glaciares
∇	Other Hydrographic Features	Andere Hydrographische Objekte	Otros Elementos Hidrográficos	Autres données hydrographiques	Outros acidentes hidrográficos

✦	Submarine Features	Untermeerische Objekte	Accidentes Submarinos	Formes de relief sous-marin	Acidentes submarinos
◻	Political Unit	Politische Einheit	Unidad Política	Entité politique	Unidade política
⌂	Cultural Institution	Kulturelle Institution	Institución Cultural	Institution culturelle	Instituição cultural
⊥	Historical Site	Historische Stätte	Sitio Histórico	Site historique	Sítio histórico
♦	Recreational Site	Erholungs- und Ferienort	Sitio de Recreo	Centre de loisirs	Área de Lazer
✈	Airport	Flughafen	Aeropuerto	Aéroport	Aeroporto
⚔	Military Installation	Militäranlage	Instalación Militar	Installation militaire	Instalação militar
❋	Miscellaneous	Verschiedenes	Misceláneo	Divers	Diversos

Column 1

San Esteban, Isla **‖** 232 28.42 N 112.36 W
San Esteban de Gormaz 34 41.35 N 3.12 W
San Fele 68 40.49 N 15.32 E
San Felice (Sankt Felix) 64 46.30 N 11.08 E
San Felice Circeo 66 41.14 N 13.05 E
San Felice sul Panaro 64 44.50 N 11.08 E
San Felipe, Chile 252 32.45 S 70.44 W
San Felipe, Col. 246 1.55 N 67.06 W
San Felipe, Méx. 232 31.00 N 114.52 W
San Felipe, Méx. 234 21.29 N 101.13 W
San Felipe, Pil. 116 15.04 N 120.04 E
San Felipe, Tx., U.S. 222 29.48 N 96.06 W
San Felipe, Ven. 246 10.20 N 68.44 W
San Felipe, Castillo de **⊥** 236 15.39 N 89.01 W
San Felipe, Cayos de **‖** 240p 21.58 N 83.30 W
San Felipe Aztatán 234 22.23 N 105.24 W
San Felipe Creek **≃** 204 33.09 N 115.46 W
San Felipe de Vichayal 248 4.52 S 81.05 W
San Felipe Indian Reservation **◄⁴** 200 35.26 N 106.26 W
San Felipe Jalapa de Díaz 234 18.04 N 96.32 W
San Felipe Nuevo Mercurio 232 24.22 N 102.06 W
San Felipe Pueblo 200 35.27 N 106.28 W
San Félix **≃** 236 8.10 N 81.51 W
San Félix, Isla **‖** 244 26.17 S 80.05 W
San Ferdinando di Puglia 68 41.18 N 16.04 E
San Fermín 196 26.20 N 104.49 W
San Fernando, Arg. 252 34.35 S 58.34 W
San Fernando, Chile 252 34.35 S 71.00 W
San Fernando, Esp. 34 36.28 N 6.12 W
San Fernando, Méx. 196 28.32 N 100.54 W
San Fernando, Méx. 200 31.16 N 110.36 W
San Fernando, Méx. 232 24.50 N 98.10 W
San Fernando, Pil. 116 16.37 N 120.19 E
San Fernando, Pil. 116 12.30 N 123.46 E
San Fernando, Pil. 116 15.01 N 120.41 E
San Fernando, Trin. 241r 10.17 N 61.28 W
San Fernando, Ca., U.S. 228 34.16 N 118.26 W
San Fernando, Ven. 246 7.54 N 67.28 W
San Fernando **□⁵** 288 34.28 S 58.34 W
San Fernando, Aeródromo **≃** 288 34.27 S 58.35 W
San Fernando Airport **≃** 280 34.17 N 118.25 W
San Fernando Creek **≃** 196 27.28 N 97.46 W
San Fernando de Atabapo 246 4.03 N 67.42 W
San Fernando de Henares 266a 40.26 N 3.32 W
San Fernando del Valle de Catamarca 288 28.28 S 65.47 W
San Fernando Mission **◄¹** 280 34.16 N 118.28 W
San Fernando Point **►** 116 16.38 N 120.17 E
San Fernando Valley **∨** 280 34.13 N 118.27 W
San Fili 68 39.20 N 16.09 E
San Filippo del Mela, It. 70 38.10 N 15.17 E
San Filippo del Mela, It. 70 38.10 N 15.17 E
Sânfjället **∧** 26 62.17 N 13.32 E
Sânfjällets Nationalpark **♦** 26 62.20 N 13.40 E
San Floriano 64 46.02 N 12.18 E
Sanford, Co., U.S. 200 37.15 N 105.54 W
Sanford, Fl., U.S. 220 28.48 N 81.16 W
Sanford, Me., U.S. 188 43.26 N 70.46 W
Sanford, Mi., U.S. 190 43.40 N 84.22 W
Sanford, N.C., U.S. 192 35.28 N 79.10 W
Sanford, Tx., U.S. 196 35.42 N 101.32 W
Sanford **≃** 162 27.22 S 115.53 E
Sanford, Mount **∧** 180 62.13 N 144.09 W
San Francesco, Convento **�'¹**, It. 66 42.28 N 12.45 E
San Francesco, Convento **�'¹**, It. 267a 42.03 N 12.46 E
San Francesco, Arg. 252 31.26 S 62.05 W
San Francisco, Col. 246 1.11 N 76.53 W
San Francisco, C.R. 236 9.49 N 85.15 W
San Francisco, El Sal. 236 13.42 N 88.06 W
San Francisco, Pan. 236 8.15 N 80.58 W
San Francisco, Pil. 116 8.30 N 125.56 E
San Francisco, Pil. 116 10.04 N 125.09 E
San Francisco, Ca., U.S. 226 37.46 N 122.25 W
San Francisco, Ca., U.S. 282 37.46 N 122.25 W
San Francisco **□⁶** 226 37.45 N 122.22 W
San Francisco **≃**, Arg. 252 23.16 S 64.03 W
San Francisco — São Francisco **≃**, Bra. 242 10.30 S 36.24 W
San Francisco **≃**, U.S. 200 32.59 N 109.22 W
San Francisco, Arroyo **≃** 288 34.43 S 58.19 W
San Francisco, Paso de **)(** 252 26.53 S 68.19 W
San Francisco, University of **�'²** 282 37.46 N 122.26 W
San Francisco Bay **c** 226 37.43 N 122.17 W
San Francisco Creek **≃** 196 29.53 N 102.19 W
San Francisco Culhuacán **≃** 286a 19.20 N 99.08 W
San Francisco de Borja 232 27.53 N 106.41 W
San Francisco de Horizonte 196 25.56 N 103.26 W
San Francisco de Lajas 234 23.07 N 105.07 W
San Francisco de la Paz 236 14.55 N 86.14 W
San Francisco del Chañar 252 29.47 S 63.56 W
San Francisco del Monte de Oro 252 32.36 S 66.08 W
San Francisco del Oro 232 26.52 N 105.51 W
San Francisco del Rincón 234 21.01 N 101.51 W
San Francisco de Macorís 238 19.18 N 70.15 W
San Francisco de Mostazal 252 33.59 S 70.43 W
San Francisco el Grande, Iglesia de **◄** 266a 40.25 N 3.43 W
San Francisco International Airport **≃** 226 37.37 N 122.23 W
San Francisco Libre 236 12.30 N 86.18 W
San Francisco Maritime National Historical Park **♦** 282 37.48 N 122.27 W
San Francisco–Oakland Bay Bridge **◄⁸** 282 37.48 N 122.22 W
San Francisco State Fish and Game Refuge **◄⁴** 282 37.35 N 122.25 W
San Francisco State University **�'²** 282 37.43 N 122.28 W
Sanfrancisco Tlalcihualcpa 234 19.18 N 99.46 W

Column 2

San Francisco Tlaltenco **◄⁸** 286a 19.17 N 99.01 W
San Francisco Zoological Gardens **♦** 282 37.44 N 122.30 W
San Francisquito Creek **≃** 282 37.28 N 122.07 W
San Franco, Cerro **◄** 236 15.25 N 87.18 W
San Fratello **►** 70 38.01 N 14.36 E
San Fratello **►** 70 38.02 N 14.34 E
Sanga, Ang. 152 11.07 S 15.22 E
Sanga, Burkina 150 11.10 N 0.10 E
Sanga, Mali 150 14.28 N 3.19 W
Sanga, Zaïre 154 7.02 S 28.21 E
San Gabriel, Ec. 246 0.36 N 77.49 W
San Gabriel, Ca., U.S. 280 33.45 N 118.06 W
San Gabriel **≃**, Ca., U.S. 280 33.45 N 118.07 W
San Gabriel **≃**, Tx., U.S. 222 30.46 N 97.01 W
San Gabriel, Isla **‖** 258 34.28 S 57.54 W
San Gabriel, North Fork **≃**, Ca., U.S. 280 34.15 N 117.52 W
San Gabriel, North Fork **≃**, Tx., U.S. 196 30.38 N 97.41 W
San Gabriel, South Fork **≃** 196 30.38 N 97.41 W
San Gabriel Arcangel, Mission **◄¹** 280 34.06 N 118.06 W
San Gabriel Chilac 234 18.19 N 97.21 W
San Gabriel Dam **◄⁶** 280 34.13 N 117.52 W
San Gabriel Mountains **∧** 228 34.20 N 118.00 W
San Gabriel Peak **∧** 280 34.15 N 118.06 W
San Gabriel Reservoir **☒** 228 34.13 N 117.51 W
Sangaĉal, mys **►** 84 40.07 N 49.30 E
San Galgano, Abbazia di **◄¹** 66 43.10 N 11.10 E
Šangaly 24 61.08 N 43.19 E
Sangamankanda Point **►** 122 7.01 N 81.52 E
Sangamner 122 19.34 N 74.13 E
Sangamon **□⁶** 219 39.47 N 89.40 W
Sangamon **≃** 194 40.07 N 90.20 W
Sangamon, South Fork **≃** 219 39.48 N 89.32 W
Sanga Puitã 255 22.40 S 55.36 W
Sangar 74 63.55 N 127.31 E
Sangar Saráy 120 34.24 N 70.38 E
Sangasanga-dalam 112 0.40 S 117.14 E
Sanga Sanga Island **‖** 116 5.04 N 119.47 E
Sangat 123 30.05 N 74.50 E
Sangatte 50 50.56 N 1.45 E
San Gavino Monreale 71 39.33 N 8.47 E
Sangay **∧¹** 246 2.00 S 78.20 W
Sangay, Parque Nacional **♦** 246 1.50 S 78.20 W
Sangayán, Isla **‖** 248 13.51 S 76.28 W
Sang Bast 128 35.59 N 59.46 E
Sangbê **◄¹** 154 6.30 N 12.28 E
Sangchis Lake **☒¹** 219 39.35 N 89.30 W
Sangchis Lake State Park **♦** 219 39.38 N 89.28 W
Sangchungshih 100 25.04 N 121.29 E
Sangeang, Pulau **‖** 115b 8.12 S 119.04 E
Sang-e Māsheh 120 33.08 N 67.27 E
San Gemini 66 42.37 N 12.33 E
San Genesio Atesino 64 46.32 N 11.20 E
Sangenjaya **◄⁸** 268 35.38 N 139.40 E
Sanger, Ca., U.S. 226 36.42 N 119.33 W
Sanger, Tx., U.S. 196 33.21 N 97.10 W
Sangerhausen 54 51.28 N 11.17 E
San Germano 240m 18.05 N 67.03 W
San Germano Vercellese 62 45.21 N 8.15 E
San Gerónimo 226 38.01 N 122.39 W
San Gerónimo, Arroyo **≃** 258 33.57 S 56.05 W
Sangerville 188 45.09 N 69.21 W
Sanggan **≃** 90 40.21 N 115.21 E
Sanggar, Teluk **c** 115b 8.20 S 118.18 E
Sangqu 112 0.08 N 110.36 E
Sangge-ri **◄⁸** 271b 37.41 N 125.05 E
Sanggin Dalai 102 38.11 N 105.17 E
Sangoana 112 3.52 S 116.48 E
Sangha **□⁵**, Centraf. 152 3.35 N 16.20 E
Sangha **≃**, Congo 152 1.00 S 16.30 E
Sangha **≃** 152 1.13 S 16.49 E
Sanghar 120 26.02 N 68.57 E
San Giacomo (Sankt Jakob in Pfitsch) 64 46.57 N 11.36 E
San Giacomo Filippo 58 46.20 N 9.16 E
Sanghe, Kepulauan **‖** 112 3.00 N 125.30 E
Sanghe, Pulau **‖** 112 3.35 N 125.32 E
Sangin dalaj nuur **☒** 88 49.17 N 99.00 E
San Gil 246 6.33 N 73.08 W
Sangiien, chrebet **∧** 88 50.18 N 96.30 E
San Gimignano 66 43.28 N 11.02 E
Sangin 58 46.38 N 8.50 E
San Gion 58 46.38 N 8.50 E
San Giorgio Canavese 62 45.20 N 7.48 E
San Giorgio della Richinvelda 64 46.03 N 12.52 E
San Giorgio del Sannio 68 41.04 N 14.51 E
San Giorgio di Lomellina 62 45.10 N 8.47 E
San Giorgio di Nogaro 64 45.50 N 13.13 E
San Giorgio di Piano 64 44.39 N 11.22 E
San Giorgio Ionico 68 40.27 N 17.23 E
San Giorgio la Molara 68 41.16 N 14.55 E
San Giorgio Lucano 68 40.07 N 16.23 E
San Giorgio Monferrato 62 45.07 N 8.23 E
San Giorgio Morgeto 68 38.23 N 16.06 E
San Giorgio Piacentino 62 44.57 N 9.44 E
San Giorgio su Legnano 266b 45.34 N 8.55 E
San Giovanni (Sankt Johann) 64 46.38 N 11.44 E
San Giovanni al Timavo (Sankt Johann in Ahrn) 64 46.58 N 11.57 E
San Giovanni a Piro 68 40.03 N 15.27 E
San Giovanni-Bianco 58 45.52 N 9.39 E
San Giovanni d'Asso 66 43.09 N 11.35 E
San Giovanni Gemini 70 37.38 N 13.39 E
San Giovanni Ilarione 64 45.30 N 11.15 E
San Giovanni in Croce 64 45.05 N 10.22 E
San Giovanni in Fiore 68 39.15 N 16.42 E
San Giovanni in Laterano **◄¹** 267a 41.53 N 12.30 E
San Giovanni in Persiceto 64 44.38 N 11.11 E
San Giovanni la Punta 70 37.35 N 15.07 E
San Giovanni Rotondo 68 41.42 N 15.44 E
San Giovanni Suergiu 71 39.07 N 8.31 E
San Giovanni Valdarno 66 43.34 N 11.32 E
San Giuliano, Lago di **☒** 68 40.37 N 16.30 E
San Giuliano Milanese 266b 45.24 N 9.17 E
San Giuliano Terme 66 43.46 N 10.26 E
San Giuseppe, It. 58 44.22 N 8.18 E
San Giuseppe, It. 70 37.58 N 13.11 E
San Giuseppe Vesuviano 68 40.50 N 14.30 E
San Giustino 66 43.33 N 12.10 E

Column 3

San Giusto, Aeroporto di **≃** 66 43.41 N 10.21 E
San Giusto Canavese 62 45.19 N 7.49 E
Sangju 98 36.26 N 128.09 E
Sangkapura 115a 5.52 S 112.40 E
Sângké **≃** 110 13.13 N 103.41 E
Sangkhai 110 14.39 N 103.52 E
Sangkulirang 112 0.59 N 117.58 E
Sângla 123 31.43 N 73.23 E
Sangley Point **►** 269f 14.30 N 120.55 E
Sāngli 122 16.52 N 74.34 E
Sanglin 100 27.54 N 114.46 E
Sangluoshu 98 37.31 N 117.43 E
Sangmélima 152 2.56 N 11.59 E
Sangngagqoiling 120 28.33 N 93.00 E
Sangnyŏng-ni 98 38.14 N 126.54 E
Sango 270 34.36 N 135.42 E
San Godenzo 66 43.55 N 11.37 E
Sângole 122 17.26 N 75.12 E
Sangolquí 246 0.19 S 78.27 W
San Gorgonio Mountain **∧** 204 34.06 N 116.50 W
San Gottardo, Passo del **)(** 58 46.33 N 8.34 E
Sangou 98 41.02 N 118.11 E
Sangre de Cristo Mountains **∧** 200 37.30 N 105.15 W
San Gregorio, Arg. 252 34.19 S 62.02 W
San Gregorio, It. 66 42.19 N 13.29 E
San Gregorio, Ca., U.S. 226 37.19 N 122.23 W
San Gregorio, Ur. 252 32.37 S 55.40 W
San Gregorio, Ur. 258 33.57 S 56.45 W
San Gregorio **◄⁸** 286a 19.15 N 99.03 W
San Gregorio, Arroyo **≃** 258 33.59 S 56.50 W
San Gregorio Creek **≃** 226 37.19 N 122.25 W
San Gregorio Magno 68 40.39 N 15.24 E
San Gregorio State Beach **♦** 282 37.19 N 122.24 W
Sangre Grande 241r 10.35 N 61.07 W
Sangro **≃** 66 42.14 N 14.32 E
Sangrūr 123 30.14 N 75.50 E
Sangsang 120 29.25 N 86.40 E
Sangshuyuan 86 42.23 N 88.30 E
Sangsues, Lac aux **☒** 190 46.29 N 77.57 W
Sangtuda 85 38.04 N 69.04 E
Sanguandian 100 31.19 N 118.05 E
Sanguang 106 31.47 N 121.16 E
Sanguanmiao 106 32.25 N 114.04 E
Sanguanyingzi 104 41.39 N 120.44 E
Sangudo 182 53.53 N 114.54 W
Sangue, Rio do **≃** 248 11.01 S 58.39 W
Sangüesa 34 42.35 N 1.17 W
Sanguinetto 64 45.11 N 11.09 E
Sanguili 104 40.45 N 124.14 E
Sangutane **≃** 156 24.07 S 33.47 E
Sangvor, Taj. 85 38.47 N 71.12 E
Sangvor, Taj. 85 38.51 N 71.06 E
Sangwa 154 5.30 S 26.00 E
Sangya 120 30.52 N 91.40 E
Sangyuanbao 105 40.15 N 115.32 E
Sangyuanbu 106 31.37 N 118.53 E
Sangyuanzhen 107 30.30 N 103.26 E
Sangzhi 100 29.18 N 110.02 E
Sangzidian 98 36.46 N 116.55 E
Sanhe, Zhg. 100 24.24 N 116.34 E
Sanhe, Zhg. 105 39.59 N 117.04 E
Sanhechang, Zhg. 107 31.22 N 106.48 E
Sanhechang, Zhg. 107 30.04 N 105.01 E
Sanhecun 98 42.28 N 129.39 E
Sanheji 100 32.42 N 117.55 E
Sanhekou 106 31.50 N 120.08 E
Sanhetun 104 42.38 N 123.38 E
Sanhezhen 100 31.30 N 117.14 E
Sanhezhuang 105 40.04 N 116.18 E
San Hipólito, Punta **►** 232 26.59 N 113.59 W
Sanhent'ai **‖** 100 23.08 N 121.25 E
Sanhsing 100 24.40 N 121.39 E
Sanhu 100 27.55 N 115.24 E
Sanhui, Zhg. 107 30.06 N 106.36 E
Sanhui, Zhg. 107 29.57 N 105.53 E
Sanhūr 142 29.25 N 30.46 E
Sanhūr al-Madīnah 142 31.07 N 30.44 E
Sani 102 31.10 N 120.46 E
Sanibel 220 26.26 N 82.01 W
Sanibel Island **‖** 220 26.27 N 82.06 W
Sânil Bherī **≃** 124 28.42 N 82.16 E
San Ignacio, Arg. 252 27.16 S 55.32 W
San Ignacio, C.R. 236 9.48 N 84.09 W
San Ignacio, Hond. 236 14.38 N 87.02 W
San Ignacio, Méx. 232 27.27 N 112.51 W
San Ignacio, Méx. 232 23.12 N 102.12 W
San Ignacio, Méx. 234 23.55 N 106.25 W
San Ignacio, Para. 252 26.52 S 57.03 W
San Ignacio, Perú 248 5.08 S 78.59 W
San Ignacio, Pil. 116 15.25 N 120.54 E
San Ignacio, Laguna **☒** 232 26.54 N 113.13 W
San Ignacio de Moxo 248 14.53 S 65.36 W
San Ignacio de Velasco 248 16.23 S 60.59 W
San Ildefonso, Cape **►** 116 16.02 N 121.59 E
San Ildefonso, Cerro **∧¹** 236 15.31 N 88.17 W
San Ildefonso Indian Reservation **◄⁴** 200 35.53 N 106.08 W
San Ildefonso o La Granja 34 40.54 N 4.00 W
San Ildefonso Peninsula **◄¹** 116 16.10 N 122.05 E
San Ildefonso Villa Alta 234 17.21 N 96.09 W
San'in-kaigan-kokuritsu-kōen **♦** 270 35.38 N 134.38 E
Sanino 265a 59.50 N 29.54 E
Sani Pass **)(** 158 29.34 S 29.19 E
San Isidro, Arg. 252 28.27 S 65.44 W
San Isidro, Arg. 252 28.27 S 58.30 W
San Isidro, C.R. 236 9.22 N 83.42 W
San Isidro, Méx. 200 31.31 N 106.18 W
San Isidro, Méx. 116 12.34 N 123.43 E
San Isidro, Nic. 236 12.56 N 86.12 W
San Isidro, Perú 286d 12.07 S 77.03 W
San Isidro, Pil. 116 11.24 N 124.21 E
San Isidro de Real, Catedral de **◄** 266a 40.25 N 3.42 W
Sanitaria Springs 210 42.09 N 75.46 W
Sanitatas 156 18.11 S 12.47 E
Sanitz 54 54.04 N 12.22 E
San Jacinto, Col. 246 9.50 N 75.08 W
San Jacinto, Méx. 232 25.29 N 103.44 W
San Jacinto, Pil. 116 12.34 N 123.44 E
San Jacinto, Ca., U.S. 226 33.47 N 116.57 W
San Jacinto **≃** 196 33.50 N 117.05 W
San Jacinto Valley **∨** 280 33.50 N 117.00 W
Sanjahšh 142 31.38 E
San Javier, Arg. 252 27.53 S 55.08 W
San Javier, Bol. 248 16.18 S 62.30 W
San Javier, Bol. 248 14.34 S 64.42 W
San Javier, Chile 252 35.36 S 71.45 W
San Javier, Méx. 196 26.16 N 99.27 W
San Javier, Ur. 252 32.41 S 58.08 W
San Javier, Ur. 252 31.30 S 60.20 W

Column 4

San Javier de Loncomilla 252 35.35 S 71.45 W
Sanjāwi 120 30.17 N 68.21 E
Sanje 154 0.46 S 31.30 E
San Jeronimito 234 17.33 N 101.20 W
San Jerónimo, Guat. 236 15.03 N 90.12 W
San Jerónimo, Méx. 234 17.08 N 100.28 W
San Jerónimo Norte 252 31.33 S 61.05 W
San Jiadian, Zhg. 105 39.58 N 116.06 E
San Jiadian, Zhg. 105 39.22 N 115.58 E
Sanjiang, Zhg. 102 25.42 N 109.23 E
Sanjiang, Zhg. 107 29.33 N 104.03 E
Sanjiang, Zhg. 107 30.31 N 103.48 E
Sanjiaocheng 102 36.47 N 104.40 E
Sanjiaopao 104 41.22 N 122.17 E
Sanjiaoshancun 104 40.42 N 122.49 E
Sanjiazhen 107 30.17 N 105.32 E
Sanjiazi, Zhg. 104 41.53 N 121.42 E
Sanjiazi, Zhg. 104 42.30 N 123.16 E
Sanjiazi, Zhg. 104 40.54 N 121.59 E
Sanjiazi, Zhg. 104 41.21 N 121.38 E
Sanjiaoyingzi 104 41.52 N 120.49 E
Sanjie, Zhg. 100 32.35 N 118.08 E
Sanjie, Zhg. 102 25.01 N 101.02 E
Sanjō 92 37.37 N 138.57 E
San Joaquín, Bol. 248 13.04 S 64.49 W
San Joaquín, Chile 286e 33.30 S 70.37 W
San Joaquín, Ca., U.S. 226 34.57 S 56.07 W
San Joaquín, Pil. 116 10.35 N 122.08 E
San Joaquín **≃**, Ca., U.S. 226 36.36 N 120.11 W
San Joaquín **≃** 226 37.51 N 121.17 W
San Joaquín **≃**, Bol. 248 13.08 S 63.41 W
San Joaquín **≃**, Ca., U.S. 226 38.03 N 121.50 W
San Joaquín, Middle Fork **≃** 226 37.32 N 119.11 W
San Joaquín, North Fork **≃** 226 37.32 N 119.11 W
San Joaquín, South Fork **≃** 226 37.26 N 119.14 W
San Joaquín Valley **∨** 204 36.50 N 120.10 W
San Jon 196 35.06 N 103.19 W
San Jorge, Arg. 252 31.54 S 61.52 W
San Jorge, El Sal. 236 13.25 N 88.21 W
San Jorge, Nic. 236 11.27 N 85.48 W
San Jorge **≃** 246 9.07 N 74.44 W
San Jorge, Bahía de **c** 200 31.12 N 113.15 W
San Jorge, Cabo **►** 248 11.01 S 58.39 W
San Jorge, Canal de — Saint George's Channel **u** 28 52.00 N 6.00 W
San Jorge, Golfo **c** 254 46.00 S 67.00 W
San Jorge Island **‖** 175e 8.27 S 159.35 E
San José, Arg. 252 27.46 S 55.47 W
San José, C.R. 236 9.56 N 84.05 W
San José, Méx. 196 28.16 N 100.15 W
San José, N. Mar. Is. 174n 15.09 N 145.43 E
San José, Para. 252 25.03 S 56.45 W
San José, Pil. 116 10.45 N 121.56 E
San José, Pil. 116 15.48 N 121.00 E
San José, Pil. 116 12.22 N 121.04 E
San José, Ca., U.S. 226 37.20 N 121.53 W
San José, Ca., U.S. 282 37.20 N 121.53 W
San José, Il., U.S. 194 40.18 N 89.36 W
San José, N.M., U.S. 200 35.23 N 105.28 W
San José, Ven. 246 10.34 N 66.57 W
San José **□⁴** 286c 10.34 N 84.30 W
San José **≃** 258 34.40 S 56.11 W
San José **≃** 258 34.15 S 56.45 W
San José **□⁷** 258 34.15 S 56.45 W
San José, Arroyo **≃** 288 34.03 S 58.19 W
San Jose, B.C., Can. 182 52.14 N 122.15 W
San Jose, Méx. 234 34.38 S 56.29 W
San Jose, Arroyo **≃** 232 28.03 N 122.30 W
San Jose, Golfo **c** 254 42.20 S 64.18 W
San Jose, Isla **‖**, Méx. 232 25.00 N 110.38 W
San Jose, Isla **‖**, Pan. 236 8.15 N 79.07 W
San Jose, Laguna **c** 240m 18.26 N 66.01 W
San Jose, Mission **◄¹** 282 37.32 N 121.55 W
San Jose, Rio **≃** 200 34.52 N 107.01 W
San Jose Arena **◄** 282 37.20 N 121.54 W
San Jose Ayuquila 234 17.58 N 97.57 W
San Jose Batuc 232 29.15 N 109.44 W
San Jose Buena Vista 236 13.49 N 90.19 W
San Jose Creek **≃** 280 34.01 N 118.03 W
San Jose de Aura 196 27.32 N 101.23 W
San Jose de Bácum 232 27.32 N 110.09 W
San Jose de Buan 116 12.02 N 125.01 E
San Jose de Chiquitos 248 17.51 S 60.47 W
San Jose de Copán 236 14.54 N 88.44 W
San Jose de Feliciano 252 30.23 S 58.45 W
San Jose de Galipán, Quebrada **≃** 286c 10.35 N 66.54 W
San Jose de Gracia 234 20.40 N 102.35 W
San Jose de Guanipa 246 8.54 N 64.09 W
San Jose de Jachal 252 30.14 S 68.45 W
San Jose de la Esquina 252 33.06 S 61.42 W
San Jose de la Parilla 234 23.44 N 104.07 W
San Jose de la Popa 196 26.10 N 100.47 W
San Jose de las Flores 234 17.20 N 95.24 W
San Jose de las Lajas 240p 22.58 N 82.09 W
San Jose de las Raices 234 24.35 N 100.14 W
San José del Cabo 232 23.03 N 109.41 W
San José del Guaviare 246 2.35 N 72.38 W
San José de Llanetes 246 10.35 N 66.54 W
San José de Lourdes 248 23.18 N 103.01 W
San José del Valle 34 36.30 N 5.48 W
San José de Mayo 234 34.20 S 56.42 W
San José de Ocuné 246 4.15 N 70.20 W
San José de Sisa 248 6.37 S 76.39 W
San José de Tiznados 246 9.23 N 67.33 W
San Jose Hills **◄²** 280 34.04 N 117.49 W
San Jose Island **‖** 196 28.10 N 96.45 W
San Jose Municipal Airport **≃** 282 37.22 N 121.56 W
San Jose State University **◄²** 282 37.20 N 121.53 W
San Juan, Arg. 252 31.32 S 68.31 W
San Juan, Dom. 238 15.52 N 88.53 W
San Juan, Guat. 236 15.04 N 104.36 W
San Juan, Méx. 116 15.01 N 120.10 E
San Juan, Perú 248 15.22 S 75.10 W
San Juan, Pil. 116 16.40 N 120.20 E
San Juan, Pil. 116 16.18 N 120.26 E
San Juan, P.R. 240m 18.28 N 66.07 W
San Juan, Ven. 246 9.47 N 71.04 W
San Juan **≃**, Arg. 252 32.17 S 67.22 W
San Juan **≃**, Méx. 232 22.07 N 98.03 W
San Juan **≃**, Méx. 196 26.22 N 98.30 W
San Juan **≃**, Méx. 234 21.25 N 78.30 W
San Juan **≃**, Perú 248 15.23 S 75.10 W
San Juan **≃**, Pil. 116 16.20 N 120.20 E
San Juan **≃**, U.S. 200 37.18 N 110.27 W
San Juan **□⁵**, Arg. 252 30.50 S 68.45 W
San Juan **≃**, Col. 246 4.03 N 77.27 W
San Juan **≃**, Méx. 232 26.22 N 98.30 W
San Juan **≃** 246 10.14 N 83.42 W

Column 5

San Juan, Cabezas de **►** 240m 18.23 N 65.37 W
San Juan, Cabo **►**, Arg. 254 54.44 S 63.44 W
San Juan, Cabo **►**, Gui. Ecu. 152 1.08 N 9.23 E
San Juan, Embalse de **☒¹** 34 40.30 N 4.15 W
San Juan, Pasaje de **u** 240m 18.24 N 65.37 W
San Juan, Pico **∧** 240p 21.59 N 80.09 W
San Juan, Port **c** 254 48.34 S 124.27 W
San Juan, Punta **►** 174z 27.03 S 109.22 W
San Juan Basin **≃¹** 200 36.15 N 108.20 W
San Juan Bautista, Méx. 196 26.58 N 101.24 W
San Juan Bautista, Para. 252 26.38 S 57.10 W
San Juan Bautista, Ca., U.S. 226 36.51 N 121.32 W
San Juan Bautista State Historical Park **♦** 226 36.51 N 121.31 W
San Juan Capistrano 228 33.30 N 117.39 W
San Juan Capistrano Mission **◄¹** 228 33.31 N 117.40 W
San Juan Cotzal 236 15.26 N 91.01 W
San Juan Creek **≃**, Ca., U.S. 226 35.40 N 120.22 W
San Juan Creek **≃**, Ca., U.S. 228 33.28 N 117.41 W
San Juan de Abajo 234 20.48 N 105.13 W
San Juan de Aragón, Bosque **♦** 286a 19.28 N 99.04 W
San Juan de Aragón, Zoológico de **♦** 286a 19.28 N 99.05 W
San Juan de Colón 246 8.02 N 72.16 W
San Juan de Dios 286c 10.35 N 66.55 W
San Juan de Guadalupe 232 24.38 N 102.44 W
San Juan de la Maguana 238 18.48 N 71.14 W
San Juan de la Vega 234 20.38 N 100.46 W
San Juan del César 246 10.46 N 73.01 W
San Juan del Monte 269f 14.36 N 121.02 E
San Juan del Norte 236 10.55 N 83.42 W
San Juan del Oro **≃** 248 21.02 S 65.19 W
San Juan de los Cayos 246 11.10 N 68.25 W
San Juan de los Lagos 234 21.15 N 102.18 W
San Juan de los Morros 246 9.55 N 67.21 W
San Juan del Río, Méx. 232 24.47 N 104.27 W
San Juan del Río, Méx. 234 20.23 N 100.00 W
San Juan del Salado **≃** 236 23.18 N 101.56 W
San Juan del Sur 236 11.15 N 85.52 W
San Juan de Lurigancho 286d 11.59 S 77.01 W
San Juan de Micay **≃** 246 3.05 N 77.32 W
San Juan de Miraflores 286d 12.11 S 76.57 W
San Juan de Payara 246 7.39 N 67.36 W
San Juan de Sabinas 196 27.55 N 101.18 W
San Juan Evangelista 234 17.54 N 95.08 W
San Juan Guichicovi 234 16.58 N 95.06 W
San Juanico 232 26.15 N 112.24 W
San Juanico 236 10.02 N 85.44 W
San Juan Indian Reservation **◄⁴** 200 36.03 N 106.04 W
San Juan Island **‖** 224 48.32 N 123.05 W
San Juan Island National Historical Park **♦** 224 48.28 N 123.00 W
San Juan Islands **‖** 224 48.36 N 122.50 W
San Juan Ixcaquixtla 234 18.27 N 97.49 W
San Juan Ixtayopan **◄⁸** 286a 19.14 N 99.00 W
San Juan Lachao 234 16.14 N 97.09 W
San Juan Mazatlán 234 17.02 N 95.25 W
San Juan Mountains **∧** 200 37.35 N 107.10 W
San Juan Nepomuceno, Col. 246 9.57 N 75.05 W
San Juan Nepomuceno, Para. 252 26.06 S 55.58 W
San Juan Peyotán 234 22.24 N 104.21 W
San Juan Quiahije 234 16.17 N 97.20 W
San Juan Sacatepéquez 236 14.43 N 90.39 W
San Juan y Martínez 240p 22.16 N 83.50 W
San Julián, Pil. 116 11.45 N 125.27 E
San Justo, Arg. 252 30.47 S 60.35 W
San Justo, Arg. 258 34.40 S 58.33 W
San Justo, Aeródromo **≃** 288 34.44 S 58.36 W
Sankaranil **◄** 150 8.56 N 10.48 W
Sankarani **≃** 150 11.31 N 8.19 W
Sankarankovil 122 9.10 N 77.33 E
Sankarpur 272b 22.01 N 88.27 E
Sánkdaha 124 22.46 N 89.10 E
Sankeda 124 22.16 N 73.32 E
Sankeshu 122 22.38 N 122.25 E
Sankeshwar 122 16.16 N 74.29 E
Sankey Brook **≃** 262 54.49 N 2.38 W
Sankh **≃** 124 22.15 N 84.48 E
Sankheda 124 22.10 N 73.35 E
Sânkosh **≃** 123 26.48 N 89.56 E
Sánkra 120 21.18 N 82.39 E
Sânkrāil 272b 22.34 N 88.14 E
Sankt Aegyd am Neuwalde 61 47.52 N 15.35 E
Sankt Andrä 61 46.46 N 14.49 E
Sankt Andrä [-vor dem Hagenthale] 61 48.19 N 16.13 E
Sankt Andrasberg 54 51.43 N 10.31 E
Sankt Anton am Arlberg 61 47.08 N 10.16 E
Sankt Augustin 56 50.46 N 7.12 E
Sankt Bartholomä **◄¹** 61 47.36 N 12.58 E
Sankt Blasien 56 47.46 N 8.07 E
Sankt Christopher-Nevis — Saint Kitts and Nevis **u¹** 238 17.20 N 62.45 W
Sankt Egiden 56 50.47 N 12.36 E
Sankt Florian **◄¹** 61 48.12 N 14.23 E
Sankt Gallen, Öst. 61 47.41 N 14.37 E
Sankt Gallen, Schw. 58 47.25 N 9.22 E
Sankt Gallen **□³** 58 47.20 N 9.08 E
Sankt Gallenkirch 61 47.00 N 9.59 E
Sankt Georgen, Dtsch. 56 48.07 N 8.20 E
Sankt Georgen, U.S. 56 47.59 N 7.47 E
Sankt Georgen, Öst. 61 44.14 N 14.55 E
Sankt Georgen am Attergau 61 47.58 N 13.30 E
Sankt Gertraud — Santa Gertrude 64 46.29 N 10.53 E
Sankt Gertrud **◄⁸** 56 53.51 N 10.40 E
Sankt Gilgen 61 47.46 N 13.22 E
Sankt Goar 56 50.09 N 7.43 E
Sankt Goarshausen 56 50.09 N 7.44 E
— Saint Helena **□²** 8 15.57 S 5.42 W
Sankt Ingbert 56 49.17 N 7.06 E

Column 6

Sankt Jakob — San Giacomo 64 46.57 N 11.36 E
Sankt Jakob im Lesachtal 64 46.41 N 12.56 E
Sankt Jakob im Rosental 61 46.33 N 14.03 E
Sankt Jakob in Defereggen 64 46.55 N 12.20 E
Sankt Johann — San Giovanni 64 46.38 N 11.44 E
Sankt Johann am Tauern 61 47.22 N 14.29 E
Sankt Johann im Pongau 200 36.15 N 108.20 W
Sankt Johann in Tirol 64 46.54 N 12.37 E
Sankt Johann in Walde 64 46.54 N 12.37 E
Sankt Kanzian 64 46.37 N 14.33 E
Sankt Leonard — San Leonardo 64 46.49 N 11.15 E
Sankt Leonhard im Forst 61 48.09 N 15.17 E
Sankt Leonhard im Pitztal 64 47.04 N 10.51 E
Sankt Lorenz **◄⁸** 54 53.51 N 10.40 E
Sankt Lorenz — Saint Lawrence **≃** 176 49.30 N 67.00 W
Sankt Lorenzen im Sebato 64 46.47 N 11.54 E
Sankt Lorenzen im Lesachtal 64 46.42 N 12.47 E
Sankt Lorenz-Golf — Saint Lawrence, Gulf of **c** 186 48.00 N 62.00 W
Sankt Lorenz-Insel — Saint Lawrence Island **‖** 180 63.30 N 170.30 W
Sankt Mang 58 47.44 N 10.21 E
Sankt Margarethen an der Raab **‖** 61 47.05 N 15.45 E
Sankt Märgen 56 48.00 N 8.05 E
Sankt Margrethen 58 47.27 N 9.36 E
Sankt Martin 64 47.28 N 13.23 E
Sankt Martin an der Raab 61 46.55 N 16.08 E
Sankt Martin in Gsies — San Martino in Casies 64 46.49 N 12.14 E
Sankt Mauritz 52 51.57 N 7.39 E
Sankt Michael im Lungau 64 47.06 N 13.38 E
Sankt Michael im Obersteiermark 61 47.20 N 15.01 E
Sankt Michel — Mikkeli 26 61.41 N 27.15 E
Sankt Moritz 58 46.30 N 9.50 E
Sankt Niklaus 58 46.11 N 7.48 E
Sankt Nikolaus — San Nicolò d'Ultima 64 46.30 N 10.55 E
Sankt Oswald 60 48.54 N 13.25 E
Sankt Peter, Dtsch. 30 54.18 N 8.38 E
Sankt Peter, Dtsch. 58 48.01 N 8.01 E
Sankt Peter **◄¹** 263 51.37 N 7.12 E
Sankt Peter am Kammersberg 61 47.14 N 14.11 E
Sankt Peter am Ottersbach 61 46.48 N 15.45 E
Sankt-Peterburg (Saint Petersburg), Ross. 76 59.55 N 30.15 E
Sankt-Peterburg (Saint Petersburg), Ross. 265a 59.55 N 30.15 E
Sankt-Petersburg, Gorod **□⁷** 265a 59.55 N 30.15 E
Sankt Peter in der Au 61 48.03 N 14.37 E
Sankt Pölten 61 48.12 N 15.37 E
Sankt-Quirinus-Dom **◄** 263 51.12 N 6.42 E
Sankt Stefan an der Gail 64 46.37 N 13.31 E
Sankt Stefan am Rosental 61 46.54 N 15.42 E
Sankt Ulrich — Ortisei 64 46.34 N 11.40 E
Sankt Valentin 61 48.10 N 14.32 E
Sankt Veit an der Glan 64 46.46 N 14.21 E
Sankt Veit im Pongau 64 47.20 N 13.09 E
Sankt-Viktors-Dom **◄** 263 51.40 N 6.27 E
Sankt Vincent — Saint Vincent and the Grenadines **u¹** 241h 13.15 N 61.12 W
Sankt Wallburg — Santa Valburga 64 46.33 N 11.00 E
Sankt-Willibrodi-Dom **◄** 56 49.28 N 7.10 E
Sankt Wolfgang im Salzkammergut 61 47.44 N 13.27 E
Sankuru **≃** 152 4.17 S 20.25 E
San Lázaro 122 22.10 S 57.55 W
San Lázaro, Cabo **►** 232 24.48 N 112.19 W
San Lázaro Race Track **◄** 269f 14.37 N 120.59 E
San Lazzaro di Savena 64 44.28 N 11.25 E
San Leandro **≃** 282 37.43 N 122.09 W
San Leandro Creek **≃** 282 37.43 N 122.09 W
San Leo 66 43.54 N 12.21 E
San Leone 222 29.29 N 94.55 W
San Leonardo (Sankt Leonhard), It. 64 46.49 N 11.15 E
San Leonardo, Méx. 196 27.28 N 104.55 W
San Leonardo 70 37.59 N 13.41 E
San Leone 70 31.48 N 114.12 E
San Liang 100 30.48 N 119.03 E
Sanlintang 100 31.46 N 119.03 E
Sanlit'ou 100 32.08 N 119.18 E
Sanlifan 100 30.51 N 115.15 E
San Lope 234 21.47 N 71.56 W
San Lorenzo, Arg. 252 26.08 S 58.46 W
San Lorenzo, Arg. 252 32.45 S 60.44 W
San Lorenzo, Bol. 248 21.26 S 64.47 W
San Lorenzo, Ec. 246 1.17 N 78.50 W
San Lorenzo, Hond. 236 13.25 N 87.27 W
San Lorenzo, It. 68 37.58 N 15.50 E
San Lorenzo, Méx. 196 25.37 N 97.35 W
San Lorenzo, Méx. 232 25.32 N 102.11 W
San Lorenzo, P.R. 240m 18.11 N 65.58 W
San Lorenzo, U.S. 196 32.42 N 110.07 W
San Lorenzo, Ven. 246 9.47 N 71.04 W
San Lorenzo **≃**, Méx. 232 24.15 N 107.24 W
San Lorenzo — Saint Lawrence, N.A. 176 49.30 N 67.00 W
San Lorenzo — Saint Lawrence, Gulf of **c** 186 48.00 N 62.00 W

ESPAÑOL

Nombre	Página	Lat.°′	Long.°′ W = Oeste
San Lorenzo, Isla I, Méx.	232	28.38 N	112.51 W
San Lorenzo, Isla I, Perú	248	12.05 S	77.15 W
San Lorenzo, Monte (Cerro Cochrane) ∧	254	47.37 S	72.19 W
San Lorenzo Bellizzi	68	39.53 N	16.20 E
San Lorenzo Creek ≃, Ca., U.S.	226	36.12 N	120.38 W
San Lorenzo Creek ≃, Ca., U.S.	282	37.39 N	122.09 W
San Lorenzo de El Escorial	34	40.35 N	4.09 W
San Lorenzo de la Parrilla	34	39.51 N	2.22 W
San Lorenzo del Vallo	68	39.40 N	16.18 E
San Lorenzo di Sebato (Sankt Lorenzen)	64	46.47 N	11.54 E
San Lorenzo in Campo	66	43.36 N	12.56 E
San Lorenzo Nuovo	66	42.41 N	11.54 E
San Lorenzo Tezonco ◆[8]	286a	19.18 N	99.04 W
San Luca	68	38.09 N	16.04 E
Sanlúcar de Barrameda	34	36.47 N	6.21 W
Sanlúcar la Mayor	34	37.23 N	6.12 W
San Lucas, Bol.	248	20.06 S	65.07 W
San Lucas, Ec.	246	3.45 S	79.15 W
San Lucas, Méx.	232	22.53 N	109.54 W
San Lucas, Ca., U.S.	226	36.08 N	121.01 W
San Lucas, Cabo ➤	232	22.52 N	109.53 W
San Luis, Arg.	252	33.18 S	66.21 W
San Luis, Cuba	240p	20.12 N	75.51 W
San Luis, Cuba	240p	22.17 N	83.46 W
San Luis, Guat.	236	16.14 N	89.27 W
San Luis, Perú	286d	12.04 S	77.00 W
San Luis, Az., U.S.	200	32.04 N	111.57 W
San Luis, Co., U.S.	200	37.12 N	105.25 W
San Luis, Ven.	246	11.07 N	69.42 W
San Luis □[4]	252	34.00 S	66.00 W
San Luis ◆[8]	286b	23.05 N	82.20 W
San Luis ≃	234	17.13 N	100.55 W
San Luis, Arroyo ≃	258	34.10 S	57.44 W
San Luís, Laguna ⊜	248	13.45 S	64.00 W
San Luis, Sierra de ⋏	252	32.40 S	65.50 W
San Luis Acatlán	234	16.48 N	98.45 W
San Luis Creek ≃	200	37.42 N	105.44 W
San Luis de la Loma	234	17.18 N	100.55 W
San Luis de la Paz	234	21.18 N	100.31 W
San Luis del Cordero	232	25.26 N	104.18 W
San Luis del Palmar	252	27.31 S	58.34 W
San Luis Gonzaga	232	24.55 N	111.16 W
San Luis Gonzaga, Bahía ⊂	232	29.48 N	114.22 W
San Luis Jilotepeque	236	14.39 N	89.44 W
San Luis Obispo	226	35.16 N	120.39 W
San Luis Obispo □[6]	226	35.30 N	120.30 W
San Luis Pass ⊂	222	29.05 N	95.08 W
San Luis Peak ∧	200	37.59 N	106.56 W
San Luis Potosí	234	22.09 N	100.59 W
San Luis Potosí □[3]	234	22.30 N	100.30 W
San Luis Reservoir ⊜[1]	226	37.07 N	121.05 W
San Luis Rey	228	33.14 N	117.20 W
San Luis Rey ≃	204	33.12 N	117.24 W
San Luis Rey, Mission ʊ[1]	228	33.14 N	117.20 W
San Luis Río Colorado	232	32.29 N	114.48 W
San Luis Soyatlán	234	20.12 N	103.18 W
San Luis State Recreation Area ♠	226	37.04 N	121.05 W
San Luis Valley V	200	37.25 N	106.00 W
Sanluri	71	39.34 N	8.54 E
San Macario	266b	45.36 N	8.47 E
Sanmaiden	270	34.34 N	135.51 E
San Mamete	58	46.02 N	9.04 E
San Mango d'Aquino	68	39.03 N	16.11 E
San Manuel, Arg.	252	37.47 S	58.50 W
San Manuel, Méx.	234	17.37 N	93.24 W
San Manuel, Az., U.S.	200	32.35 N	110.37 W
San Marcelino	116	14.58 N	120.09 E
San Marcello Pistoiese	66	44.03 N	10.47 E
San Marcial ≃	232	28.04 N	110.44 W
San Marco, Capo ➤, It.	70	37.30 N	13.01 E
San Marco, Capo ➤, It.	71	39.51 N	8.26 E
San Marco Argentano	68	39.33 N	16.07 E
San Marco dei Cavoti	68	41.18 N	14.53 E
San Marco in Lamis	68	41.43 N	15.38 E
San Marco la Catola	68	41.31 N	15.00 E
San Marcos, Chile	252	30.56 S	71.03 W
San Marcos, Col.	246	8.39 N	75.08 W
San Marcos, C.R.	236	9.40 N	84.01 W
San Marcos, El Sal.	236	13.39 N	89.11 W
San Marcos, Guat.	236	14.58 N	91.48 W
San Marcos, Hond.	236	14.24 N	88.56 W
San Marcos, Hond.	236	15.17 N	88.23 W
San Marcos, Méx.	234	16.48 N	99.21 W
San Marcos, Méx.	234	20.02 N	99.20 W
San Marcos, Méx.	234	20.47 N	104.11 W
San Marcos, Ca., U.S.	228	33.08 N	117.09 W
San Marcos, Tx., U.S.	196	29.52 N	97.56 W
San Marcos □[5]	236	15.00 N	91.55 W
San Marcos ≃	196	29.29 N	97.28 W
San Marcos, Isla I	232	27.13 N	112.06 W
San Marcos, Laguna ⊜	234	20.17 N	103.33 W
San Marcos, Universidad Nacional de ʊ[2]	286d	12.04 S	77.05 W
San Marcos Arteaga	234	17.45 N	97.58 W
San Marcos de Colón	236	13.26 N	86.48 W
San Marino, S. Mar.	66	43.55 N	12.28 E
San Marino, Ca., U.S.	280	34.07 N	118.06 W
San Marino □[1], Europe	22	43.56 N	12.25 E
San Marino □[1], Europe	66	43.56 N	12.25 E
San Martín, Arg.	252	29.14 S	65.46 W
San Martín, Arg.	252	33.04 S	68.28 W
San Martín → General San Martín, Arg.	258	34.34 S	58.32 W
San Martín, Col.	246	3.42 N	73.42 W
San Martin, Ca., U.S.	226	37.05 N	121.37 W
San Martín, Ur.	258	33.45 S	57.37 W
San Martín □[5]	248	7.00 S	76.50 W
San Martín ≃, Bol.	248	11.50 S	67.16 W
San Martín ≃, Bol.	248	13.08 S	63.43 W
San Martín ʊ[3]	9	68.07 S	67.08 W
San Martín, Arroyo ≃	258	33.49 S	57.44 W
San Martín, Cuchilla ⋏[2]	258	33.45 S	57.54 W
San Martín, Lago (Lago O'Higgins) ⊜	254	49.00 S	72.40 W
San Martín, Volcán ∧[1]	234	18.33 N	95.12 W
San Martín de Bolaños	234	21.29 N	103.58 W
San Martín de las Vacas	196	25.30 N	101.20 W
San Martín de los Andes	254	40.10 S	71.21 W
San Martin de Porras	286d	12.04 S	77.04 W
San Martín de Valdeiglesias	34	40.21 N	4.24 W
San Martín Hidalgo	234	20.27 N	103.57 W
San Martino, It.	62	45.27 N	8.47 E

FRANÇAIS

Nom	Page	Lat.°′	Long.°′ W = Ouest
San Martino (Sankt Martin), It.	64	46.47 N	11.13 E
San Martino, It.	64	45.25 N	10.35 E
San Martino Buon Albergo	64	45.25 N	11.05 E
San Martino d'Agri	68	40.14 N	16.04 E
San Martino di Castrozza	64	46.16 N	11.48 E
San Martino di Lupari	64	45.39 N	11.51 E
San Martino in Badia (Sankt Martin)	64	46.41 N	11.52 E
San Martino in Casies (Sankt Martin in Gsies)	64	46.49 N	12.14 E
San Martino in Rio	64	44.44 N	10.48 E
San Martino Valle Caudina	68	41.01 N	14.39 E
San Martín Peras	234	17.19 N	98.15 W
San Marzano di San Giuseppe	68	40.27 N	17.30 E
San Mateo, Méx.	234	22.59 N	103.30 W
San Mateo, Pil.	269f	14.42 N	121.07 E
San Mateo, Ca., U.S.	226	37.33 N	122.19 W
San Mateo, Fl., U.S.	192	29.36 N	81.35 W
San Mateo, N.M., U.S.	200	35.19 N	107.38 W
San Mateo, Ven.	246	9.45 N	64.33 W
San Mateo □[6]	226	37.25 N	122.20 W
San Mateo Atenco	234	19.16 N	99.32 W
San Mateo Bridge ◆[5]	282	37.36 N	122.13 W
San Mateo Canyon V	228	33.23 N	117.36 W
San Mateo Creek ≃	282	37.34 N	122.18 W
San Mateo del Mar	234	16.12 N	95.00 W
San Mateo Ixtatán	236	15.50 N	91.29 W
San Mateo Memorial Park ♠	282	37.17 N	122.18 W
San Mateo Point ➤	228	33.23 N	117.36 W
San Mateo Tecoloapan	286a	19.34 N	99.14 W
San Matías	248	16.22 S	58.24 W
San Matías, Golfo ⊂	254	41.30 S	64.15 W
San Mauro Castelverde	70	37.55 N	14.11 E
San Mauro Forte	68	40.29 N	16.15 E
San Mauro la Bruca	68	40.07 N	15.17 E
San Mauro Marchesato	68	39.06 N	16.56 E
San Mauro Torinese	62	45.06 N	7.46 E
San Medi, Arroyo de ≃	266d	41.28 N	2.06 E
Sanmen	100	29.06 N	121.24 E
San Menaio	68	41.56 N	15.58 E
Sanmen Wan ⊂	100	29.08 N	121.44 E
Sanmenxia (Shanxian)	102	34.45 N	111.05 E
San Michele, Sacra di ʊ[1]	62	45.11 N	7.21 E
San Michele all'Adige	64	46.12 N	11.08 E
San Michele al Tagliamento	64	45.46 N	12.59 E
San Michele di Ganzaria	70	37.17 N	14.26 E
San Michele Mondovì	62	44.23 N	7.54 E
San Michele Salentino	68	40.38 N	17.37 E
San Miguel, Arg.	252	28.00 S	57.36 W
San Miguel → General Sarmiento, Arg.	258	34.33 S	58.43 W
San Miguel, Bol.	248	16.42 S	61.01 W
San Miguel, Chile	286e	33.30 S	70.40 W
San Miguel, Ec.	246	1.44 S	79.01 W
San Miguel, El Sal.	236	13.29 N	88.11 W
San Miguel, Esp.	148	28.05 N	16.37 W
San Miguel, Méx.	232	29.10 N	101.28 W
San Miguel, Méx.	234	23.23 N	98.10 W
San Miguel, Pan.	246	8.27 N	78.56 W
San Miguel, Perú	248	13.01 S	73.58 W
San Miguel, Perú	286d	12.06 S	77.07 W
San Miguel, Pil.	116	15.09 N	120.59 E
San Miguel, Ca., U.S.	226	35.45 N	120.41 W
San Miguel ≃, Bol.	248	13.52 S	63.56 W
San Miguel (Cuilco) ≃, N.A.	236	15.56 N	92.10 W
San Miguel ≃, S.A.	246	0.08 N	75.51 W
San Miguel ≃, S.A.	248	19.15 S	59.20 W
San Miguel ≃, Co., U.S.	200	38.23 N	108.48 W
San Miguel, Cerro ∧[2]	248	19.19 S	60.36 W
San Miguel, Golfo de ⊂	246	8.22 N	78.17 W
San Miguel, Volcán de ∧[1]	236	13.26 N	88.16 W
San Miguel Arcángel, Mission ʊ[1]	226	35.44 N	120.42 W
San Miguel Bay ⊂	116	13.50 N	123.10 E
San Miguel Chimalapa	234	16.43 N	94.41 W
San Miguel Creek ≃	196	28.30 N	98.25 W
San Miguel de Allende	234	20.55 N	100.45 W
San Miguel de Cruces	232	24.25 N	105.51 W
San Miguel del Monte	258	35.27 S	58.48 W
San Miguel de Pallaques	248	7.00 S	78.51 W
San Miguel de Salcedo	246	1.02 S	78.34 W
San Miguel de Tucumán	252	26.49 S	65.13 W
San Miguel El Alto	234	21.01 N	102.21 W
San Miguel El Grande	234	17.02 N	97.37 W
San Miguel Island I, Pil.	116	13.23 N	123.48 E
San Miguel Island I, Ca., U.S.	204	34.02 N	120.22 W
San Miguel Islands II	116	7.45 N	118.28 E
San Miguelito	236	11.24 N	84.54 W
San Miguel Ixtahuacán	236	15.15 N	91.45 W
San Miguel Mountain ∧	228	32.42 N	116.56 W
San Miguel Sola de Vega	234	16.31 N	96.59 W
San Miguel Talea de Castro	234	17.22 N	96.15 W
San Miguel Tecuixiapan	234	17.58 N	99.27 W
San Miguel Tenango	234	16.16 N	95.36 W
San Miguel Totolapan	234	18.08 N	100.23 W
Sanming	100	26.14 N	117.36 E
San Miniato	66	43.41 N	10.51 E
San Murezzan → Sankt Moritz	58	46.30 N	9.50 E
Sannahed	40	59.06 N	15.09 E
Sannan	96	35.04 N	135.02 E
Sannār	140	13.33 N	33.38 E
San Narciso, Pil.	116	13.34 N	122.34 E
San Narciso, Pil.	116	15.01 N	120.05 E
Sannazzaro de'Burgondi	62	45.06 N	8.54 E
Sannicandro di Bari	68	41.00 N	16.48 E
Sannicandro Garganico	68	41.50 N	15.34 E
Sannicola	68	40.05 N	18.04 E
San Nicola, Isola I	66	42.07 N	15.30 E
San Nicola, Monte ∧	68	38.35 N	16.24 E
San Nicola Arcella	68	39.51 N	15.48 E
San Nicola da Crissa	68	38.40 N	16.17 E
San Nicolás, Cuba	240p	22.47 N	81.55 W
San Nicolás, Esp.	148	27.59 N	15.46 W
San Nicolás, Hond.	236	15.00 N	88.45 W
San Nicolás, Méx.	234	16.26 N	98.32 W
San Nicolás, Perú	248	15.13 S	75.12 W
San Nicolas, Pil.	116	18.09 N	120.38 E
San Nicolás ≃	234	19.40 N	105.14 W

PORTUGUÊS

Nome	Página	Lat.°′	Long.°′ W = Oeste
San Nicolás de los Arroyos	252	33.20 S	60.13 W
San Nicolás de los Garza	196	25.45 N	100.18 W
San Nicolas Island I	204	33.15 N	119.31 W
San Nicolò di Comelico	64	46.35 N	12.31 E
San Nicolò d'Ultimo (Sankt Nikolaus)	64	46.30 N	10.55 E
San Nicolò Ferrarese	64	44.42 N	11.42 E
San Nicolò Gerrei	71	39.30 N	9.18 E
Sannieshof	158	26.30 S	25.47 E
Sannikova, proliv Ʉ	74	74.30 N	140.00 E
Şannīn, Jabal ∧	132	33.57 N	35.52 E
Sannio, Monti del ⋏	66	41.30 N	14.45 E
Sanniquellie	150	7.22 N	8.43 W
Sannohe	92	40.22 N	141.15 E
Sannois	261	48.58 N	2.15 E
Sannūr, Wādī V	142	28.58 N	31.03 E
Sano	94	36.19 N	139.35 E
Sañogasta	252	29.18 S	67.36 W
Sanok	30	49.34 N	22.13 E
Sânon ≃	58	48.38 N	6.20 E
San Onofre	246	9.44 N	75.32 W
San Onofre Mountain ∧	228	33.22 N	117.30 W
San Pablo, Chile	254	40.24 S	73.01 W
San Pablo, Col.	246	1.40 N	77.00 W
San Pablo, Pil.	116	14.04 N	121.19 E
San Pablo, Pil.	116	7.40 N	123.27 E
San Pablo, Ca., U.S.	226	37.57 N	122.20 W
San Pablo ◆[8]	286a	19.11 N	99.04 W
San Pablo ≃, Bol.	248	14.52 S	63.42 W
San Pablo ≃, Méx.	234	18.32 N	96.01 W
San Pablo ≃, Pan.	236	7.51 N	81.10 W
San Pablo, Point ➤	282	37.58 N	122.26 W
San Pablo Autopan	234	19.21 N	99.40 W
San Pablo Bay ⊂	226	38.06 N	122.22 W
San Pablo Creek ≃	282	37.58 N	122.30 W
San Pablo Huixtepec	234	16.50 N	96.46 W
San Pablo Reservoir ⊜[1]	282	37.56 N	122.15 W
San Pablo Ridge ∧	282	37.55 N	122.15 W
San Pablo Strait Ʉ	282	37.58 N	122.26 W
San Pablo Villa de Mitla	234	16.55 N	96.24 W
Sanpāda	272c	19.04 N	73.01 E
San Pancrazio Salentino	68	40.25 N	17.50 E
San Paolo	64	46.29 N	11.15 E
San Paolo di Civitate	68	41.44 N	15.15 E
San Pascual	116	13.08 N	122.59 E
San Pasqual Indian Reservation ◆[4]	228	33.12 N	116.58 W
San Pedro, Arg.	252	33.40 S	59.40 W
San Pedro, Arg.	252	24.14 S	64.52 W
San Pedro, Arg.	252	27.57 S	65.10 W
San Pedro, Chile	252	21.57 S	68.34 W
San Pedro, Chile	252	33.54 S	71.28 W
San Pedro, Col.	246	9.24 N	75.04 W
San Pedro, C.R.	236	9.56 N	84.03 W
San Pédro, C. Iv.	150	4.44 N	6.37 W
San Pedro, Para.	252	24.07 S	56.59 W
San Pedro, Tx., U.S.	196	27.47 N	97.40 W
San Pedro, Ur.	258	34.21 S	57.51 W
San Pedro, Ven.	246	8.50 N	71.58 W
San Pedro □[5]	252	24.15 S	56.30 W
San Pedro ◆[3]	228	33.44 N	118.18 W
San Pedro ≃, Cuba	240p	21.09 N	78.30 W
San Pedro ≃, Méx.	232	30.56 N	108.08 W
San Pedro ≃, Méx.	234	21.45 N	105.30 W
San Pedro ≃, N.A.	200	32.59 N	110.47 W
San Pedro ≃, N.A.	232	17.45 N	91.25 W
San Pedro ≃, Ven.	286c	10.35 N	66.48 W
San Pedro, Arroyo ≃	258	34.21 S	57.56 W
San Pedro, Point ➤, Ca., U.S.	282	37.35 N	122.31 W
San Pedro, Point ➤, Ca., U.S.	282	37.59 N	122.27 W
San Pedro, Punta ➤	252	25.30 S	70.38 W
San Pedro, Volcán ∧[1]	252	21.53 S	68.25 W
San Pedro Amuzgos	234	16.39 N	98.06 W
San Pedro Apóstol	234	16.44 N	96.44 W
San Pedro Ayampuc	236	14.47 N	90.27 W
San Pedro Bay ⊂, Pil.	116	11.11 N	125.05 E
San Pedro Bay ⊂, Ca., U.S.	228	33.45 N	118.11 W
San Pedro Breakwater ◆[5]	280	33.42 N	118.16 W
San Pedro Carchá	236	15.29 N	90.16 W
San Pedro Channel Ʉ	228	33.35 N	118.25 W
San Pedro Creek ≃, Ca., U.S.	282	37.36 N	122.30 W
San Pedro Creek ≃, Tx., U.S.	222	31.34 N	95.14 W
San Pedro de Arriba	258	34.18 S	57.47 W
San Pedro de Atacama	252	22.55 S	68.13 W
San Pedro de Buena Vista	248	18.13 S	65.59 W
San Pedro de Curahuara	248	17.40 S	68.02 W
San Pedro de la Cueva	232	29.18 N	109.44 W
San Pedro de las Colonias	232	25.45 N	102.59 W
San Pedro del Gallo	232	25.33 N	104.18 W
San Pedro de Lloc	248	7.26 S	79.31 W
San Pedro del Norte	236	13.04 N	84.33 W
San Pedro del Paraná	252	26.46 S	56.15 W
San Pedro de Macorís	238	18.27 N	69.18 W
San Pedro El Alto	234	16.01 N	96.28 W
San Pedro Huamelula	234	16.02 N	95.40 W
San Pedro Jicayán	234	16.25 N	97.59 W
San Pedro Juchatengo	234	16.21 N	97.06 W
San Pedro Mártir ◆[8]	286a	19.16 N	99.10 W
San Pedro Mixtepec	234	16.00 N	97.07 W
San Pedro Peaks ⋏	200	36.07 N	106.49 W
San Pedro Pinula	236	14.40 N	89.51 W
San Pedro Pochutla	234	15.44 N	96.28 W
San Pedro Sacatepéquez	236	14.58 N	91.46 W
San Pedro Sula	236	15.27 N	88.02 W
San Pedro Tabasco	232	17.47 N	91.10 W
San Pedro Tapanatepec	234	16.21 N	94.12 W
San Pedro Tututepec	234	16.09 N	97.38 W
San Pedro Xalostoc	286a	19.32 N	99.05 W
San Pedro y Miquelón → Saint Pierre and Miquelon □[2]	186	46.55 N	56.20 W
San Pelayo	246	8.58 N	75.51 W
San Pellegrino	62	45.50 N	9.40 E
San Piero a Grado	66	43.41 N	10.21 E
San Piero in Bagno	66	43.51 N	11.58 E
San Pierre	216	41.12 N	86.53 W
San Pietro (Sankt Peter)	64	47.01 N	12.03 E
San Pietro, Isola di I	71	39.08 N	8.17 E
San Pietro a Maida	68	38.50 N	16.20 E
San Pietro di Cadore	64	46.34 N	12.35 E
San Pietro in Casale	64	44.42 N	11.24 E
San Pietro in Gu	64	45.37 N	11.40 E
San Pietro in Guarano	68	39.20 N	16.19 E
San Pietro in Palazzi	66	43.20 N	10.30 E
San Pietro in Vaticano ʊ[1]	267a	41.54 N	12.28 E
San Pietro Vara	62	44.20 N	9.35 E
San Pietro Vernotico	68	40.29 N	18.00 E
San Pitch ≃	200	39.03 N	111.51 W
Sanpoil ≃	202	47.53 N	118.41 W
San Policarpio	116	12.11 N	125.30 E
San Polo d'Enza	64	44.38 N	10.26 E
Sanpu	98	34.09 N	117.10 E

Sanqiao	106	30.35 N	119.58 E
San Quentin	282	37.56 N	122.29 W
San Quentin State Prison ʊ	282	37.56 N	122.28 W
Sanquhar	44	55.22 N	3.56 W
Sanquianga, Parque Nacional ♠	246	2.30 N	78.15 W
San Quintin	116	16.00 N	120.50 E
San Quintín, Cabo ➤	232	30.21 N	116.00 W
San Quirico d'Orcia	66	43.03 N	11.36 E
Sanqutan	100	27.17 N	115.04 E
Sanquzhen	107	29.39 N	105.37 E
San Rafael, Arg.	252	34.36 S	68.20 W
San Rafael, Chile	252	35.19 S	71.32 W
San Rafael, Méx.	232	25.01 N	100.33 W
San Rafael, Méx.	234	20.12 N	96.51 W
San Rafael, Ca., U.S.	226	37.58 N	122.31 W
San Rafael, N.M., U.S.	200	35.06 N	107.52 W
San Rafael, Ven.	246	10.58 N	71.44 W
San Rafael ≃, Bol.	248	18.38 S	58.55 W
San Rafael ≃, Ut,. U.S.	200	38.47 N	110.07 W
San Rafael Bay ⊂	282	37.58 N	122.28 W
San Rafael de las Tortillas	196	26.49 N	99.32 W
San Rafael del Norte	236	13.12 N	86.06 W
San Rafael del Sur	236	11.51 N	86.27 W
San Rafael Desert ◆[2]	200	38.40 N	110.30 W
San Rafael Hills ⋏[2]	280	34.10 N	118.12 W
San Rafael Mountains ⋏	204	34.45 N	119.50 W
San Rafael Oriente	236	13.23 N	88.21 W
San Rafael Swell ⋏[1]	200	38.40 N	110.45 W
San Rafael Tasajera	236	13.16 N	88.52 W
San Ramón, Arg.	252	27.42 S	64.17 W
San Ramón, Bol.	248	13.17 S	64.43 W
San Ramón, C.R.	236	10.06 N	84.28 W
San Ramón, Hond.	236	14.41 N	84.43 W
San Ramón, Perú	248	11.08 S	75.20 W
San Ramon, Pil.	116	13.16 N	124.05 E
San Ramon, Ca., U.S.	282	37.47 N	121.59 W
San Ramón, Ur.	252	34.18 S	55.58 W
San Ramon Creek ≃	282	37.54 N	122.03 W
San Ramón de la Nueva Orán	252	23.08 S	64.20 W
San Ramon Valley V	282	37.46 N	121.58 W
Sanrao	100	23.59 N	116.50 E
San-rei ∧	96	33.50 N	133.59 E
San Remigio	116	11.05 N	123.56 E
San Remo, Austl.	169	38.31 S	145.22 E
San Remo, It.	62	43.49 N	7.46 E
San Remo, N.Y., U.S.	210	40.52 N	73.13 W
San Roberto	68	38.18 N	15.44 E
San Rodrigo ≃	196	28.54 N	100.37 W
San Román ≃	236	16.21 N	90.22 W
San Román, Cabo ➤	246	12.12 N	70.00 W
San Roque, Arg.	252	28.34 S	58.43 W
San Roque, Arg.	252	30.17 S	68.41 W
San Roque, Esp.	34	36.13 N	5.24 W
San Roque, N. Mar. Is.	174n	15.15 N	145.47 E
San Roque, Pil.	269f	14.29 N	120.54 E
San Roque, Cabo → São Roque, Cabo de ➤	250	5.29 S	35.16 W
San Roque, Punta ➤	232	27.11 N	114.26 W
San Rosendo	252	37.16 S	72.43 W
San Rufo	68	40.26 N	15.28 E
San Saba	196	31.11 N	98.43 W
San Saba ≃	196	31.15 N	98.35 W
San Saep, Khlong ≅	269a	13.45 N	100.36 E
San Salvador, Arg.	252	29.16 S	57.31 W
San Salvador, Arg.	252	31.37 S	58.30 W
San Salvador, El Sal.	236	13.42 N	89.12 W
San Salvador (Watling Island) I	238	24.02 N	74.28 W
San Salvador ≃	258	33.37 S	58.06 W
San Salvador, Cuchilla ⋏[2]	258	33.56 S	57.45 W
San Salvador, Volcán de ∧[1]	236	13.44 N	89.17 W
San Salvador de Jujuy	252	24.11 S	65.18 W
San Salvador el Seco	234	19.08 N	97.39 W
San Salvatore, Monte ∧	70	37.50 N	14.03 E
San Salvatore Monferrato	62	44.59 N	8.34 E
San Salvatore Telesino	68	41.14 N	14.30 E
San Salvo	66	42.03 N	14.44 E
Sansanné-Mango	150	10.21 N	0.28 E
Sans Bois Creek ≃	196	35.20 N	94.50 W
San Sebastián, El Sal.	236	13.44 N	88.50 W
San Sebastián → Donostia, Esp.	34	43.19 N	1.59 W
San Sebastián, Guat.	236	14.34 N	91.39 W
San Sebastián, Hond.	236	14.24 N	88.42 W
San Sebastián, Méx.	234	20.47 N	104.51 W
San Sebastián, P.R.	240m	18.20 N	66.59 W
San Sebastián, Bahía ⊂	254	53.12 S	68.20 W
San Sebastián de la Gomera	148	28.06 N	17.06 W
San Sebastián del Álamo	234	21.26 N	102.21 W
San Sebastián de los Reyes	266a	40.33 N	3.38 W
San Sebastián de Yalí	236	13.18 N	86.11 W
San Sebastiano	64	45.38 N	10.16 E
San Sebastiano Curone	62	44.47 N	9.04 E
San Sebastián Tecomaxtlahuaca	234	17.21 N	98.02 W
San Sebastián Zinacatepec	234	18.20 N	97.15 W
San Secondo Parmense	64	44.55 N	10.14 E
Sansepolcro	66	43.34 N	12.08 E
San Severino Lucano	68	40.01 N	16.08 E
San Severino Marche	66	43.13 N	13.10 E
San Severo	68	41.41 N	15.23 E
Sansha	100	26.58 N	120.12 E
Sanshengchang	89	44.51 N	120.21 E
Sanshierzhan	89	53.16 N	121.49 E
Sanshijia, Zhg.	98	41.44 N	119.15 E
Sanshijia, Zhg.	98	41.05 N	119.03 E
Sanshilibao	98	39.15 N	121.48 E
Sanshiling	106	30.51 N	119.29 E
Sanshisanzhan	89	53.10 N	121.27 E
Sanshui	100	23.11 N	112.53 E
San Sigismondo (Sankt Sigmund)	64	46.49 N	11.46 E
San Simeon	226	35.39 N	121.11 W
San Simon, Méx.	204	30.30 N	115.58 W
San Simon, Az., U.S.	200	32.16 N	109.13 W
San Simón ≃, Bol.	248	13.13 S	63.31 W
San Simon ≃, Az., U.S.	200	32.50 N	109.39 W
San Simon Wash V	200	31.45 N	112.25 W
San Siro ◆[8]	266b	45.29 N	9.07 E
Sanski Most	36	44.46 N	16.40 E
Sanso	150	11.43 N	6.51 W
San Solano	252	31.29 S	65.55 W
Sansom Park Village	222	32.48 N	97.24 W
Sanson	172	40.13 S	175.25 E
San Sosti	68	39.40 N	16.02 E
San Sperate	71	39.21 N	9.00 E
Sans Souci	274a	33.59 S	151.08 E
Sans-Souci ⊥	238	19.37 N	72.12 W
Sanssouci, Schloss ʊ	54	52.24 N	13.02 E
San Stefano Ticino	266b	45.29 N	8.55 E
Santa, Perú	248	8.59 S	78.36 W
Santa, Pil.	116	17.29 N	120.26 E

Santa ≃	248	8.58 S	78.39 W
Santa, Isla del I	248	9.02 S	78.40 W
Santa Adélia	255	21.16 S	48.48 W
Santa Albertina	255	20.02 S	50.44 W
Santa Amalia	34	39.01 N	6.01 W
Santa Ana, Arg.	252	27.22 S	55.34 W
Santa Ana, Bol.	248	18.43 S	58.44 W
Santa Ana, Bol.	248	13.45 S	65.35 W
Santa Ana, Col.	246	9.19 N	74.35 W
Santa Ana, Ec.	246	1.13 S	80.23 W
Santa Ana, El Sal.	236	13.59 N	89.34 W
Santa Ana, Méx.	232	24.04 N	100.30 W
Santa Ana, Méx.	232	30.33 N	111.07 W
Santa Ana, Ca., U.S.	228	33.44 N	117.52 W
Santa Ana, Ven.	246	9.19 N	64.39 W
Santa Ana ≃, Cuba	286b	23.04 N	82.32 W
Santa Ana ≃, Ca., U.S.	228	33.38 N	117.57 W
Santa Ana, Volcán de ∧[1]	236	13.50 N	89.38 W
Santa Ana Canyon V	280	33.53 N	117.43 W
Santa Ana de Chena	286e	33.34 S	70.47 W
Santa Ana del Alto Beni	248	15.31 S	67.30 W
Santa Ana Heights	228	33.39 N	117.54 W
Santa Ana Indian Reservation ◆[4]	200	35.28 N	106.37 W
Santa Ana Island I	175e	10.50 S	162.28 E
Santa Ana Maya	234	20.00 N	101.01 W
Santa Ana Mountains ⋏	228	33.45 N	117.35 W
Santa Ana Race Track ♠	269f	14.35 N	121.01 E
Santa Ana Tlacotenco ◆[8]	286a	19.10 N	98.59 W
Santa Anita	234	20.33 N	103.27 W
Santa Anita Canyon V	280	34.12 N	118.01 W
Santa Anita Park ♠	280	34.08 N	118.03 W
Santa Anna	196	31.44 N	99.19 W
Santa Apolonia	196	25.38 N	97.59 W
Santa Bárbara, Chile	252	37.40 S	72.01 W
Santa Barbara, Col.	246	5.53 N	75.35 W
Santa Bárbara, Hond.	236	14.53 N	88.14 W
Santa Bárbara, Méx.	232	26.48 N	105.49 W
Santa Bárbara, Méx.	234	18.52 N	101.07 W
Santa Barbara, Ca., U.S.	204	34.25 N	119.42 W
Santa Bárbara, Ven.	246	3.57 N	67.06 W
Santa Bárbara, Ven.	246	7.47 N	71.10 W
Santa Bárbara □[5]	236	15.10 N	88.20 W
Santa Barbara □[6]	228	33.28 N	119.02 W
Santa Bárbara ≃	248	16.58 S	61.39 W
Santa Bárbara, Morro de ∧	287a	22.57 S	43.28 W
Santa Bárbara, Túnel ◆[5]	287a	22.56 S	43.12 W
Santa Barbara Channel Ʉ	204	34.15 N	119.55 W
Santa Bárbara do Monte Verde	256	21.58 S	43.42 W
Santa Bárbara do Sul	252	28.22 S	53.15 W
Santa Barbara do Tugúrio	256	21.15 S	43.35 W
Santa Barbara Island I	228	33.28 N	119.02 W
Santa Branca	256	23.24 S	45.53 W
Santa Branca, Represa ⊜[1]	256	23.20 S	45.50 W
Santaca	158	26.36 S	32.32 E
Santa Catalina, Arg.	252	21.57 S	66.04 W
Santa Catalina, Pil.	116	9.20 N	122.51 E
Santa Catalina, Ur.	258	33.49 S	57.29 W
Santa Catalina, Arroyo ≃	288	34.46 S	58.27 W
Santa Catalina, Gulf of ⊂	228	33.20 N	117.45 W
Santa Catalina, Isla I	232	25.40 N	110.47 W
Santa Catalina, Laguna ⊜	288	34.46 S	58.27 W
Santa Catalina Island I	228	33.23 N	118.24 W
Santa Catalina o Calovébora	236	8.47 N	81.20 W
Santa Catarina, Méx.	204	31.37 N	115.48 W
Santa Catarina, Méx.	232	25.41 N	100.28 W
Santa Catarina □[3]	252	27.00 S	50.00 W
Santa Catarina, Ilha de I	252	27.36 S	48.30 W
Santa Catarina Juquila	234	16.14 N	97.18 W
Santa Caterina di Pittinuri	71	40.06 N	8.30 E
Santa Caterina Valfurva	64	46.25 N	10.29 E
Santa Caterina Villarmosa	70	37.35 N	14.02 E
Santa Cecília	252	26.56 S	50.27 W
Santa Cesarea Terme	68	40.02 N	18.29 E
Santa Clara, Col.	246	2.43 S	69.43 W
Santa Clara, Cuba	240p	22.24 N	79.58 W
Santa Clara, Méx.	232	29.17 N	107.01 W
Santa Clara, Méx.	234	19.41 N	102.30 W
Santa Clara, Méx.	286a	19.34 N	99.04 W
Santa Clara, Ca., U.S.	226	37.20 N	121.56 W
Santa Clara, Ut,. U.S.	200	37.07 N	113.39 W
Santa Clara □[6]	226	37.20 N	121.53 W
Santa Clara ≃, Ca., U.S.	228	34.14 N	119.16 W
Santa Clara ≃, Ut,. U.S.	200	37.05 N	113.36 W
Santa Clara, Bahía de ⊂	240p	23.05 N	80.30 W
Santa Clara, University of ʊ[2]	282	37.21 N	121.56 W
Santa Clara de Olimar	252	32.55 S	54.58 W
Santa Clara Indian Reservation ◆[4]	200	35.59 N	106.10 W
Santa Clara Valley V	226	37.10 N	121.40 W
Santa Clarita	286d	12.00 S	77.01 W
Santa Clotilde	246	2.34 S	73.44 W
Santa Coloma de Cervelló	266d	41.22 N	2.01 E
Santa Coloma de Farners	34	41.52 N	2.40 E
Santa Coloma de Gramanet	266d	41.27 N	2.13 E
Santa Comba	34	43.02 N	8.49 W
Santa Comba Dão	34	40.24 N	8.08 W
Santa Cristina	64	46.34 N	11.43 E
Santa Cristina d'Aspromonte	68	38.15 N	15.58 E
Santa Croce	64	46.05 N	12.18 E
Santa Croce, Capo ➤	70	37.14 N	15.15 E
Santa Croce, Lago di ⊜	64	46.10 N	12.20 E
Santa Croce Camerina	70	36.50 N	14.31 E
Santa Croce del Sannio	68	41.23 N	14.43 E
Santa Croce di Magliano	66	41.42 N	14.59 E
Santa Croce Sull'Arno	66	43.42 N	10.47 E
Santa Cruz, Bra.	250	6.13 S	36.01 W
Santa Cruz, Bra.	255	19.56 S	40.09 W
Santa Cruz, Chile	252	34.38 S	71.22 W
Santa Cruz, C.R.	236	10.16 N	85.36 W
Santa Cruz, Méx.	200	31.14 N	110.35 W
Santa Cruz, Perú	248	6.37 S	78.57 W
Santa Cruz, Pil.	116	6.50 N	125.25 E
Santa Cruz, Pil.	116	14.17 N	121.25 E
Santa Cruz, Pil.	116	13.29 N	122.02 E
Santa Cruz, Pil.	116	13.04 N	120.43 E
Santa Cruz, Pil.	116	15.46 N	119.55 E
Santa Cruz (Tubajon), Pil.	116	10.19 N	125.33 E

Santa Cruz, Ca., U.S.	226	36.58 N	122.01 W
Santa Cruz, Ven.	246	8.25 N	71.39 W
Santa Cruz, Ven.	286c	10.26 N	67.01 W
Santa Cruz □[4]	254	49.00 S	70.00 W
Santa Cruz □[5]	248	17.30 S	61.30 W
Santa Cruz □[6]	226	36.58 N	122.01 W
Santa Cruz ◆[8], Bra.	256	22.56 S	43.41 W
Santa Cruz ◆[8], India	272c	19.05 N	72.50 E
Santa Cruz ≃, Arg.	254	50.08 S	68.20 W
Santa Cruz ≃, Cuba	286b	23.04 N	82.29 W
Santa Cruz ≃, N.A.	200	32.42 N	111.33 W
Santa Cruz, Ilha I	287a	22.52 S	43.07 W
Santa Cruz, Isla I	246a	0.38 S	90.23 W
Santa Cruz, Sierra de ⋏	236	15.40 N	89.15 W
Santa Cruz Basin ✢[1]	14	12.00 S	163.00 E
Santa Cruz Cabrália	255	16.17 S	39.02 W
Santa Cruz da Graciosa	148a	39.05 N	28.01 W
Santa Cruz das Flores	148a	39.27 N	31.07 W
Santa Cruz de Goiás	255	17.19 S	48.30 W
Santa Cruz de Juventino Rosas	234	20.39 N	101.00 W
Santa Cruz de la Palma	148	28.41 N	17.45 W
Santa Cruz de la Sierra	248	17.48 S	63.10 W
Santa Cruz de la Zarza	34	39.58 N	3.10 W
Santa Cruz del Quiché	236	15.02 N	91.08 W
Santa Cruz del Sur	240p	20.43 N	78.00 W
Santa Cruz de Mudela	34	38.38 N	3.28 W
Santa Cruz de Tenerife	148	28.27 N	16.14 W
Santa Cruz de Tenerife □[4], Esp.	34	28.20 N	16.50 W
Santa Cruz de Tenerife □[4], Esp.	148	28.15 N	17.00 W
Santa Cruz do Capibaribe	250	7.57 S	36.12 W
Santa Cruz do Piauí	250	7.09 S	41.48 W
Santa Cruz do Prata	256	21.12 S	46.45 W
Santa Cruz do Rio Pardo	255	22.55 S	49.37 W
Santa Cruz do Sul	252	29.43 S	52.26 W
Santa Cruz International Airport ⊠	272c	19.05 N	72.52 E
Santa Cruz Island I	204	34.01 N	119.45 W
Santa Cruz Islands II	14	11.00 S	166.15 E
Santa Cruz Meyehualco ◆[8]	286a	19.20 N	99.03 W
Santa Cruz Mountains ⋏	226	37.15 N	122.00 W
Santa Cruz Point ➤	116	15.44 N	119.52 E
Santa Cruz Tacache de Mina	234	17.51 N	98.07 W
Santadi	71	39.05 N	8.43 E
Santa Domenica Talao	68	39.49 N	15.51 E
Santa Domenica Vittoria	70	37.55 N	14.58 E
Sant Adrià de Besòs	266d	41.25 N	2.14 E
Santa Elena, Arg.	252	30.57 S	59.48 W
Santa Elena, Ec.	246	2.14 S	80.51 W
Santa Elena, El Sal.	236	13.22 N	88.25 W
Santa Elena, Méx.	196	27.59 N	103.56 W
Santa Elena, Méx.	232	27.28 N	102.33 W
Santa Elena, Méx.	234	18.39 N	101.34 W
Santa Elena ≃	248	15.42 S	67.13 W
Santa Elena, Bahía de ⊂	246	2.06 S	80.53 W
Santa Elena, Cabo ➤	236	10.54 N	85.57 W
Santa Elena, Golfo de ⊂	236	10.59 N	85.50 W
Santa Elena, Punta ➤	246	2.11 S	81.00 W
Santa Elena del Gomero	286e	33.29 S	70.46 W
Santa Elena de Uairén	246	4.37 N	61.08 W
Santa Elisabetta	70	37.26 N	13.33 E
Santa Eufemia	34	38.36 N	4.54 W
Santa Eugenia	34	42.33 N	9.00 W
Santa Eulalia, Esp.	34	40.34 N	1.19 W
Santa Eulalia, Guat.	236	15.45 N	91.29 W
Santa Eulària del Riu	34	38.59 N	1.31 E
Santa Fe, Arg.	252	31.38 S	60.42 W
Santa Fé, Bra.	255	15.40 S	51.16 W
Santa Fé, Bra.	255	23.01 S	51.48 W
Santa Fe, Esp.	34	37.11 N	3.43 W
Santa Fe, Hond.	236	15.55 N	86.05 W
Santa Fé, Pan.	236	8.31 N	81.05 W
Santa Fe, Pil.	116	11.09 N	123.47 E
Santa Fe, Pil.	116	16.10 N	120.57 E
Santa Fe, Pil.	116	12.10 N	122.00 E
Santa Fe, Mo., U.S.	219	39.22 N	91.49 W
Santa Fe, N.M., U.S.	200	35.41 N	105.56 W
Santa Fe □[4]	252	31.00 S	61.00 W
Santa Fé ◆[8]	286b	23.05 N	82.31 W
Santa Fe ≃, Fl., U.S.	192	29.53 N	82.53 W
Santa Fe ≃, N.M., U.S.	200	35.36 N	106.20 W
Santa Fé, Aeropuerto ⊠	286b	23.04 N	82.28 W
Santa Fe, Isla I	246a	0.49 S	90.04 W
Santa Fé, Ribeirão ≃	287b	23.24 S	46.48 W
Santa Fe Baldy ∧	200	35.50 N	105.46 W
Santa Fe Dam ◆[6]	280	34.07 N	117.58 W
Santa Fe de Bogotá	246	4.36 N	74.05 W
Santa Fe de Minas	255	16.42 S	45.26 W
Santa Fé do Sul	255	20.13 S	50.56 W
Santa Fe Flood Control Basin ≚[1]	280	34.07 N	117.58 W
Santa Fe Springs	280	33.56 N	118.04 W
Santa Filomena	250	9.07 S	45.56 W
Santa Fiora	66	42.50 N	11.35 E
Santa Flavia	70	38.05 N	13.31 E
Sant'Agata Bolognese	64	44.40 N	11.08 E
Sant'Agata de'Goti	68	41.05 N	14.30 E
Sant'Agata del Bianco	68	38.05 N	16.05 E
Sant'Agata di Militello	70	38.04 N	14.38 E
Sant'Agata di Puglia	68	41.09 N	15.23 E
Sant'Agata Feltria	66	43.52 N	12.12 E
Sant'Agata sul Santerno	66	44.26 N	11.51 E
Santa Gertrude (Sankt Gertraud)	64	46.29 N	10.53 E
Santa Gertrudis	196	26.09 N	98.44 W
Santa Giusta, Stagno di ⊜	71	39.52 N	8.35 E
Sant'Agostino	64	44.48 N	11.23 E
Sāntāhār	124	24.48 N	88.59 E
Santa Helena	250	2.14 S	45.18 W
Santa Helena de Goiás	255	17.43 S	50.35 W
Santai, Zhg.	85	39.14 N	77.42 E
Santai, Zhg.	86	44.35 N	81.18 E
Santai, Zhg.	102	31.10 N	105.02 E
Santai, Zhg.	104	41.56 N	123.11 E
Santai, Zhg.	104	41.48 N	121.53 E
Santai, Zhg.	105	38.58 N	115.49 E
Santa Inês	255	13.17 S	39.48 W
Santa Inés, Bahía ⊂	232	26.59 N	111.59 W
Santa Inés, Isla I	254	53.45 S	72.45 W
Santa Inés Ahuatempan	234	18.25 N	98.01 W
Santa Iria de Azóia	266c	38.51 N	9.05 W
Santa Isabel, Arg.	252	36.15 S	66.56 W
Santa Isabel, Arg.	252	33.54 S	61.42 W
Santa Isabel, Bra.	256	23.19 S	46.14 W
Santa Isabel, Ec.	246	3.21 S	79.19 W
Santa Isabel → Malabo, Gui. Ecu.	152	3.45 N	8.47 E
Santa Isabel, Méx.	234	23.15 N	100.52 W

≃ River	Fluß	Río	Rivière	Rio
≅ Canal	Kanal	Canal	Canal	Canal
└ Waterfall, Rapids	Wasserfall, Stromschnellen	Cascada, Rápidos	Chute d'eau, Rapides	Cascata, Rápidos
Ʉ Strait	Meeresstraße	Estrecho	Détroit	Estreito
⊂ Bay, Gulf	Bucht, Golf	Bahía, Golfo	Baie, Golfe	Baía, Golfo
⊜ Lake, Lakes	See, Seen	Lago, Lagos	Lac, Lacs	Lago, Lagos
≡ Swamp	Sumpf	Pantano	Marais	Pântano
⍓ Ice Features, Glacier	Eis- und Gletscherformen	Accidentes Glaciales	Formes glaciaires	Acidentes glaciares
⫟ Other Hydrographic Features	Andere Hydrographische Objekte	Otros Elementos Hidrográficos	Autres données hydrographiques	Outros acidentes hidrográficos
✢ Submarine Features	Untermeerische Objekte	Accidentes Submarinos	Formes de relief sous-marin	Acidentes submarinos
□ Political Unit	Politische Einheit	Unidad Politica	Entité politique	Unidade política
ʊ Cultural Institution	Kulturelle Institution	Institución Cultural	Institution culturelle	Institução cultural
⊥ Historical Site	Historische Stätte	Sitio Histórico	Site historique	Sitio histórico
♠ Recreational Site	Erholungs- und Ferienort	Sitio de Recreo	Centre de loisirs	Area de Lazer
⊠ Airport	Flughafen	Aeropuerto	Aéroport	Aeroporto
■ Military Installation	Militäranlage	Instalación Militar	Installation militaire	Instalação militar
◆ Miscellaneous	Verschiedenes	Misceláneo	Divers	Diversos

ENGLISH — Name / Page / Lat.°′ / Long.°′ · DEUTSCH — Name / Seite / Breite°′ / Länge°′ E = Ost

Santa Isabel, P.R. **240m** 17.58 N 66.24 W
Santa Isabel I **175e** 8.00 S 159.00 E
Santa Isabel ≃ **236** 15.59 N 90.00 W
Santa Isabel, Pico de ∧ **152** 3.35 N 8.46 E
Santa Isabel Creek ≃ **196** 27.39 N 99.38 W
Santa Isabel de Sihuas **248** 16.20 S 72.06 W
Santa Isabel do Araguaia **250** 6.07 S 48.19 W
Santa Isabel do Rio Prêto **256** 22.14 S 44.05 W
Santaizi **104** 41.21 N 121.36 E
Santa Josefa **116** 8.02 N 125.57 E
Santa Julia **286e** 33.30 S 70.38 W
Santa Juliana **255** 19.19 S 47.32 W
Sant'Alberto **66** 44.32 N 12.09 E
Sant'Alfio **70** 37.44 N 15.08 E
Sāntalpur **120** 23.45 N 71.10 E
Santa Luce **66** 43.28 N 10.34 E
Santa Lucía, Arg. **252** 28.59 S 59.06 W
Santa Lucía, Arg. **252** 31.32 S 68.29 W
Santa Lucía, Cuba **240p** 21.02 N 76.00 W
Santa Lucía, Cuba **240p** 22.40 N 83.58 W
Santa Lucia, It. **64** 46.28 N 10.21 E
Santa Lucia, It. **64** 45.26 N 10.57 E
Santa Lucía, Ur. **258** 34.27 S 56.24 W
Santa Lucía, Ven. **246** 8.07 N 69.46 W
Santa Lucia → Saint Lucia □[1] **241f** 13.53 N 60.58 W
Santa Lucía ≃ **258** 34.48 S 56.22 W
Santa Lucia, Cabo → Saint Lucia, Cape > **158** 28.25 S 32.25 E
Santa Lucía, Cuchilla ⋏[2] **258** 34.09 S 56.11 W
Santa Lucía Chico ≃ **258** 34.21 S 56.20 W
Santa Lucía Cotzumalguapa **236** 14.20 N 91.01 W
Santa Lucia Creek ≃ **226** 36.13 N 121.30 W
Santa Lucia del Mela **70** 38.09 N 15.17 E
Santa Lucia di Piave **64** 45.51 N 12.17 E
Santa Lucia Range ⋏ **226** 36.00 N 121.20 W
Santaluz **250** 11.15 S 39.22 W
Santa Luzia, Bra. **250** 6.53 S 36.56 W
Santa Luzia, Port. **34** 37.44 N 8.24 W
Santa Luzia I **150a** 16.46 N 24.45 W
Santa Magdalena **252** 34.30 S 63.56 W
Santa-Manza, Golfu di c **71** 41.37 N 9.22 E
Santa Margarita **226** 35.23 N 120.36 W
Santa Margarita ≃ **228** 33.14 N 117.25 W
Santa Margarita, Isla I **232** 24.27 N 111.50 W
Santa Margarita Lake ⊜[1] **226** 35.20 N 120.28 W
Santa Margarita Mountains ⋏ **228** 33.30 N 117.25 W
Santa Margherita di Belice **70** 37.41 N 13.01 E
Santa Margherita Ligure **62** 44.20 N 9.12 E
Santa María, Arg. **252** 26.41 S 66.02 W
Santa Maria, Bra. **252** 29.41 S 53.48 W
Santa Maria, C.V. **150a** 16.36 N 22.54 W
Santa María, C.R. **236** 9.39 N 83.57 W
Santa María, Méx. **196** 28.02 N 101.38 W
Santa María, Pan. **236** 8.07 N 80.40 W
Santa Maria, Pil. **116** 17.22 N 120.29 E
Santa María, P.R. **240m** 18.09 N 65.26 W
Santa Maria, Schw. **58** 46.16 N 9.09 E
Santa Maria, Schw. **58** 46.36 N 10.24 E
Santa Maria, Ca., U.S. **204** 34.57 N 120.26 W
Santa Maria I, Port. **148a** 36.58 N 25.06 W
Santa Maria I, Vanuatu **175f** 14.15 S 167.30 E
Santa Maria ≃, Bra. **252** 29.48 S 54.56 W
Santa Maria ≃, Bra. **252** 21.50 S 54.53 W
Santa María ≃, Méx. **232** 31.00 N 107.14 W
Santa María ≃, Méx. **234** 21.48 N 99.10 W
Santa María ≃, Pan. **236** 8.06 N 80.29 W
Santa Maria ≃, Az., U.S. **200** 34.19 N 113.31 W
Santa María, Bahía c **232** 25.04 N 108.06 W
Santa Maria, Cabo → Sainte-Marie, Cap >, Madag. **157b** 25.36 S 45.08 E
Santa María, Cabo >, Ur. **252** 34.40 S 54.10 W
Santa Maria, Cabo de >, Ang. **152** 13.25 S 12.32 E
Santa Maria, Cabo de >, Port. **34** 36.58 N 7.54 W
Santa Maria, Cape > **238** 23.41 N 75.19 W
Santa María, Cayo I **240p** 22.40 N 79.00 W
Santa María, Cerro ∧ **286d** 11.56 S 76.57 W
Santa Maria, Giogo di (Pass Umbrail))(**64** 46.34 N 10.25 E
Santa María, Isla I, Chile **252** 37.02 S 73.33 W
Santa María, Isla I, Ec. **246a** 1.17 S 90.26 W
Santa Maria, Isola I **71** 41.17 N 9.22 E
Santa María, Laguna de ⊜ **200** 31.07 N 107.16 W
Santa Maria, Ribeirão ≃ **250** 7.10 S 49.13 W
Santa María, Volcán ∧[1] **236** 14.45 N 91.33 W
Santa María Ajoloapan **234** 19.58 N 99.03 W
Santa Maria a Monte **66** 43.42 N 10.42 E
Santa María Asunción Tlaxiaco **234** 17.16 N 97.41 W
Santa Maria a Vico **68** 41.02 N 14.29 E
Santa María Ayoquezco **234** 16.41 N 96.50 W
Santa Maria Capua Vetere **68** 41.05 N 14.15 E
Santa María Chimalapa **234** 16.55 N 94.41 W
Santa María Colotepec **234** 15.53 N 96.55 W
Santa Maria da Boa Vista **250** 8.49 S 39.49 W
Santa Maria da Vitória **255** 13.24 S 44.12 W
Santa Maria degli Angeli **66** 43.03 N 12.34 E
Santa María de Huazamoto **234** 22.30 N 104.30 W
Santa María de Ipire **246** 8.49 N 65.19 W
Santa Maria de Itabira **255** 19.27 S 43.08 W
Santa Maria del Cedro **68** 39.45 N 15.50 E
Santa Maria della Versa **62** 44.59 N 9.18 E
Santa Maria delle Grazie ʊ[1] **266b** 45.27 N 9.10 E
Santa María del Oro **232** 25.56 N 105.22 W
Santa María de los Ángeles **234** 22.11 N 103.14 W
Santa María del Refugio **234** 23.44 N 101.14 W
Santa María del Río **234** 21.48 N 100.45 W
Santa María del Valle **234** 20.54 N 102.22 W
Santa Mariá de Mohovano **232** 26.42 N 103.39 W
Santa Maria di Galeria ◆[8] **267a** 42.01 N 12.19 E
Santa Maria di Leuca, Capo > **68** 39.47 N 18.22 E
Santa Maria di Licodia **70** 37.37 N 14.53 E
Santa Maria di Siponto ʊ[1] **68** 41.40 N 15.51 E
Santa Maria do Suaçuí **255** 18.12 S 42.25 W
Santa María Huazolotitlán **234** 16.17 N 97.56 W
Santa María Jalapa del Marqués **234** 16.30 N 95.28 W
Santa María la Real de Nieva **34** 41.04 N 4.24 W
Santa Maria Madalena **255** 21.57 S 42.01 W
Santa Maria Maggiore **58** 46.08 N 8.28 E
Santa Maria Maggiore ʊ[1] **267a** 41.53 N 12.30 E
Santa Maria Nuova **66** 43.29 N 13.18 E
Santa-Maria-Siché **36** 41.52 N 8.59 E
Santa María Tulpetlac **286a** 19.34 N 99.03 W
Santa María Xadani **234** 15.56 N 96.04 W
Santa María Zoquitlán **234** 16.33 N 96.23 W
Santa Marinella **66** 42.02 N 11.51 E
Santa Marta, Col. **246** 11.15 N 74.13 W
Santa Marta, Guat. **236** 13.58 N 91.18 W
Santa Marta, Cabo de >, Ang. **152** 13.52 S 12.25 E
Santa Marta, Cabo de >, Moç. **158** 26.05 S 32.58 E
Santa Marta, Cerro ∧ **234** 18.19 N 94.48 W
Santa Marta, Ciénaga Grande c **246** 10.50 N 74.25 W
Santa Marta Grande, Cabo de > **252** 28.38 S 48.45 W
Sant'Ambrogio **64** 45.31 N 10.50 E
Santa Mónica, Méx. **196** 28.12 N 100.37 W
Santa Monica, Ca., U.S. **228** 34.01 N 118.29 W
Santa Mónica ◆[8] **286c** 10.29 N 66.53 W
Santa Monica Bay c **228** 33.54 N 118.25 W
Santa Monica Beach State Park ♦ **280** 34.01 N 118.30 W
Santa Monica Mountains ⋏ **228** 34.05 N 118.40 W
Santa Monica Mountains National Recreation Area ♦ **228** 34.05 N 118.45 W
Santa Monica Municipal Airport ⊠ **280** 34.01 N 118.27 W
Santan **112** 0.03 S 117.28 E
Santana **255** 12.59 S 44.03 W
Santana ◆[8] **287b** 23.29 S 46.38 W
Santana ≃ **255** 19.43 S 51.02 W
Santana, Coxilha de ⋏[2] **252** 31.15 S 55.15 W
Santana, Ilha de I **250** 2.18 S 43.41 W
Santana, Ribeirão ≃ **250** 9.47 S 50.13 W
Santana da Boa Vista **252** 30.52 S 53.07 W
Santana da Vargem **256** 21.15 S 45.30 W
Santana de Caldas **256** 21.50 S 46.24 W
Santana de Cataguases **256** 21.17 S 42.33 W
Santana de Parnaíba **256** 23.27 S 46.55 W
Santana de Parnaíba □[7] **287b** 23.27 S 46.54 W
Santana do Campestre **256** 21.16 S 42.56 W
Santana do Capivari **256** 22.14 S 44.56 W
Santana do Cariri **250** 7.11 S 39.44 W
Santana do Deserto **256** 21.57 S 43.11 W
Santana do Garambéu **256** 21.36 S 44.06 W
Santana do Ipanema **250** 9.22 S 37.14 W
Santana do Livramento **252** 30.53 S 55.31 W
Santana do Matos **250** 5.57 S 36.39 W
Santander, Col. **246** 3.01 N 76.28 W
Santander, Esp. **34** 43.28 N 3.48 W
Santander, Pil. **116** 9.25 N 123.20 E
Santander □[5] **246** 7.00 N 73.15 W
Santander Jiménez **232** 24.13 N 98.28 W
Sant'Andrea, Isola I **68** 40.03 N 17.57 E
Sant'Andrea Frius **71** 39.29 N 9.10 E
Sant Andreu de la Barca **266d** 41.27 N 1.59 E
Santa Nella **226** 37.03 N 121.02 W
Santanésia **256** 22.30 S 43.49 W
Santang **100** 28.44 N 116.32 E
Sant'Angelo, Castel ⊥ **267a** 41.55 N 12.28 E
Sant'Angelo, Monte ∧ **267a** 41.56 N 12.49 E
Sant'Angelo dei Lombardi **68** 40.56 N 15.11 E
Sant'Angelo in Vado **66** 43.40 N 12.25 E
Sant'Angelo Lodigiano **62** 45.14 N 9.24 E
Sant'Angelo Muxard **70** 37.28 N 13.32 E
Sant'Angelo Romano **267a** 42.02 N 12.42 E
Santanghu **102** 44.13 N 93.22 E
Santanilla, Islas II **238** 17.25 N 83.55 W
Santa Ninfa **70** 37.46 N 12.53 E
Sant'Antimo **68** 40.56 N 14.14 E
Sant'Antine, Nuraghe ⊥ **71** 40.29 N 8.46 E
Sant'Antioco **71** 39.04 N 8.27 E
Sant'Antioco, Isola di I **71** 39.02 N 8.25 E
Sant Antoni de Portmany **34** 38.58 N 1.18 E
Sant'Antonio Abate **68** 40.43 N 14.32 E
Sant'Antonio di Santadi **71** 39.43 N 8.29 E
Sant'Antonio Morignone **64** 46.24 N 10.21 E
Santanyí **34** 39.22 N 3.07 E
Santa Panagia, Capo > **70** 37.07 N 15.18 E
Santa Paula **228** 34.21 N 119.03 W
Santa Paula Creek ≃ **228** 34.21 N 119.03 W
Santa Perpètua de Mogoda **266d** 41.32 N 2.11 E
Santapogue Creek ≃ **276** 40.40 N 73.21 W
Santa Pola, Cap de > **34** 38.12 N 0.31 W
Sant'Apollinare in Classe ʊ[1] **66** 44.22 N 12.15 E
Santaquin **200** 39.58 N 111.47 W
Santa Quitéria **250** 4.20 S 40.10 W
Santa Quitéria do Maranhão **250** 3.31 S 42.32 W
Sant'Arcangelo **68** 40.15 N 16.17 E
Santarcangelo di Romagna **66** 44.04 N 12.27 E
Sant'Arcangelo Trimonte **68** 41.10 N 14.56 E
Santarém, Bra. **250** 2.26 S 54.42 W
Santarém, Port. **34** 39.14 N 8.41 W
Santarém □[5] **266c** 38.50 N 8.56 W
Santaren Channel Ա **238** 24.00 N 79.30 W
Santa Rita, Bra. **250** 7.08 S 34.58 W
Santa Rita, Bra. **287a** 22.41 S 43.28 W
Santa Rita, Col. **246** 0.33 N 73.58 W
Santa Rita, Hond. **236** 15.09 N 87.53 W
Santa Rita, Méx. **196** 27.29 N 100.33 W
Santa Rita, Méx. **232** 28.34 N 111.42 W
Santa Rita, Pil. **116** 11.27 N 124.56 E
Santa Rita, Mt., U.S. **182** 48.42 N 112.19 W
Santa Rita, Ven. **246** 10.32 N 71.32 W
Santa Rita, Punta > **258** 34.28 S 57.52 W
Santa Rita de Caldas **256** 22.02 S 46.20 W
Santa Rita de Catuna **252** 30.57 S 66.13 W
Santa Rita de Jacutinga **256** 22.09 S 44.06 W
Santa Rita del Rucio **234** 23.04 N 100.19 W
Santa Rita do Araguaia **255** 17.20 S 53.12 W
Santa Rita do Ibitipoca **256** 21.33 S 43.55 W
Santa Rita do Sapucaí **256** 22.15 S 45.42 W
Santa Rita do Weil **246** 3.29 S 69.19 W
Santa Rita Park **226** 37.02 N 120.35 W
Santa Rosa, Arg. **252** 36.37 S 64.17 W
Santa Rosa, Arg. **252** 23.22 S 64.30 W
Santa Rosa, Bol. **248** 14.10 S 66.53 W
Santa Rosa, Bol. **248** 10.36 S 67.25 W
Santa Rosa, Bol. **248** 17.07 S 63.35 W
Santa Rosa, Bra. **252** 27.52 S 54.29 W
Santa Rosa, Bra. **255** 15.01 S 47.13 W
Santa Rosa, Col. **246** 2.31 N 68.13 W
Santa Rosa, C.R. **236** 10.51 N 85.38 W
Santa Rosa, Ec. **246** 3.27 S 79.58 W
Santa Rosa, Méx. **204** 31.59 N 116.45 W
Santa Rosa, Méx. **234** 22.18 N 104.24 W
Santa Rosa, Para. **248** 21.46 S 61.43 W
Santa Rosa, Para. **252** 26.52 S 56.49 W
Santa Rosa, Ca., U.S. **226** 38.26 N 122.42 W
Santa Rosa, N.M., U.S. **196** 34.56 N 104.40 W
Santa Rosa, Tx., U.S. **196** 26.15 N 97.50 W
Santa Rosa, Ur. **258** 34.30 S 56.03 W
Santa Rosa, Ven. **246** 8.26 N 69.24 W
Santa Rosa, Ven. **246** 7.03 N 68.28 W
Santa Rosa, Ven. **286c** 10.30 N 66.46 W
Santa Rosa □[5] **236** 14.10 N 90.18 W
Santa Rosa, Mount ∧[2] **174p** 13.32 N 144.55 E
Santa Rosa, Parque Nacional ♦ **236** 10.50 N 85.45 W
Santa Rosa, Presa ⊜[1] **234** 20.58 N 103.35 W
Santa Rosa Beach **194** 30.23 N 86.13 W
Santa Rosa Creek ≃ **226** 35.34 N 121.06 W
Santa Rosa de Aguán **236** 15.57 N 85.43 W
Santa Rosa de Amanadona **246** 1.29 N 66.55 W
Santa Rosa [de Copán] **236** 14.47 N 88.46 W
Santa Rosa de Huechuraba **286e** 33.21 S 70.41 W
Santa Rosa del Conlara **252** 32.20 S 65.12 W
Santa Rosa de Leales **252** 27.09 S 65.15 W
Santa Rosa de Lima **236** 13.37 N 87.53 W
Santa Rosa de Locobe **286e** 33.26 S 70.33 W
Santa Rosa del Palmar **248** 16.54 S 62.24 W
Santa Rosa de Osos **246** 6.39 N 75.28 W
Santa Rosa de Río Primero **252** 31.09 S 63.23 W
Santa Rosa de Sucumbíos **246** 0.22 N 77.10 W
Santa Rosa de Viterbo **246** 5.53 N 72.59 W
Santa Rosa Indian Reservation ◆[4] **204** 33.35 N 116.35 W
Santa Rosa Island I, Ca., U.S. **204** 33.58 N 120.06 W
Santa Rosa Island I, Fl., U.S. **194** 30.22 N 86.55 W
Santa Rosa Jáuregui **234** 20.44 N 100.27 W
Santa Rosalía, Méx. **196** 26.08 N 98.59 W
Santa Rosalía, Méx. **232** 27.19 N 112.17 W
Santa Rosalía, Ven. **246** 9.02 N 69.01 W
Santa Rosa Range ⋏ **204** 41.35 N 117.40 W
Santa Rosa Wash V **200** 33.00 N 112.00 W
Santa Rosita **286d** 12.03 S 76.59 W
Sant'Arsenio **68** 40.28 N 15.29 E
Šantarskije ostrova II **74** 55.00 N 137.36 E
Santa Severa **66** 42.02 N 11.57 E
Santa Severina **68** 39.09 N 16.55 E
Santa Sofia **66** 43.57 N 11.54 E
Santa Susana **228** 34.16 N 118.43 W
Santa Susana Mountains ⋏ **228** 34.20 N 118.42 W
Santa Sylvina **252** 27.49 S 61.09 W
Santa Tecla → Nueva San Salvador **236** 13.41 N 89.17 W
Santa Teresa, Bra. **255** 19.55 S 40.36 W
Santa Teresa, Méx. **196** 29.34 N 104.39 W
Santa Teresa, Méx. **200** 30.52 N 111.33 W
Santa Teresa, Méx. **232** 25.17 N 97.51 W
Santa Teresa, Méx. **234** 22.28 N 104.44 W
Santa Teresa ≃ **255** 11.47 S 48.37 W
Santa Teresa, Embalse de ⊜[1] **34** 40.40 N 5.30 W
Santa Teresa de lo Ovalle **286e** 33.23 S 70.47 W
Santa Teresa di Riva **70** 37.57 N 15.22 E
Santa Teresa Gallura **71** 41.14 N 9.11 E
Santa Tereza de Goiás **255** 13.38 S 49.01 W
Santa Terezinha **250** 10.28 S 50.31 W
Santa Valburga (Sankt Wallburg) **64** 46.33 N 11.00 E
Santa Venerina **70** 37.41 N 15.08 E
Santa Venetia **226** 38.01 N 122.31 W
Santa Vitória **255** 18.50 S 50.08 W
Santa Vitória do Palmar **252** 33.31 S 53.21 W
Santa Vittoria, Monte ∧ **71** 39.45 N 9.18 E
Santa Vittoria in Matenano **66** 43.01 N 13.29 E
Santa Ynez ≃ **204** 34.41 N 120.36 W
Santa Ynez Canyon V **280** 34.04 N 118.34 W
Santa Ysabel Indian Reservation ◆[4] **204** 33.11 N 116.41 W
Sant Bartomeu de la Quadra **266d** 41.26 N 2.02 E
Sant Boi de Llobregat **266d** 41.21 N 2.03 E
Sant Carles de la Ràpita **34** 40.37 N 0.36 E
Sant Climent de Llobregat **266d** 41.20 N 2.00 E
Sant Cugat del Vallès **266d** 41.28 N 2.05 E
Santee **228** 32.50 N 116.58 W
Santee ≃ **192** 33.14 N 79.28 W
Santee Dam ◆[6] **192** 33.24 N 80.12 W
Santee Indian Reservation ◆[4] **198** 42.45 N 97.50 W
Sant'Egidio alla Vibrata **66** 42.49 N 13.42 E
Sant'Elena **64** 45.12 N 11.43 E
Sant'Elia a Pianisi **66** 41.38 N 14.52 E
Sant'Elia Fiumerapido **66** 41.32 N 13.52 E
Sant'Elpidio a Mare **66** 43.14 N 13.41 E
Santena **62** 44.57 N 7.45 E
Santenay **58** 46.55 N 4.41 E
Santeny **261** 48.43 N 2.34 E
San Teodoro, It. **70** 37.51 N 14.42 E
San Teodoro, It. **71** 40.46 N 9.39 E
Santermo in Colle **68** 40.48 N 16.45 E
Santerno ≃ **64** 44.34 N 11.58 E
Santerre □[9] **50** 49.40 N 2.40 E
Sant'Eufemia, Golfo di c **68** 38.50 N 16.00 E
Sant'Eufemia a Maiella **66** 42.07 N 14.02 E
Sant'Eufemia d'Aspromonte **68** 38.16 N 15.52 E
Sant'Eufemia Lamezia **68** 38.55 N 16.15 E
Sant Feliu de Guíxols **34** 41.47 N 3.02 E
Sant Feliu de Llobregat **266d** 41.23 N 2.03 E
Sant Fost de Campsentelles **266d** 41.31 N 2.14 E
Sānthia, Bngl. **126** 24.03 N 89.33 E
Santhià, It. **62** 45.22 N 8.10 E
Santiago, Bol. **248** 18.19 S 59.34 W
Santiago, Bra. **252** 29.11 S 54.53 W
Santiago, Chile **252** 33.27 S 70.40 W
Santiago, Chile **286e** 33.27 S 70.40 W
Santiago → Santiago de Compostela, Esp. **34** 42.53 N 8.33 W
Santiago, Méx. **232** 23.28 N 109.43 W
Santiago, Pan. **236** 8.06 N 80.59 W
Santiago, Para. **252** 27.09 S 56.47 W
Santiago, Perú **248** 14.11 S 75.44 W
Santiago, Pil. **116** 16.41 N 121.33 E
Santiago I **150a** 15.05 N 23.40 W
Santiago ≃, Arg. **288** 34.50 S 57.57 W
Santiago ≃, Méx. **232** 25.11 N 105.26 W
Santiago ≃, S.A. **246** 4.27 S 77.38 W
Santiago, Cape > **116** 13.46 N 120.39 E
Santiago, Cerro ∧ **236** 8.33 N 81.44 W
Santiago, Isla I, Arg. **288** 34.50 S 57.53 W
Santiago, Isla I, Ec. **246a** 0.14 S 90.45 W
Santiago, Serranía de ⋏ **248** 18.25 S 59.25 W
Santiago Atitlán **236** 14.38 N 91.14 W
Santiago Chazumba **234** 18.12 N 97.40 W
Santiago Choapan **234** 17.20 N 95.57 W
Santiago Creek ≃, Ca., U.S. **228** 35.06 N 119.17 W
Santiago Creek ≃, Ca., U.S. **228** 33.46 N 117.54 W
Santiago Dam ◆[6] **280** 33.47 N 117.43 W
Santiago de Cao **248** 7.58 S 79.15 W
Santiago de Chocorvos **248** 13.50 S 75.16 W
Santiago de Chuco **248** 8.09 S 78.11 W
Santiago de Compostela **34** 42.53 N 8.33 W
Santiago de Cuba **240p** 20.01 N 75.49 W
Santiago de Cuba □[4] **240p** 20.10 N 75.55 W
Santiago de Huari **248** 19.00 S 66.48 W
Santiago de Huata **248** 16.06 S 68.53 W
Santiago de la Peña **234** 20.57 N 97.24 W
Santiago de las Vegas ◆[8] **286b** 22.58 N 82.23 W
Santiago del Estero **252** 27.47 S 64.16 W
Santiago del Estero □[4] **252** 28.00 S 63.30 W
Santiago [de los Caballeros] **238** 19.27 N 70.42 W
Santiago de Machaca **248** 17.05 S 69.16 W
Santiago de Méndez **246** 2.43 S 78.19 W
Santiago de Surco **286d** 12.09 S 77.01 W
Santiago do Cacém **34** 38.01 N 8.42 W
Santiago Island I **116** 16.24 N 119.56 E
Santiago Ixcuintla **234** 21.49 N 105.13 W
Santiago Ixtayutla **234** 16.33 N 97.39 W
Santiago Jamiltepec **234** 16.17 N 97.49 W
Santiago Juxtlahuaca **234** 17.20 N 98.01 W
Santiago Lachiguirí **234** 16.41 N 95.32 W
Santiago Larre **258** 35.34 S 59.10 W
Santiago Maravatío **234** 20.10 N 101.00 W
Santiago Papasquiaro **232** 25.03 N 105.25 W
Santiago Peak ∧, Ca., U.S. **228** 33.42 N 117.32 W
Santiago Peak ∧, Tx., U.S. **196** 29.47 N 103.25 W
Santiago Pinotepa Nacional **234** 16.19 N 98.01 W
Santiago Reservoir ⊜[1] **228** 33.47 N 117.43 W
Santiago Tepalcatlapan ◆[8] **286a** 19.15 N 99.08 W
Santiago Tulantepec **234** 20.02 N 98.22 W
Santiago Tutla **234** 17.10 N 95.26 W
Santiago Tuxtla **234** 18.28 N 95.18 W
Santiago Vázquez **258** 34.48 S 56.21 W
Santiago Yaveo **234** 17.19 N 95.42 W
Santiago Zacatepec **234** 17.11 N 95.51 W
Santiaguillo, Laguna ⊜ **232** 24.48 N 104.48 W
Santiam Pass)(**202** 44.25 N 121.51 W
San Tian Zhu (Three Indian Temples) ʊ[1] **106** 30.15 N 120.08 E
Santiao Chiao > **100** 25.02 N 121.59 E
Santiaoqiao **106** 31.36 N 121.22 E
Santi Filippo e Giacomo **70** 37.51 N 12.31 E
Santiguila **150** 12.42 N 7.26 W
Sant'Ilario d'Enza **64** 44.46 N 10.27 E
San Timoteo **246** 9.48 N 71.04 W
San Timoteo Canyon V **228** 34.04 N 117.17 W
Säntis ∧ **58** 47.15 N 9.21 E
Santissima Trinita di Saccargia ʊ[1] **71** 40.41 N 8.42 E
Santissimo ◆[8] **287a** 22.53 S 43.31 W
Santisteban del Puerto **34** 38.15 N 3.12 W
Sant Joan de Labritja **34** 39.05 N 1.30 E
Sant Joan Despí **266d** 41.22 N 2.04 E
Sant Jordi, Golf de c **34** 40.53 N 1.00 E
Sant Just Desvern **266d** 41.23 N 2.05 E
Sant Mateu del Maestrat **34** 40.28 N 0.11 E
Santō, Nihon **94** 35.21 N 136.22 E
Santō, Nihon **96** 35.19 N 134.53 E
Santo, Tx., U.S. **196** 32.36 N 98.13 W
Santo, Vanuatu **175f** 15.32 S 167.08 E
Santo Aleixo **256** 22.34 S 43.04 W
Santo Amaro, Bra. **250** 2.33 S 43.14 W
Santo Amaro, Bra. **255** 12.32 S 38.43 W
Santo Amaro ◆[8] **287b** 23.39 S 46.42 W
Santo Amaro, Ilha de I **256** 23.57 S 46.14 W
Santo Amaro das Brotas **250** 10.47 S 37.04 W
Santo Anastácio **255** 21.58 S 51.39 W
Santo André **256** 23.40 S 46.31 W
Santo Ângelo **252** 28.18 S 54.16 W
Santo Antão I **150a** 17.05 N 25.10 W
Santo Antônio, Bra. **250** 6.18 S 35.27 W
Santo António, S. Tom./P. **152** 1.39 N 7.26 E
Santo Antônio ≃, Bra. **250** 11.31 S 48.37 W
Santo Antônio ≃, Bra. **255** 17.30 S 45.37 W
Santo Antônio ≃, Bra. **287a** 22.42 S 43.37 W
Santo António, Ilha de I **156** 21.58 S 35.28 E
Santo António da Charneca **266c** 38.37 N 9.02 W
Santo Antônio da Patrulha **252** 29.50 S 50.32 W
Santo Antônio de Jesus **255** 12.58 S 39.16 W
Santo Antônio de Pádua **255** 21.32 S 42.11 W
Santo Antonio de Posse **256** 22.36 S 46.55 W
Santo Antônio do Amparo **255** 20.57 S 44.55 W
Santo Antônio do Aventureiro **256** 21.45 S 42.49 W
Santo Antônio do Içá **246** 3.05 S 67.57 W
Santo Antônio do Jardim **256** 22.07 S 46.41 W
Santo Antônio do Leverger **248** 15.52 S 56.05 W
Santo Antônio do Pinhal **256** 22.47 S 45.41 W
Santo Antônio do Rio Verde **255** 17.57 S 47.27 W
Santo Antônio do Sudoeste **252** 26.02 S 53.44 W
Santo Augusto **252** 27.51 S 53.47 W
Santo Corazón **248** 17.59 S 58.51 W
Santo Domingo, Cuba **240p** 22.35 N 80.15 W
Santo Domingo, Méx. **196** 25.38 N 101.05 W
Santo Domingo, Méx. **196** 25.48 N 104.28 W
Santo Domingo, Méx. **232** 25.32 N 112.02 W
Santo Domingo, Nic. **236** 12.16 N 85.05 W
Santo Domingo, Rep. Dom. **238** 18.28 N 69.54 W
Santo Domingo ≃, Méx. **234** 16.41 N 93.00 W
Santo Domingo ≃, Méx. **234** 17.40 N 98.07 W
Santo Domingo ≃, Méx. **234** 18.10 N 96.08 W
Santo Domingo ≃, Méx. **236** 16.15 N 91.17 W
Santo Domingo, Arroyo ≃ **204** 30.43 N 116.03 W
Santo Domingo, Isla → Hispaniola I **238** 19.00 N 71.00 W
Santo Domingo de la Calzada **34** 42.26 N 2.57 W
Santo Domingo de los Colorados **246** 0.15 S 79.09 W
Santo Domingo Indian Reservation ◆[4] **200** 35.30 N 106.25 W
Santo Domingo Nuxaá **234** 17.08 N 97.02 W
Santo Domingo Pueblo **200** 35.30 N 106.21 W
Santo Domingo Tehuantepec **234** 16.20 N 95.14 W
Santo Domingo Teojomulco **234** 16.36 N 97.14 W
Santo Domingo Zanatepec **234** 16.29 N 94.21 W
Santo Estêvão **255** 12.26 S 39.13 W
Sant'Olcese **62** 44.30 N 8.58 E
Santolea, Embalse de ⊜[1] **34** 40.47 N 0.19 W
Santo / Malo □[8] **175f** 15.20 S 166.55 E
San Tomé **246** 8.58 N 64.08 W
San Tommaso **66** 42.11 N 13.58 E
Sant'Omobono Imagna **62** 45.48 N 9.32 E
Santoña **34** 43.27 N 3.27 W
Santong ≃ **98** 42.39 N 126.03 E
Santo Nino Island I **116** 11.55 N 124.27 E
Sant' Onofrio ◆[8] **267a** 41.56 N 12.25 E
Santo Onofre ≃ **255** 12.34 S 43.12 W
Santop, Pic ∧ **175f** 18.39 S 169.03 E
Sant'Oreste **66** 42.14 N 12.32 E
Santorini → Thíra I **38** 36.24 N 25.29 E
Santorso **64** 45.44 N 11.23 E
Santos **256** 23.57 S 46.20 W
Santos, Arroyo de los ≃ **258** 35.28 S 57.29 W
Santos, Baía de c **256** 24.00 S 46.21 W
Santos Dumont **256** 21.28 S 43.34 W
Santos Dumont, Aeroporto ⊠ **256** 22.55 S 43.10 W
Santoshpur **272b** 22.40 N 88.10 E
Santo Stefano, Isola I **66** 40.47 N 13.27 E
Santo Stefano Belbo **62** 44.43 N 8.14 E
Santo Stefano d'Aveto **62** 44.35 N 9.27 E
Santo Stefano di Cadore **64** 46.33 N 12.32 E
Santo Stefano di Camastra **70** 38.01 N 14.21 E
Santo Stefano di Magra **64** 44.10 N 9.55 E
Santo Stefano Quisquina **70** 37.37 N 13.29 E
Santo Stino di Livenza **64** 45.44 N 12.41 E
Santos Tomás del Norte **236** 13.11 N 86.56 W
Santo Tirso **34** 41.21 N 8.28 W
Santo Tomás, Col. **246** 10.46 N 74.45 W
Santo Tomás, Méx. **232** 31.33 N 116.24 W
Santo Tomás, Nic. **236** 12.04 N 85.05 W
Santo Tomás, Perú **248** 6.36 S 77.48 W
Santo Tomás, Perú **248** 14.29 S 72.06 W
Santo Tomas, Pil. **116** 7.29 N 125.38 E
Santo Tomás ≃, Méx. **204** 31.32 N 116.40 W
Santo Tomás ≃, Perú **248** 13.47 S 72.09 W
Santo Tomás, Punta > **232** 31.34 N 116.42 W
Santo Tomas, University of ʊ[2] **269f** 14.37 N 120.59 E
Santo Tomás, Volcán ∧[1] **246a** 0.48 S 91.07 W
Santo Tomás y Principe → Sao Tome and Principe □[1] **152** 1.00 N 7.00 E
Santo Tomé, Arg. **252** 28.33 S 56.03 W
Santo Tomé, Arg. **252** 31.40 S 60.46 W
Santo Tomé de Guayana → Ciudad Guayana **246** 8.22 N 62.40 W
Sant'pietro, Lago di ⊜ **68** 41.01 N 15.30 E
Santpoort **52** 52.25 N 4.38 E
Sant Quirze de la Serra **266d** 41.32 N 2.05 E
Santuanjiang **106** 30.54 N 121.43 E
Santuario de Quillacas **248** 19.14 S 66.58 W
Santu Lussurgiu **71** 40.08 N 8.39 E
Santunying **105** 40.14 N 118.12 E
Sant Vicenç dels Horts **266d** 41.24 N 2.01 E
San Ubaldo **236** 11.51 N 85.20 W
Sanuki **268** 35.16 N 139.53 E
Sanuki-sammyaku ⋏ **96** 34.09 N 134.11 E
Şānūr **132** 32.21 N 35.15 E
San Valentino in Abruzzo Citeriore **66** 42.14 N 13.59 E
San Valentino Torio **68** 40.48 N 14.36 E
San Venanzo **66** 42.52 N 12.16 E
San Vendemiano **64** 45.54 N 12.20 E
San Vicente, Arg. **252** 28.30 S 64.09 W
San Vicente, Arg. **258** 34.58 S 58.22 W
San Vicente, El Sal. **236** 13.38 N 88.48 W
San Vicente □[5] **288** 34.56 S 58.24 W
San Vicente → Saint Vincent and the Grenadines □[1] **241h** 13.15 N 61.12 W
San Vicente, Cabo → São Vicente, Cabo de > **34** 37.01 N 9.00 W
San Vicente, Volcán de ∧[1] **236** 13.36 N 88.51 W
San Vicente Creek ≃ **282** 37.32 N 122.31 W
San Vicente de Alcántara **34** 39.21 N 7.08 W
San Vicente de Cañete **248** 13.05 S 76.24 W
San Vicente de Chucurí **246** 6.54 N 73.25 W
San Vicente de la Barquera **34** 43.26 N 4.24 W
San Vicente del Caguán **246** 2.07 N 74.46 W
San Vicente de Tagua-Tagua **252** 34.26 S 71.05 W
San Vicente Mountain ∧ **280** 34.08 N 118.31 W
San Vicente Reservoir ⊜[1] **228** 32.55 N 116.55 W
San Vicente Tancuayalab **234** 21.44 N 98.34 W
San Vigilio **64** 45.34 N 10.41 E
San Vigilio ʊ[1] **64** 46.37 N 11.07 E
San Vincenzo **66** 43.06 N 10.32 E
San Vito, C.R. **236** 8.50 N 82.58 W
San Vito, It. **71** 39.26 N 9.32 E
San Vito, Capo > **70** 38.11 N 12.44 E
San Vito, Serralta di ∧ **68** 38.46 N 16.22 E
San Vito al Tagliamento **64** 45.54 N 12.52 E
San Vito Chietino **66** 42.18 N 14.27 E
San Vito dei Normanni **68** 40.39 N 17.42 E
San Vito lo Capo **70** 38.10 N 12.45 E
San Vito Romano **66** 41.53 N 12.59 E
San Vito sullo Ionio **68** 38.43 N 16.25 E
Sanwa, Nihon **94** 37.07 N 138.21 E
Sanwa, Nihon **94** 36.12 N 139.49 E
Sanwa, Nihon **96** 34.42 N 133.15 E
San Xavier Indian Reservation ◆[4] **200** 32.05 N 111.08 W
Sanxi, Zhg. **100** 30.22 N 118.25 E
Sanxi, Zhg. **100** 27.42 N 120.04 E
Sanxing, Zhg. **106** 31.47 N 121.35 E
Sanxing, Zhg. **106** 31.58 N 121.07 E
Sanxingchang, Zhg. **107** 30.19 N 104.09 E
Sanxingchang, Zhg. **107** 30.32 N 104.38 E
Sanxingjie **106** 32.06 N 121.01 E
Sanyang, Zhg. **100** 28.37 N 116.15 E
Sanyang, Zhg. **100** 31.20 N 113.10 E
Sanyang, Zhg. **100** 27.57 N 114.22 E
Sanyangzhen **106** 31.55 N 121.29 E
Sanyanjing **104** 41.28 N 122.27 E
Sanyanqiao **100** 28.39 N 113.43 E
Sanyati ≃ **154** 16.49 S 28.45 E
San Ygnacio **196** 27.03 N 99.27 W
Sanyō, Nihon **96** 34.45 N 134.01 E
Sanyō, Nihon **96** 34.02 N 131.10 E
Sanyuan **102** 34.35 N 108.54 E
Sanyuanpu **98** 42.02 N 125.44 E
Sanyuhao **98** 42.30 N 117.34 E
Sanyuzhen **106** 32.08 N 121.19 E
Sanza **68** 40.15 N 15.33 E
Sanzao Dao I **100** 22.03 N 113.21 E
Sanza Pombo **152** 7.19 S 15.59 E
Sanzar ≃ **85** 40.00 N 67.40 E
San Zeno di Montagna **64** 45.37 N 10.43 E
Sanzha **98** 41.44 N 114.39 E
Sanzhan, Zhg. **89** 49.42 N 125.20 E
Sanzhan, Zhg. **89** 49.36 N 126.38 E
Sanzuodian **98** 41.36 N 118.49 E
São Benedito **250** 4.03 S 40.53 W
São Benedito ≃ **250** 9.11 S 57.02 W
São Benedito das Areias **256** 21.19 S 47.02 W
São Benedito do Rio Preto **250** 3.20 S 43.35 W
São Bento **250** 2.42 S 44.50 W
São Bento ≃ **256** 21.42 S 45.18 W
São Bento, Mosteiro de ʊ[1] **287a** 22.54 S 43.11 W
São Bento Abade **256** 21.35 S 45.04 W
São Bento de Caldas **256** 22.08 S 46.18 W
São Bento do Norte **250** 5.04 S 36.02 W
São Bento do Sapucaí **256** 22.42 S 45.43 W
São Bento do Sul **252** 26.15 S 49.23 W
São Bento do Una **250** 8.32 S 36.22 W
São Bernardino **287a** 22.40 S 43.26 W
São Bernardo **250** 3.22 S 42.24 W
São Bernardo do Campo **256** 23.42 S 46.33 W
São Bernardo do Campo □[7] **287b** 23.44 S 46.33 W
São Borja **252** 28.39 S 56.00 W
São Brás **250** 10.05 S 36.55 W
São Brás de Alportel **34** 37.09 N 7.53 W
São Braz, Cabo de > **152** 9.59 S 13.19 E
São Caetano de Odivelas **250** 0.45 S 48.02 W
São Caetano do Sul **256** 23.36 S 46.34 W
São Caetano do Sul □[7] **287b** 23.37 S 46.33 W
São Carlos **255** 22.01 S 47.54 W
São Cristóvão **250** 11.01 S 37.12 W
São Cristóvão ◆[8] **287a** 22.54 S 43.14 W
Saodatun **104** 42.02 N 123.31 E
São Domingos, Bra. **252** 26.34 S 52.32 W
São Domingos, Bra. **255** 13.24 S 46.19 W
São Domingos, Bra. **256** 21.41 S 42.47 W
São Domingos, Gui.-B. **150** 12.22 N 16.08 W
São Domingos ≃, Bra. **248** 12.28 S 64.13 W
São Domingos ≃, Bra. **255** 13.24 S 47.12 W
São Domingos ≃, Bra. **255** 19.13 S 50.44 W
São Domingos ≃, Bra. **255** 20.03 S 53.13 W
São Domingos da Bocaina **256** 21.50 S 44.01 W
São Domingos do Capim **250** 1.41 S 47.47 W
São Domingos do Maranhão **250** 5.42 S 44.22 W
São Felipe **255** 14.49 S 41.23 W
São Félix de Balsas **250** 7.08 S 44.52 W
São Félix do Araguaia **250** 11.36 S 50.39 W
São Félix do Piauí **250** 5.56 S 42.07 W
São Filipe **150a** 14.54 N 24.31 W
São Francisco **255** 15.57 S 44.52 W
São Francisco ≃, Bra. **242** 10.30 S 36.24 W
São Francisco ≃, Bra. **255** 16.09 S 40.39 W
São Francisco ≃, Bra. **256** 21.50 S 42.42 W
São Francisco ≃, Bra. **287a** 22.57 S 43.20 W
São Francisco, Baía de c **252** 26.10 S 48.34 W
São Francisco, Ilha de I **252** 26.18 S 48.37 W
São Francisco de Assis **252** 29.33 S 55.08 W
São Francisco de Goiás **255** 15.55 S 49.16 W
São Francisco de Paula **252** 29.27 S 50.35 W
São Francisco do Croará **287a** 22.42 S 43.08 W
São Francisco do Maranhão **250** 6.15 S 42.52 W
São Francisco do Piauí **250** 7.15 S 42.32 W
São Francisco do Sul **252** 26.14 S 48.39 W
São Francisco Xavier **256** 22.54 S 45.58 W
São Gabriel **252** 30.20 S 54.19 W
São Gabriel da Palha **255** 19.01 S 40.32 W
São Gabriel de Goiás **255** 15.12 S 47.34 W
São Gonçalo, Bra. **256** 21.36 S 46.19 W
São Gonçalo, Bra. **256** 22.51 S 43.04 W
São Gonçalo □[7] **287a** 22.48 S 43.01 W
São Gonçalo do Abaeté **255** 18.20 S 45.49 W
São Gonçalo do Sapucaí **256** 21.54 S 45.36 W
São Gonçalo dos Campos **255** 12.25 S 38.58 W
Sao Hill **154** 8.20 S 35.12 E
São Jerônimo **252** 29.58 S 51.43 W
São Jerônimo, Serra de ⋏[1] **255** 16.30 S 54.50 W
São Jerônimo da Serra **255** 23.43 N 50.44 W
São João **150** 11.32 N 15.26 W
São João ≃, Bra. **255** 12.27 S 51.07 W
São João ≃, Bra. **256** 22.33 S 42.29 W
São João da Barra **255** 21.38 S 41.03 W
São João da Boa Vista **256** 21.58 S 46.47 W
São João D'Aliança **255** 14.42 S 47.32 W
São João da Madeira **34** 40.54 N 8.30 W
São João da Mata **256** 21.56 S 45.56 W
São João da Ponte **255** 15.56 S 44.01 W
São João da Serra **256** 21.28 S 43.27 W
São João das Lampas **266c** 38.52 N 9.24 W
São João de Côrtes **250** 2.12 S 44.32 W
São João del-Rei **255** 21.09 S 44.16 W
São João de Meriti **256** 22.48 S 43.22 W

Symbols in the index entries represent the broad categories identified in the key at the right. Symbols with superior numbers (⋏[1]) identify subcategories (see complete key on page *I · 1).*

Symbole im Register stellen die rechts im Schlüssel erklärten Kategorien dar. Symbole mit hochgestellten Ziffern (⋏[1]) bezeichnen Unterabteilungen einer Kategorie (vgl. vollständiger Schlüssel auf Seite *I · 1).*

Los símbolos incluídos en el texto del índice representan las grandes categorías identificadas con la clave a la derecha. Los símbolos con numeros en su parte superior (⋏[1]) identifican las subcategorías (véase la clave completa en la página *I · 1).*

Les symboles de l'index représentent les catégories indiquées dans la légende à droite. Les symboles suivis d'un indice (⋏[1]) représentent des sous-catégories (voir légende complète à la page *I · 1).*

Os símbolos incluídos no texto do índice representam as grandes categorias identificadas com a chave à direita. Os símbolos com números em sua parte superior (⋏[1]) identificam as subcategorias (veja-se a chave completa à página *I · 1).*

	English	Deutsch	Español	Français	Português
∧	Mountain	Berg	Montaña	Montagne	Montanha
⋏	Mountains	Gebirge	Montañas	Montagnes	Montanhas
)(	Pass	Paß	Paso	Col	Passo
V	Valley, Canyon	Tal, Cañon	Valle, Cañón	Vallée, Canyon	Vale, Canhão
≃	Plain	Ebene	Llano	Plaine	Planície
>	Cape	Kap	Cabo	Cap	Cabo
I	Island	Insel	Isla	Île	Ilha
II	Islands	Inseln	Islas	Îles	Ilhas
⊥	Other Topographic Features	Andere Topographische Objekte	Otros Elementos Topográficos	Autres données topographiques	Outros acidentes topográficos

ENGLISH — Name, Page, Lat.°′, Long.°′ · DEUTSCH — Name, Seite, Breite°′, Länge°′ E = Ost

Name	Page	Lat.°′	Long.°′
Saurimo	152	9.39 S	20.24 E
Saur-Mogila ⊥	83	47.56 N	38.46 E
Sausalito	226	37.51 N	122.29 W
Sausar	120	21.39 N	78.47 E
Sauškin	80	49.30 N	43.32 E
Sausset-les-Pins	62	43.20 N	5.07 E
Saussy	58	47.28 N	4.57 E
Sausu	112	1.00 S	120.30 E
Saútar	152	11.06 S	18.27 E
Sauteurs	241k	12.14 N	61.38 W
Sauvas	62	44.19 N	4.09 E
Sauve	62	43.56 N	3.57 E
Sauveterre	62	44.02 N	4.48 E
Sauveterre-de-Béarn	32	43.24 N	0.56 W
Sauveterre-de-Guyenne	32	44.42 N	0.05 W
Sauvie Island I	224	45.41 N	122.49 W
Sauvo	26	60.21 N	22.42 E
Sauwald •[3]	60	48.28 N	13.40 E
Sauzal	200	31.37 N	106.18 W
Sauze di Cesana	62	44.56 N	6.51 E
Sauze d'Oulx	62	45.02 N	6.52 E
Sava, It.	68	40.24 N	17.34 E
S'ava, Ross.	80	58.01 N	46.22 E
Sava ≃	38	44.50 N	20.26 E
Sävaån ≃	40	59.45 N	17.24 E
Savage, Md., U.S.	208	39.08 N	76.49 W
Savage, Mt., U.S.	198	47.27 N	104.20 W
Savai'i I	175a	13.35 S	172.25 W
Savala ≃	80	51.03 N	41.30 E
Savalen ⊜	26	62.15 N	10.29 E
Savalou	150	7.56 N	1.58 E
Savana Island I	240m	18.20 N	65.05 W
Savana Passage ⋓	240m	18.21 N	65.04 W
Savane ≃	186	51.08 N	71.26 W
Savanna, Il., U.S.	190	42.05 N	90.09 W
Savanna, Ok., U.S.	196	34.49 N	95.50 W
Savannah, Ga., U.S.	192	32.05 N	81.06 W
Savannah, Mo., U.S.	194	39.56 N	94.49 W
Savannah, N.Y., U.S.	210	43.04 N	76.45 W
Savannah, Oh., U.S.	214	40.57 N	82.21 W
Savannah, Tn., U.S.	194	35.13 N	88.14 W
Savannah ≃	192	32.02 N	80.53 W
Savannah River Plant ʊ[3]	192	33.15 N	81.40 W
Savannah Sound	192	25.06 N	76.09 W
Savannakhét	110	16.33 N	104.45 E
Savanna-la-Mar	241q	18.13 N	78.08 W
Savanna Portage State Park ♦	190	46.51 N	93.10 W
Sāvantvādi	122	15.54 N	73.49 E
Savanūr	122	14.58 N	75.21 E
Sävar	26	63.54 N	20.34 E
Savara ≃	62	45.42 N	7.12 E
Savasse ≃	62	45.03 N	5.02 E
Savaştepe	130	39.22 N	27.40 E
Savat	130	38.21 N	40.38 E
Savcılıbüyükoba	130	39.14 N	33.41 E
Savé	150	8.02 N	2.29 E
Save (Sabi) ≃, Afr.	156	21.00 S	35.02 E
Save ≃, Fr.	32	43.47 N	1.17 E
Sāveh	128	35.01 N	50.20 E
Savelli	68	39.19 N	16.47 E
Savelugu	150	9.37 N	0.49 W
Savenay	32	47.22 N	1.57 W
Săveni	38	47.57 N	26.52 E
Saverdun	32	43.14 N	1.35 E
Savernake Forest •[3]	42	51.24 N	1.38 W
Saverne	56	48.44 N	7.22 E
Savery Creek ≃	200	41.01 N	107.27 W
Saviči, Bela.	76	52.25 N	29.03 E
Saviči, Bela.	78	51.37 N	30.17 E
Savick Brook ≃	262	53.45 N	2.47 W
Savièse	58	46.16 N	7.20 E
Savigliano	62	44.38 N	7.40 E
Savignano Irpino	68	41.14 N	15.11 E
Savignano sul Panaro	64	44.29 N	11.02 E
Savignano sul Rubicone	66	44.05 N	12.24 E
Savignone	62	44.34 N	29.12 E
Savoonga	180	63.42 N	170.27 W
Savory Creek ≃	162	23.22 S	122.37 E
Savoureuse ≃	58	47.31 N	6.51 E
Savoy	196	33.34 N	96.21 W
Savran'	78	48.09 N	30.04 E
Savruši	80	55.02 N	50.40 E
Sävsjö	26	57.25 N	14.40 E
S'avta	24	67.08 N	61.45 E
Savu Basin ✦[1]	14	9.15 S	123.15 E
Savudrija	64	45.30 N	13.30 E
Savur	130	37.33 N	40.53 E
Savusavu	175g	16.16 S	179.21 E
Savusavu Bay c	175g	16.45 S	179.15 E
Savu Sea → Sawu, Laut ⊤[2]	112	9.40 S	122.00 E
Savuto ≃	68	39.02 N	16.06 E
Savvatejevka	88	52.20 N	103.39 E
Savvino, Ross.	82	55.43 N	36.48 E
Savvino, Ross.	82	56.33 N	37.47 E
Savvo-Borz'a	88	50.46 N	118.18 E
Şawāb, Wādī aş- V	130	34.36 N	40.25 E
Sawabala Point ›	164	10.10 S	151.15 E
Sawah	112	2.23 N	115.14 E
Sawahlunto	112	0.40 S	100.47 E
Sawai	164	2.58 S	129.09 E
Sawai, Teluk c	164	2.52 S	129.12 E
Sawāi Mādhopur	124	25.59 N	76.22 E
Sawākin	140	19.07 N	37.20 E
Sawal, Gunung ∧	115a	7.12 S	108.16 E
Sawan, Indon.	115b	8.08 S	115.11 E
Sawan, Mya.	110	24.30 N	96.19 E
Sawang	114	0.45 N	103.21 E
Sawankhalok	110	17.19 N	99.50 E
Sawara	94	35.53 N	140.30 E
Sawata	92	38.00 N	138.16 E
Sawatch Range ⋏	200	39.10 N	106.25 W
Sawbridgeworth	42	51.50 N	0.09 E
Sawdā', Jabal as- ⋏[2]	146	28.40 N	15.30 E
Sawdā', Qurnat as- ∧	130	34.18 N	36.07 E
Sawdirī	140	14.25 N	29.05 E
Sawel Mountain ∧	48	54.49 N	7.02 W
Sawhāj	140	26.33 N	31.42 E
Sawi	110	10.14 N	99.07 E
Sawin, Lac ⊜	206	46.32 N	73.54 W
Sawknah	146	29.04 N	15.47 E
Şawl	142	29.21 N	31.14 E
Sawla	150	9.17 N	2.25 W
Saw Log Creek ≃	198	38.07 N	99.42 W
Saw Mill ≃	276	40.56 N	73.53 W
Sawmill Brook ≃, Ma., U.S.	283	42.34 N	70.46 W
Sawmill Brook ≃, N.J., U.S.	276	40.28 N	74.26 W
Sawmill Creek ≃, N.J., U.S.	276	40.46 N	74.05 W
Sawmill Creek ≃, Pa., U.S.	279b	40.10 N	79.58 W
Sawmill Pond Brook ≃	276	41.10 N	74.23 W
Sawmill Run ≃	285	40.07 N	75.21 W
Sawmills	154	19.31 S	28.02 E
Şawqirah, Ghubbat c	118	18.35 N	57.00 E
Sawston	42	52.07 N	0.10 E
Sawtayr ⊤[4]	140	17.03 N	30.24 E
Sawtooth National Recreation Area ♦	202	44.00 N	114.55 W
Sawtry	42	52.27 N	0.17 W
Sawu, Laut (Savu Sea) ⊤[2]	112	9.40 S	122.00 E
Sawu, Pulau I	112	10.30 S	121.54 E
Sawyer, Mi., U.S.	216	41.53 N	86.35 W
Sawyer, N.D., U.S.	198	48.05 N	101.03 W
Sawyers Hill ∧[2]	186	47.11 N	53.52 W
Sawyers Valley	168a	31.54 S	116.13 E
Sawyerville, P.Q., Can.	206	45.20 N	71.34 W
Sawyerville, Il., U.S.	219	39.05 N	89.48 W
Sawyerwood	214	41.02 N	81.27 W
Saxby ≃	166	18.25 S	140.53 E
Saxdalen	40	60.09 N	14.57 E
Saxen ⊜	40	59.46 N	14.25 E
Saxike	120	30.44 N	86.22 E
Saxilby	44	53.17 N	0.40 W
Saxis	208	37.55 N	75.43 W
Saxmundham	42	52.13 N	1.29 E
Saxon, Schw.	58	46.09 N	7.11 E
Saxon, Wi., U.S.	190	46.29 N	90.24 W
Saxonburg	214	40.45 N	79.49 W
Saxon Woods Park ♦	276	40.59 N	73.45 W
Saxony → Sachsen □[3]	30	51.00 N	13.00 E
Saxony → Sachsen □[9]	30	52.45 N	9.30 E
Saxton	214	40.12 N	78.14 W
Say	150	13.07 N	2.21 E
Sāy, Jazīrat I	140	20.42 N	30.20 E
Saya de Malha Bank ✦[4]	12	10.30 S	61.30 E
Sayama, Nihon	94	35.51 N	139.24 E
Sayama, Nihon	270	34.31 N	135.34 E
Sayama-kyūryō ⋏[2]	268	35.47 N	139.24 E
Sayán	248	11.08 S	77.12 W
Sayan Mountains (Sajany) ⋏	88	52.45 N	96.00 E
Sayansk	88	54.02 N	102.06 E
Sayaxché	232	16.31 N	90.10 W
Saybrook, Il., U.S.	216	40.25 N	88.31 W
Saybrook, Oh., U.S.	214	41.50 N	80.51 W
Saybrook Manor	207	41.17 N	72.23 W
Sayda, Dtsch.	54	50.43 N	13.25 E
Şaydā (Sidon), Lubnān	132	33.33 N	35.22 E
Şaydā □[4]	132	33.15 N	35.15 E
Şaydnāyā	132	33.42 N	36.22 E
Sayghān	120	35.11 N	67.42 E
Sayḩūt	144	15.12 N	51.14 E
Sayil ⊥	232	20.16 N	89.42 W
Saylah	142	29.21 N	30.58 E
Saylorsburg	210	40.54 N	75.19 W
Saylorville Lake ⊜[1]	190	41.48 N	93.46 W
Saylūn, Khirbat (Shiloh) ⊥	132	32.03 N	35.17 E
Säynätsalo	26	62.08 N	25.46 E
Sayō	96	35.00 N	134.22 E
Şayqal, Baḩr ⊜	132	33.40 N	37.06 E
Sayram Hu ⊜	86	44.36 N	81.13 E
Sayre, Ok., U.S.	196	35.17 N	99.38 W
Sayre, Pa., U.S.	210	41.58 N	76.30 W
Sayreville	208	40.27 N	74.21 W
Sayula	234	19.52 N	103.37 W
Sayula, Laguna de ⊜	234	20.03 N	103.31 W
Sayula de Alemán	234	17.52 N	94.57 W
Sayultepec	234	17.27 N	97.17 W
Sayville	210	40.44 N	73.04 W
Sayward	182	50.22 N	125.55 W
Saywūn	144	15.56 N	48.47 E
Saza	92	33.14 N	129.39 E
Sazanit I	38	40.30 N	19.16 E
Sazdy, Kaz.	80	46.57 N	49.19 E
Sazdy, Kaz.	86	47.22 N	61.48 E
Saze	62	43.56 N	4.41 E
Sažino	86	56.20 N	58.11 E
Sazlijka ≃	38	42.02 N	25.52 E
Sazonovo	76	59.04 N	35.14 E
Šazud	120	37.43 N	72.11 E
Sazykul', ozero ⊜	86	55.22 N	67.34 E
Sba	148	28.13 N	0.08 W
Sbeïtla	148	35.14 N	9.08 E
Sbiba	36	35.33 N	9.05 E
Scaddan	162	33.27 S	121.43 E
Scaër	32	48.02 N	3.42 W
Scafati	68	40.45 N	14.31 E
Scafell Pikes ∧	44	54.27 N	3.12 W
Scaggsville	208	39.09 N	76.54 W
Scajaquada Creek ≃	284a	42.56 N	78.53 W
Scala, Teatro alla ʊ	266b	45.28 N	9.11 E
Scala Coeli	68	39.27 N	16.53 E
Scalasaig	46	56.04 N	6.11 W
Scalby	44	54.18 N	0.27 W
Scalea	68	39.49 N	15.48 E
Scaletta Zanclea	70	38.03 N	15.28 E
Scalloway	46a	60.08 N	1.18 W
Scalpay I, Scot., U.K.	46	57.52 N	6.40 W
Scalpay I, Scot., U.K.	46	57.17 N	5.59 W
Scalp Level	214	40.14 N	78.50 W
Scalp Mountain ∧[2]	48	55.04 N	7.24 W
Scammon	198	37.16 N	94.49 W
Scammon Bay	180	61.53 N	165.38 W
Scammon Bay c	180	61.53 N	165.54 W
Scammonden Water ⊜[1]	262	53.38 N	1.56 W
Scampton	44	53.18 N	0.34 W
Scandale	68	39.07 N	16.57 E
Scandia	198	39.47 N	97.47 W
Scandiano	64	44.36 N	10.43 E
Scandicci	66	43.45 N	11.11 E
Scanlon	190	46.42 N	92.25 W
Scanno	66	41.54 N	13.53 E
Scansano	66	42.41 N	11.20 E
Scantic ≃	207	41.52 N	72.38 W
Scapa	182	51.52 N	111.59 W
Scapa Flow c	46	58.55 N	3.06 W
Scapegoat Mountain ∧	202	47.19 N	112.50 W
Ščapino	74	55.19 N	159.25 E
Ščapov	80	51.01 N	51.11 E
Ščapovo	82	55.09 N	38.11 E
Scappoose	224	45.45 N	122.52 W
Scar ≃	44	55.13 N	3.46 W
Ščara ≃	76	53.27 N	24.45 E
Scaramia, Capo ›	70	36.47 N	14.29 E
Scarba I	46	56.11 N	5.43 W
Scarborough, Austl.	168a	31.54 S	115.45 E
Scarborough, On., Can.	212	43.47 N	79.15 W
Scarborough, Trin.	241r	11.11 N	60.44 W
Scarborough, Eng., U.K.	44	54.17 N	0.24 W
Scarborough Centre •[9]	275b	43.47 N	79.16 W
Scarborough Point ›	171a	27.12 S	153.07 E
Scarborough Reef ✦[2]	116	15.08 N	117.46 E
Scardroy	46	57.31 N	4.59 W
Scargill	172	42.56 S	172.57 E
Scarinish	46	56.29 N	6.48 W
Scarisbrick	262	53.37 N	2.56 W
Scărişoara	38	44.00 N	24.35 E
Scarlino	66	42.54 N	10.51 E
Scarp I	46	58.02 N	7.08 W
Scarpe ≃	50	50.30 N	3.27 E
Scarperia	66	44.00 N	11.21 E
Scarper Peak ∧	282	37.32 N	122.26 W
Scarriff	48	52.55 N	8.31 W
Scarsdale, Austl.	169	37.40 S	143.40 E
Scarsdale, N.Y., U.S.	210	40.59 N	73.49 W
Scartaglin	48	52.10 N	9.26 W
Scarth Hill	262	53.33 N	2.52 W
Sčastje	83	48.44 N	39.14 E
Scatarie Island I	186	46.00 N	59.44 W
Scatter Creek ≃	224	46.48 N	123.06 W
Scauri, It.	66	41.15 N	13.42 E
Scauri, It.	70	36.45 N	11.58 E
Scavaig, Loch c	46	57.09 N	6.10 W
Scawfell Island I	166	20.52 S	149.36 E
Sceaux	50	48.47 N	2.17 E
Sceaux, Château de ⊥	261	48.46 N	2.18 E
Ščedrin	76	52.53 N	29.33 E
Ščedrovka	83	49.30 N	40.17 E
Ščeglovo	265a	60.02 N	30.46 E
Ščeljajur	24	65.21 N	53.21 E
Ščelkan ≃	80	50.47 N	43.33 E
Ščelkovo	76	55.55 N	38.00 E
Ščemilovo	265b	55.48 N	38.05 E
Scena	64	46.41 N	11.12 E
Scenery Hill	214	40.05 N	80.04 W
Sceptre	184	50.51 N	109.15 W
Ščerbakovo, Ross.	74	65.15 N	160.30 E
Ščerbakovo, Ross.	86	56.01 N	73.29 E
Ščerbakty	86	52.29 N	78.09 E
Ščerbinka	82	55.31 N	37.35 E
Ščerbinovka	83	48.26 N	37.50 E
Scerni	66	42.07 N	14.34 E
Scey-sur-Saône-et-Saint-Albin	58	47.40 N	5.58 E
Schaale ≃	54	53.21 N	10.49 E
Schaalsee ⊜	54	53.35 N	10.57 E
Schaan	58	47.10 N	9.31 E
Schabs → Sciaves	64	46.46 N	11.40 E
Schachendorf	61	47.16 N	16.26 E
Schaefferstown	208	40.17 N	76.17 W
Schaephuysen	263	51.26 N	6.29 E
Schaerbeek	50	50.51 N	4.23 E
Schafberg ∧	64	47.47 N	13.27 E
Schäferberg ∧[2]	264a	52.25 N	13.08 E
Schaffhausen	58	47.42 N	8.38 E
Schaffhausen □[3]	58	47.40 N	8.35 E
Schafstädt	54	51.23 N	11.46 E
Schäftlarn	64	47.59 N	11.28 E
Schagen	52	52.46 N	4.47 E
Schaghticoke	210	42.54 N	73.35 W
Schalchen	60	48.07 N	13.10 E
Schale	52	52.26 N	7.37 E
Schalkau	54	50.24 N	11.00 E
Schalke •[8]	263	51.31 N	7.05 E
Schälker Heide •[3]	263	51.24 N	7.36 E
Schalksmühle	56	51.14 N	7.31 E
Schaller	198	42.30 N	95.18 W
Schanck, Cape ›	169	38.30 S	144.53 E
S-Chanf	58	46.36 N	9.59 E
Schanfigg V	58	46.51 N	9.38 E
Schanghai → Shanghai	106	31.14 N	121.28 E
Schangnau	58	46.50 N	7.52 E
Schapbach	58	48.22 N	8.17 E
Schapen	52	52.24 N	7.33 E
Schaprode	54	54.31 N	13.10 E
Šchara, gora ∧	84	43.00 N	43.06 E
Scharbeutz	54	54.03 N	10.44 E
Schardenberg	60	48.32 N	13.30 E
Schardenberg ∧[2]	263	51.27 N	6.28 E
Schärding	60	48.27 N	13.26 E
Scharhörn I	52	53.57 N	8.25 E
Schari → Chari ≃	146	12.58 N	14.31 E
Scharmützelsee ⊜	54	52.15 N	14.03 E
Scharnhorst •[8]	263	51.32 N	7.32 E
Scharnitz	60	47.23 N	11.17 E
Scharnitzer Klause)(	64	47.24 N	11.16 E
Scharrel	52	53.04 N	7.42 E
Scharzfeld	52	51.37 N	10.22 E
Schässburg → Sighişoara	38	46.13 N	24.48 E
Schauinsland ∧	58	47.55 N	7.54 E
Schaumburg	216	42.02 N	88.05 W
Schaut	84	43.43 N	42.32 E
Schebeli → Shabeelle ≃	144	0.12 S	42.45 E
Scheessel	52	53.10 N	9.29 E
Schefferville	176	54.48 N	66.50 W
Scheggia	66	43.24 N	12.40 E
Scheggino	66	42.43 N	12.50 E
Scheibbs	61	48.00 N	15.10 E
Scheiblingstein	264b	48.16 N	16.13 E
Scheidegg	58	47.35 N	9.51 E
Scheifling	61	47.09 N	14.24 E
Scheinfeld	56	49.40 N	10.27 E
Schelde (Escaut) ≃	50	51.22 N	4.15 E
Schelklingen	58	48.22 N	9.44 E
Schell Creek Range ⋏	204	39.10 N	114.40 W
Schellenberg ∧	60	48.18 N	13.03 E
Schellsburg	214	40.03 N	78.39 W
Schelsen •[8]	263	51.09 N	6.31 E
Schenectady	210	42.48 N	73.56 W
Schenectady □[6]	210	42.47 N	73.53 W
Schenefeld	52	53.36 N	9.49 E
Schenevus	210	42.32 N	74.49 W
Schenevus Creek ≃	210	42.29 N	74.59 W
Schenkendorf	264a	52.16 N	13.35 E
Schenkenhorst	264a	52.20 N	13.12 E
Schenklengsfeld	56	50.49 N	9.50 E
Schenley	214	40.41 N	79.40 W
Schenley Park ♦	279b	40.26 N	79.56 W
Schepsdorf-Lohne	52	52.30 N	7.16 E
Schererville	216	41.30 N	87.27 W
Scherfede	52	51.32 N	9.02 E
Scherlebeck	263	51.37 N	7.08 E
Schermbeck	52	51.41 N	6.52 E
Schermerhorn	52	52.36 N	4.52 E
Schermützelsee ⊜	54	52.34 N	14.04 E
Scherpenheuvel	56	50.59 N	4.59 E
Scherpenzeel	52	52.05 N	5.30 E
Schertz	196	29.33 N	98.16 W
Schesch, Erg → Chech, Erg •[2]	148	25.00 N	2.15 W
Schesslitz	60	49.59 N	11.01 E
Schevelinger-Stausee ⊜[1]	263	51.08 N	7.26 E
Scheveningen •[8]	52	52.06 N	4.18 E
Schiedam	52	51.55 N	4.24 E
Schieder	52	51.55 N	9.09 E
Schiefbahn	56	51.14 N	6.31 E
Schiehallion ∧	46	56.40 N	4.06 W
Schierke	54	51.46 N	10.40 E
Schierling	60	48.50 N	12.08 E
Schiermonnikoog	52	53.24 N	6.10 E
Schiermonnikoog I	52	53.28 N	6.15 E
Schiers	58	46.59 N	9.41 E
Schiessen	58	48.18 N	10.14 E
Schiffdorf	52	53.32 N	8.39 E
Schiffenensee ⊜	58	46.50 N	7.10 E
Schifferstadt	56	49.23 N	8.22 E
Schiffshebewerk •[5]	263	51.37 N	7.19 E
Schihkiatschwang → Shijiazhuang	98	38.03 N	114.28 E
Schijndel	52	51.37 N	5.25 E
Schikoku → Shikoku I	92	33.45 N	133.30 E
Schildau	54	51.27 N	12.56 E
Schilde	56	51.14 N	4.34 E
Schilde ≃	54	53.26 N	10.53 E
Schildow	54	52.38 N	13.23 E
Schildwolde	52	53.14 N	6.49 E
Schiller Park	216	41.57 N	87.52 W
Schillingsfürst	56	49.17 N	10.15 E
Schillingstedt	54	51.14 N	11.11 E
Schilpario	64	46.01 N	10.09 E
Schiltach	58	48.17 N	8.20 E
Schiltigheim	58	48.36 N	7.45 E
Schimborn	56	50.03 N	9.11 E
Schimmert	56	50.55 N	5.50 E
Schinveld	56	50.57 N	5.59 E
Schinznach Bad	58	47.27 N	8.10 E
Schio	64	45.43 N	11.21 E
Schipbeek ≃	52	52.14 N	6.09 E
Schiphol, Luchthaven ⊠	52	52.17 N	4.40 E
Schipkau	54	51.31 N	13.53 E
Schirgiswalde	54	51.05 N	14.27 E
Schirmeck	58	48.29 N	7.13 E
Schirnding	54	50.05 N	12.13 E
Schisuoka → Shizuoka	94	34.58 N	138.23 E
Schjetman Reef ✦[2]	14	15.10 N	178.40 W
Schkeuditz	54	51.24 N	12.13 E
Schkoder-See → Scutari, Lake ⊜	38	42.12 N	19.18 E
Schkölen	54	51.02 N	11.49 E
Schkopau	54	51.23 N	11.59 E
Schladen	54	52.01 N	10.32 E
Schladming	64	47.23 N	13.41 E
Schlanders → Silandro	64	46.38 N	10.46 E
Schlangen	52	51.49 N	8.50 E
Schlangenbad	56	50.05 N	8.05 E
Schlänitz-See ⊜	264a	52.27 N	12.57 E
Schlanstedt	54	52.00 N	11.02 E
Schlater	194	33.38 N	90.20 W
Schlegel Lake ⊜	276	40.59 N	74.03 W
Schlei c	41	54.36 N	9.51 E
Schleiden	56	50.31 N	6.28 E
Schleife	54	51.32 N	14.32 E
Schleinitz Range ⋏	164	3.10 S	151.40 E
Schleithal	56	48.59 N	8.02 E
Schleitheim	58	47.45 N	8.29 E
Schleiz	54	50.34 N	11.49 E
Schlema	54	50.40 N	12.40 E
Schlepzig	54	52.01 N	13.53 E
Schlesien → Silesia □[9]	30	51.00 N	16.45 E
Schlesischer (Ost) Bahnhof •[5]	264a	52.30 N	13.26 E
Schleswig, Dtsch.	41	54.31 N	9.33 E
Schleswig, Ia., U.S.	198	42.09 N	95.26 W
Schleswig-Holstein □[3]	30	54.20 N	9.40 E
Schlettau	54	50.33 N	12.56 E
Schlettstadt → Sélestat	58	48.16 N	7.27 E
Schleusingen	54	50.31 N	10.45 E
Schlicke ∧	58	47.31 N	10.37 E
Schlieben	54	51.43 N	13.23 E
Schliengen	58	47.46 N	7.35 E
Schlieren	58	47.24 N	8.27 E
Schliersee	64	47.44 N	11.51 E
Schlitz	56	50.40 N	9.33 E
Schloss Holte	52	51.52 N	8.35 E
Schloss Neuhaus	52	51.44 N	8.43 E
Schlossvippach	54	51.06 N	11.08 E
Schloss Zeil	64	47.52 N	10.00 E
Schlotheim	54	51.14 N	10.39 E
Schluchsee	58	47.49 N	8.10 E
Schluchsee ⊜	58	47.49 N	8.10 E
Schlucht, Col de la)(	58	48.04 N	7.02 E
Schlüchtern	56	50.20 N	9.31 E
Schluderns → Sluderno	64	46.40 N	10.35 E
Schlüsselburg	52	52.29 N	9.04 E
Schlüsselfeld	56	49.45 N	10.37 E
Schlutup •[8]	54	53.53 N	10.48 E
Schmachtendorf •[8]	263	51.32 N	6.49 E
Schmalfeld	52	53.52 N	9.58 E
Schmalkalden	54	50.43 N	10.26 E
Schmallenberg	56	51.09 N	8.17 E
Schmalnau	56	50.27 N	9.47 E
Schmannewitz	54	51.24 N	12.58 E
Schmarsau	54	52.54 N	11.21 E
Schmelz	56	49.27 N	6.51 E
Schmida ≃	61	48.21 N	16.09 E
Schmidmühlen	60	49.16 N	11.56 E
Schmidt	56	50.39 N	6.25 E
Schmidtsdrif	158	28.41 S	24.02 E
Schmiedeberg	54	50.50 N	13.40 E
Schmiedefeld	54	50.37 N	10.49 E
Schmilka	54	50.53 N	14.14 E
Schmöckwitz •[8]	264a	52.23 N	13.39 E
Schmölln	54	50.53 N	12.20 E
Schmutter ≃	58	48.42 N	10.46 E
Schnabelwaid	60	49.49 N	11.35 E
Schnackenburg	54	53.02 N	11.32 E
Schnait	56	48.47 N	9.23 E
Schnaitsee	60	48.04 N	12.22 E
Schnaittach	60	49.31 N	11.19 E
Schnaittenbach	60	49.33 N	12.01 E
Schnakenbek	52	53.23 N	10.30 E
Schnecksville	208	40.41 N	75.36 W
Schneealpe ⋏	61	47.41 N	15.36 E
Schneeberg	54	50.36 N	12.38 E
Schneeberg ∧, Dtsch.	54	50.03 N	11.51 E
Schneeberg ∧, Öst.	61	47.47 N	15.47 E
Schneidemühl → Piła	30	53.10 N	16.44 E
Schneider	216	41.11 N	87.26 W
Schneifel ⋏[1]	56	50.15 N	6.25 E
Schneverdingen	52	53.07 N	9.47 E
Schney	56	50.10 N	11.04 E
Schober Gruppe ⋏	64	46.55 N	12.42 E
Schobüll	41	54.30 N	9.00 E
Schöckl ∧	61	47.11 N	15.28 E
Schodn'a	82	55.57 N	37.18 E
Schodn'a ≃	265b	55.50 N	37.25 E
Schœlcher	240e	14.37 N	61.06 W
Schoenbrunn Village State Memorial ⊥	214	40.27 N	81.24 W
Schofield	190	44.54 N	89.36 W
Schofield Barracks ■	229c	21.30 N	158.04 W
Schofields	274a	33.42 S	150.52 E
Schöftland	58	47.18 N	8.03 E
Schoharie	210	42.39 N	74.18 W
Schoharie □[6]	210	42.40 N	74.19 W
Schoharie Creek ≃	210	42.57 N	74.18 W
Schoharie Reservoir ⊜[1]	210	42.22 N	74.26 W
Scholen	52	52.44 N	8.46 E
Scholes	44	53.49 N	1.25 W
Schollene	54	52.41 N	12.13 E
Schöllenen V	58	46.40 N	8.35 E
Schöller •[8]	263	51.14 N	7.01 E
Schöllkrippen	56	50.05 N	9.14 E
Schöllnach	60	48.45 N	13.11 E
Scholls	224	45.24 N	122.55 W
Scholven •[8]	263	51.36 N	7.01 E
Schomberg, On., Can.	212	44.00 N	79.41 W
Schömberg, Dtsch.	56	48.47 N	8.38 E
Schömberg, Dtsch.	58	48.13 N	8.46 E
Schonach	58	48.08 N	8.11 E
Schönaich	56	48.39 N	9.03 E
Schönau, Dtsch.	56	49.26 N	8.49 E
Schönau, Dtsch.	58	47.47 N	7.53 E
Schönau, Dtsch.	64	47.37 N	12.59 E
Schönbeck	54	53.34 N	13.34 E
Schönberg, Dtsch.	54	50.31 N	11.57 E
Schönberg, Dtsch.	54	50.11 N	12.19 E
Schönberg, Dtsch.	54	53.51 N	10.56 E
Schönberg, Dtsch.	54	54.23 N	10.22 E
Schönberg, Dtsch.	60	48.50 N	13.20 E
Schönberger Strand	54	54.25 N	10.24 E
Schönberg im Stubaital	64	47.11 N	11.25 E
Schönbrunn	54	50.32 N	10.53 E
Schönbrunn, Schloss ʊ	264b	48.11 N	16.19 E
Schönbrunner Schlosspark ♦	264b	48.11 N	16.19 E
Schondra ≃	56	50.07 N	9.44 E
Schönebeck, Dtsch.	54	53.03 N	12.13 E
Schönebeck, Dtsch.	54	52.01 N	11.44 E
Schönebeck •[8]	263	51.28 N	6.56 E
Schöneberg •[8]	264a	52.29 N	13.21 E
Schöneck, Dtsch.	54	50.23 N	12.20 E
Schöneck, Dtsch.	56	50.13 N	8.52 E
Schönecken	56	50.09 N	6.27 E
Schönefeld	264a	52.23 N	13.30 E
Schöneiche	54	52.28 N	13.41 E
Schönenwerd	58	47.22 N	8.00 E
Schönerlinde	264a	52.39 N	13.27 E
Schönewalde	54	51.49 N	13.13 E
Schönfeld	264a	52.41 N	13.44 E
Schönfliess	264a	52.39 N	13.20 E
Schongau	58	47.49 N	10.54 E
Schönhagen, Dtsch.	41	54.38 N	10.01 E
Schönhagen, Dtsch.	52	51.41 N	9.33 E
Schönhausen, Dtsch.	54	52.35 N	12.02 E
Schönhausen, Dtsch.	263	51.37 N	7.38 E
Schönheide	54	50.30 N	12.31 E
Schönholthausen	56	51.11 N	8.00 E
Schöningen	54	52.08 N	10.58 E
Schönkirchen	54	54.20 N	10.15 E
Schönmünzach	56	48.36 N	8.22 E
Schonnebeck •[8]	263	51.29 N	7.04 E
Schönningstedt	52	53.32 N	10.15 E
Schönow	54	52.40 N	13.32 E
Schönsee	60	49.31 N	12.33 E
Schönthal	60	49.21 N	12.36 E
Schonungen	56	50.03 N	10.18 E
Schönwald, Dtsch.	54	50.12 N	12.05 E
Schönwald, Dtsch.	58	48.06 N	8.11 E
Schönwalde, Dtsch.	54	54.11 N	10.45 E
Schönwalde, Dtsch.	54	52.40 N	13.26 E
Schönwalde, Dtsch.	54	52.37 N	13.07 E
Schönwies	58	47.11 N	10.39 E
Schoodic Lake ⊜	188	45.21 N	68.54 W
Schoolcraft	216	42.06 N	85.38 W
Schoolhouse Run ≃	285	40.13 N	75.27 W
Schoombee	158	31.28 S	25.30 E
Schoondijke	52	51.21 N	3.32 E
Schoonebeek	52	52.40 N	6.53 E
Schoonhoven	52	51.56 N	4.51 E
Schoorl	52	52.42 N	4.41 E
Schopfheim	58	47.39 N	7.49 E
Schopfloch	56	49.07 N	10.18 E
Schopp	56	49.21 N	7.41 E
Schöppenstedt	54	52.08 N	10.46 E
Schöppingen	52	52.05 N	7.14 E
Schorfheide	54	52.56 N	13.43 E
Schorfheide •[3]	54	52.55 N	13.35 E
Schörfling	64	47.56 N	13.36 E
Schorndorf	56	48.48 N	9.31 E
Schortens	52	53.31 N	7.56 E
Schoten	50	51.15 N	4.30 E
Schötmar	52	52.04 N	8.45 E
Schotten	56	50.30 N	9.07 E
Schottland → Scotland □[8]	28	57.00 N	4.00 W
Schouten, Kepulauan II	164	0.55 S	135.55 E
Schouten Island I	166	42.19 S	148.17 E
Schouten Islands II	164	3.30 S	144.40 E
Schouwen I	52	51.43 N	3.50 E
Schrader Creek ≃	210	41.43 N	76.30 W
Schrader Range ⋏	164	5.05 S	144.15 E
Schramberg	58	48.13 N	8.23 E
Schram City	219	39.09 N	89.27 W
Schrankogel ∧	64	47.02 N	11.06 E
Schraplau	54	51.26 N	11.40 E
Schreiber	190	48.48 N	87.15 W
Schrems	61	48.47 N	15.04 E
Schrick	61	48.30 N	16.37 E
Schriever	194	29.44 N	90.48 W
Schrobenhausen	60	48.33 N	11.17 E
Schröcken	58	47.15 N	10.05 E
Schroffenstein ∧	158	27.11 S	18.42 E
Schroon ≃	188	43.29 N	73.49 W
Schroon Lake ⊜	188	43.47 N	73.46 W
Schrozberg	56	49.20 N	9.59 E
Schruns	58	47.04 N	9.55 E
Schulenburg, Dtsch.	52	52.12 N	9.47 E
Schulenburg, Tx., U.S.	222	29.40 N	96.54 W
Schuls → Scuol	58	46.48 N	10.18 E
Schultz Lake ⊜	176	64.45 N	97.30 W
Schulzendorf	54	52.22 N	13.35 E
Schulzenhöhe	264a	52.29 N	13.47 E
Schumacher	190	48.28 N	81.18 W
Schüpfheim	58	46.57 N	8.01 E
Schüren •[8]	263	51.30 N	7.32 E
Schurwald ⋏	56	48.46 N	9.29 E
Schussen ≃	58	47.37 N	9.32 E
Schussenried	58	48.00 N	9.40 E
Schüttenberg ∧[2]	61	48.05 N	16.44 E
Schutter ≃	58	48.34 N	7.50 E
Schüttorf	52	52.19 N	7.13 E
Schuyler, Ne., U.S.	198	41.26 N	97.03 W
Schuyler, Va., U.S.	192	37.47 N	78.41 W
Schuyler □[6], Il., U.S.	219	40.07 N	90.34 W
Schuyler □[6], N.Y., U.S.	210	42.23 N	76.52 W
Schuyler Lake	210	42.47 N	75.02 W
Schuylerville	210	43.06 N	73.34 W
Schuylkill □[6]	210	40.41 N	76.12 W
Schuylkill ≃	208	39.53 N	75.12 W
Schuylkill Canal ≅	285	40.14 N	75.42 W
Schuylkill Haven	208	40.37 N	76.10 W
Schwaan	54	53.56 N	12.06 E
Schwabach	60	49.20 N	11.01 E
Schwaben □[5]	58	48.15 N	10.30 E
Schwaben □[9]	30	48.10 N	9.25 E
Schwabing •[8]	60	48.10 N	11.34 E
Schwäbische Alb ⋏	58	48.25 N	9.30 E
Schwäbisch Gmünd	56	48.48 N	9.47 E
Schwäbisch Hall	56	49.07 N	9.44 E
Schwabmünchen	58	48.11 N	10.45 E
Schwabstedt	41	54.23 N	9.11 E
Schwadorf	61	48.04 N	16.35 E
Schwafheim	263	51.25 N	6.39 E
Schwagstorf	52	52.31 N	7.45 E
Schwaigern	56	49.08 N	9.03 E
Schwalenberg	52	51.52 N	9.11 E
Schwalm ≃	56	51.10 N	9.25 E
Schwalmstadt	56	50.55 N	9.11 E
Schwalmtal	56	51.13 N	6.16 E
Schwanden	58	47.00 N	9.04 E
Schwandorf	60	49.20 N	12.08 E
Schwanebeck, Dtsch.	54	52.37 N	13.32 E
Schwanebeck, Dtsch.	54	51.58 N	11.07 E
Schwanenstadt	60	48.03 N	13.46 E
Schwanenwerder •[8]	264a	52.27 N	13.10 E
Schwaner, Pegunungan ⋏	112	0.40 S	112.40 E
Schwanewede	52	53.14 N	8.35 E
Schwangau	58	47.35 N	10.44 E
Schwansen •[1]	41	54.35 N	9.50 E
Schwante	264a	52.44 N	13.05 E
Schwarme	52	52.54 N	9.01 E
Schwarmstedt	52	52.40 N	9.37 E
Schwartau ≃	54	53.56 N	10.41 E
Schwarza, Dtsch.	54	50.38 N	10.32 E
Schwarza, Dtsch.	54	50.41 N	11.19 E
Schwarza ≃, Dtsch.	54	50.41 N	11.19 E
Schwarza ≃, Öst.	61	47.43 N	16.13 E
Schwarzach, Dtsch.	60	48.55 N	12.49 E
Schwarzach, Öst.	58	47.27 N	9.45 E
Schwarzach ≃	60	49.36 N	12.08 E
Schwarzach im Pongau	64	47.19 N	13.09 E
Schwarzbach ≃, Dtsch.	56	49.16 N	7.18 E
Schwarzbach ≃, Dtsch.	263	51.19 N	6.44 E
Schwarzburg	54	50.38 N	11.12 E
Schwarze Elster ≃	54	51.49 N	12.51 E
Schwarze Laber ≃	60	49.00 N	12.03 E
Schwarzenbach am Wald	54	50.17 N	11.37 E
Schwarzenbach an der Saale	54	50.13 N	11.56 E
Schwarzenbek	52	53.30 N	10.29 E
Schwarzenberg	54	50.32 N	12.47 E
Schwarzenberg •[8]	263	51.24 N	6.42 E
Schwarzenberg Park ♦	264b	48.14 N	16.15 E
Schwarzenborn	56	50.55 N	9.27 E
Schwarzenbruck	60	49.21 N	11.14 E
Schwarzenburg	58	46.49 N	7.21 E
Schwarzenfeld	60	49.23 N	12.08 E
Schwarze Pumpe	54	51.32 N	14.20 E
Schwarzer Berg ∧[2]	263	51.41 N	7.12 E
Schwarzer Mann ∧	56	50.15 N	6.21 E
Schwarzer Regen ≃	60	49.10 N	12.50 E
Schwarzes Meer → Black Sea ⊤[2]	22	43.00 N	35.00 E
Schwarzheide	54	51.29 N	13.51 E
Schwarzkogel ∧	61	47.25 N	15.25 E
Schwarzrand ⋏	156	25.37 S	16.50 E
Schwarzriegel ∧	60	49.14 N	12.56 E
Schwarzsee	58	46.40 N	7.20 E
Schwarzwald (Black Forest) ⋏	58	48.00 N	8.15 E
Schwarzwälder Hochwald •[3]	56	49.39 N	6.55 E
Schwatka Mountains ⋏	180	67.25 N	157.00 W
Schwaz	64	47.20 N	11.42 E
Schwechat	61	48.08 N	16.29 E
Schwechat ≃	61	48.08 N	16.34 E
Schweden → Sweden □[1]	24	62.00 N	15.00 E
Schwedeneck	41	54.27 N	10.05 E
Schwedt	54	53.03 N	14.17 E
Schweez	54	53.53 N	12.24 E
Schweflinghausen	263	51.16 N	7.25 E
Schwegenheim	56	49.16 N	8.20 E
Schwei	52	53.24 N	8.21 E
Schweich	56	49.49 N	6.45 E
Schweidnitz → Świdnica	30	50.51 N	16.29 E
Schweighausen	58	48.13 N	7.57 E
Schweighouse-sur-Moder	56	48.49 N	7.44 E
Schweinfurt	56	50.03 N	10.14 E
Schweinitz	54	51.48 N	13.01 E
Schweinrich	54	53.10 N	12.37 E
Schweiz → Switzerland □[1]	58	47.00 N	8.00 E
Schweizer Nationalpark ♦	58	46.38 N	10.11 E
Schweizer-Reneke	158	27.11 S	25.18 E
Schwelm	56	51.17 N	7.17 E
Schwendi	58	48.10 N	9.58 E
Schwenke	263	51.11 N	7.26 E
Schwenksville	285	40.16 N	75.28 W
Schwepnitz	54	51.20 N	13.57 E
Schwerin, Dtsch.	54	53.38 N	11.25 E
Schwerin, Dtsch.	263	51.33 N	7.20 E
Schweriner See ⊜	54	53.45 N	11.28 E
Schwertberg	61	48.16 N	14.35 E
Schwerte	56	51.26 N	7.34 E
Schwetzingen	56	49.23 N	8.34 E
Schweyen	56	49.10 N	7.24 E
Schwieberdingen	56	48.52 N	9.04 E
Schwielochsee ⊜	54	52.03 N	14.12 E
Schwielowsee ⊜	54	52.20 N	12.57 E
Schwitten	263	51.27 N	7.48 E
Schwyz	58	47.02 N	8.40 E
Schwyz □[3]	58	47.05 N	8.40 E
Sciacca	70	37.31 N	13.03 E
Sciara	70	37.55 N	13.45 E
Sciaves (Schabs)	64	46.46 N	11.40 E
Scicli	70	36.47 N	14.42 E
Scie ≃	50	49.55 N	1.02 E
Science and Industry, Museum of ʊ	278	41.47 N	87.35 W
Sciez	58	46.20 N	6.23 E
Scigliano	68	39.08 N	16.19 E
Ščigry	78	51.53 N	36.55 E
Scilla	68	38.15 N	15.44 E
Scilly, Isles of II	42a	49.55 N	6.20 W
Ścinawa	30	51.25 N	16.27 E
Scio, N.Y., U.S.	210	42.10 N	77.59 W
Scio, Oh., U.S.	214	40.23 N	81.05 W
Scio, Or., U.S.	202	44.42 N	122.50 W
Scionzier	58	46.03 N	6.34 E
Sciota	210	40.56 N	75.19 W
Scioto □[6]	218	38.48 N	83.01 W
Scioto ≃	188	38.44 N	83.01 W
Scioto Brush Creek ≃	218	38.50 N	83.01 W
Scipio, In., U.S.	218	39.05 N	85.43 W
Scipio, Ut,. U.S.	200	39.14 N	112.06 W
Scipio Center	210	42.47 N	76.34 W
Scippo Creek ≃	218	39.31 N	82.59 W
Šćit ∧	36	44.02 N	17.47 E
Ščitkoviči	76	53.13 N	27.59 E
Scituate	207	42.11 N	70.43 W
Scituate Reservoir ⊜[1]	207	41.47 N	71.36 W
Sclafani Bagni	70	37.49 N	13.51 E
Scobey	202	48.47 N	105.25 W
Scoffera, Passo della)(	62	44.29 N	9.07 E
Scofield Reservoir ⊜[1]	200	39.47 N	111.09 W
Scoglitti •[8]	70	36.53 N	14.26 E
Ščokino	76	54.01 N	37.31 E
Scole	42	52.22 N	1.10 E
Ščolkovo	82	55.55 N	38.00 E
Scoltenna ≃	64	44.15 N	10.50 E
Scolt Head ›	42	52.58 N	0.42 E
Scone	166	32.03 S	150.52 E
Scooba	194	32.49 N	88.28 W
Scopello	62	45.46 N	8.06 E
Scordia	70	37.18 N	14.51 E
Scoresby	274b	37.54 S	145.14 E
Scorrano, It.	66	42.35 N	13.49 E
Scorrano, It.	68	40.05 N	18.18 E
Ščors	78	51.49 N	31.59 E
Ščorsk	78	48.22 N	34.06 E
Scorzè	64	45.34 N	12.06 E
Scotch ≃	206	45.27 N	74.59 W
Scotch Plains	210	40.39 N	74.23 W
Scotchtown	210	41.29 N	74.21 W
Scotia, Ne., U.S.	198	41.27 N	98.42 W
Scotia, N.Y., U.S.	210	42.49 N	73.57 W
Scotia Lake ⊜	190	47.05 N	81.23 W
Scotian Shelf ✦[4]	16	44.00 N	62.00 W
Scotia Ridge ✦[3]	18	54.00 S	50.00 W
Scotia Sea ⊤[2]	9	56.00 S	40.00 W
Scotland, On., Can.	212	43.01 N	80.22 W
Scotland, Pa., U.S.	208	39.58 N	77.35 W
Scotland, S.D., U.S.	198	43.08 N	97.43 W
Scotland, Tx., U.S.	196	33.40 N	98.28 W
Scotland □[8]	28	57.00 N	4.00 W
Scotland Neck	192	36.07 N	77.25 W
Scotland Run ≃	285	39.39 N	75.03 W
Scotlandville	194	30.31 N	91.10 W
Ščot'ovo	83	48.09 N	39.04 E
Scotrun	210	41.04 N	75.19 W
Scotsburn	186	45.39 N	62.51 W
Scotstown	206	45.32 N	71.17 W
Scott, Sk., Can.	184	52.23 N	108.50 W
Scott, Ms., U.S.	194	33.35 N	91.04 W
Scott, Oh., U.S.	216	40.59 N	84.35 W
Scott □[6], Il., U.S.	219	39.38 N	90.27 W
Scott □[6], In., U.S.	218	38.41 N	85.46 W
Scott □[6], Ky., U.S.	218	38.18 N	84.35 W
Scott ≃	204	41.48 N	123.02 W
Scott, Cape ›	182	50.47 N	128.26 W
Scott, Mount ∧, Ok., U.S.	196	34.44 N	98.32 W
Scott, Mount ∧, Or., U.S.	202	42.56 N	122.01 W
Scott Air Force Base ■	219	38.32 N	89.52 W
Scott Base ʊ[3]	9	77.50 S	166.25 E
Scottburgh	158	30.19 S	30.40 E
Scott City, Ks., U.S.	198	38.28 N	100.54 W
Scott City, Mo., U.S.	194	37.13 N	89.31 W
Scott Cove c	276	41.03 N	73.28 W
Scott Creek ≃	226	37.02 N	122.13 W
Scottdale, Mi., U.S.	216	42.03 N	86.27 W
Scottdale, Pa., U.S.	214	40.06 N	79.35 W
Scotter	44	53.29 N	0.40 W
Scott Haven	279b	40.15 N	79.47 W
Scott Island I, Ant.	9	67.24 S	179.55 W
Scott Island I, On., Can.	212	44.36 N	76.20 W
Scott Islands II	182	50.48 N	128.40 W
Scott Lake	220	25.56 N	80.13 W
Scott Mountain ∧	202	44.11 N	115.47 W
Scott Peak ∧	202	44.21 N	112.50 W
Scott Reef ✦[2]	160	14.00 S	121.50 E
Scott Run ≃	284c	38.58 N	77.12 W
Scotts	216	42.11 N	85.24 W
Scottsbluff	198	41.52 N	103.40 W
Scotts Bluff National Monument ♦	198	41.49 N	103.41 W
Scottsboro	194	34.40 N	86.02 W
Scottsburg, In., U.S.	218	38.41 N	85.46 W
Scottsburg, N.Y., U.S.	210	42.40 N	77.43 W
Scottsdale, Austl.	166	41.10 S	147.31 E
Scottsdale, Az., U.S.	200	33.30 N	111.53 W
Scotts Flat Reservoir ⊜[1]	226	39.17 N	120.55 W
Scotts Head ›	240d	15.13 N	61.23 W
Scotts Hill	194	35.31 N	88.15 W
Scotts Level Branch ≃	284b	39.22 N	76.45 W
Scottsmoor	220	28.46 N	80.53 W
Scotts Valley	226	37.03 N	122.00 W
Scottsville, Ky., U.S.	194	36.45 N	86.11 W
Scottsville, N.Y., U.S.	210	43.01 N	77.44 W

Symbols in the index entries represent the broad categories identified in the key at the right. Symbols with superior numbers (⋏[1]) identify subcategories (see complete key on page *I · 1).*

Symbole im Register stellen die rechts im Schlüssel erklärten Kategorien dar. Symbole mit hochgestellten Ziffern (⋏[1]) bezeichnen Unterabteilungen einer Kategorie (vgl. vollständiger Schlüssel auf Seite *I · 1).*

Los símbolos incluídos en el texto del índice representan las grandes categorías identificadas con la clave a la derecha. Los símbolos con numeros en su parte superior (⋏[1]) identifican las subcategorías (véase la clave completa en la página *I · 1).*

Les symboles de l'index représentent les catégories indiquées dans la légende à droite. Les symboles suivis d'un indice (⋏[1]) représentent des sous-catégories (voir légende complète à la page *I · 1).*

Os símbolos incluídos no texto do índice representam as grandes categorias identificadas com a chave à direita. Os símbolos com números em sua parte superior (⋏[1]) identificam as subcategorias (veja-se a chave completa à página *I · 1).*

∧ Mountain	Berg	Montaña	Montagne	Montanha
⋏ Mountains	Gebirge	Montañas	Montagnes	Montanhas
)(Pass	Paß	Paso	Col	Passo
V Valley, Canyon	Tal, Cañon	Valle, Cañón	Vallée, Canyon	Vale, Canhão
≚ Plain	Ebene	Llano	Plaine	Planície
› Cape	Kap	Cabo	Cap	Cabo
I Island	Insel	Isla	Île	Ilha
II Islands	Inseln	Islas	Îles	Ilhas
⊥ Other Topographic Features	Andere Topographische Objekte	Otros Elementos Topográficos	Autres données topographiques	Outros acidentes topográficos

ESPAÑOL Nombre	Página	Lat.°′	Long.°′ W = Oeste
Scott Township	279b	40.32 N	80.11 W
Scottville, Il., U.S.	219	39.29 N	90.06 W
Scottville, Mi., U.S.	190	43.57 N	86.16 W
Scourie	46	58.20 N	5.08 W
Scout Lake	184	49.22 N	106.00 W
Scrabster	46	58.37 N	3.32 W
Scranton, Ia., U.S.	198	42.01 N	94.32 W
Scranton, N.Y., U.S.	210	42.44 N	78.50 W
Scranton, N.D., U.S.	198	46.08 N	103.08 W
Scranton, Pa., U.S.	210	41.24 N	75.39 W
Scremerston	44	55.44 N	1.59 W
Screven	192	31.29 N	82.01 W
Screw	164	3.55 S	142.50 E
Scribner	198	41.40 N	96.39 W
Scridain, Loch ⊂	46	56.21 N	6.07 W
Scripps Institution of Oceanography ⊽³	228	32.52 N	117.15 W
Scrivia ≃	62	45.03 N	8.54 E
Scroggins	222	32.58 N	95.11 W
Scrooby	44	53.25 N	1.01 W
Scrub Island I	240m	18.28 N	64.31 W
Ščuči ⊕	76	53.36 N	24.45 E
Ščučinsk	86	52.56 N	70.12 E
Ščuč'e, Ross.	78	51.45 N	40.29 E
Ščuč'e, Ross.	80	51.46 N	40.29 E
Ščuč'e, Ross.	86	55.17 N	63.59 E
Ščuč'e Ozero	86	56.31 N	56.38 E
Scugcg ⊜	212	44.24 N	78.45 W
Scugog, Lake ⊜	212	44.10 N	78.51 W
Scugog Indian Reserve ◆⁴	212	44.11 N	78.54 W
Scugog Island I	212	44.10 N	78.53 W
Ščukino	82	54.28 N	37.01 E
Scunthorpe	44	53.36 N	0.38 W
Scuol (Schuls)	58	46.48 N	10.18 E
Scuppernong ≃	216	42.54 N	88.42 W
Scurcola Marsicana	66	42.03 N	13.20 E
Ščurovo	82	55.30 N	38.49 E
Scurry	222	32.31 N	96.23 W
Scutari — Shkodër	38	42.05 N	19.30 E
Scutari, Lake ⊜	38	42.12 N	19.18 E
Se ◆⁴	287b	23.33 S	46.37 W
Seabeck	224	47.38 N	122.51 W
Sea Bird Island I	49	49.15 N	121.45 W
Seabird Island Indian Reserve ◆⁴	182	49.17 N	121.42 W
Seaboard	192	36.29 N	77.26 W
Sea Bright	210	40.21 N	73.58 W
Seabrook, Md., U.S.	284c	38.58 N	76.50 W
Seabrook, N.J., U.S.	208	39.30 N	75.13 W
Seabrook, Tx., U.S.	222	29.33 N	95.01 W
Seabrook, Lake ⊜	162	30.56 S	119.40 E
Sea Cliff	210	40.50 N	73.38 W
Seacock Swamp ⊶	208	36.48 N	76.51 W
Seacombe	262	53.25 N	3.01 W
Sea Dog Island I	276	40.36 N	73.35 W
Seadrift	186	28.24 N	96.47 W
Seaford, Eng., U.K.	42	50.46 N	0.06 E
Seaford, De., U.S.	208	38.38 N	75.36 W
Seaford, N.Y., U.S.	276	40.39 N	73.29 W
Seaford, Va., U.S.	208	37.11 N	76.26 W
Seaford Creek ≃	276	40.38 N	73.29 W
Seaforth, Austl.	274a	33.48 S	151.15 E
Seaforth, On., Can.	190	43.33 N	81.24 W
Seaforth, Eng., U.K.	262	53.28 N	3.01 W
Seaforth, Loch ⊂	46	57.54 N	6.40 W
Seafox Seamount ◆³	14	30.30 S	172.45 W
Seager Wheeler Lake ⊜	184	54.27 N	103.30 W
Seagoville	222	32.38 N	93.32 W
Seagraves	196	32.56 N	102.33 W
Seaham	44	54.52 N	1.21 W
Seaholme	274b	37.52 S	144.50 E
Seahorse Breakers ◆²	112	5.30 N	112.37 E
Seahorse Point ➤	176	63.47 N	80.09 W
Seahouses	44	55.35 N	1.38 W
Seahurst	224	47.28 N	122.22 W
Sea Island I	224	49.12 N	123.10 W
Sea Islands II	192	31.20 N	81.20 W
Sea Isle City	208	39.09 N	74.41 W
Seal	260	51.17 N	0.14 E
Seal ≃	176	59.04 N	94.48 W
Seal, Cape ➤	158	34.07 S	23.25 E
Sea Lake	166	35.30 S	142.51 E
Sealand	262	53.12 N	2.58 W
Sealark Channel ⋃	175e	9.18 S	160.20 E
Seal Bay ⊂	9	71.40 S	12.25 W
Seal Beach	228	33.44 N	118.06 W
Seal Beach National Wildlife Refuge ◆⁴	280	33.45 N	118.03 W
Seal Cays II	238	21.10 N	71.38 W
Seal Cove, N.B., Can.	186	44.39 N	66.51 W
Seal Cove, Nf., Can.	180	49.56 N	56.23 W
Sealdah Railroad Station ◆⁵	272b	22.34 N	88.23 E
Seale	194	32.17 N	85.10 W
Sealevel	192	34.51 N	76.23 W
Seal Island I	186	43.25 N	66.01 W
Seal Islands II	282	38.03 N	122.03 W
Seal Lake ⊜	176	54.18 N	61.40 W
Seal Rocks II¹	282	37.47 N	122.31 W
Sealston	208	38.15 N	77.19 W
Sealy	222	29.46 N	96.09 W
Seaman	218	38.56 N	83.34 W
Seamer	44	54.14 N	0.26 W
Seanor	214	40.19 N	78.54 W
Seara	252	27.07 S	52.17 W
Searchlight	204	35.27 N	114.55 W
Searcy	194	35.15 N	91.44 W
Searles Lake ⊜	204	35.43 N	117.20 W
Sears Lake ⊜	281	42.35 N	83.39 W
Searsport	186	44.27 N	68.55 W
Sears Tower ◆	278	41.53 N	87.38 W
Searsville Lake ⊜	282	37.24 N	122.14 W
Seascale	44	54.24 N	3.29 W
Seashore State Park ◆	208	36.54 N	76.02 W
Seaside, Ca., U.S.	226	36.36 N	121.51 W
Seaside, Or., U.S.	226	45.59 N	123.55 W
Seaside Park	208	39.55 N	74.04 W
Seaside Park ◆	276	41.10 N	73.12 W
Seaton, Eng., U.K.	42	50.43 N	3.05 W
Seaton, Eng., U.K.	44	54.41 N	3.33 W
Seaton, Eng., U.K.	44	54.41 N	1.22 W
Seaton, Eng., U.K.	58	49.42 N	4.57 E
Seaton Delaval	44	55.04 N	1.31 W
Seaton Sluice	44	55.05 N	1.29 W
Seat Pleasant	284c	38.54 N	76.54 W
Seattle	224	47.36 N	122.19 W
Seattle, Mount ▲	180	60.06 N	139.11 W
Seattle Heights	224	47.48 N	122.20 W
Seattle-Tacoma International Airport ⊠	224	47.27 N	122.18 W
Seatuck National Wildlife Refuge ◆⁴	276	40.43 N	73.13 W
Seaview, Eng., U.K.	42	50.43 N	1.06 W
Sea View, Ma., U.S.	283	42.08 N	70.42 W
Seaview, N.Y., U.S.	276	40.39 N	73.09 W
Seaview, Wa., U.S.	224	46.20 N	124.03 W
Seaward Kaikoura Range ⋀	174g	42.15 S	173.30 E
Sea Roads ⋃	174g	28.13 N	177.25 W
Sea World ◆, Fl., U.S.	220	28.25 N	81.28 W
Sea World ◆, Oh., U.S.	214	41.21 N	81.23 W
Seba	112	10.29 S	121.50 E
Sébaco	236	12.51 N	86.06 W
Sebago Lake ⊜	188	43.50 N	70.35 W
Se Bai ⋍	110	15.13 N	104.47 E
Sebakor, Teluk ⊂	164	3.35 S	132.50 E
Sebalino, Ross.	82	47.22 N	43.36 E
Šebalino, Ross.	80	45.01 N	43.21 E

FRANÇAIS Nom	Page	Lat.°′	Long.°′ W = Ouest
Šebalino, Ross.	86	51.17 N	85.40 E
Sebanga	114	1.24 S	101.10 E
Sebangan, Teluk ⊂	112	3.15 S	113.30 E
Sebangka, Pulau I	112	0.07 N	104.36 E
Sebaou, Oued ≃	34	36.55 N	3.55 E
Sebarok, Pulau I	271c	1.13 N	103.48 E
Sebastian, Fl., U.S.	220	27.46 N	80.29 W
Sebastian, Tx., U.S.	196	26.20 N	97.47 W
Sebastian, Cape ➤	202	42.19 N	124.26 W
Sebastian Inlet ⊂	220	27.51 N	80.26 W
Sebastián Vizcaíno, Bahía ⊂	232	28.00 N	114.30 W
Sebastião de Lacerda	256	22.17 S	43.35 W
Sebastopol, Austl.	169	37.36 S	143.51 E
Sebastopol, Ca., U.S.	204	38.24 N	122.49 W
Sebastopol, Ms., U.S.	194	32.34 N	89.20 W
Sebatik, Pulau I	112	4.10 N	117.45 E
Sebba	150	13.26 N	0.32 E
Sebderat	144	15.26 N	36.40 E
Sébé ≃	152	1.02 S	13.06 E
Sebec Lake ⊜	188	45.18 N	69.18 W
Sebeka	198	46.38 N	95.05 W
Šebekino	78	50.25 N	36.56 E
Šebékoro	150	12.57 N	8.59 W
Šebelinka	78	49.27 N	36.30 E
Seben	130	40.24 N	31.34 E
Sebenico — Šibenik	36	43.44 N	15.54 E
Sebeş, Punta ⋀	71	39.03 N	8.50 E
Seberi	252	27.29 S	53.24 W
Seberida	112	0.43 S	102.31 E
Šeberta	88	54.40 N	99.54 E
Sebeş	38	45.58 N	23.34 E
Sebeş, Pulau I	115a	5.57 S	105.30 E
Sebes Körös (Crişul Repede) ≃	38	46.55 N	20.59 E
Sebewaing	190	43.43 N	83.27 W
Sebež	76	56.17 N	28.29 E
Sebille Manor	281	42.39 N	82.49 W
Sebinkarahisar	130	40.18 N	38.26 E
Šebiş	38	46.23 N	22.08 E
Sebnitz	54	50.58 N	14.16 E
Sebou, Oued ≃	148	34.15 N	6.40 W
Sebree	194	37.36 N	87.31 W
Sebrell	208	36.47 N	77.07 W
Sebring, Fl., U.S.	220	27.29 N	81.26 W
Sebring, Oh., U.S.	214	40.55 N	81.01 W
Sebuku, Pulau I, Indon.	112	3.30 S	116.22 E
Sebuku, Pulau I, Indon.	115a	5.53 S	105.31 E
Sebuku, Teluk ⊂	112	4.00 N	118.26 E
Seč	60	49.36 N	13.30 E
Seca, Ilha I	287a	22.50 S	43.11 W
Secane	285	39.55 N	75.18 W
Secang	115a	7.27 S	110.13 E
Secas, Islas II	236	7.58 N	82.02 W
Secaucus	276	40.47 N	74.03 W
Secchia ≃	64	45.04 N	11.00 E
Sečenovo	80	55.13 N	45.54 E
Secesh ≃	202	45.03 N	115.43 W
Sechault	56	49.16 N	4.44 E
Sechelt	182	49.28 N	123.45 W
Sec'man	76	52.32 N	40.29 E
Sechura	248	5.33 S	80.51 W
Sechura, Bahía de ⊂	248	5.42 S	81.00 W
Sechura, Desierto de ◆²	248	5.50 S	80.40 W
Seckach	56	49.26 N	9.20 E
Seckau	61	47.16 N	14.47 E
Seckau ⋃¹	61	47.16 N	14.47 E
Seclantas	252	25.18 S	66.15 W
Seclin	50	50.33 N	3.02 E
Seco ≃, Arg.	252	23.08 S	63.57 W
Seco ≃, Esp.	266d	41.30 N	2.09 E
Seco, Arroyo ≃, Ca., U.S.	226	36.25 N	121.20 W
Seco, Arroyo ≃, Ca., U.S.	280	34.05 N	118.13 W
Seco Creek ≃, N.M., U.S.	196	32.59 N	107.18 W
Seco Creek ≃, Tx., U.S.	196	29.02 N	99.08 W
Seco Island I	116	11.19 N	121.40 E
Second ≃	276	40.47 N	74.03 W
Second Cliff ▲⁴	283	42.12 N	70.43 W
Second Han-gang Bridge ◆⁵	271b	37.34 N	126.54 E
Second Herring Brook ≃	283	42.09 N	70.47 W
Second Lake ⊜	206	45.09 N	71.10 W
Second Mountain ▲	208	40.55 N	76.30 W
Second San Diego Aqueduct ≃¹	228	32.41 N	117.01 W
Second Swamp ⊶	208	37.08 N	77.12 W
Second Valley	168b	35.33 S	138.14 E
Second Watchung Mountain ▲	276	40.55 N	74.13 W
Sečovce	60	48.43 N	21.40 E
Sečovská Polianka	60	48.47 N	21.42 E
Secretário, Ribeirão ≃	256	22.14 S	43.25 W
Secretary	208	38.36 N	75.56 W
Secretary Island I	172	45.15 S	166.55 E
Section	194	34.34 N	85.59 W
Secubun Island I	5	5.06 N	120.18 E
Sécure ≃	248	15.10 S	64.52 W
Security Square ◆⁹	284b	39.19 N	76.45 W
Seda ≃	30	47.00 N	18.31 E
Seda, Lat.	76	57.40 N	25.46 E
Seda, Liet.	76	56.10 N	22.04 E
Seda, Zhg.	102	32.20 N	100.41 E
Seda ≃, P.	76	57.47 N	25.15 E
Sedah	112	10.46 S	123.12 E
Sedalia, Ab., Can.	184	51.41 N	110.40 W
Sedalia, In., U.S.	216	40.25 N	86.31 W
Sedalia, Mo., U.S.	194	38.42 N	93.13 W
Sedan, Austl.	168b	34.35 S	139.18 E
Sedan, Fr.	56	49.42 N	4.57 E
Sedan, Ks., U.S.	198	37.07 N	96.11 W
Sedanka, Cape ➤	198	53.30 N	166.10 W
Sedanka Island I	180	53.50 N	166.10 W
Sedano	34	42.43 N	3.45 W
Sedano, Tanjung ➤	115a	7.49 S	114.27 E
Sedanovo	88	56.58 N	101.28 E
Sedari, Tanjung ➤	115a	5.57 S	107.18 E
Sedayu	115a	6.59 S	112.23 E
Sedbergh	44	54.20 N	2.31 W
Sedco Hills	228	33.39 N	117.24 W
Seddin	58	52.16 N	13.07 E
Seddin-Berg ▲²	264a	52.24 N	13.40 E
Seddinsee ⊜	264a	52.23 N	13.41 E
Seddon	172	41.40 S	174.05 E
Seddonville	172	41.33 S	171.59 E
Sedé Boqer	130a	30.52 N	34.47 E
Sedel'nikovo	88	56.57 N	75.18 E
Séderon	62	44.12 N	5.32 E
Sédhiou	132	31.31 N	34.35 E

PORTUGUÊS Nome	Página	Lat.°′	Long.°′ W = Ceste
Sedini	71	40.51 N	8.4: E
Sedlčany	49	49.40 N	14.26 E
Sedley	208	36.46 N	76.56 W
Sedlice	60	49.23 N	13.56 E
Sedlitz	54	51.33 N	14.03 E
Sedlo ⋀	54	50.36 N	14.17 E
Sedn'ov	78	51.39 N	31.34 E
Šedok	84	44.13 N	40.52 E
Sedom (Scdom) ⋌	132	31.04 N	35.23 E
Sedona	200	34.52 N	111.45 W
Sedot Yam	132	32.29 N	34.53 E
Sedova, pik ▲	72	73.29 N	54.58 E
Sedovo	83	47.03 N	38.10 E
Sedovo-Vasil'jevka	83	47.14 N	38.08 E
Sedrata	36	36.08 N	7.32 E
Sedriano	62	45.29 N	8.58 E
Sedrina	62	45.47 N	9.38 E
Sedro Wooley	224	48.30 N	122.14 W
Sedrun	58	46.41 N	8.46 E
Sedtim	24	66.25 N	56.20 E
Šeduva	76	55.46 N	23.46 E
Sedziszów	30	50.04 N	21.41 E
See	58	47.05 N	10.28 E
Seebad Ahlbeck	54	53.56 N	14.11 E
Seebad Bar¨sin	54	53.57 N	14.07 E
Seebad Herngsdorf	54	53.56 N	14.08 E
Seeberg, Dtsch.	54	52.33 N	13.41 E
Seeberg, Schw.	58	47.09 N	7.40 E
Seebergsattel ⋋	61	47.38 N	15.18 E
Seeber Lake ⊜	54	52.33 N	93.03 W
Seebooben	64	44.49 N	13.30 E
Seebruck	64	47.56 N	12.28 E
Seebrugg	58	47.49 N	8.13 E
Seeburg	264a	52.31 N	13.07 E
Seefeld, Dtsch.	52	53.27 N	8.21 E
Seefeld, Dtsch.	54	52.37 N	13.40 E
Seefeld in Tirol	64	47.20 N	11.11 E
Seefin ⋀²	48	52.18 N	8.32 W
Seeg	58	47.38 N	10.36 E
Seege ≃	54	53.04 N	11.23 E
Seegefeld	264a	52.33 N	13.05 E
Seehausen, Dtsch.	54	52.06 N	11.17 E
Seehausen, Dtsch.	54	52.53 N	11.45 E
Seeheim-Jugenheim	54	49.45 N	8.38 E
Seehof	264a	52.24 N	13.17 E
Seeis	156	22.29 S	17.39 E
Seekaskootch Indian Reserve ◆⁴	184	53.43 N	109.55 W
Seekoegat	158	33.03 S	22.31 E
Seekoei ≃	158	30.18 S	25.01 E
Seekonk	207	41.48 N	71.20 W
Seelbach	58	48.18 N	7.56 E
Seeley Lake	202	47.10 N	113.29 W
Seeleys Bay	212	44.29 N	76.14 W
Seelingstädt	54	50.46 N	12.14 E
Seelow	54	52.32 N	14.23 E
Seelyville, In., U.S.	194	39.29 N	87.16 W
Seelyville, Pa., U.S.	210	41.35 N	75.17 W
Seelze	52	52.24 N	9.35 E
Seemade	144	7.10 N	48.36 E
Seemalik Butte ▲	180	60.09 N	167.08 W
Seemenbach ≃	56	50.17 N	8.59 E
Seemore Downs	162	30.42 S	125.15 E
Seen	58	47.29 N	8.46 E
Seengen	58	47.19 N	8.13 E
Seeon	64	47.58 N	12.26 E
Seer Green	260	51.37 N	0.36 W
Seergu	102	32.00 N	103.33 E
Seerhausen	54	51.16 N	13.15 E
Sées	48	48.36 N	0.10 E
Seesen	52	51.53 N	10.10 E
Seeshaupt	64	47.49 N	11.18 E
Seetal ≃	58	47.09 N	13.57 E
Seetal	152	5.20 S	13.16 E
Seetaler Alpen ⋌	61	47.05 N	14.35 E
Seevetal	52	53.23 N	9.59 E
Seewalchen am Attersee	64	47.57 N	13.35 E
Seewiesen	61	47.37 N	15.16 E
Seewinkel ◆¹	54	47.48 N	16.49 E
Seewis	58	47.00 N	9.32 E
Seez	62	45.37 N	6.48 E
Seez ≃	58	47.07 N	9.18 E
Sefaatli	130	39.31 N	34.46 E
Šefadu	148	8.39 N	10.59 W
Sefar ⋌	148	24.27 N	9.16 E
Sefare	156	23.02 S	27.28 E
Seferihisar	130	38.11 N	26.51 E
Séfeto	150	14.08 N	9.40 W
Seffern	56	50.04 N	6.30 E
Seffner	220	27.59 N	82.17 W
Sefid ⋍	123	37.26 N	49.55 E
Sefid Ābeh	123	30.56 N	60.35 E
Sefton, N.Z.	172	43.15 S	172.40 E
Sefton, Eng., U.K.	262	53.30 N	2.58 W
Sefton ⋍⁸	262	53.34 N	3.14 W
Sefton, Mount ▲	172	43.41 S	170.03 E
Sefton Park ◆	262	53.23 N	2.56 W
Segag	144	7.40 N	42.50 E
Segaliud ≃	116	5.43 N	117.55 E
Segamat ≃	112	5.27 N	119.48 E
Segangane	148	35.09 N	3.00 W
Segang	100	33.08 N	114.18 E
Segara ⊜	34	35.09 N	3.00 W
Segarcea	38	44.06 N	23.45 E
Segarka ≃	86	57.16 N	84.05 E
Segbana	150	10.56 N	3.42 E
Segem ≃	144	9.30 N	40.46 E
Segen ≃	144	4.49 N	36.57 E
Segera	164	8.15 S	143.30 E
Segeri	112	4.39 S	119.37 E
Segesta ⋋	70	37.56 N	12.50 E
Segesvár — Sighişoara	38	46.13 N	24.48 E
Segezha	22	63.44 N	34.19 E
Seggiano	66	42.56 N	11.33 E
Seggueur, Oued es ⋍	148	31.39 N	2.26 E
Ségmas	34	64.43 N	49.14 E
Segni	66	41.41 N	13.01 E
Segno	222	30.35 N	94.10 W
Segorbe	34	39.51 N	0.29 W
Ségou ⋍³	150	14.00 N	6.16 W
Ségou ⋍⁴	150	13.27 N	6.16 W
Segovary	62	62.23 N	42.57 E
Segovia, Col.	246	7.07 N	74.42 W
Segovia, Esp.	34	40.57 N	4.07 W
Segovia ⋍⁴	34	41.15 N	4.00 W
Segovia, ozero ⊜	34	50.03 N	166.10 W
Segrate	266b	45.29 N	9.19 E
Segré	50	47.41 N	0.52 W
Segre ≃	34	41.22 N	0.20 E
Seguam Island I	180	52.17 N	172.30 W
Seguam Pass ⋃	180	52.08 N	172.45 W
Séguéla	148	20.12 N	12.59 E
Seguela	150	7.57 N	6.40 W
Ségué¨a, Mali	150	14.07 N	6.44 W
Séguénéga	150	13.27 N	1.58 W
Segui	252	31.57 S	60.08 W
Seguin	196	29.34 N	97.57 W
Seguine Point ➤	276	40.31 N	74.12 W
Segula Island I	181a	52.01 N	178.07 E
Seguła ≃	150	14.18 N	6.32 E
Segundo ≃	252	31.31 N	34.35 E
Segundo	196	37.08 N	104.35 W
Segura ≃	112	1.54 N	117.47 E
Segura	34	39.50 N	6.59 W
Segura, Sierra de ⋀	34	38.00 N	2.43 W
Sehāni Kalān	272a	28.41 N	77.25 E
Sehāni Khurd	272a	28.42 N	77.25 E
Sehithwa	156	20.23 S	22.45 E
Sehlabathebe	158	29.53 S	29.05 E
Sehlabathebe National Park ◆	158	29.53 S	29.06 E
Sehma ≃	54	50.32 N	13.00 E

	Página	Lat.°′	Long.°′
Sehnde	52	52.18 N	9.57 E
Sehnkwahn	150	5.13 N	9.12 W
Sehnkwehn ≃	150	5.12 N	9.21 W
Sehore	124	23.12 N	77.05 E
Sehwän	120	26.26 N	67.52 E
Seyon-ni	98	38.20 N	127.41 E
Seia	34	40.25 N	7.42 W
Seibert	198	39.18 N	102.52 W
Seibu	268	35.50 N	139.22 E
Seiches-sur-le-Loir	32	47.35 N	0.22 W
Seidan	96	34.19 N	134.45 E
Seidersville	210	40.35 N	75.23 W
Seiersberg	61	47.01 N	15.24 E
Seifen, Ile de ⋌	32	48.02 N	4.51 W
Seifhennersdorf	54	50.54 N	14.36 E
Seignelay	50	47.54 N	3.36 E
Seigneurial, Lac ⊜	275a	45.33 N	73.20 W
Seika	270	34.46 N	135.48 E
Seikpyu	110	20.55 N	94.47 E
Seil I	46	56.18 N	5.39 W
Seiland I	24	70.25 N	23.15 E
Seilhac	32	45.22 N	1.42 E
Seiling	196	36.08 N	98.55 W
Seillans	62	43.38 N	6.38 E
Seille ≃, Fr.	56	49.07 N	6.11 E
Seille ≃, Fr.	58	46.31 N	4.56 E
Seilo	140	12.20 N	23.50 E
Sejm ≃	78	51.27 N	32.34 E
Sejm ≃	32	48.02 N	4.51 W
Sejnäi	94	35.30 N	137.42 E
Seinäjoki	26	62.47 N	22.50 E
Seine ≃, Mb., Can.	190	48.40 N	92.49 W
Seine ≃, Fr.	48	49.26 N	0.26 E
Seine, Baie de la ⊂	32	49.30 N	0.30 W
Seine-et-Marne ⋍⁵	48	48.33 N	2.35 E
Seine-Maritime ⋍⁵	48	49.45 N	1.00 E
Seine-Port	50	48.33 N	2.33 E
Seine-Saint-Denis ⋍⁵	261	48.55 N	2.30 E
Seip Mound State Memorial ⋋	218	39.15 N	83.13 W
Seipstown	208	40.35 N	75.40 W
Seis de Septiembre — Morón	258	34.39 S	58.37 W
Seishin — Ch'ŏngjin	98	41.47 N	129.50 E
Seitenstetten	61	48.02 N	14.39 E
Seitovka	82	46.43 N	48.03 E
Seitsemisen kansallispuisto ◆	26	61.58 N	23.20 E
Seixa	94	34.29 N	136.30 E
Seixal	34	38.38 N	9.06 W
Seixas, Ponta do ➤	250	7.09 S	34.47 W
Seiz	61	47.24 N	14.55 E
Seize Îles, Lac des ⊜	206	45.54 N	74.28 W
Sejaka	112	3.34 S	116.12 E
Sejerø I	41	55.53 N	11.09 E
Sejerø Bugt ⊂	41	55.50 N	11.15 E
Sejeze	62	52.24 N	9.35 E
Sejmčan	74	62.53 N	152.26 E
Sejny	30	54.07 N	23.20 E
Sejong	115b	9.02 S	116.48 E
Sejs	41	56.09 N	9.36 E
Sekadau	112	0.01 N	110.54 E
Sekake	158	30.07 S	28.27 E
Sekampung ≃	115a	5.36 S	105.50 E
Sekayam ≃	112	0.07 N	110.38 E
Sekayu	112	2.51 S	103.51 E
Seke, Ityo.	144	5.56 S	38.19 E
Seke, Tan.	154	3.20 S	33.31 E
Séke-Banza	152	5.20 S	13.16 E
Sekeladi	112	2.38 S	102.14 E
Sekenke	154	4.16 S	34.10 E
Sekerninoje	86	57.11 N	67.27 E
Seki (Nucha), Azer.	84	41.12 N	47.12 E
Seki, Nihon	94	35.29 N	136.55 E
Seki, Nihon	94	34.51 N	136.24 E
Sekid'ō-san ⋀	94	36.58 N	136.59 E
Sekigahara	94	35.22 N	136.28 E
Sekigane	94	35.22 N	133.46 E
Sekijō	94	36.14 N	139.55 E
Sekima	112	1.41 S	111.31 E
Sekinomiya	96	35.22 N	134.38 E
Sekiu	224	48.15 N	124.18 W
Sekiyado	94	36.06 N	139.47 E
Seki-zaki ➤	96	33.15 N	131.54 E
Sekoma	156	24.41 S	23.50 E
Sekondi-Takoradi	150	4.59 N	1.43 W
Sekota	144	12.38 N	39.03 E
Sekpiegu	150	9.30 N	0.22 W
Sekrenyi ≃	110	16.03 N	98.06 E
Seksna ≃	76	59.13 N	38.30 E
Sekudai	112	1.32 N	103.40 E
Sela, Pulau I	164	21.54 N	89.39 E
Sela, Ponta da ➤	256	23.54 S	45.27 W
Selabolcha	86	51.27 N	108.48 E
Sela Dingay	144	9.59 N	39.37 E
Selagskij, mys ➤	74	70.06 N	170.26 E
Selah	202	46.39 N	120.31 W
Selai ≃	114	2.13 S	103.26 E
Selajevo	88	56.56 N	97.42 E
Selama	114	5.13 N	100.42 E
Selangor ⋍³	112	3.20 N	101.30 E
Selangor ≃	114	3.13 N	101.16 E
Selangor Game Reserve ◆⁴	154	9.10 S	37.10 E
Selargius	71	39.16 N	9.10 E
Selaru, Tanjung ➤	112	4.10 S	114.38 E
Selaru, Tanjung ➤	164	8.09 S	130.55 E
Selatan, Tanjung ➤	112	4.10 S	114.40 E
Selatpanjang	114	1.00 N	102.43 E
Selawik	180	66.37 N	160.03 W
Selawik ≃	180	66.36 N	160.20 W
Selawik Lake ⊜	180	66.33 N	160.50 W
Selayar, Selat ⋃	112	5.42 S	120.28 E
Sēlba ⋋	54	50.10 N	12.08 E
Sebbeck ◆⁸	263	51.20 N	7.26 E
Se-bitz	54	50.19 N	11.44 E
Selborne	260	51.06 N	0.56 W
Selbu	26	63.11 N	11.02 E
Selby, Austl.	274b	37.55 S	145.22 E
Selby, Eng., U.K.	44	53.48 N	1.04 W
Selby, S.D., U.S.	198	45.30 N	100.01 W
Selbyville	208	38.27 N	75.13 W
Selcho	264a	52.31 N	13.06 E
Sel'co, Ross.	78	53.25 N	34.06 E
Sel'co, Ross.	62	56.26 N	36.03 E
Selçuk	130	37.56 N	27.22 E
Selden, Ks., U.S.	198	39.33 N	100.34 W
Selden, N.Y., U.S.	276	40.52 N	73.02 W
Seldovia	180	59.27 N	151.43 W
Sele ≃	66	40.29 N	14.56 E
Sele, Piana del ◆²	68	40.34 N	14.58 E
Sele, Selat ⋃	164	1.10 S	130.48 E
Selebi-Phikwe	156	22.00 S	27.50 E
Selec	273d	30.34 N	33.00 E
Selec-Choliopejon	54	45.16 N	17.34 E
Selechov	85	52.13 N	104.08 E
Selechovo	82	52.13 N	104.08 E
Selection Park	273d	26.18 S	28.27 E
Selda ≃	85	46.29 N	41.53 E
Seleç ≃	115b	8.29 S	115.02 E
Selemdagi	233b	4.22 S	15.17 E

	Página	Lat.°′	Long.°′
Selemdža ≃	89	51.42 N	126.53 E
Selemdžinsk	89	52.36 N	131.08 E
Šelemeti	80	57.27 N	48.07 E
Selendi	130	38.45 N	28.53 E
Selendum ≃	88	50.55 N	106.10 E
Selenga (Selenge) ≃	88	52.16 N	106.16 E
Selenge, Mong.	88	49.25 N	103.59 E
Selenge, Zaïre	152	1.58 S	18.11 E
Selenge ⋍⁴	88	49.30 N	106.30 E
Sclenge (Selenga) ≃	88	52.16 N	106.16 E
Selenginsk	88	52.06 N	107.01 E
Seleničė	38	40.33 N	19.38 E
Selennach ≃	74	67.48 N	144.54 E
Selennach ≃	54	54.17 N	10.26 E
Selenter See ⊜	54	54.17 N	10.28 E
Selety ≃	86	53.06 N	73.22 E
Seletyteniz, ozero ⊜	86	53.15 N	73.15 E
Selezen'ovo, Ross.	26	60.45 N	28.39 E
Selezen'ovo, Ross.	78	59.12 N	42.18 E
Selezni, Ross.	76	55.39 N	31.29 E
Selezni, Ross.	80	52.48 N	41.15 E
Selezn'ovo	76	60.45 N	28.39 E
Self Defense Fleet Headquarters ◆	268	35.18 N	139.38 E
Selfoss	24a	63.56 N	20.57 W
Selfridge	198	46.02 N	100.55 W
Selfridge Air National Guard Base ◆	281	42.36 N	82.49 W
Selghar	272c	18.57 N	73.02 E
Sel'gon	89	49.36 N	135.26 E
Šelibaby	150	15.10 N	12.11 W
Seichicho	89	50.22 N	137.38 E
Selichova, zaliv ⊂	74	60.00 N	158.00 E
Selichovo	88	55.42 N	97.41 E
Selidovo	83	48.08 N	37.18 E
Seligenthal	54	50.45 N	10.26 E
Seliger, ozero ⊜	76	57.13 N	33.05 E
Seligman, Az., U.S.	200	35.19 N	112.52 W
Seligman, Mo., U.S.	194	36.31 N	93.56 W
Selim	114	3.51 N	101.29 E
Selimbau	112	0.37 N	112.08 E
Selimiye	130	37.24 N	27.40 E
Selim River	114	3.50 N	101.24 E
Selínia	267c	37.56 N	23.32 E
Selinsgrove	208	40.47 N	76.51 W
Selinunte ⋋	70	37.35 N	12.49 E
Seliščc, Ross.	24	63.43 N	46.18 E
Selišče, Ross.	76	56.53 N	33.16 E
Selitrennoje	80	47.11 N	47.27 E
Selje	26	62.03 N	5.22 E
Seljord	26	59.29 N	8.37 E
Selk'abmeri (Bottenhavet) ⊂	26	62.00 N	20.00 E
Selke ≃	54	51.52 N	11.14 E
Selkirk, Mb., Can.	184	50.06 N	96.52 W
Selkirk, On., Can.	212	42.49 N	79.56 W
Selkirk, Scot., U.K.	44	55.33 N	2.50 W
Selkirk, N.Y., U.S.	210	42.31 N	73.48 W
Selkirk Mountains ⋌	182	51.00 N	117.40 W
Selkirk Provincial Park ◆	212	42.49 N	79.58 W
Selkirk Shores State Park ◆	212	43.33 N	76.12 W
Šelkovka	82	55.32 N	36.22 E
Šelkovskaja	84	43.30 N	46.02 E
Sella	112	2.38 S	102.14 E
Sella, Monte ▲	64	46.40 N	11.25 E
Sella, Passo di (Sellajoch) ⋋	64	46.30 N	11.45 E
Sella di Corno	66	42.21 N	13.14 E
Sellano	66	42.54 N	12.55 E
Seller Lake ⊜	184	55.00 N	94.11 W
Sellero	64	46.03 N	10.20 E
Sellers	192	34.17 N	79.28 W
Sellersburg	218	38.23 N	85.45 W
Sellersville	208	40.21 N	75.18 W
Selles-sur-Cher	50	47.16 N	1.33 E
Sellia Marina	68	38.53 N	16.43 E
Sellières	58	46.50 N	5.32 E
Sellin	54	54.22 N	13.41 E
Sells	200	31.55 N	111.52 W
Selly Oak ◆⁸	42	52.25 N	1.56 W
Selm	52	51.42 N	7.28 E
Selma, Al., U.S.	194	32.24 N	87.01 W
Selma, Ca., U.S.	226	36.34 N	119.36 W
Selma, In., U.S.	218	40.11 N	85.16 W
Selma, N.C., U.S.	192	35.32 N	78.17 W
Selman City	222	32.12 N	94.58 W
Selmer	194	35.10 N	88.36 W
Selmigerheide ◆⁸	51	51.38 N	7.47 E
Selmont	194	32.23 N	87.00 W
Selommes	50	47.46 N	1.12 E
Selon' ≃	76	58.14 N	30.52 E
Selong	115b	8.39 S	116.32 E
Selopuro	115a	8.04 S	112.11 E
Selouane	34	35.05 N	2.57 W
Selous, Mount ▲	182	62.57 N	132.31 W
Selous Game Reserve ◆⁴	154	9.10 S	37.10 E
Selsdon ◆⁸	260	51.21 N	0.04 W
Selsey	42	50.44 N	0.48 W
Selsey Bill ➤	42	50.43 N	0.48 W
Seltang	89	53.22 N	142.10 E
Seltso	78	53.22 N	34.06 E
Selters	56	50.32 N	7.46 E
Seltz	58	48.53 N	8.06 E
Selu, Pulau I	164	7.32 S	130.54 E
Selva, Arg.	252	29.46 S	62.03 W
Selva, It.	64	46.33 N	11.46 E
Selva di Cadore	64	46.27 N	12.02 E
Selvagens, Ilhas II	148	30.05 N	15.55 W
Selvas ◆²	248	5.00 S	68.00 W
Selway ≃	202	46.08 N	115.36 W
Selwyn, Mount ▲	182	56.11 N	124.59 W
Selwyn, Passage ⋃	175f	15.18 S	166.53 E
Selwyn Mountains ⋌	182	63.10 N	130.20 W
Selwyn Range ⋌	166	21.35 S	140.35 E
Selz ≃	54	49.59 N	8.19 E
Sema, Azer.	84	40.28 N	47.49 E
Semaka, Ross.	74	69.53 N	95.16 E
Semai, Pulau I	115a	5.32 S	110.40 E
Semakau, Pulau I	271c	1.12 N	103.45 E
Seman ≃	38	40.53 N	19.26 E
Semangga	164	8.31 S	140.53 E
Semangka, Teluk ⊂	115a	5.36 S	104.42 E
Semara	148	26.44 N	11.40 W
Semarang	112	6.58 S	110.25 E
Sembakung ≃	112	3.53 N	117.16 E
Sembawang	271c	1.27 N	103.50 E
Sembe	152	1.39 N	14.36 E
Sembel ≃	144	15.18 N	38.55 E
Semberong ≃	114	2.07 N	103.00 E
Sembrancher	58	46.05 N	7.09 E
Sembuli	154	10.27 S	33.58 E
Semeljci	54	45.25 N	18.40 E
Semeru, Gunung ▲	115a	8.06 S	112.55 E
Šemetcvo	76	55.39 N	35.30 E
Šemetevo	76	52.58 N	27.00 E
Semiahmoo Bay ⊂	224	48.58 N	122.48 W
Semiba¨ki	30	49.03 N	39.03 E
Semibratovo	80	57.18 N	39.32 E
Semibugry	80	46.11 N	48.16 E
Semichi Islands II	181a	52.42 N	174.00 E
Semides'atno.e	78	51.21 N	38.44 E
Semidi Islands II	180	56.07 N	156.44 W
Sem'gorsk	88	56.04 N	104.41 E
Semikarakorsk	80	54.54 N	78.20 E
Semikarakorsk	84	47.31 N	40.48 E
Semilej	80	53.57 N	45.21 E
Semilovo	80	55.04 N	42.10 E
Semiluki	78	51.41 N	39.02 E
Semiy	30	50.36 N	15.20 E
Semi'ara	68	38.20 N	15.52 E
Seminary	194	31.33 N	89.29 W
Seminoe Reservoir ⊜¹	200	42.00 N	106.50 W
Seminoe State Park ◆	202	42.05 N	106.55 W
Seminole, Fl., U.S.	220	27.50 N	82.47 W
Seminole, Ok., U.S.	196	35.13 N	96.40 W
Seminole, Tx., U.S.	196	32.43 N	102.38 W
Seminole ⋍⁶	192	30.46 N	84.50 W
Seminole Draw ⋁	196	32.27 N	102.20 W
Seminole Park	220	27.52 N	82.45 W
Semiskij chrebet ⋌	86	51.05 N	85.50 E
Semiozerce	86	49.52 N	110.23 E
Semizer'onyje	80	57.3 N	33.05 E
Semizer'onyj	88	53.44 N	120.25 E
Semipalatinsk	86	50.28 N	80.10 E
Semipalatinsk ⋍⁸	86	49.00 N	80.00 E
Semipolka	86	54.07 N	67.16 E
Semipolki	78	50.63 N	30.56 E
Semirara Island I	116	12.04 N	121.23 E
Semisopochnoi Island I	181a	52.00 N	179.35 E
Semitau	112	0.33 N	111.58 E
Semizbugy	86	50.10 N	74.56 E
Semizbugy, gora ⋀	86	50.10 N	74.58 E
Semjany	82	46.03 N	45.59 E
Semli Kalān	124	24.10 N	76.39 E
Semlow	54	54.09 N	12.37 E
Semmens Lake ⊜	184	55.03 N	94.11 W
Semmes	194	30.45 N	88.16 W
Semnān ⋍⁴	123	35.33 N	54.24 E
Semnān ⋍⁴	128	35.30 N	54.00 E
Semois ≃	56	49.53 N	4.45 E
Semonaicha	86	50.39 N	81.54 E
Sem'onc-Aleksandrovka	78	51.03 N	40.12 E
Sem'onovo	24	56.48 N	44.30 E
Sem'oncvskoje, Kaz.	86	51.20 N	70.46 E
Sem'onovka, Kyrg.	84	42.43 N	77.32 E
Sem'onovka, Ukr.	78	49.36 N	33.10 E
Sem'onovka, Ukr.	78	52.10 N	32.35 E
Sem'onovskoje, Ross.	82	55.03 N	37.46 E
Sem'oncvskoje, Ross.	80	58.16 N	38.21 E
Sema¨t	34	38.21 N	0.26 E
Semnānjung Tanjong ➤	112	7.02 N	116.45 E
Semple Lake ⊜	184	55.02 N	95.38 W
Sempol	115a	8.01 S	114.08 E
Sempolna	115a	8.26 S	112.42 E
Sempu, Pulau I	115a	8.26 S	112.42 E
Semuda	112	2.51 S	112.58 E
Šemulki ≃	154	1.14 N	30.28 E
Semur-en-Auxois	50	47.30 N	4.20 E
Semur, Moç.	154	18.53 S	34.38 E
Sena, Bol	248	11.32 S	67.11 W
Sena, Moç.	154	17.25 S	35.00 E
Sena — Seine ≃	32	49.26 N	0.26 E
Senador Amaral	256	22.35 S	46.11 W
Senador Canedo	255	16.42 S	49.05 W
Senador Cörtes	256	21.48 S	42.56 W
Senador Firmino	256	20.55 S	43.06 W
Senador Guiomard	248	10.14 S	67.36 W
Senador José Bento	256	22.40 S	46.15 W
Senador José Porfírio	250	2.39 S	51.55 W
Senador Pompeu	250	5.35 S	39.22 W
Senahú	236	15.24 N	89.49 W
Senai	114	1.36 N	103.39 E
Senaivka	261	48.30 N	1.37 E
Senaja	112	6.45 N	117.03 E
Senador, Md., U.S.	202	44.08 N	118.58 W
Senador, Or., U.S.	202	44.08 N	118.58 W
Senanayake Samudra ⊜¹	122	7.11 N	81.29 E
Senanga	156	16.07 S	23.16 E
Senang, Pulau I	271c	1.11 N	103.44 E
Senatobia	194	34.37 N	89.58 W
Sencelles	34	39.38 N	2.54 E
Senčha	78	50.15 N	32.40 E
Senec	60	48.14 N	17.24 E
Seneca, Il., U.S.	216	41.18 N	88.36 W
Seneca Creek ≃	284b	39.16 N	76.05 W
Seneca Falls	210	42.54 N	76.47 W

ENGLISH: Name — Page — Lat.°′ — Long.°′
DEUTSCH: Name — Seite — Breite°′ — Länge°′ E = Ost

Name	Page	Lat.	Long.
Seneca Lake ⊜	210	42.40 N	76.57 W
Seneca Mall ◆[9]	284a	42.50 N	78.47 W
Seneca State Park ♦	208	39.08 N	77.15 W
Senecaville Lake ⊜[1]	188	39.55 N	81.25 W
Seneffe	50	50.31 N	4.15 E
Senegal (Sénégal) □[1], Afr.	134	14.00 N	14.00 W
Senegal (Sénégal) □[1], Afr.	150	14.00 N	14.00 W
Sénégal ≃	150	15.48 N	16.32 W
Seneghe	71	40.05 N	8.36 E
Senekal	158	28.19 S	27.36 E
Senerchia	68	40.44 N	15.12 E
Senetosa, Capu di >	71	41.33 N	8.47 E
Sénez	62	43.55 N	6.24 E
Senežskoje, ozero ⊜	82	56.12 N	37.00 E
Senftenberg	54	51.31 N	14.00 E
Senga Hill	154	9.22 S	31.12 E
Sengbachstausee ⊜[1]	263	51.08 N	7.09 E
Şengejskij, ostrov I	24	68.27 N	51.05 E
Šengel'šij	86	48.33 N	57.28 E
Sengés	255	24.06 S	49.29 W
Senggarang	114	1.45 N	103.03 E
Sênggê ≃	120	32.28 N	79.44 E
Senghenydd	42	51.36 N	3.16 W
Sengilej	80	53.58 N	48.46 E
Sengkamang	114	0.42 N	101.55 E
Sengsengebirge ⋀	61	47.47 N	14.15 E
Senguer ≃	254	45.32 S	68.54 W
Sengwa ≃	154	17.07 S	28.05 E
Sengwarden	52	53.35 N	8.02 E
Senhāti	126	22.53 N	89.33 E
Senhor do Bonfim	250	10.27 S	40.11 W
Senica	30	48.41 N	17.22 E
Senigallia	66	43.43 N	13.13 E
Senirkent	130	38.07 N	30.33 E
Senise	68	40.09 N	16.18 E
Senj	36	44.59 N	14.54 E
Senja I	24	69.20 N	17.30 E
Senjitu	98	41.56 N	116.25 E
Senjō-san ∧	96	35.26 N	133.36 E
Senkaku-shotō II	90	25.45 N	124.00 E
Senkevičevka	78	50.32 N	25.02 E
Senkobo	154	17.38 S	25.58 E
Sen'kovo	83	49.31 N	37.43 E
Şenköy	130	36.05 N	36.05 E
Šenkursk	24	62.08 N	42.53 E
Senlac	184	52.29 N	109.41 W
Şenlikköy ◆[8]	267b	40.59 N	28.47 E
Senlis	50	49.12 N	2.35 E
Senlisse	261	48.41 N	1.59 E
Senmonorom	110	12.27 N	107.12 E
Senn, Ḍahr ou ⊥[4]	150	18.30 N	11.00 W
Sennaja	78	45.15 N	37.01 E
Sennan	96	34.22 N	135.17 E
Senne(Zenne) ≃	50	51.04 N	4.26 E
Sennecey-le-Grand	58	46.39 N	4.52 E
Senne II → Sennestadt	52	51.59 N	8.37 E
Sennen	42	50.04 N	5.42 W
Sennestadt	52	51.59 N	8.37 E
Senneterre	190	48.23 N	77.15 W
Senneville	275a	45.27 N	73.57 W
Sennevoy-le-Bas	50	47.48 N	4.17 E
Senno	76	54.49 N	29.43 E
Sennoj, Ross.	80	52.11 N	46.57 E
Sennoj, Ross.	80	50.16 N	43.37 E
Sennokura-yama ∧	94	36.49 N	138.50 E
Sennori	71	40.47 N	8.35 E
Sennwald	58	47.16 N	9.30 E
Sennybridge	42	51.57 N	3.34 W
Senoia	192	33.18 N	84.33 W
Senonches	50	48.33 N	1.02 E
Senones	58	48.24 N	6.59 E
Senorbì	71	39.32 N	9.08 E
Sénou	150	12.31 N	6.56 W
Sénouire ≃	62	45.11 N	3.34 E
Şenpazar	130	41.48 N	33.16 E
Šenqu → Orange ≃	156	28.41 S	16.28 E
Senqunyane ≃	158	30.03 S	28.10 E
Senriyama	270	34.47 N	135.30 E
Sens	50	48.12 N	3.17 E
Sense ≃	58	46.54 N	7.14 E
Sensée ≃	50	50.16 N	3.06 E
Sensée, Canal de la ≡	50	50.14 N	3.17 E
Sensuntepeque	236	13.52 N	88.38 W
Senta	38	45.56 N	20.04 E
Šentala	80	54.27 N	51.29 E
Sentani, Danau ⊜	164	2.36 S	140.34 E
Sentarum, Danau ⊜	112	0.51 N	112.06 E
Sentas	86	49.19 N	82.28 E
Sentelek	86	51.13 N	83.44 E
Şentery	154	5.22 S	25.45 E
Šentilj	61	46.41 N	15.40 E
Sentinel	196	35.09 N	99.10 W
Sentinel Butte ∧	198	46.53 N	103.50 W
Sentinel Peak ∧	182	54.54 N	121.57 W
Sentinel Range ⋀	9	78.10 S	85.30 W
Şentino ≃	66	43.24 N	12.59 E
Šentjur	36	46.13 N	15.24 E
Sentolo	115a	7.50 S	110.13 E
Sentosa I	271c	1.15 N	103.50 E
Sento Sé	250	9.51 S	41.51 W
Sentsū-zan ∧	96	35.09 N	133.11 E
Senyavin Islands II	14	6.55 N	158.00 E
Senye	152	1.34 N	9.50 E
Şenyurt	130	37.06 N	40.40 E
Senzaki-wan ⊂	96	34.24 N	131.15 E
Sen-zan ∧	96	34.21 N	134.51 E
Senzig	54	52.17 N	13.39 E
Senzu-dake ∧	270	34.57 N	135.52 E
Seo de Urgel	34	42.21 N	1.28 E
Seohāra	124	29.13 N	78.35 E
Seolag-san Kukrip Kongwŏn ♦	98	38.09 N	128.24 E
Seon	58	47.21 N	8.10 E
Seonāth ≃	122	21.44 N	82.28 E
Seoni	124	22.05 N	79.32 E
Seoni Mālwa	124	22.27 N	77.28 E
Seorīnārāyan	120	21.44 N	82.35 E
Seoul → Sŏul	98	37.33 N	126.58 E
Seoul Bridge ◆[5]	271b	37.32 N	126.56 E
Seoul National University ʊ[2]	271b	37.28 N	126.57 E
Seoul Stadium ♦	271b	37.35 N	127.02 E
Seoul Station ◆[5]	271b	37.34 N	126.58 E
Sepahat	114	1.34 N	101.53 E
Sepang	114	2.42 N	101.45 E
Sepanjang, Pulau I	112	7.10 S	115.50 E
Separation Creek ≃	200	41.59 N	107.28 W
Separation Point >	172	40.47 S	173.00 E
Sepasu	112	0.43 N	117.35 E
Sepatini ≃	248	7.36 S	65.24 W
Sépeaux	50	47.57 N	3.14 E
Sepetiba ◆[8]	256	22.58 S	43.42 W
Şepetiba, Baía de ⊂	256	23.00 S	43.48 W
Šepetovka	78	50.11 N	27.04 E
Sepi	175e	8.33 S	159.50 E
Sepik ≃	164	3.51 S	144.34 E
Sepino	66	41.24 N	14.37 E
Sep'o	98	38.39 N	127.22 E
Sępólno Krajeńskie	30	53.28 N	17.32 E
Sépone → Muang Xépôn	110	16.41 N	106.14 E
Sepopa	156	18.13 S	22.13 E
Sępopol	30	54.15 N	21.00 E
Sepoti ≃	248	6.43 S	61.38 W
Sepotuba ≃	248	15.56 S	57.39 W
Seppeltsfield	168b	34.30 S	138.54 E
Seppenrade	52	51.46 N	7.23 E
Sepphoris → Ẓippori	132	32.45 N	35.17 E
Seppois-le-Bas	58	47.33 N	7.10 E
Septeuil	261	48.54 N	1.41 E
Sept Frères, Lac des ⊜	206	46.20 N	75.10 W
Sept-Îles (Seven Islands)	186	50.12 N	66.23 W
Septvaux	50	49.34 N	3.23 E
Sepulga ≃	194	31.11 N	86.46 W
Sepúlveda	34	41.18 N	3.45 W
Sepulveda ◆[8]	280	34.13 N	118.28 W
Sepulveda Dam ◆[6]	280	34.10 N	118.29 W
Sepulveda Flood Control Basin ≚[1]	228	34.11 N	118.29 W
Seputih ≃	112	4.42 S	105.54 E
Sepyč	80	58.11 N	54.08 E
Sequals	64	46.10 N	12.50 E
Sequatchie ≃	192	35.02 N	85.38 W
Sequeros	34	40.31 N	6.01 W
Sequillo ≃	34	41.45 N	5.30 W
Sequim	224	48.04 N	123.06 W
Sequim Bay ⊂	224	48.03 N	123.02 W
Sequoia National Park ♦	204	36.30 N	118.30 W
Sera	96	34.36 N	133.03 E
Şera, Pulau I	164	7.40 S	131.05 E
Šerabad	128	37.40 N	67.01 E
Serachs	128	36.32 N	61.13 E
Serafettin Dağları ⋀	130	39.05 N	41.10 E
Şerafimovič	80	49.36 N	42.43 E
Šeragul	88	54.29 N	100.56 E
Seraidi	36	36.55 N	7.41 E
Seraing	56	50.36 N	5.29 E
Seraja ≃	82	56.15 N	38.45 E
Seram (Ceram) I	164	3.00 S	129.00 E
Seram, Laut (Ceram Sea) ⊤[2]	108	2.30 S	128.00 E
Serampore	126	22.45 N	88.21 E
Serang	115a	6.07 S	106.09 E
Serang ≃	115a	6.43 S	110.35 E
Serangoon	271c	1.22 N	103.54 E
Serangoon ≃	271c	1.24 N	103.56 E
Serangoon, Pulau I	271c	1.25 N	103.56 E
Serangoon Harbour ⊂	271c	1.23 N	103.57 E
Serapo	66	41.13 N	13.34 E
Serasan, Pulau I	112	2.30 N	109.03 E
Serasan, Selat u	112	2.20 N	109.00 E
Seravalle Sesia	62	45.41 N	8.19 E
Seravezza	64	43.59 N	10.13 E
Seraya, Pulau I	271c	1.16 N	103.43 E
Serayevo → Sarajevo	38	43.52 N	18.25 E
Şerayu ≃	115a	7.41 S	109.06 E
Šerbakul'	86	54.38 N	72.24 E
Serbeulangit, Pegunungan ⋀	114	3.45 N	97.50 E
Serbia → Srbija □[3]	38	44.00 N	21.00 E
Serchio ≃	64	43.47 N	10.16 E
Serdce-Kamen', mys >	180	66.57 N	171.40 W
Serdež	80	57.17 N	48.17 E
Serditoje	83	48.02 N	38.24 E
Serdo	144	11.58 N	41.18 E
Serdoba ≃	80	52.34 N	44.01 E
Serdobsk	80	52.28 N	44.13 E
Séré'ama, Mont ∧	175f	13.47 S	167.29 E
Serebr'anka, Ross.	86	57.13 N	70.42 E
Serebr'anka, Ross.	265b	55.45 N	37.55 E
Serebr'anka, Ukr.	83	48.55 N	38.08 E
Serebr'anka ≃	265b	55.47 N	37.42 E
Serebr'ansk	86	49.43 N	83.20 E
Serebr'anyj Bor ◆[8]	265b	55.48 N	37.25 E
Serebr'anyje Prudy	82	54.28 N	38.44 E
Serebrovo	88	55.24 N	97.52 E
Serechoviči	78	51.25 N	24.40 E
Sered'	30	48.17 N	17.44 E
Sereda, Ross.	76	55.54 N	35.31 E
Şereda, Ross.	80	58.00 N	40.27 E
Šeredar' ≃	82	55.56 N	39.04 E
Seredejskij	76	54.03 N	35.14 E
Seredīči	76	53.35 N	35.51 E
Seredina-Buda	78	52.11 N	34.01 E
Serednikovo, Ross.	80	55.15 N	39.40 E
Serednikovo, Ross.	265b	55.56 N	37.14 E
Seredn'ovo	265b	55.35 N	37.18 E
Seredžius	76	55.05 N	23.25 E
Şereflikoçhisar	130	38.56 N	33.33 E
Šeregeš	86	52.57 N	88.02 E
Seregno	62	45.39 N	9.12 E
Serein ≃	50	47.55 N	3.31 E
Şeremban	114	2.43 N	101.56 E
Šeremetjevka	80	55.23 N	51.32 E
Šeremetjevo, Aeroport ⊠	82	55.59 N	37.24 E
Šeremetjevskij	82	55.59 N	37.30 E
Seremuk ≃	164	1.36 S	131.46 E
Serena	216	41.29 N	88.44 W
Seren del Grappa	64	45.59 N	11.51 E
Serengeti National Park ♦	154	2.20 S	34.50 E
Serengeti Plain ≚	154	2.50 S	35.00 E
Serengka	112	1.40 S	110.40 E
Serenje	154	13.15 S	30.14 E
Şereno	256	21.19 S	42.39 W
Šereševo	76	52.33 N	24.13 E
Seret ≃	78	48.38 N	25.52 E
Serfaus	58	47.02 N	10.36 E
Ser'ga	86	57.46 N	56.52 E
Sergač	80	55.32 N	45.28 E
Sergeant	214	41.38 N	78.45 W
Sergeant Bluff	198	42.24 N	96.21 W
Sergeja Kirova, ostrova II	74	77.12 N	89.30 E
Sergejeviči	76	53.30 N	27.45 E
Sergejevka, Kaz.	86	53.51 N	67.25 E
Sergejevka, Kaz.	86	51.39 N	68.13 E
Sergejevka, Ross.	89	44.22 N	131.39 E
Sergejevka, Ross.	89	43.21 N	133.22 E
Sergejevka, Ukr.	83	48.40 N	37.22 E
Sergejevo	86	57.18 N	86.02 E
Sergen	130	41.42 N	27.42 E
Sergijevka	78	51.46 N	41.05 E
Sergijev Posad (Zagorsk)	82	56.18 N	38.08 E
Sergijevskaja, Ross.	76	60.16 N	43.54 E
Sergijevskaja, Ross.	80	50.16 N	43.47 E
Sergijevskij	80	51.56 N	51.54 E
Sergili	85	41.13 N	69.14 E
Sergines	50	48.20 N	3.15 E
Serginskij	72	62.30 N	65.38 E
Sergipe □[3]	250	10.30 S	37.30 W
Sergokala	84	42.27 N	47.40 E
Sergozero, ozero ⊜	24	66.47 N	36.42 E
Seria	112	4.39 N	114.23 E
Serian	112	1.10 N	110.34 E
Seriana, Valle V	64	45.55 N	9.55 E
Seriate	62	45.41 N	9.43 E
Seribu, Kepulauan II	115a	5.36 S	106.33 E
Seribudolok, Indon.	114	2.56 N	98.37 E
Seribudolok, Indon.	114	2.51 N	99.04 E
Sericho	154	1.05 N	39.05 E
Seridó ≃	250	6.12 S	37.10 W
Sérifontaine	50	49.21 N	1.46 E
Sérifos	38	37.09 N	24.31 E
Sérifos I	38	37.11 N	24.31 E
Sérignan-du-Comtat	62	44.11 N	4.51 E
Sérigny ≃	176	56.47 N	66.00 W
Serik	130	36.55 N	31.06 E
Seringat, Pulau I	271c	1.14 N	103.51 E
Serino	68	40.51 N	14.52 E
Serinyol	130	36.24 N	36.11 E
Serio ≃	62	45.16 N	9.45 E
Seritinga	256	21.54 S	44.30 W
Serjol	24	60.02 N	48.58 E
Serkhe, Cerro ∧	248	17.22 S	69.22 W
Serkout, Djebel ∧	148	23.30 N	6.48 E
Serkovo	82	54.28 N	38.46 E
Şerles ∧	64	47.08 N	11.23 E
Šerlovaja Gora	88	50.34 N	116.15 E
Serm ◆[8]	263	51.21 N	6.42 E
Sermaise	261	48.32 N	2.05 E
Sermaises	50	48.18 N	2.12 E
Sermaize-les-Bains	56	48.47 N	4.55 E
Serman	80	53.34 N	46.22 E
Sermata, Pulau I	164	8.13 S	128.55 E
Sermide	64	45.00 N	11.18 E
Sermilik ⊂[2]	176	65.37 N	38.03 W
Sermizelles	50	47.32 N	3.48 E
Şermoneta	66	41.33 N	12.59 E
Šerna ≃	82	55.51 N	38.34 E
Sernambetiba, Pontal de >	287a	23.02 S	43.27 W
Sernambitiba	287a	22.41 S	42.59 W
Serniki	78	51.49 N	26.14 E
Sernovodsk	80	53.56 N	51.17 E
Sernur	80	56.56 N	49.09 E
Sernyy Zavod	128	39.59 N	58.50 E
Séro	150	14.48 N	11.04 W
Serodino	252	32.37 S	60.57 W
Ser'odka	76	58.10 N	28.12 E
Seroglazka	80	47.01 N	47.29 E
Ser'ogovo	24	62.20 N	50.36 E
Serooskerke	52	51.42 N	3.50 E
Seropédica	256	22.44 S	43.43 W
Serov	86	59.29 N	60.31 E
Serovo	85	40.27 N	71.12 E
Serowe	156	22.25 S	26.44 E
Ser'oža ≃	80	55.34 N	42.29 E
Serpa	34	37.56 N	7.36 W
Serpeddi, Punta ∧	71	39.22 N	9.18 E
Serpejsk	76	54.20 N	34.59 E
Serpent, Rivière au ≃	186	49.33 N	71.14 W
Serpentine	168a	32.22 S	115.59 E
Serpentine ≃, Austl.	168a	32.33 S	115.46 E
Serpentine ≃, B.C., Can.	224	49.05 N	122.50 W
Serpentine Lakes ⊜	162	28.32 S	129.09 E
Serpentine National Park ♦	168a	32.22 S	116.01 E
Serpentine Reservoir ⊜[1]	168a	32.25 S	116.08 E
Serpent Mound State Memorial ⊥	218	39.02 N	83.26 W
Serpents Mouth u	241r	10.00 N	62.00 W
Serpnevoje	78	46.18 N	29.02 E
Serpuchov	82	54.55 N	37.25 E
Serpukhov → Serpuchov	82	54.55 N	37.25 E
Serqo → Sark I	43b	49.26 N	2.21 W
Serra	255	20.07 S	40.18 W
Serra, Monte ∧	66	43.46 N	10.33 E
Serra Branca	250	7.29 S	36.40 W
Serracapriola	68	41.48 N	15.09 E
Serrada	64	45.53 N	11.09 E
Serra da Canastra, Parque Nacional da ♦	255	20.10 S	46.40 W
Serra da Capivara, Parque Nacionl da ♦	250	8.40 S	42.15 W
Serra d'Aiello	68	39.05 N	16.08 E
Serra de'Conti	66	43.33 N	13.02 E
Serra di Corvo, Lago di ⊜[1]	68	40.51 N	16.14 E
Serradifalco	70	37.27 N	13.53 E
Serra do Navio	250	0.59 N	52.03 W
Serra dos Aimorés	255	17.46 S	40.15 W
Serra do Salitre	255	19.06 S	46.41 W
Serra dos Órgãos, Parque Nacional da ♦	256	22.26 S	43.02 W
Sérrai	38	41.05 N	23.32 E
Serramanna	71	39.25 N	8.55 E
Serramazzoni	64	44.25 N	10.47 E
Serramonte Center ◆[9]	282	37.40 N	122.28 W
Serrana	255	21.14 S	47.36 W
Serrana, Cayo de ✦[4]	236	14.23 N	80.12 W
Serra Negra	256	22.36 S	46.42 W
Serra Negra do Norte	250	6.40 S	37.24 W
Serrânia	255	21.33 S	46.03 W
Serranilla, Cayo de ✦[4]	236	15.50 N	79.50 W
Serranópolis	255	18.16 S	52.00 W
Serranos	256	21.51 S	44.30 W
Serrara	68	40.42 N	13.54 E
Serra San Bruno	68	38.35 N	16.20 E
Serra San Quirico	66	43.27 N	13.01 E
Serrastretta	68	39.01 N	16.25 E
Serrat, Cap >	36	37.14 N	9.13 E
Serra Talhada	250	7.59 S	38.18 W
Serravalle, It.	66	42.47 N	13.01 E
Serravalle, S. Mar.	66	43.57 N	12.30 E
Serravalle all'Adige	64	45.49 N	11.01 E
Serravalle Scrivia	62	44.43 N	8.51 E
Serre	68	40.35 N	15.11 E
Serre ≃	50	49.41 N	3.23 E
Serrenti	71	39.29 N	8.58 E
Serre-Ponçon, Barrage de ◆[6]	62	44.33 N	6.30 E
Serre-Ponçon, Lac de ⊜[1]	62	44.30 N	6.17 E
Serres	62	44.26 N	5.43 E
Serrezuela	252	30.38 S	65.23 W
Serri	71	39.42 N	9.08 E
Serrières	62	45.19 N	4.45 E
Serrinha	250	11.39 S	39.00 W
Serriola, Bocca)(	66	43.31 N	12.21 E
Serris	261	48.51 N	2.47 E
Serrita	250	7.56 S	39.19 W
Serro	255	18.37 S	43.23 W
Şersale	68	39.01 N	16.44 E
Šerstin	76	52.39 N	31.03 E
Šerstobitovo	86	57.16 N	78.52 E
Sertã	34	39.48 N	8.06 W
Sertânia	250	8.05 S	37.16 W
Sertãozinho	256	22.19 S	46.03 W
Sertig-Dörfli	58	46.44 N	9.51 E
Sertung, Pulau I	115a	6.06 S	105.24 E
Seru	144	7.50 N	40.28 E
Şerua, Pulau I	164	6.18 S	130.01 E
Šerubaj-Nura ≃	86	49.54 N	72.31 E
Serui	164	1.53 S	136.14 E
Seruini ≃	248	7.42 S	66.42 W
Serule	156	21.58 S	27.20 E
Serutu, Pulau I	112	1.42 S	108.45 E
Seruwai	114	4.21 N	98.10 E
Sérvia	38	40.11 N	22.00 E
Servi Burnu >	130	41.40 N	28.06 E
Servigliano	66	43.05 N	13.29 E
Servon	261	48.43 N	2.35 E
Servoz	58	45.56 N	6.46 E
Serwaru	112	8.10 S	127.42 E
Sêrxü	102	33.04 N	97.45 E
Seryševo	89	51.08 N	128.20 E
Şes, Muntele ⋀	38	47.05 N	22.30 E
Šešan	180	66.46 N	171.26 W
Sesayap ≃	112	3.36 N	117.15 E
Sesayap Lama	112	3.36 N	117.03 E
Seščа	76	53.45 N	33.23 E
Sese Islands II	154	0.20 S	32.20 E
Seseke ≃	263	51.37 N	7.32 E
Sesfontein	156	19.07 S	13.39 E
Sesheke	152	17.28 S	24.18 E
Seshu	105	39.33 N	115.37 E
Sesia ≃	62	45.05 N	8.37 E
Sesia, Val V	62	45.47 N	8.05 E
Sesibu	112	4.02 N	116.33 E
Sesimbra	34	38.26 N	9.06 W
Seskar, ostrov I	76	60.02 N	28.23 E
Şeskarö	26	65.44 N	23.44 E
Šešma ≃	80	55.27 N	51.05 E
Sesmarias ≃	256	22.28 S	44.27 W
Sesoko-jima I	174m	26.38 N	127.52 E
Sespe	228	34.23 N	118.58 W
Sespe Creek ≃	204	34.23 N	118.57 W
Sessa	152	13.56 S	20.38 E
Sessa Aurunca	68	41.14 N	13.56 E
Ses Salines, Cap de >	34	39.16 N	3.03 E
Séssé	146	11.30 N	17.34 E
Sessenheim	56	48.48 N	7.59 E
Şesta Godano	62	44.17 N	9.40 E
Šestakovka	78	48.32 N	31.58 E
Šestakovo, Ross.	82	56.21 N	35.49 E
Šestakovo, Ross.	88	56.29 N	103.59 E
Sestao	34	43.18 N	3.00 W
Šestern'a	78	47.33 N	33.16 E
Sestino	66	43.42 N	12.18 E
Sesto (Sexten)	64	46.42 N	12.21 E
Sesto Calende	62	45.44 N	8.38 E
Sesto Fiorentino	66	43.50 N	11.12 E
Sestola	64	44.14 N	10.46 E
Sesto San Giovanni	62	45.32 N	9.14 E
Sestra ≃, Ross.	80	52.11 N	49.36 E
Sestra ≃, Ross.	82	56.43 N	37.14 E
Sestriere	62	44.57 N	6.53 E
Sestri Levante	62	44.16 N	9.24 E
Sestri Ponente	62	44.25 N	8.51 E
Sestroreck	76	60.06 N	29.58 E
Sestroreckij Razliv, ozero ⊜	265a	60.04 N	30.00 E
Şestu	71	39.18 N	9.05 E
Šešupe ≃	76	55.03 N	22.12 E
Šešurga	80	57.29 N	47.35 E
Šešuvis ≃	76	55.13 N	22.15 E
Šėta, Liet.	76	55.17 N	24.15 E
Seta, Nihon	270	34.58 N	135.55 E
Seta ≃	270	34.56 N	135.54 E
Setagaya ◆[8]	268	35.39 N	139.40 E
Setail ≃	115a	8.30 S	114.21 E
Setaka	96	33.09 N	130.28 E
Setana	92a	42.26 N	139.51 E
Setapak	114	3.11 N	101.42 E
Setauket	210	40.57 N	73.07 W
Sète	62	43.24 N	3.41 E
Sete Barras	252	24.23 S	47.55 W
Sete Cidades, Parque Nacional de ♦	250	3.50 S	41.40 W
Sete de Setembro ≃	255	12.56 S	52.51 W
Sete Lagoas	255	19.27 S	44.14 W
Sete Pontes	256	22.51 S	43.05 W
Sete Quedas, Cachoeira das ⊾	250	9.27 S	56.41 W
Sete Quedas, Parque Nacional de ♦	252	24.02 S	54.12 W
Sete Rios ◆[8]	266c	38.45 N	9.10 W
Setesdal V	26	59.25 N	7.25 E
Seth Ward	196	34.13 N	101.42 W
Setī □[8]	124	29.15 N	81.00 E
Setī ≃	124	28.58 N	81.06 E
Setlagodi	158	26.16 S	25.06 E
Set Net, Punta >	236	12.28 N	83.30 W
Seto, Nihon	94	35.14 N	137.06 E
Seto, Nihon	96	33.27 N	132.15 E
Seto, Nihon	96	34.44 N	134.02 E
Setoda	96	34.18 N	133.05 E
Seto-naikai ⊤[2]	96	34.20 N	133.30 E
Seto-naikai-kokuritsu-kōen ♦	96	34.15 N	133.28 E
Seton Hall University ʊ[2]	276	40.45 N	74.15 W
Seton Lake ⊜	182	50.45 N	122.05 W
Seton Portage	182	50.43 N	122.18 W
Seto-saki >	174m	26.51 N	128.18 E
Setouchi	93b	28.10 N	129.15 E
Seto-zaki >	96	33.40 N	135.20 E
Setraki	78	49.23 N	40.49 E
Setta ≃	64	44.22 N	11.14 E
Settat	148	33.04 N	7.37 W
Settat □[4]	148	33.05 N	7.30 W
Setté Cama	152	2.32 S	9.45 E
Settecamini ◆[8]	267a	41.56 N	12.37 E
Sette-Daban, chrebet ⋀	74	62.00 N	138.00 E
Settee Lake ⊜	184	57.03 N	96.55 W
Settepani, Monte ∧	62	44.15 N	8.12 E
Settimo Milanese	266b	45.29 N	9.03 E
Settimo San Pietro	71	39.17 N	9.11 E
Settimo Torinese	62	45.09 N	7.46 E
Settimo Vittone	62	45.33 N	7.50 E
Settingiano	68	38.55 N	16.31 E
Setting Lake ⊜	184	55.00 N	98.38 W
Settle	44	54.04 N	2.16 W
Settlement Point >	169	38.25 S	145.25 E
Settlers	156	25.02 S	28.30 E
Settlers Cabin Regional Park ♦	279b	40.26 N	80.10 W
Settons, Lac des ⊜	50	47.11 N	4.04 E
Settsu	96	34.46 N	135.33 E
Setúbal	34	38.32 N	8.54 W
Setúbal □[5]	266c	38.37 N	9.00 W
Setúbal, Baía de ⊂	34	38.27 N	8.53 W
Setun' ≃	265b	55.44 N	37.33 E
Seui	71	39.50 N	9.19 E
Seúl → Sŏul	98	37.33 N	126.58 E
Seul, Lac ⊜	184	50.20 N	92.30 W
Seul Choix Point >	190	45.56 N	85.52 W
Seulimeum	114	5.22 N	95.35 E
Seulo	71	39.52 N	9.14 E
Seumanyam	114	3.45 N	96.38 E
Seurre	58	47.00 N	5.09 E
Seuzach	58	47.32 N	8.44 E
Sev ≃	76	52.24 N	34.10 E
Sevan	84	40.34 N	44.57 E
Sevan, ozero ⊜	84	40.20 N	45.20 E
Sévaré	150	14.32 N	4.06 W
Sevastopol'	78	44.36 N	33.32 E
Şevastopol'skij	86	53.08 N	65.44 E
Ševčenkovo, Ukr.	78	49.41 N	37.10 E
Ševčenkovo, Ukr.	78	45.33 N	29.20 E
Ševčenkovo, Ukr.	78	51.40 N	33.39 E
Ševčenkovo Vtoroje	78	47.29 N	36.08 E
Sevelen, Dtsch.	52	51.29 N	6.25 E
Şevelen, Schw.	58	47.07 N	9.29 E
Ševelevskaja	24	60.52 N	44.12 E
Ševelevskij Majdan	80	54.25 N	42.15 E
Seven ≃	44	54.11 N	0.52 W
Seven Caves ⊥[5]	218	39.13 N	83.23 W
Seven Creeks ≃	169	36.43 S	145.34 E
Seven Harbors	216	42.40 N	83.34 W
Sevenhill	168b	33.53 S	138.38 E
Seven Hills, Austl.	274a	33.46 S	150.57 E
Seven Hills, Oh., U.S.	214	41.23 N	81.40 W
Seven Islands → Sept-Îles	186	50.12 N	66.23 W
Seven Kings ◆[8]	260	51.34 N	0.05 E
Seven Mile	218	39.28 N	84.33 W
Seven Mile Beach National Park ♦	170	34.49 S	150.46 E
Sevenmile Bridge ◆[5]	220	24.41 N	81.11 W
Sevenmile Creek ≃	218	39.28 N	84.33 W
Sevenoaks, Eng., U.K.	42	51.16 N	0.12 E
Seven Oaks, Tx., U.S.	222	30.51 N	94.51 W
Sevenoaks □[8]	260	51.18 N	0.10 E
Sevenoaks Weald	260	51.14 N	0.12 E
Seven Palm Lake ⊜	220	25.12 N	80.44 W
Seven Persons	184	49.52 N	110.54 W
Seven Sisters	42	51.46 N	3.43 W
Seven Sisters Peaks ⋀	182	54.58 N	128.10 W
Seventy Mile House	182	51.18 N	121.24 W
Seven Valleys	208	39.51 N	76.46 W
Sévérac-le-Château	32	44.19 N	3.04 E
Severance Center ◆[9]	279a	41.31 N	81.33 W
Sever'anskij les ♦	83	48.55 N	38.00 E
Severka ≃	82	55.10 N	38.45 E
Severn, S. Afr.	158	26.36 S	22.52 E
Severn, Md., U.S.	208	39.08 N	76.41 W
Severn, N.C., U.S.	208	36.30 N	77.11 W
Severn, Va., U.S.	208	37.17 N	76.24 W
Severn ≃, On., Can.	176	56.02 N	87.36 W
Severn ≃, On., Can.	212	44.52 N	79.41 W
Severn ≃, U.K.	42	51.35 N	2.40 W
Severn, Mouth of the ≃	42	51.25 N	3.00 W
Severnaja Dvina ≃	24	64.32 N	40.30 E
Severnaja Osetija □[3]	84	43.00 N	44.15 E
Severnaja Sos'va ≃	72	64.10 N	65.28 E
Severnaja Zeml'a II	74	79.30 N	98.00 E
Severna Park	208	39.04 N	76.32 W
Severn Bridge ◆[5]	42	51.39 N	2.42 W
Severn Lake ⊜	184	53.54 N	90.48 W
Severnoje, Ross.	80	58.02 N	41.26 E
Severnoje, Ross.	80	54.06 N	52.32 E
Severnoje, Ross.	84	44.49 N	42.51 E
Severnoje, Ross.	86	56.21 N	78.23 E
Severnoje, Ukr.	83	48.04 N	38.44 E
Severn River ⊂, Md., U.S.	208	38.58 N	76.28 W
Severn River ⊂, Va., U.S.	208	37.19 N	76.25 W
Severn Tunnel ◆[5]	42	51.35 N	2.44 W
Severnyj, Ross.	24	67.38 N	64.06 E
Severnyj, Ross.	265b	55.56 N	37.33 E
Severnyje uvaly ⋀[2]	24	59.30 N	49.00 E
Severnyj Kommunar	80	58.23 N	54.02 E
Severnyj Prijut	84	43.16 N	41.51 E
Severnyj Ural ⋀	24	63.00 N	59.00 E
Severo-Bajkal'skoje nagorje ⋀[1]	88	57.00 N	111.00 E
Severočeský Kraj □[4]	30	50.30 N	14.00 E
Severodoneck	83	48.58 N	38.27 E
Severodvinsk	24	64.34 N	39.50 E
Severo-Dvinskij kanal ≡	76	59.45 N	38.22 E
Severo-Jenisejskij	74	60.22 N	93.01 E
Severo-Kazachstan □[8]	86	54.30 N	69.00 E
Severo-Kuril'sk	74	50.40 N	156.08 E
Severomoravský Kraj □[4]	30	49.45 N	17.50 E
Severomorsk	24	69.05 N	33.24 E
Severo-Mujskij chrebet ⋀	88	56.30 N	114.00 E
Severo-Sibirskaja nizmennost' ≚	74	73.00 N	100.00 E
Severoural'sk	86	60.09 N	59.57 E
Severo-Zadonsk	82	54.02 N	38.24 E
Severskaja	78	44.51 N	38.42 E
Severskij Donec ≃	72	47.35 N	40.54 E
Severskij Donec-Donbass, kanal ≡	83	48.55 N	37.45 E
Severucha	86	58.28 N	63.25 E
Severy	198	37.37 N	96.13 W
Seveso	62	45.39 N	9.09 E
Şeveso ≃	266b	45.30 N	9.12 E
Ševětin	61	49.06 N	14.35 E
Sevettijärvi	24	69.26 N	28.38 E
Sevier ≃	200	39.04 N	113.06 W
Sevier, East Fork ≃	200	38.14 N	112.12 W
Sevier Bridge Reservoir ⊜[1]	200	39.21 N	111.57 W
Sevier Desert ◆[2]	200	39.25 N	112.50 W
Sevier Lake ⊜	200	38.55 N	113.09 W
Sevierville	192	35.52 N	83.33 W
Sevilla, Col.	246	4.16 N	75.57 W
Sevilla (Seville), Esp.	34	37.23 N	5.59 W
Sevilla □[4]	34	37.25 N	5.35 W
Sevilla, Isla I	236	8.14 N	82.24 W
Seville → Sevilla, Esp.	34	37.23 N	5.59 W
Seville, Fl., U.S.	192	29.19 N	81.29 W
Seville, Oh., U.S.	214	41.00 N	81.51 W
Sevir	130	39.12 N	38.13 E
Şevketiye	130	40.05 N	27.51 E
Ševli ≃	89	54.08 N	133.04 E
Sevlievo	38	43.01 N	25.06 E
Sevran	50	48.56 N	2.32 E
Sevrej	102	43.35 N	102.12 E
Sèvres	50	48.49 N	2.12 E
Sévrier	58	45.52 N	6.08 E
Şevsk	78	52.09 N	34.30 E
Ševykan	88	54.20 N	106.49 E
Sewa ≃	150	7.18 N	12.08 W
Sewanee	194	35.04 N	85.55 W
Sewāni	123	28.55 N	75.37 E
Seward, Ak., U.S.	180	60.06 N	149.26 W
Seward, Ne., U.S.	198	40.54 N	97.05 W
Seward, N.Y., U.S.	210	42.43 N	74.37 W
Seward, Pa., U.S.	214	40.25 N	79.01 W
Seward Glacier ⊓	180	60.22 N	140.15 W
Seward Peninsula >[1]	180	65.00 N	164.00 W
Sewaren	276	40.33 N	74.15 W
Sewekow	54	53.15 N	12.39 E
Sewell, Chile	252	34.05 S	70.23 W
Sewell, N.J., U.S.	208	39.45 N	75.08 W
Sewen	58	47.48 N	6.54 E
Sewernaja-Semlja → Severnaja Zeml'a II	74	79.30 N	98.00 E
Seweweekspoort	158	33.22 S	21.25 E
Sewickley	214	40.32 N	80.11 W
Sewickley Creek ≃	279b	40.14 N	79.47 W
Sewickley Heights	279b	40.33 N	80.09 W
Sewickley Hills	279b	40.34 N	80.08 W
Sewri ◆[8]	272c	19.00 N	72.51 E
Sexcello	152	3.58 S	11.38 E
Sexsmith	182	55.21 N	118.47 W
Sexten → Sesto	64	46.42 N	12.21 E
Sextin ≃	232	25.44 N	105.14 W
Sexton	218	39.42 N	85.27 W
Sexton Island I	276	40.39 N	73.14 W
Seya ◆[8], Nihon	268	35.27 N	139.30 E
Seya ◆[8], Nihon	268	35.29 N	139.29 E
Seybaplaya	232	19.39 N	90.40 W
Seybothenreuth	60	49.54 N	11.43 E
Seybouse, Oued ≃	148	36.54 N	7.47 E
Seychellen → Seychelles □[1]	138	4.35 S	55.40 E
Seychelles □[1]	138	4.35 S	55.40 E
Seychelles Bank ✦[4]	12	4.45 S	55.30 E
Seyches	32	44.33 N	0.18 E
Seyda	54	51.53 N	12.53 E
Seydim	130	40.33 N	34.45 E
Seydişehir	130	37.25 N	31.51 E
Seyðisfjörður	24a	65.16 N	14.00 W
Seyfe Gölü ⊜	130	39.13 N	34.23 E
Seyhan ≃	130	36.43 N	34.53 E
Seyhan Barajı ⊜[1]	130	37.05 N	35.15 E
Seyitgazi	130	39.27 N	30.43 E
Seylac	144	11.21 N	43.29 E
Seymour, Austl.	169	37.02 S	145.08 E
Seymour, Ciskei	158	32.33 S	26.46 E
Seymour, Ct., U.S.	207	41.23 N	73.04 W
Seymour, In., U.S.	218	38.57 N	85.53 W
Seymour, Ia., U.S.	190	40.40 N	93.07 W
Seymour, Mo., U.S.	194	37.08 N	92.46 W
Seymour, Tx., U.S.	196	33.35 N	99.15 W
Seymour, Wi., U.S.	190	44.30 N	88.19 W
Seymour ≃	182	51.05 N	126.50 W
Seymour Inlet ⊂	182	51.03 N	127.10 W
Seymour Johnson Air Force Base ■	192	35.21 N	77.58 W
Seymour Range ⋀	224	48.40 N	124.00 W
Seymourville	194	30.27 N	91.29 W
Seyne	62	44.21 N	6.21 E
Seynod	58	45.53 N	6.05 E
Seyring	264b	48.20 N	16.29 E
Seyssel	58	45.57 N	5.49 E
Şeytan ≃	267b	41.06 N	28.59 E
Sežana	36	45.42 N	13.52 E
Sézanne	50	48.43 N	3.43 E
Şezela	158	30.24 S	30.42 E
Sežim	24	62.07 N	58.21 E
Sezimovo Ústí	30	49.23 N	14.42 E
Sezze	66	41.30 N	13.03 E
Sfax	148	34.44 N	10.46 E
Sfax □[8]	148	34.50 N	10.20 E
Sferracavallo ◆[8]	70	38.12 N	13.17 E
Sfîntu-Gheorghe	38	45.52 N	25.47 E
Sfîntu Gheorghe, Braţul ≃[1]	38	44.53 N	29.36 E
Sfîntu Gheorghe, Ostrovul I	38	45.07 N	29.22 E
Sfizef	148	35.14 N	0.15 W
Sforzesco, Castello ⊥	266b	45.28 N	9.11 E
's-Gravendeel	52	51.46 N	4.37 E
's-Gravenhage (The Hague)	52	52.06 N	4.18 E
's-Gravenzande	52	52.00 N	4.10 E
Sgritheall, Beinn ∧	46	57.08 N	5.35 W
Sgurgola	66	41.40 N	13.09 E
Sha ≃, Zhg.	98	37.31 N	117.50 E
Sha ≃, Zhg.	100	33.39 N	114.38 E
Sha ≃, Zhg.	100	26.35 N	118.02 E
Sha ≃, Zhg.	104	41.21 N	123.07 E
Sha'alav, Har ∧	132	30.04 N	35.06 E
Sha'alvim	132	31.52 N	34.59 E
Shaanxi (Shensi) □[4]	102	35.00 N	109.00 E
Sha'ar HaGolan	132	32.41 N	35.36 E
Sha'ar Menashe	132	32.27 N	35.01 E
Shab'ā	132	33.21 N	35.45 E
Shaba □[4]	154	8.00 S	27.00 E
Shābah	142	31.11 N	30.46 E
Shabakunk Creek ≃	285	40.15 N	74.43 W
Shabās al-Milḥ	142	31.12 N	30.39 E
Shabās ash-Shuhadā'	142	31.05 N	30.45 E
Shabās 'Umayr	142	31.06 N	30.48 E
Shabbona	216	41.46 N	88.52 W
Shabeellaha Dhexe □[4]	144	3.00 N	46.00 E
Shabeellaha Hoose □[4]	144	1.30 N	44.15 E
Shabeelle (Shebele) ≃	144	0.12 S	42.45 E
Shabestar	128	38.11 N	45.42 E
Shabomeka Lake ⊜	212	44.54 N	77.09 W
Shabotik ≃	190	48.50 N	85.34 W
Shabqadar	123	34.13 N	71.34 E
Shabrāmant	142	29.56 N	31.12 E
Shabshīr al-Ḥiṣṣah	142	30.52 N	31.04 E
Shabunda	154	2.42 S	27.20 E
Shabwah	144	15.22 N	47.01 E
Shache (Yarkand)	120	38.25 N	77.16 E
Shacheng	105	40.25 N	115.31 E
Shacheng Gang ⊂	100	27.10 N	120.24 E
Shackan Indian Reserve ◆[4]	182	50.17 N	121.12 W
Shackleton Ice Shelf ⊓	9	66.00 S	100.00 E
Shackleton Range ⋀	9	80.40 S	26.00 W
Shādegān	128	30.40 N	48.38 E
Shade Gap	214	40.11 N	77.52 W
Shadehill Reservoir ⊜[1]	198	45.45 N	102.15 W
Shade Mountain ∧	208	40.34 N	77.30 W
Shades Glen	210	41.11 N	75.42 W
Shadi	100	26.08 N	114.49 E
Shadian	98	35.30 N	114.26 E
Shading	102	31.20 N	94.40 E
Shadow Lake ⊜, On., Can.	212	44.43 N	78.48 W
Shadow Lake ⊜, Ma., U.S.	283	42.50 N	71.14 W
Shadow Lake ⊜, N.J., U.S.	276	40.21 N	74.06 W
Shado-Wood Village	214	40.35 N	79.12 W
Shadrinsk → Šadrinsk	86	56.05 N	63.38 E
Shadui	102	31.30 N	100.10 E
Shady Cove	202	42.04 N	122.36 W
Shady Grove, Fl., U.S.	192	30.17 N	83.37 W
Shady Grove, Tx., U.S.	222	32.48 N	97.01 W
Shady Hills	216	40.36 N	85.41 W
Shady Shores	222	33.10 N	97.02 W
Shadyside	188	39.58 N	80.45 W
Sha'f	132	32.38 N	36.51 E
Shafer, Lake ⊜	216	40.47 N	86.46 W
Shafer Butte ∧	202	43.47 N	116.05 W
Shafir	132	31.42 N	34.44 E
Shaft	128	37.12 N	49.24 E
Shafter	226	35.30 N	119.16 W
Shaftesbury	42	51.01 N	2.12 W
Shafton	279b	40.20 N	79.42 W
Shaftsburg	216	42.48 N	84.18 W
Shaftsbury	210	43.00 N	73.11 W
Shafu	100	22.25 N	113.01 E
Shag ≃	172	45.29 S	170.49 E
Shagamu	150	6.51 N	3.39 E
Shageluk	180	62.36 N	159.32 W
Shag Rocks II[1]	244	53.33 S	42.02 W
Shaguotun	104	41.10 N	120.38 E
Shāhābād, India	122	17.08 N	76.56 E
Shāhābād, India	123	30.10 N	76.53 E
Shāhābād, India	124	27.39 N	79.57 E
Shāhābād, India	272c	19.01 N	73.02 E
Shāhābād, Īrān	128	37.32 N	56.54 E
Shāhābād, Īrān	267d	35.47 N	51.31 E
Shāhāda	120	21.28 N	74.18 E
Shah Alam	114	3.04 N	101.33 E
Shahbā'	132	32.51 N	36.37 E
Shāhbandar	120	24.10 N	67.54 E
Shāhbāz Kalāt	128	26.42 N	63.58 E
Shāhbāzpur u	124	22.05 N	90.50 E
Shahdād, Namakzār-e ≚	128	30.30 N	58.30 E
Shāhdādkot	120	27.51 N	67.54 E
Shāhdādpur	120	25.56 N	68.37 E
Shāhdara, India	272a	28.30 N	77.25 E
Shāhdara, Pāk.	123	31.38 N	74.18 E
Shāhdara ◆[8]	272a	28.40 N	77.18 E
Shahdol	124	23.20 N	81.21 E
Shahe, Zhg.	98	36.56 N	114.30 E
Shahe, Zhg.	98	34.44 N	118.58 E
Shahe, Zhg.	98	37.01 N	119.43 E
Shahe, Zhg.	102	22.06 N	109.43 E
Shahedian	100	33.01 N	113.44 E
Shaheji	100	32.26 N	118.14 E
Shahepu	104	41.08 N	121.01 E
Shaheyi	98	39.53 N	118.31 E
Shaheying	104	40.50 N	120.46 E
Shahezhan	98	35.49 N	116.23 E
Shahezhen	105	40.08 N	116.15 E
Shahezi	89	46.05 N	129.20 E
Shāhganj	124	26.03 N	82.41 E
Shāhgarh, India	120	27.07 N	69.54 E
Shāhgarh, India	124	24.19 N	79.08 E
Shahḥāt	146	32.49 N	21.52 E
Shāhī Kowt	123	34.16 N	70.34 E
Shāhjahānpur	124	27.53 N	79.55 E
Shāh Jūy	120	32.31 N	67.25 E
Shāh Kot	123	31.34 N	73.29 E
Shāh Kūh ∧	128	31.37 N	59.16 E
Shāhpur, India	122	16.42 N	76.50 E
Shāhpur, Pāk.	120	28.43 N	68.25 E
Shāhpur, Pāk.	123	32.17 N	72.26 E
Shāhpura, India	120	27.23 N	75.58 E
Shāhpura, India	120	25.38 N	74.56 E
Shāhpura, India	124	23.11 N	80.42 E
Shāhpur Chākar	120	26.09 N	68.39 E
Shahrak	120	34.06 N	64.18 E
Shahr-e Bābak	128	30.07 N	55.09 E
Shahr-e Kord	128	32.19 N	50.50 E
Shahr-e Monjān	120	36.02 N	70.46 E
Shahr-e Şafā	128	31.50 N	66.22 E
Shahrestān	120	34.22 N	66.47 E
Shāhrūd ≃	128	36.40 N	49.26 E
Shahryār	128	35.28 N	51.05 E
Shahu	100	30.11 N	113.39 E
Shāhzādpur	126	24.10 N	89.36 E
Shā'ib al-Banāt, Jabal ∧	140	26.59 N	33.29 E
Shaighālu	120	31.11 N	68.49 E
Shaikou	100	27.19 N	117.35 E
Sha'īrah, Jabal ∧[2]	132	30.06 N	34.17 E
Sha'īrah, Jabal ash- ⋀	132	29.31 N	34.29 E
Shājāpur	124	23.26 N	76.16 E
Shajian	100	24.46 N	117.38 E
Shajianzi	98	41.01 N	125.26 E
Shajiazhuang	106	32.13 N	120.53 E
Shajing	100	23.36 N	114.06 E
Shajingzi	102	37.42 N	105.09 E
Shakaga-dake ∧	96	33.11 N	130.53 E
Shakaga-hana >	96	34.25 N	134.14 E
Shakaga-take-tunnel ◆[5]	96	33.27 N	130.52 E
Shakardarra	123	33.14 N	71.30 E
Shakargarh	123	32.16 N	75.10 E
Shakarpura	272a	28.46 N	77.21 E
Shakarpur Khās ◆[8]	272a	28.38 N	77.17 E

Symbols in the index entries represent the broad categories identified in the key at the right. Symbols with superior numbers (⋀[1]) identify subcategories (see complete key on page *I · 1).*

Symbole im Register stellen die rechts im Schlüssel erklärten Kategorien dar. Symbole mit hochgestellten Ziffern (⋀[1]) bezeichnen Unterabteilungen einer Kategorie (vgl. vollständiger Schlüssel auf Seite *I · 1).*

Los símbolos incluídos en el texto del índice representan las grandes categorías identificadas con la clave a la derecha. Los símbolos con numeros en su parte superior (⋀[1]) identifican las subcategorías (véase la clave completa en la página *I · 1).*

Les symboles de l'index représentent les catégories indiquées dans la légende à droite. Les symboles suivis d'un indice (⋀[1]) représentent des sous-catégories (voir légende complète à la page *I · 1).*

Os símbolos incluídos no texto do índice representam as grandes categorias identificadas com a chave à direita. Os símbolos com números em sua parte superior (⋀[1]) identificam as subcategorias (veja-se a chave completa à página *I · 1).*

	English	Deutsch	Español	Français	Português
∧	Mountain	Berg	Montaña	Montagne	Montanha
⋀	Mountains	Gebirge	Montañas	Montagnes	Montanhas
)(	Pass	Paß	Paso	Col	Passo
V	Valley, Canyon	Tal, Cañon	Valle, Cañón	Vallée, Canyon	Vale, Canhão
≚	Plain	Ebene	Llano	Plaine	Planície
>	Cape	Kap	Cabo	Cap	Cabo
I	Island	Insel	Isla	Île	Ilha
II	Islands	Inseln	Islas	Îles	Ilhas
⊥	Other Topographic Features	Andere Topographische Objekte	Otros Elementos Topográficos	Autres données topographiques	Outros acidentes topográficos

ESPAÑOL — Nombre, Página, Lat.°′, Long.°′ W = Oeste · FRANÇAIS — Nom, Page, Lat.°′, Long.°′ W = Ouest · PORTUGUÊS — Nome, Página, Lat.°′, Long.°′ W = Oeste

Nombre	Página	Lat.°′	Long.°′ W = Oeste
Shakaskraal	158	29.26 S	31.14 E
Shakawe	156	18.23 S	21.50 E
Shakeng	98	42.13 N	116.35 E
Shaker Heights	214	41.28 N	81.32 W
Shaker Heights Park ♦	279a	41.29 N	81.33 W
Shakespeare	212	43.22 N	80.49 W
Shākhen	128	33.22 N	59.32 E
Shakhty → Šachty	83	47.42 N	40.13 E
Shaki	150	8.39 N	3.25 E
Shākir, Jazīrat I	140	27.30 N	33.59 E
Shakopee	190	44.47 N	93.31 W
Shakotan-hantō ≻[1]	92a	43.20 N	140.30 E
Shakou	100	24.25 N	113.32 E
Shakshūk	142	29.28 N	30.42 E
Shaktoolik	180	64.20 N	161.09 W
Shakujii ✦[8]	268	35.45 N	139.37 E
Shakūrpur ✦[8]	272a	28.41 N	77.09 E
Shala, Lake ⊜	144	7.25 N	38.30 E
Shalalth	182	50.44 N	122.13 W
Shalatayn, Bi'r ⍑[4]	140	23.08 N	35.36 E
Shaleitian Dao I	98	39.03 N	118.44 E
Shaler Mountains ⋀	176	72.35 N	110.45 W
Shaleshanto	156	19.09 S	23.58 E
Shalford	260	51.13 N	0.34 W
Shālimah	142	31.14 N	30.52 E
Shalimar Railroad Station ✦[5]	272b	22.33 N	88.19 E
Shaling, Zhg.	104	41.09 N	122.22 E
Shaling, Zhg.	104	41.20 N	123.01 E
Shalingpu	104	41.47 N	123.11 E
Shalingzi	105	40.42 N	114.55 E
Shaliuhe, Zhg.	102	36.28 N	98.57 E
Shaliuhe, Zhg.	105	39.53 N	117.56 E
Shallotte	192	33.58 N	78.23 W
Shallowater	196	33.41 N	101.59 W
Shallow Brook ≃	276	40.21 N	74.35 W
Shallow Lake	212	44.36 N	81.05 W
Shaluhe	89	51.08 N	126.00 E
Shaluli Shan ⋀	102	30.45 N	99.45 E
Shām, Bādiyat ash- (Syrian Desert) ✦[2]	128	32.00 N	40.00 E
Shām, Jabal ash- ∧	128	23.13 N	57.16 E
Shama ≃	154	6.16 S	32.27 E
Shaman	85	38.50 N	75.36 E
Shamattawa	184	55.52 N	92.05 W
Shambe	140	7.07 N	30.46 E
Shambi	152	1.49 S	22.39 E
Shambu	144	9.40 N	37.03 E
Shambuanda	152	6.38 S	20.13 E
Shām Churasi	123	31.30 N	75.45 E
Shamei	100	24.32 N	118.25 E
Shamepūr ✦[8]	272a	28.45 N	77.09 E
Shamīl	128	27.30 N	56.53 E
Shāmli	124	29.27 N	77.19 E
Shammākh	132	30.30 N	35.30 E
Shamokin	208	40.47 N	76.33 W
Shamona Creek ≃	285	40.02 N	75.43 W
Shamrock, Fl., U.S.	192	29.38 N	83.08 W
Shamrock, Tx., U.S.	196	35.12 N	100.14 W
Shamsābād	124	27.01 N	78.08 E
Shamsher	272a	28.44 N	77.24 E
Shamva	154	17.18 S	31.34 E
Shan □[3]	110	22.00 N	98.00 E
Shanbiao	98	35.28 N	113.57 E
Shancheng	102	37.01 N	107.00 E
Shanchengzhen	98	42.23 N	125.26 E
Shandaken	210	42.07 N	74.23 W
Shandan	102	38.45 N	101.15 E
Shandatgyi	110	19.37 N	94.43 E
Shandī	140	16.42 N	33.26 E
Shandian ≃	98	42.23 N	116.21 E
Shandianhe	98	42.22 N	116.15 E
Shandīd	142	30.55 N	30.40 E
Shandon	226	35.39 N	120.22 W
Shandong	107	29.31 N	106.25 E
Shandong (Shantung) □[4]	98	36.00 N	118.00 E
Shandong Bandao (Shantung Peninsula) ≻[1]	98	37.00 N	121.00 E
Shaner	279b	40.17 N	79.47 W
Shanesville	214	40.31 N	81.39 W
Shangalume	154	10.49 S	26.34 E
Shangani	154	19.47 S	29.22 E
Shangani ≃	154	18.41 S	27.10 E
Shang'ao	106	30.41 N	119.25 E
Shangba	106	32.11 N	118.46 E
Shangbahe	100	30.40 N	115.05 E
Shangbai	106	30.29 N	119.58 E
Shangbancheng	105	40.50 N	118.03 E
Shangbatang	102	32.46 N	96.20 E
Shangcai	100	33.16 N	114.15 E
Shangcang	105	39.54 N	117.23 E
Shangchen	106	30.07 N	119.53 E
Shangcheng	100	31.48 N	115.24 E
Shangchewan	100	29.48 N	113.01 E
Shangch'iu → Shangqiu	98	34.27 N	115.42 E
Shangchuan Dao I	102	21.42 N	112.47 E
Shangdang	106	32.06 N	119.24 E
Shangdayangqi	89	51.09 N	124.02 E
Shangdian	100	34.07 N	112.23 E
Shangdianmiao	106	30.56 N	120.51 E
Shangdouying	105	40.36 N	115.33 E
Shangdu	98	41.29 N	113.34 E
Shangduichunshi	104	41.00 N	123.02 E
Shangdundu	100	27.56 N	116.15 E
Shangfu	100	28.40 N	114.59 E
Shanggaixin	102	23.25 N	100.02 E
Shanggan	100	25.56 N	119.22 E
Shanggang	100	33.30 N	120.04 E
Shanggangzi	104	42.26 N	123.03 E
Shanggao	100	28.18 N	114.54 E
Shanggecun	106	31.49 N	119.07 E
Shanggu	98	40.47 N	118.28 E
Shangguanying	98	41.18 N	117.07 E
Shanghai, Va., U.S.	208	37.37 N	76.47 W
Shanghai, Zhg.	106	31.07 N	121.22 E
Shanghai, Zhg.	106	31.14 N	121.28 E
Shanghai, Zhg.	269b	31.14 N	121.28 E
Shanghailingao	104	41.57 N	120.55 E
Shanghai Museum ᵿ	269b	31.13 N	121.28 E
Shanghai Shi (Shanghai Shih) □[7]	106	31.10 N	121.30 E
Shanghai Station ✦[5]	269b	31.15 N	121.28 E
Shanghang	100	25.06 N	116.25 E
Shanghe	98	37.19 N	117.07 E
Shanghekou	98	40.26 N	124.47 E
Shanghetou	105	39.12 N	116.59 E
Shanghewantun	104	41.42 N	123.23 E
Shang Hu ⊜	106	31.39 N	120.41 E
Shanghuang	106	31.33 N	119.34 E
Shanghuangqi	98	41.29 N	116.31 E
Shanghucun	105	40.45 N	115.45 E
Shangjao → Shangrao	100	28.26 N	117.58 E
Shangjiafen	104	41.18 N	121.10 E
Shangjiahe	98	41.51 N	124.28 E
Shangjiaodao	100	29.00 N	119.54 E
Shangjiatai	104	40.53 N	123.35 E
Shangjie	100	27.06 N	116.06 E
Shangjin	102	33.09 N	110.03 E
Shangjiuwu	100	33.59 N	113.01 E
Shangkasa	120	33.45 N	80.12 E
Shangkou	98	36.59 N	118.53 E
Shanglanjiagou	104	40.52 N	120.37 E
Shanglin, Zhg.	98	38.19 N	116.05 E
Shanglin, Zhg.	102	23.28 N	108.33 E
Shanglin, Zhg.	104	41.31 N	122.14 E
Shanglishi	100	27.52 N	113.46 E
Shangliuhezicun	104	41.28 N	123.32 E
Shangliulinzi	104	41.02 N	123.13 E
Shangmagushan	104	41.41 N	124.10 E
Shangmatai	105	39.22 N	117.15 E
Shangmatun	104	40.57 N	123.22 E
Shangmingdian	106	31.12 N	120.57 E
Shangmingju	105	39.41 N	115.12 E
Shangnan	102	33.31 N	110.45 E
Shangpandaoling	104	41.42 N	121.14 E
Shangpeibu	106	31.28 N	119.13 E
Shangping, Zhg.	100	25.57 N	117.33 E
Shangping, Zhg.	100	24.43 N	115.27 E
Shangping, Zhg.	100	24.29 N	114.38 E
Shangpuzi	104	41.37 N	121.35 E
Shangqianbu	106	30.27 N	120.04 E
Shangqiao	100	31.02 N	117.42 E
Shangqing, Zhg.	100	25.53 N	118.36 E
Shangqing, Zhg.	100	28.02 N	117.00 E
Shangqingshuicun	105	39.56 N	115.38 E
Shangqiu (Zhuji), Zhg.	98	34.27 N	115.42 E
Shangqiu, Zhg.	98	34.23 N	115.37 E
Shangrao	100	28.26 N	117.58 E
Shangshe	102	38.15 N	113.20 E
Shangshibatai	104	42.02 N	120.51 E
Shangshui	100	33.33 N	114.34 E
Shangsi	102	22.09 N	107.57 E
Shangtan	106	30.27 N	118.42 E
Shangtang	100	33.23 N	118.02 E
Shan Guan)(	100	27.30 N	117.06 E
Shangweiniuchang	104	40.54 N	120.44 E
Shangxian	102	33.51 N	109.54 E
Shangxingzhen	106	31.32 N	119.15 E
Shangxinhe	106	32.02 N	118.43 E
Shangxinqiu	104	42.27 N	121.37 E
Shangyangbao	98	42.30 N	124.14 E
Shangyangcun	106	30.48 N	118.40 E
Shangye	98	35.26 N	117.59 E
Shangyi (Nanhaoqian)	98	41.04 N	114.03 E
Shangying	89	44.10 N	127.17 E
Shangyinkou	102	32.52 N	103.04 E
Shangyou	100	25.51 N	114.30 E
Shangyou ≃	100	25.49 N	114.50 E
Shangyou Shuiku ⊜[1]	100	25.52 N	114.21 E
Shangyu	100	30.02 N	120.54 E
Shangyuan	104	41.39 N	120.55 E
Shangyun	102	23.01 N	99.50 E
Shangzhai	98	39.13 N	114.17 E
Shangzhaoshugou	104	42.12 N	121.58 E
Shangzhazi	105	40.52 N	117.42 E
Shangzhenzhuang	105	40.20 N	117.06 E
Shangzhi	89	45.13 N	127.59 E
Shangzhuangtai	105	39.41 N	115.25 E
Shanhaiguan	98	40.01 N	119.44 E
Shanhaikwan → Shanhaiguan	98	40.01 N	119.44 E
Shanhecun	89	45.38 N	128.27 E
Shanhetun	89	44.44 N	127.12 E
Shanjiazhuang	105	38.52 N	115.45 E
Shanklin	42	50.38 N	1.10 W
Shankou, Zhg.	100	26.40 N	117.46 E
Shankou, Zhg.	100	28.58 N	115.12 E
Shankou, Zhg.	100	28.48 N	114.29 E
Shankou, Zhg.	102	21.38 N	109.43 E
Shanlenggang	102	28.33 N	103.23 E
Shanli	100	29.52 N	117.21 E
Shanlian	106	30.42 N	120.19 E
Shanmenjie	106	30.40 N	118.52 E
Shanmulong	102	24.39 N	98.05 E
Shannanguan	100	31.36 N	116.52 E
Shannock	207	41.26 N	71.38 W
Shannon, Ire.	48	52.43 N	8.53 W
Shannon, N.Z.	172	40.33 S	175.25 E
Shannon, S. Afr.	158	29.08 S	26.18 E
Shannon, Ga., U.S.	192	34.20 N	85.04 W
Shannon, Il., U.S.	190	42.09 N	89.44 W
Shannon, Ms., U.S.	194	34.06 N	88.42 W
Shannon ≃	48	52.36 N	9.41 W
Shannon, Lake ⊜	224	48.37 N	121.42 W
Shannon, Mouth of the ≃[1]	48	52.30 N	9.50 W
Shannon Airport ⊠	48	52.41 N	8.55 W
Shannons Flat	171b	35.54 S	148.58 E
Shannontown	192	33.53 N	80.21 W
Shannonville	212	44.12 N	77.13 W
Shanpo	100	30.06 N	114.20 E
Shanrendong	89	46.50 N	123.08 E
Shanrenqiao	106	31.16 N	120.27 E
Shanshan	86	42.52 N	90.10 E
Shanshenmiao	105	40.45 N	117.11 E
Shanshūr	142	30.21 N	31.00 E
Shansi → Shanxi □[4]	102	37.00 N	112.00 E
Shanting	98	35.09 N	117.29 E
Shāntipur	126	23.15 N	88.26 E
Shantou (Swatow)	100	23.23 N	116.41 E
Shantung → Shandong □[4]	98	36.00 N	118.00 E
Shantung Peninsula → Shandong Bandao ≻[1]	98	37.00 N	121.00 E
Shanty Bay	212	44.25 N	79.36 W
Shanwa	154	3.10 S	33.46 E
Shanwei	100	22.47 N	115.21 E
Shanxi (Shansi) □[4]	102	37.00 N	112.00 E
Shanxian, Zhg.	98	34.48 N	116.03 E
Shanxian → Sanmenxia, Zhg.	102	34.45 N	111.05 E
Shanxiawu	100	28.52 N	113.52 E
Shanxu	102	22.21 N	107.58 E
Shanyang, Zhg.	100	26.43 N	119.13 E
Shanyang, Zhg.	102	33.35 N	109.49 E
Shanyang, Zhg.	106	31.19 N	120.16 E
Shanyao	100	25.13 N	118.55 E
Shanyaqiao	106	31.15 N	119.25 E
Shanyin	102	39.33 N	112.50 E
Shanzhangjiafen	105	40.37 N	116.44 E
Shanzui	105	40.48 N	118.13 E
Shanzuizi	104	41.55 N	120.30 E
Shaobo	100	32.30 N	119.32 E
Shaodenggao	104	42.13 N	121.47 E
Shaodian, Zhg.	98	34.08 N	118.25 E
Shaodian, Zhg.	100	33.10 N	114.18 E
Shaoguan	100	24.50 N	113.37 E
Shaogudian	98	36.57 N	115.32 E
Shaoguyingzi	104	41.33 N	120.27 E
Shaohing → Shaoxing	100	30.00 N	120.35 E
Shaohsing → Shaoxing	100	30.00 N	120.35 E
Shaojiaolou	106	31.05 N	121.32 E
Shaokuan → Shaoguan	100	24.50 N	113.37 E
Shaowu	100	27.20 N	117.28 E
Shaoxing	100	30.00 N	120.35 E
Shaoyang, Zhg.	102	27.15 N	111.28 E
Shaoyang, Zhg.	102	27.00 N	111.18 E
Shaoyun	107	29.30 N	105.57 E
Shaozihe	98	40.13 N	123.33 E
Shap	44	54.32 N	2.41 W
Shapinsay I	46	59.03 N	2.53 W
Shāpūr ≃	128	29.39 N	51.03 E
Shaq'ah, Ra's ash- ≻	130	34.19 N	35.41 E
Shaqqā	132	32.53 N	36.42 E
Shaqq al-Ju'ayfir, Wādī ∨	140	15.16 N	26.00 E
Shaqrā', Ar. Su.	128	25.15 N	45.15 E
Shaqrā, Lubnān	132	33.12 N	35.28 E
Shaqrā', Sūrīy.	132	32.54 N	36.14 E
Shaqrā', Yaman	144	13.21 N	45.42 E
Shaquan	86	44.33 N	83.25 E
Shaquzhen	107	30.33 N	103.45 E
Sharafābād	272a	28.36 N	77.23 E
Sharafkhāneh	128	38.11 N	45.29 E
Sharan Jogīzai	120	31.02 N	68.33 E
Sharatin Mountain ∧	180	57.49 N	152.41 W
Sharbatāt, Ra's ash- ≻	118	17.56 N	56.21 E
Sharbīn, Jabal ∧	132	33.43 N	36.21 E
Sharbot Lake	212	44.46 N	76.41 W
Sharbot Lake ⊜	212	44.46 N	76.41 W
Share	150	8.50 N	4.56 E
Shari	92a	43.55 N	144.50 E
Shari-dake ∧	92a	43.46 N	144.43 E
Sharīṭah, Ra's ≻	128	26.23 N	56.23 E
Shark ≃	220	25.21 N	81.05 W
Shark Bay ⊂	162	25.30 S	113.30 E
Shark Point ≻, Austl.	274a	33.55 S	151.17 E
Shark Point ≻, Fl., U.S.	220	25.23 N	81.09 W
Shark River Hills	208	40.12 N	74.03 W
Sharktooth Mountain ∧	180	58.35 N	127.57 W
Sharm ash-Shaykh	140	27.51 N	34.17 E
Sharnbrook	42	52.13 N	0.32 W
Sharnūb	142	31.01 N	30.35 E
Sharon, On., Can.	214	42.53 N	81.22 W
Sharon, Ct., U.S.	207	41.52 N	73.28 W
Sharon, Ma., U.S.	207	42.07 N	71.10 W
Sharon, N.D., U.S.	198	47.35 N	97.53 W
Sharon, Pa., U.S.	214	41.13 N	80.29 W
Sharon, Tn., U.S.	194	36.14 N	88.49 W
Sharon, Wi., U.S.	216	42.30 N	88.43 W
Sharon Center	214	41.06 N	81.44 W
Sharon Hill	285	39.54 N	75.16 W
Sharon Park	218	39.23 N	84.35 W
Sharon Springs, Ks., U.S.	198	38.53 N	101.45 W
Sharon Springs, N.Y., U.S.	210	42.48 N	74.37 W
Sharon Valley	207	41.53 N	73.29 W
Sharonville	218	39.16 N	84.24 W
Sharpe, Lake ⊜[1]	198	44.05 N	99.55 W
Sharpe Lake ⊜	184	54.24 N	93.30 W
Sharpes	220	28.25 N	80.45 W
Sharp Island I	271d	22.22 N	114.17 E
Sharpley	285	39.48 N	75.33 W
Sharp Park ♦	282	37.37 N	122.29 W
Sharp Peak ∧	116	5.58 N	125.31 E
Sharpsburg, Il., U.S.	219	39.37 N	89.21 W
Sharpsburg, Ky., U.S.	218	38.12 N	83.55 W
Sharpsburg, Pa., U.S.	279b	40.29 N	79.55 W
Sharps Hill	279b	40.30 N	79.56 W
Sharps Run ≃	285	39.54 N	74.49 W
Sharpsville, In., U.S.	216	40.22 N	86.05 W
Sharpsville, Pa., U.S.	214	41.15 N	80.28 W
Sharptown, Md., U.S.	208	38.32 N	75.43 W
Sharptown, N.J., U.S.	285	39.39 N	75.21 W
Sharqī, Al-Jabal ash- (Anti-Lebanon) ⋀	132	33.35 N	36.00 E
Sharqīyah, Aṣ-Ṣaḥrā' ash- (Arabian Desert) ✦[2]	140	28.00 N	32.00 E
Sharqpur	123	31.28 N	74.06 E
Sharshar, Jabal ∧[2]	140	23.52 N	30.20 E
Shartlesville	208	40.31 N	76.06 W
Shārūnah	142	28.36 N	30.51 E
Shārūnah, Wādī ∨	142	28.36 N	30.52 E
Shasha	144	6.20 N	35.57 E
Shashe ≃	156	22.14 S	29.20 E
Shashemene	144	7.12 N	38.43 E
Shashi	102	30.19 N	112.14 E
Shashibu	100	25.48 N	114.54 E
Shasi → Shashi	102	30.19 N	112.14 E
Shasta	204	40.36 N	122.29 W
Shasta ≃	204	41.50 N	122.35 W
Shasta, Mount ∧[1]	204	41.20 N	122.20 W
Shasta Lake ⊜[1]	204	40.50 N	122.25 W
Shatangjiang	106	31.25 N	120.01 E
Shaṭānūf	142	30.14 N	31.04 E
Shatawī	140	14.39 N	32.06 E
Shāṭi', Wādī ash- ∨	146	27.30 N	13.15 E
Shatian, Zhg.	100	25.53 N	113.44 E
Shatian, Zhg.	100	23.59 N	113.56 E
Shatila	132	33.51 N	35.30 E
Sha Tin	271d	22.23 N	114.11 E
Shatt al-Arab → Arab, Shatt al- ≃	128	29.57 N	48.34 E
Shattuck	196	36.16 N	99.52 W
Shatuji	98	35.18 N	115.45 E
Shatuosi	102	31.20 N	108.51 E
Shauck	214	40.37 N	82.40 W
Shaunavon	184	49.40 N	108.25 W
Shaver Lake	226	37.09 N	119.18 W
Shaver Lake ⊜[1]	226	37.08 N	119.17 W
Shavertown	210	41.19 N	75.55 W
Shavé Ẕiyyon	132	32.59 N	35.05 E
Shavington	44	53.04 N	2.27 W
Shaw, Eng., U.K.	44	53.34 N	2.05 W
Shaw, Ms., U.S.	194	33.36 N	90.46 W
Shaw ≃	162	20.20 S	119.17 E
Shaw Air Force Base ■	192	33.58 N	80.29 W
Shawan, Zhg.	86	44.34 N	85.48 E
Shawan, Zhg.	100	27.52 N	119.28 E
Shawan, Zhg.	107	29.25 N	103.33 E
Shawanaga Inlet ⊂	190	45.32 N	80.24 W
Shawangunk Kill ≃	210	41.41 N	74.10 W
Shawangunk Mountains ⋀	210	41.35 N	74.30 W
Shawano	190	44.46 N	88.36 W
Shawbury	42	52.47 N	2.39 W
Shaw Creek ≃	192	33.34 N	81.30 W
Shawforth	262	53.41 N	2.10 W
Shawhan	218	38.18 N	84.16 W
Shawinigan	206	46.33 N	72.45 W
Shawinigan ≃	206	46.32 N	72.46 W
Shawinigan, Lac ⊜	206	46.41 N	73.10 W
Shawinigan Falls → Shawinigan	206	46.33 N	72.45 W
Shawinigan-Sud	206	46.31 N	72.45 W
Shaw Island I	224	48.34 N	122.57 W
Shawmarī, Wādī ash- ∨	132	30.21 N	36.25 E
Shawmere ≃	190	48.20 N	82.28 W
Shawnee, Ks., U.S.	198	39.02 N	94.43 W
Shawnee, Oh., U.S.	188	39.36 N	82.12 W
Shawnee, Ok., U.S.	196	35.19 N	96.55 W
Shawnee, Lake ⊜	276	40.58 N	74.35 W
Shawnee Hills	214	40.07 N	83.09 W
Shawnee On Delaware	210	41.01 N	75.07 W
Shawnee State Park ♦	218	38.43 N	83.10 W
Shawneetown	194	37.42 N	88.11 W
Shawnī	142	30.45 N	30.55 E
Shawnigan Lake	224	48.38 N	123.35 W
Shawnigan Lake ⊜	224	48.37 N	123.37 W
Shawo, Som.	144	3.26 N	45.21 E
Shawo, Zhg.	98	34.28 N	114.37 E
Shawo, Zhg.	100	31.44 N	115.08 E
Shawo, Zhg.	100	28.52 N	114.47 E
Shawsheen ≃	283	42.42 N	71.08 W
Shawsheen Village	283	42.40 N	71.09 W
Shawtown	279b	40.20 N	79.42 W
Shawville	188	45.36 N	76.30 W
Shaxi, Zhg.	100	28.34 N	118.06 E
Shaxi, Zhg.	100	26.53 N	115.34 E
Shaxi, Zhg.	100	24.38 N	113.42 E
Shaxi, Zhg.	106	31.34 N	121.04 E
Shaxian	100	26.24 N	117.47 E
Shaxikou	100	26.33 N	118.02 E
Shaximiao	107	29.57 N	106.19 E
Shayang	100	30.42 N	112.33 E
Shaybārā I	128	25.27 N	36.48 E
Shay Gap	162	20.25 S	120.03 E
Shaykh, Jabal ash- (Mount Hermon) ∧	132	33.26 N	35.51 E
Shaykh, Wādī ash- ∨	142	28.48 N	30.55 E
Shaykh Al-Ḥadīd	130	36.30 N	36.35 E
Shaykh Miskīn	132	32.49 N	36.09 E
Shaykh Sa'd	128	32.34 N	46.17 E
Shaykh 'Uthmān	144	12.52 N	44.59 E
Shayuan	100	27.45 N	120.38 E
Shazhen	98	36.23 N	115.47 E
Shazhou	106	31.52 N	120.32 E
Shazihe	102	32.12 N	106.42 E
Shchekino → Ščokino	76	54.01 N	37.31 E
Shchelkovo → Ščolkovo	76	55.55 N	38.00 E
Shcherbakov → Rybinsk	76	58.03 N	38.52 E
She ≃	100	30.41 N	114.32 E
Sheaf ≃	44	53.23 N	1.26 W
Shea Island I	276	41.03 N	73.24 W
Sheakleyville	214	41.27 N	80.13 W
Shea Stadium ♦	276	40.45 N	73.51 W
Shebele	144	9.43 N	42.43 E
Shebele (Shabeelle) ≃	144	0.12 S	42.45 E
Sheberghān	120	36.41 N	65.45 E
Shebeshekong ≃	212	45.26 N	80.19 W
Sheboygan	190	43.45 N	87.42 W
Sheboygan ≃	190	43.45 N	87.42 W
Sheboygan Falls	190	43.43 N	87.48 W
Shebu	100	27.40 N	112.48 E
Shechem → Nābulus	132	32.13 N	35.16 E
Shechem ⊥	132	32.13 N	35.15 E
Shecheng	102	37.14 N	113.05 E
Shedd Canyon ∨	226	35.39 N	120.26 W
Shedden	214	42.44 N	81.21 W
Shediac	186	46.13 N	64.32 W
Shedin Peak ∧	182	55.55 N	127.32 W
Sheekh	144	9.56 N	45.11 E
Sheelin, Lough ⊜	48	53.48 N	7.22 W
Sheenjek ≃	180	66.45 N	144.33 W
Sheep ≃	182	50.44 N	113.51 W
Sheep Creek ≃, Ab., Can.	182	54.04 N	119.00 W
Sheep Creek ≃, U.S.	202	42.27 N	115.36 W
Sheep Creek ≃, Ut., U.S.	200	40.55 N	109.39 W
Sheep Creek ≃, Wy., U.S.	200	42.03 N	106.04 W
Sheep Haven ⊂	48	55.10 N	7.52 W
Sheepmoor	158	26.42 S	30.13 E
Sheep Mountain ∧, Az., U.S.	200	32.32 N	114.14 W
Sheep Mountain ∧, Wy., U.S.	200	43.33 N	110.32 W
Sheep Peak ∧	196	31.14 N	104.59 W
Sheepranch	226	38.13 N	120.28 W
Sheep Range ⋀	204	36.45 N	115.05 W
Sheepshead Bay ✦[8]	276	40.35 N	73.56 W
's-Heerenberg	52	51.53 N	6.15 E
's-Heerenhoek	52	51.27 N	3.46 E
Sheerness	42	51.27 N	0.45 E
Sheet Harbour	186	44.55 N	62.32 W
Shefar'am	132	32.48 N	35.10 E
Sheffield, N.Z.	172	43.23 S	172.01 E
Sheffield, Eng., U.K.	44	53.23 N	1.28 W
Sheffield, Al., U.S.	194	34.45 N	87.41 W
Sheffield, Il., U.S.	190	41.21 N	89.44 W
Sheffield, Ia., U.S.	190	42.53 N	93.12 W
Sheffield, Ma., U.S.	207	42.06 N	73.21 W
Sheffield, Oh., U.S.	214	41.25 N	82.05 W
Sheffield, Pa., U.S.	214	41.42 N	79.02 W
Sheffield, Tx., U.S.	196	30.41 N	101.49 W
Sheffield Island I	276	41.03 N	73.25 W
Sheffield Island Harbor ⊂	276	41.03 N	73.25 W
Sheffield Lake	214	41.29 N	82.06 W
Sheffield Lake ⊜	186	49.20 N	56.35 W
Shefford	42	52.02 N	0.20 W
Shefford □[6]	206	45.25 N	72.30 W
Shefu	100	26.11 N	115.22 E
Shegangshi	100	28.32 N	113.36 E
Shegaon	122	20.47 N	76.41 E
Sheho	184	51.38 N	103.12 W
Shehong	102	30.56 N	105.22 E
Shehongmiao	107	30.44 N	106.03 E
Shehy Mountains ⋀	48	51.48 N	9.15 W
Sheikh Hasan	144	12.04 N	35.53 E
Sheikhpura	124	25.09 N	85.51 E
Shekatika	186	51.17 N	58.20 W
Shekhūpura	123	31.42 N	73.59 E
Sheki → Šeki	84	41.12 N	47.12 E
Shekki → Zhongshan	100	22.31 N	113.22 E
Shek Kong	271d	22.26 N	114.06 E
Shek Kong Airfield ⊠	271d	22.27 N	114.05 E
Shek Kwu Chau I	271d	22.12 N	113.59 E
Shekou	100	30.44 N	114.20 E
Shek Uk Shan ∧	271d	22.27 N	114.18 E
Shelagyote Peak ∧	182	55.58 N	127.12 W
Shelbina	219	39.41 N	92.02 W
Shelbourne	169	36.52 S	144.01 E
Shelburn	194	39.11 N	87.24 W
Shelburne, N.S., Can.	186	43.46 N	65.19 W
Shelburne, On., Can.	212	44.04 N	80.12 W
Shelburne Bay ⊂	164	11.49 S	143.00 E
Shelburne Falls	207	42.36 N	72.44 W
Shelby, In., U.S.	216	41.11 N	87.20 W
Shelby, Ia., U.S.	198	41.30 N	95.27 W
Shelby, Mi., U.S.	190	43.36 N	86.21 W
Shelby, Ms., U.S.	194	33.57 N	90.46 W
Shelby, Mt., U.S.	202	48.30 N	111.51 W
Shelby, Ne., U.S.	198	41.11 N	97.25 W
Shelby, N.C., U.S.	192	35.17 N	81.32 W
Shelby, Oh., U.S.	214	40.52 N	82.39 W
Shelby □[6], Il., U.S.	219	39.24 N	88.48 W
Shelby □[6], In., U.S.	218	39.31 N	85.47 W
Shelby □[6], Ky., U.S.	218	38.15 N	85.13 W
Shelby □[6], Mo., U.S.	219	39.49 N	92.03 W
Shelby □[6], Oh., U.S.	216	40.17 N	84.09 W
Shelby Village	281	42.38 N	83.04 W
Shelbyville, Il., U.S.	219	39.24 N	88.47 W
Shelbyville, In., U.S.	218	39.31 N	85.46 W
Shelbyville, Ky., U.S.	218	38.12 N	85.13 W
Shelbyville, Mo., U.S.	219	39.48 N	92.02 W
Shelbyville, Tn., U.S.	194	35.29 N	86.27 W
Shelbyville, Lake ⊜[1]	219	39.30 N	88.40 W
Sheldon, Il., U.S.	216	40.46 N	87.33 W
Sheldon, Ia., U.S.	198	43.10 N	95.51 W
Sheldon, Mi., U.S.	216	42.17 N	83.28 W
Sheldon, Mo., U.S.	194	37.39 N	94.17 W
Sheldon, Tx., U.S.	222	29.52 N	95.08 W
Sheldon Brook ≃	276	41.03 N	73.52 W
Sheldon Creek ≃	212	44.07 N	79.53 W
Sheldon Point	180	62.32 N	164.52 W
Sheldon Reservoir ⊜[1]	222	29.52 N	95.10 W
Sheldonville	283	42.02 N	71.23 W
Sheldrake ≃	276	40.57 N	73.44 W
Sheldrake Lake ⊜, On., Can.	212	44.49 N	77.16 W
Sheldrake Lake ⊜, N.Y., U.S.	276	40.57 N	73.46 W
Shelikof Strait ⵖ	180	57.30 N	155.00 W
Shell ≃	184	50.58 N	101.24 W
Shell, Loch ⊂	46	58.00 N	6.30 W
Shellbrook	184	53.13 N	106.24 W
Shell Brook ≃	184	53.21 N	106.00 W
Shell Creek ≃, U.S.	200	40.56 N	108.37 W
Shell Creek ≃, Ne., U.S.	198	41.27 N	96.58 W
Shell Creek ≃, N.D., U.S.	198	47.59 N	102.17 W
Shell Creek ≃, Wy., U.S.	202	44.31 N	108.03 W
Shellen	146	9.54 N	12.00 E
Shelley, B.C., Can.	182	54.00 N	122.37 W
Shelley, Id., U.S.	202	43.22 N	112.07 W
Shellharbour	170	34.35 S	150.52 E
Shell Lake, Sk., Can.	184	53.18 N	107.04 W
Shell Lake, Wi., U.S.	190	45.44 N	91.55 W
Shell Lakes ⊜	162	29.21 S	127.25 E
Shellman	192	31.45 N	84.36 W
Shellmouth Dam ✦[6]	184	50.58 N	101.25 W
Shellow Bowells	260	51.45 N	0.20 E
Shell Rock	190	42.42 N	92.34 W
Shell Rock ≃	190	42.38 N	92.30 W
Shellrock Peak ∧	224	46.43 N	121.14 W
Shellsburg	190	42.05 N	91.52 W
Shelocta	214	40.39 N	79.18 W
Shelter, Port ⊂	271d	22.21 N	114.17 E
Shelter Island	207	41.04 N	72.20 W
Shelter Island I, H.K.	271d	22.20 N	114.17 E
Shelter Island I, N.Y., U.S.	207	41.04 N	72.20 W
Shelter Island Heights	207	41.05 N	72.21 W
Shelter Island Sound ⵖ	207	41.03 N	72.22 W
Shelton, Ct., U.S.	207	41.18 N	73.05 W
Shelton, Ne., U.S.	198	40.47 N	98.44 W
Shelton, Wa., U.S.	224	47.13 N	123.06 W
Shemanker ≃	150	8.12 N	9.45 E
Shemogue	186	46.09 N	64.11 W
Shemya Station	181a	52.43 N	174.05 E
Shenandoah, Ia., U.S.	198	40.45 N	95.22 W
Shenandoah, Pa., U.S.	208	40.49 N	76.12 W
Shenandoah, Va., U.S.	188	38.29 N	78.37 W
Shenandoah ≃	188	39.19 N	77.44 W
Shenandoah, North Fork ≃	188	38.57 N	78.12 W
Shenandoah, South Fork ≃	188	38.57 N	78.12 W
Shenandoah Heights	210	40.49 N	76.12 W
Shenandoah National Park ♦	188	38.48 N	78.12 W
Shenango	214	41.23 N	80.24 W
Shenango ≃	214	40.57 N	80.23 W
Shenango River Lake ⊜[1]	214	41.22 N	80.28 W
Shenchi	102	39.09 N	112.19 E
Shencottah	122	8.58 N	77.16 E
Shencun	106	31.04 N	118.51 E
Shendam	150	8.53 N	9.32 E
Shendang	106	30.34 N	120.49 E
Shending Shan ∧	89	46.38 N	133.28 E
Shenduncun	106	30.48 N	120.25 E
Shenfield	260	51.38 N	0.19 E
Shengang, Zhg.	100	27.20 N	116.18 E
Shengang, Zhg.	106	31.54 N	120.08 E
Shenge	150	7.55 N	12.57 W
Shengfang	105	39.04 N	116.42 E
Shenggongjing	106	31.07 N	119.48 E
Shenghongqing	100	30.12 N	114.56 E
Shengjiachi	107	30.28 N	105.03 E
Shengjiaqiao	106	31.27 N	121.24 E
Shengjiatun	104	41.14 N	121.22 E
Shengjin'gao	104	42.04 N	120.43 E
Shengou	100	34.08 N	113.13 E
Shengqing	104	41.34 N	121.36 E
Shengshan	106	30.50 N	120.15 E
Shengshui	98	35.45 N	119.39 E
Shengshuihezi	98	42.27 N	125.59 E
Shengsi Liedao II	100	30.42 N	122.20 E
Shengtian	100	27.14 N	113.06 E
Shengxian	100	29.36 N	120.48 E
Shengze	106	30.55 N	120.39 E
Shengzigou	104	41.35 N	124.04 E
Shenhu	100	24.38 N	118.39 E
Shenipsit Lake ⊜	207	41.53 N	72.26 W
Shenji	98	34.47 N	115.09 E
Shenjia	89	46.06 N	126.46 E
Shenjiadian	89	46.35 N	130.38 E
Shenjiatai	104	41.22 N	120.50 E
Shenjiawan	106	31.43 N	121.19 E
Shenjiazhuang	106	32.18 N	120.26 E
Shenjing, Zhg.	102	21.59 N	112.28 E
Shenjing, Zhg.	105	40.24 N	114.49 E
Shenjingzi	104	41.47 N	123.41 E
Shenk'eng	269d	25.00 N	121.36 E
Shenkou	100	28.42 N	116.02 E
Shenley	260	51.41 N	0.17 W
Shenmu	102	38.56 N	110.19 E
Shennan	105	38.59 N	114.56 E
Shenorock	210	41.20 N	73.44 W
Shenqiu	100	33.24 N	115.02 E
Shenquan	100	22.59 N	116.20 E
Shenquan Gang ⊂	100	22.54 N	116.18 E
Shensi → Shaanxi □[4]	102	35.00 N	109.00 E
Shenton, Mount ∧	162	28.00 S	123.22 E
Shentuan	98	35.30 N	119.17 E
Shenxian, Zhg.	98	38.01 N	115.33 E
Shenxian, Zhg.	98	36.15 N	115.41 E
Shenxing	105	39.02 N	115.19 E
Shenyang (Mukden)	104	41.48 N	123.27 E
Shenze	98	38.11 N	115.11 E
Shenzhen	100	22.34 N	114.07 E
Sheoganj	120	25.09 N	73.04 E
Sheokhāla	126	22.46 N	88.10 E
Sheopur	124	25.40 N	76.42 E
Shepard	182	50.57 N	113.55 W
Shepard Island I	9	74.25 S	132.30 W
Shepards Brook ≃	283	42.08 N	71.25 W
Shepaug ≃	207	41.28 N	73.19 W
Shepherd, Mi., U.S.	190	43.31 N	84.41 W
Shepherd, Tx., U.S.	222	30.30 N	95.01 W
Shepherd □[8]	175f	17.05 S	168.25 E
Shepherd, Îles II	175f	16.55 S	168.36 E
Shepherdstown	188	39.25 N	77.48 W
Shepherdsville	194	37.59 N	85.42 W
Sheppard Air Force Base ■	196	33.58 N	98.30 W
Sheppard Peak ∧	180	57.41 N	132.37 W
Sheppard Pond ⊜	276	41.08 N	74.13 W
Shepparton	166	36.23 S	145.25 E
Shepperd, Lake ⊜	162	29.55 S	123.09 E
Shepperton	260	51.24 N	0.27 W
Sheppey, Isle of I	42	51.24 N	0.50 E
Sheppler Hill ∧[2]	279b	40.09 N	79.49 W
Sheppton	210	40.53 N	76.07 W
Shepshed	42	52.47 N	1.18 W
Shepton Mallet	42	51.12 N	2.33 W
Shepway	260	51.15 N	0.33 E
Sheqi	100	33.03 N	112.57 E
Sherab	140	10.43 N	24.47 E
Sherada	144	7.21 N	36.32 E
Sheraden ✦[8]	279b	40.28 N	80.05 W
Sherard, Cape ≻	176	74.36 N	80.25 W
Sherborn	283	42.14 N	71.22 W
Sherborne	42	50.57 N	2.31 W
Sherborne Lake ⊜	212	45.11 N	78.47 W
Sherborne Saint John	42	51.18 N	1.07 W
Sherbro ≃	150	7.45 N	12.55 W
Sherbro Island I	150	7.45 N	12.55 W
Sherbrooke, N.S., Can.	186	45.08 N	61.59 W
Sherbrooke, P.Q., Can.	206	45.25 N	71.54 W
Sherbrooke □[6]	206	45.25 N	71.55 W
Sherbrooke Lake ⊜	186	44.40 N	64.35 W
Sherburn	198	43.39 N	94.43 W
Sherburne	210	42.40 N	75.29 W
Sherburne Reef ✢[2]	164	3.20 S	148.00 E
Sherburn in Elmet	44	53.48 N	1.15 W
Shercock	48	54.00 N	6.54 W
Shere	260	51.13 N	0.28 W
Sheridan, Ar., U.S.	194	34.18 N	92.24 W
Sheridan, Ca., U.S.	226	38.59 N	121.22 W
Sheridan, Il., U.S.	216	41.32 N	88.41 W
Sheridan, In., U.S.	218	40.08 N	86.13 W
Sheridan, Mt., U.S.	202	45.27 N	112.11 W
Sheridan, Or., U.S.	202	45.05 N	123.23 W
Sheridan, Pa., U.S.	208	40.21 N	76.14 W
Sheridan, Tx., U.S.	222	29.29 N	96.40 W
Sheridan, Wy., U.S.	202	44.47 N	106.57 W
Sheridan, Mount ∧	202	44.16 N	110.32 W
Sheridan Park ♦	284a	42.59 N	78.54 W
Sheringa	162	33.51 S	135.15 E
Sheringham	42	52.57 N	1.12 E
Sherkston	284a	42.53 N	79.08 W
Sherlock ≃	162	20.44 S	117.35 E
Sherman, Ct., U.S.	207	41.34 N	73.29 W
Sherman, Il., U.S.	219	39.54 N	89.36 W
Sherman, Ky., U.S.	218	38.44 N	84.36 W
Sherman, Ms., U.S.	194	34.21 N	88.50 W
Sherman, N.Y., U.S.	214	42.09 N	79.35 W
Sherman, Tx., U.S.	196	33.38 N	96.36 W
Sherman □[6]	224	45.25 N	120.49 W
Sherman Creek ≃	208	40.23 N	77.02 W
Sherman Mills	188	45.52 N	68.23 W
Sherman Mountain ∧	194	36.01 N	93.17 W
Sherman Oaks ✦[8]	280	34.09 N	118.26 W
Sherman Reservoir ⊜	198	41.20 N	98.55 W
Sherman Station	188	45.53 N	68.25 W
Sherpur, Bngl.	124	24.41 N	89.25 E
Sherpur, Bngl.	124	25.01 N	90.01 E
Sher Qila	123	36.06 N	74.03 E
Sherrard	190	41.19 N	90.31 W
Sherridon	184	55.07 N	101.05 W
Sherrill	210	43.04 N	75.35 W
Sherrodsville	214	40.29 N	81.14 W
Sher Shāh	123	30.06 N	71.21 E
Sherrallai	122	9.42 N	76.20 E
's-Hertogenbosch	52	51.41 N	5.19 E
Sherway Centre ✦[9]	275b	43.37 N	79.33 W
Sherwood, On., Can.	275b	43.50 N	79.31 W
Sherwood, P.E., Can.	186	46.17 N	63.08 W
Sherwood, Ar., U.S.	194	34.48 N	92.13 W
Sherwood, Md., U.S.	208	38.36 N	76.19 W
Sherwood, Mi., U.S.	216	42.00 N	85.14 W
Sherwood, N.D., U.S.	198	48.57 N	101.37 W
Sherwood, Oh., U.S.	216	41.17 N	84.33 W
Sherwood, Or., U.S.	224	45.21 N	122.50 W
Sherwood, Tn., U.S.	194	35.04 N	85.55 W
Sherwood, Lake ⊜	281	42.36 N	83.33 W
Sherwood Forest, Ca., U.S.	226	37.57 N	122.17 W
Sherwood Forest, Md., U.S.	284c	39.05 N	77.01 W
Sherwood Forest ✦[3]	44	53.08 N	1.08 W
Sherwood Island State Park ♦	276	41.07 N	73.20 W
Sherwood Manor	207	42.01 N	72.38 W
Sherwood Park, Ab., Can.	182	53.31 N	113.19 W
Sherwood Park, De., U.S.	285	39.44 N	75.39 W
Sherwood Park, N.Y., U.S.	210	42.36 N	73.43 W
Sherwood Park ♦	275b	43.43 N	79.24 W
Sherwood Point ≻	276	41.07 N	73.20 W
Sherwood Shores	196	30.36 N	98.22 W
She Shan ∧[2]	106	31.06 N	121.11 E
Sheshea ≃	248	9.36 S	74.10 W
Shesh Gāv	120	33.45 N	68.33 E
Shet Bandar	272c	18.58 N	72.56 E
Shetek, Lake ⊜	198	44.08 N	95.42 W
Shetland □[4]	46a	60.30 N	1.15 W
Shetland del Sur, Islas → South Shetland Islands II	9	62.00 S	58.00 W
Shetland Islands II	46a	60.30 N	1.15 W
Shetou	106	31.39 N	119.27 E
Shetrunji ≃	120	21.19 N	72.07 E
Shetucket ≃	207	41.31 N	72.05 W
Sheva	272c	18.56 N	72.57 E
Sheva Nhava	272c	18.58 N	72.58 E
Shevaroy Hills ⋀[2]	122	11.50 N	78.16 E
Shevington	262	53.34 N	2.42 W
Shevington Moor	262	53.35 N	2.41 W
Shewa □[4]	144	9.00 N	39.00 E
Shewa Gimira	144	7.00 N	35.50 E
Shexian, Zhg.	98	36.33 N	113.40 E
Shexian, Zhg.	100	29.53 N	118.26 E
Sheyang, Zhg.	100	33.20 N	119.38 E
Sheyang, Zhg.	100	33.46 N	120.18 E
Sheyenne	198	47.49 N	99.07 W
Sheyenne ≃	198	47.05 N	96.50 W
Sheykhābād	120	34.05 N	68.45 E
Shey-Phoksundo National Park ♦	124	29.30 N	82.45 E
Shezhu	106	31.19 N	119.16 E
Shḥīm	132	33.37 N	35.29 E
Shi ≃, Zhg.	100	32.18 N	114.31 E
Shi ≃, Zhg.	100	32.32 N	115.52 E
Shiant, Sound of ⵖ	46	57.55 N	6.25 W
Shiant Islands II	46	57.53 N	6.21 W
Shiawassee □[6]	216	42.56 N	84.09 W
Shiawassee ≃	216	43.06 N	84.10 W
Shiawassee, South Branch ≃	216	42.49 N	83.56 W
Shiba	100	32.45 N	118.07 E
Shiba ≃	268	35.47 N	139.44 E
Shibadu	102	28.01 N	110.51 E
Shibakawa	94	35.13 N	138.33 E
Shibām	144	15.56 N	48.38 E
Shiban	107	30.18 N	104.28 E
Shibanxi	107	29.17 N	103.51 E
Shibaocheng	102	39.48 N	96.10 E
Shibarni	140	14.50 N	24.25 E
Shibasaki	268	35.39 N	139.34 E
Shibata	92	37.57 N	139.20 E
Shibayama	94	35.41 N	140.25 E
Shibayama-gata ⊜	94	36.21 N	136.23 E
Shibden Hall ⊥	262	53.44 N	1.51 W
Shibecha	92a	43.17 N	144.36 E
Shibetsu, Nihon	92a	43.40 N	145.08 E
Shibetsu, Nihon	92a	44.10 N	142.23 E
Shibi	100	26.43 N	120.02 E
Shibīn al-Kawm	142	30.33 N	31.01 E
Shibīn al-Qanāṭir	142	30.19 N	31.19 E
Shibing	102	26.50 N	108.04 E
Shibishan	100	29.21 N	116.45 E
Shiblanjah	142	30.28 N	31.16 E
Shibu	98	36.45 N	119.27 E
Shibukawa	94	36.29 N	139.00 E
Shibure-yama ∧	270	34.45 N	135.05 E
Shibushi	92	31.28 N	131.07 E
Shibutsu-san ∧	94	36.54 N	139.11 E
Shibuya ✦[8]	268	35.40 N	139.42 E
Shibuzi	98	36.09 N	119.06 E
Shicha	100	28.24 N	115.50 E
Shichangyu	104	41.12 N	123.14 E
Shicheng, Zhg.	98	40.39 N	124.17 E
Shicheng, Zhg.	100	25.18 N	119.21 E
Shicheng, Zhg.	100	26.22 N	116.22 E
Shicheng Dao I	98	39.31 N	123.02 E
Shichisō	94	35.33 N	137.07 E
Shickley	198	40.25 N	97.43 W
Shickshinny	210	41.09 N	76.09 W
Shidai	100	30.20 N	117.56 E
Shidao	98	36.53 N	122.23 E
Shideng	102	26.44 N	99.11 E
Shidler	196	36.46 N	96.39 W
Shido	96	34.19 N	134.10 E
Shidong, Zhg.	107	28.59 N	105.27 E
Shidong, Zhg.	107	30.25 N	105.20 E
Shidongzigou	105	40.41 N	118.23 E
Shiel, Loch ⊜	46	56.47 N	5.35 W
Shiel Bridge	46	57.12 N	5.25 W
Shieldaig	46	57.31 N	5.39 W
Shieldhill	46	55.58 N	3.46 W
Shields ≃	202	45.43 N	110.28 W
Shiercun	106	30.31 N	119.34 E
Shi'er Shan ∧	100	29.18 N	118.08 E
Shi'erwei	106	32.15 N	119.14 E
Shifang	100	25.01 N	116.14 E
Shifnal	42	52.40 N	2.21 W
Shifo	107	29.58 N	103.50 E
Shifobao	104	41.28 N	121.27 E
Shifochang	107	30.19 N	105.07 E
Shifodian	100	32.06 N	115.46 E
Shifosi	104	42.08 N	123.20 E
Shifoya	98	40.12 N	123.10 E
Shiga, Nihon	94	36.20 N	137.59 E
Shiga, Nihon	94	35.09 N	135.55 E
Shiga □[5]	96	35.15 N	136.00 E
Shigaib	140	15.01 N	23.36 E
Shigang, Zhg.	100	32.13 N	120.58 E
Shigang, Zhg.	106	32.14 N	121.00 E
Shigangmen	269b	31.21 N	121.17 E
Shigaopu	107	30.16 N	104.01 E
Shigar ≃, Asia	123	34.39 N	75.51 E
Shigar ≃, Pāk.	123	34.39 N	75.51 E
Shigaraki	94	34.52 N	136.03 E
Shigaraki-gū ᵿ[1]	94	34.54 N	136.04 E
Shigenobu	96	33.48 N	132.50 E
Shigenobu ≃	96	33.48 N	132.41 E
Shigezhuang, Zhg.	105	38.57 N	116.19 E
Shigezhuang, Zhg.	105	38.59 N	115.36 E

Symbol	English	Deutsch	Español	Français	Português
≃	River	Fluß	Río	Rivière	Rio
≡	Canal	Kanal	Canal	Canal	Canal
⌊	Waterfall, Rapids	Wasserfall, Stromschnellen	Cascada, Rápidos	Chute d'eau, Rapides	Cascata, Rápidos
ⵖ	Strait	Meeresstraße	Estrecho	Détroit	Estreito
⊂	Bay, Gulf	Bucht, Golf	Bahía, Golfo	Baie, Golfe	Baía, Golfo
⊜	Lake, Lakes	See, Seen	Lago, Lagos	Lac, Lacs	Lago, Lagos
⩶	Swamp	Sumpf	Pantano	Marais	Pântano
⊓	Ice Features, Glacier	Eis- und Gletscherformen	Accidentes Glaciales	Formes glaciaires	Acidentes glaciares
⍑	Other Hydrographic Features	Andere Hydrographische Objekte	Otros Elementos Hidrográficos	Autres données hydrographiques	Outros acidentes hidrográficos
✢	Submarine Features	Untermeerische Objekte	Accidentes Submarinos	Formes de relief sous-marin	Acidentes submarinos
□	Political Unit	Politische Einheit	Unidad Política	Entité politique	Unidade política
ᵿ	Cultural Institution	Kulturelle Institution	Institución Cultural	Institution culturelle	Instituição cultural
⊥	Historical Site	Historische Stätte	Sitio Histórico	Site historique	Sítio histórico
♦	Recreational Site	Erholungs- und Ferienort	Sitio de Recreo	Centre de loisirs	Area de Lazer
⊠	Airport	Flughafen	Aeropuerto	Aéroport	Aeroporto
■	Military Installation	Militäranlage	Instalación Militar	Installation militaire	Instalação militar
✦	Miscellaneous	Verschiedenes	Misceláneo	Divers	Diversos

ENGLISH		DEUTSCH		
Name	Page Lat.°′ Long.°′	Name	Seite	Breite°′ Länge°′ E = Ost

ESPAÑOL			FRANÇAIS			PORTUGUÊS		
Nombre	Página	Lat.°′ Long.°′ W = Oeste	Nom	Page	Lat.°′ Long.°′ W = Ouest	Nome	Página	Lat.°′ Long.°′ W = Oeste

---

Legend (footer):

≃	River	Fluß	Río	Rivière	Rio
⊠	Canal	Kanal	Canal	Canal	Canal
๙	Waterfall, Rapids	Wasserfall, Stromschnellen	Cascada, Rápidos	Chute d'eau, Rapides	Cascata, Rápidos
ม	Strait	Meeresstraße	Estrecho	Détroit	Estreito
⊂	Bay, Gulf	Bucht, Golf	Bahía, Golfo	Baie, Golfe	Baía, Golfo
⊘	Lake, Lakes	See, Seen	Lago, Lagos	Lac, Lacs	Lago, Lagos
⊶	Swamp	Sumpf	Pantano	Marais	Pântano
⋈	Ice Features, Glacier	Eis- und Gletscherformen	Accidentes Glaciales	Formes glaciaires	Acidentes glaciares
⊥	Other Hydrographic Features	Andere Hydrographische Objekte	Otros Elementos Hidrográficos	Autres données hydrographiques	Outros acidentes hidrográficos

⊶	Submarine Features	Untermeerische Objekte	Accidentes Submarinos	Formes de relief sous-marin	Acidentes submarinos
□	Political Unit	Politische Einheit	Unidad Política	Entité politique	Unidade política
∨	Cultural Institution	Kulturelle Institution	Institución Cultural	Institution culturelle	Instituição cultural
⊥	Historical Site	Historische Stätte	Sitio Histórico	Site historique	Sítio histórico
∨	Recreational Site	Erholungs- und Ferienort	Sitio de Recreo	Centre de loisirs	Area de Lazer
⊠	Airport	Flughafen	Aeropuerto	Aéroport	Aeroporto
■	Military Installation	Militäranlage	Instalación Militar	Installation militaire	Instalação militar
⊶	Miscellaneous	Verschiedenes	Misceláneo	Divers	Diversos

Name	Page	Lat.°′	Long.°′
Sinnamary	**250**	5.23 N	52.57 W
Sinnar	**122**	19.51 N	74.00 E
Sinnemahoning Creek ≃	**210**	41.15 N	77.54 W
Sinnemahoning Creek, Bennett Branch ≃	**210**	41.20 N	78.08 W
Sinnemahoning Creek, Driftwood Branch ≃	**210**	41.20 N	78.08 W
Sinnemahoning Creek, First Fork ≃	**210**	41.19 N	78.05 W
Sinnersdorf	**56**	51.01 N	6.49 E
Sinnes	**26**	58.56 N	6.50 E
Sinni ≃	**68**	40.09 N	16.42 E
Sînnicolau Mare	**38**	46.05 N	20.38 E
Sinntal	**56**	50.18 N	9.38 E
Sinnūris	**142**	29.25 N	30.52 E
Sinnyŏng	**98**	36.04 N	128.46 E
Sino, Pedra do ∧	**256**	22.30 S	43.03 W
Sinoie, Lacul ⊜	**38**	44.38 N	28.53 E
Sinop, Bra.	**250**	11.55 S	55.35 W
Sinop, Tür.	**130**	42.01 N	35.09 E
Sinop □[4]	**130**	41.40 N	34.50 E
Sinop Burnu ≻	**130**	42.02 N	35.12 E
Sinp'a	**98**	41.24 N	127.46 E
Sinp'o	**98**	40.03 N	128.12 E
Sins	**58**	47.11 N	8.23 E
Sinsang	**98**	39.38 N	127.25 E
Sinsen	**263**	51.40 N	7.11 E
Sinsheim	**56**	49.15 N	8.53 E
Sinsiang → Xinxiang	**98**	35.20 N	113.51 E
Sinsin	**56**	50.17 N	5.15 E
Sinsi-ri	**98**	39.59 N	124.58 E
Sinskoje	**74**	61.08 N	126.48 E
Sinspelt	**56**	49.58 N	6.19 E
Sint-Amandsberg	**50**	51.04 N	3.45 E
Sintana	**38**	46.21 N	21.30 E
Sint-Andries	**50**	51.12 N	3.10 E
Sintang	**112**	0.04 N	111.30 E
Sint Annaland	**52**	51.36 N	4.06 E
Sint Annaparochie	**52**	53.16 N	5.39 E
Sint Anthonis	**52**	51.37 N	5.52 E
Sint Christoffelberg ∧[2]	**241s**	12.20 N	69.08 W
Sint-Denijs-Westrem	**50**	51.01 N	3.40 E
Sint Eustatius I	**238**	17.30 N	62.59 W
Sint-Gillis-Waas	**50**	51.13 N	4.08 E
Sint Helenabaai ⊂	**158**	32.43 S	18.05 E
Sint-Joris-Weert	**56**	50.48 N	4.39 E
Sint-Joris-Winge	**56**	50.55 N	4.52 E
Sint-Katelijne-Waver	**56**	51.04 N	4.32 E
Sint-Kruis, Bel.	**50**	51.13 N	3.15 E
Sint Kruis, Ned. Ant.	**241s**	12.18 N	69.08 W
Sint-Lenaarts	**56**	51.21 N	4.41 E
Sint Maarten	**52**	52.46 N	4.44 E
Sint Maarten (Saint-Martin) I	**238**	18.04 N	63.04 W
Sint Maartensdijk	**52**	51.33 N	4.05 E
Sint-Michiels	**50**	51.11 N	3.12 E
Sint Michielsgestel	**52**	51.38 N	5.21 E
Sint Nicolaas	**241s**	12.27 N	69.52 W
Sint-Niklaas (Saint-Nicolas)	**50**	51.10 N	4.08 E
Sint-Oedenrode	**52**	51.34 N	5.27 E
Sinton	**196**	28.02 N	97.30 W
Sintong	**114**	1.31 N	100.58 E
Sint Pancras	**52**	52.39 N	4.46 E
Sint-Pieters-Leeuw	**50**	50.47 N	4.14 E
Sintra	**34**	38.48 N	9.23 W
Sintra, Serra de ⋏[2]	**266c**	38.47 N	9.25 W
Sintra Granjo do Marquez, Aeroporto ⊠	**266c**	38.49 N	9.20 W
Sint-Truiden	**56**	50.48 N	5.12 E
Sint Willebrord	**52**	51.33 N	4.35 E
Sinú ≃	**246**	9.24 N	75.49 W
Sin'ucha ≃, Ross.	**84**	44.45 N	40.58 E
Sin'ucha ≃, Ukr.	**78**	48.03 N	30.51 E
Sin'uga	**88**	57.45 N	115.13 E
Sinŭiju	**98**	40.05 N	124.24 E
Sinujif	**144**	8.33 N	48.59 E
Sinŭp, C.M.I.K.	**98**	39.54 N	126.47 E
Sinŭp, Taehan	**98**	37.54 N	127.12 E
Sinwŏn-ni	**98**	38.13 N	125.44 E
Sinzig	**56**	50.32 N	7.15 E
Sinzing	**60**	49.00 N	12.02 E
Sió ≃, Magy.	**30**	46.20 N	18.55 E
Sio ≃, Togo	**150**	6.17 N	1.13 E
Siocon	**116**	7.42 N	122.08 E
Siófok	**30**	46.54 N	18.04 E
Sioma	**152**	16.39 S	23.30 E
Sioma Ngweze National Park ♦	**152**	17.15 S	23.20 E
Sion (Sitten)	**58**	46.14 N	7.21 E
Sionascaig, Loch ⊜	**46**	58.04 N	5.11 W
Sion Mills	**48**	54.47 N	7.29 W
Sioule ≃	**32**	46.22 N	3.19 E
Sioux Center	**198**	43.04 N	96.10 W
Sioux City	**198**	42.30 N	96.24 W
Sioux Falls	**198**	43.33 N	96.42 W
Sioux Lookout	**184**	50.06 N	91.55 W
Sioux Narrows	**184**	49.25 N	94.06 W
Sioux Rapids	**198**	42.53 N	95.09 W
Sipalay	**116**	9.45 N	122.24 E
Sipalay ≃	**116**	9.46 N	122.24 E
Sipaliwini □[5]	**250**	4.00 N	56.00 W
Sipaliwini ≃	**250**	2.22 N	56.50 W
Sipaozi	**104**	41.26 N	122.13 E
Sipapo ≃	**246**	5.03 N	67.48 W
Siparia	**241r**	10.08 N	61.30 W
Šipčenski prohod)(	**38**	42.46 N	25.19 E
Şipek	**130**	40.14 N	41.29 E
Sipes	**220**	28.48 N	81.14 W
Sipesville	**214**	40.06 N	79.06 W
Šipicyno, Ross.	**24**	61.17 N	46.28 E
Šipicyno, Ross.	**86**	56.04 N	77.18 E
Šipilovo	**82**	54.49 N	37.32 E
Siping	**89**	43.12 N	124.20 E
Sipingjie	**98**	42.31 N	125.08 E
Sipirok	**114**	1.37 N	99.16 E
Sipitang	**112**	5.05 N	115.33 E
Sipiwesk	**184**	55.27 N	97.24 W
Sipiwesk Lake ⊜	**184**	55.05 N	97.35 W
Siple ⊕[3]	**9**	75.56 S	84.15 W
Siple, Mount ∧	**9**	73.15 S	126.06 W
Siple Coast ⊥[2]	**9**	82.00 S	153.00 W
Sipocot	**116**	13.46 N	122.58 E
Sipofaneni	**158**	26.41 S	31.41 E
Sipot	**114**	4.31 N	96.02 E
Şipoteny	**38**	47.18 N	28.11 E
Šipovatoje	**78**	49.56 N	37.24 E
Sipplingen	**58**	47.47 N	9.05 E
Si Prachan	**110**	14.37 N	100.09 E
Sipsey ≃	**194**	33.00 N	88.10 W
Sipsey Creek ≃	**194**	33.53 N	88.17 W
Sipu	**98**	40.48 N	113.43 E
Sipul	**164**	5.50 S	148.45 E
Šipunovo	**86**	52.13 N	82.17 E
Šipunskij, mys ≻	**74**	53.06 N	160.02 E
Sipupus	**114**	1.25 N	99.31 E
Sipura, Pulau I	**112**	2.12 S	99.40 E
Siqian, Zhg.	**100**	22.31 N	112.52 E
Siqian, Zhg.	**100**	24.40 N	114.06 E
Siqueira Campos	**255**	23.42 S	49.50 W
Siquia ≃	**236**	12.09 N	84.13 W
Siquijor	**116**	9.13 N	123.30 E
Siquijor □[4]	**116**	9.11 N	123.34 E
Siquijor Island I	**116**	9.11 N	123.34 E
Siquirres	**236**	10.06 N	83.30 W
Siquisique	**246**	10.34 N	69.42 W
Sīra, India	**122**	13.45 N	76.54 E
Sira, Nor.	**26**	58.25 N	6.38 E
Šira, Ross.	**86**	54.29 N	89.56 E
Sira ≃	**26**	58.17 N	6.24 E
Si Racha	**110**	13.10 N	100.56 E
Siracuas	**248**	21.03 S	61.46 W
Siracusa (Syracuse)	**70**	37.04 N	15.17 E
Siracusa □[4]	**70**	37.03 N	15.00 E
Sir Adam Beck II Reservoir ⊜[1]	**284a**	43.08 N	79.04 W
Sirāhā	**124**	26.39 N	86.12 E
Šir'aj	**80**	49.34 N	44.07 E
Šir'ajevo	**78**	47.23 N	30.13 E
Sirājganj	**124**	24.27 N	89.43 E
Sir Alexander, Mount ∧	**182**	53.56 N	120.23 W
Sirāmpur	**126**	24.08 N	86.20 E
Şiran	**130**	40.12 N	39.08 E
Sirasso	**150**	9.16 N	6.06 W
Sirault	**50**	50.30 N	3.47 E
Siraway	**116**	7.34 N	122.08 E
Sirba ≃	**150**	13.46 N	1.40 E
Şīr Banī Yās I	**128**	24.19 N	52.37 E
Sir Colin Mackenzie Wildlife Sanctuary ⇸[4]	**169**	37.40 S	145.32 E
Sirdalsvatn ⊜	**26**	58.33 N	6.41 E
Sīrdān	**128**	36.39 N	49.12 E
Sirdar	**182**	49.15 N	116.37 W
Širdkoje	**78**	48.08 N	34.49 E
Sir Douglas, Mount ∧	**182**	50.44 N	115.20 W
Sire	**144**	9.00 N	36.55 E
Sir Edward Pellew Group II	**164**	15.40 S	136.48 E
Širega	**76**	60.10 N	41.15 E
Sireniki	**180**	64.25 N	173.57 W
Sirente, Monte ∧	**66**	42.09 N	13.36 E
Siret	**38**	47.57 N	26.04 E
Siret ≃	**38**	45.24 N	28.01 E
Sirevåg	**26**	58.30 N	5.47 E
Sir Francis Drake, Mount ∧	**182**	50.48 N	124.47 W
Sir Francis Drake Channel ʯ	**240m**	18.25 N	64.30 W
Sirghāyā	**132**	33.48 N	36.09 E
Sirḥān, Wādī as- V	**128**	30.30 N	38.00 E
Sirhind	**124**	30.39 N	76.23 E
Sirhind Canal ≍	**123**	30.47 N	76.01 E
Siria → Syria □[1]	**128**	35.00 N	38.00 E
Sirik, Tanjong ≻	**112**	2.46 N	111.19 E
Sirikit Reservoir ⊜[1]	**110**	17.50 N	100.30 E
Sirina I	**130**	36.21 N	26.42 E
Širinguši	**80**	53.51 N	42.46 E
Sirino, Monte ∧	**68**	40.08 N	15.50 E
Siriya-zaki ≻	**92**	41.26 N	141.28 E
Sir James MacBrien, Mount ∧	**180**	62.07 N	127.41 W
Sīrjān	**128**	29.27 N	55.40 E
Sir Joseph Banks Group II	**166**	34.32 S	136.17 E
Sirkābād	**126**	23.16 N	86.12 E
Sirkeli	**130**	40.09 N	32.52 E
Sirmaur	**124**	24.51 N	81.23 E
Sirmione	**64**	45.30 N	10.36 E
Širmovka	**78**	49.34 N	29.06 E
Sirnach	**58**	47.28 N	9.00 E
Şirnak □[4]	**128**	37.32 N	42.28 E
Siro, Jabal ∧	**140**	14.23 N	24.23 E
Sirohi	**120**	24.54 N	72.51 E
Širokaja Pad'	**89**	50.14 N	142.09 E
Širokij	**89**	49.45 N	129.30 E
Širokij Bujerak	**80**	52.07 N	47.46 E
Širokino	**83**	47.06 N	37.49 E
Širokoje, Ukr.	**78**	47.41 N	33.14 E
Širokoje, Ukr.	**83**	47.58 N	38.13 E
Širokolanovka	**78**	47.10 N	31.24 E
Širokovo	**88**	55.27 N	99.23 E
Sirolo	**66**	43.32 N	13.37 E
Sirombu	**114**	0.57 N	97.25 E
Sironj	**124**	24.06 N	77.42 E
Síros → Ermoúpolis	**38**	37.26 N	24.56 E
Síros I	**38**	37.26 N	24.54 E
Sirotino, Bela.	**76**	55.23 N	29.37 E
Sirotino, Ukr.	**83**	48.55 N	38.31 E
Sirotinskaja	**80**	49.16 N	43.39 E
Siroua, Jebel ∧	**148**	30.41 N	7.37 W
Sırpsındığı	**130**	41.46 N	26.29 E
Sirrah, Nafūd as- ⊥[8]	**128**	23.05 N	44.25 E
Sīrrī, Jazīreh-ye I	**128**	25.55 N	54.32 E
Sirsa, India	**123**	29.32 N	75.01 E
Sirsa, India	**126**	22.14 N	86.38 E
Sirsāganj	**124**	27.03 N	78.42 E
Sirs al-Layyānah	**142**	30.26 N	30.58 E
Sir Sandford, Mount ∧	**182**	51.40 N	117.52 W
Sirsi	**122**	14.37 N	74.51 E
Sirsilla	**122**	18.23 N	78.50 E
Sirsinā, Mişr	**142**	30.36 N	30.54 E
Sirsinā, Mişr	**142**	29.24 N	30.58 E
Sirsiri	**154**	4.24 N	31.53 E
Sir Thomas, Mount ∧	**162**	27.10 S	129.45 E
Siruma	**116**	14.00 N	123.15 E
Sirupa ≃	**232**	29.10 N	108.35 W
Şirvan	**130**	38.02 N	42.00 E
Şīrvān (Diyālā) ≃	**128**	33.14 N	44.31 E
Širvanskaja ravnina ≚	**84**	40.15 N	48.00 E
Širvintos	**76**	55.03 N	24.57 E
Sir Wilfrid Laurier, Mount ∧	**182**	52.47 N	119.45 W
Sir Wilfrid Laurier's Birthplace National Historic Site ⊥	**206**	45.51 N	73.45 W
Sirykrabet ⊥	**86**	44.07 N	62.35 E
Sís ≃, Guat.	**236**	14.09 N	91.39 W
Šiš ≃, Ross.	**86**	57.19 N	73.23 E
Sisa, Mount ∧	**164**	6.08 S	142.45 E
Sisaba ∧	**154**	6.09 S	29.48 E
Sisaiya Thāna	**124**	27.35 N	81.20 E
Sisak	**36**	45.29 N	16.23 E
Si Sa Ket	**110**	15.07 N	104.20 E
Šišaki	**78**	49.53 N	34.00 E
Šišakovo	**76**	60.02 N	41.30 E
Si Satchanalai	**110**	17.31 N	99.46 E
Šišchid (Kyzyl-Chem) ≃	**88**	51.21 N	96.58 E
Šiševka	**76**	58.52 N	38.52 E
Sishangcun	**105**	40.16 N	116.33 E
Sishen	**158**	27.55 S	22.59 E
Sishili	**106**	32.09 N	120.45 E
Sishilijie	**100**	29.08 N	116.44 E
Sishilipu	**105**	40.12 N	118.08 E
Sishuang Liedao II	**100**	26.42 N	120.24 E
Sishui	**98**	35.39 N	117.15 E
Sisian	**84**	39.32 N	46.02 E
Sisib Lake ⊜	**184**	52.35 N	99.22 W
Šišicy	**76**	53.13 N	27.32 E
Sisikon	**58**	46.57 N	8.42 E
Sisim ≃	**88**	55.09 N	91.54 E
Sisipuk Lake ⊜	**184**	55.45 N	101.50 W
Šiškejevo	**80**	54.12 N	44.45 E
Šiškino	**88**	52.18 N	113.35 E
Siskiyou Mountains ⋏	**204**	41.55 N	123.15 W
Siskiyou Pass)(	**202**	42.03 N	122.36 W
Şişli ⇸[8]	**267b**	41.04 N	28.59 E
Šišlovo	**82**	54.14 N	38.33 E
Sison	**116**	9.40 N	125.31 E
Sisŏphŏn	**110**	13.35 N	102.59 E
Sisquoc ≃	**204**	34.54 N	120.18 W
Sissa ≃	**115b**	8.29 S	121.18 E
Sissach	**58**	47.28 N	7.49 E
Sissano	**164**	3.00 S	142.05 E
Sisséla	**150**	10.49 N	10.37 W
Sisseton	**198**	45.39 N	97.02 W
Sisseton Indian Reservation ⇸[4]	**198**	45.40 N	97.02 W
Sissili ≃	**150**	10.16 N	1.15 W
Sisson Branch Reservoir ⊜[1]	**186**	47.16 N	67.20 W
Sissonne	**50**	49.34 N	3.54 E
Sissonville	**188**	38.31 N	81.37 W
Sīstān ⇸[1]	**128**	30.30 N	62.00 E
Sīstān va Balūchestān □[4]	**128**	28.30 N	60.30 E
Sister Bay	**190**	45.11 N	87.07 W
Sister Lakes	**216**	42.05 N	86.12 W
Sisteron	**62**	44.12 N	5.56 E
Sisters	**202**	44.17 N	121.32 W
Sistersville	**188**	39.33 N	80.59 W
Sistig	**56**	50.29 N	6.30 E
Sisto ≃	**66**	41.18 N	13.10 E
Sistranda	**26**	63.43 N	8.50 E
Sit' ≃, Ross.	**76**	58.16 N	37.54 E
Sit' ≃, Ross.	**76**	59.59 N	40.10 E
Sitabamba	**248**	8.02 S	77.44 W
Sitai, Zhg.	**85**	39.23 N	77.56 E
Sitai, Zhg.	**98**	41.16 N	114.23 E
Sitaizi, Zhg.	**104**	42.29 N	123.20 E
Sitaizi, Zhg.	**104**	41.17 N	122.16 E
Sitaizui	**105**	40.49 N	115.20 E
Sitakili	**150**	13.07 N	11.14 W
Sitalike	**154**	6.38 S	31.08 E
Sitalkuchi	**124**	26.10 N	89.11 E
Sītāmarhi	**124**	26.36 N	85.29 E
Sitampiky	**157b**	16.41 S	46.06 E
Si Tangkay	**112**	4.40 N	119.24 E
Sītāpur	**124**	27.34 N	80.41 E
Sītāpur Branch ≍	**124**	28.10 N	80.25 E
Sitārāmpur	**126**	23.43 N	86.53 E
Siteki	**158**	26.32 S	31.58 E
Sites	**226**	39.19 N	122.20 W
Si Thep ⊥	**110**	15.30 N	101.10 E
Sithoniá	**38**	35.12 N	26.07 E
Sithoniá ≻[1]	**38**	40.10 N	23.47 E
Sitidgi Lake ⊜	**180**	68.32 N	132.42 W
Sítio D'Abadia	**255**	14.48 S	46.16 W
Sítio Novo	**250**	5.51 S	46.43 W
Sitka	**180**	57.03 N	135.02 W
Sitkalidak Island I	**180**	57.10 N	153.14 W
Sitka National Historical Park ♦	**180**	57.05 N	135.15 W
Sitka Point ≻	**180**	57.00 N	135.49 W
Sitka Sound ʯ	**180**	57.00 N	135.30 W
Sitkinak Island I	**180**	56.35 N	154.12 W
Sitkinak Strait ʯ	**180**	56.39 N	154.06 W
Šitkino	**88**	56.23 N	98.21 E
Sitkovcy	**78**	48.54 N	29.12 E
Sitna ≃	**38**	47.37 N	27.08 E
Sitn'a-Ščelkanovo	**82**	54.58 N	37.59 E
Sitnica ≃	**38**	42.45 N	21.01 E
Sitniki	**80**	56.27 N	44.06 E
Sitnikovo	**86**	56.23 N	67.53 E
Sitobela	**158**	26.53 S	31.36 E
Sitona	**144**	14.28 N	37.27 E
Sitrah	**128**	26.09 N	50.38 E
Sitrah ⩡[4]	**140**	28.42 N	26.54 E
Sittard	**56**	51.00 N	5.53 E
Sitten → Sion	**58**	46.14 N	7.21 E
Sittendorf	**264b**	48.05 N	16.10 E
Sittensen	**52**	53.17 N	9.30 E
Sitter ≃	**58**	47.29 N	9.14 E
Sittingbourne	**42**	51.21 N	0.44 E
Sittoung ≃	**110**	17.10 N	96.58 E
Sittwe (Akyab)	**110**	20.09 N	92.54 E
Situ	**105**	39.20 N	115.39 E
Situbondo	**115a**	7.42 S	114.00 E
Siufaalele Point ≻	**174y**	14.17 S	169.29 W
Si'ufage	**174y**	14.14 S	169.32 W
Siulakderas	**112**	1.55 S	101.18 E
Siu Lek Yuen	**271d**	22.23 N	114.12 E
Siumbatu	**112**	2.45 S	122.03 E
Siumpu, Pulau I	**112**	5.40 S	122.31 E
Siuna	**236**	13.44 N	84.46 W
Siurgus Donigala	**71**	39.35 N	9.12 E
Siuri	**126**	23.55 N	87.32 E
Siusi (Seis)	**64**	46.32 N	11.34 E
Siuslaw ≃	**202**	44.01 N	124.08 W
Siva ≃	**80**	56.48 N	53.55 E
Sivaganga	**122**	9.52 N	78.29 E
Sivakāsi	**122**	9.27 N	77.49 E
Sivaki	**89**	52.39 N	126.45 E
Sīvand ≃	**128**	29.51 N	52.46 E
Sivas	**130**	39.45 N	37.02 E
Sivas □[4]	**130**	39.30 N	37.15 E
Sivaš ʯ	**78**	46.00 N	34.30 E
Sivaslı	**130**	38.30 N	29.42 E
Sivašskoje	**78**	46.23 N	34.34 E
Sivé	**150**	15.42 N	13.12 W
Šiveluč, vulkan ∧[1]	**74**	56.39 N	161.18 E
Siverek	**130**	37.45 N	39.19 E
Siverskij	**76**	59.21 N	30.05 E
Sivkovo	**82**	55.26 N	35.53 E
Sivomaskinskij	**24**	66.40 N	62.35 E
Sivri Ada I	**267b**	40.54 N	28.59 E
Sivrice	**130**	38.27 N	39.19 E
Sivrihisar	**130**	39.27 N	31.34 E
Sivry-Courtry	**261**	48.32 N	2.45 E
Sivry-sur-Meuse	**56**	49.19 N	5.16 E
Sīwah	**140**	29.12 N	25.31 E
Sīwah, Wāḥat ⩡[4]	**140**	29.12 N	25.31 E
Siwalik Range ⋏	**120**	31.00 N	78.00 E
Siwān	**124**	26.13 N	84.22 E
Siwang ≃	**107**	29.25 N	103.50 E
Sixaola ≃	**236**	9.34 N	82.34 W
Six Flags Great America ♦	**216**	42.21 N	87.55 W
Six Flags over Mid-America ♦	**219**	38.31 N	90.40 W
Six Flags Over Texas ♦	**222**	32.45 N	97.05 W
Six-Fours-la-Plage	**62**	43.06 N	5.51 E
Sixian	**100**	33.30 N	117.56 E
Sixitou	**100**	27.31 N	119.57 E
Six Mile Creek ≃, On., Can.	**284a**	43.15 N	79.10 W
Sixmile Creek ≃, Ky., U.S.	**218**	38.26 N	84.58 W
Sixmile Creek ≃, N.Y., U.S.	**284a**	43.17 N	78.58 W
Sixmilecross	**48**	54.34 N	7.08 W
Six Mile Lake ⊜	**212**	44.55 N	79.45 W
Sixmile Run ≃	**276**	40.28 N	74.35 W
Six Mile Water ≃	**48**	54.42 N	6.14 W
Six Nations Indian Reserve ⇸[4]	**212**	43.03 N	80.07 W
Sixshooter Draw V	**196**	30.51 N	102.33 W
Sixteen Mile Creek ≃, On., Can.	**275b**	43.27 N	79.40 W
Sixteenmile Creek ≃, Mt., U.S.	**202**	46.06 N	111.23 W
Sixth Cataract → Sablūkah, Ash-Shallāl as- ᒪ	**140**	16.20 N	32.42 E
Siyāl, Jazā'ir II	**140**	22.47 N	36.12 E
Siyāna	**124**	28.38 N	78.03 E
Siyang	**100**	33.43 N	118.41 E
Si Yat ≃	**110**	13.42 N	101.26 E
Siyeteb	**140**	18.00 N	35.01 E
Siz'absk	**24**	65.05 N	53.49 E
Sizaja	**88**	58.07 N	100.38 E
Sizhijian	**98**	42.25 N	114.36 E
Siziano	**62**	45.20 N	9.12 E
Sizilien → Sicilia I	**70**	37.30 N	14.00 E
Siziman	**89**	50.43 N	140.26 E
Siziwang Qi	**102**	41.33 N	111.31 E
Sizun	**32**	48.24 N	4.05 W
Sizuoka → Shizuoka	**94**	34.58 N	138.23 E
Sjælland I	**41**	55.30 N	11.45 E
Sjællands Odde ≻[1]	**41**	55.58 N	11.22 E
Själevad	**26**	63.18 N	18.36 E
Sjanovo	**82**	54.59 N	37.25 E
Sjenica	**38**	43.16 N	20.00 E
Sjeništa ∧	**38**	43.42 N	18.37 E
Sjoa ≃	**26**	61.41 N	9.33 E
Sjöbo	**41**	55.38 N	13.42 E
Sjøholt	**26**	62.29 N	6.48 E
Sjösa	**40**	58.46 N	17.04 E
Sjötorp	**40**	58.50 N	13.59 E
Skaby	**264a**	52.19 N	13.51 E
Skaby-Berge ∧[2]	**264a**	52.19 N	13.49 E
Skåde	**41**	56.06 N	10.13 E
Skadovsk	**78**	46.08 N	32.54 E
Skælskør	**41**	55.15 N	11.19 E
Skærbæk, Dan.	**41**	55.31 N	9.38 E
Skærbæk, Dan.	**41**	55.09 N	8.46 E
Skævinge	**41**	55.55 N	12.10 E
Skaftafell National Park ♦	**24a**	64.15 N	17.00 W
Skaftung	**26**	62.07 N	21.22 E
Skagafjörður ⊂	**24a**	65.55 N	19.35 W
Skagen	**26**	57.44 N	10.36 E
Skagern ⊜	**40**	58.59 N	14.17 E
Skagerrak ʯ	**26**	57.45 N	9.00 E
Skagersvik	**40**	58.58 N	14.06 E
Skaggs Creek ≃	**194**	36.54 N	86.04 W
Skagit □[6]	**224**	48.29 N	121.45 W
Skagit ≃	**224**	48.20 N	122.25 W
Skagit Bay ⊂	**224**	48.19 N	122.24 W
Skagway	**180**	59.28 N	135.19 W
Skaidi	**24**	70.25 N	24.30 E
Skaistkalne	**76**	56.23 N	24.39 E
Skála Oropoú	**38**	38.20 N	23.46 E
Skala-Podol'skaja	**78**	48.51 N	26.12 E
Skalat	**78**	49.26 N	25.59 E
Skalbmierz	**30**	50.19 N	20.25 E
Skälderviken	**41**	56.17 N	12.50 E
Skälderviken ⊂	**41**	56.18 N	12.38 E
Skalica	**30**	48.51 N	17.14 E
Skalino	**76**	58.32 N	40.13 E
Skalistaja, gora ∧	**84**	42.48 N	45.08 E
Skalistyj, gora ∧	**180**	68.12 N	178.10 E
Skalistyj chrebet ⋏	**84**	43.15 N	43.00 E
Skalistyj Golec, gora ∧	**88**	56.24 N	119.12 E
Skalka ⊜	**24**	66.50 N	18.46 E
Skalka, údolní nádrž ⊜[1]	**54**	50.06 N	12.19 E
Skalná	**54**	50.07 N	12.23 E
Skal'nyj	**86**	58.22 N	57.59 E
Skamania	**224**	45.37 N	122.02 W
Skamania □[6]	**224**	45.58 N	121.53 W
Skamlingsbanke ∧[2]	**41**	55.25 N	9.34 E
Skamokawa	**224**	46.16 N	123.27 W
Skanderborg	**41**	56.02 N	9.56 E
Skanderborg Sø ⊜	**41**	56.01 N	9.56 E
Skåne □[9]	**41**	55.59 N	13.30 E
Skaneateles	**210**	42.56 N	76.25 W
Skaneateles Falls	**210**	43.00 N	76.27 W
Skaneateles Lake ⊜	**210**	42.53 N	76.24 W
Skånevik	**26**	59.44 N	5.59 E
Skänninge	**26**	58.24 N	15.05 E
Skanör	**26**	55.25 N	12.52 E
Skara	**26**	58.22 N	13.25 E
Skaraborgs Län □[6]	**26**	58.20 N	13.30 E
Skaramagás	**267c**	38.01 N	23.36 E
Skärblacka	**40**	58.34 N	15.54 E
Skarð	**24a**	64.03 N	19.50 W
Skardhø ∧	**26**	62.30 N	8.45 E
Skārdu	**123**	35.18 N	75.37 E
Skärhamn	**26**	58.00 N	11.33 E
Skarhult	**41**	55.49 N	13.23 E
Skarnes	**26**	60.15 N	11.41 E
Skärplinge	**40**	60.28 N	17.46 E
Skarszewy	**30**	54.05 N	18.27 E
Skårup	**41**	55.05 N	10.42 E
Skaryszew	**30**	51.19 N	21.15 E
Skarżysko-Kamienna	**30**	51.08 N	20.53 E
Skášov	**60**	49.31 N	13.26 E
Skate Creek ≃	**224**	46.37 N	121.41 W
Skattkärr	**40**	59.25 N	13.41 E
Skaudvilė	**76**	55.24 N	22.35 E
Skaugum	**26**	59.51 N	10.26 E
Skawina	**30**	49.59 N	19.49 E
Skebobruk	**40**	59.58 N	18.36 E
Skebokvarn	**40**	59.04 N	16.42 E
Skedviken ⊜	**40**	59.46 N	18.16 E
Skedvisjön ⊜	**40**	59.35 N	15.40 E
Skeena ≃	**182**	54.09 N	130.02 W
Skeena Crossing	**182**	55.06 N	127.49 W
Skeena Mountains ⋏	**176**	57.00 N	128.30 W
Skeen Peak ∧	**222**	32.59 N	97.48 W
Skegness	**44**	53.10 N	0.21 E
Skegrie	**41**	55.24 N	13.04 E
Skei	**26**	61.38 N	6.30 E
Skeikampen	**26**	61.20 N	10.07 E
Skelde	**41**	54.51 N	9.44 E
Skeleton Coast ⊥[2]	**156**	19.15 S	12.30 E
Skeleton Coast Park ♦	**156**	19.25 S	12.55 E
Skeleton Creek ≃	**196**	35.58 N	97.25 W
Skeleton Lake ⊜	**212**	45.15 N	79.27 W
Skellefteå	**26**	64.46 N	20.57 E
Skellefteälven ≃	**26**	64.42 N	21.06 E
Skelleftehamn	**26**	64.41 N	21.14 E
Skellig Rocks II[1]	**48**	51.48 N	10.31 W
Skellytown	**196**	35.34 N	101.11 W
Skelmersdale	**44**	53.33 N	2.48 W
Skelmorlie	**46**	55.51 N	4.53 W
Skelton, Eng., U.K.	**44**	54.33 N	0.59 W
Skelton, Eng., U.K.	**44**	54.43 N	2.51 W
Skene	**26**	57.29 N	12.38 E
Skene, Mount ∧	**169**	37.25 S	146.23 E
Skepptuna	**40**	59.43 N	18.05 E
Skerne ≃	**44**	54.29 N	1.34 W
Skerpioensdrif	**158**	31.05 S	21.33 E
Skerries	**48**	53.35 N	6.07 W
Skerryvore I[2]	**46**	56.19 N	7.07 W
Skewen	**42**	51.40 N	3.51 W
Skhíza I	**38**	36.44 N	21.46 E
Ski	**26**	59.43 N	10.50 E
Skíathos	**38**	39.10 N	23.29 E
Skíathos I	**38**	39.10 N	23.28 E
Skiatook	**196**	36.22 N	96.00 W
Skibbereen	**48**	51.33 N	9.15 W
Skibby	**41**	55.45 N	11.58 E
Skibotn	**24**	69.24 N	20.16 E
Skiddaw ∧	**44**	54.38 N	3.08 W
Skidegate	**182**	53.15 N	132.00 W
Skidegate Inlet ⊂	**182**	53.14 N	132.00 W
Skidel'	**76**	53.34 N	24.15 E
Skidmore	**196**	28.15 N	97.41 W
Skien	**26**	59.12 N	9.36 E
Skierniewice	**30**	51.58 N	20.08 E
Skierniewice □[4]	**30**	52.10 N	20.15 E
Skiftet ʯ	**26**	60.15 N	21.05 E
Skihist Mountain ∧	**182**	50.11 N	121.54 W
Skikda (Philippeville)	**148**	36.50 N	6.58 E
Skikda □[5]	**148**	36.45 N	7.00 E
Skilak Lake ⊜	**180**	60.25 N	150.25 W
Skillet Fork ≃	**194**	38.08 N	88.07 W
Skillingaryd	**26**	57.26 N	14.05 E
Skillman	**276**	40.25 N	74.42 W
Škin'	**82**	55.11 N	38.30 E
Skinnastaður	**24a**	66.07 N	16.24 W
Skinner Reservoir ⊜[1]	**228**	33.35 N	117.03 W
Skinnskatteberg	**40**	59.50 N	15.41 E
Skippack	**285**	40.14 N	75.24 W
Skippack Creek ≃	**285**	40.09 N	75.27 W
Skippack Creek, West Branch ≃	**285**	40.14 N	75.23 W
Skippers	**208**	36.37 N	77.38 W
Skipskop	**158**	34.33 S	20.25 E
Skipton, Austl.	**169**	37.41 S	143.22 E
Skipton, Eng., U.K.	**44**	53.58 N	2.01 W
Skirfare ≃	**44**	54.07 N	2.01 W
Skirmish Point ≻	**171a**	27.05 S	153.13 E
Skíros	**38**	38.53 N	24.33 E
Skíros I	**38**	38.53 N	24.32 E
Skivarp	**41**	55.25 N	13.34 E
Skive	**26**	56.34 N	9.02 E
Skjálfandafljót ≃	**24a**	65.57 N	17.38 W
Skjálfandi ⊂	**24a**	66.08 N	17.38 W
Skjeberg	**26**	59.14 N	11.12 E
Skjern	**26**	55.57 N	8.30 E
Skjern ≃	**41**	55.57 N	8.40 E
Sklad	**74**	71.55 N	123.33 E
Šklov	**76**	54.13 N	30.18 E
Skniga ≃	**82**	54.53 N	37.24 E
Skobeleva, pik ∧	**85**	39.49 N	72.44 E
Skoby	**40**	60.02 N	18.01 E
Škocjanske jame ⊥[7]	**36**	45.40 N	14.00 E
Skodborg	**41**	55.25 N	9.09 E
Skodsborg	**41**	55.49 N	12.34 E
Skoenmakerskop	**158**	34.02 S	25.33 E
Škofije	**64**	45.34 N	13.48 E
Škofja Loka	**36**	46.10 N	14.18 E
Skoganvarre	**24**	69.47 N	25.06 E

ENGLISH

Name	Page	Lat.°′	Long.°′
Skoghall	**40**	59.19 N	13.26 E
Skogstorp	**40**	59.20 N	16.28 E
Skokholm Island I	**42**	51.42 N	5.16 W
Skoki	**30**	52.41 N	17.10 E
Skokie	**216**	42.02 N	87.44 W
Skokie ≃	**216**	42.05 N	87.46 W
Skokie Lagoons ⊂	**278**	42.07 N	87.47 W
Skokloster ⊥	**40**	59.42 N	17.37 E
Skokomish, North Fork ≃	**224**	47.18 N	123.14 W
Skokomish, South Fork ≃	**224**	47.18 N	123.14 W
Skokomish Indian Reservation ⇸[4]	**224**	47.21 N	123.12 W
Sköldinge	**40**	59.02 N	16.26 E
Skole	**78**	49.02 N	23.29 E
Sköllersta	**40**	59.09 N	15.20 E
Skolsta	**40**	59.40 N	17.14 E
Skolwin	**54**	53.32 N	14.35 E
Skomer Island I	**42**	51.44 N	5.17 W
Skomoroški, Ross.	**82**	54.05 N	36.57 E
Skomoroški, Ukr.	**78**	49.20 N	29.26 E
Skón	**110**	12.04 N	105.04 E
Skookumchuck ≃	**224**	46.41 N	123.00 W
Skookumchuck Reservoir ⊜[1]	**224**	47.47 N	122.42 W
Skoonspruit ≃	**158**	27.00 S	26.38 E
Skootamatta ≃	**212**	44.32 N	77.20 W
Skootamatta Lake ⊜	**212**	44.50 N	77.15 W
Skópelos, Ellás	**38**	39.02 N	26.26 E
Skópelos, Ellás	**38**	39.07 N	23.43 E
Skópelos I	**38**	39.10 N	23.40 E
Skopin	**76**	53.51 N	39.33 E
Skopje	**38**	41.59 N	21.26 E
Skórcz	**30**	53.48 N	18.32 E
Skorodnoje, Bela.	**78**	51.38 N	28.49 E
Skorodnoje, Ross.	**78**	51.05 N	37.14 E
Skørping	**26**	56.50 N	9.53 E
Skotfoss	**26**	59.12 N	9.30 E
Skotovataja	**83**	48.13 N	37.54 E
Škotovo	**89**	43.20 N	132.21 E
Skotterud	**26**	59.59 N	12.07 E
Skovby	**41**	54.53 N	10.00 E
Skövde	**26**	58.24 N	13.50 E
Skovlund	**41**	55.44 N	8.43 E
Skovorodino	**89**	53.59 N	123.55 E
Skowhegan	**188**	44.45 N	69.43 W
Skownan	**184**	51.57 N	99.36 W
Skradin	**36**	43.49 N	15.56 E
Skreen	**48**	54.15 N	8.45 W
Skreia	**26**	60.39 N	10.56 E
Skriplivka	**76**	57.32 N	30.38 E
Skrīveri	**76**	56.39 N	25.08 E
Skromberga	**41**	56.00 N	12.58 E
Skrudaliena	**76**	55.49 N	26.43 E
Skrunda	**76**	56.41 N	22.01 E
Skruv	**26**	56.41 N	15.22 E
Skrydstrup	**41**	55.14 N	9.15 E
Skudeneshavn	**26**	59.09 N	5.17 E
Skukuza	**156**	25.01 S	31.38 E
Skuleberget ∧[2]	**26**	63.05 N	18.21 E
Skulforp	**26**	58.21 N	13.49 E
Skull	**48**	51.32 N	9.33 W
Skull Creek ≃	**222**	29.32 N	96.24 W
Skull Valley	**200**	34.30 N	112.41 W
Skull Valley Indian Reservation ⇸[4]	**200**	40.24 N	112.45 W
Skultuna	**40**	59.43 N	16.25 E
Skuna ≃	**194**	33.54 N	89.41 W
Skunk ≃	**190**	40.42 N	91.07 W
Škunovka	**86**	50.45 N	55.27 E
Skuodas	**76**	56.16 N	21.32 E
Skuratovskij	**82**	54.07 N	37.36 E
Škurinskaja	**78**	46.35 N	39.22 E
Skurišenskaja	**80**	49.52 N	42.57 E
Skurup	**41**	55.28 N	13.30 E
Skutskär	**40**	60.38 N	17.25 E
Skvira	**78**	49.44 N	29.40 E
Skwentna	**180**	61.58 N	151.11 W
Skwentna ≃	**180**	62.00 N	151.08 W
Skwierzyna	**30**	52.36 N	15.30 E
Skye, Island of I	**46**	57.18 N	6.15 W
Sky Harbor Airport ⊠	**278**	42.09 N	87.51 W
Skykomish	**224**	47.42 N	121.21 W
Skykomish ≃	**224**	47.50 N	122.03 W
Skykomish, North Fork ≃	**224**	47.47 N	121.33 W
Skykomish, South Fork ≃	**224**	47.47 N	121.33 W
Sky Lake	**220**	28.28 N	81.24 W
Sky Lake ⊜	**212**	44.48 N	81.15 W
Skyland, Nv., U.S.	**226**	39.01 N	119.56 W
Skyland, N.C., U.S.	**192**	35.29 N	82.31 W
Skylight	**218**	38.25 N	85.31 W
Skyline	**284c**	38.50 N	76.54 W
Skyline Lakes ⊜	**276**	41.04 N	74.16 W
Skyllberg	**40**	58.57 N	14.59 E
Skyring, Península ≻[1]	**254**	45.58 S	74.53 W
Skyring, Seno ʯ	**254**	52.35 S	72.00 W
Sky Sailing Airport ⊠	**282**	37.30 N	121.58 W
Skytop	**210**	41.14 N	75.15 W
Skyttorp	**40**	60.05 N	17.44 E
Skyway	**224**	47.29 N	122.14 W
Slackhall	**262**	53.20 N	1.53 W
Slackwood	**208**	40.15 N	74.44 W
Slade Green ⇸[8]	**260**	51.28 N	0.12 E
Sladkij	**80**	46.10 N	42.17 E
Sladkovo	**86**	55.32 N	70.20 E
Slagelse	**41**	55.24 N	11.22 E
Slagnäs	**24**	65.34 N	18.05 E
Slagoviščí	**76**	53.57 N	35.54 E
Slaithwaite	**262**	53.37 N	1.53 W
Slamannan	**46**	55.56 N	3.50 W
Slamet, Gunung ∧	**115a**	7.14 S	109.12 E
Slaná (Sajó) ≃	**30**	47.56 N	21.08 E
Slancy	**76**	59.06 N	28.04 E
Slaney ≃	**48**	52.21 N	6.30 W
Slangerup	**41**	55.51 N	12.11 E
Slănic	**38**	45.15 N	25.57 E
Slănic Moldova	**38**	46.13 N	26.26 E
Slano	**36**	42.47 N	17.54 E
Slanské vrchy ⋏	**30**	48.50 N	21.30 E
Slaný	**54**	50.11 N	14.04 E
Šlapanice	**30**	49.10 N	16.44 E
Slaščevskaja	**80**	49.52 N	42.21 E
Śląsk → Silesia □[9]	**30**	51.00 N	16.45 E
Slastucha	**80**	51.57 N	44.32 E
Slate Bottom Creek ≃	**284a**	42.53 N	78.45 W
Slate Creek ≃, Ks., U.S.	**198**	37.08 N	97.09 W
Slate Creek ≃, Pa., U.S.	**279b**	40.28 N	79.32 W
Slatedale	**208**	40.45 N	75.40 W
Slate Hill	**210**	41.23 N	74.29 W
Slater, Ia., U.S.	**190**	41.52 N	93.40 W
Slater, Mo., U.S.	**194**	39.13 N	93.04 W
Slater Creek ≃	**200**	40.59 N	107.23 W
Slatersville	**207**	42.00 N	71.34 W
Slaterville Springs	**210**	42.24 N	76.21 W
Slatina	**38**	44.26 N	24.22 E
Slatington	**208**	40.44 N	75.36 W
Slatino	**78**	50.12 N	36.11 E
Slaton	**196**	33.26 N	101.38 W
Slattocks	**262**	53.35 N	2.10 W
Slaughter	**194**	30.43 N	91.08 W
Slaung	**115a**	8.02 S	111.24 E
Slautnoje	**74**	63.00 N	167.59 E
Slava	**89**	52.08 N	129.24 E
Slav'anka, Ross.	**89**	42.53 N	131.21 E
Slav'anka, Ukr.	**78**	48.24 N	36.43 E
Slav'anka, Uzb.	**85**	40.40 N	68.32 E
Slav'anka ≃	**265a**	59.50 N	30.32 E
Slav'anogorsk	**83**	49.02 N	37.31 E
Slav'anoserbsk	**83**	48.42 N	38.59 E
Slav'ansk	**83**	48.52 N	37.37 E
Slav'ansk-na-Kubani	**78**	45.15 N	38.08 E
Slave ≃	**176**	61.18 N	113.39 W
Slave Coast ⊥[2]	**150**	6.25 N	3.00 E
Slave Lake	**182**	55.17 N	114.46 W

DEUTSCH

Name	Seite	Breite°′	Länge°′ E = Ost
Slavgorod, Bela.	**76**	53.27 N	31.00 E
Slavgorod, Ross.	**86**	53.00 N	78.40 E
Slavgorod, Ukr.	**78**	48.06 N	35.31 E
Slavgorod, Ukr.	**78**	50.36 N	35.21 E
Slavitino	**82**	56.41 N	39.13 E
Slavkino	**80**	52.58 N	47.11 E
Slavkoviči	**76**	57.39 N	29.05 E
Slavkovský les ⋏	**54**	50.07 N	12.45 E
Slavkov u Brna	**61**	49.09 N	16.52 E
Slavnoje	**76**	54.18 N	29.27 E
Slavonia → Slavonija □[9]	**36**	45.00 N	18.00 E
Slavonice	**61**	49.00 N	15.21 E
Slavonija □[9]	**36**	45.00 N	18.00 E
Slavonska Požega	**36**	45.20 N	17.41 E
Slavonski Brod	**38**	45.10 N	18.01 E
Slavsk	**76**	55.03 N	21.41 E
Slavskoje	**78**	48.49 N	23.24 E
Slavuta	**78**	50.18 N	26.52 E
Sława	**30**	51.53 N	16.04 E
Slawi	**115a**	6.59 S	109.08 E
Sławno	**30**	54.22 N	16.40 E
Slayton	**198**	43.59 N	95.45 W
Slea ≃	**44**	53.03 N	0.12 W
Sleaford	**42**	53.00 N	0.24 W
Slea Head ≻	**48**	52.06 N	10.27 W
Sleat, Point of ≻	**46**	57.01 N	6.02 W
Sleat, Sound of ʯ	**46**	57.06 N	5.49 W
Sledge	**194**	34.25 N	90.13 W
Sledge Island I	**180**	64.29 N	166.13 W
Sled Lake ⊜	**184**	54.27 N	107.25 W
Sledmere	**44**	54.04 N	0.35 W
Slednevo	**82**	56.25 N	38.36 E
Sled'uki	**76**	53.35 N	30.22 E
Sleen	**52**	52.46 N	6.48 E
Sleeping Bear Dunes National Lakeshore ♦	**190**	44.50 N	86.08 W
Sleeping Giant State Park ♦	**207**	41.25 N	72.53 W
Sleepy Eye	**198**	44.17 N	94.43 W
Sleepy Hollow, Ca., U.S.	**226**	38.00 N	122.34 W
Sleepy Hollow, Ca., U.S.	**280**	33.57 N	117.47 W
Sleepy Hollow, Il., U.S.	**216**	42.06 N	88.24 W
Sleetmute	**180**	61.42 N	157.11 W
Sleidinge	**50**	51.08 N	3.41 E
Sleights	**44**	54.27 N	0.40 W
Sleman	**115a**	7.42 S	110.20 E
Slepino	**76**	59.11 N	29.02 E
Ślesin	**30**	52.23 N	18.19 E
Slessor Glacier ⊓	**9**	79.50 S	28.30 W
Slickville	**214**	40.27 N	79.31 W
Slidell	**194**	30.16 N	89.46 W
Slide Mountain ∧	**210**	42.00 N	74.23 W
Sliderock Mountain ∧	**202**	46.35 N	113.33 W
Sliedrecht	**52**	51.49 N	4.45 E
Slieve Aughty Mountains ⋏	**48**	53.05 N	8.35 W
Slieve Bloom Mountains ⋏	**48**	53.05 N	7.35 W
Slievekimalta ∧	**48**	52.45 N	8.16 W
Slievenamon ∧	**48**	52.25 N	7.34 W
Sligeach → Sligo	**48**	54.17 N	8.28 W
Sligo (Sligeach), Ire.	**48**	54.17 N	8.28 W
Sligo, Pa., U.S.	**214**	41.06 N	79.29 W
Sligo □[6]	**48**	54.10 N	8.40 W
Sligo Bay ⊂	**48**	54.20 N	8.40 W
Sligo Creek ≃	**284c**	38.57 N	76.58 W
Slikkerveer	**52**	51.53 N	4.37 E
Slingebeek ≃	**52**	51.56 N	6.17 E
Slinger	**190**	43.20 N	88.17 W
Šlino, ozero ⊜	**76**	57.40 N	33.23 E
Slioch ∧	**46**	57.41 N	5.22 W
Slippery Rock	**214**	41.03 N	80.03 W
Slippery Rock Creek ≃	**214**	40.51 N	80.15 W
Šlissel'burg	**265a**	59.57 N	31.02 E
Slite	**26**	57.43 N	18.48 E
Slīteres Rezervāts ♦	**76**	57.38 N	22.25 E
Sliven	**38**	42.40 N	26.19 E
Slivnica	**38**	42.51 N	23.02 E
Sloan, Ia., U.S.	**198**	42.13 N	96.13 W
Sloan, Nv., U.S.	**204**	35.56 N	115.12 W
Sloan, N.Y., U.S.	**210**	42.53 N	78.47 W
Sloan Peak ∧	**224**	48.03 N	121.20 W
Sloansville	**210**	42.46 N	74.20 W
Sloatsburg	**210**	41.09 N	74.11 W
Sloboda, Bela.	**76**	53.58 N	28.08 E
Sloboda, Ross.	**76**	55.30 N	31.51 E
Sloboda, Ross.	**78**	51.09 N	40.17 E
Sloboda, Ukr.	**78**	51.11 N	33.37 E
Slobodka, Bela.	**76**	55.41 N	27.11 E
Slobodka, Ross.	**82**	54.22 N	37.33 E
Slobodka, Ukr.	**78**	47.53 N	29.21 E
Slobodskoj	**86**	58.42 N	50.12 E
Slobodzeja	**38**	46.44 N	29.43 E
Slobodzeja-Mare	**38**	45.34 N	28.12 E
Slobozia, Rom.	**38**	44.34 N	27.23 E
Slobozia, Rom.	**38**	43.51 N	25.54 E
Slocan	**182**	49.46 N	117.28 W
Slocan Lake ⊜	**182**	49.56 N	117.22 W
Slochteren	**52**	53.12 N	6.47 E
Slocomb	**194**	31.06 N	85.35 W
Slocum	**207**	41.32 N	71.31 W
Slocum Mountain ∧	**228**	35.18 N	117.13 W
Słomniki	**30**	50.15 N	20.06 E
Slonim	**76**	53.06 N	25.19 E
Slonovka	**78**	50.39 N	37.45 E
Słońsk	**54**	52.35 N	14.50 E
Sloop Channel ʯ	**276**	40.36 N	73.31 W
Sloping Hills	**276**	40.42 N	74.34 W
Slosh Indian Reserve ⇸[4]	**182**	50.44 N	122.13 W
Sloten	**52**	52.54 N	5.38 E
Sloten ⇸[8]	**52**	52.21 N	4.48 E
Slotermeer ⊜	**52**	52.55 N	5.40 E
Slough	**42**	51.31 N	0.36 W
Slough □[8]	**260**	51.32 N	0.35 W
Slough Brook ≃	**276**	40.45 N	74.21 W
Sloughhouse	**226**	38.30 N	121.12 W
Slovakia → Slovensko □[9]	**30**	48.50 N	20.00 E
Slovakia □[1], Europe	**22**	48.30 N	20.00 E
Slovakia (Slovenská Republika) □[1], Europe	**30**	48.30 N	20.00 E
Slovan	**214**	40.21 N	80.23 W
Slovečna ≃	**78**	51.41 N	29.41 E
Slovečno	**78**	51.23 N	28.21 E
Slovenia □[1], Europe	**22**	46.15 N	15.10 E
Slovenia (Slovenija) □[1], Europe	**36**	46.15 N	15.10 E
Slovenija → Slovenia □[1]	**36**	46.15 N	15.10 E
Slovenj Gradec	**61**	46.31 N	15.05 E
Slovenska Bistrica, Slvn.	**36**	46.23 N	15.34 E
Slovenska Bistrica, Slvn.	**61**	46.23 N	15.34 E
Slovenske Gorice ⋏[2]	**61**	46.35 N	15.55 E
Slovenské rudohorie ⋏	**30**	48.45 N	20.00 E
Slovensko □[9]	**30**	48.50 N	20.00 E
Slovinka	**80**	58.02 N	43.07 E
Slowakei → Slovensko □[9]	**30**	48.50 N	20.00 E
Słowiński Park Narodowy ♦	**30**	54.40 N	17.25 E
Słubice	**54**	52.20 N	14.32 E
Sluč' ≃, Bela.	**76**	52.08 N	27.31 E
Sluč' ≃, Ukr.	**78**	51.37 N	26.38 E
Sluck	**76**	53.01 N	27.33 E
Sl'ud'anka	**88**	51.38 N	103.42 E
Sluderno (Schluderns)	**64**	46.40 N	10.35 E
Sludy	**76**	58.52 N	36.52 E
Sluis	**52**	51.18 N	3.24 E
Sluiskil	**52**	51.16 N	3.50 E

Symbols in the index entries represent the broad categories identified in the key at the right. Symbols with superior numbers (⋏[1]) identify subcategories (see complete key on page *I · 1*).

Symbole im Register stellen die rechts im Schlüssel erklärten Kategorien dar. Symbole mit hochgestellten Ziffern (⋏[1]) bezeichnen Unterabteilungen einer Kategorie (vgl. vollständiger Schlüssel auf Seite *I · 1*).

Los símbolos incluídos en el texto del índice representan las grandes categorías identificadas con la clave a la derecha. Los símbolos con numeros en su parte superior (⋏[1]) identifican las subcategorías (véase la clave completa en la página *I · 1*).

Les symboles de l'index représentent les catégories indiquées dans la légende à droite. Les symboles suivis d'un indice (⋏[1]) représentent des sous-catégories (voir légende complète à la page *I · 1*).

Os símbolos incluídos no texto do índice representam as grandes categorias identificadas com a chave à direita. Os símbolos com números em sua parte superior (⋏[1]) identificam as subcategorias (veja-se a chave completa à página *I · 1*).

∧ Mountain	Berg	Montaña	Montagne	Montanha
⋏ Mountains	Gebirge	Montañas	Montagnes	Montanhas
)(Pass	Paß	Paso	Col	Passo
V Valley, Canyon	Tal, Cañon	Valle, Cañón	Vallée, Canyon	Vale, Canhão
≚ Plain	Ebene	Llano	Plaine	Planície
≻ Cape	Kap	Cabo	Cap	Cabo
I Island	Insel	Isla	Île	Ilha
II Islands	Inseln	Islas	Îles	Ilhas
⊥ Other Topographic Features	Andere Topographische Objekte	Otros Elementos Topográficos	Autres données topographiques	Outros acidentes topográficos

Nombre	Página	Lat.°′	Long.°′ W=Oeste
Šluknov	54	51.00 N	14.27 E
Šlunj	36	45.07 N	15.35 E
Słupca	30	52.19 N	17.52 E
Słupia ≃	30	54.35 N	16.50 E
Słupsk (Stolp)	30	54.28 N	17.01 E
Słupsk □⁴	30	54.10 N	17.15 E
Slurry	156	25.43 S	25.52 E
Sl'uz-Mokr'aki	86	59.17 N	88.50 E
Sly, Oued ≃	34	36.04 N	1.08 E
Smachtino	82	54.51 N	36.25 E
Smackover	194	33.21 N	92.43 W
Smackover Creek ≃	194	33.22 N	92.24 W
Småland □⁹	26	57.20 N	15.00 E
Smålandsfarvandet ᴜ	41	55.05 N	11.20 E
Smålandsstenar	26	57.10 N	13.24 E
Smalininkai	76	55.05 N	22.35 E
Smallbridge	262	53.38 N	2.08 W
Smalleytown	276	40.39 N	74.28 W
Smallwood	210	41.40 N	74.49 W
Smallwood Reservoir ▸	176	54.05 N	64.30 W
Smallwood State Park ♦	208	38.33 N	77.12 W
Smara	148	26.44 N	11.41 W
Smartt Syndicate Dam ⊚¹	158	30.40 S	23.18 E
Smartville	226	39.12 N	121.18 W
Smeaton	184	53.30 N	104.49 W
Smeaton Bay c	182	55.20 N	130.50 W
Smečno	54	50.10 N	14.03 E
Smedby	40	58.33 N	16.16 E
Smědec	61	48.56 N	14.09 E
Smederevo	38	44.40 N	20.56 E
Smederevska Palanka	38	44.22 N	20.58 E
Smedjebacken	40	60.08 N	15.25 E
Smela	78	49.14 N	31.53 E
Sme'oje	78	50.55 N	33.36 E
Sme'ovka	84	54.47 N	49.11 E
Smeit Brook ≃, Ma., U.S.	283	42.13 N	70.58 W
Smelt Brook ≃, Ma., U.S.	283	42.00 N	70.43 W
Smelt Pond ⊜	283	41.58 N	70.43 W
Smeralda, Costa ±²	71	41.04 N	9.30 E
Smerwick Harbour c	48	52.12 N	10.24 W
Smethport	214	41.48 N	78.26 W
Smethwick	42	52.30 N	1.58 W
Smicksburg	214	40.52 N	79.10 W
Smidovič	89	48.36 N	133.49 E
Šmidta — Mys Šmidta	180	68.56 N	179.26 W
Šmidta, mys ▸	180	68.56 N	179.30 W
Šmidta, ostrov I	74	81.08 N	90.48 E
Šmidta, poluostrov ▸¹	84	54.10 N	142.40 E
Šmigiel	30	52.01 N	16.32 E
Šmilde	52	52.57 N	6.27 E
Smile	218	38.15 N	83.29 W
Smiley, Sk., Can.	184	51.37 N	109.29 W
Smiley, Tx., U.S.	222	29.16 N	97.38 W
Smiloviči	76	53.45 N	28.01 E
Smiltene	76	57.26 N	25.56 E
Smirnovskij	86	54.31 N	69.25 E
Smirnych	89	49.43 N	142.38 E
Smite ≃	44	53.04 N	0.48 E
Smith	182	55.10 N	114.02 W
Smith □⁶	202	32.20 N	95.15 W
Smith ≃, U.S.	192	36.39 N	79.45 W
Smith ≃, Ca., U.S.	204	41.56 N	124.12 W
Smith ≃, Mt., U.S.	202	47.25 N	111.29 W
Smith ≃, Or., U.S.	202	43.43 N	124.05 W
Smith, Cape ▸	190	45.48 N	81.35 W
Smith Arm c	180	66.15 N	124.00 W
Smith Bay c	180	70.51 N	154.25 W
Smithboro, II., U.S.	218	38.54 N	89.20 W
Smithfield, N.Y., U.S.	210	42.02 N	76.24 W
Smith Canyon V	198	37.46 N	103.26 W
Smith Center	198	39.46 N	98.47 W
Smith Creek ≃, S.D., U.S.	198	45.19 N	99.20 W
Smith Creek ≃, Wa., U.S.	224	46.45 N	123.53 W
Smithers, B.C., Can.	182	54.47 N	127.10 W
Smithers, W.V., U.S.	188	38.10 N	81.18 W
Smithers Lake ⊜	222	29.29 N	95.38 W
Smithfield, Austl.	168b	34.11 S	150.41 E
Smithfield, Austl.	274a	33.51 S	150.57 E
Smithfield, On., Can.	210	44.04 N	77.41 W
Smithfield, S. Afr.	158	30.09 S	26.30 E
Smithfield, Eng., U.K.	44	54.59 N	2.52 W
Smithfield, N.C., U.S.	192	35.30 N	78.20 W
Smithfield, Oh., U.S.	214	40.16 N	80.46 W
Smithfield, Pa., U.S.	214	39.48 N	79.49 W
Smithfield, Ut., U.S.	200	41.50 N	111.49 W
Smithfield, Va., U.S.	192	36.58 N	76.37 W
Smithfla:	226	38.44 N	120.45 W
Smith Haven Mall ♦¹	279	40.52 N	73.08 W
Smith Hills I	262	53.36 N	2.27 W
Smith Island I, Ant.	52	62.59 N	62.32 W
Smith Island I, N.C., U.S.	192	33.52 N	77.59 W
Smith Island I, Va., U.S.	208	37.10 N	75.51 W
Smith Island II	208	38.01 N	76.02 W
Smithland	194	37.08 N	88.24 W
Smithmill	214	40.46 N	78.25 W
Smith Mountain ⋀	192	34.17 N	117.52 W
Smith Mountain Lake ⊜¹	192	37.10 N	79.40 W
Smith: Peak ⋀	202	48.50 N	116.99 W
Smith: Peninsula ▸¹	9	74.25 S	61.15 W
Smith: Point	229	29.27 N	94.45 W
Smith Point ▸, N.S., Can.	186	45.51 N	63.25 W
Smith Point ▸, Tx., U.S.	229	29.32 N	94.45 W
Smith Point ▸, Va., U.S.	208	37.53 N	76.14 W
Smithport	214	40.50 N	78.52 W
Smith River	204	41.55 N	124.08 W
Smiths	194	32.32 N	85.05 W
Smithsburg	214	39.39 N	77.34 W
Smiths Creek	214	42.55 N	82.36 W
Smiths Falls	212	44.54 N	76.01 W
Smiths Fork ≃	200	41.23 N	110.12 W
Smiths Grove	194	37.03 N	86.12 W
Smiths Mills	276	41.01 N	74.22 W
Smith Sound ᴜ	182	51.18 N	127.48 W
Smithton, Austl.	166	40.51 S	145.07 E
Smithton, II., U.S.	219	38.24 N	89.59 W
Smithton, Pa., U.S.	214	40.09 N	79.44 W
Smithton, Mo., U.S.	279b	40.09 N	79.44 W
Smithtown	210	40.51 N	73.12 W
Smithtown Bay c	276	40.57 N	73.12 W
Smith Valley	192	38.39 N	86.12 W
Smithville, On., Can.	212	43.06 N	79.33 W
Smithville, Ga., U.S.	192	31.54 N	84.15 W
Smithville, In., U.S.	194	39.04 N	86.30 W
Smithville, Ms., U.S.	194	34.04 N	88.23 W
Smithville, Mo., U.S.	194	39.23 N	94.35 W
Smithville, N.J., U.S.	208	39.59 N	74.44 W
Smithville, Oh., U.S.	214	40.51 N	81.51 W
Smithville, Tn., U.S.	194	35.57 N	85.48 W
Smithville Flats	210	42.24 N	75.49 W
Smithville Lake ⊜¹	194	39.24 N	94.35 W
Smöger	26	58.21 N	11.13 E
Smoke Creek ≃, Nv., U.S.	198	40.18 N	104.41 W
Smoke Creek ≃, N.Y., U.S.	284a	42.49 N	78.52 W
Smoke Creek, South Branch ≃	284a	42.49 N	78.49 W
Smoke Creek Desert ≃²	204	40.30 N	119.40 W

Nom	Page	Lat.°′	Long.°′ W=Ouest
Smoke Lake ⊚	212	45.32 N	78.41 W
Smokeless	214	40.24 N	76.02 W
Smokerun	214	40.48 N	78.26 W
Smoketown	208	40.02 N	76.12 W
Smokey, Cape ▸	186	46.38 N	60.21 W
Smokey Dome ⋀	202	43.29 N	114.56 W
Smoky ≃	182	56.10 N	117.21 W
Smoky Bay	162	32.22 S	133.56 E
Smoky Cape ▸	166	30.56 S	153.05 E
Smoky Hill ≃	198	39.03 N	96.48 W
Smoky Hill, North Fork ≃	198	38.55 N	101.17 W
Smoky Lake	182	54.07 N	112.28 W
Smela I	24	63.24 N	8.00 E
Smol'anica	76	52.42 N	24.38 E
Smol'aninovo	89	43.19 N	132.28 E
Smol'any	76	54.36 N	30.04 E
Smolensk	76	54.47 N	32.03 E
Smolenskaja vozvyšennost' ⋀¹	76	54.30 N	33.00 E
Smolensk Oblast □⁴	76	55.00 N	33.00 E
Smolenskoje	86	52.20 N	85.05 E
Smoleviči	76	54.02 N	28.05 E
Smólikas ⋀	38	40.06 N	20.52 E
Smoljan	38	41.35 N	24.41 E
Smolny ᴠ	265a	59.57 N	30.24 E
Smolovka	76	55.33 N	30.13 E
Smoot	200	42.37 N	110.54 W
Smoothstone ≃	184	54.20 N	106.39 W
Smoothstone Lake ⊚	184	54.40 N	106.50 W
Smorgon'	76	54.29 N	26.24 E
Smorodovka	76	57.08 N	29.52 E
Smotrič	78	48.56 N	26.34 E
Smotrič ≃	78	48.36 N	26.38 E
Smuškovoje	80	47.20 N	45.55 E
Smyčka	82	56.04 N	35.56 E
Smygeham	41	55.21 N	13.22 E
Smygehuk ▸	41	55.21 N	13.23 E
Smyley Island I	9	72.55 S	78.00 W
Smyrna — İzmir, Tür.	130	38.25 N	27.09 E
Smyrna, De., U.S.	208	39.17 N	75.36 W
Smyrna, Ga., U.S.	192	33.53 N	84.30 W
Smyrna, N.Y., U.S.	210	42.41 N	75.34 W
Smyrna, Tn., U.S.	194	35.58 N	86.31 W
Smyrna ≃	208	39.22 N	75.31 W
Smyšľajevka	80	53.15 N	50.22 E
Smyth, Canal ᴜ	254	52.15 S	73.40 W
Smyth, Mount ⋀	176	57.54 N	124.53 W
Smythe Park ♦	275b	43.41 N	79.30 W
Smythesdale	169	37.38 S	143.41 E
Sn'adin	78	52.08 N	28.19 E
Snæfell ʟ, Ísland	24a	64.48 N	15.32 W
Snaefell ⋀, I. of Man	44	54.16 N	4.27 W
Snaefellness ▸¹	24a	64.50 N	24.00 W
Snag	180	62.24 N	140.22 W
Snaght, Slieve ⋀	48	55.12 N	7.20 W
Snagost'	78	51.21 N	34.54 E
Snahapish ≃	224	47.38 N	124.11 W
Šn'ajevo	38	53.41 N	1.02 W
Sn'ajevo	80	52.34 N	46.11 E
Snake ≃, Yk., Can.	180	65.58 N	134.10 W
Snake ≃, U.S.	202	46.12 N	119.02 W
Snake ≃, Mn., U.S.	226	39.07 N	121.43 W
Snake ≃, Mn., U.S.	198	45.49 N	92.46 W
Snake ≃, Mn., U.S.	198	48.26 N	97.07 W
Snake Bight c³	220	25.10 N	80.50 W
Snake Brook ≃	283	42.18 N	71.22 W
Snake Creek ≃, Mt., U.S.	202	48.32 N	108.53 W
Snake Creek ≃, Ne., U.S.	198	42.01 N	102.45 W
Snake Creek ≃, S.D., U.S.	198	44.58 N	98.29 W
Snake Creek, South Fork ≃	198	45.02 N	98.36 W
Snake Creek Canal ≃	220	25.57 N	80.11 W
Snake Indian ≃	182	53.11 N	118.00 W
Snake Range ⋀	204	39.00 N	114.15 W
Snake Rapids ᴸ	184	55.14 N	77.20 W
Snake River Plain ≃	202	43.00 N	113.00 W
Snake Valley ᴠ	169	37.35 S	143.35 E
Snake Valley ᴠ	204	39.20 N	113.55 W
Snaptun	41	55.49 N	10.04 E
Snares Islands II	8	48.00 S	166.30 E
Snasahögarna ⋀	24	63.13 N	12.21 E
Sn'atyn	78	48.28 N	25.34 E
Snay Pôl	110	11.40 N	105.13 E
Sneads	192	30.42 N	84.55 W
Snedsted	26	56.54 N	8.32 E
Sneedville	192	36.31 N	83.13 W
Sneek	52	53.02 N	5.40 E
Sneekermeer ⊜	52	53.05 N	5.45 E
Snee-osh-Beach	224	48.24 N	122.33 W
Sneeuberg ⋀	158	32.25 S	19.12 E
Sneeuberg ⋀	158	31.46 S	24.20 E
Snekkersten	41	56.00 N	12.36 E
Snelgrove	275b	43.44 N	79.49 W
Snelling	204	37.31 N	120.26 W
Snettisham	42	52.53 N	0.30 E
Snežaja ≃	88	51.36 N	104.38 E
Snežnik ⋀	36	45.35 N	14.27 E
Snežnoje	78	48.01 N	38.46 E
Śniardwy, Jezioro ⊚	30	53.46 N	21.44 E
Snicarte	219	40.07 N	90.14 W
Snicarte Island I	219	40.07 N	90.12 W
Snigir'ovka	78	47.06 N	32.47 E
Snina	30	48.59 N	22.07 E
Snipe Keys II	220	24.40 N	81.38 W
Snipe Lake ⊚	182	55.07 N	116.46 W
Snizort, Loch c	46	57.33 N	6.28 W
Snøde	41	55.50 N	10.55 E
Snodland	42	51.20 N	0.27 E
Snoghøj	41	55.31 N	9.43 E
Snøhetta ⋀	26	62.20 N	9.17 E
Snohomish	224	47.54 N	122.05 W
Snohomish □⁶	224	48.02 N	121.41 W
Snønipa ⋀	26	61.42 N	6.41 E
Snoqualmie	224	47.31 N	121.49 W
Snoqualmie ≃	224	47.50 N	122.03 W
Snoqualmie, Middle Fork ≃	224	47.31 N	121.46 W
Snoqualmie, North Fork ≃	224	47.31 N	121.48 W
Snoqualmie, South Fork ≃	224	47.31 N	121.48 W
Snoqualmie Falls	224	47.32 N	121.49 W
Snoqualmie Pass ᴋ	224	47.27 N	121.25 W
Snøtinden ⋀	24	66.38 N	14.00 E
Snov ≃	76	51.32 N	31.32 E
Snowbird Lake ⊚	176	60.40 N	103.00 W
Snow Canyon State Park ♦	204	37.11 N	113.42 W
Snow Creek ≃	226	37.59 N	122.53 W
Snowdon, Sk., Can.	184	53.30 N	104.41 W
Snowden, Pa., U.S.	284b	40.16 N	79.58 W
Snowdon Oaks	279a	39.04 N	76.52 W
Snowdenville	285	40.11 N	75.36 W
Snowdon ⋀	44	53.04 N	4.05 W
Snowdonia National Park ♦	28	53.00 N	3.57 W
Snowdoun	194	32.14 N	86.17 W
Snowflake	200	34.30 N	110.04 W
Snow Hill, Md., U.S.	208	38.10 N	75.23 W
Snow Hill, N.C., U.S.	192	35.27 N	77.40 W
Snowking Mountain ⋀	224	48.28 N	121.17 W
Snow Lake	184	54.53 N	100.02 W
Snow Lakes ⊚	224	47.29 N	120.45 W
Snowmass Mountain ⋀	200	39.07 N	107.04 W

Nome	Página	Lat.°′	Long.°′ W=Oeste
Snow Mountain ⋀	226	39.23 N	122.45 W
Snow Peak ⋀	202	48.35 N	118.29 W
Snows Brook ≃	283	42.47 N	71.06 W
Snow Shoe	214	41.02 N	77.57 W
Snowshoe Butte ⋀	200	44.13 N	121.22 W
Snowshoe Peak ⋀	202	48.13 N	115.41 W
Snowtown	166	33.47 S	138.13 E
Snow Water Lake ⊚	204	41.07 N	115.00 W
Snowy ≃	166	37.48 S	148.32 E
Snowy Mountain ⋀	182	43.42 N	74.23 W
Snowy Mountains ⋀	166	36.30 S	148.20 E
Snowysdie Peak ⋀	202	43.57 N	114.58 W
Snubba Range ⋀	171b	35.40 S	148.13 E
Snúol	110	12.04 N	106.25 E
Snyder, Ok., U.S.	196	34.39 N	98.57 W
Snyder, Tx., U.S.	196	32.43 N	100.55 W
Snyder □⁶	214	40.47 N	77.03 W
Snydertown	210	40.53 N	76.40 W
Soahany	157b	18.42 S	44.13 E
Soaker', Mount ⋀	172	45.23 S	167.15 E
Soalala	157b	16.06 S	45.20 E
Soalara	157b	23.36 S	43.44 E
Soaloka	157b	18.32 S	45.15 E
Sòam	98	38.01 N	126.43 E
Soamanonga	157b	23.52 S	44.47 E
Soàm ≃	123	39.13 N	71.44 E
Soan-co I	98	34.09 N	126.35 E
Soanierana Ivongo	157b	16.55 S	49.35 E
Soanindrariny	157b	19.54 S	47.14 E
Soap Creek ≃	190	45.55 N	92.14 W
Soap Lake	202	47.23 N	119.29 W
Soassiu — Tidore	108	0.40 N	127.26 E
Soatá	246	6.20 N	72.41 W
Soavina	157b	20.23 S	46.56 E
Soavinandriana	157b	19.09 S	46.45 E
Soay I	46	57.08 N	6.14 W
Soazza	58	46.22 N	9.13 E
Sob ≃	78	48.42 N	29.17 E
Sobaek-sanmaek ⋀	98	36.00 N	128.00 E
Sobat ≃	140	9.22 N	31.33 E
Sobernheim	56	49.47 N	7.38 E
Soběšice	60	49.12 N	13.41 E
Soběslav	30	49.15 N	14.44 E
Sobger ≃	164	3.44 S	140.20 E
Sobib	78	51.52 N	33.14 E
Sobinka	80	55.59 N	40.01 E
Soboba Indian Reservation ✦⁴	228	33.47 N	116.54 W
Soboko	140	6.49 N	24.50 E
Sobolevo	80	55.39 N	51.53 E
Sobolev	80	51.56 N	41.43 E
Sobolevka	78	48.56 N	29.30 E
Sobolevo	82	55.51 N	48.03 E
Sobolinc	88	53.23 N	119.42 E
Sobótka	30	50.55 N	16.45 E
Sobradinho	252	29.24 S	53.03 W
Sobradinho, Reprêsa de ⊚	250	9.40 S	42.00 W
Sobrado	34	41.02 N	8.16 W
Sobral	250	3.42 S	40.21 W
Sobrance	30	48.45 N	22.11 E
Sobrante Ridge ⋀	282	37.58 N	122.15 W
Sobrarbe ⋀¹	34	42.22 N	0.10 E
Sobue	94	35.15 N	136.43 E
Søby	41	54.56 N	10.16 E
Soča (Isonzo) ≃	64	45.47 N	13.32 E
Socairie	252	23.36 S	67.51 W
Sochie	64	46.25 N	12.52 E
Socc Giang	110	22.54 N	106.01 E
Socgorocok	78	50.11 N	38.09 E
Soch	85	39.71 N	71.02 E
Soch ≃	85	40.20 N	71.02 E
Sochaczew	30	52.14 N	20.14 E
Sochaux	58	47.31 N	6.50 E
Sochi — Sochae	120	38.25 N	77.16 E
Sochi — Soči	84	43.35 N	39.45 E
Sochondo	88	36.05 N	126.41 E
Sochondo, gora ⋀	88	49.44 N	111.05 E
Sòch'ŏng-do I	98	37.46 N	124.45 E
Sochor, gora ⋀	88	51.18 N	105.15 E
Soči	84	43.35 N	39.45 E
Social Circle	192	33.39 N	83.43 W
Social Security Administration ♦	284b	39.19 N	76.44 W
Sociedade Hípica Paulista ♦	287b	23.36 S	46.41 W
Société, Archipel de la (Society Islands) II	8	17.00 S	150.00 W
Society Hill	192	34.30 N	79.51 W
Society Islands — Société, Archipel de la II	14	17.00 S	150.00 W
Society Ridge ⋀³	14	17.50 S	151.40 W
Soco ≃	238	18.27 N	69.12 W
Socolienango	232	16.13 N	92.15 W
Socompa, Paso ᴋ	252	24.25 S	68.18 W
Soconusco, Sierra de — Madre, Sierra ⋀	236	15.20 N	92.20 W
Socorro, Bra.	256	22.36 S	46.32 W
Socorro, Col.	246	6.29 N	73.16 W
Socorro, P.R.	116	9.37 N	125.58 E
Socorro, N.M., U.S.	196	34.03 N	106.53 W
Socorro, Tx., U.S.	200	31.39 N	106.18 W
Socorro, Isla I	232	18.45 N	110.58 W
Socota	248	6.18 S	78.44 W
Socotora, Isla — Suqutrā I	118	12.30 N	54.00 E
Soc Trang	110	9.36 N	105.58 E
Socuéllamos	34	39.17 N	2.48 W
Soda Creek	182	52.21 N	126.43 E
Soda Creek ≃	226	38.48 N	122.29 W
Soda Lake ⊚, Ca., U.S.	204	35.08 N	116.04 W
Soda Lake ⊚, Ca., U.S.	226	35.15 N	119.53 W
Soda Springs	202	42.39 N	111.36 W
Soddy-Daisy	194	35.16 N	85.10 W
Sodegaura	94	35.26 N	139.57 E
Söderåsen ⋀²	41	56.04 N	13.05 E
Söderbärke	40	60.05 N	15.33 E
Söderby-Karl	40	59.53 N	18.41 E
Söderfors	40	60.23 N	17.14 E
Söderhamn	26	61.18 N	17.03 E
Söderköping	26	58.29 N	16.19 E
Södermanland □⁹	41	59.12 N	16.49 E
Södermanland □⁹	40	59.15 N	16.40 E
Södermanlands Län □⁶	40	59.12 N	16.42 E
Södra Hörken ⊚	40	60.02 N	15.02 E
Södra Råda	40	59.01 N	14.10 E
Södra Sandby	41	55.43 N	13.21 E
Södra Vi	40	57.45 N	15.48 E
Sodražica	36	45.46 N	14.38 E
Sodus	210	43.14 N	77.03 W
Sodus Bay c	210	43.15 N	76.58 W
Sodus Creek ≃	210	43.16 N	76.56 W

Nome	Página	Lat.°′	Long.°′ W=Oeste
Sodus Point	210	43.16 N	76.59 W
Sôdu-su ᴜ	98	42.05 N	129.00 E
Sodwalls	170	33.31 S	149.59 E
Sodwana Bay National Park ♦	158	27.30 S	32.39 E
Soe	112	9.52 S	124.17 E
Soeda	96	33.34 N	130.52 E
Soekmakaar	156	23.28 S	29.58 E
Soela väin ᴜ	76	58.40 N	22.35 E
Soerabaja — Surabaya	115a	7.15 S	112.45 E
Soest, Dtsch.	52	51.34 N	8.07 E
Soest, Ned.	52	52.09 N	5.18 E
Soestdijk	52	52.11 N	5.18 E
Soestdijk, Paleis ᴠ	52	52.12 N	5.15 E
Soeste ≃	52	53.10 N	7.44 E
Soesterberg	52	52.07 N	5.17 E
Soeurs, Ile des I	275a	45.29 N	73.33 W
Sofala	170	33.05 S	149.42 E
Sofala □⁵	156	19.00 S	35.00 E
Sofia — Sofija	38	42.41 N	23.19 E
Sofia ≃	157b	15.27 S	47.23 E
Sofija (Sofia)	38	42.41 N	23.19 E
Sofijevka, Ukr.	78	48.04 N	33.52 E
Sofijevka, Ukr.	78	46.33 N	34.03 E
Sofijevskij	83	48.12 N	38.52 E
Sofijsk, Ross.	89	51.34 N	139.52 E
Sofijsk, Ross.	89	52.15 N	133.58 E
Sofjanga	24	65.52 N	31.15 E
Sofje-Kondratjevka	83	48.18 N	38.12 E
Sofrino	82	55.30 N	38.11 E
Sofrino	82	56.09 N	37.56 E
Sofronovo	76	59.48 N	36.54 E
Sogakofe	150	6.00 N	0.36 E
Sogamoso	246	5.43 N	72.56 W
Sogamoso ≃	246	7.13 N	73.54 W
Soganlı	130	41.11 N	32.38 E
Soğanlı Geçidi ᴋ	130	40.33 N	40.16 E
Soğanlıköy ⋀⁸	267b	40.55 N	29.12 E
Sogcho	98	38.12 N	128.36 E
— Sokch'o	98	38.12 N	128.36 E
Sogda	89	50.24 N	132.12 E
Soledad, Col.	246	10.55 N	74.46 W
Soledad, Ca., U.S.	204	36.25 N	121.19 W
Soledad, Ven.	246	8.10 N	63.34 W
Soledad, Cerro ⋀	196	26.29 N	103.23 W
Soledad de Doblado	234	19.03 N	96.25 W
Soledad Díez Gutiérrez	234	22.12 N	100.57 W
Soledade	252	28.50 S	52.30 W
Soledad de Minas	256	22.04 S	45.03 W
Soledad Pass ᴋ	228	34.30 N	118.07 W
Soleduck ≃	224	47.55 N	124.35 W
Solemar	256	24.05 S	46.36 W
Solen	198	46.23 N	100.47 W
Solenoje	80	42.18 N	101.08 E
Sogoža ≃	76	58.28 N	39.06 E
Sogri-san Kukrip Kongwŏn ♦	98	36.33 N	127.52 E
Sogūsu Millî Parkı ♦	130	40.25 N	32.35 E
Söğüt	130	40.00 N	30.11 E
Söğütalan	130	40.09 N	30.31 E
Söğüt Gölü ⊚	130	37.03 N	29.53 E
Söğütlü	130	40.54 N	30.29 E
Sog Xian	120	31.50 N	93.45 E
Sohāg	140	26.33 N	31.42 E
— Sawhāj	140	26.33 N	31.42 E
Sohāgpur, India	124	23.19 N	81.21 E
Sohāgpur, India	124	22.42 N	78.12 E
Sohano	175e	5.27 S	154.40 E
Soharka	272a	28.35 N	77.24 E
Scheit-Tinlot	56	50.29 N	5.22 E
Schland	54	51.02 N	14.25 E
Sōhlde	52	52.11 N	10.14 E
Söhng	98	38.27 N	128.15 E
Sōhwa-ri	98	38.15 N	128.13 E
Soignies (Zinnik)	50	50.35 N	4.04 E
Soignolles-en-Brie	261	48.39 N	2.42 E
Soira ⋀	144	14.45 N	39.32 E
Soissons	50	49.22 N	3.20 E
Soisy-sous-Montmorency	261	48.59 N	2.18 E
Soisy-sur-Seine	261	48.39 N	2.27 E
Sojana	96	34.40 N	133.45 E
Sojat	120	25.55 N	73.40 E
Sŏjŏ-do I	98	34.45 N	126.05 E
Sojji Temple ᴠ¹	268	35.31 N	139.41 E
Sojitra	272a	28.13 N	77.11 E
Sòjosŏn-man c	98	39.20 N	124.50 E
Sokoto, Point ▸	154	7.33 N	40.25 E
Sŏk'o	98	53.24 N	50.08 E
Sokal'	78	50.29 N	24.17 E
Sokal'skogo, proliv ᴜ	74	79.00 N	100.25 E
Sokoto □⁵	150	14.44 N	90.48 W
Sŏkch'o	98	38.12 N	128.36 E
Soketla	154	9.55 S	24.36 E
Sokčš Passage ᴜ	154	7.01 N	158.11 E
Sokele	154	9.55 S	24.36 E
Sŏkh'o	98	38.12 N	128.36 E
Sokhós	38	40.49 N	23.21 E
Sokirany	78	48.27 N	27.25 E
Sokirincy	78	50.42 N	32.18 E
Sokna	140	29.04 N	15.48 E
Sokndal	26	58.20 N	6.16 E
Soknedal	26	62.58 N	10.12 E
Sokò, Pol.	30	53.25 N	23.31 E
Sokoka, Ross.	80	55.35 N	51.30 E
Sokol, Ross.	82	59.29 N	40.06 E
Sokol, Ross.	265b	55.48 N	37.31 E
Sokolniki Park ♦	265b	55.48 N	37.41 E
Sokol'nikovo	82	56.23 N	35.49 E
Sokolo	150	14.44 N	6.08 W
Sokologorije	82	54.09 N	32.28 E
Sokolov	54	50.09 N	12.40 E
Sokolová-Gora	80	52.19 N	48.45 E
Sokolova Pustyn'	82	55.01 N	38.26 E
Sokolovka	78	48.19 N	30.29 E
Sokolovo	82	57.53 N	36.56 E
Sokolovskij	80	52.49 N	42.26 E
Sokolów Podlaski	30	52.26 N	22.15 E
Sokol'skoje	82	57.08 N	43.13 E
Sokoto	150	13.04 N	5.16 E
Sokoto ≃	150	11.20 N	4.10 E
Sŏk'o-ri	98	37.46 N	125.27 E
Sokrutovka	80	47.57 N	46.33 E
Soksa-ri	98	40.40 N	127.17 E
Sokskij jary □¹	80	53.15 N	50.03 E
Sokukskij	76	60.39 N	30.23 E
Sokyr	85	43.49 N	74.21 E
Sol ≃	34	36.40 N	4.30 W
Sola, Costa del ±²	34	36.40 N	4.30 W
Sola, Vanuatu	175f	13.53 S	167.33 E
Sola, Zaïre	154	5.09 S	27.06 E

Nome	Página	Lat.°′	Long.°′ W=Oeste
Sola ≃	30	50.04 N	19.13 E
Solacolu	38	44.23 N	26.34 E
Solai	154	0.02 N	36.09 E
Šolaksaj	86	51.45 N	64.48 E
Solana	123	30.55 N	77.07 E
Solana Beach	220	26.56 N	82.01 W
Solander, Cape ▸	274a	34.01 S	151.14 E
Solander Island I	172	46.34 S	166.53 E
Solånea	250	6.45 S	35.39 W
Solangäri	272b	22.36 N	88.27 E
Sol'anka ≃	80	50.51 N	51.20 E
Solano	116	16.31 N	121.11 E
Solano □⁶	226	38.15 N	121.52 W
Solāpur	122	17.41 N	75.55 E
Solar, Morro ⋀²	286d	12.11 S	77.02 W
Solarino	72	37.06 N	15.07 E
Solaro	266b	45.37 N	9.05 E
Solaro, Monte ⋀	68	40.33 N	14.13 E
Solberg	26	63.47 N	17.38 E
Solberga	62	45.43 N	8.48 E
Solbiate Arno	266b	45.39 N	8.53 E
Solbiate Olona	266b	45.39 N	8.53 E
Solca, Arg.	252	30.46 S	66.28 W
Solca, Rom.	38	47.42 N	25.50 E
Solčava	64	46.25 N	14.41 E
Solda Gölü ⊚	130	37.33 N	29.42 E
Soldatskaja	84	43.48 N	43.49 E
Soldatskoje	83	40.52 N	68.56 E
Soldatsko-Stepnoje	80	49.32 N	45.30 E
Sölde ♦¹	263	51.31 N	7.35 E
Soldier Creek ≃	198	39.04 N	95.39 W
Soldier Field ♦	278	41.52 N	87.37 W
Soldier Key I	220	25.35 N	80.10 W
Soldier Point ▸	240c	17.02 N	61.41 W
Soldier Pond	186	47.09 N	68.34 W
Soldiers Grove	190	43.23 N	90.46 W
Soldotna	180	60.29 N	151.04 W
Sole, Val di V	64	46.20 N	10.45 E
Solebury	208	40.23 N	75.02 W
Solec Kujawski	30	53.06 N	18.14 E
Soledad	246	10.55 N	74.46 W
Soledad, Ca., U.S.	204	36.25 N	121.19 W
Solander	—	—	—
Solingen	52	51.10 N	7.05 E
Solih.	—	—	—
Solihull	42	52.25 N	1.45 W
Solikamsk	84	59.38 N	56.47 E
Solimões — Amazon ≃	242	0.10 S	49.00 W
Solin	36	43.33 N	16.29 E
Solingen	52	51.10 N	7.05 E
Solís de Mataojo	252	34.36 S	55.29 W
Solita	246	1.12 N	75.38 W
Sollas	46	57.39 N	7.21 W
Sollefteå	26	63.10 N	17.16 E
Sollenau	60	47.54 N	16.15 E
Soller	34	39.46 N	2.42 E
Sollerön	40	60.55 N	14.37 E
Solliès-Pont	58	43.11 N	6.02 E
Solling ⋀	52	51.45 N	9.35 E
Sollingen □⁸	263	51.29 N	7.35 E
Sollstedt	54	51.22 N	10.36 E
Solms	56	50.32 N	8.24 E
Solnce ≃	82	54.37 N	38.07 E
Solncedar	80	45.43 N	38.01 E
Solnečnogorsk	82	56.11 N	36.59 E
Solnhofen	54	48.54 N	11.00 E
Solo — Surakarta	115a	7.35 S	110.50 E
Šolochovskij	80	48.18 N	41.03 E
Solodniki	80	48.14 N	45.16 E
Solomennoje	24	61.53 N	34.22 E
Solomeo	66	43.03 N	12.17 E
Solomon, Az., U.S.	200	32.49 N	109.37 W
Solomon, Ks., U.S.	198	38.54 N	97.22 W
Solomon ≃	198	39.29 N	98.26 W
Solomon, North Fork ≃	198	39.29 N	98.26 W
Solomon, South Fork ≃	198	39.29 N	98.26 W
Solomon Basin ⋀¹	14	7.00 S	152.00 E
Solomon Islands ◉²	8	8.00 N	155.00 E
Solomon Sea ⋀²	14	8.00 S	155.00 E
Solomon's Pools — Sulaymān, Birak	128	31.41 N	35.10 E
Solon, La., U.S.	194	41.48 N	91.29 W
Solon, Me., U.S.	186	44.56 N	69.51 W
Solon, Oh., U.S.	214	41.23 N	81.26 W
Solon, Zhg.	88	46.36 N	121.13 E
Solon Springs	190	46.21 N	91.49 W
Solopaca	68	41.11 N	14.33 E

Nome	Página	Lat.°′	Long.°′ W=Oeste
Solor, Kepulauan II	112	8.25 S	123.30 E
Solor, Pulau I	112	8.27 S	123.05 E
Solotša	80	54.48 N	39.51 E
Solothurn	58	47.13 N	7.32 E
Solothurn □³	58	47.25 N	7.35 E
Solotobe	86	44.38 N	65.05 E
Solotvin	78	48.42 N	24.25 E
Solotvina	78	47.57 N	23.53 E
Soloveckie ostrova II	24	65.07 N	35.53 E
Solovjove	76	60.46 N	30.09 E
Sčlov'ovsk, Ross.	89	49.55 N	115.42 E
Sčlov'ovsk, Ross.	89	54.14 N	124.26 E
Sčlre-le-Château	50	50.10 N	4.05 E
Sčlre-sur-Sambre	50	50.18 N	4.08 E
Sdrød Strand	41	55.32 N	12.14 E
Sdsona	41	41.59 N	1.31 E
Sčt	30	46.48 N	19.00 E
Šoita, Otok I	36	43.23 N	16.15 E
Sčltånåbåd	128	36.23 N	58.02 E
Sčtau	52	52.59 N	9.49 E
Sčton ⋀	86	52.50 N	86.28 E
Sčunto ⋀	70	38.06 N	13.32 E
Sous, Mount ⋀	168a	32.28 S	116.13 E
Soutre-Pouilly	46	46.18 N	4.43 E
Sovka ≃	42	51.52 S	5.17 E
Sovkang	204	34.36 N	120.08 W
Sovarboo	40	60.24 N	15.40 E
Sovlay	210	43.03 N	76.12 W
Sovlesborg	26	56.03 N	14.33 E
Sovly vyčegodsk	24	61.21 N	46.52 E
Sovlway Firth c¹	44	54.50 N	3.35 W
Sovly	154	12.11 S	26.25 E
Sovlja	54	54.31 N	26.11 E
Sovlymér	264c	47.36 N	18.56 E
Sovlza	64	44.33 N	39.29 E
Sčma, Nihon	92	37.48 N	140.57 E
Sčma, Tür.	130	39.10 N	27.36 E
Sčmabula	154	19.41 S	29.41 E
Sčmahara-chŭtonchi, Rikujō-jieitai- ♦	94	36.23 N	138.58 E
Sčmain	50	50.22 N	3.17 E
Somalia (Somaliya) □¹, Afr.	136	6.00 N	48.00 E
Somalia (Somaliya) □¹, Afr.	144	6.00 N	48.00 E
Somalie	—	—	—
— Somalia □¹	144	6.00 N	48.00 E
Somaliland	—	—	—
Somali Republic — Somalia □¹	144	6.00 N	48.00 E
Somaliya	—	—	—
— Somalia □¹	144	6.00 N	48.00 E
Somalomo	152	3.23 N	12.44 E
Sčman	98	41.20 N	128.54 E
Somanga	154	8.24 S	39.17 E
Sombernon	46	47.18 N	4.42 E
Sombo	154	8.42 S	20.57 E
Sombor	38	45.46 N	19.07 E
Sombra	214	42.43 N	82.29 W
Sombrerete	234	23.38 N	103.39 W
Sombreretillo	196	25.59 N	99.54 W
Sombreri I	238	18.36 N	63.26 W
Sombrero Channel ᴜ	110	7.41 N	93.35 E
Sombrio	252	29.07 S	49.40 W
Sombrio, Lagoa do ⊚	252	29.12 S	49.42 W
Somcuta-Mare	38	47.31 N	23.29 E
Somdari	120	25.49 N	72.35 E
Somerares	224	48.49 N	123.54 E
Somercotes	44	53.04 N	1.22 W
Somerdale, N.J., U.S.	208	39.50 N	75.01 W
Somerdale, Oh., U.S.	214	40.34 N	81.22 W
Somer'en ≃	52	51.24 N	5.44 E
Some'o	64	60.37 N	23.32 E
Some'palu	76	57.51 N	26.48 E
Somers, Ct., U.S.	208	41.59 N	72.28 W
Somers, Mt., U.S.	207	41.59 N	72.28 W
Somers, Wi., U.S.	284	48.04 N	114.13 W
Somersby	170	33.25 S	151.17 E
Somerset, Austl.	166	41.03 S	145.49 E
Somerset, Mb., Can.	184	49.24 N	98.39 W
Somerset, Co., U.S.	200	38.55 N	107.28 W
Somerset, Ky., U.S.	192	37.05 N	84.36 W
Somerset, Ma., U.S.	284c	38.55 N	77.06 W
Somerset, Md., U.S.	207	41.46 N	71.07 W
Somerset, Oh., U.S.	214	40.44 N	71.07 W
Somerset, Pa., U.S.	214	40.00 N	79.05 W
Somerset Airport ♦	276	40.37 N	74.40 W
Somerset Center	216	42.03 N	84.25 W
Somerset East	158	32.42 S	25.35 E
Somerset Hills Airport ♦	276	40.41 N	74.32 W
Somerset Island I, Ber.	240a	32.17 N	64.52 W
Somerset Island I, N.T., Car.	176	73.15 N	93.30 W
Somerset Reservoir ⊚¹	171a	27.03 S	152.35 E
Somerset West	158	34.05 S	18.51 E
Somersham	42	52.24 N	0.01 E
Somersworth	188	43.15 N	70.51 W
Somerton, Eng., U.K.	42	51.03 N	2.44 W
Somerton, Az., U.S.	200	32.36 N	114.42 W
Somerton □⁸	285	40.06 N	75.01 W
Somerton Creek ≃	285	32.15 N	91.58 W
Somervell □⁶	202	32.15 N	97.45 W
Somerville, Austl.	168	38.13 S	145.10 E
Somerville, Ma., U.S.	207	42.23 N	71.06 W
Somerville, N.J., U.S.	208	40.34 N	74.36 W
Somerville, Oh., U.S.	218	39.34 N	84.38 W
Somerville, Tn., U.S.	194	35.15 N	89.21 W
Somerville, Tx., U.S.	222	30.21 N	96.31 W
Somerville Lake ⊚¹	222	30.18 N	96.40 W
Sčme (Szamos) ≃	38	48.07 N	22.22 E
Somespañol Mare ⋀	68	39.47 N	24.12 E
Somespañol Rece ⋀	38	47.49 N	24.41 E
Somis	228	34.16 N	119.00 W
Somm, Canal de la ≃	50	50.14 N	1.38 E

Sluk-Somm I · 165

≃ River	Fluß	Río	Rivière	Rio	♦ Submarine Features	Untermeerische Objekte	Accidentes Submarinos	Formes de relief sous-marin	Acidentes submarinos
Canal	Kanal	Canal	Canal	Canal	□ Political Unit	Politische Einheit	Unidad Política	Entité politique	Unidade política
ʟ Waterfall, Rapids	Wasserfall, Stromschnellen	Cascada, Rápidos	Chute d'eau, Rapides	Cascata, Rápidos	ᴠ Cultural Institution	Kulturelle Institution	Institución Cultural	Institution culturelle	Instituição cultural
c Bay, Gulf	Meeresstraße	Estrecho	Détroit	Estreito	⊥ Historical Site	Historische Stätte	Sitio Histórico	Site historique	Sítio histórico
⊜ Lake, Lakes	Bucht, Golf	Bahía, Golfo	Baie, Golfe	Baía, Golfo	♦ Recreational Site	Erholungs- und Ferienort	Sitio de Recreo	Centre de loisirs	Área de Lazer
≋ Swamp	See, Seen	Lago, Lagos	Lac, Lacs	Lago, Lagos	✈ Airport	Flughafen	Aeropuerto	Aéroport	Aeroporto
☒ Ice Features, Glacier	Sumpf	Pantano	Marais	Pântano	✦ Military Installation	Militäranlage	Instalación Militar	Installation militaire	Instalação militar
⊤ Other Hydrographic Features	Eis- und Gletscherformen	Accidentes Glaciales	Formes glaciaires	Acidentes glaciares	⬦ Miscellaneous	Verschiedenes	Misceláneo	Divers	Diversos
	Andere Hydrographische Objekte	Otros Elementos Hidrográficos	Autres données hydrographiques	Outros acidentes hidrográficos					

I · *166* **Somn-Sout**

ENGLISH — Name | Page | Lat.°′ | Long.°′
DEUTSCH — Name | Seite | Breite°′ | Länge°′ E = Ost

Somnitel'nyj 89 52.12 N 139.04 E
Somo ≃ 190 45.29 N 89.48 W
Somogy □6 30 46.25 N 17.35 E
Somonauk 216 41.38 N 88.40 W
Somonauk Creek ≃ 216 41.32 N 88.41 W
Somosierra, Puerto de)(34 41.09 N 3.35 W
Somosomo 175g 16.46 S 179.58 W
Somosomo Strait ⋓ 175g 16.47 S 179.58 E
Somotillo 236 13.02 N 86.55 W
Somoto 236 13.28 N 86.35 W
Somovo, Ross. 76 52.53 N 34.58 E
Somovo, Ross. 78 51.44 N 39.23 E
Sompeta 122 18.56 N 84.36 E
Somplago 64 46.21 N 13.04 E
Sompolno 30 52.24 N 18.31 E
Somport, Puerto de)(34 42.48 N 0.31 W
Sompuis 50 48.41 N 4.23 E
Somuncurá, Meseta de ⩘1 254 41.30 S 67.15 W
Somvix 58 46.44 N 8.56 E
Šomyškol' 86 46.30 N 59.53 E
Son, Ned. 52 51.31 N 5.30 E
Son, Nor. 26 59.31 N 10.42 E
Son ≃ 124 25.42 N 84.52 E
Soná 236 8.01 N 81.19 W
Sona-Bata 152 4.54 S 15.09 E
Sonādugi 126 22.47 N 90.40 E
Sonaguera 236 15.38 N 86.20 W
Sonahula 124 25.05 N 87.09 E
Sonāmarg 123 34.18 N 75.18 E
Sonāmukhi 126 23.18 N 87.25 E
Sonāpur 126 23.42 N 89.30 E
Sonar 164 2.33 S 133.00 E
Sonār ≃ 124 24.24 N 79.56 E
Sonari 272c 18.52 N 72.59 E
Sonarpur 272b 22.26 N 88.25 E
Sonātikri 272b 22.57 N 88.20 E
Sonceboz 58 47.11 N 7.11 E
Sonchamp 261 48.35 N 1.53 E
Sŏnch'ŏn 98 39.48 N 124.55 E
Soncino 62 45.24 N 9.52 E
Sondags ≃, S. Afr. 158 28.43 S 30.16 E
Sondags ≃, S. Afr. 158 33.44 S 25.51 E
Sondalo 64 46.20 N 10.19 E
Sønderå ≃ 41 54.53 N 8.59 E
Sønderborg 41 54.55 N 9.47 E
Sønderby 41 55.47 N 10.01 E
Sønder Felding 41 55.57 N 8.47 E
Sønderhav 41 54.51 N 9.30 E
Sønderjylland □6 41 55.10 N 9.15 E
Sønder Nærå 41 55.18 N 10.30 E
Sønder Omme 41 55.50 N 8.54 E
Sondershausen 54 51.22 N 10.52 E
Søndersø 41 55.29 N 10.16 E
Sondi 114 2.58 N 98.52 E
Søndre Strømfjord 176 66.59 N 50.40 W
Søndre Strømfjord ⊂2 176 66.30 N 52.15 W
Sondrio 64 46.10 N 9.52 E
Sondrio □4 58 46.10 N 10.03 E
Sonduga 76 60.08 N 41.55 E
Sone ≃ 126 21.34 N 86.54 E
Sonepur 120 20.50 N 83.55 E
Sonestown 210 41.21 N 76.33 W
Song, Malay. 112 2.01 N 112.33 E
Song, Nig. 146 9.50 N 12.38 E
Song, Thai 110 18.28 N 100.11 E
Song ≃ 100 27.02 N 118.18 E
Song'ao 100 29.36 N 121.41 E
Songbahutun 104 41.28 N 121.11 E
Song Bay Hap, Cua ⊂ 110 8.46 N 104.52 E
Songbu 100 31.05 N 114.48 E
Sŏngbyŏn-ni 98 38.03 N 125.18 E
Song Cau 110 13.27 N 109.13 E
Sŏng-ch'ŏn-gang ≃ 98 39.48 N 127.35 E
Songcun 106 30.26 N 119.43 E
Songe 26 58.41 N 9.00 E
Songea 154 10.41 S 35.39 E
Songeons 50 49.33 N 1.52 E
Songgaizhen 107 29.03 N 105.54 E
Songgang 100 22.49 N 113.51 E
Songgato ≃ 164 3.26 S 140.22 E
Songhe 100 31.10 N 113.20 E
Songhua ≃ 89 47.44 N 132.32 E
Songhuahu ⊜1 89 43.20 N 127.07 E
Songhuajiang 89 44.46 N 125.54 E
Songhwa 98 38.21 N 125.08 E
Songino 88 48.54 N 95.54 E
Sŏngjang-ni 98 41.02 N 126.50 E
Songjiachang 107 28.47 N 104.55 E
Songjiang 106 31.01 N 121.14 E
Songjiangzhen 98 42.12 N 126.56 E
Songjiapu 107 29.38 N 104.44 E
Songjiaying 105 40.38 N 115.14 E
Sŏngjin → Kimch'aek 98 40.41 N 129.12 E
Songjŏng 98 35.10 N 126.46 E
Sŏngju 98 35.55 N 128.16 E
Songkan 102 28.27 N 106.50 E
Songkhla 110 7.12 N 100.36 E
Songkhram ≃ 110 17.39 N 104.28 E
Songkou, Zhg. 100 25.48 N 118.36 E
Songkou, Zhg. 100 24.32 N 116.24 E
Songlinba 100 24.00 N 115.59 E
Songlindian 105 39.25 N 115.54 E
Songling 89 48.02 N 121.12 E
Song Ling ⩘ 98 41.10 N 120.09 E
Songmen 100 28.19 N 121.34 E
Songming 102 25.24 N 102.59 E
Sŏngmo-do I 98 37.42 N 126.18 E
Sŏngnae-ri 98 39.28 N 126.59 E
Sŏngnam 98 37.26 N 127.08 E
Sŏng-ni 98 39.38 N 127.06 E
Songnim 98 38.44 N 125.38 E
Songo 152 7.22 S 14.51 E
Songololo 152 5.42 S 14.02 E
Songot ∧ 154 3.59 N 34.28 E
Songpan 102 32.40 N 103.24 E
Song Phi Nong 110 14.13 N 100.03 E
Sŏngsa-ri 271b 37.38 N 126.52 E
Songshancun 104 41.02 N 121.09 E
Songshu 98 39.50 N 122.06 E
Songshugou 105 41.02 N 117.49 E
Songtangmiao 106 31.08 N 119.16 E
Songtao 102 28.06 N 109.05 E
Songtun 98 39.54 N 123.56 E
Šonguj 24 68.47 N 33.00 E
Songu-ri 98 37.49 N 127.09 E
Songwe, Zaïre 154 3.24 S 26.16 E
Songwe, Zaïre 154 12.25 S 29.40 E
Songwe ≃ 154 9.43 S 33.56 E
Songxi, Zhg. 100 27.33 N 118.46 E
Songxi, Zhg. 100 26.16 N 116.59 E
Songxia, Zhg. 100 25.44 N 119.36 E
Songxia, Zhg. 100 30.07 N 120.51 E
Songxian 102 34.10 N 112.05 E
Songyan 98 37.13 N 113.43 E
Songyin 106 30.54 N 121.13 E
Songyin ≃ 100 28.18 N 119.44 E
Songzhangzi 98 41.13 N 119.08 E
Songzhuang 106 32.06 N 121.17 E
Son Ha 110 15.03 N 108.34 E
Soni, Ehi ∧ 146 20.49 N 17.23 E
Sonico 64 46.10 N 10.21 E
Sonid Youqi 102 42.44 N 112.40 E
Sonid Zuoqi 102 43.58 N 113.59 E
Sonīpat 124 28.59 N 77.01 E
Sonkach 124 22.59 N 76.21 E
Sonk'ol', ozero ⊜ 85 41.50 N 75.08 E
Sonkovo 76 57.47 N 37.09 E
Son La 110 21.19 N 103.54 E
Sonmiāni 120 25.26 N 66.36 E
Sonmiāni Bay ⊂ 120 25.15 N 66.30 E
Sonnberg ∧ 264b 48.20 N 16.15 E
Sonneberg 54 50.22 N 11.10 E
Sonnefeld 56 50.13 N 11.08 E
Sonnen 60 48.41 N 13.43 E
Sonnenberg ∧2 61 47.52 N 16.28 E
Sonnewalde 54 51.42 N 13.38 E
Sonning Common 42 51.31 N 0.59 W
Sonningdale 184 52.24 N 107.40 W
Sonnino 66 41.25 N 13.14 E
Sonntagberg 61 47.59 N 14.45 E
Sono 270 34.48 N 135.55 E
Sono, Rio do ≃, Bra. 250 8.58 S 48.11 W
Sono, Rio do ≃, Bra. 255 17.02 S 45.32 W
Sonobe 96 35.06 N 135.28 E
Sonogno 58 46.21 N 8.47 E
Sonoita Creek ≃ 200 31.30 N 110.58 W
Sonoma 226 38.17 N 122.27 W
Sonoma □6 226 38.26 N 122.35 W
Sonoma Creek ≃ 226 38.10 N 122.24 W
Sonoma Mountains ⩘ 226 38.17 N 122.35 W
Sonoma Peak ∧ 204 40.52 N 117.36 W
Sonoma State Historical Park ♠ 226 38.18 N 122.28 W
Sononder 158 29.43 S 21.51 E
Sonop 158 25.39 S 27.42 E
Sonora, Ca., U.S. 226 37.59 N 120.22 W
Sonora, Tx., U.S. 196 30.34 N 100.38 W
Sonora □3 232 29.20 N 110.40 W
Sonora ≃ 232 28.48 N 111.33 W
Sonoran Desert ⊸2 16 30.00 N 113.00 W
Sonora Pass)(226 38.19 N 119.37 W
Sonostrov 24 66.09 N 34.10 E
Sonoyta 232 31.51 N 112.50 W
Sonoyta ≃ 200 31.16 N 113.26 W
Sonpār Hills ⩘2 124 24.20 N 82.15 E
Sonqor 128 34.47 N 47.36 E
Sŏnsan 98 36.16 N 128.17 E
Sonsbeck 52 51.37 N 6.22 E
Sonseca 34 39.42 N 3.57 W
Sonskyn 158 30.47 S 26.28 E
Sonsón 246 5.42 N 75.18 W
Sonsonate 236 13.43 N 89.44 W
Sonsorol Islands II 108 5.20 N 132.13 E
Sonstorp 40 58.45 N 15.36 E
Sonstraal 158 27.07 S 22.28 E
Sontag 194 31.39 N 90.12 W
Son Tay 110 21.08 N 105.30 E
Sonthofen 58 47.31 N 10.17 E
Sontra 56 51.04 N 9.56 E
Sonwān 124 27.40 N 81.45 E
Sonyea 210 42.41 N 77.50 W
Soo → Sault Sainte Marie 190 46.29 N 84.20 W
Soochow → Suzhou 106 31.18 N 120.37 E
Sooke 224 48.23 N 123.43 W
Sooke ≃ 224 48.23 N 123.42 W
Sooke Basin ⊂ 224 48.23 N 123.40 W
Sooke Lake ⊜ 224 48.33 N 123.42 W
Sooner Lake ⊜1 196 36.26 N 97.02 W
Soonwald ⩘ 56 49.55 N 7.40 E
Sooyaac 144 0.03 N 42.17 E
Sopa Sopa Head > 164 1.58 S 146.35 E
Sopchoppy 192 30.03 N 84.29 W
Soperton 192 32.22 N 82.35 W
Sop Hao 110 20.33 N 104.27 E
Sophia 192 37.42 N 81.15 W
Sopki 76 57.06 N 30.55 E
Sopockin 76 53.50 N 23.39 E
Sopot 30 54.28 N 18.34 E
Sop Pong 110 22.04 N 102.03 E
Sop Prap 110 17.53 N 99.20 E
Soprabolzano 64 46.32 N 11.24 E
Sopron 30 47.41 N 16.36 E
Sopronhorpács 61 47.29 N 16.44 E
Sopronkövesd 61 47.33 N 16.45 E
Šoptykol' 86 51.16 N 75.45 E
Sopur 123 34.18 N 74.28 E
Sŏp'yŏng-ni 98 35.01 N 127.24 E
Soquel 226 36.59 N 121.57 W
Soquel Creek ≃ 226 36.58 N 121.57 W
Sor, Ribeira de ≃ 34 39.00 N 8.17 W
Sora 66 41.43 N 13.37 E
Sorada 122 19.45 N 84.26 E
Sorae-san ∧ 271b 37.27 N 126.47 E
Soraga 64 46.22 N 11.39 E
Soragna 64 44.56 N 10.07 E
Söråker 26 62.31 N 17.30 E
Sorano 66 42.41 N 11.43 E
Šorapani 84 42.05 N 43.05 E
Soras 248 14.07 S 73.37 W
Sorata 248 15.47 S 68.40 W
Soratte, Monte ∧ 66 42.15 N 12.30 E
Sorau → Żary 30 51.38 N 15.09 E
Soraya 248 14.10 S 73.19 W
Sorbas 34 37.07 N 2.07 W
Šorbas, gora ∧ 86 47.25 N 84.12 E
Sorbhog 120 26.30 N 90.52 E
Sorbie 44 54.48 N 4.26 W
Sorbo ≃ 85 38.45 N 69.20 E
Sorbolo 64 44.51 N 10.28 E
Sorbonne ⊍2 261 48.51 N 2.21 E
Sorcier, Lac au ⊜ 206 46.42 N 73.24 W
Sordevolo 62 45.34 N 7.59 E
Sore 32 44.20 N 0.35 W
Sorel 206 46.02 N 73.07 W
Sorell 166 42.47 S 147.33 E
Sorell, Cape > 166 42.12 S 145.10 E
Sorel Point > 43b 49.16 N 2.10 W
Sörenberg 58 46.50 N 8.03 E
Sorento 219 39.00 N 89.34 W
Soreq ≃ 132 31.56 N 34.42 E
Soresina 64 45.17 N 9.51 E
Sörfjärden ⊂ 40 59.24 N 16.50 E
Sørfjorden ⊂2 26 60.24 N 6.40 E
Sørfold 24 67.28 N 15.22 E
Sörforsa 26 61.40 N 17.00 E
Sorge ≃ 41 54.21 N 9.25 E
Sorgono 71 40.01 N 9.06 E
Sorgues 62 44.00 N 4.52 E
Sorgun 130 39.49 N 35.11 E
Sori 62 44.22 N 9.06 E
Soria 34 41.46 N 2.28 W
Soria □4 34 41.35 N 2.35 W
Soriano 252 33.24 S 58.19 W
Soriano □5 258 33.45 S 57.45 W
Soriano Calabro 68 38.36 N 16.14 E
Soriano nel Cimino 66 42.25 N 12.14 E
Sorico 58 46.10 N 9.22 E
Sorido 164 1.09 S 136.03 E
Sori-do I 98 34.26 N 127.48 E
Sørli 26 64.15 N 13.45 E
Sormonne ≃ 56 49.46 N 4.40 E
Sorn 46 55.30 N 4.18 W
Sorne ≃ 58 47.22 N 7.22 E
Sorø, Dan. 41 55.26 N 11.34 E
Soro, India 120 21.17 N 86.40 E
Soro, Monte ∧ 70 37.56 N 14.42 E
Sorocaba 255 23.29 S 47.27 W
Sorocabuçu ≃ 256 23.38 S 47.13 W
Soročinka 80 47.30 N 51.44 E
Soročinsk 80 52.26 N 53.10 E
Sorcčkino 86 57.02 N 68.52 E
Soroco 240m 18.22 N 65.38 W
Sorok 88 52.20 N 100.12 E
Sorok ≃ 61 47.07 N 16.50 E
Soroka (Soroki) 38 48.09 N 28.17 E
Sorokino, Ross. 86 53.45 N 84.58 E
Sorokino, Ross. 86 54.13 N 91.31 E
Sorokošiči 78 51.12 N 30.35 E
Soroksár ⊸8 264c 47.24 N 19.07 E
Sorol I1 108 8.08 N 140.23 E
Soron 124 27.53 N 78.45 E
Sorong 164 0.53 S 131.15 E
Sororó ≃ 250 5.24 S 49.07 W
Sorot' ≃ 76 57.04 N 28.50 E
Soroti 154 1.43 N 33.37 E
Sorovskije 86 59.53 N 71.34 E
Sørøya I 24 70.36 N 22.46 E
Sorpestausee ⊜1 56 51.20 N 7.56 E
Sorraia ≃ 34 38.56 N 8.53 W
Sorrento, Austl. 169 38.20 S 144.45 E
Sorrento, It. 68 40.37 N 14.22 E
Sorrento, Fl., U.S. 220 28.48 N 81.33 W
Sorrento, La., U.S. 194 30.11 N 90.51 W
Sorris Sorris 156 20.57 S 14.50 E
Sør Rondane Mountains ⩘ 9 72.00 S 25.00 E
Sorsakoski 26 62.27 N 27.39 E
Sorsatunturi ∧ 24 67.24 N 29.38 E
Sorsele 24 65.30 N 17.30 E
Sorsk 86 54.01 N 90.12 E
Sorso 71 40.48 N 8.34 E
Sorsogon 116 12.58 N 124.00 E
Sorsogon □4 116 12.50 N 123.55 E
Sorsogon Bay ⊂ 116 12.55 N 123.55 E
Sörstafors 40 59.35 N 16.13 E
Šorsu 85 40.17 N 70.48 E
Sort 34 42.24 N 1.08 E
Šortandy 86 51.42 N 71.00 E
Sortat 46 58.33 N 3.13 W
Sortavala 24 61.42 N 30.41 E
Sortino 70 37.09 N 15.02 E
Sortland 24 68.40 N 15.20 E
Sør-Trøndelag □6 26 63.00 N 10.40 E
Sorunda 40 59.01 N 17.48 E
Sörup 41 54.43 N 9.40 E
Sõrve neem > 76 57.54 N 22.03 E
Sörvik 40 60.11 N 15.09 E
Sorviži 80 57.52 N 48.32 E
Sosa, Dtsch. 54 50.30 N 12.39 E
Sosa, Taehan 271b 37.29 N 126.47 E
Šoša ≃ 82 56.31 N 36.05 E
Sŏsan 98 36.47 N 126.26 E
Sösdala 41 56.02 N 13.40 E
Sos del Rey Católico 34 42.30 N 1.13 W
Sosedka 80 53.15 N 42.40 E
Sosedno 76 58.14 N 28.42 E
Sosenka ≃, Ross. 265b 55.35 N 37.23 E
Sosenka ≃, Ross. 265b 55.47 N 37.42 E
Sosenki 82 55.34 N 37.26 E
Sösetalsperre ⊸6 52 51.44 N 10.20 E
Soshigaya ⊸8 268 35.39 N 139.36 E
Sösjöfjällen ⩘ 26 63.53 N 13.15 E
Šoška 24 62.42 N 50.40 E
Soskovo 76 52.45 N 35.23 E
Sosna ≃ 76 52.42 N 38.55 E
Sosneado, Cerro ∧ 252 34.45 S 69.59 W
Sosnica 78 51.32 N 32.28 E
Sosnicy 76 57.38 N 30.25 E
Sosnogorsk 24 63.37 N 53.51 E
Sosnovaja Maza 80 52.30 N 47.53 E
Sosnovaja Pol'ana ⊸8 265a 59.50 N 30.09 E
Sosnovec 24 64.26 N 34.27 E
Sosnovica 76 60.21 N 40.50 E
Sosnovka, Kaz. 86 51.26 N 79.28 E
Sosnovka, Kyrg. 85 42.40 N 73.55 E
Sosnovka, Ross. 24 66.30 N 40.32 E
Sosnovka, Ross. 80 56.13 N 47.13 E
Sosnovka, Ross. 80 57.48 N 51.43 E
Sosnovka, Ross. 80 56.17 N 51.17 E
Sosnovka, Ross. 80 53.14 N 41.22 E
Sosnovka, Ross. 80 57.16 N 53.31 E
Sosnovka, Ross. 80 54.06 N 46.38 E
Sosnovka, Ross. 80 52.26 N 43.29 E
Sosnovka, Ross. 82 54.31 N 38.08 E
Sosnovka, Ross. 82 54.54 N 38.41 E
Sosnovka, Ross. 86 59.10 N 81.18 E
Sosnovka, Ross. 88 54.09 N 109.35 E
Sosnovo, Ross. 76 60.33 N 30.15 E
Sosnovo, Ross. 80 56.42 N 54.35 E
Sosnovoborsk 80 53.18 N 46.16 E
Sosnovoje 78 50.49 N 27.00 E
Sosnovo-Oz'orskoje 88 52.31 N 111.30 E
Sosnovskij 86 54.36 N 73.10 E
Sosnovskoje 80 55.48 N 43.10 E
Sosnovyj Bor, Bela. 76 52.32 N 29.36 E
Sosnovyj Bor, Ross. 76 59.55 N 29.07 E
Sosnovyj Bor, Ross. 86 57.07 N 55.03 E
Sosnovyj Solonec 80 53.17 N 49.33 E
Sosnowiec 30 50.18 N 19.08 E
Soso 194 31.45 N 89.16 W
Sosok 112 0.17 N 110.14 E
Sospel 62 43.53 N 7.27 E
Sospirolo 64 46.09 N 12.04 E
Sossusvlei ⊜ 156 24.40 S 15.23 E
Šoštanj 36 46.23 N 15.03 E
Šostka 78 51.52 N 33.30 E
Sŏsura 98 42.16 N 130.37 E
Sos'va, Ross. 72 63.40 N 62.06 E
Sos'va, Ross. 86 59.10 N 61.50 E
Sos'va ≃ 86 59.32 N 62.20 E
Sosyka ≃ 78 46.35 N 39.05 E
Sot' ≃ 80 58.00 N 40.39 E
Sota ≃ 150 11.52 N 3.24 E
Sotik 154 0.41 S 35.21 E
Sotkamo 26 64.08 N 28.25 E
Sotnicyno 80 54.17 N 41.49 E
Soto de Aldovea 266a 40.26 N 3.27 W
Soto de Pajares 266a 40.17 N 3.32 W
Soto la Marina 234 23.46 N 98.13 W
Soto La Marina ≃ 234 23.45 N 97.45 W
Soto la Marina, Barra I 232 24.10 N 97.43 W
Sotomayor 248 19.18 S 65.03 W
Sotonera, Embalse de ⊜1 34 42.05 N 0.48 W
Sotouboua 150 8.34 N 0.59 E
Sotta 71 41.32 N 9.12 E
Sottens 58 46.39 N 6.44 E
Sottern ⊜ 40 59.02 N 15.29 E
Sotteville 50 49.25 N 1.06 E
Sottile, Punta > 70a 35.30 N 12.38 E
Sotto il Monte 62 45.43 N 9.30 E
Sottomarina 64 45.13 N 12.17 E
Sottrum 52 53.06 N 9.14 E
Sottunga I 26 60.08 N 20.40 E
Souain-Perthes-lès-Hurlus 56 49.11 N 4.32 E
Souanké 152 2.05 N 14.03 E
Soubakaniédougou 150 10.28 N 5.01 W
Soubré 150 5.47 N 6.36 W
Soudan 166 20.05 S 137.00 E
Soudan → Sudan □1 140 15.00 N 30.00 E
Soude ≃ 50 48.52 N 4.10 E
Soudersburg 208 40.01 N 76.09 W
Souderton 208 40.18 N 75.19 W
Souesmes 50 47.27 N 2.10 E
Soufflay 152 2.01 N 14.54 E
Soufflenheim 56 48.50 N 7.58 E
Soufflot, Lac ⊜ 190 47.24 N 78.31 W
Souflïön 38 41.12 N 26.18 E
Soufrière 241f 13.52 N 61.04 W
Soufrière ∧, Guad. 241o 16.03 N 61.40 W
Soufrière ∧, St. Vin. 241h 13.20 N 61.11 W
Soufrière Bay ⊂, Dom. 240d 15.14 N 61.22 W
Soufrière Bay ⊂, St. Luc. 241f 13.51 N 61.04 W
Sougahatchee Creek ≃ 194 32.38 N 85.50 W
Sougne-Remouchamps 56 50.29 N 5.40 E
Souguer 148 35.12 N 1.30 E
Souhegan ≃ 188 42.51 N 71.29 W
Souillac 32 44.54 N 1.29 E
Souilly 56 49.01 N 5.17 E
Souk-el-Arba-des-Beni-Hassan 34 35.16 N 5.20 W
Souk-Khemis-du-Sahel 34 35.17 N 6.05 W
Souk Larbat Gharb 148 34.43 N 6.01 W
Sŏul (Seoul), Taehan 98 37.33 N 126.58 E
Sŏul (Seoul), Taehan 271b 37.33 N 126.58 E
Sŏul □4 98 37.34 N 127.00 E
Soulac-sur-Mer 32 45.31 N 1.07 W
Soulaines-Dhuys 58 48.22 N 4.44 E
Soulanges □6 206 45.20 N 74.15 W
Soulanges, Canal de ⩧ 275a 45.20 N 73.58 W
Soulougou 150 13.01 N 0.23 E
Soulsbyville 226 37.59 N 120.16 W
Soultzeren 58 48.04 N 7.06 E
Soultz-Haut-Rhin 58 47.53 N 7.14 E
Soultzmatt 58 47.58 N 7.14 E
Soultz-sous-Forêts 56 48.56 N 7.53 E
Soummam, Oued ≃ 34 36.45 N 5.04 E
Sound Beach 210 40.57 N 72.58 W
Sounding Creek ≃ 184 52.06 N 110.28 W
Sounding Lake ⊜ 184 52.08 N 110.29 W
Sound View Park ♠ 276 40.49 N 73.52 W
Soúnion, Ákra > 38 37.39 N 24.02 E
Soup Harbour ⊂ 212 43.51 N 77.11 W
Souppes-sur-Loing 50 48.11 N 2.44 E
Souq Ahras 148 36.23 N 8.00 E
Sources, Mont aux ∧ 158 28.46 S 28.52 E
Soure, Bra. 250 0.44 S 48.31 W
Soure, Port. 34 40.03 N 8.38 W
Sour el Ghozlane 148 36.10 N 3.45 E
Souris, Mb., Can. 184 49.38 N 100.15 W
Souris, P.E., Can. 186 46.21 N 62.15 W
Souris ≃ 198 49.39 N 99.34 W
Sourlake 194 30.09 N 94.25 W
Sourland Mountain ∧2 208 40.29 N 74.43 W
Sourou ≃ 150 12.45 N 3.25 W
Souroukaha 150 8.13 N 5.08 W
Souš 54 50.32 N 13.34 E
Sous, Oued V 148 30.27 N 9.31 W
Sousa 250 6.45 S 38.14 W
Sousânia 255 16.11 S 49.05 W
Sousas 256 22.52 S 46.59 W
Sousel 34 38.57 N 7.40 W
Sous-le-Vent, Îles → Leeward Islands II 238 17.00 N 63.00 W
Sousse 148 35.49 N 10.38 E
Sousse □8 148 35.40 N 10.30 E
Sout ≃, S. Afr. 158 31.35 S 18.24 E
Sout ≃, S. Afr. 158 33.03 S 23.28 E
Sout ≃, S. Afr. 158 28.56 S 20.40 E
South ≃, Ia., U.S. 190 41.29 N 93.20 W
South ≃, Ma., U.S. 283 42.10 N 70.43 W
South ≃, Mo., U.S. 219 39.52 N 91.26 W
South ≃, N.J., U.S. 208 40.29 N 74.23 W
South ≃, N.C., U.S. 192 34.20 N 78.03 W
South ≃, Va., U.S. 192 37.46 N 79.23 W
South ≃, Va., U.S. 208 38.02 N 77.23 W
South Acton 207 42.27 N 71.27 W
South Africa (Suid-Afrika) □1, Afr. 138 30.00 S 26.00 E
South Africa (Suid-Afrika) □1, Afr. 156 30.00 S 26.00 E
Southall ⊸8 260 51.31 N 0.23 W
South Alligator ≃ 164 12.15 S 132.24 E
Southam 42 52.15 N 1.23 W
South Amboy 208 40.28 N 74.17 W
South America ⊥1 4 15.00 S 60.00 W
South America ⊥1 18 15.00 S 60.00 W
South Amherst, Ma., U.S. 207 42.20 N 72.30 W
South Amherst, Oh., U.S. 214 41.22 N 82.14 W
Southampton, N.S., Can. 186 45.35 N 64.15 W
Southampton, On., Can. 212 44.29 N 81.23 W
Southampton, Eng., U.K. 42 50.55 N 1.25 W
Southampton, Ma., U.S. 207 42.13 N 72.43 W
Southampton, N.Y., U.S. 207 40.53 N 72.23 W
Southampton, Pa., U.S. 285 40.10 N 75.02 W
Southampton □6 208 36.42 N 77.05 W
Southampton (Eastleigh) Airport ⊠ 42 50.57 N 1.21 W
Southampton, Cape > 176 62.09 N 83.40 W
Southampton Island I 176 64.20 N 84.40 W
South Andaman I 110 11.45 N 92.45 E
South Anna ≃ 192 37.48 N 77.25 W
South Apopka 220 28.39 N 81.31 W
Southard 208 40.08 N 74.14 W
Southards Pond ⊜ 276 40.43 N 73.20 W
South Ashburnham 207 42.36 N 71.56 W
South Aulatsivik Island I 176 56.45 N 61.30 W
South Australia □3 162 30.00 S 135.00 E
South Australian Basin ✣1 14 38.00 S 126.00 E
Southaven 194 34.59 N 90.02 W
South Bald Mountain ∧ 200 40.45 N 105.41 W
South Baldy ∧ 200 33.59 N 107.11 W
South Banda Basin ✣1 14 6.30 S 127.30 E
Southbank 182 54.02 N 125.46 W
South Barre 207 42.23 N 72.05 W
South Barrington 278 42.06 N 88.07 W
South Barrule ∧2 44 54.12 N 4.40 W
South Bass Island I 214 41.39 N 82.49 W
South Bay 220 26.39 N 80.42 W
South Bay ⊂, Mb., Can. 184 56.43 N 99.00 W
South Bay ⊂, N.T., Can. 176 63.58 N 83.30 W
South Bay ⊂, On., Can. 190 45.38 N 81.50 W
South Bay ⊂, On., Can. 212 43.55 N 77.03 W
South Bay ⊂, On., Can. 212 44.52 N 79.47 W
South Bay ⊂, Fl., U.S. 220 26.42 N 80.45 W
South Bay ⊂, Va., U.S. 208 37.14 N 75.52 W
South Bay ⊂, Wa., U.S. 224 46.53 N 124.04 W
South Baymouth 190 45.33 N 82.01 W
South Beach ♠ 276 40.35 N 74.05 W
South Beacon Mountain ∧ 210 41.29 N 73.57 W
South Bedias Creek ≃ 222 30.54 N 95.42 W
South Bellingham 207 42.03 N 71.28 W
South Belmar 208 40.10 N 74.02 W
South Beloit 216 42.29 N 89.02 W
South Bend, In., U.S. 216 41.41 N 86.15 W
South Bend, Wa., U.S. 224 46.40 N 123.48 W
South Benfleet 42 51.33 N 0.34 E
South Bentinck Arm ⊂ 182 52.15 N 126.50 W
South Bethlehem 214 41.00 N 79.20 W
South Bihar Plains ⊻ 124 25.15 N 84.30 E
South Bloomfield 218 39.43 N 82.59 W
Southborough, Eng., U.K. 42 51.10 N 0.15 E
Southborough, Ma., U.S. 207 42.18 N 71.31 W
South Bosque ≃ 222 31.29 N 97.16 W
South Boston 192 36.41 N 78.54 W
South Boston ⊸8 283 42.20 N 71.03 W
South Bound Brook 276 40.33 N 74.32 W
South Bradenton 220 27.27 N 82.35 W
South Branch, Nf., Can. 186 47.55 N 59.02 W
South Branch, N.J., U.S. 276 40.33 N 74.42 W
South Brent 42 50.25 N 3.50 W
Southbridge, N.Z. 172 43.49 S 172.15 E
Southbridge, Ma., U.S. 207 42.04 N 72.02 W
South Britain 207 41.28 N 73.15 W
Southbrook, Austl. 171a 27.41 S 151.43 E
Southbrook, N.Z. 172 43.20 S 172.36 E
South Brook ≃ 285 39.52 N 75.44 W
South Brookfield 186 44.23 N 64.58 W
South Brooklyn ⊸8 276 40.41 N 73.59 W
South Bruny Island I 166 43.23 S 147.17 E
South Buganda □5 154 0.30 S 31.35 E
South Burlington 188 44.28 N 73.10 W
Southbury 207 41.28 N 73.12 W
South Butler 210 43.08 N 76.46 W
South Byfield 283 42.44 N 70.54 W
South Byron 210 43.03 N 78.04 W
South Cairo 210 42.17 N 73.57 W
South Canaan 210 41.30 N 75.25 W
South Cape > 175g 17.01 S 179.55 E
South Carolina □3, U.S. 178 34.00 N 81.00 W
South Carolina □3, U.S. 192 34.00 N 81.00 W
South Carver 207 41.50 N 70.44 W
South Castor ≃ 212 45.15 N 75.23 W
South Cave 44 53.46 N 0.35 W
South Cerney 42 51.40 N 1.56 W
South Chagrin Reservation ♠ 279a 41.25 N 81.25 W
South Channel ⋓, Pil. 116 14.20 N 120.37 E
South Channel ⋓, Mi., U.S. 190 45.38 N 84.32 W
South Channel ≃1 281 42.32 N 82.40 W
South Chaplin 207 41.46 N 72.07 W
South Charleston, Oh., U.S. 218 39.49 N 83.38 W
South Charleston, W.V., U.S. 188 38.22 N 81.41 W
South Chatham 207 41.40 N 70.01 W
South Chelmsford 283 42.34 N 71.23 W
South Chicago ⊸8 278 41.44 N 87.33 W
South China Basin ✣1 12 15.00 N 115.00 E
South China Sea ⫪2 108 10.00 N 113.00 E
South Cle Elum 224 47.11 N 120.56 W
South Coast Botanic Garden ♠ 280 33.47 N 118.21 W
South Coatesville 208 39.58 N 75.49 W
South Coffeyville 196 36.59 N 95.37 W
South Concho ≃ 196 31.21 N 100.28 W
South Corinth 210 43.12 N 73.51 W
South Corning 210 42.07 N 77.02 W
South Cotabato □4 116 6.15 N 125.00 E
South Creek ≃ 170 33.36 S 150.50 E
South Crest 273d 26.15 S 28.07 E
South Dakota □3, U.S. 178 44.15 N 100.00 W
South Dakota □3, U.S. 198 44.15 N 100.00 W
South Dandalup ≃ 168a 32.35 S 115.53 E
South Dandalup Dam ⊸6 168a 32.38 S 116.04 E
South Darenth 260 51.24 N 0.15 E
South Dartmouth 207 41.35 N 70.56 W
South Dayton 210 42.21 N 79.03 W
South Deerfield 207 42.28 N 72.36 W
South Dennis, Ma., U.S. 207 41.41 N 70.09 W
South Dennis, N.J., U.S. 208 39.10 N 74.49 W
South Dorset 210 43.13 N 73.04 W
South Dorset Downs ⩘1 42 50.40 N 2.25 W
South Dos Palos 226 36.57 N 120.39 W
South Downs ⩘1 42 50.55 N 0.25 W
South Dum Dum 126 22.37 N 88.25 E
South Duxbury 207 42.01 N 70.41 W
South East □5 156 25.00 S 25.45 E
Southeast Asia Treaty Organization Headquarters ⊍ 269a 13.45 N 100.31 E
South East Cape >, Austl. 166 43.39 S 146.50 E
Southeast Cape >, Ak., U.S. 180 62.55 N 169.42 W
Southeast Indian Ridge ✣3 6 50.00 S 110.00 E
South Easton 207 42.02 N 71.04 W
Southeast Pacific Basin ✣1 6 60.00 S 115.00 W
South East Point >, Austl. 166 39.00 S 146.20 E
South East Point >, Kiribati 174o 1.40 N 157.10 W
South Egg Harbor 208 39.31 N 74.39 W
South Egremont 207 42.09 N 73.25 W
South Elgin 216 41.59 N 88.17 W
South Elkhorn Creek ≃ 218 38.13 N 84.48 W
South El Monte 280 34.03 N 118.02 W
Southend 46 55.20 N 5.38 W
Southend Municipal Airport ⊠ 42 51.34 N 0.41 E
Southend-on-Sea 42 51.33 N 0.43 E
Southend-on-Sea □8 260 51.33 N 0.41 E
Southend Pier ⊸5 260 51.31 N 0.44 E
South English ≃ 190 41.30 N 91.56 W
Southern □4, Malaŵi 154 15.30 S 35.00 E
Southern □4, S.L. 150 8.00 N 12.15 W
Southern □4, Zam. 154 16.30 S 27.00 E
Southern □5, Bots. 156 24.45 S 24.00 E
Southern □5, Ug. 154 0.30 S 30.30 E
Southern Alps ⩘ 172 43.30 S 170.30 E
Southern California, University of ⊍2 280 34.02 N 118.17 W
Southern Cook Islands II 14 20.00 S 159.00 W
Southern Cross 162 31.13 S 119.19 E
Southern Ghāts ⩘ 122 9.30 N 77.00 E
Southern Highlands □5 164 6.00 S 143.30 E
Southern Indian Lake ⊜ 176 57.10 N 98.40 W
Southern Leyte □4 116 10.50 N 124.55 E
Southern Lueti ≃ 152 16.14 S 23.13 E
Southern Pines 192 35.10 N 79.23 W
Southern Ute Indian Reservation ⊸4 200 37.05 N 107.45 W
Southern View 219 39.46 N 89.39 W
Southern Yemen → Yemen □1 144 15.00 N 47.00 E
Southery 42 52.32 N 0.23 E
South Esk ≃, Austl. 166 41.25 S 147.08 E
South Esk ≃, Scot., U.K. 46 55.53 N 3.04 W
South Esk ≃, Scot., U.K. 46 56.42 N 2.32 W
Southesk Tablelands ⩘1 162 20.50 S 126.40 E
South Essex 207 42.38 N 70.46 W
South Euclid 214 41.31 N 81.31 W
Southey 184 50.56 N 104.30 W
South Fabius ≃ 219 39.54 N 91.30 W
South Fallsburg 210 41.42 N 74.37 W
South Farmbridge 260 51.38 N 0.41 E
South Farmingdale 276 40.43 N 73.26 W
Southfield, Ma., U.S. 207 42.06 N 73.14 W
Southfield, Mi., U.S. 216 42.28 N 83.13 W
Southfields 210 41.15 N 74.11 W
South Fiji Basin ✣1 14 26.00 S 175.00 E
Southfleet 260 51.25 N 0.19 E
South Floral Park 276 40.43 N 73.42 W
South Foreland > 42 51.09 N 1.23 E
South Fork, Co., U.S. 200 37.40 N 106.38 W
South Fork, Pa., U.S. 214 40.22 N 78.47 W
South Fort George 182 53.54 N 122.45 W
South Forty Foot Drain ⩧ 42 52.56 N 0.15 W
South Fox Island I 190 45.25 N 85.50 W
South Fulton 194 36.30 N 88.52 W
South Gate, Ca., U.S. 228 33.57 N 118.12 W
Southgate, Fl., U.S. 220 27.18 N 82.32 W
Southgate, Mi., U.S. 216 42.12 N 83.11 W
Southgate, Wa., U.S. 224 47.10 N 122.30 W
Southgate ⊸8 260 51.38 N 0.08 W
Southgate U.S.A. ⊸9 279a 41.25 N 81.32 W
South Georgia I 244 54.15 S 36.45 W
South Georgia and the South Sandwich Islands □2 244 54.00 S 38.00 W
South Gibson 210 41.44 N 75.38 W
South Glamorgan □6 42 51.30 N 3.25 W
South Glastonbury 207 41.40 N 72.35 W
South Glens Falls 210 43.17 N 73.38 W
South Grafton 207 42.11 N 71.42 W
South Grand ≃ 194 38.18 N 93.28 W
South Grand Island Bridge ⊸5 284a 43.00 N 78.56 W
South Green 260 51.37 N 0.26 E
South Greensburg 214 40.17 N 79.33 W
South Hackensack 276 40.51 N 74.02 W
South Hadley, Ma., U.S. 188 42.15 N 72.34 W
South Hadley, Ma., U.S. 207 42.15 N 72.34 W
South Hadley Falls 207 42.13 N 72.36 W
South Hamilton 207 42.36 N 70.52 W
South Hams ⊻ 42 50.22 N 3.50 W
South Hanningfield 260 51.39 N 0.31 E
South Hanover 283 42.05 N 70.51 W
South Harbor ⊂ 269f 14.33 N 120.58 E
South Hartford 210 43.21 N 73.25 W
South Harwich 207 41.40 N 70.02 W
South Hātia Island I 124 22.19 N 91.07 E
South Haven, In., U.S. 216 41.32 N 87.08 W
South Haven, Ks., U.S. 198 37.03 N 97.24 W
South Haven, Mi., U.S. 216 42.24 N 86.16 W
South Hayling 42 50.47 N 0.59 W
South Head >, Austl. 274a 33.50 S 151.17 E
South Head >, N.Z. 172 36.26 S 174.14 E
South Heart ≃ 182 55.34 N 116.11 W
South Heights 279b 40.35 N 80.14 W
South Hempstead 276 40.41 N 73.37 W
South Henderson 192 36.17 N 78.25 W
South Henik Lake ⊜ 176 61.30 N 97.30 W
South Hero 188 44.38 N 73.18 W
South Hetton 44 54.48 N 1.24 W
South Hill, N.Y., U.S. 210 42.25 N 76.33 W
South Hill, Va., U.S. 192 36.43 N 78.07 W
South Hills ⊸8 273d 26.15 S 28.05 E
South Hills Village ⊸9 279b 40.21 N 80.03 W
South Hingham 207 42.11 N 70.52 W
South Hogan Creek ≃ 218 39.03 N 84.54 W
South Holland 216 41.36 N 87.36 W
South Holston Lake ⊜1 192 36.35 N 82.00 W
South Honcut Creek ≃ 226 39.19 N 121.35 W
South Honshu Ridge ✣3 14 24.00 N 142.00 E
South Hopkinton 207 41.24 N 71.45 W
South Horr 154 2.06 N 36.55 E
South Houston 222 29.39 N 95.14 W
South Huntington 276 40.49 N 73.23 W
South Indian Basin ✣1 6 60.00 S 120.00 E
South Indian Lake 184 56.46 N 98.57 W
Southington, Ct., U.S. 207 41.35 N 72.52 W
Southington, Oh., U.S. 214 41.19 N 80.57 W
South International Falls 190 48.35 N 93.23 W
South Ionia 216 42.57 N 85.04 W
South Island I, India 122 10.03 N 72.17 E
South Island I, Kenya 154 2.38 N 36.36 E
South Island I, Micron. 175c 6.59 N 151.59 E
South Island I, N.Z. 172 43.00 S 171.00 E
South Islet I 116 8.44 N 119.49 E
South Jacksonville 219 39.42 N 90.13 W
South Kemptville Creek ≃ 212 44.54 N 75.41 W
South Kenosha 216 42.32 N 87.50 W
South Kent 207 41.40 N 73.28 W
South Kirkby 44 53.34 N 1.20 W
South Konkan Hills ⩘2 122 17.00 N 73.30 E
South Korea → Korea, South □1 98 36.30 N 128.00 E
South Ladder Creek ≃ 198 38.41 N 101.34 W
South Laguna 228 33.30 N 117.45 W
Southlake 222 32.57 N 97.09 W
South Lake ⊜, On., Can. 212 44.26 N 76.13 W
South Lake ⊜, Fl., U.S. 220 28.37 N 80.52 W
South Lake Tahoe 226 38.56 N 119.58 W
South Lancaster 207 42.26 N 71.41 W
Southland, Ky., U.S. 218 38.01 N 84.31 W
Southland, Mi., U.S. 216 42.13 N 84.24 W
Southland, Tx., U.S. 196 33.22 N 101.33 W
Southland ⊸9 282 37.39 N 122.06 W
South Laurel 284c 39.05 N 76.52 W
Southlawn, Il., U.S. 219 39.45 N 89.37 W
Southlawn, Md., U.S. 284c 38.48 N 76.59 W
South Layhill 284c 39.04 N 77.03 W
South Lebanon 218 39.22 N 84.12 W
South Lee 207 42.16 N 73.16 W
South Lima 210 42.51 N 77.41 W
South Line Island I 276 40.37 N 73.30 W
South Llano ≃ 196 30.30 N 99.46 W
South Lockport 284a 43.09 N 78.42 W
South Lorain 279a 41.27 N 82.08 W
South Loup ≃ 198 41.04 N 98.40 W
South Luangwa National Park ♠ 154 12.50 S 31.45 E
South Luconia Shoals ✣2 112 5.00 N 112.42 E
South Lynnfield 283 42.31 N 71.00 W
South Lyon 216 42.27 N 83.39 W
South Macmillan ≃ 180 63.03 N 133.18 W
South Magnetic Pole ⊸ 9 65.18 S 139.30 E
South Malosmadulu Atoll I1 122 5.10 N 72.58 E
South Manitou Island I 190 45.01 N 86.07 W
South Marsh Island I 208 38.06 N 76.02 W
South Medford 202 42.18 N 122.50 W
South Media 285 39.54 N 75.23 W
South Melbourne 274b 37.50 S 144.57 E
South Merrimack 207 42.48 N 71.33 W
South Miami 220 25.42 N 80.17 W
South Miami Heights 220 25.35 N 80.22 W
South Middleboro 207 41.49 N 70.49 W
South Milford 216 41.31 N 85.16 W
South Mills 192 36.26 N 76.19 W
South Milwaukee 216 42.54 N 87.51 W
South Mimms 260 51.42 N 0.14 W
Southminster 42 51.40 N 0.50 E
South Modesto 226 37.38 N 120.58 W
South Mokelumne ≃ 226 38.08 N 121.35 W
South Molton 42 51.01 N 3.50 W
South Monroe 216 41.54 N 83.25 W
Southmont 214 40.18 N 78.56 W
South Montrose 210 41.48 N 75.53 W
South Moose Lake ⊜ 184 53.46 N 100.08 W
South Mountain 208 39.51 N 77.29 W
South Mountain ∧, U.S. 208 39.40 N 77.30 W
South Mountain ∧, Id., U.S. 202 42.44 N 116.54 W
South Mountain Reservation ♠ 276 40.45 N 74.18 W
South Mount Vernon 214 40.23 N 82.23 W
South Nahanni ≃ 176 61.03 N 123.20 W
South Naknek 180 58.43 N 157.00 W
South Nation ≃ 188 45.34 N 75.06 W
South Negril Point > 241q 18.15 N 78.22 W
South New Berlin 210 42.31 N 75.23 W
South New Castle 214 40.58 N 80.21 W
South New River Canal ⩧ 220 26.04 N 80.12 W
South Norfolk → Chesapeake 208 36.43 N 76.15 W

Symbols in the index entries represent the broad categories identified in the key at the right. Symbols with superior numbers (⩘1) identify subcategories (see complete key on page *I · 1).*

Symbole im Register stellen die rechts im Schlüssel erklärten Kategorien dar. Symbole mit hochgestellten Ziffern (⩘1) bezeichnen Unterabteilungen einer Kategorie (vgl. vollständiger Schlüssel auf Seite *I · 1).*

Los símbolos incluídos en el texto del índice representan las grandes categorías identificadas con la clave a la derecha. Los símbolos con numeros en su parte superior (⩘1) identifican las subcategorías (véase la clave completa en la página *I · 1).*

Les symboles de l'index représentent les catégories indiquées dans la légende à droite. Les symboles suivis d'un indice (⩘1) représentent des sous-catégories (voir légende complète à la page *I · 1).*

Os símbolos incluídos no texto do índice representam as grandes categorias identificadas com a chave à direita. Os símbolos com números em sua parte superior (⩘1) identificam as subcategorias (veja-se a chave completa à página *I · 1).*

Symbol	English	Deutsch	Español	Français	Português
∧	Mountain	Berg	Montaña	Montagne	Montanha
⩘	Mountains	Gebirge	Montañas	Montagnes	Montanhas
)(	Pass	Paß	Paso	Col	Passo
V	Valley, Canyon	Tal, Cañon	Valle, Cañón	Vallée, Canyon	Vale, Canhão
⊻	Plain	Ebene	Llano	Plaine	Planície
>	Cape	Kap	Cabo	Cap	Cabo
I	Island	Insel	Isla	Île	Ilha
II	Islands	Inseln	Islas	Îles	Ilhas
⊥	Other Topographic Features	Andere Topographische Objekte	Otros Elementos Topográficos	Autres données topographiques	Outros acidentes topográficos

ESPAÑOL

Nombre	Página	Lat.°′	Long.°′ W = Oeste
South Normanton	44	53.06 N	1.20 W
South Norwalk Reservoir ⊜[1]	276	41.11 N	73.27 W
South Norwood ◆[8]	260	51.24 N	0.04 W
South Nutfield	260	51.14 N	0.08 W
South Nyack	276	41.04 N	73.55 W
South Ockendon	42	51.32 N	0.18 E
South Ogden	200	41.11 N	111.58 W
Southold	207	41.03 N	72.25 W
South Onondaga	210	42.56 N	76.13 W
South Orange	276	40.47 N	74.15 W
South Orkney Islands II	9	60.35 S	45.30 W
South Oroville	226	39.30 N	121.33 W
South Ossetia → Jugo Osetija □[9]	84	42.20 N	44.00 E
South Otselic	210	42.38 N	75.46 W
Southowram	262	53.43 N	1.50 W
South Oxhey	260	51.38 N	0.23 W
South Oyster Bay c	276	40.38 N	73.28 W
South Palo Duro Creek ≃	196	36.06 N	101.29 W
South Para ≃	168b	34.36 S	138.45 E
South Para Reservoir ⊜[1]	168b	34.42 S	138.52 E
South Paris	188	44.13 N	70.30 W
South Park	216	41.44 N	88.18 W
South Park ♦, N.Y., U.S.	284a	42.50 N	78.50 W
South Park ♦, Pa., U.S.	279b	40.19 N	80.01 W
South Pasadena, Ca., U.S.	280	34.06 N	118.08 W
South Pasadena, Fl., U.S.	220	27.46 N	82.43 W
South Pass)(	200	42.22 N	108.55 W
South Pass ʊ	175c	7.14 N	151.48 E
South Passage ʊ, Austl.	171a	27.22 S	153.26 E
South Passage ʊ, Oh., U.S.	214	41.35 N	82.45 W
South Patrick Shores	220	28.12 N	80.35 W
South Pekin	190	40.29 N	89.39 W
South Pender	224	48.45 N	123.14 W
South Pender Island I	224	48.45 N	123.10 W
South Perth	168a	31.59 S	115.52 E
South Petherton	42	50.58 N	2.49 W
South Philadelphia ◆[8]	285	39.56 N	75.10 W
South Philipsburg	214	40.53 N	78.13 W
South Pittsburg	194	35.00 N	85.42 W
South Plainfield	210	40.34 N	74.24 W
South Platte ≃	178	41.07 N	100.42 W
South Platte, North Fork ≃	200	39.25 N	105.10 W
South Point ≻, Barb.	241g	13.02 N	59.31 W
South Point ≻, Pil.	116	10.24 N	122.30 E
South Pole ◆	9	90.00 S	0.00
South Porcupine	190	48.28 N	81.13 W
Southport, Austl.	166	43.25 S	146.59 E
Southport, Austl.	171a	27.58 S	153.25 E
Southport, Eng., U.K.	44	53.39 N	3.01 W
Southport, Ct., U.S.	207	41.08 N	73.17 W
Southport, Fl., U.S.	194	30.17 N	85.38 W
Southport, In., U.S.	218	39.39 N	86.07 W
Southport, N.Y., U.S.	210	42.03 N	76.49 W
Southport, N.C., U.S.	192	33.55 N	78.01 W
South Portland	188	43.38 N	70.14 W
South Portsmouth	218	38.43 N	83.00 W
South Pottstown	208	40.14 N	75.39 W
South Prairie Creek ≃	224	47.08 N	122.10 W
South Raisin ≃	206	45.08 N	74.35 W
South Range	190	47.04 N	88.38 W
South Renovo	214	41.19 N	77.44 W
South Reservoir ⊜[1]	283	42.27 N	71.07 W
South Ribble □[8]	262	53.45 N	2.42 W
South River, On., Can.	190	45.50 N	79.23 W
South River, N.J., U.S.	208	40.26 N	74.23 W
South River c	208	38.57 N	76.29 W
South Rockwood	216	42.04 N	83.16 W
South Ronaldsay I	46	58.46 N	2.58 W
South Roxana	219	38.50 N	90.04 W
South Royalston	207	42.37 N	72.08 W
South Rukuru ≃	154	10.46 S	34.14 E
South Russell	214	41.25 N	81.21 W
South Salmara	124	25.55 N	90.01 E
South Sand Bluff ≻	158	31.19 S	30.01 E
South Sandwich Islands II	18	57.45 S	26.30 W
South Sandwich Trench ✢[1]	18	56.30 S	25.00 W
South Sandy Creek ≃	212	43.43 N	76.12 W
South San Francisco	226	37.39 N	122.24 W
South San Gabriel	280	34.03 N	118.05 W
South San Jose Hills	280	34.01 N	117.55 W
South San Ramon Creek ≃	282	37.42 N	121.55 W
South Santiam ≃	202	44.41 N	123.00 W
South Saskatchewan ≃	184	53.15 N	105.05 W
South Saugeen ≃	212	44.08 N	81.02 W
South Seaville	208	39.10 N	74.45 W
South Setauket	210	40.54 N	73.06 W
South Shafter	226	35.28 N	119.17 W
South Shetland Islands II	9	62.00 S	58.00 W
South Shields	44	55.00 N	1.25 W
South Shore	218	38.43 N	82.59 W
South Shore ◆[8]	278	41.46 N	87.35 W
South Shore Mall ◆[9]	276	40.44 N	73.15 W
South Shore Plaza ◆[9]	283	42.13 N	71.01 W
Southside	174h	2.49 S	171.43 W
South Side ◆[8]	279b	40.26 N	79.58 W
Southside Place	222	29.42 N	95.26 W
South Sioux City	198	42.28 N	96.24 W
South Skunk ≃	190	41.15 N	92.02 W
South Slocan	182	49.28 N	117.32 W
South Solon	218	39.44 N	83.36 W
South Sound ʊ	48	53.02 N	9.28 W
South Spicer Island I	176	68.06 N	79.13 W
South Standard	219	39.21 N	89.47 W
South Station ◆[5]	283	42.21 N	71.04 W
South Sterling	210	41.17 N	75.21 W
South Stony Brook	276	40.53 N	73.07 W
South Stradbroke Island I	171a	27.51 S	153.25 E
South Streator	216	40.39 N	88.23 W
South Suburban → Behāla	126	22.31 N	88.19 E
South Sulphur ≃	196	33.23 N	95.18 W
South Sunday Creek ≃	202	46.27 N	105.54 W
South Superior	200	41.45 N	108.57 W
South Swansea	207	41.43 N	71.12 W
South Taranaki Bight c[3]	172	39.40 S	174.10 E
South Tasman Rise ✢[3]	6	49.00 S	148.00 E
South Temple	208	40.24 N	75.55 W
South Thompson ≃	182	50.41 N	120.21 W
South Toms River	208	39.56 N	74.12 W
South Torrington	198	42.02 N	104.10 W
South Towanda	210	41.45 N	76.27 W
South Tucson	200	32.11 N	110.58 W
South Turkeyfoot Creek ≃	216	41.25 N	83.58 W
South Turlock	226	37.29 N	120.51 W
South Twillingate Island I	186	49.37 N	54.47 W
South Tyne ≃	44	54.59 N	2.08 W
South Ubian	116	5.11 N	120.30 E
South Uist I	46	57.15 N	7.21 W
South Umpqua ≃	202	43.20 N	123.25 W
South Valley	210	42.42 N	74.43 W
South Valley Hills ⩕[2]	285	40.00 N	75.40 W

FRANÇAIS

Nom	Page	Lat.°′	Long.°′ W = Ouest
South Valley Stream	276	40.38 N	73.44 W
South Venice	220	27.03 N	82.25 W
South Ventana Cone ∧	204	36.17 N	121.38 W
South Vestal	210	42.01 N	76.00 W
South Vietnam → Vietnam □[1]	108	16.00 N	108.00 E
Southview	214	40.20 N	80.16 W
Southview Apartments	284c	38.50 N	77.00 W
South Wabasca Lake ⊜	182	55.54 N	113.45 W
South Wales	210	42.43 N	78.35 W
South Walpole	283	42.06 N	71.15 W
Southwark ◆[8]	260	51.30 N	0.06 W
South Warren Reservoir ⊜[1]	168b	34.43 S	138.55 E
Southwater	42	51.01 N	0.21 W
South Waverly	210	41.59 N	76.32 W
South Weald	260	51.37 N	0.16 E
Southwell	44	53.05 N	0.58 W
South Wellfleet	207	41.55 N	69.59 W
South Wellington	224	49.06 N	123.53 W
Southwest	214	40.12 N	79.32 W
South West Bay c	240b	25.00 N	77.32 W
Southwest Branch ≃	284c	38.53 N	76.48 W
South Westbury	276	40.45 N	73.35 W
South West Cape ≻, Austl.	166	43.34 S	146.02 E
South West Cape ≻, N.Z.	172	47.17 S	167.28 E
Southwest Cape ≻, Ak., U.S.	180	63.18 N	171.27 W
Southwest Cape ≻, Vir. Is., U.S.	241n	17.41 N	64.54 W
Southwest Channel ʊ	220	27.34 N	82.45 W
South West City	194	36.30 N	94.36 W
South Westerlo	210	42.27 N	74.02 W
Southwest Greensburg	214	40.17 N	79.33 W
Southwest Harbor	188	44.16 N	68.19 W
Southwest Indian Ridge ✢[3]	6	30.00 S	60.00 E
Southwest Miramichi ≃	186	46.58 N	65.35 W
Southwest Museum ⊍	280	34.06 N	118.13 W
Southwest National Park ♦	166	43.15 S	146.15 E
Southwest Pacific Basin ✢[1]	6	40.00 S	150.00 W
Southwest Point ≻, Ba.	238	25.51 N	77.13 W
South West Point ≻, Kiribati	174o	1.52 N	157.33 W
Southwest Point ≻, Pap. N. Gui.	164	2.14 S	146.34 E
South Weymouth	283	42.10 N	70.57 W
South Weymouth Naval Air Station ■	207	42.09 N	70.57 W
South Whitley	216	41.05 N	85.37 W
South Whittier	280	33.57 N	118.02 W
South Wichita ≃	196	33.43 N	99.29 W
Southwick, Eng., U.K.	42	50.50 N	0.13 W
Southwick, Ma., U.S.	207	42.03 N	72.46 W
South Williamson	192	37.40 N	82.17 W
South Williamsport	210	41.13 N	76.59 W
South Wilmington	216	41.10 N	88.16 W
South Windham	188	43.44 N	70.25 W
South Windsor	207	41.49 N	72.37 W
Southwold	42	52.20 N	1.40 E
Southwood	210	42.59 N	76.08 W
Southwood Acres	207	41.59 N	72.32 W
South Woodham Ferrers	42	51.39 N	0.37 E
South Woodslee	214	42.14 N	82.43 W
South Woodstock	207	41.56 N	71.57 W
Southworth	224	47.31 N	122.30 W
South Yadkin ≃	192	35.45 N	80.27 W
South Yamhill ≃	224	45.13 N	123.08 W
South Yarmouth	207	41.40 N	70.11 W
South Yarra	274b	37.51 S	145.00 E
South Yorkshire □[6]	44	53.30 N	1.15 W
South Yuba ≃	226	39.17 N	121.12 W
South Zeal	42	50.44 N	3.54 W
Soutpan	158	28.43 S	26.04 E
Soutpansberg ⩕	156	22.55 S	29.30 E
Souttouf, Adrar ⩕	148	22.15 N	15.40 W
Souvigny	32	46.32 N	3.11 E
Souzy-la-Briche	261	48.32 N	2.09 E
Sovata	38	46.35 N	25.04 E
Soverato	68	38.41 N	16.33 E
Sovere	64	45.49 N	10.01 E
Sovereign Hill Historical Park ⊥	169	37.37 S	143.51 E
Sovereign Mountain ∧	180	62.08 N	148.36 W
Soveria Mannelli	68	39.05 N	16.22 E
Sövestad	41	55.30 N	13.47 E
Sovetašen	84	40.06 N	44.33 E
Sovetka	83	47.30 N	39.15 E
Sovetsk, Ross.	76	53.56 N	37.39 E
Sovetsk, Ross.	76	55.05 N	21.53 E
Sovetsk, Ross.	80	57.37 N	48.58 E
Sovetskaja, Ross.	80	49.00 N	42.07 E
Sovetskaja, Ross.	84	44.46 N	41.11 E
Sovetskaja, Ross.	84	44.02 N	44.03 E
Sovetskaja Gavan'	89	48.58 N	140.18 E
Sovetskich Oficerov, pik ∧	85	38.26 N	73.18 E
Sovetskij, Ross.	76	60.32 N	28.41 E
Sovetskij, Ross.	80	56.46 N	48.32 E
Sovetskij, Ross.	86	51.04 N	56.29 E
Sovetskij, Taj.	85	40.11 N	71.19 E
Sovetskij, Taj.	85	38.02 N	69.35 E
Sovetskij, Ukr.	78	45.20 N	34.56 E
Sovetskoje, Kaz.	85	42.17 N	70.15 E
Sovetskoje, Ross.	78	50.21 N	39.01 E
Sovetskoje, Ross.	80	51.27 N	46.44 E
Sovetskoje, Ross.	84	43.19 N	43.36 E
Sovetskoje, Ross.	84	42.52 N	45.41 E
Šovgenovskij	78	45.02 N	40.14 E
Sovicille	66	43.17 N	11.13 E
Sovico	266b	45.39 N	9.16 E
Søvik	26	62.33 N	6.18 E
Søvind	41	55.54 N	10.01 E
Sovpolje	24	65.18 N	43.55 E
Sow ≃	42	52.48 N	2.00 W
Sowa Pan ⊓	156	20.45 S	26.00 E
Sowek	164	0.49 S	135.30 E
Sowerby, Eng., U.K.	44	54.13 N	1.21 W
Sowerby, Eng., U.K.	262	53.42 N	1.56 W
Sowerby Bridge	44	53.43 N	1.54 W
Soweto	158	26.14 S	27.54 E
Sowjetisches Ehrenmal ⊥	264a	52.29 N	13.28 E
Soy	56	50.17 N	5.31 E
Sōya-kaikyō → La Perouse Strait ʊ	89	45.45 N	142.00 E
Sōya-misaki ≻	92a	45.31 N	141.56 E
Soyang-chŏsuji ⊜[1]	98	37.56 N	127.53 E
Soyapango	236	13.42 N	89.09 W
Soyers Lake ⊜	212	45.02 N	78.37 W
Soyet	124	24.12 N	76.10 E
Soyland Moor ◆[3]	262	53.40 N	2.02 W
Soyo	152	6.07 S	12.18 E
Soyons	62	44.53 N	4.51 E
Sož ≃, Europe	78	51.57 N	30.48 E
Soz' ≃, Ross.	82	56.48 N	36.44 E
Sozimskij	24	59.44 N	52.16 E
Šožma	24	61.56 N	40.15 E
Sozopol	38	42.25 N	27.42 E
Sozzago	266b	45.24 N	8.43 E
Spa	56	50.30 N	5.52 E
Spaatz Island I	9	73.12 S	75.00 W
Space Needle ⊍	224	47.38 N	122.23 W
Space Obelisk ⊥	265b	55.49 N	37.38 E
Spadafora	70	38.13 N	15.22 E

PORTUGUÊS

Nome	Página	Lat.°′	Long.°′ W = Oeste
Spada Lake ⊜[1]	224	47.57 N	121.40 W
Spaden	52	53.34 N	8.38 E
Spahl	56	50.39 N	9.55 E
Spaichingen	58	48.04 N	8.44 E
Spain (España) □[1], Europe	22	40.00 N	4.00 W
Spain (España) □[1], Europe	34	40.00 N	4.00 W
Spakenburg	52	52.15 N	5.23 E
Spalato → Split	36	43.31 N	16.27 E
Spalding, Austl.	166	33.30 S	138.37 E
Spalding, Sk., Can.	184	52.20 N	104.30 W
Spalding, Eng., U.K.	42	52.47 N	0.10 W
Spalding, Mo., U.S.	219	39.38 N	91.32 W
Spalding, Ne., U.S.	198	41.41 N	98.21 W
Spalt	56	49.10 N	10.55 E
Spam Island I	174h	2.48 S	171.43 W
Spanaway	224	47.06 N	122.26 W
Spandau ◆[8]	54	52.33 N	13.12 E
Spandau, Berliner Forst ◆[3]	264a	52.35 N	13.11 E
Spang	41	54.56 N	9.50 E
Spangenberg	56	51.07 N	9.40 E
Spangler	214	40.38 N	78.46 W
Spaniard's Bay	186	47.37 N	53.17 W
Spanien → Spain □[1]	34	40.00 N	4.00 W
Spanish	190	46.12 N	82.21 W
Spanish ≃	190	46.11 N	82.19 W
Spanish Camp	222	29.23 N	96.10 W
Spanish Fork	200	40.06 N	111.39 W
Spanish Lake	219	38.47 N	90.12 W
Spanish North Africa □[2], Afr.	34	35.53 N	5.19 W
Spanish North Africa □[2], Afr.	134	35.53 N	5.19 W
Spanish Peak ∧	202	44.24 N	119.46 W
Spanish Point ≻	240a	32.18 N	64.48 W
Spanish Sahara → Western Sahara □[2]	134	24.30 N	13.00 W
Spanish Town, Br. Vir. Is.	240m	18.27 N	64.26 W
Spanish Town, Jam.	241q	17.59 N	76.57 W
Spannberg	61	48.27 N	16.44 E
Sparagio, Monte ∧	70	38.03 N	12.46 E
Sparbach	264b	48.04 N	16.11 E
Spargi, Isola I	71	41.14 N	9.21 E
Sparkford	42	51.02 N	2.34 W
Sparkill	276	41.02 N	73.56 W
Sparkle Lake	210	41.18 N	73.47 W
Sparkman	194	33.55 N	92.50 W
Sparks, Ga., U.S.	192	31.10 N	83.26 W
Sparks, Nv., U.S.	226	39.32 N	119.45 W
Sparland	190	41.02 N	89.26 W
Sparlingville	214	42.58 N	82.30 W
Sparneck	54	50.09 N	11.50 E
Sparreholm	40	59.04 N	16.49 E
Sparrow Bush	210	41.23 N	74.43 W
Sparrow Lake ⊜	212	44.49 N	79.24 W
Sparrowpit	262	53.19 N	1.52 W
Sparrows Point	208	39.13 N	76.28 W
Sparrows Point ≻	284b	39.12 N	76.30 W
Sparta, On., Can.	212	42.42 N	81.05 W
Sparta → Spárti, Ellás	38	37.05 N	22.27 E
Sparta, Ga., U.S.	192	33.16 N	82.58 W
Sparta, Il., U.S.	194	38.07 N	89.42 W
Sparta, Ky., U.S.	218	38.40 N	84.54 W
Sparta, Mi., U.S.	190	43.09 N	85.42 W
Sparta, N.J., U.S.	210	41.02 N	74.38 W
Sparta, N.C., U.S.	192	36.30 N	81.07 W
Sparta, Oh., U.S.	214	40.24 N	82.42 W
Sparta, Tn., U.S.	194	35.55 N	85.27 W
Sparta, Wi., U.S.	190	43.56 N	90.48 W
Sparta Brook ≃	276	41.08 N	73.52 W
Spartak Garden ♦	265a	59.51 N	30.30 E
Sparta Lake	210	41.03 N	74.34 W
Spartanburg, In., U.S.	218	40.03 N	84.51 W
Spartanburg, S.C., U.S.	192	34.56 N	81.55 W
Spartansburg	214	41.49 N	79.41 W
Spartel, Cap ≻	34	35.48 N	5.56 W
Spárti (Sparta)	38	37.05 N	22.27 E
Spartivento, Capo ≻, It.	68	37.55 N	16.04 E
Spartivento, Capo ≻, It.	71	38.53 N	8.50 E
Spas-Demensk	76	54.25 N	34.01 E
Spas-Klepiki	80	55.08 N	40.13 E
Spass	82	55.55 N	35.55 E
Spassk-Dal'nij	89	44.37 N	132.48 E
Spasskij	86	53.42 N	59.12 E
Spasskij Zavod	86	49.32 N	73.17 E
Spasskoje, Ross.	76	53.06 N	36.24 E
Spasskoje, Ross.	80	55.52 N	45.42 E
Spasskoje, Ross.	82	54.05 N	38.28 E
Spassk-R'azanskij	80	54.24 N	40.23 E
Spas-Zaulok	82	56.29 N	36.34 E
Spáta	267c	37.48 N	23.55 E
Spátha, Ákra ≻	38	35.42 N	23.44 E
Spaulding	219	39.52 N	89.32 W
Spaulding, Lake ⊜[1]	226	39.20 N	120.37 W
Speaks	222	29.15 N	96.42 W
Spean, Glen V	46	56.53 N	4.45 W
Spean Bridge	46	56.53 N	4.54 W
Spear, Cape ≻	186	47.32 N	52.32 W
Spearfish	198	44.29 N	103.51 W
Spearman	196	36.11 N	101.11 W
Spearsville	218	39.21 N	86.11 W
Spearville	198	37.51 N	99.45 W
Spearwood	168a	32.07 S	115.47 E
Speas Artemidos (Rock Tombs) ⊥	142	27.54 N	30.52 E
Specchia	68	39.57 N	18.18 E
Spechtsbrunn	54	50.30 N	11.14 E
Spectacle Island I	283	42.19 N	70.59 W
Spectrum ♦	285	39.54 N	75.10 W
Spectrum Range ⩕	180	57.30 N	130.40 W
Spednic Lake ⊜	186	45.36 N	67.35 W
Speed	218	38.24 N	85.45 W
Speed ≃	212	43.23 N	80.22 W
Speedway	218	39.48 N	86.16 W
Speicher	58	47.24 N	9.27 E
Speichersee ⊜	60	48.13 N	11.45 E
Speightstown	241g	13.15 N	59.39 W
Speigletown	210	42.48 N	73.38 W
Speikkogel ∧	61	47.14 N	15.03 E
Speinshart	60	49.47 N	11.49 E
Speising ◆[8]	264b	48.10 N	16.17 E
Speke ◆[8]	262	53.21 N	2.51 W
Speke Gulf c	154	2.20 S	33.15 E
Speke Hall ⊥	262	53.20 N	2.52 W
Speldorf ◆[8]	263	51.25 N	6.52 E
Spellen	263	51.37 N	6.37 E
Spello	66	42.59 N	12.40 E
Spelthorne □[8]	260	51.25 N	0.28 W
Spelve, Loch c	46	56.22 N	5.46 W
Spenard	180	61.11 N	149.55 W
Spence Bay	176	69.32 N	93.31 W
Spencer, In., U.S.	194	39.17 N	86.45 W
Spencer, Ia., U.S.	198	43.08 N	95.08 W
Spencer, Ma., U.S.	207	42.14 N	71.59 W
Spencer, Ne., U.S.	198	42.52 N	98.42 W
Spencer, N.Y., U.S.	210	42.12 N	76.29 W
Spencer, N.C., U.S.	192	35.41 N	80.26 W
Spencer, Oh., U.S.	214	41.06 N	82.07 W
Spencer, S.D., U.S.	198	43.43 N	97.35 W
Spencer, Tn., U.S.	194	35.44 N	85.28 W
Spencer, W.V., U.S.	188	38.48 N	81.21 W
Spencer, Wi., U.S.	190	44.45 N	90.17 W
Spencer, Cape ≻, Austl.	166	35.18 S	136.53 E
Spencer, Cape ≻, N.B., Can.	186	45.12 N	65.55 W
Spencer, Cape ≻, Ak., U.S.	180	58.14 N	136.40 W
Spencer, Mount ∧	224	49.03 N	124.38 W
Spencer, Point ≻	180	65.18 N	166.50 W
Spencer Brook ≃	283	42.28 N	71.22 W
Spencer Creek ≃, On., Can.	212	43.17 N	79.54 W
Spencer Creek ≃, Mo., U.S.	219	39.33 N	91.20 W
Spencer Field ⊠	281	42.31 N	83.33 W
Spencer Gulf c	166	34.00 S	137.00 E
Spencer Lake ⊜	224	47.16 N	122.57 W
Spencerport	210	43.11 N	77.48 W
Spencertown	210	42.20 N	73.33 W
Spencerville, On., Can.	212	44.51 N	75.33 W
Spencerville, In., U.S.	216	41.16 N	84.55 W
Spencerville, Md., U.S.	208	39.06 N	76.58 W
Spencerville, Oh., U.S.	216	40.42 N	84.21 W
Spences Bridge	182	50.25 N	121.21 W
Spenge	52	52.08 N	8.28 E
Spennymoor	44	54.42 N	1.35 W
Spenser Mountains ⩕	172	42.15 S	172.30 E
Sperenberg	54	52.08 N	13.22 E
Sperillen ⊜	26	60.28 N	10.03 E
Sperling	224	49.08 N	122.33 W
Sperlinga	70	37.46 N	14.21 E
Sperlonga	66	41.15 N	13.26 E
Spermaceti Cove c	276	40.26 N	73.59 W
Sperone, Capo ≻	71	38.57 N	8.25 E
Sperrin Mountains ⩕	48	54.50 N	7.05 W
Sperry Creek ≃	279a	41.29 N	81.53 W
Sperry Rand Corporation ⊍[3]	276	40.45 N	73.42 W
Sperryville	188	38.39 N	78.13 W
Spessart ◆[1]	56	50.10 N	9.20 E
Spesutie Island I	208	39.27 N	76.05 W
Spétsai I	38	37.16 N	23.08 E
Spevakovka	83	49.03 N	38.54 E
Spexard	52	51.52 N	8.24 E
Spey ≃	46	57.40 N	3.06 W
Spey Bay c	46	57.41 N	3.00 W
Speyer	56	49.19 N	8.26 E
Speyerbach ≃	56	49.19 N	8.27 E
Speyside	241r	11.18 N	60.32 W
Spezia → La Spezia	62	44.07 N	9.50 E
Spezzano Albanese	68	39.40 N	16.19 E
Spezzano della Sila	68	39.18 N	16.20 E
Sphinx → Abū al-Hawl ⊥	142	29.59 N	31.08 E
Spiazzo	64	46.07 N	10.40 E
Spiceland	218	39.50 N	85.26 W
Spicer	198	45.13 N	94.56 W
Spicer Creek ≃	284a	43.02 N	78.53 W
Spicer Meadow Reservoir ⊜[1]	226	38.23 N	119.59 W
Spicheren	56	49.12 N	6.58 E
Spickard	194	40.14 N	93.35 W
Spicket ≃	283	42.42 N	71.09 W
Spieka	52	53.45 N	8.35 E
Spiekeroog I	52	53.46 N	7.42 E
Spiess Seamount ✢[3]	8	54.40 S	0.15 E
Spiez	58	46.41 N	7.39 E
Spijkenisse	52	51.51 N	4.20 E
Špikov	78	48.46 N	28.35 E
Spilamberto	64	44.32 N	11.01 E
Spilimbergo	64	46.07 N	12.54 E
Spilinga	68	38.37 N	15.54 E
Spillersboda	40	59.42 N	18.51 E
Spillimacheen ≃	182	50.55 N	116.20 W
Spillville	190	43.12 N	91.57 W
Spilsby	44	53.11 N	0.06 E
Spinazzola	68	40.58 N	16.06 E
Spīn Būldak	120	31.01 N	66.24 E
Spincourt	56	49.20 N	5.40 E
Spindale	192	35.21 N	81.55 W
Spindoli	66	43.12 N	12.54 E
Spinea-Orgnano	64	45.29 N	12.10 E
Spinetta Marengo	62	44.53 N	8.41 E
Spinnerstown	208	40.26 N	75.26 W
Spinoso	68	40.16 N	15.58 E
Spires → Speyer	56	49.19 N	8.26 E
Spirit Lake, Id., U.S.	202	47.57 N	116.52 W
Spirit Lake, Ia., U.S.	198	43.25 N	95.06 W
Spirit Lake ⊜	224	46.16 N	122.08 W
Spirit River	182	55.47 N	118.50 W
Spiritwood	184	53.22 N	107.31 W
Spiro	194	35.14 N	94.37 W
Spirovo	76	57.26 N	34.59 E
Spišská Nová Ves	30	48.57 N	20.34 E
Spitak	84	40.51 N	44.16 E
Spital am Pyhrn	61	47.39 N	14.20 E
Spithead ʊ	42	50.45 N	1.05 W
Spit Point ≻	162	20.02 S	119.00 E
Spitsbergen I	12	78.45 N	16.00 E
Spitsbergen Bank ✢[4]	12	76.00 N	23.00 E
Spittal an der Drau	64	46.48 N	13.30 E
Spittal of Glenshee	46	56.48 N	3.28 W
Spitz	61	48.22 N	15.25 E
Spitzbergen und Jan Mayen → Svalbard □[2]	12	78.00 N	20.00 E
Spitzer Berg ∧[2]	264a	52.38 N	13.35 E
Spixworth	42	52.40 N	1.20 E
Spjelkavik	26	62.28 N	6.23 E
Splavnucha	80	51.05 N	45.22 E
Splendora	222	30.14 N	95.10 W
Split	36	43.31 N	16.27 E
Split, Cape ≻	186	45.20 N	64.30 W
Split Lake ⊜	184	56.08 N	96.15 W
Splitrock Reservoir ⊜[1]	276	40.58 N	74.27 W
Spluga, Passo della (Splügenpass))(	58	46.30 N	9.20 E
Splügen	58	46.33 N	9.20 E
Splügenpass (Passo della Spluga))(	58	46.30 N	9.20 E
Spodsbjerg	41	54.56 N	10.50 E
Spofford	196	29.11 N	100.25 W
Špogi	76	56.05 N	26.44 E
Spokane	202	47.39 N	117.25 W
Spokane ≃	202	47.54 N	118.20 W
Spokane, Mount ∧	202	47.55 N	117.07 W
Spokane Indian Reservation ◆[4]	202	47.55 N	118.00 W
Spokojnaja	84	44.15 N	41.25 E
Špola	78	49.01 N	31.24 E
Spoleto	66	42.44 N	12.44 E
Spoltore	66	42.27 N	14.08 E
Spondigna	64	46.38 N	10.37 E
Spondon	42	52.54 N	1.25 W
Sponds Hill ∧[2]	262	53.19 N	2.03 W
Spóng	110	13.27 N	105.34 E
Spoon ≃	194	40.18 N	90.04 W
Spooner	190	45.49 N	91.53 W
Spořice	54	50.26 N	13.25 E
Spornitz	54	53.24 N	11.43 E
Spornoje	74	62.20 N	151.03 E
Sporovo	76	52.25 N	25.20 E
Spørring	41	56.18 N	10.09 E
Sportforum ♦	264a	52.33 N	13.29 E
Sport Hill	207	41.14 N	73.16 W
Sporting Hill	208	40.09 N	76.26 W
Sportsman's Park Race Track ♦	278	41.50 N	87.46 W
Spotorno	62	44.14 N	8.25 E
Spot Pond ⊜	283	42.27 N	71.06 W
Spotswood, Austl.	274b	37.50 S	144.53 E
Spotswood, N.J., U.S.	208	40.23 N	74.23 W
Spotsylvania	208	38.12 N	77.35 W
Spotsylvania □[6]	208	38.15 N	77.30 W
Spotsylvania Court House Battlefield ⊥	208	38.15 N	77.35 W
Sprague, Mb., Can.	184	49.02 N	95.38 W
Sprague, Wa., U.S.	202	47.18 N	117.58 W
Sprague ≃	202	42.34 N	121.51 W
Sprague, North Fork ≃	202	42.26 N	121.07 W
Sprague, South Fork ≃	202	42.26 N	121.07 W
Spragueville	207	41.53 N	71.32 W
Sprain Ridge Park ♦	276	40.59 N	73.51 W
Sprankle Mills	214	41.00 N	79.07 W
Spratly Islands II	108	10.00 N	114.00 E
Spratt Point ≻	212	44.36 N	80.01 W
Spray	202	44.50 N	119.47 W
Spray Lakes Reservoir ⊜[1]	182	50.55 N	115.20 W
Spreča ≃	38	44.45 N	18.06 E
Spreckels	226	36.36 N	121.34 W
Spreckelsville	229a	20.53 N	156.24 W
Spree ≃	54	52.32 N	13.13 E
Spreenhagen	54	52.20 N	13.52 E
Spreeufontein	158	33.22 S	20.45 E
Spreewald ◆[1]	54	51.50 N	14.05 E
Spremberg	54	51.34 N	14.22 E
Sprendlingen	56	49.51 N	7.59 E
Spresiano	64	45.46 N	12.16 E
Spring	222	30.04 N	95.25 W
Spring ≃, U.S.	194	36.52 N	94.44 W
Spring ≃, Ar., U.S.	194	36.08 N	91.05 W
Spring, North Fork ≃	194	37.18 N	94.21 W
Spring, South Fork ≃	194	36.19 N	91.30 W
Spring Arbor	216	42.12 N	84.33 W
Spring Bay c	200	41.40 N	112.50 W
Springbok	156	29.43 S	17.55 E
Springboro, Oh., U.S.	218	39.33 N	84.14 W
Springboro, Pa., U.S.	214	41.48 N	80.22 W
Spring Branch ≃	284b	39.26 N	76.35 W
Springbrook, On., Can.	275b	43.39 N	79.47 W
Springbrook, Md., U.S.	284c	39.03 N	77.00 W
Spring Brook, N.Y., U.S.	210	42.49 N	78.40 W
Spring Brook ≃	278	41.58 N	87.59 W
Springbrook Forest	284c	39.03 N	77.01 W
Springburn	172	43.40 S	171.28 E
Spring City, Pa., U.S.	208	40.10 N	75.32 W
Spring City, Tn., U.S.	192	35.41 N	84.51 W
Spring City, Ut,. U.S.	200	39.28 N	111.29 W
Spring Coulee V	198	48.31 N	100.54 W
Spring Creek, N.Z.	172	41.28 S	173.58 E
Spring Creek, Pa., U.S.	214	41.53 N	79.32 W
Spring Creek ≃, Austl.	166	24.12 S	140.58 E
Spring Creek ≃, U.S.	198	40.30 N	101.21 W
Spring Creek ≃, Ga., U.S.	192	30.54 N	84.45 W
Spring Creek ≃, Il., U.S.	216	40.49 N	87.50 W
Spring Creek ≃, Il., U.S.	219	39.52 N	89.37 W
Spring Creek ≃, Il., U.S.	278	41.32 N	88.04 W
Spring Creek ≃, Mo., U.S.	219	38.21 N	91.10 W
Spring Creek ≃, Nv., U.S.	204	39.55 N	117.50 W
Spring Creek ≃, N.D., U.S.	198	47.15 N	101.48 W
Spring Creek ≃, Pa., U.S.	214	40.56 N	77.47 W
Spring Creek ≃, Pa., U.S.	214	41.24 N	78.57 W
Spring Creek ≃, S.D., U.S.	198	45.54 N	100.18 W
Spring Creek ≃, S.D., U.S.	198	43.52 N	102.42 W
Spring Creek ≃, Tx., U.S.	222	30.02 N	95.16 W
Springdale, Nf., Can.	186	49.30 N	56.04 W
Springdale, Ar., U.S.	194	36.11 N	94.07 W
Springdale, Oh., U.S.	218	39.17 N	84.28 W
Springdale, Pa., U.S.	214	40.32 N	79.47 W
Springdale, S.C., U.S.	192	33.57 N	81.06 W
Springdale, Ut,. U.S.	200	37.11 N	112.59 W
Springdale, Wa., U.S.	202	48.03 N	117.44 W
Spring Dale, W.V., U.S.	192	37.52 N	80.48 W
Springe	52	52.12 N	9.32 E
Springer	196	36.21 N	104.35 W
Springers Brook ≃	285	39.44 N	74.41 W
Springerville	200	34.08 N	109.17 W
Springfield, N.S., Can.	186	44.38 N	64.52 W
Springfield, On., Can.	212	42.50 N	80.56 W
Springfield, N.Z.	172	43.20 S	171.55 E
Springfield, S. Afr.	158	29.02 S	22.53 E
Springfield, Co., U.S.	198	37.24 N	102.36 W
Springfield, Fl., U.S.	194	30.09 N	85.36 W
Springfield, Ga., U.S.	192	32.22 N	81.18 W
Springfield, Il., U.S.	219	39.48 N	89.38 W
Springfield, Ky., U.S.	194	37.41 N	85.13 W
Springfield, Ma., U.S.	207	42.06 N	72.35 W
Springfield, Mi., U.S.	216	42.19 N	85.14 W
Springfield, Mn., U.S.	198	44.14 N	94.58 W
Springfield, Mo., U.S.	194	37.12 N	93.17 W
Springfield, N.J., U.S.	276	40.43 N	74.18 W
Springfield, Oh., U.S.	218	39.55 N	83.48 W
Springfield, Or., U.S.	202	44.02 N	123.01 W
Springfield, Pa., U.S.	285	39.55 N	75.19 W
Springfield, S.C., U.S.	192	33.29 N	81.16 W
Springfield, S.D., U.S.	198	42.51 N	97.53 W
Springfield, Tn., U.S.	194	36.30 N	86.53 W
Springfield, Vt., U.S.	188	43.17 N	72.28 W
Springfield, Va., U.S.	284c	38.45 N	77.13 W
Springfield, Lake ⊜[1]	219	39.44 N	89.36 W
Springfield Center	210	42.50 N	74.53 W
Springfield Estates	284c	38.47 N	77.11 W
Springfield Lake ⊜	285	40.11 N	75.00 W
Springfield Lake ⊜[1]	222	31.36 N	96.33 W
Springfield Mall ◆[9]	284c	38.46 N	77.11 W
Springfield Plateau ⩕[1]	194	37.10 N	93.30 W
Springfontein	158	30.19 S	25.36 E
Spring Garden	246	6.59 N	58.31 W
Spring Garden Brook ≃	276	40.46 N	74.23 W
Spring Garden Township	208	39.57 N	76.44 W
Spring Glen, N.Y., U.S.	210	41.40 N	74.26 W
Spring Glen, Pa., U.S.	208	40.38 N	76.37 W
Spring Glen, Ut,. U.S.	200	39.39 N	110.51 W
Spring Green	190	43.10 N	90.04 W
Spring Grove, Il., U.S.	216	42.26 N	88.13 W
Spring Grove, Mn., U.S.	190	43.33 N	91.38 W
Spring Grove, Pa., U.S.	208	39.52 N	76.51 W
Springhill, N.S., Can.	186	45.39 N	64.03 W
Spring Hill, Ca., U.S.	226	39.15 N	121.03 W
Spring Hill, Fl., U.S.	220	28.33 N	82.27 W
Springhill, La., U.S.	194	33.00 N	93.28 W
Spring Hill, Pa., U.S.	214	40.23 N	78.40 W
Spring Hill, Tn., U.S.	194	35.45 N	86.55 W
Spring Hill, Tx., U.S.	222	32.34 N	94.48 W
Springhills	216	40.16 N	83.22 W
Spring Hope	192	35.56 N	78.06 W
Springhouse, B.C., Can.	182	51.55 N	122.07 W
Spring House, Pa., U.S.	285	40.11 N	75.14 W
Spring Lake, Mi., U.S.	216	43.04 N	86.11 W
Spring Lake, N.J., U.S.	208	40.09 N	74.01 W
Spring Lake, N.C., U.S.	192	35.10 N	78.58 W
Spring Lake ⊜, Mi., U.S.	216	43.06 N	86.11 W
Spring Lake ⊜, N.J., U.S.	276	40.35 N	74.25 W
Spring Lake Heights	208	40.09 N	74.01 W
Spring Mill, Oh., U.S.	214	40.54 N	82.36 W
Spring Mill, Pa., U.S.	285	40.04 N	75.17 W
Spring Mill Reservoir ⊜[1]	262	53.39 N	2.13 W
Spring Mills	210	40.51 N	77.34 W
Spring Mill State Park ♦	218	38.43 N	86.25 W
Spring Mount	208	40.17 N	75.28 W
Spring Mountains ⩕	204	36.10 N	115.40 W
Spring Pond ⊜	283	42.30 N	70.57 W
Springport, In., U.S.	218	40.03 N	85.24 W
Springport, Mi., U.S.	216	42.22 N	84.41 W
Spring Run	214	40.09 N	83.47 W
Springs	158	26.13 S	28.25 E
Springs □[5]	273d	26.14 S	28.30 E
Springs Aerodrome ⊠	273d	26.15 S	28.24 E
Springside	285	40.04 N	74.51 W
Springs Junction	172	42.19 S	172.11 E
Springsure	166	24.07 S	148.05 E
Springton	168b	34.43 S	139.05 E
Springtown	222	32.58 N	97.41 W
Springvale, Austl.	162	17.48 S	127.41 E
Springvale, Austl.	166	23.33 S	140.42 E
Springvale, Austl.	169	37.57 S	145.09 E
Springvale, Me., U.S.	188	43.28 N	70.47 W
Springvale South	274b	37.58 S	145.09 E
Spring Valley, Ca., U.S.	228	32.44 N	116.59 W
Spring Valley, Il., U.S.	190	41.19 N	89.11 W
Spring Valley, Mn., U.S.	190	43.41 N	92.23 W
Spring Valley, N.Y., U.S.	210	41.06 N	74.02 W
Spring Valley, Oh., U.S.	218	39.36 N	84.00 W
Spring Valley, Tx., U.S.	222	29.47 N	95.31 W
Spring Valley, Wi., U.S.	190	44.50 N	92.14 W
Spring Valley V	204	39.15 N	114.25 W
Spring Valley Creek ≃	204	39.20 N	114.25 W
Springview	198	42.49 N	99.44 W
Springville, Al., U.S.	194	33.46 N	86.28 W
Springville, Ca., U.S.	204	36.08 N	118.49 W
Springville, Ia., U.S.	190	42.03 N	91.26 W
Springville, N.J., U.S.	285	39.56 N	74.52 W
Springville, N.Y., U.S.	210	42.30 N	78.40 W
Springville, Pa., U.S.	210	41.42 N	75.55 W
Springville, Ut,. U.S.	200	40.09 N	111.36 W
Springwater	210	42.38 N	77.35 W
Springwood	170	33.42 S	150.33 E
Sprint ≃	44	54.22 N	2.45 W
Sprite Creek ≃	210	43.08 N	74.44 W
Sproat Lake ⊜	182	49.16 N	125.03 W
Sprockhövel	56	51.22 N	7.15 E
Sprogels Run ≃	285	40.14 N	75.37 W
Sprogø I	41	55.20 N	10.58 E
Sprötze	52	53.18 N	9.49 E
Sproul	214	40.16 N	78.28 W
Sprout Brook ≃	276	40.54 N	74.05 W
Spruce ≃	184	53.15 N	105.43 W
Spruce Brook	186	48.45 N	58.11 W
Spruce Creek	214	40.37 N	78.08 W
Spruce Creek ≃	210	43.07 N	74.46 W
Spruce Grove	182	53.32 N	113.55 W
Spruce Knob ∧	188	38.42 N	79.32 W
Spruce Knob-Seneca Rocks National Recreation Area ♦	188	38.50 N	79.20 W
Spruce Lake	184	53.32 N	109.05 W
Spruce Mountain ∧, Az., U.S.	200	34.28 N	112.24 W
Spruce Mountain ∧, Nv., U.S.	204	40.33 N	114.49 W
Spruce Pine, Al., U.S.	194	34.23 N	87.43 W
Spruce Pine, N.C., U.S.	192	35.54 N	82.03 W
Spruce Run Reservoir ⊜[1]	210	40.40 N	74.57 W
Spruce Run State Park ♦	210	40.40 N	74.56 W
Spruce Woods Provincial Park ♦	184	49.42 N	99.05 W
Spry	208	39.55 N	76.41 W
Spry Lake ⊜	212	44.44 N	81.15 W
Spulico, Capo ≻	68	39.58 N	16.39 E
Spur	196	33.28 N	100.51 W
Spurfield	182	55.13 N	114.16 W
Spurger	194	30.42 N	94.11 W
Spurn Head ≻	44	53.34 N	0.07 E
Spurr, Mount ∧	180	61.18 N	152.15 W
Sputendorf	264a	52.20 N	13.13 E
Spuzzum	182	49.41 N	121.25 W
Spy Hill	184	50.36 N	101.41 W
Spy Pond ⊜	283	42.24 N	71.09 W
Squally Channel ʊ	182	53.10 N	129.15 W
Squamish	182	49.42 N	123.09 W
Squamish ≃	182	49.45 N	123.09 W
Squam Lake ⊜	188	43.45 N	71.32 W
Square Butte Creek ≃	198	46.55 N	100.55 W
Square Lake ⊜	186	47.03 N	68.20 W
Squatec	186	47.53 N	68.43 W
Squaw Cap Mountain ∧	186	47.53 N	66.53 W
Squaw Creek ≃, Id., U.S.	202	43.51 N	116.22 W
Squaw Creek ≃, Il., U.S.	278	42.21 N	88.07 W
Squaw Creek ≃, Or., U.S.	202	44.27 N	121.20 W
Squaw Creek Lake ⊜[1]	222	32.19 N	97.47 W
Squaw Harbor	180	55.11 N	160.30 W
Squaw Hill ∧	200	41.48 N	105.02 W
Squaw Island I	284a	42.56 N	78.54 W
Squaw Peak ∧, Ca., U.S.	226	39.11 N	120.16 W
Squaw Peak ∧, Mt., U.S.	202	47.10 N	114.21 W
Squaw Rapids	184	53.41 N	103.20 W
Squaw Rapids Dam ◆[6]	184	53.40 N	103.25 W
Squaw Run ≃	279b	40.29 N	79.52 W
Squaw Valley State Recreation Area ♦	226	39.12 N	120.15 W
Squibnocket Point ≻	207	41.18 N	70.47 W
Squilax	182	50.52 N	119.35 W
Squillace	68	38.47 N	16.31 E
Squillace, Golfo di c	68	38.50 N	16.50 E
Squinzano	68	40.26 N	18.03 E
Squire	192	37.14 N	81.36 W
Squires, Mount ∧	162	26.12 S	127.28 E
Squirrel ≃	180	66.57 N	160.27 W
Squirrel Hill ◆[8]	279b	40.26 N	79.55 W
Squirrel Hill Tunnel ◆[5]	279b	40.26 N	79.55 W
Squirrel's Heath ◆[8]	260	51.35 N	0.13 E
Sragen	115a	7.26 S	111.02 E
Šramkovka	78	50.10 N	32.05 E
Srbija (Serbia) □[3]	38	44.00 N	21.00 E
Srbobran	38	45.33 N	19.48 E
Srê Âmběl	110	11.07 N	103.46 E
Sredinnyj chrebet ⩕	74	56.00 N	158.00 E
Sredna Gora ⩕	38	42.30 N	25.00 E
Sredn'aja Achtuba	80	48.43 N	44.52 E
Sredn'aja Mokla ≃	88	55.01 N	119.37 E
Sredn'aja Nanaki, gora ∧	89	52.26 N	132.50 E
Sredn'aja Ol'okma	88	55.26 N	120.33 E
Srednegorje	76	60.34 N	29.25 E
Sredneje Kujto, ozero ⊜	24	65.08 N	31.15 E
Srednekolymsk	74	67.27 N	153.41 E
Srednerusskaja vozvyšennost' ⩕[1]	72	52.00 N	38.00 E

Symbol	English	Deutsch	Español	Français	Português
≃	River	Fluß	Río	Rivière	Rio
≅	Canal	Kanal	Canal	Canal	Canal
⌊	Waterfall, Rapids	Wasserfall, Stromschnellen	Cascada, Rápidos	Chute d'eau, Rapides	Cascata, Rápidos
ʊ	Strait	Meeresstraße	Estrecho	Détroit	Estreito
c	Bay, Gulf	Bucht, Golf	Bahía, Golfo	Baie, Golfe	Baía, Golfo
⊜	Lake, Lakes	See, Seen	Lago, Lagos	Lac, Lacs	Lago, Lagos
≋	Swamp	Sumpf	Pantano	Marais	Pântano
⊓	Ice Features, Glacier	Eis- und Gletscherformen	Accidentes Glaciales	Formes glaciaires	Acidentes glaciares
⫪	Other Hydrographic Features	Andere Hydrographische Objekte	Otros Elementos Hidrográficos	Autres données hydrographiques	Outros acidentes hidrográficos
✢	Submarine Features	Untermeerische Objekte	Accidentes Submarinos	Formes de relief sous-marin	Acidentes submarinos
□	Political Unit	Politische Einheit	Unidad Politica	Entité politique	Unidade política
⊍	Cultural Institution	Kulturelle Institution	Institución Cultural	Institution culturelle	Institução cultural
⊥	Historical Site	Historische Stätte	Sitio Histórico	Site historique	Sitio histórico
♦	Recreational Site	Erholungs- und Ferienort	Sitio de Recreo	Centre de loisirs	Area de Lazer
⊠	Airport	Flughafen	Aeropuerto	Aéroport	Aeroporto
■	Military Installation	Militäranlage	Instalación Militar	Installation militaire	Instalação militar
◆	Miscellaneous	Verschiedenes	Misceláneo	Divers	Diversos

ENGLISH Name Page Lat.°′ Long.°′ — DEUTSCH Name Seite Breite°′ Länge°′ E = Ost

Name	Page	Lat.°′	Long.°′
Srednesibirskoje ploskogorje ⩘[1]	74	65.00 N	105.00 E
Srednij Ikorec	78	51.05 N	39.45 E
Srednij Kalar	88	55.51 N	117.24 E
Srednij Ural ⩘	86	58.00 N	59.00 E
Srednij Urgal	89	51.09 N	132.59 E
Srednij Vas'ugan	86	59.16 N	78.15 E
Srednyj	83	48.09 N	39.50 E
Srê Khtŭm	110	12.10 N	106.52 E
Śrem	30	52.08 N	17.01 E
Srê Moăt	110	13.18 N	107.10 E
Sremska Mitrovica	38	44.58 N	19.37 E
Sremski Karlovci	38	45.12 N	19.57 E
Srêng ≃	110	13.21 N	103.27 E
Srêpŏk ≃	110	13.33 N	106.16 E
Sretensk	88	52.15 N	117.43 E
Sretenskoje	88	56.28 N	96.25 E
Srīdharpur	126	23.04 N	89.25 E
Sri Hargobindpur	123	31.41 N	75.39 E
Sri Jayawardenepura (Kotte)	122	6.54 N	79.54 E
Srīkākulam	122	18.18 N	83.54 E
Sri Kālahasti	122	13.45 N	79.43 E
Sri Lanka □[1], Asia	118	7.00 N	81.00 E
Sri Lanka □[1], Asia	122	7.00 N	81.00 E
Srīnagar, Bngl.	126	23.32 N	90.18 E
Srīnagar, India	123	34.05 N	74.49 E
Srīnagar, India	124	30.13 N	78.47 E
Srīnagar Airport ⊠	123	34.00 N	74.52 E
Srīpur, Bngl.	126	24.12 N	90.29 E
Srīpur, Bngl.	126	23.36 N	89.24 E
Srīrampur, India	122	19.34 N	74.34 E
Srirāmpur, India	272b	22.49 N	88.29 E
Srīrangam	122	10.52 N	78.41 E
Srīvardhan	122	18.02 N	73.01 E
Srīvilliputtūr	122	9.31 N	77.38 E
Środa Śląska	30	51.10 N	16.36 E
Środa Wielkopolski	30	52.14 N	17.17 E
Srpska Crnja	38	45.43 N	20.42 E
Ssangmun-ni ♣[8]	271b	37.39 N	127.02 E
Ssuchunghsi	100	22.06 N	120.44 E
Ssup'ing → Siping	89	43.12 N	124.20 E
Staaken ♣[8]	54	52.32 N	13.08 E
Staaten ≃	164	16.24 S	141.17 E
Staaten River National Park ♦	164	16.40 S	143.00 E
Staatsburg	210	41.50 N	73.55 W
Staatz	61	48.40 N	16.29 E
Stabbursdalen Nasjonalpark ♦	24	70.06 N	24.30 E
Staberhuk ›	54	54.24 N	11.19 E
Stabroek	50	51.20 N	4.22 E
Stachanov	83	48.34 N	38.40 E
Stachy	60	49.06 N	13.40 E
Stack, Loch ⊜	46	58.20 N	4.55 W
Stack Skerry I[2]	46	59.01 N	4.31 W
Stacksteads	262	53.41 N	2.13 W
Stacyville	190	43.26 N	92.46 W
Stad-Delden	52	52.16 N	6.42 E
Stade	52	53.36 N	9.28 E
Staden, Bel.	50	50.59 N	3.01 E
Staden, Dtsch.	56	50.20 N	8.54 E
Stadion am Zoo ♦	263	51.14 N	7.07 E
Städjan ∧	26	61.55 N	12.52 E
Stadl an der Mur	61	47.05 N	13.58 E
Stadlandet ›[1]	26	62.07 N	5.18 E
Stadlau ♣[8]	264b	48.14 N	16.28 E
Stadl-Paura	64	48.05 N	13.53 E
Stadskanaal	52	53.00 N	6.55 E
Stadtallendorf	56	50.50 N	9.01 E
Stadtbergen	58	48.22 N	10.50 E
Stadthagen	52	52.19 N	9.13 E
Stadtilm	54	50.47 N	11.05 E
Städtische Rahmede	263	51.17 N	7.40 E
Stadtkyll	56	50.21 N	6.32 E
Stadtlauringen	56	50.11 N	10.22 E
Stadtlengsfeld	56	50.47 N	10.07 E
Stadtlohn	52	51.59 N	6.55 E
Stadtoldendorf	52	51.53 N	9.37 E
Stadtprozelten	56	49.47 N	9.25 E
Stadtroda	54	50.51 N	11.44 E
Stadtsteinach	54	50.09 N	11.30 E
Stadt Wehlen	54	50.58 N	14.02 E
Stadum	41	54.44 N	9.03 E
Stäfa	58	47.15 N	8.44 E
Staffa I	46	56.25 N	6.20 W
Staffanstorp	41	55.38 N	13.13 E
Staffelberg ∧	56	50.06 N	11.02 E
Staffelde	264a	52.44 N	13.00 E
Staffelsee ⊜	64	47.42 N	11.10 E
Staffelstein	56	50.06 N	11.00 E
Staffin	46	57.37 N	6.12 W
Staffora ≃	62	45.04 N	9.01 E
Stafford, Eng., U.K.	42	52.48 N	2.07 W
Stafford, Ct., U.S.	207	41.59 N	72.17 W
Stafford, Ks., U.S.	198	37.57 N	98.36 W
Stafford, N.Y., U.S.	210	42.59 N	78.04 W
Stafford, Tx., U.S.	222	29.37 N	95.34 W
Stafford, Va., U.S.	208	38.25 N	77.24 W
Stafford □[6]	208	38.25 N	77.30 W
Staffordshire □[6]	28	52.50 N	2.00 W
Stafford Springs	207	41.57 N	72.18 W
Staffordsville	188	37.49 N	82.50 W
Staffordville	207	41.59 N	72.15 W
Stagen	112	3.18 S	116.10 E
Stag Pond ⊜	276	40.59 N	74.42 W
Stahl-Berg ∧[2]	264a	52.21 N	13.46 E
Stahlbrode	54	54.14 N	13.17 E
Stahle	52	51.50 N	9.25 E
Stahnsdorf	54	52.23 N	13.13 E
Stahringen	58	47.47 N	8.58 E
Staicele	76	57.50 N	24.45 E
Staines	42	51.26 N	0.31 W
Staines Reservoirs ⊜[1]	260	51.27 N	0.30 W
Stainforth	44	53.36 N	1.01 W
Staining	44	53.49 N	2.59 W
Stainland	262	53.40 N	1.53 W
Stainmore Forest ♣[3]	44	54.30 N	2.10 W
Stains	261	48.57 N	2.23 E
Stainz	61	46.54 N	15.16 E
Stairtown	222	29.43 N	97.44 W
Stajki	78	50.05 N	30.54 E
Staked Plain → Estacado, Llano ≚	196	33.30 N	102.40 W
Stäket	40	59.28 N	17.48 E
Stakroge	41	55.53 N	8.51 E
Stalać	38	43.40 N	21.25 E
Stalbridge	42	50.58 N	2.23 W
Stalden	58	46.14 N	7.52 E
Staletti	68	38.46 N	16.32 E
Stalham	42	52.47 N	1.31 E
Stalheim	26	60.50 N	6.40 E
Stalhofen	61	47.05 N	15.16 E
Stalin → Varna, Blg.	38	43.13 N	27.55 E
Stalin → Brașov, Rom.	38	45.39 N	25.37 E
Stalin → Kuçovë, Shq.	38	40.48 N	19.54 E
Stalinabad → Dušanbe	85	38.35 N	68.48 E
Stalingrad → Volgograd	80	48.44 N	44.25 E
Stalino → Doneck	83	48.00 N	37.48 E
Stalinogorsk → Novomoskovsk	82	54.05 N	38.13 E
Stalinsk → Novokuzneck	86	53.45 N	87.06 E
Stallarholmen	40	59.22 N	17.12 E
Ställberg	40	59.59 N	14.55 E
Ställdalen	40	59.56 N	14.56 E
Stallwang	60	49.03 N	12.40 E
Stalowa Wola	30	50.35 N	22.02 E
Stalybridge	44	53.29 N	2.03 W
Stambaugh	190	46.04 N	88.37 W
Stamford, Austl.	166	21.16 S	143.49 E
Stamford, Eng., U.K.	42	52.39 N	0.29 W
Stamford, Ct., U.S.	207	41.03 N	73.32 W
Stamford, N.Y., U.S.	210	42.24 N	74.36 W
Stamford, Tx., U.S.	196	32.56 N	99.48 W
Stamford, Vt., U.S.	207	42.45 N	73.04 W
Stamford, Lake ⊜[1]	196	33.05 N	99.35 W
Stamford Bridge	44	53.59 N	0.55 W
Stamford Brige Stadium ♦	260	51.29 N	0.11 W
Stamford Harbor ⊂	276	41.02 N	73.32 W
Stamford Museum v	276	41.07 N	73.33 W
Stammbach	54	50.09 N	11.41 E
Stammersdorf ♣[8]	264b	48.18 N	16.25 E
Stammham, Dtsch.	60	48.52 N	11.28 E
Stammham, Dtsch.	60	48.15 N	12.53 E
Stammheim, Dtsch.	56	48.41 N	8.46 E
Stammheim, Schw.	58	47.38 N	8.47 E
Stampede Reservoir ⊜[1]	226	39.29 N	120.07 W
Stamping Ground	218	38.16 N	84.41 W
Stampriet	156	24.20 S	18.28 E
Stamps	194	33.21 N	93.29 W
Stams	64	47.16 N	10.59 E
Stanaford	188	37.48 N	81.09 W
Stanardsville	188	38.17 N	78.26 W
Stanberry	194	40.13 N	94.32 W
Stanborough	260	51.47 N	0.13 W
Stancija-Gorčakovo	85	40.25 N	71.45 E
Stancionno-Ojašinskij	86	55.28 N	83.53 E
Standard, Ab., Can.	182	51.07 N	112.59 W
Standard, Ak., U.S.	180	64.47 N	148.32 W
Standard, Ca., U.S.	226	37.59 N	120.20 W
Standard, Pa., U.S.	214	40.10 N	79.32 W
Standard Oil Company Refinery v[3]	282	37.57 N	122.24 W
Standard Shaft	279b	40.10 N	79.32 W
Standedge Canal Tunnel ♣[5]	262	53.34 N	2.00 W
Standedge Railway Tunnel ♣[5]	262	53.34 N	2.00 W
Standerton	158	26.58 S	29.07 E
Standiford Field ⊠	218	38.11 N	85.44 W
Standing Rock Indian Reservation ♣[4]	198	45.50 N	101.10 W
Standing Stone Creek ≃	214	40.30 N	78.00 W
Standing Stones ⊥	46	58.12 N	6.48 W
Standish, Eng., U.K.	44	53.36 N	2.41 W
Standish, Mi., U.S.	190	43.58 N	83.57 W
Standish Monument ⊥	283	42.01 N	70.41 W
Standon	42	51.53 N	0.02 E
Stanfield, Az., U.S.	200	32.52 N	111.57 W
Stanfield, Or., U.S.	202	45.46 N	119.12 W
Stanford, S. Afr.	158	34.26 S	19.29 E
Stanford, Ca., U.S.	226	37.25 N	122.08 W
Stanford, Ky., U.S.	192	37.31 N	84.39 W
Stanford, Mt., U.S.	202	47.09 N	110.13 W
Stanford Center ♣[9]	282	37.27 N	122.10 W
Stanford Heights	210	42.46 N	73.53 W
Stanford le Hope	42	51.31 N	0.26 E
Stanford Linear Accelerator v[3]	282	37.25 N	122.12 W
Stanford Rivers	260	51.41 N	0.13 E
Stanford University v[2]	282	37.26 N	122.10 W
Stanfordville	210	41.52 N	73.43 W
Stånga	26	57.17 N	18.28 E
Stångån ≃	26	58.27 N	15.37 E
Stångby	41	55.46 N	13.10 E
Stange	26	60.43 N	11.11 E
Stanger	158	29.27 S	31.14 E
Stanghella	64	45.08 N	11.45 E
Stanhope, Eng., U.K.	44	54.45 N	2.01 W
Stanhope, Ia., U.S.	190	42.17 N	93.47 W
Stanhope, N.J., U.S.	210	40.54 N	74.42 W
Staničino-Luganskoje	83	48.39 N	39.30 E
Stanislaus □[6]	226	37.39 N	121.00 W
Stanislaus ≃	226	37.40 N	121.14 W
Stanislaus, Clark Fork ≃	226	38.22 N	119.52 W
Stanislaus, Middle Fork ≃	226	38.09 N	120.21 W
Stanislaus, North Fork ≃	226	38.09 N	120.21 W
Stanislaus, South Fork ≃	226	38.04 N	120.25 W
Stanislav → Ivano-Frankovsk, Ukr.	78	48.55 N	24.43 E
Stanislav, Ukr.	78	46.34 N	32.09 E
Stanislavčik	78	48.58 N	28.07 E
Stanisławów → Ivano-Frankovsk	78	48.55 N	24.43 E
Stanke Dimitrov	38	42.16 N	23.07 E
Staňkov	60	49.34 N	13.04 E
Stanley, Austl.	166	40.46 S	145.18 E
Stanley, N.B., Can.	186	46.17 N	66.44 W
Stanley, Falk. Is.	254	51.42 S	57.51 W
Stanley, H.K.	271d	22.13 N	114.12 E
Stanley, Eng., U.K.	44	54.52 N	1.42 W
Stanley, Scot., U.K.	46	56.28 N	3.27 W
Stanley, N.Y., U.S.	210	42.49 N	77.06 W
Stanley, N.C., U.S.	192	35.21 N	81.05 W
Stanley, N.D., U.S.	198	48.19 N	102.23 W
Stanley, Va., U.S.	188	38.34 N	78.30 W
Stanley, Wi., U.S.	190	44.57 N	90.56 W
Stanley ≃	171a	27.09 S	152.32 E
Stanley, Mont ∧[2]	273b	4.19 S	15.15 E
Stanley Bay ⊂	271d	22.12 N	114.12 E
Stanley Falls ∟	154	0.30 N	25.12 E
Stanley Mills	275b	43.46 N	79.44 W
Stanley Mound ∧	271d	22.14 N	114.12 E
Stanley Park ♦, B.C., Can.	224	49.19 N	123.09 W
Stanley Park ♦, Eng., U.K.	262	53.26 N	2.57 W
Stanley Park ♦, Eng., U.K.	262	53.49 N	3.02 W
Stanley Reservoir ⊜[1]	122	11.54 N	77.50 E
Stanleyville → Kisangani	154	0.30 N	25.12 E
Stanlow	44	53.17 N	2.52 W
Stanmore ♣[8]	260	51.37 N	0.19 W
Stannards	210	42.05 N	77.55 W
Stannington	44	55.06 N	1.40 W
Stanovoj chrebet ⩘	74	56.20 N	126.00 E
Stanovoje nagorje (Stanovoy Mountains) ⩘	88	56.00 N	114.00 E
Stanovoj Kolodez'	76	52.51 N	36.16 E
Stanovoy Mountains → Stanovoje nagorje ⩘	88	56.00 N	114.00 E
Stans	58	46.57 N	8.22 E
Stansbury	168b	34.55 S	137.47 E
Stansmore Range ⩘	162	21.23 S	128.33 E
Stansstad	58	46.59 N	8.20 E
Stanstead	206	45.01 N	72.05 W
Stanstead □[6]	206	45.10 N	72.00 W
Stanstead Abbots	42	51.47 N	0.01 E
Stansted	260	51.20 N	0.18 E
Stansted Mountfitchet	42	51.54 N	0.12 E
Stanthorpe	166	28.39 S	151.57 E
Stanton, Eng., U.K.	42	52.19 N	0.53 E
Stanton, Ca., U.S.	228	33.48 N	117.59 W
Stanton, De., U.S.	208	39.43 N	75.37 W
Stanton, Ia., U.S.	198	41.05 N	95.11 W
Stanton, Ky., U.S.	192	37.50 N	83.51 W
Stanton, Mi., U.S.	190	43.17 N	85.04 W
Stanton, Mo., U.S.	219	38.16 N	91.06 W
Stanton, Ne., U.S.	198	41.57 N	97.13 W
Stanton, N.D., U.S.	198	47.19 N	101.22 W
Stanton, Tn., U.S.	194	35.27 N	89.24 W
Stanton, Tx., U.S.	196	32.07 N	101.47 W
Stantonsburg	192	35.36 N	77.49 W
Stanwell	260	51.27 N	0.29 W
Stanwell Moor	260	51.28 N	0.30 W
Stanwood	224	48.14 N	122.22 W
Stanwyck Estates	285	39.42 N	75.33 W
Stanzach	58	47.23 N	10.34 E
Stanz im Mürztal	61	47.28 N	15.30 E
Stapelburg	54	51.53 N	10.40 E
Stapelfeld	52	53.36 N	10.13 E
Staphorst	52	52.37 N	6.12 E
Stapleford	42	52.56 N	1.16 W
Stapleford Abbotts	260	51.38 N	0.10 E
Stapleford Aerodrome ⊠	260	51.39 N	0.08 E
Stapleford Tawney	260	51.40 N	0.11 E
Staplehurst	42	51.10 N	0.33 E
Staples	198	46.21 N	94.47 W
Stapleton, Al., U.S.	194	30.44 N	87.47 W
Stapleton, Ne., U.S.	198	41.28 N	100.30 W
Stąporków	30	51.09 N	20.34 E
Star', Ross.	76	53.37 N	34.09 E
Star, Ms., U.S.	194	32.05 N	90.02 W
Star, N.C., U.S.	192	35.24 N	79.47 W
Stará Boleslav	54	50.12 N	14.42 E
Starachowice	30	51.03 N	21.04 E
Stara Fužina	64	46.17 N	13.54 E
Staraja	265a	59.55 N	30.38 E
Staraja Belica, Bela.	76	54.42 N	29.38 E
Staraja Belica, Ross.	78	51.59 N	35.13 E
Staraja Belogorka	80	52.05 N	53.17 E
Staraja Derevn'a ♣[8]	265a	59.59 N	30.15 E
Staraja Duginka	82	54.20 N	38.45 E
Staraja Kriuša	78	50.12 N	41.09 E
Staraja Kulatka	80	52.43 N	47.37 E
Staraja Kupavna	82	55.48 N	38.10 E
Staraja Majačka	78	46.30 N	33.11 E
Staraja Majna	80	54.36 N	48.57 E
Staraja Poltavka	80	50.28 N	46.28 E
Staraja Porubežka	80	52.03 N	49.11 E
Staraja Račejka	80	53.22 N	48.03 E
Staraja Rudn'a	76	52.50 N	30.17 E
Staraja Russa	76	58.00 N	31.23 E
Staraja Ruza	82	55.39 N	36.20 E
Staraja Sachča	80	54.25 N	49.58 E
Staraja Sin'ava	78	49.36 N	27.37 E
Staraja Sitn'a	82	54.56 N	38.09 E
Staraja Terizmorga	80	54.16 N	44.32 E
Staraja Toropa	76	56.17 N	31.40 E
Staraja Ušica	78	48.35 N	27.07 E
Staraja Veduga	78	51.48 N	38.31 E
Staraja Vičuga	80	57.16 N	41.53 E
Staraja Vyževka	78	51.27 N	24.24 E
Staranzano	64	45.49 N	13.30 E
Stara Pazova	38	44.59 N	20.10 E
Stara Planina (Balkan Mountains) ⩘	38	42.45 N	25.00 E
Stará Role	54	50.14 N	12.47 E
Starav, Ben ∧	46	56.32 N	5.03 W
Stará Voda	60	50.00 N	12.36 E
Stara Zagora	38	42.25 N	25.38 E
Starbejevo	265b	55.55 N	37.28 E
Starbrick	214	41.50 N	79.12 W
Starbuck, Mb., Can.	184	49.46 N	97.36 W
Starbuck, Mn., U.S.	198	45.36 N	95.31 W
Starbuck, Wa., U.S.	202	46.31 N	118.07 W
Starbuck I	14	5.37 S	155.53 W
Starčenkovo	78	47.17 N	36.59 E
Star City, Sk., Can.	184	52.53 N	104.21 W
Star City, Ar., U.S.	194	33.56 N	91.50 W
Star City, In., U.S.	216	40.58 N	86.33 W
Starcross	42	50.38 N	3.27 W
Stare Czarnowo	54	53.16 N	14.45 E
Staré Sedliště	60	49.45 N	12.42 E
Starford	214	40.42 N	78.58 W
Stargard Szczeciński (Stargard in Pommern)	30	53.20 N	15.02 E
Stargo	200	33.04 N	109.21 W
Star Harbour ⊂	175e	10.47 S	162.18 E
Stari Bar	38	42.06 N	19.08 E
Starica, Ross.	76	56.30 N	34.56 E
Starica, Ross.	76	59.04 N	29.30 E
Starica, Ross.	80	48.13 N	45.56 E
Stari Grad	36	43.11 N	16.36 E
Starij R'ad	76	58.05 N	34.54 E
Starina	76	59.37 N	44.42 E
Stari Vlah ♣[1]	38	43.35 N	20.15 E
Star Junction	214	40.04 N	79.46 W
Stark □[6]	214	40.48 N	81.22 W
Starke	192	29.56 N	82.06 W
Starke □[6]	216	41.18 N	86.37 W
Starkey	210	42.32 N	76.56 W
Starkville	194	33.27 N	88.49 W
Star Lake	224	47.22 N	122.18 W
Star Mountains ⩘	164	5.05 S	141.05 E
Starnberg	60	48.00 N	11.20 E
Starnberger See ⊜	64	47.55 N	11.18 E
Starnikovo	82	55.22 N	38.24 E
Staroalejskoje	86	51.00 N	82.01 E
Starobačaty	86	54.14 N	86.07 E
Starobaltačevo	86	56.01 N	55.56 E
Starobel'sk	83	49.16 N	38.56 E
Starobeševo	83	47.44 N	38.03 E
Starobin	76	52.44 N	27.28 E
Staročerkasskaja	83	47.15 N	40.03 E
Starocuruchajtuj	88	50.12 N	119.15 E
Staroderev'ankov-Skaja	78	46.08 N	38.58 E
Starodub	76	52.35 N	32.46 E
Starod'umejevo	80	55.16 N	54.22 E
Starogan'kino	80	53.55 N	52.15 E
Starogard Gdański	30	53.59 N	18.33 E
Staroignatjevka	83	47.32 N	37.47 E
Staroje	76	59.16 N	40.40 E
Staroje Bajsarovo	80	55.31 N	53.54 E
Staroje Drožžanoje	80	54.44 N	47.34 E
Staroje Ibrajkino	80	54.52 N	51.02 E
Staroje Jaškino	80	52.49 N	52.57 E
Staroje Jermakovo	80	54.04 N	51.59 E
Staroje Oleničevo	80	45.34 N	47.11 E
Staroje Rachino	76	58.08 N	32.39 E
Staroje Šajgovo	80	54.18 N	44.26 E
Staroje Šajmurzino	80	54.45 N	47.58 E
Staroje Selo	76	55.14 N	29.54 E
Staroje Sindrovo	80	54.25 N	44.06 E
Staroje Slavkino	80	52.34 N	45.08 E
Staroje Ustje	80	53.28 N	41.51 E
Starojurjevo	80	53.21 N	40.42 E
Starokazačje	78	46.21 N	29.59 E
Starokonstantinov	78	49.46 N	27.13 E
Starokuručevo	80	55.09 N	54.04 E
Starolaspa	83	47.34 N	37.59 E
Staroleuškovskaja	78	45.59 N	39.44 E
Staromichajlovka	83	47.58 N	37.36 E
Starominskaja	78	46.31 N	39.04 E
Staromlinovka	78	47.42 N	36.49 E
Staromušta	80	55.49 N	54.14 E
Staronikolajevo	82	55.37 N	36.16 E
Staro-Podgorodneje	82	54.46 N	38.57 E
Staropokrovka	85	42.50 N	75.18 E
Staroščerbinovskaja	78	46.37 N	38.40 E
Staroseslavino	80	53.12 N	40.25 E
Starošešminsk	80	55.22 N	51.15 E
Starosiedle	54	51.50 N	14.50 E
Starosoldatskoje	86	56.12 N	72.37 E
Starosubchangulovo	86	53.06 N	57.26 E
Starotimoškino	24	53.43 N	47.32 E
Starotitarovskaja	78	45.14 N	37.09 E
Staroutkinsk	86	57.14 N	59.20 E
Staroverovka	78	49.33 N	35.42 E
Starožilovo	80	54.14 N	39.55 E
Starožil'sk	80	56.34 N	47.17 E
Star Peak ∧	204	40.32 N	118.10 W
Starr	214	41.32 N	79.22 W
Starrucca	210	41.54 N	75.28 W
Start Bay ⊂	42	50.17 N	3.36 W
Start Point ›	42	50.13 N	3.38 W
Startup	224	47.52 N	121.44 W
Starvation Reservoir ⊜[1]	200	40.15 N	110.30 W
Starved Rock State Park ♦	216	41.19 N	88.58 W
Staryj Ajbesi	80	54.57 N	47.03 E
Staryj-Ajdar	83	48.43 N	39.11 E
Staryj Bagr'až	80	54.54 N	51.39 E
Staryj Bir'uz'ak	84	44.47 N	46.54 E
Staryj Bol'ševik	265b	55.57 N	37.47 E
Staryj Čartorijsk	78	51.15 N	25.54 E
Staryj Chop'or	80	51.30 N	42.58 E
Staryj Čindant	88	50.33 N	115.33 E
Staryje Burasy	80	52.16 N	46.09 E
Staryje Dorogi	76	53.02 N	28.16 E
Staryje Maty	80	55.14 N	53.55 E
Staryje Popel'uchi	78	48.18 N	28.55 E
Staryje Senžary	78	49.25 N	34.27 E
Staryje Turdaki	80	53.55 N	45.29 E
Staryje Z'atcy	80	57.21 N	52.39 E
Staryj Kazangal	80	50.15 N	47.39 E
Staryj Kistruss	80	54.28 N	40.34 E
Staryj Krym, Ukr.	78	45.03 N	35.05 E
Staryj Krym, Ukr.	83	47.10 N	37.30 E
Staryj Lesken	84	43.20 N	43.55 E
Staryj Medved'	76	58.18 N	30.30 E
Staryj Merčik	78	49.58 N	35.46 E
Staryj Oskol	78	51.19 N	37.51 E
Staryj Sambor	78	49.27 N	22.59 E
Staryj Terek ≃	84	44.00 N	47.24 E
Staryj Tukšum	80	53.42 N	48.33 E
Starý Plzenec	60	49.42 N	13.28 E
Stary Sącz	30	49.34 N	20.38 E
Stassfurt	54	51.51 N	11.34 E
Staszów	30	50.34 N	21.20 E
State Center	190	42.01 N	93.09 W
State College	214	40.47 N	77.51 W
State Fair Grounds ♦	284b	39.27 N	76.38 W
Stateline, Ca., U.S.	226	38.57 N	119.57 W
State Line, Ms., U.S.	194	31.26 N	88.28 W
Stateline, Nv., U.S.	204	38.58 N	119.56 W
Staten Island I	276	40.35 N	74.09 W
Staten Island Mall ♣[9]	276	40.35 N	74.10 W
Statenville	192	30.42 N	83.01 W
State Park Place	219	38.40 N	90.03 W
State Road	192	36.19 N	80.52 W
Statesboro	192	32.26 N	81.47 W
Statesville	192	35.46 N	80.53 W
Stateville Correctional Center v	278	41.35 N	88.06 W
Station Peak	162	21.10 S	118.11 E
Statte	68	40.34 N	17.12 E
Statue of Liberty National Monument ♦	210	40.41 N	74.03 W
Staubbachfall ∟	58	46.35 N	7.55 E
Staufen	58	47.53 N	7.44 E
Staufenberg	56	50.40 N	8.43 E
Staughton Vale	169	37.51 S	144.17 E
Staunton, Il., U.S.	219	39.00 N	89.47 W
Staunton, Va., U.S.	188	38.08 N	79.04 W
Staunton → Roanoke ≃	192	35.56 N	76.43 W
Stavanger	26	58.58 N	5.45 E
Stave ≃	224	49.10 N	122.26 W
Stave Lake ⊜	182	49.15 N	122.21 W
Staveley	44	53.16 N	1.20 W
Stavelot	56	50.23 N	5.56 E
Stavely, Ab., Can.	182	50.10 N	113.38 W
Stavely, Eng., U.K.	44	54.22 N	2.49 W
Staveren	52	52.53 N	5.22 E
Stavern	26	59.00 N	10.02 E
Stavišče	78	49.23 N	30.12 E
Stavnoje	78	48.59 N	22.40 E
Stavropol', Ross.	72	45.02 N	41.59 E
Stavropol → Toljatti, Ross.	80	53.31 N	49.26 E
Stavropol' Kraj □[8]	84	44.38 N	43.30 E
Stavrovo	80	56.08 N	40.00 E
Stavsnäs	40	59.17 N	18.41 E
Stawell	166	37.04 S	142.46 E
Stawell ≃	166	20.38 S	142.55 E
Stawiski	30	53.23 N	22.09 E
Stawiszyn	30	51.55 N	18.07 E
Staxigoe	46	58.28 N	3.04 W
Stayner	212	44.25 N	80.05 W
Stayton	202	44.48 N	122.47 W
Stazzema	64	43.59 N	10.19 E
Steamboat	226	39.22 N	119.44 W
Steamboat Creek ≃	226	39.31 N	119.42 W
Steamboat Mountain ∧	200	41.58 N	108.58 W
Steamboat Slough ≃	226	38.11 N	121.40 W
Steamboat Springs	200	40.29 N	106.49 W
Steamburg	210	42.07 N	78.54 W
Stearns	192	36.41 N	84.28 W
Stearns Pond ⊜	283	42.37 N	71.04 W
Stębark	30	53.30 N	20.08 E
Stebbins	180	63.32 N	162.18 W
Stebl'ov	78	49.24 N	31.06 E
Stechow	54	52.38 N	12.28 E
Steckborn	58	47.40 N	8.55 E
Stederdorf	52	52.21 N	10.15 E
Stedten	54	51.26 N	11.41 E
Stedum	52	53.18 N	6.41 E
Steeg	58	47.14 N	10.17 E
Steel ≃	190	48.46 N	86.54 W
Steel City	210	40.38 N	75.20 W
Steele, Mo., U.S.	194	36.05 N	89.49 W
Steele, N.D., U.S.	198	46.51 N	99.54 W
Steele ♣[8]	263	51.27 N	7.05 E
Steele, Mount ∧	200	41.50 N	107.00 W
Steele Creek ≃, Tx., U.S.	222	31.13 N	96.19 W
Steele Creek ≃, Tx., U.S.	222	32.01 N	97.28 W
Steeles Corners	275b	43.48 N	79.25 W
Steeleville	194	38.00 N	89.39 W
Steelhead	224	49.13 N	122.19 W
Steel's Drift	158	27.21 S	29.30 E
Steels Point ›	174c	29.02 S	168.00 E
Steels Run ≃	279b	40.25 N	79.38 W
Steelton, N.Y., U.S.	284a	42.47 N	78.49 W
Steelton, Pa., U.S.	208	40.14 N	76.50 W
Steelville	194	37.58 N	91.21 W
Steenbergen	52	51.35 N	4.19 E
Steenburg Lake ⊜	212	44.50 N	77.41 W
Steenderen	52	52.04 N	6.11 E
Steens Mountain ⩘	202	42.35 N	118.40 W
Steenvoorde	50	50.48 N	2.35 E
Steenwijk	52	52.47 N	6.08 E
Steepbank ≃	184	57.01 N	111.28 W
Steephill Lake ⊜	184	55.58 N	103.08 W
Steep Holm I	42	51.21 N	3.07 W
Steeping ≃	44	53.06 N	0.18 E
Steeple Claydon	42	51.56 N	0.59 W
Steep Point ›	162	26.08 S	113.08 E
Steep Rock	184	51.26 N	98.48 W
Stefanie, Lake (Chew Bahir) ⊜, Afr.	144	4.40 N	36.50 E
Stefanie, Lake → Chew Bahir ⊜, Afr.	144	4.40 N	36.50 E
Stefansson Island I	176	73.20 N	105.45 W
Ștefan Vodă	38	44.19 N	27.19 E
Steffisburg	58	46.47 N	7.39 E
Steg	58	47.21 N	8.56 E
Stegalovka	76	52.24 N	38.19 E
Stege	41	54.59 N	12.18 E
Stegeborg	26	58.26 N	16.35 E
Stege Bugt ⊂	41	55.01 N	12.05 E
Stegelitz	54	53.08 N	13.51 E
Steger	216	41.28 N	87.38 W
Stegersbach	61	47.10 N	16.10 E
Steglitz ♣[8]	264a	52.28 N	13.19 E
Stehag	41	55.54 N	13.23 E
Stehekin	224	48.18 N	120.39 W
Stehekin ≃	224	48.21 N	120.40 W
Steiermark □[3]	30	47.10 N	15.10 E
Steigerwald ⩘	56	49.40 N	10.20 E
Steigra	54	51.18 N	11.39 E
Steilacoom	224	47.10 N	122.36 W
Steimbke	52	52.40 N	9.22 E
Stein, Dtsch.	60	49.25 N	11.01 E
Stein, Ned.	56	50.57 N	5.46 E
Stein, Schw.	58	47.33 N	7.58 E
Steina	54	51.12 N	14.01 E
Steinach, Dtsch.	54	50.25 N	11.10 E
Steinach, Dtsch.	58	48.18 N	8.04 E
Steinach, Öst.	64	47.05 N	11.28 E
Steinach ≃	54	50.11 N	11.12 E
Steinamanger → Szombathely	30	47.14 N	16.38 E
Stein am Rhein	58	47.40 N	8.51 E
Steinau	56	50.23 N	9.27 E
Steinbach, Mb., Can.	184	49.32 N	96.41 W
Steinbach, Dtsch.	56	48.43 N	8.10 E
Steinbach-Hallenberg	54	50.42 N	10.34 E
Steinberg ∧[2]	263	51.05 N	7.27 E
Steinberger Slough ≃	282	37.33 N	122.13 W
Steinbourg	56	48.46 N	7.25 E
Steindorf	61	46.42 N	14.01 E
Steinen	58	47.38 N	7.44 E
Steinernes Meer ⩘	64	47.30 N	12.58 E
Steinfeld, Dtsch.	52	52.35 N	8.12 E
Steinfeld, Dtsch.	54	50.22 N	10.44 E
Steinfeld, Öst.	64	46.45 N	13.15 E
Steinfort	56	49.40 N	5.55 E
Steinforth	263	51.09 N	6.32 E
Steinfurt	52	52.09 N	7.21 E
Steingaden	58	47.42 N	10.51 E
Steinhagen, Dtsch.	52	52.00 N	8.24 E
Steinhagen, Dtsch.	54	54.13 N	12.59 E
Steinhatchee ≃	192	29.40 N	83.24 W
Steinhausen	156	21.49 S	18.20 E
Steinhausen v[1]	58	48.01 N	9.41 E
Steinheid	54	50.28 N	11.04 E
Steinheim, Dtsch.	52	51.52 N	9.05 E
Steinheim, Dtsch.	56	48.58 N	9.16 E
Steinheim, Dtsch.	58	48.01 N	10.09 E
Steinhöfel	54	52.24 N	14.10 E
Steinhöring	60	48.05 N	12.02 E
Steinhude	52	52.27 N	9.21 E
Steinhuder Meer ⊜	52	52.28 N	9.19 E
Steinkjer	26	64.01 N	11.30 E
Steinkopf	156	29.18 S	17.43 E
Steinloge	52	52.54 N	8.19 E
Stein-Neukirch	56	50.41 N	8.03 E
Steinpass)(	64	47.39 N	12.45 E
Steinsdorf	54	52.02 N	14.40 E
Steinshamn	26	62.47 N	6.29 E
Steinstücken ♣[8]	264a	52.23 N	13.08 E
Steinwiesen	54	50.17 N	11.28 E
Stekene	50	51.12 N	4.02 E
Stekl'anka	76	59.08 N	41.37 E
Steklino	76	56.51 N	32.10 E
Steksovo	80	55.17 N	43.25 E
Stella, It.	62	44.24 N	8.30 E
Stella, S. Afr.	158	26.38 S	24.48 E
Stella, Ne., U.S.	198	40.13 N	95.46 W
Stella Niagara	210	43.12 N	79.02 W
Stella-Plage	50	50.29 N	1.35 E
Stellaquo Indian Reserve ♣[4]	182	54.03 N	124.55 W
Stellarton	186	45.34 N	62.40 W
Stelle	52	53.23 N	10.06 E
Stellenbosch	158	33.58 S	18.50 E
Steller, Mount ∧	180	60.30 N	143.02 W
Stelvio, Parco Nazionale dello ♦	64	46.30 N	10.40 E
Stelvio, Passo dello)(	64	46.32 N	10.27 E
Stemwede	52	52.25 N	8.27 E
Stenay	56	49.29 N	5.11 E
Stendal	54	52.36 N	11.51 E
Stende	76	57.09 N	22.33 E
Stenden	263	51.25 N	6.27 E
Stenhammar slott ⊥	40	59.03 N	16.31 E
Stenhouse Bay	166	35.17 S	136.56 E
Stenhousemuir	46	56.02 N	3.48 W
Stenico	64	46.03 N	10.51 E
Stenlille	41	55.32 N	11.36 E
Stenløse	41	55.46 N	12.12 E
Stenness, Loch of ⊜	46	59.00 N	3.15 W
Stenón	267c	37.58 N	23.25 E
Stenón Návstathmou ʊ	267c	37.58 N	23.33 E
Stensätra	40	60.36 N	16.44 E
Stensele	24	65.05 N	17.09 E
Stenstorp	26	58.16 N	13.43 E
Stenstrup	41	55.07 N	10.31 E
Stentrop	263	51.30 N	7.49 E
Stenungsund	26	58.05 N	11.49 E
Stepan'	78	51.10 N	26.18 E
Stepanakert	84	39.49 N	46.44 E
Stepanavan	84	41.00 N	44.23 E
Stepancevo, Ross.	80	56.08 N	41.42 E
Stepancevo, Ross.	82	56.22 N	36.10 E
Stepancy	78	49.42 N	31.18 E
Stepano-Krynka	83	47.55 N	38.21 E
Stepanovka, Ross.	80	52.04 N	53.02 E
Stepanovka, Ross.	86	57.13 N	67.26 E
Stepanovka, Ukr.	78	50.58 N	34.37 E
Stepanovo	82	55.43 N	38.28 E
Stepanovskoje	265b	55.47 N	37.10 E
Stepan Razin	84	40.24 N	49.59 E
Stepanščino	82	55.15 N	38.30 E
Stepenitz ≃	54	53.48 N	11.10 E
Stephans-Dom v[1]	264b	48.12 N	16.23 E
Stephanskirchen	64	47.51 N	12.11 E
Stephen	198	48.27 N	96.52 W
Stephen A. Forbes State Park ♦	219	38.44 N	88.46 W
Stephen F. Austin State Historic Park ♦	222	29.48 N	96.05 W
Stephens	194	33.24 N	93.04 W
Stephens, Cape ›	172	40.42 S	173.57 E
Stephens, Port ⊂	166	32.45 S	152.05 E
Stephens City	188	39.05 N	78.13 W
Stephens Creek	166	31.50 S	141.30 E
Stephens Island I	182	54.10 N	130.45 W
Stephens Knob ∧[2]	192	36.37 N	84.20 W
Stephens Lake ⊜[1]	184	56.26 N	95.07 W
Stephens Mills	210	42.23 N	77.38 W
Stephenson	190	45.24 N	87.36 W
Stephenson, Lake ⊜	222	29.35 N	94.40 W
Stephenson, Mount ∧	9	69.49 S	69.43 W
Stephens Passage ʊ	180	57.50 N	133.50 W
Stephentown	210	42.33 N	73.23 W
Stephentown Center	210	42.34 N	73.25 W
Stephenville, Nf., Can.	186	48.33 N	58.35 W
Stephenville, Tx., U.S.	196	32.13 N	98.12 W
Stephenville Crossing	186	48.30 N	58.26 W
Stepn'ak	86	52.50 N	70.50 E
Stepney ♣[8]	260	51.31 N	0.02 W
Stepnica	54	53.40 N	14.36 E
Stepnoj	80	48.56 N	45.36 E
Stepnoje, Ross.	80	51.24 N	46.52 E
Stepnoje, Ross.	84	44.17 N	44.36 E
Step Pyramid → Şaqqārah ⊥	142	29.52 N	31.14 E
Steps Point ›	174u	14.22 S	170.45 W
Steptoe Valley V	204	39.25 N	114.45 W
Stepurino	76	56.24 N	35.16 E
Sterdyń	30	52.35 N	22.18 E
Sterkaar	158	31.05 S	23.42 E
Sterkrade ♣[8]	263	51.31 N	6.51 E
Sterkspruit	158	30.32 S	27.22 E
Sterkstroom	158	31.32 S	26.32 E
Sterlibaševo	86	53.28 N	55.15 E
Sterling, S. Afr.	158	31.16 S	21.28 E
Sterling, Ak., U.S.	180	60.32 N	150.48 W
Sterling, Co., U.S.	198	40.37 N	103.12 W
Sterling, Ct., U.S.	207	41.42 N	71.49 W
Sterling, Il., U.S.	190	41.47 N	89.41 W
Sterling, Ks., U.S.	198	38.12 N	98.12 W
Sterling, Ma., U.S.	207	42.26 N	71.45 W
Sterling, Mi., U.S.	190	44.02 N	84.01 W
Sterling, Ne., U.S.	198	40.27 N	96.22 W
Sterling, N.Y., U.S.	210	43.20 N	76.39 W
Sterling, Oh., U.S.	214	40.58 N	81.51 W
Sterling, Ok., U.S.	196	34.45 N	98.10 W
Sterling, Va., U.S.	208	39.00 N	77.25 W
Sterling City	196	31.50 N	100.59 W
Sterling Creek ≃	210	43.20 N	76.42 W
Sterling Forest Lake ⊜	276	41.10 N	74.16 W
Sterling Heights	214	42.34 N	83.01 W
Sterling Junction	207	42.24 N	71.46 W
Sterling Park	282	37.41 N	122.26 W
Sterling Run	214	41.25 N	78.12 W
Sterlington	194	32.41 N	92.05 W
Sterlitamak	86	53.37 N	55.58 E
Sternberg	54	53.43 N	11.49 E
Šternberk	30	49.44 N	17.18 E
Sternstein ∧	61	48.34 N	14.16 E
Šterovka	83	48.19 N	38.57 E
Sterup	41	54.44 N	9.44 E
Sterzing → Vipiteno	64	46.54 N	11.26 E
Stęszew	30	52.18 N	16.42 E
Štětí	54	50.25 N	14.23 E
Stetson Pond ⊜	283	42.02 N	70.50 W
Stetten am kalten Markt	58	48.07 N	9.04 E
Stettin → Szczecin	30	53.24 N	14.32 E
Stettler	182	52.19 N	112.43 W
Steuben □[6], In., U.S.	216	41.38 N	85.00 W
Steuben □[6], N.Y., U.S.	210	42.20 N	77.19 W
Steubenville	214	40.22 N	80.38 W
Stevenage	42	51.55 N	0.14 W
Stevens, N.J., U.S.	285	40.05 N	74.49 W
Stevens, Pa., U.S.	208	40.13 N	76.09 W
Stevens, Lake ⊜	224	48.01 N	122.05 W
Stevens, Mount ∧	172	40.48 S	172.27 E
Stevens Creek ≃, Ca., U.S.	282	37.26 N	122.05 W
Stevens Creek ≃, S.C., U.S.	192	33.34 N	82.03 W
Stevens Creek Park ♦	282	37.17 N	122.04 W
Stevens Creek Reservoir ⊜[1]	282	37.17 N	122.05 W
Stevens Institute of Technology v[2]	276	40.44 N	74.02 W
Stevenson, Al., U.S.	194	34.52 N	85.50 W
Stevenson, Md., U.S.	284b	39.25 N	76.43 W
Stevenson, Wa., U.S.	224	45.42 N	121.53 W
Stevenson Creek ≃	162	27.06 S	135.33 E
Stevenson Entrance ʊ	180	58.45 N	152.20 W
Stevenson Lake ⊜	184	53.56 N	96.09 W
Stevens Pass)(	224	47.45 N	121.04 W
Stevens Peak ∧	202	47.27 N	115.46 W
Stevens Point	190	44.31 N	89.34 W
Stevenston	46	55.39 N	4.45 W
Stevens Village	180	66.00 N	149.05 W
Stevensville, On., Can.	284a	42.57 N	79.04 W
Stevensville, Md., U.S.	208	38.58 N	76.18 W
Stevensville, Mi., U.S.	216	42.00 N	86.31 W
Stevensville, Mt., U.S.	202	46.30 N	114.05 W
Stevensville, Pa., U.S.	210	41.46 N	76.11 W
Stevinson	226	37.20 N	120.51 W
Stevns Klint ⊥[4]	41	55.18 N	12.27 E
Steward	216	41.51 N	89.01 W
Stewardson	219	39.15 N	88.37 W
Stewart, B.C., Can.	182	55.56 N	129.59 W
Stewart, Mn., U.S.	190	44.43 N	94.29 W
Stewart ≃	180	63.18 N	139.25 W
Stewart, Cape ›	164	11.57 S	134.45 E
Stewart, Isla I	254	54.52 S	71.12 W
Stewart, Mount ∧	166	20.12 S	145.29 E
Stewart Island I	172	47.00 S	167.50 E
Stewart Islands II	175e	8.25 S	162.52 E
Stewart Lake ⊜	219	40.09 N	90.16 W
Stewart Manor	276	40.43 N	73.41 W
Stewarton	46	55.41 N	4.31 W
Stewartstown, N. Ire., U.K.	48	54.35 N	6.41 W
Stewartstown, Pa., U.S.	208	39.45 N	76.35 W
Stewartsville, Mo., U.S.	194	39.45 N	94.29 W
Stewartsville, N.J., U.S.	208	40.41 N	75.06 W
Stewartsville, Pa., U.S.	279b	40.21 N	79.46 W
Stewart Valley	184	50.36 N	107.50 W
Stewartville	190	43.51 N	92.29 W
Stewiacke	186	45.08 N	63.21 W
Steyerberg	52	52.34 N	9.01 E
Steyning	42	50.53 N	0.20 W
Steynsburg	158	31.15 S	25.49 E
Steynsrus	158	27.58 S	27.33 E
Steyr	61	48.03 N	14.25 E
Steyr ≃	61	48.02 N	14.25 E
Steyregg	61	48.17 N	14.22 E
Steytlerville	158	33.21 S	24.21 E
Stežki	80	53.06 N	41.13 E
Stezzano	62	45.38 N	9.39 E
Sthal	126	24.12 N	89.44 E
Știa	66	43.48 N	11.42 E
Štiavnické vrchy ⩘	30	48.40 N	18.45 E
Stickle Pond ⊜	276	40.59 N	74.25 W
Stickney, Eng., U.K.	44	53.05 N	0.01 E
Stickney, Il., U.S.	216	41.49 N	87.46 W
Stickney, S.D., U.S.	198	43.35 N	98.26 W
Stidsvig	41	56.12 N	13.08 E
Stiefingbach ≃	61	46.47 N	15.35 E
Stiege	54	51.40 N	10.53 E
Stiene	76	57.26 N	24.34 E
Stienitzfliess ≃	264a	52.33 N	13.43 E
Stienitz-See ⊜	264a	52.30 N	13.49 E
Stiens	52	53.15 N	5.45 E
Stiepel ♣[8]	263	51.25 N	7.15 E
Stif	148	36.09 N	5.26 E
Stif □[5]	148	36.15 N	5.10 E
Stiftskirche v[1]	263	51.23 N	7.00 E
Stige	41	55.26 N	10.25 E
Stigler	196	35.15 N	95.07 W
Stigliano	68	40.24 N	16.14 E
Stigtomta	40	58.48 N	16.47 E
Stikine ≃	180	56.40 N	132.30 W
Stikine Ranges ⩘	180	58.45 N	130.00 W
Stiklestad	26	63.48 N	11.33 E
Stilbaai	158	34.24 S	21.26 E
Stiles	210	40.40 N	75.30 W
Stiles Pond ⊜	283	42.41 N	71.02 W
Stilesville	210	42.05 N	75.24 W
Stilfontein	158	26.50 S	26.50 E
Stilís	38	38.55 N	22.36 E
Still	148	34.20 N	5.51 E
Stillaguamish ≃	224	48.11 N	122.22 W
Stillaguamish, North Fork ≃	224	48.11 N	122.07 W
Stillaguamish, South Fork ≃	224	48.11 N	122.07 W
Stillhouse Hollow Lake ⊜[1]	222	31.00 N	97.35 W
Stilling	41	56.04 N	10.00 E
Stillman Valley	216	42.07 N	89.11 W
Stillmore	192	32.26 N	82.12 W
Still Pond	208	39.19 N	76.02 W
Still Run ≃	285	39.49 N	75.18 W
Stillwater, B.C., Can.	182	49.46 N	124.18 W
Stillwater, Mn., U.S.	190	45.03 N	92.48 W
Stillwater, N.J., U.S.	210	41.02 N	74.52 W
Stillwater, N.Y., U.S.	210	42.56 N	73.39 W
Stillwater, Oh., U.S.	214	40.20 N	81.18 W
Stillwater, Ok., U.S.	196	36.06 N	97.03 W
Stillwater, Pa., U.S.	210	41.09 N	76.22 W
Stillwater ≃, Mt., U.S.	202	45.38 N	109.17 W
Stillwater ≃, Oh., U.S.	218	39.47 N	84.12 W
Stillwater Creek ≃	214	40.25 N	81.22 W
Stillwater Range ⩘	204	39.50 N	118.15 W
Stillwell, Il., U.S.	219	40.13 N	91.11 W
Stillwell, Ok., U.S.	194	35.49 N	94.38 W
Stilo	68	38.29 N	16.28 E
Stilo, Punta ›	68	38.28 N	16.36 E
Stimberg ∧[2]	263	51.40 N	7.15 E
Stimigliano	66	42.18 N	12.34 E

Symbols in the index entries represent the broad categories identified in the key at the right. Symbols with superior numbers (⩘[1]) identify subcategories (see complete key on page *I · 1*).

Symbole im Register stellen die rechts im Schlüssel erklärten Kategorien dar. Symbole mit hochgestellten Ziffern (⩘[1]) bezeichnen Unterabteilungen einer Kategorie (vgl. vollständiger Schlüssel auf Seite *I · 1*).

Los símbolos incluídos en el texto del índice representan las grandes categorías identificadas con la clave a la derecha. Los símbolos con numeros en su parte superior (⩘[1]) identifican las subcategorías (véase la clave completa en la página *I · 1*).

Les symboles de l'index représentent les catégories indiquées dans la légende à droite. Les symboles suivis d'un indice (⩘[1]) représentent des sous-catégories (voir légende complète à la page *I · 1*).

Os símbolos incluídos no texto do índice representam as grandes categorias identificadas com a chave à direita. Os símbolos com números em sua parte superior (⩘[1]) identificam as subcategorias (veja-se a chave completa à página *I · 1*).

English	Deutsch	Español	Français	Português
∧ Mountain	Berg	Montaña	Montagne	Montanha
⩘ Mountains	Gebirge	Montañas	Montagnes	Montanhas
)(Pass	Paß	Paso	Col	Passo
V Valley, Canyon	Tal, Cañon	Valle, Cañón	Vallée, Canyon	Vale, Canhão
≚ Plain	Ebene	Llano	Plaine	Planície
› Cape	Kap	Cabo	Cap	Cabo
I Island	Insel	Isla	Île	Ilha
II Islands	Inseln	Islas	Îles	Ilhas
⊥ Other Topographic Features	Andere Topographische Objekte	Otros Elementos Topográficos	Autres données topographiques	Outros acidentes topográficos

ESPAÑOL — Nombre / Página / Lat.°′ / Long.°′ W = Oeste
FRANÇAIS — Nom / Page / Lat.°′ / Long.°′ W = Ouest
PORTUGUÊS — Nome / Página / Lat.°′ / Long.°′ W = Oeste

Nombre	Página	Lat.°′	Long.°′ W = Oeste
Stimson, Mount ∧	202	48.31 N	113.36 W
Stînca-Costești, Lacul (vodochranilišče Kostešty-Stynka) ⊜[1]	38	47.55 N	27.10 E
Stinchar ≃	44	55.06 N	5.00 W
Stinear Nunataks ⋀	9	69.42 S	64.40 E
Stine Canal ≅	226	35.15 N	119.08 W
Stine Mountain ∧	202	45.44 N	113.07 W
Stingray Point ›	208	37.33 N	76.18 W
Stînișoarei, Munții ⋀	38	47.10 N	26.00 E
Stinking Water Creek ≃	198	40.22 N	101.07 W
Stinnett	196	35.49 N	101.26 W
Stintino	71	40.56 N	8.13 E
Stintonville	273d	26.14 S	28.13 E
Štip	38	41.44 N	22.12 E
Stiperstones ∧	42	52.35 N	2.56 W
Stiring-Wendel	56	49.12 N	6.56 E
Stírka ∧	60	49.24 N	13.34 E
Stirling, Austl.	162	21.44 S	133.45 E
Stirling, Austl.	168a	31.54 S	115.47 E
Stirling, Austl.	168b	35.00 S	138.43 E
Stirling, Ab., Can.	182	49.30 N	112.31 W
Stirling, On., Can.	212	44.18 N	77.33 W
Stirling, Scot., U.K.	46	56.07 N	3.57 W
Stirling, N.J., U.S.	210	40.40 N	74.29 W
Stirling, Mount ∧	162	31.50 S	117.38 E
Stirling Castle ⊥	46	56.07 N	3.57 W
Stirling City	204	39.54 N	121.31 W
Stirling Range ⋀	162	34.23 S	117.50 E
Stirling Range National Park ♦	162	34.22 S	118.00 E
Stirling Reservoir ⊜[1]	168a	33.08 S	116.03 E
Stirrat	192	37.43 N	82.00 W
Stissing Mountain ∧	210	41.57 N	73.42 W
Štitary	61	48.56 N	15.51 E
Stittsville	212	45.15 N	75.55 W
Stittville	210	43.13 N	75.17 W
Stjärnhov	40	59.05 N	17.00 E
Stjärnsund, Sve.	40	60.26 N	16.12 E
Stjärnsund, Sve.	40	58.51 N	14.55 E
Stjernøya I	24	70.18 N	22.45 E
Stjørdalshalsen	26	63.28 N	10.56 E
Stöberhai ∧	54	51.39 N	10.34 E
Stobi ⊥	38	41.33 N	21.59 E
Stochod ≃	78	51.52 N	25.38 E
Stock	260	51.40 N	0.27 E
Stock, Étang du ⊜	56	48.45 N	6.55 E
Stockach	58	47.51 N	9.00 E
Stöckalp	58	46.48 N	8.17 E
Stockamöllan	41	55.57 N	13.22 E
Stockbridge, Eng., U.K.	42	51.07 N	1.29 W
Stockbridge, Ga., U.S.	192	33.32 N	84.14 W
Stockbridge, Ma., U.S.	207	42.17 N	73.19 W
Stockbridge, Mi., U.S.	216	42.27 N	84.10 W
Stockbridge Bowl ⊜	207	42.20 N	73.19 W
Stockbridge Indian Reservation ◆[4]	190	44.52 N	88.53 W
Stockbury	260	51.20 N	0.39 E
Stockby	40	59.20 N	17.41 E
Stockdale, Oh., U.S.	218	38.57 N	82.51 W
Stockdale, Tx., U.S.	196	29.14 N	97.57 W
Stockelsdorf	54	53.54 N	10.38 E
Stöcken	54	53.00 N	10.40 E
Stockerau	61	48.23 N	16.13 E
Stockertown	208	40.45 N	75.15 W
Stockett	202	47.21 N	111.09 W
Stockheim	56	50.19 N	9.01 E
Stockholm, Sve.	40	59.20 N	18.03 E
Stockholm, Me., U.S.	186	47.02 N	68.08 W
Stockholm, N.J., U.S.	210	41.05 N	74.31 W
Stockholm, Lake ⊜	276	41.04 N	74.32 W
Stockholms Län □[6]	40	59.30 N	18.20 E
Stock Island	220	24.34 N	81.45 W
Stockland	216	40.37 N	87.36 W
Stockport, Eng., U.K.	44	53.25 N	2.10 W
Stockport, N.Y., U.S.	210	42.19 N	73.45 W
Stockport □[8]	262	53.23 N	2.08 W
Stocksbridge	44	53.27 N	1.34 W
Stockstadt	56	49.59 N	9.04 E
Stocksund	40	59.23 N	18.04 E
Stockton, Austl.	170	32.55 S	151.47 E
Stockton, Al., U.S.	194	30.59 N	87.51 W
Stockton, Ca., U.S.	226	37.57 N	121.17 W
Stockton, Il., U.S.	190	42.20 N	90.00 W
Stockton, Ks., U.S.	198	39.26 N	99.15 W
Stockton, Md., U.S.	208	38.03 N	75.24 W
Stockton, Mo., U.S.	194	37.41 N	93.47 W
Stockton, N.J., U.S.	208	40.24 N	74.58 W
Stockton, N.Y., U.S.	214	42.19 N	79.22 W
Stockton, Ut., U.S.	200	40.27 N	112.21 W
Stockton Heath, Eng., U.K.	44	53.22 N	2.34 W
Stockton Heath, Eng., U.K.	262	53.22 N	2.34 W
Stockton Metropolitan Airport ⊠	226	37.54 N	121.15 W
Stockton-on-Tees	44	54.34 N	1.19 W
Stockton Plateau ⋀[1]	196	30.30 N	102.30 W
Stockton Reservoir ⊜[1]	194	37.40 N	93.45 W
Stockton Springs	188	44.29 N	68.51 W
Stockum, Dtsch.	52	51.40 N	7.42 E
Stockum, Dtsch.	263	51.28 N	7.22 E
Stockum, Dtsch.	263	51.32 N	7.47 E
Stockum, Dtsch.	263	51.36 N	6.39 E
Stockum ◆[8]	263	51.16 N	6.44 E
Stockville	198	40.31 N	100.22 W
Stockwell	216	40.17 N	86.46 W
Stockwell, Lake ⊜	285	39.51 N	74.47 W
Stoco Lake ⊜	212	44.28 N	77.18 W
Stoczek Łukowski	30	51.58 N	21.58 E
Stod	60	49.39 N	13.10 E
Stoddard Mountain ∧	228	34.42 N	117.07 W
Stöde	26	62.25 N	16.35 E
Stodoliči	78	51.44 N	28.30 E
Stodolišče	76	54.11 N	32.39 E
Stœng Trêng	110	13.31 N	105.58 E
Stoer	46	58.12 N	5.20 W
Stoer, Point of ›	46	58.15 N	5.21 W
Stoffberg	156	25.29 S	29.49 E
Stoj, gora ∧	78	48.37 N	23.11 E
Stojba	89	52.49 N	131.43 E
Stoke	260	51.27 N	0.37 E
Stoke ≃	206	45.35 N	71.58 W
Stoke, Monts ⋀	206	45.33 N	71.42 W
Stoke D'Abernon	260	51.19 N	0.23 W
Stokenchurch	42	51.40 N	0.55 W
Stoke Newington ◆[8]	260	51.34 N	0.05 W
Stoke-on-Trent	42	53.00 N	2.10 W
Stoke Poges	260	51.33 N	0.35 W
Stokes, Mount ∧	172	41.06 S	174.06 E
Stokes Inlet c	162	33.50 S	121.08 E
Stokesley	44	54.28 N	1.11 W
Stokes Point ›	166	40.10 S	143.56 E
Stokes Range ⋀[2]	164	15.46 S	130.57 E
Stokkemarke	41	54.50 N	11.23 E
Stokksnes ›	24a	64.17 N	14.54 W
Stol ∧	38	44.13 N	22.14 E
Stolac	36	43.05 N	17.58 E
Stolbcy	76	53.29 N	26.44 E
Stolberg, Dtsch.	54	51.34 N	10.57 E
Stolberg, Dtsch.	56	50.46 N	6.13 E
Stolbišči	80	55.39 N	49.14 E
Stolboucha	86	49.59 N	84.30 E
Stolbovo	76	52.38 N	34.47 E
Stolbovoj, ostrov I	74	74.05 N	136.00 E
Stolbun	76	52.48 N	31.25 E
Stolby, zapovednik ♦	88	55.45 N	92.45 E
Stolin	78	51.53 N	26.51 E
Stollberg	54	50.42 N	12.47 E
Stöllet	26	60.24 N	13.16 E
Stol'noje	78	51.31 N	31.55 E
Stolp → Słupsk	30	54.28 N	17.01 E
Stolpe	264a	52.40 N	13.16 E
Stolpen	54	51.05 N	14.04 E
Stolper Heide ◆[3]	264a	52.39 N	13.14 E
Stolpino	80	57.24 N	42.55 E
Stolzenau	52	52.31 N	9.04 E
Ston	36	42.50 N	17.42 E
Stondon Massey	260	51.41 N	0.18 E
Stone, Eng., U.K.	42	52.54 N	2.10 W
Stone, Eng., U.K.	260	51.27 N	0.16 E
Stoneboro	214	41.20 N	80.06 W
Stone Canyon Reservoir ⊜[1]	280	34.07 N	118.28 W
Stone Corral Creek ≃	226	39.16 N	122.06 W
Stone Creek	214	40.24 N	81.34 W
Stonecutters Island I	271d	22.19 N	114.08 E
Stonefort	194	37.37 N	88.42 W
Stoneham, Ma., U.S.	283	42.28 N	71.06 W
Stoneham, Pa., U.S.	214	41.49 N	79.07 W
Stone Harbor	208	39.03 N	74.45 W
Stonehaven	46	56.57 N	2.12 W
Stonehenge	166	24.22 S	143.17 E
Stonehenge ⊥	42	51.11 N	1.49 W
Stonehill College ʊ[2]	283	42.03 N	71.05 W
Stonehouse, Eng., U.K.	42	51.45 N	2.17 W
Stonehouse, Scot., U.K.	46	55.43 N	4.00 W
Stone Indian Reserve ◆[4]	182	51.54 N	123.12 W
Stoneleigh	42	52.21 N	1.31 W
Stonelick Creek ≃	218	39.07 N	84.13 W
Stonelick State Park ♦	218	39.13 N	84.04 W
Stone Mountain	192	33.48 N	84.10 W
Stone Mountain ∧, Pa., U.S.	210	40.37 N	77.48 W
Stone Mountain ∧, Vt., U.S.	188	44.34 N	71.40 W
Stone Mountain Memorial State Park ♦	192	33.49 N	84.06 W
Stone Park	278	41.54 N	87.53 W
Stoner	182	53.36 N	122.40 W
Stoner Creek ≃	218	38.18 N	84.14 W
Stone Ridge	210	41.51 N	74.09 W
Stonerstown	214	40.13 N	78.16 W
Stones, East Fork ≃	194	35.59 N	86.27 W
Stones, West Fork ≃	194	35.59 N	86.27 W
Stones River National Battlefield ⊥	194	35.52 N	86.26 W
Stonestown ◆[9]	282	37.44 N	122.28 W
Stonevilla	279b	40.18 N	79.31 W
Stoneville	192	36.27 N	79.54 W
Stonewall, Mb., Can.	184	50.09 N	97.21 W
Stonewall, La., U.S.	194	32.16 N	93.49 W
Stonewall, Ms., U.S.	194	32.07 N	88.47 W
Stonewall, Ok., U.S.	196	34.39 N	96.31 W
Stonewall Manor	284c	38.53 N	77.14 W
Stoney Creek	212	43.13 N	79.46 W
Stoney Point ›	214	42.18 N	82.34 W
Stonington, Ct., U.S.	207	41.20 N	71.54 W
Stonington, Il., U.S.	219	39.38 N	89.11 W
Stonington, Me., U.S.	188	44.09 N	68.40 W
Stony ≃, Ak., U.S.	180	61.45 N	156.35 W
Stony ≃, Mn., U.S.	190	47.44 N	91.47 W
Stony Brook	210	40.55 N	73.08 W
Stony Brook ≃, Ct., U.S.	276	41.04 N	73.28 W
Stony Brook ≃, Ct., U.S.	276	41.08 N	73.22 W
Stony Brook ≃, Ma., U.S.	283	42.38 N	71.22 W
Stony Brook ≃, Ma., U.S.	283	42.22 N	71.16 W
Stony Brook ≃, N.J., U.S.	276	40.19 N	74.41 W
Stony Brook ≃, N.J., U.S.	276	40.56 N	74.26 W
Stony Brook Harbor c	276	40.54 N	73.10 W
Stony Brook Reservation ♦	283	42.16 N	71.09 W
Stony Creek, Ct., U.S.	207	41.15 N	72.44 W
Stony Creek, Va., U.S.	208	36.56 N	77.24 W
Stony Creek ≃, Ca., U.S.	204	39.41 N	121.58 W
Stony Creek ≃, Il., U.S.	278	41.41 N	87.51 W
Stony Creek ≃, Mi., U.S.	216	41.57 N	83.18 W
Stony Creek ≃, Mi., U.S.	216	43.00 N	84.55 W
Stony Creek ≃, N.Y., U.S.	212	43.49 N	76.14 W
Stony Creek ≃, Pa., U.S.	285	40.07 N	75.21 W
Stony Creek ≃, Va., U.S.	208	36.56 N	77.23 W
Stony Creek, Middle Fork ≃	226	39.25 N	122.31 W
Stony Creek, North Fork ≃	226	39.22 N	122.37 W
Stony Creek, South Fork ≃	226	39.22 N	122.39 W
Stony Creek Indian Reserve ◆[4]	182	53.57 N	124.07 W
Stony Creek Mills	208	40.21 N	75.52 W
Stonyford	226	39.22 N	122.32 W
Stony Gorge Reservoir ⊜[1]	226	39.34 N	122.31 W
Stony Indian Reserve ◆[4]	182	51.10 N	114.55 W
Stony Island I, Mi., U.S.	281	42.07 N	83.08 W
Stony Island I, N.Y., U.S.	212	43.53 N	76.25 W
Stony Kill ≃	210	42.24 N	73.38 W
Stony Lake ⊜, Mb., Can.	176	58.51 N	98.35 W
Stony Lake ⊜, On., Can.	212	44.33 N	78.05 W
Stony Plain	182	53.32 N	114.00 W
Stony Plain Indian Reserve ◆[4]	182	53.30 N	113.45 W
Stony Point, Austl.	169	38.22 S	145.13 E
Stony Point, Mi., U.S.	216	41.57 N	83.16 W
Stony Point, N.Y., U.S.	210	41.13 N	73.59 W
Stony Point, N.C., U.S.	192	35.51 N	81.02 W
Stony Point ›	284a	42.50 N	78.52 W
Stony Point ›[1]	212	43.52 N	76.15 W
Stony Prairie	214	41.21 N	83.10 W
Stony Rapids	176	59.16 N	105.50 W
Stony Ridge	214	41.30 N	83.30 W
Stony River	180	61.47 N	156.41 W
Stony Run	284b	39.11 N	76.42 W
Stony Run ≃	285	40.09 N	75.32 W
Stony Stratford	42	52.04 N	0.52 W
Stoober Bach ≃	61	47.27 N	16.35 E
Stop ≃	283	42.10 N	71.19 W
Stopnica	30	50.27 N	20.57 E
Stoppenberg ◆[8]	263	51.29 N	7.02 E
Stör ≃	54	53.50 N	11.29 E
Storå	40	59.43 N	15.08 E
Storå ≃	26	56.19 N	8.19 E
Stora Alvaret ≡	26	56.30 N	16.30 E
Stora Gla ⊜	26	59.30 N	12.30 E
Stora Kloten ⊜	40	59.52 N	15.16 E
Stora Le ⊜	26	59.05 N	11.53 E
Stora Lulevatten ⊜	24	67.10 N	19.16 E
Stora Mellösa	40	59.13 N	15.30 E
Stora Möja I, Sve.	26	59.26 N	18.55 E
Stora Möja I, Sve.	40	59.26 N	18.55 E
Stora Norn ⊜	40	60.14 N	15.42 E
Stora Sjöfallets Nationalpark ♦	24	67.44 N	18.16 E
Stora Skedvi	40	60.24 N	15.48 E
Stora Sundby	40	59.16 N	16.07 E
Storavan ⊜	24	65.40 N	18.15 E
Stora Vika	40	58.56 N	17.48 E
Storby	26	60.13 N	19.34 E
Stord I	26	59.53 N	5.25 E
Store Andst	41	55.29 N	9.14 E
Storebælt ʯ	41	55.30 N	11.00 E
Store Heddinge	41	55.19 N	12.25 E
Store Magleby	41	55.36 N	12.38 E
Store Merløse	41	55.33 N	11.40 E
Støren	26	63.02 N	10.18 E
Store Sotra I	26	60.18 N	5.05 E
Storeton	262	53.21 N	3.03 W
Storey □[6]	226	39.28 N	119.30 W
Storfjärden ⊜	40	60.30 N	17.23 E
Storfjorden c[2]	26	62.25 N	6.30 E
Storfors	40	59.32 N	14.16 E
Störitzsee ⊜	264a	52.23 N	13.51 E
Störkanal ≅	54	53.36 N	11.30 E
Storkerson Bay c	176	73.00 N	124.50 W
Storkerson Peninsula ›[1]	176	72.30 N	106.30 W
Storkow, Dtsch.	54	53.19 N	14.17 E
Storkow, Dtsch.	54	52.15 N	13.56 E
Storlien	26	63.19 N	12.06 E
Stormarn ◆[1]	52	53.45 N	10.20 E
Storm Bay c	166	43.10 S	147.32 E
Stormberg ∧	158	30.57 S	26.41 E
Stormberge ⋀	158	31.27 S	26.55 E
Storm King Mountain ∧	224	46.39 N	122.10 W
Storm Lake	198	42.38 N	95.12 W
Storm Mountain ∧	180	59.37 N	150.35 W
Stormont-Dundas and Glengarry □[6]	206	45.10 N	75.00 W
Štormovo	83	49.06 N	38.55 E
Stormsrivier	158	33.59 S	23.52 E
Stormsvlei	158	34.05 S	20.06 E
Stormville	210	41.34 N	73.45 W
Stornara	68	41.17 N	15.46 E
Stornarella	68	41.15 N	15.44 E
Stornorrforsen	26	63.52 N	20.03 E
Stornoway	46	58.12 N	6.23 W
Storo	64	45.51 N	10.35 E
Storoževaja	84	43.53 N	41.27 E
Storoževsk	24	61.57 N	52.16 E
Storožinec	78	48.10 N	25.43 E
Storrensjön ⊜	26	63.38 N	12.34 E
Storrington	42	50.55 N	0.28 W
Storrs	207	41.48 N	72.15 W
Storsjøen ⊜, Nor.	26	60.23 N	11.40 E
Storsjøen ⊜, Nor.	26	61.35 N	11.12 E
Storsjön ⊜, Sve.	26	62.48 N	13.07 E
Storsjön ⊜, Sve.	26	63.12 N	14.18 E
Storsjön ⊜, Sve.	40	60.34 N	16.44 E
Storsjön ⊜, Sve.	40	59.04 N	17.12 E
Storsteinsfjellet ∧	24	68.14 N	17.52 E
Storstrøm □[6]	41	55.00 N	11.55 E
Storstrømmen ʯ	41	54.58 N	11.55 E
Storstrømsbroen ◆[5]	41	54.58 N	11.50 E
Stort ≃	260	51.46 N	0.01 E
Storthoaks	184	49.22 N	101.38 W
Storuman	24	65.06 N	17.06 E
Storuman ⊜[1]	24	65.14 N	16.54 E
Storuman-See → Storavan ⊜	24	65.40 N	18.15 E
Storvarts gruve	26	62.38 N	11.31 E
Storvätteshågna ∧	26	62.07 N	12.27 E
Storvik	40	60.35 N	16.32 E
Storvindeln ⊜	24	65.43 N	17.05 E
Storvreta	40	59.58 N	17.42 E
Story	202	44.34 N	106.53 W
Story City	190	42.11 N	93.35 W
Stosch, Isla I	254	49.09 S	75.26 W
Stössen	54	51.06 N	11.55 E
Stotfold	42	52.01 N	0.14 W
Stotternheim	54	51.03 N	11.02 E
Stottville	210	42.17 N	73.44 W
Stouchsburg	208	40.23 N	76.14 W
Stough Park ♦	280	34.12 N	118.18 W
Stoughton, Sk., Can.	184	49.41 N	103.03 W
Stoughton, Eng., U.K.	260	51.15 N	0.35 W
Stoughton, Ma., U.S.	207	42.07 N	71.06 W
Stoughton, Wi., U.S.	216	42.55 N	89.13 W
Stoumont	56	50.25 N	5.48 E
Stoŭng ≃	110	12.50 N	104.19 E
Stour ≃, Eng., U.K.	42	51.52 N	1.16 E
Stour ≃, Eng., U.K.	42	50.43 N	1.46 W
Stour ≃, Eng., U.K.	42	51.18 N	1.22 E
Stour ≃, Eng., U.K.	42	52.20 N	2.15 W
Stourbridge	42	52.27 N	2.09 W
Stourport-on-Severn	42	52.21 N	2.16 W
Stout Lake ⊜	184	52.08 N	94.33 W
Stoutsville	219	39.33 N	91.51 W
Stover	194	38.26 N	92.59 W
Stow, Ma., U.S.	207	42.26 N	71.30 W
Stow, N.Y., U.S.	214	42.09 N	79.25 W
Stow, Oh., U.S.	214	41.10 N	81.27 W
Stowe, Pa., U.S.	208	40.15 N	75.40 W
Stowe, Vt., U.S.	188	44.27 N	72.41 W
Stowell	194	29.47 N	94.23 W
Stowe Township	279b	40.29 N	80.04 W
Stow Maries	260	51.40 N	0.39 E
Stowmarket	42	52.11 N	1.00 E
Stow-on-the-Wold	42	51.56 N	1.44 W
Stowupland	42	52.12 N	1.01 E
Stoyoma Mountain ∧	182	49.59 N	121.13 W
Stoystown	214	40.06 N	78.57 W
Stožec	60	48.51 N	13.50 E
Stra	64	45.25 N	12.00 E
Straach	54	51.57 N	12.35 E
Strabane, N. Ire., U.K.	48	54.49 N	7.27 W
Strabane, Pa., U.S.	214	40.15 N	80.11 W
Straberg	263	51.05 N	6.45 E
Strachan	46	57.01 N	2.32 W
Strachan Island I	164	9.00 S	142.10 E
Strachur	46	56.10 N	5.04 W
Stradbally	48	53.00 N	7.08 W
Stradbroke	42	52.19 N	1.16 E
Stradeč'	76	51.56 N	23.40 E
Stradella	62	45.05 N	9.18 E
Stradone	48	53.58 N	7.14 W
Stradovn'a, ozero ⊜	82	56.53 N	36.18 E
Straelen	56	51.27 N	6.16 E
Strafford	285	40.03 N	75.25 W
Straffordville	212	42.45 N	80.47 W
Strahan	166	42.09 S	145.19 E
Straight Creek ≃	218	38.46 N	83.55 W
Strakonice	60	49.16 N	13.55 E
Stralsund	54	54.19 N	13.05 E
Strambino	62	45.23 N	7.53 E
Strand	158	34.06 S	18.50 E
Stranda	26	62.19 N	6.54 E
Strande	54	54.26 N	10.12 E
Strandhill	48	54.17 N	8.36 W
Stranger Creek ≃	198	39.00 N	95.01 W
Strangford	48	54.22 N	5.34 W
Strangford Lough ⊜	48	54.28 N	5.35 W
Strängnäs	40	59.23 N	17.02 E
Strångsjö	40	58.54 N	16.12 E
Strangways ≃	164	14.52 S	133.50 E
Strangways, Mount ∧	162	23.02 S	133.51 E
Stranorlar	48	54.48 N	7.46 W
Stranraer	44	54.55 N	5.02 W
Strasbourg, Sk., Can.	184	51.04 N	104.57 W
Strasbourg, Fr.	58	48.35 N	7.45 E
Strasbourg, Aéroport ⊠	58	48.32 N	7.38 E
Strasburg, Dtsch.	54	53.30 N	13.44 E
Strasburg, Co., U.S.	198	39.44 N	104.20 W
Strasburg, N.D., U.S.	198	46.08 N	100.09 W
Strasburg, Oh., U.S.	214	40.35 N	81.31 W
Strasburg, Pa., U.S.	208	39.58 N	76.11 W
Strasburg, Va., U.S.	188	38.59 N	78.21 W
Straševiči	76	56.49 N	34.36 E
Strašín	60	49.08 N	13.38 E
Stråssa	40	59.45 N	15.13 E
Strassburg → Strasbourg	58	48.35 N	7.45 E
Strasshof an der Nordbahn	61	48.19 N	16.39 E
Strasskirchen	60	48.50 N	12.43 E
Strata Florida Abbey ʊ[1]	42	52.16 N	3.51 W
Stratford, On., Can.	212	43.22 N	80.57 W
Stratford, N.Z.	172	39.20 S	174.17 E
Stratford, Ca., U.S.	226	36.11 N	119.49 W
Stratford, Ct., U.S.	207	41.11 N	73.08 W
Stratford, De., U.S.	285	39.40 N	75.38 W
Stratford, Ia., U.S.	190	42.16 N	93.55 W
Stratford, N.J., U.S.	208	39.49 N	75.00 W
Stratford, N.Y., U.S.	210	43.11 N	74.42 W
Stratford, Ok., U.S.	196	34.47 N	96.57 W
Stratford, Tx., U.S.	196	36.20 N	102.04 W
Stratford, Wi., U.S.	190	44.48 N	90.04 W
Stratford Centre	206	45.47 N	71.16 W
Stratford Point ›	276	41.09 N	73.06 W
Stratford-upon-Avon	42	52.12 N	1.41 W
Strathalbyn	168b	35.16 S	138.54 E
Strathaven	46	55.40 N	4.04 W
Strathbogie Ranges ⋀	169	36.55 S	145.45 E
Strathclair	184	50.24 N	100.24 W
Strathclyde □[4]	46	56.00 N	5.15 W
Strathcona Provincial Park ♦	182	49.40 N	125.50 W
Strathdearn V	46	57.15 N	4.05 W
Strathdon	46	57.11 N	3.02 W
Strathearn V	46	56.18 N	3.45 W
Strathfield	170	33.52 S	151.06 E
Strathgordon	166	42.46 S	146.03 E
Strath Kanaird	46	57.59 N	5.11 W
Strathlorne	186	46.11 N	61.17 W
Strathminglo	46	56.16 N	3.16 W
Strathmoor ◆[8]	281	42.23 N	83.11 W
Strathmore, Ab., Can.	182	51.03 N	113.23 W
Strathmore, Ca., U.S.	204	36.08 N	119.03 W
Strathmore, N.J., U.S.	276	40.24 N	74.13 W
Strathmore V	46	56.39 N	3.00 W
Strathpeffer	46	57.35 N	4.33 W
Strathpine	171a	27.19 S	152.59 E
Strathroy	214	42.57 N	81.38 W
Strathy ≃	46	58.34 N	4.00 W
Strathy Point ›	46	58.35 N	4.02 W
Strattanville	214	41.12 N	79.19 W
Stratton, Eng., U.K.	42	50.50 N	4.31 W
Stratton, Eng., U.K.	42	51.44 N	1.59 W
Stratton, Co., U.S.	198	39.18 N	102.36 W
Stratton, Me., U.S.	188	45.08 N	70.26 W
Stratton, Ne., U.S.	198	40.08 N	101.13 W
Stratton, Oh., U.S.	214	40.32 N	80.38 W
Stratton Mountain ∧	188	43.05 N	72.56 W
Stratton Saint Margaret	42	51.35 N	1.45 W
Straubing	60	48.53 N	12.34 E
Strauch	263	51.09 N	6.56 E
Straumen	26	63.52 N	11.18 E
Straupitz	54	51.54 N	14.07 E
Strausberg	54	52.35 N	13.53 E
Straus-Berger Stadtforst ♦	264a	52.34 N	13.52 E
Strausberg-Vorstadt	264a	52.32 N	13.51 E
Straussberg	54	51.23 N	10.44 E
Straussee ⊜	264a	52.35 N	13.53 E
Straussfurt	54	51.09 N	10.59 E
Strausstown	208	40.30 N	76.11 W
Stravignano	66	43.05 N	12.49 E
Strawberry	226	38.13 N	118.35 W
Strawberry ≃, Ar., U.S.	194	35.53 N	91.13 W
Strawberry ≃, Ut., U.S.	200	40.10 N	110.24 W
Strawberry Island I	284a	42.57 N	78.55 W
Strawberry Mountain ∧	202	44.19 N	118.43 W
Strawberry Point, Ca., U.S.	282	37.54 N	122.31 W
Strawberry Point, Ia., U.S.	190	42.41 N	91.32 W
Strawberry Point ›	283	42.15 N	70.46 W
Strawberry Reservoir ⊜[1]	200	40.11 N	111.08 W
Strawberry Valley	226	39.34 N	121.06 W
Strawbridge Lake ⊜	285	39.57 N	74.57 W
Strawn	196	32.33 N	98.29 W
Straw Pump	279b	40.19 N	79.40 W
Stráž	61	49.04 N	14.54 E
Strážnice	30	48.54 N	17.18 E
Strážov	60	49.18 N	13.15 E
Strážske	30	48.53 N	21.50 E
Streaky Bay	162	32.48 S	134.13 E
Streaky Bay c	162	32.36 S	134.08 E
Streamwood	216	42.01 N	88.10 W
Streatham, Austl.	169	37.41 S	143.04 E
Streatham, B.C., Can.	182	53.52 N	126.12 W
Streatham ◆[8]	260	51.26 N	0.08 W
Streator	216	41.07 N	88.50 W
Strebersdorf ◆[8]	264b	48.18 N	16.23 E
Středočeský Kraj □[4]	30	49.55 N	14.30 E
Stredoslovenský Kraj □[4]	30	48.50 N	19.10 E
Street	42	51.07 N	2.42 W
Streeter	198	46.39 N	99.21 W
Streetman	222	31.53 N	96.19 W
Streetsboro	214	41.14 N	81.20 W
Streets Run ≃	279b	40.23 N	79.56 W
Streetsville	212	43.35 N	79.42 W
Strehaia	38	44.37 N	23.12 E
Strehla	54	51.21 N	13.13 E
Streitberg	60	49.49 N	11.13 E
Střela ≃	60	49.55 N	13.33 E
Strelasund ʯ	54	54.20 N	13.05 E
Strel'covka	83	49.18 N	39.52 E
Streleckaja Step', zapovednik ♦	83	49.16 N	40.05 E
Streleckije Vyselki	82	54.12 N	38.57 E
Strelica	78	51.37 N	38.55 E
Střelice	61	49.09 N	16.30 E
Strelitzalt	54	53.20 N	13.05 E
Strelka	86	58.05 N	93.01 E
Strelka ≃	265a	59.52 N	30.03 E
Strelka-Čun'a	74	61.45 N	102.48 E
Strelkovo	82	55.28 N	37.37 E
Strelkovoje	78	45.54 N	34.53 E
Strel'na, Ross.	24	66.06 N	38.40 E
Strel'na, Ross.	76	59.51 N	30.02 E
Strel'na ≃	24	66.04 N	38.39 E
Strel'skaja	24	59.28 N	47.47 E
Střelské Hoštice	60	49.18 N	13.46 E
Strem ≃	61	47.00 N	16.31 E
Strembo	64	46.09 N	10.44 E
Stremilovo	82	55.09 N	37.09 E
Strenči	76	57.37 N	25.41 E
Strengen	58	47.08 N	10.27 E
Strensall	44	54.03 N	1.02 W
Stresa	62	45.53 N	8.32 E
Strešen'	38	47.08 N	28.36 E
Strešin	76	52.43 N	30.05 E
Stretford	44	53.27 N	2.19 W
Stretton, Austl.	162	32.32 S	117.41 E
Stretton, Eng., U.K.	42	52.44 N	0.35 W
Stretton, Eng., U.K.	44	53.21 N	2.35 W
Streu ≃	56	50.21 N	10.16 E
Strib	41	55.32 N	9.47 E
Striberg	40	59.33 N	14.56 E
Stříbro	60	49.46 N	13.00 E
Strichen	46	57.34 N	2.05 W
Strickherdicke	263	51.29 N	7.43 E
Strickland ≃	164	6.00 S	142.05 E
Strigno	64	46.04 N	11.31 E
Strijen	52	51.45 N	4.33 E
Striker, Lake ⊜[1]	222	31.57 N	94.59 W
Strimón (Struma) ≃	38	40.47 N	23.51 E
Stringtown	218	40.05 N	86.29 W
Striven, Loch c	46	55.58 N	5.09 W
Strižament, gora ∧	84	44.46 N	42.01 E
Strižavka	78	49.19 N	28.28 E
Striži	80	58.30 N	49.13 E
Strjama ≃	38	42.10 N	24.56 E
Strobel	252	32.03 S	60.37 W
Strobel, Lago ⊜	254	48.22 S	71.12 W
Strobl	64	47.43 N	13.29 E
Strobleton	214	41.22 N	79.25 W
Strøby	41	55.23 N	12.18 E
Stroeder	254	40.11 S	62.37 W
Strofádhes, Nísoi II	38	37.15 N	21.00 E
Strogino ◆[8]	265b	55.49 N	37.25 E
Strogonof Point ›	180	56.53 N	158.49 W
Stroh	216	41.34 N	85.11 W
Ströhen	52	52.32 N	8.41 E
Stroitel'	78	50.47 N	36.26 E
Strokestown	48	53.47 N	8.08 W
Strom ≃	54	53.15 N	13.50 E
Stroma I	46	58.41 N	3.08 W
Stromberg, Dtsch.	52	51.48 N	8.12 E
Stromberg, Dtsch.	56	49.57 N	7.46 E
Stromboli, Isola I	70	38.47 N	15.13 E
Strome	182	52.48 N	112.04 W
Stromeferry	46	57.21 N	5.34 W
Strömkendorf	54	53.58 N	11.29 E
Stromness	46	58.57 N	3.18 W
Strömsberg	40	60.24 N	17.35 E
Strömsbro	40	60.42 N	17.10 E
Strömsbruk	26	61.53 N	17.19 E
Stromsburg	198	41.06 N	97.35 W
Strömsholm	40	59.32 N	16.15 E
Strömsnäsbruk	26	56.33 N	13.43 E
Strömstad	26	58.56 N	11.10 E
Strömsund	26	63.51 N	15.35 E
Strömsvattudal ⊜	26	63.56 N	15.28 E
Stromyn'	82	56.03 N	38.29 E
Strong	194	33.06 N	92.20 W
Strong ≃	194	31.51 N	90.08 W
Strong City	198	38.23 N	96.32 W
Stronghurst	190	40.44 N	90.54 W
Strongoli	68	39.15 N	17.03 E
Strongs Creek ≃	276	40.40 N	73.22 W
Strongs Neck ›[1]	276	40.58 N	73.07 W
Strongstown	214	40.33 N	78.55 W
Strongsville	214	41.18 N	81.50 W
Strongsville Airport ⊠	279a	41.19 N	81.52 W
Stronsay I	46	59.07 N	2.37 W
Stronsay Firth ʯ	46	59.02 N	2.41 W
Stronsdorf	61	48.39 N	16.18 E
Strontian	46	56.41 N	5.34 W
Strood	42	51.24 N	0.28 E
Stropkov	30	49.12 N	21.40 E
Stropnice ≃	61	48.52 N	14.30 E
Stroppiana	62	45.14 N	8.27 E
Stroud, Austl.	166	32.20 S	151.56 E
Stroud, Eng., U.K.	42	51.45 N	2.12 W
Stroud, Ok., U.S.	196	35.44 N	96.39 W
Stroudsburg	210	40.59 N	75.11 W
Strövelstorp	41	56.09 N	12.49 E
Strubenvale	273d	26.16 S	28.28 E
Strücklingen	52	53.07 N	7.40 E
Struer	26	56.29 N	8.37 E
Struga	38	41.11 N	20.40 E
Strugi-Krasnyje	76	58.17 N	29.06 E
Struisbaai	158	34.49 S	20.04 E
Struisbult	273d	26.19 S	28.29 E
Strule ≃	48	54.43 N	7.25 W
Strum	190	44.32 N	91.23 W
Struma (Strimón) ≃	38	40.47 N	23.51 E
Strumble Head ›	42	52.02 N	5.04 W
Strumica	38	41.26 N	22.38 E
Strümp	263	51.17 N	6.40 E
Strunino	82	56.23 N	38.34 E
Strupna	82	54.43 N	38.48 E
Struthers	214	41.03 N	80.36 W
Struy	46	57.24 N	4.39 W
Strydenburg	158	29.58 S	23.40 E
Strydomsvlei	158	33.10 S	23.03 E
Strydpoort	158	27.00 S	25.58 E
Stryj	78	49.15 N	23.51 E
Stryj ≃	78	49.24 N	24.13 E
Stryker, Mt., U.S.	182	48.40 N	114.46 W
Stryker, Oh., U.S.	216	41.30 N	84.24 W
Strykersville	210	42.42 N	78.27 W
Stryków	30	51.55 N	19.37 E
Stryn	26	61.55 N	6.47 E
Strynø I	41	54.54 N	10.37 E
Strypa ≃	78	48.52 N	25.26 E
Strzegom	30	50.57 N	16.21 E
Strzegowo-Osada	30	52.55 N	20.18 E
Strzelce Krajeńskie	30	52.53 N	15.32 E
Strzelce Opolskie	30	50.31 N	18.19 E
Strzelecki Creek ≃	166	29.37 S	139.59 E
Strzelecki Desert ◆[2]	166	28.00 S	140.10 E
Strzeleckie, Mount ∧	162	21.10 S	133.53 E
Strzelecki National Park ♦	166	40.14 S	148.06 E
Strzelin	30	50.47 N	17.03 E
Strzelno	30	52.38 N	18.11 E
Strzyżów	30	49.52 N	21.47 E
Stuart, Fl., U.S.	220	27.11 N	80.15 W
Stuart, Ia., U.S.	198	41.30 N	94.19 W
Stuart, Ne., U.S.	198	42.35 N	99.08 W
Stuart, Va., U.S.	192	36.38 N	80.15 W
Stuart ≃	182	54.00 N	123.32 W
Stuart, Central Mount ∧	162	21.54 S	133.27 E
Stuart, Mount ∧	224	47.29 N	120.54 W
Stuart Channel ʯ	224	48.55 N	123.45 W
Stuart Island I, Ak., U.S.	180	63.35 N	162.30 W
Stuart Island I, Wa., U.S.	224	48.42 N	123.12 W
Stuart Lake ⊜	182	54.32 N	124.35 W
Stuart Mountains ⋀	172	45.00 S	167.37 E
Stuart Range ⋀	162	29.10 S	134.56 E
Stuarts Draft	192	38.01 N	79.02 W
Stubai V	64	47.06 N	11.19 E
Stubaier Alpen ⋀	64	47.10 N	11.05 E
Stubalpe ⋀	61	47.06 N	14.54 E
Stübbecken	263	51.23 N	7.36 E
Stubbekøbing	41	54.53 N	12.03 E
Stubbenfelde	54	54.02 N	14.01 E
Stubbenkammer	54	54.35 N	13.40 E
Stubbington	42	50.50 N	1.13 W
Stubbins	262	53.39 N	2.19 W
Stubenberg	61	47.14 N	15.48 E
Stubla ≃	78	50.50 N	26.04 E
Stubner Kogel ∧	64	47.07 N	13.06 E
Studená	61	49.11 N	15.17 E
Studenec	80	54.52 N	48.16 E
Studenica, Manastir ʊ[1]	38	43.21 N	20.35 E
Studen Kladenec, jazovir ⊜[1]	38	41.37 N	25.30 E
Studholme Junction	172	44.44 S	171.08 E
Studi, Università degli ʊ[2]	266b	45.28 N	9.14 E
Studland	42	50.39 N	1.58 W
Studley	42	52.16 N	1.52 W
Stud'onoje, Ross.	80	51.36 N	53.10 E
Stud'onoje, Ross.	86	53.37 N	77.31 E
Stud'onok	78	51.42 N	34.07 E
Studsvik	40	58.46 N	17.23 E
Stugudal	26	62.54 N	11.52 E
Stugun	26	63.10 N	15.36 E
Stuhleck ∧	61	47.34 N	15.47 E
Stühlingen	58	47.44 N	8.26 E
Stuhlweissenburg → Székesfehérvár	30	47.12 N	18.25 E
Stuhr	52	53.01 N	8.45 E
Stuie	182	52.22 N	126.02 W
Stukely, Lac ⊜	206	45.22 N	72.15 W
Stukenbrock	52	51.54 N	8.39 E
Stull ≃	184	55.10 N	92.39 W
Stull Lake ⊜	184	54.23 N	92.34 W
Stülpe	54	52.02 N	13.19 E
Stumm	64	47.17 N	11.53 E
Stump Creek	214	41.01 N	78.50 W
Stump Creek ≃	276	40.28 N	74.16 W
Stumpf	263	51.06 N	7.13 E
Stump Lake ⊜	198	47.54 N	98.24 W
Stumsdorf	54	51.37 N	12.03 E
Stuorre Tjöure ∧	26	63.56 N	13.30 E
Stupart ≃	184	56.00 N	93.22 W
Stupava	61	48.17 N	17.02 E
Stupino	82	54.53 N	38.05 E
Stuppach	56	49.27 N	9.44 E
Stura ≃	62	45.09 N	8.21 E
Stura di Ala ≃	62	45.18 N	7.24 E
Stura di Demonte ≃	62	44.40 N	7.53 E
Stura di Lanzo ≃	62	45.06 N	7.44 E
Stura di Val Grande ≃	62	45.18 N	7.24 E
Stura di Viù ≃	62	45.16 N	7.26 E
Sturbridge	207	42.06 N	72.04 W
Sturdee	162	31.52 S	132.23 E
Sturge Island I	9	67.27 S	164.18 E
Sturgeon, Mo., U.S.	219	39.14 N	92.16 W
Sturgeon, Pa., U.S.	279b	40.23 N	80.13 W
Sturgeon ≃, On., Can.	190	46.19 N	79.58 W
Sturgeon ≃, Sk., Can.	184	53.12 N	105.53 W
Sturgeon ≃, Mi., U.S.	190	45.24 N	84.38 W
Sturgeon ≃, Mi., U.S.	190	45.50 N	86.41 W
Sturgeon ≃, Mi., U.S.	190	47.02 N	88.30 W
Sturgeon Bay	190	44.50 N	87.22 W
Sturgeon Bay c	184	52.00 N	97.50 W
Sturgeon Falls	190	46.22 N	79.55 W
Sturgeon Lake ⊜, Ab., Can.	182	55.06 N	117.30 W
Sturgeon Lake ⊜, On., Can.	184	55.25 N	90.55 W
Sturgeon Lake ⊜, On., Can.	212	44.28 N	78.42 W
Sturgeon Lake ⊜, Wa., U.S.	224	45.44 N	122.48 W
Sturgeon Lake Indian Reserve ◆[4], Ab., Can.	182	55.04 N	117.29 W
Sturgeon Lake Indian Reserve ◆[4], Sk., Can.	184	53.25 N	106.05 W
Sturgeon Landing	184	54.16 N	101.49 W
Sturgeon Point ›	212	42.42 N	79.03 W
Sturgis, Sk., Can.	184	51.58 N	102.32 W
Sturgis, Ky., U.S.	194	37.32 N	87.59 W
Sturgis, Mi., U.S.	216	41.47 N	85.25 W
Sturgis, Ms., U.S.	194	33.20 N	89.02 W
Sturgis, S.D., U.S.	198	44.24 N	103.30 W
Sturla	62	44.24 N	8.59 E
Sturminster Newton	42	50.50 N	2.19 W
Štúrovo	30	47.48 N	18.49 E
Sturry	42	51.18 N	1.07 E
Sturt, Mount ∧	166	29.33 S	141.42 E
Sturt Creek	162	19.10 S	128.10 E
Sturt Creek ≃	162	20.08 S	127.24 E
Sturtevant	216	42.41 N	87.53 W
Sturt National Park ♦	166	29.00 S	141.40 E
Sturt Story Desert ◆[2]	166	28.30 S	141.00 E
Sturup flygplats ⊠	41	55.34 N	13.21 E
Stürzelberg	263	51.08 N	6.49 E
Stutterheim	158	32.33 S	27.28 E
Stuttgart, Dtsch.	56	48.46 N	9.11 E
Stuttgart, Ar., U.S.	194	34.30 N	91.33 W
Stuttgart □[5]	56	49.00 N	9.45 E
Stuttgart, Flughafen ⊠	56	48.41 N	9.12 E
Stützengrün	54	50.32 N	12.31 E
Stützerbach	54	50.38 N	10.51 E
Stuyvesant	210	42.24 N	73.47 W
Stuyvesant Falls	210	42.21 N	73.44 W
Stviga ≃	78	52.04 N	27.54 E
Styal	262	53.21 N	2.15 W
Stykkishólmur	24a	65.06 N	22.48 W
Styla	83	47.41 N	37.50 E
Styr' ≃	78	52.07 N	26.35 E
Styrum ◆[8]	263	51.27 N	6.51 E
Styx ≃, On., Can.	212	44.11 N	80.57 W
Styx ≃, Al., U.S.	194	30.31 N	87.27 W
Suaçuí Grande ≃	255	18.50 S	41.46 W
Suai	112	3.48 N	113.38 E
Suain	164	3.20 S	142.55 E
Suaita	246	6.07 N	73.27 W
Suakin Archipelago II	140	18.42 N	38.30 E
Sual	116	16.04 N	120.05 E
Suan	98	38.42 N	126.22 E
Suao, Taiwan	100	24.36 N	121.51 E
Su'ao, Zhg.	100	25.38 N	119.42 E
Suapure ≃	246	6.25 N	66.23 W
Suaqui Grande	232	28.24 N	109.54 W
Suār	124	29.02 N	79.03 E
Suātala	124	23.09 N	79.02 E
Suatima	114	4.13 N	96.04 E
Šubač	76	60.22 N	38.14 E
Subačius	76	55.46 N	24.47 E
Subah	115a	6.58 S	109.52 E
Subaio	256	22.30 S	42.50 W
Subang	115a	6.34 S	107.45 E
Subansiri ≃	120	26.48 N	93.50 E
Šubarkuduk	86	49.13 N	56.34 E
Subar Laut, Pulau I	271c	1.13 N	103.50 E
Subarnapur	272b	22.58 N	88.34 E
Subarnarekha ≃	120	21.34 N	87.24 E
Šubarši	86	48.35 N	57.12 E
Subashi	85	38.22 N	74.57 E
Subasio, Monte ∧	66	43.03 N	12.40 E
Subate	76	56.01 N	25.56 E
Subay', 'Urūq as- ◆[2]	144	22.15 N	43.05 E
Subbiano	66	43.34 N	11.52 E
Subbotino	86	53.04 N	91.55 E
Subchankulovo	80	54.34 N	53.49 E
Subei	102	39.27 N	95.03 E
Subeita → Shivta, Horvot ⊥	132	30.53 N	34.38 E
Suben	60	48.25 N	13.26 E
Subhepur	272a	28.45 N	77.16 E
Subi, Pulau I	112	2.55 N	108.50 E
Subiaco	66	41.55 N	13.06 E
Subic	116	14.53 N	120.14 E
Subic Bay c	116	14.45 N	120.13 E
Subic Bay Naval Base (U.S.) ■	116	14.47 N	120.16 E
Subipur	272b	22.54 N	88.08 E
Subk al-Ahad	142	30.18 N	31.02 E
Sublette	198	37.28 N	100.50 W
Sublett Range ⋀	202	42.20 N	112.50 W
Sublime	222	29.29 N	96.48 W
Subotica	38	46.06 N	19.39 E
Suburban Airport ⊠	284c	39.05 N	76.50 W
Suburban Village	285	39.58 N	75.34 W
Suca	144	6.31 N	39.14 E
Sucarnoochee ≃	194	32.25 N	88.02 W
Succasunna	210	40.52 N	74.38 W
Succor Creek ≃	202	43.38 N	116.56 W
Suceava	38	47.39 N	26.19 E
Suceava □[5]	38	47.30 N	25.45 E
Suceava ≃	38	47.32 N	26.32 E
Sucha [Beskidzka]	30	49.44 N	19.36 E
Suchaja	88	52.32 N	107.06 E
Suchaja Volnovacha ≃	83	47.37 N	38.01 E
Suchań, Pol.	30	53.17 N	15.19 E
Suchan → Partizansk, Ross.	89	43.08 N	133.09 E
Suchana	74	68.45 N	118.00 E
Suchang	107	30.34 N	103.34 E
Süchbaatar	88	50.15 N	106.12 E
Süchbaatar □[4]	102	45.30 N	114.00 E
Suchdol ◆[8]	54	50.08 N	14.21 E
Suchdol nad Lužnicí	61	48.54 N	14.53 E
Suchedniów	30	51.03 N	20.51 E
Suchetgarh	123	32.34 N	74.40 E
Suchiapa	234	16.37 N	93.05 W

Symbol	English	Deutsch	Español	Français	Português
≃	River	Fluß	Río	Rivière	Rio
≅	Canal	Kanal	Canal	Canal	Canal
⌊	Waterfall, Rapids	Wasserfall, Stromschnellen	Cascada, Rápidos	Chute d'eau, Rapides	Cascata, Rápidos
ʯ	Strait	Meeresstraße	Estrecho	Détroit	Estreito
c	Bay, Gulf	Bucht, Golf	Bahía, Golfo	Baie, Golfe	Baía, Golfo
⊜	Lake, Lakes	See, Seen	Lago, Lagos	Lac, Lacs	Lago, Lagos
≡	Swamp	Sumpf	Pantano	Marais	Pântano
⊓	Ice Features, Glacier	Eis- und Gletscherformen	Accidentes Glaciales	Formes glaciaires	Acidentes glaciares
⊤	Other Hydrographic Features	Andere Hydrographische Objekte	Otros Elementos Hidrográficos	Autres données hydrographiques	Outros acidentes hidrográficos
✦	Submarine Features	Untermeerische Objekte	Accidentes Submarinos	Formes de relief sous-marin	Acidentes submarinos
□	Political Unit	Politische Einheit	Unidad Politica	Entité politique	Unidade política
ʊ	Cultural Institution	Kulturelle Institution	Institución Cultural	Institution culturelle	Instituição cultural
⊥	Historical Site	Historische Stätte	Sitio Histórico	Site historique	Sitio histórico
♦	Recreational Site	Erholungs- und Ferienort	Sitio de Recreo	Centre de loisirs	Area de Lazer
⊠	Airport	Flughafen	Aeropuerto	Aéroport	Aeroporto
■	Military Installation	Militäranlage	Instalación Militar	Installation militaire	Instalação militar
◆	Miscellaneous	Verschiedenes	Misceláneo	Divers	Diversos

ENGLISH Name	Page	Lat.°	Long.°	DEUTSCH Name	Seite	Breite°	Länge° E=Ost

Column 1

Suchiapa ± 234 16.36 N 93.01 W
Súchil 234 23.38 N 103.55 W
Suchiniči 76 54.06 N 35.20 E
Suchitepéquez □⁵ 234 14.25 N 91.20 W
Suchitlán 234 19.22 N 103.43 W
Suchitoto 236 13.56 N 89.02 W
Suchobezvodnoje 80 57.03 N 44.50 E
Suchoborka 24 59.06 N 49.58 E
Suchodol, Ross. 80 53.55 N 51.14 E
Suchodol, Ross. 82 54.37 N 37.22 E
Suchodol'skij 76 53.43 N 38.17 E
Suchodrev ± 82 54.44 N 35.59 E
Suchoj 80 47.06 N 41.21 E
Suchoj Jelančik ± 83 47.18 N 38.25 E
Suchoj Log 86 56.55 N 62.01 E
Suchoj Pit 58 58.48 N 92.49 E
Suchoj Sambek ± 83 47.23 N 39.07 E
Suchoj Torec ± 83 48.49 N 37.36 E
Suchona ± 24 60.46 N 46.24 E
Suchorečka 52 49.59 N 52.27 E
Suchotinka 80 52.31 N 41.35 E
Suchou 106 31.18 N 120.37 E
Suchoverkovo 76 56.37 N 35.35 E
Suchov Pervyj 80 49.59 N 43.28 E
Süchow — Xuzhou 98 34.16 N 117.11 E
Süchteln 56 51.17 N 6.22 E
Suchumi 84 43.01 N 41.02 E
Sucio ± 246 7.27 N 77.07 W
Suck ± 48 53.16 N 8.03 W
Sucker Creek ± 212 44.09 N 77.08 W
Sucker Creek Indian Reserve ◄⁴ 182 55.28 N 116.10 W
Sucker Lake @ 212 44.46 N 78.16 W
Suckling, Mount ▲ 164 9.45 S 148.55 E
Sucre, Arg. 258 34.30 S 59.07 W
Sucre, Bol. 248 19.02 S 65.17 W
Sucre, Col. 246 8.49 N 74.44 W
Sucre, Ec. 246 1.16 S 80.26 W
Sucre □³ 246 10.25 N 63.30 W
Sucre □⁵, Col. 246 9.00 N 75.00 W
Sucre □⁵, Ven. 286c 10.25 N 66.50 W
Sucúa 246 2.28 S 78.10 W
Sucuaro 246 4.34 N 68.50 W
Sucumbíos □⁴ 246 0.06 N 76.52 W
Sucunduri ± 248 5.50 S 59.32 W
Sucuriju 250 1.39 N 49.57 W
Sucuriú ± 255 20.47 S 51.38 W
Sucy-en-Brie 54 48.46 N 2.32 E
Sud, Canal du ᴜ 238 18.40 N 73.05 W
Sud, Grand Récif ◄² 175f 23.00 S 167.02 E
Sud, Pointe ► 157a 11.53 S 43.49 E
Sud, Rivière du ± 206 45.08 N 73.15 W
Suda 76 59.09 N 37.33 E
Suda ± 76 59.11 N 37.30 E
Südafrika — South Africa □¹ 156 30.00 S 26.00 E
Sudaj 76 58.58 N 43.08 E
Sudak 78 44.52 N 34.59 E
Südamerika — South America ◄¹ 18 15.00 S 60.00 W
Sudan 196 34.04 N 102.31 W
Sudan (As-Sūdān) □¹, Afr. 196 15.00 N 30.00 E
Sudan (As-Sūdān) □¹, Afr. 140 15.00 N 30.00 E
Sudan ± 10 10.00 N 20.00 E
Sudáñez 248 19.06 S 64.44 W
Sudarsan 272b 22.59 N 88.17 E
Südbahnhof ◄ 264b 48.11 N 16.23 E
Sudberg ◄⁸ 263 51.11 N 7.08 E
Sudbišči 76 52.57 N 37.39 E
Sud'bodarovka 82 52.19 N 54.07 E
Sud'brookmerland 52 53.29 N 7.24 E
Sudbury, On., Can. 190 46.30 N 81.00 W
Sudbury, Eng., U.K. 42 52.02 N 0.44 E
Sudbury, Ma., U.S. 207 42.23 N 71.25 W
Sudbury ± 283 42.28 N 71.22 W
Sudbury Center 283 42.23 N 71.25 W
Sudbury Reservoir ◄ 207 42.19 N 71.31 W
Südchinesisches Meer — South China Sea ᴛ² 108 10.00 N 113.00 E
Sudd — As-Sudd ◄¹ 140 8.00 N 31.00 E
Süd Dakota — South Dakota □³ 198 44.15 N 100.00 W
Sudd an-Na'ām, Jabal ▲ 142 29.49 N 31.43 E
Suddie 246 7.07 N 58.29 W
Sude ± 54 53.22 N 10.45 E
Süderbrarup 44 54.38 N 9.46 E
Süderlügum 41 54.52 N 8.55 E
Suderwich 263 51.37 N 7.15 E
Sudeten — Sudety ◄ 30 50.30 N 16.00 E
Sudety ◄ 30 50.30 N 16.00 E
Süd-Georgien — South Georgia I 244 54.15 S 36.45 W
Sudi 154 10.06 S 39.57 E
Sudislavl' 80 57.53 N 41.43 E
Südkamen 263 51.35 N 7.39 E
Süd-Korea — Korea, South □¹ 98 36.30 N 128.00 E
Sudersville 208 39.11 N 75.51 W
Südlicher Bug — Južnyj Bug ± 78 46.59 N 31.58 E
Südlicher Indianer-See — Southern Indian Lake @ 176 57.10 N 98.40 W
Sudislkovo 82 55.53 N 36.02 E
Sudogda 80 55.57 N 40.50 E
Sudomskaja vozvyšennost' ◄¹ 76 57.25 N 29.25 E
Sudong, Pulau I 271c 1.13 N 103.44 E
Süd-Orkney-Inseln — South Orkney Islands II 9 60.35 S 45.30 W
Sudost' ± 76 52.19 N 33.24 E
Sud-Ouest □⁵ 152 5.10 N 10.40 E
Sud-Ouest, Pointe du ► 186 49.23 N 63.36 W
Sudovaja Višn'a 78 49.49 N 23.22 E
Südradde ± 52 52.41 N 7.34 E
Süd-Sandwich-Inseln — South Sandwich Islands II 18 57.45 S 26.30 W
Süd-Shetland-Inseln — South Shetland Islands II 9 62.00 S 58.00 W
Südüd 142 30.25 N 30.54 E
Südwest-Kap — South West ◄ 166 43.34 S 146.02 E
Sudweyhe 52 52.59 N 8.53 E
Sudža 78 51.12 N 35.16 E
Sue 96 33.35 N 130.30 E
Sue ± 140 7.41 N 28.03 E
Sueca 34 39.12 N 0.19 W
Suecia — Sweden □¹ 24 62.00 N 15.00 E
Sue Creek ± 284b 39.17 N 76.24 W
Suedberg 208 40.74 N 76.28 W
Suède — Sweden □¹ 24 62.00 N 15.00 E
Suemez Island I 182 55.17 N 133.21 W
Suèvres 50 47.40 N 1.28 E
Suez — As-Suways 142 29.58 N 32.33 E
Suez, Gulf of — Suways, Khalij as- ᴄ 140 29.00 N 32.50 E
Suez Canal — Suways, Qanāt as- ᴢ 142 29.55 N 32.33 E

Column 2

Süf 132 32.19 N 35.50 E
Sufaynah 128 23.09 N 40.32 E
Suffern 210 41.06 N 74.09 W
Suffern Park 276 41.07 N 74.07 W
Suffield, Ab., Can. 184 50.12 N 111.10 W
Suffield, Ct., U.S. 207 41.58 N 72.39 W
Suffield, Oh., U.S. 214 41.01 N 81.21 W
Suffield, Canadian Forces Base ■ 184 50.15 N 111.10 W
Suffolk 208 36.43 N 76.35 W
Suffolk ◄⁸, Eng., U.K. 42 52.10 N 1.00 E
Suffolk □⁵, Ma., U.S. 207 42.21 N 71.04 W
Suffolk, Ruisseau ± 206 45.48 N 74.59 W
Süflän 128 38.17 N 45.59 E
Sufi-Kurgan 85 40.02 N 73.30 E
— Kashi 85 39.29 N 75.59 E
Suga-jima I 94 34.29 N 136.53 E
Sugana, Val ᴠ 64 46.00 N 11.40 E
Sugandha 272b 22.54 N 88.20 E
Sugandy 85 43.27 N 74.38 E
Sugano 268 35.44 N 139.56 E
Sugar ±, U.S. 190 45.24 N 89.12 W
Sugar ±, N.H., U.S. 188 43.24 N 72.24 W
Sugar ±, N.Y., U.S. 212 43.31 N 75.19 W
Sugar City 202 43.52 N 111.44 W
Sugarcreek, Oh., U.S. 214 40.30 N 81.39 W
Sugarcreek, Pa., U.S. 214 41.25 N 79.52 W
Sugar Creek ±, U.S. 216 40.47 N 87.45 W
Sugar Creek ±, Il., U.S. 194 40.09 N 89.38 W
Sugar Creek ±, Il., U.S. 219 38.28 N 89.37 W
Sugar Creek ±, Il., U.S. 219 39.48 N 89.32 W
Sugar Creek ±, In., U.S. 194 39.51 N 87.21 W
Sugar Creek ±, In., U.S. 218 39.21 N 86.00 W
Sugar Creek ±, Mi., U.S. 281 42.06 N 83.36 W
Sugar Creek ±, N.Y., U.S. 212 42.38 N 77.09 W
Sugar Creek ±, Oh., U.S. 214 40.31 N 81.28 W
Sugar Creek ±, Oh., U.S. 214 40.57 N 84.11 W
Sugar Creek ±, Oh., U.S. 218 39.27 N 83.25 W
Sugar Creek ±, Pa., U.S. 210 41.47 N 76.27 W
Sugar Creek ±, Wi., U.S. 216 42.43 N 88.19 W
Sugar Grove, Il., U.S. 216 41.45 N 88.27 W
Sugargrove, Pa., U.S. 214 41.59 N 79.21 W
Sugar Grove, Va., U.S. 192 36.46 N 81.24 W
Sugar Hill 192 34.06 N 84.02 W
Sugar Island I, On., Can. 212 44.26 N 77.17 W
Sugar Island I, Mi., U.S. 190 46.25 N 84.12 W
Sugar Land 222 29.37 N 95.38 W
Sugar Loaf 210 41.19 N 74.17 W
Sugar Loaf — Pão de Açúcar 287a 22.57 S 43.09 W
Sugarloaf ◄² 214 41.24 N 81.06 W
Sugarloaf Hill ◄ 274b 37.58 S 145.19 E
Sugarloaf Key I 220 24.40 N 81.32 W
Sugarloaf Mountain ▲, Ky., U.S. 218 38.13 N 83.32 W
Sugarloaf Mountain ▲, Me., U.S. 188 45.01 N 70.22 W
Sugar Loaf Mountain ▲, Md., U.S. 208 39.16 N 77.23 W
Sugar Loaf Mountain ▲, Ok., U.S. 208 35.02 N 94.28 W
Sugarloaf Mountain ▲² 220 28.39 N 81.44 W
Sugarloaf Peak ▲ 280 34.14 N 117.38 W
Sugar Loaf Point ►, Austl. 166 32.26 S 152.33 E
Sugar Loaf Point ►, On., Can. 284a 42.52 N 79.17 W
Sugarloaf Reservoir ◄ 169 37.41 S 145.18 E
Sugarloaf Ridge State Park ◆ 226 38.26 N 122.29 W
Sugar Notch 210 41.11 N 75.55 W
Sugar Pine Point State Park ◆ 226 39.03 N 120.07 W
Sugartown 285 40.00 N 75.31 W
Sugbai Passage ᴜ 116 5.22 N 120.33 E
Sugbay 116 7.31 N 123.19 E
Sugbuhan Point ► 116 10.04 N 126.04 E
Suggi Lake @ 184 54.22 N 102.47 W
Suginami ◄⁸ 268 35.23 N 139.38 E
Sugito 94 36.02 N 139.44 E
Şuğla Gölü @ 130 37.20 N 32.02 E
Sugnou 85 38.35 N 70.20 E
Sugod 116 12.03 N 124.09 E
Sugoj ± 74 64.15 N 154.29 E
Sugorovo 82 54.41 N 36.41 E
Sugozero 76 59.55 N 34.12 E
Sugurovo, Ross. 83 53.26 N 46.29 E
Sugurovo, Ross. 80 59.58 N 36.17 E
Sugut ± 112 6.26 N 117.43 E
Suguta ± 154 2.03 N 36.33 E
Suguti 154 1.44 S 33.39 E
Suhai Hu @ 102 38.50 N 94.00 E
Suhaitu 102 44.50 N 93.39 E
Suhār 128 24.22 N 56.45 E
Suheli Island I¹ 122 10.03 N 72.17 E
Suhl 54 50.36 N 10.41 E
Suhlendorf 54 52.55 N 10.46 E
Suhopolje 36 45.48 N 17.30 E
Suhr 58 47.23 N 8.05 E
Suhr ± 58 47.25 N 8.04 E
Suhum 150 6.05 N 0.27 W
Suhut 130 38.32 N 30.33 E
Šõi 120 28.37 N 69.19 E
Suiá-Miçu ± 250 11.13 S 53.15 W
Suianzhan 89 53.07 N 125.20 E
Suiattle ± 224 48.20 N 121.33 W
Suichang 100 28.34 N 119.14 E
Suichuan 100 26.30 N 114.32 E
Suichuan ± 100 26.30 N 114.45 E
Süide 102 37.32 N 110.12 E
Suiding 88 44.03 N 80.49 E
Suido-suigenchi ⊛¹ 270 34.54 N 135.17 E
Suidvaal 158 26.52 S 29.47 E
Suifenhe 98 44.24 N 131.10 E
Suifu, Nihon 94 36.37 N 140.29 E
Suifu — Yibin, Zhg. 107 28.47 N 104.38 E
Suigō-kokutei-kōen ◆ 94 36.00 N 140.20 E
Suigō-Tsukuba-kokutei-kōen ◆ 94 36.00 N 140.20 E
Suihua 102 46.38 N 126.59 E
Suijiang 102 28.31 N 104.07 E
Suijiang 89 48.17 N 121.12 E
Suining, Zhg. 100 33.54 N 117.56 E
Suining, Zhg. 107 30.31 N 105.34 E
Suippe ± 54 49.08 N 4.32 E
Suippes 50 49.08 N 4.32 E
Suir ± 48 52.15 N 7.00 W
Suisse — Switzerland □¹ 58 47.00 N 8.00 E
Suisun Bay ᴄ 226 38.07 N 122.02 W

Column 3

Suisun City 226 38.14 N 122.02 W
Suisun Creek ± 226 38.12 N 122.06 W
Suita 96 34.45 N 135.32 E
Suitland 284c 38.50 N 76.55 W
Suixi, Zhg. 100 33.56 N 116.46 E
Suixi, Zhg. 102 21.25 N 110.15 E
Suixian, Zhg. 100 34.26 N 115.05 E
Suixian, Zhg. 100 31.42 N 113.20 E
Suiyang, Zhg. 89 44.26 N 130.53 E
Suiyang, Zhg. 102 27.56 N 107.18 E
Suiyangdian 100 32.04 N 112.55 E
Suiza — Switzerland □¹ 58 47.00 N 8.00 E
Suize ± 58 48.08 N 5.08 E
Suizhong 102 40.20 N 120.19 E
Šuja, Ross. 24 61.55 N 34.12 E
Šuja, Ross. 80 56.50 N 41.23 E
Šuja ±, Ross. 24 61.54 N 34.15 E
Šuja ±, Ross. 80 57.56 N 43.15 E
Sujāngar 126 23.57 N 89.25 E
Sujāngarh 120 27.42 N 74.28 E
Sujāwal 120 24.36 N 68.05 E
Suji 107 29.35 N 103.57 E
Sujiabu 100 31.38 N 116.53 E
Sujiaqiao 105 39.24 N 116.10 E
Sujiatun 104 41.40 N 123.22 E
Sujiawu 105 29.48 N 104.57 E
Sujiawu 105 39.17 N 115.55 E
Sujiazui 100 33.40 N 119.29 E
Šujskoje 76 59.22 N 40.59 E
Sujutkina Kosa, mys 84 44.13 N 47.15 E
Sukabihanawa 112 9.30 S 124.57 E
Sukabumi 115a 6.55 S 106.56 E
Sukadana, Indon. 112 1.15 S 109.57 E
Sukadana, Indon. 115a 5.05 S 105.33 E
Sukadana, Teluk ᴄ 112 1.24 S 109.50 E
Sukagawa 92 37.17 N 140.23 E
Sukamandi 115a 6.20 S 107.39 E
Sukamara 112 2.43 S 111.11 E
Sukanegara 115a 7.06 S 107.07 E
Sukapura 115a 7.52 S 113.03 E
Sukaraja, Indon. 112 2.21 S 110.37 E
Sukaraja, Indon. 115a 7.27 S 108.12 E
Sukaraja, Indon. 115a 7.27 S 109.17 E
Sukarno, Pegunungan — Jaya, Puncak ▲ 164 4.05 S 137.11 E
Sukau 112 5.32 N 118.17 E
Sukchar 272b 22.42 N 88.22 E
Sukch'ŏn 98 39.24 N 125.38 E
Sukematsu 270 34.31 N 135.26 E
Sukeva 26 63.52 N 27.26 E
Sukhnah, 'Ayn ᴛ⁴ 142 29.35 N 32.15 E
Sukhothai 110 17.01 N 99.49 E
Sukhumi — Suchumi 84 43.01 N 41.02 E
Sukkertoppen (Maniitsoq) 176 65.25 N 52.53 W
Sukkozero 24 63.11 N 32.18 E
Sukla 120 27.42 N 68.52 E
Sukkwan Island I 182 55.05 N 132.45 W
Suklēra 126 23.11 N 86.21 E
Sukmanovka 78 51.47 N 41.34 E
Sukodadi 115a 7.06 S 112.19 E
Sukoharjo 115a 7.41 S 110.50 E
Sukovo 82 54.54 N 38.19 E
Sukroml'a 76 56.53 N 34.44 E
Suksun 86 57.07 N 57.24 E
Sukumo 92 32.56 N 132.44 E
Sukun, Pulau I 115b 8.07 S 122.08 E
Sukunka ± 182 55.37 N 121.37 W
Sul, Baía ᴄ 252 27.40 S 48.35 W
Sul, Canal do ᴜ 250 0.10 S 49.30 W
Sula ᴜ 26 61.08 N 4.55 E
Sula ±, Ross. 24 67.16 N 52.40 E
Sula ±, Ukr. 78 49.40 N 32.41 E
Sula, Kepulauan II 112 1.52 S 125.22 E
Sulaimān Khel 123 33.41 N 71.01 E
Sulaimān Range ◄ 120 30.30 N 70.10 E
Sulak, Ross. 84 50.52 N 48.21 E
Sulak, Ross. 84 43.16 N 47.32 E
Sulak ± 84 43.20 N 47.34 E
Sulakyurt 130 40.10 N 33.44 E
Sulat 116 11.49 N 125.27 E
Sulauan Point ► 116 8.37 N 124.29 E
Sulawesi (Celebes) I 112 2.00 S 121.00 E
Sulawesi Selatan □⁴ 112 3.30 S 120.00 E
Sulawesi Tengah □⁴ 112 1.00 N 123.00 E
Sulawesi Tenggara □⁴ 112 4.00 S 122.00 E
Sulawesi Utara □⁴ 112 0.30 N 124.00 E
Sulaymān, Birak (Solomon's Pools) I 132 31.41 N 35.10 E
Sulby 44 54.18 N 4.29 W
Sulcis ◄¹ 71 39.04 N 8.41 E
Suldalsvatnet @ 26 59.35 N 6.45 E
Süldeh 128 36.34 N 52.01 E
Sulechów 30 52.06 N 15.37 E
Sulęcin 30 52.26 N 15.08 E
Suleja 86 55.09 N 58.50 E
Sulejów 30 51.22 N 19.53 E
Sulejówek 92 52.14 N 21.17 E
Sule, Mount ▲ 164 3.25 S 142.15 E
Sule Skerry I² 46 59.05 N 4.26 W
Suleymaniye Mosque ◄¹ 267b 41.00 N 28.57 E
Süleymanli 130 37.54 N 36.50 E
Şulğino 82 53.48 N 40.14 E
Şul'ginka ± 83 49.08 N 38.56 E
Şul'gino, Ross. 82 54.33 N 37.35 E
Şulğino, Ross. 82 54.50 N 37.35 E
Sulima 150 6.58 N 11.35 W
Sulina 38 45.09 N 29.40 E
Sulina, Braţul ± 38 45.09 N 29.40 E
Sulina 38 48.54 N 40.07 E
Sulingen 52 52.41 N 8.48 E
Suliskij 24 67.52 N 40.06 E
Sulitelma ▲ 24 67.08 N 16.24 E
Sulitjelma 24 67.08 N 16.03 E
Sullana 248 4.53 S 80.41 W
Sulligent 194 33.54 N 88.08 W
Sullivan, Il., U.S. 194 39.35 N 88.36 W
Sullivan, In., U.S. 194 39.06 N 87.24 W
Sullivan, Mo., U.S. 194 38.12 N 91.09 W
Sullivan, Oh., U.S. 214 41.02 N 82.13 W
Sullivan, Wi., U.S. 216 43.00 N 88.35 W
Sullivan ◄⁶, N.Y., U.S. 210 41.39 N 74.42 W
Sullivan, Pa., U.S. 214 41.25 N 76.29 W
Sullivan Canyon ᴠ 280 34.03 N 118.30 W
Sullivan Lake @ 182 52.00 N 112.00 W
Sullivanville 210 42.14 N 76.46 W
Sully-sur-Loire 54 47.46 N 2.22 E
Sulmona 64 42.03 N 13.55 E
Sulot' ± 82 56.41 N 38.01 E
Sulphur, Yk., Can. 182 63.33 N 139.50 W
Sulphur ±, U.S. 194 31.14 N 89.10 W
Sulphur ±, U.S. 194 33.05 N 93.42 W
Sulphur Creek ± 196 33.12 N 102.17 W
Sulphur Draw ᴠ 196 33.12 N 102.17 W
Sulphur Springs, Oh., U.S. 214 40.52 N 82.52 W
Sulphur Springs, Tx., U.S. 194 33.08 N 95.36 W

Column 4

Sulphur Springs Draw ᴠ 196 32.12 N 101.36 W
Sulphur Springs Valley ᴠ 200 31.50 N 109.50 W
Sulsul 144 5.06 N 44.55 E
Sultan ± 224 47.51 N 121.48 W
Sultan ± 224 47.52 N 121.49 W
Sultana 226 36.33 N 119.20 W
Sultanahmet Mosque ◄¹ 267b 41.00 N 28.58 E
Sultan Alonto, Lake @ 116 7.53 N 124.15 E
Sultana Point ► 168b 35.08 S 137.45 E
Sultanabad ◄⁸ 267d 35.46 N 51.28 E
Sultançiftligi ◄⁸ 267h 41.02 N 29.13 E
Sultandağı 130 38.32 N 31.14 E
Sultan Dağı ▲ 130 38.58 N 27.26 E
Sultanhisar 130 38.15 N 33.33 E
Sultanhisar 130 37.53 N 28.10 E
Sultan Kudarat 116 7.17 N 124.16 E
Sultan Kudarat □⁴ 116 6.20 N 124.20 E
Sultan Mosque ◄¹ 271c 1.18 N 103.52 E
Sultānpur, India 123 31.13 N 75.11 E
Sultānpur, India 124 26.16 N 82.04 E
Sultānpur Dabās ◄⁸ 272a 28.46 N 77.03 E
Sultan sa Barongis 116 6.46 N 124.38 E
Sultan-Saly 83 47.31 N 39.35 E
Sulu 164 5.25 S 151.00 E
Sulu ◄⁴ 116 6.00 N 121.00 E
Sulu ᴜ 116 8.00 N 120.00 E
Suluan Island I 116 10.46 N 125.57 E
Sulu Archipelago II 116 6.00 N 121.00 E
Sulu Basin ◄¹ 12 8.00 N 121.30 E
Sülüklü 130 38.12 N 86.20 E
Sül'ukta 85 39.56 N 69.34 E
Sulutta 144 9.10 N 38.48 E
Suluntah 146 32.36 N 21.43 E
Suluova 130 40.47 N 35.42 E
Suluq 146 31.39 N 20.15 E
Sulusaj 85 40.00 N 36.06 E
Sulusaray 130 40.00 N 36.06 E
Sulu Sea ᴛ² 116 8.00 N 120.00 E
Suly 86 53.45 N 66.30 E
Sulz 88 48.18 N 7.51 E
Sulz am Neckar 58 48.21 N 8.37 E
Sulzano 64 45.41 N 10.05 E
Sulzbach, Dtsch. 58 49.00 N 9.30 E
Sulzbach, Dtsch. 56 49.18 N 7.07 E
Sulzbach ± 58 48.36 N 13.02 E
Sulzbach am Kocher 58 48.58 N 9.50 E
Sulzbach-Rosenberg 60 49.30 N 11.45 E
Sulzberg Bay ᴄ 9 77.00 S 152.00 W
Sulzbrunn 58 47.41 N 10.20 E
Sulze ± 52 52.22 N 10.02 E
Sulzemoos 58 48.20 N 11.19 E
Sum, Ross. 76 59.52 N 31.46 E
Sum, Ross. 88 54.51 N 95.18 E
Sumatera (Sumatra) 270 34.39 N 135.08 E
Šumadija ◄¹ 38 44.10 N 20.50 E
Sumalata 112 0.59 N 121.05 W
Sumampa 252 29.22 S 63.28 W
Sumanj 86 42.37 N 59.08 E
Sumangat, Tanjong ► 116 6.35 N 117.33 E
Sūmār 128 34.38 N 135.08 E
Sūmār 128 33.52 N 45.39 E
Sumarokovo 82 55.46 N 35.55 E
Sumas 224 49.00 N 122.15 W
Sumatera (Sumatra) I 108 0.05 S 102.00 E
Sumatera Barat □⁴ 112 0.30 S 100.30 E
Sumatera Selatan □⁴ 112 3.00 S 104.00 E
Sumatera Utara □⁴ 114 2.20 N 99.00 E
Sum'atino 82 55.00 N 36.21 E
Sumatou 107 30.28 N 104.03 E
Sumatra — Sumatera I 108 0.05 S 102.00 E
Sumava Resorts 281 41.10 N 87.26 W
Sumayh 140 12.43 N 30.50 E
Sumba I 115b 10.00 S 120.00 E
Sumba, Île I 152 1.44 N 19.32 E
Sumba, Selat ᴜ 115b 9.05 S 120.00 E
Sumbar ± 128 38.00 N 55.17 E
Sumbawa I 115b 8.40 S 118.00 E
Sumbawa Besar 115b 8.30 S 117.26 E
Sumbawanga 154 7.58 S 31.37 E
Sumbay 248 15.58 S 71.23 W
Sumbe 116 11.13 S 13.50 E
Sümber 90 46.21 N 108.20 E
Sumbilla 58 43.10 N 1.40 W
Sumbing, Gunung ▲ 115a 7.23 S 110.04 E
Sumbu National Park ◆ 154 4.00 S 120.00 E
Sumburgh Head ► 46a 59.53 N 1.20 W
Sumburgh Roost ᴜ 46a 59.49 N 1.19 W
Sumbut 80 55.33 N 50.41 E
Sumbuya 150 7.39 N 11.58 W
Sumdo 120 35.01 N 78.41 E
Sumé 250 7.39 S 36.55 W
Sumedang 115a 6.52 S 107.55 E
Sümeg 60 46.59 N 17.17 E
Sumen 38 43.16 N 26.55 E
Şümeni 115a 7.01 S 113.52 E
Sumenep 115a 7.01 S 113.52 E
Sumgait 84 40.36 N 49.38 E
Sumiainen 84 40.36 N 49.38 E
Sumicha 86 55.14 N 63.19 E
Sumida ◄⁸ 268 35.43 N 139.49 E
Sumidouro 254 22.03 S 42.41 W
Sumilao 116 8.18 N 124.57 E
Šumilinskaja 78 49.21 N 41.26 E
Suminoe ◄⁸ 270 34.36 N 135.28 E
Sumisu-jima I 92 31.27 N 140.03 E
Sumiswald 58 47.02 N 7.45 E
Sumiyoshi ◄⁸ 270 34.36 N 135.31 E
Sumiyoshi ◄⁸ 270 34.42 N 135.29 E
Sumkino 86 58.09 N 68.21 E
Sumlog ◄⁵ 116 6.53 N 126.02 E
Summer Bridge 44 54.03 N 1.41 W
Summerdale 208 40.18 N 76.56 W
Summerfield, Fl., U.S. 220 29.00 N 82.02 W
Summerfield, Mo., U.S. 219 38.17 N 91.49 W
Summerfield, N.C., U.S. 192 36.12 N 79.54 W
Summerford, Nf., Can. 186 49.29 N 54.47 W
Summerford, Oh., U.S. 218 39.55 N 83.29 W
Summerhill, Ire. 48 53.29 N 6.44 W
Summerhill, Pa., U.S. 214 40.22 N 78.46 W
Summer Island I 190 45.34 N 86.39 W
Summer Isles II 46 58.02 N 5.28 W
Summerland 182 49.36 N 119.41 W
Summerland Reserve ◆ 169 38.31 S 145.10 E
Summer Palace ◄¹ 267b 40.00 N 116.16 E
Summerseat 262 53.00 S 29.55 E
Summersville, Mo., U.S. 219 37.10 N 91.39 W
Summersville, W.V., U.S. 194 38.16 N 80.51 W
Summerton, On., Can. 275b 43.37 N 79.34 W
Summerton 192 33.36 N 80.21 W
Summerville, Ga., U.S. 192 34.28 N 85.20 W
Summerville, Pa., U.S. 214 41.06 N 79.11 W
Summerville, S.C., U.S. 192 33.01 N 80.11 W

Column 5

Summit, Eng., U.K. 262 53.40 N 2.05 W
Summit, Ak., U.S. 180 63.20 N 149.08 W
Summit, Ca., U.S. 228 34.20 N 117.25 W
Summit, Il., U.S. 216 41.47 N 87.48 W
Summit, Ms., U.S. 194 31.17 N 90.28 W
Summit, N.J., U.S. 210 40.44 N 74.21 W
Summit, N.Y., U.S. 210 42.35 N 74.35 W
Summit, S.D., U.S. 198 45.18 N 97.02 W
Summit, Wa., U.S. 224 47.10 N 122.21 W
Summit ± 214 41.05 N 81.31 W
Summit Creek ± 224 46.00 N 121.10 W
Summit Farms 284b 39.19 N 76.32 W
Summit Hill 210 40.49 N 75.52 W
Summit Lake 182 54.17 N 122.38 W
Summit Lake @ 224 48.27 N 124.07 W
Summit Mountain ▲ 204 39.23 N 116.28 W
Summit Park 276 41.09 N 74.03 W
Summit Park Mall ◄¹ 284a 43.05 N 78.56 W
Summit Peak ▲ 200 37.21 N 106.42 W
Summit Rock ▲ 172 45.25 S 170.04 E
Summit Station 208 40.34 N 76.12 W
Summitville, In., U.S. 216 40.20 N 85.38 W
Summitville, N.Y., U.S. 210 41.37 N 74.27 W
Summit 214 40.10 N 80.53 W
Summit 264d 52.41 N 13.22 E
Summter See @ 264d 52.42 N 13.23 E
Šumná 61 48.56 N 15.52 E
Sumnal 120 35.45 N 78.40 E
Sumner, Ia., U.S. 190 42.50 N 92.05 W
Sumner, Ms., U.S. 194 33.58 N 90.22 W
Sumner, Wa., U.S. 224 47.12 N 122.14 W
Sumner, Lake @¹ 172 42.42 S 172.13 E
Sumner, Lake @¹ 196 34.38 N 104.25 W
Sumner Lake State Park ◆ 196 34.38 N 104.24 W
Sumner Strait ᴜ 180 56.15 N 133.45 W
Sumoto 96 34.21 N 134.54 E
Šumpanginangae 112 4.24 S 119.36 E
Sumperk 30 49.58 N 17.00 E
Sumpiuh 115a 7.37 S 109.21 E
Sumprabum 110 26.33 N 97.34 E
Sumpter 281 42.10 N 83.29 W
Sumrall 194 31.25 N 89.32 W
Sumsar 85 41.18 N 71.19 E
Š'umsi 80 57.07 N 51.37 E
Šumskij Posad 24 64.15 N 35.25 E
Šumskoje 78 54.58 N 20.57 E
Šumšu, ostrov I 74 50.45 N 156.20 E
Sumter 192 33.55 N 80.20 W
Sumter □⁶ 220 28.38 N 82.08 W
Sumusță al-Waqf 142 28.55 N 30.51 E
Sumy 78 50.54 N 34.45 E
Sumzom 102 29.45 N 96.10 E
Sun ±, Ross. 78 55.44 N 54.16 E
Sun ±, Mt., U.S. 202 47.30 N 111.19 W
Sun ±, Zhg. 89 29.13 N 106.21 E
Suna, Kenya 154 1.05 S 34.26 E
Suna ±, Ross. 80 57.51 N 50.05 E
Sunagawa 92 43.29 N 141.55 E
Sun al-Heteimi ᴛ⁴ 132 31.05 N 34.02 E
Sun' al-Menī'ì ᴛ⁴ 132 31.07 N 34.12 E
Sunam 123 30.08 N 75.48 E
Sunamganj 120 25.04 N 91.24 E
Sunami 94 35.25 N 136.40 E
Sunapee Lake @ 188 43.23 N 72.03 W
Sunart, Loch ᴄ 46 56.41 N 5.43 W
Sunashinden 268 35.53 N 139.30 E
Sunbât 142 30.48 N 31.12 E
Sunbight 192 36.14 N 84.40 W
Sunbury, Austl. 169 37.35 S 144.44 E
Sunbury, Eng., U.K. 260 51.24 N 0.26 W
Sunbury, N.C., U.S. 192 36.26 N 76.36 W
Sunbury, Oh., U.S. 214 40.14 N 82.51 W
Sunbury, Pa., U.S. 208 40.51 N 76.47 W
Sunch'ang 98 35.23 N 127.07 E
Sunchild Indian Reserve ◄⁴ 182 52.43 N 115.24 W
Sünching 60 48.53 N 12.21 E
Suncho Corral 252 27.56 S 63.27 W
Sunch'ŏn, C.M.I.K. 98 39.26 N 125.54 E
Sunch'ŏn, Taehan 98 34.57 N 127.28 E
Sun City, Az., U.S. 200 33.35 N 112.16 W
Sun City, Ca., U.S. 226 33.42 N 117.11 W
Sun City, Fl., U.S. 220 27.40 N 82.28 W
Sun City Center 220 27.43 N 82.21 W
Suncook 188 43.07 N 71.27 W
Suncook ± 188 43.08 N 71.28 W
Sunda, Selat (Sunda Strait) ᴜ 112 6.00 S 105.45 E
Sundae 198 44.24 N 104.22 W
Sundar 112 4.54 N 115.12 E
Sundar 124 29.44 N 78.56 E
Sundarbans ◄¹ 126 21.35 N 89.20 E
Sundargarh 120 22.07 N 84.02 E
Sundarnagar 123 31.32 N 76.53 E
Sunda Shelf ◄¹ 12 5.00 N 107.00 E
Sunda Strait — Sunda, Selat ᴜ 112 6.00 S 105.45 E
Sunday Creek ± 169 37.02 S 145.05 E
Sundby, Dan. 41 54.42 N 11.48 E
Sundby, Sve. 41 54.42 N 13.02 E
Sundbyberg 41 59.22 N 17.58 E
Sundbyholm 41 59.22 N 16.24 E
Sundbyholm slott ◄¹ 41 59.22 N 16.24 E
Sunde 42 59.50 N 5.43 E
Sunderland, On., Can. 212 44.16 N 79.04 W
Sunderland, Eng., U.K. 44 54.55 N 1.23 W
Sunderland, Ma., U.S. 207 42.28 N 72.34 W
Sundern, Vt., U.S. 210 43.06 N 73.06 W
Sundern 54 51.20 N 8.00 E
Sünderup 44 54.47 N 9.27 E
Sundhausen 54 50.56 N 7.36 E
Sundi-Lutete 152 4.34 S 14.14 E
Sundown, Austl. 168 26.33 S 133.12 E
Sundown, N.Y., U.S. 210 41.54 N 74.27 W
Sundown, Tx., U.S. 196 33.27 N 102.29 W
Sundre 182 51.48 N 114.38 W
Sundre 41 57.08 N 18.26 E
Sundridge, On., Can. 212 45.46 N 79.24 W
Sundridge, Eng., U.K. 260 51.17 N 0.08 E
Sundsbruk 41 62.27 N 17.18 E
Sundsvall 24 62.23 N 17.18 E
Sundwig 263 51.23 N 7.47 E
Suneori 263 51.13 N 7.30 E
Sunfield 216 42.46 N 84.59 W
Sunfish Creek ± 218 39.01 N 80.53 W
Sunflower ± 194 32.39 N 90.32 W
Sunflower, Mount ▲ 198 39.01 N 102.02 W
Sungai ± 114 2.55 S 116.18 E
Sungaibamban 114 1.09 N 102.10 E
Sungai Bayor 114 5.15 N 100.47 E
Sungaigerong 114 3.00 S 104.52 E

Column 6

Sungai Petani 114 5.39 N 100.30 E
Sungaipinang 112 0.48 S 114.04 E
Sungairampah 114 3.29 N 99.09 E
Sungairotan, Indon. 112 1.39 S 102.51 E
Sungairotan, Indon. 112 3.06 S 104.18 E
Sungaisalak 112 0.27 S 102.59 E
Sungaiselan 112 2.24 S 105.59 E
Sungai Siput 114 4.49 N 101.04 E
Sungaitampang 114 2.20 N 100.07 E
Sungaitiram 112 0.47 S 117.12 E
Sungaj 80 48.32 N 46.46 E
Sungari — Songhua ± 89 47.44 N 132.32 E
Sungchiang — Songjiang 106 31.01 N 121.14 E
Sungezhuang 105 40.15 N 116.39 E
Sungguminasa 112 5.12 S 119.27 E
Sungi 115b 8.38 S 115.06 E
Sungi Point ► 115b 10.55 S 125.50 E
Sungkai 114 3.58 N 101.18 E
Sung Kong I 271d 22.11 N 114.17 E
Sung Noen 110 14.54 N 101.50 E
Sungsang 112 2.22 S 104.56 E
Sungshan Domestic Airport ◄ 269d 25.04 N 121.33 E
Sunglao ◄⁸ 130 40.10 N 34.23 E
Sungurlu 130 40.10 N 34.23 E
Sunja 36 45.21 N 16.34 E
Sunjiabu 106 30.55 N 118.54 E
Sunjiadizi 104 42.09 N 124.09 E
Sunjiagou 104 40.45 N 120.39 E
Sunjiajang 105 40.10 N 115.32 E
Sunjiamao 104 42.42 N 123.02 E
Sunjiawan 104 41.59 N 121.42 E
Sunjiazhai 106 30.55 N 121.52 E
Sunjikôy 114 12.20 N 29.46 E
Sunkwar, gora ▲ 86 44.15 N 73.50 E
Sunken Meadow State Park ◆ 207 40.54 N 73.16 W
Sunköll ᴄ 124 26.55 N 87.09 E
Sunland ◄⁸ 280 34.16 N 118.19 W
Sunland Park 200 32.15 N 106.45 W
Sunlight Creek ± 244 44.47 N 109.23 W
Sunlongswan 104 41.19 N 122.57 E
Sunman 218 39.14 N 85.05 W
Sunnansjö 40 60.13 N 14.57 E
Sundalsøra 26 62.40 N 8.33 E
Sunne 40 59.50 N 13.09 E
Sunnemo 40 59.55 N 13.43 E
Sunnersta 40 59.48 N 17.39 E
Sunnī, Khawr ᴠ 140 7.09 N 28.41 E
Sunningdale 260 51.24 N 0.38 W
Sunninghill 42 51.25 N 0.40 W
Sunnybrae 45 45.24 N 62.30 W
Sunny Corner 170 33.23 S 149.53 E
Sunny Crest 279 43.33 N 87.42 W
Sunnydale 224 47.28 N 122.20 W
Sunnyland 216 47.39 N 82.29 W
Sunnylvsfjorden ᴄ² 26 62.17 N 7.01 E
Sunnymead 228 33.56 N 117.14 W
Sunnyside, Nf., Can. 186 47.51 N 53.55 W
Sunny Side, Tx., U.S. 222 32.40 N 117.01 W
Sunnyside, Ut., U.S. 200 39.33 N 110.23 W
Sunnyside, Wa., U.S. 202 46.19 N 120.00 W
Sunnyside ▲ 276 41.03 N 73.52 W
Sunnyslope, Ab., Can. 182 51.40 N 113.32 W
Sunnyslope, Wa., U.S. 224 47.30 N 122.44 W
Sunnyvale, Ca., U.S. 226 37.22 N 122.02 W
Sunnyvale, Tx., U.S. 222 32.48 N 96.33 W
Sunol 226 37.36 N 121.53 W
Sunol Ridge ▲ 278 38.47 N 121.54 W
Sun Prairie 216 43.11 N 89.12 W
Sunray 196 36.01 N 101.49 W
Sunrise, Ky., U.S. 218 38.33 N 84.14 W
Sunrise, Tx., U.S. 282 31.17 N 96.53 W
Sunrise, Wy., U.S. 198 42.19 N 104.42 W
Sunrise Heights 224 42.18 N 85.09 W
Sunrise Manor 204 36.08 N 115.04 W
Sunrise Peak ▲ 226 46.20 N 121.46 W
Sun River Terrace 216 41.06 N 87.45 W
Sunset, La., U.S. 194 30.24 N 92.04 W
Sunset, Tx., U.S. 196 33.27 N 97.46 W
Sunset Bay ᴄ 214 41.09 N 79.24 W
Sunset Beach, Ca., U.S. 280 33.43 N 118.04 W
Sunset Beach, Hi., U.S. 229c 21.40 N 158.02 W
Sunset Country ◄¹ 165 35.00 S 141.30 E
Sunset Crater National Monument ◆ 200 35.18 N 111.21 W
Sunset Heights 200 31.53 N 102.22 W
Sunset Hill 276 40.35 N 80.15 W
Sunset Hills 279b 40.35 N 80.05 W
Sunset Prairie 182 55.50 N 120.48 W
Sunset Valley 282 30.14 N 97.49 W
Sunshine, Austl. 166 37.47 S 144.50 E
Sunshine, Austl. 169 37.47 S 144.50 E
Sunshine Island I 271d 22.16 N 114.03 E
Sunshine Point ► 281 42.36 N 87.42 W
Sunshine Skyway Bridge ◄ 220 27.37 N 82.39 W
Suntar 74 62.10 N 117.40 E
Suntar-Chajata, chrebet ▲ 74 62.00 N 143.00 E
Suntaug Lake @ 283 42.32 N 71.00 W
Süntel ▲ 52 52.15 N 9.28 E
Sun Temple ◄¹ 273c 29.50 N 31.15 E
Sunter, Kali ± 266 6.07 S 106.50 E
Sunti ± 272b 22.37 N 88.34 E
Suntrana 180 63.51 N 148.51 W
Suntsar 128 25.31 N 62.02 E
Suntu 144 8.06 N 36.57 E
Sun Valley, Id., U.S. 202 43.41 N 114.21 W
Sun Valley, Nv., U.S. 226 39.34 N 119.42 W
Sun Valley Center ◄⁹ 278 37.58 N 122.03 W
Sun Village 228 34.30 N 117.55 W
Sunwi-do I 98 37.44 N 125.15 E
Sunwu 102 49.27 N 127.21 E
— Jiangmen 100 22.35 N 113.05 E
Sunyani 150 7.20 N 2.20 W
Sunying 105 34.30 N 114.21 E
Sunža ± 84 43.21 N 45.00 E
Sunženskij chrebet ▲ 84 43.15 N 45.00 E
Suō-nada ᴄ² 96 33.50 N 131.30 E
Suomussalmi 24 64.53 N 28.55 E
Suonenjoki 24 62.37 N 27.08 E
Suŏntee @ 26 61.39 N 26.26 E
Suŏrva 24 67.40 N 18.12 E
Suoshu 107 31.57 N 119.00 E
Supachai 248 19.29 S 64.51 W
Supamo ± 246 6.48 N 61.50 W
Supaul 126 26.07 N 86.36 E
Supe 248 8.37 S 135.58 E

Symbols in the index entries represent the broad categories identified in the key at the right. Symbols with superior numbers (◄¹) identify subcategories (see complete key on page I · 1).

Symbole im Register stellen die rechts im Schlüssel erklärten Kategorien dar. Symbole mit hochgestellten Ziffern (◄¹) bezeichnen Unterteilungen einer Kategorie (vgl. vollständiger Schlüssel auf Seite I · 1).

Los símbolos incluídos en el texto del índice representan las grandes categorías identificadas con la clave a la derecha. Los símbolos con numeros en su parte superior (◄¹) identican las subcategorias (véase la clave completa en la página I · 1).

Les symboles de l'index représentent les catégories indiquées dans la légende à droite. Les symboles suivis d'un indice (◄¹) représentent des sous-catégories (voir légende complète à la page I · 1).

Os símbolos incluídos no texto do índice representam as grandes categorias identificadas com a chave à direita. Os símbolos com números em sua parte superior (◄¹) identicam as subcategorias (veja-se a chave completa à página I · 1).

Symbol					
▲	Mountain	Berg	Montaña	Montagne	Montanha
▲	Mountains	Gebirge	Montañas	Montagnes	Montanhas
ᴘ	Pass	Paß	Paso	Col	Passo
ᴠ	Valley, Canyon	Tal, Cañon	Valle, Cañón	Vallée, Canyon	Vale, Canhão
▶	Plain	Ebene	Llano	Plaine	Planície
►	Cape	Kap	Cabo	Cap	Cabo
I	Island	Insel	Isla	Île	Ilha
II	Islands	Inseln	Islas	Îles	Ilhas
⊥	Other Topographic Features	Andere Topographische Objekte	Otros Elementos Topográficos	Autres données topographiques	Outros acidentes topográficos

ESPAÑOL — Nombre	Página	Lat.	Long. W=Oeste
Superga, Basilica di ▪¹	62	45.05 N	7.46 E
Superior, Az., U.S.	200	33.17 N	111.05 W
Superior, Mt., U.S.	202	47.11 N	114.53 W
Superior, Ne., U.S.	198	40.01 N	98.04 W
Superior, Wi., U.S.	190	46.43 N	92.06 W
Superior, Laguna ⊘	234	16.20 N	94.55 W
Superior, Lake ⊘	190	48.00 N	88.00 W
Superior Lake ⊘	228	35.15 N	117.02 W
Superior Valley V	228	35.16 N	117.00 W
Supersano	68	40.01 N	18.14 E
Supetar	36	43.23 N	16.33 E
Suphan Buri	110	14.28 N	100.07 E
Suphan Buri ╪	110	13.29 N	100.17 E
Süphan Dağı ▲	84	38.56 N	42.50 E
Supino	66	41.37 N	13.14 E
Supiori I	124	0.45 S	135.30 E
Süpkhär	124	22.12 N	80.56 E
Supoj ⊘	78	49.36 N	31.48 E
Suponevo	107	30.40 N	103.59 E
Supoqiao	107	30.40 N	103.59 E
Supraśl	52	52.14 N	10.54 E
Supraśl ╪	30	53.04 N	22.56 E
Sup'ung ⊘	98	40.27 N	124.57 E
Sup'ung-chösuji ⊘¹	98	40.30 N	125.05 E
Supur	126	23.01 N	86.52 E
Suputinskij zapovednik ♦	89	43.40 N	132.20 E
Sūq-'Abs	140	15.55 N	43.04 E
Süq ash-Shuyūkh	128	30.53 N	46.28 E
Süq at al-Jamal	140	12.48 N	27.42 E
Suqian	100	33.09 N	118.18 E
Suqiao, Zhg.	100	34.08 N	113.47 E
Suqiao, Zhg.	105	39.03 N	116.29 E
Süq Suwayq	124	24.23 N	38.27 E
Suquamish	224	47.43 N	122.33 W
Suquträ (Socotra) I	118	12.30 N	54.00 E
Sür (Tyre), Lubnän	132	33.16 N	35.11 E
Sür, 'Umän	118	22.35 N	59.31 E
Sur, Cabo >	174z	27.12 S	109.26 W
Sur, Campos de Hielo ⋈	254	49.10 S	73.30 W
Sur, Canal ╪	288	34.37 S	58.15 W
Sur, Point >	226	36.18 N	121.54 W
Sura	80	53.53 N	45.45 E
Sura ≈	272b	22.33 N	88.25 E
Sura ≈	80	56.06 N	46.00 E
Sura, Cape >	144	11.10 N	47.30 E
Şūrāb, Pāk.	128	28.29 N	66.16 E
Şūrab, Taj.	85	40.03 N	70.33 E
Surabaya	115a	7.15 S	112.45 E
S'urachi, Nuraghe ⊥	71	40.01 N	8.33 E
Surad	142	30.59 N	30.54 E
Surag-san ▲	271b	37.42 N	127.04 E
Surahammar	40	59.43 N	16.13 E
Sürek	128	25.43 N	58.48 E
Surekarta	115a	7.35 S	110.50 E
Suramana	112	0.50 S	119.33 E
Surami	84	42.01 N	43.34 E
Şūrān, Īrān	128	27.18 N	62.04 E
Şūrān, Ross.	80	55.22 N	49.50 E
Şūrān, Sūrīy.	130	36.34 N	37.13 E
Şūrān, Sūrīy.	130	35.17 N	36.45 E
Şuran ≈	58	46.02 N	5.19 E
Şüreny	38	48.06 N	18.14 E
Surer	144	7.27 N	40.57 E
Surat, Austl.	168	27.09 S	149.04 E
Sürat, India	120	21.10 N	72.50 E
Süratgarh	123	29.19 N	73.54 E
Suret Thani (Ban Don)	110	9.08 N	99.19 E
Sureva	80	52.57 N	41.18 E
Suraž, Bela.	56	55.25 N	30.44 E
Suraż, Pol.	30	52.58 N	22.58 E
Suraž, Ross.	76	53.01 N	32.24 E
Surbiton ●⁸	260	51.24 N	0.18 W
Surbo	68	40.24 N	18.08 E
Surbourg	56	48.55 N	7.51 E
Surchan	86	46.39 N	49.38 E
Surchandarja □⁴	85	38.00 N	67.30 E
Surchandarja ≈	85	37.58 N	67.50 E
Surchdara	85	38.37 N	69.55 E
Surchob ≈	85	38.53 N	70.03 E
Surči	85	37.59 N	67.47 E
Surco ≈	286d	12.13 S	77.03 W
Surculica ≈	38	42.41 N	22.10 E
Sûre (Sauer) ≈	56	49.44 N	6.31 E
Şureanu, Munţii ▲	38	45.35 N	23.27 E
Süreksor, ozero ⊘	86	52.16 N	75.50 E
Surendorf	41	54.28 N	10.04 E
Surendranagar	120	22.42 N	71.41 E
Suresnes	261	48.52 N	2.14 E
Suretka	236	9.34 N	82.56 W
Surf City	208	39.39 N	74.09 W
Surfers Paradise	171a	28.00 S	153.25 E
Surfside, Fl., U.S.	220	25.52 N	80.07 W
Surfside, Tx., U.S.	222	28.57 N	95.17 W
Surgères	32	46.07 N	0.45 W
Surgidero	240p	22.41 N	82.18 W
Surgijn ≈	88	47.20 N	95.50 E
Surgoinsville	192	36.28 N	82.51 W
Surgut	130	38.01 N	37.59 E
Sürgücü	130	37.35 N	40.44 E
Surgut	74	61.14 N	73.20 E
Surhuisterveen	52	53.10 N	6.10 E
Suri	164	7.10 S	143.55 E
Surie	272b	22.51 N	88.33 E
Suriápet	122	17.09 N	79.37 E
Suribachi-yama ▲¹	174f	24.45 N	141.17 E
Surigao	116	9.45 N	125.30 E
Surigao ≈	116	9.45 N	125.30 E
Surigao del Norte □⁴	116	9.35 N	125.36 E
Surigao del Sur □⁴	116	9.00 N	126.00 E
Suriçao Strait ⊃	116	10.15 N	125.23 E
Surikova	86	56.59 N	91.31 E
Suriram	110	14.53 N	103.29 E
— Suriname	244	4.00 N	56.00 W
Suriname □¹, S.A.	242	4.00 N	56.00 W
Suriname □¹, S.A.	250	4.00 N	56.00 W
Surinda	88	55.13 N	113.23 E
Suring	190	44.59 N	88.22 W
Sürīyah — Syria □¹	128	35.00 N	38.00 E
S'urkum	89	50.04 N	140.31 E
S'urkum, mys >	89	50.05 N	140.41 E
Surra	56	58.58 N	50.21 E
Sürmaq	128	31.03 N	52.48 E
Surmelin ≈	54	49.04 N	3.31 E
Surnadalsøra	42	62.56 N	8.39 E
Surodadi	115a	6.53 S	109.15 E
Surovaticha	80	55.45 N	43.56 E
Surovikino	80	48.36 N	42.51 E
Surovo	88	53.50 N	105.36 E
Surprise	200	33.37 N	112.19 W
Surprise, Lake ⊘	222	29.33 N	94.41 W
Surprise Valley V	204	41.35 N	120.05 W
Surquillo	286d	12.07 S	77.02 W
Surrency	192	31.43 N	82.11 W
Surrey	198	48.14 N	101.07 W
Surrey □⁸	260	51.14 N	0.20 W
Surrey, University of ↳	260	51.14 N	0.36 W
Surrey Heath □⁸	260	51.21 N	0.40 W
Sursee	58	47.10 N	8.06 E
Sursés ⊘¹	58	46.34 N	9.36 E
Sursk	80	53.04 N	45.42 E
Surskij Majdan	80	55.01 N	46.48 E
Surskoje	80	54.30 N	46.44 E
Surt	146	31.12 N	16.35 E
Surt, Khalīj (Gulf of Sidra) ⊂	146	31.30 N	18.00 E
Surtainville	28	49.31 N	111.05 W
Surtanähu	120	26.22 N	70.00 E
Surte	26	57.49 N	12.01 E
Surtsey I	24a	63.16 N	20.32 W
Suru	164	63.55 S	144.45 W

FRANÇAIS — Nom	Page	Lat.	Long. W=Ouest
Suru	123	34.45 N	76.12 E
Surubiú ≈	250	3.58 S	48.52 W
Sürüç	130	36.58 N	38.24 E
Suruga-wan ⊂	94	34.51 N	138.33 E
Surui	256	22.40 S	43.07 W
Surui	287a	22.45 S	43.07 W
Surulangun	112	2.37 S	102.45 E
Suru-Lere ●⁸	273a	6.31 N	3.22 E
Surumu ≈	246	3.22 N	60.19 W
Surveyor Creek ≈	198	40.20 N	102.38 W
Surveyor Point >	168b	34.47 S	137.51 E
Survilliers	261	49.06 N	2.33 E
Surwold	52	53.00 N	7.30 E
Sury-le-Comtal	54	45.32 N	4.10 E
Şürýškary	74	65.54 N	65.22 E
Susa, It.	62	45.08 N	7.03 E
Susa, Nihon	96	34.37 N	131.36 E
Susâ ≈	41	55.11 N	11.46 E
Susa, Valle di V	62	45.09 N	7.10 E
Süsah	146	32.54 N	21.58 E
Susak, Otok I	36	44.31 N	14.18 E
Susaki	96	33.23 N	133.17 E
Susami	96	33.33 N	135.30 E
Susamyr	85	42.09 N	73.58 E
Susamyr ≈	85	42.08 N	74.03 E
Susamyrtau, chrebet ▲	85	42.08 N	73.15 E
Susan ≈	208	37.22 N	76.19 W
Susan	204	40.19 N	120.17 W
Susana, Port ⊂	224	48.10 N	122.25 W
Susana Knolls	228	34.16 N	118.41 W
Süsangerd	128	31.34 N	48.11 E
Susanino, Ross.	76	58.09 N	41.36 E
Susanino, Ross.	80	58.09 N	41.36 E
Susanino, Ross.	89	52.47 N	140.06 E
Susano	256	23.32 S	46.20 W
Susano ≈⁷	287b	23.35 S	46.18 W
Susanville	204	40.24 N	120.39 W
Šušary, Ross.	265a	59.46 N	30.21 E
Šušary, Ross.	265a	59.48 N	30.23 E
Susch	58	46.46 N	10.04 E
Susegana	64	45.51 N	12.15 E
Sușehri	130	40.11 N	38.06 E
Şüşef	54	54.04 N	10.43 E
Šušenskoje	86	53.19 N	91.58 E
Sušice	30	49.14 N	13.32 E
Susitna	180	61.33 N	150.30 W
Susitna ≈	180	61.16 N	150.30 W
Susleny	38	47.25 N	28.59 E
Suslonger	80	56.18 N	48.13 E
Sušn'aki Pervoje	86	57.53 N	68.47 E
Susobana ≈	94	36.37 N	138.11 E
Susoh	114	3.43 N	96.50 E
Susong	100	30.09 N	116.06 E
Susono	94	35.09 N	138.54 E
Suspiro del Moro, Puerto del ✗	34	37.04 N	3.39 W
Susquehanna	210	41.56 N	75.36 W
Susquehanna ≈⁶	210	41.50 N	75.50 W
Susquehanna ≈	188	39.30 N	78.05 W
Susquehanna, West Branch ≈	210	40.53 N	76.47 W
Susquehanna State Park ♦	208	39.36 N	76.09 W
Susques	252	23.25 S	66.34 W
Sussa ≈	152	7.22 S	17.05 E
Süssen	56	48.41 N	9.45 E
Süssenbrunn ●⁸	264b	48.17 N	16.30 E
Süsser See ⊘	54	51.30 N	11.40 E
Sussex, N.B., Can.	186	45.43 N	65.31 W
Sussex, N.J., U.S.	210	41.12 N	74.36 W
Sussex, Va., U.S.	208	36.54 N	77.16 W
Sussex, Wi., U.S.	208	43.08 N	88.13 W
Sussex ≈⁶, U.S.	208	38.42 N	75.23 W
Sussex ≈⁶, Va., U.S.	208	36.50 N	77.15 W
Sussex, Vale of V	42	54.57 N	0.17 W
Sussex Inlet	170	35.11 S	150.36 E
Sussey	54	47.13 N	4.22 E
Sustenhorn ▲	58	46.42 N	8.28 E
Susten Pass ✗	58	46.44 N	8.27 E
Susteren	52	51.04 N	5.51 E
Šustkovo	82	55.17 N	35.59 E
Susu	174m	26.47 N	128.19 E
Susubona	175e	8.18 S	159.27 E
Susui	112	4.56 N	116.41 E
Susuman	74	62.47 N	148.10 E
Susurluk	130	39.54 N	28.10 E
Susurmüsellim	130	41.06 N	27.03 E
Šušvė ≈	76	55.10 N	23.49 E
Susz	30	53.44 N	19.20 E
Sutähätä	126	22.08 N	88.07 E
Sutak	123	33.12 N	77.28 E
Sutama	35	35.47 N	138.25 E
Sut-Chol'	86	51.30 N	91.17 E
Sütçüler	130	37.30 N	30.59 E
Sutera	70	37.31 N	13.44 E
Sutersville	214	40.14 N	79.48 W
Suthat, Wat ↳¹	269a	13.45 N	100.30 E
Sutherland, Austl.	158	34.02 S	151.04 E
Sutherland, S. Afr.	158	32.25 S	20.40 E
Sutherland, Ia., U.S.	198	42.58 N	95.29 W
Sutherland, Ne., U.S.	198	41.09 N	101.07 W
Sutherland ≈	182	54.29 N	125.05 W
Sutherland Falls ↳	172	44.48 S	167.44 E
Sutherlin	204	43.23 N	123.18 W
Suthiana	272a	28.31 N	77.26 E
Sutjeska Nacionalni Park ♦	38	43.18 N	18.45 E
Sutlej (Satluj) (Langqên) ≈	120	29.23 N	71.02 E
Sutri	66	42.14 N	12.13 E
Sutrio	64	46.31 N	12.59 E
Sütschou — Xuzhou, Zhg.	98	34.16 N	117.11 E
Sütschou — Suzhou, Zhg.	106	31.18 N	120.37 E
Sutter	226	39.10 N	121.45 W
Sutter ≈⁶	226	39.08 N	121.37 W
Sutter Buttes ▲	226	39.12 N	121.50 W
Sutter Bypass ≈	226	38.47 N	121.38 W
Sutter Creek	226	38.24 N	120.48 W
Sutton, Austl.	171b	35.10 S	149.15 E
Sutton, P.Q., Can.	206	45.06 N	72.37 W
Sutton, Eng., U.K.	42	52.23 N	0.07 E
Sutton, Eng., U.K.	260	51.12 N	0.26 W
Sutton, Ma., U.S.	180	61.43 N	148.53 W
Sutton, Ne., U.S.	207	42.09 N	71.45 W
Sutton, Ne., U.S.	198	40.36 N	97.51 W
Sutton, W.V., U.S.	188	38.39 N	80.42 W
Sutton ●⁸	42	51.21 N	0.12 W
Sutton, Monts ▲	206	45.05 N	72.30 W
Sutton-at-Home	260	51.25 N	0.14 E
Sutton Bridge	42	52.46 N	0.11 E
Sutton Coldfield	42	52.34 N	1.48 W
Sutton Courtenay	42	51.39 N	1.17 W
Sutton Forest	34	34.35 S	150.19 E
Sutton in Ashfield	44	53.08 N	1.15 W
Sutton on Sea	44	53.19 N	0.17 E
Sutton on Trent	44	53.10 N	0.49 W
Sutton Place ⊥	276	51.16 N	0.33 W
Sutton Bay	190	44.58 N	85.39 W
Sutton Scotney	42	51.09 N	1.21 W
Sutton Valence	42	51.10 N	0.36 E
Sutton Veny	42	51.11 N	2.08 W
Sutton Weaver	262	53.18 N	2.41 W
Sutton West	212	44.18 N	79.22 W
Suttor ≈	166	21.25 S	147.45 E
Suttrop	56	51.27 N	8.22 E
Suttsu	92a	42.48 N	140.14 E
Sutwik Island I	180	56.34 N	157.07 W
Suulluk	86	51.46 N	58.46 E
Suurberge ▲	158	33.18 S	25.32 E

PORTUGUÊS — Nome	Página	Lat.	Long. W=Oeste
Suurbraak	158	34.00 S	20.39 E
Suure-Jaani	76	58.33 N	25.28 E
Suur Munamägi ▲²	76	57.43 N	27.04 E
Suur Fakri I	76	59.20 N	23.55 E
Suva	175g	18.08 S	178.25 E
Suvainiškis	76	56.10 N	25.17 E
Šuvalovo Oz'orki ●⁸	265a	60.02 N	30.18 E
Suva Plarina ↗	38	43.10 N	22.10 E
Suvarli	130	37.32 N	37.38 E
Suvasves ⊘	26	62.39 N	28.12 E
Šuvel'an	84	40.30 N	50.09 E
Suvereto	66	43.05 N	10.40 E
Svirica	88	53.39 N	110.00 E
Suvorka	88	56.33 N	103.24 E
Suvorov	82	54.07 N	36.30 E
Suvorovo, Ross.	82	56.07 N	35.54 E
Suvorovo, Ukr.	78	45.34 N	28.59 E
Suwa, Erit.	144	14.17 N	41.06 E
Suwa, Nihon	94	36.05 N	138.08 E
Suwa-ko ⊘	94	36.05 N	138.05 E
Suwałki	30	54.07 N	22.56 E
Suwałki □⁴	30	54.10 N	22.15 E
Suwarnaphum	110	15.33 N	103.47 E
Suwannee ≈	192	29.18 N	83.09 E
Suwannee Lake ⊘	184	56.08 N	100.10 W
Suwanose-jima I	93b	29.38 N	129.43 E
Suwanose-suidö ʌ	93b	29.32 N	129.40 E
Suwarrow I¹	14	13.15 S	163.05 W
Suwaydah	130	35.46 N	39.38 E
Suwanggong	100	32.22 N	35.50 E
Suways, Khalīj as- (Gulf of Suez) ⊂	140	29.00 N	32.50 E
Suways, Qanāt as- (Suez Canal) ╪	142	29.55 N	32.33 E
Suwŏn	98	37.17 N	127.01 E
Suwon-dong	98	29.25 N	120.07 E
Suxi	100	29.25 N	120.07 E
Suxian	100	33.38 N	116.58 E
Suya	150	9.28 N	3.11 E
Suykbulak	86	49.48 N	80.50 E
Suyo	246	4.30 S	80.00 W
Suzak	86	44.07 N	68.28 E
Suzaka	94	36.39 N	138.19 E
Suzdal'	80	56.25 N	40.26 E
Suze ≈	58	47.08 N	7.14 E
Suze-la-Rousse	62	44.17 N	4.51 E
Suzhi	98	42.17 N	113.42 E
Suzhou (Soochow)	106	31.18 N	120.37 E
Suzhuang	105	40.04 N	116.44 E
Suzi ≈	98	41.55 N	124.17 E
Suzigou ≈	105	43.26 N	118.28 E
Suz'omka	76	52.19 N	34.05 E
Suzu	94	37.25 N	137.17 E
Suzuka	94	34.51 N	136.35 E
Suzuka ≈	94	34.54 N	136.39 E
Suzuka-kokutei-kôen ♦	94	35.00 N	136.25 E
Suzuka-sammyaku ▲	94	35.00 N	136.22 E
Suzuki	268	35.43 N	139.31 E
S'uz'um	88	58.02 N	47.32 E
Suzu-misaki >	92	37.31 N	137.21 E
Suzun	86	53.47 N	82.19 E
Suzzara	64	45.00 N	10.45 E
Svaerdborg	41	55.05 N	11.54 E
Sval'ava	78	48.33 N	22.56 E
Svalbard □²	12	78.00 N	20.00 E
Svalöv	41	55.55 N	13.06 E
Svaneholm	41	55.30 N	13.28 E
Svaneke	41	55.08 N	15.09 E
Svanetskij chrebet ▲	84	42.55 N	42.42 E
Svängsta	26	56.16 N	14.46 E
Svanninge	41	55.07 N	10.15 E
Svanskog	26	59.11 N	12.33 E
Svapa ≈	76	51.44 N	34.56 E
Svappavaara	24	67.39 N	21.04 E
Švarcevskij	82	54.06 N	37.59 E
Svärdsjö	26	60.45 N	15.55 E
Svaricha	80	57.33 N	49.37 E
Svartä	26	59.08 N	14.31 E
Svartälven ≈	40	59.19 N	14.35 E
Svartär ≈	40	59.37 N	16.33 E
Svarte	41	55.25 N	13.43 E
Svartehuk ↗¹	176	71.55 N	55.00 W
Svärtinge	40	58.39 N	16.00 E
Svartisen ⋈	24	66.38 N	14.00 E
Svartsjölandet I	40	59.22 N	17.41 E
Svataj	74	67.57 N	151.54 E
Svatava ≈	54	50.11 N	12.35 E
Svatava ≈	54	50.04 N	12.18 E
Sv'atica ≈	80	58.22 N	51.43 E
Sv'atogorskaja	83	49.04 N	37.32 E
Sv'atoj Nos, mys >, Ross.	74	72.52 N	140.42 E
Sv'atoj Nos, mys >, poluostrov >¹	88	53.40 N	108.50 E
Svatovo	83	49.23 N	38.13 E
Svay Chék	110	13.48 N	102.58 E
Svay Riĕng	110	11.05 N	105.48 E
Sveafallen ↳	40	59.10 N	14.22 E
Svebolle	41	55.38 N	11.20 E
Sveča	80	58.16 N	47.32 E
Svedala	41	55.30 N	13.14 E
Svédasai	76	55.41 N	25.22 E
Sveg	26	62.02 N	14.21 E
Sveggésjön ≈¹	26	62.03 N	14.10 E
Svékšna	76	55.31 N	21.37 E
Svelgen	26	61.47 N	5.15 E
Svelvik	26	59.37 N	10.24 E
Sven'	76	53.09 N	34.21 E
Švenčionėliai	76	55.10 N	26.00 E
Švenčionys	76	55.08 N	26.10 E
Svendborg	41	55.03 N	10.37 E
Svenljunga	26	57.30 N	13.07 E
Svennevad	40	59.07 N	15.08 E
Svensby	24	69.38 N	19.53 E
Svenstavik	26	62.46 N	14.26 E
Svenstrup	26	56.59 N	9.52 E
Šventoji	76	55.06 N	24.22 E
Šventoji ≈	76	55.36 N	23.15 E
Šverbejevo	82	55.48 N	36.45 E
Sverdlovo	82	56.38 N	36.37 E
Sverdrovsk — Jekaterinburg, Ross.	86	56.51 N	60.36 E
Sverdrup, ostrov I	74	74.35 N	79.30 E
Sverige — Sweden □¹	24	62.00 N	15.00 E
Sverkestaän ≈	40	59.28 N	15.28 E
Švermov	54	50.09 N	14.05 E
Sveti Amandjel Mihajlo ●¹	38	42.07 N	21.28 E
Sveti Jovan Bigorski ↳	38	41.38 N	20.37 E
Svetilovič	76	52.48 N	31.19 E
Sveti Nikole	38	41.52 N	21.58 E
Sveti Petar u Šumi	36	45.13 N	13.55 E (?)
Svetlá nad Sázavou	30	49.44 N	15.24 E
Svetlogorsk	24	61.07 N	28.51 E
Svetlogorsk, Bela.	76	52.38 N	29.42 E
Svetlogorsk, Ross.	76	54.57 N	20.10 E
Svetlograd	72	45.20 N	42.40 E
Svetlovodsk	78	49.04 N	33.15 E
Svetlyj, Ross.	76	54.41 N	20.08 E
Svetlyj, Ross.	86	50.47 N	60.53 E
Svetlyj, Ross.	88	53.26 N	115.55 E
Svežen'kaja	80	54.01 N	43.26 E
Svidník	30	49.18 N	21.34 E

Švihov	60	49.29 N	13.17 E
Svijaga ≈	80	55.47 N	48.40 E
Svilajna≈	38	44.14 N	21.13 E
Svilengrad	38	41.46 N	26.12 E
Svindal	26	59.30 N	7.28 E
Svinecea Mare, Vîrful ▲	38	44.48 N	22.09 E
Svinesund	26	59.06 N	11.16 E
Svinninge	41	55.43 N	11.28 E
Svir'	76	54.51 N	26.24 E
Svir' ≈	76	60.30 N	32.48 E
Svirica	76	60.29 N	32.51 E
Svirsk	88	53.04 N	103.21 E
Svir'stroj	76	60.48 N	33.43 E
Sviščёv·a	80	52.51 N	43.44 E
Svišloč' Bela.	76	53.02 N	24.06 E
Svišloč' Bela.	76	53.26 N	28.59 E
Svišloč' ≈	76	53.26 N	28.59 E
Svištov	38	43.37 N	25.20 E
Svistunovka	83	49.29 N	38.20 E
Svit	30	49.03 N	20.12 E
Svitava ≈	30	49.09 N	16.38 E
Svitávka	30	49.30 N	16.37 E
Svitavy	30	49.45 N	16.27 E
Svitino	82	54.54 N	35.49 E
Svoboda, Ross.	78	51.58 N	36.17 E
Svoboda, Ross.	78	47.12 N	40.39 E
Svobodnaja	89	46.43 N	143.23 E
Svobodnyj, Ross.	83	48.32 N	37.34 E
Svobodnyj, Ross.	80	52.20 N	46.22 E
Svobodnyj, Ross.	74	51.24 N	128.08 E
Svobodnyj Port	78	46.20 N	31.51 E
Svoge	38	42.58 N	23.21 E
Svojna	82	54.09 N	36.39 E
Svol'na ≈	76	55.43 N	28.02 E
Svolvær	24	68.14 N	14.34 E
Svor	54	50.47 N	14.36 E
Svorkmo	26	63.10 N	9.45 E
Svratka ≈	61	49.11 N	16.38 E
Svržno	60	49.35 N	12.46 E
Svullrya	26	60.25 N	12.24 E
Swäbi	123	34.07 N	72.28 E
Swadlincote	42	52.47 N	1.33 W
Swaffham	42	52.39 N	0.41 E
Swain	210	42.29 N	77.51 W
Swain Reefs ✛²	166	21.40 S	152.15 E
Swainsboro	192	32.35 N	82.20 W
Swains Island I	14	11.03 S	171.05 W
Swakop ≈	156	22.38 S	14.36 E
Swakopmund	156	22.41 S	14.34 E
Swakopmund ●⁵	156	22.36 S	15.00 E
Swale ≈	260	51.21 N	0.41 E
Swale ≈	44	54.06 N	1.20 W
Swale Canyon ✛⁶	224	45.49 N	121.05 W
Swale Creek ≈	224	45.49 N	121.05 W
Swaledale ↳	44	54.25 N	1.47 W
Swallowfield	218	38.21 N	84.51 W
Swalmen	52	51.15 N	6.02 E
Swamp City	222	32.29 N	94.56 W
Swampscott	207	42.28 N	70.55 W
Swan ≈, Austl.	168a	32.03 S	115.45 E
Swan ≈, Can.	184	52.30 N	100.47 W
Swan ≈, Ab., Can.	182	55.31 N	115.17 W
Swan ≈, Mn., U.S.	190	47.01 N	93.16 W
Swan ≈, Mt., U.S.	202	48.04 N	114.05 W
Swan Acres	279b	40.33 N	80.02 W
Swanage	42	50.37 N	1.58 W
Swan Bay ⊂	169	38.14 S	144.40 E
Swan Creek ≈, Mi., U.S.	171a	28.08 S	152.13 E
Swan Creek ≈, Mi., U.S.	216	41.58 N	85.19 W
Swan Creek ≈, Oh., U.S.	216	41.58 N	83.17 W
Swan Creek ≈, N.C., U.S.	216	41.39 N	83.32 W
Swan Creek ≈, S.D., U.S.	198	45.19 N	100.15 W
Swan Creek ≈, Va., U.S.	208	37.17 N	77.15 W
Swan Creek, North Branch ≈	281	42.06 N	83.23 W
Swan Creek Point >	281	42.40 N	82.39 W
Swanee	184	50.40 N	107.44 W
— Suwannee ≈	192	29.18 N	83.09 W
Swan Hill	166	35.21 S	143.34 E
Swan Hills	182	54.43 N	115.24 W
Swan Hills ▲	182	54.48 N	115.52 W
Swanington	216	40.35 N	87.17 W
Swan Island I	169	38.15 S	144.41 E
Swan Islands — Santanilla, Islas I	238	17.25 N	83.55 W
Swank Creek ≈	224	47.07 N	120.45 W
Swan Lake, Mb., Can.	184	52.30 N	100.45 W
Swan Lake ⊘, Mt., U.S.	202	47.55 N	113.50 W
Swan Lake ⊘, Mb., Can.	184	49.20 N	98.46 W
Swan Lake ⊘, On., Can.	184	54.17 N	91.12 W
Swan Lake ⊘, Il., U.S.	219	38.57 N	90.33 W
Swan Lake ⊘, N.Y., U.S.	210	41.45 N	74.47 W
Swanland ≈	44	44.19 N	94.15 W
Swanley	260	51.24 N	0.12 E
Swanlinbar	48	54.10 N	7.42 W
Swannaroa	192	35.36 N	82.23 W
Swannaroa, Lake ⊘	276	41.01 N	74.31 W
Swan Peak ▲	202	47.43 N	113.38 W
Swanquarter	192	35.24 N	76.20 W
Swan Range ▲	202	47.50 N	113.40 W
Swan Reach	166	34.34 S	139.36 E
Swan River	184	52.06 N	101.16 W
Swansboro	192	34.41 N	77.07 W
Swanscombe	260	51.26 N	0.18 E
Swansea, Austl.	170	33.05 S	151.38 E
Swansea, Wales, U.K.	42	51.38 N	3.57 W
Swansea, Il., U.S.	219	38.32 N	89.59 W
Swansea, S.C., U.S.	192	33.44 N	81.05 W
Swansea, Wales ●⁶	42	51.38 N	3.57 W
Swansea Bay ⊂	42	51.33 N	3.52 W
Swans Island I	188	44.10 N	68.25 W
Swanson Lake ⊘¹	198	40.09 N	101.06 W
Swanton, Oh., U.S.	216	41.35 N	83.53 W
Swanton, Vt., U.S.	206	44.55 N	73.07 W
Swanville	190	45.55 N	94.38 W
Swanzey Center	207	42.49 N	72.10 W
Swarbacks Minn ≈	46a	60.20 N	1.36 W
Swarthmore	158	30.15 S	29.23 E
Swarthmore College ↳	208	39.54 N	75.21 W
Swart-Kei ≈	158	32.09 S	27.24 E
Swart-Mfolozi ≈	158	28.22 S	31.58 E
Swartruggens	158	26.08 S	26.57 E
Swartruggens ▲	158	33.02 S	19.35 E
Swartswood Lake ⊘	276	41.04 N	74.51 W
Swartswood State Park ♦	210	41.05 N	74.50 W
Swartz Creek	216	42.57 N	83.49 W
Swarupkäti	126	22.45 N	90.06 E
Swasey Peak ▲	200	39.23 N	113.19 W
Swastika	184	48.07 N	80.06 W
Swasuag Wash ≈	200	39.15 N	112.53 W
Swat ≈	123	34.20 N	71.34 E
Swatara Creek ≈	208	40.11 N	76.44 W
Swa-Tenda	152	7.09 S	17.07 E
— Shantou	100	23.23 N	116.41 E
Sväz	88	58.16 N	115.59 E

Swauk Pass ✗	224	47.21 N	120.40 W
Sway	42	50.47 N	1.37 W
Swayzee	216	40.30 N	85.49 W
Swaziland □¹, Afr.	158	26.30 S	31.30 E
Swaziland □¹, Afr.	158	26.30 S	31.30 E
Swea City	190	43.23 N	94.19 W
Swede Hill	279b	40.17 N	79.34 W
Swedeland	259	40.07 N	75.19 W
Sweden (Sverige) □¹, Europe	22	62.00 N	15.00 E
Sweden (Sverige) □¹, Europe	24	62.00 N	15.00 E
Sweden Valley	214	41.45 N	77.56 W
Swede Run ≈	285	40.02 N	74.58 W
Swedesboro	208	39.44 N	75.18 W
Swedesburg	285	40.06 N	75.20 W
Swedish Knoll ▲	200	39.16 N	111.26 W
Swedru	150	5.32 N	0.43 W
Sween, Loch ⊂	46	55.59 N	5.39 W
Sweeny Plan ≈	222	29.02 N	95.41 W
Sweeney	222	29.02 N	95.41 W
Sweeny Park ♦	284a	43.02 N	78.52 W
Sweet Briar	192	37.33 N	79.04 W
Sweetgrass	182	49.00 N	111.57 W
Sweet Grass Creek ≈	202	45.47 N	109.47 W
Sweetgrass Hills ▲²	202	48.55 N	111.30 W
Sweet Grass Indian Reserve ●⁴	184	52.44 N	108.45 W
Sweetheart Abbey ↳¹	44	54.59 N	3.38 W
Sweet Home, Or., U.S.	204	44.23 N	122.44 W
Sweet Home, Tx., U.S.	222	29.21 N	97.04 W
Sweet Springs	194	38.57 N	93.24 W
Sweet Valley	210	41.17 N	76.09 W
Sweetwater, Fl., U.S.	220	25.46 N	80.21 W
Sweet Water, Il., U.S.	219	40.03 N	89.42 W
Sweetwater, Tn., U.S.	192	35.36 N	84.27 W
Sweetwater, Tx., U.S.	196	32.28 N	100.24 W
Sweetwater ≈	200	42.31 N	107.02 W
Sweetwater Creek ≈	220	27.59 N	82.33 W
Sweetwater Creek ≈, Tx., U.S.	196	35.18 N	99.57 W
Sweetwater Creek ≈, Tx., U.S.	196	32.40 N	100.06 W
Sweetwater Mountains ▲	226	38.30 N	119.17 W
Swellendam	158	34.02 S	20.26 E
Swepsonville	192	36.01 N	79.21 W
Swerdlovsk — Jekaterinburg	86	56.51 N	60.36 E
Świdnica (Schweidnitz)	30	50.51 N	16.29 E
Świdwin	30	51.14 N	22.41 E
Świebodzice	30	50.52 N	16.20 E
Świebodzin	30	52.15 N	15.32 E
Świecie	30	53.25 N	18.28 E
Świerzawa	30	51.01 N	15.54 E
Świerzno	54	53.51 N	14.59 E
Świeta	54	53.35 N	14.36 E
Świętokrzyskie, Góry ▲	30	50.55 N	21.00 E
Świętokrzyski Park Narodowy ♦	30	50.55 N	21.00 E
Swift ≈, Eng., U.K.	42	52.23 N	1.16 W
Swift ≈, Ak., U.S.	180	61.53 N	156.18 W
Swift ≈, Ma., U.S.	207	42.12 N	72.22 W
Swift Creek ≈, Al., U.S.	194	32.26 N	86.38 W
Swift Creek ≈, N.C., U.S.	216	35.12 N	77.05 W
Swift Creek ≈, N.C., U.S.	192	35.57 N	77.35 W
Swift Current	208	50.17 N	107.50 W (?)
Swift Current Creek ≈	184	50.17 N	107.50 W
Swifton	194	35.49 N	91.07 W
Swift Reservoir ⊘¹	224	46.04 N	122.05 W
Swiftwater	210	41.06 N	75.20 W
Swilly ≈	48	54.57 N	7.42 W
Swilly, Lough ⊂	48	55.10 N	7.38 W
Swimming	276	44.05 N	74.05 W
Swimming River Reservoir ⊘¹	276	40.19 N	74.07 W
Swina ≈¹	54	53.55 N	14.17 E
Swinden Reservoirs ⊘¹	262	53.48 N	2.10 W
Swindle Island I	182	52.30 N	128.35 W
Swindon	42	51.34 N	1.47 W
Swinemünde — Świnoujście	54	53.53 N	14.14 E
Swineshead	42	52.56 N	0.09 W
Swinford	48	53.58 N	8.57 W
Swinging Bridge Reservoir ⊘¹	210	41.37 N	74.48 W
Swinomish Indian Reservation ●⁴	224	48.25 N	122.33 W
Świnoujście (Swinemünde)	30	53.53 N	14.14 E
Swinton, Eng., U.K.	44	53.28 N	1.20 W
Swinton, Eng., U.K.	44	53.31 N	2.21 W
Swinton, Scot., U.K.	44	55.43 N	2.15 W
Swisstal	56	50.45 N	6.54 E
Switzerland □⁶	218	38.45 N	85.04 W
Switzerland □¹, Europe	58	47.00 N	8.00 E
Switzerland □¹, Europe	58	47.00 N	8.00 E
Swords	48	53.28 N	6.13 W
Swords Range ▲	166	21.57 S	141.32 E
Swormville	284a	43.03 N	78.42 W
Sworton Heath	262	53.21 N	2.28 W
Syalach	74	63.16 N	124.00 E
Syam	56	46.33 N	5.40 E
Syämnagar, India	126	22.21 N	89.07 E
Syämnagar, India	272b	22.49 N	88.23 E
Syamozero ⊘	76	61.45 N	33.20 E
Syan ≈	30	50.33 N	22.50 E
Sybil Creek ≈	207	40.57 N	73.09 W
Sybille Creek ≈	202	42.07 N	105.02 W
Syburg ●⁸	275	51.25 N	7.29 E
Syčёvka	76	55.50 N	34.17 E
Syčёvka	82	55.50 N	34.17 E
Syčёva	58	59.23 N	39.42 E
Syčёv ≈	202	42.21 N	121.15 W
Sycamore, Ga., U.S.	192	31.40 N	83.38 W
Sycamore, Il., U.S.	216	41.59 N	88.41 W
Sycamore, Oh., U.S.	214	40.58 N	83.10 W
Sycamore ≈, Az., U.S.	200	33.38 N	111.40 W
Sycamore Creek ≈, Mi., U.S.	216	42.43 N	84.32 W
Sycamore Creek ≈, Oh., U.S.	214	40.58 N	83.10 W
Sycamore Gardens	280	29.14 N	100.48 W
Sycamore Island I	279b	40.33 N	79.52 W
Sycamore Slough ≈	226	38.28 N	121.33 W
Syčan ≈	204	42.47 N	121.03 W
Syčuan — Sichuan □⁴	102	31.00 N	105.00 E
Sichuan Pendi ≈	102	30.00 N	105.00 E
Sydenham, Austl.	274b	37.42 S	144.46 E
Sydenham, On., Can.	212	44.25 N	76.36 W
Sydenham, On., S. Afr.	273d	26.09 S	28.06 E
Sydenham ≈⁸, Eng., U.K.	260	51.26 N	0.03 W
Sydenham ≈, On., Can.	190	42.33 N	82.25 W

Sydenham ≈, On., Can.	212	44.35 N	80.57 W
Sydenham Lake ⊘	212	44.25 N	76.35 W
Sydenham West	274b	37.41 S	144.39 E
Sydney, Austl.	170	33.52 S	151.13 E
Sydney, Austl.	158	33.52 S	151.13 E
Sydney, N.S., Can.	186	46.09 N	60.11 W
Sydney, Fl., U.S.	220	27.58 N	82.12 W
Sydney, University of ↳	274a	33.53 S	151.11 E
Sydney Bay c, On., Can.	212	44.54 N	81.05 W
Sydney Bay c, Norf. I.	174c	29.04 S	167.57 E
Sydney Bay Bluff ▲⁴	212	44.54 N	81.07 W
Sydney Harbour Bridge ↔⁵	170	33.52 S	151.12 E
Sydney Lake ⊘	184	50.40 N	94.24 W
Sydney Mines	186	46.14 N	60.14 W
Sydney Point >	174d	0.53 S	169.36 E
Syferbult	158	26.00 S	27.20 E
Sygan	279b	40.21 N	80.08 W
Syke	52	52.54 N	8.49 E
Sykesville, Md., U.S.	208	39.22 N	76.58 W
Sykesville, Pa., U.S.	214	41.03 N	78.49 W
Sykkylven	26	62.24 N	6.35 E
Syktyvkar	24	61.40 N	50.46 E
Sylacauga	194	33.10 N	86.15 W
Sylarna ▲	26	63.02 N	12.13 E
Sylhet	120	24.54 N	91.52 E
Syloga	80	63.50 N	43.39 E
Sylt I	30	54.54 N	8.20 E
Sylva	192	35.22 N	83.13 W
Sylva ≈	86	57.39 N	56.54 E
Sylvan	224	45.30 N	122.41 W
Sylvan Beach	210	43.11 N	75.43 W
Sylvan Glen	285	40.11 N	75.42 W
Sylvan Grove	198	39.00 N	98.23 W
Sylvan Hills	194	34.53 N	92.13 W
Sylvania, Austl.	274	34.01 S	151.07 E
Sylvania, Ga., U.S.	192	32.45 N	81.38 W
Sylvania, Oh., U.S.	214	41.43 N	83.42 W
Sylvania, Pa., U.S.	210	41.48 N	76.51 W
Sylvan Lake, Ab., Can.	182	52.19 N	114.05 W
Sylvan Lake ⊘, Ab., Can.	182	52.18 N	114.05 W
Sylvan Lake ⊘, Mi., U.S.	281	42.37 N	83.20 W
Sylvan Lake ⊘, In., U.S.	216	41.29 N	85.20 W
Sylvan Lake ⊘, Mi., U.S.	281	42.37 N	83.20 W
Sylvan Pass ✗	200	44.28 N	110.08 W
Sylvan Shores	220	28.49 N	81.41 W
Sylvesterstein ●¹	54	47.34 N	11.32 E
Sylvester, Ga., U.S.	192	31.31 N	83.50 W
Sylvester, Tx., U.S.	196	32.43 N	100.15 W
Sylvester, Mount ▲²	186	48.11 N	55.04 W
Sylvia	198	37.57 N	98.24 W
Sym	74	60.20 N	88.23 E
Symmes Creek ≈	188	38.26 N	82.27 W
Symsonia	218	36.54 N	88.32 W
Syndal	274b	37.53 S	145.09 E
Syrkovo	82	56.03 N	37.38 E
Syrynyr, chrebet ▲	88	56.50 N	111.10 E
Syrtut	80	60.41 N	41.18 E
Syt'žereja	38	47.38 N	28.09 E
Syon House ⊥	260	51.29 N	0.19 W
Syosset	210	40.49 N	73.30 W
Syowa ●³	9	69.00 S	39.35 E
Syracuse — Siracusa, It.	70	37.04 N	15.18 E
Syracuse, In., U.S.	216	41.25 N	85.45 W
Syracuse, Ks., U.S.	198	37.58 N	101.45 W
Syracuse, Ne., U.S.	198	40.39 N	96.11 W
Syracuse, N.Y., U.S.	210	43.02 N	76.08 W
Syracuse Hancock International Airport ⊠, N.Y., U.S.	210	43.07 N	76.07 W
Syracuse Hancock International Airport ⊠, N.Y., U.S.	210	43.07 N	76.07 W
Syrän	80	57.22 N	50.15 E
Syrdarja	85	40.52 N	68.38 E
Syrdarja ≈	85	40.30 N	68.40 E
Syrdarja (Syr Darya) ≈	72	46.03 N	61.00 E
Syr-Dar'ya — Syrdarja ≈	72	46.03 N	61.00 E
Syre	46	58.22 N	4.14 W
Syria (Sūrīyah) □¹, Asia	118	35.00 N	38.00 E
Syria (Sūrīyah) □¹, Asia	110	16.46 N	96.15 E
Syrian Desert — Shäm, Bädiyat ash- ≈²	128	32.00 N	40.00 E
Syrie — Syria □¹	128	35.00 N	38.00 E
Syrien	128	35.00 N	38.00 E
Syrskij	76	52.34 N	39.29 E
Sysert'	86	56.29 N	60.49 E
Sysmä	26	61.30 N	25.41 E
Sysola ≈	24	61.40 N	50.53 E
Sysslebäck	26	60.44 N	12.52 E
Systä	40	59.02 N	15.38 E
Sysyg-Chem	88	52.42 N	97.14 E
Syzran'	24	53.09 N	48.27 E
Syzran' ≈	80	53.09 N	48.27 E
Szabadka — Subotica	38	46.06 N	19.39 E
Szabolcs-Szatmár-Bereg □⁶	30	48.00 N	22.10 E
Szada	264c	47.38 N	19.19 E
Szamocin	30	53.00 N	17.08 E
Szamos (Someş) ≈	38	48.07 N	22.20 E
Szamotuły	30	52.37 N	16.35 E
Szarvas	30	46.52 N	20.34 E
Szatmárnémeti — Satu Mare	30	47.48 N	22.53 E
Százhalombatta	264c	47.19 N	18.55 E
Szczawnica	30	49.26 N	20.30 E
Szczecin (Stettin)	54	53.25 N	14.32 E
Szczecinek (Neustettin)	30	53.43 N	16.42 E
Szczekociny	30	50.38 N	19.50 E
Szczuczyn	30	53.34 N	22.18 E
Szczytno	30	53.34 N	21.00 E
Szechwan — Sichuan □⁴	102	31.00 N	105.00 E
Szechwan Basin ≈	102	30.00 N	105.00 E
Szécsény	30	48.05 N	19.31 E
Szeged	30	46.15 N	20.09 E
Szeghalom	30	47.02 N	21.11 E
Székesfehérvár	30	47.12 N	18.25 E
Szekszárd	30	46.21 N	18.42 E
Szentendre	30	47.40 N	19.05 E
Szentendrei-Duna ≈	264c	47.39 N	19.04 E
Szentendrei-sziget I	264c	47.39 N	19.07 E
Szentes	30	46.39 N	20.16 E
Szentgotthárd	30	46.57 N	16.17 E
Szentpéterfa	61	47.09 N	16.29 E

Legend

	English	Deutsch	Español	Français	Português
≈	River	Fluß	Río	Rivière	Rio
╪	Canal	Kanal	Canal	Canal	Canal
↳	Waterfall, Rapids	Wasserfall, Stromschnellen	Cascada, Rápidos	Chute d'eau, Rapides	Cascata, Rápidos
⊃	Strait	Meeresstraße	Estrecho	Détroit	Estreito
⊂	Bay, Gulf	Bucht, Golf	Bahía, Golfo	Baie, Golfe	Baía, Golfo
⊘	Lake, Lakes	See, Seen	Lago, Lagos	Lac, Lacs	Lago, Lagos
⊛	Swamp	Sumpf	Pantano	Marais	Pântano
⋈	Ice Features, Glacier	Eis- und Gletscherformen	Accidentes Glaciares	Formes glaciaires	Acidentes glaciares
⊤	Other Hydrographic Features	Andere Hydrographische Objekte	Otros Elementos Hidrográficos	Autres données hydrographiques	Outros acidentes hidrográficos
✛	Submarine Features	Untermeerische Objekte	Accidentes Submarinos	Formes de relief sous-marin	Acidentes submarinos
□	Political Unit	Politische Einheit	Unidad Política	Entité politique	Unidade política
↳	Cultural Institution	Kulturelle Institution	Institución Cultural	Institution culturelle	Instituição cultural
⊥	Historical Site	Historische Stätte	Sitio Histórico	Site historique	Sítio histórico
↔	Recreational Site	Erholungs- und Ferienort	Sitio de Recreo	Centre de loisirs	Área de Lazer
✈	Airport	Flughafen	Aeropuerto	Aéroport	Aeroporto
⊠	Military Installation	Militäranlage	Instalación Militar	Installation militaire	Instalação militar
●	Miscellaneous	Verschiedenes	Misceláneo	Divers	Diversos

Name	Page	Lat.°′	Long.°′
Szeping → Siping	89	43.12 N	124.20 E
Szépművészeti Museum ♥	264c	47.31 N	19.05 E
Szerencs	30	48.09 N	21.13 E
Szigethalom	264c	47.20 N	19.00 E
Szigetszentmiklós	264c	47.21 N	19.03 E
Szilas-patak ≃	264c	47.36 N	19.06 E
Szlichtyngowa	30	51.43 N	16.15 E
Szob	30	47.50 N	18.52 E
Szolnok	30	47.10 N	20.12 E
Szombathely	30	47.14 N	16.38 E
Szprotawa	30	51.34 N	15.33 E
Sztum	30	53.56 N	19.01 E
Szubin	30	53.00 N	17.44 E
Szydłowiec	30	51.14 N	20.51 E
Szypliszki	30	54.15 N	23.05 E
T			
Ta ≃	94	36.17 N	139.54 E
Taacyn ≃	102	45.09 N	101.27 E
Taal	116	13.53 N	120.55 E
Taal, Lake ⊜	116	13.55 N	121.00 E
Taalintehdas → Dalsbruk	26	60.02 N	22.31 E
Taan ≃	100	24.24 N	120.36 E
Taancan Point ›	116	10.00 N	125.01 E
Taavetti	26	60.55 N	27.34 E
Tabacal	252	23.16 S	64.15 W
Tabacal, Quebrada ≃	286c	10.31 N	67.02 W
Tabaco	116	13.23 N	123.44 E
Tabacundo	246	0.03 N	78.12 W
Tabai ≃	164	3.01 S	135.52 E
Tabalosos	248	6.21 S	76.41 W
Tabanan	115b	8.32 S	115.08 E
Tabango	116	11.19 N	124.22 E
Tabankulu	158	30.58 S	29.19 E
Tábara	34	41.49 N	5.57 W
Tabar Island I	164	2.55 S	152.05 E
Tabar Islands II	164	2.50 S	152.00 E
Tabarka	148	36.57 N	8.45 E
Tabarz	54	50.52 N	10.31 E
Ṭabas	128	33.36 N	56.54 E
Tabasará ≃	236	8.00 N	81.39 W
Tabasco □[3]	232	18.15 N	93.00 W
Ṭabas Masīnā	128	32.48 N	60.14 E
Tabat	86	52.57 N	90.43 E
Tabatinga ≃	255	17.24 S	43.18 W
Tabayama	94	35.47 N	138.55 E
Tabayin	110	22.42 N	95.19 E
Tabb	208	37.08 N	76.29 W
Tabei	98	39.44 N	122.29 E
Tabelbala	148	29.23 N	3.15 W
Tabelbala, Kahal ⊥[8]	148	28.30 N	2.00 W
Taber	182	49.47 N	112.08 W
Taberg, Sve.	26	57.41 N	14.05 E
Taberg, Sve.	40	59.50 N	14.08 E
Taberg, N.Y., U.S.	210	43.18 N	75.37 W
Tabernacle	285	39.50 N	74.42 W
Tabi	152	8.10 S	13.18 E
Tabiang	174d	0.52 S	169.35 E
Tabiano Terme	64	44.48 N	10.02 E
Tabira	250	7.35 S	37.33 W
Tabiteuea	174t	1.25 N	173.07 E
Tabiteuea I[1]	14	1.20 S	174.50 E
Tabla	150	13.46 N	3.01 E
Tabla, Cerro de la ∧	240m	18.03 N	66.08 W
Tablada	288	34.42 S	58.32 W
Tablas, Cabo ›	252	31.51 S	71.34 W
Tablas Island I	116	12.24 N	122.02 E
Tablas Plateau ⋏[1]	116	9.43 N	122.43 E
Tablas Strait ʋ	116	12.40 N	121.48 E
Tablat	34	36.24 N	3.19 E
Table Bay ⊂	158	33.53 S	18.27 E
Table Cape ›	172	39.06 S	178.00 E
Tableland	162	17.17 S	127.00 E
Table Mountain ∧, Nf., Can.	186	47.43 N	59.13 W
Table Mountain ∧, S. Afr.	158	33.57 S	18.25 E
Table Mountain ∧, Az., U.S.	200	32.49 N	110.31 W
Table Rock	198	40.10 N	96.05 W
Table Rock Lake ⊜[1]	194	36.35 N	93.30 W
Tabletop ∧, Austl.	162	22.32 S	123.55 E
Table Top ∧, Az., U.S.	200	32.46 N	112.07 W
Tabletop Mountain ∧	171b	35.58 S	148.30 E
Tabley Mere ⊜	262	53.17 N	2.25 W
Tabligbo	150	6.35 N	1.30 E
Tablones	240m	18.15 N	65.45 W
Taboan ≃	116	17.57 N	122.11 E
Taboão, Ribeirão do ≃	287b	23.40 S	46.28 W
Taboão da Serra	256	23.38 S	46.46 W
Taboco ≃	248	19.53 S	55.58 W
Taboga	236	8.48 N	79.33 W
Tabogon	116	10.57 N	124.02 E
Tábor, Česká Rep.	30	49.25 N	14.41 E
Tabor, Ross.	74	71.16 N	150.12 E
Tabor, Ia., U.S.	198	40.53 N	95.40 W
Tabor, N.J., U.S.	276	40.52 N	74.29 W
Tabor, S.D., U.S.	198	42.56 N	97.39 W
Tabor, Mount → Tavor, Har ∧	132	32.41 N	35.23 E
Tabora	154	5.01 S	32.48 E
Tabora □[4]	154	5.15 S	32.45 E
Tabor City	192	34.08 N	78.52 W
Tabory	86	58.31 N	64.33 E
Tabou	150	4.25 N	7.21 W
Tabrīz	128	38.05 N	46.18 E
Tábua, Riacho da ≃	250	9.12 S	44.25 W
Tabuaço	34	41.07 N	7.34 W
Tabuaeran I[1]	14	3.52 N	159.20 W
Tabuão	256	21.59 S	44.02 W
Tábuas	256	22.12 S	43.37 W
Tabu-dong	98	36.03 N	128.31 E
Tabuelan	116	10.49 N	123.52 E
Tabūk, Ar. Su.	128	28.23 N	36.35 E
Tabuk, Pil.	116	17.24 N	121.25 E
Tabuleiro	256	21.22 S	43.15 W
Tabuleiro do Norte	250	5.15 S	38.07 W
Tabuny	86	52.46 N	78.45 E
Tabuse	96	33.57 N	132.03 E
Tabuyung	114	0.51 N	99.00 E
Tabwémasana, Mont ∧	175f	15.20 S	166.44 E
Täby	40	59.30 N	18.03 E
Tacagua, Quebrada ≃	286c	10.37 N	67.02 W
Tacámbaro de Codallos	234	19.14 N	101.28 W
Tacaná	236	15.14 N	92.05 W
Tacaná, Volcán ∧[1]	236	15.08 N	92.06 W
Tacañitas	252	28.38 S	62.36 W
Tacaratu	250	9.06 S	38.10 W
Taceno	58	46.02 N	9.21 E
T'ačev	78	48.02 N	23.34 E
Taché, Lac ⊜	176	64.00 N	120.00 W
Tacheng (Qoqek)	86	46.45 N	82.57 E
Tacherting	60	48.05 N	12.34 E
Tachia	100	24.21 N	120.37 E
Tachia ≃	100	24.20 N	120.33 E
Tachiaochang Airport ⊠	107	32.01 N	118.47 E
Tachiataš	72	42.22 N	59.35 E
Tachibana, Nihon	96	33.11 N	130.36 E
Tachibana, Nihon	96	33.54 N	132.17 E
Tachie ≃	182	54.40 N	124.50 W
Tachikawa	94	35.42 N	139.25 E
Tachikawa Air Base ■	268	35.43 N	139.25 E
Tachinger See ⊜	60	47.58 N	12.45 E
Táchira □[3]	246	7.50 N	72.05 W
Tachoshui	100	24.20 N	121.44 E
Tachov	60	49.48 N	12.38 E
Tachta, Ross.	80	45.54 N	42.07 E
Tachta, Ross.	89	53.08 N	139.53 E
Tachta-Bazar	128	35.57 N	62.50 E
Tachtabrod	86	52.38 N	67.34 E
Tachtakupyr	86	43.02 N	60.17 E
Tachtamygda	89	54.06 N	123.34 E
Tacima	250	6.30 S	35.39 W
Tacina ≃	68	38.56 N	16.53 E
Tacinskij	80	48.13 N	41.17 E
Taciuã, Lago ≃	246	4.29 S	60.35 W
Tacloban	116	11.15 N	125.00 E
Taclobo	116	12.20 N	122.34 E
Tacna, Perú	248	18.01 S	70.15 W
Tacna, Az., U.S.	200	32.41 N	113.57 W
Tacna □[5]	248	17.40 S	70.20 W
Tacoignières	261	48.50 N	1.40 E
Tacoma	224	47.15 N	122.26 W
Tacoma Narrows Bridge ⬥[5]	224	47.16 N	122.33 W
Taconic	207	42.02 N	73.24 W
Taconic Range ⋏	210	42.30 N	73.20 W
Taconic State Park ♠	210	42.05 N	73.34 W
Tacony ⬥[8]	285	40.02 N	75.03 W
Tacony Creek ≃	285	40.01 N	75.06 W
Tacony Creek Park ♠	285	40.02 N	75.07 W
Tacony Palmyra Bridge ⬥[5]	285	40.01 N	75.02 W
Taco Pozo	252	25.37 S	63.17 W
Tacotalpa	234	17.36 N	92.49 W
Tacotalpa ≃	234	17.50 N	92.52 W
Tacuarembó	252	31.44 S	55.59 W
Tacuarembó ≃	252	32.25 S	55.29 W
Tacuarí ≃	252	32.46 S	53.18 W
Tacuatí	252	23.27 S	56.35 W
Tacuba ⬥[8]	286a	19.28 N	99.12 W
Tacubaya ⬥[8]	286a	19.25 N	99.12 W
Tacuparé, Cachoeira L	250	5.20 S	55.50 W
Tacurong	116	6.42 N	124.42 E
Tacuru, Bra.	252	23.38 N	55.01 W
Tacuru, Bra.	255	23.38 S	55.01 W
Tacurú, Laguna ⊜	258	34.58 S	58.25 W
Tacutu (Takutu) ≃	246	3.01 N	60.29 W
Tadain	270	34.52 N	135.24 E
Tadami	92	37.21 N	139.19 E
Tadaoka	270	34.29 N	135.24 E
Tadasuni	71	40.06 N	8.53 E
Tadcaster	44	53.53 N	1.16 W
Tademaït, Plateau du ⋏[1]	148	28.30 N	2.00 E
Tadenac Lake ⊜	212	45.03 N	79.56 W
Tādepallegūdem	122	16.50 N	81.30 E
Tadía, Ciénaga de ⊜	246	6.48 N	76.49 W
Tadine	175f	21.33 S	167.52 E
Tadio, Lagune ⊂	150	5.11 N	5.15 W
Tadjemout	148	25.37 N	3.48 E
Tadjenanet	34	36.08 N	5.59 E
Tadjeraout, Oued V	148	21.17 N	1.19 E
Tadjoura	144	11.47 N	42.54 E
Tadjoura, Golfe de ⊂	144	11.42 N	43.00 E
Tadley	42	51.21 N	1.08 W
Tado	94	35.08 N	136.38 E
Tadok	114	3.58 N	96.19 E
Tadotsu	96	34.16 N	133.45 E
Tadoule Lake ⊜	176	58.36 N	98.20 W
Tadoussac	186	48.09 N	69.43 W
Tādpatri	122	14.55 N	78.01 E
Taduno	112	1.55 S	123.05 E
Tadworth	42	51.17 N	0.14 W
Tadzhikistan → Tajikistan □[1]	72	39.00 N	71.00 E
Tadžikabad	85	39.07 N	70.50 E
T'aean	98	36.46 N	126.16 E
T'aebaek-san ∧	98	37.06 N	128.55 E
T'aebaek-sanmaek ⋏	98	37.40 N	128.50 E
Taebu-do I	98	37.15 N	126.35 E
Taech'ŏn	98	36.22 N	126.34 E
Taech'ŏng-do I	98	37.49 N	124.43 E
Taedong	98	39.05 N	125.31 E
Taedong-gang ≃	98	38.42 N	125.15 E
Taegu	98	35.52 N	128.35 E
Taegu □[4]	98	35.50 N	128.35 E
Taegwan	98	40.13 N	125.12 E
Taehan-Min'guk → Korea, South □[1]	98	36.30 N	128.00 E
Taehŭksan-do I	98	34.40 N	125.25 E
Taehŭng	98	40.06 N	126.56 E
Taehwajŏn	271b	37.36 N	126.52 E
T'aein	98	35.40 N	126.55 E
Taejin	98	36.34 N	129.24 E
Taejŏn	98	36.20 N	127.26 E
Taejujŏm	98	38.24 N	127.58 E
T'aemo-san ∧	271b	37.27 N	127.04 E
Taeng ≃	110	19.06 N	98.57 E
Taer	102	34.09 N	98.50 E
Ta'erwan	100	31.49 N	113.25 E
Taeryanghwa	98	41.14 N	129.42 E
Taf ≃	42	51.47 N	4.26 W
Tafahi I	14	15.51 S	173.43 W
Tafahnā al-'Azab	142	30.36 N	31.15 E
Tafalla	34	42.31 N	1.40 W
Tafanlieh	100	21.58 N	120.46 E
Ṭafas	132	32.44 N	36.04 E
Tafāsīkh, Ghurd at- ⊥[8]	142	29.43 N	29.45 E
Tafassasset, Oued (Oued Tafassâsset) V	148	20.56 N	10.12 E
Tafassâsset, Ténéré du ⬥[2]	146	21.00 N	11.00 E
Tafea □[8]	175f	19.30 S	169.00 E
Tafelbaai → Table Bay ⊂	158	33.53 S	18.27 E
Tafelberg ∧	250	3.55 N	56.10 W
Tafermaar	164	6.51 S	134.06 E
Taff ≃	42	51.27 N	3.09 W
Tafiré	150	9.04 N	5.10 W
Tafí Viejo	252	26.44 S	65.16 W
Taflan	130	41.25 N	36.09 E
Tafna, Oued ≃	34	35.17 N	1.30 W
Tafo	150	6.13 N	0.22 W
Tafraoute	148	29.40 N	8.58 W
Taft, Īrān	128	31.45 N	54.14 E
Taft, Pil.	116	11.54 N	125.25 E
Taft, Ca., U.S.	204	35.08 N	119.27 W
Taft, Fl., U.S.	220	28.23 N	81.24 W
Taft, Ok., U.S.	196	35.45 N	95.32 W
Taft, Tx., U.S.	196	27.58 N	97.23 W
Taftān, Kūh-e ∧	128	28.36 N	61.08 E
Tafton	210	41.25 N	75.11 W
Taga, Nihon	94	35.13 N	136.17 E
Taga, Nihon	270	34.49 N	135.49 E
Taga, W. Sam.	175a	13.46 S	172.28 W
Tagabukid	116	7.00 N	126.21 E
Taga Dzong	124	27.04 N	89.53 E
Tagagawik ≃	180	66.30 N	159.00 W
Tagaj	80	54.18 N	47.39 E
Tagajō	92	38.20 N	141.00 E
Tagan	86	54.57 N	77.18 E
Tagana-an	116	9.42 N	125.35 E
Taganrog	83	47.12 N	38.56 E
Taganrogskij zaliv ⊂	78	47.00 N	38.23 E
Tagant □[4]	150	18.20 N	11.30 W
Tagânt ⬥[1]	150	18.00 N	12.00 W
Tagapula Island I	116	12.04 N	124.12 E
Tågarp	41	55.56 N	12.57 E
Tagauayan Island I	116	10.58 N	121.13 E
Tagawa	96	33.38 N	130.49 E
Tagaytay	116	14.06 N	120.56 E
Tagbara	152	5.56 N	21.09 E
Tagbilaran	116	9.39 N	123.51 E
Tagdempt → Tihert	148	35.28 N	1.21 E
Tage	164	6.20 S	143.20 E
Tageren Canal ≊	174q	9.33 N	138.09 E
Taggia	62	43.52 N	7.51 E
Taghit	148	30.55 N	2.02 W
Taghkanic Creek ≃	210	42.13 N	73.45 W
Taghmon	48	52.18 N	6.39 W
Tagig	269f	14.32 N	121.04 E
Tagig ≃	269f	14.31 N	121.05 E
T'aginka	78	46.47 N	33.04 E
Tagish Lake ⊜	180	59.45 N	134.15 W
Tagliacozzo	66	42.04 N	13.14 E
Tagliamento ≃	64	45.38 N	13.06 E
Tagliata, Monte della ∧	64	44.34 N	9.48 E
Taglio di Po	64	45.00 N	12.12 E
Tagna	88	53.36 N	101.54 E
Tagna ≃	88	53.38 N	101.53 E
Tago	116	9.02 N	126.13 E
Tago ≃	116	9.01 N	126.14 E
Tagoloan	116	8.32 N	124.45 E
Tagolo Point ›	116	8.44 N	123.23 E
Tagon Harbour ⊂	162	33.53 S	123.00 E
Tagounit	148	29.58 N	5.36 W
Tagourâret ⊤[4]	150	17.45 N	7.43 W
Tagow Bāy	120	35.42 N	66.03 E
Tagrina, Oued V	148	21.00 N	6.16 E
Taguatinga	255	12.25 S	46.26 W
Tagubanhan Island I	116	11.08 N	123.07 E
Tagudin	116	16.56 N	120.27 E
Taguedoufat V	150	14.50 N	7.42 E
Taguke	120	32.07 N	84.35 E
Tagul ≃	88	55.35 N	97.45 E
Tagula Island I	160	11.30 S	153.30 E
Tagum	116	7.28 N	125.48 E
T'agun	86	53.56 N	85.38 E
Tagun Bay ⊂	116	13.55 N	123.46 E
Tagus (Tejo) (Tajo) ≃	34	38.40 N	9.24 W
T'agyŏng-ni	98	38.04 N	126.03 E
Tah, Sebkha ⊜	148	27.45 N	12.42 W
Taha	89	47.33 N	124.14 E
Tahaa I	14	16.38 S	151.30 W
Tahakopa	172	46.31 S	169.23 E
Tahala	148	34.04 N	4.20 W
Tahan, Gunong ∧	114	4.38 N	102.14 E
Tahanaoute	148	31.24 N	7.54 W
Tahāneh-ye Ney Basteh	128	32.59 N	60.53 E
Tahara	94	34.40 N	137.16 E
Tahart	148	22.51 N	5.12 E
Tahat ∧	148	23.18 N	5.47 E
Taheke	172	35.27 S	173.39 E
Ṭāherī	128	27.42 N	52.21 E
Tahgong, Puntan ›	174n	15.06 N	145.39 E
Tahifet	148	22.58 N	5.55 E
Tahiryuak Lake ⊜	176	70.56 N	112.20 W
Tahiti I	174s	17.37 S	149.27 W
Tahkuna neem ›	76	59.07 N	22.36 E
Tāhlāb (Ṭālāb) ≃	128	28.09 N	62.45 E
Tahlequah	196	35.54 N	94.58 W
Ṭahmā wa Minshāt 'Abd as-Sayyid	142	29.38 N	31.14 E
Tahmoor	170	34.13 S	150.36 E
Tahneta Pass)(	180	61.53 N	147.20 W
Tahoe, Lake ⊜	226	39.07 N	120.03 W
Tahoe City	226	39.10 N	120.08 W
Tahoe Lake ⊜	176	70.15 N	108.45 W
Tahoe Paradise	226	38.52 N	120.01 W
Tahoe Valley	226	38.55 N	120.00 W
Tahoka	196	33.10 N	101.47 W
Taholah	224	47.20 N	124.17 W
Tahoua	150	14.54 N	5.16 E
Tahoua □[5]	150	16.00 N	5.00 E
Tahquamenon ≃	190	46.34 N	85.02 W
Tahquamenon Falls State Park ♠	190	46.29 N	85.05 W
Tahsi	100	24.57 N	121.53 E
Tahsis	182	49.55 N	126.39 W
Ṭahṭā	140	26.46 N	31.30 E
Tahtaköprü	130	39.57 N	29.39 E
Tahtsa Lake ⊜	182	53.42 N	127.26 W
Tahtsa Peak ∧	182	53.33 N	127.47 W
Tahu	100	24.26 N	120.52 E
Tahuamanu ≃	248	11.06 S	67.36 W
Tahuata I	174x	9.57 S	139.05 W
Tahulandang, Pulau I	112	2.20 N	125.25 E
Tahuna	112	3.37 N	125.29 E
Tahuofang ⊜[1]	104	41.55 N	124.07 E
Tahuya ≃	224	47.23 N	123.03 W
Ṭahwāy	142	30.22 N	30.52 E
Taï, C. Iv.	150	5.52 N	7.27 W
Tai, It.	64	46.25 N	12.20 E
Tai, Nihon	270	34.31 N	135.26 E
Tai ⬥[8]	270	34.45 N	135.00 E
Taiaçupeba	256	23.40 S	46.11 W
Tai'an, Zhg.	98	36.12 N	117.07 E
Tai'an, Zhg.	104	41.23 N	122.27 E
Tai'an, Zhg.	107	30.05 N	105.47 E
Tai'angang	106	31.43 N	121.40 E
Taiarapu, Presqu'île de ›[1]	174s	17.47 S	149.14 W
Taibai	102	34.00 N	107.18 E
Taibai Shan ∧, Zhg.	98	39.19 N	114.11 E
Taibai Shan ∧, Zhg.	102	33.54 N	107.46 E
Taibilla, Sierra de ⋏	34	38.10 N	2.10 W
Taibon Agordino	64	46.18 N	12.00 E
Taibus Qi (Baochang)	98	41.56 N	115.22 E
Taicang	106	31.26 N	121.07 E
T'aichou → Taizhou	100	32.30 N	119.58 E
Taichu → T'aichung	100	24.09 N	120.41 E
T'aichung	100	24.09 N	120.41 E
Taicunzhen	106	31.27 N	119.03 E
Taiden → Taejŏn	98	36.20 N	127.26 E
Taiei	94	35.49 N	140.25 E
Taieri ≃	172	46.03 S	170.11 E
Taif → Aṭ-Ṭā'if	144	21.16 N	40.24 E
Taigu	102	37.28 N	112.30 E
Tai Hang	271d	22.17 N	114.11 E
Taihang Shan ⋏	102	38.00 N	114.00 E
Taihape	172	39.40 S	175.48 E
Taihe, Zhg.	100	33.11 N	115.36 E
Taihe, Zhg.	100	26.49 N	114.55 E
Taihe, Zhg.	107	30.10 N	105.56 E
Taihezhen, Zhg.	89	44.47 N	123.29 E
Taihezhen, Zhg.	107	30.07 N	103.50 E
Taihezhen, Zhg.	107	30.06 N	106.03 E
Taiho	174m	26.39 N	128.07 E
Taihoku → T'aipei	100	25.03 N	121.30 E
T'aihsi	100	23.42 N	120.11 E
T'aihsien → Taizhou	100	32.30 N	119.58 E
Taihu	100	30.26 N	116.16 E
Tai Hu ⊜	106	31.15 N	120.10 E
Taijiang	102	26.32 N	108.22 E
Taijimiao	98	40.55 N	113.46 E
Taijüan → Taiyuan	102	37.55 N	112.30 E
Taikang	98	34.04 N	114.50 E
Taikkyi	110	17.19 N	95.58 E
Taikou	102	31.53 N	111.07 E
Taiko-yama ∧	96	35.46 N	135.12 E
Taikyu → Taegu	98	35.52 N	128.35 E
Tailai	89	46.23 N	123.27 E
Tai Lam Chung	271d	22.22 N	114.01 E
Tai Lam Chung Reservoir ⊜[1]	271d	22.23 N	114.01 E
Tailem Bend	166	35.16 S	139.27 E
Tailfingen	58	48.15 N	9.01 E
Tai Long, H.K.	271d	22.25 N	114.22 E
Tai Long, H.K.	271d	22.13 N	113.59 E
Tai Long Bay ⊂	271d	22.24 N	114.24 E
Taima, Nihon	96	34.30 N	135.42 E
T'aima, T'aiwan	100	22.37 N	120.59 E
Taimba	74	60.18 N	98.58 E
Taimei	100	23.19 N	114.29 E
Tai Mong Tsai	271d	22.24 N	114.18 E
Tai Mo Shan ∧	271d	22.25 N	114.07 E
Taimyr-Halbinsel → Tajmyr, poluostrov ›[1]	74	76.00 N	104.00 E
Tain	46	57.48 N	4.04 W
Tainaka	270	34.36 N	135.37 E
T'ainan	100	23.00 N	120.12 E
Taínaron, Ákra ›	38	36.22 N	22.30 E
Taining	100	26.54 N	117.09 E
Tain-l'Hermitage	62	45.04 N	4.51 E
Tai O, H.K.	100	22.15 N	113.51 E
Taio, It.	64	46.20 N	11.04 E
Taiobeiras	255	15.49 S	42.14 W
Tai Pang Wan ⊂	100	22.30 N	114.24 E
T'aipei, T'aiwan	100	25.03 N	121.30 E
T'aipei, T'aiwan	269d	25.03 N	121.30 E
T'aipei □[6]	269d	25.00 N	121.40 E
Taipei Bridge ⬥[5]	269d	25.04 N	121.30 E
T'aipeihsien	100	25.00 N	121.27 E
Taipei Institute of Technology ♥[2]	269d	25.02 N	121.32 E
Taipei New Park ♠	269d	25.03 N	121.31 E
T'aipei Shih □[7]	269d	25.05 N	121.33 E
Taiping, Malay.	114	4.51 N	100.44 E
Taiping, Zhg.	100	22.49 N	113.41 E
Taiping, Zhg.	100	30.18 N	118.12 E
Taiping, Zhg.	102	22.40 N	107.05 E
Taiping, Zhg.	107	30.24 N	103.37 E
Taipingchang, Zhg.	102	27.25 N	103.04 E
Taipingchang, Zhg.	107	30.25 N	103.46 E
Taipingchang, Zhg.	107	29.33 N	103.33 E
Taipingchang, Zhg.	107	29.53 N	106.04 E
Taipingchang, Zhg.	107	29.55 N	103.49 E
Taipingchang, Zhg.	107	30.10 N	106.21 E
Taipingchang, Zhg.	107	30.39 N	105.54 E
Taipingchuan, Zhg.	89	44.23 N	123.11 E
Taipingchuan, Zhg.	98	42.36 N	127.20 E
Taipingdian	102	32.08 N	111.45 E
Taipingkou	100	29.50 N	113.35 E
Taipingling	89	43.26 N	128.09 E
Taipingshan, Zhg.	98	40.34 N	122.25 E
Taipingshan, Zhg.	104	41.36 N	123.41 E
Taipingshao	98	40.54 N	125.08 E
Taipingsi	107	29.24 N	103.34 E
Taipingxigou	104	42.36 N	121.13 E
Taipingzhai	104	42.14 N	124.07 E
Taipingzhen, Zhg.	89	46.44 N	130.44 E
Taipingzhen, Zhg.	102	35.42 N	107.37 E
Taipingzhen, Zhg.	107	29.24 N	105.47 E
Taipingzhen, Zhg.	107	30.26 N	104.12 E
Taipingzhuang, Zhg.	104	42.38 N	123.45 E
Taipingzhuang, Zhg.	105	40.03 N	116.24 E
Taipingzhuang, Zhg.	105	40.08 N	117.36 E
Tai Po Hoi ⊂	271d	22.26 N	114.12 E
Tai Po Tsai	271d	22.21 N	114.15 E
Taipu	250	5.37 S	35.36 W
Taira, Nihon	94	36.26 N	136.57 E
Taira → Iwaki, Nihon	94	37.03 N	140.55 E
Tairetá	256	22.36 S	43.42 W
Tairiqiao	106	30.59 N	121.33 E
Tais	112	4.06 S	102.34 E
Taisen-zan ∧	96	33.06 N	131.17 E
Taisha → Izumo, Nihon	96	35.22 N	132.46 E
Taisha, Nihon	96	35.24 N	132.40 E
Taishaku-kyō ♠	96	34.53 N	133.13 E
Taishaku-zan ∧, Nihon	94	36.58 N	139.28 E
Taishaku-zan ∧, Nihon	270	34.47 N	135.07 E
Taishan, Zhg.	98	39.01 N	113.36 E
Taishan, Zhg.	102	22.16 N	112.44 E
Taishanchang	107	30.32 N	106.42 E
Taishi, Nihon	96	34.50 N	134.33 E
Taishi, Nihon	270	34.31 N	135.39 E
Taishō	96	33.12 N	132.58 E
Taishō ⬥[8]	270	34.38 N	135.27 E
Tai Shui Hang	271d	22.25 N	14.13 E
Taishun	100	27.33 N	119.43 E
Tai Tam Bay ⊂	271d	22.13 N	114.13 E
Taitao, Península de ›[1]	254	46.30 S	74.25 W
Taitapu	172	43.40 S	172.33 E
Taitō ⬥[8]	268	35.43 N	139.47 E
Tai Tong	271d	22.25 N	114.01 E
Taitouying	98	40.02 N	119.12 E
Taitō-zaki ›	94	35.18 N	140.25 E
T'aitung	100	22.45 N	121.09 E
Taivalkoski	26	65.34 N	28.15 E
Tai Wan	271d	22.10 N	114.15 E
Taiwan (T'aiwan) □[1], Asia	90	23.30 N	121.00 E
Taiwan (T'aiwan) □[1], Asia	100	23.30 N	121.00 E
T'aiwan I	100	23.30 N	121.00 E
Taiwan Strait ʋ	100	24.00 N	119.00 E
Tai Wan Tau	271d	22.18 N	114.17 E
Taixi	100	24.42 N	116.56 E
Taixian	100	32.31 N	120.09 E
Taixing	106	32.11 N	120.01 E
Taixizhen	106	31.03 N	119.49 E
Taiyang	100	30.12 N	119.19 E
Taiyanggong	271a	39.58 N	116.25 E
Taíyetos Óros ⋏	38	37.16 N	22.12 E
Ṭaiyiba	132	32.16 N	35.01 E
Taiyuan	102	37.55 N	112.30 E
Taizhao	120	30.01 N	93.08 E
Taizhou	100	32.30 N	119.58 E
Taizhou Liedao II	100	28.30 N	121.53 E
Taizi ≃	98	41.00 N	122.26 E
Ta'izz	144	13.38 N	44.04 E
Tāj al-'Izz	142	30.57 N	31.35 E
Tajarḥī	146	24.21 N	14.28 E
Tajbola	24	68.26 N	33.19 E
Tajdakovo	82	54.29 N	37.32 E
Tajerouine	36	35.54 N	8.34 E
Tajetteret, Oued V	148	21.20 N	7.22 E
Tajga	86	56.04 N	85.37 E
Tajgonos, mys ›	74	60.35 N	160.08 E
Tajgonos, poluostrov ›[1]	74	61.20 N	161.00 E
Tajikistan □[1], Asia	72	39.00 N	71.00 E
Tajikistan □[1], Asia	85	39.00 N	71.00 E
Tajikstan → Tajikistan □[1]	72	39.00 N	71.00 E
Tajima	94	37.12 N	139.46 E
Tajimi	94	35.19 N	137.08 E
Tajique	200	34.45 N	106.17 W
Tajiri	270	34.24 N	135.18 E
Tajitos	232	30.58 N	112.18 W
Tajlakdžegen	86	43.54 N	60.29 E
Tajlakovy	86	59.20 N	74.04 E
Tāj Mahal ⊥	124	27.10 N	78.03 E
Tajmura ≃	72	63.46 N	98.01 E
Tajmyr, ozero ⊜	74	74.30 N	102.30 E
Tajmyr, poluostrov ›[1]	74	76.00 N	104.00 E
Tajna	88	56.27 N	95.30 E
Tajninka	265b	55.54 N	37.45 E
Tajo → Tagus ≃	34	38.40 N	9.24 W
Tajožnyj, Ross.	86	56.09 N	94.29 E
Tajožnyj, Ross.	88	56.13 N	94.55 E
Tajpur, India	124	25.51 N	85.41 E
Tajpur, India	124	29.10 N	78.29 E
Tājpur, India	272b	22.44 N	88.16 E
Tajpur Khurd ⬥[8]	272a	28.35 N	77.03 E
Tajšet	88	55.57 N	98.00 E
Tajsojgan	80	48.19 N	53.29 E
Tajturka	88	52.51 N	103.28 E
Tajumulco, Volcán ∧[1]	236	15.02 N	91.55 W
Tajuña ≃	34	40.07 N	3.35 W
Tājūrā', Lībiyā	146	32.53 N	13.21 E
Tajura, Ross.	88	57.00 N	106.35 E
Tajura ≃	88	57.00 N	106.35 E
Tajžina	86	53.38 N	87.28 E
Tak	110	16.52 N	99.08 E
Takāb	128	36.24 N	47.07 E
Takabanare-jima I	174m	26.22 N	127.59 E
Takabara	150	11.50 N	11.30 W
Takachiho	92	32.42 N	131.18 E
Takachu	156	22.37 S	21.58 E
Takada → Bungo-takada, Nihon	96	33.33 N	131.27 E
Takada → Yamato-takada, Nihon	96	34.31 N	135.45 E
Takagi	268	35.56 N	139.35 E
Takahagi	94	36.43 N	140.43 E
Takahama, Nihon	94	34.55 N	136.59 E

ENGLISH

Name	Page	Lat.°′	Long.°′
Takahama, Nihon	94	37.00 N	136.46 E
Takahama, Nihon	96	35.29 N	135.33 E
Takahara ≃	94	36.28 N	137.15 E
Takahashi	96	34.47 N	133.37 E
Takahashi ≃	96	34.31 N	133.42 E
Takahe, Mount ∧	9	76.16 S	112.14 W
Takaido ⬥[8]	268	35.40 N	139.37 E
Takaishi	96	34.32 N	135.26 E
Takaka	172	40.51 S	172.48 E
Takakkaw Falls L	182	51.30 N	116.28 W
Takalaou	146	10.07 N	19.48 E
Takalar	112	5.28 S	119.24 E
Takamatsu, Nihon	94	36.46 N	136.43 E
Takamatsu, Nihon	96	34.20 N	134.03 E
Takami-shima I	96	34.19 N	133.41 E
Takamiya	96	34.47 N	132.44 E
Takami-yama ∧	94	34.25 N	136.05 E
Takamori	94	35.33 N	137.53 E
Takanabe	92	32.08 N	131.30 E
Takanawa-hantō ›[1]	96	33.58 N	132.56 E
Takanawa-san ∧	96	33.56 N	132.51 E
Takane, Nihon	94	36.02 N	137.29 E
Takane, Nihon	94	35.50 N	138.25 E
Takanezawa	94	36.37 N	139.59 E
Takano	96	35.02 N	132.55 E
Takanosu	92	40.13 N	140.22 E
Takao → Kaohsiung	100	22.38 N	120.17 E
Takaoka	94	36.45 N	137.01 E
Takao-kokutei-kōen ♠	94	35.38 N	139.15 E
Takao-san ∧, Nihon	94	35.38 N	139.15 E
Takao-san ∧, Nihon	270	34.49 N	135.51 E
Takapau	172	40.02 S	176.21 E
Takapuna	172	36.47 S	174.47 E
Takara-jima I	93b	29.09 N	129.13 E
Takarazuka	270	34.49 N	135.21 E
Takasago	96	34.45 N	134.48 E
Takasaki	94	36.20 N	139.01 E
Takase	96	34.10 N	133.45 E
Takase ≃	94	36.28 N	137.52 E
Takashima, Nihon	92	32.39 N	129.45 E
Takashima, Nihon	94	35.18 N	136.01 E
Taka-shima I	96	34.50 N	131.50 E
Takashippu	174m	26.24 N	127.44 E
Takasu	94	35.57 N	136.53 E
Takata → Rikuzen-takata, Nihon	92	39.01 N	141.38 E
Takata → Joetsu, Nihon	94	37.06 N	138.15 E
Takata, Nihon	96	33.06 N	130.28 E
Takatō	94	35.50 N	138.04 E
Takatomi	94	35.29 N	136.47 E
Takatori	96	34.27 N	135.48 E
Takatori-yama ∧	96	33.18 N	130.43 E
Takatori-yama ∧[2]	268	35.18 N	139.37 E
Takatsu ≃	96	34.42 N	131.49 E
Takatsuki, Nihon	94	35.28 N	136.14 E
Takatsuki, Nihon	96	34.51 N	135.37 E
Takaungu	154	3.41 S	39.51 E
Ta-kaw	110	21.36 N	98.56 E
Takayama, Nihon	94	36.08 N	137.15 E
Takayama, Nihon	94	36.37 N	138.57 E
Takayama, Nihon	94	36.40 N	138.21 E
Takayama, Nihon	270	34.45 N	135.44 E
Takayanagi, Nihon	94	37.13 N	138.38 E
Takayanagi, Nihon	268	35.25 N	139.57 E
Tak Bai	114	6.16 N	102.03 E
Takčijan	85	38.32 N	68.03 E
Takebe	96	34.52 N	133.54 E
Takefu	94	35.54 N	136.10 E
Takehara	96	34.21 N	132.55 E
Takeli	85	40.30 N	69.25 E
Takenake	120	34.11 N	81.20 E
Takengon	114	4.38 N	96.50 E
Takeno ≃	96	35.45 N	135.06 E
Takenotsuka ⬥[8]	268	35.48 N	139.48 E
Takeo	92	33.12 N	130.01 E
Takeoka	268	35.12 N	139.51 E
Tåkern ⊜	26	58.21 N	14.48 E
Takeshi	94	36.17 N	138.14 E
Take-shima I	93b	30.49 N	130.26 E
Take-shima (Tok-to) II	92	37.17 N	131.53 E
Tākestān	128	36.04 N	49.43 E
Taketa	96	32.58 N	131.24 E
Taketoyo	94	34.51 N	136.55 E
Takêv	110	10.59 N	104.47 E
Take-yama ∧[2]	268	35.13 N	139.39 E
Takhādīd ⊤[4]	128	29.59 N	44.30 E
Takhār □[4]	120	36.30 N	69.30 E
Takhatpur	124	22.09 N	81.52 E
Takhli	110	15.15 N	100.21 E
Ta Khoa	110	21.13 N	104.18 E
Takht-e Jamshīd ⊥	128	29.57 N	52.52 E
Takht-i-Bhāi	123	34.17 N	71.56 E
Tāki, India	126	22.36 N	88.55 E
Taki, Nihon	94	34.30 N	136.33 E
Taki, Nihon	96	35.16 N	132.38 E
Taki, Pap. N. Gui.	175e	6.29 S	155.50 E
Takijuk Lake ⊜	176	66.15 N	113.05 W
Takikawa	92a	43.33 N	141.54 E
Takino	96	34.56 N	134.58 E
Takipur	126	24.19 N	87.58 E
Takitimu Mountains ⋏	172	45.41 S	167.53 E
Takla Lake ⊜	182	55.25 N	125.53 W
Takla Landing	182	55.29 N	125.58 W
Takla Makan → Taklimakan Shamo ⬥[2]	90	39.00 N	83.00 E
Taklimakan Shamo ⬥[2]	90	39.00 N	83.00 E
Tako	94	35.44 N	140.28 E
Takob	85	38.50 N	68.57 E
Tako-bana ›	96	35.36 N	133.06 E
Takolekaju, Pegunungan ⋏	112	2.00 S	121.00 E
Takoma Park	284c	38.58 N	77.00 W
Takoradi → Sekondi-Takoradi	150	4.59 N	1.43 W
Takotna	180	62.56 N	156.04 W
Takow → Kaohsiung	100	22.38 N	120.17 E
Takpochao, Okso ∧	174n	15.11 N	145.45 E
Takrouna	36	36.09 N	10.20 E
Taksimo	88	51.03 N	107.50 E
Taksino	82	56.19 N	36.10 E
Takslesluk Lake ⊜	180	61.04 N	162.55 W
Taksony	264c	47.20 N	19.04 E
Taku	92	33.17 N	130.08 E
Taku ≃	180	58.26 N	133.59 W
Takuan, Mount ∧	175e	6.27 S	155.36 E
Takua Pa	110	8.53 N	98.21 E
Taku Glacier ⍓	180	58.35 N	134.10 W
Takum	150	7.17 N	9.59 E
Takuma	96	34.13 N	133.40 E
Takundi	152	4.45 S	16.34 E
Takutea I	14	19.49 S	158.18 W
Takut Tangub Bay ⊂	116	6.33 N	122.15 E
Takutu (Tacutu) ≃	246	3.01 N	60.29 W
Takuu Islands II	14	4.45 S	157.00 E
Takysie Lake	182	53.54 N	125.53 W
Tāl	123	34.55 N	72.13 E
Tala, Bngl.	126	22.46 N	89.16 E
Tāla, India	124	23.43 N	81.02 E
Tala, Méx.	234	20.40 N	103.42 W
Talā, Miṣr	142	30.41 N	30.56 E
Tala, Ur.	252	34.21 S	55.46 W
Tala, Arroyo del ≃	258	33.37 S	56.34 W
Ṭālāb (Tāhlāb) ≃	128	28.09 N	62.45 E
Talacogon	116	8.28 N	125.46 E
Talaga	112	2.11 S	125.53 E
Talagang	123	32.55 N	72.25 E
Talagante	252	33.40 S	70.56 W
Talagou	104	41.37 N	120.32 E
Ta Lai	110	11.24 N	107.23 E
Talaimannar	122	9.05 N	79.44 E
Talāja	120	21.21 N	72.03 E
Talak ⬥[1]	150	18.20 N	6.00 E
Talakag	116	8.16 N	124.37 E
Talakan	89	49.38 N	133.18 E

DEUTSCH

Name	Seite	Breite°′	Länge°′ E = Ost
Talakovka	83	47.10 N	37.43 E
Tālāla	120	21.02 N	70.32 E
Talalajevka	78	50.51 N	33.08 E
Talamanca, Cordillera de ⋏	236	9.30 N	83.40 W
Talamba	123	30.32 N	72.14 E
Talamone	66	42.33 N	11.08 E
Talana, It.	71	40.02 N	9.30 E
Talana, S. Afr.	158	28.10 S	30.15 E
Talandža	89	49.27 N	131.35 E
Talang, Gunung ∧	112	0.58 S	100.39 E
Talangbatu	112	4.06 S	105.29 E
Talangbetutu	112	2.53 S	104.41 E
Talangpadang	112	5.21 S	104.11 E
Talangrimbo	112	3.29 S	105.25 E
Talant	58	47.19 N	5.00 E
Talap	80	48.26 N	48.03 E
Talara	246	4.34 S	81.17 W
Talarrubias	34	39.02 N	5.14 W
Talas	85	42.32 N	72.14 E
Talas □[4]	85	42.30 N	72.00 E
Talas ≃	85	44.02 N	69.37 E
Talasea	164	5.20 S	150.05 E
Talasskij-Alatau, chrebet ⋏	85	42.10 N	72.00 E
Talatakoh, Pulau I	112	0.22 S	122.05 E
Tal'at al-Jamā'ah, Rujm ∧	132	30.23 N	35.30 E
Talata Mafara	150	12.35 N	6.04 E
Talaud, Kepulauan II	108	4.20 N	126.50 E
Talavera	116	15.35 N	120.55 E
Talavera de la Reina	34	39.57 N	4.50 W
Talawdī	140	10.38 N	30.23 E
Talayan	116	6.55 N	124.24 E
Tālbāndh	126	22.03 N	86.20 E
Talbingo	171b	35.34 S	148.18 E
Talbingo Reservoir ⊜[1]	171b	35.43 S	148.20 E
Talbot	169	37.11 S	143.43 E
Talbot ≃	212	44.28 N	79.10 W
Talbot, Cape ›	164	13.48 S	126.43 E
Talbot Brook	168a	32.01 S	116.40 E
Talbot Brook ≃	168a	32.10 S	116.49 E
Talbot Islands II	164	9.15 S	142.08 E
Talbot Lake ⊜, Mb., Can.	184	54.00 N	99.55 W
Talbot Lake ⊜, On., Can.	212	44.42 N	78.51 W
Talbotton	192	32.40 N	84.32 W
Talbotville Royal	214	42.48 N	81.15 W
Talbragar ≃	166	32.12 S	148.37 E
Talca	252	35.26 S	71.40 W
Talcahuano	252	36.43 S	73.07 W
Tālcher	120	20.57 N	85.13 E
Talchichitle, Isla I	232	24.59 N	108.04 W
Talco	196	33.21 N	95.06 W
Talcottville	207	41.49 N	72.30 W
Talcy, Château de ⊥	50	47.46 N	1.27 E
Taldan	89	53.40 N	124.48 E
Tāldāngra	126	23.02 N	87.06 E
Taldom	82	56.44 N	37.32 E
Taldyapan, Kaz.	80	48.07 N	47.08 E
Taldyapan, Kaz.	80	49.46 N	50.14 E
Taldyk, pereval)(	85	39.47 N	73.11 E
Taldykuduk	80	50.09 N	49.33 E
Taldy-Kurgan	86	45.00 N	78.23 E
Taldy-Kurgan □[8]	86	45.30 N	78.30 E
Tale	150	9.26 N	1.07 W
Taleex	144	9.09 N	48.26 E
Talence	32	44.49 N	0.35 W
Talent	202	42.14 N	122.47 W
Tālesh	128	37.48 N	48.55 E
Taley	152	6.40 N	16.23 E
Talgar	85	43.18 N	77.18 E
Talgar, pik ∧	85	43.05 N	77.20 E
Talgarreg	42	52.08 N	4.18 W
Talgarth	42	52.00 N	3.15 W
Ṭalḥ, 'Ilw aṭ- ∧[2]	142	28.30 N	29.38 E
Talhār	120	24.53 N	68.49 E
Tali, Pointe de ›	241o	15.56 N	61.12 W
Talia, Austl.	162	33.19 S	134.54 E
Talia, Méx.	196	25.44 N	102.26 W
Taliabu, Pulau I	112	1.48 S	124.48 E
Talian Dao I	98	39.03 N	122.52 E
Talibon	116	10.09 N	124.19 E
Talibong, Ko I	110	7.15 N	99.23 E
Talica, Ross.	76	58.44 N	41.34 E
Talica, Ross.	80	58.01 N	51.30 E
Talica, Ross.	86	57.00 N	63.43 E
Talickij Čamlyk	80	52.02 N	40.32 E
Talien → Dalian	98	38.53 N	121.35 E
Talihina	196	34.45 N	95.02 W
Tālīkota	122	16.29 N	76.19 E
Talikud Island I	116	6.56 N	125.42 E
Talim Island I	116	14.21 N	121.14 E
Talimuashili	85	39.08 N	77.03 E
Taling Chan	269a	13.46 N	100.27 E
Taliouine	148	30.36 N	7.49 W
Taliparamba	122	12.03 N	75.21 E
Tali Post	140	5.54 N	30.47 E
Talisay, Pil.	116	10.15 N	123.51 E
Talisay, Pil.	116	14.08 N	122.55 E
Talisay, Pil.	116	10.44 N	122.58 E
Talisayan	116	9.00 N	124.55 E
Talisei, Pulau I	112	1.51 N	125.05 E
Talish-Mikeyli	84	39.23 N	48.22 E
Talish Mountains (Kūhhā-ye Ṭavālesh ⋏	128	38.42 N	48.18 E
Talisker	46	57.17 N	6.27 W
Taliwang	115b	8.44 S	116.52 E
Tal'ka	76	53.22 N	28.21 E
Talkeetna	180	62.20 N	150.07 W
Talkeetna Mountains ⋏	180	62.10 N	148.15 W
Ṭalkhā	142	31.03 N	31.22 E
Talkheh ≃	128	37.52 N	45.53 E
Talladale	46	57.42 N	5.29 W
Talladega	194	33.26 N	86.06 W
Tall 'Afar	128	36.22 N	42.27 E
Tallaght	48	53.17 N	6.21 W
Tal Lah, India	126	22.19 N	87.18 E
Tallah, Miṣr	142	28.05 N	30.44 E
Tallahaga Creek ≃	194	32.55 N	88.58 W
Tallahala Creek ≃	194	31.12 N	89.05 W
Tallahassee	192	30.26 N	84.16 W
Tallahatchie ≃	194	33.33 N	90.10 W
Tall al-Abyaḍ	130	36.41 N	38.57 E
Tall al-'Amārnah (Akhetatem) ⊥	142	27.38 N	30.54 E
Tall al-Maskhūtah (Succotah) ⊥	142	30.33 N	32.07 E
Tall al-Muqayyar (Ur) ⊥	128	30.57 N	46.09 E
Tallanalla	168a	33.06 S	116.07 E
Tallangatta	166	36.13 S	147.15 E
Tallangatta Creek ≃	171b	36.15 S	147.13 E
Tallapoosa	194	33.44 N	85.17 W
Tallapoosa ≃	194	32.30 N	86.16 W
Tallard	62	44.28 N	6.03 E
Talla Reservoir ⊜[1]	46	55.29 N	3.24 W
Tall ar-Ratābah (Pithom) ⊥	142	30.32 N	32.06 E
Tall ar-Rub' (Mendes) ⊥	142	30.58 N	31.31 E
Tallassee	194	32.32 N	85.53 W
Tall as-Sulṭān ⊥	132	31.52 N	35.27 E
Tall Banī 'Umrān	142	27.40 N	30.54 E
Tall Basṭah (Bubastis) ⊥	142	30.34 N	31.31 E
Tällberg	26	60.49 N	15.00 E
Tall Bīsah	130	34.50 N	36.44 E
Tall-e Khosrow-ye Soflá	128	30.37 N	51.35 E
Talleyville	208	39.48 N	75.32 W
Tallinn	76	59.25 N	24.45 E
Tall Kalakh	130	34.40 N	36.15 E
Tall Kayf	128	36.29 N	43.08 E
Tall Kūjik	130	36.48 N	42.04 E
Tallmadge	214	41.06 N	81.27 W

Symbols in the index entries represent the broad categories identified in the key at the right. Symbols with superior numbers (⋏[1]) identify subcategories (see complete key on page *I · 1).*

Symbole im Register stellen die rechts im Schlüssel erklärten Kategorien dar. Symbole mit hochgestellten Ziffern (⋏[1]) bezeichnen Unterabteilungen einer Kategorie (vgl. vollständiger Schlüssel auf Seite *I · 1).*

Los símbolos incluídos en el texto del índice representan las grandes categorías identificadas con la clave a la derecha. Los símbolos con numeros en su parte superior (⋏[1]) identifican las subcategorías (véase la clave completa en la página *I · 1).*

Les symboles de l'index représentent les catégories indiquées dans la légende à droite. Les symboles suivis d'un indice (⋏[1]) représentent des sous-catégories (voir légende complète à la page *I · 1).*

Os símbolos incluídos no texto do índice representam as grandes categorias identificadas com a chave à direita. Os símbolos com números em sua parte superior (⋏[1]) identificam as subcategorias (veja-se a chave completa à página *I · 1).*

∧ Mountain	Berg	Montaña	Montagne	Montanha
⋏ Mountains	Gebirge	Montañas	Montagnes	Montanhas
)(Pass	Paß	Paso	Col	Passo
V Valley, Canyon	Tal, Cañon	Valle, Cañón	Vallée, Canyon	Vale, Canhão
≃ Plain	Ebene	Llano	Plaine	Planície
› Cape	Kap	Cabo	Cap	Cabo
I Island	Insel	Isla	Île	Ilha
II Islands	Inseln	Islas	Îles	Ilhas
⊥ Other Topographic Features	Andere Topographische Objekte	Otros Elementos Topográficos	Autres données topographiques	Outros acidentes topográficos

ESPAÑOL — Nombre | Página | Lat.°' | Long.°' W = Oeste
FRANÇAIS — Nom | Page | Lat.°' | Long.°' W = Ouest
PORTUGUÊS — Nome | Página | Lat.°' | Long.°' W = Oeste

Nombre	Página	Lat.°'	Long.°'
Tallman	276	41.07 N	74.06 W
Tallman Mountain State Park ♠	276	41.01 N	73.54 W
Talloires	62	45.51 N	6.13 E
Tallong	170	34.44 S	150.05 E
Tallow	48	52.05 N	8.00 W
Tallowa Dam ◆[6]	170	34.47 S	150.18 E
Tall Rāk	142	30.54 N	31.43 E
Tall Rif'at	130	36.28 N	37.06 E
Tall Salḥab	130	35.15 N	36.22 E
Tall Tamir	130	36.39 N	40.22 E
Tallula	219	39.56 N	89.56 W
Tallulah	194	32.24 N	91.11 W
Tally	80	53.08 N	53.04 E
Tally Ho	274b	37.52 S	145.09 E
Tālma	126	23.29 N	89.54 E
Talmage, Ca., U.S.	204	39.08 N	123.10 W
Talmage, Ne., U.S.	198	40.31 N	96.01 W
Talmage, Pa., U.S.	208	40.07 N	76.13 W
Talmalmo	171b	35.56 S	147.30 E
Talmas	50	50.02 N	2.20 E
Talmazy	38	46.38 N	29.40 E
Tal'menka	86	53.51 N	83.35 E
Talmine	46	58.31 N	4.26 W
Talmont	32	46.28 N	1.37 W
Tal'niki	88	52.47 N	102.24 E
Tal'noje	78	48.53 N	30.42 E
Talo ∧	144	10.44 N	37.55 E
Taloda	120	21.34 N	74.13 E
Talofofo	174p	13.21 N	144.45 E
Talofofo Bay c	174p	13.20 N	144.46 E
Taloga	196	36.02 N	98.57 W
Taloje	88	55.24 N	95.40 E
Taloje Budrukh	272c	19.05 N	73.05 E
Talok	112	1.03 N	118.48 E
Talon, Lake ⊜	190	46.18 N	79.05 W
Talonan, Tano ›	115b	9.07 S	117.02 E
Tāloqān	120	36.44 N	69.33 E
Taloro ≃	71	40.08 N	8.58 E
Talovaja	78	51.06 N	40.44 E
Talovka, Kaz.	80	50.25 N	47.35 E
Talovka, Ross.	80	49.58 N	45.01 E
Talovka, Ross.	84	44.14 N	46.36 E
Talovka, Ross.	86	51.27 N	81.54 E
Talovka, Ross.	86	57.10 N	93.09 E
Talovoje	83	48.18 N	39.40 E
Talpa	196	31.47 N	99.43 W
Talpa de Allende	234	20.23 N	104.51 W
Talquin, Lake ⊜[1]	192	30.26 N	84.33 W
Tālsa	272b	22.49 N	88.33 E
Talsarnau	42	52.54 N	4.03 W
Talsi	76	57.15 N	22.36 E
Talšik	86	53.42 N	71.53 E
Taltal	252	25.24 S	70.29 W
Taltapin Lake ⊜	182	54.19 N	125.20 W
Taltson ≃	176	61.23 N	112.45 W
Talu	112	0.14 N	99.59 E
Taludaa	112	0.20 N	123.28 E
Taluk	112	0.32 S	101.35 E
Talumphuk, Laem ›	110	8.30 N	100.10 E
Taluti, Teluk c	164	3.21 S	129.45 E
Talvik'ul'a	24	68.45 N	29.19 E
Talwandi Bhāi	123	30.51 N	74.56 E
Talwood	166	28.30 S	149.30 E
Taly	78	49.51 N	40.04 E
Ṭalyā	142	30.16 N	31.00 E
Tal-y-bont	42	52.29 N	3.59 W
Tama, Arg.	252	30.31 S	66.32 W
Tama, Nihon	94	35.37 N	139.27 E
Tama, Ia., U.S.	190	41.58 N	92.34 W
Tama ≃	94	35.32 N	139.47 E
Tama Cemetery ◆	268	35.41 N	139.31 E
Tamacuarí, Pico ∧	246	1.15 N	64.45 W
Tamadjert	148	25.36 N	7.20 E
Tamagawa, Nihon	94	37.12 N	140.24 E
Tamagawa, Nihon	96	34.01 N	132.56 E
Tamagawa ◆[8]	268	35.37 N	139.39 E
Tamagawa-josui ≃	268	35.42 N	139.35 E
Tamakautonga	174v	19.05 S	169.55 W
Tamaki	94	34.29 N	136.38 E
Tāmākośī ≃	124	27.22 N	85.59 E
Tama-kyūryō ⋏[2]	268	35.35 N	139.30 E
Tamala, Austl.	162	26.42 S	113.45 E
Tamala, Ross.	80	52.33 N	43.16 E
Tamalameque	246	8.52 N	73.49 W
Tamalave, Sierra ⋏	234	22.45 N	99.15 W
Ṭamalāy	142	30.30 N	30.51 E
Tamale	150	9.25 N	0.50 W
Tamalea	112	2.29 S	119.19 E
Tamalpais, Mount ∧	226	37.56 N	122.35 W
Tamalpais Valley	226	37.53 N	122.32 W
Tamamura	94	36.18 N	139.07 E
Taman, Indon.	115a	7.25 S	112.41 E
Taman', Ross.	78	45.13 N	36.43 E
Tamana	92	32.55 N	130.33 E
Tamana I	14	2.29 S	175.59 E
Tamaná, Cerro ∧	246	5.02 N	76.17 W
Tamana, Mount ∧[2]	241r	10.28 N	61.12 W
Tamanaco ≃	246	9.25 N	65.23 W
Tamanan	115a	8.01 S	113.49 E
Tamanar	148	31.00 N	9.35 W
Tamandourirt, Oued V	150	19.39 N	2.04 W
Tamanduateí ≃	287b	23.36 S	46.35 W
Tamanhint	146	27.13 N	14.36 E
Tamani	150	13.20 N	6.50 W
Tamaniquá	246	2.38 S	65.44 W
Taman Negara ♠	114	4.43 N	102.23 E
Tamano	96	34.30 N	133.56 E
Tamanquaré, Ilha I	246	0.28 S	64.55 W
Tamanskij zaliv c	78	45.18 N	36.45 E
Tamanthi	110	25.19 N	95.18 E
Tamanusi	112	1.48 S	121.18 E
Tamapatz	234	21.35 N	99.09 W
Tamaqua	208	40.47 N	75.58 W
Tamar ≃, Austl.	166	41.04 S	146.47 E
Tamar ≃, Nepāl	124	26.55 N	87.10 E
Tamar ≃, Eng., U.K.	42	50.22 N	4.10 W
Támara	246	5.50 N	72.10 W
Tamarac ≃	198	48.29 N	97.07 W
Tamarack Lake ⊜[1]	214	41.35 N	80.05 W
Tamarite de Litera	34	41.52 N	0.26 E
Tamaroa	194	38.08 N	89.14 W
Tamarome	164	2.54 S	133.38 E
Tamarugal, Pampa del ≡	248	21.00 S	69.25 W
Tamashima	96	34.32 N	133.40 E
Tamás	30	46.38 N	18.18 E
Tamaské	150	14.49 N	5.39 E
Tamatsukuri	94	36.06 N	140.25 E
Tamaulipas □[3]	232	24.00 N	98.45 W
Tamaya ≃	248	8.31 S	74.13 W
Tamayu	96	35.25 N	133.01 E
Tama Zoological Park ♠	268	35.39 N	139.24 E
Tamazula	232	24.57 N	106.57 W
Tamazula de Gordiano	234	19.38 N	103.15 W
Tamazulapan del Progreso	234	17.41 N	97.34 W
Tamazunchale	234	21.16 N	98.47 W
Tamba	96	35.09 N	135.25 E
Tambach-Dietharz	54	50.48 N	10.36 E
Tambacounda	150	13.47 N	13.40 W
Tambacounda □[4]	150	14.00 N	13.00 W
Tamba Dabatou	150	11.48 N	10.40 W
Tambak	115a	5.45 S	112.37 E
Tambakboyo	115a	6.48 S	111.50 E
Tamba-kōchi ⋏[1]	92	35.20 N	135.30 E
Tambakrejo	115a	7.16 S	111.36 E
Tambalan	112	3.08 N	115.34 E
Tambangsawah	112	3.02 S	102.11 E
Tambara, Moç.	154	16.45 S	34.15 E
Tambara, Nihon	96	33.54 N	133.04 E
Tāmbaram	122	12.55 N	80.07 E
Tambaú ≃	256	21.34 S	47.05 W
Tambault, Île à I	275a	45.20 N	73.51 W
Tambea	112	4.12 S	121.36 E
Tambej	74	71.30 N	71.50 E
Tambelan, Kepulauan II	112	1.00 N	107.30 E
Tambelan Besar, Pulau I	112	0.58 N	107.34 E
Tambellup	162	34.02 S	117.39 E
Tamberías	252	31.28 S	69.25 W
Tambisan, Pulau I	116	5.27 N	119.10 E
Tambler	116	6.03 N	125.09 E
Tambo, Austl.	166	24.53 S	146.15 E
Tambo, Perú	248	12.56 S	74.01 W
Tambo ≃, Austl.	166	37.51 S	147.48 E
Tambo ≃, Perú	248	17.10 S	71.51 W
Tambo ≃, Perú	248	10.43 S	73.45 W
Tamboara	255	23.09 S	52.33 W
Tambo Grande	248	4.56 S	80.21 W
Tambohorano	157b	17.30 S	43.58 E
Tamboli	112	3.57 S	121.20 E
Tambolongang, Pulau I	112	6.36 S	120.24 E
Tambopata ≃	248	12.36 S	69.11 W
Tambor	236	9.43 N	85.01 W
Tambora, Gunung ∧	115b	8.14 S	117.55 E
Tamboril	250	4.50 S	40.20 W
Tamborine	171a	27.53 S	153.08 E
Tamborine Mountain ∧[2]	171a	27.55 S	153.10 E
Tamboritha, Mount ∧	166	37.28 S	146.41 E
Tamboryacu ≃	246	2.31 S	73.40 W
Tambov	80	52.43 N	41.25 E
Tambovka, Ross.	80	47.18 N	47.23 E
Tambovka, Ross.	89	50.06 N	128.04 E
Tambov Oblast' □[4]	80	52.45 N	41.30 E
Tambre ≃	34	42.49 N	8.53 W
Tambu	112	0.02 S	119.52 E
Tambu, Teluk c	112	0.02 N	119.45 E
Tambulian Point ›	116	7.22 N	123.27 E
Tambunan	112	5.40 N	116.22 E
Tambura	140	5.36 N	27.28 E
Tamchaket	150	17.15 N	10.40 W
Tam Chuak, Laem ›	110	8.33 N	98.12 E
Tamdhas	124	28.04 N	83.14 E
Tame	246	6.28 N	71.44 W
Tame ≃	262	53.25 N	2.09 W
Tameapa	232	25.39 N	107.22 W
Tamedda, Djebel ∧	148	32.48 N	0.05 E
Tâmega ≃	34	41.05 N	8.21 W
Tameghza	148	34.23 N	7.57 E
Tamel Aike	254	48.19 S	70.58 W
Tamelelt	148	31.50 N	7.29 W
Tamenghest	148	22.56 N	5.30 E
Tamenghest □[5]	148	25.00 N	5.00 E
Tamenghest, Oued V	148	22.10 N	0.10 E
Tamenuen	164	6.27 S	139.48 E
Tamerton Foliot	42	50.26 N	4.08 W
Tamesí ≃	234	22.13 N	97.52 W
Tameside □[8]	262	53.29 N	2.03 W
Tamga, Kyrg.	85	42.09 N	77.32 E
Tamga, Ross.	89	45.34 N	133.36 E
Tamgak, Monts ⋏	150	19.11 N	8.42 E
Tamgué, Massif du ⋏	150	12.00 N	12.18 W
Tamiahua	234	21.16 N	97.27 W
Tamiahua, Laguna de c	234	21.35 N	97.35 W
Tamiami Canal ≅	220	25.47 N	80.15 W
Tamiang ≃	114	4.25 N	98.16 E
Tamica	24	64.10 N	38.05 E
Tamil Harbor c	174q	9.30 N	138.09 E
Tamil Nādu □[3]	122	11.00 N	78.15 E
Tamiment	210	41.09 N	75.02 W
Tamina	222	30.11 N	96.26 W
Tamir	88	50.24 N	107.25 E
Tamiryn ≃	88	47.48 N	102.36 E
Tamiš (Timiș) ≃	38	44.51 N	20.39 E
Tamitatoala ≃	255	11.56 S	53.36 W
Ṭāmīyah	142	29.29 N	30.58 E
Tamkūhi	124	26.41 N	84.11 E
Tam Ky	110	15.34 N	108.29 E
Tamlūk	126	22.18 N	87.55 E
Tāmma	120	25.11 N	93.42 E
Tammaro ≃	68	41.09 N	14.50 E
Tammerfors → Tampere	26	61.30 N	23.45 E
Tammisaari → Ekenäs	26	59.58 N	23.26 E
Tamms	194	37.14 N	89.16 W
Ṭammūh	273c	29.56 N	31.16 E
Tāmna	126	23.15 N	86.21 E
Tämnarån ≃	40	60.31 N	17.39 E
Tämnaren ⊜	40	60.10 N	17.20 E
Tamnum	144	15.07 N	50.49 E
Tamon ◆[8]	270	34.39 N	135.04 E
Tampa, Ang.	152	15.30 S	13.27 E
Tampa, Fl., U.S.	220	27.56 N	82.27 W
Tampa Bay c	220	27.45 N	82.35 W
Tampa International Airport ⊠	220	27.59 N	82.32 W
Tampamachoco, Laguna c	234	21.00 N	97.21 W
Tampang	112	5.54 S	104.43 E
Tampaón ≃	234	21.59 N	98.36 W
Tamparan	116	8.27 N	117.13 E
Tampere	26	61.30 N	23.45 E
Tampico, Méx.	234	22.13 N	97.51 W
Tampico, Il., U.S.	190	41.37 N	89.47 W
Tampico, In., U.S.	218	38.48 N	85.58 W
Tampin	114	2.28 N	102.14 E
Tampiquito	234	23.52 N	98.14 W
Tampulonanjing, Gunung ∧	114	1.46 N	99.24 E
Tam Quan	110	14.35 N	109.03 E
Tamra	132	32.51 N	35.12 E
Tamrau, Pegunungan ⋏	164	0.30 S	132.27 E
Tamri	148	30.43 N	9.43 W
Tamsagbulag	88	47.14 N	117.21 E
Tamsalu	76	59.10 N	26.06 E
Tamshiyacu	246	4.05 S	72.58 W
Tamsweg	64	47.08 N	13.48 E
Tamu	110	24.13 N	94.18 E
Tamuín	234	21.59 N	98.45 W
Tamuk Island I	116	6.27 N	121.49 E
Tamuning	174p	13.29 N	144.46 E
Tamura	268	35.22 N	139.22 E
Tamusuke	85	38.03 N	76.53 E
Tamworth, Austl.	166	31.05 S	150.55 E
Tamworth, On., Can.	212	44.29 N	77.00 W
Tamworth, Eng., U.K.	42	52.39 N	1.40 W
Tamyang	98	35.21 N	126.58 E
Tan ≃	100	23.57 N	115.47 E
Tana, Chile	248	19.27 S	69.57 W
Tana, Nor.	24	70.28 N	28.18 E
Tana ≃, Cuba	240p	20.42 N	77.25 W
Tana ≃, Kenya	154	2.32 S	40.31 E
T'an'a ≃, Ross.	88	58.40 N	120.30 E
Tana, Lake ⊜	144	12.00 N	37.20 E
Tanabe, Nihon	96	34.49 N	135.46 E
Tanabe, Nihon	96	33.44 N	135.22 E
Tanabi	255	20.37 S	49.37 W
Tanacross	180	63.23 N	143.21 W
Tanafjorden c[2]	24	70.54 N	28.40 E
Tanaga Island I	180	51.50 N	178.00 W
Tanaga Volcano ∧[1]	180	51.53 N	178.09 W
Tanagro ≃	68	40.38 N	15.14 E
Tanaguarena	286c	10.37 N	66.49 W
Tanagura	94	37.02 N	140.23 E
Tanah, Tanjung ›	115a	6.29 S	108.32 E
Tanahbala, Pulau I	110	0.25 S	98.25 E
Tanahgrogot	112	1.55 S	116.12 E
Tanahjampea, Pulau I	112	7.05 S	120.42 E
Tanahmasa, Pulau I	110	0.12 S	98.27 E
Tanahmerah, Indon.	112	3.41 N	117.31 E
Tanahmerah, Indon.	164	6.05 S	140.17 E
Tanah Merah, Malay.	114	2.36 N	101.48 E
Tanah Merah, Malay.	114	5.48 N	102.09 E
Tanahputih	114	1.41 N	101.03 E
Tanaka ◆[8]	270	34.42 N	134.59 E
Tanakeke, Pulau I	112	5.30 S	119.16 E
Tanakpur	124	29.05 N	80.07 E
Tan'am	128	23.09 N	56.29 E
Tanami	162	19.59 S	129.43 E
Tanami Desert ◆[2]	162	20.00 S	129.30 E
Ṭanān, Miṣr	142	30.15 N	31.14 E
Tan An, Viet	110	8.46 N	105.11 E
Tan An, Viet	110	10.32 N	106.25 E
Tanana	180	65.10 N	152.05 W
Tanana ≃	180	65.09 N	151.55 W
Tananarive → Antananarivo	157b	18.55 S	47.31 E
Tanapag	174n	15.14 N	145.45 E
Tanapag, Lagunan c	174n	15.14 N	145.44 E
Tanaro ≃	62	45.01 N	8.47 E
Tanārūt, Wādī V	146	30.08 N	9.59 E
Tanashi	94	35.44 N	139.33 E
Tanat ≃	42	52.46 N	3.07 W
Tanauan	116	11.07 N	125.01 E
Tanbar	166	25.50 S	141.55 E
Ṭanbidī	142	28.38 N	30.47 E
Tan Binh	269c	10.48 N	106.40 E
Tanbu, Zhg.	98	35.51 N	118.17 E
Tanbu, Zhg.	100	28.08 N	114.12 E
Tancarville	50	49.29 N	0.28 E
Tancarville, Canal de ≅	50	49.28 N	0.28 E
Tancha	174m	26.28 N	127.50 E
Tan Chau	110	10.48 N	105.15 E
Tancheng	98	34.37 N	118.23 E
Tanchoj	88	51.33 N	105.07 E
Tanch'ŏn	98	40.27 N	128.54 E
Tancítaro	234	19.20 N	102.22 W
Tancítaro, Pico de ∧	234	19.23 N	102.13 W
Tancochapa ≃	234	17.59 N	94.04 W
Tanda, C. Iv.	150	7.48 N	3.10 W
Tānda, India	123	31.42 N	75.38 E
Tānda, India	124	28.59 N	78.56 E
Tānda, India	124	26.33 N	82.39 E
Tānda, Pāk.	123	32.42 N	74.22 E
Tandag	116	9.04 N	126.12 E
Tandah	142	27.41 N	30.46 E
Tandai	154	19.36 S	32.48 E
Tandaj	80	47.33 N	51.30 E
Tandala	154	9.23 S	34.14 E
Tandaltī	140	13.01 N	31.52 E
Țăndărei	38	44.38 N	27.40 E
Tandaué	152	17.00 S	18.06 E
Tandian	98	40.39 N	124.46 E
Tandil	252	37.19 S	59.09 W
Tandjilé □[5]	146	9.45 N	16.30 E
Tandjilé ≃	146	9.45 N	15.50 E
Tāndliānwāla	123	31.02 N	73.08 E
Tando Ādam	120	25.46 N	68.40 E
Tando Allāhyār	120	25.28 N	68.43 E
Tando Bāgo	120	24.47 N	68.58 E
Tando Muhammad Khān	120	25.08 N	68.32 E
Tandou Bougou	152	3.32 S	10.53 E
Tandou Lake ⊜	166	32.38 S	142.05 E
Tandovo, ozero ⊜	86	55.07 N	78.02 E
Tando Zinze	152	5.22 S	12.26 E
Tandragee	48	54.20 N	6.25 W
Tandridge	260	51.14 N	0.02 W
Tandridge □[8]	260	51.17 N	0.05 W
Tandslet	41	54.55 N	9.59 E
Tandubas	116	5.10 N	120.20 E
Tandubatu Island I	116	5.13 N	120.17 E
Tandula Tank ⊜[1]	122	20.40 N	81.12 E
Tandun	112	0.36 N	100.38 E
Tāndūr	122	17.14 N	77.35 E
Tanduy ≃	115a	7.41 S	108.47 E
Taneatua	172	38.04 S	177.01 E
Tanega-shima I	93b	30.40 N	131.00 E
Taneichi	92	40.26 N	141.43 E
Tan Emellel	148	27.30 N	9.45 E
Tanete	112	4.32 S	119.36 E
Taneum Creek ≃	224	47.10 N	120.40 W
Tanew ≃	30	50.31 N	22.16 E
Taneytown	208	39.39 N	77.10 W
Tanezrouft ◆[2]	148	24.00 N	0.45 W
Tanezzuft, Wādī V	146	25.51 N	10.19 E
Tanforan Park ◆[9]	282	37.38 N	122.25 W
Tang ≃, Zhg.	98	38.45 N	115.35 E
Tang ≃, Zhg.	100	32.09 N	112.25 E
Tang ≃, Zhg.	100	33.18 N	117.46 E
Tang ≃, Zhg.	104	41.15 N	123.21 E
Tang ≃, Zhg.	105	40.43 N	116.38 E
Tanga, Ross.	88	51.02 N	111.33 E
Tånga, Sve.	41	56.12 N	12.46 E
Tanga, Tan.	154	5.04 S	39.06 E
Tanga □[4]	154	5.00 S	38.15 E
Tangail	124	24.15 N	89.55 E
Tangainony	157b	22.42 S	47.45 E
Tanga Islands II	14	3.30 S	153.15 E
Tanga Langua ›	241k	12.14 N	61.39 W
Tangalla	122	6.01 N	80.48 E
Tangamong Lake ⊜	212	44.43 N	77.51 W
Tangancícuaro [de Arista]	234	19.54 N	102.08 W
Tanganika, Lago → Tanganyika, Lake ⊜	154	6.00 S	29.30 E
Tanganjika-See → Tanganyika, Lake ⊜	154	6.00 S	29.30 E
Tanganyika, Lake ⊜	154	6.00 S	29.30 E
Tangarana ≃	246	3.02 S	75.08 W
Tangarare	175e	9.35 S	159.39 E
Tanga-shima I	96	34.40 N	134.35 E
Tangba	107	30.00 N	105.46 E
Tangchi	89	47.00 N	123.46 E
Tangchigou	104	41.04 N	124.11 E
Tangcun, Zhg.	100	29.50 N	118.54 E
Tangcun, Zhg.	100	25.26 N	113.10 E
Tangdaohe	98	40.38 N	118.58 E
Tanger (Tangier)	148	35.48 N	5.45 W
Tanger □[4]	148	35.35 N	5.50 W
Tanger ≃	54	52.33 N	11.59 E
Tangerang	115a	6.11 S	106.37 E
Tangerhütte	54	52.26 N	11.48 E
Tangerine	220	28.47 N	81.38 W
Tang'erli	105	39.09 N	116.43 E
Tangermünde	54	52.32 N	11.58 E
Tangfang, Zhg.	102	27.00 N	101.08 E
Tangfang, Zhg.	104	41.20 N	120.34 E
Tangfang, Zhg.	105	39.29 N	118.01 E
Tangfangqiao	106	31.45 N	120.50 E
Tangfeng	98	38.07 N	115.30 E
Tanggangzi	104	41.01 N	122.54 E
Tanggeasinua, Pegunungan ⋏	112	3.24 S	121.42 E
Tanggengtou	106	30.55 N	119.03 E
Tanggou	100	33.59 N	118.57 E
Tanggu	105	39.01 N	117.40 E
Tangguantun	98	38.43 N	116.55 E
Tanggul	115a	8.10 S	113.26 E
Tanggulashan (Tuotuoheyan)	120	34.05 N	92.45 E
Tanggula Shan ⋏	120	33.00 N	92.00 E
Tanggula Shankou)(	120	32.59 N	91.45 E
Tanggushiluke	120	38.45 N	80.55 E
Tanghe	100	32.43 N	112.48 E
Tanghekou	105	40.44 N	116.38 E
Tanghu	105	39.11 N	115.24 E
Tanghuang	106	31.41 N	119.25 E
Tangi	123	34.18 N	71.40 E
Tangier, N.S., Can.	186	44.48 N	62.42 W
Tangier → Tanger, Magreb	148	35.48 N	5.45 W
Tangier, Va., U.S.	208	37.49 N	75.59 W
Tangier Island I	208	37.50 N	76.00 W
Tangier Sound ʮ	208	38.02 N	75.58 W
Tangijatuo	107	29.36 N	106.39 E
Tangipahoa ≃	194	30.20 N	90.18 W
Tangjia	100	22.23 N	113.36 E
Tangjiagou	100	30.48 N	117.28 E
Tangjiang	100	25.51 N	114.44 E
Tangjiapao	104	41.59 N	122.14 E
Tangjiaqiao	106	31.24 N	119.12 E
Tangjin	98	36.54 N	126.37 E
Tangjiqiaozhen	106	31.13 N	121.31 E
Tangkahan	112	1.36 S	113.52 E
Tangkak	114	2.16 N	102.33 E
Tangkou	100	30.06 N	118.11 E
Tanglad	115b	8.47 S	115.35 E
Tanglewood, Fl., U.S.	220	26.37 N	81.53 W
Tanglewood, Tx., U.S.	222	30.30 N	96.59 W
Tanglewood ♠	207	42.21 N	73.20 W
Tangling	100	26.14 N	119.24 E
Tanglitun	104	41.45 N	123.57 E
Tangmai	102	30.08 N	95.08 E
Tangmarg	123	34.02 N	74.26 E
Tangmazhai	104	41.10 N	122.44 E
Tang Nhon Phu	269c	10.50 N	106.47 E
Tang-ni	98	34.12 N	126.52 E
Tango	96	35.44 N	135.06 E
Tango-hantō ›[1]	96	35.40 N	135.10 E
Tangowahine	172	35.52 S	173.56 E
Tangpu, Zhg.	100	29.51 N	120.47 E
Tangpu, Zhg.	100	28.28 N	114.58 E
Tangqi	106	30.29 N	120.11 E
Tangqiao	106	31.13 N	119.15 E
Tangra Yumco ⊜	120	31.00 N	86.20 E
Tangsanying	98	41.38 N	117.40 E
Tangschan → Tangshan	105	39.38 N	118.11 E
Tangse	114	5.01 N	95.55 E
Tangshan, Zhg.	105	40.10 N	116.22 E
Tangshan, Zhg.	105	39.38 N	118.11 E
Tangshan, Zhg.	106	32.05 N	119.03 E
Tang Shan ∧	106	32.03 N	119.02 E
Tangshi	106	31.33 N	120.51 E
Tangtou, Zhg.	98	35.16 N	118.35 E
Tangtou, Zhg.	102	27.42 N	108.17 E
Tangtou, Zhg.	106	31.38 N	120.19 E
Tangtouxia	100	22.50 N	114.06 E
Tangtse	120	34.02 N	78.11 E
Tanguá	256	22.44 S	42.43 W
Tangub	116	8.03 N	123.44 E
Tanguiéta	150	10.37 N	1.16 E
Tanguip Point ›	116	7.43 N	126.32 E
Tanguj	88	55.23 N	100.58 E
Tangulbei	154	0.48 N	36.17 E
Tangusu, Telukan c	116	5.27 N	119.03 E
Tangwang ≃	89	46.40 N	129.54 E
Tangxi	100	29.04 N	119.23 E
Tangxian	98	38.45 N	114.58 E
Tangxianzhen	100	31.59 N	113.07 E
Tangyan	110	22.29 N	98.24 E
Tangyi	98	36.32 N	115.47 E
Tangyin, Zhg.	98	35.55 N	114.21 E
Tangyin, Zhg.	100	27.32 N	116.16 E
Tangyuan	89	46.42 N	129.55 E
Tangzha	106	32.05 N	120.49 E
Tanhuato	234	20.17 N	102.20 W
Taniantaweng Shan ⋏	102	30.00 N	98.00 E
Tanigami ◆[8]	270	34.46 N	135.10 E
Tanigawa-dake ∧	94	36.50 N	138.56 E
Tanigumi	94	35.31 N	136.36 E
Tanimbar, Kepulauan II	164	7.30 S	131.30 E
Taninges	58	46.07 N	6.36 E
Tanintharyi □[8]	110	12.00 N	99.00 E
Tanır	130	38.26 N	36.55 E
Tanis (Zoan) ⊥	142	30.57 N	31.53 E
Tanishpa ∧	120	31.10 N	68.24 E
Tanjay	116	9.31 N	123.09 E
Tanjiafang	98	36.41 N	118.36 E
Tanjiahe	100	31.58 N	113.56 E
Tanjiang	100	24.07 N	116.32 E
Tanjiaqiao	100	30.11 N	118.15 E
Tanjil ≃	169	38.08 S	146.17 E
Tanjong Dawai	114	5.41 N	100.22 E
Tanjong Malim	114	3.41 N	101.31 E
Tanjore → Thanjāvūr	122	10.48 N	79.09 E
Tanjung, Indon.	112	2.11 S	115.23 E
Tanjung, Indon.	115a	6.52 S	108.52 E
Tanjung, Indon.	115b	8.21 S	116.09 E
Tanjungbalai	114	2.58 N	99.48 E
Tanjungbatu, Indon.	112	0.45 N	117.26 E
Tanjungbatu, Indon.	112	2.17 N	118.05 E
Tanjungbatu, Indon.	112	0.38 N	103.26 E
Tanjungenim	112	3.45 S	103.48 E
Tanjungkarang-Telukbetung	115a	5.27 S	105.16 E
Tanjunglabu	112	2.57 S	106.54 E
Tanjungmedan, Indon.	114	1.26 N	100.34 E
Tanjungmedan, Indon.	114	2.06 N	100.14 E
Tanjungmengedar	114	2.39 N	100.01 E
Tanjungpandan	112	2.45 S	107.39 E
Tanjungpinang	112	0.55 N	104.27 E
Tanjungpriok ◆[8]	269e	6.06 S	106.53 E
Tanjungpura	114	3.54 N	98.26 E
Tanjungpusu	112	0.01 S	113.30 E
Tanjungraja	112	3.21 S	104.40 E
Tanjungredep	112	2.09 N	117.29 E
Tanjungsamak	114	0.52 N	103.03 E
Tanjungselor	112	2.51 N	117.22 E
Tanjungslamat	114	3.49 N	98.20 E
Tanjunguban	112	1.03 N	104.14 E
Tānk	120	32.13 N	70.23 E
Tan Kena	148	26.33 N	9.35 E
Tan Kien	269c	10.42 N	106.35 E
Tankou	100	25.48 N	114.50 E
Tankwa ≃	158	32.20 S	19.33 E
Tanlay	50	47.50 N	4.05 E
Tann	56	50.38 N	10.01 E
Tanna	54	50.30 N	11.51 E
Tanna I	175f	19.30 S	169.20 E
Tannan	96	35.05 N	135.10 E
Tännäs	26	62.27 N	12.40 E
Tanna-tunnel ◆[5]	94	35.06 N	139.00 E
Tannay	50	47.21 N	3.36 E
Tanne	54	51.41 N	10.42 E
Tannenberg → Stębark	30	53.30 N	20.08 E
Tannenbergsthal	54	50.26 N	12.27 E
Tanner	194	34.43 N	86.58 W
Tanner, Mount ∧	182	49.40 N	118.34 W
Tannersville, N.Y., U.S.	210	42.12 N	74.08 W
Tannersville, Pa., U.S.	210	41.03 N	75.18 W
Tännesberg	60	49.32 N	12.20 E
Tännforsen ∟	26	63.27 N	12.44 E
Tannhausen	56	48.59 N	10.21 E
Tannheim	58	47.30 N	10.31 E
Tannila	26	65.29 N	25.59 E
Tannis Bugt c	26	57.40 N	10.15 E
Tannu-Ola, chrebet ⋏	74	51.00 N	94.00 E
Tannūrah, Ra's ›	128	26.40 N	50.30 E
Tano, Nihon	96	33.26 N	134.00 E
Tano, Nihon	270	34.57 N	135.36 E
Tano ≃	150	5.07 N	2.56 W
Tanon Strait ʮ	116	10.20 N	123.30 E
Tânout	150	14.58 N	8.53 E
Tanpok ≃	250	3.27 N	54.00 W
Tanque de Dolores	234	23.40 N	101.10 W
Tanque Grande, Ribeirão ≃	287b	23.25 S	46.28 W
Tan Qui Dong	269c	10.44 N	106.42 E
Tanquinho	255	11.58 S	39.06 W
T'an' Šan' → Tien Shan ⋏	90	42.00 N	80.00 E
Tansania → Tanzania □[1]	154	6.00 S	35.00 E
Tansboro	285	39.46 N	74.55 W
Tānsen	124	27.52 N	83.33 E
Tanshui	100	25.10 N	121.26 E
Tanshui ≃	100	25.11 N	121.25 E
Tansilla	150	12.26 N	4.23 W
Tánsin, Isla de I	236	15.17 N	83.54 W
Tánsin, Laguna de c	236	15.19 N	83.58 W
Tan Son Nhut Airport ⊠	269c	10.49 N	106.40 E
Tansyk	86	47.20 N	79.52 E
Ṭanṭā	142	30.47 N	31.00 E
Tantabogue Creek ≃	222	31.00 N	95.21 W
Tan-Tan	148	28.26 N	11.06 W
Tan-Tan □[4]	148	28.05 N	11.00 W
Tantangara Reservoir ⊜[1]	171b	35.45 S	148.39 E
Tan Thoi Nhut	269c	10.50 N	106.36 E
Tan Thuan Dong	269c	10.45 N	106.44 E
Tāntipāra	126	23.54 N	87.22 E
Tantō	96	35.29 N	135.00 E
Tantonville	58	48.28 N	6.08 E
Tantou, Zhg.	100	29.07 N	121.09 E
Tantou, Zhg.	100	26.03 N	119.35 E
Tantou, Zhg.	100	26.53 N	115.26 E
Tantou Shan I	100	29.11 N	122.01 E
Tantoyuca	234	21.21 N	98.14 W
Tanuku	122	16.45 N	81.42 E
Tanuma	94	36.22 N	139.35 E
Tanumshede	26	58.44 N	11.19 E
Tanunda	168b	34.32 S	138.57 E
Tan'urer ≃	180	64.44 N	174.15 E
Tanushimaru	96	33.21 N	130.41 E
Tanvald	30	50.45 N	15.19 E
Tanwax Creek ≃	224	46.52 N	122.27 W
Tanworth-in-Arden	42	52.20 N	1.50 W
Tanxi	100	28.58 N	115.38 E
Tanxia	100	23.58 N	115.34 E
Tanxu Shan I	106	30.37 N	121.37 E
Tanyang	98	36.57 N	128.21 E
Tanyeri	130	39.37 N	39.50 E
Tanyi	98	35.14 N	118.09 E
Tanymas ≃	85	38.25 N	72.39 E
Tanzania □[1], Afr.	138	6.00 S	35.00 E
Tanzania □[1], Afr.	154	6.00 S	35.00 E
Tanzanie → Tanzania □[1]	154	6.00 S	35.00 E
Tanzawa-Ōyama-kokutei-kōen ♠	94	35.30 N	139.10 E
Tanzawa-san ∧	94	35.28 N	139.10 E
Tao ≃, Zhg.	100	25.56 N	115.06 E
Tao ≃, Zhg.	102	35.52 N	103.16 E
Tao, Ko I	110	10.05 N	99.52 E
Tao'an	89	45.22 N	122.47 E
Taochong	100	31.04 N	118.06 E
Taochuan	102	25.07 N	111.06 E
Taocun	98	37.10 N	121.05 E
Taodigou	105	40.52 N	116.14 E
Tao'er ≃	89	45.42 N	124.05 E
Taoerdeng	98	40.44 N	119.02 E
Taohe	105	39.12 N	116.50 E
Taohua	106	31.23 N	120.04 E
Taohuachiyingzi	104	42.18 N	121.06 E
Taohua Dao I	100	29.48 N	122.17 E
Taohuanbuligai	104	42.13 N	122.14 E
Taohuatu	104	41.40 N	120.40 E
Taohuayuan	106	30.34 N	118.42 E
Taohuazhen	105	40.04 N	114.59 E
Taojiagou	107	29.48 N	104.48 E
Taojiahe	100	30.55 N	115.56 E
Taojialiang	104	42.36 N	121.25 E
Taolahusu	98	42.34 N	116.48 E
Taolaizhao	89	44.51 N	125.57 E
Taolakepa	120	32.05 N	85.22 E
Taole	102	38.46 N	106.40 E
Taolin	98	34.30 N	118.30 E
Taoling	100	30.21 N	118.16 E
Taoluo	98	35.17 N	119.24 E
T'aonan → Tao'an	89	45.22 N	122.47 E
Taongi I[1]	14	14.37 N	168.58 E
Taormina	70	37.51 N	15.17 E
Taos, Mo., U.S.	219	38.30 N	92.04 W
Taos, N.M., U.S.	200	36.24 N	105.34 W
Taos Pueblo	200	36.26 N	105.32 W
Taoudenni	148	22.40 N	4.00 W
Taougrite	34	36.15 N	0.55 E
Taounate	148	34.25 N	4.39 W
Taounate □[4]	148	34.30 N	4.40 W
Taoura	36	36.09 N	8.03 E
Taourirt	148	34.25 N	2.53 W
Taourirt ∧	148	24.03 N	5.02 E
Taoussa	150	16.55 N	0.35 W
Taowu	106	31.47 N	118.46 E
Taoxi, Zhg.	100	31.33 N	117.00 E
Taoxi, Zhg.	100	25.18 N	116.05 E
Taoxi, Zhg.	100	28.44 N	119.36 E
Taoxiantun	104	41.39 N	123.27 E
Taoyuan, Zhg.	100	25.48 N	117.32 E
Taoyuan, Zhg.	102	28.46 N	111.20 E
Taozhu	100	28.50 N	121.31 E
Taozhuang	106	30.58 N	120.48 E
Tapa, Eesti	76	59.16 N	25.58 E
Tapa, India	123	30.19 N	75.21 E
Tapaan Island I	116	5.28 N	120.44 E
Tapacari	248	17.31 S	66.36 W
Tapachula	232	14.54 N	92.17 W
Tapaga, Cape ›	175a	14.01 S	171.23 W
Tapah	114	4.11 N	101.16 E
Tapah Road	114	4.10 N	101.12 E
Tapaje ≃	246	2.44 N	78.07 W
Tapajós ≃	250	2.24 S	54.41 W
Tapaktuan	114	3.16 N	97.11 E
Tapalpa	234	19.57 N	103.46 W
Tapalqué	252	36.21 S	60.01 W
Tapan	112	2.10 S	101.04 E
Tapanahony ≃	250	4.22 N	54.27 W
Tapanui	172	45.57 S	169.16 E
Tapanuli, Teluk c	114	1.38 N	98.45 E
Tapasi	126	23.40 N	87.08 E
Tapauá	248	5.45 S	63.04 W
Tapauá ≃	248	5.40 S	64.21 W
Tapawera	172	41.24 S	172.49 E
Tapaz	116	11.16 N	122.32 E
Tapejara	252	28.04 S	52.00 W
Tapera	252	28.38 S	52.52 W
Taperas	248	17.54 S	60.23 W
Taperoá, Bra.	250	7.12 S	36.49 W
Taperoá, Bra.	255	13.31 S	39.06 W
Tapes	252	30.40 S	51.23 W
Tapeta	150	6.29 N	8.51 W
Taphan Hin	110	16.13 N	100.26 E
Taphoen ≃	110	14.07 N	99.25 E
Tāpi ≃, India	120	21.06 N	72.41 E
Ta Pi ≃, Thai	110	9.05 N	99.12 E
Tapiales	288	34.42 S	58.31 W
Tapiantana Channel ʮ	116	6.23 N	122.00 E
Tapiantana Group II	116	6.20 N	122.00 E
Tapiantana Island I	116	6.18 N	121.59 E
Tapiche ≃	248	4.59 S	73.51 W
Tapili	154	3.25 N	27.40 E
Tapilula	234	17.14 N	93.02 W
Taping (Daying) ≃	102	24.17 N	97.14 E
Tapini	164	8.20 S	147.00 E
Tapiraí	255	19.52 S	46.01 W
Tapirapé ≃	250	10.41 S	50.38 W
Tapiratiba	256	21.28 S	46.45 W
Tapis, Gunong ∧	114	4.03 N	102.54 E
Tapiutan Island I	116	11.12 N	119.16 E
Tapiwa	174d	0.52 S	169.35 E
Taplan National Park ♠	110	14.20 N	102.20 E
Tāplejung	124	27.21 N	87.40 E
Tapoa ≃	150	12.36 N	2.29 E
Tapol	146	8.31 N	15.35 E
Tapolca	30	46.53 N	17.27 E
Tappahannock	208	37.55 N	76.51 W
Tappal	124	28.03 N	77.35 E
Tappan	210	41.01 N	73.56 W
Tappan, Lake ⊜[1]	276	41.01 N	73.59 W
Tappan Lake ⊜[1]	214	40.21 N	81.11 W
Tappan Zee c	276	41.06 N	73.53 W
Tappan Zee Bridge ◆[5]	276	41.04 N	73.54 W
Tappen	198	46.52 N	99.38 W
Tappernøje	41	55.10 N	11.59 E
Tappi-zaki ›	92	41.15 N	140.21 E
Tappo	150	10.12 N	2.38 W
Tapps, Lake ⊜	224	47.13 N	122.09 W
Tapsiā ◆[8]	272b	22.32 N	88.22 E
Tapuaenuku ∧	172	42.00 S	173.40 E
Tapuio ≃	250	3.41 S	44.16 W
Tapul Group II	116	5.30 N	121.00 E
Tapul Island I	116	5.43 N	120.55 E
Tapun	110	18.22 N	95.27 E
Tapurucuara	246	0.24 S	65.02 W
Taputapu, Cape ›	174u	14.19 S	170.50 W
Taqāṭu' Hayyā	140	18.20 N	36.22 E
Taqian	100	29.03 N	117.03 E
Taqiao, Zhg.	100	31.28 N	118.25 E
Taqiao, Zhg.	100	28.24 N	117.02 E
Taqtaq	128	35.53 N	44.35 E
Taquara	252	29.39 S	50.47 W
Taquara ◆[8]	287a	22.55 S	43.21 W
Taquara, Serra da ∧	256	22.12 S	43.53 W
Taquaras, Ponta das ›	252	27.01 S	48.34 W
Taquari, Bra	252	29.48 S	51.51 W
Taquari, Bra	255	17.50 S	53.17 W
Taquari ≃, Bra.	248	19.15 S	57.17 W
Taquari ≃, Bra.	252	29.56 S	51.44 W
Taquari, Pantanal do ≡	248	18.20 S	56.30 W
Taquaritinga	255	21.24 S	48.30 W
Taquaruçu ≃, Bra.	248	20.30 S	55.49 W
Taquaruçu ≃, Bra.	255	21.35 S	52.07 W
Tar ≃, Kyrg.	85	40.38 N	73.26 E
Tar ≃, N.C., U.S.	192	35.33 N	77.05 W
Tara, Austl.	166	27.17 S	150.28 E
Tara, On., Can.	212	44.28 N	81.09 W
Tara, Ross.	86	56.54 N	74.22 E
Tara, Zam.	154	16.56 S	26.47 E
Tara ⋏	38	43.55 N	19.25 E
Tara ≃, Europe	38	43.21 N	18.51 E
Tara ≃, Ross.	86	56.42 N	74.36 E
Taraba ≃	146	8.30 N	10.15 E
Tarabine, Oued ti-n- V	148	20.50 N	7.25 E
Tarabuco	248	19.10 S	64.57 W
Ṭarābulus (Tripoli), Lībiyā	146	32.54 N	13.11 E
Ṭarābulus (Tripoli), Lubnān	130	34.26 N	35.51 E
Ṭarābulus (Tripolitania) □[9]	146	31.00 N	15.00 E
Tarabusi Creek ≃	281	42.24 N	83.19 W
Tarabya ◆[8]	267b	41.08 N	29.03 E
Tarach ≃	154	4.09 N	34.56 E
Taradale	172	39.32 S	176.51 E
Taragaj ≃	85	41.35 N	77.42 E
Tarāghin	146	25.59 N	14.26 E
Tarago	170	35.04 S	149.39 E
Tara Hills	282	38.00 N	122.19 W
Tarai ≡	124	26.35 N	86.40 E
Taraia	124	26.05 N	84.53 E
Taraira (Traíra) ≃	246	1.04 S	69.26 W
Tara Island I	116	12.17 N	120.22 E
Taraju	115a	7.27 S	107.59 E
Tarakan	112	3.18 N	117.38 E
Tarakan, Pulau I	112	3.21 N	117.36 E
Tarakanovka	82	55.07 N	35.44 E
Tārakeshwar	126	22.54 N	88.02 E
Taraklı	130	40.24 N	30.29 E
Taraklija, Mol.	38	46.34 N	29.06 E
Taraklija, Mol.	38	45.54 N	28.38 E
Taralga	170	34.24 S	149.49 E
Tarama	175d	24.40 N	124.41 E
Taramakau ≃	172	42.34 S	171.08 E
Taramana	112	8.10 S	124.51 E
Tarama-shima I	175d	24.39 N	124.42 E
Tarana	170	33.32 S	149.54 E
Tārānagar	123	28.41 N	75.02 E
Taranaki, Mount ∧	172	39.18 S	174.04 E
Tarancón	34	40.01 N	3.00 W
Tarandacuao	234	19.59 N	100.32 W
Taranga Island I	172	35.58 S	174.43 E
Tarangire National Park ♠	154	4.00 S	36.00 E
Tarangnan	116	11.54 N	124.45 E
Tarango, Presa ⊜[1]	286a	19.22 N	99.13 W
Taranovka	78	49.37 N	36.08 E
Taransay I	46	57.54 N	7.01 W
Taranta Peligna	66	42.01 N	14.10 E
Tarantine, Murge ◆[1]	68	40.22 N	17.40 E
Taranto	68	40.28 N	17.15 E
Taranto □[4]	68	40.37 N	17.15 E
Taranto, Golfo di c	68	40.10 N	17.20 E
Tarapacá	246	2.52 S	69.44 W
Tarapoto	248	6.30 S	76.25 W
Ṭaraq al-Hbârî ◆[1]	130	34.17 N	39.16 E
Ṭaraq an-Na'jah ◆[1]	130	34.16 N	39.53 E
Ṭaraq Sidâoui ◆[1]	130	34.33 N	39.54 E
Taraquá	246	0.06 N	68.28 W
Tarare	58	45.54 N	4.26 E
Tarariras	258	34.17 S	57.37 W
Tararua Range ⋏	172	40.46 S	175.23 E
Tarāsa Dwīp I	110	8.15 N	93.10 E
Tarašča	78	49.34 N	30.29 E
Tarascon, Fr.	32	42.51 N	1.36 E
Tarascon, Fr.	62	43.48 N	4.40 E
Tarasht ◆[8]	267d	35.42 N	51.21 E
Tarasovka, Ross.	83	49.28 N	40.05 E
Tarasovka, Ross.	265b	55.58 N	37.50 E
Tarasovka, Ukr.	83	48.21 N	37.33 E
Tarasovka, Ukr.	83	49.40 N	38.23 E
Tarasovo, Ross.	24	66.13 N	46.39 E
Tarasovo, Ross.	24	62.49 N	41.10 E
Tarasovo, Ross.	80	58.18 N	48.45 E
Tarasovo, Ross.	88	55.52 N	107.48 E
Tarasovskij	78	48.43 N	40.22 E
Tarasp	58	46.38 N	10.25 E
Tarat	148	26.13 N	9.18 E
Tarat, Oued V	148	26.09 N	9.20 E
Tarata, Bol.	248	17.37 S	66.01 W
Tarata, Perú	248	17.28 S	70.02 W
Taratai	174t	1.32 N	173.00 E
Taratakbuluh	112	0.23 N	101.27 E
Tāratanr	126	23.58 N	86.29 E
Tarauacá	248	8.10 S	70.46 W
Tarauacá ≃	248	7.19 S	70.15 W
Taravao, Baie de c	174s	17.43 S	149.17 W
Taravao, Isthme de ⊥[3]	174s	17.43 S	149.19 W
Taravo ≃	36	41.42 N	8.49 E
Tarawa I[1]	174t	1.25 N	173.00 E
Tarawera	172	39.02 S	176.35 E
Tarawera, Lake ⊜	172	38.12 S	176.27 E
Tarawera, Mount ∧[1]	172	38.14 S	176.30 E
Tarazona	34	41.54 N	1.44 W
Tarazona de la Mancha	34	39.15 N	1.55 W
Tarba	144	0.48 N	42.39 E
Tårbæk	41	55.47 N	12.36 E
Tarbagataj, Ross.	88	51.30 N	107.22 E
Tarbagataj, Ross.	88	52.07 N	109.12 E
Tarbagataj, Ross.	88	51.12 N	109.05 E
Tarbagataj, chrebet ⋏	86	47.12 N	83.00 E
Tarbat Ness ›	46	57.51 N	3.47 W
Tarbela	123	34.08 N	72.49 E
Tarbela Reservoir ⊜[1]	123	34.10 N	72.50 E
Tarbert, Ire.	48	52.32 N	9.23 W
Tarbert, Scot., U.K.	46	55.52 N	5.26 W
Tarbert, Scot., U.K.	46	57.54 N	6.49 W
Tarbert, East Loch c	46	57.52 N	6.45 W
Tarbert, Loch c	46	55.57 N	6.00 W
Tarbert, West Loch c, Scot., U.K.	46	55.48 N	5.32 W
Tarbert, West Loch c, Scot., U.K.	46	57.55 N	6.54 W
Tarbes	32	43.14 N	0.05 E
Tarbet	46	56.12 N	4.43 W
Tarbock Green	262	53.23 N	2.49 W
Tarbolton	46	55.31 N	4.29 W
Tarboro	192	35.53 N	77.32 W
Tarbū	146	26.02 N	15.10 E
Tarcăului, Munții ⋏	38	46.45 N	26.20 E
Tarcento	64	46.13 N	13.13 E
Tarchankut, mys ›	78	45.21 N	32.30 E
Tarchov Cholm, gora ∧[2]	76	57.11 N	38.25 E
Tarchovka	265a	60.04 N	29.58 E
Tarcoola	162	30.41 S	134.33 E

Symbol	English	Deutsch	Español	Français	Português
≃	River	Fluß	Río	Rivière	Rio
≅	Canal	Kanal	Canal	Canal	Canal
∟	Waterfall, Rapids	Wasserfall, Stromschnellen	Cascada, Rápidos	Chute d'eau, Rapides	Cascata, Rápidos
ʮ	Strait	Meeresstraße	Estrecho	Détroit	Estreito
c	Bay, Gulf	Bucht, Golf	Bahía, Golfo	Baie, Golfe	Baía, Golfo
⊜	Lake, Lakes	See, Seen	Lago, Lagos	Lac, Lacs	Lago, Lagos
≡	Swamp	Sumpf	Pantano	Marais	Pântano
⊓	Ice Features, Glacier	Eis- und Gletscherformen	Accidentes Glaciales	Formes glaciaires	Acidentes glaciares
⊤	Other Hydrographic Features	Andere Hydrographische Objekte	Otros Elementos Hidrográficos	Autres données hydrographiques	Outros acidentes hidrográficos
✦	Submarine Features	Untermeerische Objekte	Accidentes Submarinos	Formes de relief sous-marin	Acidentes submarinos
□	Political Unit	Politische Einheit	Unidad Politica	Entité politique	Unidade política
ᴗ	Cultural Institution	Kulturelle Institution	Institución Cultural	Institution culturelle	Institução cultural
⊥	Historical Site	Historische Stätte	Sitio Histórico	Site historique	Sitio histórico
♠	Recreational Site	Erholungs- und Ferienort	Sitio de Recreo	Centre de loisirs	Area de Lazer
⊠	Airport	Flughafen	Aeropuerto	Aéroport	Aeroporto
■	Military Installation	Militäranlage	Instalación Militar	Installation militaire	Instalação militar
◆	Miscellaneous	Verschiedenes	Misceláneo	Divers	Diversos

Tarcoon 166 30.16 S 146.43 E
Tarcutta 171b 35.17 S 147.44 E
Tarcutta Creek ≃ 171b 35.08 S 147.36 E
Tārdah 272b 22.27 N 88.31 E
Tardajos 34 42.21 N 3.49 W
Tardoki-Jani, gora ∧ 89 48.55 N 138.04 E
Tardun 162 28.48 S 115.45 E
Taredo ◆[8] 272c 19.58 N 72.49 E
Taree 166 31.54 S 152.28 E
Tareja 74 73.20 N 90.37 E
Taremert-n-Akli, Oued V 148 25.49 N 5.17 E
Tärendö 24 67.10 N 22.38 E
Tarent, Golf von → Taranto, Golfo di c 68 40.10 N 17.20 E
Tarentaise V 62 45.30 N 6.30 E
Tarento, Golfo de → Taranto, Golfo di c 68 40.10 N 17.20 E
Tarentum 214 40.36 N 79.45 W
Tarf, Garaet et ◎ 148 35.40 N 7.10 E
Ṭarfā', Baṭn aṭ- ≋ 128 23.50 N 51.27 E
Ṭarfā', Ra's aṭ- › 144 17.05 N 42.24 E
Ṭarfā', Wādī aṭ- V 142 28.25 N 30.50 E
Ṭarfāwī, Bi'r ⊤[4], Miṣr 140 22.55 N 28.53 E
Tarfawi, Bi'r ⊤[4], Sūd. 140 21.04 N 34.08 E
Tarfaya 148 27.58 N 12.55 W
Tarfside 46 56.54 N 2.50 W
Tarf Water ≃ 44 54.55 N 4.35 W
Targa 124 22.27 N 84.40 E
Targan ≃ 85 43.38 N 75.58 E
Target Rock National Wildlife Refuge ◆[4] 276 40.56 N 73.26 W
Targhee Pass)(202 44.41 N 111.17 W
Targon 32 44.44 N 0.16 W
Târgovište 38 43.15 N 26.34 E
Targuist 148 34.57 N 4.18 W
Târgu-Mureș → Tîrgu Mureș 38 46.33 N 24.33 E
Tarhjijt 148 29.05 N 9.24 W
Tarhu 102 41.09 N 107.58 E
Tarhūnah 146 32.26 N 13.38 E
Tari 164 5.50 S 143.00 E
Tarialan 86 49.47 N 91.55 E
Tariat 88 48.06 N 99.32 E
Táriba 246 7.49 N 72.13 W
Tarifa 34 36.01 N 5.36 W
Tarifa, Punta de › 34 36.00 N 5.37 W
Tariffville 207 41.54 N 72.45 W
Tarija 248 21.31 S 64.45 W
Tarija ▫[5] 248 21.30 S 64.00 W
Tarikere 122 13.43 N 75.49 E
Tariki 172 39.14 S 174.15 E
Tariku ≃ 164 3.04 S 138.09 E
Tarīm 144 16.03 N 48.59 E
Tarim ≃ 90 41.05 N 86.40 E
Tarimoro 234 20.17 N 100.45 W
Tarim Pendi ≍[1] 90 39.00 N 83.00 E
Taring 114 3.50 N 97.33 E
Tarīn Kowt 120 32.52 N 65.38 E
Taritatu ≃ 164 2.54 S 138.27 E
Tarituba 256 23.02 S 44.36 W
Tarjannevesi ◎ 26 62.07 N 24.03 E
Tarka 150 14.37 N 7.55 E
Tarka ≃ 158 32.18 S 25.44 E
Tarka, Vallée de V 150 14.00 N 6.00 E
Tarkastad 158 32.00 S 26.16 E
Tarkazy 80 53.52 N 53.39 E
Tarkhūrān 128 34.41 N 50.00 E
Tarki 84 42.56 N 47.30 E
Tarkiln 207 41.57 N 71.36 W
Tarkington Bayou ≃ 222 30.10 N 94.59 W
Tarkio 194 40.26 N 95.22 W
Tarkio ≃ 198 40.10 N 95.26 W
Tarko-Sale 74 64.55 N 77.49 E
Tarkwa 150 5.19 N 1.59 W
Tarlac 116 15.29 N 120.35 E
Tarlac ▫[4] 116 15.30 N 120.25 E
Tarlac ≃ 116 15.45 N 120.27 E
Tarland 46 57.08 N 2.52 W
Tarlee 168b 34.16 S 138.46 E
Tarleton 44 53.41 N 2.50 W
T'arlevo 265a 59.42 N 30.27 E
Tarlo ≃ 170 34.28 S 150.04 E
Tarlo River National Park ◆ 170 34.31 S 149.55 E
Tarlscough 262 53.37 N 2.52 W
Tarm 26 55.55 N 8.32 E
Tarma 248 11.25 S 75.42 W
Tarmstedt 52 53.13 N 9.04 E
Tarn ▫[5] 32 43.50 N 2.00 E
Tarn ≃ 32 44.05 N 1.06 E
Tarna ≃ 30 47.31 N 19.59 E
Tärnaby 24 65.43 N 15.16 E
Tarnak ≃ 120 31.26 N 65.31 E
Tarna Mare 38 48.04 N 23.12 E
Tårnby 41 55.38 N 12.36 E
Tarneit 274b 37.52 S 144.41 E
Tarn-et-Garonne ▫[5] 32 44.05 N 1.20 E
Tarnewitz 54 53.58 N 11.14 E
Tarnobrzeg 30 50.35 N 21.41 E
Tarnobrzeg ▫[4] 30 50.45 N 21.50 E
Tarnogród 30 50.23 N 22.45 E
Tarnogskij Gorodok 24 60.29 N 43.33 E
Tarnopol → Ternopol' 78 49.34 N 25.36 E
Tarnów, Pol. 30 50.01 N 21.00 E
Tarnów, Pol. 54 52.47 N 14.58 E
Tarnów ▫[4] 30 50.00 N 21.00 E
Tarnowskie Góry 30 50.27 N 18.52 E
Tärnsjö 40 60.09 N 16.56 E
Tarn Tāran 123 31.27 N 74.55 E
Taro ≃ 36 45.00 N 10.15 E
Taron 164 4.25 S 153.05 E
Tarong 166 26.46 S 151.51 E
Taronga Zoo ◆ 274a 33.51 S 151.15 E
Taroom 166 25.39 S 149.49 E
Tarouca 34 41.00 N 7.40 W
Taroudant 148 30.31 N 8.55 W
Ta Roun, Co ∧ 110 17.17 N 106.18 E
Tarp 41 54.40 N 9.23 E
Tarpey 226 36.47 N 119.41 W
Tarpon, Lake ◎ 220 28.07 N 82.44 W
Tarpon Springs 220 28.08 N 82.45 W
Tarporley 44 53.09 N 2.40 W
Tarqui 246 1.35 S 75.15 W
Tarquinia 66 42.15 N 11.45 E
Tarqūmiyah 132 31.35 N 35.01 E
Tarra ≃ 246 9.05 N 72.30 W
Tarrabool Lake ◎ 162 18.15 S 135.04 E
Tarrafal, C.V. 150a 16.58 N 25.19 W
Tarrafal, C.V. 150a 15.17 N 23.46 W
Tarragona 34 41.07 N 1.15 E
Tarragona ▫[4] 34 41.00 N 0.45 E
Tarraleah 166 42.18 S 146.27 E
Tarrant ▫[6] 222 32.47 N 97.18 W
Tarrant City 194 33.34 N 86.46 W
Tarrant Hinton 42 50.53 N 2.05 W
Tarrara Creek ≃ 208 36.33 N 77.10 W
Tarras 172 44.50 S 169.25 E
Tàrrega 34 41.39 N 1.09 E
Tarri 144 0.42 N 41.38 E
Tarrs 214 40.10 N 79.35 W
Tarrtown 214 40.51 N 79.31 W
Tarryall Creek ≃ 200 39.05 N 105.19 W
Tarrytown 210 41.04 N 73.51 W
Tarrytown Reservoir ◎[1] 276 41.05 N 73.51 W
Tarsus 130 36.55 N 34.53 E
Tarta 128 40.02 N 52.46 E
Tartagal, Arg. 252 22.32 S 63.49 W
Tartagal, Arg. 252 28.40 S 59.52 W
Tartaro ≃ 64 45.02 N 11.30 E
Tartas ≃ 86 55.37 N 76.44 E
Tartu 76 58.23 N 26.43 E
Ṭarṭūs 130 34.53 N 35.53 E
Ṭarṭūs ▫[8] 130 35.00 N 36.00 E
Taruaçu 256 21.37 S 42.56 W
Tarui 94 35.22 N 136.32 E
Tarum ≃ 115a 5.59 S 107.03 E
Tarumi ◆[8] 270 34.38 N 135.03 E
Tarumirim 255 19.16 S 41.59 W
Tarumizu 92 31.29 N 130.42 E
Tarumovka 84 44.03 N 46.33 E
Tarusa 82 54.43 N 37.11 E
Tarusa ≃ 82 54.44 N 37.11 E
Ṭārūṭ 142 30.32 N 31.28 E
Tarutao, Ko I 114 6.35 N 99.40 E
Tarutino, Ross. 82 55.07 N 36.56 E
Tarutino, Ukr. 78 46.12 N 29.09 E
Tarutung 114 2.01 N 98.58 E
Tarvagatajn nuruu ⋀ 88 48.20 N 99.00 E
Tarves 46 57.22 N 2.13 W
Tarvisio 64 46.30 N 13.35 E
Tarvo ≃ 248 14.47 S 61.03 W
Tarwin ≃ 169 38.42 S 145.50 E
Tarwin, East Branch ≃ 169 38.34 S 146.00 E
Tarwin, West Branch ≃ 169 38.34 S 146.00 E
Tarza 24 62.30 N 40.25 E
Tarzan 196 32.18 N 101.58 W
Tarzana ◆[8] 280 34.10 N 118.32 W
Tarzo 64 45.58 N 12.14 E
Tas 80 48.27 N 51.02 E
Tas ≃ 42 52.36 N 1.18 E
Taşağıl 130 36.55 N 31.14 E
Tašanta 86 49.43 N 89.11 E
Tasaral 86 46.20 N 73.58 E
Tašauz 72 41.50 N 59.58 E
Tašauz ▫[8] 128 40.15 N 59.00 E
Tasāwah 146 25.58 N 13.30 E
Tasbuget 86 44.48 N 65.33 E
Taschkent → Taškent 85 41.20 N 69.18 E
Taşçı 130 38.13 N 35.48 E
Taşdelen 130 38.51 N 38.31 E
Tasejeva ≃ 86 58.06 N 94.01 E
Tasejevo 86 57.12 N 94.54 E
Taseko ≃ 182 52.00 N 123.40 W
Taseko Lakes ◎ 182 51.15 N 123.35 W
Taseko Mountain ∧ 182 51.14 N 123.28 W
Tašelan 88 51.45 N 108.55 E
Tasendjanet, Oued V 148 24.36 N 1.07 E
Tāsgaon 122 17.02 N 74.36 E
Tashan, Zhg. 104 40.48 N 122.39 E
Tashan, Zhg. 104 40.51 N 120.56 E
Tashi Gang Dzong 120 27.19 N 91.34 E
Tashimalike 85 39.06 N 75.41 E
Tashiyi 100 29.43 N 112.48 E
Ṭashk, Daryācheh-ye ◎ 128 29.45 N 53.30 E
Tashkent → Taškent 85 41.20 N 69.18 E
Tāshkurghān → Kholm 120 36.42 N 67.41 E
Tashuik'u 269d 25.13 N 121.30 E
Tasikmalaya 115a 7.20 S 108.12 E
Tasīl 132 32.50 N 35.58 E
Tåsinge I 41 55.00 N 10.36 E
Tašir 84 41.07 N 44.17 E
Taširovo 82 55.25 N 36.39 E
Tasitan 85 39.17 N 76.07 E
Tåsjö 26 64.13 N 15.54 E
Tåsjön ◎ 26 64.15 N 15.47 E
Taskajevo 86 55.06 N 78.36 E
Taşkent, Tür. 130 36.55 N 32.31 E
Taškent (Tashkent), Uzb. 85 41.20 N 69.18 E
Taškent ▫[4] 85 41.00 N 69.30 E
Taškepri 128 36.18 N 62.38 E
Taşkesen 130 39.43 N 41.29 E
Taskesken 86 47.15 N 80.44 E
Taşköprü 130 41.30 N 34.14 E
Taskul 164 2.35 S 150.25 E
Taš-Kumyr 85 41.21 N 72.14 E
Taškyja 85 40.16 N 74.19 E
Tašla 80 51.47 N 52.46 E
Taşlı ≃ 267b 41.03 N 28.56 E
Tasman, Mount ∧ 172 43.34 S 170.09 E
Tasman Basin ✦[1] 6 43.00 S 158.00 E
Tasman Bay c 172 41.00 S 173.20 E
Tasmania ▫[3] 166 43.00 S 147.00 E
Tasmania I 166 42.00 S 147.00 E
Tasmanien → Tasmania I 166 42.00 S 147.00 E
Tasman Mountains ⋀ 172 41.07 S 172.33 E
Tasman Peninsula ›[1] 166 43.05 S 147.50 E
Tasman Sea ⊤[2] 14 40.00 S 163.00 E
T'asmin ≃ 78 49.05 N 32.48 E
Tășnad 38 47.29 N 22.35 E
Tasoba 80 49.47 N 49.52 E
Taşova 130 40.46 N 36.20 E
Tasrār Sharīf 123 33.52 N 74.46 E
Taşrumi 84 38.48 N 44.04 E
Tassajara Creek ≃ 282 37.41 N 121.53 W
Tassara 150 16.48 N 5.39 E
Tassdorf 264a 52.30 N 13.47 E
Tassialouc, Lac ◎ 176 59.03 N 74.00 W
Tassin-la-Demi-Lune 62 45.46 N 4.47 E
Tasso Lake ◎ 212 45.27 N 78.56 W
Tassu, Serra di lu ∧ 71 41.01 N 9.08 E
Taštagol 86 52.47 N 87.53 E
Tastiota 232 28.22 N 111.23 W
Tåstrup 41 55.39 N 12.19 E
Taštyp 86 52.48 N 89.54 E
Taşucu 130 36.19 N 33.53 E
Tasutkol'skoje vodochranilišče ◎[1] 85 43.22 N 74.00 E
Tata, Magreb 148 29.44 N 7.56 W
Tata, Magy. 30 47.39 N 18.18 E
Tata ▫[4] 148 29.40 N 7.45 W
T'at'a, vulkan ∧[1] 92a 44.21 N 146.15 E
Tataa, Pointe › 174s 17.34 S 149.37 W
Tatabánya 30 47.34 N 18.26 E
Tatahuicapan 234 18.14 N 94.45 W
Tatal 80 47.17 N 46.16 E
Tatalin ≃ 102 37.30 N 95.28 E
Tata Mailau ∧ 112 8.55 S 125.30 E
Tatamy 208 40.44 N 75.15 W
Tataouine 148 32.56 N 10.27 E
Tata Raphael, Camp ■ 273b 4.18 S 15.17 E
Tatarbunary 78 45.49 N 29.36 E
Tatarija ▫[3] 80 55.00 N 51.00 E
Tatarinka 76 55.58 N 33.54 E
Tatarino 78 50.36 N 39.07 E
Tatarinovo, Ross. 82 55.13 N 37.56 E
Tatarinovo, Ross. 82 56.34 N 38.25 E
Tatarischer Sund → Tatarskij proliv ꞵ 89 50.00 N 141.15 E
Tatarka, Bela. 76 53.16 N 28.48 E
Tatarka, Ross. 86 53.58 N 75.05 E
Tatarlar 130 41.46 N 26.55 E
Tatarovo ◆[8] 265b 55.46 N 37.26 E
Tātārpur ◆[8] 272a 28.39 N 77.07 E
Tatarsk 86 55.13 N 75.58 E
Tatarskij Kandyz 80 54.07 N 53.07 E
Tatarskij proliv (Tatar Strait) ꞵ 89 50.00 N 141.15 E
Tatarskij Sajman 80 53.18 N 47.07 E
Tatarskoje-Maklakovo 80 55.48 N 45.34 E
Tatarstan → Tatarija ▫[3] 80 55.00 N 51.00 E
Tatar Strait → Tatarskij proliv ꞵ 89 50.00 N 141.15 E
Tatau ≃ 112 3.07 N 112.49 E
Tatau Island I 164 2.50 S 152.00 E
Tataurovo, Ross. 76 58.44 N 43.20 E
Tataurovo, Ross. 80 57.48 N 49.34 E
Tataurovo, Ross. 88 51.37 N 112.56 E
Tate 192 34.25 N 84.22 W
Tate ≃ 166 17.22 S 143.44 E
Tatebayashi 94 36.15 N 139.32 E
Tate Gallery ◆ 260 51.29 N 0.08 W
Tateishi-misaki › 94 35.46 N 136.01 E
Tateiwa 94 37.05 N 139.32 E
Tateiwa-chosuichi ◎[1] 96 34.33 N 132.10 E
Tateshina 94 36.16 N 138.19 E
Tateyama, Nihon 94 34.59 N 139.52 E
Tateyama, Nihon 94 36.40 N 137.19 E
Tate-yama ∧ 94 36.35 N 137.37 E
Tathlina Lake ◎ 176 60.32 N 117.32 W
Tathlīth, Wādī V 144 20.44 N 44.17 E
Tathong Point › 271d 22.14 N 114.17 E
Tathra 166 36.44 S 149.59 E
Tatikawa → Tachikawa 94 35.42 N 139.25 E
Tatiščevo, Ross. 80 51.40 N 45.35 E
Tatiščevo, Ross. 82 56.24 N 37.31 E
Tatitlek 180 60.52 N 146.41 W
Tatla Lake 182 51.55 N 124.36 W
Tatla Lake ◎ 182 52.00 N 124.25 W
Tatlayoko Lake 182 51.39 N 124.24 W
Tatlayoko Lake ◎ 182 51.30 N 124.25 W
Tatlow, Mount ∧ 182 51.23 N 123.52 W
Tatnam, Cape › 176 57.16 N 91.00 W
Tatomi 94 35.36 N 138.31 E
Tatoosh Island I 224 48.24 N 124.44 W
Tatrang 120 38.28 N 85.35 E
Tatranský národní park ◆ 30 49.10 N 20.05 E
Tatrzański Park Narodowy ◆ 30 49.15 N 20.00 E
Tatsfield 260 51.18 N 0.02 E
Tatsuno, Nihon 94 35.59 N 137.59 E
Tatsuno, Nihon 96 34.52 N 134.33 E
Tatsunokuchi 94 36.27 N 136.35 E
Tatsuruhama 94 37.04 N 136.53 E
Tatsuyama 94 34.58 N 137.49 E
Tatta 120 24.45 N 67.55 E
Tattenhall 44 53.06 N 2.46 W
Tatton Hall ⊥ 262 53.20 N 2.23 W
Tatton Mere ◎ 262 53.19 N 2.22 W
Tatton Park ◆ 262 53.20 N 2.22 W
Tatty 85 43.12 N 73.19 E
Tatu ≃ 100 24.12 N 120.29 E
Tatuapé ◆[8] 287b 23.32 S 46.34 W
Tatuk Lake ◎ 182 53.32 N 124.15 W
Tatum, N.M., U.S. 196 33.15 N 103.19 W
Tatum, Tx., U.S. 222 32.19 N 94.31 W
Tat'ung → Datong 102 40.05 N 113.18 E
Tat'un Shan ∧ 269d 25.11 N 121.31 E
Tatvan 130 38.30 N 42.16 E
Tatzuli ≃ 100 24.08 N 121.39 E
Tau, Am. Sam. 174y 14.14 S 169.32 W
Tau, Kaz. 80 49.40 N 47.17 E
Tau, Nor. 26 59.04 N 5.54 E
Tau I 174y 14.15 S 169.30 W
Tauá 250 6.01 S 40.26 W
Taualap Pass ꞵ 175c 7.28 N 151.36 E
Taubaté 256 23.02 S 45.33 W
Tauber ≃ 56 49.46 N 9.31 E
Tauberbischofsheim 56 49.37 N 9.40 E
Taucha 54 51.23 N 12.30 E
Taučik 72 44.21 N 51.19 E
Tauern-Tunnel ◆[5] 64 47.05 N 13.05 E
Täuffelen 58 47.04 N 7.12 E
Taufkirchen 60 48.21 N 12.08 E
Taufstein ∧ 56 50.31 N 9.14 E
Taughannock Creek ≃ 210 42.33 N 76.36 W
Taughannock Falls State Park ◆ 210 42.32 N 76.35 W
Tauini ≃ 246 0.30 N 58.22 W
Taujskaja guba c 74 59.20 N 150.20 E
Taukum ◆[2] 86 44.50 N 75.30 E
Taulabé 236 14.38 N 87.59 W
Taulihawā 124 27.32 N 83.03 E
Taulov 41 55.33 N 9.37 E
Taumarunui 172 38.52 S 175.17 E
Taum Sauk Mountain ∧ 194 37.34 N 90.44 W
Taunay 248 20.18 S 56.05 W
Taunay, Cascatinha ∟ 287a 22.57 S 43.17 W
Taung 158 27.33 S 24.47 E
Taungbon 110 15.25 N 97.50 E
Taungdwingyi 110 20.01 N 95.33 E
Taunggon 110 23.38 N 96.32 E
Taunggyi 110 20.47 N 97.02 E
Taungnyo Range ⋀ 110 15.38 N 97.56 E
Taungup 110 18.51 N 94.14 E
Taungup Pass)(110 18.40 N 94.45 E
Taunsa 123 30.42 N 70.39 E
Taunsa Barrage ◆[6] 123 30.31 N 70.51 E
Taunton, Eng., U.K. 42 51.01 N 3.06 W
Taunton, Ma., U.S. 207 41.54 N 71.05 W
Taunton, N.Y., U.S. 210 43.01 N 76.13 W
Taunton ≃ 207 41.42 N 71.10 W
Taunton, Vale of V 42 51.02 N 3.08 W
Taunton Lake ◎ 285 39.51 N 74.51 W
Taunton Lakes 285 39.51 N 74.51 W
Taunus ⋀ 56 50.10 N 8.15 E
Taunusstein 56 50.08 N 8.08 E
Taupiri 172 37.37 S 175.11 E
Tauplitz 61 47.33 N 14.00 E
Taupo 172 38.41 S 176.05 E
Taupo, Lake ◎ 172 38.49 S 175.55 E
Tauragė 76 55.15 N 22.17 E
Taurak 86 51.35 N 85.01 E
Tauranga 172 37.42 S 176.10 E
Taurasi 68 41.00 N 14.57 E
Taureau, Réservoir ◎[1] 206 46.46 N 73.50 W
Tauri ≃ 164 8.08 S 146.06 E
Taurianova 68 38.21 N 16.01 E
Tauripampa 248 12.35 S 76.07 W
Taurisano 68 39.57 N 18.13 E
Taurisma 248 15.10 S 72.51 W
Tauroa Point › 172 35.10 S 173.04 E
Taurovo 86 59.36 N 73.18 E
Taurus Mountains → Toros Dağları ⋀ 130 37.00 N 33.00 E
Tauste 34 41.55 N 1.15 W
Tautira 174s 17.44 S 149.09 W
Tauxigny 50 47.13 N 0.50 E
Tauz 84 41.00 N 45.38 E
Tavaí 252 26.07 S 55.32 W
Tavajvaam ≃ 180 64.56 N 177.30 E
Tavajza 89 45.12 N 136.44 E
Ṭavālesh, Kūhhā-ye → Talish Mountains ⋀ 128 38.42 N 48.18 E
Tavanasa 58 46.45 N 9.04 E
Tavannes 58 47.13 N 7.12 E
Tavant 50 47.07 N 0.23 E
Tavares, Bra. 250 7.38 S 37.54 W
Tavares, Fl., U.S. 220 28.48 N 81.43 W
Tavares, Ilha dos I 287a 22.49 S 43.06 W
Tavarnelle Val di Pesa 66 43.33 N 11.10 E
Tavas 130 37.34 N 29.04 E
Tavastehus → Hämeenlinna 26 61.00 N 24.27 E
Tavaux 58 47.02 N 5.24 E
Tavda 86 58.03 N 65.15 E
Tavda ≃ 72 57.47 N 67.16 E
Tave ≃ 62 44.07 N 4.42 E
Tavera ≃ 64 46.29 N 11.21 E
Taverham 42 52.41 N 1.12 E
Taverna 68 39.01 N 16.35 E
Tavern Creek ≃ 194 38.19 N 92.18 W
Tavernelle, It. 64 44.18 N 10.04 E
Tavernelle, It. 66 43.00 N 12.09 E
Tavernes 62 43.36 N 6.01 E
Tavernes de Valldigna 34 39.04 N 0.16 W
Tavernier 220 25.00 N 80.30 W
Tavernole sul Mella 64 45.45 N 10.14 E
Taverny 50 49.02 N 2.13 E
Taveta, Kenya 154 3.24 S 37.41 E
Taveta, Tan. 154 9.01 S 35.37 E
Taveuni I 175g 16.51 S 179.58 W
Taviano 68 39.59 N 18.05 E
Tavil'dara 85 38.43 N 70.28 E
Tavira 34 37.07 N 7.39 W
Tavistock, On., Can. 212 43.19 N 80.50 W
Tavistock, Eng., U.K. 42 50.33 N 4.08 W
Tavn-Gašun 80 46.01 N 45.55 E
Tavolara, Isola I 71 40.54 N 9.42 E
Tavoliere ◆[1] 68 41.35 N 15.25 E
Tavolžan 86 52.44 N 77.27 E
Tavor, Har (Mount Tabor) ∧ 132 32.41 N 35.23 E
Távora ≃ 34 41.09 N 7.35 W
Tavoy → Dawei 110 14.05 N 98.12 E
Tavoy Point › 110 13.32 N 98.10 E
Tavričanka 89 43.22 N 131.52 E
Tavričeskoje 86 54.35 N 73.38 E
Tavry 265a 59.55 N 30.42 E
Tavsalayihüseynan 130 38.38 N 40.32 E
Tavşanlı 130 39.33 N 29.30 E
Tavua 175g 17.27 S 177.51 E
Tavy ≃ 42 50.16 N 4.10 W
Taw ≃ 42 51.04 N 4.11 W
Tawa 172 41.10 S 174.51 E
Tawa ≃ 124 22.48 N 77.48 E
Tawaeli 112 0.43 S 119.51 E
Tawakoni, Lake ◎[1] 222 32.55 N 96.00 W
Tawara 270 34.27 N 135.57 E
Tawarada 268 35.19 N 140.04 E
Tawaramoto 96 34.33 N 135.48 E
Tawas City 190 44.16 N 83.30 W
Tawau 112 4.15 N 117.54 E
Tawd ≃ 262 53.36 N 2.48 W
Tāwi ≃ 123 32.40 N 74.41 E
Ṭawīlah, Juzur II 140 27.35 N 33.46 E
Tawi-Tawi ▫[4] 116 5.20 N 120.00 E
Tawi-Tawi Group II 116 5.10 N 120.15 E
Tawi-Tawi Island I 116 5.10 N 120.00 E
Ṭawkar 140 18.26 N 37.44 E
Tawu 100 22.22 N 120.54 E
Ṭāwūq 128 35.08 N 44.27 E
Tāwurghā' 146 32.02 N 15.09 E
Ṭawwah Banī Ibrāhīm 142 28.05 N 30.41 E
Taxco de Alarcón 234 18.33 N 99.36 W
Taxenbach 64 47.17 N 12.58 E
Taxi 89 49.26 N 126.08 E
Taxila 123 33.44 N 72.49 E
Taxisco 236 14.04 N 90.28 W
Taxkorgan Tajik Zizhixian 120 37.49 N 75.14 E
Taxusi 102 32.58 N 98.10 E
Tay ≃, On., Can. 212 44.53 N 76.07 W
Tay ≃, Yk., Can. 180 62.34 N 134.22 W
Tay ≃, Scot., U.K. 46 56.22 N 3.21 W
Tay, Firth of c[1] 46 56.26 N 3.00 W
Tay, Lake ◎ 162 32.55 S 120.48 E
Tay, Loch ◎ 46 56.31 N 4.10 W
Tayabamba 248 8.17 S 77.18 W
Tayabas 116 14.01 N 121.35 E
Tayabas Bay c 116 13.45 N 121.45 E
Tayan 112 0.02 S 110.07 E
Tayandu, Kepulauan II 164 5.30 S 132.15 E
Tayayi 105 39.25 N 115.03 E
Tayeegle 144 4.02 N 44.31 E
Taylor, B.C., Can. 182 56.10 N 120.41 W
Taylor, Az., U.S. 200 34.27 N 110.05 W
Taylor, Ar., U.S. 194 33.06 N 93.27 W
Taylor, Mi., U.S. 216 42.14 N 83.16 W
Taylor, Mo., U.S. 219 39.56 N 91.32 W
Taylor, Ne., U.S. 198 41.46 N 99.22 W
Taylor, Pa., U.S. 210 41.23 N 75.42 W
Taylor, Tx., U.S. 222 30.34 N 97.24 W
Taylor ≃ 200 38.40 N 106.51 W
Taylor, Mount ∧, N.Z. 172 43.30 S 171.19 E
Taylor, Mount ∧, N.M., U.S. 200 35.14 N 107.37 W
Taylor Creek ≃, On., Can. 275b 43.42 N 79.20 W
Taylor Creek ≃, Il., U.S. 219 39.13 N 90.18 W
Taylor Lake Village 222 29.36 N 95.03 W
Taylor Mountain ∧ 202 44.53 N 114.13 W
Taylor Mountains ⋀ 180 60.50 N 157.20 W
Taylor Run ≃ 285 39.57 N 75.39 W
Taylors 192 34.55 N 82.17 W
Taylors Bush Park ◆ 275b 43.42 N 79.19 W
Taylors Island 208 38.28 N 76.17 W
Taylor Springs 219 39.08 N 89.30 W
Taylors Run ≃ 279b 40.11 N 79.57 W
Taylorstown 214 40.10 N 80.23 W
Taylorsville, In., U.S. 218 39.17 N 85.57 W
Taylorsville, Ky., U.S. 194 38.01 N 85.20 W
Taylorsville, Ms., U.S. 194 31.49 N 89.25 W
Taylorsville, N.C., U.S. 192 35.55 N 81.10 W
Taylorsville Dam ◆[6] 218 39.53 N 84.10 W
Taylortown, N.J., U.S. 276 40.56 N 74.24 W
Taylortown, Oh., U.S. 214 40.28 N 80.40 W
Taylortown Reservoir ◎[1] 276 40.58 N 74.22 W
Taylorville 219 39.32 N 89.17 W
Taylorville, Lake ◎[1] 219 39.30 N 89.15 W
Taymā' 128 27.38 N 38.29 E
Taymouth 186 46.11 N 66.37 W
Taymyr Peninsula → Tajmyr, poluostrov ›[1] 74 76.00 N 104.00 E
Tay Ninh 110 11.18 N 106.06 E
Taynuilt 46 56.25 N 5.14 W
Tayoltita 232 24.05 N 105.56 W
Tayport 46 56.27 N 2.53 W
Táyros 267c 37.58 N 23.42 E
Tayside ▫[4] 46 56.30 N 3.30 W
Taytay, Pil. 116 10.49 N 119.31 E
Taytay, Pil. 116 14.34 N 121.08 E
Taytay Bay c 116 10.55 N 119.35 E
Tayu 115a 6.32 S 111.02 E
Tayüan, T'aiwan 100 25.04 N 121.11 E
Tayuan, Zhg. 89 51.27 N 124.16 E
Tayyārah 140 13.12 N 30.47 E
Tayyebāt 128 34.44 N 60.45 E
Taz ≃ 72 67.32 N 78.40 E
Taza 148 34.16 N 4.01 W
Taza ▫[4] 148 34.05 N 3.45 W
Tazawa-ko ◎ 92 39.43 N 140.40 E
Tazenakht 148 30.35 N 7.12 W
Tazewell, Tn., U.S. 192 36.27 N 83.34 W
Tazewell, Va., U.S. 192 37.06 N 81.31 W
Tazhuang 105 39.55 N 117.13 E
Tazicheng 89 46.35 N 123.06 E
Tazigou ≃ 104 41.44 N 121.30 E
Tazin ≃ 176 60.26 N 110.45 W
Tazin Lake ◎ 176 59.47 N 109.03 W
T'ažinskij 86 56.07 N 88.31 E
Tāzirbū ⊤[4] 146 25.45 N 21.00 E
Tazishan 107 29.28 N 104.14 E
Tazlina 180 62.04 N 145.25 W
Tazlina Lake ◎ 180 61.50 N 146.30 W
Tazoult-Lambese 34 35.29 N 6.15 E
Tazovskaja guba c 74 69.05 N 76.00 E
Tazovskij 74 67.28 N 78.42 E
Tazovskij poluostrov ›[1] 72 68.35 N 76.00 E
Tazrouk 148 23.25 N 6.16 E
Tazumal ⊥ 236 13.59 N 89.41 W
Tāzumuddin 126 22.29 N 90.53 E
Tazungdām 102 28.02 N 97.35 E
Tbessa 148 35.28 N 8.09 E
Tbessa ▫[5] 148 35.10 N 8.00 E
Tbilisi 84 41.43 N 44.49 E
Tbilisskaja 78 45.23 N 40.12 E
Tchad → Chad ▫[1] 146 15.00 N 19.00 E
Tchad, Lac (Lake Chad) ◎ 146 13.20 N 14.00 E
Tchaguine Golo 146 10.03 N 16.19 E
Tchamba 150 9.02 N 1.25 E
Tch'ang-Cha → Changsha 100 28.12 N 112.58 E
Tchaourou 150 8.53 N 2.36 E
Tchefuncta ≃ 194 30.22 N 90.10 W
Tchékapika 152 1.17 S 16.11 E
Tcheliabinsk → Čel'abinsk 86 55.10 N 61.24 E
Tcheng-Tcheou → Zhengzhou 102 34.48 N 113.39 E
Tchentlo Lake ◎ 182 55.11 N 125.00 W
Tchériba 150 12.16 N 3.05 W
Tchesinkut Lake ◎ 182 54.05 N 125.40 W
Tchetti 150 7.50 N 1.40 E
Tchibanga 152 2.51 S 11.02 E
Tchigaï, Plateau du ⋀[1] 146 21.30 N 14.50 E
Tchikala-Tcholohanga 152 12.38 S 16.03 E
Tchin-Tabáradene 150 15.58 N 5.50 E
Tchitondi 152 4.33 S 12.08 E
Tchollire 146 8.24 N 14.10 E
Tchong-K'ing → Chongqing 107 29.34 N 106.35 E
Tchořovice 60 49.27 N 13.48 E
Tchula 194 33.10 N 90.13 W
T.C. Steele State Memorial ⊥ 218 39.08 N 86.20 W
Tczew 30 54.06 N 18.47 E
Té ≃ 110 12.27 N 106.02 E
Te, Kinh ≋ 269c 10.45 N 106.42 E
Teá ≃ 246 0.30 S 65.09 W
Teaca 38 46.55 N 24.31 E
Teacapan 234 22.33 N 105.45 W
Tea Creek ≃ 284a 43.02 N 79.06 W
Teaehoa, Pointe › 174x 9.51 S 139.01 W
Teague 222 31.37 N 96.17 W
Teahupoo 174s 17.51 S 149.13 W
Te Anau 172 45.25 S 167.43 E
Te Anau, Lake ◎ 172 45.12 S 167.48 E
Teanaway ≃ 224 47.10 N 120.50 W
Teanaway, Middle Fork ≃ 224 47.15 N 120.53 W
Teanaway, North Fork ≃ 224 47.22 N 120.53 W
Teaneck 210 40.53 N 74.00 W
Teangue 46 57.07 N 5.50 W
Teano 68 41.15 N 14.04 E
Teapa 234 17.33 N 92.57 W
Teapa ≃ 234 17.58 N 92.54 W
Te Araroa 172 37.38 S 178.22 E
Tearinibai 174t 1.35 N 172.58 E
Te Aroha 172 37.33 S 175.43 E
Teaticket 207 41.33 N 70.35 W
Tea Tree 162 22.11 S 133.17 E
Tea Tree Gully 168b 34.49 S 138.44 E
Te Atukura ∧ 174k 21.14 S 159.45 W
Te Awamutu 172 38.01 S 175.19 E
Teba, Esp. 34 36.58 N 4.56 W
Teba, Indon. 164 1.29 S 137.54 E
Tebakang 112 1.06 N 110.30 E
Tebas 256 21.35 S 42.44 W
Tebay 44 54.26 N 2.35 W
Tebbetts 219 38.37 N 91.57 W
Teberda 84 43.28 N 41.45 E
Teberdinskij zapovednik ◆ 84 43.20 N 41.45 E
Tebicuary ≃ 252 26.36 S 58.16 W
Tebicuary-Mí ≃ 252 26.26 S 56.51 W
Tebingbulan 112 3.03 S 103.44 E
Tebingtinggi, Indon. 112 0.36 N 101.36 E
Tebingtinggi, Indon. 112 3.36 S 103.05 E
Tebingtinggi, Indon. 114 3.20 N 99.09 E
Tebingtinggi, Pulau I 114 0.54 N 102.45 E
Tébourba 36 36.49 N 9.51 E
Téboursouk 148 36.28 N 9.15 E
Téboursouk, Monts de ⋀ 36 36.30 N 9.10 E
Tebra ≃ 76 56.51 N 21.12 E
Tebstrup 41 55.59 N 9.53 E
Tebulosmta, gora ∧ 84 42.33 N 45.19 E
Tebza ≃ 80 58.23 N 41.19 E
Tecalitlán 234 19.26 N 103.15 W
Tecamachalco 234 18.53 N 97.44 W
Tecate 232 32.34 N 116.38 W
Tech ≃ 32 42.36 N 3.03 E
Teche, Bayou ≃ 194 29.43 N 91.13 W
Techendorf 64 46.43 N 13.17 E
Techiman 150 7.35 N 1.56 W
Techimentia 150 7.11 N 2.02 W
Techirghiol 38 44.03 N 28.36 E
Techlé 148 21.35 N 14.58 W
Techou → Dezhou 98 37.27 N 116.18 E
Techtin 76 53.51 N 29.44 E
Tecka 254 43.29 S 70.48 W
Tecka ≃ 254 42.37 S 70.25 W
Tecklenburg 52 52.13 N 7.48 E
Teckomatorp 41 55.52 N 13.05 E
Tecolote Creek ≃ 200 35.22 N 105.15 W
Tecolotlán 234 20.13 N 104.03 W
Tecolutla ≃ 234 20.29 N 97.00 W
Tecomán 234 18.55 N 103.53 W
Tecomate, Laguna c 234 16.35 N 99.25 W
Tecominoacán 234 17.53 N 93.37 W
Tecopa 204 35.50 N 116.13 W
Tecozautla 234 20.32 N 99.38 W
Tecpan ≃ 234 17.25 N 100.40 W
Tecpan de Galeana 234 17.15 N 100.41 W
Tecpán Guatemala 236 14.46 N 91.00 W
Tecpatan 234 17.08 N 93.18 W
Tecuala 234 22.23 N 105.27 W
Tecuamburro, Volcán ∧[1] 236 14.09 N 90.24 W
Tecuautzi, Cerro ∧ 286a 19.19 N 99.00 W
Tecuci 38 45.50 N 27.26 E
Tecumseh, On., Can. 214 42.19 N 82.54 W
Tecumseh, Mi., U.S. 216 42.00 N 83.56 W
Tecumseh, Ne., U.S. 198 40.22 N 96.11 W
Tecumseh, Ok., U.S. 196 35.15 N 96.56 W
Ted Ceidaar Dabole 144 4.24 N 43.55 E
Teddington ◆[8] 260 51.25 N 0.20 W
Tédji 146 11.46 N 21.19 E
Tedori ≃ 94 36.29 N 136.28 E
Tedrow 216 41.37 N 84.13 W
Tedžen 128 37.23 N 60.31 E
Tedžen (Harīrūd) ≃ 128 37.24 N 60.38 E
Tedženstroj 128 36.55 N 60.53 E
Teec Nos Pos 200 36.56 N 109.42 W
Teeli 86 51.07 N 90.14 E
Teels Marsh ≋ 204 38.12 N 118.21 W
Teen ◎ 40 59.07 N 14.40 E
Teerijärvi → Terjärv 26 63.32 N 23.30 E
Tees ≃ 44 54.34 N 1.16 W
Tees Bay c 44 54.39 N 1.07 W
Teesdale V 44 54.38 N 2.07 W
Teesside → Middlesbrough 44 54.35 N 1.14 W
Tees-Side Airport ⊠ 44 54.31 N 1.25 W
Teeswater 212 44.00 N 81.17 W
Teeswater ≃ 212 44.18 N 81.17 W
Tefé 246 3.22 S 64.42 W
Tefé ≃ 242 3.35 S 64.47 W
Tefé, Lago ◎ 246 3.27 S 64.47 W
Tefenni 130 37.18 N 29.47 E
Tefft 216 41.12 N 86.58 W
Tefle 150 5.59 N 0.35 E
Tegal 115a 6.52 S 109.08 E
Tegalombo 115a 8.04 S 111.17 E
Tégama ◆[1] 150 15.50 N 8.12 E
Tega-numa ◎ 268 35.51 N 140.04 E
Tegel ◆[8] 54 52.35 N 13.17 E
Tegel, Berliner Forst ◆[3] 264a 52.37 N 13.16 E
Tegelen 52 51.21 N 6.09 E
Tegeler See ◎ 264a 52.35 N 13.15 E
Tegernsee 64 47.43 N 11.45 E
Tegernsee ◎ 64 47.42 N 11.45 E
Teggiano 68 40.23 N 15.32 E
Teghra 124 25.29 N 85.57 E
Tegid, Llyn ◎ 42 52.53 N 3.36 W
Tegina 150 10.05 N 6.14 E
Tegineneng 112 5.12 S 105.10 E
Tegistyk 85 44.02 N 68.22 E
Teglio 64 46.10 N 10.04 E
Tégua I 175f 13.15 S 166.37 E
Tegualda 254 41.02 S 73.26 W
Tegucigalpa 236 14.06 N 87.13 W
Tegul'det 86 57.19 N 88.10 E
Tehachapi 228 35.07 N 118.26 W
Tehachapi Creek ≃ 228 35.17 N 118.38 W
Tehachapi Mountains ⋀ 228 35.00 N 118.40 W
Tehachapi Pass)(228 35.06 N 118.18 W
Tehamiyam 140 18.20 N 36.32 E
Te Hapua 172 34.31 S 172.54 E
Tehar ◆[8] 272a 28.38 N 77.07 E
Te Haroto 172 39.08 S 176.36 E
Tehata 126 23.43 N 88.32 E
Tehek Lake ◎ 176 64.55 N 95.38 W
Teheran → Tehrān 128 35.40 N 51.26 E
Téhini 150 9.36 N 3.40 W
Tehoohaivei, Cap › 174x 9.49 S 138.54 W
Te Hope O Te Keho, Cap › 174x 10.02 S 139.06 W
Tehoru 164 3.23 S 129.30 E
Tehrān, Īrān 128 35.40 N 51.26 E
Tehrān, Īrān 267d 35.40 N 51.26 E
Tehrān ▫[4] 128 35.30 N 51.30 E
Tehrān, University of ◆[2] 267d 35.42 N 51.24 E
Tehran International Airport ⊠ 267d 35.41 N 51.19 E
Tehrān Pārs ◆[8] 267d 35.44 N 51.32 E
Tehrathum 124 27.07 N 87.32 E
Tehri 124 30.23 N 78.29 E
Tehuacán 234 18.27 N 97.23 W
Tehuacana 222 31.44 N 96.33 W
Tehuacana Creek ≃, Tx., U.S. 222 31.31 N 97.02 W
Tehuacana Creek ≃, Tx., U.S. 222 31.50 N 95.59 W
Tehuantepec 234 18.41 N 103.17 W
Tehuantepec ≃ 234 16.10 N 95.07 W
Tehuantepec, Golfo de c 234 16.00 N 94.50 W
Tehuantepec, Istmo de ⊥[3] 234 17.00 N 95.00 W
Tehuantepec Ridge ✦[3] 16 13.30 N 98.00 W
Tehuelches 254 46.56 S 67.27 W
Tehuipango 234 18.31 N 97.04 W
Tehuitzingo 234 18.21 N 98.17 W
Teià 266d 41.30 N 2.19 E
Teichl ≃ 61 47.46 N 14.10 E
Teichröda 54 50.45 N 11.18 E
Teichwolframsdorf 54 50.43 N 12.14 E
Teide, Parque Nacional del ◆ 148 28.15 N 16.30 W
Teide, Pico de ∧ 148 28.16 N 16.38 W
Teifi ≃ 42 52.07 N 4.42 W
Teifiside ◆[1] 42 52.02 N 4.22 W
Teiga Plateau ⋀[1] 140 15.38 N 25.40 E
Teign ≃ 42 50.33 N 3.29 W
Teignmouth 42 50.33 N 3.30 W
Teise ≃ 260 51.13 N 0.25 E
Teisendorf 64 47.51 N 12.49 E
Teisnach 60 49.02 N 13.00 E
Teith ≃ 46 56.08 N 3.59 W
Teixeira 250 7.13 S 37.15 W
Teixeira Pinto 150 12.10 N 13.55 W
Teixeira Soares 252 25.22 S 50.27 W
Tejakula 115b 8.08 S 115.20 E
Tejamén 232 24.48 N 105.07 W
Tejkovo 80 56.52 N 40.34 E
Tejo → Tagus ≃ 34 38.40 N 9.24 W
Tejon Creek ≃ 228 35.08 N 118.53 W
Tejon Pass)(228 34.48 N 118.52 W
Tejupan, Punta › 234 18.20 N 103.32 W
Tejupilco de Hidalgo 234 18.54 N 100.09 W
Te Kaha 172 37.44 S 177.41 E
Tekai ≃ 114 4.14 N 102.23 E
Tékakwitha, Île I 275a 45.25 N 73.42 W
Tekam ≃ 114 3.52 N 102.27 E
Tekamah 198 41.46 N 96.13 W
Te Kao 172 34.39 S 172.57 E
Tekapo, Lake ◎ 172 43.53 S 170.31 E
Te Karaka 172 38.28 S 177.52 E
Tekāri 124 24.56 N 84.50 E
Te Kauwhata 172 37.24 S 175.09 E
Tekax 232 20.12 N 89.17 W
Teke 130 41.04 N 29.39 E
Teke, ozero ◎ 86 53.48 N 73.00 E
Teke Burnu › 130 38.05 N 26.36 E
Tekeli 86 44.48 N 78.57 E
Tekeli Dağı ∧ 130 40.09 N 37.28 E
Tekes 86 43.10 N 81.43 E
Tekes ≃ 86 43.36 N 82.32 E
Tekeze (Satīt) ≃ 140 14.20 N 35.50 E
Tekirdağ 130 40.59 N 27.31 E
Tekirdağ ▫[4] 130 41.00 N 27.30 E
Tekkali 122 18.37 N 84.14 E
Tekke 130 40.43 N 36.12 E
Tekke Burnu › 130 40.02 N 26.10 E
Tekkiraz 130 40.59 N 37.08 E
Tekman 130 39.38 N 41.31 E
Tekoa 202 47.13 N 117.04 W
Tekong, Pulau I 271c 1.24 N 104.03 E
Tekong Kechil, Pulau I 271c 1.25 N 104.01 E
Tekonsha 216 42.05 N 84.59 W
Te Kopuru 172 36.02 S 173.56 E
Tekouiat, Oued V 148 22.25 N 2.35 E
Tékro ⊤[4] 146 19.30 N 20.58 E
Tekstil'ščiki 82 55.57 N 37.49 E
Tekstil'ščiki ◆[8] 265b 55.42 N 37.44 E
Teku 112 0.46 S 123.26 E
Te Kuiti 172 38.20 S 175.10 E
Tekukor, Pulau I 271c 1.14 N 103.50 E
Tel ≃ 122 20.50 N 83.54 E
Tela, Hond. 236 15.44 N 87.27 W
Tela, India 272a 28.44 N 77.20 E
Tela, Bahía de c 236 15.48 N 87.30 W
Telaga 116 6.51 N 117.03 E
Telaga, Teluk c 114 2.10 N 98.00 E
Telaga-kulon 115a 6.58 S 108.18 E
Télagh 148 34.47 N 0.34 W
Telaopengsha Shan ∧ 120 30.33 N 86.25 E
Tel Ashqelon ⊥ 132 31.39 N 34.32 E
Telavåg 26 60.16 N 4.49 E
Telavi 84 41.55 N 45.28 E
Tel Aviv ▫[5] 132 32.05 N 34.48 E
Tel Aviv-Yafo 132 32.03 N 34.46 E
Telč 30 49.11 N 15.27 E
Tel'čje 76 53.21 N 36.20 E
Telde 148 28.00 N 15.25 W
Tele ≃, Afr. 158 30.26 S 27.33 E
Tele ≃, Zaïre 152 2.48 N 23.54 E
Telechany 76 52.31 N 25.51 E
Teleckoje, ozero ◎ 86 51.35 N 87.40 E
Telefomin 164 5.10 S 141.35 E
Telegapulang 112 2.55 S 112.25 E
Telegino 80 52.55 N 44.34 E
Telegrafo, Pizzo ∧ 70 37.37 N 13.10 E
Telegraph Canyon V 280 33.55 N 117.45 W
Telegraph Cove 182 50.33 N 126.50 W
Telegraph Creek 180 57.55 N 131.10 W
Telêmaco Borba 252 24.20 S 50.40 W
Telemark ▫[6] 26 59.30 N 8.40 E
Telemba 88 52.43 N 113.16 E
Telembí ≃ 246 1.50 N 78.16 W
Telén 252 36.16 S 65.30 W
Telen ≃ 112 0.26 S 116.42 E
Telenešty 38 47.30 N 28.22 E
Teleno ∧ 34 42.21 N 6.23 W
Teleorman ▫[6] 38 44.00 N 25.15 E
Teleorman ≃ 38 43.52 N 25.26 E
Téléphone, Île du I 273b 4.20 S 15.12 E
Telerig 38 43.51 N 27.40 E
Telertheba, Djebel ∧ 148 24.10 N 6.51 E
Telescope Peak ∧ 204 36.10 N 117.05 W
Telescope Point › 241k 12.08 N 61.36 W
Telese 68 41.13 N 14.32 E
Telesterion ⊥ 267c 38.02 N 23.32 E
Telferner 222 28.51 N 96.53 W

Symbols in the index entries represent the broad categories identified in the key at the right. Symbols with superior numbers (⋀[1]) identify subcategories (see complete key on page *I · 1).*

Symbole im Register stellen die rechts im Schlüssel erklärten Kategorien dar. Symbole mit hochgestellten Ziffern (⋀[1]) bezeichnen Unterabteilungen einer Kategorie (vgl. vollständiger Schlüssel auf Seite *I · 1).*

Los símbolos incluídos en el texto del índice representan las grandes categorías identificadas con la clave a la derecha. Los símbolos con numeros en su parte superior (⋀[1]) identifican las subcategorías (véase la clave completa en la página *I · 1).*

Les symboles de l'index représentent les catégories indiquées dans la légende à droite. Les symboles suivis d'un indice (⋀[1]) représentent des sous-catégories (voir légende complète à la page *I · 1).*

Os símbolos incluídos no texto do índice representam as grandes categorias identificadas com a chave à direita. Os símbolos com números em sua parte superior (⋀[1]) identificam as subcategorias (veja-se a chave completa à página *I · 1).*

	English	Deutsch	Español	Français	Português
∧	Mountain	Berg	Montaña	Montagne	Montanha
⋀	Mountains	Gebirge	Montañas	Montagnes	Montanhas
)(	Pass	Paß	Paso	Col	Passo
V	Valley, Canyon	Tal, Cañon	Valle, Cañón	Vallée, Canyon	Vale, Canhão
≍	Plain	Ebene	Llano	Plaine	Planície
›	Cape	Kap	Cabo	Cap	Cabo
I	Island	Insel	Isla	Île	Ilha
II	Islands	Inseln	Islas	Îles	Ilhas
⊥	Other Topographic Features	Andere Topographische Objekte	Otros Elementos Topográficos	Autres données topographiques	Outros acidentes topográficos

---

≃ River	Fluß	Río	Rivière	Rio	→ Submarine Features / Untermeerische Objekte / Accidentes Submarinos / Formes de relief sous-marin / Acidentes submarinos
≈ Canal	Kanal	Canal	Canal	Canal	• Political Unit / Politische Einheit / Unidad Política / Entité politique / Unidade política
ᴸ Waterfall, Rapids	Wasserfall, Stromschnellen	Cascada, Rápidos	Chute d'eau, Rapides	Cascata, Rápidos	⬥ Cultural Institution / Kulturelle Institution / Institución Cultural / Institution culturelle / Instituição Cultural
⋃ Strait	Meeresstraße	Estrecho	Détroit	Estreito	⋅⋅ Historical Site / Historische Stätte / Sitio Histórico / Site historique / Sítio histórico
C Bay, Gulf	Bucht, Golf	Bahía, Golfo	Baie, Golfe	Baía, Golfo	◆ Recreational Site / Erholungs- und Ferienort / Sitio de Recreo / Centre de loisirs / Area ce Lazer
⊕ Lake, Lakes	See, Seen	Lago, Lagos	Lac, Lacs	Lago, Lagos	✈ Airport / Flughafen / Aeropuerto / Aéroport / Aeroporto
≋ Swamp	Sumpf	Pantano	Marais	Pântano	⊢ Military Installation / Militäranlage / Instalación Militar / Installation militaire / Instalação militar
⋈ Ice Features, Glacier	Eis- und Gletscherformen	Accidentes Glaciares	Formes glaciaires	Accidentes glaciares	⊙ Miscellaneous / Verschiedenes / Misceláneo / Divers / Diversos
⁓ Other Hydrographic Features	Andere Hydrographische Objekte	Otros Elementos Hidrográficos	Autres données hydrographiques	Outros acidentes hidrográficos	

Symbols in the index entries represent the broad categories identified in the key at the right. Symbols with superior numbers (⌂1) identify subcategories (see complete key on page I · 1).

Symbole im Register stellen die rechts im Schlüssel erklärten Kategorien dar. Symbole mit hochgestellten Ziffern (⌂1) bezeichnen Unterteilungen einer Kategorie (vgl. vollständiger Schlüssel auf Seite I · 1).

Los símbolos incluidos en el texto del índice representan las grandes categorías identificadas con la clave a la derecha. Los símbolos con numeros en su parte superior (⌂1) identifican las subcategorías (véase la clave completa en la página I · 1).

Les symboles de l'index représentent les catégories indiquées dans la légende à droite. Les symboles suivis d'un indice (⌂1) représentent des sous-catégories (voir légende complète à la page I · 1).

Os símbolos incluídos no texto do índice representam as grandes categorias identificadas com a chave à direita. Os símbolos com números em sua parte superior (⌂1) identificam as subcategorias (veja-se a chave completa à página I · 1).

Symbol	English	Deutsch	Español	Français	Português
ᴧ	Mountain	Berg	Montaña	Montagne	Montanha
ᴧ	Mountains	Gebirge	Montañas	Montagnes	Montanhas
⌣	Pass	Paß	Paso	Col	Passo
V	Valley, Canyon	Tal, Cañon	Valle, Cañón	Vallée, Canyon	Vale, Canhão
≋	Plain	Ebene	Llano	Plaine	Planície
⊁	Cape	Kap	Cabo	Cap	Cabo
I	Island	Insel	Isla	Île	Ilha
II	Islands	Inseln	Islas	Îles	Ilhas
⌂	Other Topographic Features	Andere Topographische Objekte	Otros Elementos Topográficos	Autres données topographiques	Outros acidentes topográficos

ESPAÑOL Nombre	Página	Lat.°′	Long.°′ W = Oeste
FRANÇAIS Nom	Page	Lat.°′	Long.°′ W = Ouest
PORTUGUÊS Nome	Página	Lat.°′	Long.°′ W = Oeste

Tihany ⊥ 30 46.54 N 17.53 E
Tihert 148 35.28 N 1.21 E
Tihert □5 148 35.00 N 1.45 E
Tihnāwī, Wādī at- V 142 28.11 N 30.46 E
Tihua
— Ürümqi 86 43.48 N 87.35 E
Tihuatlán 234 20.43 N 97.32 W
Tiilikkajärven kansallispuisto ♦ 26 63.38 N 28.20 E
Tijamuchi ≃ 248 14.10 S 64.58 W
Tijesno 36 43.48 N 15.39 E
Tiji 146 32.01 N 11.22 E
Tijuana 232 32.32 N 117.01 W
Tijuana ≃ 204 32.33 N 117.07 W
Tijuca ◆8 287a 22.56 S 43.14 W
Tijuca, Barra da ≃ 287a 23.01 S 43.18 W
Tijuca, Lagoa da c 287a 22.59 S 43.20 W
Tijuca, Parque Nacional da ♦ 287a 22.58 S 43.15 W
Tijuca, Pico da ∧ 287a 22.56 S 43.17 W
Tijucas 252 27.14 S 48.38 W
Tijucas do Sul 252 25.55 S 49.12 W
Tijuco ≃ 255 18.40 S 50.05 W
Tikal ⊥ 232 17.20 N 89.39 W
Tikamgarh 124 24.44 N 78.50 E
Tikaré 150 13.17 N 1.43 W
Tikchik Lakes ⊜ 180 60.07 N 158.35 W
Tikei, Île I 14 14.58 S 144.32 W
Tikhand ◆8 272a 28.31 N 77.17 E
Tikhoretsk
— Tichoreck 78 45.51 N 40.09 E
Tikitiki 172 37.48 S 178.24 E
Tiko 152 4.05 N 9.22 E
Tikokino 172 39.49 S 176.27 E
Tikrīt 128 34.36 N 43.42 E
Tikša 24 64.07 N 32.27 E
Tikšeozero, ozero ⊜ 24 66.16 N 31.53 E
Tiksi 74 71.36 N 128.48 E
Tiku 112 0.24 S 99.56 E
Til 130 38.44 N 41.49 E
Tiladummati Atoll I1 122 6.50 N 73.05 E
Tilamuta 112 0.30 N 122.20 E
Tilarán 236 10.28 N 84.59 W
Tilbalakan, Laguna c 236 15.30 N 84.17 W
Tilbanah 142 30.59 N 31.27 E
Tilburg 52 51.34 N 5.05 E
Tilbury, On., Can. 214 42.16 N 82.26 W
Tilbury, Eng., U.K. 42 51.28 N 0.23 E
Tilcara 252 23.34 S 65.22 W
Tilcha 166 29.36 S 140.54 E
Til-Châtel 58 47.31 N 5.10 E
Tilden, Il., U.S. 219 38.12 N 89.40 W
Tilden, Ne., U.S. 198 42.02 N 97.50 W
Tilden, Tx., U.S. 196 28.28 N 98.33 W
Tilden Lake ⊜ 226 38.07 N 119.36 W
Tilden Woods 284c 39.03 N 77.09 W
Tilemsès 150 15.37 N 4.44 E
Tilemsi, Vallée du V 150 16.15 N 0.02 E
Tilff 56 50.34 N 5.35 E
Tilghman Island I 208 38.42 N 76.20 W
Tilhar 124 27.59 N 79.44 E
Tilia, Oued V 148 27.27 N 0.01 W
Tiligul ≃ 78 47.04 N 30.57 E
Tiligulo-Berezanka 78 46.52 N 31.24 E
Tiligul'skij liman ⊜ 78 46.48 N 31.08 E
Tiliktino 82 56.06 N 36.36 E
Tilimsen 148 34.52 N 1.15 W
Tilimsen □5 148 35.00 N 2.00 W
Tilin 110 21.42 N 94.04 E
Tilisarao 252 32.44 S 65.18 W
Till ≃, Eng., U.K. 44 55.41 N 2.12 W
Till ≃, Eng., U.K. 44 53.16 N 0.37 W
Tillaberi 150 14.13 N 1.27 E
Tillamook 202 45.27 N 123.50 W
Tillamook □6 224 45.25 N 123.39 W
Tillamook ≃ 224 45.28 N 123.53 W
Tillamook Bay c 224 45.30 N 123.53 W
Tillamook Head > 224 45.57 N 124.00 W
Tillanchāng Dwīp I 110 8.30 N 93.37 E
Tillberga 40 59.41 N 16.37 E
Tille ≃ 58 47.07 N 5.21 E
Tillery, Lake ⊜1 192 35.17 N 80.05 W
Tilley 182 50.27 N 111.39 W
Tilli 126 23.57 N 89.57 E
Tillia 150 16.08 N 4.47 E
Tillicoultry 46 56.09 N 3.45 W
Tillicum 224 47.08 N 122.33 W
Tillières-sur-Avre 50 48.46 N 1.04 E
Tilling Bourne ≃ 260 51.13 N 0.34 W
Tillmans Corner 194 30.43 N 88.05 W
Tillson 210 41.49 N 74.04 W
Tillsonburg 212 42.51 N 80.44 W
Tillyfourie 46 57.11 N 2.35 W
Tilogne 150 15.58 N 13.36 W
Tilomar 112 9.21 S 125.08 E
Tílos I 38 36.25 N 27.25 E
Tilpa 166 30.57 S 144.24 E
Tilrhemt 148 33.10 N 3.21 E
Tilsit
— Sovetsk 76 55.05 N 21.53 E
Tilt ≃ 46 56.46 N 3.50 W
Tilton, Il., U.S. 194 40.05 N 87.38 W
Tilton, Ky., U.S. 218 38.22 N 83.45 W
Tilton, N.H., U.S. 188 43.26 N 71.35 W
Tilton ≃ 224 46.33 N 122.33 W
Tiltonsville 214 40.10 N 80.41 W
Tilzapotla 234 18.29 N 99.16 W
Tim 78 51.37 N 37.07 E
Tim ≃ 76 52.15 N 37.22 E
Ṭimā 140 26.54 N 31.26 E
Timah, Bukit ∧2 271c 1.21 N 103.47 E
Timahoe 48 53.20 N 6.49 W
Timaná 246 1.58 N 75.56 W
Timane ≃ 248 20.34 S 59.15 W
Timanskij kr'až ∧ 24 65.00 N 51.00 E
Timar 84 38.49 N 43.27 E
Timaricha 80 57.33 N 44.47 E
Timaru 172 44.24 S 171.15 E
Timaševo, Ross. 80 53.21 N 51.12 E
Timaševo, Ross. 82 55.08 N 36.29 E
Timaševsk 78 45.37 N 38.57 E
Timau, It. 64 46.35 N 13.00 E
Timau, Kenya 154 0.05 N 37.14 E
Timavo San Giovanni 64 45.48 N 13.37 E
Timay al-Amdīd 142 30.57 N 31.32 E
Timbákion 38 35.04 N 24.46 E
Timbalier Bay c 194 29.10 N 90.20 W
Timbaúba 250 7.31 S 35.19 W
Timbavati Game Reserve ◆4 156 24.27 S 31.27 E
Timbedgha 150 16.15 N 8.10 W
Timber 224 45.43 N 123.17 W
Timber Creek 164 15.39 S 130.29 E
Timber Creek ≃ 198 44.49 N 98.17 W
Timber Lake, Il., U.S. 278 42.14 N 88.07 W
Timberlake, Oh., U.S. 214 41.41 N 81.25 W
Timber Lake, S.D., U.S. 198 45.26 N 101.04 W
Timber Run ≃ 284b 39.27 N 76.52 W
Timber Trails 278 41.52 N 87.57 W
Timberview 284b 39.13 N 76.45 W
Timbío 246 2.20 N 76.40 W
Timbiras 250 4.15 S 43.57 W
Timblin 214 40.58 N 79.12 W
Timbó, Bra. 252 26.50 S 49.18 W
Timbo, Guinée 150 10.38 N 11.50 W
Timbo, Liber. 150 5.37 N 9.43 W
Timbó ≃ 287a 22.52 S 43.16 W
Timboon 169 38.29 S 142.59 E
Timbuctoo 285 40.00 N 74.49 W
Timbuktu
— Tombouctou 150 16.46 N 3.01 W
Timbun Mata, Pulau I 112 4.39 N 118.28 E
Timel'ga 86 58.53 N 76.42 E
Timelkam 60 48.00 N 13.36 E
Times Square ⊥ 276 40.45 N 74.00 W
Timétrine 150 19.27 N 0.26 W
Timétrine ⋀ 150 19.20 N 0.42 W
Timeu Creek ≃ 182 54.28 N 114.27 W
Timewell 219 40.00 N 90.52 W
Timgad ⊥ 148 35.29 N 6.28 E
Timimoun 148 29.14 N 0.16 E
Timimoun, Sebkha de ⊜ 148 29.00 N 0.05 E
Timinar 140 19.02 N 30.29 E
Timi Ouli, Ehi ∧ 146 21.08 N 16.31 E
Timir'azevo 76 55.05 N 21.37 E
Timir'azevskij 86 56.29 N 84.54 E
Timirevo 82 55.06 N 39.10 E
Timirist, Râs > 150 19.23 N 16.32 W
Timiș □6 38 45.40 N 21.20 E
Timiș (Tamiš) ≃ 38 44.51 N 20.39 E
Timiskaming, Lake ⊜ 190 47.10 N 79.25 W
Timișoara 38 45.45 N 21.13 E
Timkoviči 76 53.03 N 27.00 E
Timkovo 82 55.56 N 38.37 E
Timmendorfer Strand 54 54.00 N 10.46 E
Timmernabben 26 56.58 N 16.26 E
Timmins 190 48.28 N 81.20 W
Timmonsville 192 34.08 N 79.56 W
Timms Hill ∧2 190 45.27 N 90.11 W
Timok ≃ 38 44.13 N 22.40 E
Timon 250 5.06 S 42.49 W
Timonovo 82 56.13 N 37.02 E
Timor I 112 9.00 S 125.00 E
Timor Sea ⊤2 112 11.00 S 128.00 E
Timor Timur □4 112 8.35 S 126.00 E
Timor Trough ✢1 14 9.50 S 126.00 E
Timošino, Ross. 76 60.05 N 36.10 E
Timošino, Ross. 80 57.50 N 44.25 E
Timotes 246 8.59 N 70.44 W
Timothy Lake ⊜1 224 45.07 N 121.47 W
Timoudi 148 29.19 N 1.09 W
Timousserarène ≃ 150 16.21 N 8.07 E
Timpanogos Cave National Monument ♦ 200 40.18 N 111.52 W
Timpas Creek ≃ 198 38.02 N 103.38 W
Timpaus, Pulau I 112 1.51 S 124.01 E
Timperley 262 53.24 N 2.19 W
Timpson 194 31.54 N 94.23 W
Timpton ≃ 74 58.43 N 127.12 E
Timra 26 62.31 N 17.22 E
Timsāh, Buhayrat at- (Lake Timsah) ⊜ 142 30.34 N 32.17 E
Timsah, Lake
— Timsāh, Buhayrat at- ⊜ 142 30.34 N 32.17 E
Tims Ford Lake ⊜1 194 35.15 N 86.10 W
Timun 114 0.50 N 103.22 E
Timur 85 42.50 N 68.26 E
Timur, Banjaran ⋀ 114 5.00 N 102.30 E
Timurni 124 22.22 N 77.22 E
Tin, Ra's at- > 146 32.37 N 23.08 E
Tina ≃ 158 31.18 S 29.14 E
Tinaca Point > 116 5.33 N 125.20 E
Tinaco 246 9.42 N 68.26 W
Tinaga Island I 116 14.28 N 122.56 E
Tinah, Khalīj at- c 140 31.08 N 32.40 E
Tinahely 48 52.48 N 6.28 W
Tinaja, Punta > 248 16.14 S 73.39 W
Tinalmud 116 13.36 N 122.53 E
Tinambac 116 13.49 N 123.19 E
Tinambung 112 3.31 S 119.01 E
Ti-n-Amzi V 150 18.20 N 4.32 E
Tinapagee 166 29.28 S 144.23 E
Tinaquillo 246 9.55 N 68.18 W
Tindari, Capo > 70 38.10 N 15.03 E
Tinderry Peak ∧ 171b 35.42 S 149.16 E
Tindila 150 10.16 N 8.15 W
Tindis 126 21.35 N 86.44 E
Tindivanam 122 12.15 N 79.39 E
Tindouf 148 27.50 N 8.04 W
Tindouf, Hamada de ⋀1 148 27.30 N 9.00 W
Tindouf, Sebkha de ≍ 148 27.45 N 7.15 W
Tineba, Pegunungan ⋀ 112 1.40 S 120.25 E
Tinée ≃ 62 43.55 N 7.11 E
Tineg ≃ 116 17.38 N 120.37 E
Tineo 34 43.20 N 6.25 W
Ting ≃ 100 24.24 N 116.35 E
Tinga ∧ 146 9.21 N 23.38 E
Tingambato 234 19.30 N 101.52 W
Tinggi, Pulau I 114 2.18 N 104.07 E
Tingha 166 29.57 S 151.13 E
Tinghert, Ḥamādat (Plateau du Tinghert) ⋀1 148 29.00 N 9.00 E
Tinghert, Plateau du (Ḥamādat Tinghert) ⋀1 148 29.00 N 9.00 E
Tinghsien
— Dingxian 98 38.32 N 114.59 E
Tingkar ∧ 116 5.20 N 117.06 E
Ting Kau 271d 22.22 N 114.05 E
Tingkawk Sakan 110 26.04 N 96.44 E
Tingkou 98 36.34 N 119.46 E
Tinglev 41 54.56 N 9.15 E
Tinglin 106 30.53 N 121.17 E
Tingliuhe 98 39.34 N 118.49 E
Tingloy 116 13.40 N 120.52 E
Tingmerkpuk Mountain ∧ 180 68.34 N 162.28 W
Tingo de Saposoa 248 7.07 S 76.38 W
Tingo María 248 9.09 S 75.56 W
Tingo María, Parque Nacional ♦ 248 9.15 S 76.05 W
Tingqian 100 30.10 N 115.54 E
Tingri, Zhg. 120 28.35 N 86.38 E
Tingri, Zhg. 120 28.38 N 87.04 E
Tingsiqiao 100 29.50 N 114.12 E
Tingsryd 26 56.32 N 14.59 E
Tingstäde 26 57.44 N 18.36 E
Tingsted 41 54.49 N 11.56 E
Tinguá 256 22.36 S 43.26 W
Tingüindín 234 19.45 N 102.29 W
Tinguiririca, Volcán ∧1 252 34.49 S 70.21 W
Tingvoll 26 62.54 N 8.12 E
Tingvollfjorden c2 26 62.50 N 8.11 E
Tingwick 206 45.50 N 71.58 W
Tingwon Group II 164 2.35 S 149.45 E
Tingzitou 106 30.12 N 119.46 E
Tinharé, Ilha de I 255 13.30 S 38.58 W
Tinh Bien 110 10.36 N 104.57 E
Tinian 174n 14.58 N 145.38 E
Tinian I 174n 15.00 N 145.38 E
Tinian Harbor c 174n 14.57 N 145.36 E
Tinié 150 14.20 N 1.28 W
Tiniguiban 116 11.22 N 119.30 E
Tinitian 116 10.04 N 119.12 E
Tinjar ≃ 112 4.04 N 114.18 E
Tinjil, Pulau I 115a 6.58 S 105.47 E
Tinker Air Force Base ■ 196 35.25 N 97.24 W
Tinkers Creek ≃, Md., U.S. 284c 38.46 N 76.57 W
Tinkers Creek ≃, Oh., U.S. 214 41.22 N 81.37 W
Tinkertown 283 42.01 N 70.44 W
Tinkisso ≃ 150 11.21 N 9.10 W
Tinley Creek ≃ 278 41.39 N 87.45 W
Tinley Creek Woods ♦ 278 41.39 N 87.47 W
Tinley Park 216 41.34 N 87.47 W
Tinniswood, Mount ∧ 182 50.19 N 123.50 W
Tinnoset 26 59.43 N 9.02 E
Tinnsjø ⊜ 26 59.54 N 8.55 E
Tinogasta 252 28.04 S 67.34 W
Tinompo 112 2.09 S 121.17 E
Tínos 38 37.32 N 25.10 E
Tínos I 38 37.38 N 25.10 E
Tinqueux 56 49.15 N 3.59 E
Tin Rerhoh, Tassili ⋀ 148 20.50 N 1.35 E
Tinrhir 148 31.28 N 5.30 W
Tin Sam 271d 22.22 N 114.11 E
Tinskoj 88 56.10 N 96.55 E
Tinsley 194 32.43 N 90.27 W
Tinsukia 120 27.30 N 95.22 E
Tintagel, B.C., Can. 182 54.12 N 125.35 W
Tintagel, Eng., U.K. 42 50.40 N 4.45 W
Tintagel Head > 42 50.41 N 4.46 W
Tintaldra 171b 36.03 S 147.56 E
Tintas, Rio das ≃ 287a 22.52 S 43.28 W
Tinte, Cerro ∧ 248 22.40 S 67.02 W
Tintern Abbey ʊ1 42 51.41 N 2.40 W
Tintern Parva 42 51.42 N 2.40 W
Tintigny 56 49.41 N 5.31 E
Tintina 252 27.02 S 62.43 W
Tintinara 166 35.54 S 140.03 E
Tintioulé 150 10.13 N 9.12 W
Tinto ∧ 46 55.36 N 3.39 W
Tinto ≃ 34 37.12 N 6.55 W
Tinton Falls 276 40.19 N 74.04 W
Ti-n-Toumma ◆1 146 16.04 N 12.40 E
Tintwistle 262 53.28 N 1.58 W
Tinui 172 40.53 S 176.04 E
Tinwald 172 43.55 S 171.43 E
Ti-n-Zaouatene 150 19.55 N 2.52 E
Tinzap ≃ 120 38.23 N 77.24 E
Tio 144 14.42 N 40.58 E
Tioga, Il., U.S. 219 40.13 N 91.21 W
Tioga, N.D., U.S. 198 48.23 N 102.56 W
Tioga, Pa., U.S. 210 41.55 N 77.08 W
Tioga □6, N.Y., U.S. 210 42.06 N 76.15 W
Tioga □6, Pa., U.S. 210 41.45 N 77.17 W
Tioga ◆8 285 40.00 N 75.10 W
Tioga ≃ 210 42.09 N 77.05 W
Tioga Center 210 42.04 N 76.21 W
Tioga Pass >< 226 37.54 N 119.16 W
Tioga Terrace 210 42.03 N 76.07 W
Tiojala 24 61.10 N 23.52 E
Tioman, Pulau I 114 2.48 N 104.10 E
Tiona 214 41.45 N 79.03 W
Tione di Trento 64 46.02 N 10.43 E
Tionesta 214 41.30 N 79.27 W
Tionesta Creek ≃ 214 41.28 N 79.22 W
Tionesta Lake ⊜1 214 41.28 N 79.28 W
Tioor, Pulau I 164 4.45 S 131.45 E
Tior 140 6.23 N 31.11 E
Tioro 112 4.41 S 122.36 E
Tioro, Selat ⊔ 112 4.40 S 122.20 E
Tioroniaradougou 150 9.21 N 5.38 W
Tioughnioga ≃ 210 42.14 N 75.51 W
Tioughnioga, East Branch ≃ 210 42.36 N 76.10 W
Tipasa 34 36.35 N 2.27 E
Tipitapa 236 12.12 N 86.06 W
Tipoca, Monte ∧2 250 3.34 N 51.20 W
Tipp City 218 39.57 N 84.10 W
Tippecanoe, In., U.S. 216 41.12 N 86.06 W
Tippecanoe, Oh., U.S. 214 40.16 N 81.17 W
Tippecanoe □6 216 40.25 N 86.53 W
Tippecanoe ≃ 216 40.31 N 86.47 W
Tippecanoe, Lake ⊜ 216 41.20 N 85.46 W
Tippecanoe Battlefield State Memorial ⊥ 216 40.31 N 86.52 W
Tippecanoe River State Park ♦ 216 41.07 N 86.36 W
Tipperary, Austl. 164 13.44 S 131.02 E
Tipperary, Ire. 48 52.29 N 8.10 W
Tipperary □6 48 52.40 N 8.20 W
Tipton, Eng., U.K. 42 52.32 N 2.05 W
Tipton, Ca., U.S. 226 36.03 N 119.18 W
Tipton, In., U.S. 216 40.16 N 86.02 W
Tipton, Ia., U.S. 190 41.46 N 91.07 W
Tipton, Mi., U.S. 216 42.01 N 84.04 W
Tipton, Mo., U.S. 194 38.39 N 92.46 W
Tipton, Ok., U.S. 196 34.30 N 99.08 W
Tipton, Pa., U.S. 214 40.38 N 78.18 W
Tipton □6 216 40.17 N 86.02 W
Tipton, Mount ∧ 200 35.32 N 114.12 W
Tiptonville 194 36.22 N 89.28 W
Tip Top Mountain ∧ 190 48.16 N 85.59 W
Tiptree 42 51.49 N 0.45 E
Tiptūr 122 13.16 N 76.29 E
Tiputini ≃ 246 0.47 S 75.32 W
Tiquicheo 234 18.53 N 100.44 W
Tīra 132 32.14 N 34.57 E
Tira Chapéu, Morro ∧ 256 22.45 S 44.39 W
Tiradentes 255 21.07 S 44.11 W
Tīrah, Baḥr ≍ 142 31.03 N 31.15 E
Tīrān I 128 27.56 N 34.34 E
Tīrān, Maḍīq ⊔ 140 27.58 N 34.28 E
Tiran, Strait of
— Tīrān, Maḍīq ⊔ 140 27.58 N 34.28 E
Tirana
— Tiranë 38 41.20 N 19.50 E
Tiranë 38 41.20 N 19.50 E
Tirano 64 46.13 N 10.10 E
Tiraque 248 17.37 S 65.04 W
Tirari Desert ◆2 162 28.00 S 138.20 E
Tiraspol' 38 46.51 N 29.38 E
Tirat Karmel 132 32.46 N 34.58 E
Tirat Ẕevi 132 32.25 N 35.32 E
Tirau 172 37.59 S 175.45 E
Tire 130 38.04 N 27.45 E
Tirebolu 130 41.00 N 38.48 E
Tiree I 46 56.31 N 6.49 W
Tire Hill 214 40.16 N 78.55 W
Tires (Tiers), It. 64 46.28 N 11.31 E
Tires, Port. 266c 38.43 N 9.21 W
Tires ◆1 148 23.30 N 13.10 W
Tîrgoviște 38 44.56 N 25.27 E
Tîrgu Bujor 38 45.52 N 27.54 E
Tîrgu-Cărbunești 38 44.58 N 23.31 E
Tîrgu-Frumos 38 47.13 N 27.00 E
Tîrgu Jiu 38 45.02 N 23.17 E
Tîrgu-Lăpuș 38 47.27 N 23.52 E
Tîrgu Mureș 38 46.33 N 24.33 E
Tîrgu-Neamț 38 47.12 N 26.22 E
Tîrgu Ocna 38 46.15 N 26.37 E
Tîrgu Secuiesc 38 46.00 N 26.08 E
Tîrgusor 38 44.28 N 28.25 E
Tirhahart, Oued V 148 23.45 N 3.10 E
Tiria, Monte ∧ 71 40.23 N 9.16 E
Tirich Mīr ∧ 123 36.15 N 71.50 E
Tiriro 150 10.27 N 8.39 W
Tiris Zemmour □4 148 24.10 N 9.30 W
Tirl'anskij 86 54.14 N 58.35 E
Tirna ≃ 122 18.04 N 76.57 E
Tîrnava Mare ≃ 38 46.09 N 23.42 E
Tîrnava Mică ≃ 38 46.11 N 23.55 E
Tîrnăveni 38 46.20 N 24.17 E
Tírnavos 38 39.45 N 22.17 E
Tirnovo
— Veliko Târnovo 38 43.04 N 25.39 E
Tiro 214 40.54 N 82.46 W
Tirodi 120 21.41 N 79.42 E
Tirol □3 64 47.15 N 11.20 E
Tiroler Ache (Grossache) ≃ 60 47.51 N 12.30 E
Tirolo (Tirol) 64 46.42 N 11.10 E
Tiros 255 19.00 S 45.58 W
Tiroungoulou 146 9.34 N 22.09 E
Tīr Pol 128 34.36 N 61.15 E
Tirrenia 66 43.38 N 10.17 E
Tirreno, Mare
— Tyrrhenian Sea ⊤2 36 40.00 N 12.00 E
Tirry ≃ 46 58.02 N 4.26 W
Tirsā, Miṣr 142 29.25 N 30.49 E
Tirsā, Miṣr 273c 29.58 N 31.12 E
Tirschenreuth 60 49.53 N 12.21 E
Tirso ≃ 71 39.53 N 8.32 E
Tirsted 41 54.44 N 11.21 E
Tirstrup 41 56.18 N 10.42 E
Tīrthahalli 122 13.42 N 75.14 E
Tirua Point > 172 38.23 S 174.38 E
Tiruchchirāppalli 122 10.49 N 78.41 E
Tiruchengodu 122 11.23 N 77.56 E
Tirukkalukkunram 122 12.37 N 80.04 E
Tirukkovilūr 122 11.57 N 79.12 E
Tiruliai 76 55.47 N 23.22 E
Tirumangalam 122 9.50 N 77.59 E
Tirunelveli 122 8.44 N 77.42 E
Tirupati 122 13.39 N 79.25 E
Tiruppattūr, India 122 12.30 N 78.34 E
Tiruppattūr, India 122 10.08 N 78.37 E
Tiruppur 122 11.06 N 77.21 E
Tirūr 122 10.54 N 75.55 E
Tiruttani 122 13.11 N 79.38 E
Tirutturaippūndi 122 10.32 N 79.39 E
Tiruvalla 122 9.23 N 76.34 E
Tiruvallūr 122 13.09 N 79.55 E
Tiruvannāmalai 122 12.13 N 79.04 E
Tiruvettipuram 122 12.40 N 79.33 E
Tirūvottiyūr 122 13.09 N 80.18 E
Tiruvur 122 17.06 N 80.38 E
Tisa (Tisza) ≃ 38 45.15 N 20.17 E
Tis'ah 142 30.02 N 32.35 E
Tisaiyanvilai 122 8.20 N 77.53 E
Tisaren ⊜ 40 59.00 N 15.08 E
Tisbury 42 51.04 N 2.03 W
Tisdale 184 52.51 N 104.04 W
Tishomingo, Ms., U.S. 194 34.38 N 88.13 W
Tishomingo, Ok., U.S. 196 34.14 N 96.40 W
Tisisat Falls ⌞ 144 11.29 N 37.35 E
Ṭīsīyah 132 32.24 N 36.27 E
Tisjön ⊜ 26 60.55 N 12.58 E
Tiskilwa 190 41.17 N 89.30 W
Tiskino 86 58.05 N 83.10 E
Tiškovka 78 48.29 N 30.56 E
Tiškovo, Ross. 80 46.02 N 48.36 E
Tiškovo, Ross. 82 56.05 N 37.44 E
Tisma 236 12.05 N 86.01 W
Tisnaren ⊜ 40 58.57 N 15.57 E
Tišnevo 82 55.10 N 36.17 E
Tišnov 30 49.21 N 16.25 E
Tisovec 30 48.43 N 19.57 E
Tissa 146 7.26 N 10.16 E
Tissemsilt 148 35.35 N 1.50 E
Tissø ⊜ 41 55.35 N 11.18 E
Tīsta ≃ 124 25.23 N 89.43 E
Tisul' 86 55.45 N 88.19 E
Tisvildeleje 41 56.03 N 12.05 E
Tisza (Tisa) ≃ 38 45.15 N 20.17 E
Tiszaföldvár 30 46.59 N 20.15 E
Tiszafüred 30 47.37 N 20.46 E
Tiszavasvári 30 47.58 N 21.22 E
Tit 148 23.00 N 5.10 E
Titaf 148 27.26 N 0.13 W
Titāgarh 126 22.45 N 88.22 E
Titano, Monte ∧ 66 43.55 N 12.28 E
Titao 150 13.46 N 2.04 W
Tit-Ary 74 71.58 N 127.01 E
Titel 38 45.12 N 20.18 E
Tithwāl 123 34.24 N 73.47 E
Titicaca, Lago ⊜ 248 15.50 S 69.20 W
Titicus 207 41.18 N 73.30 W
Titi Karangan 114 5.31 N 100.37 E
Titikaveka 174k 21.15 S 159.45 W
Titilāgarh 122 20.18 N 83.09 E
Titisee-Neustadt 58 47.54 N 8.13 E
Titlis ∧ 58 46.47 N 8.25 E
Tito 68 40.35 N 15.40 E
Titonka 190 43.14 N 94.02 W
Titou 100 29.52 N 112.42 E
Titova Korenica 36 44.45 N 15.43 E
Titovka 83 48.59 N 39.44 E
Titovo, Ross. 80 53.17 N 43.41 E
Titovo, Ross. 82 54.19 N 36.56 E
Titovo, Ross. 82 55.35 N 39.07 E
Titovo Velenje 61 46.22 N 15.07 E
Titov Veles 38 41.41 N 21.48 E
Titov vrh ∧ 38 42.00 N 20.51 E
Titran 26 63.40 N 8.18 E
Tittabawassee ≃ 190 43.23 N 83.59 W
Titteri ⋀ 34 36.00 N 3.30 E
Titterstone Clee Hill ∧2 42 52.23 N 2.35 W
Titting 60 49.00 N 11.13 E
Tittling 60 48.44 N 13.23 E
Tittmoning 60 48.04 N 12.46 E
Titu 38 44.41 N 25.32 E
Titule 154 3.17 N 25.32 E
Titus □6 222 33.05 N 94.58 W
Titusville, Fl., U.S. 220 28.36 N 80.48 W
Titusville, N.J., U.S. 208 40.18 N 74.52 W
Titusville, Pa., U.S. 214 41.37 N 79.40 W
Titz 56 51.01 N 6.25 E
Tiu Chung Chau I 271d 22.20 N 114.19 E
Tiumpan Head > 46 58.16 N 6.09 W
Tiuni 120 30.57 N 77.51 E
Tiva ≃ 154 2.20 S 38.48 E
Tivaouane 150 14.57 N 16.49 W
Tiveden ⋀2 40 58.45 N 14.40 E
Tiverton, Eng., U.K. 42 50.55 N 3.29 W
Tiverton, R.I., U.S. 207 41.37 N 71.12 W
Tivoli, Gren. 241k 12.10 N 61.37 W
Tivoli, It. 66 41.58 N 12.48 E
Tivoli, N.Y., U.S. 210 42.03 N 73.54 W
Tivoli, Tx., U.S. 196 28.27 N 96.53 W
Tivoli ♦ 41 55.40 N 12.34 E
Ṭiwāl, Wādī V 146 10.22 N 22.43 E
Ṭiwāl al-'Abā ∧ 130 36.20 N 39.22 E
Tiwi, Pil. 116 13.27 N 123.41 E
Ṭīwī, 'Umān 128 22.49 N 59.16 E
Tiwuronto 115b 8.48 S 120.09 E
Tixtla de Guerrero 234 17.35 N 99.26 W
Tiyās 130 34.33 N 37.40 E
Tiyo, Pegunungan ⋀ 164 4.00 S 135.30 E
Tizapán ◆8 286a 19.20 N 99.13 W
Tizapán El Alto 234 20.10 N 103.04 W
Tizimín 232 21.10 N 88.10 W
Tizi-Ouzou 148 36.48 N 4.02 E
Tizi Ouzou □5 148 36.40 N 4.10 E
Tizmant ash-Sharqīyah 142 29.03 N 31.03 E
Tiznados ≃ 246 8.16 N 67.47 W
Tiznit 148 29.43 N 9.44 W
Tiznit □4 148 29.40 N 9.45 W
Tizoc 196 25.41 N 101.59 W
Tjällmo 40 58.43 N 15.21 E
Tjeukemeer ⊜ 52 52.54 N 5.50 E
Tjilatjap
— Cilacap 115a 7.44 S 109.00 E
Tjirebon
— Cirebon 115a 6.44 S 108.34 E
Tjolotjo 154 19.47 S 27.46 E
Tjøme I 26 59.07 N 10.24 E
Tjörn I 26 58.00 N 11.38 E
Tjörnarp 41 56.00 N 13.37 E
Tkibuli 84 42.21 N 42.59 E
Tkvarčeli 84 42.51 N 41.41 E
Tlachichuca 234 19.06 N 97.25 W
Tlacoapa 234 17.09 N 98.52 W
Tlacotalpan 234 18.37 N 95.40 W
Tlacotepec 234 17.46 N 99.59 W
Tlacuitapan 234 21.14 N 102.12 W
Tláhuac ◆8 286a 19.16 N 99.00 W
Tlahualilo de Zaragoza 232 26.07 N 103.27 W
Tlahuelilpan 234 20.08 N 99.14 W
Tlahuitoltepec 234 17.04 N 95.59 W
Tlajomulco de Zúñiga 234 20.28 N 103.27 W
Tlalchapa 234 18.24 N 100.28 W
Tlalcozotitlán 234 17.54 N 99.15 W
Tlalixtac de Cabrera 234 17.04 N 96.39 W
Tlalixtaquilla 234 17.21 N 98.28 W
Tlalnepantla 234 19.33 N 99.12 W
Tlalnepantla ≃ 286a 19.31 N 99.16 W
Tlalpan ◆8 286a 19.17 N 99.10 W
Tlalpujahua 234 19.48 N 100.10 W
Tlaltenango de Sánchez Román 234 21.47 N 103.19 W
Tl'ančetamak 80 55.28 N 52.37 E
Tlapacoyan 234 19.58 N 97.13 W
Tlapa de Comonfort 234 17.33 N 98.33 W
Tlapaneco ≃ 234 18.05 N 98.48 W
Tlapehuala 234 18.13 N 100.31 W
Tlapeng 156 23.15 S 21.49 E
Tlaquepaque 234 20.39 N 103.19 W
Tl'arata 84 42.07 N 46.22 E
Tlatlauquitepec 234 19.51 N 97.29 W
Tlaxcala □3 234 19.25 N 98.10 W
Tlaxcala [de Xicoténcatl] 234 19.19 N 98.14 W
Tlaxcoapan 234 20.05 N 99.13 W
Tlaxco [de Morelos] 234 19.37 N 98.07 W
Tlaxmalac 234 18.21 N 99.25 W
Tlazazalca 234 19.58 N 102.04 W
Tletat ed Douair 34 35.59 N 2.55 E
Tlētē Ouāte Gharbī, Jabal ∧ 130 35.20 N 39.13 E
Tlevak Strait ⊔ 182 55.03 N 132.58 W
Tlhakgameng 158 26.27 S 24.21 E
Tloch 84 42.38 N 46.28 E
Tlučiná 60 49.44 N 13.14 E
Tlumač 78 48.52 N 25.01 E
Tłuszcz 30 52.26 N 21.26 E
Tmassah 146 26.22 N 15.47 E
Tmīsān 146 27.32 N 13.19 E
Tnâot ≃ 110 11.29 N 104.57 E
Tnekvejem ≃ 180 65.50 N 177.31 E
Toa ≃ 240p 20.23 N 74.32 W
Toa Alta 240m 18.23 N 66.15 W
Toab 46a 59.53 N 1.19 W
Toa Baja 240m 18.27 N 66.15 W
Toabré ≃ 236 8.56 N 80.33 W
Toachi ≃ 246 0.08 N 79.18 W
Toahayaná 232 26.08 N 107.44 W
Toamasina 157b 18.10 S 49.23 E
Toamasina □4 157b 18.00 S 48.40 E
Toandonggu 98 40.33 N 127.35 E
Toandos Peninsula >1 224 47.43 N 122.47 W
Toano, It. 64 44.23 N 10.34 E
Toano, Va., U.S. 208 37.22 N 76.48 W
Toano Draw V 204 41.27 N 114.35 W
Toano Range ⋀ 204 40.50 N 114.20 W
Toast 192 36.30 N 80.37 W
Toa Vaca, Embalse ⊜1 240m 18.06 N 66.28 W
Toay 252 36.40 S 64.21 W
Toba, Mali 150 11.52 N 7.28 W
Toba, Nihon 94 34.29 N 136.51 E
Toba, Zhg. 102 31.18 N 97.40 E
Toba ≃ 182 50.30 N 124.15 W
Toba, Danau ⊜ 114 2.35 N 98.50 E
Tobacco ≃ 190 43.49 N 84.24 W
Tobacco Plains Indian Reserve ◆4 182 49.04 N 115.06 W
Tobacco Root Mountains ⋀ 202 45.35 N 112.00 W
Tobago I 241r 11.15 N 60.40 W
Toba Inlet c 182 50.20 N 124.50 W
Toba Kākar Range ⋀ 120 31.15 N 68.00 E
Tobalaba Eulogio Sánchez, Aeródromo ⊠ 286e 33.27 S 70.33 W
Tobalai, Pulau I 164 1.37 S 128.20 E
Tobarra 34 38.35 N 1.41 W
Tobas 252 28.08 S 62.42 W
Tobašino 80 56.56 N 47.40 E
Toba Tek Singh 123 30.58 N 72.29 E
Tobe 96 33.44 N 132.47 E
Tobejuba, Isla I 246 9.20 N 60.52 W
Tobekuduk 86 49.50 N 54.15 E
Tobelo 108 1.44 N 128.01 E
Tobelombang 112 0.57 S 122.00 E
Tobercurry 48 54.03 N 8.43 W
Tobermorey 166 22.15 S 138.00 E
Tobermory, Austl. 166 27.17 S 143.41 E
Tobermory, On., Can. 190 45.15 N 81.40 W
Tobermory, Scot., U.K. 46 56.37 N 6.05 W
Toberonochy 46 56.13 N 5.38 W
Tōbetsu 92a 43.13 N 141.31 E
Tobi I 108 3.00 N 131.10 E
Tobias 198 40.25 N 97.20 W
Tobias Barreto 250 11.11 S 38.01 W
Tobiishi-bana > 174f 24.45 N 141.17 E
Tobin, Mount ∧ 204 40.22 N 117.32 W
Tobin Lake ⊜, Austl. 162 21.45 S 125.49 E
Tobin Lake ⊜, Sk., Can. 184 53.40 N 103.35 W
Tobique ≃ 186 46.46 N 67.42 W
Tobi-shima I 92 39.12 N 139.34 E
Toblach
— Dobbiaco 64 46.44 N 12.14 E
Tobo, Indon. 164 3.34 S 130.11 E
Tobo, Sve. 40 60.16 N 17.39 E
Toboali 112 3.00 S 106.30 E
Tobol 86 52.40 N 62.39 E
Tobol ≃ 86 58.10 N 68.12 E
Toboli 112 0.43 S 120.05 E
Tobol'sk 86 58.12 N 68.16 E
Tobong-san ∧ 271b 37.42 N 127.01 E
Tobor 150 12.39 N 16.16 W
Toboso 116 10.43 N 123.31 E
Tobré 150 10.12 N 2.08 E
Tobruk
— Ṭubruq 146 32.05 N 23.59 E
Tobseda 24 68.36 N 52.14 E
Tōbu 94 36.21 N 138.20 E
Toburdanovo 80 55.22 N 47.38 E
Toby, Mount ∧ 207 42.29 N 72.32 W
Tobyhanna 210 41.10 N 75.25 W
Tobyhanna Creek ≃ 210 41.07 N 75.39 W
Tobyhanna State Park ♦ 210 41.13 N 75.25 W
Tobyš ≃ 24 65.30 N 51.00 E
Toca Grande, Morro da ∧ 287a 22.58 S 43.31 W
Tocantínia 250 9.33 S 48.22 W
Tocantinópolis 250 6.20 S 47.25 W
Tocantins □3 250 10.00 S 48.00 W
Tocantins ≃, Bra. 242 1.45 S 49.10 W
Tocantins ≃, Bra. 250 5.21 S 55.58 W
Tocantinzinho ≃ 255 13.57 S 48.20 W
Toccoa 192 34.34 N 83.19 W
Toccoa (Ocoee) ≃ 192 35.12 N 84.40 W
Toce ≃ 58 45.56 N 8.29 E
Tochapan 234 18.54 N 97.37 W
Tochcha Lake ⊜ 182 54.56 N 125.54 W
Tochigi 94 36.23 N 139.44 E
Tochigi □5 94 36.45 N 139.45 E
Tochimilco 234 18.54 N 98.34 W
Tochio 92 37.28 N 139.00 E
Tochoj 88 50.30 N 105.00 E
Tochta 24 62.14 N 48.48 E
Tochtamyš 120 37.50 N 74.39 E
Tockholes 262 53.42 N 2.31 W
Tockoje 80 52.32 N 52.45 E
Töcksfors 26 59.30 N 11.50 E
Točník 60 49.27 N 13.19 E
Toco, Chile 252 22.05 S 69.35 W
Toco, Trin. 241r 10.50 N 60.57 W
Tocoa 236 15.41 N 86.03 W
Tócome ≃ 286c 10.29 N 66.49 W
Toconao 252 23.11 S 68.01 W
Tocopilla 252 22.05 S 70.12 W
Tocos do Moji 256 22.22 S 46.06 W
Tocuco ≃ 246 9.36 N 72.15 W
Tocumwal 166 35.49 S 145.34 E
Tocuyo ≃ 246 11.03 N 68.23 W
Tocuyo de la Costa 246 11.02 N 68.23 W
Toda 94 35.48 N 139.41 E
Toda Bhīm 124 26.55 N 76.49 E
Todaiji Temple ʊ1 270 34.42 N 135.51 E
Todang-ni 271b 37.37 N 126.50 E
Toda Rāisingh 120 26.01 N 75.29 E
Todd 214 40.16 N 78.04 W
Todd ≃ 162 24.52 S 135.48 E
Todd Estates 285 39.40 N 75.43 W
Todd Fork ≃ 218 39.21 N 84.08 W
Todd Fork, East Fork ≃ 218 39.24 N 84.00 W
Toddington 42 51.57 N 0.32 W
Todd Point > 284b 39.15 N 76.27 W
Toddville, Md., U.S. 208 38.17 N 76.04 W
Toddville, N.Y., U.S. 210 41.17 N 73.53 W
Todeli 112 1.40 S 124.29 E
Todenyang 154 4.32 N 35.56 E
Todi 66 42.47 N 12.24 E
Tödi ∧ 58 46.49 N 8.56 E
Todmorden, Austl. 162 27.08 S 134.48 E
Todmorden, Eng., U.K. 44 53.43 N 2.05 W
Todoga-saki > 92 39.33 N 142.05 E
Todoromi 270 34.53 N 135.28 E
Todos Santos, Bol. 248 16.48 S 65.08 W
Todos Santos, Méx. 232 23.27 N 110.13 W
Todos Santos, Bahía c 232 31.48 N 116.42 W
Todro 154 3.21 N 30.14 E
Todtenhausen 52 52.20 N 8.56 E
Todtmoos 58 47.44 N 8.00 E
Todtmoos Au 58 47.42 N 7.58 E
Todtnau 58 47.50 N 7.56 E
Toe Head > 46 57.50 N 7.08 W
Tōei 94 35.04 N 137.41 E
T'oejo 98 39.54 N 127.46 E
Toéssé 150 11.50 N 1.16 W
Toetoes Bay c 172 46.38 S 168.43 E
Tofield 182 53.22 N 112.40 W
Tofino 182 49.09 N 125.54 W
Töfsingdalens Nationalpark ♦ 26 62.09 N 12.30 E
Tofte 26 59.33 N 10.34 E
Toften ⊜ 40 59.03 N 14.36 E
Tofterup 41 55.39 N 8.50 E
Toftlund 41 55.11 N 9.04 E
Toga 94 36.27 N 137.02 E
Toga I 175f 13.26 S 166.42 E
Togakushi 94 36.44 N 138.05 E
Togakushi-yama ∧ 94 36.46 N 138.04 E
Toganas 80 50.49 N 52.02 E
Tōgane 94 35.33 N 140.22 E
Togano, Monte ∧ 58 46.06 N 8.25 E
Togauchi 96 34.34 N 132.13 E
Togdheer □4 144 9.00 N 46.00 E
Toggenburg V 58 47.15 N 9.10 E
Togho 152 6.01 N 17.26 E
Togi 94 37.08 N 136.44 E
Togiak 180 59.04 N 160.24 W
Togiak Bay c 180 59.00 N 160.30 W
Togian, Kepulauan II 112 0.20 S 122.00 E
Togian, Pulau I 112 0.22 S 121.56 E
Töging am Inn 60 48.15 N 12.35 E
Togliatti
— Toljatti 80 53.31 N 49.26 E
Togni 140 18.04 N 35.13 E
Tōgō, Nihon 94 35.05 N 137.03 E
Tōgō, Nihon 96 35.28 N 133.53 E
Togo □1, Afr. 134 8.00 N 1.10 E
Togo □1, Afr. 150 8.00 N 1.10 E
Togochale 144 9.33 N 43.18 E
Tōgō-ike ⊜ 96 35.28 N 133.54 E
Togoron 116 12.35 N 123.37 E
Tögrög, Mong. 102 45.46 N 94.48 E
Tögrög, Mong. 102 45.32 N 102.59 E
Togtoh 102 40.22 N 111.11 E
Togučin 86 55.16 N 84.23 E
Togur 86 58.24 N 82.49 E
Togura 94 36.29 N 138.09 E
Toguzak ≃ 86 54.06 N 62.50 E
Toguzbulak 85 42.06 N 76.44 E
Togwotee Pass >< 202 43.45 N 110.04 W
Tŏgyu-san ∧ 98 35.46 N 127.40 E
Tŏgyu-san Kukrip Kongwŏn ♦ 98 35.52 N 127.45 E
Togyz 86 47.34 N 60.33 E
Tōhaku 96 35.30 N 133.40 E
Tohakum Peak ∧ 204 40.11 N 119.27 W
Tohāna 124 29.42 N 75.54 E
Tohiea, Mont ∧ 174s 17.33 S 149.49 W
Tohma ≃ 130 38.31 N 38.25 E
Toholampi 26 63.46 N 24.15 E
Tohopekaliga, Lake ⊜ 220 28.12 N 81.23 W
Tohor, Tanjong > 114 1.51 N 102.42 E
T'ohyŏn-ni 98 39.53 N 124.52 E
Toi, Nihon 94 34.54 N 138.47 E
Toi, Niue 174v 18.57 S 169.51 W
Toijala 26 61.10 N 23.52 E
Toili 112 1.27 S 122.24 E
Toi-misaki > 92 31.20 N 131.22 E
Tōin 94 35.05 N 136.35 E
Toinya 140 6.17 N 29.44 E
Toi Sar 120 31.06 N 69.54 E
Toiyabe Range ⋀ 204 39.10 N 117.10 W
Tojg 128 32.04 N 61.48 E
To-jima I 96 33.12 N 132.22 E
Tojo, Indon. 112 1.17 S 121.11 E
Tōjō, Nihon 96 34.53 N 133.16 E
Tōjō, Nihon 270 34.55 N 135.04 E
Tojtepa 85 41.03 N 69.22 E
Tōju-in ʊ1 94 35.19 N 136.04 E
Tok 180 63.19 N 142.59 W
Tok ≃ 80 52.46 N 52.22 E
Tokaanu 172 38.58 S 175.46 E
Tokachi ≃ 92a 42.44 N 143.42 E
Tokachi-dake ∧ 92a 43.25 N 142.41 E
Tokachi-heiya ≍ 92a 43.00 N 143.30 E
Tōkagi 268 35.42 N 139.56 E
Tokai, Malay. 114 6.01 N 100.24 E
Tōkai, Nihon 94 35.00 N 136.53 E
Tōkai, Nihon 94 36.27 N 140.34 E
Tokaj ≃ 78 51.18 N 41.04 E
Tokala 112 1.47 S 121.43 E
Tōkamachi 94 37.08 N 138.46 E
Tokanui 172 46.34 S 168.56 E
Tokara-kaikyō ⊔ 93b 30.10 N 130.10 E
Tokara-rettō II 93b 29.36 N 129.43 E
Tokarevka 86 50.08 N 73.12 E
Tokar Game Reserve ◆4 140 18.15 N 37.45 E
Tokar'ovka 80 51.59 N 41.09 E
Tokar'ovo, Ross. 76 55.17 N 35.04 E
Tokar'ovo, Ross. 265b 55.38 N 37.55 E
Tokashiki-jima I 93b 26.11 N 127.21 E
Tokat 130 40.19 N 36.34 E
Tokat □4 130 40.25 N 36.30 E
Tŏkchŏk-kundo II 98 37.14 N 126.07 E
Tŏkch'ŏn 98 39.46 N 126.19 E
Tokeland 224 46.42 N 123.58 W
Tokelau □2 14 9.00 S 171.45 W
Tokelau-Inseln
— Tokelau □2 14 9.00 S 171.45 W
Tokeneke Brook ≃ 276 41.03 N 73.28 W
Tŏkhŭng-ni 98 40.02 N 127.08 E
Toki 94 35.21 N 137.11 E
Toki ≃ 94 35.12 N 136.52 E
Tokio
— Tōkyō 94 35.42 N 139.46 E
Toki Point > 174a 19.19 N 166.35 E
Tokiwadaira 268 35.48 N 139.57 E
Tokke ⊜ 26 59.01 N 9.15 E
Tokko 74 59.59 N 119.52 E
Tokko ≃ 88 58.42 N 119.50 E
Toklar 130 38.26 N 36.01 E
Toklat ≃ 180 64.27 N 150.17 W
Tokma 88 58.13 N 105.42 E
Tokmak, Kyrg. 85 42.55 N 75.18 E
Tokmak, Ukr. 78 47.15 N 35.43 E
Toko 172 39.20 S 174.24 E
Tököl 264c 47.19 N 18.58 E
Tokolimbu 112 2.48 S 121.34 E
Tokomaru 172 40.28 S 175.30 E
Tokomaru Bay 172 38.08 S 178.18 E
Tokoname 94 34.53 N 136.51 E
Toko Range ⋀ 166 23.05 S 138.20 E
Tokoro ≃ 92a 44.07 N 144.05 E
Tokoroa 172 38.14 S 175.52 E
Tokorozawa 94 35.47 N 139.28 E
Tokovskoje 78 47.38 N 33.59 E
Tokrau ≃ 86 46.48 N 75.24 E
Toksook Bay 180 60.32 N 165.06 W
Toksovo 76 60.09 N 30.31 E
Tok-to (Take-shima) II 92 37.17 N 131.53 E
Toktogul 85 41.50 N 72.50 E

Symbol	English	Deutsch	Español	Français	Português
≃	River	Fluß	Río	Rivière	Rio
≍	Canal	Kanal	Canal	Canal	Canal
⌞	Waterfall, Rapids	Wasserfall, Stromschnellen	Cascada, Rápidos	Chute d'eau, Rapides	Cascata, Rápidos
⊔	Strait	Meeresstraße	Estrecho	Détroit	Estreito
c	Bay, Gulf	Bucht, Golf	Bahía, Golfo	Baie, Golfe	Baía, Golfo
⊜	Lake, Lakes	See, Seen	Lago, Lagos	Lac, Lacs	Lago, Lagos
≚	Swamp	Sumpf	Pantano	Marais	Pântano
⊠	Ice Features, Glacier	Eis- und Gletscherformen	Accidentes Glaciales	Formes glaciaires	Acidentes glaciares
⊤	Other Hydrographic Features	Andere Hydrographische Objekte	Otros Elementos Hidrográficos	Autres données hydrographiques	Outros acidentes hidrográficos
✢	Submarine Features	Untermeerische Objekte	Accidentes Submarinos	Formes de relief sous-marin	Acidentes submarinos
□	Political Unit	Politische Einheit	Unidad Política	Entité politique	Unidade política
ʊ	Cultural Institution	Kulturelle Institution	Institución Cultural	Institution culturelle	Instituição cultural
⊥	Historical Site	Historische Stätte	Sitio Histórico	Site historique	Sítio histórico
♦	Recreational Site	Erholungs- und Ferienort	Sitio de Recreo	Centre de loisirs	Area de Lazer
⊠	Airport	Flughafen	Aeropuerto	Aéroport	Aeroporto
■	Military Installation	Militäranlage	Instalación Militar	Installation militaire	Instalação militar
◆	Miscellaneous	Verschiedenes	Misceláneo	Divers	Diversos

ENGLISH — DEUTSCH

Name	Page	Lat.°′	Long.°′
Toktogul'skoje vodochranilišče ⊜[1]	85	41.50 N	72.55 E
Toku Island I	14	18.10 S	174.11 W
Tokuji	96	34.11 N	131.40 E
Tokul Creek ≃	224	47.35 N	121.50 W
Tokung	112	0.18 S	114.28 E
Tokuno-shima I	93b	27.45 N	128.58 E
Tokur	89	53.10 N	132.53 E
Tokura	270	34.58 N	135.18 E
Tokura-tōge)(	96	35.17 N	134.31 E
Tokusaga-mine ∧	96	34.26 N	131.41 E
Tokushima	96	34.04 N	134.34 E
Tokushima □[5]	96	33.45 N	134.00 E
Tokuyama, Nihon	94	35.42 N	136.29 E
Tokuyama, Nihon	96	34.03 N	131.49 E
Tokwe ≃	154	21.09 S	31.30 E
Tōkyō, Nihon	94	35.42 N	139.46 E
Tōkyō, Nihon	268	35.42 N	139.46 E
Tōkyō □[5]	94	35.45 N	139.30 E
Tokyo Bay → Tōkyō-wan c	94	35.25 N	139.47 E
Tōkyō-daigaku-uchūkūkan-kenkyūsho ʋ[3]	92	31.17 N	131.05 E
Tokyo Disneyland ♦	268	35.37 N	139.53 E
Tōkyō-kō c	268	35.37 N	139.47 E
Tōkyō-kokusai-kūkō ⊠	94	35.45 N	140.21 E
Tokyo Station -•-[5]	268	35.41 N	139.46 E
Tokyo Tower ʋ	268	35.39 N	139.45 E
Tokyo University ʋ[2]	268	35.42 N	139.46 E
Tokyo University of Education ʋ[2]	268	35.43 N	139.44 E
Tōkyō-wan (Tokyo Bay) c	94	35.25 N	139.47 E
Tokzār	120	35.52 N	66.26 E
Tol I	175c	7.22 N	151.37 E
Tolaga Bay	172	38.22 S	178.18 E
Tolala	112	2.56 S	121.06 E
Tolang	114	1.56 N	99.26 E
Tolbert	52	53.10 N	6.21 E
Tolbo Nuur	86	48.25 N	90.17 E
Tolbuchino	80	57.51 N	40.03 E
Tolderol Point ›	168b	35.22 S	139.10 E
Toldo, Pico del ∧	240p	20.30 N	74.54 W
Tole, Kaz.	85	42.40 N	70.08 E
Tolé, Pan.	236	8.14 N	81.41 W
Toledo, Bol.	248	18.10 S	67.25 W
Toledo, Bra.	252	24.44 S	53.45 W
Toledo, Bra.	256	22.44 S	46.23 W
Toledo, Col.	246	7.19 N	72.28 W
Toledo, Esp.	34	39.52 N	4.01 W
Toledo, Pil.	116	10.23 N	123.38 E
Toledo, Il., U.S.	194	39.16 N	88.14 W
Toledo, Ia., U.S.	190	41.59 N	92.34 W
Toledo, Oh., U.S.	214	41.39 N	83.33 W
Toledo, Or., U.S.	202	44.37 N	123.56 W
Toledo, Wa., U.S.	224	46.26 N	122.50 W
Toledo, Ur.	258	34.45 S	56.05 W
Toledo □[4]	34	39.45 N	4.00 W
Toledo □[5]	236	16.20 N	88.55 W
Toledo, Montes de ⋏	34	39.33 N	4.20 W
Toledo Bend Reservoir ⊜[1]	194	31.30 N	93.45 W
Toledo Express Airport ⊠	216	41.35 N	83.49 W
Tolentino	66	43.12 N	13.17 E
Tolfa	66	42.09 N	11.56 E
Tolfa, Monti della ⋏	66	42.08 N	11.54 E
Tolga, Alg.	148	34.46 N	5.22 E
Tolga, Nor.	26	62.25 N	11.00 E
Toli	86	45.57 N	83.37 E
Toliara	157b	23.21 S	43.40 E
Toliara □[4]	157b	24.00 S	45.00 E
Tolima □[5]	246	3.45 N	75.15 W
Tolima, Nevado del ∧	246	4.40 N	75.19 W
Tolimán, Méx.	234	19.36 N	103.55 W
Tolimán, Méx.	234	20.55 N	99.56 W
Tolitoli	112	1.02 N	120.49 E
Toljatti (Togliatti)	80	53.31 N	49.26 E
Tol'ka	74	64.02 N	81.55 E
Tolkmicko	30	54.20 N	19.31 E
Tolland	207	41.52 N	72.22 W
Tolland □[6]	207	41.52 N	72.22 W
Tollarp	26	55.56 N	13.59 E
Tollense ≃	54	53.54 N	13.02 E
Tollensesee ⊜	54	53.30 N	13.11 E
Tollesboro	218	38.33 N	83.34 W
Tollesbury	42	51.46 N	0.50 E
Tolleson	200	33.27 N	112.15 W
Tollhouse	226	37.01 N	119.23 W
Tolloche	252	25.30 S	63.32 W
Tølløse	41	55.37 N	11.45 E
Tollygunge -•-[8]	272b	22.30 N	88.21 E
Tolmači	76	57.26 N	35.41 E
Tolmačovo	76	58.52 N	29.55 E
Tolmezzo	64	46.24 N	13.01 E
Tolmin	36	46.11 N	13.44 E
Tolna	30	46.26 N	18.46 E
Tolna □[6]	30	46.30 N	18.35 E
Tolo	152	2.56 S	18.34 E
Tolo, Teluk c	112	2.00 S	122.30 E
Toloa, Houma ›	174w	21.17 S	175.08 W
Toločin	76	54.25 N	29.42 E
Tolokiwa Island I	164	5.20 S	147.40 E
Tolomo	89	50.03 N	137.45 E
Tolong Bay c	116	9.20 N	122.49 E
Tolongoina	157b	21.33 S	47.31 E
Tolono	194	39.59 N	88.15 W
Tolosa	34	43.08 N	2.04 W
Tolosa, Aeródromo ⊠	288	34.53 S	57.58 W
Tolovana ≃	180	64.51 N	149.45 W
Tolpuddle	42	50.45 N	2.18 W
Tolsan-do I	98	34.38 N	127.45 E
Tol'skij Majdan	80	54.57 N	44.39 E
Tolsta Head ›	46	58.20 N	6.10 W
Tolstoj, mys ›	74	59.10 N	155.12 E
Tolstoje	78	48.50 N	25.44 E
Tolstopal'cevo	265b	55.38 N	37.13 E
Tolt, North Fork ≃	224	47.42 N	121.49 W
Toltén	254	39.13 S	73.14 W
Tolten ≃	254	39.15 S	73.14 W
Tolti	123	35.02 N	76.06 E
Toltry ⋏[1]	78	49.00 N	26.10 E
Tolt-Seattle Water Supply Reservoir ⊜[1]	224	47.42 N	121.39 W
Tolú	246	9.31 N	75.35 W
Toluca	216	41.00 N	89.08 W
Toluca, Nevado de ∧[1]	234	19.08 N	99.44 W
Toluca [de Lerdo]	234	19.17 N	99.40 W
Tolvajarvi	24	62.17 N	31.27 E
Tolvdalselva ≃	26	58.10 N	8.00 E
Tolve	68	40.42 N	16.01 E
Tolwa	140	6.38 N	32.37 E
Tolworth -•-[8]	260	51.23 N	0.17 W
Tolyatti → Toljatti	80	53.31 N	49.26 E
Tolybaj	86	50.31 N	62.19 E
Tom' ≃, Ross.	86	56.50 N	84.27 E
Tom' ≃, Ross.	89	51.00 N	127.54 E
Toma	150	12.46 N	2.53 W
Tomago	170	32.50 S	151.44 E
Tomah	190	43.58 N	90.30 W
Tomahawk	190	45.28 N	89.43 W
Tomakomai	92a	42.38 N	141.36 E
Tomakovka	78	47.48 N	34.44 E
Tomani	112	4.50 N	115.55 E
Tomanivi ∧	175g	17.37 S	178.01 E
Tomar, Kaz.	86	46.24 N	75.03 E
Tomar, Port.	34	39.36 N	8.25 W
Tomari	89	47.47 N	142.03 E
Tomarovka	78	50.41 N	36.14 E
Tomarza	130	38.27 N	35.49 E
Tomás Barrón (Eucaliptus)	248	17.35 S	67.31 W
Tomasboda ∧[2]	40	59.24 N	14.58 E
Tomás Gomensoro	252	30.26 S	57.26 W
Tomašgorod	78	51.19 N	27.02 E
Tomasine ≃	190	46.40 N	76.16 W
Tomás Jofré	258	34.43 S	59.19 W
Tomášov	61	48.09 N	17.16 E
Tomašpol'	78	48.33 N	28.31 E
Tomaszów Lubelski	30	50.28 N	23.25 E
Tomaszów Mazowiecki	30	51.32 N	20.01 E
Tomatin	46	57.20 N	3.59 W
Tomatlán	234	19.56 N	105.15 W
Tomatlán ≃	234	19.50 N	105.23 W
Tomave	248	20.06 S	66.35 W
Tomazina	255	23.46 S	49.58 W
Tomba di Nerone -•-[8]	267a	41.57 N	12.27 E
Tombadonkéa	150	11.00 N	14.23 W
Tombador, Serra do ⋏[1]	248	12.00 S	57.40 W
Tomball	222	30.06 N	95.37 W
Tombe	140	5.49 N	31.41 E
Tombigbee ≃	194	31.04 N	87.58 W
Tombo, Punta ›	254	44.03 S	65.11 W
Tombôco	152	6.48 S	13.18 E
Tombolo	64	45.38 N	11.50 E
Tombos	255	20.55 S	42.02 W
Tombouctou (Timbuktu)	150	16.46 N	3.01 W
Tombouctou □[4]	150	18.20 N	3.50 W
Tombs of the Caliphs ⊥	273c	30.03 N	31.17 E
Tombstone	200	31.42 N	110.04 W
Tombstone Mountain ∧	180	64.25 N	138.30 W
Tombua	152	15.49 S	11.53 E
Tom Burke	156	23.05 S	28.00 E
Tomdoun	46	57.04 N	5.03 W
Tomé	252	36.37 S	72.57 W
Tomea, Pulau I	112	5.45 S	123.56 E
Tomé-Açu	250	2.25 S	48.09 W
Tömek	130	38.02 N	32.41 E
Tomelilla	26	55.33 N	13.57 E
Tomelloso	34	39.10 N	3.01 W
Tomerong	170	35.04 S	150.35 E
Tomhannock Reservoir ⊜[1]	210	42.51 N	73.33 W
Tomi ≃	152	5.07 N	19.19 E
Tomich	46	57.18 N	4.48 W
Tomichi Creek ≃	200	38.31 N	106.58 W
Tomifobia ≃	206	45.11 N	72.02 W
Tomiko Lake ⊜	190	46.32 N	79.49 W
Tomilino	265b	55.39 N	37.57 E
Tomini	112	0.30 N	120.32 E
Tomini, Teluk c	112	0.20 S	121.00 E
Tominian	150	13.17 N	4.35 W
Tomintoul	46	57.14 N	3.22 W
Tomio ≃	270	34.35 N	135.44 E
Tomioka	94	36.15 N	138.54 E
Tomisato	94	35.44 N	140.19 E
Tomiura	94	35.03 N	139.50 E
Tomiyama, Nihon	94	35.11 N	137.48 E
Tomiyama, Nihon	94	35.05 N	139.51 E
Tomizawa	94	35.14 N	138.29 E
T'omkino	76	55.05 N	35.01 E
Tomkins Cove	210	41.15 N	73.59 W
Tomkinson Ranges ⋏	162	26.11 S	129.05 E
Tomkinsville	208	38.19 N	76.53 W
Tomlinson Run State Park ♦	214	40.33 N	80.34 W
Tommerup Stationsby	41	55.19 N	10.13 E
Tommot	74	58.58 N	126.19 E
Tomnavoulin	46	57.18 N	3.19 W
T'omnyj	88	53.24 N	118.31 E
Tomo ≃	246	5.20 N	67.48 W
Tomobe	94	36.20 N	140.20 E
Tomogashima-suidō ʮ	96	34.17 N	135.00 E
Tomohon	112	1.19 N	124.49 E
Tömör Bulag	88	49.16 N	100.15 E
Tomori	174m	26.08 N	127.44 E
Tomori, Teluk c	112	1.58 S	121.28 E
Tompa	88	55.08 N	109.47 E
Tompkins, Nf., Can.	186	47.48 N	59.13 W
Tompkins, Sk., Can.	184	50.04 N	108.47 W
Tompkins □[6]	210	42.27 N	76.30 W
Tompkins County Airport ⊠	210	42.29 N	76.57 W
Tompkinsville	194	36.42 N	85.41 W
Tompo	112	0.56 N	120.20 E
Tom Price	162	22.41 S	117.43 E
Tom Price, Mount ∧	162	22.39 S	117.40 E
Tomptokan	74	57.06 N	133.59 E
Tomra	26	62.35 N	6.56 E
Toms ≃	208	39.57 N	74.07 W
Toms, Ridgeway Branch ≃	208	40.00 N	74.14 W
Toms Cove c	208	37.53 N	75.22 W
Toms Creek ≃	208	39.38 N	77.17 W
Tomsk	86	56.30 N	84.58 E
Tomsk Oblast' □[4]	86	58.00 N	82.00 E
Toms River	208	39.58 N	74.12 W
Tom Steed Reservoir ⊜[1]	196	34.45 N	99.00 W
Tomtabacken ∧[2]	26	57.30 N	14.28 E
Tömük	130	36.41 N	34.22 E
Tomuzlovka ≃	84	44.46 N	44.10 E
Ton	64	46.15 N	11.04 E
Tonadico	64	46.11 N	11.50 E
Tonaki-shima I	93b	26.21 N	127.09 E
Tonalá, Méx.	234	16.04 N	93.45 W
Tonalá, Méx.	234	20.37 N	103.14 W
Tonalá ≃	234	18.13 N	94.11 W
Tonale, Passo del)(	64	46.16 N	10.35 E
Tonami	94	36.38 N	136.54 E
Tonantins	246	2.47 S	67.47 W
Tonantins ≃	246	2.47 S	67.47 W
Tonara	71	40.02 N	9.10 E
Tonasket	202	48.42 N	119.26 W
Tonate	250	4.55 N	52.22 W
Tonatico	234	18.47 N	99.41 W
Tonawanda, N.Y., U.S.	210	43.01 N	78.52 W
Tonawanda, N.Y., U.S.	210	42.59 N	78.52 W
Tonawanda Channel ≃[1]	284a	43.04 N	79.00 W
Tonawanda Creek ≃	210	43.02 N	78.53 W
Tonawanda Indian Reservation -•-[4]	210	43.05 N	78.27 W
Tonawanda Island I	284a	43.02 N	78.53 W
Tonbara	96	35.05 N	132.47 E
Tonbo	110	18.31 N	95.05 E
Tonbridge	42	51.12 N	0.16 E
Tonbridge and Malling □[8]	260	51.16 N	0.20 E
Tonda	270	34.50 N	135.36 E
Tonda ≃	96	33.38 N	135.24 E
Tondabayashi	96	34.30 N	135.36 E
Tondano	112	1.19 N	124.54 E
Tønder	41	54.56 N	8.54 E
Tondhre	272c	19.05 N	73.08 E
Tondi	122	9.44 N	79.01 E
Tondibi	150	16.39 N	0.14 W
Tondidji	150	13.06 N	10.20 W
Tondi Kiwindi	150	14.28 N	2.02 E
Tondoro	156	17.45 S	18.50 E
Tone, Nihon	94	36.42 N	139.13 E
Tone, Nihon	94	35.51 N	140.09 E
Tone ≃	94	35.44 N	140.51 E
Tonekābon	128	36.49 N	50.53 E
Tone-unga ≊	268	35.54 N	139.53 E
Tonež	78	51.49 N	27.48 E
Tonga, Cam.	152	4.58 N	10.42 E
Tonga, Sūd.	140	9.28 N	31.03 E
Tonga □[1]	14	20.00 S	175.00 W
Tongaat	158	29.37 S	31.03 E
Tonga Islands II	14	20.00 S	175.00 W
Tong'an	100	24.46 N	118.08 E
Tonganoxie	198	39.06 N	95.05 W
Tong'anqiao	106	31.22 N	120.27 E
Tonga Ridge ⊹[3]	14	21.00 S	175.00 W
Tongariro, Mount ∧	172	39.08 S	175.38 E
Tongariro National Park ♦	172	39.15 S	175.30 E
Tongas	115a	7.44 S	113.06 E
Tongatapu □[8]	174w	21.10 S	175.10 W
Tongatapu I	174w	21.10 S	175.10 W
Tongatapu Group II	14	21.10 S	175.10 W
Tonga Trench ⊹[1]	14	20.00 S	173.00 W
Tongbai, Zhg.	100	32.22 N	113.24 E
Tongbai, Zhg.	105	39.35 N	116.44 E
Tongbai Shan ∧	100	32.20 N	113.14 E
Tongbai Shan ⋏	100	32.20 N	113.15 E
Tongbei	89	47.45 N	126.46 E
Tongcheng, Zhg.	100	31.03 N	116.58 E
Tongcheng, Zhg.	100	32.53 N	118.58 E
Tongcheng, Zhg.	100	29.11 N	113.49 E
Tongchengzha	100	31.30 N	118.07 E
Tongchengzhuang	105	39.22 N	117.36 E
T'ongch'ŏn	98	38.54 N	127.54 E
Tongchuan	102	35.01 N	109.01 E
Tongdao	102	26.23 N	109.23 E
Tongde	102	35.17 N	100.42 E
Tongerbao	104	41.26 N	123.02 E
Tongeren	56	50.47 N	5.28 E
Tongerlo	56	51.07 N	4.54 E
Tonggou	98	41.53 N	125.46 E
Tonggu, Zhg.	100	28.33 N	114.21 E
Tonggu, Zhg.	100	21.53 N	112.55 E
Tongguan, Zhg.	100	28.29 N	112.48 E
Tongguan, Zhg.	102	34.38 N	110.20 E
Tongguan, Zhg.	102	23.18 N	101.23 E
Tongguanyi	107	29.20 N	106.23 E
Tonghai	102	24.07 N	102.49 E
Tonghaikou	100	30.14 N	113.08 E
Tonghe, Zhg.	89	45.59 N	128.45 E
Tonghe, Zhg.	100	32.56 N	112.45 E
Tongho-ri	98	35.49 N	127.54 E
Tonghua, Zhg.	98	41.41 N	125.55 E
Tonghua (Kuaidamao), Zhg.	98	41.40 N	125.44 E
Tonghui ≃	271a	39.53 N	116.41 E
Tongi	126	23.53 N	90.24 E
Tong Island I	164	2.05 S	147.50 E
Tongjiang, Zhg.	89	47.40 N	132.30 E
Tongjiang, Zhg.	102	31.58 N	107.14 E
Tongjiangchang	107	29.37 N	103.43 E
Tongjiangkou	104	42.37 N	123.41 E
Tongjing	100	31.47 N	118.33 E
Tongjosŏn-man c	98	39.30 N	128.00 E
Tongjuzhen	98	38.36 N	117.11 E
Tongken ≃	89	46.31 N	126.22 E
Tongli	106	31.10 N	120.43 E
Tongliang	107	29.51 N	106.03 E
Tongliao	89	43.39 N	122.14 E
Tongling, Zhg.	100	30.53 N	117.46 E
Tongling, Zhg.	102	23.28 N	109.40 E
Tonglu	100	29.48 N	119.40 E
Tonglü Yunhe ≊	106	32.04 N	121.40 E
Tongmang-ni	98	37.37 N	126.26 E
Tongmu, Zhg.	100	27.57 N	113.55 E
Tongmu, Zhg.	102	24.09 N	110.04 E
Tongnae	98	35.12 N	129.05 E
Tongnan	107	30.11 N	105.48 E
Tongno-gang ≃	98	40.58 N	126.04 E
Tongo	166	30.30 S	143.45 E
Tongoa I	175f	16.54 S	168.34 E
Tongobory	157b	23.32 S	44.20 E
Tongololo Creek ≃	162	22.06 S	121.08 E
Tongoy	252	30.15 S	71.30 W
Tongqin	100	28.52 N	119.56 E
Tongquansi	107	30.23 N	104.50 E
Tongquil Island I	116	6.02 N	121.51 E
Tongren, Zhg.	102	27.38 N	109.03 E
Tongren, Zhg.	102	35.32 N	101.54 E
Tongrengchang	107	30.02 N	106.42 E
Tongsa ≃	124	26.52 N	90.57 E
Tongsa Dzong	124	27.31 N	90.30 E
Tongsan-ni	271b	37.38 N	126.53 E
Tongshan	100	29.38 N	114.29 E
Tongshi	98	35.26 N	117.43 E
Tongshuping	100	27.17 N	114.54 E
Tongta	110	21.20 N	99.16 E
Tongtai	100	32.38 N	120.47 E
Tongtan	107	28.56 N	105.17 E
Tongtian ≃	102	33.25 N	96.32 E
Tongue	46	58.28 N	4.25 W
Tongue ≃, U.S.	202	46.24 N	105.52 W
Tongue ≃, N.D., U.S.	198	48.56 N	97.18 W
Tongue ≃, Tx., U.S.	196	34.07 N	100.25 W
Tongue, Kyle of c	46	58.30 N	4.26 W
Tongue of the Ocean ⊹[1]	238	24.30 N	77.30 W
Tongue River Reservoir ⊜[1]	202	45.06 N	106.47 W
Tongwei	102	35.07 N	105.27 E
Tongxi	107	29.59 N	106.08 E
Tongxian	105	39.55 N	116.39 E
Tongxianchang	107	30.14 N	105.24 E
Tongxiang	106	30.38 N	120.32 E
Tongxin	102	37.02 N	106.09 E
Tongxinchang	107	29.42 N	106.26 E
Tongxing	107	30.35 N	106.12 E
Tongxu	98	34.29 N	114.28 E
Tongyang-ni	98	39.08 N	126.52 E
Tongyang Yunhe ≊	106	32.02 N	120.48 E
Tongyu	89	44.48 N	123.05 E
Tongyuan, Zhg.	100	28.04 N	116.08 E
Tongyuan, Zhg.	106	30.28 N	120.52 E
Tongyuanpu	104	40.49 N	123.54 E
Tongzhaipu	100	32.48 N	112.44 E
Tongzi	102	28.08 N	106.49 E
Tongzidixia	104	41.08 N	120.34 E
Tonica	216	41.12 N	89.04 W
Tonila	234	19.26 N	103.31 W
Tönisberg	263	51.25 N	6.30 E
Tönisheide	263	51.19 N	7.03 E
Tönisvorst	56	51.19 N	6.29 E
Tonj	140	7.17 N	28.45 E
Tonk	120	26.10 N	75.47 E
Tonkawa	196	36.40 N	97.18 W
Tonkin → Bac Phan □[9]	110	22.00 N	105.00 E
Tonkin, Gulf of c	110	20.00 N	108.00 E
Tonkino	80	57.23 N	46.28 E
Tonkou, Mont ∧	150	7.27 N	7.39 W
Tonkwa	110	23.36 N	96.58 E
Tônlé Sab, Bœng ⊜	110	13.00 N	104.00 E
Tonle Sap → Tônlé Sab, Bœng ⊜	110	13.00 N	104.00 E
Tonnay-Boutonne	32	45.58 N	0.42 W
Tonneins	32	44.23 N	0.19 E
Tonner Canyon V	280	33.58 N	117.48 W
Tonnerre	50	47.51 N	3.58 E
Tönnet	40	60.14 N	13.30 E
Tönning	41	54.19 N	8.56 E
Tōno	92	39.19 N	141.32 E
Tonogaya	268	35.46 N	139.22 E
Tonopah	204	38.04 N	117.13 W
Tōnoshō, Nihon	94	35.49 N	140.42 E
Tonoshō, Nihon	96	34.29 N	134.11 E
Tonosí	246	7.24 N	80.27 W
Tonota	156	21.29 S	27.29 E
Tonquish Creek ≃	281	42.21 N	83.22 W
Tons ≃	124	25.17 N	82.04 E
Tonšajevo	80	57.44 N	47.00 E
Tønsberg	26	59.17 N	10.25 E
Tönsholt	263	51.38 N	6.58 E
Tonstad	26	58.40 N	6.43 E
Tonto Creek ≃	200	33.46 N	111.15 W
Tontogany	216	41.25 N	83.44 W
Tonto National Monument ♦	200	33.34 N	111.02 W
Tonya	130	40.53 N	39.16 E
Tonypandy	42	51.38 N	3.27 W
Tonyrefail	42	51.36 N	3.25 W
Toobeah	166	28.25 S	149.52 E
Toodyay	168a	31.33 S	116.28 E
Tooele	200	40.31 N	112.17 W
Toogoolawah	171a	27.06 S	152.23 E
Tool	222	32.16 N	96.10 W
Toolik ≃	180	69.55 N	149.30 W
Tooma	171b	35.58 S	148.03 E
Tooma ≃	171b	36.04 S	148.00 E
Tooma Reservoir ⊜[1]	171b	36.04 S	148.16 E
Toomebridge	48	54.45 N	6.27 W
Toompine	166	27.13 S	144.22 E
Toomsboro	192	32.49 N	83.04 W
Toomyvara	48	52.50 N	8.02 W
Toongabbie	274a	33.47 S	150.57 E
Toora	169	38.40 S	146.20 E
Toora-Chem	88	52.28 N	96.17 E
Toorak	274b	37.51 S	145.01 E
Toormakeady	48	53.39 N	9.24 W
Toosey Indian Reserve -•-[4]	182	51.56 N	122.29 W
Toot Hill	260	51.42 N	0.12 E
Tootias	144	3.57 N	43.57 E
Tootie, Mount ∧	170	33.28 S	150.30 E
Tootsi	76	58.34 N	24.47 E
Toowoomba	171a	27.33 S	151.57 E
Topanga	228	34.06 N	118.36 W
Topanga Canyon V	280	34.05 N	118.36 W
Topanga State Park ♦	280	34.06 N	118.33 W
Topar	86	49.32 N	72.50 E
Topawa	200	31.48 N	111.49 W
Topaz Lake ⊜	226	38.41 N	119.32 W
Topçam	130	40.38 N	37.48 E
Topchānchi	126	23.54 N	86.12 E
Töpchin	54	52.10 N	13.34 E
Topčicha	86	52.49 N	83.10 E
Topeka, In., U.S.	216	41.32 N	85.32 W
Topeka, Ks., U.S.	198	39.02 N	95.40 W
Töpen	54	50.23 N	11.52 E
Topia	232	25.13 N	106.34 W
Topilejo -•-[8]	286a	19.12 N	99.09 W
Topino ≃	66	43.02 N	12.30 E
Topkanovo	82	54.43 N	38.29 E
Topkapı -•-[8]	267b	41.02 N	28.54 E
Topkapi Palace ⊥	267b	41.00 N	28.59 E
Topki	86	55.16 N	85.36 E
Topko, gora ∧	74	57.08 N	137.24 E
Topl'a ≃	30	48.45 N	21.45 E
Topley	182	54.30 N	126.18 W
Toplica ≃	38	43.13 N	21.49 E
Toplița	38	46.55 N	25.21 E
T'oploje, Ross.	76	53.37 N	37.36 E
T'oploje, Ross.	76	53.13 N	38.53 E
T'oploje ≃	83	48.47 N	39.19 E
T'oplyj Stan	80	53.58 N	50.10 E
T'oplyj Stan -•-[8]	265b	55.37 N	37.30 E
Topo ≃	286c	10.33 N	67.00 W
Topocalma, Punta ›	252	34.08 S	72.01 W
Top of Hebers	262	53.34 N	2.12 W
Topo Infiernito ∧	286c	10.33 N	66.55 W
Topol'čany	30	48.34 N	18.10 E
Topoli	80	47.59 N	51.36 E
Topolobampo	232	25.36 N	109.03 W
Topolog	38	44.53 N	28.22 E
Topolovățu Mare	38	45.46 N	21.37 E
Topolovgrad	38	42.05 N	26.20 E
Toporok	76	58.33 N	33.28 E
Topozero, ozero ⊜	24	65.40 N	32.00 E
Toppenish	202	46.22 N	120.18 W
Toppenish Creek ≃	202	46.20 N	120.11 W
Toppenish Ridge ∧	224	46.18 N	120.40 W
Toppings	262	53.37 N	2.25 W
Toprakkale	130	37.06 N	36.07 E
Tops, Mount ∧	162	21.50 S	134.00 E
Topsa	24	62.39 N	43.34 E
Topsfield	207	42.38 N	70.57 W
Topsham, Eng., U.K.	42	50.41 N	3.27 W
Topsham, Me., U.S.	188	43.55 N	69.58 W
Top Springs	164	16.38 S	131.50 E
Topton	208	40.30 N	75.42 W
Toquima Range ⋏	204	38.45 N	116.55 W
Toquop Wash V	204	36.45 N	114.11 W
Tor	144	7.51 N	33.35 E
Torahime	94	35.25 N	136.16 E
Torano Castello	68	39.30 N	16.08 E
Torawitan, Tanjung ›	112	1.46 N	124.58 E
Toraya	248	14.03 S	73.18 W
Torbalı	130	38.10 N	27.21 E
Torbat-e Ḥeydarīyeh	128	35.16 N	59.13 E
Torbat-e Jām	128	35.14 N	60.36 E
Torbay	186	47.40 N	52.44 W
Torbay □[9]	42	50.26 N	3.34 W
Tor Bay c	42	50.25 N	3.30 W
Torbejevo, Ross.	80	54.05 N	43.15 E
Torbejevo, Ross.	82	54.44 N	36.11 E
Torbert, Mount ∧	180	61.25 N	152.24 W
Torbino	76	58.35 N	32.53 E
Torbole	64	45.52 N	10.52 E
Torbreck, Mount ∧	169	37.21 S	145.57 E
Torbrook	186	44.55 N	64.59 W
Torch ≃	184	53.50 N	103.05 W
Torchany	80	55.34 N	46.36 E
Torchiarolo	68	40.29 N	18.03 E
Torch Lake ⊜	190	45.00 N	85.19 W
Torčin	78	50.46 N	24.59 E
Torcy	261	48.51 N	2.39 E
Torda → Turda	38	46.34 N	23.47 E
Tordera ≃	34	41.39 N	2.47 E
Tordesillas	34	41.30 N	5.00 W
Tordino ≃	66	42.44 N	13.59 E
Tor di Quinto -•-[8]	267a	41.56 N	12.28 E
Töre	26	65.54 N	22.39 E
Töreboda	40	58.43 N	14.08 E
Torej	88	50.33 N	104.50 E
Torekov	26	56.26 N	12.37 E
Toreno	34	42.42 N	6.30 W
Torez	83	48.01 N	38.37 E
Torfou	261	48.32 N	2.14 E
Torgau	54	51.34 N	13.00 E
Torgelow	54	53.37 N	14.00 E
Torgelower See ⊜	54	53.34 N	12.47 E
Torgo	88	58.28 N	119.50 E
Torgun ≃	80	50.15 N	46.18 E
Torhamn	26	56.05 N	15.50 E
Torhout	50	51.04 N	3.06 E
Toribulu	112	0.19 S	120.01 E
Toride	94	35.53 N	140.04 E
Torigakubi-misaki ›	94	37.10 N	138.06 E
Torigoe	94	36.21 N	136.36 E
Toriido	270	34.25 N	135.43 E
Torii-tōge)(	94	36.29 N	138.24 E
Toriki	265a	59.47 N	30.07 E
Torino (Turin)	62	45.03 N	7.40 E
Torino □[4]	62	45.08 N	7.22 E
Torino di Sangro Marina	66	42.11 N	14.32 E
Torío ≃	34	42.35 N	5.34 W
Toriparu	255	16.20 S	53.55 W
Torit	154	4.24 N	32.34 E
Toritto	68	41.00 N	16.41 E
Toriya	94	36.59 N	136.54 E
Torjun	115a	7.10 S	113.13 E
Torkestān, Selseleh-ye Band-e ⋏	128	35.25 N	64.15 E
Torkoviči	76	58.52 N	30.20 E
Torlino	86	58.53 N	63.46 E
Torment, Point ›	162	17.02 S	123.36 E
Tormentine, Cape ›	186	46.07 N	63.47 W
Tormes ≃	34	41.18 N	6.29 W
Tormestorp	41	56.07 N	13.44 E
Tormey	282	38.03 N	122.15 W
Tormini	64	45.36 N	10.29 E
Tormosin	80	48.12 N	42.42 E
Torna	24	68.04 N	44.10 E
Torna ∧	122	18.16 N	73.37 E
Tornado Mountain ∧	182	49.58 N	114.39 W
Tornal'a	30	48.27 N	20.20 E
Tornareccio	66	42.02 N	14.24 E
Tornberget ∧[2]	40	59.08 N	18.01 E
Torne ≃	44	53.36 N	0.44 W
Torneälven (Tornionjoki) ≃	24	65.48 N	24.08 E
Torne Brook ≃	276	41.08 N	74.10 W
Tornesch	52	53.41 N	9.43 E
Torneträsk ⊜	24	68.20 N	19.10 E
Torngat Mountains ⋏	176	59.00 N	64.00 W
Tornillo	200	31.27 N	106.05 W
Tornillo Creek ≃	196	29.11 N	103.00 W
Tornimparte	66	42.17 N	13.18 E
Torning	41	56.17 N	9.20 E
Tornio	26	65.51 N	24.08 E
Tornionjoki (Torneälven) ≃	24	65.48 N	24.08 E
Tornquist	252	38.06 S	62.14 W
T'orny, Ukr.	78	48.09 N	33.33 E
T'orny, Ukr.	78	50.59 N	33.59 E
T'orny, Ukr.	83	49.05 N	37.57 E
Tornyiszentmiklós	61	46.31 N	16.34 E
Toro	34	41.31 N	5.24 W
Torö I	40	58.50 N	17.50 E
Toro, Arroyo ≃	288	34.27 S	58.52 W
Toro, Cañada del ≃	258	35.16 S	59.05 W
Toro, Cerro ∧	234	19.10 N	104.27 W
Toro, Lago del ⊜	254	51.14 S	72.45 W
Toro, Punta ›	252	33.47 S	71.49 W
Torobuku	112	4.25 S	122.26 E
Torodi	150	13.18 N	1.40 E
Toro-iseki ⊥	94	34.57 N	138.24 E
Torok	146	10.03 N	14.33 E
Torokina	175e	6.14 S	155.03 E
Törökszentmiklós	30	47.11 N	20.25 E
Torola ≃	236	13.52 N	88.30 W
Torom	89	54.32 N	135.50 E
Torom ≃	89	54.36 N	135.46 E
Toroni, Nevado ∧	248	19.43 S	68.41 W
Toronto, Austl.	170	33.01 S	151.36 E
Toronto, On., Can.	212	43.39 N	79.23 W
Toronto, On., Can.	275b	43.39 N	79.23 W
Toronto, Ks., U.S.	198	37.47 N	95.56 W
Toronto, Oh., U.S.	214	40.27 N	80.36 W
Toronto, S.D., U.S.	198	44.34 N	96.38 W
Toronto □[6]	275b	43.44 N	79.24 W
Toronto, Canadian Forces Base ■	212	43.45 N	79.28 W
Toronto, University of ʋ[2]	275b	43.40 N	79.24 W
Toronto Harbour c	275b	43.38 N	79.22 W
Toronto Island Airport ⊠	275b	43.38 N	79.24 W
Toronto Lake ⊜[1]	198	37.46 N	95.57 W
Toronto Reservoir ⊜[1]	210	41.38 N	74.51 W
Toronto Zoo, Metro ♦	275b	43.49 N	79.11 W
Toro Peak ∧	204	33.32 N	116.25 W
Toropec	76	56.30 N	31.39 E
Toropovo	82	54.21 N	36.07 E
Tororo	154	0.42 N	34.11 E
Toros (Acho), Plaza de ♦	286d	12.02 S	77.02 W
Toros Dağları (Taurus Mountains) ⋏	130	37.00 N	33.00 E
Torošino	76	57.56 N	28.36 E
Torosozero	24	62.30 N	38.10 E
Torotoro	248	18.07 S	65.46 W
Toroume ∧[2]	174k	21.15 S	159.45 W
Torpa ⊥	26	57.39 N	13.16 E
Torpè	71	40.38 N	9.40 E
Torphins	46	57.06 N	2.37 W
Tor Pignatara -•-[8]	267a	41.52 N	12.32 E
Torpo	26	60.40 N	8.43 E
Torpoint	42	50.22 N	4.11 W
Torpy ≃	182	53.44 N	120.55 W
Torquay, Austl.	169	38.21 S	144.19 E
Torquay, Sk., Can.	184	49.08 N	103.31 W
Torquay, Eng., U.K.	42	50.28 N	3.30 W
Torquemada	34	42.02 N	4.19 W
Torraca	68	40.07 N	15.38 E
Torrance, Ca., U.S.	228	33.50 N	118.20 W
Torrance, Pa., U.S.	214	40.25 N	79.14 W
Torrance Lake ⊜	184	57.04 N	98.12 W
Torrance Municipal Airport ⊠	280	33.48 N	118.20 W
Torrão	34	38.18 N	8.13 W
Torre Annunziata	68	40.45 N	14.27 E
Torre Baja	34	40.07 N	1.15 W
Torrebelvicino	64	45.43 N	11.18 E
Torre Beretti	62	45.04 N	8.40 E
Torreblanca	34	40.13 N	0.12 E
Torrebruna	66	41.52 N	14.33 E
Torrecilla ∧	34	37.36 N	2.31 W
Torrecilla en Cameros	34	42.16 N	2.37 W
Torre del Campo	34	37.46 N	3.53 W
Torre del Greco	68	40.47 N	14.22 E
Torre del Lago Puccini	66	43.50 N	10.17 E
Torre de Moncorvo	34	41.10 N	7.03 W
Torre de'Passeri	66	42.14 N	13.56 E
Torre di Mosto	64	45.41 N	12.43 E
Torre di Santa Maria	64	46.14 N	9.51 E
Torredonjimeno	34	37.46 N	3.57 W
Torre Faro -•-[8]	70	38.16 N	15.39 E
Torre Gaia -•-[8]	267a	41.51 N	12.39 E
Torregrotta	70	38.11 N	15.21 E
Torrejon Air Base ■	266a	40.28 N	3.28 W
Torrejoncillo	34	39.54 N	6.28 W
Torrejón de Ardoz	34	40.27 N	3.29 W
Torrejón-Tajo, Embalse de ⊜[1]	34	39.50 N	5.50 W
Torrelaguna	34	40.50 N	3.32 W
Torrelavega	34	43.21 N	4.03 W
Torrellas, Riera de ≃	266d	41.23 N	2.01 E
Torrelles de Llobregat	266d	41.21 N	1.59 E
Torrelletes	266d	41.21 N	1.57 E
Torremaggiore	68	41.41 N	15.17 E
Torremolinos	34	36.37 N	4.30 W
Torrenieri	66	43.05 N	11.33 E
Torrens ≃	168b	34.56 S	138.30 E
Torrens, Lake ⊜	166	31.00 S	137.50 E
Torrens, Mount ∧	168b	34.52 S	138.56 E
Torrens Creek	166	20.46 S	145.02 E
Torrens Creek ≃	166	22.22 S	145.09 E
Torrens Island I	168b	34.48 S	138.32 E
Torrent, Arg.	252	28.50 S	56.28 W
Torrent, Esp.	34	39.26 N	0.28 W
Torreões	256	21.52 S	43.33 W
Torreón	232	25.33 N	103.26 W
Torre Orsaia	68	40.08 N	15.28 E
Torre Pedrera	66	44.06 N	12.31 E
Torre Pellice	62	44.49 N	7.13 E
Torreperogil	34	38.02 N	3.17 W
Torres, Arg.	258	34.26 S	59.08 W
Torres, Bra.	252	29.21 S	49.44 W
Torres, Arroyo ≃	288	34.39 S	58.45 W
Torres, Îles II	175f	13.15 S	166.37 E
Torre Santa Susanna	68	40.28 N	17.44 E
Torresdale -•-[8]	285	40.03 N	75.00 W
Torres de Alcalá	34	35.10 N	4.16 W
Torres Martinez Indian Reservation -•-[4]	204	33.35 N	116.02 W
Torres Novas	34	39.29 N	8.32 W
Torres Strait ʮ	164	10.25 S	142.10 E
Torres Vedras	34	39.06 N	9.16 W
Torretta	70	38.08 N	13.14 E
Torrette di Fano	66	43.47 N	13.07 E
Torrevella	34	37.59 N	0.41 W
Torricella	68	40.21 N	17.29 E
Torricella in Sabina	66	42.16 N	12.52 E
Torricella Peligna	66	42.01 N	14.15 E
Torricella Sicura	66	42.39 N	13.39 E
Torricelli Mountains ⋏	164	3.25 S	142.20 E
Torridge ≃	42	51.03 N	4.11 W
Torridon	46	57.33 N	5.31 W
Torridon, Loch c	46	57.35 N	5.46 W
Torriglia	62	44.31 N	9.10 E
Torrijos, Esp.	34	39.59 N	4.17 W
Torrijos, Pil.	116	13.19 N	122.05 E
Torrild	41	55.59 N	10.04 E
Torrimpietra -•-[8]	267a	41.56 N	12.13 E
Torrin	46	57.12 N	6.02 W
Tørring	41	55.51 N	9.29 E
Torrington, Ct., U.S.	207	41.48 N	73.07 W
Torrington, Wy., U.S.	198	42.03 N	104.10 W
Torrinha	255	22.26 S	48.09 W
Torrita di Siena	66	43.10 N	11.46 E
Torröjen ⊜	26	63.55 N	12.56 E
Torrox	34	36.46 N	3.58 W
Torrvarpen ⊜	40	59.42 N	14.30 E
Torsåker	40	60.31 N	16.29 E
Tor Sapienza -•-[8]	267a	41.54 N	12.35 E
Torsås	26	56.24 N	16.00 E
Torsburgen ⊥	26	57.25 N	18.43 E
Torsby	26	60.08 N	13.00 E
Tors Cove	186	47.13 N	52.51 W
Torshälla	40	59.25 N	16.28 E
Tórshavn	22	62.01 N	6.46 W
Torside Reservoir ⊜[1]	262	53.29 N	1.54 W
Torsö	40	58.47 N	13.48 E
Torsö I	40	58.48 N	13.50 E
Torteval	43b	49.27 N	2.38 W
Torto ≃	70	37.58 N	13.46 E
Tortola I	240m	18.27 N	64.36 W
Tórtolas, Cerro de las ∧	252	29.56 S	69.54 W
Tortolì	71	39.55 N	9.39 E
Tortona	62	44.54 N	8.52 E
Tortora	68	39.56 N	15.48 E
Tortoreto	66	42.48 N	13.55 E
Tortorici	70	38.02 N	14.49 E
Tortosa	34	40.48 N	0.31 E
Tortosa, Cap de ›	34	40.43 N	0.55 E
Tortue ≃	186	50.18 N	65.23 W
Tortue, Île de la I	238	20.04 N	72.49 W
Tortue, Rivière de la ≃	206	45.24 N	73.32 W
Tortuguero ≃	236	10.34 N	83.31 W
Tortuguero, Laguna c	240m	18.28 N	66.26 W
Tortuguero, Parque Nacional ♦	236	10.25 N	83.55 W
Tortuguitas	288	34.28 S	58.46 W
Tortum	130	40.19 N	41.35 E
Toru ≃	114	1.26 N	98.46 E
Toruajgyr	85	42.32 N	76.26 E
Torue	112	0.58 S	120.18 E
Torugart, pereval)(	85	40.33 N	75.20 E
Torul	130	40.35 N	39.18 E
Toruń	30	53.02 N	18.35 E
Toruń □[4]	30	53.20 N	19.00 E
Torunos	246	8.30 N	70.04 W
Torup, Sve.	26	56.58 N	13.05 E
Torup, Sve.	41	55.34 N	13.12 E
Tõrva	76	58.00 N	25.56 E
Tory	88	51.47 N	103.00 E
Tory Island I	48	55.16 N	8.14 W
Torysa ≃	30	48.39 N	21.21 E
Tory Sound ʮ	48	55.14 N	8.14 W
Toržok	76	57.03 N	34.58 E
Torzym	30	52.20 N	15.04 E
Tosa, Nihon	96	33.44 N	133.32 E
Tosa, Nihon	96	33.29 N	133.25 E
T'oša ≃	80	55.38 N	42.09 E
T'osan	98	38.18 N	126.43 E
Tosari	115a	7.53 S	112.54 E
Tosa-shimizu	92	32.46 N	132.57 E
Tosa-wan c	96	33.20 N	133.40 E
Tosayama	96	33.38 N	133.32 E
Tosa-yamada	96	33.36 N	133.41 E
Tosca	156	25.53 S	23.58 E
Toscaig	46	57.24 N	5.50 W
Toscana (Tuscany) □[4]	36	43.25 N	11.00 E
Toscano ≃	234	18.01 N	102.32 W
Toscolano	64	45.38 N	10.37 E
Tösens	58	47.01 N	10.36 E
Toses, Collada de)(	34	42.19 N	2.01 E
Tōshi-jima I	94	34.31 N	136.53 E
Toshima -•-[8]	268	35.44 N	139.43 E
To-shima I	94	34.31 N	139.17 E
Tōshō-gū ʋ[1]	94	36.46 N	139.36 E
Tosi, Indon.	115b	9.35 S	118.57 E
Tosi, It.	66	43.45 N	11.31 E
Tosilei	144	1.25 N	41.24 E
Toškalykaja, gora ∧	86	50.38 N	89.30 E
Toškovskij	83	48.46 N	38.34 E
Tosna ≃	265a	59.46 N	30.46 E
Tosno	76	59.33 N	30.53 E
Toson Cengel	88	48.47 N	98.15 E
Toson Hu ⊜	102	35.18 N	98.54 E
T'osovo	76	55.37 N	34.30 E
T'osovo-Netyl'skij	76	58.57 N	31.04 E
T'osovskij	76	58.48 N	30.52 E
Töss ≃	58	47.33 N	8.33 E
Tossens	52	53.34 N	8.16 E
Tossicia	66	42.33 N	13.39 E
Tostado	252	29.14 S	61.46 W
Tõstamaa	76	58.20 N	24.00 E
Tostedt	52	53.17 N	9.42 E
Tosterön I	40	59.25 N	17.00 E
Tostu	85	41.34 N	71.34 E
Tost uul ⋏	102	43.15 N	100.30 E
Tosu	96	33.22 N	130.31 E
Tosya	130	41.01 N	34.02 E
Totagatic ≃	190	46.05 N	92.11 W
Totak ⊜	26	59.42 N	7.57 E
Totana	34	37.46 N	1.30 W
Totānāla	126	22.05 N	87.40 E
Totatiche	234	21.56 N	103.27 W
Totban	80	46.47 N	49.06 E
Toteng	156	20.22 S	22.58 E
Tôtes	50	49.41 N	1.03 E
Totes Gebirge ⋏	30	47.42 N	13.55 E
T'otkino	78	51.17 N	34.16 E
Tot'ma	76	59.57 N	42.45 E
Totnes	42	50.25 N	3.41 W
Totness	250	5.53 N	56.19 W
Toto	152	7.08 S	14.16 E
Totonicapán	236	14.55 N	91.22 W
Totonicapán □[5]	236	15.00 N	91.20 W
Totopotomoy Creek ≃	208	37.41 N	77.13 W
Totora, Bol.	248	17.42 S	65.09 W
Totora, Bol.	248	17.49 S	68.07 W
Totoras	252	32.35 S	61.11 W
Totos	248	13.31 S	74.30 W
Tototlán	234	20.33 N	102.48 W
Totowa	210	40.54 N	74.12 W
Totoya Island I	175g	18.57 S	179.50 W
Totson Mountain ∧	180	64.26 N	157.15 W
Totsuka -•-[8]	268	35.24 N	139.32 E
Tottenham, Austl.	166	32.14 S	147.21 E
Tottenham, On., Can.	212	44.01 N	79.49 W
Tottenham -•-[8]	260	51.35 N	0.04 W
Tottenham Hotspur Football Ground ♦	260	51.36 N	0.04 W
Totten Inlet c	224	47.07 N	123.02 W
Tottenville -•-[8]	276	40.31 N	74.15 W
Totteridge -•-[8]	260	51.38 N	0.12 W
Tottington	44	53.37 N	2.20 W
Totton	42	50.56 N	1.29 W
Tottori	96	35.30 N	134.14 E
Tottori □[5]	96	35.30 N	134.00 E
Tottori-sakyū ∧[2]	96	35.31 N	134.15 E
Totuskey Creek ≃	208	37.52 N	76.45 W
Tou, Motu I	174k	21.11 S	159.48 W
Touba, C. Iv.	150	8.17 N	7.41 W
Touba, Sén.	150	14.51 N	15.53 W
Toubei	100	26.44 N	116.05 E
Toubéré Bafal	150	14.23 N	13.32 W
Toubkal, Jebel ∧	148	31.05 N	7.55 W
Toubkal, Parc National du ♦	148	31.05 N	7.55 W
Toubori	146	13.59 N	12.18 E
Touboro	152	7.43 N	15.12 E
T'ouch'eng	100	24.52 N	121.49 E
Touchet ≃	202	46.02 N	118.41 W
Touchwood Hills ⋏[2]	184	51.35 N	104.17 W
Touchwood Lake ⊜, Ab., Can.	182	54.50 N	111.23 W
Touchwood Lake ⊜, Mb., Can.	184	54.29 N	95.00 W
Toucy	50	47.44 N	3.18 E
Toudao ≃	98	42.36 N	127.11 E
Toudaogou, Zhg.	98	42.46 N	129.12 E
Toudaogou, Zhg.	104	41.37 N	121.40 E
Toudaogou, Zhg.	105	40.58 N	117.59 E
Touët-sur-Var	62	43.57 N	7.00 E
Tougan	150	13.04 N	3.04 W
Touggourt	148	33.10 N	6.00 E

Symbols in the index entries represent the broad categories identified in the key at the right. Symbols with superior numbers (⋏[1]) identify subcategories (see complete key on page *I · 1).*

Symbole im Register stellen die rechts im Schlüssel erklärten Kategorien dar. Symbole mit hochgestellten Ziffern (⋏[1]) bezeichnen Unterabteilungen einer Kategorie (vgl. vollständiger Schlüssel auf Seite *I · 1).*

Los símbolos incluídos en el texto del índice representan las grandes categorías identificadas con la clave a la derecha. Los símbolos con numeros en su parte superior (⋏[1]) identifican las subcategorías (véase la clave completa en la página *I · 1).*

Les symboles de l'index représentent les catégories indiquées dans la légende à droite. Les symboles suivis d'un indice (⋏[1]) représentent des sous-catégories (voir légende complète à la page *I · 1).*

Os símbolos incluídos no texto do índice representam as grandes categorias identificadas com a chave à direita. Os símbolos com números em sua parte superior (⋏[1]) identificam as subcategorias (veja-se a chave completa à página *I · 1).*

∧	Mountain	Berg	Montaña	Montagne	Montanha
⋏	Mountains	Gebirge	Montañas	Montagnes	Montanhas
)(	Pass	Paß	Paso	Col	Passo
V	Valley, Canyon	Tal, Cañon	Valle, Cañón	Vallée, Canyon	Vale, Canhão
≚	Plain	Ebene	Llano	Plaine	Planície
›	Cape	Kap	Cabo	Cap	Cabo
I	Island	Insel	Isla	Île	Ilha
II	Islands	Inseln	Islas	Îles	Ilhas
⊥	Other Topographic Features	Andere Topographische Objekte	Otros Elementos Topográficos	Autres données topographiques	Outros acidentes topográficos

ESPAÑOL Nombre	Página	Lat.°′	Long.°′ W = Oeste
Toughkenamon	**285**	39.50 N	75.46 W
Tougouri	**150**	13.19 N	0.31 W
Tougué	**150**	11.27 N	11.41 W
Touho	**175f**	20.47 S	165.14 E
Touiel, Oued V	**148**	31.30 N	4.46 E
Touil, Oued V	**148**	35.30 N	2.33 E
Touisset	**207**	41.43 N	71.13 W
Toukansi	**100**	29.22 N	119.06 E
Toukley	**170**	33.16 S	151.33 E
Toukoto	**150**	13.27 N	9.53 W
Toul	**58**	48.41 N	5.54 E
Toulépleu	**150**	6.35 N	8.25 W
Touliu	**100**	23.43 N	120.32 E
Toulnustouc ≃	**186**	49.35 N	68.24 W
Toulnustouc Nord-Est ≃	**186**	50.56 N	67.44 W
Toulon, Fr.	**62**	43.07 N	5.56 E
Toulon, Il., U.S.	**190**	41.05 N	89.51 W
Toulon Lake ⊜	**204**	40.01 N	118.40 W
Toulon-sur-Arroux	**32**	46.42 N	4.08 E
Touloubre ≃	**62**	43.33 N	5.02 E
Toulourenc ≃	**62**	44.14 N	5.09 E
Toulouse	**32**	43.36 N	1.26 E
Toumen Shan I	**100**	28.41 N	121.46 E
Toumfafi	**150**	15.02 N	5.38 E
Toumodi	**150**	6.33 N	5.01 W
Tounan	**100**	23.41 N	120.28 E
Tounassine, Hamada ♦[2]	**148**	28.30 N	5.00 W
Toungo	**146**	8.07 N	12.03 E
Toungoo	**110**	18.56 N	96.26 E
Toupeng	**106**	30.19 N	120.31 E
Touques	**50**	49.22 N	0.06 E
Touques ≃	**50**	49.22 N	0.06 E
Tour, Étang de la ⊜	**261**	48.40 N	1.53 E
Toura, Monts du ⋀	**150**	7.40 N	7.25 W
Touraine	**188**	45.34 N	75.47 W
Touraine □[9]	**32**	47.12 N	0.40 E
Tourakom	**110**	18.26 N	102.32 E
Tourane → Da Nang	**108**	16.04 N	108.13 E
Tourassine ⊤[4]	**148**	24.37 N	11.23 W
Tourbe ≃	**56**	49.10 N	4.52 E
Tourcoing	**50**	50.43 N	3.09 E
Touriñan, Cabo ›	**34**	43.03 N	9.18 W
Tournai	**50**	50.36 N	3.23 E
Tournan-en-Brie	**50**	48.44 N	2.46 E
Tourndo, Oued V	**148**	22.15 N	10.28 E
Tournesac ≃	**50**	47.27 N	4.01 E
Tournon	**62**	45.04 N	4.50 E
Tournus	**58**	46.34 N	4.54 E
Touros	**250**	5.12 S	35.28 W
Tou Rout	**110**	16.24 N	107.00 E
Tourouvre	**50**	48.35 N	0.40 E
Tourrette-Levens	**62**	43.47 N	7.16 E
Tours	**50**	47.23 N	0.41 E
Tours-sur-Marne	**50**	49.03 N	4.07 E
Tours-sur-Meymont	**62**	45.40 N	3.35 E
Tourteron	**56**	49.32 N	4.39 E
Tourves	**62**	43.24 N	5.56 E
Toury	**50**	48.12 N	1.56 E
Toussaint Creek ≃	**214**	41.35 N	83.04 W
Tousside, Pic ∧	**146**	21.02 N	16.25 E
Toussoro, Mont ∧	**146**	9.18 N	23.28 E
Toussus-le-Noble	**261**	48.45 N	2.07 E
Toussus-le-Noble, Aéroport de ⊠	**261**	48.45 N	2.06 E
Toustain	**36**	36.40 N	8.15 E
Toutai, Zhg.	**89**	45.40 N	124.50 E
Toutai, Zhg.	**104**	41.41 N	121.11 E
Toutaizi	**104**	42.19 N	122.49 E
Toutle	**224**	46.20 N	122.41 W
Toutle ≃	**224**	46.17 N	122.55 W
Toutle, North Fork ≃	**224**	46.23 N	122.34 W
Toutle, South Fork ≃	**224**	46.20 N	122.44 W
Toutle Mountain Range ⋀	**224**	46.20 N	122.30 W
Toutuohe	**100**	31.06 N	116.25 E
Touws ≃	**158**	33.45 S	21.11 E
Touwsrivier	**158**	33.20 S	20.00 E
Touzhan	**89**	49.27 N	119.41 E
Toužim	**60**	50.04 N	13.00 E
Töv □[4]	**88**	47.30 N	106.30 E
Tova	**24**	65.58 N	40.45 E
Tovar	**246**	8.20 N	71.46 W
Tovarkovo	**82**	54.42 N	35.57 E
Tovarkovskij	**76**	53.40 N	38.14 E
Tove ≃	**42**	52.05 N	0.38 W
Tovey	**219**	39.35 N	89.27 W
Tow	**196**	30.53 N	98.28 W
Tōwa	**96**	33.13 N	132.53 E
Towaco	**210**	40.55 N	74.20 W
Towada	**92**	40.37 N	141.13 E
Towada-Hachimantai-kokuritsu-kōen ♠	**92**	40.35 N	140.53 E
Towada-ko ⊜	**92**	40.28 N	140.55 E
Towai	**172**	35.29 S	174.08 E
Towamencin Creek ≃	**285**	40.13 N	75.23 W
Towanda, Il., U.S.	**216**	40.34 N	88.54 W
Towanda, Ks., U.S.	**198**	37.47 N	96.59 W
Towanda, Pa., U.S.	**210**	41.46 N	76.26 W
Towanda Creek ≃	**210**	41.45 N	76.26 W
Towan Head ›	**42**	50.25 N	5.07 W
Towar Gardens	**216**	42.45 N	84.28 W
Towari	**112**	4.36 S	121.29 E
Towcester	**42**	52.08 N	1.00 W
Tower	**190**	47.48 N	92.16 W
Tower City, N.D., U.S.	**198**	46.55 N	97.40 W
Tower City, Pa., U.S.	**208**	40.35 N	76.33 W
Tower Hamlets ♦[8]	**260**	51.32 N	0.03 W
Tower Hill, Austl.	**166**	22.03 S	144.36 E
Tower Hill, Il., U.S.	**219**	39.23 N	88.57 W
Towerhill Creek ≃	**166**	22.29 S	144.39 E
Tower of London ⊥	**260**	51.30 N	0.05 W
Tower Peak ∧	**226**	38.09 N	119.33 W
Towers of Silence ♁[1]	**272c**	18.58 N	72.48 E
Tower Soudan State Park ♠	**190**	47.50 N	92.15 W
Towla, Mount ∧	**154**	21.22 S	29.52 E
Tow Law	**44**	54.44 N	1.49 W
Towlī	**84**	39.11 N	47.32 E
Town ≃	**283**	42.00 N	70.57 W
Town and Country	**202**	47.42 N	117.23 W
Town Bank	**208**	39.00 N	74.56 W
Town Creek ≃, Al., U.S.	**194**	34.46 N	87.25 W
Town Creek ≃, Al., U.S.	**194**	34.24 N	86.11 W
Town Creek ≃, Oh., U.S.	**216**	41.05 N	84.25 W
Town Creek Manor	**208**	38.19 N	76.27 W
Towneley Hall ⊥	**262**	53.46 N	2.13 W
Towner	**198**	48.20 N	100.24 W
Town Estates	**285**	40.04 N	74.52 W
Town Hill ∧[2]	**240a**	32.19 N	64.44 W
Townline Tunnel ♦[5]	**284a**	42.57 N	79.15 W
Town of Niagara	**284a**	43.06 N	78.59 W
Town of Pines	**216**	41.41 N	86.58 W
Townsend, On., Can.	**212**	42.54 N	80.07 W
Townsend, De., U.S.	**208**	39.23 N	75.41 W
Townsend, Ma., U.S.	**207**	42.40 N	71.42 W
Townsend, Mt., U.S.	**202**	46.19 N	111.31 W
Townsend, Va., U.S.	**208**	37.11 N	75.57 W
Townsend, Mount ∧	**171b**	36.25 S	148.15 E
Townsend Island I	**276**	40.38 N	73.26 W
Townsends Inlet ⊂	**208**	39.07 N	74.43 W
Townshend Island I	**166**	22.15 S	150.30 E
Township Line Run ≃	**279b**	40.13 N	79.33 W
Townsville	**166**	19.16 S	146.48 E
Townville	**214**	41.41 N	79.53 W
Towrang	**170**	34.42 S	149.51 E
Towrang, Mount ∧	**170**	34.46 S	149.51 E
Towra Point ›	**274a**	34.00 S	151.10 E
Towr Kham	**123**	34.08 N	71.05 E
Towrzī, Afg.	**120**	30.11 N	65.59 E
Towrzī, Afg.	**128**	32.38 N	65.53 E
Towson	**208**	39.24 N	76.36 W

FRANÇAIS Nom	Page	Lat.°′	Long.°′ W = Ouest
Towson State College ♁[2]	**284b**	39.24 N	76.37 W
Towuti, Danau ⊜	**112**	2.45 S	121.32 E
Toxkan (Aksaj) ≃, Asia	**85**	40.55 N	78.16 E
Toxkan ≃, Zhg.	**90**	41.08 N	80.11 E
Toyah	**196**	31.19 N	103.47 W
Toyah Creek ≃	**196**	31.18 N	103.27 W
Tōya-ko ⊜	**92a**	42.35 N	140.51 E
Toyama	**94**	36.41 N	137.13 E
Toyama □[5]	**94**	36.30 N	137.30 E
Toyama-heiya ≡	**94**	36.40 N	137.15 E
Toyama-wan ⊂	**94**	36.50 N	137.10 E
Toyapakeh	**115b**	8.41 S	115.29 E
Tōyo, Nihon	**96**	33.55 N	133.05 E
Tōyō, Nihon	**96**	33.30 N	134.16 E
Toyo ≃	**94**	34.47 N	137.20 E
Toyoake	**94**	35.03 N	137.01 E
Toyoda, Nihon	**94**	34.45 N	137.49 E
Toyoda, Nihon	**268**	35.39 N	139.23 E
Toyofuta	**268**	35.53 N	139.57 E
Toyohama	**96**	34.04 N	133.38 E
Toyohara	**175d**	24.15 N	123.48 E
Toyohashi	**94**	34.46 N	137.23 E
Toyohira	**96**	34.40 N	132.24 E
Toyokawa	**94**	34.49 N	137.24 E
Toyo-kawa-yōsui ≊	**94**	34.35 N	137.03 E
Toyonaka, Nihon	**96**	34.09 N	133.42 E
Toyonaka, Nihon	**96**	34.47 N	135.28 E
Toyone	**94**	35.09 N	137.43 E
Toyono	**94**	36.43 N	138.16 E
Toyooka, Nihon	**94**	35.33 N	137.54 E
Toyooka, Nihon	**94**	34.50 N	137.52 E
Toyooka, Nihon	**96**	35.32 N	134.50 E
Toyooka, Nihon	**268**	35.11 N	139.58 E
Toyosaka, Nihon	**92**	37.56 N	139.13 E
Toyosaka, Nihon	**96**	34.34 N	132.50 E
Toyosato	**94**	36.06 N	140.02 E
Toyoshina	**94**	36.18 N	137.54 E
Toyota, Nihon	**94**	35.05 N	137.09 E
Toyota, Nihon	**94**	36.46 N	138.19 E
Toyota, Nihon	**96**	34.12 N	131.04 E
Toyota-ko ⊜	**96**	34.14 N	131.08 E
Toyotomi	**94**	35.34 N	138.33 E
Toyotsu	**96**	33.40 N	130.58 E
Toyoura	**96**	34.08 N	130.58 E
Toy's Hill	**260**	51.14 N	0.06 E
Tozer, Mount ∧	**164**	12.45 S	143.13 E
Tozeur	**148**	33.55 N	8.08 E
Tozi, Mount ∧	**180**	65.41 N	150.58 W
Tozitna ≃	**180**	65.08 N	152.23 W
Tpig	**84**	41.47 N	47.36 E
Traar ♦[8]	**263**	51.23 N	6.36 E
Trabaria, Bocca)(	**66**	43.36 N	12.14 E
Traben-Trarbach	**56**	49.57 N	7.06 E
Trabia	**70**	37.59 N	13.39 E
Trabiju	**255**	22.03 S	48.18 W
Trabuco, Arroyo ≃	**228**	33.31 N	117.40 W
Trabzon	**130**	41.00 N	39.43 E
Trabzon □[4]	**130**	40.50 N	39.50 E
Tracadie	**186**	47.31 N	64.54 W
Trachselwald	**58**	47.01 N	7.45 E
Tra Cu	**110**	9.42 N	106.16 E
Tracy, P.Q., Can.	**206**	46.01 N	73.09 W
Tracy, Ca., U.S.	**226**	37.44 N	121.25 W
Tracy, Mn., U.S.	**198**	44.14 N	95.37 W
Tracy City	**194**	35.15 N	85.44 W
Tracyton	**224**	47.36 N	122.39 W
Tradate	**62**	45.43 N	8.54 E
Trade Lake ⊜	**184**	55.22 N	103.44 W
Tradewater ≃	**194**	37.31 N	88.03 W
Trading Bay ⊂	**212**	45.15 N	78.55 W
Tradinghouse Creek Reservoir ⊜[1]	**222**	31.35 N	96.55 W
Traditional Cultures, Museum of ♁	**269f**	14.31 N	121.00 E
Trælleborg ⊥	**41**	55.23 N	11.17 E
Traer	**190**	42.11 N	92.27 W
Traessu, Monte ∧	**71**	40.28 N	8.40 E
Trafalgar, Austl.	**169**	38.12 S	146.09 E
Trafalgar, On., Can.	**275b**	43.29 N	79.43 W
Trafalgar, In., U.S.	**218**	39.24 N	86.09 W
Trafalgar, Cabo ›	**34**	36.11 N	6.02 W
Trafaria	**266c**	38.40 N	9.14 W
Trafford	**214**	40.23 N	79.45 W
Trafford □[8]	**262**	53.24 N	2.21 W
Trafford, Lake ⊜	**220**	26.25 N	81.30 W
Trafford Park	**262**	53.28 N	2.20 W
Trafoi	**64**	46.33 N	10.31 E
Tragacete	**34**	40.21 N	1.51 W
Tragliata ♦[8]	**267a**	41.58 N	12.15 E
Tragwein	**61**	48.20 N	14.37 E
Traição, Córrego ≃	**287b**	23.36 S	46.41 W
Traid	**34**	40.40 N	1.49 W
Traiguén	**252**	38.15 S	72.41 W
Traiguén, Isla I	**254**	45.35 S	73.42 W
Trail	**182**	49.06 N	117.42 W
Trail Creek	**216**	41.41 N	86.51 W
Trailer Estates	**220**	27.24 N	82.34 W
Trail Ridge ∧	**192**	30.35 N	82.05 W
Traînel	**50**	48.25 N	3.27 E
Trainer	**285**	39.50 N	75.25 W
Traipu	**250**	9.58 S	37.01 W
Traíra (Taraira) ≃	**246**	1.04 S	69.26 W
Trairão ≃	**250**	7.20 S	51.14 W
Traíras ≃	**255**	14.07 S	48.31 W
Trairi	**250**	3.17 S	39.15 W
Traisen	**61**	48.02 N	15.37 E
Traisen ≃	**61**	48.22 N	15.46 E
Traiskirchen	**61**	48.01 N	16.18 E
Traismauer	**61**	48.21 N	15.44 E
Traîtres, Baie des ⊂	**174x**	9.50 S	139.02 W
Trajouce	**266c**	38.44 N	9.20 W
Trakai	**76**	54.38 N	24.56 E
Trakt	**24**	62.44 N	51.11 E
Träkvista	**40**	59.16 N	17.47 E
Tralee	**48**	52.16 N	9.42 W
Tralee Bay ⊂	**48**	52.15 N	9.59 W
Trá Lí → Tralee	**48**	52.16 N	9.42 W
Tramatza	**71**	40.00 N	8.39 E
Tramayes	**58**	46.18 N	4.36 E
Tramelan	**58**	47.13 N	7.06 E
Tra Mi	**110**	15.20 N	108.13 E
Tramin → Termeno	**64**	46.20 N	11.14 E
Trammel	**192**	37.00 N	82.17 W
Trammel Creek ≃	**194**	36.52 N	86.23 W
Tramonti di sopra	**64**	46.18 N	12.47 E
Tramore	**48**	52.10 N	7.10 W
Tramperos Creek (Punta de Agua Creek) ≃	**196**	35.32 N	102.27 W
Tramping Lake ⊜	**184**	52.08 N	108.49 W
Tramutola	**68**	40.19 N	15.47 E
Trân	**38**	42.50 N	22.39 E
Tranås	**26**	58.03 N	14.59 E
Trancão ≃	**266c**	38.48 N	9.06 W
Trancas	**252**	26.13 S	65.17 W
Trancoso	**34**	40.47 N	7.21 W
Trand	**123**	34.38 N	72.59 E
Tranderup	**41**	54.52 N	10.22 E
Tranebjerg	**41**	55.50 N	10.36 E
Tranekær	**41**	55.00 N	10.51 E
Tranemo	**26**	57.29 N	13.21 E
Tranent	**46**	55.57 N	2.58 W
Tränental	**158**	27.09 S	19.33 E
Trang	**110**	7.33 N	99.36 E
Trangahy	**157b**	19.07 S	44.43 E
Trangan, Pulau I	**164**	6.35 S	134.20 E
Trangie	**166**	32.02 S	147.59 E
Tran Grande ≃	**116**	6.43 N	124.01 E
Trängslet	**26**	61.25 N	13.40 E
Trani	**68**	41.17 N	16.26 E
Tranmere	**262**	53.23 N	3.01 W
Trannon ≃	**42**	52.31 N	3.25 W
Tranoroa	**157b**	24.42 S	45.04 E
Tranquebar	**122**	11.02 N	79.51 E
Tranqueras	**252**	31.12 S	55.45 W
Tranquility	**218**	38.58 N	83.32 W

PORTUGUÊS Nome	Página	Lat.°′	Long.°′ W = Oeste
Tranquillity	**226**	36.38 N	120.15 W
Transantarctic Mountains ⋀	**9**	85.00 S	175.00 W
Trans-en-Provence	**62**	43.30 N	6.29 E
Transfer	**214**	41.20 N	80.26 W
Transit Airpark ⊠	**284a**	43.06 N	78.44 W
Transkei □[1], Afr.	**138**	31.20 S	29.00 E
Transkei □[1], Afr.	**158**	31.20 S	29.00 E
Transquaking ≃	**208**	38.22 N	76.00 W
Transsylvanische Alpen → Carpații Meridionali ⋀	**38**	45.30 N	24.15 E
Transtrand	**26**	61.05 N	13.19 E
Transtrandsfjällen ∧	**26**	61.17 N	13.00 E
Transvaal □[4]	**156**	25.00 S	29.00 E
Transylvania □[9]	**38**	46.30 N	24.00 E
Transylvanian Alps → Carpații Meridionali ⋀	**38**	45.30 N	24.15 E
Tranters Creek ≃	**192**	35.33 N	77.05 W
Traona	**58**	46.09 N	9.31 E
Trapalcó, Salinas de ≡	**254**	39.45 S	66.45 W
Trapani	**70**	38.01 N	12.31 E
Trapani □[4]	**70**	37.50 N	12.40 E
Traphole Brook ≃	**283**	42.10 N	71.11 W
Trappe, Md., U.S.	**208**	38.39 N	76.03 W
Trappe, Pa., U.S.	**208**	40.12 N	75.29 W
Trappenkamp	**54**	54.03 N	10.16 E
Trapper Peak ∧	**202**	45.54 N	114.18 W
Trappes	**50**	48.47 N	2.00 E
Trappeto	**70**	38.04 N	13.03 E
Trapuá ≃	**287b**	23.36 S	46.17 W
Traralgon	**169**	38.12 S	146.32 E
Traralgon Creek ≃	**169**	38.10 S	146.31 E
Traras, Monts des ⋀	**34**	35.10 N	1.40 W
Trarza □[4]	**150**	17.45 N	15.45 W
Trârza ♦[1]	**150**	18.00 N	15.00 W
Trasacco	**66**	41.57 N	13.32 E
Trasadingen	**58**	47.40 N	8.26 E
Trascăului, Munții ⋀	**38**	46.23 N	23.33 E
Trasimeno, Lago ⊜	**66**	43.08 N	12.06 E
Trask ≃	**224**	45.28 N	123.53 W
Träslövsläge	**26**	57.04 N	12.16 E
Trasna	**82**	54.45 N	38.42 E
Trás-os-Montes □[9]	**34**	41.30 N	7.15 W
Trassem	**56**	49.34 N	6.31 E
Trâstenik	**38**	43.31 N	24.28 E
Trat	**110**	12.14 N	102.30 E
Tratalias	**71**	39.06 N	8.34 E
Tratzberg, Schloss ⊥	**64**	47.23 N	11.44 E
Trauchgau	**58**	47.38 N	10.49 E
Traun	**61**	48.13 N	14.14 E
Traun ≃, Dtsch.	**60**	48.00 N	12.32 E
Traun ≃, Öst.	**30**	48.16 N	14.22 E
Traunkirchen	**64**	47.50 N	13.47 E
Traunreut	**64**	47.56 N	12.35 E
Traunsee ⊜	**64**	47.51 N	13.48 E
Traunstein, Dtsch.	**64**	47.52 N	12.38 E
Traunstein, Öst.	**61**	48.26 N	15.07 E
Traunstein ∧	**64**	47.52 N	13.50 E
Trautenstein	**54**	51.41 N	10.43 E
Travagliato	**64**	45.31 N	10.05 E
Trave ≃	**54**	53.54 N	10.50 E
Travedona	**62**	45.48 N	8.40 E
Travellers Lake ⊜	**166**	33.18 S	142.00 E
Travemünde ♦[8]	**54**	53.57 N	10.52 E
Traver	**226**	36.27 N	119.29 W
Travers, Mount ∧	**172**	42.01 S	172.44 E
Travers, Val de V	**58**	46.57 N	6.38 E
Traverse, Lake ⊜	**198**	45.43 N	96.40 W
Traverse Bay ⊂	**184**	50.40 N	96.25 W
Traverse City	**190**	44.45 N	85.37 W
Traversella	**62**	45.30 N	7.45 E
Traverse Peak ∧	**180**	65.10 N	159.12 W
Traversetolo	**64**	44.38 N	10.23 E
Travers Reservoir ⊜[1]	**182**	50.14 N	112.51 W
Tra Vinh	**110**	9.56 N	106.20 E
Travis	**222**	31.08 N	97.00 W
Travis □[6]	**222**	30.18 N	97.40 W
Travis, Lake ⊜[1]	**196**	30.27 N	98.00 W
Travis Air Force Base ■	**226**	38.16 N	121.55 W
Travnik	**36**	44.14 N	17.40 E
Trawalla	**169**	37.26 S	143.29 E
Trawbreaga Bay ⊂	**48**	55.17 N	7.18 W
Trawick	**222**	31.46 N	94.45 W
Trawsfynydd	**42**	52.54 N	3.55 W
Trayning	**162**	31.07 S	117.48 E
Trazegnies	**50**	50.28 N	4.19 E
Trbovlje	**36**	46.10 N	15.03 E
Treadwell	**210**	42.21 N	75.03 W
Treales	**262**	53.47 N	2.51 W
Treasure Island	**220**	27.46 N	82.46 W
Treasure Island I	**226**	37.48 N	122.22 W
Treasure Island Naval Station ■	**282**	37.49 N	122.22 W
Trebatsch	**54**	52.05 N	14.09 E
Trebbia ≃	**62**	45.04 N	9.41 E
Trebbin	**54**	52.13 N	13.13 E
Třebechovice pod Orebem	**30**	50.12 N	16.00 E
Trebel	**54**	52.59 N	11.20 E
Trebel ≃	**54**	53.55 N	13.01 E
Trebelsee ⊜	**54**	52.28 N	12.47 E
Třebenice	**54**	50.29 N	14.00 E
Trebgast	**60**	50.04 N	11.33 E
Třebíč	**30**	49.13 N	15.53 E
Trebinje	**38**	42.43 N	18.20 E
Trebisacce	**68**	39.52 N	16.32 E
Trebišov	**30**	48.40 N	21.47 E
Trebitz	**54**	51.45 N	12.44 E
Trebizond → Trabzon	**130**	41.00 N	39.43 E
Trebjerg ∧[2]	**41**	55.10 N	10.14 E
Třebkov	**60**	49.22 N	14.04 E
Treble Mountain ∧	**182**	55.50 N	129.51 W
Treblinka	**30**	52.39 N	22.03 E
Třeboň	**61**	49.00 N	14.47 E
Třebouň ∧	**60**	50.01 N	12.59 E
Trebsen	**54**	51.17 N	12.45 E
Trebur	**56**	49.56 N	8.25 E
Trecastagni	**70**	37.37 N	15.05 E
Trecate	**62**	45.26 N	8.44 E
Trecchina	**68**	40.02 N	15.46 E
Trece Martires	**116**	14.16 N	120.50 E
Trecenta	**64**	45.02 N	11.28 E
Tred Avon River ⊂	**208**	38.42 N	76.08 W
Tredegar	**42**	51.47 N	3.16 W
Tredici Archi, Ponte ♦[5]	**66**	41.32 N	14.57 E
Treene ≃	**41**	54.22 N	9.05 E
Trees Mills	**279b**	40.23 N	80.13 W
Treffen	**64**	46.40 N	13.52 E
Treffort	**58**	46.16 N	5.22 E
Treffurt	**56**	51.08 N	10.14 E
Trèfle, Lac du ⊜	**206**	46.36 N	73.55 W
Tregaron	**42**	52.13 N	3.55 W
Tregnago	**64**	45.31 N	11.10 E
Tregosse Islets II	**166**	17.41 S	150.43 E
Tregubovo	**76**	58.59 N	31.33 E
Tréguier	**32**	48.47 N	3.14 W
Treharris	**42**	51.41 N	3.16 W
Treherne	**184**	49.38 N	98.41 W
Trehörningsjö	**26**	63.42 N	18.48 E
Treia, Dtsch.	**41**	54.30 N	9.17 E
Treia, It.	**66**	43.19 N	13.19 E
Treig, Loch ⊜	**46**	56.50 N	4.44 W
Treinta y Tres	**252**	33.14 S	54.23 W
Treis	**56**	50.10 N	7.17 E
Trekkopje	**156**	22.18 S	14.53 E
Trélazé	**32**	47.27 N	0.28 W
Trelde Næs ›	**41**	55.37 N	9.52 E
Trelew	**254**	43.15 S	65.18 W
Trelleborg	**41**	55.22 N	13.10 E
Treloar	**219**	38.39 N	91.10 W
Tremadog	**42**	52.56 N	4.09 W
Tremblant, Lac ⊜	**206**	46.15 N	74.38 W
Tremblant, Mont ∧	**206**	46.16 N	74.35 W

Tremblay, Hippodrome du ♠	**261**	48.50 N	2.29 E
Tremblay-lès-Gonesse	**261**	48.59 N	2.34 E
Trembleur Lake ⊜	**182**	54.51 N	125.07 W
Tremecal	**255**	14.58 S	41.24 W
Tremembé	**256**	22.58 S	45.33 W
Tremezzo	**58**	45.59 N	9.15 E
Tremino	**88**	56.42 N	98.04 E
Tremiti, Isole II	**66**	42.07 N	15.30 E
Tremo La)(	**124**	27.44 N	89.12 E
Tremont, Il., U.S.	**190**	40.31 N	89.29 W
Tremont, In., U.S.	**216**	41.39 N	87.02 W
Tremont, Pa., U.S.	**208**	40.37 N	76.23 W
Tremont ♦[8]	**276**	40.51 N	73.55 W
Tremont City	**218**	40.00 N	83.50 W
Tremonton	**200**	41.42 N	112.09 W
Třemošna	**60**	49.49 N	13.20 E
Třemošná ≃	**60**	49.52 N	13.32 E
Tremp	**34**	42.10 N	0.54 E
Trempealeau	**190**	44.00 N	91.26 W
Trempealeau ≃	**190**	44.02 N	91.32 W
Tremsbüttel	**52**	53.44 N	10.18 E
Trena	**144**	10.45 N	40.38 E
Trenčín	**30**	48.54 N	18.04 E
Trendelburg	**52**	51.34 N	9.25 E
Trenel	**252**	35.42 S	64.08 W
Trêng	**110**	12.49 N	102.54 E
Trenggalek	**115a**	8.03 S	111.43 E
Trenque Lauquen	**252**	35.58 S	62.42 W
Trent, Dtsch.	**54**	54.31 N	13.15 E
Trent → Trento, It.	**64**	46.04 N	11.08 E
Trent ≃, On., Can.	**212**	44.06 N	77.34 W
Trent ≃, Eng., U.K.	**28**	53.42 N	0.41 W
Trent ≃, N.C., U.S.	**192**	35.05 N	77.02 W
Trent, Vale of V	**42**	52.44 N	1.50 W
Trent and Mersey Canal ≊	**262**	53.19 N	2.39 W
Trente et un Milles, Lac des ⊜	**188**	46.12 N	75.49 W
Trentham	**169**	37.23 S	144.19 E
Trentino-Alto Adige □[4]	**64**	46.30 N	11.20 E
Trento	**64**	46.04 N	11.08 E
Trento □[4]	**64**	46.08 N	11.07 E
Trentola-Ducenta	**68**	40.59 N	14.10 E
Trenton, N.S., Can.	**186**	45.37 N	62.38 W
Trenton, On., Can.	**212**	44.06 N	77.35 W
Trenton, Fl., U.S.	**192**	29.36 N	82.49 W
Trenton, Ga., U.S.	**192**	34.52 N	85.30 W
Trenton, Il., U.S.	**219**	38.36 N	89.40 W
Trenton, Ky., U.S.	**194**	36.43 N	87.15 W
Trenton, Mi., U.S.	**216**	42.08 N	83.10 W
Trenton, Mo., U.S.	**194**	40.04 N	93.36 W
Trenton, Ne., U.S.	**198**	40.10 N	101.00 W
Trenton, N.J., U.S.	**208**	40.13 N	74.44 W
Trenton, N.C., U.S.	**192**	35.04 N	77.21 W
Trenton, Oh., U.S.	**218**	39.29 N	84.28 W
Trenton, Tn., U.S.	**194**	35.58 N	88.56 W
Trenton, Tx., U.S.	**196**	33.26 N	96.20 W
Trenton, Canadian Forces Base ■	**190**	44.07 N	77.33 W
Trenton Channel ≃[1]	**281**	42.06 N	83.11 W
Trentwood	**202**	47.42 N	117.13 W
Trepalade	**64**	45.34 N	12.24 E
Trepassey	**186**	46.44 N	53.22 W
Trepassey Bay ⊂	**186**	46.37 N	53.20 W
Treptow ♦[8]	**54**	52.29 N	13.29 E
Trepuzzi	**68**	40.24 N	18.05 E
Trequanda	**66**	43.11 N	11.40 E
Tresa ≃	**58**	46.00 N	8.43 E
Tres Algarrobos	**252**	35.12 S	62.46 W
Tres Árboles	**252**	32.24 S	56.43 W
Tres Arroyos	**252**	38.23 S	60.17 W
Tres Cerros	**254**	48.13 S	67.33 W
Treščevo	**82**	54.11 N	37.55 E
Tresckow	**210**	40.54 N	75.58 W
Tresco I	**42a**	49.57 N	6.19 W
Três Corações	**256**	21.42 S	45.16 W
Trescore Balneario	**62**	45.41 N	9.50 E
Três Coroas	**252**	29.32 S	50.48 W
Tres de Febrero → Caseros	**258**	34.36 S	58.33 W
Tres de Febrero □[5]	**288**	34.36 S	58.35 W
Três de Maio	**252**	27.47 S	54.14 W
Tresenda	**64**	46.10 N	10.05 E
Tres Esquinas	**246**	0.43 N	75.16 W
Três Fronteiras	**255**	20.13 S	50.55 W
Treshnish Isles II	**46**	56.30 N	6.24 W
Treshnish Point ›	**46**	56.33 N	6.21 W
Três Ilhas	**256**	22.04 S	43.29 W
Tresinaro ≃	**64**	44.39 N	10.47 E
Tres Isletas	**252**	26.21 S	60.26 W
Treskino	**80**	52.40 N	44.40 E
Três Lagoas	**255**	20.48 S	51.43 W
Tres Lagos	**254**	49.37 S	71.30 W
Tres Lomas	**252**	36.27 S	62.51 W
Três Marias	**255**	18.12 S	45.14 W
Três Marias, Represa de ⊜[1]	**255**	18.12 S	45.15 W
Tres Montes, Golfo ⊂	**254**	46.54 S	75.00 W
Tres Montes, Península ›[1]	**254**	46.50 S	75.30 W
Tres Montosas ∧	**200**	34.06 N	107.28 W
Tres Morros, Alto de ∧	**246**	7.08 N	76.11 W
Tresnuraghes	**71**	40.15 N	8.31 E
Tres Padres, Pico ∧	**286a**	19.35 N	99.08 W
Tres Palacios ≃	**196**	28.45 N	96.09 W
Tres Palos, Laguna ⊂	**234**	16.46 N	99.44 W
Três Passos	**252**	27.27 S	53.56 W
Tres Picos	**234**	15.52 N	93.32 W
Tres Picos, Cerro ∧, Arg.	**252**	38.09 S	61.57 W
Tres Picos, Cerro ∧, Méx.	**234**	16.12 N	93.37 W
Tres Pinos	**226**	36.48 N	121.19 W
Tres Pinos Creek ≃	**226**	36.47 N	121.21 W
Três Pontas	**256**	21.22 S	45.31 W
Três Pontas, Cabo das ›	**152**	10.23 S	13.32 E
Tres Puntas, Cabo ›, Arg.	**254**	47.06 S	65.53 W
Tres Puntas, Cabo ›, Guat.	**236**	15.56 N	88.37 W
Três Ranchos	**255**	18.22 S	47.47 W
Tres Reyes Islands II	**116**	13.14 N	121.51 E
Três Rios, Bra.	**256**	22.07 S	43.12 W
Tres Ríos, C.R.	**236**	9.54 N	83.58 W
Tressancourt	**261**	48.55 N	2.00 E
Třešť	**30**	49.18 N	15.30 E
Tresta	**46a**	60.14 N	1.21 W
Tres Valles	**234**	18.15 N	96.08 W
Tres Vírgenes, Volcán de las ∧[1]	**232**	27.27 N	112.34 W
Tres Zapotes ⊥	**234**	18.28 N	95.24 W
Tret'akovskaja Galereja ♁	**265b**	55.45 N	37.37 E
Tretet	**114**	4.40 N	96.51 E
Trets	**62**	43.27 N	5.41 E
Tretten	**26**	61.19 N	10.19 E
Treuchtlingen	**56**	48.57 N	10.54 E
Treuen	**54**	50.32 N	12.18 E
Treuenbrietzen	**54**	52.06 N	12.52 E
Treuhandgebiet Pazifische Inseln → Trust Territory of the Pacific Islands □[2]	**14**	5.00 N	137.00 E
Trevelín	**254**	43.04 S	71.28 W
Trèves → Trier	**56**	49.45 N	6.38 E
Trevi	**66**	42.52 N	12.45 E
Treviglio	**62**	45.31 N	9.35 E
Trevignano Romano	**66**	42.09 N	12.15 E
Treviño	**34**	42.44 N	2.45 W
Treviso	**64**	45.40 N	12.15 E
Treviso □[4]	**64**	45.50 N	12.13 E
Trevor	**216**	42.30 N	88.07 W
Trevorton	**208**	40.46 N	76.40 W
Trevose	**208**	40.08 N	74.58 W
Trevose Head ›	**42**	50.33 N	5.01 W
Trevose Heights	**285**	40.09 N	74.59 W
Trévoux	**58**	45.56 N	4.46 E
Trexlertown	**208**	40.33 N	75.36 W
Trezevant	**194**	36.00 N	88.37 W
Trezzano sul Naviglio	**266b**	45.25 N	9.04 E
Trezzo sull'Adda	**62**	45.36 N	9.31 E
Trgovište	**38**	42.21 N	22.05 E
Trhomné	**60**	49.55 N	13.05 E
Trhové Sviny	**61**	48.51 N	14.39 E
Triabunna	**166**	42.30 S	147.55 E
Triadelphia Reservoir ⊜[1]	**208**	39.13 N	77.01 W
Trialeti	**84**	41.33 N	44.07 E
Trialetskij chrebet ⋀	**84**	41.45 N	43.50 E
Triana	**66**	42.47 N	11.33 E
Triánda	**38**	36.24 N	28.10 E
Triangle, Eng., U.K.	**262**	53.42 N	1.56 W
Triangle, Va., U.S.	**208**	38.32 N	77.20 W
Triangle Lake	**210**	42.32 N	74.13 W
Triangul'atorov, pik ∧	**88**	53.45 N	97.00 E
Triángulos, Arrecífes ✦[2]	**232**	20.57 N	92.16 W
Triaucourt-en-Argonne	**56**	48.59 N	5.04 E
Tribeni	**126**	22.59 N	88.24 E
Triberg	**58**	48.08 N	8.13 E
Tribes Hill	**210**	42.57 N	74.17 W
Tribobó	**287a**	22.52 S	43.01 W
Triborough Bridge ♦[5]	**276**	40.47 N	73.55 W
Tri Brata, porog ∟	**86**	57.25 N	95.39 E
Tribsees	**54**	54.05 N	12.45 E
Tribugá, Ensenada de ⊂	**246**	5.45 N	77.20 W
Tribune, Sk., Can.	**184**	49.15 N	103.50 W
Tribune, Ks., U.S.	**198**	38.28 N	101.45 W
Tribune Channel ⊔	**182**	50.50 N	126.16 W
Tribuswinkel	**264b**	48.00 N	16.16 E
Tricarico	**68**	40.37 N	16.09 E
Tricase	**68**	39.56 N	18.22 E
Tricesimo	**64**	46.10 N	13.13 E
Trichardt	**158**	26.28 S	29.13 E
Trichiana	**64**	46.05 N	12.07 E
Trichinopoly → Tiruchchirāppalli	**122**	10.49 N	78.41 E
Trichūr	**122**	10.31 N	76.13 E
Tri Cities	**222**	32.09 N	95.56 W
Tricot	**50**	49.34 N	2.35 E
Tri County Supply Canal ≊	**198**	40.49 N	100.06 W
Trida	**166**	33.01 S	145.01 E
Trident Peak ∧	**204**	41.54 N	118.25 W
Triduby	**78**	48.06 N	30.24 E
Trieben	**61**	47.29 N	14.30 E
Triebes	**54**	50.41 N	12.01 E
Triel-sur-Seine	**261**	48.59 N	2.00 E
Trient → Trento	**64**	46.04 N	11.08 E
Triepkendorf	**54**	53.17 N	13.20 E
Trier	**56**	49.45 N	6.38 E
Trier □[5]	**56**	50.00 N	6.40 E
Triesen	**58**	47.06 N	9.31 E
Trieste (Triest) (Trst)	**64**	45.40 N	13.46 E
Trieste □[4]	**64**	45.40 N	13.50 E
Trieste, Gulf of ⊂	**64**	45.40 N	13.35 E
Triesting ≃	**61**	48.05 N	16.24 E
Trieux	**56**	49.20 N	5.56 E
Triftern	**60**	48.24 N	13.01 E
Trigal	**248**	18.17 S	64.08 W
Triggiano	**68**	41.04 N	16.55 E
Triglav ∧	**64**	46.23 N	13.50 E
Triglitz	**54**	53.12 N	12.05 E
Trigna, Pizzo ∧	**70**	37.58 N	13.34 E
Trigno ≃	**66**	42.04 N	14.48 E
Trigueros	**34**	37.23 N	6.50 W
Tríkala	**38**	39.34 N	21.46 E
Trikhonís, Límni ⊜	**38**	38.34 N	21.28 E
Trikora, Puncak (Wilhelmina Peak) ∧	**164**	4.15 S	138.45 E
Tri-Lakes	**216**	41.14 N	85.26 W
Trilbardou	**261**	48.57 N	2.48 E
Trilby	**220**	28.27 N	82.11 W
Trilesy	**78**	49.59 N	29.50 E
Trillick	**48**	54.27 N	7.30 W
Trilport	**50**	48.57 N	2.57 E
Trim	**48**	53.34 N	6.47 W
Triman	**120**	29.38 N	69.05 E
Trimbach	**58**	47.22 N	7.54 E
Trimble □[6]	**218**	38.37 N	85.20 W
Trim Creek ≃	**216**	41.10 N	87.38 W
Trimdon	**44**	54.42 N	1.25 W
Trimont	**198**	43.45 N	94.42 W
Trimonte	**256**	21.43 S	42.35 W
Trin	**58**	46.50 N	9.22 E
Trinchera Creek ≃	**200**	37.19 N	105.45 W
Trincheras, Méx.	**196**	25.37 N	101.55 W
Trincheras, Méx.	**232**	30.24 N	111.32 W
Trincomalee	**122**	8.34 N	81.14 E
Trincomali Channel ⊔	**224**	48.02 N	123.30 W
Trindade	**255**	16.40 S	49.30 W
Trindade I	**244**	20.31 S	29.19 W
Třinec	**30**	49.41 N	18.40 E
Tring	**42**	51.48 N	0.40 W
Trinidad, Bol.	**248**	14.47 S	64.47 W
Trinidad, Col.	**246**	5.25 N	71.40 W
Trinidad, Cuba	**240p**	21.48 N	79.59 W
Trinidad, Hond.	**236**	14.57 N	88.45 W
Trinidad, Co., U.S.	**198**	37.10 N	104.30 W
Trinidad, Tx., U.S.	**222**	32.08 N	96.05 W
Trinidad, Ur.	**252**	33.32 S	56.54 W
Trinidad I	**241r**	10.30 N	61.15 W
Trinidad ≃	**234**	17.49 N	95.09 W
Trinidad, Golfo ⊂	**254**	49.55 S	75.25 W
Trinidad, Isla I	**252**	39.08 S	61.58 W
Trinidad and Tobago □[1], N.A.	**230**	11.00 N	61.00 W
Trinidad and Tobago □[1], N.A.	**241r**	11.00 N	61.00 W
Trinità	**62**	44.30 N	7.45 E
Trinità, Lago della ⊜	**70**	37.43 N	12.46 E
Trinità d'Agultu	**71**	40.59 N	8.54 E
Trinitapoli	**68**	41.21 N	16.05 E
Trinité, Havre de la ⊂	**240e**	14.44 N	60.58 W
Trinity, Nf., Can.	**186**	48.59 N	53.55 W
Trinity, Tx., U.S.	**222**	30.56 N	95.22 W
Trinity □[6]	**222**	31.07 N	95.10 W
Trinity ≃, Ca., U.S.	**204**	41.11 N	123.42 W
Trinity ≃, Tx., U.S.	**222**	29.47 N	94.42 W
Trinity, Clear Fork ≃	**196**	32.46 N	97.21 W
Trinity, East Fork ≃	**222**	32.30 N	96.30 W
Trinity, Elm Fork ≃	**222**	32.47 N	96.54 W
Trinity, South Fork ≃	**204**	40.54 N	123.35 W
Trinity, West Fork ≃	**196**	32.48 N	96.51 W
Trinity Bay ⊂, Nf., Can.	**186**	48.00 N	53.40 W
Trinity Bay ⊂, Tx., U.S.	**222**	29.40 N	94.45 W
Trinity Islands II	**180**	56.33 N	154.25 W
Trinity Mountain ∧	**202**	43.36 N	115.26 W
Trinity Mountains ⋀	**204**	41.00 N	122.30 W
Trinity Park ♠	**275b**	43.39 N	79.25 W
Trinity Peak ∧	**204**	40.14 N	118.45 W
Trinity Site ⊥	**200**	33.41 N	106.28 W
Trinkat Island I	**110**	8.05 N	93.30 E
Trinkitat	**140**	18.41 N	37.43 E
Trino	**62**	45.12 N	8.18 E
Trins	**64**	47.05 N	11.25 E
Trinway	**214**	40.08 N	82.00 W
Triolet	**157c**	20.03 S	57.32 E
Triolo ≃	**66**	41.40 N	15.34 E
Trion	**192**	34.32 N	85.18 W
Trionto ≃	**68**	39.37 N	16.45 E
Trionto, Capo ›	**68**	39.37 N	16.45 E
Triora	**62**	43.59 N	7.46 E
Tripa ≃	**114**	3.53 N	96.23 E
Tripi	**70**	38.03 N	15.06 E
Triplett Creek ≃	**218**	38.10 N	83.27 W
Triplett Creek, North Fork ≃	**218**	38.10 N	83.31 W
Tripoli → Ţarābulus, Lībiyā	**146**	32.54 N	13.11 E
Tripoli → Ţarābulus, Lubnān	**130**	34.26 N	35.51 E
Tripoli, Ia., U.S.	**190**	42.48 N	92.15 W
Trípolis, Ellás	**38**	37.31 N	22.21 E
Tripolis → Ţarābulus, Lībiyā	**146**	32.54 N	13.11 E
Tripolis ⊥	**130**	37.58 N	28.59 E
Tripolitania → Ţarābulus □[9]	**146**	31.00 N	15.00 E
Tripolje	**78**	50.07 N	30.46 E
Triponzo	**66**	42.50 N	12.56 E
Tripp	**198**	43.13 N	97.57 W
Trips Subdivision	**281**	42.34 N	83.25 W
Triptis	**54**	50.44 N	11.52 E
Tripura □[3]	**120**	24.00 N	92.00 E
Triquet, Lac ⊜	**186**	50.42 N	59.47 W
Trisanna ≃	**58**	47.07 N	10.30 E
Tristan da Cunha Group II	**10**	37.15 S	12.30 W
Tristan Island I	**10**	37.05 S	12.17 W
Tristán Suárez	**258**	34.53 S	58.34 W
Tristao, Îles II	**150**	10.53 N	14.58 W
Tristate Village	**278**	41.44 N	87.57 W
Triste	**34**	42.23 N	0.43 W
Triste, Golfo ⊂	**246**	10.40 N	68.10 W
Triśuli Gaṅggā ≃	**124**	27.49 N	84.47 E
Tri Ton	**110**	10.25 N	105.00 E
Tritriva	**157b**	22.46 S	46.07 E
Trittau	**52**	53.37 N	10.25 E
Trittenheim	**56**	49.49 N	6.54 E
Triuggio	**266b**	45.40 N	9.16 E
Triumph	**194**	29.20 N	89.28 W
Triunfo, Igarapé ≃	**250**	6.22 S	52.25 W
Trivandrum	**122**	8.29 N	76.55 E
Trivento	**66**	41.47 N	14.33 E
Trivero	**62**	45.40 N	8.10 E
Trivigno	**68**	40.35 N	15.59 E
Trnava	**30**	48.23 N	17.35 E
Trnovo → Veliko Târnovo	**38**	43.04 N	25.39 E
Tr'ochgolovyj Golec, gora ∧	**88**	53.22 N	107.03 E
Tr'ochizbenka	**83**	48.45 N	38.58 E
Tr'ochsv'atskoje	**82**	56.29 N	37.03 E
Trochtelfingen	**58**	48.18 N	9.14 E
Trochu	**182**	51.50 N	113.13 W
Troense	**41**	55.02 N	10.39 E
Trofa, Arroyo de ≃	**266a**	40.30 N	3.45 W
Trofaiach	**61**	47.25 N	15.00 E
Trofarello	**62**	44.59 N	7.44 E
Trögd ›[1]	**40**	59.31 N	17.15 E
Trogen	**58**	47.24 N	9.28 E
Trogir	**36**	43.31 N	16.15 E
Troglav ∧	**36**	43.57 N	16.36 E
Tröglitz	**54**	51.04 N	12.11 E
Troia	**68**	41.22 N	15.18 E
Troica	**76**	54.24 N	40.14 E
Troice-Lykovo ♦[8]	**265b**	55.47 N	37.24 E
Troick, Ross.	**86**	54.06 N	61.35 E
Troick, Ross.	**88**	57.25 N	94.50 E
Troickaja	**78**	45.08 N	38.07 E
Troickij, Ross.	**80**	50.14 N	43.03 E
Troickij, Ross.	**80**	50.14 N	43.05 E
Troickij, Ross.	**86**	50.41 N	54.38 E
Troickij, Ross.	**86**	57.03 N	63.43 E
Troickij, Ross.	**88**	54.36 N	113.09 E
Troickije Rosl'ai	**80**	53.21 N	41.24 E
Troickij Sungur	**80**	53.17 N	47.37 E
Troickij Zavod	**88**	53.27 N	102.09 E
Troicko-Charcyzsk	**83**	47.58 N	38.16 E
Troickoje, Ross.	**78**	51.17 N	41.28 E
Troickoje, Ross.	**80**	46.26 N	44.15 E
Troickoje, Ross.	**80**	53.22 N	48.23 E
Troickoje, Ross.	**80**	53.06 N	52.32 E
Troickoje, Ross.	**80**	53.23 N	52.48 E
Troickoje, Ross.	**82**	55.23 N	37.25 E
Troickoje, Ross.	**82**	54.52 N	37.07 E
Troickoje, Ross.	**83**	47.22 N	38.53 E
Troickoje, Ross.	**86**	59.07 N	58.25 E
Troickoje, Ross.	**86**	52.19 N	56.23 E
Troickoje, Ross.	**86**	52.58 N	84.40 E
Troickoje, Ross.	**89**	49.27 N	136.36 E
Troickoje, Ukr.	**78**	49.55 N	38.19 E
Troickoje, Ukr.	**78**	47.38 N	30.19 E
Troickoje, Ukr.	**83**	48.32 N	38.23 E
Troicko-Pečorsk	**24**	62.44 N	56.06 E
Troina	**70**	37.47 N	14.36 E
Troina ≃	**70**	37.49 N	14.46 E
Troisdorf	**56**	50.49 N	7.08 E
Trois Fourches, Cap des ›	**148**	35.26 N	2.58 W
Trois-Pistoles	**186**	48.07 N	69.10 W
Trois Pitons, Morne ∧	**240d**	15.22 N	61.20 W
Trois Ponts	**56**	50.22 N	5.52 E
Trois-Rivières, P.Q., Can.	**206**	46.21 N	72.33 W
Trois-Rivières, Guad.	**241o**	15.59 N	61.39 W
Trois-Rivières-Ouest	**206**	46.19 N	72.35 W
Troisvierges	**56**	50.08 N	6.00 E
Trojan	**38**	42.51 N	24.43 E
Trojanov	**78**	50.07 N	28.31 E
Trojanova Tabla ⊥	**38**	44.37 N	22.20 E
Trojanovka	**78**	51.20 N	25.17 E
Trojebratskij	**86**	54.28 N	66.01 E
Trojekurovo, Ross.	**76**	53.00 N	38.58 E
Trojekurovo, Ross.	**76**	53.25 N	39.43 E
Troldhede	**41**	55.59 N	8.45 E
Trolleholm	**41**	55.54 N	13.15 E
Trollhättan	**26**	58.16 N	12.18 E
Trollheimen ∧	**26**	62.51 N	9.05 E
Trombay ♦[8]	**272c**	19.02 N	72.57 E
Trombetas ≃	**250**	1.55 S	55.35 W
Tromelin, Île I	**138**	15.52 S	54.25 E
Tromello	**62**	45.12 N	8.52 E
Tromper Wiek ⊂	**54**	54.37 N	13.24 E
Trompia, Val V	**64**	45.44 N	10.12 E
Trompsburg	**158**	30.01 S	25.46 E
Troms □[6]	**24**	69.15 N	19.40 E
Tromsø	**24**	69.40 N	18.58 E
Trona	**204**	35.45 N	117.22 W
Tronador, Monte ∧	**254**	41.10 S	71.54 W
Troncoso	**234**	22.44 N	102.22 W
Trondheim	**26**	63.25 N	10.25 E
Trondheimsfjorden ⊂[2]	**26**	63.39 N	10.49 E
Trondheimsleia ⊔	**26**	63.30 N	9.00 E
Tronto ≃	**66**	42.54 N	13.55 E
Tronville-en-Barrois	**56**	48.43 N	5.17 E
Tronzano Vercellese	**62**	45.21 N	8.10 E
Troo	**50**	47.47 N	0.47 E
Troödos	**130**	34.55 N	32.53 E
Trooilapspan	**158**	28.40 S	21.25 E
Troon, Eng., U.K.	**42**	50.12 N	5.16 W
Troon, Scot., U.K.	**46**	55.32 N	4.40 W
Trooper	**285**	40.09 N	75.24 W
Troparevo	**82**	55.23 N	35.54 E
Tropar'ovo ♦[8]	**265b**	55.39 N	37.29 E
Tropas, Rio das ≃	**250**	6.07 S	57.28 W
Tropea	**68**	38.41 N	15.54 E
Trophy Mountain ∧	**182**	51.47 N	119.48 W
Tropic	**200**	37.37 N	112.04 W
Tropojë	**38**	42.24 N	20.10 E
Troppau → Opava	**30**	49.56 N	17.54 E
Trosa	**40**	58.54 N	17.33 E
Troškovo	**80**	57.19 N	46.05 E
Troškūnai	**76**	55.36 N	24.51 E
Trosna	**76**	52.26 N	35.46 E
Trossingen	**58**	48.04 N	8.38 E
Trostan ∧	**48**	55.03 N	6.09 W
Trost'anec, Ukr.	**78**	50.28 N	34.59 E

	English	Deutsch	Español	Français	Português
≃	River	Fluß	Río	Rivière	Rio
≊	Canal	Kanal	Canal	Canal	Canal
∟	Waterfall, Rapids	Wasserfall, Stromschnellen	Cascada, Rápidos	Chute d'eau, Rapides	Cascata, Rápidos
⊔	Strait	Meeresstraße	Estrecho	Détroit	Estreito
⊂	Bay, Gulf	Bucht, Golf	Bahía, Golfo	Baie, Golfe	Baía, Golfo
⊜	Lake, Lakes	See, Seen	Lago, Lagos	Lac, Lacs	Lago, Lagos
≡	Swamp	Sumpf	Pantano	Marais	Pântano
⊓	Ice Features, Glacier	Eis- und Gletscherformen	Accidentes Glaciales	Formes glaciaires	Acidentes glaciares
⊤	Other Hydrographic Features	Andere Hydrographische Objekte	Otros Elementos Hidrográficos	Autres données hydrographiques	Outros acidentes hidrográficos
✦	Submarine Features	Untermeerische Objekte	Accidentes Submarinos	Formes de relief sous-marin	Acidentes submarinos
□	Political Unit	Politische Einheit	Unidad Politica	Entité politique	Unidade política
♁	Cultural Institution	Kulturelle Institution	Institución Cultural	Institution culturelle	Instituição cultural
⊥	Historical Site	Historische Stätte	Sitio Histórico	Site historique	Sitio histórico
♠	Recreational Site	Erholungs- und Ferienort	Sitio de Recreo	Centre de loisirs	Area de Lazer
⊠	Airport	Flughafen	Aeropuerto	Aéroport	Aeroporto
■	Military Installation	Militäranlage	Instalación Militar	Installation militaire	Instalação militar
♦	Miscellaneous	Verschiedenes	Misceláneo	Divers	Diversos

Symbols in the index entries represent the broad categories identified in the key at the right. Symbols with superscript numbers (⪙¹) identify subcategories (see complete key on page I · 1).

Symbole im Register stellen die rechts im Schlüssel erklärten Kategorien dar. Mit hochgestellten Ziffern (⪙¹) bezeichnen Unterabteilungen einer Kategorie (vgl. vollständiger Schlüssel auf Seite I · 1).

Los símbolos incluidos en el texto del índice representan las grandes categorías identificadas con la clave a la derecha. Los símbolos con números en su parte superior (⪙¹) identifican las subcategorías (véase la clave completa en la parte superior I · 1).

Les symboles de l'index représentent les catégories indiquées dans la légende à droite. Les symboles suivis d'un indice (⪙¹) représentent les sous-catégories (voir légende complète à la page I · 1).

Os símbolos incluídos no texto do índice representam as grandes categorias identificadas com a chave à direita. Os símbolos com números (⪙¹) identificam as subcategorias (veja-se a chave completa à página I · 1).

Symbol					
▲	Mountain	Berg	Montaña	Montagne	Montanha
⋀	Mountains	Gebirge	Montañas	Montagnes	Montanhas
⋇	Pass	Paß	Paso	Col	Passo
⋁	Valley, Canyon	Tal, Cañon	Valle, Cañón	Vallée, Canyon	Vale, Canhão
≈	Plain	Ebene	Llano	Plaine	Planicie
➤	Cape	Kap	Cabo	Cap	Cabo
I	Island	Insel	Isla	Île	Ilha
II	Islands	Inseln	Islas	Îles	Ilhas
⊥	Other Topographic Features	Andere Topographische Objekte	Otros Elementos Topográficos	Autres données topographiques	Outros acidentes topográficos

ESPAÑOL — Nombre · Página · Lat.°′ · Long.°′ W = Oeste
FRANÇAIS — Nom · Page · Lat.°′ · Long.°′ W = Ouest
PORTUGUÊS — Nome · Página · Lat.°′ · Long.°′ W = Oeste

Nombre	Página	Lat.°′	Long.°′ W = Oeste
Tupelo, Ms., U.S.	194	34.15 N	88.42 W
Tupelo, Ok., U.S.	196	34.36 N	96.25 W
Tupelo National Battlefield ⊥	194	34.13 N	88.44 W
Tupi	116	6.19 N	124.57 E
Tupičov	78	51.46 N	31.26 E
Tupik	88	54.26 N	119.57 E
Tupilac	116	7.40 N	122.30 E
Tupinambarana, Ilha I	246	3.00 S	58.00 W
Tupi Paulista	255	21.24 S	51.34 W
Tupiraçaba	255	14.29 S	48.34 W
Tupiza	248	21.27 S	65.43 W
Tuplice	30	51.41 N	14.50 E
Tupman	226	35.17 N	119.21 W
Tupper	182	55.31 N	120.02 W
Tupper Lake	188	44.13 N	74.29 W
Tupperville	214	42.36 N	82.16 W
Tupungato	252	33.22 S	69.08 W
Tupungato, Cerro ∧	252	33.22 S	69.47 W
Tuqiao, Zhg.	106	31.39 N	120.24 E
Tuqiao, Zhg.	106	31.56 N	119.03 E
Tuqiao, Zhg.	107	30.24 N	105.28 E
Tuqiaozhen	107	30.32 N	104.50 E
Tuquan	89	45.26 N	121.50 E
Túquerres	246	1.05 N	77.37 W
Tuquiaochang	107	29.47 N	106.01 E
Tura, India	124	25.31 N	90.13 E
Ṭurā, Miṣr	142	29.56 N	31.16 E
Tura, Ross.	74	64.17 N	100.15 E
Tura ≃, Ross.	86	57.12 N	66.56 E
Tura ≃, Ross.	88	51.36 N	114.09 E
Turabah	144	21.13 N	41.39 E
Turabah ⊤[4]	128	28.15 N	42.55 E
Turābah, 'Ayn at- ⊤[4]	132	31.36 N	35.25 E
Turāg ≃	126	23.45 N	90.21 E
Turaiyūr	122	11.10 N	78.37 E
Turakina	172	40.02 S	175.13 E
Turakina ≃	172	40.04 S	175.08 E
Turama ≃	164	6.50 S	143.05 E
Turambhe	272c	19.04 N	73.01 E
Turan, Ross.	88	51.38 N	101.40 E
Turan, Ross.	88	52.08 N	93.55 E
Turangi	172	39.00 S	175.49 E
Turano ≃	66	42.26 N	12.47 E
Turanskaja nizmennost' ≚	86	44.30 N	63.00 E
Ṭurāq al-'Ilab ⋀[2]	130	33.55 N	38.18 E
Turate	266b	45.39 N	9.00 E
Tur'at Ghunaym	142	31.16 N	31.29 E
Ṭurayf	128	31.44 N	38.33 E
Turbaco	246	10.20 N	75.25 W
Turbacz ∧	30	49.33 N	20.08 E
Turbat	128	25.59 N	63.04 E
Turbenthal	58	47.27 N	8.51 E
Turbigo	62	45.32 N	8.44 E
Turbio ≃	234	20.19 N	101.37 W
Turbo	246	8.06 N	76.43 W
Turbotville	210	41.06 N	76.46 W
Turbov	78	49.21 N	28.44 E
Turčasovo	24	63.06 N	39.12 E
Turchi, Balata dei ›	70	36.43 N	12.02 E
Turčiansky Svätý Martin → Martin	30	49.05 N	18.55 E
Turckheim	58	48.05 N	7.17 E
Turda	38	46.34 N	23.47 E
Turdej	76	53.22 N	38.01 E
Turee Creek	162	23.37 S	118.39 E
Turee Creek ≃	162	23.35 S	117.25 E
Turek	30	52.02 N	18.30 E
Turen	115a	8.10 S	112.41 E
Turenki	26	60.55 N	24.38 E
Turfan → Turpan	86	42.56 N	89.10 E
Turfan Depression → Turpan Pendi ≗[7]	86	42.40 N	89.10 E
Turffontein ◆[8]	273d	26.15 S	28.02 E
Turffontein Race Course ♦	273d	26.14 S	28.03 E
Turgaj, Kaz.	86	49.38 N	63.28 E
Turgaj, Kaz.	86	51.46 N	72.44 E
Turgaj □[8]	86	50.00 N	65.20 E
Turgaj ≃	86	48.01 N	62.45 E
Turgajskaja ložbina V	86	51.00 N	64.30 E
Turgajskoje plato ⋀[1]	86	51.00 N	64.00 E
Turgen', Kaz.	85	43.24 N	77.36 E
Türgen, Mong.	86	50.04 N	91.36 E
Turgen' ≃	85	43.50 N	77.38 E
Turgenevka	88	53.02 N	105.41 E
Turgenevo	80	54.50 N	46.19 E
Turginovo	82	56.30 N	36.00 E
Turgojak	86	55.10 N	60.07 E
Turgoš	76	59.18 N	35.10 E
Tŭrgovishte → Târgovište	38	43.15 N	26.34 E
Turgut, Tür.	130	37.22 N	28.02 E
Turgut, Tür.	130	38.37 N	31.49 E
Turgutlu	130	38.30 N	27.43 E
Turgwi ≃	154	20.28 S	32.18 E
Turhal	130	40.24 N	36.06 E
Türi, Eesti	76	58.48 N	25.26 E
Turi, It.	68	40.55 N	17.01 E
Turia ≃	34	39.27 N	0.19 W
Turiaçu	250	1.41 S	45.21 W
Turiaçu ≃	250	1.36 S	45.19 W
Turiančajskij zapovednik ♦	84	40.40 N	47.35 E
Turij Rog	89	45.14 N	131.58 E
Turijsk	78	51.07 N	24.31 E
Turilovka	83	49.06 N	40.13 E
Turimetta Head ›	274a	33.42 S	151.19 E
Turimiquire, Cerro ∧	246	10.07 N	63.53 W
Turin, Ab., Can.	182	49.58 N	112.31 W
Turin → Torino, It.	62	45.03 N	7.40 E
Turin, N.Y., U.S.	212	43.38 N	75.25 W
Turinge	40	59.12 N	17.27 E
Turinsk	86	58.03 N	63.42 E
Turinskaja Sloboda	86	57.37 N	64.25 E
Turja ≃	78	51.48 N	24.52 E
Turka, Ross.	88	52.57 N	108.13 E
Turka, Ukr.	78	49.10 N	23.02 E
Turka ≃	88	52.56 N	108.13 E
Turkana, Lake → Rudolf, Lake ⊜	144	3.30 N	36.05 E
Türkei → Turkey □[1]	22	39.00 N	35.00 E
Türkeli Adası I	130	40.30 N	27.30 E
Turkestan	85	43.18 N	68.15 E
Turkestanskij chrebet ⋀	85	39.35 N	69.15 E
Turkestanskij kanal ≊	85	42.44 N	69.00 E
Túrkeve	30	47.06 N	20.45 E
Turkey	196	34.23 N	100.53 W
Turkey (Türkiye) □[1], Asia	22	39.00 N	35.00 E
Turkey (Türkiye) □[1], Asia	130	39.00 N	35.00 E
Turkey ≃	190	42.43 N	91.01 W
Turkey Branch ≃	284c	38.52 N	76.48 W
Turkey City	214	41.11 N	79.37 W
Turkey Creek	164	17.02 S	128.12 E
Turkey Creek ≃, On., Can.	281	42.14 N	83.06 W
Turkey Creek ≃, U.S.	198	39.58 N	96.02 W
Turkey Creek ≃, In., U.S.	278	41.31 N	87.18 W
Turkey Creek ≃, Ia., U.S.	198	41.20 N	95.05 W
Turkey Creek ≃, Ks., U.S.	198	38.53 N	97.11 W
Turkey Creek ≃, Ne., U.S.	198	40.23 N	96.53 W
Turkey Creek ≃, Ok., U.S.	196	35.58 N	97.56 W
Turkey Creek ≃, Tx., U.S.	222	30.39 N	97.05 W
Turkey Island I	284c	38.58 N	77.12 W
Turkey Point ›, On., Can.	212	42.40 N	80.21 W
Turkey Point ›, Fl., U.S.	220	25.26 N	80.19 W
Turkey Point Provincial Park ♦	212	42.40 N	80.22 W
Turkey Run State Park ♦	194	39.54 N	87.13 W
Turkeytown	279b	40.12 N	79.44 W
Türkheim	58	48.03 N	10.38 E
Turki	80	51.59 N	43.16 E
Turkish Republic of Northern Cyprus → Cyprus, North □[1]	130	35.15 N	33.40 E
Türkiye → Turkey □[1]	22	39.00 N	35.00 E
Turkmān Deh	267d	35.40 N	51.36 E
Turkmenia → Turkmenistan □[1]	72	40.00 N	60.00 E
Turkmenija → Turkmenistan □[1]	72	40.00 N	60.00 E
Turkmenistan □[1], Asia	72	40.00 N	60.00 E
Turkmenistan □[1], Asia	128	39.00 N	60.00 E
Turkmeniya → Turkmenistan □[1]	72	40.00 N	60.00 E
Turkmen-Kala	128	37.26 N	62.20 E
Turkmenskij zaliv c	128	38.54 N	53.48 E
Turk Mine	154	19.45 S	28.50 E
Türkoğlu	130	37.31 N	36.49 E
Turks and Caicos Islands □[2], N.A.	230	21.45 N	71.35 W
Turks and Caicos Islands □[2], N.A.	238	21.45 N	71.35 W
Turks Island Passage ʊ	238	21.25 N	71.19 W
Turks Islands II	238	21.24 N	71.07 W
Turks-und Caicos-Inseln → Turks and Caicos Islands □[2]	238	21.45 N	71.35 W
Turku (Åbo)	26	60.27 N	22.17 E
Turkwel ≃	154	3.06 N	36.06 E
Turlan	85	43.36 N	69.03 E
Turley	196	36.14 N	95.58 W
Turlock	226	37.29 N	120.50 W
Turlock Lake ⊜[1]	226	42.17 N	73.21 W
Turmalina	255	17.17 S	42.45 W
Turmantas	76	55.42 N	26.27 E
Turmerito, Quebrada ≃	286c	10.26 N	66.55 W
Turnagain ≃	180	59.06 N	127.35 W
Turnagain, Cape ›	172	40.29 S	176.37 E
Turnagain Arm c	180	61.00 N	150.00 W
Turnagain Island I	164	9.34 S	142.18 E
Turnau	61	47.33 N	15.20 E
Turnbull, Mount ∧	200	33.04 N	110.16 W
Turnbull, Mount ∧[2]	162	21.03 S	131.57 E
Turneffe Islands II	232	17.22 N	87.51 W
Turner, Austl.	162	17.50 S	128.17 E
Turner, Mt., U.S.	202	48.50 N	108.24 W
Turner, Or., U.S.	202	44.50 N	122.57 W
Turner ≃	162	20.21 S	118.25 E
Turner Field ⊠	285	40.13 N	75.13 W
Turners Falls	207	42.36 N	72.33 W
Turners Peninsula ›[1]	150	7.22 N	12.22 W
Turnersville, N.J., U.S.	285	39.46 N	75.03 W
Turnersville, Tx., U.S.	222	31.37 N	97.44 W
Turner Valley	182	50.40 N	114.17 W
Turnhout	56	51.19 N	4.57 E
Türnitz	61	47.57 N	15.30 E
Turnor Lake ⊜	184	56.32 N	108.38 W
Turnov	30	50.35 N	15.10 E
Tŭrnovo → Veliko Târnovo	38	43.04 N	25.39 E
Turnpike Lake ⊜	283	42.01 N	71.19 W
Turnu Măgurele	38	43.45 N	24.53 E
Turnu Roșu, Pasul)(	38	45.33 N	24.16 E
Turnu-Severin → Drobeta-Turnu Severin	38	44.38 N	22.39 E
Turobin	30	50.50 N	22.45 E
Turočak	86	52.16 N	87.08 E
Turon	198	37.48 N	98.25 W
Turon ≃	170	33.03 S	149.43 E
Turopin	78	51.00 N	24.27 E
Turopolje ≚	36	45.40 N	16.05 E
Tuross ≃	171b	36.09 S	149.39 E
Turov	76	52.04 N	27.44 E
Turovo	82	54.52 N	37.49 E
Turpan	86	42.56 N	89.10 E
Turpan Pendi (Turfan Depression) ≗[7]	86	42.40 N	89.10 E
Turques et Caicos, Îles → Turks and Caicos Islands □[2]	238	21.45 N	71.35 W
Turquía → Turkey □[1]	22	39.00 N	35.00 E
Turquie → Turkey □[1]	22	39.00 N	35.00 E
Turquino, Pico ∧	240p	19.59 N	76.50 W
Turrach	64	46.57 N	13.52 E
Turramurra	274a	33.44 S	151.08 E
Turrell	194	35.22 N	90.15 W
Turret Peak ∧	200	34.15 N	111.53 W
Turriaco	64	45.49 N	13.26 E
Turrialba	236	9.54 N	83.41 W
Turrialba, Volcán ∧[1]	236	10.02 N	83.46 W
Turriers	62	44.24 N	6.10 E
Turriff	46	57.32 N	2.28 W
Turritano ◆[1]	71	40.45 N	8.35 E
Turrubares, Cerro ∧	236	9.47 N	84.28 W
Tursi	68	40.15 N	16.28 E
Tursunzade	85	38.32 N	68.13 E
Turtas ≃	86	59.06 N	68.52 E
Turtipār	124	26.10 N	83.54 E
Turtle ≃, Mb., Can.	184	51.07 N	99.39 W
Turtle ≃, On., Can.	184	48.51 N	92.45 W
Turtle, North Branch ≃	198	47.57 N	97.35 W
Turtle Creek, N.B., Can.	186	45.58 N	64.53 W
Turtle Creek, Pa., U.S.	214	40.24 N	79.49 W
Turtle Creek ≃, Pa., U.S.	279b	40.23 N	79.51 W
Turtle Creek ≃, S.D., U.S.	198	44.55 N	98.29 W
Turtle Creek ≃, Wi., U.S.	216	42.29 N	89.03 W
Turtle-Flambeau Flowage ⊜[1]	190	46.05 N	90.11 W
Turtleford	184	53.23 N	108.56 W
Turtle Harbor Channel ʊ	220	25.15 N	80.18 W
Turtle Islands II	150	7.37 N	13.02 W
Turtle Lake, N.D., U.S.	198	47.31 N	100.53 W
Turtle Lake, Wi., U.S.	190	45.23 N	92.08 W
Turtle Lake ⊜	184	53.35 N	108.40 W
Turtle Mountain ∧[2]	184	49.00 N	100.15 W
Turtle Mountain Indian Reservation ◆[4]	198	48.51 N	99.45 W
Turtle Mountain Provincial Park ♦	184	49.03 N	100.15 W
Turtmann	58	46.18 N	7.41 E
Turton and Entwistle Reservoir ⊜[1]	262	53.39 N	2.25 W
Turton Bottoms	262	53.38 N	2.24 W
Turton Moor ◆[3]	262	53.40 N	2.29 W
Turton Tower ʋ	262	53.38 N	2.25 W
Turu ≃	74	64.38 N	100.00 E
Turua	172	37.14 S	175.34 E
Turuchan ≃	74	65.56 N	87.42 E
Turuchansk	74	65.49 N	87.59 E
Turuntajevo, Ross.	86	56.38 N	85.59 E
Turuntajevo, Ross.	88	52.12 N	107.37 E
Turusele ∧	71	40.09 N	9.34 E
Turvo	252	28.56 S	49.41 W
Turvo ≃, Bra.	255	17.46 S	50.12 W
Turvo ≃, Bra.	255	19.56 S	49.55 W
Turvo ≃, Bra.	256	22.04 S	45.42 W
Turvo ≃, Bra.	256	22.29 S	44.15 W
Turvo Grande ≃	256	21.42 S	44.22 W
Turvolândia	256	21.47 S	45.47 W
Turvo Pequeno ≃	256	21.42 S	44.22 W
Turyu-san ∧	98	41.10 N	128.47 E
Turzovka	30	49.25 N	18.39 E
Tusa	70	37.59 N	14.14 E
Tusa ≃	70	38.01 N	14.16 E
Tusas, Rio ≃	200	36.23 N	106.03 W
Tuscaloosa	194	33.12 N	87.34 W
Tuscaloosa, Lake ⊜[1]	194	33.20 N	87.35 W
Tuscania	66	42.25 N	11.52 E
Tuscany → Toscana □[4]	36	43.25 N	11.00 E
Tuscarawas	214	40.24 N	81.25 W
Tuscarawas □[6]	214	40.30 N	81.27 W
Tuscarawas ≃	214	40.17 N	81.52 W
Tuscarora, N.Y., U.S.	210	42.38 N	77.52 W
Tuscarora, Pa., U.S.	208	40.46 N	76.02 W
Tuscarora Creek ≃, N.Y., U.S.	210	42.07 N	77.14 W
Tuscarora Creek ≃, Pa., U.S.	208	40.32 N	77.23 W
Tuscarora Creek, North Branch ≃	210	42.05 N	77.18 W
Tuscarora Indian Reservation ◆[4]	210	43.09 N	78.57 W
Tuscarora Mountain ∧	188	40.10 N	77.45 W
Tuscarora Mountains ⋀	204	41.00 N	116.20 W
Tuscarora State Park ♦	208	40.48 N	76.01 W
Tuscarora Tunnel ◆[5]	214	40.05 N	77.50 W
Tuscola, Il., U.S.	194	39.47 N	88.16 W
Tuscola, Tx., U.S.	196	32.12 N	99.48 W
Tuscolo ⊥	267a	41.48 N	12.42 E
Tuscumbia, Al., U.S.	194	34.43 N	87.42 W
Tuscumbia, Mo., U.S.	194	38.13 N	92.27 W
Tuse	41	55.43 N	11.37 E
Tushan	98	34.14 N	117.51 E
Tušino ◆[8]	265b	55.50 N	37.26 E
Tuskegee	194	32.25 N	85.41 W
Tusker Rock II[1]	42	51.27 N	3.40 W
Tussey Mountain ∧	214	40.25 N	78.07 W
Tüssling	60	48.13 N	12.36 E
Tustin	228	33.44 N	117.49 W
Tustin Marine Corps Air Station (Helicopter) ■	280	33.43 N	117.50 W
Tustumena Lake ⊜	180	60.12 N	150.50 W
Tuszyn	30	51.37 N	19.34 E
Tut	130	37.48 N	37.55 E
Tuta	152	14.37 S	20.45 E
Tutaekuri ≃	172	39.30 S	176.54 E
Tutaizi	104	41.01 N	122.38 E
Tutajev	80	57.53 N	39.32 E
Tutak	84	39.32 N	42.46 E
Tutang	100	29.21 N	116.24 E
Tutbury	42	52.51 N	1.41 W
Tuthills Creek ≃	276	40.45 N	73.02 W
Tuticorin	122	8.47 N	78.08 E
Tutin	38	42.59 N	20.20 E
T'ut'kovo	82	54.37 N	38.32 E
Tutóia	250	2.45 S	42.16 W
Tutoko, Mount ∧	172	44.36 S	168.00 E
Tutong	112	4.50 N	114.40 E
Tutova ≃	38	46.06 N	27.32 E
Tutrakan	38	44.03 N	26.37 E
Tuttle, N.D., U.S.	198	47.08 N	99.59 W
Tuttle, Ok., U.S.	196	35.17 N	97.48 W
Tuttle Creek Lake ⊜[1]	198	39.22 N	96.40 W
Tuttlingen	58	47.59 N	8.49 E
Tutuala	112	8.24 S	127.15 E
Tutuban Station ◆[5]	269f	14.37 N	120.58 E
Tutu Bay c	116	5.55 N	121.12 E
Tutubu	154	5.30 S	32.41 E
Tutuí ≃	250	2.39 S	54.10 W
Tutuila I	174u	14.18 S	170.42 W
Tutūn	142	29.09 N	30.46 E
Tütüncü	130	40.04 N	27.43 E
Tutupaca, Volcán ∧[1]	248	17.01 S	70.22 W
Tutura	88	54.46 N	105.15 E
Tututalak Mountain ∧	180	67.46 N	161.10 W
Tutwiler	194	34.00 N	90.25 W
Tutzing	64	47.54 N	11.17 E
Tuul ≃	90	48.57 N	104.48 E
Tuupovaara	26	62.29 N	30.36 E
Tuurun-Poorin lääni □[4]	26	61.20 N	22.30 E
Tuusniemi	26	62.49 N	28.30 E
Tuutapu, Cerro ∧	174z	27.08 S	109.24 W
Tuva □[3]	72	52.00 N	95.00 E
T'uva-Guba	24	69.08 N	33.32 E
Tuvalu □[1]	14	8.00 S	178.00 E
Tuvutha Island I	175g	17.40 S	178.48 W
Tuwang	107	29.06 N	105.48 E
Ṭuwayq, Jabal ⋀	118	23.00 N	46.00 E
Ṭuwayyil ash-Shihāq ∧[2]	132	30.36 N	36.08 E
Tuxedo Park, De., U.S.	285	39.43 N	75.37 W
Tuxedo Park, N.Y., U.S.	210	41.11 N	74.11 W
Tuxer Alpen ⋀	64	47.10 N	11.45 E
Tuxford, Sk., Can.	184	50.35 N	105.35 W
Tuxford, Eng., U.K.	44	53.13 N	0.53 W
Tuxiaqiao	100	28.47 N	121.29 E
Tuxpan, Méx.	234	19.33 N	103.24 W
Tuxpan, Méx.	234	19.34 N	100.28 W
Tuxpan, Méx.	234	21.57 N	105.18 W
Tuxpan, Méx.	234	20.57 N	97.24 W
Tuxpan ≃	234	20.59 N	97.18 W
Tuxsun	86	42.47 N	88.38 E
Tuxtepec	234	18.06 N	96.07 W
Tuxtla Gutiérrez	234	16.45 N	93.07 W
Tuy	34	42.03 N	8.38 W
Tuy ≃	246	10.24 N	65.59 W
Tuy An	110	13.17 N	109.16 E
Tuyen Hoa	110	17.50 N	106.10 E
Tuyen Quang	110	21.49 N	105.13 E
Tuy Hoa	110	13.05 N	109.18 E
Tūysarkān	128	34.33 N	48.27 E
Tuyün → Duyun	102	26.12 N	107.31 E
Ṭuyūr, Burj aṭ- ∧[2]	140	20.55 N	27.55 E
Tuža	80	57.37 N	47.57 E
T'uzašu, pereval)(	85	42.21 N	73.48 E
T'uzbel'	85	40.34 N	73.21 E
Tuzdykol', ozero ⊜	80	49.36 N	52.20 E
Tuz Gölü ⊜	130	38.45 N	33.25 E
Tuzigoot National Monument ♦	200	34.49 N	112.01 W
Ṭūz Khurmātū	128	34.53 N	44.38 E
Tuzla, Bos.	38	44.32 N	18.41 E
Tuzla, Tür.	130	36.42 N	35.05 E
Tuzla ≃	130	39.43 N	40.16 E
Tuzla Gölü ⊜	130	39.02 N	35.50 E
Tuzlagözü	130	38.11 N	41.34 E
Tuzlov ≃	83	47.23 N	40.08 E
Tuzluca	84	40.03 N	43.40 E
Tuzlukçu	130	38.28 N	31.38 E
Tuzly	78	45.52 N	30.05 E
Tuzuntla ≃	234	18.51 N	100.44 W
Tvârdica, Blg.	38	42.42 N	25.52 E
Tvardica, Mol.	38	46.09 N	28.58 E
Tvedestrand	26	58.37 N	8.55 E
Tveitsund	26	59.01 N	8.32 E
Tver' (Kalinin)	82	56.52 N	35.55 E
Tverca ≃	76	56.52 N	35.55 E
Tver' Oblast' □[4]	76	57.00 N	34.00 E
Twain Harte	226	38.02 N	120.14 W
Twann	58	47.06 N	7.10 E
Twardogóra	30	51.22 N	17.28 E
Tweed	212	44.29 N	77.19 W
Tweed ≃	44	55.46 N	2.00 W
Tweeddale V	46	55.40 N	3.10 W
Tweede Exloërmond	52	52.55 N	6.58 E
Tweed Heads	171a	28.10 S	153.31 E
Tweedmouth	44	55.45 N	2.01 W
Tweedsmuir Provincial Park ♦	182	52.55 N	126.05 W
Tweedy Mountain ∧	202	45.29 N	112.58 W
Tweeling	158	27.38 S	28.31 E
Twee Rivieren	158	26.27 S	20.37 E
Tweespruit	158	29.11 S	27.01 E
Twello	52	52.14 N	6.06 E
Twelve Mile	216	40.52 N	86.13 W
Twelve Mile Creek ≃, On., Can.	212	43.11 N	79.16 W
Twelvemile Creek ≃, N.Y., U.S.	210	43.18 N	78.51 W
Twelvemile Island I	279b	40.32 N	79.51 W
Twelve Mile Lake ⊜, On., Can.	212	45.02 N	78.43 W
Twelve Mile Lake ⊜, Sk., Can.	184	49.29 N	106.14 W
Tweng	64	47.11 N	13.36 E
Twente ◆[1]	52	52.17 N	6.40 E
Twentekanaal ≊	52	52.15 N	6.40 E
Twentieth Century Fox Studios ʋ[3]	280	34.03 N	118.25 W
Twentyfive Mile Wash V	200	37.33 N	111.07 W
Twenty Mile Creek ≃	212	43.10 N	79.22 W
Twentynine Palms	204	34.08 N	116.03 W
Twentynine Palms Marine Corps Center ■	204	34.25 N	116.10 W
Tweya	152	0.54 S	19.05 E
Twickenham ◆[8]	260	51.27 N	0.20 W
Twilight Cove c	162	32.16 S	126.03 E
Twilight Park	210	42.11 N	74.05 W
Twillingate	186	49.39 N	54.46 W
Twimberg	61	46.55 N	14.50 E
Twin Beach	216	42.34 N	83.24 W
Twin Bridge Farm	285	39.57 N	75.33 W
Twin Bridges	202	45.32 N	112.19 W
Twin Butte Creek ≃	198	38.46 N	100.56 W
Twin Buttes ∧	202	44.20 N	122.15 W
Twin Buttes Reservoir ⊜[1]	196	31.20 N	100.35 W
Twin City	192	32.34 N	82.09 W
Twin Creek ≃	218	39.33 N	84.21 W
Twin Falls	202	42.33 N	114.27 W
Twin Heads ⋀	162	20.13 S	126.30 E
Twin Hills	180	59.23 N	159.58 W
Twin Lakes, Ca., U.S.	226	36.58 N	122.00 W
Twin Lakes, Ga., U.S.	192	30.42 N	83.12 W
Twin Lakes, In., U.S.	216	41.19 N	86.23 W
Twin Lakes, Mi., U.S.	216	42.02 N	86.04 W
Twin Lakes, Oh., U.S.	214	41.11 N	81.21 W
Twin Lakes, Pa., U.S.	210	41.24 N	74.54 W
Twin Lakes, Wi., U.S.	216	42.31 N	88.14 W
Twin Lakes ⊜, Ca., U.S.	226	38.09 N	119.21 W
Twin Lakes ⊜, Ct., U.S.	207	42.02 N	73.26 W
Twin Lakes ⊜, Wa., U.S.	224	47.55 N	120.51 W
Twin Oaks	208	39.51 N	75.26 W
Twin Peak Islands II	162	34.00 S	122.50 E
Twin Peaks	228	34.12 N	117.12 W
Twin Peaks ⋀, Ca., U.S.	282	37.45 N	122.27 W
Twin Peaks ⋀, Id., U.S.	202	44.35 N	114.29 W
Twin Rocks, Or., U.S.	224	45.36 N	123.57 W
Twin Rocks, Pa., U.S.	214	40.29 N	78.51 W
Twinsburg	214	41.18 N	81.26 W
Twin Valley	198	47.15 N	96.15 W
Twisp	202	48.21 N	120.07 W
Twiss Green	262	53.27 N	2.32 W
Twist	52	52.38 N	7.03 E
Twiste ≃	52	51.29 N	9.09 E
Twistringen	52	52.48 N	8.38 E
Twitchell Reservoir ⊜[1]	204	35.00 N	120.19 W
Twitya ≃	180	64.10 N	128.12 W
Two, Channel ʊ	220	24.50 N	80.45 W
Two Butte Creek ≃	198	38.02 N	102.08 W
Twofold Bay c	166	37.06 S	149.55 E
Two Harbors	190	47.01 N	91.40 W
Two Hills	182	53.43 N	111.45 W
Two Lakes ⊜	224	46.22 N	121.27 W
Two Medicine ≃	202	48.29 N	112.14 W
Two Mile Creek ≃, On., Can.	284a	43.16 N	79.06 W
Twomile Creek ≃, N.Y., U.S.	284a	43.01 N	78.55 W
Twong	140	8.18 N	28.20 E
Two Penny Run ≃	285	39.41 N	75.26 W
Two River Lake ⊜	184	53.52 N	91.27 W
Two Rivers	190	44.09 N	87.34 W
Two Rivers Reservoir ⊜[1]	196	33.17 N	104.45 W
Two Thumb Range ⋀	172	43.45 S	170.43 E
Two Wells	168b	34.36 S	138.30 E
Twrch ≃, Wales, U.K.	42	52.42 N	3.29 W
Twrch ≃, Wales, U.K.	42	51.46 N	3.46 W
Twyford, Eng., U.K.	42	51.29 N	0.53 W
Twyford, Eng., U.K.	42	51.01 N	1.19 W
Twymyn ≃	42	52.38 N	3.44 W
Tyabb	169	38.16 S	145.11 E
Tybee Island	192	32.01 N	80.51 W
Tybju	24	60.37 N	50.20 E
Tychy	30	50.09 N	18.59 E
Tyczyn	30	49.58 N	22.02 E
Tydal	26	63.04 N	11.34 E
Tye	196	32.27 N	99.52 W
Tyende Creek ≃	200	36.50 N	109.43 W
Tyendinaga Indian Reserve ◆[4]	212	44.11 N	77.07 W
Tyers ≃	169	38.10 S	146.26 E
Tyfors	40	60.09 N	14.12 E
Tygarts Creek ≃	218	38.43 N	82.57 W
Tygda	89	53.07 N	126.20 E
Tygda ≃	89	52.35 N	127.55 E
Tygelsjö	41	55.31 N	13.00 E
Tygh Valley	224	45.14 N	121.10 W
Tyin ⊜	26	61.17 N	8.13 E
Tyja ≃	88	55.36 N	109.20 E
Tylcen	158	32.07 S	27.05 E
Tylcesley	44	53.31 N	2.28 W
Tyler, Mn., U.S.	198	44.16 N	96.08 W
Tyler, Pa., U.S.	214	41.14 N	78.32 W
Tyler, Tx., U.S.	222	32.21 N	95.18 W
Tyler □[6]	222	30.47 N	94.32 W
Tyler, Lake ⊜[1]	222	32.13 N	95.10 W
Tyler East, Lake ⊜[1]	222	32.15 N	95.10 W
Tyler Park	284c	38.52 N	77.12 W
Tylersburg	214	41.23 N	79.19 W
Tyler State Park ♦, Pa., U.S.	208	40.14 N	74.59 W
Tyler State Park ♦, Tx., U.S.	222	32.29 N	95.14 W
Tylersville	210	41.00 N	77.25 W
Tylerton	208	37.58 N	76.01 W
Tylertown	194	31.06 N	90.08 W
Tylla	40	60.28 N	15.33 E
Tylösand	26	56.39 N	12.44 E
Tylöskog ⋀[2]	40	58.45 N	15.20 E
Tylovaj	80	57.30 N	53.47 E
Tym ≃, Ross.	74	59.25 N	80.04 E
Tym' ≃, Ross.	89	51.51 N	143.10 E
Tymna, laguna c	180	64.00 N	178.30 E
Tymochtee Creek ≃	214	40.57 N	83.16 W
Tymovskoje	89	50.51 N	142.39 E
Tymsk	86	59.24 N	80.18 E
Tynagh	48	53.09 N	8.22 W
Tyndall	198	42.59 N	97.51 W
Tyndall Air Force Base ■	194	30.04 N	85.35 W
Tyndaris ⊥	70	38.09 N	15.03 E
Tyndinskij	74	55.10 N	124.43 E
Tyndrum	46	56.27 N	4.44 W
Tyne ≃, Eng., U.K.	44	55.01 N	1.26 W
Tyne ≃, Scot., U.K.	46	56.01 N	2.37 W
Tyne and Wear □[6]	44	54.55 N	1.35 W
Tynemouth	44	55.01 N	1.24 W
Tyner	216	41.24 N	86.24 W
Tyngsboro	283	42.40 N	71.25 W
Tyngsjö	40	60.18 N	13.53 E
Tynica	78	51.08 N	32.54 E
Týn nad Vltavou	30	49.14 N	14.26 E
Tynnelsö	40	59.25 N	17.06 E
Tynset	26	62.17 N	10.47 E
Tyonek	180	61.02 N	151.17 W
Typta	88	54.35 N	104.31 E
Tyr	89	52.57 N	139.48 E
Tyre → Ṣūr, Lubnān	132	33.16 N	35.11 E
Tyre, Pa., U.S.	214	40.26 N	80.16 W
Tyresö	40	59.14 N	18.18 E
Tyret'	88	53.41 N	102.19 E
Tyrgetuj	88	51.27 N	113.46 E
Tyrifjorden ⊜	26	60.02 N	10.08 E
Tyringe	41	56.10 N	13.35 E
Tyringham	207	42.14 N	73.12 W
Tyrka	88	54.30 N	107.09 E
Tyrma	89	50.03 N	132.12 E
Tyrma ≃	89	50.29 N	131.18 E
Tyrnovo	38	48.10 N	27.40 E
Tyrnyauz	84	43.23 N	42.56 E
Tyrone, Ky., U.S.	218	38.01 N	84.50 W
Tyrone, N.Y., U.S.	210	42.25 N	77.03 W
Tyrone, Ok., U.S.	196	36.57 N	101.03 W
Tyrone, Pa., U.S.	214	40.40 N	78.14 W
Tyrone Lake ⊜	281	42.42 N	83.43 W
Tyrrell, Lake ⊜	166	35.21 S	142.50 E
Tyrrellspass	48	53.23 N	7.22 W
Tyrrhenian Sea (Mare Tirreno) ⊤[2]	36	40.00 N	12.00 E
Tyrrhenisches Meer → Tyrrhenian Sea ⊤[2]	36	40.00 N	12.00 E
Tysmenica	78	48.54 N	24.49 E
Tysnesøy I	26	60.00 N	5.35 E
Tysons Corner	284c	38.55 N	77.14 W
Tysons Corner Center ◆[9]	284c	38.55 N	77.13 W
Tysons Green	284c	38.55 N	77.15 W
Tysse	26	60.22 N	5.45 E
Tyssedal	26	60.07 N	6.34 E
Tysslingen ⊜	40	59.19 N	15.02 E
Tystberga	40	58.52 N	17.15 E
Tystrup Sø ⊜	41	55.22 N	11.35 E
Tytherington	262	53.17 N	2.08 W
Tytuvėnai	76	55.36 N	23.12 E
Ty Ty	192	31.28 N	83.38 W
Tyumen' → T'umen'	86	57.09 N	65.32 E
Tyvrov	78	49.01 N	28.30 E
Tywa ≃	54	53.13 N	14.29 E
Tywardreath	42	50.22 N	4.41 W
Tywi ≃	42	51.46 N	4.22 W
Tywyn	42	52.35 N	4.05 W
Tzaneen	156	23.50 S	30.09 E
Tzekung → Zigong	107	29.24 N	104.47 E
Tzeliutsing → Zigong	107	29.24 N	104.47 E
Tzucacab	232	20.04 N	89.03 W
Tzukung → Zigong	107	29.24 N	104.47 E
Tzupo → Boshan, Zhg.	98	36.29 N	117.50 E
Tzupo → Zibo, Zhg.	98	36.47 N	118.01 E
U			
Uaboe	174b	0.31 S	166.55 E
Uac, Mount ∧	116	12.12 N	123.40 E
Uaçá ≃	250	4.13 N	51.32 W
Uagadugu → Ouagadougou	150	12.22 N	1.31 W
Uamba	152	7.12 S	16.25 E
Uamba (Wamba) ≃, Afr.	152	3.56 S	17.12 E
Uamba ≃, Ang.	152	7.58 S	17.09 E
Uampochane	158	26.23 S	32.41 E
Uaoa Bay c	229a	20.56 N	156.16 W
Uaran → Ouarâne ◆[1]	134	21.00 N	10.30 W
Uato-Lari	112	8.45 S	126.34 E
Uatumã ≃	246	2.26 S	57.37 W
Uauá	250	9.50 S	39.28 W
Uaupés (Vaupés) ≃	246	0.02 N	67.16 W
Uaxactún ⊥	232	17.24 N	89.39 W
Ubá	255	21.07 S	42.56 W
Uba ≃	86	50.15 N	81.41 E
Übach-Palenberg	56	50.55 N	6.07 E
Ubagan ≃	86	54.24 N	64.45 E
Ubai	164	5.40 S	150.40 E
Ubaidullaganj	124	22.59 N	77.36 E
Ubaitaba	255	14.18 S	39.20 W
Ubajara	250	3.51 S	40.56 W
Ubajara, Parque Nacional de ♦	250	3.47 S	40.56 W
Ubangi (Oubangui) ≃	152	0.30 S	17.42 E
Ubatã	255	14.12 S	39.31 W
Ubaté	246	5.19 N	73.49 W
Ubatuba	256	23.26 S	45.04 W
Ubatuba, Baía de c	256	23.27 S	45.02 W
Ubauro	120	28.10 N	69.44 E
Ubay	116	10.03 N	124.28 E
Ubaye	62	44.28 N	6.22 E
Ubaye ≃	62	44.28 N	6.18 E
Ubayyiḍ, Wādī al- V	128	32.34 N	43.48 E
Ubby	41	55.37 N	11.13 E
Ube	96	33.56 N	131.15 E
Ubed' ≃	78	51.27 N	32.29 E
Úbeda	34	38.01 N	3.22 W
Uberaba	255	19.45 S	47.55 W
Uberaba ≃	255	20.07 S	48.31 W
Uberaba, Lagoa ⊜	248	17.30 S	57.45 W
Überackern	60	48.11 N	12.52 E
Über dem Wind, Inseln → Leeward Islands II	238	17.00 N	63.00 W
Uberlândia	255	18.56 S	48.18 W
Überlingen	58	47.46 N	9.10 E
Überlinger See c	58	47.45 N	9.09 E
Übersee	64	47.49 N	12.28 E
Ubiaja	150	6.38 N	6.21 E
Ubili	154	1.07 S	26.55 E
Ubin, Pulau I	271c	1.24 N	103.58 E
Ubinskoje	86	55.19 N	79.41 E
Ubinskoje, ozero ⊜	86	55.30 N	80.05 E
Ubl'a	30	48.55 N	22.23 E
Ubly	190	43.42 N	82.55 W
Uboldo	266b	45.37 N	9.00 E
Ubombo	158	27.33 S	32.00 E
Ubondo	154	0.52 S	25.37 E
Ubon Ratchathani	110	15.14 N	104.54 E
Úborsko	60	49.20 N	13.09 E
Ubort' ≃	78	52.06 N	28.28 E
Ubrique	34	36.41 N	5.27 W
Ubudiah, Masjid ʋ[1]	114	4.46 N	100.56 E
Ubundu (Ponthierville)	154	0.21 S	25.29 E
Ubur-Tochtor	88	50.06 N	113.37 E
Uča ≃, Ross.	82	56.02 N	37.37 E
Uča ≃, Ross.	265b	55.56 N	37.57 E
Ucacha	252	33.02 S	63.31 W
Uč-Adži	128	38.05 N	62.48 E
Učaly	86	54.19 N	59.27 E
Učami	74	63.50 N	96.29 E
Učaral	86	46.10 N	80.56 E
Ucayali □[5]	248	9.00 S	74.00 W
Ucayali ≃	242	4.30 S	73.27 W
Uccellina, Monti dell' ⋀	66	42.38 N	11.05 E
Uccle	50	50.48 N	4.19 E
Uch	123	29.14 N	71.03 E
Uchab	156	19.47 S	17.42 E
Uchāna	124	29.28 N	76.10 E
Uchaud	62	43.45 N	4.16 E
Uchee Creek ≃	192	32.18 N	84.57 W
Uchihara	94	36.22 N	140.21 E
Uchihata	270	34.25 N	135.27 E
Uchiko	96	33.33 N	132.39 E
Uchi Lake	184	51.05 N	92.35 W
Uchinada	94	36.39 N	136.39 E
Uchinomi	96	34.30 N	134.20 E
Uchinoura	92	31.16 N	131.05 E
Uchiumi	96	33.01 N	132.30 E
Uchiura-wan c	92a	42.20 N	140.40 E
Uchiza	248	8.29 S	76.23 W
Uchoa	255	20.56 S	49.13 W
Ucholovo	80	53.47 N	40.29 E
Ucha ≃	80	58.20 N	39.00 E
Ucha, Ross.	24	61.12 N	38.32 E
Ucha, Ross.	24	63.33 N	53.38 E
Uchte	52	52.30 N	8.54 E
Uchte ≃	54	52.46 N	11.45 E
Uchtoma	76	60.10 N	38.02 E
Uchtspringe	54	52.32 N	11.36 E
Učinskij Ryboučastok	86	60.02 N	65.10 E
Učinskoje vodochranilišče ⊜[1]	82	56.02 N	37.45 E
Uckange	56	49.18 N	6.09 E
Ückendorf ◆[8]	263	51.30 N	7.07 E
Uckermark ◆[1]	54	53.10 N	13.35 E
Uckfield	42	50.58 N	0.06 E
Üçköşe	130	40.13 N	41.00 E
Uckro	54	51.51 N	13.37 E
Učkupr'uk	85	40.33 N	71.04 E
Učkurgan	85	41.07 N	72.05 E
Ucluelet	182	48.57 N	125.33 W
Ucon	202	43.35 N	111.57 W
Üçpınar	130	37.08 N	32.16 E
Ucria	70	38.03 N	14.53 E
Üçtepeler ∧	130	39.39 N	42.41 E
Učterek	85	41.45 N	73.12 E
Úcua ≃	152	8.35 S	13.40 E
Učujevskij Majdan	80	54.33 N	44.30 E
Učur ≃	74	58.48 N	130.35 E
Uda ≃, Ross.	88	56.05 N	99.34 E
Uda ≃, Ross.	88	51.47 N	107.33 E
Uda ≃, Ross.	89	54.42 N	135.14 E
Udagamandalam	122	11.24 N	76.42 E
Udaipur	120	24.35 N	73.41 E
Udaj ≃	78	50.05 N	33.07 E
Udala	126	21.35 N	86.34 E
Udalguri	120	26.46 N	92.08 E
Udall	198	37.23 N	97.06 W
Udamalpet	122	10.35 N	77.15 E
Udankudi	122	8.26 N	78.01 E
Udaquiola	252	36.34 S	58.31 W
Udarnyj	89	49.07 N	142.09 E
Udaypur	124	26.56 N	86.31 E
Udbina	36	44.32 N	15.46 E
Udby	41	55.05 N	11.57 E
Uddeholm	40	60.01 N	13.37 E
Uddel	52	52.15 N	5.46 E
Uddevalla	26	58.21 N	11.55 E
Uddingston	46	55.50 N	4.06 W
Uddjaure ⊜	24	65.55 N	17.49 E
Udel'naja	82	55.38 N	38.03 E
Udel'naja ◆[8]	265a	60.01 N	30.19 E
Uden	52	51.40 N	5.36 E
Udenhout	52	51.37 N	5.08 E
Uder	56	51.22 N	10.05 E
Üdersdorf	56	50.09 N	6.49 E
Udgīr	122	18.23 N	77.07 E
Udhampur	123	32.56 N	75.08 E
Udhruḥ	132	30.20 N	35.36 E
Udi	150	6.19 N	7.25 E
Udimskij	24	61.09 N	45.52 E
Udine	64	46.03 N	13.14 E
Udine □[4]	64	46.10 N	13.00 E
Udmurtia → Udmurtija □[3]	80	57.00 N	53.00 E
Udmurtija □[3]	80	57.00 N	53.00 E
Udokan, chrebet ⋀	88	56.20 N	118.10 E
Udomlja	76	57.52 N	35.01 E
Udone-jima I	94	34.28 N	139.18 E
Udono	92	33.44 N	136.01 E
Udon Thani	110	17.26 N	102.46 E
Udor, Mount ∧	162	23.30 S	131.01 E
Udot I	175c	7.23 N	151.43 E
Udskaja guba c	89	54.50 N	135.45 E
Udskoje	89	54.32 N	134.26 E
Udubo	146	11.57 N	10.38 E
Udupi	122	13.21 N	74.45 E
Udy	78	50.24 N	36.03 E
Udyl', ozero ⊜	89	52.06 N	139.48 E
Udža	74	71.14 N	117.10 E
Udžary	84	40.31 N	47.39 E
Uebigau	54	51.35 N	13.18 E
Uebonti	112	0.55 S	121.38 E
Uebonti, Teluk c	112	0.50 S	121.45 E
Uecker ≃	54	53.45 N	14.04 E
Ueckeritz	54	54.00 N	14.02 E
Ueckermünde	54	53.44 N	14.03 E
Ueckermünder Heide ◆[3]	54	53.40 N	14.10 E
Ueda	94	36.24 N	138.16 E
Uedem	52	51.40 N	6.16 E
Uedesheim	263	51.10 N	6.48 E
Uegō	268	35.13 N	139.56 E
Ueharu	175d	24.25 N	123.46 E
Uehlfeld	56	49.40 N	10.43 E
Uele ≃	136	4.09 N	22.26 E
Uelen	180	66.10 N	169.48 W
Uel'kal'	180	65.32 N	179.17 W
Uelsen	52	52.30 N	6.53 E
Uelzen, Dtsch.	52	52.58 N	10.33 E
Uelzen, Dtsch.	263	51.33 N	7.44 E
Ueno, Nihon	94	36.05 N	138.47 E
Ueno, Nihon	94	34.45 N	136.08 E
Ueno, Nihon	270	34.53 N	135.14 E
Uenohara	94	35.37 N	139.07 E
Ueno Park ♦	268	35.43 N	139.46 E
Uenoshiba	270	34.33 N	135.28 E
Uerdingen ◆[8]	263	51.21 N	6.39 E
Uere ≃	154	3.42 N	25.24 E
Uetersen	52	53.41 N	9.39 E
Uettingen	56	49.48 N	9.43 E
Uetz	264a	52.28 N	12.56 E
Uetze	52	52.28 N	10.11 E
Ufa	86	54.44 N	55.56 E
Ufa ≃	86	54.40 N	56.00 E
Ufala, Punta ›	70	38.22 N	14.59 E
Uffculme	42	50.54 N	3.20 W
Uffenheim	56	49.32 N	10.14 E
Ufita ≃	68	41.09 N	14.56 E
Ufra	128	40.00 N	53.02 E
Uft'uga ≃	76	59.46 N	39.21 E
Ugab ≃	156	21.08 S	13.40 E
Ugak Bay c	180	57.25 N	152.45 W
Ugāle	76	57.16 N	22.02 E
Ugalla ≃	154	5.08 S	30.42 E
Ugamskij chrebet ⋀	85	42.00 N	70.20 E
Uganda □[1]	154	1.00 N	32.00 E
Uganik Island I	180	57.53 N	153.28 W
Ugârčin	38	43.06 N	24.25 E

Symbol	English	Deutsch	Español	Français	Português
≃	River	Fluß	Río	Rivière	Rio
≊	Canal	Kanal	Canal	Canal	Canal
⌞	Waterfall, Rapids	Wasserfall, Stromschnellen	Cascada, Rápidos	Chute d'eau, Rapides	Cascata, Rápidos
ʊ	Strait	Meeresstraße	Estrecho	Détroit	Estreito
c	Bay, Gulf	Bucht, Golf	Bahía, Golfo	Baie, Golfe	Baía, Golfo
⊜	Lake, Lakes	See, Seen	Lago, Lagos	Lac, Lacs	Lago, Lagos
≋	Swamp	Sumpf	Pantano	Marais	Pântano
⊓	Ice Features, Glacier	Eis- und Gletscherformen	Accidentes Glaciales	Formes glaciaires	Acidentes glaciares
⊤	Other Hydrographic Features	Andere Hydrographische Objekte	Otros Elementos Hidrográficos	Autres données hycrographiques	Outros acidentes hidrográficos
✦	Submarine Features	Untermeerische Objekte	Accidentes Submarinos	Formes de relief sous-marin	Acicentes submarinos
□	Political Unit	Politische Einheit	Unidad Política	Entité politique	Unicade política
ʋ	Cultural Institution	Kulturelle Institution	Institución Cultural	Institution culturelle	Instituição cultural
⊥	Historical Site	Historische Stätte	Sitio Histórico	Site historique	Sitio histórico
♦	Recreational Site	Erholungs- und Ferienort	Sitio de Recreo	Centre de loisirs	Area de Lazer
⊠	Airport	Flughafen	Aeropuerto	Aéroport	Aeroporto
■	Military Installation	Militäranlage	Instalación Militar	Installation militaire	Instalação militar
◆	Miscellaneous	Verschiedenes	Misceláneo	Divers	Diversos

Name	Page	Lat.°′	Long.°′
Ugarit ⊥	130	35.35 N	35.45 E
Ugashik	180	57.32 N	157.25 W
Ugashik Bay c	180	57.34 N	157.38 W
Ugatkyn ≃	180	68.24 N	171.30 E
Ugento	68	39.56 N	18.10 E
Ugep	150	5.48 N	8.05 E
Ugerløse	41	55.35 N	11.40 E
Uggiano la Chiesa	68	40.06 N	18.27 E
Ughaybish	140	10.52 N	31.05 E
Ughelli	150	5.29 N	5.59 E
Ugie	158	31.10 S	28.13 E
Ugie ≃	46	57.30 N	1.47 W
Ugíjar	34	36.57 N	3.03 W
Ugine	62	45.45 N	6.25 E
Uglegorsk, Ross.	89	49.02 N	142.03 E
Uglegorsk, Ukr.	83	48.19 N	38.17 E
Uglekamensk	89	43.13 N	133.11 E
Uglezavodsk	89	47.21 N	142.38 E
Uglič	76	57.32 N	38.19 E
Ugljan, Otok I	36	44.05 N	15.10 E
Uglovaja	80	57.01 N	52.57 E
Uglovka	76	58.14 N	33.31 E
Uglovoje	89	43.20 N	132.06 E
Uglovskoje	86	51.23 N	80.12 E
Ugly-Zavod	78	52.11 N	32.53 E
Ugnev	78	50.23 N	23.44 E
Ugodiči	80	57.10 N	39.30 E
Ugodskij Zavod	82	55.02 N	36.45 E
Ugol'naja, buchta c	180	63.00 N	179.20 E
Ugolnyy	180	62.58 N	179.17 E
Ugoma ∧	154	4.00 S	28.45 E
Ugovizza	64	46.31 N	13.29 E
Ugra	76	54.47 N	34.17 E
Ugra ≃	82	54.30 N	36.07 E
Ugrojedy	78	50.52 N	35.17 E
Ugr'umovo	82	55.09 N	37.40 E
Ugtaal Cajdam	88	48.17 N	105.25 E
Uguj	86	56.02 N	76.03 E
Uğurludağ	130	40.27 N	34.28 E
Ug'ut	85	41.24 N	74.50 E
Ugyak, Cape >	180	58.17 N	154.04 W
Uh (Už) ≃	30	48.34 N	22.00 E
Uha-dong	98	40.41 N	125.38 E
Uhayjibah, Jabal al- ∧	132	30.11 N	34.33 E
Uherčice	61	48.55 N	15.38 E
Uherské Hradiště	30	49.05 N	17.28 E
Uherský Brod	30	49.02 N	17.39 E
Uhingen	56	48.42 N	9.35 E
Úhlava ≃	60	49.43 N	13.23 E
Uhlenhorst	156	23.45 S	17.55 E
Uhlingen	58	47.43 N	8.19 E
Uhlman Lake ⊜	184	56.40 N	98.23 W
Uhlstädt	54	50.44 N	11.28 E
Uhrichsville	214	40.23 N	81.20 W
Uhyst, Dtsch.	54	51.11 N	14.13 E
Uhyst, Dtsch.	54	51.24 N	14.30 E
Uiche	152	12.03 S	21.02 E
Ui-do I	98	34.37 N	125.51 E
Uig	46	57.35 N	6.22 W
Uíge	152	7.37 S	15.03 E
Uíge □[5]	152	7.00 S	15.30 E
Ŭijŏngbu	98	37.44 N	127.03 E
Ŭiju	98	40.12 N	124.32 E
Uil	86	49.05 N	54.40 E
Uil ≃	80	48.36 N	52.30 E
Uilpata, gora ∧	84	42.48 N	43.48 E
Uimaharju	26	62.55 N	30.15 E
Uinebona ≃	246	5.04 N	63.01 W
Uinskoje	86	56.53 N	56.35 E
Uinta ≃	200	40.14 N	109.51 W
Uintah and Ouray Indian Reservation ◆[4]	200	40.20 N	110.20 W
Uinta Mountains ⋏	200	40.45 N	110.05 W
Uiraúna	250	6.31 S	38.25 W
Uis	156	21.08 S	14.49 E
Ŭisŏng	98	36.22 N	128.41 E
Uitenhage	158	33.40 S	25.28 E
Uitgeest	52	52.32 N	4.43 E
Uithoorn	52	52.14 N	4.50 E
Uithuizen	52	53.24 N	6.40 E
Uithuizermeeden	52	53.24 N	6.42 E
Uitspanning	158	26.46 S	29.56 E
Uj ≃, Asia	86	54.17 N	64.58 E
Uj ≃, Ross.	86	57.06 N	74.12 E
Ujae I[1]	14	9.05 N	165.40 E
Ujaly	86	44.37 N	60.57 E
Ujandina ≃	74	68.23 N	145.50 E
Ujar	86	55.48 N	94.20 E
Ujarrás ⊥	236	9.51 N	83.50 W
Ujedinenija, ostrov I	72	77.28 N	82.28 E
Ujelang I[1]	14	9.49 N	160.55 E
Ujemskij	24	64.29 N	40.50 E
Újezd, Česká Rep.	54	50.03 N	14.44 E
Újezd, Česká Rep.	60	49.26 N	13.27 E
Újezd u Brna	61	49.06 N	16.45 E
Újfehértó	30	47.48 N	21.40 E
Ujgursaj	85	40.53 N	71.03 E
Ujhāni	124	28.01 N	79.01 E
Uji	96	34.53 N	135.48 E
Uji ≃	96	34.53 N	135.42 E
Uji-guntō II	92	31.11 N	129.27 E
Ujiie	94	36.41 N	139.58 E
Ujiji	154	4.55 S	29.41 E
Uji-tawara	96	34.51 N	135.52 E
Uji-yamada → Ise	94	34.29 N	136.42 E
Ujjain	120	23.11 N	75.46 E
Újkér	61	47.28 N	16.49 E
'Ujmān	128	25.25 N	55.27 E
Újpest ◆[8]	264c	47.34 N	19.06 E
Ujście	30	53.04 N	16.43 E
Ujskoje	86	54.22 N	60.00 E
Ujum	85	38.22 N	70.51 E
Ujung	112	7.04 S	120.46 E
Ujungbatu	114	0.43 N	100.31 E
Ujungbatu, Pulau I	114	2.20 N	97.24 E
Ujungberung	115a	6.55 S	107.42 E
Ujunggading	110	0.16 N	99.33 E
Ujunggenteng	115a	7.22 S	106.24 E
Ujungkulon, Semenanjung >[1]	115a	6.45 S	105.20 E
Ujungkulon National Park ♦	115a	6.40 S	105.20 E
Ujunglamuru	112	4.40 S	119.58 E
Ujungpandang (Makasar)	112	5.07 S	119.24 E
Újvidék → Novi Sad	38	45.15 N	19.50 E
Uk	88	55.04 N	98.52 E
Uka, Nihon	174m	26.48 N	128.14 E
Uka, Ross.	74	57.50 N	162.06 E
Ukamas	158	28.02 S	19.45 E
Ukara Island I	154	1.50 S	33.03 E
Ukerewe Island I	154	2.03 S	33.00 E
Ukhaydir, Wādī V	132	30.55 N	37.01 E
Ukhra	126	23.39 N	87.14 E
Ukhrul	120	25.07 N	94.22 E
Ukhta → Uchta	24	63.33 N	53.38 E
Ukiah, Ca., U.S.	204	39.09 N	123.12 W
Ukiah, Or., U.S.	202	45.08 N	118.55 W
Ukibaru-jima I	174m	26.18 N	128.00 E
Ukiha	96	33.19 N	130.47 E
Uki Ni Masi Island I	175e	10.15 S	161.45 E
Ukmergė	76	55.15 N	24.45 E
Ukolnoi Island I	180	55.14 N	161.34 W
Ukraina → Ukraine □[1]	22	49.00 N	32.00 E
Ukraine □[1], Europe	22	49.00 N	32.00 E
Ukraine □[1], Europe	78	49.00 N	32.00 E
Ukrainka	86	54.39 N	71.20 E
Ukrainsk	83	48.06 N	37.18 E
Ukrina ≃	36	45.05 N	17.56 E
Uks'anskoje	86	55.57 N	63.01 E
Uktuz	86	55.38 N	68.30 E
Uktym	24	62.38 N	48.52 E
Uku	152	11.24 S	14.15 E
Ukui	112	0.09 S	102.11 E
Ukurejskij	88	52.24 N	116.49 E
Ukuti	154	3.39 N	33.32 E
Ukyō ◆[8]	270	35.03 N	135.42 E
Ukyr	88	49.28 N	108.52 E
Ula, India	272b	22.43 N	88.33 E
Ula, Tür.	130	37.05 N	28.26 E
Ulaanbaatar	88	47.55 N	106.53 E
Ulaanbaatar □[8]	88	47.55 N	106.53 E
Ulaanbadrach	102	44.07 N	110.11 E
Ulaan Chus	86	49.02 N	89.23 E
Ulaangom	86	49.58 N	92.02 E
Ulaan nuur ⊜	102	44.30 N	103.35 E
Ulaan Tajga ⋏	88	50.45 N	98.30 E
Ula-Chuduk	80	47.39 N	45.34 E
Ulak Island I	181a	51.22 N	179.00 W
Ulakmedan	114	2.43 N	99.38 E
Ulamba	152	9.07 S	23.40 E
Ulamona	164	5.00 S	151.15 E
Ulan, Austl.	166	32.17 S	149.44 E
Ulan, Zhg.	102	36.59 N	98.26 E
Ulan Bator → Ulaanbaatar	88	47.55 N	106.53 E
Ulanbel'	86	44.48 N	71.10 E
Ulan Buh Shamo ◆[2]	102	40.00 N	106.30 E
Ulan-Burgasy, chrebet ⋏	88	52.45 N	109.00 E
Ulan-Erge	80	46.19 N	44.53 E
Ulang ≃	236	14.27 N	83.14 W
Ulanhot → Horqin Youyi Qianqi	89	46.05 N	122.05 E
Ulānia	126	22.12 N	90.29 E
Ulanov	78	49.42 N	28.08 E
Ulanovo	78	51.46 N	34.18 E
Ulanovskij	82	54.04 N	37.51 E
Ulanów	30	50.30 N	22.16 E
Ulansuhai Nur ⊜	102	40.56 N	108.49 E
Ulan-Ude	88	51.50 N	107.37 E
Ulan Ul Hu ⊜	120	34.45 N	90.25 E
Ulan-Ušotej	88	50.45 N	105.29 E
Ular, Pulau I	271c	1.14 N	103.45 E
Ulaş	130	39.27 N	37.03 E
Ul'ašovo	24	65.27 N	56.57 E
Ulatis Creek ≃	226	38.18 N	121.00 W
Ul'atuj	88	51.09 N	116.14 E
Ulawa Island I	175e	9.46 S	161.57 E
Ulawun, Mount ∧	164	5.03 S	151.20 E
Ulaya	154	7.04 S	36.54 E
Ułazów	30	50.17 N	23.00 E
Ul'ba	86	50.16 N	83.22 E
Ul'banskij zaliv c	89	53.45 N	137.50 E
Ulchin	98	36.59 N	129.23 E
Ul'chun-Partija	88	49.56 N	112.46 E
Ulcinj	38	41.55 N	19.11 E
Ulco	158	28.21 S	24.15 E
Ulcombe	260	51.12 N	0.39 E
Ulcumayo	248	11.01 S	75.55 W
Uldum	41	55.51 N	9.36 E
Uldz ≃	88	49.56 N	115.31 E
Uleåborg → Oulu	26	65.01 N	25.28 E
Ulefoss	26	59.17 N	9.16 E
Ulen	198	47.04 N	96.15 W
Ulety	88	51.22 N	112.29 E
Ulfborg	26	56.16 N	8.20 E
Ulft	52	51.54 N	6.23 E
Ulgueira	266c	38.47 N	9.28 W
Ulhās ≃	272c	19.13 N	73.01 E
Ulhāsnagar	122	19.13 N	73.07 E
Uliast	86	48.57 N	91.17 E
Uliastaj (Džavchlant)	88	47.45 N	96.49 E
Úlice	60	49.45 N	13.09 E
Ulindi ≃	154	1.40 S	25.52 E
Ulingan	164	4.30 S	145.25 E
Ulithi I[1]	108	9.58 N	139.40 E
Ulja	74	58.51 N	141.50 E
Uljanino	82	55.21 N	38.26 E
Uljanovka, Ross.	76	59.38 N	30.46 E
Uljanovka, Ukr.	78	48.20 N	30.13 E
Uljanovka, Ukr.	78	50.58 N	34.18 E
Uljanovo, Ross.	76	53.43 N	35.32 E
Uljanovo, Uzb.	85	40.07 N	68.30 E
Uljanovsk	80	54.20 N	48.24 E
Uljanovsk Oblast' □[4]	80	53.30 N	47.30 E
Uljanovskoje, Kaz.	86	50.02 N	73.42 E
Uljanovskoje, Ross.	89	46.17 N	142.13 E
Uljuan tekojärvi ⊜	26	64.19 N	25.57 E
Ul'kajak ≃	86	48.54 N	62.00 E
Ul'kan	88	57.14 N	107.19 E
Ul'kan ≃	88	55.53 N	107.45 E
Ul'ken-Karoj, ozero ⊜	86	54.00 N	71.58 E
Ulla	76	55.14 N	29.15 E
Ulla ≃, Bela.	76	55.14 N	29.14 E
Ulla ≃, Esp.	34	42.39 N	8.44 W
Ulladulla	170	35.21 S	150.29 E
Ulladulla Head >	170	35.22 S	150.30 E
Ullāpāra	126	24.19 N	89.34 E
Ullapool	46	57.54 N	5.10 W
Ullastrell	266d	41.31 N	1.58 E
Üllendahl ◆[8]	263	51.17 N	7.11 E
Ullerslev	41	55.22 N	10.40 E
Ullervad	40	58.40 N	13.52 E
Ullin	194	37.17 N	89.11 W
Üllő	264c	47.23 N	19.21 E
Ullswater ⊜	44	54.34 N	2.54 W
Ullučaj ≃	84	42.18 N	48.08 E
Ullŭng-do I	92	37.29 N	130.52 E
Ullvettern ⊜	40	59.27 N	14.16 E
Ullvi	40	59.42 N	16.37 E
Ulm, Dtsch.	58	48.24 N	10.00 E
Ulm, Mt., U.S.	202	47.25 N	111.30 W
Ulma	38	47.53 N	25.18 E
Ul'ma ≃	89	51.54 N	129.18 E
Ulmarra	166	29.37 S	153.02 E
Ulmen	56	50.13 N	6.59 E
Ulmeni	38	45.04 N	26.39 E
Ulmer, Mount ∧	9	77.35 S	86.09 W
Ulongué	154	14.37 S	34.19 E
Ulpur	126	23.04 N	89.50 E
Ulricehamn	26	57.47 N	13.25 E
Ulrichskirchen	61	48.24 N	16.29 E
Ulrichstein	56	50.34 N	9.11 E
Ulrum	52	53.22 N	6.20 E
Ulsan	98	35.34 N	129.19 E
Ulsta	46a	60.30 N	1.09 W
Ulsteinvik	26	62.20 N	5.53 E
Ulster	210	41.51 N	76.30 W
Ulster □[6]	210	41.56 N	74.00 W
Ulster □[9]	48	54.35 N	7.00 W
Ulster ≃	56	50.51 N	9.59 E
Ulster Canal ≖	48	54.08 N	7.22 W
Ultimo, Val d' V	64	46.35 N	11.00 E
Ultraoriental, Cordillera (Serra do Divisor) ⋏	248	8.20 S	73.30 W
Ulu, Indon.	112	2.45 N	125.24 E
Ulu, Ross.	74	60.19 N	127.24 E
Ulu, Sūd.	140	10.43 N	33.29 E
Ulúa ≃	236	15.53 N	87.44 W
Ulubāria	126	22.28 N	88.06 E
Ulubat Gölü ⊜	130	40.10 N	28.35 E
Ulubey, Tür.	130	40.53 N	37.43 E
Ulubey, Tür.	130	38.25 N	29.18 E
Uluborlu	130	38.05 N	30.28 E
Uluçınar	130	36.27 N	35.51 E
Uludağ ∧	130	40.04 N	29.13 E
Ulūdāngar	272b	22.51 N	88.31 E
Uludere	128	37.27 N	42.51 E
Ulugan Bay c	116	10.07 N	118.47 E
Ulugqat	85	39.48 N	74.21 E
Uluinggalau ∧	175g	16.54 S	179.59 E
Ulujul ≃	86	57.46 N	85.30 E
Ulukışla, Kıbrıs	130	35.13 N	33.37 E
Ulukışla, Tür.	130	37.33 N	34.30 E
Ulul I	14	8.35 N	149.40 E
Ulu Laho, Bukit ∧	114	5.43 N	101.27 E
Ulunchan	88	54.51 N	111.02 E
Ulundi	158	28.17 S	31.26 E
Ulunga	89	46.31 N	136.56 E
Ulungur ≃	86	46.59 N	87.27 E
Ulungur Hu ⊜	86	47.15 N	87.20 E
Ulurijskij Golec, gora ∧	88	50.12 N	111.45 E
Uluru National Park ♦	162	25.20 S	131.00 E
Ulus	130	41.35 N	32.39 E
Ulusara	126	24.16 N	90.36 E
Ulut ≃	116	12.00 N	125.27 E
Ulutau	86	48.39 N	67.01 E
Ulutau, gora ∧	86	48.39 N	66.56 E
Ulutau, gory ⋏	86	49.00 N	67.00 E
Ulu Tiram	114	1.36 N	103.49 E
Ulu Yam	114	3.27 N	101.38 E
Ulva	272c	18.59 N	73.02 E
Ulva I	46	56.29 N	6.14 W
Ulvenhout	52	51.34 N	4.48 E
Ulverston	44	54.12 N	3.06 W
Ulverstone	166	41.09 S	146.10 E
Ulvöarna II	26	63.01 N	18.40 E
Ulvshale >[1]	41	55.02 N	12.16 E
Ulvshyttan	40	60.18 N	15.22 E
Ulvsund)(	41	54.59 N	12.11 E
Ulyanovsk → Uljanovsk	80	54.20 N	48.24 E
Ulysses, Ks., U.S.	198	37.34 N	101.21 W
Ulysses, Ne., U.S.	198	41.04 N	97.12 W
Ulysses, Pa., U.S.	214	41.54 N	77.46 W
Uly-Žilanšik ≃	86	48.51 N	63.47 E
Ulzë	38	41.41 N	19.54 E
Uma	89	52.36 N	120.37 E
Umag	36	45.25 N	13.32 E
Umaji	96	33.33 N	134.03 E
Umal'tinskij	89	51.56 N	133.36 E
Umán, Méx.	232	20.53 N	89.45 W
Uman', Ukr.	78	48.44 N	30.14 E
'Umān → Oman □[1]	118	22.00 N	58.00 E
Uman I	175c	7.18 N	151.53 E
Umanak	176	70.40 N	52.07 W
Umanak Fjord c[2]	176	70.55 N	53.00 W
Umancevo	80	47.44 N	44.16 E
Umargāon	122	20.12 N	72.45 E
Umari	250	6.38 S	38.42 W
Umari ≃	248	7.05 S	64.34 W
'Umarī, Qāʿ al- ⊜	132	31.42 N	36.57 E
Umaria	124	23.32 N	80.50 E
Umarizal	250	5.59 S	37.49 W
Umarkot	120	25.22 N	69.44 E
Umatac	174p	13.18 N	144.39 E
Umatilla, Fl., U.S.	220	28.55 N	81.39 W
Umatilla, Or., U.S.	202	45.55 N	119.20 W
Umatilla ≃	202	45.55 N	119.20 W
Umatilla, Lake ⊜[1]	202	45.44 N	120.35 W
Umatilla Indian Reservation ◆[4]	202	45.41 N	118.31 W
Umayan ≃	116	8.13 N	125.50 E
Umaze	270	34.57 N	135.03 E
Umba	24	66.41 N	34.15 E
Umbagog Lake ⊜	188	44.45 N	71.05 W
Umbai	114	2.10 N	102.20 E
Umbaúba	250	11.22 S	37.39 W
Umbelasha ≃	140	9.51 N	24.50 E
Umbertide	66	43.18 N	12.20 E
Umbogintwini	158	30.00 S	30.58 E
Umboi Island I	164	5.36 S	148.00 E
Umbrail, Pass (Giogo di Santa Maria))(	64	46.34 N	10.25 E
Umbria □[4]	66	43.00 N	12.30 E
Umbriatico	68	39.21 N	16.55 E
Umbroli	272c	19.11 N	73.06 E
Umbukul	164	2.30 S	150.00 E
Umbuzero, ozero ⊜	24	67.43 N	34.25 E
Ume ≃	154	16.40 S	28.26 E
Umeå	26	63.50 N	20.15 E
Umeälven ≃	24	63.47 N	20.16 E
Umedani	270	34.44 N	135.51 E
Umedpur	126	22.31 N	89.59 E
Umfolozi Game Reserve ◆[4]	158	28.19 S	31.50 E
Umfors	24	65.56 N	15.00 E
Umfreville Lake ⊜	184	50.18 N	94.45 W
Umfuli ≃	154	17.30 S	29.23 E
Umgungundhlovu ⊥	158	28.27 S	31.28 E
Umguza	154	19.25 S	27.51 E
Umhausen	64	47.08 N	10.56 E
Umhlanga Rocks	158	29.43 S	31.06 E
Umi	96	33.34 N	130.30 E
Umingan	116	15.56 N	120.50 E
Umkomaas	158	30.15 S	30.42 E
Umm ad-Daraj, Jabal ∧	132	32.19 N	35.48 E
Umm 'Ajārim ⊥[8]	142	30.50 N	32.49 E
Umm al-Abīd	146	27.31 N	15.02 E
Umm al-'Arā'is, Wādī V	146	26.26 N	13.55 E
Umm al-Arānib	146	26.08 N	14.45 E
Umm al-Birak	128	23.25 N	39.13 E
Umm al-Ḥawāyā, Jabal ∧	142	28.41 N	31.06 E
Umm al-Jimāl, Khirbat ⊥	132	32.20 N	36.22 E
Umm al-Khashab	144	17.21 N	42.32 E
Umm al-Qaywayn	128	25.35 N	55.34 E
Umm al-Qiṭṭayn	132	32.19 N	36.38 E
Umm al-Quṣūr	142	27.23 N	30.54 E
Ummanz	54	54.28 N	13.10 E
Umm Artah, Wādī V	142	28.41 N	32.37 E
Umm as-Sa'd ⊥	132	33.16 N	36.47 E
Umm Badr	140	14.14 N	27.57 E
Umm Balad, Wādī V	142	27.40 N	32.39 E
Umm Bayyū'd	140	12.05 N	31.40 E
Umm Bel	140	13.32 N	28.04 E
Umm Boim	140	11.43 N	25.57 E
Umm Dabbī	140	14.37 N	30.23 E
Umm Dam	140	13.45 N	30.59 E
Umm Dhibbān, Sūd.	140	14.14 N	29.37 E
Umm Dhibbān, Sūd.	140	15.26 N	32.51 E
Umm Digulgulaya	140	10.29 N	24.57 E
Umm Dīnār	142	30.12 N	31.04 E
Umm Durmān (Omdurman)	140	15.38 N	32.30 E
Umm el Faḥm	132	32.31 N	35.09 E
Ummeln	52	51.58 N	8.27 E
Ummendorf	54	52.09 N	11.11 E
Umm Habwah, Jabal ∧[2]	142	27.23 N	31.29 E
Umm Ḥamāṭ	132	31.02 N	35.46 E
Umm Jamālah	140	11.27 N	28.12 E
Umm Kaddādah	140	13.36 N	26.42 E
Umm Khunān	273c	29.55 N	31.15 E
Umm Khushayb, Wādī V	142	30.24 N	32.43 E
Umm Kuwaykah	140	13.00 N	32.17 E
Umm Lajj	128	25.04 N	37.13 E
Umm Marahik, Jabal ∧[2]	140	13.40 N	26.53 E
Umm Mirdi	140	18.59 N	33.32 E
Umm Mitmān ⊥[8]	142	30.41 N	32.30 E
Umm Qantur	140	14.17 N	31.22 E
Umm Qaṣr	128	30.02 N	47.56 E
Umm Qurayn	140	9.58 N	28.55 E
Umm Quṣayr	132	31.40 N	35.53 E
Umm Raqm, Jabal ∧	142	30.14 N	31.52 E
Umm Rīshah, Birkat ⊜	142	30.21 N	30.22 E
Umm Rumaylah ∓[4]	140	16.55 N	31.40 E
Umm Ruwābah	140	12.54 N	31.13 E
Umm Saggāt, Wādī V	140	15.15 N	23.12 E
Umm Saysabān, Jabal ∧	132	29.45 N	35.10 E
Umm Sayyālah	140	14.25 N	31.10 E
Umm Shalīl	140	10.51 N	23.42 E
Umm Shanqah	140	13.14 N	27.14 E
Umm Shuṭūr	140	7.17 N	33.14 E
Umm Sidr, Wādī V	142	27.54 N	32.33 E
Umm Sughra ∓[4]	140	15.03 N	27.12 E
Umm 'Umayd, Ra's ∧	142	27.50 N	32.19 E
Umm 'Umayyid, Bi'r ∓[4]	142	27.53 N	32.30 E
Umm 'Umayyid, Wādī V	142	27.37 N	32.41 E
Umm Urūmah I	128	25.46 N	36.32 E
Umm Walad	132	32.39 N	36.26 E
Umm Zaytah, Jabal ∧[2]	142	29.49 N	32.16 E
Umnak	180	53.17 N	168.20 W
Umnak Island I	180	53.25 N	168.10 W
Umnak Pass)(	180	53.20 N	167.45 W
Umnäs	24	65.24 N	16.10 E
Umniati	154	18.39 S	29.49 E
Umniati ≃	154	17.30 S	29.23 E
Um'ot, Ross.	80	54.08 N	42.42 E
Um'ot, Ross.	80	52.31 N	42.58 E
Umpferstedt	54	50.59 N	11.25 E
Umpqua ≃	202	43.42 N	124.03 W
Umpulo	152	12.38 S	17.42 E
'Umrān	144	15.50 N	43.56 E
'Umrānī, Wādī al- V	142	27.37 N	30.53 E
Umraniye	130	39.10 N	31.15 E
Umraniye ◆[8]	267b	41.01 N	29.05 E
Umred	122	20.51 N	79.20 E
Umreth	120	22.42 N	73.07 E
Umsini, Gunung ∧	164	1.22 S	133.45 E
Ŭmsŏng	98	36.56 N	127.41 E
Umstead State Park ♦	192	35.52 N	78.47 W
Umtanum Creek ≃	224	46.52 N	120.35 W
Umtata	158	31.35 S	28.47 E
Umtentweni	158	30.42 S	30.28 E
Umuahia	150	5.33 N	7.29 E
Umuarama	255	23.45 S	53.20 W
Umurbey	130	40.14 N	26.36 E
Umurlu	130	37.50 N	27.58 E
Umzimkulu	158	30.16 S	29.56 E
Umzingwani ≃	154	22.12 S	29.56 E
Umzinto	158	30.22 S	30.33 E
Una, Bra.	255	15.18 S	39.04 W
Una, India	120	20.49 N	71.02 E
Una, India	123	31.29 N	76.17 E
Una ≃	36	45.16 N	16.55 E
Una, Mount ∧	172	42.13 S	172.35 E
Una, Ribeirão ≃	287b	23.31 S	46.18 W
Unac ≃	36	44.30 N	16.09 E
Uña de Gato	196	25.58 N	99.41 W
Unadilla, Ga., U.S.	192	32.15 N	83.44 W
Unadilla, N.Y., U.S.	210	42.19 N	75.18 W
Unadilla ≃	210	42.20 N	75.25 W
Unaí	255	16.23 S	46.53 W
Unakami	94	35.46 N	140.45 E
Unalakleet	180	63.53 N	160.47 W
Unalaska	180	53.52 N	166.32 W
Unalaska Island I	180	53.45 N	166.45 W
Unanderra	170	34.27 S	150.52 E
Unango	154	12.50 S	35.20 E
Únanov	61	48.54 N	16.04 E
Unao	124	25.35 N	78.36 E
Unare ≃	246	10.03 N	65.14 W
Unauna, Pulau I	112	0.10 S	121.35 E
Unayyir, Ḥarrat al- ⊥[9]	128	25.20 N	37.45 E
'Unayzah, Ar. Su.	128	26.06 N	43.56 E
'Unayzah, Urd.	132	30.29 N	35.48 E
'Unayzah, Jabal ∧, Asia	128	32.12 N	39.18 E
'Unayzah, Jabal ∧, Urd.	132	30.30 N	35.47 E
Unazuki	94	36.49 N	137.35 E
Uncasville	207	41.26 N	72.06 W
Unchahra	124	24.23 N	80.47 E
Ŭnch'ŏn	98	38.34 N	125.26 E
Uncia	248	18.27 S	66.37 W
Uncompahgre ≃	200	38.45 N	108.06 W
Uncompahgre Peak ∧	200	38.04 N	107.28 W
Uncompahgre Plateau ⋏[1]	200	38.30 N	108.25 W
Uncukul'	84	42.42 N	46.48 E
Uncular	130	40.28 N	41.28 E
Unda	88	51.42 N	116.56 E
Unda ≃	88	51.25 N	116.05 E
Unden ⊜	40	58.47 N	14.26 E
Undenäs	40	58.39 N	14.25 E
Underberg	158	29.50 S	29.22 E
Under River	260	51.15 N	0.14 E
Undersåker	26	63.20 N	13.23 E
Underwood, In., U.S.	218	38.36 N	85.46 W
Underwood, N.D., U.S.	198	47.27 N	101.08 W
Underwood, Wa., U.S.	224	45.43 N	121.31 W
Undløse	41	55.36 N	11.35 E
Undory	80	54.37 N	48.25 E
Undu, Tanjung >	115b	10.05 S	120.51 E
Undu Point >	175g	16.08 S	179.57 W
Undva nina >	76	58.32 N	21.55 E
Unea Island I	164	4.55 S	149.10 E
Uneča	76	52.50 N	32.40 E
Uneča ≃	76	52.50 N	31.56 E
Uneiuxi ≃	246	0.34 S	64.58 W
Úněšov	60	49.53 N	13.09 E
Unga Island I	180	55.15 N	160.45 W
Ungama Bay c	154	2.45 S	40.20 E
Ungaran	115a	7.07 S	110.24 E
Ungarie	166	33.38 S	146.58 E
Ungarn → Hungary □[1]	30	47.00 N	20.00 E
Ungava, Péninsule d' >[1]	176	60.00 N	74.00 W
Ungava Bay c	176	59.30 N	67.30 W
Ungch'ŏn	98	35.07 N	128.44 E
Ungen' (Ungeny)	38	47.12 N	27.48 E
Unggi	98	42.20 N	130.24 E
Ungurkuj	88	50.27 N	106.58 E
Ungvár → Užgorod	78	48.37 N	22.18 E
Unhos	266c	38.50 N	9.07 W
Unhošt'	54	50.04 N	14.08 E
Uni	80	57.46 N	51.30 E
União	250	4.35 S	42.52 W
União da Vitória	252	26.13 S	51.05 W
União dos Palmares	250	9.10 S	36.02 W
Unica	24	62.38 N	34.38 E
Unicoi	192	36.11 N	82.20 W
Unicorn Branch ≃	208	39.15 N	75.52 W
Unidad Santa Fe ◆[8]	286a	19.23 N	99.15 W
Uniejów	30	51.58 N	18.49 E
Unieux	62	45.24 N	4.16 E
Unije, Otok I	36	44.38 N	14.15 E
Unimak Island I	180	54.50 N	164.00 W
Unimak Pass)(	180	54.35 N	164.43 W
Unini ≃	246	1.41 S	61.31 W
Unión, Arg.	252	35.09 S	65.57 W
Union, On., Can.	212	42.42 N	81.12 W
Unión, C.R.	236	8.36 N	83.03 W
Unión, Para.	252	24.48 S	56.33 W
Union, Il., U.S.	216	42.14 N	88.33 W
Union, Ia., U.S.	190	42.14 N	93.03 W
Union, Ky., U.S.	218	38.56 N	84.40 W
Union, La., U.S.	194	30.06 N	90.54 W
Union, Ms., U.S.	194	32.34 N	89.07 W
Union, Mo., U.S.	219	38.26 N	91.00 W
Union, N.J., U.S.	210	40.41 N	74.15 W
Union, Oh., U.S.	218	39.53 N	84.18 W
Union, Or., U.S.	202	45.12 N	117.51 W
Union, S.C., U.S.	192	34.42 N	81.37 W
Union, Wa., U.S.	224	47.21 N	123.06 W
Union, W.V., U.S.	192	37.35 N	80.32 W
Union □[6], In., U.S.	218	39.38 N	84.56 W
Union □[6], N.J., U.S.	208	40.40 N	74.11 W
Union □[6], Oh., U.S.	214	40.18 N	83.19 W
Union □[6], Pa., U.S.	210	40.58 N	76.54 W
Unión ◆[8]	258	34.53 S	56.08 W
Union Bay	182	49.35 N	124.53 W
Union Beach	208	40.26 N	74.10 W
Union Bridge	208	39.34 N	77.10 W
Union Center	210	42.09 N	76.04 W
Union City, Ca., U.S.	226	37.35 N	122.04 W
Union City, Ga., U.S.	192	33.35 N	84.32 W
Union City, In., U.S.	194	40.07 N	85.05 W
Union City, Mi., U.S.	216	42.04 N	85.09 W
Union City, N.J., U.S.	276	40.46 N	74.01 W
Union City, Oh., U.S.	216	40.11 N	84.48 W
Union City, Pa., U.S.	214	41.53 N	79.50 W
Union City, Tn., U.S.	194	36.25 N	89.03 W
Union City Dam ◆[6]	214	41.55 N	79.54 W
Uniondale, S. Afr.	158	33.40 S	23.08 E
Uniondale, In., U.S.	216	40.50 N	85.15 W
Uniondale, N.Y., U.S.	276	40.42 N	73.35 W
Union Dale, Pa., U.S.	210	41.43 N	75.30 W
Unión de Reyes	240p	22.48 N	81.32 W
Unión de San Antonio	234	21.06 N	101.58 W
Union des Émirats Arabes → United Arab Emirates □[1]	128	24.00 N	54.00 E
Unión de Tula	234	19.58 N	104.16 W
Union Flat Creek ≃	202	46.50 N	117.59 W
Union Gap	202	46.33 N	120.28 W
Union Grove, Tx., U.S.	222	32.34 N	94.55 W
Union Grove, Wi., U.S.	216	42.41 N	88.03 W
Unión Hidalgo	234	16.28 N	94.50 W
Union Hill	210	43.13 N	77.23 W
Union Lake	216	42.36 N	83.26 W
Union Lake ⊜, Mi., U.S.	216	42.03 N	85.11 W
Union Lake ⊜, Mi., U.S.	281	42.37 N	83.26 W
Union Lake ⊜, N.J., U.S.	208	39.25 N	75.03 W
Union Mills	216	41.29 N	86.46 W
Union Park	220	28.30 N	81.15 W
Union Pier	216	41.49 N	86.41 W
Union Point	192	33.36 N	83.04 W
Unionport, In., U.S.	218	40.07 N	85.06 W
Unionport, Oh., U.S.	214	40.21 N	80.51 W
Union Seamount ✦[3]	16	49.35 N	132.45 W
Union Springs, Al., U.S.	194	32.08 N	85.42 W
Union Springs, N.Y., U.S.	210	42.50 N	76.41 W
Union Station ◆[5], On., Can.	275b	43.39 N	79.23 W
Union Station ◆[5], Ca., U.S.	280	34.04 N	118.14 W
Union Station ◆[5], D.C., U.S.	284c	38.54 N	77.00 W
Union Station ◆[5], Il., U.S.	278	41.53 N	87.38 W
Uniontown, Al., U.S.	194	32.26 N	87.30 W
Uniontown, Ky., U.S.	194	37.46 N	87.55 W
Uniontown, Md., U.S.	208	39.35 N	77.06 W
Uniontown, Oh., U.S.	214	40.58 N	81.24 W
Uniontown, Pa., U.S.	188	39.54 N	79.44 W
Union Valley Reservoir ⊜[1]	226	38.50 N	120.26 W
Union Village	207	41.59 N	71.32 W
Unionville, On., Can.	275b	43.52 N	79.18 W
Unionville, Ct., U.S.	207	41.45 N	72.53 W
Unionville, In., U.S.	218	39.14 N	86.25 W
Unionville, Mi., U.S.	190	43.39 N	83.27 W
Unionville, Mo., U.S.	194	40.28 N	93.00 W
Unionville, N.J., U.S.	285	40.01 N	74.46 W
Unionville, N.Y., U.S.	210	41.18 N	74.34 W
Unionville, Oh., U.S.	214	41.47 N	81.00 W
Unionville, Pa., U.S.	285	39.54 N	75.44 W
Unionville Center	214	40.08 N	83.21 W
Uniopolis	216	40.36 N	84.05 W
Unipouheos Indian Reserve ◆[4]	184	53.52 N	110.21 W
Unisan	116	13.51 N	121.59 E
United	214	40.13 N	79.29 W
United Arab Emirates (Al-Imārāt al-'Arabīyah al-Muttaḥidah) □[1], Asia	118	24.00 N	54.00 E
United Arab Emirates (Al-Imārāt al-'Arabīyah al-Muttaḥidah) □[1], Asia	128	24.00 N	54.00 E
United Arab Republic → Egypt □[1]	140	27.00 N	30.00 E
United Kingdom □[1], Europe	22	54.00 N	2.00 W
United Kingdom □[1], Europe	28	54.00 N	2.00 W
United Kingdom Sovereign Base Area ■	130	35.00 N	33.45 E
United Nations Headquarters ʋ	276	40.45 N	73.58 W
United States □[1]	178	38.00 N	97.00 W
United States Air Force Academy ■	200	39.00 N	104.55 W
United States Coast Guard Academy ■	207	41.22 N	72.06 W
United States Merchant Marine Academy ʋ[2]	276	40.48 N	73.46 W
United States Military Academy ■	210	41.23 N	73.58 W
United States Naval Academy ■	208	38.59 N	76.30 W
United States Steel Corporation (Lorain Plant) ʋ[3], Oh., U.S.	279a	41.27 N	82.07 W
United States Steel Corporation ʋ[3], Pa., U.S.	279b	40.20 N	79.54 W
United States Steel Corporation Fairless Works ʋ[3]	285	40.09 N	74.45 W
Unity	184	52.27 N	109.10 W
Unity Reservoir ⊜[1]	279b	40.17 N	79.30 W
Universal City	196	29.32 N	98.17 W
Universal City ʋ[3]	280	34.09 N	118.21 W
Universal Mall ◆[9]	281	42.30 N	83.05 W
Universitaria, Ciudad ʋ[2]	266d	41.23 N	2.08 E
University	194	34.21 N	89.32 W
University City	219	38.39 N	90.19 W
University Gardens	276	40.46 N	73.43 W
University Heights, Ca., U.S.	226	37.26 N	122.12 W
University Heights, Oh., U.S.	279a	41.29 N	81.32 W
University Park, Il., U.S.	216	41.36 N	87.39 W
University Park, Md., U.S.	284c	38.58 N	76.57 W
University Park, N.M., U.S.	200	32.06 N	106.39 W
University Park, Tx., U.S.	222	32.52 N	96.47 W
University Place	224	47.14 N	122.32 W
University View	218	40.00 N	83.03 W
Unjha	120	23.48 N	72.24 E
Unkel	56	50.35 N	7.13 E
Unken	64	47.39 N	12.43 E
Unkurda	86	55.48 N	59.24 E
Unley	168b	34.57 S	138.35 E
Unna	52	51.32 N	7.41 E
'Unnāb, Jabal al- ∧	132	29.57 N	36.55 E
'Unnāb, Wādī al- V	132	30.11 N	36.39 E
Unnão	124	26.32 N	80.30 E
Uno, Canal Numero ≖	252	36.17 S	57.08 W
Uno, Ilha I	150	11.12 N	16.15 W
Unoke	94	36.43 N	136.42 E
Ŭnp'a	98	38.26 N	125.45 E
Unpenji-san ∧	96	34.02 N	133.44 E
Unqua Point >	276	40.39 N	73.26 W
Unquillo	252	31.14 S	64.19 W
Ŭnsan	98	39.25 N	126.01 E
Unseburg	54	51.56 N	11.30 E
Unserfrau → Madonna	64	46.43 N	10.52 E
Unsleben	56	50.22 N	10.15 E
Unst I	46a	60.45 N	0.53 W
Unstrut ≃	54	51.10 N	11.48 E
Un't	88	49.07 N	102.50 E
Unten	174m	26.41 N	128.00 E
Unterägeri	58	47.08 N	8.35 E
Unterbach, Dtsch.	263	51.12 N	6.54 E
Unterbäch, Schw.	58	46.17 N	7.48 E
Unter dem Wind, Inseln → Windward Islands II	238	13.00 N	61.00 W
Unterelchingen	58	48.27 N	10.07 E
Unterföhring	60	48.12 N	11.38 E
Unterfranken □[5]	56	50.10 N	10.00 E
Untergermaringen	58	47.56 N	10.40 E
Unterglottertal	58	48.03 N	7.56 E
Untergriesbach	60	48.35 N	13.40 E
Untergröningen	56	48.55 N	9.53 E
Untergrüne	263	51.22 N	7.39 E
Unterhaching	60	48.04 N	11.38 E
Unterhausen	58	48.26 N	9.16 E
Unterinntal V	64	47.24 N	11.47 E
Unterjettenberg	64	47.41 N	12.49 E
Unterlaa ◆[8]	264b	48.08 N	16.25 E
Unterlüss	52	52.50 N	10.17 E
Untermauerbach	264b	48.14 N	16.12 E
Untermünkheim	56	49.09 N	9.44 E
Untermünstertal	58	47.51 N	7.46 E
Unteröwisheim	56	49.08 N	8.40 E
Unterrath ◆[8]	263	51.16 N	6.47 E
Unterschächen	58	46.52 N	8.47 E
Unterschwaningen	56	49.04 N	10.37 E
Unterseen	58	46.41 N	7.51 E
Untertauern	64	47.18 N	13.30 E
Unterterzen	58	47.07 N	9.15 E
Unterthingau	58	47.46 N	10.31 E
Unterueckersee ⊜	54	53.17 N	13.51 E
Unteruhldingen	58	47.43 N	9.14 E
Unterwasser	58	47.12 N	9.19 E
Unterweissbach	54	50.37 N	11.10 E
Unterwellenborn	54	50.39 N	11.26 E
Unterwössen	64	47.44 N	12.27 E
Unterzeiring	61	47.15 N	14.31 E
Untraverket	40	60.25 N	17.18 E
Unuli Horog	120	35.06 N	91.51 E
Ünye	130	41.08 N	37.17 E
Unža	80	58.01 N	44.01 E
Unža ≃	80	57.20 N	43.08 E
Unzen-Amakusa-kokuritsu-kōen ♦	92	32.45 N	130.17 E
Unzen-dake ∧	92	32.45 N	130.17 E
Unže-Pavinskaja	86	58.53 N	64.02 E
Uojan	88	56.07 N	111.38 E
Uono ≃	94	37.15 N	138.53 E
Uo-shima I	96	34.11 N	133.19 E
Uozu	94	36.48 N	137.24 E
Upa ≃	76	54.02 N	36.15 E
Upala	236	10.47 N	85.02 W
Upanema	250	5.38 S	37.15 W
Upano ≃	246	2.45 S	78.12 W
Upata	246	8.01 N	62.24 W
Upatoi Creek ≃	192	32.22 N	84.58 W
Upavon	42	51.18 N	1.49 W
Ŭpchŏ-ri	98	37.53 N	125.09 E
Upchurch	260	51.23 N	0.39 E
Upemba, Lac ⊜	154	8.36 S	26.26 E
Upemba, Parc National de l' ♦	154	9.10 S	26.35 E
Upernavik	176	72.47 N	56.10 W
Upgant-Schott	52	53.30 N	7.16 E
Uphal	140	6.58 N	34.16 E
Upham	198	48.34 N	100.43 W
Up Holland	262	53.33 N	2.44 W
Uphusen	52	53.01 N	8.58 E
Upi	116	6.57 N	124.09 E
Upía ≃	246	4.18 N	72.45 W
Upington	158	28.25 S	21.15 E
Upire ≃	246	11.27 N	68.58 W
Upland, Ca., U.S.	228	34.05 N	117.38 W
Upland, In., U.S.	216	40.28 N	85.29 W
Upland, Ne., U.S.	198	40.19 N	98.54 W
Upland, Pa., U.S.	285	39.51 N	75.23 W
Upleta	120	21.44 N	70.17 E
Upnuk Lake ⊜	180	60.21 N	158.58 W
Upolu I	175a	13.55 S	171.45 W
Upolu Point >	229d	20.16 N	155.51 W
Uporovo	86	56.18 N	66.17 E
Upper □[4]	150	10.30 N	1.30 W
Upper Arlington	218	40.00 N	83.03 W
Upper Arrow Lake ⊜	182	50.30 N	117.55 W
Upper Artichoke Reservoir ⊜[1]	283	42.48 N	70.57 W
Upper Bay c	276	40.41 N	74.03 W
Upper Beaconsfield	274b	38.01 S	145.25 E
Upper Berkshire Valley	276	40.56 N	74.35 W
Upper Beverley Lake ⊜	212	44.37 N	76.05 W
Upper Black Eddy	210	40.35 N	75.07 W
Upper Blackville	186	46.39 N	65.52 W
Upper Brookville	276	40.51 N	73.34 W
Upper Canada Village ⊥	206	44.57 N	75.03 W
Upper Castlereagh	274a	33.43 S	150.40 E
Upperco	208	39.33 N	76.50 W
Upper Coliban Reservoir ⊜[1]	169	37.18 S	144.23 E
Upper Crystal Springs Reservoir ⊜[1]	282	37.30 N	122.20 W
Upper Darby	208	39.55 N	75.16 W
Upper Demerara-Berbice □[4]	246	5.30 N	58.20 W
Upper des Lacs Lake ⊜[1]	198	48.50 N	102.07 W
Upper Egypt → Aṣ-Ṣa'īd □[9]	140	26.00 N	32.00 E
Upper End	262	53.17 N	1.52 W
Upper Erskine Lake ⊜	276	41.06 N	74.15 W
Upper Fairmount	208	38.06 N	75.47 W
Upper Falls	284b	39.26 N	76.24 W
Upper Ferntree Gully	274b	37.54 S	145.19 E
Upper Fraser	182	54.07 N	121.56 W
Upper Ganga Canal ≖	124	29.57 N	78.12 E
Upper Gap)(	212	44.06 N	76.50 W
Upper Goose Lake ⊜	184	51.44 N	92.44 W
Upper Greenwood Lake	276	41.10 N	74.22 W
Upper Greenwood Lake ⊜	276	41.11 N	74.23 W
Upper Hat Creek	182	50.38 N	121.35 W
Upper Humber ≃	186	49.10 N	57.28 W
Upper Hutt	172	41.08 S	175.04 E
Upper Iowa ≃	190	43.29 N	91.14 W
Upper Island Cove	186	47.39 N	53.12 W
Upper Keechi Creek ≃	222	31.23 N	95.42 W
Upper Klamath Lake ⊜	202	42.23 N	122.55 W
Upper Lake	204	39.10 N	122.54 W
Upper Lake ⊜	204	41.44 N	120.08 W
Upper Lehigh	210	41.02 N	75.55 W
Upper Liard	180	60.02 N	128.55 W
Upper Machodoc Creek ≃	208	38.18 N	77.02 W
Upper Manitou Lake ⊜	184	49.24 N	92.48 W
Upper Marlboro	208	38.48 N	76.45 W
Upper Matecumbe Key I	220	24.55 N	80.39 W
Upper Moutere	172	41.16 S	173.00 E
Upper Musquodoboit	186	45.08 N	62.57 W
Upper Mystic Lake ⊜	283	42.27 N	71.09 W
Upper Nyack	210	41.07 N	73.55 W
Upper Peirce Reservoir ⊜[1]	271c	1.22 N	103.48 E
Upper Red Lake ⊜	198	48.10 N	94.40 W
Upper Rideau Lake ⊜	212	44.41 N	76.20 W
Upper River Rouge ≃	281	42.23 N	83.16 W
Upper Saddle River	276	41.03 N	74.05 W
Upper Saint Clair	279b	40.21 N	80.05 W
Upper Sandusky	214	40.49 N	83.16 W

Symbols in the index entries represent the broad categories identified in the key at the right. Symbols with superior numbers (⋏[1]) identify subcategories (see complete key on page *I · 1).*

Symbole im Register stellen die rechts im Schlüssel erklärten Kategorien dar. Symbole mit hochgestellten Ziffern (⋏[1]) bezeichnen Unterabteilungen einer Kategorie (vgl. vollständiger Schlüssel auf Seite *I · 1).*

Los símbolos incluídos en el texto del índice representan las grandes categorías identificadas con la clave a la derecha. Los símbolos con numeros en su parte superior (⋏[1]) identifican las subcategorías (véase la clave completa en la página *I · 1).*

Les symboles de l'index représentent les catégories indiquées dans la légende à droite. Les symboles suivis d'un indice (⋏[1]) représentent des sous-catégories (voir légende complète à la page *I · 1).*

Os símbolos incluídos no texto do índice representam as grandes categorias identificadas com a chave à direita. Os símbolos com números em sua parte superior (⋏[1]) identificam as subcategorias (veja-se a chave completa à página *I · 1).*

English	Deutsch	Español	Français	Português
∧ Mountain	Berg	Montaña	Montagne	Montanha
⋏ Mountains	Gebirge	Montañas	Montagnes	Montanhas
)(Pass	Paß	Paso	Col	Passo
V Valley, Canyon	Tal, Cañon	Valle, Cañón	Vallée, Canyon	Vale, Canhão
≚ Plain	Ebene	Llano	Plaine	Planície
> Cape	Kap	Cabo	Cap	Cabo
I Island	Insel	Isla	Île	Ilha
II Islands	Inseln	Islas	Îles	Ilhas
⊥ Other Topographic Features	Andere Topographische Objekte	Otros Elementos Topográficos	Autres données topographiques	Outros acidentes topográficos

ESPAÑOL Nombre	Página	Lat.°′	Long.°′ W = Oeste
Upper San Leandro Reservoir ⊜[1]	226	37.47 N	122.07 W
Upper Sheila	186	47.28 N	64.56 W
Upper Straits Lake ⊜	281	42.35 N	83.24 W
Upper Sumas	224	49.01 N	122.12 W
Upper Swan	168a	31.46 S	116.01 E
Upper Takaka	172	41.02 S	172.50 E
Upper Takutu-Upper Essequibo □[4]	246	3.00 N	59.00 W
Upper Tean	42	52.57 N	1.58 W
Upper Tooting ◆[8]	260	51.26 N	0.10 W
Upper Ugashik Lake ⊜	180	57.40 N	156.43 W
Upper Volta → Burkina Faso □[1]	150	13.00 N	1.30 W
Upper Windigo Lake ⊜	184	52.30 N	91.35 W
Upper Yarra Reservoir ⊜[1]	169	37.41 S	145.56 E
Upper Yosemite Fall ʟ	226	37.45 N	119.36 W
Uppingham	42	52.35 N	0.43 W
Uppland □[9]	40	59.59 N	17.48 E
Upplanda	40	60.14 N	17.44 E
Upplands Väsby	40	59.31 N	17.54 E
Uppsala	40	59.52 N	17.38 E
Uppsala Län □[6]	40	60.00 N	17.45 E
Upright, Cape ≻	180	60.17 N	172.15 W
Upsala → Uppsala	40	59.52 N	17.38 E
Upshi	120	33.50 N	77.49 E
Upshur □[6]	222	32.45 N	94.55 W
Upstart, Cape ≻	166	19.42 S	147.45 E
Upton, P.Q., Can.	206	45.39 N	72.41 W
Upton, Eng., U.K.	44	53.37 N	1.17 W
Upton, Eng., U.K.	44	53.13 N	2.52 W
Upton, Eng., U.K.	260	51.30 N	0.35 W
Upton, Eng., U.K.	262	53.23 N	3.06 W
Upton, Ky., U.S.	194	37.27 N	85.53 W
Upton, Ma., U.S.	207	42.10 N	71.36 W
Upton, Wy., U.S.	198	44.05 N	104.37 W
Upton Hill ∧[2]	169	36.52 S	145.27 E
Upton upon Severn	42	52.04 N	2.13 W
Uptown ◆[8]	278	41.58 N	87.40 W
Upwell	42	52.36 N	0.12 E
Upwey	274b	37.54 S	145.20 E
Uquía, Cerro ∧	246	4.22 N	63.46 W
Ur → Tall al-Muqayyar ⊥	128	30.57 N	46.09 E
Urabá, Golfo de ⊂	246	8.25 N	76.53 W
Urachi	84	42.21 N	47.36 E
Uracoa	246	9.00 N	62.21 W
Urad	54	52.15 N	14.45 E
Uradome-kaigan ♠	96	35.35 N	134.21 E
Urad Zhonghou Lianheqi	102	41.42 N	108.49 E
Uraga	268	35.15 N	139.43 E
Uraga-kō ⊂	268	35.14 N	139.44 E
Uraga-suidō ʉ	94	35.13 N	139.45 E
Uragawara	94	37.09 N	138.26 E
Urahoro	92a	42.48 N	143.39 E
Uraj	86	60.08 N	64.48 E
Urakan	88	58.38 N	106.01 E
Urakawa	92a	42.09 N	142.47 E
Ural ≃	72	47.00 N	51.48 E
Uralla	166	30.39 S	151.30 E
Ural Mountains → Ural'skije gory ⋏	72	60.00 N	60.00 E
Uralo-Kl'uči	88	56.03 N	97.28 E
Uralovo	78	52.11 N	33.34 E
Ural'sk	80	51.14 N	51.22 E
Ural'sk □[8]	80	50.00 N	51.00 E
Ural'skij	80	51.36 N	51.40 E
Ural'skije gory (Ural Mountains) ⋏	72	60.00 N	60.00 E
Urambo	154	5.04 S	32.03 E
Uran	272c	18.52 N	72.56 E
Urana	166	35.20 S	146.16 E
Urandangi	166	21.36 S	138.18 E
Urandi	255	14.46 S	42.38 W
Urangan	166	25.18 S	152.54 E
Urania, Austl.	168b	34.31 S	137.36 E
Urania, La., U.S.	194	31.51 N	92.17 W
Uranium City	176	59.34 N	108.36 W
Uranquinty	171b	35.12 S	147.15 E
Urarey	162	27.26 S	122.18 E
Urariá, Paraná ≃[1]	246	3.03 S	57.43 W
Uraricaá ≃	246	3.20 N	61.56 W
Uraricoera	246	3.27 N	60.59 W
Uraricoera ≃	246	3.02 N	60.30 W
Uras	71	39.42 N	8.42 E
Urasaki	174m	26.40 N	127.53 E
Urasoe	174m	26.15 N	127.43 E
Ura-T'ube	85	39.55 N	68.59 E
Uravakonda	122	14.57 N	77.16 E
Uravan	200	38.22 N	108.44 W
Urawa	94	35.51 N	139.39 E
Urayasu	94	35.39 N	139.54 E
'Urayfan Nāqah, Jabal ∧	132	30.22 N	34.27 E
'Urayyidah, Bi'r ⫪[4]	142	29.00 N	31.58 E
Urazmetovo	86	53.49 N	55.25 E
Urazovka	80	55.24 N	45.38 E
Urazovo	78	50.07 N	38.04 E
Urbach	56	50.53 N	7.05 E
Urban	224	48.38 N	122.40 W
Urbana, Ar., U.S.	194	33.09 N	92.26 W
Urbana, Il., U.S.	194	40.06 N	88.12 W
Urbana, In., U.S.	216	40.53 N	85.47 W
Urbana, Mo., U.S.	194	37.50 N	93.10 W
Urbana, Oh., U.S.	218	40.06 N	83.45 W
Urbancrest	218	39.53 N	83.05 W
Urbandale, Ia., U.S.	190	41.37 N	93.42 W
Urbandale, Mi., U.S.	216	44.09 N	85.11 W
Urbania	66	43.40 N	12.31 E
Urbanna	208	37.38 N	76.34 W
Urbano Noris	240p	20.36 N	76.08 W
Urbano Santos	250	3.12 S	43.23 W
Urbe	62	44.29 N	8.36 E
Urbe, Aeroporto dell' ⊠	267a	41.57 N	12.30 E
Urbiña, Peña ∧	34	43.01 N	5.57 W
Urbino	66	43.43 N	12.38 E
Urbisaglia	66	43.12 N	13.23 E
Urcos	248	13.42 S	71.38 W
Urda	80	48.47 N	47.26 E
Urdaneta	116	15.59 N	120.34 E
Urdenbach ◆[8]	263	51.09 N	6.53 E
Urdinarrain	252	32.41 S	58.53 W
Urdoma	24	61.47 N	48.32 E
Urdžar	86	47.05 N	81.38 E
Uré	246	7.46 N	75.31 W
Ure ≃, Fr.	50	48.45 N	0.11 E
Ure ≃, Eng., U.K.	44	54.01 N	1.12 W
Urečje	76	52.57 N	27.54 E
Ûrein	142	30.58 N	30.42 E
Ureki	84	41.59 N	41.46 E
Ureliki	180	64.23 N	173.15 W
Uren'	80	57.28 N	45.49 E
Uren ⊜	40	58.59 N	16.44 E
Urén ≃	236	9.33 N	82.55 W
Ureña	246	7.55 N	72.28 W
Urenui	172	39.00 S	174.23 E
Uréparapara I	175f	13.32 S	167.20 E
Ures	232	29.26 N	110.24 W
Ureshino, Nihon	92	33.06 N	129.59 E
Ureshino, Nihon	94	34.37 N	136.29 E
Ureterp	52	53.05 N	6.10 E
Urewera National Park ♠	172	38.40 S	177.00 E
Urft ≃	56	50.35 N	6.30 E
Urga → Ulaanbaatar, Mong.	88	47.55 N	106.53 E
Urga, Uzb.	86	43.35 N	58.30 E
Urgamal	88	48.29 N	94.20 E
Urgenč	72	41.33 N	60.38 E
Urgnano	62	45.35 N	9.41 E

FRANÇAIS Nom	Page	Lat.°′	Long.°′ W = Ouest
Urgučenskij Golec, gora ∧	88	53.30 N	118.08 E
Ürgüp	130	38.38 N	34.56 E
Urgut	85	39.23 N	67.15 E
Urho	86	46.48 N	89.45 E
Urho Kekkosen kansallispuisto ♠	24	68.10 N	28.30 E
Uri, India	123	34.05 N	74.02 E
Uri, It.	71	40.38 N	8.29 E
Uri □[3]	58	46.50 N	8.40 E
Uriah	194	31.18 N	87.30 W
Uriangato	234	20.09 N	101.11 W
Uribante ≃	246	7.18 N	70.44 W
Uribe	246	3.13 N	74.24 W
Uribelarrea	258	35.09 S	58.54 W
Uribia	246	11.43 N	72.16 W
Urich	194	38.27 N	94.00 W
Urick ◆[8]	265a	59.50 N	30.11 E
Urickij	86	53.19 N	65.34 E
Urickoje	78	52.02 N	38.11 E
Urie ≃	46	57.19 N	2.30 W
Urimba	152	10.56 S	16.32 E
Urión ≃[1]	288	34.24 S	58.31 W
Urique	232	27.13 N	107.55 W
Urique ≃	232	26.29 N	107.58 W
Uri-Rotstock ∧	58	46.52 N	8.33 E
Urituyacu ≃	246	4.45 S	75.28 W
Uriuaná ≃	250	2.47 S	50.29 W
Urizura	94	36.30 N	140.27 E
Urjala	26	61.05 N	23.32 E
Urk	52	52.39 N	5.36 E
Urkan ≃	89	53.27 N	126.56 E
Urkarach	84	42.11 N	47.38 E
Urla	130	38.18 N	26.46 E
Urlați	38	44.59 N	26.14 E
Urlingford	48	52.42 N	7.35 W
Urlings	240c	17.02 N	61.52 W
Urluk	88	50.03 N	107.55 E
Urma	126	23.10 N	86.15 E
Urman, Ross.	86	54.52 N	56.52 E
'Urmān, Sūrīy.	132	32.30 N	36.45 E
Urmary	80	55.42 N	47.57 E
Urmetan	85	39.27 N	68.17 E
Urmi ≃	89	48.44 N	134.16 E
Urmia → Orūmīyeh	128	37.33 N	45.04 E
Urmia, Lake → Orūmīyeh, Daryācheh-ye ⊜	128	37.40 N	45.30 E
Urmston	44	53.27 N	2.21 W
Urnäsch	58	47.19 N	9.17 E
Urnersee ⊜	58	46.55 N	8.37 E
Uroindo	248	21.41 S	64.41 W
Üröm	264c	47.36 N	19.01 E
Uromi	150	6.44 N	6.18 E
Uroševac	38	42.22 N	21.09 E
Uroyán, Montañas de ⋏	240m	18.14 N	67.02 W
Urožajnoje, Ross.	84	43.42 N	44.13 E
Urožajnoje, Ross.	84	44.47 N	44.55 E
Urquhart, Glen V	46	57.20 N	4.35 W
Urrao	246	6.20 N	76.11 W
Urr Water ≃	44	54.53 N	3.49 W
Ursa	219	40.04 N	91.22 W
Uršel'skij	80	55.41 N	40.13 E
Ursensollen	60	49.24 N	11.46 E
Ursk	86	54.27 N	85.24 E
Urspring	56	48.33 N	9.53 E
Urtazym	86	52.12 N	58.50 E
Urtigueira	252	24.12 S	50.55 W
Urt Moron	120	37.00 N	93.18 E
Uru ≃	255	15.24 S	49.36 W
Uruaçu	255	14.30 S	49.10 W
Uruana	255	15.30 S	49.41 W
Uruapan	204	31.38 N	116.15 W
Uruapan del Progreso	234	19.25 N	102.04 W
Urubamba	248	13.18 S	72.07 W
Urubamba ≃	248	10.44 S	73.45 W
Urubaxi ≃	246	0.31 S	64.50 W
Urubu ≃, Bra.	246	2.55 S	58.25 W
Urubu ≃, Bra.	250	10.51 S	49.47 W
Uruburetama	250	3.38 S	39.30 W
Urucará	250	2.32 S	57.45 W
Uruch ≃	84	43.28 N	44.06 E
Urucu ≃	246	4.11 S	63.36 W
Uruçuca	255	14.35 S	39.16 W
Uruçuí	250	7.14 S	44.33 W
Uruçuí, Serra da ⋏[2]	250	9.00 S	44.45 W
Urucuia ≃	255	16.08 S	45.05 W
Uruçui-preto ≃	250	7.20 S	44.38 W
Urucurituba	250	2.41 S	57.40 W
Urugi	94	35.16 N	137.42 E
Uruguaiana	252	29.45 S	57.05 W
Uruguay □[1], S.A.	244	33.00 S	56.00 W
Uruguay □[1], S.A.	252	33.00 S	56.00 W
Uruguay (Uruguai) ≃	252	34.12 S	58.18 W
Urugudejevskij Golec, gora ∧	88	51.25 N	102.09 E
Urul'ga	88	51.45 N	114.47 E
Urul'unguj ≃	88	50.24 N	119.08 E
Ur'um, ozero ⊜	86	54.33 N	78.30 E
Urumchi → Ürümqi	90	43.48 N	87.35 E
Ur'umkan ≃	88	52.35 N	120.08 E
Ürümqi	90	43.48 N	87.35 E
Urundel	252	23.33 S	64.25 W
Ur'ung-Chaja	74	72.48 N	113.23 E
Uruoca	250	3.20 S	40.32 W
Urup	84	43.52 N	41.09 E
Urup ≃	84	44.49 N	41.10 E
Urup, gora ∧	84	43.38 N	40.58 E
Urup, ostrov I	74	46.00 N	150.00 E
Urupá ≃	248	10.54 S	61.57 W
Urupadi ≃	250	3.51 S	57.21 W
Urupês	255	21.13 S	49.17 W
Ur'upino	88	52.46 N	120.00 E
Ur'upinsk	80	50.47 N	41.59 E
Ururicaia, Ilha I	250	1.30 S	52.05 W
Uruša	89	54.03 N	122.54 E
Urus-Martan	84	43.08 N	45.32 E
Urusovo	82	54.15 N	38.26 E
Urussanga	252	28.31 S	49.19 W
Urussu	80	54.36 N	53.24 E
Urutaí	255	17.28 S	48.12 W
Urutaí, Ilha I	250	1.07 S	51.17 W
Urutaú	252	25.42 S	63.04 W
Uruti	172	38.57 S	174.32 E
Uru Uru, Lago ⊜	248	18.10 S	67.10 W
Uruwira	154	6.27 S	31.21 E
Uryl'	86	49.15 N	86.20 E
Uryū-yama ∧	270	35.03 N	135.48 E
Uryv	78	51.07 N	39.10 E
Urzajbaš	80	54.43 N	54.23 E
Urziceni	38	44.43 N	26.38 E
Ürzig	56	49.59 N	7.01 E
Urzulei	71	40.06 N	9.30 E
Uržum	80	57.08 N	50.00 E
Us	261	49.06 N	1.58 E
Us ≃	86	52.07 N	92.15 E
Usa, Nihon	96	33.31 N	131.22 E
Usa, Ross.	86	54.03 N	88.45 E
Uša ≃, Bela.	76	54.00 N	28.55 E
Usa ≃, Ross.	24	65.57 N	56.55 E
Ušač' ≃	76	55.32 N	28.30 E
Ušači	76	55.11 N	28.37 E
Usada Island I	116	6.08 N	120.33 E
Usadel	54	53.26 N	13.11 E
Uşak	130	38.41 N	29.25 E
Uşak □[4]	130	38.35 N	29.20 E
Ušaki	76	59.29 N	30.59 E
Usakos	156	22.01 S	15.32 E
Ušakovka	83	48.48 N	39.48 E
Ušakovo, Ross.	86	56.22 N	75.41 E
Ušakovo, Ross.	89	51.55 N	126.34 E
Usambara Mountains ⋏	154	4.45 S	38.30 E
Usangu Flats ≡	154	8.30 S	34.15 E
Usanovy	86	59.28 N	73.24 E
Ušaral	85	43.54 N	70.42 E

PORTUGUÊS Nome	Página	Lat.°′	Long.°′ W = Oeste
Usarp Mountains ⋏	9	71.10 S	160.00 E
Úšava	60	49.46 N	12.40 E
Usaymir, Wādī al- V	273c	30.04 N	31.23 E
Ušba, gora ∧	84	43.08 N	42.40 E
Ušbas ≃	85	43.55 N	69.39 E
Usborne, Mount ∧	254	51.41 S	58.50 W
Ušće	38	43.28 N	20.37 E
Uščerpje	76	52.43 N	31.53 E
Uscio	62	44.25 N	9.10 E
Usedom	54	53.52 N	13.55 E
Usedom (Uznam) I	54	54.00 N	14.00 E
Useldange	56	49.47 N	5.59 E
Usellus	71	39.48 N	8.51 E
Usen' ≃	80	54.44 N	53.38 E
'Usfān	144	21.55 N	39.21 E
Ushaa	152	14.55 S	23.18 E
Ushant → Ouessant, Île d' I	32	48.28 N	5.05 W
Ushashi	154	2.00 S	33.57 E
'Ushayrah	144	21.46 N	40.38 E
Ushetu	154	4.10 S	32.16 E
Ushibuka	92	32.11 N	130.01 E
Ushiku	94	35.58 N	140.08 E
Ushimado	96	34.37 N	134.10 E
Ushuaia	254	54.48 S	68.18 W
Usibelli	180	63.51 N	148.47 W
Ušica ≃	78	48.35 N	27.08 E
Usingen	56	50.20 N	8.32 E
Usini	71	40.40 N	8.32 E
Usinsk	24	65.58 N	56.39 E
Usisya	154	11.09 S	34.11 E
Usk, B.C., Can.	182	54.38 N	128.25 W
Usk, Wales, U.K.	42	51.43 N	2.54 W
Usk, Wa., U.S.	202	48.18 N	117.16 W
Usk ≃	42	51.36 N	2.58 W
Uškanij kr'až ∧	180	65.15 N	178.35 E
Uskedal	26	59.56 N	5.52 E
Usken ⊜	40	59.39 N	15.01 E
Uskovo	265b	55.56 N	37.19 E
Üsküb → Skopje	38	41.59 N	21.26 E
Uskumru ◆[8]	267b	41.12 N	29.01 E
Uslar	52	51.39 N	9.38 E
Úslava ≃	60	49.45 N	13.24 E
Usmajac	234	19.52 N	103.34 W
Usman', Ross.	76	52.02 N	39.44 E
Usman', Ross.	89	51.29 N	134.00 E
Usmanka	80	52.49 N	51.42 E
Usmānpur ◆[8]	272a	28.41 N	77.15 E
Usmas ezers ⊜	76	57.11 N	22.10 E
Usmat	85	39.44 N	67.40 E
Usmate Velate	62	45.39 N	9.21 E
Ušmunskij Golec, gora ∧	89	51.40 N	118.35 E
Usmyn'	76	55.52 N	31.09 E
Ušna ≃	80	55.43 N	42.12 E
Usoke	154	5.06 S	32.20 E
Usolje, Ross.	80	53.23 N	49.05 E
Usolje, Ross.	82	56.49 N	38.40 E
Usolje, Ross.	86	59.25 N	56.41 E
Usolje-Sibirskoje	88	52.47 N	103.38 E
Usolka ≃	86	57.47 N	94.35 E
Uson	116	12.13 N	123.47 E
Usoro	150	5.34 N	6.13 E
Usovo	265b	55.44 N	37.13 E
Uspallata	252	32.35 S	69.20 W
Uspanapa ≃	234	17.58 N	94.29 W
Uspenka, Kaz.	86	52.54 N	77.25 E
Uspenka, Ross.	80	50.38 N	41.28 E
Uspenka, Ukr.	83	48.23 N	39.10 E
Uspenka, Ukr.	83	47.43 N	38.42 E
Uspenovka	80	51.16 N	53.36 E
Uspenskij	86	48.42 N	72.40 E
Uspenskoje	82	55.43 N	37.04 E
Usri ≃	126	24.03 N	86.23 E
Ušsaj	86	43.50 N	58.53 E
Ussassai	71	39.49 N	9.23 E
Usseglio	62	45.14 N	7.13 E
Ussel	32	45.33 N	2.18 E
Ussel ≃	56	48.44 N	11.04 E
Usshers Creek ≃	284a	43.03 N	79.02 W
Usson-en-Forez	62	45.23 N	3.56 E
Ussure	154	4.39 S	34.23 E
Ussuri (Wusuli) ≃	89	48.27 N	135.04 E
Ussurijsk	89	43.48 N	131.59 E
Ūst	123	36.56 N	72.53 E
Usta	80	57.26 N	45.40 E
Usta ≃	80	56.53 N	45.28 E
Ust'-Ajsk	86	56.07 N	57.40 E
Ustaoset	26	60.30 N	8.04 E
Ustaritz	32	43.24 N	1.27 W
Ust'-Bagar'ak	86	56.08 N	61.52 E
Ust'-Barguzin	88	53.27 N	108.59 E
Ust'-Belaja	74	65.30 N	173.20 E
Ust'-Bol'šereck	74	52.48 N	156.14 E
Ust'-B'ur'	86	53.49 N	90.15 E
Ust'-Buzulukskaja	80	50.12 N	42.10 E
Ust'-Bystr'anskaja	80	47.49 N	41.03 E
Ust'-Čaja	86	58.17 N	82.38 E
Ust'-Čaryšskaja Pristan'	86	52.24 N	83.39 E
Ust'-Čaun	74	68.47 N	170.30 E
Ust'-Choperskaja	80	49.36 N	42.24 E
Ust'-Čil'ma	24	65.27 N	52.06 E
Ust'-Čižapka	86	59.02 N	79.37 E
Ust'-Čorna	78	48.18 N	23.56 E
Ust'-Čornaja	88	52.57 N	119.02 E
Ust'-Dolyssy	76	56.09 N	29.39 E
Ust'-Doneckij	80	47.39 N	40.52 E
Ust'-Džegutinskaja	84	44.05 N	41.58 E
Úštěk	54	50.36 N	14.20 E
Ust'-Elegest	88	51.32 N	94.05 E
Uster	58	47.21 N	8.43 E
Ust'-Gr'aznucha	80	50.28 N	45.26 E
Ustica	70	38.42 N	13.11 E
Ustica, Isola di I	70	38.42 N	13.11 E
Ust'-Il'a	88	50.25 N	113.41 E
Ust'-Ilga	88	55.00 N	105.02 E
Ust'-Ilimsk	88	58.00 N	102.39 E
Ust'-Ilimskoje vodochranilišče ⊜[1]	88	57.00 N	102.15 E
Ustilug	78	50.51 N	24.09 E
Ust'-Ilyč	24	62.32 N	56.41 E
Ústí nad Labem	54	50.40 N	14.02 E
Ústí nad Orlicí	30	49.58 N	16.24 E
Ustinovka, Ukr.	78	47.57 N	32.32 E
Ustinovka, Ukr.	83	48.49 N	38.34 E
Ust'-Išim	86	57.44 N	71.10 E
Ust'-Izes	86	55.56 N	76.56 E
Ust'-Ižora	265a	59.48 N	30.36 E
Ustja ≃	24	61.30 N	42.36 E
Ust'-Javron'ga	24	63.25 N	44.21 E
Ustje, Ross.	76	60.49 N	32.49 E
Ustje, Ross.	76	59.38 N	39.43 E
Ustje, Ross.	80	57.47 N	39.47 E
Ustje, Ross.	82	55.16 N	36.20 E
Ustje, Ross.	86	57.46 N	94.42 E
Ustje-Kirovskoje	76	58.45 N	35.55 E
Ustka	30	54.35 N	16.50 E
Ust'-K'achta	88	50.32 N	106.16 E
Ust'-Kajtym	86	57.23 N	95.28 E
Ust'-Kalmanka	86	52.07 N	83.19 E
Ust'-Kamčatsk	74	56.15 N	162.30 E
Ust'-Kamenogorsk	86	49.58 N	82.38 E
Ust'-Kan, Ross.	86	50.57 N	84.45 E
Ust'-Kan, Ross.	86	56.31 N	93.48 E
Ust'-Karenga	88	54.26 N	116.30 E
Ust'-Karsk	88	52.43 N	118.48 E
Ust'-Katav	86	54.56 N	58.10 E
Ust'-Kemčug	86	57.13 N	90.30 E
Ust'-Kil'mez'	80	56.57 N	50.30 E
Ust'-Kišert'	86	57.22 N	57.15 E
Ust'-Koksa	86	50.18 N	85.36 E
Ust'-Kujda	74	70.01 N	135.36 E
Ust'-Kulom	24	61.42 N	53.40 E
Ust'-Kurd'um	80	51.39 N	46.12 E
Ust'-Kurenga	86	57.27 N	75.34 E
Ust'-Kut	88	56.46 N	105.40 E
Ust'-Labinsk	78	45.13 N	39.42 E

Ust'-Lubija	88	52.36 N	120.16 E
Ust'-Luga	76	59.40 N	28.15 E
Ust'-Lyža	24	65.44 N	56.36 E
Ust'-Maja	74	60.25 N	134.32 E
Ust'-Manja	72	62.11 N	60.20 E
Ust'-Naryk	86	54.20 N	87.25 E
Ust'-Nemda	80	57.03 N	50.22 E
Ust'-Nera	74	64.34 N	143.12 E
Ust'-Niman	89	51.23 N	132.42 E
Ust'-N'ukža	88	56.34 N	121.37 E
Uštobe	86	45.16 N	78.00 E
Ust'-Omčug	74	61.09 N	149.38 E
Ust'-Ordynskij	88	52.48 N	104.45 E
Ust'-Ordynskij Burjatskij Avtonomnyj Okrug □[8]	88	53.30 N	104.00 E
Ust'-Oz'ornaja	88	50.42 N	117.06 E
Ust'-Oz'ornoje	86	58.54 N	87.48 E
Ust'-Paden'ga	24	61.53 N	42.36 E
Ust'-Pečengskoje	76	59.47 N	42.37 E
Ust'-Pinega	24	64.11 N	41.56 E
Ust'-Pit	86	58.59 N	91.44 E
Ust'-Pogožje	80	49.28 N	44.38 E
Ustreka	76	58.38 N	34.33 E
Ust'-Reki	24	62.12 N	46.45 E
Ustroń	30	49.43 N	18.49 E
Ustrzyki Dolne	30	49.26 N	22.37 E
Ust'-Šara	76	60.13 N	33.57 E
Ust'-Ščerbedino	80	51.53 N	42.52 E
Ust'-Slav'anka ◆[8]	265a	59.50 N	30.32 E
Ust'-Šonoša	24	61.10 N	41.18 E
Ust'-Sumy	86	54.48 N	80.26 E
Ust'-Tara	86	56.41 N	74.39 E
Ust'-Tarka	86	55.34 N	75.42 E
Ust'-Tašino	89	51.07 N	129.35 E
Ust'-Tygda	89	52.35 N	127.53 E
Ust'-Tym	86	59.26 N	80.08 E
Ust'-Tyrma	89	50.29 N	131.18 E
Ust'uckoje	76	58.32 N	35.20 E
Ust'-Uda	88	54.10 N	103.03 E
Üstükran	130	39.16 N	41.17 E
Ust'-Ulagan	86	50.38 N	87.58 E
Ust'-Umal'ta	89	51.39 N	133.18 E
Ust'-Undurga	89	53.07 N	118.04 E
Ust'-Unja	24	61.48 N	57.48 E
Ust'-Urgal	89	51.09 N	132.33 E
Ust'urt, plato ⋏[1]	72	43.00 N	56.00 E
Ust'-Us	86	52.07 N	92.17 E
Ust'-Usa	24	65.59 N	56.54 E
Ust'-Uza	80	52.58 N	45.17 E
Ust'užna	76	58.51 N	36.26 E
Ust'-Vichoreva	88	56.47 N	101.24 E
Ust'-Voja	24	64.27 N	57.40 E
Ust'-Vyjskaja	24	62.57 N	46.41 E
Ust'-Vym'	24	62.14 N	50.24 E
Ust'-Zaza	88	53.10 N	111.40 E
Ust'-Žuja	88	58.48 N	118.12 E
Usu	86	44.27 N	84.37 E
Usuchčaj	84	41.25 N	47.53 E
Usuda	94	36.12 N	138.29 E
Usugli	88	52.39 N	115.16 E
Usui	96	33.34 N	130.42 E
Usuki	96	33.08 N	131.49 E
Usuki-wan ⊂	96	33.10 N	131.52 E
Usulután	236	13.21 N	88.27 W
Usumacinta ≃	232	18.24 N	92.38 W
Usumbura → Bujumbura	154	3.23 S	29.22 E
Ušumun	89	52.49 N	126.27 E
Ušur	80	57.47 N	52.58 E
Usuyŏng	98	34.35 N	126.18 E
Usu-zan ∧	92a	42.32 N	140.51 E
Usv'aty	76	55.45 N	30.45 E
Uta	71	39.17 N	8.57 E
Utah □[3], U.S.	178	39.30 N	111.30 W
Utah □[3], U.S.	200	39.30 N	111.30 W
Utah Lake ⊜	200	40.13 N	111.49 W
Utajärvi	26	64.45 N	26.23 E
Utamba	154	1.06 S	26.50 E
Utamboni ≃	152	1.00 N	9.48 E
Utan	115b	8.24 S	117.07 E
Utano	94	34.28 N	135.59 E
Utapi	156	17.31 S	15.08 E
Utashinai	92a	43.31 N	142.03 E
Utata	88	50.51 N	102.45 E
'Utaybah, Buhayrat al- ⊜	132	33.32 N	36.37 E
Ute	198	42.03 N	95.42 W
Ute ≃	248	15.28 S	65.05 W
Ute Creek ≃	196	35.21 N	103.50 W
Utegi	154	1.20 S	34.35 E
Utelle	62	43.55 N	7.15 E
Utembo ≃	152	17.06 S	22.01 E
Ute Mountain Indian Reservation ◆[4]	200	37.10 N	108.35 W
Utena	76	55.30 N	25.36 E
Utengule	154	8.57 S	35.50 E
Ute Reservoir ⊜[1]	196	36.21 N	103.31 W
Úterský potok ≃	60	49.48 N	13.06 E
Utersum	30	54.43 N	8.24 E
Utete	154	7.59 S	38.47 E
Utevka	80	52.57 N	50.58 E
Utfort	263	51.28 N	6.38 E
Uthai Thani	110	15.22 N	100.03 E
Uthal	120	25.48 N	66.37 E
U Thong	110	14.22 N	99.54 E
Uthumphon Phisai	110	15.05 N	104.08 E
Utiariti	248	13.02 S	58.17 W
Utica, Il., U.S.	216	41.20 N	89.00 W
Utica, In., U.S.	218	38.20 N	85.39 W
Utica, Ks., U.S.	198	38.38 N	100.10 W
Utica, Mi., U.S.	214	42.37 N	83.02 W
Utica, Ms., U.S.	194	32.06 N	90.37 W
Utica, Ne., U.S.	198	40.54 N	97.21 W
Utica, N.Y., U.S.	210	43.06 N	75.13 W
Utica, Oh., U.S.	214	40.14 N	82.27 W
Utica, Pa., U.S.	214	41.26 N	79.58 W
Utica → Utique ⊥	36	37.03 N	10.03 E
Utiel	34	39.34 N	1.12 W
Utikoomak Lake Indian Reserve ◆[4]	182	55.57 N	115.30 W
Utikuma Lake ⊜	182	55.50 N	115.25 W
Utila	236	16.06 N	86.54 W
Utila, Isla de I	236	16.06 N	86.56 W
Utinga	287b	23.38 S	46.32 W
Utinga ≃	255	12.34 S	41.20 W
Utique	36	37.03 N	10.03 E
Utique ⊥	36	37.03 N	10.03 E
Utirik I[1]	14	11.15 N	169.48 E
Utlängan I	26	56.01 N	15.47 E
Utl'ukskij liman ⊂[1]	78	46.15 N	35.12 E
Ut'ma	86	57.35 N	71.45 E
Utmānzai	123	34.11 N	71.46 E
Uto	92	32.41 N	130.40 E
Utö I	40	58.56 N	18.16 E
Utokota	156	17.50 S	20.22 E
Utonde	152	1.56 N	9.49 E
Utopia, Austl.	162	22.14 S	134.33 E
Utopia, Tx., U.S.	196	29.37 N	99.32 W
Utorgoš	76	58.17 N	30.15 E
Utraula	124	27.19 N	82.25 E
Utrecht, Ned.	52	52.05 N	5.08 E
Utrecht, S. Afr.	158	27.38 S	30.20 E
Utrecht □[4]	52	52.05 N	5.08 E
Utrera	34	37.11 N	5.47 W
Utroja ≃	76	57.23 N	28.09 E
Utsaladdy	224	48.15 N	122.30 W
Utsira	26	59.18 N	4.54 E
Utsjoki	24	69.53 N	27.00 E
Utsumi	96	34.21 N	133.17 E
Utsunomiya	94	36.33 N	139.52 E
Utta	80	46.23 N	46.01 E
Uttamapālaiyam	122	9.48 N	77.20 E
Uttaradit	110	17.38 N	100.06 E
Uttarkāshi	120	30.44 N	78.27 E
Uttarpara-Kotrung	272b	22.40 N	88.21 E
Uttar Pradesh □[3]	120	27.00 N	80.00 E
Uttendorf, Öst.	60	48.09 N	13.07 E

Uttendorf, Öst.	64	47.17 N	12.34 E
Uttenweiler	58	48.09 N	9.36 E
Ütterlingsen	263	51.15 N	7.45 E
Utting	60	48.02 N	11.05 E
Uttlesford □[8]	260	51.47 N	0.19 E
Uttoxeter	42	52.54 N	1.51 W
Utu	154	1.45 S	27.54 E
Utuado	240m	18.16 N	66.42 W
Utukok ≃	180	70.04 N	162.18 W
Utulei	174u	14.17 S	170.40 W
Utunomiya → Utsunomiya	94	36.33 N	139.52 E
Utupua I	14	11.16 S	166.29 E
Utva ≃	86	51.28 N	52.40 E
Utzenstorf	58	47.08 N	7.33 E
Uudenmaan lääni □[4]	26	60.30 N	25.00 E
Uulu	76	58.17 N	24.35 E
Üür ≃	88	50.18 N	101.54 E
Uurainen	26	62.30 N	25.27 E
Uusikaarlepyy (Nykarleby)	26	63.32 N	22.32 E
Uusikaupunki (Nystad)	26	60.48 N	21.25 E
Uusimaa ◆[1]	26	60.30 N	25.00 E
Uvá, Bra.	255	15.53 S	50.25 W
Uva, Ross.	80	56.59 N	52.13 E
Uvá ≃	246	3.57 N	68.24 W
Uvalda	192	33.41 N	83.25 W
Uvalde	196	29.12 N	99.47 W
Úvaly	54	50.03 N	14.47 E
Uvån ≃	40	60.01 N	13.37 E
Uvaroviči	76	52.36 N	30.44 E
Uvarovka	76	55.32 N	35.37 E
Uvarovo	80	51.59 N	42.15 E
Uvas Creek ≃	226	36.58 N	121.33 W
Uvas Reservoir ⊜[1]	226	37.05 N	121.42 W
Uvat	86	59.09 N	68.54 E
'Uvda, Biq'at V	132	29.57 N	34.57 E
Uvdal	26	60.16 N	8.44 E
Uvel'skij	86	54.26 N	61.22 E
Uvernet	62	44.22 N	6.38 E
Uvero, Punta ≻	241s	11.21 N	68.41 W
Uvinza	154	5.06 S	30.22 E
Uvira	154	3.24 S	29.08 E
Uvod' ≃	80	56.26 N	41.26 E
Uvongo Beach	158	30.51 S	30.23 E
Uvs □[4]	86	50.00 N	92.00 E
Uvs nuur ⊜	74	50.20 N	92.45 E
Uvworé ≻	175f	18.47 S	169.16 E
Uwa	96	33.20 N	132.30 E
Uwajima	96	33.13 N	132.34 E
Uwa-kai ⫪[2]	96	33.15 N	132.15 E
'Uwaybid, Jabal ∧	142	30.06 N	32.09 E
Uwayl	140	8.46 N	27.24 E
'Uwaynāt	130	35.43 N	36.05 E
'Uwaynāt, Jabal al- ∧	140	21.54 N	24.58 E
'Uwayrid, Harrat al- ▴[9]	128	27.00 N	37.30 E
Uwchland	285	40.05 N	75.42 W
Uwi, Pulau I	112	1.05 N	107.24 E
Uxbridge, On., Can.	212	44.06 N	79.07 W
Uxbridge, Ma., U.S.	207	42.04 N	71.37 W
Uxbridge ◆[8]	260	51.33 N	0.29 W
Uxmal ⊥	232	20.22 N	89.46 W
Uyak Bay ⊂	180	57.36 N	153.57 W
Uyama	270	34.50 N	135.41 E
U-yin	110	22.53 N	95.13 E
Uyo	150	5.03 N	7.56 E
Uyu ≃	110	24.51 N	94.57 E
Uyuni	248	20.28 S	66.50 W
Uyuni, Salar de ≡	248	20.20 S	67.42 W
Už (Uh) ≃, Europe	30	48.34 N	22.00 E
Už ≃, Ukr.	78	51.15 N	30.12 E
Uza ≃, Ross.	76	57.48 N	29.31 E
Uza ≃, Ross.	80	53.02 N	45.18 E
Užanicha	86	54.41 N	81.02 E
Uzas	86	57.04 N	76.55 E
Užava	76	57.14 N	21.27 E
'Uzaym, Nahr al- ≃	128	34.01 N	44.19 E
Uzbekistan □[1]	72	41.00 N	64.00 E
Uzboj ≃	128	39.30 N	55.00 E
Uzda	76	53.27 N	27.13 E
Uzdin	38	45.12 N	20.38 E
Uzerche	32	45.26 N	1.34 E
Uzès	62	44.01 N	4.25 E
Uzgen	85	40.46 N	73.18 E
Užgorod	78	48.37 N	22.18 E
Užice	38	43.51 N	19.51 E
Uzin	78	49.50 N	30.24 E
Uzkij Lug	88	50.42 N	108.01 E
Uzkoje ◆[8]	265b	55.37 N	37.32 E
Uzlovaja	76	53.59 N	38.10 E
Uzmorje	80	51.15 N	45.55 E
Uznach	58	47.14 N	9.00 E
Uznam (Usedom) I	54	54.00 N	14.00 E
Uzola ≃	80	56.32 N	43.38 E
Uz'ukovo	80	53.38 N	49.43 E
Üzümlü, Tür.	130	37.32 N	31.37 E
Üzümlü, Tür.	130	36.44 N	29.14 E
Uzun	85	38.22 N	68.03 E
Uzun Ada I	130	38.28 N	26.42 E
Uzunagač, Kaz.	85	43.13 N	76.20 E
Uzunagač, Kaz.	85	43.36 N	76.19 E
Uzunbulak	86	45.23 N	84.06 E
Uzunca ≃	267b	40.58 N	28.50 E
Uzunköprü	130	41.16 N	26.41 E
Uzunkuduk	85	40.33 N	67.11 E
Uzunkuyu	130	38.17 N	26.33 E
Uzunovo	82	54.32 N	38.37 E
Užur	86	55.20 N	89.50 E
Užventis	76	55.47 N	22.39 E
V			
Vä	26	55.59 N	14.05 E
Vaajakoski	26	62.16 N	25.54 E
Vääksy	26	61.11 N	25.33 E
Vaal ≃	158	29.04 S	23.38 E
Vaala	26	64.26 N	26.48 E
Vaaldam ⊜[1]	158	26.55 S	28.12 E
Vaalhartsdam ⊜[1]	158	28.06 S	24.55 E
Vaalkop ∧	158	31.21 S	26.31 E
Vaals	56	50.46 N	6.01 E
Vaalserberg ∧[2]	56	50.45 N	6.01 E
Vaalwater	156	24.20 S	28.03 E
Vaasa (Vasa)	26	63.06 N	21.36 E
Vaasan lääni □[4]	26	63.00 N	23.00 E
Vaassen	52	52.17 N	5.57 E
Vabalninkas	76	55.58 N	24.45 E
Vabkent	128	40.02 N	64.30 E
Vác	30	47.47 N	19.08 E
Vaca, Bol.	248	19.54 S	63.48 W
Vača, Ross.	80	55.48 N	42.46 E
Vaca, Mount ∧	226	38.24 N	122.06 W
Vacacaí ≃	252	29.55 S	53.06 W
Vaca Key I	220	24.43 N	81.04 W
Vacaria	252	28.30 S	50.56 W
Vacaria ≃, Bra.	255	16.39 S	42.45 W
Vacaria ≃, Bra.	255	21.55 S	53.59 W
Vacas, Arroyo de las ≃	258	34.00 S	58.18 W
Vacaville	226	38.21 N	121.59 W
Vacca, Kaap ≻	158	34.21 S	21.53 E
Vaccarès, Étang de ⊂	62	43.32 N	4.34 E
Vach ≃	74	60.45 N	76.45 E
Vacha	56	50.50 N	10.01 E
Vache, Île à I	238	18.05 N	73.38 W
Vaches, Île aux I	275a	45.41 N	73.40 W
Vaches, Rivière aux ≃	206	46.02 N	72.46 W
Vachrušev	89	48.59 N	142.58 E
Vachruševo	83	48.10 N	38.46 E
Vachš ≃	72	37.06 N	68.18 E
Vachšskij chrebet ⋏	85	38.35 N	69.45 E
Vachtan	80	57.58 N	46.42 E
Vači	84	42.05 N	47.13 E

Vacía Talega, Punta ≻	240m	18.27 N	65.54 W
Vacoas	157c	20.18 S	57.29 E
Vad, Ross.	80	55.32 N	44.12 E
Vad, Sve.	40	60.02 N	15.39 E
Vad ≃	80	54.33 N	42.37 E
Väddö I	40	60.00 N	18.50 E
Väden	38	45.22 N	27.56 E
Vader	224	46.24 N	122.57 W
Vadheim	26	61.13 N	5.49 E
Vādi	272c	18.56 N	73.06 E
Vadino	76	55.16 N	33.16 E
Vadinsk	80	53.43 N	43.04 E
Vadnagar	120	23.47 N	72.38 E
Vadodara	122	22.18 N	73.12 E
Vado de Cecillos	200	31.05 N	105.50 W
Vado de Piedra	196	29.50 N	104.40 W
Vado Hondo	200	31.09 N	111.22 W
Vado Ligure	62	44.17 N	8.27 E
Vadret, Piz ∧	58	46.41 N	9.57 E
Vadsbro	40	58.58 N	16.36 E
Vadsø	24	70.05 N	29.46 E
Vadstena	26	58.27 N	14.54 E
Vaduz	58	47.09 N	9.31 E
Vadvetjåkko Nationalpark ♠	24	68.35 N	18.20 E
Væggerløse	41	54.42 N	11.56 E
Værøy I	24	67.40 N	12.39 E
Vaga ≃	24	62.48 N	42.56 E
Vagaj	86	57.56 N	69.01 E
Vagaj ≃	86	57.59 N	69.01 E
Vågåmo	26	61.53 N	9.06 E
Vaganski Vrh ∧	36	44.22 N	15.31 E
Vaggeryd	26	57.30 N	14.07 E
Vaghena Island I	175e	7.26 S	157.46 E
Vaglia	66	43.54 N	11.17 E
Vaglio Basilicata	68	40.40 N	15.55 E
Vagney	58	48.01 N	6.43 E
Vagnhärad	40	58.55 N	17.30 E
Vagues	258	34.19 S	59.26 W
Váh ≃	30	47.55 N	18.00 E
Vahrn → Varna	64	46.44 N	11.38 E
Vaiano	66	43.58 N	11.07 E
Vaich, Loch ⊜	46	57.43 N	4.46 W
Vaiden	194	33.19 N	89.44 W
Vaigai ≃	122	9.21 N	79.00 E
Vaigat ʉ	176	70.11 N	53.00 W
Vaihingen an der Enz	56	48.56 N	8.58 E
Vaijāpur	122	19.55 N	74.44 E
Vaikam	122	9.46 N	76.24 E
Väike-Maarja	76	59.08 N	26.15 E
Väike Pakri I	76	59.20 N	24.00 E
Vail, Co., U.S.	200	39.38 N	106.22 W
Vail, Ia., U.S.	198	42.03 N	95.11 W
Vaila I	46a	60.12 N	1.37 W
Vailala ≃	164	7.25 S	145.25 E
Vaileka	175g	17.23 S	178.09 E
Vail Lake ⊜[1]	228	33.29 N	116.58 W
Vailly-sur-Aisne	50	49.25 N	3.31 E
Vailly-sur-Sauldre	50	47.27 N	2.39 E
Vail Mills	210	43.03 N	74.13 W
Vailoatai	174u	14.22 S	170.47 W
Vail Point ≻	212	44.43 N	80.45 W
Vails Gate	210	41.27 N	74.04 W
Vaimali	175f	16.34 S	168.11 E
Vaiņode	76	56.26 N	21.50 E
Vaiont, Lago di ⊜	64	46.16 N	12.22 E
Vaippār ≃	122	9.01 N	78.17 E
Vair ≃	58	48.27 N	5.42 E
Vairano Scalo	68	41.20 N	14.08 E
Vairao	174s	17.47 S	149.17 W
Vaires-sur-Marne	261	48.52 N	2.39 E
Vaison-la-Romaine	62	44.14 N	5.04 E
Vaitahu	174x	9.56 S	139.06 W
Vaîte	58	47.35 N	5.44 E
Vaitogi	174u	14.21 S	170.44 W
Vaitown	150	6.52 N	10.52 W
Vaitupu I	14	7.28 S	178.41 E
Vaja ≃	80	57.27 N	46.00 E
Vajgač	72	70.25 N	58.46 E
Vajgač, ostrov I	72	70.00 N	59.30 E
Vajk'	84	39.40 N	45.30 E
Vakaga □[5]	146	10.00 N	22.30 E
Vakaga ≃	146	9.48 N	21.32 E
Vākhān ≃	120	37.00 N	72.40 E
Vākhān ◆[1]	120	37.00 N	73.00 E
Vaklan	272c	19.07 N	73.06 E
Vaksdal	26	60.29 N	5.44 E
Vala ≃	80	56.59 N	51.16 E
Valaam	24	61.23 N	30.57 E
Valaam, ostrov I	26	61.22 N	30.57 E
Vålådalen	26	63.10 N	12.57 E
Valadeces	196	26.14 N	98.40 W
Valadim	154	12.22 S	36.10 E
Valais (Wallis) □[3]	58	46.10 N	7.30 E
Val-Alain	206	46.24 N	71.45 W
Valamaz	80	57.32 N	52.05 E
Valandovo	38	41.19 N	22.34 E
Valangin	58	47.01 N	6.54 E
Valap	272c	19.03 N	73.08 E
Valare, Baie ⊂	174s	17.31 S	149.46 W
Valašské Klobouky	30	49.08 N	18.01 E
Valašské Meziříčí	30	49.28 N	17.58 E
Valatie	210	42.24 N	73.40 W
Vala Ull	272c	19.02 N	73.07 E
Val-Bélair	206	46.51 N	71.26 W
Valbella	58	46.45 N	9.33 E
Vålberg	26	59.24 N	13.12 E
Valbert	56	51.07 N	7.44 E
Valbo	40	60.40 N	17.04 E
Valbondione	64	46.02 N	10.00 E
Valbonnais	62	44.54 N	5.54 E
Valbrona	58	45.53 N	9.18 E
Valcanuta ◆[8]	267a	41.53 N	12.25 E
Vâlcĕdrâm	38	43.42 N	23.27 E
Valcheta	254	40.42 S	66.09 W
Valchetta ≃	267a	41.58 N	12.30 E
Valchiusella	62	45.32 N	7.42 E
Valcivières	62	45.35 N	3.48 E
Valcourt	206	45.29 N	72.18 W
Valdagno	64	45.39 N	11.18 E
Valdahon	58	47.09 N	6.21 E
Valdai Hills → Valdajskaja vozvyšennost' ⋏[2]	76	57.00 N	33.30 E
Valdaj, Ross.	24	63.26 N	35.30 E
Valdaj, Ross.	76	57.59 N	33.14 E
Valdajskaja vozvyšennost' ⋏[2]	24	57.00 N	33.30 E
Valdarno V	66	43.35 N	11.30 E
Valdavia ≃	34	42.24 N	4.16 W
Val-David	206	46.01 N	74.12 W
Valdebeba, Arroyo de ≃	266a	41.23 N	2.10 E
Valdeblore	62	44.04 N	7.12 E
Val-de-Cães	250	1.23 S	48.29 W
Valdecañas, Embalse de ⊜[1]	34	39.45 N	5.30 W
Valdelândia	255	15.11 S	50.02 W
Val-de-Marne □[5]	261	48.47 N	2.29 E
Valdemārpils	76	57.22 N	22.35 E
Valdemarsvik	26	58.12 N	16.36 E
Valdepeñas	34	38.46 N	3.23 W
Valderaduey ≃	34	41.31 N	5.42 W
Valderas	34	42.05 N	5.27 W
Valderice	70	38.03 N	12.38 E
Valderrama	116	11.00 N	122.08 E
Valderrobres	34	40.53 N	0.09 E
Valders	190	44.03 N	87.53 W
Valdés, Península ≻[1]	254	42.30 S	64.00 W
Val-des-Bois	188	45.54 N	75.35 W
Valdese	192	35.44 N	81.33 W
Valdes Island I	224	49.04 N	123.38 W
Valdéz, Ec.	246	1.15 N	79.00 W
Valdez, Ak., U.S.	180	61.07 N	146.16 W
Valdieri	62	44.17 N	7.24 E
Val-d'Isère	62	45.27 N	6.59 E
Valdivia, Chile	254	39.48 S	73.14 W
Valdivia, Col.	246	7.11 N	75.27 W

≃ River	Fluß	Río	Rivière	Rio
≋ Canal	Kanal	Canal	Canal	Canal
ʟ Waterfall, Rapids	Wasserfall, Stromschnellen	Cascada, Rápidos	Chute d'eau, Rapides	Cascata, Rápidos
ʉ Strait	Meeresstraße	Estrecho	Détroit	Estreito
⊂ Bay, Gulf	Bucht, Golf	Bahía, Golfo	Baie, Golfe	Baía, Golfo
⊜ Lake, Lakes	See, Seen	Lago, Lagos	Lac, Lacs	Lago, Lagos
≡ Swamp	Sumpf	Pantano	Marais	Pântano
⍓ Ice Features, Glacier	Eis- und Gletscherformen	Accidentes Glaciales	Formes glaciaires	Acidentes glaciares
⫪ Other Hydrographic Features	Andere Hydrographische Objekte	Otros Elementos Hidrográficos	Autres données hydrographiques	Outros acidentes hidrográficos

✦ Submarine Features	Untermeerische Objekte	Accidentes Submarinos	Formes de relief sous-marin	Acidentes submarinos
□ Political Unit	Politische Einheit	Unidad Politica	Entité politique	Unidade política
⚘ Cultural Institution	Kulturelle Institution	Institución Cultural	Institution culturelle	Instituição cultural
⊥ Historical Site	Historische Stätte	Sitio Histórico	Site historique	Sitio histórico
♠ Recreational Site	Erholungs- und Ferienort	Sitio de Recreo	Centre de loisirs	Area de Lazer
⊠ Airport	Flughafen	Aeropuerto	Aéroport	Aeroporto
■ Military Installation	Militäranlage	Instalación Militar	Installation militaire	Instalação militar
◆ Miscellaneous	Verschiedenes	Misceláneo	Divers	Diversos

Valdobbiadene 64 45.54 N 12.00 E
Valdoie 58 47.40 N 6.51 E
Val-d'Oise □[5] 50 49.10 N 2.10 E
Val-d'Or 190 48.07 N 77.47 W
Valdorf 52 52.09 N 8.51 E
Valdosta 192 30.49 N 83.16 W
Valdoviño 34 43.36 N 8.08 W
Valdres V 26 60.55 N 9.10 E
Valdurna (Durnholz) 64 46.44 N 11.26 E
Vale, Guernsey 43b 49.29 N 2.31 W
Vale, Or., U.S. 202 43.58 N 117.14 W
Valea lui Mihai 38 47.31 N 22.09 E
Vale de Lobos 266c 38.49 N 9.17 W
Valeene 218 38.26 N 86.24 W
Valeggio sul Mincio 64 45.21 N 10.44 E
Valehouse Reservoir ⊜[1] 262 53.29 N 1.57 W
Valemount 182 52.50 N 119.15 W
Valença, Bra. 255 13.22 S 39.05 W
Valença, Bra. 256 22.15 S 43.43 W
Valença, Port. 34 42.02 N 8.38 W
Valença do Piauí 250 6.24 S 41.45 W
Valençay 50 47.09 N 1.34 E
Valence → València, Esp. 34 39.28 N 0.22 W
Valence, Fr. 62 44.56 N 4.54 E
València, Esp. 34 39.28 N 0.22 W
Valencia, Hond. 236 14.47 N 85.18 W
Valencia, Pil. 116 7.57 N 125.03 E
Valencia, Ca., U.S. 228 34.26 N 118.36 W
Valencia, Pa., U.S. 214 40.40 N 79.59 W
Valencia, Ven. 246 10.11 N 68.00 W
València □[4] 34 39.30 N 0.45 W
València, Golf de c 34 39.50 N 0.30 E
Valencia, Lago de ⊜ 246 10.15 N 67.45 W
Valencia, Quebrada ≃ 286c 10.30 N 66.46 W
Valencia de Alcántata 34 39.25 N 7.14 W
Valencia de Don Juan 34 42.18 N 5.31 W
Valencia Island I 48 51.52 N 10.20 W
Valenciennes 50 50.21 N 3.32 E
Vălenii de Munte 38 45.12 N 26.03 E
Valensole 62 43.50 N 5.59 E
Valentano 66 42.34 N 11.49 E
Valente 250 11.34 S 39.27 W
Valentigney 58 47.28 N 6.50 E
Valentin 89 43.08 N 134.17 E
Valentín Alsina ◆[8] 288 34.40 S 58.25 W
Valentine, Ne., U.S. 198 42.52 N 100.33 W
Valentine, Tx., U.S. 196 30.34 N 104.29 W
Valentine Mountain ∧ 224 48.32 N 123.56 W
Valentinovka 265b 55.55 N 37.56 E
Valenton 261 48.45 N 2.28 E
Valenza 62 45.01 N 8.38 E
Valenzano 68 41.02 N 16.53 E
Valenzuela 269f 14.42 N 120.58 E
Våler 26 60.40 N 11.50 E
Valera 246 9.19 N 70.37 W
Valérien, Mont ∧[2] 261 48.53 N 2.13 E
Vale Royal □[8] 262 53.17 N 2.37 W
Valets, Lac ⊜ 190 48.32 N 76.30 W
Valette, La → Valletta 36 35.54 N 14.31 E
Valfabbrica 66 43.09 N 12.36 E
Valflaunès 62 43.48 N 3.52 E
Valfurva 64 46.27 N 10.25 E
Valfurva V 64 46.26 N 10.26 E
Valga 76 57.47 N 26.02 E
Valge ≃ 76 59.35 N 25.42 E
Valgorge 62 44.35 N 4.07 E
Valgrisanche 62 45.38 N 7.04 E
Valguarnera Caropepe 70 37.30 N 14.23 E
Valhalla, S. Afr. 158 25.49 S 28.08 E
Valhalla, N.Y., U.S. 210 41.04 N 73.46 W
Valhalla, Lake ⊜ 276 40.56 N 74.22 W
Valiente, Península >[1] 236 9.05 N 81.51 W
Valiente, Punta > 236 9.11 N 81.55 W
Valier, Il., U.S. 194 38.01 N 89.03 W
Valier, Mt., U.S. 202 48.18 N 112.14 W
Valier, Pa., U.S. 214 40.55 N 79.03 W
Valili ∧ 175g 16.39 S 179.10 E
Valinda 280 34.02 N 117.56 W
Valinhos 256 22.57 S 47.01 W
Valjevo 38 44.16 N 19.53 E
Valka 76 57.46 N 26.00 E
Valkeakoski 26 61.16 N 24.02 E
Valkenburg 56 50.52 N 5.50 E
Valkenswaard 52 51.21 N 5.28 E
V'alki, Ross. 82 55.39 N 38.05 E
Valki, Ukr. 78 49.50 N 35.37 E
Valkininkas 76 54.21 N 24.50 E
Valla 40 59.02 N 16.23 E
Valladares 196 26.53 N 100.37 W
Valladolid, Ec. 246 4.33 S 79.08 W
Valladolid, Esp. 34 41.39 N 4.43 W
Valladolid, Méx. 232 20.41 N 88.12 W
Valladolid □[4] 34 41.40 N 4.50 W
Vallage ◆[1] 58 48.24 N 5.00 E
Vallåkra 41 55.58 N 12.52 E
Vallarsa 64 45.47 N 11.07 E
Vallata 68 41.02 N 15.15 E
Vallauris 62 43.35 N 7.03 E
Vallco Fashion Park ◆[9] 282 37.19 N 122.01 W
Valldal 26 62.20 N 7.21 E
Valldoreix 266d 41.28 N 2.04 E
Valle, Esp. 34 43.14 N 4.18 W
Valle, Lat. 76 56.30 N 24.44 E
Valle □[5] 236 13.30 N 87.35 W
Valle, Arroyo ≃ 226 37.39 N 121.54 W
Vallecas ◆[8] 266a 40.23 N 3.37 W
Valle Castellana 66 42.44 N 13.29 E
Vallecillo 196 26.40 N 99.58 W
Vallecito 226 38.07 N 120.27 W
Vallecitos 200 36.05 N 106.20 W
Vallecitos Creek ≃ 282 37.36 N 121.53 W
Vallecorsa 66 41.27 N 13.24 E
Valle Crucis Abbey ⊍[1] 42 52.59 N 3.12 W
Valle d'Aosta □[4] 36 45.45 N 7.25 E
Valle de Bravo 234 19.11 N 100.08 W
Valle de Guadalupe 234 21.00 N 102.37 W
Valle de Guanape 246 9.54 N 65.41 W
Valle de Juárez 234 19.53 N 102.51 W
Valle de la Pascua 246 9.13 N 66.00 W
Valle del Cauca □[5] 246 3.45 N 76.30 W
Valle de Olivos 232 27.12 N 106.17 W
Valle de Santiago 234 20.23 N 101.12 W
Valle de Zaragoza 232 27.28 N 105.49 W
Valle di Cadore 64 46.24 N 12.20 E
Valle di Sotto 64 46.25 N 10.21 E
Valledolmo 70 37.45 N 13.49 E
Valledupar 246 10.29 N 73.15 W
Valle Edén 252 31.50 S 56.09 W
Vallefiorita 68 38.46 N 16.27 E
Vallegrande 248 18.29 S 64.06 W
Valle Hermoso, Arg. 252 31.07 S 64.29 W
Valle Hermoso, Méx. 196 25.39 N 97.52 W
Vallehermoso, Pil. 116 10.20 N 123.19 E
Vallejo 226 38.06 N 122.15 W
Valle Lomellina 62 45.09 N 8.40 E
Vallelunga Pratameno 70 37.41 N 13.50 E
Valle Mosso 62 45.38 N 8.09 E
Vällen ⊜ 40 60.03 N 18.20 E
Vallenar 252 28.35 S 70.46 W
Vallendar 56 50.24 N 7.37 E
Vallensbæk 41 55.38 N 12.22 E
Vallentuna 40 59.32 N 18.05 E
Vallepietra 66 41.55 N 13.14 E
Valleraugue 62 44.05 N 3.38 E
Valle Redondo 204 32.31 N 116.46 W
Vallermosa 71 39.22 N 8.48 E
Vallerotonda 66 41.33 N 13.55 E
Valleroy 56 49.12 N 5.55 E
Valles → Ciudad de Valles 234 21.59 N 99.01 W
Valles Caldera ⊥[6] 200 35.52 N 106.33 W
Vallet 32 47.10 N 1.16 W
Valletta 36 35.54 N 14.31 E
Valley, Al., U.S. 194 32.49 N 85.10 W
Valley, Ne., U.S. 198 41.18 N 96.20 W
Valley, Wa., U.S. 182 48.10 N 117.43 W
Valley ≃ 184 51.21 N 99.55 W
Valley Bend 188 38.46 N 79.56 W
Valley Center, Ca., U.S. 228 33.13 N 117.02 W
Valley Center, Ks., U.S. 198 37.50 N 97.22 W
Valley City, N.D., U.S. 198 46.55 N 97.59 W
Valley City, Oh., U.S. 214 41.14 N 81.56 W
Valley Cottage 210 41.07 N 73.57 W
Valley Creek ≃, Pa., U.S. 285 40.06 N 75.28 W
Valley Creek ≃, Pa., U.S. 285 39.58 N 75.40 W
Valley Creek ≃, Tx., U.S. 196 31.43 N 100.02 W
Valleydale 280 34.06 N 117.56 W
Valley Falls, Ks., U.S. 198 39.20 N 95.27 W
Valley Falls, N.Y., U.S. 210 42.54 N 73.34 W
Valley Falls, R.I., U.S. 207 41.54 N 71.23 W
Valley Farms 200 32.59 N 111.26 W
Valleyfield 186 49.08 N 53.37 W
Valley Forge 208 40.05 N 75.28 W
Valley Forge Estates 285 40.05 N 75.26 W
Valley Forge National Historical Park ♦ 208 40.06 N 75.27 W
Valley Grove 214 40.05 N 80.34 W
Valley Head, Al., U.S. 194 34.34 N 85.36 W
Valley Head, W.V., U.S. 188 38.32 N 80.02 W
Valley Home 226 37.50 N 120.55 W
Valley Mede 284b 39.17 N 76.50 W
Valley Mills 222 31.39 N 97.28 W
Valley of Desolation National Monument ♦ 158 32.17 S 24.30 E
Valley of Fire State Park ♦ 204 36.26 N 114.30 W
Valley of the Kings ⊥ 140 25.45 N 32.37 E
Valley Park 219 38.32 N 90.29 W
Valley Plaza ◆[9] 280 34.11 N 118.24 W
Valley Springs, Ca., U.S. 226 38.12 N 120.50 W
Valley Springs, S.D., U.S. 198 43.34 N 96.28 W
Valley Station 194 38.06 N 85.52 W
Valley Stream 210 40.39 N 73.42 W
Valley Stream ≃ 276 40.39 N 73.45 W
Valley Stream State Park ♦ 276 40.41 N 73.42 W
Valleyview, Ab., Can. 182 55.04 N 117.17 W
Valley View, Il., U.S. 216 41.50 N 88.03 W
Valley View, Oh., U.S. 279a 41.23 N 81.37 W
Valley View, Pa., U.S. 210 40.38 N 76.32 W
Valley View, Tx., U.S. 196 33.29 N 97.10 W
Valley View Park 228 34.13 N 117.20 W
Vallgrund I 26 63.12 N 21.14 E
Valliant 196 34.00 N 95.05 W
Valli del Pasubio 64 45.41 N 11.15 E
Vallières 58 45.54 N 5.56 E
Vallimanca, Arroyo ≃ 252 35.40 S 60.02 W
Vallio 64 45.38 N 10.23 E
Vallirana 266d 41.23 N 1.56 E
Vallø 41 55.24 N 12.15 E
Vallo della Lucania 68 40.14 N 15.17 E
Valloire 62 45.10 N 6.26 E
Vallombrosa 66 43.44 N 11.32 E
Vallonia 218 38.50 N 86.05 W
Vallon-Pont-d'Arc 62 44.24 N 4.24 E
Vallorbe 58 46.43 N 6.22 E
Vallorcine 58 46.02 N 6.56 E
Vallouise 62 44.51 N 6.29 E
Vallromanes 266d 41.32 N 2.18 E
Valls 34 41.17 N 1.15 E
Valluga ∧ 58 47.09 N 10.12 E
Vallvidrera ◆[8] 266d 41.25 N 2.07 E
Vallvidrera, Riera de ≃ 266d 41.25 N 2.01 E
Val-Marie 184 49.14 N 107.44 W
Valmaseda 34 43.12 N 3.12 W
Valmeyer 219 38.17 N 90.18 W
Valmiera 76 57.33 N 25.24 E
Valmondois 261 49.06 N 2.12 E
Valmont 50 49.44 N 0.31 E
Valmontone 66 41.46 N 12.57 E
Valmy 56 49.05 N 4.46 E
Valognes 32 49.31 N 1.28 W
Valois 210 42.32 N 76.53 W
Valois, Baie de c 275a 45.26 N 73.47 W
Valok 78 45.47 N 34.57 E
Valona → Vlorë 38 40.27 N 19.30 E
Valongo 34 41.11 N 8.30 W
Valoria la Buena 34 41.48 N 4.32 W
Vālpārai 122 10.22 N 76.58 E
Valparaíso, Bra. 255 21.13 S 50.51 W
Valparaíso, Chile 252 33.02 S 71.38 W
Valparaíso, Méx. 234 22.46 N 103.34 W
Valparaiso, Fl., U.S. 194 30.29 N 86.29 W
Valparaiso, In., U.S. 216 41.28 N 87.03 W
Valparaiso, Ne., U.S. 198 41.04 N 96.49 W
Valparaíso □[4] 252 32.45 S 71.20 W
Valparaíso ≃ 234 22.33 N 103.39 W
Valpelline V 62 45.50 N 7.25 E
Valpovo 38 45.39 N 18.26 E
Valprato Soana 62 45.31 N 7.33 E
Valréas 62 44.23 N 4.59 E
Valrico 220 27.57 N 82.16 W
Val Roveto V 66 41.52 N 13.30 E
Vals ≃ 158 27.23 S 26.30 E
Vals, Tanjung > 164 8.26 S 137.38 E
Val-Saint-Michel 206 46.52 N 71.27 W
Valsbaai c 158 34.12 S 18.40 E
Valserine ≃ 58 46.06 N 5.50 E
Valserrhein ≃ 58 46.42 N 9.10 E
Valsertal V 58 46.37 N 9.10 E
Valsetz 202 44.50 N 123.39 W
Valsinni 68 40.10 N 16.26 E
Valsjöbyn 26 64.04 N 14.08 E
Valskog 40 59.27 N 15.57 E
Vals-les-Bains 62 44.40 N 4.22 E
Vals Platz 58 46.37 N 9.11 E
Vals-Près-le-Puy 62 45.01 N 3.52 E
Valstagna 64 45.51 N 11.39 E
Val-Suzon 58 47.25 N 4.54 E
Valtellina V 58 46.11 N 9.55 E
Valthermond 52 52.53 N 6.59 E
Valtice 61 48.44 N 16.45 E
Valtierrilla 234 20.32 N 101.08 W
Valtimo 26 63.40 N 28.48 E
Valtorta 58 45.59 N 9.32 E
Valtournanche 62 45.53 N 7.37 E
Valujec 76 52.46 N 33.23 E
Valujevka 80 46.44 N 43.43 E
Valujevo 265b 55.35 N 37.21 E
Valujki 78 50.13 N 38.08 E
Valvasone 64 45.59 N 12.52 E
Valverde 148 27.48 N 17.55 W
Valverde del Camino 34 37.34 N 6.45 W
Val Verde Park 228 34.27 N 118.40 W
Valyermo 228 34.26 N 117.50 W
Vamba ≃ 152 7.27 S 14.17 E
Vamdrup 41 55.25 N 9.17 E
Våmhus 26 61.08 N 14.28 E
Vamizi, Ilha I 154 11.02 S 40.40 E
Vammala 26 61.20 N 22.54 E
Vamori Wash V 200 31.57 N 112.21 W
Van, Tür. 128 38.28 N 43.20 E
Van, Pa., U.S. 214 41.19 N 79.40 W
Van, Tx., U.S. 222 32.31 N 95.38 W
Van □[4] 128 39.00 N 43.45 E
Vanajavesi ⊜ 26 61.09 N 24.15 E
Vanak ◆[8] 267d 35.45 N 51.23 E
Van Alstyne 196 33.25 N 96.34 W
Vanån ≃ 40 60.31 N 14.14 E
Vananda 182 49.45 N 124.33 W
Vanapa ≃ 164 9.05 S 147.10 E
Vanault-les-Dames 56 48.51 N 4.46 E
Vanavana I[1] 14 20.47 S 139.09 W
Vanavara 74 60.22 N 102.16 E
Van Buren, Ar., U.S. 194 35.26 N 94.20 W
Van Buren, In., U.S. 216 40.37 N 85.30 W
Van Buren, Me., U.S. 186 47.09 N 67.56 W
Van Buren, Mo., U.S. 194 36.59 N 91.00 W
Van Buren, Oh., U.S. 216 41.08 N 83.38 W
Van Buren □[6] 216 42.14 N 86.04 W
Van Buren Point 214 42.27 N 79.25 W
Vanč 85 38.23 N 71.26 E
Vanč ≃ 85 38.18 N 71.19 E
Vance Air Force Base ■ 196 36.21 N 97.55 W
Vanceboro 188 45.33 N 67.25 W
Vanceburg 218 38.35 N 83.19 W
Vancleave 194 30.32 N 88.41 W
Van Cortlandt Park ♦ 276 40.54 N 73.53 W
Van Cortlandtville 210 41.19 N 73.54 W
Vancouver, B.C., Can. 224 49.16 N 123.07 W
Vancouver, Wa., U.S. 224 45.38 N 122.39 W
Vancouver, Cape >, Austl. 162 35.01 S 118.12 E
Vancouver, Cape >, Ak., U.S. 180 60.33 N 165.27 W
Vancouver, Mount ∧ 180 60.20 N 139.40 W
Vancouver International Airport ⊠ 224 48.39 N 123.26 W
Vancouver Island I 182 49.45 N 126.00 W
Vancouver Island Ranges ⋀ 182 49.25 N 125.25 W
Vancouver Lake ⊜ 224 45.41 N 122.44 W
Van Daalen ≃ 164 3.05 S 138.09 E
Vandalia, Il., U.S. 219 38.57 N 89.05 W
Vandalia, Mi., U.S. 216 41.55 N 85.55 W
Vandalia, Mo., U.S. 219 39.18 N 91.29 W
Vandalia, Oh., U.S. 218 39.53 N 84.11 W
Vandalia Lake ⊜[1] 219 39.01 N 89.09 W
Vandam 84 40.57 N 47.57 E
Vandavāsi 122 12.30 N 79.37 E
Vandekerckhove Lake ⊜ 184 57.02 N 101.25 W
Vandel 41 55.42 N 9.13 E
Vandenberg Air Force Base ■ 204 34.43 N 120.33 W
Van den Bosch, Tanjung > 164 4.06 S 132.55 E
Vandenesse 58 47.13 N 4.37 E
Vanderbijlpark 158 26.42 S 27.54 E
Vanderbilt, Mi., U.S. 190 45.08 N 84.39 W
Vanderbilt, Tx., U.S. 196 28.49 N 96.37 W
Vanderbilt Mansion National Historic Site ⊥ 210 41.47 N 73.56 W
Vanderbilt Museum ⊍ 276 40.54 N 73.22 W
Vandercook Lake 216 42.11 N 84.23 W
Vandergrift 214 40.36 N 79.33 W
Vanderhoof 182 54.01 N 124.01 W
Vanderlin Island I 164 15.44 S 137.02 E
Vandervoort 194 34.22 N 94.21 W
Van Diemen, Cape >, Austl. 164 11.10 S 130.23 E
Van Diemen, Cape >, Austl. 164 16.31 S 139.41 E
Van Diemen Gulf c 164 11.50 S 132.00 E
Vandling 210 41.38 N 75.29 W
Vandoeuvre-lès-Nancy 58 48.39 N 6.11 E
Vandoies (Vintl) 64 46.49 N 11.43 E
Vändra 76 58.39 N 25.02 E
Van Duzen ≃ 204 40.33 N 124.08 W
Vandúzi ≃ 154 18.56 S 34.01 E
Vandykpark 273d 26.16 S 28.19 E
Vandžiogala 76 55.07 N 23.58 E
Vanegas 234 23.51 N 100.52 W
Vänern ⊜ 26 58.55 N 13.30 E
Vänersborg 26 58.22 N 12.19 E
Van Etten 210 42.11 N 76.33 W
Vang, Mount ∧ 9 73.56 S 68.39 W
Vanga 154 4.39 S 39.13 E
Vangaindrano 157b 23.21 S 47.36 E
Vängelälven ≃ 26 63.41 N 16.25 E
Van Gölü ⊜ 128 38.33 N 42.46 E
Vangsnes 26 61.11 N 6.38 E
Vanguard 184 49.55 N 107.20 W
Vangunu, Mount ∧ 175e 8.42 S 158.00 E
Vangunu Island I 175e 8.38 S 158.00 E
Van Hook Arm c 198 47.50 N 102.25 W
Van Horn 196 31.02 N 104.49 W
Van Horne 190 42.00 N 92.05 W
Van Hornesville 210 42.54 N 74.50 W
Vani 84 42.06 N 42.30 E
Vanier 212 45.26 N 75.40 W
Vanikolo I 14 11.39 S 166.54 E
Vaniköy ◆[8] 267b 41.04 N 29.04 E
Vanimo 164 2.40 S 141.20 E
Vanino 89 49.05 N 140.15 E
Vānīvilāsa Sāgara ⊜[1] 122 13.52 N 76.26 E
Vāniyambādi 122 12.41 N 78.37 E
Vankarem 180 67.51 N 175.50 W
Vankarem ≃ 180 67.42 N 176.17 W
Vankarem, laguna c 180 67.40 N 176.00 W
Vankaremskaja nizmennost' ≡ 180 67.30 N 176.00 W
Van Kleef Aquarium ♦ 271c 1.18 N 103.51 E
Vankleek Hill 206 45.31 N 74.39 W
Vanlay 50 48.02 N 4.01 E
Van Lear 192 37.46 N 82.45 W
Vanlue 216 40.58 N 83.28 W
Vanna I 24 70.09 N 19.51 E
Vännäs 26 63.55 N 19.45 E
Vanndale 194 35.18 N 90.46 W
Vanne ≃ 50 48.12 N 3.16 E
Vanne et du Loing, Aqueduc de ⊥[1] 261 48.36 N 2.26 E
Vannes 32 47.39 N 2.46 W
Vannes-sur-Cosson 50 47.43 N 2.13 E
Van Ninh 110 12.42 N 109.14 E
Van Norman Lakes ⊜[1] 228 34.18 N 118.28 W
Vannovka 85 42.32 N 70.21 E
Van Nuys ◆[8] 228 34.11 N 118.26 W
Van Nuys Airport ⊠ 280 34.12 N 118.29 W
Van Nuys-Sherman Oaks War Memorial Park ♦ 280 34.10 N 118.27 W
Vanoi ≃ 64 46.06 N 11.45 E
Vanoise, Massif de la ⋀ 62 45.20 N 6.40 E
Vanoise, Parc National de la ♦ 62 45.20 N 6.45 E
Van Ormer 214 40.41 N 78.30 W
Van Phong, Vung c 110 12.33 N 109.18 E
Vanport 214 40.41 N 80.20 W
Van Reenen 158 28.22 S 29.24 E
Van Reenen's Plaats 158 30.55 S 21.14 E
Van Rees, Pegunungan ⋀ 164 2.35 S 138.15 E
Vanrhynsdorp 158 31.36 S 18.44 E
Vanrook 166 16.57 S 141.57 E
Vanryndam ⊜[1] 273d 26.09 S 28.21 E
Vansant 192 37.13 N 82.05 W
Van Saun Mill Brook ≃ 276 40.55 N 74.03 W
Vansbro 40 60.31 N 14.13 E
Van Sciver Lake ⊜ 285 40.09 N 74.48 W
Van Sickle Island I 282 38.04 N 121.53 W
Vansittart Island I 176 65.50 N 84.00 W
Vansjön ⊜ 40 59.59 N 16.57 E
Vanskoje 76 58.56 N 36.52 E
Vanstadensrus 158 29.59 S 27.02 E
Vantaa (Vanda) 26 60.16 N 25.03 E
Vantaa ≃ 26 60.13 N 24.59 E
Vanthali 120 21.29 N 70.20 E
Vanua Lava I 175f 13.48 S 167.28 E
Vanua Levu I 175g 16.33 S 179.15 E
Vanua Mbalavu Island I 175g 17.40 S 178.57 W
Vanuatu □[1], Oc. 14 16.00 S 167.00 E
Vanuatu □[1], Oc. 175f 16.00 S 167.00 E
Vanves 261 48.50 N 2.18 E
Van Vleck 222 29.01 N 95.53 W
Van Voorhis 279b 40.10 N 79.58 W
Van Wert 216 40.52 N 84.35 W
Van Wert □[6] 216 40.52 N 84.35 W
Vanwyksdorp 158 33.46 S 21.28 E
Vanwyksvlei 158 30.18 S 21.49 E
Vanzaghello 266b 45.35 N 8.47 E
Vanzago 266b 45.32 N 9.00 E
Van Zandt □[6] 222 32.35 N 95.50 W
Vanzylsrus 158 26.52 S 22.04 E
Vao 175f 22.39 S 167.32 E
Vapn'arka 78 48.32 N 28.44 E
Vaqueros Creek ≃ 226 36.16 N 121.20 W
Var □[5] 62 43.30 N 6.20 E
Var ≃ 62 43.39 N 7.12 E
Vara 26 58.16 N 12.57 E
Vara ≃ 64 44.09 N 9.53 E
Varada ≃ 122 14.55 N 75.40 E
Varadero 240p 23.09 N 81.16 W
Varades 32 47.23 N 1.02 W
Varages 62 43.36 N 5.58 E
Varaita ≃ 62 44.49 N 7.36 E
Varaita, Valle V 62 44.35 N 7.10 E
Varakļāni 76 56.37 N 26.44 E
Varallo, It. 62 45.49 N 8.15 E
Varallo, It. 266b 45.40 N 8.38 E
Varāmīn 128 35.20 N 51.39 E
Vārānasi (Benares) 124 25.20 N 83.00 E
Varandej 24 68.48 N 58.00 E
Varangerfjorden c[2] 24 70.00 N 30.00 E
Varangerhalvøya >[1] 24 70.25 N 29.30 E
Varangéville 56 48.38 N 6.19 E
Varano, Lago Di c 68 41.53 N 15.45 E
Varano de'Melegari 64 44.41 N 10.01 E
Varapodio 68 38.19 N 15.59 E
Varaždin 36 46.19 N 16.20 E
Varazze 62 44.22 N 8.34 E
Varberg 26 57.06 N 12.15 E
Varces 62 45.05 N 5.41 E
Varciche 84 42.08 N 42.43 E
Vardak □[4] 120 34.15 N 68.00 E
Vardaman 194 33.52 N 89.10 W
Vardar (Axiós) ≃ 38 40.35 N 22.50 E
Varde 26 55.38 N 8.29 E
Vardenik 84 40.08 N 45.27 E
Vardenis 84 40.11 N 45.43 E
Vardenskij chrebet ⋀ 84 39.58 N 45.25 E
Vardhoúsia Óri ⋀ 38 38.44 N 22.07 E
Vardø 24 70.21 N 31.02 E
Vardūj ≃ 123 37.01 N 70.47 E
Varedo 266b 45.36 N 9.09 E
Varegovo 80 57.47 N 39.17 E
Varel 52 53.22 N 8.10 E
Varela 252 34.07 S 66.27 W
Varėna 76 54.13 N 24.34 E
Varengeville-sur-Mer 50 49.55 N 0.59 E
Varenikovskaja 78 45.07 N 37.37 E
Varenna 58 46.01 N 9.17 E
Varenne ≃ 50 49.53 N 1.08 E
Varennes 206 45.41 N 73.26 W
Varennes, Îles de II 275a 45.40 N 73.27 W
Varennes-en-Argonne 56 49.14 N 5.02 E
Varennes-Jarcy 261 48.41 N 2.34 E
Varennes-Saint-Sauveur 58 46.29 N 5.15 E
Varennes-sur-Allier 32 46.19 N 3.24 E
Varennes-sur-Amance 58 47.54 N 5.37 E
Varenovka 83 47.18 N 39.02 E
Vareš 38 44.09 N 18.19 E
Varese 62 45.48 N 8.48 E
Varese □[4] 62 45.48 N 8.40 E
Varese, Lago di ⊜ 62 45.49 N 8.45 E
Varese Ligure 62 44.22 N 9.37 E
Varèze ≃ 62 45.25 N 4.45 E
Varfolomejevka 80 50.01 N 48.12 E
Vårgårda 26 58.02 N 12.48 E
Vargas □[5] 286c 10.34 N 66.52 W
Vargaši 86 55.23 N 65.48 E
Vargem 256 22.53 S 46.25 W
Vargem, Riacho da ≃ 250 8.42 S 39.09 W
Vargem Alegre 256 22.30 S 43.55 W
Vargem do Laje 256 22.08 S 44.49 W
Vargem Grande 250 3.33 S 43.56 W
Vargem Grande ◆[8] 287a 22.59 S 43.29 W
Vargem Grande, Ribeirão da ≃ 256 22.17 S 45.40 W
Vargem Grande do Sul 256 21.50 S 46.53 W
Vargem Grande Paulista 256 23.36 S 47.01 W
Varginha 256 21.33 S 45.26 W
Vargön 26 58.22 N 12.22 E
Varigotti 62 44.11 N 8.24 E
Väringen ⊜ 40 59.26 N 15.23 E
Varirata National Park ♦ 164 9.20 S 147.20 E
Varjão 255 17.03 S 49.37 W
Varkallai 122 8.40 N 76.50 E
Varkaus 26 62.19 N 27.55 E
Varkhān ≃ 128 32.55 N 65.30 E
Varlamovo 86 54.38 N 60.40 E
Värmdölandet I 40 59.20 N 18.33 E
Värmeln ⊜ 26 59.32 N 12.54 E
Värmland □[9] 26 59.48 N 13.03 E
Värmlands Län □[6] 26 59.45 N 13.15 E
Värmlandsnäs >[1] 26 59.00 N 13.10 E
Varna, Blg. 38 43.13 N 27.55 E
Varna (Vahrn), It. 64 46.44 N 11.38 E
Varna, Ross. 86 53.24 N 60.58 E
Varna, N.Y., U.S. 210 42.27 N 76.26 W
Värnamo 26 57.11 N 14.02 E
Varnavino 80 57.24 N 45.04 E
Varnenski zaliv c 38 43.11 N 27.56 E
Varner-Hogg Plantation State Historic Park ♦ 222 29.09 N 95.37 W
Varnhem 26 58.23 N 13.39 E
Varniai 76 55.45 N 22.22 E
Varnsdorf 54 50.52 N 14.40 E
Varnville 192 32.51 N 81.04 W
Värö 26 57.16 N 12.11 E
Városliget ♦ 264c 47.31 N 19.06 E
Varpaisjärvi 26 63.22 N 27.45 E
Várpalota 30 47.12 N 18.09 E
Varpan ⊜ 40 60.38 N 15.36 E
Varresbeck ◆[8] 263 51.15 N 7.06 E
Vars, On., Can. 212 45.21 N 75.21 W
Vars, Fr. 62 44.37 N 6.41 E
Vars, Col de)(62 44.32 N 6.42 E
Vâršec 38 43.12 N 23.17 E
Varsi 62 44.40 N 9.51 E
Varsinais-Suomi ◆[1] 26 60.40 N 22.30 E
Värska 76 57.58 N 27.38 E
Varsovie → Warszawa 30 52.15 N 21.00 E
Varsseveld 52 51.57 N 6.28 E
Vårsta 40 59.10 N 17.48 E
Vartašen 84 41.06 N 47.28 E
Varto 130 39.10 N 41.28 E
V'artsil'a 24 62.11 N 30.41 E
Varty Lake ⊜ 212 44.23 N 76.48 W
Varuna ≃ 124 25.21 N 83.03 E
Varva 78 50.31 N 32.41 E
Varvarin 38 43.43 N 21.19 E
Varvarovka, Ukr. 78 48.42 N 36.02 E
Varvarovka, Ukr. 78 49.33 N 35.12 E
Varvarovka, Ukr. 83 49.05 N 38.24 E
Varysburg 210 42.46 N 78.19 W
Várzea 256 22.30 S 44.46 W
Várzea, Rio da ≃ 252 27.13 S 53.19 W
Várzea Alegre 250 6.47 S 39.17 W
Várzea da Palma 255 17.36 S 44.44 W
Varzea de Sintra 266c 38.49 N 9.24 W
Várzea Grande 248 15.39 S 56.08 W
Varzeão 252 24.34 S 49.26 W
Várzea Paulista 256 23.12 S 46.50 W
Varzi, It. 62 44.49 N 9.12 E
Varzi, Ross. 80 56.03 N 52.50 E
Varzino 24 68.19 N 38.19 E
Varzo 58 46.12 N 8.15 E
Varzob 85 38.46 N 68.49 E
Varzob ≃ 85 38.30 N 68.45 E
Varzuga 24 67.24 N 36.32 E
Varzy 50 47.22 N 3.23 E
Varzyk 85 41.07 N 71.14 E
Vas 64 45.56 N 11.56 E
Vas □[6] 30 47.05 N 16.45 E
Vasa → Vaasa 26 63.06 N 21.36 E
Vasai (Bassein) 122 19.21 N 72.48 E
Vasalemma 76 59.14 N 24.18 E
Vašana ≃ 82 54.36 N 37.10 E
Vasar 272c 19.11 N 73.09 E
Vascão, Ribeirão do ≃ 34 37.31 N 7.31 W
Vașcău 38 46.28 N 22.28 E
Väse 40 59.23 N 13.57 E
Vāshi 272c 19.04 N 72.59 E
Vashon 224 47.26 N 122.27 W
Vashon Heights 224 47.30 N 122.28 W
Vashon Island I 224 47.24 N 122.27 W
Vasilevičі 76 52.14 N 29.49 E
Vasilija, mys > 180 64.34 N 178.33 E
Vasiliká 38 40.28 N 23.08 E
Vasiliški 76 53.47 N 24.51 E
Vasiljevka, Bela. 76 52.15 N 31.31 E
Vasiljevka, Ross. 89 46.52 N 134.03 E
Vasiljevka, Ukr. 78 47.26 N 35.16 E
Vasiljevo, Ross. 24 60.46 N 38.59 E
Vasiljevo, Ross. 80 55.52 N 48.42 E
Vasiljevskij, ostrov I 265a 59.56 N 30.15 E
Vasiljevskij Moch 76 57.01 N 35.55 E
Vasiljevskoje, Ross. 80 56.56 N 41.40 E
Vasiljevskoje, Ross. 80 56.31 N 45.49 E
Vasiljevskoje, Ross. 82 55.00 N 37.25 E
Vasiljevskoje, Ross. 82 56.20 N 37.54 E
Vasil'kov 78 50.12 N 30.19 E
Vasil'kovka 78 48.13 N 36.02 E
Vasil'sursk 80 56.08 N 46.01 E
Vasis 86 57.22 N 74.44 E
Vaška ≃ 24 64.53 N 45.47 E
Vaskelovo 76 60.22 N 30.22 E
Vaskess Bay c 174o 1.51 N 157.31 W
Vaškovci 78 48.24 N 27.08 E
Vaškovcy 78 48.23 N 25.30 E
Vaslui 38 46.38 N 27.44 E
Vaslui □[6] 38 46.30 N 27.45 E
Väsman ⊜ 40 60.11 N 15.04 E
Vass 192 35.15 N 79.16 W
Vassako-Bolo, Réserve Naturelle Intégrale de la ◆[4] 146 8.10 N 19.45 E
Vassar 190 43.22 N 83.35 W
Vassdalseggi ∧ 26 59.46 N 7.10 E
Vassieux-en-Vercors 62 44.53 N 5.22 E
Vassouras 256 22.25 S 43.40 W
Vassy 50 47.34 N 4.10 E
Västanfors 40 59.59 N 15.49 E
Västerås 40 59.37 N 16.33 E
Västeråsfjärden c 40 59.34 N 16.34 E
Västerbotten □[9] 26 64.36 N 20.04 E
Västerbottens Län □[6] 24 64.00 N 17.30 E
Västerby 40 60.19 N 15.55 E
Västerdalälven ≃ 40 60.33 N 15.08 E
Västerfärnebo 40 59.57 N 16.17 E
Västergötland □[9] 26 58.01 N 13.03 E
Västerhaninge 40 59.07 N 18.06 E
Västernorrlands Län □[6] 26 63.00 N 17.30 E
Västervik 26 57.45 N 16.38 E
Västmanland □[9] 40 59.38 N 15.15 E
Västmanlands Län □[6] 40 59.45 N 16.20 E
Vasto 66 42.07 N 14.42 E
Västra Laxsjön ⊜ 40 58.54 N 14.38 E
Västra Ringsjön ⊜ 41 55.53 N 13.28 E
Västra Torup 41 56.09 N 13.29 E
Vastseliina 76 57.44 N 27.17 E
Vas'ugan ≃ 86 59.07 N 80.46 E
Vas'uganje ≡ 86 58.00 N 77.00 E
Vas'unino 82 55.15 N 37.01 E
Vašutino 265b 55.56 N 37.26 E
Vašutkiny ozera ⊜ 24 68.06 N 61.18 E
Vasvár 30 47.03 N 16.49 E
Vát 61 47.17 N 16.47 E
Vața de Jos 38 46.10 N 22.35 E
Vatan 32 47.05 N 1.48 E
Vaternish Point > 46 57.36 N 6.38 W
Vatersay I 46 56.55 N 7.32 W
Vaterstetten 60 48.07 N 11.47 E
Vatican (Cité du) → Vatican City □[1] 267a 41.54 N 12.27 E
Vatican City (Città del Vaticano) □[1], Europe 66 41.54 N 12.27 E
Vatican City (Città del Vaticano) □[1], Europe 267a 41.54 N 12.27 E
Vaticano, Capo > 68 38.38 N 15.50 E
Vatikanstadt → Vatican City □[1] 66 41.54 N 12.27 E
V'atka → Kirov 80 58.38 N 49.42 E
V'atka ≃ 80 55.36 N 51.30 E
Vatlirchvin, gora ∧ 180 68.08 N 179.52 W
Vatnajökull ⊓ 24a 64.25 N 16.50 W
Vatneyri 24a 65.38 N 23.57 W
Vätö I 40 59.49 N 18.57 E
Vatoa Island I 175g 19.50 S 178.13 W
Vatoloha ∧ 157b 17.52 S 47.48 E
Vatomandry 157b 19.20 S 48.59 E
Vatra Dornei 38 47.21 N 25.21 E
V'atskije Pol'any 80 56.14 N 51.04 E
V'atskij uval ⋀[2] 80 57.20 N 49.10 E
V'atskoje, Ross. 80 57.52 N 40.16 E
V'atskoje, Ross. 89 48.44 N 135.43 E
Vattalkundu 122 10.10 N 77.46 E
Vättern ⊜ 26 58.24 N 14.36 E
Vättersee → Vättern ⊜ 26 58.24 N 14.36 E
Vattholma 40 60.01 N 17.44 E
Vättis 58 46.55 N 9.27 E
Vatu Ira Channel ɥ 175g 17.17 S 178.31 E
Vatukoula 175g 17.31 S 177.51 E
Vatulele I 175g 18.33 S 177.37 E
Vatulino 82 55.39 N 36.09 E
Vatutino 78 49.02 N 31.04 E
Vaubecourt 56 48.56 N 5.07 E
Vauclaix 50 47.14 N 3.49 E
Vauclin, Montagne du ∧ 240e 14.33 N 60.53 W
Vaucluse 274a 33.51 S 151.17 E
Vaucluse □[5] 62 44.00 N 5.10 E
Vaucluse, Fontaine de ⊥ 62 43.55 N 5.08 E
Vaucluse, Plateau de ⋀[1] 62 44.00 N 5.22 E
Vaucouleurs 58 48.36 N 5.40 E
Vaucouleurs ≃ 261 48.59 N 1.44 E
Vaud □[3] 58 46.40 N 6.30 E
Vaudherland 261 49.00 N 2.29 E
Vaudoy-en-Brie 50 48.41 N 3.05 E
Vaudreuil (Saint-Michel-de-Vaudreuil) 206 45.24 N 74.01 W
Vaudreuil □[6] 206 45.26 N 74.15 W
Vaudreuil, Baie de c 275a 45.24 N 74.00 W
Vaufrey 58 47.21 N 6.55 E
Vaughan 212 43.47 N 79.36 W
Vaughn, N.M., U.S. 200 34.36 N 105.12 W
Vaughn, Wa., U.S. 224 47.21 N 122.46 W
Vaughnsville 216 40.53 N 84.09 W
Vaugneray 62 45.44 N 4.39 E
Vaugrigneuse 261 48.36 N 2.07 E
Vauhallan 261 48.44 N 2.12 E
Vaujours 261 48.56 N 2.35 E
Vaulovo 82 56.09 N 39.17 E
Vaulruz 58 46.37 N 6.59 E
Vaulx-en-Velin 62 45.47 N 4.56 E
Vaupés □[8] 246 0.45 N 70.30 W
Vaupés (Uaupés) ≃ 246 0.02 N 67.16 W
Vauréal 261 49.02 N 2.02 E
Vauréal, Chute ⌊ 186 49.34 N 62.42 W
Vauvenargues 62 43.33 N 5.36 E
Vauvert 62 43.42 N 4.17 E
Vauvillers 58 47.55 N 6.06 E
Vauvise ≃ 50 47.18 N 2.57 E
Vaux ≃ 50 49.33 N 4.17 E
Vaux, Ru des ≃ 261 48.42 N 2.00 E
Vauxhall 182 50.04 N 112.07 W
Vaux-le-Compte, Château de ⊥ 50 48.36 N 2.43 E
Vaux-le-Pénil 261 48.32 N 2.41 E
Vaux-lès-Saint-Claude 58 46.22 N 5.44 E
Vaux-le-Vicomte, Château de ⊥ 261 48.36 N 2.43 E
Vaux-Sous-Aubigny 58 47.39 N 5.17 E
Vaux-sur-Seine 261 49.00 N 1.58 E
Vavatenina 157b 17.28 S 49.12 E
Vava'u I 14 18.36 S 174.00 W
Vava'u Group II 14 18.40 S 174.00 W
Vavincourt 56 48.49 N 5.13 E
Vavoua 150 7.23 N 6.29 W
Vavož 80 56.47 N 51.55 E
Vavuniya 122 8.45 N 80.30 E
Vaxholm 40 59.24 N 18.20 E
Växjö 26 56.52 N 14.49 E
V'aža 78 49.16 N 41.01 E
Vaza-barris ≃ 250 11.10 S 37.10 W
Vazante 255 18.00 S 46.54 W
Vazante Grande ≃ 248 19.21 S 56.53 W
V'azemskij 89 47.32 N 134.48 E
Važgort 24 64.01 N 47.02 E
V'az'ma 76 55.13 N 34.18 E
V'az'ma ≃, Ross. 76 55.28 N 33.34 E
V'az'ma ≃, Ross. 82 56.29 N 35.49 E
V'azniki 80 56.15 N 42.10 E
Vazobe ∧ 157b 18.25 S 47.18 E
V'azovaja 80 57.39 N 45.44 E
V'azovka, Ross. 80 48.19 N 45.36 E
V'azovka, Ross. 80 51.48 N 45.47 E
V'azovka, Ross. 80 52.52 N 48.24 E
V'azovka, Ross. 80 50.52 N 43.57 E
V'azovoje, Ross. 78 51.54 N 36.59 E
V'azovoje, Ross. 78 51.09 N 37.01 E
V'azovok 78 49.11 N 31.25 E
Vazuza ≃ 76 56.10 N 34.35 E
Vazuzskoje vodochranilišče ⊜[1] 76 56.00 N 34.28 E
V'azyn' 76 54.25 N 27.10 E
Vazzola 64 45.50 N 12.23 E
Veachland 218 38.12 N 85.11 W
Veado, Ilha do I 287a 22.57 S 43.06 W
Veazie 188 44.50 N 68.42 W
Veberöd 41 55.38 N 13.29 E
Veblen 198 45.51 N 97.17 W
Vecchiano 66 43.47 N 10.23 E
Vechelde 52 52.16 N 10.22 E
Vecht (Vechte) ≃ 52 52.35 N 6.05 E
Vechta 52 52.43 N 8.16 E
Vechte (Vecht) ≃ 52 52.35 N 6.05 E
Veckerhagen 52 51.30 N 9.35 E
Vecpiebalga 76 57.08 N 25.50 E
Vecsés 30 47.25 N 19.16 E
Vecumnieki 76 56.36 N 24.31 E
Vedado ◆[8] 286b 23.08 N 82.24 W
Vedano al Lambro 266b 45.37 N 9.16 E
Vedano Olona 62 45.46 N 8.53 E
Vedāranniyam 122 10.22 N 79.51 E
Vedbæk 41 55.51 N 12.34 E
Vedder Crossing 224 49.06 N 121.57 W
Veddige 26 57.16 N 12.19 E
Vedea 38 44.47 N 24.37 E
Vedea ≃ 38 43.43 N 25.32 E
Vedelago 64 45.41 N 12.01 E
Vedène 62 43.59 N 4.54 E
Vedeno 84 42.58 N 46.05 E
Vedeseta 58 45.53 N 9.32 E
Vedevåg 40 59.32 N 15.17 E
Vedi 84 39.56 N 44.42 E
Vedia 252 34.30 S 61.32 W
Vednoje 76 57.08 N 36.10 E
Vedomša 82 56.44 N 38.21 E
Vedrovo 80 57.33 N 42.52 E
Veedersburg 194 40.06 N 87.15 W
Veen 263 51.37 N 6.27 E
Veendam 52 53.06 N 6.58 E
Veenendaal 52 52.02 N 5.34 E
Veenhuizen 52 53.03 N 6.24 E
Veenoord 52 52.43 N 6.50 E
Veere 52 51.34 N 3.40 E
Veert 52 51.33 N 6.17 E
Vefsna ≃ 24 65.50 N 13.12 E
Vega 196 35.15 N 102.26 W
Vega I 24 65.39 N 11.50 E
Vega, Arroyo de la ≃ 266a 40.31 N 3.33 W
Vega Alta 240m 18.25 N 66.20 W
Vega Baja 240m 18.27 N 66.23 W
Vega Point > 181a 51.49 N 177.16 E
Vegår ⊜ 26 58.48 N 8.47 E
Vegesack ◆[8] 52 53.10 N 8.37 E
Veghel 52 51.37 N 5.33 E
Veglie 68 40.20 N 17.58 E
Vegreville 182 53.30 N 112.03 W
Veguita 200 34.30 N 106.46 W
Vehār Lake ⊜ 272c 19.09 N 72.55 E
Vehlefanz 264a 52.43 N 13.06 E
Vehnemoor ◆[3] 52 53.05 N 8.00 E
Veigné 50 47.17 N 0.44 E
Veil, Loch ⊜ 46 56.20 N 4.25 W
Veilsdorf 54 50.24 N 10.48 E
Veinte de Noviembre 196 25.47 N 97.33 W
Veinticinco de Agosto 258 34.24 S 56.25 W
Veinticinco de Mayo, Arg. 252 35.26 S 60.10 W
Veinticinco de Mayo, Arg. 252 34.35 S 68.33 W
Veinticinco de Mayo, Ur. 258 34.12 S 56.22 W
Veintiocho de Mayo 246 3.50 S 78.52 W
Veintiocho de Noviembre 254 51.39 S 72.18 W
Veintisiete de Abril 236 10.15 N 85.45 W
Veio ⊥ 66 42.02 N 12.24 E
Veiros 250 2.05 S 52.10 W
Veisiejai 76 54.06 N 23.42 E
Veitsbronn 56 49.31 N 10.53 E
Veitsch 61 47.35 N 15.30 E
Veitschalpe ⋀ 61 47.39 N 15.30 E
Veitshöchheim 56 49.50 N 9.52 E
Vejbystrand 41 56.19 N 12.45 E
Vejdelevka 78 50.09 N 38.27 E
Vejen 41 55.29 N 9.09 E
Vejer de la Frontera 34 36.15 N 5.58 W
Vejlby 41 56.12 N 10.13 E
Vejle 41 55.42 N 9.32 E
Vejle □[6] 41 55.45 N 9.30 E
Vejle Fjord c 41 55.40 N 9.50 E
Vejprty 54 50.30 N 13.02 E
Vejrhøj ∧[2] 41 55.47 N 11.24 E
Vejrø I 41 55.02 N 11.22 E
Vekšor 24 60.33 N 49.26 E
Vel'a ≃ 82 56.31 N 37.41 E
Vela Luka 36 42.58 N 16.43 E
Velapāda 272c 18.59 N 73.04 E
Velardeña 232 25.04 N 103.44 W
Velas 148a 38.41 N 28.13 W
Velas, Cabo > 236 10.22 N 85.53 W
Velázquez 252 34.02 S 54.17 W
Velbert 56 51.20 N 7.02 E
Velburg 60 49.14 N 11.41 E
Velddrif 158 32.47 S 18.11 E
Velden, Dtsch. 60 49.37 N 11.31 E
Velden, Dtsch. 60 48.19 N 12.16 E
Velden, Öst. 61 46.37 N 14.03 E
Veldhoven 52 51.24 N 5.24 E

Symbols in the index entries represent the broad categories identified in the key at the right. Symbols with superior numbers (⋀[1]) identify subcategories (see complete key on page I · 1).

Symbole im Register stellen die rechts im Schlüssel erklärten Kategorien dar. Symbole mit hochgestellten Ziffern (⋀[1]) bezeichnen Unterabteilungen einer Kategorie (vgl. vollständiger Schlüssel auf Seite I · 1).

Los símbolos incluidos en el texto del índice representan las grandes categorías identificadas con la clave a la derecha. Los símbolos con numeros en su parte superior (⋀[1]) identifican las subcategorías (véase la clave completa en la página I · 1).

Les symboles de l'index représentent les catégories indiquées dans la légende à droite. Les symboles suivis d'un indice (⋀[1]) représentent des sous-catégories (voir légende complète à la page I · 1).

Os símbolos incluídos no texto do índice representam as grandes categorias identificadas com a chave à direita. Os símbolos com números em sua parte superior (⋀[1]) identificam as subcategorias (veja-se a chave completa à página I · 1).

∧ Mountain	Berg	Montaña	Montagne	Montanha
⋀ Mountains	Gebirge	Montañas	Montagnes	Montanhas
)(Pass	Paß	Paso	Col	Passo
V Valley, Canyon	Tal, Cañon	Valle, Cañón	Vallée, Canyon	Vale, Canhão
≡ Plain	Ebene	Llano	Plaine	Planície
> Cape	Kap	Cabo	Cap	Cabo
I Island	Insel	Isla	Île	Ilha
II Islands	Inseln	Islas	Îles	Ilhas
⊥ Other Topographic Features	Andere Topographische Objekte	Otros Elementos Topográficos	Autres données topographiques	Outros acidentes topográficos

Vele-Vicq *I* · 185

ESPAÑOL

Nombre	Página	Lat.°′	Long.°′ W = Oeste
Velebit ⩘	36	44.38 N	15.03 E
Velebitski Kanal ʮ	36	45.00 N	14.50 E
Velegož	82	54.42 N	37.16 E
Veleka ≃	38	42.04 N	27.58 E
Velemín	54	50.33 N	13.59 E
Velen	52	51.53 N	6.59 E
Velencei-tó ⊜	30	47.12 N	18.35 E
Velesa ≃	76	56.03 N	31.58 E
Velešín	61	48.50 N	14.28 E
Velestínon	38	39.23 N	22.45 E
Velet'ma	80	55.20 N	42.25 E
Velevščina	76	54.44 N	28.35 E
Vélez	246	6.01 N	73.41 W
Velez de la Gomera, Peñón de I	34	35.11 N	4.21 W
Vélez-Málaga	34	36.47 N	4.06 W
Vélez Rubio	34	37.39 N	2.04 W
Velgast	54	54.16 N	12.48 E
Vel'gija	76	58.23 N	33.59 E
Velhas, Canal do ≊	287a	22.42 S	43.22 W
Velhas, Rio das ≃	255	17.13 S	44.49 W
Veličkovo	82	54.59 N	36.46 E
Velika Gorica	36	45.43 N	16.05 E
Velikaja, Ross.	24	59.13 N	49.04 E
Velikaja, Ross.	180	64.04 N	176.12 E
Velikaja ≃, Ross.	74	64.40 N	176.20 E
Velikaja ≃, Ross.	76	57.48 N	28.20 E
Velikaja Aleksandrovka	78	47.20 N	33.18 E
Velikaja Bagačka	78	49.47 N	33.43 E
Velikaja Beloz'orka	78	47.16 N	34.42 E
Velikaja Danilovka	78	50.04 N	36.19 E
Velikaja Dymerka	78	50.36 N	30.55 E
Velikaja Gluša	78	51.49 N	25.02 E
Velikaja Kema	89	45.30 N	137.12 E
Velikaja Kochnovka	78	49.07 N	33.27 E
Velikaja Korenicha	78	46.57 N	31.54 E
Velikaja Kosnica	78	48.09 N	28.27 E
Velikaja Lepeticha	78	47.11 N	33.56 E
Velikaja Michajlovka	78	47.04 N	29.52 E
Velikaja Novos'olka	78	47.50 N	36.50 E
Velikaja Pisarevka	78	50.26 N	35.28 E
Velikaja Rublevka	78	49.53 N	34.49 E
Velikaja Vradijevka	78	47.52 N	30.35 E
Velika Kapela ⩘	36	45.15 N	15.00 E
Velika Morava ≃	38	44.43 N	21.03 E
Velika Plana	38	44.20 N	21.04 E
Velike Lašče	36	45.50 N	14.38 E
Veliki Bečkerek → Zrenjanin	38	45.23 N	20.24 E
Velikij Ber'oznyj	78	48.53 N	22.27 E
Velikij Bor	78	52.02 N	29.56 E
Velikij Burluk	78	50.05 N	37.24 E
Velikij Byčkov	78	47.58 N	24.03 E
Velikij Chutor	78	49.52 N	32.06 E
Velikij Dvor	82	56.46 N	37.25 E
Velikije Borki	78	49.32 N	25.45 E
Velikije Dederkaly	78	50.02 N	26.07 E
Velikije Kopani	78	46.29 N	32.59 E
Velikije Korovincy	78	49.59 N	28.17 E
Velikije Krynki	78	49.27 N	33.29 E
Velikije Lučki	78	48.26 N	22.35 E
Velikije Luki	76	56.20 N	30.32 E
Velikije Mosty	78	50.14 N	24.06 E
Velikije Soročincy	78	50.03 N	33.56 E
Velikij Gluboček	78	49.37 N	25.32 E
Velikij Log	83	48.15 N	39.33 E
Velikij Ust'ug	24	60.48 N	46.18 E
Velikij Žvančik	78	48.46 N	26.59 E
Veliki kanal ≊	38	45.45 N	18.50 E
Veliki Stol (Hochstuhl) ∧	61	46.26 N	14.10 E
Veliki Vitorog ∧	36	44.07 N	17.03 E
Velikoanadol'skij les ♦	83	47.42 N	37.23 E
Velikoarch-angel'skoje	78	50.51 N	40.46 E
Velikockoje	83	49.21 N	40.02 E
Velikodolinskoje	78	46.21 N	30.35 E
Velikodvorskaja	76	60.18 N	41.58 E
Velikodvorskij	80	55.15 N	40.41 E
Veliko Gradište	38	44.45 N	21.32 E
Velikoje, Ross.	76	59.32 N	36.59 E
Velikoje, Ross.	80	57.21 N	39.47 E
Velikoje, ozero ⊜, Ross.	76	57.02 N	36.34 E
Velikoje, ozero ⊜, Ross.	80	55.13 N	40.10 E
Velikonda Hills ⩘[2]	122	14.45 N	79.10 E
Velikookt'abr'skij	76	57.26 N	33.49 E
Velikoploskoje	78	47.01 N	29.40 E
Velikorusskoje	86	54.39 N	74.38 E
Veliko Târnovo	38	43.04 N	25.39 E
Velikovisočnoje	24	67.16 N	52.01 E
Velikovo	76	59.18 N	42.08 E
Velilla de San Antonio	266a	40.22 N	3.29 W
Veli Lošinj	36	44.31 N	14.30 E
Velimče	78	51.36 N	24.44 E
Vélingara, Sén.	150	15.00 N	14.40 W
Vélingara, Sén.	150	13.09 N	14.07 W
Velingrad	38	42.04 N	24.00 E
Velino ≃	66	42.33 N	12.43 E
Velino, Monte ∧	66	42.09 N	13.23 E
Velíž	76	55.38 N	31.12 E
Velížany	86	57.34 N	65.49 E
Vélizy-Villacoublay	261	48.47 N	2.10 E
Veljaminovo, Ross.	82	55.12 N	37.52 E
Veljaminovo, Ross.	82	55.53 N	36.52 E
Velká Bíteš	30	49.17 N	16.13 E
Vel'ké Kapušany	30	48.33 N	22.04 E
Velké Meziříčí	30	49.21 N	16.00 E
Velké Němčie	61	48.59 N	16.40 E
Velké Pavlovice	61	48.54 N	16.49 E
Velký Bor	60	49.22 N	13.42 E
Velký Šenov	54	51.00 N	14.25 E
Vellach ≃	61	46.35 N	14.29 E
Vella Gulf ʮ	175e	8.00 S	156.50 E
Vella Lavella I	175e	7.45 S	156.40 E
Vellano	66	43.57 N	10.43 E
Vellār ≃	122	11.29 N	79.46 E
Vellberg	56	49.05 N	9.53 E
Vellechevreux-et-Courbenans	58	47.33 N	6.32 E
Velletri	66	41.41 N	12.47 E
Vellinge	41	55.28 N	13.01 E
Vellmar	56	51.21 N	9.28 E
Vellore, On., Can.	275b	43.50 N	79.34 W
Vellore, India	122	12.56 N	79.08 E
Velm	264b	48.03 N	16.27 E
Velma	196	34.27 N	97.40 W
Vel'maj ≃	180	67.26 N	175.28 W
Velmede	56	51.21 N	8.22 E
Velo d'Astico	64	45.43 N	11.23 E
Velp	52	52.00 N	5.59 E
Velp ≃	56	50.58 N	5.05 E
Velpke	54	52.24 N	10.56 E
Velsen	52	52.27 N	4.39 E
Vel'sk	24	61.05 N	42.05 E
Vel't	24	68.03 N	49.55 E
Velten	54	52.41 N	13.10 E
Veltheim	52	52.11 N	8.58 E
Veltrusy	54	50.14 N	14.18 E
Veluwe ◆[1]	52	52.12 N	5.45 E
Veluwemeer ⊜	52	52.22 N	5.38 E
Velva, It.	62	44.16 N	9.33 E
Velva, N.D., U.S.	198	48.03 N	100.55 W
Velvary	54	50.15 N	14.15 E
Vémars	261	49.04 N	2.34 E
Vemdalen	26	62.27 N	13.52 E
Vemmenæs	41	54.59 N	10.40 E
Ven I	41	55.54 N	12.41 E
Venachar, Loch ⊜	46	56.13 N	4.19 W
Venaco	36	42.14 N	9.10 E
Venadillo	246	4.43 N	74.55 W
Venado	234	22.56 N	101.05 W
Venado, Isla I	241r	10.00 N	62.25 W
Venado, Isla del I	236	11.57 N	83.44 W
Venado Tuerto	252	33.45 S	61.58 W

FRANÇAIS

Nom	Page	Lat.°′	Long.°′ W = Ouest
Venafiorita, Aeroporto di ⊠	71	40.53 N	9.30 E
Venafro	66	41.29 N	14.02 E
Venâncio Aires	252	29.36 S	52.11 W
Venango	214	41.46 N	80.07 W
Venango □[6]	214	41.24 N	79.50 W
Venanson	62	44.03 N	7.15 E
Venant	261	48.30 N	2.06 E
Venarey-les-Laumes	58	47.32 N	4.26 E
Venaria	62	45.08 N	7.38 E
Venasca	62	44.33 N	7.24 E
Venasque	62	43.59 N	5.09 E
Vence	62	43.43 N	7.07 E
Venceslau Brás	256	22.31 S	45.21 W
Venceslau Braz	255	23.51 S	49.48 W
Vencimont	56	50.02 N	4.55 E
Venda □[1], Afr.	138	23.00 S	30.30 E
Venda □[1], Afr.	156	23.00 S	30.30 E
Venda Nova	34	41.40 N	7.58 W
Vendargues	62	43.39 N	3.58 E
Vendas Novas	34	38.41 N	8.28 W
Vendée □[5]	32	46.40 N	1.20 W
Vendéen, Bocage ◆[1]	32	46.40 N	1.30 W
Vendel	40	60.10 N	17.36 E
Vendelsö	40	59.12 N	18.12 E
Vendeuvre-sur-Barse	58	48.14 N	4.28 E
Vendičany	78	48.37 N	27.48 E
Vendin-lès-Béthune	50	50.32 N	2.37 E
Vendin-le-Vieil	50	50.28 N	2.52 E
Vendôme	50	47.48 N	1.04 E
Vendsyssel ◆[1]	26	57.20 N	10.00 E
Venecia, C.R.	236	10.22 N	84.17 W
Venecia → Venezia, It.	64	45.27 N	12.21 E
Venedig → Venezia	64	45.27 N	12.21 E
Venedocia	216	40.44 N	84.25 W
Venedy	219	38.24 N	89.39 W
Veneta, Laguna c	64	45.25 N	12.19 E
Venetia	214	40.15 N	80.03 W
Venetian Village	216	42.24 N	88.02 W
Venetie	180	67.01 N	146.25 W
Veneto □[4]	64	45.30 N	11.45 E
Venev	82	54.21 N	38.16 E
Venezia (Venice)	64	45.27 N	12.21 E
Venezia □[4]	64	45.35 N	12.34 E
Venezuela □[1], S.A.	242	8.00 N	66.00 W
Venezuela □[1], S.A.	246	8.00 N	66.00 W
Venezuela, Golfo de c	246	11.30 N	71.00 W
Venezuelan Basin ✢[1]	16	15.00 N	68.00 W
Veng	41	56.07 N	9.53 E
Vengerovka	83	48.43 N	38.24 E
Vengerovo	86	55.41 N	76.45 E
Vengurla	122	15.52 N	73.38 E
Veniaminof, Mount ∧	180	56.13 N	159.18 W
Venice → Venezia, It.	64	45.27 N	12.21 E
Venice, Fl., U.S.	220	27.05 N	82.27 W
Venice, Il., U.S.	219	38.40 N	90.10 W
Venice, La., U.S.	194	29.16 N	89.21 W
Venice, Oh., U.S.	214	41.27 N	82.46 W
Venice, Pa., U.S.	279b	40.19 N	80.14 W
Venice ◆[8]	228	34.00 N	118.29 W
Venice, Gulf of c	64	45.15 N	13.00 E
Venice Gardens	220	27.04 N	82.26 W
Venise → Venezia	64	45.27 N	12.21 E
Vénissieux	62	45.41 N	4.53 E
Venjan	26	60.57 N	13.55 E
Venjansjön ⊜	26	60.54 N	14.00 E
Venkatagiri	122	13.58 N	79.35 E
Venlo	52	51.24 N	6.10 E
Vennesla	26	58.17 N	7.59 E
Vennhausen ◆[8]	263	51.13 N	6.51 E
Venosa	68	40.57 N	15.49 E
Vénosc	62	44.59 N	6.07 E
Venosta, Val V	64	46.40 N	10.35 E
Venoste, Alpi (Ötztaler Alpen) ⩘	64	46.45 N	10.55 E
Venray	52	51.32 N	5.59 E
Vent	64	46.52 N	10.56 E
Vent, Îles du → Windward Islands II	238	13.00 N	61.00 W
Venta ≃	76	57.24 N	21.33 E
Ventanas	246	1.23 S	79.25 W
Ventasso, Monte ∧	64	44.23 N	10.17 E
Ventersburg	158	28.09 S	27.08 E
Ventersdorp	158	26.17 S	26.48 E
Venterspos	273d	26.18 S	27.39 E
Venterstad	158	30.47 S	25.48 E
Venticano	68	41.05 N	14.50 E
Ventimiglia	62	43.47 N	7.36 E
Ventimiglia di Sicilia	70	37.55 N	13.34 E
Ventnor	42	50.36 N	1.11 W
Ventnor City	208	39.20 N	74.28 W
Ventotene	66	40.48 N	13.26 E
Ventotene, Isola I	66	40.47 N	13.25 E
Ventoux, Mont ∧	62	44.10 N	5.17 E
Ventry	48	52.08 N	10.22 W
Ventspils	76	57.24 N	21.36 E
Ventuari ≃	246	3.58 N	67.02 W
Ventura (San Buenaventura)	228	34.16 N	119.17 W
Ventura □[6]	228	34.30 N	119.00 W
Ventura ≃	228	34.16 N	119.18 W
Venturina	66	43.02 N	10.36 E
Venus, Fl., U.S.	220	27.04 N	81.21 W
Venus, Pa., U.S.	214	41.22 N	79.29 W
Venus, Tx., U.S.	222	32.26 N	97.06 W
Vénus, Pointe ›	174s	17.29 S	149.29 W
Venus Bay c	169	38.40 S	145.43 E
Venustiano Carranza, Méx.	232	16.21 N	92.33 W
Venustiano Carranza, Méx.	234	19.44 N	103.47 W
Venustiano Carranza, Méx.	234	20.31 N	97.38 W
Venustiano Carranza, Bahía c	232	19.20 N	87.35 W
Venustiano Carranza, Presa ⊜[1]	232	27.30 N	100.40 W
Venzone	64	46.20 N	13.09 E
Véore ≃	62	44.49 N	4.49 E
Vép	61	47.14 N	16.44 E
Veprik	78	50.23 N	34.11 E
Vepsovskaja vozvyšennost' ⩘[1]	76	60.20 N	35.15 E
Ver ≃	42	51.42 N	0.20 W
Vera, Arg.	252	29.28 S	60.13 W
Vera, Esp.	34	37.15 N	1.52 W
Vera, Il., U.S.	219	39.02 N	89.07 W
Veracruz, Méx.	200	32.25 N	115.05 W
Vera Cruz, Pa., U.S.	208	40.30 N	75.30 W
Veracruz □[3]	234	19.20 N	96.40 W
Veracruz [Llave]	234	19.12 N	96.08 W
Veraguas □[4]	236	8.30 N	81.00 W
Verano Brianza	266b	45.41 N	9.14 E
Veranópolis	252	28.57 S	51.33 W
Verāval	120	20.54 N	70.22 E
Verba	78	50.17 N	25.37 E
Verbania	58	45.56 N	8.33 E
Verbank	210	41.44 N	73.43 W
Verbeek, Pegunungan ⩘	112	2.35 S	121.25 E
Verberg ◆[8]	263	51.22 N	6.36 E
Verberie	50	49.19 N	2.44 E
Verbicaro	68	39.45 N	15.55 E
Verbier	58	46.06 N	7.13 E
Verbilki	82	56.32 N	37.36 E
Verbinskij	83	47.53 N	40.02 E
Verbl'užka	78	48.23 N	32.54 E
Verbovskij	80	55.32 N	42.00 E
Vercelli	62	45.19 N	8.25 E
Vercelli □[4]	62	45.37 N	8.10 E
Vercel-Villedieu-le-Camp	58	47.11 N	6.24 E

PORTUGUÊS

Nome	Página	Lat.°′	Long.°′ W = Oeste
Verch'aja Irmen'	86	54.35 N	82.14 E
Verchazovka	80	50.56 N	48.46 E
Verche e Talyzino	80	55.06 N	45.49 E
Verchères	206	45.47 N	73.21 W
Verchères □[6]	206	45.45 N	73.20 W
Verchn'ačka	78	48.49 N	30.02 E
Verchn'aja Amga	74	59.30 N	126.08 E
Verchn'aja Angara ≃	88	55.42 N	109.54 E
Verchn'aja Balkarija	84	43.06 N	43.24 E
Verchn'aja Buzinovka	80	49.04 N	43.12 E
Verchn'aja Čebula	86	56.02 N	87.36 E
Verchn'aja Chava	78	51.50 N	39.56 E
Verchn'aja Chila	88	52.06 N	115.54 E
Verchn'aja Chortica	78	47.51 N	35.01 E
Verchn'aja Čuginka	83	48.55 N	39.39 E
Verchn'aja Dobrinka	80	50.46 N	45.03 E
Verchn'aja Gniluša	78	50.16 N	40.23 E
Verchn'aja Grajvoronka	78	51.41 N	37.46 E
Verchn'aja Inta	24	66.00 N	60.20 E
Verchn'aja Maza	80	52.58 N	47.56 E
Verchn'aja Orl'anka	80	53.44 N	51.04 E
Verchn'aja Pyšma	86	56.55 N	60.37 E
Verchn'aja Salda	86	58.02 N	60.33 E
Verchn'aja Serebr'akovka	80	47.21 N	42.14 E
Verchn'aja Sin'ačicha	86	57.59 N	61.40 E
Verchn'aja Sysert'	86	56.26 N	60.46 E
Verchn'aja Tajmyra ≃	74	74.15 N	99.48 E
Verchn'aja Tarka	86	56.37 N	77.30 E
Verchnaja Tereška	80	52.54 N	47.24 E
Verchn'aja Tišanka	78	51.19 N	40.32 E
Verchn'aja Tojma	24	62.13 N	45.00 E
Verchn'aja Troica	76	57.15 N	37.08 E
Verchn'aja Tura	86	58.22 N	59.49 E
Verchn'aja Zaimka	88	55.51 N	110.09 E
Verchn'aja Zima	88	53.48 N	101.47 E
Verchneaks'onovskij	80	48.21 N	42.38 E
Verchneangarskij chrebet ⩘	88	56.20 N	111.30 E
Verchne-Anikin	83	48.09 N	39.59 E
Verchnebakanskij	78	44.52 N	37.39 E
Verchneber'ozovskij	86	50.17 N	82.13 E
Verchnebuzanskij	80	46.38 N	48.02 E
Verchnecaricynskij	80	48.23 N	43.57 E
Verchnedneprovsk	78	48.39 N	34.21 E
Verchnedneprovskij	76	54.59 N	33.21 E
Verchneduvannyj	78	48.20 N	39.48 E
Verchnedvinsk	76	55.47 N	27.56 E
Verchneimbatskoje	74	63.11 N	87.58 E
Verchnejarkejevo	80	55.27 N	54.19 E
Verchneje	78	48.53 N	38.28 E
Verchneje ◆[8]	83	48.53 N	38.28 E
Verchneje Šachlovo	82	55.02 N	37.15 E
Verchneje Sinevidnoje	78	49.06 N	23.34 E
Verchnekarabachskij kanal ≊	84	39.44 N	47.57 E
Verchnemakejevka	78	49.10 N	41.03 E
Verchnemulomskoje vodochranilišče ⊜[1]	24	68.30 N	31.05 E
Verchnesadovoje	78	44.42 N	33.42 E
Verchnesjezžeje	80	52.44 N	51.15 E
Verchnespasskoje	80	52.39 N	41.47 E
Verchne-T'oploje	83	48.51 N	39.26 E
Verchnetulomskij	24	68.38 N	31.45 E
Verchneural'sk	86	53.53 N	59.13 E
Verchneusinskoje	86	52.14 N	93.01 E
Verchnevil'ujsk	74	63.27 N	120.18 E
Verchnevolynskoje	85	40.43 N	68.51 E
Verchnij Amyl	88	53.08 N	94.30 E
Verchnij Avz'an	86	53.32 N	57.33 E
Verchnij Balykle	80	49.34 N	45.10 E
Verchnij Baskunčak	80	48.14 N	46.44 E
Verchnij Byk	78	50.43 N	41.14 E
Verchnije Dvoriki	82	56.28 N	38.22 E
Verchnije Kigi	86	55.25 N	58.37 E
Verchnije Korobki	80	50.19 N	44.38 E
Verchnije Lipki	80	49.38 N	43.51 E
Verchnije Tatyšly	86	56.17 N	55.52 E
Verchnij Ikorec	78	51.11 N	39.46 E
Verchnij Karačan	80	51.24 N	41.46 E
Verchnij Krasnyj Pereval	89	46.33 N	134.37 E
Verchnij Kužebar	86	53.22 N	93.15 E
Verchnij Landech	80	56.51 N	42.36 E
Verchnij Leb'ažinskij	80	46.45 N	47.50 E
Verchnij Lomov	80	53.28 N	43.34 E
Verchnij Lomovec	76	52.13 N	38.37 E
Verchnij Mamon	78	50.10 N	40.23 E
Verchnij Most	76	57.31 N	28.50 E
Verchnij Nejvinskij	86	57.17 N	60.09 E
Verchnij Petr'ak	86	57.29 N	77.30 E
Verchnij Rogačik	78	47.14 N	34.21 E
Verchnij Šergol'džin	88	50.12 N	108.20 E
Verchnij Tagil	86	57.22 N	59.56 E
Verchnij Takermen'	80	55.39 N	52.43 E
Verchnij Trojanov Val (Upper Trajan's Wall) ⊥	38	46.35 N	29.00 E
Verchnij Ufalej	86	56.04 N	60.14 E
Verchnij Ul'chun	88	49.34 N	112.32 E
Verchnij Uslon	80	55.47 N	48.57 E
Verchnij Zub, gora ∧	86	53.45 N	89.15 E
Verchnyje Nikul'asy	76	60.25 N	30.45 E
Verchnyj Jenisej (Ulug-Chem) ≃	88	51.47 N	92.00 E
Verchnyj Nagol'čik	83	48.05 N	39.06 E
Verchojansk	74	67.35 N	133.27 E
Verchojanskij chrebet ⩘	74	67.00 N	129.00 E
Vercholensk	88	54.06 N	105.35 E
Verchopuja	24	61.34 N	41.31 E
Verchošižemje	80	58.01 N	49.07 E
Verchososna	78	50.44 N	38.14 E
Verchoturje	86	58.52 N	60.48 E
Verchoturovo	86	58.22 N	95.21 E
Verchovažje	24	60.45 N	42.00 E
Verchovcevo	78	48.29 N	34.14 E
Verchovina	78	48.09 N	24.47 E
Verchovino	76	59.33 N	43.19 E
Verchovje	76	52.49 N	37.14 E
Verchovl'an'	82	55.03 N	38.21 E
Verchozim	80	52.56 N	46.23 E
Verchubinka	86	50.29 N	82.26 E
Verclause	62	44.23 N	5.26 E
Vercors ◆[1]	62	44.57 N	5.25 E
Verdalsøra	26	63.48 N	11.29 E
Verde ≃, Bra.	248	11.54 S	55.48 W
Verde ≃, Bra.	248	13.33 S	58.01 W
Verde ≃, Bra.	250	10.27 S	42.16 W
Verde ≃, Bra.	255	15.07 S	48.40 W
Verde ≃, Bra.	255	17.05 S	46.05 W
Verde ≃, Bra.	255	18.01 S	50.14 W
Verde ≃, Bra.	255	19.11 S	50.44 W
Verde ≃, Bra.	255	19.55 S	49.45 W
Verde ≃, Bra.	255	21.12 S	51.53 W
Verde ≃, Bra.	256	21.34 S	45.31 W
Verde ≃, Bra.	256	21.38 S	47.03 W
Verde ≃, Méx.	234	16.45 N	98.07 W
Verde ≃, Méx.	234	15.59 N	97.47 W
Verde ≃, Méx.	234	21.37 N	99.15 W
Verde ≃, Méx.	234	20.42 N	103.14 W
Verde ≃, Para.	252	23.09 S	57.37 W
Verde ≃, S.A.	248	13.59 S	60.24 W
Verde ≃, Az., U.S.	200	33.33 N	111.40 W
Verde, Arroyo ≃, Arg.	254	41.56 S	65.03 W
Verde, Arroyo ≃, Bol.	248	11.25 S	66.20 W
Verde, Cape ›	238	22.50 N	74.52 W
Verde, Cerro ∧	234	20.30 N	104.36 W
Verde, Costa ⩟[2]	71	39.34 N	8.28 E
Verde Grande ≃	255	14.35 S	43.53 W
Verde Island I	116	13.33 N	121.05 E
Verde Island Passage ʮ	116	13.34 N	120.51 E
Verdello	62	45.36 N	9.37 E
Verden, Dtsch.	52	52.55 N	9.13 E

Verden, Ok., U.S.	196	35.05 N	98.05 W
Verde Pequeno ≃	255	14.48 S	43.31 W
Verdesela, Pinhal da ♦	266c	38.37 N	9.08 W
Verdi	226	39.31 N	119.59 W
Verdigre	198	42.35 N	98.02 W
Verdigre Creek ≃	198	42.42 N	98.03 W
Verdigris ≃	196	35.48 N	95.19 W
Verdinho ≃	255	17.29 S	50.27 W
Verdon	198	40.08 N	95.42 W
Verdon ≃	62	43.43 N	5.46 E
Verdon, Canal du ≊	62	43.43 N	5.57 E
Verdoy	210	42.46 N	73.48 W
Verduga	76	58.46 N	29.12 E
Verdugo Mountains ⩘	280	34.13 N	118.18 W
Verdun, P.Q., Can.	206	45.27 N	73.34 W
Verdun, Fr.	32	43.52 N	1.14 E
Verdun-sur-le-Doubs	58	46.54 N	5.01 E
Verdun-sur-Meuse	56	49.10 N	5.23 E
Verdura ≃	70	37.28 N	13.12 E
Vereb'jo	76	58.41 N	32.42 E
Vereeniging	158	26.38 S	27.57 E
Veregin	184	51.35 N	102.05 W
Vereinigte Arabische Emirate → United Arab Emirates □[1]	128	24.00 N	54.00 E
Vereinigte Königreich → United Kingdom □[1]	28	54.00 N	2.00 W
Vereinigte Staaten → United States □[1]	178	38.00 N	97.00 W
Vereja, Ross.	82	55.46 N	39.06 E
Vereja, Ross.	82	55.21 N	36.11 E
Vereja, Ross.	265b	55.37 N	38.02 E
Veremejki	76	53.46 N	31.15 E
Vereščagino, Ross.	74	64.14 N	87.37 E
Vereščagino, Ross.	80	58.05 N	54.40 E
Veresegyház	264c	47.39 N	19.17 E
Veresoč'	78	51.19 N	31.46 E
Veretje	82	54.08 N	36.17 E
Véretz	50	47.22 N	0.48 E
Verga	285	39.52 N	75.10 W
Verga, Cap ›	150	10.12 N	14.27 W
Vergara	252	32.56 S	53.57 W
Vergato	64	44.17 N	11.07 E
Vergel	196	25.39 N	103.32 W
Vergeletto	58	46.14 N	8.36 E
Vergemont Creek ≃	166	24.12 S	143.17 E
Vergennes	188	44.10 N	73.15 W
Verghereto	66	43.47 N	12.00 E
Vergiate	62	45.43 N	8.42 E
Vergons	62	43.55 N	6.35 E
Vergt	32	45.02 N	0.43 E
Vergulevka	83	48.24 N	38.32 E
Verigino	82	56.42 N	38.08 E
Verín	34	41.56 N	7.26 W
Veringenstadt	58	48.11 N	9.12 E
Verin Talin	84	40.23 N	43.53 E
Veriora	76	58.00 N	27.21 E
Veríssimo	255	19.42 S	48.18 W
Verkeerdevlei	158	28.48 S	26.48 E
Verkhneudinsk → Ulan-Ude	88	51.50 N	107.37 E
Verkhniy Ufaley → Verchnij Ufalej	86	56.04 N	60.14 E
Verkhnyaya Salda → Verchn'aja Salda	86	58.02 N	60.33 E
Verkhoyansk → Verchojansk	74	67.35 N	133.27 E
Verkykerskop	158	27.54 S	29.17 E
Verl (Senne I)	52	51.53 N	8.31 E
Vermaaklikheid	158	34.19 S	21.01 E
Vermaas	158	26.30 S	25.59 E
Vermand	50	49.52 N	3.09 E
Vermejo ≃	196	36.30 N	104.33 W
Vermelho ≃, Bra.	250	9.16 S	47.23 W
Vermelho ≃, Bra.	250	7.44 S	47.17 W
Vermelho ≃, Bra.	250	5.33 S	49.14 W
Vermelho ≃, Bra.	255	14.54 S	51.06 W
Vermenton	50	47.40 N	3.44 E
Vermette Lake ⊜	184	55.40 N	109.05 W
Vermezzo	266b	45.24 N	8.59 E
Vermiglio	64	46.18 N	10.42 E
Vermilion, Ab., Can.	182	53.22 N	110.51 W
Vermilion, Oh., U.S.	214	41.25 N	82.21 W
Vermilion □[6]	216	40.08 N	87.37 W
Vermilion ≃, Ab., Can.	184	53.44 N	110.18 W
Vermilion ≃, On., Can.	190	46.16 N	81.41 W
Vermilion ≃, Il., U.S.	216	41.19 N	89.04 W
Vermilion ≃, La., U.S.	194	29.46 N	92.09 W
Vermilion ≃, Mn., U.S.	190	48.16 N	92.30 W
Vermilion ≃, Oh., U.S.	214	41.26 N	82.22 W
Vermilion, Middle Fork ≃	216	40.12 N	87.45 W
Vermilion, North Fork ≃, Il., U.S.	216	40.49 N	88.30 W
Vermilion, North Fork ≃, Il., U.S.	216	40.13 N	87.39 W
Vermilion, South Fork ≃	216	40.49 N	88.30 W
Vermilion Bay	184	49.51 N	93.24 W
Vermilion Bay c	194	29.40 N	92.00 W
Vermilion Lake ⊜, On., Can.	184	50.03 N	92.13 W
Vermilion Lake ⊜, Mn., U.S.	190	47.53 N	92.25 W
Vermilion Pass)(	182	51.14 N	116.03 W
Vermillion	198	42.46 N	96.55 W
Vermillion ≃	198	42.44 N	96.53 W
Vermillion, East Fork ≃	198	43.44 N	97.03 W
Vermillion, West Fork ≃	198	43.44 N	97.03 W
Vermillion Bluffs ⩟[4]	200	40.50 N	108.30 W
Vermillion Creek ≃, U.S.	200	40.46 N	108.53 W
Vermillion Creek ≃, Ks., U.S.	198	39.12 N	96.13 W
Vermont, Austl.	274b	37.50 S	145.12 E
Vermont, Il., U.S.	194	40.17 N	90.25 W
Vermont □[3], U.S.	178	43.50 N	72.45 W
Vermont □[3], U.S.	188	43.50 N	72.45 W
Vermontville	216	42.37 N	85.01 W
Vernà, Pizzo di ∧	70	38.01 N	15.15 E
Vernaison	62	45.39 N	4.49 E
Vernal	200	40.27 N	109.31 W
Vernalis	226	37.37 N	121.17 W
Vernante	62	44.15 N	7.32 E
Vernayaz	58	46.08 N	7.02 E
Vernazza	62	44.08 N	9.41 E
Verndale	198	46.24 N	95.01 W
Verne	52	51.41 N	8.34 E
Verner	190	46.25 N	80.07 W
Verneuil	32	48.44 N	0.56 E
Verneuil-L'Étang	261	48.39 N	2.50 E
Verneuil-sur-Avre	50	48.44 N	0.56 E
Verneuil-sur-Seine	261	48.59 N	1.59 E
Verneukpan	158	30.00 S	21.00 E
Verneukpan ≋	158	30.00 S	21.10 E
Vernier	58	46.13 N	6.06 E
Verninge	41	55.18 N	10.13 E
Vernio	66	44.03 N	11.09 E
Vernole	68	40.17 N	18.18 E
Vernon, B.C., Can.	182	50.16 N	119.16 W
Vernon, On., Can.	212	45.10 N	75.28 W
Vernon, Fr.	50	49.05 N	1.29 E
Vernon, Al., U.S.	194	33.45 N	88.06 W
Vernon, Ca., U.S.	280	34.01 N	118.13 W
Vernon, Ct., U.S.	207	41.49 N	72.28 W
Vernon, Fl., U.S.	194	30.37 N	85.42 W
Vernon, Il., U.S.	219	38.48 N	89.05 W
Vernon, In., U.S.	218	38.59 N	85.36 W

Vernon, Mi., U.S.	216	42.56 N	84.02 W
Vernon, N.J., U.S.	210	41.11 N	74.29 W
Vernon, N.Y., U.S.	210	43.05 N	75.32 W
Vernon, Oh., U.S.	214	41.23 N	80.34 W
Vernon, Tx., U.S.	196	34.09 N	99.15 W
Vernon, Ut., U.S.	200	40.05 N	112.25 W
Vernon, Lake ⊜	212	45.20 N	79.17 W
Vernon Dam ◆[6]	207	42.46 N	72.31 W
Vernon Hills	278	42.13 N	87.58 W
Vernonia	224	45.51 N	123.11 W
Vernon Lake ⊜[1]	194	31.15 N	93.25 W
Vernon River	186	46.12 N	62.50 W
Vernouillet	261	48.58 N	1.59 E
Vernoux-en-Vivarais	62	44.54 N	4.39 E
Verny	56	49.01 N	6.12 E
Vero ≃	34	42.00 N	0.10 E
Vero Beach	220	27.38 N	80.23 W
Véroia	38	40.31 N	22.12 E
Verolanuova	64	45.19 N	10.04 E
Verolavecchia	64	45.19 N	10.03 E
Veroli	66	41.41 N	13.25 E
Verona, On., Can.	212	44.29 N	76.42 W
Verona, It.	64	45.27 N	11.00 E
Verona, Ky., U.S.	218	38.49 N	84.39 W
Verona, Ms., U.S.	194	34.11 N	88.43 W
Verona, N.J., U.S.	276	40.49 N	74.14 W
Verona, N.Y., U.S.	210	43.08 N	75.34 W
Verona, Oh., U.S.	218	39.54 N	84.29 W
Verona, Pa., U.S.	279b	40.30 N	79.50 W
Verona, Wi., U.S.	216	42.59 N	89.31 W
Verona □[4]	64	45.25 N	11.02 E
Verona Beach	210	43.12 N	75.44 W
Verona Beach State Park ♦	210	43.14 N	75.44 W
Verona Park	216	42.21 N	85.09 W
Verónica	258	35.22 S	57.20 W
Verperluda, ostrov I	265a	59.59 N	30.01 E
Verplanck	210	41.15 N	73.58 W
Verran	166	33.51 S	136.18 E
Verrazano-Narrows Bridge ◆[5]	210	40.36 N	74.03 W
Verrès	62	45.40 N	7.42 E
Verrettes	238	19.03 N	72.28 W
Verrey-sous-Salmaise	58	47.26 N	4.40 E
Verrières, Bois de ♦	261	48.45 N	2.15 E
Verrières-le-Buisson	261	48.45 N	2.16 E
Versa ≃	62	44.54 N	8.16 E
Versailles, Fr.	50	48.48 N	2.08 E
Versailles, Il., U.S.	194	39.53 N	90.39 W
Versailles, In., U.S.	218	39.04 N	85.15 W
Versailles, Ky., U.S.	218	38.03 N	84.43 W
Versailles, Mo., U.S.	194	38.25 N	92.50 W
Versailles, N.Y., U.S.	210	42.31 N	78.59 W
Versailles, Oh., U.S.	216	40.13 N	84.29 W
Versailles, Pa., U.S.	279b	40.21 N	79.51 W
Versailles, Château de ⊥	261	48.48 N	2.07 E
Versailles, Parc de ♦	261	48.49 N	2.06 E
Versailles State Park ♦	218	39.04 N	85.13 W
Verse ≃	263	51.15 N	7.46 E
Versec → Vršac	38	45.07 N	21.18 E
Versestausee ⊜[1]	263	51.11 N	7.41 E
Versien	158	27.05 S	27.52 E
Veršina Tei	86	53.20 N	89.36 E
Veršino-Darasunskij	88	52.20 N	115.32 E
Veršino-Šachtaminskij	88	51.21 N	117.50 E
Versmold	52	52.02 N	8.09 E
Versoix	58	46.16 N	6.10 E
Ver-sur-Launette	261	49.06 N	2.41 E
Vert	261	48.57 N	1.41 E
Vert, Cap ›	150	14.43 N	17.30 W
Vert'ačij	80	48.57 N	43.53 E
Verte, Île I, P.Q., Can.	186	48.02 N	69.26 W
Verte, Île I, P.Q., Can.	275a	45.34 N	73.30 W
Vertedero	240m	18.05 N	66.15 W
Verteillac	32	45.21 N	0.22 E
Vertientes	240p	21.16 N	78.09 W
Vertijevka	78	51.10 N	31.51 E
Vertkovo	82	56.07 N	36.25 E
Vert-le-Grand	261	48.34 N	2.22 E
Vert-le-Petit	261	48.33 N	2.22 E
Vertlinskoje	82	56.14 N	36.58 E
Vertou	32	47.10 N	1.29 W
Vertova	62	45.48 N	9.50 E
Vert-Saint-Denis	261	48.34 N	2.37 E
Vertus	50	48.54 N	4.00 E
Verucchio	66	43.59 N	12.25 E
Verulam	158	29.45 S	31.02 E
Verulamium ⊥	42	51.45 N	0.22 W
Verviers	56	50.35 N	5.52 E
Vervins	50	49.50 N	3.54 E
Verwall Gruppe ⩘	58	47.02 N	10.10 E
Verwood	42	50.53 N	1.52 W
Veryan	42	50.13 N	4.54 W
Verzasca ≃	58	46.09 N	8.52 E
Verzegnis	64	46.25 N	12.59 E
Verzenay	50	49.10 N	4.09 E
Verzino	68	39.19 N	16.51 E
Verzuolo	62	44.36 N	7.29 E
Verzy	50	49.09 N	4.10 E
Vesanto	26	62.56 N	26.25 E
Vesava ◆[8]	272c	19.08 N	72.48 E
Vescovato, Fr.	36	42.30 N	9.26 E
Vescovato, It.	64	45.10 N	10.10 E
Vescovo di Squillace, Roccelletta del ⊥	68	38.48 N	16.35 E
Vesdre ≃	56	50.37 N	5.37 E
Veseja	76	53.04 N	27.41 E
Veselí nad Lužnicí	30	49.11 N	14.43 E
Veselí nad Moravou	30	48.58 N	17.22 E
Veselinovo	78	47.21 N	31.14 E
Veselovskoje	86	54.00 N	78.43 E
Veselovskoje vodochranilišče ⊜[1]	80	47.00 N	41.18 E
Vésenaz	58	46.14 N	6.12 E
Vešenskaja	80	49.38 N	41.43 E
Vesgre ≃	50	48.48 N	1.36 E
Vesijärvi ⊜	26	61.06 N	25.32 E
Vesjegonsk	76	58.40 N	37.16 E
Veškajma, Ross.	80	54.04 N	47.02 E
Veškajma, Ross.	80	54.03 N	47.08 E
Veški	265b	55.56 N	37.37 E
Vesle ≃	50	49.23 N	3.38 E
Vešn'aki ◆[8]	265b	55.44 N	37.49 E
Ves'olaja Gora	83	48.43 N	39.16 E
Ves'olaja Rošča	86	53.47 N	76.22 E
Vesole, Monte ∧	68	40.24 N	15.10 E
Ves'oloje, Kaz.	85	43.19 N	77.06 E
Ves'oloje, Ross.	80	50.17 N	45.15 E
Ves'oloje, Ross.	83	47.10 N	38.45 E
Ves'oloje, Ukr.	78	47.01 N	34.55 E
Ves'olo-Voznesenka	83	47.09 N	38.20 E
Ves'olyj, Ross.	80	47.06 N	40.45 E
Ves'olyj, Ross.	83	47.20 N	39.18 E
Ves'olyje Terny	78	48.07 N	33.32 E
Ves'olyj Jar, Ross.	86	51.18 N	81.07 E
Ves'olyj Jar, Ross.	89	43.57 N	135.28 E
Ves'olyj Podol, Kaz.	86	53.31 N	65.54 E
Ves'olyj Podol, Ukr.	78	49.36 N	33.16 E
Ves'olyj Pos'olok ◆[8]	265a	59.54 N	30.28 E
Vesoul	58	47.38 N	6.10 E
Vespasiano	255	19.40 S	43.55 W
Vespolate	62	45.21 N	8.40 E
Vesta	236	9.43 N	83.03 W
Vest-Agder □[6]	26	58.30 N	7.10 E
Vestal	210	42.05 N	76.03 W
Vestal Center	210	42.02 N	76.01 W
Vestavia Hills	194	33.26 N	86.46 W
Vestbygd	26	58.06 N	6.35 E
Vesterålen II	24	68.45 N	15.00 E
Vester Egede	41	55.16 N	11.59 E
Vesterø Havn	26	57.18 N	10.56 E
Vester Skerninge	41	55.03 N	10.28 E
Vester Sottrup	41	54.57 N	9.43 E
Vestfjorden c[2]	24	68.08 N	15.00 E
Vestfold □[6]	26	59.15 N	10.10 E

Vestmannaeyjar	24a	63.26 N	20.12 W
Vestone	64	45.42 N	10.24 E
Vestreno	58	46.06 N	9.18 E
Vestsjælland □[6]	41	55.35 N	11.30 E
Vestvågøya I	24	68.15 N	13.50 E
Vésubie ≃	62	43.52 N	7.12 E
Vesubio → Vesuvio ∧[1]	68	40.49 N	14.26 E
Vesuv → Vesuvio ∧[1]	68	40.49 N	14.26 E
Vesuvio (Vesuvius) ∧[1]	68	40.49 N	14.26 E
Vesuvius → Vesuvio ∧[1]	68	40.49 N	14.26 E
Vesuvius Bay	224	48.53 N	123.35 W
Veszprém	30	47.06 N	17.55 E
Veszprém □[6]	30	47.10 N	17.40 E
Vésztő	30	46.55 N	21.16 E
Vet ≃	158	27.40 S	25.40 E
Vetapālem	122	15.47 N	80.19 E
Vetčin	76	52.27 N	28.10 E
Veterans Stadium ♦	285	39.54 N	75.10 W
Vétheuil	50	49.04 N	1.42 E
Vetju	24	62.57 N	50.44 E
Vetka	76	52.33 N	31.10 E
Vetlanda	26	57.26 N	15.04 E
Vetl'anka	80	52.52 N	51.09 E
Vetluga	80	57.51 N	45.47 E
Vetluga ≃	80	56.18 N	46.24 E
Vetlužskij, Ross.	80	57.11 N	45.07 E
Vetlužskij, Ross.	80	58.23 N	45.26 E
Vetoškino	80	57.18 N	49.44 E
Vetovo	38	43.42 N	26.16 E
Vetralla	66	42.19 N	12.03 E
Vetren	38	42.16 N	24.03 E
Vetrino	76	55.25 N	28.28 E
Vetriolo	64	46.02 N	11.18 E
Vetrişoaia	38	46.26 N	28.13 E
Větřní	61	48.46 N	14.17 E
Vetschau	54	51.47 N	14.04 E
Vettisfossen ∟	26	61.22 N	7.55 E
Vetto	64	44.29 N	10.20 E
Vettore, Monte ∧	66	42.49 N	13.16 E
Vetulonia	66	42.51 N	10.58 E
Veules-les-Roses	50	49.52 N	0.48 E
Veulettes-sur-Mer	50	49.51 N	0.36 E
Veurne (Furnes)	50	51.04 N	2.40 E
Vevay	218	38.44 N	85.04 W
Vevelstad	24	65.43 N	12.30 E
Vevenc, Khawr V	140	6.40 N	32.58 E
Vevey	58	46.28 N	6.51 E
Vex	58	46.13 N	7.24 E
Veyle ≃	58	46.18 N	4.50 E
Veynes	62	44.32 N	5.49 E
Veyrier	62	45.53 N	6.10 E
Vézelay	50	47.28 N	3.44 E
Vézelise	58	48.29 N	6.05 E
Vézénobres	62	44.03 N	4.09 E
Vézère ≃	32	44.53 N	0.53 E
Vezirköprü	130	41.09 N	35.28 E
Vezouze ≃	58	48.35 N	6.29 E
Vezza d'Oglio	64	46.14 N	10.24 E
Vezzana, Cima della ∧	64	46.17 N	11.50 E
Vezzano	64	46.05 N	11.00 E
Vezzano Ligure	64	44.09 N	9.52 E
Viacha	248	16.39 S	68.18 W
Viadana	64	44.56 N	10.31 E
Viadutos	252	27.34 S	52.01 W
Viale	252	31.53 S	60.01 W
Vialonga	266c	38.52 N	9.05 W
Via Mala V	58	46.40 N	9.26 E
Viamão	252	30.05 S	51.02 W
Viamonte	252	33.44 S	63.06 W
Vian	196	35.29 N	94.58 W
Viana	250	3.13 S	45.00 W
Viana, Ilha do I	287a	22.52 S	43.08 W
Viana del Bollo	34	42.11 N	7.06 W
Viana do Alentejo	34	38.20 N	8.00 W
Viana do Castelo	34	41.42 N	8.50 W
Vianden	56	49.57 N	6.11 E
Vianen	52	52.00 N	5.05 E
Viangchan (Vientiane)	110	17.58 N	102.36 E
Viangphoukha	110	20.41 N	101.04 E
Viar ≃	34	37.36 N	5.50 W
Viareggio	64	43.52 N	10.14 E
Viarmes	50	49.08 N	2.22 E
Viatka → Kirov	80	58.38 N	49.42 E
Viaur ≃	32	44.08 N	2.23 E
Vibank	184	50.20 N	103.55 W
Víboras, Arroyo de las ≃	258	33.57 S	58.21 W
Viborg, Dan.	26	56.26 N	9.24 E
Viborg → Vyborg, Ross.	76	60.42 N	28.45 E
Viborg, S.D., U.S.	198	43.10 N	97.04 W
Viborg □[6]	41	56.18 N	9.27 E
Vibo Valentia	68	38.40 N	16.06 E
Vibraye	50	48.03 N	0.44 E
Viburnum	194	37.42 N	91.08 W
Viby	41	55.33 N	12.02 E
Viby ◆[8]	41	56.07 N	10.10 E
Vic (Vich)	34	41.56 N	2.15 E
Vic, Étang de c	62	43.29 N	3.50 E
Vicálvaro ◆[8]	266a	40.24 N	3.36 W
Vícam	232	27.35 N	110.20 W
Vicarello	66	42.10 N	12.12 E
Vicari	70	37.49 N	13.34 E
Vicchio	66	43.56 N	11.28 E
Vicco	192	37.12 N	83.03 W
Vic-en-Bigorre	32	43.23 N	0.03 E
Vicente, Point ›	280	33.44 N	118.25 W
Vicente Casares	258	34.57 S	58.38 W
Vicente de Carvalho	256	23.56 S	46.19 W
Vicente Guerrero, Méx.	234	23.45 N	103.59 W
Vicente Guerrero, Méx.	234	18.24 N	92.53 W
Vicente Guerrero, Méx.	234	19.08 N	98.10 W
Vicente Guerrero, Presa ⊜[1]	234	24.00 N	98.45 W
Vicente López	258	34.32 S	58.28 W
Vicente López □[5]	288	34.32 S	58.30 W
Vicente Noble	238	18.23 N	71.11 W
Vicenza	64	45.33 N	11.33 E
Vicenza □[4]	64	45.40 N	11.27 E
Viceroy	184	49.27 N	105.22 W
Vichada □[5]	246	5.00 N	69.30 W
Vichada ≃	246	4.55 N	67.50 W
Vichadero	252	31.48 S	54.43 W
Vichigasta	252	29.29 S	67.31 W
Vichoreva ≃	88	56.47 N	101.22 E
Vichorevka	88	56.12 N	101.09 E
Vichra ≃	76	54.01 N	31.52 E
Vichuga → Vičuga	80	57.13 N	41.56 E
Vichuquén	252	34.53 S	72.00 W
Vichy	32	46.08 N	3.26 E
Vici	196	36.08 N	99.17 W
Vickery	214	41.23 N	82.56 W
Vicksburg, Mi., U.S.	216	42.07 N	85.31 W
Vicksburg, Ms., U.S.	194	32.21 N	90.52 W
Vicksburg, Pa., U.S.	210	40.56 N	76.59 W
Vicksburg National Military Park ♦	194	32.24 N	90.52 W
Vico	36	42.10 N	8.48 E
Vico, Lago di ⊜	66	42.19 N	12.10 E
Vico Canavese	62	45.30 N	7.47 E
Vico del Gargano	68	41.54 N	15.57 E
Vico Equense	68	40.40 N	14.25 E
Vicoforte	62	44.21 N	7.54 E
Vicopisano	66	43.42 N	10.35 E
Viçosa, Bra.	250	9.24 S	36.14 W
Viçosa, Bra.	255	20.45 S	42.53 W
Viçosa do Ceará	250	3.34 S	41.05 W
Vicosoprano	58	46.22 N	9.37 E
Vicovaro	66	42.01 N	12.54 E
Vicq	261	48.49 N	1.50 E

≃	River	Fluß	Río	Rivière	Rio
≊	Canal	Kanal	Canal	Canal	Canal
∟	Waterfall, Rapids	Wasserfall, Stromschnellen	Cascada, Rápidos	Chute d'eau, Rapides	Cascata, Rápidos
ʮ	Strait	Meeresstraße	Estrecho	Détroit	Estreito
c	Bay, Gulf	Bucht, Golf	Bahía, Golfo	Baie, Golfe	Baía, Golfo
⊜	Lake, Lakes	See, Seen	Lago, Lagos	Lac, Lacs	Lago, Lagos
≋	Swamp	Sumpf	Pantano	Marais	Pântano
⊓	Ice Features, Glaciers	Eis- und Gletscherformen	Accidentes Glaciales	Formes glaciaires	Acidentes glaciares
⊤	Other Hydrographic Features	Andere Hydrographische Objekte	Otros Elementos Hidrográficos	Autres données hydrographiques	Outros acidentes hidrográficos
✢	Submarine Features	Untermeerische Objekte	Accidentes Submarinos	Formes de relief sous-marin	Acidentes submarinos
□	Political Unit	Politische Einheit	Unidad Politica	Entité politique	Unidade política
●	Cultural Institution	Kulturelle Institution	Institución Cultural	Institution culturelle	Instituição cultural
⊥	Historical Site	Historische Stätte	Sitio Histórico	Site historique	Sítio histórico
♦	Recreational Site	Erholungs- und Ferienort	Sitio de Recreo	Centre de loisirs	Area de Lazer
⊠	Airport	Flughafen	Aeropuerto	Aéroport	Aeroporto
⊠	Military Installation	Militäranlage	Instalación Militar	Installation militaire	Instalação militar
◆	Miscellaneous	Verschiedenes	Misceláneo	Divers	Diversos

Vic-sur-Aisne 50 49.24 N 3.07 E
Vic-sur-Cère 32 44.59 N 2.37 E
Vic-sur-Seille 56 48.47 N 6.32 E
Victor, Ca., U.S. 226 38.08 N 121.12 W
Victor, Id., U.S. 202 43.36 N 111.06 W
Victor, Ia., U.S. 190 41.43 N 92.17 W
Victor, Mt., U.S. 202 46.25 N 114.08 W
Victor, N.Y., U.S. 210 42.58 N 77.24 W
Victor, Lac ⊜ 186 50.35 N 61.50 W
Victorbur 52 53.29 N 7.20 E
Victor Harbor 168b 35.34 S 138.37 E
Victoria, Arg. 252 32.37 S 60.10 W
Victoria
→ Vitória, Bra. 255 20.19 S 40.21 W
Victoria, Cam. 152 4.01 N 9.12 E
Victoria, B.C., Can. 224 48.25 N 123.22 W
Victoria, P.E., Can. 186 46.13 N 63.29 W
Victoria, Chile 252 38.13 S 72.20 W
Victoria, Gren. 241k 12.12 N 61.42 W
Victoria, Guinée 150 10.50 N 14.33 W
Victoria (Xianggang), H.K. 271d 22.17 N 114.09 E
Victoria, Malay. 112 5.17 N 115.15 E
Victoria
→ Ciudad Victoria, Méx. 234 23.44 N 99.08 W
Victoria, Pil. 116 13.12 N 121.15 E
Victoria, Pil. 116 15.35 N 120.41 E
Victoria, Rom. 38 45.45 N 24.41 E
Victoria, Sey. 138 4.38 S 55.27 E
Victoria, Ks., U.S. 198 38.51 N 99.08 W
Victoria, Tx., U.S. 196 28.48 N 97.00 W
Victoria, Va., U.S. 192 36.59 N 78.13 W
Victoria □[3] 166 38.00 S 145.00 E
Victoria □[4] 154 20.54 S 31.21 E
Victoria □[6], On., Can. 212 44.35 N 78.50 W
Victoria □[6], Tx., U.S. 222 28.55 N 97.00 W
Victoria ◆[8] 288 34.28 S 58.31 W
Victoria ≃, Austl. 160 15.12 S 129.43 E
Victoria ≃, Nf., Can. 186 48.45 N 56.40 W
Victoria ≃, Méx. 234 21.02 N 99.50 W
Victoria, Isla I 254 45.18 S 73.58 W
Victoria, Lake ⊜, Afr. 154 1.00 S 33.00 E
Victoria, Lake ⊜, Austl. 166 34.00 S 141.16 E
Victoria, Mount ∧, Mya. 110 21.14 N 93.55 E
Victoria, Mount ∧, Pap. N. Gui. 164 8.55 S 147.35 E
Victoria, Pont ◆[5] 275a 45.29 N 73.32 W
Victoria and Albert Museum ♥ 272c 18.59 N 72.50 E
Victoria Beach 184 50.43 N 96.33 W
Victoria Beach ⊥[2] 273a 6.25 N 3.25 E
Victoria de Durango
→ Durango 234 24.02 N 104.40 W
Victoria Falls 154 17.56 S 25.50 E
Victoria Falls ⌊ 154 17.55 S 25.51 E
Victoria Falls National Park ♦ 154 17.55 S 25.40 E
Victoria Gardens ♦ 272c 18.59 N 72.50 E
Victoria Harbour 212 44.45 N 79.46 W
Victoria International Airport ⊠ 224 48.39 N 123.26 W
Victoria Island I, N.T., Can. 176 71.00 N 110.00 W
Victoria Island I, Nig. 273a 6.26 N 3.26 E
Victoria Lake ⊜ 273d 26.14 S 28.09 E
Victoria Lake ⊜[1] 186 48.18 N 57.30 W
Victoria Land ◆[1] 9 75.00 S 163.00 E
Victoria Lawn Tennis Association Courts ♦ 274b 37.51 S 145.02 E
Victoria Memorial Hall ♥ 271c 1.17 N 103.51 E
Victoria Memorial Museum ♥ 272b 22.33 N 88.21 E
Victoria Nile ≃ 154 2.14 N 31.26 E
Victoria Park 168a 31.58 S 115.55 E
Victoria Park ♦, H.K. 271d 22.17 N 114.11 E
Victoria Park ♦, Eng., U.K. 262 53.23 N 2.34 W
Victoria Peak ∧, Belize 232 16.48 N 88.37 W
Victoria Peak ∧, B.C., Can. 182 50.03 N 126.06 W
Victoria Peak ∧, H.K. 271d 22.17 N 114.08 E
Victoria Peaks ∧ 116 9.22 N 118.20 E
Victoria Point 171a 27.35 S 153.18 E
Victoria Range ⋏, N.Z. 172 42.09 S 172.08 E
Victoria Range ⋏, Pil. 116 9.32 N 118.23 E
Victoria River 164 15.37 S 131.08 E
Victoria River Downs 164 16.24 S 131.00 E
Victorias 116 10.54 N 123.05 E
Victoria State Car Club Race Circuit ♦ 274b 37.45 S 145.11 E
Victoria Station ◆[5] 262 53.29 N 2.15 W
Victoria Strait ⊔ 176 69.15 N 100.30 W
Victoria Terminus ◆[5] 272c 18.57 N 72.50 E
Victoria University of Manchester ♥[2] 262 53.28 N 2.14 W
Victoriaville 206 46.03 N 71.57 W
Victoria West 158 31.25 S 23.04 E
Victorica 252 36.13 S 65.27 W
Victorino 246 2.48 N 67.50 W
Victorino de la Plaza 252 36.36 S 62.40 W
Víctor Rosales 234 22.57 N 102.42 W
Victorville 228 34.32 N 117.17 W
Victory, Mount ∧ 164 9.10 S 149.05 E
Victory Gardens 276 40.52 N 74.32 W
Victory Heights 214 41.22 N 79.46 W
Victory Hills 279b 40.11 N 79.53 W
Victory Mills 210 43.05 N 73.36 W
Victory Monument ⊥ 269a 13.46 N 100.33 E
Vičuga 80 57.13 N 41.56 E
Vicuña 252 30.02 S 70.44 W
Vicuña Mackenna 252 33.54 S 64.23 W
Vidal, Kaap ⟩ 158 28.09 S 32.33 E
Vidal Gormaz, Isla I 254 52.00 S 74.45 W
Vidalia, Ga., U.S. 192 32.13 N 82.24 W
Vidalia, La., U.S. 194 31.33 N 91.25 W
Vidal Ramos 252 27.23 S 49.22 W
Vidauban 62 43.26 N 6.26 E
Videbæk 26 56.05 N 8.38 E
Videira 252 27.00 S 51.08 W
Videle 38 44.16 N 25.31 E
Vidigueira 34 38.13 N 7.48 W
Vidim, Česká Rep. 54 50.28 N 14.31 E
Vidim, Ross. 88 56.29 N 103.09 E
Vidin 38 43.59 N 22.52 E
Vidisha 124 23.32 N 77.49 E
Vidlica 24 61.10 N 32.21 E
Vidnoje 82 55.34 N 37.41 E
Vidogošči 82 56.42 N 36.23 E
Vidor 194 30.07 N 94.00 W
Vidos ≃ 267b 40.58 N 28.53 E
Vidöstern ⊜ 26 57.04 N 14.01 E
Vidourle ≃ 62 43.32 N 4.08 E
Vidra, Rom. 38 44.16 N 26.11 E
Vidra, Rom. 38 45.55 N 26.54 E
Vidsel 24 65.51 N 20.24 E
Vidzeme □[9] 76 57.10 N 25.30 E
Vidzy 76 55.24 N 26.38 E
Vie ≃ 50 49.05 N 0.04 E
Viecht 60 48.30 N 12.04 E
Viechtach 60 49.05 N 12.53 E
Viechtwang 61 47.55 N 13.57 E
Viedma 254 40.48 S 63.00 W
Viedma, Lago ⊜ 254 49.35 S 72.35 W
Viehberg ∧ 61 48.33 N 14.37 E
Viehhausen 60 48.59 N 11.58 E
Vieil Armand ⊥ 58 47.52 N 7.10 E
Vieillard, Lac du ⊜ 190 47.23 N 78.02 W
Vieille Case 240d 15.36 N 61.24 W
Vieira do Minho 34 41.39 N 8.09 W
Viejo, Cerro ∧ 248 4.49 S 79.27 W
Viekšniai 76 56.16 N 22.31 E
Vielank 54 53.15 N 11.08 E
Viella 34 42.42 N 0.48 E
Vielle-Eglise-en-Yvelines 261 48.40 N 1.53 E
Vielsalm 56 50.17 N 5.55 E
Viels-Maisons 50 48.54 N 3.24 E
Viena
→ Vienne ≃ 32 47.13 N 0.05 E
Vienenburg 54 51.57 N 10.34 E
Vienna, On., Can. 212 42.41 N 80.48 W
Vienna
→ Wien, Öst. 61 48.13 N 16.20 E
Vienna, Ga., U.S. 192 32.05 N 83.47 W
Vienna, Il., U.S. 194 37.25 N 88.54 W
Vienna, In., U.S. 218 38.39 N 85.46 W
Vienna, Md., U.S. 208 38.29 N 75.49 W
Vienna, Mo., U.S. 194 38.11 N 91.56 W
Vienna, N.J., U.S. 210 40.52 N 74.53 W
Vienna, Oh., U.S. 214 41.14 N 80.40 W
Vienna, S.D., U.S. 198 44.42 N 97.30 W
Vienna, Va., U.S. 208 38.29 N 75.49 W
Vienna, Va., U.S. 208 38.54 N 77.15 W
Vienna, W.V., U.S. 188 39.19 N 81.32 W
Vienne, Fr. 62 45.31 N 4.52 E
Vienne
→ Wien, Öst. 61 48.13 N 16.20 E
Vienne □[5] 32 46.35 N 0.30 E
Vienne ≃ 32 47.13 N 0.05 E
Vienne-en-Arthies 261 49.04 N 1.44 E
Vienne-le-Château 56 49.11 N 4.53 E
Vientiane
→ Viangchan 110 17.58 N 102.36 E
Vientos, Paso de los ⊔
→ Windward Passage ⊔ 238 20.00 N 73.50 W
Vieques 240m 18.09 N 65.27 W
Vieques, Aeropuerto ⊠ 240m 18.07 N 65.30 W
Vieques, Isla de I 240m 18.08 N 65.25 W
Vieques, Pasaje de ⊔ 240m 18.11 N 65.37 W
Vieques, Sonda de ⊔ 240m 18.15 N 65.23 W
Vière ≃ 56 48.46 N 4.41 E
Viereck 54 53.32 N 14.02 E
Vieremä 26 63.45 N 27.01 E
Vierfontein 158 27.03 S 26.46 E
Vierhouten 52 52.20 N 5.50 E
Vieringhausen ◆[8] 263 51.11 N 7.10 E
Vierlande ◆[1] 52 53.26 N 10.14 E
Viernau 54 50.40 N 10.32 E
Viernheim 56 49.32 N 8.34 E
Vierraden 54 53.06 N 14.17 E
Viersen 56 51.15 N 6.23 E
Vierumäki 26 61.06 N 25.57 E
Vierwaldstättersee ⊜ 58 47.00 N 8.28 E
Vierzehnheiligen ♥[1] 54 50.08 N 11.02 E
Vierzon 50 47.13 N 2.05 E
Viesca 232 25.21 N 102.48 W
Viesecke 54 53.01 N 12.01 E
Vieselbach 54 51.00 N 11.08 E
Viesīte 76 56.21 N 25.33 E
Vieste 68 41.53 N 16.10 E
Vietgest 54 53.45 N 12.20 E
Vietnam □[1], Asia 108 16.00 N 108.00 E
Vietnam □[1], Asia 110 16.00 N 108.00 E
Vietnam Veterans Memorial ⊥ 284c 38.53 N 77.03 W
Vietri di Potenza 68 40.36 N 15.30 E
Vietri sul Mare 68 40.40 N 14.44 E
Viet Tri 110 21.18 N 105.26 E
Vieux-Condé 50 50.27 N 3.34 E
Vieux-Ferette 58 47.30 N 7.18 E
Vieux-Fort, P.Q., Can. 186 51.26 N 57.49 W
Vieux-Fort, Guad. 241o 15.57 N 61.43 W
Vieux Fort, St. Luc. 241f 13.44 N 60.57 W
Vieux-Fort, Pointe du ⟩ 241o 15.57 N 61.43 W
Vieux Fort Bay ⊂ 241f 13.44 N 60.58 W
Vieux-Habitants 241o 16.04 N 61.46 W
Vieux-Thann 58 47.48 N 7.08 E
Vievis 76 54.46 N 24.48 E
View Park 280 34.00 N 118.20 W
Vieytes 258 35.16 S 57.35 W
Vif 62 45.03 N 5.40 E
Vig 41 55.51 N 11.36 E
Viga ≃ 76 59.14 N 43.41 E
Vigala 76 58.43 N 24.22 E
Vigan 116 17.34 N 120.23 E
Vigarano Mainarda 64 44.50 N 11.30 E
Vigatto 64 44.43 N 10.20 E
Vigeland 26 58.05 N 7.18 E
Vigentino ◆[8] 266b 45.25 N 9.11 E
Vigersted 41 55.29 N 11.54 E
Vigese, Monte ∧ 64 44.12 N 11.06 E
Vigésima Quinta de Abril, Ponte ◆[5] 266c 38.41 N 9.11 W
Vigevano 62 45.19 N 8.51 E
Viggianello 68 39.58 N 16.05 E
Viggiano 68 40.20 N 15.54 E
Viggiù 62 45.52 N 8.54 E
Vigia 250 0.48 S 48.08 W
Vigie Airport ⊠ 241f 14.01 N 60.59 W
Vignacourt 50 50.01 N 2.12 E
Vignale 266b 45.29 N 8.36 E
Vignanello 66 42.23 N 12.17 E
Vigneulles-lès-Hattonchâtel 56 48.59 N 5.43 E
Vigneux-sur-Seine 261 48.42 N 2.25 E
Vignola 64 44.29 N 11.00 E
Vignory 58 48.17 N 5.06 E
Vignot 56 48.46 N 5.36 E
Vigny 261 49.05 N 1.56 E
Vigo 34 42.14 N 8.43 W
Vigo, Ría de ⊂[1] 34 42.15 N 8.45 W
Vigodarzere 64 45.27 N 11.53 E
Vigo di Fassa 64 46.25 N 11.40 E
Vigolzone 62 44.55 N 9.40 E
Vigone 62 44.51 N 7.30 E
Vigonovo 64 45.23 N 12.00 E
Vigo-Rendena 64 46.05 N 10.43 E
Vigrestad 26 58.34 N 5.42 E
Viguzzolo 62 44.54 N 8.55 E
Vigy 56 49.12 N 6.18 E
Vihanti 26 64.29 N 25.00 E
Vihāri 123 30.02 N 72.21 E
Vihiers 32 47.09 N 0.32 W
Vihowa 123 31.08 N 70.30 E
Vihren ∧ 38 41.46 N 23.24 E
Vihti 26 60.25 N 24.20 E
Viiala 26 61.13 N 23.47 E
Viinijärvi 26 62.39 N 29.14 E
Viinijärvi ⊜ 26 62.44 N 29.17 E
Viipuri
→ Vyborg 76 60.42 N 28.45 E
Viitasaari 26 63.04 N 25.52 E
Viivikonna 76 59.19 N 27.42 E
Vijāpur 120 23.34 N 72.45 E
Vijayawāda 122 16.31 N 80.37 E
Vijosë (Aóös) ≃ 38 40.37 N 19.20 E
Vik 40 59.44 N 17.28 E
Vik ⊥ 40 59.44 N 17.27 E
Vika 40 60.31 N 15.42 E
Vikajärvi 24 66.37 N 26.12 E
Vikārābād 122 17.20 N 77.54 E
Vikbolandet ⟩[1] 40 58.32 N 16.40 E
Vikeke 112 8.52 S 126.22 E
Viken 41 56.09 N 12.34 E
Viken ⊜ 26 58.39 N 14.20 E
Vikern ⊜ 40 59.30 N 14.55 E
Vikersund 26 59.59 N 10.02 E
Vikhroli ◆[8] 272c 19.07 N 72.56 E
Viking 182 53.06 N 111.46 W
Viking Village 218 39.05 N 84.18 W
Vikmanshyttan 40 60.17 N 15.49 E
Vikna 24 64.57 N 10.58 E
Vikna I 24 64.57 N 10.58 E
Vikramasingapuram 122 8.43 N 77.24 E
Viksøyri 26 61.05 N 6.35 E
Viktor 24 66.09 N 58.07 E
Viktorovka 86 52.51 N 62.32 E
Viktring 61 46.35 N 14.16 E
Vikulovo 86 56.49 N 70.37 E
Vil'a 80 55.15 N 42.13 E
Vila Alferes Chamusca 156 24.29 S 33.00 E
Vila Augusta 287b 23.28 S 46.32 W
Vila Babi 287a 22.42 S 43.23 W
Vila Boacaya ◆[8] 287b 23.29 S 46.44 W
Vila Caldas Xavier 154 15.59 S 34.12 E
Vila da Maganja 154 17.18 S 37.30 E
Vila da Ribeira Brava 150a 16.37 N 24.18 W
Viladecans 266d 41.19 N 2.00 E
Viladecavalls del Vallès 266d 41.33 N 1.58 E
Vila de Manica 156 18.56 S 32.53 E
Vila de Rei 34 39.40 N 8.09 W
Vila Dirce 287b 23.35 S 46.48 W
Vila do Bispo 34 37.05 N 8.55 W
Vila do Conde 34 41.21 N 8.45 W
Vila do Porto 148a 36.56 N 25.09 W
Vila Embaú 256 22.37 S 45.02 W
Vila Flor 34 41.18 N 7.09 W
Vila Fontes 156 17.50 S 35.21 E
Vila Formosa ◆[8] 287b 23.34 S 46.33 W
Vilafranca del Penedès 34 41.21 N 1.42 E
Vila Franca de Xira 34 38.57 N 8.59 W
Vila Galvão 287b 23.27 S 46.33 W
Vila Gamito 154 14.12 S 33.00 E
Vila Gomes da Costa 156 24.19 S 33.38 E
Vila Gouveia 156 18.03 S 33.11 E
Vila Guilherme ◆[8] 287b 23.30 S 46.36 W
Vilaine ≃ 32 47.30 N 2.27 W
Vila Isabel ◆[8] 287a 22.55 S 43.15 W
Vila Jaguára ◆[8] 287b 23.31 S 46.45 W
Viļaka 76 57.11 N 27.41 E
Vila Luísa 156 25.44 S 32.40 E
Vilama, Laguna de ⊜ 252 22.36 S 66.55 W
Vila Machado 156 19.18 S 34.11 E
Vila Madalena ◆[8] 287b 23.33 S 46.42 W
Vila Maria ◆[8] 287b 23.31 S 46.34 W
Vila Mariana ◆[8] 287b 23.35 S 46.38 W
Vila Matilde ◆[8] 287b 23.32 S 46.31 W
Vilanculos 156 22.01 S 35.19 E
Viļāni 76 56.33 N 26.57 E
Vila Nova ≃ 250 0.04 S 51.13 W
Vila Nova de Famalicão 34 41.25 N 8.32 W
Vila Nova de Foz Côa 34 41.05 N 7.12 W
Vila Nova de Gaia 34 41.08 N 8.37 W
Vilanova de la Roca 266d 41.33 N 2.17 E
Vilanova i la Geltrú 34 41.14 N 1.44 E
Vila Novo de Ourém 34 39.39 N 8.35 W
Vila Paiva de Andrada 156 18.44 S 34.03 E
Vila Progresso 287a 22.55 S 43.03 W
Vila Prudente ◆[8] 287b 23.35 S 46.33 W
Vila-real, Esp. 34 39.56 N 0.06 W
Vila Real, Port. 34 41.18 N 7.45 W
Vila Real de Santo António 34 37.12 N 7.25 W
Vilar Formoso 34 40.37 N 6.50 W
Vilarinho do Monte 250 1.37 S 52.01 W
Vilassar de Dalt 266d 41.31 N 2.22 E
Vilassar de Mar 266d 41.30 N 2.24 E
Vila Vasco da Gama 154 14.54 S 32.14 E
Vila Velha, Bra. 250 3.13 N 51.13 W
Vila Velha, Bra. 255 20.20 S 40.17 W
Vila Velha de Ródão 34 39.38 N 7.40 W
Vila Verde, Port. 34 41.39 N 8.26 W
Vila Verde, Port. 266c 38.50 N 9.22 W
Vila Viçosa 34 38.47 N 8.13 W
Vil'ča 78 51.22 N 29.24 E
Vilcabamba, Cordillera de ⋏ 248 12.45 S 73.20 W
Vîlcea □[6] 38 45.19 N 24.00 E
Vildbjerg 41 56.12 N 8.46 E
Vilejka 76 54.30 N 26.53 E
Vilelas 252 27.57 S 62.38 W
Vilenki 82 54.16 N 38.55 E
Vil'gort, Ross. 24 61.35 N 50.40 E
Vil'gort, Ross. 24 60.34 N 56.24 E
Vilhelmina 26 64.37 N 16.39 E
Vilhena 248 12.43 S 60.07 W
Vilija (Neris) ≃ 76 54.54 N 23.53 E
Viljandi 76 58.22 N 25.36 E
Viljoensdrif 158 26.44 S 27.55 E
Viljoenshof 158 34.40 S 19.42 E
Viljoenskroon 158 27.12 S 27.00 E
Viljoenspos 158 27.35 S 30.30 E
Vilkaviškis 76 54.39 N 23.02 E
Vil'kickogo, ostrov I, Ross. 72 73.29 N 75.50 E
Vil'kickogo, ostrov I, Ross. 74 75.44 N 152.20 E
Vil'kickogo, proliv ⊔ 74 77.55 N 103.00 E
Vilkija 76 55.03 N 23.35 E
Vilkovo 78 45.25 N 29.35 E
Villa Abecia 248 21.00 S 65.23 W
Villa Aberastain 252 31.39 S 68.35 W
Villa Acuña
→ Ciudad Acuña 232 29.18 N 100.55 W
Villa Adelina ◆[8] 288 34.31 S 58.32 W
Villa Adriana ⊥ 66 41.56 N 12.45 E
Villa Alejandrina 258 33.46 S 58.21 W
Villa Alemana 252 33.03 S 71.23 W
Villa Álvarez 234 19.14 N 103.43 W
Villa Ana 252 28.29 S 59.37 W
Villa Ángela 252 27.35 S 60.43 W
Villa Atamisqui 252 28.29 S 63.48 W
Villa Atuel 252 34.50 S 67.54 W
Villaba 116 11.13 N 124.23 E
Villa Ballester ◆[8] 258 34.32 S 58.33 W
Villabassa (Niederdorf) 64 46.44 N 12.10 E
Villabate 70 38.04 N 13.26 E
Villabé 261 48.35 N 2.27 E
Villa Bella 248 10.23 S 65.24 W
Villa Berthet 252 27.17 S 60.25 W
Villablino 34 42.56 N 6.19 W
Villa Borghese ♥ 267a 41.55 N 12.29 E
Villa Bosch ◆[8] 288 34.35 S 58.34 W
Villa Bruzual 246 9.20 N 69.06 W
Villa Cañás, Arg. 252 34.00 S 61.36 W
Villacañas, Esp. 34 39.38 N 3.20 W
Villa Carlos Paz 252 31.24 S 64.31 W
Villacarriedo 34 43.14 N 3.48 W
Villacarrillo 34 38.07 N 3.05 W
Villa Castelli, Arg. 252 29.00 S 68.11 W
Villa Castelli, It. 68 40.35 N 17.28 E
Villacastín 34 40.47 N 4.25 W
Villach 64 46.36 N 13.50 E
Villacidro 71 39.27 N 8.44 E
Villa Ciudadela ◆[8] 258 34.38 S 58.34 W
Villa Clara □[4] 240p 22.30 N 80.00 W
Villa Comaltitlan 236 15.13 N 92.35 W
Villa Concepción del Tío 252 31.19 S 62.50 W
Villa Constitución 252 33.14 S 60.20 W
Villa Cortese 266b 45.34 N 8.53 E
Villa Corzo 234 16.10 N 93.15 W
Villacoublay, Aérodrome de ⊠ 261 48.45 N 2.10 E
Villa Creek ≃ 226 35.27 N 120.58 W
Villa Cuauhtémoc, Méx. 234 19.24 N 99.34 W
Villa Cuauhtémoc, Méx. 234 22.11 N 97.50 W
Villada 34 42.15 N 4.58 W
Villa de Apaseo El Alto 234 20.27 N 100.37 W
Villa de Arista 234 22.39 N 100.50 W
Villa de Arriaga 234 21.54 N 101.23 W
Villadeati 62 45.04 N 8.10 E
Villa de Cos 234 23.17 N 102.21 W
Villa de Cura 246 10.02 N 67.29 W
Villa de Guadalupe 234 23.22 N 100.46 W
Villa del Carmen 252 32.57 S 65.03 W
Villa del Pueblito 234 20.32 N 100.27 W
Villa del Río 34 37.59 N 4.17 W
Villa del Rosario, Arg. 252 31.35 S 63.32 W
Villa del Rosario, Arg. 252 30.47 S 57.55 W
Villa de María 252 29.54 S 63.43 W
Villa de Mayo 258 34.30 S 58.41 W
Villa de Nova Sintra 150a 14.52 N 24.43 W
Villa de Reyes 234 21.48 N 100.56 W
Villa de San Antonio 236 14.16 N 87.36 W
Villa de San Francisco 236 14.10 N 86.58 W
Villa de Soto 252 30.51 S 64.59 W
Villa d'Este ⊥ 267a 41.57 N 12.48 E
Villa Devoto ◆[8] 288 34.36 S 58.31 W
Villa Diamante ◆[8] 288 34.41 S 58.26 W
Villa di Chiavenna 58 46.20 N 9.29 E
Villadiego 34 42.31 N 4.00 W
Villa Dolores 252 31.56 S 65.12 W
Villa Domínico ◆[8] 258 34.41 S 58.19 W
Villadose 64 45.04 N 11.53 E
Villadossola 58 46.04 N 8.16 E
Villa Elisa 252 32.10 S 58.24 W
Villa Elisa ◆[8] 258 34.50 S 58.05 W
Villa Escalante 234 19.24 N 101.39 W
Villa Flores 234 16.14 N 93.14 W
Villa Florida 252 26.23 S 57.09 W
Villafranca d'Asti 62 44.55 N 8.02 E
Villafranca del Bierzo 34 42.36 N 6.48 W
Villafranca de los Barros 34 38.34 N 6.20 W
Villafranca di Verona 64 45.21 N 10.50 E
Villafranca in Lunigiana 64 44.17 N 9.57 E
Villafranca Piemonte 62 44.47 N 7.33 E
Villafranca Sicula 70 37.35 N 13.17 E
Villafranca Tirrena 70 38.14 N 15.26 E
Villafrati 70 37.54 N 13.29 E
Villagarcía, Esp. 34 42.36 N 8.45 W
Villa García, Méx. 234 22.10 N 101.57 W
Village 196 35.33 N 97.33 W
Village Creek ≃ 194 35.28 N 91.19 W
Village Green 285 39.52 N 75.26 W
Villa General Roca 252 32.39 S 66.28 W
Village of Drummond Hill 285 39.43 N 75.42 W
Village of the Branch 276 40.51 N 73.11 W
Villa Gesell 252 37.15 S 56.55 W
Villa Giambruno 288 34.48 S 58.13 W
Villa González Ortega 234 22.30 N 101.55 W
Villagrán, Méx. 232 24.29 N 99.29 W
Villagrán, Méx. 234 20.31 N 100.59 W
Villagrande Strisaili 71 39.58 N 9.30 E
Villa Grazia 70 38.09 N 13.10 E
Villa Grove 194 39.51 N 88.09 W
Villaguay 252 31.51 S 59.01 W
Villa Guerrero, Méx. 234 21.59 N 103.36 W
Villa Guerrero, Méx. 234 18.52 N 99.39 W
Villa Guillermina 252 28.14 S 59.28 W
Villa Hayes 252 25.06 S 57.34 W
Villahermosa 234 17.59 N 92.55 W
Villa Hernandarias 252 31.13 S 59.59 W
Villa Hidalgo, Méx. 204 30.59 N 116.10 W
Villa Hidalgo, Méx. 234 21.40 N 102.36 W
Villa Hidalgo, Méx. 234 21.44 N 105.15 W
Villa Hidalgo Yalalag 234 17.11 N 96.11 W
Villa Huidobro 252 34.50 S 64.35 W
Villaines-la-Juhel 32 48.21 N 0.17 W
Villa Insurgentes 232 25.12 N 111.44 W
Villa Iris 252 38.10 S 63.15 W
Villa Jiménez 234 19.55 N 101.35 W
Villa José L. Suárez ◆[8] 288 34.32 S 58.35 W
Villa Juanita 234 17.47 N 95.09 W
Villa Juárez, Méx. 232 27.10 N 109.50 W
Villa Juárez, Méx. 234 22.20 N 100.17 W
Villa Krause 252 31.34 S 68.32 W
Villa La Angostura 254 40.47 S 71.40 W
Villalago 66 41.56 N 13.50 E
Villa Larca 252 32.37 S 64.59 W
Villa La Venta 234 18.10 N 94.07 W
Villalba, Esp. 34 43.18 N 7.41 W
Villalba, It. 70 37.39 N 13.50 E
Villalba, P.R. 240m 18.08 N 66.30 W
Villaldama 232 26.30 N 100.26 W
Villa Lia 258 34.07 S 59.26 W
Villalon 116 11.31 N 124.22 E
Villalón de Campos 34 42.06 N 5.02 W
Villalonga 254 39.53 S 62.35 W
Villalpando 34 41.52 N 5.24 W
Villa Lugano ◆[8] 288 34.41 S 58.28 W
Villalvernia 62 44.49 N 8.51 E
Villa Lynch ◆[8] 288 34.36 S 58.31 W
Villa Madero, Arg. 288 34.42 S 58.30 W
Villa Madero, Méx. 234 19.24 N 101.16 W
Villa Mainero 232 24.32 N 99.38 W
Villamar 71 39.37 N 8.59 E
Villa María, Arg. 252 32.25 S 63.15 W
Villa Maria, Pa., U.S. 214 41.05 N 80.30 W
Villa María del Triunfo 286d 12.10 S 76.56 W
Villa María Grande 252 31.39 S 59.54 W
Villa Martín, Bol. 248 20.46 S 67.47 W
Villamartín, Esp. 34 36.52 N 5.38 W
Villamarzana 64 45.01 N 11.41 E
Villamassargia 71 39.16 N 8.38 E
Villa Matoque 252 25.49 S 63.49 W
Villa Mazán 252 28.40 S 66.34 W
Villa Media Agua 252 31.59 S 68.25 W
Villa Mercedes 252 30.07 S 68.42 W
Villa Minozzo 64 44.22 N 10.28 E
Villamontes 248 21.15 S 63.30 W
Villa Morelos 234 20.00 N 101.25 W
Villandraut 32 44.28 N 0.23 W
Villa Nova, Md., U.S. 284b 39.21 N 76.44 W
Villa Nova, Oh., U.S. 216 40.33 N 84.26 W
Villanova, Pa., U.S. 208 40.02 N 75.20 W
Villanova d'Asti 62 44.57 N 7.56 E
Villanova Mondovì 62 44.21 N 7.45 E
Villanova Monferrato 62 45.11 N 8.28 E
Villanova Monteleone 71 40.30 N 8.28 E
Villanova sull'Arda 64 45.01 N 10.00 E
Villanova Tulo 71 39.47 N 9.13 E
Villanova University ♥[2] 285 40.02 N 75.21 W
Villa Nueva, Arg. 252 32.26 S 63.15 W
Villa Nueva, Arg. 252 32.54 S 68.47 W
Villanueva, Col. 246 10.37 N 72.59 W
Villa Nueva, Guat. 236 14.31 N 90.35 W
Villanueva, Hond. 236 15.17 N 88.00 W
Villanueva, Méx. 234 22.21 N 102.53 W
Villa Nueva, Nic. 236 12.58 N 86.49 W
Villanueva, N.M., U.S. 200 35.16 N 105.21 W
Villanueva de Córdoba 34 38.20 N 4.37 W
Villanueva de la Serana 34 38.58 N 5.48 W
Villanueva de la Sierra 34 40.12 N 6.24 W
Villanueva de los Infantes 34 38.44 N 2.59 W
Villanueva del Río y Minas 34 37.39 N 5.42 W
Villa Numancia 288 34.55 S 58.24 W
Villa Obregón 234 21.07 N 102.42 W
Villa Ocampo 252 28.28 S 59.22 W
Villa Ojo de Agua 252 29.31 S 63.42 W
Villa Oliva 252 26.01 S 57.53 W
Villa Opicina 64 45.40 N 13.49 E
Villa Oropeza 248 19.10 S 65.17 W
Villa Ottone (Uttenheim) 64 46.52 N 11.57 E
Villa Papale ♥ 267a 41.45 N 12.39 E
Villa Park, Ca., U.S. 228 33.48 N 117.48 W
Villa Park, Il., U.S. 278 41.53 N 87.59 W
Villa Park Dam ◆[6] 280 33.48 N 117.46 W
Villa Pérez 240m 18.12 N 66.47 W
Villapiana 68 39.51 N 16.28 E
Villapiana Lido 68 39.48 N 16.29 E
Villapinzón 246 5.13 N 73.36 W
Villa Potenza 66 43.19 N 13.25 E
Villaputzu 71 39.26 N 9.34 E
Villa Quinteros 252 27.14 S 65.33 W
Villa Quintilio Varo ⊥ 267a 41.58 N 12.47 E
Villa Ramírez 252 32.11 S 60.12 W
Villarcayo 34 42.56 N 3.34 W
Villar-d'Arène 62 45.02 N 6.20 E
Villard-Bonnot 62 45.14 N 5.53 E

ENGLISH — Name / Page / Lat.°′ / Long.°′

Villard-de-Lans 62 45.04 N 5.33 E
Villardefrades 34 41.43 N 5.15 W
Villar del Arzobispo 34 39.44 N 0.49 W
Villareal 116 11.34 N 124.56 E
Villa Real ◆[8] 288 34.37 S 58.31 W
Villa Regina 252 39.06 S 67.04 W
Villa Reynolds 252 33.43 S 65.23 W
Villa Rica 192 33.43 N 84.55 W
Villa Rivero 248 17.37 S 65.48 W
Villaroche 261 48.37 N 2.39 E
Villaroche ■ 261 48.37 N 2.40 E
Villa Romana del Casale ⊥ 70 37.22 N 14.20 E
Villa Rosa, Arg. 258 34.25 S 58.52 W
Villarosa, It. 70 37.35 N 14.10 E
Villar Pellice 62 44.48 N 7.09 E
Villar Perosa 62 44.56 N 7.15 E
Villarreales 196 26.07 N 100.20 W
Villarrica, Chile 254 39.16 S 72.13 W
Villarrica, Col. 246 3.58 N 74.37 W
Villarrica, Para. 252 25.45 S 56.26 W
Villarrica, Lago ⊜ 254 39.15 S 72.06 W
Villarrobledo 34 39.16 N 2.36 W
Villarrubia de los Ojos 34 39.13 N 3.36 W
Villars, Arg. 258 34.50 S 58.56 W
Villars, Schw. 58 46.18 N 7.04 E
Villars-Colmars 62 44.10 N 6.36 E
Villars-en-Azois 58 48.04 N 4.45 E
Villars-les-Dombes 58 46.00 N 5.01 E
Villars-sur-Var 62 43.56 N 7.06 E
Villa Ruiz 258 34.25 S 59.15 W
Villas 208 39.01 N 74.56 W
Villa Sáenz Peña ◆[8] 288 34.36 S 58.31 W
Villa San Andrés ◆[8] 288 34.33 S 58.32 W
Villa Sandino 236 12.03 N 84.59 W
Villa San Giovanni 68 38.13 N 15.38 E
Villa San José 252 32.12 S 58.13 W
Villa San Martín 252 28.18 S 64.12 W
Villasanta 62 45.37 N 9.18 E
Villa Santa, Montaña ∧ 236 14.12 N 86.27 W
Villa Santa Maria 66 41.57 N 14.21 E
Villa Santina 64 46.24 N 12.55 E
Villa Santo Domingo 234 23.20 N 101.44 W
Villa Santos Lugares ◆[8] 288 34.36 S 58.32 W
Villasayas 34 41.21 N 2.37 W
Villa Serrano 248 19.06 S 64.22 W
Villasimius 71 39.08 N 9.31 E
Villasis 116 15.54 N 120.35 E
Villasor 71 39.23 N 8.56 E
Villa Talavera 248 19.49 S 65.25 W
Villa Tunari 248 16.55 S 65.25 W
Villa Turdera ◆[8] 288 34.48 S 58.25 W
Villa Unión, Arg. 252 29.18 S 68.12 W
Villa Unión, Arg. 252 29.24 S 62.47 W
Villa Unión, Méx. 232 28.15 N 100.43 W
Villa Unión, Méx. 234 23.58 N 104.02 W
Villa Unión, Méx. 234 23.12 N 106.14 W
Villa Urquiza ◆[8] 288 34.34 S 58.29 W
Villa Valeria 252 34.20 S 64.55 W
Villa Vallelonga 66 41.52 N 13.37 E
Villaverde ◆[8] 266a 40.21 N 3.42 W
Villaverla 64 45.39 N 11.29 E
Villa Verona 226 39.28 N 121.33 W
Villavicencio 246 4.09 N 73.37 W
Villaviciosa 34 43.29 N 5.26 W
Villaviciosa de Córdoba 34 38.05 N 5.01 W
Villa Victoria 234 18.47 N 103.24 W
Villa Viscarra 248 17.59 S 65.36 W
Villa Vomano 66 42.37 N 13.46 E
Villazón 248 22.06 S 65.36 W
Villa Zorraquín 252 31.19 S 58.02 W
Villé 58 48.20 N 7.18 E
Villebon, Lac ⊜ 190 47.58 N 77.17 W
Villebon-sur-Yvette 261 48.42 N 2.15 E
Villeconin 261 48.31 N 2.08 E
Villecresnes 261 48.43 N 2.32 E
Villecroze 62 43.35 N 6.16 E
Ville-d'Avray 261 48.50 N 2.11 E
Ville-de-Laval
→ Laval 206 45.35 N 73.45 W
Villedieu 32 48.50 N 1.13 W
Ville-en-Tardenois 50 49.11 N 3.48 E
Villefort 62 44.26 N 3.56 E
Villefranche 58 45.59 N 4.43 E
Villefranche-de-Rouergue 32 44.21 N 2.02 E
Villefranche-sur-Cher 50 47.18 N 1.46 E
Villefranche-sur-Mer 62 43.42 N 7.19 E
Villejuif 50 48.48 N 2.22 E
Villejust 261 48.41 N 2.14 E
Ville-Marie 190 47.19 N 79.26 W
Villemaur-sur-Vanne 50 48.15 N 3.44 E
Villemeux-sur-Eure 50 48.40 N 1.28 E
Villemoisson-sur-Orge 261 48.40 N 2.19 E
Villemomble 261 48.53 N 2.31 E
Villena 34 38.38 N 0.51 W
Ville Nacíonal 234 17.50 N 96.14 W
Villenauxe-la-Grande 50 48.35 N 3.33 E
Villeneuve, It. 62 45.42 N 7.14 E
Villeneuve, Schw. 58 46.24 N 6.55 E
Villeneuve-d'Ascq 50 50.37 N 3.10 E
Villeneuve-d'Aveyron 32 44.26 N 2.02 E
Villeneuve-de-Berg 62 44.33 N 4.30 E
Villeneuve-la-Garenne 261 48.56 N 2.20 E
Villeneuve-la-Guyard 50 48.20 N 3.04 E
Villeneuve-l'Archevêque 50 48.14 N 3.33 E
Villeneuve-le-Comte 261 48.49 N 2.50 E
Villeneuve-le-Roi 50 48.44 N 2.25 E
Villeneuve-lès-Avignon 62 43.58 N 4.48 E
Villeneuve-lès-Maguelonne 62 43.32 N 3.52 E
Villeneuve-Saint-Denis 261 48.49 N 2.48 E
Villeneuve-Saint-Georges 50 48.44 N 2.27 E
Villeneuve-sous-Dammartin 261 49.02 N 2.39 E
Villeneuve-sur-Lot 32 44.25 N 0.42 E
Villeneuve-sur-Yonne 50 48.05 N 3.18 E
Villennes-sur-Seine 261 48.56 N 2.00 E
Villenoy 50 48.57 N 2.52 E
Villeny 50 47.37 N 1.45 E
Villeparisis 50 48.56 N 2.37 E
Villepinte 261 48.58 N 2.32 E
Ville Platte 194 30.41 N 92.16 W
Villepreux 261 48.50 N 2.01 E
Villequier 50 49.31 N 0.40 E
Villeron 261 49.03 N 2.33 E
Villeroy 50 48.59 N 2.47 E
Villers-Bocage, Fr. 32 49.05 N 0.39 W
Villers-Bocage, Fr. 50 49.59 N 2.20 E
Villers-Bretonneux 50 49.52 N 2.31 E
Villers-Carbonnel 50 49.52 N 2.54 E
Villers-Cotterêts 50 49.15 N 3.05 E
Villers-devant-Orval 56 49.37 N 5.19 E
Villers-en-Arthies 261 49.05 N 1.44 E
Villersexel 58 47.33 N 6.26 E
Villers-Farlay 58 47.00 N 5.45 E
Villers-la-Ville 50 50.35 N 4.32 E
Villers-le-Lac 58 47.04 N 6.40 E
Villers-lès-Nancy 58 48.40 N 6.09 E
Villers-lès-Pots 58 47.13 N 5.21 E
Villers-Outréaux 50 50.02 N 3.18 E
Villers-Saint-Paul 50 49.17 N 2.29 E
Villers-Semeuse 56 49.44 N 4.45 E
Villerupt 56 49.28 N 5.56 E
Villerville 50 49.24 N 0.08 E
Ville-Saint-Georges
→ Saint-Georges 188 46.07 N 70.40 W
Villes-sur-Auzon 62 44.03 N 5.14 E
Ville-sur-Tourbe 56 49.11 N 4.47 E
Villeta 246 5.01 N 74.28 W
Villetta Barrea 66 41.47 N 13.56 E
Villeurbanne 62 45.46 N 4.53 E
Villevaudé 261 48.55 N 2.39 E

DEUTSCH — Name / Seite / Breite°′ / Länge°′ E = Ost

Villeziers 261 48.40 N 2.10 E
Villiers 158 27.03 S 28.35 E
Villiers-Adam 261 49.04 N 2.14 E
Villiersdorp 158 34.00 S 19.19 E
Villiers-le-Bâcle 261 48.44 N 2.08 E
Villiers-le-Bel 261 49.00 N 2.23 E
Villiers-le-Sec 261 49.04 N 2.23 E
Villiers-Saint-Frédéric 261 48.49 N 1.54 E
Villiers-Saint-Georges 50 48.39 N 3.25 E
Villiers-sur-Marne 261 48.50 N 2.33 E
Villiers-sur-Morin 261 48.52 N 2.53 E
Villigst 263 51.26 N 7.35 E
Villingen-Schwenningen 58 48.04 N 8.28 E
Villisca 198 40.55 N 94.58 W
Villmanstrand
→ Lappeenranta 26 61.04 N 28.11 E
Villmergen 58 47.21 N 8.15 E
Villorba 64 45.44 N 12.14 E
Villoresi, Canale ≍ 266b 45.33 N 9.19 E
Villotta 64 45.52 N 12.45 E
Vilm I 54 54.19 N 13.32 E
Vilmnitz 54 54.21 N 13.31 E
Vilna, Ab., Can. 182 54.07 N 111.55 W
Vilna
→ Vilnius, Liet. 76 54.41 N 25.19 E
Vilnius 76 54.41 N 25.19 E
Vilosnes-sur-Meuse 56 49.20 N 5.14 E
Vilppula 26 62.01 N 24.31 E
Vils 58 47.33 N 10.38 E
Vils ≃, Dtsch. 60 49.09 N 11.58 E
Vils ≃, Dtsch. 60 48.37 N 13.11 E
Vils ≃, Europe 58 47.33 N 10.40 E
Vilsandi saar I 76 58.23 N 21.52 E
Vilsbiburg 60 48.27 N 12.12 E
Vilseck 60 49.37 N 11.48 E
Vilsheim 60 48.27 N 12.07 E
Vilshofen 60 48.39 N 13.12 E
Vil'uj ≃ 74 64.24 N 126.26 E
Vil'ujsk 74 63.45 N 121.35 E
Vil'ujskoje vodochranilišče ⊜[1] 74 62.30 N 111.00 E
Viluppuram 122 11.56 N 79.29 E
Vil'va 86 58.37 N 56.52 E
Vilvoorde 50 50.56 N 4.26 E
Vimercate 62 45.37 N 9.22 E
Vimianzo 34 43.07 N 9.02 W
Vimmerby 26 57.40 N 15.51 E
Vimodrone 266b 45.31 N 9.17 E
Vimoutiers 50 48.55 N 0.12 E
Vimpeli 26 63.09 N 23.48 E
Vimperk 60 49.03 N 13.47 E
Vimy 50 50.22 N 2.49 E
Vina 204 39.55 N 122.03 W
Vina ≃ 146 7.45 N 15.36 E
Viñac 248 12.56 S 75.47 W
Viña del Mar 252 33.02 S 71.34 W
Vinadi 58 46.55 N 10.29 E
Vinadio 62 44.18 N 7.10 E
Viñales 240p 22.37 N 83.43 W
Vinalhaven 188 44.02 N 68.49 W
Vinalhaven Island I 188 44.05 N 68.52 W
Vinantes 261 49.01 N 2.44 E
Vina Roni, Mount ∧ 175e 8.10 S 157.28 E
Vinaròs 34 40.28 N 0.29 E
Vinay 62 45.13 N 5.24 E
Vinazco ≃ 234 20.56 N 97.44 W
Vincennes, Fr. 50 48.51 N 2.26 E
Vincennes, In., U.S. 194 38.40 N 87.31 W
Vincennes, Bois de ♦ 261 48.50 N 2.25 E
Vincennes, Château de ⊥ 261 48.51 N 2.26 E
Vincennes, Étang de ⊜ 261 48.47 N 2.45 E
Vincennes Bay ⊂ 9 66.30 S 109.30 E
Vincent 194 33.22 N 86.22 W
Vincent, Point ⟩ 174c 29.00 S 167.55 E
Vincentown 208 39.56 N 74.44 W
Vinces 246 1.32 S 79.45 W
Vincey 58 48.20 N 6.20 E
Vinchiaturo 66 41.29 N 14.35 E
Vinchina 252 28.46 S 68.10 W
Vinchos 248 13.16 S 74.21 W
Vinci 66 43.47 N 10.55 E
Vinco 214 40.25 N 78.52 W
Vindeby 41 55.03 N 10.38 E
Vindelälven ≃ 24 63.54 N 19.52 E
Vindeln 26 64.12 N 19.44 E
Vinden, Mount ∧ 162 27.01 S 115.38 E
Vinderslev 41 56.15 N 9.26 E
Vinderup 26 56.29 N 8.47 E
Vindhya Range ⋏ 120 23.00 N 77.00 E
Vinding 41 55.41 N 9.35 E
Vindinge 41 55.19 N 10.45 E
Vine Brook ≃ 283 42.27 N 71.13 W
Vinegar Hill ∧ 202 44.43 N 118.34 W
Vine Grove 194 37.48 N 85.58 W
Vine Hill 282 38.00 N 122.06 W
Vineland, Mi., U.S. 216 42.03 N 86.30 W
Vineland, N.J., U.S. 208 39.29 N 75.01 W
Vinemont 194 34.14 N 86.51 W
Vine Valley 210 42.43 N 77.20 W
Vineyard Canyon V 226 35.46 N 120.41 W
Vineyard Haven 207 41.27 N 70.36 W
Vineyard Lake ⊜ 216 42.05 N 84.13 W
Vineyard Sound ⊔ 207 41.25 N 70.46 W
Vingåker 40 59.02 N 15.52 E
Vingeanne ≃ 58 47.21 N 5.29 E
Ving Ngün 110 22.37 N 99.16 E
Vinh 110 18.40 N 105.40 E
Vinhais 34 41.50 N 7.00 W
Vinhas, Ribeira das ≃ 266c 38.42 N 9.25 W
Vinh Chau 110 9.19 N 105.59 E
Vinhedo 256 23.01 S 46.59 W
Vinh Loc 269c 10.49 N 106.34 E
Vinh Long 110 10.15 N 105.58 E
Vinh Tuy, Viet 110 9.37 N 105.22 E
Vinh Tuy, Viet 110 17.24 N 106.36 E
Vinica 36 45.28 N 15.15 E
Vinita 196 36.38 N 95.09 W
Vînju Mare 38 44.26 N 22.52 E
Vinkekuil 158 32.42 S 20.27 E
Vinkeveen 52 52.13 N 4.54 E
Vinkovci 38 45.17 N 18.49 E
Vin'kovcy 78 49.02 N 27.14 E
Vinnhorst 52 52.25 N 9.43 E
Vinnica 78 49.14 N 28.29 E
Vinnica □[4] 78 49.00 N 28.45 E
Vinniki 78 49.48 N 24.08 E
Vinnitsa
→ Vinnica 78 49.14 N 28.29 E
Vinnum 263 51.41 N 7.24 E
Vinogradov 78 48.09 N 23.02 E
Vinogradovo, Ross. 82 55.25 N 38.32 E
Vinogradovo, Ross. 82 55.57 N 37.32 E
Vinogrobol' 78 51.51 N 36.26 E
Vinön I 40 59.12 N 15.43 E
Vinon-sur-Verdon 62 43.43 N 5.48 E
Vinovo 62 44.57 N 7.38 E
Vinslöv 26 56.06 N 13.55 E
Vinson Massif ∧ 9 78.35 S 85.25 W
Vinstra 26 61.36 N 9.45 E
Vintilă Vodă 38 45.28 N 26.44 E
Vinto 248 17.58 S 67.04 W
Vinton, Ia., U.S. 190 42.10 N 92.01 W
Vinton, La., U.S. 194 30.11 N 93.34 W
Vinton, Va., U.S. 192 37.16 N 79.53 W
Vintondale 214 40.28 N 78.55 W
Vintrosa 40 59.15 N 14.57 E
Viñuelas, Arroyo de ≃ 266a 40.33 N 3.33 W
Viny 76 58.22 N 32.13 E
Vinzelberg 54 52.33 N 11.40 E
Vinzili 86 56.58 N 65.46 E
Viola, Il., U.S. 190 41.12 N 90.35 W
Viola, N.Y., U.S. 276 41.08 N 74.05 W
Viola, Wi., U.S. 190 43.30 N 90.40 W
Viola, Val V 64 46.27 N 10.15 E
Violín, Isla I 236 8.51 N 83.39 W
Viols-le-Fort 62 43.45 N 3.42 E

Symbols in the index entries represent the broad categories identified in the key at the right. Symbols with superior numbers (⋏[1]) identify subcategories (see complete key on page *I · 1).*

Symbole im Register stellen die rechts im Schlüssel erklärten Kategorien dar. Symbole mit hochgestellten Ziffern (⋏[1]) bezeichnen Unterabteilungen einer Kategorie (vgl. vollständiger Schlüssel auf Seite *I · 1).*

Los símbolos incluídos en el texto del índice representan las grandes categorías identificadas con la clave a la derecha. Los símbolos con numeros en su parte superior (⋏[1]) identifican las subcategorías (véase la clave completa en la página *I · 1).*

Les symboles de l'index représentent les catégories indiquées dans la légende à droite. Les symboles suivis d'un indice (⋏[1]) représentent des sous-catégories (voir légende complète à la page *I · 1).*

Os símbolos incluídos no texto do índice representam as grandes categorias identificadas com a chave à direita. Os símbolos com números em sua parte superior (⋏[1]) identificam as subcategorias (veja-se a chave completa à página *I · 1).*

∧ Mountain	Berg	Montaña	Montagne	Montanha
⋏ Mountains	Gebirge	Montañas	Montagnes	Montanhas
)(Pass	Paß	Paso	Col	Passo
V Valley, Canyon	Tal, Cañon	Valle, Cañón	Vallée, Canyon	Vale, Canhão
≃ Plain	Ebene	Llano	Plaine	Planície
⟩ Cape	Kap	Cabo	Cap	Cabo
I Island	Insel	Isla	Île	Ilha
II Islands	Inseln	Islas	Îles	Ilhas
⊥ Other Topographic Features	Andere Topographische Objekte	Otros Elementos Topográficos	Autres données topographiques	Outros acidentes topográficos

ESPAÑOL — Nombre | Página | Lat.°′ | Long.°′ W = Oeste
FRANÇAIS — Nom | Page | Lat.°′ | Long.°′ W = Ouest
PORTUGUÊS — Nome | Página | Lat.°′ | Long.°′ W = Oeste

Nombre / Nom / Nome	Página / Page	Lat.°′	Long.°′
Viosne ≃	50	49.03 N	2.06 E
Vipava	36	45.51 N	13.58 E
Vipava ≃	64	45.54 N	13.33 E
Vipiteno (Sterzing)	64	46.54 N	11.26 E
Vipos	252	26.29 S	65.22 W
Vipperow	54	53.19 N	12.41 E
Vir, Otok I	36	44.18 N	15.04 E
Vira	58	46.08 N	8.51 E
Virac	116	13.35 N	124.15 E
Viracopos, Aeroporto de ⊠	256	23.00 S	47.08 W
Virac Point ›	116	13.31 N	124.13 E
Viradouro	255	20.53 S	48.18 W
Virago Sound ʊ	182	54.00 N	132.36 W
Viramgām	120	23.07 N	72.02 E
Virandozero	24	64.05 N	35.58 E
Viranşehir	130	37.13 N	39.45 E
Vīrarājendrapet	122	12.12 N	75.48 E
Virbalis	76	54.38 N	22.49 E
Virden, Mb., Can.	184	49.51 N	100.55 W
Virden, Il., U.S.	219	39.30 N	89.46 W
Virden, N.M., U.S.	200	32.41 N	109.00 W
Vire	32	48.50 N	0.53 W
Vire ≃	32	49.20 N	1.07 W
Virelles	50	50.04 N	4.20 E
Virelles, Étang de ⊜	50	50.04 N	4.21 E
Vireux-Molhain	56	50.05 N	4.43 E
Vîrfurile	38	46.19 N	22.31 E
Virgem da Lapa	255	16.49 S	42.21 W
Virgen	64	47.00 N	12.27 E
Vírgen del San Cristóbal ɤ[1]	286e	33.26 S	70.39 W
Vírgenes, Cabo ›	254	52.22 S	68.20 W
Vírgenes, Islas → British Virgin Islands □[2], N.A.	240m	18.30 N	64.30 W
Vírgenes, Islas → Virgin Islands □[2], N.A.	240m	18.20 N	64.50 W
Virgen Tal V	64	47.00 N	12.25 E
Virgil, On., Can.	284a	43.13 N	79.08 W
Virgil, Ks., U.S.	198	37.58 N	96.00 W
Virgil, N.Y., U.S.	210	42.31 N	76.12 W
Virgilina	192	36.33 N	78.52 W
Virgilio	64	45.07 N	10.47 E
Virgin ≃	200	36.31 N	114.20 W
Virgin, North Fork ≃	200	37.10 N	113.01 W
Virginal-Samme	50	50.38 N	4.12 E
Virgin Gorda I	240m	18.30 N	64.24 W
Virgin Gorda Peak ʌ	240m	18.30 N	64.24 W
Virginia, Austl.	168b	34.40 S	138.34 E
Virgínia, Bra.	256	22.20 S	45.06 W
Virginia, Ire.	48	53.49 N	7.04 W
Virginia, S. Afr.	158	28.12 S	26.49 E
Virginia, Il., U.S.	219	39.57 N	90.12 W
Virginia, Mn., U.S.	190	47.31 N	92.32 W
Virginia □[3]	178	37.30 N	78.45 W
Virginia Beach	208	36.51 N	75.58 W
Virginia City, Mt., U.S.	202	45.17 N	111.56 W
Virginia City, Nv., U.S.	226	39.18 N	119.38 W
Virginia Creek ≃	226	38.13 N	119.14 W
Virginia Falls ∟	180	61.38 N	125.42 W
Virginia Gardens	220	25.49 N	80.17 W
Virginia Hills	208	38.47 N	77.06 W
Virginia Key I	220	25.44 N	80.09 W
Virginia Peak ʌ	204	39.45 N	119.28 W
Virginia Ranch Reservoir ⊜[1]	226	39.20 N	121.19 W
Virginia Range ⩘	226	39.18 N	119.30 W
Virginiatown	190	48.08 N	79.35 W
Virginia Water	260	51.24 N	0.34 W
Virginia Water ⊜[1]	260	51.24 N	0.37 W
Virginie occidentale → West Virginia □[3]	188	38.45 N	80.30 W
Virgin Islands □[2], N.A.	230	18.20 N	64.50 W
Virgin Islands □[2], N.A.	240m	18.20 N	64.50 W
Virgin Islands II	240m	18.00 N	64.40 W
Virgin Islands National Park ♠	240m	18.20 N	64.45 W
Virginópolis	255	18.45 S	42.45 W
Virgin Passage c[1]	240m	18.20 N	65.10 W
Virginville	208	40.31 N	75.52 W
Virgolândia	255	18.27 S	42.18 W
Virieu	62	45.29 N	5.28 E
Virieu-le-Grand	62	45.51 N	5.39 E
Virihaure ⊜	24	67.20 N	16.35 E
Virje	36	46.04 N	16.59 E
Virkkala	26	60.12 N	24.01 E
Virklund	41	56.07 N	9.34 E
Virneburg	56	50.20 N	7.04 E
Virôchey	110	13.59 N	106.49 E
Viroflay	50	48.48 N	2.10 E
Viroin ≃	56	50.05 N	4.43 E
Virojoki	26	60.35 N	27.42 E
Víron	267c	37.57 N	23.45 E
Vironvay	50	49.12 N	1.13 E
Viroqua	190	43.33 N	90.53 W
Virovitica	36	45.50 N	17.23 E
Virpazar	38	42.15 N	19.05 E
Virrat	26	62.14 N	23.47 E
Virsbo	40	59.52 N	16.02 E
Virserum	26	57.19 N	15.35 E
Virtaniemi	24	68.53 N	28.27 E
Virton	56	49.34 N	5.32 E
Vîrtopu	38	44.12 N	23.21 E
Virtsu	76	58.34 N	23.31 E
Virú	248	8.25 S	78.45 W
Virudunagar	122	9.36 N	77.58 E
Viru-Jaagupi	76	59.15 N	26.28 E
Virulento	196	28.52 N	104.21 W
Virunga, Parc National de ♠	154	1.00 S	29.15 E
Virungu	154	7.04 S	29.46 E
Viru-Nigula	76	59.27 N	26.41 E
Virvyčia ≃	76	56.13 N	22.34 E
Viry-Châtillon	50	48.40 N	2.23 E
Vis	36	43.03 N	16.12 E
Vis ≃, Fr.	62	43.56 N	3.42 E
Vis (Fish) ≃, Namibia	156	28.07 S	17.45 E
Vis ≃, S. Afr.	158	30.53 S	20.23 E
Vis, Otok I	36	43.02 N	16.11 E
Visale	175e	9.15 S	159.42 E
Visalia	226	36.19 N	119.17 W
Visalia Airport ⊠	226	36.19 N	119.23 W
Visayan Islands II	12	11.00 N	123.30 E
Visayan Sea ⊤[2]	116	11.35 N	123.51 E
Visbek	52	52.48 N	8.19 E
Visby	26	57.38 N	18.18 E
Viscaya, Bahía de → Biscay, Bay of c	32	44.00 N	4.00 W
Viscount	184	51.57 N	105.39 W
Viscount Melville Sound ʊ	176	74.10 N	108.00 W
Visé	56	50.44 N	5.42 E
Višegrad	38	43.47 N	19.17 E
Vis-en-Artois	50	50.15 N	2.56 E
Višera ≃	76	58.34 N	31.24 E
Viserba	66	44.05 N	12.32 E
Viseu, Bra.	250	1.12 S	46.07 W
Viseu, Port.	34	40.39 N	7.55 W
Vişeu ≃	38	47.55 N	24.09 E
Vişeu de Sus	38	47.44 N	24.22 E
Vishākhapatnam	122	17.42 N	83.18 E
Vishoek	158	34.08 S	18.26 E
Visim	86	57.39 N	59.30 E
Visingsö I	26	58.03 N	14.20 E
Visitation, Île de la I	275a	45.35 N	73.40 W
Viskafors	26	57.38 N	12.50 E
Viskan ≃	26	57.14 N	12.12 E
Viškil'	80	58.05 N	48.19 E
Viskinge	41	55.40 N	11.16 E
Visl'ajevo	82	54.25 N	36.43 E
Vislanda	26	56.47 N	14.27 E
Vislinskij zaliv c	30	54.27 N	19.40 E
Vismen ⊜	40	59.17 N	14.17 E
Visnagar	120	23.42 N	72.33 E
Višn'aki	265b	55.47 N	37.54 E
Višn'akovo	82	55.45 N	38.10 E
Višnevčik	78	49.02 N	26.28 E
Visnevo	76	54.08 N	26.14 E
Višnevoje, Ross.	80	52.38 N	43.26 E
Višnevoje, Ukr.	78	48.27 N	33.56 E
Višňové	61	48.59 N	16.09 E
Višn'ovec	78	49.54 N	25.45 E
Višn'ovka, Kaz.	86	50.49 N	72.12 E
Višn'ovka, Mol.	38	46.20 N	28.26 E
Viso, Monte ʌ	62	44.40 N	7.07 E
Visoki Dečani, Manastir ɤ[1]	38	42.30 N	20.31 E
Visoko	38	43.59 N	18.11 E
Visokoi Island I	18	56.42 S	27.12 W
Visp	58	46.18 N	7.53 E
Vispa ≃	58	46.18 N	7.52 E
Visrivier	158	31.55 S	25.25 E
Vissefjärda	26	56.32 N	15.35 E
Visselhövede	52	52.59 N	9.35 E
Vissenbjerg	41	55.23 N	10.08 E
Visso	66	42.56 N	13.05 E
Vissoie	58	46.13 N	7.36 E
Vista, Ca., U.S.	228	33.12 N	117.14 W
Vista, N.Y., U.S.	210	41.12 N	73.31 W
Vista Alegre, Arg.	252	38.45 S	68.11 W
Vista Alegre, Bra.	256	21.27 S	42.35 W
Vista Alegre, Chile	286e	33.30 S	70.43 W
Vista Alegre, Perú	286d	12.09 S	77.00 W
Vista Flores	252	33.38 S	69.09 W
Vistahermosa de Negrete	234	20.16 N	102.29 W
Vista La Mesa	228	32.35 N	117.01 W
Vista Park	228	35.21 N	118.55 W
Vistina	76	59.47 N	28.29 E
Vistre ≃	62	43.40 N	4.15 E
Vistula → Wisła ≃	30	54.22 N	18.55 E
Visun' ≃	78	47.07 N	32.53 E
Vit ≃	38	43.41 N	24.45 E
Vita, Mb., Can.	184	49.08 N	96.34 W
Vita, It.	70	37.52 N	12.49 E
Vita ≃	246	6.11 N	67.31 W
Vitacura	286e	33.24 S	70.36 W
Vitali	116	7.22 N	122.18 E
Vitanje	36	46.23 N	15.18 E
Vitarte	248	12.02 S	76.56 W
Vit'azevka	78	48.01 N	31.53 E
Vite	122	17.17 N	74.33 E
Vitebsk	76	55.12 N	30.11 E
Vitebsk □[8]	76	55.20 N	29.00 E
Vitebsk Station ✦[5]	265a	59.55 N	30.21 E
Vitel, Laguna ⊜	258	35.32 S	58.07 W
Viterbo	66	42.25 N	12.06 E
Viterbo □[4]	66	42.25 N	12.05 E
Vitiaz Strait ʊ	164	5.50 S	147.20 E
Vitichi	248	20.13 S	65.29 W
Vitigudino	34	41.01 N	6.26 W
Viti Levu I	175g	18.00 S	178.00 E
Vitim	74	59.28 N	112.34 E
Vitim ≃	74	59.26 N	112.34 E
Vitimskij	88	58.14 N	113.18 E
Vitimskoje ploskogorje ⩘[1]	88	54.00 N	113.30 E
Vitinia ✦[8]	267a	41.47 N	12.24 E
Vitis	61	48.45 N	15.10 E
Vítkov	30	49.46 N	17.45 E
Vito	175e	6.02 S	155.24 E
Vítor	248	16.26 S	71.49 W
Vitor ≃	248	16.37 S	72.19 W
Vitória, Bra.	250	2.54 S	52.01 W
Vitória, Bra.	255	20.19 S	40.21 W
Vitoria (Gasteiz), Esp.	34	42.51 N	2.40 W
Vitória, Ilha da I	256	23.45 S	45.01 W
Vitória da Conquista	255	14.51 S	40.51 W
Vitória de Santo Antão	250	8.07 S	35.18 W
Vitória do Mearim	250	3.28 S	44.53 W
Vitorino Freire	250	4.04 S	45.10 W
Vitravo ≃	68	39.11 N	17.05 E
Vitré	32	48.08 N	1.12 W
Vitrey-sur-Mance	58	47.49 N	5.45 E
Vitry-aux-Loges	50	47.56 N	2.16 E
Vitry-en-Artois	50	50.20 N	2.59 E
Vitry-la-Ville	50	48.50 N	4.28 E
Vitry-le-François	56	48.44 N	4.35 E
Vitry [-sur-Seine]	50	48.48 N	2.24 E
Vitshumbi	154	0.41 S	29.23 E
Vittangi	24	67.41 N	21.36 E
Vitte	54	54.34 N	13.06 E
Vitteaux	58	47.24 N	4.32 E
Vittel	58	48.12 N	5.57 E
Vittinge	40	59.54 N	17.04 E
Vittoria, On., Can.	212	42.46 N	80.19 W
Vittoria, It.	70	36.57 N	14.32 E
Vittorio Veneto	64	45.59 N	12.18 E
Vittsjö	26	56.20 N	13.40 E
Vitulano	68	41.10 N	14.38 E
Vitznau	58	47.01 N	8.29 E
Viù	62	45.14 N	7.22 E
Vivarais □[9]	62	44.40 N	4.30 E
Vivarais, Monts du ⩘	62	44.55 N	4.15 E
Viver	34	39.55 N	0.36 W
Vivero	34	43.40 N	7.35 W
Viverols	62	45.26 N	3.53 E
Viverone, Lago di ⊜	62	45.25 N	8.02 E
Vivi ≃	74	63.52 N	97.50 E
Vivian	194	32.52 N	93.59 W
Viviers	62	44.29 N	4.41 E
Viviers-du-Lac	62	45.39 N	5.54 E
Vivione, Passo del)(	64	46.02 N	10.12 E
Vivonne	32	46.26 N	0.16 E
Vivoratá	252	37.40 S	57.39 W
Vivorillo, Cayos II	236	15.50 N	83.18 W
Viwa I	175g	17.08 S	176.54 E
Vizagapatam → Vishākhapatnam	122	17.42 N	83.18 E
Vizcaíno, Desierto de ✦[2]	232	27.40 N	113.40 W
Vizcaíno, Isla I	258	33.47 S	59.15 W
Vize	130	41.34 N	27.45 E
Vize, ostrov I	72	79.30 N	77.00 E
Vizianagaram	122	18.07 N	83.25 E
Vizille	62	45.05 N	5.46 E
Vižinada	36	45.20 N	13.46 E
Vizinga	24	61.05 N	50.04 E
Vižnica	78	48.15 N	25.12 E
Vizzini	70	37.10 N	14.53 E
Vizzola	266b	45.38 N	8.42 E
Vjulka ≃	82	56.53 N	37.57 E
Vjunka ≃	265b	55.42 N	38.01 E
Vjuny	86	55.31 N	82.55 E
Vlaanderen → Flanders □[9]	50	51.00 N	3.00 E
Vlaardingen	52	51.54 N	4.21 E
Vlachovo Březí	60	49.05 N	13.57 E
Vladař ʌ	54	50.05 N	13.14 E
Vlădeasa, Vîrful ʌ	38	46.45 N	22.48 E
Vlădeni	38	47.25 N	27.20 E
Vladičin Han	38	42.42 N	22.04 E
Vladikavkaz	84	43.03 N	44.40 E
Vladimir	80	56.10 N	40.25 E
Vladimirec	78	51.25 N	26.08 E
Vladimir Oblast' □[4]	76	56.00 N	40.30 E
Vladimirovka, Kaz.	80	50.51 N	51.08 E
Vladimirovka, Kaz.	86	53.28 N	64.02 E
Vladimirovka, Ukr.	78	47.32 N	32.55 E
Vladimirovka, Ukr.	83	47.44 N	37.23 E
Vladimirskij Tupik	76	55.42 N	33.18 E
Vladimirskoje	80	56.49 N	45.07 E
Vladimir-Volynskij	78	50.51 N	24.20 E
Vladivostok	89	43.10 N	131.56 E
Vladyčnoje	76	58.49 N	39.29 E
Vladykino ✦[8]	265b	55.52 N	37.36 E
Vlasenica	38	44.11 N	18.56 E
Vlašim	30	49.42 N	14.54 E
Vlaskovo	82	56.11 N	36.31 E
Vlasotince	38	42.58 N	22.08 E
Vlasovo, Ross.	74	70.48 N	135.00 E
Vlasovo, Ross.	82	56.38 N	38.14 E
Vlazoviči	76	53.01 N	32.18 E
Vledder	52	52.52 N	6.12 E
Vleesbaai c	158	34.16 S	21.57 E
Vleikolk	158	29.43 S	20.50 E
Vleuten	52	52.05 N	5.02 E
Vlieland I	52	53.15 N	5.00 E
Vlijmen	52	51.42 N	5.15 E
Vlissingen (Flushing)	52	51.26 N	3.35 E
Vlodrop	52	51.08 N	6.05 E
Vloesberg → Flobecq	50	50.44 N	3.44 E
Vlonë → Vlorë	38	40.27 N	19.30 E
Vlorë	38	40.27 N	19.30 E
Vlorës, Gji i c	38	40.25 N	19.25 E
Vlotho	52	52.10 N	8.51 E
Vltava ≃	30	50.21 N	14.30 E
Vnukovo	82	55.38 N	37.13 E
Vnukovo Airport ⊠	265b	55.37 N	37.17 E
Voca	196	31.01 N	99.11 W
Vochrinka	82	55.24 N	38.13 E
Vochtoga	76	58.47 N	41.07 E
Vočin	36	45.37 N	17.32 E
Vöckla ≃	64	48.00 N	13.36 E
Vöcklabruck	60	48.01 N	13.39 E
Vöcklamarkt	60	48.00 N	13.29 E
Vodla ≃	24	61.49 N	36.00 E
Vodlozero, ozero ⊜	24	62.20 N	36.55 E
Vodňany	30	49.09 N	14.11 E
Vodnjan	36	44.57 N	13.51 E
Vodnyj	24	63.32 N	53.18 E
Vodo	64	46.25 N	12.14 E
Vodosalma	24	64.29 N	30.44 E
Vodovatovo	80	55.24 N	43.34 E
Vodzimonje	80	56.49 N	51.38 E
Voël ≃	158	33.07 S	25.07 E
Voerde, Dtsch.	52	51.35 N	6.41 E
Voerde, Dtsch.	263	51.18 N	7.24 E
Vogelenzang	52	52.19 N	4.35 E
Vogelheim ✦[8]	263	51.29 N	6.59 E
Vogelkop → Doberai, Jazirah ›[1]	164	1.30 S	132.30 E
Vogel Peak → Dimlang ʌ	146	8.24 N	11.47 E
Vogelsang, Dtsch.	54	53.43 N	14.09 E
Vogelsang, Dtsch.	56	50.35 N	6.27 E
Vogelsberg ⩘	56	50.30 N	9.15 E
Vogesen → Vosges ⩘	58	48.30 N	7.10 E
Voghera	62	44.59 N	9.01 E
Vognema	76	59.59 N	38.10 E
Vogogna	58	46.01 N	8.17 E
Vogtland ✦[1]	54	50.30 N	12.05 E
Voh	175f	20.58 S	164.42 E
Vohburg an der Donau	60	48.46 N	11.37 E
Vohenstrauss	60	49.37 N	12.21 E
Vohibinany	157b	18.49 S	49.04 E
Vohilava	157b	21.04 S	48.00 E
Vohimarina	157b	13.21 S	50.02 E
Vohipeno	157b	22.22 S	47.51 E
Vohitsora	157b	23.54 S	44.17 E
Võhma	76	58.38 N	25.33 E
Vöhrenbach	58	48.02 N	8.18 E
Vöhringen, Dtsch.	58	48.16 N	10.04 E
Vöhringen, Dtsch.	58	48.20 N	8.40 E
Vöhrum	52	52.20 N	10.10 E
Vohwinkel ✦[8]	263	51.14 N	7.09 E
Voi	154	3.23 S	38.34 E
Void	58	48.41 N	5.37 E
Voight Creek ≃	224	47.06 N	122.10 W
Voikkaa	26	60.56 N	26.37 E
Voineşti	38	47.05 N	27.26 E
Voinjama	150	8.25 N	9.45 W
Voinka	78	45.52 N	33.59 E
Voire ≃	58	48.27 N	4.25 E
Voiron	62	45.22 N	5.35 E
Voise	50	48.24 N	1.43 E
Voise ≃	50	48.35 N	1.35 E
Voisenon	261	48.34 N	2.40 E
Voisins-le-Bretonneux	50	48.45 N	2.03 E
Voiteur	58	46.45 N	5.37 E
Voitsberg	61	47.03 N	15.10 E
Voja ≃	80	57.23 N	49.55 E
Vojens	41	55.15 N	9.19 E
Vojevodskoje	86	52.47 N	85.35 E
Vojkovice	54	50.15 N	13.02 E
Vojkovo, Ukr.	78	45.31 N	33.52 E
Vojkovo, Ukr.	83	48.00 N	38.02 E
Vojkovskij	83	47.46 N	38.20 E
Vojmsjön ⊜	26	64.55 N	16.40 E
Vojnić	36	45.19 N	15.42 E
Vojnica	24	65.12 N	30.15 E
Vojnilov	78	49.08 N	24.30 E
Vojtanov	54	50.06 N	12.19 E
Vojvodina □[4]	38	45.00 N	20.00 E
Voj-Vož, Ross.	24	64.20 N	55.03 E
Voj-Vož, Ross.	24	62.56 N	54.56 E
Vokeo Island I	164	3.10 S	144.05 E
Volano	66	44.48 N	12.15 E
Volant	214	41.07 N	80.16 W
Volary	60	48.55 N	13.54 E
Volcán, Arg.	252	23.54 S	65.27 W
Volcán, Pan.	236	8.46 N	82.38 W
Volcán Isluga, Parque Nacional ♠	248	19.30 S	68.30 W
Volčanka	80	52.33 N	49.59 E
Volcano, Ca., U.S.	226	38.26 N	120.37 W
Volcano, Hi., U.S.	229d	19.25 N	155.14 W
Volcano Island I	116	14.00 N	121.00 E
Volcano Islands → Kazan-rettō II	14	25.00 N	141.00 E
Volcán Poás, Parque Nacional ♠	236	10.10 N	84.15 W
Volčansk, Ross.	86	59.56 N	60.04 E
Volčansk, Ukr.	78	50.18 N	36.57 E
Volčejarovka	83	48.50 N	38.22 E
Volčenskij	83	48.14 N	40.07 E
Volchonka-Zil ✦[8]	265b	55.40 N	37.37 E
Volchov	76	59.55 N	32.20 E
Volchov ≃	76	60.08 N	32.20 E
Volčicha	86	52.02 N	80.23 E
Volčij Nos, mys ›	76	60.31 N	32.35 E
Volčja ≃	78	48.00 N	36.08 E
Volčje	78	49.14 N	22.53 E
Volčki	80	52.29 N	40.42 E
Volda	26	62.09 N	6.06 E
Volders	64	47.17 N	11.34 E
Volendam	52	52.30 N	5.04 E
Volga, Ross.	76	57.57 N	38.24 E
Volga, Ia., U.S.	190	42.48 N	91.32 W
Volga, S.D., U.S.	198	44.19 N	96.55 W
Volga ≃, Ross.	72	45.55 N	47.52 E
Volga ≃, Ia., U.S.	190	42.45 N	91.17 W
Volga-Baltic Canal → Volgo-Baltijskij kanal ≅	24	59.00 N	38.00 E
Volgino	76	58.27 N	33.52 E
Volgo, ozero ⊜	76	56.55 N	33.10 E
Volgo-Baltijskij kanal ≅	24	59.00 N	38.00 E
Volgodonsk	80	47.33 N	42.08 E
Volgo-Donskoj sudochodnyj kanal imeni V.I. Lenina ≅	80	48.40 N	43.37 E
Volgograd (Stalingrad)	80	48.44 N	44.25 E
Volgograd Oblast' □[4]	80	49.30 N	44.00 E
Volgogradskoje vodochranilišče ⊜[1]	80	49.20 N	45.00 E
Volgorečensk	76	57.30 N	41.02 E
Volissós	38	38.29 N	25.58 E
Vol'ka	76	52.47 N	25.39 E
Volkach	56	49.52 N	10.13 E
Volkel	52	51.38 N	5.40 E
Völkermarkt	61	46.39 N	14.38 E
Völkermarkter Stausee ⊜[1]	61	46.39 N	14.38 E
Völkerschlacht-Denkmal ⊥	54	51.18 N	12.24 E
Völklingen	56	49.15 N	6.50 E
Volkmarsen	56	51.24 N	9.07 E
Volkovincy	78	49.13 N	27.39 E
Volkovo, Ross.	76	59.15 N	41.27 E
Volkovo, Ross.	82	55.46 N	36.15 E
Volkovo Cemetery ✦	265a	59.54 N	30.22 E
Volkovskoje	82	54.49 N	37.13 E
Volkovysk	76	53.10 N	24.28 E
Volksdorf ✦[8]	52	53.39 N	10.10 E
Völksen	52	52.13 N	9.37 E
Volksrust	158	27.24 S	29.53 E
Vollenhove	52	52.41 N	5.58 E
Vollersode	52	53.18 N	8.56 E
Vollme	263	51.10 N	7.36 E
Vollore-Montagne	62	45.47 N	3.41 E
Vollore-Ville	62	45.47 N	3.36 E
Vollsjö	41	55.42 N	13.46 E
Volma ≃	76	53.35 N	28.19 E
Volmarstein	56	51.22 N	7.23 E
Volme ≃	263	51.24 N	7.27 E
Volmerange-les-Mines	56	49.27 N	6.05 E
Volmerswerth ✦[8]	263	51.11 N	6.46 E
Volmunster	56	49.07 N	7.21 E
Vol'naja Gorka	76	58.43 N	30.51 E
Volnay	58	47.00 N	4.47 E
Vol'nogorsk	78	48.29 N	34.01 E
Vol'noje, Ross.	80	47.09 N	47.38 E
Vol'noje, Ross.	86	54.17 N	71.21 E
Volnovacha	83	47.36 N	37.31 E
Vol'nyj	80	45.55 N	45.14 E
Vol'nyj, ostrov I	265a	59.58 N	30.14 E
Voločajevka Vtoraja	89	48.34 N	134.34 E
Voločanka	74	71.00 N	94.28 E
Voločisk	78	49.32 N	26.11 E
Volockaja	76	60.17 N	42.59 E
Volodarka, Ross.	86	52.43 N	83.38 E
Volodarka, Ukr.	78	49.31 N	29.55 E
Volodarsk, Ross.	76	56.13 N	43.10 E
Volodarsk, Ukr.	83	48.06 N	39.35 E
Volodarskij, Ross.	80	46.24 N	48.32 E
Volodarskij, Ross.	82	55.30 N	37.57 E
Volodarskij ✦[8]	265a	59.49 N	30.05 E
Volodarskoje, Kaz.	86	53.18 N	68.08 E
Volodarskoje, Ukr.	83	47.12 N	37.20 E
Volodarsk-Volynskij	78	50.37 N	28.25 E
Volodino	86	57.06 N	83.54 E
Vologda	76	59.12 N	39.55 E
Vologda ≃	76	59.17 N	40.13 E
Vologda Oblast' □[4]	24	60.00 N	40.00 E
Voloje	76	54.09 N	34.35 E
Volokolamsk	82	56.02 N	35.57 E
Volokonovka	78	50.29 N	37.51 E
Volokovaja	24	66.28 N	48.10 E
Volonga	24	67.07 N	47.41 E
Volonne	62	44.07 N	6.01 E
Volontirovka	38	46.26 N	29.37 E
Vólos	38	39.21 N	22.56 E
Vološino, Ross.	83	48.55 N	39.56 E
Vološino, Ross.	83	47.31 N	39.40 E
Vološka	24	61.20 N	40.06 E
Vološn'a ≃	82	55.51 N	35.54 E
Vološno	76	58.29 N	28.29 E
Volosoviči	76	54.46 N	28.50 E
Volosovo	76	59.26 N	29.29 E
Volosskaja Balaklejka	83	49.37 N	37.20 E
Volot	76	57.56 N	30.42 E
Volovec	78	48.43 N	23.11 E
Volovo, Ross.	76	53.35 N	38.02 E
Volovo, Ross.	78	52.03 N	37.53 E
Voložin	76	54.05 N	26.32 E
Volpago del Montello	64	45.47 N	12.07 E
Volpedo	62	44.53 N	8.59 E
Volpiano	62	45.12 N	7.46 E
Völpke	54	52.08 N	11.09 E
Völs → Fiè	64	46.31 N	11.30 E
Volsini, Monti ⩘	66	42.40 N	11.55 E
Vol'sk	80	52.02 N	47.23 E
Volstruisleegte	158	33.05 S	23.28 E
Volta □[4]	150	7.00 N	0.30 E
Volta ≃	150	5.46 N	0.41 E
Volta, Lake ⊜[1]	150	7.30 N	0.15 E
Volta Blanche (White Volta) ≃	150	9.10 N	1.15 W
Voltaggio	62	44.37 N	8.50 E
Voltago	64	46.16 N	12.00 E
Volta Grande	256	21.46 S	42.32 W
Voltaire, Cape ›	164	14.16 S	125.35 E
Volta Mantovana	64	45.19 N	10.39 E
Volta Noire (Black Volta) ≃	150	8.41 N	1.33 W
Volta Redonda	256	22.32 S	44.07 W
Volta Rouge ≃	150	10.34 N	0.30 W
Volterra	66	43.24 N	10.51 E
Vol'teva	24	64.30 N	44.12 E
Voltri	62	44.26 N	8.45 E
Volturara Appula	68	41.30 N	15.03 E
Volturara Irpina	68	40.53 N	14.55 E
Volturino	68	41.28 N	15.07 E
Volturino, Monte ʌ	68	40.25 N	15.49 E
Volturno ≃	66	41.01 N	13.55 E
Volubilis ⊥	148	34.00 N	5.30 W
Voluntown	207	41.34 N	71.52 W
Volusia □[6]	220	28.51 N	81.05 W
Vólvi, Límni ⊜	38	40.41 N	23.23 E
Volx	62	43.53 N	5.51 E
Volyn □[4]	78	51.00 N	25.00 E
Volyncy, Bela.	76	55.42 N	28.11 E
Volyncy, Ross.	80	57.48 N	45.28 E
Volyně	60	49.10 N	13.53 E
Volynka	78	51.37 N	32.26 E
Volyňka ≃	60	49.16 N	13.54 E
Volynskaja vozvyšennost' ⩘[1]	78	50.30 N	25.30 E
Volzhskiy → Volžskij	80	48.50 N	44.44 E
Volžsk	80	55.53 N	48.21 E
Volžskij, Ross.	80	53.27 N	50.07 E
Volžskij, Ross.	80	48.50 N	44.44 E
Vom	150	9.41 N	8.42 E
Vomano ≃	66	42.39 N	14.02 E
Vombsjön ⊜	41	55.41 N	13.36 E
Vomp	64	47.20 N	11.41 E
Vonavona Island I	175e	8.15 S	157.05 E
Vonda	184	52.19 N	106.06 W
Vondanka	24	59.07 N	47.49 E
Vondrozo	157b	22.49 S	47.20 E
Von Frank Mountain ʌ	180	63.33 N	154.20 W
Võnnu	76	58.17 N	27.05 E
Vonozero	76	60.22 N	34.26 E
Vonsild	41	55.27 N	9.29 E
Von Treuer Tableland ⩘[1]	162	26.38 S	122.53 E
Voorburg	52	52.05 N	4.23 E
Voordeelspan	158	29.05 S	21.32 E
Voorheesville	210	42.39 N	73.56 W
Voorne I	52	51.54 N	4.08 E
Voorschoten	52	52.07 N	4.27 E
Voorst	52	52.10 N	6.09 E
Voorthuizen	52	52.12 N	5.35 E
Vop' ≃	76	54.56 N	32.44 E
Vopnafjörður	24a	65.47 N	14.44 W
Vopnafjörður c	24a	65.52 N	14.40 W
Vörå (Vöyri)	26	63.09 N	22.15 E
Vor'a ≃, Ross.	76	54.54 N	35.01 E
Vor'a ≃, Ross.	82	55.52 N	38.13 E
Vorarlberg □[3]	58	47.15 N	9.55 E
Vorau	61	47.25 N	15.54 E
Vorbach	60	49.49 N	11.45 E
Vorbasse	41	55.38 N	9.05 E
Vorbjovo	88	57.23 N	102.18 E
Vorchdorf	60	48.00 N	13.55 E
Vörden, Dtsch.	52	52.28 N	8.05 E
Vorden, Ned.	52	52.07 N	6.18 E
Vorder-Grauspitz ʌ	58	47.03 N	9.36 E
Vorderkrimmi	64	47.14 N	12.12 E
Vordernberg	61	47.28 N	15.00 E
Vorderrhein ≃	58	46.49 N	9.25 E
Vorderriss	64	47.33 N	11.26 E
Vordingborg	41	55.01 N	11.55 E
Voreifel ⩘	56	50.15 N	7.10 E
Voreppe	62	45.18 N	5.38 E
Vorey	62	45.11 N	3.54 E
Vorga	76	53.45 N	32.45 E
Vorhalle ✦[8]	263	51.23 N	7.28 E
Vorhelm	52	51.48 N	7.56 E
Voríai Sporádhes II	38	39.15 N	23.55 E
Vøringsfossen ∟	26	60.26 N	7.15 E
Vórios Evvoïkós Kólpos c	38	38.40 N	23.15 E
Vorkuta	24	67.27 N	63.58 E
Vorlich, Ben ʌ, Scot., U.K.	46	56.17 N	4.46 W
Vorlich, Ben ʌ, Scot., U.K.	46	56.20 N	4.14 W
Vorma ≃	26	60.09 N	11.27 E
Vormholz	263	51.24 N	7.18 E
Vormsi I	76	59.00 N	23.20 E
Vorn'any	76	54.44 N	26.01 E
Vorobjevo, Ross.	82	56.11 N	35.45 E
Vorobjevo, Ross.	86	56.08 N	76.32 E
Vorobji	82	55.09 N	36.48 E
Vorobjovka	80	50.38 N	40.56 E
Vorob'jovo, Ross.	76	59.38 N	40.55 E
Vorob'jovo, Ukr.	78	45.20 N	33.15 E
Vorochta	78	48.18 N	24.36 E
Voron'	76	55.00 N	28.39 E
Voron, porog ∟	88	57.05 N	98.40 E
Vorona ≃	80	51.22 N	42.03 E
Voroncovka, Kaz.	86	48.49 N	81.32 E
Voroncovka, Ross.	78	50.37 N	40.21 E
Voroncovka, Ross.	86	59.39 N	60.14 E
Voroncovka, Ross.	88	58.51 N	112.56 E
Voroncovka, Ukr.	78	45.51 N	33.47 E
Voroncovo, Ross.	76	57.18 N	28.42 E
Voroncovo, Ross.	80	55.16 N	40.27 E
Voronej → Voronež	78	51.40 N	39.10 E
Voronež, Ross.	78	51.40 N	39.10 E
Voronež, Ukr.	78	51.46 N	33.28 E
Voronež ≃	76	51.56 N	39.25 E
Voronezh → Voronež	78	51.40 N	39.10 E
Voronež Oblast' □[4]	78	51.00 N	40.00 E
Voronežskij zapovednik ✦[4]	76	51.56 N	39.37 E
Voronino	82	56.24 N	36.52 E
Voronja ≃	24	69.10 N	35.50 E
Voronjo, Ross.	24	68.27 N	35.21 E
Voronjo, Ross.	80	58.00 N	42.01 E
Voronki, Ross.	82	55.48 N	37.16 E
Voron'ki, Ukr.	78	50.14 N	33.02 E
Voronkovo	38	47.43 N	29.08 E
Voronok	76	52.23 N	32.40 E
Voronov, mys ›	76	60.15 N	32.05 E
Voronovica	78	49.06 N	28.41 E
Voronovkova Niva	76	57.04 N	29.16 E
Voronovo, Bela.	76	54.09 N	25.19 E
Voronovo, Ross.	82	55.19 N	37.10 E
Voronovo, Ross.	86	56.01 N	83.52 E
Voropajevo	76	55.09 N	27.13 E
Voroshilov → Ussurijsk	89	43.48 N	131.59 E
Voroshilovsk → Stavropol'	72	45.02 N	41.59 E
Vorošilovgrad → Lugansk	83	48.34 N	39.20 E
Vorotajevka	80	51.56 N	47.16 E
Vorotynec	80	56.04 N	45.52 E
Vorotynsk	82	54.25 N	36.05 E
Vorovskolesskaja	84	44.23 N	42.25 E
Vorožba	78	51.12 N	34.14 E
Vorožejka	86	58.12 N	90.02 E
Vorpommern □[9]	54	53.40 N	13.45 E
Vorra	60	49.33 N	11.30 E
Vorsfelde	54	52.26 N	10.49 E
Vorskla ≃	78	48.53 N	34.06 E
Vorsma	80	55.59 N	43.16 E
Vorst, Bel.	56	51.04 N	5.01 E
Vorst, Dtsch.	56	51.18 N	6.25 E
Vørterkaka Nunatak ʌ	9	72.20 S	27.29 E
Võrtsjärv ⊜	76	58.16 N	26.03 E
Võru	76	57.50 N	27.01 E
Voruch	85	39.52 N	70.35 E
Vorzel'	78	50.33 N	30.09 E
Vosburg	158	30.33 S	22.52 E
Voschod	80	47.24 N	41.50 E
Vösendorf	61	48.07 N	16.20 E
Vosges □[5]	58	48.10 N	6.20 E
Vosges ⩘	58	48.30 N	7.10 E
Vosja	76	59.01 N	41.11 E
Voskresenka, Ross.	80	51.01 N	46.28 E
Voskresenka, Ross.	88	53.15 N	119.31 E
Voskresenki	82	54.57 N	38.04 E
Voskresenovskoje	265a	59.43 N	30.47 E
Voskresensk	82	55.19 N	38.42 E
Voskresenskoje, Ross.	76	53.12 N	38.43 E
Voskresenskoje, Ross.	76	58.54 N	38.36 E
Voskresenskoje, Ross.	76	59.26 N	37.56 E
Voskresenskoje, Ross.	76	57.49 N	37.40 E
Voskresenskoje, Ross.	80	56.51 N	45.26 E
Voskresenskoje, Ross.	80	51.51 N	46.56 E
Voskresenskoje, Ross.	82	54.07 N	37.07 E
Voskresenskoje, Ross.	82	56.20 N	38.29 E
Voskresenskoje, Ross.	86	53.08 N	56.10 E
Voskresenskoje, Ukr.	78	47.02 N	32.09 E
Voslapp	52	53.36 N	8.05 E
Voss	26	60.39 N	6.26 E
Vosselaar	56	51.19 N	4.53 E
Vossijatskoje	78	47.41 N	32.07 E
Vossman's Beacon	158	26.11 S	30.40 E
Vostočnaja Kambal'nica	24	68.18 N	46.00 E
Vostočno-Kazachstan □[8]	86	49.00 N	84.00 E
Vostočno-Kounradskij	86	47.02 N	75.07 E
Vostočno-Sibirskoje more (East Siberian Sea) ⊤[2]	12	74.00 N	166.00 E
Vostočnyj, Ross.	82	55.47 N	37.52 E
Vostočnyj, Ross.	86	58.48 N	61.52 E
Vostočnyj, Ross.	89	53.29 N	143.03 E
Vostočnyj, Ross.	89	48.17 N	142.34 E
Vostočnyj Sajan ⩘	88	53.00 N	97.00 E
Vostok I	14	10.06 S	152.23 W
Vostok ɤ[3]	9	78.30 S	106.50 E
Vostr'akovo	82	55.23 N	37.49 E
Vostrecovo	89	45.53 N	134.58 E
Vostrovo	86	52.09 N	80.38 E
Vosves	261	48.31 N	2.36 E
Votaw	222	30.26 N	94.41 W
Votice	30	49.38 N	14.39 E
Votkinsk	80	57.03 N	53.59 E
Votkinskoje vodochranilišče ⊜[1]	86	57.00 N	54.30 E
Vot'pa	86	60.13 N	62.57 E
Votuporanga	255	20.24 S	49.59 W
Voué	50	48.28 N	4.07 E
Vouga ≃	34	40.41 N	8.40 W
Vougba	152	5.10 N	23.06 E
Vougeot	58	47.10 N	4.58 E
Vouillé	32	46.39 N	0.10 E
Voujeaucourt	58	47.28 N	6.46 E
Voulangis	261	48.51 N	2.54 E
Voulou	146	8.33 N	22.36 E
Voulx	50	48.17 N	2.58 E
Voulzie ≃	50	48.25 N	3.12 E
Voutenay-sur-Cure	50	47.33 N	3.47 E
Vouvray	50	47.25 N	0.48 E
Vouvry	58	46.20 N	6.53 E
Vouziers	56	49.24 N	4.42 E
Voves	50	48.16 N	1.38 E
Vovodo ≃	140	5.40 N	24.21 E
Vowinckel	214	41.25 N	79.14 W
Voxnan ≃	26	61.17 N	16.26 E
Voyageurs National Park ♠	190	48.30 N	93.00 W
Vöyri → Vörå	26	63.09 N	22.15 E
Voža ≃	82	54.38 N	39.10 E
Vožajol'	24	62.50 N	51.17 E
Vožd' Proletariata	76	55.26 N	39.19 E
Vozdviženka, Ross.	80	53.10 N	54.14 E
Vozdviženka, Ukr.	78	47.46 N	36.05 E
Vozdviženskoje, Ross.	80	56.58 N	45.37 E
Vozdviženskoje, Ross.	80	45.50 N	43.40 E
Vozdviženskoje, Ross.	82	56.12 N	38.04 E
Vože, ozero ⊜	24	60.30 N	39.00 E
Vožega	76	60.29 N	40.12 E
Vožega ≃	76	60.33 N	39.11 E
Vožgaly	80	58.09 N	50.11 E
Vožgora	24	64.32 N	48.25 E
Voznesenje	24	61.01 N	35.27 E
Voznesenka, Kaz.	86	52.24 N	70.12 E
Voznesenka, Ukr.	78	46.51 N	35.26 E
Voznesenovka	80	46.16 N	44.21 E
Voznesensk	78	47.34 N	31.20 E
Voznesenskoje, Ross.	80	54.54 N	42.46 E
Voznesenskoje, Ross.	80	45.49 N	43.25 E
Vozroždenija, ostrov I	86	45.03 N	59.12 E
Vozroždenije	80	52.42 N	48.12 E
Vozžajevka	89	50.44 N	128.41 E
Vrå	26	57.21 N	9.57 E
Vráble	30	48.15 N	18.19 E
Vraca	38	43.12 N	23.33 E
Vračevo	82	54.53 N	39.10 E
Vrådal	26	59.20 N	8.25 E
Vrancea □[6]	38	45.45 N	27.00 E
Vrancei, Munţii ⩘	38	46.00 N	26.30 E
Vrangel'a, mys ›	89	54.17 N	138.39 E
Vrangel'a, ostrov I	74	71.00 N	179.30 W
Vranje	38	42.33 N	21.54 E
Vranov	61	48.54 N	15.49 E
Vranov [nad Topl'ou]	30	48.54 N	21.41 E
Vrbas	38	45.35 N	19.39 E
Vrbas ≃	36	45.06 N	17.31 E
Vrbovec	36	45.53 N	16.25 E
Vrbovsko	36	45.23 N	15.05 E
Vrchlabí	30	50.38 N	15.37 E
Vrede	158	27.30 S	29.06 E
Vredefort	158	27.05 S	27.16 E
Vreden	52	52.02 N	6.52 E
Vredenburg	158	32.54 S	17.59 E
Vredenburgh	194	31.49 N	87.19 W
Vredendal	158	31.41 S	18.35 E
Vreed en Hoop	246	6.48 N	58.11 W
Vreeswijk	52	52.01 N	5.05 E
Vrena	40	58.52 N	16.41 E
Vresse	56	49.52 N	4.56 E
Vreta kloster ɤ[1]	26	58.28 N	15.29 E
Vretstorp	40	59.02 N	14.52 E
Vrginmost	36	45.21 N	15.52 E
Vrhnika	36	45.58 N	14.18 E
Vriddhāchalam	122	11.30 N	79.20 E
Vriendschaps ≃	164	5.28 S	138.53 E
Vries	52	53.04 N	6.35 E
Vriezenveen	52	52.25 N	6.38 E
Vrigne-Meuse	56	49.42 N	4.51 E
Vrigstad	26	57.21 N	14.28 E
Vrilissia	267c	38.02 N	23.50 E
Vrille ≃	50	47.31 N	2.52 E
Vrin	58	46.39 N	9.06 E
Vrin ≃	50	48.00 N	3.20 E
Vrindāvan	124	27.35 N	77.42 E
Vrlika	36	43.55 N	16.24 E
Vrnograč	36	45.10 N	15.57 E
Vroeggedeel	158	28.02 S	22.32 E
Vron	50	50.19 N	1.45 E
Vrondádhes	38	38.24 N	26.08 E
Vroomshoop	52	52.27 N	6.34 E
Vrouenspan	158	27.50 S	20.24 E
Vroutek	54	50.08 N	13.24 E
Vršac	38	45.07 N	21.18 E
Vrsar	64	45.08 N	13.37 E
Vršič)(	64	46.26 N	13.44 E
Vrubovka	83	48.44 N	38.20 E
Vrubovskij	83	48.26 N	39.07 E
Vrútky	30	49.07 N	18.55 E
Vryburg	158	26.55 S	24.45 E
Vryheid	158	27.46 S	30.48 E
Vschody	76	54.42 N	34.06 E
Vselug, ozero ⊜	76	57.03 N	32.42 E
Všepadly	60	49.28 N	13.06 E
Všeruby	60	49.50 N	13.15 E
Vsetín	30	49.21 N	17.59 E
Vsevidof, Mount ʌ	180	53.07 N	168.43 W
Vsevoložsk	265a	60.01 N	30.40 E
Vtoroje Potapovo	265b	55.56 N	37.58 E
Vtoryje Levyje Lamki	80	53.17 N	41.04 E
Vuadil'	85	40.11 N	71.43 E
Vuanggava Island I	175g	18.52 S	178.54 W
Vučitrn	38	42.49 N	20.58 E
Vudor, gora ʌ	85	38.13 N	71.49 E
Vue-des-Alpes)(	58	47.04 N	6.53 E
Vught	52	51.40 N	5.17 E
Vuillafans	58	47.04 N	6.13 E
Vuillebœuf	58	46.37 N	6.34 E
Vukovar	38	45.21 N	19.00 E
Vulcan, Ab., Can.	182	50.24 N	113.15 W
Vulcan, Rom.	38	45.23 N	23.17 E
Vulcan, Mi., U.S.	190	45.46 N	87.51 W
Vulcano, Bocche di ʊ	70	38.26 N	14.57 E
Vulcano, Isola I	70	38.24 N	14.58 E
Vulcano, Monte ʌ[2]	70a	35.51 N	12.52 E
Vulci ⊥	66	42.25 N	11.35 E
Vulkanešty	38	45.41 N	28.24 E
Vulkaničeskij chrebet ⩘	78	48.30 N	23.00 E
Vulture, Monte ʌ	68	40.57 N	15.38 E
Vul'vyvejem ≃	180	66.58 N	179.10 W
Vung Tau	110	10.21 N	107.04 E
Vunindawa	175g	17.49 S	178.19 E
Vunisea Station	175g	19.03 S	178.09 E
Vuoggatjålme	24	66.36 N	16.22 E
Vuohijärvi	26	61.05 N	26.48 E
Vuohijärvi ⊜	26	61.12 N	26.42 E
Vuokatti ʌ[2]	26	64.07 N	28.14 E
Vuoksa ≃	26	61.03 N	30.11 E
Vuoksa, ozero ⊜	76	60.40 N	29.50 E
Vuoksenniska	26	61.13 N	28.49 E
Vurnary	80	55.29 N	46.58 E
Vuturu, Pizzo ʌ	70	37.56 N	14.13 E
Vuya	154	5.21 N	29.40 E
Vuyyūru	122	16.22 N	80.51 E
Vuzenica	61	46.36 N	15.10 E
Vvedenka	86	54.03 N	63.45 E
Vvedenovka	89	51.19 N	128.12 E
Vvedenskoje	82	55.42 N	36.54 E
Vyāra	120	21.07 N	73.24 E
Vyatka → Kirov	80	58.38 N	49.42 E
Vyaz'ma → V'az'ma	76	55.13 N	34.18 E
Vyazniki → V'azniki	80	56.15 N	42.10 E
Vyborg	76	60.42 N	28.45 E
Vyborgskij zaliv c	76	60.35 N	28.24 E
Výčapy	61	49.09 N	15.53 E
Vyčegda ≃	24	61.18 N	46.36 E
Vyčegodskij	24	61.16 N	46.48 E
Vychino ✦[3]	265b	55.43 N	37.48 E

≃ River	Fluß	Río	Rivière	Rio	✣ Submarine Features	Untermeerische Objekte	Accidentes Submarinos	Formes de relief sous-marin	Acidentes submarinos
≅ Canal	Kanal	Canal	Canal	Canal	□ Political Unit	Politische Einheit	Unidad Politica	Entité politique	Unidade política
∟ Waterfall, Rapids	Wasserfall, Stromschnellen	Cascada, Rápidos	Chute d'eau, Rapides	Cascata, Rápidos	ɤ Cultural Institution	Kulturelle Institution	Institución Cultural	Institution culturelle	Instituição cultural
ʊ Strait	Meeresstraße	Estrecho	Détroit	Estreito	⊥ Historical Site	Historische Stätte	Sitio Histórico	Site historique	Sitio histórico
c Bay, Gulf	Bucht, Golf	Bahía, Golfo	Baie, Golfe	Baía, Golfo	♠ Recreational Site	Erholungs- und Ferienort	Sitio de Recreo	Centre de loisirs	Area de Lazer
⊜ Lake, Lakes	See, Seen	Lago, Lagos	Lac, Lacs	Lago, Lagos	⊠ Airport	Flughafen	Aeropuerto	Aéroport	Aeroporto
≡ Swamp	Sumpf	Pantano	Marais	Pântano	■ Military Installation	Militäranlage	Instalación Militar	Installation militaire	Instalação militar
⊓ Ice Features, Glacier	Eis- und Gletscherformen	Accidentes Glaciales	Formes glaciaires	Acidentes glaciares	✦ Miscellaneous	Verschiedenes	Misceláneo	Divers	Diversos
⊤ Other Hydrographic Features	Andere Hydrographische Objekte	Otros Elementos Hidrográficos	Autres données hydrographiques	Outros acidentes hidrográficos					

ENGLISH / DEUTSCH

Name / Name	Page / Seite	Lat.°′ / Breite°′	Long.°′ / Länge°′ E = Ost
Východočeský Kraj □[4]	30	50.10 N	16.00 E
Východoslovenský Kraj □[4]	30	49.00 N	21.15 E
Vydrino, Ross.	88	51.27 N	104.39 E
Vydrino, Ross.	88	56.50 N	99.02 E
Vygoda	78	48.56 N	23.55 E
Vygoniči	76	53.08 N	34.05 E
Vygoniščì	76	52.37 N	25.55 E
Vygozero, ozero ⊜	24	63.35 N	34.42 E
Vyjezdnoje	80	55.23 N	43.47 E
Vyježžij Log	86	54.58 N	93.57 E
Vyksa	80	55.18 N	42.11 E
Vylkovo	86	53.05 N	81.26 E
Vym' ≃	24	62.13 N	50.25 E
Vyntja	86	60.31 N	67.18 E
Vypolzovo	76	57.53 N	33.42 E
Vyrica	76	59.25 N	30.21 E
Vyrnwy ≃	42	52.46 N	3.00 W
Vyrnwy, Lake ⊜	42	52.47 N	3.30 W
Vyša	80	53.52 N	42.24 E
Vyša ≃	80	54.02 N	42.06 E
Vyšehrad •[8]	54	50.01 N	14.27 E
Vyšelej	80	53.26 N	45.29 E
Vyselki	78	45.35 N	39.38 E
Vyšesteblijevskaja	78	45.12 N	37.00 E
Vyšgorodok	76	57.02 N	28.01 E
Vyška, Ross.	76	57.31 N	35.57 E
Vyška, Turk.	128	39.20 N	54.08 E
Vyskod'	76	57.46 N	30.04 E
Vyškov, Česká Rep.	30	49.16 N	17.00 E
Vyškov, Ross.	76	52.29 N	31.41 E
Vyškovskij, pereval)(	78	48.42 N	23.38 E
Vyšná Radvaň	30	49.07 N	21.56 E
Vyšneol'šanoje	76	52.08 N	37.39 E
Vyšnevolockoje vodochranilišče ⊜[1]	76	57.35 N	34.28 E
Vyšnij Voločok	76	57.35 N	34.34 E
Vysočany •[8]	54	50.05 N	14.31 E
Vysock, Ross.	76	60.36 N	28.34 E
Vysock, Ukr.	78	51.43 N	26.39 E
Vysokaja, gora ∧	89	45.59 N	136.35 E
Vysokaja Gora	80	55.56 N	49.19 E
Vysoké Mýto	30	49.57 N	16.10 E
Vysoké Tatry ⋀	30	49.12 N	20.05 E
Vysokiniči	82	54.54 N	36.55 E
Vysokogornyj	89	50.09 N	139.09 E
Vysokogorsk	89	44.23 N	135.23 E
Vysokoje, Bela.	76	52.22 N	23.22 E
Vysokoje, Kaz.	85	42.30 N	70.32 E
Vysokoje, Ross.	76	56.43 N	34.55 E
Vysokoje, Ross.	76	54.02 N	33.44 E
Vysokoje, Ross.	82	54.30 N	37.03 E
Vysokoje, Ross.	265b	55.59 N	37.09 E
Vysokopolje	78	47.29 N	33.32 E
Vysokovsk	82	56.19 N	36.33 E
Vysoký kámen ∧	61	49.06 N	15.13 E
Vyssaja Dubečn'a	78	50.44 N	30.40 E
Vyšší Brod	61	48.37 N	14.19 E
Vystupoviči	78	51.34 N	29.04 E
Vytebet' ≃	76	53.53 N	35.38 E
Vytegra	24	61.00 N	36.24 E
Vyževka ≃	78	51.41 N	24.35 E
Vzmorje	89	47.51 N	142.31 E
Vzvad	76	58.10 N	31.29 E
W			
W, Parc National du ♦	150	12.50 N	2.30 E
Wa	150	10.04 N	2.29 W
Waabs	41	54.32 N	9.58 E
Waackaack Creek ≃	276	40.27 N	74.08 W
Waadt → Vaud □[3]	58	46.40 N	6.30 E
Waajid	144	3.48 N	43.15 E
Waakirchen	64	47.46 N	11.40 E
Waal	58	48.00 N	10.46 E
Waal ≃	52	51.49 N	4.58 E
Waalre	52	51.24 N	5.26 E
Waalwijk	52	51.42 N	5.04 E
Waao	102	24.20 N	104.40 E
Waar, Meos I	164	2.05 S	134.23 E
Waarschoot	50	51.09 N	3.36 E
Waasmunster	50	51.06 N	4.05 E
Wabag	164	5.30 S	143.40 E
Wabamun	182	53.33 N	114.28 W
Wabamun Indian Reserve •[4]	182	53.30 N	114.30 W
Wabamun Lake ⊜	182	53.33 N	114.35 W
Waban	283	42.20 N	71.14 W
Waban, Lake ⊜	283	42.17 N	71.17 W
Wabana	186	47.38 N	52.57 W
Wabasca	182	56.00 N	113.53 W
Wabasca ≃	176	58.22 N	115.20 W
Wabasca Indian Reserve •[4]	182	55.53 N	113.32 W
Wabash, In., U.S.	216	40.47 N	85.49 W
Wabash, Oh., U.S.	216	40.33 N	84.45 W
Wabash □[6]	216	40.48 N	85.49 W
Wabash ≃	194	37.46 N	88.02 W
Wabasha	190	44.23 N	92.01 W
Wabasso, Fl., U.S.	220	27.44 N	80.26 W
Wabasso, Mn., U.S.	198	44.24 N	95.15 W
Wabatongushi Lake ⊜	190	48.26 N	84.15 W
Wabe Gestro ≃	144	4.17 N	42.02 E
Wabe Mena ≃	144	5.32 N	41.11 E
Wabeno	190	45.26 N	88.39 W
Wabera	144	6.26 N	40.42 E
Wabern	56	51.06 N	9.20 E
Wabigoon Lake ⊜	184	49.44 N	92.44 W
Wabowden	184	54.55 N	98.38 W
Wabrah ⫪[4]	128	27.26 N	47.22 E
Wąbrzeźno	30	53.17 N	18.57 E
Wabu	100	32.17 N	116.55 E
Wabu Hu ⊜	100	32.23 N	116.54 E
Wabuska	226	39.08 N	119.10 W
W.A.C. Bennett Dam •[6]	182	56.01 N	122.10 W
Waccamaw ≃	192	33.21 N	79.16 W
Waccamaw, Lake ⊜	192	34.17 N	78.30 W
Waccasassa Bay C	192	29.06 N	82.52 W
Wachapreague	208	37.36 N	75.41 W
Wachapreague Inlet C	208	37.35 N	75.36 W
Wachau •[1]	61	48.18 N	15.24 E
Wachenheim	56	49.26 N	8.10 E
Wachi	96	35.15 N	135.24 E
Wąchock, Klasztory ⊍[1]	30	51.05 N	21.01 E
Wachtberg	56	50.37 N	7.11 E
Wachtendonk	56	51.24 N	6.20 E
Wächtersbach	56	50.15 N	9.17 E
Wachusett Mountain ∧	207	42.29 N	71.53 W
Wachusett Reservoir ⊜[1]	207	42.23 N	71.43 W
Wacissa	192	30.21 N	83.59 W
Wackersdorf	60	49.19 N	12.11 E
Waco	222	31.32 N	97.08 W
Waco Lake ⊜[1]	222	31.34 N	97.13 W
Waconda Lake ⊜[1]	198	39.30 N	98.24 W
Waconia	190	44.51 N	93.47 W
Wacouno ≃	186	50.54 N	65.57 W
Wacousta	216	42.49 N	84.42 W
Wad	120	27.21 N	66.22 E
Wada, Nihon	94	35.02 N	140.01 E
Wada, Nihon	94	36.12 N	138.13 E
Wada, Nihon	268	35.12 N	139.38 E
Wada, Nihon	270	34.33 N	135.55 E
Wadagou	104	42.27 N	120.58 E
Wad Al-Ḥaddād	140	13.49 N	33.32 E
Wadamago	144	8.55 N	46.17 E
Wada-misaki ≻	96	34.39 N	135.11 E
Wādat Ga	120	26.57 N	97.37 E
Wadayama	96	35.19 N	134.52 E
Wad Bandah	140	13.06 N	27.57 E
Wad Ban Naqa	140	16.30 N	33.08 E
Wadbilliga National Park ♦	166	36.20 S	149.35 E
Waddān	146	29.10 N	16.08 E
Waddān, Jabal ⋀[2]	146	29.20 N	16.20 E
Waddeneilanden II	52	53.26 N	5.30 E
Waddenzee ⫪[2]	52	53.15 N	5.15 E
Wadderin	162	32.00 S	118.27 E
Waddesdon	42	51.51 N	0.56 W
Waddingham	44	53.27 N	0.31 W
Waddington, Eng., U.K.	44	53.10 N	0.32 W
Waddington, N.Y., U.S.	212	44.51 N	75.12 W
Waddington, Mount ∧	182	51.23 N	125.15 W
Waddinxveen	52	52.03 N	4.40 E
Waddy	218	38.08 N	85.04 W
Wade, Mount ∧	9	84.51 S	174.15 W
Wadebridge	42	50.32 N	4.50 W
Wadena, Sk., Can.	184	51.57 N	103.47 W
Wadena, In., U.S.	216	40.43 N	87.16 W
Wadena, Mn., U.S.	198	46.26 N	95.08 W
Wädenswil	58	47.14 N	8.40 E
Wadern	56	49.32 N	6.53 E
Wadersloh	52	51.44 N	8.15 E
Wadesboro	192	34.58 N	80.04 W
Wadeville	273d	26.16 S	28.11 E
Wadeye	164	14.13 S	129.32 E
Wadgassen	56	49.16 N	6.47 E
Wad Ḥāmid	140	16.30 N	32.48 E
Wadham Islands II	186	49.34 N	53.50 W
Wadhams	182	51.30 N	127.31 W
Wadhurst	42	51.04 N	0.21 E
Wadian	100	32.48 N	112.30 E
Wādī as-Sīr	132	31.57 N	35.49 E
Wādī Ḥalfā'	140	21.56 N	31.20 E
Wādī Jimāl, Jazīrat I	140	24.40 N	35.10 E
Wādī Mūsā	132	30.19 N	35.29 E
Wading ≃, Ma., U.S.	283	41.56 N	71.13 W
Wading ≃, N.J., U.S.	208	39.33 N	74.28 W
Wading, West Branch ≃	208	39.40 N	74.32 W
Wading River	207	40.57 N	72.50 W
Wādī Rashrāsh, Bi'r ⫪[4]	142	29.26 N	31.31 E
Wadley, Al., U.S.	194	33.07 N	85.33 W
Wadley, Ga., U.S.	192	32.52 N	82.24 W
Wad Madanī	140	14.25 N	33.28 E
Wadowice	30	49.53 N	19.30 E
Wadsworth, Il., U.S.	216	42.26 N	87.56 W
Wadsworth, Nv., U.S.	204	39.38 N	119.17 W
Wadsworth, N.Y., U.S.	210	42.49 N	77.54 W
Wadsworth, Oh., U.S.	214	41.01 N	81.43 W
Wadsworth Moor •[3]	262	53.48 N	2.02 W
Wadu I	122	5.51 N	72.58 E
Waegwan	98	35.58 N	128.24 E
Waelder	222	29.42 N	97.18 W
Waenhuiskrans	158	34.41 S	20.14 E
Wafang	98	41.44 N	118.54 E
Wafania	152	1.21 S	20.20 E
Wafrah	128	28.33 N	48.02 E
Wagadugu → Ouagadougou	150	12.22 N	1.31 W
Wāgah	123	31.36 N	74.33 E
Wagait Aboriginal Reserve •[4]	164	13.00 S	130.20 E
Wagang	102	28.04 N	103.10 E
Wagenborgen	52	53.15 N	6.56 E
Wagenfeld-Hasslingen	52	52.33 N	8.34 E
Wageningen, Ned.	52	51.58 N	5.40 E
Wageningen, Sur.	250	5.46 N	56.41 W
Wager Bay C	176	65.26 N	88.40 W
Wagerup	168a	32.55 S	115.54 E
Waggaman Heights	284c	38.49 N	76.57 W
Wagga Wagga	171b	35.07 S	147.22 E
Waggoner	219	39.23 N	89.39 W
Waghäusel	56	49.14 N	8.31 E
Wagin	162	33.18 S	117.21 E
Waging am See	64	47.56 N	12.43 E
Waginger See ⊜	64	47.56 N	12.47 E
Wägitaler See ⊜	58	47.06 N	8.55 E
Waglan Island I	271d	22.11 N	114.18 E
Wagna	61	46.46 N	15.34 E
Wagner	198	43.04 N	98.17 W
Wagner College ⊍[2]	276	40.37 N	74.07 W
Wagoner	196	35.57 N	95.22 W
Wagon Mound	196	36.00 N	104.42 W
Wagontire Mountain ∧	202	43.21 N	119.53 W
Wagontown	208	40.01 N	75.51 W
Wagrain	64	47.20 N	13.18 E
Wagram → Deutsch Wagram	61	48.18 N	16.34 E
Wagrien •[1]	54	54.15 N	10.45 E
Wągrowiec	30	52.49 N	17.11 E
Waha	146	28.16 N	19.54 E
Wahādurgañj	124	27.32 N	82.50 E
Wahai	164	2.48 S	129.30 E
Waharoa	172	37.46 S	175.46 E
Wāh Cantonment	123	33.48 N	72.42 E
Wahiawa	229c	21.30 N	158.01 W
Wāḥid	142	30.49 N	32.20 E
Wahkiakum □[6]	224	46.16 N	123.28 W
Wahlen	56	49.37 N	8.51 E
Wahlstedt	54	53.57 N	10.12 E
Wahnbachstausee ⊜[1]	56	50.48 N	7.19 E
Wahneta	220	27.57 N	81.44 W
Wahoo	198	41.12 N	96.37 W
Wahpeton	198	46.15 N	96.36 W
Wahran (Oran)	148	35.43 N	0.43 W
Wahran □[5]	148	35.30 N	0.30 E
Wahrenbrück	54	51.33 N	13.22 E
Wahrenholz	54	52.36 N	10.36 E
Währing •[8]	264b	48.14 N	16.21 E
Wahroonga	274a	33.43 S	151.07 E
Wahweap Creek ≃	200	37.02 N	111.35 W
Wai, India	122	17.56 N	73.54 E
Wai, Indon.	164	1.42 S	127.59 E
Waialeale ∧	229b	22.04 N	159.30 W
Waialua	229c	21.34 N	158.07 W
Waialua Bay C	229c	21.36 N	158.07 W
Waianae	229c	21.26 N	158.11 W
Waianae Range ⋀	229c	21.30 N	158.10 W
Waianapanapa State Park ♦	229a	20.47 N	156.01 W
Waiapu ≃	172	37.47 S	178.29 E
Waiatoto ≃	172	43.59 S	168.47 E
Waiau	172	42.39 S	173.03 E
Waiau ≃, N.Z.	172	42.47 S	173.22 E
Waiau ≃, N.Z.	172	46.12 S	167.38 E
Waiau ≃, N.Z.	172	38.58 S	177.24 E
Waibakul	115b	9.36 S	119.35 E
Waibeem	164	0.28 S	132.58 E
Waiblingen	56	48.50 N	9.19 E
Waibstadt	56	49.18 N	8.54 E
Waichagoumen	98	40.54 N	125.45 E
Waidbruck → Ponte Gardena	64	46.36 N	11.32 E
Waidhān	124	24.04 N	82.20 E
Waidhofen an der Thaya	61	48.49 N	15.18 E
Waidhofen an der Ybbs	61	47.58 N	14.47 E
Waidmannslust •[8]	264a	52.36 N	13.20 E
Waidring	64	47.35 N	12.34 E
Waiehu	229a	20.55 N	156.30 W
Waigang	106	31.22 N	121.11 E
Waigatsch → Vajgač, ostrov I	72	70.00 N	59.30 E
Waigeo, Pulau I	164	0.14 S	130.45 E
Waigoumen	98	41.24 N	116.13 E
Waihao Downs	172	44.48 S	170.55 E
Waihau Bay	172	37.37 S	177.55 E
Waihee	229a	20.56 N	156.30 W
Waihee Point ≻	229a	20.57 N	156.31 W
Waiheke Island I	172	36.48 S	175.06 E
Waihi	172	37.24 S	175.51 E
Waihola	172	46.02 S	170.06 E
Waihopai ≃	172	41.31 S	173.44 E
Waihou ≃	172	37.10 S	175.32 E
Waihuantan	106	30.25 N	118.40 E
Waika	154	2.21 S	25.43 E
Waikabubak	115b	9.38 S	119.25 E
Waikaia	172	45.44 S	168.51 E
Waikaia ≃	172	45.53 S	168.48 E
Waikanae	172	40.53 S	175.04 E
Waikane	229c	21.30 N	157.51 W
Waikapu	229a	20.51 N	156.30 W
Waikare, Lake ⊜	172	37.26 S	175.13 E
Waikaremoana, Lake ⊜	172	38.46 S	177.07 E
Waikari	172	42.58 S	172.41 E
Waikato ≃	172	37.23 S	174.43 E
Waikelo	115b	9.24 S	119.14 E
Waikerie	166	34.11 S	139.59 E
Waikiki Beach ♦	229c	21.17 N	157.50 W
Waikino	172	37.25 S	175.46 E
Waikouaiti	172	45.36 S	170.41 E
Waikuatang	106	31.20 N	120.41 E
Wailo	144	9.25 N	48.55 E
Wailua	229b	22.03 N	159.20 W
Wailua River State Park ♦	229b	22.02 N	159.21 W
Wailuku	229a	20.53 N	156.30 W
Waimahaka	172	46.31 S	168.49 E
Waimakariri ≃	172	43.24 S	172.42 E
Waimamaku	172	35.33 S	173.29 E
Waimana	172	38.09 S	177.05 E
Waimana ≃	172	38.04 S	177.00 E
Waimanalo	229c	21.21 N	157.43 W
Waimangaroa	172	41.43 S	171.46 E
Waimangura	115b	9.30 S	119.14 E
Waimarama	172	39.48 S	176.59 E
Waimate	172	44.44 S	171.02 E
Waimea, Hi., U.S.	229c	21.38 N	158.03 W
Waimea, Hi., U.S.	229d	21.57 N	159.40 W
Waimea Canyon V	229b	22.04 N	159.39 W
Waimea Canyon State Park ♦	229b	22.04 N	159.40 W
Waimes	56	50.25 N	6.07 E
Wainfleet All Saints	44	53.07 N	0.14 E
Wainganga ≃	122	18.50 N	79.55 E
Waingapu	115b	9.39 S	120.16 E
Waini ≃	246	8.24 N	59.51 W
Wainscott	260	51.25 N	0.31 E
Wainstalls	262	53.45 N	1.56 W
Wainuiomata	172	41.16 S	174.57 E
Wainunu Bay C	175g	16.55 S	178.53 E
Wainwright, Ab., Can.	182	52.49 N	110.52 W
Wainwright, Ak., U.S.	180	70.38 N	160.01 W
Wainwright, Oh., U.S.	214	40.25 N	81.25 W
Waiohau	172	38.14 S	176.51 E
Waiotira	172	35.56 S	174.12 E
Waiouru	172	39.29 S	175.40 E
Waipa ≃	172	37.41 S	175.09 E
Waipahi	172	46.07 S	169.15 E
Waipahu	229c	21.23 N	158.00 W
Waipaoa	172	38.32 S	177.54 E
Waipara	172	43.04 S	172.45 E
Waipara ≃	172	43.09 S	172.48 E
Waipawa	172	39.56 S	176.36 E
Waipiata	172	45.11 S	170.10 E
Waipio Acres	229c	21.28 N	158.00 W
Waipio Bay C	229a	20.55 N	156.13 W
Waipiro	172	38.01 S	178.20 E
Waipu	172	35.59 S	174.27 E
Waipukurau	172	40.00 S	176.34 E
Wairakei	172	38.38 S	176.06 E
Wairarapa, Lake ⊜	172	41.13 S	175.15 E
Wairau ≃	172	41.30 S	174.04 E
Wairau Valley	172	41.34 S	173.32 E
Wairio	172	46.00 S	168.02 E
Wairoa	172	39.02 S	177.25 E
Wairoa ≃	172	39.04 S	177.26 E
Waisanzao	106	30.57 N	121.52 E
Waischenfeld	60	49.51 N	11.21 E
Waïsisi	175f	19.30 S	169.22 E
Waitahanui	172	38.47 S	176.05 E
Waitahuna	172	45.59 S	169.46 E
Waitakaruru	172	37.15 S	175.23 E
Waitaki ≃	172	44.57 S	171.09 E
Waitara, Austl.	274a	33.43 S	151.07 E
Waitara, N.Z.	172	39.00 S	174.13 E
Waitara ≃	172	38.59 S	174.14 E
Waitarere	172	40.33 S	175.12 E
Waita Reservoir ⊜[1]	229b	21.55 N	159.27 W
Waitati	172	45.45 S	170.34 E
Waita-zan ∧	96	33.08 N	131.10 E
Waite Hill	214	41.37 N	81.22 W
Waitemata	172	36.56 S	174.42 E
Waite Park	190	45.33 N	94.13 W
Waitoa	172	37.37 S	175.38 E
Waitotara	172	39.48 S	174.44 E
Waitotara ≃	172	39.51 S	174.41 E
Waitpinga	168b	35.37 S	138.29 E
Waitsburg	202	46.16 N	118.09 W
Waitzen → Vác	30	47.47 N	19.08 E
Waiuku	172	37.15 S	174.45 E
Waiuta	172	42.18 S	171.49 E
Waiwera South	172	46.13 S	169.30 E
Waiwo	164	0.56 S	131.03 E
Waiya	164	3.13 S	128.55 E
Waizenkirchen	60	48.20 N	13.52 E
Wajiki	96	33.51 N	134.30 E
Wajima	92	37.24 N	136.54 E
Wajir	154	1.45 N	40.04 E
Waka, Ityo.	144	7.07 N	37.26 E
Waka, Tx., U.S.	196	36.17 N	101.03 W
Waka, Zaïre	152	1.01 N	20.13 E
Wakajabi	164	5.38 S	134.24 E
Wakakusa	94	35.36 N	138.29 E
Wakakusa-yama ∧[2]	270	34.42 N	135.52 E
Wakamatsu → Aizu-wakamatsu	92	37.30 N	139.56 E
Wakami ≃	190	47.43 N	82.22 W
Wakami Lake ⊜	190	47.29 N	82.51 W
Wakamiya	96	33.44 N	130.37 E
Wakano-ura ♦	96	34.11 N	135.11 E
Wakarusa	216	41.32 N	86.03 W
Wakarusa ≃	198	38.57 N	95.05 W
Wakasa	96	35.20 N	134.24 E
Wakasa-wan C	92	35.45 N	135.40 E
Wakasa-wan-kokutei-kōen ♦	96	35.35 N	135.30 E
Wakatipu, Lake ⊜	172	45.05 S	168.34 E
Wakatomika Creek ≃	214	40.07 N	82.00 W
Wakato-ōhashi •[5]	96	33.54 N	130.49 E
Wakaw	184	52.39 N	105.44 W
Wakaw Lake ⊜	184	52.40 N	105.35 W
Wakayama	96	34.13 N	135.11 E
Wakayama □[5]	96	34.00 N	135.20 E
Wakayanagi	92	38.46 N	141.08 E
Wake, Nihon	96	34.48 N	134.08 E
Wake, Zaïre	152	0.48 S	20.10 E
WaKeeney	198	39.01 N	99.53 W
Wakefield, N.Z.	172	41.24 S	173.03 E
Wakefield, Eng., U.K.	44	53.42 N	1.29 W
Wakefield, Ks., U.S.	198	39.12 N	97.00 W
Wakefield, Ma., U.S.	207	42.30 N	71.04 W
Wakefield, Ne., U.S.	198	42.16 N	96.51 W
Wakefield, Oh., U.S.	218	38.59 N	83.01 W
Wakefield, R.I., U.S.	207	41.26 N	71.30 W
Wakefield, Va., U.S.	192	36.58 N	76.59 W
Wakefield ≃	168b	34.10 S	138.10 E
Wakefield Forest	284c	38.50 N	77.14 W
Wake Forest	192	35.58 N	78.30 W
Wake Island □[2], Oc.	14	19.17 N	166.36 E
Wake Island □[2], Oc.	174a	19.17 N	166.36 E
Wake Island I[1]	174a	19.18 N	166.38 E
Wake Island Air Force Base ■	174a	19.17 N	166.37 E
Wake Lagoon C	174a	19.18 N	166.36 E
Wakema	110	16.36 N	95.11 E
Wakeman	214	41.15 N	82.23 W
Wakeman ≃	182	51.00 N	126.30 W
Wakenda Creek ≃	194	39.19 N	93.16 W
Wake Village	194	33.26 N	94.07 W
Wakhān → Vākhān •[1]	120	37.00 N	73.00 E
Waki	96	34.04 N	134.09 E
Wakis	164	6.13 S	150.17 E
Wakita	196	36.53 N	97.55 W
Wakkanai	92a	45.25 N	141.40 E
Wakkerstroom	158	27.24 S	30.10 E
Wakō, Nihon	268	35.47 N	139.37 E
Wako, Pap. N. Gui.	164	6.05 S	149.05 E
Wakomata Lake ⊜	190	46.34 N	83.22 W
Wakonassin ≃	190	46.28 N	81.51 W
Wakonda	198	43.00 N	97.06 W
Wakre	164	0.19 S	131.09 E
Waku Kundo	152	11.25 S	15.07 E
Wakunai	175e	5.52 S	155.13 E
Wakusimi ≃	190	49.08 N	82.17 W
Wala ≃	154	5.46 S	32.04 E
Walamba	154	13.29 S	28.45 E
Walanae ≃	112	4.08 S	119.58 E
Walang	102	28.33 N	100.54 E
Wal Athiang	140	7.42 N	29.40 E
Walawe ≃	122	6.06 N	81.01 E
Walbeck	52	51.30 N	6.15 E
Walberswick	42	52.19 N	1.39 E
Walbran Creek ≃	224	48.34 N	124.40 W
Walbridge	214	41.35 N	83.29 W
Wałbrzych (Waldenburg)	30	50.46 N	16.17 E
Walburg	222	30.44 N	97.35 W
Walbury Hill ∧[2]	42	51.21 N	1.30 W
Walcha	166	30.59 S	151.36 E
Walchensee ⊜	64	47.36 N	11.20 E
Walcheren I	52	51.33 N	3.35 E
Walchsee	64	47.39 N	12.19 E
Walcott, B.C., Can.	182	54.31 N	126.51 W
Walcott, Ia., U.S.	190	41.35 N	90.46 W
Walcott, N.D., U.S.	198	46.32 N	96.56 W
Walcott, Lake ⊜[1]	202	42.40 N	113.23 W
Walcourt	50	50.15 N	4.25 E
Wałcz	30	53.17 N	16.28 E
Wald	58	47.17 N	8.55 E
Wald •[8]	263	51.11 N	7.03 E
Waldai → Valdajskaja vozvyšennost' ⋀[2]	24	57.00 N	33.30 E
Waldaist ≃	61	48.19 N	14.34 E
Wald am Schoberpass	61	47.27 N	14.40 E
Waldbauer •[8]	263	51.18 N	7.28 E
Waldbillig	56	49.47 N	6.18 E
Waldböckelheim	56	49.49 N	7.43 E
Waldbröl	56	50.53 N	7.37 E
Waldbronn	56	48.56 N	8.29 E
Waldburg	58	47.45 N	9.43 E
Waldeck, Dtsch.	56	51.12 N	9.04 E
Waldeck, Dtsch.	60	49.52 N	11.57 E
Walden, Co., U.S.	200	40.43 N	106.16 W
Walden, N.Y., U.S.	210	41.33 N	74.11 W
Walden, Lake ⊜	281	42.39 N	83.46 W
Waldenbuch	56	48.38 N	9.07 E
Waldenburg, Dtsch.	54	50.52 N	12.36 E
Waldenburg, Dtsch.	56	49.11 N	9.38 E
Waldenburg → Wałbrzych, Pol.	30	50.46 N	16.17 E
Waldenburg, Schw.	58	47.23 N	7.45 E
Walden Pond ⊜, Ma., U.S.	283	42.26 N	71.20 W
Walden Pond ⊜, Ma., U.S.	283	42.28 N	71.00 W
Walden Ridge ∧	194	35.30 N	85.15 W
Waldershof	60	49.59 N	12.04 E
Walderslade	260	51.21 N	0.32 E
Waldfischbach	56	49.17 N	7.40 E
Waldheim, Sk., Can.	184	52.37 N	106.38 W
Waldheim, Dtsch.	54	51.04 N	13.01 E
Waldighoffen	58	47.33 N	7.19 E
Wald im Pinzgau	64	47.15 N	12.14 E
Waldkappel	56	51.08 N	9.52 E
Waldkirch	58	48.05 N	7.57 E
Waldkirchen	60	48.44 N	13.37 E
Waldkirchen am Wesen	60	48.26 N	13.49 E
Waldkraiburg	60	48.12 N	12.28 E
Waldmohr	56	49.23 N	7.20 E
Waldmünchen	60	49.23 N	12.43 E
Waldnaab ≃	60	49.36 N	12.08 E
Waldo, B.C., Can.	182	49.13 N	115.13 W
Waldo, Ar., U.S.	194	33.21 N	93.17 W
Waldo, Oh., U.S.	214	40.27 N	83.04 W
Waldoboro	188	44.05 N	69.22 W
Waldo Lake ⊜	283	42.07 N	71.03 W
Waldo Lake ⊜[1]	202	43.44 N	122.03 W
Waldon ≃	42	50.51 N	4.15 W
Waldorf	208	38.37 N	76.56 W
Waldport	202	44.25 N	124.04 W
Waldron, Sk., Can.	184	50.51 N	102.30 W
Waldron, Ar., U.S.	194	34.53 N	94.05 W
Waldron, In., U.S.	218	39.27 N	85.40 W
Waldron, Mi., U.S.	216	41.43 N	84.25 W
Waldron Island I	224	48.43 N	123.02 W
Waldsassen	60	50.00 N	12.18 E
Waldshut	58	47.37 N	8.13 E
Waldstatt	58	47.21 N	9.17 E
Waldthurn	60	49.40 N	12.20 E
Waldviertel •[1]	61	48.40 N	15.15 E
Waldwick	276	41.00 N	74.07 W
Walea, Selat ⊔	112	0.40 S	122.00 E
Walembele	150	10.30 N	1.58 W
Walensee ⊜	58	47.07 N	9.12 E
Walenstadt	58	47.07 N	9.19 E
Wales, Ak., U.S.	180	65.36 N	168.05 W
Wales, Ma., U.S.	207	42.04 N	72.13 W
Wales, Wi., U.S.	216	43.00 N	88.23 W
Wales □[8]	28	52.30 N	3.30 W
Wales Center	210	42.46 N	78.32 W
Wales Island I, B.C., Can.	182	54.45 N	130.30 W
Wales Island I, N.T., Can.	176	68.00 N	86.43 W
Walewale	150	10.21 N	0.48 W
Walgett	166	30.01 S	148.07 E
Walgreen Coast ⫫[2]	9	75.15 S	105.00 W
Walhachin	182	50.45 N	120.59 W
Walhalla, N.D., U.S.	198	48.55 N	97.55 W
Walhalla, S.C., U.S.	192	34.45 N	83.03 W
Walhalla ⊥	60	49.03 N	12.14 E
Walheim	56	50.42 N	6.10 E
Walhonding	214	40.22 N	82.09 W
Walhonding ≃	214	40.18 N	81.53 W
Wali	105	39.42 N	118.20 E
Walia	164	3.47 S	138.32 E
Walikale	154	1.25 S	28.03 E
Walincourt	50	50.04 N	3.20 E
Walis Island I	164	3.15 S	143.20 E
Walkaway	162	28.57 S	114.48 E
Walkden	44	53.32 N	2.24 W
Walkenried	54	51.35 N	10.37 E
Walker, Ia., U.S.	190	42.17 N	91.46 W
Walker, Mi., U.S.	216	43.00 N	85.46 W
Walker, Mn., U.S.	190	47.06 N	94.35 W
Walker, N.Y., U.S.	210	43.18 N	77.52 W
Walker □[6]	222	30.42 N	95.35 W
Walker ≃	204	38.54 N	118.47 W
Walker, Lac ⊜	186	50.16 N	67.09 W
Walker, Mount ∧[2]	171a	27.48 S	152.34 E
Walker Basin Creek ≃	228	35.20 N	118.47 W
Walker Bay C	158	34.30 S	19.20 E
Walker Creek ≃, Az., U.S.	200	36.58 N	109.42 W
Walker Creek ≃, Ma., U.S.	283	42.38 N	70.44 W
Walker Creek ≃, Wy., U.S.	198	43.09 N	104.52 W
Walker Lake ⊜, Mb., Can.	184	54.42 N	96.57 W
Walker Lake ⊜, Ak., U.S.	180	67.10 N	154.26 W
Walker Lake ⊜, Nv., U.S.	204	38.44 N	118.43 W
Walker Lake ⊜[1]	210	40.48 N	77.11 W
Walker Point ≻	158	34.05 S	22.57 E
Walker River Indian Reservation •[4]	204	39.00 N	118.40 W
Walkers Mill	279b	40.24 N	80.08 W
Walkersville	208	39.29 N	77.21 W
Walkerton, On., Can.	212	44.07 N	81.09 W
Walkerton, In., U.S.	216	41.28 N	86.28 W
Walkerton, Va., U.S.	208	37.43 N	77.01 W
Walkertown	192	36.10 N	80.09 W
Walker Valley	210	41.38 N	74.23 W
Walkerville	202	46.02 N	112.32 W
Walk Mill	262	53.46 N	2.12 W
Wall, Pa., U.S.	279b	40.24 N	79.47 W
Wall, S.D., U.S.	198	43.59 N	102.14 W
Wallace, Ca., U.S.	226	38.12 N	120.59 W
Wallace, Id., U.S.	202	47.28 N	115.55 W
Wallace, Ne., U.S.	198	40.50 N	101.09 W
Wallace, N.Y., U.S.	210	42.26 N	77.28 W
Wallace, N.C., U.S.	192	34.44 N	77.59 W
Wallaceburg	214	42.36 N	82.23 W
Wallace Lake ⊜	279a	41.22 N	81.52 W
Wallaceton	214	40.57 N	78.17 W
Wallacetown	214	42.38 N	81.28 W
Wallach	263	51.35 N	6.34 E
Wallachia □[9]	38	44.00 N	25.00 E
Wallacia	170	33.52 S	150.39 E
Wallal Downs	162	19.47 S	120.40 E
Wallam Creek ≃	166	28.40 S	147.20 E
Wallan	169	37.25 S	144.59 E
Wallangarra	166	28.56 S	151.56 E
Wallaroo	168b	33.56 S	137.38 E
Wallaroo Mines	168b	33.57 S	137.41 E
Wallasey	44	53.26 N	3.03 W
Wallau	56	50.56 N	8.28 E
Walla Walla	202	46.03 N	118.20 W
Walldorf, Dtsch.	54	50.36 N	10.23 E
Walldorf, Dtsch.	56	49.18 N	8.38 E
Walldürn	56	49.35 N	9.22 E
Walled Lake	216	42.32 N	83.28 W
Walled Lake ⊜	281	42.31 N	83.29 W
Wallen	216	41.09 N	85.09 W
Wallend	260	51.27 N	0.42 E
Wallenfels	54	50.16 N	11.28 E
Wallenhorst	52	52.21 N	8.01 E
Wallenpaupack, Lake ⊜	210	41.25 N	75.12 W
Waller	222	30.04 N	95.56 W
Waller □[6]	222	30.00 N	96.00 W
Wallerawang	170	33.25 S	150.04 E
Wallern im Burgenland	61	47.43 N	16.56 E
Wallers	50	50.22 N	3.24 E
Wallersdorf	60	48.44 N	12.45 E
Wallersee ⊜	64	47.55 N	13.11 E
Wallerstein	56	48.53 N	10.28 E
Wallgau	64	47.31 N	11.16 E
Wallgrove	274a	33.47 S	150.51 E
Wallhead Airport ⊠	279a	41.21 N	82.09 W
Wallingford, Eng., U.K.	42	51.37 N	1.08 W
Wallingford, Ct., U.S.	207	41.27 N	72.49 W
Wallingford, Pa., U.S.	285	39.54 N	75.22 W
Wallingford, Vt., U.S.	188	43.28 N	72.58 W
Wallington	276	40.51 N	74.06 W
Wallington •[8]	260	51.21 N	0.09 W
Wallis	222	29.37 N	96.03 W
Wallis → Valais □[3]	58	46.10 N	7.30 E
Wallis, Îles II	14	13.18 S	176.10 W
Wallis and Futuna □[2]	14	14.00 S	177.00 W
Wallisellen	58	47.25 N	8.36 E
Wallisville	222	29.50 N	94.44 W
Wallisville Lake ⊜[1]	222	29.50 N	94.45 W
Wallkill	210	41.36 N	74.11 W
Wallkill ≃, U.S.	210	41.51 N	74.03 W
Wallkill ≃, U.S.	276	41.11 N	74.35 W
Wallkill, Wildcat Branch ≃	276	41.07 N	74.36 W
Wall Lake, Ia., U.S.	198	42.16 N	95.05 W
Wall Lake, Mi., U.S.	216	42.31 N	85.24 W
Wall Lake ⊜	216	42.31 N	85.23 W
Wallmer Bridge	262	53.43 N	2.48 W
Wallmerod	56	50.29 N	7.56 E
Wallops Island I	208	37.52 N	75.27 W
Wallowa	202	45.34 N	117.31 W
Wallowa ≃	202	45.43 N	117.47 W
Wallowa Mountains ⋀	202	45.10 N	117.30 W
Walls, Scot., U.K.	46a	60.14 N	1.35 W
Walls, Ms., U.S.	194	34.57 N	90.09 W
Wallsbüll	41	54.47 N	9.14 E
Wallsend, Austl.	170	32.55 S	151.40 E
Wallsend, Eng., U.K.	44	55.00 N	1.31 W
Wallstawe	54	52.47 N	11.01 E
Wall Town Drainage Ditch ≖	216	40.26 N	88.10 W
Wallula, Lake ⊜[1]	202	46.00 N	119.00 W
Walmer, S. Afr.	158	33.59 S	25.36 E
Walmer, Eng., U.K.	42	51.13 N	1.24 E
Walmersley	262	53.37 N	2.18 W
Walney, Isle of I	44	54.07 N	3.15 W
Walnut, Ca., U.S.	228	34.01 N	117.51 W
Walnut, Il., U.S.	190	41.33 N	89.35 W
Walnut, Ia., U.S.	198	41.28 N	95.13 W
Walnut, Ks., U.S.	198	37.36 N	95.04 W
Walnut, Ms., U.S.	194	34.56 N	88.53 W
Walnut, N.C., U.S.	192	35.50 N	82.44 W
Walnut ≃	198	37.03 N	97.00 W
Walnut Canyon National Monument ♦	200	35.10 N	111.31 W
Walnut Canyon Reservoir ⊜[1]	280	33.50 N	117.45 W
Walnut Cove	192	36.17 N	80.08 W
Walnut Creek, Ca., U.S.	226	37.54 N	122.03 W
Walnut Creek, Oh., U.S.	214	40.33 N	81.43 W
Walnut Creek ≃, Ca., U.S.	280	34.03 N	118.01 W
Walnut Creek ≃, Ca., U.S.	282	37.54 N	122.03 W
Walnut Creek ≃, Ks., U.S.	198	38.21 N	98.41 W
Walnut Creek ≃, Oh., U.S.	188	39.41 N	82.59 W
Walnut Creek ≃, Tx., U.S.	222	32.38 N	97.00 W
Walnut Creek, Middle Fork ≃	198	38.32 N	100.08 W
Walnut Creek, South Fork ≃	198	38.25 N	99.53 W
Walnut Grove, B.C., Can.	224	49.11 N	122.39 W
Walnut Grove, Ca., U.S.	226	38.15 N	121.31 W
Walnut Grove, Mn., U.S.	198	44.13 N	95.28 W
Walnut Grove, Ms., U.S.	194	32.35 N	89.27 W
Walnut Heights	282	37.53 N	122.08 W
Walnut Hill	219	38.29 N	89.03 W
Walnut Lake	281	42.33 N	83.19 W
Walnut Lake ⊜	281	42.33 N	83.20 W
Walnut Park	280	33.58 N	118.13 W
Walnutport	208	40.45 N	75.35 W
Walnut Ridge	194	36.04 N	90.57 W
Walnut Springs	222	32.03 N	97.45 W
Walpert Ridge ∧	282	37.38 N	122.00 W
Walpeup	166	35.08 S	142.02 E
Walpole, Austl.	162	34.57 S	116.44 E
Walpole, Ma., U.S.	207	42.08 N	71.15 W
Walpole, N.H., U.S.	188	43.04 N	72.25 W
Walpole Island I	214	42.34 N	82.30 W
Walpole Island Indian Reserve •[4]	214	42.32 N	82.37 W
Walpole Saint Peter	42	52.42 N	0.15 E
Walsall	42	52.35 N	1.58 W
Walschleben	54	51.04 N	10.56 E
Walsden	262	53.42 N	2.06 W
Walsenburg	200	37.37 N	104.46 W
Walsh, Austl.	164	16.39 S	143.54 E
Walsh, Ab., Can.	184	49.57 N	110.03 W
Walsh, Co., U.S.	198	37.23 N	102.16 W
Walsh, Ky., U.S.	218	38.41 N	82.58 W
Walsh ≃	164	16.31 S	143.42 E
Walshaw Dean Reservoirs ⊜[1]	262	53.48 N	2.03 W
Walshville	219	39.04 N	89.37 W
Walsingham	212	42.41 N	80.32 W
Walsoorden	52	51.23 N	4.02 E
Walsrode	52	52.52 N	9.35 E
Walston	214	40.58 N	79.01 W
Walsum	52	51.32 N	6.41 E
Walt Disney World ♦	220	28.26 N	81.35 W
Waltenhofen	64	47.40 N	10.17 E
Walterboro	192	32.54 N	80.40 W
Walter F. George Lake ⊜[1]	192	31.49 N	85.08 W
Walter Reed Army Medical Center ⊍	284c	38.58 N	77.02 W
Walters	196	34.21 N	98.18 W
Waltersdorf, Dtsch.	54	50.52 N	14.38 E
Waltersdorf, Dtsch.	264a	52.22 N	13.35 E
Waltershausen	54	50.53 N	10.33 E
Waltershofen	58	47.46 N	9.55 E
Waltersville	194	32.22 N	90.52 W
Walthall	194	33.36 N	89.16 W
Waltham, Eng., U.K.	44	53.31 N	0.06 W
Waltham, Ma., U.S.	207	42.22 N	71.14 W
Waltham Abbey	42	51.42 N	0.01 E
Waltham Forest •[8]	42	51.35 N	0.01 W
Waltham on the Wolds	42	52.49 N	0.49 W
Walthamstow •[8]	260	51.35 N	0.01 W
Walthill	198	42.08 N	96.29 W
Walton, N.S., Can.	186	45.14 N	64.00 W
Walton, Eng., U.K.	42	51.24 N	0.25 W
Walton, Eng., U.K.	42	51.58 N	1.21 E
Walton, Fl., U.S.	220	27.17 N	80.15 W
Walton, In., U.S.	216	40.39 N	86.14 W
Walton, Ky., U.S.	218	38.52 N	84.36 W
Walton, N.Y., U.S.	210	42.10 N	75.07 W
Walton Hills	214	41.22 N	81.32 W
Walton-le-Dale	44	53.45 N	2.39 W
Walton on the Hill	260	51.17 N	0.15 W
Walton-on-the-Naze	42	51.51 N	1.16 E
Walton Run ≃	285	40.05 N	74.59 W
Waltonville	219	38.13 N	89.02 W
Waltrop	52	51.37 N	7.23 E
Walt Whitman Bridge •[5]	285	39.54 N	75.08 W
Walt Whitman Homes	285	39.52 N	75.11 W
Walt Whitman House State Historic Site ⊥	276	40.49 N	73.25 W
Walt Whitman Mall •[9]	276	40.50 N	73.25 W
Waltz	216	42.06 N	83.23 W
Walupt Lake ⊜	224	46.25 N	121.28 W
Walvisbaai (Walvis Bay)	156	22.59 S	14.31 E
Walvisbaai C	156	22.57 S	14.30 E
Walvis Bay → Walvisbaai	156	22.59 S	14.31 E
Walvis Bay □[8]	156	22.59 S	14.31 E
Walvis Ridge ✢[3]	10	28.00 S	3.00 E
Walwa	171b	35.58 S	147.45 E
Walwen	262	53.14 N	3.15 W
Walworth, N.Y., U.S.	210	43.08 N	77.17 W
Walworth, Wi., U.S.	216	42.31 N	88.35 W
Walworth □[6]	216	42.41 N	88.32 W
Walyunga National Park ♦	168a	31.44 S	116.04 E
Walyungup, Lake ⊜	168a	32.21 S	115.47 E
Walze	263	51.16 N	7.31 E
Walzin, Château de ⊥	56	50.13 N	4.55 E
Wama	152	12.14 S	15.33 E
Wamac	219	38.31 N	89.08 W
Wamba, Kenya	154	0.59 N	37.19 E
Wamba, Nig.	150	8.58 N	8.36 E
Wamba, Zaïre	154	2.09 N	28.00 E
Wamba (Uamba) ≃	152	3.56 S	17.12 E
Wambel •[8]	263	51.32 N	7.32 E
Wamego	198	39.12 N	96.18 W
Wamel	52	51.53 N	5.28 E
Wamesit	283	42.37 N	71.15 W
Wami ≃	154	6.08 S	38.49 E
Wamiao	100	30.49 N	113.02 E
Wamic	224	45.13 N	121.16 W
Wamma ≃	164	3.23 S	135.13 E
Wamme ≃	56	50.10 N	5.16 E
Wamplers Lake ⊜	216	42.05 N	84.09 W
Wampool ≃	44	54.54 N	3.14 W
Wampsville	210	43.04 N	75.42 W
Wampú	236	15.01 N	85.02 W
Wampú ≃	236	14.59 N	85.03 W
Wampum	214	40.53 N	80.20 W
Wampus ≃	276	41.07 N	73.43 W
Wampus Lake Reservoir ⊜[1]	276	41.09 N	73.43 W
Wamsasi	112	3.33 S	126.10 E
Wamsutter	200	41.40 N	107.58 W
Wamuran	171a	27.02 S	152.52 E
Wanaaring	166	29.42 S	144.09 E
Wanaka	172	44.42 S	169.09 E
Wanaka, Lake ⊜	172	44.30 S	169.08 E
Wanakah	210	42.45 N	78.54 W
Wanamassa	208	40.14 N	74.02 W
Wanamie	210	41.10 N	76.02 W
Wanamingo	190	44.18 N	92.47 W
Wan'an, Zhg.	100	26.56 N	117.22 E
Wan'an, Zhg.	100	26.30 N	114.49 E
Wan'an ≃	100	25.20 N	117.21 E
Wan'anchang	107	30.39 N	104.25 E
Wanapiri	164	4.33 S	135.59 E
Wanapitei ≃	190	46.02 N	80.51 W
Wanapitei Lake ⊜	190	46.45 N	80.45 W
Wanapum Lake ⊜[1]	202	47.00 N	120.00 W
Wanaque	210	41.02 N	74.17 W
Wanaque ≃	276	40.58 N	74.17 W
Wanaque Reservoir ⊜[1]	210	41.05 N	74.17 W
Wanatah	216	41.25 N	86.53 W
Wanau	164	1.22 S	132.42 E
Wanbaoshan	89	44.12 N	125.11 E
Wanbi	166	34.46 S	140.19 E
Wanblee	198	43.34 N	101.40 W
Wanborough	42	51.33 N	1.42 W
Wanchangchang	107	29.43 N	104.19 E
Wanchese	192	35.50 N	75.38 W
Wanda	158	29.36 S	24.28 E
Wandai	164	3.41 S	136.41 E
Wandana	162	32.04 S	133.49 E
Wandawega	216	42.45 N	88.40 W
Wande	98	36.21 N	116.56 E
Wanderer	154	19.37 S	29.59 E
Wandering	168a	32.40 S	116.40 E
Wandering ≃	182	55.05 N	112.30 W
Wanderup	41	54.41 N	9.20 E
Wandhofen	263	51.26 N	7.33 E
Wandingzhen	102	24.05 N	98.04 E
Wandlitz	54	52.45 N	13.26 E
Wandlitzer See ⊜	264a	52.46 N	13.27 E
Wando	98	34.18 N	126.47 E
Wan-do I	98	34.21 N	126.42 E
Wandoan	166	26.08 S	149.57 E
Wandsbek •[8]	52	53.34 N	10.04 E
Wandsworth •[8]	42	51.27 N	0.11 W
Waneta Lake ⊜	210	42.27 N	77.06 W
Wanette	196	34.57 N	97.01 W
Wanfang	104	41.57 N	122.52 E
Wanfoxia	102	40.04 N	95.55 E
Wanfried	56	51.10 N	10.10 E
Wanfu ≃	98	35.10 N	116.35 E
Wang ≃	110	17.08 N	99.02 E
Wanga	154	2.58 N	29.13 E
Wangal	164	6.10 S	134.12 E
Wanganderry, Mount ∧	170	34.20 S	150.15 E

Symbols in the index entries represent the broad categories identified in the key at the right. Symbols with superior numbers (⋀[1]) identify subcategories (see complete key on page *I · 1*).

Symbole im Register stellen die rechts im Schlüssel erklärten Kategorien dar. Symbole mit hochgestellten Ziffern (⋀[1]) bezeichnen Unterabteilungen einer Kategorie (vgl. vollständiger Schlüssel auf Seite *I · 1*).

Los símbolos incluídos en el texto del índice representan las grandes categorías identificadas con la clave a la derecha. Los símbolos con numeros en su parte superior (⋀[1]) identifican las subcategorías (véase la clave completa en la página *I · 1*).

Les symboles de l'index représentent les catégories indiquées dans la légende à droite. Les symboles suivis d'un indice (⋀[1]) représentent des sous-catégories (voir légende complète à la page *I · 1*).

Os símbolos incluídos no texto do índice representam as grandes categorias identificadas com a chave à direita. Os símbolos com números em sua parte superior (⋀[1]) identificam as subcategorias (veja-se a chave completa à página *I · 1*).

∧ Mountain	Berg	Montaña	Montagne	Montanha
⋀ Mountains	Gebirge	Montañas	Montagnes	Montanhas
)(Pass	Paß	Paso	Col	Passo
V Valley, Canyon	Tal, Cañon	Valle, Cañón	Vallée, Canyon	Vale, Canhão
≃ Plain	Ebene	Llano	Plaine	Planície
≻ Cape	Kap	Cabo	Cap	Cabo
I Island	Insel	Isla	Île	Ilha
II Islands	Inseln	Islas	Îles	Ilhas
⫫ Other Topographic Features	Andere Topographische Objekte	Otros Elementos Topográficos	Autres données topographiques	Outros acidentes topográficos

ESPAÑOL — Nombre, Página, Lat.°′, Long.°′ W = Oeste
FRANÇAIS — Nom, Page, Lat.°′, Long.°′ W = Ouest
PORTUGUÊS — Nome, Página, Lat.°′, Long.°′ W = Oeste

Nombre / Nom / Nome	Página / Page	Lat.°′	Long.°′
Wanganui	172	39.56 S	175.03 E
Wanganui ≐	172	39.56 S	175.00 E
Wang'anzhen	105	39.19 N	114.54 E
Wangaratta	166	36.22 S	146.20 E
Wangary	166	34.33 S	135.29 E
Wangbaotaicun	104	41.10 N	123.18 E
Wangbenying	105	40.28 N	116.06 E
Wangbintun	104	41.58 N	123.43 E
Wangchang, Zhg.	107	28.52 N	105.55 E
Wangchang, Zhg.	107	29.05 N	104.40 E
Wangchangtuizigou	104	41.14 N	120.32 E
Wangcheng	100	28.23 N	112.48 E
Wang Chin	110	17.53 N	99.37 E
Wangcun	98	36.41 N	117.41 E
Wangcunkou	100	28.22 N	118.59 E
Wangdain	124	29.02 N	89.15 E
Wangdalong	102	29.25 N	99.03 E
Wangdian	106	30.37 N	120.44 E
Wangdu	98	38.43 N	115.09 E
Wangdu Phodrang	124	27.29 N	89.54 E
Wange	154	2.00 S	40.55 E
Wangels	54	54.16 N	10.45 E
Wangen an der Aare	58	47.14 N	7.39 E
Wangenbourg	58	48.37 N	7.19 E
Wangen im Allgäu	58	47.41 N	9.50 E
Wangerooge	52	53.48 N	7.54 E
Wangerooge I	52	53.46 N	7.55 E
Wangersen	52	53.22 N	9.25 E
Wangfu	104	42.05 N	121.29 E
Wanggameti, Gunung ∧	115b	10.07 S	120.14 E
Wanggangpu	104	41.38 N	123.09 E
Wanggao	102	24.38 N	111.30 E
Wanggezhuang	105	40.00 N	117.52 E
Wanggil-li	271b	37.36 N	126.39 E
Wanggoutun	104	41.40 N	121.53 E
Wanghai	98	40.26 N	120.30 E
Wanghai Shan ∧	104	41.37 N	121.41 E
Wanghechenggou	104	41.52 N	121.13 E
Wang Hin, Khlong ≍	269a	13.48 N	100.35 E
Wanghu	98	39.47 N	113.54 E
Wanghuzhuang	105	38.50 N	117.05 E
Wängi	58	47.30 N	8.57 E
Wangingsha	100	22.44 N	113.33 E
Wangi Wangi	170	33.04 S	151.35 E
Wangiwangi, Pulau I	112	5.20 S	123.35 E
Wangji, Zhg.	100	34.00 N	117.46 E
Wangji, Zhg.	100	33.52 N	118.44 E
Wangjia, Zhg.	106	31.59 N	121.13 E
Wangjia, Zhg.	106	32.07 N	120.59 E
Wangjiadian, Zhg.	100	31.26 N	113.58 E
Wangjiadian, Zhg.	105	40.03 N	117.29 E
Wangjiagou	104	42.33 N	123.16 E
Wangjiajing, Zhg.	98	37.49 N	115.23 E
Wangjiajing, Zhg.	98	39.56 N	122.11 E
Wangjiang	100	30.09 N	116.41 E
Wangjiangjing	106	30.53 N	120.43 E
Wang Jian Mu (Tomb of Wang Jian) ⊥	107	30.38 N	104.04 E
Wangjiaputun	104	40.39 N	122.50 E
Wangjiapuzi, Zhg.	104	40.41 N	122.24 E
Wangjiapuzi, Zhg.	104	41.05 N	123.34 E
Wangjiaqiao	106	30.50 N	119.18 E
Wangjiashan	105	40.19 N	114.45 E
Wangjiashao	102	23.57 N	102.18 E
Wangjiatai	105	39.17 N	117.29 E
Wangjiaying, Zhg.	105	40.36 N	116.34 E
Wangjiaying, Zhg.	105	39.06 N	115.59 E
Wangjiazhai	106	31.21 N	121.37 E
Wangjiazui	106	31.16 N	120.18 E
Wangkantou	100	29.12 N	120.09 E
Wangkou	105	38.56 N	116.44 E
Wangkui	89	46.50 N	126.30 E
Wanglanzhuang	105	39.26 N	118.01 E
Wangling	100	27.13 N	113.26 E
Wangliu	100	32.25 N	115.40 E
Wangmiao	100	26.50 N	112.52 E
Wangmulazi	104	41.42 N	124.02 E
Wang Noi	110	14.13 N	100.44 E
Wangong	89	49.10 N	118.53 E
Wangpan Shan II	106	30.30 N	121.15 E
Wangpan Yang ⊂	100	30.30 N	121.46 E
Wangpingchang	107	29.17 N	105.45 E
Wangqing	89	43.20 N	129.48 E
Wangqingmen	98	41.42 N	125.23 E
Wangqingtuo	105	39.11 N	116.53 E
Wangqinzhuang	105	39.15 N	117.05 E
Wangqucun	106	31.22 N	120.19 E
Wangs	58	47.02 N	9.26 E
Wang Saphung	110	17.18 N	101.46 E
Wangshanhutun	104	42.03 N	122.37 E
Wangshi	100	33.11 N	116.04 E
Wangsi	98	38.00 N	116.55 E
Wangsim-ni ◆[8]	271b	37.36 N	127.03 E
Wangsiying	107	30.34 N	103.29 E
Wangtai, Zhg.	98	36.05 N	119.59 E
Wangtai, Zhg.	100	26.39 N	117.57 E
Wangtan	100	29.45 N	120.40 E
Wang Thong	110	16.50 N	100.26 E
Wangtian	100	25.59 N	116.04 E
Wangting	106	31.26 N	120.26 E
Wangtongshitai	104	42.05 N	123.11 E
Wangtuan, Zhg.	98	37.32 N	116.08 E
Wangtuan, Zhg.	98	37.17 N	122.04 E
Wangtuanji	100	33.12 N	116.21 E
Wangu	107	30.19 N	106.05 E
Wanguzhen	107	29.41 N	105.57 E
Wangwenzhuang	105	38.53 N	117.15 E
Wangxiangshang	106	31.29 N	120.15 E
Wangxiangtai	105	40.02 N	115.09 E
Wangxiuqiao	106	31.38 N	121.03 E
Wangyangzhen	107	29.44 N	104.14 E
Wangyedian	98	41.36 N	118.17 E
Wangyefu	98	41.50 N	118.23 E
Wangyehmiao → Horqin Youyi Qianqi	89	46.05 N	122.05 E
Wangyiguantun	104	42.36 N	123.19 E
Wangzhai	98	34.09 N	116.47 E
Wangzhimawo	105	39.39 N	117.40 E
Wangzhong	98	35.08 N	116.58 E
Wangzhuang	100	33.07 N	117.29 E
Wangzhuangbu	98	39.27 N	113.56 E
Wangzhuangji	98	34.09 N	118.23 E
Wangzhuangzi	105	39.17 N	118.14 E
Wanham	182	55.44 N	118.24 W
Wanhedian	100	32.16 N	113.16 E
Wanheimerort ◆[8]	263	51.24 N	6.46 E
Wanhsien → Wanxian	102	30.52 N	108.22 E
Wanhuyu	102	38.24 N	110.40 E
Wani	122	20.04 N	78.57 E
Wani, Gunung ∧	112	4.29 S	123.01 E
Wanica □[5]	250	5.50 N	55.10 W
Wanie-Rukula	154	0.15 N	25.32 E
Wanigela	164	9.22 S	149.10 E
Wanipigow ≐	184	51.11 N	96.18 W
Wanjiabu	100	28.51 N	115.39 E
Wanjiaqiao	106	30.25 N	119.07 E
Wanjiatun	98	40.03 N	119.51 E
Wanjindian	100	32.50 N	114.46 E
Wānkāner	120	22.37 N	70.56 E
Wankendorf	54	54.07 N	10.13 E
Wanle Weyne	144	2.37 N	44.54 E
Wanli, T'aiwan	269d	25.11 N	121.41 E
Wanli, Zhg.	106	31.06 N	120.16 E
Wanna	52	53.44 N	8.46 E
Wanna Lakes ⊜	162	28.30 S	128.27 E
Wān Namton	110	22.03 N	99.33 E
Wanne-Eickel	52	51.32 N	7.09 E
Wanneroo	168a	31.45 S	115.48 E
Wannery Creek ≐	162	22.47 S	115.43 E
Wannian	100	28.42 N	117.03 E
Wanning	110	18.53 N	110.26 E
Wannsee ◆[8]	54	52.25 N	13.09 E
Wanon Niwat	110	17.38 N	103.46 E
Wanouchi	94	35.17 N	136.38 E
Wānow	120	32.38 N	65.54 E
Wanparti	122	16.22 N	78.04 E
Wanquan	98	40.52 N	114.45 E
Wansbeck ≐	44	55.10 N	1.34 W
Wansdorf	264a	52.38 N	13.05 E
Wan-See → Van Gölü ⊜	128	38.33 N	42.46 E
Wanshan	107	30.23 N	106.06 E
Wanshouchang	107	29.26 N	105.55 E
Wanstead	172	40.08 S	176.32 E
Wanstead ◆[8]	260	51.34 N	0.02 E
Wantage	42	51.36 N	1.25 W
Wantagh	210	40.41 N	73.30 W
Wantan	102	30.03 N	110.18 E
Wantirna	274b	37.51 S	145.14 E
Wantirna South	274b	37.52 S	145.14 E
Wanxian, Zhg.	102	30.52 N	108.22 E
Wanxian, Zhg.	105	38.50 N	115.09 E
Wanyuan	102	32.04 N	108.02 E
Wanzai	100	28.06 N	114.27 E
Wanzarīk	146	27.31 N	13.29 E
Wanzhuang	105	39.34 N	116.36 E
Wanzleben	54	52.03 N	11.26 E
Wapack Range ⩕	207	42.48 N	71.52 W
Wapakoneta	216	40.34 N	84.11 W
Wapanucka	196	34.22 N	96.25 W
Wapato	202	46.26 N	120.25 W
Wapawekka Hills ⩕[2]	184	54.45 N	104.20 W
Wapawekka Lake ⊜	184	54.55 N	104.40 W
Wapella, Sk., Can.	184	50.15 N	102.00 W
Wapella, Il., U.S.	219	40.13 N	88.58 W
Wapello	190	41.10 N	91.11 W
Wapenamanda	164	5.35 S	143.55 E
Wapesi Lake ⊜	184	50.34 N	92.21 W
Wāpi	122	20.22 N	72.54 E
Wapinda	152	3.41 N	22.48 E
Wapinitia Pass)(	224	45.14 N	121.42 W
Wapisu Lake ⊜	184	55.47 N	99.11 W
Wapiti ≐	182	55.08 N	118.18 W
Wapizagonke, Lac ⊜	206	46.43 N	73.02 W
Waples	222	32.29 N	97.43 W
Wapoga ≐	164	2.42 S	136.06 E
Wappapello, Lake ⊜[1]	194	36.58 N	90.20 W
Wapping	207	41.50 N	72.33 W
Wappinger Creek ≐	210	41.35 N	73.57 W
Wappingers Falls	210	41.35 N	73.54 W
Wapsipinicon ≐	190	41.44 N	90.20 W
Waptus Lake ⊜	224	47.30 N	121.10 W
Wapus ≐	190	47.11 N	76.06 W
Wapus Lake ⊜	184	56.27 N	102.12 W
Waqf aṣ-Ṣawwān, Jibāl ⩕	132	30.53 N	36.48 E
Wāqid	142	30.42 N	30.44 E
Waqqāṣ	132	32.33 N	35.36 E
War	192	37.18 N	81.41 W
Wara	94	35.45 N	137.05 E
Warabi	94	35.49 N	139.41 E
Wārāh	120	27.27 N	67.48 E
Warakaraket I	164	2.15 S	130.36 E
Waramaug, Lake ⊜	207	41.42 N	73.22 W
Warangal	122	18.00 N	79.35 E
Wararisbari, Tanjung ≻	164	1.05 S	136.23 E
Wārāseoni	120	21.45 N	80.02 E
Waratah, Austl.	166	41.27 S	145.32 E
Waratah, Austl.	170	32.54 S	151.44 E
Waratah Bay ⊂	166	38.51 S	146.04 E
Warboys	42	52.24 N	0.04 W
Warbreccan	166	24.18 S	142.51 E
Warburg	52	51.29 N	9.08 E
Warburton, Austl.	162	26.07 S	126.35 E
Warburton, Austl.	169	37.46 S	145.41 E
Warburton, Pāk.	123	31.33 N	73.50 E
Warburton, Eng., U.K.	262	53.24 N	2.27 W
Warburton Aboriginal Reserve ◆[4]	162	24.00 S	128.15 E
Warburton Bay ⊂	176	63.50 N	111.30 W
Warburton Creek ≐	166	27.55 S	137.28 E
Warchha	123	32.25 N	71.59 E
Ward, N.Z.	172	41.50 S	174.08 E
Ward, Pa., U.S.	285	39.53 N	75.31 W
Ward ≐	166	26.32 S	146.06 E
Ward, Mount ∧	172	43.52 S	169.50 E
Warda	222	30.03 N	96.55 W
Wardcliff	216	42.43 N	84.28 W
Ward Cove	182	55.24 N	131.44 W
Warden, S. Afr.	158	27.56 S	29.00 E
Warden, Wa., U.S.	202	46.58 N	119.02 W
Wardenburg	52	53.04 N	8.11 E
Warder	54	53.59 N	10.22 E
Wardersee ⊜	54	53.58 N	10.26 E
Wardha	122	20.45 N	78.37 E
Wardha ≐	122	19.38 N	79.48 E
Ward Hill ∧[2], Scot., U.K.	46	58.54 N	3.20 W
Ward Hill ∧[2], Scot., U.K.	46	58.57 N	3.09 W
Ward Hunt, Cape ≻	164	8.05 S	149.55 E
Ward Hunt Strait ⩌	164	9.25 S	149.55 E
Wardle	44	53.39 N	2.08 W
Wardlow	182	50.54 N	111.33 W
Ward Mountain ∧	202	46.10 N	114.17 W
Wardner	182	49.25 N	115.26 W
Wardour, Vale of V	42	51.05 N	2.00 W
Wards Chapel	284b	39.24 N	76.52 W
Wards Island I	276	40.47 N	73.56 W
Ward's Stone ∧	44	54.02 N	2.38 W
Wardsville, On., Can.	214	42.39 N	81.45 W
Wardsville, Mo., U.S.	219	38.29 N	92.10 W
Wardswell Draw V	196	32.39 N	102.35 W
Wardt	52	51.41 N	6.25 E
Ware, Eng., U.K.	42	51.49 N	0.02 W
Ware, Ma., U.S.	207	42.15 N	72.14 W
Ware ≐	207	42.11 N	72.22 W
War Eagle Creek ≐	194	36.14 N	94.00 W
Waregem	50	50.53 N	3.25 E
Wareham, Eng., U.K.	42	50.41 N	2.07 W
Wareham, Ma., U.S.	207	41.45 N	70.43 W
Warehouse Point	207	41.55 N	72.37 W
Waremme	56	50.41 N	5.15 E
Waren, Dtsch.	54	53.31 N	12.40 E
Waren, Indon.	164	2.16 S	136.20 E
Warenai ≐	164	2.52 S	135.55 E
Warenda	166	22.37 S	140.32 E
Warendorf	52	51.57 N	7.59 E
Ware River ⊂	208	37.23 N	76.27 W
Ware Shoals	192	34.23 N	82.14 W
Waretown	208	39.47 N	74.11 W
Warffum	52	53.23 N	6.34 E
Warfusée-Abancourt	50	49.52 N	2.35 E
Warga	52	53.08 N	5.51 E
Wargalo	144	6.17 N	47.31 E
Wargla	148	31.59 N	5.25 E
Wargla □[5]	148	29.00 N	8.00 E
Warialda	166	29.32 S	150.34 E
Wariap	164	1.34 S	134.11 E
Warilau	164	5.24 S	134.30 E
Warilau, Pulau I	164	5.23 S	134.33 E
Warin	54	53.48 N	11.42 E
Warinanco Park ♠	276	40.39 N	74.14 W
Warin Chamrap	110	15.12 N	104.53 E
Waring Mountains ⩕	180	66.50 N	159.00 W
Wāris Alīganj	124	25.01 N	85.38 E
Warka	30	51.47 N	21.10 E
Warkopi	164	1.08 S	134.07 E
Warks Burn ≐	44	55.03 N	2.08 W
Warkworth, On., Can.	212	44.12 N	77.53 W
Warkworth, N.Z.	172	36.24 S	174.40 E
Warkworth, Eng., U.K.	44	55.21 N	1.36 W
Warland, Eng., U.K.	262	53.41 N	2.05 W
Warland, Mt., U.S.	182	48.30 N	115.17 W
Warland Reservoir ⊜[1]	262	53.41 N	2.04 W
Warley → Smethwick	42	52.30 N	1.58 W
Warley Moor Reservoir ⊜[1]	262	53.47 N	1.57 W
Warlingham	42	51.19 N	0.04 W
Warlington	42	51.39 N	1.01 W
Warman	184	52.20 N	106.34 W
Warmandi	164	0.22 S	132.39 E
Warmbad, Namibia	156	28.29 S	18.41 E
Warmbad, S. Afr.	156	24.55 S	28.15 E
Warm Baths → Warmbad	156	24.55 S	28.15 E
Warm Beach	224	48.10 N	122.21 W
War Memorial Cross ⊥	169	37.20 S	144.36 E
Warmenhuizen	52	52.43 N	4.44 E
Warmensteinach	60	49.59 N	11.47 E
Warmeriville	50	49.21 N	4.13 E
Warmington	42	52.08 N	1.24 W
Warminster, Eng., U.K.	42	51.13 N	2.12 W
Warminster, Pa., U.S.	208	40.12 N	75.06 W
Warminster Naval Air Development Center ■	285	40.12 N	75.09 W
Warm Springs, Ga., U.S.	192	32.53 N	84.40 W
Warm Springs, Mt., U.S.	202	46.11 N	112.48 W
Warm Springs, Or., U.S.	202	44.45 N	121.15 W
Warm Springs, Va., U.S.	192	38.02 N	79.47 W
Warm Springs ≐	202	44.52 N	121.04 W
Warm Springs Indian Reservation ◆[4]	224	45.00 N	121.25 W
Warm Springs Reservoir ⊜[1]	202	43.37 N	118.14 W
Warnbro Sound ⩌	168a	32.20 S	115.40 E
Warnemünde ◆[8]	54	54.10 N	12.04 E
Warner, Ab., Can.	182	49.17 N	112.12 W
Warner, N.H., U.S.	188	43.16 N	71.49 W
Warner, Ok., U.S.	196	35.29 N	95.18 W
Warner Lakes ⊜	202	42.25 N	119.50 W
Warner Mountains ⩕	204	41.40 N	120.20 W
Warner Peak ∧	202	42.27 N	119.44 W
Warner Ranch	228	33.56 N	117.13 W
Warner Robins	192	32.37 N	83.36 W
Warners	210	43.05 N	76.20 W
Warners Pond ⊜	283	42.28 N	71.24 W
Warnerville	210	42.34 N	74.30 W
Warnes, Arg.	252	34.55 S	60.31 W
Warnes, Bol.	248	17.30 S	63.10 W
Warnes Brook ≐	276	40.25 N	74.18 W
Warneton	50	50.45 N	2.57 E
Warngau	64	47.50 N	11.41 E
Warnicken → Primorje	76	54.57 N	20.02 E
Warnkenhagen	54	54.00 N	11.04 E
Warnow ≐	54	54.06 N	12.09 E
Warns	52	52.52 N	5.25 E
Warnsveld	52	52.08 N	6.13 E
Waroona	168a	32.50 S	115.55 E
Warpath ≐	184	52.21 N	98.26 W
Warra	166	26.56 S	150.55 E
Warrabri Aboriginal Reserve ◆[4]	162	21.00 S	134.20 E
Warracknabeal	166	36.15 S	142.24 E
Warr Acres	196	35.31 N	97.37 W
Warragamba Dam ◆[6]	170	33.54 S	150.36 E
Warragul	169	38.10 S	145.56 E
Warrandyte	274b	37.45 S	145.13 E
Warrandyte South	274b	37.46 S	145.14 E
Warrāq al-'Arab	273c	30.06 N	31.12 E
Warrāq al-Haḍar, Jazīrat I	273c	30.07 N	31.13 E
Warrāq al-Hadar wa Ambūtbah wa Mīt an-Naṣārā	273c	30.06 N	31.13 E
Warrawagine	162	20.51 S	120.42 E
Warrawee	274a	33.44 S	151.07 E
Warrawolong, Mount ∧	170	33.03 S	151.15 E
Warrawong	170	34.29 S	150.53 E
Warrego ≐	166	30.24 S	145.21 E
Warrego Range ⩕	166	25.00 S	146.30 E
Warren, Austl.	166	31.42 S	147.50 E
Warren, Eng., U.K.	262	53.14 N	2.10 W
Warren, Ar., U.S.	194	33.36 N	92.03 W
Warren, Il., U.S.	190	42.29 N	89.59 W
Warren, In., U.S.	216	40.40 N	85.25 W
Warren, Ma., U.S.	207	42.12 N	72.11 W
Warren, Mi., U.S.	216	42.28 N	83.01 W
Warren, Mn., U.S.	198	48.11 N	96.46 W
Warren, Mo., U.S.	219	39.47 N	91.45 W
Warren, N.J., U.S.	276	40.37 N	74.30 W
Warren, Oh., U.S.	214	41.14 N	80.49 W
Warren, Or., U.S.	224	45.49 N	122.50 W
Warren, Pa., U.S.	214	41.50 N	79.08 W
Warren, R.I., U.S.	207	41.43 N	71.16 W
Warren □[6], In., U.S.	216	40.21 N	87.17 W
Warren □[6], Mo., U.S.	219	38.45 N	91.09 W
Warren □[6], N.J., U.S.	210	40.49 N	75.05 W
Warren □[6], N.Y., U.S.	210	43.26 N	73.43 W
Warren □[6], Oh., U.S.	218	39.26 N	84.13 W
Warren □[6], Pa., U.S.	214	41.51 N	79.08 W
Warren ≐	162	34.35 S	115.50 E
Warren City	222	32.33 N	94.54 W
Warrendale	214	40.39 N	80.04 W
Warren Dunes State Park ♠	216	41.56 N	86.36 W
Warren H. Manning State Park ♠	283	42.34 N	71.18 W
Warren Park	218	39.46 N	86.03 W
Warren Peaks ⩕	198	44.29 N	104.28 W
Warrenpoint	48	54.06 N	6.15 W
Warren Point ≻	180	69.44 N	132.30 W
Warrens	190	44.07 N	90.29 W
Warrensburg, Il., U.S.	219	39.56 N	89.04 W
Warrensburg, Mo., U.S.	194	38.45 N	93.44 W
Warrensburg, N.Y., U.S.	188	43.29 N	73.46 W
Warrensville	210	41.19 N	76.57 W
Warrensville Heights	214	41.26 N	81.32 W
Warrenton, S. Afr.	158	28.09 S	24.47 E
Warrenton, Ga., U.S.	192	33.24 N	82.39 W
Warrenton, Mo., U.S.	219	38.48 N	91.08 W
Warrenton, N.C., U.S.	192	36.23 N	78.09 W
Warrenton, Or., U.S.	224	46.09 N	123.55 W
Warrenton, Tx., U.S.	222	30.01 N	96.44 W
Warrenton, Va., U.S.	188	38.42 N	77.47 W
Warrenville	216	41.49 N	88.10 W
Warrenzin	54	53.54 N	12.57 E
Warri	150	5.31 N	5.45 E
Warriedar Hill ∧[2]	162	29.06 S	117.06 E
Warriewood	274a	33.42 S	151.18 E
Warrill Creek ≐	171a	27.39 S	152.44 E
Warrington, N.Z.	172	45.43 S	170.35 E
Warrington, Eng., U.K.	44	53.24 N	2.37 W
Warrington, Fl., U.S.	194	30.23 N	87.16 W
Warrington, Pa., U.S.	285	40.15 N	75.08 W
Warrington □[8]	262	53.24 N	2.33 W
Warrington Airport ⊠	285	40.16 N	75.09 W
Warrior	194	33.48 N	86.48 W
Warrior Creek ≐	192	31.15 N	83.34 W
Warrior Reefs ✦[2]	164	9.35 S	143.10 E
Warriors Mark	214	40.42 N	78.08 W
Warrnambool	166	38.23 S	142.29 E
Warroad	198	48.54 N	95.18 W
Warrumbungle National Park ♠	166	31.20 S	149.00 E
Warsak	123	34.10 N	71.25 E
Warsaw → Warszawa, Pol.	30	52.15 N	21.00 E
Warsaw, Il., U.S.	190	40.21 N	91.26 W
Warsaw, In., U.S.	216	41.14 N	85.51 W
Warsaw, Ky., U.S.	218	38.47 N	84.54 W
Warsaw, Mo., U.S.	194	38.14 N	93.22 W
Warsaw, N.Y., U.S.	210	42.44 N	78.07 W
Warsaw, N.C., U.S.	192	34.59 N	78.05 W
Warsaw, Oh., U.S.	214	40.20 N	82.00 W
Warsaw, Va., U.S.	208	37.57 N	76.45 W
Warsaw Station ◆[5]	265a	59.54 N	30.19 E
Warschau → Warszawa	30	52.15 N	21.00 E
Warscheneck ∧	61	47.39 N	14.14 E
Warshiikh	144	2.18 N	45.48 E
Warsop	44	53.13 N	1.09 W
Warspite	182	54.06 N	112.37 W
Warstein	56	51.26 N	8.21 E
Warszawa (Warsaw)	30	52.15 N	21.00 E
Warszawa □[4]	30	52.15 N	21.00 E
Warta	30	51.42 N	18.38 E
Warta ≐	30	52.35 N	14.39 E
Wartburg, S. Afr.	158	29.25 S	30.35 E
Wartburg, Tn., U.S.	192	36.06 N	84.35 W
Wartburg ⊥	54	50.58 N	10.18 E
Wartenberg	60	48.24 N	11.59 E
Wartenberg ◆[8]	264a	52.34 N	13.31 E
Warth	58	47.15 N	10.11 E
Warthan Creek ≐	226	36.08 N	120.20 W
Warthe → Warta ≐	30	52.35 N	14.39 E
Wartin	54	53.15 N	14.09 E
Warton, Eng., U.K.	44	54.09 N	2.47 W
Warton, Eng., U.K.	44	53.45 N	2.54 W
Warton Aerodrome ⊠	262	53.45 N	2.54 W
Wartrace	194	35.31 N	86.20 W
Wartsberg ∧[2]	263	51.25 N	6.29 E
Waru	164	3.24 S	130.40 E
Warud	120	21.28 N	78.16 E
Warunta, Laguna de ⊜	236	15.23 N	84.05 W
Waruta ≐	164	3.18 S	140.08 E
Warwick, Austl.	171a	28.13 S	152.02 E
Warwick, P.Q., Can.	206	45.56 N	71.59 W
Warwick, Eng., U.K.	42	52.17 N	1.34 W
Warwick, Md., U.S.	208	39.25 N	75.46 W
Warwick, N.Y., U.S.	210	41.15 N	74.21 W
Warwick, R.I., U.S.	207	41.41 N	71.22 W
Warwick ≐	208	37.05 N	76.33 W
Warwick Castle ⊥	42	52.17 N	1.34 W
Warwick Channel ⩌	164	13.51 S	136.16 E
Warwick Farm Racecourse and Motor Race Track ♠	274a	33.55 S	150.57 E
Warwickshire □[6]	42	52.13 N	1.37 W
Warza	54	51.00 N	10.41 E
Wasaga Beach	212	44.31 N	80.01 W
Wasagu	150	11.25 N	5.49 E
Wasatch Mountain State Park ♠	200	40.33 N	111.31 W
Wasatch Plateau ⩕[1]	200	39.20 N	111.30 W
Wasatch Range ⩕	200	40.40 N	111.35 W
Wasāwewāla	123	30.28 N	73.40 E
Wasbank	158	28.24 S	30.05 E
Wasbister	46	59.10 N	3.07 W
Wascana Creek ≐	184	50.39 N	104.55 W
Wäschenbeuren	56	48.46 N	9.41 E
Wasco, Ca., U.S.	226	35.35 N	119.20 W
Wasco, Or., U.S.	224	45.35 N	120.41 W
Wasco □[6]	224	45.10 N	121.12 W
Wase	150	9.06 N	9.59 E
Wase ≐	146	8.27 N	10.06 E
Waseca	190	44.04 N	93.30 W
Waseda University ʊ[2]	268	35.42 N	139.43 E
Wasekamio Lake ⊜	184	56.45 N	108.45 W
Wasen	58	47.03 N	7.48 E
Wasgomuwa National Park ♠	122	7.40 N	80.45 E
Washademoak Lake ⊜	186	45.48 N	65.58 W
Washago	212	44.45 N	79.20 W
Washburn, Il., U.S.	190	40.55 N	89.17 W
Washburn, Me., U.S.	186	46.47 N	68.09 W
Washburn, N.D., U.S.	198	47.17 N	101.01 W
Washburn, Wi., U.S.	190	46.40 N	90.53 W
Washburn ≐	44	53.54 N	1.39 W
Washburn, Mount ∧	202	44.48 N	110.25 W
Washburn Lake ⊜	176	70.03 N	106.50 W
Washdyke	172	44.21 S	171.14 E
Washicoutai	186	50.17 N	60.42 W
Washiga-take ∧	94	35.56 N	136.58 E
Wāshīm	122	20.06 N	77.09 E
Washimiya	94	36.06 N	139.40 E
Washington, Eng., U.K.	44	54.55 N	1.30 W
Washington, Ca., U.S.	226	39.22 N	120.48 W
Washington, Ct., U.S.	207	41.37 N	73.18 W
Washington, D.C., U.S.	208	38.53 N	77.02 W
Washington, D.C., U.S.	284c	38.53 N	77.02 W
Washington, Ga., U.S.	192	33.44 N	82.44 W
Washington, Il., U.S.	190	40.42 N	89.24 W
Washington, In., U.S.	194	38.39 N	87.10 W
Washington, Ia., U.S.	190	41.17 N	91.41 W
Washington, Ks., U.S.	198	39.49 N	97.03 W
Washington, Ky., U.S.	218	38.36 N	83.48 W
Washington, La., U.S.	194	30.36 N	92.03 W
Washington, Mi., U.S.	214	42.44 N	83.02 W
Washington, Mo., U.S.	219	38.33 N	91.01 W
Washington, N.J., U.S.	210	40.45 N	74.58 W
Washington, N.C., U.S.	192	35.31 N	77.01 W
Washington, Pa., U.S.	214	40.10 N	80.14 W
Washington, Tx., U.S.	222	30.20 N	96.10 W
Washington, Ut., U.S.	200	37.07 N	113.30 W
Washington, Va., U.S.	188	38.42 N	78.09 W
Washington □[6], Il., U.S.	219	38.21 N	89.23 W
Washington □[6], In., U.S.	218	38.36 N	86.06 W
Washington □[6], N.Y., U.S.	210	43.15 N	73.27 W
Washington □[6], Or., U.S.	224	45.33 N	123.07 W
Washington □[6], Pa., U.S.	214	40.10 N	80.15 W
Washington □[6], R.I., U.S.	207	41.28 N	71.35 W
Washington □[6], Tx., U.S.	222	30.15 N	96.20 W
Washington □[6], Wi., U.S.	216	43.14 N	88.15 W
Washington □[3], U.S.	178	47.30 N	120.30 W
Washington □[3], U.S.	202	47.30 N	120.30 W
Washington, Lake ⊜, Fl., U.S.	220	28.07 N	80.45 W
Washington, Lake ⊜, Wa., U.S.	224	47.37 N	122.15 W
Washington, Mount ∧	188	44.15 N	71.15 W
Washington Court House	218	39.32 N	83.26 W
Washington Crossing	208	40.17 N	74.52 W
Washington Crossing State Historic Site ⊥	208	40.17 N	74.53 W
Washington Depot	207	41.38 N	73.18 W
Washington Heights ◆[8]	276	40.52 N	73.56 W
Washington Island	190	45.23 N	86.55 W
Washington Island I	190	45.23 N	86.55 W
Washington Memorial Chapel ʊ[1]	285	40.06 N	75.26 W
Washington Mills	210	43.03 N	75.16 W
Washington Monument ♠	284c	38.53 N	77.03 W
Washington Monument State Park ♠	208	39.30 N	77.38 W
Washington National Airport ⊠	208	38.51 N	77.02 W
Washington-on-the-Brazos State Historic Park ♠	222	30.20 N	96.09 W
Washington Park	219	38.38 N	90.05 W
Washington Park ♠, Il., U.S.	278	41.48 N	87.37 W
Washington Park ♠, Oh., U.S.	279a	41.27 N	81.40 W
Washington Pass)(	224	48.32 N	120.39 W
Washington Place	218	39.47 N	86.01 W
Washington Rock State Park ♠	276	40.37 N	74.28 W
Washington's Headquarters ⊥	285	40.06 N	75.28 W
Washington Terrace	200	41.10 N	111.58 W
Washington Township	276	40.54 N	74.00 W
Washington Valley	276	40.48 N	74.32 W
Washington Valley Reservoir ⊜[1]	276	40.36 N	74.34 W
Washingtonville, N.Y., U.S.	210	41.26 N	74.10 W
Washingtonville, Oh., U.S.	214	40.54 N	80.46 W
Washingtonville, Pa., U.S.	210	41.03 N	76.40 W
Washita ≐	196	34.12 N	96.50 W
Washoe □[6]	226	39.22 N	119.43 W
Washoe Lake ⊜	226	39.16 N	119.48 W
Washougal	224	45.34 N	122.21 W
Washougal ≐	224	45.35 N	122.23 W
Washow Bay ⊂	184	51.22 N	96.47 W
Washtenaw □[6]	216	42.15 N	83.50 W
Washtucna	202	46.45 N	118.18 W
Wāshuk	128	27.44 N	64.48 E
Wasian	164	1.54 S	133.17 E
Wasilków	30	53.12 N	23.12 E
Wasilla	180	61.35 N	149.26 W
Wasior	164	2.43 S	134.30 E
Wasiri	112	7.35 S	126.38 E
Wāsiṭ □[4]	128	32.45 N	45.25 E
Waskada	184	49.06 N	100.46 W
Waskaganish	176	51.30 N	78.45 W
Waskahigan ≐	182	54.45 N	117.12 W
Waskaiowaka Lake ⊜	184	56.30 N	96.20 W
Waskatenau	182	54.07 N	112.47 W
Waskesiu Lake ⊜	184	53.56 N	106.10 W
Waskom	194	32.29 N	94.04 W
Wąsosz	30	51.34 N	16.42 E
Waspam	236	14.44 N	83.58 W
Waspuk ≐	236	14.38 N	84.26 W
Wasquehal	50	50.40 N	3.09 E
Wassaic	210	41.48 N	73.35 W
Wasselonne	58	48.38 N	7.27 E
Wassen	58	46.42 N	8.36 E
Wassenaar	52	52.07 N	4.24 E
Wassenberg	56	51.06 N	6.08 E
Wasseralfingen	56	48.52 N	10.06 E
Wasserbillig	56	49.44 N	6.30 E
Wasserburg am Inn	60	48.04 N	12.13 E
Wasserkuppe ∧	56	50.30 N	9.56 E
Wasserkurl	263	51.33 N	7.38 E
Wasserleben	54	51.55 N	10.44 E
Wassertrüdingen	56	49.02 N	10.35 E
Wassigny	50	50.01 N	3.36 E
Wass Lake ⊜	184	53.40 N	95.25 W
Wassmannsdorf	264a	52.22 N	13.28 E
Wassou	150	10.02 N	13.39 W
Wassy	58	48.30 N	4.57 E
Wast Water ⊜	44	54.26 N	3.18 W
Wasu	164	6.00 S	147.15 E
Wasum	164	6.05 S	149.20 E
Wasungen	54	50.40 N	10.22 E
Watabeag Lake ⊜	190	48.14 N	80.32 W
Watampone (Bone)	112	4.32 S	120.20 E
Watamu Marine National Park ♠	154	3.23 S	40.00 E
Waṭan, Wādī al- V	142	30.26 N	31.49 E
Watansopeng	112	4.21 S	119.53 E
Watapi Lake ⊜	184	55.18 N	109.35 W
Watarai	94	34.26 N	136.37 E
Watarase ≐	94	36.13 N	139.42 E
Wataru I	122	5.43 N	73.23 E
Watatic, Mount ∧	207	42.42 N	71.53 W
Watauga	222	32.51 N	97.15 W
Watchet	42	51.12 N	3.20 W
Watch Hill	207	41.18 N	71.51 W
Watchung	276	40.38 N	74.27 W
Watchung Reservation ♠	276	40.41 N	74.23 W
Water	262	53.44 N	2.14 W
Waterbeach	42	52.16 N	0.11 E
Waterberg	156	20.28 S	17.13 E
Waterberge ⩕	156	24.30 S	28.00 E
Waterberg Plateau Park ♠	156	20.30 S	17.00 E
Waterbury, Ct., U.S.	207	41.33 N	73.02 W
Waterbury, Vt., U.S.	188	44.20 N	72.45 W
Waterdale	158	30.40 S	24.02 E
Wateree ≐	192	33.45 N	80.37 W
Wateree Lake ⊜[1]	192	34.25 N	80.50 W
Waterend, Eng., U.K.	260	51.47 N	0.30 W
Water End, Eng., U.K.	262	53.41 N	2.15 W
Waterfall, Austl.	170	34.08 S	151.00 E
Waterfall, Pa., U.S.	214	40.08 N	78.04 W
Waterford, On., Can.	212	42.56 N	80.17 W
Waterford (Port Láirge), Ire.	48	52.15 N	7.06 W
Waterford, S. Afr.	158	33.05 S	25.00 E
Waterford, Ca., U.S.	226	37.38 N	120.46 W
Waterford, Ct., U.S.	207	41.20 N	72.09 W
Waterford, In., U.S.	216	41.40 N	86.50 W
Waterford, Mi., U.S.	216	42.42 N	83.24 W
Waterford, N.Y., U.S.	210	42.47 N	73.40 W
Waterford, Pa., U.S.	214	41.56 N	79.59 W
Waterford, Wi., U.S.	216	42.45 N	88.12 W
Waterford □[6]	48	52.10 N	7.40 W
Waterford Harbour ⊂	48	52.10 N	6.55 W
Waterford Mills	216	41.33 N	85.50 W
Waterford Works	208	39.43 N	74.50 W
Watergate Bay ⊂	42	50.27 N	5.05 W
Watergrasshill	48	52.01 N	8.21 W
Watergrove Reservoir ⊜[1]	262	53.39 N	2.08 W
Waterhen ≐	184	54.38 N	107.47 W
Waterhen Lake ⊜, Mb., Can.	184	52.06 N	99.34 W
Waterhen Lake ⊜, Sk., Can.	184	54.28 N	108.25 W
Waterhouse Range ⩕	162	24.01 S	133.25 E
Wateringbury	260	51.15 N	0.25 E
Wateringen	52	52.02 N	4.16 E
Water Island	276	40.41 N	73.02 W
Waterkloof	158	30.19 S	25.18 E
Waterloo, Austl.	164	16.38 S	129.18 E
Waterloo, Austl.	168a	33.20 S	115.47 E
Waterloo, Austl.	168b	33.59 S	138.53 E
Waterloo, Bel.	50	50.43 N	4.23 E
Waterloo, On., Can.	212	43.28 N	80.31 W
Waterloo, P.Q., Can.	206	45.21 N	72.31 W
Waterloo, S.L.	150	8.20 N	13.04 W
Waterloo, Eng., U.K.	44	53.28 N	3.02 W
Waterloo, Al., U.S.	194	34.55 N	88.03 W
Waterloo, Il., U.S.	219	38.20 N	90.08 W
Waterloo, In., U.S.	216	41.25 N	85.01 W
Waterloo, Ia., U.S.	190	42.29 N	92.20 W
Waterloo, N.Y., U.S.	210	42.54 N	76.51 W
Waterloo, Wi., U.S.	216	43.11 N	88.59 W
Waterloo □[6]	212	43.30 N	80.30 W
Waterloo Bay ⊂	168b	35.08 S	137.26 E
Waterloo State Recreation Area ♠	216	42.22 N	84.20 W
Waterlooville	42	50.53 N	1.02 W
Waterman, Il., U.S.	216	41.46 N	88.46 W
Waterman, Wa., U.S.	224	47.34 N	122.35 W
Waterman Mountain ∧	228	34.20 N	117.56 W
Waterman Wash V	200	33.21 N	112.31 W
Water Mill	207	40.55 N	72.21 W
Waterport	210	43.20 N	78.16 W
Waterport Pond ⊜[1]	212	43.19 N	78.16 W
Waterproof	194	31.48 N	91.23 W
Waterside	214	40.11 N	78.23 W
Waterside Park	276	40.56 N	73.20 W
Watersmeet	190	46.16 N	89.10 W
Waterton ≐	182	49.32 N	113.16 W
Waterton-Glacier International Peace Park ♠	202	48.47 N	113.45 W
Waterton Lakes National Park ♠	182	49.05 N	113.50 W
Watertown, Ct., U.S.	207	41.36 N	73.07 W
Watertown, Ma., U.S.	207	42.22 N	71.11 W
Watertown, N.Y., U.S.	212	43.58 N	75.54 W
Watertown, S.D., U.S.	198	44.53 N	97.06 W
Watertown, Wi., U.S.	216	43.11 N	88.43 W
Waterval-Boven	156	25.40 S	30.20 E
Watervale	168b	33.57 S	138.38 E
Water Valley, Ms., U.S.	194	34.09 N	89.37 W
Water Valley, N.Y., U.S.	284a	42.42 N	78.51 W
Water View	208	37.43 N	76.36 W
Waterville, N.S., Can.	186	45.03 N	64.41 W
Waterville, P.Q., Can.	206	45.16 N	71.54 W
Waterville, Ire.	48	51.49 N	10.13 W
Waterville, Ks., U.S.	198	39.41 N	96.44 W
Waterville, Me., U.S.	188	44.33 N	69.37 W
Waterville, Ma., U.S.	207	42.40 N	72.04 W
Waterville, Mn., U.S.	190	44.13 N	93.34 W
Waterville, N.Y., U.S.	210	42.55 N	75.22 W
Waterville, Oh., U.S.	216	41.30 N	83.43 W
Waterville, Pa., U.S.	210	41.19 N	77.22 W
Waterville, Wa., U.S.	202	47.38 N	120.04 W
Watervliet, Mi., U.S.	216	42.11 N	86.15 W
Watervliet, N.Y., U.S.	210	42.43 N	73.42 W
Watervliet Reservoir ⊜[1]	210	42.43 N	73.58 W
Wates, Indon.	114	1.00 N	100.16 E
Wates, Indon.	115a	7.55 S	112.07 E
Wates, Indon.	115a	7.51 S	110.10 E
Watford, On., Can.	214	42.57 N	81.53 W
Watford, Eng., U.K.	42	51.40 N	0.25 W
Watford □[8]	260	51.40 N	0.25 W
Watford City	198	47.48 N	103.16 W
Wa'th	140	8.10 N	32.07 E
Wathaman ≐	184	57.16 N	102.52 W
Wathaman Lake ⊜	184	56.55 N	103.43 W
Wathena	198	39.45 N	94.56 W
Watheroo	162	30.17 S	116.04 E
Watheroo National Park ♠	162	30.14 S	115.52 E
Wathlingen	52	52.32 N	10.09 E
Wath upon Dearne	44	53.29 N	1.20 W
Wati	120	28.02 N	96.59 E
Watino	182	55.43 N	117.37 W
Watkins Glen	210	42.22 N	76.52 W
Watkins Glen International Raceway ♠	210	42.20 N	76.55 W
Watkins Glen State Park ♠	210	42.22 N	76.55 W
Watkins Island I	284c	39.02 N	77.17 W
Watkins Lake ⊜	281	42.40 N	83.22 W
Watkinsville	192	33.51 N	83.24 W
Watlaar	164	5.28 S	133.07 E
Watling Island — San Salvador I	238	24.02 N	74.28 W
Watlington	42	51.37 N	1.00 W
Watoga State Park ♠	188	38.07 N	80.05 W
Watonga	196	35.50 N	98.24 W
Watonwan ≐	198	44.04 N	94.07 W
Watopeka ≐	206	45.34 N	72.00 W
Watou	50	50.51 N	2.37 E
Wat Phai Tan, Khlong ≍	269a	13.48 N	100.33 E
Watrous, Sk., Can.	184	51.40 N	105.28 W
Watrous, N.M., U.S.	200	35.47 N	104.58 W
Watsa	154	3.03 N	29.32 E
Watseka	216	40.46 N	87.44 W
Watsi Kengo	152	0.48 S	20.33 E
Watson, Austl.	162	30.29 S	131.31 E
Watson, Sk., Can.	184	52.07 N	104.31 W
Watson, In., U.S.	218	38.22 N	85.41 W
Watsonia	274b	37.43 S	145.05 E
Watson Lake	180	60.07 N	128.48 W
Watsons Bay	274a	33.51 S	151.17 E
Watsons Creek	274b	37.40 S	145.13 E
Watsons Creek ≐	274b	37.43 S	145.16 E
Watsontown	210	41.05 N	76.51 W
Watsonville	226	36.54 N	121.45 W
Watt	222	31.39 N	96.51 W
Watten	50	50.50 N	2.13 E
Watten, Loch ⊜	46	58.29 N	3.19 W
Wattens	64	47.17 N	11.36 E
Wattenscheid	56	51.29 N	7.08 E
Wattenwil	58	46.46 N	7.30 E
Wattignies	50	50.35 N	3.03 E
Wattiwarriganna ≐	162	28.57 S	136.10 E
Wattle Flat	170	33.08 S	149.41 E
Wattle Glen	274b	37.40 S	145.11 E
Wattle Park ♠	274b	37.50 S	145.07 E
Watt Mountain ∧	240d	15.19 N	61.19 W
Watton	42	52.35 N	0.48 E
Wattrelos	50	50.42 N	3.13 E
Watts ◆[8]	280	33.56 N	118.15 W
Watts Bar Lake ⊜[1]	192	35.48 N	84.39 W
Watts Branch ≐	284c	39.03 N	77.15 W
Wattsburg	214	42.00 N	79.49 W
Watts Island I	208	37.48 N	75.53 W
Watts Mills	192	34.31 N	82.02 W
Wattville	273d	26.13 S	28.18 E
Wattwil	58	47.18 N	9.06 E
Watu	152	3.18 S	20.03 E
Watubela, Kepulauan II	164	4.35 S	131.40 E
Wat Wat	164	4.29 S	152.21 E
Watzekopf ∧	58	46.59 N	10.48 E
Watzmann ∧	64	47.33 N	12.55 E
Wau	164	7.20 S	146.45 E
Waubach	56	50.55 N	6.03 E
Waubaushene	212	44.45 N	79.42 W
Waubaushene Channel ⩌	212	44.46 N	79.45 W
Waubay	198	45.19 N	97.18 W
Waubay Lake ⊜	198	45.25 N	97.25 W
Waubesa, Lake ⊜	216	43.01 N	89.20 W
Waubra	169	37.21 S	143.39 E
Waubuno Creek ≐	212	42.58 N	81.08 W
Wauchope, Austl.	162	20.36 S	134.15 E
Wauchope, Austl.	166	31.27 S	152.44 E
Wauchula	220	27.32 N	81.48 W
Wauconda, Il., U.S.	216	42.15 N	88.08 W
Wauconda, Wa., U.S.	182	48.43 N	119.00 W
Wauconda, Wa., U.S.	202	48.43 N	119.00 W
Waugh	184	49.40 N	95.13 W
Waugh Mountain ∧	202	45.29 N	114.47 W
Waukara, Bukit ∧	112	1.15 S	119.42 E
Waukaringa	166	32.18 S	139.26 E
Waukarlycarly, Lake ⊜	162	21.25 S	121.50 E
Waukegan	216	42.21 N	87.50 W
Waukena	226	36.08 N	119.31 W
Waukesha	216	43.00 N	88.13 W
Waukesha □[6]	216	43.02 N	88.20 W
Waukomis	196	36.16 N	97.53 W
Waukon	190	43.16 N	91.28 W
Waulsort	56	50.13 N	4.52 E
Waura	224	47.22 N	122.38 W
Waurakee	216	43.11 N	89.27 W
Wauneta	198	40.25 N	101.22 W
Waupaca	190	44.21 N	89.05 W
Waupecan Creek ≐	216	41.20 N	88.28 W
Waupoos Island I	212	43.59 N	76.58 W
Waupun	190	43.38 N	88.43 W

≐	River	Fluß	Río	Rivière	Rio
≍	Canal	Kanal	Canal	Canal	Canal
⌊	Waterfall, Rapids	Wasserfall, Stromschnellen	Cascada, Rápidos	Chute d'eau, Rapides	Cascata, Rápidos
⩌	Strait	Meeresstraße	Estrecho	Détroit	Estreito
⊂	Bay, Gulf	Bucht, Golf	Bahía, Golfo	Baie, Golfe	Baía, Golfo
⊜	Lake, Lakes	See, Seen	Lago, Lagos	Lac, Lacs	Lago, Lagos
⁝	Swamp	Sumpf	Pantano	Marais	Pântano
⊓	Ice Features, Glacier	Eis- und Gletscherformen	Accidentes Glaciales	Formes glaciaires	Acidentes glaciares
⫪	Other Hydrographic Features	Andere Hydrographische Objekte	Otros Elementos Hidrográficos	Autres données hydrographiques	Outros acidentes hidrográficos

✦	Submarine Features	Untermeerische Objekte	Accidentes Submarinos	Formes de relief sous-marin	Acidentes submarinos
□	Political Unit	Politische Einheit	Unidad Politica	Entité politique	Unidade política
ʊ	Cultural Institution	Kulturelle Institution	Institución Cultural	Institution culturelle	Instituição cultural
⊥	Historical Site	Historische Stätte	Sitio Histórico	Site historique	Sitio histórico
♠	Recreational Site	Erholungs- und Ferienort	Sitio de Recreo	Centre de loisirs	Area de Lazer
⊠	Airport	Flughafen	Aeropuerto	Aéroport	Aeroporto
■	Military Installation	Militäranlage	Instalación Militar	Installation militaire	Instalação militar
◆	Miscellaneous	Verschiedenes	Misceláneo	Divers	Diversos

Name	Page	Lat. °′	Long. °′
Wauregan	207	41.44 N	71.54 W
Waurika	196	34.10 N	97.59 W
Waurika Lake ⊜[1]	196	34.15 N	98.05 W
Wausa	198	42.29 N	97.32 W
Wausau	190	44.57 N	89.37 W
Wausaukee	190	45.22 N	87.57 W
Wauseon	216	41.32 N	84.08 W
Waushakum Pond ⊜	283	42.16 N	71.26 W
Wautoma	190	44.04 N	89.17 W
Wauwa	154	3.27 N	27.21 E
Wauwatosa	216	43.02 N	88.00 W
Wauzeka	190	43.05 N	90.52 W
Wave Hill	162	17.29 S	130.57 E
Waveland, Ma., U.S.	283	42.17 N	70.53 W
Waveland, Ms., U.S.	194	30.17 N	89.22 W
Waveney ≐	42	52.28 N	1.45 E
Waver ≐	44	54.52 N	3.17 W
Waverley, Austl.	169	37.53 S	145.10 E
Waverley, Austl.	274a	33.54 S	151.16 E
Waverley, N.Z.	172	39.46 S	174.38 E
Waverley, S. Afr.	158	31.58 S	26.28 E
Waverley, Ma., U.S.	283	42.23 N	71.11 W
Waverley ✦[8]	273d	26.08 S	28.04 E
Waverly, Al., U.S.	194	32.44 N	85.35 W
Waverly, Fl., U.S.	220	27.59 N	81.37 W
Waverly, Il., U.S.	219	39.35 N	89.57 W
Waverly, Ia., U.S.	190	42.43 N	92.28 W
Waverly, Ks., U.S.	198	38.23 N	95.36 W
Waverly, Mi., U.S.	216	42.44 N	84.33 W
Waverly, Mn., U.S.	190	45.04 N	93.57 W
Waverly, Mo., U.S.	194	39.12 N	93.31 W
Waverly, Ne., U.S.	198	40.55 N	96.31 W
Waverly, N.Y., U.S.	210	42.00 N	76.31 W
Waverly, Oh., U.S.	218	39.07 N	82.59 W
Waverly, Pa., U.S.	210	41.32 N	75.42 W
Waverly, Tn., U.S.	194	36.05 N	87.47 W
Waverly, Va., U.S.	208	37.02 N	77.05 W
Waverly Hall	192	32.41 N	84.44 W
Wavre	56	50.43 N	4.37 E
Wavrin	50	50.34 N	2.55 E
Wāw	140	7.42 N	28.00 E
Wāw ≐	140	7.03 N	27.13 E
Wawa, On., Can.	190	47.59 N	84.47 W
Wawa, Nig.	150	9.55 N	4.25 E
Wawa, Sūd.	140	20.26 N	30.21 E
Wawa ≐	236	13.53 N	83.28 W
Wawaka	216	41.27 N	85.28 W
Wāw al-Kabīr	146	25.20 N	16.43 E
Wawanesa	184	49.36 N	99.41 W
Wawarsing	210	41.46 N	74.21 W
Wawasee, Lake ⊜	216	41.24 N	85.41 W
Wawayanda State Park ♦	276	41.11 N	74.26 W
Wawiag ≐	190	48.25 N	91.07 W
Wawoi ≐	164	8.01 S	143.33 E
Waworada, Teluk c	115b	8.44 S	118.51 E
Wawota	184	49.55 N	102.00 W
Waxahachie	222	32.23 N	96.50 W
Waxahachie, Lake ⊜[1]	222	32.20 N	96.49 W
Waxhaw	192	34.55 N	80.44 W
Waxuecun	106	31.07 N	121.38 E
Waxweiler	56	50.05 N	6.22 E
Way, Lake ⊜	162	26.48 S	120.18 E
Waya I	175g	17.18 S	177.08 E
Wayabula	108	2.17 N	128.12 E
Wayaopu	106	30.33 N	118.53 E
Waycross	192	31.12 N	82.21 W
Wayi	154	5.11 N	30.10 E
Wayland, Ia., U.S.	190	41.08 N	91.39 W
Wayland, Ky., U.S.	192	37.26 N	82.48 W
Wayland, Ma., U.S.	283	42.21 N	71.21 W
Wayland, Mi., U.S.	216	42.40 N	85.38 W
Wayland, N.Y., U.S.	210	42.34 N	77.35 W
Wayland, Oh., U.S.	214	41.10 N	81.04 W
Waylyn	192	32.51 N	79.59 W
Waymansville	218	39.04 N	86.03 W
Waymart	210	41.34 N	75.24 W
Wayne, Ab., Can.	182	51.23 N	112.39 W
Wayne, Mi., U.S.	216	42.16 N	83.23 W
Wayne, Ne., U.S.	198	42.13 N	97.01 W
Wayne, N.J., U.S.	210	40.55 N	74.16 W
Wayne, N.Y., U.S.	210	42.28 N	77.06 W
Wayne, Oh., U.S.	214	41.18 N	83.28 W
Wayne, Ok., U.S.	196	34.55 N	97.18 W
Wayne, Pa., U.S.	208	40.02 N	75.23 W
Wayne, W.V., U.S.	188	38.13 N	82.26 W
Wayne □[6], Il., U.S.	219	38.25 N	88.40 W
Wayne □[6], In., U.S.	218	39.50 N	84.54 W
Wayne □[6], Mi., U.S.	216	42.14 N	83.12 W
Wayne □[6], N.Y., U.S.	210	43.04 N	77.00 W
Wayne □[6], Oh., U.S.	214	40.48 N	81.56 W
Wayne □[6], Pa., U.S.	210	41.34 N	75.16 W
Wayne City	194	38.20 N	88.35 W
Wayne Lakes	218	40.01 N	84.39 W
Waynesboro, Ga., U.S.	192	33.05 N	82.00 W
Waynesboro, Ms., U.S.	194	31.40 N	88.38 W
Waynesboro, Pa., U.S.	208	39.45 N	77.34 W
Waynesboro, Tn., U.S.	194	35.19 N	87.45 W
Waynesboro, Va., U.S.	192	38.04 N	78.53 W
Waynesburg, Oh., U.S.	214	40.40 N	81.15 W
Waynesburg, Pa., U.S.	188	39.53 N	80.10 W
Waynesfield	216	40.36 N	83.59 W
Wayne State University ʊ[2]	281	42.21 N	83.04 W
Waynesville, Il., U.S.	194	40.15 N	89.08 W
Waynesville, Mo., U.S.	194	37.49 N	92.12 W
Waynesville, N.C., U.S.	192	35.29 N	82.59 W
Waynesville, Oh., U.S.	218	39.32 N	84.05 W
Waynoka	196	36.34 N	98.52 W
Waynoka, Lake ⊜[1]	218	38.55 N	83.47 W
Wayoh Reservoir ⊜[1]	262	53.39 N	2.24 W
Waza	146	11.25 N	14.34 E
Waza, Parc National de ♦	146	11.20 N	13.40 E
Wazah	120	33.22 N	69.26 E
Wāzah Khwāh	120	32.12 N	68.21 E
Waziers	50	50.23 N	3.07 E
Wāzin	146	31.57 N	10.40 E
Wazīrābād	123	32.27 N	74.07 E
Wazirābād ✦[8]	272a	28.43 N	77.14 E
Wāzirpur ✦[8]	272a	28.41 N	77.10 E
Wazuka	96	34.47 N	135.55 E
Wazuka ≐	270	34.45 N	135.53 E
Wda ≐	30	53.25 N	18.29 E
We, Pulau I	114	5.51 N	95.18 E
Wea Creek ≐	216	40.24 N	86.57 W
Weagamow Lake ⊜	184	52.53 N	91.22 W
Weald Park ♦	260	51.38 N	0.14 E
Wealdstone ✦[8]	260	51.36 N	0.20 W
Weam	164	8.40 S	141.08 E
Wear ≐	44	54.55 N	1.22 W
Wearhead	44	54.45 N	2.13 W
Wearyan ≐	164	15.57 S	136.51 E
Weatherford, Ok., U.S.	196	35.31 N	98.42 W
Weatherford, Tx., U.S.	222	32.45 N	97.47 W
Weatherford, Lake ⊜[1]	222	32.47 N	97.41 W
Weatherly	210	40.56 N	75.50 W
Weatogue	207	41.51 N	72.49 W
Weaubleau	194	37.53 N	93.32 W
Weaver, Austl.	168b	34.56 S	137.40 E
Weaver, Al., U.S.	194	33.45 N	85.48 W
Weaver, Tx., U.S.	222	33.10 N	95.25 W
Weaver ≐	44	53.18 N	2.43 W
Weaverham	44	53.16 N	2.35 W
Weaver Lake ⊜	184	52.45 N	96.35 W
Weavertown	279b	40.16 N	80.11 W
Weaverville, Ca., U.S.	204	40.43 N	122.56 W
Weaverville, N.C., U.S.	192	35.41 N	82.33 W
Webau	54	51.10 N	12.04 E
Webb, Sk., Can.	184	50.11 N	108.12 W
Webb, Ms., U.S.	194	33.56 N	90.20 W
Webb Brook ≐	283	42.32 N	71.14 W
Webb City	194	37.08 N	94.27 W
Webber Lake ⊜	184	54.28 N	94.00 W
Webberville	216	42.40 N	84.10 W
Webbwood	190	46.16 N	81.53 W
Weber ≐	200	41.13 N	112.16 W
Weber, Mount ʌ	182	55.32 N	128.31 W
Weber City	192	36.37 N	82.33 W
Weber Creek ≐	226	38.46 N	121.00 W
Weber Hill	219	38.27 N	90.34 W
Weberi Bekera	144	9.39 N	39.03 E
Webster, Ab., Can.	182	55.26 N	118.42 W
Webster, Fl., U.S.	220	28.36 N	82.03 W
Webster, In., U.S.	218	39.54 N	84.57 W
Webster, Ma., U.S.	207	42.03 N	71.52 W
Webster, N.Y., U.S.	210	43.12 N	77.25 W
Webster, Pa., U.S.	214	40.11 N	79.50 W
Webster, S.D., U.S.	198	45.19 N	97.31 W
Webster, Wi., U.S.	190	45.52 N	92.22 W
Webster City	190	42.28 N	93.48 W
Webster Crossing	210	42.40 N	77.38 W
Webster Groves	219	38.35 N	90.21 W
Webster Lake ⊜	216	41.19 N	85.41 W
Websters Corners, B.C., Can.	224	49.13 N	122.30 W
Websters Corners, N.Y., U.S.	284a	41.47 N	78.45 W
Webster Springs	188	38.28 N	80.24 W
Weches	222	31.33 N	95.14 W
Wechmar	54	50.53 N	10.47 E
Wechselburg	54	51.00 N	12.47 E
Weda	108	0.21 N	127.52 E
Wedau ✦[8]	263	51.24 N	6.48 E
Wedau, Sportpark ♦	263	51.25 N	6.47 E
Weddell Island I	254	51.55 S	61.00 W
Weddell Sea ⊤[2]	9	72.00 S	45.00 W
Wedderburn	166	36.25 S	143.37 E
Wedding ✦[8]	54	52.33 N	13.22 E
Weddinghofen	263	51.36 N	7.37 E
Wedel	52	53.35 N	9.41 E
Wedemark	52	52.33 N	9.44 E
Wedge, Central Mount ʌ	162	22.51 S	131.50 E
Wedge Mountain ʌ	182	50.10 N	122.50 W
Wedgeport	186	43.44 N	65.59 W
Wedgewood	219	38.47 N	90.17 W
Wedmore	42	51.14 N	2.49 W
Wedowee	194	33.18 N	85.29 W
Wedron	216	41.26 N	88.46 W
Weduar, Tanjung >	164	6.00 S	132.50 E
Wedweil	140	9.00 N	27.12 E
Wedza	154	18.35 S	31.35 E
Weebo	162	28.01 S	121.03 E
Weed	204	41.25 N	122.23 W
Weed Heights	226	38.59 N	119.12 W
Weedon	206	45.42 N	71.28 W
Weedon Beck	42	52.14 N	1.05 W
Weedon Island I	220	27.51 N	82.36 W
Weed Patch	228	35.19 N	118.55 W
Weed Patch Hill ʌ[2]	218	39.10 N	86.13 W
Weedsport	210	43.02 N	76.33 W
Weedville	214	41.17 N	78.30 W
Weehawken	276	40.46 N	74.01 W
Weeim, Pulau I	164	1.29 S	130.14 E
Wee Jasper	171b	35.09 S	148.41 E
Weekapauq	207	41.20 N	71.45 W
Weeki Wachee Spring ♦	220	28.32 N	82.35 W
Weeki Wachee Swamp ≡	220	28.31 N	82.37 W
Weeks Point >	276	40.53 N	73.39 W
Weekstown	208	39.35 N	74.36 W
Weelde	56	51.25 N	5.00 E
Weeley	42	51.51 N	1.07 E
Weel Shimbirro	144	2.23 N	44.16 E
Weems	208	37.39 N	76.26 W
Weende	52	51.33 N	9.55 E
Weenen	158	28.57 S	30.03 E
Weener	52	53.10 N	7.21 E
Weeney Bay c	274a	34.01 S	151.10 E
Weeping Water	198	40.52 N	96.08 W
Weequahic Lake ⊜	276	40.42 N	74.12 W
Weert	52	51.15 N	5.43 E
Weesatche	222	28.51 N	97.27 W
Weesby	41	54.50 N	9.08 E
Weesow	264a	52.39 N	13.43 E
Weesp	52	52.17 N	5.02 E
Weetfeld ✦[8]	263	51.38 N	7.49 E
Weethalle	166	33.53 S	146.38 E
Weeting	42	52.27 N	0.37 E
Weeton	262	53.48 N	2.56 W
Weetulta	168b	34.15 S	137.38 E
Wee Waa	166	30.14 S	149.26 E
Weeze	52	51.37 N	6.12 E
Wefensleben	54	52.11 N	11.09 E
Weferlingen	54	52.19 N	11.02 E
Wegberg	56	51.08 N	6.16 E
Wegdraai	158	28.50 S	21.52 E
Wegeleben	54	51.53 N	11.10 E
Wegendorf	264a	52.36 N	13.45 E
Wegenstedt	54	52.23 N	11.11 E
Wegeringhausen	56	51.02 N	7.45 E
Weggis	58	47.02 N	8.26 E
Węgliniec	30	51.17 N	15.13 E
Węgorzewo	30	54.14 N	21.44 E
Węgorzyno	30	53.32 N	15.33 E
Węgrów	30	52.25 N	22.01 E
Wegscheid	60	48.36 N	13.48 E
Wehdel	52	53.30 N	8.48 E
Wehebach Stausee ⊜[1]	56	50.45 N	6.20 E
Wehingen	58	48.08 N	8.47 E
Wehofen ✦[8]	263	51.32 N	6.46 E
Wehr	58	47.37 N	7.54 E
Wehringhausen ✦[8]	263	51.21 N	7.27 E
Wehrsdorf	54	51.03 N	14.22 E
Wei ≐, Zhg.	98	36.51 N	115.43 E
Wei ≐, Zhg.	98	37.05 N	119.28 E
Wei ≐, Zhg.	102	34.30 N	110.20 E
Weichang (Zhuizishan)	98	42.00 N	117.32 E
Weichsel → Wisła ≐	30	54.22 N	18.55 E
Weichselboden	61	47.40 N	15.10 E
Weichuan	98	34.17 N	113.58 E
Weicun	106	31.59 N	119.55 E
Weida	54	50.45 N	12.04 E
Weida ≐	54	50.47 N	12.06 E
Weiden am See	61	47.55 N	16.52 E
Weidenberg	60	49.57 N	11.43 E
Weiden in der Oberpfalz	60	49.41 N	12.10 E
Weidenstetten	56	48.33 N	9.59 E
Weidhausen	54	50.12 N	11.08 E
Weidling	264b	48.17 N	16.19 E
Weidlingau ✦[8]	264b	48.13 N	16.13 E
Weidlingbach	264b	48.16 N	16.15 E
Weidlingerbach ≐	264b	48.18 N	16.20 E
Weifang	98	36.42 N	119.04 E
Weigelstown	208	39.59 N	76.49 W
Weihai	98	37.28 N	122.07 E
Weihaiwei → Weihai	98	37.28 N	122.07 E
Weihmichl	60	48.36 N	12.03 E
Weihnachtsinsel → Christmas Island □[2]	112	10.30 S	105.40 E
Wei Island I	164	3.20 S	144.25 E
Weijiagou	105	40.28 N	115.08 E
Weijiatang	106	31.25 N	118.55 E
Weijiazhuang	105	39.37 N	116.22 E
Weijiazui	100	30.29 N	117.20 E
Weijingtang	106	31.17 N	120.39 E
Weikersheim	56	49.29 N	9.54 E
Weil ≐	56	50.28 N	8.16 E
Weil am Rhein	58	47.37 N	7.38 E
Weilburg	56	50.29 N	8.15 E
Weil der Stadt	56	48.45 N	8.52 E
Weiler	58	47.36 N	9.55 E
Weilerbach	56	49.29 N	7.37 E
Weilerswist	56	50.45 N	6.50 E
Weilheim	64	47.50 N	11.08 E
Weilheim an der Teck	56	48.37 N	9.32 E
Weilmoringle	166	29.15 S	146.51 E
Weilmünster	56	50.26 N	8.22 E
Weimar, Dtsch.	54	50.59 N	11.19 E
Weimar, Dtsch.	56	51.22 N	9.23 E
Weimar, Ca., U.S.	226	39.02 N	120.58 W
Weimar, Tx., U.S.	222	29.42 N	96.46 W
Weinan	102	34.29 N	109.29 E
Weinböhla	54	51.10 N	13.34 E
Weinel Cross Roads	279b	40.37 N	79.37 W
Weiner	194	35.37 N	90.53 W
Weinfelden	58	47.34 N	9.06 E
Weingarten, Dtsch.	56	49.05 N	8.31 E
Weingarten, Dtsch.	58	47.48 N	9.38 E
Weinheim	56	49.33 N	8.39 E
Weining, Zhg.	102	26.43 N	104.18 E
Weining, Zhg.	104	41.21 N	123.49 E
Weinsberg	56	49.10 N	9.17 E
Weinsberger Wald ✦[3]	61	48.30 N	14.50 E
Weinviertel ✦[1]	61	48.38 N	16.25 E
Weipa	164	12.41 S	141.52 E
Weippe	202	46.22 N	115.56 W
Weir, India	124	27.01 N	77.11 E
Weir, Ks., U.S.	198	37.18 N	94.46 W
Weir, Ms., U.S.	194	33.16 N	89.17 W
Weir ≐, Austl.	166	28.50 S	149.06 E
Weir ≐, Mb., Can.	184	56.54 N	93.21 W
Weir ≐, Ma., U.S.	283	42.16 N	70.53 W
Weir, Lake ⊜	220	29.00 N	81.57 W
Weir River	184	56.49 N	94.04 W
Weirsdale	220	28.58 N	81.55 W
Weirton	214	40.25 N	80.35 W
Weisburd	252	27.18 S	62.36 W
Weisburg	218	39.13 N	85.03 W
Weischlitz	54	50.26 N	12.02 E
Weisendorf	56	49.37 N	10.49 E
Weiser	202	44.15 N	116.58 W
Weiser ≐	202	44.15 N	116.59 W
Weishan (Xiazhen), Zhg.	98	34.52 N	117.09 E
Weishan, Zhg.	100	29.20 N	120.25 E
Weishan, Zhg.	100	29.41 N	120.48 E
Weishan, Zhg.	102	25.15 N	100.20 E
Weishancheng	100	32.34 N	113.24 E
Weishanhe	104	40.47 N	123.31 E
Weishan Hu ⊜	98	34.40 N	117.15 E
Weishanzhuang	105	39.40 N	116.25 E
Weishi	98	34.25 N	114.11 E
Weismain	54	50.05 N	11.14 E
Weisner Mountain ʌ	194	34.02 N	85.40 W
Weissach	56	48.50 N	8.55 E
Weissbriach	64	46.41 N	13.15 E
Weisse Elster ≐	54	51.26 N	11.57 E
Weissenbach	264b	48.05 N	16.13 E
Weissenbach am Lech	58	47.26 N	10.39 E
Weissenberg	54	51.11 N	14.40 E
Weissenborn	54	50.52 N	13.25 E
Weissenbrunn	54	50.12 N	11.20 E
Weissenburg	58	46.39 N	7.28 E
Weissenburg in Bayern	56	49.01 N	10.58 E
Weissenfels	54	51.12 N	11.58 E
Weissenhorn	58	48.18 N	10.09 E
Weissensee	54	51.11 N	11.04 E
Weissensee ✦[8]	264a	52.33 N	13.27 E
Weissensee ⊜	64	46.42 N	13.22 E
Weissenstadt	54	50.06 N	11.53 E
Weissenstein, Dtsch.	56	48.42 N	9.53 E
Weissenstein, Öst.	64	46.41 N	13.44 E
Weissenstein ʌ	58	47.15 N	7.31 E
Weissenstein Tunnel ✦[5]	58	47.12 N	7.23 E
Weissenthurm	56	50.24 N	7.27 E
Weisser Main ≐	60	50.04 N	11.24 E
Weisser Nil → White Nile ≐	140	15.38 N	32.31 E
Weisser See → Beloje, ozero ⊜	76	60.11 N	37.37 E
Weisser Stein ʌ	56	50.23 N	6.20 E
Weisses Meer → Beloje more ⊤[2]	24	65.30 N	38.00 E
Weisse Spitze ʌ	64	46.52 N	12.21 E
Weissfluh ʌ	58	46.50 N	9.48 E
Weisshorn ʌ	58	46.06 N	7.42 E
Weissig	54	51.05 N	13.52 E
Weisskugel (Palla Bianca) ʌ	64	46.48 N	10.44 E
Weiss Lake ⊜[1]	192	34.15 N	85.35 W
Weissmeer-Ostsee Kanal → Belomorsko-Baltijskij kanal ≊	24	62.48 N	34.48 E
Weissport	210	40.50 N	75.42 W
Weisstannen	58	46.59 N	9.21 E
Weisswasser	54	51.30 N	14.38 E
Weisweiler	56	50.50 N	6.19 E
Weitang	105	40.24 N	117.24 E
Weitang ≐	104	42.19 N	122.18 E
Weitendorf	54	53.54 N	12.16 E
Weitensfeld	61	46.51 N	14.11 E
Weiterstadt	56	49.54 N	8.35 E
Weitian	100	27.43 N	118.46 E
Weitin	54	53.34 N	13.12 E
Weiting	106	31.22 N	120.47 E
Weitmar ✦[8]	263	51.27 N	7.12 E
Weitnau	58	47.38 N	10.07 E
Weitou	100	24.34 N	118.34 E
Weitra	61	48.42 N	14.54 E
Weituo	107	30.03 N	106.08 E
Weitzgrund	54	52.11 N	12.32 E
Weiwan	98	36.43 N	115.54 E
Weixdorf	54	51.09 N	13.48 E
Weixi, Zhg.	102	27.14 N	99.12 E
Weixi, Zhg.	107	30.12 N	106.39 E
Weixian, Zhg.	98	36.57 N	115.15 E
Weixian, Zhg.	98	36.22 N	114.56 E
Weixian (Hanting), Zhg.	98	36.52 N	119.07 E
Weixin	102	27.48 N	105.06 E
Weiyuan	107	29.33 N	104.39 E
Weiyuan ≐	102	22.50 N	100.20 E
Weiyuankou	100	30.09 N	115.15 E
Weiyuanpu	98	42.39 N	124.16 E
Weiz	61	47.13 N	15.37 E
Weizhen	98	37.17 N	114.44 E
Weizhou Dao I	102	21.03 N	109.04 E
Weizhou Wan c	100	24.34 N	118.30 E
Weizhuang	105	39.02 N	115.20 E
Weizi	98	40.04 N	123.10 E
Weizigou, Zhg.	104	42.25 N	122.47 E
Weizigou, Zhg.	104	42.05 N	120.34 E
Weizigoumen	98	41.58 N	116.49 E
Weiziyu	98	41.29 N	124.31 E
Wejherowo	30	54.37 N	18.15 E
Wekiva ≐	220	28.52 N	81.23 W
Wekiwa Springs State Park ♦	220	28.43 N	81.27 W
Wekoewa Punt >	241s	12.14 N	68.24 W
Wekusko Lake ⊜	184	54.45 N	99.50 W
Welaka	192	29.28 N	81.40 W
Welbourn Hill	162	27.21 S	134.06 E
Welch, Ok., U.S.	196	36.52 N	95.05 W
Welch, Tx., U.S.	196	32.56 N	102.08 W
Welch, W.V., U.S.	192	37.25 N	81.35 W
Welch Creek ≐	282	37.32 N	121.51 W
Welches	224	45.19 N	121.57 W
Welch Peak ʌ	224	49.10 N	121.36 W
Welcome, On., Can.	212	43.58 N	78.21 W
Welcome, Mn., U.S.	198	43.40 N	94.37 W
Welcome, S.C., U.S.	192	34.49 N	82.26 W
Welcome Lake ⊜	212	45.25 N	78.25 W
Welcome Monument ⊥	269e	6.11 S	106.49 E
Welden	58	48.27 N	10.40 E
Weldiya	144	11.50 N	39.41 E
Weldon, Sk., Can.	184	53.00 N	105.08 W
Weldon, Il., U.S.	219	40.07 N	88.45 W
Weldon, N.C., U.S.	192	36.25 N	77.35 W
Weldon, Tx., U.S.	222	31.01 N	95.34 W
Weldon ≐	194	40.06 N	93.38 W
Weldona	198	40.20 N	103.58 W
Weldon Brook ≐	276	40.58 N	74.35 W
Weleetka	196	35.20 N	96.08 W
Welega □[4]	144	9.40 N	35.50 E
Weleri	115a	6.58 S	110.04 E
Welfare Island I	276	40.45 N	73.57 W
Welgedag	273d	26.12 S	28.30 E
Welhamgreen	260	51.44 N	0.13 W
Welheim ✦[8]	263	51.32 N	6.59 E
Weligama	122	5.58 N	80.25 E
Welikaja → Velikaja ≐	76	57.48 N	28.20 E
Welkenraedt	56	50.40 N	5.59 E
Welker Seamount ✤[3]	16	55.07 N	140.20 W
Welkite	144	8.15 N	37.50 E
Welkom	158	27.59 S	26.45 E
Well	52	51.34 N	6.06 E
Welland	212	42.59 N	79.15 W
Welland ≐, On., Can.	212	43.04 N	79.03 W
Welland ≐, Eng., U.K.	42	52.52 N	0.03 W
Welland Canal ≊	212	43.03 N	79.13 W
Welland Junction	284a	42.57 N	79.14 W
Wellard	168a	32.19 S	115.50 E
Wellaune	54	51.34 N	12.33 E
Wellborn, Fl., U.S.	192	30.13 N	82.49 W
Wellborn, Tx., U.S.	222	30.32 N	96.18 W
Wellerode	56	51.14 N	9.34 E
Wellers Bay c	212	44.00 N	77.34 W
Wellers Creek ≐	278	42.03 N	87.53 W
Wellesbourne	42	52.12 N	1.35 W
Welles Harbor c	174g	28.12 N	177.26 W
Wellesley, On., Can.	212	43.28 N	80.45 W
Wellesley, Ma., U.S.	207	42.17 N	71.17 W
Wellesley ≐	168a	33.17 S	115.44 E
Wellesley College ʊ[2]	283	42.18 N	71.19 W
Wellesley Hills	283	42.19 N	71.17 W
Wellesley Island I	212	44.19 N	75.58 W
Wellesley Islands II	164	16.42 S	139.30 E
Wellesley Island State Park ♦	212	44.19 N	76.01 W
Wellesley Lake ⊜	180	62.30 N	139.50 W
Wellfleet	207	41.56 N	70.02 W
Well Hill	260	51.21 N	0.09 E
Wellin	56	50.05 N	5.07 E
Welling ✦[8]	260	51.28 N	0.07 E
Wellingborough	42	52.19 N	0.42 W
Wellinghofen ✦[8]	263	51.28 N	7.29 E
Wellington, Austl.	166	32.33 S	148.57 E
Wellington, B.C., Can.	224	49.13 N	124.01 W
Wellington, On., Can.	212	43.57 N	77.21 W
Wellington, N.Z.	172	41.18 S	174.47 E
Wellington, S. Afr.	158	33.38 S	18.57 E
Wellington, Eng., U.K.	42	52.43 N	2.31 W
Wellington, Eng., U.K.	42	50.59 N	3.14 W
Wellington, Co., U.S.	200	40.42 N	105.00 W
Wellington, Il., U.S.	216	40.32 N	87.41 W
Wellington, Ks., U.S.	198	37.15 N	97.22 W
Wellington, Mo., U.S.	194	39.08 N	93.58 W
Wellington, Nv., U.S.	226	38.45 N	119.22 W
Wellington, Oh., U.S.	214	41.10 N	82.13 W
Wellington, Tx., U.S.	196	34.51 N	100.12 W
Wellington, Ut,. U.S.	200	39.32 N	110.44 W
Wellington □[6]	212	43.50 N	80.30 W
Wellington, Isla I	254	49.20 S	74.40 W
Wellington Bay c, N.T., Can.	176	69.30 N	106.30 W
Wellington Bay c, On., Can.	212	43.56 N	77.21 W
Wellington Channel ꓤ	176	75.00 N	93.00 W
Wellington Point	171a	27.29 S	153.15 E
Wellington Reservoir ⊜[1]	168a	33.24 S	116.01 E
Wellington Station	186	46.27 N	64.00 W
Wellman, Ia., U.S.	190	41.27 N	91.50 W
Wellman, Tx., U.S.	196	33.03 N	102.26 W
Wells, B.C., Can.	182	53.06 N	121.34 W
Wells, Eng., U.K.	42	51.13 N	2.39 W
Wells, Mi., U.S.	190	45.47 N	87.04 W
Wells, Mn., U.S.	190	43.44 N	93.43 W
Wells, Nv., U.S.	204	41.06 N	114.57 W
Wells, N.Y., U.S.	210	43.24 N	74.17 W
Wells, Tx., U.S.	222	31.29 N	94.56 W
Wells □[6]	216	40.44 N	85.11 W
Wells, Lake ⊜	162	26.43 S	123.10 E
Wells, Mount ʌ	168a	32.42 S	116.20 E
Wells, Mount ʌ[2]	162	17.26 S	127.14 E
Wellsboro	210	41.44 N	77.18 W
Wells Bridge	210	42.22 N	75.15 W
Wellsburg, Ia., U.S.	190	42.27 N	92.56 W
Wellsburg, N.Y., U.S.	210	42.00 N	76.43 W
Wellsburg, W.V., U.S.	214	40.16 N	80.36 W
Wells Cathedral ʊ[1]	42	51.13 N	2.39 W
Wellsford	172	36.17 S	174.31 E
Wells Gray Provincial Park ♦	182	52.20 N	120.00 W
Wells Lake ⊜	184	57.15 N	101.00 W
Wells-next-the-Sea	42	52.58 N	0.51 E
Wells Point >	284b	39.17 N	76.23 W
Wells State Park ♦	207	42.09 N	72.05 W
Wells Tannery	214	40.05 N	78.10 W
Wellston, Oh., U.S.	188	39.07 N	82.31 W
Wellston, Ok., U.S.	196	35.41 N	97.03 W
Wellsville, Ks., U.S.	198	38.43 N	95.04 W
Wellsville, Mo., U.S.	219	39.04 N	91.34 W
Wellsville, N.Y., U.S.	210	42.07 N	77.56 W
Wellsville, Oh., U.S.	214	40.36 N	80.38 W
Wellsville, Pa., U.S.	208	40.03 N	76.56 W
Wellsville, Ut,. U.S.	200	41.38 N	111.55 W
Wellton	200	32.40 N	114.08 W
Welmel ≐	144	5.38 N	40.47 E
Welmen	263	51.39 N	6.41 E
Welney	42	52.31 N	0.15 E
Welo □[4]	144	11.50 N	40.20 E
Welper	263	51.25 N	7.12 E
Wels	61	48.10 N	14.02 E
Welsberg → Monguelfo	64	46.45 N	12.06 E
Welschbillig	56	49.51 N	6.34 E
Welse ≐	54	53.10 N	14.18 E
Welsford	186	45.27 N	66.20 W
Welsh	194	30.14 N	92.49 W
Welshpool, Austl.	169	38.39 S	146.26 E
Welshpool, Wales, U.K.	42	52.40 N	3.09 W
Welsickendorf	54	51.54 N	13.08 E
Welsleben	54	52.00 N	11.38 E
Weltenburg	60	48.54 N	11.50 E
Welver	52	51.38 N	7.57 E
Welverdiend	158	26.23 S	27.16 E
Welwitschia	156	22.23 S	14.55 E
Welwyn Garden City	42	51.50 N	0.13 W
Welwyn Hatfield □[8]	260	51.47 N	0.12 W
Welzheim	56	48.53 N	9.38 E
Welzow	54	51.34 N	14.10 E
Wem	42	52.51 N	2.44 W
Wema	152	0.26 S	21.38 E
Wembere ≐	154	4.10 S	34.11 E
Wembley	182	55.09 N	118.18 W
Wembley ✦[8]	260	51.33 N	0.18 W
Wembley Stadium ♦, S. Afr.	273d	26.14 S	28.03 E
Wembley Stadium ♦, Eng., U.K.	260	51.33 N	0.17 W
Wembury	42	50.19 N	4.05 W
Wemding	56	48.52 N	10.43 E
Wemeldinge	52	51.31 N	4.00 E
Wemme	224	45.20 N	121.57 W

ENGLISH

Name	Page	Lat. °′	Long. °′
Wemperhardt	56	50.09 N	6.05 E
Wemyss Bay	46	55.53 N	4.54 W
Wen ≐, Zhg.	98	35.28 N	118.32 E
Wen ≐, Zhg.	98	36.38 N	119.22 E
Wen'an	105	38.52 N	116.28 E
Wen'an Wa ≡	105	38.54 N	116.37 E
Wenas Creek ≐	224	46.42 N	120.35 W
Wenatchee	202	47.25 N	120.18 W
Wenatchee ≐	202	47.27 N	120.19 W
Wenatchee, Lake ⊜	224	47.49 N	120.47 W
Wenatchee Mountains ⋏	202	47.20 N	120.45 W
Wenchang	110	19.41 N	110.48 E
Wencheng	100	27.50 N	120.05 E
Wenchi	150	7.42 N	2.07 W
Wenchow → Wenzhou	100	28.01 N	120.39 E
Wendaohezi	104	41.46 N	124.09 E
Wendel	279b	40.18 N	79.41 W
Wendell, Id., U.S.	202	42.46 N	114.42 W
Wendell, N.C., U.S.	192	35.46 N	78.22 W
Wendelsheim	56	49.46 N	7.59 E
Wendelstein	60	49.21 N	11.08 E
Wendelstein ʌ	64	47.42 N	12.00 E
Wendelville	284a	43.04 N	78.47 W
Wenden, Dtsch.	52	52.19 N	10.30 E
Wenden, Dtsch.	56	50.57 N	7.51 E
Wenden, Az., U.S.	200	33.49 N	113.32 W
Wendeng	98	37.12 N	122.04 E
Wendesi	164	2.25 S	134.13 E
Wendilou	104	41.13 N	121.08 E
Wendisch Rietz	54	52.13 N	14.01 E
Wendish Baggendorf	54	54.04 N	12.56 E
Wendji	152	0.04 S	18.10 E
Wendland ✦[1]	54	53.00 N	11.10 E
Wendo	144	6.38 N	38.27 E
Wendover, Eng., U.K.	42	51.46 N	0.46 W
Wendover, Ut,. U.S.	200	40.44 N	114.02 W
Wenduine	50	51.18 N	3.05 E
Wenebegon ≐	190	46.53 N	83.12 W
Wenebegon Lake ⊜	190	47.24 N	83.08 W
Wenfang	100	28.02 N	117.19 E
Weng	60	48.40 N	12.23 E
Weng ≐	100	24.10 N	113.24 E
Weng'an	102	26.53 N	107.22 E
Wengbo	120	31.23 N	86.40 E
Wengcheng	100	24.23 N	113.51 E
Wengdang	124	28.50 N	90.03 E
Wenge	152	0.03 N	24.01 E
Wengen, Dtsch.	58	47.41 N	10.09 E
Wengen, Schw.	58	46.36 N	7.56 E
Wengern	263	51.24 N	7.21 E
Wengjiabu	106	30.23 N	120.21 E
Wengong	107	30.11 N	104.09 E
Wenguantun	104	41.53 N	123.30 E
Wengyang	100	28.03 N	120.58 E
Wengyuan	100	24.21 N	114.08 E
Wenham	207	42.36 N	70.53 W
Wenham Lake ⊜	283	42.35 N	70.53 W
Wenham Swamp ≡	283	42.37 N	70.55 W
Wenheng	100	25.42 N	116.45 E
Wenī	124	28.21 N	83.34 E
Wenigzell	61	47.26 N	15.47 E
Wenjiachang	107	30.41 N	103.55 E
Wenjiang	107	30.42 N	103.49 E
Wenjiangban	100	26.01 N	117.51 E
Wenjiazhen	100	28.20 N	116.05 E
Wenling	100	28.22 N	121.20 E
Wenlock	164	13.06 S	142.58 E
Wenlock ≐	164	12.02 S	141.55 E
Wenlock Edge ⊥[4]	42	52.30 N	2.40 W
Wenlong	100	24.48 N	114.54 E
Wenmingsi	100	25.33 N	113.20 E
Wennigsen	52	52.16 N	9.34 E
Wenning ≐	44	54.07 N	2.39 W
Wennington ✦[8]	260	51.30 N	0.13 E
Wenniu	102	24.18 N	104.31 E
Wenns	58	47.10 N	10.44 E
Wenona, Il., U.S.	216	41.03 N	89.03 W
Wenona, Md., U.S.	208	38.08 N	75.57 W
Wenonah	208	39.47 N	75.08 W
Wenquan, Zhg.	86	44.59 N	81.04 E
Wenquan, Zhg.	100	23.37 N	113.43 E
Wenquansi	104	41.20 N	124.04 E
Wenshan	102	23.30 N	104.20 E
Wenshang	98	35.44 N	116.29 E
Wenshui, Zhg.	102	28.28 N	106.30 E
Wenshui, Zhg.	102	37.28 N	112.01 E
Wensickendorf	264a	52.45 N	13.23 E
Wensleydale V	44	54.19 N	2.00 W
Wensum ≐	42	52.37 N	1.19 E
Went ≐	44	53.39 N	0.59 W
Wentorf	52	53.30 N	10.15 E
Wentworth, Austl.	166	34.07 S	141.55 E
Wentworth, N.C., U.S.	192	36.24 N	79.46 W
Wentworth, S.D., U.S.	198	43.59 N	96.57 W
Wentworth Falls	170	33.43 S	150.22 E
Wentworth Park	273d	26.07 S	27.48 E
Wentworthville	274a	33.48 S	150.58 E
Wentzville	219	38.48 N	90.51 W
Wenxi	102	35.26 N	111.11 E
Wenxian	102	32.58 N	104.46 E
Wenxingchang	107	29.52 N	106.29 E
Wenyu ≐	105	39.56 N	116.40 E
Wenzenbach	60	49.05 N	12.12 E
Wenzhou	100	28.01 N	120.39 E
Wenzhu	100	27.01 N	113.58 E
Wenzhuangzicun	104	42.16 N	123.51 E
Weobley	42	52.09 N	2.51 W
Weohyakapka, Lake ⊜	220	27.49 N	81.25 W
Wepener	158	29.46 S	27.00 E
Wépion	56	50.25 N	4.52 E
Weppersdorf	61	47.35 N	16.26 E
Wequetequock	207	41.21 N	71.52 W
Wera ≐	115b	8.20 S	120.43 E
Werbellin	54	52.53 N	13.41 E
Werbellinsee ⊜	54	52.54 N	13.40 E
Werben	54	52.52 N	11.58 E
Werbomont	56	50.23 N	5.41 E
Werchojansker Gebirge → Verchojanskij chrebet ⋏	74	67.00 N	129.00 E
Werda	156	25.15 S	23.16 E
Werdau	54	50.44 N	12.22 E
Werden ✦[8]	263	51.23 N	7.00 E
Werder, Dtsch.	54	52.23 N	12.56 E
Werder, Ityo.	144	6.58 N	45.20 E
Werder ✦[1]	54	53.40 N	13.25 E
Werdohl	56	51.15 N	7.45 E
Were Ilu	144	10.37 N	39.28 E
Werfen	64	47.28 N	13.11 E
Weri	164	3.12 S	132.38 E
Werkel	56	51.09 N	9.18 E
Werkendam	52	51.49 N	4.53 E
Werl	52	51.33 N	7.54 E
Werlaburgdorf	52	52.04 N	10.34 E
Werl-Aspe	52	52.04 N	8.43 E
Werleshausen	56	51.19 N	9.54 E
Werlte	52	52.51 N	7.41 E
Wermelskirchen	56	51.08 N	7.13 E
Wermsdorf	54	51.17 N	12.56 E
Wern ≐	56	50.02 N	9.44 E
Wernadinga	166	18.07 S	139.58 E
Wernberg, Dtsch.	60	49.32 N	12.10 E
Wernberg, Öst.	64	46.37 N	13.56 E
Werne	52	51.40 N	7.38 E
Werne ✦[8]	263	51.29 N	7.18 E
Werneck, Bra.	256	22.13 S	49.22 W
Werneck, Dtsch.	56	49.59 N	10.05 E
Werneuchen	54	52.38 N	13.44 E
Wernigerode	54	51.50 N	10.47 E
Wernitz	264a	52.34 N	12.55 E
Wernsdorf	264a	52.22 N	13.43 E
Wernsdorfer See ⊜	264a	52.23 N	13.42 E
Wernshausen	54	50.43 N	10.21 E
Wernstein	60	48.30 N	13.28 E
Werra ≐	30	51.26 N	9.39 E

DEUTSCH

Name	Seite	Breite °′	Länge °′ E = Ost
Werribee	169	37.54 S	144.40 E
Werribee ≐	169	37.59 S	144.41 E
Werribee Gorge State Park ♦	169	37.40 S	144.21 E
Werribee South	169	37.56 S	144.42 E
Werries	52	51.41 N	7.53 E
Werrington	274a	33.45 S	150.46 E
Werris Creek	166	31.21 S	150.39 E
Werschweiler	56	49.27 N	7.13 E
Wersten ✦[8]	263	51.11 N	6.49 E
Wertach	58	47.36 N	10.25 E
Wertach ≐	58	48.24 N	10.53 E
Wertheim	56	49.46 N	9.31 E
Werther, Dtsch.	52	52.04 N	8.24 E
Werther, Dtsch.	54	51.29 N	10.46 E
Wertingen	56	48.34 N	10.41 E
Wervershoof	52	52.44 N	5.09 E
Wervik	50	50.47 N	3.02 E
Wervin	262	53.15 N	2.52 W
Werwaru	164	8.13 S	128.11 E
Weschnitz ≐	56	49.43 N	8.24 E
Weseke	52	51.54 N	6.51 E
Wesel	52	51.40 N	6.38 E
Wesel-Datteln-Kanal ≊	263	51.38 N	6.36 E
Wesenberg	54	53.17 N	12.58 E
Wesendahl	264a	52.36 N	13.49 E
Wesendorf	52	52.35 N	10.31 E
Weser ≐	52	53.32 N	8.34 E
Weser-Elbe-Kanal (Mittellandkanal) ≊	54	52.16 N	11.41 E
Weser-Ems □[5]	52	52.45 N	8.00 E
Wesergebirge ⋏	52	52.15 N	9.10 E
Wesham	262	53.48 N	2.53 W
Wesickaman Creek ≐	285	39.44 N	74.43 W
Wesī Śahar	124	28.15 N	84.23 E
Weskan	198	38.52 N	101.57 W
Weslaco	196	26.09 N	97.59 W
Weslemkoon Lake ⊜	212	45.02 N	77.25 W
Wesley, Dom.	240d	15.34 N	61.19 W
Wesley, Ia., U.S.	190	43.05 N	93.59 W
Wesleyville, Nf., Can.	186	49.09 N	53.34 W
Wesleyville, Pa., U.S.	214	42.08 N	80.00 W
Wessel, Cape >	164	10.59 S	136.46 E
Wesseling	56	50.49 N	6.58 E
Wessel Islands II	164	11.30 S	136.25 E
Wesselsbron	158	27.50 S	25.23 E
Wesselsvlei	158	27.23 S	23.47 E
Wessington	198	44.27 N	98.41 W
Wessington Springs	198	44.04 N	98.34 W
Wessobrunn	64	47.52 N	11.01 E
Wesson	194	31.42 N	90.23 W
Wessum	52	52.05 N	6.58 E
West, Ms., U.S.	194	33.11 N	89.46 W
West, Tx., U.S.	222	31.48 N	97.05 W
West ≐, N.Y., U.S.	210	42.41 N	77.22 W
West ≐, Vt., U.S.	188	42.52 N	72.33 W
West Abington	207	42.05 N	70.58 W
Westacres	216	42.35 N	83.26 W
West Acton	207	42.28 N	71.28 W
West Alexander	214	40.06 N	80.31 W
West Alexandria	218	39.44 N	84.31 W
Westall, Point >	162	32.55 S	134.04 E
West Allen ≐	44	54.55 N	2.19 W
West Allis	216	43.01 N	88.00 W
Westalton	219	38.51 N	90.13 W
West Amityville	276	40.41 N	73.26 W
West Andover	207	42.39 N	71.09 W
West Athens	280	33.55 N	118.18 W
West Atlantic City	208	39.23 N	74.28 W
West Babylon	210	40.43 N	73.21 W
Westbahnhof ✦[5]	264b	48.11 N	16.20 E
West Baines ≐	164	15.36 S	129.58 E
West Bangor	210	40.52 N	75.14 W
Westbank	182	49.50 N	119.38 W
West Bank □[9]	132	31.40 N	35.15 E
West Barnstable	207	41.42 N	70.22 W
West Barrington	207	41.44 N	71.20 W
West Bay, N.S., Can.	186	45.43 N	61.10 W
Westbay, Fl., U.S.	194	30.17 N	85.52 W
West Bay c, Fl., U.S.	194	30.16 N	85.47 W
West Bay c, Tx., U.S.	222	29.15 N	94.57 W
West Bay Shore	276	40.42 N	73.16 W
West Belmar	208	40.10 N	74.02 W
West Bend, Ia., U.S.	198	42.57 N	94.26 W
West Bend, Wi., U.S.	190	43.25 N	88.11 W
West Bengal □[3]	124	24.00 N	88.00 E
West Bergholt	42	51.55 N	0.51 E
West Berlin	208	39.48 N	74.56 W
West Bernard Creek ≐	222	29.23 N	95.58 W
Westbevern	52	52.01 N	7.47 E
West Bhāgīrath Plain ≚	126	23.30 N	88.00 E
West Bijou Creek ≐	198	39.51 N	104.08 W
West Billerica	283	42.33 N	71.19 W
West Blocton	194	33.07 N	87.07 W
West Bloomfield	210	42.54 N	77.32 W
West Bolivar	214	40.23 N	79.10 W
Westborough	207	42.16 N	71.37 W
Westbourne	184	50.09 N	98.35 W
West Bow Creek ≐	198	42.46 N	97.08 W
West Boxford	283	42.42 N	71.04 W
West Boylston	207	42.22 N	71.47 W
West Bradenton	220	27.30 N	82.37 W
West Branch, Ia., U.S.	190	41.40 N	91.20 W
West Branch, Mi., U.S.	190	44.16 N	84.14 W
West Branch Reservoir ⊜[1]	210	41.25 N	73.42 W
West Branch State Park ♦	214	41.07 N	81.05 W
Westbridge	182	49.10 N	118.59 W
West Bridgewater	207	42.01 N	71.00 W
West Bridgford	42	52.56 N	1.08 W
West Bristol	285	40.06 N	74.53 W
West Bromwich	42	52.31 N	1.56 W
Westbrook, Austl.	171a	27.36 S	151.52 E
Westbrook, On., Can.	212	44.16 N	76.38 W
Westbrook, Ct., U.S.	207	41.17 N	72.26 W
Westbrook, Me., U.S.	188	43.40 N	70.22 W
Westbrook, Mn., U.S.	198	44.02 N	95.26 W
Westbrook, Tx., U.S.	196	32.21 N	101.01 W
West Brook ≐	276	41.04 N	74.18 W
West Brookfield	207	42.14 N	72.08 W
Westbrookville	210	41.30 N	74.34 W
West Burlington, Ia., U.S.	190	40.49 N	91.09 W
West Burlington, N.Y., U.S.	210	42.42 N	75.11 W
West Burra I	46a	60.05 N	1.21 W
Westbury, Eng., U.K.	42	52.41 N	2.57 W
Westbury, Eng., U.K.	42	51.16 N	2.11 W
Westbury, N.Y., U.S.	276	40.45 N	73.35 W
Westbury-on-Severn	42	51.50 N	2.24 W
West Butte ʌ	202	48.57 N	111.32 W
Westby, Austl.	171b	35.30 S	147.25 E
Westby, Mt., U.S.	198	48.52 N	104.03 W
Westby, Wi., U.S.	190	43.39 N	90.51 W
West Cache Creek ≐	196	34.13 N	98.23 W
West Caicos I	238	21.39 N	72.28 W
West Calder	46	55.52 N	3.35 W
West Caldwell	276	40.50 N	74.18 W
West Cameron	208	41.06 N	75.15 W
West Camp	210	42.07 N	73.56 W
West Canada Creek ≐	188	43.01 N	74.58 W
West Cape >	172	45.54 S	166.26 E
West Cape Howe >	162	35.08 S	117.36 E
West Cape May	208	38.56 N	74.56 W
West Carlisle	196	33.35 N	101.56 W
West Caroline Basin ✤[1]	14	4.00 N	138.00 E
West Carrollton	218	39.40 N	84.15 W
West Carson	280	33.57 N	118.23 W
West Carthage	212	43.58 N	75.36 W

Symbols in the index entries represent the broad categories identified in the key at the right. Symbols with superior numbers (⋏[1]) identify subcategories (see complete key on page I · 1).

Symbole im Register stellen die rechts im Schlüssel erklärten Kategorien dar. Symbole mit hochgestellten Ziffern (⋏[1]) bezeichnen Unterabteilungen einer Kategorie (vgl. vollständiger Schlüssel auf Seite I · 1).

Los símbolos incluidos en el texto del índice representan las grandes categorías identificadas con la clave a la derecha. Los símbolos con numeros en su parte superior (⋏[1]) identifican las subcategorías (véase la clave completa en la página I · 1).

Les symboles de l'index représentent les catégories indiquées dans la légende à droite. Les symboles suivis d'un indice (⋏[1]) représentent des sous-catégories (voir légende complète à la page I · 1).

Os símbolos incluídos no texto do índice representam as grandes categorias identificadas com a chave à direita. Os símbolos com números em sua parte superior (⋏[1]) identificam as subcategorias (veja-se a chave completa na página I · 1).

Symbol	English	Deutsch	Español	Français	Português
ʌ	Mountain	Berg	Montaña	Montagne	Montanha
⋏	Mountains	Gebirge	Montañas	Montagnes	Montanhas
✕	Pass	Paß	Paso	Col	Passo
V	Valley, Canyon	Tal, Cañon	Valle, Cañón	Vallée, Canyon	Vale, Canhão
≚	Plain	Ebene	Llano	Plaine	Planície
>	Cape	Kap	Cabo	Cap	Cabo
I	Island	Insel	Isla	Île	Ilha
II	Islands	Inseln	Islas	Îles	Ilhas
⊥	Other Topographic Features	Andere Topographische Objekte	Otros Elementos Topográficos	Autres données topographiques	Outros acidentes topográficos

West-Whit I · 191

ESPAÑOL — Nombre | Página | Lat.°′ | Long.°′ W = Oeste
FRANÇAIS — Nom | Page | Lat.°′ | Long.°′ W = Ouest
PORTUGUÊS — Nome | Página | Lat.°′ | Long.°′ W = Oeste

West Catfish Creek ≃ 212 42.46 N 81.04 W
West Channel ≃[1] 180 68.51 N 136.10 W
West Chelmsford 283 42.37 N 71.23 W
Westchester, Il., U.S. 216 41.51 N 87.52 W
West Chester, Pa., U.S. 208 39.57 N 75.36 W
Westchester, Va., U.S. 284c 38.51 N 77.16 W
Westchester □[6] 210 41.02 N 73.46 W
Westchester ◆[8], Ca., U.S. 280 33.55 N 118.25 W
Westchester ◆[8], N.Y., U.S. 276 40.51 N 73.52 W
West Chester Airport ⊠ 285 39.59 N 75.35 W
Westchester County Airport ⊠ 207 41.04 N 73.43 W
Westchester Creek ≃ 276 40.48 N 73.51 W
Westchester Estates 284c 38.47 N 76.55 W
Westchester Station 186 45.37 N 63.40 W
West Chester University of Pennsylvania ⚲[2] 285 39.57 N 75.36 W
West Chicago 216 41.53 N 88.12 W
West Clandon 260 51.15 N 0.30 W
West Clarksville 210 42.08 N 78.15 W
West Clear Creek ≃ 200 34.34 N 111.51 W
West Cleddau ≃ 42 51.46 N 4.54 W
Westcliffe 200 38.08 N 105.27 W
Westcliffe ◆[8] 273d 26.11 S 28.02 E
Westcliff-on-Sea 260 51.32 N 0.41 E
West College Corner 218 39.34 N 84.48 W
West Collingswood Heights 285 39.59 N 75.07 W
West Columbia, S.C., U.S. 192 33.59 N 81.04 W
West Columbia, Tx., U.S. 222 29.08 N 95.38 W
West Concord, Ma., U.S. 207 42.27 N 71.23 W
West Concord, Mn., U.S. 190 44.09 N 92.53 W
West Conshohocken 285 40.04 N 75.19 W
West Cote Blanche Bay ⊂ 194 29.40 N 91.45 W
Westcott 260 51.13 N 0.22 W
Westcott Cove ⊂ 276 41.02 N 73.30 W
West Covina 228 34.04 N 117.56 W
West Creek 208 39.38 N 74.18 W
West Creek ≃, In., U.S. 216 41.12 N 87.30 W
West Creek ≃, Pa., U.S. 214 41.30 N 78.15 W
Westdale, Ma., U.S. 283 42.01 N 70.59 W
Westdale, N.Y., U.S. 210 43.23 N 75.49 W
West Danby 210 42.19 N 76.32 W
West Davenport 210 42.27 N 74.58 W
West Deane Park ♠ 275b 43.40 N 79.34 W
West Decatur 214 40.56 N 78.17 W
West Delaware Aqueduct ≊[1] 210 41.52 N 74.31 W
Westdene ◆[8] 273d 26.11 S 27.59 E
West Dennis 207 41.39 N 70.10 W
West Derby ◆[8] 262 53.26 N 2.54 W
West Derry 214 40.20 N 79.20 W
West Des Moines 190 41.34 N 93.42 W
West Ditch ≊ 276 40.56 N 74.19 W
West Dolores ≃ 200 37.35 N 108.21 W
West Drayton ◆[8] 260 51.30 N 0.29 W
West Duffins Creek ≃ 212 43.51 N 79.04 W
West Duxbury 283 42.03 N 70.47 W
West Easton 210 40.41 N 75.14 W
West Eaton 210 42.51 N 75.39 W
Westecunk Creek ≃ 208 39.37 N 74.16 W
West Edmeston 210 42.46 N 75.17 W
West Edmondale 284b 39.18 N 76.43 W
West Elizabeth 279b 40.17 N 79.54 W
West Elk Mountains ⋏ 200 38.40 N 107.15 W
West Elk Peak ∧ 200 38.43 N 107.13 W
West Elkton 218 39.35 N 84.33 W
West Ellicott 214 42.05 N 79.16 W
West Elmira 210 42.04 N 76.50 W
West End, Ba. 238 26.41 N 78.58 W
West End, Eng., U.K. 260 51.44 N 0.04 W
West End, Eng., U.K. 260 51.20 N 0.38 W
West End, Ar., U.S. 194 34.13 N 92.03 W
West End, Il., U.S. 216 42.17 N 89.09 W
West End, N.Y., U.S. 210 42.28 N 75.05 W
West End, N.C., U.S. 192 35.14 N 79.34 W
West End ◆[8], Eng., U.K. 260 51.32 N 0.24 W
West End ◆[8], Pa., U.S. 279b 40.27 N 80.02 W
Westende, Bel. 50 51.10 N 2.46 E
Westende, Dtsch. 263 51.25 N 7.24 E
Westendorf 64 47.26 N 12.13 E
Westenfeld ◆[8] 263 51.28 N 7.09 E
Westenholz 52 51.45 N 8.28 E
Westenschouwen 52 51.41 N 3.42 E
Westerbauer ◆[8] 263 51.20 N 7.23 E
Westerblokker 52 52.39 N 5.08 E
Westerbönen 263 51.36 N 7.46 E
Westerbork 52 52.51 N 6.37 E
Westerburg 56 50.33 N 7.58 E
Westercelle 52 52.36 N 10.05 E
Westerdale 46 58.27 N 3.30 W
Westeregeln 54 51.57 N 11.23 E
Westerham 42 51.16 N 0.05 E
Westerhausen 54 51.48 N 11.03 E
Westerholt 52 51.36 N 7.05 E
Westerholz ◆[3] 263 51.32 N 7.28 E
Westerkappeln 52 52.18 N 7.52 E
Westerland 30 54.54 N 8.18 E
Westerlo, Bel. 56 51.05 N 4.55 E
Westerlo, N.Y., U.S. 210 42.31 N 74.03 W
Westerly 207 41.22 N 71.49 W
Western 198 40.23 N 97.11 W
Western □[4], Ghana 150 5.30 N 2.30 W
Western □[4], Kenya 154 0.30 N 34.35 E
Western □[4], Sol.Is. 175e 8.00 S 157.00 E
Western □[4], Zam. 152 16.00 S 24.00 E
Western □[5], Pap. N. Gui. 164 7.00 S 142.00 E
Western □[5], Ug. 154 1.00 N 31.00 E
Western ≃ 166 22.22 S 142.25 E
Western Area □[4] 150 8.20 N 13.00 W
Western Australia □[3] 160 25.00 S 122.00 E
Western Branch ≃ 284c 38.55 N 76.48 W
Western Canal ≊ 226 39.28 N 121.35 W
Western Channel ʮ 98 34.40 N 129.00 E
Western Cove ⊂ 168b 35.43 S 137.38 E
Western Desert → Gharbīyah, Aṣ-Ṣaḥrā' al- ◆[2] 140 27.00 N 27.00 E
Western Division □[5] 175g 18.00 S 177.30 E
Western Ghāts ⋏ 122 14.00 N 75.00 E
Western Highlands □[5] 164 5.45 S 144.30 E
Western Isles □[4] 46 57.40 N 7.00 W
Westernport 188 39.29 N 79.02 W
Western Port ⊂ 169 38.22 S 145.20 E
Western Port Bay ⊂ 169 38.15 S 145.20 E
Western Sahara □[2], Afr. 134 24.30 N 13.00 W
Western Sahara □[2], Afr. 148 24.30 N 13.00 W
Western Samoa □[1], Oc. 14 13.55 S 172.00 W
Western Samoa □[1], Oc. 175a 13.55 S 172.00 W
Western Sayans → Zapadnyj Sajan ⋏ 74 53.00 N 94.00 E
Western Shore 186 44.32 N 64.19 W
Western Springs 278 41.48 N 87.54 W
Westernville 210 43.18 N 75.23 W
Westerschelde ⊂[1] 52 51.25 N 3.45 E
Westerstede 52 53.15 N 7.55 E
Westervelt 219 39.29 N 88.52 W
Westerville 214 40.07 N 82.55 W
Westerwald ⋏ 56 50.40 N 7.55 E
West European Basin ✢[1] 10 47.00 N 15.00 W
West Exeter 210 42.48 N 75.09 W
West Fairview 208 40.16 N 76.54 W
Westfalen □[9] 52 51.50 N 7.30 E
Westfalenhalle ⚲ 263 51.30 N 7.27 E
West Falkland I 254 51.50 S 60.00 W
West Falls 210 42.42 N 78.41 W
West Falmouth 207 41.36 N 70.38 W
West Fargo 198 46.52 N 96.54 W
West Farleigh 260 51.15 N 0.27 E
West Farmington 214 41.23 N 80.58 W
Westfield, Eng., U.K. 42 50.55 N 0.35 E
Westfield, Il., U.S. 194 39.27 N 88.01 W
Westfield, In., U.S. 218 40.02 N 86.07 W
Westfield, Ma., U.S. 207 42.07 N 72.45 W
Westfield, N.J., U.S. 210 40.39 N 74.20 W
Westfield, N.Y., U.S. 214 42.19 N 79.34 W
Westfield, Pa., U.S. 210 41.55 N 77.32 W
Westfield, Tx., U.S. 222 30.01 N 95.24 W
Westfield, Wi., U.S. 190 43.53 N 89.29 W
Westfield ≃ 207 42.05 N 72.35 W
Westfield, Middle Branch ≃ 207 42.16 N 72.52 W
Westfield, West Branch ≃ 207 42.13 N 72.52 W
Westfield Center 214 41.01 N 81.55 W
West Fiord ⊂[2] 176 76.02 N 90.00 W
Westford, Ma., U.S. 283 42.34 N 71.26 W
Westford, N.Y., U.S. 210 42.39 N 74.48 W
West Fork 194 35.55 N 94.11 W
West Foxboro 283 42.05 N 71.17 W
West Frankfort 194 37.53 N 88.55 W
West Friesland ◆[1] 52 52.45 N 4.50 E
West Frisian Islands → Waddeneilanden II 52 53.26 N 5.30 E
West Fulton 210 42.34 N 74.28 W
Westgate, Austl. 166 26.35 S 146.12 E
Westgate, Mi., U.S. 216 43.03 N 85.42 W
Westgate on Sea 42 51.23 N 1.21 E
West Genesee Terrace 210 43.03 N 76.16 W
West-Ghats → Western Ghāts ⋏ 122 14.00 N 75.00 E
West Gilgo Beach 276 40.37 N 73.25 W
West Glacier 202 48.29 N 113.58 W
West Glamorgan □[6] 42 51.35 N 3.35 W
West Glens Falls 210 43.18 N 73.43 W
West Glenville 210 42.56 N 74.04 W
West Goshen 207 41.49 N 73.15 W
West Granby 207 41.57 N 72.50 W
West Grand Lake ⊜ 188 45.15 N 67.50 W
West Groton 207 42.36 N 71.37 W
West Grove 208 39.49 N 75.49 W
Westham 208 37.35 N 77.32 W
West Ham ◆[8] 260 51.31 N 0.01 E
West Hamburg 208 40.33 N 76.00 W
West Ham Football Club ♠ 260 51.32 N 0.02 E
Westham Island I 224 49.05 N 123.10 W
West Hamlin 188 38.17 N 82.11 W
Westhampton, N.Y., U.S. 207 40.49 N 72.39 W
Westhampton, Va., U.S. 284c 38.54 N 77.11 W
West Hanningfield 260 51.40 N 0.30 E
West Hanover 283 42.07 N 70.53 W
West Harbor ⊂ 276 40.54 N 73.32 W
West Harrison 218 39.15 N 84.49 W
West Hartford 207 41.45 N 72.44 W
West Hartland 207 42.00 N 72.58 W
Westhausen 56 48.53 N 10.11 E
Westhaven, Ca., U.S. 204 41.03 N 124.06 W
West Haven, Ct., U.S. 207 41.16 N 72.57 W
Westhaven, Il., U.S. 278 41.35 N 87.51 W
West Haverstraw 210 41.12 N 73.59 W
West Hazleton 210 40.57 N 75.59 W
Westhead 262 53.34 N 2.51 W
West Hebron 210 43.14 N 73.22 W
West Heidelberg 274b 37.45 S 145.02 E
Westheim 56 49.03 N 9.44 E
West Helena 194 34.33 N 90.38 W
Westhemmerde 263 51.33 N 7.47 E
West Hempstead 276 40.42 N 73.39 W
West Henrietta 210 43.02 N 77.40 W
West Hickory 214 41.34 N 79.25 W
Westhill 46 57.09 N 2.17 W
West Hill ◆[8] 275b 43.46 N 79.11 W
Westhofen 263 51.25 N 7.31 E
Westhoff 222 29.12 N 97.28 W
Westhoffen 58 48.36 N 7.26 E
West Hollywood, Ca., U.S. 228 34.05 N 118.21 W
West Hollywood, Fl., U.S. 220 26.01 N 80.10 W
Westholme 224 49.52 N 123.42 W
West Homestead 279b 40.24 N 79.55 W
Westhope, N.D., U.S. 198 48.54 N 101.01 W
Westhope, Oh., U.S. 216 41.18 N 83.57 W
West Horndon 260 51.34 N 0.21 E
West Horsley 260 51.16 N 0.27 W
Westhoughton 262 53.33 N 2.32 W
West Hoxton 274a 33.55 S 150.49 E
West Humber ≃ 212 43.44 N 79.33 W
West Humble 260 51.15 N 0.20 W
West Huntington 276 40.42 N 73.18 W
West Hurley 210 42.00 N 74.06 W
Westhuyzen 158 27.30 S 25.27 E
West Hyde 260 51.37 N 0.30 W
West Ice Shelf ⍓ 9 67.00 S 85.00 E
Westick 263 51.35 N 7.38 E
Westig 263 51.22 N 7.45 E
West Indies II 230 19.00 N 70.00 W
Westindische Inseln → West Indies II 230 19.00 N 70.00 W
West Irian → Irian Jaya □[4] 164 5.00 S 138.00 E
West Island I, Austl. 164 15.36 S 136.34 E
West Island I, Ma., U.S. 207 41.36 N 70.50 W
West Islip 210 40.42 N 73.18 W
West Jan Mayen Ridge ✢[3] 10 71.00 N 13.00 W
West Jefferson, N.C., U.S. 192 36.24 N 81.29 W
West Jefferson, Oh., U.S. 218 39.56 N 83.16 W
West Jordan 200 40.36 N 111.56 W
Westkapelle, Bel. 50 51.19 N 3.18 E
Westkapelle, Ned. 52 51.32 N 3.27 E
West Keansburg 276 40.27 N 74.09 W
West Kettle ≃ 182 49.07 N 119.00 W
West Kilbride 46 55.42 N 4.51 W
West Kill 210 42.13 N 74.31 W
West Kingsdown 42 51.21 N 0.17 E
West Kingston 207 41.28 N 71.33 W
West Kirby 44 53.22 N 3.10 W
Westkirchen 52 51.53 N 8.02 E
West Kittanning 214 40.49 N 79.32 W
West Lafayette, In., U.S. 216 40.25 N 86.54 W
West Lafayette, Oh., U.S. 214 40.16 N 81.45 W
Westlake, La., U.S. 194 30.15 N 93.15 W
Westlake, Oh., U.S. 214 41.27 N 81.55 W
Westlake, Tx., U.S. 222 32.59 N 97.12 W
West Lake ⊜, On., Can. 212 43.56 N 77.17 W
West Lake ⊜, Fl., U.S. 220 25.12 N 80.49 W
West Lake ⊜, N.J., U.S. 276 40.58 N 74.22 W
West Lamma Channel ʮ 271d 22.13 N 114.04 E
West Lancashire □[8] 262 53.35 N 2.50 W
Westland, Mi., U.S. 216 42.19 N 83.24 W
Westland, Pa., U.S. 214 40.17 N 80.16 W
Westland Center ◆[9] 281 42.20 N 83.23 W
Westland National Park ♠ 172 43.30 S 170.10 E
Westlands 207 42.37 N 71.20 W
West Lanham Hills 284c 38.57 N 76.53 W
West Laramie 200 41.18 N 105.37 W
West Lawn 284c 38.52 N 77.11 W
West Lebanon, In., U.S. 216 40.16 N 87.23 W
West Lebanon, Pa., U.S. 214 40.35 N 79.22 W
West Leechburg 214 40.37 N 79.37 W
Westleigh, S. Afr. 158 27.31 S 27.21 E
Westleigh, Eng., U.K. 262 53.30 N 2.31 W
West Leipsic 216 41.07 N 84.00 W
Westley 226 37.33 N 121.12 W
West Leyden 212 43.28 N 75.28 W
West Liberty, Ia., U.S. 190 41.34 N 91.15 W
West Liberty, Ky., U.S. 192 37.55 N 83.15 W
West Liberty, Oh., U.S. 216 40.15 N 83.45 W
West Liberty, Pa., U.S. 214 41.00 N 80.03 W
West Liberty, W.V., U.S. 214 40.10 N 80.35 W
West Liberty ◆[8] 279b 40.24 N 80.01 W
Westliche Sahara → Western Sahara □[2] 148 24.30 N 13.00 W
Westliche Sierra Madre → Madre Occidental, Sierra ⋏ 232 25.00 N 105.00 W
Westline 214 41.47 N 78.46 W
West Linn 224 45.21 N 122.36 W
West Linton 46 55.46 N 3.22 W
West Little Owyhee ≃ 202 42.28 N 117.15 W
Westlock 182 54.09 N 113.52 W
West Lorne 214 42.36 N 81.36 W
West Los Angeles ◆[8] 280 34.03 N 118.28 W
West Lulworth 42 50.38 N 2.15 W
West Lunga ≃ 154 13.06 S 24.39 E
West Lunga National Park ♠ 154 12.55 S 25.10 E
Westmalle 52 51.18 N 4.41 E
West Malling 42 51.18 N 0.25 E
West Malling Aerodrome ⊠ 260 51.16 N 0.24 E
West Manayunk 285 40.01 N 75.14 W
West Manchester 218 39.54 N 84.37 W
West Mansfield, Ma., U.S. 207 41.59 N 71.14 W
West Mansfield, Oh., U.S. 216 40.24 N 83.32 W
West Mariana Basin ✢[1] 14 15.00 N 137.00 E
West Mayfield 214 40.47 N 80.20 W
West Meadowview 216 41.08 N 87.52 W
Westmeath □[6] 48 53.30 N 7.30 W
West Medway 207 42.08 N 71.25 W
West Melbourne 220 28.04 N 80.39 W
West Memphis 194 35.08 N 90.11 W
West Meon 42 51.01 N 1.05 W
Westmere 210 42.41 N 73.52 W
West Mersea 42 51.47 N 0.55 E
West Miami 220 25.45 N 80.17 W
West Middlesex 214 41.10 N 80.27 W
West Middletown 214 40.15 N 80.25 W
West Midlands □[6] 42 52.30 N 2.00 W
West Mifflin 214 40.22 N 79.52 W
West Milford 210 41.07 N 74.22 W
West Millbury 207 42.11 N 71.48 W
West Mill Creek ≃ 222 29.55 N 96.17 W
West Milton, Oh., U.S. 218 39.57 N 84.19 W
West Milton, Pa., U.S. 210 41.01 N 76.52 W
West Milwaukee 216 43.00 N 87.58 W
West Mineola 222 32.41 N 95.31 W
Westminster, Ca., U.S. 228 33.45 N 118.02 W
Westminster, Co., U.S. 200 39.50 N 105.02 W
Westminster, Md., U.S. 208 39.34 N 76.59 W
Westminster, Ma., U.S. 207 42.32 N 71.54 W
Westminster, Oh., U.S. 216 40.42 N 83.58 W
Westminster, S.C., U.S. 192 34.39 N 83.05 W
Westminster ◆[8] 260 51.30 N 0.09 W
Westminster Abbey ⚲[1] 260 51.30 N 0.07 W
Westminster Mall ◆[9] 280 33.45 N 118.01 W
West Modesto 226 37.37 N 121.02 W
West Monroe 194 32.31 N 92.08 W
Westmont, Ca., U.S. 280 33.56 N 118.18 W
Westmont, Il., U.S. 278 41.47 N 87.58 W
Westmont, N.J., U.S. 285 39.54 N 75.02 W
Westmont, Pa., U.S. 214 40.18 N 78.57 W
West Monterey 214 41.03 N 79.39 W
West Montreal ≃ 190 47.56 N 80.39 W
West Moors 42 50.49 N 1.55 W
Westmoreland, Ks., U.S. 198 39.23 N 96.24 W
Westmoreland, N.Y., U.S. 210 43.07 N 75.24 W
Westmoreland, Tn., U.S. 194 36.33 N 86.14 W
Westmoreland, Va., U.S. 208 38.04 N 76.34 W
Westmoreland □[6], Pa., U.S. 214 40.18 N 79.33 W
Westmoreland □[6], Va., U.S. 208 38.10 N 76.50 W
Westmoreland City 214 40.20 N 79.41 W
Westmoreland State Park ♠ 208 38.09 N 76.50 W
Westmorland 204 33.02 N 115.37 W
Westmount 206 45.29 N 73.36 W
West Mountain ∧ 188 43.51 N 74.43 W
West Mud Creek ≃ 222 32.07 N 95.10 W
West Mustang Creek ≃ 222 29.04 N 96.26 W
West Nab ∧ 262 53.35 N 1.53 W
West Nanticoke 210 40.13 N 76.01 W
West New Britain □[5] 164 5.45 S 149.30 E
West Newbury 207 42.48 N 70.59 W
West Newton, Ma., U.S. 283 42.21 N 71.14 W
West Newton, Pa., U.S. 214 40.12 N 79.46 W
West New York 276 40.47 N 74.00 W
West Nicholson 154 21.06 S 29.25 E
West Nishnabotna ≃ 198 40.39 N 95.37 W
West Nodaway ≃ 194 40.38 N 95.01 W
West Norriton 208 40.08 N 75.22 W
West Norwood ◆[8] 260 51.26 N 0.06 W
West Novaya Zemlya Trough ✢[1] 10 73.30 N 50.00 E
West Nueces ≃ 196 29.16 N 99.56 W
West Nyack 210 41.06 N 73.58 W
West Okaw ≃ 219 39.32 N 88.42 W
Weston, Austl. 170 32.49 S 151.28 E
Weston, Malay. 112 5.13 N 115.36 E
Weston, Eng., U.K. 262 53.19 N 2.44 W
Weston, Co., U.S. 200 37.07 N 104.50 W
Weston, Ct., U.S. 207 41.12 N 73.22 W
Weston, Id., U.S. 202 42.02 N 111.58 W
Weston, Ma., U.S. 207 42.22 N 71.18 W
Weston, Mi., U.S. 216 41.46 N 84.06 W
Weston, Mo., U.S. 194 39.24 N 94.54 W
Weston, Ne., U.S. 198 41.11 N 96.44 W
Weston, Oh., U.S. 216 41.20 N 83.47 W
Weston, Or., U.S. 202 45.48 N 118.25 W
Weston, Pa., U.S. 210 40.57 N 76.09 W
Weston, W.V., U.S. 188 39.02 N 80.28 W
Weston □[8] 275b 43.43 N 79.31 W
Westonaria 273d 26.19 S 27.39 E
West Oneonta 210 42.28 N 75.07 W
Westönnen 52 51.33 N 7.58 E
Weston Reservoir ⊜[1] 283 42.21 N 71.18 W
Westons Mill Pond ⊜ 276 40.28 N 74.25 W
Westons Mills 210 42.04 N 78.23 W
Weston-super-Mare 42 51.21 N 2.59 W
Weston upon Trent 42 52.45 N 2.02 W
West Orange, N.J., U.S. 276 40.47 N 74.14 W
West Orange, Tx., U.S. 194 30.05 N 93.46 W
Westover, Md., U.S. 208 38.07 N 75.42 W
Westover, Pa., U.S. 214 40.45 N 78.40 W
Westover, Tn., U.S. 194 35.36 N 88.52 W
Westover, W.V., U.S. 188 39.38 N 79.58 W
Westover Air Force Base ■ 207 42.12 N 72.33 W
Westoverledingen 52 53.10 N 7.28 E
Westowne 284b 39.17 N 76.43 W
West Palm Beach 220 26.42 N 80.03 W
West Palm Beach Canal ≊ 220 26.38 N 80.03 W
West Paris 188 44.19 N 70.34 W
West Park 210 41.48 N 73.58 W
West Paterson 276 40.53 N 74.11 W
West Pawlet 210 43.21 N 73.15 W
West Peckham 260 51.15 N 0.22 E
West Pensacola 194 30.25 N 87.16 W
Westphalia, Ks., U.S. 198 38.10 N 95.29 W
Westphalia, Mi., U.S. 216 42.55 N 84.47 W
Westphalia, Mo., U.S. 219 38.26 N 91.59 W
West Pittsburg, Ca., U.S. 226 38.01 N 121.56 W
West Pittsburg, Pa., U.S. 214 40.55 N 80.21 W
West Pittston 210 41.19 N 75.47 W
West Plains 194 36.43 N 91.51 W
West Point, Ca., U.S. 226 38.23 N 120.31 W
West Point, Ga., U.S. 192 32.52 N 85.11 W
Westpoint, In., U.S. 216 40.21 N 87.03 W
West Point, Ia., U.S. 190 40.43 N 91.27 W
West Point, Ky., U.S. 194 37.59 N 85.56 W
West Point, Ms., U.S. 194 33.36 N 88.39 W
West Point, Ne., U.S. 198 41.50 N 96.42 W
West Point, N.Y., U.S. 210 41.23 N 73.57 W
West Point, Oh., U.S. 214 40.43 N 80.42 W
West Point, Pa., U.S. 285 40.12 N 75.18 W
West Point, Va., U.S. 208 37.31 N 76.47 W
West Point ∧ 180 64.57 N 144.40 W
West Point ›, Austl. 166 35.01 S 135.57 E
West Point ›, P.E., Can. 186 46.37 N 64.25 W
West Point Lake ⊜[1] 192 33.00 N 85.10 W
West Pond ⊜ 276 40.53 N 73.38 W
Westport, Nf., Can. 186 49.47 N 56.38 W
Westport, N.S., Can. 186 44.16 N 66.21 W
Westport, On., Can. 212 44.41 N 76.26 W
Westport, Ire. 48 53.48 N 9.32 W
Westport, N.Z. 172 41.45 S 171.36 E
Westport, Ct., U.S. 207 41.08 N 73.21 W
Westport, In., U.S. 218 39.10 N 85.34 W
Westport, Ky., U.S. 218 38.28 N 85.28 W
Westport, Ma., U.S. 207 41.37 N 71.04 W
Westport, Or., U.S. 224 46.07 N 123.22 W
Westport, Pa., U.S. 214 41.18 N 77.51 W
Westport, Wa., U.S. 224 46.53 N 124.06 W
West Portland 224 45.25 N 122.45 W
West Portland Park 224 45.21 N 122.37 W
Westport Point 207 41.31 N 71.04 W
West Portsmouth 218 38.45 N 83.01 W
West Prairie ≃ 182 55.30 N 116.31 W
West Puente Valley 280 34.04 N 117.59 W
West Pullman ◆[8] 278 41.41 N 87.39 W
Westpunt › 241s 12.37 N 70.03 W
West Pymble 274a 33.46 S 151.08 E
West Quoddy Head › 188 44.49 N 66.57 W
West Rand 273d 26.07 S 27.45 E
Westray I 46 59.18 N 3.00 W
Westray Firth ʮ 46 59.12 N 2.55 W
West Redding 207 41.19 N 73.26 W
Westrem 50 50.58 N 3.52 E
Westrich ◆[1] 56 49.15 N 7.20 E
West Richfield 214 41.14 N 81.39 W
West Richland 202 46.18 N 119.20 W
West River ⊥ 208 38.52 N 76.31 W
West Road ≃ 182 53.19 N 122.52 W
West Rosebud Creek ≃ 202 45.29 N 109.27 W
West Roxbury ◆[8] 283 42.17 N 71.09 W
West Rupert 210 43.14 N 73.14 W
West Rutland 188 43.35 N 73.02 W
West Ryde 274a 33.48 S 151.05 E
West Sacramento 226 38.34 N 121.31 W
West Saint Marys ≃ 186 45.15 N 62.04 W
West Saint Modeste 186 51.36 N 56.42 W
West Salem, Il., U.S. 194 38.31 N 88.00 W
West Salem, Oh., U.S. 214 40.58 N 82.06 W
West Salem, Wi., U.S. 190 43.53 N 91.04 W
West Salt Creek ≃ 200 39.13 N 108.54 W
Westsamoa → Western Samoa □[1] 175a 13.55 S 172.00 W
West Sand Lake 210 42.39 N 73.37 W
West Saugerties 210 42.07 N 74.03 W
West Sayville 276 40.43 N 73.05 W
West Sayville County Park ♠ 276 40.43 N 73.06 W
West Scenic Park 220 27.55 N 81.39 W
West Scotia Basin ✢[1] 18 57.00 S 53.00 W
West Seneca 210 42.50 N 78.45 W
West Sepik □[5] 164 4.00 S 141.30 E
West Shoal Lake ⊜ 184 50.20 N 97.41 W
West Siberian Plain → Zapadno-Sibirskaja ravnina ⩸ 72 60.00 N 75.00 E
Westsibirisches Flachland → Zapadno-Sibirskaja ravnina ⩸ 72 60.00 N 75.00 E
West Side Canal ≊ 226 35.19 N 119.23 W
West Side Tennis Club ♠ 276 40.43 N 73.51 W
West Simsbury 207 41.52 N 72.51 W
West Slope 224 45.29 N 122.45 W
West Spanish Peak ∧ 200 37.23 N 104.59 W
West Springfield, Ma., U.S. 207 42.06 N 72.37 W
West Springfield, Pa., U.S. 214 41.57 N 80.29 W
West Springfield, Va., U.S. 208 38.46 N 77.13 W
West Stewartstown 206 44.59 N 71.31 W
West Stockbridge 207 42.20 N 73.22 W
West Stony Creek ≃ 210 43.15 N 74.13 W
West Suffield 207 41.59 N 72.41 W
West Sunbury 214 41.00 N 79.54 W
West Sussex □[5] 42 50.55 N 0.35 W
West Swanzey 207 42.52 N 72.20 W
West Terre Haute 194 39.27 N 87.27 W
West-Terschelling 52 53.21 N 5.13 E
West Thompson Lake ⊜[1] 207 41.57 N 71.54 W
West Thurrock 260 51.29 N 0.16 E
West Tiana 207 40.52 N 72.33 W
West Tilbury 260 51.29 N 0.24 E
West Tisbury 207 41.22 N 70.40 W
West Toodyay 168a 31.33 S 116.27 E
West Torrens 168b 34.56 S 138.32 E
Westtown, N.Y., U.S. 210 41.20 N 74.32 W
Westtown, Pa., U.S. 285 39.56 N 75.33 W
West Townsend 207 42.40 N 71.44 W
West Turffontein ◆[8] 273d 26.16 S 28.02 E
West Union, Ia., U.S. 190 42.57 N 91.48 W
West Union, Oh., U.S. 218 38.47 N 83.32 W
West Union, W.V., U.S. 188 39.17 N 80.46 W
West Union Creek ≃ 282 37.25 N 122.16 W
West Unity 216 41.35 N 84.26 W
West University Place 222 29.43 N 95.26 W
West Upton 207 42.10 N 71.37 W
Westvale 210 43.02 N 76.13 W
West Valley, Mt., U.S. 202 46.08 N 113.01 W
West Valley, N.Y., U.S. 210 42.24 N 78.37 W
West Valley City 200 40.42 N 111.57 W
West Vancouver 182 49.22 N 123.12 W
West View 214 40.31 N 80.02 W
West View Amusement Park ♠ 279b 40.31 N 80.02 W
Westview Heights 207 41.33 N 73.05 W
Westville, N.S., Can. 186 45.34 N 62.43 W
Westville, In., U.S. 216 41.32 N 86.54 W
Westville, N.H., U.S. 207 42.49 N 71.07 W
Westville, N.J., U.S. 285 39.52 N 75.07 W
Westville, Oh., U.S. 218 40.07 N 83.51 W
Westville, Ok., U.S. 194 35.59 N 94.34 W
Westville, Pa., U.S. 214 41.13 N 78.50 W
Westville Center 206 44.57 N 74.24 W
Westville Grove 285 39.51 N 75.07 W
Westville Lake ⊜[1] 207 42.05 N 72.05 W
Westville Oaks 285 39.51 N 75.08 W
West Virginia □[3], U.S. 178 38.45 N 80.30 W
West Virginia □[3], U.S. 188 38.45 N 80.30 W
West-Vlaanderen □[4] 50 51.00 N 3.00 E
West Walker ≃ 226 38.53 N 119.10 W
West Wallsend 170 32.54 S 151.35 E
Westward Ho90 42 51.02 N 4.15 W
West Wareham 207 41.47 N 70.45 W
West Warren 207 42.12 N 72.14 W
West Warwick 207 41.42 N 71.31 W
West Water ≃ 46 56.47 N 2.38 W
West Webster 210 43.12 N 77.29 W
Westwego 194 29.54 N 90.08 W
West Wellow 42 50.58 N 1.35 W
West Whittier 280 33.59 N 118.03 W
West Wickham ◆[8] 260 51.22 N 0.01 W
West Willington 207 41.52 N 72.18 W
West Willow 216 42.14 N 83.34 W
West Windsor 210 42.06 N 74.46 W
West Winfield, N.Y., U.S. 210 42.53 N 75.11 W
West Winfield, Pa., U.S. 214 40.48 N 79.42 W
Westwold 182 50.28 N 119.45 W
Westwood, Ca., U.S. 204 40.18 N 121.00 W
Westwood, In., U.S. 218 39.55 N 85.25 W
Westwood, Ma., U.S. 207 42.12 N 71.14 W
Westwood, Mi., U.S. 216 42.13 N 85.38 W
Westwood, N.J., U.S. 210 40.59 N 74.01 W
Westwood, Pa., U.S. 214 40.13 N 78.56 W
Westwood ◆[8] 280 34.04 N 118.27 W
Westwood Lakes 220 25.44 N 80.22 W
Westworth Village 222 32.45 N 97.25 W
West Wyalong 166 33.55 S 147.13 E
West Wycombe 42 51.39 N 0.49 W
West Yarmouth 207 41.39 N 70.14 W
West Yegua Creek ≃ 222 30.20 N 96.52 W
West Yellow Creek ≃ 194 39.38 N 93.04 W
West Yellowstone 202 44.39 N 111.06 W
West York 208 39.57 N 76.45 W
West Yorkshire □[6] 44 53.45 N 1.40 W
Wetan, Pulau I 164 7.54 S 129.32 E
Wetar, Pulau I 112 7.48 S 126.18 E
Wetar, Selat ʮ 112 8.20 S 126.30 E
Wetaskiwin 182 52.58 N 113.22 W
Wete 154 5.04 S 39.43 E
Wethau 54 51.08 N 11.52 E
Wetherby 44 53.56 N 1.23 W
Wetherill Park 274a 33.51 S 150.54 E
Wethersfield 207 41.43 N 72.40 W
Wethmar 263 51.37 N 7.33 E
Wetiko Hills ⋏[2] 184 54.30 N 92.20 W
Wetluga → Vetluga ≃ 80 56.18 N 46.24 E
Wetmore 198 39.38 N 95.48 W
Wet Mountains ⋏ 200 38.00 N 105.10 W
Weto 152 7.57 N 7.50 E
Wetten 52 51.34 N 6.17 E
Wetter, Dtsch. 56 50.54 N 8.43 E
Wetter, Dtsch. 56 51.23 N 7.23 E
Wetter ≃ 56 50.18 N 8.49 E
Wetterau ◆[1] 56 50.15 N 8.50 E
Wetteren 50 51.00 N 3.53 E
Wetterhorn ∧ 58 46.39 N 8.08 E
Wetterstein Gebirge ⋏ 64 47.25 N 11.05 E
Wettigan 110 18.57 N 95.21 E
Wettin 54 51.35 N 11.48 E
Wettingen 58 47.28 N 8.19 E
Wettringen 52 52.12 N 7.19 E
Wetumka 196 35.14 N 96.14 W
Wetumpka 194 32.32 N 86.12 W
Wetwang 44 54.01 N 0.34 W
Wetzikon 58 47.19 N 8.47 E
Wetzlar 56 50.33 N 8.29 E
Wetzstein ∧[2] 54 50.27 N 11.27 E
Wevelgem 50 50.48 N 3.10 E
Wevelinghoven 56 51.06 N 6.37 E
Wewahitchka 192 30.06 N 85.12 W
Wewak 164 3.35 S 143.40 E
Wewelsfleth 52 53.50 N 9.24 E
Wewer 52 51.41 N 8.42 E
Wewoka 196 35.09 N 96.29 W
Wexford, Ire. 48 52.20 N 6.27 W
Wexford, Pa., U.S. 214 40.38 N 80.03 W
Wexford □[6] 48 52.20 N 6.40 W
Wexford ◆[8] 275b 43.45 N 79.18 W
Wexford Harbour ⊂ 48 52.20 N 6.24 W
Wey ≃ 42 51.23 N 0.28 W
Weyakwin Lake ⊜ 184 54.30 N 106.00 W
Weyanoke 284c 38.48 N 77.09 W
Weyarn 64 47.51 N 11.48 E
Weyauwega 190 44.19 N 88.56 W
Weybridge 42 51.23 N 0.28 W
Weyburn 184 49.41 N 103.52 W
Weyer ◆[8] 263 51.10 N 7.01 E
Weyer Markt 61 47.52 N 14.41 E
Weyersheim 56 48.43 N 7.48 E
Weyhausen 52 52.47 N 10.23 E
Weyhe 52 52.59 N 8.52 E
Weymouth, N.S., Can. 186 44.25 N 66.00 W
Weymouth, Eng., U.K. 42 50.36 N 2.28 W
Weymouth, Ma., U.S. 207 42.13 N 70.56 W
Weymouth, N.J., U.S. 208 39.30 N 74.46 W
Weymouth, Cape › 164 12.37 S 143.27 E
Weymouth Back ≃ 283 42.15 N 70.55 W
Weymouth Fore ≃ 283 42.16 N 70.56 W
Weymouth Great Pond ⊜ 283 42.12 N 71.02 W
Wezemaal 56 50.57 N 4.46 E
Wezep 52 52.27 N 6.00 E
Whakatane 172 37.58 S 177.00 E
Whakatane ≃ 172 37.57 S 177.00 E
Whalan 274a 33.45 S 150.49 E
Whale Creek ≃ 276 40.27 N 74.13 W
Whaley Bridge 44 53.20 N 1.59 W
Whaley Lake 210 41.33 N 73.40 W
Whaleysville 208 38.23 N 75.18 W
Whaleyville 208 36.37 N 76.41 W
Whalley 44 53.50 N 2.24 W
Whalom 207 42.34 N 71.44 W
Whalsay I 46a 60.20 N 0.59 W
Whangaehu ≃ 172 40.03 S 175.06 E
Whangamata 172 37.12 S 175.52 E
Whangamomona 172 39.09 S 174.44 E
Whanganui National Park ♠ 172 39.20 S 175.00 E
Whangara 172 38.34 S 178.13 E
Whangarei 172 35.43 S 174.19 E
Whangaruru Harbour ⊂ 172 35.22 S 174.21 E
Whaplode 42 52.48 N 0.02 W
Wharfe ≃ 44 53.51 N 1.07 W
Wharfedale V 44 54.01 N 1.56 W
Wharles 262 53.49 N 2.50 W
Wharton, N.J., U.S. 210 40.53 N 74.34 W
Wharton, Oh., U.S. 214 40.52 N 83.21 W
Wharton, Tx., U.S. 222 29.18 N 96.06 W
Wharton, W.V., U.S. 188 37.54 N 81.40 W
Wharton □[6] 222 29.17 N 96.13 W
Wharton Basin ✢[1] 12 21.00 S 100.00 E
Wharton Lake ⊜ 176 64.00 N 99.55 W
Wharton State Forest ♠ 285 39.45 N 74.40 W
Whataroa 172 43.17 S 170.25 E
Whatatutu 172 38.23 S 177.50 E
What Cheer 190 41.24 N 92.21 W
Whatcom □[6] 224 48.48 N 121.59 W
Whatcom, Lake ⊜ 224 48.43 N 122.20 W
Whately 207 42.26 N 72.38 W
Whatley 194 31.39 N 87.42 W
Whatshan Lake ⊜ 182 50.00 N 118.03 W
Whauphill 44 54.49 N 4.29 W
Wheao ≃ 172 38.34 S 176.39 E
Wheatfield 216 40.33 N 87.06 W
Wheatland, Ca., U.S. 226 39.00 N 121.25 W
Wheatland, Ia., U.S. 190 41.49 N 90.50 W
Wheatland, Pa., U.S. 214 41.12 N 80.28 W
Wheatland, Wy., U.S. 200 42.03 N 104.57 W
Wheatland Hills 208 40.02 N 76.21 W
Wheatland Reservoir ⊜[1] 200 41.52 N 105.36 W
Wheatley, On., Can. 214 42.06 N 82.27 W
Wheatley, Eng., U.K. 42 51.44 N 1.08 W
Wheatley, Ar., U.S. 194 34.54 N 91.06 W
Wheatley Hill 44 54.45 N 1.23 W
Wheaton, Il., U.S. 216 41.51 N 88.06 W
Wheaton, Md., U.S. 208 39.02 N 77.03 W
Wheaton, Mn., U.S. 198 45.48 N 96.29 W
Wheaton Plaza ◆[9] 284c 39.02 N 77.03 W
Wheaton Regional Park ♠ 284c 39.03 N 77.02 W
Wheat Ridge 200 39.45 N 105.04 W
Wheelbarrow Peak ∧ 204 37.27 N 116.05 W
Wheeler, In., U.S. 216 41.30 N 87.10 W
Wheeler, Ms., U.S. 194 34.34 N 88.36 W
Wheeler, Tx., U.S. 196 35.26 N 100.16 W
Wheeler ≃, P.Q., Can. 176 57.02 N 67.13 W
Wheeler ≃, Sk., Can. 184 57.20 N 105.30 W
Wheeler Air Force Base ■ 229c 21.29 N 158.03 W
Wheeler Dam ◆[6] 283 42.48 N 71.12 W
Wheeler Island I 282 38.05 N 121.56 W
Wheeler Lake ⊜[1] 194 34.40 N 87.05 W
Wheeler Peak ∧, Ca., U.S. 226 38.25 N 119.17 W
Wheeler Peak ∧, Nv., U.S. 204 38.59 N 114.19 W
Wheeler Peak ∧ N.M., U.S. 200 36.34 N 105.25 W
Wheeler Ridge 228 35.06 N 119.01 W
Wheelersburg 218 38.43 N 82.51 W
Wheelers Hill 274b 37.55 S 145.11 E
Wheeling, Il., U.S. 216 42.08 N 87.55 W
Wheeling, W.V., U.S. 214 40.03 N 80.43 W
Wheeling Creek ≃ 214 40.03 N 80.41 W
Wheelock 222 30.54 N 96.24 W
Wheelock ≃ 44 53.12 N 2.26 W
Wheelton 262 53.41 N 2.36 W
Wheelwright, Arg. 252 33.47 S 61.13 W
Wheelwright, Ky., U.S. 192 37.19 N 82.43 W
Wheelwright Park ♠ 283 42.15 N 70.49 W
Wheeny Creek ≃ 170 33.26 S 150.50 E
Whela Creek ≃ 162 26.17 S 116.50 E
Whelan, Mount ∧[2] 166 23.25 S 138.54 E
Whelpleyhill 260 51.44 N 0.33 W
Whernside ∧ 44 54.14 N 2.23 W
Whetstone Creek ≃ 214 40.23 N 83.03 W
Whetstone Gulf State Park ♠ 212 43.44 N 75.27 W
Whickham 44 54.56 N 1.41 W
Whidbey Island I 224 48.15 N 122.40 W
Whidbey Island Naval Air Station ■ 224 48.17 N 122.37 W
Whiddon Down 42 50.43 N 3.51 W
Whigham 192 30.52 N 84.19 W
Whigville 207 41.43 N 72.56 W
Whim Creek 162 20.50 S 117.50 E
Whinham, Mount ∧ 162 26.04 S 130.15 E
Whippany 210 40.49 N 74.25 W
Whippany ≃ 276 40.51 N 74.21 W
Whirl Creek ≃ 212 43.28 N 81.12 W
Whirlwind Reefs ✢[2] 164 4.42 S 148.16 E
Whiskey Peak ∧ 200 42.18 N 107.35 W
Whiskeytown-Shasta-Trinity National Recreation Area ♠ 204 40.45 N 122.15 W
Whisky Chitto Creek ≃ 194 30.31 N 92.55 W
Whiston 262 53.25 N 2.50 W
Whitacres 207 41.48 N 72.39 W
Whitaker 279b 40.24 N 79.53 W
Whitakers 192 36.06 N 77.42 W
Whitbourne 186 47.25 N 53.32 W
Whitburn, Eng., U.K. 44 54.57 N 1.22 W
Whitburn, Scot., U.K. 46 55.52 N 3.42 W
Whitby, On., Can. 212 43.52 N 78.56 W
Whitby, Eng., U.K. 44 54.29 N 0.37 W
Whitby, Eng., U.K. 262 53.17 N 2.54 W
Whitby Abbey ⚲[1] 44 54.28 N 0.38 W
Whitchurch, Eng., U.K. 42 51.53 N 0.51 W
Whitchurch, Eng., U.K. 42 51.14 N 1.20 W
Whitchurch, Eng., U.K. 42 51.52 N 2.39 W
Whitchurch, Eng., U.K. 42 52.58 N 2.41 W
Whitchurch-Stouffville 212 43.58 N 79.15 W
Whitcombe, Mount ∧ 172 43.13 S 170.55 E
White, Ga., U.S. 192 34.16 N 84.44 W
White, S.D., U.S. 198 44.26 N 96.38 W
White □[6] 216 40.45 N 86.46 W
White ≃, B.C., Can. 182 50.23 N 115.35 W
White ≃, On., Can. 190 48.33 N 86.16 W
White ≃, N.A. 180 63.11 N 139.36 W
White ≃, U.S. 194 33.53 N 91.03 W
White ≃, U.S. 198 43.45 N 99.30 W
White ≃, U.S. 200 40.04 N 109.41 W
White ≃, Az., U.S. 200 33.44 N 110.13 W
White ≃, In., U.S. 194 38.25 N 87.44 W
White ≃, Mi., U.S. 190 43.25 N 86.21 W
White ≃, Nv., U.S. 204 37.42 N 115.10 W
White ≃, Or., U.S. 224 45.14 N 121.04 W
White ≃, Tx., U.S. 196 33.14 N 100.56 W
White ≃, Vt., U.S. 188 43.37 N 72.20 W
White ≃, Wa., U.S. 224 47.12 N 122.15 W
White ≃, Wa., U.S. 224 47.50 N 120.49 W
White ≃, Wi., U.S. 190 46.36 N 90.42 W
White ≃, Wi., U.S. 216 42.41 N 88.17 W
White, East Fork ≃, Az., U.S. 200 33.47 N 110.00 W
White, East Fork ≃, In., U.S. 194 38.33 N 87.14 W
White, Lake ⊜ 162 21.05 S 129.00 E
White, Lake ⊜[1] 218 39.07 N 83.02 W

Symbol	English	Deutsch	Español	Français	Português
≃	River	Fluß	Río	Rivière	Rio
≊	Canal	Kanal	Canal	Canal	Canal
∟	Waterfall, Rapids	Wasserfall, Stromschnellen	Cascada, Rápidos	Chute d'eau, Rapides	Cascata, Rápidos
ʮ	Strait	Meeresstraße	Estrecho	Détroit	Estreito
⊂	Bay, Gulf	Bucht, Golf	Bahía, Golfo	Baie, Golfe	Baía, Golfo
⊜	Lake, Lakes	See, Seen	Lago, Lagos	Lac, Lacs	Lago, Lagos
⩸	Swamp	Sumpf	Pantano	Marais	Pântano
⍓	Ice Features, Glacier	Eis- und Gletscherformen	Accidentes Glaciales	Formes glaciaires	Acidentes glaciares
⍑	Other Hydrographic Features	Andere Hydrographische Objekte	Otros Elementos Hidrográficos	Autres données hydrographiques	Outros acidentes hidrográficos
✢	Submarine Features	Untermeerische Objekte	Accidentes Submarinos	Formes de relief sous-marin	Acidentes submarinos
□	Political Unit	Politische Einheit	Unidad Politica	Entité politique	Unidade política
⚲	Cultural Institution	Kulturelle Institution	Institución Cultural	Institution culturelle	Instituição cultural
⊥	Historical Site	Historische Stätte	Sitio Histórico	Site historique	Sitio histórico
♠	Recreational Site	Erholungs- und Ferienort	Sitio de Recreo	Centre de loisirs	Area de Lazer
⊠	Airport	Flughafen	Aeropuerto	Aéroport	Aeroporto
■	Military Installation	Militäranlage	Instalación Militar	Installation militaire	Instalação militar
◆	Miscellaneous	Verschiedenes	Misceláneo	Divers	Diversos

I · 192 Whit-Will

ENGLISH / DEUTSCH

Name	Page	Lat.°'	Long.°'
White, North Fork ≃, Az., U.S.	200	33.47 N	110.00 W
White, North Fork ≃, Co., U.S.	200	39.58 N	107.38 W
White, South Fork ≃	200	39.58 N	107.38 W
White, West Fork ≃	224	47.07 N	121.37 W
White Bay c	186	50.00 N	56.30 W
White Bear Indian Reserve ◆4	184	49.45 N	102.15 W
White Bear Lake	190	45.03 N	93.00 W
Whitebear Lake ⊜	184	51.05 N	108.05 W
White Bluff	194	36.06 N	87.13 W
White Breast Creek ≃	190	41.24 N	93.02 W
White Butte ∧	198	46.23 N	103.19 W
Whitecap Lake ⊜	184	56.54 N	95.14 W
White Cap Mountain ∧	188	45.35 N	69.13 W
White Castle	194	30.10 N	91.08 W
White Center	224	47.31 N	122.21 W
White Chuck ≃	224	48.11 N	121.27 W
White City, Fl., U.S.	220	29.53 N	85.13 W
White City, Ks., U.S.	198	38.47 N	96.44 W
White City Stadium ♦	260	51.31 N	0.14 W
White Clay Creek ≃, U.S.	198	43.12 N	102.48 W
White Clay Creek ≃, U.S.	285	39.42 N	75.37 W
White Cliffs, Austl.	162	28.26 S	122.57 E
White Cliffs, Austl.	166	30.51 S	143.05 E
White Cloud	190	43.33 N	85.46 W
White Cloud Island I	212	44.50 N	80.58 W
Whitecoomb ∧, N.Z.	172	45.36 S	169.05 E
White Coomb ∧, Scot., U.K.	44	55.26 N	3.20 W
Whitecourt	182	54.09 N	115.41 W
White Creek	210	42.58 N	73.18 W
White Creek ≃, In., U.S.	218	38.58 N	86.01 W
White Creek ≃, Wa., U.S.	224	46.01 N	121.08 W
White Deer, Pa., U.S.	210	41.05 N	76.52 W
White Deer, Tx., U.S.	196	35.26 N	101.10 W
White Deer Creek ≃	210	41.05 N	76.53 W
White Earth ≃	198	48.09 N	102.42 W
White Earth Indian Reservation ◆4	198	47.18 N	95.50 W
White Esk ≃	44	55.12 N	3.10 W
Whiteface	196	33.36 N	102.37 W
Whiteface ≃	190	46.58 N	92.48 W
Whiteface Mountain ∧	188	44.22 N	73.54 W
Whitefield, Eng., U.K.	44	53.33 N	2.18 W
Whitefield, N.H., U.S.	188	44.22 N	71.36 W
Whitefish	202	48.24 N	114.20 W
Whitefish ≃	190	45.55 N	86.57 W
Whitefish Bay	216	43.06 N	87.54 W
Whitefish Bay c, On., Can.	184	49.26 N	94.14 W
Whitefish Bay c, N.A.	190	46.40 N	84.50 W
Whitefish Lake ⊜, Ab., Can.	182	54.22 N	111.55 W
Whitefish Lake ⊜, Mb., Can.	184	55.34 N	93.13 W
Whitefish Lake ⊜, N.T., Can.	176	62.41 N	106.48 W
Whitefish Lake ⊜, On., Can.	190	48.03 N	84.29 W
Whitefish Lake ⊜, On., Can.	212	45.18 N	79.47 W
Whitefish Lake ⊜, On., Can.	212	44.31 N	76.14 W
Whitefish Lake ⊜, Ak., U.S.	180	61.21 N	160.00 W
Whitefish Lake ⊜, Mt., U.S.	202	48.27 N	114.22 W
White Fish Lake Indian Reserve ◆4	182	54.20 N	111.45 W
Whitefish Point	190	46.45 N	84.59 W
Whitefish Point >	190	46.45 N	85.00 W
Whitefish Range ⋏	202	48.40 N	114.26 W
Whiteford	208	39.42 N	76.20 W
Whiteford Point >	42	51.38 N	4.14 W
White Fox	184	53.27 N	104.05 W
White Fox ≃	184	53.32 N	104.00 W
Whitegate	48	51.50 N	8.14 W
White Gull Creek ≃	184	53.44 N	104.20 W
Whitehall (Paulstown), Ire.	48	52.41 N	7.01 W
Whitehall, Scot., U.K.	46	59.07 N	2.37 W
White Hall, Ar., U.S.	194	34.16 N	92.05 W
White Hall, Il., U.S.	219	39.26 N	90.24 W
White Hall, Md., U.S.	208	39.37 N	76.37 W
Whitehall, Mi., U.S.	190	43.24 N	86.20 W
Whitehall, Mt., U.S.	202	45.52 N	112.05 W
Whitehall, N.Y., U.S.	188	43.33 N	73.24 W
Whitehall, Oh., U.S.	218	39.58 N	82.53 W
Whitehall, Pa., U.S.	214	40.21 N	79.59 W
Whitehall, Wi., U.S.	190	44.22 N	91.18 W
Whitehaven, Eng., U.K.	44	54.33 N	3.35 W
White Haven, Pa., U.S.	210	41.03 N	75.46 W
Whitehead	48	54.46 N	5.43 W
White Holme Reservoir ⊜1	262	53.41 N	2.02 W
Whitehorse, Yk., Can.	180	60.43 N	135.03 W
White Horse, N.J., U.S.	208	40.11 N	74.42 W
White Horse, Vale of V	42	51.37 N	1.37 W
Whitehorse Hill ∧2	42	51.34 N	1.34 W
Whitehouse, Scot., U.K.	46	57.13 N	2.37 W
Whitehouse, N.J., U.S.	210	40.37 N	74.46 W
Whitehouse, Oh., U.S.	216	41.31 N	83.48 W
White House, Tn., U.S.	194	36.35 N	86.49 W
Whitehouse, Tx., U.S.	222	32.13 N	95.14 W
White House ⊍	284c	38.54 N	77.02 W
White House Station	210	40.36 N	74.46 W
White Island I, Ant.	9	66.44 S	48.35 E
White Island I, N.T., Can.	176	65.50 N	84.50 W
White Island I, N.Z.	172	37.31 S	177.11 E
White Lake, Mi., U.S.	281	42.41 N	83.33 W
White Lake, N.Y., U.S.	210	41.40 N	74.50 W
White Lake, S.D., U.S.	198	43.43 N	98.42 W
White Lake, Wi., U.S.	190	45.09 N	88.45 W
White Lake ⊜, On., Can.	190	48.48 N	85.36 W
White Lake ⊜, On., Can.	212	44.47 N	76.45 W
White Lake ⊜, On., Can.	212	45.18 N	76.31 W
White Lake ⊜, On., Can.	212	44.27 N	77.03 W
White Lake ⊜, La., U.S.	194	29.45 N	92.30 W
White Lake ⊜, Mi., U.S.	281	42.40 N	83.34 W
Whiteland	218	39.33 N	86.05 W
Whitelaw	182	56.07 N	118.04 W
Whiteley Village	260	51.21 N	0.26 W
White Lick Creek ≃	218	39.30 N	86.23 W
White Lick Creek, East Fork ≃	218	39.35 N	86.22 W
White Lick Creek, West Fork ≃	218	39.38 N	86.23 W
Whiteman Air Force Base ■	194	38.44 N	93.34 W
Whiteman Airpark ⊠	280	34.15 N	118.25 W
Whiteman Range ⋏	164	5.50 S	149.55 E
Whitemans Creek ≃	212	43.10 N	80.21 W
Whitemark	166	40.07 S	148.01 E
White Marsh	284b	39.23 N	76.26 W
Whitemarsh Run ≃	284b	39.22 N	76.25 W
White Meadow Lake	210	40.55 N	74.31 W
White Meadow Lake ⊜	276	40.55 N	74.31 W
White Mills	210	41.32 N	75.12 W
White Mountain	180	64.41 N	163.24 W
White Mountain Peak ∧	204	37.38 N	118.15 W
White Mountains ⋏, U.S.	204	37.30 N	118.15 W
White Mountains ⋏, Az., U.S.	200	33.45 N	109.40 W
White Mountains ⋏, N.H., U.S.	188	44.10 N	71.35 W
Whitemouth	184	49.57 N	95.59 W
Whitemouth ≃	184	50.07 N	96.02 W
Whitemouth Lake ⊜	184	49.14 N	95.40 W
Whitemud ≃	184	50.15 N	98.37 W
Whiten Head >	46	58.34 N	4.36 W
White Nile (Al-Baḥr al-Abyaḍ) ≃	140	15.38 N	32.31 E
White Nile Dam → Jabal al-Awliyā', Khazzān ◆6	140	15.14 N	32.29 E
White Oak, Md., U.S.	284c	39.02 N	77.00 W
White Oak, Pa., U.S.	279b	40.20 N	79.48 W
White Oak, Tx., U.S.	222	32.32 N	94.52 W
White Oak ≃	192	34.40 N	77.07 W
White Oak Creek ≃, Oh., U.S.	218	38.47 N	83.57 W
White Oak Creek ≃, Tx., U.S.	194	33.16 N	94.39 W
White Oak Creek, East Fork ≃	218	39.00 N	83.53 W
White Oak Creek, North Fork ≃	218	39.00 N	83.53 W
White Oak Lake ⊜1	194	33.40 N	93.10 W
White Oak Regional Park ♦	279a	40.21 N	79.47 W
White Pass)(, N.A.	180	59.38 N	135.05 W
White Pass)(, Wa., U.S.	224	46.38 N	121.24 W
White Pigeon	216	41.47 N	85.38 W
White Pine, Mi., U.S.	190	46.45 N	89.35 W
Whitepine, Mt., U.S.	182	47.45 N	115.29 W
White Pine, Tn., U.S.	192	36.06 N	83.17 W
White Pines, Ca., U.S.	226	38.18 N	120.21 W
White Pines, Il., U.S.	278	41.57 N	87.57 W
White Plains, Md., U.S.	208	38.35 N	76.56 W
White Plains, N.Y., U.S.	210	41.02 N	73.45 W
White Plains, N.C., U.S.	192	36.26 N	80.38 W
White Pond ⊜	283	42.26 N	71.23 W
White River, On., Can.	190	48.35 N	85.15 W
Whiteriver, Az., U.S.	200	33.50 N	109.57 W
White River, S.D., U.S.	198	43.34 N	100.44 W
White River Junction	188	43.38 N	72.19 W
White Rock	224	49.02 N	122.49 W
White Rock Creek ≃, Ks., U.S.	198	39.55 N	97.51 W
White Rock Creek ≃, Tx., U.S.	222	30.54 N	95.16 W
White Rock Creek ≃, Tx., U.S.	222	32.43 N	96.44 W
White Rock Lake ⊜1	222	32.50 N	96.44 W
White Rocks ∧	192	36.40 N	83.27 W
Whiterocks ≃	200	40.26 N	109.55 W
White Roding	260	51.48 N	0.16 E
White Russia → Belarus □1	22	53.50 N	28.00 E
Whitesail Lake ⊜	182	53.30 N	127.00 W
White Salmon	224	45.43 N	121.29 W
White Salmon ≃	224	45.43 N	121.31 W
Whitesand ≃	184	51.34 N	101.55 W
White Sands Beach	207	41.18 N	72.09 W
White Sands Missile Range ■	200	32.23 N	106.28 W
White Sands National Monument ♦	200	32.46 N	106.20 W
Whitesboro, N.J., U.S.	208	39.02 N	74.51 W
Whitesboro, N.Y., U.S.	210	43.07 N	75.17 W
Whitesboro, Tx., U.S.	196	33.39 N	96.54 W
Whitesburg	192	37.07 N	82.49 W
White Sea → Beloje more ⩪2	24	65.30 N	38.00 E
White Settlement	222	32.45 N	97.27 W
Whiteshell Provincial Park ♦	184	50.00 N	95.25 W
Whiteside	219	39.11 N	91.01 W
Whiteside, Canal ⊔	254	53.55 S	70.15 W
White's Landing	214	41.25 N	82.54 W
White Springs	192	30.19 N	82.45 W
White Stone	208	37.38 N	76.23 W
Whitestone ◆8	276	40.47 N	73.49 W
White Stone Lake ⊜	184	56.25 N	97.31 W
Whitestown	218	39.59 N	86.20 W
White Sulphur Springs, Mt., U.S.	202	46.32 N	110.54 W
White Sulphur Springs, N.Y., U.S.	210	41.48 N	74.50 W
White Sulphur Springs, W.V., U.S.	192	37.47 N	80.17 W
Whites Valley	210	41.42 N	75.22 W
Whitesville, Ky., U.S.	194	37.40 N	86.52 W
Whitesville, N.Y., U.S.	210	42.02 N	77.45 W
Whitesville, W.V., U.S.	188	37.58 N	81.31 W
White Swan	224	46.22 N	120.43 W
Whiteswan Lakes ⊜	184	54.05 N	105.10 W
Whitevale	212	43.53 N	79.09 W
White Valley	214	40.25 N	79.36 W
Whiteville, N.C., U.S.	192	34.20 N	78.42 W
Whiteville, Tn., U.S.	194	35.19 N	89.08 W
White Volta (Volta Blanche) ≃	150	9.10 N	1.15 W
Whitewater, Ks., U.S.	198	37.57 N	97.08 W
Whitewater, Mt., U.S.	202	48.45 N	107.37 W
Whitewater, Wi., U.S.	216	42.50 N	88.43 W
Whitewater ≃, U.S.	218	39.10 N	84.47 W
Whitewater ≃, Ca., U.S.	204	33.30 N	116.03 W
Whitewater ≃, Mo., U.S.	194	37.01 N	89.43 W
Whitewater, Dry Fork ≃	218	39.11 N	84.47 W
Whitewater, East Fork ≃	218	39.24 N	85.01 W
Whitewater Baldy ∧	200	33.20 N	108.39 W
Whitewater Bay c	220	25.16 N	81.00 W
Whitewater Creek ≃, N.A.	202	48.30 N	107.11 W
Whitewater Creek ≃, Ga., U.S.	192	32.21 N	84.03 W
Whitewater Creek ≃, Wi., U.S.	216	42.52 N	88.45 W
Whitewater Lake ⊜, Mb., Can.	184	49.15 N	100.20 W
Whitewater Lake ⊜, Wi., U.S.	216	42.47 N	88.42 W
Whitewater State Park ♦	218	39.36 N	84.58 W
White Woman Creek ≃	198	38.25 N	100.54 W
Whitewood, Austl.	166	21.28 S	143.36 E
Whitewood, Sk., Can.	184	50.20 N	102.15 W
Whitewood, S.D., U.S.	198	44.27 N	103.38 W
Whitewood, Lake ⊜	198	44.20 N	97.18 W
Whitewright	196	33.30 N	96.23 W
Whitfield	42	51.09 N	1.18 E
Whithorn, Jam.	241q	18.15 N	78.02 W
Whithorn, Scot., U.K.	44	54.44 N	4.25 W
Whitianga	172	36.50 S	175.42 E
Whiting, In., U.S.	216	41.40 N	87.29 W
Whiting, Ia., U.S.	198	42.07 N	96.08 W
Whiting, Ks., U.S.	198	39.35 N	95.36 W
Whiting, N.J., U.S.	208	39.57 N	74.22 W
Whiting, Wi., U.S.	190	44.29 N	89.33 W
Whiting Bay	46	55.29 N	5.06 W
Whiting Field Naval Air Station ■	194	30.43 N	87.02 W
Whitingham	207	42.47 N	72.53 W
Whitinsville	207	42.06 N	71.40 W
Whitland	42	51.50 N	4.37 W
Whitley □6	216	41.10 N	85.29 W
Whitley Bay	44	55.03 N	1.25 W
Whitley City	192	36.43 N	84.28 W
Whitley Row	260	51.15 N	0.09 E
Whitman	207	42.04 N	70.56 W
Whitman Mission National Historic Site ⊥	202	46.01 N	118.30 W
Whitmans Pond ⊜	283	42.12 N	70.57 W
Whitman Square	208	39.45 N	75.03 W
Whitmire	192	34.30 N	81.36 W
Whitmore Lake	216	42.25 N	83.46 W
Whitmore Lake ⊜	281	42.26 N	83.45 W
Whitmore Mountains ⋏	9	82.35 S	104.30 W
Whitmore Village	229c	21.30 N	158.01 W
Whitner Heights	226	36.37 N	119.32 W
Whitney, On., Can.	212	45.30 N	78.14 W
Whitney, Pa., U.S.	214	40.15 N	79.24 W
Whitney, Tx., U.S.	222	31.57 N	97.19 W
Whitney, Lake ⊜1	222	31.55 N	97.23 W
Whitney, Mount ∧	204	36.35 N	118.18 W
Whitney Point	210	42.19 N	75.58 W
Whitney Point Lake ⊜1	210	42.25 N	75.55 W
Whitney Woods Reservation ♦	283	42.13 N	70.51 W
Whitstable	42	51.22 N	1.02 E
Whitsunday Island I	166	20.17 S	148.59 E
Whittaker	216	42.08 N	83.36 W
Whittemore, Ia., U.S.	198	43.03 N	94.25 W
Whittemore, Mi., U.S.	190	44.14 N	83.48 W
Whittier, Ak., U.S.	180	60.47 N	148.42 W
Whittier, Ca., U.S.	228	33.58 N	118.01 W
Whittier, N.C., U.S.	192	35.26 N	83.22 W
Whittier Narrows Dam ◆6	280	34.01 N	118.04 W
Whittier Narrows Flood Control Basin ⊜1	280	34.02 N	118.04 W
Whittingham	44	55.24 N	1.54 W
Whittington	42	52.52 N	3.00 W
Whittle, Cap >	186	50.11 N	60.08 W
Whittle Hill ∧2	262	53.40 N	2.16 W
Whittle-le-Woods	262	53.41 N	2.38 W
Whittlesea, Austl.	169	37.31 S	145.07 E
Whittlesea, Ciskei	158	32.10 S	26.50 E
Whittlesey	42	52.34 N	0.08 W
Whittlesey, Mount ∧2	190	46.18 N	90.37 W
Whitwell	194	35.12 N	85.31 W
Whitwick	42	52.44 N	1.21 W
Whitworth	44	53.40 N	2.10 W
Whitworth Peak ∧	224	49.05 N	121.13 W
Wholdaia Lake ⊜	176	60.43 N	104.10 W
Whonock	224	49.11 N	122.28 W
W. Howard Frankland Bridge ◆5	220	27.56 N	82.35 W
Whyalla	166	33.02 S	137.35 E
Whycocomagh	186	45.59 N	61.07 W
Whymper, Mount ∧	224	48.57 N	124.10 W
Wiang Pa Pao	110	19.22 N	99.30 E
Wiang Phan	110	20.26 N	99.53 E
Wiarton	212	44.45 N	81.09 W
Wiasi	150	10.21 N	1.20 W
Wiau Lake ⊜	182	55.23 N	111.18 W
Wiawso	150	6.12 N	2.29 W
Wiay I	46	57.23 N	7.13 W
Wiązów	30	50.49 N	17.11 E
Wibaux	198	46.59 N	104.11 W
Wiblingen ◆8	58	48.21 N	9.58 E
Wiblingwerde	263	51.18 N	7.37 E
Wichian Buri	110	15.39 N	101.07 E
Wichita	198	37.41 N	97.20 W
Wichita ≃	196	34.07 N	98.10 W
Wichita Falls	196	33.54 N	98.29 W
Wichita Mountains ⋏	196	34.45 N	98.40 W
Wichlinghofen ◆8	263	51.27 N	7.30 E
Wick	46	58.26 N	3.06 W
Wick ≃	46	58.27 N	3.05 W
Wickatunk	276	40.21 N	74.14 W
Wickede	52	51.29 N	7.52 E
Wickede ◆8	263	51.32 N	7.37 E
Wickenburg	200	33.58 N	112.43 W
Wickepin	162	32.46 S	117.30 E
Wicker Memorial Park ♦	278	41.34 N	87.28 W
Wickett	196	31.34 N	102.59 W
Wickford	42	51.38 N	0.31 E
Wickham, Austl.	162	20.31 S	117.08 E
Wickham, P.Q., Can.	206	45.45 N	72.30 W
Wickham, Eng., U.K.	42	50.54 N	1.10 W
Wickham ≃	164	16.22 S	131.06 E
Wickham, Cape >	166	39.36 S	143.57 E
Wickham Bishops	260	51.47 N	0.40 E
Wickham Market	42	52.09 N	1.22 E
Wickiup Reservoir ⊜1	202	43.40 N	121.43 W
Wickliffe, Ky., U.S.	194	36.58 N	89.05 W
Wickliffe, Oh., U.S.	214	41.06 N	80.43 W
Wickliffe, Oh., U.S.	214	41.36 N	81.27 W
Wicklow	48	52.59 N	6.03 W
Wicklow □6	48	53.00 N	6.30 W
Wicklow Head >	48	52.58 N	6.00 W
Wicklow Mountains ⋏	48	53.02 N	6.24 W
Wickrath	56	51.07 N	6.24 E
Wicksteed Lake ⊜	190	46.46 N	79.40 W
Wicomico	208	37.17 N	76.31 W
Wicomico □6	208	38.22 N	75.36 W
Wicomico ≃	208	38.13 N	75.55 W
Wicomico Church	208	37.49 N	76.23 W
Wiconisco	208	40.34 N	76.41 W
Wiconisco Creek ≃	208	40.32 N	76.58 W
Wid ≃	56	51.45 N	0.27 E
Widas ≃	115a	7.30 S	112.08 E
Widden Brook ≃	170	32.32 S	150.22 E
Widdern	56	49.19 N	9.25 E
Widdert ◆8	263	51.08 N	7.04 E
Widdop Reservoir ⊜1	262	53.48 N	2.06 W
Widdrington Station	44	55.15 N	1.36 W
Wide Bay c, Pap. N. Gui.	164	5.05 S	152.05 E
Wide Bay c, Ak., U.S.	180	57.20 N	156.25 W
Widecombe in the Moor	42	50.35 N	3.48 W
Widemouth Bay	42	50.47 N	4.32 W
Widen	188	38.27 N	80.51 W
Widener College ⊍2	285	39.52 N	75.21 W
Wide Open	44	55.03 N	1.38 W
Widerøe, Mount ∧	9	72.08 S	23.30 E
Wide Ruin Wash V	200	35.13 N	109.52 W
Widford	260	51.43 N	0.27 E
Widgeegoara Creek ≃	166	27.30 S	145.55 E
Widgiemooltha	162	31.30 S	121.34 E
Widnes	44	53.22 N	2.44 W
Wi-do I	98	35.36 N	126.17 E
Widodaren	115a	7.25 S	111.14 E
Widuchowa	54	53.10 N	14.25 E
Widur	124	27.55 N	85.10 E
Wiebelskirchen	56	49.22 N	7.11 E
Więcbork	30	53.22 N	17.30 E
Wieck	54	54.06 N	13.26 E
Wied ≃	56	50.26 N	7.27 E
Wieda	54	51.38 N	10.34 E
Wiederitzsch	54	51.24 N	12.22 E
Wiedlisbach	58	47.15 N	7.39 E
Wiefelstede	52	53.15 N	8.07 E
Wiehe	54	51.16 N	11.25 E
Wiehengebirge ⋏	52	52.20 N	8.40 E
Wiehl	56	50.57 N	7.31 E
Wiek	54	54.37 N	13.17 E
Wieleń	30	52.54 N	16.10 E
Wielichowo	30	52.08 N	16.21 E
Wieliczka	30	49.59 N	20.04 E
Wielkopolska ◆1	30	51.50 N	17.20 E
Wielkopolski Park Narodowy ♦	30	52.15 N	16.50 E
Wieluń	30	51.14 N	18.34 E
Wiemelhausen ◆8	263	51.28 N	7.13 E
Wien (Vienna), Öst.	61	48.13 N	16.20 E
Wien (Vienna), Öst.	264b	48.13 N	16.20 E
Wien □3	61	48.12 N	16.22 E
Wien ≃	264b	48.13 N	16.23 E
Wien, Universität ⊍2	264b	48.13 N	16.22 E
Wiener Berg ⋏2	264b	48.10 N	16.22 E
Wienerherberg	264b	48.03 N	16.33 E
Wiener Neudorf	61	48.05 N	16.19 E
Wiener Neustadt	61	47.49 N	16.15 E
Wiener Neustädter Kanal ≚	61	48.05 N	16.22 E
Wienerwald ⋏	61	48.10 N	16.00 E
Wienhausen	52	52.35 N	10.11 E
Wien-Schwechat, Flughafen ⊠	61	48.07 N	16.33 E
Wiepke	54	52.36 N	11.20 E
Wieprz ≃	30	51.34 N	21.49 E
Wieprza ≃	30	54.26 N	16.22 E
Wieprz-Krzna, Kanał ≚	30	51.56 N	22.56 E
Wiera ≃	56	50.55 N	9.10 E
Wierden	52	52.22 N	6.35 E
Wieren	54	52.53 N	10.39 E
Wiergate	194	31.00 N	93.42 W
Wieringermeer ◆1	52	52.45 N	5.00 E
Wieringerwerf	52	52.51 N	5.02 E
Wieruszów	30	51.18 N	18.08 E
Wierzyca ≃	30	53.51 N	18.50 E
Wies	61	46.43 N	15.16 E
Wies ⊍1	58	47.40 N	10.53 E
Wiesa	54	50.36 N	13.01 E
Wiesau	60	49.55 N	12.11 E
Wiesbaden	56	50.05 N	8.14 E
Wiescheid ◆8	263	51.08 N	6.59 E
Wiescherhöfen ◆8	263	51.39 N	7.46 E
Wiese ≃	58	47.35 N	7.35 E
Wiesede	52	53.27 N	7.46 E
Wieselburg	61	48.08 N	15.09 E
Wiesen	58	46.43 N	9.43 E
Wiesenburg	54	52.07 N	12.26 E
Wiesenfeld	56	51.16 N	10.06 E
Wiesensteig	56	48.34 N	9.37 E
Wiesent ≃	60	49.42 N	11.05 E
Wiesentheid	56	49.47 N	10.20 E
Wieseth ≃	56	49.10 N	10.39 E
Wiesloch	56	49.17 N	8.42 E
Wiesmoor	52	53.25 N	7.43 E
Wieting	61	46.52 N	14.32 E
Wietmarschen	52	52.31 N	7.07 E
Wietze	52	52.39 N	9.50 E
Wietzen	52	52.43 N	9.04 E
Wigan	44	53.33 N	2.38 W
Wigan □8	262	53.32 N	2.35 W
Wiggensbach	58	47.44 N	10.14 E
Wigger ≃	58	47.18 N	7.53 E
Wiggington	260	51.47 N	0.38 W
Wiggins, Co., U.S.	198	40.13 N	104.04 W
Wiggins, Ms., U.S.	194	30.51 N	89.08 W
Wiggins Fork ≃	202	43.27 N	109.28 W
Wigglesworth	44	54.01 N	2.17 W
Wight, Isle of I	42	50.40 N	1.20 W
Wigmore, Eng., U.K.	42	52.19 N	2.51 W
Wigmore, Eng., U.K.	260	51.21 N	0.35 E
Wignehies	50	50.01 N	4.00 E
Wigston	42	52.36 N	1.05 W
Wigton	44	54.49 N	3.09 W
Wigtown	44	54.52 N	4.26 W
Wigtown Bay c	44	54.46 N	4.15 W
Wijalpurā	124	26.55 N	85.51 E
Wijchen	52	51.48 N	5.43 E
Wijhe	52	52.24 N	6.07 E
Wijk aan Zee	52	52.29 N	4.35 E
Wijk bij Duurstede	52	51.58 N	5.20 E
Wil	58	47.27 N	9.03 E
Wilbarger Creek ≃	222	30.11 N	97.23 W
Wilber	198	40.28 N	96.57 W
Wilberforce, Austl.	170	33.33 S	150.50 E
Wilberforce, Oh., U.S.	218	39.42 N	83.52 W
Wilberforce Falls L	176	67.07 N	108.47 W
Wilbraham	207	42.07 N	72.25 W
Wilbur	202	47.45 N	118.42 W
Wilburton	196	34.55 N	95.18 W
Wilcannia	166	31.34 S	143.23 E
Wilcock, Península >1	254	50.40 S	74.00 W
Wilcox, Sk., Can.	184	50.07 N	104.44 W
Wilcox, Ne., U.S.	198	40.21 N	99.10 W
Wilcox, Pa., U.S.	214	41.34 N	78.41 W
Wilcox, Tx., U.S.	222	30.27 N	96.22 W
Wilcox, Mount ∧	207	42.13 N	73.16 W
Wildalpen	61	47.39 N	14.59 E
Wildau	54	52.19 N	13.38 E
Wildbad im Schwarzwald	56	48.45 N	8.32 E
Wildberg, Dtsch.	54	52.52 N	12.37 E
Wildberg, Dtsch.	56	48.37 N	8.44 E
Wildboarclough	262	53.13 N	2.02 W
Wildcat Canyon Regional Park ♦	282	37.56 N	122.17 W
Wildcat Creek ≃, Ca., U.S.	282	37.57 N	122.23 W
Wildcat Creek ≃, In., U.S.	216	40.28 N	86.52 W
Wildcat Creek, Middle Fork ≃	216	40.25 N	86.46 W
Wildcat Creek, South Fork ≃	216	40.26 N	86.48 W
Wildcat Hill ∧2	184	53.17 N	102.30 W
Wild Coast ⊥2	158	32.30 S	28.45 E
Wilde ◆8	288	34.42 S	58.20 W
Wildegg	58	47.25 N	8.11 E
Wildeman ≃	164	5.33 S	139.13 E
Wildemann	52	51.49 N	10.17 E
Wildenbruch	264a	52.17 N	13.04 E
Wildenfels	54	50.40 N	12.35 E
Wildenstein	58	47.59 N	6.58 E
Wildenthal	54	50.27 N	12.37 E
Wilder	202	43.40 N	116.54 W
Wilderness	158	34.00 S	22.36 E
Wilderness of Judaea (Midbar Yehuda) ◆2	132	31.30 N	35.18 E
Wilderness State Park ♦	190	45.42 N	84.57 W
Wildersville	194	35.46 N	88.21 W
Wildervank	52	53.04 N	6.51 E
Wildeshausen	52	52.54 N	8.26 E
Wildfield	212	43.49 N	79.44 W
Wildflecken	56	50.23 N	9.54 E
Wildfontein	158	31.04 S	24.50 E
Wildhaus	58	47.12 N	9.22 E
Wildhay ≃	182	54.02 N	117.20 W
Wildhorn ∧	58	46.21 N	7.22 E
Wildhorse Creek ≃, U.S.	198	40.36 N	102.00 W
Wild Horse Creek ≃, Ok., U.S.	196	34.32 N	97.10 W
Wild Horse Creek ≃, Wy., U.S.	198	44.39 N	106.08 W
Wild Horse Draw V	196	31.11 N	104.50 W
Wild Horse Hill ∧2	168a	33.12 S	116.40 E
Wildhorse Lake ⊜	202	48.58 N	110.00 W
Wild Horse Plains	168b	34.22 S	138.17 E
Wildnest Lake ⊜	184	55.00 N	102.20 W
Wildon	61	46.53 N	15.31 E
Wild Rice ≃, Mn., U.S.	198	47.20 N	96.50 W
Wild Rice ≃, N.D., U.S.	198	46.45 N	96.47 W
Wild Rice, South Branch ≃	198	47.12 N	96.38 W
Wildrose, N.D., U.S.	198	48.37 N	103.11 W
Wild Rose, Wi., U.S.	190	44.10 N	89.14 W
Wildseeloder ∧	64	47.26 N	12.32 E
Wildspitze ∧	64	46.53 N	10.52 E
Wildstrubel ∧	58	46.24 N	7.32 E
Wildwood, Ab., Can.	182	53.37 N	115.14 W
Wildwood, Fl., U.S.	220	28.51 N	82.02 W
Wildwood, Il., U.S.	216	42.21 N	88.00 W
Wildwood, N.J., U.S.	208	38.59 N	74.48 W
Wildwood, Pa., U.S.	214	40.36 N	79.58 W
Wildwood, Lake ⊜	276	41.09 N	74.32 W
Wild Wood Beach	284b	39.15 N	76.25 W
Wildwood Canyon Park ♦	280	34.13 N	118.17 W
Wildwood Crest	208	38.58 N	74.50 W
Wiley	224	46.33 N	120.39 W
Wilfersdorf	61	48.35 N	16.38 E
Wilge ≃, S. Afr.	158	25.34 S	29.10 E
Wilge ≃, S. Afr.	158	27.03 S	28.20 E
Wilgena	162	30.46 S	134.44 E
Wilgespruit ≃	273d	26.07 S	27.52 E
Wilhelm, Lake ⊜1	214	41.23 N	80.08 W
Wilhelm, Mount ∧	164	5.45 S	145.05 E
Wilhelmina Gebergte ⋏	250	3.45 N	56.30 W
Wilhelminakanaal ≚	52	51.47 N	4.51 E
Wilhelminaoord	52	52.53 N	6.10 E
Wilhelmina Peak → Trikora, Puncak ∧	164	4.15 S	138.45 E
Wilhelmsburg	61	48.06 N	15.36 E
Wilhelmsburg ◆8	52	53.30 N	10.00 E
Wilhelmshaven	52	53.31 N	8.08 E
Wilhelmshöhe, Schloss ⊥	56	51.21 N	9.22 E
Wilhelmshorst	54	52.19 N	13.03 E
Wilhelmstadt ◆8	264a	52.31 N	13.11 E
Wilhelmstal	156	21.54 S	16.19 E
Wilhelmstein, Schloss ⊥	52	52.28 N	9.18 E
Wilis, Gunung ∧	115a	7.52 S	111.48 E
Wilkau-Hasslau	54	50.40 N	12.31 E
Wilkerson Pass)(	200	39.02 N	105.32 W
Wilkes-Barre	210	41.14 N	75.52 W
Wilkes-Barre Scranton Airport ⊠	210	41.20 N	75.45 W
Wilkesboro	192	36.08 N	81.09 W
Wilkes Island I	174a	19.18 N	166.34 E
Wilkes Land ◆1	9	69.00 S	120.00 E
Wilkeson	224	47.06 N	122.02 W
Wilket Creek ≃	275b	43.43 N	79.21 W
Wilket Creek Park ♦	275b	43.43 N	79.21 W
Wilkhaven	46	57.52 N	3.45 W
Wilkie	184	52.25 N	108.43 W
Wilkinsburg	214	40.26 N	79.51 W
Wilkinson	218	39.53 N	85.36 W
Wilkinson Lakes ⊜	162	29.40 S	132.39 E
Wilkins Sound ⊔	9	70.15 S	73.00 W
Wilkins Township	279b	40.25 N	79.50 W
Will □6	216	41.32 N	88.05 W
Will, Mount ∧	180	57.31 N	128.46 W
Willacoochee	192	31.20 N	83.02 W
Willamette ≃	202	45.39 N	122.46 W
Willamette, Middle Fork ≃	202	44.01 N	123.01 W
Willamette, North Fork ≃	202	43.46 N	122.32 W
Willamina	224	45.04 N	123.29 W
Willamina Creek ≃	224	45.05 N	123.28 W
Willandra Billabong Creek ≃	166	33.08 S	144.06 E
Willapa	224	46.40 N	123.39 W
Willapa ≃	224	46.42 N	123.50 W
Willapa Bay c	224	46.37 N	124.00 W
Willard, Mo., U.S.	194	37.18 N	93.25 W
Willard, N.M., U.S.	200	34.35 N	106.01 W
Willard, N.Y., U.S.	210	42.40 N	76.52 W
Willard, Oh., U.S.	214	41.03 N	82.44 W
Willard, Ut,. U.S.	200	41.24 N	112.02 W
Willard, Wa., U.S.	224	45.48 N	121.38 W
Willard, Punta >	232	28.50 N	113.15 W
Willards	208	38.23 N	75.20 W
Willaston, Austl.	168b	34.36 S	138.45 E
Willaston, Eng., U.K.	262	53.18 N	3.00 W
Willaumez Peninsula >1	164	5.05 S	150.05 E
Willcox	200	32.15 N	109.49 W
Willcox Playa ⊜	200	32.08 N	109.51 W
Willebadessen	52	51.37 N	9.02 E
Willebroek	50	51.04 N	4.22 E
Willem Pretorius Game Reserve ◆4	158	28.16 S	27.13 E
Willemsoord	52	52.49 N	6.05 E
Willemstad, Ned.	52	51.42 N	4.26 E
Willemstad, Ned. Ant.	241s	12.06 N	68.56 W
Willerburn Acres	284c	39.03 N	77.10 W
Willeroo	164	15.17 S	131.35 E
Willer-sur-Thur	58	47.51 N	7.05 E
Willerswalde	54	54.07 N	13.08 E
Willesden ◆8	260	51.33 N	0.14 W
Willet	210	42.28 N	75.55 W
Willett Pond ⊜	283	42.11 N	71.14 W
Willey Creek ≃	279a	41.25 N	81.25 W
William, Lac ⊜	206	46.07 N	71.34 W
William, Mount ∧, Austl.	166	37.17 S	142.36 E
William, Mount ∧, Austl.	169	37.13 S	144.47 E
William, Mount ∧2	168a	32.57 S	116.07 E
William Bill Dannelly Reservoir ⊜1	194	32.10 N	87.10 W
William Boyce Regional Park ♦	279b	40.28 N	79.45 W
William Girling Reservoir ⊜1	260	51.37 N	0.02 W
William H. Harsha Lake ⊜1	218	39.02 N	84.07 W
William Lake ⊜	184	53.50 N	99.25 W
Williamnagar	124	25.30 N	90.35 E
William Patterson College ⊍2	276	40.56 N	74.12 W
William P. Gleason Park ♦	278	41.33 N	87.21 W
William Preston Lane Jr. Memorial Bridge ◆5	208	39.00 N	76.28 W
Williams, Austl.	168a	33.01 S	116.52 E
Williams, Az., U.S.	200	35.14 N	112.11 W
Williams, Ca., U.S.	226	39.09 N	122.08 W
Williams, Ia., U.S.	190	42.29 N	93.32 W
Williams, Mn., U.S.	198	48.46 N	94.57 W
Williams □6	214	41.35 N	84.33 W
Williams ≃, Austl.	166	20.04 S	141.08 E
Williams ≃, Austl.	168a	32.59 S	116.24 E
Williams ≃, Austl.	170	32.45 S	151.45 E
Williams, Cape >	9	70.29 S	164.05 E
Williams Air Force Base ■	200	33.18 N	111.40 W
Williams Bay	216	42.34 N	88.32 W
Williamsburg, On., Can.	212	44.58 N	75.15 W
Williamsburg, In., U.S.	218	39.57 N	84.59 W
Williamsburg, Ia., U.S.	190	41.39 N	92.00 W
Williamsburg, Ky., U.S.	192	36.44 N	84.09 W
Williamsburg, Ma., U.S.	207	42.23 N	72.43 W
Williamsburg, Mo., U.S.	219	38.55 N	91.42 W
Williamsburg, Oh., U.S.	218	39.03 N	84.03 W
Williamsburg, Pa., U.S.	214	40.27 N	78.12 W
Williamsburg, Va., U.S.	208	37.16 N	76.42 W
Williamsburg ◆8	276	40.42 N	73.57 W
Williamsburg Bridge ◆5	276	40.43 N	73.58 W
Williams Center	216	41.26 N	84.36 W
Williams Creek ≃, Austl.	274a	33.57 S	150.58 E
Williams Creek ≃, In., U.S.	218	39.36 N	85.09 W
Williamsdale	171b	35.35 S	149.09 E
Williamsfield	214	41.32 N	80.32 W
Williams Fork ≃	200	40.26 N	107.39 W
Williams Lake	182	52.08 N	122.09 W
Williams Lake Indian Reserve ◆4	182	52.07 N	122.00 W
Williams Mountain ∧2	194	34.15 N	94.33 W
Williamson, N.Y., U.S.	210	43.13 N	77.11 W
Williamson, W.V., U.S.	192	37.40 N	82.16 W
Williamson □6	222	30.40 N	97.32 W
Williamson ≃	202	42.28 N	121.57 W
Williamson, Mount ∧	204	36.39 N	118.18 W
Williamson Head >	9	69.09 S	157.49 E
Williamsport, Nf., Can.	186	50.32 N	56.19 W
Williamsport, In., U.S.	216	40.17 N	87.17 W
Williamsport, Oh., U.S.	214	39.35 N	83.07 W
Williamsport, Pa., U.S.	210	41.14 N	77.00 W
Williamston, Mi., U.S.	216	42.41 N	84.16 W
Williamston, N.C., U.S.	192	35.51 N	77.03 W
Williamston, S.C., U.S.	192	34.37 N	82.28 W
Williamstown, Austl.	168b	34.40 S	138.53 E
Williamstown, Austl.	169	37.52 S	144.54 E
Williamstown, On., Can.	206	45.08 N	74.35 W
Williamstown, Ky., U.S.	218	38.38 N	84.33 W
Williamstown, Ma., U.S.	207	42.42 N	73.12 W
Williamstown, N.J., U.S.	208	39.41 N	74.59 W
Williamstown, N.Y., U.S.	212	43.26 N	75.54 W
Williamstown, Pa., U.S.	208	40.34 N	76.37 W
Williamstown, Vt., U.S.	188	44.07 N	72.32 W
Williamstown, W.V., U.S.	188	39.24 N	81.27 W
Williamstown Junction	285	39.45 N	74.56 W
Williamstown Lake ⊜1	218	38.41 N	84.32 W
Williamsville, Il., U.S.	219	39.57 N	89.32 W
Williamsville, N.Y., U.S.	210	42.57 N	78.44 W
Williamtown	170	32.49 S	151.50 E
Willich	56	51.16 N	6.33 E
Willikies	240c	17.05 N	61.42 W
Willimantic	207	41.42 N	72.12 W
Willimantic ≃	207	41.43 N	72.12 W
Willingale	260	51.44 N	0.19 E
Willingboro	208	40.01 N	74.52 W
Willingdon, Ab., Can.	182	53.50 N	112.08 W
Willingdon, Eng., U.K.	42	50.47 N	0.15 E
Willingdon, Mount ∧	182	51.45 N	116.15 W
Willingen	56	51.17 N	8.37 E
Willingham	42	52.19 N	0.04 E
Willington, Eng., U.K.	42	52.50 N	1.33 W
Willington, Eng., U.K.	44	54.43 N	1.41 W
Willis, Mi., U.S.	216	42.09 N	83.33 W
Willis, Tx., U.S.	222	30.25 N	95.28 W
Willis ≃	192	37.41 N	78.07 W
Willisau	58	47.07 N	8.00 E
Willis Group II	164	16.18 S	150.00 E
Willis Island I	186	48.48 N	53.42 W
Williston, S. Afr.	158	31.20 S	20.53 E
Williston, Fl., U.S.	192	29.23 N	82.26 W
Williston, N.D., U.S.	198	48.08 N	103.38 W
Williston, Oh., U.S.	214	41.36 N	83.20 W
Williston, S.C., U.S.	192	33.24 N	81.25 W
Williston Lake ⊜1	176	55.40 N	123.40 W
Williston Park	276	40.45 N	73.38 W
Willisville	194	37.59 N	89.35 W
Willis Wharf	208	37.30 N	75.48 W
Williton	42	51.10 N	3.20 W
Willits	204	39.24 N	123.21 W
Willmar	198	45.07 N	95.02 W
Willmersdorf	264a	52.40 N	13.41 E
Willmore Wilderness Provincial Park ♦	182	53.45 N	119.00 W
Willoughby, Austl.	170	33.48 S	151.12 E
Willoughby, Oh., U.S.	214	41.38 N	81.25 W
Willoughby, Cape >	166	35.51 S	138.07 E
Willoughby Bay c	240c	17.02 N	61.44 W
Willoughby Hills	214	41.35 N	81.25 W
Willow, Ak., U.S.	180	61.45 N	150.03 W
Willow, Mi., U.S.	216	42.07 N	83.24 W
Willow, N.Y., U.S.	210	42.05 N	74.14 W
Willow ≃, Ab., Can.	182	55.58 N	113.55 W
Willow ≃, B.C., Can.	182	54.03 N	122.21 W
Willow ≃, Mn., U.S.	190	46.40 N	93.35 W
Willow ≃, Wi., U.S.	190	44.59 N	92.46 W
Willowbrook, Sk., Can.	184	51.13 N	102.47 W
Willow Brook, Ca., U.S.	280	33.54 N	118.13 W
Willowbrook, Il., U.S.	278	41.46 N	87.56 W
Willowbrook, Md., U.S.	284c	39.02 N	77.11 W
Willow Brook ≃, On., Can.	212	43.53 N	80.16 W
Willow Brook ≃, Eng., U.K.	42	52.32 N	0.24 W
Willow Brook ≃, N.J., U.S.	276	40.20 N	74.10 W
Willowbrook Mall ◆9	276	40.53 N	74.15 W
Willowbrook Park ♦	276	40.36 N	74.09 W
Willow Bunch	184	49.24 N	105.37 W
Willow Bunch Lake ⊜	184	49.27 N	105.28 W
Willow City	198	48.36 N	100.17 W
Willow Creek, Ca., U.S.	204	40.56 N	123.38 W
Willow Creek, Mt., U.S.	202	45.49 N	111.38 W
Willow Creek ≃, Ab., Can.	182	49.46 N	113.21 W
Willow Creek ≃, On., Can.	212	44.25 N	79.53 W
Willow Creek ≃, U.S.	226	37.09 N	119.27 W
Willow Creek ≃, Ca., U.S.	226	39.22 N	122.05 W
Willow Creek ≃, Il., U.S.	216	41.42 N	89.10 W
Willow Creek ≃, In., U.S.	216	41.15 N	85.08 W
Willow Creek ≃, Mi., U.S.	281	42.20 N	83.25 W
Willow Creek ≃, Mt., U.S.	202	48.10 N	111.11 W
Willow Creek ≃, Mt., U.S.	202	48.09 N	106.38 W
Willow Creek ≃, Mt., U.S.	202	46.28 N	108.28 W
Willow Creek ≃, Nv., U.S.	204	38.10 N	116.35 W
Willow Creek ≃, N.D., U.S.	198	48.34 N	100.48 W
Willow Creek ≃, Oh., U.S.	279a	41.20 N	82.03 W
Willow Creek ≃, Or., U.S.	202	44.00 N	117.13 W
Willow Creek ≃, Or., U.S.	202	45.48 N	120.01 W
Willow Creek ≃, Ut., U.S.	200	40.02 N	109.45 W

Symbols in the index entries represent the broad categories identified in the key at the right. Symbols with superior numbers (⋏1) identify subcategories (see complete key on page I · 1).

Symbole im Register stellen die rechts im Schlüssel erklärten Kategorien dar. Symbole mit hochgestellten Ziffern (⋏1) bezeichnen Unterabteilungen einer Kategorie (vgl. vollständiger Schlüssel auf Seite I · 1).

Los símbolos incluídos en el texto del índice representan las grandes categorías identificadas con la clave a la derecha. Los símbolos con numeros en su parte superior (⋏1) identifican las subcategorías (véase la clave completa en la página I · 1).

Les symboles de l'index représentent les catégories indiquées dans la légende à droite. Les symboles suivis d'un indice (⋏1) représentent des sous-catégories (voir légende complète à la page I · 1).

Os símbolos incluídos no texto do índice representam as grandes categorias identificadas com a chave à direita. Os símbolos com números em sua parte superior (⋏1) identificam as subcategorias (veja-se a chave completa à página I · 1).

∧ Mountain	Berg	Montaña	Montagne	Montanha
⋏ Mountains	Gebirge	Montañas	Montagnes	Montanhas
)(Pass	Paß	Paso	Col	Passo
V Valley, Canyon	Tal, Cañon	Valle, Cañón	Vallée, Canyon	Vale, Canhão
≍ Plain	Ebene	Llano	Plaine	Planície
> Cape	Kap	Cabo	Cap	Cabo
I Island	Insel	Isla	Île	Ilha
II Islands	Inseln	Islas	Îles	Ilhas
⊥ Other Topographic Features	Andere Topographische Objekte	Otros Elementos Topográficos	Autres données topographiques	Outros acidentes topográficos

ESPAÑOL — Nombre | Página | Lat.°′ | Long.°′ W = Oeste
FRANÇAIS — Nom | Page | Lat.°′ | Long.°′ W = Ouest
PORTUGUÊS — Nome | Página | Lat.°′ | Long.°′ W = Oeste

Nombre	Página	Lat.°′	Long.°′ W = Oeste
Willow Creek, North Fork ≃	226	37.13 N	119.30 W
Willow Creek, South Fork ≃	226	39.32 N	122.10 W
Willowdale ◆[8]	275b	43.47 N	79.26 W
Willowdale State Forest ♠	283	42.40 N	70.54 W
Willowdene	273d	26.18 S	29.57 E
Willowemac	210	41.55 N	74.41 W
Willowemoc Creek ≃	210	41.53 N	74.48 W
Willow Glen ◆[8]	282	37.18 N	121.53 W
Willow Grove	208	40.08 N	75.06 W
Willow Grove Naval Air Station ■	208	40.12 N	75.08 W
Willow Grove Park ♠	285	40.08 N	75.08 W
Willow Hill	214	40.06 N	77.48 W
Willowick	214	41.37 N	81.28 W
Willow Lake	198	44.37 N	97.38 W
Willow Lake ⊜, N.T., Can.	176	62.11 N	119.10 W
Willow Lake ⊜, N.Y., U.S.	276	40.43 N	73.50 W
Willowlake ≃	176	62.52 N	123.08 W
Willow Metropolitan Park ♠	281	42.08 N	83.22 W
Willowmore	158	33.17 S	23.29 E
Willow Park	222	32.45 N	97.39 W
Willowra	162	21.15 S	132.35 E
Willowra Aboriginal Reserve ◆[4]	162	21.15 S	132.35 E
Willow Reservoir ⊜[1]	190	45.45 N	89.50 W
Willow Ridge Estates	284a	43.01 N	78.49 W
Willow River	182	54.04 N	122.28 W
Willow Run, De., U.S.	285	39.44 N	75.37 W
Willow Run, Mi., U.S.	216	42.14 N	83.35 W
Willow Run, Va., U.S.	284c	38.49 N	77.10 W
Willow Run Airport ⊠	281	42.14 N	83.32 W
Willows	226	39.31 N	122.11 W
Willow Springs, Ca., U.S.	228	34.53 N	118.18 W
Willow Springs, Il., U.S.	278	41.44 N	87.51 W
Willow Springs, Mo., U.S.	194	36.59 N	91.58 W
Willow Springs, Pa., U.S.	279b	40.19 N	79.44 W
Willow Street	208	39.59 N	76.17 W
Willowvale	158	32.16 S	28.30 E
Willow Woods	284c	38.50 N	77.16 W
Will Rogers Beach State Park ♠	280	34.01 N	118.30 W
Will Rogers State Park ♠	280	34.03 N	118.31 W
Willroth	56	50.34 N	7.31 E
Wills, Lake ⊜	162	21.25 S	128.51 E
Wills Creek ≃, Austl.	166	22.43 S	140.02 E
Wills Creek ≃, Oh., U.S.	188	40.09 N	81.55 W
Wills Creek Lake ⊜[1]	214	40.08 N	81.45 W
Willseyville	210	42.17 N	76.23 W
Willshire	216	40.45 N	84.48 W
Wills Point	222	32.43 N	96.01 W
Willston	284c	38.52 N	77.09 W
Willunga	168b	35.17 S	138.33 E
Wilmar	194	33.37 N	91.55 W
Wilmer, Al., U.S.	194	30.49 N	88.21 W
Wilmer, Pa., U.S.	285	40.07 N	75.32 W
Wilmer, Tx., U.S.	222	32.35 N	96.41 W
Wilmerding	279b	40.23 N	79.48 W
Wilmersdorf ◆[8]	264a	52.30 N	13.19 E
Wilmette	216	42.04 N	87.43 W
Wilmington, Austl.	166	32.39 S	138.07 E
Wilmington, Eng., U.K.	260	51.26 N	0.12 E
Wilmington, De., U.S.	208	39.44 N	75.32 W
Wilmington, Il., U.S.	216	41.18 N	88.08 W
Wilmington, Ma., U.S.	207	42.32 N	71.10 W
Wilmington, N.C., U.S.	192	34.13 N	77.56 W
Wilmington, Oh., U.S.	218	39.26 N	83.49 W
Wilmington, Vt., U.S.	188	42.52 N	72.52 W
Wilmington ◆[8]	280	33.47 N	118.16 W
Wilmington Manor	285	39.41 N	75.35 W
Wilmington Manor Gardens	285	39.40 N	75.34 W
Wilmore, Ky., U.S.	192	37.51 N	84.39 W
Wilmore, Pa., U.S.	214	40.23 N	78.43 W
Wilmot, Ar., U.S.	194	33.03 N	91.34 W
Wilmot, Oh., U.S.	214	40.39 N	81.38 W
Wilmot, S.D., U.S.	198	45.24 N	96.51 W
Wilmot, Wi., U.S.	216	42.31 N	88.11 W
Wilmot Woods ♠	278	42.18 N	87.56 W
Wilmslow	44	53.20 N	2.15 W
Wilna → Vilnius	76	54.41 N	25.19 E
Wilnecote	42	52.36 N	1.40 W
Wilnsdorf	56	50.49 N	8.09 E
Wilpattu National Park ♠	122	8.20 N	80.00 E
Wilpen	214	40.17 N	79.12 W
Wilpshire	262	53.47 N	2.28 W
Wilsall	202	45.59 N	110.39 W
Wilsdruff	54	51.05 N	13.32 E
Wilseder Berg ʌ[2]	52	53.10 N	9.56 E
Wilseyville	226	38.23 N	120.31 W
Wilshamstead	42	52.05 N	0.27 W
Wilson, Austl.	166	32.00 S	133.22 E
Wilson, Ar., U.S.	194	35.34 N	90.02 W
Wilson, Ct., U.S.	207	41.48 N	72.38 W
Wilson, Il., U.S.	278	42.21 N	87.54 W
Wilson, Ks., U.S.	198	38.49 N	98.28 W
Wilson, La., U.S.	194	30.55 N	91.06 W
Wilson, N.Y., U.S.	210	43.18 N	78.49 W
Wilson, N.C., U.S.	192	35.43 N	77.54 W
Wilson, Ok., U.S.	196	34.09 N	97.25 W
Wilson, Pa., U.S.	208	40.41 N	75.14 W
Wilson, Tx., U.S.	196	33.19 N	101.44 W
Wilson ≃, Austl.	164	16.47 S	128.17 E
Wilson ≃, Austl.	166	27.38 S	141.24 E
Wilson ≃, Or., U.S.	224	45.28 N	123.53 W
Wilson, Cape ≻	176	66.59 N	81.28 W
Wilson, Mount ʌ, Az., U.S.	200	35.59 N	114.37 W
Wilson, Mount ʌ, Ca., U.S.	280	34.13 N	118.04 W
Wilson, Mount ʌ, Co., U.S.	200	37.51 N	107.59 W
Wilson, Mount ʌ, Nv., U.S.	204	38.15 N	114.23 W
Wilson, Mount ʌ, Or., U.S.	224	45.04 N	121.39 W
Wilson, Mount ʌ[2], Austl.	162	20.14 S	127.39 E
Wilson, Mount ʌ[2], Austl.	168b	35.13 S	138.38 E
Wilson, Point ≻, Austl.	169	38.05 S	144.30 E
Wilson, Point ≻, Wa., U.S.	224	48.08 N	122.45 W
Wilson Cliffs ⏏[4]	162	22.03 S	127.09 E
Wilson Creek ≃, Tx., U.S.	222	33.07 N	96.35 W
Wilson Creek ≃, Wa., U.S.	202	47.25 N	119.07 W
Wilson Lake ⊜[1], Al., U.S.	194	34.49 N	87.30 W
Wilson Lake ⊜[1], Ks., U.S.	198	38.57 N	98.40 W
Wilson Range ⋀	162	28.50 S	124.25 E
Wilson Run ≃, De., U.S.	285	39.48 N	75.35 W
Wilson Run ≃, Pa., U.S.	279b	40.13 N	79.37 W
Wilsons Beach	186	44.56 N	66.56 W
Wilson's Creek National Battlefield ♠	194	37.06 N	93.27 W
Wilsons Promontory ≻	166	38.55 S	146.20 E
Wilsons Promontory National Park ♠	166	39.00 S	146.25 E
Wilsonville, Il., U.S.	219	39.04 N	89.51 W
Wilsonville, Ne., U.S.	198	40.06 N	100.06 W
Wilsonville, Or., U.S.	224	45.18 N	122.46 W
Wilster	52	53.55 N	9.22 E
Wilthen	54	51.06 N	14.24 E
Wilton, Eng., U.K.	42	51.05 N	1.52 W
Wilton, Ct., U.S.	207	41.11 N	73.26 W
Wilton, Me., U.S.	188	44.35 N	70.13 W
Wilton, N.H., U.S.	207	42.50 N	71.44 W
Wilton, N.Y., U.S.	210	43.11 N	73.45 W
Wilton, N.D., U.S.	198	47.09 N	100.46 W
Wilton, Wi., U.S.	190	43.48 N	90.31 W
Wilton ≃	164	14.45 S	134.33 E
Wilton Creek ≃	212	44.12 N	76.56 W
Wilton Farm Acres	284b	39.18 N	76.50 W
Wilton Manors	220	26.09 N	80.08 W
Wiltshire □[6]	42	51.15 N	1.50 W
Wiltz	56	49.57 N	5.55 E
Wiluna	162	26.36 S	120.13 E
Wimapedi ≃	184	55.27 N	99.07 W
Wimauma	220	27.42 N	82.17 W
Wimberley	196	30.00 N	98.06 W
Wimbleball Reservoir ⊜[1]	42	51.04 N	3.28 W
Wimbledon	198	47.10 N	98.27 W
Wimbledon ◆[8]	260	51.25 N	0.12 W
Wimbledon Common ♠	260	51.26 N	0.14 W
Wimborne Minster	42	50.48 N	1.59 W
Wimereux	50	50.46 N	1.37 E
Wimmelburg	54	51.31 N	11.30 E
Wimmenau	56	48.55 N	7.25 E
Wimmera ≃	169	36.55 S	142.56 E
Wimmis	58	46.41 N	7.38 E
Winagami Lake ⊜	182	55.38 N	116.45 W
Winam c	154	0.15 S	34.35 E
Winamac	216	41.03 N	86.36 W
Winburg	158	28.37 S	27.00 E
Winburne	214	40.57 N	78.08 W
Wincanton	42	51.04 N	2.25 W
Wincham	262	53.16 N	2.29 W
Winchcombe	42	51.57 N	1.58 W
Winchelsea, Austl.	169	38.15 S	143.59 E
Winchelsea, Eng., U.K.	42	50.55 N	0.42 E
Winchendon	207	42.41 N	72.02 W
Winchester, On., Can.	212	45.06 N	75.21 W
Winchester, N.Z.	172	44.12 S	171.17 E
Winchester, Eng., U.K.	42	51.04 N	1.19 W
Winchester, Ca., U.S.	228	33.42 N	117.05 W
Winchester, Id., U.S.	202	46.14 N	116.37 W
Winchester, Il., U.S.	219	39.37 N	90.27 W
Winchester, In., U.S.	218	40.10 N	84.58 W
Winchester, Ky., U.S.	192	37.59 N	84.10 W
Winchester, Ma., U.S.	283	42.27 N	71.08 W
Winchester, N.H., U.S.	207	42.46 N	72.23 W
Winchester, Oh., U.S.	218	38.56 N	83.39 W
Winchester, Tn., U.S.	194	35.11 N	86.06 W
Winchester, Tx., U.S.	222	30.01 N	97.01 W
Winchester, Va., U.S.	188	39.11 N	78.10 W
Winchester Cathedral ♁[1]	42	51.04 N	1.19 W
Winchmore Hill	260	51.39 N	0.39 W
Winchmore Hill ◆[8]	260	51.38 N	0.06 W
Wind ≃, Yk., Can.	180	65.49 N	135.18 W
Wind ≃, Wa., U.S.	224	45.43 N	121.47 W
Wind ≃, Wy., U.S.	202	43.35 N	108.13 W
Windang	170	34.32 S	150.53 E
Windau → Ventspils	76	57.24 N	21.36 E
Windber	214	40.14 N	78.50 W
Wind Cave National Park ♠	198	43.32 N	103.25 W
Windeck	56	50.48 N	7.37 E
Winder	192	33.59 N	83.43 W
Winder, Lake ⊜	220	28.15 N	80.51 W
Windera	166	26.03 S	151.50 E
Windermere, B.C., Can.	182	50.30 N	115.58 W
Windermere, Eng., U.K.	44	54.23 N	2.54 W
Windermere, Fl., U.S.	220	28.30 N	81.32 W
Windermere ⊜	44	54.22 N	2.56 W
Windermere Lake ⊜	190	47.56 N	83.47 W
Winder Village	285	40.06 N	74.52 W
Windfall, Ab., Can.	182	54.11 N	116.15 W
Windfall, In., U.S.	216	40.21 N	85.57 W
Windgap	210	40.51 N	75.18 W
Windham, Ct., U.S.	207	41.41 N	72.09 W
Windham, N.H., U.S.	283	42.48 N	71.18 W
Windham, N.Y., U.S.	210	42.19 N	74.15 W
Windham, Oh., U.S.	214	41.14 N	81.02 W
Windham □[6], Ct., U.S.	207	41.55 N	71.55 W
Windham □[6], Vt., U.S.	207	42.50 N	72.43 W
Windham Manor	284c	39.04 N	77.00 W
Windhoek	156	22.34 S	17.06 E
Windhoek □[5]	156	22.30 S	17.00 E
Windigo ≃	184	53.22 N	91.48 W
Windigo Lake ⊜	184	52.35 N	91.32 W
Windisch	58	47.29 N	8.13 E
Windischeschenbach	60	49.48 N	12.09 E
Windischgarsten	61	47.44 N	14.20 E
Wind Lake	216	42.49 N	88.09 W
Wind Lake ⊜	216	42.50 N	88.09 W
Windlass Run ≃	284b	39.24 N	76.24 W
Windleite ʌ	54	51.22 N	10.56 E
Windlesham	260	51.22 N	0.40 W
Windley Key I	220	24.57 N	80.35 W
Windmill Point ≻, On., Can.	284a	42.52 N	79.01 W
Windmill Point ≻, Mi., U.S.	281	42.22 N	82.55 W
Windmill Point ≻, Va., U.S.	208	37.37 N	76.17 W
Windom, Mn., U.S.	198	43.51 N	95.07 W
Windom, N.Y., U.S.	210	42.47 N	78.48 W
Windom Peak ʌ	200	37.37 N	107.35 W
Windorah	166	25.26 S	142.39 E
Windorf, Dtsch.	60	48.37 N	13.13 E
Windorf, Öst.	61	48.27 N	14.02 E
Window Rock	200	35.40 N	109.03 W
Wind Point	216	42.47 N	87.45 W
Wind River Indian Reservation ◆[4]	202	43.26 N	109.00 W
Wind River Peak ʌ	200	42.42 N	109.07 W
Wind River Range ⋀	200	43.05 N	109.25 W
Windrush ≃	42	51.42 N	1.25 W
Windsbach	56	49.14 N	10.50 E
Windsor, Austl.	168b	34.25 S	138.20 E
Windsor, Austl.	170	33.37 S	150.49 E
Windsor, Nf., Can.	186	48.57 N	55.40 W
Windsor, N.S., Can.	186	44.59 N	64.08 W
Windsor, On., Can.	214	42.18 N	83.01 W
Windsor, On., Can.	281	42.18 N	83.01 W
Windsor, P.Q., Can.	206	45.34 N	72.00 W
Windsor, Eng., U.K.	42	51.29 N	0.38 W
Windsor, Ca., U.S.	204	38.33 N	122.49 W
Windsor, Co., U.S.	200	40.28 N	104.54 W
Windsor, Ct., U.S.	207	41.51 N	72.38 W
Windsor, Il., U.S.	194	39.26 N	88.35 W
Windsor, In., U.S.	218	40.09 N	85.12 W
Windsor, Mo., U.S.	194	38.31 N	93.31 W
Windsor, N.J., U.S.	208	40.15 N	74.35 W
Windsor, N.Y., U.S.	210	42.05 N	75.39 W
Windsor, N.C., U.S.	192	35.59 N	76.56 W
Windsor, Oh., U.S.	214	41.32 N	80.56 W
Windsor, Pa., U.S.	208	39.54 N	76.35 W
Windsor, Vt., U.S.	188	43.29 N	72.23 W
Windsor, Va., U.S.	208	36.48 N	76.44 W
Windsor, Wi., U.S.	216	43.13 N	89.20 W
Windsor, Gare ◆[5]	275a	45.30 N	73.34 W
Windsor, University of ♁[2]	281	42.18 N	83.04 W
Windsor Airport ⊠	214	42.17 N	82.58 W
Windsor and Maidenhead □[8]	260	51.28 N	0.37 W
Windsor Castle ⊥	42	51.29 N	0.36 W
Windsor Forest	192	31.58 N	81.07 W
Windsor Forest ◆[3]	42	51.27 N	0.43 W
Windsor Great Park ♠	260	51.27 N	0.37 W
Windsor Heights	214	40.12 N	80.40 W
Windsor Hills	280	33.59 N	118.21 W
Windsor Locks	207	41.55 N	72.37 W
Windsor Race Course ♠	260	51.29 N	0.39 W
Windsor Raceway ♠	281	42.15 N	83.05 W
Windsor Terrace	284b	39.19 N	76.43 W
Windsorton	158	28.16 S	24.44 E
Windsorville	207	41.53 N	72.32 W
Windthorst	196	33.34 N	98.26 W
Windward Islands II	238	13.00 N	61.00 W
Windward Passage ʊ	238	20.00 N	73.50 W
Windy Hills	285	39.48 N	75.35 W
Windy Lake ⊜	184	54.22 N	102.35 W
Windy Peak ʌ, Co., U.S.	200	38.21 N	106.16 W
Windy Peak ʌ, Wa., U.S.	202	48.56 N	119.58 W
Windy Run ≃	284c	38.54 N	77.05 W
Winefred ≃	184	56.02 N	110.36 W
Winefred Lake ⊜	182	55.30 N	110.35 W
Winejok	140	9.01 N	27.34 E
Winesburg	214	40.37 N	81.42 W
Winfield, Ab., Can.	182	52.58 N	114.26 W
Winfield, Al., U.S.	194	33.55 N	87.49 W
Winfield, Il., U.S.	216	41.52 N	88.10 W
Winfield, Ia., U.S.	190	41.07 N	91.25 W
Winfield, Ks., U.S.	198	37.14 N	96.59 W
Winfield, Mo., U.S.	219	38.59 N	90.44 W
Winfield, N.J., U.S.	276	40.38 N	74.17 W
Winfield, Tx., U.S.	222	33.10 N	95.07 W
Winfield, W.V., U.S.	188	38.31 N	81.53 W
Wing	198	47.08 N	100.16 W
Wing ≃	198	46.29 N	94.58 W
Wingate, Eng., U.K.	44	54.44 N	1.23 W
Wingate, Md., U.S.	208	38.16 N	76.04 W
Wingate, N.C., U.S.	192	34.59 N	80.26 W
Wingate Mountains ⋀	164	14.29 S	130.42 E
Wingates	262	53.34 N	2.32 W
Wingdale	210	41.39 N	73.34 W
Wingecarribee ≃	170	34.23 S	150.07 E
Wingecarribee Reservoir ⊜[1]	170	34.34 S	150.30 E
Wingello	170	34.42 S	150.09 E
Wingene	50	51.04 N	3.16 E
Wingen-sur-Moder	56	48.55 N	7.22 E
Wingerworth	44	53.12 N	1.26 W
Wingham, Austl.	166	31.52 S	152.22 E
Wingham, On., Can.	212	43.53 N	81.19 W
Wingham, Eng., U.K.	42	51.17 N	1.13 E
Wing Lake Shores	281	42.33 N	83.17 W
Wingles	50	50.29 N	2.51 E
Wingo	194	36.38 N	88.44 W
Wings Field ⊠	285	40.08 N	75.16 W
Wingst	52	53.43 N	9.03 E
Winhole Channel ʊ	276	43.37 N	73.48 W
Winhöring	60	48.16 N	12.39 E
Winifred	202	47.33 N	109.22 W
Winifreda	252	36.15 S	64.14 W
Winisk	176	55.15 N	85.12 W
Winisk ≃	176	55.17 N	85.05 W
Winisk Lake ⊜	176	52.55 N	87.22 W
Wink	196	31.45 N	103.06 W
Winkana	110	15.44 N	98.01 E
Winkelman	200	32.59 N	110.46 W
Winkelpos	158	27.35 S	26.49 E
Winkler, Mb., Can.	184	49.11 N	97.56 W
Winkler, Tx., U.S.	222	31.56 N	96.13 W
Winklern	64	46.52 N	12.52 E
Winlaw	182	49.37 N	117.34 W
Winlock	224	46.29 N	122.56 W
Winneba	150	5.25 N	0.36 W
Winnebago, Il., U.S.	190	42.15 N	89.14 W
Winnebago, Mn., U.S.	190	43.46 N	94.09 W
Winnebago, Ne., U.S.	198	42.14 N	96.28 W
Winnebago □[6]	216	42.17 N	89.06 W
Winnebago ≃	190	43.03 N	92.57 W
Winnebago, Lake ⊜	190	44.00 N	88.25 W
Winnebago Indian Reservation ◆[4], Ne., U.S.	198	42.15 N	96.31 W
Winnebago Indian Reservation ◆[4], Wi., U.S.	190	44.15 N	90.38 W
Winnecke, Mount ʌ[2]	162	18.47 S	130.20 E
Winnecke Creek ≃	162	18.35 S	131.34 E
Winneconne	190	44.06 N	88.42 W
Winneconnet	283	41.59 N	71.08 W
Winneconnet Pond ⊜	283	41.58 N	71.08 W
Winnekendonk	52	51.36 N	6.17 E
Winnekenni Park ♠	283	42.47 N	71.04 W
Winnemucca	204	40.58 N	117.44 W
Winnemucca Lake ⊜	204	40.09 N	119.20 W
Winnenden	56	48.53 N	9.24 E
Winner	198	43.22 N	99.51 W
Winnetka	216	42.06 N	87.44 W
Winnetka ◆[3]	280	34.13 N	118.35 W
Winnett	202	47.00 N	108.21 W
Winnfield	194	31.55 N	92.38 W
Winnibigoshish, Lake ⊜	190	47.27 N	94.12 W
Winnie	194	29.49 N	94.23 W
Winning	162	23.09 S	114.32 E
Winningen, Dtsch.	54	51.49 N	11.26 E
Winningen, Dtsch.	56	50.18 N	7.31 E
Winnipeg	184	49.53 N	97.09 W
Winnipeg ≃	184	50.38 N	96.19 W
Winnipeg, Lake ⊜	184	52.00 N	97.00 W
Winnipeg Beach	184	50.31 N	96.58 W
Winnipegosis	184	51.39 N	99.56 W
Winnipegosis, Lake ⊜	184	52.30 N	100.00 W
Winnipesaukee, Lake ⊜	188	43.35 N	71.20 W
Winnsboro, La., U.S.	194	32.09 N	91.43 W
Winnsboro, S.C., U.S.	192	34.22 N	81.05 W
Winnsboro, Tx., U.S.	222	32.57 N	95.17 W
Winnsboro, Lake ⊜[1]	222	32.55 N	95.21 W
Winnsboro Mills	192	34.21 N	81.05 W
Winnweiler	56	49.34 N	7.51 E
Winona, Ks., U.S.	198	39.03 N	101.14 W
Winona, Mi., U.S.	190	46.52 N	88.55 W
Winona, Mn., U.S.	190	44.03 N	91.38 W
Winona, Ms., U.S.	194	33.28 N	89.43 W
Winona, Mo., U.S.	194	37.00 N	91.19 W
Winona, Oh., U.S.	214	40.50 N	80.54 W
Winona, Tx., U.S.	222	32.29 N	95.10 W
Winona Lake, In., U.S.	216	41.13 N	85.49 W
Winona Lake, N.Y., U.S.	210	41.31 N	74.03 W
Winona Lake ⊜	216	41.13 N	85.50 W
Winooski	188	44.29 N	73.11 W
Winooski ≃	188	44.30 N	73.15 W
Winooski, North Branch ≃	188	44.15 N	72.35 W
Winschoten	52	53.08 N	7.02 E
Winscombe	42	51.18 N	2.50 W
Winsen, Dtsch.	52	52.41 N	9.54 E
Winsen, Dtsch.	52	53.22 N	10.12 E
Winsford, Eng., U.K.	42	51.06 N	3.33 W
Winsford, Eng., U.K.	44	53.12 N	2.32 W
Winshill	42	52.48 N	1.36 W
Winside	198	42.10 N	97.10 W
Winslow, Eng., U.K.	42	51.57 N	0.54 W
Winslow, Az., U.S.	200	35.01 N	110.41 W
Winslow, Me., U.S.	188	44.32 N	69.37 W
Winslow, N.J., U.S.	285	39.39 N	74.52 W
Winslow Reef ✤[2]	14	1.36 S	174.57 W
Winsted, Ct., U.S.	207	41.55 N	73.03 W
Winsted, Mn., U.S.	190	44.57 N	94.02 W
Winston, Fl., U.S.	220	28.01 N	82.00 W
Winston, Or., U.S.	202	43.07 N	123.24 W
Winston Churchill Memorial ♁	219	38.52 N	91.58 W
Winston Creek ≃	224	46.30 N	122.40 W
Winston-Salem	192	36.05 N	80.14 W
Winsum	52	53.19 N	6.31 E
Wintego Lake ⊜	184	55.33 N	102.52 W
Winter	190	45.49 N	91.00 W
Winter Beach	220	27.43 N	80.25 W
Winterberg, Dtsch.	56	51.11 N	8.32 E
Winterberg, Dtsch.	263	51.17 N	7.18 E
Winterberg ʌ[2]	263	51.20 N	7.13 E
Winterberge ⋀	158	32.28 S	26.15 E
Winterbourne Abbas	42	50.43 N	2.34 W
Winter Creek ≃	280	34.12 N	118.02 W
Winterfeld	54	52.44 N	11.14 E
Winter Garden	220	28.33 N	81.35 W
Winter Gardens	228	32.50 N	116.56 W
Winter Harbor	188	44.23 N	68.05 W
Winter Harbour	182	50.31 N	128.02 W
Winterhaven, Ca., U.S.	204	32.44 N	114.38 W
Winter Haven, Fl., U.S.	220	28.01 N	81.43 W
Winter Hill ʌ[2]	262	53.38 N	2.31 W
Wintering ≃	198	48.12 N	100.34 W
Wintering Lake ⊜	184	55.24 N	97.42 W
Winter Island I, N.T., Can.	176	66.14 N	83.04 W
Winter Island I, Ca., U.S.	282	38.03 N	121.51 W
Winter Island I, Ma., U.S.	283	42.32 N	70.52 W
Winterlingen	58	48.11 N	9.07 E
Winter Park, Fl., U.S.	220	28.35 N	81.20 W
Winter Park, N.C., U.S.	192	34.12 N	77.53 W
Winterport	188	44.38 N	68.51 W
Winters, Ca., U.S.	226	38.31 N	121.58 W
Winters, Tx., U.S.	196	31.57 N	99.57 W
Winters Bayou ≃	222	30.22 N	95.06 W
Winters Canal ≅	226	38.32 N	121.58 W
Wintersdorf	54	51.03 N	12.21 E
Winterset, Ia., U.S.	190	41.19 N	94.00 W
Winterset, Oh., U.S.	214	40.06 N	81.25 W
Winter Springs	220	28.41 N	81.18 W
Winters Run ≃	208	39.26 N	76.18 W
Winterstown	208	39.50 N	76.37 W
Wintersville	214	40.22 N	80.42 W
Winterswijk	52	51.58 N	6.44 E
Winterthur, Schw.	58	47.30 N	8.43 E
Winterthur, De., U.S.	285	39.48 N	75.35 W
Winterthur Museum ♁	285	39.48 N	75.36 W
Winterton, Nf., Can.	186	47.58 N	53.20 W
Winterton, S. Afr.	158	28.46 S	29.35 E
Winterton, Eng., U.K.	44	53.39 N	0.36 W
Winterton-on-Sea	42	52.43 N	1.42 E
Winterville, Ga., U.S.	192	33.58 N	83.16 W
Winterville, Ms., U.S.	194	33.30 N	91.03 W
Winterville, N.C., U.S.	192	35.31 N	77.24 W
Winthrop, Ct., U.S.	207	41.21 N	72.29 W
Winthrop, Ia., U.S.	190	42.28 N	91.44 W
Winthrop, Me., U.S.	188	44.18 N	69.58 W
Winthrop, Ma., U.S.	283	42.22 N	70.59 W
Winthrop, Mn., U.S.	190	44.32 N	94.21 W
Winthrop, Wa., U.S.	182	48.28 N	120.11 W
Winthrop, Lake ⊜	283	42.11 N	71.25 W
Winthrop Harbor	216	42.28 N	87.49 W
Wintinna	162	27.44 S	134.07 E
Wintinna Creek ≃	162	27.47 S	134.14 E
Winton, Austl.	166	22.23 S	143.02 E
Winton, N.Z.	172	46.09 S	168.20 E
Winton, S. Afr.	158	27.29 S	22.34 E
Winton, Ca., U.S.	226	37.23 N	120.37 W
Winton, N.C., U.S.	192	36.23 N	76.55 W
Winton, Wa., U.S.	224	47.44 N	120.44 W
Wintzenheim	58	48.04 N	7.17 E
Winwick	262	53.26 N	2.36 W
Winz	263	51.23 N	7.09 E
Winzenberg	263	51.06 N	7.38 E
Winzer	60	48.44 N	13.04 E
Winzermark	263	51.23 N	7.08 E
Wipper ≃, Dtsch.	54	51.17 N	11.10 E
Wipper ≃, Dtsch.	54	51.47 N	11.42 E
Wipper ≃, Dtsch.	263	51.07 N	7.24 E
Wipperdorf	54	51.28 N	10.42 E
Wipperfeld	263	51.05 N	7.19 E
Wipperfürth	56	51.07 N	7.23 E
Wippra	54	51.34 N	11.16 E
Wirātnagar	124	26.29 N	87.17 E
Wirendranagar	124	28.35 N	81.38 E
Wireton, Il., U.S.	278	41.40 N	87.42 W
Wireton, Pa., U.S.	279b	40.34 N	80.14 W
Wirgañj	124	27.00 N	84.52 E
Wiriagar ≃	164	2.17 S	132.52 E
Wirksworth	44	53.05 N	1.34 W
Wirosari	115a	7.05 S	111.05 E
Wirral □[8]	262	53.22 N	3.05 W
Wirral ≻[1]	44	53.20 N	3.03 W
Wirraminna	166	31.12 S	136.15 E
Wirrulla	162	32.24 S	134.31 E
Wisbech	42	52.40 N	0.10 E
Wisby → Visby	26	57.38 N	18.18 E
Wiscasset	188	44.00 N	69.39 W
Wischhafen	52	53.46 N	9.19 E
Wisconsin □[3], U.S.	178	44.45 N	89.30 W
Wisconsin □[3], U.S.	190	44.45 N	89.30 W
Wisconsin ≃	190	43.00 N	91.10 W
Wisconsin, Lake ⊜[1]	190	43.24 N	89.43 W
Wisconsin Dells	190	43.37 N	89.46 W
Wisconsin Dells V	190	43.41 N	89.49 W
Wisconsin Rapids	190	44.23 N	89.49 W
Wiscoy	210	42.30 N	78.05 W
Wisdom	202	45.37 N	113.27 W
Wisdom, Lake ⊜	164	5.20 S	147.05 E
Wise	192	36.58 N	82.34 W
Wise □[6]	222	33.07 N	97.40 W
Wise ≃	202	45.48 N	112.57 W
Wiseman	180	67.25 N	150.06 W
Wisemans Ferry	170	33.24 S	150.59 E
Wises Landing	218	38.35 N	85.25 W
Wishart	184	51.34 N	104.00 W
Wishaw	46	55.47 N	3.56 W
Wishek	198	46.16 N	99.33 W
Wishkah ≃	224	46.58 N	123.45 W
Wishram	224	45.39 N	120.57 W
Wiske ≃	44	54.15 N	1.26 W
Wisła	30	49.40 N	18.52 E
Wisła ≃	30	54.22 N	18.55 E
Wisley Aerodrome ⊠	260	51.18 N	0.28 W
Wisley Gardens ♠	260	51.19 N	0.29 W
Wisłok ≃	30	50.13 N	22.32 E
Wisłoka ≃	30	50.27 N	21.23 E
Wismar, Dtsch.	54	53.53 N	11.28 E
Wismar, Guy.	246	6.00 N	58.18 W
Wismarbucht c	54	53.57 N	11.25 E
Wisner, La., U.S.	194	31.58 N	91.39 W
Wisner, Ne., U.S.	198	41.59 N	96.54 W
Wissahickon Creek ≃	285	40.01 N	75.12 W
Wissant	50	50.53 N	1.40 E
Wissembourg	56	49.02 N	7.57 E
Wissen	56	50.47 N	7.43 E
Wissenkerke	52	51.35 N	3.45 E
Wissey ≃	42	52.33 N	0.21 E
Wissinoming ◆[8]	285	40.01 N	75.04 W
Wissmar	56	50.38 N	8.41 E
Wissous	261	48.44 N	2.20 E
Wister	194	34.58 N	94.43 W
Wisznice	30	51.48 N	23.12 E
Witbank	158	25.56 S	29.07 E
Witberge ⋀	158	30.45 S	27.32 E
Witbooisvlei	156	25.04 S	18.27 E
Witchekan Lake ⊜	184	53.25 N	107.35 W
Witches Falls National Park ♠	171a	27.56 S	153.10 E
Witch Hazel	224	45.30 N	122.46 W
Witdraai	158	26.58 S	20.45 E
Witfield	273d	26.11 S	28.12 E
Witham	42	51.48 N	0.38 E
Witham ≃	44	53.06 N	0.13 W
Withamsville	218	39.03 N	84.16 W
Withens Clough Reservoir ⊜[1]	262	53.42 N	2.02 W
Witheridge	42	50.55 N	3.42 W
Withernsea	44	53.44 N	0.02 E
Witherspoon, Mount ʌ	180	61.23 N	147.12 W
Withington ◆[8]	262	53.26 N	2.14 W
Withington Green	262	53.14 N	2.18 W
Withlacoochee ≃, U.S.	192	30.24 N	83.10 W
Withlacoochee ≃, Fl., U.S.	192	29.00 N	82.45 W
Withnell	262	53.42 N	2.34 W
Withokspruit ≃	273d	26.19 S	28.21 E
Witjira National Park ♠	162	26.25 S	135.40 E
Wit-Kei ≃	158	32.09 S	27.24 E
Witkoppies ʌ	158	27.44 S	29.20 E
Witkowo	30	52.27 N	17.47 E
Witless Bay	186	47.16 N	52.50 W
Witley	42	51.09 N	0.38 W
Wit-Mfolozi ≃	158	28.22 S	31.58 E
Witney	42	51.48 N	1.29 W
Witnica	30	52.40 N	14.55 E
Wit Nossob ≃	156	23.05 S	18.45 E
Witpoort	158	27.10 S	26.08 E
Witrivier	156	24.40 S	31.00 E
Witry-lès-Reims	50	49.18 N	4.07 E
Witsand	158	34.24 S	20.50 E
Witt	219	39.15 N	89.20 W
Wittabrenna Creek ≃	166	29.20 S	142.43 E
Witteberg ⋀	158	28.40 S	28.02 E
Witteberge ⋀	158	33.18 S	20.36 E
Wittelsheim	58	47.49 N	7.15 E
Witten	56	51.26 N	7.20 E
Wittenau ◆[8]	264a	52.35 N	13.20 E
Wittenberg, Dtsch.	54	51.52 N	12.39 E
Wittenberg, Wi., U.S.	190	44.49 N	89.10 W
Wittenberge	54	53.00 N	11.44 E
Wittenburg	54	53.31 N	11.04 E
Wittenheim	58	47.49 N	7.20 E
Wittenoom	162	22.17 S	118.19 E
Wittensee ⊜	41	54.23 N	9.45 E
Wittering	42	52.37 N	0.27 W
Wittgensdorf	54	50.53 N	12.52 E
Wittichenau	54	51.23 N	14.14 E
Wittingen	54	52.43 N	10.44 E
Wittislingen	56	48.37 N	10.25 E
Wittlaer	56	51.19 N	6.44 E
Wittlich	56	49.59 N	6.53 E
Wittman	208	38.47 N	76.17 W
Wittmar	54	52.07 N	10.38 E
Wittmund	52	53.34 N	7.47 E
Witton Park ♠	262	53.45 N	2.31 W
Wittow ≻[1]	54	54.38 N	13.19 E
Wittstock	54	53.10 N	12.29 E
Witu	154	2.23 S	40.26 E
Witu Islands II	164	4.40 S	149.25 E
Witvlai	156	22.23 S	18.32 E
Witwatersrand, University of the ♁[2]	273d	26.12 S	28.02 E
Witwatersrand Gold Mine ◆[7]	273d	26.12 S	28.11 E
Witwatersrant ◆[1]	158	26.00 S	27.00 E
Witzenhausen	56	51.20 N	9.51 E
Witzhelden	263	51.07 N	7.06 E
Witzputz	156	27.25 S	17.43 E
Wiveliscombe	42	51.03 N	3.19 W
Wivenhoe	42	51.52 N	0.58 E
Wivenhoe Reservoir ⊜[1]	171a	27.20 S	152.35 E
Wiwa Creek ≃	184	50.02 N	106.31 W
Wixom	216	42.31 N	83.32 W
Wiżajny	30	54.23 N	22.51 E
Wizernes	50	50.43 N	2.14 E
Wjatka → V'atka ≃	80	55.36 N	51.30 E
W. Kerr Scott Reservoir ⊜[1]	192	36.07 N	81.15 W
Wkra ≃	30	52.27 N	20.44 E
Wladiwostok → Vladivostok	89	43.10 N	131.56 E
Władysławowo	30	54.49 N	18.25 E
Wleń	30	51.01 N	15.40 E
Wlingi	115a	8.05 S	112.19 E
Włocławek	30	52.39 N	19.02 E
Włocławek □[4]	30	52.30 N	19.05 E
Włodawa	30	51.34 N	23.32 E
Włoszczowa	30	50.52 N	19.59 E
Wnion ≃	42	52.45 N	3.54 W
Woady Yaloak ≃	169	38.06 S	143.33 E
Wobaer	85	39.19 N	75.32 E
Wöbbelin	54	53.24 N	11.30 E
Woburn	207	42.28 N	71.09 W
Woburn ◆[8]	275b	43.46 N	79.13 W
Woburn Sands	42	52.01 N	0.39 W
Woden, Austl.	171b	35.22 S	149.08 E
Woden, Tx., U.S.	222	31.30 N	94.32 W
Wodgina	162	21.11 S	118.40 E
Wodonga	166	36.07 S	146.54 E
Wodzisław Śląski	30	50.00 N	18.28 E
Woensdrecht	52	51.26 N	4.18 E
Woerdeke	85	39.41 N	77.53 E
Woerden	52	52.05 N	4.54 E
Woerth	56	48.56 N	7.45 E
Woëvre ◆[1]	56	49.05 N	5.40 E
Wofosi	105	40.09 N	115.18 E
Wo Fo Si (Temple of the Sleeping Buddha) ♁[1]	105	40.01 N	116.12 E
Wognum	52	52.41 N	5.01 E
Wohlde	41	54.24 N	9.17 E
Wohlen	58	47.21 N	8.17 E
Wohlensee ⊜	58	46.58 N	7.20 E
Wohlford, Lake ⊜[1]	228	33.10 N	116.59 W
Wohlthat Mountains ⋀	9	71.35 S	12.20 E
Wohra ≃	56	50.49 N	8.55 E
Woi	140	7.53 N	31.10 E
Woincourt	50	50.04 N	1.32 E
Woippy, Dtsch.	56	49.09 N	6.09 E
Woippy, Fr.	56	49.09 N	6.09 E
Wojcieszów	30	50.58 N	15.56 E
Wokalup	168a	33.06 S	115.53 E
Wokam, Pulau I	164	5.37 S	134.30 E
Wokha	120	26.06 N	94.16 E
Woking, Ab., Can.	182	55.35 N	118.46 W
Woking, Eng., U.K.	42	51.20 N	0.34 W
Woking □[8]	260	51.19 N	0.32 W
Wokingham	42	51.25 N	0.51 W
Wokingham Creek ≃	166	22.19 S	142.30 E
Wolbach	198	41.24 N	98.24 W
Wolbeck	52	51.55 N	7.43 E
Wolbrom	30	50.24 N	19.46 E
Wolcott, Ct., U.S.	207	41.36 N	72.59 W
Wolcott, In., U.S.	216	40.45 N	87.02 W
Wolcott, N.Y., U.S.	210	43.13 N	76.48 W
Wolcott Creek ≃	210	43.17 N	76.50 W
Wolcottsburg	210	43.04 N	78.38 W
Wolcottsville	210	43.07 N	78.31 W
Wolcottville	216	41.32 N	85.22 W
Wołcza ≃	54	53.58 N	14.53 E
Wołczenica ≃	54	53.52 N	14.44 E
Wołczyn	30	51.01 N	18.03 E
Woldberg ⋀[1]	52	52.25 N	5.55 E
Woldegk	54	53.27 N	13.35 E
Woldingham	260	51.17 N	0.02 W
Woleai I[1]	108	7.21 N	143.52 E
Woleu-Ntem □[4]	152	1.30 N	12.00 E
Wolf ≃, On., Can.	190	48.49 N	88.30 W
Wolf ≃, U.S.	194	35.09 N	90.04 W
Wolf ≃, Ks., U.S.	198	39.54 N	95.11 W
Wolf ≃, Ms., U.S.	194	30.21 N	89.18 W
Wolf ≃, Wi., U.S.	190	44.11 N	88.48 W
Wolf, Isla I	246a	1.23 N	91.49 W
Wolf, Volcán ʌ[1]	246a	0.02 N	91.20 W
Wolfach	58	48.17 N	8.13 E
Wolf-Bay	186	50.16 N	60.08 W
Wolf Creek, Mt., U.S.	202	47.00 N	112.04 W
Wolf Creek, Or., U.S.	202	42.41 N	123.23 W
Wolf Creek ≃, U.S.	196	36.35 N	99.30 W
Wolf Creek ≃, Ca., U.S.	226	39.02 N	121.08 W
Wolf Creek ≃, Co., U.S.	200	40.12 N	108.29 W
Wolf Creek ≃, In., U.S.	216	41.15 N	87.07 W
Wolf Creek ≃, Ia., U.S.	190	42.20 N	92.09 W
Wolf Creek ≃, Mt., U.S.	198	48.05 N	105.40 W
Wolf Creek ≃, Mt., U.S.	202	47.37 N	109.38 W
Wolf Creek ≃, Oh., U.S.	214	41.16 N	83.11 W
Wolf Creek ≃, Pa., U.S.	214	41.03 N	80.07 W
Wolf Creek ≃, S.D., U.S.	198	43.21 N	97.37 W
Wolf Creek ≃, S.D., U.S.	198	44.42 N	98.40 W
Wolf Creek Lake ⊜[1]	198	38.14 N	95.41 W
Wolf Creek Pass)(	200	37.29 N	106.48 W
Wolf Creek State Park ♠	219	39.30 N	88.41 W
Wolfdale	214	40.12 N	80.17 W
Wolfe □[6]	206	45.45 N	71.30 W
Wolfeboro	188	43.35 N	71.12 W
Wolfe City	196	33.22 N	96.04 W
Wolfegg	58	47.49 N	9.47 E
Wolfe Island	212	44.12 N	76.26 W
Wolfe Island I	212	44.12 N	76.20 W
Wolfe Lake ⊜	212	44.40 N	76.30 W
Wolfen	54	51.40 N	12.16 E
Wolfenbüttel	52	52.10 N	10.32 E
Wolfenden, Mount ʌ	182	50.26 N	127.33 W
Wolfenschiessen	58	46.55 N	8.24 E
Wolfertschwenden	58	47.53 N	10.16 E
Wolfforth	196	33.30 N	102.01 W
Wolfgangsee ⊜	64	47.44 N	13.26 E
Wolfhagen	56	51.19 N	9.10 E
Wölfis	54	50.48 N	10.46 E
Wolf Island I	212	44.33 N	78.15 W
Wolflake, In., U.S.	216	41.20 N	85.30 W
Wolf Lake, Mi., U.S.	216	43.15 N	86.06 W
Wolf Lake ⊜, Ab., Can.	182	54.42 N	110.59 W
Wolf Lake ⊜, On., Can.	212	44.44 N	78.11 W
Wolf Lake ⊜, Yk., Can.	180	60.40 N	131.40 W
Wolf Lake ⊜, U.S.	278	41.40 N	87.31 W
Wolf Lake ⊜, N.J., U.S.	276	40.57 N	74.42 W
Wolf Mountain ʌ	180	65.17 N	154.02 W
Wolfpassing	264b	48.19 N	16.11 E
Wolf Point	202	48.05 N	105.38 W
Wolframs-Eschenbach	56	49.14 N	10.43 E
Wolfratshausen	64	47.54 N	11.25 E
Wolf Rock I[2]	28	49.57 N	5.49 W
Wolf Run	214	40.30 N	80.54 W
Wolfsberg	61	46.51 N	14.51 E
Wolfsberg ʌ[2]	263	51.38 N	6.27 E
Wolfsburg	54	52.25 N	10.47 E
Wolf's Castle	42	51.54 N	4.58 W
Wolfsegg am Hausruck	60	48.06 N	13.40 E
Wolfstein	56	49.35 N	7.36 E
Wolftrap Creek ≃	284c	38.58 N	77.17 W
Wolf Trap Farms for the Performing Arts ♠	284c	38.56 N	77.16 W
Wolfurt	58	47.28 N	9.45 E
Wolfville	186	45.05 N	64.22 W
Wolga → Volga ≃	72	45.55 N	47.52 E
Wolgan ≃	170	33.12 S	150.28 E
Wolgast	54	54.03 N	13.46 E
Wolgograd → Volgograd	80	48.44 N	44.25 E
Wolgograder Stausee → Volgogradskoje vodochranilišče ⊜[1]	80	49.20 N	45.00 E
Wolhusen	58	47.04 N	8.04 E
Wolin	30	53.50 N	14.35 E
Wolin I	54	53.55 N	14.31 E
Woliński Park Narodowy ♠	30	53.55 N	14.30 E
Wolkenstein	54	50.39 N	13.04 E
Wolkersdorf	61	48.23 N	16.31 E
Wölkisch	54	51.13 N	13.21 E
Wolkramshausen	54	51.25 N	10.44 E
Wollangambe ≃	170	33.21 S	150.35 E
Wollaston	42	52.15 N	0.40 W
Wollaston, Islas II	254	55.40 S	67.30 W
Wollaston Beach ⏏[2]	283	42.17 N	71.01 W
Wollaston Lake ⊜, On., Can.	212	44.50 N	77.50 W
Wollaston Lake ⊜, Sk., Can.	176	58.15 N	103.20 W
Wollaston Peninsula ≻[1]	176	70.00 N	115.00 W
Wollemi Creek ≃	170	33.13 S	150.31 E
Wollemi National Park ♠	166	32.50 S	150.30 E
Wollogorang	166	17.13 S	137.57 E
Wollombi	170	32.56 S	151.09 E
Wollombi Brook ≃	170	32.33 S	151.04 E
Wollondilly ≃	170	33.57 S	150.26 E
Wollongong	170	34.25 S	150.54 E
Wöllstein	56	49.49 N	7.58 E
Wolmaransstad	158	27.12 S	26.13 E
Wolmirsleben	54	51.57 N	11.29 E
Wolmirstedt	54	52.15 N	11.37 E
Wolnzach	60	48.36 N	11.37 E
Wołomin	30	52.21 N	21.14 E
Wołów	30	51.21 N	16.39 E
Wolowaru	115b	8.46 S	121.54 E
Wolseley, Sk., Can.	184	50.25 N	103.19 W
Wolseley, S. Afr.	158	33.26 S	19.12 E
Wolsey	198	44.24 N	98.28 W
Wolsingham	44	54.44 N	1.52 W
Wolsztyn	30	52.08 N	16.06 E
Wolterdingen	52	53.02 N	9.50 E
Woltersdorf, Dtsch.	54	52.24 N	12.22 E
Woltersdorf, Dtsch.	54	52.26 N	13.45 E
Woluogu	105	39.40 N	117.46 E
Woluwe-Saint-Lambert (Sint-Lambrechts-Woluwe)	56	50.51 N	4.24 E
Wolvega	52	52.53 N	6.00 E
Wolverhampton	42	52.36 N	2.08 W
Wolverine	190	45.16 N	84.36 W
Wolverine Lake	281	42.33 N	83.29 W
Wolverine Loon Lake ⊜	281	42.33 N	83.30 W
Wolverine Mountain ʌ	180	65.20 N	149.51 W
Wolvertem	50	50.57 N	4.18 E
Wolverton	42	52.04 N	0.50 W
Wolwehoek	158	26.55 S	27.48 E
Wölzerbach ≃	61	47.08 N	14.23 E
Wolziger See ⊜	54	52.16 N	13.50 E
Woman ≃	190	47.57 N	82.19 W
Wombarra	170	34.16 S	150.58 E
Wombat, Mount ʌ	169	36.51 S	145.40 E
Wombeyan Caves ⏏[5]	170	34.18 S	149.56 E
Wombourne	42	52.32 N	2.11 W
Wombwell	44	53.31 N	1.24 W
Womelsdorf	208	40.22 N	76.11 W
Women's Rights National Historical Park ♠	210	42.54 N	76.47 W

Symbol	English	Deutsch	Español	Français	Português
≃	River	Fluß	Río	Rivière	Rio
≅	Canal	Kanal	Canal	Canal	Canal
ᒪ	Waterfall, Rapids	Wasserfall, Stromschnellen	Cascada, Rápidos	Chute d'eau, Rapides	Cascata, Rápidos
ʊ	Strait	Meeresstraße	Estrecho	Détroit	Estreito
c	Bay, Gulf	Bucht, Golf	Bahía, Golfo	Baie, Golfe	Baía, Golfo
⊜	Lake, Lakes	See, Seen	Lago, Lagos	Lac, Lacs	Lago, Lagos
⩩	Swamp	Sumpf	Pantano	Marais	Pântano
⍓	Ice Features, Glacier	Eis- und Gletscherformen	Accidentes Glaciales	Formes glaciaires	Acidentes glaciares
⊤	Other Hydrographic Features	Andere Hydrographische Objekte	Otros Elementos Hidrográficos	Autres données hydrographiques	Outros acidentes hidrográficos
✤	Submarine Features	Untermeerische Objekte	Accidentes Submarinos	Formes de relief sous-marin	Acidentes submarinos
□	Political Unit	Politische Einheit	Unidad Politica	Entité politique	Unidade política
♁	Cultural Institution	Kulturelle Institution	Institución Cultural	Institution culturelle	Institução cultural
⊥	Historical Site	Historische Stätte	Sitio Histórico	Site historique	Sitio histórico
♠	Recreational Site	Erholungs- und Ferienort	Sitio de Recreo	Centre de loisirs	Area de Lazer
⊠	Airport	Flughafen	Aeropuerto	Aéroport	Aeroporto
■	Military Installation	Militäranlage	Instalación Militar	Installation militaire	Instalação militar
◆	Miscellaneous	Verschiedenes	Misceláneo	Divers	Diversos

ESPAÑOL · FRANÇAIS · PORTUGUÊS

Nombre / Nom / Nome	Página / Page	Lat.°′	Long.°′ W = Oeste / W = Ouest
Xavante ≐	250	11.23 S	49.41 W
Xavantes ≐	250	10.40 S	50.41 W
Xavantina	255	21.15 S	52.48 W
Xa Vo Dat	110	11.09 N	107.31 E
Xaxim	252	26.56 S	52.31 W
Xcalak	232	18.16 N	87.50 W
X-Can	232	20.50 N	87.43 W
Xelva	34	39.45 N	0.59 W
Xenia, Il., U.S.	219	38.38 N	88.38 W
Xenia, Oh., U.S.	218	39.41 N	83.55 W
Xénô	110	16.35 N	104.50 E
Xercavins, Arroyo de ≐	266d	41.30 N	2.02 E
Xerém	256	22.33 S	43.18 W
Xeres — Jerez de la Frontera	34	36.41 N	6.08 W
Xertigny	58	48.03 N	6.24 E
Xeruã ≐	248	6.03 S	67.50 W
Xhumo	156	21.07 S	24.42 E
Xi ≐, Zhg.	100	24.34 N	117.30 E
Xi ≐, Zhg.	100	25.14 N	118.03 E
Xi ≐, Zhg.	100	30.21 N	115.06 E
Xi ≐, Zhg.	102	42.20 N	100.20 E
Xi ≐, Zhg.	102	22.25 N	113.23 E
Xi ≐, Zhg.	104	41.15 N	123.32 E
Xi ≐, Zhg.	104	41.30 N	121.26 E
Xi ≐, Zhg.	107	30.26 N	103.48 E
Xiaang	106	30.45 N	120.07 E
Xiaba	100	24.54 N	116.06 E
Xiabai, Zhg.	106	31.12 N	119.50 E
Xiabai, Zhg.	106	30.29 N	120.00 E
Xiabanghu	100	30.31 N	112.38 E
Xiabian	104	40.51 N	120.30 E
Xiabuji	100	28.19 N	116.20 E
Xiacang	105	39.47 N	117.24 E
Xiache	100	24.40 N	115.08 E
Xiachengzi	89	44.41 N	130.27 E
Xiachuan Dao I	102	21.40 N	112.37 E
Xiacun	105	40.21 N	116.14 E
Xiadao	100	26.34 N	118.16 E
Xiadian, Zhg.	98	37.06 N	120.19 E
Xiadian, Zhg.	100	31.26 N	114.17 E
Xiadian, Zhg.	105	39.57 N	116.55 E
Xiadianjie	100	25.13 N	118.27 E
Xiafeidi	98	42.18 N	124.21 E
Xiafu, Zhg.	100	25.01 N	113.41 E
Xiafu, Zhg.	100	23.52 N	115.45 E
Xiagaixin	102	22.36 N	99.59 E
Xiagang	106	31.55 N	120.13 E
Xiagezhuang	98	36.41 N	120.25 E
Xiaguan, Zhg.	98	39.07 N	114.09 E
Xiaguan, Zhg.	102	25.34 N	100.14 E
Xiaguan, Zhg.	106	32.06 N	118.44 E
Xiaguanjunchang	104	41.28 N	121.40 E
Xiaguanpi	100	24.04 N	117.06 E
Xiagucheng	102	36.47 N	102.53 E
Xiagucun	106	30.56 N	119.09 E
Xiahada	104	41.58 N	124.08 E
Xiahailangzhai	104	41.35 N	123.46 E
Xiahe	102	35.18 N	102.30 E
Xiahuangjintun	104	41.57 N	123.48 E
Xiahuayuan	105	40.29 N	115.17 E
Xiajiabaozi	98	42.16 N	124.37 E
Xiajialou	104	42.25 N	123.39 E
Xiajiang	100	27.32 N	115.08 E
Xiajiangdun	106	31.14 N	120.24 E
Xiajiangwu	106	30.29 N	119.00 E
Xiajiayuan	106	32.13 N	120.38 E
Xiajiezi	102	27.28 N	101.35 E
Xiajin	98	36.55 N	115.57 E
Xiakou	100	28.28 N	118.31 E
Xialianggang	105	39.14 N	115.07 E
Xialufang	102	31.11 N	103.38 E
Xiamaguan	102	37.14 N	106.28 E
Xiamen (Amoy)	100	24.28 N	118.07 E
Xiamen Gang c	100	24.19 N	118.10 E
Xiamianzhen	107	30.08 N	106.32 E
Xiamin'ansutai	104	41.54 N	120.53 E
Xiamocun	106	31.09 N	119.22 E
Xi'an (Sian)	102	34.15 N	108.52 E
Xian ≐	107	29.22 N	104.44 E
Xianchenggu	98	36.53 N	115.17 E
Xiandu	100	25.04 N	117.44 E
Xianfeng, Zhg.	100	25.42 N	117.53 E
Xianfeng, Zhg.	102	29.41 N	109.02 E
Xiang ≐, Zhg.	100	25.35 N	115.49 E
Xiang ≐, Zhg.	102	29.00 N	112.56 E
Xiang'an	100	31.12 N	117.46 E
Xiangcheng, Zhg.	100	33.28 N	114.53 E
Xiangcheng, Zhg.	100	33.53 N	113.29 E
Xiangcheng, Zhg.	102	28.59 N	99.45 E
Xiangcheng, Zhg.	106	31.29 N	120.44 E
Xiangfan	102	32.03 N	112.01 E
Xiangfuguan	100	28.30 N	115.26 E
Xiangfusi	107	30.06 N	104.24 E
Xianggang — Victoria	271d	22.17 N	114.09 E
Xianggongshi	100	28.25 N	113.32 E
Xianggongzhuang	105	39.48 N	118.19 E
Xianghe	105	39.46 N	116.59 E
Xiangheguan	100	33.08 N	113.26 E
Xianghuazhen	106	31.31 N	121.43 E
Xiangjia, Zhg.	106	31.20 N	120.31 E
Xiangjia, Zhg.	106	31.19 N	120.23 E
Xiangjiachang	107	30.08 N	104.18 E
Xiangkhoang	110	19.20 N	103.22 E
Xiangkhoang, Plateau de ✗[1]	110	19.30 N	103.10 E
Xiangning	102	36.01 N	110.45 E
Xiangride	102	36.02 N	98.08 E
Xiangshan, Zhg.	100	29.28 N	121.51 E
Xiangshan, Zhg.	105	39.59 N	116.12 E
Xiangshan Gang c	100	29.38 N	121.48 E
Xiangshizhen	107	29.17 N	105.09 E
Xiangshui, Zhg.	100	23.15 N	114.10 E
Xiangshui, Zhg.	100	34.12 N	119.34 E
Xiangtan	100	27.51 N	112.54 E
Xiangtang	100	28.26 N	115.58 E
Xiangxiang	102	27.43 N	112.27 E
Xiangyang	105	39.13 N	115.25 E
Xiangyangkou	105	40.06 N	115.47 E
Xiangyin	100	28.40 N	112.53 E
Xiangyuan	102	36.32 N	113.00 E
Xiangyun	102	25.30 N	100.30 E
Xiangzhenpu	100	30.52 N	117.21 E
Xiangzhou, Zhg.	98	36.12 N	119.24 E
Xiangzhou, Zhg.	102	23.55 N	109.49 E
Xiangzhu	100	29.02 N	120.04 E
Xianinggang	100	28.20 N	112.56 E
Xianjiang	100	27.48 N	120.30 E
Xianju	100	28.51 N	120.44 E
Xianning	100	29.53 N	114.13 E
Xiannongtan Stadium ♠	271a	39.52 N	116.23 E
Xiannübu	100	25.36 N	114.40 E
Xianru	89	43.11 N	128.02 E
Xianshichang	107	28.43 N	105.44 E
Xianshui ≐	102	30.05 N	110.59 E
Xianshuigu	105	38.59 N	117.23 E
Xiantan, Zhg.	107	29.21 N	104.53 E
Xiantan, Zhg.	107	28.50 N	106.12 E
Xiantang	100	23.48 N	114.46 E
Xianxia Ling ✗	100	28.30 N	118.46 E
Xianxian	98	38.13 N	116.06 E
Xianyang, Zhg.	100	28.02 N	118.30 E
Xianyang, Zhg.	102	34.22 N	108.42 E
Xianyou	100	25.23 N	118.40 E
Xianzhong	100	28.36 N	113.48 E
Xiao ≐	100	28.11 N	120.14 E
Xiao'an ≐	107	29.59 N	106.13 E
Xiao'ao	100	26.14 N	119.39 E
Xiaoazhang	102	23.42 N	104.58 E
Xiaobangniulu	104	41.34 N	122.46 E
Xiaobeigou	104	41.55 N	120.46 E
Xiaobeihe, Zhg.	104	42.39 N	123.58 E
Xiaobeihe, Zhg.	104	41.22 N	122.50 E
Xiaocaohu	86	43.06 N	88.30 E
Xiaochangshan Dao I	98	39.12 N	122.41 E
Xiaocheng	100	26.20 N	119.47 E
Xiaochengdu	106	30.59 N	120.04 E
Xiaochengzi, Zhg.	89	46.33 N	122.54 E
Xiaochengzi, Zhg.	89	42.56 N	123.12 E
Xiaochi	100	30.33 N	116.23 E
Xiaochikou	100	29.46 N	115.59 E
Xiaodanyang	106	31.38 N	118.43 E
Xiaodong	102	22.14 N	108.39 E
Xiao'ergou	89	49.12 N	123.42 E
Xiaofangshen	104	42.13 N	123.54 E
Xiaofanshan	105	40.16 N	115.19 E
Xiaofen	106	31.45 N	119.39 E
Xiaofeng	106	30.36 N	119.32 E
Xiaogan	100	30.55 N	113.54 E
Xiaogangkou	100	28.14 N	115.50 E
Xiaogaojiatun	104	41.02 N	121.59 E
Xiaogencaigangzi	104	41.48 N	122.42 E
Xiaogu	107	29.08 N	104.01 E
Xiaoguai	86	45.13 N	85.02 E
Xiaogushan	98	39.49 N	123.12 E
Xiaohaizhen	106	31.58 N	120.59 E
Xiaohaladaokou	98	42.37 N	119.32 E
Xiaohan	98	35.48 N	114.52 E
Xiaohe	106	32.01 N	119.52 E
Xiaohei Shan ∧	102	24.42 N	98.55 E
Xiaohekou	102	33.19 N	107.25 E
Xiaoheyan	98	42.26 N	119.38 E
Xiaoheying	102	32.37 N	104.23 E
Xiao Hinggan Ling (Lesser Khingan Range) ✗	89	48.45 N	127.00 E
Xiaohongmen	271a	39.49 N	116.26 E
Xiaohu	100	27.20 N	118.14 E
Xiaohuying	98	41.09 N	117.13 E
Xiaoji, Zhg.	98	36.45 N	121.01 E
Xiaoji, Zhg.	100	27.08 N	113.15 E
Xiaoji, Zhg.	100	32.38 N	119.48 E
Xiaojiachang	107	30.18 N	106.28 E
Xiaojiagang	100	31.06 N	113.55 E
Xiaojialing	100	29.35 N	116.32 E
Xiaojiang	100	25.08 N	114.59 E
Xiaojianji	100	33.23 N	116.29 E
Xiaojiawu	105	39.36 N	116.36 E
Xiaojiayingzi	98	40.17 N	118.47 E
Xiaojieling	100	31.36 N	115.09 E
Xiaojin	102	31.00 N	102.21 E
Xiaojingfang	105	39.22 N	116.34 E
Xiaojiu	89	45.15 N	127.47 E
Xiaokaoshantun	104	42.10 N	123.53 E
Xiaokuli	89	50.18 N	120.20 E
Xiaokunshan	106	31.02 N	121.07 E
Xiaolan	100	22.41 N	113.14 E
Xiaoliangshan	104	42.05 N	122.32 E
Xiaoling, Zhg.	89	45.20 N	127.18 E
Xiaoling, Zhg.	104	42.18 N	123.23 E
Xiaoling ≐	104	41.06 N	121.07 E
Xiaolingzi	104	41.07 N	123.19 E
Xiaolinzhuang	104	41.36 N	124.01 E
Xiaolipu	98	36.24 N	116.35 E
Xiaolongtan	102	23.51 N	103.10 E
Xiaoluan ≐	98	41.36 N	117.05 E
Xiaolüzhuang	106	31.57 N	119.25 E
Xiaomei	100	27.50 N	118.58 E
Xiaomei Guan)(	100	25.17 N	114.17 E
Xiaomiaozi	98	41.24 N	114.25 E
Xiaonanhai	107	29.23 N	106.27 E
Xiaopikou	98	35.47 N	115.53 E
Xiaopingyang	102	23.22 N	109.13 E
Xiao Qaidam He ⊜	102	37.30 N	95.12 E
Xiaoqiao	100	26.57 N	118.30 E
Xiaoqiaotou	106	30.43 N	119.27 E
Xiaoqing ≐	98	37.17 N	118.52 E
Xiaoqingchuizi	104	42.30 N	123.39 E
Xiaoquandong	102	41.14 N	95.26 E
Xiaosanjiazi	104	42.34 N	123.23 E
Xiaosha ≐	104	41.13 N	122.45 E
Xiaoshakou	100	29.58 N	113.16 E
Xiaoshan	106	30.10 N	120.15 E
Xiaoshangqiao	100	33.43 N	113.58 E
Xiaoshi	100	27.27 N	116.49 E
Xiaoshixiang	100	30.36 N	116.38 E
Xiaoshu	106	30.48 N	119.46 E
Xiaoshun	100	29.11 N	119.51 E
Xiaosigou	98	40.53 N	118.33 E
Xiaosijia	104	42.24 N	120.46 E
Xiaotang	98	41.38 N	119.33 E
Xiaotanghe	98	42.04 N	127.10 E
Xiaotao	100	25.46 N	117.08 E
Xiaotazi	104	42.17 N	123.08 E
Xiaotian	100	31.12 N	116.33 E
Xiaotianji	100	32.45 N	115.36 E
Xiaotun	104	42.24 N	123.44 E
Xiaotunzicun	104	41.14 N	123.20 E
Xiaowa	104	41.03 N	122.04 E
Xiaowan	100	26.53 N	116.36 E
Xiaowangmiao	100	29.41 N	121.21 E
Xiaowutai Shan ∧	105	39.51 N	115.09 E
Xiaowutai Shan ✗	105	39.50 N	115.00 E
Xiaoxi	100	25.48 N	115.21 E
Xiaoxi ≐	106	32.15 N	120.24 E
Xiaoxian	98	34.11 N	116.56 E
Xiaoxincheng	105	39.24 N	115.11 E
Xiaoxintian	271a	39.58 N	116.22 E
Xiaoxizhen	106	30.51 N	119.50 E
Xiaoyangjiadian	104	42.23 N	122.24 E
Xiaoyangqi	89	50.48 N	124.12 E
Xiaoyantai	104	41.26 N	123.10 E
Xiaoyaozhen	100	33.46 N	114.16 E
Xiaoyi	102	37.10 N	111.46 E
Xiaoying, Zhg.	98	37.18 N	118.04 E
Xiaoying, Zhg.	105	40.12 N	116.33 E
Xiaoyingcun	105	39.28 N	116.41 E
Xiaoyuan	107	30.00 N	104.56 E
Xiaozhan	105	38.55 N	117.25 E
Xiaozhang ≐	105	39.47 N	117.22 E
Xiaozhongdian	102	27.40 N	99.46 E
Xiaozhuang	104	41.30 N	121.27 E
Xiaozhujiawan	106	31.24 N	121.01 E
Xiapu, Zhg.	100	26.52 N	120.01 E
Xiapu, Zhg.	100	27.49 N	114.26 E
Xiaqialafangzi	104	41.48 N	121.44 E
Xiaqi Dao I	100	29.42 N	122.15 E
Xiaqiubao	98	37.01 N	119.54 E
Xiasantumen	105	38.50 N	114.48 E
Xiashe	106	30.33 N	120.11 E
Xiashesi	100	27.46 N	112.57 E
Xiashi — Haining	106	30.32 N	120.41 E
Xiashu	106	32.11 N	119.10 E
Xiashuerfowei	89	50.23 N	120.47 E
Xiashuiquan	104	41.52 N	123.38 E
Xiataizi	105	40.37 N	117.45 E
Xiatang, Zhg.	100	33.45 N	112.39 E
Xiatang, Zhg.	106	31.29 N	118.41 E
Xiatangtian	106	30.55 N	120.12 E
Xiataohuatu	104	41.42 N	120.36 E
Xiawa	98	42.39 N	120.35 E
Xiawajiang	106	30.59 N	121.51 E
Xiawaziyu	104	41.15 N	123.38 E
Xiaxi	106	31.43 N	119.45 E
Xiaxian	102	35.11 N	111.15 E
Xiaxiangcheng	102	28.42 N	99.59 E
Xiaxikou	100	26.15 N	118.59 E
Xiaxinhe	106	31.40 N	119.31 E
Xiayang, Zhg.	100	28.48 N	119.41 E
Xiayang, Zhg.	100	26.46 N	117.59 E
Xiayang, Zhg.	100	24.39 N	116.52 E
Xiayi	98	34.14 N	116.06 E
Xiaying, Zhg.	98	37.03 N	119.25 E
Xiaying, Zhg.	105	40.10 N	117.25 E
Xiayunling	105	39.43 N	115.44 E
Xiazhang	98	36.08 N	116.57 E
Xiazhen	100	28.39 N	118.21 E
Xiazhuang, Zhg.	98	35.28 N	118.43 E
Xiazhuang, Zhg.	100	27.22 N	119.01 E
Xiazhuang, Zhg.	105	39.54 N	117.01 E
Xiazhuang, Zhg.	105	39.38 N	115.26 E
Xiazikou	105	39.01 N	115.25 E
Xiban	107	30.32 N	106.12 E
Xibaqianmou	104	40.59 N	121.35 E
Xibeiyingzi	104	41.55 N	121.38 E
Xibo ≐	98	42.17 N	118.57 E
Xibu	100	31.46 N	118.17 E
Xicang	106	31.34 N	120.29 E
Xichang, Zhg.	102	27.58 N	102.13 E
Xichang, Zhg.	104	42.15 N	124.12 E
Xicheng	89	48.10 N	125.29 E
Xichong	102	31.00 N	105.52 E
Xicicun	105	39.29 N	116.08 E
Xico	234	19.25 N	97.00 W
Xicoténcatl	234	23.00 N	98.56 W
Xicotepec de Juárez	234	20.17 N	97.57 W
Xictle, Volcán ∧[1]	286a	19.14 N	99.14 W
Xicun	100	27.46 N	114.14 E
Xidachuan	98	41.46 N	127.34 E
Xidapo	89	43.12 N	130.02 E
Xidaying	105	39.41 N	116.14 E
Xidian	100	29.32 N	121.26 E
Xiditou	105	39.16 N	117.23 E
Xidongting Shan ∧	106	31.07 N	120.16 E
Xié ≐	246	0.54 N	67.11 W
Xiecun	105	39.00 N	115.31 E
Xiedian	100	33.27 N	113.28 E
Xiefang	100	26.12 N	116.41 E
Xieji	98	34.32 N	115.29 E
Xiejia	98	42.24 N	125.42 E
Xiejiagangzi	104	41.55 N	122.20 E
Xiejiapu	106	31.15 N	119.09 E
Xiejunmiao	107	30.15 N	103.40 E
Xielipuke	120	31.30 N	82.45 E
Xiemachang	107	29.46 N	106.22 E
Xiemata Shan ∧	89	50.28 N	120.47 E
Xiepu	100	30.02 N	121.37 E
Xieqiao, Zhg.	106	32.03 N	120.22 E
Xieqiao, Zhg.	106	30.29 N	120.34 E
Xietang	106	31.18 N	120.44 E
Xiexi	106	31.54 N	118.54 E
Xiexinggou	104	41.51 N	121.05 E
Xifei ≐	100	32.38 N	116.39 E
Xifeng, Zhg.	98	42.43 N	124.40 E
Xifeng, Zhg.	102	27.02 N	106.30 E
Xifengkou	105	40.24 N	118.19 E
Xifocun	104	41.26 N	122.33 E
Xigangzi	89	49.58 N	127.20 E
Xigaolizhuangzi	104	41.40 N	122.55 E
Xigaotan	98	38.18 N	116.13 E
Xigaotun	98	40.27 N	122.36 E
Xigazê	120	29.17 N	88.53 E
Xiguanjiatun	104	42.35 N	123.10 E
Xiguanyingzi	104	41.50 N	120.37 E
Xihaikou	104	40.50 N	121.05 E
Xihan ≐	102	33.30 N	106.02 E
Xihe, Zhg.	100	31.01 N	118.28 E
Xihe, Zhg.	100	31.41 N	113.27 E
Xihe, Zhg.	102	34.01 N	105.17 E
Xiheying	105	39.53 N	114.42 E
Xihezhuang	105	39.20 N	118.02 E
Xi Hu ⊜	106	30.15 N	120.08 E
Xihua	100	33.47 N	114.31 E
Xihuangcang	106	31.43 N	121.40 E
Xihuanzidong	104	41.31 N	122.28 E
Xihuashan, Zhg.	100	25.28 N	114.20 E
Xihuashan, Zhg.	105	40.07 N	116.54 E
Xihuishan	104	41.41 N	122.38 E
Xiis	144	10.53 N	46.54 E
Xiji, Zhg.	102	35.58 N	105.44 E
Xiji, Zhg.	105	39.49 N	116.52 E
Xijialong	102	23.31 N	103.51 E
Xijiang	100	25.50 N	115.49 E
Xijiansharzi	104	40.47 N	120.48 E
Xi Jiao Airfield ⊠	271a	39.58 N	116.15 E
Xijiapuzitun	104	41.26 N	123.50 E
Xijir Ulan Hu ⊜	120	35.12 N	90.18 E
Xikou, Zhg.	89	46.40 N	120.40 E
Xikou, Zhg.	100	28.52 N	119.11 E
Xikou, Zhg.	100	25.26 N	118.45 E
Xikou, Zhg.	100	29.44 N	118.02 E
Xikou, Zhg.	100	29.14 N	114.24 E
Xikou, Zhg.	100	29.11 N	114.23 E
Xikou, Zhg.	106	30.40 N	118.41 E
Xikouxu	100	25.24 N	117.03 E
Xikouzi	89	53.06 N	120.40 E
Xilai	107	30.20 N	103.29 E
Xilaiqiao	106	32.03 N	119.54 E
Xilaizhen	106	32.07 N	120.25 E
Xilin	120	28.33 N	87.48 E
Xi Ling (Western Tombs) ⊥	105	39.24 N	115.18 E
Xilintuo	120	30.08 N	88.04 E
Xilitla	234	21.20 N	98.58 W
Xiliuhe	105	38.58 N	116.32 E
Xiliushuyingzi	104	42.25 N	121.54 E
Xilókastron	38	38.05 N	22.38 E
Xiluga ≐	98	42.21 N	118.38 E
Xiluncun	89	47.08 N	126.26 E
Ximagou	105	40.16 N	117.50 E
Ximakou	100	30.33 N	113.47 E
Ximalatu	89	47.00 N	122.01 E
Ximalin	98	40.48 N	114.29 E
Ximiao	102	41.09 N	100.17 E
Ximucheng	104	40.42 N	122.54 E
Xin ≐	100	28.37 N	116.40 E
Xin'an, Zhg.	89	43.46 N	125.40 E
Xinan, Zhg.	100	25.26 N	117.35 E
Xin'an, Zhg.	100	26.44 N	116.13 E
Xin'an, Zhg.	100	23.02 N	114.56 E
Xin'an, Zhg.	105	39.09 N	116.38 E
Xin'an, Zhg.	106	31.47 N	120.09 E
Xin'an, Zhg.	106	31.30 N	120.22 E
Xin'an ≐	100	29.33 N	118.58 E
Xin'andian	100	32.37 N	114.03 E
Xin'andu	100	30.52 N	116.53 E
Xin'anji	100	33.22 N	115.13 E
Xin'anjiang Shuiku ⊜[1]	100	29.27 N	119.06 E
Xin'anpu	104	42.39 N	123.27 E
Xin'anqiao	106	32.16 N	121.07 E
Xin'ansuo	102	23.16 N	103.27 E
Xin'anzhen, Zhg.	89	44.06 N	123.46 E
Xin'anzhen, Zhg.	105	39.45 N	117.32 E
Xi'nanzhuang	105	40.48 N	118.23 E
Xinavane	156	25.02 S	32.47 E
Xinba, Zhg.	98	34.27 N	119.09 E
Xinba, Zhg.	100	30.24 N	116.52 E
Xinba, Zhg.	106	32.08 N	120.39 E
Xinba, Zhg.	106	32.16 N	119.45 E
Xinbao'an	105	40.27 N	115.24 E
Xin Barag Youqi (Altan Emel)	88	48.41 N	116.53 E
Xin Barag Zuoqi (Amgalang)	88	48.14 N	118.18 E
Xinbin, Zhg.	98	41.42 N	125.02 E
Xinbin, Zhg.	106	30.56 N	121.04 E
Xinbo	98	42.19 N	117.44 E
Xincai	100	32.44 N	114.59 E
Xincang, Zhg.	106	30.25 N	120.42 E
Xincang, Zhg.	106	30.44 N	121.11 E
Xinchang, Zhg.	100	29.30 N	120.53 E
Xinchang, Zhg.	102	28.03 N	103.46 E
Xinchang, Zhg.	102	25.10 N	104.18 E
Xinchang, Zhg.	106	31.42 N	121.46 E
Xinchang, Zhg.	106	31.02 N	121.38 E
Xinchang, Zhg.	107	30.29 N	106.21 E
Xinchang, Zhg.	107	30.16 N	104.29 E
Xinchang, Zhg.	107	29.20 N	104.15 E
Xinchang, Zhg.	107	29.38 N	104.33 E
Xinchangzi	107	29.40 N	103.46 E
Xincheng, Zhg.	100	25.34 N	114.36 E
Xincheng, Zhg.	102	24.09 N	108.46 E
Xincheng (Gaobeidian), Zhg.	105	39.20 N	115.51 E
Xincheng, Zhg.	105	38.59 N	117.33 E
Xincheng, Zhg.	106	32.17 N	119.14 E
Xincheng, Zhg.	106	30.48 N	120.36 E
Xinchengzi	104	42.03 N	123.30 E
Xinchepaizi	86	44.55 N	84.30 E
Xincunji	100	32.53 N	115.31 E
Xindai	106	30.49 N	121.05 E
Xindi	104	42.21 N	120.31 E
Xindian, Zhg.	89	45.55 N	127.50 E
Xindian, Zhg.	98	37.07 N	114.49 E
Xindian, Zhg.	98	37.29 N	118.28 E
Xindian, Zhg.	100	33.07 N	112.38 E
Xindian, Zhg.	100	31.33 N	115.16 E
Xindian, Zhg.	100	33.38 N	113.51 E
Xindian, Zhg.	100	29.40 N	113.40 E
Xindian, Zhg.	105	40.11 N	116.11 E
Xindian, Zhg.	105	40.47 N	116.49 E
Xindian, Zhg.	105	39.10 N	116.27 E
Xindian, Zhg.	107	29.19 N	105.40 E
Xindianbu	100	32.24 N	116.22 E
Xindianzi, Zhg.	105	40.04 N	118.01 E
Xindianzi, Zhg.	107	28.49 N	103.35 E
Xindianzi, Zhg.	107	29.03 N	103.46 E
Xindianzi, Zhg.	107	29.52 N	106.06 E
Xindianzi, Zhg.	107	29.46 N	105.11 E
Xindianzi, Zhg.	107	29.43 N	104.01 E
Xindu	102	23.59 N	111.46 E
Xinfatuncun	104	41.13 N	122.28 E
Xinfeng, Zhg.	100	25.24 N	114.56 E
Xinfeng, Zhg.	100	27.26 N	116.40 E
Xinfeng, Zhg.	100	33.19 N	120.30 E
Xinfeng, Zhg.	100	24.04 N	114.12 E
Xinfeng, Zhg.	100	24.05 N	116.53 E
Xinfeng, Zhg.	106	31.09 N	118.40 E
Xinfeng, Zhg.	106	32.05 N	119.34 E
Xinfeng, Zhg.	106	30.43 N	120.55 E
Xinfeng ≐	100	23.42 N	114.42 E
Xinfeng Shuiku ⊜[1]	100	23.52 N	114.30 E
Xing'an, Zhg.	89	48.49 N	121.45 E
Xing'an, Zhg.	102	25.37 N	110.31 E
Xin'gang, Zhg.	106	31.56 N	120.57 E
Xingang, Zhg.	106	32.03 N	120.25 E
Xing'antun	89	51.31 N	120.08 E
Xingcheng	104	40.37 N	120.43 E
Xingguo	100	26.21 N	115.19 E
Xinghai	102	35.31 N	99.36 E
Xinghe	98	40.48 N	113.58 E
Xinghua	100	32.57 N	119.50 E
Xinghua Wan c	100	25.20 N	119.20 E
Xingjing	102	29.43 N	102.59 E
Xingkai Hu (ozero Chanka) ⊜	89	45.00 N	132.24 E
Xingliu	100	33.04 N	115.41 E
Xinglong, Zhg.	100	32.05 N	112.51 E
Xinglong, Zhg.	102	35.38 N	106.08 E
Xinglong, Zhg.	105	40.26 N	117.34 E
Xinglong, Zhg.	107	30.36 N	106.20 E
Xinglong, Zhg.	107	30.20 N	106.07 E
Xinglongchang, Zhg.	107	30.25 N	104.06 E
Xinglongchang, Zhg.	107	29.34 N	106.09 E
Xinglongchang, Zhg.	107	29.54 N	105.26 E
Xinglongcun	89	49.50 N	125.12 E
Xinglongdian, Zhg.	104	42.16 N	124.00 E
Xinglongdian, Zhg.	104	41.59 N	123.03 E
Xinglonggou, Zhg.	104	41.46 N	120.38 E
Xinglonggou, Zhg.	104	40.45 N	123.08 E
Xinglongpao	89	46.27 N	125.47 E
Xinglongtai	104	42.30 N	123.48 E
Xingning	100	24.09 N	115.45 E
Xingou, Zhg.	100	30.41 N	113.57 E
Xingou, Zhg.	100	30.08 N	112.56 E
Xingren	102	25.27 N	105.13 E
Xingrenbu	102	37.06 N	105.12 E
Xingshanbao	89	45.30 N	125.45 E
Xingtai	98	37.04 N	114.29 E
Xingtan	100	22.46 N	113.07 E
Xingtang	98	38.26 N	114.33 E
Xingtian	100	27.30 N	118.02 E
Xingu ≐	242	1.30 S	51.53 W
Xinguan	100	33.38 N	118.05 E
Xingwenping	102	29.24 N	103.23 E
Xingxian	102	38.36 N	111.15 E
Xingxing	106	30.39 N	121.09 E
Xingyi, Zhg.	98	38.18 N	115.01 E
Xingyi, Zhg.	102	25.06 N	104.58 E
Xingzhuangzi	105	40.34 N	115.00 E
Xingzi	100	29.28 N	116.01 E
Xinhe, Zhg.	98	37.32 N	115.14 E
Xinhe, Zhg.	100	28.30 N	121.27 E
Xinhe, Zhg.	105	39.03 N	117.37 E
Xinhe, Zhg.	106	31.59 N	121.21 E
Xinhekou	89	48.22 N	130.45 E
Xinheng	100	23.38 N	116.18 E
Xinhezhen	106	31.35 N	121.31 E
Xinhezhuang	106	31.10 N	118.46 E
Xinhua	102	27.37 N	111.02 E
Xinhuai ≐	100	34.23 N	120.05 E
Xinhuang	106	30.37 N	120.55 E
Xinhui	100	22.32 N	113.02 E
Xining (Sining)	102	36.38 N	101.55 E
Xiniu, Zhg.	100	24.10 N	113.07 E
Xiniu, Zhg.	106	31.25 N	120.07 E
Xiniuguchengzi	104	41.01 N	122.24 E
Xinji, Zhg.	98	35.19 N	115.36 E
Xinji, Zhg.	100	33.24 N	114.44 E
Xinji, Zhg.	105	40.04 N	118.21 E
Xinji, Zhg.	105	39.52 N	117.10 E
Xinjiaji	98	36.56 N	116.59 E
Xinjian, Zhg.	100	28.46 N	120.02 E
Xinjian, Zhg.	100	28.34 N	115.47 E
Xinjian, Zhg.	106	31.33 N	119.39 E
Xinjiang, Zhg.	100	24.29 N	113.52 E
Xinjiang, Zhg.	102	35.40 N	111.11 E
Xinjiang, Zhg.	106	32.05 N	120.40 E
Xinjianglang	106	30.58 N	120.54 E
Xinjiang Uygur Zizhiqu (Sinkiang) □[4]	90	40.00 N	85.00 E
Xinjiapu	105	40.32 N	115.57 E
Xinjiazhuang	105	40.31 N	114.58 E
Xinjie	102	26.48 N	101.15 E
Xinjieji	89	52.08 N	126.24 E
Xinjin (Pulandian), Zhg.	98	39.24 N	121.58 E
Xinjin, Zhg.	107	30.25 N	103.49 E
Xinjingzi	86	42.13 N	87.36 E
Xinjuntun	105	39.39 N	117.57 E
Xinkai ≐	89	43.37 N	123.36 E
Xinkaigang	106	31.55 N	120.56 E
Xinkengdong	100	26.09 N	113.46 E
Xinle (Dongchangshou)	98	38.24 N	114.47 E
Xinli	89	44.41 N	126.45 E
Xinlitun, Zhg.	89	43.34 N	125.18 E
Xinlitun, Zhg.	104	42.00 N	122.09 E
Xinlitun, Zhg.	104	42.15 N	122.51 E
Xinlizhuang	105	39.17 N	116.10 E
Xinmin	104	42.00 N	122.48 E
Xinmintun	104	41.39 N	123.02 E
Xinning	102	26.19 N	110.45 E
Xinping	102	24.06 N	101.58 E
Xinpu	100	24.31 N	116.08 E
Xinqianhu	98	37.59 N	118.15 E
Xinqiao, Zhg.	106	31.32 N	119.04 E
Xinqiao, Zhg.	106	31.04 N	121.18 E
Xinqiao, Zhg.	107	29.32 N	106.28 E
Xinqiao, Zhg.	107	30.10 N	103.50 E
Xinqiao, Zhg.	107	30.33 N	105.33 E
Xinqiaotou	106	31.00 N	119.24 E
Xinqiaozhen	107	29.36 N	103.39 E
Xinqiu	98	41.53 N	119.41 E
Xinqizhou	100	28.56 N	115.50 E
Xinqu	86	44.57 N	85.15 E
Xinquan	100	25.23 N	116.38 E
Xinsanyu	106	31.58 N	120.07 E
Xinshao	102	27.11 N	111.20 E
Xinshengzhen	107	29.29 N	104.39 E
Xinshi, Zhg.	106	30.37 N	120.19 E
Xinshi, Zhg.	106	32.04 N	120.02 E
Xinshizhen, Zhg.	102	28.39 N	104.02 E
Xinshizhen, Zhg.	107	30.20 N	104.35 E
Xinshu ≐	98	34.41 N	119.12 E
Xintai	98	35.54 N	117.44 E
Xintaimen	98	40.50 N	120.23 E
Xintaizi, Zhg.	104	41.06 N	122.42 E
Xintaizi, Zhg.	104	42.07 N	123.36 E
Xintang, Zhg.	100	23.08 N	113.36 E
Xintang, Zhg.	102	30.13 N	109.30 E
Xintang, Zhg.	106	31.02 N	119.59 E
Xintangcun	106	31.53 N	119.31 E
Xintanpu	100	29.43 N	114.54 E
Xintian	102	25.53 N	112.05 E
Xintun	104	42.11 N	123.45 E
Xinvi	105	40.04 N	118.21 E
Xinwei	100	25.21 N	115.48 E
Xinwen (Suncun)	98	35.53 N	117.40 E
Xinxian, Zhg.	100	31.38 N	114.51 E
Xinxian, Zhg.	102	38.25 N	112.48 E
Xinxiang	98	35.20 N	113.51 E
Xinxim ≐	250	7.57 S	53.20 W
Xinxing, Zhg.	89	43.16 N	129.48 E
Xinxing, Zhg.	100	22.40 N	112.52 E
Xinxing, Zhg.	102	19.57 N	109.32 E
Xinxu, Zhg.	100	22.52 N	114.20 E
Xinxu, Zhg.	100	24.57 N	117.34 E
Xinyang	100	32.08 N	114.04 E
Xinyao	100	27.39 N	118.52 E
Xinye	100	32.33 N	112.21 E
Xinyi (Xin'anzhen), Zhg.	98	34.22 N	118.21 E
Xinyi (Dongzhen), Zhg.	102	22.13 N	110.50 E
Xinyi ≐	100	34.29 N	119.49 E
Xinying	102	35.03 N	105.35 E
Xinyu	100	27.49 N	114.57 E
Xinyuan	86	43.08 N	82.31 E
Xinzao	100	23.02 N	113.26 E
Xinzha	102	23.41 N	101.09 E
Xinzhai, Zhg.	98	39.24 N	118.46 E
Xinzhai, Zhg.	98	36.24 N	118.37 E
Xinzhai, Zhg.	102	24.33 N	99.08 E
Xinzhan	100	33.33 N	114.50 E
Xinzhang	105	39.05 N	116.46 E
Xinzhangzi	105	40.45 N	117.50 E
Xinzhao	102	39.32 N	107.52 E
Xinzhazhen	106	31.50 N	119.52 E
Xinzhen, Zhg.	98	35.37 N	114.03 E
Xinzhen, Zhg.	105	39.01 N	116.22 E
Xinzhen, Zhg.	106	31.24 N	121.24 E
Xinzheng	100	34.25 N	113.43 E
Xinzhou, Zhg.	100	30.50 N	114.47 E
Xinzhou, Zhg.	102	19.48 N	109.18 E
Xinzhuang, Zhg.	98	35.05 N	117.56 E
Xinzhuang, Zhg.	271a	39.56 N	116.31 E
Xinzhuangtou	105	39.25 N	115.45 E
Xinzhuangzi, Zhg.	104	41.05 N	121.23 E
Xinzhuangzi, Zhg.	105	40.14 N	116.59 E
Xinzhuangzi, Zhg.	105	40.32 N	115.10 E
Xinzhuangzi, Zhg.	105	38.52 N	117.21 E
Xinzhuangzi, Zhg.	105	39.20 N	118.25 E
Xinzo de Limia	34	42.03 N	7.43 W
Xiongdi Yu II	100	23.33 N	117.40 E
Xiongjiachang	102	26.31 N	105.39 E
Xiongxian	105	38.59 N	116.05 E
Xiongyuecheng	98	40.10 N	122.08 E
Xipamanu (Chipamanu) ≐	248	10.43 S	67.50 W
Xiping, Zhg.	100	28.27 N	119.29 E
Xiping, Zhg.	100	33.23 N	114.02 E
Xiping'anhe	104	40.47 N	122.01 E
Xiqia	106	31.03 N	119.37 E
Xiqilichiquan	89	49.59 N	119.27 E
Xiqin	100	26.33 N	118.06 E
Xiqing Shan ✗	102	35.30 N	101.30 E
Xique-Xique	250	10.50 S	42.44 W
Xisanshilipu	100	32.40 N	117.31 E
Xisantai	98	39.38 N	121.37 E
Xishan, Zhg.	100	28.34 N	115.37 E
Xishan, Zhg.	105	39.38 N	118.10 E
Xishanqiao	106	31.57 N	118.43 E
Xishanxicun	105	40.01 N	116.50 E
Xisha Qundao (Paracel Islands) II	108	16.30 N	112.15 E
Xishijiazi	104	41.46 N	120.55 E
Xishiqiao	106	31.53 N	120.06 E
Xishu	98	36.41 N	113.49 E
Xishui	100	30.27 N	115.13 E
Xishuiyu	105	40.25 N	116.16 E
Xisuhupu	104	41.41 N	123.14 E
Xitai	98	40.37 N	120.12 E
Xitan	100	23.47 N	117.08 E
Xitang	106	30.57 N	120.53 E
Xitangqiao, Zhg.	106	31.49 N	120.38 E
Xitangqiao, Zhg.	106	30.37 N	121.01 E
Xitaoyuan	104	40.57 N	122.11 E
Xiti	120	33.27 N	82.48 E
Xitianmu Shan ∧	106	30.21 N	119.25 E
Xitiao ≐	106	30.57 N	120.10 E
Xiting	106	32.07 N	121.00 E
Xitole	150	11.43 N	14.50 W
Xituan	105	39.29 N	115.47 E
Xiu ≐	100	29.13 N	115.56 E
Xiujiangpu	104	41.17 N	123.02 E
Xiuning	100	29.47 N	118.10 E
Xiushan	102	28.29 N	108.52 E
Xiushui	100	29.04 N	114.33 E
Xiushui ≐	104	42.03 N	122.58 E
Xiushuihe	104	42.22 N	123.01 E
Xiuyan	98	40.17 N	123.18 E
Xiva	34	39.28 N	0.43 W
Xiwei	100	25.22 N	117.46 E
Xiweizigou	104	42.01 N	121.59 E
Xiwenquan	107	29.42 N	106.07 E
Xiwu	100	29.40 N	121.30 E
Xiwukou	106	30.24 N	118.54 E
Xixabangma Feng ∧	124	28.22 N	85.50 E
Xixi	100	26.45 N	118.42 E
Xixia	102	33.22 N	111.28 E
Xixian, Zhg.	100	32.21 N	114.44 E
Xixian, Zhg.	102	36.43 N	110.52 E
Xixiang	102	32.48 N	107.55 E
Xixiangyang	105	39.33 N	116.02 E
Xixiaojie	104	40.42 N	122.12 E
Xixiashu	106	31.57 N	119.49 E
Xixing	106	30.11 N	120.13 E
Xixona	34	38.32 N	0.30 W
Xiyang, Zhg.	98	37.37 N	113.42 E
Xiyang, Zhg.	100	25.50 N	117.25 E
Xiyang, Zhg.	106	31.49 N	120.43 E
Xiyang, Zhg.	106	31.52 N	119.23 E
Xiyang Dao I	100	26.32 N	120.04 E
Xiyangji	100	33.25 N	116.22 E
Xiyangjiao	106	31.43 N	120.23 E
Xiyangshugou	104	40.41 N	122.44 E
Xiyangzhuang	106	31.50 N	119.22 E
Xiyingzi	104	41.55 N	122.34 E
Xiyou	98	37.24 N	119.56 E
Xiyushi	106	30.36 N	119.26 E
Xizang Zizhiqu (Tibet) □[4]	90	32.00 N	88.00 E
Xizhi ≐	100	23.04 N	114.31 E
Xizhimen Station ◆[5]	271a	39.56 N	116.21 E
Xizhong Dao I	98	39.26 N	121.17 E
Xizhou	100	29.29 N	121.39 E
Xizi	98	41.48 N	119.16 E
Xochiapa	234	17.39 N	95.46 W
Xochicalco ⊥	234	18.48 N	99.19 W
Xochimilco ◆[8]	286a	19.16 N	99.06 W
Xochimilco, Lago de ⊜	286a	19.16 N	99.06 W
Xochipala	234	17.48 N	99.39 W
Xochistlahuaca	234	16.47 N	98.15 W
Xochitlán	234	19.59 N	97.36 W
Xoka	120	29.58 N	93.48 E
Xom Binh Phuoc	269c	10.40 N	106.47 E
Xom Xoai Minh	269c	10.42 N	106.50 E
Xu ≐	100	28.17 N	116.05 E
Xuancheng	106	30.58 N	118.45 E
Xuan'en	102	30.00 N	109.20 E
Xuanfeng	100	27.42 N	114.08 E
Xuang ≐	110	19.58 N	102.15 E
Xuanhan	102	31.24 N	107.43 E
Xuanhua	105	40.37 N	115.03 E
Xuanhuadian	100	31.42 N	114.29 E
Xuanhui ≐	98	38.07 N	117.45 E
Xuanjiabao	106	32.17 N	120.01 E
Xuanjiangying	98	41.25 N	116.45 E
Xuan Loc	110	10.56 N	107.14 E
Xuantan	107	29.12 N	105.34 E
Xuan Thoi Thuong	269c	10.52 N	106.34 E
Xuanwei	102	26.07 N	104.05 E
Xuanzhuang	105	39.29 N	118.07 E
Xubu	98	40.02 N	113.43 E
Xuchang, Zhg.	100	34.03 N	113.49 E
Xuchang, Zhg.	107	29.06 N	104.31 E
Xucheng	98	35.56 N	116.27 E
Xuchilquitongo	234	17.15 N	96.53 W
Xucun	106	30.27 N	120.22 E
Xudazhuang	100	33.44 N	117.53 E
Xuddun	144	9.09 N	47.28 E
Xuddur	144	4.07 N	43.54 E
Xueao	100	29.27 N	121.30 E
Xuebu	106	31.43 N	119.22 E
Xuecheng	98	34.50 N	117.16 E
Xuedian, Zhg.	100	34.04 N	113.04 E
Xuedian, Zhg.	100	34.30 N	113.44 E
Xuefanggou	104	41.57 N	121.01 E
Xuefeng	100	33.21 N	118.22 E
Xuehu	98	34.08 N	116.27 E
Xueshan Zhang ∧	100	24.24 N	113.37 E
Xueshuiwen	89	49.10 N	129.45 E
Xuetangpuzi	104	40.38 N	123.53 E
Xueyanqiao	106	31.30 N	120.06 E
Xuezhen	106	31.35 N	118.38 E
Xuguanzhen	106	31.23 N	120.30 E
Xuguichenxiaodian	106	32.07 N	121.20 E
Xuguit Qi (Yakeshi)	89	49.17 N	120.41 E
Xuji	100	31.50 N	116.22 E
Xujiabu	100	29.27 N	116.18 E
Xujiadong	100	25.54 N	113.02 E
Xujiadu	100	28.18 N	114.44 E
Xujiagou	104	42.17 N	124.04 E
Xujiapuzi	104	40.44 N	123.18 E
Xujiatou	106	31.19 N	119.25 E
Xujiazhai, Zhg.	106	31.11 N	121.46 E
Xujiazhai, Zhg.	269b	31.23 N	121.17 E
Xuliying	105	39.28 N	116.02 E
Xun ≐, Zhg.	89	49.27 N	128.55 E
Xun ≐, Zhg.	102	23.28 N	111.18 E
Xungru	120	29.15 N	84.49 E
Xunhe	89	49.18 N	128.04 E
Xunhua	102	35.49 N	102.26 E
Xunjiansi	105	40.50 N	116.04 E
Xunke	89	49.35 N	128.25 E
Xunle	102	25.17 N	108.12 E
Xunmukou	98	34.03 N	114.42 E
Xunshansuo	98	37.10 N	122.29 E
Xunwu	100	24.58 N	115.38 E
Xunwu ≐	100	24.28 N	115.26 E
Xunxian	98	35.43 N	114.31 E
Xupu, Zhg.	102	27.44 N	110.24 E
Xupu, Zhg.	106	31.45 N	120.54 E
Xushe	106	31.24 N	119.39 E
Xushi	106	31.40 N	120.57 E
Xushui	105	39.02 N	115.39 E
Xutian	98	34.10 N	114.03 E
Xuwan	100	27.55 N	116.31 E
Xuwen	102	20.21 N	110.11 E
Xuxiandai	106	30.40 N	120.47 E
Xuxiang	106	31.33 N	120.13 E
Xuyen Moc	110	10.34 N	107.25 E
Xuyi	100	33.01 N	118.29 E
Xuyong	102	28.10 N	105.24 E
Xuzhou (Süchow)	98	34.16 N	117.11 E
Xuzhuang	106	31.09 N	120.32 E
Y			
Yaak	182	48.50 N	115.42 W
Yaan	102	30.03 N	103.02 E
Yaapeet	166	35.46 S	142.03 E
Yaaq-Baraawe	144	1.57 N	43.11 E
Yaba ◆[8]	273a	6.30 N	3.23 E
Yaba College of Technology ʋ[2]	273a	6.32 N	3.23 E
Ya'bad	132	32.27 N	35.10 E
Yabakei	96	33.27 N	131.07 E
Yabassi	152	4.28 N	9.58 E
Yabe	96	33.09 N	130.49 E
Yabe ≐	96	33.06 N	130.26 E
Yabelo	144	4.54 N	38.05 E
Yablis	236	14.10 N	83.49 W
Yablonovy Range — Jablonovyj chrebet ✗	88	53.30 N	115.00 E
Yabrīn ⊤[4]	128	23.17 N	48.58 E
Yabrūd	130	33.58 N	36.40 E
Yabu, Nihon	96	35.22 N	134.47 E
Yabu, Nihon	174m	26.36 N	127.57 E
Yabucoa	240m	18.03 N	65.53 W
Yabuki	94	37.12 N	140.19 E
Yabuli	89	44.55 N	128.35 E
Yacambu, Parque Nacional ♠	246	9.40 N	69.42 W
Yacaré Norte, Riacho ≐	252	22.43 S	58.14 W
Yacheng	110	18.25 N	109.11 E
Yachi ≐	102	27.18 N	107.15 E
Yachimata	94	35.39 N	140.19 E
Yachiyo, Nihon	94	35.43 N	140.07 E
Yachiyo, Nihon	94	36.10 N	139.53 E
Yacimiento Río Turbio	254	51.32 S	72.18 W
Yaco	248	17.09 S	67.24 W
Yaco (Iaco) ≐	248	9.03 S	68.34 W
Yacolt	224	45.51 N	122.24 W
Yacuiba	248	22.02 S	63.45 W
Yacuma ≐	248	13.38 S	65.23 W
Yacyretá, Isla I	252	27.25 S	56.30 W
Yada ≐	96	35.38 N	134.37 E
Yādgīr	122	16.46 N	77.08 E
Yadkin ≐	192	35.23 N	80.03 W
Yadkinville	192	36.08 N	80.39 W
Yad Mordekhay	132	31.35 N	34.34 E
Yadong	124	27.29 N	88.55 E
Yādūdah	132	32.40 N	36.04 E
Yaenengu	152	2.28 N	23.15 E
Yaeyama-rettō II	175d	24.20 N	124.00 E
Yāfā	132	32.41 N	35.17 E
Yafran	146	32.04 N	12.31 E
Yaftābād	267d	35.39 N	51.19 E
Yafuquan	85	39.12 N	76.09 E
Yagachi-shima I	174m	26.40 N	128.01 E
Yağcılar	130	39.25 N	28.23 E
Yageg	144	3.16 N	44.00 E
Yagi	96	35.04 N	135.32 E
Yagishiri-tō I	92a	44.26 N	141.25 E
Yağlıca Dağı ∧	84	40.18 N	43.18 E
Yago	234	21.50 N	105.04 W
Yagonde	152	0.02 N	22.41 E
Yagoona	274a	33.55 S	151.02 E
Yagoua	146	10.20 N	15.14 E
Yagradagzê Shan ∧	120	35.12 N	95.20 E
Yaguachi Nuevo	246	2.07 S	79.41 W
Yaguajay	240p	22.19 N	79.14 W
Yaguala ≐	236	15.25 N	86.40 W
Yaguará	246	2.40 N	75.31 W
Yaguaraparo	246	10.34 N	62.49 W
Yaguarí	252	31.31 S	54.58 W
Yaguarón (Jaguarão) ≐	252	32.39 S	53.12 W
Yaguas ≐	246	2.45 S	70.04 W
Yagur	132	32.44 N	35.04 E
Yahagi ≐	94	34.50 N	136.59 E
Yahagong	102	28.24 N	99.11 E
Yahara ≐	190	42.48 N	89.07 W
Yahata — Kitakyūshū	96	33.53 N	130.50 E
Yahe, Zhg.	89	45.24 N	130.24 E
Yahe, Zhg.	106	31.44 N	119.52 E
Yahila	152	0.13 N	24.28 E
Yahk	182	49.05 N	116.05 W
Yahmūm al-Asmar, Jabal ∧	142	29.56 N	31.38 E
Yaho	268	35.41 N	139.27 E
Yahōga-take ∧	96	33.04 N	130.50 E
Yahongqiao	105	39.45 N	117.51 E

	English	Deutsch	Español	Français	Português
≐	River	Fluß	Río	Rivière	Rio
⊼	Canal	Kanal	Canal	Canal	Canal
L	Waterfall, Rapids	Wasserfall, Stromschnellen	Cascada, Rápidos	Chute d'eau, Rapides	Cascata, Rápidos
ʊ	Strait	Meeresstraße	Estrecho	Détroit	Estreito
c	Bay, Gulf	Bucht, Golf	Bahía, Golfo	Baie, Golfe	Baía, Golfo
⊜	Lake, Lakes	See, Seen	Lago, Lagos	Lac, Lacs	Lago, Lagos
≡	Swamp	Sumpf	Pantano	Marais	Pântano
⊓	Ice Features, Glacier	Eis- und Gletscherformen	Accidentes Glaciales	Formes glaciaires	Acidentes glaciares
⊤	Other Hydrographic Features	Andere Hydrographische Objekte	Otros Elementos Hidrográficos	Autres données hydrographiques	Outros acidentes hidrográficos
✦	Submarine Features	Untermeerische Objekte	Accidentes Submarinos	Formes de relief sous-marin	Acidentes submarinos
□	Political Unit	Politische Einheit	Unidad Politica	Entité politique	Unidade política
ʋ	Cultural Institution	Kulturelle Institution	Institución Cultural	Institution culturelle	Instituição cultural
⊥	Historical Site	Historische Stätte	Sitio Histórico	Site historique	Sítio histórico
♠	Recreational Site	Erholungs- und Ferienort	Sitio de Recreo	Centre de loisirs	Area de Lazer
⊠	Airport	Flughafen	Aeropuerto	Aéroport	Aeroporto
■	Military Installation	Militäranlage	Instalación Militar	Installation militaire	Instalação militar
◆	Miscellaneous	Verschiedenes	Misceláneo	Divers	Diversos

ENGLISH / DEUTSCH

Name	Page / Seite	Lat.°′ / Breite°′	Long.°′ / Länge°′ E = Ost
Yahualica	**234**	21.08 N	102.51 W
Yahuma	**152**	1.05 N	23.13 E
Yahyalı	**130**	38.07 N	35.22 E
Yai ≃	**114**	5.02 N	101.47 E
Yai, Khao ∧, Asia	**110**	12.27 N	99.26 E
Yai, Khao ∧, Thai	**110**	15.25 N	99.20 E
Yainax Butte ∧	**202**	42.20 N	121.16 W
Yaita, Nihon	**94**	36.48 N	139.56 E
Yaita, Nihon	**268**	35.57 N	140.03 E
Yaitopya → Ethiopia □[1]	**144**	9.00 N	39.00 E
Yaizu	**94**	34.52 N	138.20 E
Yajiang	**102**	30.02 N	101.05 E
Yaka	**130**	41.15 N	34.01 E
Yakacık	**130**	36.47 N	36.10 E
Yakacık ◆[8]	**267b**	40.55 N	29.13 E
Yakage	**96**	34.37 N	133.35 E
Yakak, Cape ›	**180**	51.38 N	177.00 W
Yakapınar	**130**	37.00 N	35.36 E
Yakarta → Jakarta	**115a**	6.10 S	106.48 E
Yake-dake ∧	**94**	36.14 N	137.35 E
Yake-yama ∧	**94**	36.55 N	138.03 E
Yakhchāl, Afg.	**120**	31.47 N	64.41 E
Yakhchāl, Afg.	**128**	31.47 N	64.41 E
Yakima	**202**	46.36 N	120.30 W
Yakima □[6]	**224**	46.34 N	121.03 W
Yakima ≃	**202**	46.15 N	119.02 W
Yakima Firing Center ■	**202**	46.44 N	120.10 W
Yakima Indian Reservation ◆[4]	**224**	46.16 N	121.03 W
Yakkan ≃	**96**	33.34 N	131.22 E
Yakmach	**128**	28.45 N	63.51 E
Yako	**150**	12.58 N	2.16 W
Yakō ◆[8]	**268**	35.32 N	139.41 E
Yakobi Island I	**180**	58.00 N	136.30 W
Yakoma	**152**	4.05 N	22.27 E
Yakou	**100**	24.46 N	118.46 E
Yakuendai	**268**	35.43 N	140.03 E
Yakuluku	**154**	4.20 N	28.48 E
Yakumo	**92a**	42.15 N	140.16 E
Yakuno	**96**	35.19 N	135.00 E
Yakushi-dake ∧	**94**	36.28 N	137.33 E
Yakushi-ji υ[1]	**94**	36.25 N	139.53 E
Yaku-shima I	**93b**	30.20 N	130.30 E
Yakutat	**180**	59.33 N	139.44 W
Yakutat Bay ⊂	**180**	59.40 N	140.00 W
Yakutat Seamount ✚[3]	**16**	35.15 N	48.00 W
Yakutia → Jakutija □[3]	**74**	67.00 N	125.00 E
Yakutsk → Jakutsk	**74**	62.00 N	129.40 E
Yala, Ghana	**150**	10.07 N	1.52 W
Yala, Thai	**110**	6.33 N	101.18 E
Yalaha	**220**	28.44 N	81.48 W
Yalahau, Laguna ⊂	**232**	21.30 N	87.15 W
Yalakdere	**130**	40.36 N	29.33 E
Yalata	**162**	31.29 S	131.52 E
Yalata Aboriginal Reserve ◆[4]	**162**	31.30 S	131.45 E
Yalca, Laguna ⊜	**258**	35.34 S	57.55 W
Yalding	**260**	51.13 N	0.26 E
Yale, B.C., Can.	**182**	49.34 N	121.26 W
Yale, Mi., U.S.	**190**	43.07 N	82.47 W
Yale, Ok., U.S.	**196**	36.06 N	96.41 W
Yale, Va., U.S.	**208**	36.50 N	77.17 W
Yale, Lake ⊜	**220**	28.54 N	81.45 W
Yale, Mount ∧	**200**	38.51 N	106.18 W
Yale Lake ⊜[1]	**224**	46.00 N	122.12 W
Yalgar ≃	**162**	26.09 S	117.57 E
Yalgoo	**162**	28.20 S	116.41 E
Yalgorup National Park ♠	**168a**	32.55 S	115.41 E
Yali	**152**	0.04 N	21.03 E
Yaliji	**98**	36.06 N	114.56 E
Yalikamba	**152**	1.17 S	22.30 E
Yalinga	**152**	6.31 N	23.15 E
Yalisere	**152**	0.11 N	22.33 E
Yalleroi	**166**	24.04 S	145.45 E
Yallourn	**169**	38.11 S	146.21 E
Yallourn North	**169**	38.09 S	146.22 E
Yalnızçam Dağları ⋀	**84**	41.10 N	42.25 E
Yalobusha ≃	**194**	33.33 N	90.10 W
Yaloká	**152**	5.19 N	17.05 E
Yalong ≃	**102**	26.37 N	101.48 E
Yaloupi ≃	**250**	2.47 N	52.28 W
Yalova	**130**	40.39 N	29.15 E
Yalta → Jalta	**78**	44.30 N	34.10 E
Yalu	**89**	48.34 N	122.09 E
Yalu (Amnok-kang) ≃, Asia	**98**	39.55 N	124.22 E
Yalu ≃, Zhg.	**89**	46.56 N	123.30 E
Yalufi	**152**	0.45 N	24.26 E
Yalvaç	**130**	38.17 N	31.11 E
Yalwal Creek ≃	**170**	34.50 S	150.23 E
Yamachiche	**206**	46.16 N	72.50 W
Yamachiche ≃	**206**	46.16 N	72.48 W
Yamada, Nihon	**92**	39.28 N	141.57 E
Yamada, Nihon	**94**	35.49 N	140.36 E
Yamada, Nihon	**94**	36.34 N	137.05 E
Yamada, Nihon	**96**	33.33 N	130.47 E
Yamada → Tosa-yamada, Nihon	**96**	33.36 N	133.41 E
Yamada, Nihon	**174m**	26.26 N	127.47 E
Yamada, Nihon	**270**	34.31 N	135.39 E
Yamada, Nihon	**270**	34.48 N	135.32 E
Yamada ≃	**270**	34.47 N	135.04 E
Yamaga, Nihon	**96**	33.01 N	130.41 E
Yamaga, Nihon	**96**	33.27 N	131.30 E
Yamagata, Nihon	**92**	38.15 N	140.20 E
Yamagata, Nihon	**94**	36.38 N	140.24 E
Yamagata, Nihon	**94**	36.10 N	137.52 E
Yamagawa	**92**	31.12 N	130.39 E
Yamaguchi, Nihon	**94**	35.33 N	137.33 E
Yamaguchi, Nihon	**96**	34.10 N	131.29 E
Yamaguchi, Nihon	**270**	34.50 N	135.15 E
Yamaguchi □[5]	**96**	34.20 N	131.30 E
Yamaguchi-chosuichi ⊜[1]	**268**	35.46 N	139.25 E
Yama-Hita-Hiko-san-kokutei-kōen ♠	**96**	33.25 N	131.02 E
Yamakawa	**96**	34.04 N	134.15 E
Yamakita	**94**	35.21 N	139.05 E
Yamakuni	**96**	33.24 N	131.02 E
Yamakuni ≃	**96**	33.37 N	131.12 E
Yamalia → Jamalo-Neneckij □[3]	**72**	67.00 N	75.00 E
Yamām, Jabal al- ∧	**132**	30.02 N	35.28 E
Yamamoto, Nihon	**96**	34.07 N	133.44 E
Yamamoto, Nihon	**270**	34.38 N	135.38 E
Yamanaka	**94**	36.15 N	136.22 E
Yamanakako	**94**	35.24 N	138.52 E
Yamanaka-ko ⊜	**94**	35.25 N	138.52 E
Yamanashi	**94**	35.40 N	138.40 E
Yamanashi □[5]	**94**	35.30 N	138.30 E
Yamanouchi	**94**	36.44 N	138.25 E
Yamasaki	**96**	35.00 N	134.33 E
Yamashina ◆[8]	**270**	34.58 N	135.49 E
Yamashiro, Nihon	**94**	34.45 N	135.49 E
Yamashiro, Nihon	**96**	33.57 N	133.45 E
Yamaska (Saint-Michel)	**206**	46.00 N	72.55 W
Yamaska □[6]	**206**	46.00 N	72.45 W
Yamaska ≃	**206**	46.06 N	72.56 W
Yamaska, Mont ∧[2]	**206**	45.27 N	72.52 W
Yamaska Nord ≃	**206**	45.17 N	72.51 W
Yamaska Sud-Est ≃	**206**	45.17 N	72.55 W
Yamate	**270**	34.30 N	135.27 E
Yamatengwumulu	**102**	38.38 N	97.05 E
Yamato, Nihon	**94**	35.48 N	136.54 E
Yamato, Nihon	**94**	35.29 N	139.29 E
Yamato, Nihon	**94**	37.10 N	138.56 E
Yamato, Nihon	**96**	33.08 N	130.26 E
Yamato ≃	**96**	34.36 N	135.26 E
Yamato-Aogaki-kokutei-kōen ♠	**94**	34.40 N	135.50 E
Yamato-kōriyama	**96**	34.38 N	135.47 E
Yamato-takada	**96**	34.31 N	135.45 E
Yamatsuri	**94**	36.52 N	140.25 E
Yamazaki	**268**	35.56 N	139.54 E
Yamba	**166**	29.26 S	153.22 E
Yambata	**152**	2.26 N	21.58 E
Yambéring	**150**	11.49 N	12.21 W
Yambio	**154**	4.34 N	28.23 E
Yambol → Jambol	**38**	42.29 N	26.30 E
Yamboyo	**152**	0.40 N	22.18 E
Yambrasbamba	**248**	5.45 S	77.54 W
Yambuya	**154**	1.16 N	24.33 E
Yamdena, Pulau I	**164**	7.36 S	131.25 E
Yame	**96**	33.28 N	130.34 E
Ya Men ⊂	**100**	22.09 N	113.05 E
Yamenkou	**105**	39.53 N	116.12 E
Yamenying	**89**	43.25 N	122.19 E
Yamethin	**110**	20.26 N	96.09 E
Yamhill	**224**	45.21 N	123.11 W
Yamhill □[6]	**224**	45.15 N	123.20 W
Yamhill ≃	**224**	45.14 N	123.00 W
Yamia	**150**	13.24 N	10.18 E
Yamizo-san ∧	**94**	36.56 N	140.17 E
Yamma Yamma, Lake ⊜	**166**	26.20 S	141.25 E
Yamoussoukro	**150**	6.49 N	5.17 W
Yampa	**200**	40.09 N	106.54 W
Yampa ≃	**200**	40.32 N	108.59 W
Yampa Plateau ⋀[1]	**200**	40.25 N	109.00 W
Yamparaez	**248**	19.10 S	65.10 W
Yamsay Mountain ∧	**202**	42.56 N	121.22 W
Yamu	**102**	43.48 N	94.48 E
Yamuna ≃	**120**	25.25 N	81.50 E
Yamuna Bridge ◆[5]	**272a**	28.40 N	77.14 E
Yamunānagar	**124**	30.07 N	77.18 E
Yamzho Yumco ⊜	**120**	28.58 N	90.44 E
Yan	**114**	5.48 N	100.22 E
Yan ≃, S. Lan.	**122**	8.55 N	81.01 E
Yan ≃, Zhg.	**102**	36.24 N	110.28 E
Yanac	**166**	36.08 S	141.26 E
Yanacachi	**248**	16.23 S	67.43 W
Yanachaga-Chemillen, Parque Nacional ♠	**248**	10.10 S	75.20 W
Yanadani	**96**	33.32 N	133.01 E
Yanagawa	**96**	33.10 N	130.24 E
Yanagi	**270**	34.25 N	135.56 E
Yanagimoto	**270**	34.34 N	135.51 E
Yanahara	**96**	34.55 N	134.05 E
Yanaha-shima I	**174m**	26.54 N	127.56 E
Yanahuara	**248**	16.24 S	71.33 W
Yanai	**96**	33.58 N	132.07 E
Yanaka	**268**	35.24 N	140.01 E
Yanam	**122**	16.44 N	82.13 E
Yan'an	**102**	36.36 N	109.28 E
Yanaoca	**248**	14.13 S	71.26 W
Yanarsu	**130**	38.02 N	41.33 E
Yanbian	**102**	26.55 N	101.30 E
Yanbu	**100**	23.05 N	113.10 E
Yanbuʻ al-Baḥr	**128**	24.05 N	38.03 E
Yanbutou	**100**	29.52 N	115.04 E
Yanceyville	**192**	36.24 N	79.20 W
Yanchang	**102**	36.31 N	110.08 E
Yancheng, Zhg.	**100**	33.36 N	113.57 E
Yancheng, Zhg.	**100**	33.24 N	120.09 E
Yanchep	**168a**	31.33 S	115.41 E
Yanchep National Park ♠	**168a**	31.32 S	115.40 E
Yanchi, Zhg.	**102**	37.52 N	107.22 E
Yanchi, Zhg.	**105**	40.02 N	115.53 E
Yanchuan	**102**	36.56 N	110.05 E
Yanco	**166**	34.36 S	146.25 E
Yanco Creek ≃	**166**	35.16 S	145.07 E
Yanda Creek ≃	**166**	30.28 S	145.45 E
Yandal	**162**	27.33 S	121.07 E
Yandama Creek ≃	**166**	30.00 S	140.10 E
Yandé, Île I	**175f**	20.03 S	163.49 E
Yande Aboriginal Reserve ◆[4]	**162**	21.35 S	118.45 E
Yandev	**150**	7.20 N	9.01 E
Yandina	**175e**	9.07 S	159.13 E
Yandja	**152**	1.41 S	17.43 E
Yandongi	**152**	2.51 N	22.16 E
Yandoon	**110**	17.02 N	95.39 E
Yandua Island I	**175g**	16.49 S	178.18 E
Yandun	**102**	42.20 N	94.09 E
Yanfeng	**102**	25.53 N	101.01 E
Yanfolila	**150**	11.11 N	8.09 W
Yang ≃, Thai	**110**	15.44 N	104.00 E
Yang ≃, Zhg.	**105**	40.24 N	115.20 E
Yangambi	**154**	0.47 N	24.28 E
Yangan, Austl.	**171a**	28.12 S	152.13 E
Yang'an, Zhg.	**98**	37.38 N	117.09 E
Yan'gang	**100**	26.02 N	116.22 E
Yangarakata	**154**	3.01 N	30.28 E
Yangasa Levu I	**175g**	18.57 S	178.26 W
Yangbajain	**120**	30.06 N	90.33 E
Yangce	**100**	32.58 N	113.14 E
Yangcha	**98**	41.11 N	126.15 E
Yangchang	**107**	30.22 N	103.42 E
Yangcheng, Zhg.	**102**	35.29 N	112.25 E
Yangcheng, Zhg.	**106**	31.24 N	120.47 E
Yangcheng Hu ⊜	**106**	31.26 N	120.47 E
Yangchiang → Yangjiang	**102**	21.51 N	111.56 E
Yangch'ŏn ◆[8]	**271b**	37.34 N	126.51 E
Yangchow → Yangzhou	**100**	32.24 N	119.26 E
Yangchu	**98**	37.11 N	120.47 E
Yangch'üan → Yangquan	**98**	37.52 N	113.36 E
Yangchun	**102**	22.10 N	111.46 E
Yangcun, Zhg.	**100**	28.07 N	117.40 E
Yangcun, Zhg.	**100**	23.26 N	114.30 E
Yangcun, Zhg.	**105**	39.09 N	115.50 E
Yangcunqiao	**100**	29.36 N	119.28 E
Yangdachengzi	**89**	43.59 N	124.25 E
Yangdalinzi	**98**	42.38 N	125.07 E
Yangdang	**100**	32.23 N	112.39 E
Yangdian	**106**	31.08 N	119.45 E
Yang'erzhuang	**98**	38.18 N	117.30 E
Yangfang	**105**	40.07 N	116.07 E
Yangfangpu	**105**	40.48 N	115.01 E
Yangfengang	**105**	39.07 N	116.52 E
Yangfenzhen	**106**	30.28 N	120.03 E
Yanggang Do □[4]	**98**	41.15 N	128.00 E
Yangganzhen	**106**	31.00 N	119.15 E
Yanggao	**98**	40.25 N	113.44 E
Yanggezhuang	**105**	40.09 N	116.48 E
Yanggong-ni	**271b**	37.39 N	126.37 E
Yanggu, Taehan	**98**	38.06 N	127.59 E
Yanggu, Zhg.	**98**	34.44 N	114.48 E
Yanggu, Zhg.	**98**	36.08 N	115.48 E
Yangguanpu	**100**	32.13 N	115.31 E
Yanghang	**106**	31.22 N	121.26 E
Yanghe	**100**	33.47 N	118.23 E
Yanghexi	**102**	29.39 N	108.40 E
Yanghu	**100**	32.34 N	116.30 E
Yanghua	**107**	30.11 N	104.45 E
Yanghua ≃	**107**	30.09 N	104.42 E
Yangi-Yul' → Jangijul'	**85**	41.07 N	69.03 E
Yangji, Zhg.	**98**	36.44 N	113.56 E
Yangji, Zhg.	**98**	34.25 N	116.06 E
Yangji, Zhg.	**100**	34.19 N	119.28 E
Yangjia, Zhg.	**98**	34.19 N	119.28 E
Yangjia, Zhg.	**106**	30.41 N	120.15 E
Yangjiachang, Zhg.	**107**	29.23 N	104.21 E
Yangjiachang, Zhg.	**107**	29.45 N	105.21 E
Yangjiafeng	**100**	30.49 N	112.47 E
Yangjiagou	**105**	39.18 N	117.54 E
Yangjiajie	**107**	30.18 N	104.39 E
Yangjian	**106**	31.39 N	120.33 E
Yangjiang	**102**	21.51 N	111.56 E
Yangjiaogou	**98**	37.16 N	118.50 E
Yangjiaqiao, Zhg.	**100**	27.44 N	112.46 E
Yangjiaqiao, Zhg.	**106**	31.53 N	121.42 E
Yangjiaqiao, Zhg.	**106**	32.02 N	121.26 E
Yangjiatao	**105**	39.49 N	117.51 E
Yangjiawopu	**104**	42.21 N	122.57 E
Yangjiazeng	**105**	40.12 N	117.04 E
Yangjiazhangzi	**104**	40.48 N	120.33 E
Yangjie	**102**	24.49 N	100.22 E
Yangjishi	**100**	26.39 N	113.14 E
Yangkou	**100**	26.47 N	117.51 E
Yangkoushi	**100**	28.39 N	118.53 E
Yanglinjie	**100**	29.07 N	113.27 E
Yangliupu, Zhg.	**100**	30.52 N	118.37 E
Yangliupu, Zhg.	**107**	30.09 N	104.03 E
Yangliuqing	**105**	39.08 N	117.01 E
Yangloudong	**100**	29.31 N	113.44 E
Yanglousi	**100**	29.30 N	113.38 E
Yangluo	**100**	30.41 N	114.34 E
Yangluomayu	**104**	40.47 N	122.54 E
Yangmachang	**107**	30.39 N	103.45 E
Yangma Dao I	**98**	37.28 N	121.37 E
Yangmahe	**107**	30.29 N	104.31 E
Yangmeisi	**100**	25.42 N	114.30 E
Yangmiao, Zhg.	**98**	34.11 N	114.53 E
Yangmiao, Zhg.	**106**	30.51 N	120.49 E
Yangmingshan ◆[8]	**269d**	25.09 N	121.33 E
Yangming Shan ∧	**102**	26.03 N	111.56 E
Yangmugou, Zhg.	**98**	40.36 N	124.28 E
Yangmugou, Zhg.	**104**	41.11 N	123.50 E
Yangmulin	**105**	40.06 N	115.12 E
Yangon (Rangoon)	**110**	16.47 N	96.10 E
Yangon □[8]	**110**	16.50 N	96.10 E
Yangor	**174b**	0.31 S	166.54 E
Yangpingguan	**102**	32.51 N	106.09 E
Yangpu	**100**	27.14 N	119.08 E
Yangp'yŏng	**98**	37.30 N	127.29 E
Yangp'yŏng-ni	**98**	40.53 N	127.58 E
Yangqi	**106**	31.23 N	119.57 E
Yangquan	**98**	37.52 N	113.36 E
Yangriwan	**102**	31.37 N	110.49 E
Yangsan	**98**	35.21 N	129.03 E
Yangshan, Zhg.	**98**	41.13 N	120.24 E
Yangshan, Zhg.	**98**	35.13 N	116.13 E
Yangshan, Zhg.	**102**	24.28 N	112.38 E
Yangshigangzi	**104**	41.42 N	122.59 E
Yangshitun	**104**	42.06 N	123.44 E
Yangshu	**106**	31.39 N	120.08 E
Yangshugemen	**105**	40.55 N	118.18 E
Yangshugoudonggou	**104**	41.43 N	120.41 E
Yangshuling	**98**	41.02 N	118.47 E
Yangshuo	**102**	24.45 N	110.24 E
Yangtan	**106**	30.42 N	119.11 E
Yangtian Zhang ∧	**100**	24.37 N	115.38 E
Yangting	**98**	37.24 N	122.07 E
Yangtou	**100**	23.26 N	115.24 E
Yangtze → Chang ≃	**90**	31.48 N	121.10 E
Yanguan	**106**	30.26 N	120.32 E
Yangwan, Zhg.	**100**	28.22 N	116.46 E
Yangwan, Zhg.	**106**	31.03 N	120.22 E
Yangxi, Zhg.	**100**	30.11 N	118.39 E
Yangxi, Zhg.	**100**	27.18 N	114.10 E
Yangxian	**102**	33.03 N	107.47 E
Yangxiang, Zhg.	**106**	31.29 N	119.35 E
Yangxiang, Zhg.	**106**	31.12 N	121.01 E
Yangxiangtun	**104**	40.58 N	122.48 E
Yangxiaodian	**100**	31.46 N	116.45 E
Yangximu ≃	**104**	42.04 N	123.00 E
Yangxin, Zhg.	**98**	37.39 N	117.34 E
Yangxin, Zhg.	**100**	29.51 N	115.12 E
Yangxiudian	**271a**	39.44 N	116.32 E
Yangyang	**98**	38.04 N	128.36 E
Yangyuan (Xicheng)	**98**	40.01 N	114.10 E
Yangze	**100**	26.57 N	118.23 E
Yangzhong	**106**	32.16 N	119.49 E
Yangzhou	**100**	32.24 N	119.26 E
Yangzhuang	**100**	33.36 N	118.58 E
Yangzhujuanzi	**104**	41.38 N	122.46 E
Yangzi	**100**	31.19 N	112.36 E
Yangzishao	**98**	42.28 N	126.09 E
Yanhaiyingzi	**104**	41.52 N	123.05 E
Yanhe, Zhg.	**100**	31.16 N	115.07 E
Yanhe, Zhg.	**102**	28.37 N	108.35 E
Yanhecheng	**105**	40.04 N	115.43 E
Yanheying	**98**	40.02 N	119.03 E
Yanhui	**98**	37.54 N	113.51 E
Yanina → Ioánnina	**38**	39.40 N	20.50 E
Yanji, Zhg.	**98**	34.41 N	115.27 E
Yanji, Zhg.	**98**	42.57 N	129.32 E
Yanji (Longjing), Zhg.	**98**	42.47 N	129.26 E
Yanji, Zhg.	**98**	34.17 N	115.39 E
Yanjia	**104**	40.57 N	121.41 E
Yanjiabao	**106**	32.19 N	120.07 E
Yanjiadian	**98**	39.48 N	121.49 E
Yanjiahe	**100**	31.48 N	114.50 E
Yanjiajie	**104**	41.02 N	121.32 E
Yanjiao	**105**	39.56 N	116.48 E
Yanjiapu	**105**	39.52 N	118.00 E
Yanjiatuozi	**104**	42.27 N	123.47 E
Yanjiawopeng	**104**	40.59 N	121.17 E
Yanjin	**98**	35.11 N	114.11 E
Yanjing, Zhg.	**102**	29.00 N	98.34 E
Yanjing, Zhg.	**107**	29.56 N	106.21 E
Yankalilla	**168b**	35.28 S	138.21 E
Yankalilla Bay ⊂	**168b**	35.28 S	138.15 E
Yankari Game Reserve ◆[4]	**146**	9.45 N	10.30 E
Yankdŏk	**98**	39.14 N	126.41 E
Yankee Lake	**210**	41.35 N	74.33 W
Yankee Springs State Recreation Area ♠	**216**	42.38 N	85.30 W
Yankee Stadium ♠	**276**	40.50 N	73.56 W
Yankeetown	**220**	29.01 N	82.42 W
Yankton	**198**	42.52 N	97.23 W
Yankton Indian Reservation ◆[4]	**198**	43.10 N	98.22 W
Yanling, Zhg.	**98**	34.07 N	114.11 E
Yanling, Zhg.	**106**	31.54 N	119.30 E
Yanliumiao	**100**	32.01 N	116.52 E
Yanmeimeizi	**105**	39.42 N	115.03 E
Yanna	**166**	26.56 S	146.03 E
Yannarie ≃	**162**	22.28 S	114.48 E
Yanqi	**90**	42.00 N	86.15 E
Yanqian, Zhg.	**100**	24.54 N	116.14 E
Yanqian, Zhg.	**100**	26.15 N	117.28 E
Yanqianhu	**104**	42.16 N	123.12 E
Yanqiao	**106**	31.41 N	120.17 E
Yanqidoumen	**106**	31.17 N	118.42 E
Yanqing	**105**	40.28 N	115.58 E
Yanque	**248**	15.39 S	71.39 W
Yanrey	**162**	22.31 S	114.48 E
Yanshan, Zhg.	**98**	38.05 N	117.13 E
Yanshan, Zhg.	**100**	28.18 N	117.41 E
Yanshan, Zhg.	**102**	23.41 N	104.21 E
Yan Shan ⋀	**105**	40.20 N	117.40 E
Yanshankou	**105**	39.59 N	117.42 E
Yanshi	**100**	25.17 N	117.10 E
Yanshi ≃	**100**	25.20 N	117.17 E
Yanshou	**89**	45.28 N	128.20 E
Yansi	**100**	29.48 N	118.20 E
Yanṭā	**132**	33.36 N	35.57 E
Yantabulla	**166**	29.21 S	145.00 E
Yantai (Chefoo), Zhg.	**98**	37.33 N	121.20 E
Yantai, Zhg.	**105**	39.47 N	116.38 E
Yantan, Zhg.	**100**	28.28 N	120.44 E
Yantan, Zhg.	**100**	28.55 N	120.11 E
Yantan, Zhg.	**107**	29.17 N	104.52 E
Yantian, Zhg.	**100**	26.53 N	119.53 E
Yantian, Zhg.	**100**	27.21 N	114.22 E
Yantic ≃	**207**	41.31 N	72.05 W
Yantietang ⩸	**106**	31.49 N	120.46 E
Yanting	**102**	31.19 N	105.23 E
Yantis	**222**	32.56 N	95.35 W
Yantongshan, Zhg.	**89**	43.17 N	126.00 E
Yantongshan, Zhg.	**105**	40.42 N	115.06 E
Yanu	**164**	9.57 S	148.25 E
Yanwangshan	**104**	41.36 N	123.57 E
Yanweigang	**98**	34.30 N	119.48 E
Yanxi	**100**	24.46 N	117.47 E
Yanxia	**100**	29.34 N	114.50 E
Yanxidu	**100**	26.51 N	114.58 E
Yanxing	**102**	25.23 N	101.42 E
Yan Yean Reservoir ⊜[1]	**169**	37.33 S	145.08 E
Yanyegongsi	**106**	32.02 N	121.41 E
Yanyuan	**102**	27.29 N	101.32 E
Yanzhou	**98**	35.33 N	116.50 E
Yanziji	**106**	32.09 N	118.49 E
Yanzijiao	**102**	23.38 N	100.12 E
Yanzikou	**102**	27.31 N	105.21 E
Yao, Centraf.	**152**	5.19 N	19.36 E
Yao, Nihon	**96**	34.37 N	135.36 E
Yao, Tchad	**146**	12.51 N	17.34 E
Yao Airport ⊠	**270**	34.36 N	135.36 E
Yao'an	**102**	25.32 N	101.12 E
Yaoba	**107**	28.45 N	105.39 E
Yaocun, Zhg.	**98**	36.12 N	113.50 E
Yaocun, Zhg.	**98**	35.41 N	116.57 E
Yaocun, Zhg.	**105**	39.09 N	115.32 E
Yaodafangshen	**104**	42.27 N	122.59 E
Yaoerwan	**105**	40.49 N	115.27 E
Yaogongbu	**100**	29.51 N	120.18 E
Yaohongcaopao	**104**	40.55 N	122.26 E
Yaohuamen	**106**	32.08 N	118.52 E
Yaohuangdi	**104**	41.32 N	122.48 E
Yaojiaji	**100**	31.14 N	114.22 E
Yaojiaqiao	**106**	32.10 N	119.46 E
Yaojiatun	**104**	41.18 N	121.57 E
Yaojiawopeng	**104**	41.47 N	122.25 E
Yaojie	**102**	36.26 N	102.59 E
Yaoling	**100**	24.49 N	113.58 E
Yaolugou	**98**	40.34 N	119.24 E
Yaoluzi	**104**	41.26 N	121.34 E
Yaopi	**100**	26.52 N	113.38 E
Yaopu	**100**	32.14 N	118.20 E
Yaoqianhutun	**104**	41.32 N	123.36 E
Yaoshizhen	**107**	30.11 N	105.30 E
Yaotou	**100**	26.38 N	114.48 E
Yaotsu	**94**	35.28 N	137.09 E
Yaotun, Zhg.	**89**	49.28 N	127.30 E
Yaotun, Zhg.	**104**	40.59 N	122.18 E
Yaotutun	**104**	42.06 N	123.29 E
Yaoundé	**152**	3.52 N	11.31 E
Yaowan	**98**	34.12 N	118.03 E
Yaowangmiao	**98**	40.47 N	120.10 E
Yaoxian	**102**	34.56 N	108.53 E
Yaoya ≃	**236**	13.28 N	84.14 W
Yao Yai, Ko I	**110**	8.00 N	98.35 E
Yaozhan	**89**	52.53 N	125.13 E
Yap I	**174q**	9.31 N	138.06 E
Yapacaní	**248**	16.45 S	64.18 W
Yapacani ≃	**248**	16.00 S	64.25 W
Yapakopra	**164**	4.24 S	135.05 E
Yapehe	**152**	0.13 S	24.27 E
Yapei (Tamale Port)	**150**	9.10 N	1.10 W
Yapen, Pulau I	**164**	1.45 S	136.15 E
Yapen, Selat µ	**164**	1.30 S	136.10 E
Yapero	**164**	4.59 S	137.11 E
Yapeyú	**252**	29.28 S	56.49 W
Yaphank	**207**	40.50 N	72.56 W
Yappar ≃	**166**	18.22 S	141.16 E
Yapraklı	**130**	40.46 N	33.47 E
Yap Trench ✚[1]	**14**	8.30 N	138.00 E
Yaqian	**100**	26.38 N	114.30 E
Yaʻqūb	**140**	12.29 N	25.11 E
Yaque del Norte ≃	**238**	19.51 N	71.41 W
Yaqui ≃	**232**	27.37 N	110.39 W
Yaquina ≃	**202**	44.37 N	124.04 W
Yara	**240p**	20.16 N	76.57 W
Yaracuy □[3]	**246**	10.20 N	69.10 W
Yaraka	**166**	24.53 S	144.04 E
Yaratuar	**164**	2.58 S	134.40 E
Yarbasan	**130**	38.59 N	28.49 E
Yarcombe	**42**	50.52 N	3.05 W
Yardea	**166**	32.23 S	135.32 E
Yardımcı	**130**	37.00 N	38.59 E
Yardımcı Burnu ›	**130**	36.13 N	30.25 E
Yardley	**208**	40.14 N	74.50 W
Yardville	**208**	40.10 N	74.39 W
Yare ≃	**42**	52.35 N	1.44 E
Yarí ≃	**246**	0.23 S	72.16 W
Yariga-take ∧	**94**	36.20 N	137.39 E
Yārik	**123**	32.06 N	70.47 E
Yarīm	**144**	14.29 N	44.21 E
Yaring	**110**	6.52 N	101.22 E
Yaritagua	**246**	10.05 N	69.08 W
Yarkand → Shache	**120**	38.25 N	77.16 E
Yarkand → Yarkant ≃	**90**	40.28 N	80.52 E
Yarkant (Yarkand) ≃	**90**	40.28 N	80.52 E
Yarker	**212**	44.23 N	76.46 W
Yarkhūn ≃	**123**	36.17 N	72.30 E
Yarlarweelor	**162**	25.35 S	117.59 E
Yarle Lakes ⊜	**162**	30.15 S	131.27 E
Yarloop	**168a**	32.57 S	115.54 E
Yarlung → Brahmaputra ≃	**120**	24.02 N	90.59 E
Yarma	**130**	37.49 N	32.54 E
Yarmouth, N.S., Can.	**186**	43.50 N	66.07 W
Yarmouth, Eng., U.K.	**42**	50.42 N	1.29 W
Yarmouth → Great Yarmouth, Eng., U.K.	**42**	52.37 N	1.44 E
Yarmouth, Me., U.S.	**188**	43.48 N	70.11 W
Yarmouth, Ma., U.S.	**207**	41.42 N	70.13 W
Yarmu	**164**	4.18 S	142.17 E
Yarmūk, Nahr al- ≃	**132**	32.38 N	35.34 E
Yarra ≃	**169**	37.51 S	144.54 E
Yarra Bend Park ♠	**274b**	37.48 S	145.01 E
Yarra Glen	**169**	37.40 S	145.23 E
Yarragon	**169**	38.12 S	146.04 E
Yarra Junction	**169**	37.47 S	145.37 E
Yarraloola	**162**	21.34 S	115.52 E
Yarram	**166**	38.33 S	146.41 E
Yarraman	**171a**	26.50 S	151.59 E
Yarrangobilly	**171b**	35.39 S	148.28 E
Yarrangobilly ≃	**171b**	35.48 S	148.23 E
Yarrangobilly Caves ⊥[5]	**171b**	35.44 S	148.29 E
Yarraville	**274b**	37.49 S	144.53 E
Yarrawonga	**166**	36.01 S	146.00 E
Yarra Yarra Lakes ⊜	**162**	29.40 S	115.47 E
Yarrow, B.C., Can.	**224**	49.05 N	122.02 W
Yarrow, Scot., U.K.	**46**	55.32 N	3.01 W
Yarrow ≃	**262**	53.40 N	2.49 W
Yarrowee ≃	**169**	37.48 S	143.56 E
Yarrow Point	**224**	47.39 N	122.13 W
Yarrow Reservoir ⊜[1]	**262**	53.38 N	2.34 W
Yarrow Water ≃	**46**	55.34 N	2.51 W
Yarrunga, Lake ⊜[1]	**170**	34.45 S	150.20 E
Yarty ≃	**42**	50.47 N	3.01 W
Yarumal	**246**	6.58 N	75.24 W
Yasa	**152**	3.42 S	21.24 E
Yasaka, Nihon	**96**	35.39 N	135.07 E
Yasaka, Nihon	**96**	34.46 N	132.04 E
Yasa-Lokwa	**152**	5.15 S	19.24 E
Yasato	**94**	36.14 N	140.12 E
Yasawa I	**175g**	16.47 S	177.31 E
Yasawa Group II	**175g**	17.00 S	177.23 E
Yasendu	**152**	0.27 N	24.20 E
Yashanjie	**106**	30.51 N	119.03 E
Yashbum	**144**	14.19 N	46.56 E
Yashi	**150**	12.23 N	7.54 E
Yashikera	**150**	9.46 N	3.28 E
Ya-shima I	**96**	33.44 N	132.09 E
Yashima ♠	**96**	34.23 N	134.08 E
Yashio	**268**	35.49 N	139.51 E
Yashiro	**96**	34.55 N	134.58 E
Yashiro-jima I	**96**	33.55 N	132.15 E
Yāsīn	**123**	36.21 N	73.19 E
Yasku	**146**	12.20 N	12.30 E
Yasothon	**110**	15.45 N	104.08 E
Yass	**166**	34.50 S	148.55 E
Yassıada I	**267b**	40.51 N	29.00 E
Yassy → Iaşi	**38**	47.10 N	27.35 E
Yasu, Nihon	**94**	35.03 N	136.01 E
Yasu, Nihon	**96**	33.32 N	133.45 E
Yasuda	**96**	33.26 N	133.59 E
Yasugi	**96**	35.26 N	133.15 E
Yāsūj	**128**	30.40 N	51.36 E
Yasun Burnu ›	**130**	41.08 N	37.41 E
Yasuní ≃	**246**	0.56 S	75.23 W
Yasuni, Parque Nacional ♠	**246**	0.50 S	76.15 W
Yasuoka	**94**	35.22 N	137.50 E
Yasuura	**96**	34.17 N	132.45 E
Yasuzuka	**94**	37.08 N	138.28 E
Yata	**248**	13.20 S	66.35 W
Yata ≃, Bol.	**248**	10.29 S	65.26 W
Yata ≃, Centraf.	**146**	10.23 N	22.45 E
Yatabe	**94**	36.02 N	140.04 E
Yatağan	**130**	37.20 N	28.09 E
Yatakala	**150**	14.48 N	0.22 E
Yata-Ngaya, Réserve de Faune de la ◆[4]	**146**	9.15 N	23.30 W
Yāṭar	**132**	33.09 N	35.20 E
Yatate-yama ∧	**92**	34.10 N	129.10 E
Yaté	**175f**	22.09 S	166.57 E
Yates □[6]	**210**	42.40 N	77.03 W
Yatesboro	**214**	40.48 N	79.20 W
Yates Center	**198**	37.52 N	95.43 W
Yates City	**190**	40.46 N	90.00 W
Yathata Island I	**175g**	17.15 S	179.32 W
Yathkyed Lake ⊜	**176**	62.41 N	98.00 W
Yating	**102**	25.03 N	106.05 E
Yatomi	**94**	35.06 N	136.43 E
Yatsuga-take ∧	**94**	35.59 N	138.23 E
Yatsuga-take-chūshin-kōgen-kokutei-kōen ♠	**94**	36.03 N	138.20 E
Yatsuka	**96**	35.17 N	133.42 E
Yatsuo	**94**	36.34 N	137.08 E
Yatsushiro	**92**	32.30 N	130.36 E
Yatsushiro-kai ⊂	**92**	32.20 N	130.25 E
Yaṭṭah	**132**	31.27 N	35.05 E
Yatta Plateau ⋀[1]	**154**	2.00 S	38.00 E
Yatton	**42**	51.24 N	2.49 W
Yatuá ≃	**246**	1.43 N	66.30 W
Yatusiro → Yatsushiro	**92**	32.30 N	130.36 E
Yauca	**248**	15.40 S	74.32 W
Yauca ≃	**248**	15.41 S	74.31 W
Yauco	**240m**	18.02 N	66.51 W
Yauco ≃	**240m**	17.59 N	66.48 W
Yauco, Embalse de ⊜[1]	**240m**	18.07 N	66.50 W
Yauli	**248**	11.41 S	76.06 W
Yaundé → Yaoundé	**152**	3.52 N	11.31 E
Yaupi	**246**	2.59 S	77.50 W
Yauri	**248**	14.47 S	71.29 W
Yautepec	**234**	18.53 N	99.04 W
Yau Tong	**271d**	22.18 N	114.13 E
Yauyos	**248**	12.24 S	75.57 W
Yāval	**120**	21.10 N	75.42 E
Yavarí (Javari) ≃	**242**	4.21 S	70.02 W
Yavarí Mirim ≃	**246**	4.31 S	71.44 W
Yavaros	**232**	26.42 N	109.31 W
Yavatmāl	**122**	20.24 N	78.08 E
Yaven Yaven Creek ≃	**171b**	35.06 S	147.46 E
Yavero ≃	**248**	12.06 S	72.57 W
Yavi	**130**	39.48 N	36.13 E
Yaví, Cerro ∧	**246**	5.32 N	65.59 W
Yavita	**246**	2.55 N	67.26 W
Yaviza	**246**	8.11 N	77.41 W
Yavne	**132**	31.53 N	34.45 E
Yavuzeli	**130**	37.20 N	37.33 E
Yavuzkemal	**130**	40.43 N	38.21 E
Yaw ≃	**110**	20.55 N	94.49 E
Yawahara	**268**	35.59 N	140.01 E
Yawata, Nihon	**96**	34.52 N	135.42 E
Yawata → Kitakyūshū, Nihon	**96**	33.53 N	130.50 E
Yawata, Nihon	**268**	35.32 N	140.08 E
Yawatahama	**96**	33.27 N	132.24 E
Yaxchilán ⊥	**232**	16.54 N	90.58 W
Yaxi	**102**	27.32 N	106.45 E
Yaxian	**110**	18.20 N	109.30 E
Yaxigang	**106**	31.23 N	119.10 E
Yaxley	**42**	52.31 N	0.16 W
Yayama	**152**	1.16 S	23.07 E
Yayladağı	**130**	35.56 N	36.01 E
Yayladere	**130**	39.14 N	40.03 E
Yaylak	**130**	37.23 N	38.20 E
Yayouta	**150**	8.11 N	8.30 W
Yayuan	**98**	41.47 N	126.11 E
Yazd	**128**	31.53 N	54.25 E
Yazd □[4]	**128**	32.00 N	54.30 E
Yazi	**98**	37.04 N	121.17 E
Yazichangcun	**104**	41.16 N	122.26 E
Yazıhan	**130**	38.36 N	38.11 E
Yazmān	**123**	29.08 N	71.45 E
Yazoo ≃	**194**	32.22 N	91.00 W
Yazoo City	**194**	32.51 N	90.24 W
Ybbs ≃	**61**	48.10 N	15.06 E
Ybbs an der Donau	**61**	48.11 N	15.05 E
Ybbsitz	**61**	47.56 N	14.53 E
Ybor City	**220**	27.57 N	82.27 W
Ybycuí	**252**	26.01 S	57.03 W
Yding Skovhøj ∧[2]	**41**	56.00 N	9.48 E
Ydstebøhavn	**26**	59.08 N	5.15 E
Ydžid Parma ⋀	**24**	63.06 N	58.15 E
Ye	**110**	15.15 N	97.51 E
Yea	**169**	37.13 S	145.26 E
Yea ≃	**169**	37.11 S	145.23 E
Yeading ◆[8]	**260**	51.32 N	0.24 W
Yeadon, Eng., U.K.	**44**	53.52 N	1.41 W
Yeadon, Pa., U.S.	**285**	39.56 N	75.15 W
Yeagertown	**208**	40.38 N	77.34 W
Yealm ≃	**42**	50.18 N	4.03 W
Yealmpton	**42**	50.21 N	3.59 W
Yebawgyi	**110**	18.40 N	94.35 E
Yebbi-Bou	**146**	20.58 N	18.04 E
Yébigué, Enneri ∨	**146**	22.04 N	17.49 E
Yèbles	**261**	48.38 N	2.46 E
Yebyu	**110**	14.15 N	98.12 E
Yecapixtla	**234**	18.53 N	98.52 W
Yecheng	**120**	37.54 N	77.25 E
Yech'ŏn	**98**	36.40 N	128.26 E
Yecla	**34**	38.37 N	1.07 W
Yécora	**232**	28.20 N	108.58 W
Yedashe	**110**	19.09 N	96.21 E
Yedi Göller Milli Parkı ♠	**130**	40.50 N	31.30 E
Yedikule ◆[8]	**267b**	40.59 N	28.55 E
Yedikule ⊥	**267b**	40.59 N	28.55 E
Yédinga, Ouadi ∨	**146**	15.46 N	20.05 E
Yedseram ≃	**146**	12.30 N	14.05 E
Yeed	**144**	4.33 N	43.02 E
Yeeda	**162**	17.36 S	123.39 E
Yeelanna	**166**	34.09 S	135.45 E
Yeelirrie	**162**	27.17 S	120.06 E
Yeernuozha Hu ⊜	**120**	32.30 N	89.30 E
Yegor'yevsk → Jegorjevsk	**82**	55.23 N	39.02 E
Yegros	**252**	26.24 S	56.25 W
Yegua Creek ≃	**222**	30.23 N	96.18 W
Yeguas, Punta ›	**258**	34.55 S	56.19 W
Yeguas, Río de las ≃	**34**	37.22 N	4.45 W
Yehliu	**269d**	25.12 N	121.41 E
Yehliu Chia ›	**269d**	25.13 N	121.42 E
Yehud	**132**	32.02 N	34.53 E
Yei	**154**	4.05 N	30.40 E
Yei ≃	**140**	6.15 N	30.13 E
Yeji, Ghana	**150**	8.13 N	0.39 W
Yeji, Zhg.	**100**	31.52 N	115.55 E
Yekaterinburg → Jekaterinburg	**86**	56.51 N	60.36 E
Yekaterinodar → Krasnodar	**78**	45.02 N	39.00 E
Yekaterinoslav → Dnepropetrovsk	**78**	48.27 N	34.59 E
Yekokora ≃	**152**	1.20 N	20.21 E
Yekumbo	**152**	1.02 S	23.27 E
Ye Kyun I	**110**	18.37 N	93.47 E
Yela Island I	**160**	11.21 S	154.09 E
Yelarbon	**166**	28.34 S	150.45 E
Yelcho, Lago ⊜	**254**	43.18 S	72.18 W
Yele	**150**	8.25 N	11.50 W
Yelets → Jelec	**76**	52.37 N	38.30 E
Yélimané	**150**	15.08 N	10.34 W
Yell I	**46a**	60.36 N	1.06 W
Yellandu	**122**	17.36 N	80.20 E
Yellow ≃, U.S.	**194**	30.33 N	87.00 W
Yellow ≃, In., U.S.	**216**	41.16 N	86.50 W
Yellow ≃, Ia., U.S.	**190**	43.05 N	91.11 W
Yellow ≃, Wi., U.S.	**190**	44.58 N	91.18 W
Yellow ≃, Wi., U.S.	**190**	43.59 N	90.03 W
Yellow ≃, Wi., U.S.	**190**	46.01 N	92.22 W
Yellow → Huang ≃, Zhg.	**90**	37.32 N	118.19 E
Yellow Breeches Creek ≃	**208**	40.13 N	76.51 W
Yellow Creek ≃, U.S.	**194**	33.34 N	88.20 W
Yellow Creek ≃, Co., U.S.	**200**	40.10 N	108.24 W
Yellow Creek ≃, Oh., U.S.	**214**	40.34 N	80.40 W
Yellow Creek ≃, Tn., U.S.	**194**	36.26 N	87.34 W
Yellow Creek, North Fork ≃	**214**	40.33 N	80.42 W
Yellow Creek State Park ♠	**214**	40.35 N	79.02 W
Yellowdine	**162**	31.18 S	119.39 E
Yellow Grass	**184**	49.49 N	104.08 W
Yellowhead Pass)(	**182**	52.53 N	118.28 W
Yellow House Draw ∨	**196**	33.35 N	101.50 W
Yellowknife	**176**	62.27 N	114.21 W
Yellowknife ≃	**176**	62.31 N	114.19 W
Yellow Lake ⊜	**212**	44.20 N	75.36 W
Yellow Medicine ≃	**198**	44.44 N	95.25 W
Yellow Mountain ∧	**166**	32.30 S	146.51 E
Yellow Sea ᴛ[2]	**90**	36.00 N	123.00 E
Yellow Springs	**218**	39.48 N	83.53 W
Yellowstone ≃	**178**	47.58 N	103.59 W
Yellowstone, Clarks Fork ≃	**202**	45.39 N	108.43 W
Yellowstone Falls ᒪ	**202**	44.43 N	110.30 W
Yellowstone Lake ⊜	**202**	44.25 N	110.22 W
Yellowstone National Park	**202**	44.59 N	110.42 W
Yellowstone National Park ♠	**202**	44.30 N	110.35 W
Yellowtail Dam ◆[6]	**202**	45.12 N	107.57 W
Yell Sound µ	**46a**	60.32 N	1.15 W
Yellville	**194**	36.13 N	92.41 W
Yelm	**224**	46.56 N	122.36 W
Yelma	**162**	26.30 S	121.40 E
Yelvertoft	**166**	20.13 S	138.53 E
Yelverton	**42**	50.30 N	4.05 W
Yelwa	**150**	10.51 N	4.46 E
Yema ≃	**102**	41.25 N	95.10 E
Yemadu	**86**	43.36 N	81.50 E
Yemagong	**124**	29.28 N	89.06 E
Yemaotai	**104**	42.20 N	122.53 E
Yemassee	**192**	32.41 N	80.51 W
Yematan	**102**	34.40 N	98.16 E
Yemen (Al-Yaman) □[1], Asia	**118**	15.00 N	47.00 E
Yemen (Al-Yaman) □[1], Asia	**144**	15.00 N	47.00 E
Yemen, People's Democratic Republic of → Yemen □[1]	**144**	15.00 N	47.00 E
Yemen, República Popular Democrática del → Yemen □[1]	**144**	15.00 N	47.00 E
Yémen, République démocratique populaire du → Yemen □[1]	**144**	15.00 N	47.00 E
Yen	**152**	2.27 N	12.41 E
Yenagoa	**150**	4.55 N	6.19 E
Yenakiyevo → Jenakijevo	**83**	48.14 N	38.13 E
Yenangyaung	**110**	20.28 N	94.52 E
Yenanma	**110**	19.46 N	94.48 E
Yen Bai	**110**	21.42 N	104.52 E
Yen Chau	**110**	21.03 N	104.18 E
Yench'eng → Yancheng	**100**	33.24 N	120.09 E
Yenchi → Yanji	**98**	42.57 N	129.32 E
Yenda	**166**	34.15 S	146.11 E
Yende Millimou	**150**	8.53 N	10.11 W
Yendéré	**150**	10.12 N	4.58 W
Yendi	**150**	9.26 N	0.01 W
Ye-ngan	**110**	21.09 N	96.27 E
Yenge ≃	**152**	0.55 S	20.40 E
Yengema	**150**	8.43 N	11.10 W
Yengisar	**85**	38.57 N	76.03 E
Yengo	**152**	0.22 N	15.29 E
Yengo, Mount ∧	**170**	32.59 S	150.51 E
Yéni	**150**	13.26 N	2.59 E
Yeniçağa	**130**	40.46 N	32.02 E
Yenice, Tür.	**130**	39.45 N	28.55 E
Yenice, Tür.	**130**	39.55 N	27.18 E
Yenice, Tür.	**130**	36.59 N	35.03 E
Yenice, Tür.	**130**	41.11 N	32.19 E
Yenice ≃	**130**	41.35 N	32.03 E
Yenicekale	**130**	37.37 N	36.37 E
Yeniceoba	**130**	38.53 N	32.48 E
Yenierenköy	**130**	35.32 N	34.11 E
Yenifoça	**130**	38.44 N	26.51 E
Yenikapı ◆[8]	**267b**	41.00 N	28.57 E
Yeniköy	**130**	39.46 N	28.00 E
Yeniköy ◆[8]	**267b**	40.59 N	28.53 E
Yenimehmetli	**130**	39.26 N	32.10 E
Yenipazar, Tür.	**130**	37.48 N	28.12 E
Yenipazar, Tür.	**130**	40.11 N	30.31 E
Yenişehir	**130**	40.16 N	29.39 E
Yenisey → Jenisej ≃	**72**	71.50 N	82.40 E
Yennadon	**224**	49.14 N	122.34 W
Yenne	**62**	45.42 N	5.46 E
Yennora	**274a**	33.52 S	150.58 E
Yenshuichen	**100**	23.20 N	120.16 E
Yentna ≃	**180**	61.34 N	150.28 W
Yeo ≃, Eng., U.K.	**42**	51.02 N	2.49 W
Yeo ≃, Eng., U.K.	**42**	51.01 N	3.50 W
Yeo ≃, Eng., U.K.	**42**	50.45 N	3.36 W
Yeola	**122**	20.02 N	74.29 E
Yeo Lake ⊜	**162**	28.04 S	124.23 E
Yeoman	**216**	40.40 N	86.43 W
Yeoval	**166**	32.45 S	148.40 E
Yeovil	**42**	50.57 N	2.39 W
Yeoville ◆[8]	**273d**	26.12 S	28.04 E
Yepachic	**232**	28.26 N	108.23 W
Yeppoon	**166**	23.08 S	150.45 E
Yerba Buena, Montaña ∧	**236**	14.05 N	87.26 W
Yerba Buena Island I	**282**	37.48 N	122.22 W
Yères ≃	**50**	50.02 N	1.19 E
Yerevan → Jerevan	**84**	40.11 N	44.30 E
Yerilla	**162**	29.28 S	121.49 E
Yering	**274b**	37.41 S	145.23 E
Yerington	**226**	38.59 N	119.09 W
Yerington Indian Reservation ◆[4]	**226**	39.05 N	119.12 W
Yerkes	**285**	40.10 N	75.27 W
Yerkes Astronomical Observatory υ[3]	**216**	42.34 N	88.34 W
Yerkesik	**130**	37.07 N	28.17 E
Yerköy	**130**	39.38 N	34.29 E
Yerlisu	**130**	40.46 N	26.39 E
Yermasóyia	**130**	34.43 N	33.05 E
Yermenonville	**261**	48.33 N	1.37 E
Yermo	**204**	34.54 N	116.49 W
Yeroḥam	**132**	31.00 N	34.55 E
Yerolimín	**38**	36.28 N	22.24 E
Yèrre ≃	**50**	48.01 N	1.16 E
Yerres	**50**	48.43 N	2.30 E
Yerres ≃	**50**	48.43 N	2.27 E
Yerseke	**52**	51.29 N	4.02 E
Yerupaja, Nevado ∧	**248**	10.16 S	76.54 W

Symbols in the index entries represent the broad categories identified in the key at the right. Symbols with superior numbers (⋀[1]) identify subcategories (see complete key on page *I · 1*).

Symbole im Register stellen die rechts im Schlüssel erklärten Kategorien dar. Symbole mit hochgestellten Ziffern (⋀[1]) bezeichnen Unterabteilungen einer Kategorie (vgl. vollständiger Schlüssel auf Seite *I · 1*).

Los símbolos incluídos en el texto del índice representan las grandes categorías identificadas con la clave a la derecha. Los símbolos con numeros en su parte superior (⋀[1]) identifican las subcategorías (véase la clave completa en la página *I · 1*).

Les symboles de l'index représentent les catégories indiquées dans la légende à droite. Les symboles suivis d'un indice (⋀[1]) représentent des sous-catégories (voir légende complète à la page *I · 1*).

Os símbolos incluídos no texto do índice representam as grandes categorias identificadas com a chave à direita. Os símbolos com números em sua parte superior (⋀[1]) identificam as subcategorias (veja-se a chave completa à página *I · 1*).

∧ Mountain	Berg	Montaña	Montagne	Montanha
⋀ Mountains	Gebirge	Montañas	Montagnes	Montanhas
)(Pass	Paß	Paso	Col	Passo
∨ Valley, Canyon	Tal, Cañon	Valle, Cañón	Vallée, Canyon	Vale, Canhão
≚ Plain	Ebene	Llano	Plaine	Planície
› Cape	Kap	Cabo	Cap	Cabo
I Island	Insel	Isla	Île	Ilha
II Islands	Inseln	Islas	Îles	Ilhas
⊥ Other Topographic Features	Andere Topographische Objekte	Otros Elementos Topográficos	Autres données topographiques	Outros acidentes topográficos

ESPAÑOL Nombre	Página	Lat.°′	Long.°′ W = Oeste
Yerushalayim (Al-Quds) (Jerusalem)	132	31.46 N	35.14 E
Yerushalayim □[5]	132	31.45 N	35.00 E
Yerville	50	49.40 N	0.54 E
Yesa, Embalse de ⊜[1]	34	42.36 N	1.09 W
Yesan	98	36.41 N	126.50 E
Yeshenpu	104	40.51 N	122.32 E
Yeshiva University ⚜[2]	276	40.51 N	73.55 W
Yeshvi	272c	18.55 N	73.03 E
Yeşil ≃	130	41.24 N	36.35 E
Yeşilçonlu	130	40.13 N	28.06 E
Yeşildere	130	37.09 N	33.31 E
Yeşilhisar	130	38.21 N	35.06 E
Yeşilkent	130	36.59 N	36.10 E
Yeşilköy	130	40.57 N	28.49 E
Yeşilköy Burnu ›	267b	40.57 N	28.50 E
Yeşilova	130	37.30 N	29.46 E
Yeşiltepe	130	37.12 N	33.02 E
Yeşilyazı	130	39.20 N	39.05 E
Yeşilyurt	130	38.18 N	38.15 E
Yeso	196	34.26 N	104.36 W
Yeso Creek ≃	196	34.13 N	104.15 W
Yesŏng-gang ≃	98	37.53 N	126.24 E
Yessentuki → Jessentuki	84	44.03 N	42.51 E
Yeste	34	38.22 N	2.18 W
Yes Tor ∧	42	50.42 N	4.00 W
Yesud HaMa'ala	132	33.03 N	35.36 E
Yetholme	170	33.27 S	149.49 E
Yetman	166	28.54 S	150.46 E
Yetminster	42	50.53 N	2.33 W
Yetsou I	152	2.08 S	10.42 E
Yettem	226	36.29 N	119.16 W
Yetti	164	3.00 S	140.53 E
Yetti ◆[1]	148	26.10 N	7.50 W
Ye-u	110	22.46 N	95.26 E
Yeu, Île d' I	32	46.42 N	2.20 W
Yevpatoriya → Jevpatorija	78	45.12 N	33.22 E
Yexian, Zhg.	98	37.13 N	119.54 E
Yexian, Zhg.	100	33.37 N	113.20 E
Yexie	106	30.56 N	121.19 E
Yextla ≃	234	18.00 N	100.06 W
Yeysk → Jejsk	78	46.42 N	38.16 E
Yeyuan	98	36.22 N	118.27 E
Yeywa	110	21.41 N	96.24 E
Yezd → Yazd	128	31.53 N	54.25 E
Yeze Hu ⊜	106	31.08 N	120.40 E
Yezhuang	105	39.10 N	116.18 E
Yezhuhe	105	40.53 N	118.13 E
Ygatimí	252	24.05 S	55.30 W
Ygnacio Canal ≋	282	37.55 N	122.03 W
Yguazú ≃	252	25.20 S	55.00 W
Yhú	252	24.59 S	55.59 W
Yi	98	42.08 N	118.48 E
Yi ≃, Ur.	252	33.07 S	57.08 W
Yi ≃, Zhg	98	34.07 N	118.15 E
Yi ≃, Zhg.	100	34.10 N	112.10 E
Yi ≃, Zhg.	105	39.14 N	115.46 E
Yi'an	89	47.55 N	125.20 E
Yiannitsá	38	40.48 N	22.25 E
Yíaros I	38	37.37 N	24.43 E
Yibao	106	30.25 N	119.53 E
Yibin (Ipin)	107	28.47 N	104.38 E
Yibug Caka ⊜	120	33.00 N	86.25 E
Yibutan	107	28.54 N	104.40 E
Yicanghe	100	32.47 N	120.43 E
Yichang (Ichang)	102	30.42 N	111.17 E
Yicheng, Zhg.	98	34.46 N	117.37 E
Yicheng, Zhg.	98	36.48 N	114.17 E
Yicheng, Zhg.	102	31.43 N	112.07 E
Yichexun	102	26.50 N	103.28 E
Yichuan, Zhg.	100	34.26 N	112.24 E
Yichuan, Zhg.	102	36.04 N	110.06 E
Yichun, Zhg.	90	47.42 N	128.55 E
Yichun, Zhg.	100	27.50 N	114.23 E
Yicun	105	38.57 N	115.37 E
Yidan	89	43.24 N	125.25 E
Yidie	102	37.08 N	110.30 E
Yidu, Zhg.	98	36.41 N	118.28 E
Yidu, Zhg.	102	30.22 N	111.22 E
Yidun	102	29.56 N	99.22 E
Yiewsley ◆[8]	260	51.31 N	0.28 W
Yifag	144	12.02 N	37.44 E
Yifeng, Zhg.	100	33.19 N	113.47 E
Yifeng, Zhg.	100	28.26 N	114.46 E
Yigaolou	106	30.56 N	120.20 E
Yiğılca	130	40.58 N	31.27 E
Yiğitler	130	39.52 N	26.37 E
Yigou	98	35.51 N	114.20 E
Yihe	100	23.50 N	114.53 E
Yihechang	107	30.23 N	106.24 E
Yi He Yuan (Summer Palace) ⚜	105	40.00 N	116.16 E
Yihezhuang, Zhg.	98	37.53 N	118.23 E
Yihezhuang, Zhg.	104	41.15 N	122.57 E
Yihuang	100	27.34 N	116.10 E
Yihuang ≃	100	28.05 N	116.18 E
Yijiangzhen	100	30.55 N	118.28 E
Yijiawan	100	27.58 N	113.01 E
Yijiazi	104	42.29 N	122.41 E
Yijingpu	105	40.08 N	117.47 E
Yijinqiao	100	30.54 N	117.12 E
Yijun	102	35.24 N	109.00 E
Yikengaolu	102	42.17 N	98.19 E
Yikou	100	26.45 N	117.00 E
Yilaha	89	48.50 N	125.10 E
Yilan	89	46.19 N	129.34 E
Yilaxi	89	43.47 N	126.08 E
Yıldız Dağı ∧	130	40.08 N	36.56 E
Yıldız Dağları ⩘	38	41.50 N	27.30 E
Yıldızeli	130	39.52 N	36.38 E
Yilehuli Shan ⩘	89	51.20 N	124.30 E
Yili	107	30.45 N	105.58 E
Yiliang, Zhg.	102	24.58 N	103.07 E
Yiliang, Zhg.	102	27.35 N	104.01 E
Yiliekede	89	48.51 N	121.37 E
Yilin	100	33.36 N	119.37 E
Yiling	100	32.30 N	119.46 E
Yiliping	120	37.55 N	93.30 E
Yilliminning	162	32.54 S	117.22 E
Yilong, Zhg.	89	47.28 N	125.23 E
Yilong, Zhg.	102	31.34 N	106.19 E
Yilong, Zhg.	102	25.20 N	103.14 E
Yimachi	104	42.11 N	122.15 E
Yimatu	104	41.55 N	121.25 E
Yimen, Zhg.	100	33.39 N	116.02 E
Yimen, Zhg.	102	24.43 N	102.10 E
Yimuhe	89	52.45 N	120.07 E
Yin ≃, Mya.	110	20.04 N	95.01 E
Yin ≃, Zhg.	98	42.19 N	118.37 E
Yinan (Jiehu)	98	35.37 N	118.30 E
Yinbaing	110	17.25 N	97.46 E
Yinchuan	102	38.30 N	106.18 E
Yindarlgooda, Lake ⊜	162	30.45 S	121.55 E
Yindi	154	1.35 N	27.40 E
Yinfang	105	39.07 N	114.52 E
Ying ≃	100	32.30 N	116.32 E
Yingcheng	100	30.57 N	113.32 E
Yingchengzi, Zhg.	89	44.08 N	125.56 E
Yingchengzi, Zhg.	98	38.58 N	121.23 E
Yingchengzi, Zhg.	104	41.50 N	124.04 E
Yingchengzi, Zhg.	104	42.22 N	124.14 E
Yingde	100	24.12 N	113.24 E
Yingen	102	41.09 N	104.45 E
Yingfang	105	40.14 N	116.17 E
Yinggehai	110	18.31 N	108.44 E
Yinghe	100	32.16 N	116.31 E
Yingjin ≃	98	42.20 N	119.19 E
Yingkoshih ≃	269d	25.06 N	121.43 E
Yingkou, Zhg.	104	40.40 N	122.14 E
Yingkou (Dashiqiao), Zhg.	104	40.38 N	122.30 E
Yingpan, Zhg.	102	25.48 N	106.18 E
Yingpan, Zhg.	102	24.44 N	99.38 E
Yingpanjie	102	25.27 N	98.24 E
Yingqiao	100	33.58 N	113.39 E
Yingshan, Zhg.	100	30.45 N	115.39 E

FRANÇAIS Nom	Page	Lat.°′	Long.°′ W = Ouest
Yingshan, Zhg.	100	31.38 N	113.50 E
Yingshan, Zhg.	102	31.08 N	106.31 E
Yingshang	100	32.38 N	116.15 E
Yingshouyingzi, Zhg.	105	40.33 N	117.38 E
Yingshouyingzi, Zhg.	105	40.49 N	117.55 E
Yingtan	100	28.14 N	117.00 E
Yingtaogou	104	42.08 N	121.57 E
Yingtaoyuan	104	41.10 N	123.05 E
Yingtian	100	28.50 N	112.56 E
Yingxiangjie	107	29.24 N	105.11 E
Yingxianpu	104	41.20 N	121.31 E
Yining (Kuldja)	86	43.54 N	81.21 E
Yinjiadai	105	32.03 N	120.07 E
Yinjiang	102	28.02 N	108.28 E
Yinjiawopeng	104	42.34 N	121.01 E
Yinkeng	100	26.14 N	115.34 E
Yinliu	105	39.59 N	117.23 E
Yinmabin	110	22.05 N	94.54 E
Yinmahe	89	44.07 N	125.44 E
Yinmatu ≃	98	40.57 N	117.43 E
Yinnietharra	162	24.39 S	116.11 E
Yinnyein	110	16.48 N	97.23 E
Yinong	102	30.19 N	101.01 E
Yinping	98	34.15 N	118.39 E
Yinqiaotou	106	31.52 N	119.13 E
Yin Shan ⩘	102	41.48 N	109.00 E
Yinshanzhen	107	29.41 N	104.58 E
Yinwogou	98	41.55 N	117.55 E
Yinxian	100	29.50 N	121.38 E
Yinxiang	106	31.55 N	118.49 E
Yinxianji	100	32.07 N	116.32 E
Yinyangjie	104	42.16 N	121.23 E
Yinyuan	102	23.26 N	101.54 E
Yinzhan'ao	100	23.33 N	113.07 E
Yio Chu Kang	271c	1.23 N	103.51 E
Yi'ong	102	30.17 N	94.51 E
Yi'ong ≃	120	29.56 N	95.10 E
Yi Pak	271d	22.19 N	114.00 E
Yipinchang	107	29.17 N	106.34 E
Yipinglang	102	25.11 N	101.51 E
Yiqian	100	26.34 N	116.11 E
Yirba Muda	144	6.12 N	38.42 E
Yirga Alem	144	6.52 N	38.22 E
Yirkā	132	32.57 N	35.13 E
Yirol	140	6.33 N	30.30 E
Yirrkala	164	12.14 S	136.56 E
Yirshi	89	47.20 N	119.45 E
Yirwa	140	7.47 N	27.15 E
Yisaduo	102	28.50 N	96.44 E
Yishan, Zhg.	100	27.32 N	120.32 E
Yishan, Zhg.	102	24.40 N	108.35 E
Yishui	98	35.50 N	118.41 E
Yishun	271c	1.26 N	103.50 E
Yisikan	89	49.09 N	124.47 E
Yisra'el → Israel □[1]	132	31.30 N	35.00 E
Yisuhe	100	27.46 N	112.54 E
Yitajing	102	42.32 N	94.12 E
Yitang, Zhg.	98	35.10 N	118.16 E
Yitang, Zhg.	100	31.06 N	113.42 E
Yíthion	38	36.45 N	22.34 E
Yiting	100	29.15 N	119.57 E
Yitm, Wādī al- V	132	29.34 N	35.01 E
Yitong	89	43.20 N	125.17 E
Yitong ≃	98	42.40 N	125.58 E
Yitulihe	89	50.38 N	121.34 E
Yiwu, Zhg.	100	29.18 N	120.04 E
Yiwu, Zhg.	102	43.15 N	94.45 E
Yiwu, Zhg.	102	22.00 N	101.28 E
Yiwulü Shan ⩘	104	41.42 N	121.42 E
Yixi	100	23.45 N	116.38 E
Yixian, Zhg.	100	29.55 N	117.56 E
Yixian, Zhg.	104	41.32 N	121.15 E
Yixian, Zhg.	105	39.21 N	115.29 E
Yixiken	89	52.57 N	125.40 E
Yixing	106	31.22 N	119.50 E
Yixingbu	105	39.12 N	117.12 E
Yixingchang	107	30.37 N	106.38 E
Yixu	100	26.02 N	119.16 E
Yixun ≃	98	41.16 N	117.35 E
Yiyang, Zhg.	100	28.23 N	117.25 E
Yiyang, Zhg.	102	28.36 N	112.20 E
Yiyang, Zhg.	102	34.30 N	112.10 E
Yiyuan (Nanma)	98	36.11 N	118.08 E
Yiyuankou	98	40.10 N	119.35 E
Yizhang	100	25.26 N	112.56 E
Yizheng	106	32.16 N	119.12 E
Yizikong	102	25.38 N	104.28 E
Yizre'él	132	32.33 N	35.20 E
Yizre'el, 'Émeq ≡	132	32.36 N	35.14 E
Ylakiai	76	56.17 N	21.51 E
Yläne	26	60.53 N	22.55 E
Ylihärmä	26	63.09 N	22.47 E
Yli-Kitka ⊜	26	66.08 N	28.30 E
Ylimarkku → Övermark	26	62.33 N	21.30 E
Ylistaro	26	62.57 N	22.31 E
Ylivieska	26	64.05 N	24.33 E
Ylöjärvi	26	61.33 N	23.36 E
Ymeray	261	48.31 N	1.42 E
Ymir	182	49.17 N	117.13 W
Yndin	24	61.24 N	55.10 E
Yngaren ⊜	40	58.52 N	16.35 E
Yngen ⊜	40	59.44 N	14.18 E
Yntaly	86	48.58 N	70.55 E
Ynykčanskij	74	60.15 N	137.43 E
Yoakum	222	29.17 N	97.09 W
Yobi, Indon.	164	1.43 S	138.04 E
Yobi, Indon.	164	1.42 S	136.27 E
Yockanookany ≃	194	32.40 N	89.40 W
Yoco	246	10.36 N	62.24 W
Yocona ≃	194	34.11 N	90.11 W
Yōda	268	35.24 N	139.25 E
Yoder	216	40.55 N	85.10 W
Yodo ≃	96	34.41 N	135.25 E
Yodoe	96	35.28 N	133.26 E
Yodogawa ◆[8]	270	34.42 N	135.28 E
Yoe	208	39.55 N	76.39 W
Yōga ◆[8]	268	35.38 N	139.38 E
Yogo	94	35.33 N	136.12 E
Yog Point ›	116	14.06 N	124.12 E
Yoğuntaş	130	41.50 N	27.04 E
Yogyakarta	115a	7.48 S	110.22 E
Yogyakarta □[4]	115a	7.45 S	110.30 E
Yoho National Park ♠	182	51.26 N	116.30 W
Yoichi	92a	43.12 N	140.41 E
Yojoa, Lago de ⊜	236	14.50 N	88.00 W
Yŏju	98	37.18 N	127.37 E
Yōka	96	35.24 N	134.46 E
Yokadouma	152	3.31 N	15.03 E
Yōkaichi	94	35.06 N	136.12 E
Yōkaichiba	94	35.42 N	140.33 E
Yokamba	152	0.01 N	22.17 E
Yokana	152	0.45 N	22.53 E
Yokawa	96	34.52 N	135.06 E
Yokchi-do I	98	34.38 N	128.15 E
Yokkaichi, Nihon	94	34.58 N	136.37 E
Yokkaichi, Nihon	96	33.32 N	131.20 E
Yoko	152	2.36 S	20.06 E
Yokoate-jima I	93b	28.48 N	129.00 E
Yokohama, Nihon	94	35.27 N	139.39 E
Yokohama, Nihon	268	35.27 N	139.39 E
Yokohama-kō ⊂	268	35.27 N	139.39 E
Yokohama National University ⚜[2]	268	35.25 N	139.36 E
Yokohama Park Baseball Ground ♠	268	35.26 N	139.39 E
Yokolo	152	0.36 S	23.04 E
Yokonuma	268	35.58 N	139.27 E
Yokoshiba	94	35.40 N	140.28 E
Yokosuka	94	35.18 N	139.40 E
Yokosuka District Naval Headquarters ■	268	35.17 N	139.39 E
Yokosuka-kō ⊂	268	35.18 N	139.39 E
Yokosuka Naval Base ■	94	35.18 N	139.41 E
Yokota, Nihon	96	35.10 N	133.06 E
Yokota, Nihon	268	35.23 N	140.01 E
Yokota, Nihon	270	34.40 N	135.55 E

PORTUGUÊS Nome	Página	Lat.°′	Long.°′ W = Oeste
Yokota Air Base ■	268	35.45 N	139.21 E
Yokote	92	39.18 N	140.34 E
Yola	146	9.12 N	12.29 E
Yolaina, Serranías de ⩘	236	11.40 N	84.20 W
Yolboyu	130	37.55 N	40.00 E
Yolo	226	38.44 N	121.48 W
Yolo □[6]	226	38.41 N	121.46 W
Yolo ≃	273b	4.19 S	15.20 E
Yolo Bypass ≃	226	38.25 N	121.40 W
Yolombó, Col.	246	6.36 N	75.01 W
Yolombo, Zaïre	152	1.32 S	23.15 E
Yolonga	152	1.36 S	23.12 E
Yom ≃	110	15.52 N	100.16 E
Yombi	152	1.26 S	10.37 E
Yomou	150	7.34 N	9.16 W
Yona	174p	13.25 N	144.47 E
Yonabaru	174m	26.12 N	127.45 E
Yonago	96	35.26 N	133.20 E
Yonaguni	175d	24.27 N	122.57 E
Yonaguni-shima I	175d	24.27 N	123.00 E
Yonaha-dake ∧[2]	174m	26.43 N	128.13 E
Yŏnan	98	37.55 N	126.10 E
Yoncalı	130	39.01 N	38.15 E
Yoncalla	202	43.35 N	123.16 W
Yŏnch'on ◆[3]	271b	37.38 N	127.04 E
Yoneshiro ≃	92	40.13 N	140.01 E
Yonezawa	92	37.55 N	140.07 E
Yŏngam	98	34.48 N	126.40 E
Yongamp'o	98	39.55 N	124.24 E
Yŏngan, C.M.I.K.	98	41.15 N	129.30 E
Yong'an, Zhg.	100	25.58 N	117.22 E
Yongan, Zhg.	107	30.44 N	106.16 E
Yong'an, Zhg.	107	29.13 N	104.46 E
Yong'an ≃	100	28.52 N	121.04 E
Yonganbao	98	40.15 N	119.52 E
Yong'anchang	107	30.24 N	103.58 E
Yong'anshi	100	28.13 N	113.19 E
Yŏngbyŏn	98	39.49 N	125.48 E
Yongchang, Zhg.	100	29.13 N	119.20 E
Yongchang, Zhg.	102	38.17 N	101.59 E
Yongchangzhen	106	31.42 N	121.44 E
Yongcheng	100	33.58 N	116.21 E
Yongch'ŏn, C.M.I.K.	98	39.59 N	124.28 E
Yŏngch'ŏn, Taehan	98	38.07 N	127.05 E
Yŏngch'ŏn, Taehan	98	35.58 N	128.56 E
Yongch'ŏn-dong	98	41.18 N	129.40 E
Yongchuan	107	29.21 N	105.54 E
Yongchun	100	25.21 N	118.21 E
Yongdeng	102	36.48 N	103.14 E
Yongdian	98	40.34 N	124.48 E
Yongding	100	24.46 N	116.43 E
Yongding ≃, Zhg.	100	24.42 N	116.34 E
Yongding ≃, Zhg.	105	39.20 N	117.04 E
Yongdingmen Station ◆[5]	271a	39.52 N	116.23 E
Yŏngdŏk	98	36.26 N	129.23 E
Yŏngdong	98	36.10 N	127.48 E
Yŏngdŭngp'o ◆[8]	271b	37.32 N	126.54 E
Yongfeng, Zhg.	100	29.44 N	116.49 E
Yongfeng, Zhg.	100	27.19 N	115.24 E
Yongfengchang	107	30.33 N	105.05 E
Yongfu	100	25.05 N	117.20 E
Yonggang	98	38.52 N	125.21 E
Yonggangonch'ŏn	98	38.53 N	125.14 E
Yonggi	98	36.24 N	128.24 E
Yongguzhai	98	34.05 N	116.50 E
Yonghe	100	28.18 N	113.51 E
Yongheshi	100	28.18 N	113.51 E
Yonghŭng	98	39.32 N	127.13 E
Yŏnghŭng-do I	98	37.16 N	126.28 E
Yŏnghŭng-man ⊂	98	39.15 N	127.30 E
Yongi	89	43.40 N	126.30 E
Yŏngil-man ⊂	98	36.02 N	129.26 E
Yongji	102	34.51 N	110.29 E
Yongjia, Zhg.	100	28.11 N	120.42 E
Yongjia, Zhg.	107	29.34 N	106.01 E
Yŏngjong-do I	98	37.30 N	126.31 E
Yŏngju	98	36.50 N	128.37 E
Yongkang, Zhg.	100	32.32 N	117.24 E
Yongkang, Zhg.	100	28.53 N	120.02 E
Yongkou	100	26.16 N	118.19 E
Yongle, Zhg.	89	45.45 N	125.12 E
Yongle, Zhg.	105	39.32 N	115.59 E
Yongle ≃	100	26.54 N	113.12 E
Yongledian	105	39.43 N	116.46 E
Yonglong	106	31.34 N	121.48 E
Yonglonghe	100	30.46 N	112.48 E
Yŏngmi-dong	98	39.40 N	125.31 E
Yongnian (Linmingguan)	98	36.47 N	114.30 E
Yongnianchang	107	29.08 N	104.51 E
Yongning, Zhg.	100	24.43 N	118.42 E
Yongning, Zhg.	102	38.20 N	106.17 E
Yongning, Zhg.	102	22.42 N	108.50 E
Yongning, Zhg.	102	27.47 N	100.38 E
Yongningcheng	105	40.34 N	116.11 E
Yongningjian	98	39.56 N	121.48 E
Yong Peng	114	2.01 N	103.04 E
Yongping, Zhg.	100	28.12 N	117.45 E
Yongping, Zhg.	102	25.28 N	99.33 E
Yongqing, Zhg.	105	39.19 N	116.29 E
Yongqing, Zhg.	107	30.00 N	105.27 E
Yongquan	100	28.46 N	121.19 E
Yongren	102	26.08 N	101.40 E
Yŏngsan-gang ≃	98	34.54 N	126.32 E
Yongsan-ni	98	38.52 N	125.56 E
Yŏngsanp'o	98	34.58 N	126.44 E
Yongshan	102	28.15 N	103.24 E
Yongshanqiao	100	29.06 N	117.17 E
Yongsheng	102	26.42 N	100.43 E
Yongshou	102	34.43 N	108.05 E
Yongshun	102	28.57 N	109.41 E
Yongshunchang	107	30.06 N	105.26 E
Yongtai	100	25.54 N	118.58 E
Yŏngwŏl	98	37.12 N	128.28 E
Yŏngwŏn	98	39.49 N	126.32 E
Yongwŏn-ni	98	40.41 N	128.42 E
Yongxin, Zhg.	100	26.56 N	114.18 E
Yongxin, Zhg.	107	28.59 N	106.32 E
Yongxing, Zhg.	98	40.11 N	123.52 E
Yongxing, Zhg.	100	26.08 N	113.06 E
Yongxing, Zhg.	102	39.08 N	110.31 E
Yongxing, Zhg.	106	31.56 N	120.55 E
Yongxing, Zhg.	107	30.13 N	105.06 E
Yongxing, Zhg.	107	30.34 N	105.35 E
Yongxingchang, Zhg.	107	29.02 N	104.34 E
Yongxingchang, Zhg.	107	29.37 N	106.23 E
Yongxingchang, Zhg.	107	30.20 N	103.44 E
Yongxiu	100	29.04 N	115.49 E
Yŏngyang, Taehan	98	36.40 N	129.07 E
Yongyang, Zhg.	100	26.57 N	114.46 E
Yŏngyn	98	39.18 N	125.34 E
Yongyŏn-ni	98	40.44 N	126.09 E
Yongzhai	100	27.59 N	115.26 E
Yŏnhŭi-ri	271b	37.33 N	126.41 E
Yŏnhwa-san ∧	98	40.46 N	127.23 E
Yonibana	150	8.26 N	12.14 W
Yonkers	210	40.55 N	73.53 W
Yonkers Raceway ♠	276	40.55 N	73.52 W
Yonne □[5]	50	47.55 N	3.45 E
Yonne ≃	32	48.23 N	2.58 E
Yono	94	35.53 N	139.38 E
Yŏnp'yŏng-yŏlto II	98	37.38 N	125.40 E
Yonsei University ⚜[2]	271b	37.34 N	126.56 E
Yoo, Enneri V	146	19.24 N	16.38 E
Yoontow	144	0.08 S	42.34 E
Yopal	246	5.21 N	72.23 W
Yop'o-ri	98	38.50 N	125.33 E
Yopurga	85	39.15 N	76.45 E
Yoqne'am	132	32.39 N	35.07 E
Yorba Linda	228	33.53 N	117.48 W
Yorii	94	36.07 N	139.12 E
Yorishima	96	34.29 N	133.35 E
York, Austl.	168a	31.53 S	116.46 E
York, On., Can.	212	43.41 N	79.29 W
York, S.L.	150	8.17 N	13.11 W
York, Eng., U.K.	44	53.58 N	1.05 W
York, Al., U.S.	194	32.29 N	88.17 W
York, In., U.S.	216	41.41 N	84.49 W
York, Ne., U.S.	198	40.52 N	97.35 W
York, N.Y., U.S.	210	42.52 N	77.53 W
York, N.D., U.S.	198	48.18 N	99.34 W
York, Pa., U.S.	208	39.57 N	76.43 W
York, S.C., U.S.	192	34.59 N	81.14 W
York □[6], On., Can.	212	43.55 N	79.25 W
York □[6], Pa., U.S.	208	39.58 N	76.44 W
York □[6], Va., U.S.	208	37.15 N	76.40 W
York ≃, On., Can.	212	45.20 N	77.35 W
York ≃, P.Q., Can.	186	48.49 N	64.34 W
York ≃, Va., U.S.	208	37.15 N	76.23 W
York, Cape ›	164	10.42 S	142.31 E
York, Kap ›	16	75.53 N	66.12 W
York, Vale of V	44	54.10 N	1.20 W
Yorkana	208	39.59 N	76.35 W
York Center, Il., U.S.	278	41.52 N	87.59 W
York Center, Oh., U.S.	216	40.24 N	83.27 W
Yorkdale Centre ◆[9]	275b	43.44 N	79.27 W
Yorke Peninsula ›[1]	166	35.00 S	137.30 E
Yorketown	168b	35.02 S	137.36 E
York Factory	184	57.00 N	92.18 W
Yorkfield	278	41.52 N	87.56 W
York Haven	208	40.06 N	76.42 W
Yorklyn	285	39.48 N	75.40 W
York Minster ⚜[1]	44	53.57 N	1.04 W
York New Salem	208	39.54 N	76.47 W
Yorkshire, N.Y., U.S.	210	42.31 N	78.28 W
Yorkshire, Pa., U.S.	208	39.59 N	76.41 W
Yorkshire, Va., U.S.	208	38.47 N	77.27 W
Yorkshire Dales National Park ♠	44	54.13 N	2.10 W
Yorkshire Wolds ⩘[2]	44	54.00 N	0.40 W
York Sound Ʉ	160	14.50 S	125.05 E
York Springs	208	40.00 N	77.07 W
Yorkton	184	51.13 N	102.28 W
Yorktown, In., U.S.	218	40.10 N	85.29 W
Yorktown, Tx., U.S.	222	28.58 N	97.30 W
Yorktown, Va., U.S.	208	37.14 N	76.30 W
Yorktown ◆[9]	278	41.51 N	88.01 W
Yorktown Battlefield ⊥	208	37.13 N	76.31 W
Yorktown Heights	210	41.16 N	73.46 W
Yorktown Manor	207	41.38 N	71.26 W
York Township Airport ⊠	278	41.51 N	88.02 W
York University ⚜[2]	275b	43.47 N	79.30 W
Yorkville, Il., U.S.	216	41.38 N	88.26 W
Yorkville, Mi., U.S.	216	42.23 N	85.24 W
Yorkville, N.Y., U.S.	210	43.06 N	75.16 W
Yorkville, Oh., U.S.	214	40.09 N	80.43 W
Yorkville ◆[8]	275b	43.40 N	79.24 W
Yoro, Hond.	236	15.09 N	87.07 W
Yoro, Mali	150	14.17 N	2.08 W
Yōrō, Nihon	94	35.18 N	136.33 E
Yoro □[5]	236	15.15 N	87.15 W
Yōrō ≃	94	35.32 N	140.04 E
Yoroi-zaki ›	94	34.24 N	136.55 E
Yoron-jima I	93b	27.02 N	128.26 E
Yōrō-no-taki ∟	94	35.17 N	136.32 E
Yorosso	150	12.22 N	4.47 W
Yosemite Creek ≃	226	37.44 N	119.36 W
Yosemite National Park	226	37.45 N	119.35 W
Yosemite National Park ♠	226	37.51 N	119.33 W
Yoshida, Nihon	94	36.02 N	139.02 E
Yoshida, Nihon	94	34.46 N	138.15 E
Yoshida, Nihon	96	33.16 N	132.33 E
Yoshida, Nihon	96	34.40 N	132.42 E
Yoshida, Nihon	96	35.10 N	132.51 E
Yoshida ≃	96	34.03 N	131.02 E
Yoshii, Nihon	94	36.15 N	138.59 E
Yoshii, Nihon	96	33.20 N	130.45 E
Yoshii, Nihon	96	34.38 N	133.26 E
Yoshii, Nihon	96	34.55 N	134.06 E
Yoshii, Nihon	270	34.53 N	135.03 E
Yoshii ≃	96	34.36 N	134.03 E
Yoshikawa, Nihon	94	37.13 N	138.25 E
Yoshikawa, Nihon	94	35.53 N	139.51 E
Yoshikawa, Nihon	270	34.55 N	135.28 E
Yoshimi	94	36.02 N	139.27 E
Yoshino, Nihon	96	34.21 N	135.51 E
Yoshino, Nihon	96	34.06 N	134.23 E
Yoshino ≃, Nihon	94	34.22 N	135.40 E
Yoshino ≃, Nihon	96	34.05 N	134.36 E
Yoshinodani	94	36.17 N	136.39 E
Yoshino-Kumano-kokuritsu-kōen ♠	92	34.07 N	135.55 E
Yoshioka	94	36.27 N	139.01 E
Yoshiumi	96	34.09 N	133.03 E
Yoshiwa	96	34.29 N	132.09 E
Yoshkar-Ola → Joškar-Ola	80	56.38 N	47.52 E
Yosowilangun	115a	8.15 S	113.18 E
Yos Sudarso, Pulau (Frederik Hendrikeiland) I	164	7.50 S	138.30 E
Yŏsu	98	34.46 N	127.44 E
Yotausito	248	16.03 S	63.03 W
Yōtei-zan ∧	92a	42.49 N	140.49 E
Yotsukaidō	94	35.39 N	140.10 E
Yotvata	132	29.53 N	35.03 E
You ≃, Zhg.	100	26.23 N	118.27 E
You ≃, Zhg.	102	22.50 N	108.06 E
You ≃, Zhg.	102	28.27 N	110.24 E
Youanmi	162	28.37 S	118.49 E
Youbou	224	48.53 N	124.13 W
Youcheng	100	29.14 N	116.48 E
Youfang	106	32.09 N	119.50 E
Youghal	48	51.57 N	7.51 W
Youghal Bay ⊂	48	51.52 N	7.50 W
Youghiogheny ≃	214	40.22 N	79.52 W
Yougoslavie → Yugoslavia □[1]	22	44.00 N	21.00 E
Youhe	100	32.19 N	113.50 E
Youjidong	104	42.12 N	121.07 E
Youkounkoun	150	12.32 N	13.08 W
Youlan	100	28.34 N	116.10 E
Young, Austl.	166	34.19 S	148.18 E
Young, Sk., Can.	184	51.47 N	105.46 W
Young, Az., U.S.	200	34.06 N	110.57 W
Young, Ur.	252	32.41 S	57.38 W
Young America	216	40.34 N	86.20 W
Younghusband Peninsula ›[1]	166	36.00 S	139.30 E
Youngs ≃	224	46.10 N	123.49 W
Youngs, Lake ⊜	224	47.25 N	122.07 W
Youngs Creek	218	38.29 N	86.30 W
Youngs Creek ≃	219	39.21 N	91.51 W
Youngs Rock I[2]	174e	25.03 S	130.07 W
Youngstown, Ab., Can.	182	51.32 N	111.13 W
Youngstown, Fl., U.S.	192	30.21 N	85.26 W
Youngstown, N.Y., U.S.	210	43.14 N	79.03 W
Youngstown, Oh., U.S.	214	41.05 N	80.38 W
Youngstown Municipal Airport ⊠	214	41.15 N	80.41 W
Youngsville, La., U.S.	194	30.05 N	91.59 W
Youngsville, N.Y., U.S.	210	41.48 N	74.54 W
Youngsville, N.C., U.S.	192	36.01 N	78.28 W
Youngsville, Pa., U.S.	214	41.51 N	79.19 W
Youngwood	214	40.14 N	79.34 W
Youngwood Park ♠	279b	40.14 N	79.36 W
Yountville	226	38.24 N	122.22 W
Youshashan	120	38.08 N	91.10 E
Youssoufia	148	32.16 N	8.33 W
Youtingpu	107	29.26 N	105.45 E
Youville ◆[8]	275a	45.33 N	73.39 W
Youxi, Zhg.	100	28.45 N	121.06 E
Youxi, Zhg.	100	26.11 N	118.09 E
Youxi, Zhg.	107	29.12 N	106.09 E
Youxian	100	27.00 N	113.21 E
Youxizhen	107	30.35 N	106.18 E
Youyang	102	28.58 N	108.41 E
Youyi	89	46.44 N	131.44 E
Youyu	102	40.09 N	112.32 E
Youzhagou	106	31.04 N	118.46 E
Youzhou	105	40.09 N	115.42 E
Yoweragabbie	162	23.13 S	117.39 E
Yŏyang-ni	98	37.30 N	128.43 E
Yozgat	130	39.50 N	34.48 E
Yozgat □[4]	130	39.40 N	35.10 E
Ypacaraí	252	25.23 S	57.16 W
Ypané ≃	252	23.29 S	57.19 W
Ypé Jhú	252	23.54 S	55.20 W
Yport	50	49.44 N	0.19 E
Ypres → Ieper	50	50.51 N	2.53 E
Ypsilanti	216	42.14 N	83.36 W
Ypsilanti East	216	42.15 N	83.35 W
Yreka	204	41.44 N	122.38 W
Yrgajty ≃	85	43.03 N	74.43 E
Yron ≃	56	49.10 N	5.52 E
Ysabel Channel Ʉ	164	2.00 S	150.00 E
Ysbyty Ystwyth	42	52.20 N	3.48 W
Yser (IJzer) ≃	50	51.09 N	2.43 E
Ysieux, Ruisseau l' ≃	261	49.09 N	2.22 E
Yssche ≃	56	50.49 N	4.38 E
Yssel → IJssel ≃	52	52.35 N	5.50 E
Ysselmeer → IJsselmeer Ŧ[2]	52	52.45 N	5.25 E
Yssingeaux	62	45.08 N	4.07 E
Ystad	41	55.25 N	13.49 E
Ystalyfera	42	51.47 N	3.47 W
Ysterfonteinpunt ›	158	33.22 S	18.09 E
Ystrad ≃	44	53.13 N	3.20 W
Ystrad Aeron	42	52.11 N	4.11 W
Ystradfellte	42	51.48 N	3.34 W
Ystradgynlais	42	51.47 N	3.45 W
Ystwyth ≃	42	52.24 N	4.05 W
Ytambey ≃	252	24.46 S	54.24 W
Ythan ≃	46	57.18 N	2.00 W
Ytre Arna	26	60.26 N	5.30 E
Ytterharnäs	40	60.39 N	17.21 E
Ytterhogdal	26	62.12 N	14.51 E
Yttermalung	40	60.35 N	13.50 E
Ytterselö	40	59.23 N	17.15 E
Yttre Hållsfjärden ⊂[2]	40	59.08 N	17.40 E
Yttygran, ostrov I	180	64.36 N	172.40 W
Yū	96	34.02 N	132.13 E
Yu ≃	102	23.24 N	110.05 E
Yu, Pulau I	164	0.03 S	129.36 E
Yu'alliq, Jabal ∧	140	30.22 N	33.31 E
Yuam ≃	110	17.47 N	97.45 E
Yuan → Red ≃, Asia	110	20.17 N	106.34 E
Yuan ≃, Zhg.	100	28.09 N	115.34 E
Yuan ≃, Zhg.	102	28.58 N	111.49 E
Yuan'an	102	31.04 N	111.26 E
Yuanao	100	26.29 N	119.48 E
Yuanbachang	107	29.44 N	105.27 E
Yuanhua	106	30.25 N	120.46 E
Yuanjiang	102	23.34 N	102.03 E
Yuankeng	100	26.48 N	117.44 E
Yüanli	100	24.27 N	120.39 E
Yüanlin	100	23.58 N	120.34 E
Yuanling	102	28.20 N	110.16 E
Yuanmou	102	25.38 N	101.54 E
Yuanshancun	106	31.08 N	120.20 E
Yuanshi	98	37.45 N	114.32 E
Yuantan, Zhg.	100	32.47 N	112.53 E
Yuantan, Zhg.	100	23.39 N	113.12 E
Yuantongsi	107	30.13 N	104.15 E
Yuantouzhu	106	31.32 N	120.14 E
Yuanxiang	98	34.14 N	115.19 E
Yuanxiangzhen	106	31.39 N	119.15 E
Yuanxing	107	30.36 N	104.59 E
Yuanyang (Yangwu), Zhg.	98	35.04 N	113.57 E
Yuanyang, Zhg.	102	23.12 N	102.52 E
Yuanyangpu	107	30.10 N	105.15 E
Yuanyangqiao	107	29.41 N	106.33 E
Yuasa	96	34.02 N	135.11 E
Yuat ≃	164	4.25 S	143.55 E
Yuba	102	29.27 N	97.42 E
Yuba □[6]	226	39.16 N	121.17 W
Yuba ≃	226	39.07 N	121.36 W
Yuba City	226	39.08 N	121.36 W
Yubara	96	35.12 N	133.45 E
Yubara-chosuichi ⊜	96	35.13 N	133.43 E
Yūbari	92a	43.04 N	141.59 E
Yūbari-sanchi ⩘	92a	43.15 N	142.20 E
Yubdo	144	9.00 N	35.22 E
Yūbetsu	92a	44.14 N	143.37 E
Yūbetsu ≃	92a	44.14 N	143.37 E
Yucaipa	228	34.02 N	117.02 W
Yucatán □[3]	232	20.50 N	89.00 W
Yucatán, Canal de Ʉ	238	21.45 N	85.45 W
Yucatan Peninsula (Península de Yucatán) ›[1]	232	19.30 N	89.00 W
Yucca	200	34.52 N	114.08 W
Yucca Lake ⊜	204	36.59 N	116.01 W
Yucca Mountain ∧	204	36.56 N	116.29 W
Yucca Valley	204	34.07 N	116.35 W
Yuchaozhuang	105	39.35 N	117.50 E
Yucheng, Zhg.	98	36.56 N	116.39 E
Yucheng, Zhg.	106	30.32 N	120.51 E
Yuci	102	37.45 N	112.41 E
Yuda	92	39.20 N	140.50 E
Yudaokou	98	42.14 N	116.48 E
Yudi Shan ∧	89	52.17 N	121.52 E
Yudong	106	32.02 N	121.22 E
Yudu	100	25.59 N	115.24 E
Yue ≃	107	28.50 N	104.21 E
Yuebo	107	29.03 N	104.12 E
Yuecheng	100	32.39 N	114.49 E
Yuechi	107	30.33 N	106.26 E
Yuejiatun	104	41.10 N	120.43 E
Yuejiawopeng	104	41.35 N	122.20 E
Yuekou	100	30.32 N	113.03 E
Yuelai	106	31.56 N	121.27 E
Yuelaichang, Zhg.	107	29.44 N	106.32 E
Yuelaichang, Zhg.	107	28.53 N	106.22 E
Yuemenpu	107	30.28 N	106.34 E
Yuendumu	162	22.16 S	131.49 E
Yuendumu Aboriginal Reserve ◆[4]	162	22.20 S	131.47 E
Yuen Long	271d	22.26 N	114.02 E
Yuepu	106	31.25 N	121.26 E
Yueqing	100	28.08 N	120.58 E
Yuewang	106	31.33 N	121.09 E
Yuexi, Zhg.	100	30.50 N	116.24 E
Yuexi, Zhg.	102	28.42 N	102.28 E
Yueyang	100	29.23 N	113.06 E
Yuezi	100	24.54 N	115.02 E
Yufa	105	39.31 N	116.19 E
Yufeng	107	30.37 N	105.11 E
Yufu-dake ∧	96	33.17 N	131.24 E
Yufuin	96	33.15 N	131.20 E
Yugan	100	28.41 N	116.41 E
Yugawara	94	35.09 N	139.04 E
Yuge	96	34.15 N	133.12 E
Yugoslavia (Jugoslavija) □[1], Europe	22	44.00 N	21.00 E
Yugoslavia (Jugoslavija) □[1], Europe	38	44.00 N	21.00 E
Yugou	100	33.42 N	118.55 E
Yuguan	98	39.56 N	119.22 E
Yuguo	104	41.52 N	123.15 E
Yuhang (Linping)	106	30.25 N	120.18 E
Yuhebu	102	38.01 N	109.37 E
Yuhu	100	27.53 N	120.08 E
Yuhuaizhuang	105	39.24 N	117.40 E
Yuhuan	100	28.10 N	121.12 E
Yuhuan Dao I	100	28.08 N	121.12 E
Yuhuang Ding ∧	98	36.50 N	121.21 E
Yui	94	35.06 N	138.34 E
Yuin	162	27.58 S	116.02 E
Yujiachang	107	29.57 N	104.04 E
Yujiacun	106	31.45 N	121.48 E
Yujiang	100	28.11 N	116.47 E
Yujiaqiao	106	31.30 N	119.25 E
Yujiawan	86	44.32 N	86.45 E
Yukarıbey	130	39.15 N	27.06 E
Yukarıdudullu ◆[8]	267b	41.02 N	29.09 E
Yuke	98	37.58 N	115.39 E
Yūki, Nihon	94	36.18 N	139.53 E
Yuki, Nihon	96	34.29 N	132.16 E
Yuki, Nihon	96	34.46 N	133.17 E
Yuki, Nihon	96	33.46 N	134.36 E
Yukon, Ok., U.S.	196	35.30 N	97.45 W
Yukon, Pa., U.S.	214	40.13 N	79.41 W
Yukon □[4], Can.	176	64.00 N	135.00 W
Yukon □[4], Can.	180	64.00 N	135.00 W
Yukon ≃	180	62.33 N	163.59 W
Yukon Flats ≡	180	66.30 N	146.00 W
Yukou	105	40.12 N	117.00 E
Yukuhashi	96	33.44 N	130.59 E
Yulan	210	41.31 N	74.56 W
Yulao	102	23.31 N	111.46 E
Yulara	162	25.14 S	131.04 E
Yule ≃	162	20.41 S	118.17 E
Yule Bay ⊂	9	70.44 S	166.40 E
Yule Island I	164	8.50 S	146.30 E
Yuli, Nig.	146	9.42 N	10.17 E
Yüli, T'aiwan	100	23.20 N	121.18 E
Yuli, Zhg.	98	37.00 N	121.25 E
Yuliang	100	29.52 N	118.30 E
Yuliangpu	89	43.26 N	121.55 E
Yulin, Zhg.	102	22.36 N	110.07 E
Yulin, Zhg.	102	38.20 N	109.29 E
Yulin, Zhg.	110	18.16 N	109.32 E
Yulincun	105	40.12 N	116.42 E
Yul-li	98	38.52 N	126.13 E
Yulong	107	29.58 N	104.22 E
Yuma, Az., U.S.	200	32.43 N	114.37 W
Yuma, Co., U.S.	198	40.08 N	102.43 W
Yuma, Bahía de ⊂	238	18.21 N	68.35 W
Yuma Marine Corps Air Station ■	200	32.40 N	114.38 W
Yuma Proving Ground ■	204	33.05 N	114.25 W
Yumare	246	10.37 N	68.41 W
Yumbel	252	37.08 S	72.32 W
Yumbi, Zaïre	152	1.53 S	16.32 E
Yumbi, Zaïre	154	1.14 S	26.14 E
Yumbo	246	3.35 N	76.28 W
Yumen (Laojunmiao)	102	39.56 N	97.51 E
Yumenzhen	102	40.17 N	97.07 E
Yumesaki	96	34.58 N	134.42 E
Yumezaki ≃	96	34.47 N	134.39 E
Yumin	86	46.02 N	82.37 E
Yumurtalık	130	36.49 N	35.45 E
Yun ≃	100	30.43 N	114.04 E
Yuna, Austl.	162	28.20 S	115.00 E
Yuna, Nihon	174m	26.46 N	128.12 E
Yuna ≃	238	19.12 N	69.37 W
Yunak	130	38.49 N	31.45 E
Yunan (Ducheng)	102	23.11 N	111.29 E
Yunaska Island I	180	52.40 N	170.50 W
Yuncao	100	31.26 N	118.04 E
Yuncheng, Zhg.	98	35.35 N	115.54 E
Yuncheng, Zhg.	102	35.00 N	110.59 E
Yundamindra	162	29.07 S	122.02 E
Yundanyingzi	104	42.00 N	121.34 E
Yunderup	168a	32.35 S	115.46 E
Yunfeng Ding ∧	106	30.56 N	120.02 E
Yungas ◆[1]	248	16.00 S	67.45 W
Yungay, Chile	252	37.07 S	72.01 W
Yungay, Perú	248	9.09 S	77.44 W
Yungchi → Jilin	89	43.51 N	126.33 E
Yungchia → Wenzhou	100	28.01 N	120.39 E
Yungho	269d	25.01 N	121.31 E
Yungning → Nanning	102	22.48 N	108.20 E
Yung Shue Wan	271d	22.14 N	114.06 E
Yunhe → Peixian, Zhg.	98	34.21 N	117.59 E
Yunhe, Zhg.	100	28.06 N	119.34 E
Yunjin	107	29.06 N	105.40 E
Yunkai Dashan ⩘	102	22.30 N	111.00 E
Yun Ling ⩘	102	27.20 N	99.20 E
Yunlong, Zhg.	102	25.50 N	99.17 E
Yunlong, Zhg.	107	30.31 N	104.46 E
Yunluchang	107	29.45 N	105.57 E
Yunmeng	100	31.02 N	113.41 E
Yunmenling	100	25.15 N	115.49 E
Yunmenzhen	107	30.06 N	106.20 E
Yunnan □[4]	102	24.00 N	101.00 E
Yunnanfu → Kunming	102	25.05 N	102.40 E
Yunotan	94	37.14 N	139.01 E
Yunotsu	96	35.05 N	132.21 E
Yunta	166	32.35 S	139.33 E
Yunting	106	31.53 N	120.19 E
Yunwu Shan ∧	98	41.07 N	116.34 E
Yunxi, Zhg.	100	29.28 N	113.16 E
Yunxi, Zhg.	102	32.49 N	110.13 E
Yunxian, Zhg	102	24.30 N	100.03 E
Yunxian (Yunyang), Zhg.	102	32.49 N	110.49 E
Yunxiao	100	24.04 N	117.20 E
Yunyan ≃	100	34.39 N	119.18 E
Yunyang, Zhg.	100	33.28 N	112.42 E
Yunyang, Zhg	102	30.58 N	109.05 E
Yunzalin ≃	110	17.23 N	97.40 E
Yunzhong	100	29.13 N	117.40 E
Yunzhou	98	41.01 N	115.44 E
Yuping	102	27.07 N	108.47 E
Yuqi	106	31.43 N	120.11 E
Yuqia	102	38.07 N	94.35 E
Yuqian'gou	104	41.41 N	121.28 E
Yuqiao Shuiku ⊜[1]	105	40.02 N	117.33 E
Yuqing	102	27.05 N	107.44 E
Yura, Nihon	96	33.57 N	135.07 E
Yura, Perú	248	16.11 S	71.40 W
Yura ≃	96	35.31 N	135.17 E
Yurano-hara ›	96	33.01 N	132.23 E
Yurécuaro	234	20.20 N	102.18 W
Yurga → Jurga	86	55.42 N	84.51 E
Yuri-jima I	96	33.51 N	132.32 E
Yurimaguas	248	5.54 S	76.05 W
Yuriria	234	20.12 N	101.09 W
Yuriria, Laguna de ⊜	234	20.15 N	101.06 W
Yuruarí ≃	246	6.44 N	61.40 W
Yurubi, Parque Nacional ♠	246	10.25 N	68.42 W
Yürük	130	40.56 N	27.04 E
Yurumanguí ≃	246	3.27 N	77.21 W
Yurungkax ≃	120	37.00 N	79.55 E
Yuryev → Tartu	76	58.23 N	26.43 E
Yusala, Laguna ⊜	248	14.05 S	67.12 W
Yuşa Tepesi ∧[2]	267b	41.09 N	29.05 E
Yuscarán	236	13.55 N	86.51 W
Yushan, Zhg.	100	26.54 N	118.36 E
Yushan, Zhg.	100	28.41 N	118.15 E
Yushan, Zhg.	100	33.19 N	113.41 E
Yü Shan ∧, T'aiwan	100	23.28 N	120.57 E
Yu Shan ∧, Zhg.	100	26.06 N	115.20 E
Yushanzhen	102	29.38 N	108.19 E
Yushu, Zhg.	89	44.46 N	126.34 E
Yushu (Jiegu), Zhg.	102	33.01 N	97.00 E
Yushugou	86	44.07 N	87.05 E
Yushulinzi, Zhg.	98	41.30 N	119.07 E
Yushulinzi, Zhg.	98	40.59 N	125.57 E
Yushupu	104	41.10 N	122.08 E
Yushutai, Zhg.	89	43.30 N	124.17 E
Yushutai, Zhg.	104	41.42 N	123.26 E
Yushuwan	105	40.04 N	115.35 E
Yusichang	107	29.14 N	105.25 E
Yūsofābād ◆[8]	267d	35.44 N	51.25 E
Yuste, Monasterio de ⚜[1]	34	40.08 N	5.45 W
Yūsuf, Bahr ≋	142	29.18 N	30.50 E
Yusufeli	130	40.50 N	41.33 E
Yusuhara	96	33.23 N	132.55 E

≃	River	Fluß	Río	Rivière	Rio
≋	Canal	Kanal	Canal	Canal	Canal
∟	Waterfall, Rapids	Wasserfall, Stromschnellen	Cascada, Rápidos	Chute d'eau, Rapides	Cascata, Rápidos
Ʉ	Strait	Meeresstraße	Estrecho	Détroit	Estreito
⊂	Bay, Gulf	Bucht, Golf	Bahía, Golfo	Baie, Golfe	Baía, Golfo
⊜	Lake, Lakes	See, Seen	Lago, Lagos	Lac, Lacs	Lago, Lagos
≡	Swamp	Sumpf	Pantano	Marais	Pântano
ℸ	Ice Features, Glacier	Eis- und Gletscherformen	Accidentes Glaciales	Formes glaciaires	Acidentes glaciares
Ŧ	Other Hydrographic Features	Andere Hydrographische Objekte	Otros Elementos Hidrográficos	Autres données hydrographiques	Outros acidentes hidrográficos
✢	Submarine Features	Untermeerische Objekte	Accidentes Submarinos	Formes de relief sous-marin	Acidentes submarinos
□	Political Unit	Politische Einheit	Unidad Politica	Entité politique	Unidade política
⚜	Cultural Institution	Kulturelle Institution	Institución Cultural	Institution culturelle	Instituição cultura
⊥	Historical Site	Historische Stätte	Sitio Histórico	Site historique	Sitio histórico
♠	Recreational Site	Erholungs- und Ferienort	Sitio de Recreo	Centre de loisirs	Area de Lazer
⊠	Airport	Flughafen	Aeropuerto	Aéroport	Aeroporto
■	Military Installation	Militäranlage	Instalación Militar	Installation militaire	Instalação militar
◆	Miscellaneous	Verschiedenes	Misceláneo	Divers	Diversos

Symbols in the index entries represent the broad categories identified in the key at the right. Symbols with superior numbers (ʌ¹) identify subcategories (see complete key on page *I · 1*).

Symbole im Register stellen die rechts im Schlüssel erklärten Kategorien dar. Symbole mit hochgestellten Ziffern (ʌ¹) bezeichnen Unterabteilungen einer Kategorie (vgl. vollständiger Schlüssel auf Seite *I · 1*).

Los símbolos incluidos en el texto del índice representan las grandes categorías identificadas con la parte superior (ʌ¹) identifican las subcategorías (véase la clave completa en la página *I · 1*).

Les symboles de l'index représentent les catégories indiquées dans la légende à droite. Les symboles suivis d'un indice (ʌ¹) représentent des sous-catégories (voir légende complète à la page *I · 1*).

Os símbolos incluídos no texto do índice representam as grandes categorias identificadas com a parte superior (ʌ¹) identificam as subcategorias (veja-se a chave completa à página *I · 1*).

ʌ	Mountain	Berg	Montaña	Montagne	Montanha
⋌	Mountains	Gebirge	Montañas	Montagnes	Montanhas
⋋	Pass	Paß	Paso	Col	Passo
⋁	Valley, Canyon	Tal, Cañon	Valle, Cañón	Vallée, Canyon	Vale, Canhão
≃	Plain	Ebene	Llano	Plaine	Planície
⋗	Cape	Kap	Cabo	Cap	Cabo
₪	Island	Insel	Isla	Île	Ilha
₪₪	Islands	Inseln	Islas	Îles	Ilhas
±	Other Topographic Features	Andere Topographische Objekte	Otros Elementos Topográficos	Autres données topographiques	Outros acidentes topográficos

Key map of regional atlas coverage

For a complete depiction of *all* scales and map series, see the REGIONAL INDEX MAPS, pp. *xiii-xv.*

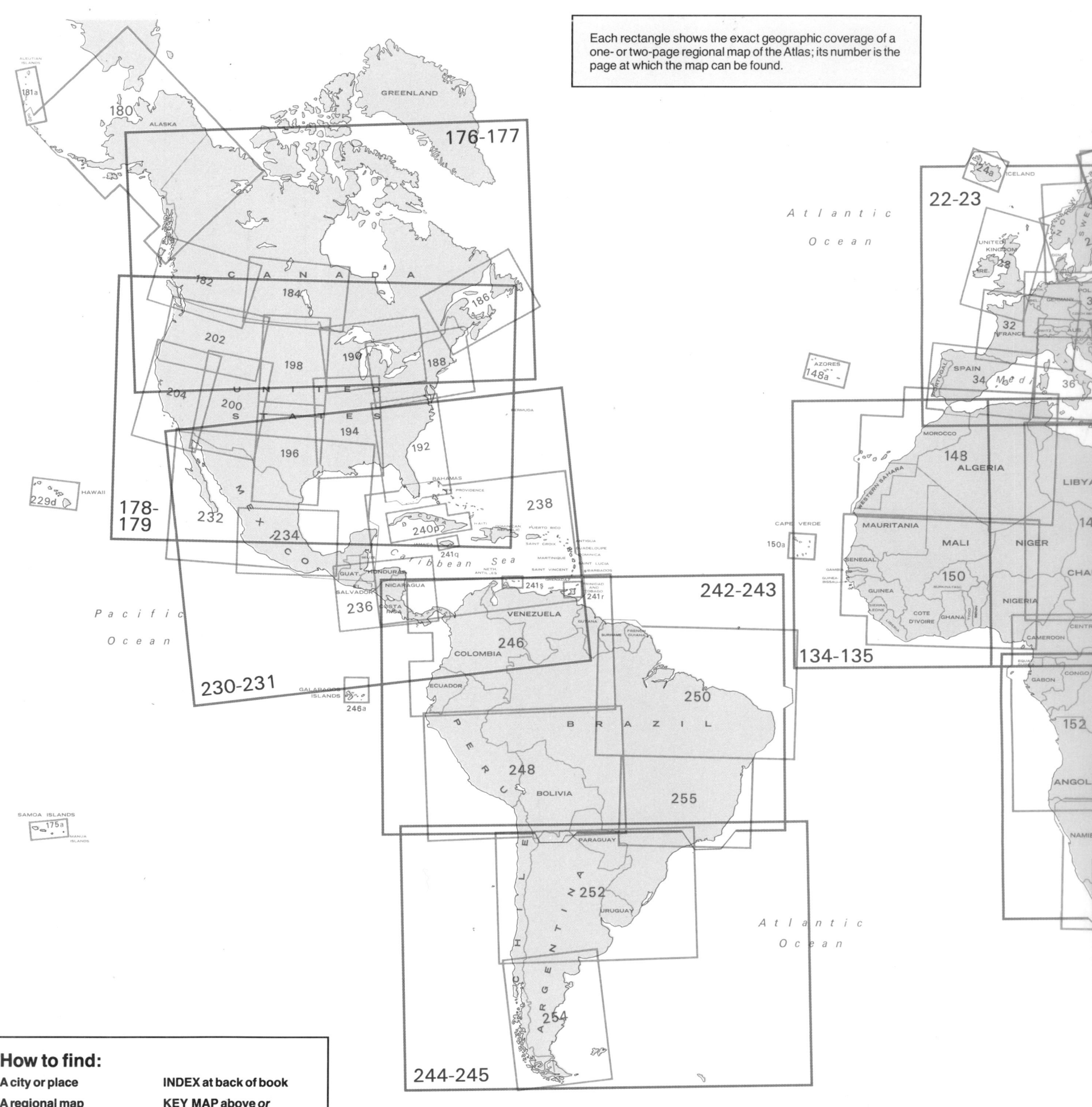

Each rectangle shows the exact geographic coverage of a one- or two-page regional map of the Atlas; its number is the page at which the map can be found.

How to find:

A city or place	INDEX at back of book
A regional map	KEY MAP above *or* alphabetical LIST OF MAPS, pp. *vi-ix*
A country or state	KEY MAP above.
A physical feature (lake, mountain, river)	SELECTED MAP REFERENCES, p. *xvi*
Meaning of map symbols, typographic conventions, etc.	LEGEND TO MAPS, pp. *x-xii*
Population of a country, state, etc.	WORLD INFORMATION TABLE, pp. 296-299
Population of a city	POPULATION OF CITIES AND TOWNS, pp. 301-316
World patterns of economic and human geography	WORLD SCENE, pp. *xvii-xl (See summary at right)*

Exact geographic coverage of each regional map
See the KEY MAP above or the REGIONAL INDEX MAPS, pp. *xiii-xv.*

Quick reference to the major places in the atlas
See the alphabetical LIST OF PLACES opposite the Title Page.

Symbols on the maps and what they mean
See LEGEND TO MAPS, pp. *x-xii.*